FINAL STRIKE

JASON KASPER

SEVERN RIVER
PUBLISHING

Copyright © 2025 by Regiment Publishing.

All rights reserved.

No part of this book may be reproduced in any form or by any electronic or mechanical means, including information storage and retrieval systems, without written permission from the author, except for the use of brief quotations in a book review.

Severn River Publishing
SevernRiverBooks.com

This is a work of fiction. Names, characters, businesses, places, events and incidents are either the products of the author's imagination or used in a fictitious manner. Any resemblance to actual persons, living or dead, or actual events is purely coincidental.

ISBN: 978-1-64875-647-4 (Paperback)

ALSO BY JASON KASPER

American Mercenary Series
Greatest Enemy
Offer of Revenge
Dark Redemption
Vengeance Calling
The Suicide Cartel
Terminal Objective

Shadow Strike Series
The Enemies of My Country
Last Target Standing
Covert Kill
Narco Assassins
Beast Three Six
The Belgrade Conspiracy
Lethal Horizon
Congo Nightfall
Rogue Frontier
Final Strike

Spider Heist Thrillers
The Spider Heist
The Sky Thieves
The Manhattan Job
The Fifth Bandit
The Stormridge Con

Standalone Thriller
Her Dark Silence

To find out more about Jason Kasper and his books, visit
Jason-Kasper.com

To David
2023 can burn in hell

"Out of suffering have emerged the strongest souls; the most massive characters are seared with scars."
-Khalil Gibran

"Careful who you fuck with."
-David Rivers

1

Worthy's first thought after pulling his parachute ripcord was that he was in deep shit.

He was already low—which was more or less the point of a HALO jump—and instead of feeling the gentle tug of an unfurling canopy catching air, he was thrust into a violent, uncontrollable spiral in the time it took him to flinch.

Sky and earth whipped across his night vision in stark shades of green, nausea gripping him as he came to terms with his circumstances. Parachute lines had somehow flipped over the canopy during deployment, causing one side to collapse while the other inflated asymmetrically, turning him into a puppet at the hands of an exceedingly ruthless master.

The landscape rushed up to meet him with frightening speed, his attempt to reach up for his steering toggles like trying to part a rushing river with his bare hands. There would be no dislodging the line by pumping his brakes, no reaching them in the first place. The disorienting spiral made it impossible to so much as look up and assess the carnage overhead, and he tried to reach for his cutaway handle only to find that the intense G-forces were pinning his hands to his sides and inhibiting his ability to think as much as move.

Worthy's breathing had gone from slow and controlled to sharp, staccato bursts, the pure air from his O2 bottle tinged with a plasticky odor from the oxygen mask clinging to his face like a lobster. The relentless turning squeezed the clarity from his thoughts until they blurred, broke, and then scattered in every direction. His arms felt leaden as he fought against the overwhelming centrifugal force, each spin sending a wave of dizziness crashing over him and causing his vision to tunnel ever further toward a single pinprick. Seconds of full consciousness remained to turn the tides on his situation, a possibility that seemed much further away than the rapidly approaching earth below.

For Worthy, this was a particularly catastrophic development in an already hellish night.

Heated undergarments and insulated outerwear could only do so much to keep you warm when exiting a plane into subarctic temperatures at 25,000 feet, and the thin-blooded Georgia native had already been freefalling for close to three minutes with biting wind slicing through his protective gear, numbing his skin as he approached the ground at 120 miles per hour.

Strapped atop the multi-layered snowsuit was not only his parachute harness but a weapons case with his trusty HK416 and, inverted from his waist, the anvil of a rucksack practically bursting at the seams at maximum tensile strength, containing everything he'd need to fight and survive for days or weeks on end without hope of resupply.

That collective weight made the rotational pressure of his spin all the more difficult to overcome as he forced both hands to the cutaway handle on his right side, barely managing to grasp the hollow metal tubing and using the last of his waning strength and cognition to pull it down and out.

The twin risers connected to his shoulders detached and he fell free of his main parachute. Any relief from this success, however, was short-lived. Instead of stopping his brutal rotation, the temporary victory only intensified it. Worthy was now a rag doll caught in a cyclone, limbs flailing uncontrollably in a desperate attempt to stabilize himself.

And while there was no question that he had to pull his reserve, doing so now would only send the parachute into a hopelessly tangled mess of lines and risers that may or may not be wrapped around his body.

Wind noise that had formerly stabilized at a loud roar was now a discordant, pulsating scream, the sound oscillating wildly with each frantic spin and underscored by a new sound—the high-pitched chirping of his audible altimeter screaming that he was passing through the hard deck for saving his own life. If he continued at his current velocity, an automatic activation device would fire the reserve for him, although it would be too hopelessly twisted to offer much in the way of deceleration before he made landfall. At best he'd be turned into a vegetable in a full-body cast.

Worthy forced his pelvis down and arms out wide, trying to fight the uncontrolled spin. The world kept rotating, his night vision displaying the warbling blur of a line dividing dark and light that could only be the horizon. But gradually—agonizingly slowly—his momentum around the axis of his body's center of gravity began to lessen.

Now. It had to be now. He still wasn't stable enough to reliably deploy his reserve, but if he didn't do exactly that in the next two seconds, then stability would be the least of his concerns.

With a final surge of effort, he brought his left hand to the reserve handle and pulled. The emergency chute deployed with a jolt, the canopy snapping open above him with far greater speed than his main parachute had. His body swung like a pendulum beneath the life-saving fabric. Worthy spun like a ballet dancer until his risers could wrap around each other no more, then flipped back to the right with increasing speed.

He had stabilized just enough to think straight, but his reserve parachute was billowing above the twisted risers and steering lines. Unless he fixed that in record time, he'd hit the ground with bone-crunching force. Bringing both hands behind his helmet to grasp the risers just below the point where their wrap began, he pulled them apart with maximum strength of effort.

To this he added the most undignified of parachutist corrective procedures, a frenzied sequence of kicks that rivaled the fastest efforts of a Tour de France contender in the home stretch.

The combination of outward pressure on the risers and bicycle kicks turned his body into a lever to unwind the twist, sending him into a left-hand pivot. Worthy had no idea how low he was, no depth perception with which to gauge his altitude beyond the darkness of earth swallowing his view from bottom to top. He could only prepare for the canopy to fully open and fly him straight; after that, he'd forgo any effort to gain control of his steering toggles in the interests of dropping his rucksack on its lowering line before the eighty-pound mass dramatically increased the chances of injury upon impact.

A final clockwise rotation ensued before he slowly reversed direction—the risers were now fully untangled—and Worthy yanked the release handle to detach the rucksack and send it falling on its tether.

He was about to bring both hands upward to gain control of his parachute when he heard the thudding percussion of the ruck bouncing off the ground, and his last act before making landfall was to bring his feet and knees together and shield his face with both arms.

As the ground surged up, a single thought crossed Worthy's mind.

So this is how it ends.

2

Cancer crested the small hill with the grace of a predatory cat, his boots finding purchase on the loose gravel without so much as a single misstep. The cold air of the desert plains was scarcely an afterthought—the exertion of a hasty ruck march had sufficiently warmed his body, and no temperatures at 3,000 feet above sea level could match the subzero hell his team had plummeted through before deploying their parachutes an hour earlier.

The landscape unfurled before him, ghostly and surreal through the green glow of his night vision device. His view was bathed in shades of emerald and black that highlighted every rock, scrub, and ridge in eerie detail.

Crouching low at the summit, he caught his breath. The high ground offered a clear vantage point of the surrounding area. The jagged outline of mountains loomed in the distance, their peaks cutting into the night sky and standing watch over the vast desert floor that stretched beneath them.

Cancer's gaze swept across the terrain, systematically identifying sectors of fire. The rocky and uneven ridgeline to the northeast provided natural cover—an ideal approach for anyone trying to get the drop on them. He marked it in his mind, assigning it as a priority. To the northwest, a dry riverbed carved its way through the valley, its banks steep and riddled with potential hiding spots. Anyone moving through there would be forced into a bottleneck, but it also meant they'd be harder to spot until they were close.

He adjusted his stance, the familiar weight of his suppressed HK417 rifle steadying him as he scanned further south. There, the ground sloped gently away into the valley, the terrain more open and sliced by a dirt road. It was the most vulnerable sector for the enemy, a place where any movement would be visible from a distance, and therefore an ideal sector for the least experienced of his combat-hardened teammates.

Keying his radio, he spoke in a low and controlled voice. "Angel, you're covering south. Doc, northeast. Last sector is northwest."

In other settings he'd have simply used his infrared laser to delineate exact positions, but not tonight—not when the risk of being spotted by opponents with night vision was so perilously high.

The green shadows of his four teammates appeared one at a time atop the hill, three of them seamlessly moving to their assigned security positions while the remaining man approached and knelt beside him.

No words were exchanged. Cancer checked the positioning of each man to ensure the security perimeter was fully occupied, then transmitted, "Drop rucks." He sat down, leaned back, and stripped off his shoulder straps, then recovered his rifle with newfound agility after shedding the pack. He moved swiftly toward the largest figure among his ranks.

Reilly was already in the prone, adjusting his position to find what little comfort there was to be had on the rocky ground.

Taking a knee, Cancer quietly asked, "How're you holding up?"

"Hard part's over," the medic replied. "I can carry a ruck all night and day, but that jump was—"

"Colder than a witch's tit in a brass bra."

"Yeah. That."

"Just don't fall asleep on me out here."

"Feels like I'm lying on a bed of broken glass. Staying awake won't be a problem."

"Good." Cancer moved out then, remaining crouched as he made a semicircle to the next man.

"Ian. What's good."

The intelligence operative took a final pull of water from the flexible hose emerging from his ruck. "Easy part's over. I'd rather jump again than haul this ruck all night."

"The green tick will suck the life out of you," Cancer agreed. "But you've got no one to blame but yourself."

"Why's that?"

"You're an intel guy. Could've found a desk job. The rest of us didn't have a choice."

"That's fair."

Ian's reply served as an unwitting final comment as Cancer departed, moving to complete his rotation with the final man on perimeter security.

Cancer's check-ins with each man served a more practical purpose than casual banter. He was not only verifying sectors of fire but also checking for any delayed reactions or slurred speech that could indicate exhaustion, hypothermia, dehydration, and anything and everything else that men of paramilitary caliber would view as a sign of weakness to be suppressed at all costs.

He came upon the final figure lying in a security position, this one covering the dry riverbed to the northwest.

Dropping to a knee, Cancer said, "Hey, man. You ready to quit, or what?"

His counterpart's real name took a minor amount of effort to remember; in addition to being the newest team member, Jalal Hassan preferred responding to Hass. The man snickered at the inquiry.

"I've been ready to quit every time I've ever put on a ruck. Haven't found the balls to go through with it yet."

Cancer asked, "Miss your team?"

"Do you miss Worthy?"

"Not in the least."

Hass paused. "Damn, I guess that backfired."

"Don't worry. I mean, sure, we're not as by-the-book as your guys."

"Or as professional, or as disciplined."

"Goes without saying. But we've always come out on top by playing it fast and loose. You're gonna be fine."

"Unless your team's luck is about to run out."

"*Our* team," Cancer corrected him. "You're playing for the winning side now. And if we die, we die together."

The statement hung in the air as Cancer left, making for the center of the formation where his final teammate was adjusting the angle of a mobile satellite antenna resting atop its tripod.

David Rivers didn't look up as Cancer approached, instead procuring his radio hand mic for the inevitable report to headquarters.

"Guys are good," Cancer said, taking a seat. "Now get your bullshit over with so we can keep moving."

"Don't tell me what to do."

"If you were worth a shit as a team leader, I wouldn't have to."

"I blame my second-in-command for all my shortcomings," David quipped, then keyed his radio mic and spoke again.

"Raptor Nine One, this is Suicide Actual. Infiltration complete. Time: zero one three zero. Location: alpha alpha two. All men, weapons, and equipment accounted for. No enemy contact. Preparing to move to checkpoint one, how copy?"

The team leader listened intently to some return transmission, then looked up without speaking.

"What?" Cancer asked.

David's night vision device tilted as he cocked his head. "She just said ENDEX."

"ENDEX? As in, end exercise?"

"Yeah."

"There's no way."

David radioed, "Raptor Nine One, say again." He listened again for the response before confirming, "Suicide Actual, copy."

Then he released a long breath and concluded in a resigned tone, "She just said it again: ENDEX. We need to make our way to the road—they're sending a truck to pick us up."

3

I stepped into the room and was struck, as I always was, by the brightness—fluorescent lights hummed overhead, illuminating every cubic inch of the spacious interior.

The walls were covered with evidence of our planning process. Satellite images and intel reports were tacked up alongside whiteboards filled with radio frequencies and brevity codes, checkpoint grids and timelines, equipment inventories and contingency plans. Most notable of all were the maps of varying scales marked with flight paths, parachute landing zones, and ground routes leading to and from twin objectives. I'd committed a shocking amount of this information to memory whether I wanted to or not, having lived and breathed operational specifics for weeks on end.

My entrance was greeted by a booming Southern voice calling out the announcement reserved for the arrival of a superior officer.

"Room, atten-*tion!*"

During my time in the military, such a declaration was followed by the scrape of chairs as everyone leapt to their feet.

In a room full of CIA contractors, however, the outcome was a series of snickers as I faced the row of seated men to identify my pointman—or, I thought, my former pointman.

"Worthy," I responded, "I heard you fucked up your jump as usual. Add that to your tree landing in the Congo, and I think it's time for you to consider alternate methods of infiltration."

There was a mocking "ooooh" of fake shock from the men seated beside him, or at least some of them.

Griffin remained impervious to humor, sitting erect and motionless without the faintest trace of expression. He was as unflappable a leader as I'd ever met or heard of, though his team didn't share his stoic nature. Munoz, Washington, and Keller appeared thrilled at the outset of verbal hostilities, however good-natured, and Worthy answered with his typical self-deprecating charm.

"That jump makes strike two for me, no doubt about it. Parachutes just aren't my thing."

I continued into the room, making way for Cancer, Reilly, Ian, and Hass to enter behind me.

It was that last man in our group who altered the ranks from everything we'd known before. Since this mission would require a JTAC-qualified individual for each team—that was, joint terminal attack controller, an expert in managing aircraft and calling in airstrikes—we'd been forced to switch up our usual team structure.

Griffin's team had two JTACs, Munoz and Hass, and my team had none.

The one-man swap of Hass and Worthy had thus been an unfortunate necessity, and I exchanged a parting shot with my former teammate.

"Try to fix yourself before we pull off this mission for real."

"If we do at all," Munoz replied. "Not sure why they called off our training, but it can't be for anything good."

That brought me to a momentary halt. The operation we'd spent the better part of two months preparing for couldn't have been officially canceled.

Could it?

As my men made their way to their seats, shit-talking with the members of our sister team every step of the way, I approached Griffin and said, "We would've heard by now if they called off the op. Did your guys do anything different this time?"

"No. It was textbook, same as the first full mission profile."

"Same here. If we were in trouble for the way we do business, it should have come up by now."

"Unless," Griffin proposed, "this has something to do with Pakistan."

That comment caught me off guard, though in retrospect it seemed an obvious implication. Griffin was a model leader, no doubt about it. And while I was certainly no slouch, my team had a tendency of accomplishing our overseas missions via an imaginative range of acts that violated every conceivable CIA restriction, all of which were then covered up by the lies, half-truths, and omissions of fact that characterized my official reporting to headquarters.

Our last mission to Pakistan had involved both my team and Griffin's, but I was the overall ground force commander, and my moral leniency in doing whatever it took to accomplish the mission hadn't exactly tightened up while we hunted a stolen nuclear warhead.

But none of that had come up in the after-action mission review—in fact, the CIA had offered both myself and Griffin the Intelligence Star, a valor award that we both said we'd accept only if everyone on our teams received it as well. The outcome had been that no one had gotten it at all. And now that I found myself questioning what facts against us could have possibly emerged since our return to the US three months ago, I had no idea.

"Well, shit," I said, knocking twice on the table and addressing Griffin's entire team. "My guys already know the drill—ask for a lawyer and refer all questions to me. I've been training to be a scapegoat my entire career."

Griffin said nothing, nor did I leave him any time to do so before heading to my chair.

I took a seat beside Cancer and asked, "You think we got burned, or what?"

The sniper ran a hand over his close-cropped hair, scratching an itch at the back of his head.

"No way. We've run ten real-world missions without getting fried. If they were going to burn us at the stake, it would've happened before we came to Nevada."

Then he leaned closer and added, "Besides, think of how much money they spent on this bullshit."

He wasn't wrong, I thought.

As far as full mission profile exercises went, shooters like myself had the simplest role: show up, get briefed, plan, and execute our task. They always involved a physical suckfest, to be sure, but at least no one would be shooting at us.

At least, not with real bullets.

The bulk of the work fell to the CIA. They'd selected the Nevada Test and Training Range for its simulated air defenses, and had then gone on to reserve the training area and airspace, constructed and modified buildings to serve as mock objectives, arranged Farsi-speaking role-players, and made the training as realistic as possible. All of this was done without broadcasting the actual specifics of the ultimate mission to any of the dozens of people involved in supporting us, and keeping their evaluators and medical support discreetly out of sight.

Then there was the not-insignificant matter of the infiltration and exfiltration platforms, the former of which required political approval along with an astronomical sum of taxpayer dollars whose exact amount I didn't want to begin to contemplate.

I asked, "So what do you think—"

My inquiry ended with the appearance of a new arrival to the room, this one a middle-aged Taiwanese American woman in outdoor attire that she looked remarkably uncomfortable in. Meiling Chen. The head of Project Longwing, the highly compartmentalized targeted killing program whose action arm was represented by myself and the nine men seated alongside me.

All banter ceased at the instant of her arrival, though rather than acknowledge us in the slightest, she continued to a chair as a second figure entered.

Chen's appearance was unwelcome, though not surprising—she'd been back and forth between CIA Headquarters and Nevada since our team's arrival here, and regardless of location remained the voice on the other end of our satellite radio.

But the gentleman in his seventies who entered now had no cause to be here and an abundance of reasons to distance himself from our program altogether. His dress shirt and pressed khakis were far too formal for the current setting and yet somehow far beneath him. I'd only met Senator Gossweiler in person once, although I'd seen him on TV many more times, and never without an immaculate suit.

A shock of silver hair was combed back neatly over his ghostly blue eyes as he squared off at the front of the room and faced us.

"Tom Gossweiler. You boys know who I am?"

A few men nodded and I glanced at Reilly, who remained stock still and appeared just as surprised as I was.

Gossweiler needed no introduction, though his name was almost never spoken within the confines of Project Longwing. As the Chairman of the US Senate Select Committee on Intelligence, he was the highest ranking politician who knew of our program—other than the president, who'd signed the executive order tacitly allowing assassinations against rising terrorist leaders. But only Gossweiler oversaw our operations, and to hear Chen tell it, even occasionally inserted himself in the operations center when things went wrong.

His gaze swept over us for a few moments. "Good. Then we can dispense with further introductions. Let's get down to business."

What that business was, I almost didn't want to know.

"I know you boys have drilled this mission so much that you could do it in your sleep. In fact, you're already 'go' for launch—I validated your operational concept after the last full mission profile. But we had the birds scheduled for one more night, and as you can imagine, I didn't want to waste that considerable expense. Now that you're done with the jump, I'm sending all of you home five days early. After that, you'll have your regular leave period as scheduled. Spend some extra time with your families before you head out to do the job."

Still, no one spoke, although the elation was palpable. In a world where the training was always going to get worse before it got worse, a sudden and unexpected reprieve was unheard of. I thought of Laila, and considered whether my wife would drop dead with shock when I told her I'd be home early.

"Now for the bad news," he continued. "We've been operating on a loose leash courtesy of an administration that's up for re-election this fall, and whether or not we could've continued became a moot point the second our program was blasted all over *The New York Times*. We can all thank the Chinese for that, but the damage is done. I regret to tell you that the calls for a formal investigation are gaining steam. As of this morning, both the SSCI and the House Intelligence Committee are launching inquiries. They're going to dig deep—into the legality, oversight, you name it. We're looking at public hearings, classified sessions, the works."

The chairman's frustration was evident in his voice. "Bottom line, we're going to lose our executive order. We would've already, if I hadn't made a very strong case that you boys are the best option to discreetly neutralize the current target individual. But I regret to inform you that your upcoming mission for Project Longwing will be the last. The moment your teams are safely recovered, the program is going to be dissolved. You'll receive a severance, your contracts will be null and void, and you'll never work for the CIA again."

He let that sink in for a moment, and my concern went from the status of our planned operation to my teammates.

I had, after all, already made my decision to retire. That much was no secret among my team or Chen. Only Reilly had likewise chosen to leave the Agency upon conclusion of our contract, and for the same reason I had.

Ian wanted to continue working in the CIA, albeit as an analyst. Worthy and Cancer had yet to voice any intentions. Now that the decision was being made for all three men, I had no idea how or if they'd cope. At this point in our working relationship, I couldn't envision Cancer as a civilian any more than I could imagine him as a nuclear physicist.

Gossweiler went on, "I came here to tell you this personally out of respect for your accomplishments and sacrifice on behalf of the United States, because you saved my daughter, and because points one and two are causing me to unwittingly inherit a son-in-law." He cut his eyes to Reilly, whose face was turning an ever-deeper shade of crimson. "This is my last chance to get you boys out the door, and I'm taking it. There's no bigger target than the one you're going after. Malek's first swing at a terrorist operation was the damn near successful theft of a nuclear warhead. We know he remains operational. He is the single most dangerous enemy of our country, Target Number One without so much as a close second. And if we don't take him off the battlefield, a whole lot of innocent civilians are going to pay the price."

After a final pause, he concluded, "So make this job count."

4

Wilmington, North Carolina, USA

"Don't lie," Olivia said. "I know your work trips mainly involve sipping Mai Tais and staring at the local women."

Reilly tried not to cringe. "If you knew about the hellholes we go to, you wouldn't be worried about other women—"

"I'll bet every raid has a beautiful woman being held hostage by Libyan terrorists, completely at your mercy, breathless at the sight of you."

"Only the once. Lucky me."

"It's okay," she assured him. "I don't care where you get hungry, so long as you eat at home."

He smiled at this, then chuckled.

The bench on which they sat was solid and unyielding, its dark wood smooth from years of use, reflecting a subtle sheen under the soft overhead lights. He ran a palm along the rich wood to take her hand, and they intertwined their fingers as he watched her.

Reilly hadn't tired of Olivia Gossweiler since they started dating, and thought he never would. Her chestnut hair was styled in a neat bob that framed her face just below a soft jawline, her warm and inviting hazel eyes locked onto his. They sparkled with a lively personality that exemplified everything he loved about her.

He said, "Trust me, Liv, the only thing I'll be craving out there is the flight home."

Olivia leaned closer, her voice softening. "You're always so focused on coming back in one piece. Sometimes I wonder if you ever think about what it does to you—what it takes away."

He hesitated, caught off guard by the shift in her tone. "What do you mean?"

"I mean, you're out there patching up your teammates, making sure everyone survives. But who's looking out for you?"

"Everyone looks out for me. I'm super lovable."

Her gaze intensified. "I know you think you're tough. I do, too. But you're a healer before you're a warrior, Reilly."

That was the exact opposite of priorities for a special operations combat medic, he thought, but said nothing as she continued.

"You've been doing this job long enough, and I'm glad it's almost done."

The faint murmur of voices drifted from nearby, mingling with the occasional echo of footsteps on the polished floor, creating a rhythm that was both comforting and slightly unnerving in its constancy.

"Me too," he said. "I've been counting down the days since we decided I'd get out. But look on the bright side: the job brought me to you, didn't it?"

She released a tittering laugh, then tried to suppress it as the sound echoed down the muted beige walls of the corridor.

In reality he'd thrown himself on her before his teammates entered the room with guns blazing during an emergency hostage rescue, and their first real conversation had been on the bench of an MH-6 helicopter spiriting them between the peaks of Libya's Green Mountains.

When asked how they met, of course, they couldn't exactly describe such an inauspicious and classified beginning for a budding romance. Instead, they'd settled on the story that a mutual friend had introduced them.

Olivia composed herself and asked, "Do you remember what you said to me on the helicopter?"

"Sure," he said matter-of-factly. "I profiled you as an aid worker. Said you probably own more than one pair of BIRKENSTOCK sandals and consider granola a major food group. I mean, now I know you actually wear Tevas, but I was right about the granola and you can't take that away from me—"

"That's not what I mean. You told me to see a psychiatrist when I got back, that with trauma the hangover comes later." She lowered her voice as a suit-clad man hustled past, the heels of his dress shoes echoing down the corridor. "And you were right."

"Of course I was. I wouldn't tell anyone to start therapy if I wasn't in it myself."

She gave a slight nod. "Whatever you're going over there to do, it's going to be tough. I don't know who's taking care of you when you're gone, or if anyone is at all. But as soon as you're home, that job is mine and mine alone. I've had enough to unpack from being a hostage for one week. You've seen a lot more than I have or ever will, and we've both got a lot of healing left to do. We're going to get through it together. Just come back to us in one piece, okay?"

Reilly's gaze dropped to her stomach, then rose back to her eyes. He'd been elated ever since she'd shared her news, knew at that moment that his life had been inexorably changed for the better. The reality of what "us" meant now weighed on him more than ever. There was more at stake—more to fight for, more to return to—provided he could make it back alive.

He almost jumped when the door beside them swung open, and a young female clerk stepped into the hall and spotted them.

"Reilly and Olivia?"

They stood in unison and she gestured for them to enter. "It's time."

She vanished inside as Olivia looked at him and shrugged. "Here goes nothing."

And while today's modest festivities were and would forever remain hidden from their parents—and Senator Gossweiler in particular—right now, Reilly was looking forward to the coming minutes more than anything else in life.

He smiled and cocked his elbow. Olivia slid a hand around his arm and together they strolled past a brass plaque beside the door that read *CITY HALL WEDDING CHAPEL*.

5

Moultrie, Georgia, USA

Worthy jammed the flat end of a pry bar beneath the edge of a rotted plank, straining against the resistance as he worked it free from the weathered fence. The wood groaned in protest, splintering under the pressure. He shifted his grip, pushing harder, inch by inch, until the plank began to give.

The cool Georgia morning air brushed against his face as he worked. March in Moultrie meant the earth was beginning to warm, but a lingering chill still clung to the air. Wild grasses swayed gently under the breeze, interspersed with patches of clover in the field behind his farmhouse. He'd purchased the home from his parents, who'd practically sold it to him for a song. It was one of several such structures on their sprawling property, the rest of which were used to host guests for his father's services as a hunting guide.

Repairing the fence was physical, grounding work—something to keep his hands busy while his thoughts wandered through the uncertainties ahead.

With a final grunt, Worthy wrenched the board free, sending a shower of decayed wood fibers to the ground. He tossed the plank aside when a flicker of movement caught his eye. He straightened up, the pry bar in his hand, and turned to scan the field beyond the fence.

At first, it was just a shape in the distance, barely distinguishable from the shadows cast by the rising sun. Then it came into focus—a deer, limping across the open field. While it had already shed its antlers, he could tell from its size and build that it was a mature buck. It dragged one of its hind legs, each step a slow, labored effort, the animal's body trembling with exhaustion. Dark smears along its flank confirmed for him that it had been hit by a car, probably along the county road.

He lowered the pry bar to the ground and removed his work gloves, tossing them atop the rotted board as he considered the 1911 pistol on his belt. Two hundred meters separated him from the wounded deer, and he gave a weary sigh as he began the trek across the field. Worthy had grown up hunting, although he'd given it up entirely around the same time his career dictated the pursuit of human quarry. He saw enough killing on any given mission to last a lifetime, and now had no intentions of ever killing another animal.

But doing so was better than letting the buck suffer any more.

He completed a few paces before the deer collapsed, its ribs heaving in the morning light. Worthy picked up the pace, determined not to draw this out any longer than necessary for his benefit as much as the buck's, and then his phone buzzed in his pocket.

The vibration broke his concentration and he slowed, slipping the phone out to see the name on the display. He decided to let the call go to voicemail and found himself answering it instead, bringing the phone to his ear.

"Speak of the devil," he said, forcing himself to keep walking. "I was going to call you today."

A woman responded, "Good timing, then."

Worthy had been enamored with Jelena Bradić since meeting her on the job in Serbia—technically through the mutual acquaintance of a black market arms dealer, although that particular individual's remains were currently at the bottom of the Sava River.

He continued, "I've got some time off. Thought we could get together."

"I'm in the middle of my recertifications. Maybe in a few days."

"Your place or mine?"

"The Ritz in Tysons Corner, if you can make it up here."

"I'd love to," he replied. The relationship between him and the beautiful CIA officer had been casual, to say the least. It was one of two secrets he'd kept from his team—the other was his hobby of poetry—but unlike poetry, for which Cancer would give him no small amount of hell if he ever found out, Worthy was uncertain why he never told them about his relationship.

Fear of failure, perhaps.

Worthy continued his slow, measured pace across the field, keeping his eyes on the animal. "One more thing. I'm...I'm retiring next month."

There was a pause, and he could hear the shift in her tone when she finally spoke. "Your choice?"

"Yes and no. I'm not dreading it, I'll put it that way. I was thinking maybe we could get out together. Or, you know, close to it."

The words had spilled out more freely than he'd expected, and when silence followed he hastily added, "Or at least see each other more often."

Jelena's voice softened, but there was an edge to it, like she was choosing each word with care. "Worthy, I don't know what I'd do if I got out." Another pause, this one stretching painfully. "And I'm not sure I want to find out."

"Okay then," he said, feeling his jaw clench.

"Okay."

Worthy came to a stop at the buck, its labored breathing a harsh, wet rasp that cut through the quiet. Its tawny coat, once majestic, was streaked with dirt and darkened by blood, the fur clinging tightly to ribs that heaved with every shallow breath. Three of its legs twitched against the ground in a futile attempt to rise. The fourth lay twisted at an unnatural angle, its joint swollen and bent where the impact had shattered bone.

"So," he asked hopefully, "I'll see you in DC?"

Another pause, this one longer. The buck tried and failed to lift its head, eyes rolling toward him with a frantic, desperate edge.

Jelena answered, "You know what, I'll probably be too busy."

Swallowing hard, he said the only words that came to mind. "I guess this is goodbye, then."

"It is," she said resolutely. "Goodbye, Worthy."

Worthy put the phone away, his palm finding the grip of his 1911 in its holster. He closed his eyes briefly, felt his heart thudding.

Then he opened his eyes and drew the pistol in a smooth motion, locking eyes with the deer.

With a final, quiet exhale, he whispered, "Sorry, brother."

6

Phoenix, Arizona, USA

Ian took a sip of scotch and set his glass on the small table beside him, the ice cubes rattling softly.

The living room was a sanctuary of quiet reflection, bathed in the warm, flickering glow of the fireplace. The flames danced gently behind the iron grate, casting shadows that wavered across the room's carpeted floor. The heat from the fire had settled into the space, creating a cocoon of warmth that contrasted with the cold Arizona night.

A gravelly voice asked, "So what do you really want to talk about? I know by now I'll only get that if I start feeding you scotch."

Ian looked at the man in the recliner beside him.

Grant Greenberg was more well-known as "Mad Dog," a moniker he'd earned in Vietnam. His face was weathered, the lines etched deeply into his skin like a roadmap of conflicts and hardships. And his eyes, though softened by age, still held a sharpness—a piercing green that reflected the flickering firelight.

Ian had grown up in the shadow of this man, his father, although the number of people who made the connection between their last names lessened as time went by.

"My program," Ian said, "is getting shut down. I'm about to be force-retired from the Agency."

His father made a soft grunt. "I don't suppose this would have anything to do with that article I read in *The New York Times*?"

"It would."

"Damn," he said. "Didn't think I saw you on that cover photo."

"You didn't. I was at a second objective."

"Couldn't have been more important than stopping the warhead, I imagine."

Ian considered how to address that veiled inquiry for further information. He had no need to keep secrets from his dad, and the walls surrounding them were a testament to that.

A shadow box displayed a collection of medals—Silver Stars, Bronze Stars, and four Purple Hearts among them, along with a slew of plaques from Special Forces.

The only indication of his father's later service in the CIA's Ground Branch program came in the form of framed photographs: images of him with men whose faces were blacked out, the backgrounds unspecified locations ranging from jungle to desert, and one of a much older Grant Greenberg shaking hands with Afghan tribal leaders shortly after 9/11.

Ian said, "I was with a couple other guys going after the mastermind of that nuke theft. And we got him—or at least, we thought we did. Turned out he was disguised as a bodyguard and made it out."

He hesitated, then added, "And now we're about to go after him for real."

His father sat up, hands propped on the armrests of the recliner, the veins prominent under the thin skin. "How can I help?"

"You can't. Not with the mission, I mean."

Grant rocked back in his recliner. "And yet, here you are."

"Because I don't know what to do next. I always figured that my program would be shut down at some point, or that I'd be rotated out of it. But I planned on continuing on as an analyst. Now the CIA's getting rid of us for good, and I don't even have that."

His father drew a long breath and sighed before he spoke.

"I should've known you'd be an intel guy. Since you were a boy, you were...relentlessly inquisitive, is the way I used to put it. Hounded the hell out of me to explain how everything worked, made your mother and I read you so many books our eyes bled. When you were older you wanted all the war stories, too."

"So?"

"So right now, you need something else to put your mind to. Because those wheels aren't going to stop turning."

"But no three-letter agency is going to hire me—"

"Who said you have to go back to alphabet soup? Plenty of jobs to be had outside the government. Public sector, private sector, consulting work, you name it. What's wrong with that?"

Ian felt himself smirk. "Dad, when you've hunted a nuclear warhead, it's hard to settle for a corporate job."

There was a clank of ice as his father lifted his glass without taking a drink from it. "I know that the job is more important to you than anything else, at least right now. But the Agency leaves everyone behind at some point, not just you. And intel's not going to keep you warm at night during the decades you'll have left. Neither does any of this shit." He waved his glass to indicate the relics of his military and Agency service on the walls, the amber liquid catching the light from the fire. "Not an hour goes by that I don't wish your mother were still here, God rest her soul."

His father set his drink down with a thud, the sound barely resonating before he continued, "Son, it may be time to think about settling down."

There it was, Ian thought, letting his gaze drift toward the fire. The demand for grandkids was never stated outright, but when you knew how to read between the lines of Grant's advice—which Ian did, all too well—the subtext was clear enough.

Taking another pull of scotch, Ian said, "I've had a few chances to do that. But I burned all those bridges a long time ago."

"Doesn't mean you can't build a new one."

Ian nodded distantly, saying nothing until his father spoke again.

"All right, you don't care about my domestic advice. Fair enough. So let's get back to your future employment. There's only one job I want you to scratch off the list, right fucking now."

"Dad—"

"You never told me much about your Agency work. So be it. But before that, you wouldn't tell me shit about shit, and that's a dark side you don't want to go back to."

He was alluding to a period of time that Ian tried not to think about, which his father accurately assessed involved heavy work in the criminal mercenary realm.

Ian said, "I'm not that guy anymore...that guy is dead." The defense seemed hollow, but it was nonetheless the only one he could conjure at present.

His father's voice was forceful. "Then who are you now?"

"I don't know, Dad," Ian said. "I don't know."

7

Newark, New Jersey

The motel room was dimly lit, a flickering neon sign casting red light through the curtains in an erratic rhythm. A slight chill crept through the drafty window, and the heater clicked and hummed, trying to warm the space.

Cancer always drove to Newark for such forays—the police here had bigger problems to worry about than his recreational activities—and booked his rooms under a fake ID reserved for the purpose. He wasn't going to change his lifestyle just because he worked for the government now.

He sat on the edge of the bed, a takeout container balanced on his lap, using chopsticks to navigate his chow mein with a beer in his free hand. The TV played an encore presentation of *Die Hard*, a classic, and Bruce Willis was currently bursting onto the rooftop of Nakatomi Plaza with his signature Beretta. One of the greatest action set pieces in Hollywood history was about to occur, Cancer thought.

Next to him, Kayla reclined against the headboard, nonchalantly picking at her food. They'd known each other for a couple of years now—she wasn't just a face in a crowd. She worked nights at a diner off Route 21 but picked up extra cash when times were tight. Their arrangement was simple and unspoken, a blend of familiarity and distance that suited them both.

Kayla said, "You know, I could quote this entire movie by heart."

Cancer raised an eyebrow. "Prove it."

She adopted a gruff tone and spoke in unison with Bruce Willis. "'Get downstairs, all of you! The whole fuckin' roof is wired to blow!'"

"Not bad."

She shrugged. "It's the best Christmas movie ever made."

"Damn straight. Food all right?"

She dipped a spring roll into sweet chili sauce. "M&T keeps getting better and better. It's the Cadillac of Chinese restaurants."

"At least in Newark."

"Definitely. Thanks for thinking of it."

"Small comforts," he began, pausing to listen to an exchange in the next room. A man and a woman were having it out, their voices rising as an argument escalated.

Cancer grabbed the remote, turning up the TV volume. "Reminds me of childhood. They've got domestic bliss compared to my parents."

The man next door started shouting then, his voice audible even over the soundtrack of *Die Hard*. Kayla was tense now.

"You okay?" he asked.

"Fine," she said a bit too quickly. "Just brings back memories."

The man shouted a string of curses, followed by the sound of something heavy smashing against the wall. The pitch of the woman's voice turned from annoyance to genuine fear, and then she screamed.

Cancer finished his beer.

There was no shift in his thoughts—it was more like the flip of a light switch, his quiet fury igniting at once. His sense of calm had dissolved in full.

And now that it was gone, there'd be no turning back.

Bruce Willis was now unrolling a firehose, about to take his flying leap off the roof of Nakatomi Plaza. Goddammit, Cancer thought. He loved this part.

Setting his beer bottle on the carpet, he placed his Styrofoam food container on the worn comforter beside him. He glanced around for a napkin, found one and wiped his mouth, then placed all his trash in a plastic takeout bag and tied the top.

Then he retrieved his wallet, keys, and the backpack containing everything he'd packed for the overnight stay, pulling the straps over his shoulders and tightening them snug.

"Get ready to go," he told Kayla.

Cancer strolled to the doorway, disengaging the deadbolt and chain lock as he took in both the arrangement of furniture in the room and the particulars of the door construction.

The second-floor balcony brought with it a cold breeze as he closed the door behind him, its surface bathed in the red light of the motel sign. He set his bag of trash down, walked to the room where the muffled argument continued, then pounded on the door and announced, "Police. Open up."

Cancer stood close enough to the eyehole so only his face was visible, listening to a man's hushed whisper. He heard the clack of the deadbolt, and the door opened a few inches, stopping when the chain lock went taut.

Cancer could only make out a glimpse of the figure on the other side, but in this case one glimpse was enough.

The man was over six feet tall, a thick and tattooed forearm gripping the edge of the door like it might snap under his hold. A sliver of his broad chest strained beneath a flannel shirt, a disheveled beard hanging low on his jaw. His eyes—bloodshot with alcohol and probably one or more other choice substances—darted over Cancer's civilian clothes, registering that this new entrant to his night was no cop.

Cancer smiled. "Hey."

Then he wheeled away and drove a hard mule kick into the locking side of the door. The chain snapped under the force, propelling the panel of solid-core wood into the man's face.

The door ricocheted back and Cancer shouldered it open to find the man had been knocked on his ass, dazed, a gash across his forehead— freebie concussion to get this started. His wife and/or girlfriend screamed in the corner, a detail noticed and forgotten as Cancer dragged over the room's heavy chair, using it to prop the door open before striding over to deliver a hard stomp to his adversary's sternum that knocked the wind out of him in one wheezing gasp.

Now it was time for the fun part.

He savagely kicked the man in his ribs, causing him to roll onto his side. Cancer stepped over him and grabbed the nearest wrist. With an ironclad grip, he wrenched the man's thick arm behind his back, twisting it upward at a sharp angle. A low, guttural groan ensued as the pain of straining tendons tore through the man's body.

"Get up," Cancer instructed, though words were fully redundant at this point. Now it was a simple matter of leverage, which he applied generously, angling the arm in his grasp until the man had to scramble to his feet to relieve the pressure. He struggled upward against the pain as Cancer kept the angle tight, applying even more pressure—he could snap the man's wrist like dry wood—but instead, he maneuvered to shift the man's weight as he forced him the rest of the way upward.

Then Cancer drove the man forward, keeping the arm locked behind his back and stepping in close, his shoulder pressing into the man's broad back, using his own body to keep his victim moving. Every step was fueled by momentum as the man stumbled in front of him, unable to resist the force driving him toward the open door.

The man's feet barely had time to find purchase before Cancer shoved him harder, propelling him across the threshold. They crashed out onto the balcony, and with a final surge of power, Cancer rammed him forward. The man's chest slammed into the steel railing with bone-cracking force. The impact was brutal—Cancer felt the give in the man's ribs beneath the pressure, a sickening yet satisfying crack that caused him to double over the edge.

Cancer finally released the arm to grab the man's belt and the back of his collar, keeping his stomach pinned to the railing before hooking one leg around the man's shins and sweeping his legs out from under him.

He was already dead weight, and with a burst of strength, Cancer used simple momentum to heave the top-heavy man over the side with the words, "Oopsie daisy."

The former opponent was sent into an ungraceful front flip over the railing. The back of his skull clipped the concrete balcony on the far side, after which his body made another forward rotation on the way down.

Now—wait for it, Cancer thought—the man landed face-first atop the roof cargo box of a Jeep Cherokee parked below. The cargo box cracked, and its demolisher rolled weakly sideways before freefalling the short distance between cars onto the cracked asphalt of the parking lot.

Not bad for thirty seconds of effort.

"I'm calling the cops!" the woman shrieked from inside the motel room.

"Find a better boyfriend," Cancer shot back, turning to see that his own date for the night was standing on the balcony, eyes wide with horror, hands over her mouth.

"We should go now," he said.

Kayla screamed, "You psycho!"

"Relax," he assured her, lifting his shirt to expose the Glock 27 holstered inside his waistband. "If I wanted to kill him, I'd have killed him."

His well-intentioned attempt at comforting her failed. The mere sight of the weapon caused her to retreat into their motel room and slam the door, locking it behind her.

Both women were now more scared of him than they were of the man who'd just gone over the edge, an abusive scumfuck who would gladly beat the shit out of either or both of them. The disparity both alarmed and confused Cancer. He snatched his bag of fingerprint-laden takeout trash and moved quickly down the balcony, toward the stairs. A lifetime of violence had turned him into a man wholly unable to blend into normal society. And yet, normal society was all he'd have left in a few weeks—provided he didn't get killed on the upcoming mission, a possibility that now looked more and more appealing.

Was he having a crisis of identity? Cancer wasn't sure. He was only certain of one thing at the moment, and gave voice to the thought by way of muttering under his breath while taking the stairs two at a time.

"There goes my last chance to get laid before infil."

8

Charlottesville, Virginia, USA

My daughter sat across from me at the dinner table, her curly brown hair a wild halo around her face, framed by the leftover birthday decorations still taped to the walls—streamers and balloons now slightly deflated.

Langley's brown eyes were locked onto mine with a seriousness that seemed too heavy for a girl who'd just turned nine. "Why do you have to leave tomorrow?"

I paused to set my burger down, suddenly noticing how her jiu-jitsu academy T-shirt looked far too big on her thin frame. "I told you, sweetheart. It's for work, but it'll be my last trip before I retire and find a new job."

Her brow furrowed. "What's that going to be?"

"My next job," I clarified, "is to take you guys to Grand Cayman for spring break. I'll worry about the rest later. Money is no object—I married a doctor, remember?"

Laila, seated beside me, raised an eyebrow as she sipped her wine, the deep red contrasting with her green eyes and the loose blonde waves cascading over her shoulders. "You married a pediatrician, not a heart surgeon."

I glanced at my glass of water, an unappetizing dinner companion now that I'd quit drinking alcohol. "True, but you're still the one with the medical degree."

My three-month-old son Jackson, all chubby cheeks and wide, curious eyes, let out a high-pitched squeal, his tiny hands waving aimlessly. One brushed against the brightly colored plastic rings on the tray of his reclining high chair, and a ring tumbled to the floor, joining the spit-soaked bibs scattered beneath him. Rivers family dinners had never been formal, and yet were never so chaotic as they were since Jackson's arrival.

I sighed, shaking my head with a smile. "Correction," I said, "my next job is being a full-time housekeeper cleaning up after Jackson."

Langley paused to eat a fry, having already finished her second burger —both vegan patties by her own preference—in record time. She was about to have another growth spurt, I thought, and she looked at me with relentless focus. "How long will you be gone?"

"A couple weeks, give or take."

"Where will you be going?"

"Langley." My wife's voice was gentle but firm, a warning in her tone. Her hand reached out, resting lightly on mine, grounding me in the moment.

My daughter was undeterred, waiting.

"Well?"

I gave her a gentle smile, trying to keep my tone light. "A very boring place to do very boring things. And if you keep asking questions, I'll make you come with me."

Langley's eyes brightened, a small smile tugging at her lips. "I'd like that."

Laila leaned back in her chair, her gaze shifting to Jackson. She smiled softly, almost to herself, before changing the subject. "You know, I've been wondering what kind of person Jackson's going to turn out to be."

I glanced over at my son. His tiny hands continued waving aimlessly, knocking the bottle against the tray of his reclining high chair, sending droplets of breast milk splattering across the surface.

"It's hard to say," I replied, watching as he giggled at the mess he was making. "Maybe a food critic."

Laila proposed, "Or a chef with his own kitchen disasters."

My daughter looked from me to her brother, then back again. "I don't know. I see a lot of you in him, Dad. Strong. Stubborn. But a big heart."

"For his sake, I hope he takes after his mother," I said, though my thoughts were drifting.

As my wife continued to talk about Jackson's possible future—his first steps, his first words, his first day of school—my mind wandered to the mission ahead. I'd offered to quit the CIA the moment my wife told me she was pregnant. Laila had quickly told me not to, just not to renew my contract. In that moment, however, I'd been perfectly willing to do either.

But now, upon grasping the enormity of the mission ahead, I was immeasurably grateful she hadn't taken me up on my initial offer. The thought of leading this operation was terrifying, but far less so than the prospect of letting some other team leader run it. No matter how seasoned my possible stand-in could be, no one had the commitment to these men that I did, no one else had forged a bond spanning our time as mercenaries up to employment as Agency contractors. Whatever this mission would take to bring them home alive, I was willing to pay the cost.

Laila's voice brought me back to the moment. "Or maybe he'll be like Langley."

"Nine going on nineteen?" I asked. "Or maybe you're talking about him skipping a grade. Langley, are you sure you want to go straight to fifth? That's dangerously close to middle school."

"Wouldn't you?" my daughter asked.

"Langley, I know we haven't spent much time discussing my academic career. But I assure you I was in no danger of anyone ever asking me to skip a grade."

"Now now," Laila began, more for our daughter's benefit than my own, "your dad is humble. After all, he went to West Point."

I snorted. "After three applications and a year at the prep school. In retrospect it was like fighting to get into prison."

A troubling thought occurred to me then. The previous night, I'd had a dream of a ship being tossed in the waves of a cataclysmic storm. I was familiar enough with that scene, though I hadn't dreamt it since my mercenary days. It wasn't a good omen then, and was even less so now.

Langley abruptly asked, "Why did you guys stop dating in college?"

For all her charm, my daughter wasn't in the habit of pulling verbal punches whenever a thought occurred to her, a trait she probably got from me.

My wife and I glanced at each other at the same moment, each expecting the other to field the inquiry. Laila's expectant stare told me it was my turn.

"Well," I said, glancing at the plates around me. "Dinner was excellent. Who wants leftover cake?"

I rose and made my way to the entrance of the dining room—I'd clear the table later, now an every-meal duty with my wife constantly taking care of Jackson—and paused for a moment to look back at my family.

Laila was beautiful and accomplished, my daughter was a rising star at school and in martial arts, and my son, while too young to have much in the way of a discernible personality, was half composed of my genetics and therefore represented a total wild card.

Before I disappeared into the kitchen, Langley asked, "Dad, can I have two pieces?"

My wife's reply was immediate. "No, honey. That's too much."

"You know what?" I said thoughtfully. "It's a special occasion. Request approved."

9

Whiteman Air Force Base, Missouri, USA

Reilly carefully unwrapped his pre-mission Snickers bar, wondering if the smell of metal and aviation fuel would affect his single greatest guilty pleasure in life.

But the first bite brought with it the smooth richness of chocolate that quickly gave way to slightly salty caramel. The crunch of roasted peanuts added a satisfying contrast, balancing the sweetness with a savory note, while the nougat—oh Lord, the nougat—tied the entire symphony together with its soft, airy texture.

His reverie was interrupted by David appearing beside him.

"One hour until we load," the team leader said. "Last chance to propose the bet. Everyone else is in, but we're not going to pick up the slack if you're not. I need a final answer. Remember, this affects all of us."

Reilly swallowed his mouthful of candy bar.

"I'm in."

David swiftly departed on a beeline for the other team, who stood in a tight circle beside their equipment on the opposite side of the hangar. They looked, he thought, like an Olympic bobsled crew awaiting their turn in the chute.

Even from this distance there was a measured precision in their stance as Griffin led a verbal rehearsal with calm authority. Munoz, Worthy, Keller, and Washington listened intently, immediately responding when asked a question, their expressions focused.

Turning to glance behind him, Reilly found his own team more like a group of street kids who may or may not have been vaguely considering a pickup game of basketball at some point in the day.

Cancer was sprawled beside his gear bags, a boonie cap pulled low over his eyes as he slept. Hass was sitting up, at least, cross-legged and listening to earbuds as he arranged solitaire cards on the polished concrete floor. Ian was swiping through his Agency phone, looking like any other civilian doom scrolling through social media although he was undoubtedly reviewing mission data—for the intelligence operative, there was no other option.

Reilly directed his gaze forward, taking another bite of his Snickers. They weren't in Nevada for training, not anymore. This was the real deal, or would be soon, and the climate-controlled hangar in which he stood was at Whiteman Air Force Base in Missouri. It seemed an unlikely location from which to launch a covert operation. But there were two very good reasons for its use, and both loomed before him now.

To the uninitiated, the pair of B-2 Spirit stealth bombers could practically be mistaken for alien craft.

Each plane was shaped like a 52-meter flying wing, with a boomerang shape and an eerily flat profile save for the subtle bulge of the cockpit rising smoothly from the center and extending into the bomb bay. Four low, wraparound pilot windows near the nose were about the only indication that human hands were required to fly them at all, every curve and facet seamlessly integrated into the aircraft's sleek, predatory design.

The angular, bat-like silhouettes of the B-2s dominated the space, matte charcoal surfaces seeming to absorb the light and giving the bombers an almost spectral presence.

Every exterior surface was coated in multiple layers of material designed to reduce its detectability, some absorbing radar waves at different frequencies while others reduced infrared signature. Even the aircraft frames themselves were made of advanced composite materials far less detectable than metal, and together with cutting-edge avionics, Spirit pilots could hit their targets with incredible precision in the most heavily defended areas in the world.

Only 21 of the aircraft were built, with twenty remaining after a sensor issue caused one to crash on takeoff.

That meant Reilly was now looking at ten percent of America's remaining B-2 fleet.

"You okay?" Ian asked.

Reilly hadn't even heard him approach—the deep, rumbling hum of ground power units precluded that, providing electricity without draining the aircraft's internal batteries.

"Yeah," he said, taking another bite of his Snickers and speaking with his mouth half-full. "Yeah, sure. Just, you know, thinking. We've done six training jumps out of these, and I still can't believe the Threshold Blade program exists."

"I can," Ian said, sounding unimpressed.

"Well, I mean...but, why?"

The intelligence operative shrugged. "Because the B-2 is specialized to the point of irrelevance. Think about it: two missions in Kosovo '99, three nights during the invasion of Afghanistan and 11 in Iraq. Three missions in Libya, two against the Gaddafi regime and another one against ISIS camps in 2017. Add it up, man. Compared against the price of the fleet, each real-world bomb drop has cost about as much as a single aircraft. That's two billion with a B. Is it any wonder they looked for alternate uses?"

Reilly said nothing, and for a moment they both watched the pilots moving methodically around the bombers for their pre-flight checks. Maintenance personnel worked in sync with the pilots, inspecting the aircraft's undercarriage, testing control surfaces, and verifying the integrity of the bomb bay doors.

Ian abruptly added, "Besides, the US either has or soon will have high-altitude long-range stealth drones that can deliver munitions without risking an aircrew. I wouldn't be surprised if there are other programs similar to this one."

The medic couldn't imagine what other efforts could possibly rival the one they were talking about.

Threshold Blade began as a compartmentalized test program that found a new use for the pair of B-2 Spirits before them, which stood alone with a few key modifications that enabled their use in military freefall operations.

Nearly all of these centered on converting the bomb bay into a space for jumpers, to include a system that could pressurize and depressurize a space originally designed to hold munitions—of particular importance when the flight time between takeoff and jump would total fifteen hours—and pre-breath consoles supplying oxygen throughout the flight. But the most expensive components were new drop doors that, rather than exposing the entire bomb bay to the open sky, would give the jumpers space to safely exit.

And before Reilly and Ian could further their discussion, David was on his way back from the other team. He made a beeline for them before stopping to ask, "What are you guys talking about?"

Reilly waved his remaining Snickers toward the B-2s. "The program that modified these birds."

"Meh," David said. "It's nothing new."

"It kind of is, though."

The team leader crossed his arms and replied, "Look, Jack Singlaub re-rigged the bay door of a B-26 and did the first jump from a bomber. Then he increased the length of his freefalls until he was pulling a few thousand feet off the ground, and boom, the HALO jump was born. That was during the Korean War. 1951, I think."

"But..." Reilly began. "But these are *stealth*."

"Whatever you got to tell yourself, brother."

Ian asked, "Did they take the bet?"

David glanced over at Griffin's team and back again, then nodded.

"Sure did. Whichever team positively identifies the target gets a case of beer. Per man."

Reilly still felt uneasy about sending both teams to a pair of geographically disparate objectives. There would be no hasty reinforcement of one another if shit hit the fan.

But at the moment Reilly wanted to think about anything and everything but his teammates' chances of survival and, as a close second, his own.

He finished his Snickers and crumpled the wrapper. "I'm going to throw this away and take a leak. Peace."

After a short walk, Reilly pushed open the restroom door, stepping into the dimly lit space. The sound of the GPUs outside faded slightly as the door closed behind him.

To his surprise, a man was washing his hands at the sink—one of the B-2 pilots, his flight suit entirely devoid of patches.

"Which team are you flying?" Reilly blurted.

"Griffin's," the pilot replied. "That you?"

"No, I'm with Rivers. Good luck out there, though."

"You too."

Reilly moved past him to the urinals, unbuttoning his fly as he said, "I don't know how you guys can do this."

"Do what?" the pilot asked, ripping off a paper towel from the dispenser.

"Fly round trip from Missouri to the Middle East and back again with midair refuelings and no pilot rotations. I've stayed awake for 30 hours on missions more than a few times. But I wasn't in a seat the whole time flying round trip in a bomber, either."

The pilot sounded incredulous. "They don't give you Go Pills?"

Reilly's flow stopped abruptly, his eyes narrowing.

"Modafinil," the pilot clarified.

"Is that like Dexedrine?" he asked, hastily buttoning his fly.

"Newer. Better."

Reilly moved to the sink. "I'm a medic. Can you tell me what it does?"

"What *doesn't* it do? Let's see, after a half hour or so you'll be more focused than you've ever been in your life. A few hours after that and any amount of coffee will feel like a downer. Twelve hours later it's starting to wear off, and you take another one. Rinse and repeat. But the comedown is hard. We come off the mission, take the downers they give us, and crash for two, maybe three days. It's heavy, but the only way we can do our jobs."

Reilly dried his hands, then took a step closer and lowered his voice. "You have any more of that stuff?"

10

25,000 feet over South Khorasan Province, Iran

Worthy sat on the cold, hard floor inside the modified bomb bay.

The low hum of the B-2 Spirit's engines was a constant reminder of the stealth platform slicing through the night over enemy territory. The bay's modification from one designed to cradle deadly ordnance into an improvised troop compartment had resulted in a cavernous space lit by red lights that cast an ethereal glow across the interior and, at present, Brent Griffin.

The team leader was positioned beside the closed jump door in the bottom of the bay, wearing full combat gear designed for the high-altitude mission. His black, non-reflective thermal jumpsuit was made from flame-resistant fabric, its seams reinforced to withstand the brutal conditions of the fall. Over the suit, he wore a tactical vest rigged with essential gear—magazines, grenades, medical supplies—along with a suppressed HK416 rifle strapped barrel-down to his side. This equipment was secured in part by his parachute harness, although the bulk of his gear was in the gargantuan rucksack strapped from waist to knees.

A matte gray helmet covered his head and an oxygen mask most of his face. A hose extended from the mask to a portable oxygen tank strapped to his chest, vital for surviving the thin air at 25,000 feet. His aerodynamic helmet was equipped with a night vision device currently flipped up and away from his eyes.

Griffin suddenly held up his index and middle fingers—two minutes from drop—then extended his arm to his side, palm up, and lifted it to shoulder height.

That motion was the command to stand up, and while there was no standing to full height in the confines of the bomb bay, Worthy rose to a kneeling position, feeling the movement of Washington behind him, checking his primary and reserve pins and oxygen pressure gauge. Worthy would have been doing the same to the man at his front if there was one—but tonight, on the last mission of his life, he'd be the first one out the door.

They'd spent most of the fifteen-hour flight seated in rigid fold-down chairs in the spartan but functional space, the walls around him layered in radar-absorbent material. Racks for gear, now empty, were tightly secured and cushioned against the vibrations of the flight, the center of the space open for movement. The team had previously breathed from an onboard system called the pre-breathe console, saturating their blood with oxygen to prevent hypoxia.

But they'd recently transferred their hoses to their individual oxygen bailout bottles, which would sustain them through the jump, or at least until they descended below 10,000 feet where the air was thick enough to breathe.

The interior space erupted with the whoosh of depressurization, bringing a sudden, cataclysmic temperature drop. Frigid air sliced through his thermal gear within seconds, accompanied by a dramatic surge in wind and engine noise and the ear-popping drop in air pressure. He could see frost forming on the floor, a dismal reminder that the real cold would begin after he exited the aircraft.

He flexed his fingers, trying to keep the blood flowing, and turned to take one last look at the rest of his team.

AJ Washington gave him a nod, followed by Daniel Munoz, and, in trail, Logan Keller. Their eyes conveyed a businesslike formality not unlike the other men of Project Longwing in the moments before a mission infil, and

Worthy thought that being assigned here had an oddly familiar quality. Both teams had bonded in blood in Yemen and Pakistan, and despite being forced to switch sides, he felt as at home here as he did beside David, Cancer, Reilly, and Ian.

Directing his gaze forward, he watched Griffin place a hand to his chest, then extend it to his side, and finally raise it in a salute-type gesture in the command for the jumpers to move to the rear.

One minute out.

Worthy tightened the straps securing the rucksack to his front, lowered his goggles over his eyes followed by his night vision device, and then shuffled forward to a strip of luminescent tape marking the one-meter threshold from the jump door. The red lighting extinguished then, leaving him to view the space in the murky green hues of his night vision.

A fast exit was critical. The instant that jump door was open, the B-2's radar cross section would go from near invisible to a blaring beacon. And as soon as the team had leapt out, the pilots had to remotely close the door and execute a complex series of evasive maneuvers across varying altitudes on their way out of Iranian airspace.

Every second the team took to spill out of the hatch increased the risk to the aircraft and its two men in the cockpit, and Worthy was determined not to be a weak link in that equation.

Griffin made a thumbs up at his side, then hoisted the hand over his head—15 seconds from drop, and the signal to stand by that Worthy mirrored before shuffling forward to the second and final strip of luminescent tape.

With a mechanical whir, the jump door lifted slightly and began sliding to the left.

The original clamshell design had been replaced with the reinforced lateral panel that opened now, splitting the belly of the aircraft with mechanical precision. Simultaneously, the metal extension of a retractable platform lowered to ensure the team was well clear of the aircraft's structure when they jumped.

A blast of frigid air surged into the bay, slamming into him with the force of a physical blow. The wind roared, an all-consuming howl that drowned out everything else, filling his ears with the sound of raw, untamed power. It tore at his gear, the straps vibrating violently against his body as if the very air was trying to rip him apart.

The temperature plummeted further, the biting cold seeping through his gloves, his suit, every layer he wore. His eyes watered behind his goggles, the green-tinted world a blur of shifting shadows and turbulent skies.

Worthy's heart pounded, the adrenaline flooding his system, sharpening his senses. He was acutely aware of the vast emptiness now yawning beneath him, the ground somewhere far below, hidden in the darkness. This was the edge of everything—of the mission, of safety, of the known world. The void beckoned, an abyss ready to swallow him whole.

He turned his attention to Griffin, whose eyes were fixed on a red LED light beside the door. In the next ten seconds it would extinguish to be replaced by a green one, and the team leader would give the next hand signal, extending both arms to his sides in what would be the final command.

The jump door was still sliding open when a shrill alarm blared—brace for impact—though the noise had barely begun when Worthy was thrown sideways, the B-2 shuddering violently and then lurching to the left. A deep, ominous boom of the impact reverberated through the bomb bay, a sickening sound that seemed to come from everywhere and nowhere at once. Worthy's shoulder slammed against the cold metal floor as the aircraft jolted and yawed. His hands instinctively grabbed for something, anything, to hold onto, his mind racing to catch up with what his body already knew: they'd been hit.

Then the entire world tilted as the B-2 banked sharply, losing altitude. The wind, already fierce, became a screaming maelstrom, whipping through the partially open bomb bay with terrifying speed, snatching at loose gear and threatening to tear apart the aircraft. A howling groan rose in volume from loud to deafening, making it impossible to hear anything else as Worthy tried to right himself and make it to the jump door, but it was too late.

"Last call," he murmured into his oxygen mask.

In a flash, the interior of the plane erupted into a searing inferno. Jet fuel, ignited by the missile's impact, surged through the aircraft, flames racing from the cockpit and devouring everything in their path. The heat was searing and instantaneous, and his last glimpse was of Brent Griffin engulfed in flames, body writhing in agony as the fire consumed him.

11

Ian hurtled into the void, the jump platform disappearing beneath him as the freezing wind tore at his body, a violent, all-encompassing force that shoved the breath from his lungs as he catapulted free of the bird.

For long seconds he did little more than try to establish a stable body position, arching his pelvis as hard as he could. The B-2 was far from purpose-built for parachutists, and exiting its modified jump door with a full combat load was far from graceful; the earth and sky whipped through his night vision, followed by a glimpse of the stealth bomber's flying wing shape as it banked in violent evasive maneuvers.

He moved his body against the chaotic forces, striving for control, for the position that would bring him stability in this unforgiving void a hair below the stratosphere. The world spun and then steadied, horizon leveling out. But the cold remained, biting deep, making his joints ache, his fingers numb even through the gloves. It was the kind of cold that didn't just sting —it gnawed, relentless, a reminder that he was plunging through an altitude where humans weren't meant to survive.

The thin line between life and death up here was a few layers of insulated fabric atop an electric-heated base layer woefully insufficient to the task at hand, and a mask feeding him precious oxygen. The rush of wind was a constant scream as he tumbled through the sky, his body a tiny speck against the vast, frozen blackness.

Ian stabilized as he neared his terminal velocity of 120 miles per hour, and then he stole a glance down to see his night vision goggles painting the scenery below in an otherworldly green. The raw, alien landscape of Iran sprawled beneath him, jagged and unforgiving. It was a stark contrast to the sterile, map-like images he'd been studying. The ground was still miles away, yet it loomed in his vision like an ever-present force drawing him in.

Scattered clusters of lights marked towns and villages, each one teeming with people completely oblivious to the covert parachute infiltration in progress. A single light flicked on and off amid the rest, this one only visible under night vision—Hass had been the first one out the jump door, and as the low man had activated the infrared strobe on his helmet. Now he was waiting, a fixed point in the chaos, allowing the others to swoop in and form up.

Ian arched his pelvis harder, straightening his legs to the extent necessary to steer himself across the wind in an oblique approach. He wasn't far now but there was no beating Cancer, the second one to jump, currently a black shadow that glided toward Hass.

Speed mattered more than precision in the initial approach, and Ian didn't flatten his arch until he was almost level with the two men. Then he edged his elbows back toward his sides, using the angle of his legs to glide toward the two men as they swelled in his field of view.

With a final adjustment, he reached out with his left hand, firmly gripping Cancer's right wrist as the sniper released his grip on Hass and edged outward to expand the center of the formation to accommodate a third man. In the same fluid motion, Hass reached over and took hold of Ian's right forearm, locking the trio together in a stable grouping while keeping the altimeters on their left wrists visible. Ian checked his now, watching the needle glide counterclockwise against the luminescent dial.

Eighteen thousand feet and falling.

There was no mistaking Reilly for anyone else on the team, either on the ground or in midair. He had a larger build, for one, to which he'd added considerable muscle mass through his hobby-slash-obsession with weight lifting. The medic's approach was effective if indelicate—he came zooming in with so much speed that Ian was afraid the formation was about to be knocked apart like bowling pins.

But Reilly slowed in the final seconds, bumping the collective mass of linked men but not dividing them as Cancer and Hass spread their grip.

That left one team member missing, and Ian saw him a moment later.

David carved through the air with the grace of an owl, effortlessly gliding downward in a pivoting arc that turned into a swooping approach toward the formation. The team leader may not have had as many military freefall jumps as some on the team, but he had hundreds upon hundreds of skydives, many of which were with a four-way competition skydiving team at West Point. He could fly circles around anyone else up here, and at the moment, he was.

Ian watched David whip a fast 360-degree turn above their cluster, remaining just beyond the outer edge of their boots to maintain his airflow, accomplishing absolutely nothing beyond showing off. But the demonstration ended in seconds as he dropped between Ian and Hass, joining the star formation as the fifth man.

Now they were united and stable, and needed only to remain that way—without a consolidated fall, the extreme winds at altitude could cause them to drift a kilometer or more from one another before it was time to pull their ripcords. The figures around him appeared as masked monsters, breathing oxygen through hoses and strapped down with an immense amount of tactical and parachute equipment yet floating on a bed of air, bodies silhouetted against the faint glow of distant stars.

And while the five of them were linked together in physical hold as well as purpose, Ian's thoughts drifted to a sixth man, present somewhere amid the remote wilderness of Iran.

Soren Malek.

His dossier was more sparse than any Ian had ever seen, though he strongly suspected the CIA knew far more than they had chosen to tell the team. There was no reason to hide the information—Malek was behind the theft of a Hatf 8 nuclear warhead from a Pakistani Air Force base, and the race to stop that 12-kiloton device from leaving the country had very nearly cost the lives of every shooter on both teams freefalling into Iran tonight.

That was all that Ian or anyone else needed to know to solidify their commitment to the operation in progress, and yet the Agency had chosen to reveal little else beyond the fact that Malek headed an upstart terrorist organization whose motives were unclear.

And, of course, every conceivable detail required to kill him.

Malek had only had two known locations, both separate compounds he would appear at with seemingly no rhyme or reason between sometimes lengthy absences to parts unknown. And while the CIA could verify which facility he was at whenever he appeared there, they also couldn't drop a 2,000-pound bomb or send a Tomahawk cruise missile within Iran's territorial boundaries without an international incident. There could be no US fingerprints on the kill, and yet the compounds themselves were far too robust for the Project Longwing teams to raid.

The solution was a precision airstrike whose ingenious delivery method couldn't be tied back to America, and that required knowing at which exact point in a given facility Malek was located. Not even the CIA could determine that remotely, although they were all too happy to provide extremely specialized equipment that their Project Longwing teams could employ to guide the strike.

That meant separate jumps for Griffin's and David's teams, both of which would move to their assigned objective and establish surveillance. Once Malek was pinpointed, the winning team would call in the surgical airstrike—hence the necessity for a JTAC on each team, and swapping Worthy for Hass—and all Americans present would begin exfil the moment their target was killed.

At least, if everything went according to plan.

If not, there was no one on earth Ian trusted more than the Americans freefalling through Iranian airspace with him, as well as those on Griffin's team now making the same infiltration 60 kilometers to their southwest.

Ian checked his altimeter to see that they were falling below 9,000 feet, the reduced altitude equally apparent by subtle changes—the air becoming just a touch thicker, the cold easing its hold bit by bit as they continued their controlled descent toward the earth.

There was another more prominent shift as well. The ground below, once a blurred patchwork of indistinct shapes from 25,000 feet, continued to sharpen with startling clarity. Features that had been little more than vague outlines now emerged in detail—roads snaking through the desert, clusters of buildings nestled in valleys, gnarled strips of jagged hills. The horizon, once a distant line at the edge of the world, now loomed larger, eclipsing the sky with ever-greater speed as the ground rushed up to meet them. No longer an abstract map, the terrain had become a living, breathing landscape they were about to set foot on.

Provided, of course, that no one had a parachute mishap in the interim.

He watched his altimeter needle crest 5,000 feet as the audible altimeter in his helmet chirped its first notification. Letting go of Cancer's arm as everyone else released their grip on one another, Ian spun 180 degrees and began tracking away. It was a clumsy process with his bulky rucksack, but one he did to the best of his abilities by sweeping his arms to his sides like retracted wings and locking his knees.

With his head angled downward, the wind buffeted him away from the center of the formation. Each of the five jumpers gained as much distance from one another as possible in an ever-expanding diameter before they deployed their parachutes.

Ian tracked for 14 seconds before his audible altimeter gave the 2,500-foot warning. Arching his back, he slowed his forward momentum and brought his arms close to his body. The roar of the wind eased as he reached for the ripcord on his right side and pulled.

A sharp tug signaled the parachute deploying above him, transitioning him from freefall to a controlled descent. As the harness tightened around his chest and thighs, Ian glanced up to ensure the canopy was fully open. So far, so good.

After confirming the airspace around him was clear, he tested his canopy with quick turns to either side, then pulled down on both steering toggles. The wind softened to a gentle hum.

Resuming full flight, he scanned his surroundings and spotted another parachute to his left, about 400 feet below. Ian steered to form up behind it, then looked over both shoulders to see two more canopies doing the same.

One jumper was unaccounted for. Ian's heart quickened as he scanned the sky until he finally spotted the missing man high above them—he must have had a slammer of a parachute deployment. But his canopy was open, and he was making tight turns to descend more quickly.

Ian directed his gaze forward, zeroing in on the parachute ahead. Its operator was making subtle adjustments to his steering, leading the team on the downwind leg of a flight pattern toward the sandy clearing of the landing zone ahead.

12

CIA Headquarters
Special Activities Center, Operations Center F2

Meiling Chen sat at her workstation in the OPCEN, her eyes sweeping over the bustling room. This was the nerve center of Project Longwing, especially during a high-stakes mission like this one. It resembled a control room from a science fiction movie, with countless screens and a frenetic energy that filled the air.

The descending rows of tiered seating stretched before her, filled with staff members buzzing with low chatter, fingers tapping on keyboards, analysts hunched over screens. Every face was tense, the air thick with the gravity of the mission's events.

Although an hour had passed, the B-2 shootdown hung over them like a storm cloud.

She'd already fielded calls from the CIA's Ground Branch Chief, Director of the Special Activities Center, and the Deputy Director of Operations, all of whom wanted little more than clarification of her initial report—what else could they do? The National Security Council was already in damage control mode, preparing a response for the inevitable victorious announcement from the Iranian regime.

Her gaze came to rest on the central screen at the front of the room, currently depicting satellite imagery of their area of operations in eastern Iran. The bird's-eye view of the landscape was dotted with navigational checkpoints of ground routes, green rectangles of parachute landing zones, and dotted flight paths for the infiltration aircraft, one of which had already circled out of Iranian airspace.

The line marking the other plane's journey halted abruptly at the exit point.

Chen had occupied this desk over the course of three previous missions, although when she thought back over the untold memories of planning, execution, and post-mission analysis, all that stood out were the tactical crises. Of which there had been many.

The greatest of these mishaps was the theft of a nuclear warhead, and stopping it had been a dizzying high point that would be surpassed by no other save, perhaps, the death of the mastermind behind the operation. Up until the shootdown, she'd fully expected that triumph to occur within the week, and now the prospect was eclipsed entirely by the death of two Air Force pilots and five CIA paramilitary contractors.

Not to mention, she thought, the loss of a $2 billion stealth aircraft in what would soon become an international media debacle.

Down the tiered seating, Lucios called out, "Preliminary report just came in. We've got some details on the B-2 shootdown."

"Let's hear it," Chen said as the rest of the staff fell silent. She was already dreading the prospect of what was to follow. By now they had, of course, speculated a full range of possible explanations.

And given the CIA's exhaustive accounting of Iranian military assets and their exact location on an ongoing basis, to say nothing of the precise mission planning to ensure that the B-2's technology and flight path would evade every air defense asset capable of detecting it, the list was perilously short.

It was possible that Iran had developed a new, advanced passive radar system that leveraged the signals from other sources instead of emitting one itself. Or, even less plausible, a local air defense network incorporating radar, infrared, and optical sensors with an AI-driven data fusion capability. It would have to prioritize low probability of intercept radar profiles such as the fleeting signature of a modified bomb bay door opening, which was possible at least in theory.

But any new Iranian technology would have had to be developed or obtained while kept completely offline and untested to avoid detection by Western intelligence services, which left perhaps the most troubling possibility of all: an intelligence leak.

Lucios scrolled through the report and began, "The B-2's onboard system transmitted the lock-on data seconds before the impact. It was engaged by an S-400."

The room went still.

Chen was familiar enough with the nomenclature. The S-400 was one of the most advanced mobile long-range surface-to-air missile systems in the world, capable at least on paper of detecting and engaging a B-2 during a parachutist drop.

There was, however, just one problem.

She said, "What is a Russian S-400 doing in Iran? How could we have missed that?"

Lucios shook his head, still focused on the report.

"The DA assesses that the only explanation is a covert acquisition. Russia was likely seeking to bolster its allies' defenses without direct confrontation with the West, and to avoid provoking further geopolitical tensions they probably supplied the unit as one of several sent in multiple shipments with false labels. All components would have gone through multiple intermediary countries to mask their origin, and were assembled later at Iranian military facilities."

Chen frowned. "Every indication we had was that Iran was focused on upgrading their existing systems, not acquiring new capabilities. Their military drills and routine maintenance have backed up that assertion."

"Correct, ma'am, but the report speculates that could have been part of a counterintelligence campaign. Any incoming S-400s would have been kept offline during transport and setup. No electronic emissions, no chatter. If so, there was nothing for us to pick up. The launch vehicles are roughly the size of a semi and just as mobile, so they're not difficult to hide from satellite surveillance. Iran must have chosen to deploy them away from the fixed sites we've been monitoring. Without any human intelligence to contradict our existing collection methods, there's no way we could've known."

Chen leaned back, her fingers tapping the desk, her eyes fixed on him. "How could the air defense operators have achieved a lock so fast?"

"The S-400 is built for this," Lucios said, voice steady. "It has anti-stealth UHF radar capable of detecting a B-2 with an open bay door. They knew what to look for, and as soon as they saw that radar cross-section, they fired."

There was precedent for such trigger-happy air defense engagements, she knew—the Iranian military had once mistakenly downed a Boeing 737 shortly after it had taken off from the largest airport in the country.

But the B-2 shootdown site was nowhere near major air defense installations, and Chen's face hardened as she processed the implications of this disparity.

"This was planned. They knew we were coming."

"Or," Lucios pointed out, "Malek knew that Iran had accepted a covert delivery of S-400s, and leveraged the same government connections that he used to secure safe haven to ensure one of those systems was emplaced within effective range of his facilities. In my assessment, that explanation is more likely than premeditation. While the S-400 was locking onto the jump door event with Griffin's aircraft, it missed the other."

He paused, then added, "I believe that if there was advance notice of the operation, both B-2s would now be down."

That was cold consolation at present, Chen thought. No one from either ground team had ever been killed on a mission, and now five were gone in a single catastrophic event.

Five more remained, all presumably alive after having successfully jumped over Iran. She wouldn't know for sure until they reached their secondary assembly area and made their first radio transmission.

And once they did, she faced the sickening task of notifying David Rivers that he and his men were now alone in Iran.

13

"Raptor Nine One," I transmitted, "this is Suicide Actual."

I released the transmit switch on my satellite handset, glancing about with my night vision to see the figures of my team in a tight perimeter across the hilltop.

Their exact placement wasn't my concern—Cancer handled security while I was setting up communications, and no one could do it better—but there was a strange, detached sense of déjà vu after reaching this same moment so many times in Nevada.

And while the cold desert air stung my face in both locations, there were a few key differences.

Dust and dry earth filled my nostrils, mingling with the faint scent of camelthorn and sagebrush. It was a far cry from the pungent juniper in the desert where we had trained for this mission, as were the distant howls of jackals.

Back in Nevada, the air had been crisp and dry, but it lacked the heavy, oppressive weight of this Iranian night. The sights were familiar—rocky hills and sparse shrubs that gave way to jagged rocks, with my night vision device casting the barren landscape in a muted green light. Here, however, everything felt foreign and menacing. Even the rocks seemed sharper, as if the landscape itself was ready to cut us down. This was the real deal. No more full mission profiles, no more practice runs. We were in hostile terrain, pure and simple.

"*Suicide Actual,*" Chen replied over my handset, "*Raptor Nine One.*"

"Infiltration complete. Time: zero one one five. Location: alpha alpha two. All men, weapons, and equipment accounted for. No enemy contact, preparing to move to checkpoint one. How copy?"

Everything prior to this had gone about as routinely as it had on our training runs, from linking up just off the landing zone to caching our parachute equipment. The 1.6-kilometer foot movement to this point had passed without the slightest indication of human, much less enemy, presence, confirming that for once, the intelligence assessments we'd based our planning off of had been spot-on.

Chen replied, "*Suicide Actual, Raptor Nine One. Copy all.*"

When she didn't immediately offer further comment, I asked, "What's the status of the other team?"

No response.

"Mayfly," I said, "what's the status of the other team?"

"*Their bird was shot down.*"

My first thoughts didn't extend to the team inside the plane. Instead I was gripped by complete disbelief over what she was telling me. The flight paths had been carefully set so there would be no air defense assets capable of detecting, much less engaging, a B-2 Spirit. And while the CIA was certainly capable of mistakes, such a critical oversight was simply beyond the realm of possibility.

I quickly struck the idea from my mind. If the other plane had been shot down, the particulars of how and why weren't my concern.

The men, however, were.

"Where?"

"*Just before the exit point.*"

"Did anyone make it out?"

"*No.*"

The last time I'd conducted this post-infiltration report was in Nevada, and my transmission had been rewarded with an order to end the training exercise. Now, both the pilots and the other team were dead.

Or were they?

I mashed my transmit switch. "How can you be sure?"

"*Because,*" Chen replied, "*the jump door wasn't fully open, and the plane came apart after the impact. The wreckage is spread across a 20-kilometer area so far, and the Iranians are in the process of recovering debris so small they haven't yet decided whether they hit a plane or a drone.*"

"If the plane came apart, then jumpers could have made it out."

"*Everyone on the team carried a satellite radio. None have been used to contact us. If you'd survived a shootdown, wouldn't the first thing you did be to notify us of your location?*"

"Doesn't mean they've had time to do it yet."

"*Be that as it may, every minute that passes without a SATCOM transmission proves my point.*"

"Maybe they're busy hauling ass to their linkup point. If I'd managed to land and knew I had two local assets with vehicles a few kilometers away, I might not bother stopping to contact you either."

Chen paused, then responded, "*Their assets stopped responding to our attempts to contact them shortly after the shootdown. They've fled the area, and for good reason.*"

"Stand by," I shot back, as if all this was her fault.

What could I do—tell Hass first? He'd potentially lost four teammates. But they were as much teammates to my men as him, and Worthy had been with us for a hell of a lot longer. And even if I could decide, should I waste the time required going man to man? Could I do this over radio, or would that be a cold and heartless response akin to notifying someone of a death in the family by text?

I keyed my team radio. "Cancer."

My second-in-command arrived and knelt at my side within seconds, moving quicker upon hearing the urgency in my voice. I relayed everything Chen had told me in the fewest words possible. Whatever time we did have was desperately needed to reach our local assets before the end of the linkup window, and every second that wasn't spent achieving that would be dedicated to this private counsel before the entire team found out.

Cancer's response to my words was first silence, then a nod, and finally, a statement.

"We can still do it."

"Do what?" I asked.

"The mission, fuckface."

"How? We're allotted five days to be on the ground, with a maximum extension of three days if we don't get positive identification by then. Malek's gone over a week without showing his face at one objective or the other. That's why we needed two teams in the first place. Losing Griffin's team just cut our odds of success in half."

He put a hand on my shoulder. "If we stuck to our original plan, sure. But we're not going to be running into buildings with guns blazing, man. It's remote surveillance and calling in an airstrike. We're on our way to link up with two local assets driving two vehicles. So we split our team. Three guys handle our target, the rest go to Griffin's."

I considered that for a moment. It was clearly the right tactical play, or would've been if I'd been able to consider the situation at least somewhat objectively. And while emotions were getting the better of me, Cancer had no such limitations—or at least, none that he was willing or able to display.

But there was one adjustment that my heart demanded more than my head.

"We're only sending two guys to our team's target. You and Ian. The rest of us go to the second."

"Why?"

"Because if the bird got shot down near the exit point, there's only one evasion corridor any jumpers could use. And while Reilly and Hass are running surveillance, I'm going to search for survivors."

"I thought she said there wasn't any SATCOM contact."

"That's why I'll need an asset and his vehicle. I'll drive the main roads in the corridor and try to raise them on FM. The survival radios can't transmit far, and our team radios aren't much better. Until I've done sweeps to try and pick them up, we can't know for sure and we're not accepting their death as a fact."

Cancer gave an amused grunt. "Do I need to clarify that you can't tell Chen, or is that obvious by now?"

"It's obvious. Get the guys ready. I'll send Chen an update about us dividing our team and break the news to our guys while we're on the move."

He vanished from my side then, leaving me to transmit to Chen.

"I need detailed information about the spread of debris by the next time I check in. The other team was supposed to travel by vehicle quite a ways before their surveillance point, but I don't want to take any chances with Iranian military activity."

"*What do you mean,*" she asked, "'*take any chances?' It's too far from your objective to—*"

"We'll transition to split teams. Cancer and Angel will cover our main target. Myself, Doc, and Rain Man will move to the second. One local asset and one vehicle per split team."

"*Malek's not dumb. He may have fled the area entirely.*"

"Maybe. But there's only one way to find out, and we're already here. This is our final strike, and I'm not going to waste it. We're continuing mission. Over."

Chen didn't reply immediately, and I heard a distant shrill wail arise to be greeted by another, then many more. The jackals were howling again.

She said at last, "*Good copy. We'll be prepared to support and standing by.*"

"Suicide Actual, out."

I packed up my satellite antenna, then donned my rucksack as quickly as I could so I wouldn't keep my men waiting. By now they were all on a knee, fully kitted up, waiting for my word to move.

"Let's go," I transmitted over our team frequency.

Hass led us out, disappearing over the edge of the hilltop as pointman. It was him I was worried about the most.

I followed him, boots crunching over sand and shale rock on a descent for the next leg of our dismounted movement. Sweeping the terrain with my night vision, I heard the footfalls of Ian, Reilly, and finally Cancer behind me. We had about an hour remaining until the beginning of our linkup window with the pair of local nationals who'd be awaiting our arrival, and three hours until they left with or without us. In the meantime we'd have 2.9 kilometers to cover—not a problem if we didn't encounter any obstacles, but still tight enough that a sprained ankle, much less enemy contact, would put us in a world of hurt.

Waiting until we reached the low ground and a relatively flat expanse of terrain, I keyed my team radio.

"All right, guys," I said, releasing a deep sigh. "I've got some really shitty news."

14

Cancer stood on the rocky incline, scanning downhill through the green haze of his night vision device. He peered into the darkness, searching for any sign of movement, any glint of metal, any shadow that seemed out of place. The hill stretched out below him like a steep, jagged descent into the unknown, its rough terrain punctuated by boulders and scrub. For a moment it seemed as if he were the only soul in this barren stretch of Iran.

But the illusion shattered when he turned to face the slope and found his team moving steadily uphill, each man pulling himself up over rocks and boulders. Their forms were mere shadows against the terrain—no accident, as the infiltration was planned for a night with zero moon illumination to conceal the twin aircraft as much as the jumpers exiting them. Now that his team was on the ground, the profound darkness continued to work in their favor. Stars formed a glimmering panorama above, but couldn't penetrate the black void of the landscape. His teammates would be near impossible to spot from a distance even with good night vision, although that visual stealth was belied by the nonstop stream of whispered communications over the team frequency.

Hass transmitted, "*Hundred meters to the crest.*"

"Good," Reilly replied. "*We'll be lucky if no one breaks a leg climbing up this shit. And this'll be the last easy thing we'll do all mission.*"

"It sounds like you're doubting the plan," Cancer noted, bringing up the rear of the formation as he followed the medic's path between boulders.

David paused to brace himself against a boulder, his breath heavy in the cold night air. *"The plan's the best we can do under the circumstances."*

"I get that," Reilly continued. *"But splitting up our team puts everyone under a lot more risk."*

Normally, the team frequency would be near silent when they were this close to a linkup with local assets—a critical juncture where danger loomed as large as the potential payoff. But after the loss of Griffin's team, the net remained alive with almost nonstop back-and-forth ever since they'd stepped off from their last assembly area.

It was normally Cancer's prerogative to shut down any unnecessary conversation. Instead he let it go, adding his voice to the fray for one simple reason: if the guys were arguing and talking shit over the radio, they weren't stuck in a mental and emotional death spiral over the B-2 shootdown and all that it represented.

He transmitted, "We're not being paid to do half the job. The other team can't cover their objective, so it's on us. Simple as that."

Ian responded after pulling himself atop a rock slab, *"It's as simple as that as long as we don't get fucked in the process and double the number of US casualties."*

"So Malek should get a free pass? After the rest of our guys got killed?"

"The rest of our guys?" David shot back. *"Some of them, maybe. Until I get on the ground in the evasion corridor and try to raise them on comms, we're not declaring that team dead. Or any one of them, for that matter."*

No one would argue that point, Cancer knew, and for long moments all he heard from his team was the scrape of boots and gear, punctuated by the occasional grunt of effort as they navigated the jagged rocks and boulders on their way uphill.

But the conversational pause was too much for Reilly to bear for long. *"And I'm with you on that. But you taking off by yourself leaves a pair of two-man elements out there alone, and one of them won't have an asset or a vehicle because you'll have taken it in the search."*

Ian asked, *"Would you prefer we leave any survivors to fend for themselves?"*

"I'd prefer if we took the whole team to search for them."

There was a brief pause before David pointed out, "*So would Malek.*"

"*Seventy-five meters to the crest,*" Hass transmitted.

Cancer adjusted his grip on his rifle as he climbed. "The decision has been made. We've got two objectives to cover, so we pull double duty."

"*Triple,*" Reilly interjected.

"What?"

"*Triple duty. Suicide's taking off on his own, and that's a third line of effort—*"

"I don't care. Whatever. Shut up. Point is, we've only got so much time on the ground. We take our eyes off one objective and we could lose Malek. We don't go hunt for survivors from the shootdown and we could be leaving our guys to die alone. We have to do all of it at once."

Ian paused atop a boulder, turning to help Reilly up as he transmitted, "Suicide, you really think some of them might have made it out of the bird?"

"*For all we know,*" the team leader replied, "*that missile could've blown the tail off the bird and sent the entire team spilling out. They were almost at the exit point, so everyone was hooked up to their personal oxygen bottles and ready to jump. If it got hit ten or twenty minutes earlier, it'd be a different story. But until proven otherwise, I'm assuming all of them made it.*"

Cancer pushed his rifle back on its sling to grip Reilly's outstretched arm, then worked the soles of his boots up a sharply slanting rock face before reaching the top. The medic abandoned him to proceed forward, and Cancer paused to conduct another rearward security sweep before keying his mic.

"If all of them made it, I'm going to give them hell. Because this would be the second time we had to save their bacon."

Ian said, "*Don't forget they saved ours in Pakistan. No one on Griffin's team owes us anything, not anymore. They paid their debt in full.*"

"*True,*" David allowed. "*That being said, if they're alive I'll never let them hear the end of this. They're stocking our team room with beer until the end of time.*"

Cancer considered letting that comment slide—everyone present had enough to worry about.

But his particular brand of raw candor got the best of him once again, and he transmitted the obvious. "We're not going to have a team room much longer, remember?"

"*Shit.*" David sighed. "*That's right.*"

Another pause before Reilly said, "*Hell of a mission, this one. Last job, a shootdown, and no matter how anything else shakes out, we're coming out of this unemployed.*"

David's response was firm. "*Them's the breaks. And I daresay the future of our careers is dead last on our list of priorities right now.*"

He wasn't wrong, Cancer thought. And the first priority wasn't establishing surveillance on two objectives, or even searching for any men from Griffin's team who may or may not have miraculously made it out of the bird.

It was their linkup.

Asset linkups were a delicate process. David would make initial contact and exchange bonafides while the rest of the team remained hidden from view, taking aim in the event their assets turned against them or had unwittingly led an enemy force to the location. Only once David gave the all-clear would the team consolidate, executing a well-practiced search for tracking devices on the assets and their vehicles before loading their gear and departing.

This sequence of events existed for good reason and was never, ever deviated from; if the linkup went as planned, they'd be spirited away from the area of their infiltration, and if it went bad, they'd be stranded if not hunted, and their every move would be an emergency action or reaction. It was like watching a space-bound rocket at the moment of launch—in 120 seconds, it would successfully leave the Earth's atmosphere or be destroyed in a cataclysmic explosion, with no options in between.

And that, in a nutshell, was a local asset linkup. Every damned time.

Hass's next transmission ended the thought. "*Fifty meters to the crest.*"

Reilly replied, "*Rain Man, how are you holding up? You've been awfully quiet.*"

"*No,*" Hass said, "*I've been calling out our remaining distance at regular intervals, kind of like you would on a tactical patrol. But it seems like I'm the only one who remembers we're on a fucking mission here.*"

Touché, Cancer thought, although it was David who formally acknowledged that fact. "*He makes a good point.*"

Reilly chuckled. "*Ha. I see what you did there.*"

"What?"

"'Good point.' Because he said something insightful, but he's also our pointman, so it's like, what do you call it...a pun, I think."

Ian quickly corrected him. "Double entendre. Dual meaning of the word 'point.'"

"Enough," Cancer snapped. "Both of you. Suicide, I'm moving forward. Rain Man, slow it down and stop once you're 25 meters from the crest."

He accelerated his walking pace, legs burning in protest as he slipped past Reilly and whispered, "You're on rear security, asshole."

It was Cancer's show now—the linkup point would be visible from the top of the hill, and as team sniper he'd be the first team member with eyes-on.

The designated meeting place was an abandoned caravanserai, a ruined fortress that once accommodated caravans of people and goods making their way along ancient trade routes. For the pair of local assets that meant ample cover and concealment, but for the team it represented crumbling structures that would require careful observation for anything out of the ordinary.

Cancer wordlessly made his way past Ian, accelerating uphill so he could establish his sniper position with minimal impact to the team's pace. The worst of the rockfall was below them now—the remaining slope was an easy if steep expanse relatively free of ankle-snapping obstacles. His rucksack, previously an unwelcome burden, now felt lighter with the knowledge that he'd be able to strip it off soon.

"*Twenty-five meters out,*" Hass transmitted. "*I'm stopping.*"

By then Cancer was coming alongside David, who said nothing but slapped the sniper on the ass as he passed. The team leader's white-knuckled fixation on the prospect of survivors from the other team had been a source of mild consternation for Cancer, who knew at a gut level that no one had or could make it through the insubstantial jump door in the floor of a B-2 after a surface-to-air missile strike. Particularly, he thought, at an altitude that demanded the highest level of life support and thermal equipment for a human being to survive in the first place.

But if a few driving passes along the evasion corridor were all it took to get the split teams arrayed at both objectives, he was content to let David cling to his fantasy for the time being. That much was certainly preferable to arguing with the team leader, particularly when the rest of their men existed in a fragile state of uncertainty and grief.

Hass was just ahead, kneeling as he awaited the sniper's arrival. Cancer could see the crest of the hill neatly dividing the blackness of earth from the starry sky beyond, and scanned the uneven barrier for a divot suitable for him to establish a line of sight to the linkup point below.

He'd just located a prime prospect when the crumble of loose rock and dirt beneath his boots vanished amid the echoing booms of gunfire from the low ground beyond the hill—a sudden development that assured him beyond all doubt that no trap awaited his team at the linkup point.

While enemy fighters of one flavor or another had just tipped their hand, the only possible explanation was grim. The team, after all, could battle and kill their way out of an armed confrontation.

But the two local assets were Iranian locals vetted and recruited by the CIA for their ability to travel throughout the province for work purposes. Nowhere in their job description or career history was any military experience that would lend itself to survival in the tactical realm; that much was the team's responsibility, although their ability to make good on that arrangement only extended as far as their physical proximity to the two poor bastards who'd just been gunned down in cold blood. That meant they'd already divulged every aspect of their involvement in the CIA's plan, and in that moment killing all witnesses to their confessions became just as important to the survival of Cancer's team as not getting shot in the coming engagement.

He charged up the hill as David issued his orders over the team frequency.

"Angel, on me, we're going straight ahead. Rain Man, Doc, flank right."

No words were necessary for Cancer, whose task was the only one that wouldn't change in the coming engagement. Few things were more critical now than a sniper on the high ground, maintaining a God's-eye view of the engagement area with whatever precision fire was required to gain the upper hand. And while Cancer was all too willing to provide just that, first he had to reach the crest.

Straining to defy gravity as he made his way up the final stretch of the slope, he heard another rattle of automatic weapons from the caravanserai. At last he reached the upper limits of the hill, his mind racing with anticipation of what he had to do.

Now, the killing could begin.

Reilly ran down the far side of the slope with Hass at his side, both men taking in their first view of the linkup area-turned-tactical objective.

The ancient caravanserai now existed in a state of near-total ruin, its structures collapsed in heaps of mud-brick within a crumbling perimeter wall. A few outlying sections of wall and the remnants of smaller buildings dotted the surrounding area, along with Peugeot and Renault SUVs—the two vehicles belonging to their local assets.

The downhill race continued as Reilly made a semicircle to the right of the objective, too focused on placing his footfalls to note what was happening below save the fact that the gunfire had abruptly ended. Beyond that detail he was entirely reliant on Cancer, who transmitted a moment later.

"*I dropped two, and half a dozen or so flushed into the ruins. Looks like they're heading for a pair of trucks on the right flank, but my view is blocked by a stone wall. Doc, Rain Man, you guys had better cut them off.*"

That last order was nonnegotiable. Even if the now-dead drivers hadn't crumbled under a tactical interrogation—which they most certainly had—if any of the enemy made it out, they'd spread word that a night vision-equipped force had attempted a linkup with two drivers in the middle of nowhere. It didn't take a vast leap of logic to deduce that a military or paramilitary element had infiltrated the area. Apart from scaring Malek into hiding, the team would go from operating in a denied area to doing so while hunted. Either development would at best irreconcilably end their mission in Iran.

Reilly hazarded a glance toward the target only long enough to identify the trucks Cancer had referenced. They were stationary between the perimeter wall and a lower stretch of dilapidated dirt and stone, the tops of their cabs visible from his current position but not much else. The sniper hadn't been exaggerating when he said he couldn't obtain a direct line of sight. Both trucks were directly in the path that Reilly and Hass were to approach at the conclusion of their flanking maneuver, and it remained unclear whether either man would be able to make a shot against them from ground level.

Their run continued as they rounded the caravanserai, moving ever further down the slope at the quickest pace they could maintain without losing their footing and rolling downhill. Progress would be quicker if they abandoned their rucksacks at the top of the crest, but that would leave them too far separated from their equipment and needing to climb back up to retrieve it. The tradeoff of keeping their rucks on was worth it for that reason alone, and any hindrance to speed was mitigated by the fact that gravity was now on their side.

And, mercifully enough, the terrain itself.

A majority of this far slope was loose sand and gravel, allowing Reilly to easily avoid scrub brush and patches of jagged rock. They were moving faster than he expected, although it remained uncertain whether the pace would be sufficient for them to reach the trucks before the enemy fighters did.

But such considerations were little more than abstractions filed away in the back of his mind. The vast majority of his focus was directed to more immediate priorities, namely reaching the low ground in the most expeditious manner possible. The transition from a routine ground patrol complete with conversational radio transmissions to laser-focused tactical mode was instantaneous, an irreversible flip of a Pavlovian light switch that came at the first gunshot.

He heard Hass's footfalls beside him as both men reached the lower boundaries of the hill, setting foot on a flat stretch crossed by stream beds that had long since dried to a fine layer of sand. They were still circling the objective, now offset from the corner of the four-sided caravanserai walls.

The next step was to complete their semicircle to the target's right flank, and Reilly kept the roofs of the pickup cabs in sight as he rounded the completion of his flanking maneuver.

Cancer's voice exploded through his radio earpieces.

"Doc, get to the trucks right fucking now or you'll be too late."

That admonition served to transition the medic's movement from circling run to a straight-line sprint—he could still make out the upper reaches of two pickup cabs over the mud wall, but that was where his view ended. By the time he and Hass could reach the wall itself, the enemy would have fled unmolested. His only hope was to scare them away from the vehicles before it was too late, and there was exactly one way to do that with his suppressed weapon.

Coming to a halt and activating his infrared laser, Reilly opened fire at the top of one driver's-side window, then the next.

The crack of shattering glass seemed to have the intended effect as Cancer transmitted, "*They're heading back into the ruins.*"

That was all the notice Reilly and Hass needed to strip off their rucksacks, letting the massive packs slam into the dirt behind them. They leveraged their newfound lightness to descend on their prey as fast as they could, closing with the remains of the mud wall blocking the pickups from view.

Reilly scrambled atop the debris, staying low as he searched for the backsides of retreating men waiting to be shot.

He made out one fighter kneeling behind a pile of rocks, though as he took aim his laser and his view of the target vanished amid a blinding white glare. Reilly fired three subsonic bullets that pivoted the light source downward, where its broad spread narrowed beneath a falling enemy fighter—his enemy's rifle had a taclight attached to its upper receiver, and now that the weapon and its owner were removed from the battlefield, Reilly's night vision once again exposed the remnants of the caravanserai.

The silhouettes of men appeared as flitting shadows darting back into the ruins, and both he and Hass engaged them the best they could, the beams of their infrared lasers sweeping back and forth with momentary pauses as they fired rounds.

Then the caravanserai was utterly still as if no one had been there at all, the only evidence that men were inside coming in the form of distant shouts.

He transmitted, "Suicide, Angel, they're all inside—we're ready to reinforce your assault."

Ian came to a stumbling halt behind the Renault SUV standing between him and the caravanserai, dropping to a knee to strip off his rucksack straps while clumsily transferring his suppressed HK416 from one hand to the next.

David was doing the same thing at the Peugeot to the left, his ruck hitting the ground just before he replied to Reilly's transmission.

"Copy, we just got here," the team leader replied, breathing heavily. It was a somewhat embarrassing admission—by distance, he and Ian should have arrived on scene long before Reilly and Hass's flanking maneuver was complete. But a veritable minefield of jagged rocks and thorny bushes littered the straight-line approach, slowing their progress as they dodged countless obstacles.

David continued, "Rain Man, move to the northeast corner to watch for squirters. Doc, head for us and reinforce the assault along the southeast wall. Cancer, break down and—"

"*Already moving,*" Cancer transmitted back.

Ian peered out from the Renault, his attention drawn to dark splashes of blood on the remains of a wall before him. Beneath this grisly display was a crumpled body, clearly felled in a gangland-style execution, that had been shot up and then some. Ian assessed the corpse's physical build and what was left of his face, determining beyond reasonable doubt that it was one of their local assets.

Where was the other?

"One asset is missing," he transmitted, which was all he had time to do before Reilly came over the net.

"*In position.*"

"Assault," David ordered.

It was a spectacularly understated command given what they were about to do. Ian had glimpsed the objective on his way downhill, and any protocol of unified room clearing had no place here. Instead they'd have to remain spread out, advancing in a single front and playing the rest by ear.

Ian rose and moved forward, noting the caravanserai looked very different than it had from higher up on the hill.

At ground level the ancient structure appeared as a maze of decay, with walls that had crumbled and roofs that had long since fallen under the weight of time. Broken stone pillars jutted out of the ground like skeletal remains as he identified the main entrance through the perimeter wall, now collapsed into a heap of rubble.

But there was no shortage of entry points via gaps in the wall and breaches where mortar turned to dust, and Ian slipped toward one before glancing to either side—David was to his left and Reilly to his right, each man spaced out by fifteen meters or more. Depending on the layout within the caravanserai, Ian thought, it could be the last time he saw them until the assault was complete.

Then he was alighting on a crumbled section of wall, crouching low as he swept his HK416 across the space beyond.

Partially collapsed arches framed doorways to abandoned rooms, now nothing more than empty shells. He could see flashes of light and hear muffled shouts echoing through the structure, a sure indication that the remaining enemy fighters had taken positions deeper inside, using the rubble as cover.

He set foot within the caravanserai and moved behind the remains of a stone column, the first piece of cover among the many he'd have to move between in a cautious advance. Large stones and debris littered the ground, providing no shortage of places to maneuver between but also potential hiding spots for anyone lying in wait. The team had the advantage of night vision, but that didn't preclude an enemy fighter from waiting until he heard someone approaching before unleashing an automatic burst at near point-blank range.

And who were these fighters, anyway? There were no organized extremist groups in South Khorasan Province save Baluchi separatists, drug traffickers, and criminal gangs, none of which had any cause whatsoever to discover, much less interrogate and execute, ostensible civilian drivers this far from civilization.

By then he was making his way through a courtyard cluttered with debris, piles of stones, and wooden beams that had fallen from the upper levels. The air was thick with the smell of dust and old earth, each breath a reminder of the centuries that had passed since the caravanserai had been a bustling stopover in the desert. Now it was a battleground, every corner and crevice a potential threat as he and his teammates moved ever closer toward the ruin's heart. He caught a glimpse of David between rubble to his left, the team leader passing in and out of sight like a ghost. The clearance had proceeded so silently thus far that it was entirely possible the enemy was unaware that armed men were inside the caravanserai to kill them— and no sooner had this thought occurred than Ian's breath caught in his throat as a muffled voice reached his ears from up ahead.

Ian crossed from one piece of cover to the next, advancing quietly before pausing to listen.

He could make out the distinct tone of someone speaking with authority, issuing orders. The words themselves were lost in the echoes of the old stone walls, but the intent was unmistakable. Several enemy fighters were consolidated, and now Ian had to find their location before they dispersed.

Making another bound forward, he stopped behind a thick, partially collapsed wall and strained his ears, focusing on the sounds and scanning the grainy green image ahead. Another fragment of conversation caused him to focus on a partially intact archway leading into a darkened room just ahead, its entrance flanked by the remains of wooden beams.

Ian ducked down and opened a pouch on his tactical vest. Pulling out a fragmentation grenade, he gripped it tightly in his gloved hand. His eyes flicked toward David's last known position, then back to the archway.

This was his best chance.

He keyed his radio and whispered, "Frag out," before pulling the pin with a practiced motion. Rising just enough to clear the wall, he lobbed the grenade toward the archway. The metal sphere sailed through the air, disappearing into the darkness beyond the opening.

Ducking back behind the wall, he heard muffled shouts of alarm before the grenade exploded in a thunderclap of noise and light that split the night apart, shaking and illuminating the entire courtyard for a split second before the echo rumbled across the caravanserai.

Rising to brace his HK416 atop the wall, Ian took aim through the shockwave that rattled loose stones and debris only to find a plume of sand pouring out of the archway. It formed a wall that blocked his view entirely —until a single staggering form lunged out of the cloud like a zombie, a mortally wounded enemy fighter who had survived the blast for reasons that defied explanation. Ian thumbed a pressure switch on his rifle to send an infrared laser spearing through the night toward the man's chest, then drilled two rounds that dropped the impossible survivor in his tracks.

The grenade's echo was still reverberating when a chorus of shouts erupted to his left, followed by unsuppressed gunfire.

David's voice came over the net with five urgent words.

"*Left flank, I need support.*"

Ian rose and made his way toward the team leader, but the ever-spreading cloud of sand from the grenade blast eclipsed him and forced him to slow before he nonetheless struck his shin on an immobile cube of stone. With the view through his night vision now a uniform haze of dull green, he knew he'd be too late to help—and before he could transmit words to that effect, Cancer transmitted with a tone of supreme confidence if not elation.

"*I got you, brother. Sit tight.*"

Cancer mounted a pile of stone and descended the opposite side, then darted through the dust of the caravanserai.

His night vision reduced this ancient world to shades of green and black, among which the sand cloud from Ian's grenade hung thick in the air and blurred the ruins into a chaotic smear. Cancer didn't need perfect clarity. What he needed was a signpost directing him to David's position, and as he ran between fallen pieces of cover he got his wish in the form of glowing lights to the far left of the courtyard.

They served as a beacon to direct his charge, and he bounded from a fallen column to a collapsed building in search of a better vantage point. As he moved, another crack of automatic gunfire ripped through the air, and Cancer caught sight of his team leader crouched behind a broken stone trough barely large enough to conceal him. Three enemy fighters moved in, the lights on their weapons glaring bright against the darkness and bobbing with each step they took. Their carelessness was a mixed blessing —they were giving away their positions but blinding David in the process, and if the team leader so much as exposed himself to turn the tables he'd be gunned down in an instant.

No matter, Cancer thought.

Bloodlust was a specialty of his, and getting in position was not only the hard part but the only hard part of what he had to do next. Split-second reactions honed over countless combat missions would take care of the rest, and he made a final break for a chunk of fallen masonry before dropping to a knee beside its jagged edges.

His suppressed HK417 seemed to aim itself, its infrared laser barely visible amid the glare but nonetheless centered on the chest of the nearest fighter the instant it was activated. Cancer fired twice, and while it seemed inconceivable that he'd missed, his target dove to the side and behind an overturned cart as if guided by premonition alone. Was he wounded? Had to be, and before Cancer could so much as transition his aim to the next opponent, the searing glare of taclights being wielded in his direction forced him behind cover.

The masonry exploded with bullet strikes, spraying debris into the air. Cancer was moderately chagrined, though far from out of the fight. Suppressors dramatically reduced muzzle flashes but didn't eliminate them completely, and the flickering glow of his two fired shots may as well have been a star cluster against the pitch-black caravanserai.

And while the good news was that if they were firing at him, they weren't firing at David, that wasn't good enough. Cancer was determined not to cede a single kill to his team leader.

He aimed at the ground to his left and fired his taclight, casting a momentary gleam as bait for any overeager fighters before extinguishing the glow and lunging right to take aim off the opposite side of the masonry.

The incoming bullets were immediate, a pair of abbreviated bursts transpiring in unison as bullets whipped off the ground before the enemy had realized their mistake.

By then it was too late to save them—Cancer had the rightmost man in his sights, his infrared laser spearing a direct line between the collarbones that guided three subsonic rounds that sailed true. The enemy fighter stumbled backward in a flailing fall, and hadn't yet hit the ground before

Cancer was back behind cover, this time rising above it just enough for his barrel to clear the masonry.

The remaining man had learned his lesson and was racing behind a pile of rubble when a laser gleamed across his shoulders, the beam shuddering as the rifle it was attached to blasted near-silent rounds that sent the fighter sprawling dead just shy of his intended cover.

It was a clean engagement, and would have been a satisfying end for Cancer save one inconvenient detail: he hadn't fired the shots.

Glancing right, he found a teammate in tactical gear and night vision making his way through the debris. Fucking Ian, he thought, and eager to take point on the assault while there was still a reasonable chance of having enemy left to kill, he transmitted, "Clear. Moving."

Then Cancer was off, scrambling around the masonry and speeding past David as the team leader rose from the insubstantial cover of his stone trough. The fleeting visuals of the gunfight thus far assured Cancer that two fighters posed no threat, both of them having eaten enough rounds to the right areas to be incapacitated if not dead. There remained, however, one enemy fighter whose presence on the battlefield plagued him to no end.

He slowed before the overturned cart, transitioning his aim sideways before slipping past the edge.

The first man he'd shot at was lying on his back, a single bullet wound in his chest, rifle abandoned at his side in lieu of a cell phone that he held to his ear. Cancer was dismayed that he'd only delivered one of the two bullets he'd previously fired, and somewhat surprised that the man had managed to survive long enough to attempt a call for backup.

Rectifying both emotions was as simple as firing a pair of bullets, one into the fighter's chest beside the first and a second into the bridge of his nose. Cancer reloaded and ducked down to snatch the device—there would be no further time to search the bodies—then ended the call and pocketed the phone before darting left to continue leading the assault.

This was more like it, he thought as he moved. Now they were turning the tables on these fuckers.

Except these fuckers weren't the ones who took out Griffin's team—the CIA hadn't templated any enemy forces out here, had selected the drop zones and linkup points for specifically that reason. And while the Agency in its infinite wisdom was wrong about that detail on the other plane's exit point, the untrained fighters Cancer had just battled had no affiliation with whatever sophisticated opposition had successfully executed a high-altitude missile strike.

But cathartic release was cathartic release, and Cancer was getting his now.

He sprinted through the shifting dust and shadows, weaving between the crumbling remnants of the caravanserai and scanning for any signs of human life. The jagged edges and broken arches around him cast distorted shapes in the green glow of his night vision.

Ahead, he spotted a narrow passageway, half-obscured by a fallen stone archway and leading to what looked like a partially intact room, one of the few spaces in the ruins that hadn't collapsed completely. The archway had crumbled inward, its stones scattered across the ground, creating an uneven path leading into the darkened space beyond.

Cancer approached the entrance cautiously, instinct drawing him deeper into the space with his rifle raised, eyes scanning the dim recesses. The room was dark, with a small, narrow slit of a window high up on one wall. His night vision revealed a floor strewn with debris—chunks of stone, splintered wood, and piles of sand that had blown in over the years.

He moved with deliberate steps, the silence of his approach almost unnerving amid the distant sounds of the ongoing battle. Each footfall was measured, his senses heightened, alert for any movement or sound that might indicate an enemy's presence. He edged around a large slab of fallen masonry, the rifle's barrel leading the way, ready to fire at the first sign of a threat.

As he rounded the corner, he spotted a cluster of old wooden crates stacked haphazardly against the far wall. Their surfaces were marred with deep gouges and cracks, evidence of the weight of time and neglect. Cancer's heart rate quickened as he moved closer, his focus narrowing to the potential danger they concealed. The crates were large enough to hide a person, and he knew better than to assume the enemy wouldn't use every possible hiding spot.

He circled around, keeping his back to the wall, rifle steady. He moved past the crates, sweeping his rifle to clear the space behind them, expecting an ambush. The air was thick with dust, the silence pressing in on him as he advanced, each step bringing him closer to whatever might be lurking in the shadows.

Suddenly, a faint rustling sound reached his ears, coming from behind the crates. Cancer tensed, finger hovering over the trigger, ready to fire. He edged around the corner, eyes locked on the source of the noise.

Behind the crates, in a darkened corner of the room, he saw him. The man was cowering, visibly shaking as he shielded his head with his hands. Cancer could feel the fear radiating off him, the uncertainty that gripped him even in the darkness. He was unarmed, a fact that wouldn't have inconvenienced Cancer in the least save for a single radio transmission he'd almost forgotten.

"Hey, asshole," he said.

When the man gained the inner strength to lower his hands and open his eyes, Cancer continued.

"You our driver?"

15

The man at the wheel beside me steered with one hand while dipping the other into a bag of Pofak, Iranian-style cheese puffs. Even under the subtle glow of the Peugeot SUV's headlights reflecting off the signs on Highway 95, I could see the crumbs pouring onto his knitted wool sweater.

Sensing my judgment and/or disapproval, the driver spoke in an unmistakably Iranian accent.

"Sorry," he said over the crinkle of the foil-lined pouch as he reached for another handful. "I eat when I am stressed."

Judging by his physique, I thought, that was a fairly regular occurrence.

We were assigned two local assets for this mission, both selected for jobs requiring extensive travel across various regions. Omid Nasiri was a civil engineer tasked with inspecting and evaluating construction sites, infrastructure projects, and maintenance efforts. His duties included assessing bridges and public utilities in both urban and rural areas, and this gave him strategic access to transportation hubs, military bases, and industrial sites—ironclad excuses for him to be damned near anywhere he wanted, whenever he wanted, all with implied consent from the Iranian government.

Unfortunately for us, Nasiri had been shoved against the caravanserai wall and shot.

That left us with Shayan Farrokhi, a pudgy dork whose appearance and mannerisms were so at odds with the other men in the vehicle as to be almost comical. If I saw him in America, I'd have instantly assumed he lived in his parents' basement among a smuggler's hoard of *Star Wars* paraphernalia.

Reilly asked from the backseat, "Hey Shayan, you have any more Pofak?"

"Of course," the driver said with his mouth half full. Nudging me with an elbow as if I were his personal assistant, he continued, "Glove box."

I sighed drearily, then opened the compartment to find not one but three bags of the children's snack waiting for me. Selecting a parcel, I turned to hand it to Reilly.

The medic eagerly accepted it before ripping the pouch open, and Hass met my eyes with a *what the fuck* expression. I shrugged.

Turning forward, I gazed through the Peugeot's windshield and said, "So that's Birjand."

"It is," Shayan replied. "The largest city in South Khorasan. It was an important trade center during the Safavid and Qajar dynasties—surely you can guess why." Without waiting for a response, he continued, "A very strategic location on the trade routes between Iran, India, and the Arabian Peninsula."

I said nothing, instead taking in the sight before me. Birjand had first appeared as a distant glow on the horizon, breaking the monotony of the desert's darkness. Now that we were closer, the city began to take shape—low-rise buildings with flat roofs emerged, their architecture simple and utilitarian, and the faintly illuminated domes and minarets from mosques pierced the modest skyline.

We were descending into the valley where Birjand sprawled. The streets were almost deserted at three a.m., with only a few cars and motorbikes passing us.

Shayan said, "We are approaching the interchange with Highway 68. Where would you like me to—"

"Stay on 95 southbound," I cut him off. "Take us east around the city."

"And then?"

"I'll provide further instructions when you need them."

"I understand that," Shayan conceded, crumpling his now-empty snack bag and stuffing it in a cupholder. Wiping a hand on his sweater, he continued, "But beyond the financial compensation—which was...generous—and ten days of work, I was not informed of my role."

It was a good thing he wasn't informed, I thought.

Standard security protocol to prevent leaks continued to work in our favor: as far as Shayan was concerned, the fact that Cancer and Ian had taken the Renault SUV to parts unknown was all part of the original plan, minus the loss of their driver. They were now Split Team One, currently traveling northbound on the same highway toward our original objective. I'd have loved to convince myself that they were alone and unafraid, but there was nothing about this mission that wasn't terrifying even before the series of events that had ended in those two driving themselves without so much as a local asset to help them navigate South Khorasan Province.

Now, I simply had to pitch the requirements of the remaining Americans and myself without in any way alluding to the fact that a $2 billion US stealth aircraft had been shot down roughly sixty kilometers south of our linkup site.

Until, of course, that news hit the mainstream media—but I'd cross that bridge when I came to it.

I answered him, "My two colleagues will need to be dropped off. Then you and I will be spending a lot of time driving around."

"Why?"

"Let's just say it has to do with mobile scans, and leave it at that."

Shayan was all too happy to do so, and I reflected on the fact that a vague reference to "mobile scans" would be of far greater comfort to my driver than the reality that I'd be blindly attempting radio contact with any survivors from an aircraft shootdown.

But then the driver asked, "Where will we be driving?"

I was quiet for a moment, noting that the sound of Shayan eating had been seamlessly replaced by Reilly as he accepted the torch. "I'll tell you when you need to know."

Our driver shook his head. "Dropping men off is one thing. As is driving in the populated areas near Birjand. But if I am to be spending a lot of time driving with an American in the automobile, it will attract attention. The roads are not as empty as they used to be, and we must avoid unnecessary scrutiny from police. Certain areas here are controlled by local tribes, and if they see an unfamiliar vehicle driving through repeatedly, they will ask questions. Some roads are only safe to travel during the day. Others have checkpoints. Do you understand why I wish to know?"

That much was a fair point. And there wasn't much for me to lose by giving him slightly more information—after all, he wouldn't be unsupervised before then.

"Not far from here," I said. "In the mountains. Parvand Range."

Shayan nodded, seeming assured that everything I'd just told him was part of a well-laid plan.

I, however, was increasingly uncertain to what extent I was deluding myself about the prospect of survivors. Even if I'd been willing to write off the occupants of the destroyed B-2 as a combat loss, the immense strain of separating my team across two objectives weighed heavily on me. Removing myself from that equation in the hopes that one or more men from Griffin's team were out there, alive, despite the fact that no one had managed a SATCOM transmission to the Agency in the hours since the shootdown, took our degree of risk to a whole new level.

And yet remove myself I would, and not out of any logic or probability that I was right.

Instead, the hunt for evading Americans simply had to happen. I couldn't cope with any other outcome, couldn't even conceive of it. And while no one on my team had explicitly told me not to attempt what I was about to do, I more or less was going rogue by virtue of not informing Chen of my plans. Sometimes it was better to beg forgiveness than ask permission, as the saying went, although I wouldn't beg. Or bend.

If anyone was alive out there, I was damn sure going to find them.

"You know," Shayan blurted, "there is a legend of a hidden citadel used by exiled rulers from various Persian dynasties. According to lore, it was a sanctuary for kings and princes who fled during strife and invasions. Particularly during the periods of the Arab conquest and the later Mongol invasions. The citadel was built to be self-sustaining and hidden from the main trade routes. This place is called *Arg-e Pādshāhān-e Parākande*, the Citadel of the Scattered Kings, and some say it still holds treasures and forgotten scrolls from the ancient rulers."

Lucky Ian was in the other vehicle, I thought. He'd have derailed our entire mission by going down historical rabbit holes, and probably even been able to educate his fellow nerd on obscure aspects of Iranian history.

Reilly cleared his throat uncomfortably.

"Was there...my God, Shayan, was there a point to any of that?"

The driver gave a sly look over his shoulder. "Can you guess the reported location of the ruins?"

Hass's voice from the backseat was monotone. "Oh, I don't know...the Parvand Range?"

"Precisely!" Shayan said. "Of course the citadel's existence has never been proven, but there have been numerous accounts across the centuries. One of the earliest mentions was during the reign of the Saffarid dynasty, when an explorer claimed to have found remnants of a fortified structure deep in the Parvand Range. His writings, however, were lost to time."

"I thought," Hass began, "that you were a surveyor."

Strictly speaking, this was true—Shayan's official role was to map out land for agricultural and industrial purposes. And while the requirements for land surveys and verifying geographic data gave him the flexibility to move somewhat freely in South Khorasan Province, strategic sites were strictly off limits. Which wasn't a problem unless, as had been the case with many Project Longwing missions to date, we ended up far off the grid of our planned area of operations.

Replying to Hass, Shayan said, "I *am* a surveyor."

"Then why do you sound like Indiana fucking Jones?"

"Ah. My father was a cultural preservationist. Heritage preservation, you understand? He took me to historical locations, museums, archaeological sites, that sort of thing. I inherited his fascination with the history of my land. And local lore, of course."

"Of course," I said, desperately hoping that his previous verbal rampage would be the last one I had to endure during our partnership but suspecting that wouldn't be the case. "Too bad you're stuck with us. We've got a guy in the Renault who would give you a run for your money in talking about this stuff."

"Perhaps I will get to meet him before you go."

"Perhaps," I agreed.

Although if that were the case, I observed ruefully, it meant that my entire team was fucked.

16

Ian cinched his rucksack straps tight, the weight settling on his shoulders before he recovered his rifle and gave a final scan of the cargo space to ensure they'd left nothing behind. Satisfied, he lowered the tailgate until it clicked into position, the sound joining the faint ticking of the engine as the Renault SUV cooled in the predawn stillness.

He'd barely turned before his night vision was filled by the imposing silhouette of Cancer, who kept his voice low.

"It's almost four o'clock, we've got about an hour until twilight. We need to be in a hide site before the light catches us. Keep up."

Then the sniper was off, negotiating a steep trail snaking its way up a slope of exposed rock as Ian made a final 360-degree sweep.

They'd driven hard to reach the quarry, which Ian assessed from satellite imagery to be the best spot to abandon the Renault without drawing attention. The original plan would have seen them dropped off by local assets who would remain on call, but the bloodbath at the caravanserai forced their hand into the current arrangement.

Nonetheless, the unanticipated change of plans seemed to be paying off —the old mining site was a wide, dusty scar in the landscape whose rocky terrain and cold breeze offered perfect cover for stashing the vehicle. Within a few hours it would be as coated in sand as its surroundings and, if discovered, would leave precious little indication of how long it had been left there, or why.

Ian set off after Cancer, who was setting a near-unsustainable pace to the surface level. They had a long way to go until they reached the surveillance point for their team's original objective, and the more ground they could cover before dawn, the less they'd have to travel after sunset the following night. The daylight hours in between would be relegated to staying hidden, rotating from sleep to guard shifts and back again, and recovering from the all-night infiltration before entering the next phase of the mission.

But until they'd established a hide site, every second counted.

Ian pushed himself to keep up with Cancer's determined footsteps, his breath coming in increasingly labored gasps as they quickly ascended the trail. The weight of his gear seemed to increase with every meter covered, sweat forming beneath his gear despite the cold air burning in his lungs as they climbed higher. Ever since leaving the caravanserai he'd been dreading the arrival of the morning's first light spilling over their vulnerable forms, exposing them to enemy observation. Now, he regarded the coming dawn as a merciful end to the blistering pace Cancer had set.

But the physical strain was the least of Ian's problems.

Far worse was the mental and emotional strain of the second team's loss, a weight that closed in around him like a thick and impenetrable fog. Ian had endured losses before, and plenty of them. But none had hit him this hard, and that wasn't solely due to the number of men who'd vanished in one fell swoop.

His team had saved Griffin's in Yemen, and they'd eagerly returned the favor in Pakistan. That made Munoz, Keller, Washington, and Griffin himself far more than brothers-in-arms. They were brothers, period, and any consolation afforded by the limited duration of his working relationship with them was far outweighed by its intensity.

And that was before he considered Worthy.

Ian hadn't been able to envision working without his pointman until the teams' personnel swap had forced him to do so, and that alone had been hard enough to stomach. Worthy had always been a constant—steady, unflinching in the face of opposition, pragmatic when the odds against them seemed overwhelming. He was the kind of man who anchored the rest of them, who could navigate the worst terrain and toughest situations without ever losing his head. Ian had depended on him more times than he could count, and now...now there was a gaping hole where Worthy should be.

It would have been possible, at least in theory, for Ian to delude himself into thinking that some of the men had survived. He knew better, of course, although he certainly didn't fault David for clinging onto hope, however threadbare it may be. But the team leader's search for missing parachutists would come up empty, and when it did there would be a dreaded radio transmission declaring that all five men were dead. That proverbial nail in the coffin may well leave Ian's team worse off than they were when they heard about the B-2 shootdown, and he knew it would occur in the next 24 hours. Ian ended the consideration with the self-assurance that he'd survived worse before.

But no sooner had this thought crossed his mind than he realized he hadn't.

The coming seconds jarred him back to reality—Cancer's form, previously blending with the inky green and black shadows along the trail, was suddenly silhouetted against the horizon overhead before vanishing altogether.

"*Get up here*," Cancer transmitted.

Ian kept his eyes on the path, feeling the pressure to move fast and stay silent as he closed the distance with his legs practically screaming in protest.

He reached the top to find the sniper crouching, facing forward, and Ian dropped to a knee beside him while gasping for air.

The landscape before them was a chaotic tangle of knotted hills rising and falling in tight, irregular waves. To the northeast, the hills gave way to a single, enormous slope that swept upward, dividing the earth from the unblinking, star-laden sky in a sharp, clean line.

No lights, no movement. Just the endless undulations of rock and shadow.

"There," Cancer whispered, nodding toward the distant hill that dwarfed all others. "That's where Malek's compound is. We've got fifty minutes, tops, before we have to hole up for the day. That won't amount to much if we go straight ahead. I want to flank east to that ridge, then follow the high ground as far as we can."

Ian found the ridge in question, his gaze tracing its length and then comparing it to the surrounding terrain. Searching for better options and finding none, he said, "Straight-line azimuth through the canyons is a no-go. You're right, we drift off course to stay on the high ground. Drop off the crest to find a hide site facing west for satellite comms."

"Comms," Cancer agreed, "and the data shot."

"What data shot?"

"You can't be that tired."

Ian's shoulders sagged. "Right."

He'd completely forgotten about the fucking phone. Cancer had nearly thrown it at him after the caravanserai gunfight, and Ian slipped the captured device into a Faraday pouch without a second thought.

Aside from further delaying sleep, perhaps the worst part of having to transmit the data to the CIA was that it wouldn't result in anything useful to their current mission. At best it could illuminate some militia network for future Agency efforts, but that wouldn't help anyone in the attempt to kill Malek and get the hell out of Iran.

That thought marked the end of the momentary conferral, with Ian serving as a proxy for their now-absent team leader.

Cancer stood and bounded forward as Ian swept for threats behind them and, with a frustrated grunt, rose to continue his pursuit.

17

"The Directorate of Analysis report is in," Chen's communications officer announced, turning to lock eyes with her across the OPCEN. "It's got everything they've found so far from the captured cell phone."

The hum of tense chatter filling the room ceased at once. Rows of analysts who had previously been hunched over their screens sat erect, waiting to receive the information.

Chen replied, "You provide the facts. Lucios, I want your analysis."

"Yes, ma'am," Lucios replied, accessing the report on his computer.

The communications officer began, "The enemy force from the caravanserai was Jaish al-Adl."

This opening line caused her to recoil—the militant Sunni group operated across multiple provinces in Iran.

But South Khorasan wasn't one of them.

The fact that they were this far from their typical areas of operation didn't just surprise her, it sent alarm bells ringing for her, and apparently Lucios as well.

He interjected, "They're primarily in Sistan and Baluchistan Provinces. We've had zero reports of them operating so far north. The fact that they were is an anomaly, but paired with them forcibly interdicting our local assets at a remote location means something else entirely."

"Which is?"

"They're hired muscle for Malek. Peripheral security for his area of operations, most likely." Lucios continued scanning the report. "Which is corroborated by how they were paid—we've got a financial lead."

Chen directed her gaze to the front of the OPCEN. The central display still showed satellite imagery, although the icons had been adjusted. Gone were the B-2 flight paths and shootdown site of the destroyed bomber, replaced by two inverted teardrop icons marking the hide sites of Split Teams One and Two, both remaining concealed during the daylight hours before resuming their march toward their respective objectives.

There had previously been a shaded column snaking its way across the hills of the Parvand Range, marking the evasion corridor for Griffin's team. But after ten hours had elapsed without satellite radio contact, Chen had ordered it removed from the imagery. It only mocked the unspoken truth hanging in the air: all five men were dead.

She asked, "And does this financial lead trace all the way to Malek?"

"Possibly. Cellular network analysis provided a vector to multiple bank accounts where Jaish al-Adl received payments that were funneled through a highly sophisticated network to cover the trail. Whoever's running these transactions knows what they're doing. It reeks of a professional financial broker."

"A broker." Chen's eyes flicked toward Lucios, narrowing in thought. "Someone in Malek's core group?"

The intelligence operative nodded. "Given the proximity to his hideouts and Jaish al-Adl's likely role in providing security to insulate the network, we're well outside the bounds of coincidence."

Chen absorbed this information. It was as though the ground had shifted beneath them, expanding the scope of the mission. Financial brokers for terrorist organizations were notoriously hard to find, at least if they remained alive long enough to hone their craft.

"If we can identify the broker," she ventured, "we can take down the elements of Malek's network that would survive his death. Because unless I'm mistaken, that broker is likely responsible for the entire web of financial transactions supporting Malek's activities across Iran and beyond."

The communications officer chimed in again, "The accounts lead to a mix of businesses, charities, and shell companies. Some are legitimate, but others are outright fronts. And they're all tied back to the same financial trail. The DA has identified several of the front companies involved, but the pattern is what's critical here. The payments go back months—at least six, possibly more."

"That long?" Chen asked. "Malek's been running these operations for months without us knowing the extent of his network?"

Lucios leaned over his workstation. "We've been focused on him as the central node, but it's becoming clear that this network is decentralized, with the broker acting as a key facilitator. Malek's smart—he's keeping himself at arm's length."

Then he turned to her, his face tight with focus. "And it's not just Jaish al-Adl. We're seeing payments that touch other groups too, all low-level, mostly regional players. This broker is orchestrating the whole thing, making sure Malek's network stays operational without tipping anyone off."

Chen's gaze locked onto the satellite imagery once more. South Khorasan Province stretched out across the screen, but her focus was far beyond the topography now. Malek wasn't just a figurehead hiding in Iran; he was the centerpiece of something far more intricate.

She said, "Track every transaction: front companies, charities, offshore accounts. Trace it all. Screen our backlogs of communications intercepts from Malek's facilities for any coded references that could relate to this broker. Find out where he operates from, physically and digitally. We need his identity and current location, and we need it fast."

When she received blank stares from some of her staff, she clarified her thinking on the matter.

"The B-2 shootdown is going to hit the news any minute now, and it's quite possible that Malek already knows. If he suspects the presence of a second team—and with a Jaish al-Adl security element dead near one of his hideouts, he already might—he could alter his pattern of life or worse, vanish entirely. If Rivers's team can't get Malek, maybe I can get approval for them to go after the broker. Because at some point the Seventh Floor will order a full mission abort and hard exfil out of Iran."

In truth, Chen was surprised that it hadn't occurred already.

Not only had no one above her called off the operation, but the pressure for a successful outcome had increased. The B-2 shootdown had escalated this mission into something bigger—justifying the loss now hinged on completing the original objective, and the CIA had doubled down on that goal. If Malek was off the table, Chen needed to offer her superiors some way to achieve meaningful effects against Malek's network.

"So get to work," she concluded, watching her staff resume their flurry of activity before checking a digital display on the wall, neat rows of red numbers displaying multiple time zones from Eastern to Iran Standard Time.

The clocks ticked mercilessly, each second drawing herself, the staff, and the remaining ground team ever closer to a point of no return.

18

Reilly lay flat in the dirt beneath the rock overhang, a natural hide site on the hillside that required only some minor excavation with a collapsible shovel to accommodate two men and their equipment.

That process was completed minutes earlier, and not a second too soon with the approach of dawn. South Khorasan's barren landscape stretched endlessly in all directions, bathed in a cold, muted blue as the first hint of BMNT—beginning morning nautical twilight—crept over the horizon ahead of sunrise. The air was cool, the temperature lingering in the low fifties, and Reilly could feel the chill through his sleeves as he transmitted via his newly erected satellite antenna.

"Raptor Nine One, this is Doc. Split Team Two in position, grid to follow."

Chen replied, *"Doc, Raptor Nine One, send your location."*

Reilly relayed the alphanumeric grid identifier followed by ten digits, then waited until Chen repeated the sequence back to him before responding, "Good copy, awaiting guidance."

"No indications of the target's presence at either facility. I'll let you know as soon as there's any change. Confirm your equipment is functional and complete the mapping procedure."

"We're about to," Reilly said impatiently. "Doc, out."

Setting down the handset, he momentarily considered how long he'd be in the prone under a rock. It was arguably preferable, however, to the all-night movement to get into position.

He sighed. "Well, that was easy. I thought she'd ask why David wasn't on the line. Didn't even have to give her the excuse about—"

"Stop stalling." Hass was in the prone beside him, carefully arranging a ruggedized black case. "Main building. Ready?"

Reilly drew his own black case nearer, its appearance identical to Hass's in every way except size. Taking a breath, he said, "Yeah. On three?"

"On three," Hass agreed. "One, two—"

Both men unzipped their cases in unison, flipping open the lids and reaching for the equipment inside in a well-practiced procedure they'd done many times before. Never under such a time crunch per se, Reilly thought, but competitive natures didn't go away merely because they were doing so under real-world circumstances.

Reilly erected a tripod before retrieving the Aegis-R4.

The device was smaller than it had any right to be, roughly the size of two stacked laptops though with enough heft to remind him that it was no ordinary piece of gear. Just the latest bit of CIA magic, but even the newest toys required a bit of manual assembly. After locking the Aegis onto its tripod, he plugged in a tablet and powered on the unit before glancing over at Hass, who was busy doing the same with the Sentinel-9.

The Aegis blinked to life with a familiar hum, its screen dim in the pre-dawn darkness. Reilly's fingers moved over the tablet's touchscreen controls, zooming in the optics on the oasis compound 1.2 kilometers to their southeast.

Under night vision, the buildings were little more than dark silhouettes against the sand, blurred splotches amid clusters of palm trees. But on the Aegis's screen, the walls of the main building were not only visible but transparent—and then, Hass spoke.

"Done. Compound mapped, main building in focus."

Reilly hung his head, then lowered his hands from the screen. "Best out of three?"

"No way."

"The Aegis takes longer to boot up—"

"Dude," Hass said firmly. "You picked scissors, I picked rock. There's no going back on that. It's bro code."

Reilly hesitated, then conceded defeat.

"Fuck. Go ahead and start triage."

He watched the tablet screen beside him, its green glow bathing Hass's face as he adjusted its parameters.

The Sentinel-9 was only slightly larger than Reilly's device, and was likewise supported by a tripod. But its function was entirely different—it was a GSR, ground surveillance radar, capable of providing high-resolution movement tracking within and around a building.

While it could cast a wide net for area detection, Hass had adjusted the parameters to narrow the scope to a single structure whose interior was now mapped and displayed as a blurry blueprint that went in and out of focus as the Sentinel sent out its radar in pulses.

"There they are," Hass said, and Reilly leaned closer to watch the blips on the tablet screen. They were small at first, then more defined. The radar was picking up movement in the building, tracking bodies as they moved.

Or didn't.

"Most are stationary, but there's a pair of bogeys in the front section. Start there and I'll label the buildings."

Reilly resumed his manipulation of the controls on his tablet, picking up where Hass had left off.

While the Sentinel was capable of scanning wide, casting its invisible net over the entire compound, its resolution stopped at identifying clusters of activity within a given building. It was far too general for guiding an airstrike.

That was where the Aegis-R4 came in.

Rather than utilizing ground surveillance radar, Reilly's device relied on through-wall imaging radar—TWIR for short—to provide detailed 3D imaging of internal spaces. That included the number of occupants, movement patterns, and their precise locations within a structure.

And while operating the Aegis was like looking through a drinking straw, it paired with the Sentinel like peanut butter and jelly. Hass could scan wide enough to identify activity within the entire compound, and once an area of concern was identified, Reilly could get as much detail as needed. The technology was staggering, he thought: he was looking through walls a kilometer away.

"Mapping the ground floor," Reilly said, although in truth the task was being performed by an AI-assisted interface that outlined the room layout and labeled each space on a gridded reference graphic. As the system pulsed, he saw faint outlines—shapes, furniture, and the movement of two men coming to a stop in what looked like a kitchen.

"They're pouring coffee," he noted, "in room 1-Echo."

Hass leaned closer, eyes flicking between the Aegis's screen and his own GSR display. "This shit is insane."

"Robot superpowers," Reilly agreed. "When the machines turn on us, it's going to be one hell of a battle."

"Agreed. Let's get this done and shut everything down."

It was an unglamorous end to all the technological fanfare. They'd map the structures and document the number and location of inhabitants, then power down the twin units to conserve battery. And then wait.

And wait.

And wait.

No further action was necessary or even possible, at least until the Agency's signal intelligence efforts revealed Malek's arrival. If and when that happened, the split team would locate and track him continuously, right up until the arrival of a precision airstrike during the hours of darkness.

Reilly thought aloud, "It'd be a whole lot easier if they could just level the building. I wish they weren't so damned touchy about leaving a US signature on this one."

Hass nodded beside him. "Agreed. But you have to admit, the Agency's airstrike solution is pretty elegant."

"That it is," the medic said appreciatively. "That it is."

19

"Vehicles inbound," Cancer said. He abandoned his Sentinel-9 for another piece of equipment mounted to a tripod, this one infinitely more familiar to him.

Aligning the spotter scope to center the view on a pair of SUVs churning a thin trail of dust on the mountain road, he adjusted the magnification to keep them in view amid the frigid early glow of dawn. "Two Land Cruisers, ten-meter interval, looks like they're headed for Building Four—you got them on the Aegis?"

"Yeah," Ian said beside him, "go ahead."

Cancer reached for the satellite handset and transmitted, "Raptor Nine One, Split Team One, Cancer."

The men were situated near the slit of a modest cavern amid the rocky high ground, barely high enough for them to stand doubled over at its tallest point but nonetheless palatial by hide site standards.

"Raptor Nine One," Cancer repeated, "come in."

While waiting for a response, he tracked the 4×4s until they vanished behind a sand-colored building, one of several in the secluded compound he and Ian had been surveilling for the past six hours. As best as they could tell from radar imaging of the facilities, the structures included a command center, barracks, and storage units, all within a heavily fortified perimeter built into the base of a mountain.

The objective would have been impossible to approach undetected, much less target with a ground strike—which was just as well, because if an attack occurred here it would be from the sky.

"This is Raptor Nine One," Chen responded over the handset, "*go ahead.*"

"Be advised, we've got a pair of Land Cruisers that just arrived at Objective One. Need you to monitor their comms to confirm or deny they're transporting Malek."

"*We're still intercepting, no traffic yet. But the captured phone gave us a lead on a major financial broker—it could be him arriving, and he may be a viable alternate target if Malek doesn't show.*"

"Copy," Cancer replied, releasing the transmit button to address Ian. "She says it could be a big-time financier. Alternate target. Looks like the phone I snatched wasn't so useless after all."

Ian was bundled in all the cold weather gear he'd packed, and didn't so much as glance up from the Sentinel display. "I never said it was."

"You seemed awfully inconvenienced by having to rip the data."

"Blame it on the lack of sleep."

"I haven't slept any more than you, and I didn't turn into an asshole."

"No," Ian agreed, "because you've always been an asshole."

"But at least I'm consistent—"

"Six people disembarking the vehicles, two guys from Building Four outside to meet them."

Cancer transmitted, "Half a dozen guys got out of the Land Cruisers, two-man reception party, Building Four."

"Copy," Chen responded. "*Comms intercepts confirm positive identification—Malek is at Objective One. Need you to monitor his pinpoint location.*"

"That's him," Cancer said to Ian. "Game time."

"Got it," Ian confirmed.

Cancer barely had time to key his handset and say, "We're on it," before his CIA superior spoke again, this time with a far more troubling transmission.

"*Suicide, come up on comms.*"

This caused him to wince, and he strained to hear the return transmission.

"*This is Rain Man, Split Team Two. Suicide got some kind of stomach bug, he's puking his guts out at the moment. I'll relay.*"

Cancer wondered if Chen would buy that particular lie. David was out hunting for survivors, and had been since dropping off the other split team. Though after 17 hours of searching without results, it was time to throw in the towel on that effort—more so now that the primary target was in their sights.

"All right," Chen replied. "*Tell him to pull your split team and consolidate on Objective One. Cancer, I need you and Angel to start working up the airstrike. Historically Malek has spent the night at a minimum, but that's not to say he won't leave for some reason. I want the attack to occur as soon as it's dark enough for the aircraft to approach undetected.*"

Cancer nodded. "Agreed. Will keep you posted on his movements. Split Team Two, out."

Then, to Ian, he said, "Still got them?"

"All interior now, Building Four, Room One Charlie."

"Cool." Cancer returned to the tablet of his Aegis, tapping the controls to pan his view toward the location. He managed to pick up the blurry figures of one seated man receiving what appeared to be a detailed brief by three others standing at the wall before him.

Not bad for surveillance from 1,395 meters away, he thought. Cancer was used to operating around this range as a sniper, and slightly farther when behind the scope of a .338 Lapua or .50 caliber rifle. But those night vision and thermal optics paled in comparison to the X-ray radar vision afforded by the CIA, and he watched the men on his objective out of curiosity as much as to gain a second point of view to support Ian's. The military adage that two was one and one was none had already paid off—without packing a second set of Sentinel and Aegis units, his team would have been unable to cover both targets.

Cancer said, "You know, I half expected Malek to be a ghost as soon as that stealth bomber went up in smoke."

"The thought had crossed my mind," Ian replied. "If the CIA knew where to find you, why go anywhere you've been before? The answer's obvious: because there's something bigger at play."

"Such as?"

"Imminent attack, most likely. And a big one at that. Vital enough to outweigh the risks of him coming back here. But that's not what concerns me most."

Cancer watched the intelligence operative, waiting for him to finish the thought.

Ian glanced over to lock eyes with him. "Whatever he's working on, there's a very real possibility that he's going to accelerate it now."

"Really?"

"Really," he replied, looking back at his tablet. "And I'm not the only one to suspect that. Why else do you think the Agency would let us continue the mission after an entire team got killed?"

Cancer's watch beeped—5:30. He reached for the radio tethered to the satellite antenna by way of a cable. Dialing the settings to an alternate frequency known only to his team, he transmitted.

"Split Team One, up."

Hass replied, "*Split Team Two on call. Nothing yet.*"

"So much for fuckin' punctuality."

Then a third voice broke over the net.

"*Net call, this is Suicide. I've driven the entire range, hit every comms window so far with negative results. Any updates from the objectives?*"

"Yeah," Cancer replied. "First, Mayfly is tracking some financial broker she's all hot and bothered about. Doesn't matter now, though, because our guy just popped on Objective One. We need to have everyone consolidated here by nightfall, before the airstrike."

David should have been elated by this news. Malek's appearance was a godsend, a surefire ticket to an airstrike that would accomplish their mission at almost zero further risk to the team. And once it was done, only exfil remained.

Instead, Cancer thought, the team leader sounded like a kid who'd just watched their puppy get hit by a car.

"*Shit. Okay. How much time do I have?*"

"How much time?" Cancer asked, incredulous. "Let's see...Split Team

Two will have to make their way to the road, then you're going to have to pick them up and head to our vehicle drop-off at the quarry. And your foot movement to our surveillance site is going to be a bitch. We took a ridge most of the way, but you guys will have to make the trip in broad daylight. That means staying in the low ground, and that's going to triple your distance at least. So how much time do you have? None. You've covered the entire evasion corridor, and sunrise is in fifteen minutes. The other team's gone, now start focusing on the rest of us."

There was a pause before David responded.

"*Copy. Rain Man, you and Doc need to head toward the pickup site. I'm going to run the corridor until the next comms window, and then I'll be on my way for pickup. Give me an hour.*"

Cancer muttered to Ian, "That fucker wants another hour."

"Of course he does," the intelligence operative replied. "But he's still the team leader. Let him have it."

Hass transmitted, "*Split Team Two copies all,*" and then Cancer gave his parting shot.

"Split Team One, copy. Don't waste any more time."

"*One more hour,*" David said, "*then I'll be on my way. Scout's honor.*"

20

"Any Talon Element," I transmitted over the team FM frequency, "Suicide Actual."

Then I lifted the survival radio from the Peugeot's cupholder and repeated the process, hearing no return message from either.

I checked my watch—two minutes past six.

"Let me guess," Shayan said from the driver's seat. "Nothing?"

"Patience, man. Patience."

"I have been patient for a day and night."

"Then you shouldn't be bothered by another few minutes."

We were now well over an hour past sunrise, the early morning light bouncing off rocky outcrops, painting them in shades of amber and gold. The Peugeot SUV's engine hummed as we wound through the narrow, crumbling roads of the Parvand Mountains.

Jagged peaks loomed on both sides, the terrain in between a mix of harsh browns and muted grays, dotted with scraggly bushes that looked like they had been fighting the desert for centuries. Here and there, small patches of snow clung to the higher ridges, stubbornly refusing to melt.

Shayan and I had seen it all before.

We'd spent an entire day covering the Parvand Range. After reaching the far end we'd doubled back, and spent most of the night going in the other direction—but now that the sun was up, our Peugeot SUV was doubly suspicious to anyone who'd seen it before.

The trail wound uphill, and Shayan commented, "If the Citadel of the Scattered Kings does exist, it is likely near here. The higher the location, the more secure."

He was groggy, practically slurring his speech. I'd let him sleep three hours the previous night while I stood guard, continuing my attempts at radio contact in case any survivors happened to wander into FM range.

Shayan continued, "There are many references, you know. Several Persian poets referenced a hidden stronghold in the mountains, and my father always said that—"

"Dude," I cut him off, "I'm glad you have a hobby. Under other circumstances I'd grab a shovel and help you look for the fucking place. But we're working."

"Perhaps if you let me listen to the car radio, I would not need to make conversation."

"I told you, I need to listen for transmissions."

The reality was that I needed to keep him blissfully unaware of our true purpose in the Parvand Range. Since I was certain the Iranian government either had announced the B-2 shootdown on the world stage or would very soon, I'd forbidden Shayan from turning on the SUV's radio and hearing any local news that would trumpet a victory over the Great Satan. As far as he was concerned, I was simply trying to make up for lost radio contact with an unspecified US element that he didn't have a need to know further specifics about.

I keyed my mic and transmitted, "Any Talon element, this is Suicide Actual."

Before I could repeat the process on the survival radio, Shayan asked, "Left or right?"

Looking up, I saw a Y-intersection ahead, the dual paths split by a wedge-shaped rock face. We'd covered both sides of the obstacle twice so far. But this was it, I thought—the final decision point of my rescue attempt, after which I'd have no choice but to leave the mountains, pick up Reilly and Hass from their linkup point, and focus solely on killing Malek.

The fact that the choice was completely arbitrary added insult to injury.

We were within the evasion corridor, and I had no further information with which to base my decision.

"Left."

Shayan obeyed, veering the Peugeot through the split and continuing onto a rocky trail. We passed a few crumbling structures, long since abandoned, their stone walls blending into the mountainside. A few goats dotted the hillside, clinging to the steep slopes with impossible balance, their herder nowhere in sight. The dirt road was cracked and rough, patches of dirt accumulating in mounds as if nature was slowly reclaiming what man had abandoned.

Then I repeated my attempt to contact survivors, hoping against hope that I'd hear a response.

Besides the SATCOM that had yet to yield any results, any survivors would have two additional means to communicate: the normal team FM, and smaller, shorter-range survival radios as a backup. Conserving the batteries for both was of the utmost importance while on evasion with no hope of resupply, and there was a very specific protocol for that. The radios would be turned on for the first ten minutes of every hour for the first 24 hours, then every even-numbered hour for the next 24. Once 72 hours elapsed, those communications windows would reduce to four times daily: twelve, three, six, and nine.

Since only thirty hours had passed since the shootdown, the survivors would be on the even-numbered hour schedule. So while I'd demanded another hour for my search, I was actually buying time for this ten-minute window to attempt radio contact.

I checked my watch: four minutes remained.

"Village ahead," Shayan warned me.

I pulled the checkered scarf over the bridge of my nose as we rounded a bend, and suddenly the village came into view, clinging to the mountainside like it had been carved out of the rock. Mud-brick houses, faded to the same dusty brown as the earth, clustered together in uneven rows. Flat roofs, some with crude satellite dishes, others with bundles of firewood stacked high, blended into the landscape so well that you could almost miss them if you weren't paying attention.

A narrow dirt road cut through the middle, winding between the houses, and a few sparse trees, gnarled and twisted from the harsh winds, dotted the edges of the village. Smoke curled lazily from a couple of chimneys, the smell of burning wood faint in the crisp air, though my attention was drawn to the people.

Two men stood near one of the houses, bundled in worn coats, their faces weathered from years of sun and wind. They glanced up as we passed, eyes narrowed, but didn't wave. Both were suspicious of us to be sure—they'd seen the Peugeot the day before, I was certain, and the SUV stood out like a clown at a funeral against the usual traffic of old trucks and rusted-out sedans, all looking like they'd been through the ringer more than once.

"Any Talon Element, Suicide Actual." By now the words were automatic, little more than white noise. How many times had I repeated that phrase in the past eighteen hours? I wasn't sure, though I added one more now over the survival radio.

Shayan asked, "How much longer?"

At this point I dreaded the sight of my watch, each second tick representing diminishing odds that my passes through the mountains had served any purpose whatsoever.

"Thirty-four seconds," I said testily, repeating my transmission sequence.

No response.

I'd continue attempting radio contact on our way out of the Parvand Range, but if anyone was left alive, they wouldn't be listening to receive the transmission.

"Any Talon element, Suicide Actual."

My watch face flicked from 6:09 and 59 seconds to 6:10 even.

The sight enraged me, and knowing that this was my last transmission with any chance of hitting home, I mashed my transmit button and abandoned all radio protocol.

"This is Suicide," I practically yelled. "Is anyone fucking out here?"

And as if spurred by my profanity, a faint voice spoke through a burst of static.

"*Suicide, Racegun.*"

21

The sound of David's voice hit Worthy like a jolt of electricity.

At first it felt like a ghost speaking through the radio, something he wasn't sure was real. There was an immediate sense that he was dreaming this up, that his mind was playing tricks on him after so many hours of silence, fear, and exhaustion. But as the words registered he felt a relief so sharp that it hurt. David's transmission represented a tether to the world that Worthy thought had forgotten him, a voice that cut through the isolation like a hand pulling him back from the edge of hopelessness.

"Where are you?" Worthy asked, and received only a crackle of static in return.

Keying his radio again, he said, "Go back to where you were, I can't hear you."

David replied, *"How about now?"*

"Good," Worthy said, scrambling for his GPS. "Stand by for my location."

After an all-night movement along his evasion corridor, Worthy had tucked himself into a shallow ravine hidden beneath a rock overhang. The Parvand Mountains offered little in the way of lush cover, but what they lacked in greenery they made up for in craggy terrain and deep, shadowed crevices. The walls of the ravine were uneven, worn smooth in places by ancient winds and time, but jagged enough to keep him obscured from outside view. The rock under him was cold, hard against his back, and he transmitted his grid location as clearly as he could enunciate for fear that David would lose radio contact once more.

"*Got it,*" David confirmed. "*I'm about three hundred meters to your southeast, on the road. White Peugeot SUV.*"

Worthy was about to transmit back when the sound of men's voices reached him. He peeked out from his hiding place to find an Iranian military patrol making their way up the rocky hillside. There were at least a dozen men spread out in a loose formation, navigating the uneven terrain in desert camouflage fatigues. Their somewhat casual movements assured him that they weren't on the hunt for a survivor—at least, not yet.

David asked, "*Hey man, you still got me?*"

Tucking himself behind cover, Worthy replied, "Patrol is moving in from the north—I could've used that info."

"*I didn't know. I can't exactly ask our boss for updates, I'm not supposed to be here. Military?*"

"Looks like conventional infantry, probably came up the hill searching for wreckage. This may be a hot exfil. Did you bring the whole team?"

"*Lone Ranger, baby. Except for Shayan, he's my Tonto. Who's with you?*"

"It's just me."

He let that sink in, and when David didn't respond, Worthy whispered, "How'd you know I made it?"

"*I didn't.*"

Now it was Worthy's turn to process the words, and once he did, he said, "All right, I'm going to make a run for it."

He considered leaving his rucksack, and decided against it—on the off chance that he could make it to David without getting spotted, having all his equipment on his person was the difference between a clean getaway and leaving definitive proof that at least one American was on the ground in Iran. That would in turn bring a massive search that would very likely compromise his entire team, and Worthy wasn't about to let that happen.

Sliding his arms through the ruck's shoulder straps, he verified the location of the quick release tabs near the bottom attachment point. He'd ditch the thing on the run if needed.

Grabbing his rifle and hazarding another glance from his hiding place, he saw only a few trailing men sweeping west of his position and missing him entirely—the patrol leader had chosen the easier terrain, assuring Worthy that his adherence to evader best practices, namely finding the most inaccessible places to hide, had paid off.

But that didn't mean he wouldn't get shot in the back.

Worthy took a deep breath, steadying his nerves. He waited until the last Iranian soldier disappeared over a rocky ridge before slowly emerging from his cramped hiding spot beneath the overhang. His legs protested as he stretched them out, muscles stiff from hours of consecutive movement followed by remaining completely stationary in the cold shadows.

Crouching low, he scanned the rugged landscape, searching for the safest route southeast toward David's position on the road. The terrain was a chaotic jumble of wind-sculpted sandstone and loose scree, treacherous footing that would make moving quickly and quietly difficult to say the least.

Worthy set off, picking his way carefully across the uneven ground, mindful of every footfall. Loose pebbles skittered down the slope with each step, their rattle amplified in the mountain stillness. He froze, heart pounding, straining his ears for any signs that the patrol had detected him. But the only sound was the low moan of wind through the ravines.

He pressed on, following the contours of the land, using boulders and shadowed gullies for cover and panting breaths of crisp, thin mountain air tinged with cold as he continued toward David. Worthy was under extreme pressure to escape undetected, though even as the stress weighed on him he couldn't deny the fact that this was the easiest part of the mission thus far.

If spinning under a wildly malfunctioning canopy on his last training jump had been terrifying, then freefalling out of the B-2 with his gear partially on fire was a plunge into pure, unrelenting horror.

He'd planned on pulling his parachute at high altitude and toughing out the cold in the interests of putting as much distance as possible between himself and the site of the shootdown.

But the B-2 was a disintegrating comet trailing flame and raining debris across the sky, and he'd had no choice but to fall well clear of it for fear of being struck by one of the pieces of radar-absorbing composite flipping end over end in all directions.

How had the bird been shot down? Worthy had no idea, still didn't, and the focus of his concentration beyond trying not to get hit by wreckage was to watch the aircraft in the hopes that one or more of his teammates would appear in the night, where the freezing air and high-altitude winds would extinguish the flames licking at their gear. But no figures came tumbling from the jump door. No one else had survived.

There was only him.

Worthy figured he was free of risk from a debris strike by 18,000 feet, and was dangerously close to pulling his ripcord for a long-range canopy flight when a new thought brought him up short. Even with its jump door open, the radar cross section of the B-2 should have been minimal, and if an air defense system had somehow detected the plane, then so too could it pick up an open parachute.

And while a man-sized target was unlikely to get hit by a missile, they could easily track his flight all the way to his touchdown point. He'd be captured by an Iranian defense element in short order to become international news as an American captive, and a spy at that.

So he'd chosen to continue falling, plummeting through the airspace to carry out his original intention of a low opening jump. The entire point of pulling low was to evade radar detection, and now he didn't have a choice. Judging by the terrain below he was several kilometers east of his team's intended landing zone, and he'd used what little canopy flight he had to fly toward his evasion corridor, touching down in the desert at the southwest tip of the Parvand Range.

Worthy crested a rise and caught sight of the road below, a thin ribbon of asphalt winding through the barren mountains. He couldn't make out David's vehicle yet but quickened his pace regardless, boots crunching on the loose scree as he half-ran, half-skidded down the slope toward salvation. Three hundred meters had never seemed so far. Each step required full concentration to keep from losing his footing and tumbling head over heels.

"I'm about halfway to you," he transmitted on the move.

The ability to make radio contact felt liberating in the extreme—

upon caching his parachute equipment and moving into the hills, he'd discovered the extent of the fiery debris that hit him in the plane. A smoldering fragment had sheared off a single tip of his mobile satellite antenna, and that was all it took to render the entire device useless. Worthy had tried tying the remaining rod into position with cord, but his transmissions to his team, the CIA, and anyone else who would listen went unanswered.

But not all radio transmissions were a good thing.

David's response to the progress update caused Worthy to increase his pace at the expense of all noise discipline.

"It may be your turn to save my ass," the team leader said. "We've got two carfuls of armed men boxing us in—you'd better hurry."

"What are they saying?" I asked Shayan, quickly working the handle to roll down the passenger window.

"If we do not step out of the vehicle, they will open fire."

This was a hell of a predicament, I thought. I'd been so concerned for Worthy's safety, for remaining at the exact point where I'd managed to maintain tenuous radio contact with my missing teammate, that I'd completely disregarded any tactical considerations for myself and my driver. Rocky slopes flanked us on both sides—too steep to climb without a fight and a hell of a place to get boxed in.

The two vehicles pinning us into position had arrived near simultaneously, a mid-size SUV blocking the path to our rear and some kind of Jeep Wrangler knockoff with a Suzuki badge cutting us off from the front.

Doors flung open. Three men stepped out of each vehicle, armed with a collective assortment of rifles ranging from an old Mauser bolt-action to an SKS and multiple AK-47s. They moved with the confidence of people who had done this before—maybe not exactly this, but something close enough. One of them, a gaunt man with a wild beard and darting eyes, barked his orders in Farsi.

The sun was inching higher over the rugged horizon, gradually illuminating the narrow dirt road where we'd parked. Dust from the vehicles' abrupt stops still billowed around us, catching the morning light in a haze that made everything feel surreal.

"Roll down your window," I instructed Shayan. "Tell them we're leaving, and that we'll pay and pay well for them protecting the route."

Shayan obeyed, his voice quavering for a few stammered sentence fragments before the leader cut him off, shouting even louder than before.

"We must step out of the car," Shayan translated. "Now. Or else we are dead."

Stepping out was going to be problematic—I was attired in civilian clothes, my Caucasian features only partially obscured by the checkered scarf pulled high over my nose. My tactical vest was on the floorboard at my feet, although its trio of rifle magazines were stowed in my pockets for just such an occasion...and my true lifeline, the suppressed HK416, was and needed to remain inside.

Because while being surrounded by six men was all well and good in a Hollywood scenario, in the real world at least one of them would get the best of me sooner rather than later. And Shayan's fat ass didn't stand a chance.

"Put one hand up," I said, doing so myself as I continued, "and open your door with the other. Step out very, very slowly."

Shayan had begun to comply when I added, "When the shooting starts, you crawl under this car and don't come out until I tell you." I pulled the handle and eased my door open, taking final note of my rifle's exact orientation for a split-second grab when the time came.

Delaying that moment for as long as possible was now my number one priority.

The Peugeot's engine was off, and the ticking of the cooling metal filled the silence as I exited the vehicle, putting both hands skyward, my boots crunching onto a crumble of rocks.

There were more shouts from the leader. While I waited for him to shut the fuck up and Shayan to translate, I glanced to my front and rear as casually as I could manage under the circumstances, taking in the positions of the men and the orientation of their barrels catching the morning light.

The fighters to my rear were spread wide, flanking their vehicle in a rough semicircle, rifles at the ready. Up front, the men from the Suzuki were in a narrow triangle pointing our way, the leader in the center. I took in the mix of shalwar kameez, pakol caps, ammunition bandoliers, and field jackets, along with the age range from a wiry teenager with a patchy attempt at a beard to a couple of grizzled fighters old enough to be my grandfather. This assured me they weren't military, which was of limited consolation when I knew for a fact that an Iranian infantry patrol was within a half kilometer to my north.

So who were these guys? Militia. Hired guns. Bandits. The distinctions were academic. All I needed to know was whether they were going to pull the trigger if we didn't play along, and Shayan's next translation assured me that the answer to that query was a resounding yes.

"He says you are an American spy from the plane...from some plane that exploded...I do not understand. But they want to take you alive."

"Tell him I'm a Russian arms dealer," I said evenly. "And that I have money. Lots of it."

"He will take your money when he wishes, I assure you. And the government will pay him far more."

"Dude. Whose side are you on?"

Two of the fighters to my front broke from their positions and approached at a rapid clip, rifles at the ready. The first was the wiry teenager, scurrying forward with his Mauser bobbing erratically in his grip.

Beside him strode a battle-hardened fighter with a thick black beard streaked with gray, his face a roadmap of scars and sun-weathered creases. He moved with the easy grace of a man who had spent a lifetime in the unforgiving mountains, the AK-47 in his hands as natural an extension of his body as his own limbs.

Another shout from the leader and Shayan said, "Get on the ground, now. Do it, Suicide."

Time to earn my callsign, I thought, preparing to move for my rifle when a scream from the hill to my left split the air.

"HEY!"

Diving toward the vehicle, I snatched my rifle with an uncanny speed born of sheer necessity as bullets pummeled into the open passenger door. I leveled my weapon through the window frame, ignoring the teenager to blast five subsonic rounds at the older man whose AK-47 barrel spewed a final glare of flame before going silent.

His partner was still trying to overcome panic, fumbling with his rifle as I took aim at the bearded leader now scrambling for the cover of his vehicle. Two shots sent him sprawling, the sound of unsuppressed gunfire behind me failing to ignite any corresponding degree of fear—Worthy was dealing with those men, I knew, and I used my final seconds of forward visibility to drill the teenager's abdomen with three sloppily aimed rounds before I pivoted backward while dropping to a knee.

The SUV parked there had become the Alamo for the lone fighter I could make out who had survived Worthy's onslaught, a twenty-something man in his prime who was just now realizing that the attacker on the hill was no longer the only threat he had to worry about.

Our barrels found one another almost in unison, though his frantic attempt to defend himself resulted in him firing his SKS wide, while my HK416 aligned itself seamlessly before gently bucking with the recoil of three rounds. One split the wrist of his firing hand while the other two struck diagonally across his chest, and as he went down I registered Worthy racing down the hill, calling out to me as he moved.

"Get the front!"

I rose and spun, clearing the passenger door and making for the Suzuki.

Two bodies were strewn on the ground, the older fighter dead and bleeding out while the gut-shot teenager writhed in the dirt, his Mauser locked in the grip of one hand before and after I delivered a close-range headshot as I passed.

Sweeping left of the Suzuki, I searched for the leader to find a trail of scraped dirt laced with blood. Upon rounding the vehicle I found him lying in a crumpled heap, his life seeping away in a crimson pool that soaked the sand and rocks. He'd since abandoned his AKM rifle, and now his chest heaved in shallow, rapid breaths, each one a gurgling struggle as blood frothed at the corners of his mouth.

Coming to a stop and taking aim between his feverish eyes, I unceremoniously fired a final round that put him out of his misery. He'd started the fight and I'd just ended it, and I executed a lightning-fast reload on my way back to the Peugeot to assess our situation.

Worthy was already on the road, clearing the rear SUV, and as glad as I was to see him alive, the reunion was more rushed than I would've preferred.

The Iranian military patrol was now moving toward the sound of gunshots like moths to flame. Even if we were gone before they arrived—and we damned well better be—the nearby villagers would be all too eager to report a suspicious SUV that had made multiple passes through the Parvand Range. That meant Shayan's Peugeot was fully burned, and before long the two enemy vehicles would be too, whether they had bullet holes or not.

At this point the half-dozen blood-splattered corpses were merely icing on the evidentiary cake of American presence, and the only decision that remained was how many cars we'd take with us.

I knelt to find Shayan wedged between the ground and the undercarriage of his Peugeot.

"Get behind the wheel and follow me out," I said. "I'll drive the Suzuki."

Then I rose and called out to Worthy, "You take the rear truck. Let's go."

I was halfway to the Suzuki when I heard his shouted response.

"It's nice to see you, too."

22

Ian lay prone, eyes fixed on the tablet display of the Sentinel radar monitor in his hide site. The harsh afternoon light slanted across the Parvand Mountains as Cancer lay beside him, eyes flicking between the Aegis-R4 and his spotter scope.

Cancer asked, "You still think it's him?"

The Sentinel's tablet display showed the compound's interior glowing in shades of green, its radar revealing a network of rooms and hallways. One figure remained fixed in Room 1-Foxtrot, isolated.

Ian replied, "If Room 1F is the command post, and I'm pretty sure it is, then yeah. He hasn't left for anything more than a piss break. They brought him his lunch there, and he's the only one who hasn't rotated out at some point since the Land Cruisers arrived. I'd say that narrows it down."

"Let's hope you're right." Cancer scanned the compound through his spotter scope, taking in every detail and watching for changes with a sniper's precision. "Wouldn't want to disappoint Affinity Gold."

This was the second time the team had brushed shoulders with the highly classified CIA program; now that Project Longwing was being shut down, Ian thought, it would be the last.

Affinity Gold employed officers of foreign descent, sent back to their birth countries to broker purchases from black-market arms dealers. Posing as representatives of larger trafficking organizations, they infiltrated the illicit weapons trade with the twofold mission of providing a steady stream of unattributable weapons for America's covert arming of allies and removing major threats from the black market.

Chief among that latter list were unmanned aerial vehicles, typically crude Iranian-manufactured drones supplied to Russia, the Houthis in Yemen, and Hezbollah in Lebanon that had one way or another ended up for sale to the highest bidder. But Iran's most lethal UAVs were reserved for its own military operating abroad in places like Syria, where, fortunately for the CIA, four Shahed-129s had been captured by ISIS.

Without any means of operating the Iranian equivalents of US MQ-1 Predators, complete with advanced surveillance and targeting systems to include electro-optical and infrared sensors, ISIS had promptly sold the aircraft to the black market, where a pair of Middle-Eastern-born Affinity Gold officers were all too happy to negotiate their purchase.

Ian glanced at the horizon, where heat shimmered off the rocky slopes. "How's the weather looking?"

Consulting the tablet beside him, Cancer said, "High winds start in an hour and begin dying down at seventeen hundred. Looks like they'll be twenty to thirty knots, dropping to ten around sunset. Light and variable by midnight. Nothing that would affect the airstrike."

"It's not the airstrike I'm worried about." Ian stared at his screen. "If there's going to be a sandstorm this afternoon, it could fuck with my radar readings."

"I thought the software automatically labeled everyone by height and body composition."

"It does, but—"

"And it auto-logs their locations throughout the day, right?"

"Yeah."

Cancer didn't bother looking up from his spotter scope. "Then stop overthinking it. If you're going to sweat anything, sweat air defense."

"Air defense is the easy part. Our birds will be flying too low."

The quartet of Shahed-129 drones that Ian referenced had come complete with anti-tank missiles, and the fleet had languished in the custody of the CIA's Armor and Special Programs Department for years. It was held in reserve for a mission demanding its unique capabilities, a requirement that had gone unmet until Soren Malek was located in Iran.

And since the means with which to conduct a covert attack that would eliminate a single man within a building were severely limited indeed, the CIA had simply removed all serial numbers on the unmanned aircraft before increasing and optimizing the already extensive payload of the precision Sadid-1 missiles. All debris from the airstrike would tell the story of Iranian-made drones launching Iranian projectiles—there would be no US aerial or cruise missile fragments, only evidence pointing to an internal operation.

The illusion was vital, leaving both the Iranian government and Malek's own allies to question whether a rogue faction or a Quds Force element was responsible. Anyone who suspected better would be wholly unable to prove it.

Ian recalibrated his radar, zooming out slightly to track movements in the surrounding rooms. Malek's presence hadn't shifted. Each room glowed, tagged and labeled, his mind running through potential scenarios. "Assuming he stays in 1-Foxtrot, do you think we should stick with the primary strike pattern?"

Four Shahed-129s equipped with four Sadid-1 missiles each gave them sixteen precision munitions to be directed at the team's pinpoint instruction, although the CIA had generated a number of possible variations to account for building architecture surrounding Malek's location at the time of the attack.

"That's our best bet," Cancer said, laying it out as if reading from a manual. "Missiles one through four on target. Five through eight in a cross pattern ten meters from initial impact, nine through twelve in a square formation to fill the gaps, thirteen through sixteen back on target. Two seconds between impacts, five seconds between volleys, 39 seconds from first detonation to last. If Malek can survive that, he deserves to live."

Ian visualized the sequence. Each missile hitting its mark, surgical in its destruction. It was as close to an unassailable kill as they could get under the circumstances...and when that thought segued into how long he and Cancer would be out here on their own, he suddenly checked his watch.

"It's 11:32," he said.

Cancer begrudgingly adjusted the satellite radio frequency, then lifted his handset and transmitted, "Suicide, Cancer."

Ian didn't expect a response—they'd been attempting hourly check-ins ever since their last radio contact with David just before sunrise. Their last five transmissions had come and gone without response, either from their team leader or from Reilly and Hass, the latter of whom should have been picked up by the former long before now. In the best-case scenario, that pickup had already been coordinated via FM communications, and all three men were simply too busy covering ground to worry about stopping to set up a mobile satellite antenna.

But there were a whole lot of possibilities that fell well short of that ideal outcome, and each unanswered transmission was a more damning reminder of the possibility that Ian and Cancer were now the only two survivors from both teams.

And while Ian couldn't hear a return transmission now, the shock on his partner's face left no doubt that not only had there been one, but whatever the content, it was something unexpected.

Cancer's hands flew to the radio, which he put in speaker mode before snatching the handset once more.

"Say again."

Then a metallic voice filled the hide site. "*Split Team One, this is Racegun.*"

Ian's heart jolted. For a second, he forgot where he was—forgot the unyielding stone beneath him, the tension in his muscles from hours of stillness. The words echoed in his head, almost impossible to process. Worthy was alive. He'd survived the shootdown along with God only knew what else in the hours since, and now he'd been reunited with his original team.

Cancer replied, "You better not be fucking with us."

"*Nope,*" Worthy transmitted back, his Southern drawl unmistakable. "*It's me. In the flesh. But I'm the only one who made it out, so don't get too excited.*"

"We're changing your callsign to 'Lazarus.'"

"*No, we're not. Here's Suicide.*"

A rush of emotion hit Ian, a cocktail of relief, shock, and something darker—guilt. He'd already made peace with Worthy's death, had tucked it away with every other unspoken loss that had come before. It was a necessary compartmentalization, a survival mechanism. Now, after hearing Worthy's voice on the other end, the impact of this new reality struck him like a physical blow.

"Remind me again," David's voice emitted through the radio speaker, "who was it that said to abandon the search before that last comms window—me or you? I can't recall."

Cancer asked, "Did you already pick up Doc and Rain Man?"

"Sure did. We're all on the way."

"Mayfly's freaking out. We were all starting to think you were dead. What took you so long?"

"We had a dustup in the Parvand Range while picking up Racegun. Shayan's vehicle got burned, so we had him buy a couple more from a village outside Birjand. We're now on the way in the two cringiest-named vehicles on the planet: a Tata Safari and a Chery Tiggo. I'm not making those up."

"Yes," Cancer said, "you are."

"I'm really not. Is Malek still on the objective?"

"Yes, and that means we need to consolidate before the airstrike. Mayfly wants it going down as soon as possible after nightfall. Where are you guys at?"

There was a pause as David double-checked his information, then replied, "About 90 minutes out from the quarry. We're planning to leave one vehicle there, and have Shayan on call with the other one. Still think we can make a foot movement to your location in broad daylight?"

Cancer nodded. "All you gotta do is stay in the low ground. By the time you reach the quarry there should be a sandstorm to cover your movement, which won't hurt. You've got a long walk to the grid I gave you earlier, but that puts you right in the valley behind us, out of sight from the objective. Once the airstrike is complete, me and Angel will haul ass to your location. All six of us move out to the quarry together, you call in Shayan, and then it's a drive to our exfil. When are you going to break the news to Mayfly?"

Ian and Cancer locked eyes, a knowing grin creeping across the sniper's face at the sound of David's response.

"Right now. Switch frequencies and enjoy the show."

23

Chen transmitted, "Split Team One, this is Raptor Nine One."

The lack of a response within seconds of her transmission irritated her, as it always did. But now, Cancer and Ian simply had no reason not to respond—they'd been sitting in a hide site all day and would remain there until the airstrike was complete, and as a result should have been tuned in to their satellite radio's command net at all times.

Unless something bad had happened.

"Split Team One," she repeated. "Raptor Nine One."

The atmosphere in the OPCEN was tense, a maze of glowing monitors and huddled analysts. Its usual hum of tension had sharpened to a knife's edge; the air was heavy with the unspoken understanding that they were teetering on the brink. Workstations encircled Chen, each staffed by analysts whose eyes flicked between screens, fingers dancing over keyboards as they parsed data streams and decrypted intercepted communications. The room smelled faintly of stale coffee and stress, a space that had been lived in for far too many hours. Iran had yet to publicly announce the shootdown in a delay that was, per the CIA's best information, the result of conferring with Russia and China to coordinate a unified diplomatic response. Only when they'd collectively decided how to best portray

Iran as the victim of unprovoked US aggression, she knew, would the information be brought to the world stage.

"Cancer, Angel, this is Mayfly. Come in—"

"*This is Cancer,*" a voice responded. "*Go ahead.*"

Chen's shoulders eased slightly, the tight coil of anxiety loosening but not disappearing. "Are you all right?"

"*Yeah,*" he said. "*Are you?*"

Her fingers tapped rhythmically against the desk, a small release of the tension that had been building since her—and her Agency superiors'—decision to inexorably alter the mission at hand. "We've been tracking down Malek's financial broker via a series of payments linked to the purchase of a luxury property in Birjand. The owner is a man named Dariush Navidi, an Oxford-educated global asset manager that we've assessed to be the individual we've been looking for. I've just sent a data shot with all the information for Angel to take a look."

"*Okay, he will. But we've got Malek in our sights, seven hours until sunset, and not enough drones for a secondary strike against some money guy in Birjand. I'm failing to see the relevance.*"

Chen's gaze drifted back to the central display. The icon marking the Split Team One's position now felt like a tiny, fragile beacon in a vast sea of hostility. It was the final chess piece in a game with no second chances.

"Navidi's not just a 'money guy,'" she responded. "He's the keystone in Malek's entire network. Taking out Malek is the immediate priority, yes. But without addressing the financial arm, any ongoing operations could continue."

She steeled herself for what she was about to say—or rather, for Cancer's reaction to it. "And the relevance is that we've intercepted communications that Obsidian, a codename that we now know to be Navidi, will be summoned to meet with Malek at Objective One."

The sniper's response was spoken in a flat monotone indicative of thinly veiled disgust. "*When.*"

"Tomorrow night."

"*That's interesting, because by tomorrow night there's not going to be much of Objective One left standing.*"

She glanced at the analysts seated below her, their screens filled with scrolling data feeds. They had been working nonstop, piecing together the fragments that would justify this operation's high cost.

Then she said, "I'm delaying the airstrike."

"Delaying—are you fucking kidding me? You don't even know if Malek will be here then."

"If Navidi is being summoned to meet him, he'll be there."

"Last I checked, international terrorists ain't exactly famous for their routine and consistency. If you want to keep us out here an extra 24 hours, you must really be looking to increase the number of dead Americans because—"

His transmission was cut off not by her but by the voice of David Rivers.

"Cancer," the team leader said, "I'll take it from here. Mayfly, this is Suicide Actual."

She asked, "What's your status?"

David replied, "An hour and a half from the quarry. I'm with Split Team Two and Racegun, who was alive this whole time."

"Racegun—he's alive? How did you find him?"

"By running a few sweeps of the evasion corridor. His SATCOM antenna was damaged, so we made contact via FM. We had a gunfight in the Parvand Range, six enemy killed in action during our linkup."

She took two panting breaths. "Please don't tell me they were Iranian military."

"No. Bandits or militia who thought that I was a spy from the shootdown. There was a military patrol in the area, though, so if they were unaware of US presence before, they're not now. Has Iran gone public about destroying a B-2 yet?"

"Not yet. We're braced for the big announcement."

"Right," he continued. "They're tweaking the press release to include photographs of dead bodies—minus the weapons, of course—surrounded by 5.56mm shell casings. They're going to sell it as US operatives slaughtering Iranian civilians twenty kilometers from the shootdown. That puts the entire country on the lookout for us, and a bounty on our heads that couldn't be bigger. So here's the deal."

"Excuse me?"

"I said 'here's the deal,' and you'd better listen close because I'm not fucking around. We've already lost four shooters plus two pilots. Barely got Racegun back, *and it's a miracle we're this close to having everyone consolidated in one place for an airstrike with damn near 100% odds of killing Malek, which is why we came here in the first place. My men will stay on target outside the objective tonight, and tonight only. By midnight we're making our way to exfil whether you've sent the airstrike or not."*

Chen reeled from the sheer insubordination—and the audacity, my God—of his remarks. She was used to some coded play-by-play over satellite radio, every transmission of which was recorded in the mission transcript to be scrutinized by her superiors. But in this case her superiors were hellbent on maximizing the deliverable results of an operation that had thus far yielded anything but, and she replied with absolute authority from this foundation of support.

"That decision is not yours to make. If I say you remain for an additional night, then you will remain—"

"Or what?" David shot back. "You'll fire us? The program's already done for. And good luck bringing legal action that will confirm The New York Times article that everyone's been trying to bury, especially in the wake of a half-dozen Americans dead and Iran parading wreckage of a $2 billion stealth bomber through cheering crowds in the streets of Tehran. I've got nothing to lose, and if you want to test me on that, go right ahead. Because there's nothing I won't do to get my men out of here alive, and by this time tomorrow we'll be so far from Objective One that you'll be praying the Iranians don't find us before you do."

24

Reilly trudged across the narrow channel of low ground between desert hills, eyes straining behind his shooting glasses as the sandstorm raged.

Gusts whipped into the canyon, hurling grit and stinging sand against his exposed skin. He could barely make out Worthy up front, a shadowy figure moving with purpose. David was just behind the pointman, a dark shape that appeared and disappeared in the swirling chaos.

The landscape was a blur of shifting shadows and muted colors, the rocky outcrops rising on either side of their path. At times, the sandstorm cleared enough to give Reilly a fifty-meter view of the undulating hills, the crests barely discernible against the gray-orange haze of the sky. Then the storm would tighten its grip without warning, reducing his world to a narrow corridor sphere of three meters in any direction. It felt like moving through a tunnel of sand, the world around him a disorienting mix of swirling grit and fleeting glimpses of the terrain ahead.

"*Split Team One,*" David transmitted, "*Suicide.*"

The radio call went unanswered as had those before it, delivered in regular intervals as they closed with Cancer and Ian's hide site.

Each man moved in a staggered column, rucksacks swaying with each step. Reilly could feel the weight of his pack digging into his shoulders, the straps cutting into his body with every lurch across the shifting sand. His

HK417 was gripped tightly in his hands, ready to snap up at the first sign of danger if the visibility would grace him with the ability to detect it. The storm made their approach stealthy but also robbed them of their greatest asset—situational awareness.

He glanced back over his shoulder at Hass, the rearguard, a barely perceptible figure lost in the sand-filled air.

Hass was unquestionably hurting from the loss of Griffin, Keller, Washington, and Munoz, though he'd done his best to conceal that fact. Reilly sensed his own teammates were no less impacted, particularly by Munoz's death—they'd done damn near an entire mission with him in Yemen—but they were nonetheless facing a very different reality. While they previously felt like the world was coming down over their heads, now they may as well have been immortal. His team had been through so much together that despite the losses of this mission so far, Worthy's recovery made it seem like nothing could stop them.

Not even the storm.

David transmitted once more, "Split Team One, Suicide."

And this time, at last, he received a response.

"Cancer here, I've got you—what's your location?"

"About three-quarters of the way, we just passed Checkpoint Five."

"Outstanding. How's the storm treating you?"

"Shitty," David admitted, *"but if it gets us to our staging area without us getting spotted, I'll take it."*

"For sure. Keep me posted."

The wind howled a low, mournful sound that filled Reilly's ears. It came in erratic bursts, gusting hard enough to make him hunch his shoulders against the force. Dust clouded his vision, settling on his face and making every breath an effort through the fabric of his scarf. He squinted through his shooting glasses, eyes watering as he blinked away the granules that managed to slip past.

Then the sandstorm lifted for a heartbeat, a swirling veil of dust parting just enough to give Reilly a glimpse ahead.

Worthy suddenly dropped to a knee, his suppressed HK416 against his shoulder as he opened fire at some unseen enemy that answered almost immediately with the harsh bark of unsuppressed fire. The sound crashed through the channel like a wave, triggering a surge of adrenaline in Reilly's veins, his heartbeat pounding in his ears like a war drum as he sought the cover of a rock-laden mound beside him and took aim into the swirling sand ahead.

"Break contact." David's voice came through the radio, sharp and direct.

Cancer came over the net almost immediately. "*Moving to support, ETA six minutes.*"

Then Worthy emerged from the sand, racing past Reilly while reloading—the pointman must have gone through his first magazine in record time. This left David to continue the fight, trying to slow the enemy's progress to buy time and space for their withdrawal.

They were so close to making it to their destination, Reilly thought, so close to reuniting with Ian and Cancer, and the circumstances of this new compromise remained unclear. Was this a random collision with a routine enemy patrol? An ambush? The latter seemed unlikely by virtue of a lack of gunfire coming from overhead, though before he could pursue the thought his focus centered on his team leader, momentarily visible through a swirling cloud. David was firing in short bursts before abruptly rising and retreating toward the medic, his boots kicking up clouds of sand.

Reilly was up, HK417 pressed against his shoulder, eyes scanning the shifting currents of sand ahead with the concerned realization that he hadn't actually seen the enemy yet—judging by the fact that David had ordered a fighting retreat rather than an advance, there was a considerable number of them somewhere ahead. But perhaps Worthy and the team leader had managed to fend them off entirely. Maybe, Reilly thought, he should empty a magazine into the haze and run, or even run without firing to conserve his ammo.

Then he saw them.

Dimly visible figures of men were darting forward between the sparse cover, a disciplined front line advancing through the chaos. Reilly fired the moment he identified his opponents, engaging each target with three to five rounds before transitioning to the next. The roar of return fire erupted, although the points of impact were indistinguishable by sight or sound; they couldn't see him any better than he could them and probably even less, judging by the fact that he was stationary while they were moving forward.

But they were unmistakably experienced fighters, advancing in pairs, one group laying down suppressive fire while the others moved. He caught glimpses of faces obscured by scarves, eyes hidden behind goggles. They moved too fast, too confidently. They weren't militia, he realized. They were something else entirely.

Reilly rotated his selector lever to fully automatic as they closed in despite his best efforts. He managed three quick bursts before his magazine ran dry, the rifle's bolt locking back with a mechanical clack that he felt rather than heard.

Then he was off, rising and sprinting backward while hugging the opposite canyon wall to allow his final teammate a clear field of fire. Hass didn't hesitate, blasting subsonic rounds from his HK416 as Reilly ejected his mag on the move, recovering a new one and slamming it into place as he passed the trail man who'd just taken the lead in this fight against an unknown enemy force.

"They're still coming at us hard," he transmitted, seeking a visual on David to his front as his split team made their escape, desperately running back to the quarry.

Worthy moved swiftly, his rifle tucked against his shoulder as he retraced his steps through the winding terrain. The sandstorm had returned in full force, reducing visibility to almost nothing. He could hear the wind howling through the canyon, its gusts tearing at his clothes and mask. Reilly's last transmission had been clear—the enemy was still on them, closing fast, and his team's best bet was to outpace the threat long enough to reach terrain that was advantageous enough to set up a hasty ambush.

The pointman passed one narrow outlet to his left, a sliver of an escape route twisting away into the unknown. But Worthy ignored it, staying on the course they'd taken earlier. He trusted the path they knew, the one they had scouted on their approach. Every other option was a gamble that would take them farther from their vehicles and, therefore, the only chance of escape.

Ahead, the canyon narrowed briefly before opening into a wider, rock-strewn flat. He pushed forward, forcing his legs to pump harder against the weight of his rucksack and the sand dragging at his boots. The gusts eased for a moment, and in that fleeting stillness, he saw them—dark figures emerging from the swirling haze ahead, moving like ghosts in the storm.

Worthy dropped to one knee, sighted down his HK416, and squeezed the trigger. The rifle thumped against his shoulder with each bullet fired, the suppressor muting each shot well below the threshold of the wind noise. The lead enemy figure staggered back, collapsing into the dust, and Worthy engaged a second with similar results.

But then the return fire came, thunderous and unsuppressed, bullets ricocheting off the rocks around him. He adjusted his aim, firing again, this time more frantically as the enemy bounded forward, relentless. Their shapes became clearer in the fleeting gaps of the sandstorm, their movements methodical, trained—and there were more of them than he had anticipated.

He rose to retreat, nearly colliding with David. The team leader could divine their situation well enough from context, taking cover to engage their opponents in a seamless transition into a second break contact drill that would send the team back the way they'd come yet again.

Then and only then did Worthy have time to key his radio. The team had exactly one way out now—the canyon outlet he'd passed moments earlier—and if a third enemy force was closing in from that direction, they'd have no choice but to fight their way through a narrow channel that reduced the odds of success to near zero.

"Enemy front and rear," he transmitted, "we're taking the path east. Follow me."

He reloaded on the move, knowing there was precious little else he could say. With his teammates alternately bounding in a two-way retreat and firing at one of two enemy contingents squeezing the noose ever tighter, and the storm presenting varying degrees of visibility with each passing second, it would be a free-for-all trying to get everyone reoriented in the new direction of movement.

All Worthy knew for sure was that he'd be the one to blaze the trail, and when he reached the one and only path leading away from the twin enemy forces, he took it at a run.

Now he was in uncharted territory, the ability to simply retrace his steps removed once and for all. Each break in the swirling sand brought with it new lines of sight along with an almost paralyzing fear of more shadowy enemy figures beyond—but he proceeded unhindered, gaze sweeping his surroundings as he desperately tried to recall the canyon layout from his route planning.

He'd scanned the satellite imagery hours earlier, and there was no time to stop and check his phone for confirmation. But Worthy was a pointman at heart, and identifying every primary and alternate path was his bread and butter. They'd passed Checkpoint Five just before making contact with the enemy, and his mind presented an overhead view of that point in the imagery almost as sharply as if he saw it in front of him.

His current path weaved its way to a Y-intersection. The left side was wider and thus appeared the obvious choice, but it was a false god—within a few hundred meters it reached a dead end. Following the narrower channel to the right was the only way, a lifeline extending southeast and rejoining the network of canyons.

David transmitted, *"Check in."*

"Racegun, point."

"Doc, I'm on the trail now."

"Rain Man, I made the turnoff. Haven't seen anyone yet."

"Keep going," David transmitted. *"I think I'm the last man."*

No delineated order of movement, Worthy thought, and no patrol formation. Just a wild sprint into oblivion, and he was now the only one who could get his team out alive.

The sandstorm raged on as Worthy approached the critical juncture, the swirling dust obscuring his vision in fits and starts. With each fleeting lull, the forking paths revealed themselves in greater clarity. A broad avenue stretched to the left, its wide berth an enticing respite from the suffocating narrows they'd just escaped. And to the right, a jagged crevice, so tight at this point that only a single file could navigate its twisting depths.

In that ephemeral moment of decision, Worthy's eye caught a glint of light dancing off the left-hand canyon wall, the tease of an exit bathed in sunshine and promise. It lulled the mind with visions of an easy egress, of circumventing the enemy's snare and breaking free. But Worthy's memory held firm against the temptation, an inviolable image of the path from the satellite imagery emblazoned in his mind.

"Passing the Y-juncture," he transmitted. "Follow it right, the narrower canyon—the other way's a dead end." Knowing full well that the opposite appeared true, and that each man would have to negotiate the intersection without the benefit of seeing the teammate to his front, he reiterated, "Stay right, stay right, stay right."

He entered the narrower canyon and continued moving, the fatigue of running with his rucksack taking its toll despite the adrenaline.

Worthy tried to focus, bringing his mind back to the memory of planning the route and its attendant checkpoints. What lay on the path ahead? Beyond the intersection he'd just passed, the pathways became blurry in his memory. He consigned himself to defeat on this point—he could proceed as far as the next canyon juncture before he'd have to check his phone for real.

But that was a problem for a future he'd be lucky to live long enough to see. For now, there was no enemy ahead and his team was on the one and only escape route. Worthy would take it as far as he could before reassessing the best way back to the quarry and their vehicles.

His radio earpieces crackled to life.

"*Doc, I'm past the intersection.*"

Seconds later, Hass transmitted. "*Rain Man, I made it through, staying right. Eyes-on Doc.*"

Good, Worthy thought as he ran, the path ahead widening slightly. Now all he needed was confirmation from David to be assured that everyone remained on the correct route.

And when the team leader didn't transmit, Worthy did.

"Suicide."

Nothing.

"Suicide," he repeated, momentarily considering whether or not to reverse course and search for the missing team leader, "where the fuck are you?"

I surged forward, muscles burning from the strain, sweat and sand stinging my eyes behind my shooting glasses. The wind whipped the sand into a frenzy, obscuring my vision one moment and then parting like a curtain the next to reveal the terrain ahead.

As I rounded a bend, the canyon walls fell away on either side. The path diverged into two channels, splitting like a serpent's forked tongue.

"*Suicide*," Worthy transmitted.

To the left, the way was wide and inviting, the sandstone walls worn smooth by eons of wind and water. It curved gently out of sight, promising an easy route. Thanks to Worthy, I recognized the deception it concealed— a dead end waiting to swallow me whole, to leave me cornered and defenseless against the enemy closing in.

The path to the right was narrow and treacherous, and no man in his right mind would dare take it if not for Worthy's transmission. He'd already saved the lives of both Reilly and Hass. I desperately wanted to add my name to that tally but needed to assess whether we were still being pursued before committing to a full-blown retreat as last man.

"*Suicide*," Worthy implored, "*where the fuck are you?*"

I scrambled behind the largest rock I could find, kneeling to watch my trail as I keyed my mic in response. "Just cleared the intersection, staying right. Keep going."

It was a lie, of course, but a white one. I simply couldn't risk my teammates trying to come back for me.

Leveling my HK416 back the way I'd come, I scanned for enemy fighters and considered how long I should wait. If they'd followed me headlong, they would be upon me in seconds. If any more time elapsed, then they'd have likely thought better of their pursuit and backed off, potentially long enough for me to join my men and make our escape.

In a single instant the first enemy fighter appeared and fell, but not by my hand—Cancer had arrived on the high ground to deal himself into the fight.

That the sniper had managed to translate our radio transmissions into his own route along the high ground based on a single checkpoint reference was a miracle in itself. Doing so while on the move through a sandstorm transcended the abilities of even the most trained soldiers, but that kind of work was more or less Cancer's superpower.

Another two fighters appeared before me, moving low and cautiously, and now it was my turn. I drilled one with subsonic rounds, then the next, a torrent of sand swirling between us before I could assess my shots.

And in the seconds before visibility cleared once more, I considered my options.

Normally Cancer's presence alone would be sufficient to turn the tables, but with the intermittent visibility I couldn't rely on the sniper to achieve much more than sporadic kills. And there were far too many enemy fighters for that alone to make a difference. If these men were interested in self-preservation they would have backed off already, called in reinforcements, and tried to encircle us at some point further along in the terrain.

Instead they'd pursued a relentless onslaught, a nightmare-grade scenario for my team. They weren't going to stop coming until they ran us down.

The decision was made for me.

When the next enemy appeared, this time a three-man element, I didn't fire at all. There were too many behind them for me or Cancer or both of us to kill, and at this point I didn't even want to try.

I wanted to be seen.

Rising from my covered position in full view of the men, I darted left down the wider, dead-end trail.

Gunshots erupted behind me, none hitting in the storm's haze. The sound was a victory, however Pyrrhic, indicating that priority number one had been accomplished—the enemy would follow me rather than pursue my teammates, all of whom were now at liberty to make their way back to the vehicles however they could. As far as the bad guys were concerned, they were chasing our entire element rather than a lone decoy.

For me, though, the storm's howl and the increasing distance between me and my teammates amplified the reality that I was heading into near certain death with only one way out.

Ahead, the path widened so much that I momentarily second-guessed Worthy's advice. Had he gotten it wrong, reversed the routes in his mind?

But the basin of sand into which I soon entered was surrounded on all sides by rock walls sloping steeply into sheer cliffs. Worthy had remembered the route all right, and I was at the dead end he'd promised.

I looked up, seeing only waves of sand. Cancer was up there somewhere, and my only hope now was to climb like lightning and hope he'd have the visibility to shoot any enemy off my back.

But it only took a few seconds for me to realize that option was off the table.

Every slope became too steep for me to negotiate without climbing gear, much less with only my hands and feet to aid the effort. I yanked the quick release snaps on my ruck straps, feeling the anchor fall free of my back while identifying the highest point I could reach.

Slinging my rifle, I took off like a shot and scrambled upward with all the speed I could muster. Escape was no longer a possibility but establishing the most entrenched fighting position I could was nonetheless an enticing prospect, and I hauled myself onto a rock ledge before grabbing my HK416 and situating myself into the prone. The enemy could still get me and they certainly would, but I was going to make them pay dearly for that outcome.

A few seconds of whipping sand elapsed before I could make out the entrance to the basin of my last stand, and once I did, I oriented my rifle and took aim.

I expected to hear a transmission from Cancer, who was surely overhead by now and fully aware of what was about to go down. When he didn't contact me, I knew it was for the same reason that I had lied to my teammates about following them on the path to freedom—neither of us wanted them to compromise their escape after learning the monstrous truth of my actions.

Panic should have set over me then; instead, there was a Zen-like calm, an eerie tranquility that was wholly alien in my Stateside life much less in combat. I didn't think of my young daughter, my infant son, or my loving wife. The world back home was wholly compartmentalized from my current reality, and instead my mind mapped out a play-by-play of how I could go about killing as many men as possible before they took me down.

One last trip into the void, I thought, my final gunfight. The element of sacrifice wasn't lost on me—I just didn't care. My team would be safe, and I wouldn't. It was as simple as that, a clinical exchange of one life for five. Simple, and nothing that any of my men wouldn't do under the same circumstances.

Sand swirled around me, and I saw the enemy enter the basin and close in as silhouettes in the storm.

I opened fire with a generous number of rounds per each spotted enemy, seeking to exploit each moment of visibility before it was taken from me. Between my suppressor and my elevated position atop the ledge they'd have a hell of a time spotting me, though it was a matter of time before the tactical advantage swung the other way with violent finality.

The sand swirled and parted, granting me fleeting glimpses of the approaching fighters before obscuring them once more. I squeezed off controlled bursts, feeling the rifle jerk against my shoulder. One man crumpled, then another, and then both disappeared in a cloud brought forth by a new gust of wind.

When it cleared I saw another fighter rolling limply to a stop, felled by Cancer's lethal marksmanship. The sniper was still out there, an invisible guardian picking off targets of opportunity.

I acquired a new target in the dancing sand. *Pop pop pop*. Miss. Adjust. Fire again. This time the man spun and fell, and my next trigger squeeze yielded no corresponding shot—my weapon had gone empty without me realizing it. Reloading as the sand thinned for a precious few seconds, I continued my attempts to thin the horde. At least six men had made it into the basin, totally undaunted by the loss of their comrades.

Then muzzle flashes strobed in the swirling haze, the only indication of foes I couldn't see at the moment. They unleashed a barrage that hammered around me, chipping the stone as ricochets flew. I instinctively pressed myself into the stone below, elevating myself only enough to return fire. One of my barrages found its mark, a new assailant toppling into the sand only to be replaced by two more rushing forward to take his place.

Return fire cracked past, peppering my position. A shape darted between boulders and I tracked it, firing just as the wind parted the sandy veil. The man crumpled, a spray of crimson misting the air. Another of Cancer's shots had found its mark. We were giving better than we were getting, at least for the moment, and it wasn't until my view was obscured once more that I realized all the incoming gunfire had ended.

A retreat? I wouldn't be that lucky. They knew they had me dead to rights, and that assumption was confirmed with my next clear view—the enemy was closer now, waves of men sprinting across the basin as I engaged the closest two targets.

Things happened quickly after that, the gusts of wind accelerating in staccato bursts that provided and then removed my visibility like a strobe light. A sudden movement to my left—I swiveled, rifle snapping to target, finger tightening on the trigger until I broke a clean shot and everything turned to a gray-brown fog around me.

They were moving up the rocks now, closing in fast. The next target was to my right and the next, my front. Each man I identified and shot at was closer than the last. Why didn't they just spray and pray, I wondered? They had the numbers to take me out whether they saw me through the sand or not.

It didn't matter now. With grim determination, I resolved to fight to my last breath. I would make them kill me at point-blank range, force them to end it here on this desolate patch of rock and sand. It was the only choice I had left, the only way to buy time for my team to make it to safety.

I only hoped that Cancer was having better luck than I was.

Cancer peered through the scope of his accurized HK417, his finger resting on the trigger. He had a second's worth of clear line of sight into the basin, where David was a lone figure amid the swirling haze, the enemy forming a semicircle on the rocks around him and tightening their collective grip. Cancer pulled the trigger, sending a round into the shoulder of a fighter who'd ventured too close to David's position. The man slid down the slope, but there were far too many of his comrades for the hit to make a difference. The enemy fighters were bounding forward like wolves scenting blood.

Cursing under his breath, Cancer realigned the crosshairs on the next target. The sandstorm made it difficult to maintain a steady aim, gusts whipping across his face and forcing him to blink against the grit. He fired again, the shot slicing through the chaos to drop another fighter in his tracks. But this was like bailing water from a sinking ship; every man he felled was replaced by another, and then another still. A relentless wave of trained killers driven by a singular purpose.

David was doing his best to hold them off, gaining second after precious second for the rest of the team to cover more distance. Cancer knew it, felt the weight of it with every shot he fired. But he also knew the brutal truth —there were too many. His mind raced through the calculus of death. If he aimed too long, he'd lose the next target to the storm's veil. If he fired too quickly, he'd miss his chance.

When the sand next cleared he saw the cluster of enemy fighters, closing in on David's position, still moving up the rocks. They were close— too close. Cancer lined up a shot but before he could fire, a burst of gunfire cracked from below, rock fragments spraying against his face as bullets slammed into his cover.

Cancer pulled back from the edge, relocating a few meters before popping out again, the world narrowing to a deadly game of angles. He had to choose between taking out the men targeting him or trying to save David, and it was no choice at all. He caught a glimpse of his team leader and redirected his aim to see the enemy fighters closing the distance, scrambling over the rocks like ants.

David fired at one man and Cancer another, but no one was shooting at the besieged team leader.

The realization struck Cancer like a thunderbolt—they wanted David alive. It was the only explanation for their restraint, the only reason they hadn't simply obliterated his position with overwhelming firepower. The irony of it was sickening. After all the lives the team had taken under David's guidance, all the blood on their hands, the enemies were going to deny the team leader a warrior's death. Instead he'd be dragged off to some desolate facility, tortured and interrogated until he either broke or his captors tired of him. It was a fate worse than death, and one that Cancer had no intention of allowing.

He peered through his scope again, his crosshairs settling on the point between David's shoulder blades. The team leader didn't have the presence of mind to consider swallowing his barrel, but Cancer could do it for him. At this range, with his skill, the shot was a certainty—a swift end. His finger hovered over the trigger, the weight of the moment pressing down like a physical force. Could he do it? Could he pull the trigger on his own team leader to spare him a worse fate? The chaos faded into the background as he wrestled with the decision. If the roles were reversed, would David hesitate?

In the end, however, he diverted his aim and fired at an enemy fighter instead. A new burst of fire chipped at the edge of his cover, and before he could so much as flinch, the entire basin was engulfed in a massive, roiling cloud of sand and dust.

The sandstorm intensified with unnatural fury, as if the very desert itself had risen up to eclipse the battlefield and everyone in it. Visibility dropped to zero in an instant, the winds howling as Cancer squinted against the stinging grit, his eyes watering as he strained to catch any glimpse of movement below.

But there was nothing to see, just an impenetrable wall of airborne particles whipping past in a frenzied maelstrom. The entire world had vanished, replaced by a seething, churning cloud.

Cancer relocated and hunkered low, pulling his shemagh tight across his face as he waited for a break in the storm. Seconds ticked by with agonizing slowness, turning a single minute or less into what felt like hours. He was supposed to be the overwatch, the guardian angel as he'd been so many times before.

And he was failing.

When the winds finally died down, the scene below had transformed entirely—the enemy were halfway out of the basin now, scurrying away with their prize.

Two men dragged David's unconscious body through the sand, and by the time Cancer could take aim, the sandstorm spared him the misery of having to watch what he knew would transpire.

His options in that moment boiled down to trying to pursue the element, picking them off one at a time while taking fire in return, or dedicating his every effort to safeguarding the rest of his team however he could.

It was a soul-crushing decision. David was the closest thing he had to a brother; the two men were connected by a burden of leadership forged in blood and battle, tempered by the unspoken understanding that each would die for the other without hesitation.

But Cancer was no longer just a sniper. His position as second-in-command of the only surviving Project Longwing team had just evaporated. Full leadership, once David's domain, had been thrust upon him.

He rose and transmitted, "Angel, break down and prepare to move, I'm coming back for you and we'll move out to the quarry together. Everyone else, make it to your vehicles and get out of here. From now on, I'm in command."

Worthy's response sounded panicked. *"Where is Suicide?"*

An uneasy silence passed before Cancer replied.

"They took him."

25

Senator Gossweiler sat alone in his expansive office, the early morning sun bleeding through the windows. The muted glow of a flat-screen television provided the only other illumination, its flickering images reflecting off the glass fronts of bookcases lined with legislative volumes and political biographies. He leaned forward in his high-backed leather chair, eyes fixed on the live broadcast unfolding on CNN.

On the screen, a solemn procession was taking place in Tehran. A stern-faced Iranian general in a dress uniform adorned with a chest full of medals guided Ayatollah Khamenei and the president through a cordoned-off area beneath a vast, domed ceiling. Rows of long tables draped in vibrant Iranian flags were covered with twisted metal fragments and scorched debris—the unmistakable wreckage of a downed aircraft.

The camera zoomed in on a piece of charred fuselage bearing the faint outline of a US Air Force insignia. The general gestured emphatically toward it, his voice resolute as he spoke in Farsi. A translator's voiceover cut in, "This is evidence of the American aggression against our sovereign nation. The B-2 bomber was shot down after it violated our airspace without declaration of war, disregarding all international laws."

Gossweiler's jaw tightened as the broadcast shifted to images of somber civilians gathered around flag-draped coffins. The footage was interspersed with blurred-out photographs of corpses in the dirt—alleged civilian victims of an unprovoked American attack.

An American news anchor took the screen then, speaking in a grave tone.

"Iranian officials claim that in addition to the downed aircraft, US forces have caused civilian casualties during alleged incursions into Iranian territory. They are accusing the United States of war crimes and are calling for an emergency session of the United Nations Security Council."

Gossweiler rubbed his temples, feeling the weight of the situation pressing down on him. The political ramifications were immense—calls for retaliation, heightened tensions, possible escalation into open conflict. With worldwide coverage of the catastrophic turn of events in Iran, his responsibilities had just increased tenfold. As the Chairman of the Senate Select Committee on Intelligence, he was the highest political oversight directly involved with Project Longwing. *The New York Times* exposé had lit a fuse, and while not publicly affiliated with the shootdown in Iran—yet, at least—this was the explosion that he'd be held accountable for.

The television continued its relentless coverage. Now, the Iranian general was leading the president and Ayatollah past the wreckage, pausing to examine a display of the bomber's black box and other sensitive equipment. Reporters jostled for position, flashes illuminating the scene as the president turned and spoke. "Let this be a warning," he declared, his words echoed by the translator. "Iran will not stand idly by while foreign powers violate our sovereignty and endanger our people."

A sudden ring pierced the room, startling him. He glanced at his desk where his secure line vibrated insistently, the caller ID displaying the word RESTRICTED.

He took a deep breath, muted the television, and then steeled himself as he picked up the phone.

"I'd ask for good news," he said, his voice strained, "but I think we're past that."

Chen responded tentatively. "I'm afraid so, Senator. And we've had a... a development that I'm calling to inform you of."

"Let's hear it," he replied, a hollow sensation settling in his gut.

"The men of Split Team Two were on their way to the hide site approximately two hours ago when they encountered heavy enemy contact. They were split up, and Rivers was captured."

"Captured?" he nearly shouted back, a surge of anxiety coursing through him. "Dead or alive?"

"Alive, Senator. The enemy went to great lengths to ensure that."

"So I'm about to see his face on CNN along with every other damn thing," he said, his grip tightening on the phone.

"Senator, the team assesses that he wasn't captured by the military. Given the proximity to the objective, it was likely a security element belonging to Malek."

"Where is the team now—or what's left of them?" he asked, struggling to keep his composure.

"They're consolidated, Senator, at an abandoned farmstead. All five men are there, along with their local asset. I just heard from them, or I would've told you sooner. They abandoned their hide site with no loss of sensitive equipment."

"And Malek?" He stared at the muted TV, the images blurring as his mind raced.

"Both objectives went dark, and we believe they've been abandoned entirely. To the best of our knowledge, Malek has gone into hiding."

"Even if we find him, there's no team to guide the airstrike. This mission is dead in the water. Is the exfil intact?"

"It is, Senator, although we'll have to adjust the linkup point and route to account for the possibility that Rivers is tortured into providing information."

"Of course he's going to be tortured into providing it. Christ, Chen," he muttered, a wave of nausea hitting him.

He closed his eyes for a moment, then spoke firmly. "Listen, I need to speak with the CIA Director immediately. Because I'm about to be called onto the carpet before the President."

"Understood, Senator."

The enormity of the situation pressed down on him, but there was no time to lose.

"In the meantime," he said, opening his eyes to his spacious office, "order the remaining team members to begin their exfil from Iran. Get them out of there—now. The mission is aborted."

26

A sharp, throbbing pain pulsed at the base of my skull as I blinked awake.

Harsh light from an exposed bulb overhead stabbed into my eyes, forcing me to squint. I tried to lift a hand to shield my face but found my wrists handcuffed to the arms of a heavy wooden chair. A thick strap crossed my chest, pinning me in place, and ropes bit into my ankles where they were bound to the chair's legs.

I took a slow, measured breath, letting my eyes adjust to the glare. The air was stale, carrying the scent of damp concrete and diesel—generator fumes. No windows, just four walls of chipped plaster.

Memories flooded back: the attack in the canyon, drawing the enemy away so my team could escape. Had they made it out? If anyone could get the team to safety, it was Cancer—provided he'd survived the attempt to defend me. Whoever had taken me alive moved with precision and skill, likely Malek's people. Former Quds Force, perhaps.

I shifted my focus inward, assessing for injuries. Aside from the headache and some bruises, everything seemed intact. I was wearing a pair of fatigue pants, a promising indication that my well-hidden tools for escaping cuffs and other restraints were still on my person with one notable exception.

The pants weren't mine.

Nor was the high-end, moisture-wicking T-shirt covering my torso. This was an unexpected turn of events—one of many on the mission thus far—but still preferable to waking up in an orange jumpsuit. I tried to check the time only to find that my watch was gone.

But I had more pressing priorities. Horrific torture was imminent. They'd want intel on the team, our mission, who'd sent us and why. Standard procedure. My SERE training surfaced: survival, evasion, resistance, and escape. The first step of capture was to survive it in the first place, and I'd unwittingly accomplished that despite killing as many of my attackers as possible.

And until resisting interrogation became necessary, my thoughts turned to escape. The hum of the generator confirmed I was in a remote location, probably an isolated compound. Unquestionably preferable to being held in an urban facility. I hadn't been sold to the Iranian government, at least not yet—this was no prison cell.

I scanned the room again, noting the single metal door reinforced with rivets. No obvious weaknesses. The light bulb's wiring snaked along the ceiling, disappearing into a small hole—no help there.

Suddenly footfalls moved down the hall, heading toward me at a rapid clip.

I heard the shuffle of men outside—guards in the hall—and then the door swung open, followed by a man entering my room so quickly that I thought he was going to attack me.

But the tall figure striding inside lifted a metal folding chair from its position against the wall, opened it, and set it down directly to my front in one smooth motion before taking a seat.

He was thin, athletic, and had the build of a marathon runner and a sharpness to his features that bordered on gaunt. His skin was tanned, pulled taut across his high cheekbones, and his dark eyes were framed by a pair of thin, wire-rimmed glasses that gave him an air of academic detachment. Hair, streaked with gray, was slicked back meticulously, and he wore khakis and a thin button-down shirt. A SIG Sauer P226 rested against one hip, the only overt indication of his lethality—at least, until I looked at his opposite side. There, hanging from his belt, was a sheathed knife that I recognized all too well. It was my Winkler. He crossed his legs, leaning back slightly to watch me.

Soren Malek.

His voice was smooth, neutral—and, most disturbingly of all, unquestionably American. "So you're the one causing all this trouble."

"Trouble?" I asked. "I'm just a Canadian journalist, caught in the wrong place at the wrong time. Can I have some water?"

"You may, David Rivers, in time."

That brought me up short. The Geneva Convention dictated that captives provide their name, rank, and service number, but I hadn't exactly carried dog tags or an ID card with me when I parachuted out of a bomber over Iran.

Malek seemed amused by my confusion.

"There is nothing the Chinese government hasn't hacked, and very little information among it that I don't have access to. You know who I am, Mr. Rivers, and it's only right that I be extended the same courtesy."

I glanced down at the fingertips on my right hand, found them smudged with black ink.

Malek went on, "We couldn't take the risk of leaving your clothes on. After searching them, it seems our concern was not unjustified. One of my men donated a partial uniform. I hope it's sufficient."

"More than sufficient," I replied evenly. "Be careful with the wristwatch you took, though. It's got a laser and a flamethrower—you've seen movies."

"Indeed I have."

Silence stretched between us. He studied me, and I returned the favor.

Then Malek asked, "Did you know I was American?"

Should I lie? "No. The dossier they gave us was pretty thin."

He gave a knowing nod. "I can already see the wheels turning. Wondering how one of your countrymen could end up in my position."

I hesitated. "I'd be lying if I said the thought hadn't crossed my mind."

"Perhaps," he offered, "you'd have been more comfortable if I was a true believer carving a righteous Islamic caliphate out of an immoral capitalist lapdog state."

"At the very least, it would explain your goal in Pakistan."

"Pakistan, yes. Where you very nearly killed me. I saw you, you know."

"And I saw you. The ruse with the bodyguards and the decoy VIP was a good one."

He almost smiled, a fleeting expression that vanished as quickly as it appeared. "It was, wasn't it?"

"But the theft that you were fleeing...a bit dramatic, don't you think?"

"Perhaps. But I imagine you mistook my intentions."

"Unless you stole that nuclear warhead for research purposes, I don't think there's much I could misunderstand. Killing innocent people has never appealed to me."

"Nor has it appealed to me. If you think I intended to target civilians, think again."

"Unless you planned to set it off in the middle of the Sahara, I don't see how that makes much difference. It wasn't exactly a precision weapon."

Malek removed his glasses.

"I understand why the CIA withheld my nationality," he said, procuring a cleaning cloth from his shirt pocket and rubbing the lenses in precise circular motions. "The CIA's Phoenix Program, Mr. Rivers, killed between twenty thousand and forty thousand suspected Communist supporters during the Vietnam War."

"I'm familiar."

He held his glasses up to the light, evaluating them for smudges. "One detail you may not be so familiar with is that there were quite a few American citizens among the targets. Those targets were provided to only the most seasoned American soldiers, and yet the refusal rate was close to sixty percent. Another twenty percent of such missions failed, the majority of which were statistically due to deliberate error. The successful kills from a fellow countryman had mixed outcomes—half of the assassins requested immediate assignment outside the Phoenix Program."

"And the other half were sociopaths," I said.

"Were they?" he asked, sliding his glasses on and neatly folding his cleaning cloth. "By that logic, you would be a sociopath as well for agreeing to terminate me. As would your teammates."

That final word caused me to tense, first out of concern for the men whose fates remained uncertain. A close second was that while any previously planned locations would have been shifted at the moment of my capture, I was going to endure considerable torture before anyone on Malek's side would believe that fact if they would at all.

Malek picked up on my discomfort, pocketing his cleaning cloth with a disarming smile.

"Relax, Mr. Rivers. As you must have guessed by now, we are not at any of my previous facilities. If there was a thread that could tie me to this location, we would not be here either. No one will be coming for you. I know there were one or more survivors from the shootdown. The dead bodies along a logical evasion corridor in the Parvand Range made that clear enough. But they or them, along with your team, are currently on their way to an emergency exfiltration point. I have no intentions of stopping them, nor any reason to do so."

My nostrils flared, my gaze falling once more upon the Winkler knife before I forced myself to look up. "With as much respect as a man tied to a chair can offer, you'll forgive my skepticism."

"I already have one captive. Why would I expend resources to gain more—for information? I already know everything I need to know. Project Longwing is nothing but a name, and one already exposed by the media. America will do away with it and shift those capabilities to a new program. Different name, different shooters, same purpose. DoD or Agency, it doesn't matter. I am well aware of the opposition against me, although after the loss of a B-2"—he made a mournful *tsk-tsk* sound—"I suspect it will be some time before my former country regains the political appetite for a direct apprehension."

"Lucky you," I said.

"Indeed. And I know the question you are asking right now."

"About the water?"

He fixed his gaze on me with an almost recriminatory intensity. "If I don't need information on who you work for or what you were doing here, and if I have no intentions of harming your teammates, then what am I planning to do with you? Vengeful torture? Execution propaganda? Selling you to the Iranian government for a hostage exchange?"

"I assumed you'd keep me here because I'm an excellent conversationalist."

"None of the above, Mr. Rivers."

"I'll bite," I said, feeling my jaw settle. "What do you plan to do with me?"

He leaned forward, elbows on his knees, fingers interlaced.

"A topic for our next conversation."

Then he stood, looming over me.

"Water," he called to the men outside. "And food. Our guest must be famished."

And with that, Soren Malek exited the room as quickly as he'd entered.

27

"There's just one thing we're not considering," Ian said.

Worthy asked, "What's that?"

"David could already be dead."

The house on the abandoned farmstead was a skeletal husk, its stone walls riddled with gaps where doors and windows once stood. Evening wind swept through these openings, carrying the chill down from the mountains. Sand coated the floor, swirling in tiny eddies as it caught the last rays of sunlight filtering through the shattered frames.

Ian sat beside the satellite radio, its cable snaking out through a missing doorway to the antenna propped outside. Worthy and Cancer stood nearby, gazing through the vacant window arches as the discussion progressed. Their shadows stretched across the dirt floor as the sun dipped low, painting the sky in deep reds and purples.

Swallowing hard, Ian continued, "I mean, think about it: how can we possibly know he's still alive?"

Cancer peered through the doorway at the horizon, where the wrinkled hills melded with the darkening sky. "I can't begin to tell you how many men they sacrificed rather than kill him. Whatever Malek offered or threatened, it worked. Believe me, David's alive."

They'd already transmitted news of David's capture and their current location and status to Chen, who, true to form, had offered nothing in the way of consolation or tactical support. Instead, she said she had to make some calls before doing the unthinkable.

She put them on hold.

Now they were in an interlude that was the mission equivalent of listening to elevator music, but the time wasn't wasted. With Reilly and Hass standing guard outside, the remaining men had formed a command cell of sorts—Cancer as ground force commander, Ian as his consigliere, and Worthy...well, Worthy simply refused not to be included. The pointman knew well enough that David alone had risked his life to search the evasion corridor, and now that he was missing, Worthy was dead set on returning the favor.

The pointman looked out at the barren landscape. "What now? We don't have a lead to follow even if we wanted to."

Ian exchanged a knowing look with Cancer. "I wouldn't say that."

Worthy turned, the scrape of his boots against the floorboards echoing in the space. "How could we possibly—"

"Chen fucked up," Cancer said. "She sent us the full dossier on Malek's financier, including his address."

"Navidi," Ian noted. "Dariush Navidi."

Worthy asked, "You think he knows where they took David?"

"Directly? Probably not. But he handles the money, buys properties for Malek. One of those properties is a fallback spot, and if David's still alive then that's where he's being held. We grab Navidi, and we get that information out of him one way or another."

"Unless he's fled."

Ian shook his head distantly. "As far as Navidi knows, the CIA hasn't identified him, let alone his location. He was set to meet Malek tomorrow night. Now that Malek's on the run, he probably ordered Navidi to sit tight and wait for word."

"Which," Worthy pointed out, "could come anytime."

Cancer's silhouette was rigid against the dimming light. "Exactly. That's why we need to move on him now, tonight."

"Where is he?"

"Birjand. Couple hours from here. So we're all in agreement. And I know Reilly and Hass are on board." Cancer looked at Ian, shadows hiding his expression. "Aren't you supposed to play devil's advocate?"

Ian paused, then sighed. "I can make a strong case that going after David is the worst possible thing we could do. But I'd be lying if I said I agreed with it."

The satellite radio came to life, the sound from its speaker slicing through the stillness. Chen's voice emerged from the static.

"Any Suicide Element, Raptor Nine One."

Cancer strode over, and Ian handed him the mic. "Cancer here."

"The mission is aborted." Chen's tone was flat. *"We've arranged an alternate exfil. I need you to proceed to a new linkup with all personnel and equipment."*

Outside, the wind whipped through the gaps in the walls. Ian's stomach knotted—here it comes, he thought.

Cancer replied, "We're not going anywhere except after Suicide."

"This isn't my decision." Chen's voice was strained. *"Orders from the highest levels."*

Ian caught Cancer's eye. "We'll need her help eventually. Be diplomatic."

The acting team leader nodded in seeming agreement, deflating before he keyed the mic again. "Yeah, well, the highest levels can go fuck themselves."

Silence stretched on the line. If the air hadn't felt charged before, it was now.

Cancer continued, "Look, I realize this sucks for you. First you couldn't get us to stay, and now you can't get us to leave. But you might want to try spending a day in combat before you have an opinion about how we should handle our business. Now, do you have any intel that will help us out?"

"Intel? The...the whole world is staring at the B-2 wreckage, the dead bodies. You want intel? It's an international firestorm, that's the intel. We have nothing on Suicide's location and neither do you. You can't locate him."

Cancer stared into the darkness. "Watch me. I'll let you know when we need support. Cancer, out."

After he tossed down the handset, Cancer's next actions were as fluid as changing magazines in a gunfight—he retrieved a pack of cigarettes, procured one, and sparked it before pocketing his lighter in one seamless series of movements.

Exhaling a cloud of smoke at the farmhouse ceiling, he spoke.

"Fuck it—let's go to Birjand."

28

"Five minutes out," Worthy transmitted, adjusting the HK416 between his knees and looking up from his phone's navigation display.

The streets of Birjand were mostly empty at this hour, although the sporadic passage of civilian vehicles allowed his team's pair of vehicles to blend in well enough. Dim streetlights cast uneven patches of light onto the paved streets, their faint glow reflecting off the stone facades of old buildings.

Shayan was behind the wheel of the Tata SUV, guiding them through narrow streets as he spoke. "This area was a crossroads of trade on the Silk Road. During the eleventh century, a wealthy merchant caravan set out from Birjand and mysteriously vanished into the desert, not far from where we are now. Some say it was lost in a sandstorm, but no trace was ever found. That means somewhere, the silk, spices, and gold are out there, waiting to be discovered."

Worthy looked at the driver in confusion, waiting for some relevance. When none came, he asked, "What the fuck are you talking about?"

Hass mercifully intervened from the backseat. "He does this. Random segues into local lore. It's like a glitch."

Shayan didn't look away from the road ahead. "Or a feature. My father was a cultural preservationist, and taught me the history of—"

"That's great," Worthy cut him off. "But we've got bigger things to worry about."

Undaunted, Shayan switched tack with eagerness. "This part of the city was built during the Safavid era. You can see—"

Worthy didn't even turn his head. "Not now," he said, cutting the driver off mid-sentence. "Just focus. You see something out of place, let us know. Until then, silence is a virtue."

He saw a minaret jutting above the skyline ahead and checked his phone to verify the landmark. "Right turn after the mosque."

Shayan negotiated the intersection as ordered, and Worthy looked behind him to see that the Chery SUV containing Ian, Cancer, and Reilly still followed at a distance.

Turning back in his seat, he checked his phone and transmitted, "Three minutes."

The dashboard clock read 21:47. Still a little ways off, but not much. The vehicle bounced slightly as they crossed a pothole, skirting the edge of a dried-up irrigation canal. Here, the road widened into an empty square where faded signs of a bazaar were barely visible in the ambient glow of streetlights. Worthy stole a glance at Shayan, who was keeping his eyes on the road but still looked like he wanted to say something.

Scanning the streets, Worthy mentally calculated escape routes, side alleys they could use if stopped by Iranian authorities or worse.

He checked his phone again, the familiar task of navigation as the team's pointman giving him some small measure of control over a situation that felt like it was slipping further away with each passing city block.

They were now minutes away from parking their vehicles to embark on a stealthy raid of Dariush Navidi's residence. Ian would remain with the second vehicle while Cancer and Reilly quietly breached whatever entry point they could find at the front of the house. Worthy and Hass, meanwhile, would enter through the back, and neither element would leave until the broker was in custody and his family—if he had any, he thought, because Chen had omitted that detail—was restrained and left in place.

With any luck the incursion would end with a spirited drive toward a pre-established interrogation site where Navidi would tell them everything they wanted to know, whether he was willing to talk or not.

"Left up here," he said, and Shayan had barely begun the turn when Hass spoke from the backseat.

"Holy shit," he muttered. "Feels like we're on a whole other planet."

The neighborhood of Parandshahr was a world apart from the older parts of Birjand. Wide, clean streets stretched ahead of them, lined with palm trees and sleek, modern streetlights.

Gated homes rose on either side, their facades illuminated by discreet landscaping lights. The buildings were a mix of luxurious villas and upscale apartment complexes, their polished stone and glass exteriors reflecting the wealth of their occupants. Each property boasted private gardens, some with fountains trickling gently in the night. The neighborhood had the unmistakable quiet of affluence, the kind of silence that only money could buy.

Worthy transmitted, "Two minutes."

Cancer replied from the rear vehicle, "*I bet these rich fucks have never seen a gun in their life. Navidi's in for a rude awakening.*"

"True," Worthy replied. "But I'm not so sure this will go according to plan. I've got a weird feeling about this one."

"*Could be worse.*"

"How?"

"*Could be daytime.*"

That much was true, Worthy thought—there was no question they were going in blind, tracking a lead they barely understood. But Malek's broker was their only shot at finding David, and while it was a long shot to say the least, making the attempt under night vision was far better than the alternative.

Navidi's house was close now, hidden somewhere among the maze of upscale residences.

"Right turn," he said, keying his mic. "Target street ahead."

Then, without facing his driver, he continued, "Keep a constant speed when we pass by. We're just taking a look. Don't speed up and definitely don't slow down, all right?"

"I understand," Shayan allowed, wheeling the Tata SUV through the turn.

He kept his eyes forward as they glided past one high-walled villa, its ornate gate shadowed under a canopy of trees, then another.

Worthy checked his phone and transmitted, "Five houses down, on the left, twenty seconds."

He was gaining his first view of the perimeter well when Navidi's gate swung open on automated hinges.

"Slow down," he announced.

"But you said—"

"Slow down," Worthy repeated with more force, then transmitted to his teammates, "Gate's opening, black sedan pulling out and turning toward us."

Cancer replied, "*Gotta be him. Block him from the front, I'll take care of the rest. We're taking him on the street.*"

"Stay in your lane," Worthy said to Shayan, "until I tell you. Then swing over and block this car from the front, bumper-to-bumper."

He ditched his phone in the cupholder, assuming a two-handed grip on his HK416 as he watched the sedan approach, its blinding headlights illuminating the cab. It was a BMW 7 Series, a status symbol for a financial broker but nothing so exotic as to garner unwanted attention, and Worthy held his breath until it was two car lengths away before speaking again.

"Now!" he said, bracing himself as Shayan swung the SUV into the opposite lane.

His vehicle and the BMW braked at the same time, though too late to avoid a collision— the front fenders smashed into one another, jolting the occupants of both.

Cancer's SUV glided past Worthy's passenger window, veering left to block the BMW at its rear quarter panel.

With the target vehicle pinned, the team spilled out of both trucks— Worthy and Hass from the front, Reilly and Cancer from the rear, weapons raised as they closed in on the German sedan.

Reilly's boots hit the pavement before the Chery SUV had come to a full stop.

He was closest to the BMW's driver door, and swung his HK417 up in the tight space to sweep the taclight over the cab. The vehicle was unoccupied save the driver, and Reilly was reaching for the door handle when the dazed man seemed to regain his senses all at once.

The car's locks clicked down and Navidi, his face illuminated by the glow of the dashboard, looked to the rearview mirror as he threw the car into reverse and mashed the gas.

The BMW's wheels spun frantically, a desperate whine filling the air as rubber battled asphalt. Smoke began to rise, carrying with it the acrid stench of burnt rubber—and while the SUV didn't budge, Reilly had no intention of finding out how long that would last.

He slammed the buttstock of his rifle into the driver's window, striking hard at the lower right corner where the glass met the frame.

The glass held.

Navidi seemed oblivious to the impact, singularly focused on his escape. He shifted into drive and accelerated into the bumper of the equally immobile Tata SUV to his front. The BMW's rear tires spun ever faster, their shrieks rising in pitch, as Reilly repeated the strike with his buttstock, harder this time, causing a spiderweb of cracks to spread across the glass.

A third blow was all it took for the window to shatter inward, showering Navidi with fragments and creating an opening for Reilly's next move.

He drove a swift, left-handed blow across the broker's temple, causing his head to snap sideways against the headrest. Releasing his fist, Reilly swept his palm to find the handle, popped it, and then flung the door open before pushing his rifle back on its sling.

The broker raised his hands defensively as Reilly unbuckled the seatbelt and grabbed Navidi with both hands, wrenching him free from the vehicle like a rag doll. That process was barely complete when Cancer greeted their new captive with a savage, close-range uppercut to the kidney —Navidi collapsed in Reilly's grasp, leaving the medic to haul him toward the open door of the SUV.

The medic was about to shove him inside when he realized the options at hand. They could leave Navidi's BMW and whatever intelligence it contained in place, all to serve as evidence that he'd been forcibly apprehended.

Option two was what he did now.

"Keys," he said, and Cancer understood immediately. He dug through Navidi's pockets to procure the BMW FOB, and once it was secure, Reilly slung the broker into the Chery's backseat. Cancer followed the captive inside, but not before handing off the key.

That left the medic to greet his new ride, the BMW's engine still idling, its headlights casting a stark glare that extended as Shayan reversed his Tata SUV away from the interdiction site.

Reilly slid into the BMW's driver seat, the leather creaking beneath his weight as he settled atop the scattered fragments of safety glass. The cabin was filled with the distinctive scent of fresh, high-end leather, brushed aluminum accents and dark wood trim gleaming in the vehicle's red-orange ambient light.

It was a major upgrade from the utilitarian SUV now pulling away with Navidi inside, although Reilly didn't have time to linger on that fact. He slammed his door shut and shifted, reversing toward the taillights of his former vehicle.

A hard crank of the hand-stitched leather steering wheel brought the BMW's rear end into the driveway it had just departed, and Reilly braked just shy of the still-closing gate before shifting again and pulling forward, turning onto the street and accelerating to catch up with Cancer's Tata SUV.

He adjusted his rearview mirror to find the headlights of Shayan's vehicle following behind him, then closed the gap with the lead vehicle by way of a gentle push on the pedal that sent the V-8 twin turbo working harder than he anticipated. Braking before a rear-end collision, he assumed a careful interval that he maintained by looking over the BMW's large touchscreen display that showed a navigation map.

"*He's going down,*" Cancer transmitted. "*Doc, your pocket rocket is working.*"

Reilly smiled faintly—the term referred to the syringes he'd staged in the seatbacks of both vehicles, both spares to complement the ones on his person. Each contained 300 milligrams of ketamine and five milligrams of midazolam, a combination that would put Navidi out like a light.

Cancer continued, "*Racegun, find us a place to search and ditch the BMW on our way to the interrogation point.*"

"Copy," the pointman replied, leaving Reilly to add his two cents.

Speaking over the whistle of cold wind through the missing driver's window, he transmitted, "Do we really have to ditch it, though?"

Cancer replied, "*Tracking and theft recovery, asshole.*"

And while Reilly prematurely mourned the loss of the most luxurious vehicle he'd ever had the opportunity to ride in, much less drive, on a mission abroad, the good far outweighed the bad.

They were now one massive step closer to locating David, and in such smooth fashion that Reilly almost felt like he'd dreamt up the entire event. His team had planned on a surreptitious raid, and instead, within thirty seconds of the BMW leaving its gated estate, it was as if Navidi had never been there at all.

29

A rumble echoed in the room as the heavy metal door swung open, and Malek stepped inside with an air of composed authority. The dim light cast sharp shadows across his lean frame, highlighting the angular features of his face and the glint in his dark eyes. Dressed in clean civilian clothes, he seemed almost out of place against the stark, utilitarian backdrop of the cell. The only nod to his status as a terrorist was the holstered SIG pistol that I'd seen him with before.

And, of course, my Winkler knife, worn in an insult that made me too angry to bring up for fear of losing control.

He settled into the chair across from me and asked, "You have been well taken care of, I trust? The food is to your liking?"

"Better than I expected," I acknowledged.

"And my guards have been courteous? Treated you with respect and dignity?"

"They have."

"Very good. Then let's talk, shall we?"

It was hard to tell if he was being serious or not—there was a veil separating his thoughts from his expression, now an impenetrable mask.

I must have been far easier to read, plagued as I was by a twinge of irritation as I fought to keep my expression neutral. The chains binding my wrists rattled softly as I shifted in the chair, the cold metal against my wrists a stark reminder of my predicament.

"Consider me a captive audience. What are we talking about?"

"I believe the CIA is a good place to start."

Well this was fucking great, I thought. This was where the roundabout dialogue would, at some point, seamlessly transition into well-hidden probes for information.

"What about the CIA?" I asked.

"The truth, of course. They overthrow democratically elected governments whenever it suits their interests—installing dictators in Iran to control oil, sparking civil war in Guatemala to protect US business, and backing brutal regimes in places like Chile, all for corporate profits. They targeted civil rights leaders and activists through Operation CHAOS, tortured their own citizens with MKUltra's mind-control experiments. I could go on, of course."

"You could," I agreed, "endlessly. You're trying to make me believe that the CIA is dirty as hell and always has been. Well congratulations, I already do. You've won. Now what?"

A subtle flicker of surprise crossed his face, quickly masked by a thoughtful expression. He rested his elbows on his knees, fingertips pressed together as he regarded me intently. "If your vision is so clear, why do you serve it?"

"My service only applies to what I can control. Namely my team, which, I might add, tries to kill the right person without collateral damage."

"You value your team, your code—what if that could extend to something greater?"

"Such as?"

"America, Mr. Rivers."

So I wasn't going to be probed for information, or even tortured—at least, not yet. Instead, I was undergoing something that was arguably worse.

Political indoctrination.

Malek was feeding me his personal ideology and would continue to do so, slowly and systematically, to get me to side with him and ultimately serve his cause.

Every topic of conversation, every selectively included fact, would be designed to chip away at my loyalty, to make me question my own beliefs. Isolation and psychological pressure were classic tactics. But the main ingredient was time, and with no one coming to save me and no possibility for escape, Malek had that in droves.

I knew what was happening. But resisting it, day after day, was a whole different battle. The smart move would have been to keep my responses extremely subtle. But subtlety was never my strong suit.

"Before you waste your breath," I said, "I should mention that every vestige of patriotism I had evaporated somewhere in the course of my first deployment. I'm not the kind of guy who runs off into the sunset singing Jody cadence while toting an American flag. But we come from the same country, and she's better than a lot of the alternatives on the world stage right now."

"America," he replied, his tone measured, "was founded on genocide and built by slavery. Of the 50 states, 48 were formed due to the genocide of the indigenous people. Hawaii was gained after a group of American businessmen, with the support of US military forces, overthrew its monarchy. And Alaska was purchased."

I pointed out, "Trace any country's roots back far enough, and you're going to find bloodshed. Some more recent than others. But as long as the world isn't run by the Nazis, I think we've succeeded in some small measure. Don't you?"

Malek adjusted his glasses, the light casting a glint across the lenses as he settled back into his chair. The tension in the room was palpable, the air thick with the unspoken weight of ideology clashing between us. His gaze never left mine, piercing and unyielding.

"You present me with WWII, Mr. Rivers? And with a straight face, no less. Let us not forget that the US watched the Allies get slaughtered in wholesale quantities by the Axis powers, with no intention of helping beyond financial and military aid until Pearl Harbor. This was largely due to the isolationist view of the American population, the same segment of people that will today point to defeating the Nazis as their only defense against everything I've just said. Along with, of course, vague references to freedom despite the fact that while the US makes up four percent of the global population, she incarcerates twenty percent of prisoners worldwide. All her own citizens."

Malek spoke with a measured calmness, each word carefully enunciated as if he were presenting an irrefutable argument in a courtroom. In reality, he was making an interesting twist to the formula of political indoctrination. He wasn't lying, only stacking the facts in his favor.

In SERE training it was forbidden to engage in a battle of wits against your interrogator. But my wits were all I had left, and without the possibility of ever getting out of here, I decided to make my own rules.

"I'm no fan of mass incarceration. Or the War on Drugs, or a hell of a lot of other things our country does. But I have to side with Churchill. 'Democracy is the worst form of government, except all those other forms that have been tried from time to time.'"

Malek didn't hesitate. "A more fitting comparison for our purposes is Thoreau. 'Disobedience is the true foundation of liberty.' The paradox of patriotism, Mr. Rivers, is that love for one's country often necessitates dissent against its actions. The structures you defend, whether the CIA or America, are not as impregnable as they seem. Change is inevitable—whether we guide it or become casualties of it is the real question."

"Guide it?" I asked. "We're two guys in the middle of the desert. Don't get me wrong, I have no doubt you can manage your fair share of terrorist attacks. But that tactic has never resulted in meaningful change at the national level, now has it?"

"You seem to forget Algeria and Afghanistan."

"Exceptions that prove the rule. And except for the fact that they start with the letter A, neither country had anything in common with America."

He leaned forward, resting his elbows on his knees, fingers interlaced.

"Both countries fell because foreign powers exploited them, just as America is exploited by corporate interests. Insurgents used guerrilla tactics to overcome superior military strength. Public anger fueled those fights, and the same discontent in America can and will spark an insurgency. Terrorism achieves far more than simple violence. When properly applied as a tactic, it unravels the system from within."

His eyes bored into mine, searching for any sign of agreement or doubt as he continued.

"The Roman Empire collapsed under the weight of internal corruption, political instability, and an overextended military, much like the America of today. The elites grew disconnected from the people increasingly affected by economic inequality, just as corporate greed and political divisions now erode the US. When empires rot from the inside, their fall becomes inevitable. America is already teetering on the same edge, heading toward collapse."

"Even if you're right," I said, "the Roman Empire lasted a thousand years. This metaphor means you're going to have to wait another 700 years or so."

He chuckled softly, the sound devoid of genuine mirth. "What I am trying to accomplish certainly won't be accomplished in my lifetime. But there is no America anymore, Mr. Rivers. Just corporations holding control, the CIA beholden to capital, the military industrial complex undermining the democratic process exactly as Eisenhower warned in his farewell address."

I shifted against my restraints. His conviction was unsettling—not because I agreed, but because I could see the unwavering belief fueling his actions. "So you want to wade into this mess and try to wrangle something out of it that more closely resembles America at its inception. Do I have that right?"

"A restart, yes. By amplifying existing issues to hasten an ongoing collapse. This will be a process of chiseling away, not so that I or anyone currently working for me will personally reap the rewards, but so that our children's children will benefit from a new future. One where America exists as more than a marketing concept."

"Well," I said, "this is all fascinating. I wouldn't hold your breath on me wishing you luck, but I don't think luck will help you anyway. The CIA's got your number, and if you ever leave Iran, it's going to be the shortest trip you've ever taken."

"Of that I have no doubt. But you have no idea the extent of support I have operating behind the scenes in America. No idea at all, Mr. Rivers."

"I suppose I'll have to take your word on that."

He raised his eyebrows, his face now carefree. I wondered if our session was over and if so, which of us had won.

Instead he replied, "Not at all. I am happy to demonstrate, but that is up to you."

His gaze was unwavering, and there was a weight behind his words that hinted at something far more sinister than abstract philosophy.

"Demonstrate...how? And how is this up to me?"

Malek drew a breath, released it in an ecstatic sigh. Whatever he was about to say, this was the moment he'd been waiting for.

"You will join my cause and begin your service in the upheaval that is already far in progress within the next eight hours. Or, as an alternative, I will detonate multiple synchronized explosive devices in the Main Concourse of Grand Central Terminal in New York while you watch live on CNN. The choice is yours, Mr. Rivers."

30

"Flumazenil," Reilly explained, depressing the plunger on the syringe. "Reverses the effects of the midazolam sedation."

Cancer asked, "How long?"

"A minute. Maybe two."

"Wonderful. Go pull security with the guys."

The medic took his syringe and departed, his footsteps echoing in the cavernous space.

Red lens headlamps provided the only light, the dim glow barely illuminating the narrow tunnel ahead and behind. Rough walls streaked with white deposits glistened faintly, every surface encrusted with salt. The ceiling was barely high enough to stand, supported by thick, weathered wooden beams.

And leaning against the nearest beam, restrained at the wrists and ankles, was Dariush Navidi.

He didn't seem to mind Reilly's injection—the captured broker was currently motionless and, with the exception of some murmured sentence fragments in Farsi, had remained that way ever since Cancer drugged him at the impromptu interdiction point.

"This better work," Cancer said.

Ian sat cross-legged in front of Navidi, his digital voice recorder prepped. "If it doesn't, we're out of options. Especially after you pissed off our boss. You could've told her we agreed to exfil, bought us some time."

"Not enough to make a difference. And if you're not persuasive enough with this fuck"—he nudged Navidi with the toe of his boot—"then I sure as shit will be."

Ian nodded. He'd previously been all too quick to point out that Iran had some of the world's largest salt reserves, and the extensive database on his encrypted field laptop yielded a few abandoned mines in the area.

This one was outside Amirabad, the closest such location to Birjand and therefore the obvious choice. With David getting tortured, Malek alive and well, and the team trying to avoid capture while fully rogue from the CIA, there was no time to waste.

Cancer unsheathed his Winkler knife, kneeling to slice the flex cuffs binding Navidi's wrists together. The ankle restraints would remain in place, and Cancer stood before resting the tip of his blade against the base of the man's neck.

Navidi's eyes fluttered halfway open, his head lolling drowsily.

When the broker came to, his first reaction was to scramble upward—and then, feeling the blade of Cancer's knife, he fell back down and looked about wildly.

"*Khodaaya, koja hastam?*"

Cancer rounded his front, standing beside Ian so their captive could see the knife. "English. We speak English in this bitch."

Navidi looked about with desperation in his eyes. "*Man nemifahmam.*"

"Your name," Ian said, "is Dariush Navidi. Global asset manager currently under the employ of Soren Malek. Educated at Oxford, and if that institution taught you how to lie, then they didn't do a very good job."

Navidi exhaled then, lowering his head into his hands.

"Where am I?"

Cancer was all too happy to field that inquiry.

"Where you're at now is a whole lot better than where you will be if you don't tell us everything you want to know. A man can lose a gallon and a half of blood before dying." He tilted his blade upward and mused, "And I can draw that out one drop at a time if I need to."

Staring up at the weapon, Navidi appeared first disoriented and then scared. "There is no need. Please—I will cooperate."

Cancer returned his Winkler to its sheath, and Ian began the interrogation in earnest. "I need to know where Malek is right now."

"How can I know this?"

"Because," Ian replied, "you were responsible for acquiring Malek's properties. One of those was the fallback site he's currently at. And right now you're going to provide every location you know about."

Navidi nodded quickly, eager to comply. "A desert compound south of the Parvand Range. Another built into the base of a mountain, seventy kilometers northeast of Birjand. These I purchased for him. I do not know the exact points, but perhaps I could locate them on a map."

There was no need—Navidi had just described both original Project Longwing objectives.

"What else?" Ian asked.

"That is all I know."

Cancer interceded, "Well if that's all you're going to say, I can start carving you to pieces until it jogs your memory."

Turning his palms upward, the broker pleaded, "Please, I purchased these properties. But that is it, that is all."

Ian went on, "We know Malek traveled between those two sites. But he spent a whole lot of time somewhere else, and unless you can tell me some other locations, there's nothing I can do for you."

Cancer leered, a bad cop who was all too happy to play the role.

Navidi swallowed, gaze darting around the mine. "I am certain he has other sites. But he is a careful man, and would not trust one individual with all this information."

"That information is kept somewhere."

Navidi's face brightened with a sudden recollection. "Yes, there is one such place, a central hub that I know of in Tabas. I never worked there directly, as someone else negotiated the purchase. But I did arrange transport of equipment there."

"What equipment?"

"I have no idea. But there were many shipments, all smuggled through a series of cutouts."

"Fine. Where is this place?"

"As I said," Navidi replied warily, "I never worked there directly. I could access the shipment records, perhaps, but I do not have my laptop. There is no way I can remember everything, you see?"

"So the information is on your computer."

"My laptop, yes. But I do not have it—"

Cancer walked behind the column, then lifted a leather satchel and slammed it into Navidi's chest.

"You do now. Make it fast."

Reilly had found the satchel during his hasty search of the BMW sedan, along with a whole lot of Iranian currency and not much else. And now that they'd ditched the car, having never so much as set foot in Navidi's house, the sum total of their ability to locate much less rescue David Rivers was now riding on whether or not that laptop held the information they were looking for.

The odds of which, Cancer noted, were looking pretty good at present.

Navidi barely managed to hold onto the satchel, horrified rather than relieved at the sight of it. Thus far he'd only revealed information he knew with great confidence that his captors already possessed; now, he'd have to cross the line into outright treason against a man and organization that had paid for his entire lifestyle. The consequences for such an infraction would be far worse than simply fatal, both for him and anyone he knew or was even distantly related to, and right now Cancer had to assure him that his immediate fate could be far worse.

Cancer watched Navidi power on his laptop, then type in a password that must have been twenty characters in length—lowercase letters, uppercase letters, numbers, special characters, the whole lot. A final keystroke caused the screen to fully illuminate.

Navidi hesitated then, his hands beginning to tremble. "How do I know you will not kill me if I tell you?"

Cancer shot him a leering grin. "I'll kill you right now if you don't."

Ian was more conciliatory in his approach, his voice an almost soothing cadence. "You have my word, no harm will come to you if this location provides the information we're looking for."

"If?"

"I don't trust many people," Cancer said, "and you ain't one of them. If you think we're going to cut you loose and hope that you were telling the truth, think again."

Kneeling to bring his face close to the broker, he continued, "We're not going to kill you, because you're coming with us."

31

The door swung open with a low creak, and three men stepped into the room. I watched them closely, sizing each one up in seconds.

The first was a young white guy, couldn't have been older than his early thirties and by far the youngest of the trio. Tall and lean, with tousled hair. His eyes flickered with a quick, darting energy.

Behind him, a Latino man, older—mid-fifties, maybe. Stocky, with the kind of build that said he'd been through hell and walked back out the other side. Unmistakable military bearing, full tattoo sleeves on both arms peering out from the edges of his shirt cuffs.

The last guy, Black, smooth as glass. His every movement was deliberate, calm. He didn't need the intimidation game; he'd already won by virtue of his mere presence.

Two of them set up foldout chairs in front of me, and the third—Mr. Intimidation—eased into the one already waiting as he spoke.

"Mr. Malek asked us to stop by." His voice was low and measured. "He'd like us to give you some insight into why we're here. You may ask us any and all questions you wish."

Raising an eyebrow, I said, "Sure. Here's the first: what is this supposed to be, a support group meeting for Traitors Anonymous?"

I expected them to bristle at my shrewd observation, to fire back with their words and/or fists. At this point, I didn't much give a shit which it was—I was so far off the reservation of my interrogation training that I had nothing to lose. All those formal techniques worked well in theory. When your captor knew your identity, however, along with the fact that you'd come to Iran to kill him, playing dumb wasn't a viable strategy.

But instead of demonstrating immediate defensiveness upon hearing my remark, these men laughed—a low, familiar chuckle. Had they been through this routine before?

The older man, the military one, shook his head. "More like the start of a bad joke. A white guy, a Mexican, and a Black dude walk into an interrogation room..."

Another round of laughs. Cutting through the humor, I voiced my sole demand. "I need to talk to Malek."

Several hours had already passed since he'd made his threat, and while I had no means of gauging the exact time remaining, I didn't intend to test my captor on whether or not he had the means and men in place to blow up Grand Central Terminal. Based on what I'd seen in Pakistan, he most definitely did.

My statement caused the laughter to subside, and quickly. I wondered if they knew what Malek had said to me, and figured they must.

"That's a no-go," said the Latino military man. "Mr. Malek will come to see you when he's ready. Ethan, you're up."

The youngest of the three nodded and I sized him up again—pale skin, neatly combed brown hair that was already thinning at the crown. Something about him screamed entitlement, but there was a hollow look in his eyes.

"David," he began, "I'm Ethan. I spent fifteen years working as a policy advisor on Capitol Hill. Got my start at Yale, interned for a senator, worked my way up. I drafted major legislation on healthcare and defense, sat in meetings with lobbyists from every industry you can imagine. And I found out that's where the real power is, not in Congress. It's in the boardrooms of Big Pharma, defense contractors, and insurance giants.

"I saw it all up close. I...I sat in those rooms when the suits came in, pushing for policies that would kill meaningful reform. I watched elected officials—even the ones I used to think had some integrity—take their marching orders from the same companies bankrolling their re-election campaigns. They wrote checks, and our job was to write laws that kept their profits high and the public in the dark."

At this point I vaguely wondered if he was some role player with fake credentials sent in by Malek. I couldn't press him or any of them too far, had to make Malek believe I was a prospective convert in the interests of stopping the New York City attack as much as keeping myself alive.

And my family, I thought. What would become of them if I refused Malek's offer?

I asked, "What's the worst thing you saw?"

Ethan scoffed. "Sure, I mean...where to begin. Big Pharma's a case study in how this shit goes wrong. An entire industry designed to make billions off of people's suffering. Take the opioid crisis—they flooded the market despite known addictiveness, got 800,000 people addicted to heroin once they couldn't get the pills anymore, and then made billions off Narcan to stop overdoses. Life-saving HIV meds, insulin, cancer treatments—Americans pay up to ten times more than in Canada or Europe. That's all because Big Pharma lobbies to block price controls and tweaks formulas to block generics, all for profit.

"We had legislation on the table—price caps, subsidies, the works. You know what happened? Lobbyists for the pharmaceutical industry came in with their campaign donations, their promises of post-political careers, and that bill died in committee. We killed it. And that wasn't a one-time thing—it's the system, and it's meant to stay broken. Part of that is due to the revolving door. These Congressmen retire and six months later, they're sitting on the board of the companies they were regulating. It's even worse in the defense sector—"

The Latino man cut him off.

"Stay in your lane, young pup. We'll get there."

I watched Ethan closely. "It's a long way from DC to Iran. How'd you end up involved in this?"

He gave a slight shake of his head. "First I hit my breaking point. A senator I worked for—Walter Davenport, Illinois—asked me to bury a study showing that our healthcare policy was killing people. Looked me dead in the eye and told me it was 'politically inconvenient' to release it.

Before that I blamed the politicians and lobbyists, the entire system. But then I realized I'd been part of the problem myself.

"A week later I was at one of those insider events—cocktails, canapés, the usual bullshit. This consultant I barely knew approached me, said he could tell I was losing faith. He offered a different way to make change, real change. That's how I got my first introduction to Mr. Malek's people."

If true, I thought, Malek's recruitment network was not only well-placed but extremely proficient. DC was a hotbed for foreign intelligence collection, and not an easy place for such efforts to go unnoticed.

I asked, "And what, exactly, do you think you're doing to solve the problem now?"

"America isn't the country we thought it was. But it can be."

He exhaled slowly, his eyes focused on mine with sober acceptance. "Malek's the only one with a plan to make that happen."

"I'll go next," the Latino man said, before I had time to formulate a response to the policy advisor's chilling final comments.

By now I was assured that these people were the real deal—not actors, not role players— although that certainty came from a gut-level instinct more than any logical conclusion.

I focused on the man I'd assumed by his bearing to be former military. He had the look of someone who'd seen it all. Late forties, maybe fifty. Black hair cropped close, streaked with gray at the temples, barrel chest and thick arms.

"Name's Hector Alvarez," he began. "Grew up Oakland, in a neighborhood they don't put in recruitment posters. Half my cousins were locked up before they were 18. The other half? Running from the law or dead. All over weed, David. The same thing that's now a $100 billion industry. But back then, if you were Black or Latino and caught with it, they threw the book at you. White boys in the suburbs? They got probation, if that."

Hector leaned back, his tone factual.

"I had family and friends locked up for decades over a couple grams. Ever seen the inside of a private prison? It's about profit. They lobby for laws that fill cells. Stricter sentences, mandatory minimums. Every person they lock up makes them money. Doesn't matter if it's for a bullshit drug charge. They need those beds full, and we were the fodder."

He shook his head.

"I thought I'd escape all of it by joining the Marines, and stayed all the way to Sergeant Major. Served in Vietnam Parts 2 and 3, AKA Afghanistan and Iraq. Same story. We fought for nothing. I watched my men—kids, really, most of them just out of high school—get blown to pieces so America could fund its military industrial complex by playing puppet master over countries that didn't want us there. You've been to war, so you know. Right or wrong?"

I said nothing, unwilling to agree and thus make myself complicit in whatever the hell Malek had going on out here.

Hector's voice sharpened. "It wasn't until I got out that I realized how fucked our military truly is. We spend a whole lot of time desensitizing our young men and women to killing, making them do whatever they're told without question, turning them into the fighting machines we want. And when we're done with them, there's no integration with society. They're just dumped.

"I was in hell after getting out, man. PTSD doesn't cover it." His hands were clenching into fists now. "If accountants killed themselves at twice the rate of anyone else, who'd sign up for that job? No one. But raise kids in a world where they're told it's noble, wave enough flags in their faces, and keep hammering home how honorable it is to serve, they'll keep marching straight into the meat grinder. That's what our military does. It's been feeding that machine from day one."

I considered his words, then said, "If you're trying to undermine the military, terrorism is a shitty way to do it—"

"I wasn't finished," he cut me off, speaking with surprising restraint given the hot-button topic I was trying to press. "Right after I got out, they took my mom. She lived in America for over 30 years. Worked, paid taxes, never even got a speeding ticket. But when deportations ramped up, she got caught in the net. No criminal record, no reason—just didn't have the right papers. That was my breaking point."

Hector leaned forward, his eyes hard. "You said if I wanted to undermine the military, terrorism was a shitty way to do it. And you're right. But our target here isn't the military, it's the entire power structure. That doesn't happen without bloodshed, and you'd better goddamn believe we're going to do it with as little loss of civilian life as possible. As for everyone else... well, they're fair game."

"And how," I asked, "did you end up here?"

That question seemed to relax him, though I couldn't fathom why. He blinked twice, his face softening as if he was recalling a fond memory.

"After they took my mom, I hit rock bottom. Eventually put down the bottle long enough to go to a veterans support group. After a few months the facilitator pulled me aside, told me there were others who saw the truth and were ready to do something about it. And now I'm here."

First a political defector and now a military one, I thought. If what these men were saying was true, Malek had found the fissures of discontent in American society and placed his recruiters there.

The question remained, however—how widespread was his operation?

I looked at the final man. "And you?"

He was Black, probably in his early forties, with an air of polished authority that left me utterly clueless as to his background. Definitely not a combat vet, and I suspected he wasn't political, either. He had too much easy confidence for either. He carried himself like he still belonged at the top of the food chain.

"My name is Richard Hargrove. I graduated top of my class at Harvard, got my MBA at Stanford. For the last decade, I was the Senior Vice President of Global Business Development & Strategy at Lockheed Martin."

That caught me off guard—the last person I would have expected to find in a terrorist syndicate was a business mogul, particularly one with a background in national defense.

"My job was to secure the contracts that kept wars going. We worked directly with the Pentagon, Congress, and the State Department, lobbying for interventions in Afghanistan, Iraq, and Syria to keep the money flowing. More boots on the ground meant more demand for tanks, missiles, drones, and the hardware that made us billions.

"Hell, we invented this system. Funneled tens of millions into lobbying to make sure Congress voted in our favor. When politicians left office, half of them ended up working for us. Generals would call for wars in uniform, and then profit off them as corporate execs. We say these wars are about democracy and protecting America, but at their core they're about profit. I sat in those rooms, saw it all firsthand. We didn't care who we were fighting or how many died. Peace doesn't pay. War does. And every time we secured another contract, stock prices went up."

My eyes narrowed. "If you really were the—what was your position?"

"Senior Vice President. Global Business Development & Strategy."

"Right. That. By the way, can you fit all that on a business card?"

He grinned slightly, the first crack in his veneer. "Small font, David. Tiny."

"You must have taken one hell of a pay cut."

The grin faded. "You've got no idea. Can't put a price on a clean conscience, though. Know what my responsibilities were under that job title? Making sure Congress rubber-stamped defense budgets, year after year. When the public got tired of one military intervention, we pivoted to the next. Our job was never about stopping terrorism, fake WMDs, drugs, or anything else. It was about endless war, endless profit however we could justify it. That cost me my family, but I kept reaching for that golden ring until I couldn't anymore."

I nodded. "And now that you're serving a terrorist organization, is your conscience clean?"

"The bigger picture from this angle is quite a bit different. This is about *a* war, not endless war. What I did before...let's just say I wasn't just complicit. I orchestrated it. It's on me to atone for that."

"And how did you find your way to Malek?"

"Through a colleague. The first one I confided in after deciding I was done with Lockheed. I didn't make it straight to Mr. Malek, of course. But his people funneled me through meetings. Polygraph, psychological evaluation. Turns out"—he gestured to the men beside him—"I wasn't alone. Every American in this building and a whole lot more in the States have seen the system from the inside. Our eyes are open."

I wanted to retort, to deliver the usual sardonic quips that came to mind when I was faced with authority figures of any kind. Two things stopped me.

One, the only way I could stop a bombing—if there was a way at all, definitely not a sure thing considering I was dealing with Soren Malek—was to convince him I'd willingly serve his cause.

And two, nothing these men said wasn't factual. The difference between us was that I disagreed with what they planned to do about it. Given the only part of Malek's operation I was aware of to date involved the theft of a nuclear warhead, these people were to be taken seriously.

I said, "Let's assume your plan works. In your perfect world, what's going to happen?"

Hargrove responded at once, speaking with the absolute authority he'd projected since entering the room.

"David, right now our country is a corporate dictatorship, and a violent one at that. A phoenix rises from the ashes, and America will too.

"But first"—Hargrove let the silence stretch, his eyes locked on mine—"she must burn."

32

"You should have told me," Shayan said bitterly.

He kept his eyes forward, hands steady on the wheel, refusing to so much as glance at the passenger seat.

"If we'd told you," Worthy asked, "would it have helped?"

Silence ensued as the Tata SUV's headlights cut through the pre-dawn darkness, their beams carving out a narrow path along the winding stretch of Route 68. On either side of the road, the landscape rose into jagged, semi-mountainous terrain, the rocky outcrops dotted with sparse scrub that clung to life in the cracks and crevices.

Finally Shayan said, "I would have known what I was getting into."

Hass replied from the backseat. "Whether you knew or not, you'd be in it regardless—"

"But not uninformed," the driver shot back. "Now I know why Suicide would not let me listen to the radio."

The downside of cutting their local asset loose on their way to Cancer and Ian's hide site, Worthy knew, was that it allowed him to get caught up on current events. If Shayan had previously suspected the Iranian military patrol in the Parvand Range to be a random training maneuver, now he knew the truth. An American aircraft had been shot down, and the only reason the driver continued to fulfill his supporting role, however reluctantly, was that he'd personally witnessed the firefight that his government claimed to be the wanton slaughter of civilian men.

"Yeah," Worthy agreed, "now you know why he wouldn't let you listen to the radio. But you also know what he risked to come get me, and if he hadn't I'd either be dead by now or wishing I was."

Hass added, "Besides, we already made it past Deyhuk and that was the most dangerous spot on the route. We've only got another hour left to go."

Shayan heaved a discontented sigh. "One hour until Tabas, yes. Then what? Then you do battle and hope to survive. Still it will not be over."

"We saved your life, bro."

"Two days ago," the driver shot back. "And I would be in your debt if you had not been trying to get me killed ever since."

Worthy said, "Just take it easy. The sooner we do what we need to do, the sooner you're on your way with a boatload of cash."

"A dead man cannot spend money."

"Then don't die," Worthy answered, checking his mirror to see the Chery Tiggo three hundred meters back, driven by Ian and occupied by Reilly and Cancer.

And, of course, their prisoner.

However bad this was for Shayan, Dariush Navidi had it worse. He was an unpaid prisoner bearing the weight of accountability for the raid ahead, and if it ended up being a dry hole—whether or not the broker knew that in advance—then he'd be at the mercy of a team skilled in extending anything but.

Worthy thought that Shayan had resigned himself to acceptance, but then the driver began, "If either of you were in my position, it would be clear that—"

"Enough," Hass shouted, silencing the outburst. "We're in the same danger as you are. And everyone but you lost a shitload of friends to get here. We don't expect you to be happy about that, but if you think we're going to feel sorry for you, then think again. You're getting paid a hell of a lot more than we are for this, and when you're back to your day job and researching obscure local history we're going to be facing the widows and children of our teammates. So man the fuck up."

That seemed to do the trick, Worthy noted, silencing the driver entirely. An unsettling quiet followed as a gust of wind picked up, sweeping dust across the road, the dry scrub whispering against the rocks on either side of them. The faintest hint of dawn hadn't yet crept into the horizon, leaving the land shrouded in a heavy, inky blackness. Worthy saw the glow of a faraway village to their left, briefly erased by the headlights of a cargo truck that swept past in the opposite direction. Then they were alone again, left with the hum of the engine and the weight of the mission pulling them deeper into the heart of hostile territory.

The road began to rise gently, the semi-mountainous terrain more pronounced now, casting shadows in the Tata's headlights that made the landscape seem like a hostile, watchful giant. Worthy's eyes flicked from his mirror to the windshield as they rounded a bend and he spotted a cluster of dim lights. They weren't the kind that came from any town or village. They were too isolated, too orderly. A pit formed in his stomach as reality clicked —however low their chances of slipping past, they'd be even worse if he ordered Shayan to stop and reverse. That course of action would flag the vehicle as prey, and given the enemy force ahead, they wouldn't escape that designation.

Worthy keyed his radio and said, "Checkpoint," leaning forward in the passenger seat to get a better view. "Military. Too late for us, you guys need to stop."

Cancer transmitted, *"Negative, we're coming to back you up."*

Ahead, the scene unfolded in sharp detail. Four trucks were parked on the right side of the road, their hulking forms blocking nearly half of the narrow highway. Two smaller armored vehicles were positioned on the opposite side, their dark, angular profiles bristling with mounted machine guns.

Iranian soldiers, at least two dozen of them, moved around the trucks, some clustered in loose groups, others patrolling with their rifles slung over their shoulders.

Shayan's voice shook. "What do we do?"

"Nothing," Worthy said firmly, pulling his shemagh over the lower half of his face. "Just slow down and keep driving until they make us stop."

His mind raced, and he keyed his mic again. "Four trucks on the right, a pair of armored personnel carriers on the left. Twenty-plus dismounts. We'll exit right, try and take out the turret gunners and move to the high ground. Cancer, you've got the left flank."

He stopped there, because there was nothing else to say. They were hopelessly outnumbered, and anything beyond their initial response would be determined on a second-by-second basis. At best the team would flee together on foot, avoiding total slaughter—for as long as they could while being hunted by the Iranian State.

Worthy picked up his HK416 and gripped the door handle. Hass had already shifted to the passenger side of the backseat—the initial fight would be up close and personal, and at this point that was their only chance of making it out on foot.

The nearest soldiers were now five meters in front of their vehicle, rifles slung low, smoking and chatting like they didn't have a care in the world. Further up, near the armored trucks, a pair of soldiers were leaning against the vehicles, eyes on the road, but they didn't seem alarmed. The gunners in the armored vehicles were still in their hatches, machinegun barrels tilted upward. A few soldiers were on the opposite side of the road, their backs turned to the approaching Tata. All it would take was one of them to look too closely.

One of the Iranian soldiers lifted a hand, as if to stop them—and then he waved his arm lazily, signaling for them to pass.

Worthy keyed his mic. "They're letting us through."

His pulse quickened as they neared. The path through the vehicles was narrow, barely wide enough to squeeze through. As they passed, his eyes flicked toward the soldiers. Their expressions were casual—too casual. They were just doing their jobs, unaware of who was in the vehicle. But all it would take was one sharp-eyed officer to look through the windshield and notice a passenger trying to hide his face, and this whole thing would fall apart.

They rolled through, tension thickening the air inside the SUV. The soldiers didn't give them a second glance. The Tata Safari passed between the trucks like a ghost.

But now there was the Chery behind them.

"They're not going to make it," Hass muttered, watching the rearview mirror. "A second vehicle out here is too suspicious."

Worthy said to Shayan, "Keep rolling, but go slow. When I tell you to stop, me and Hass are going to get out. You kill the headlights and drive off, wait for our call."

His eyes were fixed on the Chery Tiggo in his mirror. The sight of another vehicle following so closely would set off alarms. The Iranian soldiers may have been complacent at the moment, but they weren't stupid.

"Come on," Worthy muttered under his breath. "Come on, make it."

The Chery approached the military convoy, headlights bouncing slightly on the uneven road. From where Worthy sat, it looked like a disaster waiting to happen. He saw the soldiers tense, the gunners shift in their hatches. The soldiers standing near the trucks turned, eyes narrowing as they caught sight of the second vehicle. Worthy's heart pounded with anticipation of the inevitable. Once the Iranians stopped Cancer's truck, it wouldn't be a firefight—it would be a slaughter.

But that wouldn't stop the team from dealing out their own personal brand of hell while they still could.

Shayan's voice was tight with fear. "They are about to be questioned."

The Chery slowed slightly as it neared the soldiers. Worthy held his breath, waiting for the right moment to give Shayan the order to stop. Time seemed to stretch, the seconds crawling as he waited for the first explosion of gunfire.

At the last second, one of the soldiers waved the second vehicle through with the same disinterest. The Chery passed, sliding between the trucks with barely enough room to breathe.

"*We're clear*," Cancer transmitted.

Worthy exhaled slowly. They were still alive. Both vehicles.

"Jesus," Hass muttered, his voice barely above a whisper.

The convoy behind them faded into the rearview mirror, swallowed by the darkness of the mountains as the Chery continued along the road. Worthy turned to exchange a glance with Hass, the weight of their narrow escape settling in.

"That was too close," Worthy said quietly.

"Yeah," Hass replied with an incredulous expression, his posture finally easing. "But we made it."

Shayan started on another tirade against the recklessness of his American employers, but only for a moment. When Worthy and Hass shouted, "Shut the *fuck* up," in unison, their reluctant local asset obeyed.

33

Reilly moved swiftly through the predawn darkness as he followed Worthy, Hass, and Cancer, their feet kicking up puffs of fine sand as they moved toward the small building.

The night was still, the only sound the low hum of wind turbines scattered across the landscape. Their white towers rose 150 meters, steel surfaces gleaming faintly in the moonlight. Massive blades turned slowly, cutting through the air with an eerie, rhythmic whoosh, like the labored breath of a sleeping giant. In perfect rows, the turbines stretched into the distance, their silhouettes stark against the night sky.

The wind farm was vast, spread out across the arid plains outside the town of Tabas. To the untrained eye this would seem like a desolate place, just another attempt at modern energy harnessing in a forgotten part of the world. But the address Navidi had given them pointed directly to the building ahead, and with no other leads to follow, Reilly could only hope there was more to it than met the eye.

The structure was squat and nondescript, its concrete walls stained by years of exposure to the harsh desert elements. A faded sign near the door was the only distinguishing feature, and once he was a few meters out, Worthy slowed his approach to allow his teammates to close the distance behind him.

The pointman stopped short of the door, flattening himself against the wall along with the rest of the men as Reilly slipped around him and traded his HK417 for the crowbar slid through a loop in his tactical vest.

The door wasn't fortified, just a simple exterior lock. Reilly slid the crowbar's flattened end into the narrow space between the door and the frame, working it in slowly before applying steady pressure. The metal creaked in protest, giving little by little until the lock popped loose with a groaning snap. Grabbing the handle, Reilly pulled the door open and stepped aside.

Worthy slipped through the gap in an instant, followed by Hass and Cancer by the time the medic tossed down the crowbar and resumed a two-handed grip on his rifle.

Then Reilly moved inside, clearing the centerline past the doorway and cutting right toward Worthy amid the scents of sweat, dust, and stale air.

His aim instinctively locked onto the shapes of two men scrambling out of their cots.

"*Dast-ha*," Cancer shouted. "Hands, motherfuckers."

The men were only half-awake, caught off guard by the sudden entry of four Americans. Both of the occupants reacted sluggishly, still groggy from sleep, their movements slow and panicked. One of them, a thin, bearded man, raised his hands halfway, eyes darting around in confusion without the benefit of night vision. The other man, heavier-set, reached instinctively toward the floor where a rifle lay half-hidden by the cot.

Worthy's HK416 unleashed a series of muffled hisses, his subsonic bullets punching through the larger man's chest. Cancer fired a heartbeat later, their now-dead target rolling fully off his cot as Reilly watched the remaining man. They needed him alive, though any possibility of that outcome vanished as his hands moved beneath the wool blanket.

Reilly fired a controlled pair of shots at his chest, and Hass followed the brief salvo with a short-range headshot for good measure as their teammates' lasers momentarily converged on the body, then fanned outward in a secondary sweep of the room.

A clatter of expended brass came to a stop amid the faint whirr of the turbines and the breaths of his teammates. Reilly took in the building's scant interior with the thought that if his team had been expecting some kind of intelligence windfall here, they were about to be sorely disappointed.

The room was small, cramped, barely enough space for the cots, a rusted metal table, and a few scattered maintenance tools. It appeared to be a place for a couple of workers to crash in between shifts, their gear strewn about in the corner, a toolbox kicked over near the door. The only suspicious thing about it was the presence of the men's weapons—how common that was in Iran, he had no idea—and the fact that they'd reached for them rather than comply may well have been nothing more than a panicked response to their circumstances.

Now they were dead, the team members moving about the space to search through rusting pipes, oil-stained rags, a few outdated manuals on a sagging metal bookshelf on the back wall. Nothing felt out of place, and that fact seemed just as evident to Cancer as he transmitted.

"Two EKIA," he said, and Reilly wondered whether the addition of "enemy" to the acronym for killed in action was an overstatement.

Then the sniper continued, "Angel, get your ass in here."

"Coming in," Ian replied without keying his radio, speaking loudly enough to be heard.

He'd been loosely trailing his team's formation, one arm grasping Navidi's bicep as they jogged toward the doorway. The broker's wrists were flex cuffed at the small of his back, his mouth gagged—although not for long—and while he'd been compliant thus far, Ian handled him roughly to ensure he stayed that way.

Releasing his grip, Ian gave Navidi a shove to the back that sent him stumbling through the doorway. Hass intercepted him and pulled down the gag as Ian stepped inside and asked, "What do we got?"

"You're looking at it," Cancer replied, patting down a corpse lying face down on the floor. Another body, chest and headshot, rested on a cot where a blanket had been cast aside to reveal a pistol.

Ian took in the room's surroundings at a glance, the ordinary details slipping past his focus. The pile of oil-stained rags and tools were all peripheral noise to him—the room was too small, too isolated to be the central hub for whatever Malek had been moving large shipments of unspecified equipment to. It was possible that the items had since been transferred elsewhere, but Navidi had said the shipments were already smuggled through a series of cutouts, which left open another tantalizing prospect.

Hass said, "Start talking."

"How should I know?" Navidi replied, panicked. "As I said, I have never been here—"

"Gag him," Ian said, moving for the tall bookshelf at the back of the room. What caught his attention wasn't the manuals haphazardly piled there, but the fact that the bookshelf itself had wheels at the bottom. He scanned the floor to find track marks in the dust, and thrust the shelving unit aside to find the missing piece of the puzzle.

The door-sized panel on the wall was easy to miss, its facade matching exactly the cinder blocks around it, the seam barely detectable. There was no handle and Ian pressed the right side instead, disengaging a push-to-open latch and causing the panel to pop open by a few inches— which was all Ian had time to observe before Worthy grasped his shoulder and moved him sideways, taking up the number one man position beside the door as he edged it further open.

"Stairs," he said quietly.

Cancer replied, "Take it."

Worthy was on the move before Cancer had finished speaking, followed by Hass and Reilly. Ian turned to grab hold of Navidi as Cancer disappeared through the hidden door.

Then he was struck with his dilemma.

Waiting behind while his four teammates assaulted a small building was one thing, but now they were descending into parts unknown. He had to back them up without leaving Navidi unsupervised. If he followed too closely, the broker's clumsy movements could cost them the element of surprise; too far, and he'd be unable to lend his rifle to the fight.

He settled on a compromise, waiting a few seconds before muscling Navidi into a narrow stairwell that stretched into darkness. Whatever waited below wasn't one story below ground level, but two—the stairs seemed to go on endlessly, and he'd barely begun his descent when his pulse spiked like a bloodhound on the trail.

The faint smell of ozone and cooling electronics wafted up from below. No dry hole, this, and he intuitively sensed that they were about to find exactly what they'd come here for. Anyone below would be a guaranteed hostile, and even if his teammates had to slaughter everyone to clear the space—a not-unlikely possibility, given his working experience with them—he felt more than confident that with Navidi at hand to interpret any findings of a thorough search, they'd uncover a follow-on location that, with any luck, would lead them to David.

And Malek.

Ian guided his captive down, moving slowly at first until Navidi had figured out the spacing of the stairs and then picking up the pace. They made it ten steps down, then twelve, before gunfire erupted below.

Bullets popped off the walls on either side of the stairway, ricochets hissing through the air. Ian reflexively crouched down, as did his teammates.

But Navidi didn't, and before Ian could drag him down the broker fell of his own accord, crashing to the stairs in a lifeless heap.

There was no time to mourn the loss of the only man who could decipher the inner workings of Malek's operation—the incoming gunfire was cut short by the muffled whiffs of his teammates' suppressed response, and the stack below him surged forward.

Ian rose and stepped over Navidi's body, then raced down the stairs after his team.

Cancer flipped his night vision upward on its mount as the team divided down the middle—there was a well-lit T-intersection at the base of the stairs, and each man alternated direction across it with blinding speed.

And since Worthy, in the lead, had gone right, that left Cancer following Hass to the left.

He sidestepped the body of a guard slumped against the corner. The man had fired almost blindly around the edge with an American M4 of all possible weapons, and Worthy had to lunge sideways to achieve an effective angle of fire—an effort that paid off, given the half-dozen bullet holes whose exit wounds now oozed a satisfying puddle of blood on the dusty concrete floor.

Then Cancer was in the left-side corridor, taking up a position on the opposite wall from Hass as both men moved beneath fluorescent lighting. They now had effective cross coverage down the hall, a short stretch with only two doors.

The first of these was ajar, and some wily bastard had awaited the sound of their footsteps before popping out from the kneeling position, the barrel of his assault rifle making a sudden appearance.

Cancer had been aiming at the far door and Hass beat him to the punch. A flurry of subsonic rounds were airborne by the time the sniper adjusted his aim, claiming the only consolation prize to be had in the form of two quick shots that ended up being redundant—Hass had ventilated the emerging guard well enough, his body falling to push the door fully open and leaving a smear of blood on the surface as he collapsed.

Then Hass was entering the room, with Cancer on his heels as they cleared their respective corners before sweeping their aim to the center.

It was cleared at a glance, containing nothing more than stacks of large tough boxes and dust rising in the air, disturbed by their entry.

Cancer pivoted toward the door and beat Hass back to the hall, coming to a stop at the remaining door that had been closed and stayed that way—no guard popping out like a suicidal Jack-in-the-Box this time, although he heard the faintest hum of electricity from within.

That sound put Cancer even more on edge than he already was. No abandoned storage room, and its contents were about to be revealed. Hass leaned around him and tested the handle, which turned in his grasp. He pushed the door inward and stepped back, clearing the way for Cancer to make his entry.

The sniper did so with the maximum possible speed, shouldering past the door in a crouch and button-hooking right to find an empty corner.

He was exactly a half step inside the door when gunfire rang out, a deafening roar in the confined space that caused Cancer to instinctively duck even further and whip sideways, firing at the noise before he so much as saw the source. Hass wouldn't have hesitated, nor could he step into the doorway with bullets flying out. Cancer was alone, his subsonic rounds thudding harmlessly into the opposite wall before he identified the man he was now locked in a battle to the death with—a battle whose outcome would be determined within the next two seconds.

The guard had positioned himself behind an overturned steel desk in the corner, using it as cover and perching his M4 atop it. He hadn't, however, anticipated how quickly Cancer would react.

Now kneeling, Cancer adjusted his point of aim in tandem with his target, his subsequent bullets hitting low and puncturing the desktop. The next shot would establish a clear winner and Cancer took the milliseconds required to make his count, aligning his sights with the profile of the guard's shoulders and head. Cancer faced one of the absurd thoughts that occurred mid-combat, this one from a trip to the Gettysburg Museum where a display of two molded rounds explained, *These two bullets met in midair above Culp's Hill.*

But no similarly probability-defying feat would occur today—the guard's head snapped backward and he dropped out of sight following Cancer's next shot, after which a hail of gunfire simultaneously popped into the desk as Hass entered the room.

Cancer scrambled upright, continuing his clearance alongside his teammate to find that they were alone in the room. But the adrenaline didn't subside, and the space wasn't empty—Hass rounded the desk and fired another two rounds at the fallen guard while Cancer marveled at the sight before him.

Banks of servers lined the far wall, their matte black surfaces humming quietly. Cables snaked across the floor, and the faint glow of LEDs blinked intermittently in the darkness. Large screens on the wall displayed seemingly random lines of code as cooling fans whirred steadily, pushing stale, slightly metallic air around the enclosed space.

He wasn't sure what he was looking at, but this was no makeshift operations center or rudimentary command post. The equipment was high-end, industrial-grade tech, the kind of setup designed for far more than basic communications although its true purpose eluded him and his limited knowledge of such technology. Even without fully grasping the implications, he knew they had found something important.

Before he or Hass could process the sight, the sound of automatic gunfire echoed from deeper in the sublevel. Their earpieces crackled to life with an incoming transmission.

"*Support,*" Worthy transmitted, "*right hallway, we're pinned, need backup asap—*"

The message ended with the clap of an explosion, its noise reverberating toward them as Cancer and Hass turned to sprint down the hall.

34

The grenade blast shook the room, its sheer force sending a shockwave through the cramped kitchen. Worthy felt the explosion in his bones, echoing violently across the steel countertops and heavy-duty appliances behind which he'd taken cover, the decibel cutoff in his radio earpieces only doing so much to protect his hearing from total annihilation. Only then did he register the searing fragments of shrapnel burning his right side.

"*I'm good*," Ian transmitted from his hiding place behind an industrial-grade oven he'd pushed aside, followed by Reilly echoing the same.

"Me too," Worthy transmitted, although he was certain both teammates bore minor injuries as bad or worse than his own—nothing that took their attention off the imminent urge for survival, save the shared and unspoken recognition that their cover was insufficient for protecting them from further grenades.

Then the gunfire resumed, bullets cracking off every exposed surface and ricocheting across the room.

Their attackers were clearly experienced in close-quarters battle—they'd simply waited for the team to flush into the first room, then executed an unconventional response by taking up positions in the hallway to isolate them while they were inside. The effort had commenced with the guards firing blindly through the doorway of the lone exit, and Worthy knew at that moment that he, Reilly, and Ian were utterly fucked.

"They're firing from the hall," he transmitted for Cancer and Hass's benefit. "Must be at least three, four."

No response.

He felt a trickle of fluid across his right cheek that could have been either sweat or tears, and wiped it away to find that it was blood.

Gunfire echoed in the doorway as the guards continued to fire, the relentless barrages making it impossible for him and his teammates to so much as raise their heads without getting lit up. That meant the guards outside were firing and reloading in succession, secure in the knowledge that their quarry was pinned.

Worthy gritted his teeth, barely able to hear his own thoughts over the gunfire. Pots and pans littered the floor, and the appliances that had saved their lives now seemed like a cage, trapping them while their enemies had free rein to finish them off.

Another explosion would do the trick if they didn't move soon—and yet, all they could do now was hunker down and hope like hell Cancer and Hass arrived before the guards finished the pinned men off.

The barrage at their doorway faltered, then went silent.

Cancer transmitted, *"They flushed to the room across the hall—move, now."*

Worthy did so at once, scrambling to lead the way toward the door as Reilly and Ian followed him.

The transmission meant that Worthy and his men could make it inside the room before Cancer and Hass, and he desperately wanted to exploit the advantage of the guard retreat while he still could. Every passing second would allow them time to seek cover and take aim against their pursuers, and Worthy sought to minimize that span of time as much as he could.

He cleared the doorway at a run, identifying two enemy dead as well as the room across the hall before charging toward it amid the thud of footsteps from within.

Any hesitation would be counterproductive in the extreme, and Worthy's fear took a distant second to the urgency of the situation as he slipped through the doorway and cut right with the desperate hope that his teammates had kept pace.

The room was larger than the others, a living quarters hastily converted into a defensive stronghold. Personal belongings were scattered across the floor, and three guards were darting behind furniture that would serve as makeshift barricades.

Worthy managed to shoot one of them twice in the back before he had a chance to make it, firing the opening shots before the enemy realized he was in the room.

The advantage of surprise ended there as the remaining two men reacted, diving behind cover as the team flooded into the room. Worthy had seen their hiding places—a couch and a standing wardrobe at the far side—and by now he was well familiar with the enemy's willingness to fire blindly around objects without exposing themselves.

And while the rules of room clearing were ironclad for a reason, Worthy made the split-second decision that improvisation was in order lest his teammates fall victim to the hidden guards.

He turned before reaching his corner, making an oblong race across the room and compromising the American sectors of fire in the interests of removing the threats himself. In his sudden burst of speed, however, he found himself unable to stop.

The attempt at a skidding halt took him beyond the edge of the standing wardrobe, where the entrenched guard was only then raising his weapon around the nearest side. The barrel nearly struck Worthy in the process, missing him by inches as he kept his weapon angled low to dodge the obstacle before firing three subsonic rounds that shredded into the standing guard's leg. It was an almost point-blank engagement that came and went in the course of Worthy's skid, and the guard fell to reveal his final comrade behind the couch, now spinning to confront the sudden appearance of an American assaulter.

Worthy tried to drop to a knee, but his momentum was too great to overcome with any semblance of finesse. He crashed to his side instead, straining to bring his suppressor to bear on the remaining enemy fighter while still sliding across the floor.

He fired once, then twice more, registering that one or more of his rounds had sailed into the guard's abdomen.

Then Worthy's head struck the back wall, bringing him to a painful stop amid a high-pitched ringing that erupted in both ears simultaneously. He strained to see through blotches of bright color that obscured his vision, managed to deliver another trio of bullets that turned the guard from gut-shot to dead.

But his fight wasn't over. The guard he'd shot in the leg was now on his back, swinging his rifle atop his body to engage his assailant as Worthy desperately tried to slither into a position affording him a proper point of aim.

He never had the chance.

The wounded guard's body jolted as if he were being electrocuted, convulsing with the impact of bullets that seemed like they were never going to stop coming. Ian stood beside the wardrobe, erring on the side of caution as he fired a seemingly endless succession of shots that only ended when the guard's lifeless arms were splayed out on the ground, his rifle abandoned.

Ian ended his fire then, looking like an angel of death with flecks of blood from grenade shrapnel dotting his face and body.

"Racegun," he said, reloading, "what the fuck?"

Rather than explain his improvised and reckless maneuver, Worthy scrambled to his feet as the blotches of color in his vision began to subside. The room was clear, but not the sublevel—one room still remained, and as he moved to exit the room he saw Reilly leaving first, disappearing into the hall before the flashing figures of Hass and Cancer sped past to back him up.

Reilly closed with the final doorway, a sense of horror descending upon him now that he was in the lead.

He'd been in more similar situations than he could recount, and yet this one felt alien to him—he was married now, had no reason to be running around Iran with or without a suppressed weapon. Thoughts like this produced hesitation that could kill a man as surely as lack of experience could, and yet he couldn't tamp the notion down.

And despite his best efforts, he felt himself stalling for the briefest of steps just before the doorway.

Muscle memory took over then, along with a deep subconscious instinct that he had better pull himself together before condemning Olivia, his bride, to a memorial ceremony at CIA Headquarters.

Till death do us part.

Then he was inside the room, a desire for self-preservation tearing him apart as he feverishly scanned for targets against a backdrop of distractions that bordered on sensory overload. There were glowing monitors displaying streams of code, flickering maps and screens flashing with shifting data and diagrams. The room felt chaotic, alive with technology, and while his upper body was neatly sweeping his rifle across the space, Reilly's mind struggled to catch up.

He identified a figure at the far end of his initial sector of fire, damn near in a blind spot. And with the full realization that he may have been too late, he pivoted the final few degrees and fired.

To his immense relief, the hasty shot turned out to be a miraculous feat of reaction, pummeling into the target's side. The man staggered backward, a hand instinctively clutching at the wound as his knees buckled, sending him crashing into a bank of monitors. Blood began to seep through his fingers, spreading rapidly across his shirt.

Reilly refrained from a follow-up shot to continue his movement to the room's corner, making way for his teammates to spill inside and finish the job. It was only after he'd come to a stop and swept for further threats and found none that he realized no one else had fired—everyone's footsteps came to a halt before Reilly's gaze found his target.

The man he'd shot, now bleeding out on the floor, was entirely unarmed.

This newfound knowledge momentarily froze Reilly in place, and then he darted to the wounded man with the frantic hope that he could still be saved. He hadn't yet scrutinized the room's interior in full, though the details he'd observed told him that his team had reached some vital nerve center of a command post. Everyone else in the sublevel and the building above had been armed guards, a considerable security element to protect this room—and the lone man on duty to operate the equipment here, who was unquestionably the only one who could give them the information they needed to locate David.

"You'd better save him," Ian said as Reilly fell to his knees before the casualty, his training and experience as a medic taking over.

His casualty was thin, with a pale complexion that suggested more time spent in front of screens than outdoors. His dark hair was disheveled, the sweat beading on his forehead, and his eyes were wide with shock, darting from Reilly's face to his own bloodied torso.

The bullet had entered just below the ribs on the man's right side, leaving a small hole in the fabric of his shirt, now stained crimson. And since there was no corresponding flood on the floor beneath him, the subsonic 7.62mm round hadn't passed through at all; instead, it had tumbled through the man's body, wreaking havoc. The blood pooling around the man's hand was dark, rich with oxygen, and his breathing resulted in a shallow, unilateral rise and fall of his chest.

Reilly could tell at a glance the extent of internal devastation—punctured kidney, collapsed lung. Massive hemorrhaging in the abdominal cavity, blood spilling into the pleural space. He shifted the man's hand aside, applying pressure to the wound as if there was a chance of stopping the blood flow.

"You with me?" he asked, trying to elicit any response that would indicate the man was capable of answering questions.

But he was too far gone, panting, eyes going in and out of focus from pain.

"Doc," Ian said, his tone sharper now, "you'd better save him."

Reilly removed his hands and opened his aid pouch, withdrawing a syringe and pulling the cap off with his teeth. With his other hand, he procured a small vial and drove the needle into the rubber stopper. Inverting the vial, he pulled back the plunger, watching the amber liquid fill the barrel, carefully checking the measurement hashmarks.

Five to 10 milligrams of morphine would relieve moderate pain such as fractures or bullet wounds. An amputation warranted 10 to 15, while extreme trauma—multiple amputations, for instance, or catastrophic internal organ damage—required a dose that put the patient at significant risk for near-fatal respiratory depression, up to 20 milligrams.

Reilly loaded his syringe with 30.

He gave the syringe a quick flick to dislodge any air bubbles, then pressed the plunger gently to expel them. The action was automatic, rehearsed to the point that he couldn't not do it. Without hesitation, he slid the needle through the man's shirt and into the deltoid muscle, depressing the plunger with steady pressure.

Injecting it would bring almost immediate pain relief, followed by hypoxia, then coma, and finally death in the most merciful circumstances now possible.

Reilly had already killed the man when he shot him; now, he was simply putting him out of his misery.

Ian's voice sounded faraway, distant.

"That was morphine, wasn't it?"

"Yeah," Reilly answered, removing the needle and watching the syringe fall from his hand. Without looking over his shoulder, he asked, "Did I just fuck us?"

"Yeah," Ian replied, feeling a chill run up his spine. "You did."

Cancer asked, "Where's Navidi?"

"Dead on the stairs."

"We found a bunch of tech equipment in the left hallway, servers or something—"

Ian held up a hand to stop him.

"I know. This, all of this, is what Navidi delivered." His eyes swept over the room, taking in the blinking screens, the whirring servers, and the endless streams of data scrolling across the monitors.

Ian considered how he could possibly summarize what he realized upon entering the room. He pointed to a screen with a map of the US where countless icons marked specific locations, some of which were connected by frail red lines. "Infrastructure targets—power grids, pipelines, transportation hubs, communication relays."

Swinging his hand to another screen, he continued, "AI algorithms. Processing information, compiling reports. Running attack scenarios."

"AI?"

"And the computer systems to train and refine it," he said, turning to face his team.

Cancer looked like he was watching corpses rise from the dead. Hass was visibly pale, and Worthy wiped a trickle of blood off the side of his face from one of many hopefully minor shrapnel wounds. Reilly hadn't fared much better, and was pocketing the dead man's phone while scanning the men head to toe in the search for injuries while ignoring his own.

Ian knew that he had his fair share of cuts and probably metal shards embedded under his skin, had felt their collective pain after the grenade blast. At the time it had been cause for alarm.

But now, seeing the contents of this room, he just didn't care.

Locking eyes with Cancer, he said, "Believe me, everything I've just said is barely scratching the surface."

The acting team leader responded by addressing not Ian but everyone else.

"Site exploitation, combat resupply," he said. "Phones and grenades are top of the list. Make it fast."

Hass, Worthy, and Reilly departed at once. They'd barely left the room before Cancer took a step closer, lowering his voice to ask, "It's that bad?"

Ian shook his head. "It's worse."

In truth, the servers weren't just handling basic information, they were running high-level algorithms, cross-referencing massive datasets, analyzing US infrastructure, and identifying vulnerabilities. The AI was designed to map out critical sectors: the electrical grid, water supplies, internet backbones, and transportation networks. Every system was connected and Malek's AI was pinpointing weak spots, planning cascading failures that could paralyze entire regions with a single strike.

The AI was constantly updating, learning in real time, adjusting strategies based on new data. It had the power to coordinate multiple attacks—cyber or physical—on the most vital arteries of American infrastructure. One calculated strike could send shockwaves through the country, causing chaos that would take weeks, maybe months, to recover from.

Or longer, if recovery was possible at all.

Cancer threw up his hands. "Well, do your intel shit—exploit this, find David."

Ian let his gaze drift across the consoles, taking in the finer details in case he missed something up to this point.

But everything he saw only confirmed the conclusions he'd already reached.

"The systems are locked down with military-grade encryption. It's all remotely controlled. Any intel we need is stored off-site and probably locked behind biometric access."

"Then there's nothing to lose by trying. Do your best; at least pull some data we can send to the Agency."

Ian paced before the desks and consoles. "No paper trail, and nothing on the computers that I can access without a hell of a lot of equipment that I don't have."

He stopped abruptly in front of the only item there that was bizarrely out of place—a tarnished bronze coin that he picked up, finding it heavier than it looked. One side bore the worn image of flames rising in detailed, curving lines, surrounded by faded inscriptions too worn for him to make out.

"We'll have to use grenades," Ian said. "Destroy what we can."

He stared at the coin in his hand. "But we won't get all of it."

35

The night was pitch black, broken only by jagged flashes of lightning tearing through the sky. In those brief moments, the ocean below came into view—a churning, violent expanse. Waves towered and crashed, tossing a ship barely holding together, its masts shattered, sails whipping in twisted, useless rags.

I felt Laila's hand slip through mine but I couldn't see her. Another bolt of lightning revealed the ship, now climbing an impossible wave, its broken form rising higher and higher, suspended in agonizing slow motion. My children, Jackson and Langley—they were with me somehow, their presence hanging in the air.

A final flash illuminated the towering wall of water. The ship lurched sideways, nearing the crest, suspended for a heartbeat before the wave crashed down with a thunderous roar, swallowing it whole. Darkness rushed in and a sharp, searing pain ripped through my chest.

I flinched awake, my breathing ragged. Sweat soaked my shirt, cold against my skin, and I blinked in the harsh light, disoriented.

The room was quiet except for the low hum of distant machinery. My wrists ached from the metal cuffs biting into my skin. Slowly, my vision cleared, and I saw him.

Malek.

He sat across from me, composed, as if he'd been watching me sleep for some time. His eyes were calm, unblinking behind his glasses, like nothing in the world could touch him.

"Good morning," he said.

"Is it?" I asked, clearing my throat. "I'd like to say there's no place in the world I'd rather be, but...well, this is about rock bottom."

"I wouldn't say that, Mr. Rivers. You could be in a grave."

I yawned, leaned my head back, tried to get my bearings. "My point stands."

Then I remembered my team, Malek's last line suddenly weighing heavy. He'd found them, I thought, killed them all, and was about to tell me—but that wouldn't be enough. I was going to be forced to see pictures of their corpses, grisly images I wouldn't be able to unsee in whatever time I had left.

Instead, my captor brushed a speck of dirt off one thigh and crossed his legs. "You slept quite fitfully."

"Where do we stand on New York?"

"Ah, Grand Central."

The nonchalance in his voice made my stomach tighten. His calm demeanor set my teeth on edge, as if the stakes weren't high enough already. I straightened up in the chair, though the cuffs pulled against my wrists, biting into my skin as he continued.

"You know what I'm offering. Your future—your family's future. It's quite simple, really. Agree to my arrangement, and the attack will be called off. You spoke with several of my men, and if you maintain any doubt as to the extent of my abilities, then there is little else I can do to persuade you."

"I never doubted your abilities. But I'm surprised at the scope of your recruitment network."

"You overestimate the scope," he said, with an almost casual wave of his hand. "I don't need hundreds of recruiters, just the right ones. My methods are... selective. Targeted. You see how?"

"No."

"Artificial intelligence, Mr. Rivers. A self-learning system that analyzes patterns across digital communications, from encrypted messaging apps to social media chatter. It picks up on linguistic cues—disillusionment, resentment, cognitive dissonance—and cross-references those against personal histories, employment data, even psychological profiles. Targeting the right person, you see, is far more efficient than casting a wide net."

Holy shit, I thought, this guy was good. "Impressive."

"And once I find the right people...well, you must have guessed the scope of my network."

"I have, but let's not overestimate my powers of speculation. I'd like to hear it from you."

Malek leaned back slightly, adjusting his glasses with a careful hand. His movements were slow, calculated. "For every man you met earlier, I have three dozen more who never leave the States in the course of their duties. I don't need many Americans in my inner circle, you see. My most valuable assets remain in service to their country as well as the cause."

"Military?"

"Military, of course. And intelligence, government agencies, private corporations. Insider knowledge goes a long way when paired with the massive data processing power of artificial intelligence. Of course, none of my sleeper agents are more important than those employed in overseeing and managing infrastructure. I have compelling contacts in the highest levels of classified power grid management, any one of whom can trigger a cascading blackout that will continue as long as I wish."

This conversation was steering around to my role, I knew, and my concern increasingly gravitated toward my family. Malek had to know he couldn't turn me into a true believer overnight, and didn't have to—all he needed was leverage, and the three greatest avenues to gaining that were in the suburbs of Charlottesville, Virginia.

"And how do you ensure their compliance?" I asked.

"Compliance isn't the issue. The people who work for me merely require the opportunity, and I provide them with the biggest one of all."

His eyes flicked toward the ceiling for a moment, as though he was weighing his words carefully. "Of course, I must have certain safeguards in place."

"Safeguards," I repeated, leaving the door open for him to outline the murder of spouses and children.

"Once hired, of course, I have certain expectations of my people. They understand their roles, as well as the consequences if they fail to comply."

Malek was looking right at me when he said it, and I knew the implication. If I refused to go along with his plan, or agreed and then deviated in the slightest, my family would be next. Given what I'd seen of his operation so far, I had no reason to suspect he was bluffing. Even if I agreed to work for him only to get the hell out of here, my future attempts to inform the CIA or anyone else of his plans, however surreptitiously, wouldn't go unnoticed.

He continued, "But we must consider the net positive, Mr. Rivers. You can return to your family, watch your children grow up as you enjoy retirement. They will be safe—an outcome I cannot ensure if you refuse." He paused, letting that line settle in as a torrent of hot rage filled my face. Malek's eyes never wavered from mine. "All I ask is for your cooperation. The occasional favor, you see. Small, insignificant tasks that align with your normal routine."

"Such as?"

"Gathering information, first and foremost. You still have contacts, Mr. Rivers—valuable ones. I may ask you to rekindle certain relationships as an avenue to establish new ones. Some of these people will be instrumental in arranging things discreetly. Safehouses, transportation, covert financial transfers, perhaps the movement of equipment without raising attention."

This was really happening, I thought. He was seeding the deal, and each favor he so trivially mentioned was an act of slavery that would lead me deeper into the abyss, entangling me in his web.

Malek's tone, however, remained conversational, almost soothing. "Every man and woman I employ supports the recruitment effort, of course. It may come to pass that I send you a prospective name, along with instructions for making contact. In that event, your role is a few conversations, some foundational assessment, and then, if instructed, to direct them to the next step in their journey."

"What about my journey?" I asked. "My government knows I've been captured, and even if I wasn't unattributable—which I am—I can't exactly waltz through Customs to get back."

"Don't trouble yourself with the particulars. Getting you back will be no trouble at all."

"Forgive me if I need some convincing, but I don't see how."

He gave a slight sigh as if dismissing the concern outright. "You were captured and held by a splinter faction of Jaish al-Adl. The first indications of this will be communications about a detained foreign operative leaked over channels that I know to be monitored. A hostage video will find its way to the CIA, and your release will be facilitated through a non-governmental entity in order to keep this event out of the media."

I nodded. "Okay. But assuming I make it back, there's going to be a lengthy reintegration process."

"Obviously. You will have a clearly delineated narrative of your time in captivity, from which you will not deviate in the slightest."

"That doesn't account for the poly."

I almost regretted the words as soon as I'd said them, but it needed to be addressed. I'd unquestionably face a polygraph upon returning, and being found out there would condemn my family as surely as refusing Malek outright.

He paused, watching for my reaction before continuing. "Your reintegration screening will be handled by the Special Activity Center's senior polygraph examiner. I'll withhold the name since you two have never met, but trust that she will ensure that you pass."

Not a good look for the Agency if he was telling the truth, I thought, and the confidence with which he spoke assured me that he was.

"I hope you're right about that."

"I am," he assured me, "although there will be no deceiving the polygraph you must take for me."

He smiled at my surprise. "Mr. Rivers, you did not think that a verbal agreement would be sufficient to shed your restraints and give you free rein in this facility, did you? Your compliance will be assessed at several points throughout your training, and again before you are released. You do not need to be ideologically aligned, of course, merely...willing to do what must be done."

I wanted to speak but couldn't find the words, and his voice filled the silence once more.

"The alternative is that the attack against Grand Central Station commences in"—he checked his watch—"32 minutes."

Lowering his wrist, he continued, "And by then, you won't have a family to return to. Do you understand?"

I was barely holding it together now, my thoughts screaming at me to do something, anything, to stop this.

But what could I do? Banking on Grand Central Station being an elaborate bluff wasn't an option, nor was gambling with my family's safety. I had no doubt that Malek's description of my role as a sleeper agent was genuine, although I fully expected an eventual order to kill someone as part of my continued employment. I'd be a puppet in his hands if my family was in the crosshairs.

I had to agree, *had to*, and the nauseating irony of the situation wasn't lost on me. After all, I'd begun my career with Project Longwing by stopping an attack against America.

Now I was tasked with facilitating one.

Not a single attack, I corrected myself, but countless ones whose sum total would kill far more civilians than I'd saved in the course of my duties with the CIA. Whether Malek succeeded in his ultimate goal or not, whether that occurred in my lifetime or not, was beside the point.

My thoughts drifted to the faces of my family. Laila, loving and supporting me despite the sheer depth of darkness that raged within, and the sacrifices she'd had to endure while I was running around the world with a suppressed weapon. Langley's hopeful eyes looking to me as a hero, a best friend, and my son Jackson's utter reliance on me as a father.

If there was anything on Earth I wasn't willing to do in order to save them, it was this. And yet even when faced with the deaths of countless innocents and the potential collapse of the very country that I'd served for better or worse, I didn't flinch in the slightest. Faced with the greatest existential dilemma of my life, my family came first.

"Okay," I said, watching his eyes bore into mine. "I'll do it."

36

Cancer sat among the rocky terrain, the barren desert stretching out beneath him in muted shades of tan and gray. The sun was still rising across the rugged landscape, the cool morning air already hinting at the heat that would soon come. He gripped the satellite radio handset, hesitated, then pressed it to his ear.

"Raptor Nine One, this is Cancer."

Chen's voice came through the radio speaker, calm and measured, though it lacked the urgency Cancer was hoping for. He scowled.

"*My previous order stands.*"

Cancer glanced at Ian, sitting cross-legged and listening intently. The intelligence operative looked deep in thought, face covered in cuts from the debris kicked up by the grenade blasts at the AI facility beneath the windfarm. Hass knelt beside him, looking as worn as Cancer felt.

He replied, "I'm not calling about your goddamned order. I'm calling to see if you've found any information from those phones."

There was a brief pause on the other end. Cancer's jaw clenched as the wind shifted, carrying the dry scent of sand and rock.

"*I already told you, we haven't.*"

Cancer wanted to stand and pace the ridgeline, the radio suddenly feeling like an anchor weighing him down. His eyes tracked the distant, empty horizon, his mind racing through their next steps—unless Chen had some new development, there was only one thing he could do.

"Don't hold out on me," he said. "If you want us out of Iran, then help us find Suicide."

The sound of Chen's measured breathing on the other end irritated him more than her words when they came.

"*The cell phone data revealed exactly zero information on new locations. Network analysis reveals what appears to be personal contacts, nothing that's led us any higher up the chain to Malek. The best we can tell is that they didn't even receive orders over these devices.*"

The wind kicked up dust as Cancer paused, eyes sweeping over the figures of Worthy and Reilly at their security positions, then Ian. Only Hass looked back at him, a silent question in his gaze. What next?

Chen continued, "*The trail is cold. We have no further information to go off of. Your orders remain: you are to be at the linkup point at zero one hundred hours, and you will begin exfil at that time. Don't make this any harder than it already is.*"

Cancer scanned the barren land below, an unspoken fury simmering just beneath his skin. He wanted to push back, demand something—anything—but what was there to say?

"I'd have a hell of a time figuring out how to make this any harder. Cancer, out."

He placed the handset down and cast a glance toward the east, where the sun now hung just above the horizon, painting the rocky landscape in sharp relief.

"So?" Hass asked. "What's it going to be, boss?"

Cancer lit a cigarette, trying to conceal the tremor in his hands. "We stay here. If Chen hasn't provided any further intelligence by nightfall, we move to the linkup. We'll be in Turkmenistan by this time tomorrow, America three days after that. And that's the end of our Project Longwing careers."

"And David," Hass said. "We can't leave him here."

The statement caused Cancer's face to drop into an expressionless mask, the stone-cold look that normally predicated extreme violence.

"You think I want to? Give me one way to find him and I'll call off the exfil right now. Go ahead, you fuck. Tell me what I'm missing."

Silence ensued while he took another drag and exhaled the smoke from his lungs. Then he continued, "I didn't think so. What's our alternative? You want to go native, see if we can find jobs in Tabas? If we run any lower on ammo we'll be using enemy weapons. And I'm fine doing that if there's anywhere to go, anything to find, but there isn't, is there?"

Hass looked at Ian as if seeking backup, but the intelligence operative maintained a frigid silence, his eyes unfocused. Then Hass said, "I haven't been running with you guys for very long. So let me ask, what would David do if the roles were reversed?"

"He'd make the same shitty call that I'm making. He wouldn't be any happier about it, but he wouldn't keep the team around to die in Iran, either. Getting five men back home is better than zero. I don't like this any better than you do. The best we can do in the meantime is bluff and hope she finds something useful."

"Until nightfall."

Cancer blew another stream of smoke into the morning air. "That's right, asshole, until nightfall. We've already dodged terrorist shitheads, the Iranian military, and Malek's people. Our luck's not going to hold much longer."

"So that's it, then."

"Yeah," Cancer said, flicking the ash off the end of his cigarette. "That's it."

Ian rose and stalked off uphill.

His job at a time like this was to be the man with the answers, the insights, piecing together clues against his massive repository of intelligence to drive the team's next actions.

But he found himself in the rare position not only of having nothing to contribute—which was understandable enough—but being solely responsible for letting Malek's artificial intelligence operation run uncontested.

He circled around a boulder, seeking a place to sit alone that was within the security perimeter and wouldn't silhouette him against the sky. Finding a flat section of rock, Ian took a seat and set his rifle down. Then he rocked back and forth before going still.

He squinted against the sunrise, the barrenness of the entire landscape now reflecting his team's own lack of options. The situation had been going from bad to worse ever since their infil, and Ian had made no meaningful contributions to change that.

Retrieving the coin from his pocket, he looked blankly at the worn images and text. This item, this stupid fucking scrap of metal, was the only thing he had to show for the entire raid that risked the lives of his teammates. Now that the cell phones were found to be useless and the bulk of Malek's AI left intact, they may as well have not conducted an operation at the wind farm at all.

His thoughts were broken by the sound of footsteps coming up the hill.

Expecting Cancer, Ian looked over to snap that he wanted to be left alone. Instead he saw Hass approaching, and found that his attitude immediately shifted. Hass had lost his entire team and would forever face the fallout from that event by way of survivor's guilt that had probably set in already.

Ian said nothing as Hass took a seat beside him.

"Hey man, you all right?"

"No," Ian said quietly. "You?"

"No. You should get some sleep while you can."

"So should you."

Hass snickered. "I can't sleep."

"Neither can I."

A beat of silence followed, and Ian began fidgeting with his hands.

"What's that?" Hass asked.

For a moment Ian didn't know what he was talking about, then realized that Hass was staring at the coin. Ian held it up for him to see. "I found it during our last raid."

Hass looked at the coin for a moment, then snatched it away and rose.

"Come with me."

Ian followed his purposeful steps toward a rock overhang; beneath it, a portly figure was stuffed into a team sleeping bag.

Hass dropped to a knee and forcefully shook the man. "Shayan, wake up."

He had to repeat the process before the Iranian man finally roused from his slumber, and the only indication that he was awake came when he spoke in a voice thick with sleep.

"What do you want?"

"Take a look at this."

Shayan rolled over halfway, accepting the coin and squinting at it. After flipping it over, he handed it back. "Yes, it is authentic."

"I didn't ask if it's authentic," Hass said. "What is it?"

Shayan rolled back over. "The image on one side is a fire temple, the other an ancient leader. This coin is from the Sassanid era. A Zoroastrian stronghold before the Islamic conquest. You can find these for sale in Pir Hajat. Most are fakes. This one is real. I am sorry to inform you that they are not particularly rare."

Ian asked, "What's Pir Hajat?"

"Pir Hajat Rural District. Northwest of here. Many Zoroastrian ruins, many excavations."

Hass handed the coin back to Ian. "There you go. Unless, you know, you have any better ideas."

Ian was off like a flash, striding toward the satellite radio with long bounds.

When he reached it he waved Cancer away, kneeling to grasp the handset.

"Raptor Nine One, this is Angel."

Chen replied, "*Go ahead.*"

"We have new intelligence indicating Malek is at a fallback location in Pir Hajat Rural District."

She was quiet for a moment. "*What intelligence?*"

"Something we just pieced together from our previous raid," he said, handing the coin to Cancer and jerking his head toward Shayan. "We need you to direct surveillance against remote facilities consistent with his previously known strongholds. Once you get a hit, and you will, we'll set up surveillance to confirm positive identification. And then the airstrike occurs as planned."

"What's your level of fidelity on this?"

"Hundred percent," Ian lied, determined to voice enough conviction for her to take this seriously. "Start running surveillance and you'll see that I'm right. We've got about twelve hours until nightfall, and that's how long you have to pinpoint a location for us to go in after."

Chen hesitated. "*We'll give it a shot.*"

"You've got to do better than that. Don't you get it? This is our chance to complete the mission we came here for. We've already lost a lot of men to this, and now's our chance to kill Malek before heading home. You wanted us to get him. I'm telling you that we can. Pir Hajat District. Malek's there. Get to work."

He'd barely finished the transmission before Cancer transmitted over the team frequency.

"Net call, we've got a lead on Malek's general location. Long shot, but we're working on a pinpoint location. Plan on moving out at nightfall to establish surveillance. I know we're all running on fumes, but we're going to have to delay exfil and push through one more night."

"*Who needs sleep?*" Reilly transmitted back from his guard position. "*I've got Modafinil.*"

"The fuck is that?"

The medic explained, "*Go pills. Got them off a B-2 pilot back at Whiteman Air Force Base. At least twelve hours of full energy. We can pop them at sunset and run through the night, easy.*"

"We've been out here for three days with minimal sleep."

"*I know. I've been with you.*"

Cancer looked at Ian, his eyes narrowing. "And you've had those in your pocket this whole time?"

"Well, yeah."

Ian keyed his mic. "Doc, what the fuck?"

Reilly was unapologetic. "*He only gave me five.*"

37

I lay on the mattress, the room quiet except for the soft rustle of pages as I read. My body, for the first time in days, felt rested. I wasn't hungry, my stomach full from the last meal. The stillness was unnerving, but my mind clung to the book in my hands, soaking in every word.

Agreeing to Malek's deal, however reluctantly, had bought me an upgrade to a room/cell that was palatial compared to my previous accommodations—no longer was I shackled to a chair.

Instead I had freedom of movement within these four walls, a mattress, crate of water bottles, abundant food and snacks, and a latrine bucket in the corner.

And, of course, the reading material.

My mind was desperate to soak up any and all stimulation after the increasing isolation of my captivity, and it hadn't taken me long to pore through the stack with increasing fascination.

I'd found titles like *Perpetual War for Perpetual Peace* and *Democracy: America's Deadliest Export*. Noam Chomsky was well-represented, as were various historians and academics.

I now read the shortest book of the group, its spine so narrow that it couldn't hold the title that I found the most interesting of all. That distinction was reserved for the cover and its blood-red letters.

War is a Racket.

I'd nearly finished the entire thing in the course of an hour, and found that it underscored nearly everything at the core of Malek's discontent. War was continually perpetuated by a small group of American elites—corporations, politicians, arms manufacturers—who manipulated public opinion on military interventions through patriotic rhetoric. Industry thus made astronomical sums of money off government contracts while soldiers received low pay and almost no support after returning home, and the suffering of those who went to war and the profits of those who didn't increased in direct proportion with one another. A fairly accurate representation of the world I'd known since 9/11.

I could easily dismiss the book as propaganda, pure and simple, selectively chosen by Malek to present a narrow and highly biased viewpoint.

There was just one problem: the author was Smedley D. Butler, a Marine Corps general and two-time Medal of Honor recipient, and the book was written in 1935.

The muffled thump of an explosion caused me to sit up, dropping my book as the echo spread through the building. My pulse quickened, ears straining for more, but the silence held—until it didn't. A rapid burst of gunfire followed, distant but unmistakable.

I shot up from the mattress, eyes locking on the door. It was reinforced steel, not something that would give easily. I waited, counting the seconds, my mind racing through possibilities. Another explosion, closer this time, reverberated through the walls, rattling the metal bucket in the corner.

Then, the unmistakable scrape of a bolt being thrown back. The door swung open, and two guards rushed in, weapons raised. I threw my hands up, not comprehending their sudden aggression. Both were Americans, the same men who brought me food and emptied my latrine bucket.

Now they were in a near-panic, and forcing my wrists into handcuffs that they threaded through a metal loop on the wall.

"What's going on?" I asked.

It was no use—they were gone as quickly as they arrived, bolting my door shut and leaving me shackled in place. I pulled against the restraints, frustration mixing with the growing sound of chaos. The gunfire was closer now, echoing through the compound in sharp, staccato bursts. An explosion rocked the building again, dust drifting from the ceiling.

Was this some militia attack? Was the Iranian government raiding the facility? No, I thought, Malek had all of the above in his pocket and his safe haven status was proof of that.

My mind raced—there was only one explanation for the noise closing in on me.

A hostage rescue.

It was hard to comprehend the sheer sense of hope that dawned on me then. There were no standing US military or paramilitary elements operating in Iran, and Chen certainly wasn't sending backup to recover an unattributable contractor. That meant it was my team shooting their way through the building, drawing nearer with each passing second.

For a second I wondered how they could have possibly found me, and then the thought was eclipsed by the sheer audacity of their presence. There were five of them against who the fuck knew how many of Malek's fighters. It was a suicide mission, plain and simple, but even if they and I were slaughtered in the process, nothing—nothing—could ever remove the sense of unity I felt with them in that moment.

Hass, Worthy, Reilly, Ian, and Cancer were in the building, were here with me right now, and no matter the outcome they were going to deal the maximum amount of death and destruction to reach my cell.

I heard the shouts of men outside, more gunfire, running footfalls. They were close now, another explosion causing me to wince, followed by shots in the hall outside.

"In here!" I shouted at the top of my lungs. "I'm in here!"

Then the gunfire subsided, along with the racing footsteps. Holy hell, I thought, had my team actually killed everyone or, at a minimum, forced them to retreat? Or had all my men been killed? Neither would have surprised me, and my first indication that I faced the former rather than the latter came with the sound of a man's voice outside my door.

"David?"

I couldn't identify the speaker through the steel door, but I didn't need to.

"I'm in here, alone."

The metal bolt screeched, and I was almost delirious with ecstasy as I watched the door open to reveal a lone figure in the hall.

I inhaled and held the breath, pressed my forehead against the chipped surface of the wall, and released a shuddering exhale.

"Thank you," Malek began, striding into my cell, "for permitting me that indulgence, Mr. Rivers."

He unlocked the handcuffs and my wrists fell away from the metal loop. I staggered a few steps back, staring blankly at him and then the hallway beyond the door. My guards were back in position as if nothing had happened.

Malek pocketed the cuffs, then the keys. "Flashbangs and blank ammunition, I'm afraid. It was an unfortunate, but necessary, demonstration."

My gaze fell to the SIG pistol on his hip, and I had to force myself to look away. I didn't attack him, didn't react at all. How could I? My family would pay for the slightest infraction on my part, and Malek knew it as well as I did. He'd effectively neutered any chance I had at resistance, much less escape, with that looming threat more than any restraints or security measures.

I didn't want to bring this evil any closer to them, almost wished that Malek would execute me and leave them be as an alternative to terrorism and high treason on an ongoing basis.

But of course, he wasn't going to do that. I was more valuable to him alive.

"Why?" I asked.

"My parents named me Soren after Søren Kierkegaard. Are you familiar?"

I should have stood face to face with him, not ceding to any indication of weakness, however subtle.

Instead I stumbled away from the wall and fell to a seat on my mattress, placing my head in my hands without responding.

"He was a Danish philosopher, and one whose work is deeply important to me. Kierkegaard is credited with coining the phrase 'leap of faith,' although he did not use those exact words. He believed that true faith requires a leap beyond rationality and reason, into the unknown. Do you see the significance?"

I didn't look up. "No."

"Then I will explain," Malek went on. "This leap cannot be made on behalf of someone else, nor can it be fully explained or justified to others. It is a solitary act that requires the individual to confront their own doubts, fears, and uncertainties, and to then choose faith over skepticism. Not a belief, then, but an existential commitment. The total surrender of one's will to something greater."

Running my hands through my hair, I clasped the back of my neck, staring at the floor. "Let me guess: you view the destruction of America as your leap of faith."

"Not mine, Mr. Rivers, but *ours*. You made a deal—"

"I had no choice," I shot back, finally glaring up at him.

His tone was that of a schoolteacher reprimanding a rebellious student. "Indeed you did. You could have prioritized your nation above your family. If America was everything she claims to be, then the death of three individuals as well as yourself would be an insignificant cost to sustain a beacon of hope and freedom to which the rest of the world should aspire.

"But deep down, you knew the truth. I merely placed you in a situation where you would be forced to confront this core belief, however subconsciously. If you truly deemed America worthy of saving, you would have chosen differently."

"No," I said, "I wouldn't have. Any father would sign a deal with the devil to save his family."

Malek leaned a shoulder against the wall, folding his arms. "I am not the devil, Mr. Rivers, but an accelerationist. America is an oppressive, crumbling institution, and instead of resisting we must intensify her contradictions to expedite the inevitable breakdown."

"Why did you take my knife?"

"This?" he asked, pulling it from its sheath and examining the blade with great interest. "It's an incredible weapon. Loyal as my guard force is to me, I suspect it would have been pilfered if I didn't take it under my direct control. And I couldn't risk it being lost. Because"—he sheathed the knife—"when we part ways, I will return it to you."

"You'd goddamn better."

He smiled, then glanced at the book beside my mattress. "I see you have been reading Butler. How appropriate. Have you or anyone at the CIA guessed my target for the nuclear warhead I obtained in Pakistan?"

I was momentarily at a loss on whether I should reply or not. What were the alternatives? Argue? Ignore him? Neither would help my family.

"DC," I said.

Malek gave a soft chuckle at this, grinning at me with a subtle shake of his head.

"The national capital does not require twelve kilotons to be dealt with. I intended to strike at the heart of the US military industrial complex. Not DC, Mr. Rivers, but LA."

His smile broadened and then faded, probably as he recalled that my team had contributed to stopping his warhead from leaving Pakistan.

Then he assumed the faraway look of recalling a particularly fond memory.

"A detonation in El Segundo would hit Lockheed Martin, Northrop Grumman, and Raytheon, all of them the lifeblood of America's war machine, all of them working ceaselessly to ensure that conflict remains the most profitable industry in the world. And if that detonation occurred, the ripple effects across the defense and aerospace industries would have been catastrophic. Unnecessary, given what's to come, but a symbolic blow nonetheless."

I clapped my hands together a few times, to his seeming alarm.

"Yeah. Good work, Malek, that'd be a hell of a statement. Unfortunately it would also be a 'symbolic blow' to a half million innocent civilians, so you'll understand if I don't lose any sleep over the fact that the nuke was stopped."

He recoiled slightly. "Of course. Not now, at least. Not with your current level of understanding, or lack thereof. In time, however, you will see the fight ahead as your true legacy—one you will never receive formal credit for, but one that elevates the world and humanity in the long run. When you realize the true insidiousness of the US military industrial complex, I expect you'll change your tune."

"I don't know if you're familiar with 9/11," I replied, raising my voice for emphasis, "but catastrophic terrorist attacks aren't synonymous with the lean years for defense contractors."

"With one key distinction. This time the government will have no foreign boogeyman to point to, no xenophobic war cries against people abroad. Because when I launch my offensive, and launch it I shall, my acceptance of credit for the attacks will reveal that the threat has arisen from within. Unlike 9/11, Mr. Rivers, Congress will not sing 'God Bless America.' In fact, shortly after I tip my hand there will not be a Congress left to sing—as I said, I can handle the national capital without twelve kilotons."

The weight of this entire situation hit me at once. Suddenly I was less concerned about the fate of the US government than I was about my own shock and outrage at what had occurred minutes earlier, a ploy designed to bring my hopes to a dizzying high point before pulling out the rug in a twisted mindfuck.

I said, "You didn't need to stage a false hostage rescue. I've already played into your hands."

"I had your commitment, yes, albeit only to protect your wife and children. And it's true, that alone would be sufficient to serve my ends. But before we proceed with your training, I must grant you a final understanding."

"Which is?"

Malek strolled to the open doorway, finding the cuffs and keys and handing both to a guard outside.

Then he put his hands in his pockets and turned to face me.

"There is no going back, Mr. Rivers. Not for either of us."

He vanished as the steel door swung shut, closing with a thud and sealed by the bolt being slid home once more.

38

Lucios announced, "Ma'am, we've just turned up a lead."

Meiling Chen looked up sharply from her desk. The air in the OPCEN was thick with tension, and had been since the team had gone rogue seventeen hours earlier. Added to this was the collective weight of long hours and growing pressure as her analysts worked without result to track every flicker of intel that could point them toward Soren Malek.

Chen sat at the center of it all, her arms crossed tightly against her chest, her eyes now fixed on Lucios.

"How promising?" she asked.

"Better than we could have hoped. We intercepted a burst transmission that matches the encrypted pattern Malek used to communicate with his inner circle before he went dark. The frequency hopping is identical, and the transmission window lines up with the timeframes we've seen in previous intel from his known strongholds."

Chen leaned forward, her eyes narrowing as Lucios continued.

"The signal's encrypted, of course, but the metadata is a match. Duration, size, and even the relay route point to the same kind of activity we tracked before the team went in. It's short, under five seconds, but it's the most promising signature we've seen."

This was the first win her program had in some time, she thought.

When Cancer had first refused her order to exfil, she'd maintained a face of stoic professionalism to her staff.

Then she had excused herself, made the short walk to her private office, and had a near-panic attack on the couch.

Somewhere in the course of her sobbing hyperventilation it had occurred to her that her career was finished along with Project Longwing. She was already awaiting an unknown reassignment. And no program director could recover from a ground element going rogue, namely because such a situation was inconceivable in the first place. The fact that she'd lost all control over a team who'd repeatedly refused her orders to exfil made her a unique specimen among her peers, and one who wouldn't fare well once this was all over with.

It had taken her twenty minutes to regain control of her breathing, during which her phone had rung four times.

Now her heart was pounding again as she processed the implications of Lucios's words. "Talk me through the location."

Brian Sutherland, the Joint Terminal Attack Controller for Project Longwing, took over.

"It's Target Number Three of the six we've been scanning," he said, pulling up the satellite view on the main screen. "It's isolated. Fits the profile of his previous facilities. Rural, off the grid, easily defensible."

Chen's attention wasn't drawn to the main building so much as the compound walls surrounding it. "My God, that's fortified."

Sutherland shrugged. "To a ground attack, yes. But the building is one story, and imagery is consistent with traditional adobe construction common in South Khorasan. Thick mud-brick walls reinforced with straw, and the ceiling is likely a timber frame with wooden beams covered in mud and plaster. Sturdy enough to withstand the extreme temperatures and sandstorms of the region, but it'll fold like a suit bag under a Sadid-1 missile impact. Two or three will definitely do the job and Hass has got sixteen to work with—if Malek's there at the time of launch, they'll punch his ticket for sure."

"Okay. You've analyzed the patterns?"

"I have. Hass holds the ultimate judgment call, but to my eye the primary strike pattern will be the best bet. Four sets of four missiles, first set on target, then a cross pattern ten meters out. Third set in a square formation and the last set back on target, 39 seconds from start to finish and no US munitions in sight. Afterward, the drones will fly to their deaths in the Caspian Sea."

Chen cut her gaze to Jamieson. "Any issues with the exfil?"

"No, ma'am," the operations officer replied. "Only change required is bumping the exchange point to Nastanj. The team will transfer to vehicles, cut Shayan loose, and the exfil drivers will take them three hours to the original smuggler crossing west of Serakhs, Turkmenistan. After that, they're home free."

"And finally," she said, feeling her shoulders tense, "is there anything prohibiting us from ordering the team to set up surveillance outside the compound to establish positive identification of Malek?"

Gregory Pharr, the Agency lawyer assigned to ensure legal compliance with every aspect of their operations, shook his head. "No, ma'am, we're well within our operational authorities."

His voice assumed a playful tone. "Although the team hasn't been keen on following orders lately, so you may want to frame it as a suggestion."

Her smoldering glance caused him to look away in short order.

Chen lifted her satellite hand mic, then paused.

Her career was back on track, or very nearly so. If they could pull this off, manage to take out Soren Malek despite the setbacks of an aircraft shootdown, it would be the biggest comeback in Special Activities Center history.

And she would be at the helm.

Keying her mic, she began, "Cancer, this is Raptor Nine One."

39

Cancer swept his HK417 from left to right, scanning the compound ahead under cover of darkness.

His team was clustered beneath a rock overhang in an impromptu hide site they'd occupied minutes before. They were eight hundred meters southeast of their objective, although his thermal scope rendered the distance almost null and void.

Their target compound was an isolated fortress set against the barren expanse of desert—tall, solid mud-brick walls stood at least three meters high. No barbed wire or guard towers visible, but that didn't mean the place was unguarded.

The central building was a one-story structure with a flat roof peppered with long-range antennas. Scattered around it were smaller outbuildings, sheds mostly, their squat forms half hidden in the shadows of the walls. No lights, no movement, and that was perhaps the most suspicious factor of all.

There were no visible signs of life, but the place felt alive—watching.

Or maybe, he thought, he was simply too amped up from the Modafinil Reilly had given him. Sleep wouldn't be necessary, not tonight.

"We're mapped," Ian said beside him.

Cancer lowered his rifle and then his night vision over his eyes, looking over to see the intelligence operative squinting at the display of the Aegis-R4. The tablet showed the results of the through-wall imaging radar, a fuzzy 3D imaging of the building interior beset by the glowing forms of men.

Ian continued, "Main building is packed. Couple dozen people that I've made out so far, most appear to be guards. But there are three men seated together at desks, and you better believe one of them's Malek."

"What about—"

"Two of the guards are stationed outside a room. One figure confined inside. He's done pushups, paced, and then done more pushups. It's David."

Cancer felt a mixed wave of relief and fear sweep over him. The odds against them locating the missing team leader were astronomical, and yet they'd found a way—and knowing that less than a kilometer separated them from David somehow made him feel farther away than ever.

Ian asked, "Should we tell Chen?"

"Are you serious?" Cancer replied. "She thinks we're playing ball, so let's not fuck with that. Where's Malek's command post?"

"Two rooms down from the holding cell. If we send the airstrike against Malek, we kill David in the process."

Reilly looked up from his position beside Ian, where he manned the Sentinel-9 and its ground imaging radar. "We can't breach that wall and raid that place, not with five guys."

"I know," Cancer said through gritted teeth.

Worthy, crouched on his opposite side, spoke in a low drawl. "Malek's got some heavy action cooking. We know that from his AI. If we don't take him out now, tonight, there's going to be major consequences in the homeland."

Hass whispered behind them, "Major consequences, sure. But we'd kill David."

Silence fell over them, and Cancer used his scope to perform another scan of the objective. The walls seemed interminably high, the main building all but impenetrable. He felt the weight of command bearing down on him, knew that there were no good options but plenty of bad ones.

Worthy said, "You know what we have to do."

"Yeah," Cancer said. "I know."

Reaching for his satellite handset, he spoke with grim resolve. "I'll notify headquarters. Hass, start setting up the airstrike."

40

Hass's voice crackled over the team net, calm and steady. *"Ten seconds to Time on Target."*

Worthy's pulse quickened, his hand tightening around the grip of his rifle. Reilly already had the Tata Safari in gear, the engine rumbling beneath them. In the backseat, Cancer adjusted his equipment one last time, ready for what was coming. They all were.

"Go," Cancer said.

Reilly didn't need to be told twice. His foot slammed down on the gas and the Tata lurched forward, tires kicking up dust as they sped away from the cover of the ridge. Behind them Ian followed in the Chery Tigo.

The terrain was rough, the ridgeline a shadowy barrier between them and the compound. Worthy kept his eyes forward, the horizon barely visible in his night vision. This was really happening, he thought with an almost insuppressible sense of disbelief.

They cleared the ridge in seconds, the landscape opening up before them as Reilly turned toward the compound and accelerated. From one kilometer out, it appeared as a single, distant monolith.

Hass's voice came through again. *"Time on Target."*

Worthy felt his breath hitch as the first missile explosion rocked the compound. A fireball bloomed, lighting up the desert like a flash of lightning before going dark to reveal a cloud of dust rising into the air. He saw it all in incredibly vivid detail—the Modafinil had him as alert as he'd ever been without any corresponding jitteriness, and he now felt like he was on a transcendent plane beyond mere adrenaline.

The mission was on.

While two seconds were supposed to elapse between missile impacts, the remaining trio of munitions from the first drone's volley seemed to occur in rapid-fire explosions—whether due to a tighter timing than anticipated or a result of Worthy's racing perceptions, he couldn't be sure.

Debris and smoke flew from the compound, the shuddering sound of the explosions reaching them by the time the initial Shahed-129 drone flew clear of the engagement area to make way for the second.

"Eight hundred meters out," he transmitted, only now fully accepting his team's current reality.

They'd not only lied to Chen, but the entire Agency.

Malek was at the farthest point in the building from where his team had claimed, and Hass had adjusted the strike pattern accordingly. While the CIA believed they were taking Malek out, the team's real goal was to create a breach in both the wall and building without killing David in the process.

It was their only chance to rescue him.

The second missile volley slammed into place in rapid succession, a cross pattern this time, spreading the destruction wider. Each strike was a blinding flash in Worthy's night vision that subsided to be quickly replaced by another, the team's plan clicking into place one blast at a time.

He keyed his radio and said, "Six hundred meters," by the time the third volley began to impact, its missiles forming a square formation that, by the final missile explosion, had dropped a section of the compound wall by turning it into rubble within the blink of an eye.

"Four hundred meters, wall's down," he transmitted. The sound of the blasts reached them far quicker now as the SUV closed the distance, barreling toward a final confrontation that could only end in total victory or total defeat.

They'd also withheld the most crucial piece of information from Chen: David was inside. His proximity to Malek resulted in the unspoken truth that if they failed, the terrorist leader would go free. This entire attempt was a gamble and a large one at that, the team betting it all on red for their own survival and David's.

But it was their only play.

The next volley came in like hammer blows, each missile tearing into the compound with deafening force. Worthy watched the first explosion send a geyser of dust and debris from the building into the air, the sound reaching him along with the blast this time, a crack like thunder that shook both the vehicle and the ground below.

Another missile followed, driving into the corner of the building they sped toward now, turning the entire section into a collapsing mass of mudbrick and timber. Worthy could see the debris twisting through the air, the black shapes of shattered beams silhouetted against the glowing chaos.

"Two hundred meters." Worthy's voice was tight, heart hammering in his chest.

The third missile struck and the roof of the building continued to fall in on itself like a house of cards.

But time slowed to a crawl as the final missile found its mark, the flash of its blast visible through the gap in the compound wall. Its shockwave hit them with such force that it rattled the vehicle and rolled through him like a tidal wave of energy. Dust plumed out from the building in massive clouds, curling into the air above it like an ever-expanding storm.

The crack of the missile impact lingered in the air, mixing with the rising roar of the SUV's engine as Worthy focused on the immense devastation ahead, the smoke so thick now that even through his night vision the scene seemed otherworldly, an abyss of swirling sand and shattered remnants through which they were about to make entry.

Hass transmitted, "*Rounds complete,*" followed immediately by Worthy calling out, "One hundred meters."

The sixteen missile impacts had surely killed some of the guards Ian had identified with the imaging radar of his Aegis-R4, but the bulk of Malek's people were consolidated in the northwest side in the largely untouched section of the building. Worthy estimated about fifteen remaining guards to contend with, not to mention support personnel, a collective force that outnumbered the team more than three to one. The team's only option was to turn the building ahead into Thermopylae, and then kill everyone inside but David.

Worthy suddenly realized that he had a white-knuckled grip on his rifle, that every muscle in his body was coiled. His vehicle was inside of fifty meters now, and Reilly began to brake.

"We can make it," he said.

The ruins of the wall ahead made that seem a dubious prospect—the Tata Safari was a 4×4 vehicle designed for off-road use, though its engineers had likely never considered the need for driving up and over the smoldering rubble of a recently decimated swath of mud-brick.

But the only alternative was to stop short of the wreckage, costing them perhaps twenty meters and valuable seconds before they made entry.

"Do it," Cancer said.

The Chery Tigo behind them couldn't negotiate that obstacle—if the first SUV could at all without getting stuck—and it would be up to Worthy, Reilly, and Cancer to establish an initial foothold in the building before Ian and Hass made the remainder of the journey on foot.

Worthy braced himself against the dash as his vehicle hit the rubble, the front tires jolting upward as Reilly pressed the gas and the SUV violently climbed over the remains of the compound wall. The rough ascent rattled every bone in Worthy's body, the windshield cracking somewhere in the process of the vehicle cresting the heap of debris.

Then the Tata lurched downward on the other side, its front bumper scraping the ground before the tires bounced hard, violently jostling the vehicle on its suspension. Reilly floored the accelerator as they barreled through the dust clouds. The building loomed ahead, a third or more of its sprawling expanse now reduced to smoking ruins. Flames flickered along the edges of the wreckage, casting a faint orange glow through the rising haze.

Worthy's mind raced, eyes darting over the wreckage as they closed the final distance. It was a mess of collapsed walls, timber beams splintered and scattered, chunks of roof hanging precariously over what remained. He scanned for any point of entry, his night vision filtering through the chaos, searching for a breach that could lead them inside.

Exterior doors were a last-ditch option, representing the most likely places for boobytraps and fortified defenses. But it appeared that formal entrances would be unnecessary—Worthy saw the remains of what had once been a room, still partially intact, its walls crumbling inward. A single doorway was visible through the haze, promising access deeper into the remaining building.

He assessed the remaining section of roof above it, wondering if it would hold long enough for them to get inside and finding himself wanting for a conclusive answer.

"Breach point," he transmitted, "straight past the wall, exposed room."

Worthy gripped his door handle. They were ten meters out. Seven, five. Reilly slammed on the brakes, and Worthy flung his door open.

Then he leaped out, his suppressed HK416 raised as he charged over the wreckage, Cancer on his heels.

The destruction was so total at this side of the building that only fragments of rooms remained, sections of the ceiling precariously hanging above what used to be walls. A sharp smell of charred mud-brick and burnt timber filled the air, clinging to the back of his throat as Worthy navigated the rubble below with his pulse thundering in his ears.

The world around him blurred. Flames crackled amid clouds of whirling smoke as he remained laser-focused on the doorway ahead, adrenaline coursing through him like wildfire.

It was hotter with each passing step, the temperature rising as he scrambled over the wreckage of what had once been the building's roof, the heat from the missile strikes still radiating from its collapsed surfaces. He tread over slabs of debris as quickly as he could, the jagged remains of mud-brick and timber splinters crunching beneath his boots as he slipped under an intact section of roof. The interior was a landscape of shadow and ruin, dimly lit by flaming wreckage. Burning wood mixed with dust and smoke created a suffocating haze that stung his eyes.

But he made it into the room or what was left of it, gained stable footing, and charged toward the doorway only to see a shadow appear beyond it—a man with his weapon held loosely as he tried to assess the damage of the airstrike. His eyes locked on Worthy with stunned shock, the expression both comical and a surefire indicator that he hadn't been expecting a ground attack in any form.

Worthy shot him three times in the chest, dropping him in place before leading the way into the building.

Reilly plunged through the partially demolished room in pursuit of Worthy and Cancer as they slipped through the first doorway. As the driver, it had taken him the longest to disentangle himself and his weapon from the vehicle, and now he faced the very real concern that he wouldn't be able to back them up fast enough.

He flipped his night vision upward on its mount, ceding his visibility to the taclight mounted on his rifle. Trying to negotiate the debris ahead would have been impossible otherwise.

Before he'd made it to the door, he heard Cancer's transmission.

"Angel, go left inside the doorway—we're heading right."

"Copy," Ian replied.

They had a decent understanding of the building interior from the ground surveillance and through-wall imagery radar, although sixteen Sadid-1 missiles had done significant remodeling to the floor plan.

But the right side boasted the most direct route to David's holding area, and despite the chaos and unconventional nature of the current effort, this was still a hostage rescue—and every second that elapsed was one more that Malek could exploit to kill his captive, if he or one of his guards hadn't done so already.

Then Reilly was through the doorway, sidestepping a corpse and finding himself in a T-intersection. He caught a glimpse of his teammates before confronting the dubious honor of trying to pull rear security while following them in the other direction, a task he managed only with periodic rearward glances while trying not to trip and eat shit on the rubble below his feet.

Darkness pressed in from all sides, cut only by the trio of taclights as he, Cancer, and Worthy made their way down the hall. The air was thick with the dust of freshly shattered stone and mud-brick swirling in front of his light like smoke. He swept his rifle across the space, its beam cutting through the cloud, revealing jagged piles of debris and fractured beams above. Every step sent small pieces of rubble skittering ahead, each noise dwarfed by the pops of flame and a groaning sound as the remaining walls shifted for the first time in decades.

There were no sounds of combat yet, but Reilly knew it wouldn't last long. It never did. Worthy and Cancer were moving swiftly ahead, their figures dim shapes as they moved deeper into the belly of the building. Ian transmitted, *"We're in, moving left,"* and Reilly caught a glimpse of the intelligence operative and Hass momentarily appear in the hallway behind him before they slipped around a corner and vanished.

He turned forward at the sound of Worthy and Cancer dislodging loose building material with their boots, and found they'd just cleared a pile of rubble blocking the hallway. It was a mound of broken bricks and twisted metal, evidence of a building that was barely holding itself together after the airstrike. Reilly clambered atop it, the shifting debris crunching loudly beneath his weight.

The fact that he was the heaviest member of the team by far added another layer of unease to the already fragile ground. He was halfway across when the unstable footing began to slide in all directions, loose bricks shifting as the entire pile threatened to give way.

Reilly leaped the final few feet, landing hard on the other side as the debris pile collapsed into itself in a muffled crash of stone and plaster. Worthy and Cancer were already flowing around a corner ahead, and he raced to catch up.

The two men now moved down either wall of the next corridor, their taclights sweeping the dust-filled space. This space felt different—heavier, like it was holding itself together by sheer willpower.

A loud crack rang out above, and Reilly barely had time to glance upward before the ceiling split under its own weight. A heavy timber beam, loosened by the earlier missile strikes, came crashing down toward him.

His boots skidded on the debris-strewn floor as he threw himself to the side with a quick reaction time bolstered by Modafinil, narrowly dodging the massive beam as it slammed into the ground with a hollow thud. Its impact reverberated through the floor and sent up a fresh cloud of dust and splintered wood. Reilly hit the floor hard, gasping for breath as the air filled with the acrid scent of plaster and decay. Why, he wondered, did this kind of crazy shit only happen to him?

Scrambling to his feet, he found his unsympathetic teammates proceeding without so much as a look back in his direction. To his front, Worthy abruptly dropped to a knee and opened fire toward a far doorway.

Racing behind Worthy with his rifle aimed at the doorway, Reilly took the lead, coming to a stop at the entrance and waiting until Cancer appeared at the opposite side and lowered his barrel.

Reilly slipped into the next room and cut left to find that the door had swung inward toward a wall directly to his front. He shouldered past it only to feel the door bounce back into him, the first indication that someone had sought refuge in the corner.

By then Worthy's taclight was gleaming through the darkness as he moved to support Cancer, and making the educated guess that both men could handle security for the time being, Reilly slammed his considerable mass into the door before kneeling, pushing it inward with his boot, and bringing his rifle up.

The HK417 was a long weapon, made more so by the suppressor. Reilly had to lean back to place the tip against the wood door, and then he fired four times, walking his rounds upward with each shot.

A muffled groan preceded the door pushing against his foot, and Reilly shifted to fling it closed.

The man who fell to the ground without the benefit of a door pinning him in place nearly hit Reilly on his way down, and the medic delivered a pair of follow-up shots to his chest to find that he was well equipped with a chest rack and a bullpup assault rifle, his face betraying Iranian features.

Rising to follow his teammates, Reilly instead heard a shout from the next doorway. Cancer and Worthy were on the far wall, granting the medic the only possibility of cross coverage on the new danger area. He continued moving when a metal cylinder flew into the room, and he had just enough time to hit the deck and close his eyes before the flashbang grenade bounced off a wall and exploded with a blinding white light that he could see through his eyelids.

The concussive blast felt like someone had detonated a bomb inside his skull. Even with his radio earpieces, his hearing rang so loud it felt like his eardrums had been punctured.

There was no time to hesitate—why the guards here possessed flashbangs was beyond him at present, but the use of one could only mean that they were about to make entry. He struggled to take aim at the doorway against a nauseating wave of disorientation.

But automatic gunfire was already ringing out, the crack of rounds on the walls overhead oddly muted above his ringing head. Activating his taclight would expose his position but also blind them, and he took the calculated risk in the same instant as Worthy and Cancer.

His heart pounded as he saw the illuminated figures of men pouring into the room, their movement leaving visual traces in his compromised vision as he fired quickly, sloppily, trying to take them out before they could return the favor.

The room turned into a cyclone of incoming and outgoing rounds slamming into and off of the walls as both sides engaged one another simultaneously, each firing as quickly as they could.

With the effects of the flashbang still bouncing through his skull, Reilly saw little more than shadows and muzzle flashes, each of which were met with his suppressed fire as he chewed through the remaining contents of his 20-round magazine far too fast for comfort.

A sudden burning sensation erupted in his left shoulder. The pain hit a split second later, searing hot and radiating through his entire arm. His body jolted with the shock of it, though he kept his mind focused as much as he could—he'd been struck by a ricochet, and he could deal with it later if he was still around by then.

He fired again and again, struggling to center his shots through the blinding smoke and dust as more bullets ripped overhead. Every squeeze of the trigger was a desperate attempt to cut down the shapes moving in the haze, and while he felt the thud of bodies hitting the floor there was no time to process it. The gunfire was unrelenting, rounds still slicing through the dust-choked air. He fought to see straight, to steady his shots as the silhouettes danced in and out of his fading vision while his shoulder throbbing in rhythm with his racing heartbeat.

Finally a single man remained directly in his line of sight, and Reilly pulled his trigger only to find there was no slack—his ammunition had finally run out. Before he could so much as roll to his side and reach for a fresh magazine, the enemy fighter was fully illuminated in the glow of Worthy's taclight, jolting as he absorbed subsonic rounds and then fell forward, dead.

Silence fell in the aftermath, shots echoing as the literal and proverbial dust settled. The pain in Reilly's shoulder gave way to a fiery, stabbing ache, the slick warmth of blood seeping through his shirt as he made good on his reload. His vision returned as he saw the floor strewn with bodies, the acrid stench of gunpowder hanging heavy in the air.

If the remaining guard force had any doubt that a ground attack was underway, it was now gone in full—and his team needed to resume their forward progress before it was too late.

Cancer was on his feet first, moving toward the doorway with a speed that indicated he desperately hoped these fighters weren't the last ones they'd find tonight.

Cancer halted at the doorway, observing first that the space beyond was a hallway extending in only one direction, and second, that a gory trail of blood led out of the room. Someone had made it out, and the sight heightened his senses with anticipation.

He glided out of the room, his taclight illuminating the cracked and buckling walls on either side, but there was no enemy to be seen. Then, lowering his HK417, he spotted not one but two enemy attempting to crawl away.

The first made a pain-stricken effort to roll onto his back and raise his rifle, and he got it first. Cancer didn't slow his pace, delivering a single bullet to his chest but no more, now all too aware of his dwindling ammunition supply.

But the remaining survivor was the real prize, cowering and pleading in Farsi. Probably begging for his life, although Cancer's mastery of the language ended at a few key phrases woefully unsuited for entering into a meaningful exchange. The sniper hadn't broken stride, was close enough for a knife kill but denied the pleasure by virtue of the hallway ahead, and he settled for putting a bullet into the man's upper lip before aiming forward once more.

Worthy and Reilly followed close behind, their taclights cutting through air thick with dust, beams bouncing off the jagged edges of rubble. But Cancer was already a few steps ahead, slipping through the shadows with razor-sharp alertness. Modafinil aside, he reveled in this—the thrill, the rush of adrenaline that came from reaching the edge between life and death and then pursuing it as far as he could.

But this was his first tangle with a building whose structural integrity was on its last legs, and he frowned at the sight of a partially collapsed ceiling whose deposits caused the hallway to narrow ahead. It would require a single-file passage, a death trap if ever he'd seen one, and he wondered why the enemy who'd stormed into the previous room hadn't simply waited to ambush them at this bottleneck.

Because, he decided, they didn't realize the team had made it so far. If, of course, they'd realized there was a team inside at all. The glow from the taclights had tipped them off and forced their hand in a hasty assault that had, as they'd learned soon thereafter, become the last mistake they'd ever make.

Cancer moved down the center of the hallway, using the rubble ahead to conceal himself somewhat as he advanced, hearing the soft crunch of his teammates' boots on the debris behind him—a sound that soon came from his front as well.

He raised his rifle to aim at a flash of movement ahead, a man who'd just stumbled into the hallway. Cancer was about to fire when his taclight reflected off the long barrel of a belt-fed machinegun being leveled at the waist, and he darted behind the rubble a moment before a deafening burst of automatic fire ripped through the space.

The stream of bullets sheared through the air with near-simultaneous supersonic cracks, its path heralded by the green tracers whose streaks blended into a single unified rope. Crouching behind the pile of debris and glancing behind him, he half expected to find Worthy and Reilly painted across the wall and floor—but both men had followed him behind cover, having wisely intuited that if a man of Cancer's disposition had gotten the hell out of the way, then they had better do so as well.

Another machinegun burst thwacked into the rubble they hid behind now, the gunner trying and failing to penetrate the cover as rounds pirouetted overhead. Weighed down with his weapon and ammo, the machine gunner had been slow to move and thus late to the party that had slaughtered his teammates.

Cancer and his men were safe for now, but also pinned. This was his assault fucked, and he reached for a grenade before seeing the problem therein.

The ceiling over the machine gunner's position was already bowing downward, threatening to break. A grenade blast could well result in a blocked hallway, and while Cancer wasn't averse to survival at all costs, he instead decided to test another option first.

Leaning back, he fired single shots that chipped away at the damaged ceiling, until his sixth round succeeded in dislodging a table-sized chunk that fell free and then rocketed downward to elicit a bloodcurdling scream.

Cancer clambered upward, cresting the debris and shining his taclight to find that gravity and luck had caused the section of ceiling to fall across the writhing machine gunner's legs. A controlled pair of well-aimed shots did the rest, ending the man's agony for good.

"Go," he said, unwilling to cede his elevated vantage point.

Worthy and Reilly flowed back into the gap between the rubble and the wall, proceeding under the sniper's cover until they'd reached the far side of the obstacle. Cancer was about to climb down and reload when he spotted movement ahead, and opened fire in unison with his teammates— two, maybe three enemy fighters had emerged from the lone doorway at the end of the hall, scrambling back inside before the team scored any kill shots. Perhaps they'd wounded one, but tonight wounding wouldn't be enough.

Cancer scrambled backward off the rubble, reloading in the time it took for him to negotiate the obstacle and dart through the remainder of the bottleneck. Worthy and Reilly had not only held their ground but continued advancing along the left wall, closing the distance toward the door with their taclights off. Cancer couldn't resist momentarily activating his own light as he passed the dead machine gunner.

The section of rooftop that had fallen was thicker than he'd realized, not only pinning the man's legs but pulverizing every bone from the hips down. It was a combat first for the sniper, and such events were increasingly rare for him by this point in his career.

His bragging rights would have to wait, however, and he transmitted before catching up with his teammates.

"Hold at the door and I'll take care of them."

It was a tactical precaution born of noise discipline—something as undignified as a shout would signal his team's position, although that detail hadn't been taken into consideration by the presumed leader of the enemy force in the room ahead.

A man was screaming orders in Farsi, an air of desperation in his voice. His troops were probably in disarray, wildly overestimating the number of attackers in the building, and Cancer sought to exploit that fear and confusion while he still could.

But not by entering and clearing the room as usual.

The odds of eating one or, more likely, many bullets by trying to advance in such a manner were simply too great, and Cancer caught up with Reilly and Worthy as they stopped outside the door in compliance with his order.

Pushing his rifle back on its sling and reaching for a frag grenade in his tactical vest, he pulled the pin and held the spoon in place with his thumb.

"Give me some light," he whispered.

Reilly activated his taclight, its beam spearing an oblong path across the space ahead and illuminating the doorway. Cancer adjusted his grip, letting the spoon fly off and making a mental two-second count as he stepped beside Worthy and hurled the device inside the room with the words, "Adios, fuckers."

If the enemy inside was expecting a flashbang, they were about to be sorely disappointed—but it didn't appear that was the case, judging by the sudden shouts as Cancer grabbed his rifle and slipped behind Reilly.

A single man feared the blast more than the prospect of his enemies outside, darting into the hallway and Worthy's sector of fire as the pointman drilled him twice. His third shot missed entirely, an embarrassing lapse in accuracy that would've been unforgivable save the circumstances.

The guard's body was flung into the far wall with astonishing speed by the force of the blast within the room, a clap of light and sound whose characteristic echo was suddenly underscored by a deeper, more ominous resonance—something far more dangerous.

Worthy yelled, "Back!"

Cancer turned to scramble down the hallway, making room for his teammates' retreat as a violent rumble shook the floor beneath them, reverberating through the walls like an earthquake.

The ceiling creaked above them as they ran, the entire hallway trembling as heavy timber beams cracked under the weight of the blast. Chunks of plaster and brick crumbled to the ground in jagged pieces, one of which struck Cancer on the shoulder as he moved.

The cave-in started from the room—he could hear it, the unmistakable crunch of stone collapsing inward, one section of the wall giving way to another. It was an audible cascade of rock, timber, and brick folding in on itself until the collective roar ceased in one fell swoop, projecting its vibrating echo down the hall.

Cancer stopped and turned, the ambient glow of his taclight illuminating the dust- and sweat-streaked faces of Reilly and Worthy as they panted for breath.

The trio looked back toward the room—or, to put a finer point on it, the former room—only to find that the view was blocked by a wall of slabs that had once been the roof. Sand continued to pour across it, glimpses of the night sky visible through the rising dust.

"Hey," Cancer said, pointing his taclight at the dead machine gunner beside him. "You guys see that shit?"

Reilly shook his head. "Timing, man."

The response was an unwelcome reminder of their circumstances. Cancer had kept his men alive, however narrowly, but he'd also blocked their ability to advance.

He transmitted, "Right side, dead end. Angel, try not to throw any grenades—we're coming to reinforce."

Ian crept forward with his suppressed HK416 steady in his hands, the green glow of his night vision goggles painting the room in an eerie hue.

After Cancer's transmission, he'd wondered what kind of a mess the other team element had gotten into—the structural integrity on this side of the building was sound, allowing a stealthy and thus far uncontested advance. Ian and Hass had begun their clearance expecting an ambush at any moment. Given the size of the guard force before the airstrike, it seemed impossible that they'd be exempt from enemy contact.

But Ian soon remembered that Cancer's side of the building was the quickest route to the area of the missile strikes, and thus the logical avenue to send a team of defenders. The distant rattle of automatic fire and ultimately an explosion had only confirmed this suspicion.

Ian brushed the thoughts aside, continuing to move forward while Hass did the same on the far side. The air here was thick, almost suffocating, with the unmistakable stench of opium. It clung to the inside of his throat, the smell seeping into his lungs with each breath.

The room was a bulk storage chamber, the walls lined with large burlap sacks. Each was stuffed with bricks of raw opium, no doubt smuggled in from Afghanistan. Metal containers, stacked waist-high, held processed heroin, the labels scrawled in Farsi marking it as ready for transport. A significant source of financing for Malek's empire, Ian thought.

He advanced carefully, his eyes sweeping each shadow for movement. Hass moved with the same fluidity, his own HK416 raised as they reached the wall and converged on the single doorway. Angling his barrel down, Ian let Hass flow inside and then did the same. Both men cleared their respective corners before pivoting toward the center, their steps near silent.

And then, Ian realized that narcotics were merely the tip of the iceberg for Soren Malek.

The enormous shapes of industrial-grade printing presses loomed against the walls, rendered silent when the attending generator was knocked out. Banded stacks of freshly printed US dollars lay haphazardly on nearby tables, along with sophisticated engraving plates for more bills.

The scale of the operation was staggering—this wasn't a backyard forgery ring, it was professional, government-level precision.

His eyes flicked over the equipment as he moved, mentally calculating the sheer volume of counterfeit money that Malek must have pushed into circulation. But before he could process it all, the door at the far end of the room swung open with a sharp metallic creak.

Dim light flooded in—one or more generators must have continued providing power deeper in the building—and the glow silhouetted a man in combat gear that Hass fired at first with no more effect than knocking him backward slightly.

"Contact!" the man shouted, struggling to raise his rifle as Ian's infrared laser locked onto his torso and then dropped. The only explanation for Hass's inability to kill him on sight was the presence of an armored plate on the man's gear, and Ian's first two shots of the raid sent subsonic rounds into the pelvis instead.

His target crumpled to his knees and grunted, "You traitors," before Hass picked him off with a headshot that sent the man sprawling on the ground. The clatter of footfalls sounded from the next room. Four or five men at least, which left Ian and Hass outgunned and outmanned during the imminent assault.

No coordination was needed, and both of them scrambled for defensive positions behind the nearest counterfeit presses. Judging by the size, the machinery would be well equipped to absorb bullets. Ian aimed at the doorway in anticipation of what came next.

He caught his first sight of one man darting inside, then another, and fired at waist level for the second that elapsed before the roar of gunfire filled the air with a return salvo that impacted his cover and forced him back. Both men he'd seen wore tactical gear and body armor, their faces obscured by night vision goggles. They could see his and Hass's infrared lasers, further increasing the odds against the two men.

Ian flipped his own night vision up before exposing himself once more, this time with his taclight blazing. He scanned for targets but the assaulters must have taken cover behind machinery as well.

The roar of gunfire shattered the air and Ian took cover, this time transmitting in a harsh whisper.

"We're pinned," he said, "need support asap."

"*Still moving*," Cancer replied over the net with seeming indifference.

Ian pressed his back tighter against the equipment, the odds of survival shrinking with each passing second. He exchanged a quick glance with Hass—both of them knew they were outmanned and outgunned. The situation was spiraling, and Ian could feel the weight of it crushing down on them.

When he heard the whisper of footfalls, Ian risked exposure to take aim. The glare of his taclight was met by three more and he aborted the effort before the hissing pop of incoming rounds impacted his machine.

He sucked in a breath. If they didn't make a move soon, it was over.

And at that exact moment, Reilly transmitted.

"*You guys need to hit the deck. Like, now.*"

The order was confusing to say the least—the remainder of the team should have been taking up positions behind the far doorway, achieving angles of crossfire and selectively firing at the entrenched assaulters.

But Ian complied nonetheless, dropping into the prone as Reilly's transmission suddenly made complete sense.

A machinegun opened fire behind him, from the direction he and Hass had entered the room. The deafening roar seemed to split the room in two as a stream of green tracers appeared and then cut back and forth. Bullets ripped through the counterfeiting equipment, shredding the far printing presses and stacks of counterfeit dollars. Sparks flew as rounds struck metal and machinery, sending shreds of fake cash fluttering into the air like confetti.

Then the gun went quiet, but only for a moment—the scramble of footfalls from the assaulters preceded another wild burst, this time aimed down the centerline of the room. When it ended, the flashing figures of two team members darted past, followed in short order by Reilly's hulking figure, now armed only with his primary rifle. Whatever machinegun the medic captured, Ian decided as he reloaded, had finally run out of ammo.

He rose and proceeded forward with Hass to find that Worthy, Cancer, and Reilly had stopped at the last covered positions, and were in the process of delivering single shots to the enemy bodies now prostrate on the floor. They held their fire as Ian and Hass bounded past, setting up on the next doorway and flowing inside.

No threats, Ian saw at a glance, and he moved toward the far side while processing the sights around him.

The walls were plastered with posters and flags, all bearing the insignia of militant groups that Ian knew too well—the three H's of Hamas, Hezbollah, and the Houthis. The vibrant, defiant imagery stood out starkly under the overhead lighting.

A long table ran the length of the room, stacked with bomb-making materials and scattered printouts of IED diagrams. Boxes of cell phones and pagers completed the picture that made the purpose of the room all too clear. Malek was working with Iran, using the military expertise of his forces to train, equip, and arm foreign extremist organizations in exchange for safe haven.

It was bigger than Ian had thought. Much bigger.

But there was no time to dwell on it. Ian closed with the next doorway, slightly ajar, and waited until the footfalls of his teammates fell silent and he felt a squeeze on his shoulder.

Ian shouldered through the doorway, moving straight ahead to his corner and instead colliding with a man who pinned his weapon down. Trying to wrestle it away was futile, and firing now had just as good a chance of blowing his own foot off as hitting his opponent.

Releasing one hand from his weapon to draw his Winkler knife, Ian found himself looking into the terrified eyes of a pale-skinned man with neatly combed hair. No fighter at all but an analyst, and one who shouted, "Wait!" before Ian raised his arm and plunged his blade into the base of the man's neck.

A gurgling, choking gasp followed, during which Ian felt his enemy's grip release. Assuming a two-handed grip on his rifle once more, Ian stepped back and placed his suppressor against the dying man's sternum before ripping loose three rounds that finished the job.

The body collapsed before him, and Ian sought to resume his clearance only to find that his team was almost finished flowing into the room, securing sectors of fire in every direction. After reloading, Ian knelt to withdraw his knife from the young man's neck, sheathing the

Winkler blade while it was still slick with the warm blood of his dead opponent.

Then he heard an alarmed cry from deeper in the room, and whipped sideways to see a Black man shakily rising from behind a row of desks laden with radios and communications equipment. Worthy and Cancer were aiming at him as he stood fully, hands raised, pleading for his life in perfect English. Another American.

Ian knew what came next by virtue of the fact that his teammates said nothing in response—no orders to turn away and drop to his knees for flex cuffs, only a beat of silence. They had no time to restrain him, no time for anything but a relentless forward sweep in search of David.

Worthy held his fire but Cancer didn't, his suppressor whiffing with two shots that caused the man to crash out of sight.

Ian felt the weight of it settle in his gut, but they couldn't stop now. There was no time to process what they had just done. The urgency of rescuing David pressed against them like a vise.

Then the team was on the move, and Ian pursued them while mentally recalling the building layout. He'd spent more time staring at the Aegis imagery than anyone else, and a moment later he transmitted.

"Next room, door right, that's the holding cell."

His teammates were moving on before Ian could catch up, and to his surprise there was no sound of gunfire; by the time he reached the doorway, they'd already cleared the next room and were moving into David's holding area.

Ian knew as soon as his radio crackled that they'd found him.

But instead of the word "jackpot," Cancer said, *"Angel, get in here."*

Jogging forward, Ian cut right and slipped into the room that should have contained their missing team leader. Had he misremembered which room held the captive? Or, he thought, was David dead already, having been executed in the course of the raid?

The first possibility was removed as soon as Ian took in the room's interior—a metal loop on the wall for restraint, and a mattress on the floor along with bottled water, piles of books, and a latrine bucket. He breathed stale air with the unmistakable scent of body odor.

But no David.

Ian's eyes swept the room again, desperately searching for any sign of where David could have gone, any clue left behind. But there was nothing. Just the emptiness, the cold reality settling in.

Cancer spoke in a hollow tone.

"Where the fuck is he?"

My wrists were handcuffed behind my back, the chain held in place by the leg of a heavy metal table that, try as I might, I was unable to shift in the slightest. This spot on the floor in the command post had been my final resting place ever since Hector and three guards had dragged my ass in here shortly after the first missile explosions.

The room was suffocating, cluttered with tactical maps, scattered files, and the persistent hum of equipment, a facade of order growing thinner by the second as chaos raged outside.

Malek stood by the radio console, his back to me. I could see the tension in his shoulders, the subtle twitch in his hand as he reached for the hand mic. His world was crumbling around him, and the control he'd so confidently wielded was slipping through his fingers.

He pressed the mic to his lips, voice calm, but I could hear the undercurrent of frustration. "Command post to Alpha team, respond."

I was in a state of mild shock that my team had somehow managed to find Malek, and certain that they were unaware of my presence here when the first rockets from the airstrike rained down on the building. For lack of options, I'd simply waited for my imminent death at the hands of an Iranian-produced Sadid missile.

But the subsequent sounds of gunfire assured me that not only did my men know I was here, but they were coming for me—an immense reassurance that grounded me after days of captivity, and one that gave me no small measure of comfort even though I knew how this would end.

Malek tried again. "Command post to Bravo team."

Nothing but dead air in response.

The roar of a machinegun minutes earlier convinced me that my team had been decimated, but still the gunfire drew nearer. Those crazy bastards were still fighting their way through the building, I knew, though they'd never be able to move fast enough to save me.

"Command post to Charlie. Status report."

Malek lowered the hand mic, staring at it like he could elicit a response through sheer force of will. For a second, I thought he'd smash the thing against the wall, but he just set it down, slower than he probably wanted to. His eyes flicked toward me. I could practically see him calculating, weighing his options.

I said, "You seem tense. Does that mean the attack isn't a hoax this time?"

He forced a small, cold smile. "I think not."

"There's still time to run."

"Across the open desert, to be taken out by a drone strike?"

"There aren't any more drones, I told you—"

"And I will face my fate with my eyes open, if this is to be my end."

I shook my head. "It doesn't have to be. Cut me loose. I'll tell them to pull back. They're here for me, not you."

He shook his head, perplexed. "Why hasn't the CIA abandoned you? I researched your program. You're unattributable."

"I am," I said, my voice steady despite the adrenaline pulsing in my veins. "But not to my team."

Malek paused, considering my words more carefully than I expected. His eyes darkened as something shifted in his expression, though whether it was doubt or some new calculation, I couldn't tell. The weight of what I'd said hung between us, and I saw a crack in his certainty. He realized, maybe for the first time, that my team wasn't coming for any greater mission—they were coming for me. No matter the cost.

He removed his glasses and placed them on the table behind me.

Not a good sign.

I added, "If you want to stay alive, you'd better get that pistol off your hip and sit down beside me."

Malek's eyes met mine, dark and unreadable, but there was no denying the reality closing in around him.

Another burst of gunfire, closer now. His gaze flicked toward the door, then back to me. "You know," he said with an edge of dark fatalism in his voice, "men like us... we have a death wish, whether we admit it or not."

"Speaking for myself," I replied, "yeah, I guess I do. Or did."

It wasn't a lie. I'd spent most of my life toeing the line between life and death, voraciously pursuing situations that made survival feel like a coin toss. But that was before I had a wife and daughter, and now a son.

He sounded as if my answer confirmed something for him. "My own death wish is alive and well," he said, his voice growing quieter, more intense. "But I have vowed not to be killed by my enemies."

Malek's hand moved slowly, deliberately, as he pulled the SIG from its holster. The sound of metal sliding against leather felt too loud in the room, even with the chaos outside. My heart rate ticked up, my gaze following the pistol as far as I could until its barrel came to rest against my head.

My thoughts immediately turned to my family—not returning to them seemed like the cruelest trauma I could possibly inflict, and I was determined not to relinquish my fate to death as long as there was air in my lungs to change Malek's mind.

"You're not afraid of dying," I said, my voice steady, cutting through the tension in the room. "But you're terrified that none of this has meant anything."

Outside, the gunfire drew closer. The sound of boots was now audible, and he and I both knew it wasn't his men. It didn't matter—all of this was background noise to the exchange between us.

I continued, "You don't want to admit it, but that's what this is really about, isn't it? You're afraid. Afraid that all of this... your cause, your philosophy... it was for nothing. I get that. We both know it's over. But you don't have to take me with you."

I could sense that his control was slipping, the final threads of his plan fraying as he stood there, gun in hand, trying to hold onto something that was already lost.

The door rattled with another burst of gunfire outside. My team was so close, but it didn't matter. Malek's hand was trembling, the SIG still pressed to my head as he spoke.

"My cause will outlive us both."

I closed my eyes, knowing the next three seconds would decide everything. "I agreed to your deal, and you said I'd make it back to my family."

After a brief pause, I said the last words I'd ever speak to Soren Malek.

"Are you going back on your word?"

Worthy conducted an alternate failure drill—two shots to the pelvis, one to the head—against his latest opponent, an older, barrel-chested Latino man with body armor who'd damn near taken him out in the process. He was transitioning to the next target, already being engaged by a teammate, when the pointman's clearance ground to a crashing halt.

There had been so much gunfire over the course of this objective, and yet the most terrifying sound was what came next.

A single pistol shot from the room ahead.

David had just been executed.

Worthy took off at a sprint, abandoning any notion of urban combat tactics as he darted across the room to leave any remaining enemy to his teammates. He was too late to save his team leader, but as long as his executioner was alive, there was time to make him suffer. Tremendously.

His men completed their clearance and stopped shooting as Worthy threw open the door and sidestepped inside, sweeping his rifle across the space and stopping when his eyes found a dead body.

It was Soren Malek, pistol still in his hand, the back of his head blown off as blood and brain matter soaked into the rug beneath him.

Beside the body was David—handcuffed to the leg of a table, breathing heavily, but alive.

"You good?" Worthy asked.

"I am now."

Worthy lowered his rifle and nodded toward Malek. "What'd you do, talk to him about your kids until he couldn't take it anymore?"

David sighed. "I just started using your accent, and he pulled a Hitler right after that—"

His words cut off as Cancer shouted from the doorway.

"Hey, asshole. Don't you *ever* run off by yourself like that—"

"Relax, you old bastard," David said dismissively. "We're all retiring after this."

Worthy knelt beside him. "Let me get those handcuffs picked."

"Don't bother. Keys are in his pocket."

As Worthy patted down Malek to find the keyring, he noticed David's knife. Disgusted, he wrenched off Malek's belt to retrieve it. "This fucker took your Winkler?"

"He said he'd give it back. And wasn't I bailing your ass out a few days ago? Didn't expect you to return the favor so fast."

Worthy leaned over to unlock the handcuffs. "Don't say I never did anything for you."

David brought his arms to his front, rubbing his wrists and grabbing the Winkler before rising stiffly. Worthy helped him upright as the rest of the team poured in.

Reilly nearly tackled the team leader with a bear hug, then lifted him off the ground. "Hey, you made it!" Then the medic winced. "Damnit, forgot about the ricochet."

It was Reilly's first mention of being hit—they'd have to patch him up on the way out, Worthy thought.

David grunted as he was set down. "And now I've got a few broken ribs to show for it. Thanks for that."

Hass strode over to greet him, while Ian ignored the newly liberated hostage completely.

He was in his element, removing a trash bag from his kit and whipping it open to begin stuffing laptops and hard drives inside as fast as his hands could move. All of the above was catnip for an intelligence operative, and David called out, "Nice to see you too."

Ian didn't respond, probably didn't hear him in the first place.

Cancer slapped Ian's shoulder and said, "You've got ten seconds and we're out of here."

David recovered the pistol and its holster from Malek's discarded belt. "You bring a rifle for me or what?"

"No," Worthy said, leading David toward their teammates as they staged at the door for their return trip to the vehicles. "But don't worry, you'll find plenty lying around on the way out."

41

"You ready?" I asked, impatiently waving the radio handset.

"Almost," Reilly replied, continuing to adjust the satellite antenna on the hood of the vehicle.

I assessed the view through my new night vision device, a prize captured off a dead guard.

The other SUV was parked directly behind mine, Shayan in the driver's seat, as the rest of my team pulled security. I caught sight of Cancer looking back at me—he was still pissed that I'd gone off alone to divert the enemy away from our team during the sandstorm, the silences during our brief interactions since leaving the decimated compound icy at best. Whatever, I thought. He'd get over it.

Or not.

The wind whistled softly through the jagged rocks, bringing with it the dry, gritty scent of dust and earth. We'd parked both vehicles deep in a crevice between massive boulders, hidden from view on one side by the natural rock formation and thick scrub that grew around its edges.

On the other side was the low slope of a mountain range that, despite its relatively modest height, looked rather imposing by virtue of the fact that it stood between us and the village of Nastanj, where our exfil drivers were waiting to take us into Turkmenistan.

But first, we needed to verify the exfil plan was intact.

Reilly made a final adjustment to the antenna and checked the radio. "You're good."

I keyed my handset and spoke.

"Did you miss me?"

A pause, and a long one, before Chen replied.

"*Say again.*"

"This is Suicide Actual. Did you miss me?"

The response to this wasn't a response at all. Or at least, not a verbal one.

Instead I heard the static-laced sound of applause—Chen was holding her transmit switch down so I could hear the reaction from her staff at the OPCEN, and I felt a triumphant smile cross my face. The approval or lack thereof from anyone at CIA Headquarters meant precious little to me, but the fact that I'd been rescued by my team...well, that had replaced the emotional exhaustion of captivity with an almost overwhelming sense of freedom.

Chen transmitted, "*This is where you give me an explanation. And a status report.*"

Right. "Team is consolidated at Checkpoint Two, no major injuries. Malek is dead. I happened to escape in the confusion. We're ready to move to exfil."

"Copy," she said, her tone suddenly businesslike in the extreme. "*The Iranian military has blocked off all routes surrounding the compound as they respond to the airstrike. You can no longer drive to Nastanj.*"

I adjusted the gear on my torso. Normally my tactical kit felt like little more than a second skin, but the awkward fitting of my current plate carrier reflected its selection—the least blood-splattered of options I'd found among the dead guards on my way out. No one else on my team had body armor, and I made no attempt to reconcile that. If I could stay safer on behalf of my family, then that's what I'd do.

Malek's SIG pistol was now on my hip, a trophy I'd keep until the day I died. And Worthy hadn't been kidding when he said I'd have plenty of rifles to choose from on our way out of the compound. Among the plethora of swanky assault rifles, I had ultimately chosen an M4 carbine. It was the weapon I carried into combat as an 18-year-old Ranger, and it would now see me through the last mission of my gunslinging career. A fitting choice, or at least I thought so—and with my Winkler knife once more attached to my kit, I felt damn near invincible.

I keyed my handset and replied, "I had a feeling this wouldn't be as easy as I'd hoped."

"*It would have been,*" Chen said, "*if your team had left after the airstrike. As planned.*"

"But then you'd miss the pleasure of my company. Am I correct that we'll have to do a foot movement east, over the mountains?"

"*You are. Eight kilometers straight-line distance, closer to thirteen on foot if my operations officer is correct. And it will have to be quick. Exfil window ends at zero nine, and if you haven't made it by then we have no assurances the drivers will return for another linkup cycle. Especially given the extent of the Iranian response. Inform Shayan of the roadblocks and get rid of him.*"

"He wouldn't keep pace with us anyway. We're moving. Will check in prior to Nastanj. Suicide Actual, out."

I passed the handset over to Reilly for him to pack up the satellite antenna, then transmitted over the team net.

"Roads are blocked. Racegun, plan a route through the mountains. We're heading out to Nastanj on foot. Hard time for linkup is zero nine if we want to make it out. Grab what we need from the trucks. Shayan's on his own."

Cancer took over the rest, first heading over to Hass to relay my brief—I'd inherited our newest team member's radio, a necessary theft that he hadn't objected to.

As my teammates began extracting their packs from the vehicles, I headed to the rear truck and leaned toward the open driver's window.

"You're officially released from your duty," I said.

Shayan looked flustered. "Already?"

"Iranian military is blocking all the roads leading out. You can't risk getting caught with Americans. Wait here for an hour, then head for a local village and lie low for a day or two. We won't leave any evidence in either vehicle, so your cover story is your cover story, full stop."

He gave a slight nod, shifting uneasily in the driver's seat. "And what about you? You and the others?"

There was a reason we never told local assets any more than we absolutely had to—Shayan had no idea about Nastanj, our linkup with the exfil drivers, or anything else beyond having to comply with our every demand.

I glanced at my teammates already consolidating to move out. Cancer was performing a final sweep of the SUV interiors, using a red light to ensure every trace of our presence had been removed.

Then I said, "We'll take care of ourselves. I can't thank you enough for all your help."

Before I could continue, Ian appeared at my side and handed the driver three stacks of bills.

"Cash bonus," he explained. "Courtesy of Dariush Navidi. Don't spend it all in one place. Stay safe, Shayan."

The driver took the money and said, "You are neglecting one thing, my friend."

Ian fished through a pocket and procured a large coin of some kind that he held up with the words, "I was hoping you'd forget about it."

Shayan smiled and took it from him. "I told you it was authentic."

If he got caught, we all knew, things could spiral quickly. But the remaining truck wasn't big enough to hold all of us and Shayan knew that just as well as anyone else. He'd be able to infer we were crossing over the mountains easily enough—now we had to do so and make our linkup before anyone else could figure that out.

I followed Ian toward the rest of our team until he stopped abruptly, turning to hold up the digital voice recorder he used during field interrogations.

"Take this," he said. "When you get a chance on patrol, start narrating your time in captivity. Everything you saw and heard, and most definitely everything Malek said. I need to get it on record while it's still fresh."

I rolled my eyes and took it from him.

"Sure, I'll do that in my abundant free time."

Hass, Worthy, and Reilly were assembled with their rucksacks on. Cancer was in the process of donning his, followed by Ian, while I would be delightfully unencumbered—save my armored plates, of course—in what was quite possibly the sole benefit of being captured.

"Same order of movement," Cancer said. "Worthy, hard drive uphill. You can slow the pace once we're on the high ground."

"You got it," the pointman said.

The landscape suddenly looked ghostly in my night vision, the mountains somehow ominous in a way they had never been before. Had I ever actually expected a seamless movement to exfil? Perhaps, I thought, if only by virtue of this being my team's last hurrah. But we'd just been dealt a parting shot by Murphy's law: anything that can go wrong will go wrong. Not even an unexpected patrol across mountainous terrain, however, could bring down my spirits.

I was free.

Then I realized the team was waiting, and became suddenly aware that Cancer was the ground force commander no longer.

"Let's move," I said, and our patrol began.

42

Worthy led his team across the mountains as the sun began to crest over the jagged peaks around him.

He scanned the surrounding terrain in a never-ending cycle, continuously searching for vantage points concealing hidden opponents and prioritizing features to take cover behind for every conceivable angle of enemy fire. All of the above were part and parcel of his role as pointman, a task that had gotten more difficult in the last twenty minutes.

The Modafinil that Reilly had provided before the airstrike was already wearing off, and his sharp senses were beginning to cede their razor edge to the cumulative fatigue and exhaustion that had been building ever since he'd bailed out of a destroyed B-2 bomber three days ago.

But Worthy was no stranger to operating in such circumstances, and drew upon his innate reserves of strength to stay as focused as he could manage beneath the ever-brightening sky. The air was crisp, and small patches of green sprouted between the rocks—a reminder that spring had come to South Khorasan. Tiny shoots of grass struggled against the rocky soil, and here and there, delicate white blossoms clung to the hard ground as if nature itself was determined to break through.

He noted the ground falling away ahead, the possible paths diverging to either side. And while he had a rough idea of what lay ahead from his hasty route planning against the satellite imagery, the map, as ever, was not the terrain.

"Short halt," he transmitted. "I need to check this out."

Glancing backward, he saw his teammates lower themselves to a knee, dropping their rucksacks one at a time and alternating which direction they faced to provide security in every direction except his. They appeared just as weary as he was, particularly Reilly, who'd done a heroic job of carrying his gear despite the fact that they'd recently dug a bullet ricochet out of his left shoulder.

Worthy took off his own rucksack, grateful for the reprieve. He moved forward at a careful walk, then a crouch, and finally dropped into the prone to slither forward on his belly, his tactical vest scraping against cold rocks until he stopped at the edge.

And then, he got his first sight of the village below.

It had been little more than a grainy blur on his satellite imagery and the in-person view wasn't much more illuminating—a handful of buildings clustered together, with a small mosque standing at its center. There wasn't a person in sight, although their presence was indicated by thin wisps of smoke from the cooking fires inside a few homes as well as the goats and donkeys milling about in pens.

He set his rifle down and pulled out his compact field binoculars, scanning for any movement he'd missed before turning his attention to the surrounding terrain.

"Suicide," he transmitted, "we've got a decision point here."

"*Moving*," David replied.

Worthy lowered his binoculars and appraised the grander landscape around them, searching for alternatives and finding none.

Their movement through the mountains thus far had been plagued by impassable terrain, every necessary compromise in their path costing them time and funneling them closer to the village ahead. The team had traveled just over seven kilometers in total, and roughly six remained between them and their exfil drivers. They were close, but time was not on their side.

He checked his watch. 5:23 a.m.

That left them with just over three and a half hours to complete the journey to Nastanj and, now that the sun was up, immeasurably more risk in doing so. Particularly, he thought, given a human population below. Civilian at best, and at worst...well, the team's fight may not have been finished just yet.

The sound of movement behind him preceded the arrival of David at his side, and then Cancer.

Worthy handed the binoculars to his team leader, who took in the sight below.

"The way I see it," Worthy began, "we can't bypass the village entirely. Unless you want to follow that ridge to the right, which'll add an hour minimum, maybe two or three depending on how the terrain shakes out. High ground to the left is worse, there's no way we're making it through."

"Shit," David muttered, passing the binoculars to Cancer.

The sniper had barely raised them to his eyes before narrating his thoughts.

"We miss that linkup window, and the odds of never seeing our drivers again are close to a hundred percent. They're still local assets. The drivers for Griffin's team wouldn't even answer the Agency's calls after the Iranian military showed up, and now that the roads to our west are blocked"—he lowered the binoculars and handed them back—"we'll be lucky if they're still in Nastanj by the time we get there."

David keyed his radio. "Angel, we're looking at the village now. Livestock, a few fires, can't see anyone. Who's down there?"

Ian transmitted back, "*Farmers and herders, most likely. It's safe to say none of them have the Iranian military on speed dial, but they could have ties to smuggling or black market networks. Unlikely there are any Jaish al-Adl fighters, but there could be some scouts or sympathizers. Beyond that, it's hard to say.*"

Then Cancer spoke.

"Tick-tock, asshole."

Worthy expected David to be a hesitant shell of his former self, at least for a few days following his rescue.

But the team leader seemed grounded if not enthusiastic.

"Take us right, into the low ground. We've got plenty of rocks to stay behind until we hit the western edge of the village, and even then it's going to be a short exposure before we're back behind cover. Seventy-five meters, 80 maybe, and we take turns covering it at a run. The longer we wait, the more people down there will be awake. If either of you has any issues with that, speak now or forever hold your peace."

Worthy nodded, his gut tightening. It wasn't the decision he wanted to hear, but it was the right one if they wanted to get out of Iran alive. The clock was ticking, and the village was a wildcard they'd simply have to navigate around rather than avoid entirely. He glanced over at Cancer, who gave a slight grunt.

"Best we're gonna get." Then he transmitted, "Ruck up. We're skirting the village to the south, high risk, there will be running involved."

David and Cancer slid backward in unison, easing themselves backward to return to the team.

Worthy still held the binoculars in his hand, and gave the village one last look. The fires still burned, curling smoke into the air. But the silence... the silence remained heavy, oppressive, like the calm before a storm.

Whatever was waiting for them, they'd face it soon enough.

Putting his binoculars away, he cradled his rifle in his elbows and pushed himself back from the edge.

43

Ian crouched low in the ravine, moving with as much silence as he could manage while his team slipped forward. The village loomed just beyond the rocks to their left, an ominous cluster of buildings, the tallest rooftops stark in the early morning light.

"*Ten meters,*" Worthy transmitted.

And while the pointman's tone indicated a routine update, the message was anything but.

They'd managed to stay hidden up to this point, but the moment of exposure was drawing closer—and with it, a sense of unease gnawed at Ian. Eighty meters was an incredible distance when running in full combat gear with ruck, and even more so when fully exposed to a village and its occupants.

Ian could make out the lapse in rock cover ahead, and David transmitted steady as ever. "*We'll stop before we break cover. Worthy goes first, then everyone else in 20-meter intervals. Barrels on the village until it's your turn to run, then pick up security on the far side. Cancer and Doc, I want your eyes on the buildings until the bitter end. Rain Man's in charge of controlling the flow for everyone else.*"

"*Copy,*" Cancer replied.

Worthy came to a stop beside the final rock cover, dropping to a knee along with David, and Ian closed the distance to do the same.

As they waited for the rest of their teammates to arrive, they scanned the path ahead.

Each man would be running across an expanse of loose rock and scrub brush, the only cover between them and the village coming by way of small boulders strewn across the periphery. None were big enough to stand or even kneel behind, which meant anyone on the move if this went bad would be forced into the prone. Not great. The path even made a C-shape toward the village, coming dangerously close to the peripheral buildings before arcing outward again.

"Doesn't look that bad," David whispered.

Worthy turned back with a quizzical expression. "Hell, I'd say it looks *exactly* that bad."

Hass arrived next, grunting as he dropped to a knee. "Damn. That's rough."

Then Reilly, who moved in front of Worthy. His assessment wasn't much different. "Shit. Lot of ground to cover."

Cancer was last, moving to the front and taking up a position at the very edge of their current cover.

"Fuck," he said matter-of-factly. "All right, let's get this over with. Worthy, you ready?"

The pointman's lack of enthusiasm was now evident in his tense posture as much as his voice. "Guess so."

After a nod from David, Hass spoke a single word that propelled the plan into motion.

"Go."

Cancer and Reilly pivoted around the edge, leveling their HK417s toward the buildings beyond. Worthy rose and, with a sharp inhale, took off at a run.

His feet pounded against the ground, building all the momentum he was capable of while weighed down by gear as David and Ian crept forward and stopped.

Cancer said, "No movement. Doc?"

"Nothing," Reilly replied.

Ian's heart was racing as he watched Worthy's receding figure. He was fifteen meters out now, moving fast. The distance between the rest of the team and their next concealment seemed to stretch with each passing step.

"Go," Hass said.

Then David was gone, darting off after the pointman with the clatter of loose rock.

Ian moved beside Cancer and Reilly, crouching at their backsides, a dense lump forming in his throat as he swallowed against a dry mouth. The silence gnawed at him. It felt unnatural, although when he appraised his instincts for any premonitions of good or bad fortune, his mind was silent.

He leaned out to take a glance at the buildings to his left.

A few two-story buildings, but nothing taller than that. Small houses, livestock pens, and narrow alleys that cut through the village below electrical cables. He caught a glimpse of a mosque, heard the distant bleating of goats. The air was still and heavy, pregnant with inactivity. Maybe that was an indicator that something was off, or maybe it simply meant that most of the village was asleep.

"Go," Hass said.

Ian stood and took off, his boots kicking up small bits of gravel as he sprinted across the open ground, his rucksack thumping against his back, the shoulder straps resisting his forward drive. His heart pounded from the sudden burst of speed as much as the exposure, mind racing through every possible threat the village could be hiding and finding that list growing longer than his initial assessment to David.

Buildings passed in a blur, although he didn't venture any more than a periodic sideward glance for fear of losing his footing. Worthy was well over halfway across, the team frequency in his earpieces silent for lack of anything to report.

Ian was keenly aware of the low boulders to the left of his path, his mind seamlessly locking onto one, then the next, as a source of salvation for him to dive behind at the sound of gunfire. A rooster's sudden call sounded like it was broadcast through a loudspeaker—his senses were on full alert, the survival instinct typical of high-stakes combat situations alive and well within his chest.

David was past the halfway point now, coming up on the closest point to the village. Worthy was three-quarters of the way across, seconds away from establishing security on the far side. Hass would be starting his run any moment now, and Ian felt a flash of relief that they were actually going to pull this off, that within the next few minutes he'd be chastising himself for the bout of anxiety.

A sharp crack split the air.

Ian registered a cluster of pebbles to his front exploding in all directions from the bullet strike, and his body reacted before his mind had fully caught up.

He threw himself down beside a meter-high rock, the force of his impact sending a shockwave of pain that was soon forgotten. His breath came in shallow, rapid bursts as he writhed his arms free of his ruck and pressed himself flat against the ground, trying to become as small a target as possible.

Cancer transmitted, "*Sniper, second floor—*"

The net went silent at the blast of another shot, and a seemingly endless second went by before Cancer spoke again.

"*Shit, he's got me dialed in. Sniper, second floor of the building next to Suicide.*"

Another shot followed, its echo ripping across the ravine.

"*Just tried to get an angle,*" Worthy said. "*Nearly got my head blown off. Guy's good.*"

Ian glanced right to see David in the prone behind whatever meager cover he could find, hazarding one glance before ducking back. When no shot followed, he took a longer look.

To the left, Ian saw that Hass was with Cancer and Reilly. He hadn't even made it far enough to find cover before being driven back, and now the entire team was pinned down in a worst-case scenario.

Cancer came over the net again. "*He's deep in the room, firing out the center window. I barely saw the muzzle flash. Not sure any of us will be able to hit him.*"

Grenade launchers were one of the many pieces of equipment the team had left behind in the States for lack of packing space, although Ian wasn't sure they'd help—if the sniper remained this quick to react, even a unified charge would result in three team members killed, at least. They couldn't stay pinned like this, but there was no safe way forward.

Any attempt to move now would be suicidal, but the next man to transmit specialized in such undertakings.

David's voice came over the radio, clear and resolute. *"Relax, guys. I'm in his blind spot. I'll take care of it."*

"*Don't you dare,*" Cancer began, but it was too late.

David was already up and moving, and quickly at that—his figure flashed toward the village at a sprint as Ian watched in utter disbelief. If he was wrong about the length or angle of the sniper's blind spot, the next shot would be fatal. Ian eased out from behind his cover, desperate to achieve a line of sight to the second-floor window to cover his team leader's advance.

And when another gunshot blasted through the air, Ian was certain that David Rivers was dead.

But the round slammed off the boulder Ian was hidden behind and he aborted the effort, every muscle at maximum tension before he forced himself to breathe again.

Then he keyed his radio and admitted, *"That was for me."*

David's response was livid.

"*Stop exposing yourselves,*" the team leader transmitted, his words choppy with panted breaths. "*Just give me...three minutes...and I'll give you... a dead sniper.*"

No one could move to aid him, not without getting killed in the process. The degree of sheer helplessness was overwhelming, and yet when Ian searched for any alternatives to waiting and hoping, he found none.

Whatever happened next, David was on his own.

I sprinted into the village with my M4, moving through the stench of manure and burning wood.

Chickens scattered in a panicked flutter as I moved between rough stone buildings, their crumbling walls lined with drying herbs and faded prayer flags that fluttered weakly in the morning breeze. The alleyway was strung with ropes that held up laundry and tarps, all of them visual obstacles that I darted between in my race toward a head-to-head confrontation with the sniper.

I slipped past the final strung tarp to register a flash of movement, the barrel of my M4 locking onto it without any conscious effort whatsoever. It was a scrawny brindle dog with ribs jutting from its sides, skittering past with its tail between its legs.

Then I was at the corner of the two-story building where my target waited. With no back door I was forced to the front, exposing me to buildings that I quickly scanned for signs of life only to find none. That much was typical for civilian homes in this part of the world after gunshots rang out, and a solid indicator that my prospects for survival were looking good for the moment.

Rounding the edge of the building, I began my final advance toward the door, weathered and scarred, its frail planks harvested from the sparse trees in the surrounding mountains some time ago. Rusted iron nails held the boards together, the collective panel bearing cracks and splinters, woefully unsuited to withstanding what was about to come.

I was going to kick that fucker apart.

But when I was perhaps a meter out, it creaked open of its own accord. The face of a young man appeared, a teenager at best, peering at the surrounding village before whipping toward me.

It was supremely bad timing on his part, but superlative on mine. The muzzle of my M4 practically grazed his forehead at the moment I fired a single shot.

The 5.56mm round tore through the young man's skull, instantly pulverizing bone and shredding brain matter into a gruesome spray that splattered across the weathered wood of the door. One eye now dangled from its socket by a glistening strand of nerves as I grabbed his shoulder and threw him toward the street, then moved through the entryway streaked with rivulets of crimson blood.

I entered the room to find a mess of confusion. Rifles lay scattered, knocked over in haste; boots were still unlaced, and men were either partially dressed or hurriedly pulling on their gear.

My first glance told me everything I needed to know about the source of my team's current troubles. These were no hardened terrorists but smugglers of one flavor or another, and this was their safehouse.

The entire situation was, I realized, a misunderstanding of epic proportions.

They thought my team was here for them, possibly that we were some competing group out to steal their drugs or take over their operation. In reality all they had to do was let us pass—and since that hadn't happened, they were going to pay.

Five men in total, some only recently awakened, all of them in the process of gearing up for a ground assault against my men that they'd never be able to execute. None had body armor, but I did. And I was the only one in the room who had been expecting gunplay on such an immediate timeline.

All of that information was processed within a split second of my entrance, and now came the fun part—which of them was going to get it first?

That honor was reserved for the most capable of the group, ex-military by my assessment, his AK-47 slung and in his grasp after he'd abandoned the kneeling effort to tie his combat boots.

Two shots through his sternum, both fatal, before I transitioned to a forty-something bearded man in jeans reaching for his rifle on a table beside him. A trio of clean trigger pulls ensured he'd never complete the act, and he bowled over the surface instead while I shifted my aim to the next two contestants, both of equal priority in this gunfight that would only end one way.

The first had been in the process of donning a magazine carrier when I entered, the second stuffing a radio into the pocket of his field jacket. Neither had their weapons in arm's reach. I gave the latter man a single 5.56mm round to the chest, his comrade two, and then shifted back to the first to deliver a final bullet.

That left me with the final enemy fighter, if you could call him that, who was the least intimidating of all the half-formed threats I'd just dealt with.

His retreat had begun upon seeing me step through the door, and he'd only just cleared the next doorway in the time it took me to kill the rest of his team. A gentleman in his twenties, as best I could tell, and I pulled the trigger before he could dart out of sight entirely.

He went momentarily rigid as the round speared into his lower back, my first shot that hadn't been textbook perfect but nonetheless sufficient to halt him in place, to say the least.

The echo of my gunfire faded to the satisfying percussion of human bodies hitting the floor, and I lowered my rifle to perform a follow-up sweep. Had anyone survived? Merely been wounded? Nope, I decided, all these men had since departed save the one I dealt with now.

My runner was flat on his stomach, suddenly shrieking like a child awakened by a nightmare but literally and figuratively paralyzed against further use of his legs. That didn't stop him from trying to pull himself away on his elbows, not registering that he had nowhere to go, his panic absolute.

It took me three steps to get an angle of fire on the back of his head, where I sent a single round that splayed him out for the last time.

Another sweep to confirm no emerging threats and I knew beyond all doubt that I had 19 rounds remaining—how? I'd never been able to count my shots before, and I reloaded, pocketing the partially spent magazine and finding the stairs to my left.

The sniper was still on the second floor, and the lack of further sound brought an intuitive certainty that he and I were now alone in the building. Whoever he was, he'd had more than sufficient notice to stage an ambush against me. It didn't matter, I thought. He'd almost taken out my teammates and would be held to account for that. I was coming for him, and nothing in this building, this village, or the entire world would slow me down.

I made my way to the staircase, knelt, and then peered upward.

No sniper in sight, although the stairs ended at a wall leading left. Only one way for an ascending man to move, and that meant he had a covered firing position to take out whoever approached. No flip of the coin, not for either of us. There was only one way I could move and both of us knew it as well as the other. I had no grenades, hadn't thought to ask if my teammates did, and that narrowed my options—this would be a rifle-on-rifle engagement, and mine was more than suitable for the task.

The M4 was merely an additional limb at this point, and one that I employed with just as much precision as my arms and legs. Maybe more. Using it now felt like coming home, back to my roots as a Ranger private, back to the beginning of my mercenary career.

Without further thought, I charged up the stairs.

My boots thudded heavily against the stone steps, the sound ricocheting off the walls as I made no effort to mask my approach. I wanted him to hear me. Every footfall was a message: I'm coming for you.

The top of the staircase loomed ahead, a blind corner to the left that grew nearer with each passing step.

There was no room for error now. If I failed, my team would come into the village whether I was alive or dead, would enter this building to get me or my body no matter how many of them the sniper managed to eliminate in the process. They'd gone against far greater odds in rescuing me from Malek, but this time it would cost them far more.

I had to succeed.

Three stairs to go, and I cleared two of them in a bound.

At the final step I grabbed the edge of the wall with my left hand, twisting my body in the opposite direction as I threw myself to the ground. My chest slammed into the floor, the momentum causing me to slide across the dusty ground, directly into the sniper's kill zone with one important distinction: I was now a prone target.

And a moving one, at that.

My slide continued as I tried to take aim, knowing that we faced one another—me sliding low, barely above the floor, and him aiming at chest level to defend himself before it was too late. It wouldn't take him long to adjust his point of aim, maybe a second.

But one second was all I needed.

Everything slowed as I glided across the floor, elbows scraping as they supported my M4. Dust particles swirled lazily in the air, catching the weak sunlight that filtered through a window. The world around me blurred at the edges as I spotted and then focused on an heirloom chest before me.

It was ornately decorated but battered from years of use, the only piece of cover in sight. And sure enough there was a shadow behind it, the low profile of a man's shoulder and head above the long barrel of a rifle that erupted into a brilliant starburst of flame.

A thunderous boom shook the space, and I felt the air shift as the round sailed overhead. My right shoulder struck the wall, ending my slide in one jolting halt as I adjusted my aim, and he adjusted his.

My M4's front sight post and rear aperture slowly aligned with the shadowy outline of the head behind the trunk, my finger curled around the trigger. Each millisecond of this process stretched into an eternity as I watched the sniper's barrel continue its downward arc toward me, the black void of the muzzle growing larger as it angled toward my face.

I had time for one shot before being killed and I tried to make it fast—but time had slowed to a very thin stream, the pad of my index finger compressing the curved metal of my trigger against what felt like enormous resistance.

The world around me had fallen away completely, my entire existence narrowed down to this one critical instant.

Then the trigger broke and my firing pin slammed forward. A controlled explosion erupted within the chamber, the rapidly expanding gasses propelling the bullet down the barrel at supersonic speed.

But I wasn't the only one who fired—the thunder of my outgoing round was met by one in return, and while the fact that I was hearing it should've been evidence enough that it was a miss, I felt wholly unconvinced until a round tore into the floor inches from my left side.

The world snapped back into focus as I realized my opponent was no longer visible, the echo of the shots fading to the thudding of my heartbeat as I saw a new detail ahead.

A gruesome abstract painting of blood and brain matter flecked with bits of bone now oozed down the wall just above the heirloom chest.

It was over.

Or almost over, I thought, leaping to my feet amidst the sound of shallow, ragged breaths. I cleared the rest of the space to find a table set back from the window, its surface topped with a foam sleeping pad, one side pinned by a sandbag bearing a U-shaped depression— the position from which the sniper had fired at my team.

I rounded the trunk to find a Dragunov SVD rifle on the floor, its wooden stock worn so smooth from decades of use that it appeared polished. The slender scope atop it was chipped and scratched, but had clearly served its purpose well.

Beside the gun was its owner.

He must have been in his seventies, an uneven gray beard clinging to his jawline and thinning in patches. A keffiyeh was loosely wrapped around his neck, its once vibrant pattern now muted and frayed. But his eyes hadn't been dulled with age, hazel irises locked on mine in a hollow stare as his chest heaved with weak gasps.

Half of his skull had been blown away, the jagged edges of shattered bone visible beneath the shredded skin, blood pouring from the gaping wound. His body twitched uncontrollably as he tried and failed to move.

I could have left him for dead, and if he'd managed to kill one of my teammates, I probably would have.

But he'd played his part well, an admirable opponent who both warranted and had won my respect. He deserved a warrior's death.

I raised my M4 and graced him with the last words of wisdom he'd ever hear.

"Careful who you fuck with."

Then I fired, and turned to jog back toward the stairs as I transmitted.

"Sniper down. It's a smuggling safehouse, they were about to send a ground assault. Think I got them all."

I was taking the stairs downward two at a time when Cancer responded, *"Copy, we're moving forward to secure you."*

"Just stay put," I told him, moving through the carnage of my slaughter on the first floor and peering out the doorway for threats. "I'm on my way out."

"Fuck that," Cancer said resolutely. *"We're moving to you."*

That son of a bitch, I thought, exiting the building and sweeping my rifle across the street as I slipped to the corner.

The last thing I wanted now was to make them come after me once again. We didn't have much farther to go to our linkup for exfil. Even if someone called for reinforcements from the smuggling network, the villages were few and far between out here in the mountains. We'd be long gone by the time any more enemy arrived.

I moved back to the alley, negotiating the laundry and tarps on my way back out, scanning for movement.

And when I pushed my way past a strung sheet, I found it—a figure in a window that I took aim at, fully willing at this point to fire at the slightest provocation, or even no provocation at all.

But the wide-eyed face watching me from his home belonged to a boy of ten or twelve. He looked terrified and I gave him a friendly wave, continuing forward to see my entire team charging across the short distance from their trail toward me.

Worthy was moving the fastest, with Hass a close second. Ian was making an admirable effort and Reilly, despite his muscle mass, was managing to stay ahead of Cancer. No way that heavy smoker was beating anyone, I thought. The sight of them brought a sense of immense strength and protection. There was nothing these men wouldn't do for me, and nothing I wouldn't do for them—we were a brotherhood within a brotherhood, warriors who had seen it all together and were about to depart combat for the last time.

I was running forward to meet them when I spun sideways, my legs tangling beneath me. Stumbling, I barely caught myself from falling and then collapsed entirely.

My ears were ringing, some cataclysmic roar registering but sounding muffled and distant. I looked back to the window to see the boy I'd waved at lowering an AK-47 before darting out of view.

The pain hit a split second later, white hot and searing. It radiated out from my heart, stealing my breath away as I looked down to find my chest awash with blood pouring forth in staggering amounts.

I watched the sight with detachment, a strange numbness overtaking my body and mind as I rolled onto my back in the dusty street. A golden and blue sky spun above me and my vision tunneled, the pain fading entirely. My body wasn't my own anymore, just a distant, flickering image as the world blurred and twisted.

The light dimmed, and then—nothing.

44

Cancer opened the aid pouch on his kit, falling to his knees beside David.

The team leader was lying on his back, either unconscious or dead, and Cancer moved the M4 away before setting his own rifle down.

For once in his life, he didn't concern himself with security—the other team members were already forming a tight perimeter around the casualty save Reilly, who unslung his aid bag on David's opposite side.

Retrieving his medical shears, Cancer cut David's blood-soaked plate carrier at the shoulders and sides, pulling the front panel off. Underneath, the shirt was saturated, the red staining it and sticking to his skin. With the dark uniform and tactical kit, it was impossible to say if it was the bright red of an artery. And if the blood was pooling under the surface, he wouldn't be able to see it at all.

Cancer ripped the shirt apart to see blood pouring from a dark, ragged hole in the flesh.

The bullet had punched through just beneath the right collarbone, so close to the armored plate it was a miracle it had hit flesh. High on the chest, right where the lung sat, far too close to the heart for comfort. A gunshot wound just below the clavicle was almost always fatal, in part due to the proximity of a cluster of major arteries—the subclavian artery that curved under the collarbone, and the pulmonary arteries carrying blood from the heart to the lungs. If the former was clipped, there was a small chance Reilly could keep David alive.

But if the latter had been damaged, no medic in the world would be able to save him.

Cancer had barely exposed the wound before Reilly wiped away the blood with a wad of gauze and tore open an occlusive chest seal. The transparent, dinner plate-sized piece of adhesive plastic gleamed as he pressed it down firmly, the small tube of a one-way air valve centered directly over the bullet hole to allow air to escape from the chest cavity.

Reilly ran his hands under David's back, inspecting his palms afterward. "No exit wound."

So the bullet was still inside, Cancer thought, which meant it had bounced inside David's body and possibly shredded vital organs and vessels in the process. The risk of internal bleeding was increased tenfold.

Reilly's hands moved quickly, tilting David's jaw back to keep the airway open. Cancer procured a needle from his aid pouch as the medic pressed his ear to David's chest, listening intently.

Cancer could already see David's shortness of breath, a neck vein bulging on his injured side. Hemothorax. The accumulation of blood was compressing his lung.

Reilly said, "Needle thoracostomy," and Cancer handed him the 14-gauge dart with a one-way air valve. Reilly uncapped it and punctured just beneath the collarbone, into the second intercostal space. He advanced the needle far enough to penetrate the chest wall, then removed it to leave the catheter in place and its valve exposed outside. A small amount of blood came out, but no more—the lung was still collapsing.

The medic's next course of action was to grab a scalpel and drive it into David's side, below the armpit, using the lower rib of the fifth intercostal space as a cutting board to make a one-inch incision through the muscle.

The medic plunged his index finger through the gash, twisting it around to perform a hasty thoracotomy. A torrent of blood flooded out, relieving the pressure on David's lung. Reilly applied another vented chest seal to allow blood to escape without the risk of air entering.

"Tibial IO," the medic continued, reaching into his aid bag.

Cancer used his shears to cut through the fabric of David's pant leg, exposing the shin just below the knee. What came next was on the very short list of things that always made Cancer cringe just at the thought.

Reilly now held a medieval device, a large-bore, hollow needle designed to pierce bone, and positioned it carefully just below David's knee. With a firm grip and precise aim, he drove the needle into the tibia, using controlled pressure until he felt the tip pop through bone and reach the marrow inside.

Once Reilly confirmed the needle was properly positioned, he inserted a syringe filled with a tranexamic acid and lidocaine flush into the IO access port. Upon depressing the plunger as hard as he could to create cavitation inside the marrow, David's limbs twitched violently. The pain was unbearable even though he was unconscious, and Reilly continued the procedure by pulling slightly back on the plunger to confirm marrow was present. Then he connected an IV bag to the needle's port via a fluid line. Lactated Ringer's solution began flowing immediately into the bone marrow, replenishing David's circulating volume. Reilly applied a blood cuff to the bag to squeeze it, then kept it elevated for a moment to ensure the flow was steady.

He retrieved a strip of elastic webbing, looping it around the fluid bag and fastening it to David's shoulder to keep it elevated. It wasn't ideal, but it would hold for what came next. Cancer moved to the aid bag, his hands darting to the outside pouch to find a small, tightly folded bundle—a lightweight, compact field litter—secured with compression straps. He unclipped it in one quick motion and pulled the litter free, the material barely adding weight to his grip as he pivoted toward David's opposite side.

The litter unfolded with a practiced snap of his wrists, its tough nylon fabric unfurling smoothly to revealing its full size. Cancer laid it flat beside David, ensuring none of the handles on each side were pinned underneath. It was long enough to support the man's full frame, wide enough to offer the stability they needed for extraction.

By then, Reilly was checking David's chest and pulse again, his ear pressed close to listen for the sounds of breath.

"How bad?" Cancer asked, moving to David's feet.

"Not looking good," Reilly said, taking up a kneeling position at David's head. "On three."

They counted in sync, "One, two, three," and together, they lifted their team leader from the legs and shoulders, careful not to disturb the fluid line as they shifted him over the litter and laid him down again.

Then Cancer was suddenly aware of the village around him, the alley in which his team clustered, the laundry and tattered sheets drifting from ropes between the buildings. He'd been so intent on aiding David that it hadn't occurred to him that he was now in command once more—he and his men were in a village in Iran in broad daylight, their rucksacks abandoned along the trail, five and a half kilometers remaining to the linkup point and an ever-dwindling amount of time to get there.

Then his focus shifted to the building beside him.

He hadn't seen the shot, but knew from watching David's fall where it had come from. Was the shooter still inside? Maybe, maybe not. He recalled a statement that David had made on a previous mission.

You put a bullet into one of ours, and you live long enough to regret it. But no further.

A deep and insatiable bloodlust rose within him then, a shuddering desire for revenge at all costs. He wanted to enter the building, single-handedly if necessary, to hunt for the shooter and, if he'd escaped, take his release on whomever he found. To continue prowling the rest of the buildings until he'd killed every male occupant big enough to hold a weapon.

To burn this entire fucking village to the ground.

But none of that would help David, and in that moment, Reilly's medical assessment loomed heavier than any enemy threat.

Not looking good.

"Angel," Cancer snapped, putting away his shears. "Rain Man. You're carrying. Let's go."

His functional team had just been reduced from six to five, which made specifying any further roles unnecessary. Ian and Hass would man the front carrying handles of the litter and Reilly the rear, allowing the medic full visibility over his casualty and the ability to call a halt when and if needed.

Worthy, as ever, would remain the pointman, and Cancer rear security; they were the only two who'd be able to react to a threat with any immediacy whatsoever, a grim prospect made worse by the fact that David would either live or die as a result of his wound.

The team leader still wore Malek's pistol on his belt, and Cancer grabbed the M4. They'd leave his plate carrier, could no longer afford any excess weight, but the rifle—for some reason, the rifle would stay. Dropping the magazine and locking the bolt to the rear to eject the final round, he lay the M4 at David's side. If Reilly had any objection to that, he didn't voice it.

Ian and Hass took hold of the front carrying handles, awaiting their order from Reilly.

"On three."

Cancer didn't hear the rest, instead circling to the rear and sweeping his HK417 across the buildings. Worthy was doing the same, focusing on the greatest danger area until they'd left sight of the village. The trio of men had lifted David in the litter and were moving swiftly back toward the trail, where they'd recover their rucksacks and continue their movement to the linkup point with whatever time they had left.

Ian asked, "How's he doing?"

Cancer fielded the inquiry before Reilly could.

"Stable," the sniper said. "He's gonna be fine."

45

Reilly squeezed a bag of blood, forcing the contents through the IO port and into David's bone marrow. It was the second time he'd done this, both bags in the emergency transfusion coming from Worthy. Still, David's condition hadn't improved—he continued to bleed internally.

The cool mountain air brushed against Reilly's sweat-soaked skin as he forced the blood inside. The plateau around them was a precarious refuge, its surface perched above a narrow valley. Early morning light filtered over the rocky landscape, casting a muted glow on the tufts of grass and the small clusters of white and purple spring blossoms swaying in the breeze. Under any other circumstances it would have seemed peaceful, Reilly thought as he finished his transfusion. When the last of Worthy's blood was gone, the medic hooked up another bag of Lactated Ringer's.

The pain from his ricochet injury was long forgotten, and Reilly pressed his stethoscope against David's chest. He listened for the reassuring sound of air moving through the wounded lung. It was weak, but there. The hemothorax he'd relieved earlier was still holding, for now. Reilly pressed two fingers to David's neck, feeling for the pulse—thin, but steady. David's skin had taken on a pale hue, it wasn't cold yet.

Reilly had initially believed he could save David, albeit not by much.

His last flicker of hope for a possible save, however, had been extinguished upon upgrading his finger thoracotomy to a chest tube. When the bleeding still hadn't stopped, he knew his team leader was doomed. Administering a full liter of blood was a last-ditch option, and it had failed. As an O positive bearer, Worthy was the only team member compatible with David's O negative. Taking any more blood from Worthy would remove him from the fight completely, and if the two bags' worth hadn't helped, neither would a third. Reilly had nothing left in his aid bag to give, had exhausted every possibility and wracked his brain several times over only to conclude that there was nothing else he could do.

Around them, the scene remained quiet. Cancer and Worthy held positions to cover the direction they'd come from, while Ian and Hass kept watch on the path ahead. The mountains loomed in every direction, their craggy faces softened by the first light of morning. Wind rustled gently through the sparse brush, at odds with the growing urgency tightening in Reilly's chest.

He checked David's wrist again, feeling the faint pulse as he carefully monitored the flow of the fluids through the IV line. They could only hold off the inevitable for so long. The plateau, the blossoms, the quiet wind—all of it faded from Reilly's awareness as his focus narrowed on the fragile life beneath his hands.

He glanced at David's face. Sweat had begun to form along the team leader's hairline. His skin was still pale, but now it felt colder under Reilly's touch. David's body was losing too much blood internally for the fluids alone to keep him going for long. The color was draining from his face, his lips turning a faint shade of gray.

Reilly checked the pulse again. This time, it was weaker, more irregular. David's heart was racing to compensate for the blood loss, but it couldn't hold out forever. Things were turning south faster than Reilly wanted to admit, the internal damage was far worse than what he could treat out here. Hypovolemic shock was creeping in fast—David's pulse was weak, erratic, and his heart couldn't sustain the effort much longer.

He was focused on adjusting the IV line when a faint groan slipped from David's lips. His head twitched to the side and his eyelids fluttered, as if struggling to open against some invisible weight. Reilly stilled, looking down at him. Not fully alert, but David was coming around, fighting his way back from the fog of unconsciousness. His body had clawed its way back from the edge, for now.

"David?" Reilly said, leaning in closer, his voice low but clear. "Can you hear me?"

David's eyes cracked open, the faintest slivers of awareness behind them, but they were unfocused, glassy, as if the world wasn't quite coming into view yet. His breathing remained shallow, each rise of his chest uneven, but there was a flicker of life. Reilly watched him closely, the strain visible on David's face—his body wasn't ready to let him wake up fully yet, but it was trying.

"Come on, stay with me," Reilly urged, pushing for a response. He leaned in closer, pressing two fingers to David's neck to feel the pulse again. It was still weak, still erratic, but there. That was enough for now.

David's eyes moved slightly, blinking sluggishly against the sunlight filtering over the plateau.

Reilly said, "You're still here. Good." David wasn't fully back yet, but this was something. His lips parted slightly, as if he was trying to speak, but no sound came. The effort alone told Reilly that David was still fighting.

With a steady hand, Reilly adjusted the flow of the fluids, knowing David's body needed everything it could get. He was hanging on by a thread. Reilly could feel it in every shallow breath David took as much as the coldness of his skin.

"David, I'm gonna give you something for the pain," Reilly said, grabbing the morphine from his aid bag. He paused for a second, watching for any sign of response, but David's eyes remained unfocused as Reilly drew 5 milligrams into his syringe.

"If that's morphine," David rasped, "you can forget it."

I came to slowly, the world around me creeping back into focus.

My body felt like it was pinned down, heavy and immobile, but the pain—it was sharp, unforgiving. Every breath I took sent a searing bolt through my chest. The burning ache spread with each shallow inhale, and I could feel the ragged edges of my right lung struggling to work. It wasn't just discomfort; it was deep, visceral agony that seemed to pulse with every beat of my heart.

Reilly asked, "How's your pain level? Where does it hurt?"

"Eleven and everywhere," I managed. "Our guys?"

"Everyone's fine, David. They're all here."

I blinked to see the sky overhead, the sight jolting a memory loose—the shot. It hit me like a hammer, and I could feel it all over again. The men on the first floor of the safehouse weren't a surprise, and killing the sniper had been a tactical masterpiece. I'd raced into that village expecting resistance. What I didn't expect was the boy—a kid, barely older than my daughter, with a rifle too big for him. Brainwashed extremist, or simply a child trying to defend his home? Surely the latter, I decided, and I suddenly felt a deep, unbidden sorrow for him. He'd have to live with that memory for the rest of his life, and no matter who he thought I was at the time he pulled the trigger, he'd endured trauma at a much younger age than I'd been when I first killed a man.

Reilly asked, "Do you know where you are?" He was trying to assess my cognitive state, although judging by every sensory perception and instinct since I'd regained consciousness, mental clarity was the least of my worries.

"Fucking Iran. How far to the linkup?"

"Just over three kilometers."

"Time?"

A pause as he checked his watch. "7:14."

"Shit. We've got to move."

"We can't move you, David. Not like this. You've already taken a liter of blood and Worthy's got nothing left to give. If we try to move you like this, you won't make it to the linkup."

I winced with pain. My body was struggling to keep going, and Reilly knew that as well as I did. "Aren't you supposed to tell me I'm doing great?"

He considered that. "Probably."

"Garbage medic, man. Look, it's getting tough to breathe...bring the guys around."

"David," he began, although no words followed.

"Do it," I said, closing my eyes again. "And do it fast."

I heard him speaking quietly over the radio, thought *Christ, this is how* it ends. In the hills of Iran, of all places. How many countries had I done battle in? More than I cared to recount, and if this was to be the last, then so be it.

Someone crouched beside me, and Hass's voice reached my ears.

"Hey Boss, how are you doing?"

My eyelids fluttered open. "God, you always were a handsome fuck. Thanks for saving our asses in Libya. I'm sorry about your team, I—I wish it would've worked out differently."

"They wouldn't have made it this far without you."

I sensed a brief exchange between him and Reilly, after which Hass took my hand and squeezed it.

"Safe travels, brother. See you in Valhalla."

Then he was gone, my unoccupied mind left to lapse into a swirling descent. For a moment I was a Ranger private, maneuvering against a sniper in Afghanistan—my first gunfight, wasn't it? How appropriate that the same situation would be my last, and then, a flashing memory of leaping from the door of an MC-130 on a combat jump into Iraq.

"David," a voice said.

"Ian." I smiled despite the grueling pain. "You better not get killed. You're...you're the only one who's been with me since, since the beginning."

"Yeah," he said, his voice choked.

"At least one of us from the first team made it all the way through." I strained to see his face—streaked with tears, bottom lip trembling. "You look adorable. Don't let Cancer see you crying. He'd have a field day."

"David," he said, "I can't...I can't say everything you mean to me."

"No worries. It's mutual, believe me. Stay safe, all right?"

He leaned forward and pressed his forehead against mine, then disappeared with a sob.

Ian was always so emotional, I thought, and the beginning of our relationship came to mind. Serving on a mercenary team in a criminal syndicate. Oh God, the darkness of those days. The darkest period of my life, my impulse for self-destruction a bottomless pit. And now that I faced death in full, I felt a mix of emotions. One part of me thought that I was just getting to the good stuff, a life with my family free of the violence.

Another part of me felt relief.

This life, everything up to this point, had been so goddamned hard. So much suffering, much of it self-inflicted whether I realized it at the time or not.

"—hear me?"

I opened my eyes at the sound of the drawl, realizing I'd missed the opening line. Not good.

"I gave you your callsign," I pointed out.

"Yeah," Worthy replied, nodding. "Yeah, you did."

When I'd met him he was a bodyguard with a tricked-out pistol, back when...back when I was working my way up the ladder of a criminal syndicate to kill its leader. An act of revenge, of vengeance, that now seemed of pitiable insignificance against the scope of my life.

I said, "Get the guys out of here safe. I know you will. Thanks for the blood. If Reilly..." I struggled to raise my voice. "If Reilly was half the medic that you are a pointman, I wouldn't be in this mess."

Worthy laughed, alighting a hand on my shoulder. "Life's not going to be the same without you, Boss."

"Don't I know it. Carry on, though, will you?"

"Always." He squeezed my shoulder, then released it. "We'll raise a beer to you, brother. All of us, once we get out of here."

"Have one for me."

I vaguely heard him departing, felt a rush of emotions more than memories as the journey inward, backward, continued. Traveling the world to shoot people before they shot me, toppling the kingpin I'd dedicated my life to killing, my descent into a darkness that I embraced wholeheartedly with a mercenary career where, paradoxically, I had found the first traces of light.

Langley, then a five-year-old girl who I vowed to protect the moment she became an orphan. I'd planned on retiring then, until a woman who called herself Duchess offered me the opportunity to head my own paramilitary team. The CIA would choose the targets, she said, but I could choose my own people. The names that came immediately to mind belonged to the same men who followed me into Iran—each handpicked from those I had served alongside as mercenaries—and every mission of my Agency career had confirmed I'd chosen wisely. Ian, Cancer, Reilly, and

Worthy had saved my life as well as each other's, and each time we'd emerged from the fray of combat as a unified team.

Now, I'd never see any of them again.

Langley's face appeared to me then, my beautiful daughter, an angel who'd saved me and continued to do so every day. I wondered what she'd be when she grew up.

"I told you not to run off alone, asshole."

Cancer's face loomed over mine, his eyes intense, an angry old man until the bitter end.

"Yeah," I said. "You did. Time to hang up my spurs."

His features softened, face betraying a fissure in his otherwise ironclad composure. "You want a smoke?"

"Hard pass. Maybe next time. You've got my family, right?"

"We all do. Anything they need, for life. Count on it."

Swallowing, I said, "I figured. Don't...don't make any moves on Laila, or I'll haunt your ass."

"Challenge accepted."

Laila's face appeared then. That poor woman. What had I dragged her through, what would she suffer after my death? It was okay, I thought, Langley would carry her through it. I'd done everything I could to be the husband my wife deserved, tried to open my heart to her, and nonetheless wondered how much I'd succeeded.

Priorities.

I said, "Get the boys out of here, all right?"

"I will. We've got time."

"Don't waste any. Now beat it, you fuck. I don't want the last thing I smell to be cigarettes."

He ruffled my hair. "You're a good kid. A better team leader. We're gonna miss you."

"You better. Later, Cancer."

"Later."

He'd barely departed before I saw Jackson, only a few months into his own journey through the world. Leaving him behind would be the hardest for me, and the easiest for him. He'd have no memory of me, while my own life had been so immeasurably enriched by his. What legacy was I leaving behind? Only the spoken word of Laila and Langley, who would now shape everything he knew of his father.

My level of pain ramped up even further, a racking misery taking hold of me as a frigid chill extended from my heart out to my extremities.

"Is it getting colder?" I asked.

Reilly sighed. "No. No, it's not."

"Huh. Must be the hypovolemic shock."

"David, I can give you something for the pain."

"Morphine?"

"Yeah. Morphine."

My face grew tight, contorting with agony. "Thirty milligrams, the big ride?"

"It's ready, David. If you want it."

My limbs were now freezing, fingers numb, my body failing. Each breath felt more shallow, more like I was drawing air through a straw. I was aware that my time was running short, but my mind remained lucid.

I said, "Nah. Nah, let's squeeze every...last second out of this one. You ever get qualified in last rites?"

"You never struck me as religious."

"Me neither. We'll settle for this—you've got Olivia. I'd say don't fuck that up...but I know you won't. You two will make a beautiful family." I gasped. "Nothing's better than kids, Reilly. You're going to have to live that for both of us, yeah?"

"Yeah," he said, "I will."

I wouldn't be able to talk for long, I knew. "Hey."

"Yeah?"

"What are...what are some cool...last words? I never thought this through."

A pause. "How about, 'Suicide Actual, out?'"

"No."

"I mean, like your radio transmissions—"

"No, yeah, I get it. Just a little..." I sucked in another breath. "Dunno. Trite."

My awareness began flickering. This entire event felt like a culmination, and I suddenly recalled all the depression, the impulse for self-destruction, the sheer anger and hatred at myself and the world that had teemed through me during my mercenary days. What had it gotten me?

Nothing whatsoever, though the rewards after I let it go had been profound. My wife, my daughter and son, a new lease on life, and, no less importantly, the men surrounding me now. Though any sense of separation between the best of my friends and the worst of my enemies faded from me at that moment, whatever awaited me on the other side, I was going to meet it now.

"All right," I managed, my body desperate for oxygen, lungs unable to cope. "Shit, this is my sendoff. Last call."

A series of gasping, irregular breaths signaled my body's last attempts to survive. I now sounded, I thought, exactly like the old sniper I'd mortally wounded in my final gunfight. Karma had circled quickly on this one. What a bitch.

My chest burned, and every inhale became a battle. Darkness was creeping in at the edges of my vision as I pushed back for as long as I could, unaware if Reilly was speaking, and if so, what he was saying.

"Reilly," I gasped, seized by an urgent need to speak. "Tell the guys."

I heard his response, but just barely.

"Yeah, David?"

I had only seconds left, maybe less. My body was shutting down, the fight almost over. Blackness was about to swallow me whole and I tried to push the words out, every ounce of my remaining strength focused on forcing them past the tightness in my throat. I was headed into the unknown, and everything or nothing awaited me at the end. These would be the last words I'd ever speak.

"I love you fuckers."

46

Worthy was on point, leading his team downhill out of the mountains and toward the linkup point, when Cancer's voice came over his radio earpieces.

"*We're not going to make it.*"

Progress had been slow with three men on litter duty, each of them performing a clockwise rotation around it at periodic intervals. Worthy was exempt by virtue of the fact that he'd given a liter of blood, which made his trek all the more difficult. He'd been battling fatigue and lightheadedness, and the bag of saline Reilly had administered did little to quell his utter dehydration.

But the team was determined to carry David's body with them to the linkup point, then in the exfil vehicles into Turkmenistan.

Worthy transmitted back, "We can't leave him out here."

"We have to," Cancer said in response. "*Two kilometers to cover and just over an hour to make it there. That's max pace for this terrain. It's out of our hands. Halt movement.*" Then he added, "*This is as good a place as any.*"

Worthy turned, wind whipping his face as he assessed the validity of that last statement.

The plateau jutted out over a steep drop, the jagged cliffs below falling away into the valley like a broken staircase of stone. From here, he could see for miles—across the vast, empty expanse of desert and mountains stretching into the distance, their craggy peaks barely softened by the late morning light.

Cancer, Hass, and Ian eased the litter down, and Reilly converged from his position on rear security before dropping his rucksack with the rest of the men. Reluctantly, Worthy did the same and approached the body.

David was motionless on the litter, his chest no longer rising with breath, the stillness unnerving in a way that hit harder than any wound ever had. His face, pale and slack, had taken on a grayish hue, the color drained away by the hour that had passed since his death. His lips were slightly parted, blood dried in the corners of his mouth, and his eyes—though closed—seemed sunken, as if the life that had once burned behind them had already retreated deep into the shadows.

Blood that had soaked his body was now dark and congealed, the once-bright red turning almost black. The bullet wound near his collarbone, which Reilly had tried so hard to treat, still oozed faintly, but the bleeding had slowed to a trickle, a macabre reminder that there was nothing left to pump the blood through his veins.

There was an eerie quiet about him now—an unnatural stillness that hadn't existed in David's life. The tension, the drive that always seemed to hum beneath the surface, was gone, replaced by the hollow calm of a man who no longer existed in the world around him.

The team didn't look much better.

They surrounded David's body in silence, their faces etched with the weariness of men who had given everything and still lost. Worthy scanned their expressions—each one different, but the same hollow look lingered in all of them. Reilly knelt beside the litter, his head hung low, staring at David's chest as if willing it to rise again. His hands, stained up to the wrists in David's blood, were flexed and tensed, as if searching for something to do now that there was nothing left. The medic had been hit the hardest by this mission, still bearing the superficial cuts of a narrowly dodged grenade blast, along with a ricochet to his left shoulder, and on top of it all, watching David die under his care despite his best efforts.

Cancer stood rigid, his face set like stone, but there was no masking the quiet rage simmering just below the surface. His gaze was fixed on the horizon, but Worthy knew he wasn't seeing anything out there—he was reliving every moment of their time at the village, searching for something he could have done differently, something that might have changed this outcome.

Ian looked stunned, eyes wide. His face was laced with cuts and he kept shaking his head, as though trying to wake from a bad dream, his lips moving silently like he was talking to himself. He hadn't said a word since David's death, his mind somewhere far away, trying to process the unthinkable until he finally knelt to retrieve his digital voice recorder from David's pocket.

Hass stood slightly apart, his arms folded over his rifle, face pinched and drawn. He looked like he couldn't quite believe that David was really gone, his eyes darting from the body to the ground and back again. But the longer he stood there, the more the reality sank in, his shoulders slowly sagging under the weight of it all.

For a moment, no one spoke. They didn't need to. The grief was thick in the air between them, the disbelief still settling in like a slow-moving storm. They'd all lost men before, but not like this.

Not David.

Cancer said, "We dig, right here."

The cliff's edge loomed only a few meters away, and Worthy felt the gravity of the place. It was exposed, no shelter from the wind or the heat, but it had a quiet kind of finality. There were no trees here, no flowers—just stone and sky. The world around them was vast, endless, and indifferent. In some strange way, it felt right.

The men knelt in unison, digging into the earth with their hands. The ground was unforgiving, sunbaked and cracked in places, with very little give to it. It wasn't the kind of place you could dig with your hands—too much stone, too little soil. They continued nonetheless, excavating a grave that was far too shallow for David's body.

They lowered the field litter into it regardless, situating their team leader as best they could.

Reilly asked, "Should we bury him with his Winkler?"

"Fuck no," Cancer said. "Give it to me."

The medic did so at once. David still wore Malek's pistol on his hip, and there seemed to be an unspoken agreement to leave it with him. Worthy laid the M4 at his side before speaking.

"Rocks."

It was the only feasible option for David's final resting place. Loose and weathered stones were abundant here, and the team began laying them over the body in a tomb of sorts, starting with his boots and working their way upward.

No one wanted to cover his face and Worthy was the first to do so, concealing his last glimpse of David. The features were frozen in a shroud of death, looking not peaceful so much as painfully determined. Worthy felt a tug of emotion as he watched the face of his team leader vanish stone by stone. The man had carried them through so much, had personally gone after Worthy when he was otherwise left for dead after the shootdown. It pained him immensely to do what he did now, and yet there was no other way.

The concealment was complete within minutes, ending when they surrounded the grave.

Reilly began, "Rest in peace, brother—"

Cancer wasn't having it.

"You want to honor him? Don't get stranded in Iran. We're fighting the clock. Worthy, move as fast as you fucking can. Everyone else, you better keep pace. Let's go."

Worthy turned and moved to his rucksack, scanning the horizon as he moved. The emptiness of the valley below was a reminder of just how far they still had to go. But here, at least, David would be laid to rest with a view that seemed to stretch forever. It wasn't much, but it was all they had.

Shouldering his pack with the rest of his team, Worthy took his HK416 into his hands and pulled in a breath of cold mountain air.

Then he set off, resuming his route toward their destination and looking over his shoulder to steal one last glance at David's final resting place.

The grave disappeared behind him as the path curved, the rocks fading into the earth until the hillside finally eclipsed it from view.

47

Longwing Isolation Facility
Rockingham County, North Carolina

Ian stood in the team's isolation facility, his eyes scanning the near-empty room. The once-cluttered space, filled with the hum of mission planning, briefing sessions, and the chaotic energy of a team constantly preparing for the next operation, now felt hollow. Tables were stripped of gear, rolling chairs scattered in disarray, and the computers they'd huddled around, analyzing satellite imagery, were long gone. An Agency cleanup crew had already seen to the recovery of all sensitive items, including the team's weapons, night vision, and every scrap of issued tactical equipment.

The team had already packed up their personal effects, leaving only those belonging to David Rivers.

Walking to the back room, Ian watched as Reilly crouched beside David's locker, pulling out boots and folding up the clothes. It didn't feel right, boxing up what little remained of David's possessions, but it was something that had to be done. Someone had to pack this all up for Laila, and that wasn't an easy task. Yet he and Reilly had volunteered, neither man wanting to send the other in alone for such a task.

The medic looked up at him now, pausing for a moment. "What do you think the Agency's going to do with this place now that we're gone?"

"I don't know," Ian said. "Another team, probably. Different program, or the same program under a new name."

Reilly's phone rang, the sudden sound jarring in the quiet room. He glanced at the display and frowned. "Shit. I've got to take this."

He stepped away, answering with a brisk, "Reilly."

Ian moved forward, sliding one of the packing boxes aside with his foot and stopping before the locker.

A row of worn fatigues hung neatly, untouched since the team's departure for Iran. He'd save those for last. On the floor of the locker, David's workout gear sat in a crumpled pile—worn T-shirts, faded and sweat-stained. Ian picked up each item carefully, folding them with slow precision, his hands methodical even though his mind was distant. One at a time they went into the box as he kept packing, listening to the medic's half of the conversation.

"You want my honest opinion?" Reilly's voice cut back into the silence as he paced near the door.

The weeks following the team's return to the States had been eventful, to say the least.

Armed with the computers recovered from Malek's command post, the CIA's cyber division had hacked the remnants of the AI facility to retrieve its data, which revealed the extent of the man's reach. In addition to narcotics trafficking, counterfeiting, and training Iranian militant proxies, he'd been plotting cyberattacks, sanctions evasion networks, cryptocurrency manipulation, and funding terrorist camps in four countries across the Middle East and Africa.

The man had been busy.

After recovering what they needed, the CIA shut the AI operations down via a tailored malware program, after which the FBI had gone on the warpath to dismantle Malek's insider network. Dozens of arrests were made across military and government organizations, and even within the CIA itself. Protective details for the team's families lasted one week in total before the threat was eliminated entirely, and the world had moved on free of Soren Malek.

Ian couldn't have cared less.

David was gone. Project Longwing was over. The team was done for, at least in a formal capacity.

"Wait one," Reilly said, lowering the phone and looking at Ian. "What do you think about Chen?"

Ian chuckled. "Before or after she hung Griffin's team out to dry in Yemen, then sent us into the same slaughterhouse knowing we'd probably be killed or captured on infil? Because if you're asking about after, I'd say she deserves to die about as much as Malek."

Reilly returned the phone to his ear.

"No," he said, his voice sharp and decisive. "Not at all. Not in the least. And everyone on my team would agree with me."

Reilly ended the call, stuffing his phone back into his pocket before looking at Ian with a quizzical expression.

"Who was that?" Ian asked, glancing up from the box.

"Senator Gossweiler."

Ian raised an eyebrow. "What did he want?"

"The truth about Chen," Reilly replied, his voice flat. "She's up for reassignment."

"And?"

"And," Reilly said, pausing for a moment, "I think I just ended her career."

Ian considered that, then nodded and returned to folding David's clothes. "Good for you."

They continued packing together until the locker was empty—fatigues, scuffed sets of boots, and running shoes that had seen better days were all placed into boxes, then sealed with tape. After shuttling the boxes to the planning area, they stood at the doorway to the locker room. The job was done, but the feeling of finality lingered, heavy in the air between them.

Then, for the last time, Ian turned off the light.

They lingered in the planning area with bittersweet remembrance, appraising the empty space. Everything was packed now, nothing remaining for them to remove.

Except, of course, everything on the trophy wall.

Ian and Reilly turned to face it in unison.

Reilly asked, "What should we do with all this stuff?"

"Split it up, I suppose. Whoever wants it."

Some of the objects were nailed into its surface, others displayed on shelves. The two men took in the sight, a visual record of their team's missions.

An ISIS flag from Syria. A PPSh-41 submachine gun stamped with its facility of production in the USSR, recovered from slain bandits in China.

Next was a pair of fatigue pants hanging from a nail—David's, worn in Nigeria—with a bullet hole through the left cargo pocket, a shot that didn't so much as break his skin.

A sawed-off 12-gauge shotgun carried by their target in a chase that spanned Colombia and Venezuela.

Their next mission had yielded several trophies. A ceremonial sword that their target had vowed to use to decapitate his hostage, Olivia, and a dagger that he was going to use to carve out her heart. Both remained unbloodied while their target had not. On another shelf was Reilly's armored plate with three bullets embedded in it, signed in metallic marker by everyone on the team along with their callsign. All were from Libya, the first time they'd operated with Hass.

A leather-wrapped flask bearing another target's initials, recovered in Serbia. Dangling from another nail was a necklace with a cimaruta pendant, a miniature tree whose branches ended in a key, crescent moon, dagger, and rose. It had been worn by Fulvio Pagano, the terrorist mastermind who went by the name of Erik Weisz. Killed in action in Yemen, where Ian's team had first met Griffin's.

A black gorilla hood ornament from the Democratic Republic of the Congo, and a nazzar battu bracelet with a single bead serving as a glass eye. It was intended for protection, and transported along with the nuclear warhead that Soren Malek had stolen in Pakistan.

The final memento had been obtained by Reilly, a camera snapshot now prominently displayed in a framed, glossy 8×10 on the trophy wall. In honor of their final mission, the medic had printed out a few dozen copies and festooned the entire facility with them, taping them to every flat surface, where they remained until the rest of the team had packed up.

In the photo, Hass strode in traditional Libyan garb, his face blacked out. The features of the individual trailing him needed no modification—they were already hidden by a niqab covering everything but the eyes, along with a long-sleeve black dress that extended all the way to the ground. It was attire worn by some Muslim women to express their religious identity and modesty, although the hysterical part was the identity of the person beneath it as he slipped past a surveillance camera.

David Rivers.

Reilly gave a low whistle. "It's hard to believe how much shit we took overseas."

"Yeah," Ian agreed.

Then he asked thoughtfully, "Did we bring anything back from Iran?"

Ian drew a breath, then let it out in a long exhale.

"No," he said. "But we lost a lot."

48

CIA Headquarters

The Director stood behind a podium emblazoned with the CIA seal, addressing the crowd of men and women seated before him.

"These men embodied the highest ideals of duty, selflessness, and sacrifice, serving their country without hesitation and without question..."

A row of easels stood at the front, each displaying a photograph of one of the men lost—Brent Griffin, AJ Washington, Daniel Munoz, Logan Keller, and David Rivers.

Families sat in neat rows, their dark attire blending into the somber atmosphere. A woman with soft brown hair pulled back in a neat bun clutched a crumpled tissue, her red eyes fixed on the floor. Across the aisle, a lady with a bright blue scarf wrapped around her neck sat very still, her trembling hands folded in her lap. In the row ahead, a tall woman with elegant earrings held a small photo frame against her chest, gazing at it with a sad smile as she brushed her thumb over the glass; beside her, a restless child fidgeted until she gently placed a hand on his knee to calm him.

The Director's words continued to fill the room, measured and clear.

"...their courage was not just in the missions they completed, but in the quiet resolve they carried every day, knowing the risks and accepting them with unwavering dedication."

Chairs creaked softly as some in the crowd shifted, the soft noises of crying spouses drifting through the air. Mostly a hushed reverence, save the speaker.

"The sacrifices they made weren't just their own; you, their families, sacrificed as well. Sharing in the burden of service that we now honor..."

Langley shifted in her seat, her uncomfortable low-heeled loafers not quite reaching the floor. The room was too quiet, and the man's words seemed to float over her head. She didn't understand why everything felt so cold, why everyone spoke in hushed tones.

She glanced at the family members again, this time focusing on the children. A boy about her age clutched a worn teddy bear, his eyes red and puffy as he leaned into his mother's side. A little girl with blonde braids sat swinging her legs slowly, staring blankly ahead while her mother rested a hand on her shoulder. Did they all feel the same confusing mix of sadness and numbness that she did? Langley wondered if they missed their dads as much as she missed hers. Did they also hope that maybe, just maybe, this was all a mistake and their dads would walk through the door?

But deep down, she knew that wouldn't be the case. Dad was gone. And while her heart ached at his loss, it wasn't herself she was most concerned about now.

Her mother sat rigid beside her, back straight, holding baby Jackson in her lap. Langley's three-month-old brother stirred now and then, shifting in the unfamiliar surroundings but far too young to understand where they were or why. He whimpered softly and Mom adjusted his blanket, then his pacifier, pressing him gently against her chest.

"Their legacy will live on through the work we continue, through the lives they touched, and through the example they set for all of us."

Her mother's expression was one of exhaustion, her shoulders seeming to carry a weight they hadn't before. She'd seen her mom pretend to be okay before, but now it seemed like she might start crying if she didn't keep holding Jackson close.

Langley reached over to grasp her mother's hand, exchanging fleeting eye contact and a subtly faked smile. Her eyes flickered to Jackson, now examining the lights on the ceiling in rapt fascination, and back to her father's picture on the easel.

The photograph showed him in the maternity suite, holding a newborn Jackson. Her father's smile was wide, beaming with joy as he cradled her baby brother to his chest, the white hospital bracelet still on his wrist, eyes alight with new life.

"As we leave here today, let us carry their courage and dedication within us, keeping their legacy alive in all that we do."

Then the speech was over—finally—and the Director moved from widow to widow, trailed by a group of assistants handing him items to give them, one at a time.

When he reached Langley and her family, he leaned down to exchange quiet words with her mom. He was older, suit was perfectly pressed with a CIA lapel pin, smelling of cologne that was a little too strong for the room. It felt like he wanted to be somewhere else, which made Langley feel uncomfortable.

A folded American flag was the first thing to be passed from his assistants to him, then to her mom, who accepted it with one hand and then passed it to Langley so she could cradle Jackson. Langley felt the weight of the fabric, the rough texture, and wondered why the man had given it to her mom. Could a flag bring Dad back?

Another item changed hands before reaching her in turn.

It was a leather-wrapped box, open to expose a felt interior in which a circular medallion was set. The CIA crest on a star ringed with the words CENTRAL INTELLIGENCE AGENCY– FOR VALOR.

The other families had received it too, and it didn't make her feel any better. It wasn't Dad. She closed the box a little too hard, the click louder than she expected. The man glanced her way, and she quickly looked down, her cheeks warming.

Then the Director rose and said his final farewells, whisking out of the room followed by his assistants. A woman in professional attire took the podium and thanked the families for coming, going on to announce a reception with refreshments in the lobby.

"Refreshments," her mother said under her breath. "Are they serious?"

Langley had been surprised by how at home she'd felt walking into CIA

Headquarters. It felt somehow familiar to her, like a place she'd been in a dream. Even the town in which the buildings were located was her namesake, a coincidence too odd for her to ignore.

A group of men approached before she and her mother could rise. No Agency staff members, Langley could tell at once—they moved like athletes, and each appeared quite ill at ease in their suits, as if it was their first time wearing them.

They spoke with her mother one at a time, then her.

The first man was balding, lean, wiry with smart eyeglasses, and he knelt before her like she was a queen. "Hey, Langley. I'm Ian. Your dad and I go back a long, long way. And while I can't begin to apologize for what happened to him…I can promise you that…I will always, always…"

She put a hand on his shoulder.

"Thank you," she said. "We'll be here for you too, Mr. Ian."

Next was a short and stocky man, dropping to a knee with a smile and speaking in a pronounced Southern drawl.

"Do you remember me?" he asked.

She shook her head and his smile faded, but only a bit.

"I protected you when you were little. I'll do it for the rest of your life. Whatever you need, it's done."

He made way for a bulky meathead of a man in a suit that was almost comically small. When he knelt his eyes were still above hers, but there was nothing imposing in his demeanor—quite the opposite, in fact. Boyish features and a voice to match.

"Your dad was…he was something else, Langley. You're lucky to have him as a father." He looked horrified at his own words, quickly correcting himself. "To *have* had him as a father…I mean…I didn't mean it like that."

"I know what you meant," she said. "Thank you."

A grizzled-looking man with close-cropped silver hair was leaning down, speaking to her mom and offering her a rectangular case. Langley's mother held up a hand to stop him, and said, "She deserves to get it from you." Clearing his throat uncomfortably, he took a step over and knelt before her. He looked uncomfortable, like he didn't know how to talk to kids.

Langley cut him off before he could speak.

"You're Cancer."

He looked taken aback. "How do you know who I am?"

"Because," she explained, "you smell like cigarettes. Not in a bad way, just...faint. Dad talked about you a lot."

"All good, I hope—"

"Naw. Not really. He said you were a grumpy old man." That caused him to grin, almost laugh, and she continued, "But that you were *his* grumpy old man. And that you always brought the boys back home."

His face grew solemn then, dead serious. "I wish I could've brought your father back."

"The enemy gets a vote. Dad used to say that too."

Cancer nodded distantly, then raised the rectangular case, turning it to face her before undoing the clasps and opening the lid.

"This belonged to your father. It's yours now."

She peered inside the foam-padded interior to see a sheathed knife.

Her heart fluttered as she picked it up and examined it, grasping the handle and sliding it out of its sheath.

The knife was sleek, matte black, razor sharp with a long false edge. On the blade, just above the hilt, were the stamped words WINKLER KNIVES and an engraved serial number—*001*.

"Damn," she said breathlessly, tilting the blade in the space between them. "This was Dad's?"

He nodded.

This was more like it, she thought. Holding the knife made her feel closer to Dad. It was something he had used, something that was a part of him.

Cancer said, "Whatever you decide to do in life, you're carrying forward his legacy now. That's a big responsibility, and I know you're up for it. I see him in your eyes."

Langley nodded distantly, the sum total of her attention almost completely absorbed by the blade before her. She held up the knife for her mom to see, and her enthusiasm was met with an increasingly concerned glance directed first at her, then at Cancer.

He and Langley gave the same helpless shrug in unison, met each other's sparkling eyes once more, and smiled.

The Stormridge Con
SPIDER HEIST #5

The Sky Thieves went dark. Now an unseen enemy wants them back in the spotlight.

After dismantling their biggest rival, the Sky Thieves scattered, each hoping to disappear. But when a surveillance drone tracks Blair Morgan and her husband, Sterling, to a secluded beach in the Maldives, their quiet escape turns into a high-speed getaway.

Back in the U.S., their crewmates Alec and Marco are blindsided—framed for a series of high-tech heists they didn't commit. Someone with unlimited resources is pulling the strings, turning elite thieves into fugitives. Desperate and determined, the Sky Thieves reunite and begin their search for answers. Someone has them backed into a corner and they want to know who.

With time running out and their reputations to clear, the Sky Thieves must pull off the ultimate con: a high-stakes infiltration against impossible odds. But as they crack impenetrable security, dodge ruthless enforcers, and outmaneuver federal agents, Blair faces an even greater threat—an old enemy with unfinished business.

Get your copy today at
Jason-Kasper.com

30% Off your next paperback.

Thank you for reading. For exclusive offers on your next paperback:

- **Visit SevernRiverBooks.com** and enter code **PRINTBOOKS30** at checkout.
- Or scan the QR code.

Offer valid for future paperback purchases only. The discount applies solely to the book price (excluding shipping, taxes, and fees) and is limited to one use per customer. Offer available to US customers only. Additional terms and conditions apply.

ABOUT THE AUTHOR

Jason Kasper is the USA Today bestselling author of the Spider Heist, American Mercenary, and Shadow Strike thriller series. Before his writing career he served in the US Army, beginning as a Ranger private and ending as a Green Beret captain. Jason is a West Point graduate and a veteran of the Afghanistan and Iraq wars, and was an avid ultramarathon runner, skydiver, and BASE jumper, all of which inspire his fiction.

Sign up for Jason Kasper's reader list at
Jason-Kasper.com

jasonkasper@severnriverbooks.com

THE CAMBRIDGE GREEK LEXICON

VOLUME II
K–Ω

Edited by
J. Diggle (Editor-in-Chief)
B. L. Fraser
P. James
O. B. Simkin
A. A. Thompson
S. J. Westripp

CAMBRIDGE
UNIVERSITY PRESS

University Printing House, Cambridge CB2 8BS, United Kingdom
One Liberty Plaza, 20th Floor, New York, NY 10006, USA
477 Williamstown Road, Port Melbourne, VIC 3207, Australia
314–321, 3rd Floor, Plot 3, Splendor Forum, Jasola District Centre, New Delhi – 110025, India
103 Penang Road, #05-06/07, Visioncrest Commercial, Singapore 238467

Cambridge University Press is part of the University of Cambridge.
It furthers the University's mission by disseminating knowledge in the pursuit of
education, learning, and research at the highest international levels of excellence.

www.cambridge.org
Information on this title: www.cambridge.org/9780521826808
DOI: 10.1017/9781139050043

© The Faculty Board of Classics of the University of Cambridge 2021

This publication is in copyright. Subject to statutory exception
and to the provisions of relevant collective licensing agreements,
no reproduction of any part may take place without the written
permission of Cambridge University Press.

First published 2021
Reprinted 2021

Printed in the United Kingdom by TJ Books Limited, Padstow, Cornwall

A catalogue record for this publication is available from the British Library.

Set ISBN 978-0-521-82680-8 Hardback
Volume I ISBN 978-1-108-83699-9 Hardback
Volume II ISBN 978-1-108-83698-2 Hardback

Cambridge University Press has no responsibility for the persistence or accuracy
of URLs for external or third-party internet websites referred to in this publication
and does not guarantee that any content on such websites is, or will remain,
accurate or appropriate.

Authors and Editions

The following list records all the authors who are cited in this Lexicon, the works for which they are cited (if they are cited for only a selection), their abbreviated names, and the editions which have been taken as providing the standard text. It does not include commented editions of parts of these authors, unless they also contain what is taken as the standard text.

Some of these editions were published during the course of the Lexicon's composition, so that only partial use of them has been possible. Thus, while West's *Iliad* has been taken as the standard text since its publication, not all traces of an outdated text may have been eradicated from work done before that date. The same is true, to a much greater extent, of his *Odyssey*, and of Wilson's Herodotus. In the case of some authors, no one text has been treated as standard, more than one edition is listed, and independent judgement has been applied.

There are some limitations to the coverage of authors in this list. Very brief fragments of verse are usually ignored. So too are fragments of the orators and of Aristophanes. Coverage of tragic fragments is limited to the selection in the OCT; of Aristotle, to the seven works listed; of the New Testament, to Gospels and Acts; of the Presocratics (Heraclitus, Parmenides, Empedocles, Democritus), to those quoted (other than merely referred to) in Kirk–Raven–Schofield. A few other exclusions are noted under the author names.

(i) Collections frequently cited

Budé	Collection Budé, Les Belles Lettres, Paris
Kirk–Raven–Schofield	G. S. Kirk, J. E. Raven, M. Schofield, *The Presocratic Philosophers*, 2nd edn, Cambridge 1983 (1st edn G. S. Kirk and J. E. Raven, 1957)
OCT	Oxford Classical Text, Oxford
Teubner	Bibliotheca Teubneriana, Stuttgart/Leipzig/Berlin
Page, *PMG*	D. L. Page, *Poetae Melici Graeci*, Oxford 1962
Page, *SLG*	D. L. Page, *Supplementum Lyricis Graecis*, Oxford 1974
West, *IEG*	M. L. West, *Iambi et Elegi Graeci*, 2nd edn, Oxford 1989–92

(ii) Authors, abbreviated names, editions

A.	Aeschylus	D. L. Page, OCT 1972; M. L. West, Teubner 1990
A.*fr.*		J. Diggle, *Tragicorum Graecorum Fragmenta Selecta*, OCT 1998
Aeschin.	Aeschines	M. R. Dilts, Teubner 1997
Alc.	Alcaeus	E. Lobel–D. L. Page, *Poetarum Lesbiorum Fragmenta*, Oxford 1955; Page, *SLG* pp. 77–102
Alcm.	Alcman	Page, *PMG* pp. 2–91, *SLG* pp. 1–3
Anacr.	Anacreon	Page, *PMG* pp. 172–235, *SLG* pp. 103–4; West, *IEG* vol. 2, pp. 30–4

AUTHORS AND EDITIONS

Anan.	Ananius	West, *IEG* vol. 2, pp. 34–6
And.	Andocides	G. Dalmeyda, Budé 1930
Antipho	Antiphon	L. Gernet, Budé 1923
Apollod.Lyr.	Apollodorus	Page, *PMG* p. 364
Ar.	Aristophanes	N. G. Wilson, OCT 2007
AR.	Apollonius Rhodius	H. Fränkel, OCT 1961
Archil.	Archilochus	West, *IEG* vol. 1, pp. 1–108
Ariphron	Ariphron	Page, *PMG* pp. 422–3
Arist.	Aristotle	*Athenaion Politeia*, M. Chambers, Teubner 1986; *Ethica Eudemia*, R. R. Walzer–J. M. Mingay, OCT 1991; *Ethica Nicomachea*, I. Bywater, OCT 1894; *Metaphysica*, W. Jaeger, OCT 1957; *De Arte Poetica*, R. Kassel, OCT 1965; *Politica*, W. D. Ross, OCT 1957; *Ars Rhetorica*, W. D. Ross, OCT 1959
Arist.*eleg.*		West, *IEG* vol. 2, pp. 44–5
Arist.*lyr.*		Page, *PMG* pp. 444–5
Asius	Asius	West, *IEG* vol. 2, p. 46
B.	Bacchylides	H. Maehler, 11th edn, Teubner 2003
Bion	Bion	A. S. F. Gow, *Bucolici Graeci*, OCT 1952, pp. 153–65; J. D. Reed, Cambridge 1997
Call.	Callimachus	R. Pfeiffer, Oxford 1949–53; H. Lloyd-Jones–P. Parsons, *Supplementum Hellenisticum*, Berlin–New York 1983, pp. 89–144; *Hecale*, A. S. Hollis, 2nd edn, Oxford 2009; *Aetia*, A. Harder, Oxford 2012; *The Fifth Hymn*, A. W. Bulloch, Cambridge 1985; *Hymn to Demeter*, N. Hopkinson, Cambridge 1984
Call.*epigr.*		A. S. F. Gow–D. L. Page, *Hellenistic Epigrams*, Cambridge 1965, vol. 1, pp. 57–74
Callin.	Callinus	West, *IEG* vol. 2, pp. 47–50
Carm.Pop.	Carmina Popularia	Page, *PMG* pp. 450–70
Castorio	Castorion	Page, *PMG* p. 447
Corinn.	Corinna	Page, *PMG* pp. 326–45
Critias	Critias	West, *IEG* vol. 2, pp. 52–6
D.	Demosthenes	M. R. Dilts, OCT 2002–9 (excl. 61 *Erotikos*); W. Rennie, OCT vol. 3, 1931 (*Exordia*)
Democr.	Democritus	Kirk–Raven–Schofield pp. 402–33
Demod.	Demodocus	West, *IEG* vol. 2, pp. 56–8
Diagor.	Diagoras	Page, *PMG* pp. 382–3
Din.	Dinarchus	N. C. Conomis, Teubner 1975
Dionys.Eleg.	Dionysius Chalcus	West, *IEG* vol. 2, pp. 58–60
E.	Euripides	J. Diggle, OCT 1981–94
E.*Cyc.* (*Cyclops*)		ibid.
E.*fr.*		J. Diggle, *Tragicorum Graecorum Fragmenta Selecta*, OCT 1998
E.*lyr.fr.*		Page, *PMG* p. 391
Eleg.adesp.	Elegiaca adespota	West, *IEG* vol. 2, pp. 7–15
Emp.	Empedocles	Kirk–Raven–Schofield pp. 280–321
Eumel.	Eumelus	Page, *PMG* p. 361
Even.	Evenus	West, *IEG* vol. 2, pp. 63–7
Hdt.	Herodotus	C. Hude, 3rd edn, OCT 1927; N. G. Wilson, OCT 2015

Heraclit.	Heraclitus	Kirk–Raven–Schofield pp. 181–212
Hermipp.	Hermippus	West, *IEG* vol. 2, pp. 67–9
Hermoloch.	Hermolochus	Page, *PMG* p. 447
Hes.	Hesiod	*Theogony*, M. L. West, Oxford 1966; *Works and Days*, M. L. West, Oxford 1978; *Scutum*, F. Solmsen, OCT 1970
Hes.*fr.*		R. Merkelbach–M. L. West, *Fragmenta Hesiodea*, Oxford 1967
hHom.	Homeric Hymns	M. L. West, Loeb Classical Library, Harvard University Press, Cambridge MA 2003 (excl. Hymn 8 to Ares). See also section (iii) below.
Hippon.	Hipponax	West, *IEG* vol. 1, pp. 109–71; H. Degani, 2nd edn, Teubner 1991
Hom.	Homer	See Il. and Od. The label is sometimes used to include hHom. (see section (iii) below).
Hyp.	Hyperides	F. G. Kenyon, OCT 1907
Iamb.adesp.	Iambica adespota	West, *IEG* vol. 2, pp. 16–28
Ibyc.	Ibycus	Page, *PMG* pp. 144–69, *SLG* pp. 44–73
Il.	Homer, Iliad	T. W. Allen, Oxford 1931; M. L. West, Teubner 1998–2000
Ion	Ion	Page, *PMG* pp. 383–6; West, *IEG* vol. 2, pp. 79–82
Is.	Isaeus	W. Wyse, Cambridge 1904; P. Roussel, Budé 1922
Isoc.	Isocrates	G. Mathieu–E. Brémond, Budé 1928–62; B. G. Mandilaras, Teubner 2003
Lamprocl.	Lamprocles	Page, *PMG* pp. 379–80
Lasus	Lasus	Page, *PMG* pp. 364–6
Licymn.	Licymnius	Page, *PMG* pp. 396–8
Lycophronid.	Lycophronides	Page, *PMG* p. 446
Lycurg.	Lycurgus	N. C. Conomis, Teubner 1970
Lyr.adesp.	Lyrica adespota	Page, *PMG* pp. 484–551, *SLG* pp. 106–51
Lys.	Lysias	C. Carey, OCT 2007
Melanipp.	Melanippides	Page, *PMG* pp. 392–5
Men.	Menander	H. Sandbach, 2nd edn, OCT 1990
Mimn.	Mimnermus	West, *IEG* vol. 2, pp. 83–92
Mosch.	Moschus	A. S. F. Gow, *Bucolici Graeci*, OCT 1952, pp. 132–52
NT.	New Testament	Gospels and Acts, E. Nestle–K. Aland, *Novum Testamentum Graece*, 28th edn, Stuttgart 2012
Od.	Homer, Odyssey	T. W. Allen, 2nd edn, OCT 1917–19; M. L. West, Teubner 2017
Panarces	Panarces	West, *IEG* vol. 2, pp. 93–4
Parm.	Parmenides	Kirk–Raven–Schofield pp. 239–62
Philox.Cyth.	Philoxenus Cytherius	Page, *PMG* pp. 423–32
Philox.Leuc.	Philoxenus Leucadius	Page, *PMG* pp. 433–41
Pi.	Pindar	B. Snell–H. Maehler, 8th edn, Teubner 1987
Pi.*fr.*		H. Maehler, Teubner 1989
Pl.	Plato	C. A. Duke et al., OCT vol. 1 1995; J. Burnet, OCT vols 2–5 1901–7; *Respublica*, S. R. Slings, OCT 2003
Plb.	Polybius	T. Büttner-Wobst, Teubner 1882–1905 (excl. book 34)
Plu.	Plutarch	*Vitae Parallelae*, K. Ziegler, 2nd, 3rd or 4th edn, Teubner 1964–71
Pratin.	Pratinas	Page, *PMG* pp. 367–9
Praxill.	Praxilla	Page, *PMG* pp. 386–90

S.	Sophocles	H. Lloyd-Jones–N. G. Wilson, 2nd edn, OCT 1990; R. D. Dawe, 3rd edn, Teubner 1996
S.*eleg.*		West, *IEG* vol. 2, pp. 165–6
S.*fr.*		J. Diggle, *Tragicorum Graecorum Fragmenta Selecta*, OCT 1998
S.*Ichn.* (*Ichneutai*)		ibid.
S.*lyr.fr.*		Page, *PMG* pp. 380–1
Sapph.	Sappho	E. Lobel–D. L. Page, *Poetarum Lesbiorum Fragmenta*, Oxford 1955; Page, *SLG* pp. 74–6, 87–102
Scol.	Scolia	Page, *PMG* (Carmina Convivialia) pp. 472–82
Semon.	Semonides	West, *IEG* vol. 2, pp. 98–114
Simon.	Simonides	Page, *PMG* pp. 238–323; West, *IEG* vol. 2, pp. 114–37
Sol.	Solon	West, *IEG* vol. 2, pp. 139–65
Stesich.	Stesichorus	Page, *PMG* pp. 95–141, *SLG* pp. 5–43; M. Davies–P. J. Finglass, Cambridge 2014
Telesill.	Telesilla	Page, *PMG* pp. 372–4
Telest.	Telestes	Page, *PMG* pp. 419–22
Terp.	Terpander	Page, *PMG* pp. 362–3
Th.	Thucydides	H. S. Jones–J. E. Powell, OCT 1942
Theoc.	Theocritus	A. S. F. Gow, 2nd edn, Cambridge 1952
Theoc.*epigr.*		A. S. F. Gow–D. L. Page, *Hellenistic Epigrams*, Cambridge 1965, vol. 1, pp. 183–91
Thgn.	Theognis	West, *IEG* vol. 1, pp. 172–241
Thphr.	Theophrastus	*Characters*, J. Diggle, Cambridge 2004
Tim.	Timotheus	Page, *PMG* pp. 399–418; J. H. Hordern, Oxford 2002
Timocr.	Timocreon	Page, *PMG* pp. 375–8
Tyrt.	Tyrtaeus	West, *IEG* vol. 2, pp. 169–84
X.	Xenophon	E. C. Marchant, OCT 1900–20
Xenoph.	Xenophanes	West, *IEG* vol. 2, pp. 184–91

(iii) *Further conventions used in citations*

Authors cited by collective or genre labels

Att.orats.	Attic orators	3 or more orators
Eleg.	Elegy	3 or more authors (as in West, *IEG*); occasionally 2
Hellenist.poet.	Hellenistic poets	3 or more of Call., AR., Theoc., Mosch., Bion
Iamb.	Iambic	2 or more authors (as in West, *IEG*)
Lyr.	Lyric	3 or more authors
Trag.	Tragedy	A., S., E. (all three)

Use of Hom. *and* hHom.
The label Hom. indicates both Il. and Od. The label Il. + excludes Od., while Od. + excludes Il. The label Hom. is sometimes also used to cover hHom., but only when Hom. is immediately followed by Hes. A list beginning Hom. Hes. hHom. (all of the same genre) would allow only three further citations (on the principle that a list will be limited to six), and curtailment of hHom. allows more room for citation of authors representing different genres.

Authors citing other authors or texts
When an author or text not included in the above list is cited by an author who is included, a label indicating the source of the quotation is generally added to the name of the quoting author. Thus,

Plu.(quot.com.) indicates a quotation by Plutarch from a comic poet (for example, a fragment of Aristophanes, a fragment of Menander not covered by the edition cited above [Sandbach 1990], or a fragment of a different comic poet); and Aeschin.(quot.epigr.) indicates a quotation by Aeschines of an epigram by an author not included in that list. Similarly, Plu.(quot. E.) indicates a quotation of a fragment of Euripides not covered by the edition cited above [Diggle 1998]. Quotations from non-literary sources are given in a similar style: for example, Hdt.(oracle), D.(law).

Abbreviations

For the abbreviations of authors' names, see the Authors and Editions section above.

•	introduces a Greek quotation giving an illustrative example of what has already been described in general terms	com.	comic, comedy (as a genre)
		compar.	comparative
		compl.cl.	complement clause
		concr.	concrete
		conj.	conjunction
abstr.	abstract	connot.	connotation
acc.	accusative	constr.	construction
acc.pers.	accusative of person	contr.	contracted, contraction
act.	active (voice)	contrastv.	contrastive meaning or emphasis
AD	*anno domini*	copul.	copulative
adj.	adjective	correlatv.	correlative
adjl.	adjectival	cpd.	compound
adv.	adverb	ctxt.	context
advbl.	adverbial		
Aeol.	Aeolic (dialect)	dat.	dative
aor.	aorist	dbl.	double
aor.2	second aorist	def.art.	definite article
app.	apparently	demonstr.	demonstrative
appos.w.	in apposition with	derog.	derogatory
approx.	approximately	desideratv.	desiderative
archit.	architectural term	dial.	dialect(al)
art.	(definite) article	diect.	diectasis
assoc.w.	associated with	dimin.	diminutive
astron.	astronomical term	dir.	direct
athem.	athematic	dir.q.	direct question
Att.	Attic (dialect)	dir.sp.	direct speech
		disyllab.	disyllabic
BC	before Christ	du.	dual
betw.	between	dub.	dubious reading
Boeot.	Boeotian (dialect)	dub.cj.	dubious conjecture
C.	century	E.	east
c.	circa	el.	element
causatv.	causative	eleg.	elegy (as a genre)
cf.	compare (Lat. *confer*)	ellipt.	elliptical(ly)
cj.	conjecture	emph.	emphasis, emphatic
cl.	clause	enclit.	enclitic
cogn.acc.	cognate accusative	ep.	epic (dialect or genre)
collectv.	collective	epigr.	epigram
colloq.	colloquial(ly)	ep.Ion.	epic-Ionic

epith.	epithet	lit.	literal(ly)
equiv.	equivalent	loanwd.	loanword
esp.	especially	loc.	locative
etym.	*see* pop.etym.	log.	term in logic
euphem.	euphemism, euphemistic(ally)	lyr.	lyric (as a genre)
excl.	excluding		
exclam.	exclamation	m.	masculine noun or proper name
		masc.	masculine
f.	feminine noun or proper name	math.	mathematical term
fem.	feminine	medic.	medical term
fig.	figurative(ly)	Megar.	Megarian (dialect)
fr.	from	meton.	metonymical(ly)
fr.	fragment	*metri grat.*	*metri gratia* (for the sake of the metre)
freq.	frequent(ly)		
fut.	future	mid.	middle (voice)
		mid.pass.	middle–passive
gen.	genitive	mid.sens.	middle sense (of a passive form)
gener.	general(ly)	milit.	military term
geom.	geometrical term	mock-ep.	comic use of epic language or creation of epic forms
Gk.	Greek (language)		
gramm.	grammatical term	mock-trag.	comic use of tragic vocabulary
		mod.	modern
hyperbol.	hyperbole, hyperbolic(ally)	monosyllab.	monosyllabic
		movt.	movement
imperatv.	imperative	Mt.	Mount
impers.	impersonal	mt.	mountain
impf.	imperfect	mus.	musical term
incl.	including	mythol.	in mythology, mythological
indecl.	indeclinable		
indef.	indefinite	N.	north
indic.	indicative	n.	neuter noun or proper name
indir.	indirect	naut.	nautical term
indir.q.	indirect question	neg.	negative
indir.sp.	indirect speech	neut.	neuter
inf.	infinitive	nom.	nominative
instr.	instrumental	nr.	near
intensv.	intensive	num.	numeral, numerical
interj.	interjection		
intern.acc.	internal accusative	occas.	occasionally
interpr.	interpretation, interpreted	oft.	often
interrog.	interrogative	opp.	as opposed to
intr.	intransitive	opt.	optative
Ion.	Ionic (dialect)	orig.	original(ly)
Iran.	Iranian (languages)	oxymor.	oxymoron
iron.	ironic(ally)		
irreg.	irregular	parenth.	parenthetic(ally)
iteratv.	iterative	parox.	paroxytone
		partitv.	partitive
kg	kilogram	pass.	passive (voice)
		pass.sens.	passive sense (of a middle form)
Lacon.	Laconian (dialect)	patronym.	patronymic
Lat.	Latin (language)	pcl.	particle
leg.	legal term		

pejor.	pejorative	S.	south
perh.	perhaps	*satyr.fr.*	satyric fragment
periphr.	periphrasis, periphrastic	sb.	substantive
pers.	person(al)	Semit.	Semitic (languages)
personif.	personified, personification	sens.	sense
pf.	perfect	sg.	singular
philos.	philosophical term	shd.	should
phr.	phrase	sim.	similar(ly)
pl.	plural	sp.	speech
pleon.	pleonastic(ally)	specif.	specific(ally)
plpf.	pluperfect	statv.	stative
poet.	in poetic language	sthg.	something
poet.pl.	poetic plural	sts.	sometimes
pop.etym.	(by) popular etymology	subj.	subjunctive
possessv.	possessive	superl.	superlative
postpos.	postpositive	syllab.	syllable, syllabic
predic.	predicate, predicative(ly)		
prep.	preposition(al)	tm.	in tmesis, tmetic
pres.	present	tr.	transitive
prfx.	prefix	trag.	tragedy (as a genre)
privatv.	privative	transf.epith.	transferred epithet
prob.	probably	transl.	translating, translation (of)
pron.	pronoun	trisyllab.	trisyllabic
proparox.	proparoxytone		
provb.	proverb	uncert.	uncertain
provbl.	proverbial(ly)	uncontr.	uncontracted
ptcpl.	participle, participial	understd.	understood
		usu.	usual(ly)
q.	question		
quadrisyllab.	quadrisyllabic	var.	variant
quinquesyllab.	quinquesyllabic	vb.	verb
quot.	quoting, quotation	vbl.	verbal
		v.l.	variant reading (Lat. *varia lectio*)
R.	River	voc.	vocative
redupl.	reduplicated		
ref. to	referring to, in reference to	W.	west
reflexv.	reflexive	w.	with
relatv.	relative	wd.	word
reltd.	related to	wkr.sens.	weaker sense
rhet.	rhetorical term		

K κ

κᾱ *dial.enclit.pcl.*: see ἄν¹
καβαίνω *dial.vb.*: see καταβαίνω
καββάλλω *ep.vb.*: see καταβάλλω
Κάβειροι ων *m.pl.* [loanwd.] Kabeiroi (gods of a mystery cult in N. Aegean, esp. Lemnos, Miletos and Samothrace) Hippon. A.(title) Hdt. Call.*epigr.*
κάγκανος ον *adj.* (of firewood) **dry** Hom. hHom. AR. Theoc.
καγχαλάω *contr.vb.* | ep.3pl. (w.diect.) καγχαλόωσι, ptcpl. καγχαλόων, fem. καγχαλόωσα | **laugh** (in exultation, satisfaction or derision) Hom. AR. | see also ἐπικαγχαλάω
κἀγώ: crasis for καὶ ἐγώ
κάδ *dial.prep.*: see κατά
καδδίζομαι *pass.vb.* [κάδδιχος] | pf.inf. κεκαδδίσθαι | ‖ PF. (of a person) **be excluded by vote** Plu.
κάδδιχος ου *m.* [κάδος] **jar** (used as an improvised voting-urn) Plu.
κάδδραθον (ep.aor.2): see καταδαρθάνω
καδίσκος ου *m.* [dimin. κάδος] **urn for receiving jurors' ballots, voting-urn** Ar. Att.orats.
Καδμο-γενής ές *adj.* [Κάδμος; γένος, γίγνομαι] (of the people of Thebes) **of the Kadmeian race** A. E.; (of Herakles, as born at Thebes) S.
Κάδμος ου *m.* Kadmos (mythol. founder of Thebes in Boeotia, said to have come fr. Phoenicia) Od. Hes. Thgn. +
—**Καδμεῖος** (also **Καδμέιος** Pi.) ᾱ (Ion. η) ον, Ion. **Καδμήιος** η ον *adj.* **1** (of an endeavour) **of Kadmos** E. **2** (of the city, land, walls of Thebes) **of or belonging to Kadmos** (or his descendants), **Kadmeian** Hes. Pi. Trag.; (of persons, the people) Pi.*fr.* Hdt. S. E. Theoc.; (of the kingship) S.; (of the limbs) **of Kadmeians** E. ‖ MASC.PL.SB. **Kadmeian men, Kadmeians** Hom. Hes. Pi. Hdt. Trag. Lys. + ‖ FEM.PL.SB. **Kadmeian women** S.
3 ‖ FEM.SB. **Kadmeia** (the citadel of Thebes) Att.orats. X. Plb. Plu.
4 (of a form of the Greek alphabet used at Thebes, described as similar to Ionian, and believed to have been brought fr. Phoenicia by Kadmos) **Kadmeian** Hdt.
5 (of a garment) in the Theban style, **Kadmeian** E.; (provbl., of a ruinous victory) Hdt. Pl.; (of education) Pl.
—**Καδμειῶνες** ων *m.pl.* **descendants of Kadmos, Kadmeians** Il.
—**Καδμηίς** ίδος *f.* **daughter of Kadmos** (ref. to Semele) Hes. hHom.; (ref. to Autonoe) Call. ‖ ADJ. (of the land) **Kadmeian** Hes. Th.
κάδος ου *m.* **1 jar, urn** (esp. for water or wine) Archil. Anacr. Hdt. S.*fr.* Ar. D.; **well-bucket** (of bronze or earthenware) Ar. Men.; (gener., ref. to containers which can be nested inside each other) Pl.
2 voting-urn Ar.
κάδος *dial.n.*, **κάδω** *dial.vb.*: see κήδος, κήδω
Κάειρα *fem.adj.*: see under Κᾱ́ρ²

καήμεναι (ep.aor.2 pass.inf.): see καίω
καθ-ά *conj.* [κατά; ἅ, see under ὅς¹] (introducing comparisons or citing an authority) **in the same way as** (someone has said or done), **as, just as** X. D. Arist. Plb. NT.
—**καθάπερ**, Ion. **κατά περ** *conj.* [ἅπερ, see under ὅσπερ] (introducing comparisons or citing an authority) **just as** Hdt. Th. Ar. Att.orats. +
—**καθαπερεί**, Ion. **κατά περ εἰ** *conj.* **as if** (sthg. were the case) Hdt. Pl. Plb.
—**καθαπερανεί** (also **καθάπερ ἄν εἰ**) *conj.* **just as if** (sthg. were the case) Pl. Plb.
καθ-αγίζω, Ion. **καταγίζω** *vb.* | Ion.fut.inf. καταγιεῖν |
1 sanctify (by burning); **burn as a sacrificial offering** —*animals, parts of them* Hdt. Pl. —*spoils of war (ref. to persons,* W.DAT. *to a god)* Hdt. —*grain, an eel* Ar. Men.; (gener.) **burn** —*incense* Hdt. Plu.; (fig.) **consecrate** —*a cup (by drinking its contents)* Ar. ‖ PASS. (of parts of animals) be burned (as a sacrificial offering) Hdt.; (of incense) Hdt.; (of a fruit, as an intoxicant) Hdt.
2 cremate —*a dead body* Plu.
καθ-αγνίζω *vb.* **1 make holy or pure, sacrifice** (on a fire) —*a mixture of food* E.
2 purify by funeral rites; (fig., of animals) **purify, sanctify** —*corpses (by eating them)* S. ‖ PASS. (of a dead person) be purified —W.DAT. *by fire* E.
καθαιμακτός όν *adj.* [καθαιμάσσω] (of a corpse) **bloodstained** E.
καθ-αιμάσσω *vb.* | pf.pass.ptcpl. καθημαγμένος | **make bloody, stain with blood** —*a person's flesh, head, neck (by killing or injuring him)* E. —*one's hand and sword* Plu.; (of a slaughtered animal, in a purifying rite) —*a person* A.; (of a charioteer) —*a horse's tongue and jaws (w. the bit)* Pl.; (of a murder) —*the pedestal of a statue* Plu. ‖ PF.PASS.PTCPL.ADJ. (of a toga) bloodstained Plu.
καθ-αιματόω *contr.vb.* **make bloody, stain with blood** —*the head, hair, cheek (of an enemy)* E. —*one's own hand (in killing someone)* E.; (of a murdered baby) —*an altar* Ar.(mock-trag.)
κάθ-αιμος ον *adj.* [αἷμα] (of wounds, human flesh being eaten) **bloodstained, gory** E.
καθαίρεσις εως *f.* [καθαιρέω] **1 breaking down, demolition** (of a fortress, city walls, or sim.) Th. Isoc. X.; (fig., of Roman rule) Plb.; **breaking up** (of precious objects) D.
2 (medic.) **wasting away** (of a person's body) Plu.
3 disintegration (of liquid particles, ref. to melting) Pl.
καθαιρετέος ᾱ ον *vbl.adj.* (of Athenian power) **to be overthrown** Th.
καθαιρέτης ου *m.* **overthrower** (W.GEN. of enemies) Th.
καθαιρετός ή όν *adj.* (of a skill) **able to be achieved** (by practice) Th.
καθ-αιρέω, Ion. **καταιρέω** *contr.vb.* | aor.2 καθεῖλον, Ion. κατεῖλον, ep.3sg.subj. καθέλῃσι, ep.inf. (tm.) κατὰ ... ἐλέειν

καθαίρω

| Ion.pf.pass.ptcpl. καταραιρημένος | **1 take down, lower** —*sails* Od. —*a signal* And. Plb.; (mid.) —*masts* Plb.
2 lower (the eyelids); **close** —*the eyes (of a dead person)* Hom.(sts.tm.)
3 take down, remove —*a basket (fr. someone's head)* Ar. —*a burden (fr. someone's back)* Ar. —*a severed head (fr. a gate)* Hdt. —*a person (fr. a cross)* Plb. NT. —*a child (fr. a horse)* Plb. —*money, a statue (fr. the Acropolis)* Ar. Lycurg.
4 (sts.mid.) **take down, remove** (fr. a peg or place of storage) —*a yoke, weapons, utensils, documents, firewood* Il.(tm.) Hdt. Ar. X. Arist. Call.
5 take down, remove —*legal tablets (fr. public display, signifying the revocation of a law)* Arist. Plu. —*pillars (recording an alliance)* D.; **annul, revoke** —*laws, decrees, agreements (by removing the pillars on which they are inscribed)* Th. Lys. D. Arist. || PASS. (of a law or decree) be revoked Th. Lys.
6 take down (fr. trees), **pick** —*apples* Theoc.; **get down** —*a bird* (w. ἐκ + GEN. *fr. a tree, by catching it*) Theoc.
7 (of witches) **draw down** —*the moon (fr. the sky)* Ar. Pl.
8 (in wishes, of Hades, the earth) **drag down, swallow up** —*a person* S.(tm.) E.(tm.)
9 pull down, demolish, destroy —*cities, walls, buildings* Hdt. E. Th. Att.orats. Pl. +; || PASS. (of walls or sim.) be demolished Th. Lys. X. +; (of precious objects) be destroyed D.
10 (of a person or god, death, time, misfortune) **overpower, conquer, destroy** —*a person, people, city, army* Od. Simon. Pi. Hdt. Trag. Th. +; (of old age) **impair, ruin** —*someone's beauty* Archil. || PASS. (of a city) be conquered S.; (of a person) be brought low (by misfortune) Pl.; be impaired —w.ACC. *in one's senses* Plu.
11 (specif.) **bring down, depose, overthrow** —*a ruler or powerful person* Hdt. E. Th. Aeschin. Plb. Plu.; **put an end to** —*someone's power* Hdt. Th. Aeschin. || PASS. (of a ruler) be brought down Hdt. D.; (of an empire) be destroyed Hdt. Th.
12 (of a boxer) **lay low, fell** —*an opponent* Theoc.; (fig., of a person) —*a maxim (envisaged as a boxing or wrestling opponent)* Pl.
13 (leg., of an argument, a voting-token) **condemn** —*a person* E. Lys.; (gener., of a lot) **constrain** —*someone* (W.INF. *to do sthg.*) S.
14 reduce (in bulk or importance); **make** (W.ACC. one's body) **waste away** (by dieting) Plu.; (of a litigant) **play down, belittle** —*contracts* Arist.
15 take away, remove —*woodwork, bricks (fr. houses)* Th. —*a tray (fr. a person)* Ar.; (of Zeus) —*the breath (fr. someone's chest, i.e. kill him)* Pi. || PASS. (of valuables) be removed (fr. a temple) Hdt.; (of a temple) be stripped —W.GEN. *of its magnificence* NT.
16 get rid of, eliminate —*piracy (sts. W.GEN. fr. the sea)* Th.; **bring to an end** —*someone's misfortune* E.
17 catch, grasp —*someone* (W.GEN. *by their ears*) Theoc.; **apprehend** —*someone* (w. ἐν + DAT. *in an act of folly*) S.; (wkr.sens., of sleep, mistiness of vision) **take hold of** —*a person* Od.(tm.) AR.(tm.) || PASS. be caught —W.NOM.PTCPL. *committing an offence* S.
18 (of pursuers) **overtake, catch** —*an enemy ship* Hdt.; (of a horseman) —*a person on foot* X. || PASS. (of a person) be caught (by pursuers) Hdt.
19 (of an athlete) **achieve** —*one's ambition* Pi.; **win** —*contests* Plu. || MID. (of states) **accomplish** —*their business* (W.DAT. *by bloodshed, by negotiation*) E. || PASS. (of great things) be achieved Hdt.

καθαίρω *vb.* [καθαρός] | fut. καθαρῶ | aor. ἐκάθηρα, ep. κάθηρα, later Att. ἐκάθᾱρα || MID.: fut. καθαροῦμαι | aor. ἐκαθηράμην || PASS.: aor. ἐκαθάρθην | pf.ptcpl. κεκαθαρμένος |
1 cleanse —*drinking-vessels, furniture* Od. —*a dead body* Od. —*one's face* (w. a cosmetic) Od. —*corn* (by winnowing) X.; **refine** —*gold* Pl. || PASS. (of a corpse's stomach) be cleaned out (by embalmers) Hdt.
2 clean away —*dirt (fr. one's body or clothes)* Hom. —*polluting blood (fr. someone's hand)* A. —W.DBL.ACC. *blood, fr. a corpse* Il.
3 purify (by ritual washing or fumigation) —*a sacrificial cup* Il. —*a person (fr. the pollution of murder or sim.)* Hdt. Ar. —*a city, house, deme, island* Hippon. Hdt. Th. Att.orats. Arist. Thphr.; (by regular rites and lustrations) —*initiates, a sacrificial offering, or sim.* D. Plu. || MID. **purify oneself** (after a funeral, a homicide) Hdt. Pl. D.; (gener., ref. to practising philosophy, eliminating sthg. fr. one's mind, correcting a factual error) Pl. || PASS. (of a person) be purified Heraclit. Hdt. Pl.
4 (gener.) **purify, cleanse** —*land and sea (of dangers)* S. Plu. —*a city (of harmful persons, certain kinds of music)* Pl.; (iron.) —*the soul (of virtues)* Pl.; (colloq.) **beat up** —*someone* Men. Theoc.
5 (of Apollo, doctors) **effect a purge** (sts. w. κάτω *down below*, i.e. *in the bowels*, by laxatives; sts. w.gener.ref. to healing) Pl.; (of the Socratic method of argument) **purge** —*the soul (compared w. medical treatment for the body)* Pl.; (of a herdsman) **apply** —W.COGN.ACC. *a purge (by removing unhealthy and inferior animals)* Pl.; (fig.) **purge, eliminate** —*dangers (fr. a land)* S.; **cut back, prune** —*a healthy vine-branch* NT. || PASS. be purged (by a laxative) Thphr.

καθ-άλλομαι *mid.vb.* [κατά] | aor.2 ptcpl. καθαλόμενος | (of a person) **leap down** (fr. a horse) X.; (of a horse) **jump down** (fr. a height) X.; (of a tempest) **swoop down** Il.

καθᾱμέριον *dial.neut.adv.*: see under καθημέριος

κάθαμμα ατος *n.* [καθάπτω] that which is fastened; (fig.ref. to a tangle of misunderstanding) **knot** (W.GEN. of words) E.

καθανύτω, καθανύω Att.vbs.: see κατανύω

καθ-άπαξ *adv.* **1 once and for all, permanently** Od. D. Arist. Plu.
2 completely, unconditionally D. Arist. Plb. Plu.; (quasi-adjl., of enemies) **utter, complete** D.
3 (neg.phr.) οὐδὲ καθάπαξ (or sim.) *not even once* Plb.

καθάπερ, καθαπερεί, καθαπερανεί *conjs.*: see under καθά

καθαπτός ή όν *adj.* [καθάπτω] (of Dionysus) **equipped, arrayed** (W.DAT. w. thyrsos and fawnskin) E.*fr.*

καθ-άπτω, Ion. **κατάπτω** *vb.* | aor. καθῆψα | fut.mid. καθάψομαι || pf.pass.ptcpl. καθημμένος | **1 fasten, attach** —*a garment* (W.DAT. *around a person's shoulders*) S. —*a bracelet* (W.GEN. *to someone's body*) E. —*guy-ropes* (W.PREP.PHR. *to the ground*) X. —*the base of a crane (to a fixed object)* Plb.; (intr., of a snake) **fasten** —W.GEN. *onto a person's hand* NT. || PF.PASS. (of a hanged person) be fastened —W.DAT. *by a noose* S.
2 || MID. **dress** —*one's body* (W.DAT. *in an outfit*) E.; **put** —*a wreath* (W.PREP.PHR. *on one's brow*) Theoc.epigr. || PASS. be dressed —W.DAT. *in a fawnskin* S.*Ichn.*
3 || MID. (sts. as ptcpl., w. main vb. φημί or sim.) **address or accost** —*persons* (sts. W.DAT. w. *sweet or harsh words*) Hom. Hes. —*one's own heart* Od.
4 || MID. **make a verbal attack** —W.GEN. *on persons* Hdt. Th. Pl. X. Plu.; **humiliate** —W.GEN. *someone (by demoting him)* Plu.

5 ‖ MID. (of troops) **harass** —W.GEN. *a rearguard* Plb.
6 ‖ MID. **fasten upon, clasp** —W.GEN. *a baby (in one's arms)* Theoc.; (intr., of a dye) **take hold** Plu.; (fig.) **embrace** —W.GEN. *tyranny and force* Sol.
7 ‖ MID. **call as witness, appeal to** —W.GEN. *gods, persons* Hdt.

καθάρειος (also **καθάριος**) ον *adj.* [καθαρός] (of persons) **neat, tidy** (in appearance, behaviour) Arist.; (of weaponry) Plb.; (of the preparation of food) Men.

—**καθαρείως** (also **καθαρίως**) *adv.* **1 neatly** —*ref. to pouring wine* X.
2 clearly —*ref. to showing or understanding sthg.* Plb.

καθαρειότης (also **καθαριότης**) ητος *f.* **1** bodily cleanliness, **hygiene** Hdt.; **purity** (of emotions, fr. sensory and other activities) Arist.; (of the Spartan manner of speech) Plu.
2 (gener.) **goodness, wholesomeness** (of food) Plu.; **neatness** (of papyrus-garlands) Plu.

καθαρεύω *vb.* **1** (of places, circumstances) **be free from pollution** Pl. D.(oath) Plu.; (gener., of a household, city, country) **be free** —W.GEN. *fr. crimes, meanness* Plu. —*fr. lamentation, an execution during a festival* Plu.
2 (of persons, oft. in neg.phr.) **be free from pollution, be pure** X. —W.DAT. *in body* Aeschin. —W.ACC. *in mind* Ar.; (gener.) **be free** —W.GEN. or ἀπό + GEN. *fr. one's corporeal nature, dissolute acts* Pl. Plu.; (fig., of a politician) **keep one's hands clean** —W.PREP.PHR. *in financial matters* Plb.

καθαρίζω *vb.* | aor. ἐκαθάρισα | **1** (of persons) **wash, clean** —*cups and plates* NT.
2 (of God) **make pure** —*food* NT. —*persons' hearts* NT.
3 heal —*someone (fr. leprosy)* NT. ‖ PASS. **be healed** NT.

καθάριος *adj.*, **καθαριότης** *f.*: see καθάρειος, καθαρειότης

καθαρισμός οῦ *m.* [καθαρίζω] **purification** (of the hands or body, ref. to ritual cleansing) NT.; (of a leper, after being healed) NT.; (of parents, after childbirth) NT.

κάθαρμα ατος *n.* [καθαίρω] **1** ‖ COLLECTV.PL. residue from a purificatory sacrifice, **leavings, dregs** A.
2 ‖ COLLECTV.PL. purification ritual E.; (gener.) **cleansing** (of sea and land, fr. monsters and other dangers, by Herakles) E.
3 (concr.) **purified area** (ref. to the meeting-place of the Assembly) Ar.
4 (pejor., ref. to a person) **piece of filth, scum** Ar. Att.orats. Men. Plu.

καθ-αρμόζω, Ion. **καταρμόζω** *vb.* **1 join or fit** (one thing to another); **fasten, fit** —*a noose* (W.DAT. *to one's neck*) E. —*parts of an animal-skin (to parts of one's body)* E.
2 fit in place —*a stone (in a wall)* Hdt. —*hair* (W.PREP.PHR. *beneath a headband*) E. —*timber and tiles (to make rafts)* Plb. ‖ PASS. (of charioteers' whips, when not in use) **be set in place** —W.PREP.PHR. *on the horses' yokes* E.
3 close up —*wounds* E.

καθαρμός οῦ *m.* [καθαίρω] **1 ritual cleansing** (fr. pollution); (sg. and pl.) **purification** (of a person or object) Trag. Pl.; (of a place) S. Plb. Plu.; (of an army) X. Plb. Plu.
2 purificatory rite (for initiation into the Mysteries or sim.) E. Pl. D.
3 (concr., ref. to a person) purificatory offering, **scapegoat** (W.GEN. *for a country*) Hdt.
4 purgation (of the body, by medicines) Pl.; (fig., of a poet, through writing a poem) Pl.; (of the soul, through philosophy) Pl. Plu.
5 purge (of a herd, by removing unhealthy animals) Pl.; (of the state, ref. to ostracism or sim.) Pl. Plb. Plu.

καθαρός ά (Ion. ή) όν, Aeol. **κόθαρος** ᾱ ον *adj.* **1 made free from dirt or stain** (by washing or cleansing); (of persons, parts of the body) **clean** Xenoph. Hdt. E.*Cyc.* +; (of clothes) Od. Archil. Ar.; (of a face-cloth) Ar.; (of a bowl, cup) Anacr. Xenoph.; (of a floor, dwelling, or sim.) Xenoph. E. Men.
2 (of a cauldron, sulphur) having a cleansing or purifying effect, **cleansing, purifying** Pi. Theoc.
3 free from moral defilement or the stain of crime (esp. bloodshed); (of persons, their hands, a city, populace, house) **clean, pure, untainted** Trag. Th. Att.orats. Pl. +; (phr.) καθαρὸς (τὰς) χεῖρας *without blood on one's hands* Hdt. Att.orats. Pl.
4 (of places) **pure, free** (W.GEN. fr. pollution, murderers, evils, or sim.) Antipho Lys. Pl. X.; (of a soul, fr. evils and desires) Pl.; (gener., of persons) **innocent** (sts. W.GEN. of a charge, blame) Antipho; (of wrongdoing) Pl.
5 having received ritual purification; (of a person, a house) **purified, pure** A. E. Pl.; (of the air, by fumigation) E.
6 pure (in terms of religious requirements); (of persons, animals, altars, foodstuffs, or sim.) **pure, free from taint** A. Hdt. +; (of an animal) **untainted** (W.GEN. by certain defects) Hdt.
7 (gener.) **pure** (through association w. divinity); (of the seed of a god) **pure** Pi.; (of words, addressed to gods) Xenoph.; (of specified days) **holy** (opp. ἀποφράδες *inauspicious*) Pl.
8 free from admixture or contamination; (gener., of things) **pure, unadulterated** Heraclit. Pl. X. +; (of gold, silver) **pure, unalloyed** B.*fr.* Hdt.; (colloq., of money) **good** Theoc.
9 (of water) **pure, clear** Xenoph. E. Pl Plb.; (of a river, opp. muddy) Hdt.; (fig., of a mind) **serene, untroubled** E.
10 (of light) **pure, clear** Alc. Pi. Parm. Pl.; (of the sheen on the surface of gold) Thgn.; (of the world of Forms) Pl.; (of the sound of a bird) Ar.
11 (of modesty, excellence) **pure, unsullied** A.*fr.* Pi.; (of hatred, benefits) **pure, unmixed** Pl. Men.; (fig., of a misanthrope) **pure, absolute, total** Ar.
12 free from dishonesty or error; (of a mind) **pure, sincere, honest** Thgn. Scol. Pi. E.; (of a sceptre, meton. for royal rule) **just** Pi.; (of a touchstone) **true, reliable** Pi.*fr.*; (of financial calculations on an abacus) D.
13 (of oracles) **clear, unambiguous** E.; (of speech) **plain, frank** Ar.
14 ‖ NEUT.SB. **sound or fit part** (W.GEN. of an army) Hdt.
15 born of unmixed stock; (of citizens) **pure** (W.DAT. in descent) Arist.; (of a populace, a military force) consisting of true-born citizens, **pure-blooded** E. Th.
16 clear of obstructions; (of a place, path, or sim.) **clear, open** Pi. Hdt. X. Hellenist.poet.; (of ground, vines) **free** (W.GEN. of weeds) X.; (prep.phrs.) ἐν καθαρῷ *in a clear space, on open ground* Il. Pi. S.(dub.); (app.) *in a place clear of people (i.e. in private)* Ar.; διὰ καθαροῦ *through unobstructed land (ref. to a river flowing)* Hdt.
17 (fig., of a form of execution) **clean** (i.e. quick and easy, opp. slow and painful) Od.

—**καθαρῶς** *adv.* **1** in a manner that entails physical or ceremonial purity, **purely** —*ref. to washing, sacrificing* Hes. hHom.
2 in a manner that incurs no taint of pollution, **without taint** E.
3 in a manner that incurs no taint of dishonour, **honestly** Thgn. Pl. X. D. Arist. +
4 clearly —*ref. to speaking, explaining, understanding* E. Ar. Isoc. Pl. Arist. Plu.

καθαρότης

5 by unmixed descent, **truly, wholly** —*ref. to being a citizen or of a certain nationality* Hdt. Lys. D.
6 without obstruction (fr. the terrain), **freely** —*ref. to running* X.
7 **with a clean sweep, in one go** —*ref. to birds eating sthg. up* Ar.

καθαρότης ητος *f.* 1 **cleanliness** (of a place) Pl.; **purity** (of bodily appearance) X.; (of colours; of aither, compared w. air) Pl.; (in music) Pl.
2 **honesty** (in financial matters) Plb.

καθ-αρπάζω *vb.* [κατά] **snatch, grab** —*a sword (fr. a hand), armour, a shield (fr. its hook)* E. Ar.

καθάρσιος ον *adj.* [καθαίρω] 1 cleansing from guilt or defilement; (epith. of Zeus) **purificatory** Hdt. AR.; (of the presence of Dionysus) S.; (of fire, barley grains) E. Plu.; (of the Lupercalia; of February as the month in which this festival was held) Plu.
2 (of Apollo, sacrificial victims) **offering purification** (W.GEN. of a house) A. E.; (of sacrificial equipment, W.DAT. for someone) E.; (of Apollo, a priest, W.DAT. for someone, W.GEN. fr. blood-guilt) A.
3 (of bloodshed) **able to be cleansed** A.
4 ‖ NEUT.SB. purification (fr. blood-guilt) Hdt.; (concr.) purificatory offering Aeschin. Plu.

κάθαρσις εως *f.* 1 **cleaning** (W.GEN. of a horse's body) X.; (of corn, by winnowing) Pl.
2 cleansing from guilt or defilement, **purification** (of a person, a place) Hdt. Th. Pl. Arist. Plu.; (of the soul, by truth) Pl.
3 (medic.) clearing of morbid humours; **evacuation** (of blood) D.; **purging** (of the body) Pl. Arist. Plu.; (fig., ref. to removing pity and fear, through their representation in tragedy) **catharsis** Arist.

καθαρτής οῦ *m.* 1 (ref. to a military engineer) **clearer** (W.GEN. of rivers) Plu.
2 (ref. to an avenger) **purifier** (W.GEN. of a house) S.; (ref. to a poet, envisaged as Herakles, W.GEN. of a land) Ar.
3 (fig., ref. to a sophist) **purger** (W.GEN. of false opinions) Pl.

καθαρτικός ή όν *adj.* 1 able to cleanse or purify; (of a substance, app.ref. to soda) **cleansing** (sthg., W.GEN. fr. oil and earth) Pl.
2 (of an art, assoc.w. intellectual discrimination) **purifying** Pl.; (of melodies, ref. to their effect on people) Arist.
‖ NEUT.SB. purification (as part of the art of discrimination) Pl.

καθαρῶ (fut.): see καθαίρω

καθ-αυαίνω *Ion.vb.* (of Sirius) **dry up** —*people* Archil.

καθάψομαι (fut.mid.): see καθάπτω

καθ-έδρα ᾱς *f.* [κατά] 1 **chair** or **seat** Plb.; (specif.) **rowers' bench** (on a ship) Plb.; **trader's bench** NT.
2 ancestral position of authority, **seat** (W.GEN. of Moses) NT.
3 place in which a hare habitually rests, **form** X.
4 (milit.) **encampment** (outside a stronghold, by an attacking force) Th. Plu.

καθ-έζομαι *mid.vb.* | impf. and aor.2 ἐκαθεζόμην (Th. +), also καθεζόμην (Hom. +) | fut. καθεδοῦμαι | 1 **take one's seat, sit down** (oft. W.ADV. or PREP.PHR. in a place, on a seat, bed, or sim.) Hom.(sts.tm.) Hes. S. E. Th. +; (of a god, a ruler) —W.PREP.PHR. *on a throne, in a place of authority* A. E.; (of suppliants) —*at a temple, altar, hearth* Th. And. Lys. Ar.; (of a tutelary goddess) **settle** (in a place) A.
2 (of officials) **take one's seat** —W.PREP.PHR. *for the examination of accounts* Aeschin.; (of the presiding officers of an assembly) **gain one's position** —W.PREP.PHR. *by intrigue* Aeschin.
3 be or remain seated, **be seated, sit** Hom. Hes. Thgn. Pi.*fr.* Th. Ar. +; (on a horse) X. —w. πρόχνυ *on one's knees (ref. to crouching)* Il.; (of suppliants, sts. W.PREP.PHR. at an altar) E. Th. D.; (of magistrates, jurors, arbitrators, the Council, while performing their duties) Att.orats.
4 **sit idle** (opp. be active, do one's duty) X. D. Men. Plu.; (fig., of a poet, envisaged as a fighter waiting to compete) Ar.
5 (of an army) **pitch camp, encamp** Th. X.; (of a group of soldiers) **take up position** Th. Plu.

καθέηκα (ep.aor.): see καθίημι
καθείατο (ep.3pl.impf.mid.): see κάθημαι
καθείληφα (Att.pf.): see καταλαμβάνω
καθεῖλον (aor.2): see καθαιρέω
καθειμαρμένος (pf.pass.ptcpl.): see καταμείρομαι
καθεῖμεν (1pl.athem.aor.), **καθειμένος** (pf.pass.ptcpl.): see καθίημι
καθείργνῡμι, καθείργω Att.vbs.: see κατείργω
κάθειρξις εως Att.*f.* [κατέργω] **shutting in, repression** (W.GEN. of one's desires) Plu.
καθεῖσα (aor.), **καθεισάμην** (aor.mid.): see καθίζω
καθεῖσαν (3pl.athem.aor.), **καθεῖτο** (3sg.plpf.pass.): see καθίημι
καθεκτέον (neut.impers.vbl.adj.): see κατέχω
καθεκτός ή όν, Boeot. **κάθεκτος** ᾱ ον *adj.* [κατέχω] 1 (in neg.phr., of persons, their feelings) **able to be restrained** or **controlled** D. Plu.; (of a city in turmoil, sedition) Plu.
2 (of political power) **able to be retained** (W.DAT. by the people) Plu.
3 (of a person) **gripped** (W.DAT. by grief) Corinn.

καθ-ελίσσω, Aeol. **κατελίσσω**, Ion. **κατειλίσσω** *vb.* [κατά] | Ion.3pl.plpf.pass. κατειλίχατο | **wrap, swathe, bind up** —*wounds, a mummified body (w. linen bandages)* Hdt. ‖ MID. **bind up** —*one's hair (in a headband)* Sapph.; **swathe oneself** —W.DAT. w. *strips of cloth (around the neck)* Plu. ‖ PASS. have (W.ACC. one's legs) swathed —W.DAT. w. *cloths* Hdt.

καθ-έλκω, Ion. **κατέλκω** *vb.* | aor. καθείλκυσα | 1 **draw down** (to the sea), **launch** —*ships* E. Th. Ar. Isoc. Pl. +; (of a state) **send out** (to sea) —*a fleet* Ar. D. Plb. ‖ PASS. (of ships) be launched Hdt. Th.
2 (of a heavy object, fig.ref. to a line of poetry) **pull down** (a scale-pan) Ar.; (of money, placed in the scales) —*rational argument* (W.PREP.PHR. *towards itself, i.e. outweigh it*) D.; (of a short poem) **outweigh** (in benefit) —*a long one* Call.

καθέμεν (ep.1pl.athem.aor.): see καθίημι

καθ-εξῆς *adv.* 1 **in order, one after another** —*ref. to visiting places, describing events* NT.
2 (quasi-adjl., of persons) **coming next in time, subsequent** NT.; (prep.phr.) ἐν τῷ καθεξῆς *afterwards* NT.

κάθεξις εως *f.* [κατέχω] 1 **maintaining, preservation** (of imperial rule) Th.
2 **holding in, restraining** (of one's breath, emotions) Arist.

καθέξω (fut.): see κατέχω

καθ-έρματα των *n.pl.* **earrings** Anacr.

καθ-έρπω *vb.* | aor. καθείρπυσα | 1 (of a person) **go down** —W.PREP.PHR. *to a place* Ar.; (of a young man's sideburns, as they grow) —*past his ears* X.; (fig., of a person's heart) —*into his bowels* Ar.
2 (of Pytho) **extend** or **stretch down** —W.PREP.PHR. *fr. a river* Call.

κάθες (athem.aor.imperatv.), **κάθεσαν** (ep.3pl.athem.aor.): see καθίημι

κάθεσα, κάθεσσα (ep.aor.), **καθεσσάμην** (dial.aor.mid.): see καθίζω

καθεστηκότως *pf.ptcpl.adv.*: see under καθίστημι
καθεστήξω (fut.pf.), **καθεστώς** (pf.ptcpl.): see καθίσταμαι
καθέσω (fut.): see καθίζω
κάθετον, **καθέτω** (2du. and 3sg. athem.aor.imperatv.): see κάθημαι
κάθετος ον *adj.* [καθίημι] let down; (prep.phr.) πρὸς κάθετον (w. γραμμήν *line* understd.) *vertically* Plu.(quot.epigr.)
καθ-εύδω, Ion. **κατεύδω** *vb.* | impf. καθηῦδον (Ar. Pl.), also ἐκαθεῦδον (Lys. +), ep. καθεῦδον | fut. καθευδήσω ‖ neut.impers.vbl.adj. καθευδητέον | **1** (of persons, animals, birds) **sleep, go to sleep** or **be asleep** Hom. Anacr. Hippon. Thgn. A. Hdt. + ‖ NEUT.PTCPL.SB. *state of sleep* Heraclit.
2 go to bed or **be in bed** (w. a sexual partner) Od. Ar.
3 (of soldiers, the Council, or sim.) **pass a night** (in a place) And. Ar. X.
4 (fig.) **be asleep** (mentally or spiritually) Pl.; **take one's ease, be idle** A. Ar. Pl. X. D. Plu.
5 (fig., of fallen city walls) **lie sleeping** (on the ground, opp. be made to get up, i.e. be rebuilt) Pl.; (of hopes, laws) **be dormant** E. Plu.
καθ-ευρησιλογέω (or **καθευρεσιλογέω**) *contr.vb.* (of rhetoricians) **invent clever arguments** Plb.
καθ-εψιάομαι *mid.contr.vb.* **amuse oneself** (at another's expense); **mock, jeer at** —W.GEN. *someone* Od.
καθ-έψω *vb.* **1 boil down**; (fig., of a profligate person) **digest** —*money* Ar.
2 (fig.) **calm down, soothe** —*a high-spirited horse* X.
κάθη (2sg.mid.): see κάθημαι
καθ-ηγεμών, Ion. **κατηγεμών**, όνος *m.* **1 one who leads or shows the way; guide** Plb. Plu.; (W.GEN. *on a journey, march*) Hdt. Plu.; (specif.) **pilot** (providing navigational help for ships) Plb.
2 one who gives guidance or exercises influence (in matters of behaviour); **guide, adviser** (for political policy) Plb.; **promoter** (W.GEN. *of virtuous conduct*) Plu.; **prompter, instigator** (W.GEN. *of evil conduct, a plan*) Hdt. Plb.
3 ‖ PL. (ref. to one's ancestors) **leaders** or **founders** (W.GEN. *of a family line*) Plu.; **guides** (W.GEN. *for one's own life*) Plu.
καθ-ηγέομαι, Ion. **κατηγέομαι** *mid.contr.vb.* **1 lead the way, act as a guide** Hdt. Th. Plb. —W.PREP.PHR. *to a place* Hdt. —W.GEN. *on an expedition* Plu. —W.NEUT.ACC. *in an enterprise* X.; **lead, guide** —W.DAT. *persons* (W.PREP.PHR. *to a place*) Hdt. —(W.ACC. *on a route*) Hdt.
2 act as guide to (i.e. in relation to) —*a reef, a river* Hdt. Pl.
3 give guidance (over conduct); (of a priestess) **give advice** —W.DAT. *to someone* Hdt.
4 take the lead, come first (in a procession) Plb.
5 (of a commander) **go at the head** —W.GEN. *of his army* Plb.; **lead** —W.DAT. *a wing* Plb. ‖ PTCPL.ADJ. (of a wing) *leading, advance* Plb.
6 have charge —W.GEN. *of a state* Plu.
7 take a lead (in doing sth.); **introduce** —*a religious practice* Hdt.; **found** —*an oracle* Hdt.; **break new ground** —W.NOM.PTCPL. *in doing sth.* Hdt.; (gener.) **take the initiative** X.
8 make a beginning —W.GEN. *to a speech* Pl.; (of a subject of study) **be preliminary** —W.GEN. *to others* Pl.
καθηγήτειρα ᾱς *f.* **guide** (W.GEN. *on a journey*) Call.
καθηγητής οῦ *m.* **teacher** NT.
καθ-ηδυπαθέω *contr.vb.* **squander on indulgent pleasures** —*money, time* X. Plu.
καθῆκα (aor.): see καθίημι
καθ-ήκω, Ion. **κατήκω** *vb.* **1** (of a person) **come down** (fr. higher ground) —W.PREP.PHR. *to the market-place* Plu.

2 come down (to fight or compete), **enter a contest** A. Plu.
3 (of a territory, its people) **reach down, extend** —W.PREP.PHR. *to the sea* Hdt. Th. X. Plb. Plu.; (gener.) **extend downwards** (sts. W.PREP.PHR. *to a place*) Hdt. X.
4 (of succession to a kingdom) **devolve** —W.PREP.PHR. *on someone* Plu.
5 (of activities) **come in due course**; (of a turn to speak, military duty, dice-throw) **come round** —W.DAT. or PREP.PHR. *for someone* Aeschin. D. Plb. Plu.; (of a task) **devolve** (as a duty) —w. ἐπί + ACC. *on someone* D.
6 (of things) **duly arrive** (as appropriate or prescribed); (of a time for sth.) **arrive** X. Plu.; (of a time of life appropriate for a task) Arist.; (of a regular meeting) **fall due** D.; (of a festival) Plu. —W.PREP.PHR. *on specified days* Plu.
‖ PTCPL.ADJ. (of the time or day for an event) **appropriate, prescribed** Aeschin. D.; (of the time needed for doing sth.) S.; (of a political meeting) **regular** Plb.
7 (of circumstances) **pertain, be relevant** —W.DAT. *to someone* Hdt. ‖ PTCPL.ADJ. (of circumstances) **current** Hdt. ‖ NEUT.PL.PTCPL.SB. **current circumstances** Hdt.
8 (of things) **have a connection** (w. someone or sth.); (of a law) **relate** —w. πρός + ACC. *to sth.* Arist.; (of things) **belong** —W.DAT. *to someone* Plb.; (of money) **be due** (to someone) Plb.
9 (of regulations, a style of dress) **be suited to** or **appropriate for** —W.DAT. *someone or sth.* Arist. Plb.
‖ PTCPL.ADJ. (of activities or circumstances) **appropriate** Arist. Plb. ‖ NEUT.SB. **what is appropriate** Plb.
10 ‖ IMPERS. **it is appropriate** or **a duty** (to do sth.) D. Plu. —W.DAT. + INF. *for someone to do sth.* Lys. X. Plb. Plu. —W.ACC. + INF. Hdt. X. NT. ‖ NEUT.PL.PTCPL.SB. **appropriate** or **appointed tasks, duties** X. D. Plb.
—**καθηκόντως** *ptcpl.adv.* **appropriately** Plb.
καθ-ηλόω *contr.vb.* [ἧλος] **nail down** —*a statue* (W.PREP.PHR. *onto its pedestal*) Plu. ‖ PASS. (of a gangway) **be nailed together** —W.DAT. *w. planks* (i.e. *be made of planks nailed together*) Plb.
κάθ-ημαι, Ion. **κάτημαι** *mid.vb.* [ἧμαι] | only pres. and impf. ‖ PRES.: 2sg. κάθησαι, later κάθη (NT.), Ion. κάτησαι, Ion.3pl. κατέαται | imperatv. κάθησο, later κάθου (Men. NT.), 3sg. καθήσθω | subj. καθῶμαι, opt. καθήμην | IMPF.: ἐκαθήμην, 2sg. καθῆσο (E.), 3sg. καθῆτο, also καθῆστο (Hom. +), κάθητο (D. +), Ion. κατῆστο, 3pl. ἐκάθηντο, also καθῆντο, ep. καθείατο (or καθήατο), Ion. κατέατο |
1 (of gods, persons) **be seated, sit** (in a place, on a seat, horse, or sim.) Hom. +; (of suppliants) S. E. Ar.; (of a statue, i.e. the figure it represents) Hdt. Arist. ‖ MASC.PL.PTCPL.SB. **seated spectators** (in the theatre) Thphr.
2 (of officials, judges, jurors, or sim., while performing their duties) **sit** or **be in session** Thgn. Ar. Att.orats. Pl. +; (of the Council, a military assembly) X. D. ‖ MASC.PL.PTCPL.SB. **persons in session** (ref. to members of the Assembly, jurors, other officials) Th. And. Ar. D. Thphr.
3 (of persons, troops, commanders, freq.pejor.) **sit idle** Hom. A. Hdt. E. Th. Ar. +
4 (of a commander, an army, troops, ships) **be encamped** or **stationed** (in a place) Hdt. E. Th.; (of a commander) —W.ACC. *on the brow of a hill* E.; (gener., of persons) **be based** or **live** —W.PREP.PHR. *in a place* Hdt.
5 (of persons) **remain, continue** —W.PREP.PHR. *in a certain place* or *condition* Od. Pi. Hdt. +
6 occupy oneself, be employed, work —W.PREP.PHR. *at a craft* Hdt. —*at the banker's table* Isoc. D. —*in a doctor's surgery* Aeschin. —*in a brothel* Att.orats.

καθημερείᾱ ᾱς *f.* [καθημέριος] **daily routine** (of a soldier) Plb.

καθ-ημέριος ᾱ ον *adj.* [ἡμέρᾱ] (quasi-advbl., of a fate afflicting a city) **daily, day by day** S.

—**καθᾱμέριον** *dial.neut.adv.* **daily, day by day** E.

—**καθημερινός** ή όν *adj.* (of activities) **daily** NT. Plu.

καθημμένος (pf.pass.ptcpl.): see καθάπτω

καθήνυσα (Att.aor.): see κατανύω

κάθηρα (ep.aor.): see καθαίρω

καθ-ησυχάζω *vb.* (of a group of people) **remain silent** Plb.

καθῆψα (aor.): see καθάπτω

καθ-ιδρύω *vb.* | ep.3sg.impf. καθίδρυε | **1 cause to sit down, seat** —*a person* Od. ‖ PASS. **take one's seat** —W. ἐς + ACC. *in a ship* Theoc.
2 establish, settle —*persons, an animal* (W.PREP.PHR. or ADV. *in a place*) E. Plu. ‖ PASS. (of persons) **settle down** —W.ADV. *somewhere* Ar. ‖ STATV.PF.PASS. **be settled** —W.PREP.PHR. *in a city* Pl.; (of troops) **be established or encamped** —W.PREP.PHR. *on a mountain* Th.
3 ‖ MID. **establish, set up** —*a statue, an altar* (*in a place*) E. D.(quot.epigr.) ‖ STATV.PF.PASS. (of a god, ref. to his statue) **be established, stand** —W.DAT. *on a headland* E.Cyc.; (of a temple) —W.PREP.PHR. *on a hill* Plb.; (of a sacred spear) —*in a palace* Plu.

καθ-ιερεύω *vb.* **sacrifice** —*persons* Arist. Plu.; (hyperbol., of lovers) —*themselves, their beloved* Pl.

καθ-ιερόω, Ion. **κατιρόω** *contr.vb.* | aor. καθιέρωσα, Ion. κατίρωσα | **1 consecrate, dedicate** (sts. W.DAT. to a god) —*a temple, property, land, booty, or sim.* Hdt. Att.orats. Pl. Plu. —*oneself* (*to death, on behalf of one's country*) Plu.; (intr.) **perform a consecration** Plu. ‖ PASS. (of things) **be consecrated or dedicated** (sts. W.DAT. to a god) Pl. Is. D. Plb. Plu.; (of Vestal Virgins, their bodies) Plu.; (of a person, as if a sacrificial animal) —W.DAT. *to Erinyes* A.
2 (of a lawgiver) **give a sacred character to, sanctify** —*a generally held view* Pl. ‖ PASS. (of a law, treaty) **be sanctified** Pl. Plb.

καθιέρωσις εως *f.* **consecration, dedication** (of buildings, booty, or sim.) Aeschin. Plu.; (of Vestal Virgins) Plu.

καθιερωτέος ᾱ ον *vbl.adj.* (of kinds of song and dance) **to be consecrated** (in a state) Pl.

καθ-ιζάνω, Aeol. **κατισδάνω** *vb.* **sit down, take one's seat** Od. Sapph. A. Thphr.; (of bees) **settle** —W.PREP.PHR. *on plant-shoots* Isoc.

καθ-ίζω, Ion. **κατίζω** *vb.* | impf. καθῖζον, ep. κάθιζον, later also ἐκάθιζον | fut. καθέσω, later καθιῶ (X. +), Ion. κατίσω, dial. καθιξῶ ‖ AOR.: καθεῖσα, ep. κάθεσα, also κάθεσσα, Aeol. κάτεσσα, Ion. κατεῖσα (or κατῖσα), dial. κάτιξα, later also ἐκάθισα | inf. καθέσαι, ep. καθέσσαι, later also καθίσαι | ptcpl. καθέσᾱς, ep. καθέσσᾱς, Ion. κατίσᾱς, dial. καθίξᾱς, later also καθίσᾱς | Ion.imperatv. κάτισον ‖ MID.: fut. καθιζήσομαι, also καθίσομαι (NT.) | aor. καθεισάμην, dial. καθεσσάμην (Pi.), also ἐκαθισάμην, ep. ἐκαθισσάμην and καθισσάμην (Call. AR.) |
1 cause to sit down, sit, seat —*someone* (sts. W.PREP.PHR. *on a seat or sim.*) Hom.(sts.tm.) Hes. Hdt. S. Ar. Isoc. +; **set** —*someone* (W.PREP.PHR. *upon a throne, as king*) X.; (of a charioteer) **bring down** —*a team of horses* (*onto their haunches*) Pl.
2 cause (a group of persons) **to sit down; call to a sitting, convene** —*an assembly, a court, jurors* Od. Ar. Pl. D.; **assemble** —*a crowd of spectators* hHom.; **institute** —*a council* (W.PREDIC.SB. *as guardian of the laws*) Plu.
3 post, station —*a lookout, sentries, troops, or sim.* (*in a place*) Od. Hdt. E. Th. X. Plu.; **set** —*an ambush* Plu.; **encamp** —*one's army* E. Th. X.
4 establish, found —*a precinct* Alc. ‖ MID. **set up** —*a statue* Pi. —*shrines, altars* Call. AR.
5 set, settle —*someone* (*in a house, city, land, or sim.*) Il.(sts.tm.) Hdt. E. AR.(mid.)
6 put in a certain condition, set —*persons* (W.PREDIC.PTCPL. *weeping*) Pl. X.
7 (intr.) **seat oneself** (in order to judge, debate, preside, or sim.); **sit down** (sts. W.PREP.PHR. *in a place, on a seat*) Hom. +; (mid.) Il.(tm.) Ar. Pl. D. Call. Theoc.
8 take one's seat, be seated, sit Hom. +; (of a suppliant) —W.ACC. *at an altar* E.; (of Apollo) —*at the earth's navel, on his prophetic seat* E.; (of judges, officials, while performing their duties) Hdt. Pl. D.; (of the Council, members of an assembly) **sit, meet** (in a place) Arist. AR.
9 (of ships) **run aground** Plb.
10 (of a person) **remain** (in a city) NT.

καθ-ίημι, Ion. **κατίημι** *vb.* | pres.: ῑ in Hom., usu. in Att. | AOR.1: καθῆκα, ep. καθέηκα, Ion. κατῆκα | ATHEM.AOR.: 1pl. καθεῖμεν, ep. κάθεμεν, 3pl. καθεῖσαν, ep. κάθεσαν | imperatv. κάθες, 3sg. καθέτω, 2du. κάθετον (hHom.) ‖ PASS.: pf.ptcpl. καθειμένος, ep. καταειμένος (AR.) | 3sg.plpf. καθεῖτο |
1 propel downwards; (of Zeus) **send down** —*a thunderbolt, drops of blood* Il.(tm.); (of a person) **bring down** —*a club* (W.PREP.PHR. *on someone's head*) E.; **plunge** —*a sword* (W.PREP.PHR. *through someone's body*) E. —*an arrow* (*into one's throat*) Th. —*a thyrsos* (*into the ground*) E. —*a stake* (*into a fire*) E.Cyc.; (fig.) —*a person* (*into sleep, by knocking him unconscious*) E.; **cast** (W.ACC. oneself) **down** (*onto the ground, a couch*) Plu.; **cast** —*a lot* (*into a helmet*) S.; (intr., of a person, envisaged as a storm-wind) **sweep down** Ar.
2 cause or allow to fall downwards (*into water*); **cast, plunge, sink** —*oneself, animals, objects* (*into the sea, a river, or sim.*) Il. Hdt. E. Arist. Plu.; **let down, lower** —*anchors, a sounding-line, a pole* Hdt. —*a fishing-line* Plu.; (intr.) **plunge** —W.PREP.PHR. *into a communal bath* Plb. ‖ PASS. (of a sounding-line, fishing nets) **be let down** Hdt. Plu.
3 cause (liquids) **to flow downwards; pour** —*libations* E. —*poison* (*into a drink*) E. —*water* (*into stoups*) E.; **allow** (W.ACC. wine) **to pass down** —W.GEN. *one's throat* Il.; (intr., of rivers) **flow downwards, descend** Pl.
4 bring down to a lower position; let down, lower —*sails* Od. hHom. A. —*a person, oneself* (fr. *a wall, roof, into a well*) E. Ar. NT. —*ropes* (fr. *windows*) Plu. —*a ladder* (fr. *a ship*) E. —*a club* (*into a child's hand*) E. —*objects* (*into a pit*) X. —*a portcullis* Plb. —*a ship's grappling machine* Plb. —*one's spear* (*into the attack position*) X.; (of a bird, envisaged as a soldier) —*its beak* Ar.; (of ships, i.e. rowers) —*their oars* (so as to stop the ship) Th. ‖ PASS. (of a person, an object) **be lowered** (fr. a height) Plb. NT. Plu.
5 lower (a part of the body); **lower** —*one's hands* (*to one's knees, to the ground*) Hdt. Plb.; (of a person on a bed) —*his legs* (*to the ground*) Pl.; (of a rider) —*his buttocks* (*onto a horse*) X.; (of birds) —*their beaks* (*into a drink*) E.; **let** (W.ACC. one's knees) **sink** (*to the ground*) E.; (intr.) **sink** —W.PREP.PHR. *to one's knees* Plu. ‖ PASS. (of a mare's udder) **be made to sink downwards** Hdt. ‖ PF.PASS.PTCPL.ADJ. (of a leather phallus) **hanging down** Ar.
6 (of women) **let down** —*their hair* E. Ar.; (of a man) **let** (W.ACC. his beard) **grow** Plu.(also mid.); (of a woman, dressed as a man) **sport** —*a beard* Ar.; (of a pillar, in a vision, being transformed into a man) **grow** —*hair* E.

καθίστημι

‖ PF.PASS.PTCPL. (of a woman's hair) let down AR.; (of a beard) allowed to grow Plu.

7 extend (W.ACC. city walls) **down** (to the sea) Plu. —W.PREP.PHR. *to the sea* Th. ‖ PASS. (of walls) be extended down (to a place) Th. ‖ PF.PASS.PTCPL. (of mountains) extending down —W.PREP.PHR. *to the sea* Pl.

8 (of the creator god) **make** (W.ACC. veins) **extend downwards** (in the body) Pl. ‖ PASS. (of a nozzle) be extended down (fr. a beam) Th.

9 let (W.ACC. one's cloak) **trail down** —W.PREP.PHR. *as far as one's ankles* D.; **let** (W.ACC. reins) **rest** —W.PREP.PHR. *on a horse's withers* X. ‖ PASS. (of a horse's bit) be allowed to drop —W.PREP.PHR. *towards the front of its mouth* X.

10 (intr., of a mountain) **slope downwards** Plu. ‖ PF.PASS.PTCPL.ADJ. (of an isthmus) sloping AR.

11 (of a commander) **bring down** (fr. high ground) —*an army* (W.PREP.PHR. *into a region, onto level ground*) Plb.; (intr.) **come down** (into a region) Plb.

12 take down (to the sea), **launch** —*ships* (W.PREP.PHR. *into a specific sea*) Plu.

13 send down (to a place of competition), **enter** —*a chariot team* Th. Isoc. Plu.; (fig., of Sophocles) —*a drama* Plu. ‖ PASS. (of an expeditionary force) be sent to fight Hdt.

14 (w.connot. of underhand behaviour) **send in, suborn** —*rumour-mongers* D. —*spokesmen or sim.* (*to act on one's behalf*) Plu.

15 (fig.) **dangle** (before someone) —*a bait* (*ref. to an appealing story*) E. —*an excuse, an argument* Ar. D.; (gener.) **set down** —*a proposal* Plu.

16 set, lay —*an ambush* Plb.

17 bring or receive back —*exiles* X.

καθ-ικετεύω, Ion. **κατικετεύω** vb. **1** plead, beg, implore Hdt. E.(mid.) Plu. —W.ACC. + INF. someone to do sthg. Plu.

2 plead or beg for —sthg. (W.GEN. *fr. someone*) E.

καθ-ικνέομαι mid.contr.vb. ‖ fut. καθίξομαι ‖ aor.2 καθικόμην ‖ **1** (of sorrow) **come upon** —*someone* Od.; (of a person) **reach, touch** —W.DBL.ACC. *someone, in his heart* (W.DAT. *w. a rebuke*) Il.

2 (of an aggressor) come down on, **strike** —W.GEN. *someone* (W.ACC. *on the head*, W.DAT. *w. a whip*) S. —(W.DAT. *w. a staff, thongs, a sword, one's fist*) Men. Plu.

3 attain, achieve —W.GEN. *a goal* Plb.; (intr.) **achieve one's goal** Plb.

καθ-ίκω vb. **go down** (perh. to Hades) Call.

καθ-ιμάω contr.vb. **let down by a rope** —*a person, oneself* Ar. Men.

καθῖξα (dial.aor.), **καθίξω** (dial.fut.): see καθίζω

καθ-ιππάζομαι, Ion. **κατιππάζομαι** mid.vb. **1** (of cavalry) **overrun** —*a region* Hdt.

2 (fig., of Apollo, new divinities) **ride roughshod over** —*old goddesses, ancient laws* A.

καθ-ιππεύω vb. mount a cavalry charge against, **ride down** —*an army* E.

καθ-ιπποτροφέω contr.vb. **squander money on keeping horses** Is.

καθισσάμην (ep.aor.mid.): see καθίζω

καθ-ίστημι, Ion. **κατίστημι** vb. —also (pres.) **καθιστάνω** (Plb. NT.) ‖ The tr. senses are given first: act. (pres., impf., fut., aor.1, later pf.), mid. (in all tenses), pass. (aor. and pf.). For intr. senses (mid., except aor.; also act.athem.aor., pf., plpf., fut.pf.) see καθίσταμαι below. ‖ imperatv. καθίστη, ep. καθίστᾱ ‖ 3sg.impf. καθίστη ‖ aor.1 κατέστησα, dial. κατέστασα ‖ later pf. καθέστακα (Hyp.) ‖ MID.: aor. κατεστησάμην ‖ PASS.: aor. κατεστάθην ‖ pf.ptcpl. καθεσταμένος (Plb.), inf. καθεστάσθαι (Plb.) ‖

1 cause (someone or sthg.) to stand or be placed; **help** (W.ACC. someone) **to stand** S.; **set up, erect** —*towers, a trophy* Th. Critias; **set down** (in its place) —*a bowl* Il.; (gener.) **stand, station, place** —*persons or things* (freq. W.ADV. or PREP.PHR. *somewhere*) E. Th. Ar. + ‖ MID. **set in position** —*a sail* (W.DAT. *w. ropes*) hHom. —*a mast and oars* E. —*a target* Critias

2 bring to a standstill, **halt** —*one's ship* Od.

3 conduct (someone) to a position; **bring** or **take** —*someone* (W.ADV. or PREP.PHR. *somewhere*) Od. Hdt. E. Th. +; **place** —*a woman* (w. ἐπί + ACC. *in a brothel*) Antipho ‖ PASS. be brought —w. εἰς + ACC. *to a place* Archil.

4 bring —*someone* (W.DAT. *to a ruler*, w. ἐς + ACC. *for questioning*) Hdt. —(w. εἰς + ACC. *to trial*) Att.orats. Pl.; **present, offer** —*oneself* (*for trial*) Th.

5 (act. and mid.) **post, station** —*guards, lookouts* Hdt. Th. Lys. Ar. +; **establish** —*settlers, a colony, a garrison* (*in a place*) Th.

6 (sts.mid.) **appoint, nominate** —*a ruler, commander, jurors, sureties, or sim.* Hdt. Th. Ar. Att.orats. + —*someone* (W.PREDIC.SB. *as a ruler or sim.*) Hdt. Ar. Att.orats. + —(w. εἰς + ACC. *to a position of authority*) E. Lys. Isoc. —(W.INF. *to do sthg. or be such and such*) Hdt. Is. ‖ AOR. and PF.PASS. be appointed (freq. W.PREDIC.SB. as such and such) Hdt. Att.orats. X. Plb. Plu. —w. εἰς + ACC. *to an office* Isoc. D. —W.INF. *to do sthg.* X.

7 (act. and mid.) **set up, establish, institute** —*a tribunal, laws, customs, rites, a type of government, or sim.* A. Hdt. E. Th. Ar. Att.orats. + ‖ AOR.PASS. (of laws, practices, forms of government) be established Isoc. X. D.

8 (wkr.sens.) **provide, furnish** —*remedies, a choice, security* (W.DAT. *for someone*) E. Th. ‖ MID. **make for oneself** —*a living* (W.PREP.PHR. *fr. certain activities*) Hdt.; **begin, set afoot** —*a war* E.; **institute** —*a legal action* (w. ἐπί + ACC. *against someone*) D.; (of a fleet) **effect** —*its departure* A.

9 (act. and mid.) **arrange, organise** —*matters, places* (sts. W.ADV. or PREP.PHR. *in a certain way*) E. Th. Lys.

10 bring, put —*someone or sthg.* (w. εἰς + ACC. *into a certain state*) E. Th.(also mid.) Att.orats. +; **place** —*someone* (w. ἐν + DAT. *in a certain state*) Antipho Pl. X. —(w. ἔξω + GEN. *beyond blame*) Antipho —(w. εἰς + ACC. *in a particular class of persons*) X.

11 make, render —*someone or sthg.* (W.PREDIC.ADJ. or SB. *such and such*) Pratin. Trag. Th.(also mid.) Att.orats. +; **leave** —*someone* (W.PTCPL. *weeping*) E. ‖ AOR.PASS. (of agreements) be rendered —W.PREDIC.ADJ. *invalid* Isoc.

12 cause —*someone* (W.INF. *to do sthg.*) E. Th. —W.INF. (*persons*) *to teach* (W.DAT. *in certain subjects, i.e. institute teaching of them*) Pl.

—**καθίσταμαι**, Ion. **κατίσταμαι** mid.vb.‖ For tr. uses of the mid. see καθίστημι above (aor. κατεστησάμην is always tr.). ‖ also ACT. (intr.): athem.aor. κατέστην, 3pl. κατέστησαν, dial. κατέσταν (Pi.) ‖ pf. καθέστηκα, Ion. κατέστηκα, 1pl. καθεστήκαμεν, also καθέσταμεν, 2pl. καθεστήκατε, also καθέστατε, 3pl. καθεστήκᾱσι, also καθεστᾶσι, Ion. κατεστᾶσι (or κατεστέᾱσι), inf. καθεστάναι, ptcpl. καθεστηκώς, also καθεστώς, Ion. κατεστεώς ‖ plpf. καθεστήκειν, 3sg. καθειστήκει, Ion. κατεστήκεε, 3pl. καθεστήκεσαν, also καθέστασαν, Ion. κατέστασαν ‖ fut.pf. καθεστήξω ‖ PASS.: aor. (w.mid.sens.) κατεστάθην, ep.3pl. κατέσταθεν ‖

καθό

1 take up a position, **come and stand, stand** —W.ADV. or PREP.PHR. *in or at a certain place* Sol. Thgn. Hdt.; (of the sun) —*in mid heaven* S.; (of soldiers) **take up position** E. Th. || AOR.PASS. (of a soldier) take one's stand Archil.; (of the gods) —W.DAT. *against the Titans* Hes.
2 (of a speaker, about to deliver a formal oration) **stand forth** A. Pi. Hdt. E. —w. ἐπί + ACC. *before his audience* Hdt. Th.; (gener., of a person) **come** —w. ἐς + ACC. *into someone's presence* Hdt. || AOR.PASS. (of a god, about to deliver a prophecy) stand forth E.
3 (of troops, colonists, or sim.) **come and establish oneself** (sts. w. ἐς + ACC. at a place) Hdt. Th.
4 (gener., of troops) **go** or **come** —W. ἐς + ACC. *into position, their former positions, to their camp* Hdt. Th. || PF. (of a person) have come —W.ADV. *to a place* S.
5 come —W.PREP.PHR. *to war, battle, a contest* (freq. W.DAT. *w. someone*) Hdt. E. Th.
6 turn —W.PREP.PHR. *to flight* Th. —*to action, an activity* Th.; **have recourse** —W.PREP.PHR. *to a strategy* Th.; **return** —W.PREP.PHR. *to the old ways of life* Ar.; (of a dispute) **develop** —W.PREP.PHR. *into war* E.
7 come (into a certain condition); **be thrown, fall** —w. εἰς + ACC. *into panic, desperation, distress, enmity, danger, or sim.* Hdt. E. Th. Att.orats. +; **come to be** —w. ἐν + DAT. *in dispute* (w. someone) Antipho; **go** (W.ADVBL.PHR.) *back again*) —w. ἐς + ACC. *to a former state* Hdt.; **get** (w. πάλιν *back*) —W.DAT. *in a certain state* (i.e. *revert to it*) E. || STATV.PF. and PLPF.ACT. be placed, be —w. ἐν or ἐπί + DAT. *in a certain state* Hdt. E. Th. + —W.DAT. S.
8 (of an oracle, a city, garrison, navy, form of government, alliance, or sim.) **be established** or **set up** Hdt. Th. Ar. +; (wkr.sens., of an assembly) **be convened** Th.; (of a trial) **be set afoot** Antipho; (of a remedy, form of behaviour) **be devised** Th.
9 (of persons) become established (in a certain role); **set oneself up, establish oneself** (as a ruler) Th. —W.PREDIC.SB. *as a ruler, commander, or sim.* Hdt. E. Isoc.; (of a ruler or sim.) **be appointed** Hdt. Th.; (of a person) —W.PREDIC.SB. *as ruler* Hdt.; **enter** —w. ἐς + ACC. *into an office* Th. || STATV.PF. and PLPF.ACT. have set oneself up, act —W.PREDIC.SB. *as a pirate* Hdt.; have been appointed —W.PREDIC.SB. *as a doctor* Hdt.; have authority —w. ἐπί + DAT. *over certain persons* Arist.
10 (gener., of persons or things) **come to be, become** —W.PREDIC.SB. or ADJ. *such and such* Hdt. S. E. Th. Att.orats. + || STATV.PF., PLPF. and FUT.PF.ACT. have become, be —W.PREDIC.SB. or ADJ. *such and such* Hdt. S. E. Th. +
11 (of purchases) **amount** —W.GEN. *to a certain sum* And.
12 (of events or circumstances) **come about**; (of war) **break out** Th.; (of a disturbance) **arise** Th.; (of a feeling of gratitude) **result** Th.; (of affairs) **turn out** —W.ADV. *well* (W.DAT. *for someone*) Hdt. || STATV.PF. and PLPF.ACT. (of a siege, war, lamentation, flight, or sim.) be afoot, be in progress, be current Hdt. Th.; (of certain winds) have set in Hdt. || PF.PTCPL.ADJ. (of a war, a time of year) current Th. || NEUT.PL.PTCPL.SB. app., present circumstances S.
13 || STATV.PF., PLPF. and FUT.PF.ACT. (of things) be in a fixed or settled condition; (of laws, customs, practices, or sim.) **have become established, be fixed, prevail** Hdt. S. E. Th. || IMPERS.PF. it is established practice, it is normal —W.ACC. + INF. *that someone shd. do sthg., that sthg. shd. happen* Th. || PF.PTCPL.ADJ. (of a constitution, laws, practices) established, existing Hdt. S. Th. Ar.; (of a number or amount, a manner) regular, usual, customary Hdt. Th. || NEUT.SG.PTCPL.SB. established or normal practice Th.

|| NEUT.PL.PTCPL.SB. established laws or customs Hdt. Isoc. Pl. +; traditional views E.
14 (of a lake) settle down, **become calm** Ar.; (of a commotion) **subside** Hdt.; (of a situation) **calm down, become settled** Lys. || PF.PTCPL.ADJ. (of a sea) calm Plb.; (of a breeze) settled Ar.; (of a period of life, ref. to middle age) Th.; (of a person's expression) composed Plu.
—**καθεστηκότως** *pf.ptcpl.adv.* **in a settled** or **composed state of mind** Arist.
καθ-ό *relatv.adv.* [ὅ¹, see ὅς¹] **1** to the extent that, **in so far as** Lys. Arist. Plb. Plu.
2 for this reason, **hence, therefore** Pl.
καθ-οδηγέω *contr.vb.* **act as guide** (for soldiers) Plu.
κάθ-οδος, Ion. **κάτοδος**, ου *f.* [ὁδός] **1** journey down, **descent** (to Hades) Anacr. Call.(dub.); (fr. a hill) Plu.
2 journey back, **return** (usu. fr. exile) Hdt. E. Th. Att.orats. Pl. +
καθολικός ή όν *adj.* [καθόλου] (of a statement, narrative, or sim.) **general** (opp. specific or detailed) Plb.
—**καθολικῶς** *adv.* | compar. καθολικώτερον | **in general terms** or **from a general point of view** Plb.
καθ-όλου *adv.* [ὅλος] **1** on the whole, in general terms, generally X. Arist. Plb.
2 (quasi-adjl., of a statement, narrative, or sim.) **general** Arist. Plb.; (of first principles) **universal** Arist.
3 || NEUT.SB. (w.art.) the general, the universal (opp. the particular) Arist. || NEUT.PL.SB. universal truths (as themes of poetry) Arist.
4 altogether, completely Plb.; (in neg.phr.) **at all** D. Plb.
καθ-ομιλέω *contr.vb.* **1** (of a ruler or commander) bring into association or friendly relations (w. oneself), **win over, conciliate** —*the wealthy class* Arist. —*peoples, the masses* Plu.
2 || PF.PASS.PTCPL.ADJ. (of an opinion) generally accepted Plb.
καθ-ομολογέω *contr.vb.* **1** agree (sts. W.ACC. to a proposition) Pl.; **make an agreement** (over the terms of a contract) And.; (tr.) **agree to** —*an amount of interest* (on a loan) D.
2 (of a father) **betroth** —*his daughter* (W.DAT. *to someone*) Plu. || MID. **agree to, accept** —*a woman* (W.PREDIC.SB. *as wife*, W.DAT. *for one's son*) Plu. || PF.PASS. (of a woman) be betrothed —W.DAT. *to someone* Plu.
καθ-οπλίζω *vb.* equip with weapons, **put under arms** —*persons* Isoc. Aeschin. Plb. Plu.; (fig.) **arm** —(perh.) *a strategy or plan* S.(dub.) || MID. **arm oneself** Plb. Plu.
|| PF.PASS.PTCPL.ADJ. fully armed X. Plb. NT. Plu.
καθόπλισις εως *f.* process of putting on armour, **arming** X. Plb.
καθοπλισμός οῦ *m.* **armour** (of a soldier) Plb.
καθ-οράω, Ion. **κατοράω** *contr.vb.* | impf. καθεώρων, Ion.3sg. κατώρα | fut. κατόψομαι | aor.2 κατεῖδον | pf. καθεώρᾱκα || 3sg.pf.pass. κατῶπται || neut.impers.vbl.adj. κατοπτέον | **1 look down** (fr. a height) Il. Hdt. Plu. —W.PREP.PHR. *upon a place* Il.(mid.); (tr.) **look down upon** or **see** (fr. above) —*persons, places, things* Il.(mid., tm.) Hdt. E. Ar. Pl. X. Plu.; (of the sun) —*mortals* Sol. Thgn. Hdt. E.; (of philosophers, envisaged as gods) —*human life* Pl.
2 (gener.) **have** or **catch sight of, see** —*someone or sthg.* hHom. Hdt. Trag. Th. Ar. +; (mid.) Hdt. S. E.(dub.) || PASS. (of persons or things) be seen or be visible Hdt. Th. +
3 look at, inspect, examine —*sthg.* Hdt. —(W.INDIR.Q. *to see whether sthg. is the case*) Hdt.; **look** (for the purpose of inspection) —w. εἰς + ACC. *at sthg.* Hdt.(mid.) Plu.; **make an inspection** (of a situation) Hdt.

4 look into (or down into), **fathom** —*the mind of Zeus (envisaged as bottomless)* A.
5 see mentally, **see** —W.ADVBL.PHR. *further than others* (W.DAT. *w. one's mind*) Isoc.; (tr.) **see, perceive, discern** —W.ACC. *sthg.* Thgn. S. Isoc. Pl. + —W.INDIR.Q. or COMPL.CL. *what* (*or whether sthg., or that sthg.*) *is the case* Pi. E. Isoc. Pl. +

καθ-ορμίζω *vb.* | *aor.* καθώρμισα | *aor.mid.* καθωρμισάμην | *aor.pass.* (w.mid.sens.) καθωρμίσθην | **1 bring to anchor** —*a fleet* (w. εἰς + ACC. *at a place*) Plu.; (fig.) **land** —*oneself* (*in trouble*) A.
2 || MID.PASS. (of ships, sailors) **come to anchor, put in** (freq. W.PREP.PHR. *at a place*) Th. Isoc. Plb. Plu.

καθ-οσιόω *contr.vb.* **1 hallow** or **purify** —*a city* (*by performing religious rites*) Plu.
2 || MID. (of a goddess) **sanctify** or **consecrate for oneself, dedicate** —*a victim* (W.DAT. *for one's altar*) E. || PASS. (of offerings) **be consecrated** —W.DAT. *on an altar* Ar.
3 || PF.PASS. **be in a state of sanctity**; (of a tribune) be **consecrated** —W.DAT. *to the people* Plu.; (of kingship) —W.PREP.PHR. *to the gods* Plu.

καθ-ότι *conj.* [ὅστις] | in earlier Att. authors καθ' ὅτι, Ion. κατ' ὅτι; see ὅστις 6 | **1 in so far as, on the ground that, because** Plb. NT. Plu.
2 in the same way as Arist. Plu.
3 in what way, how Plu.

κάθου (mid.imperatv.): see κάθημαι

καθ-υβρίζω, Ion. **κατυβρίζω** *vb.* **1 treat brutally** or **dishonourably, abuse, outrage** (by actions or words) —*persons, their bodies, a country* S. E. Ar. Plu. —W.GEN. *persons* S. —W.DAT. Hdt.; **mock, jeer at** —W.DAT. *someone's afflictions* S.; (intr.) **behave brutally** S. Plu. || PASS. be treated brutally Plu.
2 demean —*a dignified occasion* Plu.

καθ-υγραίνω *vb.* (of marshy terrain) **make very wet, soak** —*persons* Plu.

κάθ-υγρος ον *adj.* [ὑγρός] (of terrain) **very wet, sodden** Plb.

κάθ-υδρος ον *adj.* [ὕδωρ] (of a bowl) **full of water** S.

καθ-υπάρχω *vb.* (of things) **be present** or **available** Plb.; (of a land) **be** —W.PREDIC.ADJ. *in a certain condition* Plb.

καθ-υπερακοντίζω *vb.* (fig., of the gods) **completely outshoot** (W.NOM.PTCPL. *in bragging*) —*the Giants* Ar.

καθ-υπερέχω *vb.* (of troops) **be greatly superior** —W.DAT. *in some quality* Plb.

καθ-ύπερθε(ν), Ion. **κατύπερθε**, Aeol. **κατέπερθεν** *adv. and prep.* **1** (ref. to movt.) **from above** or **down from above** Hom. Alc.
2 (ref. to location) **higher up, above, on top** Hom. hHom. Thgn. Xenoph. Hdt. Th. +; (as prep.) **on top** —W.GEN. *of an object or place* Hdt. AR.; **above, higher than** —W.GEN. *a place* Hdt.
3 (ref. to geographical position) **further beyond** (a place); **inland** Il. AR.; **to the north** Hdt. AR.; (quasi-adjl., of places, a route) **northern** Hdt.; (as prep.) **inland** —W.GEN. *fr. a place* Hdt. Call.; **north** —W.GEN. *of a place* Od. hHom.; **upstream** —W.GEN. *fr. a place* Hdt. || NEUT.SB. (w.art., sg.pl.) **the region or regions further inland** or **to the north** Hdt.; (W.GEN. of others) Hdt.
4 (ref. to status or power) **in a position of superiority** Hdt. —W.GEN. *over someone or sthg.* Hes.*fr.* Thgn. Pi. Hdt. S.
5 (as prep., ref. to time) **before** —W.GEN. *certain events* Hdt.; (quasi-adjl., of ancestors) **earlier** Hdt.

καθ-υπέρτερος ᾱ ον, Ion. **κατυπέρτερος** η ον *compar.adj.*
1 (of a god's strength) **superior** A.; (epith. of Zeus) **who holds the upper hand** Theoc.

2 (of people, esp. troops, their fortunes) **superior, stronger** Hdt. Th.; **having the upper hand, victorious** (W.GEN. over opponents) Hdt. X. Theoc. Plu.; **in control** (W.GEN. of a citadel) Plu.
3 (fig., of a person) **rising above** (W.GEN. superstition) Plu.

—καθυπέρτατος η ον *Ion.superl.adj.* || FEM.SB. **highest part** (W.GEN. of a country) Hdt.

καθ-υπνόω, Ion. **κατυπνόω** *contr.vb.* **go to sleep** Hdt. X. || PF.PASS.PTCPL.ADJ. **fast asleep** Hdt.

καθ-υποκρίνομαι *mid.vb.* (of an actor) **overcome** (W.ACC. an audience) **by one's performance** D.

καθ-υστερέω *contr.vb.* **1 be late** (in doing sthg.) Plb. Plu.; **arrive late** Plb.; **be** or **arrive too late** —W.GEN. *for sthg.* Plb.
2 fall behind (on a journey or in pursuit) Plb. Plu.
3 be inferior (to someone) —W.DAT. *in some respect* Plb.; **be badly off** —W.DAT. *in resources* Plb.
4 (of pay) **be in arrears** Plb.

καθ-υφίημι *vb.* **1** (pejor.) **give up** (someone or sthg.); **give up, surrender** —*allies, an opportunity for action* (W.DAT. *to an enemy*) D.; **betray** or **compromise** —*a city's interests* Lys.(cj.) D. || MID. **shirk, abandon** —*one's responsibilities* D.; (fig., of exhausted and famished soldiers) **let go of, abandon** —*themselves* (i.e. give up the will to go on) Plb.
2 (of a collusive or dishonest litigant) **abandon, drop** —*a lawsuit* D.; (intr.) **abandon one's lawsuit** D.; (tr.) **connive at the loss of** —*items in dispute* D.
3 || MID. (of a magistrate, suspected of being bribed) **scale down** —*someone's fine* Plu.
4 || MID. (intr.) **give way, yield** —W.DAT. *to an opponent* X. Men.

κάθω *dial.vb.* (for κάθημαι, imitating barbarian speech) **remain, stay** (where one is) Tim.

καθ-ώς *conj.* [κατά, ὡς] **1 in the same manner that, just as** Plb. NT.
2 to the extent that, as much as Plb. NT.
3 when NT.
4 (introducing an indir. statement) **how** NT.

καί *conj. and adv.* | The wd. has two main functions: (as conj.) connective (1-2) and (as adv.) additive or emphatic (3-6). It is also combined w. other pcls. (7). Only the most common applications are illustrated. |
1 (connecting wds. or cls.) **and** Hom. +; καί ... καί *both ... and* Il. + | For τε (...) καί *both ... and* see τε[1] 3.
2 (after wds. expressing likeness) • γνώμῃσι ἐχρέωντο ὁμοίῃσι καὶ σύ *they had the same opinion as you* Hdt.
3 (additive) **also, too** or **even** Hom. +
4 (emph.) **actually, in fact, indeed** Hom. +
5 (intensifying, esp. w. quantitative advs. or adjs.) Hom. + • καὶ μάλα *very much indeed* Thgn. + • καὶ παντὶ ῥᾴδιον *easy for anyone at all* Pl.
6 (introducing a main cl., esp. following a temporal cl.) Hom. + • ἀλλ' ὅτε τέτρατον ἦλθεν ἔτος ..., καὶ τότε δή ... *but when the fourth year arrived ..., then ...* Od.
7 (w. a pcl.) esp. καὶ γάρ (see γάρ F), καὶ δή (see δή E 2), καὶ μήν (see μήν[1] 7-8), καί ... περ (see περ[1] 5)

καικίας ου *m.* **north-easterly wind, north-easter** Plu.; (fig.ref. to an informer) Ar.

καινίζω *vb.* [καινός] | *aor.* ἐκαίνισα | **1 make for the first time, devise, invent** —*a net* (*to entrap a person*) A.(dub.); **formulate in novel terms** —*prayers* E.
2 experience for the first time, accept as a new burden —*the yoke of slavery* A.; (of a house) **experience** (W.ACC. sthg.) **new** S.
3 be first to experience, be first victim of —*the bull of Phalaris* Call.

καινολογίᾱ ᾱς *f.* [λέγω] inventive use of language (by a dishonest informant), **fictional narrative** Plb.

καινο-παθής ές *adj.* [πάθος] (of calamities) **bringing new sufferings** S.

καινο-πηγής ές *adj.* [πήγνῡμι] (of a shield) **newly put together, newly made** A.

καινο-πήμων ονος *masc.fem.adj.* [πῆμα] (of slave-girls) **enduring fresh misery** A.

καινοποιέω *contr.vb.* **1 make (sthg.) new; renew, begin again** —*a war* Plb.; **reinvigorate** or **re-equip** —*troops* Plb.; **revive** —*people's hopes, their enthusiasm* Plb. ‖ PASS. (of war, people's anger or reputation) **be renewed** or **revived** Plb.
2 renew the memory of, expose again —*people's misdeeds* Plb.
3 do (sthg.) new; (of Fortune) **change** —*many things, the world* Plb.; (intr.) **change events** Plb. ‖ IMPERS.PASS. **new things happen** Plb. ‖ AOR.PASS.PTCPL.ADJ. (of an event) **newly brought about, novel** S.

καινοποιητής οῦ *m.* **inventor of novelties** (ref. to a cook) X.

καινοποιΐᾱ ᾱς *f.* **change** (W.PREP.PHR. in political leadership) Plb.

καινοπρεπεστέρως *compar.adv.* [πρέπω] **in a rather novel way** Arist.

καινός ή όν *adj.* **1 of recent origin or occurrence** (opp. old or belonging to the past); (of events, news, or sim.) **new, recent, fresh** Hdt. Trag. Ar. +
2 replacing that which formerly existed; (of a name, marriage, law, or sim.) **new, fresh** S. E. Ar. Isoc.; (of rain) Ar.; (of a ruler, husband, wife) E.; (of gods) Ar. Pl. X. Aeschin.
3 (of actions associated with political change, **subversive, revolutionary** Plu. [cf. Lat. *res nouae, revolution*]
4 not previously existing or known; (of things) **new, novel** B. Trag. Th. Ar. +; (of a son) **newly found** E.; (prep.phr., ref. to building walls) ἐκ καινῆς *afresh* Th.
5 (of a person) **novel** (W.ACC. in one's thinking) Ar.; (of a servant of the Muses, a guide, commander, host, guest, as fulfilling that role for the first time) **new, fresh** B. S. E.; (of a man, as first of his family to attain a magistracy) Plu. [equiv. to Lat. *nouus homo*]
6 (quasi-advbl., of a person arriving) **newly, recently** E.*fr.*
7 (of things) **not commonly met with** (freq. w.connot. of being unwelcome), **strange, unheard of, unsettling** E. Antipho D.

—**καινῶς** *adv.* **in a new way, with originality** Isoc. Pl.

καινότης ητος *f.* **1 newness** (of appearance), **freshness, modernity** (of old works of art) Plu.
2 novelty (in an argument or speech) Th. Isoc.; (of an invention, an art-form, or sim.) Plu.
3 unfamiliarity (of things, to people) Plu.
4 strangeness (of a person's behaviour) Plu.

καινοτομέω *contr.vb.* [καινοτόμος] **1 cut a new seam** (in a mine) X. ‖ IMPERS.PASS. **a new seam is cut** X.
2 (gener.) **make innovations** Ar. Pl. Arist. Plb. Plu. —W.PREP.PHR. in religious matters Pl.; (tr.) **originate, newly devise** —*a rite, practice, change of wording, or sim.* Ar. Pl. Arist. Plb. Plu. ‖ PASS. (of activities) **be subject to innovation** Pl. D. Plu. ‖ NEUT.PL.PASS.PTCPL.SB. **innovations** Plu.
3 (in political ctxt.) **stir up change, be seditious** Arist. Plb.

καινοτομίᾱ ᾱς *f.* **1 cutting of a new seam** (in a mine) Hyp.
2 innovating (in customs, language, politics, or sim.) Pl. Plb. Plu.
3 sedition, rebellion Plb.
4 novelty, strangeness (of an event) Plb.

καινο-τόμος ον *adj.* [τέμνω] ‖ NEUT.SB. **originality, inventiveness** (of Socrates' discourses) Arist.

καινουργέω *contr.vb.* [καινουργός] **1 adopt a new policy** —W.PREP.PHR. *in relation to certain people* X.
2 (tr.) **newly devise** —*sthg.* E.; **be innovative** —W.ACC. *in competitive events* (i.e. devise new forms of them) X.; **be new and strange** —W.ACC. *in speech* (i.e. say sthg. new and strange) E.

καινουργίᾱ ᾱς *f.* (in political ctxt.) **innovation, change** Isoc.

καινουργός οῦ *m.* [ἔργον] (pejor.) **initiator** (W.GEN. of obsequious behaviour) Plu.

καινόω *contr.vb.* **1 inaugurate** —*a building* Hdt.
2 ‖ MID. (in political ctxt.) **be innovative** —W.ACC. *in ideas* Th. ‖ PASS. (of a state's institutions) **be reformed** Th.

καίνυμαι *mid.vb.* ‖ only impf., pf. and plpf. ‖ 3sg.impf. ἐκαίνυτο ‖ pf. (w.pres.sens.) κέκασμαι, ptcpl. κεκασμένος, dial. κεκαδμένος (Pi.) ‖ 3sg.plpf. (w.impf.sens.) ἐκέκαστο, also ep. κέκαστο ‖ **1 surpass, be superior to** —*someone* (usu. W.DAT. *in a skill or quality*) Hom. Hes. AR. —(W.INF. *in doing sthg.*) Od.; (of a fragrance) —*another* Mosch.
2 (intr.) **be pre-eminent, excel** —W.DAT. *in a skill or quality* Hom. Hes. Ion Ar. AR. —(W.GEN. *among people*) Il. —W.INF. *in doing sthg.* AR.; (of a bow) —*in shooting powerfully* Stesich.
3 ‖ PF. (of Pelops) **have** (W.ACC. his shoulder) **distinguished** or **furnished** —W.DAT. *w. ivory* (i.e. have an ivory shoulder) Pi.; (of a king) **be equipped** —W.DAT. *w. bodyguards* E.; (of Argus) —*w. unsleeping eyes* Mosch.; (of an army) —W.ADV. *well* A.(dub.)

—**καίνῡμι** *act.vb.* ‖ only 3sg.imperatv. καινύτω ‖ (of deception) **prevail over** —*someone* (W.ACC. *in his mind*) Emp.

καίνω *vb.* [reltd. κτείνω] ‖ fut. κανῶ ‖ aor.2 ἔκανον ‖ **kill, slay** —*persons, animals* Scol. Timocr. Trag. X. Call. Theoc. ‖ PASS. **be killed** A. E.

καίπερ (also **καί περ** Il. Hes. AR.) *conj.* **1 despite** —W.PTCPL. (or W.PREDIC.PHR., the ptcpl. being understd.) *sthg. being the case* (i.e. *although it is*) Hom. + ‖ For καί ... περ (the usual order in ep.) see περ¹ 5.
2 (introducing a main cl.) **and yet** —W.INDIC. *sthg. is the case* Plb.

καίριος ᾱ (Ion. η) ον (also ος ον) *adj.* [καιρός] **1 in the right place** ‖ NEUT.SB. **right** or **critical place** (to strike w. a weapon, so as to cause death), **vital part** (of a body) Il. X. ‖ SUPERL. **most vital part** X.
2 (of a wound or blow) **at the critical place, mortal, fatal** A. Hdt. E. X. Plb. Plu.
3 appropriate (to a given situation); (of a prayer) **appropriate, proper** Thgn.; (of speedy action, fear of punishment) S.; (of words, thoughts, arguments, or sim.) **apposite, to the point** S. Pl. X. Plb. ‖ NEUT.SG.SB. **what is right** Pl. X. ‖ NEUT.PL.SB. (ref. to speech) **what is to the point** A. E.; (ref. to action) **what is correct** S.
4 favourable or **effective** (as being appropriate to the needs of a situation); (of circumstances) **favourable** A.; (of a plan, an accomplishment) **appropriate, effective** A. Hdt. E.; (prep.phr.) πρὸς τὸ καίριον *appropriately, effectively* S. ‖ NEUT.PL.SB. **favourable circumstances** Th.
5 appropriate (in time); (of drought) **in due season** Emp.; (quasi-advbl., of a person arriving) **at the right time, opportunely** S. E.

—**καίρια** *neut.pl.adv.* **appropriately** —*ref. to joining in laughter* (at a symposium) Call.*epigr.*

—**καιρίως** *adv.* ‖ compar. καιριωτέρως (X.) ‖ **1 fatally** —*ref. to wounding* or *being wounded* A. Plb.
2 in a manner appropriate for the situation or time, appropriately, opportunely A. E.; **to the point, effectively** —*ref. to speaking* Plb.
3 ‖ COMPAR. **to greater advantage** X.

καιρόεις εσσα εν *adj.* [καῖρος *row of loops, by which the warp threads were attached to the loom*] | only contr.Ion.fem.gen.pl. καιρουσσέων (cj., for καιροσέων) | (of cloths) **closely** or **tightly woven** Od.

—**καίρωμα** ατος *n.* **woven garment** Call.

—**καιρωτός** ή όν *adj.* (prob. of garments) **closely** or **tightly woven** Call.

καιρός οῦ *m.* **1 appropriate degree** or **amount, due** or **appropriate measure** (sts.opp. excess) Hes. Thgn. A. Pi. E. Critias +; (prep.phrs.) καιροῦ πέρα *beyond the appropriate measure, unduly* A.; παρὰ καιρόν Th. Pl. Plu.; ὑπὲρ καιρόν And. X.; κατὰ καιρόν *to the right degree, appropriately* Pi. **2 appropriate goal** (as that which is aimed at, hit or missed) S. Pl.; (prep.phr.) πρὸ καιροῦ *short of the mark (ref. to a missile falling)* A. **3** that which is appropriate to (or needful in) the circumstances, **appropriateness, propriety, rightness** Pi. Trag. Th. +; καιρός (w. ἐστί, sts.understd.) *it is appropriate* (sts. W.INF. *to do* sthg.) S. E. Th. +; (prep.phrs.) κατὰ καιρόν *appropriately* Pi. Pl. +; ἐν καιρῷ B.*fr.* S. Th. +; μετὰ καιροῦ Th.; πρὸς καιρόν *to the point, effectively, appropriately* S. Pl. Plb. NT.; παρὰ καιρόν *inappropriately* Thgn. Pi. E. + **4 appropriate** or **right time** (sts. W.INF. *to do* sthg.) Hdt. Trag. Th. Ar. +; (prep.phrs.) ἐν καιρῷ *at the right time, opportunely* A. E. Th. +; εἰς (ὁ) καιρόν Hdt. S. E. +; κατὰ καιρόν Hdt. Ar. +; ἐπὶ καιροῦ D.; σὺν καιρῷ Plb. Plu.; (also advbl.phrs.) καιρῷ E.; καιρόν S. E.*fr.*; καιρὸν ... οὐδένα *not at the right time* E.; ἀπὸ καιροῦ *inopportunely* Pl. **5 favourable time** (for doing sthg.), **opportunity** Pi. Trag. Th. + **6 favourable circumstances** or **consequences, advantage** E.; (prep.phrs.) ἐς καιρόν *advantageously (ref. to things turning out)* E.; (of a person) ἐν καιρῷ (w. εἶναι or γίγνομαι) *come in useful* (W.DAT. *for someone*) X. **7 point in time, time** (assoc.w. a specific event) Hdt. Th. +; **critical time** Th. X. +; (gener.) **time** or **period of time** Arist. Men. Call.*epigr.* Theoc. Plb. +; (prep.phrs.) ἐπὶ καιροῦ, πρὸς καιρόν *on the spur of the moment (ref. to acting, speaking)* Plu. **8 vital part** (of the body); (prep.phr.) ἐς καιρόν *in the vital part, mortally (ref. to being wounded)* E. | see καίριος 1–2

καιρουσσέων (Ion.fem.gen.pl.): see καιρόεις

καιροφυλακέω *contr.vb.* [καιρός, φύλαξ] **1 watch for an opportune moment for** —*employment (of leisure)* Arist. **2 watch for a bad moment for** —*a city (i.e. wait for a disadvantage on which to capitalise)* Hyp. D.

καίρωμα *n.*, **καιρωτός** *adj.*: see under καιρόεις

καί-τοι *pcl.* [τοι¹] **1** (adversative, introducing an objection or reservation) **and yet, but** Hdt. Trag. Th. Ar. Att.orats. + **2** (connective) **and indeed, and in fact** S. Att.orats. Pl. X. + **3** (concessive, w.ptcpl., equiv. to καίπερ) **although** Simon. Lys. Ar. Pl. Plb. Plu.

καίω, Att. **κάω** *vb.* | ep.inf. καιέμεν | impf. ἔκαιον, ep. καῖον, Att. ἔκαον | fut. καύσω, also καύσομαι (Ar.), dial. καυσῶ (Call.) | AOR.: ἔκαυσα, ep. ἔκηα, also κῆα | ep.inf. κῆαι (v.l. κεῖαι) | ep.imperatv. κεῖον | ep.1pl.subj. κείομεν (v.l. κή-), 3sg.opt. κήαι, 3pl. κήαιεν | ep.masc.pl.ptcpl. κήαντες (v.l. κείαντες), Att. κέαντες (A. S.) | AOR.MID.: ep.3pl. κείαντο (v.l. κή-), ptcpl. κειάμενος (v.l. κη-) | PASS.: aor. ἐκαύθην | aor.2 ἐκάην, ep.inf. κάημεναι | pf. κέκαυμαι |
1 kindle, ignite, light —*a fire, pyre, lamp* Hom. A. Hdt. Th. X. + ‖ MID. **light for oneself** —*a fire* Hom.; **have** (W.ACC. *a fire*) **lit** Od. ‖ PASS. (of a fire, pyre, lamp, torch) **be alight,** **burn, blaze** Hom. Pi. Hdt. Ar. +; (of shooting stars) Ar.; (fig.ref. to a prophet) NT. **2 set on fire, burn** —*persons, places, objects* Il. B. E. Ar. Pl. + ‖ PASS. **be** or **be set on fire, burn** Hom. Hes. Pi. Hdt. Lys. Ar. + ‖ PF.PASS.PTCPL.ADJ. (of a stake, a forest) **burnt** E.*Cyc.* Th. **3 consume by burning** (on a funeral pyre), **burn** —*corpses, bones* Il. S. Is. Men. Call. AR. + ‖ PASS. (of corpses) **be burned** Hom. Pi. Hdt. Th. Pl. Plu. **4 burn** —*sacrificial offerings* Hom. Hes. Thgn. Ar. Hellenist.poet. ‖ PASS. (of sacrifices) **be burned** Pl. D. **5** (of enemy troops) **burn** —*land (i.e. crops)* X.; (intr.) X. **6** (of the sun) **burn, scorch** —*people, places* Hdt. E.*fr.*; (intr.) Pl. ‖ PASS. (of a hound's feet) **be burned** (by heat) X. **7** (of snow) **burn, blister** —*a hound's nose and feet* X. **8** (medic.) **cauterise** —*persons, parts of the body* Hdt.; (intr.) A. Pl. X. ‖ PASS. **be cauterised** Pl. **9** ‖ PASS. (of the insides of a sick person) **burn** Th.; (wkr.sens., of the body) **be warmed** (by ingestion of food) Pl. **10** ‖ PASS. (fig., of a person) **be inflamed** —W.PREP.PHR. *by someone, by love* Call. Theoc.; **burn** (w. desire for sthg. or w. indignation) —W.ACC. or PREP.PHR. *in one's heart* Pi. Ar.; (of a lover's heart) —W.DAT. w. *desire (for someone)* Sapph.; (of lust) —w. *violence* Pl.; (of a listener's heart, w. enthusiasm) NT.

κάκ *dial.prep.*: see κατά

κακαγγελέω *contr.vb.* [κακάγγελος] **bring bad news** D.(quot.trag.)

κακ-άγγελος ον *adj.* [κακός] (of a tongue) **bringing bad news** A.; (w. indeterminable sb.) Call.

κακ-άγγελτος ον *adj.* [ἀγγέλλω] (of sorrows) **brought as ill tidings** S.

κακᾱγορίᾱ *dial.f.*, **κακάγορος** *dial.adj.*: see κακηγορία, κακήγορος

κακανδρίᾱ ᾱς *f.* [ἀνήρ] **unmanliness, cowardice** S. E.

κακεντρέχεια ᾱς *f.* [κακεντρεχής] **malice, viciousness** Plb.

κακ-εντρεχής ές *adj.* **adept in evil, malicious, vicious** Plb.

κάκη ης *f.* **1 baseness, wickedness** E. Pl. **2 faint-heartedness, cowardice** A. E. Ar. Pl.

κακηγορέω *contr.vb.* [κακήγορος] **speak ill of, abuse, slander** —*someone* Pl.; (intr.) **be abusive** Pl. Arist. ‖ PASS. (of a concept) **be slandered** or **reviled** Pl.

κακηγορίᾱ, dial. **κακᾱγορίᾱ**, ᾱς *f.* **abuse, slander** Pi. Att.orats. Pl. Arist.

κακ-ήγορος, dial. **κακάγορος**, ον *adj.* [ἀγορεύω] (of a tongue) **abusive, slanderous** Pl. ‖ MASC.PL.SB. **slanderers** Pi.

κακίᾱ ᾱς, Ion. **κακίη** ης *f.* **1 moral badness, baseness, wickedness, depravity, vice** (freq.opp. ἀρετή *virtue*) Thgn. S. Att.orats. Pl. X. + **2 faint-heartedness, cowardice** Th. Att.orats. Pl. Plu. **3** (wkr.sens.) **poor quality, faultiness** Lys. Pl. **4 bad reputation, ill-repute, dishonour** Th. **5 trouble, misfortune** NT.

κακίζω *vb.* | fut. κακιῶ | aor. ἐκάκισα ‖ aor.pass. ἐκακίσθην | **1 call** (someone or sthg.) **bad**; (gener.) **find fault with, abuse, reproach** —*persons, their behaviour* Ar.(cj.) Pl. X. D. Plu.; **blame** —*fortune* D. ‖ PASS. **be maligned** —W.DAT. *because of bad luck* Th. **2** (specif.) **accuse** (W.ACC. *someone*) **of cowardice** Hdt. Pl. —W.COMPL.CL. *on the ground that he failed to do sthg.* Th.; **make** (W.ACC. *someone*) **open to a charge of cowardice** E. ‖ PASS. **be open to a charge of cowardice** Il. E. Pl.; **be accused of cowardice** —W.PREP.PHR. *by someone* Th.

κάκιστος (superl.adj.), **κακίων** (compar.adj.): see κακός

κακκᾶ *interj.* [κάκκη] | acc. κακκᾶν (as though declinable sb.) | kakka, shit (a baby's cry) Ar.
κακκαβίς ίδος *f.* partridge Alcm.
κάκκαβος ου *m.* three-legged pot Philox.Leuc.
—**κακκάβιον** ου *n.* [dimin.] little pot Philox.Leuc.
κακκείω *ep.vb.*: see κατακείω
κάκκη ης *f.* shit Ar.
κακκῆαι (ep.aor.inf.): see κατακαίω
κακκτείνω *ep.vb.*: see κατακτείνω
κακό-βιος ον *adj.* [κακός, βίος] (of a people) with a poor quality of life Hdt. X. Plu.
κακοβουλέομαι *pass.contr.vb.* [κακόβουλος] | aor.ptcpl. κακοβουληθείς (cj.) | (of a person's soul) be the victim of evil designs E.
κακοβουλίᾱ ᾱς *f.* wicked scheming, evil plotting Plu.
κακό-βουλος ον *adj.* [βουλή] (of persons) ill-advised E. Ar.; (of thinking) S.*fr.*
κακό-γαμβρος ον *adj.* [γαμβρός] (of grief) over an evil brother-in-law E.
κακο-γάμιον ου *n.* [γάμος] (leg.) improper marriage (as a crime at Sparta) Plu.
κακο-γείτων ονος *m.* 1 neighbour to one's misery S.
2 evil neighbour Call.
κακό-γλωσσος ον *adj.* [γλῶσσα] 1 (of a woman) with an evil tongue Call.
2 (of a cry) of evil import, ill-omened E.
κακοδαιμονάω *contr.vb.* [κακοδαίμων] be possessed by an evil spirit, be mad or deluded, act irrationally Ar. Att.orats. X. Men.
κακοδαιμονέω *contr.vb.* 1 be ill-fated, be down on one's luck X. Men.
2 act irrationally Plu. [perh. κακοδαιμονάω]
κακοδαιμονίᾱ ᾱς, Ion. **κακοδαιμονίη** ης *f.* 1 ill fortune, misery Hdt. Antipho X. Plu.
2 possession by an evil spirit, irrational behaviour, delusion, madness Ar. X. D.
κακο-δαίμων ον, gen. ονος *adj.* 1 (sts. w. note of contempt rather than commiseration) ill-fated, wretched E. Ar. Pl. Men. Plu.
2 possessed by an evil spirit, mad, deluded Antipho D. Men.
3 (of a spirit) malign Ar.
κακοδικίᾱ ᾱς *f.* [δίκη] perversion of justice Pl.
κακοδοξέω *contr.vb.* [κακόδοξος] have a bad reputation X.
κακοδοξίᾱ ᾱς *f.* bad reputation Pl. X. Plu.
κακό-δοξος ον *adj.* [δόξα] (of a person) with a bad reputation Thgn. X.; (of a victory) disreputable, discreditable E.
κακο-είμων ον, gen. ονος *adj.* [εἷμα] (of beggars) poorly clothed, shabbily dressed Od.
κακοεργίᾱ *f.*, **κακοεργίη** *ep.Ion.f.*: see κακουργίᾱ
κακοεργός *ep.adj.*: see κακοῦργος
κακοζηλωσίᾱ (v.l. **κακοζηλίᾱ**) ᾱς *f.* [ζῆλος] misplaced ambition, affectation, bad taste Plb.
κακοήθεια (also perh. **κακοηθίᾱ**) ᾱς, Ion. **κακοηθίη** ης *f.* [κακοήθης] wickedness of character, malevolence, malice Att.orats. Pl. X. Arist. Plb. Plu. || pl. displays of malice Isoc. Aeschin.
κακοήθευμα ατος *n.* [κακοηθεύομαι] nasty trick Plu.
κακοηθεύομαι *mid.vb.* [κακοήθης] play a nasty trick (on someone) Men.
κακο-ήθης ες *adj.* [ἦθος] 1 (of persons) having an evil character or disposition, malicious, wicked Ar. Isoc. D. Arist. Men. Plu.; (of a person's conduct, arguments) Aeschin. D. Plu. || neut.sb. evil character Pl. Plu.
2 (of keys w. multiple teeth) nasty Ar.

—**κακοήθως** *adv.* 1 maliciously Plu.
2 with a nasty trick, deviously Men.
κακοηθιστέον *neut.impers.vbl.adj.* [κακοηθίζομαι act maliciously] it is necessary for there to be malicious behaviour Arist.
κακοθημοσύνη ης *f.* [τίθημι] bad management, disorderliness Hes.
κακό-θρους ουν Att.*adj.* [θρόος] (of a rumour) evil-sounding, slanderous S.
κακοθῡμίᾱ ᾱς *f.* [θῡμός] ill will, malevolence Plu.
Κακο-ίλιος ου *f.* accursed Ilios (i.e. Troy) Od.
κακοκερδείη ης Ion.*f.* [κέρδος] dishonest gain Thgn.(pl.)
κακό-κνημος, dial. **κακόκνᾱμος**, ον *adj.* [κνήμη] (of Pans, a person) with ugly shins Call. Theoc.
κακοκρισίᾱ ᾱς *f.* [κρίνω] bad judgement Plb.
κακολογέω *contr.vb.* [κακολόγος] speak ill of, malign, slander, abuse —someone or sthg. Att.orats. NT.; (intr.) speak abusively D.
κακολογίᾱ ᾱς, Ion. **κακολογίη** ης *f.* 1 baseness of speech or expression Pl.
2 slander, abuse Hdt. X.
κακο-λόγος ον *adj.* evil-speaking, slanderous Pi. Arist. Plu.; speaking ill (w.gen. of people) Arist. || masc.sb. slanderer Arist. Thphr.
κακό-μαντις εως *masc.fem.adj.* [μάντις] 1 (of an Erinys, a person's spirit) predicting evil A.
2 || masc.sb. evil prophet AR.
κακο-μέλετος ον *adj.* [μελέτη] (of a cry) concerned with disaster, woeful A.
κακο-μηδής ές *adj.* [μήδεα¹] plotting evil, mischief-making hHom.
κακό-μητις ιος *masc.adj.* [μῆτις] with evil schemes, plotting, wicked E.
κακομηχανέω *contr.vb.* [κακομήχανος] plan trouble Plb.
κακο-μήχανος, dial. **κακομάχανος**, ον *adj.* [μηχανή] (of persons, Eros, strife) planning evil, trouble-making Hom. B. Mosch.
κακόν *n.*: see under κακός
κακονοέω *contr.vb.* [κακόνους] show ill will —w.dat. towards someone Lys.
κακόνοια ᾱς *f.* ill will, malice Lys. X. D. Plu.
κακονομίᾱ ᾱς *f.* [κακόνομος] bad government X.
κακό-νομος ον *adj.* [νόμος] | superl. κακονομώτατος | (of a people) poorly governed, badly organised Hdt.
κακό-νους ουν Att.*adj.* [νόος] | masc.nom.pl. κακόνοι | bearing ill will, ill-disposed, unfriendly, hostile (freq. w.dat. towards someone or sthg.) Th. Ar. Att.orats. X. Arist. Plu.
κακό-νυμφος ον *adj.* [νύμφη, νυμφίος] 1 entailing evil in relation to marriage; (oxymor., of the blessing) of a marriage that brings disaster E.
2 || masc.sb. evil husband E.; unlucky bridegroom E.
κακό-ξεινος ον Ion.*adj.* [ξένος²] | compar. κακοξεινώτερος | (of a host) unfortunate in one's guests Od.
κακοξενίᾱ ᾱς *f.* poor hospitality, inhospitableness Plu.
κακο-ξύνετος ον *adj.* [συνετός] clever in a bad way || compar. cleverer for the worse Th.
κακοπάθεια (also **κακοπαθίᾱ**) ᾱς *f.* [κακοπαθέω] suffering, hardship Antipho Th. Isoc. Arist. Plb. Plu.
κακοπαθέω *contr.vb.* [πάθος] suffer harm or hardship Democr. Th. Att.orats. X. Arist. Men. +; (of philosophers) get into difficulties —w.prep.phr. concerning a particular theory Arist.
κακοπαθητικός ή όν *adj.* (of a person) of the kind able to suffer hardship, hardy, enduring Arist.

κακοπαθῶς *adv.* in a state of hardship —*ref. to living* Arist.
κακο-πατρίδᾱς ᾱ *dial.masc.adj.* [πατήρ] born of ignoble ancestors, **low-born** Alc.
κακό-πατρις ιδος *fem.adj.* | acc. κακόπατριν | (of a woman) **of low birth** Thgn.
κακο-πινής ές *adj.* [πίνος] (of a person) **vile and filthy** S.
κακοποιέω *contr.vb.* [κακοποιός] **1** act wickedly, **do wrong or harm** Ar. X. Arist. NT.
2 (tr., of troops) do harm to, **inflict damage on** —*enemies, their land, ships, equipment* X. Plb. Plu.; **harass** —*an enemy's march* Plb.; (intr.) **inflict damage** Plb.
3 perform badly (tasks which one has been shown how to perform well) X.
κακοποιίᾱ ᾱς *f.* **harmful action** Isoc.(pl.)
κακο-ποιός όν *adj.* [ποιέω] doing wrong or harm; (of persons) **wicked, harmful** Arist. Plb.; (of a disgrace) Pi.
κακο-πολῑτείᾱ ᾱς *f.* **misgovernment** (of a country) Plb. Plu.
κακο-πονητικός ή όν *adj.* [πονέω] (of a person's physical condition) **unfit for hard work** Arist.
κακό-ποτμος ον *adj.* [πότμος] (of persons, their fortunes) **ill-fated** A. B. E.
κακό-πους πουν, gen. ποδος *adj.* [πούς] (of a horse) **with bad feet** X.
κακοπρᾱγέω *contr.vb.* [reltd. πράσσω] fare badly, **suffer misfortune or adversity** Th. Arist.
κακοπρᾱγίᾱ ᾱς *f.* **1 misfortune, adversity** Th. Arist. Plb. Plu.
2 misdeed, wrongdoing Isoc.
κακοπρᾱγμονέω *contr.vb.* [κακοπράγμων] **engage in wrongdoing** Plb. Plu.
κακοπρᾱγμοσύνη ης *f.* **wrongdoing, unscrupulousness** D. Plb.
κακο-πρά̄γμων ον, gen. ονος *adj.* [πράσσω] evil-doing, **wicked, unscrupulous** Isoc. X. Arist. Plb.
κακορραφίη ης *Ion.f.* [ῥάπτω] **evil scheming, villainy** Hom.
κακο-ρρέκτης εω *Ion.m.* [ῥέζω] | dat.pl. κακορρέκτῃσι | **evildoer, villain** AR.
κακορρημοσύνη ης *f.* [κακορρήμων] **abusive language** Plb.
κακο-ρρήμων ον, gen. ονος *adj.* [ῥῆμα] (of prophecy) **telling of evil** A.
κακορροθέω *contr.vb.* [ῥοθέω] utter noisy abuse; (tr.) **slander, defame** —*a person, a city* E. Ar. || PASS. (of a person) **be abused or slandered** E.fr.
κακός ή (dial. ά̄) όν *adj.* | compar. κακίων, ep. κακίων, also ep. κακώτερος | superl. κάκιστος | see also χείρων, χείριστος | **1** (of persons) lacking excellence (in respect of physical characteristics); **poor, unimpressive** (W.ACC. in appearance or stature) Hom.
2 lacking excellence (in respect of ancestry), **low-born, of humble birth, ignoble** Il. +
3 lacking courage, **cowardly, craven** Hom. +
4 lacking strength, **powerless, feeble** Od.
5 lacking excellence among one's kind; (of a charioteer, archer, doctor, or sim.) **bad, poor, ineffective, unskilled** Hom. +; (gener.) **poor, bad** (W.ACC. or DAT. in reasoning) S.; (W.INF. at learning) S.
6 (of things) of inferior quality, **poor, bad, worthless** Od. +
7 (w. moral connot., of persons) **wicked, evil** Hom. +; (of a person's mind) Od.+; (of actions, schemes, or sim.) Hom. +
8 entailing evil, harm or misfortune; (of things, circumstances, emotions) **evil, harmful, cruel** Hom. +; (of a daimon) **unkind, hostile** Od.+; (of luck) **bad** Hdt.
9 (of speech) **foul, insulting, abusive** Hom. +
—**κακόν** οῦ *n.* **1** evil (that is suffered), **harm, trouble, misery, misfortune, disaster** Hom. +

2 evil (that is done to others), **evil, harm, trouble** Hom. +
3 || PL. evil words, **reproaches, abuse** Hdt. Trag. +
4 (ref. to an action or circumstance) **bad thing** Hom. + • οὐ ... τι κακὸν βασιλευέμεν *it is no bad thing to be a king* Od.
5 pest, nuisance (ref. to a person) Hom. +; **nasty swarm** (W.GEN. of birds) Ar.
—**κακῶς** *adv.* | compar. κάκῑον, superl. κάκιστα | **1** in a manner that entails suffering, **miserably, unhappily, painfully** Hom. +
2 in a manner that is morally evil, harmful or offensive, **wickedly, harmfully, offensively, abusively** Hom. +
3 in an imperfect, unsuccessful or mistaken manner, **badly, poorly, wrongly** Semon. Hdt. Trag. +
4 ignobly —*ref. to being born* Hdt.
5 (w. intensifying force) **severely, badly** —*ref. to being hungry, going mad* Hdt.
6 (w.vbs. connoting death or destruction) **wretchedly, horribly** A. Hdt. E. +
7 (coupled W.ADJ. κακός, esp. in imprecations) S. + • κακὸς κακῶς ἄθαπτος ἐκπέσοι χθονός *may the wretch be cast wretchedly unburied out of the land* S. • κακὸς κακῶς ἀπώλετο *the miserable man died a miserable death* D.
κακό-σῑτος ον *adj.* [σῖτος] **with a poor appetite for food** Pl.
κακο-σκελής ές *adj.* [σκέλος] (of horses) **with weak legs** X.
κάκ-οσμος ον *Att.adj.* [ὀδμή] (of a dung-beetle) **foul-smelling** Ar.
κακο-σπλάγχνος ον *adj.* [σπλάγχνον] **faint-hearted, cowardly** A.
κακοστομέω *contr.vb.* [κακόστομος] **speak ill of, abuse** —*someone* S.
κακό-στομος ον *adj.* [στόμα] (of talk) **foul-mouthed, offensive** E.
κακό-στρωτος ον *adj.* [στρωτός] (of ships' walkways) **badly spread, with poor bedding** A.
κακοσχημονέστατα *neut.pl.superl.adv.* [σχῆμα] **in a most undignified or improper manner** Pl.
κακό-σχολος ον *adj.* [σχολή] (of winds that prevent sailing) **bringing unwelcome idleness** A.
κακοτεχνέω *contr.vb.* [κακότεχνος] **engage in dishonest, unscrupulous or criminal acts** Hdt. Antipho D. Men.
κακοτεχνίᾱ ᾱς, Ion. **κακοτεχνίη** ης *f.* **dishonest or discreditable behaviour** Heraclit.; (in legal ctxt.) **unscrupulous or criminal behaviour** Pl. D.
κακό-τεχνος ον *adj.* [τέχνη] (of a trick) **planned with evil intent, malicious** Il.
κακότης ητος, dial. **κακότᾱς** ᾱτος *f.* **1** poor or inferior state, **badness, poorness** (opp. excellence) Hes. Thgn.
2 cowardice, cravenness Hom. A. Hdt. Th.
3 misery, distress, hardship Hom. Hes. Eleg. Lyr. Hdt. S. AR.; **disaster, ruin** Hom.
4 evil-doing, **wickedness, depravity, crime** Il. Hes. Sol. Thgn. Hdt. Antipho
κακοτροπεύομαι *mid.vb.* [κακότροπος] **behave dishonestly or unscrupulously** Plb.
κακοτροπίᾱ ᾱς *f.* evil behaviour, **wickedness, depravity** Th.
κακό-τροπος ον *adj.* [τρόπος] (of a person) **with evil ways** Sapph.
κακοτυχέω *contr.vb.* [κακοτυχής] **be unfortunate** Th.
κακο-τυχής ές *adj.* [τύχη] (of persons, their destiny) **unfortunate, ill-fated** E. || NEUT.SB. **ill fortune** E.
κακουργέω *contr.vb.* [κακοῦργος] | impf. ἐκακούργουν | aor. ἐκακούργησα | pf.pass.ptcpl. κεκακουργημένος | **1** do wrong, **commit a harmful or criminal act** E. Th. Ar. Att.orats. Pl. X. + || PASS. (of actions) be performed

wrongfully or harmfully D. || NEUT.PL.PF.PASS.PTCPL.SB. unscrupulous or criminal actions D.
2 (tr.) **wrong, maltreat, do harm to** —*persons* Th. Pl. X. D. —*a city, land, property* E. Pl. Plu. —*laws* D.; **damage** —*an enterprise* Plu.
3 (of troops) **cause damage** Th. X.; (tr.) **inflict damage on** —*the enemy* X. —*land, a city, a country* Th. X. Plu. || PASS. (of a country) **be ravaged** Th.
4 (of a disputant) **act unscrupulously** (in argument) Pl. Arist.; (tr.) **maltreat** —*an opponent or argument* Pl.
5 (of a horse) **behave badly, be vicious** X.; (wkr.sens., of sweat, when dripping into the eyes) **cause trouble** X.

κακούργημα ατος *n.* **wrong, harmful** or **unscrupulous act** Att.orats. Pl. Arist. Plu.

κακουργίᾱ, also **κακοεργίᾱ**, ᾱς, ep.Ion. **κακοεργίη** ης *f.*
1 wrong or **harmful behaviour, wrongdoing, criminality, crime** Od. Th. Att.orats. Pl. +; **maltreatment** (of a city) Pl.
2 vicious behaviour (of a horse) X.

κακουργικός ή όν *adj.* (of unjust acts) **of the criminal kind** Arist.

κακοῦργος, ep. **κακοεργός**, ον *adj.* [ἔργον] **1 doing wrong** or **harm**; (of persons, their actions) **criminal, wicked** Hdt. S. E. Att.orats. X. Arist. || MASC.FEM.SB. **criminal** E. Th. Att.orats. Pl. X. Theoc. + || NEUT.SB. **wrongdoing** E.
2 (of a person) **harmful** (w.GEN. to others, oneself, a city) Pl. X.
3 (of things) causing wrong or harm; (of a hungry belly) **mischievous, annoying** Od.; (of Bacchic rites) **pernicious** E.; (of behaviour, attitudes, desires) **injurious** Pl.; (of rumours) **ill-intentioned** Th.; (of an argument) **unscrupulous** D.

—**κακούργως** *adv.* **dishonestly** Plu.

κακουχίᾱ ᾱς *f.* [ἔχω] **1 process of doing wrong** or **causing harm, criminal** or **injurious behaviour** Pl.; **maltreatment** (w.GEN. of one's country) A.
2 bad conditions, hardship (suffered by troops) Plb.

κακό-φατις ιδος *fem.adj.* [φάτις] (of a cry) **ill-sounding, ill-omened** A.

κακο-φραδής ές *adj.* [φράζω] (of a person) **bad in counsel, ill-counselling** Il. Sol. AR. [or perh. **bad in perception**, *imprudent*]

κακοφραδίη ης Ion.*f.* **lack of care, negligence** hHom. [or perh. **lack of perception,** *folly*]

κακοφρονέω *contr.vb.* [κακόφρων] (of a daimon) **bear ill will** A.

κακό-φρων ον, gen. ονος *adj.* [φρήν] **1** (of a person, a people) **ill-minded, evil-thinking, malignant** Simon. E.; (of the fruit of the mind) Pi.*fr.*; (of streams) **hostile** (to people) S.(dub.cj. for εὔ-)
2 wrong-thinking, imprudent, foolish S.
3 (of a concern) **thinking of troubles, grim-minded** A.

κακο-φυής ές *adj.* [φυή] **having innate badness, evil-natured** (W.PREP.PHR. in one's soul) Pl.

κακό-χαρτος ον *adj.* [χαρτός] (of Strife, Envy) **rejoicing over misfortune** Hes.

κακο-χράσμων ον, gen. ονος *dial.adj.* [app. χράομαι] (of a community) perh. **difficult to deal with** Theoc.(dub.)

κακό-ψογος ον *adj.* [ψόγος] (of a city) **given to malicious fault-finding** Thgn.

κακοψυχίᾱ ᾱς *f.* [ψυχή] **weakness of spirit, faint-heartedness, cowardice** Pl.

κακόω *contr.vb.* **1** (in military ctxt.) **harm, damage** —*a place, a populace, its forces, its prospects* Il. Th. X. D. Plu.; (intr.) **cause damage** Th. || PASS. (of a populace, city or country, troops) **be damaged, harmed** or **ruined** Il. A. Hdt. Th. X. +
2 harm, injure, maltreat —*a person* Od. A. E. Pl. D. NT. —*a populace* Lys. Arist.; **ruin** —*a house* (i.e. *a family*) A.*fr.* Hdt.; (of a disease) **afflict** —*a person's body* Plu. || PASS. (of a person) **be harmed, injured** or **maltreated** Hdt. Trag. Antipho Pl. Is. Plu.; **be wronged** E.; **be afflicted** or **debilitated** (by a plague, drugs) Plu.
3 speak ill of, malign —*persons* Plu.; **embitter, poison** —*a person's mind* (w. κατά + GEN. *against someone*) NT.
4 ruin, corrupt —*political life* Hdt. || PASS. (of a person's virility) **be ruined** or **destroyed** A.; (of a person's good qualities) **be impaired** —W.PREP.PHR. *by disasters* Plu.; (of a tree's roots) **be destroyed** (by cutting) Plu.
5 trouble, distress —*a person* Od. || PASS. **suffer hardship** or **distress** Od. Hdt. S. E. Plu.; (of a country, a populace) Hdt. And.; (of a horse) X.
6 (of a god) **disfigure, make unsightly** —*a mortal* Od. || PASS. **be made unsightly** —W.DAT. *by brine* Od.

κακτείνω *ep.vb.*: see κατακτείνω

κακτός οῦ *f.* **a kind of spiky plant, thistle, thorn** Theoc.

κακύνομαι *mid.vb.* [κακός] **1 be bad** or **behave badly** Pl.
2 feel disgraced or **degraded** —W.DAT. or ἐπί + DAT. *by sthg.* E.

κακχέει (dial.3sg.): see καταχέω

κάκωσις εως *f.* [κακόω] **1 causing of harm** or **damage; harming** (W.GEN. of an enemy) Th.; **oppression** (of a people) NT.
2 maltreatment (W.GEN. of a person) X.; (leg., of parents, an heiress, orphan, orphan's estate) Att.orats. Arist.; **maladministration** (of a Roman province) Plu.
3 damage, injury, suffering (of troops being attacked) Th.
4 || PL. **injuries** or **afflictions** (W.GEN. of the body) Arist.
5 degradation or **reduction to misery** (of a person) Th.

κακώτερος (ep.compar.adj.): see κακός

κᾶλα ων *n.pl.* [perh.reltd. καίω] **1 logs** (for burning) hHom. Call.
2 timbers (for joinery) Hes.
3 (as Lacon.wd.) **timbers** (meton. for ships) Ar. X. Plu.

κάλαθος ου *m.* **basket** (w. a narrow base and wide rim) Ar. Arist.; (used in ritual) Call.

—**καλαθίσκος** ου *m.* [dimin.] **small basket** Ar. Theoc.

καλαμαίᾱ ᾶς *f.* [καλάμη] (appos.w. μάντις) **a kind of grasshopper, praying mantis** Theoc.

καλαμευταί ᾶν *dial.m.pl.* [κάλαμος] **limed-reed hunters** (of cicadas) Theoc.

καλάμη ης, dial. **καλάμᾱ** ᾱς *f.* **1 corn-stalk** Call. Theoc.; (used to make an aulos) Theoc.; (collectv.sg.) **straw** (in a field) Il. X. Call. Plu.; **stubble** (left after reaping) Od. Arist.
2 straw (as a commodity) Hdt. X.

καλαμη-τόμος ον *adj.* [τέμνω] (of a sickle) **for cutting corn** AR.

καλαμη-φόρος ον *adj.* [κάλαμος, φέρω] (of a person) **carrying a reed** X.

καλαμίνθη ης *f.* [reltd. μίνθη] **a kind of odoriferous plant, catmint** Ar.

καλάμινος η ον *adj.* [κάλαμος] (of houses, boats, bows, arrows) **made of reed** or **cane** Hdt.

καλαμίσκος ου *m.* [dimin. κάλαμος] **reed-stalk** (used as a phial) Ar.

καλαμίτης ου *m.* (appos.w. ἥρως *hero*) perh. **man who uses the splint** (ref. to an Athenian hero assoc.w. medicine) D.

καλαμόεις εσσα εν *adj.* (of panpipes) **made of reeds** E.

κάλαμος ου *m.* **1 reed** (as the growing plant) Alc. X. Theoc. Plb. NT.; (collectv.sg.) **reeds** Hdt. Plu.

2 reed (as the material for roofs, mats, boats) Hdt.; (for huts) Plb.; (for baskets) Th.; (for wreaths) Ar.; (for bedding) Plu.; (for panpipes and auloi) Theoc. Plu.; (used to support the arms of a lyre) hHom.; (to suck wine fr. jars) X.
3 (specif., ref. to objects made of reed) **mat** Pl.; **pipe** (sg. and pl., ref. to the aulos) Carm.Pop. Pi. Telest. Mosch.; (sg. and pl., ref. to panpipes) E.; **rod** (for fishing) Pl. Theoc. Plu.; **limed twig** (used by fowlers) Bion; **pen** Pl. Plu.; **arrow** Mosch.; (gener.) **stick** NT. Plu.
4 stalk (of wheat) X.

καλαμό-φθογγος ον *adj.* [φθόγγος] ‖ NEUT.PL.SB. tunes played on reeds (i.e. panpipes) Ar.

καλάνδαι ῶν *f.pl.* [Lat. *kalendae*] **first day** (W.GEN. or ADJ. of a particular month) Plu.

κᾰλᾰ́-πους ποδος *m.* [κᾶλα, πούς] wooden mould in the shape of a human foot, **shoemaker's last** Pl.

καλάσῐρις ιος *Ion.f.* [loanwd.] **kalasiris** (Egyptian tunic, w. tassels or fringes at the bottom) Hdt.

—Καλασίριες ίων *Ion.m.pl.* **Kalasiries** (members of a class of Egyptian soldiers who wore such a tunic) Hdt.

καλαῦροψ οπος *f.* **staff** (of a herdsman, used as a throwing-stick to control cattle) Il. AR.

καλέω *contr.vb.* —also **κάλημμι** *Aeol.vb.* | Ion.nom.pl.ptcpl. καλεῦντες | ep.inf. καλήμεναι | impf. ἐκάλουν, Ion. ἐκάλεον, ep. κάλεον, Aeol.3sg. ἐκάλη | iteratv.impf. καλέεσκον, also κάλεσκον | fut. καλῶ, Ion. καλέω, also καλέσω (NT.) | aor. ἐκάλεσα, ep. ἐκάλεσσα, also κάλεσσα | pf. κέκληκα ‖ PASS.: ep.Ion.3pl.impf. καλεῦντο | 3sg.iteratv.impf. καλέσκετο | fut. κληθήσομαι, also καλοῦμαι | fut.pf. (w.fut.sens.) κεκλήσομαι | aor. ἐκλήθην | pf. κέκλημαι, ep.3pl. κεκλήαται, Ion. κεκλέαται, opt. κεκλήμην, 2sg. κέκληο, 1pl. κεκλήμεθα | plpf. ἐκεκλήμην, ep.3pl. κεκλήατο |
1 (act. and mid.) **call, summon** —*persons, gods* (freq. W.ADV. or PREP.PHR. *to a place, to oneself, to an activity,* or W.PREDIC.SB. *as a helper* or sim.) Hom. Hes. Pi. Hdt. Trag. + —W.INF. *to do sthg.* Il. hHom. Pi. S. E.; (intr., of fate) Pl. ‖ PASS. be summoned Hdt. S. E. + —W.ACC. *to a council* Il.
2 summon (for the purpose of hospitality); **invite** —*persons* Od. Alc. Thgn. —(W.ADV. *to one's house*) Od. —(W.PREP.PHR. *to a meal*) Pi. Hdt. E. X. + —(W.PREDIC.ACC. *to be sharer in a meal*) E. ‖ PASS. be invited Archil. Pl. —W.PREP.PHR. *to a meal* Thgn. Hdt. + —*to someone* (i.e. *his house*) D.
3 (of circumstances) **prompt** (an action); (of vengeance and murder) **call for, demand, require** —*vengeance and murder* E.; (of a critical moment) —*a certain kind of person* D. —W.ACC. + INF. *someone to do sthg.* S. E.; (of a taste of wine) **invite** —*a purchase* E.*Cyc.*
4 call (to a god, to come and help) Sapph.; (tr.) **call upon, invoke** —*a god or supernatural agent* Pi. Hdt. Trag. + —(W.PREDIC.SB. *as witness*) S. E. —(W.INF. *to do sthg.*) S. ‖ MID. **invoke** —*a god* A.; **call down** —*curses* (W.DAT. *on someone*) S. ‖ PASS. (of a god) be invoked A. E.
5 call out to —*a person, a land* Hdt. Trag. Ar.; (of a swan) —*its dead father* E.; **call out** —*someone's name* E. —W.DIR.SP. *sthg.* S. E. ‖ PASS. (of a name) be called out D.; be mentioned E.
6 (leg., of a magistrate) **summon** —*someone* (W.PREP.PHR. *to court*) D.; (intr.) **issue a summons** D.; **call into court** —*a case* Ar.; (intr.) **call a case** Ar. ‖ MID. **issue** —W.COGN.ACC. *a summons* Antipho ‖ PASS. (of a case) be called Ar. D.
7 ‖ MID. (leg., of a plaintiff) **summon** (a person) to appear in court (on a specified day); **summon** —*someone* Ar. —(W.GEN. *on a certain charge*) Ar. —(W.PREP.PHR. *before a magistrate*) Pl.; (intr.) **issue a summons** Ar. D.
8 (of a court official) **call** —*a witness* Att.orats.; (of a plaintiff) Aeschin. D. ‖ MID. (of a plaintiff) **issue a summons** (to a witness, to appear later in court) Pl.; (of plaintiff and defendant) **summon** or **collect** —*testimonies and evidence* A. ‖ PASS. be summoned (as a witness) Pl.
9 call (a person, place or thing, by a name, title or description); **call** —*someone or sthg.* (W.PREDIC.SB. or ADJ. *such and such*) Hom. + —(W.ACC. ὄνομα + defining adj. or sim. *by a certain name*) Od. E. Pl. —(W. ἐπ᾽ ὀνόματος, ἐπ᾽ ὀνόματι *by a certain name*) Plb. NT.; **give** —*a name* (w. the name itself in apposition, W.DAT. *to sthg.*) Pl. —(W. ἐπί + DAT. *to sthg.*) Pl.
10 call —*someone* (W. εἶναι + PREDIC.ADJ. *so as to be of the same name, i.e. give him the same name*) Pi. —(W.COMPL.CL. *that he is of illegitimate birth, i.e. call him a bastard*) S.
11 ‖ PASS. (freq. STATV.PF. and FUT.PF.) **be called, named** or **known as** —W.PREDIC.SB. or ADJ. *such and such* Hom. + —W.GEN. *someone's child* Pi. S. E.; be called —W.ACC. ὄνομα *by (a certain) name* Pi. Hdt. E. —W.GEN. *after* (i.e. *by the name of*) *someone* Pi. E. —W.DAT. Pi.; (of a name, w. the name itself in apposition) be given —W.DAT. *to a place* E. ‖ PTCPL. (w.art.) so-called Hdt. + • ὁ ἱερὸς καλούμενος πόλεμος *the so-called Sacred War* Th.
12 ‖ PASS. (of places) be located (somewhere) with (such and such) a name Il. + • ἔνθα ἡ Τριπυργία καλεῖται *where there is the place called Tripyrgia* X.; (also act.) • ἔνθ᾽ Ἀρείας πόρον ἄνθρωποι καλέοισι *where there is the place which men call Areia's Ford* Pi.

καλήτωρ ορος *m.* **crier** (ref. to a king's herald) Il.

καλῐᾱ́ ᾶς, Ion. **καλῐή** ῆς, Aeol. **καλῐᾱ́** ᾱς (Theoc.) *f.* **1 barn, granary** Hes. AR.
2 hut (for habitation) Hes. Call.
3 bird's nest Theoc.
4 (pl. for sg.) **lair** (of a porcupine) Call.

καλῐᾱ́ς άδος *f.* **shrine, temple** Plu.

καλίκιος *m.*: see κάλκιος

καλινδέομαι *mid.contr.vb.* [perh.reltd. ἀλινδέομαι, κυλίνδω] | only pres. and impf. | **1** move in an aimless or unsteady manner; (of a vagrant, trapped warriors) **roam, drift** Hdt. Plu.; (of plague-ridden persons) **stagger about** Th.; (of persons or horses) **stumble, tumble** —w. κατά + ACC. *down a steep slope* X.; (of performing bears) **lurch** or **dance about** Isoc.; (of a religious worshipper) D.
2 (pejor.) **loiter** —W.PREP.PHR. *around lawcourts, on the rostrum* Isoc.; (fig., of unclaimed sculptures) —*in a workshop* Is.
3 occupy oneself obsessively —W.PREP.PHR. *in certain pursuits* Isoc. —*in trying to acquire a skill* X.

κᾰ́λινος η ον *adj.* [κᾶλα] (of houses) **wooden** AR.

καλίστρᾱ ᾱς *f.* [app.reltd. καλινδέομαι] **rolling** (of a horse, in sand after exercise) X.

καλιστρέω *contr.vb.* [καλέω] **call out to** —*passers-by* D. —*a god* Call.; **summon** —*a feared creature* (to scare a naughty child) Call.

κάλκιος (also **καλίκιος, κάλτιος**) ου *m.* [Lat. *calceus*] **shoe** Plb. Plu.

κάλλαια ων *n.pl.* **wattles** (of a cockerel, i.e. its fleshy pendent lobes) Ar.

καλλείπω *ep.vb.*: see καταλείπω

καλλι-βλέφαρος ον *adj.* [κάλλος, βλέφαρον] (of the brightness) **of beautiful eyes** E.

καλλι-βόᾱς ᾱ *dial.masc.adj.* [βοή] (of an aulos) **fair-sounding** Lyr.adesp. S. Ar.

καλλί-βοτρυς υ *adj.* [βότρυς] (of the narcissus) **with beautiful clusters** (of flowers) S.

καλλί-βωλος ον *adj.* [βῶλος] (of a mountain) **with fine** or **rich soil** E.

καλλι-γάλᾱνος ον *dial.adj.* [γαλήνη] (of a face) **beautifully serene** E.

καλλι-γένεθλος ον *adj.* [γενέθλη] (of a town, i.e. its people) **with beautiful offspring** Corinn.

καλλι-γέφῡρος ον *adj.* [γέφῡρα] (of a river) **with fair bridges** E.

καλλί-γραπτος ον *adj.* [γραπτός] (of votive offerings) **finely painted** A.*satyr.fr.*

καλλι-γύναιξ αικος *masc.fem.adj.* [γυνή] (of a country or city) **with beautiful women** Hom. Hes. hHom. Lyr.adesp. Pi.

καλλί-δενδρος ον *adj.* [δένδρεον] (of a region) **with fine trees** Plb.

καλλι-δίνᾱς ᾱ *dial.masc.adj.* [δίνη] (of a river) **with beautiful eddies** E.

καλλί-διφρος ον *adj.* [δίφρος] (of horses) **with a beautiful chariot** E.

καλλι-δόναξ ακος *masc.fem.adj.* (of a river) **with beautiful reeds** E.

καλλιεπέομαι *mid.contr.vb.* [καλλιεπής] | *pf.pass.ptcpl.* κεκαλλιεπημένος | **1** (of a poet) **use fine language** (in inappropriate circumstances) Arist. || PF.PASS.PTCPL. (of expressions) **beautifully formulated** Pl.
2 make fancy claims —W.COMPL.CL. *that sthg. is the case* Th.

καλλι-επής ές *adj.* [ἔπος] (of a poet) **using beautiful language** Ar.

καλλιερέω, Ion. **καλλῑρέω** *contr.vb.* [ἱερός] | *aor.pass.* (w.mid.sens.) ἐκαλλιερήθην | **1** perform a sacrifice so as to gain favourable omens; (pres., impf., fut.) **sacrifice for favourable omens** (sts. W.DAT. to a god) Pl. X. D.(oracle) Arist. —*an animal* D.(oracle); (mid.) Hdt. Ar.
2 (aor., pf., plpf., also impf.) perform a sacrifice giving favourable omens, **sacrifice with favourable omens** (sts. W.DAT. to a god) Att.orats. X. Arist. Plb. Plu. —*an animal* Theoc. —*oneself* Plu.; (mid.) Isoc. X. Plu.; (aor.pass., w.mid.sens.) X. Men.
3 (aor., of a sacrifice) **give favourable omens** Hdt. || IMPERS. (impf. and aor.) **the omens prove favourable** —W.DAT. *for someone* Hdt. —(w. ὥστε + INF. *to do sthg.*) Hdt. —W.ACC. + INF. *for someone to do sthg.* Hdt.

καλλι-ζυγής ές *adj.* [ζεύγνυμι] (fig., of a team of three goddesses) **beautifully yoked** E.

καλλί-ζωνος ον *adj.* [ζώνη] (of women) **beautifully girdled** Hom. Hes.*fr.* hHom. B.

καλλί-θριξ τριχος *masc.fem.adj.* [θρίξ] **1** (of a horse) **with a beautiful mane** Hom. Hes. hHom.
2 (of sheep) **with beautiful fleeces** Od.

καλλί-καρπος ον *adj.* [καρπός¹] **1** (of a country) **with fine crops, fertile** A. E. Plb. Plu.
2 (of bryony) **bearing fine fruit** E.; (of an oak) Plu.

καλλι-κέρᾱς ᾱτος *masc.fem.adj.* [κέρας] | *acc.* καλλικέρᾱν | (of a heifer) **with beautiful horns** B.

καλλι-κόμᾱς ᾱ *dial.masc.adj.* [κόμη] (of hair) **with beautiful tresses** E.

καλλί-κομος ον *adj.* (of women, goddesses) **with beautiful hair** Hom. Hes. Lyr. Ar.

καλλι-κρᾱνος ον *dial.adj.* [κρήνη] (of a spring) **with beautiful waters** Pi.*fr.*

καλλι-κρήδεμνος ον *adj.* [κρήδεμνον] (of a woman) **with a beautiful head-dress** Od.

καλλί-μορφος ον *adj.* [μορφή] **with beautiful form**; (of a man's body) **handsome** E.; (of a group of children) **good-looking** E.

κάλλιμος ον *adj.* **1** (of a man's skin) **handsome, attractive** Od.
2 (of children) **beautiful, good-looking** hHom.
3 (of a voice) **beautiful** Od.
4 (of gifts) **fine, splendid** Od.
5 (of a wind) **fair, favourable** Od.

καλλί-νᾱος ον *adj.* [νάω] (of a stream, lake, spring) **fair-flowing** E. AR.

καλλί-νῑκος ον *adj.* [νίκη] **1** (of persons) **glorious in victory, triumphant** Pi. E. Ar. Men.; (W.GEN. over one's enemies, over a riddle) E.; (of a city's fortifications) E.
2 (of a statue, a crown) **for a glorious victory** E.; (of the renown, the joy) **of a glorious victory** Pi.
3 (of a song) **of victory, of triumph** Pi. E.
|| MASC.FEM.NEUT.SB. **song of victory or triumph** Pi. E.
4 (of warfare, a contest, a weapon) **victorious, triumphant** E.

κάλλιον, **καλλιόνως** (compar.advs.): see καλῶς, under καλός

Καλλιόπη ης, dial. **Καλλιόπᾱ**, also **Καλλιόπεια** (Stesich.), ᾱς *f.* **Kalliope** (one of the nine Muses, sts. specified as the Muse of Epic Poetry) Hes. hHom. Lyr. Pl. +

καλλί-παις παιδος *masc.fem.adj.* [παῖς¹] **1 having or consisting of beautiful children**; (of a crowning glory) **of fine children** (for a father) E.; (of a family's destiny) **blessed with fine children** A.; (of a place) Lyr.adesp.(dub.); (fig., of a man, ref. to his speeches) Pl.
2 (of Persephone) **who is a beautiful child** E.

καλλι-πάρηος ον *Ion.adj.* —also perh. **καλλιπάρᾱος** ον (B., cj.) *dial.adj.* [παρήιον] (of a woman or goddess) **with beautiful cheeks** Hom. Hes. B.

καλλι-πάρθενος ον *adj.* [παρθένος] **1** (of streams) **with beautiful maidens** (i.e. water-nymphs) E.
2 (of the neck) **of a beautiful maiden** E.(dub.)

καλλι-πέδῑλος ον *adj.* [πέδῑλον] **with beautiful sandals** hHom.

καλλί-πεπλος ον *adj.* [πέπλος] (of a woman) **with a beautiful robe** Pi. E.

καλλί-πηχυς υ *adj.* [πῆχυς] **with a beautiful forearm** E.

καλλι-πλόκαμος ον *adj.* (of a woman or goddess) **with beautiful hair** Hom. Hes.*fr.* hHom. Pi. E.

καλλί-πλουτος ον *adj.* [πλοῦτος] (of cities) **splendidly rich** Pi.

καλλί-πνοος ον *adj.* [πνοή] (of an aulos) **with beautiful breath** Telest.

καλλί-πολις εως *f.* [πόλις] **fair city** Pl.

κάλλιπον (ep.aor.2): see καταλείπω

καλλι-πόταμος ον *adj.* (of the water) **of a beautiful river** E.

καλλι-πρόσωπος ον *adj.* [πρόσωπον] **fair-faced** Anacr. Philox.Cyth.

καλλί-πρωρος ον *adj.* [πρῷρα] **1** (of a ship) **with a beautiful prow** E.
2 (fig., of a child) **fair-faced** A.; (wkr.sens., of a mouth) **beautiful** A.

καλλί-πυργος ον *adj.* [πύργος] (of a city or land, ref. to Thebes) **with fine towers** E.; (fig., of wisdom) **finely towering** Ar.

καλλι-πύργωτος ον *adj.* [πυργόω] (of cities) **with fine towers** E.

καλλί-πωλος ον *adj.* [πῶλος] (of a land) **with fine horses** Pi.

καλλι-ρέεθρος (also **καλλιρρέεθρος** E.) ον *adj.* [ῥέεθρον] **1** (of a spring, a river) **fair-flowing** Od. Hes. hHom. E.
2 (of a place) **with fine streams** Od.(dub.)

καλλῑρέω *Ion.contr.vb.*: see καλλιερέω

καλλί-ρροος, also **καλλίροος**, ον *adj.* —also **καλλιρόᾱς** ᾱ (B.) *dial.masc.adj.* [ῥόος] (of rivers, springs, their waters) fair-flowing Hom. Hes. Thgn. Lyr. A. Pl.(quot.); (fig., of breath) Pi.

καλλι-στάδιος ον *adj.* [στάδιον] (of a running-track) **with a beautiful course** E.

καλλιστεῖον ου *n.* [καλλιστεύω] **1 prize for beauty** E. 2 ‖ PL. (ref. to a captive woman) **fairest prize** (for military valour) S.

καλλίστευμα ατος *n.* **1 pre-eminent beauty** (of a woman) E. 2 ‖ PL. **fairest offerings** (W.DAT. for a god, ref. to female captives) E.

καλλιστεύω *vb.* [κάλλιστος] **1** (of a woman, man, animal, chariot) **be most beautiful** or **attractive** Hdt. Thphr. Plu.; (of a river) E.; (mid., of a region) E. 2 (of a woman, her body, gifts) **surpass in beauty** —W.GEN. *all women, all gifts* Hdt. E.(mid.)

καλλι-στέφανος ον *adj.* [κάλλος] (of a goddess) **with a beautiful garland** hHom. Tyrt.; (of festivities) **fair-garlanded** E.

κάλλιστος (superl.adj.): see καλός

καλλί-σφυρος ον *adj.* [σφυρόν] (of a woman or goddess) **with beautiful ankles** Hom. Hes. hHom. Alcm. Simon.

καλλί-τεκνος ον *adj.* [τέκνον] (of a parent) **with beautiful children** Arist.*eleg.* Plu.

καλλιτεχνίᾱ ᾱς *f.* [τέχνη] **beauty of workmanship** Plu.

καλλί-τοξος ον *adj.* [τόξον] **with a beautiful bow** E.

καλλι-φεγγής ές *adj.* [φέγγος] (of Dawn, the Sun, sunlight) **shining beautifully** E.

καλλί-φθογγος ον *adj.* [φθόγγος] (of songs, a lyre) **with a beautiful voice** E.; (of a loom, ref. to the noise of the κερκίς *pin-beater*) E.

καλλί-φλοξ ογος *masc.fem.adj.* [φλόξ] (of a sacrificial offering) **producing a bright flame** E.

καλλί-φωνος ον *adj.* [φωνή] (of an actor) **with a beautiful voice** Pl.

καλλί-χορος ον *adj.* [χορός] **1** (of a city, a land) **with beautiful dancing-places** Od. hHom. Pi. B. E. Corinn. 2 (of girls, dolphins) **dancing beautifully** E. 3 (of singing, festivity) **with beautiful dancing** E.*fr.* Ar.; (of garlands) **for beautiful dances** E.

—**Καλλίχορος** ου *m.* —or perh. **Καλλίχορον** ου *n.* **Kallichoros** or **Kallichoron** (sacred well nr. Eleusis) hHom. E. Call.

—**Καλλίχορος** ον *adj.* (of the waters) **of Kallichoros** E.

καλλίων (compar.adj.): see καλός

καλλονή ῆς, *dial.* **καλλονά** ᾶς *f.* [κάλλος] **1 beauty** (of persons, goddesses, animals, objects) E. Pl. Plb.; (personif., as a deity) **Beauty** Pl. 2 **good quality** (of wool, flax) Hdt.

κάλλος εος (ους) *n.* [καλός] **1 physical beauty, beauty** (of men, women, deities, animals) Hom. hHom. Thgn. Lyr. Hdt. Trag. +; **prize for beauty** E. 2 **beauty** (of created or natural objects, places) Il. Hdt. Critias Isoc. Pl. +; (of the soul, learning) Pl. Arist.; (of achievements) Hdt. Isoc. Plu.; (of self-control) Plu.; (of proportion or sim.) Pl. Arist.; (of words, phrases) Pl. Arist.; (pejor., of deceptive words) E.*fr.*(pl.) 3 (concr.) **substance used for beautification, cosmetic** Od. 4 **thing of beauty** (ref. to a person) S. X.; (pl., ref. to fabrics) A.; (ref. to created or natural objects) Pl. D. Call. 5 (wkr.sens.) app. **good condition** (of ships) Th.

καλλοσύνᾱ ᾱς *dial.f.* **beauty** (of a woman) E.

κάλλυντρον ου *n.* [καλλύνω] implement for sweeping (a house) clean, **broom** Plu.

καλλύνω *vb.* [κάλλος] **1 make beautiful, beautify** —*a city* Archil.; (of the moon) —*its face* S.*fr.* 2 **put a fair complexion on, gloss over** —*a discreditable act* S. Pl. 3 ‖ MID. **put on a show of vanity** Pl. 4 **sweep clean** —*a house* Thphr. ‖ PASS. (of ground) be swept clean Plb.

καλλύσματα των *n.pl.* **sweepings, dust** Thphr.(cj.)

καλλ-ωπίζω *vb.* [ὤψ] **1** cause (someone or sthg.) to have a beautiful appearance; **beautify** —*a city* (sts. envisaged as a woman) Plu.; **embellish** or **prettify** —*a name* (by changing its letters) Pl. ‖ MID. **smarten oneself up** Pl. Plu. ‖ PASS. (of a word) be prettified Pl. ‖ PF.PASS.PTCPL.ADJ. (of women) **made up, wearing make-up** Ar. X.; (of men) **smartly dressed** Plb.; (of a house or room) **decorated** or **furnished attractively** X. 2 ‖ MID. **pride oneself** —W.DAT. or ἐπί + DAT. *on sthg.* Pl. X. Plu. —W.COMPL.CL. or ὡς + PTCPL. *on sthg. being the case* Pl. —W.INF. *on doing sthg.* Plu. 3 ‖ MID. (of a horse) **show off, make a good impression** X.; (of a city) **put on a show of vanity** Arist. 4 ‖ MID. **be coy** or **mock-modest** —W.DAT. or πρός + ACC. *w. someone* Pl. —W.INF. *about doing sthg. or not wishing to do sthg.* Plu.

καλλώπισμα ατος *n.* **1 object of beautiful appearance, thing of beauty, work of art** Plu. 2 ‖ PL. (pejor., ref. to certain concepts) **mere ornaments** or **embellishments** Pl.

καλλωπισμός οῦ *m.* **1 creation of a beautiful appearance, ornamentation, decoration, adornment** (of the body) Pl. X. Plb.; **prettification** (of language) Pl. 2 **showing off, making a display** (by a person) Pl. Plb.; (by a horse) X.

καλλωπιστής οῦ *m.* (pejor.) **one who puts on a beautiful appearance, dandy** Isoc. Arist.

καλοκᾱγαθίᾱ (also written **καλοκἀγαθίᾱ**) ᾱς *f.* [καλός καὶ ἀγαθός, see καλός 10] **good and honourable nature, excellent character** (of a person) Att.orats. X. Arist. Plb. Plu.; (of a city, a people) D. Plb.

καλοκᾱγαθικός ή όν *adj.* (of a person) **of a good and honourable nature, of an excellent character** Plu.; (of a person's principles) **honourable** Plb.

—**καλοκᾱγαθικῶς** *adv.* **in an honourable spirit** Plu.

κᾶλον *n.sg.*: see κᾶλα

κᾶλο-πέδῑλα ων *n.pl.* [κᾶλα, πέδιλον] **wooden shoes, clogs** Theoc.

καλοποιέω *contr.vb.* [καλός] **do what is good** or **right** NT.

καλός ή (dial. ᾱ), Aeol. **κάλος** ᾱ ον *adj.* —also **κᾱλός** ή (dial. ᾱ) όν (Hom. +) *adj.* | *compar.* καλλίων, Att. καλλίων | *superl.* κάλλιστος | **1** beautiful in appearance; (of men, women, deities, animals, their bodies, parts of the body) **beautiful, handsome, good-looking** Hom. + 2 (of places, features of the natural world) **beautiful, fair** Hom. + 3 (of created things, such as clothes, weapons, buildings) **beautiful, handsome, fine** Hom. + 4 (of a voice, singing, or sim.) **beautiful** Hom. + 5 (as a term of general commendation, of things or circumstances) good (in terms of quality, practical usefulness or capacity to satisfy or give pleasure), **good, excellent, fine** Hom. +; (also iron.) Trag. + 6 (specif., of a wind) **favourable** Od.; (of sacrifices or omens) **good, auspicious, propitious** A. Hdt. E. Th. +; (of coinage) **genuine** (opp. counterfeit) X. 7 ‖ NEUT.IMPERS. (w. ἐστί, sts.understd.) **it is a good time** —W.INF. *to do sthg.* S. Th. Ar.; (also prep.phr.) ἐν καλῷ S. E.

κάλος

8 (prep.phrs.) ἐν καλῷ *in a good place, in the right spot* Ar. X. Theoc. Plu.; (W.GEN. *for sthg., i.e. some purpose*) X.; *under favourable circumstances* Th. Plb.; *at the right moment, opportunely* E. Pl.; (also) εἰς καλόν S. E. Pl. X. Men.
9 (w. moral connot., of things said or done) **good, noble, honourable, fitting, proper** Hom. + || NEUT.IMPERS. (w. ἐστί, sts.understd.) *it is good, right,* or sim. (freq. W.INF. *to do sthg.*) Hom. +
10 (phr., of a man combining moral excellence w. good birth or social status, freq. as sb.) καλὸς (or καλός τε) κἀγαθός (or καὶ ἀγαθός) *fine and good, upstanding, decent* Hdt. Th. Ar. Att.orats. Pl. X. +; (of a woman) Plu.; (iron., of a man) Aeschin. Men.; (iron., of a woman) Men.; (of actions, abstr. qualities) Isoc. Pl. X.; (of an island) *beautiful and productive* Hdt.; (of an oil-flask) *perfectly good* Ar.

—**καλόν** *neut.sg.adv.* **1 beautifully** Hom. Hes. hHom. E.*Cyc.* Hellenist.poet.
2 (w.art.) **beautifully** Call.*epigr.* Theoc.; **dearly** —*ref. to being loved* Theoc.

—**καλά**, dial. **κᾱλά** *neut.pl.adv.* **1 beautifully** Call. AR.
2 decently, properly, well Hom. Call. Theoc.
3 with good consequences, **well, happily** Hom. Call.*epigr.*
4 with good judgement, **rightly, sensibly** Od.

—**καλῶς**, Aeol. **κάλως**, dial. **κᾱλῶς** (B.) *adv.* | compar. κάλλιον, Att. κάλλῑον, also καλλιόνως (Pl.) | superl. κάλλιστα | **1** in a manner that is beautiful, excellent, correct or appropriate, **beautifully, rightly, properly, admirably** Alcm. +; (iron.) S. E. +
2 in a fortunate or successful manner, **happily, successfully, well** Hdt. Trag. +
3 in a manner or to a degree that is thorough, **thoroughly, fully** S. E. +
4 (w. moral connot.) **nobly, honourably, decently** Od. Hdt. Trag. +
5 (in expressions of approval or thanks) in a manner that is satisfying or deserving of gratitude, **pleasingly, satisfyingly, gratifyingly** S. + • καλῶς λέγεις (or ἔλεξας) *you speak (spoke) pleasingly or gratifyingly (i.e. thank you for your words)* S. E. Ar. • καλῶς γε ποιῶν, ὅστις ἦν *thanks to him, whoever he was* Ar.
6 (ellipt., in approval) **good!, well said!** E. Ar. D.
7 (ellipt., in acceptance) **thank you!** Men.; (also impers.) καλῶς ἔχει Men.
8 (ellipt., in polite refusal) **no, thank you!** Ar.; (also) κάλλιστα Ar.; (impers.) καλῶς ἔχει (μοι) Men.; ἔχει κάλλιστα Theoc.

κάλος[1] *m*.: see κάλως[1]
κάλος[2] Aeol.*adj*.: see καλός
κάλπις ιδος *f.* | acc. κάλπιν, also κάλπιδα (Pi.) | **1 pitcher, jar** (for water) Od. hHom. Pi. E. Ar. X. Hellenist.poet.; (for oil) Call.; (for unguents) Plb.; (for voting-pebbles) Corinn.
2 urn (for bones or ashes) Plb. Plu.

κάλτιος *m*.: see κάλκιος

καλύβη ης, dial. **καλύβᾱ** ᾱς *f.* [perh.reltd. καλύπτω] **1 hut** Hdt. Th. Theoc. Plu.
2 chamber (of a bride) AR.

—**καλύβιον** ου *n.* [dimin.] **hut** Plu.

καλυκο-στέφανος ον *adj.* [κάλυξ] (of a goddess, a woman) **garlanded with flower-buds** B.

καλυκ-ῶπις ιδος *fem.adj.* [ὤψ] (of a woman) **with eyes like flower-buds** hHom. B.*fr.*

κάλυμμα ατος *n.* [καλύπτω] **1** that which covers or conceals (the head or body, freq. pl. for sg.), **head-dress, head-scarf** or **veil** (of a woman or goddess) Il. hHom. A. B. E. Ar.
2 (fig.) **veil** (concealing the future) B.
3 covering, shroud (for a man's head, assoc.w. sorrow or shame) S.; (for a corpse) S.; (ref. to a man's garment, perh. cloak) Anacr.; (ref. to a robe used by Clytemnestra to entrap Agamemnon) A.

κάλυξ υκος *f.* **1 seed-pod, pod, sheath** (of fruit or grain) A. Hdt. S. Ar. Plu.
2 flower-bud; bud (of a rose) hHom. Theoc.
3 || PL. **buds** (ref. to jewellery, perh. earrings in the shape of flower-buds or rosettes) Il. hHom. Call.

καλυπτός ή όν (also ός όν Ar.) *adj.* [καλύπτω] **1** (of a woman) **shrouded** or **veiled** (W.DAT. *in a robe*) Ar.(mock-trag.)
2 (of objects) **hidden, concealed** S.*fr.*
3 (of fat, on bones offered in sacrifice) **covering, concealing** S.

καλύπτρᾱ ᾱς, Ion. **καλύπτρη** ης *f.* **1** covering (for the head of a woman or goddess), **head-dress, head-scarf** or **veil** Hom. Hes. Ibyc. A. Parm. Pl. +
2 headgear, hat (of a man) Call.
3 cover, lid (of a quiver) Hdt.
4 (fig.) **veil** (of darkness) A.

καλύπτω *vb.* | fut. καλύψω | aor. ἐκάλυψα || PASS.: aor. ἐκαλύφθην | pf. κεκάλυμμαι | **1** cover up or envelop (for concealment or protection); (of a god) **cover, shroud** —*a person, a place* (W.DAT. *in darkness, mist, a cloud*) Il. E.; (of darkness, mist, a cloud) —*persons, a house* A. AR. || PF. or PLPF.PASS. (of persons, places, ships) **be covered** or **shrouded** —W.DAT. *in mist, clouds* Hom. Hes. hHom.
2 cover, protect —*a ship* (W.DAT. *w. spears and shields, against overhead attack by birds*) AR.; (of a piece of armour) —*part of the body* X.; (mid., of a warrior) —*his body* (W.DAT. *w. a shield*) Tyrt. || PF. or PLPF.PASS. **be covered** or **protected** —W.DAT. *by bronze armour, a shield* Il.
3 cover up, shroud —*a corpse* (usu. W.DAT. *w. a sheet, a robe*) Il. S. E. || PF.PASS.PTCPL. (of a corpse) **shrouded** Men.
4 cover up (beneath the ground); (of Tartaros) **cover, envelop** —*a deposed god* A.; (of earth) —*the dead* A. Lycurg.; (of persons) —*the dead, their bodies* (usu. W.DAT. *w. earth, a tomb, i.e. bury them*) Pi. Trag.; (of death) —*a person's body* E.; (hyperbol., of hills) **cover, bury** —*persons* NT. || PASS. (of corpses) **be covered** —W.DAT. *w. earth* E.
5 cover up (w. clothing or sim.); **cover** —*one's face* (w. *one's cloak*) Od. —*one's back* (W.DAT. *w. a leopard-skin*) Il. —*one's breasts* (w. *one's robe*) E. —*a person* (w. *a cloak*) Archil. —*a baby* (W.PREP.PHR. *in animal-skins*) hHom.; (of sandals) —*feet* Sapph. || MID. **cover up** —*one's face, head, flesh* (W.DAT. *w. a garment*) Hes. hHom. AR.; **cover** or **shroud oneself** —W.DAT. *w. a garment, a head-dress* Il. AR. —*w. leaves* Od.; **shroud one's head** (in *one's cloak*) Od. Thgn. Ar. AR.
|| PF.PASS.PTCPL. **covered up** —W.DAT. or PREP.PHR. *by a sheep's fleece, in one's cloak, over one's head* Hom. hHom.; *with one's head shrouded* X.
6 cover up, wrap up —*bones* (W.DAT. *in cloths*) Il. —*entrails* (*in an ox's stomach*) Hes.
7 (of death, the darkness of sleep or death, grief, a cloud of grief) **cover, envelop** —*a person, the eyes* Hom. Hes.*fr.* hHom. B.; (of a person) —*another* (W.DAT. *in the darkness of death, i.e. kill him*) Il.
8 (of a wave) **cover, envelop** —*a person, a fish* Hom.; (of the sea) **engulf** —*a ship* Men. || PASS. (of a ship) **be engulfed** —W.PREP.PHR. *by waves* NT.
9 (gener.) **cover** or **overlay** (sthg., usu. W.DAT. *w. sthg. else*); (of persons or gods) **cover** —*a corpse, sacrificial bones* (W.DAT. *w. animal fat*) Hom. Hes. AR. —*the earth* (w. *snow, a*

cloud) Il. —*a beach* (w. *sand*) Il. —*a tomb* (w. *vine-clusters*) E. ‖ PASS. (of arrows) be covered —W.DAT. w. *feathers* Hes. ‖ PF.PASS.PTCPL. (fig., of a deed) shrouded —W.DAT. *in danger* Pi.

10 conceal from sight, **conceal, hide** —*a person* S. —*a lamp* (W.DAT. *in a container*) NT. —*light* (w. *darkness*) Pi.*fr*.; (of a lion) **veil, hood** —*its eyes* (*by lowering its brow*) Il. ‖ PASS. (of persons, things, behaviour) be concealed Od. Plu. ‖ PF.PASS.PTCPL. concealed Hom. Ar.(cj.) NT.

11 conceal from the knowledge of others, **conceal, hide** —*things heard, a crime, an accomplishment, thoughts, feelings* Pi. S. E.; (of a miserable fate) —*persons* (*by condemning them to live in obscurity*) AR.

12 cause (sthg.) to be a protection or covering; **hold** (W.ACC. a shield, a garment) **as a cover** —W.PREP.PHR. *around or before someone, before one's chest* Il.; (of a river) **pour** (W.ACC. silt) **as a covering** —W.DAT. *over a corpse* Il.

13 (fig.) cast a veil of dishonour over, **cloud the fame of** —*a city* S.; (of another's fame) **overshadow** —*a person* AR.

κάλχᾱ ᾱς *dial.f*. [reltd. κάλχη *purple shellfish, murex*] a kind of purple flower Alcm.

καλχαίνω *vb*. make or be purple; (fig.) **be darkly troubled in one's mind, brood deeply** —w. ἀμφί + DAT. *over children in one's care* E. —W.ACC. *over news* S. ‖ cf. πορφύρω 2

Κάλχας αντος *m*. Kalkhas (seer accompanying the Greek expedition to Troy) Il. Hes.*fr*. Trag.

καλῴδιον ου *n*. [dimin. κάλως¹] **rope, cord** Th. Ar. Men. Plb. Plu.

κάλως¹ ω *m*. (*also f*. Ibyc.) | acc. κάλων ‖ PL.: ep.nom. κάλωες (AR.) | acc. κάλως, ep. κάλωας (AR.) | dat. κάλως | —also **κάλος** ου (Od. Hdt. Plb. Plu.) *m*. | acc. κάλον ‖ PL.: acc. κάλους | dat. κάλοις | **1 rope, sheet** or **halyard** (as part of a ship's rigging) Ibyc. AR. Plu.

2 (specif., pl.) **brailing-rope, brail** (used to set the effective area of a sail, by raising and lowering its bottom edge) Od. Hdt. Plb. Plu.; (in phr., *let out the brails*, ref. to using the full sail) E.; (fig., ref. to making a great effort) E. Ar. Pl. | see ἐκτείνω 6, ἐξίημι 3

3 rope or **cable** (used for towing a ship) Hdt. Th. Ar.; (as a sounding-line) Hdt.; (ref. to a stern-cable) E.; (used w. various mechanisms on deck) Plb.

4 rope (used as a noose) Hdt. Ar.

κάλως² *Aeol.adv*.: see under καλός

καλω-στρόφος ου *m*. [κάλως¹, στρέφω] one who makes ropes by twisting (thread), **rope-maker** Plu.

κάμ *dial.prep*.: see κατά

καμάκινος η ον *adj*. [κάμαξ] (of a spear) app. **cane-shafted** X.

κάμαξ ακος *f*. **1 pole** (supporting vines) Il. Hes.

2 shaft (of a spear, meton. for spear) A. E. Plu.(oracle)

καμάρη ης *Ion.f*. **covered cart** Hdt.

καματηρός ά (Ion. ή) όν *adj*. [κάματος] **1** causing or caused by weariness; (of old age) **wearisome** hHom.; (of fatigue) Ar.; (of panting) **from weariness** AR.

2 (of soldiers) **worn out, exhausted** or **unwell** Hdt.

κάματος ου *m*. [κάμνω] **1** (sg. and pl.) toilsome effort, **toil, labour** Hom. Hes. Pi. S. E. Critias +

2 (sg.) effect of toil, **weariness, exhaustion, fatigue** Hom. hHom. Hdt. E. AR. Plu.

3 physical and emotional suffering, **distress** AR.

4 condition of being unwell, **illness** Simon.

5 (concr.) product of toil, **labour, hard work** (of oneself or others) Hom. Hes. Thgn.; (W.GEN. of the lathe, ref. to an aulos) A.*fr*.

καματώδης ες *adj*. **1** (of summer, i.e. its heat; of a boxer's blows) causing physical tiredness, **fatiguing** Hes. Pi.

2 (of cares) causing emotional weariness, **wearisome** Pi.*fr*.

καμεῖν (aor.2 inf.): see κάμνω

κάμηλος ου *f*. [Semit.loanwd.] **1 camel** A. Hdt. Ar. X. +

2 (collectv.) corps of camels, **camelry** (in an army) Hdt.

κάμῑνος ου *f*. **1 oven** (for roasting) Hdt.

2 kiln (for firing bricks, earthenware) Hdt. Critias Call. Plu.

3 furnace (for smelting, metalwork) X. Call.

4 furnace (W.GEN. of fire, ref. to Hell) NT.

—καμῑνόθεν *adv*. **from the furnace** Call.

καμῑνώ όος *f*. | only dat. καμῑνοῖ | (pejor., appos.w. γραῦς) **oven-woman** Od.

καμμονίη ης *ep.Ion.f*. [reltd. καταμονή] **power of endurance** Il.

κάμμορος ον *ep.adj*. [κατά, μόρος] (of a person) **ill-fated, unlucky, unhappy** Od. AR.

καμμύω *vb*.: see καταμύω

κάμνω *vb*. | fut. καμοῦμαι, ep.inf. καμέεσθαι (AR.) | aor.2 ἔκαμον, ep. κάμον, inf. καμεῖν, ep. καμέειν (AR.) | pf. κέκμηκα, ptcpl. κεκμηκώς, dial. κεκμᾱκώς (Theoc.), ep. κεκμηώς (gen. κεκμηῶτος, also κεκμηότος) |

1 toil, labour, strive, exert oneself Hom. E. Th. Hellenist.poet. Plu.

2 (tr.) **labour to create** —*clothes, armour, ships, a city, or sim.* Hom. B. AR.(also mid.) Theoc. —*an island* (W.PREDIC.ADJ. *furnished w. fine buildings*) Od.(mid.); **labour to win** —*captive women* Il.(mid.)

3 (wkr.sens.) labour over, **undertake, accomplish** —*an act* AR.(also mid.)

4 (intr.) **grow weary, become tired** or **exhausted** (freq. W.PTCPL. fr. doing sthg.) Hom. Hdt. E. Ar. X. Arist. +; (in neg.phr., esp. a command or wish) **tire** —W.PTCPL. *of doing sthg*. A. Pi. B. E. Ar. Pl. + —W.DAT. *in expenditure* (i.e. of spending) Pi. ‖ PF. and PLPF. be weary, tired or exhausted Hom. Th. Hellenist.poet. Plu.

5 be sick, ill or **unwell** Hdt. S. Th. Ar. Att.orats. Pl. + —W.COGN.ACC. w. *a sickness* E. Arist.; **suffer from an ailment** —W.ACC. *in the eyes, the body* Hdt. Pl. ‖ AOR. fall ill Hdt. Att.orats. X. Men. Plu. —W.ACC. w. *a sickness* Pl. —W.DAT. Plu.

6 (gener., of persons, troops, ships) **suffer, be in trouble** or **distress** Pi. Hdt. Trag. Ar. AR.; **be in difficulties** —W.DAT. *over free time* (i.e. be pressed for time) E.

7 (of abstr. things) be deficient; (of fruitfulness) **fail** A.; (of misfortunes) **abate** E.; (of an argument) **be weak** E.; (of a journey) **founder** (i.e. be held up) E.

8 ‖ AOR.PTCPL. (of persons) deceased, **dead** Hom. AR.; (masc.pl., as sb.) **dead men** Hom. Alcm. A. Theoc.

9 ‖ MASC.PL.PF.PTCPL.SB. (w.art.) **the dead** A. E. Th. Pl. Arist.

καμπή ῆς *f*. [κάμπτω] **1 bend, curve** (in a river) Hdt.

2 turning-post (of a racecourse) E. Ar. Pl.; (fig., ref. to a headland) A.*satyr.fr*.; (fig., ref. to the beginning of the second stage of a plan of action) E.

3 reversal of direction, **turn** Pl.

4 bending, flexion (of parts of the body) Pl.; **joint** (in the body) Arist.

5 bend or **curvature** (opp. straightness) Plu.

6 (mus.) **bend, twist, turn** (in a scale, rhythm or tuning, ref. to a modulation) Ar.

κάμπιμος η ον *adj*. **1** (fig., of courses or laps, completed by a fugitive envisaged as a charioteer) round a turning-post, **turning, back-and-forth** E.

2 (of cycles of years) **turning, revolving** E.(cj.)

καμπτήρ ῆρος *m.* **1** **turning-post** (at either end of a racecourse); (in ctxt.) **finishing-post** Arist.
2 **turning-point** (for an army's wing, as it adopts a position at angles to the main body) X.

καμπτός ή όν *adj.* (of limbs) **flexible** Pl.

κάμπτω *vb.* | fut. κάμψω | aor. ἔκαμψα ‖ PASS.: aor. ἐκάμφθην | pf.ptcpl. κεκαμμένος ‖ The sections are grouped as: (1–5) bend or curve (things), (6–12) make a curving movement, (13–14) humble or sway (persons). |
1 force into an arched or angular shape, **bend** —*a spit* Ar. —*saplings* Theoc. —*the branch of a tree* (W.PREP.PHR. *towards the ground*) E. ‖ PASS. (of objects, trees) **be bent** X. Arist. Theoc. Plb. Plu. ‖ PASS.PTCPL.ADJ. (pres., of a piece of wood) **bent** Pl.; (pf., of a line) Arist.
2 create by bending, **bend into shape** —*a felloe* (i.e. wheel-rim) Il. —(fig.) *felloes of words* Ar.
3 (of a wounded soldier) **bend, double over** —*his flanks and stomach* E. —*his body* Plu. ‖ MID. (of a person) **bend, flex** —*one's limbs* Pl. ‖ MID.PASS. (of an acrobat) **bend oneself** —W.PREP.PHR. *backwards* X.; (of the body) **bend** (at the joints) Pl.
4 (of a horse) **bend** —*its knees* (in walking) X. —*its legs* (W.PREP.PHR. *at the knees*) X.
5 (of a person) **bend** —*one's knee or knees* (so as to sit and rest) Il. A. E. AR.; (of a bird, in alighting after flight) A. Call.; (of a person) **rest** —*one's limbs* (by sitting) S.; (intr.) bend the knee, **sit down, rest** S. E.; **allow** (W.ACC. one's knees and arms) **to sag** (fr. exhaustion) Od.
6 make a curving movement (around a turning-post, in a race); (intr., of a charioteer, horse, runner) **go round the turning-post** S. X. Plu.; **make a turn** —W.PREP.PHR. *around the turning-post* Theoc.; (of a sea-monster, envisaged as a charioteer) **round** —W.COGN.ACC. *the turning-post* (of an island, fig.ref. to a headland) A.satyr.fr.(cj.); (tr., of a runner or charioteer, envisaged as rounding or having rounded the turning-post) **run** —*the second leg* (of a two-leg race) A.; **run or complete** —*a course* B.; (fig.) —*a second journey* (i.e. do sthg. a second time) Call. —*the last part* (W.GEN. of life, i.e. die) E.; **run the last leg of** —*life* (i.e. die) S. E.; **bring an end to** —*troubles* E.
7 (gener., of a horse or rider) **make a turn** X. Plu.
8 (of troops) **wheel** —W.PREP.PHR. *around a turning-point* X.
9 (of sailors) **double round** (a landmark); **round** —*a headland* Hdt. Plb. Plu. —*a bay* Hdt.; **double** —W. περί + ACC. *round a headland* Ar. Plb.; **make a turn** (round a headland) Plb.
10 (gener., of a person) **double** —W.ADV. *back* E.; **turn round, double back** Men.
11 (wkr.sens.) **follow** —*a path, lane* Call. Theoc.*epigr.*
12 (mus.) **make** —W.COGN.ACC. *a bend* (i.e. a modulation in scale, rhythm or tuning) Ar.
13 cause (someone) to bend or stoop; (fig., of a god) **bow down, bring low, humble** —*an arrogant mortal* Pi. ‖ PASS. (of a person) **be bent** (opp. upright, w. both physical and moral connot.) Pl.; **be bowed down** (by a misfortune) Plu. —W.DAT. *by sufferings* A.; (fig., of snow) **be humbled** (by being stored underground for use in cooling wine) Simon.
14 ‖ PASS. **be swayed** (by an argument or plea) Th. Pl. Plu.; **give way, relent** (in one's attitude) Plu.

καμπύλος η ον *adj.* **1** (of a bow) **bent, curved, curving** Hom. hHom. AR.; (of a chariot, ref. to its front rail) Il. Hes. A. Pi.; (of a plough) hHom. Sol.; (of a wheel) Il.; (of a line, staff, mason's rule) Ar. Plu.; (of a quarry's tracks) X.; (of objects seen in water) Pl.; (fig., of a song) Pi.*fr.*

2 ‖ NEUT.SB. **curvedness, curvature** Arist.; (concr.) **curved line, curve** Arist.

καμψι-δίαυλος ον *adj.* **rounding the turning-post in a two-leg race**; (fig., of a hand playing on a stringed instrument) **coursing up and down** Telest.

καμψί-πους ποδος *masc.fem.adj.* [πούς] (of an Erinys) **bending the foot** (i.e. leg), **swift-footed** A.

κάμψις εως *f.* **1 bending** (of limbs) Pl.
2 joint (of a limb or sim.) Arist.

κάν *dial.prep.*: see κατά

κἄν: crasis for καὶ ἄν (or ἄν)

καναφόρος *dial.f.*: see κανηφόρος

καναχά-πους ποδος *dial.masc.fem.adj.* [πούς] (of a horse) **with clattering hooves** Alcm.

καναχέω *contr.vb.* [καναχή] (of a bronze basin) **ring out** Od.; (tr., of Orpheus) —*a melody* (w. his lyre) AR.

καναχή ῆς, dial. **καναχά** ᾶς *f.* **1 ringing sound, clang** (of armour) Il. Tyrt. B. S.
2 ringing strains (of musical instruments) hHom. Pi. B. S.
3 clatter, din (of galloping mules) Od.
4 sound of gnashing (of teeth) Il. Hes.

καναχηδά *adv.* **1 with a roar** —*ref. to rivers flowing* Hes. Call. AR.
2 with ringing notes —*ref. to a victor's headband* (meton. for a song of victory) *being embellished* Pi.

καναχής ές *adj.* (of tears) **splashing** A.

καναχίζω *vb.* (of timbers, the earth) **ring out, resound** (w. blows, hoof-beats) Il. Hes.

κάνδαυλος, also **κάνδυλος**, ου *m.* [loanwd.] a kind of Lydian stew Men.

κάνδυς υος *m.* [loanwd.] sleeved Persian overgarment, **jacket, coat** X. Plu.

κανδύτᾱνες ων *m.pl.* containers for storing clothes, **trunks, chests** Men.

κάνεον (also ep. **κάνειον**) ου, Att. **κανοῦν** οῦ *n.* [κάνναι]
1 basket (for serving food) Hom. Hdt. Philox.Leuc. Theoc.
2 basket (for barley grains and sacrificial implements, sts. carried in a procession) Od. E. Th. Ar. Aeschin. D. +; (made of gold) E.(dub.)
3 bowl, dish (of gold or bronze, for food) Hom.

κάνης ητος *m.* **reed-mat** Plu.

κανηφορέω *contr.vb.* [κανηφόρος] (of a young girl) **serve as basket-carrier** Ar. Arist.; (fig., of a sieve, white w. flour, envisaged as the young girl whitened w. cosmetics) Ar.

κανηφορία ᾶς *f.* **act of serving as basket-carrier** Pl.

κανη-φόρος, dial. **καναφόρος**, ου *f.* [κάνεον, φέρω] **basket-carrier** (ref. to a young girl who carried the basket, containing items needed for a sacrifice, in a religious procession) Ar. Theoc.

κάνθαρος ου *m.* **1 dung-beetle** Hippon. S.*Ichn.* Ar. Plu.; (w. play on sense 3) Ar.; (gener.) **beetle** (as a pest of fig trees) Theoc.
2 mark in the form of a scarab-beetle, **scarab-mark** (under the tongue of a sacred calf in Egypt) Hdt.
3 a kind of light boat, **vessel, schooner** (w. play on a further sense *drinking-cup*) Men.

κανθήλια ων *n.pl.* **panniers, saddle-bags** (carried by a pack-animal) Ar. Plb.

κανθήλιος ου *m.* (sts. appos.w. ὄνος *donkey*) **pack-ass** Ar. Pl. X.

κανθοί ῶν *m.pl.* **corners of the eye**; (gener.) **eyes** Call.

κάνθων ωνος *m.* [reltd. κανθήλιος] **donkey, pack-ass** Ar.; (w. play on κάνθαρος 1) Ar.

κάνναβις ιος Ion.f. [loanwd.] | acc. κανναβιδα | hemp-plant, hemp (as a source of fibre for clothing, its seeds burned to make a vapour-bath) Hdt.

κάνναθρον ου n. [κάνναι] rush-work carriage X. Plu.

κάνναι ῶν f.pl. [app.loanwd.] **1** reeds, canes (for making huts) Plb.
2 cane-fence, row of canes (around a statue) Ar.

καννεύσας (ep.aor.ptcpl.): see κατανεύω

κανονίζω vb. [κανών¹] evaluate, regulate —*one's actions* (W.DAT. *by reference to pleasure and pain*) Arist.

κανονίς ίδος f. column of slots (in a jury-selection machine) Arist.

κανοῦν Att.n.: see κάνεον

κάνυστρον ου n. [reltd. κάνναι] basket (of wicker) Carm.Pop.

κανῶ (fut.): see καίνω

Κάνωβος ου m. Canopus (city in Egypt, at the western corner of the Nile Delta) A. Hdt. Plb. Plu.

—**Κανωβικός** ή όν adj. (of a mouth of the Nile) at Canopus, Canopian Hdt. Plu.

—**Κανωβίς** ίδος fem.adj. (of the shore) of Canopus Sol.

—**Κανωβίτης**, also **Κανωπίτης**, ου, dial. **Κανωπίτᾱς** ᾱ (Call.) masc.adj. (of the shore) of Canopus Call.; (of fishermen) Plu. || SB. god of Canopus (ref. to Sarapis) Call.epigr.

κανών¹ όνος m. **1** rod (across the inside of a shield, to strengthen it) Il.
2 loom-rod (ref. to one of two horizontal bars used to separate alternate warp-threads) Il. Ar. Call.
3 shaft (of a spear, w. play on sense 2) Ar.
4 straight-rule (for drawing geometric figures) Ar. Pl. Arist.
5 rule, ruler (of a mason or carpenter, for measuring or checking straightness) E. Pl. X. Aeschin. Arist. +; (fig., W.GEN. for verbal expressions, in a poetry contest) Ar.
6 (fig.) marker, guide (ref. to a beam of sunlight, perh. as providing the illumination by which to get a clear view of events and assess them) E.
7 standard against which one makes an assessment, standard, yardstick, criterion Democr. Att.orats. Arist. Plb. Plu.

κανών² (aor.2 ptcpl.): see καίνω

Κανωπίτης masc.adj.: see under Κάνωβος

κάπ dial.prep.: see κατά

κάπετον (dial.aor.2): see καταπίπτω

κάπετος ου f. **1** ditch, trench Il. Mosch.
2 grave S.

κάπη ης f. food-trough, manger (for horses or cattle) Hom. S.*Ichn*.

καπηλείᾱ ᾱς f. [καπηλεύω] selling of goods (esp. fr. a shop or market-stall, sts. seen as a degrading or dishonest profession), retail trading Pl. X. Arist.

καπηλεῖον ου n. tavern Lys. Ar. Isoc. X. Arist. Plu.

καπηλευτικά ῶν n.pl. retail-trade matters Pl.

καπηλεύω vb. [κάπηλος] **1** engage in retail trading Hdt. Isoc. Pl.; (tr.) sell, peddle —*wine* Hippon.; (of sophists) —*doctrines* Pl.; (fig.) do petty traffic in —*a war* (i.e. *make it a minor concern*) A.
2 (fig., of a king) turn to petty profit —*all one's dealings* Hdt.; (intr., of an ascetic) act like a huckster (i.e. make a deceiving show) —w.DAT. *in one's diet* E.

καπηλικός ή όν adj. (of business, money-making) in retail trade Pl. Arist. || FEM. or NEUT.SB. retail trade Pl. Arist.

—**καπηλικῶς** adv. in the manner of a huckster; (of a heavily made-up old woman, w. ἔχειν) be vamped up for sale Ar.

καπηλίς ίδος f. tavern-keeper or barmaid Ar. Plu.

κάπηλος ου m. **1** local retail trader (opp. import and export merchant), market-trader, shopkeeper or huckster Hdt. Lys. Ar. Pl. X. Arist. +; seller (W.GEN. of weapons) Ar.; (of intellectual wares, pejor.ref. to a sophist) Pl.; (fig.) peddler (W.GEN. of wickedness) D.
2 (specif.) tavern-keeper Ar. Pl. Plu.

καπίθη ης f. [loanwd.] Persian grain-measure (equiv. to two Attic khoinikes) X.

κάπνη ης f. [καπνός] smoke-hole, chimney Ar.

καπνιάω contr.vb. | ep.3pl. (w.diect.) καπνιόωσι | smoke out —*a swarm of bees* AR.

καπνίζω vb. | ep.aor. κάπνισσα | pf. κεκάπνικα | **1** raise smoke, get a fire going Il.
2 (of cooks) annoy with smoke —*persons* D.
3 || PF. (of an oven, w. secondary ref. to female genitals) be sooty (fr. smoke, also ref. to dark pubic hair) Ar.

καπνο-δόκη ης Ion.f. [δέχομαι] smoke-hole, chimney Hdt.

καπνόομαι pass.contr.vb. (of a sacked city, a man struck by lightning) be turned into smoke, go up in smoke Pi. E.

καπνός οῦ m. **1** smoke Hom. +; (W.GEN. of incense, of a particular kind of wood) Hes.fr. Hdt. E. Ar.; (W.ADJ. *of an enemy*, ref. to their campfires) Plu.; (ref. to a smoking fire, extinguished w. water) Pi.; (meton., ref. to a kiln) Plb.; (ref. to soot, as sullying clothes) Od.; (fig., ref. to slander, as sthg. that sullies) Simon.; (as a symbol of what is impermanent or insubstantial) S. E. Ar. Pl.; (in provb. *flee fr. the smoke into the fire*) Pl.
2 vapour (ref. to steam, mist, sea-spray) Hom. Ar. Pl.

καπνώδης ες adj. (of air) smoke-like, misty, foggy Plb.

κάπος dial.m.: see κῆπος

κάππα indecl.n. [Semit.loanwd.] kappa (letter of the Greek alphabet) Ar. Plb. Plu.; (ref. to its sound) Pl.

Καππαδόκης ου m. man from Cappadocia, Cappadocian Plu. || PL.SB. Cappadocians (as a population or military force) Hdt. X. Plb. Plu.

—**Καππάδοκες** ων m.pl. Cappadocians Plu.

—**Καππαδοκίᾱ** ᾱς, Ion. **Καππαδοκίη** ης f. Cappadocia (region in central Asia Minor) Hdt. X. Men. Plb. NT. Plu.

καππαύω dial.vb.: see καταπαύω

κάππεσον (ep.aor.2), **κάππετον** (dial.): see καταπίπτω

κάππιον (ep.aor.2): see καταπίνω

καπ-πυρίζω dial.vb. [κατά, πῦρ] | aor.fem.nom.ptcpl. καππυρίσασα | (of laurel leaves) burn, catch fire Theoc.

καπράω contr.vb. [κάπρος] | only fem.ptcpl. καπρῶσα | (of a sow) want the boar; (fig., of an old woman) be on heat Ar.

κάπριος ον adj. **1** || MASC.SB. (oft. appos.w. σῦς) boar Il. Alc. AR.
2 (of a ship's prow) in the shape of a boar's head Hdt.

κάπρος ου m. (sts. appos.w. σῦς) boar (sts.ref. to a domestic pig) Hom. +

κάπτω vb. gobble up (food) Ar.; (of birds) —*insects* Ar.

καπυρός ά όν adj. [reltd. καπνός] **1** (of thistledown) dry, fluffy Theoc.
2 (of a fever, ref. to lovesickness) desiccating, parching Theoc.
3 (of the voice of the Muses, fig.ref. to a poet) app. clear, pure Theoc.

καπφθίμενος (dial.athem.aor.mid.ptcpl.): see καταφθίνω

κάρ¹ dial.prep.: see κατά

κάρ² καρός sb. | only gen.sg., gender indeterminate | (as exemplifying sthg. negligible) perh. louse Il.

κάρ³ n.: see ἐπικάρ

κάρ, Κάρ¹ dial.f.: see κήρ

Κάρ² Κᾱρός *m.* **Carian** (inhabitant of Caria) Hdt. Th. Ar. D. Plu.; (notable as mercenaries, hence oft. provbl. in ctxt. of letting another bear a risk on one's behalf) Archil. E.*Cyc.* Pl. Plb. ‖ PL.SB. Carians (as a population or military force) Il. Simon. Hdt. Th. Critias Ar. +

—**Κάειρα** ᾱς (Ion. ης) *fem.adj.* (of a woman) **Carian** Il. Hdt. Call.; (of a style of dress) Hdt.

—**Κᾱρίᾱ** ᾱς, Ion. **Κᾱρίη** ης *f.* **Caria** (region of SW. Asia Minor) Hdt. Th. Ar. Isoc. +

—**Κᾱρικός** ή όν *adj.* **1** (of customs, an army, the language or race) of or relating to the Carians, **Carian** Hdt. Plu.; (of a war, i.e. against the Carians) Plb.
2 (of music, a helmet-crest) of Carian style or origin, **Carian** Alc. Ar. Pl.

—**Κᾱρίνη** ης *f.* **Carian woman** Plu.

—**Κάριος** ᾱ (Ion. η) ον *adj.* (epith. of Zeus) **of the Carians, Carian** Hdt.

—**Καρίων** ωνος *m.* **Carion** (i.e. Carian boy, a common slave-name) Ar. Aeschin. Men.

κάρα *n.* | only nom.acc. (Stesich. Pi. Trag. Ar.), and dat. κάρᾳ (Trag.) | —also **κάρη** ητος (also ήατος) *ep.Ion.n.* | dat. κάρητι, καρήατι ‖ PL.: nom.acc. κάρητα, also κάρᾱ (hHom.) | dat. καρήασι | —also **κάρη** ης (Thgn. Call. Mosch.) *Ion.f.* [reltd. κρᾱ́ς, κάρηνα]
1 head (of a person, god, monster or animal) Hom. Hes. Stesich. Thgn. Pi. Trag. +; (in dat., in ctxt. of decreeing or assenting to sthg., i.e. w. *a nod*) hHom. Call.; (ref. to a person's head w. its hair, esp. W.ADJ. *white* or *grey*) Il. Tyrt. Anacr. Trag.; (as that on which punishment or disaster falls) Trag. Mosch.; (as that which is sworn by) S. E. Call. AR.; (meton. for a person's life) S.; (W.GEN. of a person or animal, periphr. for person or animal) Il. S. E. Plu.(oracle); (W.ADJ. or GEN., in addresses) Trag.
2 head, bloom (of a flowering plant) hHom.
3 (fig.) **head, top** (of a throne) A.
4 peak (of a mountain) Hes. Call. AR.

καραδοκέω *contr.vb.* [δοκέω] **1 wait anxiously** or **expectantly** E. Plu.; **look expectantly** —w. εἰς + ACC. *towards someone* Ar.
2 (tr.) **wait** or **watch for** —*a signal, breeze, orders, threatened blows, an outcome*, or sim. E. X. Plb. Plu. —*a person* Plb.
3 wait to see —W.INDIR.Q. *what will be the case* Plb. Plu. —W.ACC. + INDIR.Q. *how sthg. will turn out* Hdt. E.

κάρᾱνα *dial.n.pl.*: see κάρηνα

καρᾱνιστήρ ῆρος *masc.fem.adj.* (of punishment) **by beheading** A.

καρᾱνιστής οῦ *masc.adj.* (of death) **by beheading** E.

κάρᾱνον *dial.n.*: see under κάρηνα

κάρᾱνος ου *m.* [app.loanwd.] **commander, chief** X.

καρᾱνόω *contr.vb.* [κάρηνα] **bring to a head, complete** —*a deed* A. ‖ PASS. (of a tale) **be completed, culminate** A.

καρατομέω *contr.vb.* [κάρᾱτομος] **behead** —*a person, a Gorgon* E.

κάρᾱ-τομος ον *adj.* **1** (of slaughter, devastation) **by beheading** E.
2 (of locks of hair) **cut from the head** S.

—**καρᾱτόμος** ον *adj.* (of Perseus) **cutting off the head** (W.GEN. of a Gorgon) E.*fr.*

κάρβᾱνος ον *adj.* —also **καρβᾱ́ν** ᾶνος *masc.fem.adj.* (of speech, a person, hand) **foreign, barbarian** A. S.*satyr.fr.*

καρβάτιναι ῶν *f.pl.* **rawhide sandals** X.

καρδαμίζω *vb.* [κάρδαμον] **talk about cress** Ar.

κάρδαμον ου *n.* a kind of peppery herb, **cress** Ar. X.; (phr.) βλέπειν κάρδαμα **have a look as peppery as cress** Ar.

καρδίᾱ (also dial. **κραδίᾱ**) ᾱς, Ion. **καρδίη** (also ep.Ion. κραδίη) ης *f.* [κῆρ] **1 heart** (of a person, ref. to the physical organ in the chest) Il. +; (of a god, person or animal, as the seat of emotions, bravery) Hom. +; (as the seat of one's true feelings) E. Ar. Call. Theoc. NT. Plu.; (as the seat of the mind and will) Hom. +; (as the seat of one's memory) AR.; (meton. for a person's feelings, desires or character) Mimn. E. Pl. NT. Plu.; (meton. for life) E.
2 (meton.) **spirit, resolve, pluck** (of a person or animal) Archil. Thgn. A. Pi. E. Plu.
3 (meton.) **desire of one's heart, earnest wish** or **desire** S. E.
4 (fig.) **bosom** (of the earth, in ctxt. of burial) NT.

καρδιο-γνώστης ου *m.* **knower of hearts** (ref. to God) NT.

καρδιό-δηκτος ον *adj.* [δάκνω] (of the power of a malign daimon) **gnawing away at the heart** A.

καρδιο-φύλαξ ακος *m.* **chest-guard, breastplate** Plb.

κάρδοπος ου *f.* **dough-trough, kneading-tray** Ar. Pl.

καρῇ (3sg.aor.2 pass.subj.): see κείρω

κάρη *ep.Ion.n.* (also *Ion.f.*), **καρήατα** (ep.Ion.n.pl.), **καρήατος** (ep.Ion.gen.sg.): see κάρᾱ

καρηβαρέω *contr.vb.* [κάρᾱ, βαρύς] **be heavy-headed, be dizzy** or **drowsy** (fr. poison, loss of blood) Plu.; (fr. perplexity) Plu.(quot.com.)

κάρηνα ων *ep.Ion.n.pl.* —also **κάρᾱνα** ων (A.) *dial.n.pl.* [κάρᾱ] **1 heads** (of persons, Gorgons, animals) Hes. hHom. A. AR.; (W.GEN. of persons, animals, the dead, periphr. for persons etc.) Hom. Hes.*fr.* hHom.
2 tops, peaks (of mountains) Hom. Hes.*fr.* hHom. AR.
3 topmost parts, citadel (W.GEN. of a city) Il. Hdt.(oracle)

—**κάρηνον** ου *ep.Ion.n.sg.* —also **κάρᾱνον** *dial.n.sg.* **head** (of a god, an animal) hHom. Mosch.

κάρητι (ep.Ion.dat.), **κάρητος** (gen.): see κάρᾱ

κάρι (Aeol.dat.): see κῆρ

Κᾱρίᾱ *f.*, **Κᾱρίη** *Ion.f.*, **Κᾱρικός** *adj.*, **Κᾱρίνη** *f.*, **Κάριος** *adj.*, **Καρίων** *m.*: see under Κάρ²

κᾱρίς, dial. **κωρίς**, ίδος *f.* **shrimp, prawn** Semon. Ar.

καρκαίρω *vb.* (of the earth) **rumble, resound** —W.DAT. w. *the feet of charging warriors* Il. [or perh. *shake, quake*]

καρκίνος ου *m.* **1 crab** Hippon. Scol. S.*Ichn.* Ar. Pl. X.
2 pair of pincers, tongs E.*Cyc.*
3 malignant tumour, cancer D.

Καρνεῖος, dial. **Καρνήιος** (Pi.), ου *m.* **1 Karneios** (epith. of Apollo) Pi. Call.
2 Karneios (appos.w. μήν², name of a Spartan month) E. Th. Plu.

—**Κάρνεια** (also **Κάρνεα** Theoc.) ων *n.pl.* **Karneia** (Spartan festival of Apollo, held in the month of Karneios) Hdt. Th. Theoc.

καρόομαι *pass.contr.vb.* [κάρος] **be stunned** (by a wound to the head) Plu. ‖ PF. (of snakes) **lie senseless** —W.DAT. *in death* Theoc.

καρός (gen.): see κάρ²

κᾱρός, Κᾱρός¹ (dial.gen.): see κῆρ

Κᾱρός² (gen.): see Κάρ²

κάρος ου *m.* **stupor, dizziness, swooning-fit** AR. Plu.

καρπαίᾱ ᾱς *f.* a kind of narrative dance (fr. NE. Greece) X.

καρπάλιμος η (dial. ᾱ) ον *adj.* (of feet) **swift, quick** Il. hHom. Ar. AR. Theoc.; (of the jaws of a shrieking Gorgon) Pi.

—**καρπαλίμως** *adv.* **swiftly, quickly** Hom. Hes. hHom. AR.

καρπείᾱ ᾱς *f.* [καρπεύω] **revenue** or **profit** (fr. a territory) Plb.

καρπεύω *vb.* [καρπός¹] **harvest the crops of, cultivate, farm** —*an area of land* Plb.

καρπίζω *vb.* **1** (of Demeter) **make fruitful** —*the earth* (W.DAT. w. *crops*) E.; (of rivers) —*a place* E.
2 ‖ MID. (fig., of chastity) **reap, garner** —*a good reputation* E.

κάρπιμος ον adj. **1** (of myrtle-branches) **bearing fruit** Ar.; (of crops, summer, the earth) **fruitful** A. E. Theoc. ‖ NEUT.PL.SB. **crops** Ar.
2 (fig., of persons) **fruitful, ripe, lucrative** (for extorting) Ar.
3 (of possessions) **productive, profitable** Arist.

καρπογονίᾱ ᾱς f. [γίγνομαι] **bearing of fruit** (by trees) X.

καρπόομαι mid.contr.vb. **1** gather in a harvest; **harvest** —crops Pl. X.; (fig., of persons, cities) **garner** —profits, advantages, honours, or sim. X. D. Plu. —pleasure, wisdom Pl.; (of persons, their actions) **reap** —disaster, criticism Pl.
2 (of persons, populations) **harvest the crops of** —fields, a country A. Hdt. Pl. X.; (fig., of a wise man) **harvest** —a furrow of good judgement (W.PREP.PHR. in his mind) A.; (of a person) **reap the fruits of** —wrongdoing A.
3 enjoy the fruits of —a land A. Th. Att.orats. X. Plb. Plu.; **receive the proceeds of** —workshops, ports, slaves, estates, or sim. X. D. Plu.; (specif.) **enjoy the revenue** or **profit from** —a sum of money, an estate Is. D.; (of a land) **enjoy the benefit of** —rainwater Pl.; (fig., of a person) **enjoy the dividends of** —the honoured memory of one's father-in-law Plu.
4 profit from, exploit for gain —persons, populations, things, events Lys. Ar. X. D.; (intr.) **rake in profits** Ar.
5 enjoy the possession of —estates, goods, money Pl. X. Is. D. Arist. Plu.; **enjoy, possess** —freedom, honours, a certain fate A.fr. E. Th. X. Hyp. Plu.
6 enjoy, take delight in —good news, a certain pleasure A. S. Pl.

—**καρπόω** act.contr.vb. **bear fruit**; (fig., of hubris) **produce** —a crop of calamity A.

καρπο-ποιός όν adj. [ποιέω] (of Demeter) **crop-producing** E.

καρπός¹ οῦ m. | usu. collectv.sg. | **1** (pl. and collectv.sg.) agricultural produce, **fruits, crops, produce** Hom. +; (fig., of the kingdom of heaven) NT.
2 (specif., ref. to corn) **fruit, crop, produce** (sts. W.GEN. of Demeter) Hom. +
3 fruit or **crop** (oft. W.GEN. of a particular plant or tree) Hom. +; (ref. to cotton) Hdt.; (ref. to nectar, collected by bees) AR.; (fig., of one's loins, ref. to offspring) NT.
4 (gener.) **fruit, crop, produce** (W.GEN. of Dionysus, the vine, or sim., ref. to wine) Il. Pi.fr. Hdt.; (of the olive, ref. to oil) A. Pi.; (of the bee, ref. to honey) E.fr.
5 crop-bearing plants, crops (oft. ref. to cornfields) Il. +
6 crop of produce (fr. a season of farming), **crops, harvest** Hes. +
7 bringing in of crops, harvest (as a seasonal event) Ar. NT.
8 (fig.) that which is ripe (and ready to be plucked), **fruit, blossom** (of youth) Mimn. Pi.
9 (fig.) **produce, bounty, fruit** (of poetry, wisdom, one's mind, labours, a course of action) Pi. Ar. Pl. X. D. +; **crop, fruit** (of a wrongful action) A. Pi.fr. NT.; (of a person, ref. to his deeds) NT.
10 (fig., ref. to sthg. accruing to a person) **harvest** (consisting of pain, honour, gratitude) E. Isoc. Men.
11 (fig.) **fruition** (of prophecies or sim.) A.
12 revenue (fr. an estate) Is. Arist.; **earnings** (made by a person) Plu.

καρπός² οῦ m. **wrist** (sts. W.GEN. of a person's hand) Hom. hHom. E. X. D.

καρπο-τελής ές adj. [καρπός¹, τέλος] (of the earth) **producing a harvest, fecund, fruitful** A.

καρπο-φάγος ον adj. [φαγεῖν] (of animals) **herbivorous** (opp. carnivorous) Arist.

καρποφορέω contr.vb. [καρποφόρος] (of plants, the earth) **produce a crop, bear fruit** X. NT.; (fig., of persons, envisaged as seeds) NT.

καρπο-φόρος ον adj. [καρπός¹, φέρω] **1** (of trees) **fruit-bearing** Hdt. X.
2 (of regions, the earth) **crop-bearing, fertile** Pi. E.
3 (of Demeter) **bringing the harvest, fruitful** Ar.; (of seasons) NT.
4 (of youth) **fertile, fecund** (i.e. destined to bear children) E.

καρπόω contr.vb.: see under καρπόομαι

καρπώματα των n.pl. **ripening fruits** (w. sexual connot.) A.

κάρπωσις εως f. **fruits of taxation, revenue** (fr. a province) X.

καρρέζω ep.vb.: see καταρρέζω

κάρρων Lacon.compar.adj.: see κρείσσων

κάρτα adv. [κράτος] **1 very much** Hippon. Scol. Hdt. Trag. Democr. Call.; (modifying an adj. or adv.) **very** Hdt. Trag. Pl. Theoc.
2 (esp. in phr. ἦ κάρτα, καὶ κάρτα or καὶ τὸ κάρτα) **indeed, truly** Hdt. Trag. Ar.; (in predictions or sim.) **surely** Trag.

καρταί-πους ποδος m. [πούς] **sturdy-footed animal** (ref. to a bull) Pi.

καρτερ-αίχμᾱς ᾱ dial.masc.adj. [καρτερός, αἰχμή] (of Herakles) **mighty with the spear** Pi.

καρτερέω contr.vb. **1 be steadfast, hold out** (esp. in the face of danger, hardships, temptation) S. E. Th. Isoc. Pl. + —W.PREP.PHR. against hardship, temptation, or sim. Isoc. Pl. —W.NEUT.PL.ADV. fearsomely S.
2 endure (hardships, punishment) E. Pl. X. Plu. —W.PREDIC.ADJ. going without food X. —W.PTCPL. doing sthg. E. Isoc. Pl. X. Aeschin. +; **bear** —W.INF. to do sthg. Plu.; (tr.) **endure** —hardships, frustrations, ill-treatment, or sim. A.fr. E. Isoc. X. Arist. + ‖ PF.PASS. (of a person's plight) **have been endured to the end** (i.e. his endurance is now over) E.
3 show self-restraint Isoc. Pl. X.; (esp. in neg.phr.) **hold one's peace, restrain oneself** (opp. take action) Arist. Plb. Plu.
4 persevere (in an endeavour) Pl. —W.PTCPL. in doing sthg. E. Th. Pl. X. Plu.
5 (wkr.sens.) **persist** (in thinking sthg.) Pl. —W.PTCPL. in doing sthg. E.
6 (of a battle) **be fiercely fought** E.

—**καρτερούντως** ptcpl.adv. **resolutely** —ref. to facing misfortune Pl.

καρτέρημα ατος n. **act of enduring, endurance, perseverance** (by the soul) Pl.

καρτέρησις εως f. **process of enduring, endurance** (sts. W.GEN. of hardships) Pl.

καρτερίᾱ ᾱς f. **1 quality of enduring, endurance** Isoc. Pl. X. Hyp. Plb.
2 capacity for endurance, fortitude, hardiness, self-control Isoc. Pl. X. Arist. Plu.

καρτερικός ή όν adj. [καρτερός] **1** (of persons) **able to endure hardships, hardy** X. Arist. Plu.; (of a city, ref. to its population) Arist.
2 (of persons) **willingly enduring hardships, austere** Isoc.

—**καρτερικῶς** adv. **austerely** —ref. to living Arist.

καρτερο-βρέντᾱς ᾱ dial.masc.adj. [βρέμω] (of Zeus) **with mighty thunder** Pi.fr.

καρτερό-θῡμος ον adj. [θῡμός] **1** (of gods, warriors, the winds) **stout-hearted** Hom. Hes.
2 (of Conflict, Ares) **hard-hearted** Hes. B.

καρτερός ά (Ion. ή) όν adj. [κράτος, reltd. κρατερός] **1** (of gods, persons, animals) **strong, mighty** Hom. Hes.fr. hHom.

καρτερούντως

A. Pi. Hdt.(oracle) +; (W.INF. in killing enemies) Il.; (of deeds) Theoc.
2 (of weapons, an animal's claws) **strong, powerful** hHom. B. Hdt.; (of a weapon, fig.ref. to poetry) Pi.; (of a phrase, in a poetic contest) Ar.
3 (of a stone) **weighty, massive** Pi.
4 (of bonds, defensive structures) firmly resistant, **strong** hHom. AR. Mosch. Plu.; (of earth) **firm** (W.INF. so as to bear weight) Plu.
5 (of military positions) **strong, well-defended** Hdt. Th. X. Plu. || NEUT.SB. strong defensive position Th. Plu.
6 (of oaths) **strong, firm** Hom. hHom. Pi.; (of evidence) Plu.
7 (of necessity) **strong** B.; (of worry) **intense, overpowering** Pi.
8 (of a crash) **mighty, deafening** A.
9 (of a wound) **severe** Il.
10 (of fighting) **fierce** Pi. Hdt. Th. Plb. Plu.; (of a siege) **intense, tight** Plu. || NEUT.SUPERL.SB. fiercest part (of a battle) Plu.
11 (w.neg.connot., of a person's spirit) **aggressive, forceful** Sol.; (of deeds) **savage, violent** Il. || NEUT.SB. force, violence A. Hdt.; (esp. in prep.phrs.) full force, utmost effort E. Ar. Pl. Theoc.
12 (of a god, a person, their spirit) **steadfast** Il. Thgn. Ar. Call. Mosch.; (of a horse's temperament) X. || NEUT.SB. steadfastness (of a person's disposition) Plu.
13 (of a person) **hardy** X.; (w.neg.connot.) **austere** Isoc.
14 (of persons, the arrogance of the Titans) **stubborn, intransigent** A. Pl.; (of a crown, fig.ref. to a cause of misplaced pride) Thgn.
15 (of persons) **masterful** (W.INF. at talking) Pl.
16 (of persons) **powerful** (socially or politically) Od.; **possessing mastery** (W.GEN. over persons, a place) Archil. Theoc.; **in control** (W.GEN. of one's tongue and mind) Thgn.
—**καρτερῶς** adv. **1 soundly, deeply** —ref. to sleeping Hdt.
2 closely —ref. to keeping a prisoner under guard Plu.
καρτερούντως ptcpl.adv.: see under καρτερέω
καρτερό-χειρ χειρος masc.fem.adj. [χείρ] (of Ares, an athlete) **strong-handed** hHom. B.
κάρτιστος η ον ep.superl.adj. [κρατύς, reltd. κράτιστος] (of Zeus) **mightiest** (W.GEN. of all gods) Il.; (of the eagle, W.GEN. of birds) Il.; (of warriors, sts. W.GEN. of men, Greeks) Il. Hes.; (of a battle against warriors) **mightiest, fiercest** (that one has ever fought) Il.
κάρτος ep.n., **καρτύνω** ep.vb.: see κράτος, κρατύνω
κάρυα ων n.pl. **nuts** (as a foodstuff) Ar. Philox.Leuc. X. Thphr. Theoc.
Καρύαι (or **Κάρυαι**) ῶν f.pl. **Karyai** (town in Laconia, site of a temple to Artemis) Th. X. Call.
—**Καρυάτιδες** ων f.pl. **Karyatids** (female worshippers of Artemis, who danced w. baskets on their heads) Plu.
καρυκεύω vb. [καρύκη rich sauce made from blood] **make into a sauce** —eggs, flour, honey Men. || PASS. (of dishes of food) be served in sauce Men.
καρύκινος η ον adj. (of robes) the colour of blood-sauce, **maroon** X.
καρυκοποιέω contr.vb. (fig., of a demagogue) **serve up sauce** (app.ref. to using elaborate or rabble-rousing language) Ar.
κᾶρυξ (or **κᾶρῡξ**) dial.m.: see κῆρυξ
κᾱρύσσω dial.vb.: see κηρύσσω
καρφαλέος η ον ep.adj. [κάρφω] (of straw) **dry** Od.
—**καρφαλέον** neut.adv. **harshly** —ref. to a shield clanging Il.
κάρφη ης f. **straw, hay** X.

καρφολογέω contr.vb. [κάρφος, λέγω] **pluck off** —a piece of straw (fr. a person's hair, as an obsequious gesture) Thphr.
κάρφος εος (ους) n. [κάρφω] **1 piece of straw** or **twig** Hdt. Ar. AR.; (as exemplifying sthg. small and insignificant) Ar. NT.
2 small clay token (ref. to the tesserae used in the Roman army), **pass, ticket** Plb.
καρφυρά ᾶς f. nest of straw and twigs, **nest** (of a bird) E.
κάρφω vb. | aor. ἔκαρψα | **1 dry out** —cowhides (to make them usable) S.Ichn.; (of the sun) **scorch** —someone's skin Hes. || PASS. (of Egypt) suffer from drought Call.
2 (of a goddess) **shrivel, make wrinkled** —someone's skin Od. || PASS. (of skin) be shrivelled —W.DAT. in wrinkles Archil.
3 (of Zeus) **wither, blast** —arrogant people Hes. || PASS. (of a woman) waste away —W.DAT. w. a pitiful fate AR.
καρχαλέος η ον ep.adj. [app.reltd. καρφαλέος, perh. by pop.etym.] **1** (of persons) **parched** (W.DAT. w. thirst) Il. AR.
2 (of dogs) **ravenous** AR.
καρχαρ-όδους οντος masc.fem.adj. [κάρχαρος jagged, ὀδούς] (of dogs, a sickle) **with jagged teeth** Il. Hes. B. Ar. || MASC.SB. sharp-toothed monster (com.ref. to a politician) Ar.
καρχάσιον dial.n.: see καρχήσιον
καρχηδονίζω vb. [Καρχηδών] (of a Sicilian city) **side with the Carthaginians** (against Rome) Plu.
Καρχηδών όνος f. **Carthage** (Phoenician colony on the coast of N. Africa) Hdt. Th. Ar. Isoc. Pl. +
—**Καρχηδόνιος** ᾱ (Ion. η) ον adj. **1** (of persons) from Carthage, **Carthaginian** Hdt. Plb. Plu.; (of flax) X.; (of a ship) Plb. || MASC.PL.SB. Carthaginians Hdt. Th. Isoc. Pl. X. +
2 || FEM.SB. region of Carthage Plu.
—**Καρχηδονιακός** ή όν adj. (of a port) **Carthaginian** Th.
καρχήσιον, dial. **καρχάσιον**, ου n. **1** a kind of drinking-cup, **goblet** Sapph.
2 structure at the top of a ship's mast (to which the sailyard was raised), **mast-head** Pi. E. Plu.(pl.); (ref. to part of a machine, to which a yard-arm was attached) Plb.
κασαλβάζω vb. [κασαλβάς] (of a woman) **behave like a whore** Hermipp.; (of a demagogue) app., shout whore's curses at, **rail at** —generals Ar.
κασαλβάς άδος f. **prostitute**; (pejor., ref. to a lascivious old woman) **whore** Ar.
κασᾶς ᾶ m. [Semit.loanwd.] **cloth, blanket** (for a horse) X.
κασία ᾱς, Ion. **κασίη** ης f. **cassia, cinnamon** (as a spice or incense) Sapph. Hdt. Melanipp.
κασιγνήτη ης, dial. **κασιγνήτᾱ** ᾱς f. [reltd. καί; γίγνομαι] | dial.gen.pl. κασιγνητᾶν | **sister** Hom. Hes. Lyr. Trag. AR.; (fig., W.GEN. of the vine, ref. to the fig) Hippon.; (of Delos, ref. to another site assoc.w. Artemis) Pi.
κασίγνητος ου m.f. | fem.du. κασιγνήτω | **1** (m.) **brother** Hom. + || PL. (gener.) brethren, kinsmen Hom. Hdt. E.Cyc. Call.(dub.); (ref. to kindred peoples) Hdt. || ADJ. (of the head) of a brother S.
2 || FEM.DU. sisters S. || ADJ. (of the head) of a sister E.
κάσις ιος m.f. **1** (m.) **brother** Lyr.adesp. Trag.
2 (f.) **sister** Anacr. E. Call.; (fig., W.GEN. of mud, ref. to dust) A.; (of fire, ref. to smoke) A.
Κασσάνδρᾱ ᾱς, Ion. **Κασσάνδρη** ης f. **Cassandra** (daughter of Priam and Hecuba, taken to Greece by Agamemnon after the fall of Troy; famous for her gift of prophecy but cursed to be disbelieved) Hom. Lyr. A. E. Plu.
κασσίτερος, Att. **καττίτερος**, ου m. **tin** metal, **tin** (esp. as a component of armour) Il. Hes. Hdt. Pl. Arist. Plb.

—**Κασσιτερίδες** ων f.pl. (appos.w. νῆσοι) **Tin Islands** (app.ref. to a part of Britain, perh. the Isles of Scilly) Hdt.

Κασταλίᾱ ᾱς, Ion. **Κασταλίη** ης f. **Kastalia** (sacred spring below Mt. Parnassos, assoc.w. the Muses) Pi. B. Hdt. S. E.

—**Κασταλίς** ίδος fem.adj. (of a nymph) **Kastalian** Theoc.

καστόριαι ῶν f.pl. [perh.reltd. Κάστωρ] **Kastorian hounds** (ref. to a breed of dog) X.

καστόρνῡμι ep.vb.: see καταστόρνῡμι

κάστωρ ορος m. **beaver** Hdt.

Κάστωρ ορος m. **Kastor** (son of Leda by Tyndareos or Zeus, brother of Helen and Polydeukes) Hom. + | see also Διόσκοροι

—**Καστόρειος** ον adj. (of a hymn, ref. to a Spartan battle-song) **to Kastor, Kastorian** Pi. Plu.

κάσχεθε (ep.3sg.aor.2): see κατέχω

κασώρειον ου n. [reltd. κασαλβάς] **brothel** Ar.

κατά, dial. **κάτ** (w. assimilation to κάδ before δ, κάκ before γ and κ, κάμ before μ, κάν before ν, κάπ before π, κάρ before ρ) prep. | W.ACC. and GEN. | sts. following its noun (w. anastrophe of the accent), e.g. Λυκίην κάτα in Lycia Il. |

—A | space or location |
1 down in, in —W.GEN. the earth, water Pi. Hdt. Trag. +
2 in, at or **near** —W.ACC. a place Hdt. Trag. +
3 (ref. to wounding) **in** or **on** —W.ACC. a part of the body Il.
4 (ref. to knowing, feeling pain) **in** —W.ACC. the heart or soul Hom.
5 everywhere in, throughout —W.ACC. a place Hom. +
6 opposite, facing —W.ACC. someone or sthg. Hdt. +
7 (ref. to an island being located) **off** —W.ACC. a region Th.
8 before —W.ACC. the eyes E. Ar. X.
9 in the company of, among —W.ACC. people Hdt. +
10 (phrs., W.ACC.) κατὰ κέρας in the flank; κατὰ κεφαλήν overhead; κατὰ πόδας at the heels; κατὰ πρύμναν at the stern; κατὰ χώραν in place (see κέρας 11, κεφαλή 1, πούς 13, πρύμνα 4, χώρα 6); (W.GEN.) κατὰ νώτου behind the back, in the rear (see νῶτον 1)

—B | movt. or direction |
1 down into —W.GEN. the earth, Il. + —W.ACC. the waves Il.
2 down through —W.GEN. the nostrils Il.
3 down over —W.GEN. the head, back, shoulders, eyes, hands, or sim. Hom. +; (phrs.) κατὰ χειρός (χειρῶν) over the hands (ref. to pouring water) Philox.Leuc. Ar. Men. Plu.; κατὰ κρῆθεν over the head (see κρῆθεν 1)
4 down from —W.GEN. heaven, mountains, rocks, walls, horses, or sim. Hom. + —eyes (ref. to tears flowing) Il. +; (phrs.) κατ' ἄκρας from top to bottom, completely; κατὰ κρῆθεν from head to foot (see ἄκρα 4, κρῆθεν 1)
5 (ref. to scattering) **among** —W.ACC. tents and ships Il.; **over** —W.GEN. an island Plb.
6 along into, into —W.ACC. a group of people Il.
7 down along, down, on —W.ACC. a stream, track, or sim. Hom. +
8 to (as a goal) —W.GEN. a vestibule S.
9 along with, with, on —W.ACC. the wind Trag.
10 over, across —W.ACC. the sea Hom. +
11 everywhere in, throughout —W.ACC. a city Od. +
12 within, in —W.ACC. a city, house, or sim. Hom. +
13 (ref. to acting w. hostility) **against** —W.GEN. someone Trag. +

—C | time |
1 in the course of, during —W.ACC. the day, night Hdt. Trag. | for καθ' ὕπνον during sleep see ὕπνος 4
2 by (i.e. every) —W.ACC. day, year S. E. Th. Ar. +
3 at or **around** —W.ACC. a certain time Hdt. | for κατὰ καιρόν at the right time see καιρός 4
4 in the time of —W.ACC. someone Hdt. X. D.
5 for the duration of, throughout, for —W.GEN. all time Lycurg.

—D | distribution |
1 (ref. to dividing, separating or arranging) **into, in, by** —W.ACC. tribes, villages, groups, or sim. Il. +
2 by —W.ACC. oneself, itself (i.e. separately or independently) Il. +; (a certain number, unit or amount) • κατ' ἔπος word by word Ar. • κατὰ κεφαλήν per head Arist. • (ref. to ships sailing) κατὰ μίαν (ναῦν) one by one (i.e. in column) Th. Plb. | see also ἀνήρ 6, βραχύς 17, εἷς 5, ἕκαστος 4, ζυγόν 11, μέρος 7, 15, μικρός 11, μίτος 3
3 (ref. to paying a specified amount of tax) **on** —W.ACC. (every) twenty-five minae D.

—E | purpose |
1 for the purpose of, for —W.ACC. sthg. Od. +
2 in search of, after —W.ACC. sthg. Od. +

—F | manner |
1 comparable in manner or appearance to, like —W.ACC. someone or sthg. A. Pi. Hdt. +
2 in conformity or **accordance with** —W.ACC. one's mind or will, due order, custom, law, or sim. Il. + —one's ability Hes. Hdt. Th. + —oneself (i.e. one's station) A.; (phrs.) κατ' αἶσαν in due measure; κατὰ δίκην justly; καθ' ἑκουσίαν voluntarily; κατὰ λόγον proportionately, rationally; κατὰ φύσιν naturally (see αἶσα 4, δίκη 2, ἑκούσιος 3, λόγος 4, 12, φύσις 8, 12) | see also διαδοχή 8, δυνατός 8, καιρός 1, 3, κόσμος 7, κράτος 1, μοῖρα 8, νόμος 1, ὀρθός 16, πρόθεσις 5, στάθμη 5, σχῆμα 10
3 (in quotations) **according to** —W.ACC. an author Ar. Pl.

—G | basis or cause |
1 on account of, by reason of —W.ACC. sthg. A. Hdt. Th. Pl. +; (phr.) κατὰ γλῶσσαν by hearsay S.
2 by the will of —W.ACC. a divinity Pi. E. Ar.

—H | attendant circumstances |
in —W.ACC. war, battle Il.

—I | means or manner |
1 (ref. to swearing) **by** —W.GEN. someone or sthg. Lys. Ar. D.; **over** —W.GEN. victims Th. Arist.
2 (phrs.) κατὰ κράτος (also κατὰ τὸ ἰσχυρόν) by force; κατὰ σπουδήν with eager haste; κατὰ σχολήν in a leisurely way; κατὰ τάχος with speed (see κράτος 1, ἰσχυρός 3, σπουδή 1, 3, σχολή 1, τάχος 5)

—J | specification |
1 in respect of, concerning —W.ACC. someone or sthg. A. Hdt. E. + —W.GEN. Pl.
2 (ref. to speaking or sim.) **about** —W.GEN. someone or sthg. Pl. Aeschin. Arist.

—K | extent |
(phrs.) κατὰ βραχύ to a brief extent; κατὰ μικρόν to a small extent; κατὰ πάντα in all respects, completely; κατὰ τὸ πλεῖστον for the most part (see βραχύς 17, μικρός 11, πᾶς 9, πλεῖστος 4)

καταβάδην adv. [καταβαίνω] **with one's feet downwards, upright** —ref. to standing (opp. reclining) Ar.

κατα-βαθμός, Att. **καταβασμός**, οῦ m. **place where a river descends rapidly; rapids, cataract** (of the Nile) A. Plb.

κατα-βαίνω, dial. **καβαίνω** (Alcm.) vb. | fut. καταβήσομαι || ATHEM.AOR.: κατέβην, dial. κατέβᾱν, 3pl. κατέβησαν, ep. κατέβαν | ep.1pl.subj. καταβείομεν (v.l. καταβήομεν) | ptcpl. καταβάς | ep.inf. καταβήμεναι | imperatv. κατάβηθι, also κατάβᾱ (Ar. Men.) | pf. καταβέβηκα || EP.MID.AOR. (w.act.sens.): 3sg. κατεβήσετο, imperatv. καταβήσεο, 3sg.subj. καταβήσεται | ep.3sg.aor.mid. (tm.) κατὰ ... βήσατο (AR.) || neut.impers.vbl.adj. καταβατέον || The sections are

καταβακχιόομαι

grouped as: (1–8) go down (usu. fr. a higher to a lower place), (9–12) step down (fr. a raised position), (13–16) go towards an end point. |

1 (of persons, gods, sts. things) move downwards, **go or come down, descend** Od. + —W.GEN., PREP.PHR. or ADV. *fr. a place* Hom. + —W.ACC. *to a place* Od. Pi. E. —W.DAT. *to a person or place* Pi. Ar. —W.ACC. or PREP.PHR. *by a ladder, a particular route* Od. + —W.ACC. *fr. an upper storey* Od.

2 go down (to earth); (of gods, other celestial beings) **go or come down, descend** (sts. W.ADV. or PREP.PHR. fr. heaven) Hom. Hes. Alcm. Ar. Pl. NT.; (of natural phenomena, such as winds, rain or fire) Il. NT.

3 go down (beneath the earth); **go down, descend** (to the underworld) X. —W.ACC., ADV. or PREP.PHR. *to Hades* Od. Hdt. S. Mosch.; (ref. to dying) Anacr. Thgn. Pi. E.

4 go down (fr. a northerly place); **go south** —W.PREP.PHR. *to a country* NT.

5 (specif., of persons, armies, funds) **go or come down** (fr. the Persian capital, towards territories nearer the coast) Hdt. Th. Att.orats. X. Plu.

6 (of a country's boundaries) **run down** (to the coast) Pl.

7 (of woven cloth) **come down** (i.e. be taken down, when finished) —w. ἀπό + GEN. *fr. the loom* Theoc.

8 come (for a specific occasion), **turn up** Pi. Plu. —W.PREP.PHR. *for a contest* Pi. Isoc. Plu.; (specif.) **enter a contest** Hdt. S. Isoc. Pl. X.

9 step down (fr. a raised position); **get down** (oft. W.PREP.PHR. fr. a chariot, wagon, bed, or sim.) Il. +; (ep.aor.mid.) AR.(tm.)

10 (specif.) **dismount** (fr. a horse) Ar. X. Plb. Plu. —w. ἀπό + GEN. *fr. a horse* X. ǁ PF. be dismounted (ref. to having given up a cavalry post) Arist. —w. ἀπό + GEN. *fr. horses (ref. to having given up riding)* D. ǁ PASS. (of a horse) be dismounted from X.

11 (of a speaker, after giving a speech) **step down** (sts. w. ἀπό + GEN. fr. the platform) Ar. Att.orats. Plu.

12 (fig.) step down (fr. office), **retire** Plu.

13 go towards an end point; (of a lineage, a person listing one) **go down** —w. εἰς + ACC. *to a particular person* Hdt. Plu.

14 proceed (towards a goal) Pi. —w.ACC. τέλος *towards a goal* Pi.; (of reasoning) —w. ἐπί + ACC. *to a particular conclusion* Pl.

15 end up —W.PTCPL. or ἐς + ACC. *talking about sthg.* Hdt.

16 (of times of marriages) **conform, correspond** —w. εἰς + ACC. *to guidelines of age (for men and women)* Arist.

κατα-βακχιόομαι *mid.contr.vb.* [βάκχιος] (fig., of a city, i.e. its inhabitants) **consecrate oneself to Bacchus** —W.DAT. w. *branches of oak or pine* E.

κατα-βάλλω, ep. **καββάλλω** *vb.* | fut. καταβαλῶ | aor.2 κατέβαλον, ep. κάββαλον | pf. καταβέβληκα ǁ MID.: dial.2sg.impf. κατεβάλλευ ǁ PASS.: aor. κατεβλήθην | pf. καταβέβλημαι ǁ neut.impers.vbl.adj. καταβλητέον ǁ The sections are grouped as: (1–3) cast down (by throwing or striking), (4) pull or tear down (material things), (5–8) destroy or overthrow (persons or non-material things), (9–12) throw (persons or things) into a particular place or condition, (13–14) throw aside, (15) let fall, (16) move down, (17–18) put down, (19) lay down (foundations), (20) lay down in store, (21) pay (money), (22) make public. |

1 cast down by throwing; **throw down** —*persons or things (oft. W.ADV. or PREP.PHR. to the ground, into the sea, or sim.)* Il. Hes. X. AR. Plu.; (of a horse) —*its rider* Hdt. X. Plu.; (of a wrestler) —*his opponent* Ar. Pl. Plu.; (fig., of a person, goddess or argument, envisaged as a wrestler) Ar.(tm.) Pl. Plu.; (fig., of a man, envisaged as a wrestler) **force down** —*a woman (for sexual intercourse)* Ar. Men. ǁ MID. **throw oneself down** —W.PREP.PHR. *into bed* Theoc. ǁ PASS. (of objects) be thrown down Alc.(tm.) X. Plu.

2 cast down by striking, **strike down** —*sacrificial victims* E. Isoc. Plu.; (of armed persons, falling rocks) —*persons, animals* Il.(tm.) Hes. Hdt. Th. +

3 knock down (by accident), **knock over** —*objects* E.Cyc. Th. Plu.; **overturn** (on purpose) —*lamps* Plu.

4 knock down (so as to destroy); **pull down** —*statues, trophies* Hdt. X. Plu.; (of persons, earthquakes, gales, floods) **tear down, demolish** —*walls, buildings, cities* Il. Hdt. Th. Isoc. X. +; **mow down** —*corn (w. a scythe)* Theoc. ǁ PASS. (of statues) be pulled down Plu.; (of buildings) be torn down Lycurg.

5 destroy the power or effectiveness (of persons or things); **bring down, ruin** —*persons, states, their ambition* Plu.; **overturn** —*laws, traditions* E. Plu.

6 overthrow, overwhelm, vanquish —*enemies* Plu.; (fig.) **defy** —*wintry weather (w. warmth and wine)* Alc.

7 cast down —*a person (w. ἀπό + GEN. fr. his hopes)* Pl. —(w. εἰς + ACC. *to nothingness*) Hdt.

8 humiliate, abase —*a person* Plu.; **discredit, diminish** —*oracles, persons, their achievements* Hdt. Plb. Plu. ǁ PF.PASS. (of persons) be abased Isoc.

9 throw (a person, into a place); **throw, cast** —*a person (w. εἰς + ACC. into jail)* Hdt. Plu. —(*into a mill*) E.Cyc.; (of fate) **cast ashore** —*a person (W.ADV. at a place)* Od. ǁ PASS. be thrown —w. εἰς + ACC. *into jail* Plu.

10 throw (persons or things, into a particular condition); **throw, cast, lead** —*persons, situations (w. εἰς + ACC. into confusion, disaster, or sim.)* E. Pl. Plu. —*a person (into disreputable activities)* Plu.; (of an argument) —*a person (into a foolish belief)* Pl.

11 (wkr.sens.) **cast, plunge** —*oneself (w. εἰς + ACC. into a forest)* Plu.; (intr.) **plunge** (into a forest) Plu.

12 throw, introduce —*a false notion (w. εἰς + ACC. into philosophy)* Plu.

13 throw aside, discard —*objects, refuse* Ar. Arist. Plu.

14 abandon, give up —*enterprises, hopes, notions* Isoc. Pl. D. Men. Plu.

15 let fall, drop —*persons, animals, objects* Il. Men. AR.(sts.tm.) Plu.; (of grasses) **shed** —*seeds* X.; (of an archer) **let down, suspend** —*a quiver (W.ADV. behind him)* Hes. ǁ PF.PASS. (of a horse's reins) be allowed to drop (i.e. be held loosely) X.

16 move to a lower position; **lower, take down** —*sails* Thgn.(tm.); (of troops) **lower, level** —*their spears (to engage the enemy)* Plb.; (of persons, gods, animals) **lower** —*their eyes, eyebrows, ears, head* Od. hHom.(tm.) E.Cyc. X. Plu.; (of a young man) **have** (w.ACC. the first hairs of his beard) **growing down** —W.PREP.PHR. *fr. his temples* Theoc.

17 put or set down —*objects (oft. W.PREP.PHR. in a place)* Il. E. Ar. X. Plu.; (fig.) —*laws (w. εἰς + ACC. on a firm foundation)* Pl. ǁ PF.PASS. (of armour) lie placed on the ground Alc.(tm.)

18 put down (into the ground); **sow** —*crops (i.e. the seeds for them)* Men.; (fig.) —*the seed of a policy (W.PREP.PHR. in a state)* D.

19 ǁ MID. lay down (foundations); **lay down** —*a keel (as the first step in building a ship)* Pl.; **lay down the foundations of** —*buildings, ships* Plb. Plu.; (fig.) **begin** —*a lament, literary work* E. Plb. —W.INF. *to sing* Call. ǁ PASS. (fig., of the foundations of a person's birth, the beginnings of a war) be laid E. Plu.

20 put down (in store, for future use); **lay down, deposit** —provisions (W.DAT. *for an army*) Hdt. ‖ PASS. (of written evidence) be deposited (in a courtroom) D.

21 put down (money, in payment); **pay** —*money* (*to persons, the state, peoples*) Th. Att.orats. Pl. Arist. +; (fig., of a lake) —*money* (ref. *to the proceeds fr. the sale of its fish,* w. ἐς + ACC. *into a royal treasury*) Hdt. ‖ PASS. (of money) be paid D. Arist.

22 app., set down (in the public domain, i.e. make public); **publish, spread** —*a rumour, an accusation* Hdt. E. Plu. ‖ PASS. (of teachings, arguments) be set down or made public (sts. in writing) Pl. Arist.

—**καταβεβλημένως** *pf.pass.ptcpl.adv.* **in a lowly and ignoble manner** —*ref. to living* Isoc.

κατα-βάπτομαι *pass.vb.* (of iron) **be dipped** or **immersed** —W.DAT. *in vinegar* (*during manufacture*) Plu.

κατα-βαρέω *contr.vb.* (of wrestlers) **overpower** —*opponents* Plu. ‖ PASS. (of troops) be overpowered Plb.

κατα-βαρύνομαι *pass.vb.* (of eyes) **become heavy** (w. sleep) NT.

καταβάς (athem.aor.ptcpl.): see καταβαίνω

κατάβασις εως (Ion. ιος) *f.* [καταβαίνω] **1** **downward path, descent, way down** (oft. W.GEN. or ἀπό + GEN. fr. a place) Hdt. Th. X. Plb. NT. Plu.
2 downward journey, **descent** X. Plb.; (to the underworld) Hdt. Isoc.

καταβασμός Att.m.: see καταβαθμός

καταβατέον (neut.impers.vbl.adj.): see καταβαίνω

καταβάτης ου *m.* [καταβαίνω] one who jumps down from a chariot (to fight); **mounted infantryman** Pl.

κατα-βεβαιόομαι *mid.contr.vb.* (of a historian) strongly assert, **insist** —W.ACC. + INF. *that sthg. is the case* Plu.

καταβεβλημένως *pf.pass.ptcpl.adv.*: see under καταβάλλω

καταβείομεν (ep.1pl.athem.aor.subj.), **κατάβηθι** (athem.aor.imperatv.), **καταβήμεναι** (ep.athem.aor.inf.), **καταβήσεο** (ep.aor.mid.imperatv.), **καταβήσεται** (ep.3sg.aor.mid.subj.), **καταβήσομαι** (fut.mid.): see καταβαίνω

κατα-βιάζομαι *mid.vb.* **1 subdue by force, overpower** —*enemies* Plu.; (fig., of a commander's ambition) —*enemies, regions, circumstances* Plu. ‖ PASS. be subdued by force Plu.
2 (of conspirators) **coerce** —*a people* Th.; (of persons) **override** —*nature* Plu.

κατα-βιβάζω *vb.* cause to come down; **bring** or **send down** —*persons, cattle* (oft. W.PREP.PHR. *to or fr. a place*) Hdt. Th. X. Plb. Plu.; **force** or **entice down** —*enemy troops* (*fr. a hill*) Th. X.; (fig., of a statesman) —*a city* (W.PREP.PHR. *to the sea, i.e. persuade it to develop its navy*) Plu. ‖ PASS. (of persons) be led down (to a place) Plu.; (fig., of a city of unbelievers) be sent down —W.PREP.PHR. *to Hell* NT.

καταβιβαστέος ᾱ ον *vbl.adj.* (of persons) **to be sent down** (to a cave, fig.ref. to the world of ignorance) Pl.

κατα-βιβρώσκω *vb.* | athem.aor. κατέβρων | **1 devour completely, eat up** —*a sheep* Men. ‖ PF.PASS. (of a harvest) be eaten up Hdt.
2 (gener.) **eat** —*food* hHom. ‖ PASS. (of a corpse) be eaten —W. ὑπό + GEN. *by worms* Hdt.
3 ‖ PASS. (of matter) be consumed (by decay) Pl.

κατα-βῑνέω *contr.vb.* | pidgin Gk. καταβεβίνησι (cj.), app. for 3sg.pf.pass. καταβεβίνηται | ‖ PASS. (fig., of a quiver) be fucked away (i.e. be lost through its owner's womanising) Ar.

κατα-βιόω *contr.vb.* | fut. καταβιώσομαι | athem.aor. κατεβίων | aor.1 κατεβίωσα (Plb. Plu.) | **spend one's days,** **live one's life** —W.PREDIC.SB. *as a private citizen* Pl. Plu. —w. ἐν + DAT. *in a particular place or condition* Pl. Plb. Plu.; **live** —W.COGN.ACC. *one's life* Pl.; (specif.) **live out** —*the rest of one's life* (*in a particular manner*) Isoc. Men. Plu. ‖ AOR.1 and FUT. live out one's life Plu.

κατα-βλακεύω *vb.* harm as a result of neglect, **mismanage** —*a person's affairs* X.

κατα-βλάπτω *vb.* **do substantial harm to** —*a person* Pl. D.; **inflict** —W.COGN.ACC. *damage or injury* Pl. D.; (wkr.sens., of arguments in a speech) **harm** —*one another* Arist. ‖ PASS. (of a city) be harmed —w. ὑπό + GEN. *by a person* Aeschin.; (of a person) suffer damage D. —W.ACC. *to one's interests* hHom.

κατα-βλέπω *vb.* **look down** (fr. above) —W.PREP.PHR. *on people fighting* Plu.; (of the evening star) **look down on** —W.ACC. *an island* Call.

κατάβλημα ατος *n.* [καταβάλλω] (philos.) **overthrow, dethronement** (of the senses) Democr.

καταβλητέον (neut.impers.vbl.adj.): see καταβάλλω

καταβλητικός ή όν *adj.* (of a manoeuvre) **liable to topple** (an enemy fr. his horse) X.

κατα-βληχάομαι *mid.contr.vb.* (of goats) **bleat** Theoc.

κατα-βλώσκω *vb.* **go down** —W.ACC. *to a town* Od. —W.PREP.PHR. *fr. a town* AR.; (of a river) **flow down** (to the sea) AR.

κατα-βοάω *contr.vb.* | fut. καταβοήσομαι, Ion. καταβώσομαι | **1** (of a voice) **shout** (W.ACC. a pitiful cry) **down** —W.DAT. *to spirits in the underworld* S.(tm.)
2 (of a statesman) **shout down** —*an opponent* Ar.
3 (of persons) **raise an outcry, shout angrily** Plu. —W.GEN. *at someone* Plu.; (specif.) **denounce, complain against** —W.GEN. *persons, peoples* (sts. W.COMPL.CL. *as doing sthg.*) Hdt. Th. Plu. —W.ACC. *a person's conduct* Plu.

καταβοή ῆς *f.* **1 outcry** (W.GEN. against persons) Th.
2 (specif.) **denunciation** (of a person) Th.

καταβόησις εως *f.* **outcry** (against a person's conduct) Plu.

καταβολή (also **κατηβολή** Pl.) ῆς, dial. **καταβολά** ᾶς *f.* [καταβάλλω] **1** laying down of foundations; (fig.) **beginnings, first foundation** (of success, tyranny, dynasties, the universe) Pi. Plb. NT. Plu.; **outset, beginning** (of a literary work) Plb.; (prep.phr.) ἐκ καταβολῆς *from the outset* (ref. *to doing sthg.*) Plb.; *from scratch* (ref. *to building ships, inventing stories*) Plb.
2 **down-payment, payment** (of money, esp. in instalments) D. Arist.
3 **onset, attack** (usu. W.GEN. of a disease or sim.) Pl. D.; **affliction** (ref. to a disease) Plu.

κατά-βορρος ον *adj.* [βορέας] (of a region) **sheltered from the north wind** Pl.

κατα-βόσκω *vb.* (of a shepherd) **feed one's herds on, use as pasture** —*a place* Theoc. ‖ MID. (fig., of a plague) **feed on, consume** —*herds* Call.

κατα-βόστρυχος ον *adj.* (of a young man) **with flowing locks** E.

κατα-βρέχω *vb.* **1 drench** —*a person, one's chin* (w. perfume, water) Anacr. Plu. —*a city* (W.DAT. *w. honey, fig.ref. to song*) Pi. ‖ PASS. (of a person) get drenched (by rain) Ar.
2 (fig.) **quench** —*a boast* (W.DAT. *w. silence*) Pi.

κατα-βρίθω *vb.* **1** (of sheep) **be weighed down** —W.DAT. *w. wool* Hes.; (of branches) —*w. fruit* Theoc.
2 (fig., of a king) **outweigh** —*other kings* (W.DAT. *in riches*) Theoc.

κατα-βρόξαι (also **καταβρῶξαι** AR.) *aor.inf.* [reltd. βρόχθος] **gulp down** —*a potion* Od.; (of the Harpies) —*food* AR.

κατα-βροχθίζω vb. swallow —a coin (by mistake) Ar.; **gulp down** —food Ar.; (fig., of a statesman) —parts of lawsuits (as opportunities for profit) Ar.

κατα-βρύκω vb. **chomp down** —food Hippon.

κατα-βυρσόω contr.vb. [βύρσα] **1 cover with hides** —the upper parts of a warship (for protection in battle) Th. **2 skin, flay** —a corpse Plu.

καταβώσομαι (Ion.fut.mid.): see καταβοάω

κατάγαιος Ion.adj.: see κατάγειος

καταγγελεύς έως m. [καταγγέλλω] **proclaimer** (of foreign gods) NT.

καταγγελία ᾶς f. **official proclamation, announcement** Plu.

κατ-αγγέλλω vb. **1 denounce, reveal** —a plot X. **2 announce, proclaim** —war, measures, events Lys. Plb. Plu.; (of the Apostles) —Jesus, his teachings, or sim. NT. ‖ PASS. (of the word of God, forgiveness) be proclaimed NT.; (of a commander) be announced —W.INF. to be marching on a city Plu.

κατάγγελτος ον adj. (of a people) made public, **reported** (to their enemies, W.PTCPL. as doing sthg.) Th.

κατά-γειος, Ion. **κατάγαιος,** ον adj. [γῆ] **1** (of rooms, tunnels, dwellings) **underground, subterranean** Hdt. Pl. X. Plu. ‖ NEUT.SB. cavern Pl. **2** (of a bird) **terrestrial** (i.e. flightless) Hdt.

καταγέλαστος ον adj. [καταγελάω] (of persons or things) inviting ridicule, **laughable, ridiculous** Hdt. Ar. Att.orats. Pl. X. +; (w. ὑπό + GEN. in the eyes of someone) Isoc. Pl. Plu.

—καταγελάστως adv. ǀ superl. καταγελαστότατα ǀ **1** in a manner inviting ridicule, **ridiculously** Pl. X. Aeschin. Plu. **2 contemptibly** Aeschin.

κατα-γελάω contr.vb. **laugh scornfully** E. Ar. Isoc. Pl. X. +; **ridicule, make fun of, mock** —W.DAT. someone or sthg. Hdt. —W.GEN. Hdt. Ar. Att.orats. Pl. +(w. ὡς + PTCPL. as being idiotic or sim.) Pl. Plu. ‖ PASS. be mocked A. Th. Isoc. Pl. + —W. ὑπό + GEN. by someone Hdt. Ar. Pl.

κατά-γελως ωτος m. [γέλως] **1 scornful laughter, derision, mockery** Ar. X. D.; (concr., ref. to symbols of office, as shaming the wearer) A. **2 ridiculousness** (of a situation) Pl.

κατα-γέμω vb. (of places) **be crammed full** —W.GEN. w. people, spoils Plb.

κατα-γηράσκω vb. —also **καταγηράω** (Pl. +) contr.vb. ǀ aor.1 κατεγήρασα ǀ ep.3sg.athem.aor. κατεγήρᾱ ǀ **grow old** Od. Hdt. E. Ar. Att.orats. +

κατα-γιγαρτίζω vb. [γίγαρτον] (fig.) **squeeze the pips out of** —a slave-girl (i.e. have sex w. her) Ar.

κατα-γιγνώσκω, dial. **καταγῑνώσκω** (Plb. Plu.) vb. **1** perceive a negative quality or circumstance; **detect** —a shortcoming (W.GEN. in someone) Ar. X. D. Plu. —a plot X. —W.ACC. + INF. that someone is doing sthg. wrong X.; **recognise, be forced to concede** —W.COMPL.CL. that sthg. is the case Th. **2** (wkr.sens.) **notice, realise** —sthg. X. —W.COMPL.CL. that sthg. is the case X. **3** form an unfavourable conclusion; **conclude** —W.ACC. + INF. that sthg. unfortunate is the case Isoc. Pl. Din.; **deem** —W.GEN. a person, oneself (W.INF. to be flawed, incapable, or sim.) Th. Isoc. Pl. X.; **suspect** —W.NEUT.ACC. + COMPL.CL. that sthg. is the case Pl. ‖ PASS. (of a person) be deemed —W.INF. to deserve punishment Plu.; be suspected —W.INF. of doing wrong Hdt. **4 form an unfavourable opinion** (of someone) Th. Plb. Plu. —W.GEN. of someone or sthg. Pl. X. Thphr. Plb. Plu. —(W.COMPL.CL. as doing or having done sthg. bad) Pl. D. Plu. ‖ PASS. (of a person) be despised Plb. **5** attribute a negative quality to a person; **impute** —cowardice, malice, or sim. (usu. W.GEN. to someone) Hdt. Att.orats. Pl. X. + **6 denounce, condemn** —W.ACC. someone's actions or character D. Plb. Plu. —W.GEN. a person (oft. W.INF. or COMPL.CL. as doing sthg. wrong) Isoc. Pl. Din. Plb. Plu. **7 convict, find guilty** —W.GEN. a person (oft. W.ACC. or INF. of committing a particular crime) Th. Att.orats. X. Arist. Plu.; **prove** (W.GEN. oneself) **guilty** (esp. by fleeing trial) Att.orats. Plb. Plu. ‖ PASS. be found guilty Th. And. X. D.(law) Plu. —W.INF. of doing wrong X. —W.PREDIC.SB. of being a murderer Antipho. **8 impose** (as a sentence) —death, exile, imprisonment, a fine, or sim. (W.GEN. on a person) Th. Att.orats. Arist. Plu. —exile (W.GEN. on oneself) Lycurg. Plb. ‖ PASS. be sentenced —W.GEN. to death Din.; (of death, a fine) be imposed as a sentence And.(decree) Isoc. —W.GEN. on a person Att.orats. X. Plu. **9 issue a guilty verdict** X. Aeschin. D. Arist. Plu. —W.GEN. in a case Isoc.; **find** (W.ACC. a person) **guilty** —W.INF. of doing wrong Plu.; **issue** —a verdict (W.GEN. of murder) Antipho; **decide** —a case (sts. W.GEN. against a person) Ar. Is. D. ‖ PASS. (of a crime) be passed sentence upon Lycurg.; (of a person's guilt) be confirmed by a court Arist.; (of a case) be given a guilty verdict Att.orats. Plu.; (wkr.sens., of a case) be decided A.

καταγίζω Ion.vb.: see καθαγίζω

κατ-αγῑνέω Ion.contr.vb. (of wagons) **bring down** —timber (W.PREP.PHR. fr. hills) Od.; (of a person) **cause** (W.ACC. fugitives) **to come down** (fr. a hilltop sanctuary) Hdt.

κατα-γίνομαι dial.mid.vb. [γίγνομαι] **remain occupied** —w. ἐν + DAT. in hunting Plb.

κατα-γλωττίζω Att.vb. [γλῶσσα] **kiss with the tongue** (i.e. give a French kiss); (fig., of a demagogue) **tongue** —lies (W.GEN. over someone) Ar. ‖ PF.PASS.PTCPL. (of a city) French-kissed —W.PREP.PHR. by a demagogue Ar.; (as adj., of a song, i.e. lascivious, saucy) Ar.

καταγλωττίσματα των n.pl. **kisses involving the tongue, French kisses** Ar.

κάταγμα ατος n. [κατάγω 7] **roll of carded wool** (ready to be spun into thread), **clump of wool** S. Ar. Pl.

κατάγνῡμι, also **καταγνύω** vb. [κατά, ἄγνυμι] ǀ fut. κατάξω, also κατεαξῶ (NT.) ǀ aor. κατέαξα, 3sg.subj. κατάξῃ, inf. κατάξαι, ep.2sg.opt. καυάξαις, ep.masc.pl.ptcpl. καυάξαντες ǀ pf. κατέᾱγα, Ion. κατέηγα ǀ aor.2 pass. κατεάγην, subj. κατᾱγῶ, also κατεαγῶ (NT.) ǀ

1 (of gods, persons, a wave) **break to pieces** —objects, ships Hom. Hes. Th. Ar. Pl. +; (fig., of debaters) **break up** —concepts, classes of things Pl. ‖ PASS. and PF.ACT. (of ships, objects) be broken to pieces Hdt. Ar. Pl. Plb. Plu.; (fig., of a person envisaged as a pot) Ar.

2 (specif.) **break, fracture** —someone's legs or skull Lys. Ar. X. Men. NT. ‖ PASS. and PF.ACT. (of limbs, the skull) be fractured Pl. D. NT.; (of a person) suffer a fracture Pl. —W.PARTITV.GEN. to one's skull Ar. Pl. —W.ACC. to one's skull or collar-bone E.Cyc. Att.orats. Thphr.; get battered —W.ACC. on one's ears (fr. boxing) Pl.

3 (gener.) inflict fractures on, **injure** —a person D.; **chop down** —a tree Arist.; **wreck, destroy** —one's native land E.

4 (wkr.sens., of manual trades) **weaken** —the soul X. ‖ PF. (of persons) be effeminate Plu.

κατάγνωσις εως *f.* [καταγιγνώσκω] **1** act of finding guilty, **condemnation** (of a person, by a court) Th. D. Arist.; **sentence** (W.GEN. of death) X.
2 (gener.) **censure, condemnation** (of a person) Plb.
3 low opinion (W.GEN. of an enemy's weakness) Th.
κατα-γοητεύω *vb.* (of a ruler, a statesman) render spellbound, **hold in thrall** —*a people* X. Plu.
κατά-γομος ον *adj.* [γόμος] (of ships) **heavily laden** Plb.
κατ-αγοράζω *vb.* (of a merchant) **buy up, purchase** —*wares* D.
κατ-αγορεύω *vb.* **1 inform against, denounce** —*a person, a plot, its ringleader* (W.DAT. or PREP.PHR. *to someone*) Th. X. —W.GEN. *people (to a tyrant)* Arist.
2 (gener.) **disclose, tell** (sthg.) —W.DAT. *to someone* Ar.
καταγραφή ῆς *f.* [καταγράφω] **1 outline** (of a figure moulded in relief) Pl.
2 (sg. and pl.) **enrolment** (of soldiers) Plb.; (concr.) **register, roll** (of soldiers) Plb.
κατα-γράφω *vb.* **1** (of unborn lions) **scratch, lacerate** (their mother's womb, w. their claws) Hdt.
2 cover with writing, **write on** —*a podium* Plu.; (fig., of the voice of Orpheus) **inscribe** —*writing-tablets* E.
3 write down —W.ACC. or DIR.SP. *a message, a line of verse* (w. εἰς + ACC. *on the ground, a wall*) Plb. Plu.; (intr.) **write** —w. εἰς + ACC. *on the ground* NT. ‖ PASS. (of laws, treaties, official records) be written down Pl. Plb. Plu.; (of messages, a name) be written —w. ἐν + DAT. *on walls, a discus* Plu.
4 assign in writing, allocate —*a residence (to a person)* Plu.
5 add to a list, **enrol** —*troops, sailors, conspirators* Plb. Plu.; **raise by enrolment** —*legions* Plb. Plu. ‖ PASS. (of persons) be put on a list Plb. Plu.; (of troops) be enrolled Plb.; (of legions) be raised by enrolment Plb.
κατ-άγχω *vb.* **strangle** —*someone* Plu.
κατάγω (aor.2 pass.subj.): see κατάγνυμι
κατ-άγω *vb.* | The sections are grouped as: (1–9) bring down (fr. above), (10–11) bring down (fr. the sea, to land), (12–14) bring in, (15–18) bring back. |
1 bring down (towards the ground), **pull down** —*a person, tree-top, lever* E. Plb. Plu. ‖ PASS. (of suspended objects) be made to descend Plu.
2 pull downwards, pull down, pull off —*robes, a covering* Ar. Plu.; **tug on** —*a person's beard* Plu.
3 bring down (fr. the sky); (of sorcerers, a mystic) **call down** —*Zeus, an eagle* Plu.
4 cause to go down (to the underworld); (of Hades, Hermes, death) **take down** —*persons, souls* (sts. W.PREP.PHR. *to the underworld*) Od. Pi. E.; (of a taskmaster, necessity) **send down** —*a person* (W.PREP.PHR. *to Hades*) Od. E.; (of a person, w. play on sense 15) **send home** —*persons (i.e. to the underworld, by killing them)* E.
5 bring downhill (esp. to a city or the coast); **lead down** —*persons (to a place)* Il. Hdt. E. X. NT. Plu.; **lead or drive down** —*animals* Hom.; **bring down** —*objects, supplies* Hdt. Pl. AR. Plu.; (of a ravine) **channel down** —*a river (to the sea)* AR. ‖ PASS. make one's way down (to a place) Plu.
6 bring down (fr. a northerly place); **bring down** —*a person (fr. Macedonia)* Plu.
7 draw down (into a thread), **spin** (wool) Pl.
8 ‖ PASS. (of news) be brought down —W.DAT. *to a sea god* Call.
9 ‖ PASS. (of a person's genealogy) be traced down Plu.
10 bring down (fr. the sea, to land); (of persons, winds) **bring to land** —*persons, ships, cargo* Od. Isoc. X. D. NT. Plu.; (of a ship) —*persons* Call.; (of gales, a time of day) —*waves* Plu.; (intr., of sailors, ships) **put in to shore** Od. X.

‖ IMPERATV. (fig., addressed to persons visiting a sick-bed) perh., **draw in!** E. ‖ MID. (of sailors, ships) **put in to shore** Od. Hdt. Ar. Pl. X. —W.ACC. *at a place* S. ‖ PASS. (of persons, ships, things) be brought to land Hdt. Lycurg. D. Men. Plb. Plu.
11 force to shore —*captured ships, sailors* Att.orats. Plb. Plu. ‖ PASS. (of captured ships, sailors) be taken to shore D. Plb.
12 bring in (to a house or lodging); **take in** —*a person (as a guest)* Plu. ‖ MID. **arrive for a stay, take lodging** —W.PREP.PHR. *at a place* X. Aeschin. D. ‖ PASS. be admitted as a guest X. Plu.
13 (gener., of persons, circumstances) **bring in** —*a person* (oft. W.PREP.PHR. *to a place*) NT. Plu. ‖ PASS. (of persons or things) be brought in (to a place) D.
14 bring —*a city* (W.PREP.PHR. *into danger*) Th.; **introduce** —*an argument (into a discussion)* Pl.
15 bring back (to home); (of persons, circumstances) **bring back** —*persons (esp. exiles)* Timocr. A. Hdt. Th. Critias Ar. +; (fig.) —*exiled elements of the soul* Pl. ‖ PASS. (of persons, esp. exiles) be brought back X. Plb.; make one's way back (fr. overseas) Plb.
16 (gener.) **bring back** (fr. elsewhere) —*objects, news* Od.(tm.) Semon.
17 (specif., of a commander) **bring back** (fr. a war), **gain, win** —*spoils, victories, triumphs* Plb. Plu. ‖ PASS. (of a triumph) be brought back (i.e. won) —W.PREP.PHR. *fr. a war* Plu.
18 bring back (to a former condition); **restore** —*a deposed ruler* Hdt. E. Th. Isoc. Plb. Plu. —*the people (i.e. democratic rule)* Att.orats. —*a city* (w. εἰς + ACC. *to itself, after a time of chaos*) Plu. —*an earlier situation* Plu.
καταγωγή ῆς *f.* **1 putting in** (of ships, to a port) Th. Plb.
2 lodging (of travellers, in a place) Hdt.
3 rest-stop (on a journey, climb, or sim.) Hdt. Pl. X.
4 restoration (of a deposed king, to his throne) Plb.
καταγώγιον ου *n.* **guest-house, hostelry** Th. Pl. X. Plu.
καταγωγίς ιδος *f.* **dress, robe** (of a woman) Sapph.
κατ-αγωνίζομαι *mid.vb.* (of a competitor) **overpower** —*an opponent* Plu.; (gener., of commanders, persons, qualities) **defeat, win out against** —*enemies, rivals, qualities* Men. Plb. Plu. ‖ PASS. be overcome (by an opponent or enemy) Plb. Plu.
κατα-δαίνυμαι *mid.vb.* **gobble down, devour** —*barley-cakes* Theoc.
κατα-δάκνομαι *pass.vb.* **be bitten** (by insects) Theoc.(tm.)
κατα-δακρύω *vb.* **weep over** —*someone or sthg.* X. Plu.; (intr.) **weep bitterly** E. Tim. X. Plu.
κατα-δακτυλικός ή όν *adj.* [δάκτυλος] **inclined to give the finger** (i.e. make an obscene gesture, W.GEN. to a certain kind of person) Ar.
κατα-δαμάζομαι *mid.vb.* **subdue, defeat** —*enemy troops* Th.
κατα-δαμαλίζω *vb.* (fig., of a blast of wind) **overwhelm, destroy** —*a person's life* Pi.(tm.)
κατα-δάμναμαι *mid.vb.* **destroy** —*cows' heads and hooves* (W.DAT. *w. fire*) hHom.
κατα-δαπανάω *contr.vb.* **1 exhaust by consuming, use up** —*resources, provisions* X. Arist.; **consume by oneself** —*possessions, delicacies (opp. share them out)* X. ‖ PASS. (of funds) be completely spent Hdt. X.
2 (of troops) **use up** —*the weight of one's blankets* (w. εἰς + ACC. *on provisions, i.e. bring food in one's pack instead of blankets*) X.
κατα-δάπτω *vb.* (of wild beasts) **tear to pieces** —*a slain man* Hom. [or perh. *devour*] ‖ PASS. (fig., of a person's heart) be torn (by bad news) Od.
κατα-δαρθάνω *vb.* | aor.2 κατέδαρθον, ep. κατέδραθον, also κάδδραθον | **1 sleep** or **go to sleep** Od. Th. Ar. Pl. X. +
2 go to bed (i.e. have sex) —W.PREP.PHR. *w. someone* Ar. Pl.

κατα-δατέομαι *mid.contr.vb.* | ep.3pl.fut. (tm.) κατὰ ... δάσονται | (of wild beasts) **tear to pieces** (and devour) —*a person* Il.

καταδεής ές *adj.* [καταδέω²] **1** entirely lacking; (of jars) **devoid, emptied** (W.GEN. of their contents) Hdt. **2** (of a person, a tomb) **inferior, substandard** Pl. Aeschin. || COMPAR. (of persons, things) inferior (oft. W.GEN. to someone or sthg.) Att.orats. Arist. Plb.
—**καταδεέστερον** *neut.compar.adv.* —also **καταδεεστέρως** *compar.adv.* **1** to an inferior standard, **less well** (oft. W.GEN. than someone or sthg., than one's wishes) Isoc. X. Lycurg. **2** less prosperously Isoc. D.

κατα-δείδω *vb.* | aor. κατέδεισα | **be frightened by** —someone or sthg. Th. And. D. Plu.; **be too scared** (to do sthg.) D. —W.INF. to do sthg. Th.; **be terrified** Th. Ar. Plu.

κατα-δείκνῡμι *vb.* | aor. κατέδειξα, Ion. κατέδεξα || Ion.3sg.plpf.pass. κατεδέδεκτο | **1** discover and make known, **discover** (a fact) Hdt. —*places* Hdt. || PASS. (of a route) be discovered —W.PTCPL. to be disadvantageous Hdt. **2** (of gods, persons, a city) **introduce** —a practice or sim. (oft. W.DAT. or PREP.PHR. to persons, mankind) Ar. Isoc. Pl. D. Arist. +; **teach** (persons) —W.INF. to do sthg. Hdt. Ar. Aeschin. || PASS. (of a custom) be introduced D. Plu.

κατα-δειλιάω *contr.vb.* | aor. κατεδειλίᾱσα | **1 show cowardice** (in battle) Plu.; **be afraid** —w. πρός + ACC. at the prospect of a voyage Plu.
2 leave undone through cowardice, **flinch from** —a mission X.

καταδέκομαι *dial.mid.vb.*: see καταδέχομαι

κατα-δέρκομαι *mid.vb.* | act.aor.2 κατέδρακον || aor.pass. (w.mid.sens.) κατεδέρχθην | **1** (of the sun) **gaze down** —W.PREP.PHR. on land and sea hHom.
2 (tr., of the sun) **gaze down on** —persons Od. Ibyc.; (of Hera) —Olympos Lyr.adesp.
3 (of a person) **behold** —a city Pi. || AOR.PASS. (fig., of Herakles) behold —the blossoming of madness (i.e. begin to go mad) S.

κατάδεσις εως *f.* [καταδέω¹] **binding by spells** Pl.

κατά-δεσμος ου *m.* [δεσμός] **binding by spells** Pl.

κατα-δεύω *vb.* [δεύω¹] (of a person, a raincloud) **soak** —clothes (w. wine, rain) Il. Hes.(tm.); (of a river) **water, irrigate** —a plain E. || MID. **get** (W.ACC. one's ears) **wet** (in the rain) Hes.

κατα-δέχομαι, dial. **καταδέκομαι** *mid.vb.* **1** (of earth, reservoirs, bones in the body) **receive, absorb** —water, nourishment Pl.; (of a person) —the blood of a murdered person (W.DAT. in the folds of one's cloak) Plu.; (fig.) —beautiful things (w. εἰς + ACC. into one's soul) Pl.
2 (of the designers of a state) **allow in, admit** —poetry Pl.
3 (of cities, peoples, a court) **take or allow back** —exiles Hdt. Att.orats. Arist. —a person (on a council, the list of citizens) Aeschin. D.; (fig., of a person) —exiled elements of one's soul Pl.

κατα-δέω¹ *contr.vb.* **1** tie on, attach, **fasten** —sthg. (sts. W.PREP.PHR. to sthg., W.DAT. w. a rope or sim.) Hom. Hdt. Pl. || PASS. (of a person) be bound —W.PREP.PHR. to a wheel Plu.
2 (specif.) **tether** —an animal (oft. W.PREP.PHR. to sthg., in a place) Hom. Anacr. Hdt. Pl. X. +; (fig., of creator gods) —the appetite (envisaged as an animal, W.ADV. in the stomach) Pl. || PASS. (of an animal) be tethered Hdt.
3 || MID. **fasten to oneself** —a noose E. || PF.PASS. have (W.ACC. one's eyes) bound (w. a blindfold) Hdt.
4 bind, bandage —wounds NT. || MID. **bind up** —one's whole body and face (W.DAT. in hides and skins, as protection fr. pests) Hdt. || PF.PASS. have (W.ACC. one's legs) bandaged Plu.
5 close by binding, **fasten, seal up** —a pouch (W.DAT. w. a string) Od.; **seal up, lock** —chests Hdt.
6 restrain with bonds, **tie up** —a person Od.; **shackle, imprison** —persons Hdt. Th. Plu. || PASS. (fig., of the soul) be held imprisoned —w. ὑπό + GEN. by the body Pl.; (fig., of a person) be bound or constrained —W.PREP.PHR. in a state of fear E.
7 (of gods) **hold back** —the winds, their courses, the course of a boat Od. Call.
8 || MID. **bind by a spell** —a person (sts. W.DAT. or PREP.PHR. w. charms, rites) Theoc.
9 (of oracles, soothsayers) **convict** —a person (W.INF. of committing perjury, being a thief) Hdt.

κατα-δέω² *contr.vb.* (of an army, fleet, journey, the side of a pyramid) **fall short by** —W.GEN. a certain small amount (oft. W.GEN., PREP.PHR. or μή + INF. fr. being a certain total number, distance or length) Hdt.
—**καταδέομαι** *mid.contr.vb.* | 3sg.aor.pass.opt. (w.mid.sens.) καταδεηθείη | **make a request** —W.GEN. of someone Pl.

κατά-δηλος ον *adj.* [δῆλος] **1** (of things, animals) able to be clearly seen, **visible** (sts. W.DAT. to someone) Th. Ar. X. Plu.; (fig., of a group of people, to the mind's eye) Pl.
2 (of facts, qualities) **clear, obvious, apparent** Th. Pl. X. Plu.; (of persons, sts. things) κατάδηλος εἶναι (or sim.) be clearly —W.NOM.PTCPL. doing sthg. S. Isoc. Pl. X. Plu. —w. ὅτι + INDIC. Pl. X. —W.INF. Th. —w. ὡς ἄν + OPT. Pl. || NEUT.IMPERS. (w. γίγνεται or sim., sts.understd.) it is clear —W.COMPL.CL. or INDIR.Q. that sthg. (or what) is the case Pl. X.
3 (of persons, wrongdoings) **exposed, found out** Hdt. Pl. || NEUT.SB. obviousness, detectability (of plotters) Th.

κατα-δημαγωγέομαι *pass.contr.vb.* **1** (of petitioners to a king) **be won over by flattery** Plu.
2 (of a statesman) **be outdone in courting popular favour** Plu.
3 (of a king) **be thwarted by demagogues** Plu.

κατα-δημοβορέω *contr.vb.* [δημοβόρος] (of the inhabitants of a city) consume as a populace, **communally feast on** —a person's possessions (to save them fr. enemy hands) Il.

κατα-διαιρέω *contr.vb.* | aor.2 mid.inf. καταδιελέσθαι | || MID. (of a nation) **cause division among** —confederate cities Plb.

κατα-διαιτάω *contr.vb.* (of courts or sim.) **decide against** (one party, in an arbitration case) D. —W.GEN. someone Is. D.; **issue** —W.INTERN.ACC. a ruling or fine (esp. for default) D. || MID. obtain as a ruling (in an arbitration case) —a fine, a judgement (W.GEN. against someone) Lys. D.

κατα-διαλλάσσομαι *pass.vb.* **be reconciled** (w. a rival) Ar.

κατα-δίδωμι *vb.* (of a sea) **flow out, feed** —w. ἐς + ACC. into a strait Hdt.; (app., of marshes) **give out, issue** (into the sea) Plu.

κατα-δικάζω *vb.* **1** (of persons, jurors, courts) **issue a guilty verdict, pass judgement** (oft. W.GEN. against someone) Pl. X. Aeschin. Arist. NT. —W.ACC. of a fine, a certain sentence Hdt. Att.orats. Arist. Plb. —W.INF. to suffer the death penalty X.; **condemn** —the innocent NT.; (wkr.sens., of observers) **judge** —W.COMPL.CL. that someone was right to do sthg. X.
2 || MID. (of persons or peoples bringing a lawsuit) **obtain a judgement** (oft. W.GEN. against a person or people) Th. Lys. Pl. D. —W.ACC. of a fine, a guilty verdict Th. Pl. D. Plu.
3 || PASS. (of persons) be condemned, be found guilty And. Pl. Arist. Plb. NT. Plu.; (of a fine, a judgement) be awarded (sts. W.GEN. against someone) X. Is.

κατα-δίκη ης *f.* **1** judgement of a court (against someone), **conviction** Plb. NT. Plu.; (W.GEN. for embezzlement) Plu.
2 (specif.) sum of money imposed as a judgement, **fine** Th. D. Plu.; **award** (to a plaintiff, to be paid by a defendant) D.
κατάδικος ον *adj.* (of persons) **convicted, condemned** Plu.
κατα-διώκω *vb.* **1 pursue, chase** —*persons, ships* (sts. W.PREP.PHR. *to a place*) Th. X. Plb. Plu. ‖ PASS. be pursued Plu.
2 chase back —*persons, ships* (sts. W.PREP.PHR. *to a place*) Th. Plb. Plu. ‖ PASS. (of ships) be chased back (to land) Th.
3 chase off, chase away —*troops* X. Plb.
4 go in search of —*a person* NT.; **hunt down** —*a wanted man* Plu.
5 (of a people) **seek after, aim for** —*convenience* (in their method of doing sthg.) Plb.
κατα-δοκέω *contr.vb.* **1** harbour a suspicion, **suspect** —*someone* (of being a certain person) Hdt. —W.ACC. + INF. that someone is doing sthg. Hdt.; **imagine** —W.INDIR.Q. what is the case Hdt. ‖ PASS. be held in suspicion Antipho; be suspected —W.INF. + PREDIC.SB. of being a murderer Antipho
2 have an expectation, **suspect, expect** (sthg.) Hdt.
κατα-δοξάζω *vb.* **1** harbour a suspicion or belief, **suspect** —W.ACC. + INF. that sthg. is the case X.
2 have an expectation, **expect** —W.ACC. + INF. that sthg. is the case Plu.
κατα-δουλόω *contr.vb.* **1** ‖ MID. **enslave** —*persons* E. Lys. X. Arist. Plu.
2 (act. and mid.) reduce to subjection, **make subject, enslave** —*peoples, cities, regions, or sim.* (sts. W.DAT. *to a foreign power or ruler*) Hdt. Th. Att.orats. Pl. X. + ‖ PASS. (of peoples, regions) be made subject (to someone) Hdt. Att.orats. Plu.
3 ‖ MID. (of persons, fear, corruption, avarice) **render subservient** —*persons* Isoc. Pl. X. Aeschin. Plu. —*good qualities of the soul* (sts. W.DAT. *to some bad quality*) Pl.; (of bad omens) **subdue** —*a person's spirits* Plu.; (of a malady) —*democracy* Pl.
4 (act. and mid.) **hold in thrall** —*persons* (esp. by inspiring love or admiration) Pl. Men. ‖ PASS. be held in thrall —w. ὑπό + GEN. by a person, wisdom Pl.
καταδούλωσις εως *f.* **enslavement, subjugation** (W.GEN. of a people, a region) Th. Pl.
καταδοχή ῆς *f.* [καταδέχομαι] **1** act of receiving back, **allowing back** (of exiles) Pl.
2 reception (of ambassadors) Plb.(cj.) | see καταλογή
κατα-δραμεῖν *aor.2 inf.* | The pres. and impf. are supplied by κατατρέχω. | **1** (of persons, cavalry) **run down, rush down** (usu. W.PREP.PHR. fr. a height, to the shore, or sim.) Hdt. Th. Ar. X. Men. Plu.; (wkr.sens.) turn up at a rush, **rush** —W.PREP.PHR. *at someone* NT. Plu.
2 (of troops, commanders) **overrun** —*a region* Th. Plb. Plu.
3 (of a ship) **put in at** —*a port* Call.
4 (of a person) **roam over** —*mountains* Call.
5 (fig.) **run down, be disparaging about** —*a nation* Pl.
κατα-δρέπω *vb.* **pluck** —*leaves, fruit* (fr. trees) Hdt. Pl.
καταδρομή ῆς *f.* [καταδραμεῖν] **1 hostile incursion, raid** (by troops) Th. Lys. X. Plb. Plu.
2 (fig.) **attack** (on writers, someone's theory or character) Pl. Aeschin. Plb.
κατάδρομος ον *adj.* (of buildings) **ravaged** (W.DAT. by fire and enemy spears) E.
κατάδρυμμα ατος *n.* [καταδρύπτομαι] **tearing** (of one's skin w. one's nails, in mourning) E.
κατα-δρύπτομαι *mid.vb.* **tear** —*one's cheeks* (in mourning) Hes.(tm.)

κατα-δυναστεύω *vb.* **1** (of opponents' wealth) **prevail over** —*a person facing a jury* X.
2 ‖ PASS. be possessed —w. ὑπό + GEN. by the Devil NT.
καταδύνω *vb.*: see καταδύω
κατάδυσις εως *f.* [καταδύω] **hiding-place, den** (of an animal) Plu.
κατα-δύω, also **καταδύνω** *vb.* [δύω¹] | aor.1 (causatv.) κατέδυσα | athem.aor. κατέδῦν | **1 dive down** —W.PREP.PHR. *to the sea-bed or sim.* Thgn. Theoc.
2 (of the sun) **go down, set** Hom. Hes. hHom. Hdt.(mid.) Plu.
3 go down underground; (of persons) **go down** (sts. W.PREP.PHR. beneath the earth) Hdt. Pl. ‖ MID. **go down** —W.PREP.PHR. to the underworld (i.e. die) Od.
4 (act. and mid.) **plunge into** —*a throng, a battle* Il. Hes.
5 (act. and mid.) **slip in among** —*a crowd* Hom.; (of a rumour, when its source is sought) **slip away into** —*the throng* Plu.
6 (act. and mid.) **make one's way in** —W.PREP.PHR. *to a place* Hom. hHom. Pl.; (of rhythm, harmony, anarchy) —*to the soul or sim.* Pl.; (of snakes) **creep in** —W.PREP.PHR. *to a place* Plu.
7 (act. and mid.) **put on** —*armour, clothes* Hom. Mosch.
8 (act. and mid.) **go down** (into concealment), **duck down** —W.PREP.PHR. *into bedclothes, holes* hHom. X.; **hide away** Ar. Pl. D. Plu. —W.PREP.PHR. *in a place* Hdt. Pl. Aeschin. Theoc. +
9 (act. and mid.) **run off into hiding, take refuge** —W.PREP.PHR. *in a place* Anacr. Plb. Plu.; (fig.) —w. εἰς + ACC. *in a deceptive show of behaviour* Plu.; (wkr.sens.) **run off** —W.PREP.PHR. *to one's lover's bosom* Plu.
10 (act. and mid., of persons, animals, objects) **sink down** (sts. W.PREP.PHR. in the ground, snow, or sim.) X. Plb. Plu.
11 (fig., act. and mid.) **sink down** (fr. shame, sts. W.PREP.PHR. under the ground) X. —W.DAT. *because of one's conduct* D.
12 (act. and mid., of persons, an island) **be submerged, sink** X. —W.PREP.PHR. *in the sea* Hdt.
13 (act. and mid., of ships, sailors) **sink** Hdt. Th. Pl. D. Plb.; (wkr.sens., of ships) **founder, be disabled** X.; (of sailors) **have one's ship disabled** X.
14 (aor.1, of friends) **cause to set, see down** —*the sun* (W.DAT. in conversation) Call.*epigr.*
15 (aor.1, of strong medicine) **sink** —*a person's faculties* (W.PREP.PHR. to the depths, i.e. render him incapacitated) Plu.
16 (aor.1, of judgemental people) **cause to sink into the ground from shame, mortify, render prostrate** —*a person* (W.DAT. w. chagrin) X.
17 (aor.1) **cause to sink in the sea, immerse** —*a person* (to drown him) Plu.
18 (aor.1) **sink** —*ships, sailors* Hdt. Th. Ar. X. D. +; (wkr.sens.) **disable** —*a ship* Th.; (fig.) —*the ship of state* D.
κατ-άδω, also **καταείδω** *vb.* (of foreign priests) **chant incantations** —W.DAT. *to the wind* Hdt.; (tr., of a priestess) **chant** —*foreign incantations* E.
κατα-δωροδοκέω *contr.vb.* (act. and mid., of officials) **take bribes** Lys. Ar. Arist.; perh. **betray for bribes** —W.GEN. *one's city* Ar.
καταείδω *vb.*: see κατάδω
καταειμένος¹ (ep.pf.mid.pass.ptcpl.): see καταέννῡμι
καταειμένος² (ep.pf.pass.ptcpl.): see κάθημι
καταείνυον (ep.3pl.impf.): see καταέννῡμι
κατα-είσομαι *ep.fut.mid.vb.* [εἴσομαι²] | 3sg.aor. καταείσατο | (of a spear) **speed down** —W.GEN. *into the ground* Il.

κατα-έννῡμι, also **καταεινύω** *ep.vb.* | 3pl.impf. καταείνυον (v.l. καταείνυσαν) ‖ aor.mid.ptcpl. καταεσσάμενος | pf.mid.pass.ptcpl. καταειμένος | **shroud, cover** —*a corpse* (W.DAT. *w. shorn hair*) Il. ‖ PF.MID.PASS.PTCPL. (of a mountain, a place) clad —W.DAT. *in forests* Od. hHom.; (fig., of a person) wrapped —W.DAT. *in sufferings* Ibyc.

καταέρρω *Aeol.vb.*: see **καταίρω**

κατ-αζαίνω *vb.* [reltd. ἄζω] | 3sg.iteratv.aor. καταζήνασκε | (of a god) make dry, **dry up** (a lake) Od.

κατα-ζεύγνῡμι, also (pres. and impf.) **καταζευγνύω** *vb.*
1 attach with a yoke, **yoke** —*the strength of horses* (W.PREP.PHR. *to a chariot*) Pi.
2 control or subdue by yoking; (fig., of a conqueror) **yoke** —*Greece* Plu. ‖ PASS. (of the sea) be yoked (ref. to the bridging of the Hellespont) Tim.; (fig., of cities) come under the yoke (of a rigid constitution) Pl.
3 ‖ PASS. (of a woman) be confined (in a chamber) S.; (of a people) be constrained —W. ὑπό + GEN. *by necessity* Hdt.
4 (of troops) come to a halt (on a journey), **pitch camp** Plb. Plu.

κατα-ζευγοτροφέω *contr.vb.* [ζεῦγος, τρέφω] **use up money on raising chariot teams** Is.

καταζευξις εως *f.* [καταζεύγνῡμι] act of pitching camp, **encamping** (by an army) Plu.

κατα-ζώννῡμαι *mid.vb.* secure (one's dress) with a belt; (of women) **gird up** —*their tunics* Plu.; (of Bacchants) —*fawnskins* (W.DAT. *w. snakes, serving as belts*) E.

κατα-ζώω *vb.* | Att.3sg. καταζῇ, Att.inf. καταζῆν | Att.aor.inf. καταζῆσαι (Plu.) | **1** keep living, **live** —*a holy life* E.; **live one's life, spend one's days** —W.PREP.PHR. *in certain activities, in someone's company* Pl. Arist. Plu. —W.PTCPL. *being looked after* Men.
2 ‖ AOR. live out —*one's life* (i.e. the remainder of it, W.PREP.PHR. *among certain people*) Plu.

κατ-άημι *vb.* | dial.3sg.aor.mid. καταήσσατο | ‖ MID. (of a goddess) **breathe down** —*joy* (w. 2ND ACC. *on a person*) Alc.(dub.)

κατα-θαμβέομαι *mid.contr.vb.* ‖ PF. (of a general) be in awe of —*an enemy commander* Plu.; (of a city) —*a ruler's power* Plu.

κατα-θάπτω, ep. **καθθάπτω** *vb.* **bury** —*a corpse, bones* Il. A. Lys. D. Mosch.

κατα-θαρρέω *Att.contr.vb.* [θαρσέω] **1** (of commanders, troops) **be confident** (of military success or sim.) Plb.; (of persons) **be bold, show no fear** Arist.(dub.)
2 (of troops) behave with confidence, **be audacious** Plb.

—κατατεθαρρηκότως *Att.pf.ptcpl.adv.* **boldly** Plb. Plu.; (pejor.) **overconfidently** Plb.

κατα-θαρρύνω *Att.vb.* [θαρσύνω] **give encouragement** (to someone) —w. πρός + ACC. *concerning the future* Plu.

κατα-θεάομαι *mid.contr.vb.* **1 look down on, observe** —*troops, a battle* (w. ἀπό + GEN. *fr. a hill, a wall*) X.
2 look at closely, inspect —*persons, places* X. Plu.; (intr.) **look around** X.
3 look over in one's mind, **consider** —*a matter* X. —W.ACC. + INDIR.Q. *how sthg. is the case* X.; **go through** —*people on a list* X.

καταθείομεν (ep.1pl.athem.aor.subj.): see **κατατίθημι**

κατα-θέλγω *vb.* **1** subdue with spells, **bewitch** —*animals* Od.
2 charm —*a person* Mosch. Plu.

καταθεματίζω *vb.* [reltd. κατατίθημι] **invoke a curse** (on oneself) NT.

κατα-θέω *contr.vb.* [θέω¹] | only pres. | **1** run down; (of troops, cavalry) **charge down** (usu. W.PREP.PHR. fr. a high place) Th. X.
2 (of ships) sail rapidly in, **speed in** —W.PREP.PHR. *to a port* X.; (fig., of persons envisaged as ships) —*into a camp* Plu.
3 (of troops, commanders) **go out on a foray** X.; (tr.) **make a foray over** —*a land* Th. X. D.; **raid** —*cities* X.
4 (fig.) **run down, criticise** —*a person* Pl.

κατα-θεωρέομαι *pass.contr.vb.* (of cookery and medicine) be examined carefully or contrastively, **be scrutinised** —w. ὑπό + GEN. *by the soul* Pl.

κατ-ᾱθλέω *contr.vb.* **1** (fig., of a commander) **wrestle to the ground** —*an enemy commander* Plu.
2 ‖ PF. (of soldiers) be physically well-trained Plu.

κατα-θλίβομαι *pass.vb.* | aor.2 κατεθλίβην | (of vapour) **be compressed** (in the earth, to make water) Plu.

κατα-θνῄσκω (or **-θνήσκω**), ep. **κατθνῄσκω**, Aeol. **κατθναίσκω** *vb.* | fut. κατθανοῦμαι (E.) | aor.2 κατέθανον, ep. κάτθανον, Aeol.inf. κατθάνην | pf. κατατέθνηκα, ep.3sg.opt. κατατεθναίη, ep.masc.gen.sg.ptcpl. κατατεθνηῶτος |
1 (of persons, their bodies) **die** or **be killed** Il. Sapph. Alc. Trag. Ar.(quot. E.) + ‖ AOR. and PF. have died, be dead Hom. Archil. Mimn. Sapph. Trag. +
2 (of things, incl. living creatures) pass out of existence, **die** Emp.; (fig., of honey, exemplifying the end of all sweetness) Mosch.; (of a goddess's beauty) —w. σύν + DAT. *along w. her lover* Bion

κατα-θνητός ή όν *adj.* (of men, women) **mortal** Hom. Hes. hHom. Thgn.; (in neg.phr., of a god) Il. ‖ MASC.PL.SB. mortals hHom.

κατα-θορυβέομαι *pass.contr.vb.* (of a speaker) **be shouted down** Pl.

κατα-θραύω *vb.* **1 break up, shatter** —*substances* (*into small particles*) Plu. ‖ PASS. (of a substance) be broken up Pl.
2 (wkr.sens.) **split up, divide** —*a herd of animals* Pl.

κατα-θρηνέω *contr.vb.* **lament** E. Plu.; (tr.) **mourn** —*a person* (W.DAT. *w. songs*) E.*fr.*

κατα-θρῴσκω (or **-θρώσκω**) *vb.* | aor.2 κατέθορον | (of a goddess) **leap down** (fr. Olympos to earth) Il.(tm.); (of a person) —w. ἀπό + GEN. *fr. a horse* Hdt.; **jump down from** —W.ACC. *a wall* Hdt.

κατ-αθῡμέω *contr.vb.* (of persons) **lose heart** X.

κατα-θύμιος ᾱ (Ion. η) ον (also ος ον Call.) *adj.* [θυμός] **1** (of death, an instruction to be communicated) present in the thoughts, **in the mind** (W.DAT. *of a person*) Hom.
2 (of companions, outcomes, actions, omens fr. a sacrifice) in accordance with one's tastes or wishes, **agreeable, pleasing** (W.DAT. *to a person*) Thgn. Hdt. Call.; (of a Muse, to Zeus) Eumel.

κατα-θύω *vb.* [θύω¹] **1 offer in sacrifice** —*animals, a person* (sts. W.DAT. *to a god*) Hdt. X. Plu.
2 offer to a god —*a harvest, a tithe* X. Plu.

κατα-θωρᾱκίζομαι *pass.vb.* (of horses) **be clad in armour** X.

καταιβάτης ου *masc.adj.* [καταβαίνω] **1** (of a thunderbolt) **plunging** (fr. the sky) A.
2 (of the river Acheron) **flowing down** (to the underworld) E.
3 ‖ SB. Descender (epith. of Zeus; applied to a deified king at the place, dedicated to him, where he first stepped down fr. his chariot onto Athenian soil) Plu.

—καταιβάτις ιδος *fem.adj.* (of a path) **leading downwards** (to earth fr. Olympos, to Hades fr. earth) AR.

καταιβατός ή όν *adj.* (of an entrance to a cave) **providing a way down** (W.DAT. *for people*) Od.

καταῖγδην *ep.adv.* [καταΐσσω] **moving violently downwards** AR.

κατ-αιγίζω *vb.* [αἰγίς²] (of a wind, its howl) **rush down in a storm** A.*fr.* Plu.; (fig., of the winds of war) A.

καταιγίς ίδος *f.* storm descending from above, **storm, gale** Plu.

κατ-αιδέομαι *mid.pass.contr.vb.* **1 have respect for** —*Zeus, a person, a soul* Hdt. S. E. Ar. X.
2 feel shame about —*one's fate* E.; (intr.) **feel ashamed** E. —w.INF. *to do sthg.* Plu.
3 refrain out of shame, **forbear** —w.INF. *to do sthg.* E.

κατ-αιθαλόω *contr.vb.* (of Zeus, the fire of his thunderbolt, a commander of fire-bearing eagles) reduce to soot, **burn to ashes** —*persons, buildings* E. Ar.; (of Iris, perh. w. play on a fig. sense *inflame with desire*) —*a person* Ar. ǁ PASS. (of Troy) be burned to ashes E.

κατ-αιθύσσω *vb.* **1** (of a warrior's hair) flutter down, **cascade** —w.ACC. *over his back* Pi.
2 (fig., of Kastor, as bringer of good weather to sailors) send fluttering down, **shed** —*calm* (w.ACC. *over a place*) Pi.

κατ-αίθω *vb.* **1 burn to ashes** —*buildings, a log* A. E. —*a person* E. Ar. ǁ PASS. (of Troy, its buildings) be burned to ashes —w.DAT. *by fire* E.
2 (fig., of love) **consume** —*a person* Theoc. ǁ PASS. be consumed by love —w. ἐπί + DAT. *for someone* Theoc.

καταικίζω *vb.*: see κατακίζω

καταίνεσις εως *f.* [καταινέω] pledging in marriage, **betrothal** (of one's daughter) Plu.

κατ-αινέω *contr.vb.* | aor. κατήνεσα, Ion. καταίνεσα, dial. καταίνησα (Pi.) | **1 agree to** —*a request or proposition* Hdt.; (intr.) **agree** (to sthg.) Hdt. Plb. —w.DAT. or ἐπί + DAT. *to sthg.* Hdt. Th. —w.INF. *to do sthg.* Pi. —w.ACC. + INF. *that sthg. shd. be the case* Hdt.
2 (of a city, an oracle) **grant** —*sthg.* (w.DAT. *to someone*) S. Plu.
3 promise, pledge —*freedom* (w.DAT. *to someone*) S.*Ichn.*; (intr.) **promise** (to do sthg.) A. —w.INF. *to do sthg.* S.
4 pledge in marriage, **betroth** —*one's daughter* (w.DAT. *to a man*) E. Plu.

καταῖξ ῖκος *ep.f.* [καταΐσσω] violent squall descending from above; **gale, gust** (w.GEN. of wind) Call. AR.

καταιρέω *Ion.contr.vb.*: see καθαιρέω

κατ-αίρω, Aeol. **καταέρρω** *vb.* | Aeol.imperatv. (tm.) κὰδ ... ἄερρε | aor. κατῆρα | **1 take down** —*drinking-cups* (fr. *where they are stored*) Alc.(tm.)
2 ǁ PASS. (of a person's arm) be lowered X.
3 (intr., of birds, persons envisaged as birds) **swoop down** —w.PREP.PHR. *on a place* Ar. Plu.; (of persons, compared to birds) **fall** —w. εἰς + ACC. *into the hands of the enemy* Plu.
4 (of troops) **march down** —w.PREP.PHR. *to a place* Plb.
5 (of ships, sailors) sail in, **put in** Th. —w.PREP.PHR. *at a place* Th. Pl. Plb. Plu. —w.ACC. Plu.
6 (gener., of persons, migratory birds) **turn up, arrive** —w.ADV. or PREP.PHR. *at a place* E. Plu.

κατ-αισθάνομαι *mid.vb.* perceive the nature of, **recognise the truth about** —*one's marriage* S.

κατ-αίσιος ον *adj.* (of a deed) **righteous** A.

κατ-αΐσσω (also **καταΐσσω**) *ep.vb.* [ᾄσσω] **1** (of Harpies) **swoop down** AR. ǁ MID. (of air) **rush down** (into the body, during respiration) Emp.
2 (of a deity, in the form of pure consciousness) **dart through** —*the cosmos* (w.DAT. *w. swift thoughts*) Emp.

καταισχυντήρ ῆρος *m.* [καταισχύνω] one who defiles, **desecrator** (of a house) A.

κατ-αισχύνω *vb.* **1 bring dishonour upon** —*oneself, one's family, ancestors, native land, or sim.* Od. Alc. A. E. Ar.

Att.orats. +; (of things, events) —*persons, cities* Thgn. Plu.; (intr., of a person) **behave dishonourably** —w.ACC. *in a matter* Plu.; (of actions) **bring disgrace** Arist.
2 bring into disrepute —*one's argument* Pl.; **dishonour, make a mockery of** —*one's promises* (opp. *honour them*) Pl.
3 (of the passage of time) **make shameful** (to the debtor) —*a debt of gratitude owed to someone* Pi.
4 sully —*one's reputation, achievements, noble birth, the glory of one's ancestors, or sim.* Sol. Hdt. Trag. Att.orats. Plb. Plu. —*a banquet* (by behaving shamefully) Od.
5 defile —*a sacred offering* Stesich.; (of a poppy) —*its beautiful appearance* (by wilting) Stesich.; (of poverty) —*a person's body and mind* Thgn.
6 do dishonour to —*a god, the laws of hospitality* E. D. —*a noble man* E.
7 (specif.) do dishonour to a person (by seduction or rape); **defile** —*a woman* E. Lys. Isoc. Men. Plb. Plu. —*a man* (by hiring him for sex) D.; defile by indecent behaviour, **defile** —*oneself, one's body, one's virginity* Aeschin. Plu.
8 ǁ MID. **feel shame** —w.ACC. *before men, the gods* S. ǁ PASS. (of persons) be put to shame Th. NT. —w.ACC. *before another's courage* Isoc.; be ashamed —w.INF. *to do sthg.* Isoc.

καταίσχω *ep.vb.*: see κατίσχω

κατ-αιτιάομαι *mid.contr.vb.* **1 accuse, blame, reproach** —*persons, one another* Hdt. X.
2 (specif.) bring an accusation against, **charge** —*a person* (w. *wrongdoing*) D. ǁ PASS. be accused Th. Plb. —w.INF. *of doing sthg.* X.
3 allege (sthg.) as an accusation; **allege** —*ignorance* (on someone's part) Th. —w.NEUT.ACC. *certain things* D.

καταῖτυξ υγος *f.* **leather helmet** Il.

κατ-αιωρέομαι *pass.contr.vb.* | Ion.3pl.impf. κατηωρεῦντο | (of tassels) **hang down** (fr. a bag) Hes.

κατα-καίνω *vb.* | fut. κατακανῶ | aor.2 κατέκανον | pf. κατακέκονα | **kill** —*persons, animals* S. X.

κατα-καίριος ον *adj.* (of a spear-wound) **fatal** Il.

κατα-καίω, Att. **κατακάω** *vb.* | ep.inf. κατακαιέμεν | aor. κατέκαυσα, ep. κατέκηα, ep.inf. κατακῆαι, κακκῆαι, 1pl.subj. κατακείομεν (v.l. κατακήομεν) | pf. κατακέκαυκα ǁ PASS.: fut. κατακαυθήσομαι | aor. κατεκαύθην | aor.2 κατεκάην, Lacon.inf. κατακαάμεν (Plu., quot.) |
1 burn to ashes —*bodies, objects, buildings, places* Hom. Callin. Hdt. Th. Isoc. X. +; (of God) —*chaff* (fig.ref. to sinners) NT.; (of wind in a thundercloud) **burn up** —*itself* (fr. friction) Ar.; (intr., of a person) **burn things down** Men. ǁ PASS. (of bodies, objects, places) be burned to ashes Hom.(tm.) Hdt. Th. Pl. +; (of gold) be melted in a fire Plu.
2 (specif.) **burn alive** —*persons* Hdt. Th. Men. Plb. ǁ PASS. be burned alive Hdt. Ar. X.
3 (intr., of the sun) **scorch** Men.
4 scorch, singe —*someone* (w.DAT. *w. a torch*) Ar.; (hyperbol., of an exploding haggis) —*a person's face* Ar.
5 (fig., of circumstances) **inflame** —*persons* (w.DAT. *w. jealousy*) Plu.
6 ǁ PASS. (of a fire) burn out Il.(tm.); (fig., of the flame of tyranny) Plu.(quot.)

κατα-καλέω *contr.vb.* **1 call down** —*a person* (fr. *an attic room*) Plu.
2 call back, recall —*exiles* Plb.
3 ǁ MID. **invite** —*immigrants* (w.ADV. *to a place*) Plu. ǁ PASS. be summoned or called —w.PREP.PHR. *fr. a place* Th.
4 call on, invite, urge —*a person* (w.INF. *to do sthg.*) Plu.
5 ǁ MID. **call upon, invoke** —*a god or gods* Isoc. Plu.

κατα-καλύπτω *vb.* | tm. in Hom. Hes. AR. | **1** (of Zeus) conceal by covering, **hide from view** —*a mountain* (W.DAT. *w. clouds*) Il.; (of persons) —*another person, a door* (*w. a screen or sim.*) X. Plu. —*objects* Plu. ‖ PASS. (of objects) be hidden from view Hdt.; (of planets, by eclipses or sim.) Pl. **2 cover up** —*a corpse, a statue* Plu. ‖ MID. (specif.) **cover with one's cloak** —*one's head* Od.; (intr.) **cover one's head** Hdt. ‖ PASS. (of a statue) be covered up X.; (of a person) have one's head covered with one's cloak Pl. **3 cover** —*sacrificial offerings* (W.DAT. *w. fat*) Il. Hdt.(tm.) AR.; (of earth) —*persons, a race of men* (*in death*) Il. Hes.; (of death, darkness) —*persons, their eyes* Il. A.(tm.) E.

κατα-κάμπτω *vb.* **1** (of the influence of thoughts) **bend, twist** —*the lobe and ducts of the liver* (*w.* ἐκ + GEN. *away fr. their proper position*) Pl.; (of a god) —*parts of the world soul* (*w.* εἰς + ACC. *into a circle*) Pl.; (of a poet) **bend into shape, compose the melodic twists and turns of** —*lines of sung verse* Ar.
2 ‖ PASS. (fig., of jurors) be bent away from straight conduct, be swayed —w. πρός + ACC. *to shameful acts* Aeschin.

κατα-κάρφομαι *pass.vb.* (of leaves) **become withered** A.

κατακάσα ης *f.* [app.reltd. κασαλβάς] (pejor., ref. to a woman who betrayed her father for love) **prostitute** Call.

κατα-καυχάομαι *mid.contr.vb.* (fig., of a growing branch on a tree) **boast over, lord it over** —*broken branches* NT.

κατακάω *Att.vb.*: see κατακαίω

κατά-κειμαι *mid.pass.vb.* [κεῖμαι] **1** (of persons) **lie down** (oft. W.PREP.PHR. on a bed or sim.) Il. hHom. Hdt. Ar. Pl. X. +; (specif.) **lie asleep in bed** Plb. Plu.; (fig., of ruined walls, envisaged as being asleep) **lie** —W.PREP.PHR. *on the ground* (opp. *be woken up*, i.e. *rebuilt*) Pl.
2 lie sick in bed Hdt. D. Thphr. NT. Plu.
3 lie down in bed (w. a person, usu. w. sexual connot.) Lys. Ar. Pl.
4 lie back (on a couch or sim.), **recline** (esp. at a dinner) Thgn. Lys. Ar. Pl. X. + —W.ADJ. or PREP.PHR. *in a particular seat at a banquet* Ar. Pl. X. Thphr. Men.
5 (of corpses, slain animals) **lie prostrate** Od. Tyrt. Theoc. Plu.
6 (of headlands) **slope down** —w. πρός + ACC. *to the sea* Pi.
7 (of animals) **lurk, crouch** —W.PREP.PHR. *in a thicket* Hom.
8 (of persons) **lie idle** (when action is called for) Callin. Ar. X. Men.
9 (of sufferings, evil thoughts) **lie quiet, lie contained** —W.ADV. or PREP.PHR. *in a person's heart* (opp. *be expressed*) Il. Thgn.
10 (of objects) **lie, sit** —W.PREP.PHR. *on a floor* Il.; (of the scales of justice) **sit waiting, be ready** —W.ADV. *in a place* (W.DAT. *for adversaries at law*) hHom.
11 (of possessions, resources) **lie in storage, be stored up** —W.DAT. or PREP.PHR. *for a person, in his house* Hes.
12 be dedicated —W.DAT. *to virtue* (W.ACC. *in all one's efforts*) Pi.

κατακείομεν (ep.1pl.aor.subj.): see κατακαίω

κατα-κείρω *vb.* **1** ‖ MID. **cut off all the hair from, shave bare** —*one's head* Hdt.
2 (fig.) **deplete, use up** —*a person's house, livestock, resources* Od.

κατα-κείω, also **κακκείω** *ep.vb.* [κείω¹] **go off to bed** Hom.

κατακέκαυκα (pf.): see κατακαίω

κατακέκονα (pf.): see κατακαίνω

κατα-κελεύω *vb.* give a command, **call out a signal** (to a herald) Ar.; **call out a beat** (to rowers) Ar.

κατα-κεντέω *contr.vb.* (of a god) **pierce, puncture** —*skin* (*in creating the body*) Pl.

κατακέντημα ατος *n.* **puncture** (of the skin) Pl.

κατα-κερδαίνω *vb.* (of military officers) **derive corrupt profit** (fr. their commission) X.

κατα-κερματίζω *vb.* (fig., of a participant in a discussion) **divide up into small pieces** —*virtue* Pl. ‖ PASS. (of a nation's wealth) be divided up —w. εἰς + ACC. *into small shares* Plu.; (fig., of entities, classes of things) Pl.

κατα-κερτομέω *contr.vb.* **taunt, mock** —*a person* Hdt.

κατακῆαι (ep.aor.inf.): see κατακαίω

κατα-κηλέω *contr.vb.* **1** ‖ PASS. **be spellbound or captivated** Pl. —w. ὑπό + GEN. *by a person* Plu. —W.DAT. *by a person's good qualities* Plu.; **be held in thrall** —W.DAT. *by idleness, pleasure* Plu.
2 soothe with charms, allay —*a catastrophe* S. ‖ PASS. (of an infatuation) be allayed —W.DAT. *by reason* Plu.

κατα-κηρόω *contr.vb.* **cover with wax** —*a corpse* (to embalm it) Hdt. ‖ PASS. (of a corpse) be covered with wax Hdt.

κατα-κηρύσσω *vb.* **1** ‖ PASS. (of verdicts) be proclaimed Plb.
2 (of a public auctioneer) **announce the acceptance of a bid; knock down** —*an estate* (w. εἰς + ACC. *to a bidder*) Plu.

κατ-ακίζω *vb.* | fut.mid. κατακιοῦμαι ‖ pf.pass. κατῄκισμαι | ‖ MID. **disfigure** —*one's body* (w. one's nails, fr. grief) E. ‖ PASS. (of weapons) be tarnished (by smoke) Od.

κατα-κλαίω *vb.* **1 weep and wail** E. Plu.
2 bewail, weep over —*one's fate* Plu.
3 (act. and mid.) **lament over, mourn** —*a person* E. Ar. Plb.

κατα-κλάω *contr.vb.* | aor. κατέκλασε, ep.3sg. (tm.) κατὰ ... κλάσσε | **1 break in two, snap** —*spears, plants, staffs, equipment* Il. Hes.fr. Pi. Hdt. D. Plu. ‖ PASS. (of spears, a spearhead) be broken in two Il. Plu.
2 break off —*the tops of reeds* (for bedding) Plu.
3 break into pieces —*loaves, fish* (to share out) NT.
4 (wkr.sens.) cause to bend down, **bend** —*a bull's neck* (W.PREP.PHR. *to the ground*) Theoc.(tm.)
5 (fig., of grief, a terrible sight, a pleading woman) **break** —*a person's mind or spirit* AR.(tm.) Plu. ‖ PASS. (of a person's courage or spirit) be broken Od. Plu.; (of a person) be shattered —W.ACC. *in one's mind* (W.DAT. *by a morbid passion*) E.
6 (of a person weeping) cause to break down, **reduce to tears** —*persons* Pl. ‖ PASS. (of a goddess) be moved (by entreaties) Call.

κατάκλειστος ον *adj.* [κατακλείω] (of judges) enclosed in a chamber, **sequestered** (to ensure impartiality) Plu.; (of a young man or woman) **cloistered** (at home) Call. Plu.

κατα-κλείω, Att. **κατακλῄω**, dial. **κατακλάω**, Ion. **κατακληίω** *vb.* [κλείω¹] | dial.3sg.aor.mid. κατεκλήξατο | **1 shut, close** —*gates, the lid of a chest* Hdt. Plu.
2 close the doors of, close up —*a carriage* X.; **close, lock up** —*temples, a shop* Hdt. ‖ PASS. (of temples) be closed Hdt.; (of a dungeon) —W.DAT. *by a boulder* (*serving as a door*) Plu.
3 lock away —*objects* (sts. w. εἰς + ACC. *in a place*) X. Arist. Plu.; (fig.) **safeguard** —*a sum of public money* (W.DAT. *w. a decree*) And.; (of a lawmaker) —*laws* (w. εἰς + ACC. *for a hundred years*) Arist. ‖ PASS. (of valuables) be locked away Ar.
4 lock up, shut in —*a person, oneself* (sts. W.PREP.PHR. *in a room or sim.*) X. Men. NT. Plu. ‖ MID. shut oneself away Plu. —W.PREP.PHR. *in a room or building* X. Plu.; (of a bridegroom) shut away with oneself —*one's bride* (*in the marriage chamber*) Theoc. ‖ PASS. (of persons) be shut up —W.ADV. or PREP.PHR. *in a house, a chest* Theoc. Plu.

κατακολουθέω

5 (of a ruler) **confine** —*a population* (w. εἰς + ACC. *within a citadel*) Plu.; (fig.) —*oneself* (*in one's own city*) X.; (specif., of troops, commanders) **pen in, trap** (*by military action*) —*enemy troops, commanders, or sim.* (usu. w. εἰς + ACC. *in a place*) Th. X. Hyp. Arist. Plu. || PASS. (of troops, commanders, populations) be penned in (usu. w. εἰς + ACC. *in a place*) Th. Att.orats. X. Arist. Plu.; (of wind) be trapped —w. εἰς + ACC. *inside clouds* Ar.

6 (fig., of a statesman) **confine** —*a general* (w. εἰς + ACC. *to a senatorial post, so as to curtail his military activities*) Plu.; (of a commander, a rhetorical technique) **trap** —*enemies, opponents* (w. εἰς + ACC. *in a hopeless situation*) Plu.; (of a people, a person) **bind** —*people* (W.INF. *to do sthg.*, W.DAT. *by means of a law*) D. —(w. εἰς + ACC. *to an agreement*) Aeschin. || PASS. (of a city) be trapped —w. εἰς + ACC. *in a dangerous position* D.; (of a person) be constrained —w. εἰς + ACC. *to a desperate course of action* (w. ὑπό + GEN. *by necessity*) Plu.

7 (wkr.sens.) **enclose** (a corpse, in a wooden case) Hdt.; **sheathe** —*a sword* Plu.; **include** —*a piece of private business* (W.DAT. *in a decree*) D.

κατακληΐς ep.f.: see κατακλῄς

κατα-κληρονομέω contr.vb. (of God) apportion as an inheritance or entitlement, **assign** —*land* (*to the Jews*) NT.

κατα-κληρόομαι mid.contr.vb. (of a prince) receive as one's allocation, **take over** —*royal power* Plu.

κατα-κληρουχέω contr.vb. 1 (of a commander) **portion out** —*land* (W.DAT. *to troops*) Plu.

2 (act. and mid., of conquerors, participants in a coup) **divide amongst one another** —*land, estates* Plb. || PASS. (of land) be divided up —w. ὑπό + GEN. *by invaders* Plb.

κατα-κλῄς ῇδος, ep. **κατακληΐς** ῖδος f. [κλείς] 1 **latch** (of a door) Ar.

2 container, **quiver** (W.GEN. *for arrows*) Call.

κατακλήω Att.vb.: see κατακλείω

κατα-κλίνω vb. 1 **lay down** —*a spear* (W.PREP.PHR. *on the ground*) Od.; **lay down** or **lower** —*rods of office* (*to show submission to the will of the people*) Plu.

2 **lay down** (on a bed or sim.) —*persons, animals* (*esp. to sleep*) Ar. X. Men. Plu. —*oneself* Plu. || PASS. lay oneself down (on a bed, the ground, or sim., esp. to sleep) Ar. Pl. X. Hyp. Men. Plu.; (of a corpse) lie prostrate Plb.

3 (specif.) lay down for intercourse, **bed** —*one's husband* (W.ADV. *on the ground*) Ar. || PASS. go to bed (w. a sexual partner) Ar. Pl.

4 cause to recline (usu. in a company of diners), **seat** —*dinner guests or sim.* Hdt. Pl. X. NT. Plu. || PASS. recline (esp. on a couch, usu. at a banquet) Hdt. Ar. Pl. X. D. +

5 lay low, **overthrow, topple** —*a tyrant* Thgn.

6 || PASS. (of a valley) slope down —W.ADV. *inland* AR.

κατάκλισις εως (Ion. ιος) f. 1 act of reclining at table, **taking of a seat** (at a banquet) Pl. Arist.

2 (concr.) **banquet** Hdt.

3 way of sitting, **posture at table** (of an actor) Plu.

4 act of seating (a person or persons), **seating, offering of a seat** (to guests, elders) Pl. Arist. Plu.

κατα-κλύζω vb. | fut. κατακλύσω, ep. κατακλύσσω (Pi.) | 1 (of deities) send a flood upon, **flood** —*the earth* (w. *a deluge*) Pi. Pl.; **drench** —*a region* (W.DAT. *w. rainwater*) Plu.

2 (of water, rivers, the sea, blood fr. a massacre) **flood** —*the earth, a region* Pi. Hdt. Th. AR.(tm.) Plu.; (intr., of a river) **be in flood** Plu. || PASS. (of regions) be flooded (by a river) Plu.; be drenched —w. ὑπό + GEN. *by rainstorms* Isoc.

3 (of pipes) **pour forth in a flood** —*perfumed oil* Plu.; (intr., of a wave) **come flooding in** Pl.

4 (of waves) overwhelm in flood, **flood over** —*a person* Archil.(sts.tm.) —*a pebble* Pi.; (of a wave, fig.ref. to a problematic claim) **overwhelm, drown** —*a person* (W.DAT. *in laughter and scorn*) Pl.; (fig., of a deity) —*prosperity* (W.PREP.PHR. *in waves of troubles*) E.; (of Odysseus) —*the Cyclops* (*by befuddling him w. wine*) E.Cyc. || PASS. (of a person) be overwhelmed (by a wave, fig.ref. to a problematic claim) Pl.; (of a city) —W.DAT. *by a wave of invaders* A.

5 overwhelm with abundance; (fig., of generous benefactors) **inundate** —*a person's subsistence* (W.DAT. *w. abundance*) X.; (pejor., of a person) **swamp** —*a town* (W.DAT. *w. costly luxuries*) E. || PASS. (of a statesman) be overwhelmed (i.e. corrupted) —W.DAT. *by foreign gold* Plu.

6 || PASS. (of a clod of earth) be carried off by a wave —w. ἐκ + GEN. *fr. a ship* Pi.

7 obliterate by washing away; (of rain) **wash away** —*tracks of animals* X.; (fig., of a statesman) —*the achievements of one's predecessors* (W.DAT. *w. public projects*) Plu.; (of a love-potion) —*a person's senses* Plu. || PASS. (of personal convictions) be washed away —w. ὑπό + GEN. *by other people's opinions* Pl.

8 **rinse out** —*a bathtub* Ar.

κατακλυσμός οῦ m. **flood, deluge** (ref. to mythol. events) Pl. Plb. Plu.; (specif., ref. to the biblical flood) NT.; (fig., W.GEN. of diseases ravaging a city) Pl.; (ref. to the passage of time, as washing away earlier events) D.

κατα-κλύω vb. **hear** —*a sound* S.Ichn.

κατα-κνάπτω vb. (fig., of a person) **tear to shreds** —*one's hopes* E.

κατα-κνάω contr.vb. | aor. κατέκνησα | dial.2sg.aor.opt.mid. (tm.) κατὰ … κνάσαιο (Theoc.) || aor.pass. κατεκνήσθην | 1 (fig., of a cheese-grater, envisaged as quartermaster) **grate out** —*provisions* (W.DAT. *for troops*) Ar. || PASS. (fig., of a person) be grated —w. ἐν + DAT. *in a savoury sauce* Ar.

2 || MID. **scratch to shreds** —*one's skin* (W.DAT. *w. one's nails*) Theoc.

κατα-κνίζω vb. 1 (of teachers of oratory) **mangle** —*someone's speeches* Isoc.

2 || PASS. be utterly tormented (by love) Ar.

κατα-κνώσσω vb. **sleep, slumber** AR.

κατα-κοιμάω contr.vb. 1 **put to bed** —*a person* (*in a shrine, to receive an oracular dream*) Hdt.; (fig.) **lull, put to sleep** —*one's eyes* (*ref. to blinding them fr. the truth*) S.

2 || PASS. go to bed, lie down to sleep Il. Hdt. Plb. Plu.

3 || PASS. (w. sexual connot.) go to bed —W.PREP.PHR. *w. a woman* Il.

4 cast into the sleep of death; (fig., of oblivion, in neg.phr.) **obliterate** —*divine laws* S.

5 || PASS. (of a fire) die down Plu.

κατα-κοιμίζω vb. 1 **put to bed** —*persons* Pl. X.; (specif.) **lull to sleep** —*children* Pl.

2 || PASS. go to bed, lie down to sleep Plb.

3 **sleep through** —*the day, one's sentry duty* Hdt. X.

κατα-κοινωνέω contr.vb. 1 **work in partnership** —W.DAT. *w. someone* D.

2 **share out** —*a state's affairs* (w. *a foreign ruler*) Aeschin.

κατά-κοιτος ον adj. [κοίτη] in bed; (fig., of love) **at rest** (i.e. not tormenting a person) Ibyc.

κατ-ακολουθέω contr.vb. 1 **follow behind, follow** Plb. NT. —W.DAT. *persons, a swineherd's call* Plb. NT.

2 act in accordance with, **follow, obey** —W.DAT. *a person, advice* Plb.; **follow, take into account** —W.DAT. *the natural strengths of a site* (*in making camp*) Plb.

κατακολπίζω

3 (of a historian) accept as an authoritative guide, **follow** —W.DAT. *a writer, his version of events, a document* Plb. Plu.
4 follow (a prescribed ritual); **complete** —W.DAT. *a sacrifice* Plu.

κατα-κολπίζω *vb.* [κόλπος] sail into a bay; **sail in** —w. ἐς + ACC. *to a place* Th.

κατα-κολυμβάω *contr.vb.* **dive underwater** Th.

κατακομιδή ῆς *f.* [κατακομίζω] transportation to the coast, **sending off** (of goods for export) Th.

κατα-κομίζω *vb.* **1 bring down, transport, convey** —*goods, a ship, a person's ashes* (sts. W.PREP.PHR. *to a place*) Th. Lycurg. Plu.; (gener.) **transport** —*goods* (W.DAT. *in ships*) Pl. || PASS. **be conveyed** —W.ACC. *along a road* (W.PREP.PHR. *in a litter*) Din.
2 **bring in** —*women, children, livestock* (sts. W. εἰς + ACC. *to a city, for safety*) Lycurg. D. Plu.
3 **bring in to port** or **bring back** —*ships* (sts. W.ADV. or PREP.PHR. *to a place*) Aeschin. D.; (gener.) **bring** —*a ship* (*to a place*) D. || PASS. (of a ship) **be brought back** —W.PREP.PHR. *to a place* D.

κατά-κομος ον *adj.* [κόμη] (of the cheek of a young man, envisaged as a bullock) covered with hair, **hirsute** E.

κατακονά ᾶς *dial.f.* [κατακαίνω] act of killing, **destruction** (W.GEN. of a person's life) E.

κατα-κονδυλίζομαι *pass.vb.* [κόνδυλος] (of a person) **be punched** Aeschin.

κατ-ακοντίζω *vb.* **strike down with javelins** —*persons, horses* Hdt. Th. X. D. Plb. Plu. || PASS. **be struck down with javelins** X. Plu.

κατά-κοπος ον *adj.* [κόπος] (of a person, a dog) **tired out** Plu.

κατα-κόπτω *vb.* **1 cut to pieces, break up** —*precious objects* Plu. —*a tiled roof* Plb.; (specif.) **cut up for bullion** —*objects of precious metal* X. D. Plu.; **cut up for coinage** or **strike into coinage** —*gold or silver bullion* Hdt. || PASS. (of objects of precious metal) **be cut up for bullion** Plu.
2 **cut up for cooking, cut up** —*meat, animals, a person* Hdt. Pl. Men. Theoc. Plu.; **divide up** —*an empire* (envisaged as a carcass) Plu. || PASS. (of birds) **be cut up** (for cooking) Ar.
3 (of a madman) **cut** —*oneself* (W.DAT. *w. stones*) NT. || PASS. (of a veteran) **be cut** or **scarred** —W.ACC. *on his whole body* (w. ὑπό + GEN. *w. wounds*) Plu.
4 || PASS. (of trees) **be chopped down** X. Arist.
5 **cut down, kill, slaughter** —*animals* Th. D.; **strike, chop** —*an ox's neck* (W.DAT. *w. an axe*) AR.(tm.) || PASS. (of animals, persons) **be killed with a sword or knife** Hdt. X. D. Plu.
6 **cut down in battle, kill** —*enemies* Hdt. X. D. Plb. Plu.; **massacre** —*civilians* Th. X. || PASS. **be cut down in battle** Th. X. Plb. Plu.; **be hacked about** (by enemy troops) Plb.; (wkr.sens., ref. to being wounded) Hdt.
7 **cut down to a man, obliterate, wipe out** —*a regiment* D. || PASS. (of regiments) **be wiped out** Plu.
8 || PASS. (of wool) **be ravaged** —w. ὑπό + GEN. *by moths* Ar.
9 (of riders) **wear** or **tire out** —*horses* X. || PASS. (of a chef) **be worn out** (w. play on sense 2) Men.
10 **annoy, exasperate** —*a person* Men.

κατα-κορής ές *adj.* [κορέννυμι] **1** (of a person) **filled to satiety, overfull** (W.DAT. *w. strong drink*) Pl.
2 (of the use of epithets in poetry, time spent in someone's company) **excessive** Pl. Arist.
3 (of loose talk) **immoderate, unrestrained** Pl.; (of persons, in a particular respect) Plb.; (quasi-advbl., of a person making threats) **without restraint** Tim.
4 (of a shade of black) **intense, deep** Pl.

κατά-κορος ον *adj.* [κόρος¹] (of ritual ceremonies) lacking moderation, **extravagant** Plu.

—κατακόρως *adv.* **1 without restraint, immoderately** D. Plu.
2 **excessively** Arist. Plb. Plu.
3 **furiously** —*ref. to shouting war-cries* Plb.

κατα-κοσμέω *contr.vb.* **1 fit** —*an arrow* (w. ἐπί + DAT. *to a bow-string*) Il.
2 **deck out** —*troops* (W.DAT. *in fine armour*) Plb.; (wkr.sens.) **furnish** —*a person* (W.DAT. *w. more dignified pursuits*) Ar. || MID. **deck oneself out** —W.DAT. *in armour* Plb. || PASS. **be decked out** —W.DAT. *in armour* X. Plb.
3 **adorn** —*helmets* (w. gold and silver) Plu.; (fig.) —*one's beloved* (envisaged as a statue of a god) Pl.
4 **set in order** —*persons, things, one's fortunes* Od. Pl. Plu.; **regulate** —*one's frame of mind* Plu. || PASS. (of persons, things, the world) **be set in order** Pl.
5 (of a group of people) **set in harmony** —*themselves* (i.e. act in unison) Plu. || MID. **fall into line** Plu. —w. εἰς + ACC. w. *someone's opinion* Plu. || PASS. (of a person's voice) **be harmonised** —W.DAT. *w. his life* Plu.

κατακόσμησις εως *f.* **1 orderly running, arrangement, order** (of the world) Pl.
2 **well-ordered condition** (of a person's soul) Pl.

κατ-ακούω *vb.* **1** (esp. in neg.phr.) **be able to hear, hear** (sthg.) Th. Pl. Arist. Plu. —W.ACC. or GEN. *a sound, someone's words* E. Th. Ar. Pl. Plu. —W.GEN. *persons* (i.e. their words) Pl. D. Plu. —W.GEN.PTCPL. *someone playing the aulos* Arist. || PASS. (of a speaker) **be heard** Plu.
2 **listen in, eavesdrop** (on an interrogation) Plu.
3 (of tribes) **obey, be subject to** —W.GEN. or DAT. *a person, a nation* Hdt. D.

κατα-κράζω *vb.* | *fut.pf.* (w.fut.sens.) κατακεκράξομαι | defeat by screeching; (of a person) **shout down** —*an opponent* Ar.

κατα-κρατέω *contr.vb.* **1 have mastery over** —W.GEN. *territory, love, one's appetite, a flood of tears* Hippon. Pl. Plb. —*the Greek language* Plb.
2 **prevail against** —W.GEN. *enemies, an attack* Plb.; **gain the upper hand** (in a battle, a trial of strength) Hdt. Plb.
3 **prevail, win out** (against threats to one's authority) Th.; (of a stream, in giving its name to a river also fed by other streams) Hdt.
4 (gener.) **conquer** (a steep climb) Plu.; **succeed** (in doing sthg.) Plb. —W.GEN. *in one's aim* Plb.

κατα-κρεμάννῡμι *vb.* **1 hang** —*a lyre* (w. ἐκ + GEN. *fr. a peg*) Od.; (of Artemis) **hang up** —*her bow and arrows* (after use) hHom.
2 **suspend** —*a corpse* (w. κατά + GEN. *fr. a wall*) Hdt. || PASS. (of a horse's legs) **hang suspended** —W.PREDIC.ADJ. *in the air* Hdt.

κατα-κρεουργέομαι *Ion.pass.contr.vb.* [κρεουργός] (hyperbol., of a soldier) **be butchered, be hacked to pieces** Hdt.

κατα-κρημνάομαι *pass.contr.vb.* [reltd. κατακρίμναμαι] (of grapes) **hang down** (fr. a vine) hHom.

κατα-κρημνίζω *vb.* [κρημνός] **1 throw off a cliff** —*a person* NT. Plu. || PASS. **be thrown off a cliff** D. Plu.
2 **push off a cliff** —*fellow soldiers* (in a panicked retreat) Plu.; (of the wind) —*donkeys* X. || PASS. **fall off a cliff** X.
3 (gener.) **throw down, hurl** —*oneself, others* (w. ἀπό + GEN. *fr. a roof*) Plb.; **throw overboard** —*sailors* X.
4 **pull down, topple** —*riders* (w. ἀπό + GEN. *fr. their horses*) Plb.

κατα-κρίμναμαι *pass.vb.* (of clouds) **sag down** (w. rain) Ar.

κατα-κρίνω vb. **1 condemn, sentence** —persons Plb. NT. —(W.GEN. to death) Plb. —(W.INF. to suffer a certain penalty) Hdt. NT. ‖ PASS. be condemned E. X. Plb. NT. —W.GEN. to death Plb. —W.INF. to die X. Plu.; (of legal cases) be decided (by passing a sentence) Antipho; (of a death sentence) be passed —W.DAT. on a person Hdt.
2 (fig., of people's age) **convict** (them) Antipho; (of fate) **condemn** (all men) —W.INF. to die Isoc.; (hyperbol., of a person) **sentence to death** —a suitor (by rejecting him) Theoc.
3 ‖ PASS. (of Apollo) be deemed —W.INF. to be such and such Pi.fr.

κατα-κροταλίζω vb. (of Amazons, performing a war-dance) make a drumming sound, **drum** —W.DAT. w. their feet Call.

κατα-κρούω vb. **knock** (on objects, to attract bees) Pl.

κατα-κρύπτω vb. | aor. κατέκρυψα | aor.2 κατέκρυβον (Plu.) | **1 hide, conceal** —persons, things (sts. W.DAT. or PREP.PHR. in a place) Hom. Hippon. Pi. Hdt. Pl. Plu. —one's intentions or activities Od. —one's wickedness (W.DAT. w. wealth) Thgn.
2 disguise —oneself Od. —(W.DAT. in another's armour) Plu.
3 (of a deity) **shroud** —persons (W.DAT. in night) Od. —a city (in dark grief) A.
4 cover —seeds (w. earth) Hes.; (fig., of the dust of the grave) —the successes of the living Pi.; (specif., of persons) **bury** —bodies (W.PREP.PHR. in the earth) X. ‖ PASS. (of an underground chamber) be covered (w. earth) Plu.; (of grain) —W.PREP.PHR. by rainwater X.; (of a statue) —W.DAT. by a robe Hdt.

κατακρυφά ᾶς dial.f. **means of concealing** (information) S.

κατα-κρώζω vb. (of birds, fig.ref. to detractors) **screech at** —a statesman Ar.

κατακτάμεν and **κατακτάμεναι** (ep.athem.aor.infs.), **κατακτάμενος** (ep.athem.aor.mid.ptcpl.): see κατακτείνω

κατα-κτάομαι mid.contr.vb. **1** gain possession of, **acquire, win** —advantages, wealth, power, territory S. Isoc. Pl. X. Arist. +
2 incur —accusations Th.

κατα-κτεατίζομαι mid.vb. gain possession of, **acquire, get** —a toy (fr. someone) AR.

κατα-κτείνω, ep. **κακκτείνω, κακτείνω** vb. | fut. κατακτενῶ, ep. κατακτενέω, also κατακτανέω | aor. κατέκτεινα | aor.2 κατέκτανον, ep. κάκτανον | ep.athem.aor.: 3sg. κατέκτα, 3pl. κατέκταν, ptcpl. κατακτάς, inf. κατακτάμεν, κατακτάμεναι, κακκτάμεναι | pf. κατέκτονα ‖ MID. ep.athem.aor.ptcpl. (w.pass.sens.) κατακτάμενος ‖ PASS.: ep.3pl.aor. κατέκταθεν | (of persons, gods, animals) **kill** —persons, animals Hom. Hes. Alc. Hippon. B. Hdt. + ‖ PASS. be killed Hom.

κατάκτησις εως f. [κατακτάομαι] act of gaining or taking possession, **acquisition** (of power, territory) Plb. Plu.

κατακτός ή όν adj. [κατάγω] brought down; (of a game of kottabos) **in which the target is knocked down** Ar.

κατα-κυβεύω vb. squander in dice-playing, **gamble away** —one's fortune Lys. ‖ PASS. (of money) be gambled away Aeschin.

κατα-κυλίνδομαι pass.vb. (of persons, a helmet) **tumble down** (fr. a high place) Hdt. —W.PREP.PHR. fr. one's horse X.

κατα-κῡμοτακής ές adj. [κῦμα, τήκω] (of winds) **dispersing the waves** Tim.

κατα-κύπτω vb. (of persons) **bend** or **stoop down** Il. Men. NT.

κατα-κῡριεύω vb. **1** (of rulers) **have authority** —W.GEN. over a people NT.
2 (of a possessed man) **overpower** —W.GEN. exorcists NT.

κατα-κῡρόω contr.vb. **1** (of officials) **ratify** (the sale of an exiled man's estate) Arist. ‖ PASS. (of a death sentence) be ratified S.
2 ‖ PASS. (of a person) be confirmed —W.DAT. in a sentence of death E.

κατα-κωλύω vb. **1 hold back, stop** —persons (sts. W.INF. fr. going somewhere or doing sthg.) X. D. Plu. —the state (fr. becoming too powerful) Plu. ‖ PASS. be stopped (fr. hanging oneself) And. —W.INF. fr. sailing X. —W.GEN. fr. a voyage D.; be stopped (in one's flight), be intercepted —w. ὑπό + GEN. by enemies X.
2 (wkr.sens.) **hold up, delay** —persons X. D. —W.INF. having dinner Ar.

κατα-κωμάζω vb. (fig., of divine retribution) **bring a revel of destruction** —W.DAT. into a house E.

κατ-αλαζονεύομαι mid.vb. **1 boastfully say** —sthg. D. —W.COMPL.CL. that sthg. is the case Plu.
2 make exaggerated claims —w. περί + GEN. about someone or sthg. Isoc.

κατα-λαλέω contr.vb. **1 tell as gossip, blab** —things Ar.
2 speak badly of, **criticise, malign** —a person, a decree Plb. ‖ PASS. be maligned —w. ἐπί + DAT. for sthg. Plb.

κατα-λαμβάνω vb. | fut. καταλήψομαι, Ion. καταλάμψομαι | aor.2 κατέλαβον | pf. κατείληφα, Att. καθείληφα (Ar.), Ion. καταλελάβηκα ‖ PASS.: aor. κατελήφθην, Ion. κατελάμφθην ‖ The sections are grouped as: (1) take hold physically, (2–8) take possession or control, (9–15) come upon, encounter or find, (16–17) afflict or befall, (18–21) compel or restrain, (22) convict. |
1 take hold of, grasp, clasp —a sheep's back Od.(tm.) —a person's hands (to pin him down) Plu.
2 take possession or control of, seize —people's money Ar. —power, the command of an army Hdt. Th. And. ‖ PASS. (of power) be seized Th.
3 seize, capture —a city, military position, or sim. Hdt. Th. Ar.(sts.tm.) Att.orats. Plb. Plu.; (fig., of desires) —the citadel of a person's soul Pl. ‖ PASS. (of places) be captured Th. Att.orats. +
4 take up, occupy —a seat, site, land, camp Th. Ar. Isoc.
5 capture, catch —persons, cattle Hdt. Ar. X. ‖ PASS. (of persons, cattle) be caught Th. Pl. X.
6 app., take control of, **incapacitate** —someone's eye (W.DAT. w. one's hand, i.e. block its vision) Pl. ‖ PASS. (of an eye) be incapacitated Pl.
7 grasp with the mind, **grasp, comprehend** —W.INDIR.Q. how sthg. happened Plb. ‖ MID. **realise** —W.COMPL.CL. that sthg. is the case NT.
8 ‖ MID. (of a writer) take up for oneself, **handle, treat** —a subject Hdt.
9 catch up with, overtake —persons in flight, ships Hdt. Ar. X.; (of sounds, planets) —other sounds, planets Pl.; (fig., of arguments) —debaters Pl.; (intr., of pursuers) **catch up** X. ‖ PASS. (of persons in flight, moving objects) be caught up Hdt. Pl. Plb.
10 (specif., of falling rocks) **catch, hit** —persons Hdt. ‖ PASS. be run down or hit (by a chariot out of control) X.
11 (wkr.sens.) **come across, encounter** —persons Hdt. Isoc. Pl. X. ‖ PASS. (of enemies) be encountered Th.
12 catch out —a person (W.PTCPL. doing sthg.) Ar. ‖ PASS. be caught —W.PTCPL. doing sthg. E.Cyc. D. —W.PREP.PHR. in adultery NT.; be caught by surprise Plu.
13 (gener.) **find** —a person (W.PTCPL. + PREDIC.ADJ. to be such and such) Isoc. Pl.
14 (specif.) find on arrival, **find, discover** —persons, things (W.PTCPL. or ADV. in a particular condition) Hdt. Th. Ar.

καταλαμπτέος

Att.orats. Pl. X. ‖ PASS. be found or caught —w.PTCPL. *in a particular condition* X.
15 (intr.) **arrive in time** (for sthg.) Hdt.
16 (of afflictions, such as death, disease, weariness, grief) **take hold of, overcome** —*persons* Hom. Hdt.
17 (of events and circumstances, usu. unwelcome ones) **befall** —*persons, cities* Hdt. E. Th. Ar. Att.orats. +; (intr.) Hdt. Th.
18 (of necessity) **compel** —*someone* (*oft.* W.INF. *to do sthg.*) Hdt. Isoc. Pl. ‖ IMPERS. it becomes necessary —W.ACC. + INF. *for someone to do sthg.* Hdt. ‖ PASS. be compelled Hdt. Th. —W.INF. *to do sthg.* And.; (of practices, decisions) be enforced Pl. Arist.
19 (specif.) **bind** —*someone* (W.DAT. *w. an oath, sts.* W.INF. *to do sthg.*) Hdt. Th. ‖ PASS. be bound (by an oath) Th.
20 hold back, restrain —*oneself* Hdt.; **check, stop** —*investigators, people quarrelling* Hdt. —*a fire, disputes, an enemy's increasing power* Hdt.
21 dissuade —*someone* (sts. w. μή + INF. *fr. doing sthg.*) Hdt.
22 convict, condemn —*a defendant* Antipho ‖ PASS. be convicted (sts. W.GEN. by a law) Antipho

καταλαμπτέος *Ion.vbl.adj.*: see καταληπτέος

κατα-λάμπω *vb.* **1** (of daylight, the sun, the moon, its light) **shine down** hHom.(dub., v.l. ἐπι-) E. Plu. —W.GEN. *on things* Pl.; (fig., of truth and reality) Pl.; (tr., of daylight) **illuminate** —*a person* (*wishing to remain under cover of darkness*) Plu. ‖ PASS. (of persons) be shone down upon —w. ὑπό + GEN. *by the sun* X.; (of places) be illuminated (by the sun) E. Plu.
2 (gener., of lamps) **light up** —*streets* Plu. ‖ PASS. (of a plain) be lit up —W.DAT. *by campfires* Plu.

κατ-αλγέω *contr.vb.* feel great pain in one's heart, **be aggrieved** S. Plb.

καταλέγμενος (ep.athem.aor.mid.ptcpl.): see καταλέχομαι

κατα-λέγω *vb.* | aor. κατέλεξα | PASS.: aor. κατελέχθην | aor.2 κατελέγην | pf.ptcpl. κατειλεγμένος, also καταλελεγμένος (Plu.) ‖ The sections are grouped as: (1–5) tell or recount, (6–7) count, (8–9) select. |
1 recount, tell —*sthg.* (*oft.* W.DAT. *to someone*) Hom. Hes. Emp. Hdt. AR. Theoc. —W.COMPL.CL. OR INDIR.Q. *what is the case, how sthg. happened, or sim.* Hom.; **tell** (sthg.) Call. —W.DAT. *to someone* Od. Hdt.
2 describe, tell about —*sthg.* (*oft.* W.DAT. *to someone*) Od. Hdt. Ar. Plu. —W.ACC. + INDIR.Q. *someone, whether he is doing sthg.* Od. ‖ PASS. (of things) be mentioned or described Hdt.
3 give instructions —W.DAT. *to someone* (W.INF. *to do sthg.*) Od.
4 (specif.) **list** —*a series of things or events* Hdt. Lys. Ar. ‖ PASS. (of persons, things) be listed Hdt.
5 read out, recite —*verses, records, a list of names* Hdt. Pl. X. Arist. —W.PARTITV.GEN. *fr. a set of oracles* Hdt.
6 calculate, reckon up —*the number of one's friends* X.
7 reckon, count —*a person* (W.PREDIC.ADJ. *as rich*) Pl. —W.COMPL.CL. *when someone does such and such* (W.PREDIC.SB. *as a good deed*) X.
8 pick out, select, appoint —*persons* (*for a particular post or duty*) Hdt.(mid.) Th. Pl. X. Arist. + —(W.INF. *to do sthg.*) X. ‖ PASS. be appointed (to an office) Pl. Plu. —w. εἰς + ACC. *to the Senate* Plu. —W.PARTITV.GEN. *as one of the trierarchs* Is.
9 (act. and mid.) **enlist, enrol** —*persons* (for a duty) X. Arist. —(w. εἰς + ACC. *into an army, navy, or sim.*) Th. Lys. —(*on an official blacklist*) Lys.; (intr.) **make an official register** (of citizens) Lys.; (specif.) **conscript, levy** —*soldiers* Th. Lys. Isoc. X. Plu. —*an army* X.; (intr.) **levy troops** Plu. ‖ PASS. be enlisted or conscripted (for military service or sim.) Hdt. Lys. Pl. D. + —W.PREP.PHR. *into an army or sim.* Lys. X. —W.PREDIC.NOM. *as a soldier* Lys. Plu. —W.PARTITV.GEN. *as one of the infantry* Lys.

κατα-λείβω *vb.* **1** ‖ PASS. (of tears) be shed, flow down E.; (of water) trickle down Theoc. —W.PREP.PHR. *fr. a rock* Hes. Theoc.; (gener., of honey) drip, ooze Il.
2 wear out in weeping —*one's body* E. ‖ PASS. (of a person) be worn out in weeping —W.DAT. *fr. sufferings* E.

κατ-άλειπτος ον *adj.* [ἀλείφω] (of persons) **anointed** (W.DAT. w. perfumed ointment) Ar.

κατα-λείπω, ep. **καλλείπω** *vb.* | aor.1 κατέλειψα (NT.) | aor.2 κατέλιπον, ep. κάλλιπον | 3sg.iterativ.aor.2 καταλίπεσκε (Hdt.) |
1 leave behind in a place, leave behind —*persons, animals, things* Hom. hHom. Tyrt.(sts.tm.) Sapph. Hdt. E. + —*persons, troops, ships* (W.PREDIC.ACC. *as guards, hostages, settlers, or sim.*) Hdt. Th. Ar. X. ‖ PASS. (of persons, ships, things) be left behind (in a place) Hdt. E. Th. Ar. X.; (of a person, troops) —W.PREDIC.NOM. *as a caretaker ruler, a garrison* Hdt. X.
2 leave behind, depart from —*a place* Il. Hdt. AR.(tm.)
3 (act. and mid.) leave behind after one's death, **leave behind** —*a wife, children, descendants* Il. Hdt. Ar. Att.orats. Pl. + —*persons* (W.PREDIC.SB. *as heirs*) Isoc. Is. —*the need to be avenged* Antipho —*grief, sorrow* (W.DAT. *for one's friends or family*) Od. Sol. Lys. Ar. —W.INF. (*enough money*) *to be buried* (i.e. to pay for one's funeral) Ar. ‖ PASS. (of persons) be left (after someone's death) Isoc. —W.PREDIC.SB. OR ADJ. *as an orphan, an heir, penniless* Isoc.
4 (specif.) **leave as an inheritance** (oft. W.DAT. for one's children, descendants, or sim.) —*property, land, a legacy* Od. Ar. Att.orats. Pl. X.; (gener., of persons, achievements) **leave to posterity** —*a legacy, memorial, good reputation, writings, or sim.* Hdt. Th. Isoc. ‖ PASS. (of money, a political or educational system) be left as an inheritance Isoc. Is.; (of glory, achievements, or sim.) be left as a legacy or memorial Th. Isoc.
5 leave abandoned, abandon —*persons, places, things* Hom. Archil. A. Hdt. S. Th. + ‖ PASS. (of persons) be left to one's fate Th.
6 leave neglected or unfinished, leave —*things* (usu. W.PREDIC.ADJ. *unattended, unfinished, or sim.*) Od. Hes. Ar. X.; **leave off from, give up** —*an activity, a speech* Isoc. X. ‖ PASS. (of things) be left —W.PREDIC.ADJ. *unfinished* Th.
7 (act. and mid.) **leave remaining, leave** —*possibilities, an opening, an escape route, or sim.* Od. Hdt. Th. Isoc. Pl. X. + ‖ PASS. (of persons, things) be left over, remain Hes.*fr.* Th. Ar. Att.orats. X.; (to be dealt with in the future) And. X.
8 ‖ MID. (of the gods) **reserve** —*knowledge* (*of sthg.*, W.DAT. *for themselves alone*) X.

κατάλειψις εως *f.* leaving behind, **bequeathing to posterity** (of writings, by statesmen) Pl.

καταλεκτέος ᾱ ον *vbl.adj.* [καταλέγω] (of a list) **to be compiled** Pl.

κατα-λεπτολογέω *contr.vb.* **quibble away to nothing** —*a rival's utterances* Ar.

κατα-λεύω *vb.* **stone to death** —*persons* Hdt.(sts.tm.) Th. Ar. X. Lycurg. D. + ‖ PASS. be stoned to death Hdt. X. Aeschin. Plu.

κατα-λέχομαι *ep.mid.vb.* | fut. καταλέξομαι | 3sg.aor. κατελέξατο | athem.aor.: 3sg. κατέλεκτο, inf. καταλέχθαι, ptcpl. καταλέγμενος | **lie down** (esp. on a bed, to sleep) Hom. Hes.

κατ-αλέω *contr.vb.* | ep.3pl.aor. (tm.) κατὰ ... ἄλεσσαν | **grind to powder, grind up** —*wheat, dried locusts* Od. Hdt.

κατα-λήγω vb. 1 (of evils, tumults, anger) **abate, subside** A. Plb.; (gener., of a season) **end** Plb.
2 (of a river's course) **come to an end** Plu.
∥ NEUT.SG.PTCPL.SB. **furthest part** (of a sea) Plb.
∥ NEUT.PL.PTCPL.SB. **borders, outskirts** (of a region) Plu.

κατα-λήθομαι ep.mid.vb. [λανθάνω] **completely forget** —W.GEN. *dead comrades* Il.

καταληπτέος ᾱ ον, Ion. **καταλαμπτέος** η ον vbl.adj. [καταλαμβάνω] 1 (of an enterprise) **to be achieved** (W.DAT. w. daring and good timing) Plu.
2 (of a wrongdoer) **to be dealt with** (W.DAT. by death) Hdt.

καταληπτικός ή όν adj. (of a politician) **good at repression** (W.GEN. of a noisy mob) Ar.

καταληπτός ή όν adj. 1 (of grief) **taking hold** (of a house) E.
2 (of a person) **captivated, obsessed** (W.DAT. by money) Plb.
3 (of concepts) **able to be grasped, comprehensible** Plb.
4 (of goals) **to be achieved** (W.DAT. by certain means) Th.

κατα-λητουργέω contr.vb. **use up on public services** —*vast sums* D.

καταλήψιμος ον adj. [καταλαμβάνω] (of a defendant) **deserving to be convicted** Antipho

κατάληψις εως f. 1 **seizing, occupying** (of regions, cities, military positions, by troops or commanders) Att.orats. Pl. Plb. Plu.; (prep.phr., ref. to an enemy fleet) ἐν καταλήψει *within capturing-distance* Th.
2 (philos.) act of grasping (w. the mind), **apprehension** Plu.
3 **quashing** (of opponents in a debate) Ar.

κατα-λιθάζω vb. **stone to death** —*persons* NT.

κατα-λιθόω contr.vb. [λίθος] **stone to death** —*persons* D.

κατα-λιμπάνω vb. [λείπω] 1 **leave behind, abandon** —*a person* Sapph.
2 **cause to remain behind** (when one leaves), **leave** —*troops* (W.PREP.PHR. *in a place*) Th.

κατα-λῑπαρέω contr.vb. **make a successful plea** (to someone) Men.

καταλλαγή ῆς f. [καταλλάσσω] 1 **reconciliation** (w. enemies) D. Arist.; **settling** (of a war) Ar.; (fig., of a curse) A.
2 **exchanging** (of money, fr. one currency to another) D.

καταλλακτικός ή όν adj. (of persons) **inclined to reconciliation, forgiving, conciliatory** Arist.

κατ-αλλάσσω, Att. **καταλλάττω** vb. 1 ∥ MID. **exchange, trade** —*sthg.* (w. πρός + ACC. or ἀντί + GEN. *for sthg. else*) Pl. Arist.; (specif.) **exchange for currency, trade in** —*gold* D. Plu.(act.)
2 **reconcile** —*warring parties* Hdt.; **make peace** (for a people) Hdt. ∥ MID. **settle** —*one's conflicts* Hdt. ∥ PASS. **be reconciled** (w. enemies, one another) X. D. Arist. —W.DAT. or πρός + ACC. w. *enemies* E. Th. Pl.; **be converted** —W.GEN. fr. *one's anger* (W.DAT. *against the gods*) S.

κατ-άλληλος ον adj. [ἀλλήλων] 1 (of troop formations) **in corresponding positions, in alignment** (w. the front line) Plb.
2 (of events) **contemporary** (w. each other) Plb.
—**κατάλληλα** neut.pl.adv. **at the same time** (sts. W.DAT. as sthg.) —*ref. to things happening* Plb.; (quasi-adjl., of events) **contemporary** (w. each other) Plb.

κατ-αλοάω contr.vb. ∣ impf. κατηλόων ∣ 1 **beat to death** —*captives* Aeschin.
2 (of charging cavalry) **crush to pieces** —*troops, armour* X.

καταλογάδην adv. [καταλέγω] 1 **in conversation** (opp. in one's literary compositions) Pl.
2 **in prose** (opp. verse) Pl.; (quasi-adjl., of writings) Isoc. Pl.

καταλογεύς έως m. official who enrols people (as assemblymen, knights), **keeper of the rolls, registrar** Lys. Arist.

καταλογή ῆς f. app. **respect, honour** (accorded to ambassadors) Plb.(dub., cj. καταδοχή)

κατα-λογίζομαι mid.vb. 1 **enumerate by calculation, calculate, tally up** —*a population* (i.e. its size) X.
2 (specif.) **enter as a debit or credit in one's accounts, chalk up** —*a favour* (w. πρός + ACC. *to someone, i.e. expect future remuneration for it*) D.
3 (wkr.sens.) **assess** —W.ACC. + COMPL.CL. *an army, how it fared in battle* X.
4 **calculate, reckon** —W.COMPL.CL. *that sthg. is the case* Is.
5 **reckon, count** —*persons, acts* (w. ἐν + DAT. *in the category of the unjust, the virtuous*) X. Aeschin. —*sthg.* (W.PREDIC.ADJ. *as such and such*) Aeschin.

κατάλογος ου m. [καταλέγω] 1 **list** (of persons) Aeschin.; (specif.) **list, catalogue** (of ships, ref. to the description of the Greek fleet in Homer's *Iliad*) Th. Arist. Plu.
2 **genealogical list** (of ancestors), **family tree** Pl.
3 **official register** (of citizens, conscripts, or sim.) Th. Ar. Att.orats. Pl. X. +
4 **official list of regulations** (for those funding triremes) D.
5 **act of enrolling conscripts for military service, enrolment, conscription** Plu.

κατά-λοιπος ον adj. [καταλείπω] 1 (of persons) **left behind** (in a place), **left over, remaining** (after others have left) D.
2 (of things, tasks) **left over, remaining** (after others have been dealt with) Pl. Plb.
3 (of actions) **subsequent** Plb.

κατ-αλοκίζομαι mid.vb. (hyperbol., of mourners) **make furrows** (in their cheeks) —W.DAT. w. *their nails* E.(tm.)

κατα-λούομαι mid.vb. ∣ 2sg. καταλόει ∣ **use up on bathing** —*one's father's money* Ar.

καταλοφάδεια ep.adv. [κατά, λόφος] ∣ ᾱ metri grat. ∣ **across the neck** (i.e. over one's shoulders) —*ref. to carrying a slain deer* Od.

κατα-λοχίζω vb. **assign to companies; enrol** —*boys, slaves* (w. εἰς + ACC. *into a cadet corps, a fighting force*) Plu. ∥ PASS. (of troops) **be enrolled into companies** Plu.

καταλοχισμός οῦ m. **formation of companies** Plu.

κατάλυμα ατος n. [καταλύω] (sg. and pl.) **lodging-place, guest-room, quarters** Plb. NT.; **guest-house** NT.

κατα-λῡμαίνομαι mid.vb. (of a manager) **damage completely, ruin, wreck** —*a person's estate* X.; (of troops) —*roofs* (W.DAT. w. *fire*) Plb.; (of manual labour) —*people's bodies* X.

καταλύσιμος ον adj. [καταλύω] (of an evil) **able to be undone** or **brought to an end** S.

κατάλυσις εως (Ion. ιος) f. 1 **disbanding** (of a gathering) X.; **dismissal** (of cavalry after a display) X.; (specif.) **dissolution, disbandment** (of an army) X. Plu.
2 **breaking up, destruction** (of a bridge) Plb.
3 **ending** (of a war) Th. Isoc. X. Arist. Plb. Plu.
4 **overthrow** (of a regime, ruler, or sim.) Th. Att.orats. Pl. +
5 (gener.) **ending** (of someone's life, a political cycle) X. Plu.; **end** (of persons, ref. to their death) Plb.
6 (ref. to malign influences or circumstances) **cause of ruin, undoing** (of virtue, an enterprise, a person's authority) X. D. Plu.
7 act of taking up quarters, **lodging** (in a place) E. Pl. Plb.; (specif.) **encamping** (of an army) Plu.
8 (concr.) **lodging-place, lodgings** (for travellers, soldiers, or sim.) Hdt. Pl. Plb. Plu.; (gener.) **dwelling, residence** Plb. Plu.

καταλύτης ου m. **one who takes up lodgings, guest, boarder** (ref. to travellers, troops) Plb. Plu.

κατα-λύω vb. **1** untie, unyoke —horses (fr. a chariot) Od.; cut down —a suspended corpse Hdt.
2 dismantle —tents Plb. ‖ PASS. (of tents) be dismantled Plu.
3 disband, break up —an army, a society, fleet, gathering Hdt. Th. X. D. Plb. Plu. ‖ PASS. (of an army, fleet, group) be disbanded Lys. D. Plb. Plu.
4 resolve, settle —complaints Th.; write off or make amends for —one's earlier wrongdoings Th.
5 (act. and mid.) resolve, bring to an end —hostilities, a war Hdt. Th. And. Ar. X. +; (intr.) end hostilities, make peace Hdt. Th. —W.DAT. or πρός + ACC. w. a people Hdt. Th. ‖ PASS. (of wars) be brought to an end Th. X. Plu.
6 (gener.) bring to an end —one's life, troubles E.(also mid.) X. Plu. —a speech, an activity Att.orats. Pl. X.
7 give up —an activity Isoc. X. D. Plb. Plu.
8 stop (before the proper time), curtail —sentry duty Ar. Pl. —guarding the state (compared to sentry duty) Arist.
9 abolish —laws, practices, institutions, or sim. Hdt. Th. Att.orats. X. +; cancel —a procession Plu. ‖ PASS. (of laws, practices, offices) be abolished Th. Att.orats. Arist. Plu.
10 (of gods, persons, natural forces) bring down, destroy —cities, temples Il. E. NT. ‖ PASS. (of buildings) be brought down NT. Plu.
11 (of persons, things, situations) bring down, ruin —persons, empires, prosperity, or sim. Hdt. Th. Ar. Att.orats. X. + ‖ PASS. (of persons, things) be ruined Att.orats. Pl. X. +; (of people's vigour, in old age) Arist.
12 (specif.) depose —rulers, officials Th. Att.orats. Pl. Arist. Plu. —(W.GEN. fr. their rule) X.; (fig.) —the prophets NT.; overthrow —a regime Hdt. Th. Ar. Att.orats. Pl. + ‖ PASS. (of rulers, officials) be deposed Hdt. Th. X. Aeschin. Plu. —W.GEN. fr. their rule Hdt. Arist.; (of regimes) be overthrown Th. Att.orats. Pl. +
13 ‖ MID. take one's rest —W.DAT. in death E.
14 (of commanders, armies, travellers) come to a halt, make a stop (at a place) Pl. X. Plb. Plu.
15 take up lodgings (oft. w. παρά + DAT. w. someone) Th. Pl. Aeschin. D. Thphr. Men. +

κατα-λωβάω contr.vb. mutilate, dismember —captives Plb.
κατα-λωφάω, ep. **καταλωφέω** (AR.) contr.vb. **1** (of a person's heart) find relief or respite —W.GEN. fr. evils Od.(tm.)
2 (tr., of sleep) provide respite to, relieve —a person (W. ἐκ + GEN. fr. suffering) AR.
κατα-μαλακίζομαι pass.vb. become soft or enervated X.
κατα-μανθάνω vb. **1** learn, find out (sthg.) X. Arist. —sthg. (sts. w. ἐκ + GEN. fr. some source) Att.orats. Pl. X. + —W.ACC. + PTCPL. that sthg. is the case And. Pl. X. —W.INDIR.Q. or COMPL.CL. how (or the fact that) sthg. is the case Att.orats. Pl. +
2 understand (sthg.) Pl. —sthg. X. —W.COMPL.CL. that, how or why sthg. is the case Plb. Plu.
3 (of dogs) recognise, know —a person Pl.
4 find out by observing, perceive, observe (sthg.) X. Men. Plu. —sthg. Isoc. Pl. X. Men. + —W.COMPL.CL. or ACC. + PTCPL. that sthg. is the case Hdt. Pl. X. D. +
5 get the measure of by examining, scrutinise —someone or sthg. Hdt. Plu.
6 think about, consider —W.ACC. + PTCPL. or INDIR.Q. that (or how) sthg. is the case Men. NT.
κατα-μαντεύομαι mid.vb. predict, divine —the future Plb. —(w. ἐκ + GEN. fr. the past) Arist.
κατ-αμάομαι mid.contr.vb. heap up —dirt Il.
κατα-μαργέω Ion.contr.vb. [μαργάω] be thoroughly mad —W.DAT. w. envy Hdt.

κατα-μάρπτω vb. **1** catch up with, run down —a fleeing enemy Il.; (fig., of tricks, justice) —a person, a wrongdoer Thgn. Pi.
2 (wkr.sens.) catch up with —a person walking ahead Il.
3 grab, seize —a person, a fawn Thgn. Pi.; (of the earth) swallow up —a charioteer, his horses Pi.(tm.)
4 (of old age, hardship) grip —a person Od.(tm.) Hes.
κατα-μαρτυρέω contr.vb. **1** give evidence (against a person) Att.orats. Plu. —W.GEN. against a person Att.orats. NT. Plu.; (of facts, documents) provide damning evidence —W.GEN. against a person Antipho Lys. —W.GEN. of someone's wrongdoing Is. Plu. ‖ PASS. (of a person) be testified against Antipho Aeschin.
2 give evidence of, testify to —wrongdoing or sim. Plu.
3 state in evidence (sts. W.GEN. against a person) —W.INTERN.ACC. false testimony, true facts, or sim. Att.orats. NT. —W.INF. that he has done sthg. D. —W.INF. that one has done sthg. D. Plu. —W.COMPL.CL. that sthg. is the case Lycurg. D. Plu. ‖ PASS. (of testimony) be given in evidence (sts. W.GEN. against someone) Att.orats.
4 (wkr.sens., of a play) speak against, contradict —W.GEN. another play (i.e. the version of events presented in it) Plu.
κατα-μάχομαι mid.vb. defeat in battle —enemies Plu.
κατ-αμάω contr.vb. (fig., of a cleaver, an Erinys and derangement, as representing disaster for a house) mow down —a ray of hope S.(tm.)
κατ-αμβλύνω vb. (fig.) take the edge off, blunt —someone's passion S.
κατα-μεθύσκω vb. | aor.ptcpl. καταμεθύσας | make (W.ACC. someone) drunk Hdt. Pl. ‖ PASS. be made drunk, get drunk Plb.
κατα-μείγνῡμι (also written **καταμίγνῡμι**) vb. —also (pres. and impf.) **καταμειγνύω**, **καταμιγνύω**, **καταμίσγω** **1** mix in (sthg., w. sthg. else); combine, incorporate —sthg. (W.DAT. or PREP.PHR. w. or into sthg. else) D. Plb. Plu. —persons (into a larger group or sim.) Ar. Plu. ‖ PASS. (of persons or things) be incorporated —W.DAT. or PREP.PHR. into other things, among other groups X. Plb. Plu.
2 intersperse —troops (W.DAT. among elephants, persons) Plu. ‖ PASS. (of flowers) be interspersed —W.DAT. w. grass hHom.; (of a person's red complexion) —W.DAT. w. whiteness Plu.; (of a person's character, a timeless spirit) be infused, be pervasive (in a person's words or works) Plu.
3 temper —one's nature, one's mind (W.DAT. or εἰς + ACC. w. education, clear air) Ar. Plu.
4 put in a situation of interaction; allow (W.ACC. persons) to associate —W.DAT. or εἰς + ACC. w. a population or group D. Plu.; get (W.ACC. oneself) involved —W.DAT. w. people, in civil disturbances Plu. ‖ PASS. mingle, interact —W.DAT. w. the public Plu.
κατα-μείρομαι pass.vb. | pf.ptcpl. καθειμαρμένος | ‖ PF.PTCPL. (of events) ordained by fate Plu.
κατα-μελετάω contr.vb. **1** train oneself in —the art of writing eulogies Pl.
2 develop, cultivate —one's faculties of perception Pl. ‖ PASS. (of bravery) be cultivated Pl.
3 ‖ PASS. (of philosophical calculations) be carried out Pl.
κατ-αμελέω contr.vb. be entirely neglectful, neglect, disregard —W.GEN. persons or things Isoc. Pl. X. —W.NEUT.ACC. nothing X.; (intr.) be remiss or neglectful S. Pl. X. Is. ‖ PASS. (of persons or things) be neglected or disregarded Isoc. Plu.
κατα-μελιτόω contr.vb. (fig., of a bird) fill with honey (i.e. w. sweet song) —a thicket Ar.

κατα-μέλλω vb. delay, procrastinate Plb.
κατάμεμπτος ον adj. [καταμέμφομαι] (of old age) found fault with, **deplorable, accursed** S.
—**κατάμεμπτα** neut.pl.adv. **in a manner to be found fault with** S.
κατα-μέμφομαι mid.vb. | aor.pass. (w.mid.sens.) κατεμέμφθην | **1 find fault with, reproach, criticise** —oneself (sts. w.PTCPL. or ὡς + PTCPL. for doing sthg.) Th. Pl. X. Plu. —one's own overcautiousness Plu. —persons, things, events Anacr. X. Aeschin. D. Plb. —persons (w.PTCPL. or ὡς + PTCPL. for doing sthg.) Plb. Plu. —(w.PREP.PHR. because of sthg.) D. Plb. —(w.GEN. for their behaviour) Plu.
2 find wanting, have no confidence in, mistrust —oneself, one's powers, or sim. Pi. Th. Att.orats. X.
καταμέμψις εως f. **criticism, reproach** Th.
κατα-μένω vb. **1 stay on, remain behind** (usu. w.ADV. or PREP.PHR. in a place, opp. leave) Thgn. Hdt. Lys. Ar. +; (specif.) **stay at home** (opp. go somewhere) Aeschin. Plu.; **stay and settle** (sts. w.ADV. in a place) Hdt. X. Plb.
2 (of an army) **come to a halt** —w.ADV. in a place Plb.
3 (of a commander) **make a stand** —w.ADV. in a place X.
4 (of travellers) **stay, lodge** —w.ADV. in a place NT.
5 (of money) **stay, remain** —w. ἐν + DAT. in a city Plu.; (of troops) —in the equipment of mercenaries (opp. take up the arms of the infantry) X.; (of estates) —w.DAT. or ἐν + DAT. in the possession of people X. Plu.
6 (of persons) **remain, be left over** (in an army, after a purge) X.; (of a system of administration) **remain in existence** X.
7 (of a person) **hold back, wait** (opp. do sthg.) Men.
κατα-μερίζομαι pass.vb. (of things) **be shared out** or **distributed** —w.DAT. among people X.
κατα-μετρέω contr.vb. **1 measure out, apportion** —grain (w.DAT. to troops) Hdt.
2 measure out the plan of, plot out —a temple, the features of a garden X. Plu. —part of an army camp (w.DAT. w. lines) Plb.
3 (intr., of component parts) **provide a measurement** (of the whole) Arist.
καταμέτρησις εως f. **plotting out** (of a site) Plb.
κατα-μηλόω contr.vb. [μήλη medical probe] **insert a probe**; (fig.) **insert** —the funnel of a voting-urn (into a thieving official, to make him vomit up what he has stolen) Ar.
κατα-μηνύω vb. **1 give incriminating information against, inform against** —w.GEN. someone Lys. —w.ACC. Plu.
2 divulge, reveal —a secret, a plot (sts. w.DAT. or PREP.PHR. to someone) A. Plu.
3 reveal —oneself (w.COMPL.CL. as being a certain person) Hdt. —w.INDIR.Q. what is the case D.; **give a sign** (that sthg. is the case) X.
4 (of a stele) **indicate** —boundaries (w.PREP.PHR. w. an inscription) Hdt.
κατα-μιαίνω vb. | Aeol.aor.masc.nom.ptcpl. καταμιάναις |
1 defile, sully —one's lineage (w.DAT. w. lies) Pi.; (of flaws) —noble things Pl.
2 || MID. (of a mourner) **disfigure oneself** Hdt.
καταμίγνῡμι, καταμιγνύω vbs.: see καταμείγνῡμι
κατα-μιμνήσκομαι mid.vb. **make mention** —w.GEN. of sthg. Call.(tm., dub.)
καταμίσγω vb.: see καταμείγνῡμι
κατα-μισθοφορέω contr.vb. **1 use up by paying out as salaries, dole out** —public money Ar.
2 use up on mercenaries —one's resources Aeschin.
κατάμομφος ον adj. [καταμέμφομαι] (of portents) such as may be found fault with, **to be deplored** A.

καταμονή ῆς f. [καταμένω] **delay, wait** (before doing sthg.) Plb.
κατα-μονομαχέω contr.vb. **defeat in single combat** —an opponent Plu.
κατάμονος ον adj. [καταμένω] (of a state of war, honours awarded to someone) **persisting, continuing** Plb.
κατ-αμπέχω vb. (of troops) **cover up** —their helmets (to avoid detection) Plu.
κατ-αμπίσχω vb. (of the gods) **encompass, cover** —a man who dies bravely (w.DAT. w. earth that lies lightly on him) E.
κατάμυσις εως f. [καταμύω] **closing of the eyes** Plu.
κατ-αμύσσω vb. (of a dog) **tear, scratch** —someone's skin Theoc.(tm.); (mid., of a person) —one's hand, forehead, nose Il. Hdt.
κατα-μυττωτεύομαι Att.pass.vb. (fig., of a city) be completely mashed up, **be turned into mincemeat** (by war) Ar.
κατα-μύω vb. | aor. κατέμυσα | —also **καμμύω** vb. | aor. ἐκάμμυσα (NT.) | **1** (of persons, animals) **close** —their eyes X. NT.; (intr.) **close one's eyes** X. Men.
2 (specif.) close one's eyes in sleep, **doze off** Ar.
κατ-αμφικαλύπτω vb. **wrap around as a covering, wrap** —a cloak (w.DAT. around one's head) Od.(tm.)
κατα-μωκάομαι mid.contr.vb. [μωκάομαι mock] **make a laughing-stock** —w.GEN. of someone Plu.
καταμώκησις εως f. **act of making a laughing-stock, exposure to ridicule** (of persons, deeds) Plb.
κατ-αναγκάζω vb. **1 compel** —someone (w.INF. to do sthg.) Th. Is. Plu. —land and sea (to become theatres of war) Th. || PASS. (of persons) be compelled (sts. w.INF. to do sthg.) Th.
2 || PF.PASS.PTCPL.ADJ. (of oaths) extracted under compulsion E.; (of sufferings, situations) unavoidable Plb. Plu.
3 || PASS. be constrained —w.DAT. by bonds E.
κατα-ναίω vb. | aor. κατένασσα || aor.pass. κατενάσθην |
1 || AOR. (of gods) **settle, install** —persons, deities, Titans, a lion (w.DAT., PREP.PHR. or ADV. in a place) Hes. A.(mid.) B.
2 || AOR.MID. or PASS. (of persons) **settle, come to live** —w.ACC. in a place Hes.fr. —w.PREP.PHR. somewhere E. Ar. AR.
3 || AOR. **build, establish** —an altar B.
κατ-αναλίσκω vb. | impf. κατανήλισκον (Plu.) | aor. κατηνάλωσα (Isoc.), also καταναλ- and κατανηλ- (Plu.) | pf. καταναλωκα and κατανηλ- (Plu.) | 3sg.plpf. κατανηλώκει (Pl.), also καταναλ- (Plb.) |
1 exhaust by spending, use up, spend —money, resources (oft. w. εἰς + ACC. on sthg.) Isoc. Pl. X. Hyp. Plu. || PASS. (of money, resources) be used up Isoc. Plu. —w. εἰς + ACC. on sthg. Plu.
2 exhaust by eating up; use up —one's horses (w.PTCPL. by eating them) Plu.; **consume, eat up** —provisions Plu.; (of a mouse) —its offspring Plu.
3 (gener.) **use up** —explanations (w. εἰς + ACC. on natural phenomena) Arist. —troops (by deploying them on ships) Plu.; **exhaust** —one's vigour (w. εἰς + ACC. on oratory) Plu.; **vent** —one's anger (opp. nurture it) Plu. || PF. (intr., of a mixture) run out, be used up Pl.
4 reduce to nothing; dissipate —a river (by diverting it) Plu.; (of time, warring nations) **use up** (i.e. kill off) —persons Plb. Plu.; (wkr.sens., of a commander) **wear out** —an enemy (w.DAT. through delaying tactics) Plu. || PASS. (of a river) be dissipated —w.PREP.PHR. in marshes Plu.; (of corpses, living things) be reduced to nothing (fr. death and decay) Pl. Plu.; (of a military force, a group of people) be used up (i.e. killed in various campaigns) Plu.

κατανάσσω 764

5 use up in a particular activity; **use up** —*time* (*sts.* W.PTCPL. *in doing sthg.*) Plu.; **devote** —*one's life, free time* (w. εἰς + ACC. *to someone or sthg.*) Isoc. Lycurg.
6 waste —*time* (w. ἐν + DAT. *on sthg.*) Plu. —*certain qualities* (w. εἰς + ACC. *on sthg.*) Plu. ‖ PASS. (of an opportunity for glory) **be lost** —w. εἰς + ACC. *to someone else* Plu.
κατα-νάσσω *vb.* | aor. κατέναξα | **stamp down** —*earth* (*to make a path*) Hdt.
κατα-ναυμαχέω *contr.vb.* **defeat in a sea-battle** —*commanders, peoples, troops, fleets* Att.orats. X. Plu. ‖ PASS. **be defeated at sea** Isoc. Plu.
κατα-νείφω (also **κατανίφω**) *vb.* | aor. κατένειψα | **1** (of storms) **shower down snow** Plu.
2 ‖ IMPERS. **it is snowing** Ar.
3 ‖ PASS. (of mountains) **be covered with snow** Plu.
κατα-νέμω *vb.* **1** (of gods, commanders, councils) **divide up** —*a land, people, army* (w. 2ND ACC. or εἰς + ACC. *into parts*) Pl. X. Plu.
2 divide up and distribute, **parcel out** —*a region, buildings* (W.DAT. *to people*) Hdt. Th. Isoc. Plu. ‖ PASS. (of land) **be parcelled out** —W.DAT. *to soldiers* Plu.
3 ‖ MID. (of peoples, military forces) **parcel out for occupation** —*a region* Att.orats. Pl. —(w. εἰς + ACC. *for winter quarters*) Plu.; (of days) **take a share of** —*time* (W.ADJ. + PREP.PHR. *equally w. nights, i.e. be of equal length*) Plu.
4 assign, allocate —*seats, sleeping-quarters* (W.DAT. *to persons*) Aeschin. D. Plu. —*people, demes* (w. εἰς + ACC. *to demes, tribes*) Hdt. D.(decree) ‖ PASS. (of people) **be distributed by allocation** (around a city) Pl.
5 assign —*a person* (w. εἰς + ACC. *to the ranks of heroes or villains*) Aeschin. Plb.
6 ‖ PASS. (specif., of horses) **be put to pasture** —w. ἐν + DAT. *in a place* Plu.
7 ‖ MID. and AOR.PASS. (of a fire) **spread** —w. εἰς + ACC. *to huts* Plb.; (of leprosy) **spread over** —*someone's body* Plu.; (of a plague) **ravage** —*a population's youth and strength* Plu.
κατα-νεύω *vb.* | fut. κατανεύσομαι | ep.aor.ptcpl. καννεύσᾱς |
1 make a signal by nodding, nod, signal (sts. W.DAT. w. one's head) Od. —W.DAT. *to someone* (sts. W.INF. *to do sthg.*) Od. Plb. NT.
2 nod in agreement (to a question) Ar. Pl. Plb.
3 (of persons; of gods, esp. Zeus) **nod in assent to a request, give a nod of assent** (sts. W.DAT. w. one's head or locks, oft. W.DAT. to someone) Hom. hHom. Hdt. Ar. Men. Plb. —w. ἐπί + DAT. *to sthg.* hHom. —w. ὡς + SUBJ. *that one will do sthg.* Il. —W.INF. or ὥστε + INF. *to do sthg.* Hom. hHom. Pi. —W.ACC. + INF. *that sthg. shd. be the case* Il.; (wkr.sens., of an army, a commander) **agree** —W.INF. *to do sthg.* Plb.
4 vow, promise (sthg.) Call. —W.ACC. + INF. *that sthg. will be the case* Bion —W.INTERN.ACC. *a particular promise* Il.
5 vow to give, promise —*gifts, glory, victory, a certain fate* (W.DAT. *to someone*) Hom. B.
κατα-νεφόω *contr.vb.* [νέφος] (of mist) **cover with cloud** —*mountain peaks* Plu.
κατα-νέω[1] *contr.vb.* [νέω²] | ep.3pl.aor.mid. (tm.) κατὰ ... νήσαντο | ‖ MID. (of the Fates) **spin out** —*a destiny* (W.DAT. *for someone*) Od.
κατα-νέω[2] *contr.vb.* [νέω³] **pile up, heap** —*frankincense* (W.PREP.PHR. *on an altar, to burn it*) Hdt.
κατανήλισκον (impf.), **κατανήλώκει** (3sg.plpf.), **κατανήλωσα** (aor.): see καταναλίσκω
κατ-ανθρακόομαι *pass.contr.vb.* ‖ PF. (of a person's body) **be burned to cinders** S.; (of the Cyclops) **have** (w.ACC. his eye) **burned to cinders** E.*Cyc.*

κατα-νίσσομαι *ep.mid.vb.* [νίσομαι] **1** (of a stream) **go down, descend** —W.ADV. *to a plain* AR.
2 (of Dionysus) **come back** —W.ACC. *to Thebes* (fr. *India*) AR.(cj.)
κατ-ανίσταμαι *mid.vb.* | athem.aor.act. κατανέστην | **rise up against** —W.GEN. *critics, enemies, authorities* Plb.
κατανίφω *vb.*: see κατανείφω
κατα-νοέω *contr.vb.* **1 apprehend, understand** —*a matter, a statement* Hdt. Pl. Arist. Men. Plb.; (intr.) **learn** —w. περί + GEN. *about sthg.* Plb.
2 learn, study —*a subject, language, natural phenomena* Th. Pl. Plu. ‖ PASS. (of phenomena) **be studied** Pl.
3 ascertain, work out —*sthg.* Pl. Arist. Plb.
4 perceive, notice —*sthg.* Th. Lys. Pl. X. Plb. + —W.ACC. + PTCPL. *that sthg. is the case* Th. Pl. X. Arist. +; **realise** —W.COMPL.CL. *that* (or *how*) *sthg. is the case* Isoc. Pl. X. Arist. Plb. ‖ PASS. (of a person's true character) **be recognised** (by people) Plu.
5 bear in mind —*sthg.* Pl. X. —W.COMPL.CL. *that sthg. is the case* Pl. X.
6 consider in one's mind, reflect on —*sthg.* Th. Pl. X. Plu. —W.INDIR.Q. *whether, why or how sthg. is the case* Th. X. —W.ACC. + COMPL.CL. NT.; (intr.) **reflect** X. —w. περί + GEN. *on a matter* X.
7 look closely at —*an object* NT. Plu.
κατανόημα ατος *n.* **strategy, idea** (for making money) Arist.
κατανόησις εως *f.* **1** act or result of discerning; **perception, identification** (of a person's character) Plu.; **familiarity** (w. one's own body) Pl.
2 impression (formed by someone, about sthg.) Plu.
3 discernible class (of diseases) Pl.
κατ-άνομαι *ep.pass.vb.* [ἀνύω] (of provisions) **be used up, be consumed** Od.
κατα-νομοθετέω *contr.vb.* (of a principle underlying a lawcode) **make laws against** (objections), **counter-legislate** Pl.
κατα-νοστέω *contr.vb.* **return from exile** Plb.
κατα-νοτίζω *vb.* (of lamentation) **moisten** —*the eyes* E.(tm.)
κάτ-αντα *adv.* [ἄντα] (ref. to movt.) **downhill** Il.
κατ-αντάω *contr.vb.* **1 arrive** —W.PREP.PHR. *at a place* NT.
2 arrive —W.PREP.PHR. *at a particular conclusion* Plb. —*at a goal* NT.; **focus** —W.PREP.PHR. *on a particular topic* Plb.; **finally come** —W.PREP.PHR. *to a particular action, argument or target* Plb.; (of regimes, audacity) **end up, result** —W.PREP.PHR. *in a particular condition or outcome* Plb.
3 (of crimes) **fall** —W.PREP.PHR. *into particular categories* Plb.
κατ-άντης ες *adj.* [ἄντα] **1** (of ground) **sloping downwards** Plu.; (of a ship on rollers) AR.; (of a building, W.DAT. in its roof) Plu. ‖ NEUT.SB. **downward slope** X. Arist. Theoc.; (prep.phrs.) εἰς τὸ κάταντες **downhill** X. Bion; ἐπὶ κάταντες **downwards** Pl.
2 (fig., of a path) **downhill** (i.e. easy) Ar. Plu.; (quasi-advbl., ref. to events moving, i.e. quickly and easily, W.PREP.PHR. *to a good outcome*) E.
3 (w.neg.connot., of a path of lax government) **downhill** (i.e. on a slippery slope) Plu.
4 (w.neg.connot., of persons) **acquiescent, easily induced** (W.PREP.PHR. *to some action*) Plu.
κατ-αντικρύ *adv. and prep.* **1 straight down** (W.GEN. fr. a roof) —*ref. to falling* Od.
2 directly opposite (usu. W.GEN. fr. a place) —*esp. ref. to places being situated* Th. Pl. Plb. Plu.; (quasi-adjl., of places,

objects, usu. W.GEN. fr. a place) Th. Ar. Pl. X. Plb. ‖ NEUT.SB. (w.art., esp. in prep.phrs.) opposite side (of somewhere or sthg.) Pl.; far end (of a bridge) Plb.
3 in direct opposition or **comparison** —*ref. to presenting conflicting statements* Arist.
4 directly contrary; **in defiance** (W.GEN. of a person) AR. ‖ FEM.SB. (w.art.) contrary view or position (to that held by another person) Arist.
5 directly in front (of a person) Pl.; (quasi-adj., of a person) Pl.; (prep.phrs.) ἐκ τοῦ καταντικρύ *from head-on (ref. to troops attacking)* X.; εἰς τὸ καταντικρύ *straight forwards (ref. to proceeding)* Pl.
6 straight on (opp. at a slant) —*ref. to looking, applying a seal* Pl.
7 (emph.) **outright, out-and-out** —*ref. to persons having a certain national identity* Th.

κατ-αντίον *adv. and prep.* **1 over on the opposite side, opposite** (W.GEN. or DAT. fr. a place) Hdt.; (quasi-adj., of a place) Hdt.
2 on the opposing side (of a battle) —*ref. to a person dying* S.

κατ-αντιπέρᾱν *prep.* **opposite** —W.GEN. *a place* Plb.

κατ-αντλέω *contr.vb.* pour down (liquid) over; (fig.) **pour down** —*words* (W.GEN. or κατά + GEN. *over someone, the ears*) Ar. Pl.

κατα-νύσσομαι *pass.vb.* be stabbed or wounded; (fig.) **be deeply pained** —W.ACC. *in one's heart* NT.

κατ-ανύω, Att. **καθανύω**, **καθανύτω** (X.) *vb.* | aor. κατήνυσα, Att. καθήνυσα | pf. κατήνυκα | **1** accomplish a journey; **cover, travel** —*a certain distance, a course* Hdt. X. Plu. —W.PREP.PHRS. *fr. one place to another* NT.
2 finish one's journey, **arrive** X. Plu. —w. εἰς + ACC. *at a place* X. —*(fig.)* w. ἐπί + ACC. *at (the accomplishment of) one's plan* Plb.
3 reach —W.GEN. *a friendly hostess* S.; (fig.) —*another's state of mind (i.e. come to that same state)* E.
4 accomplish —*a deed* E.
5 (of an army) **procure** —*provender* Plb.

κατάξαι (aor.inf.): see κατάγνυμι

κατα-ξαίνω *vb.* | aor. κατέξηνα ‖ PASS.: aor. κατεξάνθην | pf.inf. κατεξάνθαι | **1** comb or card (wool); (fig.) **tear to shreds, lacerate** —*persons, their bodies* (w. *stones*, w. εἰς + ACC. *into rags*) Ar. —(W.DAT. w. *rods*) Plu. —*one's horse (fr. riding it through rocky areas)* Plu.; (of mountain heights) —*a woman's hair (when she is flung fr. them)* E.; (of a snake's tail, attempting to lead its body) **cause** (W.ACC. *the head*) **to be lacerated** (because it cannot see where it is going) Plu. ‖ PASS. be torn to shreds —W.DAT. *by stones, missiles* Trag.
2 (fig., of breezes preventing sailing) **wear down, waste away** —*the flower of Argos (i.e. its warriors)* A. ‖ PASS. (of a person) be reduced to nothing —W.DAT. *by fire* E.; be wasted away (by sickness) E. —W.DAT. *by labour, weeping* E.

κατα-ξενόομαι *pass.contr.vb.* **be received as a guest** A.

κατα-ξηραίνομαι *pass.vb.* (of fleshy matter) **become dry** Pl.

κατ-αξιοπιστέομαι *mid.contr.vb.* [ἀξιόπιστος] **ask to be taken on trust in one's criticism** —W.GEN. *of persons* Plb.

κατ-άξιος ον *adj.* **1** (of a person, actions, esp. in neg.phr.) **worthy** (sts. W.GEN. of someone) S. E. Men.
2 (of a person) **deserving** (W.GEN. of someone, as a colleague) S.

—καταξίως *adv.* **in a manner that is appropriate** (sts. W.GEN. to sthg.) Plb.

κατ-αξιόω *contr.vb.* **1** (oft. in neg.phr.) **consider** (W.ACC. a person) **worthy** —W.GEN. *of a response* Plb. —W.INF. *to share in sthg.* D.; **consider** (W.ACC. a battle) **deserving** —W.GEN. *of a battle-plan* Plb. ‖ PASS. (of persons or things) be considered worthy —W.GEN. *of sthg.* Plb.; (of persons) —W.INF. *to do sthg.* NT.
2 (of persons, Justice) **hold in esteem** —*a person* A.(mid.) Plb. ‖ PASS. (of a deed) be held in esteem Plb.
3 consider it right (that sthg. shd. be the case) S. Pl. —W.INF. *to do sthg.* A.

καταξίωσις εως *f.* **high esteem, respect** (for persons) Plb.

κατάξω (fut.): see κατάγνυμι

κατα-παγίως *adv.* **steadily, continuously** —*ref. to living in a place* Isoc.

κατα-παιδεραστέω *contr.vb.* **use up on pederasty, squander on chasing boys** —*an inheritance* Is.

κατα-παλαίω *vb.* **outwrestle** —*a person* Plu.; (fig., of a defendant) —*a legal opponent* Ar.; (of a commander) —*enemy kings* Plu.; (of arguments) —*fears, a debater* E. Pl. ‖ PASS. be outwrestled Plu.

κατα-πάλτης, also **καταπέλτης**, ου *m.* [πάλλω] (milit.) machine that shoots darts, **catapult** Arist. Plb. Plu.

—καταπελτικός ή όν *adj.* **1** (of missiles) **for catapults** Plb. Plu.
2 ‖ NEUT.PL.SB. catapults Plb.

κατάπαστος ον *adj.* [καταπάττω] **1** (of a victor) **strewn, bedecked** (W.DAT. w. *garlands*) Ar.
2 (of a robe) **embroidered** Ar.

κατα-πατέω *contr.vb.* **1** (of a farmer) **tread into the ground** —*seed* (W.DAT. *by the use of his pigs*) Hdt.
2 (of persons, animals) injure or destroy by treading down, **trample underfoot** —*cornfields, tracks, pearls* X. NT. —*persons, animals* Th. X. Plb. NT. ‖ PASS. (of persons or things) be trampled underfoot (by persons, elephants) Hdt. Th. X. D. +; be trampled to death Plu.; (fig., of a small body of troops) be trampled over (i.e. trounced) —w. ὑπό + GEN. *by an army* Hdt.
3 (fig., of persons, political regimes) **trample underfoot, ride roughshod over** —*oaths, laws, principles, or sim.* Il.(tm.) Pl. ‖ PASS. (fig., of stupid people's brains) be trampled —w. ἐν + DAT. *in their heels (opp. being in their heads)* D.

κατα-πάττω *Att.vb.* [πάσσω] **sprinkle** —*ash* (w. κατά + GEN. *over a table*) Ar.; (fig.) **strew** —*a place* (W.GEN. w. *ideas*) Ar. ‖ PASS. (of a person) be sprinkled (w. *flour*) Ar.

κατάπαυμα ατος *n.* [καταπαύω] that which brings to an end; (ref. to a warrior who exacts revenge) **finisher** (W.GEN. of *grief*) Il.

κατάπαυσις εως (Ion. ιος) *f.* **1** act of bringing to an end; **ending** (of a king's reign, by deposition) Hdt.; **deposing** (of tyrants) Hdt.
2 act of staying; **dwelling** (of God, in a temple) NT.

κατα-παύω, dial. **καππαύω** (Pi.) *vb.* **1** cause to cease (fr. sthg.); **check, restrain, stop** —*persons, musical instruments* Hom. Hdt. E. Ar. Men. Plu. —(W.GEN. *fr. an activity*) Il. Pl. NT. Plu. —*the Muses (i.e. cease fr. musical activities)* E.
2 (euphem., of a warrior's spear) **put a stop to** (i.e. kill) —*a person* Il.
3 cause (sthg.) to cease; **bring to an end, stop, end** —*an activity, condition, emotion* Hom. + ‖ PASS. (of illnesses) be stopped —W.DAT. *by doctors' remedies* D.
4 cause (someone) to be removed (fr. office); **remove** —*someone* (W.GEN. *fr. power, kingship*) Hdt. X. Plu.; **remove from power, depose** —*rulers, officials, the people (in a democracy)* Hdt. Th. X. Aeschin.(quot.epigr.)

καταπεδάω

5 ‖ MID. **cease, desist** (fr. doing sthg.) Pi.*fr.* Dionys.Eleg. Ar. X. Arist.

κατα-πεδάω *contr.vb.* **bind with shackles**; (of fate, Ruin) **shackle, trammel** —*a person* Hom.(tm.); (of sleep) **bind** —*eyes* (W.DAT. *w. gentle bonds*) Mosch.(tm.)

κατ-απειλέω *contr.vb.* (of threats) **menacingly utter** —*futile words* S.(dub.) ‖ NEUT.PL.PF.PASS.PTCPL.SB. **threats** S.

κατά-πειρα ᾱς *f.* [πεῖρα] **attempt** (to achieve sthg.) Plb.

κατα-πειράζω *vb.* **1 make trial of** (someone's views, by questioning); **sound out** —W.GEN. *someone* Plb. —(W.INDIR.Q. *about how much he would pay for sthg.*) Plb. **2 test** (by provocation); **test out** —W.GEN. *persons, an enemy* Plb.; **provoke** —W.GEN. *an enemy* Plb. **3 make trial of** (by military engagement); **test the strength of, attack** —W.GEN. *enemies* Plb.; **make an attempt on** —W.GEN. *a city* Plb. **4** (gener.) **attempt to influence** —W.ACC. *a vote* Lys.; **try to achieve** —W.GEN. *one's hopes, the deliverance of a people* Plb.; (intr.) **make an attempt, try** Plb.

κατα-πειρητηρίη ης *Ion.f.* [πειράομαι] **sounding-line, plumb-line** (to test the depth of a sea or river) Hdt.

κατα-πελεμίζω *ep.vb.* | 3sg.aor. (tm.) κὰδ ... πελέμιξε | (of a boxer) **bring** (W.ACC. *his heavy fist*) **crashing down** —W.PREP.PHR. *on an opponent* AR.

κατα-πελτάζω *vb.* | fut. καταπελτάσομαι | **overpower with peltasts, overrun with light infantry** —*a region* Ar.

καταπέλτης *m.*, **καταπελτικός** *adj.*: see καταπάλτης

κατα-πέμπω *vb.* **1** (of Zeus) **send down** —*a Titan* (W.PREP.PHR. *to Hades*) Hes. **2** (of Persian kings; gener., of kings, commanders) **send down from the capital city, send out, despatch** —*persons* (*to a place*) Att.orats. X. Plu. —*an army* (*as a relief force*) Plu. ‖ PASS. **be sent out** —W.PREDIC.NOM. *as a regional governor* X. **3 send out, send** —*letters, gifts* (oft. W.DAT. *to people*) Aeschin. Plu. ‖ PASS. (of gifts) **be sent** —W.DAT. *to a person* (*by the king of Persia*) Arist. **4 send out, promulgate** —*treaties, an offer of peace* X. Plu.; **send out instructions** —W.ACC. + PREDIC.ADJ. *that a city shd. be under the control* (*of another city*) D. ‖ PASS. (of terms of peace) **be sent out** (by a king) Plu.

καταπεπταμένος (pf.pass.ptcpl.): see καταπετάννῡμι

καταπεπτηυῖα (ep.fem.pf.ptcpl.): see καταπτήσσω

καταπέπωκα (pf.): see καταπίνω

κατά περ *Ion.conj.*: see under καθά

κατα-πέρδομαι *mid.vb.* | act.aor.2 κατέπαρδον | **fart at** —W.GEN. *persons, Poverty* (to show one's contempt) Ar.; (fig., of a wine-filled donkey-jug) —*an empty cup* (i.e. glug when poured into it) Ar.

κατα-περίειμι *vb.* [περίειμι¹] **surpass** —W.GEN. *rivals* (W.DAT. *in certain qualities*) Plb.

κατα-περονάω *contr.vb.* **attach by putting rivets through, rivet** —*a spear-head* (*to a shaft*, W.DAT. *w. clamps*) Plb.

κατα-πέσσω *vb.* **1 swallow, choke down** —*one's anger* Il. **2 digest, be content with** —*great wealth* Pi.

κατα-πετάννῡμι *vb.* | pf.pass.ptcpl. καταπεπταμένος | **cover by draping over, cover, drape** —*persons, their heads, a courtyard* (W.DAT. *w. cloths, nets, a sail*) Ar. Pl. ‖ PASS. (of horses) **be draped** (i.e. caparisoned) —W.DAT. *w. cloth* X.; (of a street) **be covered over** —W.DAT. *w. sails* (*as a canopy*) Plu.; (of a sail) **be spread over** (a place, as a canopy) Plu.

καταπέτασμα ατος *n.* **veil, curtain** (of a Jewish temple, enclosing the Holy of Holies, i.e. the inner sanctum) NT.

κατα-πέτομαι *mid.vb.* | athem.aor. κατεπτάμην | aor.2 ptcpl. καταπτόμενος | pf.act. κατέπτηκα (Men.) | **1** (of birds, persons envisaged as winged) **fly down** (sts. W.PREP.PHR. *to or fr. a place, through the air*) Stesich. Hdt. Ar. **2** (fig., of a wrongdoer) **flit down** —W.ADV. *fr. a place* Men.

κατα-πετρόομαι *pass.contr.vb.* **be stoned to death** X.

καταπεφρονηκότως *pf.ptcpl.adv.*: see under καταφρονέω

κατα-πήγνῡμι *vb.* —also (pres.) **καταπηγνύω** (Arist.) | 3sg.athem.aor.mid. (w.pass.sens.) κατέπηκτο | **1 fix in the ground or sea-bed**; **fix, plant** —*posts, spears, or sim.* (sts. W.DAT. OR PREP.PHR. *in a place, the sea, a river*) Il. Hdt. Th. Ar. Arist. + ‖ PASS. and PF.ACT. (of logs, a stele, an arrow) **be planted** (in the ground) Il. Hdt. Plu. **2** ‖ PF.ACT. (of animals) **be frozen stiff** (in snow and ice) Plb. **3** | AOR.PASS. (of a person) **catch a chill** Plu.

κατα-πηδάω *contr.vb.* **leap down** —W.PREP.PHR. *fr. a horse or chariot* X. Plu. —*into a well, a boat* Men. Plu.; (of a horse, at a rider's command) X.

κατα-πιαίνομαι *pass.vb.* | pf.ptcpl. καταπεπίασμένος | (of animals) **be fattened, grow fat** Pl.

κατα-πίμπλημι *vb.* **1 fill up the entirety of a space; fill** —*a place* (W.GEN. *w. corpses, slaughter, or sim.*) Plu.; **cover** —*a chair and podium* (W.GEN. *w. graffiti*) Plu.; **cram** —*one's writings* (W.GEN. *w. self-praise*) Plu. ‖ PASS. (of a place) **be filled** —W.GEN. *w. persons, corpses* Plu.; (of a formation of troops) **be choked** —W.GEN. *by others fleeing the front-lines* Plu.; (of a person) **be covered** —W.GEN. *w. gore* Plu.; (of soldiers) **get** (W.ACC. *their tents*) **filled** —W.GEN. *w. mud and water* Plu. **2 fill with an emotion or condition; fill** —*persons, troops, a camp* (W.GEN. *w. despair, commotion, or sim.*) Plu. ‖ PASS. (of persons) **be filled** —W.GEN. *w. lawlessness* Pl.; (of a region) **be overwhelmed** —W.GEN. *by a shocking event* Plu. **3** (of a populace) **fill to satiety, flood** —*itself* (W.GEN. *w. gold and silver*) Plu. ‖ PASS. (of persons) **be laden down** —W.GEN. *w. spoils* Plu.; **be gorged** —W.GEN. *w. public money* Plu.

κατα-πίμπρημι *vb.* | aor. κατέπρησα ‖ PASS.: aor. κατεπρήσθην | pf.inf. καταπεπρῆσθαι | **burn down** —*buildings, cities, ships* Plu. ‖ PASS. (of buildings, cities) **be burned down** Plu.; (of persons) **be burned to death** Plb. Plu.

κατα-πίνω *vb.* | fut. καταπίομαι, also καταπιοῦμαι (Plu.) | aor.2 κατέπιον, ep. κάππιον / pf. καταπέπωκα ‖ PASS.: fut. καταποθήσομαι | aor. κατεπόθην |
1 (of persons, gods, animals) **swallow** —*food, objects, persons, gods* Hes. +; (fig., of an informer) —*lawsuits* Ar.; (of persons) —*bait* (ref. *to bribes, tempting offers*) Plb. ‖ PASS. (of food, objects) **be swallowed** Hdt. Plu. **2** (of a wave) **swallow up, engulf** —*a ship* Thgn.(tm.) ‖ PASS. (of a city) **be swallowed up** (by the sea, a crack in the earth) Plb. Plu.; (of water) **be absorbed or soaked up** (by soil) Pl. **3** (fig., of persons) **guzzle up** —*money* Ar.; (of a heavy cloak) —*a huge amount of wool* (in its making) Ar.; (specif., of a person) **drink away** —*one's inheritance* Aeschin. Plu. **4** (fig., of a regional power) **swallow up** —*a city* Plu.; (of persons) **swallow whole, eat for breakfast** (i.e. utterly defeat) —*persons* Ar. ‖ PASS. (of persons) **be eaten for breakfast** (i.e. utterly defeated) Ar. **5** (fig., of a person's soul) **imbibe, absorb** —*Euripides* Ar. **6** (fig.) **swallow down, choke back** —*one's anger* Men.

κατα-πίπτω *vb.* | aor.2 κατέπεσον, ep. κάππεσον, dial. κάππετον, also κάπετον (Pi.), ep.inf. καππεσέειν (Mosch.) |
1 (of persons, animals, objects) **fall down** (oft. W.PREP.PHR. *fr. or upon sthg.*) Il. +; (fr. one's horse) X.; (provbl.) καταπεσεῖν ἀπ' ὄνου *fall off a donkey* (on one's head, as a

possible explanation for bizarre or idiotic behaviour) Ar.; (of a wrestler) **fall** (i.e. be thrown by one's opponent) X.; (of persons) **collapse to the ground** (fr. fear or despair) Archil. Ar. NT.; (specif.) **collapse in a faint, swoon** Men.
2 (of persons, animals) **fall down dead** (esp. in battle) Hom. +; **die** —w. πρός + GEN. *at someone's hands* A.
3 (of buildings) **collapse** Th. And. Arist.; (of ashes) **settle** Il.
4 (of ships) **keel over** —W.PREDIC.ADJ. *sideways* Plb.
5 (of persons) **jump** —W.DAT. *into the sea* Od. —W.PREP.PHR. *fr. a ladder* Ar.
6 (fig., of persons' spirits) **sink** —W.PREP.PHR. *to their feet* Il.; (of persons, a people, an argument) **fall** —w. εἰς + ACC. *into despondency, slavery, discredit* Pl. X.
7 ‖ PF. (of a person's lineage) **be lowly** Plu.

κατα-πιστεύω *vb.* **have complete confidence** —W.DAT. *in one's endeavours or military strength* Plb.; **trust** (a person) Plu.

κατα-πιστόομαι *mid.contr.vb.* **give assurances, vouch** (w. ὑπέρ + GEN. for someone) —w. πρός + ACC. *to a person* Plu.

καταπίστωσις εως *f.* act of making a promise, **pledge** (betw. lovers) Plu.

κατα-πιττόω *Att.contr.vb.* [πίσσα] **cover with pitch** —*a person* (*as preparation for burning him alive*) Ar. ‖ PASS. **be covered with pitch** Pl.

καταπλαγής ές *adj.* [καταπλήσσω] (of persons) **alarmed, intimidated** (by an enemy) Plb.; (w. μή + SUBJ. that sthg. might happen) Plb.; (periphr.w. γίγνομαι) **be afraid of** —W.ACC. *an attack* Plb.

κατα-πλάσσω, Att. **καταπλάττω** *vb.* **1 plaster over, smear** —*a person's eyelids* (w. ointment) Ar. —*a crocodile's eyes* (W.DAT. *w. mud*) Hdt.(tm.) —*an ointment* (W. 2ND ACC. *over one's face and body*) Hdt.
2 ‖ PF.PASS. (of a way of life) **be shaped by deception or pretence** D.(cj.)

καταπλαστός όν *adj.* (of medicine) **smeared on, in the form of a poultice** or **ointment** Ar.

—καταπλαστόν οῦ *n.* app. **bandage** or **sticking-plaster** (*concealing the wound of love*) Men.

καταπλαστύς ύος *f.* layer of ointment applied to the face and body (of a woman), **beauty mask** Hdt.

κατα-πλέκω *vb.* **1 plait** —*rushes* (*to make clothing*) Hdt.
2 (fig.) **tie up, conclude** —*a speech, one's life* Hdt.
3 implicate —*a person* (W.DAT. *in treachery*) Hdt.
4 ‖ PASS. (of a narrative) **be made tangled or over-complicated** —W.DAT. *by elaboration* Arist.

κατα-πλέω *contr.vb.* —also **καταπλώω** *Ion.vb.* [πλέω¹] **1** (of commanders, sailors, ships) **sail in** (W.ADV. or PREP.PHR. *to a place*) Od. Hdt. Th. Att.orats. X. Plb. +; (of goods) **come in by sea** —W.ADV. or PREP.PHR. *to a place* D. Arist.
2 sail back (to a place) Th. Att.orats. X. Plb. Plu. —W.ADV. or PREP.PHR. *to* (or *sts. fr.*) *a place* Hdt. Th. Att.orats. X. + —W.PREP.PHR. *to face trial* Th. D.
3 sail downstream —w. κατά + ACC. *down a river* Th.; **sail down** —W.ACC. *a river* Hdt.
4 (of fish) **swim downstream** —w. ἐς + ACC. *to the sea* Hdt.

κατά-πλεως ων, gen. ω *adj.* [πλέως] **1** (of a city) **completely full** (W.GEN. of corpses) Plu.; (of a casualty of battle) **riddled** (W.GEN. + ACC. w. spears, in his body) Plu.
2 (of a man, his chin, clothes) **completely covered** (W.GEN. in blood, mud) X. Plu.

καταπληκτικός ή όν *adj.* [καταπλήσσω] **1** (of persons or things) **terrifying, intimidating** Plb. Plu.
2 (wkr.sens., of persons, their appearance, a historian's treatment of a subject) **impressive, imposing** Plb. Plu.

—καταπληκτικῶς *adv.* **in a terrifying** or **intimidating manner** Plb.

κατα-πλήξ ῆγος *masc.fem.adj.* **1 amazed, dumbstruck** Lys.
2 cowed, disheartened Plu.
3 (wkr.sens.) **fearful, timid** Plu.; **diffident** Arist.

κατάπληξις εως *f.* **1** state of being cowed; **abject fear** (of a population) Th.; **awe** (of Rome, felt by her allies) Plb.
2 act of striking terror (into people), **intimidation** Plb.
3 dismay, consternation (felt by people) Th. Plb. Plu.
4 (wkr.sens.) **diffidence** (of a person) Arist.

κατα-πλήσσω, Att. **καταπλήττω** *vb.* ‖ pf.ptcpl. καταπεπληγώς ‖ aor.2 pass. κατεπλάγην, ep. κατεπλήγην ‖ neut.impers.vbl.adj. (w.pass.sens.) καταπληκτέον ‖
1 (of persons, armies, circumstances) **terrify, intimidate, cow** —*persons, their spirits, enemy forces, cities, or sim.* Th. X. D. Arist. Plb.; (also mid.) Plb. Plu.; (of Zeus) —*a people* (W.DAT. *w. thunder*) X. ‖ PASS. **be terrified, intimidated** or **cowed** (sts. W.ACC., DAT. or PREP.PHR. by sthg.) Il. Th. X. D. +; **be awestruck** or **amazed** (sts. W.ACC. at sthg.) Plb. Plu.
2 ‖ NEUT.PF.PTCPL.SB. **cowed state** (of an army) Plu.

καταπλοκή ῆς *f.* [καταπλέκω] **interweaving** (of sinew, skin and bone, around the fingers) Pl.

κατά-πλους ου *Att.m.* [πλόος] **1 sailing to land, landing** (of ships, persons) Th. Din. Plb.
2 sailing back, return voyage X. D. Plb.

κατα-πλουτίζω *vb.* (of a commander) **enrich** —*his troops* Hdt. —(W.DAT. *w. gifts*) X.

κατα-πλύνω *vb.* **1 wash** —*a horse's head* (W.DAT. *w. water*) X.
2 ‖ PF.PASS. (fig., of a practice) **be washed away** (i.e. discontinued) Aeschin.

κατάπλυσις εως *f.* **washing** (of a horse's legs) X.

καταπλώω *Ion.vb.:* see καταπλέω

κατα-πνέω *contr.vb.* —also **καταπνείω** *ep.vb.* **1** (of a goddess) **breathe down, blow** —*sweet breezes* (W.GEN. *onto a land*) E. —*desire* (w. κατά + GEN. *on women's bodies, to make them attractive to men*) Ar. —W.NEUT.ADV. *sweetly* (*upon a person*) hHom.; (of winds) **blow** —W.NEUT.ADV. *most pleasantly* Plu.
2 (fig., of a person's old age) **breathe, instil** —*the heaven-sent persuasive power of song* (*into a person*) A.
3 inspire by breathing on; (of a warrior) **inspire** —*Troy* E.

καταποθήσομαι (fut.pass.): see καταπίνω

κατα-ποικίλλω *vb.* **1** (of an orator) skilfully decorate, **adorn** —*a speech* (W.DAT. *w. fine arguments*) Isoc. ‖ PASS. (of temples) **be adorned** (w. mythol. scenes) —w. ὑπό + GEN. *by sculptors* Pl.
2 (of a malignant humour) **speckle** —*the body* (*w. white patches*) Pl.

κατα-πολεμέω *contr.vb.* **bring down** or **defeat in war** —*commanders, armies, peoples, regions* Th. Isoc. X. D. Plb. Plu. ‖ MID. **get** (W.ACC. an enemy) **defeated in war** —W.DAT. *by others* Plb. ‖ PASS. **be defeated in war** Th. Isoc. Pl. X. +

κατα-πολῑτεύομαι *mid.vb.* **thwart by political machinations** —*rivals, laws, a people's avarice* D. Plu.

κατα-πονέω *contr.vb.* **1 work hard at** —*a task* Men.
2 prevail by force (over persons) Plu. ‖ PASS. (of persons, a kingdom) **be overcome by force** Plb. Plu.; (of a people) **be exhausted** (by war) Aeschin.
3 ‖ PASS. **be mistreated** or **abused** (by an overlord) NT.; (of Herakles) **be racked with pain** —W.DAT. *fr. a poisoned cloak* Plb.

κατά-πονος ον *adj.* [πόνος] **1** (of an athlete, his strength) **worn out, exhausted** Plu.; (of a commander) **worn down** (by

campaigning) Plu.; (of warring peoples, w. ὑπό + GEN. by each other) Plu.
2 (of bad poetry and paintings) **laboured** Plu.
κατα-ποντίζω vb. **1 send to the bottom of the sea** —*grain (by scuttling a ship)* D.
2 (specif.) **drown in the sea, throw overboard** —*persons* Lys. D. Plb. Plu. ‖ PASS. **be thrown overboard** Plb. NT. Plu.
3 ‖ PASS. (of a person) **sink in the sea, drown** NT.
καταποντισμός οῦ m. **throwing overboard** (of persons, as a method of killing them) Isoc.
καταποντιστής οῦ m. **one who drowns** (others) **in the sea, pirate** Isoc. D.
κατα-ποντόω contr.vb. [πόντος] **1 send to the bottom of the sea, throw overboard** —*iron, a corpse* Hdt. Antipho ‖ PASS. (of a corpse) **be thrown overboard** Antipho
2 kill by throwing overboard, drown —*a person* Hdt.
3 ‖ PASS. (of persons) **be lost at sea, be drowned** Pl. Plu.
κατα-πορεύομαι mid.vb. ‖ aor.pass. (w.mid.sens.) κατεπορεύθην ‖ **come back from exile** (sts. W.PREP.PHR. to or fr. a place) Plb.
καταπόρνευσις εως f. [καταπορνεύω] **act of forcing into prostitution, prostitution** (of captured women) Plu.
κατα-πορνεύω vb. **force into prostitution, make a prostitute of** —*townswomen, one's daughters* Hdt. Plu.
κατάποσις εως f. [καταπίνω] **swallowing** or **absorption** (of liquids, nourishment) Pl.
κατα-πράττω Att.vb. [πρᾱ́σσω] **accomplish, achieve** —*sthg.* Isoc. X. D. Plb.; **gain** —*power* X.; **bring it about** —w. ὥστε and ACC. + INF. *that someone shd. do sthg.* X. ‖ MID. **accomplish for oneself** —*sthg.* D. Plu. ‖ PASS. (of deeds, goals) **be achieved** X.; (of tasks, proposals) **be carried out** X. D.
κατα-πρᾱ́ῡνω, Ion. **καταπρηΰ́νω** vb. **1** (of pleasant odours) **soothe** —*parts of the body* Pl.
2 (of persons) **calm** —*people's anger, distress, or sim.* AR. Plb. Plu.
3 calm down, placate —*angry or distressed persons or crowds, restive cities or peoples* Isoc. Pl. X. Plb. Plu. —*persons* (W.GEN. or ἐκ + GEN. *fr. anger or harshness*) Plu. ‖ PASS. (of persons listening to poetry) **be made calm** —W.ACC. *in their dispositions* Plu.
4 (of orators or sim.) **render amenable** —*a group of people* Isoc. X. Arist. Plu.
κατα-πρεσβεύω vb. **send a delegation against** (a particular group, to a regional power) Plb.
κατα-πρηνής ές Ion.adj. [πρᾱνής] (of hands) **turned downwards** (w. open palms, in ctxts. of using the flat of one's hand) Hom. hHom.
κατα-πρίω vb. **1 saw up** —*logs of wood* Hdt.
2 (provbl., of a miser) **split** —*a cumin seed* Theoc.
κατα-προδίδωμι vb. **1 hand over, betray** —*a city* (W.DAT. *to foreigners*) Hdt.; (of officials) **betray** —*their responsibilities* Lys.; (wkr.sens.) **give up, throw away** —*military advantages* Th.
2 leave in the lurch —*one's allies or sim.* Hdt. Th.; (intr.) **turn traitor** (by abandoning one's allies or troops) Th.; (wkr.sens.) **let down** —*a playwright* (by awarding him last place) Ar. ‖ PASS. **be left in the lurch** Hdt. Th.
κατα-προίεμαι mid.vb. **allow to be lost, give away** —*public money* (W.DAT. *to thieves*) Plu.; **let go, lose** —*an opportunity* Plb.; **ruin** —*one's personal fortune, shared enterprises* Plb.
κατα-προίξομαι, Ion. **καταπροΐξομαι** fut.mid.vb. [reltd. προίξ] (in neg.phr.) **will get away scot-free** —W.GEN. *fr. a person* Archil. Ar. —W.PTCPL. *w. doing or having done sthg.* Hdt. Ar.

κατα-προλείπω vb. **leave behind** —*one's comrades* AR.
κατα-προτερέομαι pass.contr.vb. **be completely inferior** —W.DAT. *in military prowess* Plb.; **be no match** —W.DAT. *for one's attackers* Plb.
κατα-προχέω contr.vb. **pour down** —*tears* (W.GEN. *over one's cheeks*) AR.
καταπτακών (aor.2 ptcpl.): see καταπτήσσω
κατά-πτερος ον adj. [πτερόν] (of Night, the Gorgons) **winged** A. E.
κατα-πτερόω contr.vb. **furnish with plumage**; (fig., of Zeus) **cover** —*a woman* (W.DAT. *w. a horse's coat*) E.fr.
κατα-πτήσσω vb. ‖ aor.2 ptcpl. καταπτακών ‖ ep.athem.aor.3du. καταπτήτην ‖ pf. κατέπτηχα, ep.fem.ptcpl. καταπεπτηυῖα ‖ **1** (of persons, animals) **cower, crouch in terror** Hom. A. S.fr. Lycurg.; (phr.) πόδα καταπτήσσειν *run for cover* S.fr.
2 (of a goddess of death) **be hunched** —W.DAT. *fr. hunger* Hes.
3 (fig., of people's hatred and fear of a tyrant) **lurk in hiding, be repressed** D.; (of a political faction) **be cowed** Plu.; (gener., of persons) **be terrified** Plu.
4 (wkr.sens., of persons) **be apprehensive** —W.PREP.PHR. *about the future* Plu.
καταπτόμενος (aor.2 mid.ptcpl.): see καταπέτομαι
κατάπτυστος ον adj. [καταπτύω] (of persons, monsters, a crime) **despicable** A. E. D. Din.
κατα-πτυχής ές adj. [πτύσσω] (of a dress) **with ample folds, full** Theoc.
κατα-πτύ́ω vb. **spit** (at a person) Ar.; **spit on** —W.GEN. *a person* (to show one's contempt) D.; (fig.) —*a hostile power, bribe-taking* Aeschin.
κατάπτω Ion.vb.: see καθάπτω
κατα-πτώσσω vb. (of warriors) **cower, crouch in terror** Il.
κατα-πτωχεύω vb. **make a beggar of, reduce to penury** —*one's husband* Plu. ‖ PASS. **be reduced to penury** Plu.
καταπῡγοσύνη ης f. [καταπύγων] **habit of taking a passive role in male homosexual intercourse**; (derog.) **pathic debauchery** Ar. Plu.(quot.com.)
κατα-πύ́γων ονος masc.adj. ‖ compar. καταπυγωνίστερος ‖ **1** (of men, boys) **taking a passive role in homosexual intercourse**; (derog.) **faggoty** Ar. ‖ SB. **pathic, faggot** Ar.
2 (gener., of birds) **shameless, degraded** Ar.
κατα-πύ́θω vb. (of the might of Helios) **cause to rot away, rot to nothing** —*a dying monster* hHom. ‖ PASS. (of wood) **rot away** Hes.fr. —W.DAT. *in the rain* Il.
κατά-πυκνος ον adj. [πυκνός] (of a plant) **forming a dense clump, thick, luxuriant** Theoc.epigr.
κατα-πυκνόω contr.vb. **1 densely cover** —*a wall* (W.DAT. *w. holes*) Plu.; **cram, pack** —*a city* (W.DAT. *w. a multitude of model citizens*) Plu.
2 (of the ground) **compress, condense** —*vapour and air* (thus producing water) Plu.
κατα-πυρπολέω contr.vb. **burn down** —*a district* Plb. ‖ PASS. (hyperbol., of a person) **be burned to ashes** Ar.
κατάρᾱ ᾱς, Ion. **κατάρη** ης f. [καταράομαι] **1 curse, imprecation** (uttered by a person) A. Hdt. Pl. Plb. Plu.
2 suffering inflicted as divine punishment, curse (affecting a country) Hdt.
καταραιρημένος (Ion.pf.pass.ptcpl.): see καθαιρέω
κατ-αράομαι, ep. **κατᾱράομαι** mid.contr.vb. **1 utter a curse** Il. Lys. Ar. X. D. Plu. —W.DAT. *on a person, object, country* Hippon. Hdt. Ar. Isoc. Pl. X. + —W.ACC. *on a person, a tree* NT.
2 invoke, call down —*sufferings* (oft. W.DAT. *on a person*) Od. Pl. D. Plu.; **pray** —W.ACC. + INF. *that someone shd. die* Thgn. Plb.

3 ‖ PASS. (of sinners) be accursed (in the eyes of God) NT.; (wkr.sens., of an object) be accursed or wretched Plu.

κατ-αράσσω, Att. **καταράττω** vb. | aor. κατήραξα | fut.mid. (w.pass.sens.) καταρράξομαι (Plu., perh. better καταράξομαι) | **1 smash to pieces** —*a cup* Hippon. ‖ PASS. (of military forces) be smashed to pieces Plu.(dub.)
2 drive in rout —*troops* (sts. w. εἰς + ACC. *to a place*) Hdt. D. Plu. ‖ PASS. (of troops) be driven in rout Th.

κατάρᾱτος ον adj. [καταράομαι] **1** (of a wrongdoer) declared accursed, **cursed** (by someone) E. D.
2 (gener., of persons, their old age) **cursed, blighted** B.*fr.* S. Ar.
3 (of persons, a monster, a disease) **accursed, abominable** E. Ar. D. Din. Call.
4 (wkr.sens., of shoes) **wretched, blasted** Ar.

κατ-αργέω contr.vb. **1 be idle** —W.ACC. *w. one's hand* E.
2 (of a barren fruit tree) **fruitlessly occupy, waste** —*the ground* NT.

κατάργματα των n.pl. [κατάρχω] **1 preliminary rites** (at a sacrifice) E.
2 sacrificial offerings E. Plu.

κατ-αργυρόομαι pass.contr.vb. [ἄργυρος] **1** (of military equipment, battlements) **be coated with silver** Hdt. Plu.
2 (of a person) **be bribed with silver** S.

κατ-άρδω vb. **1** (of a spring) **water, irrigate** —*a place* Plu.
2 (fig., of a playwright) shower with flattery, **soft-soap** (a populace) Ar.

καταρέζω ep.vb.: see καταρρέζω

κατάρη Ion.f.: see κατάρᾱ

κατα-ρῑγηλός όν adj. (of war, weapons, ships) **shudder-inducing, terrifying** Hom.

κατ-αριθμέω contr.vb. **1 count** —*things* (W.PREDIC.NUM. *as being of a certain number*) Pl. —*someone* (W.PREDIC.NUM.ADJ. *as having a certain number*, W.PREP.PHR. *in a group*) Plu.
2 (usu.mid.) **count up, enumerate, list** —*persons, things, actions* Isoc. Pl. Aeschin. Plu.
3 ‖ MID. present as the result of numerical calculation, **reckon up** —W.COMPL.CL. *that sthg. is the case* Pl. Aeschin.
4 (usu.mid.) **count, include** —*someone or sthg.* (W.PREP.PHR. *in a particular group or class*) Pl.(act.) Plb. Plu. ‖ PASS. be counted or included —W.PREP.PHR. *in a particular group or class* E. Hyp. Arist. NT.
5 ‖ MID. **reckon, classify** —*someone* (W.PREDIC.ADJ. *as such and such*) Pl.

κατ-αρκέω contr.vb. **1** (of a single day) **be sufficient** —W.DAT. *for someone* (W.INF. *to do sthg.*) E.
2 (of a region) **be self-sufficient** —W.PTCPL. *in providing all necessities* Hdt.

καταρμόζω Ion.vb.: see καθαρμόζω

κατ-αρνέομαι mid.contr.vb. **strongly deny** —w. μή + INF. *that one has done sthg.* S.

κατ-αρόω contr.vb. **plough up** —*farmland* (W.DAT. *w. oxen*) Ar.

κατα-ρρᾱθῡμέω (or **καταρρᾱθῡμέω**) contr.vb. [ῥᾳθυμέω] (of athletes) be idle from complacency, **slack off** X.; (of a commander, the public) **be remiss, neglect one's responsibilities** X. D. Din. ‖ PASS. (of things) be lost through neglect D.

κατα-ρρᾱκόω contr.vb. [ῥάκος] | pf.pass.ptcpl. κατερρακωμένος | (hyperbol., of a person) **be torn to shreds** S.

καταρράκτης (or **καταρράκτης**) ου masc.adj. [καταρράττω] (of a threshold, ref. to a cleft in the ground) **leading downwards** S.

2 ‖ SB. **portcullis** Plb. Plu.
3 ‖ SB. a kind of diving bird; perh., **tern** Ar.

—**Καταρρήκτης** εω Ion.m. **Plunging Torrent** (as the name of a river) Hdt.

καταρρακτός ή όν adj. (of a door) **opening downwards** (i.e. a trapdoor) Hdt.(cj.) Plu.

καταρράξομαι (fut.mid.): see καταράσσω

κατα-ρράπτω vb. [ῥάπτω] **1 sew up, stitch** —*a severed head* (w. εἰς + ACC. *into an ass's hide*) Plb. —*a gemstone* (*into a belt*) Plu. ‖ PASS. (of a raft's wooden frame) be woven —W.DAT. *w. plaited rushes* Hdt.(dub.)
2 (fig., of a god) **devise** —*a fate* (W.DAT. *for someone*) A.

κατα-ρράττω Att.vb. [ῥάσσω] (of a waterfall) **plunge down** —w. εἰς + ACC. *onto rocks* Plb.

κατα-ρρέζω, ep. **καταρέζω**, **καρρέζω** vb. [ῥέζω] (of persons, esp. women) **stroke, pat** —*a person* (oft. W.DAT. *w. one's hand*) Hom. Call. AR.

καταρρεπής ές adj. [καταρρέπω] (of a wave) app., weighing or pressing down, **overpowering** AR. [also interpr. as *from the opposite direction*]

κατα-ρρέπω vb. [ῥέπω] **1** (of fate) cause to sink (in the scales of fortune), **cast down** —*persons* S.
2 (of one element in a balanced political system) sink down, **decline, go under** Plb.

κατα-ρρέω contr.vb. [ῥέω] | aor.2 pass. (w.act.sens.) κατερρύην | **1** (of rivers, water) **flow downhill** D. Plu. —W.PREP.PHR. *past or into a place, into the sea* X. Plb. Plu.; (fig., of food eaten by an insatiable man) **flow down** (into his stomach) —W.PREP.PHR. *as though into the sea* Call.
2 (of tears) **flow** AR.(tm.); (of blood) —w. ἐκ + GEN. *fr. a wound* Il.; (of phlegm) —*fr. the head* Hdt.
3 (of shrines) **drip, run** —W.DAT. *w. blood* E.; (mid.pass., of a spear) Plu.
4 (of persons) **rush down** Ar. —W.PREP.PHR. *to a place* Plb.
5 (of a wind) **blow down** —W.DAT. *on people* Plb.
6 (of prizes or sim.) **fall** (as one's share) —w. ἐς + ACC. *to a person or god* Theoc. Bion
7 (act. and aor.2 pass., of persons, fruits, shorn hair) **fall down** (sts. W.PREP.PHR. *to the ground*) Anacr. Th. Ar. X. Plu.
8 (fig., of achievements) **fall to pieces** D.

κατα-ρρήγνῡμι, also **καταρρηγνύω** vb. [ῥήγνῡμι] | pf. κατέρρωγα ‖ aor.2 pass. κατερράγην | **1 smash to pieces** or **tear down** —*a bridge, house, or sim.* Hdt. E.; (of anarchy) **cause** (W.ACC. *the rout of troops*) **by breaking** (their ranks) S. Plu. (of structures) come crashing down Hdt. Th. Plu.; (wkr.sens., of soil) crumble Hdt.
2 tear to pieces —*clothes* Aeschin. D. Plu. ‖ MID. **tear** —*one's clothes* (*in mourning or sim.*) X. Plu. ‖ PASS. (of dogs' feet) be torn (by rough ground) X.
3 ‖ PASS. and PF.ACT. (of streams of tears) **burst forth** —W.PREP.PHR. *fr. the eyes* E.; (of thunder, storms, or sim.) **break out** Hdt. Plb. Plu.; (of a war) Ar.; (of applause) Plb.; (of a place) **erupt** —w. ὑπό + GEN. *w. applause and shouting* Plb.

κατα-ρρῑγέω contr.vb. [ῥῑγέω] **shudder** —W.INF. *to contemplate sthg.* AR.

κατα-ρρῑζόω contr.vb. [ῥῑζόω] (of the bonds uniting body and soul) **make rooted, make a foundation for** —*living things* (W.PREP.PHR. *in bone marrow*) Pl. ‖ PASS. (of plants) be rooted (in the ground) Pl.; (of the component elements of hair) become rooted —W.PREP.PHR. *under the skin* Pl.

κατα-ρρικνόομαι pass.contr.vb. [ῥικνός] | only pf.ptcpl. κατερρικνωμένος | (of a tortoise) **be shrivelled** or **stiffened** —W.DAT. *in its carapace* S.Ichn.

κατα-ρρῑνάω contr.vb. [ῥίνη] | pf.pass.ptcpl.

καταρρῑνόω κατερρῑνημένος | (fig., of a poet's phrases) be well filed down, **be well trimmed** Ar.

κατα-ρρῑνόω contr.vb. [reltd. ῥῑνός] | pf.pass.ptcpl. κατερρῑνωμένος | (fig., of troops) be covered with hide, **be toughened** A.(cj.)

κατα-ρρίπτω vb. [ῥίπτω] **1** (of troops) **tear down** —*palaces* Plu.
2 (of a popular uprising) **overturn** —*a government* A.

καταρροϊκός ή όν adj. [κατάρρους] (of sicknesses) **taking the form of catarrh** Pl.

κατάρρους ου Att.m. [καταρρέω] sickness producing a running nose, **catarrh** Pl. Plu.

κατα-ρροφέω contr.vb. [ῥοφέω] **take a gulp** (sts. W.PARTITV.GEN. of wine) X.

καταρρυής ές adj. [καταρρέω] (of sacrificial offerings of meat) **streaming, dripping** (w. fat) S.

κατα-ρρυπαίνω vb. [ῥυπαίνω] (of failure, flaws) **sully, defile** —*noble achievements, blessings* Isoc. Pl.; (of persons) —*oneself, one's home, a country's deeds* (W.DAT. or PREP.PHR. w. base actions, accusations) Isoc. Pl. Arist.

κατάρρυτος (also **κατάρυτος** E.) ον adj. [καταρρέω] **1** (of gardens, groves, a region) **well-watered, irrigated** E. Plu.
2 (of the Nile Delta) **alluvial** Hdt.
3 (of mountainous regions) **melting** (W.DAT. w. snow) E.
4 (of a tiled roof) **sloping** Plb.

καταρρωδέω Ion.contr.vb.: see κατορρωδέω

καταρρώξ ῶγος masc.fem.adj. [καταρρήγνῡμι] (of cliffs) **jagged** S.

κάταρσις εως f. [καταίρω] **landing-place** (for ships) Th. Plu.

κατ-αρτάω contr.vb. **1 hang up** —*armour* (sts. W.PREP.PHR. on a trophy) Plu. || PASS. (of ribbons) be suspended (fr. a wreath) Plu.
2 || PF.PASS.PTCPL.ADJ. (of monarchy, as an institution) **properly regulated** Hdt.

κατ-αρτίζω vb. **1 make ready** —*nets, supplies* Plb. NT.; **equip, fit out** —*ships* Plb. || PASS. (of troops) be put in formation Hdt.; be made ready (for a voyage) Plb.; (of persons, a people) be given training or experience NT. —W.DAT. *in rowing* Plb.
2 || MID. (of God) **procure** —*praise* (W.PREP.PHR. *fr. the mouths of children*) NT.
3 set right —*a restive populace, an intransigent person* Hdt. Plu.

κατάρτισις εως f. **training, education** (of a boy) Plu.

καταρτιστήρ ῆρος m. **settler** (of a dispute), **mediator** Hdt.

κατάρτῡσις εως f. [καταρτύω] **breaking-in** (of horses) Plu.

κατ-αρτύω vb. **1 attach** —*oars* (W.DAT. *to rowlocks*) AR.
2 arrange, effect —*sthg.* S.
3 || PASS. (of good qualities) be integrated or assimilated (by a person) Pl.
4 || PASS. and PF.ACT. (of horses) be tamed or disciplined S.; (fig., of a person, a child's faculties) A. Pl.; (wkr.sens., of persons' minds) be matured Sol. Plu.

κατάρυτος adj.: see κατάρρυτος

κατ-αρχαιρεσιάζω vb. **canvass against** —*a candidate* Plu.

καταρχή ῆς f. [κατάρχω] act of beginning, **beginning** (oft. W.GEN. of a war, attack, speech, or sim.) Plb.

κατ-άρχω vb. **1** (act. and mid.) **begin, start** —W.ACC. or GEN. *a song, discussion, war, journey, action* Alcm. Carm.Pop. Trag. Ar. Pl. + —W.INF. *to do sthg.* Plb.; **take the lead** (in an action) Pi.fr. Pl. X. Plb. —W.GEN. *in a journey, an action* S. X. || MID. (intr., of winter) **begin** E. Plb. || PASS. (of a dance, a lament) be started E.
2 begin with —*a person, a god's title* (*as the subject of a song or lament*) E. Call.

3 || MID. (specif.) begin a sacrifice (by performing preliminary rites); **begin with** —*certain rites* Od.; **begin** —W.GEN. *a sacrifice* E. X. Plu.
4 || MID. consecrate (a victim) by performing preliminary rites; **begin the sacrifice of, consecrate** —W.GEN. *victims* Hdt. E. Ar. D. Plu.; (intr.) **perform a consecration** Hdt. E. And. Plu. || PASS. (of a person's body) be consecrated —W.DAT. *to a goddess* E.
5 || MID. (fig., ref. to committing murder) **perform a sacrifice** E. Plu.

κατα-σβέννῡμι vb. | aor.1 κατέσβεσα | athem.aor. κατέσβην | pf. κατέσβηκα | **1** (of a person, god, water, rain) **put out, extinguish** —*a fire, lamps, a pyre* Il.(sts.tm.) Ar. X. Plu.; (fig., of a laboured rhetorical conceit) —*a fire* Plu. || ATHEM.AOR. (of a fire) die down, go out Hdt. || PASS. (of fires, burning things) be extinguished Plu. Pl. Plu.
2 (specif.) cool with liquid, **quench** —*the temper of hot steel* (W.DAT. w. vinegar, to make it brittle and unworkable) Plu.
3 (of rain) **slake** —*the dryness of desert sands* Plu.
4 (fig., of a person, a legal claim) **dry up** —*a sea, life-source* A. || PF. (intr., of streams of tears) have dried up A.
5 (of persons, a rule; of a storm, fig.ref. to strong action) **quash, stamp out** —*uprisings, conspiracies, insolent behaviour, incest* S. Pl. Plu. || PASS. (of arrogance) be quashed X.
6 (of old age) **extinguish, quench** —*a person's dynamism* Plu. || PASS. (of sensations, a woman's former beauty, a commander's power) fade Pl. Plu.; (of a storm) die down Plu.
7 (of persons, gods) **calm, allay** —*uproar, conflict, fear, or sim.* S. E. X. Plu.; (of oil) —*a sick man's aversion fr. food* Pl. || PASS. (of uproar, commotion, a person's spirit) be calmed Pl. X. Men. Plb.

κατα-σείω vb. **1** (of a siege-engine) **shake to pieces** —*a large part of a building* Th.
2 wave back and forth, dangle —*bait* (*on a fish-hook*) Theoc.; **wave in the air** —*one's hand or cloak* NT. Plu.; **wave, gesture** (oft. W.DAT. w. one's hand) Plb. NT. —W.DAT. *to persons* X. NT. —(W.INF. *to be quiet*) NT.

κατα-σεύομαι mid.vb. | ep.3sg.athem.aor. κατέσσυτο | (of a wave) **sweep down** —*a river channel* Il.

κατα-σημαίνομαι mid.vb. **1 close with a seal** (as protection against tampering) —*letters, legal documents* Pl. X. D. Arist. —*money, treasure* X. Plu.; (fig.) —*promising young men* (*as though treasure*) Pl. || PASS. (of documents, jars) be sealed D. Plu.
2 (of officials) **note down, record** —*persons nominated for office* Pl. || PASS. (of names) be recorded Pl. Arist.

κατα-σήπω vb. **1 allow** (W.ACC. possessions) **to rot away** X.
2 || PASS. and PF.ACT. (of objects, corpses) rot away Pl. X. Plu.; (fig., of an old woman) Ar.
3 || PASS. be wasted away —w. ὑπό + GEN. *by disease* Plu.

κατ-ασθμαίνω vb. (of a horse) pant in impatience, **champ** —W.GEN. *at the bit* A.

κατα-σῑγάω contr.vb. **keep silent** Pl.

κατα-σικελίζω vb. [Σικελοί] (of a dog) **eat in Sicilian style** —*a cheese* (i.e. feast on it like the proverbially sybaritic Sicilians) Ar.

κατα-σῑτέομαι mid.contr.vb. **feed off, eat** —*dead bodies* Hdt.

κατα-σιωπάω contr.vb. **1 keep silent** Isoc. D. Arist. Plb. Plu. —W.ACC. *about sthg.* Plu. || PASS. (of achievements) be passed over in silence Isoc.
2 (act. and mid., of a herald or sim.) **obtain silence** (fr. a crowd) X. —W.ACC. *fr. a crowd* Plb.; (of conspirators) **ensure the silence of** —*a person* (*by threats*) X.

κατα-σκάπτω vb. | pf. κατέσκαφα ‖ aor.pass. κατεσκάφην | **demolish, raze** —*cities, buildings, walls, or sim.* (sts. W.PREP.PHR. *to the ground*) Hdt. Trag. Th. Ar. Att.orats. +; **lay waste to, destroy** —*a region* S. E. Plu. ‖ PASS. (of buildings, cities, or sim.) **be demolished** Hdt. E. Att.orats. +

κατασκαφή ῆς *f.* **1** act of digging; **burial** (of the dead) A.; (concr.) **grave** S.
2 demolition, destruction (of buildings, cities, walls, or sim.) Trag. Th. Lys. Tim. Aeschin.

κατασκαφής ές *adj.* (of a dwelling-place, ref. to an underground chamber) **dug out** S.

κατα-σκεδάννῡμι vb. **1** sprinkle upon or over; **pour** —*chamber-pots* (over people) D. —*a basket of dung* (W.PREP.PHR. *over someone's head*) Plu. —*sauce* (W.PREP.PHR. or perh. GEN. *over food*) Ar.
2 (fig.) **spatter down, pour** —*one's wickedness, vile behaviour* (W.GEN. *on a person, a place*) D. Plu.; (of poets, an improper marriage) —*criticism, a charge of licentiousness, or sim.* (*on a person*) Plu.
3 spread —*a rumour* Pl. ‖ PASS. (of a rumour) **be spread** Lys. Pl.

κατα-σκελετεύομαι pass.vb. [σκελετός] (fig., of young men's dispositions) **become desiccated** —w. ἐπί + DAT. *fr. the study of dry doctrines* Isoc.

κατα-σκέλλω vb. | pf. κατέσκληκα | ‖ PF. (of an animal hide) **be shrivelled up** Plu. ‖ PASS. (of persons) **waste away** (fr. disease) A.

κατ-ασκέομαι pass.contr.vb. (of a person's diet or training regime) **be intensive** Plu.

κατα-σκέπτομαι mid.vb. | For pres. and impf., earlier authors (before Plb. Plu.) use κατασκοπέω. | **1** (of commanders, troops, hunters, ships) **reconnoitre** —*a location or situation* Th. X. Plb. Plu. —W.INDIR.Q. *what an enemy is doing, where or whether sthg. is the case* Th. X. Plb.
2 (intr., of ships) **conduct reconnaissance** Plb.; (of a person) **assess the situation** (in a place) Plu.

κατα-σκευάζω vb. | The sections are grouped as: (1–2) equip or supply (w. sthg.), (3) provide or supply (sthg.), (4–6) prepare or organise, (7–9) create (material things), (10–16) bring about (non-material things), (17–18) effect (sthg.) by underhand means, (19–21) render (sthg., such and such). |
1 (act. and mid.) **equip, furnish** —*soldiers, ships, animals* (*oft.* W.DAT. *w. armour, equipment, or sim.*) Hdt. X. D. Plb.; **supply** —*a region* (w. *crops, livestock, or sim.*) X. ‖ PASS. (of persons, ships) **be equipped, supplied or furnished** (sts. W.DAT. w. *servants, weapons, or sim.*) Att.orats. Pl. X.; (of farms, a region, w. livestock or sim.) Th. Pl. X.; (of buildings, w. furniture, objects) Hdt. X. Plb.; (of cities, regions, w. fortifications, amenities) X. Plb.
2 (of gods) equip with essentials, **provide for** —*mortals* X. ‖ PASS. (of persons) **be provided for** Pl. X.
3 (act. and mid.) **provide, supply** —*rowers, equipment, supplies* (for ships, troops, persons) Pl. D. Plb. —*lands, an empire* (W.DAT. *for someone*) Plb. ‖ PASS. (of equipment, resources) **be provided** (oft. W.DAT. or PREP.PHR. for persons) Pl. X. D.
4 (act. and mid.) **make ready, prepare** —*a region, cities, things* (for war or sim.) Th. X. —*persons* (for responsibilities) X.; (of gods) —*man's body and soul* (W.INF. *to bear physical discomforts*) X.; (intr.) **make preparations** —W.INF. or ὡς + FUT.PTCPL. *to do sthg.* X. ‖ PASS. (of troops, places) **be made ready** (for war or sim.) Th. Plb.; (of a tent, for someone to stay in) X.; (of persons) **be fully prepared** —w. ὥστε + INF. *to do sthg.* X.
5 ‖ MID. **prepare** —*a deed* D. ‖ PASS. (of a siege) **be made ready** Th.
6 (act. and mid., of gods or persons) **organise, manage** —*men's daily lives, a situation* Pl. Arist. ‖ PASS. (of a ship) **be managed or run** —W.ADV. *in a certain way* Pl.
7 (act. and mid.) **construct** —*buildings, ships, furniture, weapons, objects* Th. Att.orats. Pl. X. Plb. ‖ MID. **construct for oneself** —*a tomb* Hdt. ‖ PASS. (of buildings, bridges, or sim.) **be constructed** Hdt. Pl. X. Plb.
8 (act. and mid.) **form, create** —*a cavalry force, a fleet* X. Plb. —*a seating arrangement* Pl.; **establish** —*a state, democracy, institutions* Th. Att.orats. Pl. + ‖ PASS. (of a cavalry force) **be formed** X.; (of empires) **be established** X.; (of soothsayers) **be produced** (fr. a certain type of people) Pl.
9 ‖ MID. (of troops) **set up** —*camp* Th.; (intr.) **unpack** (baggage, i.e. encamp) X.
10 devise —*a treaty, strategy, course of action* Att.orats.
11 (act. and mid.) **secure, obtain** (sts. W.DAT. for oneself) —*a legal ruling* D. —*an income* And. X. D. —*a particular trade* D. —*free time* X.; **win** —*glory* Pl.
12 bring about —*an outcome, a situation, or sim.* Att.orats. Pl. X. Plb.
13 ‖ MID. establish oneself, **set up home** or **shop** (in a place) Th. Lys. ‖ PASS. (of persons) **be established** (in the mining business) X.
14 ‖ PASS. (wkr.sens., of persons or things) **be constituted** —W.ADV. or PREP.PHR. *in a particular way* Pl. X. Plb.
15 (philos.) **create by constructive argument, postulate** —*a theory or sim.* Arist.; (intr.) **construct an argument** Arist.
16 (of poets, theorisers) **postulate, imagine** —*a scene, event, entity* Pl. Arist.
17 concoct, fabricate —*a pretext, false evidence, or sim.* Att.orats. X.; **intimate, make out** —W.COMPL.CL. *that sthg. is the case* D. ‖ PASS. (of evidence or sim.) **be concocted** D.
18 (act. and mid.) **work on, corrupt, suborn** —*persons* D. Arist. Din. Plb.; **subvert, manipulate** —*a political situation* Plb. ‖ PASS. (of persons) **be suborned** D.
19 (act. and mid.) **make, render** —*persons or things* (W.PREDIC.ADJ. or SB. *such and such*) Isoc. X. D. Arist. Plb.
20 dispose —*an audience* (W.ADV. *favourably, towards oneself*) Arist.
21 (of speakers, writers, or sim.) **render by depiction, represent** —*persons or things* (W.PREDIC.ADJ. or SB. *as being such and such*) Pl. D. Arist.

κατασκεύασμα ατος *n.* **1 contrivance, fabrication** (of accusations, a will) D.; **scheme, stratagem** D.
2 political measure or **institution** Arist.
3 design, construction (of a bronze bull) Plb.
4 (concr.) **building** D. Plb. Plu.; **construction, edifice** (ref. to siege-works or sim.) Plb.
5 item of household furniture, **object, piece** (esp. ref. to valuables) Plb.

κατασκευασμός οῦ *m.* **contrivance** or **subterfuge** D.

κατασκευαστέος ᾱ ον vbl.adj. (of a cavalry force) needing to be formed, **necessary** X.

κατασκευαστικός ή όν *adj.* (philos., of arguments) of the constructive kind, **establishing propositions** (opp. refuting them) Arist.

κατασκευή ῆς *f.* | The sections are grouped as: (1–7) act of making ready, equipping or organising, (8–9) act of constructing or creating, (10–13) manner of construction

κατασκηνάω

or organisation, (14–19) result of construction or organisation, (20–24) resources or equipment. |
1 act of making ready, **preparation** (for a war or sim.) Th. Plb. Plu.
2 (specif.) **unpacking** (of baggage, by troops) X.
3 act of fitting out, **equipping** (of farms) Plu.; **decking out, enhancing** (of a city, w. new buildings or sim.) Plu.
4 act of working (on sthg.); **restoration** (of a wall, statue, or sim.) Plb.; **development, refinement** (of a system, a style of government) Plb. Plu.; **tackling** (of a mathematical problem) Plu.
5 act of managing, **management** (of resources, personal or political affairs) Pl. X. D. Plu.; **running** (of a state) Pl.; **implementation** (of laws) Pl.; **political engagement, civic work** Pl.
6 provision (of food, weapons, or sim.) Pl. Plb. Plu.; **deployment** (of siege-engines) Plb.
7 assembling, **collecting** (of books) Plu.; **acquisition, cultivation** (of friends, allies) Plb.
8 act of making, **construction** (of buildings, ships, or sim.) Pl. Lycurg. Arist. Plb. Plu.; **production, manufacturing** (of weapons, ladders, or sim.) Plb. Plu.; **production, writing** (of works of literature) Plb.; **bringing about** (of treachery, benefits) Arist. Plu.
9 act of setting up, **establishment** (of a state, legal system, or sim.) Pl. Plb. Plu.; **formation, shaping** (of the nature of a person's soul) Pl.; **fostering, encouragement** (of commerce) D.
10 manner of construction, **design** (of buildings, objects) Plb. Plu.; **architecture** (of a city) Plb. Plu.; (specif.) **fine style** (of an object's workmanship) Plu.; **fine architecture** (of buildings) Plu.; **clever construction, intricate structure** (of a play's plot, an author's prose) Plb. Plu.
11 layout, **topology** (of a piece of land or geographical feature) Plb. Plu.
12 manner of arrangement, **set-up** (of a state or sim.) Pl.; **type** (of governments, souls) Pl.; **style** (of a person's life) Isoc. Pl. Plu.; (specif.) fine style, **airs and graces** (of a person's conduct) Plu.
13 (gener.) state of affairs, **situation, condition** E. Isoc. Pl. X. Plb.
14 construction work Isoc.; (concr.) **construction** (ref. to buildings, fortifications, or sim.) Plb. Plu.; (collectv.sg.) **buildings** (of a town) Th. Plb. Plu.; (specif.) **building** Th. Isoc. Arist.
15 work, **oeuvre** (ref. to a book) Plb.
16 system of operation, **strategy, policy** X.
17 stratagem, **ruse** Aeschin. Din.
18 preparatory section, **introduction** (of a book) Plb.
19 education, **experience** (of a person) Plb.; **lessons** (of history) Plb.
20 resources (ref. to ships, food, weapons, or sim.) Isoc. Pl. D. Plb.
21 (pl. and collectv.sg.) **equipment** (of soldiers, sailors, doctors, cooks, or sim.) Th. X. Arist. Plb. Plu.
22 (specif.) stock of a farm, **livestock** Plb.
23 (pl. and collectv.sg.) **household objects, furnishings** Th. Pl. X. Is. D. Arist. +; **fittings** (of a roof) Plu.; (specif.) **fine decor** Pl. X. Plu.
24 provision of entertainment, **hospitalities** X. Arist.
κατα-σκηνάω contr.vb. (of troops, commanders) pitch one's tent, **encamp** (usu. W.ADV. or PREP.PHR. in a place) X.; (mid., of the souls of the dead, in the underworld) Pl.
κατα-σκηνόω contr.vb. **1** (of troops, commanders) pitch one's tent, **encamp** (usu. W.ADV. or PREP.PHR. in a place) X. Plb. Plu.
2 (of a person's soul) **dwell** —W.PREP.PHR. in hope (of divine salvation) NT.; (of birds) **lodge, nest** —W.PREP.PHR. in a tree NT.
κατασκήνωμα ατος n. covering, **robe** (used as a bath-robe or shroud) A.
κατασκήνωσις εως f. **1** act of taking up quarters, **lodging** (by persons, in a place) Plb. Plu.
2 dwelling-place, **nest** (for birds) NT.
κατα-σκήπτω vb. **1** (of a thunderbolt, supernatural fires, clouds) **rush** or **shoot down** —W.ADV. or PREP.PHR. on a place Plu.; (of a stroke of fate, a person's or god's anger) A. —W.DAT. or PREP.PHR. on a person or place Hdt. E. Plb.; (of a disease) **descend, seize** —W.PREP.PHR. on a person's extremities Th.
2 (tr., of persons, gods) **bring down** —anger, vengeance (W.DAT. on a person) E. Plu.
3 call down, **importune** —goddesses (W.DAT. w. prayers) S.
κατα-σκιάζω vb. | fut. κατασκιῶ | **1** (of a grove) **cast shade over** —a place Plu.; (of garlands) —people's faces Plu.; (of hair) —a person's shoulders or neck Archil. Anacr.(tm.); (of Giants) —Titans (W.DAT. w. missiles) Hes.(tm.) || PF.PASS. have (W.ACC. one's face) shaded (by a veil) Men.
2 shroud —a dead man (W.DAT. w. earth) S.; (of a god) **cover** —bones (W.DAT. w. flesh) Pl.
3 drape (W.ACC. tapestries) **as a shade** (over a tent-frame) E.
κατα-σκιάω contr.vb. (of a tree's branches) **cast shade over** —a whirlpool Od.
κατα-σκιόεις εσσα εν adj. (of a grove) **shaded** (W.DAT. by laurels) Stesich.(cj.).
κατά-σκιος ον adj. [σκιά] **1** (of places) **shaded** (usu. W.DAT. by trees or sim.) Pi.fr. Hdt. S. Plu.; (of a person, by a wreath worn on his head) A.; (of seated suppliants, by branches held in their hands) A.
2 (wkr.sens., of animal hides) **covered** (W.DAT. w. fur) Hes.
3 (of ivy, helmet-plumes) **casting shade** A. E. Ar.
κατα-σκοπέω contr.vb. | Only pres. and impf. (other tenses are supplied by κατασκέπτομαι). | **1** (of troops) conduct a thorough inspection of, **inspect** —their weapons Plb.; (of a commander) **reconnoitre** —enemy troops, a piece of ground Plu.(also mid.); **observe** —W.INDIR.Q. where one's troops are hard-pressed E.
2 || MID. (of a vain woman, a proud man) **scrutinise** —oneself X. Aeschin.
κατασκοπή ῆς f. **1 reconnaissance** (by scouts or sim.) E. Th. X. Plb. Plu.; (W.GEN. of a situation) Aeschin.; **observation** (by a commander) Plu.
2 inspection (of ships, stores of bullion) Th. X.
3 act of keeping watch, **lookout** S.
κατασκοπικός ή όν adj. [κατάσκοπος] || NEUT.PL.SB. reconnaissance ships Plu.
κατάσκοπος ου m. [κατασκοπέω] **1 spy** Hdt. E. X. Aeschin. D. +; (W.GEN. on persons, their deeds, a place, or sim.) Hdt. E. Th. Ar. +; (W.GEN. sent by a person, an enemy force) E. Plu.
2 scout (in an army) Hdt. Th. X. Plb. Plu.; (appos.w. ναῦς) reconnaissance ship Plu.; (w. ναῦς understd.) Plu.
3 inspector, **investigator** (appointed by a ruler or sim.) Hdt. Th. Plb.
κατα-σκώπτω vb. **mock, jeer at** —persons Hdt. Plu.; (intr.) **jeer** Hdt.
κατα-σμῑκρίζω vb. [σμῑκρός] **belittle, play down the value of** (an object or service rendered) Arist.

κατα-σμύχω vb. **1 burn up** —*enemy ships* (W.DAT. *w. fire*) Il.(tm.)
2 (fig., of Eros) cause to smoulder, **inflame** —*a person* (w. *lovesickness*) Theoc. ‖ PASS. (fig., of the loser of a contest) be seared (w. *chagrin*) Theoc.
κατα-σοφίζομαι mid.vb. (of a king) **behave craftily towards** —*a subject people* NT.
κατ-ασπάζομαι mid.vb. **shower kisses on** —*a person, a burial urn* Plu.
κατα-σπαράττω Att.vb. **tear to pieces** —*a branch, a book* Ar. Plb.
κατα-σπάω contr.vb. **1 pull down** —*statues, grappling-hooks, a wreath* Plb. Plu. —*a robe* (w. ἀπό + GEN. *fr. someone's shoulders*) Plu.; **drag down** —*a person, a corpse* (usu. w. ἀπό + GEN. *fr. a podium, chariot, bier, or sim.*) Plb. Plu. —(W.GEN. *by the hair*) Ar. ‖ PASS. (of signal-flags) be taken down Th.; (of a person) be dragged down —w. ἀπό + GEN. *fr. a horse, a podium* X. Plu.
2 ‖ PASS. (of limbs) be stretched out (in a particular pose) X.
3 (specif.) drag down to the sea, **launch** —*ships* Hdt. Plu.
4 pull down, demolish —*buildings* Plb. ‖ PASS. (of tents) be pulled down Plu.
5 gulp down —*food* Ar.
6 (of rampaging elephants) **break up** —*lines of troops* Plb.
κατα-σπείρω vb. **1 sow** —*gold-dust* (*in a field, as though corn*) Plu.; (fig.) —*troubles* (W.DAT. *for a person*) S. ‖ PASS. (of land) be sown Plu.
2 beget —*a child* E.; (of love and desire) **sow, implant** —*embryos* (W.PREP.PHR. *in the womb, compared to a field*) Pl.
3 scatter —*corpses* (*in a place*) Plu.
4 shower down —*missiles* (W.GEN. *on an enemy fort*) Plu.; (of a breeze) —*flowers* (*on an army*) Plu.; (wkr.sens., of a land) **shed** —*a breeze* (W.DAT. *on sailors*) Plu.
5 spread —*rumours* Plu. ‖ PASS. (of notions) be widely spread —W.PREP.PHR. *among all mankind* Pl.
κατάσπεισις εως f. [κατασπένδω] **pledging** (of soldiers, to die w. their commander) Plu.
κατα-σπένδω vb. **1 pour a libation** Hdt. Plu. —W.DAT. *to a god* Plb.; (tr.) **pour a libation on** —*oneself* (*prior to self-immolation*) Plu.; (fig.) **pour a libation to** —*a dead man* (W.DAT. *w. one's tears*) E. ‖ PASS. (of a victim) have a libation poured over one (prior to sacrifice) Plu.
2 pour —*libations* (W.PREP.PHR. *over a tomb*) E.; (of Athena) —*ambrosia* (*over someone's head*) Ar.
3 pledge —*oneself* (*to die w. one's commander*) Plu.
κατα-σπέρχω vb. **1** (of a warrior) **press, harry** —*bandits* (W.DAT. *w. a spear*) Ar.(quot. E.); (of a favourable wind) **urge on** —*sailors* (*to embark*) AR.
2 (intr., fig., of an enemy's fearsomeness) **be impressive** —W.DAT. *to the eye and ear* Th.
κατα-σπεύδω vb. **hasten along** —*a matter, a war* Aeschin. Plu.; **eagerly press on with** —*the pursuit of fleeing enemies* Plu.
κατα-σποδέω contr.vb. **cast down in the dust** (i.e. kill) —*a man* (W.DAT. *w. an axe*) Ar. ‖ PASS. be struck down (in battle) A.
κατα-σπουδάζομαι pass.vb. **be over-serious** Hdt.
κατα-στάζω vb. **1** (of persons, animals) **drip, shed** —*blood, tears, or sim.* E. AR. —(W.GEN. *down one's cheek*) E.; **ooze** (liquid) —W.ACC. *fr. one's foot* (W.DAT. *due to disease*) S.; (of a horse's headgear) **drip** —W.DAT. *w. foam* E.
2 (of blood, sweat, tears) **drip down** Men. —W.ACC. *a person, a cheek* S. E. —W.GEN. *a tomb, an altar* E.

κατα-στασιάζω vb. **1** (intr., of statesmen) **form factions** Plu.; (tr.) **form a faction against** —*a statesman, a council* Plu.; **form a counter-faction against** —*a plotter* Plu. ‖ PASS. (of persons) be the object of factional rivalry D. Arist. Plu.
2 overthrow by conspiracy —*a statesman, a government* Plu. ‖ PASS. be overthrown by conspiracy Plu.
κατάστασις εως (Ion. ιος) f. [καθίστημι] **1** act of appearing before a court or assembly; **audience** (given to envoys) Hdt.
2 staging, putting on (of choruses) A. Ar.
3 (leg.) **production in court** (W.GEN. of items needing to be seen) Is. D. Arist. | see ἐμφανής 10
4 payment (of bail, security) D.; (concr.) **allowance** (paid to citizens serving in the cavalry) Lys.
5 act of establishing, **establishment** (of laws, a system of government, or sim.) S. Th. Pl. Arist. Plb. +; (of legal guardianship) Arist.; **initiation** (of negotiations) D.
6 appointment (of officials) Pl. Arist. Plb. Plu.; **method of appointment** Isoc. Arist. Plu.
7 restoration (of sthg. to its original condition) Pl. Arist.
8 resolution, settling (of a matter) Plb. Plu.
9 act of quieting, **calming** (of anger, rebellions) Arist. Plb.
10 sustained effort (of wrestlers, a person's oratory) Pl. Plu.
11 situation, state of affairs (faced by a person, nation, army, or sim.) E. Th. Att.orats. Pl. X. +
12 established condition, nature (of mankind, peoples) Hdt. Pl.; **status** (of a state, as a member of a confederacy) Plb.
13 (specif.) **political set-up, system of government** (of a state or sim.) Hdt. Isoc. Pl. X. Arist. Plb. +; **established order** (of a system of government) Isoc. Pl. Plb.
14 normal state, usual appearance (of the features of a person's face) E.; **established routine** (of a person's activities) Hdt.; **established order** (of troops on the battlefield) Plu.; (concr.) **position** (of troops, on a specific occasion) Plb.
15 enduring condition; stillness, depths (of night) E.
16 stability (of a government or sim.) Plb. Plu.
17 enduring calm, tranquillity (in times of peace) Plb. Plu.
καταστάτης ου m. one who sets right; **restorer** (of a royal house) S.
καταστατικός ή όν adj. of the kind which quietens or calms ‖ NEUT.SB. calming power (of a certain type of poetry) Plu.
κατα-στεγάζω vb. cover with a top layer, **roof over, cover** —*a canal, a litter* Pl. Plu.; **form a roof by covering** —*wooden planks* (W.DAT. *w. rushes*) Hdt.
καταστέγασμα ατος n. **covering** (ref. to a giant stone slab serving as the roof of a temple) Hdt.
κατά-στεγος ον adj. [στέγη] (of courtyards, passageways, or sim.) **roofed over** Hdt. Pl. Men. Plb.
κατα-στείβω vb. **tread on** —*a flower, holy ground* Sapph. S.
κατα-στέλλω vb. **1 put in order** —*a person* (ref. to hair or garments) E. Ar.
2 put things right for —*a woman* E.(dub.)
3 ‖ PASS. (of the task of overseeing young women) be organised (by a ruler) Plu.
4 make calm, quieten down —*an angry mob* NT. ‖ PASS. be calmed NT.
κατα-στένω vb. lament E. —W.PREP.PHR. *over sthg.* E. —*persons, circumstances* S. E.(sts.tm.)
κατάστερος ον adj. [ἄστρον] (of the sea) app., **covered with stars, starry** Tim.(dub.)
καταστεφής ές adj. [καταστέφω] **1** (of a suppliant's branch) **wreathed** (w. wool) E.; (of vines) **crowned** (W.DAT. *w. leaves*) AR.
2 (of a person) wearing a garland, **wreathed** S.

κατα-στέφω *vb.* deck with garlands, **wreathe** —*persons, animals, objects* E. Plu.; (fig., of a suppliant) —*a person* (W.DAT. *w. one's hands*) E. ‖ MID. deck oneself with a garland Plu. ‖ PASS. (of persons, objects) be wreathed Aeschin. —W.DAT. *w. wool, myrtle* Plu.

κατάστημα ατος *n.* [καθίστημι] **1 system of government** Plb. **2 restrained demeanour** (of a person) Plu.

καταστηματικός ή όν *adj.* **restrained, decorous** (W.DAT. in one's looks and bearing) Plu.

κατά-στικτος ον *adj.* [στικτός] (of fawnskins) **dappled** E.

καταστολή ῆς *f.* [καταστέλλω] **modesty, restraint** (of a person's style of dress) Plu.

κατα-στόρνῡμι, ep. **καστόρνῡμι** *vb.* | ep.fem.ptcpl. καστορνῦσα | fut. καταστορῶ | aor. κατεστόρεσα, ep.3pl. (tm.) κὰδ ... στόρεσαν | —also **καταστρώννῡμι** *vb.* | aor. κατέστρωσα, also 3pl. κατεστρώννυσαν (X., dub., cj. κατέστρωσαν) | 3pl.plpf.pass. κατέστρωντο |
1 spread out —*blankets, fleeces* (on chairs, a ship's deck) Od.(sts.tm.)
2 cover by spreading, strew —*a grave* (W.DAT. *w. stones*) Il. —*a staircase* (w. wool, to muffle footsteps) Plu.
3 mow down, fell —*an enemy* X. —*persons* (W.DAT. *w. an arrow*) E. ‖ PASS. be mown down —W.DAT. *by troops* Hdt.
4 (gener.) **utterly defeat, vanquish** —*enemies* Hdt.; (fig.) —*an opponent* Ar.(cj.)
5 smooth or **level out** —*inequality* Plu.; **calm** —*a troubled city* Plu.; (of a commander, defeat) **dampen down, quell** —*rebellions, a person's ambition* Plu.

κατα-στοχάζομαι *mid.vb.* **guess at, infer** —*sthg.* Plb.

κατ-αστράπτω *vb.* **1** (of Zeus) **hurl down lightning** —w. κατά + ACC. *on a place* S. ‖ IMPERS. there is lightning Plu.
2 (tr., of a storm) **dazzle with lightning** —*people's eyes* Plu.

κατα-στρατηγέω *contr.vb.* outdo in generalship, **outmanoeuvre** —*an enemy commander* Plu. ‖ PASS. be outmanoeuvred Plu. —w. ὑπό + GEN. *by an enemy commander* Plu.

κατα-στρατοπεδεύω *vb.* (tr., of a commander) **encamp** —*one's forces* (usu. W.PREP.PHR. *in a place*) X. Plb.; (intr.) **encamp, make camp** (sts. W.ADV. or PREP.PHR. in a place) X.(mid.) Plb. Plu.

κατα-στρεβλόω *contr.vb.* **torture** —*a person* Plu.

κατα-στρέφω *vb.* **1 turn upside-down** —*one's hand, clods of earth* Plu.; (specif.) **turn** —*crops* (w. the plough, i.e. plough them into the soil) X. ‖ PASS. (of a wreath) be turned upside-down Plu.
2 fling upside-down, overturn —*tables and benches* NT.; (of a god) —*an island* hHom. ‖ PASS. (of ships) be flung upside-down (by a siege-engine) Plb.
3 (of an orator) **throw into disarray** —*a city* Ar.; (of a person) **bring to ruin** —*a kingdom* Plb.; (of Fortune) —*someone's plans* Din. ‖ PASS. (of a kingdom) be brought to ruin Plb.
4 ‖ MID. (of peoples, commanders, military forces, or sim.) **conquer, subdue** —*peoples, cities, regions, kings* Hdt. Th. Ar. Att.orats. X. +; **force** —*peoples, kings* (w. ἐς + ACC. *into paying tribute*) Hdt. —(W.INF. + PREDIC.ACC. *into being a tribute-paying state*) Hdt.; (fig., of a person) **overcome** —*a sickness* (ref. to a morbid passion) E. ‖ PASS. (of peoples, cities, regions) be conquered or subdued Hdt. Th. Isoc. X.; be forced —w. ἐς + ACC. *into paying tribute* Hdt.; (of a person) —W.INF. *into obeying someone* A.
5 turn (sthg.) **in a certain direction; turn** —*one's words* (W.ADV. or PREP.PHR. *to a certain aim*) A. Aeschin.; **redirect** —*an illustrious career* (W.PREP.PHR. *towards seeking pleasure*) Plu.

6 (intr., of words) **lead on** —w. ἐπί + ACC. *to action* Plu.; (of a day) **incline, draw on** —w. εἰς + ACC. *to a certain hour* Plu.
7 bring to a conclusion —*a speech, discussion, book, or sim.* Plb.; (intr., of a dynasty, year) **come to an end** Plu. ‖ MID. (of a military force) **bring to a successful conclusion** —*a campaign* Plb.
8 ‖ PF.PASS.PTCPL.ADJ. (of λέξις *style of writing*) brought to a conclusion (i.e. periodic, opp. εἰρομένη *paratactic*) Arist. | see εἴρω¹ 2
9 come to the end of —W.ACC. *one's life* (i.e. die) Plb. Plu.; (intr.) **end one's life, die** Plu.

καταστροφή ῆς *f.* [καταστρέφω] **1 overturning** (of established laws) A.
2 subjugation, conquest (of cities, peoples, regions) Hdt. Th.
3 resolution (of a situation) A.; **denouement** (of a play) Plb.
4 outcome, conclusion (of events) Plb.
5 end (of a book, discussion, series of events, an author's lies) Plb.
6 end (of a person's life) S. Men. Plb.; (of a person, ref. to his death) Th. Plb.

κατάστρωμα ατος *n.* [καταστόρνῡμι] **deck** (of a ship) Hdt. Th. Pl. X. D. +

καταστρώννῡμι *vb.*: see καταστόρνῡμι

κατα-στυγέω *contr.vb.* **be aghast** (on hearing bad news) Il. Hes.*fr.*; (tr.) **be horror-struck at** —*a monstrous giant* Od.

κατα-στύφελος ον *adj.* [στυφελός] (of rocks) **craggy, rugged** Hes. hHom.

κατα-στωμύλλομαι *mid.vb.* | pf.pass.ptcpl. κατεστωμυλμένος | **rattle off** —*arguments* Ar.
‖ PF.PASS.PTCPL.ADJ. (of a person) seduced by idle chatter Ar.

κατα-σύρω *vb.* **1** (of troops) **lay waste to** —*land, cities, regions* Hdt. Plb.
2 (of an accuser) **drag off** —*a person* (w. πρός + ACC. *to a judge*) NT.

κατα-σφάζω *vb.* **slaughter by throat-cutting, kill** —*a horse* Plu.; **execute** —*persons* Hdt. Plb.; (gener.) **slay, butcher** —*persons* Plb. NT. ‖ PASS. be slain or butchered Trag. X. Plb. Plu.; (of troops or sim.) be massacred E. Plb. Plu.

κατα-σφρᾱγίζομαι, Ion. **κατασφρηγίζομαι** *pass.vb.* **1** (of statements or objects) **be marked with a seal** (to prove their authenticity) E.*fr.*; (fig., of a divine decree) **be sealed** —W.DAT. *w. oaths* Emp.
2 (of urns) be closed up with a seal, **be sealed shut** —w. ὑπό + GEN. *by officials* Isoc.; (of statements) **be sealed away** —W.PREP.PHR. *in folded pages* A.

κατα-σχεδιάζω *vb.* speak or act in an offhand manner; **make slapdash statements** —W.GEN. *about sthg.* Plb.

κατασχεθεῖν (ep.aor.2 inf.): see κατέχω

κατάσχεσις εως *f.* [κατέχω] **appropriation** (of territory) NT.; **dispossession** (of peoples, i.e. appropriation of their territory) NT.

κατάσχετος ον *adj.* **1** (of intentions) **held back** (i.e. kept secret) S.
2 (of persons) **possessed** (W.DAT. by Bacchic frenzy, a fixation) Plu.

κατα-σχηματίζω *vb.* (of would-be wise men, a king) **deck out** —*oneself* (in a certain way) Isoc. Plu. ‖ PASS. (of citizens) be moulded —W.DAT. *by role-models* Plu.

κατασχήσω (fut.2): see κατέχω

κατα-σχίζω *vb.* **1 tear into pieces** —*robes, sandals, texts* Ar. Plu.; **split into pieces** —*wooden doors, a chest, a trough* Ar. Plu. ‖ PASS. (of a robe) be torn into pieces Anacr.(tm.)
2 break open —*doors, gates* X. D. Plu.

κατα-σχολάζω vb. **1** lag behind —W.GEN. *a due time* S. **2** spend in leisure —*one's time* Plu.
κατα-σωρεύω vb. make into a heap, **pile up** —*a mass of weapons* Plu. ‖ PASS. (of corpses) be piled up Plu.
κατα-σώχω Ion.vb. [ψώχω] **grind up** —W.GEN. *pieces of wood* (W.PREP.PHR. *on a stone*) Hdt. ‖ PASS. (of wood) be ground up Hdt.
κατατάκω dial.vb.: see κατατήκω
κατατάμνω dial.vb.: see κατατέμνω
κατα-τανύω vb. | ep.3pl.aor. καττάνυσαν | (of sailors) **tighten** —*the sheets* hHom.
κατάτασις εως f. [κατατείνω] act of spreading out, **spreading** (of liquid, over a flat surface) Pl.
κατα-τάττω Att.vb. [τάσσω] **1 assign** —*a person* (W.PREP.PHR. *to a particular position or office*) Lys. Pl. X. D. Plu. —*soldiers* (*to a particular place*) Plb. ‖ PASS. be appointed —W.PREP.PHR. *to the Senate* Plu.
2 set down in writing, **draw up** —*a decree, pronouncement* Plu. —(W.PREP.PHR. *in a letter*) Plb.; (wkr.sens.) **include** —sthg. (W.PREP.PHR. *in a book, letter, or sim.*) Plb. Plu. ‖ MID. **draw up, arrange** —*a loan* (W.DAT. *w. someone*) D. ‖ PASS. (of a decree) be drawn up —W.PREP.PHR. *on a tablet* Plb.; (of decrees, matters) be included —W.PREP.PHR. *in a book or sim.* Plb. Plu. ‖ IMPERS.PASS. it is set down (in a treaty) —W.COMPL.CL. *that someone shd. do sthg.* Plb.
κατα-ταχέω contr.vb. [τάχος] **move** or **act quickly** Plb.; **be quick enough, be in time** Plb. —W.PTCPL. *for doing sthg.* Plb.; (tr.) **be quicker than** —*others* Plb.
κατατεθαρρηκότως Att.pf.ptcpl.adv.: see under καταθαρρέω
κατα-τείνω vb. **1 pull tight** —*ropes, a horse's reins* Il.(tm.) Hdt. X. Plu.; (of air, in the body) —*tendons* Pl.; (intr., of a charioteer) **pull on the reins** Plu.; (fig., of a statesman) Plu. **2** pull tight with a rope ‖ PASS. (of a cow) be pulled —W.DAT. *by a rope* Plu.; (of a person) be stretched —W.PREP.PHR. *on a rack* Plu.
3 (fig.) **drive up** —*valuables at auction* (W.PREP.PHR. *to a high price*) Plu.
4 cause to stretch out, **lay out** —*persons* (W.PREP.PHR. *on the ground*) Plu. ‖ PASS. (of creatures, water) lie stretched or spread out —W.PREP.PHR. *on the ground* Pl.
5 lay out in a straight line; **extend** (i.e. dig) —*trenches* Hdt.; (fig., of orators) **draw out** —*a racecourse-length of a speech* Pl.; (intr., of walls, ridges, or sim.) **stretch out, extend** —W.PREP.PHR. *to a place* Hdt. X. Plb. Plu.
6 (intr.) **strain oneself, go all out** (in doing sthg.) Pl.; (of passions) **strain** Pl. ‖ MID.PASS. (of a person or horse) **exert oneself** Plu.; (of a physical mass) **resist, strain** (against an external force) Pl.; (of a penis) **be at high tension** Ar.
7 (intr.) **press one's case** (in speaking) E. X. ‖ PASS. (of arguments) be pressed hard E.
κατα-τέμνω, dial. **κατατάμνω** vb. **1 cut off** —sthg. (w. ἐκ + GEN. *fr. sthg. else*) Pl. ‖ PASS. (of strips of linen) be cut Hdt.
2 ‖ PASS. (of mine-shafts, canals) be cut out (i.e. dug) X.; (of stone quarries) be hewn out —w. ἐς + ACC. *for pyramids* Hdt.
3 cut to pieces, **cut up** (meat) Ar. —*meat, objects* Hdt. X. Men. Plu. —*oneself, one's head* X. Aeschin. —*a body* Pl.; (fig.) **dissect** —*a topic under discussion* Pl. ‖ PASS. (of persons, meat) be cut into pieces Ar.
4 (fig.) **tear a strip off** (i.e. berate) —*a person* Pl. Hyp.
5 divide up —*a location* (w. *canals, streets*) Hdt. Arist. —*a people* (W.COGN.ACC. *into subdivisions*) Plu. ‖ PASS. (of regions) be divided up Hdt. —W.ACC. *w. canals, streets* Hdt.

κατα-τετραίνομαι pass.vb. (of cavities in the lungs) be full of holes, **be porous** Pl.
κατα-τήκω, dial. **κατατάκω** vb. **1** cause to melt away; (of a wind) **melt** —*snow* Od.; (of caustic soda) **dissolve** —*flesh* Hdt.; (of fire) —*particles of air* Pl. ‖ PASS. and PF.ACT. (of snow) melt away Od.; (of flesh, particles) be dissolved Hdt. Pl.
2 (fig., of a person) cause (W.ACC. one's eyes) **to melt** —W.DAT. *in tears* Theoc.epigr.
3 cause to waste away; (of a soul engrossed in some pursuit) **waste away** —*the body* Pl. ‖ PASS. and PF.ACT. (of a person) waste away (fr. longing or despair) Od. S.(tm.) Ar. X. Theoc.
κατα-τίθημι vb. | ep.3pl.athem.aor. κάτθεσαν, ep.1pl.athem.aor.subj. καταθείομεν, ep.athem.aor.inf. κατθέμεν ‖ MID.: ep.athem.aor.imperatv. κάτθεο, ptcpl. κατθέμενος ‖ The sections are grouped as: (1–15) set down, (16–18) set aside, (19–25) set in store, (26–29) hand over. |
1 (act. and mid.) **set down, put down** —*objects, persons* (oft. W.ADV. or PREP.PHR. *on the ground, a chair, or sim.*) Hom. Hes. Hdt. E.*Cyc.* Ar. X. + ‖ PASS. (of objects, a body) be set down (on the ground) X. Plu.
2 (specif.) set down in dedication, **place** —*a wreath, a branch* (W.PREP.PHR. *on an altar or sim.*) And. Call. Theoc.
3 lay out —*a corpse* (*for burial*) Hom. Bion
4 set out, serve —*a meal* Ar. Call.
5 (wkr.sens., of horses) **lower, lean** —*their heads* (W.PREP.PHR. *over someone*) Il.; (of a hare) **rest** —*its head* (W.PREP.PHR. *on its forelegs*) X.
6 (specif.) **set forth as a prize** —*a valuable object* Hom. Theoc.
7 (of sailors) set down on shore, **disembark** —*a person* (*in a place*) Od.; (of gods) **set down** —*a dead man* (W.PREP.PHR. *in a place*) Il.
8 set down (in the ground), **bury** —*a body* (W.PREP.PHR. *in a particular country*) Plu.
9 plant —*trees or sim.* Pl.
10 lay down (i.e. build) —*a road* Pi.
11 plant, erect —*a stele* (W.ADV. *in a place*) Th.; **put up** —*a decree, treaty* (W.PREP.PHR. *in a place*) Isoc. Pl. D.
12 lay down —*laws* (W.DAT. *for a city*) X.; **make available** —*benefits, freedom, or sim.* (W.PREP.PHR. *for everyone, for common enjoyment*) Hdt. Ar. Pl. X. Hyp. D.
13 ‖ MID. **assign, give** —*names* (sts. W.DAT. *to things*) Parm.; (of a boar) **inflict, direct** —*its anger* (W.PREP.PHR. *on someone*) X.; (of persons) **devote** —*one's efforts, attention, free time* (W.PREP.PHR. *to sthg.*) Plu.; **set** —*one's mind* (W.INF. *to do sthg.*) Parm.
14 (of the creator god) **set, place** —*the mouth* (W.ADV. *in a particular position*) X.; (of a person) **put** —*a point of difference* (W.PREP.PHR. *out in the open*) Pl.; **relegate** —*individual interests* (W.PREP.PHR. *to a position of lesser importance*) Pl. ‖ MID. **assign** —*a hill* (W.PREP.PHR. *to a position of honour*) Theoc.; (of a god) **consign** —*people* (w. ἐν + DAT. *to a state of ignorance*) X.
15 ‖ MID. **commit** —*things, facts, opinions* (W.PREP.PHR. *to writing, memory, or sim.*) Pl. Call. Plu.; **set down, record** (a debt) Thphr.
16 (act. and mid.) **set aside** (i.e. take off) —*clothes, a garland* hHom. Pi. Ar. Plu.; **lay down** —*weapons, objects* Hom. hHom. Ar. X. Plu.; (fig.) —*a burden* (ref. *to supreme power*) X.; (of a court official) **put down** (a text, i.e. stop reading it out) D.
17 ‖ MID. (fig.) **set to one side** —*arguments, precedents* Pl.; **put aside** —*one's anger or sim.* Thgn. Ar. Plu.; **give up** —*high office* Plu.; **lay aside** (i.e. stop waging) —*war* Th. Lys. D. Plu.

κατατῑλάω

18 ‖ PASS. (of a situation) be resolved —W.ADV. *in a reasonable manner* Th.
19 (act. and mid.) set in store, **stow away** —*goods, objects* Od. Hes. Hdt. Ar. Pl. X.; (fig.) —*a blessing, good advice* Thgn.; (specif.) **bury** —*treasure* Hdt. Ar.; (wkr.sens.) **put, stow** —*a drug, a valuable object* (W.DAT. *in a box, one's belt*) AR. Plu.; (of a goddess) **shut away** —*an old man* (W.PREP.PHR. *in a room*) hHom.
20 (act. and mid.) **store up** —*goods, money* Hes. Lys. Pl. X.; (of the days of one's life) —*evils* S.
21 ‖ MID. (fig.) store up for oneself, **earn, win** —*gratitude or sim.* (usu. W.DAT. or PREP.PHR. *fr. someone*) Hdt. Th. Att.orats. Pl. X. NT. —*glory, an ally* Hdt. Th. Pl. X.; **incur** —*hatred* Lys.
22 ‖ MID. deposit for safekeeping, **deposit** —*money, documents, valuables* (W.PREP.PHR. *w. someone*) Att.orats. X. Plu.; (fig., of death) **put** —*someone's accomplishments* (W.PREP.PHR. *in a safe place*) Plu. ‖ PASS. (of money) be deposited —w. παρά + DAT. *w. someone* Men.
23 ‖ MID. **commit** —*a friendship* (W.PREP.PHR. *to the gods, i.e. swear to it in sacred oaths*) X.; (of a trait possessed by a person) **leave** —*a record of itself* (w. παρά + DAT. *w. someone, i.e. in his mind*) Pl.
24 ‖ MID. (of persons or gods) **install, lodge** —*hostages, persons, livestock* (usu. W.PREP.PHR. *in a place*) Hdt. Th. Ar. Isoc. Pl. X. +; (also act.) Theoc.; **place** —*a statue* (W.PREP.PHR. *in a temple*) Hdt.
25 ‖ MID. **send** —*persons, troops* (W.ADV. or PREP.PHR. *to prison, distant lands*) D. Plu.
26 (act. and mid.) **hand over, give up** —*possessions* Ar. Plu.
27 hand over, **pay** —*money* (*to a person, city, god*) Hdt. Th. Ar. Att.orats. Pl. X. —*a penalty* (*ref. to a fine or sentence*) D.; **spend** —*money* (w. εἰς + ACC. *on sthg.*) Aeschin.; **invest** —*money* (w. εἰς + ACC. *in sthg.*) Hyp. Plu.; (fig.) **pay up on, make good** —*one's promises* S.
28 **hand back, repay** —*money* D.
29 (act. and mid.) **render** —*praise* (W.DAT. *to a victorious athlete*) Pi.; **do** —*a favour* (W.DAT. *for someone*) D.

κατα-τῑλάω contr.vb. defecate over, **crap on** —W.GEN. *a pillar, shrine, person* Ar. ‖ PASS. be crapped on —W.DAT. *by birds* Ar.

κατατίλλω vb.: see τίλλω 6

κατα-τιτρώσκω vb. severely **wound** —*persons, horses, oneself* X. Plb. Plu. ‖ PASS. be severely wounded Plu. —W.ACC. *on one's body* D. Plu.

κατα-τοκίζομαι pass.vb. **be bankrupted by interest payments** Arist.

κατα-τολμάω contr.vb. 1 **take bold action** —W.GEN. *against an enemy* Plb.; **make an impudent bid** —W.GEN. *for supreme power* Plb.; **treat with impudence** —W.GEN. *a city* Plb. —*(fig.) propriety* Plb.
2 (intr.) **behave audaciously** Plb.; **have the audacity** —W.INF. *to do sthg.* Plb.

κατατομή ἧς f. [κατατέμνω] cut-away area, **recess** (ref. to part of an auditorium) Hyp.

κατα-τοξεύω vb. **shoot down** (w. an arrow) —*a person* Hdt. Th. Plu.; (fig.) —*a personif. argument* (W.DAT. *w. assertions and axioms*) Ar. ‖ PASS. (of men, horses) be shot down X.

κατα-τραυματίζω, Ion. **κατατρωματίζω** vb. 1 inflict a wound on, **wound, disable** —*soldiers* Th. Plb. —*oneself* Arist. ‖ PASS. (of soldiers, elephants) be wounded Hdt. Th. Plb.
2 inflict crippling damage on, **disable, cripple** —*ships* Th.

κατα-τρέχω vb. ǀ Only pres. and impf. (other tenses are supplied by καταδραμεῖν). ǀ 1 **run down** (fr. a high position) Hdt. X.
2 (of sailors) come to shore, **sail in** —W.PREP.PHR. *to a port* Plb.
3 (of troops, commanders) **overrun, invade** —*a region, a city* Plb. Plu.
4 **criticise, denounce** —W.GEN. *one's fellow writers* Plb.

κατα-τριᾱκοντουτίζω vb. [τριᾱκοντούτης, perh. w. play on τρία, κοντός] take up for thirty years; **give a thirty-year poking to** —W.GEN. *thirty-year Truces* (*personif. as desirable women*) Ar.

κατα-τρίβω vb. ǀ pf. κατατέτρῑφα ǀ 1 (of a spinner) **rub, smooth out** —*yarn* (W.PREP.PHR. *on her knee*) Theoc.
2 (of orators) **wear smooth** —*the podium* Isoc.; (of persons) **wear out** —*clothes* Thgn. Pl.; (of a soul) —*a body* (*envisaged as a garment*) Pl. ‖ PASS. (of clothes, straps, tools) be worn out Pl. X.; (fig., of persons, animals, esp. by war) Ar. Isoc. X. Plu.
3 **use up** —*possessions, money* Isoc. X.; **spend, waste** —*time, a day, one's life* (usu. W.PTCPL. *doing sthg.*) Att.orats. Pl. Arist. Men. +; (of studies) **take up** —*someone's time* X.

κατα-τρῡ́ομαι pass.vb. ǀ pf. κατατέτρῡμαι ǀ (of horses) **be worn out** —w. ὑπό + GEN. *by a journey* X.

κατα-τρῡ́χω vb. 1 (of a chieftain, a guest) **use up the resources of** —*people* Hom.
2 (of a beloved) wear out, **make pine away** —*a young man* Theoc. ‖ PASS. (of parents) be worn out —W.DAT. *by care* E.

κατα-τρώγω vb. ǀ aor.2 κατέτραγον ǀ (of persons, animals, insects) **gobble up** —*figs* Ar. Theoc.; **nibble at** —W.GEN. *fruits* Plu.

κατατρωματίζω Ion.vb.: see κατατραυματίζω

κατα-τυγχάνω vb. (of persons, a city, the art of divination) meet with success, **be successful** (sts. W.DAT. or PREP.PHR. in an undertaking) D. Plu.; (of a city's location) **be felicitous** Arist.(dub.)

κατ-αυγασμοί ὦν m.pl. [αὐγάζω] **shinings** (of the moon, ref. to its phases) Plu.

κατ-αυδάω contr.vb. speak out or against, **announce** or **denounce** (sthg.) S.

κατ-αῦθι adv. in that place, **there** AR.

κατ-αυλέω contr.vb. (of persons, the art of music) **charm with aulos-playing** (a person's soul) Pl.; (fig., of mothers) **lull into a trance** —W.GEN. *babies* (*w. lullabies*) Pl.; (fig., of Madness) **mesmerise** —*a person* (W.DAT. *w. fear*) E. ‖ PASS. (of a person) be charmed by aulos-playing Pl. Call.; (fig., of an island) Plu.

κατ-αυλίζομαι mid.pass.vb. be or go indoors, **take up lodging** (in a place) Hippon. S. Plu.; (of soldiers) **go to one's quarters** E.; (of soldiers, commanders) **encamp** (in a place) X. Plb. Plu.

κατ-αυτόθι adv. 1 in that place, **there, on that very spot** AR. Theoc.
2 at that very place and time, **there and then** AR.
3 in this place, **here, on this very spot** AR.

κατ-αυχέω contr.vb. (of a commander) **exult** —W.DAT. *in the number of his ships* A.

κατα-φαγεῖν aor.2 inf. ǀ Other tenses are supplied by κατέδω and κατεσθίω. ǀ 1 (of persons, animals) **eat, devour** —*sthg.* Hdt. Ar. X. D. +
2 (fig., of soldiers) **have for breakfast** —*enemies* (i.e. make short work of them) X.
3 **consume, use up** —*an inheritance or sim.* Hippon. Aeschin. Men. NT.
4 (fig., of religious zeal) **consume** —*a pious man* NT.

κατα-φαίνω vb. 1 reveal the truth of, **prove** —*a saying* Pi.
2 ‖ PASS. (of objects, landmarks) be or become visible (sts. W.DAT. *to someone*) hHom. Th. AR. Theoc. Plu.; (of a

commander) arrive on the scene —W.PREDIC.ADJ. w. one's full forces Plu.

3 ‖ PASS. (of facts, consequences) be or become apparent (sts. W.DAT. to someone) Hdt. Pl. ‖ IMPERS. it seems apparent (W.DAT. to someone) Pl. Men. —W.ACC. + INF. *that sthg. is the case* Hdt. Pl.

4 ‖ PASS. (of persons, their features) appear (sts. W.DAT. to an onlooker) —W.PREDIC.ADJ. *such and such* Pl. X. Theoc. Plu.

5 ‖ PASS. (of persons or things) seem (sts. W.DAT. to one considering them) —W.PREDIC.ADJ. or SB. *such and such* Pl. X. D. Men. —W.PTCPL. or INF. *to be or be doing sthg.* Hdt. Pl.

κατεφάμιξα (dial.aor.): see καταφημίζω

καταφανής ές adj. **1 clearly visible to the eye**; (of persons, things, places) **visible** (sts. W.DAT. to persons) Th. Pl. X. Plu.; (of a monument) **prominent, conspicuous** Plu.; (of places) **exposed, open** X. ‖ NEUT.SB. **open sight, visibility** (of sthg.) X.

2 (of a night) **clear, bright** Plu.

3 (of facts, qualities) **clear, apparent, obvious** Att.orats. Pl. X. +; (of persons or things, W.PTCPL. or COMPL.CL. in doing or being sthg.) Th. Att.orats. Pl. X. Arist. + ‖ NEUT.IMPERS. (w. ἐστί, γίγνεται, or sim.) **it is apparent** —W.COMPL.CL. *that sthg. is the case* Hdt. Att.orats. Pl. X. Plu.

4 (of things) **discernible** Pl.; **straightforward, comprehensible** Pl. D.

5 (of things) **known** (W.DAT. to persons) Pl. Men. Plb. Plu.; **publicly known** Att.orats. Plb.

6 (of persons or things) **revealed, found out** (esp. in wrongdoing) Aeschin. Plb. Plu.

—**καταφανῶς** adv. | compar. καταφανέστερον | **1 clearly** Th. Ar. Isoc. D. Plb.

2 publicly, openly Is.

κατάφαρκτος *Att.adj.*: see κατάφρακτος

κατα-φαρμακεύω vb. **1** ‖ PASS. (of a person's mouth) be bewitched —w. ὑπό + GEN. *by someone* Pl.

2 administer drugs to —*a woman* (*to render her infertile*) Plu.

κατα-φαρμάσσω vb. **bewitch, render spellbound** —*a person* (W.DAT. *w. Platonic philosophy*) Plu.

κατάφασις εως f. [κατάφημι] (philos.) **positive statement, affirmation** Arist.

κατα-φατίζω vb. **pledge** —W.INF. *to do sthg.* Arist. Plu.

κατα-φαυλίζω vb. **regard as paltry** —*a banquet* Plu.

καταφερής ές adj. [καταφέρω] **1** (of land) **sloping, steep** Plb.; (of the sun) **sinking, setting** Hdt.

2 (of a person) **inclined, prone** (w. πρός + ACC. *to drink*) Plu.

κατα-φέρω vb. **1 carry down** (fr. a higher to a lower place); **carry downhill** —*an object* (W.PREP.PHR. *to a place*) Th. Plu.; (of grief) **carry down** —*a person* (W.PREP.PHR. *to Hades*) Il.; (of dew) —*scents* (*into the ground*) X. ‖ PASS. (of furniture) **be brought downstairs** D.

2 ‖ PASS. (of persons) **come downhill** Plb.; (of rivers) **flow downhill** Plb.

3 bring down from above; (of an Erinys) **bring down** —*her foot* (*on wrongdoers*) A.; (of warriors) —*their swords* (*in a slashing movement*) Plu.; **strike a downwards blow** —W.DAT. *w. a battle-axe* Plu.

4 (of a river) **carry downstream** —*a cradle* Plu.; (of Athens, envisaged as a flood) **sweep along** —*persons, things* Isoc. ‖ PASS. (of objects) **be carried downstream** Hdt. Plu.

5 (of storms, wind) **drive ashore** —*ships, sailors* (sts. W.PREP.PHR. *to a place*) Th. Plb. ‖ PASS. (of ships, sailors) **be driven ashore** (sts. W.PREP.PHR. *by a storm or pursuers*) Th. Plb.; **rush ashore** —W.ACC. *to a place* Plu.; (of persecuted men, envisaged as storm-tossed sailors) **rush in** —W.ACC. *to a commander's camp* Plu.

6 (wkr.sens., of a sea-swell) **drive** —*sailors* (W.PREP.PHR. *betw. rocks*) AR. ‖ PASS. (of persons) **travel across the sea** —W.PREP.PHR. *to a place* Plu.

7 carry back, take home —*goods* Ar.; (fig.) **bring in, add** —*extra years* (W.PREP.PHR. *to one's lineage*) Plu.

8 lay down, pay —*money* (sts. W.DAT. *to someone*) Plb. Plu.

9 deliver (charges, a vote) against (someone); **lay** —*charges* NT.; **cast** (W.ACC. *a vote*) **in condemnation** NT.; **indict** —*a city* Plu.

10 (of troops) **bring down, destroy** —*towers* Plb.

11 ‖ PASS. (of persons, objects) **fall down** (sts. W.PREP.PHR. *to the ground, on someone or sthg., fr. the sky*) Plb. Plu.

12 ‖ PASS. (of the sun, moon) **sink, set** Plu.; (of day) **draw to an end** Plu.; (of a lamp) **burn down** Plu.

13 ‖ PASS. (of persons) **sink, fall** —W.PREP.PHR. *into a sickness* Plu. —W.DAT. or PREP.PHR. *into sleep* NT. Plu.

14 ‖ PASS. (of persons) **be brought down or reduced** —W.PREP.PHR. *to a certain fate, condition, course of action* Isoc. Plb.; **be led** —W.PREP.PHR. *to a certain conclusion or decision* Isoc. Thphr. Plb.; (of circumstances) —*to a certain outcome* Plu.

κατα-φεύγω vb. **1 flee for refuge** (fr. danger) E. Plb. Plu. —W.ADV. or PREP.PHR. *to a person or place* Hdt. Th. Att.orats. Pl. X. Arist. +; **seek shelter** (fr. a storm, summer heat) —W.ADV. or PREP.PHR. *in a place* X. Plu.

2 (wkr.sens., of persons or things) **seek refuge** —W.PREP.PHR. *in a particular circumstance* Pl.; **appeal** (for protection) —W.PREP.PHR. *to jurors, the people, their sympathy or goodwill* Att.orats. Plu.

3 fall back, rely —W.PREP.PHR. *on a defence, pretext, hope of salvation, or sim.* Att.orats. Pl. Plb. Plu. —*on persons* (esp. as support for one's version of events) Att.orats. Plu.

4 have recourse, resort —W.PREP.PHR. *to a court, judge, action or strategy, certain pleasures* Att.orats. Pl. Arist. +

κατάφευξις εως f. **flight to safety** (by ships) Th.

κατά-φημι vb. **assert one's agreement, agree** (w. a statement) S. D.; (philos.) **make an assertion** or **affirmation** (opp. a neg. statement) Arist.; **affirm** or **assert** —*sthg.* Arist.

κατα-φημίζω vb. | dial.aor. κατεφάμιξα | **1 declare, assert** Plu. —W.ACC. + INF. *that sthg. is the case* Pi. ‖ IMPERS.PF.PASS. **it is asserted** —W.COMPL.CL. *that sthg. is the case* Plb.

2 ‖ PASS. (of places, things) **be pledged or dedicated** —W.DAT. *to a god, a dead person* Plb. Plu.

κατα-φθατέομαι mid.contr.vb. [φθάνω] (of a goddess) **be first to take possession of, stake a claim on** —*a land* A.

κατα-φθείρω vb. **1** (of a god) **destroy** —*an army* A.; (of troops, commanders) **lay waste to** —*lands, cities, crops, buildings* Pl. Plb. Plu.; (of diseases) **ravage** —*herds* Theoc. ‖ PASS. (of armies) **be destroyed** A. Plb.; (of lands, buildings) **be laid waste** Plb. Plu.

2 (of troops, commanders) **kill** —*persons* Plb. ‖ PASS. (of troops) **be killed** Plb.

3 (of persons, nations) **bring ruin upon, ruin** —*a city, a nation* S. Plb. ‖ PASS. (of a nation's prosperity) **be ruined** A. Plb.; (of persons) **be ruined or doomed** Plb.

4 (of commanders) **suffer the loss of** —*troops, captured livestock* Plb. Plu. ‖ PASS. (of armies) **suffer losses** Plb.

5 ‖ PASS. (of persons, nations) **be corrupted** (by bribery, debauchery, or sim.) Hyp. Men.; (of armies) **be ruined or marred** (by disaffection, disorder, or sim.) Plb.

κατα-φθινύθω vb. (of gales) **destroy** —*fields of crops* Emp.; (of Demeter) —*honours due to the gods* hHom.

κατα-φθίνω vb. | fut. καταφθείσω (Od., v.l. καταφθίσω) | aor. κατέφθισα | pf. καταφθίνηκα (Plu.) ‖ MID.: athem.aor. κατεφθίμην, dial.ptcpl. καπφθίμενος, inf. καταφθίσθαι (καταφθεῖσθαι AR.) |
1 ‖ MID. (of the sun's light) **wane** (at evening) A.
2 ‖ MID. (of supplies, strength) **run out, be used up** Od.
3 (of a person, the body) **waste away** Plu. —W.DAT. *fr. disease, old age* S. E.; (fig., of woes, a land) **dissolve away** S. E.; (of the fruits of someone's words) **come to nothing** Pi.
4 ‖ MID. (of a person, the body) **perish, die** Hom. Hes. Simon. Emp. Trag. AR. —W.DAT. *fr. a thunderbolt, a certain fate* S. E.
5 (tr., of a god) cause to perish, **destroy** —*a person* Od. —*long-standing arrangements* A.

καταφθορά ᾶς *f.* [καταφθείρω] **1 destruction** (of crops, cities, buildings, regions) Plb.; (of people, by persons likened to wild beasts) Plu.; **ruin** (of Greece) Plb.; **breakdown** (of one's mind) A.
2 annihilation, death (of a person) E.; **loss** (of troops, animals) Plb.

κατα-φιλέω contr.vb. **kiss affectionately or repeatedly, shower kisses on** —*a person, head, hands, feet, an object* X. Men. Plb. NT. Plu.; (wkr.sens.) **kiss** —*a person, hand* Plu. ‖ PASS. **be kissed** —w. ὑπό + GEN. *by a person* Thphr. Plu.

κατα-φλέγω vb. **burn to ashes** —*houses, towns, ships, objects* Hes. AR. Plu. ‖ PASS. (of things) **be burned to ashes** Th. Plu.; (of a person) —w. ὑπό + GEN. *by lightning* Plu.

κατα-φοβέω contr.vb. (of a people) **terrify** —*an enemy* Th. ‖ PASS. (of persons) **be terrified** Th.; (wkr.sens.) **be worried** —W.COMPL.CL. *that sthg. is the case* Ar.

κατάφοβος ον *adj.* (of life under a tyranny) **in a state of fear, fearful** Plu.; (of persons) **afraid** Plu.; (w. ὑπέρ + GEN. for sthg.) Plb.; (w.ACC. of someone or sthg.) Plb.; (w. μή + SUBJ. *that sthg. might happen*) Plb.

κατα-φοιτάω contr.vb. (of lions) **regularly venture down** (fr. the hills, to prey on an army) Hdt.

κατα-φονεύω vb. (of persons; fig., of a mountain) **kill, slaughter** —*persons* Hdt. E. Plb. ‖ PASS. **be killed** —w. ὑπό + GEN. *by persons* (W.DAT. *w. stones*) E.

καταφορά ᾶς *f.* [καταφέρω] **1 downward stroke, slash** (of a sword) Plb. Plu.
2 cascade (of water over a precipice) Plb.; **sinking** (of objects thrown into the sea) Plb.; **setting** (of the sun) Plb.
3 way down, descent (fr. a mountain) Plb.
4 act of falling asleep, **dozing off** Plu.
5 passing out (fr. a snakebite) Plu.

κατα-φορέω contr.vb. **1** (of a river) **carry downstream** —*grains of gold* Hdt. ‖ PASS. (of gold) **be carried downstream** —w. ὑπό + GEN. *by a river* Hdt.
2 (fig., of a person) **hurl down** (on one's audience) —*a huge arithmetical calculation* (envisaged as a flood) Pl.

κατα-φράζω vb. **1** ‖ MID. **take heed of** —*sthg.* Hes.
‖ AOR.PASS. (w.mid.sens.) **notice** —W.ACC. + PTCPL. *someone doing sthg.* Hdt.
2 ‖ MID. **think, reckon** —W.COMPL.CL. *that sthg. will be the case* Sol.; **plot, devise** —*destruction* (W.DAT. *for an enemy*) Stesich.
3 (of Time) **declare** —*the truth about sthg.* Pi.

καταφρακτος, Att. **κατάφαρκτος**, ον *adj.* [καταφράσσομαι] **1** (of a person) **enclosed** (W.PREP.PHR. in a prison of rock) S.
2 (of ships) covered over with a deck, **decked** Th. Plb. ‖ FEM.SB. **decked ship** Plb. Plu.

3 (of cavalry) **armoured, mail-clad** Plb. Plu. ‖ FEM.SG. and MASC.PL.SB. **armoured cavalry** Plu.

κατα-φράσσομαι pass.vb. [φράσσω] **1** (of troops, horses) **be armoured** Plu. —W.DAT. *w. bronze, iron plate, or sim.* Plu.
2 (of military positions, a commander) **be defended** or **ringed** —W.DAT. *by troops* Plu.

κατα-φρονέω contr.vb. **1** think badly of, **hold in contempt** —W.GEN. *persons, things, oneself* Att.orats. Pl. X. Arist. Men. + —(w. ὡς + PTCPL. or ADJ. *as being such and such*) Isoc. Pl.; **treat with contempt, show one's disdain for** —W.GEN. *persons* Isoc. Pl. Men. NT. Plu. —W.ACC. E. ‖ PASS. (of persons or things) **be held in contempt** (sts. w. ὑπό + GEN. *by someone*) Att.orats. Pl. X. Arist. +
2 have no regard for —*the gods, laws, commands, or sim.* E. Att.orats. Pl. X.; **be dismissive** (about sthg.) Th. Isoc. Pl. D. —W.GEN. *of enemies, dangers, things* Th. Lys. Isoc. Pl. X. + —W.ACC. Th.
3 (specif.) show nonchalance towards a threat, **be dismissively confident** (about enemies, dangers, or sim.) Th. Isoc. X. —W.DAT. *in one's superiority in numbers, forces, or sim.* X.; **arrogantly presume** —W.INF. *to be such and such* Hdt. Th. X. —W.NEUT.ACC. *certain things* Hdt.
4 ignore —W.GEN. *an unconvincing stratagem* Plb.; (of a horse) —*a smooth bit* X.; **spurn** —W.GEN. *honours, wealth, or sim.* Isoc. Pl. Is.
5 set one's mind on, be bent on acquiring —W.ACC. *tyrannical power* Hdt.

—**καταπεφρονηκότως** pf.ptcpl.adv. **contemptuously** D.

καταφρόνημα ατος *n.* **disdain, contempt** Th.

καταφρόνησις εως *f.* **1 holding in contempt; contempt, disdain** (for persons) Arist.; **arrogant disregard** (for an institution, its commands, sacred laws, or sim.) Pl. Plb.; **nonchalance** (in the face of an enemy, oft. w.connot. of overconfidence) Th. Plb. Plu.
2 condition of being held in low esteem, **scorn, contempt** Plb.

καταφρονητής οῦ *m.* **one who is contemptuous** NT.; (W.GEN. of death, i.e. a brave man) Plu.

καταφρονητικός ή όν *adj.* (of persons, their speech or behaviour) **condescending, contemptuous** (oft. W.GEN. towards someone or sthg.) Arist.

—**καταφρονητικῶς** *adv.* **1 condescendingly, contemptuously** —*ref. to addressing or treating people* Pl. Plu.; **with arrogant disregard** —*ref. to destroying property* D.
2 (specif.) with nonchalant dismissiveness (towards an enemy), **nonchalantly** X. Plu.

κατα-φροντίζω vb. **think away** —*one's cloak* (i.e. *forfeit it to sophists, in return for instruction in thinking*) Ar.

κατα-φρύγω vb. (of lightning) **burn to ashes** —*persons* Ar. ‖ PASS. (fig., of a woman) **burn or be consumed** —W.ACC. *w. love* Theoc.

κατα-φυγγάνω vb. (of troops) **flee** —w. πρός + ACC. *to a place* Hdt.; (fig., of one swearing a false oath) **flee to safety, take refuge** —w. εἰς + ACC. *in people's trust of oaths* Aeschin.

καταφυγή ῆς *f.* [καταφεύγω] **1 seeking of refuge** (W.GEN. by ships, in a place) Th.
2 place of refuge E. Th. Isoc. X. +
3 source of safety, means of escape (oft. W.GEN. fr. danger or sim.) Hdt. E. Th. Tim. Att.orats. +; (ref. to adoption) **escape, way out** (W.GEN. fr. being heirless) Is.
4 shelter W.GEN. fr. the heat of summer, provided by trees or sim.) Plu.; (concr., ref. to a country villa) **retreat** Plu.
5 (ref. to friends, laws, or sim.) **recourse** (for people in need) Att.orats. Arist. Men. Plu.

κατα-φῡλαδόν adv. [φῡλή] **divided according to tribe** Il.
κατα-φυλάσσω vb. **watch closely, monitor** —someone's steps Ar.(dub., see παραφυλάσσω 3)
κατα-φυλλοροέω dial.contr.vb. [φυλλορροέω] (fig., of an athlete's fame, envisaged as a victor's wreath) **shed leaves, lose verdancy** Pi.
κατα-φυτεύω vb. **plant** —a market-place (W.DAT. w. trees) Plu.
κατά-φυτος ον adj. [φύω] (of a piece of land) **planted with crops, cultivated** Plb.; (of paths) **lined with trees** Plu.
κατα-φωράω contr.vb. **1 unmask, expose** —plotters Th.; (of an unconvincing pretext) **give away** (a plotter) Th.
2 discover, catch out —someone (W.PTCPL. double-dealing) Plu.; (wkr.sens.) **detect** —a person's soul (W. ὡς + PTCPL. as existing) X.
κατάφωρος ον adj. (of a person) **unmasked, exposed** (W.GEN. in one's true opinions) Plu.
κατα-χαίρω vb. **rejoice in spiteful triumph** (at a people's plight) Hdt.; **exult over** —W.DAT. a captive enemy Hdt.
κατα-χαλκεύομαι pass.vb. (of iron) **be beaten** or **worked** (by a blacksmith) Plu.
κατα-χαλκόομαι mid.contr.vb. (fig., of a person, envisaged as a ram) **have** (W.ACC. one's horns) **covered with bronze** (to armour them) Hdt.
κατά-χαλκος ον adj. [χαλκός] (of a shield) **covered with bronze** E.; (fig., of a plain, i.e. full of armed warriors) E.
κατα-χαρίζομαι mid.vb. **1 indulge** (the body or soul) Pl.; (of demagogues) —W.DAT. public opinion Isoc.
2 (of jurors, witnesses, or sim.) **do a favour** (sts. W.DAT. to someone) Lys. D.; **give as a favour** (sts. W.DAT. to someone) —money, condemned men Lys. Plu.
3 show favouritism (sts. W.DAT. to someone) —W.ACC. in one's judgements or sim. Pl. Aeschin. Arist. Din.
κατάχαρμα ατος n. [καταχαίρω] (ref. to a person) **source of gloating** (for one's enemies) Thgn.
κατα-χέζω vb. (of a lizard) **crap on** —W.GEN. a person Ar.
κατα-χείριος ον adj. (of an oar) **fitting the hands** AR.
κατα-χειροτονέω contr.vb. (of jurors, the Assembly, or sim.) **vote against by a show of hands, vote to condemn** —W.GEN. a person Att.orats. —(W.COGN.ACC. w. a vote) Aeschin. —(W.ACC. to death) Lys. D. Plu. —(W.INF. as having done sthg.) D. ‖ PASS. (of wrongdoers) be condemned by a general vote Plu. ‖ IMPERS.PASS. a vote of condemnation is passed —W.GEN. against a person D.
καταχειροτονίᾱ ᾱς f. **vote of condemnation** (by the Assembly) Aeschin. D. Arist.
κατα-χέω contr.vb. —also **καταχεύω** ep.vb. | dial.3sg. κακχέει |
1 pour (a liquid) over (usu. W.DAT., GEN. or PREP.PHR. someone or sthg.); **pour** —a liquid (over a person, head, body, animals, objects) Il.(sts.tm.) Alc.(tm.) Hdt. Ar. Pl. +; (fig., of a god) **shower** —wealth, health (on or over someone) Il. Ar. ‖ MID. **pour a shower** (of water or wine) —W.GEN. or κατά + GEN. over oneself, one's clothes Pl. Thphr. ‖ PASS. (of perfume) be poured —W.GEN. over someone's head Plb.; (of blood) pour down —W.DAT. on roofs Hdt.(tm., oracle)
2 (gener.) **pour** —a liquid (W.PREP.PHR. into a container) Hdt. Pl.(mid.); (fig., of music) **flood** —sounds (W.GEN. into a person's soul) Pl. ‖ MID. **pour** or **have poured for oneself** —W.PARTITV.GEN. some soup Plu.
3 ‖ MID. (fig.) **pour out, squander** —gold (W.GEN. on oneself, one's children, one's kingdom) Plu.
4 ‖ MID. (specif.) cause to be melted down, **melt down** —gold Hdt.

5 cast (sthg. non-liquid, usu. W.DAT. or GEN. or κατά + GEN. over someone or sthg.); **shower, scatter** —confetti of nuts and fruit (over a person) Ar. D.; (of gods, other non-personal agents) **cast, shed, spread** —a mist (over a person, an animal, the eyes or head, mountain peaks) Hom.(sts.tm.) Archil.(tm.) Pi. —sleep, beauty, relief fr. pain (over a person, the body) Od.(sts.tm.) Theoc. —an itching disease (over people's heads) Hes.fr.(tm.); (fig.) —a ruinous illness (over someone's finances) Ar. ‖ PASS. (of sleep, dizziness, numbness, grief) be cast, be shed, spread —W.DAT. or GEN. or κατά + GEN. over persons, their eyes or hands Il.(tm.) Ar. Pl.; (of fire) —over a ship Il.(tm.); (of grey hairs) spread down —w. ἐκ + GEN. fr. someone's head hHom.
6 ‖ MID. (fig., of a statesman) **cause** (W.ACC. country dwellers) **to pour** —W.PREP.PHR. inside the city walls (for safety in wartime) Plu.
7 (fig.) **let out a flood of** —blasphemy (W.GEN. over sacred offerings) Pl.; **pour, cast** —reproaches (W.DAT. on someone) Od.(sts.tm.); **bring** —shame, disgrace (W.DAT. or GEN. on someone) Od.(tm.) Pl. AR.(tm.); (of a fast horse, on slower horses) Il.
8 (of a cicada) **pour forth** —its song Hes. Alc.
9 cause (tears) **to pour down; shed** —tears Hom.(tm.) Hes.fr.(tm.) E.(tm.) AR.(tm.) ‖ PASS. (of eyes) be flooded —W.DAT. w. tears E.
10 (of Zeus, a wind) **pour down, shed** (sts. W.ADV. or PREP.PHR. on the ground) —raindrops, snow Hom. —W.COGN.ACC. a fall of leaves Call.(mid.); (of a hawk) —feathers (fr. a seized dove) Od.(tm.) ‖ PASS. (of a ship's rigging) be cast down, tumble —W.PREP.PHR. into the hold Od.
11 let fall —reins, a thyrsos, one's robe (sts. W.ADV. or PREP.PHR. to the ground) Il.(sts.tm.) ‖ MID. (of a woman) **let down, unloose** —her hair Call.
12 (of a god) **sweep down** —a wall (W.PREP.PHR. into the sea) Il.
13 ‖ MID. (of a woman) **pour, scatter** —objects (W.GEN. fr. a chest, W.DAT. into her lap) AR. ‖ PASS. (of objects) be scattered or strewn about Hdt.

κατα-χήνη ης f. [reltd. χάσκω] **act of showing scorn or mockery, snubbing** (of wealth, the haughty) Ar.
κατα-χηρεύω vb. **spend in prolonged widowhood** —one's life D.
κατ-ᾱχής ές dial.adj. [ἠχή] (of running water) **echoing, resounding** Theoc.
κατα-χθόνιος ᾱ (Ion. η) ον adj. (of Zeus, ref. to Hades) **of the underworld** Il.; (of goddesses) AR.
κατα-χορδεύω vb. (fig., of a deranged man) **cut up as if sausages, slice into pieces** —his belly Hdt.
κατα-χορηγέω contr.vb. **1 squander on staging choruses** —a large sum of money Lys.
2 (gener., of rulers, commanders) **spend lavishly, use up** —their fortunes Plu.; **spend vast sums** —w. εἰς + ACC. on banquets, their soldiers, or sim. Plu. —W.PARTITV.GEN. of their own money (W.DAT. on their soldiers) Plu. ‖ PASS. (of armour) be provided at great expense (by a commander, for his soldiers) Plu.
κατα-χόω contr.vb. **1 bury in the ground**; (of troops) **bury** —wagons (W.PREP.PHR. up to the axles) Plu.
2 bury by heaping (sthg.) on top; (of a sand-storm) **bury** —persons Hdt. Plu.; (hyperbol., of assailants) —the enemy (under a hail of missiles) Hdt. —a person (W.DAT. w. stones, i.e. by stoning him) Ar.(tm.); (fig., of a speaker) —his

καταχραίνω

audience (W.DAT. *w. words*) Pl. ‖ PASS. (of a woman) be buried —W.DAT. *by shields* (*thrown upon her*) Plu.
3 (fig., of side-issues) bury so as to conceal, **bury, swamp** —*the original argument* Pl. ‖ PASS. (of early deeds) be buried —W.DAT. *by subsequent achievements* Plu.; (of the original shapes of words) —w. ὑπό + GEN. *by people elaborating them* Pl.

κατα-χραίνω vb. (of dust fr. racing horses) make dirty, befoul —*a horse running behind* B.

κατα-χράομαι mid.contr.vb. **1** make use of —W.DAT. *sthg.* (oft. W.PREP.PHR. *for a particular purpose*) Isoc. Pl. D. Plu. ‖ PASS. (of melodies) be used —w. εἰς + ACC. *for songs* Pl.
2 deploy —W.DAT. *an argument* (*esp. in a lawcourt*) Pl. D. Men.; (intr.) allege, insist —W.COMPL.CL. *that sthg. is the case* D.
3 use up —W.DAT. or ACC. *food, honours* (sts. w. εἰς + ACC. *on sthg.*) Pl. Plu.; (of a writer) exhaust, do to death —W.DAT. *a topic* Isoc.; (specif.) spend —W.DAT. or ACC. *money* (oft. w. εἰς + ACC. *on sthg.*) Att.orats. Plu. ‖ PASS. (of topics) be exhausted Isoc.
4 (euphem.) do away with (i.e. kill) —W.DAT. or ACC. *persons* Hdt. Aeschin. Plb.; (hyperbol.) destroy, ruin —W.DAT. *a person* Men. ‖ PASS. be put to death Hdt.
5 make improper use of, misuse —W.DAT. or ACC. *names, things, reputations* Isoc. Pl. Is. Plb. Plu.

—καταχράω act.contr.vb. (of a horse's mane) be sufficient, serve —w. ἀντί + GEN. *for a helmet-crest* Hdt. ‖ IMPERS. it is sufficient (W.DAT. *for someone*) —W.INF. or COMPL.CL. *to do sthg., if someone shd. do sthg.* Hdt.

κατα-χρέμπτομαι mid.vb. (of a Muse) spit on —W.GEN. *sub-standard chorus directors* Ar.

κατά-χρεος ον adj. [χρέος] in debt, owing money Plb.

κατα-χρῡσόω contr.vb. **1** cover with gold, gild —*objects* Hdt.; (fig.) —*one's city* (w. *fine buildings*) Plu. ‖ PASS. (of battlements, a shrine) be covered with gold Hdt.
2 (fig.) glorify —*a person* Ar.

κατα-χρώζομαι pass.vb. | pf. (tm.) κατά ... κέχρωσμαι | (of a sacked city) be stained —W.ACC. *w. soot-marks* E.(tm.)

καταχύδην adv. [καταχέω] copiously —*ref. to drinking* Anacr.

κατάχυσμα ατος n. **1** sauce poured over a dish of food, gravy, sauce Ar.
2 ‖ PL. confetti of nuts and fruit showered over a bride or new slave Ar. D.

κατα-χωνεύω vb. [χοανεύω] melt down —*jewellery, gold vessels* D. Din.

κατα-χωρίζω vb. (of a commander) draw up in ranks, place in position —*troops* X.; (of a housekeeper) —*items of kitchenware* X.; (intr., of a commander) assign troops to their places X. ‖ PASS. (of troops) take up position X.

κατα-ψακάζω (also **καταψεκάζω** Plu.) vb. (of persons) sprinkle —*a street* (W.DAT. *w. a liquid*) Plu.; (of dew, drizzle) fall in drops (on people) A.

κατα-ψάλλομαι pass.vb. (of an island) be serenaded by stringed instruments Plu.

κατα-ψάω contr.vb. **1** stroke soothingly, stroke, caress —*an animal, person or child, their head* Hdt. Ar. Pl. X. Plb. Plu.
2 (fig.) treat with flattering respect —*envoys, a foreign ruler* Plb.

κατα-ψεύδομαι mid.vb. **1** falsely accuse —W.GEN. *persons, a council* (sts. W.ACC. *of certain things, w. certain accusations*) Att.orats. Pl. Plb. Plu. —(W.COMPL.CL. *of being ungrateful*) D.; make false accusations (sts. W.ACC. *of a certain kind, usu.*

w. κατά + GEN. *against a person*) Att.orats. Arist. Plu. ‖ PASS. (of accusations) be falsely alleged Antipho
2 (of persons, a decree) tell lies about —W.GEN. *persons, gods, things* Ar. Pl. Aeschin. Hyp.; falsely allege —W.ACC. *certain things* Plu. —W.COMPL.CL. *that sthg. is the case* E.
3 (gener.) misrepresent —W.GEN. *persons, gods, places, things* Pl. D. Plb. —*the art of music* (W.COMPL.CL. *as having no criterion of right or wrong judgement*) Pl.

κατα-ψευδομαρτυρέω contr.vb. give false testimony against —W.GEN. *a person* X. ‖ MID. make use of false testimony D. ‖ PASS. be falsely testified against Pl. Is. D.

κατα-ψηφίζομαι mid.vb. **1** (of jurors, assemblies, statesmen) vote against, reject —W.GEN. *laws, proposals* D. Plu.
2 vote against, vote to convict (someone) Att.orats. Pl. Arist. Plu. —W.GEN. *a person* (sts. W.ACC. *for a particular crime*) Att.orats. Pl. X. Arist. Plu. —*a people* Plu.; sentence —W.GEN. *a person* (W.ACC. *to death*) Att.orats. Pl. X. Plu.; (fig.) —*one's country* (*to death and servitude*) Lycurg. ‖ PASS. (of persons) be convicted Pl. X. D. Din.; be sentenced —W.GEN. *to death or exile* Pl. —w. εἰς + ACC. *to a fine* Aeschin.(law); (of crimes) be condemned or given a guilty verdict —w. ὑπό + GEN. *by jurors* Lycurg.; (of a sentence) be passed or pronounced Th. Lys. X. —W.GEN. *on a person* Plu.; (of death) be imposed as a sentence —W.GEN. *on a person* Plu. —(w. ὑπό + GEN. *by Nature, ref. to human mortality*) X.
3 (of jurors) vote in condemnation, vote —W.INF. or ACC. + INF. *to do sthg., that sthg. shd. be done* Att.orats.
4 (of philosophers) condemn —W.GEN. *the Universe* (*as being inconstant*) Arist.
5 (of citizens) vote in favour (of a proposal) Arist.; (wkr.sens., of literary critics) accept, endorse (a statement or proposition) Arist.

καταψήφισις εως f. conviction (of wrongdoers) Antipho

κατα-ψήχω vb. **1** stroke —*one's beard* (W.DAT. *w. one's hand*) Call.
2 rub down, curry-comb, groom —*horses* E.
3 soothe, calm (a person) —W.DAT. *w. tender words* AR.
4 ‖ PASS. (of a clump of wool, tissues in the body) dissolve away, disintegrate S. Pl.

κατάψῡξις εως f. [καταψῡχω¹] condition of being cold, coldness Arist.

κατα-ψῡχω¹ vb. | aor. κατέψῡξα ‖ pf.pass. κατέψυγμαι |
1 make cold, cool —*a person's tongue* (w. *water*) NT.
2 (fig., of a commander) cool the ardour of —*his troops* Plu. ‖ PF.PLPF.PASS. (of old or jaded men) be chilled in spirit Arist. Plu.

κατα-ψῡχω² vb. | pf.pass. κατέψυγμαι | ‖ PF.PASS. (of land) be dry or arid Plu.

κατέᾱγα (pf.), **κατεάγην** (aor.2 pass.), **κατέᾱξα** (aor.), **κατεάξω** (fut.): see καταγνῡμι

κατέαται and **κατέατο** (Ion.3pl.pres. and impf.mid.): see κάθημαι

κατέβην (athem.aor.), **κατεβήσετο** (ep.3sg.aor.mid.): see καταβαίνω

κατεβίων (athem.aor.): see καταβιόω

κατεβλακευμένως pf.pass.ptcpl.adv. [βλακεύω] sluggishly, idly —*ref. to going somewhere* Ar.

κατέβρων (athem.aor.): see καταβιβρώσκω

κατ-εγγυάω contr.vb. **1** pledge, betroth —*one's sister or daughter* (W.DAT. *to someone*) E. ‖ PASS. pledge or commit oneself —W.INF. *to do sthg.* Plb.
2 pledge or give as security (on a loan) —*slaves, a ship* D.

3 demand (a sum of money as) security from, **hold to bail** —*arraigned persons, foreigners* Pl. D. Plb. Plu. ‖ PASS. be held to bail D. —W.COGN.ACC. Pl.

κατεγγύη ης *f.* money given as security, **bail** D.

κατέδαρθον (aor.2): see καταδαρθάνω

κατέδεισα (aor.): see καταδείδω

κατέδεξα (Ion.aor.): see καταδείκνυμι

κατέδραθον (ep.aor.2): see καταδαρθάνω

κατέδρακον (aor.2): see καταδέρκομαι

κατ-έδω *vb.* | pres. only in ep. | fut. κατέδομαι | pf. κατεδήδοκα | The aor. is supplied by καταφαγεῖν. See also κατεσθίω. | **1** (of persons, gods) **devour** —*food, offerings* Ar. —*human flesh* Emp.(tm.) —*dung* Ar.; (of animals, pests) —*slain men, plants, food* Hom. Ar. ‖ PASS. (of a person's flesh) be eaten away (by maggots) Plu.
2 (fig., of an angry man) **eat** —*a person* (sts. W.PTCPL. *alive, i.e. give him a thrashing*) Men.
3 gnaw at, consume —*one's heart* (*in anger or grief*) Il.
4 consume —*someone's resources* Od.; **squander** —*one's inheritance* Aeschin.
5 ‖ PASS. (of precious stones, in neg.phr.) be corroded Pl.

κατεέργνυμι, κατεέργω ep.vbs.: see κατείργω

κατέηγα (Ion.pf.): see κατάγνυμι

κατ-εθίζω *vb.* make customary, **institute as a regular custom** —*festivals and rituals* (W.DAT. *for a population*) Plb.

κατέθορον (aor.2): see καταθρώσκω

κατ-είβω ep.vb. **1** shed —*tears* Od.; (intr., of love) **flow down, flood** (into someone's heart) Alcm. ‖ PASS. (of tears) flow down Ar. —W.GEN. *a person's cheeks* Il.; (of water, streams, rivers) flow downwards Hom. hHom. Theoc.
2 ‖ PASS. (fig., of a person's life) flow away, be wasted Od.
3 ‖ PASS. (of a person) melt —W.ACC. *in one's heart* (*fr. love*) AR.; (of a person's heart) AR.

κατεῖδον (aor.2): see καθοράω

κατ-είδωλος ον *adj.* [εἴδωλον] (of a city) **full of pagan idols** NT.

κατ-εικάζω *vb.* **1** form an impression of, **conjecture, suspect** —*sthg.* Hdt.
2 ‖ PASS. show a resemblance —W.DAT. *to the ways of the Egyptians* (W.ACC. *in one's lifestyle*) S.

κατειλεγμένος (pf.pass.ptcpl.): see καταλέγω

κατ-ειλέω[1] *contr.vb.* ‖ PASS. (of troops) be hemmed in together Hdt. —W.ADV. or PREP.PHR. *in a place* Hdt.; huddle together (on a peak) Plu.

κατ-ειλέω[2] *contr.vb.* (of a horseman) **wrap up** —*a horse's bit* (*in cloth, to make it softer*) X.

κατείληφα (pf.): see καταλαμβάνω

κατειλίσσω Ion.vb.: see καθελίσσω

κατεῖλον (Ion.aor.2): see καθαιρέω

κατ-ειλυσπάομαι mid.contr.vb. [ἰλυσπάομαι] (of a woman) **wriggle** or **crawl down** (a rope) Ar.

κατ-ειλύω *vb.* [εἰλύομαι] **1 wrap** —*dead bodies* (w. ἐν + DAT. *in oxhides*) AR.
2 (of a river god) **cover** —*a dead man* (W.DAT. w. *sand*) Il.(tm.) ‖ PASS. (of mountains) be covered —W.DAT. w. *sand* Hdt.

κάτ-ειμι *vb.* [εἶμι] | Only pres. (oft. w.fut.sens.) and impf. Other tenses are supplied by κατέρχομαι. | **1** (of persons, their souls, animals) **go down** —W.ADV. or PREP.PHR. *to the underworld* (*in death*) Il. Hes. E. —*into the earth* (*in death*) Pl. —*into another phase of life* (*ref. to dying*) E.; (into an underground chamber) S. Plu.
2 (of persons, horses) travel downhill, **come** or **go down** Plu. —W.ADV. or PREP.PHR. *to a place* Hom. Hdt. X. Plu. —*to the sea, a river, a ship* AR. Plu.; (wkr.sens.) —W.ACC. or PREP.PHR. *to a place* Od. Ar. X. Call. Plu.; (specif.) **come down to the forum** (as a candidate for public office) Plu.
3 (of a goddess) travel southwards, **come down** —W.ADV. *fr. Euboea* (*to the Cyclades*) Call.
4 (of a ship) **come to shore** —W.PREP.PHR. *in a place* Od.
5 (of wind and waves) **come in** (to a gulf) —W.PREP.PHR. *fr. the high sea* Plu.
6 (of mist, clouds, heat, darkness) **come down, descend** Ar. —W.PREP.PHR. *on a place, fr. heaven, or sim.* Plu.; (of an anvil) **fall down** —W.PREP.PHR. *fr. heaven, to earth, to hell* Hes.; (of a river) **flow down, descend** —W.PREP.PHR. *fr. a region* Plu.; (of wine) —*into the body* Hdt.
7 (of winds) come down (fr. the heavens), **start to blow** Th. Plu.
8 (of a river) **come down in flood** Il. Plu.
9 (of grey hairs) **come down** (into a man's beard) Ar.; (of reproaches) **fall** —W.DAT. *on a person* Hdt.; (of words, reports) **spread** —W.PREP.PHR. *to the general public* Plu.; (of laughter) —*fr. the audience to the jury* Plu.
10 (of persons) **come back, return** Hdt. Men. Plu. —W.ADV. or PREP.PHR. *to or fr. a place, a military campaign* Od. Hdt. E. Plu.; (of a sacred basket, brought back to a temple after a ritual) Call.; (specif., of persons) **return from exile** (sts. W.ADV. or PREP.PHR. *to a place*) A. Hdt. Th. Att.orats. +; (fig., of poetry, freedom, democracy) Pl. Plu.

κατ-εῖπον aor.2 *vb.* —also **κατεῖπα** aor.1 *vb.* **1 inform against, denounce** (a person) Hdt. E.*fr.* Lys. Isoc. Arist. —W.GEN. *a person* Ar. D. Plu.; **incriminate** —W.GEN. *oneself* Antipho —(W.COMPL.CL. *as having done sthg.*) D.; (gener.) **tell tales on** —W.GEN. *a person* Pl. Plu. —(W.COMPL.CL. *that he is doing sthg.*) X.
2 disclose, expose, reveal (sthg.) Antipho Ar. Plu. —*wrongdoing, plots, or sim.* E. And. Lys. Ar. Plu. —*spies, wrongdoers, supposititious children* And. Ar. Arist.; **reveal, tell** —*the truth* (*esp. in a courtroom*) Att.orats.
3 (gener.) reveal in speech, **reveal, tell** (sthg.) Hdt. E. Lys. Plu. —*sthg.* E. Ar. Isoc. X. Plu. —W.INDIR.Q. or COMPL.CL. *what* (or *that sthg.*) *is the case* E. Ar. Isoc.

κατ-είργω, Att. **καθείργω,** ep. **κατεέργω** *vb.* —also Att. **καθείργνυμι,** Ion. **κατέργνυμι,** ep. **κατεέργνυμι** *vb.* | ep.3sg.impf. (tm.) κατὰ ... ἔεργυ | ep.aor. κατέερξα ‖ MID.: poet.aor.2 imperatv. κατειργαθοῦ (A.) ‖ The basic senses of the vb. are *shut in* and *restrain*. The aspirated forms (καθείργω, καθείργνυμι) are restricted to section 1 and perh. 2. See also εἴργω. |
1 shut in, confine —*persons, animals, things* (*in a building or enclosure*) Od.(tm.) hHom. Anan. Hdt. E. Th. Ar. + —*the moon* (*in a box*) Ar.; (fig.) —*knowledge* (*in the soul*) Pl.; (of human eyelids) —*the force of fire* (envisaged as generated fr. the eyes) Pl. ‖ PASS. (of persons) be confined (in an enclosure, house, prison) X. Men. Plu.; (of bile or heat, in the body) Pl. Plu.
2 press hard —*an enemy* (W.DAT. w. *war by land and sea*) Th. ‖ PASS. (of people) be under pressure (fr. others) Th.; be blockaded —W.DAT. *by ships* Th.; (fig., of political actions) be constrained —W.DAT. *by threatening circumstances* Th.
3 keep in check, restrain —*an Erinys* E. —*a crowd* A.(mid.) —*one's own verbosity* Pl. —*vices, ambitions* Plu.; **hold back, hinder** —*someone* E.; **prevent** —W.ACC. + INF. *corpses fr. receiving burial* E.

κατειρύω Ion.vb.: see κατερύω

κατ-είρω *vb.* [εἴρω[2]] | fut. κατερῶ, Ion. κατερέω | pf. κατείρηκα ‖ PASS.: fut.pf. (w.fut.sens.) κατειρήσομαι ‖ The

aor. is supplied by κατεῖπον, pres. by καταλέγω or καταγορεύω. |
1 inform against, denounce —W.GEN. *persons* Lys.(decree) —W.ACC. *plotters* Hdt.; (gener.) **tell tales on** —W.GEN. *a person* Pl. X.
2 reveal in speech, tell, reveal —W.ACC. or INDIR.Q. *sthg. or what is the case* Pi.*fr.* Hdt. E. Ar. Isoc.; (of birds) **reveal** (through omens) —*profitable enterprises* Ar.; (of persons) **speak, say** —*a certain name* Ar. || PASS. (of the truth) be told Hdt.

κατ-ειρωνεύομαι *mid.vb.* **1** (of a ruler) **be falsely modest about, dissemble** —*one's power* (W.DAT. *w. simplicity of life, dress and behaviour*) Plu.
2 speak dissemblingly to —*a person* Plu.; (intr.) **speak or write dissemblingly** Plu.
3 speak words of mocking irony Plu. —W.ACC. *to a person* Plu.
4 make light of, mock —*persons, an oracle, serious matters* Plu.

κατεῖσα (Ion.aor.): see καθίζω
κατεκάην (aor.2 pass.): see κατακαίω
κατέκανον (aor.2): see κατακαίνω
κατεκαύθην (aor.pass.), **κατέκαυσα** (aor.), **κατέκηα** (ep.aor.): see κατακαίω
κατεκλάξατο (dial.3sg.aor.mid.): see κατακλείω
κατ-εκλύω *vb.* put at ease, lull —*an enemy* (*i.e.* cause him to let his guard down) Plb.
κατέκρυβον (aor.2): see κατακρύπτω
κατέκτα (ep.3sg.athem.aor.), **κατέκταθεν** (ep.3pl.aor.pass.), **κατέκτανον** (aor.2), **κατέκτονα** (pf.): see κατακτείνω

κατ-ελαύνω *vb.* **1 propel downwards; row to shore, bring down** —*ships* (W.ADV. *into a harbour*) Plu.
2 thrust down; (of a man) **have sex with, screw** —W.GEN. *a woman* Ar. —W.ACC. *a man* Theoc.

κατ-ελέγχω *vb.* **1 expose as a sham** —*one's fine appearance* Tyrt.(tm.) —(W.DAT. *by one's deeds*) Pi.(tm.); (of one's mind) —*oneself* (W.ACC. *in one's fine appearance*) Hes.
2 (of athletes) **disgrace** —*illustrious ancestors, their prowess* Pi.

κατ-ελεέω *contr.vb.* **have pity on** —*persons, their sufferings* And. Lys. Pl. Plb.

κατέλεκτο (ep.3sg.athem.aor.mid.), **κατελέξατο** (ep.3sg.aor.mid.): see καταλέχομαι
κατελεύσομαι (fut.mid.), **κατελήλυθα** (pf.): see κατέρχομαι
κατέλιπον (aor.2): see καταλείπω
κατελίσσω *Aeol.vb.*: see καθελίσσω
κατέλκω *Ion.vb.*: see καθέλκω
κατ-ελπίζω *vb.* **have great hopes** —W.FUT.INF. *of doing sthg.* Hdt. Plb.

κατελπισμός οῦ *m.* **great hope** (of profiting fr. sthg.) Plb.

κατ-εναίρω *vb.* | aor.2 κατήναρον | ep.aor.1 mid. κατενηράμην | (act. and mid., of a god, a warrior) **kill, slay** —*a person, a serpent* Od. Call.; (hyperbol.) **take the life from, doom** —*a living person* S.

κατ-έναντα, also **κατέναντι** (NT.) *adv.* in a facing position; (as prep., ref. to a deer coming) **up against, face to face with** —W.GEN. *a lion* Pl.(quot.lyr.); (ref. to sitting) **opposite** —W.GEN. *a place* NT., (quasi-adjl., of a village) **facing, in front** (sts. W.GEN. *of a person*) NT.

κατ-εναντίον *neut.sg.adv.* in a facing position; (as prep., ref. to going) **up against, face to face with** —W.GEN. or DAT. *a warrior, a god* Il. Hes.; (ref. to sitting) **opposite** —W.GEN. *a place* Hdt. Theoc.; (quasi-adjl., of a headland) **facing** —W.GEN. *the Great Bear* (*i.e.* North) AR.

—**κατεναντία** *neut.pl.adv.* (as prep., quasi-adjl., of land) **facing** —W.GEN. *an island* AR.

κατέναξα (aor.): see κατανάσσω

κατ-εναρίζομαι *pass.vb.* (of persons, flocks) **be slain** —W.PREP.PHR. *by a warrior, his hand* A. S.

κατενάσθην (aor.pass.), **κατένασσα** (aor.): see καταναίω

κατ-ενήνοθε *ep.3sg.pf.* | 3pl. κατενήνοθεν | (of hair, tear-stained dust) **be spread down over** —*someone's shoulders* Hes. hHom.

κατένωπα *adv.*: see ἐνῶπα

κατεξάνθην (aor.pass.): see καταξαίνω

κατ-εξανίσταμαι *mid.vb.* | athem.aor.act. κατεξανέστην | (of a horse) **rear up, show fierce resistance** —W.GEN. *against its handlers* Plu.; (of a politician) —*against opponents* Plu.; (of a people) —W.GEN. *in a war* Plu.

κατ-εξουσιάζω *vb.* (of leaders) **exert authority over** —W.GEN. *people* NT.

κατ-επαγγέλλομαι *mid.vb.* **make a promise** —W.DAT. or πρός + ACC. *to someone* Aeschin. D. —W.INF. or COMPL.CL. *to do sthg.* Aeschin. —W.ACC. *about the future* Aeschin.

κατ-επάδω *vb.* **1 render spellbound by means of incantations, charm** —*serpents* Plu.
2 (fig.) **render spellbound, mesmerise** —*young people* (by education and indoctrination) Pl. —*a person* (W.DAT. *w. Platonic philosophy*) Plu.; **befuddle** —*a debating partner* Pl.

κατεπάλμενος (ep.athem.aor.mid.ptcpl.): see κατεφάλλομαι
κατέπαρδον (aor.2): see καταπέρδομαι

κατ-επείγω *vb.* **1** (of old age) **weigh heavily upon, afflict** (a person) Il.(tm.); (of a military campaign) **be a burden** (for a state) Plu. || PASS. (of a people) **be hard pressed** —W.DAT. *by a war* Plb.
2 press on the heels of, pursue —*a fleeing crowd* Plu.; (of creditors) **press, chase up** —*a debtor* D.
3 hasten the occurrence of, precipitate —*a war, an execution* Plu.; (of a clock) **urge on** (a person giving a timed speech in court) Pl.; (intr., of a person) **make haste** Ar. —W.INF. *to do sthg.* Hdt.; (wkr.sens.) **be eager** —W.INF. *to do sthg.* X.
4 urge on —*persons* (sts. W.INF. *to do sthg.*) Th. Plb. Plu.
5 (of matters, circumstances) **press, impel** —*someone* (W.INF. *to do sthg.*) D.; **constitute a pressing reason** —w. τὸ μή + INF. *not to do sthg.* Pl. —w. ἐπί + ACC. *for securing one's own interests* D.; **press, call out** —W.INF. *to be discussed or dealt with* Isoc.
6 (of matters, tasks, commands) **be pressing** or **urgent** Isoc. Pl. X. Plb. Plu.; (of the time of day, the season, an impending festival or harvest, someone's age) **be a pressing consideration** D. Plb. Plu. || IMPERS. there is a pressing need (for someone, to do sthg.) Isoc.
7 (of matters) **be of vital importance** Isoc. || IMPERS. it is of vital importance —W.ACC. + INF. *that a city shd. do sthg.* Isoc.
8 (of supplies, expenditure, or sim.) **be a pressing need** Plb.; (iron., of courtesans) —W.ACC. *for a ruler* Plu. || PASS. (of a people) be in pressing need —W.GEN. *of an alliance* Plb.; (iron., of a ruler) *of courtesans* Plb.

κατέπερθεν *Aeol.adv.*: see καθύπερθε(ν)
κατέπεσον (aor.2): see καταπίπτω
κατ-έπεφνον *ep.redupl.aor.2 vb.* [θείνω] (of persons, gods, wild beasts, an axe) **kill, slay** —*persons, monsters, animals* Hom. Hes.*fr.* hHom. B. S. Hellenist.poet.

κατέπηκτο (3sg.athem.aor.mid.): see καταπήγνῡμι
κατέπιον (aor.2): see καταπίνω
κατ-επιορκέομαι *mid.contr.vb.* **lose** (w.ACC. a lawsuit) through perjury (by an opponent) D.
κατεπλάγην (aor.2 pass.), **κατεπλήγην** (ep.): see καταπλήσσω
κατεπόθην (aor.pass.): see καταπίνω
κατέπρησα (aor.): see καταπίμπρημι
κατεπτάμην (athem.aor.mid.), **κατέπτηκα** (pf.): see καταπέτομαι
κατ-εργάζομαι *mid.vb.* **1** (of crafts, craftsmen) **work with, use** —*ivory, metal, stone, other materials* D. Plu.
2 apply one's efforts to, **work at, devote oneself to** —*a particular discipline* Pl.; **use one's efforts** (to do sthg.) Plu.
3 (specif., of persons, bees) apply one's efforts to create, **make, produce** —*walls, ships, syrups, honey* Hdt. And.; (of a river) **create** —*a channel* Plb.
4 (of educators) **make** —*children* (W.PREDIC.ADJ. *coarse*) Arist.; (of motion) —W.ACC. + INF. *people be rational* Pl.
5 (of persons, gods, Greece) **perform, accomplish** —*a task, goal, great deeds* Hdt. S. E. Th. Ar. Att.orats. + —*good services* (W. 2ND ACC. *for one's city*) And. Aeschin.; **cause** —W.ACC. + INF. *sthg. to be the case* X.; (intr.) **be responsible** (for a victory) Lys. || PASS. (of deeds) **be performed or accomplished** (sts. W.DAT. by someone) Hdt. E. Att.orats. Plb. Plu.
6 secure by one's efforts, **win, achieve** —*power, victory, peace, a benefit, or sim.* Hdt. Th. And. Isoc. Pl. +; **gain, attain** —*one's own doom* S. —*blood fr. a dragon* (i.e. make it bleed) E.; (of persons, trust, a war) **bring about, secure** —*peace, freedom, benefits* (W.DAT. *for peoples, cities, regions*) E. And. Lys. X. Plu.; (intr.) **garner achievements** —W.DAT. *for oneself* Hdt.; **achieve one's aims** Arist.; **prevail, be successful** (in a war, a lawsuit, one's studies) Hdt. And. Ar. X. || PASS. (of benefits) **be won or attained** Hdt. Antipho Isoc.
7 bring to an end —*a war* Plu.
8 win over —*a person* Hdt. X. Plu.; **persuade** —*a person* (W.INF. *to do sthg.*) X. Plu. || PASS. (of a woman) **be won over** —W.DAT. *by a suitor* Hdt.
9 (of persons, peoples, time) **defeat, overpower** —*persons, monsters, powers* Hdt. S. Th. Isoc. Plu.; **conquer** —*a region* Hdt. || PASS. **be conquered** Hdt. Plu.; (of a city) **be destroyed** —W.DAT. *by fire* E.
10 (of a circumstance) **finish off, put paid to** —*a person* Call.*epigr.*; (specif., of persons, a war-horse) **kill** —*persons, animals* Hdt. E. X. Plu. —*oneself* Hdt. || PASS. **be killed** Plu.
11 (of horses) work on, **chew up** —*food* Plu. || PASS. (of land) **be worked over** —W.DAT. *w. a mattock* A.
κατέργνῡμι *Ion.vb.*: see κατείργω
κατ-ερείκω *vb.* | aor. κατήρειξα | **1** || MID. **tear to pieces, tear** —*one's clothes* (in mourning) Sapph. A. Hdt.
2 (fig., of a millstone) **grind to pieces** —*someone's anger* Ar.
κατ-ερείπω *vb.* | aor.2 κατήριπον | pf. κατερήριπα | **1** (of an apparition) **knock down, cast down in ruins** —*a city* Pi.*fr.*; (intr., of an earthquake) **wreak destruction** Plu. || PASS. (of a land) **be ruined or sacked** E.
2 (of circumstances) **reduce to a wreck, overwhelm** —*a person* Plu.
3 (intr., pf. and aor.2, of a wall) **collapse, fall in ruins** Il.; (of the products of agriculture) **be destroyed** (by a flood) Il.; (of a tree) **come crashing down** AR.; (of a person) **fall down** —W.PREP.PHR. *into a pool* Theoc.
κατ-ερεύγομαι *mid.vb.* | aor.2 κατήρυγον | (of a thick woollen cloak) **belch out** (W.NEUT.ACC. a blast of heat) at —W.GEN. *a person* Ar.

κατ-ερέφω *vb.* **cover with a roof; cover** —*tents* (W.DAT. *w. branches*) Plu.; (of troops) —*one another* (w. their shields) Plu. || MID. **make a roof for, roof over** —*one's house* (W.DAT. *w. tiles*) AR.; (intr., of tortoises) **have a roof** (i.e. their shells) Ar.
κατερέω (Ion.fut.): see κατείρω
κατερήριπα (pf.): see κατερείπω
κατ-ερητύω *vb.* **keep or hold back** —*a person* (W.PREP.PHR. *in a place*) Hom. —*someone's journey* S.; **stop** (someone, fr. weeping or arguing) Od. AR.
κατερικτός ή όν *adj.* [κατερείκω] **ground to pieces** || NEUT.PL.SB. **milled pulses** (ref. to peas, lentils, or sim.) Ar.
κατερράγην (aor.2 pass.): see καταρρήγνῡμι
κατερρύην (aor.2 pass.): see καταρρέω
κατέρρωγα (pf.): see καταρρήγνῡμι
κατ-ερῡκάνω *vb.* **hold back** —*a person* (*wishing to depart*) Il.
κατ-ερῡ́κω *vb.* (of persons, shame) **hold back, keep** —*a person* (fr. leaving) Hom. Thgn. —(fr. doing sthg.) Hom. AR. —(W. ἀπό + GEN. fr. good things) Ar. || PASS. **be held back** (oft. W.DAT. or PREP.PHR. in a place) Od.
κατ-ερύω, Ion. **κατειρύω** *vb.* | ep.aor.mid.ptcpl. (tm.) κὰδ ... ἐρυσσάμενος | **1** || MID. **pull down** —*a sail* AR.(tm.)
2 haul down —*a boat* (W.PREP.PHR. *to the sea*, W.DAT. *w. levers*) Od. || PASS. (of a boat) **be launched** Od.
3 tow —*wrecked ships* (W.PREP.PHR. *to a harbour*) Hdt.
κατ-έρχομαι *mid.vb.* | fut. κατελεύσομαι | aor.2 κατῆλθον, ep. κατήλυθον | pf. κατελήλυθα | The impf. and usu. fut. are supplied by κάτειμι. | **1** (of gods, heroes, persons, their souls) **go down** —W.ACC. or PREP.PHR. *to the underworld* (esp. at death) Hom. Hes.*fr.* E. Bion; **go down** (to the underworld) E. Ar. —w. ἐπί + ACC. *in search of a poet* Ar.; (of gods) **come down** —W.PREP.PHR. *fr. Olympos, the heavens* Il. hHom.
2 travel downhill; (of persons) **travel down** —W.GEN. *a river* AR.; **come or go down** (oft. W.GEN. or PREP.PHR. fr. a mountain or sim.) AR. NT. Plu. —w. ἐπί + ACC. *to the sea, a river, a ship* Od. Theoc. Plu.; (wkr.sens.) —W.ADV. or εἰς + ACC. *to a place* Od. Hdt. Lys. Ar. Call. +
3 (specif.) **come to shore** (in a ship) Od. hHom. —W.ACC. *at a place* E. AR. Plu.
4 (of a rock) **sink or fall down** Od.; (specif., winds) **come down** (fr. the heavens), **start to blow** AR.
5 (of a river) **come down in flood** Hdt. Th. Call.
6 (of a person) continue in time, **reach** —w. εἰς + ACC. *the third generation* (i.e. live to see it) Plu.
7 come back, return (oft. W.ADV. or PREP.PHR. to a place) Hdt. Isoc. X. AR. Plu.; (specif.) **return from exile** (oft. W.ADV. or PREP.PHR. to a place) A. Hdt. S. Th. Ar. Att.orats. +; **be brought back from exile** —w. ὑπό or διά + GEN. *by a person or political faction* Th. Aeschin.
κατερῶ (fut.): see κατείρω
κατέσβεσα (aor.), **κατέσβηκα** (pf.), **κατέσβην** (athem.aor.): see κατασβέννῡμι
κατ-εσθίω *vb.* | The fut. and pf. are supplied by κατέδω, the aor. by καταφαγεῖν. | **1** (of animals, monsters) **devour, gobble up** —*animals, plants, food, people* Hom. Scol. Hdt. E.*Cyc.* Ar. Isoc. +; (of fire, envisaged as a living thing) —*fuel* Hdt.; (of persons, gods, esp. w.connot. of greed) —*food, offerings* Semon. Hdt. Ar. D. —*a foe's helmet-crest* (envisaged as a fighting-cock's comb) Ar.; (intr., of a person) **eat ravenously** Hippon. || PASS. (of food, animals) **be eaten up or devoured** Hdt.; (of fuel) **be consumed** (by fire) Hdt.
2 (fig., of corrupt officials, parasites, or sim.) **consume** —*public funds, other people's money* Ar. NT.; **squander on banquets** —*one's inheritance* D.

κατέσκληκα (pf.): see κατασκέλλω
κάτεσσα (Aeol.aor.): see καθίζω
κατέσσυτο (ep.3sg.athem.aor.): see κατασεύομαι
κατεστεώς (Ion.pf.ptcpl.), **κατέστην** (athem.aor.): see καθίσταμαι
κατέστρωσα (aor.): see καταστόρνῡμι
κατ-εστυμμένος η ον *pf.pass.ptcpl.* [στύφω *contract, draw together*] || NEUT.SB. (fig.) **astringency** (of a person) Plu.
κατέσχεθον (ep.aor.2), **κατέσχηκα** (pf.), **κατέσχον** (aor.2): see κατέχω
κατέτραγον (aor.2): see κατατρώγω
κατεύγματα των *n.pl.* [κατεύχομαι] **prayers** (to a god) A. S.; **imprecations** (ref. to curses or prayers that a god shd. inflict punishment) A. E.
κατ-ευδοκέω *contr.vb.* **be thoroughly impressed** —W.DAT. *by someone* Plb.
κατεύδω Ion.vb.: see καθεύδω
κατ-ευημερέω *contr.vb.* (of a politician) **enjoy great success** —w. παρά + DAT. *among his fellow citizens* Aeschin.
κατ-ευθῡ́νω *vb.* **1** (of an eagle) **keep on a straight course** —*its flight* Plu.
2 put on a straight course; (fig., of oligarchs, educators) **straighten out** —*the masses, children's natures* Pl. Plu.; (of officials) **put back on track** —*a person* (w. εἰς + ACC. *to his proper course in life*) Pl.; (of God) **guide** —*people's feet* (W.PREP.PHR. *in the path of peace*) NT.; (of a god) **steer** —*a situation* (W.PREP.PHR. *to a successful conclusion*) Plu.
|| PASS. (of movements, the borders of a plain) **be made straight** Pl.
3 (of an official) **issue corrective punishment against, sentence** —W.GEN. *a person* (W.ACC. *to a fine*) Pl.
κατ-ευκαιρέω *contr.vb.* **have a good opportunity** (to do sthg.) Plb.
κατ-ευκηλέω *contr.vb.* [εὔκηλος] (of night) **bring peaceful calm to** —*the world* AR.
κατ-ευνάζω *vb.* **1** (of a commander) **put to bed** (i.e. assign sleeping-quarters to) —*an allied commander* E.; (fig., of Night) —*the Sun* S. || PASS. (of persons) **lie down to sleep** Il. Plu.; (specif.) **be assigned sleeping-quarters** E.
2 (fig., of a deity) **put to rest** (i.e. bring about the death of) —*a person* S. E.
3 (of windless air) **calm** —*the sea* AR.(tm.)
κατευναστής οῦ *m.* **attendant of the bedchamber, valet** Plu.
κατ-ευνάω *contr.vb.* | dial.aor. κατηύνᾱσα | **1** (of Sleep) **put to bed, lull to sleep** —*gods* Il.; (fig.) **calm** —*the waters of Okeanos* Il. || PASS. (of persons) **lie down to sleep** Od.
2 (fig.) **lay to rest** (i.e. end) —*one's life* E.(tm., cj.)
3 (fig.) **soothe** or **staunch** —*ulcerous bleeding* (W.DAT. *w. herbs*) S.
κατ-ευστοχέω *contr.vb.* **1** (of an archer) **hit the target** Plu.
2 (fig., of persons) **be successful** (in an enterprise) Plb.
κατ-ευτρεπίζω *vb.* **set in order, arrange** —*persons, things* Ar. X.
κατ-ευτυχέω *contr.vb.* (of persons) **enjoy good fortune, be successful** Arist. Plu.; (of commanders, forces, a litigant) **be victorious** Plu.; (of an orator) **win the day** —W.DAT. *w. a proposal* Plu.
κατ-ευφημέω *contr.vb.* (of a crowd) **voice one's support for, cheer** —*a person* Plu.
κατευχή ῆς *f.* [κατεύχομαι] **prayer, supplication** (to a god) A. Plu.; (to a person, as though a god) Plu.
κατ-εύχομαι *mid.vb.* **1** utter a prayer, **pray** (sts. W.DAT. *to a god* or *gods, one's dead father*) A. Hdt. S. Plb. Plu. —W.DIR.SP. *sthg.* E. —W.INTERN.ACC. *a certain prayer* Hdt. S. —W.ACC. + INF. *that someone may do sthg., that sthg. might happen* A. Hdt. S. Pl. Plu.
2 (tr.) **pray for** —*a particular outcome* (W.DAT. *for someone, a city*) A. E.
3 (wkr.sens.) **beg, implore** —*someone* (W.INF. *to do sthg.*) Theoc.
4 **utter a curse** (sts. W.ACC. *of a certain nature*) E. —W.GEN. or DAT. or κατά + GEN. *against someone* Pl. Plu.
5 **vow** —W.INF. *to do sthg.* E.*fr.*
6 **boast** —W.FUT.INF. *that one will do sthg.* Theoc.
κατ-ευωχέομαι *mid.contr.vb.* **dine well on, feast on** —*sthg.* Hdt.
κατ-εφάλλομαι *mid.vb.* | ep.athem.aor.ptcpl. κατεπάλμενος | **leap down** —W.PREP.PHR. *fr. a chariot* Il.; (of a towering wave) **plunge down** —W.PREP.PHR. *on a ship* AR.
κατεφθίμην (athem.aor.mid.), **κατέφθισα** (aor.): see καταφθίνω
κατ-εφίσταμαι *mid.vb.* | athem.aor.act. κατεπέστην | (of the Jews) **rise up against** —W.DAT. *a Christian preacher* NT.
κατ-έχω *vb.* | Aeol.3sg.impf. κατῆχε | fut. καθέξω, also fut.2 κατασχήσω | aor.2 κατέσχον, also ep.aor.2 κατέσχεθον, inf. κατασχεθεῖν, 3sg. κάσχεθε | pf. κατέσχηκα
|| neut.impers.vbl.adj. καθεκτέον || The sections are grouped as: (1) hold down, (2-5) hold back, (6) hold steadily, (7-12) hold in one's hands, possession or mind, (13-15) have an abode or location, (16-22) have under control or in subjection, (23) bring to shore, (24) achieve an aim, (25) prevail, (26) be current. |
1 hold down, hold low —*one's head* Od.; **pull down** —*a veil* (W. κατά + GEN. *over someone's head*) Hes.
2 hold (someone or sthg.) **back; hold back, restrain** —*persons, their hands, horses' galloping, the winds* (sts. W. ὥστε μή + INF. *fr. doing sthg.*) Sol. Lyr. Hdt. Trag. +; **curb** or **hold in check** —*excess, evil plans, or sim.* Sol. A. B. E. Arist.
|| PASS. (of persons, peoples, desires) **be held in check** Th. Pl.; **be prevented** —w. μή + INF. *fr. doing sthg.* Th.
3 hold back (oneself or things of one's own); **hold back** —*tears, laughter, anger, or sim.* Thgn. Pi. Trag. Pl. +; **hide** —*one's intentions* Th.; **restrain** —*oneself, one's hands* (sts. W. μή + INF. *fr. doing sthg.*) Hdt. Ar. Pl. Men.; (intr.) **restrain oneself** Hdt. S. Men. Plu. —w. τὸ μή + INF. *fr. doing sthg.* Pl.; (specif.) **hold one's peace, keep silent** Hdt.; (of a wind) **abate** Ar.
4 hold back (in a place); **hold** or **keep back, detain** —*persons, a god, ships, an army* (sts. W.PREP.PHR. *in a place*) Hom. Hdt. S. E. Th. X. —*a sword* (*in its scabbard*) Pi.; (intr.) **linger, stay** —W.ADV. *in a place* Th. || MID. **delay, tarry** —W.ADV. *in a place* Od. Hdt. || PASS. **be detained** —W.PREP.PHR. *in a place* S.; (of troops) **be held back** (by enemies) Th.
5 hold back (by delay); **put off, delay** —*an action* Th.; (of an actor) **keep waiting** —*an audience* Plu.
6 hold steadily or **continuously; hold, keep** —*one's hand* (W.PREP.PHR. *over an enemy's head, i.e. in domination*) E.
7 hold in one's hands or **possession; keep hold of** —*a branch, sword, person* Hippon. Trag. Ar.; **possess** —*riches, land, power* Hdt. Th. Isoc. Is. || MID. **keep for oneself** —*money* Hdt.
8 (of Herakles) **hold, support** —*the heavens* (*on his shoulders*) E.; (of a person) **carry** —*luggage* Ar.
9 (of the earth) **hold, contain** —*a person* (*in death*) Hom. Archil.(tm.) Hdt.(oracle); (of a piece of land) —*houses* Plb.; (of a temple) —*the navel-stone of the earth* E.

10 keep hold of (opp. give up or lose) —*a lamentable life* S. —*one's good fortune* Isoc.; (wkr.sens.) **nurture** —*a hope* E.; **keep** —*watch* E.; app. **engage in** —*transgressions and perjury* Thgn.
11 keep in one's mind; hold —*a person* (W.DAT. *in one's thoughts*) S.; **know by heart, remember** —*lessons, a verse of Homer* Isoc. Thphr.
12 have a firm hold of (w. the mind); **grasp, understand** —*a particular point or issue* Pl. Men.
13 have an abode or location; (of persons, gods, animals) **occupy, inhabit** —*a region, sacred grove, tomb* Pi.*fr.* Hdt. Trag. Ar. Isoc. X.; (of a military force) **occupy, fill** —*a strait* (W.DAT. *w. ships*) Hdt.; (intr., of a person) **lodge** —W.PREP.PHR. *in someone's house* E.; (of troops) **be present** (as an occupying force) Th.
14 (of leprous patches) **extend all over, cover** —*people's skin* Hes.; (of night, day, clouds, the sun, or sim.) **fill** —*the sky, the land, a place* Od. A. Ar.; (of sounds, heat, light, processions) —*a place* Hes. hHom. Alc. A. B. Hdt. +; (of a person) —*a place* (W.DAT. *w. cries, sounds*) S. E. ‖ PASS. (of a house) be filled —W.DAT. *w. weeping* Hdt.
15 (of locks of hair) **surround** —*a god's face* hHom.; (of dust) **cover** —*a corpse* S. ‖ MID. **cover** —*one's face* (W.DAT. *w. one's hands*) Od.; **wrap oneself** —W.DAT. *in a cloak* Il. ‖ PASS. (of persons, the moon) be shrouded —W.DAT. *by clouds, mist* Hom.
16 (of rulers, commanders, troops, peoples) **have control over** —*territory, peoples, situations* Il. Hdt. Th. Ar. Isoc. +; (intr., of a person) **be in control** —W.PREP.PHR. *in a city* Th. ‖ PASS. (of territory) be held (by an army, a people) Th. Isoc. X.
17 (esp. aor. and fut.2) **get one's hands on, get possession of** —*objects, money* Hdt. E. And. Ar. Isoc.; **seize control of** —*territory, power, or sim.* Hdt. S. E. Th. Ar. +; (intr., of a faction) **seize control** (in a city) Arist.
18 (esp. aor. and fut.2) **subdue, overcome** —*a people, Zeus' power, the Sphinx's power* S. E. Th.
19 hold in subjection —*cities, peoples* A. Th. Isoc. ‖ PASS. be held in subjection Hdt. Th.
20 (of an orator, an actor) **hold in thrall** —*the masses, an audience* E. Plu.; (of love) —*a person* Plu. ‖ PASS. be held spellbound —W.DAT. or PREP.PHR. *by music, passions, or sim.* Pi. E. Th.; be possessed (by a god) Pl. —W.PREP.PHR. *by a god, Homer* E. Pl. X.; (wkr.sens.) be preoccupied —w. ἐπί + DAT. *w. sthg.* X.
21 (of conditions or circumstances) **control, hold sway over** —*persons or places* Thgn.(sts.tm.) Pi. Hdt. S. E. Th. + ‖ PASS. (of a ruler) be beset —W.DAT. *by war, political trouble* Isoc.; (of military forces) be occupied (by threats, wars, or sim.) Th.; (of persons) be controlled or gripped —W.DAT. or PREP.PHR. *by circumstances or emotions* E. Th. Tim. Isoc. Pl. X.; be bound —W.DAT. *by oaths* (W.INF. *to do sthg.*) Hdt.
22 (of enemies) press hard, **harry** —*persons, a people* E. Th. X.; (of hunters) **drive** —*hounds* X. ‖ PASS. (of deer) be pressed hard (in the chase) X.
23 bring to shore —*a ship* (W.PREP.PHR. *at a place*) Hdt. —*a person* S.(cj.); (intr., of sailors, ships) **come in to shore** E. Th. —W.ADV. or PREP.PHR. *at a place* hHom. S. E.*Cyc.* Antipho Th. +; **land at** —W.ACC. *a place* Hdt. E. Ar. (fig., of a premonition) **come to land** —W.ADV. *successfully* (*i.e. have a fortunate outcome*) S.
24 achieve, accomplish —*sthg.* E. Th. And. Isoc.; **succeed** (in one's aims) E. Th. Lys.

25 prevail over, outdo —*persons* (*in a competition*) Hdt.; (intr., of persons or things) prevail over others, **prevail** Thgn. E. Ar.
26 (of stories) **be current** Th. And. Plu.; (of earthquakes) **be ongoing** (in a region) Th.; (tr., of a style of dress) **be current among** —*people* Th.

κατηβολή *f.*: see καταβολή
κατηγεμών Ion.*m.*, **κατηγέομαι** Ion.mid.contr.vb.: see καθηγεμών, καθηγέομαι
κατηγορέω contr.vb. [κατήγορος] | neut.impers.vbl.adj. κατηγορητέον | **1 speak against, criticise, condemn, denounce** (persons or things) Pl. Plb. —W.GEN. *persons, deeds, things* Th. Ar. Att.orats. Pl. +; **accuse** —W.GEN. *someone* (W.ACC. *of stupidity, madness, certain thoughts*) E. Pl. X. Is.
2 (specif.) **deliver a speech of accusation** (in a lawcourt) Ar. Att.orats. Pl.; (of persons; fig., of sycophancy) **bring a lawsuit, be the accuser** or **plaintiff** Att.orats. Pl. Arist. Plb.; **act as a public prosecutor** Ar.
3 (of persons, written testimony, a personif. doctrine) **make an allegation of wrongdoing** (esp. in a lawcourt); **make an accusation** (sts. W.ACC. on a specific charge) Hdt. Th. Ar. Att.orats. + —W.GEN. *against someone* Hdt. S. E. Ar. Att.orats. + —(W.COMPL.CL. *of having done sthg.*) Att.orats. Pl. X. —w. κατά + GEN. *against someone* X.; **allege** (sthg.) Is. —W.COMPL.CL. *that sthg. is the case* Th. Att.orats. Pl. + ‖ PASS. (of persons) be accused (of wrongdoing, in a lawsuit) Antipho And. —W.COMPL.CL. *of having done sthg.* X.; (of criticisms, charges of wrongdoing) be laid as an accusation Att.orats. Pl. Plb. —W.GEN. *against someone* S. Th. Att.orats. Pl. ‖ IMPERS.PASS. an accusation is made —W.GEN. *against someone* (sts. W.INF. or COMPL.CL. *of having done sthg.*) Hdt. Lys. X.
4 file an objection (against someone, in a court determining eligibility for citizenship) Is.; (tr.) **challenge** —*an audit* Arist.
5 (of persons, their arguments) **give evidence against, incriminate, implicate.** —W.GEN. *a person, oneself* (sts. W.COMPL.CL. *as having done sthg.*) Lys. Pl. X. Plb.; (of a sword) **be incriminating** S.; (of witnesses) **give evidence of wrongdoing** Ar.; (tr.) **attest to** —*an event* (*i.e. that it happened*) Antipho
6 (of a person's face) **betray, reveal** —W.GEN. *one's joy at sthg.* A.; (of youthfulness of body) —W.ACC. *a person's age* X.; (of the name of a river, a garment) —W.COMPL.CL. *that it is Greek, foreign* Hdt.; (of a person) **reveal** (sthg., to someone) X. ‖ IMPERS. it demonstrates —W.COMPL.CL. *that sthg. is the case* Pl.
7 (philos.) **define as an attribute or dependent feature; predicate** —W.ACC. *a quality* (W.GEN. or ἐπί + GEN. *of sthg.*) Arist. ‖ PASS. (of qualities, things) be predicated Arist. —W.GEN. or PREP.PHR. *of sthg.* Arist.
‖ NEUT.PL.PASS.PTCPL.SB. **predicates, categories** (of predicates) Arist.

κατηγόρημα ατος *n.* **1 accusation, charge** (against a person) Att.orats. Pl. Plb. Plu.; **objection** (against a potential khoregos) Pl.
2 (philos.) **quality** or **property that is attributed** (to sthg.), **predicate** Arist.
3 class of attributes or **qualities, category of predicates** Arist.

κατηγορίᾱ ᾱς *f.* **1 accusation** (of wrongdoing, sts. W.GEN. against someone) Hdt. Th. Att.orats. Pl. +; (specif.) **indictment, prosecution** (of a person) Att.orats. Plu.; (gener.) **criticism, denunciation** Arist. Thphr. Plb. Plu.

κατηγορικός

2 (philos.) attribution of a particular quality or property (to sthg.), **predication** Arist.
3 quality or property attributed (to sthg.), **predicate** Arist.
4 class of attributes or qualities, **category of predicates** Arist.

κατηγορικός ή όν *adj.* [κατήγορος] ‖ MASC.SB. **denouncer, state informer** Plu.

κατ-ήγορος ου *m.* [reltd. ἀγορεύω] 1 one who brings an accusation of wrongdoing (esp. in a court or assembly), **accuser** (sts. W.GEN. of a person) S. Att.orats. Pl. X. Arist. +; (ref. to the entire populace) Din.; (fig., ref. to one's conscience) Plb.
2 (specif.) accuser appointed by the state, **public prosecutor** Isoc. Arist. Din. Plu.
3 **exposer** (sts. W.GEN. of wrongdoers, their deeds) Hdt. Att.orats.; (fig., ref. to hearsay, laziness, one's own tongue) A. X. Aeschin.
4 (ref. to an additional name given to a person) **indicator** (W.GEN. of one's beauty) Plu.

κατῆκα (Ion.aor.): see καθίημι

κατήκισμαι (pf.pass.): see κατακίζω

κατ-ήκοος ον *adj.* [ἀκούω] 1 ‖ MASC.SB. **informer** Hdt.; (gener.) **hearer** (of news about sthg.) S.*Ichn.*
2 (of children, wives, slaves, soldiers, citizens) **obedient** (sts. W.GEN. to someone or sthg.) Hdt. S. Pl. X. Plu.; (of the appetite or sim., W.GEN. to reason) Pl. Arist.
3 (of peoples, regions) **subject** (usu. W.GEN. to a people or ruler) Hdt.

κατήκω *Ion.vb.*: see καθήκω

κατῆλθον (aor.2), **κατήλυθον** (ep.aor.2): see κατέρχομαι

κατήλιψ ιφος *f.* [app. κατά, 2nd el.uncert.] app. **high shelf** (in a house) Ar.

κατ-ηλογέω *contr.vb.* [ἀλογέω] **regard as inconsequential, pay no attention to, disregard** —*a law, a section of a fortification* Hdt.; **have no concern for** —*someone's affairs* Hdt.

κατηλόων (impf.): see καταλοάω

κατηλυσίη ης *Ion.f.* [κατέρχομαι] act of descending; **arrival, onset** (of a wind) AR.

κάτημαι *Ion.mid.vb.*: see κάθημαι

κατ-ημύω *vb.* (of young plants) **droop, wilt** AR.; (of persons) **be dejected** —W.ACC. *in their hearts* AR.

κατηνάλωκα (aor.): see καταναλίσκω

κατήναρον (aor.2): see καταναίρω

κατήορος ον *Ion.adj.* [καταίρω] (of a strap) **hanging down** (fr. a belt) AR.

κατ-ηπιάομαι *pass.contr.vb.* [ἤπιος] | ep.3pl.impf. (w.diect.) κατηπιόωντο | (of pains) **be soothed** Il.

κατῆρα (aor.): see καταίρω

κατήραξα (aor.): see καταράσσω

κατ-ηρεμίζω *vb.* (of a commander) **calm down** —*troops* X. ‖ PASS. (of troops) **be calmed down** X.

κατ-ηρεφής ές *adj.* [ἐρέφω] 1 (of a wave) **arching overhead** Od.
2 (of houses, tombs, docks, beehives) **roofed** Il. Hes. S.; (W.DAT. w. stone, a roof) Hes. E. Pl.; (of caves) **vaulted** Od. S.; **canopied** (W.DAT. w. laurels) Od.; (of trees, w. leaves) Theoc.
3 (of a mountain) **covered** (W.DAT. w. trees) Plu.; (of a table, W.GEN. w. dishes) Anacr.; (of a warrior's foot) **protected** (by a shield) A.

κατ-ήρης[1] ες *adj.* [ἀραρίσκω] (of a woman) **furnished** (W.DAT. w. a cloak, i.e. dressed in it) E.; (of wine, w. an aroma) E.

κατ-ήρης[2] ες *adj.* [app. ἐρέσσω] (of a ship) **equipped with oars** Hdt.; (of a row of oars) **fitted, set in place** E.(dub.)

κατήριπον (aor.2): see κατερείπω

κατήρυγον (aor.2): see κατερεύγομαι

κατήφεια ᾶς, Ion. **κατηφείη** ης *f.* [κατηφής] 1 **hanging of one's head in dejection, dejection, despondency** Th. AR. Plu.; **source of dejection** Il.
2 **hanging of one's head in shame, shame** Il. Plu.; **source of shame** Il. Plu.

κατηφέω *contr.vb.* (of persons, a city) **be downcast, be despondent** Hom. Call.*epigr.* AR.

κατ-ηφής ές *adj.* [app. κατά, 2nd el.uncert.] 1 (of persons, their eyes or face) **downcast, dejected** E. Men. AR. Plu.
2 **shamed, disgraced** Od.

κατηφιάω *contr.vb.* | ep.ptcpl. (w.diect.) κατηφιόων | **be downcast, be despondent** AR.

κατηφών όνος *m.* (ref. to a person) **source of shame, disgrace** Il.

κατῆχε (Aeol.3sg.impf.): see κατέχω

κατ-ηχέομαι *pass.contr.vb.* **be informed, be told** (sthg.) —w. περί + GEN. *about a person or topic* NT.; **be instructed** —W.ACC. *in the path of the Lord* NT.

καθάπτω *ep.vb.*: see καταθάπτω

κατθέμεν (ep.athem.aor.inf.), **κατθέμενος**, **κάτθεο** (ep.athem.aor.mid.ptcpl. and imperatv.), **κάτθεσαν** (ep.3pl.athem.aor.): see κατατίθημι

κατθνᾴσκω *Aeol.vb.*, **κατθνῄσκω** *ep.vb.*: see καταθνῄσκω

κατ-ιάπτω *vb.* (of a distraught woman) **utterly ruin, damage, spoil** —*her complexion* (fr. *weeping*) Od.(tm.); **fret away** —*her soul* Mosch.(tm.)

κατίζω *Ion.vb.*: see καθίζω

κατίημι *Ion.vb.*: see καθίημι

κατ-ιθύνω *vb.* 1 (of a kind of rudder) **keep straight, keep on course** —*a barge* Hdt.; (of Poseidon) **guide** —*a voyage* Mosch.
2 (of Poseidon) **smooth** —*the waves* Mosch.

κατικετεύω *Ion.vb.*: see καθικετεύω

κατ-ικμαίνομαι *mid.vb.* | aor. κατικμηνάμην | **drench oneself** —W.DAT. w. *warm water* Call.

κατ-ιλύομαι *pass.vb.* [ἰλύς] | aor. κατιλύθην | (of cornplants) **be covered in mud** X.

κατ-ιόομαι *pass.contr.vb.* [ἰός³] (of metal) **be tarnished** NT.

κατιππάζομαι *Ion.mid.vb.*: see καθιππάζομαι

κατιρόω *Ion.contr.vb.*: see καθιερόω

κάτισα (Ion.aor.), **κάτισον** (Ion.aor.imperatv.): see καθίζω

κατισδάνω *Aeol.vb.*: see καθιζάνω

κατίστημι *Ion.vb.*: see καθίστημι

κατ-ισχάνω *vb.* **hold back, keep in check** —*one's thoughts* Od.(tm.)

κατ-ισχναίνω *vb.* | fut.mid. κατισχνανοῦμαι | 1 (of Erinyes) **cause to wither, shrivel up** —*a person* (W.DAT. w. *their breath*) A. ‖ MID. (of Prometheus) **waste away** A.; (of a person) **lose weight** (by dieting) Pl.
2 (medic.) **reduce** (a swelling); (fig., of the Muses) **cure** —*love* (envisaged as a malady) Call.*epigr.*

κάτ-ισχνος ον *adj.* [ἰσχνός] (of a person) **very thin** Plu.

κατ-ισχύω *vb.* 1 **come to full strength** —W.ACC. *in one's body* S.
2 **prevail over** (someone) **by force; force** —*a person* (*into doing sthg.*) Men.; (fig., in neg.phr., of the gates of Hades) **prevail over** —W.GEN. *the Church of Christ* NT.; (of troops, a political faction) **get the upper hand** Plb.; (of a warring state's decisions) **win the day, secure victory** Plb.; (of persons, their shouts) **prevail** (in an assembly) Plb. NT.
3 (specif.) **prevail with a proposal** —W.INF. *to do sthg.* Plb.; (of particular desires or ambitions) **be prevalent** —W.PREP.PHR. *in people's lives, politics* Plb.

4 be strong enough, **be able** —W.INF. *to escape disaster* NT.

κατ-ίσχω, ep. **καταΐσχω** *vb.* **1** (of a charioteer) **keep in check, restrain** —*his horses* Il.; (of a person) —*his envy* X.; (of a king) **detain** —*someone's ships* Hdt. ‖ MID. **keep back for oneself** —*a captive girl (as a concubine)* Il.
2 hold —*one's head* (W.ADV. *low*) Alc.
3 ‖ PASS. (of an island) **be occupied, be taken up** —W.DAT. *by flocks and ploughland* Od.
4 (of sailors, a fleet) **bring to land, put in** —*one's ships* (W.PREP.PHR. *at a place*) Od. Hdt. AR.; (intr.) **put in to shore** —W.DAT. or PREP.PHR. *at a place* Th.
5 (intr., of a beam of light) **travel down** —W.PREP.PHR. *fr. heaven* Hdt.

κάτοδος Ion.*f.*: see κάθοδος

κάτ-οιδα *pf.vb.* [οἶδα] **1 be aware of, know about** —*sthg.* S. E.; **know** (sthg.) S. E. —W.INF. (*so as to be able*) *to tell someone* S. —W.INDIR.Q. or COMPL.CL. *what* (*or that sthg.*) *is the case* S. E.
2 remember —W.COMPL.CL. *that sthg. is the case* S.
3 be aware of (someone or sthg.) as existing; **be familiar with, know of** —*someone* S. E. —*sthg.* E.
4 have understanding or insight (into sthg.); **understand** (a situation) A. —*sthg.* S. Pl.; **know well, be familiar with** —*the constellations, a route* A. Pl.

κατ-οικέω *contr.vb.* | pf.pass.ptcpl. κατῳκημένος, Ion. κατοικημένος | **1 found, establish** —*a city* Isoc. ‖ PASS. (of cities, states) **be founded or established** S. Pl. D. Arist.
2 impose a new order upon, **refound, colonise** —*a city* Hdt.
3 (of persons, populations) **settle in** —*a place* E. Th. Isoc. X.; (intr.) **settle** —W.ADV. or PREP.PHR. *in a place* Th. Isoc. Lycurg. Plu.
4 (of persons, gods, animals) **dwell in, live in** —*a place* S. E. Att.orats. Arist. +; (intr.) **dwell, live** (in a place) Ar. Pl. X. Arist. + —W.ADV. or PREP.PHR. *in a place* E. Th. Att.orats. Pl. +; (of evil spirits, one's conscience) —*in a person, the soul* Plb. NT. ‖ PASS. (of cities) **be inhabited** —w. ὑπό + GEN. *by certain peoples* Plb.
5 ‖ PASS. (of populations) **live** —W.PTCPL. *scattered and mixed w. others* Pl. ‖ PF.PLPF.PASS. **be settled, dwell** (in a place) Hdt. —W.ACC. *in a place* Hdt. —W.ADV. or PREP.PHR. Hdt. Th.
6 (of cities) **occupy** —*a particular place* Isoc.; (intr.) **be situated** —W.PREP.PHR. *in a place* E. Pl.; (of the stomach) —W.ADV. *in a particular part of the body* Pl.
7 (intr., of cities) **be established** Pl.
8 ‖ PASS. (of cities) **be situated** —W.PREP.PHR. *in a place* D.; (pf.) Hdt.

κατοίκησις εως *f.* **1** act of settling in a place; **settling, settlement** (of a region) Plu.
2 act of living in a place, **residence** Th.
3 place of settlement or habitation, **dwelling-place** Pl. NT. Plu.; **seat, location** (of the liver, in the body) Pl.

κατοικίᾱ ᾱς *f.* **1** place where people are settled; **settlement, colony** (esp. of former soldiers) Plb. Plu.
2 (gener.) place where people live, **settlement, community** Plb. NT.
3 founding of a settlement; **settling** (in a region) Plb.; **founding** (of cities) Plu.

κατ-οικίζω *vb.* **1 found, establish** —*a city, colony* Pi. Th. Ar. Pl. X. Plu.; (fig.) —*oneself* (*on the model of the ideal state*) Pl.; (intr.) **found a state** Pl.; **found colonies** Pl. ‖ PASS. (of cities) be founded Isoc. Pl. Arist.; (of a population) be organised into a state Pl. D.
2 (of states, peoples, rulers, gods) **re-establish, restore** —*a city, its population* E. Th. Pl. Aeschin. Din. Plu.; **repopulate** —*a city* (*w. new settlers, esp. after conquering it*) Th. Plu. ‖ PASS. (of cities) be restored Th. D.; be relocated —w. εἰς + ACC. *in a place* Pl.
3 settle people in, **colonise** —*a place* Hdt. Th. Isoc. Pl.; (of gods) **populate** —*a region* Pl. ‖ PASS. (of places) be settled with people (esp. by a state or ruler) Th.
4 (of states, peoples, rulers, gods) **settle or resettle** —*people* (oft. W.PREP.PHR. *in a city or region*) A. Hdt. Th. Isoc. Pl. Plu. —(W.DAT. *in a region*) S.; **settle** (people, in a place) Th. ‖ PASS. (of populations) be settled (oft. W.PREP.PHR. in a place) Pl. —W.DAT. or ὑπό + GEN. *by a ruler* Pl. Plu. ‖ PF.PASS. (of persons, peoples) be settled, dwell —W.PREP.PHR. *in a certain place* Pl.; (of the soul) be situated, reside —W.PREP.PHR. *in a certain part of the body* Pl.
5 (of gods, rulers, persons) **install** —*persons, their spirits, War* (W.ADV. or PREP.PHR. *in a place*) Hdt. S. E.*fr.* Ar. —*the soul, its components* (*in a particular part of the body*) Pl.; (of Zeus) **bring** —*womankind* (W.PREP.PHR. *into the world*) E.; (of Prometheus) **instil** —*hopes* (W.PREP.PHR. *in people*) A. ‖ PASS. (of a woman) be installed —W.ADV. *in a place* Is.
6 (of persons, peoples) **settle in** —*a place* A. E. ‖ MID. **settle** —W.PREP.PHR. *in a place* Th. Isoc. ‖ PASS. (of persons, peoples) settle —W.ADV. or PREP.PHR. *in a place* Pi.*fr.* Hdt. E. Th. Pl.; (of the soul) take up residence —W.ADV. *in a body* Pl.

κατοίκισις εως *f.* **1** settling (of a region) Pl.; **founding** (of a city) Pl.
2 re-establishment, **restoration** (of a city, a population) Th. D.
3 (concr.) **settlement** (ref. to a colony) Pl.

κατοικισμός οῦ *m.* act of establishing a settlement or colony; **settlement** (sts. W.GEN. of a region) Pl. Plu.

κατ-οικοδομέω *contr.vb.* **1 put up buildings** Plu.; (tr.) put up buildings on, **build on** —*roads, public land* X. Arist.
2 app. **trap inside a building, imprison** —*a person* Is.

κατ-οικονομέω *contr.vb.* successfully deal with, **take care of** —*a piece of business* Plu.

κάτ-οικος ου *m.* [οἶκος] **colonist, settler** (in Egypt) Plb.

κατ-οικοφθορέω *contr.vb.* (of expensive military activities) completely use up the resources of, **bankrupt** —*a city* Plu.

κατ-οικτίζω *vb.* | aor.pass. (w.mid.sens.) κατῳκτίσθην |
1 feel pity for, take pity on —*persons, their sufferings* Trag.; (in neg.phr., of tearing) —*garments* A.; (intr., of persons, a god) **feel pity** (for a person) A. S.; (of words) **express pity** S.
2 ‖ MID. and AOR.PASS. **lament** Hdt. E.; (tr.) **lament over** —*a defeated army* A.

κατ-οικτίρω (also written **κατοικτείρω**) *vb.* **feel pity for, take pity on** —*a person, an animal* Hdt. S. E. Ar. X. Arist.; (intr.) **feel pity** (for someone) Hdt. E.

κατοίκτισις εως *f.* [κατοικτίζω] sympathy (for a person's suffering), **compassion, pity** X.

κάτ-οικτος ον *adj.* [οἶκτος] full of pity; (quasi-advbl., of a person lamenting) **piteously** A.(cj.)

κατ-οιμώζω *vb.* **lament over, mourn** —*a dead person* E.; **weep for** —*oneself* (*over a missed opportunity*) Plb.

κατοινόομαι *pass.contr.vb.* [κάτοινος] ‖ PF. be drunk, be intoxicated Pl.

κάτ-οινος ον *adj.* [οἶνος] **drunk, intoxicated** E. Plu.

κατ-οιχνέω *contr.vb.* (of a sound) **travel over** —W.GEN. *a place* S.*Ichn.*

κατ-οίχομαι *mid.vb.* (of persons) **be departed** (i.e. dead) D. Plu.(oracle)

κατ-οκνέω *contr.vb.* **hold back timidly, shrink back** (sts. W.INF. fr. doing sthg.) A. S. Th. Isoc. +; (wkr.sens.) **hold back**

κατοκωχή

(sts. W.INF. fr. doing sthg.) Isoc. D. Plu.; **be reluctant** —W.INF. *to do sthg.* Th.

κατοκωχή ἧς *f.* [κατέχω] act of holding in an entranced state; **possession** (of poets, by the Muses) Pl.

κατοκώχιμος η ον *adj.* **1** (leg., of a plot of land) held back, **held as a security** Is.
2 (of persons) liable to be captivated or held in thrall, **susceptible** (W.PREP.PHR. to influences, activities) Arist.

κατ-ολιγωρέω *contr.vb.* **be utterly neglectful** Plb. —W.GEN. *of someone or sthg.* Lys. Plb.

κατ-ολισθάνω *vb.* | ep.aor.2 κατόλισθον | (of a ship, being launched) **slide down** —w. ἔσω + GEN. *into the sea* AR.

κατ-όλλυμι *vb.* (of enemy ships) **destroy** —*young men* Tim.(tm.) ‖ PF. (of a nation's youth) have perished A.(tm.)

κατ-ολολύζω *vb.* (of Conflict) **utter a shrill cry of triumph** —W.GEN. *over a victim* A.

κατ-ολοφύρομαι *mid.vb.* **lament** (over a situation) E. —W.ACC. *over someone or sthg.* E. X. Plb.

κατ-όμνυμι *vb.* (act. and mid.) take a solemn oath (to do sthg., or attesting to the truth of sthg.); **swear** (sts. W.COGN.ACC. an oath, sts. W.DAT. to someone) Hdt. E. Ar. Arist. —W.ACC. *by a god, a river, one's life, or sim.* (sts. W.INF. *to do sthg.*) E. Ar. —W.ACC. + INF. *that sthg. is or will be the case* Ar. D.

κατ-ονίνημι *vb.* | 2sg.aor.mid.opt. κατόναιο | ‖ MID. (w. sexual connot.) **obtain gratification** —W.GEN. *for oneself* Ar.

κατ-ονομάζω *vb.* **1 name** —*a city* (W.PREDIC.SB. w. *a particular name*) Plb. ‖ PASS. (of emotions) be named or classified —W.DAT. *according to a particular principle* Arist.
2 ‖ PASS. (of a woman) be betrothed —W.DAT. *to a man* Plb.

κατ-όνομαι *mid.vb.* | aor.pass. (w.mid.sens.) κατωνόσθην | regard or treat with disrespect, **denigrate** —*someone or sthg.* Hdt.

κάτ-οξυς εια υ *adj.* [ὀξύς] very sharp; (of shouting) **shrill, strident** Ar.

κατ-οπάζω *vb.* (of shamelessness) **drive away** —*decency* Hes.

κατόπιν *adv.* [κατόπισθεν] **1** in the rear, **behind** (esp.ref. to following someone) Th. Ar. X. Plb. Plu.; (quasi-adjl., of persons, regions, things) Th. Plb. Plu.; (as prep.) **behind** —W.GEN. *someone or sthg.* Ar. Pl. Plb. Plu.
2 afterwards Plb. Plu.; (as prep.) **after** —W.GEN. *a particular event or point in time* Pl. Plb. Plu.; (quasi-adjl., of a day, a year) **subsequent, following** Plb. Plu.; (of praise) **belated** Plu.

κατ-όπισθε(ν) *adv.* **1 from behind** —*ref. to wounding or snatching at a person or animal* Hom.
2 in the rear, **behind** (esp.ref. to following) Hom. hHom. Archil. E. Pl.(quot.poet.) Plu.(oracle); (as prep.) **behind** —W.GEN. *someone or sthg.* Il. AR.
3 (quasi-adjl., of an argument) **following, subsequent** Pl.
4 in the future, **hereafter** or **thereafter** Od. hHom. Thgn. Pl.

κατοπτέον (neut.impers.vbl.adj.): see καθοράω

κατ-οπτεύω *vb.* **1 spy on, observe** —*someone* Plu. ‖ PASS. be observed or detected S. —W.PREP.PHR. *by enemy forces* S. Plb.; be revealed (as wearing make-up) —W.PREP.PHR. *by a bath* X.
2 (esp. in military ctxt.) **observe, survey** —*locations, enemy forces* Plb.; (intr.) **scout around, make a survey** Plb. ‖ PASS. (of a region) be surveyed or explored Plb.
3 observe, investigate —*a situation* Plb.; (intr.) **make an investigation** Plb.

κατοπτήρ ῆρος *m.* [καθοράω] **scout, spy** (in an army) A.

κατόπτης ου, dial. **κατόπτας** ᾱ *m.* **observer** (of events) hHom. Ar.; (specif.) **spy** (sts. W.GEN. on a foreign land, an enemy fleet) A. Hdt. E.

κάτοπτος ον *adj.* **1** (of places, things) **visible** Th. Lys.
2 (of a headland) **looking down** (over a gulf) A.

κάτ-οπτρον (also **κάτροπτον**) ου *n.* [ὄπωπα, see ὁράω] **mirror, looking-glass** (usu. ref. to a handheld implement of polished bronze) E. Ar. Pl. X. Call. Plb. +; (fig., ref. to that which reflects or shows the truth) A. E. Arist.(quot.)

κατοράω *Ion.contr.vb.*: see καθοράω

κατ-οργιάζω *vb.* **initiate** —*a city* (*into religious observances*) Plu.

κατ-ορθόω *contr.vb.* **1** set upright, **hold erect** —*one's body* E.
2 make straight, **lay straight** —*a contorted body* E.; **straighten** —*a child's limbs* (by massage or sim.) Pl.
3 set on a straight path, **hold steady** —*a spear* X.
4 (fig., of persons or gods) **set straight** —*the base part of human nature* Pl.; **set on a right course** —*one's mind* S.; (of words, knowledge) —*persons, the use of wealth* S. Pl.; (intr., of persons) **be on the right path** (sts. W.DAT. OR PREP.PHR. in a certain matter) Pl. ‖ PASS. (of education) be set up in the right way Pl.; (of a person) be set on the right path —W.DAT. *in one's mind* A. ‖ PF.PASS. (of events) have been properly treated —W.DAT. *by historians* Plu.
5 (of persons, gods, fortune) **bring to a successful conclusion** —*an undertaking* E. Ar. Isoc. Pl. D. +; (specif.) **win** —*a lawsuit, battle, war* Lys. D. Plb. Plu. —*a victory* Plu. ‖ MID. **gain a successful conclusion for** —*an undertaking* (w. διά + GEN. *through the agency of a person*) Plu. ‖ PASS. (of undertakings) be successfully carried out Th. Isoc. X. D. Plb. Plu.; (gener., of things) be successful, go well B. Hdt. E. Th. Arist. Plb.
6 (intr.) **be successful** (sts. W.DAT. OR PREP.PHR. in an undertaking) Th. Ar. Att.orats. Pl. +; (of undertakings, words) **be successful** (in their aims) Th. Arist. Din. Men.; (specif., of persons) **be victorious** (sts. W.DAT. OR PREP.PHR. in a contest, lawsuit, battle, war) Th. Isoc. X. D. Plb. Plu.; (gener., of persons, countries) **prosper, do well** Th. Att.orats. Plb.

κατόρθωμα ατος *n.* **success** (ref. to a particular achievement) Plb. Plu.; (specif.) **victory** (in a battle or war) Plb. Plu.

κατόρθωσις εως *f.* **1 restoration** (of political order in a city) Plb.
2 improvement (of a situation) Plb.
3 success (esp. in battle) Aeschin. Arist. Plb. Plu.

κατορθωτικός ή όν *adj.* (of good men) **liable to do well** Arist.; (of a commander) **successful** (in battles) Plu.

κατ-ορούω *vb.* (of a god, a horseman) **rush** or **leap down** —W.PREP.PHR. *fr. or into a place* hHom. X.

κατ-ορρωδέω, Ion. **καταρρωδέω** *contr.vb.* **1** (of persons, commanders, armies, populations) **be afraid** or **terrified** Hdt. Plb. —w. ὑπέρ + GEN. *for oneself, for Greece* Hdt. —w. μή + SUBJ. *that sthg. may happen* Hdt.
2 (tr.) regard with terror, **be terrified by** —*a dream, portent, enemy forces* Hdt. Plb.; **be afraid of** —*impending danger, invasion, a risky engagement* Hdt. Plb.

κατ-ορύσσω, Att. **κατορύττω** *vb.* **1 bury in the ground; bury, inter** —*a dead person or animal, their bones* Th. Ar. Pl. X. Plu. —*a person* (W.PTCPL. *alive, esp. as a sacrifice or ritual punishment*) Hdt. X. Plu.; (gener.) **bury** —*faeces* Ar. ‖ PASS. (of a person or body) be buried Ar. Pl. —W.PTCPL. *alive* E. Plu. —(fig.ref. *to having a meaningless life, after the death of one's son*) Antipho; (of honours) be made defunct —W.DAT. *by laws and decrees* Plu.
2 bury (for safekeeping) —*money, valuables, the god Wealth* Hdt. Ar. X. Men. ‖ PASS. (of money or sim.) be buried D. Plu.; (of wine, in jars, to preserve it) X.

3 ‖ PF.PASS. (of gold) lie buried in the ground (as nuggets or veins in rock) Pl.
4 sink or partially bury, **bury** —*wrongdoers* (W.PREP.PHR. *up to the neck, in a mire*) Hdt. Pl. ‖ PASS. (of cobblestones, stakes) be sunk (in the ground) X. Plb.; (fig., of the eye of the soul) —W.PREP.PHR. *in a mire* Pl.

κατ-ορχέομαι *mid.contr.vb.* taunt (W.ACC. an enemy) **with a mocking dance** Hdt. Plu.

κατ-ουδαῖος ον *adj.* [οὖδας] **1** (of a giant) **under the ground, in the depths of the earth** Call. ‖ MASC.PL.SB. Subterraneans (a fabled race of Africans) Hes.*fr.*
2 (of a trench) **sunk in the earth** hHom.

κατ-ουλάς άδος *fem.adj.* [reltd. κατειλέω²] (of a pitch-black night) **all-enveloping, shrouding** AR.

κατ-ουρέω *contr.vb.* (fig.) **piss on** —W.GEN. *a person (i.e. treat him w. contempt)* Ar.

κατ-ουρίζω *vb.* convey (to a destination) with a fair wind; (of a prophecy) **bring to fulfilment** —*events* S. [or perh. intr., of events, *come to fulfilment*]

κατ-ουρόω *contr.vb.* [οὖρος¹] **sail with a fair wind** Plb.

κατ-οχεύς ῆος *ep.m.* that which holds back; **bolt** (of a door) Call.

κατοχή ῆς *f.* [κατέχω] **1** restriction, **confinement** (of a person, to a particular place) Hdt.
2 **possession** (of a person by a god, in a mystic rite) Plu.

κάτοχος ον *adj.* **1** (of a person) **held fast** (W.DAT. by sleep) S.; (of evils) **kept in check, confined** (W.DAT. in the earth) A.
2 (of a warlike race) **subject** (W.DAT. to Ares) E.
3 (of persons) **possessed** (by a god) Plu.; **gripped, held in thrall** (w. ὑπό + GEN. by delight) Plu.
4 holding fast; (of a person) **retentive** (in memory) Plu.

κατόψιος ον *adj.* [κατόψομαι, see καθοράω] **1** (of routes) **in sight, visible** AR.
2 (of the Acropolis) **facing, overlooking** (W.GEN. the land of Troizen) E.

κατ-οψοφαγέω *contr.vb.* ‖ PASS. (of money) be used up on fine dining Aeschin.

κάτροπτον *n.*: see κάτοπτρον

καττά, **καττάδε**, dial. for κατὰ τά, κατὰ τάδε

καττάνυσαν (ep.3pl.aor.): see κατατανύω

καττίτερος *Att.m.*: see κασσίτερος

κάττυμα ατος *Att.n.* [καττύω] **sole of a shoe** Ar.

καττύω *Att.vb.* sew soles on shoes, **make shoes** Pl. ‖ PASS. (of shoes) be resoled or stitched back together Thphr.; (fig., of a ploy, envisaged as a shoe) be stitched together Ar.

καττῶ: dial. for κατὰ τοῦ

κατυβρίζω *Ion.vb.*, **κατύπερθε** *Ion.adv.*, **κατυπέρτερος**, **κατυπέρτατος** *Ion.adjs.*, **κατυπνόω** *Ion.contr.vb.*: see καθ-

κάτω *adv.* [κατά] | The sections are grouped as: (1–3) downwards, (4) upside-down, (5–10) down below, (11–12) at the bottom, (13) underneath, (14–15) subsequent, (16–17) down (opp. ἄνω up). |
1 with a downwards movement, **downwards** Il. Pi. Hdt. Trag. Th. +; (specif.) **downstairs** Hdt. Lys. D.; **downhill** Hdt. Pl. X. +; **down underground** Hdt. S.; **down to the underworld** Hdt. Trag. Ar.
2 in a downwards direction, **downwards** —*esp. ref. to pointing, looking, bowing one's head* Od. Hdt. E. Ar. Thphr. AR. +; (specif.) **downhill** —*ref. to a path leading* Plu.; (quasi-adjl., of paths) Heraclit. Pl.
3 (phr.) τὰ κάτω **outward leg** (*of a race running down and back up a racecourse*) Pl.
4 **upside-down** —*ref. to turning objects* Hdt. Ar. —*ref. to turning a situation* Hdt. | see also 17
5 in a low position, **down low** —*ref. to holding one's head* Alc.; **down below** —*ref. to placing sthg., being situated* Hdt. X. Hyp. D. Arist. NT.; (quasi-adjl., of persons or things) Hdt. Pl. Men.; (specif.) **downstairs** (in a house) Lys.
6 (quasi-adjl., of persons, places) at a lower altitude, **downhill** Pl. Plu.
7 (specif.) **down by the sea** (opp. inland) Th.; (quasi-adjl., of regions, their inhabitants) Hdt. Th. X. Men. Plu.
8 (quasi-adjl., of regions) **to the south** Hdt. Plu.
9 **down on earth** (opp. up in heaven or the air) Ar. Pl. NT.; (quasi-adjl., of persons or things) Pl. NT.
10 **down in the underworld** Hes. Pi.*fr.* S. E. Ar.; (quasi-adjl., of gods, persons, things) Hdt. Trag. Att.orats. Call.*epigr.*
11 at the bottom or lower end (of sthg.) Tyrt. Pi. E. Pl. X. +; (quasi-adjl., of jaws, bowels, parts of sthg.) **lower** Hdt. Ar. Pl. X. Plb.; (phr.) τὸ κάτω **lower part** (*of sthg.*) Xenoph. Hdt. Pl. +; **bottom** (*of a trench or pit*) Hdt. Ar. X.; τὰ κάτω **lower parts, lower half** (*of a person, animal, thing*) Hdt. S.*satyr.fr.* Ar. Pl. +; **lower storey, ground floor** (*of a house*) Lys.
12 at the bottom of the digestive tract, **down below** —*ref. to evacuating the bowels* Pl. X. Thphr.
13 **underneath** (sthg.) Ar. X. Plu.; (quasi-adjl., of a layer of ice) Plb.; **underground** S. Ar.; (as prep.) **under** —W.GEN. *the earth* Alc. Trag.
14 further down in a sequence; (quasi-adjl., of things) **belonging to a lower level** (in classification or derivation) Pl. Arist.; (as prep., ref. to being seated at dinner) **down** (by one place) —W.GEN. *fr. someone* Pl.
15 (quasi-adjl., of time) **subsequent, later** Plu.; (prep.phr.) εἰς τὸ κάτω (of generations) *in the future* Pl.
16 ἄνω (τε καὶ) κάτω *up and down, back and forth, this way and that* A. + | see ἄνω 14
17 ἄνω (τε καὶ) κάτω *upside-down, in total disorder* E. + | see ἄνω 15

—**κατωτέρω** *compar.adv.* **1** (ref. to movt.) **further downwards** Ar. Pl.; (wkr.sens.) **further** (W.GEN. than a certain place) Hdt.
2 **lower down, in a lower position** X.; (quasi-adjl., of a horse's leg-bones, W.GEN. than the fetlocks) X.
3 **lower, younger** (than a certain age) NT.

—**κατωτάτω** *superl.adv.* **lowest down, at the very bottom** Hdt. Arist.

—**κατώτατα** *neut.pl.superl.adv.* **at the very bottom** (of a trench) Hdt.

κάτωθεν (also **κάτωθε** Theoc.) *adv.* **1** from a lower position, **up from below** E. Th. Ar. Pl. Plu.
2 **up from the underworld** A. Ar.
3 **from lower ground** Th. Theoc. Plu.
4 **from underneath** —*ref. to removing earth* Th.
5 in a lower position, **down below** S. Pl. D. Arist. Plu.; (as prep.) **below** —W.GEN. *a wall* Th.
6 **down below in the underworld** S. E. Ar. Plu.(quot.com.)
7 **further downstream** Pl.
8 **further down, later** (in a sequence of generations) Pl.
9 at the bottom Hdt. Th. X. Plb. Plu.; (phr.) τὰ κάτωθεν **lower parts** (*of a house, ship, animal, or sim.*) Pl. X. D.
10 **underneath** Hdt. X.

κατ-ωθέω *contr.vb.* **push down, cast down** —*an impaled enemy* Il.(tm.)

κατω-κάρᾱ *adv.* with head down, **upside-down** —*ref. to being hung* Pi.*fr.* Ar.; **head-first** —*ref. to being thrown* Ar.

κατωμάδιος ᾱ (Ion. η) ον *adj.* [κατωμαδόν] **1** (of a pouch, a key) **hanging from the shoulder** Call. Mosch.
2 (of a discus) **swung from the shoulder** Il.

κατ-ωμαδόν *adv.* [ὦμος] **1 down from the shoulder** —*ref. to a quiver hanging* AR. **2 with a downward sweep of the arm** —*ref. to lashing a horse* Il.

κατωμοσίη ης *Ion.f.* [κατόμνῡμι] **swearing of an oath** Hdt.

κατ-ωμόχανος ον *adj.* [ὦμος, χάσκω] (of a man) **gaping all the way to the shoulders** (fr. stupidity, or perh. sodomy) Hippon.

κατω-νάκη ης *f.* **rough garment of sheepskin or with a sheepskin hem; sheepskin tunic** (worn by slaves and peasants) Ar.; (fig., ref. to bushy pubic hair) Ar.

κατωνόσθην (aor.pass.): see κατόνομαι

κατῶρυξ υχος *masc.fem.adj.* [κατορύσσω] **1** (of the stones of a building) **sunk into the ground** Od. **2** (of a vault; of early men, living in caves) **underground** A. S. ‖ FEM.SB. **underground vault or chamber** S.; (for storing treasure) E.

κατώτατα *neut.pl.superl.adv.*, **κατωτάτω** *superl.adv.*, **κατωτέρω** *compar.adv.*: see under κάτω

κατώτερος ᾱ (Ion. η) ον *compar.adj.* [κάτω] (of persons) **under, younger than** (W.INDECL.NUM. sixty) Call.

κατω-φαγᾶς ᾶ *m.* [φαγεῖν] **one who eats with the head down, gobbler** (as an invented name for a bird) Ar.; (ref. to a glutton) Ar.

κατω-φερής ές *adj.* [φέρω] (of a piece of ground) **sloping downwards** X.; (of a dog's head) **pointing downwards** X.; (of a mountain path) **steep** Plb.

καυάξαις (ep.2sg.aor.opt.), **καυάξαντες** (ep.masc.pl.aor.ptcpl.): see κατάγνῡμι

καύης εω *Ion.m.* [Lydian loanwd.] **priest** Hippon.

Καύκασος ου *m.* **Caucasus** (mt. range NE. of the Black Sea; sts.ref. to one huge peak, prob. Mt. Elbrus) A. AR. Theoc. Plb. Plu.

—**Καύκασις** ιος *Ion.m.* **Caucasus** (ref. to Mt. Elbrus) Hdt.

—**Καυκάσιος** ᾱ (Ion. η) ον *adj.* (of mountains, crags, a nymph) **of the Caucasus, Caucasian** Hdt. AR.; (of a sea, ref. to the Black Sea) AR.

καυλός οῦ *m.* **1 stalk** (of a plant) Ar. AR.; (fig.) **juiciest parts** (of magistrates' audits, as opportunities for profit) Ar. **2 shaft** (of a feather) Pl. **3 socket** (of a spear-head) Il.

καῦμα ατος *n.* [καίω] **1 burning heat** (of the sun) Il. +; (fr. fire, thunderbolts) Hes.; (in the underworld) Pl. **2 overheating** (of a person's body) Pl. **3 inflammation** (of the body, due to illness) Th. Pl. X. **4** (pl., concr.) **ember** (of burnt offerings) Pl.

καυματίζομαι *pass.vb.* (of plants) **be scorched by the sun** NT.

καυνάκης ου *m.* [loanwd.] **a Persian style of thick woollen cloak, burnous** Ar.

Καῦνος ου *f.* **Kaunos** (city in Caria) Hdt. Th. Plb. Plu.

—**Καύνιος** ᾱ ον *adj.* **1** (of a person) **Kaunian** Plu. ‖ MASC.PL.SB. **Kaunians** (as a population or military force) Hdt. Plb. Plu. **2 of Kaunos** (after whom the city was named, lover of his sister Byblis); (provbl., of love, i.e. incest) **Kaunian** Arist.

καυσία ᾶς *f.* **soft hat with a flat top and deep circular rim** (esp. worn by Macedonians), **kausia** Men. Plb. Plu.

καύσιμος ον *adj.* [καίω] (of things) **combustible, inflammable** Pl. X.

καῦσις εως (Ion. ιος) *f.* **1 act of burning, burning** (of sacrificial victims) Hdt. **2** (specif.) **cauterisation** (as a medical treatment) Isoc. Pl. Arist. **3 heat** (as a bodily sensation) Pl.

καῦσος ου *m.* **burning fever** Arist.

καύστειρα ης *fem.adj.* (fig., of battle) **burning, blazing** Il.

καυστός *adj.*: see καυτός

Καΰστριος (also **Κάϋστρος**) ου *m.* **Kaystros** (river in Lydia) Il. Hdt. X.

—**Καΰστριος** ᾱ ον *adj.* (of plains, a meadow) **by the river Kaystros** Ar. Call.

καύσω (fut.): see καίω

καύσων ωνος *m.* [καίω] **burning heat** (of the sun) NT.

καυτήρ ῆρος *m.* (ref. to a tyrant) **burner** (of people, W.DAT. in a bronze bull) Pi.

καυτός (also **καυστός**) ή όν *adj.* **1** (of a wooden stake) **burnt, charred** E.*Cyc.* **2** (of oil) **inflammable** Arist.

καυχάομαι *mid.contr.vb.* | imperatv. καυχῶ | **1 boast, brag** Sapph. Pi. Theoc. NT. —W.INF. *of doing sthg.* Hdt.; **exult** NT. —W.PREP.PHR. *about sthg.* NT.; **be proud and boastful, be cocksure** Theoc. **2 mock** —w. εἰς + ACC. *at someone's young age* Arist.

καύχη ης *f.* **proud boast** Pi.

καύχημα, dial. **καύχᾱμα**, ατος *n.* **1 proud boast** Pi. **2 boasting** Plu.

Κᾱφῑσός *dial.m.*: see Κηφῑσός

καχάζω *vb.* | dial.fut. καχαξῶ | **laugh out loud, laugh** —W.INTERN.ACC. *hurtful laughs* S.(v.l. βακχάζω) —*a great laugh* (in triumph, w. κατά + GEN. *over someone*) Theoc.; **laugh and joke** S.*Ichn.*(cj.) —w. μετά + GEN. w. *someone* Ar.

καχασμός οῦ *m.* **laughter** (ref. to merrymaking) Ar.(pl.)

καχεκτέω *contr.vb.* [καχέκτης] (of a people) **be disaffected** Plb.

καχ-έκτης ου *masc.adj.* [κακός, ἔχω] (of troops, allies, citizens) **disaffected, discontented** Plb.

καχεξίᾱ ᾱς *f.* **1 bad physical condition, unhealthiness** (sts. W.GEN. of the body) Pl. X. Arist. Plb.; (of horses) Plb. **2 insalubriousness** (of a person's lifestyle) Plb. **3 bad state** (of political affairs, in a place) Plb. **4 disaffection** (of cities in an alliance) Plb.

καχ-εταιρίη ης *Ion.f.* [ἑταιρία] **bad company** Thgn.

καχλάζω *vb.* **1** (of a river, a shore) **make a rushing or splashing sound, splash, murmur** AR. Theoc.; (of a cup) —W.DAT. w. *wine* Pi.; (of a wave) **seethe** —W.ACC. w. *foam* E. **2** (of a wave) **crash** AR.; (fig., of a wave of evils or warriors) —W.PREP.PHR. *against a city* A.

κάχληξ ηκος *m.* [reltd. καχλάζω] (collectv.sg.) **shingle** (on a beach) Th.

κάχρυς υος *f.* [reltd. κέγχρος] | acc.pl. κάχρῡς | **parched barley** Ar. Plu.(quot.com.)

καχ-ύποπτος ον *adj.* [κακός] (of persons) **suspicious, mistrustful** Pl. Arist.

καχ-υπότοπος ον *adj.* [ὑποτοπέω] (of a lover's possessiveness) **suspicious, mistrustful** Pl.

κάω *Att.vb.*: see καίω

κε *dial.enclit.pcl.*: see ἄν[1]

κεάζω *vb.* [reltd. κείω[2]] **split, chop up** —*firewood* Od.; (of Zeus) **smash to pieces** —*a ship* (w. *his thunderbolt*) Od.; (of a spear) —*a person's bones* Il. ‖ PASS. (of firewood) be chopped up Od.; (of a person's head) be split (by a spear, sword, rock) Il. AR.; (of a ship) be smashed to pieces (by a storm) AR.

κέαντες (Att.masc.nom.pl.aor.ptcpl.): see καίω

κέαρ *n.*: see κῆρ

κέαται (Ion.3pl.mid.pass.), **κέατο** (ep.3pl.impf.): see κεῖμαι

κεβλή ῆς *f.* [κεφαλή] **head** (of a person) Call.

κεβλή-πυρις ιδος *f.* [πῦρ] a kind of small bird; perh. firecrest Ar.

κεγχρεών ῶνος *m.* [app. κέγχρος] area or structure forming part of a mine; perh. **foundry, furnace-room** (of a silver-mine) D.

κέγχρος ου *m.* [reltd. κέρχνος] **1** (sg. and pl.) **millet** (as a crop or grain) Hes. Hdt. X. Plb.; (specif.) **millet seed** (ref. to a single grain) Hdt.
2 small grain-like object ‖ PL. **granules** (ref. to fish eggs) Hdt.

κέγχρωμα *n.*: see κέρχνωμα

κεδάννῡμι *vb.* [reltd. σκεδάννῡμι, κίδνημι] | ep.aor. ἐκέδασσα ‖ PASS.: aor. ἐκεδάσθην | ep.3sg.plpf. κεκέδαστο | (of a god, warrior, boar) **scatter** —*men, troops, hounds* Hom.; (of a flood) **sweep** or **wash away** —*embankments* Il. ‖ PASS. (of troops, the beams of a broken ship) **be scattered** or **dispersed** Il. AR.; (of an enemy force) **be divided** —W.ADV. *into two factions* AR.

κεδάομαι *pass.contr.vb.* —also **κεδαίομαι** *pass.vb.* | 3pl. (w.diect.) κεδόωνται | (of a person) **be torn to pieces** AR.; (of a population) **be split** —W.DAT. *by disagreement* AR.

κεδνός ή (dial. ἅ) όν *adj.* **1** (of persons, their attitudes) **loyal, faithful** Hom. Hes. hHom. A. B. E.; (of an army, its service to the nation) A.; (of a seer, helmsman, the steering of a city) **trusty, reliable** A. Pi. E.
2 (of persons, the gods, their traits or achievements) **noble, good** Hes. A. Pi.
3 (of advice) **reliable, helpful** A.; (of deeds, events) **beneficial, positive** S. E.; (of news) **welcome** A. E.
4 (of persons) **beloved, dear** Hom. Hes. hHom. Pi. B. E.

κεδρίη ης *Ion.f.* [κέδρος] **cedar-oil** (used in embalming) Hdt.

κέδρινος η ον *adj.* (of a chamber, chest, couch, the framework of a palace) **of cedar-wood** Il. E. Theoc. Plb.

κεδρίς ίδος *f.* **juniper berry** Ar.

κέδρος ου *f.* **1 cedar tree** Hdt.
2 cedar-wood Od. Hes.*fr.* Hdt. E. Theoc.*epigr.*
3 (specif.) **cedar-wood chest** (esp. as a coffin) E. Theoc.

κεδρωτός ή όν *adj.* (of the timbers of a building) **of cedar-wood** E.

κειάμενος (ep.aor.mid.ptcpl.), **κείαντο** (ep.3pl.aor.mid.): see καίω

κείαται (Ion.3pl.mid.pass.), **κείατο** (ep.3pl.impf.): see κεῖμαι

κεῖθεν *adv.*, **κεῖθι** *adv.*: see ἐκεῖθεν, ἐκεῖθι

κεῖμαι *mid.pass.vb.* | 3pl. κεῖνται, Ion. κέαται, also κείαται, ep. κέονται | 3sg.subj. κέηται, ep. κεῖται, 3sg.opt. κέοιτο | imperatv. κεῖσο, 3sg. κείσθω | ptcpl. κείμενος | impf. ἐκείμην, dial. κείμᾱν, 3pl. ἔκειντο, Ion. ἐκέατο, ep. κέατο, also κείατο | 3sg.iteratv.impf. κέσκετο | fut. κείσομαι, dial. κεισεῦμαι ‖ The sections are grouped as: (1–4) be recumbent or prostrate, (5–13) lie or be situated, (14–15) lie idle or undisturbed, (16) be stored away, (17–22) be laid down or established. |
1 (of persons, animals) **be recumbent, lie down** (oft. W.PREP.PHR. on the ground, in a place, in a certain position) Hom. +; (of a Titan) **lie stretched out** —W.PREP.PHR. *over a huge distance* Od.
2 (specif.) **lie asleep, lie down to sleep** Od. +
3 lie dead Hom. + —W.PREP.PHR. *in the underworld* Pi. S. E.; **lie buried** (oft. W.PREP.PHR. in a tomb, in a particular place) Od. +
4 lie prostrate (fr. sickness, old age, a blow to the head, or sim.) Hom.; (of a wall) **be broken down** —w. ὑπό + GEN. *by time* Hdt.; (fig., of persons, their spirits, things) **be brought low** (by disaster, suffering, or sim.) Od. +
5 (of objects) **lie, sit** (oft. W.ADV. or PREP.PHR. in a particular place) Hom. +
6 (of buildings, cities, islands, or sim.) **be situated** —W.ADV., PREP.PHR. or INTERN.ACC. *in a particular location* Od. +
7 (of emotions) **sit, lie** —W.PREP.PHR. *in someone's heart* Od. Sol.; (of an outcome) **rest** —W.PREP.PHR. *in the lap of the gods* Hom.
8 (of objects) **sit** (on top), **rest** —W.PREP.PHR. *on sthg.* Hes. +
9 (of a sword, a stone) **sit suspended, hang** —W.PREP.PHR. *around someone's shoulders, over someone's head* Hes. Alc.
10 (of persons, success, situations) **be dependent, depend** —W.DAT. or PREP.PHR. *on a person, a god* Archil. Pi. S.
11 (of a person) **be subject** —W.PREP.PHR. *to necessity* E.
12 (of persons) **remain, stay** —W.PREP.PHR. *in a place* Hom. +; (of persons or things) —W.PTCPL. or PREP.PHR. *in a particular condition* Hom. +
13 (of persons) **reside** —W.ACC. *in a certain place* S.
14 lie or **sit idle** Il. —W.ACC. *w. resting feet* E.*fr.*; (of an evil) **lie dormant** S.
15 (of persons or things) **lie undisturbed, be at rest** A. Pl.; (of a bow, a shield) **lie unused** Hom.; (of a person, corpse, dog, objects) **lie neglected** Hom. Semon.
16 (of valuable objects) **be stored away** —W.PREP.PHR. *in a place* Hom. +; (of money) **be deposited** (sts. W.PREP.PHR. in a fund or bank) Ar. Isoc. —W.DAT. *for someone* Thphr.; (fig., of a benefit) **be stored up** —W.DAT. *for someone* Th. Pl.
17 be laid down or **established**; (of laws) **be laid down** E. +; (of penalties) **be stipulated** or **prescribed** E. Th. Lys.; (of customs duties) —W.DAT. *to someone* (*i.e. to pay them*) D.; (of an end or outcome) **be fixed** or **determined** Sol. +
18 (gener.) **be put forward**; (of valuables, money, or sim.) **be offered** (as a prize or reward, oft. W.PREP.PHR. in a contest) Il. +; (of a contest) **be set up, be organised** S.; (of ideas, arguments) **be set out** Arist.
19 (wkr.sens., of victory, supremacy) **reside** —W.DAT. *w. someone* Pi. S.
20 be established as true; (of facts, propositions) **be established** or **agreed upon** Pl.
21 be in established use; (of a name, a term) **be in use** (as a designation) —W.DAT. *for a person, place, thing* Hdt. Ar. Pl. X. —w. ἀπό + GEN. *because of a certain fact* Arist.; (specif., of a name) **be given** —W.DAT. *to a girl* (w. ὑπό + GEN. *by her father*) Is.
22 have an established and continuing existence; (specif., of a will) **continue to apply, be valid** —W.DAT. *for someone* Is.; (of a person, i.e. his name) **be** —W.PREP.PHR. *on men's lips* Thgn.; (of things, situations) **be, exist** (sts. W.ADV. in a certain condition) —W.DAT. *for people* S. +

κειμᾶν (dial.impf.mid.pass.): see κεῖμαι

κειμήλιον ου *n.* [reltd. κεῖμαι] (usu.pl.) **precious object kept in store** (in a house or sim.), **treasure, valuable possession** Hom. Hes.*fr.* Xenoph. Hdt. S. E.*fr.* Pl. +; (fig., ref. to good advice, noble deeds, a patron goddess) E.

—**κειμήλιος** ᾱ ον *adj.* (fig., of aged relatives) **kept as a prized possession** (in a house) Pl.

κεινός *Ion.adj.*: see κενός

κεῖνος *demonstr.pron. and adj.*: see ἐκεῖνος

κείνως *demonstr.adv.*: see under ἐκεῖνος

κείομεν (ep.1pl.aor.subj.), **κεῖον** (ep.aor.imperatv.): see καίω

Κεῖος *adj.*: see under Κέως

κειρίᾱ ᾱς *f.* **1** (sg. and pl.) **bedstead made of knotted cords, rope bed** Ar. Plu.

κειρύλος

2 strip of cloth used as a bandage, **wrapping** (to bind the hands and feet of a corpse) NT.

κειρύλος ου *m.* [κείρω, w. play on κηρύλος *kingfisher*] **kingsnipper** (an invented name for a bird, w.connot. of its being a barber) Ar.

κείρω *vb.* | fut. κερῶ, Ion. κερέω | aor. ἔκειρα, ep. ἔκερσα, also κέρσα, inf. κεῖραι ‖ MID.: dial.imperatv. κείρευ | aor. ἐκειράμην, ep. ἐκερσάμην ‖ PASS.: aor. ἐκέρθην | aor.2 ἐκάρην, 3sg.subj. καρῇ ‖ MID.PASS.: pf. κέκαρμαι, inf. κεκάρθαι |
1 cut off —*beams, branches* Il. S.; (of a boar) **cut through** (w. its tusks) —*the sinews of a man's leg* AR.
2 (of Ajax) create by slashing, **slash out** —W.INTERN.ACC. *a slaughter of beasts* S.
3 cut off, shave off —*one's hair* (esp. in mourning) Il. Thgn. Hdt.; (of dead warriors) **cause the cutting of** —*their wives' hair* E.; (fig., of city walls) **shear off** —*a child's hair* (i.e. cause it to be sheared off by impact w. the ground when he is thrown fr. them) E. ‖ MID. **cut off, shave off** —*one's hair, beard, moustache* (esp. in mourning, sts. w. ἐπί + DAT. *for someone*) Hom. Archil. A. Hdt. E. Call. +; (of Eros) **have** (W.ACC. his wings) **clipped** Call.*epigr.* ‖ PASS. (of hair) be shorn off Pi. E.
4 cut the hair off, shave —*oneself* (esp. in mourning) Hdt. Plu.; **cut the mane off, crop** —*horses* Hdt. Plu.; **shear** —*a sheep* NT. ‖ MID. **cut the hair off** —*oneself, one's head* NT. Plu.; (intr.) **cut off one's hair** Il. Hdt. E. Lys. +; (gener.) **have one's hair cut** —W.ACC. or ADV. *in a certain way* Hdt. Thphr. Call. Theoc. Plu. ‖ PASS. (of persons, their heads) be shaved E. X. Plu.
5 cut down —*trees, corn* hHom. AR. Plu. —*the Sown Men* (as though corn) AR.; (fig.) **cut, harvest** —*sweet grass* (W.PREP.PHR. *fr. a girl's bed*) Pi. ‖ PASS. (of corn, reeds) be cut or harvested Plb. Plu.
6 cut down the vegetation of a region; level, clear —*a plain, a mountain* (so that troops can pass) Hdt. —*land and sea* (fig.ref. to destroying enemy forces) A.; **lay waste to** —*a place* Hdt. Th. Pl. Plu. ‖ PASS. (of vineyards, farmland, regions) be laid waste Thgn. Hdt.
7 (of a god) **destroy** —*persons* A. S.*fr.*
8 (of vultures, fish, eels) **tear at** —*a person's entrails* Hom.; (of brambles) **scratch** —*Aphrodite* Bion
9 (of a donkey) **eat up** —*corn* Il.; (of unwanted guests) **consume** —*someone's wealth* Od.

κεῖσε *demonstr.adv.*: see ἐκεῖσε

κεισεῦμαι (dial.fut.mid.pass.), **κείσθω** (3sg.imperatv.), **κεῖσο** (2sg.imperatv.), **κείσομαι** (fut.): see κεῖμαι

κείω[1] *ep.vb.* [desideratv. κεῖμαι] | inf. κειέμεν, ptcpl. κείων, also κέων | **wish to lie down in bed, wish to sleep** Od. ‖ PTCPL. (w.vbs. of motion) going to bed Hom.

κείω[2] *vb.* [reltd. κεάζω] **split, chop** (firewood) Od.

κεκαδήσομαι (fut.pf.mid.): see κήδω

κεκαδήσω (ep.redupl.fut.), **κέκαδον** (ep.redupl.aor.2): see χάζω

κεκαδμένος (dial.pf.mid.ptcpl.): see καίνυμαι

κεκάδοντο (ep.3pl.redupl.aor.2 mid.): see ὑποχάζομαι

κεκαθαρμένος (pf.pass.ptcpl.): see καθαίρω

κεκάλυμμαι (pf.pass.): see καλύπτω

κεκαμμένος (pf.pass.ptcpl.): see κάμπτω

κέκαρμαι (pf.mid.pass.): see κείρω

κέκασμαι (pf.mid.), **κέκαστο** (ep.3sg.plpf.mid.): see καίνυμαι

κέκαυμαι (pf.pass.): see καίω

κεκαφηώς *ep.pf.ptcpl.* [perh.reltd. ἀποκαπύω] (of a wounded or exhausted person) **gasping out** —*one's spirit* (i.e. having fainted) Hom.

κέκηδα (pf.): see κήδω

κέκλᾱγα (dial.pf.), **κέκλαγγα** (pf.), **κεκλάγξομαι** (fut.pf.mid.): see κλάζω

κέκλαυμαι (pf.mid.pass.): see κλαίω

κεκλέαται (Ion.3pl.pf.pass.), **κεκλήαται** (ep.3pl.pf.pass.), **κεκλήατο** (Ion.3pl.plpf.pass.): see καλέω

κέκλεο (ep.redupl.aor.2 mid.imperatv.), **κέκλευ** (dial.): see κέλομαι

κέκληγα (pf.), **κεκληγών** (ep.pf.ptcpl.): see κλάζω

κεκλήισμαι (ep.pf.pass.): see κληίζω

κέκληκα (pf.), **κέκλημαι** (pf.pass.), **κεκλήσομαι**[1] (fut.pf.pass.): see καλέω

κέκλημαι (Att.pf.pass.), **κεκλήσομαι**[2] (Att.fut.pf.pass.): see κλείω[1]

κέκλικα (pf.), **κέκλιμαι** (pf.pass.): see κλίνω

κέκλομαι *mid.vb.*, **κεκλόμην** (ep.redupl.aor.2 mid.): see κέλομαι

κέκλοφα (pf.): see κλέπτω

κέκλυθι and **κέκλυτε** (2sg. and pl.redupl.athem.aor. imperatv.): see κλύω

κεκμᾱκώς (dial.pf.ptcpl.), **κέκμηκα** (pf.), **κεκμηώς** (ep.pf.ptcpl.): see κάμνω

κέκομμαι (pf.pass.), **κεκοπώς** (ep.pf.ptcpl.): see κόπτω

κεκόρεσμαι (pf.pass.), **κεκόρημαι** (Ion.pf.pass.), **κεκορηότε** (ep.du.pf.ptcpl.): see κορέννυμι

κεκορυθμένος (pf.pass.ptcpl.): see κορύσσω

κεκοτηώς (ep.pf.ptcpl.): see κοτέω

κεκράανται (ep.3sg.pf.pass.): see κραίνω

κέκρᾱγα (pf.): see κράζω

κεκράγματα των *n.pl.* [κράζω] **rantings** (of demagogues) Ar.

κεκραγμός οῦ *m.* **bellowing** (of a crowd) E.

κεκράκτης ου *m.* **ranter** (ref. to a demagogue) Ar.

κέκρᾱμαι (pf.pass.): see κεράννυμι

κέκρανται (3sg.pf.pass.): see κραίνω

κεκραξι-δάμᾱς αντος *m.* [κράζω, δάμνημι, w. play on name Ἀλκιδάμᾱς *Alkidamas*] (ref. to a demagogue) **all-conquering ranter** Ar.

κεκράξομαι (fut.pf.mid.), **κέκραχθι** (pf.imperatv.): see κράζω

κέκρημαι (Ion.pf.pass.): see κεράννυμι

κέκρῑγα (pf.): see κρίζω

κέκρικα (pf.), **κέκριμαι** (pf.pass.): see κρίνω

Κέκροψ οπος *m.* **Kekrops** (mythical founder-king of Athens, sts. described as half-serpent) Hdt. E. Th. Ar. Isoc. Pl. +

—**Κεκροπίδαι** ῶν *m.pl.* **1 descendants of Kekrops, Athenians** Hdt. S.*lyr.fr.* E. Call.; (sg.) Ar.
2 Kekropians (ref. to members of the Kekropian tribe, one of the ten tribes of Athens) D. Plu.

—**Κεκρόπιος** ᾱ (Ion. η) ον *adj.* **1** (of crags, a land, the Agora) **of Kekrops, Kekropian** (i.e. Athenian) E. Men. AR. Plu.(quot.eleg.)
2 ‖ FEM.SB. **land of Kekrops** (ref. to Athens) E. Arist.*eleg.*

—**Κεκροπῆθεν** *Ion.adv.* **from the land of Kekrops** Call. AR.

—**Κεκροπίς** ίδος *fem.adj.* (of a tribe) **Kekropian** Antipho Ar.

κέκρυμμαι (pf.pass.): see κρύπτω

κεκρύφαλος ου *m.* [κρύπτω] **1 hairnet** (worn by women) Il. Ar.
2 bag-shaped net; purse, belly (of a hunting net) X.
3 criss-crossing web, network (of cables, attached to the ropes of a siege-engine) Plu.

4 interlocking straps of a bridle, **headstall, bridle** (for a horse) X.

κεκρύφαται (Ion.3pl.pf.pass.): see κρύπτω

κέκτημαι (pf.mid.): see κτάομαι

κέκυθον (ep.redupl.aor.2): see κεύθω

κελαδεινός ή όν, dial. **κελαδεννός** ἅ όν adj. [κέλαδος] **1** (of the West Wind) **roaring, howling** Il.; (of gorges) **echoing** hHom.; (of words, songs) **resounding** Pi.; (of violent arrogance) **noisy, blustering** Pi.
2 (of the Graces) **resounding, melodious** Pi.
3 (epith. of Artemis) **of the noisy hunt** Il. Hes.fr. hHom.
—**κελαδεινά** neut.pl.adv. **noisily, with echoing roar** —ref. to rivers flowing AR.

κελαδέω contr.vb. | dial.3pl. κελαδέοντι (Pi.) | fut. κελαδήσω, also κελαδήσομαι (Pi.) | aor. ἐκελάδησα, ep. κελάδησα, dial.inf. κελαδέσαι (Pi.) | **1** make a loud or resounding noise; (of waves) **crash** Ar.; (of water) **babble** Sapph.; (of birds) **sing** Stesich. Ar. Theoc.; (of bells, trumpets, a battle-song) **ring out, sound** E.; (tr., of the aulos) **utter** —a sweet sound E.
2 (of persons) **shout, cheer** Il. Theoc.; (of a baby) **cry out** A.; (of Greece) **utter** —a cry E.; (of Apollo) —oracles E.
3 (of poets, singers, Muses, their voices) **sing out** Pratin. —W.PREP.PHR. about heroes, valour Pi.; **sing** —songs, hymns Simon. Pi. B. E.; **sing about, celebrate** (sts. W.DAT. in song) —gods, heroes, victories, or sim. Lyr. A. E. Ar. Tim.

κελάδημα ατος n. **echoing roar** (of winds, rivers) E. Ar.

κελαδῆτις ιδος fem.adj. (of a voice) **resounding** (in song) Pi.

κέλαδος ου m. **1** loud tumult, **uproar** (of battle or sim.) Hom. Hes.
2 clamour, **din** (of shouting, wailing, drunken singing) A. E.; (specif.) **shout, roar** A. S. AR.
3 resounding noise (of music, a lyre, singing, an oracle) Lyr.adesp. A. Pi. E.

κελάδων οντος ptcpl.adj. (of rivers, seas) **echoing, roaring** Il. B. Ar. AR.

κελαιν-εγχής ές adj. [κελαινός, ἔγχος] (epith. of Ares) **with a dark spear** Pi.

κελαι-νεφής ές adj. [νέφος] **1** (epith. of Zeus) **of the dark clouds** Hom. Hes. hHom. Pi.fr.
2 (of plains, darkness) **black-clouded** Pi.
3 (of spilt blood) **dark** Hom.

κελαινό-βρωτος ον adj. [βιβρώσκω] (of Prometheus' liver) **darkened from being eaten** (by Zeus' eagle) A.(dub., cj. κελαινόχρωτος dark-coloured)

κελαινόομαι pass.contr.vb. (fig., of a person's innards) be darkened, **turn black** (w. despair, on hearing sthg. pitiful) A.

κελαινός ή (dial. ἅ) όν adj. **1** dark from the absence of light; (of night, a hiding-place, the underworld) **dark** Il. A. E. AR.; (of eyes) **darkened** (in death) S.
2 dark in colour; (of water, earth, storms, mist, smoke, or sim.) **dark, black** Il. Hes. hHom. Emp. Trag. AR.; (of animals, objects, ships) Il. Trag. AR.; (of weapons, spilt blood) Hom. Hes. S. E. AR.
3 (of Egyptians, Aithiopians) **dark-skinned** A. Theoc.
4 dark and ominous; (of Erinyes) **dark** A.; (w.ACC. in complexion) E.; (of a fierce man's heart) **dark, grim** Hes.

κελαινο-φαής ές adj. [φάος] (of the gloom of night) **dark-gleaming** Ar.(mock-trag.)

κελαινό-φρων ον, gen. ονος adj. [φρήν] **dark-minded, black-hearted** A.

κελαινό-χρως ωτος masc.fem.adj. [χρώς] **dark-coloured**; (fig., of a person's heart) **dismal, black with despair** A.

κελαινόχρωτος adj.: see κελαινόβρωτος

κελαιν-ώψ ῶπος masc.fem.adj. [ὤψ] (of Colchians) **dark-faced, swarthy** Pi.

—**κελαινωπᾶς** ᾶ dial.masc.adj. (of a person's soul) **dark in appearance, black** S.

—**κελαινῶπις** ιδος dial.fem.adj. (of a cloud of mist) **dark in appearance, black** Pi.

κελαρύζω vb. [prob.reltd. κέλαδος] | dial.aor. κελάρυξα (Pi.) | **1** (of water, a stream) **murmur, babble** Il. Theoc.
2 (of blood, milk, wine) **gush forth** hHom. —W.PREP.PHR. fr. a wound, animals' udders Il. Lyr.adesp.; (of water) **stream** or **drip** —W.PREP.PHR. fr. a drenched man's head Od.

κελέβη ης, dial. **κελέβᾱ** ᾶς f. **bowl** (for wine, hot water) Anacr. Call. Theoc.

κελέοντες ων m.pl. **side-beams** (of a loom) Theoc.

κελευθο-ποιός όν adj. [κέλευθος, ποιέω] (of the sons of Hephaistos, ref. to the Athenians) **road-building** (ref. to making a route for Apollo to Delphi) A.

κέλευθος ου f. | nom.pl. κέλευθοι, also neut.nom.acc.pl. κέλευθα | **1** path, road, track Hom. Hes. hHom. Pi. Trag. Hellenist.poet.; (pl., fig., of the sea) Hom. hHom. Pi. AR. Mosch.; (of sleep, travelled by an apparition) A.
2 open path, **passable way** (by which one can travel, esp.ref. to a cleared route on a battlefield) Il. A. Pi. AR.
3 route taken, **path, route, course** (of a person, god, animal) Hom. hHom. Archil. A. Pi. Emp. +; (fig., of a poet or speaker, their words, a report) Pi. B. E. Call.
4 (specif.) marks on the ground left by a walker, **track** hHom.; trail left by a ship, **wake** AR.
5 fixed or habitual route, **course, path** (of the sun, moon, stars, a river) Od. S. E. AR.; (fig., of justice) B.; place which one frequents, **haunt, domain** (of the gods) Il.
6 (fig.) **path** (of righteousness or sim., followed by a person or city) Simon. Pi.; **way** (of life) Emp.
7 route between two points, **route, journey** (ref. to a particular itinerary) Od. B. S. E. AR.
8 route to a particular destination, **way** Call. AR.; (fig.) course of action leading to a particular outcome, **path** (to glory or sim.) Xenoph. Pi. B. E.
9 journey (made by a person, god, ship, horses) Hom. Hes. Thgn. Pi. Trag. AR. +; (specif.) **expedition** (by heroes or sim.) A. AR.
10 act of travelling, **passage** (across a sea) AR.
11 motion, **coursing** (of winds) Hom.
12 characteristic mode of travelling, **way of travelling** (of a blind man) S.; **gait** (of a wolf, ref. to walking on all fours) E.

κέλευσμα, also **κέλευμα**, ατος n. [κελεύω] **1** command, **order** (fr. a general, master, god, city) Trag.
2 shouted command, **signal** (to soldiers, rowers) A. Hdt. E. Th.; **call, command** (to hounds, a horse) S.Ichn. Pl. X.; **cry of summons** (fr. a baby to its nurse) A.
3 shout of encouragement, **exhortation** E.

κελευσμός οῦ m. **1** command, order (fr. a god, a person) E.
2 shout of encouragement, **exhortation** E.

κελευσμοσύνη ης f. **command, order** (fr. a ruler) Hdt.

κελευστής οῦ m. crewman who shouts orders to rowers, **rowing-master, boatswain** E. Th. Ar. Pl. +

κελευστικός ή όν adj. **relating to giving orders to rowers** || FEM.SB. boatswain's art Pl.

κελευτιάω contr.vb. | ep.ptcpl. (w.diect.) κελευτιόων | **shout exhortations, urge on** (warriors in battle) Il.

κελεύω vb. | fut. κελεύσω, ep.inf. κελευσέμεναι | aor. ἐκέλευσα, ep. κέλευσα | pf. κεκέλευκα || pf.pass. κεκέλευσμαι | **1** urge on —persons, horses Hom.; **give shouts**

of encouragement —W.DAT. *to persons* Il.; (wkr.sens.) **call out** —W.DAT. *to persons* Od.
2 urge (someone, to do sthg.) Hdt. Lys. X. —*someone* (W.INF. *to do sthg.*) Th. Lys.; **propose** —W.ACC. + INF. *that sthg. shd. be the case* D.
3 (of persons, one's heart, the law, justice) **command, bid, ask** (someone, to do sthg.) Hom. + —*someone* (usu. W.INF. *to do sthg.*) Hom. +; **order** —*people* (w. ἐπί + ACC. *against a person, to arms*) X. ‖ PASS. (of persons) be ordered (to do sthg.) Hdt. +
4 command —*sthg.* (sts. W.ACC. or DAT. *of someone*) Hom. + —W.ACC. + INF. *that sthg. shd. be the case, that someone shd. do sthg.* Antipho Arist.; **give commands** Il. —W.DAT. *to persons, horses* Hom. Hes. hHom. —(W.INF. *to do sthg.*) Hom. ‖ PASS. (of actions) be ordered Hdt. +
5 (specif., of a boatswain) **call out instructions** —W.DAT. *to rowers* Pl.; **give the signal for** —W.ACC. *a certain course or action* E. ‖ PASS. (of instructions) be shouted (by a boatswain) Th.

κέλης ητος *f.* [κέλλω] **1 fast horse** (for riding), **racehorse, mount** Alcm. Hdt. Lys. Ar. Pl.; (appos.w. ἵππος) Od. Plu.
2 a kind of fast ship, clipper Hdt. Th. Ar. X. Plb.

κελησάμην (dial.aor.1 mid.), **κελήσομαι** (fut.mid.): see κέλομαι

κελητίζω *vb.* [κέλης] **1 ride** —W.DAT. *on horses* Il.
2 (of a woman, in sexual ctxt.) **straddle** (a man) Ar.

κελήτιον ου *n.* [dimin. κέλης] **small fast ship, clipper** Th.

κέλλω *vb.* [reltd. ὀκέλλω] | fut. κέλσω | aor. ἔκελσα | **1** (of sailors) **bring to shore** —*a ship, a person, one's voyage* (sts. W.DAT. or PREP.PHR. *in a particular place*) Od. S. E.; (of a seer) **direct to shore** —*a crew* AR.
2 bring one's ship to land at —*a shore, a city* A. E.
3 (intr., of sailors, ships) **come to shore** Od. AR. —W.DAT. or PREP.PHR. *in a particular place* A. E. AR.
4 (fig., of a person) **find a safe haven** (in a place) A. E.
5 (fig.) **end one's voyage** (i.e. die) E.

κέλομαι, also **κέκλομαι** (AR.) *mid.vb.* | fut. κελήσομαι | dial.2sg.impf. ἐκέλευ (Theoc.) | dial.aor.1 κελησάμην (Pi.) | redupl.aor.2 ἐκεκλόμην, ep. κεκλόμην, imperatv. κέκλεο, dial. κέκλευ (Pi.) |
1 call out Hes. AR. —W.DAT. *to persons, horses* Hom. Hes. hHom. —(W.DIR.SP. *sthg.*) Hom. hHom. Call. —(W.INF. *to do sthg.*) Hom. AR.
2 call upon —*a god* Il. hHom. A. S. AR. —*gods* (W.PREDIC.SB. *as witnesses or by a certain name*) AR.
3 name —*a child* (W.PREDIC.SB. *w. a certain name*) Pi.
4 (of persons, gods, a person's heart, stomach) **give an order** Hom. Simon. —W.INF. *to do sthg.* Hom. Hes. Sapph. AR.; **order, command, bid** —*someone* (usu. W.INF. *to do sthg.*) Hom. Hes. Archil. Alc. A. Pi. +; (of a person's heart) **urge** (him) —w. ἐπί + DAT. *against someone* (i.e. to attack him) Il.
5 (wkr.sens.) **give advice, make a recommendation** Hom. AR. —W.INF. *to do sthg.* AR.; **invite** —*someone* (W.INF. *to do sthg.*) AR. Theoc.
6 (of the sun's rays, the force of kneading) **compel, prompt** (wax, to soften) Od.

Κελτοί ῶν *m.pl.* **Celts** (people of Spain, Gaul, N. Italy and E. Europe, as a population or military force) Hdt. Pl. X. Arist. + ‖ SG. **Celtic man** Plb. | see also Γαλάται
—**Κελτίᾱ** ᾱς *f.* **land of the Celts** (ref. to Gaul and N. Italy) Plb.(treaty)
—**Κελτικός** ή όν *adj.* **1** of or relating to the Celts; (of a people, clothing) **Celtic** Plu.; (of wars) **Celtic, Gallic** Plu.; (of an invasion, the sacking of a city) **by the Celts** Plu. ‖ NEUT.PL.SB. **Celtic invasion** (of Rome, c.387 BC) Plu.
2 ‖ FEM.SB. **territory of the Celts** (in Gaul and N. Italy) Plb. Plu.
—**Κελτός** ή όν *adj.* (of Ares, meton. for a war) **Celtic** Call.

κέλυφος εος (ους) *n.* (pl., fig.ref. to old men serving as jurors) **husk, shell, pod** (W.GEN. *of affidavits*) Ar.

κέλωρ ωρος *m.* **son** E.

κεμαδο-σσόος ον *ep.adj.* [κεμάς, σεύω] (of Artemis) **driving deer in flight, deer-chasing** Call.

κεμάς άδος *f.* **young deer, deer** Il. Call. AR.

κεν *dial.enclit.pcl.*: see ἄν¹

κεν-αγγής ές *adj.* [κενός, ἄγγος] (of weather that prevents sailing) **causing jars to be empty, exhausting one's supplies** A.

κενανδρίᾱ ᾱς *f.* [κένανδρος] **lack of men** (in a city, after war) A.

κέν-ανδρος ον *adj.* [κενός, ἀνήρ] (of a city) **empty of men, lacking menfolk** A. S.

κενεᾱγορίᾱ ᾱς *dial.f.* [ἀγορεύω] **empty talk** (of fools) Lyr.adesp.

κενε-αυχής ές *ep.adj.* [αὔχη] **full of empty boasts, vainglorious** Il.

κενέβρεια ων *n.pl.* **flesh of dead animals, carrion** Ar.

κενεμβατέω *contr.vb.* [κενός, ἐμβαίνω] **step into a hole**; (of birds) **fall into a hole** (in the air, split by a loud noise) Plu.

κενεός, κενεόφρων *ep.adjs.*: see κενός, κενόφρων

κενεών ῶνος *m.* **hollow between the waist and the ribs, flank** (of a person, horse, hound) Hom. X. Theoc.

κενέωσις *dial.f.*: see κένωσις

κενοδοξέω *contr.vb.* [κενόδοξος] (of philosophers) **show conceited pride** —w. περί + ACC. *in invention of paradoxes* Plb.

κενοδοξίᾱ ᾱς *f.* **conceit, vanity** (of a person) Plb.

κενό-δοξος ον *adj.* [κενός, δόξα] **conceited, vain** Plb.

κενολογέω *contr.vb.* [λόγος] **talk emptily, engage in pointless discussion** Arist.

κενός, Ion. **κεινός**, ep. **κενεός**, ή (dial. ᾱ) όν *adj.* **1** (of things) **empty** (of their usual contents); (of containers, ships, houses, tables, a helmet) **empty** Il. Hdt. S. E. Ar. Isoc. +; (of a purse, coffer, treasury) Isoc. Theoc. Plu.; (of a person's belly, mouth) Ar.; (of hands, sts. W.GEN. *of spoils, wealth, weapons*) Od. Hdt. E. Pl. Call.*epigr.* + ‖ NEUT.SB. **empty part** (of a threshing-floor) X.
2 (of persons, objects, places) **devoid** or **bereft** (W.GEN. *of sthg.*) S. E. Pl. X. +; (of a military force, W.GEN. *of allies*) E.
3 (of places, houses, ships, chariots) **empty** (sts. W.GEN. *of people*) Il. hHom. Hdt. S. E. Th. +; (of a bed, chair, fireside, tomb, shroud, bier) Hdt. S. E. Th. X. +; (of a lair, a nest) S. Plu.
4 (of a place in the ranks) **unfilled** Aeschin.
5 (of a writing-tablet) **blank** Hdt.
6 (of a portion of space) **empty** Emp. Pl. ‖ NEUT.SB. **space, gap** (betw. objects) E.; **empty space** Pl.; (specif.) **vacuum** (opp. air) Pl. Plu.; (philos.) **void** (opp. matter) Democr. Arist. Plu.
7 (of persons) **empty-handed** Hom. A. Hdt. S. Pl. X. +; (specif.) **penniless, broke** Men.
8 (of persons) **empty-bellied** (opp. full) X. NT.; (opp. pregnant) Pl. Plu.
9 (of a lioness) **bereft** (of cubs) S.; (of Loves, of Adonis) Bion
10 (of a troubled person's eyes) **blank, joyless** AR.
11 lacking substance; (of boasts, threats, notions, or sim.) **idle, empty** Od. Pi. S. E. Ar. Pl. +; (of pleasures, honours, activities, or sim.) **empty, worthless** E. X. Aeschin. D. +; (of a noise) **meaningless, unimportant** E.; (of goodwill, a marriage, a pretext, or sim.) **sham** E. Aeschin. D. Men. Plu.
12 (of fears) **groundless, baseless** E. X. ‖ NEUT.SB. **false alarm** (in war) Th. Arist. Plb.

13 (of hopes) **futile** Hes. Simon. Pi. Trag. Att.orats. +; (of toils, actions, desires, discussions, joy) **fruitless** Pi. S. E. Isoc. Pl. D. +; (of retching, panting for breath, sea-storms, a bowshot, a spear-throw) **ineffectual** A. E.fr. Th. AR. Plu.; (prep.phr.) διὰ κενῆς *in vain* E. Ar.; *pointlessly, fruitlessly* Th. Arist. Men. Plb.

14 (of persons) devoid of substance or sense, **empty, foolish** Pi. S. E. Plb.

15 (of persons, their ambition, pride) showing empty conceit, **vain** Pi.fr. Pl. Plu.

—**κενά**, ep. **κενεά** *neut.pl.adv.* to no purpose, **in vain** Pi. S. E.fr.

—**κενῶς** *adv.* **1 to no purpose** —*ref. to stating sthg.* Arist.
2 out of vanity —*ref. to saying sthg.* Plu.

κενοταφέω *contr.vb.* [τάφος] give an empty tomb to, **honour with an empty burial** —*a person lost at sea, his body* E.

κενοτάφιον ου *n.* empty tomb, **cenotaph** (for unrecovered war-dead) X.

κενότης ητος *f.* **1 emptiness** (in the soul, ref. to ignorance) Pl.
2 empty space (within a substance) Pl.

κενοφροσύνη ης *f.* [κενόφρων] **vanity, conceit** (of a ruler) Plu.

κενό-φρων, ep. **κενεόφρων**, ον, gen. ονος *adj.* [φρήν] (of persons, the common people) empty-headed, **foolish** Thgn. Pi.fr.; (of plans, a saying) Simon. A.; (of pride) **foolish, vain** Pi.

κενόω *contr.vb.* | aor. ἐκένωσα | **1 make empty; empty** —*temples* (*of contents*) E. —*one's hands* (W.GEN. *of valuables, by giving them away*) E.; (of persons, a hunter, a plague) —*a place* (W.GEN. *of goats, people, by killing them*) A. E. Call.epigr.; (of bad qualities) **purge** —*the soul* (W.GEN. *of good qualities*) Pl. ‖ PASS. (of persons, creatures, their bodies) be empty (fr. hunger or thirst) Pl.; be made empty —w. ὑπό + GEN. *by fire and air* Pl.; (of a space) be left empty (by removal of its contents) Th. Pl. X. Plu.; (of a walled town) be emptied —W.GEN. *of everything* (*by its inhabitants*) Hdt.
2 (of a ruler) render empty of people, **depopulate** —*a region* A. ‖ PASS. (of houses) be rendered empty of people (by a plague) S. Th.; (of ships) be left unmanned Th.
3 render empty by leaving, **vacate** —*a place* E.

κένσαι (ep.aor.inf.), **κέντᾱσα** (dial.aor.): see κεντέω

Κενταύρειος ᾱ ον *adj.* [κένταυρος] (of the race) **of Centaurs** E.

κενταυρικός ή όν *adj.* (of a throng of people) **centaur-like** (in appearance or behaviour) Pl.

—**κενταυρικῶς** *adv.* like a centaur (i.e. fiercely) —*ref. to charging at a door* Ar.

Κενταυρομαχίᾱ ᾱς *f.* [μάχομαι] **battle against the Centaurs** Plu.

κενταυρο-πληθής ές *adj.* [πλῆθος] (of a battle) **against a huge throng of centaurs** E.

κένταυρος ου *m.* **1 centaur** (member of a savage race generally represented as half-man, half-horse; oft. ref. to famous individuals such as Chiron and Nessos) Od. hHom. Pi. B. S. Ar. +
2 ‖ PL. Centaurs (famous for their battle w. the Lapiths) Hom. Hes. Thgn. Xenoph. E. Isoc. +

κενταυρο-φόνος ον *adj.* [θείνω] (of Herakles) **centaur-slaying** Theoc.

κεντέω *contr.vb.* | aor. ἐκέντησα, dial. κέντᾱσα (Theoc.), ep.inf. κένσαι | **1 prick with a goad, apply the goad to** —*a horse* Il. —*a person* (*envisaged as an ox or horse*) Thgn. Ar.
2 prick with a sharp object, **prick, jab** —*a person, his eyes* Hdt. E. Arist. Plu. ‖ PASS. be pricked (esp. as a torture) Th. X.

3 stab with a sword, **stab** —*a person, his neck, the air* S. E. Pl. Plb. ‖ PASS. be stabbed Plu.

4 (of a bee) **sting** —*Eros* Theoc.; (of persons, envisaged as wasps) —*persons, their eyes, fingers* Ar. Pl. ‖ PASS. be stung —W.ACC. *in the mouth and eyes* Ar. —(fig.) *in the face and eyes* (w. ὑπό + GEN. *by clever arguments, envisaged as hornets*) Ar.

5 (of a bed of rock) **prick, chafe** —*Typhon's back* Pi.; (in neg.phr., of a kiss fr. a beardless man) **prickle** Theoc. ‖ PASS. (of the soul) be chafed (by growing feathers) Pl.

κέντημα ατος *n.* sharp tip for stabbing, **point** (of a sword) Plb.

κεντρ-ηνεκής ές *adj.* [κέντρον; ἐνεγκεῖν, see φέρω] (of horses) **driven by** or **enduring the goad** Il.

κεντρίζω *vb.* **1 prod with a goad** —*a person* (*envisaged as a horse*) X.
2 (of love) **spur on** —*a person* (W.INF. *to do sthg.*) X. ‖ PASS. be spurred on —w. ὑπό + GEN. *by competitiveness* X.

κεντρο-δάλητις ιδος *dial.fem.adj.* [δηλέομαι] (of pains) **from the torturing sting** (of a gadfly) A.

κέντρον ου *n.* [κεντέω] **1** pointed stick, **goad** (to drive on horses or cattle) Il. Pi. S. E. Pl. +; (to torture a person) Hdt. Ar.; (ref. to the sting of a gadfly) A.; (to drive on a person) Sol. Thgn. Pl.; (fig., phr.) πρὸς κέντρα λακτίζειν (or sim.) *kick against the pricks* A. Pi. E. NT.
2 that which inflicts pain; **barb** (of slander or sim., fr. someone's tongue) E.; (of suffering) A. S.
3 that which spurs on by causing pain; **goad** (of love, Aphrodite) E.; **pricking** (of desire) Pl.
4 that which spurs on, **goad** (to action) Pi.fr. Trag. Plu.; **stimulating effect** (of songs, a person's charisma) Plu.
5 sting (of a wasp, bee, scorpion) Ar. Pl. D. Call.; (fig., of a person) Pl. Plu.
6 spur (on a cockerel's heel) Plu.
7 pointed implement, **pin** AR.
8 point (of a javelin) Plb.; (pl., of a sea-god's tail-flukes) AR.; **pointed base** (of a spinning-top) Pl.
9 central point, **centre** (of a circle, an arrangement of triangles, mirrors) Pl. Plu.

κεντρόω *contr.vb.* **1 prick with a goad** —*a dead body* Hdt.
2 ‖ PF.PASS. (of drones, fig.ref. to people) have been equipped with a sting Pl.

κέντρων ωνος *m.* (pejor.) **one who deserves** (or bears the marks of) **punishment** or **torture** Ar.

κεντυρίων ωνος *m.* [Lat. *centurio*] **centurion** (officer in the Roman army) Plb.; (as a guard at the cross of Jesus) NT.

κέντωρ ορος *m.* [κεντέω] one who applies the goad; (ref. to a people) **driver, spurrer on** (of horses) Il.(pl.)

κένωμα ατος *n.* [κενόω] **empty area** (in the layout of an army camp) Plb.; **gap** (in a line of troops) Plu.

κένωσις εως, dial. **κενέωσις** ιος *f.* **1 emptiness** (opp. fullness) Pl.
2 emptying (opp. filling) Pl.
3 emptying, flooding (of the sea, over a plain) Pi.

κέοιτο (3sg.opt.), **κέονται** (ep.3pl.): see κεῖμαι

Κέος *dial.f.*: see Κέως

κέπφος ου *m.* a kind of sea-bird (regarded as thoughtless and excitable); (ref. to a person) **gull, booby** Ar. Call.

κεράασθε (ep.2pl.mid.imperatv.): see κεράω¹

κερα-ελκής ές *adj.* [κέρας, ἕλκω] (of oxen) **pulling the plough with the horns** (i.e. wearing a head-yoke) Call. | see κερεαλκής

κεραίᾱ ᾱς, Ion. **κεραίη** ης *f.* **1** that which resembles a horn; **horn, tip** (of a crescent-shaped curve) Plu.

κεραΐζω

2 projecting beam or spar, **yard-arm** (supporting a ship's sail) A. AR. Plb. Plu.; **beam, spar** (of a crane or sim., fr. which sthg. is hung) Th. Plb. Plu.; **projecting spike, side-branch** (of a stake in a palisade) Plb.; (gener.) **beam, log** Th.
3 projecting spur of a mountain, **spur** Plu.
4 small stroke projecting (fr. a letter of the Hebrew alphabet); **hook, serif** (ref. to the smallest detail of a written text) NT.

κεραΐζω vb. **1 sack, pillage** —cities, villages Hom. Hes.fr. Hdt. ‖ PASS. (of cities, a king's chambers) be laid waste Il.; (of marriage beds) be wrecked —W.DAT. by deaths E.
2 **destroy, sink** —ships Hdt. ‖ PASS. (of ships) be sunk Hdt.
3 (of a warrior) **slay and pillage, wreak havoc** (among an enemy) Il.; (tr., of lions) **wreak havoc on, prey on** —sheep-pens, camels, a population Il. Hdt. Theoc.; (of a warrior, a huntress) **kill** —enemies, animals Il. Pi.; (of Zeus) **conquer, bring down** —Typhon Pi.fr.
4 **plunder, carry off** —belongings, helpless victims Hdt.; (intr.) **plunder, steal** Hdt.

κεραϊστής οῦ m. **plunderer, robber** hHom.

κεραίω ep.vb.: see κεράω¹

κεραμεία ᾱς f. [κεραμεύς] manufacture of clay vessels, **art of the potter, pottery** Pl.

κεραμεικός ή όν adj. **1** (of a wheel) of a potter, **potter's** X.
2 ‖ MASC.SB. Potters' Quarter (district in Athens) Th. Ar. Pl. X. Is. Plu.

κεραμεῖον ου n. **potter's workshop** Aeschin.

κεραμεοῦς ᾶ οῦν Att.adj. —also **κεράμεος** ᾱ ον adj. [κέραμος] (of vessels, plates, bricks, a model chariot) made of fired clay, **clay** Pl. X. Plb. Plu.

κεραμεύς έως m. | nom.pl. κεραμῆς | **1** maker of clay vessels, **potter** Il. Hes. Ar. Pl. Arist. Call. +
2 ‖ PL. (specif., at Athens) workers of the Potters' Quarter Ar.; (meton.) Potters' Quarter Pl. Aeschin. D.

κεραμεύω vb. **make pots** Pl.; (tr.) **make, mould** —pots Ar. —(fig.) the state Ar.; (fig.) **make pots out of** —the potter Pl. ‖ PASS. (of a pot) be moulded or made —w. ὑπό + GEN. by a potter Pl.

κεραμεών ῶνος m. earthenware jar, **wine-jar** Ar.

κεραμικός ή όν adj. **1** (of the spinning of a wheel) **of the potter** Ar. ‖ FEM.SB. art of the potter Pl.
2 ‖ NEUT.SB. (collectv.sg.) tiling, tiles (of a roof) Plu.

κεράμινος η ον adj. (of vessels) **earthenware, ceramic** Hdt.

κεράμιον ου n. clay jar, **jar** (for liquids, salted fish) Hdt. Pl. X. D. Men. +

κεραμίς ίδος f. **1** clay tile, **tile** Th. Ar. Pl. X. Plb. Plu.; (made of silver) Plb.; (collectv.sg.) **tiling, tiles** Arist.
2 ‖ ADJ. (of soil) clay Pl.

κέραμος ου m. **1** baked clay, **terracotta** (as the material of pots or sim.) Hdt. Pl.
2 clay jar, **jar** (for wine) Il. Alc. Xenoph.; (of bronze, in which Ares was imprisoned) Il.
3 (collectv.sg.) clay vessels, **pottery, crockery** Hdt. Critias Ar. Men.
4 (collectv.sg.) **tiling, tiles** (of a roof) Th. Ar. X. AR. Plb. Plu.; (pl.) NT. Plu.; (sg., fig.ref. to a tortoise's shell) Ar.

κεραμωτόν οῦ n. **tiled roof** Plb.

κεράννῡμι, also **κεραννύω**, **κίρνημι**, Aeol. **κέρνᾱμι** vb. —also **κιρνάω** contr.vb. | dial.inf. κιρνάμεν, 3pl.imperatv. κιρνάντων, Aeol.ptcpl. κέρναις | aor. ἐκέρασα, ep. κέρασα, κέρασσα ‖ PASS.: aor. ἐκεράθην, also ἐκεράσθην | pf. κέκρᾱμαι, Ion. κέκρημαι ‖ see also κεράω¹, κεραίω |
1 prepare by mixing, **mix** —wine (w. water, for drinking), a bowl of wine Od. Xenoph. Lyr. Ion Hdt. Th. + —nectar, poison Od. Mosch. Plu. —bathwater Od. ‖ MID. **mix** —a bowl of wine, a libation Od. AR. ‖ PASS. (of wine, a honey drink) be mixed or diluted (w. water) E.Cyc. Even. Pl. X. Arist. +; (of ambrosia) Sapph. ‖ IMPERS.PASS. wine is (being) mixed Men. ‖ MASC.PF.PASS.PTCPL.SB. mixed (i.e. diluted) wine Ar. Arist. Plu.
2 create by blending, **put together, concoct** —men's characters or souls Pl.; **devise** —a boast, an argument, a constitution Pi. Pl. Plu. ‖ PASS. (of foam) be created by mixing, be whipped up Pi.
3 (of persons, gods, destiny, time, circumstances) **blend together, combine** —different things, qualities Pl. Plu. —a thing or quality (W.DAT. or πρός + ACC. w. sthg.) E. Pl. Plu. ‖ PASS. (of things, substances, entities) be combined or mixed together (sts. W.DAT. or PREP.PHR. w. sthg.) Pi. E. Pl. D. Arist. Plu.; be a combination (of different things or qualities) A. Th. Pl. X.
4 (of a bitter spring) mingle with, **contaminate** —a river Hdt.
5 ‖ PASS. be present as an admixture; (of sickness, old age, friendship, profit) be present (usu. W.DAT. in a person or thing) Pi. E. Pl.
6 (of persons) **mix, infuse** —a spring (W.DAT. w. wine, honey) X. Plu. ‖ PASS. (of persons) be infused —W.DAT. w. youthfulness, nobility Pi. Pl.; (of a region) —w. darkness Pl.
7 render softer by dilution; (of persons) **temper** —their rough nature Plb.; (of Peace) —people's minds (W.DAT. w. gentler feelings) Ar. ‖ PASS. (of a person's nature) be tempered —W.DAT. by certain attributes Plu.
8 ‖ PASS. (of seasons, the climate of a place, persons, a political system) be constituted or tempered (oft. W.ADV. in a certain way) Hdt. Pl. X. Arist. Plu.; (of persons, their spirit or body, a political constitution) be suited —w. πρός + ACC. for sthg. Arist. Plu.

κεραο-ξόος ον adj. [κέρας, ξέω] (of a craftsman) carving horn, **working with horn** Il.

κεραός ά́ (Ion. ή) όν adj. **1** (of animals) **horned** Hom. Hes. Hellenist.poet.; (of the crescent moon) Mosch.
2 (of walls) **made of horn** Call.

κέρας αος (contr. ως, Ion. εος, Att. ᾱτος) n. | dat. κέρα (Il. Th.), Att. κέρατι, Ion. κέρεϊ ‖ PL.: nom.acc. κέρᾱτα, Ion. κέρεα, ep. κέρα (always before vowel, perh. κέρα') | dat. κέρασι, ep. κεράεσσι, Att. κέρᾱσι, poet. κεράασι (AR.) |
1 horn (of an animal) Hom. hHom. Hdt. S. E. Ar. +; (pl., of a lyre) E.; (sg., W.GEN. of Amaltheia, ref. to the Horn of Plenty) Anacr. Philox.Leuc.; (of salvation, fig.ref. to a strong ruler) NT.; (fig.phr., of a poet) ἐς κέρας θυμοῦσθαι put anger into one's horns (i.e. rage angrily) Call.
2 vessel made from a hollowed animal horn, **drinking-horn** Pi.fr. Philox.Leuc. X. Plu.
3 trumpet made from a hollowed animal horn, **horn** (esp. for giving signals in battle) X. Plu.
4 bow (as made fr. or resembling a horn) Call.epigr. Theoc.
5 (sg. and pl.) **horn** (as a material) Od.; (ref. to the Gates of Horn, through which true dreams pass, opp. the Gates of Ivory, for false ones) Od. Pl.; (as exemplifying a hard material) Od. Thphr.
6 piece of horn (as part of a fish-hook) Hom.
7 hairstyle resembling a horn, **cornate hair** Il.
8 branch (of a river) Hes. Pi.fr. Th. AR.; τὸ Κέρας the Horn (ref. to the Golden Horn, the inlet of the Bosporos at Byzantium) Plb.
9 horn (of the crescent moon) AR.(pl.)
10 peak (of a mountain) X.; **tip** (of a pole) Plb.
11 wing (of an army or fleet) A. Hdt. E. Th. Ar. X. +; (prep.phrs.) κατὰ κέρας in the flank (ref. to attacking, being

attacked) X. Plb. Plu.; ἐπὶ κέρας *to the wing* (ref. *to wheeling round*) X. Plb.; *in column, in a line* (ref. *to marching, sailing*) Hdt.; (also) ἐπὶ κέρως Th. X.

12 column, line (of troops or ships) X.

κερασ-βόλος ον *adj.* [βάλλω] (of seeds) struck by the hoof (of a farm animal, supposedly rendering them tough and resistant to boiling); (fig., of persons) **stubborn, inflexible** Pl.

κέρασσα (ep.aor.): see κεράννυμι

κεράστης ου *m.* [κέρας] **1 horned one** (ref. to a ram) E.*Cyc.*
2 ∥ ADJ. (of a deer, a beetle) **horned** S.

κεραστίς ίδος *fem.adj.* (of Io, transformed into a cow) **horned** A.

κερασ-φόρος ον *adj.* [φέρω] (of animals, Io) having horns, **horned** E. Pl.

κεράτινος η ον *adj.* (of plectrums, cups) **made of horn** Pl. X.

κεράτιον ου *n.* [dimin. κέρας] **1** trumpet made from a hollowed animal horn, **horn, cow-horn** Plb.
2 seed-pod of the carob tree, **carob-pod** NT.

κερατό-φωνος ον *adj.* [φωνή] (of a chord played on a stringed instrument) sounding like a horn, **resounding** Telest. [or perh. *struck w. a horn plectrum*]

κερατώδης ες *adj.* (of a hill) horned, **peaked** Call.

κεραυν-εγχής ές *adj.* [κεραυνός, ἔγχος] (epith. of Zeus) having a lightning-bolt as a spear, **wielding the lightning-bolt** B.

κεραύνιος ᾱ ον (also ος ον) *adj.* **1** (of death, a strike) **from a lightning-bolt** A. E. Call.; (of the fire, light) **of a lightning-bolt** E.
2 (of persons) **struck by a lightning-bolt** S. E.

κεραυνο-βίας ᾱ *dial.masc.adj.* [βίᾱ] (epith. of Zeus) **mighty with the lightning-bolt** B.*fr.*

κεραυνοβολέω *contr.vb.* [κεραυνοβόλος] (of Zeus) **hurl the lightning-bolt** Plu.

κεραυνο-βόλος ον *adj.* [βάλλω] (of thunder) **striking with the lightning-bolt** E.

κεραυνο-βρόντης ου *masc.adj.* [βροντή] (epith. of Zeus) **thundering with the lightning-bolt** Ar.

κεραυνός οῦ *m.* **thunderbolt, lightning-bolt** (esp. as the weapon of Zeus) Hom. Hes. Lyr.adesp. Pi. Hdt. Trag. +; (fig., ref. to the weapon of Perikles' tongue) Plu.

κεραυνο-φαής ές *adj.* [φάος] (of the fire) **of a blazing lightning-bolt** E.

κεραυνο-φόρος ον *adj.* [φέρω] (of Eros, a king in a painting) **wielding the lightning-bolt** Plu.

κεραυνόω *contr.vb.* (of Zeus, the gods) **strike with a lightning-bolt** —*the race of giants, proud creatures* Hdt. Pl. ∥ PASS. be struck by a lightning-bolt Hes. Pi. Pl. Plu.

κεραύνωσις εως *f.* striking by lightning, **lightning-strike** Plu.

κεράω[1] *ep.contr.vb.* —also **κεραίω** *ep.vb.* [κεράννυμι] ∣ MID.: 2pl.imperatv. (w.diect.) κεράασθε, 3pl.subj. κέρωνται ∣ 3pl.impf. (w.diect.) κερόωντο ∣ (act. and mid.) **mix together, mix** —*wine* (w. *water, for drinking*) Hom. ∥ PASS. (of different races of creatures) be mingled together Emp.

κεράω[2] *contr.vb.* [κέρας] (of troops) **position oneself on the wings** (of an army) Plb.

Κέρβερος ου *m.* **Cerberus** (monstrous canine guardian of the underworld) Hes. Ar. Isoc. Pl. +

κερδαίνω *vb.* [κέρδος] ∣ fut. κερδανῶ, Ion. κερδανέω ∣ aor. ἐκέρδᾱνα, also ἐκέρδηνα (Hes. Hdt.), ἐκέρδησα (Hdt. NT.) ∥ MID.: fut. κερδήσομαι (Hdt.) ∣
1 make a profit Hdt. S. Th. Ar. Att.orats. + —W.ACC. *of a certain nature, size or amount* Hes. Hdt. S.*fr.* Ar. Att.orats. +; **gain, accrue** —W.COGN.ACC. *profit* S. Pl.

2 gain, win —*praise, fame, victory, a benefit, a change in circumstances* Pi. S. E. Lys. Pl. + —*tears, injury, loss* E. NT.; **win over** —*persons, their hopes* Plb. NT.; **save oneself, avoid** —*a long voyage* Plu.

3 gain advantage, benefit (fr. sthg.) S. E. Ar. Att.orats. + —W.DAT. *fr. sthg.* A. Hdt. E. —W.PTCPL. *by doing sthg.* A. Hdt. E. Th. Ar. Pl. ∥ MID. gain for oneself, **gain** —*some benefit, nothing* Hdt.

κερδαλέος ᾱ (Ion. η) ον, contr. **κερδαλοῦς** ῆ οῦν (Archil.) *adj.* **1** (of persons, their words, thoughts) **crafty, cunning** Od. hHom. Call.; (of a fox) Archil. Pl.; (of plans, words) **shrewd, astute** Il. AR.

2 (of persons, gods) concerned only with personal gain, **avaricious** hHom. Arist.

3 (of things, actions, circumstances) **profitable, lucrative** Ar. Isoc. Pl. X. ∥ NEUT.SB. personal gain Plu.

4 (gener.) **advantageous, beneficial** A. Pi. Hdt. Th. Isoc. + —**κερδαλέως** *adv.* ∣ compar. κερδαλεώτερον ∣ **for personal advantage** Th.; **profitably** X.

κερδαλεό-φρων ον, gen. ονος *adj.* [φρήν] **1 crafty-minded** Il.
2 thinking only of personal gain, **greedy-minded** Il.

κερδίων ον *compar.adj.* (of circumstances, options, the truth) more advantageous, **better** Hom. Stesich. Pi. Hdt.(oracle) S. AR. Theoc.; (without compar. force) **advantageous, profitable** Hom. ∣ see also κῡδίων, under κύδιστος

—**κέρδιστος** η ον *superl.adj.* **1** (of a person) **most crafty** Il.
2 (of an option) most advantageous, **best** A.

κέρδος εος (ους) *n.* **1** ∥ PL. wiles, craftiness Hom.
2 (sg. and pl.) **desire for profit** Thgn. Lyr. A. E. Th. Att.orats. +
3 financial or material gain, **profit, reward** Od. Hes. Archil. Alc. Eleg. Pi. +
4 benefit, advantage Hom. Hes. Thgn. Pi. B. Hdt. +

κερδοσύνη ης *f.* **guile, cunning** Hom. AR.

κερδώ όος *f.* ∣ acc. κερδώ ∣ dat. κερδοῖ ∣ **fox** Pi.(cj.); (fig., ref. to a cunning person) Ar.

κέρεα (Ion.nom.acc.pl.): see κέρας

κερε-αλκής ές *Ion.adj.* [κέρας, ἀλκή] (of a bull) **strong-horned** AR.(v.l. κεραελκής)

κέρεϊ and **κέρεος** (Ion.dat. and gen.): see κέρας

κερέω (Ion.fut.): see κείρω

κερκιδο-ποιική ῆς *f.* [κερκίς, ποιέω] **art of making pin-beaters** Arist.

κερκίζω *vb.* (of a weaver) **bring together the weft-threads** (on a loom, w. a pin-beater) Pl.; (of a pin-beater) Pl. Arist.

κερκίς ίδος *f.* **1** pointed rod for bringing together the weft-threads (on a loom), **pin-beater** (as the characteristic tool of the weaver, sts. interpr. as *shuttle*) Hom. Lyr.adesp. S. E. Ar. Pl. +; (envisaged as a bard, fr. the twanging sound which it produced fr. the warp-threads) Ar.(quot. E.)
2 comb (for the hair) AR.
3 shin (of a person) AR. Plu.
4 aspen tree Call.

κερκιστικός ή όν *adj.* of or relating to the pin-beater ∥ FEM.SB. art of weaving Pl.

κέρκος ου *f.* **1 tail** (of an animal) E.*fr.* Ar. Pl. Plu.
2 penis Ar.

κέρκουρος ου *m.* a kind of ship, **galley** Hdt.

κερκύδιλος *m.*: see κροκόδειλος

Κέρκῡρα (also **Κόρκυρα** Isoc.) ᾱς (Ion. ης), Boeot. **Κόρκουρα** ᾱς *f.* **Corcyra** (island off the W. coast of Greece, mod. Corfu) Hdt. Th. Att.orats. X. Call. +; (as the name of its mythol. foundress) Corinn. AR.

—**Κερκῡραῖος** ᾱ ον *adj.* **1** (of persons) **from Corcyra, Corcyraean** D.; (of ships) Plu.; (of wings, fig.ref. to a large whip of the type carried by officials fr. the island) Ar.; (of a settlement) **on Corcyra** Call. || MASC.PL.SB. Corcyraeans (as a population or military force) Hdt. Th. X. D. Plb. Plu.
2 || FEM.SB. Corcyra Th.(dub.)
—**Κερκῡραϊκός** ή όν *adj.* || NEUT.PL.SB. events on Corcyra Th.

Κέρκωψ ωπος *m.* **1** || PL. Kerkopes (mischievous dwarfs defeated and captured by Herakles) Hdt.
2 (colloq., pejor.ref. to a person) **Kerkops** Aeschin.

κέρμα ατος *n.* [κείρω] small cut piece; (pl. and collectv.sg.) **coins of low value, loose change** Ar. NT. Plu.

κερματίζω *vb.* (fig., of persons, fire) **cut up into small pieces** —*things, concepts* Pl. || PASS. (of things, substances, concepts) be cut up into small pieces Pl.

κερμάτιον ου *n.* [dimin. κέρμα] (collectv.sg.) **loose change** (as a sum of money) Men. Plu.(sts.pl.)

κερματιστής οῦ *m.* **money-changer** NT.

κέρνᾱμι *Aeol.vb.*: see κεράννῡμι

κερο-βάτᾱς ᾱ *dial.masc.adj.* [κέρας, βαίνω] (of Pan) walking on horn, **with hooves of horn** Ar.

κερό-δετος ον *adj.* [δέω¹] (of bows) **bound with horn** (i.e. strengthened w. strips of it) E.

κερόεις εσσα εν, contr. **κερούς** οῦσσα οῦν *adj.* (of animals, Io) having horns or antlers, **horned** Anacr. Pi.*fr.* E. Call.

κερο-πλάστης ου *m.* [πλάσσω] one who dresses hair in the shape of horns, **hairstylist** Archil.

κεροτυπέω *contr.vb.* [τύπτω] butt with the horns || PASS. (fig., of ships) be buffeted —W.DAT. *by a tempest* A.

κερουλκός όν *adj.* [ἕλκω] (of a bow) **horn-drawn** E. | cf. κερόδετος

κερουτιάω *contr.vb.* [κερόεις] toss one's horns or antlers; (fig., of a personif. populace, flattered by an orator) **preen oneself, strut around proudly** Ar.

κερουχίς ίδος *fem.adj.* [κέρας, ἔχω] (of goats) having horns, **horned** Theoc.

κερο-φόρος ον *adj.* [φέρω] (of cows) having horns, **horned** E.

κερόωντο (ep.3pl.impf.mid.): see κεράω¹

κέρσα (ep.aor.): see κείρω

κερτομέω *contr.vb.* [κέρτομος] **1 mock** —*a person, a god, Bacchic rites* Od. hHom. A. E. AR. —*someone* (w. ὡς + COMPL.CL. *as being guilty of sthg.*) hHom. —(perh. w. 2ND ACC. *for sthg.*) Pi.*fr.* —(W.PREDIC.ADJ. *as being such and such*) Theoc.; (intr.) **mock, jeer** Hom. Hes. hHom. S. E. AR. —w. ἐπί + DAT. *at the dead* Archil. || PASS. (of a country) be mocked —W.PREDIC.ADJ. *as being reckless* E.
2 provoke —*wasps* Il.

κερτόμησις εως *f.* **mockery** S.

κερτομίη ης *Ion.f.* **mocking and insulting speech, mockery, taunting** Hom. AR.

κέρτομος, also **κερτόμιος**, ον *adj.* (of words, choruses, anger) **mocking, insulting** Hom. Lyr.adesp. Hdt. S.; (of the infant Hermes) **insolent** hHom.; (of a joy) **delusive** E.
|| NEUT.PL.SB. taunts Od. Hes. AR.

κερχνής ῆδος *f.* **kestrel** Ar.

κέρχνος ου *m.* [reltd. κέγχρος] app., millet seed, **millet** S.Ichn.

κέρχνωμα ατος *n.* app. **embossed rim** (of a shield) E.(cj., for κέγχρωμα)

κερῶ (fut.): see κείρω

κέρωνται (ep.3pl.mid.subj.): see κεράω¹

κέρως (gen.): see κέρας

κέσκετο (3sg.iteratv.impf.mid.pass.): see κεῖμαι

κεστός ή όν *adj.* [κεντέω] (of Aphrodite's breast-band) **embroidered** Il. || MASC.SB. embroidered band (of Aphrodite) Call. Bion

κέστρᾱ ᾱς *f.* a kind of fish; **barracuda** Ar. [or perh. *pike*]

κευθάνω *vb.* [κεύθω] **hide, conceal** (a person) Il.

κευθμός οῦ *m.* **1** || PL. hollow depths (of the sea, the earth) Il. AR.
2 secret hollow, hiding-place Call.

κευθμών ῶνος *m.* **1** hollow depths, **depths** (of Tartaros, the dead, ref. to the underworld) A. E.; (of the sea) A.*satyr.fr.*
2 secret hollow, hiding-place (in a cave, the earth) Od. Hes.; **lair, den** (of a monster or animal) Hes. AR.; **sty, stall** (of a pig) Od.
3 cave, hollow (in a rock, the earth) hHom. Stesich. Pi.*fr.* AR.; (as the site of a shrine) A. E.*Cyc.*
4 valley, glen (in a mountainous region) Pi. Hdt.(oracle) E.

κεῦθος εος *n.* **1** || PL. hollow depths (of the earth, usu.ref. to the underworld) Hom. Hes. hHom. Thgn. A. Pi.; (sg., W.GEN. of the dead, ref. to the underworld) S.; (sg., of the sea) AR.
2 secret hollow, hiding-place A. E.*fr.*
3 recess, innermost part (of a house) E.

κεύθω *vb.* | fut. κεύσω | ep.aor.2 κύθον | ep.redupl.aor.2 κέκυθον | pf. κέκευθα | ep.3sg.plpf. κεκεύθει | **1** (of persons) **hide from view, hide, conceal** —*an object* Hes.*fr.* Ion; (of a cave, the earth, wreaths, a folded writing-tablet) **contain secretly, conceal** —*someone or sthg.* Hes. hHom. E. || PASS. (of a tripod) lie hidden —W.DAT. *in the earth* AR.
2 (of persons, their minds) **conceal, keep secret** (opp. reveal) —*emotions, thoughts, plans, news, facts* Hom. hHom. Trag. AR.; **repress** —*tears, laughter* Od. A.
3 keep (W.ACC. someone) **in the dark** (about sthg.) Od. hHom. AR.
4 (of earth, a funerary urn) **conceal, contain** —*a dead person, ashes* Od. Trag. Th.(quot.epigr.) Aeschin.(quot. Il.) || PASS. (of a person) lie hidden —W.DAT. *in Hades* Il.
5 (wkr.sens., of persons, a city) **harbour, have** —*a plan, an idea, hatred, understanding* Od. E.
6 (of houses, a city, ship, the world, or sim.) **contain** —*persons, animals, things* Hom. Hes.*fr.* S. E.
7 (intr., of a location, the moon) **be hidden** S. AR.
8 (of a dead person, his qualities) **lie hidden** —W.PREP.PHR. *in Hades* S.; **lie buried** A. —W.PREP.PHR. *in the ground* A. S.
9 (of blood) **be contained** (within the body) Emp.

κεφαλά *dial.f.*, **κεφάλᾱ** *Aeol.f.*: see κεφαλή

κεφάλαιον ου *n.* [κεφαλή] **1 head** (of an animal, as a cooked dish) Philox.Leuc.
2 bulb (of a radish) Ar.
3 highest point (of a location) X.
4 that which crowns, **culmination** (of a series of deeds, injustices, or sim.) Att.orats. Plb.
5 conclusion, upshot (of an argument, a discussion) Is. Arist.; **end result** (of a situation) Att.orats.
6 that which is most important; **chief item** (in a series of questions) Pl.; **key function** (of persons, an army, rhetoric, education) Pl. D.; **chief intention** (of persons, their actions) Plu.; **key passage, extract** (fr. a poet's works) Pl.; **chief point** (of a story, agreement, accusation, discussion, text) Pi. Th. Att.orats. Pl. +; **chief** (of a group of demagogues; ref. to the large-headed Perikles, w. play on *head*) Plu.(quot.com.)
7 that which summarises, **summary statement** Aeschin. Plb.; (prep.phrs.) ἐν κεφαλαίῳ (or κεφαλαίοις) *in summary* Th. Att.orats. Pl. X. Arist. Plb.; (also) ἐπὶ κεφαλαίου (or κεφαλαίων) Att.orats. Arist. Plb.

8 sum total (of money, troops, years, threats, houses) Lys. Pl. D. Thphr. Plb. Plu.
9 capital sum (of money, oft. opp. interest) Pl. Aeschin. D. NT. Plu.
—**κεφάλαιος** ᾱ ον *adj.* (of a poetic phrase) **crowning, momentous** (w. play on being head-breaking to an opponent) Ar.
κεφαλαιόω *contr.vb.* (of speakers) describe in summarised form, **sum up** —*disadvantages, a type of person* Th. Pl.(mid.); (intr.) Th. ‖ PASS. (of causes) be summarised Arist.
κεφαλαιώδης ες *adj.* (of verbal accounts or descriptions) in summary form, **summarised** Plb.
—**κεφαλαιωδῶς** *adv.* **summarily, in summary form** Arist. Plb.
κεφαλαίωμα ατος *n.* **sum total** (of people) Hdt.
κεφαλ-αλγής ές *adj.* [κεφαλή, ἄλγος] (of foodstuffs) **causing a headache** X.
κεφαλή ῆς, dial. **κεφαλά** ᾶς, Aeol. **κεφάλᾱ** ᾶς *f.* | ep.gen.dat.sg.pl. κεφαλῆφι | **1 head** (of a person, god, monster, animal, statue) Hom. Hes. Eleg. Lyr. Hdt. Trag. +; (as the ruler of the body) Pl. Plu.; (prep.phrs.) ἐπὶ κεφαλήν *headfirst, headlong* Hdt. Pl. Men. Plu.; *impetuously* Hyp. D.; κατὰ κεφαλήν *overhead, from above* X. Plb.; (also) ἐκ κεφαλῆς Plu.
2 (prep.phr.) εἰς κεφαλήν *on one's head* (*in ctxts. of punishment, disaster or responsibility falling on a person*) Od. Hdt. E. Ar. Pl. D. +
3 head of hair; (phr.) κεφαλὴ περίθετος *artificial hair, wig* Ar.
4 head (meton. for a person's mind) Pi. Ar.
5 head (meton. for life, esp. as put at risk) Hom. B. Hdt. Pl. Plu.
6 head (meton. for a person, god or monster, sts. in voc., esp. w.adj.) Hom. Hes. Pi. Hdt. E. +; (meton. for a person, in a count) Hdt.; (prep.phr.) κατὰ κεφαλήν *per head, per person* Arist.
7 (meton. for stature) κεφαλῇ *in height* (*ref. to being taller or shorter*) Il.; (as a unit of measurement) *by a head* (*ref. to being taller*) Pl.; (*ref. to beating someone in a race*) X.
8 head of a skeleton, skull Hdt.
9 head, bulb (of garlic, an onion) Ar. Plb. Plu.
10 highest or projecting part; tip (of an arrow) Stesich.; **top** (of a plant) X.; (sg. and pl.) **ramparts** (of a fortification) X.; (pl., in names for mountain passes) **peak** Hdt. Th. X. Plb. Plu.; **brim** (of a wine-cup, a milk-pail) Alc. Theoc.; **rim** (of a broken jar) Ar.; **head** (of a liver, ref. to the caudate lobe) Plu.
11 mouth (of a river) Call.; (pl., of a gulf) Plu.
12 ‖ PL. **headwaters** (of a river, i.e. its source) Hdt.
13 principal part; primary stone (of a corner, i.e. a cornerstone) NT.; **capital** (of a country) Plu.; **header, summary** (as the introduction to a speech) Arist.; **crowning part, conclusion** (of a story, a debate) Pl.; **completion, fulfilment** (of a calendrical cycle, a branch of learning, an undertaking, a military expedition) Pl. Arist. Plu.
κεφαλ-ηγερέτα ᾱ *dial.m.* [ἐγείρω] **head-gatherer** (i.e. skilled persuader, com.ref. to Perikles, w. play on νεφεληγερέτα *cloud-gatherer*) Plu.(quot.com.)
κεφαλιόω *contr.vb.* **strike the head of** —*a slave* NT.
κεφαλίς ίδος *f.* app. **tip, toe-cap** (of a shoe) Arist.
Κεφαλλήν ῆνος *m.* **1** ‖ PL. Kephallenians (as a population or military force) Hom. Hes.*fr.* S. E. Th. +
2 man from Kephallenia (ref. to Odysseus) S.
—**Κεφαλληνίᾱ** ᾱς, Ion. **Κεφαλληνίη** ης *f.* **Kephallenia** (island off the W. coast of Greece) Hdt. Th. X. D. Plb.
—**Κεφαλλήνιοι** ων *m.pl.* **Kephallenians** Plb.

κεχάνδει (ep.3sg.plpf.), **κεχανδώς** (ep.pf.ptcpl.): see χανδάνω
κεχάραγμαι (pf.pass.): see χαράσσω
κεχάρηκα (pf.), **κεχάρημαι** (pf.mid.), **κεχαρήσω** (fut.pf.): see χαίρω
κεχαρισμένως *pf.mid.pass.ptcpl.adv.*: see under χαρίζομαι
κεχαρμένος (pf.mid.ptcpl.), **κεχαρόμην** (ep.redupl.aor.2 mid.): see χαίρω
κέχηνα (pf.): see χάσκω
Κεχηναῖοι ων *m.pl.* [χάσκω] gaping fools, **Simpletonians** (as com. substitute for Ἀθηναῖοι *Athenians*) Ar.
κέχλᾱδα *dial.pf.vb.* [perh.reltd. καχλάζω] **1** app., make exuberant noise; (of a victory-chant, castanets, a blazing torch) **swell, surge** Pi.
2 (of heroes) **swell, brim** —W.DAT. *w. youth* Pi.
κεχόνδει (ep.3sg.plpf.), **κεχονδώς** (ep.pf.ptcpl.): see χανδάνω
κέχρηκα (pf.): see χράω, under χράομαι
κέχρημαι (pf.mid.), **κεχρήσομαι** (fut.pf.mid.): see χράομαι
κέχυμαι (pf.pass.), **κέχυντο, κέχυτο** (ep.3pl. and 3sg. plpf.pass.): see χέω
κεχωρισμένως *pf.pass.ptcpl.adv.*: see under χωρίζω
κέχωσμαι (pf.pass.): see χόω
κέων (ep.ptcpl.): see κείω¹
Κέως ω, dial. **Κέος** ου *f.* | acc. Κέω, also Κέων (Plb.), dial. Κέον | dat. Κέῳ | **Keos** (island in the Cyclades) Pi. B. Hdt. Pl. X. +
—**Κεῖος**, dial. **Κήιος**, ᾱ (Ion. η) ον *adj.* **1 of or from Keos**; (of persons) **Kean** Hdt. Ar. Pl. Call. Theoc. Plu.; (of a nightingale, fig.ref. to a poet) B. ‖ MASC.PL.SB. **people of Keos, Keans** (as a population or military force) B. Hdt. Th. Isoc. Pl. Men.
2 (of poetic creativity) of the Keans, **Kean** B.; (of poetic nonsense, as an insult) Timocr.
κῆ *Aeol.demonstr.adv.*: see ἐκεῖ
κη *Ion.enclit.adv.*: see πη
κῆ *Ion.interrog.adv.*: see πῇ
κῆα (ep.aor.), **κῆαι** (ep.aor.inf.), **κήαι** (ep.3sg.aor.opt.), **κήαντες** (ep.masc.pl.aor.ptcpl.): see καίω
κηδείᾱ ᾱς, Ion. **κηδείη** ης *f.* [κηδεύω] **1 connection by marriage** (betw. people or groups) E. X. D. Arist. Plb.
2 care shown to a dead body; funeral rites, funeral AR. Plu.
3 mourning, lamentation AR.
κήδειος (also **κήδεος** Il.) ον *adj.* [κῆδος] **1** (of brothers) dearly loved, **dear, close** Il.; (of a dead man, W.DAT. to someone) Il.
2 (of the rearing of children) with love and care, **caring** E.
3 (of offerings, lamentations) **at a funeral, over a tomb** A. E.
κηδεμονεύς έως *m.* [κηδεμών] **one who takes care, carer** (of a child, an old man) AR.
κηδεμονίᾱ ᾱς *f.* activity of looking after another; **care** (for a person) Pl. Hyp. Plu.; act of taking care, **care** (W.GEN. τοῦ + INF. that no one shd. suffer) Plu.
κηδεμονικός ή όν *adj.* (of a person) of the kind who has concern for another's interests, **protective, benevolent** Plb. Plu. ‖ NEUT.SB. care or concern (for someone) Plb.
—**κηδεμονικῶς** *adv.* **1** with concern for another's well-being, **benevolently** Plb.
2 with proper care, reverently —*ref. to burying someone* Plb.
κηδεμών όνος *m.* [κῆδος] **1 one who takes care** (of the funeral of a dead kinsman or comrade), **mourner** Il. AR. Theoc.*epigr.*
2 one who takes care (of another); **carer** (for a sick man) Men.

κήδεος *adj.*: see κήδειος

3 one who cares (about persons or places); **sympathiser, faithful friend** Thgn. A. S.; (specif.) **protector, patron** (of a person, city, land, mankind) S. Ar. Att.orats. Pl. X. Call. Plu.; **guardian** (of a woman) X. Men. AR.
4 one who takes an active interest; **one who cares** (W.GEN. about living and thinking) Pl.
5 relative by marriage, **in-law** E. Mosch.

κήδεος *adj.*: see κήδειος

κηδεστής οῦ *m.* relative by marriage, **in-law** (esp. ref. to a father-, son- or brother-in-law) E. Ar. Att.orats. Pl. X. +; (ref. to a stepfather or stepbrother) A.*satyr.fr.* D.

κηδεστία ᾱς *f.* fact or condition of being related by marriage, **connection by marriage, family tie** (betw. people) X.

κήδευμα ατος *n.* [κηδεύω] **1** connection by marriage, family tie E. Pl. Plu.
2 relative by marriage, **in-law** S. E.

κηδεύω *vb.* **1 take care of, look after** —*a person, city* S. E.; **tend to, treat** —*someone's illness* E.
2 give a funeral to, bury —*persons, a dog* E. Plb. Plu.; (intr.) bury (a person), **take part in a funeral** Plb. || PASS. be given a funeral, be buried S. Plu.
3 ally oneself in marriage (w. persons, i.e. one's in-laws); **forge marriage ties** —W.DAT. *w. someone* E. D. Arist. Plu. —W.ADV. or PREP.PHR. *of a good or appropriate nature* (*i.e. w. a suitable family*) A. E.; (gener.) **be related by marriage, be an in-law** —W.DAT. *to someone* Men.
4 make (W.ACC. someone) **a relation by marriage** E. || PASS. (fig., of a river) be linked to a marriage (by supplying water for the bride's ritual bath) E.
5 marry —*a goddess* E.*fr.*; **make** —W.COGN.ACC. *a particular marriage* (*i.e. marry a particular person*) S.

κήδιστος η ον *superl.adj.* [κῆδος] (of friends, in-laws) **dearest, closest** (oft. W.DAT. to a person) Hom.

κῆδος, *dial.* **κᾶδος**, εος *n.* **1 concern, compassion** (for a person) Hom. Thgn. Pi. AR.
2 sorrow, grief Hom. Hes. Thgn. A. Pi. S. +
3 mourning (for a dead person) Archil. Stesich. Pi. Hdt.
4 funeral Hdt. E. Isoc. Arist. Plu.
5 that which one cares about, **concern, preoccupation** Od. Pi.
6 cause for concern (ref. to a threat posed by someone) Od.
7 cause of sorrow, affliction, misfortune Hom. Hes. Alcm. Archil. B. Pl. +
8 connection by marriage (sts. W.GEN., DAT. or εἰς + ACC. to a person) Pi. Hdt. Trag. Th. AR. Plu.; (w. play on sense 2) A.; (gener.) **marriage, match** E.

κηδοσύνη ης *f.* **1 grief, distress** AR.
2 longing, yearning (for a voyage) AR.

κηδόσυνος ον *adj.* (of a person's steps) **anxious, sorrowful** E.

κήδω, *dial.* **κάδω** *vb.* | iteratv.impf. κήδεσκον | fut. κηδήσω | pf. κέκηδα (Tyrt.) || MID.: pres. κήδομαι, dial. κάδομαι, dial.imperatv. κάδευ | 3sg.iteratv.impf. κηδέσκετο | aor.imperatv. κήδεσαι (A.) | fut.pf. κεκαδήσομαι (Il.) |
1 (of gods, persons, an arrow, wound, storm) **cause distress to, torment** —*a god, a person, his spirit, animals, a river god's streams, a household* Hom.; (specif., of gods, persons, ships) trouble with attacks, **harass, harry** —*persons, a people, cities* Il. Call. —(W.DAT. *w. arrows*) Il.; (of possessions) **be a source of anxiety for** —*a person* Hes.
2 || PF. (of a city) be in distress —W.DAT. *w. longing* (*for a dead man*) Tyrt.
3 || MID.PASS. (of gods, persons) **be distressed, be grieved** Hom. hHom.; **be vexed, be riled** Il.
4 || MID.PASS. feel concern and anxiety, **be concerned** (for someone) Il. —W.GEN. *for a people, a fleet* Il. Lys. —W.COMPL.CL. *in case sthg. shd. happen* Hdt. Pl.
5 || MID.PASS. (of gods, persons, peoples, institutions) be concerned for the interests or safety (of persons or things); **care** (about someone) Od. Arist. —W.GEN. *about persons, peoples, cities, regions, things, one's own life* Hom. Hdt. S. Th. Ar. +; (w.neg.connot.) **be on the side** —W.GEN. *of an enemy state* X.
6 || MID.PASS. (of gods, persons, animals) take protective care of, **look after** —W.GEN. *persons, households, a farm, city* Od. A. Pi. S. Isoc. + —*someone's sustenance* (*i.e. by giving food*) Od. S. Ar. —*public money* Isoc. +; (w.neg.connot.) **be overprotective** —W.GEN. *of one's money* Pl.

κηθάριον ου *n.* **voting-urn, ballot-box** (meton.ref. to jury service and the payment received for it) Ar.

κῆθι *Aeol.demonstr.adv.*: see ἐκεῖθι

Κήϊος *dial.adj.*: see under Κέως

κηκίς ῑδος *f.* **1** oozing liquid; **ooze, dripping flow** (of blood, purple dye, molten pitch, juice fr. burning meat) A. S.
2 (specif.) ink extracted from oak-galls, **gall dye, ink** D.

κηκίω, ep. **κηκίω** *vb.* (of seawater, sweat, blood) **gush or ooze forth** (oft. W.PREP.PHR. fr. someone's mouth and nostrils, temples, a wound) Od. S. AR.; (of smoke) **billow forth** AR.; (of the sea) **bubble, surge** —W.DAT. or ACC. *w. foam* AR.

κῆλα *n.pl.* [perh.reltd. κηλέω] | only nom.acc. | perh., means by which a god's miraculous power is manifested or deployed, **signs of divine power** (ref. to Apollo's plague-bearing arrows) Il.; (ref. to Zeus' thunder and lightning) Hes.; (ref. to snowflakes sent by Zeus) Il.; (gener., ref. to visible manifestations of Apollo's presence) hHom.; (ref. to notes played on the lyre) Pi. [usu.interpr. as *shafts, missiles*]

κήλεος, also **κήλειος**, η ον *ep.adj.* [app.reltd. καίω] (of fire) **burning, blazing** Hom. Hes.

κηλέω *contr.vb.* **1** put in a trance, **render spellbound** —*gods, persons, animals* (sts. W.DAT. *w. songs*) E. Pl. Plu. || PASS. be put in a trance, —W.DAT. or ὑπό + GEN. *by Sirens, persons, animals*) Pi.*fr.* Pl. X. Aeschin. Arist.; (of rocks) be bewitched —W.DAT. *by music* E.*fr.*
2 (esp. of skilled speakers) **entrance, captivate** —*persons* (sts. W.DAT. *w. words*) E. Pl. Plu. || PASS. be held spellbound (sts. W.DAT. or ὑπό + GEN. *by persons, poetry, skilled oratory*) Pl. Plu.
3 (w.neg.connot.) lull into inactivity, **beguile** —*one's own spirit* Pl. || PASS. (of gods, persons) be beguiled —W.DAT. or ὑπό + GEN. *by gifts, pleasures, laziness, low prices* Pl. Aeschin. D.

κηληθμός οῦ *m.* **enchantment, captivation** (gripping the audience of a speaker or bard) Od. AR.

κηλήματα των *n.pl.* **bewitchments, enchantments** (of love, an alluring woman) Ibyc. E.

κήλησις εως *f.* **1** act of bewitching with spells, **charming** (of snakes, pests, diseases) Pl.
2 act of rendering spellbound, **captivating** (of an audience) Pl. Plu.
3 power to enchant, **captivating power** (of metre, rhythm, harmony) Pl.

κηλήτειρα ης *Ion.f.* soother, **propitiator** (of Hades, ref. to farmland deliberately left fallow) Hes.(cj.)

κηλητήριος ᾱ ον *adj.* (of a substance) **able to act as a charm** (W.GEN. on someone's mind) S.; (of offerings) **full of magical power** E.

κηλῑδόω *contr.vb.* [κηλίς] (of certain gods) inflict degradation upon, **defile** —*their fathers* (W.DAT. *w. chains*) E.

κηλίς ίδος *f.* **1 spot, stain** (of blood, soot, dirt, on an object, garment or person) S. E. Thphr.; (on a land, fr. a poisonous blight) A.; **spot, speckle** (on the skin, fr. poison) Plu.
2 (fig.) **stain** (of impiety or dishonour, on a person, life or career) S. E. Antipho X. Plu.
κῆλος εος *n.* **beam, timber** (of a ship) Hes.*fr.*
κήλων ωνος *m.* **male animal in rut**; (appos.w. ὄνος) **rutting donkey** Archil.
κηλώνειον, Ion. **κηλωνήιον**, ου *n.* **tilting beam** (w. attached bucket) for drawing water from a well, **shadoof** Hdt. Men.
κημός οῦ *m.* **1 muzzle** (to stop a horse fr. biting) X.
2 conical wickerwork funnel; **funnel of a ballot-box** (into which votes are cast) Ar.; (fig., inserted in the throat of a corrupt official, to make him vomit up what he has taken) Ar.; (gener.) **ballot-box** Ar.
3 funnel-shaped object, **cone, funnel** (ref. to a ship-mounted flame-thrower) Plb.
κημόω *contr.vb.* **muzzle** —*a horse* X.
κήνοθεν Aeol.demonstr.adv.: see ἐκεῖθεν
κῆνος dial.demonstr.pron. and adj.: see ἐκεῖνος
κῆνσος ου *m.* [Lat. *census*] **poll-tax** (on Roman subjects) NT.
κήξ κηκός *f.* a kind of sea-bird; perh. **tern** Od.
κήομεν (ep.1pl.aor.subj.): see καίω
κήπευμα ατος *n.* [κηπεύω] **that which is tended or cultivated** ‖ PL. **plants, gardens** (of the Graces) Ar.
κηπεύω *vb.* [κῆπος] **cultivate, grow** —*plants* Plu.; (of Reverence) **tend, nurture** —*a sacred meadow* (W.DAT. w. river waters) E.; (of a mother) **care for, cherish** —*her child's hair* E.
κηπίον ου *n.* [dimin. κῆπος] **small garden** or **orchard** Plb.; (fig., ref. to a dispensable appendage of land) **mere garden** Th.
κῆπος, dial. **κᾶπος**, ου *m.* **1 garden, orchard** Hom. Hdt. E. Ar. Att.orats. +; (ref. to the plot of land surrounding a house) Pl. D. Plu.; (fig., ref. to a sacred precinct) Pi. E.; (ref. to mythol. groves, esp. of the Graces, Muses, or sim.) Ibyc. Pi. Ar. Pl.; (gener., ref. to a fertile piece of land) Pi. Hdt. E. Aeschin.; (fig., ref. to texts as flowerbeds of ideas) Pl.; (ref. to a woman's genital area) Archil.
2 ‖ PL. **gardens** (W.GEN. of Adonis, ref. to plants grown in pots or baskets for his festival) Pl.; (without GEN.) Men. Theoc.
κηπ-ουρός οῦ *m.* [οὖρος²] **one who looks after a garden** or **orchard, gardener** Plb. NT. Plu.
κήρ κηρός, dial. **κάρ** κᾱρός *f.* | dat. κηρί, Aeol. κᾶρι |
1 (personif.) Goddess of Fate, **Doom, Fate** Il. Hes. Alc. AR. ‖ PL. **Keres, Fates** (sts. identified w. Erinyes) Hes. Mimn. Carm.Pop.(dub.) Emp. Trag. AR. +
2 (sg. and pl.) **doom, fate** (for persons) Hom. +; (for fish) Il.; (specif.) way of meeting one's end, **fatal accident** Plu.
3 (gener.) **destiny, fate** (of a person) Alc. Trag.
4 source of doom or suffering, **curse, plague, blight** (ref. to persons, monsters, envy, or sim.) A. E. Democr. Plu.
5 (wkr.sens.) source of contamination, **blemish, taint** (ref. to character flaws or sim.) Pl. Plu.
κῆρ, also **κέαρ** (Pi. +) *n.* [reltd. καρδίᾱ] | dat. κῆρι | only nom.voc.acc. and dat.sg. | **1 heart** (of a person, ref. to the physical organ in the chest) Il.; (of a god, person or animal, as the seat of emotions or bravery) Hom. Thgn. Pi. B. Trag. +; (as the seat of the senses) Il.; (w. pers. name in GEN., meton.ref. to a person) Il.; (in voc., meton.ref. to a person) Call.*epigr.*
2 heart, core (W.GEN. of the soul, w. play on κηρός *wax*, as receiving impressions) Pl.

—**κηρόθι** *adv.* **in one's heart, with all one's heart** —*ref. to being angered, hating, loving or honouring someone* Hom. Hes. hHom.
κηραίνω *vb.* [κήρ] **1** (of beasts and men) **destroy, ruin** —*the tender fruits of summer* A.
2 (intr.) **be distressed** E.
κηρεσσι-φόρητος ον *adj.* [φορητός] (of dogs, fig.ref. to the Greeks at Troy) **driven by the Fates** Il.
κήρινος η (dial. ᾱ) ον *adj.* [κηρός] **1** (of the fruits) **of the honeycomb** (i.e. honey) Alcm.
2 (of blocks or pieces) **of wax** Pl.; (of figurines, funeral wreaths) **made of wax** Ar. Pl.; (of letters) **written in wax** (i.e. on writing-tablets) Arist. ‖ NEUT.SB. **block or piece of wax** Pl.
3 (fig., of children, men's souls) **malleable like wax, impressionable** Pl.
κηρίον ου *n.* **comb of cells** (made by bees, sts.ref. to the honey inside), **honeycomb** Hes. hHom. Hippon. Pi.*fr.* Hdt. Ar. +; **nest** (made by wasps) Hdt.
κηρι-τρεφής ές *adj.* [κήρ, τρέφω] (of mankind) **born to misery** Hes.
κηρό-δετος ον *adj.* [κηρός, δέω¹] (of a reed, ref. to a panpipe) **fixed together with wax** E.; (of a breath, ref. to music played on the panpipe) Theoc.*epigr.*
κηρο-ειδής ές *adj.* [εἶδος¹] (of substances) **wax-like** Pl.
κηρόθι *adv.*: see under κῆρ
κηρο-πλάστης ου *m.* [κηρός, πλάσσω] **maker of wax models**; (ref. to the creator god) **fashioner** (of the human race) Pl.
κηρό-πλαστος ον *adj.* [πλαστός] (of reed-pipes) **fashioned with wax** (i.e. held together by it) A.
κηρός οῦ *m.* **1 beeswax, wax** Od. +
2 wax comb, honeycomb Theoc. Mosch.
κηρο-χυτέω *contr.vb.* [χυτός] melt and cast wax; **mould** (objects) **in wax** Ar.
κήρυγμα ατος *n.* [κηρύσσω] **1 proclamation** (by a god) S.*Ichn.* E.*fr.*; (by a ruler, commander, state, usu. announced by an official herald) Hdt. S. E. Th. Att.orats. +; (specif., ref. to a summons to conscripts or sim.) S. Ar. Plb. Plu.; (ref. to an announcement of honours awarded to a person) Aeschin. D. Plu.
2 (gener.) **announcement** (of news, by a person) E.
3 preaching (by a holy man) NT.
κηρύκαινα ης *f.* [κῆρυξ] **female announcer** Ar.
κηρυκείᾱ ᾱς, Ion. **κηρυκηίη** ης *f.* [κηρυκεύω] **delivery of official announcements** (by a herald, on behalf of a state) Hdt. Pl.
κηρύκειον, Ion. **κηρυκήιον**, ου *n.* **herald's staff** Hdt. Th. X. D. +; (meton. for diplomacy and negotiation, opp. war) Plb.
κηρύκευμα ατος *n.* **announcement, report** (fr. a scout to a commander) A.
κηρῡκεύω *vb.* [κῆρυξ] **1 be a herald, deliver official announcements** (for a state) Aeschin.
2 (tr., of Hermes) **proclaim** —*good things* (W.DAT. *to men*) A.; (of persons) **announce** —*a death sentence, a message fr. a foreign power* E. Pl.
κηρῡκικός ή όν *adj.* (of the class) **of heralds** Pl.; (of the art) **of the herald** Pl.
κήρῡλος ου *m.* a kind of sea-bird; app. **kingfisher** Alcm. Archil.; (personif.) Mosch.
κῆρυξ (or perh. **κήρῡξ**), dial. **κᾶρυξ** (or perh. **κάρῡξ**), ῡκος *m.* **1 announcer** (of news, messages and orders, appointed by a ruler or commander), **herald** Hom. +; (as a subordinate among nobles, tasked w. preparing meals or sim.) Hom.; (in an army, responsible for calling troops to duties, meals, or

κηρύσσω

sim.) Hdt. X.; (ref. to the cockerel, as announcer of dawn) Ar.; (fig.ref. to a poet) Sol. Pi. Tim. Plu.
2 herald, messenger (of the gods, ref. to Hermes) Hes. hHom. A. Pi.; (of the dead, ref. to the screech-owl) Hippon.; (of Zeus, ref. to the eagle) E.; (of Aphrodite, ref. to Youthfulness) Pi.
3 (gener.) **announcer** (W.GEN. of news, knowledge, or sim.) E. Ar. Pl.
4 (specif.) **envoy** (fr. a foreign power, esp. during hostilities) A. Hdt. E. Th. Ar. +
5 official whose task is to make announcements, **announcer** (of winners in athletic or poetic competitions, or sim.) Pi. E.*lyr.fr.* Ar. Tim. Pl. Call.*epigr.*
6 crier, public announcer (of decrees, legal notices, arrest warrants, announcements fr. individuals) E. Ar. Pl. Arist. +
7 herald, marshal (as an official in the Assembly) Ar. Att.orats. Pl. X. Arist.
8 herald in religious ceremonies; **herald** (of initiates in the Mysteries) X. Plu. ‖ PL. Heralds (a clan in Athens w. hereditary rights to religious offices) Th. Att.orats. Arist. Plu.
9 (specif.) **auctioneer** Hdt. Ar. Plu.

κηρύσσω, Att. **κηρύττω**, dial. **κᾱρύσσω** vb. | fut. κηρύξω, dial. κᾱρύξω, also κᾱρυξῶ, dial.3pl. κᾱρύξοντι | aor. ἐκήρυξα, dial. ἐκάρυξα ‖ PASS.: fut. κηρυχθήσομαι, also κηρύξομαι | aor. ἐκηρύχθην | pf. κεκήρυγμαι |
1 (of heralds, rulers, persons, gods, birds, a tomb) **announce, proclaim** —sthg. (sts. W.DAT. to people) Trag. Th. Pl. Call.*epigr.* Plb. NT. —W.INTERN.ACC. *a message* E. —W.COMPL.CL. *that sthg. is the case* A.*satyr.fr.* S. Th.; (intr.) **make a proclamation** Il. A. E.; **deliver proclamations and messages, serve as a herald** Il. ‖ PASS. (of news, crimes, rewards) be announced (esp. by a herald) S. E. Antipho Th. And. +; (of a person) be proclaimed —w. ἀπό + GEN. (*to be*) *fr. a noble family* E.
2 (of heralds, persons, songs, a family's fame) **proclaim** —W.ACC. + INF. *a chariot to be victorious* Pi.; **proclaim as victor** —*a person* B.; **publicly honour** —*a person* Aeschin.; (causatv.) cause to be honoured, **win honour for** —*a person, city* Pi. ‖ PASS. be proclaimed —W.PREDIC.ADJ. *victorious* E. —W.PTCPL. *victorious* (W.DAT. or ACC. *in a contest*) X. Plb.; be proclaimed as victor X.; be publicly honoured E. Att.orats. X.
3 ‖ PASS. be announced as a wanted criminal Antipho D.
4 denounce —*a person* (W.PREDIC.ADJ. *as evil, shameless, loud-mouthed*) S.
5 (of a herald) publicly inquire, **ask** —W.INDIR.Q. *what* (*or whether sthg.*) *is the case* And. D.; **publicly name** —*someone* (W.INDIR.Q. *to find out where he is*) Ar.
6 (of heralds, rulers, persons; sts. quasi-impers., w. κῆρυξ understd.) **command, decree** —*sthg.* (sts. W.DAT. *to someone*) Trag. X. —W.COMPL.CL. *that someone shd. do sthg.* Hdt. D. Arist.; **give the command** —W.INF. or DAT. + INF. (*to people*) *to do sthg.* Pi. E. Ar. Pl. X. —W.ACC. + INF. *that people shd. do sthg.* Th. Ar. X. Plb. ‖ PASS. (of things) be ordered E. —W.INF. *to be done* S. ‖ IMPERS.PASS. the order is given —W.INF. *to have dinner* X.
7 (milit.) **call for, requisition** —*all available beasts of burden* X.
8 (of heralds, persons) **summon** —*troops, persons* (sts. W.ADV. *to battle, an assembly*) Hom.; (intr.) **summon the troops, sound the call to assembly** Hom. ‖ PASS. (of a person) be summoned —W.ACC. *to sentry duty* E.; (of assemblies, councils) be convened Alc.
9 (of Hermes, a person) **summon, invoke** —*gods* E. —(W.INF. *to hear one's prayers*) A.; **call out** —W.DAT. *to someone* A. —(W.INF. *to hear one's prayers*) A.

10 make public announcements (of goods for sale), **be an auctioneer** (seen as a lowly occupation) D. Thphr.; (tr.) **auction** —*goods* Hdt. ‖ PASS. (of goods) be announced —W.INF. *to be on sale* Hdt.
11 (of a holy man) **preach** NT.

κηρωτή ῆς f. [κηρός] waxy ointment, **liniment** Ar.
κήτειος ᾱ ον adj. [κῆτος] (of the backs) **of sea-monsters** (ridden by Nereids) Mosch.
κῆτος εος (ους) n. **sea-monster** (ref. to mythol. beasts) Hom. Ar. AR. NT.; (gener., ref. to seals, dolphins, large fish) Hom. Hdt. Mosch. Plu.
κητώεις εσσα εν adj. (of a region) perh. **full of chasms** Hom.
κηφήν ῆνος m. stingless and unproductive bee, **drone** (oft. fig.ref. to work-shy people) Hes. Ar. Pl. X.; (fig.ref. to a decrepit and useless old person or animal) E.
κηφηνώδης ες adj. (of squalid desires for wealth, profit, or sim.) like drones in a hive, **drone-like** Pl.
Κηφισιεύς έως (contr. ῶς) m. **man from Kephisia** (a deme in Attica) Att.orats. Pl.
—**Κηφισίᾱσι** dat.pl.adv. **in Kephisia** Aeschin.
Κηφισός, dial. **Κᾱφισός**, οῦ m. **1 Kephisos** (river in Boeotia feeding Lake Kopais) Il. hHom. Pi. Hdt. X. Plu.; (as a river god) Hdt. Corinn.
2 Kephisos (river in Attica) S. E. X. Plu.; (as a river god) E. Lycurg.
—**Κηφίσιος**, dial. **Κᾱφίσιος**, ᾱ ον adj. (of the waters) **of Kephisos** Pi.
—**Κηφισίς**, dial. **Κᾱφισίς**, ίδος fem.adj. **1** (of a lake, ref. to Kopais) **Kephisian** Il. hHom.
2 ‖ SB. daughter of Kephisos (ref. to the nymph Kopais) Pi.
κη-ώδης ες adj. [reltd. καίω, ὄζω] (of a woman's lap) perfumed with incense, **sweet-smelling, fragrant** Il.
κνώεις εσσα εν adj. (of a room) perfumed with incense, **sweet-smelling, fragrant** Od.
κιβδηλείᾱ ᾱς f. [κιβδηλεύω] act of adulterating or counterfeiting, **adulteration** (of goods for sale) Pl.
κιβδήλευμα ατος n. instance of adulteration or counterfeiting, **adulteration** (of goods for sale) Pl.
κιβδηλεύω vb. [κίβδηλος] **counterfeit** —*coins* Arist.; **adulterate** —*goods for sale* Pl.; (fig.) **concoct** —*an appealing story* E. ‖ PASS. (of coins or goods) be counterfeited or adulterated Ar. Pl.
κιβδηλίᾱ ᾱς f. counterfeiting; (fig.) **dishonesty** (W.GEN. in life) Ar.
κίβδηλος ον adj. **1** (of coinage, precious metals) **counterfeit, debased** Thgn. E. X. Plb.; (fig., of a city, envisaged as coinage) D.
2 (of goods for sale) **counterfeit** or **adulterated** Pl.; (fig., of justice) **sham** Arist.
3 (of honours) **spurious** Pl.; (of prophecies) **false** Hdt.; (of a financial calculation of interest) **incorrect** Pl.
4 (of an oracle) **deceptive** Hdt. ‖ NEUT.SB. deceptiveness (of noble birth, as a criterion of moral probity) E.
5 (of persons, their nature or conduct) **dishonest, deceitful** Thgn. E. Pl.; (of acts, business practices) Anacr. Pl. Plu.
6 (of the letter *s*, ref. to its sound) **false, imperfect** Pi.*fr.*
κίβισις εως f. leather pouch, **pouch, bag** Hes. Alc. Call.
κιβώτιον ου n. [dimin. κιβωτός] small wooden chest, **box** (for storage) Ar. X. D. Arist. Plu.; (for collecting ballots) Arist.
κιβωτός οῦ f. **1** wooden chest, **box, chest** (for storing valuables or household items) Lys. Ar. Arist. Thphr. Plu.
2 ark (built by Noah) NT.
κιγκλίζω vb. jerk (sthg.) about repeatedly; (fig., in neg.phr.) **fiddle with** —*a good life* Thgn.

κιγκλίς ίδος *f.* **1** latticed wooden gate; (specif., at Athens) **gate** (to the Council-chamber or courtroom) Ar. D.
2 wooden railing, **railing** Plu.
3 instrument of torture; **rack** (meton., ref. to torture) Plu.

κιγχάνω *vb.*: see κιχᾰ́νω

κίδναμαι *pass.vb.* [reltd. σκίδναμαι, κεδάννῡμι] | only pres. and impf. | (of sunlight, dawn) **spread** —W.PREP.PHR. *over the sea, the earth* Il. Mimn. AR.; (of a sweet fragrance) —*over a hill, a region* hHom. Pi.; (of a shout) —*into the air* AR.; (of wind) **spread all around** Simon.

Κιθαιρών, Boeot. **Κιθηρών**, ῶνος *m.* **Kithairon** (mountain in the range dividing Boeotia fr. Attica) Pi. Hdt. Trag. Th. +

—**Κιθαιρώνειος** ᾱ ον *adj.* (of the rocky uplands) **of Kithairon** E.

—**Κιθαιρώνιος** ᾱ ον (also ος ον) *adj.* **1** (epith. of Hera) **of Kithairon** Plu.
2 (of echoes) **from Kithairon** Ar.

—**Κιθαιρωνίς** ίδος *fem.adj.* (of a pass) **over Kithairon** Hdt.

κιθάρᾱ ᾱς, Ion. **κιθάρη** ης *f.* [κίθαρις] **kithara, lyre** (esp. ref. to the box-lyre, w. more strings and a louder sound than the archaic round-based λύρα or φόρμιγξ) Hdt. E. Pl. Arist. Plu.; (meton., ref. to its music) Thgn. E. AR. Plu.

κιθαραοιδότατος *superl.adj.*: see under κιθαρῳδός

κιθαρίζω *vb.* | Aeol.inf. κιθαρίσδην | (of gods, persons, plectrums) **play the lyre** (ref. either to the archaic φόρμιγξ or to the κιθάρα) Il. hHom. Alcm. Pi. Hdt. E. +; **play lyre-music** —W.DAT. *on the lyre* Hes. hHom. X.

κίθαρις εως (also ιδος E.*fr.*) *f.* [reltd. κιθάρᾱ] **kithara, lyre** Od. hHom. Alc. Pi. E.*fr.* Ar. +; (meton., ref. to its music) Hom. hHom.

κιθάρισις εως *f.* [κιθαρίζω] **1** art of playing the lyre, **lyre-playing** Pl. Arist.
2 lyre music Pl.

κιθαρίσματα των *n.pl.* lyre music Pl.

κιθαρισμός οῦ *m.* playing of the lyre, **lyre-playing** Call.

κιθαριστής οῦ, dial. **κιθαριστᾱ́ς** ᾶ *m.* lyre-player Hes. hHom. Alcm. Pl. +; (ref. to a music teacher) Ar. Pl. X.

κιθαριστικός ή όν *adj.* skilled at playing the lyre Pl.; (of the art) **of the lyre-player** Pl. || FEM.SB. art of the lyre-player Pl.

κιθαριστύς ύος *f.* art of playing the lyre, **lyre-playing** Il.

κιθαρῳδέω *contr.vb.* [κιθαρῳδός] **sing to the accompaniment of the lyre** Pl.

κιθαρῳδίᾱ ᾱς *f.* **singing to the accompaniment of the lyre** Pl.

κιθαρῳδικός ή όν *adj.* (of songs) **sung to the accompaniment of the lyre** Ar. Pl. || FEM.SB. singing to the accompaniment of the lyre Pl.

κιθαρ-ῳδός οῦ *m.* [κιθάρᾱ, ἀοιδή] one who sings to the accompaniment of the lyre, **kitharode** (esp. ref. to a professional musician) Hdt. Pl. Aeschin. Arist. Plu.; (ref. to Orpheus, w.neg.connot. of his profession being unheroic) Pl.; (com.ref. to a cockerel) Ar.

—**κιθαραοιδότατος** η ον *superl.adj.* **best at singing to the accompaniment of the lyre** Ar.

Κιθηρών Boeot.*m.*: see Κιθαιρών

κιθών Ion.*m.*, **κίθων** Aeol.*n.*: see χιτών

κίκι *indecl.n.* [Egyptian loanwd.] a kind of vegetable oil, **castor-oil** (used in lamps) Hdt. Pl.

κίκιννοι ων *m.pl.* curls of hair, **locks, ringlets** (as a fashionable male hairstyle) Ar. Theoc.

κικκαβαῦ *interj.* (representing a bird's call) **kikkabau!** Ar.

κικκαβίζω *vb.* (of owls) **hoot** or **screech** Ar.

κικλήσκω (or **κικλῄσκω**) *vb.* [reltd. καλέω] **1 call, summon** —*persons, a god* Hom. hHom. —(w. εἰς + ACC. *to an assembly, a dance*) Il. Ar. —*Poseidon* (w. ἐκ + GEN. *fr. the sea*) Theoc.; **invite** —*persons* (*to a wedding*) Call.
2 call upon, invoke —*deities, a dead man* Il. Hes. B. Trag. Call. —(W.PREDIC.SB. *as a helper*) AR. —(W.INF. *to do sthg.*) Il.
3 call —*a god, person, place, thing* (W.PREDIC.ACC. *by a certain name or description*) Hom. Hes. A. Pi. E. Call. + —*a day* (*by its true name*) Hes. || PASS. (of gods, persons, places, things) be called —W.PREDIC.NOM. *by a certain name or description* Od. hHom. A. Emp. E.*fr.* AR. —W.GEN. (*son*) *of a person* E.

Κικυννεύς έως *m.* | nom.pl. Κικυννῆς | **man from Kikynna** (an Attic deme) Ar.

—**Κικυννόθεν** *adv.* **from Kikynna** Ar.
—**Κικυννοῖ** *adv.* **at Kikynna** Lys.

κῖκυς υος *f.* **strength, vigour** (possessed by a person) Od. hHom.

Κίλιξ ικος *m.* | ep.dat.pl. Κιλίκεσσι | **1** || PL. **Cilicians** (ref. to the inhabitants of Cilicia in SE. Anatolia, as a population or military force) A. Hdt. E. Th. X. +; (ref. to the inhabitants of a region in the Troad) Il.
2 Cilician man Hdt. X. Plb. Plu.
3 || ADJ. (of Typhon) Cilician Pi.

—**Κίλισσα** ης *f.* **1 Cilician woman** X.; (as the name of a slave) A.
2 || ADJ. (of ships) Cilician Hdt. Plu.

—**Κιλίκιος** ᾱ (Ion. η) ον *adj.* **1** (of a cave, city, region; of gates, ref. to a coastal pass) **Cilician** A. Pi. Hdt. Plb. Plu. || FEM.SB. Cilicia Hdt. Att.orats. X. Plb. +
2 || MASC.PL.SB. Cilicians (as a population) Hdt.

κιλλίβᾱς αντος *m.* wooden stand or easel; **stand** (for a shield) Ar.

κιμαῖος ου *m.* mulberry juice Hippon.

Κιμβερικός ή όν *adj.* (of women's garments) of the Kimberian type, **Kimberian** (ref. to an expensive and fashionable style of dress, app.fr. a place name) Ar.

κίμβιξ ικος *m.* **miser, skinflint** Arist.

Κιμμέριος ᾱ (Ion. η) ον *adj.* **1** || MASC.PL.SB. **Cimmerians** (a mythol. race living at the ends of the earth) Od.; (a historical race living in Crimea and Anatolia) Callin. Hdt. Plu.
2 (of a region, a strait, city walls) **Cimmerian** (ref. to the Crimean peninsula and the Strait of Kerch) Hdt.

—**Κιμμερικός** ή όν *adj.* (of an isthmus, a strait) **Cimmerian** A. Plb. Plu.

Κιμώλιος ᾱ ον *adj.* (of earth, ref. to fuller's earth, a type of clay w. detergent properties) **from Kimolos** (an island in the Aegean), **Kimolian** Ar.

κιναβράω *contr.vb.* (of goats) **be rank-smelling** Ar.

κίναδος εος (ους) *n.* **fox**; (fig., ref. to a cunning person) **fox** S. Ar. Att.orats. Men. Theoc.

κινάθισμα ατος *n.* **fluttering** (of birds) A. [or perh. *massing together*]

κιναιδίᾱ ᾱς *f.* [κίναιδος] **deviancy** (esp.ref. to passive male homosexuality) Aeschin.

κίναιδος ου *m.* male taking a passive role in homosexual intercourse; (derog.) **sodomite, faggot** Pl. Aeschin.

κινάμωμον *n.*: see κιννάμωμον

κίνασις dial.*f.*: see κίνησις

κινδύνευμα ατος *n.* [κινδυνεύω] **risky undertaking** S. E. Pl.

κινδῡνευτής οῦ *m.* **risk-taker, adventurer** Th.

κινδῡνευτικός ή όν *adj.* **prone to take risks** Arist.

κινδῡνεύω *vb.* [κίνδυνος] **1** incur jeopardy (for sthg. or someone); **run a risk** —W.DAT., ἐν + DAT. or περί + GEN. *w. one's life, other people's children, a city, country, possessions, or sim.* Hdt. Ar. Att.orats. Pl. +; (provbl.) —*w. a*

κίνδυνος

Carian (i.e. let someone else bear the risk on one's behalf) E.*Cyc.*; **take, run** —W.COGN.ACC. *a risk* Antipho Lys. Pl. ǁ PASS. (of reputations, money, an estate, a city's interests) *be put at risk* Th. D.; (of a risk) *be taken or incurred* Pl. ǁ IMPERS.PASS. *a risk is taken* Antipho Th.

2 lay oneself open to (a certain) risk; **run the risk** —W.GEN. or περί + GEN. *of death, enslavement, prosecution, or sim.* Att.orats. ǁ PASS. (of a reversal of fortunes) *be a risk* —W.DAT. *for people* Th.

3 put oneself in danger, **take a risk** Hdt. E. Ar.; (specif.) **risk one's life** (esp. in war) Th. Lys. X. Is. Arist.

4 carry out a risky and daring act, **take a chance** Hdt. Th. Ar.; take the chance of, **risk** —W.PTCPL. *doing sthg.* Th. ǁ PASS. (of deeds) *be ventured* Pi. —w. ὑπό + GEN. *by people* Lys.

5 (specif.) stake one's fortune on the battlefield; **go to war** Isoc. —w. πρός + ACC. *against enemy forces* Hdt. X. —w. περί + GEN. *for one's kingdom or native land, a territorial possession* Hdt. D.

6 face danger (in the courtroom), **be on trial** Att.orats.

7 (of persons, military positions, towns, lands) **be in danger** (of death, conquest, destruction, or sim.) Hdt. Antipho Th. Isoc. Plb.; **face** —W.COGN.ACC. *dangers* Att.orats. Pl.

8 be in danger —W.INF. *of losing one's life, suffering a defeat, or sim.* Hdt. Th. Ar. Pl. X. —W.PTCPL. *of losing one's children* Th.

9 (wkr.sens.) **stand a good chance** —W.INF. *of doing or being sthg.* Hdt. Th. Pl. X. —W.PTCPL. *of doing sthg.* Th. ǁ IMPERS. (in dialogue, agreeing w. a statement) *there is a good chance* (of sthg.), *it would seem to be the case* Pl.

κίνδῡνος ου *m.* **1 danger, risk** Eleg. A. Pi. Hdt. E. +; (W.GEN. or περί + GEN. *to one's life, children, city, or sim.*) Th. Att.orats. Pl. +; (W.GEN. *posed by sthg.*) E. Th.; (W.INF. *of being destroyed or sim.*) Hdt. E.

2 (esp.pl.) **danger** (ref. to a specific threat faced by a person, people, city, or sim.) Thgn. A. Pi. Hdt. E. Th. +

3 (specif.) military encounter, **battle, fighting** Plb. Plu.

4 hazarding, risking (of one's life, empire, or sim.) Plu.

5 process of being put at risk (in the courtroom), **trial** Lys. D. Plb.; (fig., W.GEN. *of wisdom, ref. to a contest of wits*) Ar.

κινδῡνώδης ες *adj.* (of ventures, wars, paths down a mountain) **dangerous, perilous** Plb. Plu.

κῑνέω contr.vb. —also Aeol. **κίνημι** vb. [reltd. κίνυμαι] | Aeol.ptcpl. κίνεις | aor. ἐκίνησα, Aeol.masc.ptcpl. κινήσαις ǁ MID.: fut. (w.pass.sens.) κινήσομαι ǁ PASS.: dial.imperatv. κινεῦ, Ion.ptcpl. κινεύμενος | aor. ἐκινήθην, ep. κινήθην, ep.3pl. ἐκίνηθεν ǁ neut.impers.vbl.adj. κινητέον ǁ The sections are grouped as: (1–3) cause to move forward, (4–10) stir into motion or activity, (11–14) cause agitated motion or disturbance, (15–20) change by movement (fr. one place or condition to another). |

1 cause to move forward; (of gods, persons) **set in motion** —*a cloud, a person* Il. Ar.; (of persons, animals; of a ship, envisaged as a person) —*one's foot* (i.e. make a journey) E.; (intr., of commanders) move one's troops forward, **advance** Plb. Plu. ǁ PASS. (of gods, persons) *move forward* Il. E.; (of troops, commanders) *advance* S. E. Th. X. D.

2 (milit.) **mobilise, move** —*an army, a fleet* Th. ǁ PASS. (of troops, ships) *be mobilised* Hdt. Th.; *carry out a manoeuvre* Th.

3 (of madness, terrors) **drive on** —*a person* A. E.; (of the rising sun) **urge on** —*a warrior* S.

4 (of persons, gods, animals) stir into motion or activity, **move** —*their eyes, limbs, bodies, oars, reins* Od. hHom. Semon. Hdt. S. E. + ǁ PASS. *move* Semon. Hdt. Ar. Isoc. Pl. +

5 take up, handle, brandish —*arms, a spear* E. Th.; (of Bacchants) —*the thyrsos* E. ǁ PASS. (of a thunderbolt, a spear) *be brandished* Pi.*fr.*

6 rouse —*wasps* (fr. their nest) Il. —*sleeping persons, their eyes or body* Hom. E.; (of Hermes) —*souls of the dead* Od.; (of aulos-playing) **rouse, spur on** —*a dolphin* Pi.*fr.*; (of a person) —*a bee* (fig.ref. to a poet, commissioned to write an ode) B. ǁ PASS. *be roused* (fr. sleep) E.

7 (of wind) **stir up** —*a wave* Il.; (of persons or things) —*someone's pain, one's own anger* S. E. Ar. —*a war, political strife* Th. Pl. ǁ PASS. (of a whirlwind) *be stirred up* S.

8 spur on —*a comrade* (W.DAT. w. threats) S.; **provoke** —*the minds of the gods* Ar. ǁ PASS. *be spurred on or fired up* (to action) Il. Ar. X. —w. πρός + ACC. *to diligence* X. ǁ PF.PASS.PTCPL.ADJ. *app., well-versed, expert* (w. περί + ACC. *in sthg.*) Th.

9 rouse to speech or song; **incite, provoke** —*a person, a mouth* (to speak) S. Pl. X. —*angry words, a speech* S. E.; (of shepherds) **rouse** —*their panpipes* E.*fr.*; (of dawn) **bring forth** —*birdsong* S.

10 initiate —*an action, a debate* Th. Pl.; **develop, set out** —*an idea* (in one's mind), *propositions* Ar. Pl. ǁ PASS. (of actions, events) *be initiated* Th. Ar.

11 cause agitated motion or disturbance; **shake** —*one's head, helmet-crest* Hom. Tyrt. E.; **rattle** —*a barred door* Od.

12 (of wind) **ruffle** —*a cornfield, the sea* Il. Sol.; (of ploughmen) **break** or **churn up** —*the earth* X. ǁ PASS. (of sea, land) *be churned up* hHom. Simon. X.; (specif., of places, the earth) *be shaken by an earthquake* Hes.*fr.* hHom. Hdt. Th.

13 (of persons, plotters, disasters) **throw into turmoil** —*an army, city, region, its political affairs* E. Th. Ar. ǁ PASS. (of armies, cities, regions) *be thrown into turmoil* Il. E. Th. Isoc. Pl. +; (of a person) *be frenzied* Pl.

14 (colloq.) engage in vigorous sexual activity; (of a man) **screw, fuck** —*a woman, a boy* Ar.; (intr.) Ar. ǁ PASS. (of men) *be fucked* (by men) Ar. | see also βινέω

15 move (fr. one place to another), **move** —*a person, objects, a military camp* Il. Alc. S. Th. Ar. + ǁ PASS. (of things, a military camp) *be moved* Hdt. X.

16 interfere with sacred things; **disturb, remove** —*sacred objects, temple funds, temple ruins, or sim.* Hdt. E. Th. Isoc. —W.PARTITV.GEN. *some of a temple's funds* Th.

17 (fig.) **desecrate** —*holy secrets* (by revealing them) S. ǁ PASS. (of secrets) *be desecrated* —W.DAT. *in speech* S.

18 move, disturb —*a woman lying down, things at rest* E. Pl.; **drive** —*Bacchants* (W.PREP.PHR. *fr. a mountain*) E.

19 (provbl.) **move** —*every stone or thing* (i.e. leave no stone unturned) Hdt. E.; (in neg.phr.) —*a single twig* (i.e. not move a muscle) Ar. ǁ PASS. (of a stinking plant) *be disturbed* (ref. to unwise interference) Ar.

20 tamper with, alter, change —*ancestral customs, laws, an agreement, medical treatment, or sim.* Thgn. Hdt. Antipho Isoc. Arist. ǁ PASS. (of a temple) *be altered* Hdt.; (of laws, rules, the science of medicine) Pl. Arist.

κῑνηθμός οῦ *m.* **movement** (of the Clashing Rocks) Pi.

κίνημα ατος *n.* **1 movement** (made by persons, their bodies, animals, objects) Theoc. Plb. Plu.; (of a person's features, ref. to facial expressions) Plu.; **bearing, deportment** (of a person) Plu.

2 movement (of a tribe or sim., esp. in an armed uprising) Plb. Plu.

3 uprising, insurrection (among troops, a people) Plb. Plu.; **disturbance** (in a city, military camp, or sim.) Plb. Plu.

4 (ref. to a person's actions) **cause of insurrection, agitating force** Plu.

κίνημι Aeol.vb.: see κῑνέω

κίνησις, dial. **κίνᾱσις**, εως f. **1 movement** (of persons, animals, their limbs, objects, heavenly bodies, or sim.) Th. Pl. X. Arist. Plb. Plu.; (of music or the voice, ref. to melody) Pl.; (fig., of or within the soul, the mind; esp. ref. to emotions, impressions) Democr. Pl. Arist. Plu.; **speed** (of sounds, as relating to their pitch) Pl.
2 movement, manoeuvre (of troops in battle) Plb. Plu.
3 (gener.) **movement, motion** (oft.opp. στάσις or ἠρεμία *rest*) Pl. Arist. Plu.; (ref. to processes involving change, as being motion fr. one state to another) Arist. Plu.
4 (specif.) **physical exercise** Pl. Arist. Plu.(pl.)
5 way of moving, **movement, gestures, deportment** (of a person) Arist. Plu.; (specif.) way of walking, **gait, pace** Plb. Plu.
6 movement of the senses, **sense-impression, emotion** Arist.
7 impact, effect (of rhythms, music, heat) Arist.
8 handling (of weapons, by troops) Plb.
9 capacity to throw a missile, **range** (of a war-machine) Plu.
10 political or military action; **action** (taken by a state, conspirators) Th. Plu.; **mobilisation** (of sides in a war) Th.
11 political upheaval (in a city or region) Arist. Plb. Plu.; **insurrection** (among troops, a people) Plb. Plu.; **commotion, turmoil** (in a place, among a people) Plb. Plu.
12 disturbance, agitation (of the ground, the air) Plu.
13 development from one state to another, change Arist. Plu.

κῑνητέος ᾱ ον vbl.adj. **1** (of an enemy) **to be impelled** (w. εἰς + ACC. to battle) Plu.
2 (of laws) **to be changed** Arist.

κῑνητήρ ῆρος m. (ref. to Poseidon) **mover** (W.GEN. of the earth and sea) hHom. Pi.

κῑνητήριος ᾱ ον adj. **1** (of a gadfly) **driving on** (a cow) A.
2 (of harsh words) **provocative** (W.GEN. of anger) A.

κῑνητής οῦ m. **1 mover, instigator** (of new words) Ar.
2 agitator, stirrer of sedition Plb.

κῑνητιάω contr.vb. [desiderativ., reltd. βῑνητιάω] (of women) **want a fuck** Men.

κῑνητικός ή όν adj. **1** (of water) of the kind which moves, **mobile, fluid** Pl.
2 (of entities) **capable of causing motion** (in other things) Arist. Plu.; (of parts of an animal's body) **used in moving, locomotory** Arist.
3 (of rhythms, metres) suited to movement, **lively** (opp. sedate) Arist.
4 (of a woman's appearance) **arousing, alluring** X.
5 (of a person's manner) **able to stir emotion** (W.GEN. in the populace) Plu.
6 (of persons, troops, slander) **seditious** Plb.

κῑνητός ή όν (also ός όν) adj. **1** (of things) **able to be moved** Pl. Arist.
2 able to be changed, mutable, variable Arist.

κιννᾱμώμινος ον adj. [κιννάμωμον] (of oil) **perfumed with cinnamon** Plb.

κιννάμωμον (also κινάμωμον) ου n. [Semit.loanwd.] **cinnamon** (ref. to the twigs and bark of the tree, used as a spice and in perfumes) Hdt. Plu.

κίνυγμα ατος n. [κῑνύσσομαι] (ref. to Prometheus, chained to a rock) **object of buffeting** (by the elements) A.

κίνυμαι ep.mid.vb. [reltd. κῑνέω] | only pres. and impf. | 3pl.impf. κίνυντο | **1** (of a person) **stir oneself, move about** Hom. AR.; (of a sleeping giant) **shift oneself** —W. εἰς + ACC. *onto one's shoulder* Call.
2 (of troops) **move, advance** (sts. W.ADV. or PREP.PHR. into battle) Il. AR.
3 (of a wind) **blow** AR.
4 ‖ PASS. (of perfumed oil) **be shaken** (to spread its fragrance) Il.; (of sand, trees, a pillar) **be moved** (sts. W.PREP.PHR. by the wind) AR.

κῑνύρομαι mid.vb. [κινυρός] **1** (fig., of the bridles of war-horses) perh. **bellow** —*slaughter* A.(dub.)
2 (of persons, goddesses, birds) **wail in lamentation, lament** A.*satyr.fr.* Ar. AR. Mosch. —W.DIR.SP. *sthg.* Bion; (tr.) **lament over, mourn** —*a dead man, his poetry* Call. Mosch.

κινυρός ά (Ion. ή) όν adj. **1** (of a cow protecting its calf) perh. **lowing, bellowing** Il. [or perh. *fiercely defensive*]
2 (of a lament) **plaintive** AR.

κῑνύσσομαι pass.vb. [κίνυμαι] **be tossed around** (by hopes and fears) A.

κινώπετον ου n. **dangerous wild animal, beast** Call. [or perh. specif. *serpent*]

κῑό-κρᾱνον ου n. [κίων, κρανίον¹] **head of a column, capital** X.

κίον (ep.aor.2): see κίω

Κίρκη ης, dial. **Κίρκᾱ** ᾱς f. **Circe** (daughter of Helios, sorceress able to turn men into animals) Od. Hes. Alcm. E. X. +

κιρκ-ήλατος ον adj. [κίρκος¹, ἐλαύνω] (of a nightingale) **chased by a hawk** A.

κίρκος¹ ου m. **hawk, falcon** Hom. Stesich. A. S.*fr.* AR.

κίρκος² ου m. **circus** (ref. to a public entertainment at Rome) Plb. Plu.

κιρκόω contr.vb. [κρίκος] (of Hephaistos) **encircle, shackle** —*a person's legs* (w. *leg-irons*) A.

κιρνάω contr.vb., **κίρνημι** vb.: see κεράννῡμι

Κίρρα f., **Κίρρᾱθεν** adv., **Κιρραῖος** adj.: see Κρῖσα

κίς (or perh. **κῖς**) κιός m. **small wood-boring pest**; perh. **weevil** Pi.*fr.*

κίσηρις εως f. **pumice-stone** Arist.

κίσθος ου m. a kind of plant, **cistus, rock-rose** Theoc.

κίσσα, Att. **κίττα**, ης (dial. ᾱς) f. **jay** or **magpie** Ar. Theoc.

κισσ-ήρης ες adj. [κισσός, ἀραρίσκω] (of the slopes of Mt. Nysa, assoc.w. Dionysus) **covered in ivy** S.

κίσσινος η ον adj. (of wreaths, sprigs) **of ivy** Pi.*fr.* E.; (of a wine-cup) **of ivy-wood** E. Tim.; (of the thyrsos) **wreathed in ivy** E.

Κίσσιος ᾱ ον adj. **1** (of persons, walls, a citadel, gate, region) of Kissia (a region in Persia, w. Susa as its capital), **Kissian** A. Hdt. ‖ MASC.PL.SB. **Kissians** (as a population or military force) Hdt. Plb.
2 (as the name of one of the gates of Babylon) facing the city of Kish, **Kissian** Hdt.

κισσο-δαής ές adj. [κισσός, δαῆναι] (of Dionysus) **familiar with ivy** Pi.*fr.*

κισσο-κόμης ου masc.adj. [κόμη] (of Dionysus) having hair wreathed with ivy, **ivy-haired** hHom.

κισσός, Att. **κιττός**, οῦ m. **1 ivy** (ref. to the plant and its foliage, esp. used as wreaths for Dionysus, his worshippers, banqueters) hHom. Pi.*fr.* Trag. Ar. Pl. X. +; (as an example of that which clings) S. E. Theoc.
2 ivy-wood (as the material of a drinking-bowl) E.*Cyc.*

κισσο-φόρος, Att. **κιττοφόρος**, ον adj. [φέρω] (of Dionysus) ivy-bearing, **wreathed in ivy** Pi. Ar.; (of banquets) **with wreaths of ivy** E.; (gener., of glades) **full of ivy** E.

κισσο-χαίτᾱς ᾱ dial.masc.adj. [χαίτη] (of Dionysus) ivy-haired, **wreathed in ivy** Pratin.

κισσόω contr.vb. (of a worshipper of Dionysus) **wreathe with ivy** —*one's head* E.

κισσύβιον ου *n.* [reltd. κισσός by pop.etym.] **drinking-bowl** Od. Call. Theoc.

κίστη ης, dial. **κίστα** ᾱς *f.* **basket, hamper** (for food) Od. S.*fr.* Ar. Call. Theoc. Plu.; (carried in ritual processions) Theoc. Plu.

κιστίς ίδος *f.* **basket, hamper** (for food) Ar.

κιστο-φόρος ου *m.* [φέρω] **carrier of a basket** (in a ritual procession) D.

κίταρις εως *f.* [Semit.loanwd.] a kind of head-dress worn by Persian kings, **royal turban** Plu.

κίττα Att.*f.*: see κίσσα

κιττάω Att.contr.vb. [κίσσα] behave like a magpie; (gener.) **have a craving** —w.GEN. *for sthg.* Ar. —w.INF. *to do sthg.* Ar.

κιττός Att.*m.*, **κιττοφόρος** Att.adj.: see κισσός, κισσοφόρος

κιχάνω (also **κιγχάνω** Trag.) vb. | impf. ἐκίχανον, ep. κίχανον | ep.fut.inf. κιχησέμεν (AR.) | aor.1 ptcpl. κιχήσᾱς (B.) || AOR.2: ἔκιχον, ep. κίχον | ptcpl. κιχών | subj. κίχω, ep.3sg. κίχησι | 3sg.opt. κίχοι || EP.ATHEM.AOR.: 2sg. ἐκίχεις, 3du. κιχήτην, 1pl. ἐκίχημεν | inf. κιχῆναι, κιχήμεναι | ptcpl. κιχείς | subj. κιχείω, 1pl. κιχείομεν | opt. κιχείην | MID.: κιχᾰ́νομαι | fut. κιχήσομαι | ep.3sg.aor.1 κιχήσατο | ep.athem.aor.ptcpl. κιχήμενος || Mid. and act. are used without distinction of sense. |

1 (of persons, gods, horses, rushing water) **catch up with** —*persons, horses, a ship, or sim.* Hom. Pi. Hellenist.poet.; (provbl., of the slow) —*the quick* Od.

2 (specif.) catch up with and detain (or kill); (of persons, hunting dogs) **catch** —*a person, an animal* Hom. E.; (provbl.) —*that which flees fr. one* B.

3 (of persons, gods) go up to, **approach, reach** —*persons, a corpse* Hom. Pi. B. Bion; (of Scylla, W.DAT. w. her heads) Od.

4 (of a warrior) **reach, hit** —*an enemy* (W.DAT. *w. one's spear*) Il.; (of a spear) —*an enemy* Il.

5 (of persons) **arrive at, reach** —*a place* Il. hHom. S. E.

6 reach a certain point in time; **reach, come through to, see** —*the end of a war* Il.

7 (of death, fate, justice, evil deeds) **catch up with** —*someone* Hom. Eleg. Simon. Mosch.; (of Hermes, as conductor of souls, meton. for death) A.; (of hunger, thirst, madness, darkness, pollution, need) **grip, afflict** —*someone* Il. Archil. E. AR.; (of an end to troubles) **come to** —*someone* Thgn.; (intr., of fear, fate) **come, arrive** Archil. S.

8 (of persons) **meet, encounter, find** —*someone* (oft. W.PREP.PHR. *in a place*) Hom. S. E. AR. —*wailing and lamentation* Il.; (fig.) —*Justice* B.

9 find —w.ACC. + PTCPL. *someone doing sthg.* Hom. Pi. —w.ACC. + PREDIC.ADJ. *someone in a certain state* Hom. Hes. Pi. —w.GEN. + PREDIC.ADJ. S.

κίχλη ης, dial. **κίχλᾱ** ᾱς *f.* —also **κιχήλᾱ** ᾱς (Ar.) dial.*f.* **thrush** (esp. eaten as a delicacy) Od. Ar. Men. Plu.

κιχλίζω vb. (of boys, young women) **giggle** Ar. Theoc.

κιχρᾱ́ς (ptcpl.), **κίχρασθαι** (mid.inf.), **κίχρημι** vb.: see χράω, under χράομαι

κίω vb. [reltd. κίνυμαι] | 2sg. κίεις (A.) | aor.2 (or impf.) ἔκιον, ep. κίον | aor.2 (or pres.) imperatv. κίε, ptcpl. κιών | (of persons, gods) **go** or **come** (sts. W.ADV. or PREP.PHR. to or fr. someone or somewhere) Hom. Hes. A. B. AR. Theoc.; (of ships) Il.

κίων ονος *m.f.* | dat.pl. κίοσι, also κιόνεσσι (Pi.) | **1** supporting pillar, **pillar, column** (in a house, palace or portico) Od. +; (in a temple or public building) Pi.*fr.* +; (mythol., supporting the sky, held steady by Atlas) Od. A.; (supporting the island of Delos) Pi.*fr.*; (ref. to the Pillars of Hercules) Pi.; (ref. to a mountain, envisaged as a pillar) Pi. Hdt.; (pinning down Prometheus) Hes.; (fig., ref. to a warrior, an island) **pillar of support** (W.GEN. or DAT. for people, a place) Pi.

2 free-standing pillar, **pillar, column** (topped by a statue) Plb. Plu.; (as a marker or milestone) Plu.; (of earth, in a hunter's pit-trap) X.

κλαγγαίνω vb. [κλαγγή] (of Erinyes, envisaged as hounds) **cry out, yelp, bark** A.

κλαγγάνω vb. (of a lyre) **ring forth** S.*Ichn.*

κλαγγέω contr.vb. | dial.3pl. κλαγγεῦντι | (of dogs) cry out, **yelp, bark** Theoc.

κλαγγή ῆς, dial. **κλαγγᾱ́** ᾶς *f.* **1 loud inarticulate sound** (of animals or persons); **screeching** (of birds, Harpies) Il. AR. Plu.; **clamour** (of wild beasts, pigs, hounds) Od. hHom. A. Pi.*fr.* X.; (of people, spirits of the dead) Il. AR.

2 loud vocal sound (of singing or lamentation); **shrieking** (of a woman, sts.ref. to songs of lament) A. E.; **shouting** (of men, ref. to a paean to Apollo) S.

3 resonant noise, **twang** (of a bow) Il.; (of a stringed instrument) Telest.

κλαγγηδόν adv. **with strident cries** —*ref. to flocks of birds settling* Il.

κλαδαρός ᾱ́ όν adj. (of spears) lacking rigidity, **pliant** (as a mark of poor quality) Plb.

κλάδος ου *m.* | dat. κλάδῳ, also κλαδί | gen.pl. κλαδέων (Philox.Leuc., cj.) | dat.pl. κλάδοις, also κλάδεσι | **1** leafy branch, **branch, sprig, frond** (growing on a tree or sim.) E. Ar. Theoc. Bion NT.; (cut fr. a tree, esp. carried by a suppliant or woven into a wreath) Hdt. Trag. Ar.(quot. Scol.) Philox.Leuc. Arist. +; (used as a crowbar) E.; (fig.ref. to a javelin) B.; (pl., fig.ref. to wings growing fr. a creature's back) Emp.

2 (fig.) **scion** (of Enyalios, ref. to a warrior) Ibyc.

κλαδός (dial.gen.): see κλείς

κλάζω vb. [κλαγγή] | fut. κλάγξω | aor.1 ἔκλαγξα | aor.2 ἔκλαγον | pf. κέκληγα (dial. κέκλᾱγα), also κέκλαγγα, ptcpl. κεκληγώς (ep. κεκλήγων, pl. κεκλήγοντες), also κεκλαγγώς (X.), κεκλαγώς (Plu.) || mid.fut.pf. κεκλάγξομαι (Ar.) |

1 make a loud inarticulate sound; (of birds) **cry out, screech** Il. Hes. Stesich. S. Hellenist.poet. +; (of dogs) **yelp, howl** Od. Ar. X. Theoc.

2 (of wind) **howl** Od. AR.; (of the sea) **roar** B.; (of Zeus) **peal forth** —w.ACC. *w. a thunderclap* Pi.

3 (of arrows in a quiver) **rattle** Il.; (of wheel-hubs) **screech** A.; (of bells on a shield, a horse's bridle) **ring out** —w.ACC. *a fearful noise, a clang of metal* A. E.; (of a trumpet) —*a song of war* B.

4 make a loud articulate sound; (of persons, gods, a Muse) **cry out, shout** Hom. Hes. Alcm. A. S. AR. —w.DIR.SP. *sthg.* E. AR. —w.ACC. (representing dir.sp.) *'War'* A. —*'Zeus'* (w. 2ND ACC. *in a song of victory*) A. —w.ACC. *a lament, news, advice* A. Pi.*fr.*

5 make a sound on a musical instrument; **make music** hHom. —w.DAT. *w. the lyre* E.

κλᾴζω dial.vb. [κλείω¹] | fut. κλᾴξω | **lock** or **bar** —*a door* Theoc.

κλᾱΐδος (dial.gen.): see κλείς

κλᾴθρον dial.*n.*: see κλεῖθρον

κλᾱΐς dial.*f.*: see κλείς

κλαίω, Att. **κλάω**, perh. Aeol. **κλαΐω** vb. | dial.3pl. κλαίοντι, ep.3sg.subj. κλαίῃσι (unless κλαίησι), ep.2sg.opt. κλαίοισθα | iteratv.impf. κλαίεσκον | fut. κλαύσω (Theoc. NT.), κλαιήσω (Hyp.), Att. κλᾱήσω (D.) | aor. ἔκλαυσα || MID.: fut. κλαύσομαι, also κλαυσοῦμαι | aor. ἐκλαυσάμην | fut.pf.

κεκλαύσομαι ‖ pf.mid.pass. κέκλαυμαι, ptcpl. κεκλαυμένος ‖ The usu. fut. is mid. κλαύσομαι. |
1 (of persons, gods, animals, Justice, rivers, a city) **weep and wail** (fr. sadness, distress, or sim.) Hom. Hes. Archil. Emp. Hdt. Trag.(also mid.) + —W.PREP.PHR. *over someone or sthg.* E. D. Plb. NT. —W.GEN. *over someone* A. E.; (tr.) **weep over** —*someone or sthg.* Hom. Archil. Thgn. Trag. Hellenist.poet. Plu. —w. αἰαῖ *crying 'aiai'* Bion; (mid.) S. ‖ PASS. (of misfortunes) be wept over Mosch.
2 (of persons, animals, rivers) **mourn** —*a dead person, his music, a city* Hom. Stesich. Thgn. Trag. X. +; (intr.) **mourn, grieve** (for a dead person) Thgn. S. E. | PASS. (of persons) be mourned A.
3 shed tears; cry, weep Ar. —W.DAT. *w. tears* Alc. D. —W.ACC. *a flood of tears* Theoc.; (fr. joy) X.
4 lament loudly; wail —W.ADV. *shrilly* Hom. —w. πρός + ACC. *to the heavens* Il. —*to someone* Ar. —W.INTERN.ACC. *a lament* Ar.
5 (esp. in threats, usu. fut.) be made to cry, **be brought to tears** or **suffer** (usu. w.connot. of coming to regret one's actions) Trag. Ar. Pl. D. Men.
6 (imperatv.) **go to hell, go hang** Ar.; (phr.) κλαίειν κελεύειν (or λέγειν, or sim.) *tell* (W.ACC. *someone*) *to go to hell* Hippon. Hdt. E.*Cyc.* Ar.

κλᾶμμα Aeol.n.: see κλῆμα

κλάξ κλακός *dial.f.* [κλείς] **key** (to unlock a chest) Theoc.

κλαξῶ (dial.fut.): see κλᾴζω

κλάριον ου *dial.n.* [κλῆρος] document pledging land as security for a loan, **mortgage document** Plu.

κλάριος ᾱ ον *dial.adj.* (epith. of Zeus) app. **allotting** (justice, destinies, or sim.) A.

κλᾱρο-παληδόν *dial.adv.* [πάλλω] **in the casting of lots** —*ref. to being dealt a particular fate* Stesich.

κλᾶρος *dial.m.*, **κλᾱρόω** *dial.contr.vb.*: see κλῆρος, κληρόω

κλάς *dial.f.*: see κλείς

κλάσις εως *f.* [κλάω] **1** act of breaking into pieces; **breaking** (of bread, to share it out at a meal) NT.
2 act of interrupting; **breaking** (of a circle, ref. to skewing the movement of sthg.) Pl.
3 break (in a formation of troops in battle) Plu.

κλάσματα των *n.pl.* **broken pieces** (of branches, spears, benches) X. Plb. Plu.; (of bread) NT.

κλάσσα (ep.aor.): see κλάω

κλαστάζω *vb.* prune (vines); (fig.) **trim down to size** —*generals* Ar.

κλαυθμονή *f.*: see κλαυμονή

κλαυθμός οῦ *m.* [κλαίω] tearful wailing, **lamentation** Hom. A. Hdt. Arist. NT. Plu.

κλαυθμυρισμός οῦ *m.* [κλαυμυρίζομαι] tearful wailing, **whimpering** (of a child) Plu.

κλαύματα των *n.pl.* [κλαίω] fits of tearful wailing, **weeping and wailing** A.; (fig., ref. to punishments or misfortunes that will bring tears to the eyes) S. And. Ar. X.

κλαυμονή (or perh. **κλαυθμονή**) ῆς *f.* fit of tearful wailing, **crying** (of a child) Pl.

κλαυμυρίζομαι *mid.vb.* (of a baby) **have a crying fit, whimper** Men.

κλαυσιάω *contr.vb.* [desiderativ. κλαίω] (fig., of a door) **want to weep and wail** (i.e. be asking for a beating) Ar.

κλαυσί-γελως ωτος *m.* [γέλως] tearful laughter, **laughter that brings tears to the eyes** X.

κλαυσί-μαχος ου *masc.adj.* [μάχη, w. play on name Λάμαχος] (of a man) **lamenting battles** Ar.

κλαύσομαι, also **κλαυσοῦμαι** (fut.mid.), **κλαύσω** (fut.): see κλαίω

κλαυτός ή όν *adj.* (of a situation) **to be wept over** A. S.

κλάω *contr.vb.* | aor. ἔκλασα, ep. κλάσα, also (in tm.) κλάσσα ‖ PASS.: aor. ἐκλάσθην | pf. κέκλασμαι | **1 break off** —*a branch* (w. ἐκ + GEN. *fr. a bush*) Od. ‖ PASS. (of young plants) be broken off —W.ADV. *at the root* AR.
2 break in two or into pieces, **break** —*a javelin, pillar* Plu. —*bread, fish* (*to share w. others*) NT. ‖ PASS. (of an arrow-shaft, spears, a wooden peg) be broken in two Il. Plb. Plu.; (of objects) be broken into pieces Arist.; (of a pillar of support) be broken (fig.ref. to the fall of a king) Plu.
3 ‖ PASS. (of the movement of a comet) be interrupted or erratic (opp. straight) Plu.

κλάω *Att.vb.*: see κλαίω

κλέα (neut.pl.): see κλέος

κλεεννός *dial.adj.*: see κλεινός

κλεηδών *Ion.f.*: see κληδών

κλεῖα (neut.pl.): see κλέος

κλειδίον ου *n.* [dimin. κλείς] **key** (to a door) Ar. Men.

κλείζω *dial.vb.*: see κλῄζω

κλεῖθρον, Att. **κλῇθρον**, Ion. **κλήϊθρον**, dial. **κλάϊθρον**, ου *n.* [κλείω¹] **1 keyhole** (of a door) hHom.
2 that which closes (a door); **bar** or **bolt** A. E. Ar. X. Plu.; (fig., on the eyes of a sleeper) Pi.
3 (gener.) **barred door, door** S. E.; (pl., ref. to the gates of Thebes) E.
4 barrier, breakwater (along a coast) Plu.

κλεινός, dial. **κλεεννός**, also **κλεννός** (Alcm.), ή (dial. ά) όν *adj.* [κλέος] **1** (of persons, gods, places, things) **famous, illustrious, glorious** Sol. Scol. Lyr. Hdt. Trag. Critias +; (iron., of a murderer) S. E.; (of a marriage, i.e. to a noble husband) Pi.
2 (of a deed) bringing glory, **glorious** E.

—**κλεινά** *neut.pl.adv.* **illustriously** —*ref. to leading an army* E.

κλείξω (dial.fut.): see κλῄζω

κλείς ειδός, Att. **κλῇς** ῃδός, Ion. **κληίς** ῖδος, dial. **κλᾱΐς** ῖδος, also **κλάς** ᾳδός *f.* [κλείω¹] | acc. κλεῖν, also κλεῖδα (NT. Plu.) | acc.pl. κλεῖς, also κλεῖδας | **1 bar** or **bolt** (on a door) Hom. Parm. E. Call. AR.; (fig., on a person's tongue or mind) S. E.
2 key (to open the bolt of a locked door) Hom. hHom. A. E. Lys. +; (to unlock a chest) D.; (to the Kingdom of Heaven) NT.
3 (fig., ref. to the control of access) **key** (W.GEN. to counsels, wars, love, marriage) Pi. Ar.; (to knowledge) NT.; (to Cyprus, ref. to a headland) Hdt.; (to the Black Sea, ref. to the Bosporos) E.
4 clasp (of a brooch) Od.
5 collar-bone (of a person) Il. S. And. X. D. Arist. +
6 peg to which an oar is fastened, **thole-pin, rowlock** Hom.
7 bench on which rowers sit, **rowing-bench** Lyr.adesp. AR.

κλεισιάδες (sts. written **κλῑσιάδες**) ων *f.pl.* [κλεισίον] pair of doors at the front of a house, **front door** Plu.; (fig.) **entrance-way** (into Greece, for the invading Persians) Hdt.; (into public life, for an ambitious man) Plu.; (to military success against an enemy) Plu.

κλεισίον (sts. written **κλῑσίον**) ου *n.* [κλίνω] **1 lean-to shed, hut** Lys. D.
2 entrance-chamber, vestibule (of a Roman house) Plu.

κλειτός ή (dial. ά) όν *adj.* [κλέω] **1** (of persons, places, a breed of horses) **famous, illustrious** Il. Hes. Mimn. Pi. Hdt.(oracle)
2 (of sacrifices) bringing glory, **glorious** Il. Hes. Thgn. Pi. Men.

κλειτύς (sts. written **κλῑτύς**) ύος *f.* [κλίνω] | acc. κλειτύν, also κλειτῦν (Od.) | acc.pl. κλειτῦς (Il.) | **sloping ground, hillside** Hom. S. E.; **side** (W.ADJ. or GEN. of a mountain) S. E.

κλείω[1], Att. **κλῄω**, Ion. **κληίω** vb. | fut. κλείσω, Att. κλήσω | aor. ἔκλεισα, Att. ἔκλησα, Ion. ἐκλήϊσα | pf. κέκλεικα || PASS.: aor. ἐκλείσθην | pf. κέκλειμαι, Att. κέκλημαι, Ion. κεκλήϊμαι | Att.fut.pf. κεκλήσομαι |
1 close by barring or locking, **close, bar, lock** —doors, city-gates Od. E. Th. Ar. Pl. + —(W.DAT. w. a bar, a key) Od. Arist. —towers (ref. to city-gates) E. —door-bolts Od. —a chest Thphr. || PASS. (of doors, city-gates) be barred Th. Ar. X. Men. +
2 close by barring or locking the doors, **close up, lock** —houses, buildings Aeschin. D. Plu. —the Kingdom of Heaven NT. || PASS. (of buildings, rooms) be closed (w. doors and gates) Hdt. Men. Plb. NT. Plu.; (fig., of the right of speech) be barred —W.DAT. by legal penalties D.
3 close —a quiver hHom. —one's mouth E. Ar.; (fig.) —a person's breast (after looking into his soul) Scol.; (of sleep) —someone's eyes Lyr.adesp.
4 close off, block off —sea-channels, a harbour, a pass A. Th. D.; **blockade** —trading-ports D. || PASS. (of trading-ports) be closed (by a blockade) Lys. D.
5 || PASS. (fig., of the sky) be sealed tight (ref. to being rainless) —W.PREP.PHR. for a certain period of time NT.
6 (of collars) **encircle** —horses' necks E. || PASS. (of a city) be encircled —W.DAT. w. fortifications A.
7 lock up, shut away —a person (W.ADV. or PREP.PHR. in a place) E. || PASS. (of a person) be bound —W.DAT. w. ropes (W.ACC. on the hands) E.; (fig.) —w. oaths E.; be caught —W.DAT. in a net (fig.ref. to a trap) E.
κλείω[2] ep.vb.: see κλέω
Κλειώ, also **Κλεώ**, οῦς f. [κλέος] | voc. Κλειοῖ, Κλεοῖ | **Clio** (one of the nine Muses, sts. specified as the Muse of History) Hes. Pi. B. Call.
κλέμμα ατος n. [κλέπτω] **1** that which is stolen (ref. to goods or money), **stolen property** E. Pl. X. D.; (ref. to a woman abducted by a god) A.fr.
2 instance of stealing, **theft** Ar.
3 act of deception or fraud Aeschin. D.
4 stratagem (in war) Th.
—**κλεμμάδιον** ου n. [dimin.] that which is stolen, **item of stolen property** Pl.
κλεννός dial.adj.: see κλεινός
κλέος n. [reltd. κλύω] | only nom.acc.sg., and nom.acc.pl. κλέα, also κλεῖα (Hes.) | **1 glorious fame** (of a person, god, people or nation, their valour or accomplishments) Hom. Hes. Archil. Eleg. Lyr. Hdt. +; (of a place, river, event or thing) Hom. Lyr. A. Th. AR.; (concr.) **honour** (to a dead warrior, ref. to a pyre) Il.
2 || PL. glorious deeds (W.GEN. ἀνδρῶν of men, or sim.) Hom. Hes. hHom. AR. Theoc. Plu.
3 reputation (of a person or people) Pi. Hdt. E. Th.
4 report, rumour (oft. W.GEN. about a person or event) Hom. hHom. A. Pi. S. AR.
κλέπτης ου m. [κλέπτω] one who steals, **thief** Il. Hdt. S.Ichn. E. Ar. Att.orats. +; (W.GEN. of fire, ref. to Prometheus) A.; **robber** (W.GEN. of a person) S.; stealer (of public money), **embezzler** Att.orats. Pl.
κλεπτικός ή όν adj. relating to theft || FEM.SB. thievery Pl.
κλεπτίστατος η ον superl.adj. (of a servant) **most thievish** Ar.
κλεπτοσύνη ης f. thieving, thievery Od.
κλέπτω vb. | fut. κλέψω | aor. ἔκλεψα, ep. and dial. κλέψα | pf. κέκλοφα || PASS.: aor. ἐκλέφθην | aor.2 ἐκλάπην | pf. κέκλεμμαι || neut.impers.vbl.adj. κλεπτέον |
1 (of persons, gods, animals) **steal** —valuables, food, money Hes. hHom. Pi. Hdt. Trag. + —public money Ar. Att.orats. + —a ship's oar-hole (i.e. the public money allotted to the rower) Ar. —funeral rites (fr. the dead, i.e. deprive them of proper burial) E.; (of desire) —someone's senses Archil. || PASS. (of objects, livestock, money) be stolen Thgn. Hdt. Ar. Pl. +
2 (intr., of persons or gods) commit theft, **steal** Semon. Eleg. Hdt. S. Ar. + —W.PARTITV.GEN. fr. a herd of horses, a store of meat, public funds, someone's estate Il. Ar. X.(mid.) —fr. someone Arist.; (phr.) κλέπτον βλέπειν look thievish Ar. || PASS. be robbed (of sthg.) Pl.
3 (of a person or god) take away by stealth, **smuggle away** —a corpse, a person Il. S. E. Corinn. NT.; (of Helen) **secretly lower** —her body (fr. the walls of Troy) E.; (of a commander) **secretly transport** —troops Plu.
4 (of persons or gods) **carry off, abduct** —a woman Pi. Ar. Corinn. —an old man S. —a witness Antipho || PASS. (of a dead woman) be carried away (into the heavens) —w. ὑπό + GEN. by the Dioscuri Call.
5 obtain by unfair means, **steal** —a marriage, victory Theoc. Plu.
6 obtain by stealth or cunning, **seize by stealth** —a situation (i.e. command of events) Plu.; (specif., of troops, commanders) **take by stealth** —a military position X. —W.PARTITV.GEN. part of a mountain X.
7 stealthily commit —evil acts S. Pl.; **stealthily spread** —rumours S.
8 (of persons, gods, allure) **deceive** —persons, gods, their minds, ears Il. Hes. Semon. Thgn. A. Pi. +; **betray** —a friendship Thgn.; (of persons, poetic cleverness) **practise deceit** —W.DAT. w. words Pi. S. E. Aeschin. —W.ACC. in a certain matter S. || MID. **deceive** —one's own mind E. || PASS. be deceived S. E. Arist. —W.DAT. by time (i.e. be foolish due to old age) S.
9 hide, conceal —objects, an unborn child, mistakes, one's fear Pi. E. X. —one's troops (fr. the enemy) X. —oneself Plu.; (of a court) **keep secret** —its decisions Pl. || PASS. (of love, the sun during an eclipse, literary artifice) be concealed Pi.fr. Arist.; (of regions, fr. someone, i.e. be unknown to them) Hdt.
κλεψί-φρων ον, gen. ονος adj. [φρήν] (of Hermes) **thievish-minded** hHom.
κλεψ-ύδρα ᾱς, Ion. **κλεψύδρη** ης f. [ὕδωρ] **1** vessel with a perforated base and narrow mouth (used as a pipette to transfer liquid fr. one container to another), **strainer-jug** Emp.
2 vessel with a perforated base (filled w. water and used to measure time by its slow emptying), **water-clock** Ar. Arist.
Κλεώ f.: see Κλειώ
κλέω contr.vb. —also **κλείω** ep.vb. [reltd. κλέος, καλέω] | Lacon.fem.ptcpl. κλέωά (Ar.) | **1** (of poets, singers, the Muses, a person, a poem) tell the fame of, **celebrate** (oft. W.DAT. in song) —gods, heroes, persons, their deeds or attributes, a city, an event Od. Hes. hHom. Stesich. Pi.fr.(mid.) E. + —W.ACC. + RELATV.CL. mythol. figures, what they suffered Call.epigr. —W.ACC. + INF. how a mythol. hero did sthg. B. AR.; (intr., of the Muses) **confer fame** —W.DAT. in songs Hes. || PASS. (of heroes, gatherings) be celebrated S. —w. ἐν + DAT. in music Pi.; (of Athena, Priam) be famous —W.DAT. for wisdom Hom.
2 (of persons, recounting a local tradition) **say, claim** —W.ACC. + INF. that sthg. is the case AR.
3 call —a person, god, place or thing (W.PREDIC.ADJ. or SB. by a certain name) Call. AR.; (of the Argonauts) **name** —an island (W.PREDIC.SB. by a certain name) AR. || PASS. (of a

place) be called —w.predic.nom. *by a certain name* Call. AR.

κλήδην *adv.* [καλέω] **by name** —*ref. to summoning someone* Il.

κληδουχέω *Att.contr.vb.* [κληδοῦχος] (of a woman) **be a temple-guardian** —w.dat. *for a goddess* E.

κληδοῦχος ου *Att.m.* [κλείς, ἔχω] (ref. to Eros) **holder of the keys** (to the chamber of Aphrodite) E.; **keeper, guardian** (of a temple, ref. to a priest or priestess) A. E.; **protectress** (of Athens, ref. to Athena) Ar.

κληδών, Ion. **κλεηδών**, ep. **κληηδών**, όνος *f.* [καλέω]
1 prophetic utterance (ref. to an omen derived fr. another's words) Od. A. Hdt. Call.*epigr.* Plb. Plu.; (personif., as an object of worship) Plu.; (gener.) **omen** Hippon.
2 story or piece of news conveyed orally, report, rumour Od. Hdt. Trag. And.
3 reputation (of a person) S. E.; (specif.) good reputation, **fame** Simon. A. AR.
4 call, summons (to a person or god) A. E.
5 that by which one is called, **appellation, name** A.

κλῄζω, ep. **κληΐζω** (Call. AR.), dial. **κλεΐζω** *vb.* [reltd. κλέος, καλέω] | *fut.* κλῄσω, dial. κλεΐξω ‖ *ep.pf.pass.* κεκλήϊσμαι, perh. also ἐκλήϊσμαι | *ep.3sg.plpf.* ἐκλήϊστο |
1 (of poets, Muses, gods, choruses, persons) **tell the fame of, celebrate** —*gods, their attributes, a person, place, Olympic victory* hHom. Pi. E. Ar. AR. ‖ PASS. (of the Argo) be celebrated (in song, by a woman) E.*fr.*; (of Helen) be infamous —w.compl.cl. *for doing sthg.* E.
2 (of people) **say, tell, relate** —w.acc. + aor.inf. *that a deity did sthg.* E. ‖ PASS. (of reports, stories) be told —w.prep.phr. *by people* A. S. AR.; (of events, deeds) be spoken about E. AR.; (of a person) be reported —w.predic.sb. or adj. *as being in a certain role or condition* S. E.
3 (of a person, a land) **call** —*a person or god* (w.predic.adj. or sb. *by a certain description*) S. E. ‖ PASS. (of persons, places) be called —w.predic.adj. or sb. *by a certain name or description* (oft. ref. to their role or lineage) S. E. Call. AR.; (of the Perseidai) be named —w. ἀπό + gen. *after Perseus* X.; (of a name) be used as an appellation —w.predic.adj. *that is double* (i.e. referring to two people) E.

κληθήσομαι (fut.pass.): see καλέω

κλήθρη ης *Ion.f.* **alder tree** Od.

κλῆθρον *Att.n.*: see κλεῖθρον

κληΐζω *ep.vb.*: see κλῄζω

κλήϊθρον *Ion.n.*: see κλεῖθρον

κληΐς *Ion.f.*: see κλείς

κληϊστός *ep.adj.*: see κλῃστός

κληΐω *Ion.vb.*: see κλείω[1]

κλῆμα, Aeol. **κλᾶμμα**, ατος *n.* [κλάω] **1 cut vine-branch** Ar. Pl. Plb. Plu.; (planted in the ground) X. Call.(cj.); (ref. to a centurion's cudgel) Plu.; (gener.) **vine-branch** (on the plant) Alc. NT.
2 ‖ PL. (fig.) **shoots** (w.gen. of a democratic government) Aeschin.(quot. D.)

κλημάτινος η ον *adj.* (of a fire) **of vine-branches** Thgn.

κληματίς ίδος *f.* vine-branch used as firewood, **stick of firewood** Th. Ar. Men.

κληματόομαι *mid.contr.vb.* (of a vine) **grow branches** or **shoots** S.*fr.*

κληρονομέω *contr.vb.* [κληρονόμος] **1 be the inheritor of, inherit** —w.gen. *an estate, a woman* (treated as part of the estate under Athenian law) Att.orats. Arist. —*a father's friendships, honours or loss of rights* Isoc. D. —*one's ancestors' pledges* (i.e. be bound by them) Lycurg. —w.acc. *an estate* Plu.; (intr.) be the inheritor (of an estate), **be an heir** D.
2 (gener.) gain as one's entitlement; (of the meek, the righteous) **inherit** —*the earth, the Kingdom of Heaven* NT.; (of the patriotic kings of old) **have a rightful share in** —w.gen. *their native land* Lycurg.; (of a ruler) **receive as one's share** (in an undertaking) —w.acc. *a wasteland* Plb.
3 obtain for oneself (sthg. which was not originally one's own); (of jurors) **inherit, incur by proxy** —w.gen. *someone's wickedness* (by refusing to condemn him) D.; (of lawmakers, politicians) —*the prestige and privileges of Athens* D.; (of a people) **inherit, become the new owners of** —w.acc. *the territory of a deported population* Plb.
4 (wkr.sens.) **incur** —w.gen. *disgrace* D.; **obtain** —w.acc. *a bad reputation* Plb. —*the credit for a success* Plb.; **receive, be given** —w.acc. *a certain name* Plb. —*eternal life* NT.

κληρονομίᾱ ᾱς *f.* **1** right of inheritance (of someone's estate or sim.), **inheritance** Att.orats. Arist. Men. NT. Plu.; **right of sole possession** (of the name of pleasure, as claimed by physical pleasures) Arist.
2 (concr.) that which is inherited, **inheritance, bequest** (of property, money) NT. Plu.

κληρο-νόμος ου *m.* [κλῆρος, νέμω] **1 heir** (of a person) or **inheritor** (of a person's estate) Att.orats. Pl. D. Arist. +; (phr.) ἐν πίστει κληρονόμος **trustee** (of an estate left to a girl) Plu.
2 heir, inheritor (of a parent's reputation or loss of rights) Isoc. D.; (of one's ancestors' high principles) Plb.; (of a departing person's side of an argument) Pl.; (of a style of poetry) Mosch.; (of a consulship or tyranny, i.e. its style of governance) Plu.; (of a grievance against a wrongdoer) D.; (pejor.) **true heir** (of a shameful practice) Aeschin.

κληρο-παλής ές *adj.* [πάλλω] (of portions of meat) **assigned by casting lots** hHom.

κλῆρος, dial. **κλᾶρος**, ου *m.* **1** object or token used in the casting of lots, **lot** Hom. Pi. S. Pl. Call. +; (used in divination, to determine the will of the gods) Pi. E. Pl.
2 casting of lots (to allocate a task, fate, privilege, esp. DAT. κλήρῳ *by lot*) Hom. Hdt. Trag. Ar. Pl. X. +
3 allocation (of a woman's fate, by her captors) E.; **allocation of territory** (to peoples, by destiny) Plu.
4 that which is allotted, **allotted fate, lot** E. Ar.; **allotted share** (of a kingdom) Hes.*fr.* A. E.; (in Christ's ministry) NT.
5 (concr.) piece of land allotted to a particular person (by the state), **allotment of land** Hdt. Th. Pl. Arist. Plu.; (gener.) **parcel of land** Pl.
6 allotted territory (of a people) A. Call.; **realm** (of a king) AR.
7 land owned by an individual, **landholding, estate** (of a person) Hom. Hes. Pi. Hdt. Pl. Arist. +
8 property and possessions of an individual, **estate** (esp. as an inheritance) Hes. Hippon. Thgn. Att.orats. Pl. +; (fig.) **inheritance** (ref. to the tradition of tragic drama) Ar.(dub.)
9 inheritance case, inheritance suit D.(law)

κληρουχέω *contr.vb.* [κληροῦχος] (of persons) hold an allotment of land (in a colony), **be a settler in** —*a region* Hdt.; (fig., of gods) **hold territory** —w. κατά + acc. *in a region* Pl.

κληρουχίᾱ ᾱς *f.* **1** allotment of land (to the landless poor) Plb. Plu.; (specif.) **allotment of overseas land** (to settlers) Isoc. Plu.; (w.gen. in a certain place) Arist.
2 colony of settlers Plu.

κληρουχικός ή όν *adj.* **1** (of a law) concerning the allotment of land Plu.
2 (of land) **for allocation to settlers** Ar.
3 (of an Athenian) **living overseas as a settler** D.

κληροῦχος ου *m.* [κλῆρος, ἔχω] **1** (ref. to an old person) **possessor of an allotted share** (w.GEN. of many years) S. **2 possessor of an allotment of land**; **settler** (sent to one of Athens' foreign possessions) Hdt. Th. Aeschin. D. Plu.

κληρόω, dial. **κλᾱρόω** contr.vb. **1 hold a lottery** (to select officials) Arist. —w.GEN. *for inheritance cases* (*to assign trial dates*) D.(law); (tr.) **hold a lottery among** —*tribes* (*to select jurors, conscript soldiers*) Arist. Plb.
2 ‖ MID. **take part in a lottery**; (gener., of persons) **cast lots** (to decide sthg.) A. X. D. Plb. Plu.; (specif.) **enter one's lot** (in an official lottery, sts. W.GEN. or ACC. for a particular office) Att.orats. Arist.; (to be allocated a free dinner) Ar.
3 select by lot; (of rulers, officials, persons, the luck of the draw) **select by lot** (sts. W.GEN. or ἐκ + GEN. fr. a particular group) —*officials, jurors* Pl. Arist. Plu. —*persons* (*for a particular task or fate*) Hdt. E. Ar. Pl. Arist. + ‖ MID.PASS. (of persons) **be selected by lot** (for an office) Pl. D. —w.ACC. *for a particular office* Arist.; (specif., of officials, jurors, a chorus director) D. Arist. Plu.
4 assign by lot; (of rulers, officials, a casting of lots) **assign by lot** —*magistracies* (*to persons*) Isoc. D. —*areas of land* (w. εἰς + ACC. *to tribes*) Arist.; (of Apollo) —*oracular responses* E.; (of commanders) —*sections of a fleet* (W.DAT. *among one another*) Th. —*captured horses and equipment* (*to cavalry regiments*) X.(mid.) ‖ MID. (of the Argonauts) **assign by lot** (among themselves) —*the oars* (*i.e. rowing places*) Call.
‖ PASS. (of captive women) **be assigned by lot** (to someone, as slaves) E.; (of governors) —w. εἰς + ACC. *to a particular province* Plu.
5 ‖ MID. **receive by lot**; (of citizens) **receive an allotment** (of a portion of land) Pl.; (of captive women) **be allotted** —w.ACC. *a master* E.
6 allot (a person, to a patron deity); (of fate) **allot** —*persons* (W.DAT. *to Zeus*) Pi. ‖ MID.PASS. (of Aphrodite) **be allotted** (to someone) Ar.
7 ‖ MID. **receive an allotted fate**; (of a person) **be assigned, be fated** —w. ἐκ + GEN. *by the gods* (W.INF. *to write tragedies*) Call.

κλήρωσις εως *f.* **choosing by lot** (of officials, jurors) Isoc. Pl.; **allocation** (of reincarnations, of who lives and who dies) E. Pl.

κληρωτήριον ου *n.* **randomised allocation device, lottery machine** (for selecting jurors) Ar. Arist.

κληρωτός ή όν *adj.* (of officials, jurors, priests) **chosen by lot** Att.orats. Pl. Arist. Plu.

κλῆς Att.*f.*: see κλείς

κλῆσις εως *f.* [καλέω] **1 act of calling** (to a person or animal); **call** (to a hound) X.; **salutation** (to a person) Pl.
2 act of calling upon a person, call, request (for help, fr. an ally) Plb.
3 act of summoning, summons (fr. a king) X.
4 (leg.) **call to a witness or defendant to appear at court**; **summons, writ, subpoena** Antipho X. D. Arist.; **issuing of summonses** Ar.
5 invitation (to dinner) X. D. Plu.
6 calling of a person or thing by a certain name, appellation, name Pl. Plu.

κλῇσις εως *f.* [κλείω¹] **1 act of closing off, blocking** (of a harbour) Th.
2 that which closes off (a harbour), **barrier, obstruction** (ref. to ropes holding together a line of ships) Th.

κληστός, ep. **κληϊστός**, ή όν *adj.* (of doors) **closed** Od.; (of temples) **shut** (w. barred doors) Th.; (of a harbour) **closed off, enclosed** Th.

κλήσω¹ (fut.): see κλῄζω
κλήσω² (Att.fut.): see κλείω¹

κλητέος ᾱ ον *vbl.adj.* [καλέω] (of persons or things) **to be called** (by a certain name or description) Pl.

κλητεύω *vb.* [κλητήρ] **1** (leg.) **call as an unwilling witness, issue a summons to, subpoena** —*a person* Lycurg. D.
2 act as witness to the serving of a summons, witness the serving of a summons Ar. D. —W.DAT. *for a person* (*i.e. the plaintiff*) Ar. —w.ACC. *on a person* D.
3 act as witness that a summons has been served, bear witness to the serving of a summons —w.ACC. *w. false testimony* D.

κλητήρ ῆρος *m.* [καλέω] **1 one who calls or summons, announcer, herald** (ref. to a town-crier or sim.) A.
2 one who summons, summoner, caller-up (of an Erinys) A.
3 (leg.) **witness to the serving of a summons** (sts. w.neg.connot. of making trouble for others) Ar. Pl. D. Men.
4 one who brays, donkey Ar.; (w. play on sense 3) Ar.

κλητός ή όν *adj.* **1** (of persons) **summoned, invited** (to one's house) Od.; (to a banquet) Aeschin. NT.
2 called up, chosen, selected (for a mission) Il.

κλήτωρ ορος *m.* **witness to the serving of a summons** D.

κλήω Att.vb.: see κλείω¹

κλίβανος *m.*: see κρίβανος

κλίθην (ep.aor.pass.): see κλίνω

κλίμα (or perh. **κλίμα**) ατος *n.* [κλίνω] **1 slope** (of a hill or mountain range) Plb. Plu.
2 orientation (of a city, towards the north) Plb.
3 region of the earth at a certain latitude, zone Plu.
4 (gener.) **region** (of a country) Plb.

κλιμάκιον ου *n.* [dimin. κλίμαξ] **little ladder** Ar.; **toy ladder** (for a pet bird) Thphr.

κλιμακίς ίδος *f.* **ladder** Plb. Plu.

κλῑμακο-φόρος ου *m.* [φέρω] **ladder-carrier** (in a contingent of troops preparing to storm a city) Plb.

κλιμακτήρ ῆρος *m.* **rung of a ladder** E.

κλιμακωτός ή όν *adj.* (of an approach to a city) **stepped** (w. footholds cut into the rock) Plb.

κλῖμαξ ακος *f.* [κλίνω] **1 ladder** (esp. for ascending to a roof, scaling city walls, descending fr. a ship) Od. Archil. A. E. Th. +; (fig., in ctxt. of ascending to the height of prosperity) E.
2 fixed ladder or stairway by which the upper floor of a house is reached, **ladder** or **stairway** Od. E. Lys.; **stairway, ascent** (to Olympos) Pi.*fr.*; (sg. and pl.) **flight of stairs, staircase** Plu.
3 ladder or **rack** (to which a person is tied for torture) Ar.
4 horizontal runged structure, gangway Plb.
5 wrestling move where an opponent is gripped from the back, ladder hold S.

κλῖνα (ep.aor.): see κλίνω

κλινάριον ου *n.* [dimin. κλίνη] **bed** or **mattress** (on which a sick person is laid) NT.

κλίνειος ᾱ ον *adj.* [κλίνη] (of wood) **for making couches** D.

κλίνη ης, dial. **κλίνᾱ** ᾱς *f.* [κλίνω] | Lacon.nom.pl. κλίναι (Alcm.) | **1 couch** (on which one sits or reclines, esp. at a banquet) Alcm. Lyr.adesp. Hdt. E. Ar. +; **bed** (on which one lies or sleeps) Hdt. Th. Ar. Att.orats. +
2 portable bed, stretcher (on which an incapacitated person is carried) And. NT.
3 bier (on which a corpse is laid or carried) Hdt. Th. Pl. Plu.; (of stone, in a tomb) Pl.

κλινήρης ες *adj.* [ἀραρίσκω] **confined to one's bed, bed-ridden** Plu.

κλίνθην (ep.aor.pass.): see κλίνω

κλινίδιον ου *n*. [dimin. κλίνη] **1 couch, bed** (on which one lies or sleeps) Ar. Plu.
2 portable bed, **litter** (on which a commander is carried) Plu.; **stretcher** (on which an incapacitated man is carried) Plu.

κλινίς ίδος *f*. **couch** (on which one sits or reclines) Ar.

κλινοκοσμέω contr.vb. (of a ruler) **adorn one's couches with soft furnishings** (as a sign of unmanliness) Plb.

κλινο-πετής ές *adj*. [πίπτω] confined to one's bed, **bed-ridden** X.

κλινο-ποιός οῦ *m*. [ποιέω] **couch-maker** Pl. D.

κλινουργός οῦ *m*. [ἔργον] **couch-maker** Pl.

κλιντήρ ῆρος *m*. [κλίνω] **couch, bed** (on which one lies or sleeps) Od. Hellenist.poet. Plu.

κλίνω *vb*. | fut. κλινῶ | aor. ἔκλινα, ep. κλῖνα, ep.3sg.subj. κλίνησι (or κλίνῃσι), imperatv. κλῖνον | pf. κέκλικα (Plb. NT.) ‖ MID.: aor. ἐκλινάμην ‖ PASS.: fut. (in cpds.) -κλιθήσομαι, also -κλινήσομαι | aor. ἐκλίθην (ep. κλίθην), also ἐκλίνθην (ep. κλίνθην), ep.3pl. ἔκλιθεν, ep.3du. κλινθήτην | aor.2 (in cpds.) -εκλίνην | pf. κέκλιμαι, 3pl. κέκλινται, Ion. κεκλίαται, ptcpl. κεκλιμένος | ep.plpf. 3sg. κέκλιτο, 3pl. κέκλιντο |
1 cause (someone or sthg.) to turn in some direction; **turn** —*one's eyes, face* (W.ADV. or PREP.PHR. *to the side, the ground*) Il. NT. —*one's foot* (*i.e. steps*, W.PREP.PHR. *out of a place*) S.; (of creator gods) **bend** —*veins* (W.PREP.PHR. *around the human head*) Pl. ‖ PASS. turn oneself to the side Il. Theoc.; (of a child) turn —W. πρός + ACC. *to its nurse's bosom* Il.; (of a person's neck) be twisted or bent —W. εἰς + ACC. *to the left* Plu.; (of a person) veer —W.ADV. *to one side or other* (*in his path through life*) Thgn.; (of an object) —W.ADV. *in a certain direction* Pl.
2 (intr., of troops, commanders) **turn, wheel about** —W.PREP.PHR. *to the left or right* Plb. Plu.
3 ‖ PASS. (of a sea-gulf, coastline) curve —W.PREP.PHR. or ADV. *beyond a cape, in another direction* AR. ‖ PF.PASS. (of regions, places) be oriented, face —W.ADV. or PREP.PHR. *in a certain direction* Plb. Plu.; (of the hair of a horse's coat) X.
4 turn (someone or sthg.) towards a certain state or course of action; (of Fortune) **turn** —*all affairs* (W.PREP.PHR. *in a single direction*) Plb.; (intr., of a city, events) **take a turn** —W.PREP.PHR. *for the worse* X. —*in someone's favour* Plb. ‖ PASS. (of a musician) turn or devote oneself —W.DAT. *to a melody* Pi.
5 turn in the opposite direction; (of a god) **turn around** —*a battle* Il.; (of warriors) **put to flight** —*enemies* Hom. E. AR.; (intr., of persons, troops) **turn around** —W.PREP.PHR. *in flight* S.*Ichn*. Plb.; **turn in flight** Plb. ‖ PASS. (of troops) be put to flight Plu.
6 force open —*doors* S. ‖ PASS. (of doors) be swung open E.
7 cause (sthg.) to incline (at an angle to the upright); (of troops) **level** —*spears* Plu. ‖ PASS. (of spears) be levelled Plu.
8 ‖ PASS. (of a basin, a wounded man, his head) lean, tip —W.ADV. *to the side* Hom.; (of a ship) list to the side Thgn.; (of a city wall, a siege-tower) lean to the side X. Plu.; (fig., of a land) totter (fr. civil strife) Sol.
9 lean —*an object* (W.DAT. or πρός + ACC. *against a post, wall, or sim.*) Hom. —*a wrecked chariot* (*against a tree, or perh. on the ground*) hHom. ‖ MID. **lean oneself** —W.DAT. *against a post* Od. ‖ PASS. (usu.pf., of persons, objects) lean —W.DAT. or PREP.PHR. *against a post, wall, or sim.* Hom. hHom. Archil. Hdt. AR. Theoc.; (of Herakles) —*against two continents* (*i.e. grasping the Pillars of Hercules*) S.(dub.);

(fig., of a person) lean for support (on someone) S.; (fig., of a musician) be supported —W.DAT. *by a song* (*i.e. play along to it*) Pi.
10 cause (sthg.) to incline downwards; (of Zeus) **tilt** —*the scales* (*of fate in a battle*) Il.; (of sailors) —*a ship* (W.ADV. + PREP.PHR. *downwards, on rollers, to be launched*) AR.; (of a day, an error) **bring down** —*the fortunes of a person or city* S. Plu.; (of a bird) **droop** —*its wings* Plu.(quot.poet.); (of a person) —*one's head* NT.; (intr., of the sun, stars) **sink, set** AR.; (of a day, a watch of the night) **come to an end** Plb. NT. ‖ PASS. (of personif. Asia) be brought down —W. ἐπί + ACC. *to her knees* A.; (of a person) fall back, sink —W.PREP.PHR. *into someone's arms* S. —*into a coma* AR.
11 ‖ PASS. (usu.pf.) (of capes, islands) slope down —W.DAT. or PREP.PHR. *to the sea* Od. hHom. AR.; (of persons, a city) be situated by the edge —W.DAT. or PREP.PHR. *of a sea, marsh, ford, plain* Il. Thgn. Pi. Call.
12 lay down —*one's limbs* (*on the ground*) AR. —*one's head* (*to rest*) NT. —*a person* (sts. W.PREP.PHR. *on a bed or sim.*) Archil. S. E. Theoc.; **make** (W.ACC. dinner guests) **recline** Hdt.; (fig.) **put to rest** —*old Bacchus* (W.PREP.PHR. *in a bowl, ref. to decanting wine*) Men.; (intr.) **lay oneself down, recline** E. Ar. ‖ PASS. (of persons) lie down or recline Hom. Archil. Simon. Hdt. S. E. +
13 lower —*a ship's mast* (*to the deck*) AR.
‖ PF.PASS.PTCPL.ADJ. (of a ship's mast) lowered AR.
14 ‖ PF.PLPF.PASS. (of armour, leaves) lie on the ground Hom. Plu.; (fig., of a land) be prostrate (fr. misfortune) Plu.

κλισία ᾱς, Ion. **κλισίη** ης *f*. **1 structure for resting in; hut** (of a herdsman or farmer) Hom. hHom.; **hut or tent** (of the Greek warriors at Troy) Hom. B. S.; (pl., ref. to the military camp on the beach at Troy) Hom. E.
2 piece of furniture for resting on; **couch** (to sit on) Od.; (to sleep on) hHom. Call.; (for reclining at dinner) Pi. Call. Plu.; (ref. to a nuptial bed) E.
3 group of people reclining to eat a meal, **group of diners** NT.

—**κλισίηθεν** Ion.adv. **from a tent** Il.

—**κλισίηνδε** Ion.adv. **to a tent** Il.

κλισιάδες *f.pl*.: see κλεισιάδες

κλίσιον *n*.: see κλείσιον

κλίσιον ου *n*. [κλίνω] (app.collectv.) **row of lean-to sheds, outbuildings** (around a farmhouse) Od.

κλίσις εως *f*. **1** lying (or placing) in a reclining position; **reclining** (of a person, on a couch) Plu.; **laying down** (W.GEN. of one's limbs, on the ground) E.
2 act of bending or curving, **bending** (on one knee, by troops in a defensive formation) Plu.
3 bending to one side, **inclining** (of a person's neck) Plu.; **angled positioning** (of lamps arranged in decorative patterns) Plu.
4 act of turning, **wheeling** (of troops or cavalry in battle) Plb. Plu.

κλισμίον ου *n*. (pl. for sg.) **couch** (ref. to a nuptial bed) Call.

κλισμός οῦ *m*. (*also f*. Theoc.) **couch** (on which one sits or reclines) Hom. hHom. E. Call. AR.; (on which a dead man is laid) Thgn. Theoc.

κλίτεα ων *n.pl*. [reltd. κλειτύς] **cliffs** AR.

κλιτύς *f*.: see κλειτύς

κλοιός, Att. **κλῳός**, οῦ *m*. **1 collar** (of wood, to restrain a dog or person) E.*Cyc*. Ar. X. Plb. Plu.
2 piece of jewellery worn round the neck, **necklace** (of gold) E.*Cyc*.

κλονέω contr.vb. [κλόνος] **1** (of warriors, personif. Fear and Panic) drive before one in confusion, **drive in a confused throng, put to flight** —warriors Il. Hes. Mimn. Ar.; (of lions, wild beasts, hawks) —herds, doves Il. AR.; (of the winds) **drive forward** —clouds, a fire Il. Hes. ‖ PASS. (of warriors) be driven in confusion (by an enemy) Il.; (of shipwrecked men, grains of sand) be tossed around —W.DAT. *by waves and tempests* Semon. Pi.
2 (of warriors) **throw into turmoil** —a battlefield Il.; (intr.) **create turmoil** (among the enemy) Il. —W.PREP.PHR. *on a battlefield* B. ‖ PASS. (of warriors, horsemen) gather in a confused throng Il.; (of fish, bees) Hes. AR.
3 (of a boxer) **batter, pummel** —opponents Pi.; (of the elements; of disasters, compared to waves) —a person S.; (of Orpheus) **vigorously strum** (the lyre) AR. ‖ PASS. (of a headland) be battered (by storms) S.

κλόνος ου *m.* **1 chaotic throng, thronging mass** (of warriors in battle, spears) Il. Hes. Alcm. A.; (of dancing worshippers) Pi.*fr.*
2 commotion (in the bowels) Ar.

κλοπαῖος ᾱ ον *adj.* [κλοπή] **1** (of objects, cattle, women) acquired by theft, **stolen** Trag.
2 (of acts) **of theft** Pl.

κλοπεύς έως *m.* **1 thief** (of cattle, weapons) S.
2 perpetrator of stealthy deeds; (ref. to a person's mind) **criminal** S.

κλοπή ῆς, dial. **κλοπᾱ́** ᾶς *f.* [κλέπτω] **1 theft** (of objects, a woman) Trag. Ar. Att.orats. Pl. X. +; **embezzlement** (of public funds or sim.) Ar. Att.orats. Pl. Plu.
2 stealthy removal (of one's feet, fr. a place) S.
3 stealth (of an escape or sim.) S. E.
4 deceptive behaviour, **deceit** S. E. Aeschin.; **tricking** (of an enemy, in war) Plb.

κλοπικός ή όν *adj.* (of Hermes) **crafty, deceitful** (in speech) Pl.

κλόπιος η ον *Ion.adj.* [κλοπός] (of words) like those of a thief, **deceitful** Od.

κλοπός οῦ *m.* [κλέπτω] **thief, stealer** (W.GEN. of cows) hHom.

κλοτοπεύω *vb.* perh. **talk fruitlessly, waste time talking** Il.

κλύδων ωνος *m.* [κλύζω] **1** (collectv.sg.) **strong waves, choppy waters** (on the sea) Od. Trag. Th. Tim. Thphr. AR. +; (on a lake, river, or sim.) NT. Plu.; (fig.ref. to political disturbance or external threats affecting the ship of state) Pl. Plu.
2 (fig.) **surging sea** (of fighting or fleeing soldiers, galloping horses) S. E. Plu.; (W.GEN. or ADJ. of troubles, conflict, war) Trag.; **tumult** (ref. to political disturbance) D.; (ref. to anguish) E.

κλυδωνίζομαι *pass.vb.* **be tossed about** (on a rough sea) NT.

κλυδώνιον ου *n.* [dimin. κλύδων] **rough waters** (of the sea) E.; (fig., affecting the ship of state) A.; **flood, wave** (W.GEN. of anguish, affecting a person) E.

κλύζω *vb.* | iteratv.impf. κλύζεσκον | ep.fut. κλύσσω | aor. ἔκλυσα ‖ PASS.: aor. ἐκλύσθην | pf. κέκλυσμαι | **1** (of waves, the sea, or sim.) **wash over** —an island, a shore, a person hHom. AR. Theoc.; (intr., of waves) **splash, break** AR.
—W.PREP.PHR. *on a shore* Il.; (of suffering, envisaged as a wave) **surge up** A. ‖ PASS. (of headlands) be washed (by the sea) AR. Plu.
2 (of a sea-swell) **wash forward, bear off** —a ship (W.PREP.PHR. *across the sea*) AR. ‖ PASS. (of the sea, a river) surge with waves Hes.; surge forward —W.PREP.PHR. *upon a shore* Il.; surge up —W.PREP.PHR. *under the impact of a boulder, a mass of people* Od. Plu.
3 (of a person) **rinse out** —a cup X.; (intr.) **splash water** —W.PREP.PHR. *into the ears* (to wash away a scandalous proposal) E. ‖ PASS. (of a wooden cup) be washed (i.e. treated) —W.DAT. *w. wax* (to make it waterproof) Theoc.
4 (of the sea, a rainstorm) **wash away, carry off** —a broken oar, crops, fields AR. Plu. —evil deeds or sim. E.; (of a goddess, after a hunt or chariot-ride) **wash off** (W.DAT. w. river water) —dirt (fr. herself), sweat and dust (fr. horses) Call.

κλῦθι (athem.aor.imperatv.): see κλύω

κλύμενος η ον *adj.* [κλύω] (of an infatuation) **famous** or **infamous** Theoc.

κλυσι-δρομάς άδος *fem.adj.* [κλύζω] (of a breeze) **racing and drenching** (w. spray) Tim.

κλύσμα ατος *n.* **1 enema** (of a medicine or embalming fluid) Hdt.
2 that which is washed (by the sea), **beach, shore** Plu.

κλυστήρ ῆρος *m.* **enema syringe** (used in embalming) Hdt.

Κλυταιμήστρᾱ (sts. written **Κλυταιμνήστρα**) ᾱς, Ion. **Κλυταιμήστρη** (also **Κλυταιμνήστρη**) ης *f.* **Clytemestra** or **Clytemnestra** (murderous wife of Agamemnon) Hom. Hes.*fr.* Pi. Trag. Arist.; (as generic name for such a wife) Antipho

κλῦτε (2pl.athem.aor.imperatv.): see κλύω

κλυτο-εργός όν *adj.* [κλυτός, ἔργον] (of Hephaistos) **famous for craftsmanship** Od.

κλυτό-καρπος ον *adj.* [καρπός¹] (of victory-wreaths) **bearing famous fruit** Pi.

κλυτό-μαντις ιος *masc.fem.adj.* [μάντις] (of Pytho) **famous for prophecy** Pi.*fr.*

κλυτό-μητις ιος *masc.fem.adj.* [μῆτις] (of Hephaistos) **famous for skill** (as a craftsman) hHom.; (of Paian, as a healer) Lyr.adesp.

κλυτό-πωλος ον *adj.* [πῶλος] (of Hades) **having famous horses** or **famous for horses** Il.; (of Poseidon) Pi.

κλυτός ή (dial. ᾱ́) όν (also ός όν) *adj.* [κλύω] **1** widely heard or spoken of; (of gods, persons, peoples, their names, lineage, lives, destinies) **of noble fame, illustrious** Hom. Hes. Pi. B. AR. Mosch.; (of places) Hom. Pi. B. S. E. AR. +; (of warriors) **famous** (W.DAT. w. the spear) Hom.; (of a city, for garlands and horses, i.e. victories in the games) Pi.; (of a musician, W.ACC. for his voice) Hes.*fr.* | For ὄνομα κλυτός see ὀνομάκλυτος.
2 conferring glory; (of gifts, spoils, honours, songs of praise, or sim.) **glorious** Hom. Hes. A.(cj.) Pi. S.; (of works, deeds, skills) Od. Hes. hHom. AR.
3 having a natural splendour; (of armour, clothes, places, palaces) **glorious, splendid** Hom. Hes.; (of the earth, the sky, Okeanos, a star, a swallow) Od. Hes. Lyr. S.; (of persons, peoples, the dead) **noble** Hom. hHom.; (of sheep, goats) **fine** Od. S.
4 (of an Erinys) **infamous** A.

κλυτο-τέχνης ου *masc.adj.* [τέχνη] (of Hephaistos) **famous for craftsmanship** Hom. Hes.*fr.* hHom.

κλυτό-τοξος ον *adj.* [τόξον] (of Apollo) **famous with the bow** Hom. B.

κλύω *vb.* | aor.2 ἔκλυον, ep. κλύον | athem.aor.imperatv. κλῦθι, also redupl. κέκλυθι, 2pl. κλῦτε, also redupl. κέκλυτε | **1** (of gods, persons) listen and be receptive, **listen** (to persons, their prayers, advice, or sim.) Hom. Hes. Archil. Lyr. Trag. + —W.GEN. *to persons, their prayers or advice* Hom. Hes. Lyr. Emp. Trag. + —W.DAT. *to persons* Hom. Hes. Eleg.

Lyr.adesp. Melanipp. —W.ACC. *to words, prayers, entreaties* Il. A. Pi. B. S.

2 (of persons) **heed, obey** —W.GEN. *rulers, fate, one's mind* Trag. Tim.; (of a ship) —W.GEN. *its rudder* A.

3 hear (persons, their words) Trag. Ar. —W.GEN. *a person, message, sound* Hom. hHom. Trag. Ar. Theoc. —W.ACC. *news, voices, sounds* Hom. Hes.*fr.* Pi. Emp. Trag. Ar. + —W.ACC. + GEN. or PREP.PHR. *sthg., fr. someone* Hom. Trag. AR. —W.ACC. + PTCPL. *that sthg. is the case* B. Trag. —W.ACC. + INF. E.; **hear about, learn of** —W.ACC. *sthg.* A. Call. AR. —W.GEN. S.

4 (pres., w.pf.sens.) **have heard** (sthg.) Trag. —W.GEN. *sthg.* S. —W.ACC. E. —W.ACC. + GEN. or PREP.PHR. *sthg., fr. someone* S. E.; **have heard about, know** (sthg.) E. —W.ACC. + PTCPL. *that sthg. is the case* S.

5 recognise, know (sthg.) Od.

6 (of persons, a city) **be spoken of** —W.ADV. *well or badly* Trag.

κλώζω *vb.* (of an audience) make a noise of disapproval, **boo** —*a person entering the theatre* D.

Κλῶθες ων *f.pl.* [κλώθω] **Spinners** (ref. to the Moirai, goddesses of Fate, i.e. Klotho, Lakhesis and Atropos) Od. —**Κλωθώ** οῦς *f.* **Klotho** (spinner of the thread of a mortal's life) Hes. Lyr. Pl.

κλώθω *vb.* | aor.pass. ἐκλώσθην | spin (fibres into thread); (of a woman) **spin** —*flax* (*into linen thread*) Hdt. ‖ PASS. (of individual destinies) be spun (by Klotho) Pl.; (of necessity) —W.DAT. *for a person* Lyr.adesp.

κλωμακόεις εσσα εν *adj.* (of a place) full of rocks, **rocky, craggy** Il.

κλών ωνός *m.* **branch** or **sprig** (of a tree) S. E. Pl. X. Call. Plu.; (as carried by a suppliant, or placed on an altar or tomb) S. E.

κλῳός Att.*m.*: see κλοιός

κλωπεία ᾱς *f.* [κλωπεύω] stealing of property, **thieving** Isoc. Pl.; **plundering** (by troops) Pl. Plu.

κλωπεύω *vb.* [κλώψ] **1 be a thief, engage in thieving** X.
2 (tr.) **kidnap, capture** —*people* X.

κλώπιος η ον Ion.*adj.* (of a bandit) **thieving** or **stealthy** AR.

κλωπικός ή όν *adj.* characteristic of a thief; (of footsteps) **stealthy** E.; (of an ambush) E.

κλωσμός οῦ *m.* **clucking** (w. the tongue, made by a rider to urge on a horse) X.

κλωστήρ ῆρος *m.* [κλώθω] **1 spindle** (on which thread is wound) AR. Theoc.
2 cord (of a fishing net) A.; **skein** (of spun yarn) Ar.
3 thread of fate, destiny Plu.(oracle)

κλωστός ή όν *adj.* (of a cord) **spun, braided** E. Plu.

κλώψ ωπός *m.* [κλέπτω] **thief, robber** Hdt. E. Pl. X. Plu.

κνᾱκο-μιγής ές dial.*adj.* [κνῆκος *safflower*, μείγνῡμι] (of chickpeas) **mixed with safflower** Philox.Leuc.

κνᾱκός dial.*adj.*: see κνηκός

κνάκων ωνος dial.*m.* [κνηκός] a kind of tawny-coloured animal, **tawny buck** (ref. to a goat) Theoc.

κνᾶμα dial.*f.*: see κνήμη

κνᾱμίδες (Aeol.nom.pl.): see κνημίς

κνᾱμός dial.*m.*: see κνημός

κνάπτω (also **κνάμπτω** Pl.) *vb.* | aor.pass.ptcpl. κναφθείς | card (wool) or full (cloth, i.e. rake it w. sharp combs); (of demons in the underworld) **lacerate, tear the flesh of** —*wicked men* Pl. ‖ PASS. (of persons) be lacerated or mangled (by physical injuries) A.(cj.) S.; (by pain) A.(cj.) | see also γνάπτω

κνάσαιο (dial.2sg.aor.opt.mid.): see κατακνάω

κναφεῖον (also **γναφεῖον**), Ion. **κναφήιον**, ου *n.* [κναφεύς] **fuller's shop** (where garments were taken to be cleaned) Hdt. Lys. Aeschin. Plu.

κναφεύς (also **γναφεύς**) έως *m.* **fuller** A. Hdt. Ar. Att.orats. Pl. +

κναφευτικός (also **γναφευτικός**) ή όν *adj.* (of the art) **of being a fuller** Pl.

κναφεύω (or **γναφεύω**) *vb.* **be a fuller** Ar.

κνάφος ου *m.* [κνάπτω] **fuller's comb, carding-comb** Hdt.

κνάω contr.*vb.* | ptcpl. κνῶν | ep.3sg.impf. (in tm.) κνῆ ‖ MID.: 3sg. κνᾶται (Plu.), inf. κνῆσθαι (Pl.) | (of a horse) **scratch** —*its head* (*against sthg.*) X. ‖ MID. (of a person) **scratch oneself** (to cure an itch) Pl. Plu.; (tr.) **scratch** —*one's head* Plu.

κνεφάζω *vb.* [κνέφας] (of a god's anger) **cast darkness over** —*a bridle* (fig.ref. to the Greek army besieging Troy) A.

κνεφαῖος ᾱ ον *adj.* **1** (of the underworld, the far west) **dark, murky** A. E.
2 (quasi-advbl., of persons performing an activity) **in darkness, before dawn** Hippon. Ar. X.

κνέφαλλον, Aeol. **γνόφαλλον**, ου *n.* **cushion** Alc.

κνέφας αος (also ους Ar., ατος Plb.) *n.* | dat. κνέφᾳ (X.) |
1 dusk, twilight Hom. AR. Plb.
2 darkness (of night) A. E. AR.
3 morning twilight, **half-light, dawn** Ar. X.

κνῇ (ep.3sg.impf.): see κνάω

κνήθω *vb.* [κνάω] rub or tickle (sthg.) ‖ PASS. be itching —W.ACC. *in one's hearing* (*i.e. to hear sthg.*) NT.

κνηκίς ίδος *f.* [κνηκός] **speck of white** (in a blue sky) Call.

κνηκός ή όν, dial. **κνᾱκός** ά όν *adj.* (of a satyr's beard, a goatskin) **yellow, tawny-coloured** S.*Ichn.* Theoc.

κνήμ-αργος ον *adj.* [κνήμη, ἀργός] (of oxen) **white-legged** Theoc.

κνήμη ης, dial. **κνᾶμα** ᾱς *f.* lower part of the leg, **shin** Hom. +; (of a horse) X.

κνημῑδο-φόρος ον *adj.* [κνημίς, φέρω] (of Lycian troops) wearing shin-pads, **armoured with greaves** Hdt.

κνημίς ῖδος *f.* [κνήμη] | Aeol.nom.pl. κνᾱμίδες | **shin-pad, greave** (ref. to armour) Il. Hes. Alc. E. Ar. +; **leather leggings** (worn by a gardener) Od.

κνημός, dial. **κνᾱμός**, οῦ *m.* foothill or spur of a mountain, **mountain ridge** or **spur** Hom. Hes.*fr.* hHom. AR. Bion

κνησιάω contr.*vb.* [desideratv. κνάω] **feel the need to scratch** (an itch) Pl. —W.ACC. *one's head* Pl.; (fig.) **feel an itch** (ref. to a desire for sex) Ar.

κνῆσις εως *f.* **1 scratching** (of an itch) Pl.
2 need to scratch; **itching, irritation** (of the gums of a teething infant) Pl.

κνῆσμα ατος *n.* **1** | PL. (fig.) scrapings, shavings (W.GEN. of speeches, opp. fully fashioned ones) Pl.
2 sting, bite (fr. an insect) X.

κνηστίς ίδος *f.* **comb** (worn in the hair) Plu.

κνῆστις ιος Ion.*f.* | dat. κνήστῑ | **1 grater** (for cheese) Il.
2 spine, backbone (of an animal) Od.(v.l. ἄκνηστις)

κνίδᾱ ᾱς dial.*f.* [perh. κνίζω] **stinging nettle** Theoc.

Κνίδος ου *f.* **Knidos** (city in Caria) hHom. A. Hdt. Th. +
—**Κνίδιος** ᾱ (Ion. η) ον *adj.* of or from Knidos; (of persons) **Knidian** Hdt. Th. Plu.; (of territory) Hdt. ‖ FEM.SB. territory of the Knidians, **Knidia** Th. Call. ‖ MASC.PL.SB. **Knidians** (as a population or military force) Hdt. Th. Plb. Plu.

κνίζω *vb.* | fut. κνίσω | aor. ἔκνισα, dial. κνίσα, perh. also ἔκνιξα ‖ PASS.: aor. ἐκνίσθην | pf. κέκνισμαι | **1** cause pain or irritation, as if by scratching, stinging or chafing; (w. aggressive connot.) **scratch** or **sting** —*a person* (w. *insults*)

κνῖσα Ar.; **scratch at** —*a rival poet's words* Ar.; (of expenses) **chafe, damage** —*people's hopes* Pi. ‖ PASS. (of a woman) be **distressed** Pi.
2 (of persons, their words, circumstances) **irritate, annoy** —*a person, mind, god* Hdt. S. E. Theoc.; (intr., of excess) Pi. ‖ PASS. **be irritated or annoyed** E. Men.
3 (of love) **torment, stir, arouse** —*a person or mind* Pi. B. Hdt. Plu.; (of a coy lover) **tease, provoke** —*someone* Theoc.; (of joy) **stir, thrill** —*someone* Pi. ‖ PASS. **be tormented** (by love) Men. Theoc.
4 (of words, an event) **provoke** —*anger, a person* (W.INF. *to rouse his anger*) Pi.; (of a wish to do sthg.) **spur on** —*a person* E.

κνῖσα, Ion. **κνίση**, ης, dial. **κνῖσᾶ** ᾶς *f.* **1** fragrant steam and smoke from burnt offerings, **smell of sacrifice, savour of roasting meat** Hom. hHom. Hippon. Pi. Ar. Pl. AR.
2 (concr.) **sacrificial fat** (ref. to the layer of fat which was an important part of the traditional sacrifice) Hom. A.; (gener., as an ingredient of sausages) Od.

κνῑσάω contr.vb. | inf. κνῑσᾶν, also κνῑσῆν (D., oracle) | **fill with the smell of burnt offerings, make fragrant with the smoke of sacrifice** —*the streets* Hes.*fr.* Ar. D. —*altars* E.; (intr.) **make the smoke of sacrifice rise up** —W.DAT. *on altars* D.(oracle)

κνῑσήεις, dial. **κνῑσάεις**, εσσα εν adj. (of a house, procession, smoke) **fragrant with the smell of sacrifice** Od. Pi. AR.

κνισμός οῦ *m.* [κνίζω] **torment** (of unrequited love) Ar.

κνῑσο-κόλαξ ακος *m.* [κνῖσα] **one who flatters to obtain the fat of a sacrifice, parasite** Asius

κνῑσωτός ή όν *adj.* [reltd. κνῖσα] (of sacrifices) **fragrant with the smoke of burnt offerings** A.

κνίψ κνῑπός *m.* **small wood-boring pest; perh. mite** Ar.

κνόος *m.*: see χνόος²

κνοώσσω dial.vb.: see κνώσσω

κνύζα ης *f.* **fleabane** (a kind of herb) Theoc.

κνυζέομαι mid.contr.vb. | dial.3pl. κνυζεῦνται (Theoc.) | (of dogs) **whine, whimper** S. Ar. Theoc.; (of infants) Theoc.

κνυζηθμός οῦ *m.* **whining, whimpering** (of dogs, wild beasts) Od. AR.

κνύζημα ατος *n.* **whining, whimpering** (of infants) Hdt.

κνυζός ή όν *adj.* (of a woman) perh. **wrinkled** Anacr.

κνυζόω contr.vb. (of a goddess) **make bleary** (in appearance) —*someone's eyes* Od.

κνῦμα ατος *n.* [κνύω] **scratching, scrabbling** (of fingers, against a door) Ar.

κνύος εος *n.* **itch** Hes.*fr.*

κνύω vb. | impf. ἔκνυον | **scratch** —*a door* (w. *one's fingers, to get the attention of someone inside*) Ar.

κνώδαλον ου *n.* **creature or beast** (esp.ref. to monsters and dangerous animals) Od. Hes. hHom. Alcm. Pi. Trag. Theoc.; **beast, brute** (ref. to satyrs, Erinyes) A.; (fig.ref. to a person) Ar.

κνώδων οντος *m.* **blade** (of a sword) S.; (meton. for sword) S. ‖ PL. **barbs** (on the blade of a hunting spear) X.

Κνωσός οῦ *f.* | freq. v.l. Κνωσσός | **Knosos or Knossos** (chief city of Crete) Hom. hHom. B. Pl. Call. Plb.

—**Κνωσσόθεν** adv. **from Knossos** AR.

—**Κνώσιος** ᾱ ον adj. | freq. v.l. Κνώσσ- | (of a person, the Minotaur) **of or from Knossos, Knossian** B. Hdt. E. Pl. Plb.; (of one's home city) Pi.; (of dances) S. ‖ MASC.PL.SB. **men of Knossos, Knossians** (as a population or military force) B. Pl. Plb.

κνώσσω, dial. **κνοώσσω** vb. (of persons) **sleep, slumber** Od. Simon. Pi. Hellenist.poet. Plu.(quot.poet.); (of an eagle) Pi.

κοάλεμος ου *m.* **moron, idiot** Ar.; (as the name of a supposed deity) Ar.; (as a nickname for a person) Plu.

κοάξ interj. (representing a frog's croak) **koax!** Ar.

κοβᾰλικεύματα των *n.pl.* [κόβᾱλος] **dishonest tricks** Ar.

κοβᾰλικός ή όν adj. (of bribes) **wicked, dishonest** Timocr.

κόβᾱλος ου *m.* **scoundrel** Ar.; (pl., as supposed deities) Ar.

—**κόβᾱλος** η ον adj. ‖ NEUT.PL.SB. **dishonest tricks** Ar.; (ref. to a kind of poetry) Ar.

κόγχη ης *f.* **1** a kind of shellfish, **clam, mussel, conch** X.
2 case or cover protecting the seal on a document (made fr. or resembling a shell), **shell-case** Ar.

κόγχος ου *m.* (also *f.* Plb.) **1** a kind of shellfish; (gener.) **sea-shell** Call.*epigr.*
2 object resembling a sea-shell, **boss** (on a shield) Plb.

κογχυλιάτης ου *m.* **stone containing fossil shells, shell marble** (as a building material) X.

κογχύλιον ου *n.* [dimin. κόγχη] **sea-shell** Hdt.

κοδράντης ου *m.* [Lat. quadrans] **penny** (Roman bronze coin of small value) NT.

κοέω contr.vb. **notice, recognise** —W.COMPL.CL. *that sthg. is the case* Call.; (intr., in neg.phr.) **notice** (sthg.) Anacr.(cj.)

κόθᾰρος Aeol.adj.: see καθαρός

κόθεν Ion.interrog.adv., **κοθέν** Ion.enclit.adv.: see πόθεν, ποθέν

κόθορνος ου *m.* **a kind of footwear; slip-on boot** (esp. worn by women, and oft. w.connot. of unmanliness) Hdt. Ar. Plu.; (as nickname for a traitor, fr. its fitting either foot) X. Plu.

κόθουρος ου adj. [οὐρά] (of drones in a beehive) **with docked tails, stingless** Hes.

κοΐ interj. (representing a pig's grunt) **oink!** Ar.

κοΐζω vb. | fut. κοΐξω | (of persons) **oink like a pig** Ar.

κοίη Ion.fem.dat.adv.: see under ποῖος

Κοιηΐς *f.*: see under Κοῖος

κοικύλλω vb. perh. **act or talk like a fool** Ar.

κοιλαίνω vb. [κοῖλος] | aor. ἐκοίλᾱνα, Ion. ἐκοίληνα | **make hollow, hollow out** —*a wooden beam* Th.; (of birds) —*a lump of myrrh* Hdt.; **dig** —*a grave* Theoc. ‖ PASS. (of a stone) **be hollowed out** (by dripping water) Bion; (of mirrors) **be made concave** Plu.

κοιλάς άδος *f.* **hollow place, hollow, valley** Plb. Plu.

κοιλία ᾱς, Ion. **κοιλίη** ης *f.* **1 abdominal cavity** (fr. which the intestines are removed) Hdt.
2 belly, stomach (as being empty, receiving food, or sim.) Ar. Pl. Arist. NT. Plu.; **bowels** (as affected by disease) Th. Plu.; (sg. and pl., specif.) **stomach or intestines** (of a person or animal) Hdt. Ar. Pl. Plb.; **tripe** (as a foodstuff) Ar.
3 (gener.) **belly, abdomen** Ar. Plu.; (incl. the womb) NT.
4 pot-belly (of a fat man) Plb.

κοιλιακός ή όν adj. (of disorders) **of the bowels** Plu.

κοιλιο-πώλης ου *m.* [πωλέω] **tripe-seller** Ar.

κοιλο-γάστωρ ορος masc.fem.adj. [γαστήρ] **1** having a hollow belly; (of a shield) **hollow, concave** A.
2 (of wolves) **hungry, ravenous** A.

κοιλό-πεδος ου adj. [πέδον] (of a sacred grove) **situated in a hollow** Pi.

κοῖλος, dial. **κόϊλος**, η (dial. ᾱ) ον adj. | compar. κοιλότερος, dial. κοϊλώτερος (Anacr.) | **1** (of objects, buildings, caves) **containing an internal cavity, hollow** Hom. +; (of ships) Hom. Hes. Ibyc. Pi. E.*Cyc.* Hellenist.poet.; κοίλη ναῦς **hollow of a ship** (ref. to its hold) Hdt. X. D.; (w. ναῦς understd.) Theoc. ‖ COMPAR. (of a ship) **more capacious** (than other ships) Plu. ‖ NEUT.SB. **hollow space or cavity** (inside an object) Ar.
2 (of a bed for transporting a sick person) providing ample space, **deep, capacious** S.

3 (of a naval formation) containing open spaces, **open** (opp. densely arrayed) Plb.

4 (of places, regions) forming a hollow between mountains, **valleyed** Hom. + ‖ NEUT.SB. valley or dale Ar. X.

5 Κοίλη Συρία *Koile Syria* (*ref. to the entire region inland fr. the Levantine coast, perh. orig.ref. to the smaller valleyed area betw. the mt. ranges of Lebanon and Anti-Lebanon*) Plb. Plu.

6 (of stormy seas) sunk low (beneath towering waves), **with hollow troughs, plunging** AR. Plb. Plu.

7 (of roads, rivers, places) situated in a hollow, **low-lying, sunken** Il. + ‖ NEUT.SB. sunken place or natural hollow (in the ground) Hdt. Th. Pl. X. Plb. Plu.

8 (of shields, beaches, harbours, objects) exhibiting an inward curvature, **curving inwards, concave** Od. +; (of Argos, ref. to its location in the hollow of a gulf) **recessed** S.; (of a hand) **cupped** Ar.; (of forced doors) **bulging inwards** S.; κοῖλος ἄργυρος *hollow silverware* (*ref. to bowls, plates*) Arist. Plu. ‖ NEUT.SB. hollow (of a harbour) Th.; (abstr.) concaveness Arist. ‖ NEUT.PL.SB. hollow (of the belly, as the target of a spear) E.

9 (of a doorway) constructed with sunken panels, **coffered, panelled** Theoc.

κοιλότης ητος *f.* **1** concavity (of objects, curves) Arist.

2 hollow nature, **lowness** (of a piece of ground) Plu.

3 (concr.) **hollow** (in the ground, a boulder) Plb. Plu.

κοιλ-όφθαλμος ον *adj.* [ὀφθαλμός] (of a horse) **sunken-eyed** X.

κοίλωμα ατος *n.* hollowed-out place, **hollow** (in a cliff) Plu.; **canyon** Plb.; **basin** (into which rivers flow) Plb.

κοιλ-ῶνυξ υχος *masc.fem.adj.* [ὄνυξ] (of horses) **hollow-hoofed** Stesich.

κοιλ-ωπός όν *adj.* [ὤψ] (of a cleft in a rock) hollow-faced, **hollow** E.

κοιμάω *contr.vb.* [κεῖμαι] | aor. ἐκοίμησα, ep. κοίμησα, dial. ἐκοίμασα ‖ ep.3sg.aor.mid. κοιμήσατο ‖ PASS.: aor. ἐκοιμήθην, ep. κοιμήθην, dial. ἐκοιμάθην ‖ The aor.mid. is confined to ep. | **1** (of gods) put to sleep, **lull** (sts. W.DAT. to sleep) —*a person* Od.; (of Sleep) **close** —*a person's eyes* Il.; (of a helmsman, in neg.phr.) —*his eyes* A.; (of a deer) **put to bed** —*her fawns* Od.; (of a host, a commander) **settle for the night** —*guests, troops* Od. E.

2 (euphem., of Death) **put to sleep** —*a person* E.

3 (of gods) **make calm, quieten** —*winds, waves, or sim.* Hom. A. E. Call. AR.; (fig., of persons) —*a sacred flame* (*w. incense*) A.; (fig.) —*the flame of love* Call.; (of gods, persons) **soothe** —*pains, wounds* Il. S. ‖ PASS. (of appetites) be assuaged Pl.

4 make quiet, **silence** —*one's voice* Plu.

5 ‖ MID.PASS. (esp.aor.) **lie down to sleep, go to bed** Hom. Hdt. Pl. X. Thphr.; (esp.pres.) **sleep** (oft. W.PREP.PHR. w. a person, in a particular place or manner) Hom. +; **fall into** or **sleep** —W.INTERN.ACC. *a certain kind of sleep* X. Plu.

6 ‖ MID.PASS. (euphem.) **fall into** or **sleep** —W.INTERN.ACC. *the sleep of death* Il. Call.*epigr.*; **go to sleep, be asleep** (in death) S. NT.

7 ‖ MID.PASS. (w. sexual connot., of gods, persons) **go to bed** —W.DAT. or PREP.PHR. *w. someone* Hes. Pi. E. Ar.; (of animals) **mate** hHom.

8 ‖ MID.PASS. (of a watchman) **pass the night** (at his post) A.

κοιμήματα των *n.pl.* **1 sleeps, naps** (of a baby) S.*Ichn.*

2 (w. sexual connot.) **nights spent together** S.

κοίμησις εως *f.* act of sleeping, **night's sleep** (in a particular place) Pl.; **rest** (W.GEN. of sleep, opp. that of death) NT.

κοιμίζω *vb.* | aor. ἐκοίμισα | **1** (of a goddess) **lay down to sleep** —*a baby* (W.PREP.PHR. *in a cradle*) Call.; (of Sleep) **lull to sleep** —*a person* Licymn.; (of mandrakes) **put to sleep** —*humans* X.; (of a beloved) **cause** (W.ACC. a spurned lover) **to sleep** —W.ADV. *in a certain way* (*i.e. badly*) Call.*epigr.*; (of a watchman, in neg.phr.) **rest** —*his eyes* E. ‖ PASS. (of a person) sleep —W.PREP.PHR. *at someone's side* E.; (fig., of base appetites) be lulled to sleep Pl.

2 (fig., of warriors) **rest** —*their swords* (*i.e. sheathe them*) E.

3 (of gods, spirits) **take to eternal rest** (in Hades) —*a person, the Titans* S. E.

4 (of winds) **calm** —*the sea* (*by ceasing to blow*) S.; (of persons or things) **assuage** —*anger, pain, grief* Pl. X. ‖ PASS. (of griefs, in neg.phr.) be assuaged —W.DAT. *by words or the law* Hyp.

5 (of gods) **silence** —*speech and boasting* Anacr. E.

κοινάν *dial.m.*, **κοινᾱνίᾱ** *dial.f.*: see κοινῶν, κοινωνία

κοινάω *dial.contr.vb.*: see κοινόω

κοινεών *m.*: see κοινῶν

κοινῇ *adv.*: see under κοινός

κοινοβουλέω *contr.vb.* [κοινός; βουλή, βουλεύομαι] (of commanders) **deliberate together** X.

κοινοβούλιον ου *n.* **joint council** (ref. to an assembly of councillors) Plb.

κοινοβωμίᾱ ᾱς *f.* [βωμός] **shared altar-ground** (of several gods) A.

κοινο-γενής ές *adj.* [γένος, γίγνομαι] (of a species) **able to breed together, interbreeding** Pl.

κοινογονίᾱ ᾱς *f.* [γίγνομαι] **hybridising, interbreeding** (of animals) Pi.

κοινό-λεκτρος ου *masc.fem.adj.* [λέκτρον] (of a wife, concubine) **sharing the bed** (of a husband, lover) A.

κοινο-λεχής οῦς *masc.fem.adj.* [λέχος] (of a man) **sharing the bed** (of a woman) S.

κοινολογέομαι *mid.contr.vb.* [λόγος] | aor.pass. (w.mid.sens.) ἐκοινολογήθην (Plb.) | (of leaders, envoys, councillors, or sim.) **deliberate together** (oft. W.DAT. or PREP.PHR. w. someone, w. περί or ὑπέρ + GEN. about sthg.) Hdt. Th. Pl. X. D. +

κοινολογίᾱ ᾱς *f.* session of deliberation, **group discussion, conference** Plb. Plu.; **discussion, conversation** (betw. two people) Plu.

κοινό-πλους ουν Att.*adj.* [πλόος] (of a crew of sailors) **making a common voyage, sailing together** S.

κοινό-πους πουν, gen. ποδος *adj.* [πούς] (of an arrival) **of people travelling together** S.

κοινοπρᾱγέω *contr.vb.* [πράσσω] (of persons, nations) **act in concert, join forces, form an alliance** (sts. W.DAT. w. someone) Plb. Plu.; **conspire** —w. περί + GEN. *in a certain matter* Plb.

κοινοπρᾱγίᾱ ᾱς *f.* acting in common, **alliance** (oft. W.DAT. or PREP.PHR. w. a commander, nation, or sim.) Plb.; **cooperation** (W.GEN. of nations, allies, or sim.) Plb. Plu.

κοινός ή (dial. ά) όν (also ός όν S. E.) *adj.* | compar. κοινότερος | superl. κοινότατος | **1** (of circumstances, actions, afflictions) pertaining to all members of a group, **shared, common** (sts. W.DAT. or GEN. among persons or things) Pi. Hdt. Trag. Th. Att.orats. Pl. +; (prep.phr.) ἐν κοινῷ *in common, shared, equally* E. Att.orats. Pl. X. + ‖ NEUT.SB. common cause (of a particular group) E.

2 (of benefits, resources) available to all members of a group, **shared** (sts. W.DAT. among persons or things) Pi. Trag. Pl. +; (prep.phr.) ἐπὶ κοινᾶς *communally* Philox.Leuc.; (of a house, the sea) **available, open** (W.DAT. to persons) And. | For κοινὸς Ἑρμῆς see Ἑρμῆς 4.

κοινότης

3 (of actions, decisions, shouts) made by all members of a group, **collective, joint** Hdt. Trag. Th. Pl. +; (of a meal) ἐκ κοινοῦ *at shared expense* Hes.
4 (of persons, their blood, achievements) linked by ancestry, **related, kindred** Pi. Trag.; linked by a particular connection, **partnered** S. Ar.
5 (of objects, circumstances) pertaining to all members of a political community, **public** E. Th. Att.orats. Pl. + || NEUT.SB. the people A. Th. || NEUT.PL.SB. public affairs, politics E. Att.orats. Thphr.
6 (of situations, political debate) **of public interest** Pl. Arist. || NEUT.SB. common good (of a population), public interest Isoc. Arist.
7 (of assets) owned by the community as a whole, **public** (opp. private) X. Arist. || NEUT.SB. (sg. and pl.) public funds Hdt. Th. Ar. Att.orats. X. || NEUT.SB. public treasury Th. Ar.
8 (of events) in the sight or knowledge of the public, **publicly known** E.; (prep.phrs.) ἐς (τὸ) κοινόν *publicly, openly* A. E. Ar. Pl. X. D.; ἐν (τῷ) κοινῷ *in public* E. Att.orats. || NEUT.PL.SB. public life (of a person) Att.orats.
9 (of decisions, actions, entities) representing all members of a political community X. Plb. || NEUT.SB. the state Hdt. Th. Ar. Att.orats. Pl. X. || NEUT.SB. alliance, league (ref. to a confederacy of cities) Hdt. Th. Plb.(sts.pl.)
10 relating to the official representatives of a political community || NEUT.SB. (sg. and pl.) government (sts.ref. to the assembly, as the seat of government) Hdt. Th.
11 applying to all alike; (of definitions) **general, universal** (opp. specific) Arist.; (of a coinage) **universally valid** Pl.
12 (of persons) treating all alike, **impartial, showing no favouritism** Th. Att.orats. Arist.; (of leaders, nations, or sim.) neutral (esp. in a war) Th. Att.orats. || COMPAR. (of fortunes in war) more balanced or even Th.
13 (of a location) **equally accessible** (W.GEN. fr. all sides) Arist.; (of persons) **open to all** (not just the rich) X.; **friendly to all, sociable** Isoc.
14 (of a system of government) of benefit to people in general, **egalitarian** Isoc.
15 (of resources, opportunities) available to people in general; (of food) **ordinary** (opp. the fine food of the rich) Alcm.
16 (of knowledge) current among the general population, **general** (opp. specialised) Arist. Plb.
17 (of circumstances) **widespread, commonly found** Arist.; (of sayings, expressions) **commonplace, popular** Men.
18 (pejor., of a prostitute) available to all alike, **common** Plb.(quot.)
19 (of proscribed foodstuffs, unwashed hands) **impure, profane** NT.
—κοινῇ *adv.* **1 collectively, jointly, together** (sts. W.DAT. or PREP.PHR. w. someone or sthg.) *—ref. to doing or sharing in sthg.* Hdt. S. E. Th. Ar. Att.orats. +
2 for the state as a whole *—ref. to sthg. being of benefit or sim.* Att.orats. Arist. Plb.; **on behalf of the state, officially** *—ref. to acting* Att.orats. Arist. Plb. Plu.
3 publicly (opp. in private) Att.orats. Pl. X. Arist. Plb. Plu.
4 in general (opp. in specific cases) Arist.
—κοινῶς *adv.* **1 collectively, jointly** E. Th. X. Lycurg. Plu.
2 for the state as a whole Th. Isoc.
3 on equal terms (W.DAT. for both parties in an agreement) Isoc.
4 impartially *—ref. to discussing an issue* D.
5 in an ordinary manner (and without special favouritism) *—ref. to treating someone* Plu.
6 in general (opp. in specific cases) Plu.

κοινότης ητος *f.* **1 sharing** (of one's resources, w. comrades or fellow citizens) Arist.; **communal nature** (of meals, at Sparta) Plu.; **homogeneity** (of the diet of all Spartans) Plb.
2 equality (among citizens, as a principle of democracy) And.
3 openness, accessibility (of a public figure) X.
4 universality, **standard nature** (of Athenian Greek, compared to other dialects) Isoc.
5 point in common, common feature (shared by people or things) Pl. Plb. Plu.

κοινό-τοκος ον *adj.* [τόκος] (of a person of noble birth, ref. to a brother) **born of the same parents** (as oneself) S.

κοινοτροφικός ή όν *adj.* [τρέφω] (of the science) **of raising whole groups** (of animals) Pl.; (fig., W.GEN. of people, by a ruler) Pl.

κοινο-φιλής ές *adj.* [φιλέω] (of a feeling) **of love for one's fellow citizens** A.

κοινό-φρων ον, gen. ονος *adj.* [φρήν] (of persons) **having intentions in common** (W.DAT. w. someone) E.

κοινόω, dial. **κοινάω** (Pi.) *contr.vb.* | aor.ptcpl. κοινώσας, dial. κοινάσας || dial.fut.mid. κοινάσομαι | **1** give a share (of sthg.) to another; (of rulers) **share** *—power, a title* (w. someone) Th. Plu.(mid.); (of a legislator) **make communal** *—ownership of property* Arist. || MID. **merge** *—one's estate* (W.DAT. w. another's) Is.
2 || MID. have (sthg.) in common; (of persons) **share, have a joint stake in** *—*W.ACC. OR GEN. *a thing, event or circumstance* (oft. W.DAT. w. someone) S. E. Lys. X. Plu.; (of things) *—a quality or circumstance* (w. sthg.) Pl.(also act.); (of persons) **coincide, agree** *—*W.DAT. *in their opinions* Arist. || PASS. (of a concubine) be given a share *—*W.DAT. *in a bed* (w. a wife) E.; (of a substance) *—in a particular quality* Pl.
3 || MID. (of persons, cities) **enter into a collaboration, join forces** *—*W.DAT. *w. a person, a foreign power* Pl. Is.; **cooperate** *—*W.ACC. *in an enterprise, plan, military campaign* E. Th. Pl. Is. D.; (pejor.) **conspire** Is. Plu. || PASS. (of rhythm and melody) be brought into partnership *—*W.DAT. *w. each other* Pl.
4 || MID. (of persons) **take counsel** (w. one another) A. *—*W.DAT. *w. someone* B.(act.) E. Pl. X. Plu.; (tr.) **discuss** *—a matter* (W.DAT. *w. one another*) Plb.
5 (act. and mid.) share one's knowledge or intentions; **tell, divulge** *—sthg.* (W.DAT. or PREP.PHR. *to someone*) A. E. Th. Ar. Pl. Men. +; **commit, entrust** *—a song* (*to voices and the lyre*), *a journey* (*to the night, i.e. travel secretly*) Pi.; (intr.) communicate (a piece of information), **give a briefing** *—*W.DAT. *to someone* (sts. W.PREP.PHR. *about sthg.*) A. Th. Pl. X. Plb. Plu.
6 (act., of persons) make impure, **defile** *—a holy place, the Lord's works* NT.; (of proscribed foods, impure behaviour or speech) *—a person* NT.

κοινών, also **κοινεών**, ῶνος, dial. **κοινᾶν** ᾶνος *m.* **partner, companion, collaborator** (in an undertaking) X.; (W.GEN. in a child, i.e. its birth; ref. to Zeus, as co-father w. a mortal) E.; (ref. to a person's own mind) Pi.

κοινωνέω *contr.vb.* **1** (of persons, states) **form a partnership** or **alliance** X. Arist. *—*W.DAT. *w. a person, people, a state* Att.orats. Pl. Plb. Plu.; (of animals, in a fable) Ar.
2 (of persons) **associate** *—*W.DAT. *w. someone* E. *—*W.ACC. *in a relationship of a certain kind* Pl.; **have a sexual relationship** *—*W.DAT. *w. someone* Pl.; (of persons lacking true knowledge, their souls) **be in communion, be closely tied** *—*W.DAT. *w. the body* Pl.; (of a dead man) **be part of, be**

incorporated into —W.GEN. *the earth* X. ‖ PASS. (of rituals) be combined or accompanied —W.DAT. *w. prayers* Pl.
3 (of persons, animals, states, an organisation) **work together** or **in unison, cooperate, collaborate** Pl. X. Arist. —W.DAT. *w. someone* (W.GEN. *in a certain matter*) Att.orats. Arist. Plb. Plu. —W.DAT. or PREP.PHR. *in a deed, a crime, sedition* Plb. Plu.
4 (of persons, states) take part along with others, **participate in, take part in** —W.GEN. *an action, ritual, discussion, military campaign, civic life* E. Att.orats. Pl. X. Arist. Men. + —*a treaty, alliance, or sim.* Th. X. D. Plb. Plu.; (of female nature) **be an equal participant** —W.DAT. *w. male nature* (W.PREP.PHR. *in all kinds of work*) Pl.
5 (of persons or things) take part in a wider or universal activity; **partake in** —W.GEN. *an activity, way of life, quality or circumstance* Pl. X. Arist. Plu.
6 (of persons) come to share in, **be privy to** —W.GEN. *a piece of news* A.
7 be a partner in, share in —W.GEN. *a business, property, sum of money, burial plot* (W.DAT. *w. someone*) Att.orats. X. —*success, failure, risks, a particular fate, someone's ambitions* A. E. Att.orats. X. Plb. Plu.
8 give a share (of sthg., to someone); **share** —W.GEN. *food, drink, resources* (oft. W.DAT. *w. someone*) Ar. X. D. Plb. Plu.
9 have (sthg.) in common (w. others); **share** —W.GEN. *a condition, circumstance, opinion* (oft. W.DAT. *w. someone*) Trag. Att.orats. Pl. X. Arist. +; (of pleasures) —W.PREP.PHR. *in a mixed nature* Pl.
10 (of persons) **be in accord, agree** Pl. —W.GEN. *on sthg.* Pl.
11 (of things) **have** (W.ACC. sthg., nothing) **in common** —W.DAT. *w. sthg. else* X. Arist.; (of a phenomenon) **be related** or **connected** —W.DAT. *to sthg.* Att.orats. Pl.
κοινώνημα ατος *n.* **1 collaborative enterprise** Pl.
2 connection, tie (betw. persons, cities, peoples) Arist. Plu.
κοινώνησις εως *f.* act of sharing, **shared recognition** (by states, of children w. dual citizenship) Pl.
κοινωνίᾱ, dial. **κοινᾱνίᾱ** (Pi.), ᾱς *f.* **1** condition of having (sthg.) in common; **sharing** (of property, dogs, wives, children, glory, laws) Pl. X. Arist. Plb. Plu.
2 connection, association, relationship (of one person or thing w. another) E. Ar. Pl. D. Plu.
3 interaction (of people or things, w. one another) Pi. Pl. Arist. Plu.; **closeness** (betw. people) D.; **fellowship** (betw. Christians) NT.; **relationship** (betw. husband and wife, or sim.) Plu.; (w. sexual connot.) E.; (specif.) **sexual intercourse** Plu.
4 partnership, agreement (betw. people, esp. in business) Att.orats. Pl. X. Arist. Plu.; (betw. states or rulers) D. Plb. Plu.; **collusion, conspiracy** (w. someone, in a matter) Aeschin. Plu.
5 group with shared circumstances or characteristics; **group, set** (of people or things) E. Pl.; **community** Pl. Arist.
6 association, organisation (ref. to a guild, society, or sim.) Pl. Is.; **state institution** Pl. Plu.
7 alliance, federation (of states or sim.) Th. D. Plb.
κοινωνικός ή όν *adj.* **1** relating to cooperation; (of a god, persons, their relationships, virtues) **social, cooperative** Arist. Plb. Plu.
2 (of persons) **holding joint ownership** (of an estate) D.
3 (of lawsuits) **relating to business partnerships** Arist.
—**κοινωνικῶς** *adv.* **equitably, with benefit to all** —*ref. to using one's success* Plb.
κοινωνός οῦ *m.f.* **1** one who shares in a deed or circumstance; (ref. to persons, also fig.ref. to objects, abstr. qualities) **partner** (oft. W.GEN. or PREP.PHR. *in a certain matter*) Trag. Th. Att.orats. Pl. X. +
2 associate (esp. of a businessman, politician, ruler, or sim.) Att.orats. Arist. Plb. NT. Plu.
3 crony (of a dishonest official) Ar.
κοιν-ωφελής ές *adj.* [κοινός, ὄφελος] (of a ruler) of benefit to all, **working for the common good** Plu.
Κοιο-γενής ές *adj.* —also **Κοιογένεια** ης (AR.) *Ion.fem.adj.* [Κοῖος; γένος, γίγνομαι] (of Leto) **born to Koios** Pi.*fr.* AR.
κοῖος *Ion.interrog.adj.*: see ποῖος
Κοῖος ου *m.* **Koios** (Titan, father of Leto) Hes. hHom. Pi.
—**Κοιηίς** ίδος *f.* **daughter of Koios** (ref. to Leto) Call.
κοιρανέω *contr.vb.* [κοίρανος] | iteratv.impf. κοιρανέεσκον |
1 (of chieftains, Ares) **be in command** (of warriors, esp. in battle) Il.
2 (of kings, leaders, Zeus, an Amazon queen) **be ruler** (sts. W.GEN. or PREP.PHR. *in a place*) Hom. hHom. A. AR. —W.DAT. *in a land* AR. —*over people, the gods* A. AR.; (of the Nemean lion) **hold sway, be master** —W.GEN. *in a place* Hes. ‖ PASS. (of lands) be ruled —W.DAT. *by a king* Call.
3 (of the gods) **preside over** —W.ACC. *dances and feasts* Pi.
κοιρανίδαι ῶν *m.pl.* **lords, rulers** (of a city) S.
κοίρανος ου *m.* **1 leader, commander** (of soldiers) Il. E.
2 lord, ruler (W.GEN. of the immortals, ref. to Zeus) Hes.*fr.*; (of the dead; of night and eternal sleep, ref. to Hades) hHom. Lyr.adesp.; (usu. W.GEN. or ADJ. of a city or region) hHom. Trag. Ar. Call.; (as a title of Alexander the Great) Plu.; (derog., W.GEN. of beggars and wayfarers) Od.
κοιτάζομαι *mid.vb.* [κοίτη] | dial.3sg.aor. κοιτάξατο | **go to bed, sleep** —W.PREP.PHR. *in a place* Pi. Plb. Plu.
κοιταῖος ᾱ ον *adj.* **1** (of persons) **staying the night** (W.PREP.PHR. in a certain place) Plb.
2 ‖ NEUT.SB. **lair, den** (of an animal) Plu.
κοίτη ης, dial. **κοίτᾱ** ᾱς *f.* [κεῖμαι] **1 bed** Od. Hdt. S. E. Pl. +; (ref. to a marital bed, meton. for marriage) S.
2 sleeping-place, den (of a deer) Call.
3 bed (meton.ref. to sleep) X.
4 going to bed, bedtime Hdt.
5 (fig.) **resting, abeyance** (of the winds) Pl.
κοιτίς ίδος *f.* **box, chest** (for storing jewellery) Men.
κοῖτος ου *m.* **1** act of going to bed, **bed, sleep, rest** Od. Hes. Hdt. E. Theoc.
2 sleeping-place, bed Od. A.*fr.* Theoc.
3 roosting-place (for a bird) Od. Theoc.
κοιτών ῶνος *m.* **bedchamber** NT.
κόκκινος η ον *adj.* [κόκκος] (of clothes, a blushing man) **scarlet, bright red** Men. NT.
κόκκος ου *m.* **seed** (of a pomegranate) hHom. Hdt. Call.; (of mustard) NT.; **grain** (of wheat) NT.
κόκκῡ *interj.* **1** (as the call of the bird) **cuckoo!** Ar.
2 (as a call to action, by a person) **cuckoo!, quick now!** Ar.
κοκκύζω, dial. **κοκκύσδω** *vb.* | pf. κεκόκκυκα | **1** (of a cuckoo) make a call, **cuckoo** Hes. Ar.; (of a cockerel) **crow** Ar. Theoc.
2 (of a person) make the sound cuckoo, **say cuckoo** Ar.
κοκκύ-μηλον ου *n.* [κόκκῡξ or κόκκος, μῆλον²] **plum** Hippon.
κόκκῡξ ῡγος *m.* **cuckoo** Hes. Anacr. Ar. Plu.; (fig.ref. to a foolish person) Ar.
κολάζω *vb.* | fut. κολάσω | aor. ἐκόλασα ‖ MID.: fut. κολάσομαι, also κολῶμαι ‖ PASS.: fut. κολασθήσομαι | aor. ἐκολάσθην | pf.ptcpl. κεκολασμένος ‖ neut.impers.vbl.adj. κολαστέον | **1** (of persons, their souls) **correct, curb** —*their passions, base desires* Pl. ‖ PASS. (of base desires or sim.) be

corrected or curbed Pl. Arist.; (of strong wine, excess salt in soil) be tempered (by dilution w. water or sim.) Pl. X.
2 (of slave-owners, commanders, parents) inflict salutary punishment upon, **discipline** (w. physical violence or sim.) —*one's slaves, troops, children* Ar. Pl. X.; (of a rider) —*his horse* X. ‖ PASS. (of persons, animals) be disciplined Th. Pl. X. Arist.
3 (act. and mid., of judges, rulers, gods, the state, laws) **punish** —*wrongdoers, crimes, arrogance* (oft. W.DAT. w. penalties, fines, exile, death) E. Th. Ar. Att.orats. Pl. X. + —*a wrongdoer* (W.GEN. *for a crime*) Th. Ar.; (of fear) **be a punishment for** —*wrongdoers* X. ‖ PASS. be punished (oft. W.DAT. w. a particular penalty) Th. Ar. Att.orats. Pl. X. + —W.DAT. *by fear of punishment* Plu.
4 (act. and mid., of rulers, states, troops) punish (by defeat in battle or sim.), **teach a lesson to** —*enemies, their hostility or arrogance* Th. Pl. Plb. —*an opponent* (*by beating him up*) Ar. ‖ PASS. (of an invading force) be taught a lesson (i.e. defeated in battle) Th.
5 (of persons) **chastise, admonish** —*a person* (sts. W.DAT. or ACC. w. words) S.

κολακείᾱ ᾱς f. [κολακεύω] **1 flattery, sycophancy** Att.orats. Pl. Arist. Plu.
2 fawning behaviour Pl. Aeschin. D. Plb.
3 cultivation (of the masses), **winning of favour** Plu.

κολάκευμα ατος n. **act of flattery** X. Plu.

κολακευτικός ή όν adj. relating to flattery ‖ FEM.SB. art of flattery Pl.

κολακεύω vb. [κόλαξ] **1 be a flatterer** or **sycophant** Isoc. Pl. X. D. Plu.
2 behave (towards someone) in a flattering or fawning way; **flatter** Ar. Isoc. Pl. X. D. + —*someone* X. D. Plu. —*a ruler's prosperity* Plb.; (of demagogues) —*the masses* And. Isoc. Plu.; (of orators, statesmen, envoys, allies, foreign powers) —*a people, state, ruler* Att.orats. Pl. X. Plb. Plu.; (of biography) —*its subjects, their deeds* Plu.; (of deeds) **be flattering** (to the doer) Plu. ‖ PASS. (of persons, rulers, the masses) be flattered X. Aeschin. D. Arist. Plb. Plu.
3 (of a womaniser) cajole with flattery, **flatter, seduce** —*women* Plu.; (of pleasures) **beguile** —*men's souls* Pl.
4 behave in a servile manner (towards someone); **pander to** —*the army, the masses, foreign powers, persons* Isoc. Plu.
5 (of a girl) **behave reverently towards** —*nymphs* Men.

κολακικός ή όν adj. **1** (of rhetoric, enticements) with the aim of flattery, **flattering** Pl.; (of the art) **of flattery** Pl.
2 (of persons, their qualities) **flattering, obsequious** Arist.(dub.) Men. Plb.

κόλαξ ακος m. **1** one who flatters to win favour, **flatterer, sycophant** (oft. W.GEN. of a rich and powerful person) Ar. Att.orats. Pl. Arist. Thphr. Men. +
2 (appos.w. ψόφος) *coaxing* or *cajoling call* (*of a herdsman*) S.*Ichn.*

κόλασις εως f. [κολάζω] **1 act of punishing, punishment** (of wrongdoers, slaves, soldiers, peoples) Th. Pl. Arist. Plb. Plu.; (of sinners, in the afterlife) NT.
2 (ref. to a particular instance) **punishment, penalty** Plb. Plu.
3 corrective treatment (of the sick, as analogous to the punishment of wrongdoers) Arist.

κόλασμα ατος n. **punishment, penalty** (administered to wrongdoers, soldiers) X. Plu.

κολασμός οῦ m. **punishment, penalty** (administered to wrongdoers) Call. Plu.

κολαστέος ᾱ ον vbl.adj. (of wrongdoers) **to be punished** or **corrected** Pl.

κολαστήριον ου n. **correction, chastisement** (of persons) X.

κολαστής οῦ m. (ref. to gods, rulers, commanders, one's own conscience) **punisher** (of wrongdoers, their deeds) Trag. Lys. Plu.; (pl., ref. to jurors) Lys.; (ref. to death, i.e. capital punishment) Pl.

κολαστικός ή όν adj. (of the art) **of corrective punishment** Pl.

κολαφίζω vb. **punch with the fist, punch** —*a person* NT.

κολεόν, ep. **κουλεόν**, οῦ n. **sheath for a sword** or **dagger, scabbard** Hom. Pi. Hdt. S. E. X. +

κολετράω contr.vb. **trample** or **stamp on** —*a person* Ar.

κόλλα ης f. **glue** (made fr. cowhide or sim.) Hdt. E.*fr.* Arist.; (pl., ref. to the unifying force of Harmony, acting on life-forms) Emp.

κόλλαβος ου m. a kind of **bread roll** or **cake, bun** Ar.

κολλάω contr.vb. [κόλλα] | aor. ἐκόλλησα, dial. ἐκόλλᾱσα |
1 attach with glue or a glue-like agent; (of the creator god, substances in the body) **glue** —*the flesh* (w. πρός + ACC. *to the bones*) Pl. —*the sinews* (W.PREP.PHR. *around the neck*) Pl.; (fig., of a man, in a riddle) —*bronze* (ref. to a cupping-glass, w. ἐπί + DAT. *to a person*) Arist.(quot.poet.) ‖ PASS. (wkr.sens., of dust) be stuck or adhere —W.DAT. *to persons* NT.
2 (fig.) join (things) together as with glue; (of a Muse) **glue** or **join together** —*gold, ivory and rosemary* (*to make a crown, fig.ref. to a song*) Pi.; (of a writer) —*words* (w. πρός + ACC. *to one another*) Pl.; (of longing, in a relationship) —*differing natures* Pl.; (app., of a river) —*a group of houses* (*by enabling the transport of building materials*) Pi. ‖ PASS. (of conspiracies) be glued together Ar.
3 (fig., of distress) make fixed and immobile, **stick fast** —*someone's knees* Call.
4 firmly join (persons, to other persons or things) ‖ PASS. (of a family) be glued fast —w. πρός + DAT. *to disaster* A.; (wkr.sens., of persons) be joined or attached —W.DAT. *to one's wife* (*in marriage*) NT.; attach oneself —W.DAT. *to a person, group* (i.e. go and join them) NT.

κολλήεις εσσα εν adj. having parts glued or joined together; (of lances, chariots) **close-jointed** Il. Hes.

κόλλησις εως f. **attaching** (of one thing to another, as if w. glue) Arist.; **welding** or **soldering** (of metal) Hdt.

κολλητός ή όν adj. consisting of parts glued or joined together; (of textiles) **glued together** (W.DAT. w. adhesives) Pl.; (of chariots, doors) **close-jointed** Hom. Hes.*fr.* E.; (of a lance, W.DAT. w. metal bands) Il.; (of a vessel-stand) **welded** or **soldered** Hdt.

κολλῑκο-φάγος ον adj. [κόλλιξ, φαγεῖν] (of a person) **bread-roll-eating** Ar.

κόλλῑξ ῑκος m. **bread roll** Hippon.

κολλομελέω contr.vb. [κόλλα, μέλος] (fig., of a poet, envisaged as a carpenter) **join together into melodies** —*words* Ar.

κόλλοψ οπος m. **lyre-peg** (for tuning the strings) Od. Pl.; (fig., W.GEN. of one's anger, in ctxt. of slackening the peg, i.e. toning down one's anger) Ar.

κολλυβιστής οῦ m. [κόλλυβος] **money-changer** NT.

κόλλυβος ου m. **small bronze coin of low value** (used by money-changers), **penny** Ar. Call.

κολλῡ́ρᾱ ᾱς f. **bread roll** or **bun** Ar.

κολλώδης ες adj. [κόλλα] resembling glue, **glutinous, slimy** Pl.

κολοβός όν adj. [reltd. κόλος] **1** (of persons, animals) **maimed, missing a limb** X. Arist.; (of animals) **lacking** (W.GEN. horns) Pl.

2 (of things) **missing a piece** Arist.; (of a metrical unit in poetry) **truncated, missing a syllable** Arist.

κολοβότης ητος *f.* **shortness** (W.GEN. of breath, as a physical infirmity) Plu.

κολοβόω *contr.vb.* **1** cut off the limbs or extremities from, **mutilate** —*captives* Plb.
2 (of God) cut short (in duration), **shorten** —*a period of time* NT. ‖ PASS. (of a period of time) be cut short NT.

κολόβωμα ατος *n.* piece taken away, **missing part, amputated part** (of an object or entity) Arist.

κολοί-αρχος ου *m.* [κολοιός, ἄρχω] **jackdaw-leader** (in the kingdom of the birds) Ar.

κολοιός οῦ *m.* **1** a kind of crow, **jackdaw** Il. Pi. Ar. Thphr. Plu.; (pejor., ref. to a person) Plb.(quot.)
2 (provb.) κολοιὸς παρὰ (ποτὶ) κολοιόν *jackdaw next to jackdaw* (*i.e. birds of a feather flock together*) Arist.

κολόκῡμα ατος *n.* [reltd. κῦμα] **sea-swell** or **huge wave** Ar.

κολοκύντη ης, dial. **κολοκύντᾱ** ᾱς *f.* a kind of edible gourd, **gourd** Alc.; (fig.ref. to large lumps of discharge in the eyes) Ar.

κόλον ου *n.* **large intestine** ‖ PL. **intestines** (of an animal, eaten as tripe) Ar.

κόλος ον *adj.* **lacking an extremity;** (of cattle, goats) **hornless** Hdt. Theoc.; (of a spear) having the point lopped off, **docked, headless** Il.

κολοσσός οῦ *m.* **1 giant statue** (of a human figure, made of stone, wood or bronze) Hdt. Theoc. Plb. Plu.; (specif.ref. to the Colossus of Rhodes) Plb.
2 (gener.) **statue** A.

κολοσυρτός οῦ *m.* [perh.reltd. σύρω] **1 loud and disordered crowd, noisy throng** (of huntsmen and their dogs, people) Il. Ar.
2 loud and disordered commotion, **tumult** (of a gale) Hes.

κολουραῖος η ον *Ion.adj.* [κόλουρος] **with a section missing;** (of a stone) **hollow** Call.

κόλ-ουρος ον *adj.* [κόλος, οὐρά] **with tail cut short;** (of an aged bird) **with missing tail-feathers** Plu.

—**κόλουρις** ιδος *f.* animal with a docked tail, **dock-tailed creature** Timocr.

κόλουσις εως *f.* [κολούω] act of cutting short, **lopping** (of ears of corn) Arist.; (ref. to ostracism) **docking, curtailing** (of threats to the state) Plu.

κολούω *vb.* [κόλος] **1 lop off** —*ears of corn, someone's fingers* Hdt. Theoc.; (fig.) **prune** —*a person* (*envisaged as a tree, ref. to curtailing his power*) Plu.
2 cut short, cut off —*one's work* (W.ADV. *in the middle*) Il.; **hold back** —*gifts* Od.
3 hamper, curtail —*one's own prosperity, the enjoyment of it* Od. Plu.; **curtail the power of** —*rites* (*by performing them incorrectly*) AR.; (of persons, rulers, the state, the penalty of ostracism) **check, curtail** —*a person, council, state, their power, ambitions, or sim.* Hdt. Pl. Arist. Plu.; (fig.) —*a maxim* (i.e. *discredit it*) Pl. ‖ PASS. (of persons, an army, a state's power or confidence) be checked or curtailed A. Th. Pl. Plu.

κολοφών ῶνος *m.* **finishing touch** (to an argument or story) Pl.

κολπίᾱς ου *masc.adj.* [κόλπος] (of a robe) **hanging in folds** A.

κόλπος ου *m.* **1** (sg. and pl.) **fold at the lap of a garment** (formed where it loops over the belt), **lap-fold** (of a dress or robe, usu. a woman's) Il. Pi. Hellenist.poet. Plu.; (of a woman's dress, soaked w. her tears) Il. A. AR. Mosch.; (forming a pocket used to carry or conceal items) Hom. A. Hdt. E. Ar. D. +; (in which one spits to avert evil) Thphr. Men. Call. Theoc.; **fold** (of the aigis worn by Athena) A.
2 (sg. and pl.) area of the body covered by the lap-fold, **lap, bosom** (usu. of a mother or nurse, where a child or animal is nurtured or sheltered) Il. hHom. Thgn. Isoc. Hellenist.poet. Plu.; (of a goddess, where a child is raised) Il. hHom. Alc. AR.; (where a lock of hair is cherished) Call.; (of a love-poet, where Eros is raised) Mosch.; (of a man or woman, in which a lover or sim. rests the head) Ar. AR. NT. Plu.; (of a powerful man, fig.ref. to nepotistic favouritism) Plu.; (of Abraham, God the Father) NT.
3 bosom (of a beautiful woman) Ar. Theoc.
4 womb (of a woman) E. Ar. Call.
5 bosom (of the earth, esp. as holding the dead) Melanipp. D.(quot.epigr.) Plu.(oracle); (of a sea goddess, ref. to the ocean depths) Tim.
6 capacious depths, bosom (of the sea) Hom.; (of the air) Pi.
7 curving recess of the coast, bay, gulf Pi. Hdt. E. Ar. AR. +
8 gulf of water between enclosing coasts, gulf Hom. hHom. A. Hdt. Th. X. +
9 valley, glen Pi. S. Ar. X.
10 capacious hollow, hold (of a ship) E.; **recess, cavity** (in the ground, in a cave) Plu.
11 curving hollow (of a hunting net) X.; (of a line of troops) Plu.; (of a line drawn on the ground) Plu.

κολπόω *contr.vb.* (of sailors) cause to swell, **belly out** —*their sails* (W.DAT. *in the wind*) B. ‖ PASS. (of a woman's dress) billow —W.DAT. *fr. her shoulders* Mosch.

κολπώδης ες *adj.* (of a coastal area) perh. **curving, gulf-like** E.; (of a coastal voyage) **following a course around a gulf** Plb.

κόλπωμα ατος *n.* **curving hollow** (of the centre of a battle-line) Plu.

κολυμβάς άδος *f.* [κολυμβάω] **olive swimming in brine, pickled olive** Call.

κολυμβάω *contr.vb.* | dial.inf. κολυμβῆν | **1** (of persons) **dive** —W.PREP.PHR. *into the sea, a well* Anacr. Pl.; (of the river Alpheios, supposedly flowing under the sea) Mosch.
2 (of persons) **swim** NT.

κολυμβήθρᾱ ᾱς *f.* pool for diving, **bathing pool** Pl. NT. Plu.

κολυμβητήρ ῆρος *m.* one who dives, **diver** A.

κολυμβητής οῦ *m.* **diver** Th. Pl.

κολυμβητικός ή όν *adj.* relating to diving ‖ FEM.SB. art of diving Pl.

κολυμβίς ίδος *f.* —also **κόλυμβος** ου *m.* a kind of diving bird; prob. **grebe** Ar.

Κόλχοι ων *m.pl.* people of Colchis (coastal region E. of the Black Sea), **Colchians** Pi. Hdt. E. X. AR. Theoc. +

—**Κόλχος** ον *adj.* (of Medea, a river) of or from Colchis, **Colchian** Hdt. Pl.

—**Κολχικός** ή όν *adj.* (of linen) **from Colchis** Hdt. ‖ FEM.SB. land of Colchis Plu.

—**Κολχίς** ίδος *fem.adj.* (of the land, language, a city, a ship) **Colchian** A. Hdt. X. AR.; (of a woman) Simon. Hdt. AR. ‖ SB. Colchian woman E. AR.; land of Colchis Hdt. X. Plu.

κολῳάω *contr.vb.* [app.reltd. κολοιός] make a clamorous din; (of a person) **bicker and shout** Il.

κολῶμαι (fut.mid.): see κολάζω

κολώνη ης, dial. **κολώνᾱ** ᾱς *f.* **1 hill** Il. Pi. AR. Theoc.; **mountain** (ref. to Athos) Call. AR.
2 mound (of earth, ref. to a burial mound) Il. S.

κολωνίᾱ ᾱς *f.* [Lat. *colonia*] **colony** (of Rome) NT.

κολωνός οῦ *m.* **1 hill** Hes.*fr.* hHom. Hdt. AR.
2 heap, mound (of stones or earth) Hdt. X. Plu.

Κολωνός οῦ *m.* Kolonos (Attic deme, site of a temple to Poseidon) S. E. Th. Ar. Aeschin.

—Κολωνῆθεν *adv.* (quasi-adjl., of a person) **from Kolonos** D.

κολῳός οῦ *m.* [κολῳάω] **clamour, uproar** (of argument and bickering) Il. AR.; (of warriors shouting) AR.

κόμᾱ *dial.f.*: see **κόμη**

κόμαρος ου *f.* **arbutus tree** Ar. Theoc.

κομαρο-φάγος ον *adj.* [φαγεῖν] (of a kind of bird) **eating the arbutus fruit** Ar.

κομάω *contr.vb.* [κόμη] | dial.3pl. (w.diect.) κομόωντι (Theoc.), ep.masc.nom.pl.ptcpl. (w.diect.) κομόωντες | aor. ἐκόμησα, dial.3sg.opt. κομάσαι (Theoc.) ‖ pf.pass.ptcpl. κεκομημένος |
1 (of persons, usu. men) **grow the hair long, be long-haired, have long hair** (freq. among foreign tribes and the heroes of epic, but at Athens oft. w.connot. of swaggering militarism, dandified luxury or Spartan sympathies) Anacr. Hdt. Lys. Ar. Pl. X. + —w.ACC. **on one's head** Hom. Hdt. Plu. —w.ADV. or ACC. **at the back, on one side** Il. Hdt. —w.ACC. **on one's chin** X. —w.DAT. w. **golden locks** Call. —**in a Scythian top-knot** Plu.; (of a person's head) Plu.
2 (of horses) **have a long mane** X. —w.DAT. **of golden hair** Il.
3 (of persons) cultivate the long hair and swaggering manner of the equestrian class, **adopt a long-haired swagger** —w. ἐπί + DAT. w. *a view to seizing power* Hdt.; (gener.) **preen oneself, behave arrogantly** Ar.
4 (fig.) **bristle with foliage or vegetation;** (of trees, plants) **bloom, bristle** Call. Theoc. —w.DAT. w. *leaves* AR. Theoc.; (of plains) Plu. —w. *ears of corn* hHom. ‖ PASS. (of a mountain) **be densely clothed** —w.DAT. w. *forest* Call.

κομέω *contr.vb.* | 3du.imperatv. κομείτων | iteratv.impf. κομέεσκον | (of persons, goddesses) **tend to, look after, take care of** —*persons or animals* Hom. Hes. hHom. Call. AR. ‖ PASS. (of a child) **be looked after or raised** AR.

κόμη ης, dial. **κόμᾱ** ᾱς *f.* **1** (pl. and collectv.sg.) **hair** (on the head), **hair, tresses, locks** (of a man, woman or deity) Hom. hHom. Archil. Lyr. Hdt. Trag. +; (cut off and offered to the dead) Hom. Thgn. S. E. Pl.; (fig., w.GEN. of a mist) Pi.*fr.*
2 (phr.) κόμαι πρόσθετοι **added hair** (i.e. wig, worn by Medes) X.
3 long hair (of an Athenian dandy or Spartan) Ar. Plu.
4 (specif.) **lock of hair** Call.
5 (fig.) **foliage** (of an olive tree) Od.

κομήτης ου *masc.adj.* **1** (of men, a corpse) **long-haired** Hdt. Pl.; (w.connot. of being vain and self-satisfied) Iamb.adesp. Ar. Plu.
2 (gener., of men) **having hair** (opp. being bald) Pl.; (of a woman's pubic area) **hairy** Ar.
3 (fig.) abundant in foliage (of a meadow) **leafy, grassy** E.; (of a thyrsos) **tressed, wreathed** (w.DAT. w. *ivy*) E.
4 (fig., of an arrow) having trailing feathers, **feathered** S.
5 ‖ SB. **long-tailed star, comet** Plu.

κομιδή ῆς, dial. **κομιδᾱ́** ᾱς *f.* [κομίζω] **1 attention to needs, tending, care** (of plants, animals, old men, wayfarers) Hom. Theoc.
2 (concr.) **necessities of life, provisions** (on a ship) Od.
3 act of providing supplies (to persons); **provision, supplying** (of necessities, to troops) Th.
4 payment (of salaries or sim.) Plb.
5 conveyance, transport (of supplies, esp. by ship) Th. Plu.; **importing** (of supplies) Isoc.
6 act of sending by ship; **sending** (of tribute) Call.
7 act of carrying by hand; **carrying** (of supplies, by troops or persons) Arist. Plb.
8 act of carrying back supplies; **harvesting** (of crops) X. Arist. Plb.; **acquisition** (of grain) Plu.
9 act of regaining (a person or thing); **rescuing** (of a person, on the battlefield) Pi.; **regaining, recovery** (of a person, a territorial possession, property, human remains) Hdt. D. Plb. Plu.; **recovery, collection** (of debts) D. Arist.; **repayment** (of money) Plb.
10 act of receiving or acquiring; **receiving** (of salaries) Plb.
11 act of transporting or being transported by ship; **transport** (of persons, troops, barges) Hdt. Th. X. Plb.
12 act of being transported or travelling back (esp. by ship); **return** (of persons) Hdt. AR. Plu.

κομιδῇ *dat.adv.* **1 exactly, precisely** Pl. D.; (as a reply) **quite so!** Ar. Pl.
2 completely, entirely Ar. Att.orats. Pl. Arist. Men. Plu. ‖ NEG.PHR. **not at all, not one bit** D. Plu.
3 exceedingly, extremely D. Plb. Plu.

κομίζω *vb.* [κομέω] | fut. κομιῶ, ep. κομίσσω (AR.) | aor. ἐκόμισα, ep. ἐκόμισσα, κόμισσα, dial. ἐκόμιξα | pf. κεκόμικα ‖ MID.: fut. κομιοῦμαι | aor. ἐκομισάμην ‖ PASS.: aor. ἐκομίσθην ‖ neut.impers.vbl.adj. κομιστέον ‖ The sections are grouped as: (1–3) look after, (4–6) bring or take in, (7–13) bring, receive or take back, (14–16) receive or obtain, (17–21) bring or convey, (22–23) carry away. |
1 (act. and mid.) **tend to, look after** —*children, animals, persons* Hom. Hes. hHom. A. AR. ‖ PASS. **be looked after** Od.
2 (of women) **attend to** —*a household, a task* Hom.
3 (act. and mid.) **look after, keep safe** —*valuables, possessions* Od. Hes. Hdt. —*a land* (w.DAT. *for future generations*) Pi.; (of songs and stories) **save, preserve** —*people's deeds* Pi.
4 (act. and mid.) **take in, welcome** —*persons* (*into one's house, city, or sim.*) Od. A. E. Th. Att.orats.; (gener.) **bring in** —*a person* (*to a place*) S.
5 bring in —*supplies, materials* (*to a place*) Hdt. Pl. X. Arist.; **introduce** —*a practice or doctrine* Isoc. Pl.(mid.) Arist.; **instil** —*courage* (w.DAT. *in one's troops*) A. ‖ PASS. (of goods) **be brought in** (to a city or sim.) Hdt. Pl. X.; (of books, poems, a legend, a ritual procedure) Pl.
6 ‖ MID. (specif.) **take in, harvest** —*crops* Hes. Hdt.; (fig.) —*the fruits of one's labours, another's compassion* X. D.
7 (act. and mid.) **bring back with one, bring back** —*hunted animals* Pi. —*persons, ships* Pi. S. E. Th. X.; (of spirit-guides) **lead back** —*a soul* (*fr. the underworld*) E. Pl. ‖ PASS. (of captives or sim.) **be taken back** (to a place) Th.
8 ‖ PASS. **travel or come back** (to a place) Hdt. Th.
9 (act. and mid.) **bring back** (to safety), **bring back, recover** —*captives, war dead, or sim.* Il. Th. Isoc. X. —*a goddess* (*fr. the battlefield*) Il. —*a person* (*fr. the underworld, fr. death*) Pi. E. —*a chariot* (*fr. a dangerous race*) Pi.; **rescue** —*a person* (*fr. danger*) Ar. ‖ PASS. (of troops) **be brought back safely** Th.
10 (act. and mid.) **bring back for burial** —*a corpse* Hdt. Trag. X. Is.; **bring home** —*a soul* (i.e. a dead person's body) Pi. ‖ PASS. (of a body, bones) **be brought back for burial** Hdt. Th. Pl. X. Is.
11 restore —*a person's life* Pi.
12 ‖ MID. **receive back, get back** —*one's son* (*fr. the sophists*) Ar. —*one's son* (*as a corpse*) X.; **welcome back** (into one's house) —*a widowed daughter* Is.
13 (act. and mid.) **regain, recover** —*possessions, territory, honours, rights, borrowed goods* Pi. Th. Ar. Att.orats. Pl. X. +; (of troops) **recover, retrieve** —*their shields* X.
14 ‖ MID. **receive, obtain** —*thanks, gratitude* Th. Att.orats. X. Men. —*vengeance* Lys. —*rewards, benefits, honours, rights,*

goods, money S. Th. Ar. Att.orats. Pl. + —*pain* (*as punishment for crimes*) Pl.; **acquire** —*interest* (*on a loan*), *profit* (*fr. an investment*) Att.orats. Pl.; (of a military force) —*a person* (*as leader*) Th. ‖ PASS. (of money) be acquired Isoc.
15 win —*victories, praise* Pi. S.
16 (act. and mid., of a warrior) **receive, take** —*a spear* (oft. W.DAT. or PREP.PHR. *in one's flesh*) Il.
17 bring —*an object* (*to a place or person*) Hom. Hdt. S. E. Th. Ar. + ‖ PASS. (of objects, money) be brought or fetched Is.
18 take along with one, carry, transport —*objects, a letter* Hdt. E. Th. Att.orats. Pl. X. + —*a sick or wounded man, a baby* X. Thphr. Call.; (of wagons, horses) —*persons, water* Hdt. X.; (of a ship) —*supplies* (*for the crew*) X. ‖ PASS. (of a sick or wounded man) be carried Pl. X.
19 lead, escort —*a person, group, fleet, or sim.* Hdt. S. E. Th. Ar. Pl. +; (fig., of a patron nymph) —*a city* (W.DAT. *on a voyage of freedom*) Pi.; (of fate) —*a person* (*to a place*) Ar. Pl. ‖ PASS. (of persons) be led or escorted (to a place) S. Th. And. X.
20 convey, send —*persons, a fleet, objects* (*to a place*) Hdt. Th. Isoc. Pl. X.; (of a breeze) —*ships* (sts. W.PREP.PHR. *across the sea*) E. Arist.; (of a god) —*a person* (*to a particular fate*), *a hostile power* (*to assail a people*) Pl.
21 (act. and mid.) **convey, take** —*oneself, one's feet* (*to a place or in a certain direction*) S. E. —(fig.) *one's foot* (W.PREP.PHR. *fr. the mire of ruin*) A. ‖ PASS. be conveyed, travel (by ship) Hdt. Th. X.; (of ships) travel, sail —W.INTERN.ACC. *a certain journey* Th.; (gener., of persons) travel —W.PREP.PHR. *to a place or person* Hdt. Th. X.; come or go (to a place) A. E.
22 pick up and take away, pick up —*a fallen object* Il.
23 (act. and mid.) **carry off** (esp. as spoils) —*armour, livestock, valuables* Il. Hdt. S. E. Th. +; **carry away** (in one's mind) —*a goddess's teachings* Parm.

κομίσκα ᾶς *dial.f.* [dimin. κόμη] (collectv.sg.) **hair, tresses** (of a girl) Alcm.

κομιστέος ᾱ ον *vbl.adj.* [κομίζω] (of fruits) **to be harvested** A.

κομιστήρ ῆρος *m.* **1** one who leads or escorts, **escorter** (of a girl, to be sacrificed) E.
2 one who brings or supplies, **supplier** (of building materials) Plu.

κομιστής οῦ *m.* **1 escort** (for a person, ref. to a group of nymphs) E.
2 one who takes to burial, **arranger of burial** (for the dead) E.

κόμιστρα ων *n.pl.* **1 means of bringing back** (W.GEN. a person, an animal) A.*fr.* E.
2 means or **way of saving** (W.GEN. someone's life) A.

κομιῶ (fut.): see κομίζω

κόμμα ατος *n.* [κόπτω] **1** result of striking or issuing of coins, **coinage, mintage** (ref. to a particular type or issue) Ar.; (fig., ref. to a batch of newly invented gods) Ar.
2 stamp, design (on a coin, as an indication of its value) Ar.; (fig., ref. to the nature and appearance of a person) Ar.

κόμμι *indecl.n.* [Egyptian loanwd.] **gum** (fr. the acacia tree) Hdt. Arist.

κομμός οῦ *m.* [κόπτω] **1** (sg. and pl.) **beating** (of one's chest, in mourning) A. Bion
2 song of lament (shared by chorus and actor in a tragic drama) Arist.

κομμωτικός ή όν *adj.* [κομμόω *embellish, adorn*] relating to adornment ‖ FEM.SB. art of beautifying (oneself, w. cosmetics or sim.) Pl.

κομμώτρια ᾱς *f.* **personal attendant** (ref. to a lady's maid or sim.) Ar. Pl.

κομόωντες (ep.masc.nom.pl.ptcpl.), **κομόωντι** (dial.3pl.): see κομάω

κομπάζω *vb.* [κόμπος] **1 boast, brag** Trag. Lys. Call. Plu. —W.INF. *that one did sthg. or is such and such* A. E. —W.NOM.PTCPL. *of doing sthg.* E. Plu. —W.ACC. + INF. *that sthg. is the case* E. —W.COMPL.CL. X. Plu.; **say** (W.ACC. sthg.) **boastfully** A. S. X.; **boast about** —*sthg.* A. S. Lys.
2 ‖ MID. **make a boast** B.; (fig., of Terror, on the battlefield) **vaunt oneself** A.
3 ‖ PASS. be extolled —W.PREDIC.SB. or ADJ. *as such and such* E.

Κομπασεύς έως *m.* person from the (imaginary) deme of Kompos, **Braggadocian** Ar.

κομπάσματα των *n.pl.* **boasts** A. Ar.

κομπασμός οῦ *m.* **boasting, bragging** Plu.

κομπαστής οῦ *m.* **boaster, braggart** Plu.

κομπέω *contr.vb.* **1** (of struck bronze) **ring out** Il.
2 (of persons) **boast, brag** Pi. Hdt. S. —W.ACC. + INF. *that sthg. is the case* E.; **say** (W.ACC. sthg.) **boastfully** S.; **boast about** —*sthg.* A. S. ‖ PASS. (of soldiers) be boasted of —W.PREDIC.ADJ. *as being so many* (in number) Th.
3 noisily allege (sthg.) E.; **rant about** —*sthg.* E.

κομπολᾱκέω *contr.vb.* [λᾱκέω] (of a playwright) **make a bombastic din** Ar.

κομπολᾱκύθης (or perh. **κομπολᾱ́κυθος**) ου *m.* [κομπολᾱκέω, also reltd. ληκυθίζω] (as a supposed species of bird) **big-mouthed boastard** Ar.

κομπός οῦ *m.* **boaster, braggart** E. Call.

κόμπος ου *m.* **1 din, noise** (of boars clashing their tusks, marching feet, jangling bells on a shield) Hom. E.; (of singers) Pi.*fr.*
2 boast (made by a person) Hdt. Trag. Th. Aeschin. Plu.; **exaggeration** Plu.; **ostentation** (in the works of a sculptor) Plu.
3 boast (about a person), **praise** Pi.

κομπο-φακελο-ρρήμων ον, gen. ονος *adj.* [φάκελος, ῥῆμα] (of Aeschylus) **uttering bundles of boastful words** Ar.

κομπώδης ες *adj.* (of persons, shouts, or sim.) **boastful** Th. Plu. ‖ NEUT.SB. **boastfulness** Th. Plu.

κομψείᾱ ᾱς *f.* [κομψεύω] **nicety, subtle point, quibble** (in a philosophical discussion) Pl.

κομψ-ευρῑπικῶς *adv.* [κομψός, Εὐρῑπίδης] **in a smart Euripidean way** Ar.

κομψεύω *vb.* **1 quibble** or **talk glibly about** —*sthg.* S.
2 ‖ MID. (freq. iron. or pejor.) **make a clever** or **subtle point** Pl.; **subtly point out** —W.COMPL.CL. *that sthg. is the case* Pl.
3 ‖ MID. **dress up, gloss over** —*wicked behaviour* E.
4 ‖ PASS. (of a tool) be ingeniously devised Pl.

κομψο-πρεπής ές *adj.* [πρέπω] (of verbal artistry) **clever-looking, stylish** Ar.

κομψός ή όν *adj.* **1** (as a term of commendation, but sts. w. a note of irony; of persons) **clever, smart, subtle** Timocr. E.*Cyc.* Ar. Pl. X. Men.; (of an idea, plan, argument, or sim.) Ar. Philox.Leuc. Pl. Plu. ‖ NEUT.SG.SB. **cleverness, subtlety** (of Socrates' discourses) Arist. ‖ NEUT.PL.SB. **subtleties** (of behaviour, speech) E. Pl.
2 (gener., of a young man, a baby) **fine, lovely** Men.; (of a feature of the landscape) **delightful, exquisite** Pl.
3 (specif., of a person) **refined** (in taste or behaviour) Plb.; **discriminating, critical** Plu.; **polished, accomplished** (W.INF. in public speaking) Plu.
4 (pejor., of a person) **smart, clever** E.; (of talk, artistic pursuits) E. ‖ NEUT.PL.SB. **over-cleverness** Arist.(quot. E.)

κομψότης

5 (perh. iron., of works of art) **elegant, exquisite** Plu.; (pejor., of a cloak) **smart, fancy** Aeschin.; (of speech) **over-refined, affected** Plu.
—κομψῶς *adv.* | compar. κομψότερον, also κομψοτέρως (Isoc.) | **1 neatly, deftly** Ar. X.
2 in a sophisticated or **polished style** —*ref. to composing a speech* Isoc.
3 cleverly, subtly Ar. Pl. Arist. Plu.; (pejor.) E.*fr.*
4 (compar., w. ἔχειν) **be better** (*in health*) NT.
κομψότης ητος *f.* **1 stylistic refinement** (of a speech) Isoc.
2 refinement or **delicacy** (of behaviour) Plu.
3 cleverness, smartness (W.GEN. of a remark) Plu.
κοναβέω *contr.vb.* [κόναβος] (of struck metal, a lyre) **ring out** Il. hHom.; (of the earth, ships, a house) **echo, reverberate** (w. thunder, shouting, a sneeze) Hom. Hes.
κοναβίζω *vb.* (of struck metal) **ring out** Il.; (of the earth, a house) **echo, reverberate** (w. footsteps, wailing) Hom.
κόναβος ου *m.* **din** (of dying men, splintering ships, clashing shields, a storm) Od. A. AR.
κόνδυ υος *n.* [loanwd.] **drinking-cup, tankard** Men.
κόνδυλος ου *m.* (sg. and pl.) **knuckle** (meton. for a punch w. the clenched fist) Ar. Aeschin. D. Call. Plu.
κονία ᾶς, Ion. **κονίη** ης *f.* [κόνις] | sts. ῑ *metri grat.* | **1** (sg. and pl.) **dust** (of the ground, esp. on a battlefield) Hom. Hes. Alc. Eleg. A. E. +; (sullying a person or animal) Hom. AR.; (ref. to a dust-cloud in the air) Hom. Simon.; (specif.) **dust-storm** or **sand-storm** Hes.
2 mud, sand (of a river-bed) Il.
3 (gener.) **land** (opp. sea) Pi.(dub.) [perh. *fem.adj.*, see κόνιος, also χέρσος 3]
4 ‖ PL. **dust and ashes** (of a hearth) Od.
5 alkali prepared from wood-ash, **washing-soda, detergent** (app. also used as soap) Ar. Pl.
κονιατός ή όν *adj.* [κονιάω] (of water-tanks) **lined with plaster** X.
κονιάω *contr.vb.* [κόνις] | pf.pass.ptcpl. κεκονιᾱμένος | **1 coat with plaster, plaster, whitewash, stucco** —*walls, buildings* D. ‖ PF.PASS.PTCPL.ADJ. (of walls, buildings, tombs) plastered, whitewashed or stuccoed NT. Plu.
2 ‖ PASS. (of hills) be covered with dust Plu.
κονι-ορτός οῦ *m.* [ὄρνῡμι] **1 dust raised or stirred up, dust-cloud** (esp. caused by soldiers or horsemen) Hdt. Th. Ar. X. Plb. Plu.; **ash-cloud** Th. Plu.; **dust-storm** or **sand-storm** (caused by a wind) Pl. Plu.; (gener.) **dust** (of the road) NT.
2 (pejor., as nickname for a person) **dust-cloud** D.
κόνιος ᾱ ον *adj.* (of dry land, opp. sea) **dusty** Pi.(dub.) [perh. *fem.sb.*, see κονίᾱ 3]
κονί-πους ποδος *m.* [πούς] ‖ DU. or PL. **dusty-foot shoes** (ref. to light sandals) Ar.
κόνις εως (also εος (E.*Cyc.*), Ion. ιος) *f.* | also nom. κόνῑς | acc. κόνιν, also κόνῑν | dat. κόνει, ep.Ion. κόνι (before a vowel) |
1 dust (of the ground) Il. +; (in which a slain man lies, or on which blood is shed) Il. A.; (in the air, raised by soldiers, horsemen, or sim.) Hes. B. Trag. Lyr.adesp. Plu.
2 (specif.) **dust** (sprinkled on a corpse, as part of the rites before cremation) S. E.; (ref. to the soil which covers a buried body) Pi. S. E. Th.(quot.epigr.)
3 dust (exemplifying that which is innumerable) Il. Lyr.adesp.
4 (collectv.) **ashes** Od. hHom. Theoc.; (poured over one's head in mourning) Hom.; (ref. to the remains of a cremated body) Call.*epigr.*
5 sand (covering the floor of a gymnasium, and for wrestlers to sprinkle on themselves before fighting) Plu.

κονίσαλος ου *m.* **1 dust-cloud** (on a battlefield) Il.
2 Konisalos (a priapic deity) Ar.
κονίστρᾱ ᾱς *f.* **sanded area** (for wrestling) Thphr.(cj.) Call.
κονίω *vb.* | fut. κονίσω | aor. ἐκόνῑσα ‖ pf.pass. κεκόνῑμαι |
1 (of galloping horses) **raise a cloud of dust** —W.GEN. *on a plain* Hom. Hes.; (of an advancing army) A.; (tr., of fleeing soldiers) **raise a cloud of dust over** —W.ACC. *a plain* Il.; (fig., of Wealth, envisaged as either on the battlefield or in the wrestling arena) **raise dust from** —*the ground* A. ‖ MID. **raise the dust** (by hurrying on an errand) Ar.
2 (of Ares, struck to the ground in battle) **sully** (W.ACC. his hair) **with dust** Il. ‖ PASS. (of the head of Hector, dragged behind a chariot) be sullied with dust Il.
‖ PF.PASS.PTCPL.ADJ. (of fleeing warriors) covered in dust Il.; (of a reaper) Hes.; (of a person, fr. hurrying on the road) Ar.
3 ‖ PF.PASS.PTCPL.ADJ. (fig., of ivy) dotted —W.DAT. w. *clusters of flowers* Theoc.(dub.)
κοννέω *contr.vb.* **know, be familiar with** —*someone's language or jealous nature* A.
κοντός οῦ *m.* **1 long pole** (usu. assoc.w. boats and ships, esp. used for manoeuvring) Od. Hdt. E. Th. Plb. Plu.
2 long spear or **pike** (used by Parthian soldiers) Plu.
κοπάζω *vb.* [κόπος] (of a wind or storm) **die down, abate** Hdt. NT.
κόπανον ου *n.* [κόπτω] **chopper, cleaver** (as a weapon) A.
κοπετός οῦ *m.* **breast-beating** (by mourners) Plu.; **sound of lamentation** or **mourning** NT. Plu.
κοπιάω *contr.vb.* [κόπος] | aor. ἐκοπίᾱσα | **1 grow weary, become tired** Ar. Men. NT.; (fig.) —W.PTCPL. *of receiving benefits* Plu.; **be worn out** —w. ὑπό + GEN. *by one's blessings* Ar.
2 work hard, toil NT. —W.ACC. *at sthg.* NT.
κοπίς ίδος *f.* [κόπτω] **1 chopper, cleaver** (used for butchering animals) E. Plu.; (appos.w. μάχαιρα *knife*) E.*Cyc.*; (W.GEN. of the nether gods, fig.ref. to the means by which they destroy mortals) S.(cj.)
2 (fig., as a name applied by an orator to a rival speaker) **cleaver** (W.GEN. of one's speeches) Plu.(quot. D.)
3 a kind of bladed weapon, scimitar (esp. assoc.w. Persians) X. Plu.; **sabre** (of a cavalryman) X.; perh. **battle-axe** (of a Gaul) Plu.
κόπις ιδος *m.* (ref. to Odysseus) perh., **chopper** (of logic), **glib talker** E.
κόπος ου *m.* **1 delivering of a blow, blow, strike** (w. a weapon) Ar.(quot. A.)
2 beating (of the head or breast w. the hands, by mourners) A. E.
3 buffeting (W.GEN. by a storm) Pl.(cj.)
4 (sg. and pl.) state of weariness, **exhaustion, fatigue** S. E. Th. Ar. Pl. X. +
5 exhausting work, **exertion, toil** Ar. NT.
6 (wkr.sens.) **trouble, difficulty, annoyance** NT.
κοππατίᾱς ου *masc.adj.* [κόππα *koppa*, a letter used in early forms of the Greek alphabet] (of a horse) **branded with a koppa** Ar.
κοπρ-αγωγέω *contr.vb.* [κόπρος, ἀγωγός] | Lacon.inf. κοπραγωγῆν | **carry dung** (i.e. manure the fields, w. further ref. to anal intercourse) Ar.
Κόπρειος ᾱ ον *adj.* [Κόπρος, name of an Attic deme] (of a person) **belonging to the deme Kopros, Koprian** Is.; (w. play on κόπρος *dung*) **Shittian** Ar.
κοπρέω *contr.vb.* —or perh. **κοπρίζω** *vb.* | masc.nom.pl. fut.ptcpl. κοπρήσοντες (v.l. κοπρίσσοντες) | **spread dung on** —*land* Od.

κοπρίᾱ ᾶς, Ion. **κοπρίη** ης f. dunghill, compost heap NT. || COLLECTV.PL. dung, muck Semon.

κόπρια ων n.pl. dung, excrement (of persons or animals) NT. Plu.

κοπρίζω vb.: see κοπρέω

κοπρο-λόγος ου m. [λέγω] dung-collector Ar. Arist.

κόπρος ου f. **1** dung, excrement (of persons or animals, oft. as manure) Hom. Semon. Hdt. Ar. Pl. X. +; **fertiliser, compost** (made fr. hay) X.
2 dunghill, compost heap X. Men.
3 (meton.) **cattle-yard** or **cowshed** Hom. Call.

κοπροφορέω contr.vb. [κοπροφόρος] **dump in manure** or **dump manure on** —a person Ar.

κοπρο-φόρος ον adj. [φέρω] (of a basket) **for carrying dung** X.

κοπρώδης ες adj. tainted with dung; (of wax) **mixed with dirt, dirty** Pl.

κοπρών ῶνος m. **shithouse, latrine** Ar. D.

κόπτω vb. | fut. κόψω | aor. ἔκοψα, ep. κόψα | pf. (in cpds.) -κέκοφα | ep.pf.ptcpl. κεκοπώς (Od.), Aeol. κεκόπων (Il., dub.) || PASS.: aor.2 ἐκόπην | pf. κέκομμαι | **1 strike with a blow, strike, hit** —a person, a part of the body, an animal, an object (sts. W.DAT. w. one's hand, a staff, weapon, or sim.) Hom. Hippon. A. Ar. AR. Theoc.; (of a snake) **strike at** (i.e. bite) —an eagle Il.
2 strike so as to kill (a sacrificial victim); **strike** or **strike down** —an animal Od. E.; (intr.) **deliver a blow** —W.PREP.PHR. behind the horns (of an ox) Il. || PASS. (of a person, envisaged as a sacrificial victim) **be struck down** A.
3 (gener.) **slaughter** —animals (for food) X.; **cut down** —enemy soldiers Hdt. Plu. || PASS. (of animals) be slaughtered Plb.
4 (of the Cyclops) **strike, dash** —someone (W.PREP.PHR. against the ground) Od.
5 (fig., of Love, envisaged as a smith) **strike** —someone (W.DAT. w. a hammer) Anacr. || PASS. (fig., of a person) be struck —W.GEN. out of one's wits A.
6 (usu.mid.) **beat** —one's head (under intense emotion) Il. Hdt. Men.(act.) —one's forehead (in mourning) Hdt.; (intr.) **beat one's breast** (in mourning) Ar. Pl. Men. NT. Plu.; (tr.) **mourn for** —someone Ar. NT.; (act.) **strike** —W.COGN.ACC. blows (to the breast or head, in mourning) A.
7 knock on —a door And. Ar. X. D. Men. Plu.; (intr.) **knock** Ar. Men. Plu.
8 (of rowers) **strike** —the water (w. oars) Call. AR.; (of a sea-monster, w. its fins) AR.
9 || PASS. (of the ground) **be struck** (by the hands or feet of persons summoning up the dead) A.; (of dust) —w. ὑπό + DAT. beneath or by chariots and horses' hooves Hes.; (of the sea, armour) —W.DAT. by wind, hail or rain Theoc. Plu.
10 (of the bone-structure of a horse's legs) **jolt** —its rider X.; (of a sea-current) **knock** —a ship (W.PREDIC.ADJ. fr. side to side) AR. || PASS. (of a rider) be jolted X.
11 (of Hephaistos) **hammer, forge** —rivets, chains Hom.
12 strike, mint —coins Hdt.(also mid.) Plu. || PASS. (of coins) be struck Ar. Plu.
13 (of draught-animals) **crush** —grain X.; (of persons) —a fruit Plb.; app. **make** (by crushing sesame seeds) —a sesame cake Men. || PF.PASS.PTCPL.ADJ. (of linseed) crushed Th.
14 (gener.) **damage by striking, batter, smash** —enemy ships (by ramming) Th. Plu.; **mutilate** —sacred objects D. || PASS. (of ships) be battered Th.
15 (fig., of a person) **wear down, weary, bore** —someone (usu. by one's loquacity) D. Men. Plu. || PASS. (of a populace)

be worn down —W.DAT. by constant military service D.
16 strike (so as to cut), **slash** —wickerwork shields (W.DAT. w. swords) X.; (mid.) —one's forehead (w. a knife) Hdt. || PF.PASS.PTCPL. (of letters) cut or carved —w. ἐν + DAT. on bark Call.
17 cut (into pieces), **cut up, chop** —wood AR. Plu. —fruit, rushes Hdt. —meat Thphr. AR.; (of the Cyclops, W.DAT. w. his teeth) E.Cyc.; (fig., of anxiety) **cut short** —someone's sleep Theoc. || MID. cut for oneself, **cut** —planks (w. ἐκ + GEN. fr. the wood of a certain tree) Hdt. || PASS. (of water, when mixed w. earth) be broken up, disintegrate Pl. || PF.PASS.PTCPL. (of a plant) chopped up Hdt.
18 cut off —someone's hands and feet Od. —someone's head (w. ἀπό + GEN. fr. his neck) Il. —branches (fr. trees) NT.
19 cut down —trees (esp. as a hostile act) Th. X. Call. Plu.; cut down the trees of, **level, lay waste to** —a region, fields X. Men. Plu.; (intr.) **cut down trees, level a region** X. || PASS. (of trees) be cut down Ar. Plu.; (of a region) be levelled or laid waste X.

κοπώδης ες adj. [κόπος] (of a feast-day) **exhausting** Plu.

κόρα, Κόρᾱ dial.f.: see κόρη¹

κορακῖνος ου m. [κόραξ] a kind of small fish; **raven-fish** (perh. so named fr. being black) Ar.

κόραξ ακος m. **1 raven, crow** (freq. noted as an aggressive scavenger and feeder on corpses) Hes.fr. Thgn. A. Pi. Hdt. Ar. +; (as colloq. curse) ἐς κόρακας (oft. w.imperatv. βάλλε, ἔρρε, or sim.) **go to the crows!** (i.e. go to hell!) Archil. Lys. Ar. Thphr. Men.
2 machine which lowers a gangplank for boarding enemy ships, **raven** Plb.

κοράσιον ου n. [dimin. κόρη¹] **girl** NT.

κορβᾶν indecl.sb. [Semit.loanwd.] **offering** (to God) NT.

—**κορβανᾶς** ᾶ m. **temple treasury** NT.

κορδακίζω vb. [κόρδαξ] (fig., ref. to behaving in a vulgar and unsuitable manner) **dance the kordax** Hyp.

κορδακικός ή όν adj. || COMPAR. (of the trochaic metre) **more appropriate for the kordax** (i.e. relatively lacking in dignity) Arist.

κορδακισμός οῦ m. (pejor.) **dancing of the kordax** D.

κόρδαξ ᾱκος m. a kind of obscene dance (assoc.w. the comic stage, performed by drunken persons), **kordax** Ar. Thphr.

Κόρεια ων n.pl. [Κόρη, under κόρη¹] **festival of Persephone** Plu.

κορέννῡμι vb. | fut. κορέσω, ep. κορέω | aor. ἐκόρεσα, ep. ἐκόρεσσα (Theoc.) | ep.masc.nom.du.pf.ptcpl. κεκορηότε || MID.: aor. ἐκορεσάμην, ep. ἐκορεσσάμην, κορεσσάμην || PASS.: aor. ἐκορέσθην, ep. κορέσθην, ep.3pl. ἐκόρεσθεν (Ar.) | pf. κεκόρεσμαι, Ion. κεκόρημαι |
1 satisfy (a bodily appetite); (of a slain warrior) **sate, satiate, glut** —dogs and birds (sts. W.DAT. w. his fat and flesh) Il.; (of a ruler) —an enemy (W.GEN. w. blood) Hdt.; (of wild beasts) —their mouths (W.GEN. w. human flesh) S.; (of a fisherman, w. his catch) —many people Il.; (of food) —a person Theoc.
2 satisfy (a desire); **satisfy, sate** —someone, one's heart (w. wealth or power) Eleg. A. —one's desire (for wealth) Plb.; (of girls) —their hearts (W.DAT. w. play) AR.
3 || AOR.MID. and PASS. **have one's fill** (of food) Hes. AR. —W.GEN. of food, drink, or sim. Hom. Hes. E. AR. NT. —of love A.satyr.fr. —of war Il. Ar.(mock-ep.) —W.PTCPL. of weeping or sim. Hom.; (of animals) Il. —W.GEN. of food, pasture, or sim. Hom. Thgn. Theoc. —W.DAT. hHom. Thgn.
4 || AOR.MID. **become wearied** (W.ACC. in one's hands) —W.PTCPL. fr. cutting trees Il.

κορεύματα

5 ‖ PF.PASS. and EP.PF.ACT. have had one's fill, have had enough (of food, war) Ar. X. —W.GEN. *of food, music, troubles* Od. Hes. Theoc. —*of a person* Sapph. —W.PTCPL. *of being cooped up* Il.; (of animals) —W.GEN. *of grass* Od. AR.; (of a lion) —*of slaughter* Plu.
6 ‖ PF.PASS. be glutted or sated —W.DAT. *w. wealth* Thgn. —*w. insolence and envy* Hdt.

κορεύματα των *n.pl.* [κορεύομαι] **maidenhood, virginity** E.

κορεύομαι *pass.vb.* [κόρη¹] | fut. κορευθήσομαι | **pass one's maidenhood** E. [or perh. *pass from maidenhood (on marriage)*]

κορέω¹ *contr.vb.* | pf.pass.ptcpl. κεκορημένος | **1 sweep** —*a room* Od. D.
2 ‖ FEM.PF.PASS.PTCPL.ADJ. (w. τρίς, of a woman, app. w. sexual connot.) *thrice-swept* Anacr.

κορέω² (ep.fut.): see κορέννυμι

κόρη¹, Ion. **κούρη**, ης, dial. **κόρα, κούρα**, also **κώρα** (Corinn. Theoc. Bion), ᾱς *f.* [reltd. κόρος²] **1 young woman, girl, maiden** Hom. Hes. Thgn. Lyr. Hdt. Trag. +; (appos.w. παῖς *child*) *young girl* Lys. Ar. D. Men.; (w. ἀδελφή) *young sister* Th. Isoc.; (specif.) **virgin** S.
2 **unmarried or virgin goddess or demigoddess** (regardless of age), **maiden** (ref. to Athena, Artemis) Hes. hHom. Pi. B. S. E. Ar.; (ref. to the Graiai, Graces, Erinyes) B. Trag.; (ref. to the Sphinx) S.; (ref. to Lakhesis) Pl.; (ref. to nymphs) Od. Hes.(cj.) Pi. E.
3 **daughter** (of a person or deity) Hom. Hes. Hippon. Thgn. Lyr. Trag. +
4 **small votive statue in female form, figurine** Pl.
5 **image reflected in the pupil of the eye, reflected image** Pl.
6 **pupil** (of the eye) Emp. Pl. ‖ PL. (gener.) **pupils or eyes** Ion S.*fr.* E. Ar.; (meton.) **glances** E.

—**Κόρη**, Ion. **Κούρη**, ης, dial. **Κόρα, Κούρα**, ᾱς *f.* Daughter (of Demeter, ref. to Persephone), **Kore** Archil. Lyr. Hdt. E. Ar. +

κόρη² ης *f.* [prob.loanwd.] **long sleeve, foresleeve** (of Persian ceremonial dress, extending over the hand) X.

κόρημα ατος *n.* [κορέω¹] **broom** Ar.

κορθύνω *vb.* [κόρθυς] | ep.aor. κόρθυνα | (of Zeus) **gather up** —*his strength* Hes.

κορθύομαι *pass.vb.* | ῡ AR. | (of waves) **be heaped up high** Il. AR.

κόρθυς υος *f.* **heap or swathe** (of scythed corn) Theoc.

κορίαννα ων *n.pl.* (collectv.) **coriander** (ref. to the plant or its seeds) Ar.

κορίζομαι *mid.vb.* [reltd. κόρη¹, κόρος²] **treat (someone) like a child**; (specif., of a father) **speak affectionately** (to his baby son) Ar.

Κόρινθος ου *f.* (sts. *m.*) **1 Corinth** (city of the Peloponnese, adjoining the Isthmos) Il. Hes.*fr.* Simon. Pi. Hdt. S. +
2 Διὸς Κόρινθος *Korinthos son of Zeus* (as a catchphrase, app. mocking a reiterated claim by Corinthians about the ancestry of their mythical founder, i.e. *the same old story*) Pi. Ar. Pl.

—**Κορινθόθι** *ep.adv.* **at Corinth** Il.

—**Κορίνθιοι** ων *m.pl.* **men of Corinth, Corinthians** (as a population or military force) Simon. Hdt. Th. Ar. +; (ref. to bedbugs, w. play on κόρις *bedbug*) Ar.

—**Κορίνθιος** ᾱ (Ion. η) ον *adj.* **1 of or belonging to Corinth**; (of the city or land) **of Corinth** Simon. S. E.; (of men or women) **Corinthian** Pi. Hdt. S. E. Th. +; (of prostitutes) Ar. Pl. ‖ FEM.SB. **territory of Corinth** Th. X. Arist. Plu.
2 **of or characteristic of Corinth or the Corinthians**; (of ships, coins, clothing, or sim.) **Corinthian** Hdt. Th. Ar. X. Plu.; (of wild celery, used as a garland at the Isthmian games) Pi.

—**Κορινθιακός** ή όν *adj.* (of the gulf) **of Corinth, Corinthian** X. Plb.; (of a war, political disturbances) Isoc. Men.

κόριον ου *n.* [dimin. κόρη¹] (in voc. address) **dear girl** Theoc.

κόρις εως *m.* **bedbug** Ar.

κορίχιον ου *n.* [dimin. κόρη¹] (in voc. address) **little girl** Ar.(cj.)

κορκορυγή ῆς *f.* (sg. and pl., in military or political ctxt.) **tumult, uproar** A. Ar.

Κόρκυρα *f.*, **Κόρκουρα** Boeot.*f.*: see Κέρκυρα

κορμός οῦ *m.* [κείρω] **1 trunk** (of a tree) Od.
2 **sawn-off trunk, log** Hdt. E. Ar.
3 **piece of timber** (W.ADJ. ναυτικός *belonging to a ship*), **plank, spar, timber** E.

κορο-πλάθος ου *m.* [κόρη¹, πλάσσω] **moulder of figurines** Pl.; (as a derog. term for a sculptor) Isoc.

κόρος¹ ου *m.* [κορέννυμι] **1 state of having one's fill, satiety, sufficiency, enough** (usu. W.GEN. of food, drink, battle, love, lamentation, or sim.) Hom. Archil. Heraclit. Pi. E. Pl. +
2 (gener.) **abundance, plenty** (opp. poverty) Hes.; (W.GEN. of purple dye) Alcm.
3 **satisfaction, sating** (W.GEN. of a desire) Plb.
4 (pejor.) **state of having more than one's fill, surfeit, excess, more than enough** (sts. W.GEN. of sthg.) Eleg. A. Pi. E. Plb. Plu.; (as begetter of ὕβρις *insolence*) Sol. Thgn.; (personif.) **Excess** (as child of Ὕβρις) Pi. Hdt.(oracle)
5 (prep.phr.) ἄχρι κόρου **to excess, ad nauseam** D.

κόρος², Ion. **κοῦρος**, dial. **κῶρος** (Theoc. Bion), ου *m.* [reltd. κόρη¹] **1 young man, youth** or **boy** Hom. Hes.*fr.* hHom. Lyr. Emp. Parm. +; (pl., ref. to warriors) Hom. E.
2 **son** (of a person or god) Od. hHom. Pi. S. E. Arist.*lyr.* +

κόρος³ ου *m.* [κορέω¹] **broom** Bion (dub.)

κόρος⁴ ου *m.* [Semit.loanwd.] **unit of dry measure** (approx. 400 litres); **measure** (W.GEN. of grain) NT.

κόρρη, Att. **κόρρη**, ης, dial. **κόρρα** (Alc.), **κόρρα** (Theocr.), ᾱς *f.* [κείρω] **1** (sg.) **temple or temples** (of the head, esp. as the target of a blow) Il. Alc. Pl. D. Call. Theoc.
2 (gener.) **head** Emp.
3 ‖ PL. **hair** A.(dub.)

κόρταλον *n.*: see κρόταλον

Κορύβαντες (also **Κύρβαντες** Call.) ων *m.pl.* **Corybants** (minor Phrygian divinities attendant upon Cybele; sts. identified w. the Kouretes, and assoc.w. Dionysus; worshipped at Athens w. ecstatic dancing and the music of drums and the aulos) E. Ar. Pl. Men. Call.

κορυβαντιάω *contr.vb.* (of a worshipper) **be possessed by the Corybants** (i.e. be in a state of manic possession) Ar. Pl. Plb.; (fig., of a person) **be off one's head** Men.

κορυβαντίζω *vb.* **induce Corybantic possession** (in a person, to cure a mental disorder) Ar.

κορυδός οῦ *f.* —**κόρυδος** ου *m.* —also **κορυδαλλίς** ίδος *f.* —**κορυδαλλός** οῦ (dial. ῶ) *m.* [perh.reltd. κόρυς] **lark, crested lark** Simon. Ar. Pl. Theoc. Plu.

κορυζάω *contr.vb.* [κόρυζα *snot*] **1 have a runny nose, drivel** (w. play on sense 2) Pl.
2 (fig.) **talk drivel** Men.; (of cities) **behave with drivelling idiocy** Plb.

κόρυθα (acc.sg.): see κόρυς

κορυθ-άϊξ ῑκος *masc.fem.adj.* [κόρυς, ἄσσω] (of a warrior) perh. **with flashing helmet** Il.

κορυθ-αίολος ον *adj.* [αἰόλος] (of Hector, Ares) **with glittering helmet** Il.; (of contests) Ar.(mock-ep.)

κόρυμβος ου *m.* [reltd. κορυφή] | neut.nom.acc.pl. κόρυμβα | **1 uppermost point**; app. **stern-post** (W.GEN. of a

ship, equiv. to ἄφλαστον) Il. E. ‖ PL. (for sg.) tip (W.GEN. ἀφλάστοιο of the stern-post) AR.; perh., bow-post (equiv. to ἀκροστόλιον, meton. for a ship's bows) A.
2 summit (W.GEN. of a burial mound, a mountain) A. Hdt.
3 cluster (of flowers, perh. on a branch) Mosch.

κορύνη ης, dial. **κορύνᾱ** ᾱς f. [perh.reltd. κόρυς] | also freq. ῡ | club (of wood, used as a weapon) Hdt. E. Arist. Hellenist.poet. Plu.; (made of iron) Il.; (ref. to a countryman's staff) Theoc.

κορυνήτης ου m. one who fights with a club, **club-wielder** Il.

κορυνη-φόροι ων m.pl. [φέρω] **club-bearers** (ref. to the bodyguard of the tyrant Peisistratos) Hdt. Arist. Plu.

κορύπτῑλος ου m. [κορύπτω] animal which strikes with the head, **head-butter** (ref. to a goat) Theoc.

κορύπτω vb. [κορυφή] (of a goat) strike with the head, **butt** —a person Theoc.

κόρυς υθος f. [reltd. κορυφή] | acc. κόρυθα, also κόρυν | ep.dat.pl. κορύθεσσι | **1 helmet** (usu. of metal w. horsehair crest) Hom. Hes. Tyrt. S. AR. Theoc.
2 crest (of hair, on a bullock's head) E.

κορύσσω vb. | dial.inf. κορυσσέμεν (Pi.) | ep.3sg.impf. κόρυσσε ‖ MID.: ep.3du.impf. κορυσσέσθην | aor.ptcpl. κορυσσάμενος ‖ PASS.: pf.ptcpl. κεκορυθμένος |
1 ‖ MID. equip oneself with a helmet; (gener., of a warrior) **arm oneself** (sts. W.DAT. w. bronze or sim.) Hom. —w. ἐπί + DAT. against someone AR.; (fig., of a wife) —w. ἐς + ACC. for battle Semon. ‖ PF.PASS.PTCPL. armed or equipped AR. —W.DAT. w. bronze Hom. —W.ACC. in golden armour E.; (fig., of goddesses) —W.DAT. for a beauty contest E.
2 ‖ PF.PASS.PTCPL. (of spears) tipped (usu. W.DAT. w. bronze) Hom.
3 (fig.) arm, equip —one's life (W.DAT. w. good planning) Pi.
4 (of a commander, Athena, Strife) **prepare for** or **direct** —fighting or sim. Il. Hes. Pi. E. —(W.PREP.PHR. against a person) Ibyc.
5 cause (sthg.) to rise into a crest; (of a river god) **raise into a crest, raise high** —his swell Il. ‖ MID. (of a wave) **rise high, rear up** Il. AR.; (of Strife) Il.; (of flames, clouds) AR. Theoc.

κορυστής οῦ, dial. **κορυστᾱ́ς** ᾶ m. helmeted or armed man, **warrior** Il. Alcm. B.

κορυφαίᾱ ᾱς f. [κορυφή] part of a bridle which fits over a horse's head, **headstall** X.

κορυφαῖον ου n. top (of a hunting net) X.

κορυφαῖος ου m. **1** one who is in chief position, **leader, head** (of a community or faction) Hdt. Pl. Plb. Plu.
2 (specif.) **chorus-leader, koryphaios** Arist.
3 person in prime position (in the public baths, app. as being nearest to the fire) Ar.
4 ‖ ADJ. (of a cap) perh., rising to a peak (ref. to Lat. apex, a kind of mitre worn by Roman priests) Plu.

κορυφή ῆς, dial. **κορυφᾱ́** ᾶς f. **1** top of the head, **crown** (of a person, god or animal) Il. hHom. Lyr. Hdt. E. Pl. +; (gener.) **head** E. Pl. Call.
2 (meton.) nod (of Zeus' head) A.
3 (sts.pl. for sg.) **summit, top, peak** (of a mountain or sim.) Hom. Hes. Thgn. Lyr. A. Hdt. +; (of a tomb) E.; (of a city, ref. to its citadel) Alc. E. Plb.; (prep.phr.) κατὰ κορυφήν from the heights (ref. to troops entering a territory) Th.
4 (gener.) top (of a jar) Sol.; (of a pillar, ladder, structure, roof, or sim.) Pl. Plb. Plu.
5 apex, tip (of a triangle, wedge, the Nile Delta) Pl. Plb.
6 (fig.) summit, peak, crown (of achievements, athletic contests, possessions, cities) Pi. Plu.
7 essence, central point (of a statement, philosophical argument) Pi. Pl.

κορυφόω contr.vb. **1** ‖ MID.PASS. (of a wave) **rise to a peak** Il.; (of the summit of achievement) **reach a peak** —W.DAT. for kings (i.e. be attainable only by them) Pi.
2 build (W.ACC. a skylight) **as the topmost feature** —W.PREP.PHR. on a temple Plu.

κορώνεως ω Att.f. [κορώνη] **crow-fig tree** (app. named fr. the grey or black colour of its fruit) Ar.

κορώνη ης, dial. **κορώνᾱ** ᾱς f. **1 crow** (ref. to the hooded crow) Hes. Archil. Stesich. Carm.Pop. Ar. +
2 (sts. W.ADJ. εἰναλίη of the sea) a kind of sea-bird; app. **shearwater** or **cormorant** Od.
3 curved or hooked object (app. as resembling a crow's beak); **hook** (at the tip of a bow, around which the string was looped) Hom. B. Theoc.; (of a plough-shaft) AR.; **door-handle** Od.

κορωνιάω contr.vb. | neut.nom.acc.pl.ptcpl. (w.diect.) κορωνιόωντα | **1** (of corn-stalks) **curve, bend** (fr. the weight of the ears) Hes.
2 (fig., of a person) perh., hold one's head high (like a proud horse), **be presumptuous** Plb.

κορωνίς ίδος fem.adj. **1** (of ships) having an upward curve (at bow and stern), **curved** Hom. [or perh. beaked, having a beak-shaped projection at the prow]
2 (of cattle) **with curved horns** Theoc.
3 ‖ SB. wreath, garland (as having a curved shape) Stesich.

κορωνός ή όν adj. (of an ox) app., with head held high, **proud** Archil.

κοσκινό-μαντις εως m.f. [κόσκινον, μάντις] one who tells fortunes by using a sieve, **sieve-diviner** Theoc.

κόσκινον ου n. sieve Semon. Ar. Pl. Plb. Plu.

κοσκυλμάτια ων n.pl. [perh.reltd. σκύλλω] **scraps of leather** (fr. a tanner's workshop) Ar.

κοσμέω contr.vb. [κόσμος] | ep.3du.impf.mid. κοσμείσθην | ep.3pl.aor.pass. κόσμηθεν, also ἐκόσμηθεν (Pi.) | **1** adorn (a person or part of the body, freq. W.DAT. w. clothes, jewellery, garlands, or sim.); **adorn, deck out, dress up** —a person (esp. a woman or goddess), the body Hes. hHom. Pi. B. Hdt. E. + ‖ MID. adorn —one's body (w. robes or sim.) E.; (intr.) adorn or **dress oneself** hHom. Hdt. E. Ar. ‖ PASS. be adorned or dressed hHom. Pi.fr. Hdt. E.
2 (specif.) dress —a corpse (in funeral garments) S. E. Is.
3 fit out (w. armour or sim.); **equip** or **furnish** —troops (W.DAT. w. bronze) E. ‖ MID. equip —one's body (W.DAT. w. armour) E.; (intr.) **equip oneself** (w. armour) E. Isoc. ‖ PASS. be equipped —W.DAT. w. armour S. E. Pl.; (of cavalry horses) be caparisoned —W.ADV. beautifully Hdt.; (gener., of a state) be furnished —W.DAT. w. troops and cavalry Th.
4 ‖ MID. (of Spartans) **spruce up** —their heads (by combing their hair) Hdt.
5 adorn (an object); **adorn, decorate** —a house (W.DAT. w. spoils, tripods) A. Pi. —statues (w. votive tablets) A. —a corpse (w. paint) Hdt.; (of bronze) —a house Critias ‖ PASS. (of a temple) be decorated or adorned —W.ADV. in a certain way Hdt. —W.DAT. w. spoils E.; (of a ceiling) —w. helmets Alc.; (of a pond) —w. a stone border Hdt.; (of a corselet) —w. gold and cotton thread Hdt.
6 (fig., of a poet or speaker) **adorn, embellish, dress out** —one's narrative, arguments, sentiments (sts. W.DAT. w. fine phrases or sim.) E. Th. Isoc. X. —oneself (w. empty words) Pl.; (pejor.) **gloss over, disguise** —wrongdoings, weaknesses, or sim. E.; (intr.) **use stylistic embellishments** Th. Isoc. ‖ PASS. (of speeches) be dressed up Pl. —W.DAT. w. fine phrases Th.
7 do honour to, add lustre to, **glorify** —persons, places, achievements (esp. w. songs of praise, speeches, or sim.) Thgn.

κόσμημα

Pi. B. Dionys.Eleg. Th. Ar. +; (fig., of a warrior) —*Ares* (W.DAT. w. *his spear*) E.; (gener.) **adorn** or **embellish** —*rituals* (W.DAT. w. *sacred dances*) E.*fr*.; (of a dramatist) —*tragic nonsense* (*by using fine words*) Ar.
8 honour (the dead) with due ceremony; **honour** —*a dead person* (W.DAT. w. *ritual washing, burial rites*) S. E.; **tend** —*a grave* E. X.; **accord the honour** —W.INTERN.ACC. *of burial* S. ‖ PASS. (of a dead person) be duly honoured E. Th.
9 arrange (troops) in order; **draw up in formation, marshal** —*one's troops* Il.(also mid.) Theoc. ‖ PASS. (of troops) be marshalled or arranged (in a certain formation) Il. Hdt. Pl. X.
10 ‖ PASS. be assigned (to a certain category); (of persons) be treated as belonging —w. ἐς + ACC. *to a particular nation* Hdt.; (of regions) —*to a particular province* Hdt.
11 control, discipline —*someone, oneself* S. E.*fr*.; **train** —*someone* (W.PREP.PHR. *for warfare*) E.*fr*.; (of doctors and trainers) **keep in order** —*a person's body* Pl.
‖ PF.PASS.PTCPL.ADJ. (of a person) orderly, disciplined Pl.
12 put (things) in order; **arrange, get ready** —*a meal* Od. —*a table* (*for a meal*) X. —*an urn* (W.PREP.PHR. *for burial*) S. —*a fine entertainment* Theoc. ‖ PASS. (of a feast) be arranged Pi.; (gener., of places, activities) be arranged or organised (sts. W.ADV. *in a certain way*) Hdt. ‖ NEUT.PL.PTCPL.SB. established system, proper order of things S.
‖ PF.PASS.PTCPL.ADJ. (of the finished creation of an artist or artisan) well-ordered Pl.
13 create (by proper arrangement), **fashion** —*a garland* E.; (of a poet) —*a song* hHom.
14 conduct in an orderly way, **manage, direct** —*a city* (W.ADV. *well, securely*) Hdt. Th. —*one's tasks* Hes. —*festivities, a burial* Sol. E.; (of the mind) —*all things* Pl.
15 hold the office of kosmos (a magistrate in Crete) Arist. Plb. | see κόσμος 22

κόσμημα ατος *n*. (pl. and collectv.sg.) **decorative trappings** (worn by a soldier) Pl. X.

κόσμησις εως *f*. **1 orderly arrangement** (of buildings) Pl.
2 organised event, **ceremonial occasion** Pl.
3 cosmetic treatment (of women's hair or skin) Plu.

κοσμητήρ ῆρος *m*. **director** (W.GEN. of fighting, ref. to a commander) Aeschin.(quot.epigr.) Plu.(quot.epigr.)

κοσμητής οῦ *m*. **1 director** (W.PREP.PHR. in war, ref. to a commander) Aeschin.(quot.epigr.) Plu.(quot.epigr.)
2 organiser (W.GEN. of ranks, ref. to a company commander) Pl.; (of a city, ref. to a legislator) Pl.; (gener., of a public event) Pl.
3 marshal, supervisor (of ephebes, at Athens) Arist.
4 cosmetician (of a foreign ruler) X.

κοσμητικός ή όν *adj*. ‖ FEM.SB. art of decoration or adornment Pl.

κοσμητός ή όν *adj*. (of vegetable-beds) well-ordered, **tidy, neat** Od.

κοσμήτωρ ορος *m*. **1 marshal** (of troops, ref. to a commander) Hom.; **director** (of fighting) Pi.*fr*.
2 supervisor, guardian (of a boy) AR.

κόσμια ων *n.pl*. [dimin. κόσμος] **insignia** (of a king or praetor) Plu.

κόσμιος ᾱ ον (also ος ον Pl.) *adj*. [κόσμος] **1** (of a soldier) **orderly, disciplined** X.
2 (of a system of government) **orderly, well-regulated** Isoc. Pl. Plu.; (of expenditure) Pl. ‖ NEUT.SB. orderliness Pl. Plu.
3 (of housing provided in a city) kept within appropriate limits (of size or quality), **moderate, reasonable** Pl.
4 (w. moral connot., of persons, their character, conduct, or sim.) **orderly, well-behaved, decent, respectable** Ar.

Att.orats. Pl. X. Arist. Lycophronid. +; (of testimony) **respectable** or **decorous** (in expression) Aeschin. ‖ NEUT.SB. propriety, decorum S. Pl. Plu.
5 (specif., of citizens) **law-abiding** Att.orats. Pl.

—**κοσμίως** *adv*. **1 in an orderly manner** or **in proper order** Ar. X. Plu.
2 (usu. w. moral connot.) in the proper manner, **decently, properly, appropriately** Ar. Att.orats. Pl. +

κοσμιότης ητος *f*. (usu. w. moral connot.) **orderly behaviour, propriety, decorum** Ar. Pl. D. Arist.

κοσμοποιέω contr.*vb*. (of philosophers) **explain the creation of the universe** Arist.

κοσμοποιίᾱ ᾶς *f*. **creation of the universe** Arist.

κοσμό-πολις ιδος *m*. [πόλις] **city-magistrate** (at Lokroi) Plb.

κόσμος ου *m*. | The wd. has four main senses: (1–7) orderly arrangement, (8–18) adornment, (19–21) world-order, (22) a Cretan official. |
1 act or result of creating an ordered structure; **fashioning, construction** (W.GEN. of the Trojan Horse) Od.
2 composition (W.GEN. of words or a song, ref. to a poem or its creation) Sol. Simon. Pi.*fr*. Parm. Lyr.adesp.(cj.)
3 organisational structure, **constitution, regime** (of a state) Hdt. Th. Pl.
4 fixed arrangement, **established system** (of behaviour, at a royal court, or in a civic ctxt.) Hdt. Th.; **established** or **normal use** (W.GEN. of a metal) Hdt.(dub.); (gener.) **orderliness** (opp. randomness, in actions) Th.
5 regular or appropriate arrangement (of troops); **proper place** (in a formation, for a soldier) Th.; (concr.) **orderly formation** Th.; (advbl.acc.) τὸν αὐτὸν κόσμον *in the same formation* Hdt.
6 proper and disciplined behaviour, **good order, discipline** (in military ctxt.) Thgn. Hdt. Th. D.; (in civic ctxt.) E. Isoc.
7 (prep. and advbl.phrs., ref. to position or behaviour) κατὰ κόσμον *in proper order* Hom. hHom. Parm. X. AR.; *in the proper manner* Hom. hHom. Sol. Hippon. Th. +; κόσμῳ *in proper order* Od. Hdt. Ar. Pl. +; *in good order* or *in a disciplined manner* Il. A. Th.; *in the proper manner* A. Pi.; ἐν κόσμῳ *in good order* or *in a disciplined manner* Pl. X. Arist. Plb. Plu.; οὐδενὶ κόσμῳ *in disorder* or *disarray* or *in an ill-disciplined manner* Hdt. Th. Plb.; *at random, chaotically* Th.; οὐδένα κόσμον *in disorder* Hdt.
8 (collectv.sg.) **adornment, finery** (usu. of a woman, ref. to jewellery, garments, or sim.) Il. Hes. hHom. Hdt. Trag. +; (gener.) **attire, dress** A. ‖ PL. adornments, ornaments Isoc. Pl. +; accoutrements, attire (of a prophetess) A.; (for the statue of a goddess) E.
9 (specif.) **proper adornment** (for a corpse, ref. to funeral garments) E.
10 (ref. to an individual item) **adornment, decoration, ornament** (for a woman) Sapph. B.; (for a horse) Il. Pi.; (ref. to a garland, for a victor in the games) Pi.; (fig., ref. to an impressively dressed husband, for his wife) X.; (ref. to an attractive boy, in a chorus) E.
11 (collectv.sg.) **accoutrements, gear** (of a warrior, ref. to his armour) Trag.; **equipment** (for a hunting hound) X.
12 decoration (for a temple, ref. to votive offerings) A.*satyr.fr*.; (for a tree, ref. to gold ornaments) Hdt.; (collectv.sg.) **furnishings** (of a room) Hdt.
13 ornamentation, embellishment (in written language or style) Isoc. Arist.
14 (gener.) **impressive appearance** (of troops) Hdt.; **beauty, radiance** (of the moon) hHom.

15 source of adornment or lustre; (ref. to troops) **ornament, glory** (of their country) A.; (ref. to a person, W.DAT. for his city) Pi.; (ref. to the olive, for Athens) E.; (ref. to magnanimity) **crowning glory** (W.GEN. of virtues) Arist.
16 (gener.) **honour, distinction, glory** (granted to or won by a person or city) Simon. A.(pl.) Pi. B. Ar. +
17 rendering of honour (by a particular act); **honour** (W.GEN. for the dead, ref. to mourning) E.; **tribute** (W.GEN. of gifts, wedding songs) E.; (ref. to a victory ode) Pi.
18 (wkr.sens.) **credit** (accruing to a person fr. behaving in a particular way) Hdt. S. Th.
19 natural order (of the world or universe); **order** (W.GEN. of immortal nature) E.fr.; **world-order** Heraclit.
20 (concr.) **universe, cosmos** Emp. Isoc. Pl. X. +; **firmament, sky, heavens** Isoc. Plb.
21 (gener.) **world** (sts.ref. to earth, opp. heaven) NT.; (ref. to mankind) **whole world** NT.
22 kosmos (title of a Cretan official) Arist.

κόσος *Ion.interrog.adj.*: see πόσος

κόσσυφος, Att. **κόψιχος**, ου *m.* **blackbird** Lyr.adesp. Theoc.*epigr.*

κοταίνω *vb.* [κότος] (of Zeus) **be angry** A.

κότε *Ion.interrog.adv.*, **κοτέ** *Ion.enclit.adv.*: see πότε, ποτέ

κότερος *Ion.interrog.adj.*: see πότερος

κοτέω *ep.contr.vb.* [κότος] | aor.ptcpl. κοτέσᾱς | pf.ptcpl. κεκοτηώς ‖ MID.: 3pl.impf. κοτέοντο | aor.: 3sg. κοτέσσατο, ptcpl. κοτεσσάμενος, 3sg.subj. κοτέσσεται |
1 (act. and mid., of persons or gods) **bear resentment, feel anger** or **rage** (freq. W.DAT. against someone) Hom. Hes. hHom. Call. AR. —W.DAT. **at someone's behaviour** Pi.fr. —W.ACC. or GEN. **over sthg.** Il. —W.PREP.PHR. **over someone** Hes.; (of wild animals, sts. W.DAT. against each other) Hes.
2 ‖ PF.ACT.PTCPL.ADJ. (of the heart of a person or god) **resentful, angry** Hom. AR.; (of bulls) AR.

κοτήεις εσσα εν *adj.* (of a god) **resentful, angry** Il.

κοτινη-φόρος ον *adj.* [κότινος, φέρω] (of the R. Alpheios) **bearing wild olives** (fr. Olympia, where they were used for victory-garlands) Mosch.

κότινος ου *m.* (*also f.* Theoc.) **wild olive** (ref. to the tree, its foliage or its wood) Ar. AR. Theoc. Plu.

κοτινο-τράγος ον *adj.* [τρώγω] (of birds) **feeding on wild olives** Ar.

κότος ου *m.* **resentment, anger, wrath** (of a person or god) Hom. A. Pi. E. Ar.(mock-trag.); (fig., W.GEN. of hurricanes) A.; (personif.) Emp.

κοττάβεια (also **κοττάβια**) ων *n.pl.* [κότταβος] (collectv.) **prize in the game of kottabos** Arist. Call.

κοτταβίζω *vb.* **play the game of kottabos** Ar.

κότταβος ου *m.* **kottabos** (a game played at symposia, in which dregs fr. a wine-cup were aimed at a target) Anacr. Pi.fr. Dionys.Eleg. Critias Ar. Philox.Leuc.

κοτύλη ης *f.* **1** small drinking-vessel, **cup** Hom.; **pot** (for honey) Plu.(quot.poet.)
2 (as a unit of liquid or dry measure, approx. a quarter of a litre) **cupful** Hdt. Th. Ar. Pl. Men. Plu.
3 cup-joint (in the body), **hip-joint** Il.
4 ‖ PL. **cymbals** or **castanets** A.fr.

κοτυληδών όνος *f.* | ep.gen.dat.sg.pl. κοτυληδονόφιν | **1** cup-shaped object ‖ PL. **suckers** (of an octopus) Od.
2 cup-joint (in the body), **hip-joint** Ar.

κοτυλ-ήρυτος ον *adj.* [ἀρύω] (of spilt blood) **able to be drawn off in cupfuls** (i.e. copious) Il.

κοτυλίσκιον ου *n.* [dimin. κοτύλη] **little cup** Ar.

κοῦ *Ion.interrog.adv.*, **κου** *Ion.enclit.adv.*: see ποῦ, που

κουλεόν *ep.n.*: see κολεόν

Κούπρις *Boeot.f.*: see Κύπρις

κουρά ᾶς, Ion. **κουρή** ῆς *f.* [κείρω] **1 cutting** (W.GEN. of a person's hair) Hdt.; **haircut** (ref. to its style) Pl. Thphr. Plu. ‖ PL. **shearing** (of a horse's mane) S.fr.
2 cropped hair (of a mourner) E.
3 cut lock (W.GEN. of hair) A.
4 lopping (of branches) Pl.

κούρᾱ, **Κούρᾱ** *dial.f.*: see κόρη¹

κουρεακός ή όν *adj.* [κουρεῖον] (pejor., of gossip) **characteristic of the barber's shop** Plb.

κουρεῖον ου *n.* [κουρεύς] **barber's shop** Lys. Ar. D. Thphr. +

κούρειον ου *n.* [κουρά, unless reltd. κόρος²] **sacrifice** or **offering** (made during the Apatouria, when a child was entered on the phratry-list, prob. on the day called Κουρεῶτις) Is.

κουρεύς έως *m.* [κουρά] **barber** Lys. Pl. Plu.

κουρεύτρια ᾱς *f.* **female hairdresser** Plu.

Κουρεῶτις ιδος *f.* [reltd. κουρεῖον] **Koureotis** (name given to the third day of the Apatouria, perh. fr. the dedication of a lock of hair by a child when entered on the phratry-list) Pl.

κουρή *Ion.f.*: see κουρά

κούρη, **Κούρη** *Ion.f.*: see κόρη¹

κούριος η ον *Ion.adj.* [κόρη¹] (of the bloom of a woman's beauty) **youthful** hHom.

κούρητες ων *Ion.m.pl.* [κόρος²] **young men** (ref. to warriors) Il.

—**Κούρητες** (also **Κούρητες**) ων *Ion.m.pl.* —also **Κώρειτες** ων *Boeot.m.pl.* **1 Kouretes** (demigod warriors, who helped to raise the infant Zeus on Crete) Hes.fr. E. Corinn. Call. AR. Plu.(sg.); (assoc.w. the Cretan mother-goddess Rhea, and identified w. the Corybants) E.; (ref. to worshippers impersonating them in rituals) E.fr. Plu.
2 Kouretes (ancient tribe of Greeks, neighbours and enemies of the Aetolians) Il. Hes.fr. B. AR.

κουριάω *contr.vb.* [κουρά] **1 grow** (W.ACC. one's beard) **long** Semon.
2 have cropped hair Plu.

κουρίδιος η ον *Ion.adj.* [κόρη¹] | dial.acc. κουριδίᾱν (Stesich.) | **1** (of a wife) having the status of virgin (at the time of marriage), **lawful, wedded** Hom. hHom. Stesich. Eleg. Hdt. AR.; (of a husband, who marries such a woman) Hom. hHom.; (of the title) **of lawful husband** Call. ‖ MASC.SB. **husband** Od.
2 (of a bed, house, bridal chamber) **marital, nuptial** Hom. Ar. AR.; (of love) **married** (i.e. betw. married persons) AR.

κουρίζω *Ion.vb.* [κόρος², κόρη¹] **1 be a boy** (in age) Od. Call. AR.; **be a girl** Call. AR.
2 (of the baby Zeus) **make childish sounds** Call. AR.
3 (tr., of nymphs) **raise from boyhood** —men (i.e. raise boys into men) Hes.

κουρικός ή όν *adj.* [κουρά] (of scissors) **for cutting the hair** Plu.

κούριμος η ον *adj.* **1** (of a lock of hair) **cut off** A. E.
2 (of a mourner's head) with hair cut off, **shorn** E.
3 (fig., of the appearance of a city deprived of its battlements) **shorn** (i.e. mournful) Plu.

κουρίξ *adv.* **1 by the hair** —ref. to dragging someone Od.
2 perh. **so as to tear one's hair** —ref. to pulling at one's locks AR.

κουρίς ίδος *f.* **female hairdresser** Plb.

κουρο-βόρος ον *dial.adj.* [κόρος², βιβρώσκω] relating to the devouring of boys; (of clotted blood) **of devoured boys** A.

κοῦρος *Ion.m.*: see κόρος²

κουροσύνᾱ ᾱς *dial.f.* **boyish prowess** (of the young Herakles) Theoc.

κουρότερος η ον *Ion.compar.adj.* (of a man) **more youthful, younger** Hom. Hes. AR.; (of a woman) AR. ‖ MASC.PL.SB. **younger men** AR.

κουρο-τόκος ον *dial.adj.* (of women) **who have borne boys** E.

κουρο-τρόφος ου *dial.f.* [τροφός] (epith. of Hekate) **nurse of the young, rearer of children** Hes. AR. Theoc.; (of Leto) Theoc.; (of Peace) Hes. E.; (perh. of Aphrodite) Archil.; (ref. to an unspecified goddess) Ar.; (ref. to Ithaca, the earth) Od. Sol.; (W.ADJ. *hateful*, ref. to Faction) Pi.*fr.*; (specif., ref. to Delos) **nurse** (W.GEN. of Apollo) Call.

—κουροτρόφος ον *adj.* (of a prize of war, fig.ref. to captive Trojan girls) **rearing children** (W.DAT. for Greece) E.

κουστωδίᾱ ᾱς *f.* [Lat. *custodia*] **guard-detail** (of soldiers) NT.

κουφίζω *vb.* [κοῦφος] ‖ fut. κουφιῶ ‖ aor. ἐκούφισα ‖ **1** (intr., of a ship's cargo) **be light** E.; (of soil, opp. be heavy in clods) Hes.
2 make lighter, **lighten** *—ships (by offloading cargo)* Plb. NT.; (intr., of a naval force) **lighten oneself** (by leaving heavier ships behind) Th. ‖ PASS. (of ships) be lightened Plb.
3 give relief (fr. a weight); (of Zeus) **lighten, relieve** *—the earth* (W.GEN. *of a troublesome mass of mortals*) E.
4 lighten (what is burdensome or distressing); **lighten, alleviate, ease** *—misfortunes, suffering, love* D. Theoc. Plu.; (intr., of words) **offer relief** or **comfort** Plu. ‖ PASS. (of a war) be made less burdensome Plb.
5 give relief (fr. what is burdensome or distressing); **relieve** *—a person (of the weight of grief, of an obligation)* X. Plb. Plu. —(W.GEN. *of talk, i.e. spare him the need for it*) E.; (intr.) **feel relief** (fr. sickness or pain) S. ‖ PASS. be relieved (of obligations, grief, worries) E. Th. Arist. Call. Plb. Plu. —W.GEN. *of obligations* Plb.; (of a person's body, sts. W.GEN. of sickness) E. Plu.
6 (tr.) **lift up** *—a person* S. *—a scabbard* Theoc. *—a ship's prow* (w. *a grappling engine*) Plb.
7 bear lightly *—a bronze shield* E.; **carry** (W.ACC. *someone*) **lightly** (through the air) Ar. ‖ PASS. (of a soul) be carried lightly aloft —W.DAT. *on wings* Pl. —w. ὑπό + GEN. *by Justice* Pl.; (fig., of a person) be made conceited —W.DAT. *by someone's deferential behaviour* Plu.
8 (of a fawn, a shaken lot) **lightly make** *—a leap (i.e. leap lightly)* S. E.; (of a person on the edge of a rock, compared to a bird) **lightly hold** *—a poised position (i.e. be lightly poised)* E.

κούφισις εως *f.* **alleviation** (of sufferings) Th.

κουφίσματα των *n.pl.* (collectv.) **support** (for an old man, W.GEN. fr. another's hand) E.

κουφισμός οῦ *m.* making lighter, **lessening, reduction** (of a city's population) Plu.; (W.GEN. of jealousy) Plu.

κουφολογίᾱ ᾱς *f.* [κοῦφος, λέγω] **vain** or **boastful talk** Th.

κουφό-νοος ον, contr. **κουφόνους** ουν *adj.* [νόος] (of birds, desires, naivety) **empty-minded, thoughtless** A. S.

κοῦφος η (dial. ᾱ) ον *adj.* **1** of little weight; (of things) **light** hHom. E. Pl. X. Arist. Plu.; (fig., of rumour, renown, envisaged as a burden, W.INF. to lift up or bear) Hes. X.; (of earth, a tomb) **weighing lightly** (upon a buried person) E. Call.*epigr.* Theoc.*epigr.*; (of ships) **lightly laden** Th.
2 (of troops) **light-armed** Plb. Plu.
3 (of food) not weighing heavily (on the stomach), **light** Philox.Leuc.(dub.) Arist.
4 (of a fawn) not ponderous in movement, **light, nimble** AR.; (of feet, steps, wings, running, leaping) Lyr. Trag. Ar. AR. Theoc.
5 (of a hand) with a light touch, **light, gentle** Pi. AR.; (of breezes) S.; (of a remedy) **mild** Theoc.
6 (of athletic contests, physical exercises, military service, tasks) **light, not burdensome** E. X. Arist. Plb.; (of an expense) E.; (of cares) Theoc.
7 (of a victor, the exercise of kingship) **mild, not oppressive** Isoc. X.
8 (of offences) not grave, **light, minor** Pl. AR.
9 (of an achievement) entailing little effort, **easy** Pi.; (of a gift, a favour) **easily granted** A. Pi.
10 (of persons) **unburdened, untroubled, cheerful** X. Arist.
11 (iron., of a poet, envisaged as a winged creature) **light and airy** Pl.
12 (pejor., of a person) **light-headed, empty-headed** Men.; (of thoughtlessness) S.; (of the mind of a person or bird) **empty** Thgn. Simon. Pi.
13 (of a shadow) **insubstantial, fleeting** S.; (of ambitions; of persuasion, as a technique) **lightweight** B. Ar.; (of hopes, words) **vain, empty** Sol. Th. Pl.

—κοῦφα *neut.pl.adv.* **lightly, nimbly** Il. Hes. Lyr. Ar.

—κούφως *adv.* **1 lightly** *—ref. to being armed or equipped* Th. X.
2 feebly, without force *—ref. to stabbing oneself* Plu.
3 lightly, nimbly *—ref. to moving* A. X.
4 lightly, easily *—ref. to bearing trouble or sim.* Hdt. E. Pl. Plu.
5 easily *—ref. to accomplishing sthg.* A.
6 light-heartedly *—ref. to speaking* Od.

κουφότης ητος *f.* **1 lightness** (as a quality, opp. heaviness) Pl. Arist.; (of specific things) Pl. Plu.
2 nimbleness, agility Plu.
3 levity (of a person) Plu.; **foolishness** or **vanity** Plu.

κόφινος ου *m.* **basket** Ar. X. Thphr. NT. Plu.

κοχλίᾱς ου *m.* [κόχλος] **1 snail** (as food) Men.; (collectv.sg.) Theoc.
2 mechanical snail (ref. to an automaton) Plb.

κόχλος ου *m.* (*also f.* AR.) [reltd. κόγχος] **conch shell** AR.; (blown as a trumpet) E. Theoc. Mosch.

κοχυδέω *contr.vb.* ‖ iteratv.impf. κοχύδεσκον ‖ (of sweat) **stream forth** —w. ἐκ + GEN. *fr. someone's brow* Theoc.

κοχώνη ης *f.* ‖ nom.acc.du. κοχώνᾱ ‖ ‖ DU. **buttocks** or **crotch** Ar.

κόψιχος *Att.m.*: see κόσσυφος

Κόωνδε *ep.adv.*, **Κόως** *ep.f.*: see Κῶς

κρααίνω *ep.vb.*: see κραίνω

κράατα (ep.neut.nom.acc.pl.), **κράατι** (dat.sg.), **κράατος** (gen.sg.): see κράς

κράβαττος ου *m.* **mattress, pallet** (used as a bed) NT.

κραγέτᾱς ᾱ *dial.m.* [κράζω] (appos.w. κολοιός *jackdaw*) **squawker, screecher** Pi.

κράγος ου *m.* (pejor.) **screech** (of a demagogue) Ar.

κραδαίνω *vb.* [κραδάω] ‖ aor. ἐκράδᾱνα (Plu.) ‖ aor.pass. ἐκραδάνθην (Plu.) ‖ **1** make (sthg.) quiver; **brandish** *—a spear* E. Plu.; **shake** *—one's helmet crests* Ar.(mock-trag.) ‖ PASS. (of a spear) quiver (on piercing a person's body or the ground) Il.; (of cavalrymen's lances, fr. the movement of their horses) Plb.; (of ladders, a siege-engine) shake, wobble Plu.
2 shake *—a child (whom one is holding in the air)* Plu. ‖ PASS. shake —W.ACC. *in one's body (fr. fear)* Plu.; reel (under a blow) Plu.

3 (of a hurricane) **shake** —*the earth* (w. ἐκ + GEN. *fr. its foundations*) A.; (fig., of a military threat) **set** (W.ACC. *a region*) **quivering** (w. *alarm*) Plu. ‖ PASS. (of a region) be set quivering Plu.

κραδάω *contr.vb.* | only ptcpl. κραδάων | **brandish** —*a spear* Hom.

κράδεμνον *dial.n.*: see κρήδεμνον

κράδη ης *f.* **fig-branch** Hes. Hippon. Ar. Men.; (pl., meton. for a fig crop) Ar.

κραδίᾱ *dial.f.*, **κραδίη** *ep.Ion.f.*: see καρδίᾱ

κράζω *vb.* | fut. κράξω (NT.) | aor. ἔκρᾱξα (NT.), also ἐκέκρᾱξα (NT.) | aor.2 (in cpds.) -έκραγον | pf. (w.pres.sens.) κέκρᾱγα, imperatv. κέκραχθι, pl. κεκράγετε | plpf. (w.impf.sens.) ἐκεκράγειν ‖ fut.pf.mid. (w.fut.sens.) κεκράξομαι |
1 (of persons, freq. of public speakers) **make a noisy utterance, cry out, shout, bawl, yell** A. Ar. Att.orats. X. Men. +
—W.DIR.SP. *sthg.* Ar. NT. —W.ACC. *'shoes'* Ar.
—W.NEUT.PL.ACC. *arrogant words, just and unjust words* S. Ar. —W.COMPL.CL. or ACC. + INF. *that sthg. is the case* Ar. D. Plu.; (of a baby) Men.
2 call out —W.ACC. + INF. *for someone to do sthg.* Ar.
3 (fig., of soup, in an upset stomach) **trumpet out** —παππάξ (*i.e. the noise of a fart*) Ar.; (of shores) **cry out** (supposedly as a prosaic synonym for Homeric βοάω) Arist.; (of stones) NT.
4 (of a person, envisaged as a dog) **yelp** —W.NEUT.PL.ADV. *terrifyingly* Ar.; (of frogs) **croak** Ar.

κραίνω, also ep. **κρᾱαίνω** (or **κραιαίνω**) *vb.* | ep.3sg.impf. ἐκράαινε (v.l. ἐκραίαινε) | fut. κρανῶ, Ion. κρανέω | aor. ἔκρᾱνα, ep. ἔκρηνα, also ἐκρήηνα, ep.inf. κρῆναι, also κρηῆναι, imperatv. κρῆνον, also κρήηνον ‖ MID.: Ion.fut.inf. (w.pass.sens.) κρανέεσθαι ‖ PASS.: fut. κρανθήσομαι | aor. ἐκράνθην, ep.3pl. ἐκράανθεν (Theoc.) | 3sg.pf. κέκρανται, ep. κεκράανται (AR.) |
1 fulfil (a request, prophecy, or sim.); (of a god or person) **fulfil** —*a wish, prayer, command, promise, threat* (sts. W.DAT. *for someone*) Hom. hHom. A. Pi. E. —*a prophetic dream* Mosch. ‖ PASS. (of a curse, a prophecy) be fulfilled A. E.
2 bring (an event) **to fulfilment;** (usu. of gods) **accomplish, bring about** —*an event or outcome* Pi. B. Emp. Trag. AR.; (intr., of gods) **achieve a result** Od.; (of ruin) **come to fulfilment** A. ‖ PASS. (of an event, purpose or result) be accomplished, achieved or brought about (usu. by gods) Il. A. Pi. E. AR. Theoc.; (of a contest) be decided E.
3 ordain (w. guarantee of fulfilment in the future); (of gods, oracles, prophetic dreams) **ordain, decree, determine** —*an event or outcome* Hom. hHom. A. E.; **deliver** —*prophecies* E. ‖ PASS. (of an outcome) be ordained (by Zeus) A.; (of a decree of the gods) be ratified E.; (of a god's gift) have a fixed purpose E.; (of a person) be ordained (by the gods) —W.INF. *to do sthg.* Pi.*fr.*
4 (of persons, esp. in a civic ctxt.) **ordain, decree, determine** —*sthg., everything* S. E. —W.ACC. + INF. *that sthg. shd. be the case* A.; **ratify** —*a proposal, legal judgements* A. E. ‖ PASS. (of honours) be ordained —W.DAT. *for a god* E.; (of a vote) be passed A. E.
5 (of persons) **have authority, be in control** Od. Lycurg.(oath, cj.) —W.GEN. *over a country, an army* S.; **wield** —W.ACC. *the sceptre* S.
6 (of Hermes) perh. **speak with authority about** —*the gods, the earth* hHom.

κραιπαλάω *contr.vb.* [κραιπάλη] **1 suffer from the after-effects of heavy drinking, have a hangover** Ar. Pl.
2 (gener.) **be in a state of drunkenness, be drunk** Plb. Plu.

κραιπάλη ης *f.* **1 all-night drinking-party, drinking-bout** Ar. [or perh. ref. to its after-effects, i.e. *hangover*]
2 (gener.) state of being drunk, **drunkenness** Men. NT.

κραιπαλό-κωμος ον *adj.* [κῶμος] (of a crowd) **of revellers with hangovers** Ar.

κραιπνός ή όν *adj.* **1** (of divine beings, heroes) **moving with speed, swift, rapid** Il. Pi. Hdt.(oracle); (of feet) Hom. A. AR.; (of leaping or jumping) S.*Ichn.* E.; (of horse-riding) Plu.(quot.epigr.); (of winds) Od. hHom.; (of arrows) Pi. AR.; (of the Clashing Rocks) Pi.; (of a melody) AR.
2 (of a young man's mind) **quick** Il.

—**κραιπνά** *neut.pl.adv.* **swiftly** Hom.

—**κραιπνῶς** *adv.* **swiftly** Hom. AR.

κραιπνό-συτος ον *adj.* [σεύω] (of a winged chariot) **speeding swiftly** A.

κραιπνο-φόρος ον *adj.* [φέρω] (of winds) **giving swift conveyance** (to a winged chariot) A.

κράκτης ου *m.* [κράζω] | voc. κρᾶκτα | (pejor., ref. to a politician) **bawler** Ar.

κράμβη ης *f.* **cabbage** Hippon. Anan.

κράμβος η ον *adj.* app., dry; (fig., of the mouth of a poet, envisaged as a cook) perh. **fastidious** Ar. [or perh. *loud*]

κράνᾱ *dial.f.*: see κρήνη

κραναή-πεδος ον *ep.adj.* [κραναός, πέδον] (of Delos) **with rocky terrain** hHom.

Κραναΐδαι *m.pl.*: see under κραναός

κρανάϊνος *adj.*: see κρανέϊνος

κραναός ά (Ion. ή) όν *adj.* **1** (of Ithaca) **rocky, rugged, craggy** Hom.; (of Delos) hHom. Pi.; (of other islands) Il. AR.
2 (of the citadel of Eleusis) hHom.; (of Athens) Pi.; (of Tiryns) Mosch.

—**Κραναά** ᾶς *f.* **Kranaa** (as the name for Athens or the Acropolis) Ar.; (also pl., unless masc.pl. *Kranaans*) Ar.

—**Κραναός** οῦ *m.* **Kranaos** (mythol. founder of Athens) A.

—**Κραναΐδαι** ῶν *m.pl.* **descendants of Kranaos** (ref. to the Athenians) E.

—**Κραναοί** ῶν *m.pl.* **Kranaans** (name of the original inhabitants of Athens) Hdt.

κράνεια ᾱς (Ion. ης) *f.* **1 cornelian cherry, cornel tree** Hom. Plu.
2 cornel wood (as the material of a bow or spear) E.*fr.* X. Plu.

κρανέϊνος (v.l. **κρανάϊνος**) η ον *adj.* | ῑ *metri grat.* hHom. | (of a bow, javelin, lance) **of cornel wood** hHom. Hdt. X.

κρανέω (Ion.fut.), **κρανθήσομαι** (fut.pass.): see κραίνω

Κρανίδες ων *dial.f.pl.* [κρήνη] **nymphs of the springs** Mosch.

κρανίον[1] ου *n.* [reltd. κάρᾱ, κρᾶς] **upper part of the head, cranium, skull** (of a person or animal) Il. Pi. E.*Cyc.* Pl. Plu.

κρανίον[2] ου *dial.n.* [dimin. κρήνη] **little spring** Pi.*fr.*

κρανίς *dial.f.*: see κρηνίς

κρανοποιέω *contr.vb.* [κρανοποιός] (fig., of a playwright, using military terms) **make helmets** Ar.

κρανο-ποιός οῦ *m.* [κράνος, ποιέω] **helmet-maker** Ar.

κράνος εος (ους) *n.* **helmet** A. Hdt. E. Ar. X. +; (fig., ref. to a warship's ram) Tim.

κράντορες ων *m.pl.* [κραίνω] men in charge, **leaders, chiefs** (W.GEN. *of a land*) E.

κρανῶ (fut.): see κραίνω

κρᾶς (also **κρᾶτα**) κρατός *n.* (sts. *m.f.*) [reltd. κάρᾱ] | SG.: masc.nom. κρᾶς, neut. κρᾶτα (S.) | acc. κρᾶτα (neut. S. E., masc. or fem. E., indeterminate Od. Pi. E. +) | neut.gen. κρᾱτός (also fem. E.), ep. κράᾱτος | neut.dat. κρᾱτί, ep. κράᾱτι ‖ PL.: neut.nom.acc. κρᾶτα, ep. κράᾱτα | also masc.

κρᾶσις or fem.acc. κρᾶτας (E.) | neut.gen. κρᾶτων | neut.dat. κρᾶσί | ep.neut.gen.dat.sg.pl. κράτεσφι ‖ see also κρῆθεν |
1 head (of a person, animal, monster) Hom. Hes. Lyr. Trag. Ar. Men. +; (as that on which disaster falls) Od. S.; (W.ADJ. *my*, ref. to oneself) S.
2 peak, summit (of a mountain) Il.
3 head (of a harbour, ref. to its inmost part) Od.
4 top, upper rim (of a mixing-bowl, wine-jar) S. Theoc.

κρᾶσις εως n. Ion. **κρῆσις** ιος f. [κεράννῡμι] **1 process of mixing together, mixing, blending** (of substances) Emp. Pl. Arist.
2 combining (of music and gymnastics) Pl.
3 mixing, preparation (of medicines) A.
4 admixture (of moisture w. air, of sthg. sweet w. water) E.fr. Arist.
5 (concr.) **mixture, blend** (of substances) Pl.; (of wine and water, as a libation) Call.(cj.)
6 combination (of things or conditions) Sapph.(dub.) Pl. X. Plu.
7 composition, make-up (of a substance) Emp. Arist.; (of the human body) Parm.
8 (specif.) **constitution, temperament** (of persons, their bodies) Arist. Plu.; (w.connot. of temperature) Plu.
9 prevailing weather, climate (of a place, in each season) Pl. Plu.; **temperature** (of soil) Plu.

κράσπεδα ων n.pl. **1 fringes** (W.GEN. of tufts of wool, on a Spartan's cloak) Ar. ‖ SG. **edge, border, hem** (of a cloak) Theoc. NT. Plu.
2 tassels (worn on their cloaks by Jews) NT.
3 edges (of a sail) E.
4 edges (of mountains, ref. to their lower slopes) X.
5 edges (of a military force, ref. to its flanks or wings) E. X.

κρασπεδόομαι pass.contr.vb. | 3sg.pf. κεκρασπέδωται | (of a woven garment) **be fringed** —W.DAT. w. serpents (i.e. images of them) E.

κρᾶτα (nom.acc.sg.pl.): see κρᾶς

κραται-βολος ον adj. [κραταιός, βάλλω] (of rocks) **thrown with force** E.

κραται-γύαλος ον adj. [γύαλον] (of cuirasses) **strong-plated** Il.

κραταιΐς (or **Κραταιΐς**) f. | only nom. | app. **force, weight** (or personif. *Force, Mighty One*, causing Sisyphos' rock to roll downhill) Od.
—**Κραταιΐς** f. | only acc. Κράταιιν | **Krataiis** (mother of Scylla) Od. AR.

κραταί-λεως ων, gen. ω adj. [λᾶας] (of ground) **with hard rocks, rocky** A. E.

κραταιόομαι mid.pass.contr.vb. (of a growing child) **become strong** NT. —W.DAT. *in spirit* NT.

κραταιός ά (Ion. ή) όν adj. [κράτος] **1** (of persons, their strength, hands) **powerful, mighty** Hom. hHom. Lyr. Trag.; (of a lion) Il.; (of a spear, bow) Pi. Plu.; (of fate) Il. Hes.fr.
2 (of fighting) **fierce, stubborn** Plb.
3 (of a statement) **effective** Pi.

κραταί-πεδος ον adj. [πέδον] (of a floor) **with a hard surface, hard** Od.

κραταί-ρινος ον adj. [ῥινός] (of a tortoise) **tough-skinned** Hdt.(oracle)

κρᾶτας (acc.pl.): see κρᾶς

κρατερ-αύχην ενος masc.fem.adj. [κρατερός, αὐχήν] (pejor., of a horse) app. **with a thick neck** Pl.

κρατερός ά (Ion. ή) όν adj. [κράτος, reltd. καρτερός] | ep.fem.dat.sg. κρατερῆφι | **1** (of persons, esp. warriors; of deities, demigods, monsters) **strong, powerful, mighty** Hom. Hes. A. Pi. B. Hdt.(oracle) +; (of a person's hands) Od. Pi. AR.; (of animals, parts of their bodies) Hom. Hes. Thgn. AR.; (of the strength of persons, monsters, animals) Hom. Hes. Thgn. B. AR.; (of the strength of a fire) **fierce** Od.
2 (of weapons) **strong, powerful** Hom. hHom. Sol.; (of a hammer) Il.; (of iron, perh. w. additional connot. of *hard*) Hes.; (of nails, bolts) Pi. AR.; (of bonds) Hom. Hes. A.
3 (of ground) **hard** hHom.; (of the human head, ref. to its physical composition) Pl.
4 (of fighting, conflict, or sim.) **powerful, fierce** Hom. Hes. Mimn. B. AR.; (of a contest, wrestling) **tough** Od. B.
5 (of compulsion) **strong** Hom. Hes. Thgn. B. Parm. Hdt.(oracle) +; (of endurance) **firm** Archil.
6 (of pain, grief, madness, trembling, fear) **intense, overpowering** Hom.; (of hunger) Call.
7 (of speech, instructions, reproach) **stern, strict, firm** Il.

—**κρατερῶς** adv. **1 with physical strength, strongly, powerfully** Hom. AR.; **firmly, stoutly** —ref. to resisting Il.
2 firmly, forcefully —ref. to speaking Il.
3 intensely, fiercely —ref. to being angry Il.

κρατερό-φρων ον, gen. ονος adj. [φρήν] **1** (of persons, demigods) **stout-hearted** Hom. Hes. Callin. AR.; (of Poseidon, Athena) Stesich. Ibyc.
2 (of wild animals, monsters, the spirit of primeval men) **fierce-hearted** Il. Hes.

κρατερ-ῶνυξ υχος masc.fem.adj. [ὄνυξ] **1** (of horses, mules) **strong-hoofed** Hom.
2 (of wolves, lions) **strong-clawed** Od.

κράτεσφι (ep.neut.gen.dat.sg.pl.): see κρᾶς

κρατευταί ῶν ep.m.pl. **stone or metal supports for spits of meat** (on either side of a hearth), **cooking-stands** Il.

κρατέω contr.vb. [κράτος] **1** (of persons, gods) **be strong or powerful** Il. Hes.; (of a warrior) **show one's might** Il.
2 have command or **control** (freq. W.GEN. over persons, places, things) Hdt. Trag. Th. +
3 (specif.) **rule** Od. hHom. Trag. —W.GEN. *over people, a populace, region, or sim.* Hom. Trag. —W.DAT. *over gods, men, the dead* Od. —W.DAT. *in or over a place* Pi. —W.ACC. *over a land* A.; (of the vote of the people) **have sovereign power** A. ‖ MASC.PTCPL.SB. (usu. w.art.) **ruler** Hdt. Trag. ‖ NEUT.PTCPL.SB. (w.art.) **ruling power** E. Pl. Arist. ‖ PASS. (of a person) **be ruled** (opp. rule) E.
4 (aor.) **seize power** Sol. A.fr.
5 (esp. in military ctxt.) **have the upper hand, be victorious, triumph** Hdt. Trag. Th. +; **overcome, defeat** —W.ACC. or GEN. *enemies or sim.* Hdt. E. Th. + ‖ PASS. **be defeated** E. Th.
6 (of athletes) **be victorious** Pi. —W.DAT. *in a contest* Pi. —W.ACC. B. E.; **defeat** —W.ACC. *opponents* Pi. ‖ PASS. **be defeated** A.
7 (of a tribe) **be best** (though not victorious) —W.ACC. *in a choral contest* D.
8 (of a disputant) **prevail** (in an argument) Hdt. E.; (of a legal case, a proposal) A. Th.; (of the good, divine will, chance) A. S.; (of novel things) Th.
9 (of a report) **prevail, be current** A. S. Plb.
10 ‖ IMPERS. **it is better** —W.INF. *to die* A. E.
11 (of persons, gods, things) **get the better of, prevail over, overcome, master** —W.ACC. or GEN. *someone or sthg.* Trag. Th. + ‖ PASS. (of persons) **be mastered or overcome** A. —W.DAT. or PREP.PHR. *by sleep* A. Hdt. —*by foolhardiness, pleasures* A. Pl.; **be condemned** —W.DAT. *by a vote* E.
12 (of persons or things) **outdo, surpass** —W.ACC. or GEN. *someone or sthg.* A. Pi. E. Th. +; (of a serpent) **exceed** (in size) —W.ACC. *a ship* Pi.

13 (usu.aor.) **take possession of** (sts. by force) —W.GEN. *persons, places, things* Hdt. S. Th. + ‖ PASS. (of persons) be captured Th.
14 ‖ PASS. (wkr.sens., of things) be achieved or attained Th. Arist.
15 take hold of —W.GEN. *someone's hand* NT. —W.ACC. *someone* (W.GEN. *by the hand*) NT.
16 take into custody —W.ACC. *a person* Plb. NT.

κρᾱτήρ, Ion. **κρητήρ**, ῆρος *m.* [κεράννῡμι] **1 krater, mixing-bowl** (a large vessel in which wine was diluted w. water before drinking) Hom. +
2 (ref. to the vessel and its contents) **bowl of wine** (as being mixed, offered, drunk, or sim., oft. in ritual ctxt.) Hom. +
3 bowl (W.GEN. of milk) Theoc.
4 (fig.) **mixing-bowl** (filled w. evils by a criminal and drunk by him) A.; (W.GEN. for evils, ref. to an informant) Ar.; (for songs, ref. to a chorus-trainer) Pi.; (of or for the Muses' songs, ref. to a poetical offering) Pi.
5 bowl-shaped hollow (in a rock), **basin** S.

κρᾱτηρίζω *vb.* ply (W.ACC. Dionysian initiates) **with a bowlful** (of wine) D.

κρᾱτησί-μαχος ον *adj.* [κρατέω, μάχη] (of the might of the Dioscuri) **victorious in battle** Pi.

κρᾱτησί-πους πουν, gen. ποδος *adj.* [πούς] (of an athlete) **victorious in the foot-race** Pi.

κρᾱτήσ-ιππος ον *adj.* [ἵππος] (of a chariot) **with victorious horses** Pi.

κρᾱτί (neut.dat.sg.): see κρᾶς

κρᾰτιστεύω *vb.* [κράτιστος] **1** (of persons or animals) **be best, be supreme, excel** X. Plu.; (of Helios) —W.PREP.PHR. *in seeing* S.
2 ‖ PTCPL.ADJ. (of a word) perh., choicest or most powerful Pi.*fr.*
3 be superior —W.GEN. *to others* And. Isoc. X.

κράτιστος η (dial. ᾱ) ον *superl.adj.* [κρατύς, reltd. κάρτιστος] **1** (of Zeus, Athena, Wealth) **mightiest** (sts. W.GEN. of the gods) Pi. Ar. ‖ MASC.SB. mightiest one (ref. to Zeus) Pi.*fr.*
2 (of mythol. persons) **mightiest** (W.GEN. of heroes, Greeks, Greece) Pi. S. E.
3 (of combatants) **strongest** Th. Isoc. ‖ NEUT.SG.SB. best or strongest part (of military forces) Th. X.; (pl., of allied communities) Th.
4 (of a man, as described by an obsequious person) **most excellent** Thphr.; (as honorary epith. of a Roman official) NT.; (in voc., as a polite address) NT. ‖ MASC.PL.SB. (also NEUT.COLLECTV.SG.SB.) aristocrats or ruling class (in a state) X.
5 (gener.) **best** (in quality, desirability, usefulness, or sim.); (of persons, things, circumstances, courses of action) **best** (sts. W.GEN. of persons or things, sts. W.ACC., DAT. or PREP.PHR. in a particular respect) Pi. Hdt. S. E. Th. Critias +; (of a person, W.INF. at doing sthg.) Antipho Th. Pl. X. Plu.; (W.PTCPL.) X. ‖ NEUT.SG.SB. most important part (of philosophy) X. ‖ NEUT.PL.SB. best parts (of a region or country) Th. X.
6 ‖ IMPERS.NEUT.SG. or PL. (w. ἐστί or sim., sts.understd.) it is best —W.INF. *to do sthg.* Trag. Th. Ar. Att.orats. Pl. +
7 (advbl.phr.) τὰ κράτιστα *most strongly* Th.; (prep.phr.) ἀπὸ τοῦ κρατίστου *from the best possible motive* Plb.
—**κράτιστα** *neut.pl.adv.* **best** (in quality) Th. X. Plb. Plu.; (in desirability or utility) E. Th. Ar.

κρᾱτός (fem.neut.gen.sg.): see κρᾶς

κράτος, ep. **κάρτος**, Aeol. **κρέτος**, εος (ους) *n.* | ep.Ion.gen. **κάρτευς** (Hes.) | **1** physical strength, **strength, might** (of a god, person or animal) Hom. Hes. hHom. Simon. S. E.; **strength, hardness** (of iron) Od.; **power** (of lightning) S.
2 (prep.phrs.) κατὰ κράτος **strongly, powerfully, with all one's might** (ref. to fighting or sim.) Th. Pl. X. +; **by force** (ref. to capturing a city or sim.) Th. Isoc. Pl. +; (fig.) **firmly, decidedly** (ref. to being proven guilty or wrong) D. Plu.; ἀνὰ κράτος **with all one's might** X. Plu.
3 might, power, authority (of a god, esp. Zeus) Il. Hes. Archil. Thgn. A. Pi. +
4 (personif., as a deity) **Power, Might** Hes. A.
5 power, authority (of persons, sts. W.GEN. over persons or things) hHom. Pi. Trag. Pl. +; (W.ADJ. ἐμόν *over me*) E.
6 (specif.) sovereign or political power, **power, authority, control, rule** Od. Alc. Eleg. Hdt. Trag. Th. +; (W.GEN. over a country, its people, over the sea) Hdt. Trag. Th.
7 (milit.) **command** Hdt.; (W.GEN. of an army) Hdt.
8 (ref. to a god or person) one who holds power, **power, authority** A. E.
9 mastery, supremacy, success, victory (in battle, the games or other endeavours; sts. paired w. νίκη *victory*) Hom. Hes. A. Pi. B. S. Th. + ‖ PL. mighty or victorious deeds (of a warrior or athlete) S.

κρᾰτύνω, ep. **κᾰρτύνω** *vb.* | Boeot.3sg. κρατούνῐ | aor. ἐκράτῡνα, ep. ἐκάρτῡνα | **1 make physically strong, toughen, harden** —*feet* (of persons and horses) X. ‖ PASS. (of Spartan babies) be toughened —W.ACC. *in their constitution* Plu.
2 (act. and mid.) **strengthen, fortify** —*cities, walls, buildings* Hdt. Th. —*one's roof* (against bad weather) AR. ‖ PASS. (of walls) be strengthened —W.DAT. *w. battlements* Call.(cj.)
3 ‖ MID. (of troops) **strengthen** —*their ranks* (by closing up) Il. Hes.
4 (of air, pressing against the lower aperture of a container) app. **hold firm, support** —*the surface of the water inside* Emp.
5 strengthen, reinforce —*a king* (W.DAT. w. bodyguards) Hdt.; (of a king) —*himself* (W.DAT. *by the use of his absolute power*) Hdt.; (mid., of a commander) —*cities* (w. garrisons) Plu.; (of boxers) —*their hands* (w. oxhide bindings) Theoc.; (of the Cyclopes) —*Zeus* (w. the thunderbolt) AR.; (of a king) —*his rule* Plu. ‖ PASS. (of a king) be strengthened or reinforced (in his power) —W.DAT. *by an oracle* Hdt.
6 ‖ MID. (of persons) **confirm, cement** —*their pledges of mutual loyalty* (W.DAT. *by complicity in crimes*) Plu.
7 ‖ MID. (of a commander) **firmly establish, secure** —*his power* (in a country) Plu.; **secure control of** —*a region* (sts. W.DAT. *for himself*) Plu.
8 (of a king, a people) **have power** or **control over, rule** —W.ACC. *a land, a city, its altar* A. —W.GEN. *a land* S. E.; (of Zeus) —W.ACC. *all things* S.; (of gods or persons) **exercise, wield** —W.INTERN. or COGN.ACC. *power* (*of a certain kind*) A. E.; (intr.) **rule** Trag. ‖ PASS. (of a city) be ruled —W.PREP.PHR. or DAT. *by one man, a mob* E.
9 have control or **be master of** —W.GEN. *a bow* S. —*another's weapons* S. —*the means of one's subsistence* S.; (of a god) —W.ACC. *a woman's bed* Corinn.
10 (of a warrior-seer) **win** —W.INTERN.ACC. *first place* (W.DAT. *w. the spear and in augury*) S.
11 apply one's strength (to an object); **vigorously throw** —*javelins* Pi.; **grip tightly** —*an oar* (W.DAT. w. *one's hands*) AR.; (mid.) —*one's levelled spear* (W.PREP.PHR. w. *both hands*) Plu.

κρατύς έος *ep.masc.adj.* [κράτος] (epith. of Argeiphontes, i.e. Hermes) **mighty** Hom. hHom.

κράτων (neut.gen.pl.): see κράς

κραυγάζω *vb.* [κραυγή] **1** (of a dog) **yelp** Pl.(quot.lyr.) **2** (of persons) **yell, shout** D. NT. —W.DIR.SP. *sthg.* NT.

κραυγάνομαι *mid.vb.* (of a baby) **bawl** Hdt.

κραυγή ῆς, dial. **κραυγά** ᾶς *f.* **shouting** E. Th. Att.orats. X. +

κραῦρος ᾱ ον *adj.* | compar. κραυρότερος | (of bone, pottery) **brittle** Pl.

κρε-άγρᾱ ᾱς *f.* [κρέας, ἀγρέω] **meat-hook** (for extracting meat fr. a stew-pot) Ar.; (gener.) **hook** (attached to a well-rope, to hold a bucket) Ar.

κρεάδιον (sts. written **κρεᾴδιον**) ου *n.* [dimin. κρέας] **scrap of meat** Ar. X. Men. Plu.

κρεανομέω *contr.vb.* [κρεανόμος] **give a share of meat** (fr. a sacrifice) —W.DAT. *to someone* Is. ‖ MID. (of Bacchants) **divide up among each other** —*parts of a dismembered body* Theoc.

κρεα-νόμος ου *m.* [κρέας, νέμω] **one who apportions meat, server, carver** E.*Cyc.*

κρέας κρέως *n.* | also dial.nom. κρῆς (Ar.) ‖ PL.: nom.acc. κρέα, also perh. κρεῖα (Timocr., cj.) | gen. κρεῶν, ep. κρειῶν, also κρεάων (hHom.) | dat. κρέασι, also ep. κρέεσσι (Hdt., oracle) | **1 flesh, meat** (of an animal) Hes. Anan. E.*Cyc.* Ar. Theoc.; **piece of meat** (cut fr. an animal) Od. Hippon. Hdt. Th. Ar. Thphr. + | COLLECTV.PL. **meat** (cut fr. an animal) Hom. hHom. Semon. Thgn. Timocr. Pi. +; (cut fr. a person) Od. A. Hdt. E.*Cyc.*

2 (in voc. address, fig.ref. to a person) **hunk of meat** Ar.

3 ‖ PL. (fig.) **skin, bacon** (of a person, as risked in battle) Ar.

κρεαφαγέω *contr.vb.*: see κρεοφαγέω

κρεγμός οῦ *m.* [κρέκω] **strumming** (of a lyre, w. a plectrum) AR.

κρείοισα *Aeol.f.*: see κρέουσα

κρεῖον[1] ου *n.* [κρέας] **meat-platter** (for carving or serving) Il.

κρεῖον[2] (ep.voc.): see κρέων

κρείουσα, Κρείουσα *ep.f.*: see κρέουσα

κρείσσων, Att. **κρείττων**, Ion. **κρέσσων**, Lacon. **κάρρων** (Alcm. Plu.), ον, gen. ονος *compar.adj.* [reltd. κράτος]

1 having greater physical strength; (of persons or animals) **stronger, more powerful** (sts. W.GEN. than others) Hom. Hes. Alcm. A. Pi. Antipho

2 (of a commander, army, city, or sim.) having greater military strength, **stronger, more powerful** Hdt. E. Th. +

3 (of gods) **mightier, more powerful** (than other gods or than mortals) hHom. Thgn. Trag.; (of the mind of Zeus) Il. ‖ MASC.SB. (w.art.) the mightier one (ref. to Zeus) A. ‖ MASC. and NEUT.PL.SB. higher powers (ref. to the gods) E. Pl.

4 (of things, abstr. forces) **stronger, more powerful** (freq. W.GEN. than others) Thgn. Heraclit. A. Pi. Hdt. E. +

5 (of combatants) proving the stronger, **superior, victorious** Hom.; (of ships) Th.

6 (of persons) having greater authority or status, **more powerful** (sts. W.GEN. than others) Il. Trag. Pl. +; having a **greater right** (W.INF. to do sthg.) Od. ‖ MASC.PL.SB. one's **betters** Hdt. ‖ NEUT.SG. or MASC.PL.SB. **stronger side or party** Th.

7 (gener.) **superior or preferable** (in quality, desirability, usefulness, or sim.); (of persons, animals, things, situations, courses of action) **better** (freq. W.GEN. than others) Od. Hes. Thgn. Anan. Pi. Hdt. Trag. +

8 ‖ NEUT.IMPERS. (w. ἐστί or sim., sts.understd.) **it is better** —W.INF. *to do sthg., that sthg. shd. happen* (sts. W. ἤ + INF. *than to do sthg. else*) Hdt. Trag. Th. +

9 (of a person, w.vb. *is* or *was*, in place of impers. constr.) **better** —W.PTCPL. *doing sthg.* (i.e. *it would be better if he were doing sthg.*) S.; (of a trial) —W. μή + PF.PTCPL. *not having taken place* Aeschin.

10 stronger (than some temptation or influence, i.e. able to overcome it); (of persons) **having mastery** (W.GEN. over one's desires and appetites) X.; (over oneself, i.e. one's desires) Pl.; **impervious** (W.GEN. to bribery, ethical considerations) Th.; **unresponsive** (W.GEN. to education) Arist.

11 (of things) **greater** (in amount or degree); (of blessings) **greater** (W.GEN. than sorrows) Pi.; (of present toils, than past ones) E.

12 (of things) surpassing (some limit, norm or capacity); (of a city) **greater** (W.GEN. than its reputation) Th.; (of a calamity, than expectation) Th.; (of deeds, than wonders, i.e. immeasurably wonderful) E.; (w. ἤ + INF. than one may describe, i.e. defying description) E.; (of the height of a net) **too great** (W.GEN. for leaping out from) A.; (of deeds, for one's capabilities) X.; (for hanging, i.e. deserving a greater punishment) S.; (of beauty, the nature of a disease, for words, i.e. defying description) Th. X.; (of a sight, for seeing, i.e. greater than the eyes can bear) E.; (of a person's mind and tongue, for one's time of life, i.e. mature for one's years) Pi.

—**κρεῖσσον**, Ion. **κρέσσον** *neut.compar.adv.* **1 more powerfully** (W.GEN. than fire) S.

2 to a greater extent, **more** (w. ἤ + DAT. than in words, i.e. than can be described) —*ref. to being fortunate* E.

3 better (W.GEN. than someone else) —*ref. to judging* Hippon.

—**κρεισσόνως** *compar.adv.* with greater physical force, **more powerfully** —*ref. to defending oneself against attack* Antipho

κρειῶν (ep.gen.pl.): see κρέας

κρείων *ep.m.*: see κρέων

κρεκάδια ων *n.pl.* [κρέκω] **tapestries** (as wall-hangings) Ar.

Κρεκοπίς *fem.adj.*: see under κρέξ

κρέκω *vb.* | Aeol.inf. κρέκην | **1** (of a weaver) perh., **strike a web** (w. a κερκίς *pin-beater*); (gener.) **weave** —*a web, garments* Sapph. E.

2 perh., strike a lyre (w. a plectrum); (of a lyre-player) **strike up** —*a tune* Theoc.*epigr.*

3 sing (to an accompaniment); (of singers) **give voice to** —*a song* (to the accompaniment of harps) Telest.; (of swans) —*a cry* (to the accompaniment of wings beating) Ar.; (of a woman, in ctxt. of weaving) —*a song* (perh. to the accompaniment of a pin-beater) E.*fr.*

4 (gener.) **play** —*the aulos* Ar.

κρεμάθρᾱ ᾱς *f.* [κρεμάννυμι] **lifting-hook** (suspended fr. a rope) Ar. Arist.

κρεμάννῡμι *vb.* [reltd. κρίμνημι] | fut. κρεμῶ, 3sg. κρεμᾷ, inf. κρεμᾶν, ep.1sg. (w.diect.) κρεμόω | aor. ἐκρέμασα, ep. κρέμασα ‖ MID.: aor.inf. κρεμάσασθαι (Hes.) ‖ PASS.: κρέμαμαι, also κρεμάννυμαι (X.), subj. κρέμωμαι, opt. κρεμαίμην | impf. ἐκρεμάμην, ep.2sg. ἐκρέμω and κρέμω (or ἐκρέμαο and κρέμαο) | fut. κρεμήσομαι | aor. ἐκρεμάσθην |

1 fasten to a higher support, hang up —*an object* (on a peg, wall, or sim.) Ar. Pl. X. Plu.; (fig., of Socrates, himself hanging in a basket) —*his mind* (to communicate w. the supposedly intelligent air) Ar. ‖ PASS. (of an object) **be hung up** —W.PREP.PHR. *on a peg* Ar. ‖ PASS.PTCPL. (of an object) **hanging** (on a wall or sim.) Hdt. Plu.

2 (specif.) **hang up** (in a temple, as a dedication) —*captured weapons* Il. Plu.(quot.epigr.) ‖ PASS. (of dedicated objects) **be hung or be hanging** (in a temple, on its walls) Pi. Hdt. Plu.

3 hang up (w.connot. of putting away, out of use) —*a boat's rudder* (*in the off-season*) Hes.(mid.) Ar. —*one's shield* (*in peacetime*) Ar. ‖ PASS. (of a shield) be hung up Ar.
4 cause to hang downwards (fr. a higher support); (of gods) **hang down, suspend** —*a rope* (*fr. heaven*) Il.; (of sailors) —*a ship's anchor* (W.PREP.PHR. *above the prow*) Pi. ‖ PASS. (of a person) be hung or suspended —W.PREP.PHR. + ADV. *by the feet, upside down* Ar.
5 ‖ PASS. be attached (to sthg.) so as to hang downwards; (of quivers) be hung (under shields) Hdt.; (of corpses, fr. trees) AR.; (of rings, fr. a horse's bit) X.; (of a noose, a millstone, around someone's neck) Plb. NT.; (of soldiers, unable to extricate themselves fr. palings) be left hanging X.; (of a ship's storm-beaten tackle) Theoc. ‖ PASS.PTCPL. (of persons or objects) hanging, dangling (sts. w. ἐκ + GEN. fr. sthg.) Hdt. X. NT. Plu.
6 ‖ PASS. (fig., of a situation) hang —w. ἐκ + GEN. *by a rotten thread* Plu.
7 hang (sthg.) over (a person or place); (of Zeus) **hang, suspend** —*a stone* (W.DAT. *over Tantalos*) Pi. ‖ PASS. (of the stone of Tantalos) be hung —W.PREP.PHR. *over an island* Archil.; (of mountains) loom —W.PREP.PHR. *over a river* X.(dub.); (fig., of blame) hang —W.DAT. *over someone* Pi.; (of errors) —W.PREP.PHR. *around people's minds* Pi.
8 ‖ PASS. be held suspended in a raised position; (of a person) be suspended (in the air) Pl.; (of a ship, lifted fr. the water by a mechanical device) Plu.; (hyperbol., of a rider) —w. ἐπί + GEN. *on a horse* X.; (of a wall) be left suspended (above excavated tunnels) Plb.; (fig., of the mind) be left in suspense Arist.
9 hang up —*a person* (*esp. a slave, usu. by the wrists or feet, or on a board or gibbet, for punishment or torture*) Ar. Men. Plu.; (by the testicles, in a sadistic threat) Ar.; (on a cross) NT. ‖ PASS. be hung up Il. Ar.; (on a cross) NT.
10 hang —*a person* (*to death, in a noose*) Arist. Plu. —*oneself* Ar. ‖ PASS. be hanged E. Ar. Theoc. Plu.
11 ‖ PASS. (of a woman) hang on, be attached —w. πρός + GEN. *to someone's feet* (*in supplication*) Ar.
12 ‖ PASS. (fig., of a lover) be attached —w. ἐκ + GEN. *to his lover's body* (*opp. his mind*) X.; (of a person's soul) —*to private possessions* Pl.
13 ‖ PASS. (fig., of a skill) hang, depend —W.ADV. *on a certain source of inspiration* Ar.; (of the law) —w. ἐν + DAT. *on a commandment* NT.; (of evils and blessings) be derived —w. ἐκ + GEN. *fr. love* Thgn.
κρεμάς άδος *fem.adj.* (of a crag) **overhanging** A.
κρεμαστός ή όν *adj.* **1** (of a noose) **hanging, suspended** S. E.; (of armour, fr. pegs) E.; (of body parts, fr. branches) E.; (of a hammock) Plu.
2 (of a person) **hanging** (fr. a noose) S.; **hung up** (alive, as punishment) S.
3 ‖ NEUT.PL.SB. (w. σκεύη understd.) hanging gear, rigging (of a ship, ref. to ropes, sails, anchors) X.; (provbl. or colloq.phr.) κρεμαστῶν τρίβων *knowing the ropes* Ar.
κρέμβαλα ων *n.pl.* **clackers, castanets** Lyr.adesp.
κρεμβαλιαστύς ύος *f.* **clacking** (of castanets) hHom.(dub., v.l. βαμβαλιαστύς)
κρεμόω (ep.fut.), **κρεμῶ** (fut.): see κρεμάννυμι
κρέξ κρεκός *f.* **1 a kind of bird; perh. corncrake** Hdt. Ar.
2 [perh. a different wd.] **lock of hair** Call.
—**Κρεκοπίς** ίδος *fem.adj.* (of a tribe of birds, w. play on Κεκροπίς *Kekropian*, name of an Athenian tribe) **Corncrakopian** Ar.(cj.)

κρεό-βοτος ον *adj.* [κρέας, βόσκω] (of the Amazons) **fed on meat** A.(dub., cj. κρεοβόρος *meat-eating*)
κρεοδαισίᾱ (sts. written **κρεωδαισίᾱ**) ᾱς *f.* [κρεοδαίτης] **distribution of meat** Plu.
κρεο-δαίτης ου *m.* [δαίομαι²] **meat-carver** (in the service of a king) Plu.
Κρέοισα *dial.f.*: see under κρέουσα
κρεοκοπέω *contr.vb.* [κόπτω] (of troops, the Cyclops) cut up (as if meat), **butcher** —*human limbs* A. E.*Cyc.*
Κρεοντίς *dial.f.*: see under κρέων
κρεο-πώλης ου *m.* [πωλέω] **meat-seller, butcher** Thphr.
κρεουργηδόν Ion.*adv.* [κρεουργός] **like a butcher** —*ref. to soldiers dismembering people* Hdt.
κρεουργός όν *adj.* [κρέας, ἔργον] (of a festal day) **of butchery** (i.e. on which a sacrificial feast was held) A.
κρέουσα, ep. **κρείουσα**, Aeol. **κρέοισα**, ης (dial. ᾱς) *f.* [κρέων] **ruler, queen** (epith. of Artemis, Demeter, Rhea, sts. w. μέγα + GEN. or DAT. in great power among goddesses or women) Hellenist.poet.; (ref. to a woman, Calypso) Hes.*fr.* AR.; (W.GEN. of Sicily, ref. to Demeter) B.; (of Olympos, ref. to Hera) Call.; (W.GEN. among women, ref. to a concubine of Priam) Il.
—**Κρέουσα**, ep. **Κρείουσα**, Aeol. **Κρέοισα**, ης (dial. ᾱς) *f.*
1 Creusa (a naiad nymph) Pi.
2 Kreousa (mother of Ion) Hes.*fr.* E.
3 Kreousa (mother of Aigeus) B.
κρεοφαγέω (sts. written **κρεαφαγέω**) *contr.vb.* [κρεοφάγος] **eat meat** Plb.
κρεο-φάγος ον *adj.* [κρέας, φαγεῖν] (of a people) **meat-eating** Hdt.
κρέσσων Ion.*compar.adj.*: see κρείσσων
κρέτος Aeol.*n.*: see κράτος
κρεωδαισίᾱ *f.*: see κρεοδαισίᾱ
κρεῶν (gen.pl.), **κρέως** (gen.sg.): see κρέας
κρέων, ep. **κρείων**, οντος *m.* | ep.voc. κρεῖον | (epith. of Zeus) **lord, ruler, mighty one** hHom. A.; (of Poseidon) Hom. Hes.*fr.* Call.; (of a river god) Il.; (ref. to kings or warriors, esp. Agamemnon) Hom. Ibyc. Pi. AR.; (w. εὐρύ *far and wide*, ref. to Poseidon, Agamemnon) Hom.; (W.GEN. of the heavens, ref. to Zeus) Pi.; (of the sea, ref. to Poseidon) E. ‖ PL. lords (ref. to the gods) Hom.
—**Κρέων** οντος *m.* **1 Creon** (successor of Oedipus as ruler of Thebes) Od. Trag. D. Arist. Plu.
2 Creon (ruler of Corinth, killed by Medea) E.
—**Κρεοντίς** ίδος *dial.f.* **daughter of Creon** (of Thebes, ref. to Megara, wife of Herakles) Pi.
κρήγυος ον (Ion. η ον) *adj.* **1** (of a prophecy) **good, honest** Il.; (of a person) Theoc.*epigr.*
2 (perh. of a ship) **good** Archil.; (of a teacher) **proficient** Pl.
3 (of a statement) **true** Theoc.
—**κρηγύως** *adv.* **well** —*ref. to being taught* Call.
κρή-δεμνον, dial. **κράδεμνον**, ου *n.* [app. κρᾱ́ς, δέω¹] **1** (sg. and collectv.pl.) **head-dress, head-scarf** (worn by a woman or goddess) Hom. hHom. E.
2 ‖ PL. (fig.) battlements, ramparts (of a city) Hom. hHom. B.; (collectv.sg.) Hes.
3 lid, seal or **stopper** (of a wine-jar) Od.
4 ‖ PL. app., head-rest (ref. to the ground) E.
κρῆναι (ep.aor.inf.), **κρῆνον** (ep.aor.imperatv.): see κραίνω
κρῆθεν ep.*adv.* [κρᾱ́ς] **1** (prep.phr.) κατὰ κρῆθεν *down over one's* (or *another's*) *head* —*ref. to drawing down a head-dress, letting drip ambrosia* Hes. hHom.; *down from the top*

κρημνοποιός

(*of trees*) —*ref. to fruit hanging* Od.; (fig.) *from head to foot, utterly* —*ref. to being overwhelmed by grief* Il. [sts. interpr. as κατ' ἄκρηθεν, equiv. to κατ' ἄκρης]
2 (prep.phr.) ἀπὸ κρήθεν *from the head* (*of a person*) —*ref. to beauty emanating* Hes.
κρημνο-ποιός οῦ *m.* [κρημνός, ποιέω] (fig., ref. to Aeschylus, as creator of imposing and rugged words) **cliff-maker** Ar.
κρημνός οῦ *m.* **1 steep side**, **bank** (of a trench, river, lake, sea) Il. Pi. Hdt.
2 sheer face (of a mountain or sim.), **cliff** Pi.*fr.* Hdt. S. E. Th. Ar. +
κρημνώδης ες *adj.* **1** (of a region, ravine, hill, route, or sim.) **steep, precipitous** Th. Plb. Plu.
2 ‖ NEUT.SB. **steepness** (of a bank or sim.) Plu.; (concr.) **precipitous part** (of a place) Th. Plu.
κρῆναι (ep.aor.inf.): see κραίνω
κρηναῖος ᾱ ον *adj.* [κρήνη] **1** (of nymphs, water, or sim.) **of** or **from a spring** Od. Hdt. Trag. AR.
2 (as the name of one of the gates of Thebes) **Krenaian** (prob. nr. the spring of Dirke) E.
κρήνη ης, dial. **κράνᾱ** ᾱς *f.* **spring** (esp. as a source of drinking-water) Hom. +
—**κρήνηνδε** *adv.* **to a spring** Od. AR.
κρηνίς, dial. **κρᾱνίς**, ῖδος *f.* **1 spring** (of water) E. Call. Theoc.
2 (fig.) **wellspring** (W.GEN. of troubles) A.(cj.)
κρῆνον (ep.aor.imperatv.): see κραίνω
κρηπίς ῖδος *f.* **1** (sg. and collectv.pl.) **foundation** (for a superimposed structure); **base** (of an altar, a tomb) Hdt. S. E. Plu.; (of a wall, fortress) X.; (of a statue, ref. to its plinth) E. Theoc.; (fig., of a mountain, ref. to the adjoining region) E.
2 base, platform (of a temple, ref. to the raised area supporting the columns) Arist.; (sg. and pl., specif.ref. to the stepped area on the outside of the columns) **steps** E. ‖ PL. **foundations** (supporting the pillars of a house) E.; (app. of temples) Pi.*fr.*
3 (fig.) **secure base** or **foundation** (of a family, political system, freedom, troubles, virtue, or sim.) A.(dub.) Pi.*fr.* E. Pl. X. Plu.; (of wise words, ref. to a speech) Pi.; (W.GEN. or DAT. for songs, ref. to a prelude or sim.) Pi.
4 border (of stone, around a lake) Hdt.
5 quay (of a harbour) Plb. Plu.
6 heavy shoe (ref. to a thick sole, attached to the foot by laces, sts. studded w. nails, worn esp. by soldiers and travellers) X. Theoc. Plb. Plu.
Κρής *masc.adj.*: see under Κρῆτες
κρής *dial.n.*: see κρέας
κρησέρα ᾱς *f.* **flour-sieve** Ar.
Κρήσιος *adj.*: see under Κρῆτες
κρῆσις Ion.*f.*: see κρᾶσις
Κρῆσσα *fem.adj.*: see under Κρῆτες
κρησφύγετον ου *n.* [2nd el.app.reltd. φεύγω] **place of refuge** Hdt.
Κρῆτες ῶν *m.pl.* [Κρήτη] **people of Crete, Cretans** (as a population or military force) Hom. hHom. Pi. B. Hdt. Th. +; (as provbl. liars) Call. Plb. Plu. ‖ SG. **Cretan man** X. +
—**Κρής** ητός *masc.adj.* **of or belonging to Crete**; (of men, archers) **Cretan** Th. Att.orats. Pl. X. +; (of a style of music or dance) Pi.*fr.*; (of a tomb) Call.
—**Κρῆσσα** ης (dial. ᾱς) *fem.adj.* (of women) **Cretan** Hdt. S. E.; (of a city, a festival) Call. ‖ PL.SB. **Cretan women** Sapph.(or Alc.)
—**Κρήσιος** ᾱ ον *adj.* **(of the land) of Crete, Cretan** E.; (of the sea, N. of Crete) S.; (of persons or things) E. Plu.; (of rhythms) Lyr.adesp.

—**Κρητικός** ή όν *adj.* **1 of or relating to Crete or the Cretans**; (of the sea, N. of Crete) **Cretan** B. Th. Plb. Plu.; (of customs, laws, a political system, way of life) Archil. Hdt. Pl. Arist. Plb. Plu.; (of hunting dogs) X.; (of songs, artefacts, or sim.) A. Ar. Plu. ‖ NEUT.SG.SB. **Cretan robe** (app. a short, light garment worn by men) Ar.
2 (of a war) **against Crete** (fought by Rhodes, c.155 BC) Plb. ‖ NEUT.PL.SB. **Cretan war** (fought by Rhodes, c.205–200 BC) Plb.
3 (of persons, their behaviour, or sim.) **characteristic of Cretans, Cretan** (i.e. dishonest or cunning) Plb. Plu.
—**Κρητικῶς** *adv.* **in Cretan style** —*ref. to dancing* Ar.
Κρήτη ης, dial. **Κρήτᾱ** ᾱς *f.* **Crete** (island S. of Greece) Hom. +; (pl.) Od.
—**Κρήτηνδε** *adv.* **to Crete** Od.
—**Κρήτηθεν** *adv.* **from Crete** Il. hHom. Call.
—**Κρηταῖος** ᾱ ον *adj.* (of a cave, mountain, plain) **Cretan** Call. AR.
—**Κρηταιεῖς**, ep. **Κρηταιέες** (also **Κρηταέες**), έων *m.pl.* **Cretans** Call. AR. Plb.
κρητήρ Ion.*m.*: see κρᾱτήρ
Κρητίζω *vb.* [Κρῆτες] (provbl.) **act like a Cretan**
—W.PREP.PHR. **against a Cretan** (i.e. *play someone at his own game, by behaving w. dishonesty or cunning*) Plb. Plu.
Κρητικός *adj.*: see under Κρῆτες
κρητισμός οῦ *m.* (pejor.) **Cretan behaviour** (i.e. dishonesty or cunning) Plu.
κρῖ *n.* [reltd. κρῖθαί] | only nom.acc. | **barley** Hom. hHom.
κριβανίτης ου *masc.adj.* [κρίβανος] **1** (of oxen) **roasted in an oven** Ar.
2 ‖ SB. (w. ἄρτος bread understd.) **oven-baked loaf** Ar.
κρίβανος (also **κλίβανος** Hdt. NT.) ου *m.* **clay container used as an oven** (esp. for baking bread), **kiln, oven** Hdt. Ar. NT.
κριβανωτός οῦ *m.* **oven-baked loaf** Alcm. Ar.
κρίζω *vb.* | ep.aor.2 κρίκον | pf. κέκριγα | **1** (of a chariot-yoke) **creak** Il.
2 (of barbarians or barbarian gods) **shriek** Ar.
κριηδόν *adv.* [κριός] **like a ram** —*ref. to charging at a door* Ar.
κριθαί ῶν (Ion. έων) *f.pl.* [reltd. κρῖ] **barley** (as a grain or a crop in the field) Hom. +; (used to make beer, by non-Greeks) A. Hdt.; (ritually sprinkled over a sacrificial offering) Ar.
—**κριθή** ῆς *f.* **barley-corn** (colloq.ref. to a penis) Ar.
κριθάω contr.*vb.* (of a horse) **be fed on barley** (i.e. be well fed) A.
κρίθην (dial.aor.pass.), **κριθῆναι** (aor.pass.inf.), **κριθήσομαι** (fut.pass.): see κρίνω
κριθίασις εως *f.* [κριθαί] **disease of horses caused by eating too much barley, barley surfeit** (app.ref. to laminitis) X.
κρίθινος η ον *adj.* (of bread) **made from barley** Hippon. X. NT.; (of wine, ref. to beer) X.
κρῑθο-τράγος ον *adj.* [τρώγω] (of birds) **barley-eating** Ar.
κρῑθοφαγία ᾱς *f.* [φαγεῖν] **diet of barley** (as a punishment for Roman soldiers) Plb.
κρίκον (ep.aor.2): see κρίζω
κρίκος ου *m.* **1 ring** (used in linking a wagon-yoke to the pole) Il.; (attached to a sail, to thread ropes through) Hdt.
2 bangle (as jewellery) Arist. Plu.
κρίμα (also perh. **κρῖμα** A.) ατος *n.* [κρίνω] **1 decision, judgement** (on a specific issue) A.(dub.)
2 passing of judgement, judgement, condemnation (of persons, sts. by God) NT.

3 (leg.) **ruling, verdict** (of a tribunal) Plb.; **sentence** (W.GEN. of death) NT.

κρίμνημι vb. [reltd. κρεμάννῡμι] | act. only in cpds. ἀνακρίμνημι, ποτικρίμνημι | mid.pass. κρίμναμαι | ‖ MID.PASS. (of clouds, fig.ref. to grief) **hang** —W.PREP.PHR. *over someone's eyes* A.; (of a suppliant) **hang on, cling** —w. ἐκ + GEN. *to someone's cheeks* E.

κρίμνον ου n. [κρῖ, κρῖθαί] **barley** (as an ingredient in a bowl of gruel) Call.

κριμνώδης ες adj. ‖ NEUT.PL.ADV. like barley —*ref. to snow falling* Ar.

κρίνον ου n. | nom.acc.pl. κρίνεα (Hdt.), also κρίνα (Theoc. NT.) | dat.pl. κρίνεσι (Ar.) | **lily** Hdt. Ar. Theoc. NT.; (ref. to the Egyptian water-lily) Hdt.

κρίνω, Aeol. **κρίννω** vb. | fut. κρινῶ | aor. ἔκρῑνα | pf. κέκρικα ‖ MID.: fut. (sts. w.pass.sens.) κρινοῦμαι | aor. ἐκρινάμην ‖ PASS.: fut. κριθήσομαι | aor. ἐκρίθην, dial. κρίθην (Pi.), ep.3pl. ἔκριθεν (AR.), dial. κρίθεν (Pi.), ep.aor.ptcpl. κρινθείς, inf. κριθῆναι, ep. κρινθήμεναι (AR.) | pf. κέκριμαι ‖ neut.impers.vbl.adj. κριτέον ‖ The sections are grouped as: (1-3) separate, distinguish, divide, (4-5) choose, (6-10) determine (esp. the outcome of a dispute, (11-18) make a decision or judgement, (19-21) give a legal judgement, (22) interrogate. |

1 (of Demeter) **separate** (fr. each other) —*grain and chaff* Il. ‖ PASS. (of persons) separate, part (fr. each other) Pi.; (of fire) be separated off (fr. other elements) Emp.

2 distinguish (fr. each other) —*the true and the false, the noble and the base, good and bad people* Simon. Pl. X. —*truth (fr. falsehood)* Hes.; (of Ares) —*friend (fr. foe)* B.; (mid.) —*opposites* Parm. ‖ PF.PASS.PTCPL.ADJ. (of offspring) distinguished (fr. one another), distinct Hes.; (of powers, honours) Pi.

3 (of a commander) **divide up** —*troops* (W.PREP.PHR. *by tribes and clans*) Il.; **marshal** —*troops* Il.; (intr.) **marshal one's troops** Il.

4 (act. and mid.) **pick out, select, choose** —*persons, animals (for their excellence)* Hom. ‖ PASS. (of an athlete) be marked out or distinguished —W.DAT. *for his talent* Pi. ‖ PF.PASS.PTCPL.ADJ. (of persons or animals) choice, select Od. Hdt.

5 (act. and mid.) **choose** —*persons (for a task)* Hom. A. ‖ PASS. (of persons) be chosen Hom. ‖ PF.PASS.PTCPL.ADJ. (of guards) specially chosen Il.

6 determine (the outcome of an event, esp. a conflict); (of a god; of the sword, i.e. warfare) **decide** —*the outcome (of fighting)* B. E.; (of Ares, W.PREP.PHR. w. his dice) A.; (of charioteers) —*a combat* Od.; (of a commander) **win** —*a battle* Plb.; (intr., of a person's inherited destiny) **decide the outcome** —W.PREP.PHR. *in all actions* Pi. ‖ PASS. (of a combat) be decided Od.; (of an army, meton. for its fortune in combat) E.; (of battles) —W.DAT. *by men's hearts (rather than bodies)* X.

7 decide (a dispute or legal issue); (of a judge or sim.) **decide, settle, judge** —*disputes* Od.; **give** —W.COGN.ACC. *crooked judgements, straight judgement, or sim.* Il. Hes. A. ‖ PASS. (of a trial) be decided A.

8 ‖ PASS. (of the valour of mortals) be determined —W.PREP.PHR. *by the gods* Pi. ‖ PF.PASS. (of a rule of conduct) have been determined, be fixed or set —W.DAT. *for mortals* (w. πρός + GEN. *by a god*) Thgn.; (of the end of mortals' lives) Pi.; (of a person's judgement) Thgn. ‖ PF.PASS.PTCPL.ADJ. (of a wind, coming fr. Zeus) fixed or set (i.e. settled or steady) Il.; (of labours) decided (i.e. ended) Pi.

9 ‖ MID. arrange a division or settlement; (of the gods) **come to a settlement** —W.DAT. w. *the Titans* (W.GEN. *over privileges*) Hes.; (of gods and mortals, w. each other) Hes.

10 ‖ MID. range oneself on the opposite side (to another), **contend** (in battle) Hom.; **dispute** (in argument) Ar. —W.DAT. w. *someone* E. —W.PREP.PHR. *over sthg.* Hdt. —(W.DAT. *at law, i.e. go to arbitration*) Th.

11 make a decision or **judgement** Hdt. Trag. Th. +; **make** —W.COGN.ACC. *a decision that is righteous* A.

12 judge, consider —W.COMPL.CL. *that sthg. is the case* Pi. —W.ACC. + INF. A. Hdt. + —W.INDIR.Q. *what or whether sthg. is the case* Hdt. Trag. + —*someone or sthg.* (W.PREDIC.ADJ. *as such and such*) S. E. Th. + ‖ PASS. (of persons or things) be judged —W.PREDIC.ADJ. *as such and such* Hdt. S. Th. +

13 form a judgement about, **judge** —*things, circumstances* S. E. Th. + —*an expectation* (W.PREP.PHR. *before the event, i.e. prejudge the outcome*) S.

14 interpret —*bird-omens* Hes. —*dreams* A. Hdt. E.; **judge** (fr. dreams) —W.INDIR.Q. *what events are destined to happen* A. —W.ACC. + INF. *that sthg. will be the case* A. ‖ MID. **interpret, expound** —*dreams* Il.

15 rank —*competitors, their speed and strength* B. E.; decide the result of, **judge** —*a competition* Ar. ‖ PASS. (of women) be judged —W.ACC. *in terms of beauty* Alc.; (of a competition) E.

16 adjudge, assign —*victory (in a contest,* W.DAT. *to someone)* S. ‖ PASS. (of a happy homecoming) be assigned or awarded —W.DAT. *to someone* Pi.

17 judge (by an explicit criterion); **judge, evaluate** —*someone* (w. πρός + ACC. *in relation to oneself*) D. —*happiness (in relation to money)* Isoc. ‖ PASS. (of things) be judged —w. πρός + ACC. *in relation to other things* Pl.

18 judge in favour of, **favour, choose, prefer** —*a candidate or competitor* Hdt. E. Ar. —*an argument or proposal* E. X. —*prosperity that attracts no envy* A. —*sthg.* (w. πρό + GEN. *ahead of sthg. else*) Pl. ‖ PASS. (of a person) be preferred or favoured Hdt.

19 (leg.) **be judge, give judgement** (freq. W.ACC. *in a lawsuit*) A. Hdt. E. Th. +

20 bring to trial —*someone* (sts. W.GEN. or περί + GEN. *on a particular charge*) Th. Att.orats. + ‖ PASS. be brought to trial Th. Att.orats. +

21 pass judgement on, judge —*someone* Th. D. NT. ‖ PASS. have judgement passed on one, be judged NT.; (specif.) receive a verdict (W.PREDIC.ADJ. *of equal votes*, i.e. equally for and against) A.; be condemned —W.INF. *to be put to death* D.

22 (gener.) **question, interrogate** —*someone* S.

κριοκοπέω contr.vb. [κριός, κόπτω] **attack** (W.ACC. a tower) **with a battering-ram** Plb.

κριο-πρόσωπος ον adj. [πρόσωπον] (of statues of an Egyptian god identified w. Zeus) **ram-faced** Hdt.

κριός οῦ m. **1 male sheep, ram** Od. Thgn. Pi. Hdt. +
2 battering-ram X. Plb. Plu.
3 (fig., w. play on both senses, ref. to a rejected lover battering a woman's door) **butting ram** Thphr.

Κρῖσα (also **Κρίσα** Pi.), Ion. **Κρίση** (hHom.), ης (dial. ᾱς) f. —also **Κίρρα** ᾱς f. **Krisa** or **Kirrha** (town SW. of Delphi, esp. assoc.w. the Pythian games) Il. hHom. Pi. B. S. +

—**Κίρρᾱθεν** adv. **from Kirrha** Pi.

—**Κρισαῖος** (also **Κρισαῖος** Pi.) ᾱ ον adj. —also **Κιρραῖος** ᾱ ον adj. (of the region, plain, hill, vales, gulf) **of Krisa** or

Kirrha Pi. Hdt. S. Th. Att.orats. ‖ MASC.PL.SB. people of Krisa or Kirrha hHom. Aeschin. D. Plu.

κρίσις εως (Ion. ιος) *f.* [κρίνω] | Ion.dat.sg. κρίσῑ | **1 choice, selection** (of persons, for political office) Arist. **2 decision, conclusion, outcome** (of a war) Th. Plb. **3 decision, judgement, verdict** (of gods or persons, sts. W.GEN. or PREP.PHR. about sthg.) A. Pi.*fr.* B.(cj.) Parm. Hdt. Isoc. +; (prep.phr.) κατὰ κρίσιν *by choice, advisedly* Plb. **4** (leg.) **settlement** (of a dispute), **arbitration** Th. **5 trial** (by jury or sim.) Th. Att.orats. Pl. + **6 legal judgement, verdict** Th. Att.orats. +; (phr.) ἡμέρα κρίσεως *day of judgement* NT. **7 judging, assessment, test** (of persons or things competing or compared w. each other) Hdt. S. E. Ar. + **8 trial** (of strength or skill); **test, trial** (W.GEN. or PREP.PHR. of or in athletic contests) Pi.; (W.GEN. of the foot-race) S.; (of archery) S.; (of hands, feet, horses, in the games) Call. **9 adjudication, award** (W.GEN. of the arms of Achilles) Pl.; (as title of a play by Aeschylus) Arist.

κρισσός οῦ *m.* **varicose vein** (in a horse's leg) X.

κριτέον (neut.impers.vbl.adj.): see κρίνω

κριτήριον ου *n.* [κριτής] **1 means of judging or evaluating, criterion** Pl. Arist. **2 means of deciding a legal case, legal procedure** Pl. **3 court of arbitration, tribunal** (for disputes betw. countries) Plb.

κριτής οῦ *m.* [κρίνω] **1** (gener.) **one who gives a judgement or assessment** (of persons or things), **judge, assessor, arbiter** A. Hdt. E. Th. Att.orats. + **2 one who decides on the winner** (of a competition), **judge, umpire** S. Ar. Isoc. +; (specif., of a dramatic or musical competition) Ar. Att.orats. Pl. + **3** (leg.) **person with judicial authority, judge** NT. Plu.; (specif., ref. to the early leaders of the Jewish people) NT. **4 interpreter** (of dreams, inspired utterances) A. Pl. **5 critic** (of literary works) Plb. **6 supporter, endorser** (of a theory) Arist.

Κριτίᾱς ου *m.* **Critias** (Athenian elegiac poet and dramatist, one of the Thirty Tyrants, associate of Socrates, c.460–403 BC) Att.orats. Pl. X. Arist. Plu.

κριτικός ή όν *adj.* **1 relating to judging or evaluating**; (of a skill, a branch of intellectual science) **based on judgement, evaluative** Pl.; (of understanding, as a faculty) Arist. **2** (of persons, their understanding) **skilled in judgement or evaluation** (W.GEN. of sthg.) Arist. **3 relating to making legal judgements**; (of an office) **judicial** (opp. deliberative) Arist. **4** ‖ MASC.SB. app., **scholar** Plb.

κριτός ή όν *adj.* **1** (of warriors, umpires) **specially chosen, select, choice** Hom. B.; (of a bride, a spoil of war) S. **2** (of a person, a people) **distinguished** Pi.

κροαίνω *vb.* [reltd. κρούω] (of a galloping horse) **stamp, thud** Il.

κροκάλαι ῶν *f.pl.* **pebbles** (on a beach); (collectv.) **shingle, seashore** E.

κρόκεος ᾱ ον *adj.* [κρόκος] **1** (of a garment) **saffron-coloured** Pi.(v.l. κροκόεις) E. **2** (of petals) **of the crocus** E.

κρόκη ης, dial. **κρόκᾱ** ᾱς *f.* [κρέκω] | also acc.sg. κρόκα (Hes.) | **1** (collectv.) **threads woven horizontally between the vertical warp-threads of a web, weft** Hes. Carm.Pop. Hdt. Pl. Arist. + **2 thread** (ref. to a single strand) Plu. ‖ PL. **threads** (of a worn-out garment) E.*satyr.fr.* **3** (collectv., ref. to the finished products) **weaving, woven cloth** Ar. ‖ PL. (specif.) woven cloaks Pi.; woven cloths S.

κροκήιος η ον *ep.Ion.adj.* [κρόκος] (of the flower) **of the crocus** hHom.

κροκίζω *vb.* (of the colour and odour of a kind of marble, when rubbed) **resemble saffron** Plu.

κρόκινος η ον *adj.* (of a perfumed ointment) **made from saffron** Plb.

κροκό-βαπτος ον *adj.* [βαπτός] (of a Persian slipper) **saffron-dyed** A.

κροκο-βαφής ές *adj.* [βάπτω] (of the blood of a terrified person) **saffron-dyed** (i.e. turned yellow by fear, like his complexion) A.

κροκόδειλος (or perh. **κροκόδῑλος**), also **κερκύδῑλος** (Hippon.), ου *m.* **1 lizard** Hippon. Hdt. **2 crocodile** Hdt.

κροκόεις εσσα εν *adj.* [κρόκος] (of garments) **saffron-coloured** Sapph. E.; (of ivy, its fruit) Theoc. ‖ NEUT.PL.SB. saffron garments Ar. | see also κρόκεος 1

κροκό-πεπλος ον *adj.* [πέπλος] (of Dawn) **with saffron-coloured robe** Il.; (of demigoddesses) Hes. Alcm.

κρόκος ου *m.* **1 crocus** Il. hHom. Pi.*fr.* S. Hellenist.poet. **2 saffron** (ref. to a spice, of orange-yellow colour, derived fr. the flower of the crocus, used as a dye) Ar.; (meton., ref. to a dyed robe) A.

κροκύς ύδος *f.* [reltd. κρόκη] **flock of wool** (plucked fr. a cloak) Hdt. Thphr. Plu.

κροκώδης ες *adj.* [κρόκη] (of cross-threads, fig.ref. to the composition of a person's temperament) **weft-like** (i.e. more soft or relaxed than one composed of the tauter warp-threads) Pl.

κροκωτίδιον ου *n.* [dimin. κροκωτός] **fancy saffron gown** Ar.

κροκωτός ή όν *adj.* [κρόκος] **1** (of Herakles' swaddling-clothes) **saffron-coloured** Pi. **2** ‖ MASC.SB. **saffron gown** (worn by women) Ar.; (worn by Dionysus) Ar.

κροκωτο-φορέω *contr.vb.* **wear a saffron gown** Ar.

κρόμμυον, ep. **κρόμυον**, ου *n.* **onion** Hom. Hdt. Ar. X. Plu.

κρομμυ-οξυρεγμίᾱ ᾱς *f.* [ὀξύς, ἐρεύγομαι] **acidic belching caused by eating onions, sour onion belch** Ar.

Κρόνος ου *m.* **1 Kronos** (a Titan, son of Gaia and Ouranos, whom he castrated w. a sickle; ruler of the gods, overthrown by his son Zeus; his reign provbl. for a golden or very remote age) Hom. + **2** (pejor., ref. to a person) **Kronos, Old Fogey** Ar. Pl.; (specif., as nickname of the philosopher Diodorus) Call.*epigr.* **3 Saturn** (ref. to the Roman god) Plb. Plu. **4 Saturn** (ref. to the planet) Arist.

—**Κρονίδης** ου (ep. ᾱο, Ion. εω), dial. **Κρονίδᾱς**, Aeol. **Κρονίδαις**, ᾱ *m.* **1 son of Kronos** (ref. to Zeus) Hom. Hes. Eleg. Lyr. Hdt.(oracle) E. + **2** ‖ PL. **sons of Kronos** (ref. to Zeus, Poseidon, Hades) Call.

—**Κρονίων** ωνος (also ονος) *m.* | sts. ῑ *metri grat.* | **son of Kronos** (ref. to Zeus) Hom. Hes. hHom. Tyrt. Pi. Theoc.

—**Κρόνιος** ᾱ (Ion. η) ον *adj.* **1 of or relating to Kronos**; (of a sickle) **of Kronos** (used to castrate Ouranos) Call.; (of a hill, nr. Olympia) Pi.; (of a sea, ref. to the Adriatic) AR. ‖ NEUT.SB. **hill of Kronos** (nr. Olympia) Pi. X. **2** (of laws) **of Kronos** (i.e. very old) Call. ‖ NEUT.PL.SB. (pejor.) **antediluvian attitudes** Ar. **3** ‖ MASC.SB. **son of Kronos** (ref. to Zeus) A. Pi. B. E.; (ref. to Poseidon) Pi.; (ref. to Pan) E.

κρούω

4 ‖ MASC.SB. Kronios (as the name of a month, equiv. to Hekatombaion, in which the festival of Kronos was celebrated) Plu.
—**Κρόνια** ων *n.pl.* **festival of Kronos** D.; (at Rome) **Saturnalia** Plu.
—**Κρονιάδες** ων *f.pl.* (at Rome) **Saturnalia** Plu.
—**Κρονικός** ή όν *adj.* **1** (of equality of rights) **existing in the age of Kronos** Plu.
2 (of the mental blindness of old men) **prehistoric, antediluvian** Ar.; (of a poet's subjects) **hoary, outdated** Pl.
3 (of the Roman festival) **of the Saturnalia** Plu.

κρόσσαι ῶν (ep. ἄων) *f.pl.* **1** structures forming part of a fortified wall; perh. **supporting courses** (for battlements) Il.
2 stepped sides, **steps** (of a pyramid) Hdt.

κροσσωτός ή όν *adj.* (of a general's cloak) **fringed with tassels, tasselled** Plu.

κροταλίζω *vb.* [κρόταλον] **1** (of women) **play the castanets** Hdt.
2 make (sthg.) **rattle**; (of galloping horses) **rattle along** —*empty chariots* Il.

κρόταλον (also **κόρταλον** E.*fr.*, cj.) ου *n.* [reltd. κρότος] **1** ‖ PL. **clappers, castanets** (esp. as used in the rites of Cybele) hHom. Sapph. Pi.*fr.* Hdt. E. Lyr.adesp. Plu.
2 (fig., ref. to a person) **chatterbox, noisy prattler** E.*Cyc.* Ar.

κρόταφος ου *m.* **1** (usu.pl.) side of the forehead, **temple** Hom. Hes. Anacr. Pi.*fr.* Hdt. E. +
2 brow (of a mountain) B. ‖ PL. **mountain peaks** A.

κροτέω *contr.vb.* [κρότος] **1** make a percussive noise (by causing things to strike against each other); (of horses) cause to rattle (over the ground), **rattle along** —*empty chariots* Il. hHom.; (of a shipwrecked sailor) **gnash together, chatter** —*his teeth* Hippon. ‖ PASS. (of the bit of a champing horse) be made to rattle, clank AR.
2 strike one's hands together (in accompaniment to music or singing); **clap** —*one's hands* Hdt.; (intr.) —W.DAT. *w. one's hands* Thphr.
3 clap (in applause); **clap** —*one's hands* X.; (intr.) **clap, applaud** Pl. X. D. Thphr. Plu. —W.ACC. *a person* Plu. ‖ PASS. (of a person, a proposal) **be applauded** Plb. Plu.
4 (pejor., of a woman) **make a clatter, play percussion** —W.DAT. *w. potsherds* Ar.
5 strike (an object, to make a noise); **beat, drum on** —*a cauldron* (*in mourning*) Hdt.; **strum** —*a lyre* Theoc.
6 strike (without the explicit purpose of making a noise); **beat** —*one's sides* (W.DAT. *w. one's elbows, in imitation of a fighting-cock*) D.; (of a Bacchant) —*the ground* (*w. a thyrsos*) E.; (of singers or dancers) —*the ground* (*w. their feet*) Pi.*fr.* AR.(v.l. κρούω); (of horses, w. their hooves) Plu.
7 beat metal ‖ PASS. (of a foundation of gold, fig.ref. to the subject matter of a song) **be wrought** Pi.*fr.*; (fig., of a person) —w. ἐκ + GEN. *fr.* **trickery** Theoc.

κρότημα ατος *n.* app., object of beaten metal; (fig. and pejor., ref. to Odysseus, W.ADJ. **wily**) **piece of work** E.

κροτησμός οῦ *m.* **beating, pounding** (on a shield, by an enemy) A.

κροτητός ή όν *adj.* **1** (of chariots) **rattling** S.
2 (of a person's head) **beaten** (by blows) A.

κρότος ου *m.* **1** percussive noise (made by striking one thing against another); **beating, stamping** (of feet, in a dance) E. Ar.
2 clapping (of hands, in accompaniment to music, singing or dancing) Ar.; (in applause) Pl. X. D. Men. Plb. Plu.
3 clacking (W.GEN. of castanets) E.*fr.*
4 clanging (of weapons, by troops celebrating victory) Plu.

κροτών ῶνος *m.* a kind of parasitic insect, **tick** Men.

κροῦμα ατος *n.* [κρούω] **1 blow** (to the strings of a musical instrument, w. the fingers or a plectrum) ‖ PL. **notes** (of a lyre) Ar.(quot. E.) Pl.
2 (w. sexual connot.) **knocking, banging** Ar.

κρουνός οῦ *m.* [perh.reltd. κρήνη] **1 spring** (as the source of a stream) Il. Pi. Men.
2 stream, jet (of water) S.; (of blood, fr. a wound) E.; (of fire, fr. a volcano) Pi.; (fig.) **torrent** (of words) Ar.

κρουνο-χυτρο-ληραῖον ου *n.* [χύτρος, λῆρος] (ref. to a person, app. a teetotaller) **streaming bucket of nonsense** Ar.

κρούνωμα ατος *n.* (collectv.) **springs** or **streams** (of water) Emp.

κρουσιδημέω *contr.vb.* [κρούω, δῆμος] (fig., of a politician, seen as a trader who 'knocks' the scales or a measuring-jar, i.e. tampers w. them in some way) **give a short measure to the people** Ar.

κροῦσις εως *f.* **1 striking** (of a rider's foot against a horse's flanks, to spur it on) Plu.
2 knocking (of arms and armour, against each other, while being transported) Plu.
3 striking (of lyre-strings, w. a plectrum) Plu. ‖ PL. (gener.) **musical performance** (of aulos-players) Plb.
4 punchy point-making (as a technique in oratory) Ar.

κρουσματικός ή όν *adj.* [κροῦμα] of the kind produced by striking a stringed instrument; (fig., of words) **merely musical** (opp. articulate or meaningful) Plb.

κρουστικός ή όν *adj.* [κρούω] (of a politician) **skilled in punchy point-making** Ar.

κρουφάδᾱν *Boeot.adv.*, **κρούφιος** *Boeot.adj.*: see κρυφηδόν, κρύφιος

κρούω *vb.* **1 strike** (w. an object); (of a rider) **strike** —*the flanks of chariot-horses* (*w. a whip*) E.*fr.*; (of a trainer) —*a horse* (W.DAT. *w. a stick*) X.; (of a seer, in a rite of purification) —*a person* (*w. laurel*) Call.; (of a person) —*the hilt of his sword* (*w. his hand*) Plu.
2 (w. aggressive connot.) **strike, kick** —*a person, an animal* (W.DAT. *w. one's leg, foot*) Ar. AR.; **swat** —*someone* (*envisaged as a gadfly*) Pl.; (of a boxer) **punch** —*an opponent* Pl.; (fig., of disputants) **pummel** —*arguments* (W.DAT. *w. other arguments*) Pl.
3 strike (one thing against another, so as to make a noise); (of soldiers, persons performing a war-dance) **strike, beat** —*their shields* (W.DAT. *w. other weapons*) X. Plu.; **clash together** —*their shields, weapons* X. Plu. ‖ PASS. (of weapons) be knocked (accidentally) —W.PREP.PHR. *against each other* Th.
4 strike together, clap —*one's hands* E.
5 strike —*lyre-strings* (W.DAT. *w. a plectrum*) Pl.; (gener., of an aulos-player) **make music** Carm.Pop.
6 strike —*a bronze pot* (*so as to make it ring*) Pl.; (fig.) **tap** (i.e. test by tapping) —*qualities and entities* (*envisaged as pots*) Pl.
7 knock on —*a door* E.*fr.* Ar. Pl. X. NT.; (fig., w. sexual connot.) Ar.; (fig., of a personif. turd, impatient to be let out through the anus) Ar.; (intr.) **knock** (on a door) NT. ‖ PASS. (of a door) be knocked on Pl.
8 cause (sthg.) to strike (against sthg.); **strike** —*a torch* (*against the ground*) E.; (of a dancer) **stamp, beat** —*one's foot* E. —(w. ἐν + DAT. *on the ground*) E.
9 strike, stamp upon, beat —*the ground* (W.DAT. *w. one's foot*) Plu.; (of a horse) AR. | see also κροτέω 6
10 ‖ MID. (of sailors, W.ADVBL.ACC. πρύμναν **sternwards**) **row astern, back water** Th. Plu.; (act.) Plb. | see also ἀνακρούω 2

κρύβδα *adv.* [κρύπτω] **1 secretly, in secret** Pi.; (quasi-adjl., of a gift) given secretly, **secret** A.
2 (as prep.) **without the knowledge** —W.GEN. *of someone* Il.
κρύβδην, dial. **κρύβδᾱν** *adv.* **1 secretly, in secret** Od. Lys. Ar. Pl. Theoc.; (ref. to voting) Att.orats. Pl.; (quasi-adjl., of a vote) cast secretly, **secret** Lys. D.
2 (as prep.) **without the knowledge** —W.GEN. *of someone* Pi.
κρυερός ά (Ion. ή) όν (also ός όν Hes.) *adj.* [κρύος] **1** (of frost) **ice-cold, chilly** Alc.; (of a city) Ar. || NEUT.PL.SB. icy coldness Ar.
2 (fig., of Hades) **chill, chilling** Hes.; (of warfare, panic, lamentation, ruin, or sim.) Hom. Hes. Ar. Plu.(quot.epigr.); (of a king's command) AR.
κρῡμός οῦ *m.* **1 freezing weather, icy cold, frost** Hdt. Call. Bion; (concr.) **frozen ground** Hdt.
2 (medic.) abnormal state of bodily coldness, **chill** Call.
κρυόεις εσσα εν *adj.* (fig., of Tartaros) **chill, chilling** Hes.; (of Rout, panic, battle, death, disaster) Il. Hes. Lyr.; (of an oracle) Pi.; (of the Black Sea) AR. | see also ὀκρυόεις
κρύος εος (ους) *n.* **1 freezing weather, icy cold, frost** Hes. Bion Plu.
2 (fig.) **icy sting** (of a lash) A.; **chill** (of terror) A.
3 (medic.) abnormal state of bodily coldness, **chill** Plu.
κρυπτάδιος ᾱ (Ion. η) ον (also ος ον A.) *adj.* [κρύπτω] (of lovemaking) **secret** Il. Hes. Mimn.; (of plots) AR.; (of fighting) **stealthy** A. || NEUT.PL.SB. secret thoughts (of Zeus) Il.
κρυπτείᾱ ᾱς *f.* **secret service** (ref. to a Spartan institution by which young men infiltrated and policed the Helots) Pl. Plu.
κρυπτεύω *vb.* **1** (of the gods) **conceal** —*the slow pace of time* (*i.e. delay their vengeance, to catch wrongdoers unawares*) E.
2 (intr., of soldiers) **lie hidden** X.
3 || PASS. (of a person) be ambushed E.
κρυπτήριον ου *n.* place where a prisoner is hidden away, **dungeon** E.*fr.*(cj.)
κρυπτός ή (dial. ᾱ́) όν *adj.* **1 hidden from sight**; (of persons or things) **hidden, concealed** Hdt. E. Ar. X. AR.; (w. ἀπό + GEN. fr. someone) E.
2 hidden from knowledge; (of things, circumstances, activities) **secret** Il. Hes.*fr.*(cj.) Pi. E. Call. NT.; **kept secret** (W.GEN. fr. someone) E.; (prep.phr.) ἐν (τῷ) κρυπτῷ *in secret* NT. || NEUT.SB. secretiveness, lack of transparency (of the Spartan political system) Th. || NEUT.PL.SB. secrets E. Men.
3 (quasi-advbl., of a person arriving) **in secret** E.
4 || MASC.PL.SB. officials acting clandestinely, **secret police** Pl.
5 (of a person's boyhood) **secluded** (W.GEN. fr. sorrows) S.
6 (of footsteps) **stealthy, furtive** E.
7 (of words with hidden meaning, **cryptic, obscure** E.; with hidden intentions, **deceptive** S.
κρύπτω *vb.* | 3sg.iteratv.impf. κρύπτεσκε, also κρύπτασκε | fut. κρύψω | aor. ἔκρυψα, ep. κρύψα || PASS.: fut. κρυφήσομαι | aor. ἐκρύφθην, ep. κρύφθην, ep.3pl. ἔκρυφθεν (E.) | aor.2 ἐκρύφην, also ἐκρύβην (NT.), ptcpl. κρυφείς | pf. κέκρυμμαι, Ion.3pl. κεκρύφαται, inf. κεκρύφθαι |
1 hide from sight; hide, conceal —*persons or things* Hom. + —(W.ACC. *fr. someone*) hHom. Thgn.; (also mid.) S. || MID. **conceal oneself, hide** Heraclit. S. E. || PASS. (of persons or things) be hidden from sight Hes. +
2 remove from sight (so as to get rid of); (of Zeus) **put away** —*a race of mortals* (*by destroying them*) Hes.; (of Hera) —*the lame Hephaistos* (*by throwing him fr. heaven*) Il.
3 cause to disappear (beneath the earth); (of Zeus) **hide away, entomb** —*Amphiaraos and his chariot* (*by opening up the earth beneath them*) Pi. —*Prometheus* (*under a fall of rock*) A.; (of a chasm in the earth, created by Poseidon) —*Erekhtheus* E. || PASS. (of the Titans, Typhon, Amphiaraos) be hidden away (beneath the earth) Hes. Hdt. S.
4 bury, inter —*a person, a body* (*usu.* W.DAT. or PREP.PHR. *beneath the earth, in a tomb, or sim.*) Pi. Hdt. S. E. Th. || PASS. (of persons, animals) be buried —W.DAT. *in the ground* Hdt. S. E. || PF.PASS.PTCPL. (of a corpse) buried S.
5 put underground, **bury** —*a sword* S. E.; (of a boar, when rooting for food) —*its snout* (W.PREP.PHR. *beneath the earth*) Stesich.
6 (of things) provide concealment; (of soil) **conceal, cover** —*buried men* A.; (of soldiers' greaves) —*pegs* (*on which they are hung*) Alc.
7 cover up for protection; **cover, protect** —*someone* (W.DAT. *w. a shield*) Il. —*one's head* (*w. a helmet*) Il. —*one's body* (*w. armour*) E. || PASS. be hidden —W.PREP.PHR. *by one's shield* Il.
8 cover up (w. clothing); **cover, shroud, envelop** —*a person, a corpse, someone's* (*or one's own*) *head or face* (*usu.* W.DAT. *w. a garment*) A. E. —*someone's feet* (W.DAT. *in fur boots*) Hippon. || MID. **cover** —*one's head* (W.DAT. *w. a veil*) S. || PASS. (of a coward) be concealed —W.PREP.PHR. *under a cloak* S.; (of a sick man) —*inside blankets* E.
9 keep from being known; **conceal, keep secret** —*facts, news, circumstances* Od. + —(W.ACC. *fr. someone*) Trag. Lys. Ar.; **keep** (W.ACC. someone) **uninformed** (about sthg.) E.
|| MID. **conceal** —*the truth* S. || PASS. (of things) be kept secret Od. Hdt. S.*Ichn.* E. + —w. ἀπό + GEN. *fr. others* Od.
|| PF.PASS.PTCPL.ADJ. (of a prayer to a god, questions put to seers) secret S. E.; (of drugs) E.; (of words) with hidden meaning Thgn.
10 (wkr.sens., of gods) **fail to expose** —*criminal actions* S.
11 (app.intr.) hide oneself; (of Argos' eyes) **close** E.(dub.)
κρυστάλλινος η ον *adj.* [κρύσταλλος] (of writing-tablets) **made from rock-crystal** Plu.
κρυσταλλό-πηκτος ον *adj.* [πηκτός] (of winds) **freezing, icy** E.
κρυσταλλο-πήξ πῆγος *masc.fem.adj.* (of a river) **frozen solid with ice** A.
κρύσταλλος ου *m.* **1 ice** Hom. Hdt. S.*satyr.fr.* Th. Pl. Arist. +
2 rock-crystal (as exemplifying that which is bright) Theoc.
κρυφᾷ *dial.adv.*: see κρυφῇ
κρύφα *adv.* [κρύπτω] **1 secretly, in secret** Pi. Th. X. Call. Plu.
2 (as prep.) **without the knowledge** —W.GEN. *of someone* Th. Plu.
κρυφαῖος ᾱ ον (also ος ον E.*fr.*) *adj.* [κρύφα, κρυφῇ] **1 hidden from sight**; (of a corpse) **hidden, concealed** E.*fr.*; (of wealth) Pi.; (of a sword) S.; (of channels in the body, ref. to veins) Pl.
2 hidden from knowledge; (of sorrow, a sickness, dances) **hidden, secret, private** A. E.; (of activities) **secret, covert, clandestine** A. E. Pl. X. Plu.; (prep.phr.) ἐν τῷ κρυφαίῳ *in secret* NT.
—**κρυφαῖα** *neut.pl.adv.* **secretly, covertly** E.
—**κρυφαίως** *adv.* **secretly, covertly** A. S.*Ichn.*(cj.) Plu.
κρυφείς (aor.2 pass.ptcpl.): see κρύπτω
κρυφῇ, dial. **κρυφᾷ** *adv.* **secretly** Pi. S. X.
κρυφηδόν *adv.* —also **κρουφάδᾱν** Boeot.*adv.* **secretly** Od. Corinn.
κρύφιος, Boeot. **κρούφιος**, ᾱ ον (also ος ον E. Th.) *adj.*
1 hidden from sight; (of a serpent) **hidden, concealed** S.; (of the submerged part of a structure) Th.
2 hidden from knowledge; (of feelings, a pregnancy) **hidden, secret, covert** Pi. E.; (of lovers' talk, a sexual union, a vote) Hes. Lyr. S. E.

3 (quasi-advbl., of a person arriving, being equipped w. a sword, a ship being moored) **in secret, secretly** E.

κρυφός οῦ *m.* **1 concealment, secrecy** Pi.
2 perh., that which covers, **covering** Emp.

κρυψί-νους ουν *adj.* [νόος] hiding one's true feelings or intentions, **dissembling, insincere** X.

κρύψις εως *f.* **hiding, concealment** (of persons or things) E. Arist. Plb. Plu.

κρωβύλος ου *m.* **1** knot of hair on the top of the head, **top-knot** (pinned w. a brooch, as an old Athenian fashion) Th.
2 tuft (on a leather helmet, as worn by a foreign tribe) X.

κρώζω *vb.* | aor. ἔκρωξα | **1** (of a crow or raven) **caw** Hes. Ar. —w.neut.acc. or dir.sp. *sthg.* Ar. Call.*epigr.*; (of a crane) Ar.
2 (pejor., of a person, compared to an unknown bird) **squawk, screech** or **croak** Hippon.; (of a person) —w.acc. *sthg.* Ar.

κρωσσός οῦ *m.* **1 bucket, pail** (for liquids, esp. water) S. E. Theoc.
2 pitcher or **jar** (for unguents) Plu.
3 urn (for cremated bones) Mosch.

κτάμεναι, κτάμενος (ep.athem.aor.inf. and mid.ptcpl.), **κτανεῖν** (aor.2 inf.), **κτανέω** (ep.fut.), **κτάνον** (ep.aor.2): see κτείνω

κτάομαι mid.contr.*vb.* | fut. κτήσομαι | aor. ἐκτησάμην, ep. κτησάμην | pf. κέκτημαι, also ἔκτημαι, Ion.3pl. ἐκτέαται, inf. κεκτῆσθαι, also ἔκτησθαι, subj. κέκτωμαι, opt. κεκτήμην | plpf. ἐκεκτήμην, also ἐκτήμην | fut.pf. κεκτήσομαι, also ἐκτήσομαι || pass.: aor. ἐκτήθην, ptcpl. κτηθείς || neut.impers.vbl.adj. κτητέον |
1 acquire (material things); **get, gain, obtain** —*land, money, objects, slaves, or sim.* Hom. + || statv.pf., plpf., fut.pf. **possess, have** —*material things* Il. + || masc. or fem. ptcpl.sb. **owner, master or mistress** (of a slave) Ar. Pl. Men. || pass. (of things) be acquired Th.; (of a person, as a slave) E.
2 acquire (non-material things); **get, gain, obtain** —*power, skill, courage, or sim.* S. E. Th. +; **win** —*gratitude, goodwill, or sim.* S. E. +; **make** —*someone's mind* (w.predic.adj. *well-disposed*) S. || statv.pf., plpf., fut.pf. **possess, have** —*power, moral qualities, or sim.* E. Th. + —*a certain lifestyle* Semon. E.
3 acquire (persons); **get, gain, win** —*a wife* Od. —*a woman* (as wife) E. —*friends, allies* S. E. Th. —*someone* (w.predic.sb. or adj. as a *master, friend, enemy, or sim.*) E. X.; **have** —*children* (w. ἐκ + gen. by a particular woman) S. E. || statv.pf., plpf., fut.pf. **have** —*friends, allies, enemies* E. And. Pl. + —*someone* (w.predic.adj. *as an ally, friend, husband, slave*) E. —*the gods* (as enemies) E. || masc.ptcpl.sb. **possessor, owner** (of a wife, ref. to a husband) A. E.
4 bring upon oneself (sthg. unfavourable); **incur, provoke** —*anger, hostility, censure, calamity, or sim.* S. E. Th. + || statv.pf. or fut.pf. **have** —*the taint of pollution, bloodguilt, troubles* A. E.
5 acquire, earn, win —*a bad reputation* E. —(ellipt., a *reputation for*) *impiety, indifference* S. E. —(the prize for) *beauty* E. || statv.pf. or fut.pf. **have** —*a certain reputation* E. —(ellipt., a reputation for) *cowardice* E.

κτᾶσθαι (ep.athem.aor.mid.inf.): see κτείνω

κτέανα ων *n.pl.* [reltd. κτέατα] **1 possessions, goods, property** (of a person or city) Hes. Eleg. A. Pi. E. AR. Theoc.; (ref. to personal attributes, such as youth and a sound mind) Thgn.
2 || sg. **possession** (ref. to a lyre) Pi. S.*Ichn.*

κτέατα των *ep.n.pl.* [κτάομαι] | dat.pl. κτεάτεσσι | **possessions, goods, property** Hom. Thgn. Pi. AR. Theoc.

κτεάτειρα ᾱς *f.* (ref. to Night) **winner** (w.gen. of great glories) A. [also interpr. as *possessor* of great ornaments, i.e. the moon and stars]

κτεατίζω *ep.vb.* | aor. κτεάτισσα || mid.: 3sg.pf. ἐκτεάτισμαι, 3sg.plpf. ἐκτεάτιστο | **1 acquire, gain, obtain** —*material things* Od. Theoc.(also mid.) —*a woman* (as a spoil of war) Il. || pf.plpf.mid. **have acquired for oneself, possess** —*material things* hHom. Call.
2 make one's own —*a piece of land* (by cultivating it) Od.
3 || mid. **bring under one's control, conquer** —*tribes* AR.

κτείνω *vb.* | ep.subj. κτείνωμι | iteratv.impf. κτείνεσκον | fut. κτενῶ, ep. κτενέω, also κτανέω (dub.) | aor. ἔκτεινα, Aeol.ptcpl. κτένναις | aor.2 ep. κτάνον, ep. κτανῶν, inf. κτανεῖν | ep.athem.aor.: 3sg. ἔκτα, also ἔκτᾱ (E.), 1pl. ἔκταμεν, 3pl. ἔκταν, inf. κτάμεναι, 1pl.subj. κτέωμεν || mid.: ep.athem. aor.inf. (w.pass.sens.) κτάσθαι, ptcpl. κτάμενος || pass.: ep.3pl.athem.aor. ἔκταθεν |
1 kill —*persons or animals* Hom. + || pass. (of persons or animals) **be killed** Hom. +
2 (intr., of an illness) **prove fatal** Th.
3 (of boldness of spirit) **be responsible for the death of, kill** —*a lion* Il.; (of love) —*a person* Theoc.

κτείς κτενός *m.* [perh.reltd. πέκω] **1 comb** (for the hair) Pi.*fr.* Call. Plu.
2 || pl. **fingers** (of the hand) A.

κτενίζω *vb.* | pf.pass. ἐκτένισμαι | **1** || mid. **comb** —*one's hair* Hdt. || pass. (of hair) **be combed** Semon.
2 groom —*a horse's coat* (w.dat. w. a horse-comb) E.

κτενισμός οῦ *m.* **combing** (of a woman's hair) E.

κτενῶ (fut.): see κτείνω

κτέρεα έων *ep.n.pl.* [perh.reltd. κτέατα] | dat. κτερέεσσι | **gifts for the dead, funeral honours** (ref. to offerings or rites) Hom. AR. Mosch.; (specif.) **winding-sheets, shroud** AR.
—**κτέρας** *ep.n.sg.* | only nom.acc. | **gift** or **possession** Il. AR.

κτερεΐζω *vb.* | aor. ἐκτερέιξα | **perform funeral rites for** —*a person* Il. Call. AR.; **honour** —*a dead person* (w.dat. w. funeral games) Il.

κτερίζω *vb.* | fut. κτεριῶ | **perform funeral rites for** —*a person* Il. S. E.

κτερίσματα των *n.pl.* **funeral offerings** S. E.

κτέωμεν (ep.1pl.athem.aor.subj.): see κτείνω

κτῆμα ατος *n.* [κτάομαι] **1 possession, acquisition** (ref. to a material object, esp. a valuable one) Od. S. E. Pl. X. +; (specif.) **prize** (ref. to a captured woman) S.; **chattel** (ref. to a slave) E.; (ref. to a human being, as the property of the gods) Pl. || pl. **possessions, acquisitions, goods, property** Hom. Hes. Hdt. Trag. Att.orats. +
2 possession, asset (ref. to an abstr. entity, such as freedom, or to a trait of character or mental attribute, such as obstinacy, good sense) Hdt. S. E. Isoc. Pl. X. +; (ref. to a good friend) Hdt.; (ref. to a historical work, as having lasting value) Th.; **acquisition, prize** (w.gen. of victory) S.
3 piece of land, estate, property Men. NT. Plu. || pl. **landed property, real estate** Th. D. Men.

κτηματικός ή όν *adj.* (of persons) **property-owning** or **land-owning** Plb. Plu.

κτηνηδόν *adv.* [κτῆνος[1]] **like cattle** —*ref. to savages copulating* (i.e. *promiscuously*) Hdt.

κτῆνος[1] εος (ους) *n.* **1 farm animal, beast** (such as an ox or sheep) Hdt. X.; (used for riding, ref. to a horse, donkey or mule) NT. Plu.
2 || collectv.pl. **livestock, cattle** hHom. A. Hdt. Pl. X. Arist. +
3 || pl. app., **possessions, goods, property** Hes.*fr.*

κτῆνος[2] ου *m.* **property, wealth** Hes.*fr.*

κτηνοτροφίᾱ ᾱς *f.* [κτῆνος[1], τρέφω] **cattle-breeding** Plu.

κτήσιος ᾱ ον *adj.* [κτῆσις] **1** belonging (to someone) as a possession; (of goods) **in one's possession** A.; (of a sheep) **from one's own flock** S.; (of a person's wits) **native** S.*fr.* **2** (epith. of Zeus) **protecting property** A. Att.orats.; (of his altar) A.

κτῆσις εως (Ion. ιος) *f.* [κτάομαι] **1** act of acquiring, **acquisition** (of money, knowledge, friends, territory, or sim.) Th. Ar. Att.orats. Pl. +
2 act of achieving, **accomplishment** (of a deed) S.
3 state of possessing, **possession** (of wealth, virtue, a right, or sim.) S. Th. Att.orats. Pl. +; (of sons) Pl.
4 ownership (as a concept) Arist.; **claim of ownership** (of sthg.) X.
5 (collectv.sg.) **possessions, property** Hom. Hdt. S. Critias X. Is. +; (pl.) Hdt. Isoc. Plb. Plu.; (sg.) **territorial possessions** (of a city) X.

κτητέος ᾱ ον *vbl.adj.* (of legal currency) **to be possessed** (by the citizens of a state) Pl.

κτητικός ή όν *adj.* **1** (of persons) **acquisitive** (W.GEN. of things) Isoc.
2 (of an art) **of acquisition, acquisitive** Pl. Arist.

κτητός ή όν *adj.* **1** (of material things) **able to be acquired** or **attained** Il. Isoc.; (of non-material things, such as skill and good sense) Pl. Arist.
2 (of a wife, a servant) **acquired** (as a chattel) Hes. Pl.
|| NEUT.PL.SB. acquisitions or possessions E.
3 (of a certain kind of life, in neg.phr.) able to be possessed, **to be had** (W.DAT. by someone) E.
4 (of Eros, certain bodily senses) to be possessed, **worth possessing** Pl.

κτήτωρ ορος *m.* **owner** (of a house or plot of land) NT.

κτίδεος η ον *Ion.adj.* [ἴκτις] (of a helmet) **of marten skin** Il.

κτίζω *vb.* | fut. κτίσω | aor. ἔκτισα, ep. κτίσα, also ἔκτισσα and κτίσσα || MID.: ep.aor. ἐκτισσάμην, dial.3du. κτισσάσθᾱν || PASS.: ep.3pl.opt. κτιζοίατο (A.) | aor. ἐκτίσθην, dial. κτίσθην | pf. ἔκτισμαι, ep.ptcpl. κτίμενος (A.) |
1 (of mythol. ancestors, a mother-city, colonists, or sim.) found a settlement in, **found, settle, colonise** —*a place* Il. Hes.*fr.* Pi.(also mid.) Hdt. E. Th. + || PASS. (of a place) be colonised Hdt. Th.
2 found, establish —*a city, colony* Od. A. Pi. B. Hdt. Th. + || PASS. (of cities) be founded Hdt. E.*fr.* Th. Pl. +
3 establish, set up —*an altar, sanctuaries* Pi. —*a festival, games* Pi.(also mid.) —*regular sacrifices* Th. —*a hero* (*as the object of worship*) Hdt. || PASS. (of feasts) be established A.
4 (gener.) **create, build** —*a tomb* S. || PASS. (of a wall) be built Pi. || EP.PF.PASS.PTCPL.ADJ. (of a portal or vault, W.ADV. καλῶς) **well-built** A. | cf. εὐκτίμενος
5 bring into being; (of Zeus) **create** —*a child* A.; (of Poseidon) —*the horse's bit* S.; (of painters) —*people and things* (i.e. *representations of them*) Emp.; (mid., of Deucalion and Pyrrha) —*a people* (*out of stones*) A.
6 perform —*an act* A. S.
7 make, render —*someone or sthg.* (W.PREDIC.ADJ. *such and such*) A. E.

κτιλόομαι *mid.contr.vb.* [κτίλος] (of Scythian men) **tame** —*the Amazons* Hdt.

κτίλος ον *adj.* [app.reltd. κτίζω] **1** (of animals) **tame, domesticated** Emp.
2 || MASC.SB. tame animal, ram (ref. to the bellwether, trained to lead the flock, to whom leaders of troops are compared) Il.; (fig., ref. to a priest of Aphrodite) Pi.

κτίσις εως *f.* [κτίζω] **1 founding** (of a city or colony) Th. Isoc. Plb. Plu.; (of a shrine) Aeschin.; (of a constitution) Plu.
2 establishment, settling (of an incoming race, in a country) Th.
3 accomplishment, achievement, feat Pi.
4 creation (of the world, by God) NT.
5 that which is created; **creation** (ref. to the world) NT.

κτίσμα ατος *n.* **foundation, settlement** (ref. to a city) Call. Plb.

κτίστης ου *m.* **founder** (of a city) Call. Plu.; (of one's country, hyperbol.ref. to one who saves it fr. destruction) Plu.

κτιστός ή όν *adj.* (of stones) **cut** or **smoothed** hHom. [or perh. *set in place*]

κτιστύς ύος *f.* **founding** (of a city) Hdt.

κτίστωρ ορος *m.* **coloniser** (of a land) E. Ar.; **founder** (of a city) Ar.(quot. Pi.)

κτίτης ου *m.* **inhabitant** (W.GEN. of a city) E.

κτυπέω *contr.vb.* [κτύπος] | aor. ἐκτύπησα, ep. κτύπησα | aor.2 ἔκτυπον, ep. κτύπον | **1** make a loud or resonant sound; (of Zeus) **boom, crash** (w. thunder) Hom. Hes. S.; (of the Cyclops, w. a noise imitating thunder) E.*Cyc.*
2 (of trees, falling or crushed by the impact of a boulder) **crash** Il.; (of the sea) **roar** Pl.
3 (of a war-horse's bells) **make a din** —W.ACC. *of terror* E.; (of an aulos) **sound forth** E.; (of a sound of music or singing) **ring out** B.
4 (of a person, a crowd) **make a loud noise** Ar. Tim.; (gener., in neg.phr.) **make a noise** hHom. E.; (specif.) **stamp** (on the ground) —W.DAT. w. *one's feet* Ar.
5 make a responsive sound; (of the sky, cliffs, earth) **resound, echo** (w. thunder, shrieks) S. E. AR.; (of a house, w. running footsteps, unbarring of doors, preparations for a sacrifice) E.; (of boxers' chins, w. blows) AR.
6 cause (sthg.) to resound (by striking it); **beat, thump** —*the ground* (w. *one's hands, to invoke the spirits of the dead*) E.; —(W.DAT. w. *one's foot*) Plu.; (of horses, w. their hooves) Hes.; (of worshippers of Dionysus) —*drums* E. —*the thyrsos* (*against the ground, in a dance*) E.
7 || MID.PASS. (of shoes) **resound** —W.DAT. w. *rhythmic tread* Ar.(mock-trag.); (of an echo) Ar.

κτύπημα ατος *n.* **blow, thud** (by a mourner's hand, on the head) E.

κτύπος ου *m.* **1** loud or resonant sound; **crash** (of thunder) Il. A. S. Plu.; (of falling buildings or rocks) E. Plu.; (of ships colliding) Th.
2 crash, clang (of weapons or armour) A. E. X.
3 beating (of head or breast, by a mourner's hands) A. E.; **knocking** (W.GEN. at a door) A.
4 beating (of rain) A.; **pounding** (of waves against a headland) S.; **roar** (of a rough sea) Plu.
5 clatter, thud, stamp (of horses' hooves) Il. hHom. Ar. X.; (of feet) Hom. S. E. Ar.
6 beating (of a drum) E.; **clacking** (of castanets) E.*fr.*
7 blare (of trumpets) B.; **sound** (of an aulos, a lyre) E.
8 noise, din (of battle) Hom. Hes. Tyrt.; (of racing-chariots) S.; (of hammering, woodcutting, metalwork) A. Ar. Call.
9 (gener.) **sound, noise** (made by persons) Od. S. E. Pl. X. Plu.

κυαθίζω *vb.* [κύαθος] **ladle out** (wine) Plu.; (fig., of Archimedes) **ladle up** (water) —W.DAT. w. *ships* (*by hauling them out of the sea w. a mechanical device*) Plb. Plu.

κύαθος ου *m.* **1 ladle** (used to serve wine) X. Call.*epigr.*
2 (as a liquid measure, approx. 45 centilitres) **ladleful** (of wine, water) Anacr.; (fig., of peace, envisaged as an unguent) Ar.
3 (medic.) **cupping-glass** (for the relief of bruises and swellings) Ar.

κυαμευτός ή όν *adj.* [κυαμεύω] (of persons) **chosen by lot** X. Plu.

κυαμεύω *vb.* [κύαμος] **choose** (W.ACC. officials) **by lot** Arist. ‖ PASS. be chosen by lot D.(oath)

κύαμος ου *m.* **1** (usu.pl.) **bean** Il. Hdt. Ar. Pl. Theoc. + **2 lottery-bean, lot** (as used in appointing officials, the successful candidate drawing the white bean) Hdt. Th. And.(law) Ar. X. Arist. +

κυαμο-τρώξ ῶγος *m.* [τρώγω] (ref. to a person) **bean-muncher** Ar.

κυάν-αιγις ιδος *fem.adj.* [κυάνεος, αἰγίς¹] (epith. of Athena) **with dark aigis** Pi.

κυαν-άμπυξ υκος *masc.fem.adj.* (of Thebe, personif. Delos) **with dark headband** Pi.*fr.* Theoc.

κυαν-ανθής ές *adj.* [ἄνθος] (of a stormy sea) **dark-hued** B.

κυάν-ασπις ιδος *masc.fem.adj.* [ἀσπίς¹] (of warriors) **with dark-coloured shield** Anacr.

κυαν-αυγής ές *adj.* [αὐγή] (of Hades' brows) **dark-gleaming** E.; (fig., of dithyrambs, ref. to their obscure style) Ar.

Κυάνεαι (fem.pl.): see κυάνεος 9

κυαν-έμβολος ον *adj.* (of ships, their prows) **dark-beaked** E. Ar.

κυάνεος ᾱ (Ion. η) ον, also contr. **κυανοῦς** ῆ οῦν (Pl., perh. A.) *adj.* [κύανος] | ep. ῡ *metri grat.* | **1** (of designs on a shield) **depicted in black** or **dark-blue gloss** Il.
2 (of a colour, painted or dyed objects) **glossy black** or **dark-blue** Hdt. Pl. AR.
3 naturally dark and lustrous; (of hair, beards, eyes and eyelids, the brows of Zeus) **black, dark** Hom. Hes. hHom. Ibyc. AR.; (of Poseidon's horses) E.; (of a raven's plumage, cattle) hHom. Call. AR.; (of Africans) Hes.; (of a plant) Theoc.
4 (of seawater, a swallow) **dark** or **dark-blue** Simon. AR.
5 having a black or dark appearance; (of ranks of warriors) **black, dark** Il.; (of a ship) E.; (of the earth) Pi.*fr.*
6 made black or dark (by absence of light); (of clouds, usu. supernatural, enveloping and concealing a person or place) **black, dark** Hom. Hes.; (fig., of a cloud, W.GEN. of warriors, death) Il. B.; (of darkness, night, the night sky) Simon. Tim. Lyr.adesp. AR.; (of a thicket) Pi.
7 (of the sea-bed, turbulent water) **black, dark** Od. E.
8 (w. sinister connot., esp. as assoc.w. the underworld or death); (of the gates of Hades, Charon's boat) **black, dark** Thgn. Theoc.; (of mourning garments) Il. hHom.; (of robes worn in nocturnal or sinister rituals) Pl. AR.; (of the Gorgon's blood, a serpent's coils, its gaze) A. AR. Theoc.; (of serpents, the Fates, as depicted on a shield) Hes.
9 (of the Clashing Rocks) **dark** E. AR. Theoc. ‖ FEM.PL.SB. **Dark Islands** or **Rocks** (at the entrance to the Black Sea, identified w. the Clashing Rocks) Hdt.; (also app. neut.pl.sb.) Lycurg. D. Plu.

κυανο-ειδής ές *adj.* [εἶδος¹] (of river-water) **dark** or **dark-blue** E.

κῡανό-πεζα ης *fem.adj.* [πέζα] (of a table) **with feet of black** or **dark-blue gloss** Il.

κῡανό-πεπλος ον *adj.* [πέπλος] (of goddesses) **dark-robed** Hes. hHom.

κυανο-πλόκαμος ον *adj.* (of women, goddesses) **dark-haired** B.

κυανό-πλοκος ον *adj.* [πλόκος] (of Thetis) **dark-haired** Pi.*fr.*

κυανό-πρῳρος ον (also ᾰ ον B.) *adj.* —also **κυανοπρώρειος** ον (Od.) *adj.* [πρῷρα] (of ships) **dark-prowed** Hom. hHom. B.

κυανό-πτερος ον *adj.* [πτερόν] (of a bird, a cicada) **dark-winged** Hes. E.

κύανος ου (also **κυανός** οῦ Pl.) *m.* **1** glossy black or dark-blue substance used in decorating (either enamel, i.e. glass-paste, or niello, a metallic alloy), **black** or **dark-blue gloss** Hom. Hes. Pl. Mosch.
2 perh. **lapis lazuli** (a bright blue mineral, used as a pigment) Pl.

κυανό-στολος ον *adj.* [στολή] (of Aphrodite, in mourning) **dark-robed** Bion

κυανοῦς *contr.adj.*: see κυάνεος

κυάν-οφρυς υος *masc.fem.adj.* [ὀφρῦς] (of a woman) **dark-browed** (as an attractive feature) Theoc.

κῡανο-χαίτης ου *masc.adj.* [χαίτη] | ep.nom. κῡανοχαῖτα |
1 (epith. of Poseidon) **dark-haired** Hom. Hes. hHom.; (of Hades) hHom.
2 (of a horse) **dark-maned** Il. Hes.

κυανο-χίτων ωνος *masc.fem.adj.* [χιτών] (of a person) **with dark** or **dark-blue tunic** Pi.*fr.*

κυανό-χροος ον *adj.* —also **κυανόχρως** ων, gen. ωτος *adj.* [χρώς] (of waves, the sea-bed) **dark-hued** E. Arist.(quot.); (of hair) E.

κυαν-ῶπις ιδος *fem.adj.* [ὤψ] (of a woman or goddess) **dark-eyed** Od. Hes. Anacr.; (of ships, ref. to the eyes painted on their bows) A. B.

κύβδα *adv.* [κύπτω] **bent over, bottom up** —*ref. to a woman engaged in sexual intercourse* Archil. Ar. —*ref. to a satyr (compared to a monkey) farting at someone* S.*Ichn.* —*ref. to a person being dragged by the arse* Ar.

κυβεῖᾱ ᾱς *f.* [κυβεύω] (usu.pl.) **dice-playing, gambling** Pl. X. Arist. Men.

κυβεῖον ου *n.* **gambling den** Aeschin.

Κυβέλη ης, dial. **Κυβέλᾱ** ᾱς *f.* —also **Κυβήβη** ης *f.* **Cybele, Cybebe** (Anatolian goddess, sts. known as Great Mother or Mountain Mother) Hippon. Pi.*fr.* Hdt. E. Ar. Call. Theoc.

κυβερνάω *contr.vb.* **1** (of a helmsman) **steer** —*a ship* Od. Pl. X. D. +; (intr.) **be a helmsman, steer** Ar. Pl. X. Arist. + ‖ PASS. (of ships) be steered (by a helmsman) Pl.; (fig.) —W.DAT. by Fortune Pi.
2 (fig., of persons, gods, Virtue, Fortune, or sim.) **steer, direct, guide, govern** —*persons, cities, affairs, or sim.* Lyr. Parm. Pl. Men. Plu. —(app.) W.GEN. Pl.(quot.); (intr., of justice) **act as a guide** (for a prosecutor) Antipho ‖ PASS. (of chariots) be steered Pl.; (of persons, a kingdom, an army, activities) be directed or governed (usu. W.DAT. or PREP.PHR. by someone or sthg.) Heraclit. Pi. S. Pl. X. Plb.

κυβερνήσια ων *n.pl.* **festival in honour of the helmsman** (of the ship which took Theseus to Crete and back) Plu.

κυβέρνησις εως, dial. **κυβέρνᾱσις** ιος *f.* **1 steering** (of a ship, as the helmsman's responsibility) Pl.; (fig., in political ctxt.) Plu.
2 (fig.) **guidance, direction, governance** (W.GEN. of persons, cities) Pi.(pl.) Plu.

κυβερνητήρ, dial. **κυβερνᾱτήρ**, ῆρος *m.* **helmsman** (of a ship) Od. AR.; (fig., for a ruler, ref. to a god) Pi.; (for an athlete, ref. to his trainer) Pi.

κυβερνητήριος ᾱ ον *adj.* (of the work) **of a helmsman** (fig.ref. to the governance of a city) Plu.(oracle)

κυβερνήτης ου (Ion. εω), dial. **κυβερνᾱ́τᾱς** (also **κυβερνήτᾱς** B.) ᾱ *m.* **1 helmsman** (of a ship) Hom. +; (fig., ref. to the ruler of a city) Thgn. E.; (ref. to the supreme deity) Pl.; (of the soul, ref. to the mind) Pl.
2 steersman (of horses, ref. to a charioteer) B.

κυβερνητικός ή όν *adj.* **1** (of skill) **in steering** Pl. ‖ FEM.SB. **art of steering, helmsmanship** Pl. Arist. Plb.; (fig., W.GEN. of people) Pl.; (also neut.sg. and pl.sb.) Pl. Arist.
2 (of a person or mind) **experienced in helmsmanship** Pl. X.

κυβευτής οῦ *m.* [κυβεύω] **dice-player, gambler** X. Aeschin. Arist. Plu.

κυβευτικός ή όν *adj.* **1** (of the apparatus) **for dice-playing** Aeschin.
2 (of a person) **skilled at dice-playing** Pl.

κυβεύω *vb.* [κύβος] **1 play dice, gamble** (usu. regarded as a disreputable activity) Ar. Isoc. X. Aeschin. Thphr. +
2 (fig.) **gamble, run a risk** E. Pl.

Κυβήβη *f.*: see Κυβέλη

κυβικός ή όν *adj.* [κύβος] (of the shape) **of a cube** Pl.

κυβιστάω, Ion. **κυβιστέω** (Mosch.) *contr.vb.* **1** (of a wounded charioteer) **plunge head over heels, somersault** (fr. his chariot) Il.
2 (of performers) **turn somersaults** Pl. X.; (of puppies) X.
3 (of eels and fish) **plunge up and down** Il.; (of a dolphin) **leap, gambol** —W.PREP.PHR. *over the sea-swell* Mosch.

κυβιστητήρ ῆρος *m.* one who turns somersaults, **tumbler, acrobat** (as a performer) Hom.; (ref. to a warrior falling fr. a chariot) E.

κύβος ου *m.* **1** ‖ PL. **dice** (for gambling) Hdt. Pl. Arist. Plu.
2 ‖ PL. (meton., ref. to the game) **dice** Hdt. Lys. Ar. Aeschin. Plb. Plu.
3 ‖ PL. (in fig.ctxts.) **dice** (envisaged as thrown by one taking a risk) E.; (as thrown by a god or Fortune) A. E.; (also sg.) Men. Plu.
4 (specif.) side of a die marked with a single spot, **one, ace** Ar.(app.quot. E.) Pl.
5 cube (ref. to a black or white ballot inserted into a machine used to allot jurors) Arist.
6 (geom.) **cube** Pl. Arist.
7 (math.) cubed number, **cube** Pl. Plu.

κυδάζομαι *mid.vb.* | ep.2sg.aor. ἐκυδάσσαο | **insult, revile** *—someone* AR. ‖ PASS. **be reviled** —W.DAT. *by people* S.

κυδαίνω *vb.* [κύδος] | aor. ἐκύδηνα, dial. ἐκύδᾱνα | **1** (of a god) **confer glory on, do honour to** *—a person* Hom. AR.; **restore to glory** *—a wounded warrior* (by healing his wounds) Il.
2 (of a ruler, a victorious athlete) **confer glory on** *—a city* Pi.
3 do honour to *—persons* (by compliments or material gifts) Il. Hes. Plu. *—the dead* (by sacrifices or other tributes) AR.; **gratify** *—someone's heart* (by a show of honour) Od.; **do honour** (to someone, by one's speech) AR.
4 (of a city) **hold in honour, extol** *—military prowess* Plu.

κυδάλιμος η (dial. ᾱ) ον *adj.* **1** (of persons) **glorious, renowned** Hom. Hes. AR.; (of a goddess) Alc.
2 (of the heart of a person, lion or boar) **glorious, noble** Hom.

κυδάνω *vb.* [reltd. κυδαίνω] **1** (of a god) **confer glory on** *—the Trojans* Il.
2 (intr., of warriors) **win glory, be triumphant** Il.

κῡδι-άνειρα ης *ep.fem.adj.* [κύδος, ἀνήρ] **1** (of battle, the place of assembly) **where men win glory** Il.
2 (of Sparta) **renowned for men** Ibyc.

κυδιάω *ep.contr.vb.* | w.diect.: 3pl. κῡδιόωσι, ptcpl. κῡδιόων, iteratv.impf. κῡδιάασκον | also ptcpl. κῡδιόων (hHom.) |
1 (of gods) **glory, exult, be triumphant** Il.; (of a leader) **bear oneself proudly** Il.; (of maidens) hHom.; (of a stallion) Il. AR.
2 (of persons) **glory, exult** —W.DAT. *in their prosperity, military might, youthful vigour* Hes. hHom. AR.; (of sacred cattle) *—in their golden horns* AR.
3 (of a horse) **boastfully rely** —w. ἐπί + DAT. *on a goddess* AR.

κύδιμος η ον *adj.* (epith. of Hermes) **glorious, renowned** Hes. hHom.; (gener., of children) Hes.*fr.*; (of the Olympic games) Pi.

κύδιστος η ον *superl.adj.* [κῡδρός] **1** (of Zeus, goddesses, rulers, freq. voc.) **most glorious** or **renowned** Hom. Hes. hHom. Ar.(quot. A.) AR. Theoc.
2 (of a particular virtue) **most highly regarded** Thgn.
3 (of sufferings) **most honourable** (W.GEN. of sufferings, i.e. least undesirable) A.

—κυδίων ον *compar.adj.* ‖ NEUT.IMPERS. (w. ἐστί understd.) **it is more creditable, it is better** —W.INF. *to do sthg.* E.(dub., cj. κέρδιον)

κυδοιδοπάω *contr.vb.* [perh.reltd. κυδοιμός] (of persons, a ferret) **create havoc** or **confusion** Ar.

κυδοιμέω *contr.vb.* [κυδοιμός] (of warriors) **create havoc** (in battle) Il.; (tr., of Zeus) **create havoc among** *—the gods* (by attacking them in rage) Il.

κυδοιμός οῦ *m.* **1 confusion, uproar, havoc** (on the battlefield) Il. Ar.(mock-trag.) AR. Plb.; (caused by Eros) Anacr.(pl.); (personif.) **Havoc** Il. Hes. Emp. Ar.
2 brawling of fighting-cocks) Theoc.(pl.)

κῦδος εος *ep.n.* **1 splendour, glory** (of a god, esp. Zeus) Il.
2 glory, renown (attained esp. by warriors, rulers, athletes, freq. assoc.w. victory, sts. conferred by a god) Hom. Hes. Eleg. Lyr. A. Hdt. +
3 (concr., ref. to a person or object) **source of glory** (for others); (ref. to Nestor, Odysseus) **glory, pride** (W.GEN. of the Achaeans) Hom.; (ref. to Hector, W.DAT. for the Trojans) Il.; (ref. to a horse's ornament, for its rider) Il.

κῡδρός ά (Ion. ή) όν *adj.* | compar. κῡδρότερος | **1** (of a goddess or demigoddess) **glorious, esteemed** Hom. Hes. hHom. A.*fr.* AR.; (of a god or demigod) hHom. Alcm.; (of a mortal woman) Od.
2 ‖ COMPAR. (of a victorious athlete) **more glorious** or **esteemed** Xenoph.; (of a hope) **loftier** B.
3 (of a person) **self-confident** or **exultant** (in appearance or manner) X.; (of a horse's bearing) **confident, proud** X.
‖ NEUT.SB. **proud bearing** (of a horse) X.

—κῡδρότερον *compar.adv.* **more lustily, with greater gusto** (W.GEN. than one's companions) *—ref. to drinking* Ion

Κυδωνίᾱ ᾱς, Ion. **Κυδωνίη** ης *f.* **Cydonia** (city on the NW. coast of Crete, mod. Chania) Hdt. Th.

—Κύδωνες ων *m.pl.* men or people of Cydonia, **Cydonians** Od. Call.

—Κυδωνιᾶται ῶν *m.pl.* **Cydonians** Th. Plb.

—Κυδωνικός ή όν *adj.* (of a man) **from Cydonia** Theoc.

—Κυδώνιος ᾱ ον *adj.* **1** (of Artemis' bow) **Cydonian** Call.
2 (of an apple, ref. to a quince) **Cydonian** Stesich. Plu.; (of an apple tree, ref. to a quince tree) Ibyc.; (fig., of a girl's breasts, i.e. like quinces) Ar.

κυέω *contr.vb.* | see also κύω | **1** (of a woman) **be pregnant** Ar. Pl. D. + —W. ἐκ + GEN. *by someone* Hdt. Att.orats. ‖ AOR. **become pregnant** Hdt. Ar. Men. Plu. —W. ἐκ + GEN. *by someone* Plu.
2 (tr.) **be pregnant with** *—a child* Il.; (of a mare) *—a mule* Il.
‖ AOR. **become pregnant with, conceive** *—a child* Pl. ‖ PASS. (of a foetus) **be carried in the womb** Pl.
3 (fig., of a man) **be pregnant** (in his mind, sts. W.NEUT.ACC. w. certain thoughts) Pl.; (of a person's mind) —W.NEUT.ACC. *w. a thought* X.

Κύζικος ου *f.* **Cyzicus** (Greek city on the S. coast of the Propontis) Hdt. Th. X. +

—Κυζικηνός ή όν *adj.* **1** (of persons) **from Cyzicus** Hdt. Th. + ‖ MASC.PL.SB. **men** or **inhabitants of Cyzicus** Hdt. X. +
2 (of staters) from Cyzicus, **Cyzicene** (ref. to a type of electrum coin, widely circulated in Greece) Lys. D.
‖ MASC.SB. **Cyzicene stater** Lys. X. D.

—**Κυζικηνικός** ή όν *adj.* (of the colour of a terrified soldier) **Cyzicene** (i.e. as pale as an electrum coin) Ar.

κύημα ατος *n.* [κυέω] that which grows in the womb, **foetus** Pl.; (fig., ref. to the engendering of beauty in the soul) Pl.

κύησις εως *f.* **1 conception** Pl.
2 pregnancy Plu.

Κυθέρεια ᾱς (Ion. ης), Aeol. **Κυθήρηα** ᾱς *f.* —also **Κυθήρᾱ** ᾱς (Bion) *f.* [Κύθηρα] goddess of Cythera, **Cytherea** (ref. to Aphrodite) Od. Hes. Sapph. Thgn. A. Hellenist.poet. +

κυθη-γενής ές *adj.* [κεύθω; γένος, γίγνομαι] (of Dionysus) **born in secret** Call.

Κύθηρα ων *n.pl.* **Cythera** (island off the SE. coast of the Peloponnese, mythical birthplace of Aphrodite) Hom. Hes. Hdt. Th. Ar. +

—**Κυθηρόθεν** *adv.* **from Cythera** Il.

—**Κυθήριος** ᾱ (Ion. η) ον *adj.* **1** (of the island) **of Cythera** Hdt. ǁ FEM.SB. **island of Cythera** X.
2 (of persons) **from Cythera** Il. ǁ MASC.PL.SB. **men or inhabitants of Cythera** Th. X.

Κυθηρο-δίκης ου *m.* [δίκη] **commissioner for Cythera** (title of a Spartan official) Th.

κύθον (ep.aor.2): see κεύθω

κύθρος Ion.m.: see χύτρος

κυΐσκομαι mid.pass.vb. [κύω] (of women, animals, fish) **become pregnant, conceive** Hdt. Pl.; (of fish) **be impregnated** —w. ἐκ + GEN. **by milt** Hdt.

κυκάω contr.vb. | ep.ptcpl. (w.diect.) κυκόων | **1 stir** —*milk* (mixed w. fig-juice, to curdle it) Il. —*brine* (W.DAT. *for crabs, i.e. in preparation for boiling them*) Ar.
2 mix (ingredients, to make a κυκεών gruel drink); **stir together, mix** —*barley, cheese and honey* (W.DAT. *w. wine*) Od.; **stir a mixture** (of these) —W.DAT. *w. wine* Il. ǁ MID. **mix oneself a gruel drink** Ar.
3 ǁ PASS. (of particles of matter, elements in a poem) **be mixed or jumbled together** Pl.
4 stir or agitate (waters); **stir up** —*muddy water* Ar. ǁ PASS. (of a river, its waters, the sea, a whirlpool) **be stirred up, seethe** Hom. hHom. AR.; (fig., of a wave of crashed chariot-horses) **surge in confusion** S.
5 (fig., of a person's tongue) **stir up** —*sthg. evil* (W.INF. *to say*) Sapph.; (of a person) —*turmoil, trouble* Ar. Men.; (intr.) **stir up trouble** Ar. ǁ PASS. (of trouble) **be stirred up** Men.
6 (fig., of a politician) **stir up, shake up** —*the Council, Greece* Ar.; (of a military commander) —*the world* Plu.
7 throw (persons or things) **into disorder**; (of Zeus) **throw into turmoil** —*everything* (W.DAT. *w. blizzards and thunderstorms*) A. ǁ PASS. (of troops, chariot-horses) **be thrown into confusion** Il.; (of drowned men) **be tossed about in confusion** (by the waves) A.; (of people who have fallen into a whirlpool) Pl.
8 throw (a situation) **into confusion**; (of disputants) **confuse** —*everything* Pl. ǁ PASS. (of a political situation) **be thrown into confusion** Ar.
9 harass —*a person* Ar.; **interfere with** —*sacred hearths* (w. secondary connot. of vaginas) Ar. ǁ PASS. (of a person) **be harassed** —W.PREP.PHR. *by an official* Ar.; (fig., of a person, the heart) —W.DAT. *by troubles, diseases* Archil. Sol.

κυκεών ῶνος *m.* | acc. κυκεῶνα, ep. κυκειῶ and κυκειῶ | **gruel drink** (a mixture of grain and liquid, sts. cheese, oft. seasoned w. herbs, esp. assoc.w. poor or country persons) Hom. hHom. Hippon. Ar. Pl. Thphr. +

κύκηθρον ου *n.* **instrument for stirring**; (fig., ref. to a person) **stirrer, troublemaker** Ar.

κύκησις εως *f.* **mixing together** (of different substances) Pl.

κυκησί-τεφρος ου *m.* [τέφρᾱ] (derog.) **ash-stirrer** (ref. to a bath-keeper or launderer, alluding to the use of wetted ash as a detergent) Ar.

κυκησμός οῦ *m.* **confusion, mix-up** S.*Ichn.*

κύκλα (neut.pl.): see κύκλος

κυκλάμῑνος ου *f.* **a kind of plant, cyclamen** Theoc.

κυκλάς άδος *fem.adj.* [κύκλος] (of the time of a festival) **coming round, recurring** E.

—**Κυκλάδες** ων *fem.pl.adj.* (of νῆσοι *islands*, sts.understd.) **Cycladic** (ref. to the Cyclades, encircling Delos) Hdt. E. Th. Isoc. Call. Theoc. +; (of cities on those islands) E.

κυκλέω contr.vb. | In general, the vb. refers to moving in a circle, by contrast w. κυκλόω, which refers to forming a circle. Some forms of these vbs. are identical. |
1 convey by means of wheels, wheel —*corpses* (W.DAT. *w. oxen and mules, i.e. on wagons drawn by them*) Il.
2 move (sthg.) **in a circle**; **move** (W.ACC. one's feet, steps) **in a circle** (i.e. pace around) S. E. Ar.; (of a traveller, uncertain whether to proceed) **turn** (W.ACC. oneself) **full-circle** (i.e. reverse one's course twice) S.
3 turn (W.ACC. one's face, eye) **around** (i.e. look this way and that) E. Ar.
4 (fig.) **cause to go around, circulate** —*an argument* Pl.; (of speech) —*everything* Pl.; (intr., of arguments) **circulate** Plu.
5 (fig.) **revolve, turn over** —*a plan* (in one's mind) Plu.
6 ǁ MID. (of a wave of trouble) **circle round, encircle** —*someone* S.
7 ǁ MID.PASS. (of things) **have circular motion**; (of a spindle, the universe) **revolve, rotate** Pl.
8 ǁ MID.PASS. (of things) **move or be made to move in a circle**; (of objects) **rotate or be rotated** —W.DAT. *on or by pivots* E.; (fig., of a person's heart) **whirl round** —W.DAT. *in eddies* (app.ref. to throbbing w. agitation) A.
9 ǁ MID.PASS. (of things) **move in an ever-revolving cycle**; (of a person's fate) **revolve** —W.PREP.PHR. *on Fortune's wheel* (i.e. change repeatedly) S.*fr.*; (of nights and days) **come round** S.; (of sufferings) E.; (of time) **go round** (i.e. elapse) Pl.

κύκλησις εως *f.* **1 rotation** (of the cosmos, as producing the cycle of night and day) Pl.
2 time-cycle, epoch Pl.

κυκλικός ή όν *adj.* [κύκλος] (of a kind of poem) **cyclic** (i.e. like those of the epic cycle, which related early mythic stories) Call.*epigr.*

κυκλιο-διδάσκαλος ου *m.* [κύκλιος] **director of a circular** (i.e. dithyrambic) **chorus, dithyrambic poet** Ar.

κύκλιος ᾱ ον (also ος ον E.) *adj.* [κύκλος] **1** (of lake-water) **moving in a circle, circling** E.; (of the whirling of a bull-roarer) E.
2 (of a group of dancers) **in a circular formation or moving in a circle, circular or circling** E.; (specif., of the chorus which performed the dithyramb) **circular, dithyrambic** Lys. Ar. X. Aeschin. Plu.; (of boys) **performing in the dithyrambic chorus** Plu.; (of songs) **for a dithyrambic chorus** Ar.

—**κύκλιον**, also **κύκλια** *neut.sg. and pl.adv.* **in a circle** —*ref. to dancing* E. Call.

Κυκλοβόρος ου *m.* **Kykloboros** (a loud torrential stream nr. Athens) Ar.

—**Κυκλοβορέω** contr.vb. (of a politician) **roar like Kykloboros** Ar.

κυκλόεις εσσα εν *adj.* (of the seat of a goddess, fig.ref. to a city's agora) **circular** S.

κύκλος ου *m.* | also neut.nom.acc.pl. κύκλα | The sections are grouped as: (1) circle, (2) circular configuration (of

persons or things), (3-9) circular body or object, (10-11) group of persons forming a circle, (12-14) circular area, (15) circular path or motion, (16-17) cycle (of things recurring), (18) sequence of poems, (19-20) advbl. and prep.phrs. |
1 circular figure, **circle** Hdt. Ar. Pl. +
2 circular configuration (of persons or things); **circle** (of hunters) Od.; (of seats) Il.; (of metal or oxhide, on a shield) Il.; (of ships) Th.; (periphr., W.GEN. of a person's arms, i.e. encircling arms) E. || NEUT.PL. app., circles or bands (of gold, on the surface of a ball) AR.
3 (concr.) object or body having a circular shape; **wheel** Il. Pi. Parm.; **hoop** (of an acrobat) X.; app. **circular disc** (of wood, shaped on a lathe) Pl. || COLLECTV.NEUT.PL. set of wheels (on a vehicle) Il. Theoc.
4 (periphr.) **circle** (W.GEN. of a shield, i.e. round shield) A. E. Ar.(mock-trag.); (without GEN.) **shield** A. E.
5 (periphr.) **circle** (W.GEN. of a basket, i.e. round basket) E.; (of a cake, i.e. round cake) Ar.; (W.ADJ. *of feathers*, ref. to a fan) E.
6 orb, disc (W.GEN. of the sun, moon) Hdt. Trag.; (W.ADJ. *of the full moon*) E.; (without GEN., ref. to the moon) Hdt. || NEUT.PL. crescents (of the horned moon, as if its rim were cut in two) Mosch.
7 orb (W.GEN. of the eye) S.; (without GEN.) **eye** S.
8 circuit-wall (of a city) Hdt. X.; (specif., of Athens) Hdt. Th. Isoc. X. D.; (of the Peiraieus) D.; (of a military camp) Th.; (periphr.) **circle, circuit** (W.GEN. of a wall) Hdt.
9 || PL. **coils** (of a serpent) Call.; (neut.) AR.
10 group of persons forming a circle; **circle, ring** (of persons engaged in discussion) S. E. X.; (of spectators) Pi. B.; (of symposiasts) Critias
11 circle (of dancers, ref. to their formation, also to the pattern of their dance) Ar. Call. AR.; (of islands surrounding Delos, envisaged as dancers) Call.
12 circular space (W.GEN. of an agora) E.
13 circle or **sphere** (ref. to the universe) Emp.
14 vault (W.GEN. of heaven, the sky) Hdt. E.; (without GEN.) S. Ar.; (W.GEN. of night, ref. to the night sky) S.
15 circular path or motion, **orbit** (of the sun, moon, planets) Pl.
16 recurring period of time, **cycle** (W.GEN. of the seasons) Hdt.; (W.GEN. or ADJ. of a year) E.; (W.GEN. of a month) E.; (without GEN., ref. to a month or year) Ar.
17 recurring sequence of events, **cycle** Emp.; (W.GEN. of human fortunes) Hdt.
18 cycle (ref. to a collection of early epic poems, arranged in sequence to make a narrative extending fr. the creation of the world to the end of the Heroic Age) Arist.
19 (advbl. and prep.phrs.) κύκλῳ *in a circle* or *all around* Od. +; (as prep.) *around* —W.GEN. *a place* Hdt. X. D.; ἐν κύκλῳ *in a circle* or *all around* S. E. Th. +; (as prep.) *around* —W.GEN. *an altar, a place* E. Th.
20 (quasi-adjl.) Pi. + • τὸ κύκλῳ πέδον *the plain round about* Pi. • τὰ κύκλῳ ἔθνη *the surrounding peoples* X. • τὰ κύκλῳ *peripheral matters* Arist.
—**κυκλόθεν** *adv.* **right round** —*ref. to a road bordering a plot of land* Lys.
—**κυκλόσε** *adv.* **in a circle** —*ref. to people gathering or standing* Il.
κυκλο-σοβέω *contr.vb.* (of dancers) perh. **show off** (W.ACC. *their swift steps*) **in a circular dance** Ar.
κυκλο-τερής ές *adj.* [app.reltd. τετραίνω] **1** (of objects) **rounded, round, circular** Hdt. X.; (of a harbour) Hes.; (of the neck) Pl.; (of an eye) Hes.; (of a star, sphere, the shape and structure of the universe) Emp. Ar. Pl.; (of a mountain, the earth depicted on a map, a shape traced on the ground) Hdt. Plu.
2 (of a grove of poplars) **forming a circle** (around a fountain) Od.; (of a trench, around a city) Plu.
3 (predic., of a bow being stretched) **into an arc** (when the string is drawn back) Il.
κυκλοφορία ᾱς *f.* [φέρω] **circular motion** Arist.
κυκλόω *contr.vb.* | see also κυκλέω | **1** (of the river Okeanos) form a circle round, **encircle** —*the world* E.; (of people) **gather round** —*someone* NT. || MID. (of persons) **encircle** —*someone* Call.(cj.); (intr.) **gather in a circle** X. —W.PREP.PHR. *around sacrificial victims* X. || MID.PASS. (of a city wall) **form** or **be built in a circle** Plu. || PASS. (of a ditch) be made to form a circle —w. περί + ACC. *around a plain* Pl.
2 (w. hostile connot., of troops, commanders, or sim.) **encircle, surround** —*enemy troops* Plb.; (fig.) **envelop** —*a city* (W.DAT. *w. war*) E.(dub.) || MID. **encircle** —*enemy troops, a city, house, person* A. Hdt. Th. Ar. X. Plu.; (intr.) **form a circle** (around persons or a place) Hes.*fr.* —W.PREP.PHR. *around a city* X.; (of sailors, i.e. their ships) **adopt a circular formation** Hdt. || PASS. (of troops, a city) be encircled (by enemy troops) Th. X. Plb. NT. Plu.
3 || MID. (of nymphs) **encircle** or **move in a circle around** —*a goddess* (W.PREP.PHR. *in a dance*) Call.; (intr., of an individual, in a group of dancers) **circle** —W.PREP.PHR. *around an altar* Call.; (of swans) —*around an island* Call.
4 cause (sthg.) to form an arc (opp. a complete circle); (perh. of an eagle; of Zephyrus) **wheel** (W.ACC. *one's wings*) **in an arc** Archil. Call.; (of a discus-thrower) **swing** —*his hand* Pi. || MID. (of a branch, when pulled towards the ground, compared to a bow being stretched and to a wheel being traced in outline) **form an arc, curve** E.
5 (of winds) **cause** (W.ACC. *the sea*) **to rise up in an arc** Plb. [unless fr. κυκλέω]
6 (of Odysseus) **rotate** —*a stake* (*in the Cyclops' eye*) E.*Cyc.*(dub., cj. κυκλέω)
κύκλωμα ατος *n.* **1** circular object, **circle** (W.ADJ. *of stretched hide*, ref. to a hand-drum) E.
2 wheel (of Ixion) E.(dub.)
κύκλωσις εως *f.* **1** act of encircling, **encirclement** (of enemy troops) Th. X. Plu.
2 state of being encircled, **encirclement** (by enemy troops) Plu.
3 (concr.) **surrounding force** Th. Plu.
4 act of making one's way round (a place); **circuitous crossing** (of a mountain range, avoiding the regular path) Plu.
5 (concr.) **circuitous path** Plu.
κυκλωτός ή όν *adj.* (of protection for the body, ref. to a shield) **rounded, circular** A.; (of an item of food) Philox.Leuc.
κύκλ-ωψ ωπος (also οπος Emp.) *masc.fem.adj.* [κύκλος, ὤψ] (of the moon) round-eyed or round-faced, **round, spherical** Parm.; (of the pupil of the eye) Emp.
Κύκλωψ ωπος *m.* **1** || PL. **Cyclopes** (mythol. race of large, strong and uncivilised beings in human form, usu. one-eyed) Od. Tyrt. Pi.*fr.* E.*Cyc.* Th. Pl. +; (as builders of the walls of Mycenae and Tiryns) B. E. || SG. **Cyclops** (ref. to Polyphemos, son of Poseidon, blinded by Odysseus) Od. E.*Cyc.* Theoc. Plu.; (as wooer of Galateia) Ar. Hellenist.poet.; (as nickname given to a man, for his looks) Plu.
2 || PL. **Cyclopes** (ref. to Arges, Brontes and Steropes, one-eyed sons of Ouranos and Gaia, blacksmiths who made Zeus' thunderbolts) Hes. E. Call. AR.

—**Κυκλώπιον** ου *n*. [dimin.] (as voc. address to Polyphemos) **dear little Cyclops** E.*Cyc*.
—**Κυκλώπιος** (also **Κυκλώπειος**) ᾱ ον *adj*. **1** (of the jaws) **of the Cyclops** (ref. to Polyphemos) E.*Cyc*.
2 (of walls, a gateway, at Mycenae or Argos) **Cyclopean** (i.e. built by the Cyclopes) Pi.*fr*. E.; (of the land or city of Mycenae or Argos) E.; (of the hands) **of the Cyclopes** (as builders) E.
—**Κυκλωπίς** ίδος *fem.adj*. (of a hearth, meton. for the palace in which it stands) **Cyclopean** E.
—**Κυκλωπικῶς** *adv*. **in the manner of the Cyclopes** —*ref. to living by one's own personal rules* Arist.
κύκνειον ου *n*. [κύκνος] **swan-song** (fig.ref. to a final appeal) Plb.
κυκνό-μορφος ον *adj*. [μορφή] (of each of the Graiai) having the appearance of a swan, **with swan-white hair** A.
κυκνό-πτερος ον *adj*. [πτερόν] (of a vision, app.ref. to Helen) **swan-plumed** (alluding to her birth fr. the union of Leda w. Zeus as a swan) E.(dub.)
κύκνος ου *m*. **swan** (assoc.w. Apollo, noted for its song, and sts. said to sing most beautifully when about to die) Il. +
Κύκνος ου *m*. **1 Cycnus** (son of Poseidon, Trojan ally, killed by Achilles) Pi. Ar. Isoc. Arist. Theoc.
2 Cycnus (son of Ares, killed by Herakles) Hes. E. Plu.
—**Κύκνεια** ᾱς *dial.fem.adj*. (of Herakles' fight) **against Cycnus** Pi.
κυκῶν (ep.ptcpl.): see κυκάω
κυλικεῖον ου *n*. [κύλιξ] piece of furniture for storing cups and other vessels, **dresser, cabinet** Thphr.
κυλινδέω *contr.vb*.: see κυλίνδω
κυλίνδησις εως *f*. [κυλινδέω] **1 constant involvement** (w. ἐν + DAT. in debates) Pl.
2 (pejor.) **cavorting** (w. women) Plu.
κύλινδρος ου *m*. **1 rolling stone, runaway boulder** AR. [or perh. *rolling log*]
2 cylinder (as a container) Plu.
κυλίνδω *vb*. —also **κυλινδέω** (Ar. Pl. X. Plu.) *contr.vb*. | aor. ἐκύλισα (Call. Theoc.) | 3pl.iteratv.impf.mid. κυλινδέσκοντο (Pi.) | aor.pass. ἐκυλίσθην || see also κυλίω | **1 put into rolling motion** (at sea); (of a wave) **roll along** —*a swimmer, a corpse* Od.; (of a wind) —*a wave* Od. Iamb.adesp.; (fig., of a god) **roll** —*disaster* (envisaged as a wave, W.DAT. *upon someone*) Il. || MID. (of waves) **roll on** Hom. Alc. AR.
|| MID.PASS. (fig., of disaster) **roll** or **be brought rolling** —W.DAT. *upon someone* Hom.
2 (of sea-swell) **roll, churn** —*sand* (W.ADV. *fr. the sea-bed*) S.
3 || PASS. (of hopes, envisaged as ships) be tossed —W.ADVS. *up and down* Pi.
4 put into rolling motion (on the ground); (of persons, a torrent) **roll** —*boulders* X. Theoc.; (of a god) **roll over** —*slaughtered cows* hHom.; (of a person hanging himself) —*the stone on which he is standing* Theoc. || MID. (of a boulder, a helmet; of a human trunk, compared to a log) **roll** (over the ground) Hom. Hes.; (of water) Pl.; (of lava, torrents, down a mountain) Pi. AR.; (gener., of things) **roll about** (on the ground) Semon. Pl. Theoc. || PASS. (of boulders) be rolled (down a hillside) X.
5 roll —*an on-stage actor* (W.ADV. *inside, i.e. into the stage-building, on the ekkuklema*) Ar. || PASS. (of Ixion) be rolled round (on his wheel) Pi.
6 put into rolling motion (in the air); (of a wind) **roll along** —*clouds* Theoc. || MID. (of clouds) **roll along** Ar.; (of smoke) Call.

7 || MID. (gener., of the Clashing Rocks) **roll** (together) Pi.
8 || MID. (of days) **roll by** Pi.
9 (app., of persons) **hurl** —*someone* (W.PREP.PHR. *fr. a seat*) Call. || PASS. (of a charioteer) be hurled or tossed (in an accident) —W.PREP.PHR. *fr. a chariot* S.
10 (fig., of a person) **roll forth, set in motion** —*a thought* Pi. —*hope* (W. ἐκ + GEN. *after hope*) Plu.
11 || MID. (of persons) **roll about** (on the ground, fr. grief) Hom.; (in grovelling adulation) Ar.; (fig.) **toss about** —W.PREP.PHR. *in a state of helplessness* Thgn.; (of a person, the public interest) perh., roll about helplessly, **flounder** Ar.; (pejor., of persons) **wallow** —W.PREP.PHR. *in ignorance, moral abasement* Pl.
12 || MID. (of a wounded horse or serpent) **roll about, writhe** Il. hHom.; (of wounded soldiers) Plu.
13 || MID. (pejor., of a person, a soul) **drift around** Pl. Plu.; (fig., of a written work, a spoken word) Ar. Pl.; (of conventional beliefs) —W.PREP.PHR. *betw. two extremes* Pl.
κύλιξ ικος *f*. | dat.pl. κύλιξι, dial. κυλίκεσσι | **drinking-cup, cup** (usu. for wine; sts. meton. for cup of wine, or gener. for wine) Iamb. Eleg. Lyr. Hdt. S. E. +
κυλίχνη ης, dial. **κυλίχνᾱ** ᾱς *f*. **cup** (for wine) Alc.
—**κυλίχνιον** ου *n*. [dimin.] **little jar** (of ointment) Ar.
κυλίω *vb*. [κυλίνδω] | only pres. and impf. | **1** (of snakes) **roll, slide** —*their bellies* (W.PREP.PHR. *along the ground*) Theoc.
2 || MID. (of a person suffering a convulsive fit) **roll about** (on the ground) NT.; (of bathers, in spilt unguent) Plb.; (of aulos-players) **spin around** (to imitate a discus) Arist.; (pejor., of townspeople) **drift around** —W.PREP.PHR. *in the centre of the city* Arist.
Κυλλήνη ης, dial. **Κυλλάνᾱ** ᾱς *f*. **1 Cyllene** (mt. in Arcadia, birthplace of Hermes) Il. hHom. Alc. Hippon. Pi. S.; (nymph to whom this mt. was sacred) S.*Ichn*.
2 Cyllene (harbour town on the coast of Elis in the NW. Peloponnese) Th. Ar. X. Plb.
—**Κυλλήνιος**, dial. **Κυλλάνιος**, ᾱ ον *adj*. **1** (epith. of Hermes) of mount Cyllene, **Cyllenian** Od. Hes.*fr*. hHom. Hippon.; (of a ridge, a crag) S. Call.
2 (of a person) from Cyllene (in Elis), **Cyllenian** Il.
κυλλῆστις ιος *Ion.m*. a kind of Egyptian bread (made fr. spelt) Hdt.
κυλλο-ποδίων ονος *m*. [κυλλός, πούς] (as nickname of Hephaistos) **cripple-foot** Il.
κυλλός ή όν *adj*. (of a hand, a foot) **deformed, crippled** Ar.; (of a person) NT.
κυλοιδιάω *contr.vb*. [κύλα *parts of the face under the eyes*, οἰδέω] | ep.masc.nom.pl.ptcpl. (w.diect.) κυλοιδιώωντες |
1 have a swelling under the eye, have a black eye Ar.
2 have bags under the eyes (fr. lovesickness or sleeplessness) Theoc.
κῦμα ατος *n*. [κύω] | dat.pl. κύμασι, dial. κῡμάτεσσι (Pi.) |
1 that which swells; **wave** (on the sea, a lake or river) Hom. +
2 flow, current (of a river, Okeanos) Hom.
3 || PL. and COLLECTV.SG. **swell, surge** (of the sea) Hom. +
4 || PL. and COLLECTV.SG. (gener.) **waves** (ref. to the sea or its surface) Hom. +
5 wave (exemplifying that which is unresponsive to persuasion or force) A. E.; (exemplifying that which is uncountable) AR. Theoc.
6 (fig., usu. W.GEN.) **wave** (of warriors attacking a city) A.; (of battle) Tyrt.; (of disaster, troubles, madness, bitter feelings) Trag.; (of Hades, i.e. death) Pi.; (pl., ref. to turbulent circumstances) E.

7 that which grows in the womb, **foetus, embryo** A. AR.
8 produce (of the earth) A.

κῡμαίνω *vb.* | aor.pass. ἐκῡμάνθην | **1** (of a sea) swell with waves, **swell, surge** Hom. Hes.; (of the current of a lake or river) AR.; (of liquid) **move in waves** —W.ADVS. *up and down* Pl. ‖ PASS. (of a sea) be made to swell, be churned up —W.DAT. *by a strong wind* Plu.
2 (of a cooking-pot) **seethe, boil** Call.
3 (fig., of the bloom of a person's youth) **be at the peak** Pi.; (of words, people's souls) **swell, seethe** A. Pl.
4 (of a person) be at the mercy of the waves; (fig.) **toss** —W.DAT. *in one's misfortunes* Tim. ‖ PASS. be tossed —W.DAT. *by desire* Pi.*fr*.
5 (fig., of a populace, a city, troops) **be in a turbulent** or **restless state** Plu.
6 (fig., of a war) swell up like a threatening wave, **loom** Plu.

κῡματίᾱς ου, Ion. **κῡματίης** εω *masc.adj.* **1** (of a sea or strait) full of waves, **billowing, turbulent** A. Hdt.
2 (of a wind) **causing waves** Hdt.

κῡματο-ᾱγής ές *adj.* [ἄγνῡμι] (of disasters) **breaking like waves** (over someone) S.

κῡματο-πλήξ ῆγος *masc.fem.adj.* [πλήσσω] (of a headland) **wave-beaten** S.

κῡματόω *contr.vb.* **1** (of a wind) **engulf** (W.ACC. a plain) **with waves** (of sand) Plu.
2 ‖ PASS. (of the sea) be turned into a tidal wave (ref. to a tsunami) Th.

κῡματ-ωγή ῆς *f.* [app.reltd. ἄγνῡμι] place where waves break, **seashore** Hdt. Democr.

κῡματώδης ες *adj.* (of a beach) **wave-beaten** Plu.

κύμβαλον ου *n.* —also **κύμβαλος** ου (Call.) *m.* **cymbal** X. Men. Call.

κύμβαχος[1] ου *m.* [app.reltd. κύμβη *cup* or *bowl*] perh. **curved plate** (of a helmet) Il.

κύμβαχος[2] ον *adj.* (quasi-advbl., of a person falling) **headlong, head-first** Il. Call.

κυμβίον ου *n.* [dimin. κύμβη *cup* or *bowl*] **small cup** D.

κύμινδις ιδος *m.f.* | acc. κύμινδιν (Il.) | an unknown kind of bird Hippon. Ar.; (called χαλκίς by the gods) Il.

κύμῑνον ου *n.* **cumin** (ref. to the seed, used for seasoning) Thphr. NT.; (provbl., w. καταπρίειν) *split cumin* (i.e. be a miser) Theoc.

κυμῑνο-πρίστης ου *m.* [πρίω] **cumin-splitter** (ref. to a miser) Arist.

κυμῑνοπρῑστο-καρδαμο-γλύφος ον *adj.* [κάρδαμον, γλύφω] (of a person) **cumin-splitting-cress-paring** (fig.ref. to an utter miser) Ar.

κῡμο-δέγμων ον, gen. ονος *adj.* [κῦμα, δέχομαι] (of a headland) receiving the waves, **where the waves break** E.

κῡμο-κτύπος ον *adj.* (of the Aegean) **with crashing waves** E.*fr*.

κυνᾱγέτᾱς *dial.m.*, **κυνᾱγετέω** *dial.contr.vb.*: see κυνηγ-

κυνᾱγέω *dial.contr.vb.* —also **κυνηγέω** (Plb. Plu.) *contr.vb.* [κυνᾱγός] **1 go hunting, hunt** Bion Plu.; (fig., of Argus) **hunt down** —*Io* A.(cj.) ‖ PASS. (hyperbol., of a person) be hunted (by one's lover) Plu.
2 ‖ PASS. (of a region) be hunted in Plb.

κυνᾱγίᾱ ᾱς *dial.f.* —also **κυνηγίᾱ** ᾱς (Arist. +) *f.* (sg. and pl.) **hunting expedition, hunt** E. Arist. Plb Plu.; (for a person) S.

κυν-ᾱγός οῦ *dial.m.f.* —also **κυνηγός** οῦ (Plb. Plu.) *m.* [κύων, ἄγω] one who leads a pack of hunting hounds, **huntsman** E. Call. Theoc. Plb. Plu.; (pl., fig.ref. to the Greeks searching for Helen) A.; **huntress** (ref. to Artemis) S. Ar.; (ref. to Atalanta, Prokris) E.

κυν-άγχης εω Ion.*m.* [ἄγχω] (epith. of Hermes, as patron of thieves) **guard-dog throttler** Hippon.

κυν-αγωγός οῦ *m.* app., one who leads hounds (out to a hunt), **dog-handler** X.

κυν-αλώπηξ εκος *f.* **dog-fox** (nickname of a disreputable person) Ar.

κυνά-μυια ης Ion.*f.* [μυῖα] **dog-fly** (as a term of abuse for a goddess) Il.

κυνάριον ου *n.* [dimin. κύων] **1 little dog** or **puppy** Pl. X. Thphr.
2 (gener.) **dog** NT. Plu.

κυνάς άδος *f.* **dog's hair** (pejor., ref. to a poor-quality sheepskin) Theoc.

κυνέᾱ ᾱς (also contr. **κυνῆ** ῆς), Ion. **κυνέη** ης, Aeol. **κυνίᾱ** ᾱς *f.* [κύνεος] **1** dogskin (app. used to make caps); (specif., as worn by warriors) **helmet** (of bullhide, marten-skin, or other leather) Il. Hdt.; (of metal, or of leather fitted w. plates) Hom. Hes. Tyrt. Alc. Hdt. +; (of wood) Hdt.
2 cap or **helmet** (W.GEN. of Hades, conferring invisibility on its wearer) Il. Hes. Ar. Pl.
3 hat (worn by travellers, for protection fr. the elements) B. S. Ar.; (worn by a goatherd) Lycophronid.; (of goatskin, worn by a gardener) Od.

κύνειος ᾱ ον *adj.* [κύων] **1** (of a leash) **for a dog** Ar.; (of a death) **like that of a dog** (i.e. horrible or painful) Ar.
2 (of sausages or sim.) **made of dog-meat** Ar.

κύνεος η ον Ion.*adj.* (of persons, their minds or hearts) having the characteristics of a dog, **shameless** Il. Hes. AR.

κυνέω *contr.vb.* | fut. κυνήσομαι | aor. ἔκυσα, ep. ἔκυσσα, also κύσα, κύσσα | **1 kiss** (as a greeting or sign of affection) —*a person, head, hands* Hom. E. Ar. AR. —*a bull* Mosch. —*the ground, one's bed* Od. E. AR. —W.DBL.ACC. or ACC. + GEN. *a person, on the head or hand* Od. AR. —*someone's knees* (in gratitude or supplication) Hom.
2 kiss (amorously) —*a person, lips* Ar. AR. Theoc. —*a lover's doorpost* Theoc.; (hyperbol.) —*a drink of wine* E.Cyc.; (of wine, envisaged as a lover) —*a drinker* E.Cyc.

κυνῆ *f.*: see κυνέᾱ

κυνηγεσίᾱ ᾱς *f.* [κυνηγετέω] (pl.) **hunting expedition, hunt** Plb.

κυνηγέσιον ου *n.* **1 hunting team** (ref. to huntsmen and their hounds) Hdt.
2 (sg. and pl.) **hunting expedition, hunt** Pl. X. Plu.; (staged as a public spectacle in the Roman circus) Plu.
3 ‖ COLLECTV.PL. hunting (as an activity or pursuit) E. Isoc. Pl. X. Plb. Plu.
4 hunting-ground X.
5 (fig.) **hunt** (after an attractive man) Pl.; (after courage, to identify and define it) Pl.; **hunting down** (W.GEN. of people, ref. to a military campaign waged as a sport) Plu.

κυνηγέσσω *vb.* [κυνηγέτης] | only aor.subj. κυνηγέσω | **hunt for, track down** —*stolen cattle* S.*Ichn*.

κυνηγετέω, dial. **κυνᾱγετέω** *contr.vb.* **1 hunt with hounds, hunt, go hunting** Ar. Pl. X. Men.(cj.) Plb. Plu.; (tr.) **hunt** —*game* Aeschrn. Plb.
2 be on the trail (of lost animals, a person) S. —W.COGN.ACC. *in pursuit of someone* E.; (tr.) **hunt down** —*fugitives* Plu. ‖ PASS. (of a person) be hunted down —W.PREP.PHR. *by someone* Plu.

κυν-ηγέτης ου, dial. **κυνᾱγέτᾱς** ᾱ *m.* [κύων, ἡγέομαι] one who leads a pack of hunting hounds, **huntsman, hunter** Od. S.*Ichn*. E. Pl. X. Men. +; (fig., ref. to a wrestler, in pursuit of a prize) Pi.

κυνηγετικός ή όν *adj.* **1** ‖ MASC.SB. one who hunts with hounds, huntsman Pl. Plu.; (as the title of a treatise) X. **2** ‖ FEM.SB. art of hunting with hounds Pl.

κυνηγέω *contr.vb.*, **κυνηγίᾱ** *f.*: see κυνᾱγ-

κυνήγιον ου *n.* [κυνᾱγός] **1** hunting expedition, hunt Plb. **2** hunting scene (ref. to a sculpture) Plu.

κυνηγός *m.*: see κυνᾱγός

κυνηδόν *adv.* [κύων] like a dog —*ref. to licking plates clean, snaffling up scraps of food* Ar.

κυν-ηλασίη ης *Ion.f.* [ἐλαύνω] sending on of hounds, **hunting with hounds** Call.

κυνήποδες ων *m.pl.* [app. κύων, πούς] **fetlocks** (of a horse) X.

Κύνθος ου *m.* **Cynthus** (mt. on Delos, against which Leto supported herself when she gave birth to Apollo and Artemis) hHom.

—**Κύνθιος** ᾱ ον *adj.* (of the hill, cliff, rock) **of Cynthus** hHom. Pi.*fr.* E. Ar.; (epith. of Apollo) **Cynthian** Call.

—**Κυνθιάς** άδος *fem.adj.* (of goats) **of Mount Cynthus** Call. ‖ PL.SB. Cynthian goats Call.*epigr.*

κυνίᾱ *Aeol.f.*: see κυνέᾱ

κυνίδιον ου *n.* [dimin. κύων] **1** young dog, **puppy** Ar. Pl. X. Plu. **2** (pejor.) cur, mutt Ar. Arist.

κύνικλος ου *m.* [Lat. *cuniculus*] **rabbit** Plb.

κυνικός ή όν *adj.* [κύων] having the characteristics of a dog; (as nickname of Diogenes, 4th-C. BC teacher, after whom a tradition of thought and behaviour was named) **Cynic** Plu. ‖ NEUT.SB. Cynic-like quality (of a person's outspokenness) Plu.

κυνίσκη ης *f.* [dimin. κύων] **little hound** (of Artemis) Ar.

κυν-όδους οντος *m.* [ὀδούς] **canine tooth** (of a horse) X.

κυνοδρομέω *contr.vb.* [δρόμος] **1** (of hunters) **run with the hounds** X. **2** (fig., of persons) **run about like hounds** (searching for one another) X.

κυνοδρομίη ης *Ion.f.* running with hounds, **hunting with hounds** Call.

κυνο-θαρσής (also **κυνοθρασής** A.) ές *adj.* [θάρσος, θράσος] (of men or women) **as brazen as a dog** A. Theoc.

κυνο-κέφαλος ου *m.* [κεφαλή] | -κέφᾰλος (unless -κέφαλλος) *metri grat.* Ar. | **1** dog-headed ape, **baboon** Ar. Pl. **2** ‖ PL. dog-headed creatures (app. human, in Africa) Hdt.

κυνο-κλόπος ου *m.* [κλέπτω] **dog-stealer** Ar.

κυνοκοπέω *contr.vb.* [κόπτω] beat like a dog, **thrash** —*someone's back* Ar.

κυνο-ραιστής οῦ *m.* [ῥαίω] dog-destroyer, **flea** or **tick** Od. Arist.

κυν-ορτικός όν *adj.* [ὄρνῡμι] (of a whistling call) **for urging on hounds** S.*Ichn.*

κυνός (gen.): see κύων

Κυνόσαργες εος (ους) *n.* **Kynosarges** (site on the outskirts of Athens, w. a gymnasium for the use of non-Athenians) Hdt. And. D. Plu.

κυνόσ-βατος ου *f.* [κύων, βάτος¹] **evergreen rose** Theoc.

Κυνοσουρίς ίδος *f.* **Kynosurian hound** (ref. to a breed of Spartan hunting dog) Call.

κυνο-σπάρακτος ον *adj.* [σπαράσσω] (of a corpse) **mangled by dogs** S.

κυνοῦχος ου *m.* [ἔχω] **leather bag** or **sack** (for carrying hunting nets) X.

κυνό-φρων ον, gen. ονος *adj.* [φρήν] (of a woman) **with the heart of a bitch** (w.connots. of shamelessness and villainy) A.

κύντερος ᾱ ον *compar.adj.* [κύων] more doglike (in lack of shame or human feelings); (of things, in neg.phr.) **more shameless** or **outrageous** (W.GEN. than a woman, a specified goddess, the belly) Hom.; (of sufferings, deeds, circumstances) **more ignominious** or **cruel** (than others) Od. hHom. AR.

—**κύντατος** η ον *superl.adj.* (of a person) **most shameless** or **offensive** AR.; (of sufferings, deeds, circumstances) **most ignominious** or **cruel** Il. hHom. E. Call. AR.

κυν-υλαγμός οῦ (or **κυνύλαγμος** ου) *m.* **barking of dogs** Il.(dub.) Stesich.

κυν-ώπης ου *masc.adj.* [ὤψ] | voc. κυνῶπα | (of a man, in an abusive address) **dog-faced** (i.e. shameless) Il.

—**κυνῶπις** ιδος *fem.adj.* (of a woman or goddess) **dog-faced** (i.e. shameless) Hom. Plu.(quot.com.); (of Erinyes, ref. to their appearance) E.

κύον (voc.sg.): see κύων

κύπαιρος *dial.m.*, **κυπαιρίσκος** *dial.m.*: see κύπειρος

κυπάρισσος, Att. **κυπάριττος**, ου *f.* **cypress** (ref. to the tree or its wood) Od. Pi.*fr.* Hdt. E.*fr.* Pl. Theoc. +

—**κυπαρίσσινος**, Att. **κυπαρίττινος**, η ον *adj.* (of timbers, buildings, objects) **of cypress wood** Od. Pi. Th. Pl. X. Theoc. +

κύπασσις ιδος *m.* [loanwd.] a kind of garment, **tunic** Alc.

—**κυπασσίσκος** ου *m.* [dimin.] **tunic** Hippon.

κύπειρος, Ion. **κύπερος**, ου, dial. **κύπαιρος** ω (Alcm.) *m.* —also **κύπειρον** ου (Hom.) *n.* a kind of semi-aquatic plant; **galingale** Hom. hHom. Alcm. Hdt. Ar. Call. Theoc.

—**κυπαιρίσκος** ω *dial.m.* [dimin.] **galingale** Alcm.

κύπελλον ου *n.* **drinking-cup, goblet** Hom. AR.

Κύπρις, Boeot. **Κούπρις**, ιδος *f.* [Κύπρος] | acc. Κύπριν, also Κύπριδα (Il. Ibyc.) | Cyprian goddess, **Kypris** (as title of Aphrodite) Il. Hes.*fr.* Eleg. Lyr. Emp. Trag. +; (appos.w. Ἀφροδίτη) hHom.; (meton. for love, passion) A. B.*fr.* Emp. E. Ar.

Κυπρο-γενής έος (οῦς) *fem.adj.* [γένος, γίγνομαι] (epith. of Aphrodite) **Cyprus-born** (ref. to her emerging fr. sea-foam at Paphos) Hes. hHom. Thgn. ‖ SB. Cyprus-born Goddess Sol. Thgn. Pi. Lyr.adesp.; (adj. or sb.) Stesich.

—**Κυπρογένεια**, Aeol. **Κυπρογένηα**, ᾱς *f.* **Cyprus-born Goddess** Lyr. Theoc. Bion Plu.(quot.); (appos.w. Ἀφροδίτη) Ar.

Κύπρος ου *f.* **Cyprus** (island in the E. Mediterranean) Hom. +

—**Κυπρόθε** *adv.* **from Cyprus** Call.

—**Κύπρονδε** *adv.* **to Cyprus** Il.

—**Κύπριος** ᾱ ον *adj.* **1** of or from Cyprus; (of persons, cities, rites) **Cyprian, Cypriot** Hippon. A. Hdt. Isoc. Pl. + ‖ MASC.PL.SB. Cyprians, Cypriots (as a population or military force) Pi. Hdt. Th. Lys. X. + **2** (of an epic poem) **Cyprian** (i.e. prob. by a poet fr. Cyprus) Hdt. ‖ NEUT.PL.SB. *Cypria* (ref. to the poem) Hdt. Arist. **3** ‖ FEM.SB. Cyprian goddess (ref. to Aphrodite) Pi.

κυπτάζω *vb.* [κύπτω] keep oneself bent forwards; **be busy, bustle** —w. περί + ACC. *around a place* Ar.; (of a wife, perh. w. sexual connot.) —*around her husband* Ar.; (of cowardly troops) —*around a dead man* (*stripping his armour, as a pretext for avoiding a fight*) Pl.

κυπτός ή όν *adj.* (fig., of a message) **bent, distorted, crooked** A.

κύπτω *vb.* [reltd. κῡφός,] *aor.* ἔκυψα | *pf.* κέκῡφα | **1** bend one's body, **bend down, stoop** Hom. Ar. NT. Plu.; (to pass through a doorway) X.

Κυράνᾱ

2 (of a woman, prob.ref. to adopting a sexual position) **bend over, go down on all fours** Hippon.
3 bend one's head (sts. W.ADV. or PREP.PHR. downwards or towards the ground); **lower** or **hang one's head** (fr. grief) Hdt. D. Plu.; (fr. shame) Ar. Plu.; (to avoid eye contact) Ar. Thphr. Plu.; (like cattle, fr. brutishness) Pl.; (aggressively, like a bull ready to butt) Ar.; (as the posture of a wrestler, a tired runner) Ar.
4 ‖ PF.PTCPL.ADJ. (of an ox's horns) curving downwards Hdt.

Κυράνᾱ *dial.f.*: see Κυρήνη

Κύρβαντες *m.pl.*: see Κορύβαντες

κυρβασίᾱ ᾱς, Ion. **κυρβασίη** ης *f.* [loanwd.] peaked head-dress (worn by Persians and Scythians) Hdt.; (fig., ref. to a cock's comb) Ar.

κύρβις εως (Ion. ιος) *m.f.* **1** ‖ PL. (at Athens) kyrbeis (ref. to objects, perh. wooden boards, inscribed w. Solon's laws) Lys. Ar. Pl. Arist. Plu.
2 (pejor., ref. to a person) **walking law-book** Ar.
3 (gener.) **tablet** or **pillar** (w. an inscription) Call.; (pl.) AR.

Κύρειος *adj.*: see under Κῦρος

κυρέω *contr.vb.* [κύρω] | fut. κυρήσω | aor. ἐκύρησα |
1 chance upon, come across, find —*a person, a corpse* E. —*people* (W.PTCPL. *doing sthg.*) E. —W.GEN.PTCPL. *people dining* Pi.
2 meet with, experience —W.GEN. *an undesirable marriage* A. S. —*dishonour, wretched treatment, indifference* A. Hdt. S. —*a fate, an occurrence* (W.ADJ. *of a particular kind*) A. E.; **face** —W.GEN. *a trial (at law)* Hdt.; (fig.) **be caught** —W.GEN. *in a net (ref. to an unwelcome fate)* A.
3 hit the mark, be accurate (usu. W.PTCPL. in saying sthg.) A. S.
4 attain, achieve, gain —*sthg.* (*usu. welcome or desired*) A. E. —W.GEN. B. Hdt. Trag. Theoc.; **gain, find** —W.GEN. *persons, children* (W.ADJ. *of a certain kind*) A. Hdt. Theoc.
5 (of good or bad things) **happen, come about** (sts. W.DAT. *for someone*) S. E.; (of a war, situation, fortune) **turn out** —W.ADV. *in a particular way* Trag.
6 (of persons or things, usu. w. no notion of coincidence) **happen to be** or **be** —W.PREDIC.ADJ. or SB. *such and such* Trag. —W.ADVBL. or PREP.PHR. *in a particular place or situation* Trag.; **happen** —W.PTCPL. *to be doing or to have done sthg., or to be such and such* Trag. Ar.(quot. A.)
7 (of things) **pertain, relate** —w. πρός + ACC. *to sthg.* Plb.

κυρηβάζω *vb.* [perh.reltd. κυρίσσω] (fig., of a person, envisaged as a ram) **butt** —w. πρός + ACC. *against someone's leg* (*i.e. be kicked or obstructed by it*) Ar.

κυρήβια ων *n.pl.* **bran** (fr. wheat and barley) Ar.

Κυρήνη ης, dial. **Κυράνᾱ** ᾱς *f.* | sts. ῡ | **1 Cyrene** (nymph abducted by Apollo and taken to Libya, to become patroness and mythic foundress of an eponymous colony) Hes.*fr.* Pi. Call. AR.
2 Cyrene (Libyan colony of Thera, ref. either to the city or to its surrounding territory) Pi. Hdt. Th. +

—Κυρηναῖος ᾱ (Ion. η) ον *adj.* | ῡ Call. | **1** (of the city or region) **of Cyrene** Hdt.
2 (of persons or things) of or from Cyrene, **Cyrenaean** Hdt. X. D. + ‖ MASC.PL.SB. Cyrenaeans (as a population or military force) Hdt. Th. +

κῡρίᾱ ᾱς *f.* [κύριος] **authority, control** (W.GEN. or περί + GEN. over sthg.) Plb.

κυριεύω *vb.* **1** (of persons or peoples) **have power, control** or **authority** —W.GEN. *over persons, lands, the sea,* *everything* X. Plb. NT. Plu.; (of a husband) —*over a household* Arist.; (of the voice of law rather than the threats of an individual, in a happy city) —*over people* Hyp.
2 ‖ AOR. **take possession or control** —W.GEN. *of persons, places, or sim.* D. Plb. Plu.

κύριος ᾱ (Ion. η) ον (also ος ον) *adj.* [reltd. κῦρος] **1** (of gods, rulers, officials, individuals) **having power, control** or **authority** (freq. W.GEN. over persons, places, things) Pi. Trag. Th. Ar. Att.orats. Pl. +; **having authority** (W.INF. to do sthg.) A. E. Th. Att.orats. +; **acting with authority** (W.PTCPL. in doing sthg.) Th. Plb.; **having authority to decide** (W.INDIR.Q. what shd. be the case) X. Is.; (W.ACC. + INF. that sthg. shd. be the case) Pl.
2 ‖ NEUT.SB. **supreme authority** or **sovereign power** (in a state) Arist. ‖ NEUT.PL.SB. **authorities** (ref. to persons or their offices) S. D. Arist.; (abstr.) **authority, power** (of deities) A.(dub.)
3 (of things) having authority, validity or effectiveness; (of a law, decree, verdict, agreement, will, adoption) **binding** E. Th. Att.orats. Pl. +; (of speech, feelings, attitudes, opinions, or sim.) **authoritative** or **valid** Pi. E. Pl. Is. +; (of refutation, as a process) **powerful, effective** Pl.; (fig., of conspirators, ref. to sleep and weariness) A.
4 (of a meeting of the Assembly reserved for the most important business) **principal** Arist.; (perh., wkr.sens.) **regular, scheduled** (opp. extraordinary) Ar.
5 determined by authority (divine or human); (of an ending, a purificatory sacrifice) **ordained** A. Pi.; (of a tomb, ref. to a mountain) **appointed** (for a child, by the parents who exposed it to die there) S. ‖ NEUT.SB. **app., ordained fate** A.*fr.*
6 (of a day) **appointed** (for a particular event) A. Hdt. E.; (of a month) Pi. ‖ FEM.SB. **appointed day** D.
7 (of words) **regular, current, ordinary** (opp. archaic or figurative) Arist.; (specif., of nouns) **proper** (i.e. denoting a person or place) Plb.
8 (of virtue) **properly defined, in the true sense** Arist.
—κύριος ου *m.* **1** (gener.) man with authority or responsibility (in a certain situation), **master** A. S. Ar.; (specif., of a house) A. Men. NT.; **owner** (of a slave) Antipho X. Arist. Men. NT.; (leg.) **guardian** (of a woman or child) Ar. Att.orats. X. Men.
2 ‖ VOC. (as a term of respectful address) **sir** NT.
3 Lord (ref. to God or Jesus) NT.; (ref. to a Roman emperor) NT.; (in voc. address to an angel) NT.

—κυρίως *adv.* **1 with exercise of power, control or authority; under complete control** —*ref. to taking cities* Isoc.; **with supreme authority** —*ref. to a court imposing penalties* Arist.; (wkr.sens.) **completely** Plb.
2 validly, with full authority or **right** (in terms of the law) S. Att.orats. Pl. Men.; (w. ἔχειν, of a law) *have authority, be valid* A.
3 properly, precisely, exactly —*ref. to seeing the truth* Pl. —*ref. to explaining sthg.* Plb.
4 in the true sense, properly speaking Pl. Arist. Plb.

κυρίσσω, Att. **κυρίττω** *vb.* (of bulls or goats) **butt** —*a person, each other* (sts. W.DAT. *w. their horns*) Pl.; (fig., of wave-tossed corpses) **knock against** —*the rocky land* A.

κυρκανάω *contr.vb.* [reltd. κυκάω] **mix** (food or drink); (fig.) **cook up, devise** —*a ruse, a deadly plot* Ar.

κύρμα ατος *n.* [κυρέω] **1 that which one comes across;** (ref. to persons) **prey, spoil, booty** (W.DAT. for animals, birds, fishes, enemy soldiers) Hom. AR.

2 (ref. to a cunning rogue) perh., one who takes advantage of every opportunity, **go-getter** Ar.

Κύρνος ου *f.* Kyrnos (island off NW. Italy, mod. Corsica) Hdt. Call. Plb. Plu.

—**Κύρνιοι** ων *m.pl.* men or inhabitants of Kyrnos, **Kyrnians** Hdt. Plb.

κῦρος εος (ους) *n.* [κυρόω] **1** (in political or military ctxt.) **supreme power** or **authority** (sts. W.GEN. or PREP.PHR. over someone or sthg.) A. Hdt. Th. Pl. Arist.
2 (concr.) **that which has authority** (W.GEN. + INF. over musical standards, to make decisions about them) Pl.
3 validation or confirmation, **guarantee** (W.GEN. of future good fortune) S.
4 perh. **ordained** or **decisive conclusion** (of events) S.

Κῦρος ου *m.* **1** Cyrus (the Great, Persian king, 6th C. BC) A. Hdt. Th. Isoc. Pl. X. +
2 Cyrus (Persian prince, killed in battle in 401 BC, while attempting to depose his brother w. the help of Greek mercenaries) Th. Isoc. Pl. X. D. Plu.

—**Κύρειος** ᾱ ον *adj.* (of an army, a camp) **of Cyrus** (the prince) Isoc. X. || MASC.SB. **Cyrus' troops** X.

κυρόω contr.vb. [κῦρος] **1** act with authority; **make** (W.ACC. a statement) **with authority** (i.e. state authoritatively or decisively) A.; (intr., of a statement) **carry authority** or **be decisive** A.
2 determine with authority; **take a final decision on, settle** —*a disputed issue* Hdt.; (of a judge or jury) **decide** —*a case* A.
|| PASS. (of a final decision) be authorised (by an assembly) A.; (of an issue, the outcome of a conflict) be finally decided A. Hdt. Th. || IMPERS.AOR.PASS. a final decision was taken —W.INF. *to do sthg.* Hdt. || IMPERS.STATV.PLPF.PASS. the final decision was —W.INF. *to do sthg.* Hdt.
3 (of a father) come to a decision about, **confirm, authorise** —*his daughter's marriage* Hdt. || STATV.PLPF.PASS. (of a marriage) have authorisation —W.DAT. *fr. the bride's father* Hdt.
4 (in political or legal ctxt.) **confirm, ratify** —*a law, proposal, treaty, penalty, or sim.* Th. Lys. D. Arist. Plb. Plu.
|| PASS. (of laws, proposals, contracts, or sim.) be ratified And. D. Arist. Plb. Plu.
5 (gener.) confirm (sthg.) as valid; (of a daimon) **confirm** —*the destiny of a soul* Pl.; (of a ruler, by his behaviour) —*his reputation for cruelty* Plb.; (of Zeus) **ratify** —*a request* Ar.; (of Poseidon) **ordain** —*a boundary* E.
6 || MID. (of a particular art) **accomplish** —*its ends* (W.DAT. *through speech*) Pl.
7 || PASS. (of a human sacrifice) be carried out E.

κυρσάνιος ου *Lacon.m.* **young man, youth** Ar.

κύρτη *f.*: see κύρτος

κυρτός ή όν *adj.* **1** forming a curve; (of a man's shoulders) curved (towards his chest), **curved, hunched** Il.; (of an angry lion's spine, compared to a bow) **arched** Theoc.; (of a dolphin's back) Lyr.adesp.; (of a wheel being traced in outline by the τόρνος, *peg-and-string device*) **curving** E.; (of a headland) AR.
2 (of a wave) curved (at the crest), **curving, curling, arched** Il. AR.
3 (of the front surface of a shield) **convex** Plb. || NEUT.SB. convex side, outer edge (of a curve) Arist.

—**κυρτόν** neut.adv. **with arching waves** —*ref. to sea foaming* Mosch.

κύρτος ου *m.* —also **κύρτη** ης (Hdt.) *f.* **wickerwork trap, creel** (for catching lobsters, eels or fish) Hdt. Theoc.; (compared w. the structure of the human body) Pl.

κυρτόω contr.vb. [κυρτός] **1** form into a curve or arc; (of an angry bull) **arch** —*its back* E.; (of a horse) —*its head* X.
|| MID. (of a horse) app. **arch the neck** X.
|| AOR.PASS.PTCPL.ADJ. (of a wave) arched Od.
2 || MID.PASS. (of a human body) **be bent** (opp. upright) X.; (of palm trees, compared to pack-asses) **bend** (under their load) X.
3 || PASS. be made convex; (of a sail) be made to bulge (w.ADV. *in the middle*) —W.DAT. *by the wind* AR.

κύρτωμα ατος *n.* **convex face, bulge** (of a battle formation) Plb.

κύρω *vb.* [reltd. κυρέω] | impf. ἔκυρον, ep. κῦρον | fut. κύρσω | aor. ἔκυρσα | **1** (of a lion) **chance upon, come across, find** —W.DAT. *a carcass* Hes.; (of a charioteer) **crash into, hit** —W.DAT. *another chariot* Il.; (of troops) **encounter, come face to face with** —W.GEN. *enemy forces* A.; (of a river channel) **meet with, find** —W.GEN. *low ground* AR.
2 (of a goddess's head) **reach** —W.GEN. *the roof of a house* hHom.; (of a person, envisaged as a bird) —*a cloud* S.; (of a tree, a headland, rocks) —W.DAT. *the sky* Call. AR.
3 **meet with, experience** —W.DAT. *good or bad fortune, disaster* Il.(mid.) Hes.
4 (of a person, envisaged as an archer) successfully aim at, **hit** —W.GEN. *the mark* A.
5 **gain, acquire** —W.GEN. *a suitor, wife, mother, child* (w.ADJ. *of a particular kind*) A. E. —*sthg.* (usu. welcome or desired) Trag.
6 find —W.GEN. *someone* (W.PREDIC.ADJ. *hostile*) A.
7 (of things) **happen, come about** S.
8 (of persons) **happen** —W.PTCPL. *to be doing sthg.* S.; **chance** (to do sthg.) AR.
9 (of a thing) **be** —W.PREP.PHR. *in a certain place* Parm.

κύρωσις εως *f.* [κυρόω] **1 final decision** (of an issue under discussion) Th.
2 means of achieving an end, **efficacy** (of oratory) Pl.

κύσα, κύσσα (ep.aor.): see κυνέω

κύσθος ου *m.* female genitals, **cunt** Ar.

κυσί (dat.pl.): see κύων

κύστις εως *f.* **bladder** (of a person, as an organ in the body) Il. Pl.; (fr. an animal, inflated like a balloon) Ar.

κύτισος ου *f.* **moon-trefoil** Call. Theoc.

κύτος εος (ους) *n.* **1** rounded hollow object (esp.ref. to its outer surface or internal space); **bowl** or **belly** (W.GEN. of a tripod, cauldron) Alcm. E.; (of a shield, ref. to its convex shape) A.(dub.); (of a cuirass) Ar.(mock-trag.); (specif., without GEN.) **cuirass** E.; **hull** or **hold** (of a ship) Plb.
2 (gener.) **container** (ref. to a vessel or urn, for liquids, ballots, ashes) A. S. Men.; (ref. to a basket) E.; (W.GEN. of the soul, ref. to the body) Pl.; (of the head, ref. to the skull) Pl.; (specif., without GEN.) **skull** Pl.
3 (periphr.) **encasement** (W.GEN. of the trunk of the human body, i.e. encasing trunk) Pl.; (specif., without GEN.) **trunk, torso** S. Pl.; **outer structure** (W.GEN. of a wickerwork trap, as an analogy for the framework of the human body) Pl.; (fig.) app. **main body** (W.GEN. of a city) Plb.

κύτταρος ου *m.* [κύτος] **1 cell** (as home of a grub, in a honeycomb or wasps' nest) Ar.
2 catkin Ar. [or perh. **acorn-cup**.]
3 (fig.) **vault, dome** (W.GEN. of heaven) Ar.

κυφ-αγωγός όν *adj.* [κυφός] (of a horse) **with head bent low** (as it moves) X.

κυφός ή όν *adj.* [κύπτω] **1** (of an old person, a back) **bent, stooping** Od. Ar. AR.
2 (of a plough) **crooked, curved** Thgn.

κύφων ωνος *m.* **1** instrument of punishment that holds the victim in a bent position, **pillory, stocks** Ar. Arist. Plu.
2 (app.meton.) **punishment, pain** Men.

κυψέλη ης *f.* large earthenware container for storing grain, **grain-bin** Hdt. S.*fr.* Ar.

Κύψελος ου *m.* **Kypselos** (first tyrant of Corinth, 7th C. BC, supposedly so named because his mother hid him in a κυψέλη when a baby, to save his life) Hdt. Arist. Plu.
—**Κυψελίδαι** ῶν *m.pl.* **descendants of Kypselos, Kypselids** (ref. to the ruling family of Corinth) Thgn. Hdt. Pl. Arist.

κύω *vb.* [reltd. κυέω] | aor. ἔκῡσα | Forms of the pres. may be ascribed (w. change of accent) to the commoner κυέω. |
1 (pres., of women, female animals) **be pregnant** Hdt.(oracle) Pl. X. Arist. Plu. —w. ἐκ + GEN. *by someone* Plu.; (said as an insult, of a man) —*by his lover* Arist.; (fig., of a city about to produce a tyrant) Thgn.; (of all the natural world, in springtime) Bion
2 (tr.) **be pregnant with** —*a child* Plu.; (of a hare) —*a litter* X.
3 ‖ AOR. (causatv., of rain) **make pregnant, impregnate** —*the earth* A.*fr.*
4 ‖ AOR.MID. (of a woman) **become pregnant, conceive** Hes.

κύων κυνός *m.f.* | voc. κύον | dat.pl. κυσί, ep. κύνεσσι | **1 dog, bitch, hound** Hom. +
2 (in oaths, esp. as sworn by Socrates) νὴ (or μὰ) τὸν κύνα *by the dog* Ar. Pl.
3 (as a contemptuous term for a shameless person, esp. a woman) **dog, bitch** Hom. +
4 (as a mythol. creature or attendant of a deity) **hound** (pl., w.GEN. of Madness) E.; (pl., ref. to Erinyes) Trag.; (fig., ref. to the Sphinx, the Hydra) S. E.; (w.GEN. of Zeus, ref. to an eagle, griffin, Harpy) A. AR.; (of Cybele, ref. to Pan) Pi.*fr.*
5 (fig., ref. to a person) **watchdog, guard-dog** (sts. w.GEN. of a place) A. Ar.; (w.GEN. of the people, ref. to a politician) D. Thphr.
6 (w.art., ref. to Diogenes) **the Dog, the Cynic** Arist.
7 dog (w.GEN. of Orion, ref. to the dog-star, i.e. Sirius) Il.; (w.ADJ. σείριος) A.; (without GEN. or ADJ.) Arist. Plb.
8 a kind of marine animal; perh. **dogfish, shark** Od.

κω *Ion.enclit.adv.:* see πω

κῶας αος *n.* | PL.: nom.acc. κώεα, dat. κώεσι | **sheepskin, fleece** (as bedding or to sit on) Hom. hHom. AR. Theoc.; (ref. to the Golden Fleece) Mimn. Pi. Hdt. AR. Theoc.

κωβιός οῦ *m.* a kind of fish; **gudgeon** Semon. Pl. Men.

κωδάριον ου *n.* [dimin. κῶας] **little sheepskin** Ar.

κώδεια ᾱς *f.* **poppy-head** Il.

κῴδιον ου *n.* [dimin. κῶας] **sheepskin, fleece** (as bedding or to sit on) Ar. Pl. Men.

κώδων ωνος *m.* (*also f.*) **1 bell** Plu.; (carried by a town watchman making his rounds) Th. Plu.; (carried by a town-crier) D.; (attached to a shield, a war-horse) A. E.
2 (*f.*) **war-trumpet** S.
3 (*f.*, ref. to a woman or female animal) perh. **bawler** Ar.(dub.)

κωδωνίζω *vb.* **test by ringing** (to listen for the quality of the sound); (fig.) **test** —*a tragedian's output* Ar. ‖ PASS. (of coinage) **be tested** Ar.

κωδωνό-κροτος ον *adj.* [κρότος] (of the sound) **of jangling bells** (on a shield) E.

κωδωνο-φαλαρό-πωλος ον *adj.* [φάλαρα, πῶλος] (of warriors depicted in tragedies) **with bells on the harness-brasses of one's horse** Ar.

κωδωνο-φορέω *contr.vb.* (of a watchman, on patrol round a city wall) **carry a bell** Ar. ‖ PASS. (of a city wall) **be patrolled with a bell** Ar.

κώθων ωνος *m.* [app. Lacon.] **drinking-cup, mug** (esp. assoc.w. soldiers on campaign) Archil. Ar. X. Plu.; (meton. for a drinking-bout) Plu.

κωθωνίζομαι *mid.pass.vb.* **engage in hard drinking, get drunk** Plb.

κώκῡμα ατος *n.* [κωκύω] **wail, lament** Trag.

κωκῡμός οῦ *m.* (ref. to a mouse) **cause of wailing, trouble, pest** (w.DAT. for people) Call.

κωκῡτός οῦ *m.* **wailing, lamentation** Il. Simon. Pi. Trag.
—**Κωκῡτός** οῦ (also **Κώκῡτος** ου Od.) *m.* **Kokytos, River of Lamentation** (in the underworld) Od. A. B. E. Ar. Pl.

κωκύω *vb.* | ῡ in pres. (Ar. Bion), ῠ in pres. and impf. (Hom. Mosch.) | aor. ἐκώκυσα, ep. κώκυσα | **1** (usu. of women or goddesses) **utter a cry of grief, shriek, wail** Hom. hHom. Emp. Mosch. Bion Plu.; (of a man, fr. a beating) Ar.; (phr., in a curse) κωκύειν (τινα) κελεύειν *tell (someone) to go to hell* Ar.
2 (tr., of women) **wail for, lament** —*a dead person* Od. S. —*someone's fate, a bed that is empty* (*through death*) A. S.; (mid., of men) —*their singed hair* Ar.

κωλ-ακρέτης ου *m.* [app. κωλῆ or κῶλον, ἀγείρω] **pay-clerk** (one on a board of ten officials responsible for paying jurors and others) Ar. Arist.

κωλῆ ῆς *f.* [κῶλον] **1 thighbone** (together w. its flesh), **haunch, ham** (of an animal, as food or a sacrificial offering) Xenoph. Ar.; (as part of a person's body) Ar.
2 rump (of a hare) X.

κωλήν ῆνος *f.* **haunch** (of an animal, as food) Plu.

κώληψ ηπος *f.* app. **back of the knee** (as a vulnerable spot) Il.

Κωλιάς άδος *fem.adj.* **1** ‖ SB. **Kolias** (promontory nr. Athens, site of a temple of Aphrodite) Ar. D. Call. Plu.
2 (of the beach) **of Kolias, Kolian** Hdt.; (of women) Hdt.(oracle)
3 ‖ SB. **Kolian goddess** (ref. to Aphrodite) Ar.

κῶλον ου *n.* **1 limb** (of the body) Trag. Pl.
2 (specif., sts. sg. for pl.) **leg** Hippon. Trag. Ar. Pl.
3 thigh (of an animal, as a sacrificial offering) A.
4 leg (ref. to the return part of the diaulos race) A.
5 side (of a building) Hdt. Pl.
6 limb (w.GEN. of a sling, ref. to one of two thongs) Plb.
7 clause (as a unit in a sentence) Arist.

κώλῡμα ατος *n.* [κωλύω] **1** that which hinders or prevents (an activity), **hindrance, impediment, obstacle** E. Th. X. Plb. Plu.; (w.GEN. to sthg.) Pl. Plu.; (w.INF. or μή + INF. to doing sthg. or to sthg. happening) Th.
2 (specif.) **preventive measure** (against flames) Th.

κωλύμη ης *f.* **hindrance, prevention** (sts. w.GEN. of sthg.) Th.

κωλῡσιεργέω *contr.vb.* [ἔργον] (of the Senate) **hinder operations, be obstructive** Plb.

κώλῡσις εως *f.* **hindering** or **preventing** (sts. w.GEN. of sthg.) Pl. Arist. Plu.

κωλῡτήριος ᾱ ον *adj.* (of an act) **preventive** (of sthg.) A.*satyr.fr.*

κωλῡτής οῦ *m.* **1** (ref. to a person) **preventer** or **obstructor** (usu. w.GEN. of someone or sthg.) Th. D.
2 (ref. to a sandbank) **impediment, obstruction** (to ships) Pl.

κωλῡτικός ή όν *adj.* (of things, circumstances) likely to hinder or prevent, **preventive** (sts. w.GEN. of sthg.) X. Arist.

κωλύτωρ ορος *m.* (ref. to an image nailed to a building) **deterrent** (w.GEN. of travellers) A.*satyr.fr.*

κωλύω *vb.* | sts. ῠ in pres. and impf. (Sapph. Pi. Ar. Men.) | aor. ἐκώλῡσα | pf. κεκώλῡκα ‖ PASS.: fut. κωλῡθήσομαι (Plb.), also κωλύσομαι (Th.) | aor. ἐκωλύθην | pf. κεκώλῡμαι ‖ neut.impers.vbl.adj. κωλῡτέον |

1 (of persons or things) **hinder** or **prevent** —*someone* (oft. W.INF. or μή + INF. *fr. doing sthg.*) Sapph. Pi. Hdt. E. Th. + —(W. τό + INF.) S. —(W.GEN. *fr. an action*) X. NT. —*sthg.* E. Th. Lys. + —(W.INF. *fr. doing sthg.*) Hdt.; (intr.) **stand in the way, be an obstacle** S. E. Th. + ∥ PASS. (of persons) be hindered or prevented (oft. W.INF. or μή + INF. fr. doing sthg.) E. Antipho Th. + —W.PTCPL. *fr. doing sthg.* Th. —W.GEN. *fr. an action* Plb.; (of things) Th.
2 (of laws) **forbid** (usu. W.ACC. or ACC. + INF. sthg., persons fr. doing sthg., or sim.) Democr. X. Is. D.; (of lawmakers) **deter** —*wrongdoers* Arist.; (of a command) —*people* (w. ἀπό + GEN. *fr. wrongdoing*) X.
3 (specif., of a Roman tribune) **use one's power of veto** Plu.
4 debar, exclude —*someone* (W.GEN. *fr. a contest*) X.; **keep away** —*someone* (w. ἀπό + GEN. *fr. a person*) X.
5 withhold —*sthg.* (w. ἀπό + GEN. *fr. someone*) NT.

κῶμα ατος *n.* **1 deep sleep** (induced by supernatural or other extraordinary means), **trance, coma** Hom. Hes. Alcm. Sapph. Pi.
2 deep sleep (naturally induced) AR.
3 perh. **lethargy** or **unconsciousness** (W.GEN. of sleep) Theoc.*epigr.*
4 numbness, torpor (of a person dying or fainting) AR.

κωμάζω, dial. **κωμάσδω** *vb.* [κῶμος] | fut. κωμάσω, also κωμάσομαι, dial. κωμάξομαι (Pi.) | aor. ἐκώμασα, dial. ἐκώμαξα (Pi.) |
1 take part in communal revelry; (of young men, at a public celebration) **revel, make merry** (to the accompaniment of the aulos) Hes.
2 (specif., of men) **take part in a drunken revel** (either at a symposium or more freq. roaming the streets at night, sts. gate-crashing on individuals or drinking-parties), **revel** or **go revelling** Alc. Thgn. E. Lys. Pl. X. + —W.PREP.PHR. *to a woman* (w. the aim of pounding at her door or serenading her) Is. Thphr. Theoc. —W.DAT. Anacr.; (fig., of persons behaving in a reckless, disrespectful or unseemly manner) Plu.
3 take part in a celebratory revel (in the ctxt. of an athletic victory); (of a victor, his friends, a poet) **go revelling in celebration** (sts. W.PREP.PHR. to a place) Pi.; (tr., of a poet, people's voices) **celebrate with revelry** —*a victorious athlete* Pi.; (of the victor) —*the festival* (*in which he was victorious*) Pi.; (of his friends) —*Zeus* (*as patron of the festival*) Pi. ∥ PASS. (of victorious athletes) be celebrated with revelry B.
4 (of a military victor) **celebrate** —W.INTERN.ACC. *w. a song of victory* E.
5 (gener., of a poet) **offer a song of celebration** —W.DAT. *to gods and heroes* Pi.
6 app. **be a reveller** —W.PREP.PHR. *in the processions* (*at the Dionysia*) D. | see κῶμος 8

κώμ-αρχος ου *m.* [κώμη, ἄρχω] **village headman** (in Anatolia) X.

κωμαστής οῦ *m.* [κωμάζω] **reveller** Pl. X.; (appos.w. Dionysus) Ar.

κώμη ης *f.* **1 village** (usu. ref. to an unwalled settlement, opp. πόλις *city* or *town*) Hes. Hdt. Th. Att.orats. Pl. +
2 district (of a city) Isoc. Pl.

κωμήτης ου *m.* **1 inhabitant of a village, villager** Pl. X. Call.
2 (gener.) **townsman, inhabitant** (W.GEN. of a land) E.
3 fellow townsman, neighbour Ar.

—κωμῆτις ιδος *f.* **fellow townswoman, neighbour** Ar.

κωμικός ή όν *adj.* [κῶμος] **1 relating to comic drama**; (of a poet, actor, chorus, mask, the stage) **comic** Aeschin. D. Arist. Thphr.(dub.) Plu.; (fig., of a witness to victory, ref. to a mask dedicated by an actor or dramatist) Call.*epigr.* ∥ MASC.SB. **comic dramatist** Plb. Plu. ∥ NEUT.SB. **quotation from a comedy** Plu.
2 (of behaviour) **comic, amusing** Plu.

κωμό-πολις εως *f.* [κώμη, πόλις] **small town** NT.

κῶμος ου *m.* **1** occasion of communal revelry (assoc.w. feasting, dancing, singing, drinking), **revel, merrymaking** hHom. Hdt. E.
2 (specif.) revelry (by drunken men, either at a symposium or more freq. roaming the streets at night, sts. gate-crashing on individuals or drinking-parties), **revel** Thgn. Pratin. E.*Cyc.* Ar. Pl. X. +; (going to the house of one's beloved, w. the intention of pounding at the door or performing a serenade) Is. Bion; (accompanied by women, to the houses of their male lovers) Plu.; (gener.) **riotous behaviour** Plu.
3 (collectv., ref. to a group of persons in the streets) **revel-band** Thgn.; (of satyrs, accompanying Dionysus to a woman's house) E.*Cyc.*(cj.); (fig., W.GEN. of Erinyes, who have drunk blood) A.; (of doves, whose arrival interrupts a feast) E.; (ref. to Bacchants) E.; (ref. to an army) E.
4 singing by revellers, **song of revelry** E.*Cyc.*
5 celebratory revel (for a victorious athlete, involving the victor, his friends, or the poet who sings his praises), **victory-revel** Pi. B. Call.
6 festive celebration (in honour of a deity, ref. to song and dance) Ar.; **festive band** (of persons singing in honour of a goddess) E.; (singing the praises of a bride and groom) E.
7 (app.oxymor.) **celebration** (by mourners, ref. to a funeral lament) E.
8 revel (app. as an event at the Dionysia) D.(law) | see κωμάζω 6

κῶμῡς ῦθος *f.* **bundle, sheaf** (of hay) Theoc.

κωμῳδέω contr.vb. [κωμῳδός] **1** (of a dramatist) **tell in comedy** —*the honest truth* Ar. ∥ NEUT.PL.PASS.PTCPL.SB. **things represented in comedy** Pl.
2 (of a dramatist) **make the subject of comedy, satirise, lampoon, ridicule** —*someone or sthg.* Ar. Pl. X. Arist. Plu. ∥ PASS. (of a person) be ridiculed in comedy X. Plu.
3 (of persons) **treat in the manner of a comic dramatist, ridicule, make fun of** —*someone or sthg.* Lys. Ar. Pl. Plu.; (intr.) **poke fun** Ar. ∥ PASS. (of persons) be ridiculed Ar.

κωμῳδήματα των *n.pl.* **subjects for comic treatment** Pl.

κωμῳδίᾱ ᾱς *f.* **comic drama, comedy** (ref. either to a single play or to the genre) Ar. Isoc. Pl. Arist. Theoc.*epigr.* Plu.

κωμῳδικός ή όν *adj.* of or relating to comic drama; (of verses, a chamber-pot, behaviour, a performance) **comic** Ar. Pl. ∥ NEUT.PL.SB. **comic material** Ar.

κωμῳδιο-γράφος ου *m.* [κωμῳδίᾱ, γράφω] **writer of comedies** Plb.

κωμῳδοδιδασκαλίᾱ ᾱς *f.* [κωμῳδοδιδάσκαλος] act of putting on a comedy, **staging of a comedy** Ar.

κωμῳδο-διδάσκαλος ου *m.* [κωμῳδός] teacher or trainer of a comic chorus (usu. the poet himself), **comic dramatist** Ar. Isoc. Arist.

κωμῳδολοιχέω contr.vb. [λείχω] app., be one who licks like a comic performer; (fig.) **jest obsequiously, suck up** —w. πρός + ACC. *to a successful person* Ar.

κωμῳδο-ποιητής οῦ *m.* **comic poet** Ar.

κωμῳδο-ποιός οῦ *m.* [ποιέω] **comic poet** Pl. Arist. Plu.

κωμ-ῳδός οῦ m. [κῶμος, ἀοιδή] **1 comic performer** (ref. to an actor) Plu.; (ref. to a member of the chorus) Arist. ‖ PL. comic performers (actors or chorus members or both) Arist. **2 comic poet** Pl. **3** ‖ COLLECTV.PL. (meton., ref. to the plays themselves) comedies Lys. Pl. X. Arist.; (ref. to the occasion) comic performances Aeschin. D.(law)

κώνειον, Ion. **κωνῆον**, ου n. **1 hemlock** (ref. to the plant) Plu.; (ref. to the prepared juice as a poison, esp. as the official method of execution at Athens) And. Lys. Ar. Pl. X. Arist. **2 fennel rod** (being used to draw geometrical figures in sand) Call.

κῶνος ου m. **pine cone** Theoc.

κώνωψ ωπος m. **gnat** or **mosquito** A. Hdt. Ar. NT.

Κῷος adj.: see under Κῶς

Κῶπαι ῶν f.pl. **Kopai** (town in Boeotia) Il.

—**Κωπαΐς** ίδος, contr. **Κωπᾷς** ᾷδος fem.adj. **1 of or near Kopai**; (appos.w. λίμνη) *Lake Kopais* Hdt. **2** (of eels; of girls, fig.ref. to eels) **from Lake Kopais, Kopaic** Ar. ‖ SB. Kopaic eel Ar.

κωπεύς έως (Ion. έος) m. [κώπη] | Att.nom.pl. κωπῆς, Ion. κωπέες | ‖ PL. **timber for making oars, oar-spars** Hdt. And. Ar.

κώπη ης, dial. **κώπᾱ** ᾱς f. **1 handle** (of an oar); (gener.) **oar** Od. Pi. Hdt. Trag. Th. Ar. +; (meton. for a ship) E.; (meton. for a fleet) E. **2 handle, shaft** (of a key) Od. **3 hilt** (of a sword) Hom. Tyrt. S. E. **4 shaft** (of a firebrand) E.Cyc.

κωπήεις εσσα εν adj. (of a sword) **furnished with a hilt, hilted** Il. AR.

κωπηλατέω contr.vb. [ἐλαύνω] **1 pull an oar, row** Plb. **2** (of a carpenter) **ply, drive** —a drill (W.DAT. *by a double thong, i.e. a strap wound around the drill body, w. its two ends pulled alternately, so that the drill spins backwards and forwards*) E.Cyc.

κωπ-ήρης ες adj. [ἀραρίσκω] **1** (of a vessel) **equipped with oars, oared** E. Th.(treaty) Plu.; (of a military force) E.fr.; (of a company of men, periphr. for rowers) E. ‖ NEUT.SB. **rowing-boat** Plu. **2** (of a ship's armament, ref. to its full complement) **of oars** A.

κωπίον ου n. [dimin. κώπη] **oar** or **paddle** Ar.

κώρᾱ dial.f.: see κόρη¹

Κώρειτες Boeot.m.pl.: see Κουρῆτες, under κούρητες

κωρίς dial.f.: see κᾱρίς

κῶρος dial.m.: see κόρος²

Κωρυκαῖος ου m. [Κώρυκος *Korykos* (city on the coast of Cilicia, in S. Turkey)] **man from Korykos** (provbl. for an eavesdropper) Call.

Κωρύκιος¹ ᾱ ον adj. (of a kind of crocus) **from Korykos, Korykian** AR.

Κωρύκιος² ᾱ (Ion. η) ον adj. (of a cave on Mt. Parnassos, assoc.w. nymphs and Pan) **Corycian** Hdt.; (of the mountain, its peaks) E.; (of nymphs) S. Call. AR.

—**Κωρυκίς** ίδος fem.adj. (of the cave) **Corycian** A.

κώρυκος ου m. **1 leather bag** (for provisions) Od. Ar. **2 punch-bag** Dionys.Eleg. Arist.(quot.com.)

Κώρυκος ου m. **Korykos** (Lydian town, on the Erythrai peninsula opposite Chios) hHom. Th.

κῶς Ion.interrog.adv., **κως** Ion.enclit.adv.: see πῶς, πως

Κῶς Κῶ f. | also ep.nom. Κόως (hHom. Theoc.) | acc. Κῶν, also Κῶ | **Cos** (island in the Aegean, off the coast of Caria, also ref. to its main city) Il. hHom. Hdt. Th. +

—**Κόωνδε** ep.adv. **to Cos** Il.

—**Κῷος** ᾱ (Ion. η) ον adj. (of persons) **from Cos, Coan** Hdt. Pl. Plb.; (of wine) D. ‖ MASC.PL.SB. men of Cos, Coans (as a population or military force) Hdt. Plu.

κωτιλίζω vb. [κωτίλος] (of birds) **chatter, prattle** Call.

κωτίλλω vb. **1 chatter, prattle** Sol. —*sthg. foolish* Thgn. —W.NEUT.PL.ACC. w. *wily* or *soft words* Hes. Thgn. —w. *endless talk* Theoc. **2 flatter, cajole** Thgn. —*someone* Thgn. S.

κωτίλος η (dial. ᾱ) ον adj. **1** (of persons) **talkative** Thgn. Theoc.; (of birds) Anacr. Call. **2** (of a Muse, meton. for music) perh. **beguiling** Lyr.adesp.

κωφός ή όν adj. **1** (of a weapon) **blunt, ineffective** Il. E.fr. **2** (of the earth) **lacking sensibility, senseless, inert, dumb** Il. **3** (of a sea-swell, a wave) **giving off no sound, silent, noiseless** Il. Alcm. AR.; (of undisturbed ground, opp. that which is being tunnelled under) Hdt. **4** (of a harbour, ref. to a permanent characteristic) app. **quiet** (by contrast w. a busy one nearby) X. **5** (of persons) unable to speak, **dumb, mute** Hdt. Ar. NT.; (of a poet who does not speak on a given theme) **as good as dumb** Pi. **6** (of persons, animals) unable to hear, **deaf** hHom. A. S.*Ichn.* Pl. X. +; (fig., of winds, to a person's words) Call. **7** lacking comprehension (of things heard); (fig., of persons, their intellect, or sim.) **deaf, uncomprehending** Parm. S. Pl.; (gener., of persons) **helpless** Plu. **8** (of rumours, a narrative) conveying no clear information or meaning, **unclear, obscure, vague** S. Plb.

κωφότης ητος f. **deafness** Pl.; (fig.) **incomprehension** D.

Λ λ

λάᾱ dial.f.: see λεία
λᾶας λᾶος m. | acc. λᾶαν, also λᾶα (Call.) | dat. λᾶι ‖ du.nom. λᾶε ‖ PL.: nom. λᾶες, gen. λάων, ep.dat. λάεσσι —also **λᾶος** ου m. (f. Corinn.) | SG.: only gen. λάου (S.) ‖ PL.: nom. λᾶοι (Call.), acc. λάους (Hes.fr. Simon.), Boeot.fem.dat. λᾶῦς |
1 loose stone, **stone, rock, boulder** (esp. used as a missile) Hom. Simon. E. Corinn. Hellenist.poet.; (rolled uphill by Sisyphos in the underworld, as an eternal punishment) Od.
2 piece of stone (used in construction), **stone** Hom. hHom. Call.
3 mass of stone (as a natural feature in the landscape), **stone, rock** S.; (created through metamorphosis of objects or living beings) Hom. B.fr. Call.
4 ‖ PL. (w. play on λᾱός people, ref. to humans created through metamorphosis of stones thrown by Deukalion, son of Prometheus, and his wife Pyrrha) **stone-people** Hes.fr. Call.
λάβᾱ Aeol.f.: see λαβή
λάβδα indecl.n. [Semit.loanwd.] **1 labda, lambda** (letter of the Greek alphabet) Pl. [The spelling λάμβδα is post-classical.]
2 (euphem.) **do the L** (i.e. λαικάζω perform fellatio) Ar.
Λάβδακος ου m. **Labdakos** (king of Thebes, grandson of Kadmos, father of Laios and grandfather of Oedipus) Hdt. S. E.
—**Λαβδάκειος** ᾱ ον adj. (of the son) **of Labdakos** (ref. to Laios) S.; (of the house, i.e. descendants) S.
—**Λαβδακίδαι** ῶν (dial. ᾶν) m.pl. sons or descendants of Labdakos, **Labdakids** Pi. S. E.(dub.) Call.
λάβε (aor.2 imperatv.), **λαβέ** (Att.), **λαβεῖν** (aor.2 inf.), **λάβεσκον** (iteratv.aor.2): see λαμβάνω
λαβή ῆς, Aeol. **λάβᾱ** ᾱς f. [λαμβάνω] **1** act of taking in the hand, **receiving, acceptance** (W.GEN. of money) A.
2 (concr.) that which affords a grip for the hand; **handle** (of a container) S. Ar.; **hilt** (of a sword) Alc. D. Plu.
3 hold, grip (on an opponent, in wrestling) Plu.; (fig, in argument or other kind of contention, usu.ref. to an opening or opportunity gained or conceded) A. Ar. Pl. D. Plu.
4 (gener.) **hold, grip** (on an object) Plu.; (on a person, taken by a disease) Plu.; (over a city, by a commander defending it) Plu.
5 ‖ PL. (in military ctxt.) **grips, grappling** (ref. to hand-to-hand fighting) Plu.; (fig.) **clutches** (of an enemy commander) Plu.
λάβῃσι (ep.3sg.aor.2 subj.): see λαμβάνω
λαβίς ίδος f. [λαμβάνω] **rivet** (for fastening a spear-head to the haft) Plb.
λάβοισα, λαβοῖσα (Aeol. and dial.fem.aor.2 ptcpl.): see λαμβάνω
λαβόλιον ου n. [λάβολος] **stoning** (as a form of execution) Alc.(dub.)

λᾱ́-βολος ον adj. [λᾶας, βάλλω] (of a person) **deserving to be stoned** Alc.
λάβον (ep.aor.2): see λαμβάνω
λαβρ-αγόρης εω Ion.m. [λάβρος, ἀγορεύω] **reckless talker** Il.
λάβρᾱξ ᾱκος m. **large carnivorous fish, sea-bass** Ar.
λαβρεύομαι mid.vb. [λάβρος] **talk recklessly** Il.
λάβρος ον adj. **1** (of wind, rain, waves, rivers) **rushing, turbulent, violent** Hom. hHom. A. Hdt. E. AR. +; (of the neck of the Hellespont, fig.ref. to its channel) Tim.
2 (of fire, flames, smoke) **fierce, raging** Pi. E. AR.
3 (of a serpent's jaws) **fierce, ferocious, violent** Pi. E.; (of a knife-blade) E.Cyc.; (of Zeus' thunderbolt) E.
4 (of persons) **boisterous, impetuous, reckless** Thgn. Pi.; (W.DAT. in indiscriminate speech) Pi.; (of a person's speech) S.
—**λάβρως** adv. **furiously** Alc. Thgn. A. Lyr.adesp.
λαβροστομέω contr.vb. [στόμα] **speak recklessly** or **impetuously** A.
λαβρό-συτος ον adj. [σεύω] (of Io) **rushing furiously** A.
λαβύρινθος ου m. **1 large building with elaborate and complicated passageways** (fr. which it is difficult to find a way out), **labyrinth** (in Egypt, built early in the 2nd millennium BC, as a memorial for rulers) Hdt.; (at Knossos, built by Minos to confine the Minotaur) Call. Plu.
2 (fig.) **labyrinth, maze** (ref. to a tortuous argument) Pl.
3 cage, trap (of woven rushes, used in fishing) Theoc.
λάβω (aor.2 subj.), **λαβών** (aor.2 ptcpl.): see λαμβάνω
λαγαρίζομαι mid.vb. [λαγαρός] (of persons) app. **become thin** or **emaciated** Ar.
λαγαρός ά όν adj. **1** (of dancing-girls) **slim** Ar. [or perh. loose-limbed, lithe]
2 (of a hound's flanks) app. **hollowed, curved** X.; (of part of a horse's neck) X. [or perh. loose, flexible]
3 (of parts of the terrain) **hollow** X. [or perh. narrow]
4 (of pillars) **thin, narrow** Plu. ‖ NEUT.SB. perh., **weakly fortified section** (of a wall) Plu.
λᾱγέτᾱς ᾱ dial.m. [λᾱός, ἡγέομαι] **leader of the people** Pi.
λάγινος η (dial. ᾱ) ον adj. [λαγώς] (of a creature) **of the hare family** A.
λάγιον ου n. [dimin. λαγώς] **young hare, leveret** X.
λαγνείᾱ ᾱς f. **lechery** X. Arist.
λαγο-δαίτᾱς ᾱ dial.m. [λαγώς, δαίνυμι] (ref. to an eagle) **devourer of a hare** A.
λαγοθηρέω contr.vb. [θήρᾱ] **be a hare hunter, hunt hares** Ar.
λαγός Ion.m.: see λαγώς
λαγχάνω vb. | fut. λήξομαι, Ion. λάξομαι | aor.2 ἔλαχον, ep. ἔλλαχον, λάχον, inf. λαχεῖν | ep.redupl.aor.2 subj.: 2pl. λελάχητε, 3pl. λελάχωσι | pf. εἴληχα, dial. λέλογχα, 3sg. λέλογχε, also λελόγχει (Theoc.), 3pl. λελόγχᾱσι (Od.), also

λαγωβολίη

λελάχᾱσι (Emp.) | plpf. εἰλήχειν ‖ PASS.: aor. ἐλήχθην | pf. εἴληγμαι ‖ neut.impers.vbl.adj. ληκτέον |
1 engage in the drawing of lots (as a process for determining priority, duties, or sim.); (of an individual) draw the winning lot, **be chosen by lot** Hom. Hdt. S. E. Th. Ar. + —W.INF. *to do sthg.* Il. Hdt. Th.; **be chosen** —W.DAT. πάλῳ, κλήρῳ *by drawing of lots* A. Hdt.; (of soldiers) **be allotted** —W.PREP.PHR. *to a specified station* Il. A.; (tr.) **draw** —*a lot* Sapph. A.
2 (at Athens) draw a lot (for a public office or other responsibility); **be chosen by lot** (sts. W.DAT. κυάμῳ *by lot*) Ar. Att.orats. + —W.PREDIC.SB. *as a magistrate, priest, or sim.* Ar. Att.orats. —W.INF. *to hold an office, be a member of the Council* Hdt. Ar. Pl. D.; (tr.) **have assigned to one by lot** —*an office* Ar. Att.orats.; (intr.) **make appointments by lot** Isoc.
3 receive through a drawing of lots (one's share of sthg. taken fr. the enemy); **obtain by lot** —*goods, women, a portion of spoils* Hom. E. ‖ PF. (intr., of captives) have been allotted —W.PREP.PHR. or ADV. *to individual persons or collectively* E. —W.INF. *to serve as someone's slave* E. ‖ PF.PASS. (of captives) have been assigned by lot E.
4 (of Poseidon, Hades, Zeus) **gain by drawing of lots** —*the sea, underworld, heaven* (W.INF. *to dwell in*) Il.; (of a person) **have assigned to one** (W.DAT. κλήρῳ *by lot*) —*a country* A. E.; (intr., of a group of persons) **draw lots** —W.PREP.PHR. *for sthg.* (*to decide who shall have it*) NT.
5 (of a chorus director) **have assigned to one by lot** —*a poet* Antipho
6 (intr., without actual drawing of lots) have (a place) allocated to one; (of goats) **be allocated** —W.PREP.PHR. *to ships* (*i.e. distributed among them*) Od. ‖ PF. (of fire) have been allocated a place —W.PREP.PHR. *in some region of the universe* Pl.; (of a virtue) —*in a person's nature* E.
7 receive as one's share (in a division or distribution) —*captured property and slaves* Hdt. —*money* Hdt. —*a land* Isoc.; (intr.) **receive one's due share** (of a meal) Od.
8 have apportioned to one (by the gods, fate, or no specific agent), **be allotted, gain, obtain** —*prosperity, glory, honour, sufferings, lands, material goods, or sim.* Xenoph. Pi. B. Hdt. Trag. + —W.COGN.ACC. μοῖραν, μέρος *a share or portion* (sts. W.GEN. *of sthg.*) Thgn. +; (of gods) **receive** —*their rightful honours* Il. —*a libation* E.(dub.) —*religious rites* AR.; (w. relationship betw. subject and object reversed, of inherited wealth) **be apportioned to** —*a person* Pi.
9 (gener.) **gain, obtain** —W.GEN. *gifts, funeral rites* Hom. —*garlands* Pi. —*honour* Thgn. S. —*virtue, beauty, good sense* Thgn. A. —*one's patrimony, a second life* E. —*health, the Graces* (meton. *for their gifts*) B. —*a glorious death* Th. —*sleep* Hdt. X. —*a meal* X. —*a stupid master* Hippon. —*an ally* S.; (w. relationship betw. subject and object reversed, of anxieties) **be the allotment** —W.GEN. *of persons* Thgn.
10 (causatv., in ep.redupl.aor.) **give** (W.ACC. a dead person) **a due share** —W.GEN. *of fire* (*i.e. cremate him*) Il.
11 (of deities) receive (a privilege or function) as one's allotment (fr. Zeus or the Fates); **receive** —*one's portion, an honour* Od. Hes. hHom. Pi.; (of Helios) —*daily toil* Mimn. ‖ STATV.PF. be in possession of —W.GEN. *a long life* Emp.
12 (of deities) receive (a place) as one's allotment (freq. w.connot. of taking tutelary responsibility for it); (of individual gods) **receive** —*a specific city or region* hHom. Pi. Pl. Hellenist.poet.; (of Hestia) —*civic buildings* Pi.; (of unspecified gods) —*a land* Hdt.; (of nymphs) —W.GEN. *spring waters* Pi.
13 (of deities) receive (a particular human activity) as one's area of concern; (of Hades) **be allotted** —*mourning and wailing* Stesich.; (of Persephone) —*head-beating* (*by mourners*) E.; (of Eunomia) —*festivities* B.; (of Erinyes) —*actions involving blood and lamentation* A. E. —*mortal affairs* (W.INF. *to manage*) A.
14 (of deities or other agents) receive (a person) as one's responsibility; (of Mnemosyne) **be allotted** —*Hermes* hHom.; (of Apollo) —*archers and singers* Call.; (of Aphrodite) —*a particular woman* Ar.; (of a daimon) —*a person, a person's fate* Lys. Pl. Theoc.; (of a hateful fate, an unhappy destiny) —*a person* Il. E. AR.; (of impoverishment) **become the lot of** —*slanderers* Pi.
15 (leg.) gain permission to bring (a lawsuit, app. reflecting the fact that the presiding magistrate decided the order of hearing by lot); **initiate, bring** (sts. W.DAT. against someone) —W.ACC. δίκην (sts. understd.) *a lawsuit* (sts. W.GEN. defining the alleged crime, matter at issue, or item for which a claim is being made) Att.orats. Pl. +; (also) —w. κρίσιν *a suit* Pl. —w. ἔγκλημα *a charge* D. —W.COGN.ACC. λῆξιν Is. ‖ PF. (fig.) have earned the right to prosecute —W.GEN. *for murder* (*i.e. to avenge it by killing the murderer*) E. ‖ PASS. (of lawsuits) be authorised or brought Att.orats. ‖ IMPERS.PASS. a case is authorised or brought Is. D.

λαγωβολίη ης *Ion.f.* [λαγωβόλον] **hare-hunting** Call.

λαγω-βόλον ου *n.* [λαγώς, βάλλω] curved stick for throwing at hares; **throwing-stick** (also used as a club or cudgel) Theoc.

λαγῴδιον ου *n.* [dimin. λαγώς] young hare, **leveret** Ar.

λαγών όνος *f.* [reltd. λαγαρός] **1** (usu.pl.) area between the ribs and the hip (of a person or animal), **flank, side, waist** E. Ar. X. Hellenist.poet.
2 flank (of a mountain, cliff) Call.(pl.) Plu.

λαγῷος ᾱ ον *adj.* [λαγώς] (of the meat) **of a hare** Ar. ‖ NEUT.PL.SB. (w. κρέα understd.) hare-meat Ar. Philox.Leuc.

λαγώς ώ (or **λαγῶς** ῶ) Att.m. | acc.sg. λαγών (Ar.), also λαγώ (X.) | PL.: nom. λαγῷ, acc. λαγῶς | —also ep. **λαγωός**, Ion. **λαγός**, οῦ *m.* | dial.acc.pl. λαγός (Hes.) | hare Hom. +; (exemplifying timidity or cowardice) D. Plu.

λάδανον *n.*: see λήδανον

λᾶδος εος *dial.n.* **light dress** (of a woman) Alcm.

λάε (ep.3sg.impf.): see λάω

Λᾱέρτης ου (Ion. εω, ep. ᾱο), dial. **Λᾱέρτᾱς** ᾱ *m.* —also **Λᾱέρτιος** (contr. **Λᾱρτιος**) ου *m.* Laertes (father of Odysseus) Od. Hes.fr. S. E. Ar. +

—Λᾱερτιάδης ου (Ion. εω), dial. **Λᾱρτιάδᾱς** ᾱ *m.* son of Laertes (ref. to Odysseus) Hom. E.

λάζομαι *mid.vb.* —also (pres.) **λάζυμαι** (hHom. E. +) *mid.vb.* [reltd. λαμβάνω] | dial.imperatv. λάζευ and λάσδεο (Theoc.) | ep.3pl.opt. λαζοίατο | ep.3sg.impf. λάζετο | **1 take hold of** —*a weapon, reins, gifts, or sim.* (freq. W.DAT. w. one's hands) Hom. E. AR. Theoc. —*a person* (W.ADV. *in one's arms*) Il. —*a baby* E. —W.GEN. *a cup* Ar.; (of fallen enemies) —W.ACC. *the earth* (W.ADV. w. *their teeth, i.e. 'bite the dust'*) Il. AR.
2 lay hands on, apprehend, seize —*a person* hHom. E.
3 (wkr.sens.) **take, draw** —*perfumed oil* (W.PREP.PHR. *fr. a flask*) Theoc.
4 take —*one's words* (W.ADV. πάλιν *back, i.e. retract them*) Il.; **keep** —*one's words* (W.ADV. πάλιν *back, i.e. leave them unspoken*) Od.

λάθᾱ *dial.f.*: see λήθη

λᾱθ-άνεμος ον *dial.adj.* [λήθω, see λανθάνω] (of a time of year) escaping the winds, **windless** Simon.

λαθεῖν (aor.2 inf.), **λᾱθέμεν** (dial.inf.): see λανθάνω

λαθητικός ή όν adj. [λανθάνω] (of wrongdoers) **likely to be undetected** Arist.

λαθι-κηδής ές adj. —also perh. **λαθικάδεος** ον Aeol.adj. [κῆδος] (of a mother's breast) causing forgetfulness of troubles, **care-relieving** Il.; (of wine) Alc.

λᾱθί-πονος ον dial.adj. [λήθω, see λανθάνω; πόνος] **forgetful of one's troubles** S.; (of a person's life) made to forget troubles, **relieved** (w.GEN. of pains) S.

λαθι-πορφυρίς ίδος f. [λανθάνω, app. πορφυρίων] a kind of marsh-hen (w. timid habits); **purple gallinule** Ibyc.

λαθί-φθογγος ον adj. [φθόγγος] (of death) having or causing forgetfulness of speech, **speechless** Hes.

λαθιφροσύνη ης f. [φρονέω] **forgetfulness** AR.

λαθοίατο (ep.3pl.aor.2 mid.opt.), **λαθόμην** (ep.aor.2 mid.), **λάθον** (ep.aor.2): see λανθάνω

λᾶθος εος dial.n. [reltd. λήθη] **forgetfulness, oblivion** Theoc.

λάθρᾱ (also **λάθρᾰ** hHom.), Ion. **λάθρη** adv. [λανθάνω] **1** in a manner which escapes notice, **without anyone else knowing, secretly, in private, stealthily** Hom. +
2 (as prep.) **without the knowledge** —w.GEN. of someone Il. +

λαθράδᾱν dial.adv. **without the knowledge** —w.GEN. of someone Corinn.

λαθραῖος ᾱ ον (also ος ον) adj. **1** escaping the notice of others; (of sexual relations) **secret, clandestine, furtive** E.fr. Plu.; (of childbirth, meton. for a child) E.; (of a person's gaze) S.; (of wrongdoing) S. Arist.; (of undertakings or activities) Plb. Plu.
2 escaping the notice of a particular victim; (of destruction) **stealthy, underhand** A.; (of cunning) Ar.(perh.quot. A.); (of a fatal contest, disaster) **unforeseen, unsuspected** S.; (of a person's death, ref. to his murder) And.
3 (of swords) **concealed** E.
4 (of persons) **prone to secrecy** Pl.

—λαθραίως adv. | superl. λαθραιότατα | **1** without the knowledge of others, **secretly** S. E. Antipho Pl. Plb. Plu.
2 without one's own knowledge, **unawares, without warning** A.

λάθριος ον adj. **1** (of thefts) **secret, furtive** S.Ichn.; (of a child, ref. to its birth) Men.; (of adulterous desires) Men.; (of kisses, lovemaking) Bion
2 (quasi-advbl., of Envy speaking) **privately** Call.

—λάθρια neut.pl.adv. **secretly** Call.

λάθω dial.vb., **λαθών** (aor.2 ptcpl.): see λανθάνω

λᾶι (dat.sg.): see λᾶας

λάιγξ ιγγος f. [λᾶας] **1 pebble** Od.
2 stone, boulder AR.

λαιδρός ά (Ion. ή) όν adj. (of a person's spirit, a crow) **shameless, impudent** Call.

Λᾱίειος adj.: see under Λάϊος

λαίθαργος ον adj. (of dogs) app. **guileful, treacherous** Hippon. Ar.(mock-oracle)

λαικάζω vb. | fut. λαικάσομαι | (of a man) perform fellatio, **suck cocks** Ar.; (as a crude imprecation) οὐ λαικάσει; **won't you go and suck cocks?** Men.

λαικαστής οῦ m. **fellator, cock-sucker** Ar.

—λαικάστρια ᾱς f. **cock-sucker** (ref. to a prostitute) Ar. Men.

λαῖλαψ απος f. **sudden and violent gusting of wind, squall, tempest** Hom. hHom. Semon. A. Plb. NT. Plu.

λαιμαργία ᾱς f. [app. λαιμός, μάργος] app., greediness of throat, **gluttony** Pl. X. Plu.

λαιμάττω Att.vb. [λαιμός] **eat greedily** or **voraciously** Ar.

λαιμάω contr.vb. (of a person's mouth, compared to a heron's) **be voracious** Hippon.

λαιμόρρυτος adj.: see αἱμόρρυτος

λαιμός οῦ m. **1 throat** (of a person, pierced in battle or cut in slaughter) Hom. E. AR.; (caught in a noose, for death by hanging) E. AR.; (assoc.w. the passage of food or drink) Il. E. Plu.; (meton., ref. to the voice) Theoc.
2 throat (of an animal, cut in slaughter) A.fr. E. Ar. AR.

λαιμό-τμητος ον adj. [τμητός] **1** (of the Gorgon's head) **severed at the throat** E.
2 (of sufferings) connected with cutting the throat, **throat-cutting** Ar.(mock-trag.)

λαιμο-τόμᾱς ᾱ dial.m. [τέμνω] (ref. to Perseus) **throat-cutter** E.

λαιμοτομέω contr.vb. **cut the throat** —w.ACC. of a person Plu. —of sacrificial animals AR.; (intr.) AR.

λαιμο-τόμος ον adj. (of a hand, sword) **throat-cutting** E. Tim.

—λαιμότομος ον adj. **1** (of a person) **with the throat cut** E.; (of heads) **severed at the throat** E.
2 (of drops of blood) **from the cutting of the throat** E.

λαΐνεος ᾱ ον adj. [λᾶας] (of structures) made or built of stone (either hewn fr. rock or constructed fr. cut blocks), **of stone** Il. AR. Theoc.; (of a product of building-work) **in stone** E.

λάϊνος η ον adj. **1** (of structures) made or built of stone (sts. ref. to marble), **of stone** Hom. hHom. B. Parm. S. E. +; (of bowls and jars) Od.
2 (fig., of a coat) **of stones** (ref. to death fr. stoning, as a punishment) Il.
3 (of a cave, as a natural feature) hollowed out of the rock, **rocky** hHom. Theoc.
4 (fig., of a person) **stone-like, hard-hearted** Theoc.

λαῖον ου n. app. **end of the ploughshare** (pressed down by the foot at the start of ploughing) AR.

λαιός ά (Ion. ή) όν adj. **1** on the left side (opp. right); (of a hand, arm, shoulder, foot) **left** E. AR.; (provbl., of the hand which takes, opp. that which gives) Plb. || FEM.SB. **left hand** Carm.Pop. AR. Theoc.
2 (ref. to relative position or direction) λαιᾶς χειρός **on the left-hand side** A.
3 (of the side of a ship) **left, left-hand** E.; (of the wing of an army) E. Plb. || NEUT.SB. (sg. and pl.) **left wing** (of an army) Plb.

Λάϊος, contr. **Λᾱος** (Pi.), ου m. **Laios** (king of Thebes, son of Labdakos and father of Oedipus) Pi. Hdt. Trag. Pl. Arist. Plu.

—Λᾱίειος ᾱ ον adj. (of a son, the murder) **of Laios** S.

λᾱίς dial.f.: see ληίς

λαισήιον ου n. [perh.reltd. λάσιος] light shield covered in animal hide and hair, **light shield, buckler** Il. Scol. Hdt.

Λαιστρῡγόνες ων m.pl. **Laestrygonians** (mythical race of cannibal giants, usu. regarded as inhabiting Sicily) Od. Th. Plb.(quot.); (sg., of an individual) Od.

—Λαιστρῡγόνιος η ον Ion.adj. (of a city, the race) **Laestrygonian** Od. Hes.fr.

λαῖτμα ατος n. [perh.reltd. λαιμός] **1** expanse of deep open water; **open sea, deep waters** (sts. w.GEN. of the sea) Hom. Hes. hHom. AR. Theoc.
2 app. **deep pool** (of blood, w.GEN. of an animal) Ar.

λαίφη ης f. [reltd. λαῖφος] **ragged garment** Call.

λαῖφος εος (ους) n. **1** a kind of garment (perh. of animal-skin or coarse cloth, assoc.w. poor or country people), **ragged garment, sheet** Od. hHom.; (wrapping a baby, in a cot) hHom.

λαιψηροδρόμος

2 (sg. and pl.) **sailcloth, sail** hHom. Alc. Lyr.adesp. Trag. Call. AR.

λαιψηρο-δρόμος ον *adj.* [λαιψηρός] (epith. of Achilles) **swift-running** E.

λαιψηρός ά όν, Aeol. **λαίψηρος** ᾱ ον *adj.* [perh.reltd. αἰψηρός] **1** moving swiftly; (of persons, their knees) **swift, nimble** Il. Sapph.; (of their feet) Pi. B. E.; (of the wings of a bird or goddess) Archil. AR.
2 (of arrows, the course of the winds) **swift** Il.; (of a wind) **brisk, stiff** AR.
3 (of the jaws of man-eating horses) **ravening** E.
4 performed or completed swiftly; (of a foot-race) **swift, rapid** Pi.; (of wars) Pi.
—**λαιψηρά** *neut.pl.adv.* **swiftly** —*ref. to moving* Il. AR.; **briskly** —*ref. to a wind blowing* AR. ; **nimbly** —*ref. to leaping* E.

λακάζω *vb.* [reltd. λάσκω] **shriek** A.

Λάκαινα *fem.adj.*: see under **Λάκων**

λᾱ-καταπῡ́γων ονος *m.* [intensv.prfx.] (ref. to a politician) **utter faggot** Ar.

Λακεδαίμων ονος *f.* [reltd. **Λάκων**] **Lacedaemon** (old and more formal name for Sparta, used of the city or the surrounding territory) Hom. +; (appos.w. γῆ *land*) E.

—**Λακεδαιμόνιος** ᾱ (Ion. η) ον *adj.* (of a man or woman) **Lacedaemonian** Pi. Hdt. E. Th. + ‖ MASC.PL.SB. people of Lacedaemon, **Lacedaemonians** Pi. Hdt. Th. +

λακεῖν (aor.2 inf.): see **λάσκω**

λακέρυζα ης *fem.adj.* [reltd. λάσκω] (of crows) **raucous** Hes. Stesich. Ar.(quot. Hes.) AR.; (of a bitch) Lyr.adesp.

λᾱκέω *contr.vb.* [reltd. λάσκω] **1** (of bay leaves) **crackle** (in a fire) Theoc.
2 (of a person, falling down dead) **split open** —W.ADJ. *at the middle* NT. ‖ cf. διαλᾱκέω

λακήσομαι (fut.mid.): see **λάσκω**

λακίς ίδος, Aeol. **λάκις** ιδος *f.* **1** (sg. and pl.) act of tearing into pieces, **tearing, rending** (of clothes, in mourning) A.
2 ‖ PL. results of tearing, **tears, rents** (in sail-cloth) Alc.; (w.GEN. in clothes, periphr. for torn clothing) A. Ar.(mock-trag.)

λακίσματα των *n.pl.* torn pieces, **tatters** (w.GEN. of clothes, periphr. for tattered clothes) E.

λακκαῖος ᾱ ον *adj.* [λάκκος] (of water) **from a cistern** Thphr.

λακκό-πλουτοι ων *m.pl.* [πλοῦτος] **pit-wealth people** (ref. to the descendants of a man whose wealth came fr. treasure found hidden in a storage-pit) Plu.

λακκό-πρωκτος ου *m.* [πρωκτός] (hyperbol., ref. to a passive male homosexual) **one with an anus like a storage-pit, cistern-arse** Ar.

λάκκος ου *m.* **storage-pit** (sunk in the ground and lined, esp. for water or wine; small for personal use, or as large as a pond); **pit, tank, cistern, reservoir** Hdt. Ar. X. Aeschin. D. Plu.

λάκον (ep.aor.2): see **λάσκω**

λακ-πάτητος ον *adj.* [λάξ, πατέω] (fig., of joy) **trampled underfoot** S.

λακτίζω *vb.* [λάξ] | dial.inf. λακτιζέμεν (Pi.) | aor. ἐλάκτισα | pf. λελάκτικα | **1 kick** —*a person* Ar. X. Plu.; (of animals) —*a person, another animal* Pl. X. Plu.; (provbl., of a person) —*one who has fallen* (i.e. *add insult to injury*) A. ‖ PASS. **be kicked** —W.PREP.PHR. *by a horse* X. Plu.
2 strike (sthg.) by kicking; **kick** —*a door* (*to attract attention*) Ar.; (of a person felled by a blow or weapon) —*the ground, an object* (W.DAT. *w. one's feet*) Od.; (of a baby hidden in a pot, as if in the womb) —*the pot's belly* Ar. (fig., of a terrified person's heart) —*the midriff* A.; (of flame) —*the sky* (W.DAT. *w. smoke*) Pi.
3 kick (sthg.) contemptuously or dismissively; (fig.) **kick** —*the altar of Justice* (W.PREP.PHR. *into oblivion*) A.; kick aside, **spurn, repudiate** —*a debt of gratitude* E.
4 (intr.) kick (in opposition or defiance); (of a horse) **kick, kick out** (as a habitual trait) X.; (provbl., of persons) —W.PREP.PHR. *against the goad* (i.e. *fight back*) A. Pi. E. NT.; (fig., of sailors) —*against the swell of the sea* E.

λάκτισμα ατος *n.* **kicking over** (W.GEN. of a meal, i.e. table, in revulsion) A. ‖ PL. **stamping** (on the ground) S.*Ichn.*

λακτιστής οῦ *m.* (ref. to a horse) **kicker** (as a habitual trait) X.

Λάκων ωνος *masc.adj.* [reltd. **Λακεδαίμων**] (of a man, ref. to an inhabitant of Lacedaemon, i.e. Sparta) **Laconian** Pi. Hdt. Th. Ar. + ‖ SB. (sg. and pl.) **Laconian man, Laconian** Hdt. Ar. Pl. +

—**Λάκαινα** ης (dial. ᾱς) *fem.adj.* **1** (of a woman) **Laconian** Thgn. Hdt. E. Ar. Plu.; (of a group of girls) Pi.*fr.*; (of a Muse) Ar.; (of the land, the chief city) Hdt. E.; (of hunting-hounds) Pi.*fr.* S. Pl. X.; (of a kind of hat or cap) B.
2 ‖ SB. **Laconian woman** E. Plu.; (pl.) S.(title) Theoc.
3 ‖ SB. **Laconian land, Laconia** X.

Λακωνίζω *vb.* **1 be Laconian, Laconise** (ref. to imitating the customs or supporting the political interests of Sparta) Isoc. Pl. X. D. Plu.
2 speak in the Laconian dialect Plu.

Λακωνικός ή (dial. ᾱ́) όν *adj.* **1** of or belonging to the Laconian people or land; (of persons) **Laconian** Ar. Pl. X. Plu.; (of cities, the land) Hdt. Th. X. Plb.; (of an army, troops, ships) Hdt. Th. X. Plu.; (of hounds) Thphr.; (of a monument, wealth, poetry, or sim.) Th. Plu. ‖ FEM.SB. **Laconian land, Laconia** Hdt. Th. And. Ar. Isoc. + ‖ MASC.PL.SB. **Laconians** Ar. X.
2 (in military ctxt.) relating to the Laconians; (of a defeat) **suffered by the Laconians** Hdt.; (of a war) **against the Laconians** Arist. Plb. ‖ NEUT.SG.SB. **Laconian sphere of influence** Hdt. ‖ PL. **activities in Laconia** Aeschin.
3 of the Laconian kind or in the Laconian style; (of a door-key) **Laconian** Ar. Men.; (of a knife, cup) X. Plu.; (of the σκυτάλη *despatch-staff*) Ar.; (of a liquid quarter-measure) Hdt.; (of a meal, dance-steps) Hdt.; (of items of food) Ar.; (of reins, meton. for shoe-straps) Ar.(mock-trag.) ‖ FEM.PL.SB. (w. ἐμβάδες understd.) **Laconian-style shoes** Ar.
4 (of the constitution, customs or way of life) **Laconian** Pl. X. Arist. Plb. Plu. ‖ NEUT.SB. **Laconian style** (W.GEN. of exercising authority) Plu.
5 (of a style of speech, characterised by brevity) **Laconic** Pl. Arist. Plu. ‖ NEUT.SB. **Laconian style** (W.GEN. of conversation) Plu.

—**Λακωνικόν** *adv.* **in the Laconian manner** —*ref. to showing an attitude of bravado* Ar.

—**Λακωνικῶς** *adv.* **1 in the Laconian manner** —*ref. to fighting bravely and to the death* Plb.
2 in Laconic style, Laconically —*ref. to speaking briefly* Plu.

Λακωνίς ίδος *fem.adj.* (of the land) **Laconian** hHom.; (of an island-colony) Call.

Λακωνισμός οῦ *m.* [Λακωνίζω] **sympathy or support for Laconian interests** (by an individual or a state), **pro-Laconian sympathies, Laconism** Isoc. X. Plu.

Λακωνιστής οῦ *m.* **1 supporter of Laconian interests** ‖ PL. **pro-Laconians** X.
2 imitator of Laconian customs; (as a person's nickname) **Laconist** Plu.

Λακωνομανέω contr.vb. [Λάκων, μαίνομαι] be mad about the Laconians (i.e. have excessive sympathy for their customs and attitudes), **be Laconia-crazy** Ar.

λαλαγέω contr.vb. [reltd. λαλέω] | dial.3pl. λαλαγεῦντι |
1 (pejor., of a poet) **chatter, babble, prattle** Pi.
—W.NEUT.ACC. *on a particular theme* Pi.
2 (of birds, cicadas) **chatter, chirrup** Theoc.

λαλάζω vb. (of a person, talking while drinking, and compared to the waves of the sea) **babble** Anacr.
|| PTCPL.ADJ. (pejor., of a writer) babbling Call.(v.l. ἀλαζών)

λαλέω contr.vb. **1** talk (informally or privately), **talk, chat, chatter** Ar. X. D. Thphr. Men. Theoc. || PASS. (of things) be talked about Ar. Men.
2 (pejor.) indulge in unnecessary, unwanted or unprofitable talk, **prattle, babble** Ar. Pl.
3 (gener.) **talk, speak, converse** (usu. W.DAT. to or w. someone) D. Thphr. Men. Plb. NT. Plu.
4 (tr.) **speak** —*words, the truth, or sim.* (sts. W.DAT. *to someone*) NT. || PASS. (of things) be spoken NT.
5 (fig., of a musician) **discourse** —W.DAT. *on a wind instrument* Theoc.
6 (of grasshoppers, birds) **chatter, chirrup** Theoc. Mosch.; (of trees) **whisper** (W.DAT. to one another) —W.ACC. *about someone's wedding* Theoc.; (of hyacinths) **speak** —*letters written on their petals* Mosch.

λάλημα ατος n. **1 chatter** (of Eros) Mosch.
2 (pejor., ref. to a person) **chatterer, prattler** S. E.(dub.)

λάλησις εως f. **chattering** (W.GEN. of the nether regions, ref. to farting) S.*satyr.fr.* [or perh. about the nether regions of the earth, ref. to scientific discourse]

λαλητικός ή όν adj. (of a person) of the chattering kind, **talkative** Ar.

λαλιά ᾶς f. **1** (pejor.) idle talk, **chatter, prattle, gossip** Ar. Aeschin. Men. Plb. Plu.
2 (wkr.sens.) **talk** or **conversation** (about someone or sthg.) Plb.
3 that which is said (by a person), **words, speech** NT.
4 characteristic way of speaking, **manner of speaking** NT.

λάλλαι ῶν f.pl. [app.reltd. λαλέω] app., those which make a noise (when brushed against each other by waves), **pebbles** (on the bed of a spring) Theoc.

λαλο-βαρύοψ οπος masc.fem.adj. [λάλος, βαρύς, ὄψ] (pejor., of a reed-pipe) **with a deep-voiced prattle** Pratin.

λάλος ον adj. [λαλέω] | compar. λαλίστερος | superl. λαλίστατος | **1** (usu.pejor.) **talkative, loquacious** E. Ar. Pl. Arist. Thphr. Men. +; (of the noise made by a pot being tested) **babbling** Ar. || COMPAR. (of a person) more twittering (W.GEN. than swallows) Thphr.
2 || NEUT.SB. casual talk, conversation Plu.

Λάμαχος ου m. **Lamakhos** (Athenian general, died 414 BC) Th. And. Ar. +

—**Λαμαχίππιον** ου n. [dimin. ἵππος] (voc.) **dear little equestrian Lamakhos** Ar.

λαμβάνω vb. | fut. λήψομαι, Ion. λάμψομαι, dial.2sg. λαψῇ (Theoc.), later λήμψομαι (NT.) || AOR.2: ἔλαβον, ep. λάβον, also ἔλλαβον, iterativ. λάβεσκον | ptcpl. λαβών, dial.fem. λαβοῖσα (Call. Theoc.), Aeol.fem. λάβοισα | imperativ. λάβε, Att. λαβέ || subj. λάβω, ep.3sg. λάβῃσι | inf. λαβεῖν || pf. εἴληφα, Ion. λελάβηκα || plpf. εἰλήφειν || MID.: aor.2 ἐλαβόμην, ep.3sg. ἐλλάβετο, ep.redupl.inf. λελαβέσθαι || PASS.: fut. ληφθήσομαι | aor. ἐλήφθην, Ion. ἐλάμφθην | pf. εἴλημμαι, also λέλημμαι (Trag.), Ion. (in cpds) -λέλαμμαι || neut.impers.vbl.adj. ληπτέον || The vb. describes the processes of taking, acquiring and receiving, in a wide range of applications (physical, mental and figurative). |
1 take (with or in one's hand or hands), **take hold of, grasp** —*objects, persons, parts of their bodies* Hom. + —*a person* (W.PARTITV.GEN. *by a part of the body or clothing*) Hom. + —W.GEN. *an object or person* Hom. —W.DBL.GEN. *a person, by a part of the body* Od.
2 || MID. **lay hands on, grasp, clasp** —W.GEN. *an object, person, part of the body* Od. Hdt. S. E. Ar. + —W.DBL.GEN. *a person, by a part of the body* Ar. Pl. —W.ACC. *a person* Od.
3 || MID. (fig.) **lay into, attack** —W.GEN. *someone* (W.ADV. *harshly, i.e. w. abuse or blows*) Hdt.; **find fault with** —W.GEN. *someone* Pl.
4 (of a bird or animal) **take hold of, grasp, seize** —*prey* Il. Hes. Pi. —*a bird* (W.GEN. *by its wing*) Il.; (of a fisherman) **catch** —*fish* Od. Hdt.
5 take possession of by force, seize, capture —*objects, persons, cities, ships, or sim.* Hom. + || PASS. (of persons, cities, or sim.) be seized or captured Hdt. Trag. Th. +
6 catch, find out, detect —*a criminal* S.; **catch, find** —*someone* (W.PTCPL. *doing sthg.*) Hdt. + || PASS. be caught —W.PTCPL. *doing sthg.* Hdt. E. + —W.PREDIC.SB. *as an adulterer* Lys. Is.
7 find, consider —*someone* (W.PREDIC.ADJ. *pious, hostile*) S. E. || PASS. be found —W.PREDIC.ADJ. *evil* S.
8 take, grasp —*an opportunity* A. E. || MID. **grasp, seize** —W.GEN. *power* S. —*an opportunity* Is.; (of a soul) —*the truth* Pl.
9 take (by process of law), **exact** —*a penalty, vengeance, or sim.* E. Att.orats.
10 gain a hold over (a person, by some non-physical constraint); **bind** —*someone* (W.DAT. *under pledges and oaths*) Hdt. —(W.PREDIC.ADJ. *under a curse, an oath*) S. Aeschin.
11 (of emotions, mental or bodily states, sicknesses, death, or sim.) **take hold of, come over, seize** —*persons, parts of the body* Hom. +; (of great danger, in neg.phr.) perh. **engage** —*a coward* Pi. || PASS. (of persons) be seized or overcome —W.DAT. or PREP.PHR. *by sickness, troubles, perplexity, or sim.* Hdt. S. E. +
12 (of darkness) **come over, occupy** —*the sky* A.; (intr., of the appropriate time) **come on, arrive** Th.
13 take up (for wearing), **put on, don** —*clothes* Hdt.; (fig.) **take** —*a yoke* (W.PREDIC.ADJ. *on one's neck*) Pi.
14 take in, receive hospitably —*a traveller* Od. —*a suppliant* S.
15 (of a military force) **take in, contain** —*a certain number of troops* Plb.
16 take or **reach** (a location); **take possession of** or **occupy** —*a tower, platform* E. —*a cave* E.Cyc. || MID. (of troops) **gain, reach** —W.GEN. *mountains* Th.; (of ships) —*an island* Th.
17 (of a person travelling) **get** or **keep** —*a place* (W.PREP.PHR. *on one's right or left*) Hdt. Th.; (of a river) **skirt round** —*an army* (W.PREP.PHR. *in the rear, i.e. be behind it*) Hdt.
18 acquire, obtain, get —*persons (as colleagues or helpers), troops, ships, material objects, wealth, rule, or sim.* Od. +; (of a lion) —*a meal* Il.; (of an inanimate object or dead person, in a vision or hypothetical ctxt.) —*a voice* Trag.
19 win —*a prize, glory* Hom. Hdt. S. E.
20 acquire (what is given to one), **receive** —*a ransom, money, gifts, food, clothing, or sim.* Il. + —*one's deserts* Hdt. —*a favour, gratitude* E. —*a pledge, an oath* E. X. Arist. —*an*

Λάμια

account (i.e. reckoning) X. D. —*punishment, penalties* Hdt. D.; (of a wall, house) **acquire** —*battlements* Hdt.
21 (gener.) acquire (sthg. desirable); **obtain, get, gain** —*excellence, help, delight, a respite fr. labours, a journey home, or sim.* Thgn. Simon. Pi. S. E. + —*strength, courage, composure* Trag. —*one's spirits* (W.ADV. *back again*) Od.
22 acquire (sthg. undesirable); **get, incur, suffer** —*pain, poverty, toil, sickness, reproaches, blame, or sim.* Thgn. Hdt. S. E. Th. +
23 (wkr.sens.) **receive, get** —*a sight (of sthg.), a verbal greeting* S.; (periphr., of a person) **get** —*a beginning (i.e. begin)* E.; (of a wall) —*height (i.e. be made higher)* Th.; (of certain arts) —*advancement (i.e. be advanced)* Isoc. | for πεῖραν λαμβάνειν *get (i.e. make) a test*, see πεῖρα 2
24 (specif.) **obtain, get** —*a woman (as sexual partner)* Hdt. —(*in marriage*) Semon. E. Isoc. X. Men.; (of a father) —*someone's daughter* (W.DAT. *for one's son*) Men.
25 receive (as produce or profit); **get, obtain** —*wine* (W.PREP.PHR. *fr. one's land*) Ar. —*money (fr. public office)* Pl.
26 acquire by purchase, **buy** —*sthg.* Ar. X.
27 conceive (thoughts or feelings); **take** —*thought* (W.GEN. *of sthg.*) Pi.; **entertain** —*a notion (of sthg.)* E.; **feel** —*fear, reverence, anger, concern* Trag.
28 obtain (by application of one's mental faculties), **ascertain, determine** —*a measurement* (W.ADV. *in a certain way*) Th. —*the magnitude of a crime* (W.ADV. *by a certain criterion*) Lycurg. —*the cause (of sthg.)* Pl. —*the truth (about sthg.)* Antipho
29 take in, apprehend, understand (W.DAT. or PREP.PHR. w. one's mind) —*someone's words or actions* Hdt. —*an abstr. entity* Pl. —W.COMPL.CL. *that sthg. is the case* Hdt. X. Plb. || PASS. (of an abstr. entity) be apprehended —W.DAT. *by a particular sense* Pl.
30 take something (in a particular manner); **take, respond to** —*an oracle* (W.ADV. *in a certain way*) Hdt. —*someone's words (in a hostile spirit)* Th. —*a situation* (W.ADV., DAT. or PREP.PHR. *seriously, w. suspicion, compassion, anger, fear, or sim.*) E. Th. Plb. Plu.; **treat, handle** —*an undertaking* (W.ADV. *in a certain way*) Hdt. || PASS. (of a situation) be taken —W.ADV. *lightly* E.*fr.*
31 take, interpret, regard —*sthg.* (W.PREDIC.ADJ. or SB. *as such and such*) Th. Arist. —(w. ὡς + PREDIC.ADJ.) Arist.
32 (intr.) **form an interpretation** or **assumption** (sts. W.ADV. *in a certain way*) Arist. —W.PREP.PHR. *about sthg.* Arist. —(W.INDIR.Q. *as to what it is*) Arist. —W.COMPL.CL. *that sthg. is the case* Arist.

Λάμια ᾱς *f.* [λαμρός] Lamia (fabled monster that ate human flesh, invoked to terrify children) Ar. Men.

Λᾱμνιακός, Λᾱμνιάς, Λάμνιος *dial.adjs.,* **Λᾱμνόθεν** *dial.adv.,* **Λᾶμνος** *dial.f.*: see Λῆμνος

λαμπαδαρχίᾱ ᾱς *f.* [λαμπάς, ἄρχω] **superintendence of torch-races** (as a leitourgia, i.e. public duty) Arist.

λαμπαδηφορίη ης *Ion.f.* [λαμπαδηφόρος] **carrying of torches, torch-race** (by relay teams, ref. to that held at the festival of Hephaistos at Athens) Hdt.

λαμπαδη-φόρος ου *m.* [λαμπάς, φέρω] **torch-bearer** (as a competitor in a relay race) Men.; (fig., ref. to a person passing on a beacon-signal fr. one station to the next) A.

λαμπάδιον ου *n.* [dimin. λαμπάς] **1 little torch** Pl. Plu. **2 bandage** Ar.

λαμπαδοῦχος ον *adj.* [ἔχω] (of day) having the torch (of the sun), **light-bringing** E.

λαμπάς άδος *f.* [λάμπω] **1 torch** (of burning wood, to provide light or ignition, freq. carried in ritual processions, dances and ceremonies) Trag. Th. Ar. Men. Theoc. +
2 torch (carried in a relay race) Ar. Arist.; (ref. to a beacon-signal, envisaged as such a torch) A.; (in a simile envisaging life as a torch, passed on fr. generation to generation) Pl.; **torch-race** Hdt. And. Ar. Pl. X. Is. +
3 torch (W.GEN. of the sun) Parm. E.; (without GEN., ref. to the sun) S. || PL. fiery rays (W.GEN. of the sun) E.
4 || PL. torches (in the sky, ref. to meteors, comets or lightning) A.; flashes, bolts (of lightning) E.; (sg., ref. to a meteor or fireball) Plu.
5 oil-lamp, **lamp** NT.
6 || ADJ. (of the shores of Eleusis, at the festival of the Mysteries) torch-lit S.

λαμπετάω *contr.vb.* | only ep.ptcpl. (w.diect.) λαμπετόων | (of fire, stars) **shine, gleam** Hom. Hes. AR.

λαμπηδών όνος *f.* **shine, lustre** (of bronze weapons) Plu.

λαμπρός ά (Ion. ή) όν *adj.* **1 bright** (w. one's own light); (of the sun, moon, stars, their light or other attributes) **bright, shining, gleaming, radiant** Il. Hes. hHom. Trag. Th. +; (gener., of light) A. Pi.; (of lightning, its flashes) Sol. Pi. S.; (of fire, flames) B. X.; (of the Dioscuri, envisaged as St Elmo's fire) Alc.; (of the sparkle of a girl's face) Sapph.; (of the eye of a personif. lamp) Ar.(mock-trag.)
2 bright (w. reflected light); (of metal armour and weapons) **bright, shining** Il. Alc. A. E.; (of the stamp on a silver coin) E.; (of a mirror) E.; (of armed warriors) **gleaming, glittering** E.; (of a person, W.DAT. w. gold, i.e. jewellery) E.
3 having a bright surface or texture; (of a tunic or cloak) with a bright sheen, **shiny** Od. Thphr.; (of skin; of persons, ref. to their skin) Hdt. Ar.; (of a fleece) Pi.; (of clothes, after washing) Anacr.; (of a temple entrance, after sweeping) E.; (of a Roman toga, worn by a candidate for office) **white** Plb.
4 (of water, air, sky) **bright, clear** A. E. Ar. X.; (of daylight) Plb.
5 (of a person's eyes or sight) **bright** (opp. dimmed by blindness) S. E.
6 (of sounds) **clear, distinct** Pl.; (of a voice, a herald's words) **loud and clear** E. D. Plu.
7 (of a wind) **fresh, strong** A. Hdt. Plb. Plu.; (fig., of a person, envisaged as a wind) Ar.; (gener., of a commander) **keen, vigorous** E.; (of fighting) Plb.
8 (of animal tracks, evidence, circumstances) **clear, unambiguous** Trag. X.; (of a victory) **decisive** Th.
9 (of persons, their attributes, ref. to external appearance) **resplendent, radiant, dazzling** S. E. Th. Ar. +; (of clothes) **splendid** E.; (of an expensively dressed woman's outdoor excursions) **flamboyant** D.
10 (of horses, ref. to their appearance) **impressive, magnificent** Lys. X. Is.
11 (of persons, ref. to their demeanour) **beaming, radiant** S. X.
12 (fig., of persons) **dazzling** (W.DAT. in their good fortune) E.; (app.colloq.) **sitting pretty, in clover** Men.
13 (of persons, ref. to their ancestry, reputation or merits) **illustrious, distinguished, renowned** Hdt. E. Th. Att.orats. +; (of a person's life, death, character, valour) **glorious** Hdt. S. E. || NEUT.SB. splendour, distinction (of people) Pi.
14 (of activities, events, circumstances) **splendid, glorious** Hdt. S.*Ichn.* Th. Ar. +; (of words of praise) S.
15 (of passages of poetry, poetic style) **brilliant, dazzling** Ar. Arist.

—**λαμπρόν** *neut.adv.* **1 brightly** —*ref. to a star or armour shining* Il.

2 with bright eyes (opp. downcast or shifty) —*ref. to looking* Pi.
3 loud and clear —*ref. to singing a paean* X.
4 brilliantly —*ref. to performing on the lyre* Arist.
—**λαμπρῶς** *adv.* | compar. λαμπρότερον, superl. λαμπρότατα | **1 in a clearly visible or open manner, clearly, unambiguously, openly, overtly** A. Th.
2 energetically, fiercely Th. X. Plb. Plu.
3 impressively, splendidly, gloriously Att.orats. Pl. X. Arist. +
λαμπρότης ητος *f.* **1 brightness** (of the sun) NT.; **sheen** (of oil, honey) Plu.
2 brilliance, splendour (of troops, their equipment, or sim.) Th. X. Plb. Plu.; (of a young man's looks) Plu.; (of a person's lifestyle) Plu.
3 dazzling ability or **display** (of a prancing horse) X.
4 clarity (of a singer's voice) Plu.
5 clarity (of a false rumour) Plu.
6 sharpness, brilliance (of mental abilities) Plb.
7 distinction, eminence, renown Hdt. Th. Isoc. D. Plu. ‖ PL. distinctions, accolades Th. Isoc. Plu.
λαμπροφωνίη ης *Ion.f.* [λαμπρόφωνος] **clarity of voice** Hdt.
λαμπρό-φωνος ον *adj.* [φωνή] **having a voice that is clear** D.
λαμπρύνω *vb.* | aor.mid. ἐλαμπρυνάμην ‖ 3sg.pf.pass. λελάμπρυνται | **1** ‖ MID. **make bright, polish** —*one's weapons and armour* X. ‖ PASS. (of a shield) **be polished** X.
2 (fig., of honours) **burnish** —*certain kinds of character* Plu.
3 ‖ PASS. (of a blind man) **be given light** —W.ACC. *in the eyes* (i.e. have his sight restored) Ar.(quot. S.); (of a sleeping mind) —W.DAT. *by the eyes* (i.e. be able to see in dreams) A.(dub.)
4 ‖ MID. (of criticism of someone's behaviour) **become loud and clear** E.
5 (of a rider) **show off the brilliance of** —*his horse* X.
6 ‖ MID. (sts. pejor. or iron.) **make a brilliant impression** (by one's lavish expenditure or generosity) Arist. Plu. —W.DAT. *w. one's chariot and fine clothing* E. —*w. one's luxurious house and furnishings* Plu.
7 ‖ MID. **perform brilliantly** or **distinguish oneself** —W.ACC. or DAT. or ἐν + DAT. *in some activity* Th. Ar. Plu.; (gener.) **gain renown** (because of a notable deed) Plu.
λαμπτήρ ῆρος *m.* [λάμπω] **1 light-giver, lamp** (ref. to a portable brazier, holding burning wood) Od. A. E.; (ref. to a watch-fire in a camp) S. E.; (ref. to a beacon-fire) A.; (ref. to a lantern) Emp. E. X. Plu.
2 ‖ PL. **fiery rays** (W.GEN. of the sun) E.
λαμπτηρουχίᾱ ᾱς *f.* [ἔχω] **holding of lamps, deployment of beacon-fires** A. [or perh. *station for beacon-fires*]
λάμπω *vb.* | iteratv.impf. λάμπεσκον | fut. λάμψω | aor. ἔλαμψα | pf.(w.pres.sens.) λέλαμπα (E.) | **1** (act. and mid.) **give off light**; (of the sun, moon, dawn, stars) **shine, gleam** hHom. Sapph. Sol. Pi. E. Ar. +; (of light, lightning, fire, flames, torches, lamps) Il. hHom. B. Emp. S. E. +; (of precious metal and stones, in the dark) Hdt.
2 (act. and mid.) **give off reflected or borrowed light**; (of weapons and armour) **shine, gleam** Hom. E. AR. Plu.; (of warriors, usu. W.DAT. in their armour or w. bronze) Il. Hes. Stesich. B.; (of places, objects, buildings, gold, jewellery, sts. W.DAT. or PREP.PHR. w. light or sim.) Il. Hes. hHom. B. Ar. X. +; (of a balding man's forehead) Ar. Theocr.; (of a cliff) **blaze** —W.INTERN.ACC. *w. the light of torches* E.; (fig., of a person) —W.DAT. *w. a two-edged tongue* Ar.
3 (act. and mid., of persons, monsters, serpents, their faces or eyes, hyperbol. or in supernatural ctxt.) **shine, be ablaze** (sts. W.DAT. w. fire) Il. Hes. Ar. AR. NT.
4 (of persons, ref. to their external appearance or inherent excellence) **shine forth in splendour, be radiant** Pi. S. Ar. AR.(sts.mid.); (of a bull, compared to a star) Theocr.; (of a person's excellence, fame, deeds) **shine forth** Pi. E.; (of youthful vigour) E.; (of city-states) **blaze forth** (w. success) Plb.
5 (of Justice) **shine forth** (in dark places) A.; (of Persuasion, W.ADJ. *silver*, meton. for coinage used as a bribe) Anacr.; (of light, fig.ref. to prosperity) A.; (of beauty, grace, pleasure) Pl. Ariphron Lyr.adesp.; (wkr.sens., of a matter) **be set in a clear light** B.
6 (tr., of a person luring a ship onto rocks) **flash** —*a treacherous star* (fig.ref. to a deceptive beacon-signal) E.
7 (of a message, hymn, lamentation) **sound forth loud and clear** S.
λαμυρίᾱ ᾱς *f.* [λαμυρός] **forwardness, impertinence, cheek** (of a woman, public performers) Plu.
λαμυρός ά όν *adj.* **1** perh., with a rapacious appetite; (of a lion's teeth) **ravenous** Theocr.
2 (of a person) **avid** (W.PREP.PHR. for popular acclaim) Plu.; (of conduct in public life) perh. **self-seeking** Plu.
3 (of a woman) **flirtatious, cheeky** Plu.
4 (of a donkey's look) perh. **impudent** Plu.
—**λαμυρώτερον** *compar.adv.* **rather frankly** or **grossly** —*ref. to speaking* (about sexual matters) X.
λάμψομαι (Ion.fut.mid.): see λαμβάνω
λανθάνω *vb.* —also **λήθω**, dial. **λᾱ́θω** *vb.* | impf. ἐλάνθανον, ἔληθον, ep. λῆθον, iteratv. λήθεσκον | fut. λήσω, dial. λᾱσῶ (Theocr.), Aeol.inf. λᾱ́σην | aor.2 ἔλαθον, ep. λάθον, ptcpl. λαθών, inf. λαθεῖν | ep.redupl.aor.2 subj. λελάθω, opt. λελάθοιμι | pf. λέληθα, Aeol.ptcpl. λελάθων | plpf. ἐλελήθειν, Att. ἐλελήθη, 3sg. ἐλελήθει, Ion. ἐλελήθεε, dial. ἐλελάθει | MID.: fut. λήσομαι, dial. λᾱσεῦμαι (Theocr.) | dial.aor.1 ptcpl. λᾱσάμενος (Mosch.) | aor.2 ἐλαθόμην, ep. λαθόμην, ep.3pl.opt. λαθοίατο | ep.redupl.aor.2: 3pl. λελάθοντο, 3sg.imperatv. λελαθέσθω, 3sg.opt. λελάθοιτο, inf. λελαθέσθαι | pf. λέλησμαι, ep. λέλασμαι, ep.ptcpl. λελασμένος | fut.pf. (w.fut.sens.) λελήσομαι (E.) | PASS.: dial.aor.inf. (w.mid.sens.) λασθῆμεν (Theocr.) |
1 (of persons or things) **escape notice** or **detection** Hom. + —W.NOM.PTCPL. *doing sthg. or happening* (i.e. act or happen without being noticed) Il. +; (also ep.redupl.aor.2 mid.) Hes.; (w. inverse constr., the ptcpl. expressing the idea of escaping notice) • ἆλτο λαθών *he leapt without being noticed* Il.
2 escape one's own notice, be unaware, fail to realise —W.NOM.PTCPL. *that one is doing sthg.* Hdt. Ar. Theocr.
3 (tr.) **escape the notice of, fail to be detected by** —*someone* Hom. + —(W.NOM.PTCPL. *doing sthg. or happening*) Hom. + ‖ IMPERS. **it escapes the notice of** —*someone* (to do sthg., that sthg. is the case, or sim.) Il. + —(W.INF. *to do sthg., i.e. one forgets or omits to do it*) Pi. Plu.
4 (ep.redupl.aor.2) **cause** (W.ACC. someone) **to forget** —W.GEN. *sthg.* Il. Lyr.adesp.
5 ‖ MID. **cease** or **fail to think of**; **forget** —W.GEN. *someone* or *sthg.* Hom. + —W.INF. *to do sthg.* Theocr.; **be forgetful** (of someone or sthg.) Il. +
6 ‖ FUT.MID. (w.pass.sens., of an evil) **be forgotten** S.
—**λεληθότως** *pf.ptcpl.adv.* **1 secretly, stealthily** Plu.
2 imperceptibly, unconsciously —*ref. to sthg. happening* Plu.

λᾱνός *dial.f.*: see ληνός

λάξ *adv.* [reltd. λακτίζω] **with the heel** or **foot** (sts. reinforced by ποδί) —*ref. to stepping upon or kicking someone or sthg.* Hom. Hippon. Thgn. A. AR. Theoc.; (fig.) **underfoot** —*ref. to trampling or being trampled* (i.e. *treating or being treated w. disrespect*) Hippon. Thgn. A.

λᾱξευτός ή όν *adj.* [λᾶας, ξέω] (of a tomb) **hollowed out of rock** NT.

λάξις *Ion.f.*: see λῆξις[1]

λάξομαι (Ion.fut.mid.): see λαγχάνω

λαο-δάμᾱς αντος *masc.adj.* [λᾱός, δάμνημι] (epith. of Ares) **who subdues peoples** A.

λᾶοι (nom.pl.): see λᾶας

λῶον *dial.n.*: see λήιον

λαο-παθής ές *adj.* [λᾱός, πάθος] (of sorrows) **suffered by the people** A.(dub.)

λαο-πόρος ον *adj.* (of a device, ref. to a bridge of boats) **providing a passage for troops** A.

λᾱός οῦ, Ion. and Att. **λεώς** ώ *m.* | sg. and pl. in all usages |
1 (in military ctxt.) group of men, **host, army, troops** Hom. Hes. Archil. Tyrt. Hdt. Trag. +
2 group of men under a leader, **retinue, followers** Hom. Pi.; **group, band** (of settlers or colonists) Hdt. Pl. Call. Plu.
3 people under (or contrasted with) a ruler, **people, subjects, common folk** Hom. +
4 people sharing a distinct identity (as defined by ADJ., as *country, seafaring, poor*), **people, folk** Il. S. Ar.
5 people as a community or living in a specific place, **people, population** Hom. +
6 people sharing a geographical or ethnic identity (sts. defined by ADJ. or by name in GEN.), **people, nation** Pi. Hdt. Trag. +
7 people as a crowd (esp. in public gatherings), **people** Hom. +; (w. imperatv., in a formal summons to listen, be silent or be present) Trag. Ar. Plu.
8 (gener.) **people, men, folk** Hom. +

λᾶος (gen.sg.): see λᾶας

Λᾶος *m.*: see Λάιος

λαο-σεβής ές *adj.* [λᾱός, σέβω] (of a dead king) **worshipped by the people** Pi.

λαο-σσόος ον *ep.adj.* [σεύω] **1** (epith. of a god or warrior) **who rouses armies** Hom. Hes.
2 (of contests) **which bring the people together** Pi.

λαοτομέω *dial.contr.vb.* [λήιον, τέμνω] **cut the crop, reap** Theoc.

λαο-τρόφος ον *adj.* [λᾱός, τρέφω] **1** (of a city) **caring for its people** Pi.
2 (of a responsibility) **of care for the people** Pi.

λάου (gen.sg.), **λάους** (acc.pl.): see λᾶας

λαο-φθόρος ον *adj.* [λᾱός, φθείρω] (of factional conflict) **people-destroying, ruinous** Thgn.

λαο-φόνος ον *adj.* [θείνω] (of a warrior, spear) **people-killing, murderous, deadly** B. Theoc.

λαο-φόρος, Ion. and Att. **λεωφόρος**, ον *adj.* [φέρω] **carrying the people**; (of a road) **that is a public highway** Il. E. Theoc.; (of city-gates) **that serve as a public thoroughfare** Hdt. || FEM.SB. **public highway** Pl. Plu.; (fig., ref. to a prostitute) Anacr.

λάπᾱ ᾱς *dial.f.* **scum** (on liquids); (gener.) **glutinous mud, slime** (pervading the underworld) A.

λαπαδνός ή όν *adj.* [reltd. ἀλαπαδνός] (of a person) **weakened, powerless** A.

λαπάζω *vb.* [reltd. ἀλαπάζω] | only fut. λαπάξω | **ravage, devastate** —*a city, its defenders* A.

λαπάρη ης *Ion.f.* [λαπαρός] **soft part of the body between ribs and hip** (esp. as vulnerable to injury), **flank, side** Il. Hdt. AR.

λαπαρός ά όν *adj.* (of a hare's flanks) **supple** X.

Λαπίθαι ῶν (ep. ἄων, dial. ᾶν) *m.pl.* **Lapiths** (ancient Thessalian tribe, noted for their battle w. the Centaurs) Hom. Hes. Pi. E. Isoc. AR. +

—Λαπίθης ου (Ion. εω, ep. ᾱο) *m.sg.* **1** (as proper name) **Lapithes** (ancestor of the Lapiths) Hes.fr. Call.
2 (as ethnic name, ref. to one who is descended fr. the tribe) **Lapith** Hdt.

λάπτω *vb.* | fut. λάψω | (of wolves) **lap up** —*water* (W.DAT. w. *their tongues*) Il.

λᾱρῑνός ή όν *adj.* (of a bull, an ox) **fattened** Xenoph. Ar.; (fig., of a speech) Ar.

Λαρῑσο-ποιοί ῶν *m.pl.* [reltd. Λάρῑσα *Larisa* (city in Thessaly), ποιέω] **makers of cauldrons of the Larisaean type** Arist.(quot.)

λάρκος ου *m.* **container** (for storing charcoal and other goods), **basket** Ar.

—λαρκίδιον ου *n.* [dimin.] **container** (envisaged as a child), **dear little basket** Ar.

λάρναξ ακος *f.* **1 storage-container, chest, box** Il. B. Hdt. Theoc. Plu.
2 container (for the bones of a cremated corpse); **casket** (made of gold) Il.; **coffin** (of wood) Th.
3 chest (in which a person is set adrift on the sea) Hes.fr. Simon. AR.; (in which a person is imprisoned) Theoc.

λᾱρός όν *adj.* | superl. λᾱρώτατος | **1 pleasant to the senses**; (of a meal, wine) **pleasing, delicious** Hom. AR.; (of blood, to a mosquito) Il.; (of the scent of meadow-grass, to a bull) Mosch.
2 (of a word, spoken by a girl in love) **sweet** AR.

λάρος ου *m.* **seagull** Od. Ar.; (exemplifying greed and thievishness, fig.ref. to a person) Ar.

Λᾱρτιάδᾱς *dial.m.*: see Λαερτιάδης, under Λαέρτης

Λάρτιος *m.*: see Λαέρτης

λαρυγγίζω *vb.* [λάρυγξ] | fut. λαρυγγιῶ | **1** (of a person) **make a full-throated noise, bellow** D.
2 throttle, strangle —*politicians* Ar. [or perh. *out-bellow*]

λάρυγξ υγγος *m.* **larynx** (upper part of the windpipe); (gener.) **throat** E.Cyc. Ar.

λᾱσάμενος (dial.aor.mid.ptcpl.): see λανθάνω

λάσανα ων *n.pl.* **supports for holding cooking-pots over a fire, pot-props** Ar.

λάσδεο (dial.mid.imperatv.): see λάζομαι

λᾱσεῦμαι (dial.fut.mid.), **λάσην** (Aeol.fut.inf.): see λανθάνω

λασθαίνω *vb.* [λάσθη] **insult, mock** —*someone* Hippon.

λάσθη ης *f.* **insult, mockery** Hdt.

λασθῆμεν (dial.aor.pass.inf.): see λανθάνω

λασι-αύχην ενος *masc.fem.adj.* [λάσιος, αὐχήν] **1** (of a Centaur, bear, horse) **having a shaggy neck, shaggy-maned** hHom. S.; (of a lionskin) Theoc.
2 (of the hair of Aeschylus, envisaged as a wild beast) **on a shaggy neck** Ar.

λάσιος ᾱ (Ion. η) ον *adj.* **1 covered thickly with hair**; (of a sheep, its belly) **woolly** Hom. Theoc.; (of other animals, parts of their bodies) **hairy, shaggy** Hdt. S. Pl. X. Theoc.; (of bees) Theoc.
2 (of Silenos, the Cyclops, his eyebrow) **hairy, shaggy** Call. Theoc.; (of a person or head) Ar. Pl.; (of a warrior's chest) Il.; (of a warrior's heart, as being in such a chest) Il.

3 (of hair on a giant's chest, on a person's head) **shaggy** Call. Plu.; (of a horse's mane) AR.; (of goatskin thongs) Plu.
4 covered thickly with foliage; (of trees, branches, a copse) **thickly leaved, leafy** Hellenist.poet.; (of ground, pasture, a hillside) **overgrown, bushy, wooded** Pl. X. AR. Plu.; (of the primeval earth) Emp. ‖ NEUT.PL.SB. thick undergrowth X.

λάσκω *vb.* | fut. λακήσομαι | aor.1 ἐλάκησα (Ar.) | aor.2 ἔλακον, ep. λάκον, inf. λακεῖν | pf. (w.pres.sens.) λέλακα, Ion. λέληκα, ep.fem.ptcpl. λελακυῖα ‖ MID.: ep.3pl.redupl. aor. λελάκοντο |
1 make a sharp sound; (of weapons and armour) **ring** (w. blows) Il.; (of bones struck in battle) **crack** Il.; (of a burning forest) **crackle** Hes.; (of the hubs of chariot-wheels) **squeal, screech** A.
2 (of animals) give a shrill or rasping cry; (of a bird in pursuit of its prey, or caught by a predator) **shriek, scream** Il. Hes.; (of a girl, envisaged as an owl) **screech** Alcm.; (of a woman, envisaged as a dog) **yelp, yap** Semon.; (of Scylla) Od. ‖ MID. (of dogs) **bark** hHom.
3 (of persons) **shriek, cry out** —W.INTERN.ACC. *a shout, cry of triumph* A. E.; (of a land) —W.NEUT.ADV. *in lamentation* A.; (of singers, Echo) **raise a cry** E.
4 (of gods, prophets, messengers, or sim.) **speak with authority, proclaim** A. Ar.(mock-trag.) —W.INTERN.ACC. *an oracular message, a lie, disaster, or sim.* Trag. Ar. —W.ACC. + INF. *that sthg. is or will be the case* A. S.
5 (gener., of persons) **speak forcefully, sound forth** Ar.(cj.); **utter, declare, proclaim** —W.INTERN.ACC. *sthg.* Trag. Ar.; **shout** —*sthg.* (W.ACC. *at someone*) E.

Λᾶσος ου *m.* **Lasus** (lyric poet, fr. Hermione, 6th C. BC) Hdt. Ar.

λάσταυρος ου *m.* (pejor.) **passive male homosexual, pathic** Men. Plb.(quot.)

λαστρίς *dial.f.*: see ληστρίς

λᾱσῶ (dial.fut.): see λανθάνω

λάταγες ων *f.pl.* **last drops of wine** (thrown fr. a cup, in the game of kottabos) Alc. Critias Call.

Λᾱτογενής *dial.adj.*, **Λᾱτογένεια** *dial.fem.adj.*, **Λᾱτοΐδᾱς** *dial.m.*: see under Λητώ

λᾱτομέω *contr.vb.* [λᾶας, τέμνω] **hew out** —*a tomb* (w. ἐν + DAT. *in a rock*) NT. ‖ PASS. (of a tomb) be hewn —W. ἐκ + GEN. *out of a rock* NT.

λᾱτομίαι ῶν *f.pl.* **stone-quarries** Plu.

λατρείᾱ ᾱς *f.* [λατρεύω] **1** condition of owing service (to someone); (pejor.) **subservience, servitude** (to a divine or human master) A. S. Plu.; **domestic service** (by a wife) Plu. ‖ PL. acts of servility Plu.
2 (w. neutral or positive connot.) **service** (performed for a god, by a cup-bearer or temple-attendant) E.; (gener.) **service, devotion** (to a god) Pl.; (to God) NT. ‖ PL. acts of service (to the gods) Pl.

λάτρευμα ατος *n.* **1** ‖ PL. acts of servitude (to a human master) S.
2 ‖ PL. acts of service (to a god, by worshippers, ref. to offerings) E.
3 (ref. to a person) **slave** E.

λατρεύω *vb.* [λάτρον] **1** perform servile labour, **work as** or **like a slave** Sol. X. —W.DAT. *for someone* S. E. —W.COGN.ACC. *in servitude* Plu.; (fig.) **be a slave** —W.DAT. *to sufferings* S. —*to beauty* Isoc.; (of Prometheus) —*to a rock* A.
2 serve voluntarily, **be a devoted servant of** —W.DAT. *the laws* X.
3 (of a temple-attendant) **serve** (sts. W.DAT. a god) E.

—W.COGN.ACC. *w. fine toil* E.; (of female slaves) **serve, wait upon** —W.ACC. *a priestess and her altars* E.
4 worship (sts. W.DAT. God) NT.

λάτριος ᾱ ον *adj.* **1** (of a wage) **for menial services** Pi.
2 (predic., of a city, being handed over) **for servitude, into slavery** Pi.

λάτρις ιος *m.f.* **1 hired servant; hireling, servant** (of a household or an individual master, sts. derog. or ref. to a slave) Thgn. S. E. Arist.(quot.trag.) Call.; (of an army, ref. to a messenger) E.; **servant, attendant** (of a god, in a temple) E.; (W.GEN. of the gods, of Zeus, ref. to Hermes or Iris as messengers) S.*satyr.fr.* E.
2 app. **wage** Call.

λάτρον ου *n.* **1 payment, rent** (for lodging) A.(pl.)
2 payment or **reward** Call.

Λᾱτώ *dial.f.*: see Λητώ

λαυκανίη (or **λευκανίη**) ης Ion.*f.* **throat** or **gullet** (of a person) Il. AR.

—λαυκανίηνδε (or **λευκανίηνδε**) Ion.*adv.* **to the mouth** —*ref. to lifting food* AR.

λαύρᾱ ᾱς, Ion. **λαύρη** ης *f.* **1 passageway** (in a palace) Od.
2 alley, back street (in a town) Hippon. Pi. Hdt. Ar.; **lane** (out of town) Theoc.*epigr.*
3 passage (betw. cliffs, leading into a cave) Plu.

Λαύρειον ου *n.* [perh.reltd. λαύρᾱ] **Laureion** (hilly region of southern Attica, w. rich silver-mines) Hdt. Th. And.

—Λαυρειωτικός ή όν *adj.* of or relating to Laureion; (of silver coins, revenue fr. the mines) **Laureian** Ar. Plu. ‖ FEM.SB. Laureian region Plu.

λᾶῦς (Boeot.dat.pl.): see λᾶας

λαφυγμός οῦ *m.* [λαφύσσω] **gluttony** Ar.

λαφύκτης ου *m.* **indulgent squanderer, spendthrift** Arist.

λάφυρα ων *n.pl.* **1 spoils, booty** (seized in war) Trag. X. Plb. Plu.; (also collectv.sg.) Plb.; (sg., ref. to a single item) Plu.
2 ‖ SG. **right of plunder** Plb.

λαφῡραγωγέομαι *mid.contr.vb.* [ἀγωγή] **carry off as spoils** —*an enemy's goods* Plu.

λαφῡροπωλεῖον (or **λαφῡροπώλιον**) ου *n.* [λαφυροπώλης] **market for selling booty** Plb.

λαφῡροπωλέω *contr.vb.* **sell booty** X.; (tr.) **sell as booty, sell off** —*plunder* Plb.

λαφῠρο-πώλης ου *m.* [πωλέω] **official in charge of selling booty** (in the Spartan army) X. Plu.

λαφύσσω *vb.* [reltd. λάπτω] (of lions) **gulp down** —*blood and entrails* Il.

λαχαί ῶν *f.pl.* [λαχαίνω] **excavations** (W.GEN. of an ancestral tomb) A. [or perh.reltd. λαγχάνω, *allotted portion*]

λαχαίνω *vb.* | aor. ἐλάχηνα | **create by digging, dig out** —*a trench* Mosch. —*springs* AR.

λάχανα ων *n.pl.* **plants** (w. leaves that are cooked and eaten as a vegetable), **pot-herbs, vegetables** Ar. Philox.Cyth. Pl. Thphr. NT. Plu.; (sg.) D. NT.

λαχανισμός οῦ *m.* **gathering of vegetables** (by foragers) Th.

λαχανοπωλήτρια ᾱς *f.* [πωλητής] **female vegetable-seller, greengrocer** Ar.

λαχανόπωλις ιδος *f.* [πωλέω] **female vegetable-seller, greengrocer** Ar.

λάχεια *fem.nom.adj.* (of a shore, an island, w. sense uncert.) Od.

λαχεῖν (aor.2 inf.): see λαγχάνω

Λάχεσις εως *f.* [λαγχάνω] **1 Lakhesis** (one of the three Moirai, allotter of the length of a mortal's life) Hes. Pi. Lyr.adesp. Pl.
2 (as common noun) **allotted destiny** Hdt.(oracle)

λαχμός οῦ *m.* **wool, fleece** (of a sheep) Od.(v.l. λάχνος)
λάχνη ης, dial. **λάχνᾱ** ᾱς *f.* **1 hair** (on a person's head, perh. envisaged as woolly or bristly) Il.; (on the chest) Call.; (gener., on the body) AR.
2 down (of a first beard, on the cheeks) Od. ‖ PL. downy hairs (of such a beard) Pi.
3 hair or **fur** (on an animal's hide) Hes. AR.
4 tuft of wool (plucked fr. a fleece) S.
5 nap or **pile** (of a woollen cloak) Il.
λαχνήεις, dial. **λαχνάεις**, εσσα εν *adj.* **1** (of Centaurs, the chests of Hephaistos and Typhon, the head of a sea-god) **hairy, shaggy** Il. Pi. AR.
2 (of a boar's hide) **bristly** Il.; (of thatch) Il.
3 (of groves) **bristling with foliage** Ibyc.
λαχνό-γυιος ον *adj.* [γυῖα] (of wild animals) **shaggy-limbed** E.
λαχνόομαι *pass.contr.vb.* (of a young man's chin) **be covered with hair** Sol.
λάχνος *m.*: see λαχμός
λαχνώδης ες *adj.* (of ground) **downy, soft** (W.GEN. w. grass) E.*Cyc.*
λάχον (ep.aor.2): see λαγχάνω
λάχος εος (ους) *n.* [λαγχάνω] | nom.acc.pl. λάχη, also λάχεα (E.) | **1** that which is allotted (by the gods); **allotted domain** (of a god) Pi. Call.; **allotted fate** (of a demigod) Pi.; **allotted function** or **role** (of Erinyes) A.; (of a king) A.
2 allotment, allocation (of a function, to a god) A.
3 allotment, portion, share (W.GEN. of good and bad fortune for mortals, granted by the gods) Thgn.
4 (gener.) **lot, fate, destiny** (for a person, prescribed by an oracular god) E.
5 that which is allotted by humans, **allotted share** or **portion** (W.GEN. of spoils) A.; (of sacrificed or captured animals) X.
6 portion, part (of day or night, equiv. to one third of either) AR. Mosch.
λαψῇ (dial.2sg.fut.mid.): see λαμβάνω
λάω *ep.vb.* | only ptcpl. λάων, 3sg.impf. λάε | (of an eagle) **look, gaze** —W.ADV. **keenly** hHom.; (tr., of a dog) perh. **transfix with a stare** —*a fawn* Od. [or perh. **seize, grip**]
λαώδης ες *adj.* [λαός] (of invitations to dinner) **addressed to members of the public** Plu.
λέαινα *f.*: see under λέων
λεαίνω, ep. **λειαίνω** *vb.* [λεῖος] | fut. λεανῶ, ep. λειανέω | aor. ἐλέηνα (Hdt.), ep. λείηνα | **1 make smooth** (by removing irregularities or obstacles); **smooth, make smooth** —*a bow of horn* Il. —*a path* (*for horses*)*, a dance-floor* Hom. —*rocky ground* Plb. —*wrinkles in leather* Pl.; (of taste-particles) —*roughened parts of the tongue* Pl. ‖ MID. (pejor., of a man) **make one's body smooth** (by depilation) Plb. ‖ PASS. (of the bodies and cheeks of rejuvenated persons) **be made smooth** (by loss of wrinkles and hair) Pl.; (of substances) —W.DAT. *by the warmth of the mouth* Pl.
2 (fig., of Lawfulness) **make smooth** —*the rough* Sol.; (of an emissary) **put a smooth gloss on** —*the proposal which he is bringing* Hdt.
3 make smooth by grinding (w. pestle and mortar), **grind to a powder** —*dried fish* Hdt.; (intr., of the molars) **grind** (food) X.
4 (of troops) make level (w. the ground), **level, raze** —*vegetation* Hdt.
λέβης ητος *m.* | dial.dat.pl. λεβήτεσσι (Pi.) | **1** large metal bowl (for boiling liquids), **cauldron** (freq. as a valuable possession, prize, gift or offering) Hom. hHom. Pi. Hdt. E. Men. +; (used as a brazier) Th.; (used as a percussion instrument) Hdt. Call.
2 metal bowl (for water, usu. for washing the hands or feet), **basin** Od. AR. Bion; (ref. to a bath) A.
3 urn (for the ashes of the dead) A. S.; (used to store a garment) S.
—λεβήτιον ου *n.* [dimin.] **pot** (for cooking) Men.
λεγεών (also **λεγιών**) ῶνος *f.* [Lat. *legio*] **legion** NT. Plu.
λεγνωτός ή όν *adj.* [λέγνον *coloured border*] (of a garment) **with coloured border** Call.
λέγω *vb.* | fut. λέξω | aor. ἔλεξα ‖ MID.: aor. ἐλεξάμην | ep.athem.aor. ἐλέγμην, 3sg. λέκτο ‖ PASS.: fut. λεχθήσομαι, also λέξομαι | aor. ἐλέχθην, also (in cpds.) -ελέγην | pf. λέλεγμαι, also (in cpds.) -είλεγμαι | fut.pf. λελέξομαι ‖ neut.impers.vbl.adj. λεκτέον ‖ The sections are grouped as: (1–5) collect, choose, count, (6) tell of, (7–19) speak, say. |
1 (act. and mid.) **gather up, collect** —*stones, bones, firewood, or sim.* Hom. Pi. AR.
2 choose, determine —*a number* (*of religious festivals*) Pl. ‖ MID. **pick out for oneself, select, choose** —*persons* Hom. ‖ PASS. (of persons or things) **be chosen** Il. Pl.
3 ‖ MID. (of a naval leader) **review, muster** —*his crew* Pi.
4 count up, number —*persons* Il.(mid.) A.; **reckon up, count, calculate** —*the number of a group of persons or things* Od.(mid.) Pi.
5 count, include —*someone or sthg.* (W.PREP.PHR. *among a particular group*) Od.(mid.) A. E.; **rate, reckon** —*someone* (W.ADV. **nowhere**, i.e. of no account) S. —*nights of love* (W.INTERROG.ADV. *where*, i.e. of what account?) E.(cj.) —*sthg.* (W.PREDIC.SB. *as gain*) S. ‖ MID. **count** or **include oneself** —W.PREP.PHR. *among certain persons* Od. ‖ PASS. (of persons or things) **be counted** or **reckoned** —W.PREP.PHR. *among certain persons or things* Il. E. X. Call.; (of a city) —W.GEN. *among cities of a certain kind* E.
6 tell of, speak about, relate, mention —*sthg.* Od. +; (mid.) Il. ‖ PASS. (of a story or sim.) **be told** Pi. +
7 speak, talk (freq. W.DAT. or PREP.PHR. to someone, or about sthg., or W.ADV. **thus, well**, or sim.) Pi. Hdt. Trag. + ‖ MID. (of persons) **talk** (to one another) Il.
8 (specif.) **speak, make a speech** (in court, the Assembly, or other public or formal ctxt.) S. E. Th. Att.orats. +; **plead** —*a case* Ar. Att.orats. ‖ PASS. (of a case) **be pleaded** Plu.
9 (gener.) **say, utter, speak** —W.ACC. or DIR.SP. *certain words* Hom.(also mid.); (pleon., w. another vb. of speech) εἶπε λέγων, ἔλεγε φάς (or sim.) Hdt. S. + ‖ PASS. (of things) **be said** or **spoken** Pi. Hdt. Trag. +; (advbl.acc.) τὸ λεγόμενον *as the saying goes* Th. Pl.
10 say, declare —W.INF. or ACC. + INF. *that one* (or *someone*) *is doing sthg., that sthg. is the case* hHom. Pi. Hdt. Trag. + —W.COMPL.CL. or INDIR.Q. *that sthg.* (or *what*) *is the case* Hdt. Trag. + ‖ PASS. (of persons or things) **be said** —W.INF. *to be doing sthg., to be such and such* Pi. S. + ‖ IMPERS.PASS. it is said —W.ACC. + INF. *that sthg. is the case* Pi. Hdt. +
11 speak of, describe —W.ACC. + PTCPL. *someone as doing sthg., or as such and such* Trag. ‖ PASS. **be spoken of** or described —W.NOM.PTCPL. *as doing sthg.* E.; (of a deposed god, in neg.phr.) —W.NOM.PTCPL. *as existing formerly* A.
12 (of a person, named at the beginning of a letter or document) **declare** or **state in words, say** —*sthg.* Hdt.; (of a message or inscription) Hdt. Th.
13 (phrs.) λέγειν τι *say something of substance, talk sense* S. Pl. X.; οὐδὲν λέγειν *talk nonsense* Hdt. Ar. Pl. Thphr.

14 speak, address —w.dbl.acc. *an abusive remark* (*or sim.*) *to someone* Hdt. +; **speak of** —w.acc. + adv. *someone in a certain way* (e.g. *abusively or kindly*) Thgn. +
15 identify precisely (what has been previously mentioned), **mean, signify** —*someone or sthg.* Trag. Att.orats. +
16 (of persons, by their words; of a name, phrase, or sim.) **mean, intend, imply** —w.acc. or compl.cl. *sthg., that sthg. is the case* Ar. Pl. D.; (of a dream, an oracle) **signify** —*sthg.* Ar. Pl.; (intr.) πῶς λέγεις; *what do you mean?* Pl.
17 designate, describe —*someone or sthg.* (w.predic.adj. or sb. *as such and such*) Hdt. Trag. +
18 give an order —w.inf. or w.dat. or acc. + inf. (*to someone*) *to do sthg.* Trag. +; (of the law) **dictate** (sthg.) D.
19 read out, read aloud (fr. a book) Pl. —w.acc. *a law* Att.orats.

λεηλασίᾰ ᾱς, Ion. **λεηλασίη** ης *f*. [λεηλατέω] **1** act of pillage, **plundering, raid** X. Plu.
2 result of pillage, **spoils** AR.

λεηλᾰτέω contr.vb. [λείᾱ, ἐλαύνω] **1** drive away booty (orig.ref. to cattle); (gener.) **pillage, take plunder** S. E. X. Plb. Plu.; (tr.) **take** (w.acc. sthg.) **as plunder** X.
2 pillage, plunder —*a city, region* Hdt. Plb. Plu. —*people* Plb.

λείᾱ ᾱς, Ion. **ληίη** ης, dial. **λᾱ́ᾱ** ᾱς (Pi.) *f*. **1 plunder, spoil, booty** Pi. Hdt. S. E. Th. Isoc. +; (ref. to cattle) S. Plb. Plu.; (ref. to captives) E. Plb. Plu.; (provbl.) Μυσῶν λεία *booty from the Mysians* (ref. to sthg. *there for the taking*) D. Arist.
2 prey (captured by hunters, fig.ref. to soldiers) E.

λειαίνω ep.vb.: see λεαίνω

λείβω vb. | aor. ἔλειψα | **1** pour (an offering to the gods); **pour a libation** Hom. Sapph. —w.cogn.acc. A. E.(also mid.) —w.acc. *of wine* Hom. Hes. AR. —*of honey* AR.
2 (gener.) **shed** —*tears* Hom. Trag. Call. AR.; (of Erinyes) **drip** —w.cogn.acc. *a foul drip* (*of blood, fr. their eyes*) A.; (of hair) —*fragrant oil* Call. || mid. **pour forth** —*a stream of tears* A. || pass. (of tears) be shed E. X.; (of foam) drip —w.prep.phr. *around a boar's mouth* Hes.; (of a viscous fluid, fr. the bones) Pl.; (fig., of a lament) be poured forth Pi.
3 || pass. (of persons) stream —w.dat. *w. tears* E.; stream with tears E. Ar. Mosch.
4 (fig.) **liquefy, dissipate** —*one's emotions* (by listening to the wrong kind of music) Pl.

λείηνα (ep.aor.): see λεαίνω

λεῖμαξ ακος *f*. [reltd. λειμών] **meadow** E. Lyr.adesp.

λεῖμμα ατος *n*. [λείπω] **remaining part** (of an uncompleted task) Plu.(dub.) || pl. remnants (of a child, served up as a meal) Hdt.

λειμών ῶνος *m*. [reltd. λιμήν, λίμνη] **1 meadow** (ref. to well-watered land, rich in grass and flowers) Hom. Hes. Thgn. Lyr. Hdt. Trag. +; (fig., ref. to a place where poetic inspiration or spiritual nourishment may be gathered) Ar. Pl.; (pejor., ref. to a source of rich pickings) Pl.
2 meadow (in the underworld, as the haunt or place of judgement for souls) Od. Pi.*fr.* Emp. Pl.
3 (fig.) **meadow** (ref. to the female pubic region) E.*Cyc.*

λειμωνιάς άδος *fem.adj*. (of a nymph) **of the meadows** S. AR.

λειμώνιος ᾱ ον *adj*. **1** of or relating to a meadow; (of dew) **of the meadow** A.; (of flowers) Theoc.
2 (of a marshy plain) like a meadow, **meadowy** AR.

λειμωνόθε(ν) *adv*. **from a meadow** or meadows Il. Theoc.

λειο-γένειος ον *adj*. [λεῖος, γένειον] (of men) smooth-chinned, **beardless** Hdt.

λεῖος ᾱ (Ion. η) ον *adj*. **1** free from roughness or surface irregularities; (of a poplar tree, ref. to its trunk) **smooth** Il.; (of objects and entities, such as slabs, pots, wax, particles of matter) hHom. Pl. X. Arist. AR. Plu.; (of the condition or sensation) **of smoothness** Pl. || neut.sb. smoothness or that which is smooth Pl. Arist.
2 (of ground, plains, roads, surfaces) **smooth** Hom. Hes. Hdt. Pl. X. +; **clear** (w.gen. of rocks) Od.
3 (of textiles) having a surface that is not ornamented with brocade, **not brocaded, plain** Th.; (of a woven fabric, fig.ref. to a well-integrated community) **smooth, seamless** Pl.
4 (of persons, parts of the body) having a smooth skin, **smooth-skinned, hairless** Thgn. S.*Ichn.* Pl.; (of livestock) **smooth-headed, hornless** Pl.; (provb., ref. to attempting an impossible task) θεῖναι λεῖον τὸν τρηχὺν ἐχῖνον *make the prickly hedgehog smooth* Ar.
5 (of a sea or stretch of water) **smooth, calm** A.*satyr.fr.* Hdt. Plu.
6 (of hills) app. **gently sloping** X.
7 (of words of persuasion) **smooth, soft** A.; (of sounds, speech) Pl.
8 (of a breeze) **soft, gentle** Ar.
9 (of a person) **in an amenable mood** Theoc.; (of a teaching method) **gentle** Pl. || neut.sb. easy-going nature, softness (of a person's character) Pl.

—λείως *adv*. **1** with easy or gentle movement, **smoothly** —ref. to dragging a ship Plu. —ref. to making progress in one's education Pl.
2 mildly, gently —ref. to prattling Sol.

λειότης ητος *f*. **smoothness** (as an attribute of things) Arist.; (specif., of sacrificial entrails, as a favourable sign in divination) A.; (of rocks, mirrors, shiny surfaces, particles of matter) Pl.; (of a horse's bit) X.; (of the skin, through depilation, w.connot. of unmanliness) Pl. Plu.

λείουσι (ep.dat.pl.): see λέων

λείπω vb. | fut. λείψω | aor.2 ἔλιπον, ep. λίπον, also ἔλλιπον (Call. AR.), ptcpl. λιπών, inf. λιπεῖν | pf. λέλοιπα || mid. (sts. w.pass.sens.): fut. λείψομαι | aor.2 ἐλιπόμην, ep. λιπόμην | ep.3sg.athem.aor. ἔλειπτο (AR.) || pass.: fut. λειφθήσομαι | aor. ἐλείφθην | pf. λέλειμμαι | 3sg.plpf. ἐλέλειπτο, ep. λέλειπτο | fut.pf. λελείψομαι || neut.impers.vbl.adj. λειπτέον || The sections are grouped as: (1–7) leave behind, (8–11) leave remaining, (12–16) leave out or be lacking, (17–19) fall short. |
1 (of departing persons) **leave behind** —*persons or things* (freq. w.adv. or prep.phr. *in a place*) Hom. + || pass. be left behind Hom. +; (wkr.sens.) stay behind (when others depart) Hom. Hdt.
2 || pass. (of persons, charioteers, horses, sheep, birds) be left behind or outdistanced (freq. w.gen. by others) Hom. A. E. Th.
3 (w.pejor.connot.) **leave behind, forsake, abandon** —*persons or things* Il. + —*a long relationship* E.; (of a soldier) **desert** —*his post* Pl.; (fig.) **stray from, fail to live up to** —*one's true nature* S.
4 depart from, leave —*a place* Hom. +; (of a warrior) —*the fighting* Il.
5 (of a dying person) **leave** —*life, the light of day, or sim.* Il. +; (of life, spirit) —*persons or animals, their bodies* Hom. || statv.pf. (of a person's spirit) be gone Od.
6 leave behind (after death) —*children, possessions* Hom. + —*glory* A. —*grief* (w.dat. *for a survivor*) S.; (mid.) —*a memorial* Hdt. —*children* (w.predic.sb. *as one's successors*) Plu. || pass. (of persons) be left behind (as successors, avengers) Hom.; (of possessions, as an inheritance) Thgn.; (of glory) —w.dat. *for oneself* Hdt.; (of grief) —*for others* Il.; (of a family) be left —w.predic.adj. *less distinguished* Hes.

λειριόεις

7 (of a killer) **leave behind** —*grief* (W.DAT. *for the victim's father*) Il.; (mid.) —*avengers* (*for himself, ref. to the victim's children*) E.
8 leave (sthg.) remaining; **leave** —*a gap* (*betw. buildings*) Hdt. —*a task* (W.DAT. *for someone*) X.; (in neg.phr.) —*a single drop or scrap* (*of wine or meat*) E.Cyc. || PASS. (of things) be left over or remain (freq. W.DAT. for someone) Il. +
9 || IMPERS.PASS. there remains the possibility —W.ACC. + INF. *that sthg. is the case* Pl.
10 leave (sthg.) incomplete; **leave** —*a task* (W.PREDIC.ADJ. *unfinished*) Hes. || PASS. (of a ship) be left —W.PREDIC.ADJ. *half-burnt* Il.
11 leave (sthg.) untouched or unharmed; (in neg.phr., of snow, rain, waves) **leave alone** —*a rock* Il. S.; (usu. in neg.phr.) **leave alive** or **standing, spare** —*a person, house, or sim.* Archil. Hdt. Pl. X. || PASS. (of persons) be left alive, survive (after others have died) Hom. Hdt. S. X.; (of ships) remain (after others have been destroyed) A.; (of troops) —W.GEN. *fr. warfare* (*i.e. survive it*) A.; (of a population) be left —W.PREDIC.ADJ. *independent* (*by an imperial power*) Th.
12 leave out (of one's thoughts or actions); **neglect, spurn** —*a suggested mode of transport* E.; **omit, ignore** —*a house* (*i.e. fail to visit it*) Theoc.; **leave unpaid, default on** —*instalments of tribute, debt repayments* X. D.; **fail to give** —*evidence* D.; **refuse to take** —*an oath* D.
13 leave off (an activity); (of a prosecutor) **drop** —*a case* Arist.; (of a speaker) **finish** —*a story* Call.
14 (of arrows) **fail, run out for** —*someone* Od.
15 (intr., of misfortune) **depart, be gone** —W.PREP.PHR. *fr. persons, a house* S. E.; (of strife) **leave off, cease** —W.PREP.PHR. *in cities* E.; (of persons or things) **be wanting, lacking** or **missing** Pl. Plb. NT. || STATV.PF. (of a person's possessions, sureness of step) have gone, be lost Od. E.
16 || PASS. be left without or deprived of —W.GEN. *friends, possessions* Pi. S.; (wkr.sens.) be without, lack —W.GEN. *children, sound judgement* S. E.; (in neg.phr., of a grieving person) —*laments* S.
17 (of an amount) **fall short** (sts. W.GEN. of a certain figure) Lys. Plb.; (of things) —w. τὸ μή or τοῦ μή + INF. *of being or doing such and such* S. Plb.
18 || PASS. fall short (usu. W.GEN. of someone, W.ACC., DAT. or PREP.PHR. in a certain respect or quality) Hdt. S. E. Th. + —W.GEN. *in a battle* A. —W.PTCPL. *in doing sthg.* N.
19 || PASS. fall short (of achieving sthg.); miss, be too late for —W.GEN. *an opportunity, event, or sim.* Hdt. E. X.; fail —W.GEN. *in a task* Hdt.; fail to understand or be aware of —W.GEN. *someone's intentions, a people's customs* E.; fail to heed —W.GEN. *a request* S.; (of a commander, a candidate for office) fail, be defeated Plb. Plu. || IMPERS.PASS. there is a deficiency (in an argument) Pl.

λειριόεις εσσα εν *adj.* [λείριον] rich in the qualities of a lily; (of the voices of the Muses or cicadas, w.connot. of delicacy or clarity) **lily-like** Il. Hes.; (of a man's skin, w.pejor.connots. of paleness and delicacy) **lily-white** Il.

λείριον ου *n.* **lily** (prob.ref. to the White or Madonna Lily) hHom. AR. Mosch.

λείριος ον *adj.* **1** (of the eyes of boys and maidens) **lily-like** (w.connot. of softness or brightness) B.; (of the voices of the Sirens, w.connot. of beauty or clarity) AR.
2 (app. of the stalk of a flower) perh. **pliant, supple** Pi.

λεϊστός *ep.adj.*: see ληιστός

λειτουργέω *contr.vb.*: see λῃτουργέω

λειτούργημα ατος *n.* [λῃτουργέω] **act of public service** (by a Spartan king) Plu.

λειτουργία *f.*: see λῃτουργία

λειτουργός οῦ *m.* **1** (in Greek states) one who performs a leitourgia, **public servant** Plu.
2 (in military ctxt.) one who performs assigned manual duties, **workman, pioneer** Plb. Plu.

λειφθήσομαι (fut.pass.): see λείπω

λειχήν ῆνος *m.* **1** disease of the skin, **ulcer, canker** A.
2 fungal growth on the ground, **canker, blight** (causing barrenness in plants and women) A.

λείχω *vb.* | aor. ἔλειξα | (of persons or animals) **lick** or **lick up** —*liquids* A. Hdt. Ar. Call. —*honey* Theoc. —*ambrosia, cakes* Ar. —*dust* Hdt.

λείψανον ου *n.* [λείπω] **1** that which remains or is left behind; **remnant** (of a ship) E.; (of a land-mass) Pl.; (of a people or group, ref. to a single person) E. Plu.; (of desire and affection) Plu.; (pejor., ref. to an old man) **relic** (W.GEN. of a man) E.
2 || PL. remains, remnants (of a defeated army) Plb. Plu.; (of objects, places) Plu.; (of a meal) AR.; (of a person's strength, a city's power) Ar. Plu.; (of ancient knowledge) Arist.; (fig., of wars, ref. to small and scattered conflicts, envisaged as corpses left for animal predators) Plu.
3 || PL. remains (W.GEN. of a dead person, ref. to a corpse, bones or ashes) S. Pl. Plu.; (of good men, ref. to their accomplishments or fame) E.
4 (in neg.phr.) **scrap, trace** (of a person's clothing or corpse) Plu.

λεκάνη ης *f.* [reltd. λέκος] **bowl, basin** Ar. Philox.Leuc. Plu.

—λεκάνιον ου *n.* [dimin.] **little bowl, dish** (W.GEN. of meat) Ar.

λεκάριον ου *n.* [dimin. λέκος] **dish** (of food) X.

λεκιθίτᾱς ᾱ *dial.m.* [λέκιθος] app., variety of bread or cake made from pulses, **pulse-bread** Carm.Pop.

λεκιθόπωλις ιδος *f.* [πωλέω] **porridge-seller** Ar.

λέκιθος ου *m.* **gruel, porridge** (of pulses or cereals) Ar.

λέκος εος Ion.n. **bowl, dish** (W.GEN. of wheat) Hippon.

λεκτέος ᾱ ον *vbl.adj.* [λέγω] (of things) **to be spoken** or **spoken about** Isoc. Pl. X. D.

λεκτικός ή όν *adj.* [λεκτός] **1** (of persons) **skilled in speaking, eloquent** X.
2 || FEM.SB. art of speaking Pl.
3 (of iambic metre) related to ordinary speech, **speakable** Arist.; (of a tone of voice) **conversational** Arist.
4 (of the delivery) **of the spoken word** (opp. song) Plb.

λέκτο[1] (ep.3sg.athem.aor.mid.): see λέγω

λέκτο[2] (ep.3sg.athem.aor.mid.): see λέχομαι

λεκτός ή όν *adj.* [λέγω] **1** (of stones) **gathered, picked up** Hes.*fr.*
2 (of persons) **hand-picked, specially chosen, select** Trag. || MASC.PL.SB. select members (W.GEN. of a band of heroes) AR.
3 (of an event or circumstance, in neg.phr.) able or fit to be spoken of, **describable** E. Ar.; (pejor., of all things, i.e. anything, however disgraceful) able to be spoken, **speakable** (W.DAT. by someone) S.

λέκτρον ου *n.* [λέχομαι] | freq. pl. for sg. | **1 bed** Hom. Pi. Trag. AR. Theoc.
2 marriage bed (oft. meton. for marriage) Od. Pi. Trag. Corinn. Men. Hellenist.poet.
3 liaison, sexual union (outside marriage) E.
4 perh., product of one's union, **child, offspring** AR.

—λέκτρονδε *adv.* **to bed** Od.

λελαβέσθαι (ep.redupl.aor.2 mid.inf.), **λελάβηκα** (Ion.pf.): see λαμβάνω

λελαθέσθαι (ep.redupl.aor.2 mid.inf.), **λελάθοντο** (3pl.), **λελάθοιμι** (act.opt.), **λελάθω** (subj.), **λελάθων** (Aeol.pf.ptcpl.): see λανθάνω

λέλᾱκα (pf.), **λελάκοντο** (ep.3pl.redupl.aor.mid.), **λελακυῖα** (ep.fem.pf.ptcpl.): see λάσκω

λέλασμαι (ep.pf.mid.): see λανθάνω

λελάχᾱσι (3pl.pf.), **λελάχητε**, **λελάχωσι** (2 and 3pl. ep.redupl.aor.2 subj.): see λαγχάνω

λέλειμμαι (pf.pass.), **λέλειπτο** (ep.3sg.plpf.pass.), **λελείψομαι** (fut.pf.pass.): see λείπω

λελέξομαι (fut.pf.pass.): see λέγω

λέληθα (pf.), **λεληθότως** pf.ptcpl.adv.: see λανθάνω

λέληκα (Ion.pf.): see λάσκω

λέλημμαι (pf.pass.): see λαμβάνω

λελήσομαι (pf.mid.), **λελήσομαι** (fut.pf.mid.): see λανθάνω

λελήσομαι (pf.pass.): see λήζομαι

λελίημαι ep.pf.vb. | usu.ptcpl. λελιημένος | also 2sg. λελίησαι (Theoc.), 3sg.plpf. λελίητο (AR.) | **1 be eager** Il. AR. —w. ὄφρα + OPT. *to do sthg.* Il. —W.INF. Hellenist.poet. —W.GEN. *for a place* (*i.e. to reach it*) AR.
2 (of air outside a container) **be eager to go** —W.ADV. *inside* Emp.

λέλιμμαι (pf.mid.): see λίπτω

λελογισμένως pf.pass.ptcpl.adv.: see under λογίζομαι

λέλογχα (dial.pf.): see λαγχάνω

λέλοιπα (pf.): see λείπω

λέμβος ου m. **1 small boat** (carried by a larger vessel) Lycurg. D.; (of a fisherman or other individual) Theoc. Plu.
2 light warship Plb.

λέμμα ατος n. [λέπω] **1** that which is peeled or stripped off; **shell** (of an egg) Ar.
2 film, membrane (put on human flesh by the creator god, as the original form of human skin) Pl.

λέμφος ου m. mucous discharge from the nostrils; (fig., pejor.ref. to a man) **snotty-nose, drivelling idiot** Men.

λέντιον ου n. [Lat. *linteum*] **linen cloth, towel** NT.

λέξασθαι (ep.aor.mid.inf.), **λεξάσθην** (3du.), **λεξάσθων** (3pl.imperatv.), **λέξεο** (ep.athem.aor.mid.imperatv.), **λέξεται** (ep.3sg.aor.mid.subj.): see λέχομαι

λέξις εως f. [λέγω] **1** act or process of speaking, **speaking, speech** (sts. opp. song, dance or action) Pl.
2 manner of speaking, **diction** Pl. Arist. Plu.
3 manner of expressing oneself (in speech or writing), **style** Isoc. Pl. Arist.
4 unit of expression, **word** or **phrase** Arist. Plb. Plu.; (gener.) **statement, remark** Plu.
5 (prep.phr.) κατὰ λέξιν *word for word* Plu.; (introducing a quotation) *in the following words* Plu.

λέξο (ep.athem.aor.mid.imperatv.): see λέχομαι

λέξομαι[1] (fut.pass.), **λέξον**[1] (aor.act.imperatv.), **λέξω** (fut.): see λέγω

λέξομαι[2] (ep.fut.mid. and aor.subj.): see λέχομαι

λέξον[2] (ep.aor.imperatv.): see λέχω, under λέχομαι

λεοντ-άγχης ου m. [λέων, ἄγχω] | voc. λεοντάγχα | (epith. of Herakles) **lion-strangler** Call.*epigr.*

λεόντειος ᾱ ον adj. (of the claws) **of a lion** Plu.; (of the skin, used as a bed) Theoc.

λεόντεος ᾱ (Ion. η) ον adj. (of milk) **from a lioness** Alcm.
—**λεοντέη** ης Ion.f. —also **λεοντῆ** ῆς Att.f. **lionskin** (worn as a garment) Hdt. Ar. Pl. Plu.

λεοντο-μάχᾱς ᾱ dial.m. [μάχη] (epith. of Herakles) **lion-fighter** Theoc.*epigr.*

λεοντο-φυής ές adj. [φύω] | Att.acc. λεοντοφυᾶ | (of a captured animal, ref. to a cub) **born of a lion** E.

λεοντώδης ες adj. (of a person's temperament) **lion-like** Arist. Plu. || NEUT.SB. lion-like quality (in human nature or a particular man) Pl. Plu.

λέπαδνον ου n. one of a pair of leather straps fastening the yoke to the neck of a chariot-horse; (usu.pl., ref. to both) **yoke-strap, harness-strap, halter** Il. Anacr. A. Ar.; (fig., W.GEN. of necessity, ref. to an inescapable constraint) A.; (of a bride, ref. to a marriage arranged by a father for his son) E.*fr.*

λεπαῖος ᾱ ον adj. [λέπας] (of ground, a glen, hilltop) **craggy, rugged** E.

λέπ-αργος ον adj. [λέπος skin (or sim.), λέπω; ἀργός] (of a hawk) **with shiny coat** (i.e. white-feathered) S.*fr.*; (as the name of a young calf) Theoc.

λεπάς άδος f. **limpet** (as exemplifying that which clings) Ar.

λέπας n. | only nom. and acc. | **crag, cliff** or **mountainside** A. E. Th.; (in fig.ctxt.) πρὸς λέπας *uphill* (*ref. to dragging sthg., w.connot. of effort and difficulty*) E.

λεπαστή ῆς f. app., deep drinking-cup, **goblet** Ar.

λεπιδωτός ή όν adj. [reltd. λεπίς] **1** (of a crocodile's skin) covered with scales, **scaly** Hdt. || MASC.SB. a kind of fish (found in the Nile), scale-fish Hdt.
2 (of a cuirass) covered with metal plates, **plated** Hdt.

λεπίζω vb. [λεπίς] **strip the plating from** —*objects* (*covered w. precious metals*) Plb.

λεπίς ίδος f. [λέπω] **1** (collectv.sg.) **plating** (of metal, prob. on a cuirass) Hdt.; (on the rim of a shield) Plu.; (pl., ref. to a decorative covering of precious metal on buildings) Plb. Plu.
2 || PL. **scales** (on animals) Emp.(dub., cj. φλονίδες); (fig., as falling fr. the eyes when one sees a truth) NT.

λέπρᾱ ᾱς, Ion. **λέπρη** ης f. [λεπρός] **1** a kind of skin disorder; perh. **psoriasis** or **eczema** Hdt. Thphr.
2 contagious skin disease, **leprosy** NT.

λεπράς άδος fem.adj. (of a rock) **rough, rugged** Theoc.

λεπρός ά όν adj. [λέπω] (of persons) with a contagious skin disease, **with leprosy** NT. || MASC.SB. **leper** NT.

λεπταλέος ᾱ (Ion. η) ον adj. [λεπτός] **1** (of a garment) **thin, fine, delicate** AR.
2 (of a Muse, meton. for poetry) **slim, slender** (i.e. delicate, refined) Call.
3 (of a singer's voice) perh. **high-pitched, shrill** Il.; (of wailing) AR.
—**λεπταλέον** neut.adv. **shrilly** —*ref. to panpipes playing* Call.

λεπτό-γεως ων adj. [γῆ] (of Attica) **having light** or **thin soil** Th.

λεπτό-δομος ον adj. [δέμω] (of the cables of a bridge) constructed of thin strands, **finely spun** A.

λεπτό-θριξ τριχος adj. [θρίξ] (of an eagle's tresses, i.e. plumage) of fine hair, **finely feathered** B.

λεπτό-λιθος ον adj. [λίθος] (perh. of sands) **covered with little stones** (i.e. pebbles) Scol.

λεπτολογέω contr.vb. [λεπτολόγος] reason subtly, **quibble, split hairs** Ar.

λεπτο-λόγος ον adj. (of minds) **subtly reasoning** Ar.

λεπτό-μιτος ον adj. [μίτος] (of a cloak) made of fine threads, **finely spun** E.

λεπτό-πρυμνος ον adj. [πρύμνα] (of a ship) **slender-sterned** B.

λεπτός ή (dial. ά) όν adj. [λέπω] **1** (of barley) stripped of the husk, **husked, peeled** Il.
2 forming a thin layer; (of bronze, oxhide) **thin** Il. Pi.; (of bronze plates) Plb.; (of a membrane) AR.; (of an acorn's shell) Theoc.
3 forming a light layer; (of dust, ashes) **light** S. Ar.

λεπτότης

4 consisting of small particles; (of dust) **fine** Il.
5 consisting of or made from thin fibres; (of yarn, threads, a web, a spider's web) **fine, delicate** Od. Hdt. E. Philox.Leuc. X.; (of garments, fabrics) **of fine texture, delicate** Hom. hHom. Emp. E. X. +; (of manufactured products) **in delicate fabrics** Aeschin.; (gener., of clothing) **light, thin** (opp. coarse, thick) Th. Pl. Thphr.
6 **slight in width**; (of an entrance, path, strait) **narrow** Od. Alcm. Theoc. Pl.; (of a ship's prow) **slender** Th.
7 of small cross-section; (of a cord) **thin, slender** Il. Theoc.; (of a tube) Hippon.; (of a reed) E. Ar.(cj.); (of a myrtle tree) Philox.Leuc.; (of a spear) Plb.; (of a finger) Pl.; (of a hare's neck) X.
8 (of persons) having little flesh, **thin, lean, skinny** Ar. Arist. Thphr. Theoc. Plu.; (of a person's hand, chest) Hes. Ar.; (of cattle, wild animals) Hdt. X. Men. Theoc.; (fig., of the framework of a land, envisaged as the human body) Pl.
9 (of men, in high summer) **weak, feeble** Alc.
10 having a low density; (of soil) **fine, light** X.; (of a piece of earth) Pl.; (of natural elements, odours) **rarefied** Pl.
11 (milit., of an army's wing) lacking depth or density, **forming a thin line** Plu.; (prep.phr.) ἐπὶ λεπτόν *in a thin line* X. Plb.
12 (gener.) small (for its kind); (of boats) **small, little** Hdt. Th. D. Plb. Plu.; (of ladders) Ar.; (of headlands, rocks) Hdt. Plu.; (of a cake) Anacr.; (of a bird) Plu.
13 small (by nature); (of grains of wheat) **small** Ar.; (of scraps of a garland) Theoc.; (of a baby's ear) Simon.; (of a gnat's intestine) Ar.; (of particles of matter) **fine, tiny** Pl.
14 (of a coin) **small** (in size and value) Plu. ‖ NEUT.SB. **small coin** (of low value) NT.
15 (of persons) of slender means, **poor** Plb. Plu.
16 (of an animal's scent) **slight, faint** X.; (of heat) Pi.; (of light) AR.
17 small in degree; (of a person's capacity for decisive thought) **slight** Il.; (of hope, a chance of safety) A.fr. Ar. Pl.; (in fig.ctxt., of a turn of the scales) S.fr.
18 slight or light (w.connot. of delicacy or softness); (of down on the cheeks) **light, delicate** Call.; (of fire, fig.ref. to a sensation stealing beneath a lover's flesh) Sapph.; (of a person's mind) perh. **delicate, sensitive** Sapph.
19 (of the whirring of a gnat's wings) **light, gentle** A.; (of the current of a channel) E.; (of a footstep) **quiet** E.
20 refined (in matters of logic or speech); (of a mind, a thinker) **subtle** E. Ar.; (of talk, arguments, thoughts, or sim.) E. Antipho Ar. Call.*epigr.* Plu.
21 (of the music of the nightingale) **delicate** or **subtle** E.fr.
—**λεπτόν** *neut.sg.adv.* 1 **gently** or **delicately** —*ref. to birds twittering* Ar.
2 **faintly, weakly** —*ref. to breathing one's last* Bion
—**λεπτά** *neut.pl.adv.* 1 **faintly** —*ref. to seeing* E.
2 app. **briefly** —*ref. to glancing* Theoc.
—**λεπτῶς** *adv.* 1 **subtly** —*ref. to thinking* Pl.(quot.poet.)
2 **weakly** (so as to be brittle) —*ref. to metal being forged* Plu.
λεπτότης ητος *f.* 1 **fineness, slenderness, thinness** (of things) Pl.
2 **thinness, leanness** (of the body) Pl.
3 **rarefied quality, thinness** (of air) Pl.
4 **lack of viscosity, thinness** (of a liquid) Pl. Plu.
5 **fineness, delicacy, lightness** (of textiles) Plu.
6 **lightness** (of shields) Plu.
7 **fineness of logic, subtlety** (W.GEN. of the mind) Ar.
λεπτουργέω *contr.vb.* [λεπτουργής] 1 **do finely crafted work** (in wood or metal) Plu.

2 (fig.) make fine distinctions (in speech), **talk subtly, quibble** E. Pl.
λεπτουργής ές *adj.* [ἔργον] (of a garment) **finely worked** hHom.
λεπτο-ψάμαθος ον *adj.* (of the mouth of the Nile) **with fine sands** A.
λεπτύ́νω *vb.* 1 (of a commander) **make into a thin line** —*a troop formation* Plb.
2 (intr., of a person) **become thin** Theoc. ‖ MID. (of runners, boxers) **keep oneself thin** or **underdeveloped** —W.ACC. *in one's shoulders or legs* X.
3 ‖ PASS. (of air) **become thin** or **rarefied** Plu.
λεπύ́ριον ου *n.* [λέπω] **shell** (of an acorn) Theoc.
λέπω *vb.* **peel** or **strip** | only in cpds. ἀπολέπω, ἐπιλέπω, περιλέπω
Λέρνα ης (dial. ᾱς) *f.* **Lerna** (region in Argolis, famous for its springs and fertile pastures, the mythol. home of the Hydra, killed by Herakles) Hippon. A. E. AR. Plu.
—**Λερναῖος** ᾱ (Ion. η) ον (also ος ον E.) *adj.* (of the shore, waters) **of Lerna, Lernaian** Pi. E.; (of the Hydra) Hes. S. E. AR. Plu.
λεσβιάζω *vb.* [Λέσβος] (of a Muse) **behave in a Lesbian manner** (i.e. w. the lyric artistry characteristic of the musicians and poets, and w. the sexual behaviour characteristic of the women, ref. to fellatio) Ar.
λεσβίζω *vb.* | fut.inf. λεσβιεῖν | **treat in a manner characteristic of Lesbian women**; (of a woman) **fellate** —*a man* Ar.
Λέσβος ου *f.* **Lesbos** (island off the NW. coast of Asia Minor, esp. assoc.w. music and lyric poetry) Hom. +
—**Λεσβόθεν** *adv.* **from Lesbos** Il.
—**Λέσβιος** ᾱ (Ion. η) ον *adj.* 1 (of a man or woman) **of** or **from Lesbos, Lesbian** Semon. Sapph. Pi.fr. Hdt. Pl. Plu.
‖ MASC.PL.SB. **Lesbians** (as a population or military force) Alc. Hdt. Th. +
2 of or relating to Lesbos or the Lesbians; (of products, artefacts, a paean, building style) **Lesbian** Archil. Hdt. Th. Arist. Call.*epigr.*
—**Λεσβιάς** άδος *f.* **woman of Lesbos** Alc.
—**Λεσβίς** ίδος *fem.adj.* (of women) **from Lesbos, Lesbian** Il.
λεσχάζω *vb.* [λέσχη] **talk** or **gossip about** —*trivial or malicious things* Thgn.
λεσχαίνω *vb.* **talk** —*nonsense* Call.
λέσχη ης, dial. **λέσχα** ᾱς *f.* 1 app. **gathering place, public lounge** (as a resort for travellers or idlers) Od. Hes.; (at Sparta, ref. to a place or building where people met to converse) Plu.
2 **talk, conversation, discussion** Hdt. Trag. Call. Plu.; (pejor.) **idle talk, gossip** E.
3 **conference** (W.GEN. of elders) S.
λεσχηνεύομαι *mid.vb.* **hold a conversation** —W.DAT. *w. a house* (as an example of pointless behaviour) Heraclit.
λευγαλέος ᾱ (Ion. η) ον *adj.* [reltd. λυγρός] 1 (of a beggar) **wretched, miserable, pitiable** Od.; (of sufferings, pains) Od. AR.
2 (pejor., of persons, their mind or words) **wretched, contemptible** Hom.; (of a manner of death) **pitiful, demeaning** Hom.
3 (of an animal's haunts) **miserable, dismal** Hes.
4 (of war, circumstances, emotions, or sim.) **grievous, baneful, grim** Il. Hes. Thgn. AR.
5 (predic., of a person or thing) turning out **painful** (for someone), **disastrous** AR.

–λευγαλέως adv. **1** in a sorry state —ref. to being forced to retreat Il.; **wretchedly, pitifully** —ref. to being killed AR. **2 painfully, grimly** —ref. to routing an enemy AR.

λεύκᾱ dial.f.: see λεύκη

λευκαθέω contr.vb. [λευκός] | only masc.gen.pl.ptcpl. λευκαθεόντων | (of teeth) **be white** Hes.

λευκαίνω vb. **1** (of rowers) **whiten** —the sea (W.DAT. w. oars, the splash of oars) Od. E.Cyc.; (intr., of the sea) **be whitened** (by rowers) E.fr. || PASS. (of a ship's wake) **show white** AR. **2** (of dawn and the rising sun) **bring a white gleam to** —the light of day E. **3** (of advancing age) **bring whiteness** (to a person's hair) Theoc.

λευκ-ανθής ές adj. [ἄνθος] having a white bloom; (of a man's head, ref. to his hair) **tinged with white** S.; (of smoke) **billowing white** Pi.

λευκανθίζω vb. (of soldiers) **be coloured white** (fr. chalking their bodies) Hdt.

λευκανίη Ion.f., **λευκανίηνδε** Ion.adv.: see λαυκανίη

Λευκάς[1] άδος fem.adj. (w. πέτρα, πέτρη) **White or Leucadian Rock** (name of a landmark on the route to Hades) Od.; (provbl., as a place fr. which persons committing suicide leapt into the sea) Anacr. E.Cyc.

Λευκάς[2] άδος f. **Leukas** (island off the W. coast of Greece) Th. +

λεύκ-ασπις ιδος masc.adj. [λευκός, ἀσπίς[1]] | acc. λεύκασπιν | (epith. of the warrior Deiphobos) **having a white shield** (uncert. whether fr. paint, linen covering or a pale silver alloy), **white-shielded** Il.; (of an Argive army) Trag.; (of Carian, Carthaginian and Macedonian troops) X. Plu.

λεύκη ης, dial. **λεύκᾱ** ᾱς f. **1 white poplar** And. Ar. Theoc.; (ref. to the branches and leaves used for garlands) D. Theoc. **2** a kind of skin disease, **white disease** (distinguished fr. λέπρα) Hdt.; (distinguished fr. ἀλφός) Pl.

λευκ-ήρετμος ον adj. [ἐρετμόν] (of a warship) **white-oared** E.

λευκ-ήρης ες adj. [ἀραρίσκω] (of a beard) **white** A.

Λευκιππίδες ων f.pl. **daughters of Leukippos** (brother of Tyndareos, ref. to the wives of the Dioscuri, w. a cult at Sparta) E.

λεύκ-ιππος ον adj. [ἵππος] (of gods, heroes or warriors, a people) **having a white horse or horses, white-horsed** Lyr.; (of the Spartan Dioscuri; cf. λευκόπωλος) E.; (of Dawn) B.fr. Theoc.; (of a competitor in a chariot-race) S.; (transf.epith., of the streets of a people) Pi.

λευκίτᾱς ᾱ dial.m. (ref. to a goat) **white one** Theoc.

λευκογραφέω contr.vb. [γράφω] **draw in white on a dark ground** (or perh. draw in black on a white ground); **draw** (w.ACC. an image) **in black and white** Arist.

Λευκοθέᾱ ᾱς, Ion. **Λευκοθέη** ης f. **Leukothea** (sea-goddess, formerly Ino, the mortal daughter of Kadmos) Od. Pi. E. Arist. Plu.

λευκό-θριξ τριχος masc.fem.adj. [θρίξ] **1** having white hair; (of a ram) **white-fleeced** Ar.; (of horses) **white-coated** Call. **2** (of braids of wool) consisting of white hair, **white-haired** E.

λευκο-θώρᾱξ ᾱκος masc.adj. (of Persian cavalrymen) **with white cuirass** X.

λευκό-ιον ου n. [ἴον] a kind of flower; perh. **white stock** or **snowdrop** Theoc.

λευκο-κύμων ον, gen. ονος adj. [κῦμα] (of beaches) **with white surf** E.

λευκό-λινον ου n. [λίνον] a kind of flax or hemp (used for ropemaking); **white flax** Hdt.

λευκό-λοφος ον adj. [λόφος] (of a helmet, its wearer) **white-crested, white-plumed** Anacr. Ar.

–λευκολόφᾱς ᾱ dial.m. (ref. to a warrior) **white-plumed one** E.

λευκό-πεπλος ον adj. [πέπλος] **1** (of women) **white-robed** Corinn. **2** (of a day) **for wearing white clothes** (because a feast-day) Hippon. [or perh. auspicious] | see λευκός 1

λευκό-πετρον ου n. [πέτρᾱ] **bare rock** Plb.

λευκό-πηχυς υ adj. [πῆχυς] (of women) with white or pale arms; (transf.epith., of women's hands) **pale** E.

λευκο-πληθής ές adj. [πλῆθος] (of the Assembly) **crowded with white** (ref. to the complexions of women attending it covertly) Ar.

λευκό-πους ποδος masc.fem.adj. [πούς] **1** (of Bacchants) **pale-footed** E.Cyc. **2** (of a horse) **white-footed** Plu. **3** || MASC.PL.SB. (ref. to soldiers) white-footed ones (perh. honorific or w.connot. of having dusty feet) Ar.

λευκό-πτερος ον adj. [πτερόν] **1** having white feathers or wings; (fig., of a snow-storm) **white-feathered** A.; (of Dawn, ref. to the horses of her chariot) **white-winged** E. **2** (of a ship) **white-sailed** E.

λευκό-πωλος ον adj. [πῶλος] **1** having a white horse or horses; (epith. of the Spartan Dioscuri, Kastor and Polydeukes) **white-horsed** Pi.; (epith. of the Theban Dioscuri, Amphion and Zethos) E. | see λευκός 6 **2** (of day, ref. to the Sun's chariot) **drawn by white horses** A. S.; (of a four-horse chariot) Plu.

λευκός ή (dial. ά) όν adj. [reltd. λεύσσω] **1** (of sunlight, the sky) **bright, shining, clear** Od. E.; (of a day, esp. as following night or unhappiness, usu. w. further connot. auspicious, happy) A. S. Call.; (of spring, w. same connot.) Call. Theoc.; (of other seasons) Call.; (of a day, w.connot. of auspicious explained as deriving fr. the use of white and black beans in casting lots) Plu. **2** (of the eye, face or rays of Dawn) perh. **pale** E. Theoc. **3** (of water, streams, a calm sea) **bright, clear, limpid** Hom. Hes. Thgn. Lyr.adesp. A. E. Call. **4** (of metal objects) **bright, shining** Il.; (of gold, ref. to electrum) **white** Hdt. **5** having a white colour; (of snow, ivory, Parian marble, an egg, sts. as exemplifying pure whiteness) **white** Hom. Hes. Sapph. Pi. Trag. Pl. Theoc.; (of milk, cream cheese, porridge) Hom. Alcm. A. Pi. E. Philox.Leuc. +; (of products or phenomena of the natural world, such as stones, barley, beets, salt, flowers, clouds) Il. Hes. hHom. Ar. X. Call. Theoc.; (of foam, surf, eddies) Hes. E. AR.; (of teeth, bones, ivory) Hom. Hes. Pi. Emp. Ar. Thphr.; (of semen, the brain) Archil.(cj.) Hdt. S.; (of garments, sails, or sim.) Hom. Hes. Thgn. Hdt. A. E.; (of a building, made of marble) Hdt.(oracle); (of places, perh.fr. the colour of their stone or rock) Il. E. **6** (of animals, birds, their hair, coat or feathers) **white** Il. hHom. Carm.Pop. Hdt. Ar. X. +; (of horses, usu. as a mark of quality or beauty) Il. Hippon. Hdt. E. Ar. X. +; (as cult title, of the two horses of Zeus, ref. to Amphion and Zethos; cf. λευκόπωλος) E.fr.; (of a chariot-team) E.; (of horsehair plumes) Alc. **7** || NEUT.SB. white (as a colour) Ar. Pl. X. Arist.; (sg. and pl.) white clothing Ar. **8** having become white (fr. being differently coloured); (of persons, objects) **white, pale** (w. dust) Il.; (of buildings) **whitened** (by painting) Hdt.; (of hair, by dyeing) Pl.; (of a woman, by make-up) X. | see also στάθμη 2

λευκοστεφής 868

9 (of hair, the head) **white** (fr. old age) Tyrt. Anacr. B.*fr.* S. E. Pl. +; (of a person or body, ref. to their hair, sts. W.DAT. fr. old age) S. E. Call.
10 (of women) having a white or pale complexion (fr. keeping out of the sun, as a positive quality), **pale-complexioned, fair-skinned** Ar. Men. Theoc.; (of parts of their bodies) Hom. B. S. E. Call. AR.
11 (of men, their complexion, freq. pejor., w.connot. of effeminacy or lack of outdoors activity) **pale, fair** E. Ar. Pl. X. Men. Theoc.; (of a warrior's unexposed flesh) Il.
12 (fig., of a person's mind) perh. **young, raw, lacking sense** Pi.

λευκο-στεφής ές *adj.* [στέφω] (of branches, carried by suppliants) **white-wreathed** (w. wool) A.

λευκό-στικτος ον *adj.* [στικτός] (of horses' coats) **flecked with white** E.

λευκό-σφυρος ον *adj.* [σφυρόν] (of a goddess) **pale-ankled** Theoc.

λευκότης ητος *f.* **whiteness** Hdt. Pl. Arist. Plu.

λευκό-τροφος (or **λευκοτρόφος**) ον *adj.* [τρέφω] (of myrtleberries) **white-nourished** (i.e. grown fr. the myrtle's blossom) Ar. [or perh. *white and nourishing*]

λευκο-φαής ές *adj.* [φάος] (of sand) **gleaming white** E.

λευκο-φορῑνό-χροος ον *adj.* [φορίνη, χρώς] (of ribs of meat) perh. **encased in white fat** Philox.Leuc.

λεύκ-οφρυς υος *masc.fem.adj.* [ὀφρύς] with white brow; (fig., of a market-place, adorned w. Parian marble) **white-fronted** Hdt.(oracle)

λευκο-χίτων ωνος *masc.fem.adj.* [χιτών] (fig., of wheat) **white-jacketed** Lyr.adesp.

λευκό-χρως ων *adj.* [χρώς] | acc. λευκόχροα | **1** (of a man) **pale-skinned** Theoc.*epigr.*; (w.pejor.connot.) Men.
2 (of hair) white in colour (fr. old age), **white** E.

λευκόω *contr.vb.* **1** || MID. **whiten** —*helmets, wooden shields* X.
2 || PF.PASS.PTCPL. (of a wall, tablet or board) whitened (for writing on w. charcoal) Pl. D. Arist.
3 || PASS. (of a man, ref. to his head) be made white —W.DAT. *w. myrtle-garlands* Pi.

λευκ-ώλενος ον *adj.* [ὠλένη] (of goddesses and women) **white-armed** (w.connot. of beauty) Hom. Hes. hHom. Lyr.

λεύκωμα ατος *n.* [λευκόω] **whitened board** (on which to write a temporary notice in charcoal) Lys. D.

λευρός ᾱ́ όν *adj.* **1** (of ground) **flat, level, smooth** Od. A. Hdt.(oracle); (of rock, a sandy shore) A. E.; (of streets) Call.; (of a path through the air) A.
2 (of a sword) **smooth** Pi. [or perh. as penetrating flesh, *smooth-gliding*]

λεύσιμος ον *adj.* [λεύω] relating to stoning; (of the hand) **of one who stones** E.; (of punishment, death) **by stoning** E.; (of curses) **that call for stoning** A.; (of a murder) **to be avenged by stoning** A.; (pleon.) λευσίμῳ πετρώματι *by stoning with rocks* E.

λευσμός οῦ *m.* **stoning** (as a punishment) A.

λεύσσω *vb.* [reltd. λευκός] | only pres. and impf. | impf. ἔλευσσον, ep. λεῦσσον | iteratv. λεύσσεσκον | **1 have sight of, see, observe** —*someone or sthg.* Hom. Emp. Trag. Ar.(quot. A.) AR. Theoc.
2 look or **gaze upon, inspect, examine** —*sthg.* Il. E.
3 (intr.) **look, gaze** S. E. —W.ADV. or PREP.PHR. *in a certain direction, at or towards a person or place, over the sea, into a mirror* Hom. S. E.
4 see, look upon —*the sun, light, day* (*periphr. for being alive*) Pi. Trag. Ar.; (intr.) **see the light** (i.e. be alive) S.
5 (intr.) have sight, **see** —W.NEUT.PL.ADV. *faintly* E.
6 see (as an outcome), **find** —*rest fr. labours* E.(cj.)
7 have a look (of a particular kind); **look, stare, glare** —W.COGN.ACC. *w. a serpent's look* A. —W.NEUT.ACC.ADV. (sg. and pl.) *fiercely, dreadfully* E.; **have a look of** —W.ACC. *murder* Theoc.
8 look with the mind, **look** —W.ADVS. *ahead and behind* (i.e. *to the future and the past*) Il.; **observe, consider** —*circumstances* Od. —W.COMPL.CL. *that sthg. is the case* Il. E.; (of Pythagoras) be able to see (mentally), **see** —*all things that exist* Emp.

λευστήρ ῆρος *m.* [λεύω] **1** one who pelts with stones (as a punishment), **stoner** E.; (appos.w. μόρος) *death by stoning* A.
2 (derog.) app. **mere stone-thrower** (ref. to the potential usurper of a kingdom) Hdt.(oracle)

λευχειμονέω *contr.vb.* [λευκός, εἷμα] **wear white clothes** Pl. Plu.

λεύω *vb.* | fut. λεύσω || aor.pass. ἐλεύσθην | **pelt with stones** (as a punishment, or out of hatred or contempt), **stone** —*a person or body* Hippon. A.*fr.* Hdt. Th. —*a tomb* E. || PASS. be stoned S. E.

λεχαῖος ᾱ (Ion. η) ον *adj.* [λέχος] **1** (of chicks) belonging to the nest, **nestling** A.
2 (of greenery) usable for a bed, **for bedding** AR.

λεχε-ποίης *Ion.masc.fem.adj.* [app. λέχος; ποίᾱ] | only acc. λεχεποίην, dat. λεχεποίῃ | app., with beds of grass; (of cities) **nestling in grass, grassy** Il. hHom.; (of a river) **with grassy banks** Il. Hdt.(oracle)

λεχ-ήρης ες *adj.* [λέχος, ἀραρίσκω] **bedridden** E.

λεχθήσομαι (fut.pass.): see λέγω

λέχομαι *ep.mid.vb.* | fut. λέξομαι | AOR.1: 3sg. ἐλέξατο, 3du. λεξάσθην, subj. λέξομαι, 3sg. λέξεται, 3pl.imperatv. λεξάσθων, inf. λέξασθαι | ATHEM.AOR.: 3sg. ἔλεκτο, also λέκτο, imperatv. λέξο, also λέξεο |
1 lie down (esp. on a bed, to sleep) Hom. Hes.
2 camp out, bivouac (in a place) Il.

—**λέχω** *act.vb.* | aor. ἔλεξα, imperatv. λέξον | **provide a bed for** —*someone* Il.; (of Sleep) **lay to rest** —*the mind of Zeus* Il.

λέχος εος (ους) *n.* | freq. pl. for sg. | **1 bed** (as a place for sleeping, resting or sexual intercourse; sts. meton. for the last) Hom. Hes. Lyr. Trag. AR. Mosch.
2 marriage bed (sts. meton. for marriage) Hom. Hes. Alc. Pi. Trag. Ar. +
3 spouse or **partner** Sapph. S. E. Theoc.
4 bier (for a corpse) Hom. Plu.
5 nest (of a bird) A. S.

—**λέχοσδε** *adv.* **to bed** Hom.

λέχριος ᾱ ον (also ος ον Call.) *adj.* **1** (quasi-advbl., of a person stepping or falling) **sideways** S. E.; (of a person sleeping, w. head inclined) **to one side** Call.
2 (of the heads of dogs on the hunt) **slanting, inclined** (W.PREP.PHR. *towards the ground*) X.
3 (fig., of a person's situation or undertakings) **awry, amiss** S.

λέχρις *adv.* **1 to one side** —*ref. to inclining one's head* AR.
2 leaning forwards —*ref. to crouching over a stream* AR.
3 at an angle (to another) —*ref. to buildings standing* AR.

λεχώ οῦς *f.* [λέχος] woman having given birth or about to give birth, **woman in childbirth** E. Ar. Thphr.

λεχώιος ον *adj.* (of purificatory baths) **for a woman who has just given birth** AR. || NEUT.SB. childbed (W.GEN. of a goddess, ref. to a region where she gave birth) Call.

λεχωΐς ΐδος *f.* woman having given birth or about to give birth, **woman in childbirth** Call. AR.

λέων οντος *m.* | ep.dat.pl. λείουσι | **lion** Hom. +; (fig., ref. to a person or god, as exemplifying savagery, fearlessness or strength) Il. A. Hdt.(oracle) E. Ar. Pl.; (provbl.) ξυρεῖν λέοντα *shave a lion (i.e. attempt a risky undertaking)* Pl.

—**λέαινα** ης (dial. ᾱς) *f.* **lioness** Hdt. S. E. Call. Theoc.; (fig., ref. to a woman, as exemplifying savagery) A. E. Men.; (as adopting a crouching posture in sexual intercourse) Ar.

λεωργός όν *adj.* [perh. λέως; ἔργον] perh., ready to do anything; (of persons) **villainous** or **reckless** A. X.; (of actions) Archil.

λεώς Ion. and Att.*m.*: see λαός

λέως *Ion.adv.* [reltd. λείως, under λεῖος] **completely**; (in neg.phr.) **at all** Archil.

λεω-σφέτερος ον *Ion.adj.* [λαός] (predic., of a person who is given the status) **belonging to one's own people** (i.e. as a fellow citizen) Hdt.

λεωφόρος *Ion. and Att.adj.*: see λαοφόρος

λῇ (dial.3sg.indic. and subj.): see λῶ

λήγω *vb.* | ep.inf. ληγέμεναι | fut. λήξω | aor. ἔληξα, ep. ἔλληξα (AR.) | **1 cease, desist** (fr. doing sthg.) Il. Hes.*fr.* A. S. Ar. X. + —w.GEN. *fr. activities, emotions, or sim.* Hom. Hes. Thgn. B. S. E. Ar. + —*fr. slaughter* (w.ACC. *w. one's hands, i.e. restrain them fr. slaughter*) Od. —w.PREP.PHR. *fr. work* AR.; **relent, slacken** —w.ACC. *in one's fury* Il.; **stop** —w.PTCPL. *doing sthg.* Hom. hHom. Trag. Pl. X. + —w.INF. Lyr.adesp.
2 (of wind, rain) **cease, stop** A. Pi. B. X. AR.; (of activities, happenings, emotions, or sim.) Carm.Pop. Pi.*fr.* S. E. Th. Ar. +; (of days, seasons, years, the bloom of youth) **come to an end** Hdt. S. Th. Pl. X. D. +; (of a cask of wine) **run out** Hes.
3 (of a path, region, mountain range, walls under construction) **come to an end** Hdt. Th. Call.

Λήδᾱ ᾱς, Ion. **Λήδη** ης *f.* **Leda** (mother of Helen, Clytemnestra and the Dioscuri) Od. +

λήδανον (also **λάδανον**) ου *n.* [loanwd.] **rock-rose resin** (an aromatic resin fr. the rock-rose bush) Hdt.

ληδάριον ου *n.* [dimin., reltd. λᾶδος] **light garment** (worn in summer), **light cloak** Ar.

λήζομαι, Ion. **ληίζομαι** *mid.vb.* [λεία] | ep.fut. ληίσσομαι | aor. ἐλησάμην, Ion. ἐληισάμην, ep.3sg. ληίσσατο, ep.3sg.subj. ληίσσεται || PASS.: Ion.aor.ptcpl. ληισθείς | pf. λέλησμαι |
1 acquire plunder (through violence, in war, or as a way of life), **plunder, pillage** Hdt. Th. Lys. X. Plb. Plu.; (tr.) —*places, people* Hdt. Th. And. D. X. Plb. Plu. || PF.PASS. have had (w.ACC. one's wife) carried off as plunder E.
2 take as plunder, **plunder, carry off** —*persons, cattle, property* Hom. Hdt. E. D. Plb. || PASS. (of a woman) be carried off as plunder E. AR.
3 (gener.) **steal** —*wealth* (*through deceit, perjury*) Hes. Hdt.
4 (wkr.sens.) **win, acquire** —*a wife* Hes. Semon.
5 (of animals) **scavenge for food** X.

ληθαῖος ᾱ ον *adj.* [λήθη] **1** (of the wing of Sleep) **bringing forgetfulness** Call.
2 (of a song, sung in the underworld) associated with the region of Lethe, **Lethean** Mosch. | see λήθη 5

ληθάνω *ep.vb.*: see ἐκλανθάνω

λήθη ης, dial. **λάθᾱ** ᾱς *f.* [λανθάνω] **1 state or act of forgetting** or no longer caring about things past, **forgetfulness, obliviousness** Il. Thgn. Pi. Isoc. Pl. X. +; (w.GEN. of someone or sthg.) Sapph. Pi. Hdt. S. E. Th. +
2 inability to remember (as a disorder), **loss of memory** Th.
3 state of being universally forgotten, oblivion, obscurity Pi. S. X.
4 (personif., as a deity) **Lethe, Forgetfulness, Neglect** Hes.; **Obliviousness** (w.GEN. to troubles) E.
5 (as the name of a plain in the underworld) **Lethe** Ar. Pl.

λήθω *vb.*: see λανθάνω

ληιάς άδος *Ion.f.* [λήζομαι] | ep.dat.pl. ληιάδεσσι | **woman taken as plunder, captive woman** AR.; (appos.w. γυνή) Il.

ληι-βότειρα ης *Ion.fem.adj.* [λήιον, βοτήρ] (of a wild sow) **crop-consuming** Od.

ληίζομαι *Ion.mid.vb.*: see λήζομαι

ληίη *Ion.f.*: see λεία

λήιον, dial. **λᾶον**, ου *n.* **standing corn, crop** Hom. Hes. Thgn. Hdt. Theoc.

ληίς, dial. **λαΐς** (A.), ίδος *f.* [λήζομαι] **1 plunder, spoil, booty** Hom. hHom. A. X. AR.
2 (without connot. of plunder) **livestock, cattle** Hes. AR. Theoc.

ληιστήρ ῆρος *Ion.m.* one who practises robbery with violence (by land or sea), **robber, brigand, bandit, pirate** Od. hHom. AR.

ληιστής *Ion.m.*: see λῃστής

ληιστός ή όν *Ion.adj.* —also **λεϊστός** ή όν *ep.adj.* (of cattle, flocks) **able to be won by plundering** Il.; (of a person's life, in neg.phr.) Il.

ληιστύς ύος *Ion.f.* **plundering, pillaging** Hdt.

λήιστωρ ορος *Ion.m.* **bandit, pirate** Od.

ληῖτις ιδος *Ion.f.* **1** (epith. of Athena) **goddess of the spoils** Il.
2 (appos.w. κούρη) **woman taken as plunder, captive** AR.

λήιτον ου *Ion.n.* [reltd. λαός] **public building, town hall** (as Achaean wd. for πρυτανεῖον) Hdt.; (as equiv. to δημόσιον 4, under δημόσιος) Plu.

ληκάομαι *pass.contr.vb.* (of a woman) **be fucked** Ar.

ληκτέον (neut.impers.vbl.adj.): see λαγχάνω

ληκυθίζω *vb.* [λήκυθος] (of the Muse of tragedy) **speak bombastically** Call.

ληκύθιον ου *n.* [dimin. λήκυθος] **little oil-flask** Ar. D.

λήκυθος ου *f.* **oil-flask** (esp. used in the gymnasium, or as a grave-gift for the dead) Od. Ar. Pl. Arist. Thphr. +

λῆμα ατος *n.* [λῶ] **1 strong will or spirit** (directed to some purpose), **will, spirit, determination** A. Pi. E. Call. Plu.
2 (gener., qualified by an adj. such as *noble, tyrannical, shameless*) **temperament, character, spirit** Pi. Trag. Ar. Call.
3 (without a qualifying adj.) **brave** or **bold spirit** A. Hdt. E. Ar.
4 (pejor.) **proud** or **insolent spirit** S. Ar.

ληματίας ου *m.* **strong-spirited man** Ar.

λημάω *contr.vb.* [λήμη] **be blear-eyed** Ar.; (fig., of old men) —w.ACC. *in their mind* (*i.e. have no power of discernment*) Ar.

λήμη ης *f.* **1 infection** or **malady in the eyes, bleariness** Ar.; (fig., in relation to the mind) Ar.
2 (fig., ref. to Aigina) **eyesore** (w.GEN. of the Peiraieus) Arist. Plu.

λῆμμα ατος *n.* [λαμβάνω] **1 receipt** (of money), **income** Att.orats. Pl. Plu.
2 (gener., sts. pejor.) **gain, profit** S. Att.orats. Pl. Arist. Plu.
3 (log.) statement taken as given, **premise, assumption** Plu.
4 theme undertaken (in a written work or speech), **argument, subject** Plb.

λημνίσκος ου *m.* [perh.reltd. λῆνος] **band, ribbon** (assoc.w. a victor's garland) Plb. Plu.

Λῆμνος, dial. **Λᾶμνος**, ου *f.* **Lemnos** (island in the NE. Aegean) Hom. +

—**Λαμνόθεν** *dial.adv.* **from Lemnos** Pi.

—**Λήμνιος**, dial. **Λάμνιος**, ᾱ (Ion. η) ον *adj.* **1** (of a man or woman) **of** or **from Lemnos, Lemnian** Pi. Hdt. Is. D. Arist.

λήμψομαι

|| MASC.PL.SB. Lemnians (as a population or military force) Th.
2 of or relating to Lemnos or the Lemnians; (of the land, shore) **Lemnian** S. E.*fr.*; (of fire, fr. a volcano on the island) B. S. Ar.; (of a ship) Hdt.; (of vines) Ar.; (of songs, ref. to their once being sung there) E.*fr.*
3 (of a crime, as a byword for atrocity) **Lemnian** (ref. to the murder of their husbands by Hypsipyle and the Lemnian women) A. Hdt.; (ref. to the later murder of Athenian mothers and children on Lemnos by their Pelasgian husbands) Hdt.
—**Λημνιάς**, dial. **Λάμνιάς**, άδος *fem.adj.* (of women) **Lemnian** Pi. AR. || PL.SB. Lemnian women AR.
—**Λάμνιακός** ά όν *dial.adj.* (of hills) **Lemnian** Call.
λήμψομαι (fut.mid.): see λαμβάνω
λῆν (dial.inf.): see λῶ
λῆναι ῶν *f.pl.* [perh.reltd. ληνός] **maenads, Bacchants** Heraclit. Theoc.(title)
Λήναια ων *n.pl.* [app. λῆναι] **Lenaia** (Dionysiac festival at Athens, incl. a dramatic contest) Ar.
—**Λήναιον** ου *n.* **Lenaion** (precinct of Dionysus in Athens, where the Lenaia festival was held) Ar. Pl. D.(law) Arist.
Ληναΐζω *vb.* **celebrate the Lenaia** Heraclit.
Ληναΐτης ου *masc.adj.* (of clamour) **typical of the Lenaia** (i.e. festive, joyous) Ar.
Ληναιών ῶνος *m.* **Lenaion** (name of a month in Ionian states, equiv. to Attic Gamelion, late January to February, during which the Lenaia festival was held) Hes.
ληνός, dial. **λᾱνός**, οῦ *f.* **1 wine-vat, wine-press** Theoc. NT.
2 || PL. watering-troughs (for cattle) hHom.; (perh., gener.) vats or troughs (on a farm) Theoc.
λῆνος εος *n.* **1 wool** (wreathing a suppliant's olive-branch) A.
2 || PL. wool (fr. the golden-fleeced ram) AR.
ληξι-αρχικός όν *adj.* [λῆξις¹] (of a register, maintained by demes, containing the names of those who are eligible for appointment to office by lot) **for allotment to office** Att.orats.
λῆξις¹ εως, Ion. **λάξις** ιος *f.* [λαγχάνω] **1 selection by lot** (W.GEN. for a political office) Pl.; (app.concr.) section chosen for office by lot (fr. a larger group), **selected section** Arist. | see λαγχάνω 2
2 (concr.) **allotment** (ref. to a piece of land received by an individual in a distribution by the state) Pl. | see λαγχάνω 7
3 territory (occupied by a people, through historical inheritance) Hdt.
4 act of allotting, **allotment** (by the gods, of specific regions, as the responsibility of an individual god) Pl.; (concr.) **allotted region** Pl. | see λαγχάνω 12
5 act of allotting, **allotment** (of kings, to Zeus, i.e. as his responsibility) Call. | see λαγχάνω 14
6 (leg., w. δίκης, sts.understd.) granting of permission to bring a lawsuit (app. reflecting the fact that the order of hearing was decided by lot); **filing of a lawsuit** Att.orats. Pl.; (phr.) λῆξις κλήρου *suit claiming an estate, inheritance claim* Is. D. Arist. | see λαγχάνω 15
λῆξις² εως *f.* [λήγω] **cessation** (W.GEN. of sufferings) A.; **lessening, dropping** (W.GEN. of winds) AR.
λήξομαι (fut.mid.): see λαγχάνω
λήξω (fut.): see λήγω
ληπτέος ᾱ ον *vbl.adj.* [λαμβάνω] **1** (of persons) **to be grasped** Men.(cj.)
2 (of the better option) **to be adopted** Pl.; (of a line of argument, a metrical form) Arist.
3 to be grasped (by the mind); (of an argument or concept) **to be taken** or **regarded** (in a certain way) Arist.; (of a limit) **to be assumed** Arist. | see λαμβάνω 31–32
ληπτικός ή όν *adj.* (of persons) **of the acquisitive kind** Arist.
ληπτός ή όν *adj.* **1** (of a person, an animal, a place) **able to be seized** or **captured** Pl. Plu.
2 (of things) **able to be apprehended** (W.DAT. by reason and thought) Pl.
ληρέω *contr.vb.* [λῆρος] **1 speak foolishly, talk nonsense** S. Ar. Att.orats. Arist. Men. Plb. Plu. —W.COGN.ACC. Ar.
2 talk beside the point, speak irrelevantly Aeschin. D.
ληρήματα των *n.pl.* **nonsensical remarks** Pl.
λῆρος ου *m.* **1** (sg. and pl.) foolish talk or notion, **nonsense** Ar. Pl. Aeschin. Men. NT.; (sg., as predic., ref. to a statement) Aeschin. Thphr.; (ref. to a person, i.e. to a story about him) Pl.; (ref. to money, as a concept) Arist.
2 (predic., ref. to a person) **foolish prattler** Pl.
3 (collectv.sg., as predic., ref. to persons or things) **rubbish, trash** Ar. Men.; (w. πρός + ACC. compared w. sthg. else) Ar. Pl. X. || PL. trashy things Ar.; things of no importance, trifles D.
ληρώδης ες *adj.* (of a person) **full of empty prattle** Pl.; (of a verbal expression) **nonsensical** Arist.
λῇ (dial.3sg.indic. and subj.): see λῶ
λησί-μβροτος ον *adj.* [λανθάνω, βροτός] (of gods or humans) **taking people unawares** (by theft or cheating) hHom. [or perh. λησίμβροτος, reltd. λήζομαι, *robbing people*]
λησμοσύνη ης, dial. **λησμοσύνᾱ** ᾱς *f.* [λανθάνω] state of being forgetful or no longer caring, **forgetfulness** (W.GEN. of troubles, wars) Hes. S.
λήσομαι (fut.mid.): see λανθάνω
ληστ-άρχης ου *m.* [ληστής, ἄρχω] **bandit chief** Plu.
ληστεία ᾱς *f.* [ληστεύω] **1 robbery with violence** (as a way of life, on land or sea), **banditry, brigandage, piracy** Th. Pl. X. Arist. Plb.
2 (as a practice in war) **plundering, marauding, pillage** Th. Plb. Plu. || PL. plundering raids Th. X. Plb. Plu.
ληστεύω *vb.* [ληστής] **1** (of troops) conduct plundering raids, **plunder, pillage** Th. D. —*a territory* Th. Plb. || PASS. (of people, a territory) be subject to plundering raids Th.
2 (of a people) **practise banditry** or **brigandage** Plu.; (of an individual) **rob** (w. violence) —*passers-by* Plu.
ληστήριον ου *n.* **1 band of robbers** or **marauders** X. Aeschin. Plu.
2 band of pirates Plu.
ληστής οῦ, Ion. **ληιστής** έω *m.* [λήζομαι] **1** (sg. or pl.) one who commits robbery with violence (as a way of life or on a specific occasion), **robber, bandit, brigand** B. S. E. Th. Ar. Att.orats. +; **pirate** hHom. Hdt. S. E.*Cyc.* Th. Att.orats. +
2 (pl.) one who engages in raids on an enemy (by land or sea), **raider, marauder, plunderer** Th. Ar. X.
3 (sg., ref. to a specific person) **robber, thief, usurper** (W.GEN. of someone's kingdom) S.; (fig.) **pirate** (W.GEN. in politics) Aeschin.
ληστικός ή όν *adj.* **1** (of a ship) equipped for use in raiding, **pirate** D.
2 || FEM.SB. art of raiding Pl.
3 || NEUT.SB. piratical activity, piracy Th.
—**ληστικώτερον** *compar.adv.* **more for the purpose of piracy** (than regular naval warfare) —*ref. to building ships, undertaking an expedition* Th.
λῆστις εως *f.* [λανθάνω] **forgetfulness** (of cares) S. Critias; (W.GEN. of troubles) E.*Cyc.*
ληστρικός ή όν *adj.* [ληστής] **1** (of ships) **equipped for**

raiding (opp. regular naval tactics) Th. Plu.; (of a military force) **of bandits** or **marauders** (opp. a regular army) Plu. **2** (of a ship) of the kind used by pirates, **pirate** Plu.; (of a dagger) **of the kind used by bandits** Plu.; (identified w. Latin *dolo*) Plu.
3 (of a people, way of life) **devoted to banditry** or **brigandage** Arist. ‖ NEUT.PL.SB. piratical activities, piracy Plu.
—**ληστρικώτερον** *compar.adv.* **more for plunder** (than any other purpose) Plu.; **more by raiding** or **marauding** (than regular military tactics) Plu.
ληστρίς, dial. **λαστρίς**, ίδος *f.* **1** (sts. appos.w. ναῦς or τριήρης) **pirate ship** D. Plu.
2 (ref. to a woman, as a term of general abuse) **thief** Theoc.(cj.); (appos.w. γυνή) **bandit** Plu.
λήσω (fut.): see λανθάνω
λῆτε (dial.2pl.indic. and subj.): see λῶ
λήτειρα ης *Ion.f.* [reltd. λαός, λήιτον] **public priestess** Call.
Λητοΐδης *m.*: see under Λητώ
λητουργέω (later **λειτουργέω**) *contr.vb.* [reltd. λαός, λήιτον; ἔργον] **1** (esp. at Athens) **undertake a leitourgia, take on a public office, perform a public service** (freq. W.COGN. or INTERN.ACC.) Att.orats. Arist. Thphr. —W.DAT. *for one's city or fellow citizens* Att.orats. X.
‖ NEUT.PL.PF.PASS.PTCPL.SB. public services D.
2 (gener.) **serve the public good** (in some other way) Lys. D. Arist.
3 (of slaves or subordinates) **perform a service** —W.DAT. *for a master or superior* Arist. Plb.
4 serve (by prayer or worship) —W.DAT. *God* NT.
λητουργίᾱ (later **λειτουργίᾱ**) ᾱς *f.* **1** (esp. at Athens) **leitourgia, liturgy, public service** (ref. to a duty imposed on the rich, requiring the contribution of funds to equip a trireme, train a chorus, provide a banquet, or sim.) Att.orats. Pl. Arist. Thphr. Plu.
2 (gener.) **service** (to another) Arist.; (to the community) Plu.; (to the gods, by the community) Arist.; (to God, by a priest) NT.
3 (esp. in military ctxt.) **task, duty** Plb. Plu.
Λητώ, dial. **Λᾱτώ**, οῦς (also dial. όος) *f.* ǀ voc. Λητοῖ, dial. Λᾱτοῖ ǀ acc. Λητώ, dial. Λᾱτώ, Ion. Λητοῦν ǀ dat. Λητοῖ, dial. Λᾱτοῖ ǀ **Leto** (mother of Apollo and Artemis) Hom. +
—**Λητοΐδης** ου (ep. ᾱο AR.), dial. **Λᾱτοΐδᾱς** (also **Λᾱτοΐδᾱς** Pi. B.) ᾱ *m.* **son of Leto** (ref. to Apollo) Hes. hHom. Thgn. Lyr. Ar. Call. +
—**Λητῷος** ᾱ ον *adj.* **1** (of the daughter) **of Leto** (ref. to Artemis) S.
2 ‖ NEUT.SB. **temple of Leto** Arist.
—**Λητωιάς** άδος *f.* **daughter of Leto** (ref. to Artemis) Call.
—**Λητωίς** ίδος *f.* **daughter of Leto** (ref. to Artemis, sts. appos.w. κούρη) Call. AR.
—**Λᾱτογενής** ές *dial.adj.* —also **Λᾱτογένεια** ᾱς *dial.fem.adj.* [γένος, γίγνομαι] (of a child) **born of Leto** (ref. to Artemis) A. E.
ληφθήσομαι (fut.pass.): see λαμβάνω
λῆψις εως *f.* [λαμβάνω] **1** act of taking, **capture, seizure** (of persons, a city, enemy territory, ships) Th. Arist. Plb.
2 act of receiving, **receipt** (of money, wages) Pl.
3 act of getting or acquiring, **acquisition** (of money, benefits, or sim.) Arist.
4 adoption (of an appropriate choice) Plu.
λήψομαι (fut.mid.): see λαμβάνω
λιάζομαι *mid.vb.* ǀ aor.pass. ἐλιάσθην, ep. λιάσθην, 3pl. λίασθεν ǀ 3sg.plpf. λελίαστο ǀ **1** (intr.) **turn aside**
—W.PREP.PHR. *away fr. people, a place* Hom. —W.ADV. *to a place* Il. Emp.
2 (of a warrior) **move to one side, swerve** (to avoid an attack) Il.
3 (of a person) **slip away** (fr. somewhere) —W.PREP.PHR. *to a person* E.; (of a departing phantom) Od.
4 (gener.) **move away, go off, depart** AR.
5 depart —W.PREP.PHR. *fr. life* AR.
6 (of the surge of the sea) **move aside, fall back** (to let divinities pass) Il.
7 (of a wounded warrior) **sink down, collapse** Il. ‖ STATV.PF. lie fallen Mosch.
8 (of a dying bird's feathers) **droop** Il.
λιάζω *vb.* [λίαν] act in a way that is excessive, **overdo things** —W.COGN.ADV. *overly* Archil. Anacr.
λίᾱν (also **λίᾰν**), Ion. **λίην** (also **λίην**) *adv.* **1** to a great or excessive degree; (intensv., w.adj., adv. or prep.phr.) **exceedingly, very, too** Hom. + • λίην πολλοί *all too many* Il. • λίαν σαφῶς *very clearly* Ar. • λίην ... νηῶν ἑκάς *too far from the ships* Od.
2 (w.vb.) **exceedingly, very much, too much** Hom. + • λίην ἄχθομαι *I am very greatly distressed* Il. • μὴ λίαν στένε *do not lament too much* S.
3 (prefixed to a statement, adding emphasis) καὶ λίην **certainly, truly, indeed** Hom. • καὶ λίην τοι ἐγώ γε παρέσσομαι *I shall certainly stand by you* Od.
4 (quasi-adjl., w. noun) A. + • ἡ λίαν δυσπραξία *extreme misfortune* E. • αἱ πρὸς τοὺς τυράννους αὗται λίαν ὁμιλίαι *this excessive familiarity with tyrants* D. ‖ NEUT.SB. (w.art.) **excess, immoderation** (of behaviour, grief) E.
λιαρός ή όν *Ion.adj.* **1** (of blood, water) **warm** Hom. AR.; (of a cow's milk) Theoc.; (of tears) AR.
2 (of winds) **soft, gentle** Od. AR.; (of sleep) Il.
λίβα (acc.sg.): see λίψ¹, λίψ²
λίβανος ου *f.* [Semit.loanwd.] **1 frankincense tree** Pi.*fr.* Melanipp. Hdt.
2 a kind of aromatic resin, frankincense (burned as incense, esp. as an offering to the gods and at the beginning of a symposium) Sapph. Pi.*fr.* Emp. E. NT.
λιβανωτός οῦ *m.* (*also f.* Men.) **frankincense** Sapph. Xenoph. Pi.*fr.* Hdt. Antipho Ar. +
λιβανωτο-φόρος ον *adj.* [φέρω] (of trees, regions) **frankincense-producing** Hdt.
λιβάς άδος *f.* [λείβω] **1 outpouring** (of a liquid); **trickling** or **gushing stream** (fr. a fountain or spring) E. Call.; **flowing stream** (of a river) S.
2 ‖ PL. **drops** or **streams** (W.GEN. of spring water) A.; (of tears) E.; (of electrum, ref. to the tears of the Heliades) AR.; (of milk) AR.
λιβός (gen.sg.): see λίψ¹, λίψ²
λίβος ους *n.* [λείβω] **drop** or **fleck** (W.GEN. of blood, on the eyes) A.(cj.) ‖ PL. **streaming tears** A.
Λιβυ-άρχης ου *m.* [Λιβύη, ἄρχω] **governor of Libya** Plb.
Λιβύη ης, dial. **Λιβύᾱ** ᾱς *f.* **1 Libya** (ref. to the land west of the Nile, or gener. to the whole continent of Africa) Od. Pi. Hdt. E. Th. Ar. +
2 Libya (daughter of Epaphos, after whom the land was supposedly named) A. Isoc.
—**Λιβύᾱθε** *dial.adv.* (ref. to a person's origin) **from Libya** Theoc.
—**Λιβυκός** ή όν *adj.* **1** or relating to Libya (sts. ref. to Africa); (of a person, the race, language, regions, the sky) **Libyan** Hdt. E.*fr.* Plu.; (of a bird, goat, elephant, fig) Ar. Theoc. Plb. Plu.; (of a style of chariot construction) X.; (of a kind of

Λιβυρνικός 872

fable) Arist.; (of the sea, off the coast of N. Africa) Men. Plb. Plu.; (of an account) **of Libya** Hdt.; (of events, a war) **in Libya** Plb. Plu.
2 (of a triumph) **in a war against Libya** Plu.

Λιβυρνικός ή όν *adj.* [Λιβυρνοί *Liburnians (Illyrian people on the NE. Adriatic coast)*] ‖ NEUT.SB. **Liburnian ship** (ref. to a kind of light fast-sailing warship) Plu.

Λιβυρνίς ίδος *fem.adj.* **1** (of islands, in the NE. Adriatic) **Liburnian** AR.
2 ‖ SB. **Liburnian warship** Plu.

Λίβυς υος *masc.adj.* [Λιβύη] | acc.pl. Λίβυας, also Λίβῡς | **of or relating to Libya** (sts.ref. to Africa); (of a man) **Libyan** Hdt. S. Th. Plb. Plu.; (of the aulos, i.e. made fr. the wood of the lotus tree) E. ‖ SB. **Libyan man, Libyan** Pi. Hdt. ‖ PL. **people of Libya, Libyans** Hdt. Th. X. +

—**Λίβυσσα** ης (dial. ᾱς) *fem.adj.* (of a woman) **Libyan** Pi.; (of the Gorgons) E.; (of soil) Plu.(oracle) ‖ SB. **Libyan woman** Hdt. Call.

—**Λιβυστικός** ή όν *adj.* (of women) **Libyan** A.; (of stories, a word) A. Hdt.; (of the sea) AR.

—**Λιβυστίς** ίδος *fem.adj.* (of the land) **Libyan** AR.; (of a gazelle) Call.

Λιβυ-φοίνῑκες ων *m.pl.* [Φοῖνιξ] **Libyphoenicians** (Phoenician inhabitants of N. Africa) Plb.

λίγα *adv.*: see under λιγύς

λιγαίνω *vb.* [λιγύς] **1** emit a clear or penetrating sound; (of heralds) **cry out, proclaim** —W.ACC. + INF. *that persons are to do sthg.* Il.
2 (of a mourner) **utter a piercing cry** A.
3 (of a lyre-player) **sound forth** AR.; (of a singer) —W.ACC. *a particular melody* Mosch. Bion

λίγδην *adv.* app. **with a glancing blow** —*ref. to striking someone w. a weapon* Od.

λιγέα *neut.pl.adv.*, **λιγέως** *adv.*: see under λιγύς

λίγεια (fem.adj.), **λίγηα** (dial.fem.adj.): see λιγύς

λιγνυόεις εσσα εν *adj.* [λιγνύς] (of smoke) **sooty, murky** AR.

λιγνύς ύος, dial. **λίγνυς** υος (Call.) *f.* **thick** or **sooty smoke** S. Ar. Call. AR. Plb.; (snorted out by Typhon) A.

λίγξε *ep.3sg.aor.* [perh.reltd. λιγύς] (of a bow) **twang** Il.

λιγού *Boeot.neut.sg.adv.*: see λιγύ, under λιγύς

λιγουρο-κώτιλος ον *Boeot.adj.* [λιγυρός, κωτίλος] (of a poet's voice) **clear and coaxing** Corinn.

λιγουρός *Boeot.adj.*: see λιγυρός

λιγυ-ᾱχής ές *dial.adj.* [λιγύς, ἠχή] (of a lyre) **clear-sounding** B.(cj.)

Λίγυες ων *m.pl.* **Ligurians** (inhabitants of NW. Italy and S. France) A.*fr.* Hdt. Th. Pl. +

—**Λίγυς** υος *masc.adj.* (of an army) **Ligurian** A.*fr.*

—**Λιγυστίς** ίδος *fem.adj.* (of Circe) **Ligurian** E.; (of islands) AR.

—**Λιγυστικός** ή όν *adj.* (of shields) of the Ligurian kind, **Ligurian** Plb. ‖ FEM.SB. **Ligurian land, Liguria** Plb.

λιγυ-κλαγγής ές *adj.* [λιγύς, κλαγγή] (of choruses, a bowstring) **ringing out clearly** B.

λιγυ-μακρόφωνος ον *adj.* [μακρός, φωνή] (of heralds) **with clear far-reaching voice** Tim.

λιγύ-μολπος ον *adj.* [μολπή] (of mountain-nymphs) **clear-singing** hHom.

λιγυ-πνοιός όν *ep.adj.* [πνοή] (of winds) **shrill-blowing, whistling** Hom.

λιγυρός, Boeot. **λιγουρός**, ά (Ion. ή) όν *adj.* [reltd. λιγύς] **1** having a clear or high-pitched sound; (of a poet) **clear-voiced** Corinn.; (of a bird) Il.; (of song or sim.) Od. Hes. hHom. Sapph. AR. Theoc.; (of a panpipe, the lyre, its sound) **clear-toned** Hes. Sapph. B.; (fig., of a whetstone, envisaged as sharpening a poet's tongue) **clear-sounding** Pi.; (of a river, assoc.w. singing) **tuneful** Mosch.
2 (of cries of grief) **shrill** E.
3 (of winds, their blasts) **shrill, whistling** Il.; (of a whip) Il. S.
4 (of a person) app. **clear** or **fluent** (in speech) Isoc.
5 (of the tail of a hunting hound) perh. **whip-like** X.

—**λιγυρόν** *neut.adv.* **shrilly** —*ref. to a place echoing to the sound of cicadas* Pl.

—**λιγυρῶς** *adv.* **with a clear voice** —*ref. to singing* Theoc.

λιγύς λίγεια (dial. λίγηα Alcm.) λιγύ *adj.* **1** having a clear or high-pitched sound; (of an orator) **clear-voiced** Hom.; (of Muses, Sirens) Od. hHom. Lyr. Pl. AR. Theoc.; (of a nightingale) A. S.; (of singing) B. AR.; (of a lyre, panpipe, the sound of an aulos) **clear-toned** Hom. hHom. E. Call. AR.; (of a path of words) **clear-sounding** Pi.; (of the sound of the cicada) **clear** Call.
2 (of cries of grief) **shrill** A.
3 (of winds) **shrill, whistling** Hom. AR.

—**λιγύ**, Boeot. **λιγού** *neut.sg.adv.* **1 with clear tones** —*ref. to singing* Hes. Corinn.
2 shrilly —*ref. to crying out in grief* A. Mosch.
3 shrilly, with a whistling sound —*ref. to a wind blowing* Od.

—**λιγέα** *neut.pl.adv.* **1 with clear tones** —*ref. to singing* Thgn.
2 shrilly —*ref. to chicks screeching* AR.

—**λιγέως** *adv.* **1 with a clear voice** —*ref. to speaking* Il.; **with clear tones** —*ref. to playing the lyre* hHom.; **distinctly** —*ref. to a shield resonating* Hes.
2 shrilly —*ref. to lamenting* AR.; **loudly** —*ref. to weeping* Hom.
3 shrilly, with a whistling sound —*ref. to winds blowing* Il.
4 app. **in sad tones** —*ref. to speaking* AR.

—**λίγα** *adv.* **1 with clear tones** —*ref. to singing* Od. hHom. Alcm. Thgn. —*ref. to playing the lyre* AR.
2 shrilly —*ref. to crying out in grief* Hom. AR.
3 shrilly —*ref. to a wind blowing* AR.

Λίγυς *masc.adj.*, **Λιγυστικός** *adj.*, **Λιγυστίς** *fem.adj.*: see under Λίγυες

λιγυ-σφάραγος ον *adj.* [λιγύς; σφαραγέομαι, σφαραγίζω] (of lyres) **clear-toned** Pi.*fr.*

λιγύ-φθογγος ον *adj.* [φθόγγος] (of heralds) **clear-voiced** Hom.; (of a nightingale, other birds, their song) B. Ar. Theoc.*epigr.*; (of a bee, fig.ref. to a poet) B.; (of an aulos) **clear-toned** Thgn.

λιγύ-φωνος ον *adj.* [φωνή] **1** (of the Hesperides; of a girl, fig.ref. to a lyre) **clear-voiced** Hes. hHom.; (of a nightingale) Sapph. Theoc.
2 (of a bird of prey) **shrill-voiced** Il.

λίην (also **λίην**) *Ion.adv.*: see λίαν

λιθάζω *vb.* [λίθος] **1** (of soldiers, as a military tactic) **throw stones** (against an enemy) Plb.
2 (tr.) **stone** —*a person (to death)* NT.

λίθαξ ακος *masc.fem.adj.* (of a rock) perh., bristling with projecting stones, **rough, jagged** Od.

λιθάς άδος *f.* | ep.dat.pl. λιθάδεσσι | **piece of stone, stone** (used in constructing a building) Od.; (thrown as a missile) Od.; (collectv.sg.) **hail of stones** (as missiles) A.

λιθάω *contr.vb.* (medic.) **suffer from stones** (in the body) Pl.

λίθεος ᾱ (Ion. η) ον *adj.* (of a threshold, looms) made of stone, **of stone** Hom.

λιθίᾱ (or **λιθείᾱ**) ᾱς *f.* **stonework** or **building-stones** Plb.

λιθίδιον ου *n.* [dimin. λίθος] **small precious stone, gem** Pl.

λίθινος η (dial. ᾱ) ον *adj.* [λίθος] **1** consisting of or made from stone; (of buildings, statues, pillars, or sim.) **of stone** Pi. Hdt. Th. Ar. Att.orats. Pl. +; (of offspring, ref. to people created out of the stones thrown by Deukalion and Pyrrha) Pi. ‖ NEUT.PL.SB. **stone figures** X.
2 (of a decision) **recorded on stone** Pi.
3 (of death) **stony** (caused by looking at the Gorgon's head, which turns the looker to stone) Pi.
4 (of ἀρτήματα *pendants*) λίθινα χυτά *of cast stone* (*ref. to glass*) Hdt.
—**λιθίνως** *adv.* (fig.) **in a stony** or **fixed manner** —*ref. to looking at someone* (*as if at a Gorgon*) X.
λιθοβολέω *contr.vb.* [λιθοβόλος] **stone** —*a person* (*to death*) NT.
λιθο-βόλος ου *m.* [βάλλω] **stone-thrower** (ref. to a military catapult) Plb. ‖ PL. **stone-throwers** (ref. to a detachment of troops) Th. Pl.
—**λιθόβολος** ον *adj.* (of a bloody death) **caused by casting stones, by stoning** E.
λιθό-δερμος ον *adj.* [δέρμα] (hyperbol., of persons under torture) **with skin as hard as stone, thick-skinned** Arist.(dub.)
λιθο-ειδής ές *adj.* [εἶδος¹] (of an enclosing structure in the body, ref. to the spine) **with the appearance of stone, stone-like** Pl.
λιθο-κόλλητος ον *adj.* [κολλητός] **1** (of a horse's metal bit) **set with stones** (to make it more painful) S.
2 (of cups, armour, jewellery) **set with precious stones** Thphr. Plu.
λιθο-κόπος ου *m.* [κόπτω] **stone-cutter, mason** D.
λιθό-λευστος ον *adj.* [λεύω] **1** (of a violent death) **by stoning** S.
2 (of a lover's soul, envisaged as a runaway) **deserving to be stoned, damnable** Call.*epigr.*
λιθολόγημα ατος *n.* [λιθολόγος] **stones laid by a mason, stone-masonry** X.
λιθο-λόγος ου *m.* [λέγω] **stone-mason, mason** Pl.; (attached to an army, for building fortifications) Th. X.
λίθος ου *m.* (sts. *f.*) **1 stone, rock** (as a natural feature of the landscape) Hom. +
2 piece of detached stone, **stone, rock, boulder** Hom. +; (as a missile) Il. +; (ref. to a discus) Od.
3 large rock or stone block, **rock** (used as a seat) Hom.; (ref. to a speaker's platform, esp. in the Assembly) Ar. Plu.; (in the Athenian agora, where archons, arbitrators and certain witnesses swore oaths) D. Arist. Plu.
4 stone, pebble (used as a piece in a board-game) Alc. Theoc.
5 large block (esp. of regular shape, hewn fr. stone, for use in building), **stone block** Hdt. Th. Pl. +; (*f.*) **gravestone** Call.*epigr.*
6 stone as a material (for use in building), **stone** Hom. +; (w.ADJ. λευκός *white*) **marble** Hdt.; (w. Πάριος) *Parian marble* Pi. Hdt.; (*f.*, w. Παρία) Theoc.; (w. πώρινος) *tufa* Hdt.
7 stone, rock (in comparisons, as exemplifying immutability, insensitivity or absence of life) Hom. Thgn. Pl. Theoc.; (ref. to a person, as exemplifying stupidity) Ar.; (provbl.) λίθον ἕψειν *boil a stone* (*ref. to trying to persuade an obstinate person*) Ar.
8 (usu. *f.*) a kind of stone (w. special properties); **stone** (w.ADJ. διαφανής *transparent*, ref. to glass) Ar.; (w.ADJ. Ἡρακλεία *from Herakleia*, ref. to a lodestone) Pl.; (appos.w. σμάραγδος) *emerald* Hdt.; (w.ADJ. Λυδία *Lydian*, ref. to a touchstone) B.*fr.*; (without ADJ., ref. to a touchstone) Pl.

λιθο-σπαδής ές *adj.* [σπάω] (of a sealed tomb) **with the stones torn away** S.
λιθό-στρωτος ον *adj.* [στρωτός] (of a chamber) spread with stones, **rock-floored** S.
—**Λιθόστρωτον** ου *n.* **Paved Way** (name of a public space in Jerusalem) NT.
λιθο-τομίαι ῶν (Ion. έων) *f.pl.* [λιθοτόμος] **stone-quarry** Hdt. Th. X. D.
λιθο-τόμος ον *adj.* [τέμνω] **stone-cutter** X.
λιθουργεῖον ου *n.* [λιθουργός] **stone-mason's** or **sculptor's workshop** Is.
λιθουργός οῦ *m.* [ἔργον] man working in stone or marble, **stone-mason** Th. Ar. Plu.; **sculptor** Arist.
—**λιθουργός** όν *adj.* (of iron tools) **for stone-working** Th.
λιθοφορέω *contr.vb.* [λιθοφόρος] **carry stones** (for building operations) Th.
λιθο-φόρος ον *adj.* [φέρω] **1** (of wagons) **stone-carrying** Plu.
2 ‖ MASC.SB. **stone-carrier** (ref. to a military catapult) Plb.
λιθώδης ες *adj.* (of ground, a road) **stony** Hdt. X.; (fig., of an element in a person's nature) Pl.
λικμάω *contr.vb.* **1** (intr.) perform the operation of winnowing (i.e. separate the chaff fr. the grain, by throwing them to the wind or shaking them in a winnowing-basket), **winnow** Il. X.; **winnow out** —*chaff* X.
2 (in fig.ctxt., of a stone) app. **crush** —*a person* NT.
λικμητήρ ῆρος *m.* **winnower** Il.
λικνῖτις ιδος *fem.adj.* [λίκνον] | acc. λικνῖτιν | (of nursing) **for one in the cradle** S.*Ichn.*
λίκνον ου *n.* [reltd. λικμάω] basket of wickerwork used in winnowing, **winnowing-basket** (carried in sacred processions, as a symbol of fertility) Call. Plu.; (used as a cradle for the baby Hermes) hHom.; (made of gold, for the baby Zeus) Call.
λικνο-φόρος ου *m.f.* [φέρω] **carrier of the winnowing-basket** (in a sacred procession) D.
λικριφίς *adv.* [reltd. λέχριος] **to one side, sideways** —*ref. to moving quickly* (*to avoid a weapon*) Il.; **from the side, obliquely** —*ref. to a boar charging* Od.
Λικύμνιος ου *m.* **Licymnius** (dithyrambic poet, fr. Chios, late 5th C. BC) Arist.
—**Λικύμνιος** ᾱ ον *adj.* (of words) of Licymnius, **Licymnian** Pl.
λιλαίομαι *ep.mid.vb.* | only pres. and impf. | **1 eagerly desire** —W.INF. or ACC. + INF. *to do sthg., that sthg. shd. happen* Hom. Hes. AR. Theoc.; (fig., of a spear) —W.INF. *to be glutted w. flesh* Il.
2 be eager (for sthg.) AR. —W.GEN. *for sthg.* Hom. Hes.
3 make one's way quickly —W.ADV. *to a place* Od.
λῑμαίνω *vb.* [λῑμός] | aor. ἐλίμηνα | (of armies, animals) **be short of food, go hungry** Hdt.
λιμενήοχος ον *ep.adj.* [λιμήν, ἔχω] (of a headland) **protecting a harbour** AR.
λιμενο-σκόπος ον *adj.* [σκοπέω] | dial.masc.fem.gen. λιμενοσκόπω | (epith. of Zeus, Artemis) **watching over harbours** Call.
λιμήν ένος *m.* [reltd. λειμών] | dat.pl. λιμέσι, ep. λιμένεσσι | **1 harbour** (natural or man-made, esp. as a place of refuge or shelter) Hom. +; **haven** (W.GEN. fr. the sea, i.e. providing shelter fr. it) Od. Hes. hHom.
2 (fig.) haven (fr. sthg. unwelcome); **haven, refuge, shelter** (W.GEN. fr. troubles, toils) A. Critias; (fr. a storm of troubles, ref. to a person) E.

λῑμηρός

3 (fig.) haven (for sthg.); **haven, refuge** (W.GEN. for someone's plans, ref. to a person) E.
4 (gener.) haven (as a goal or destination); **haven** (W.GEN. of Hades) S.; (for birds, ref. to a place where they gather) S.; (fig., for someone's cries of woe) S.; (ref. to a marriage) S.
5 (fig.) haven (consisting in some source of support); **haven** (W.GEN. of wealth) A. E.; (of comradeship) S.

λῑμηρός ά όν *adj.* [λῑμός] (of a lover's passion) **threatening starvation** (fr. his lack of appetite or of gainful employment) Theoc. ‖ NEUT.PL.SB. meagre scraps of food Call.

λιμνάζω *vb.* [λίμνη] (of a river, a liquid) **form a lake** Plu.

Λίμναι ῶν *f.pl.* **1** Limnai, Marshes (name of an area of Athens, app. near the Acropolis, w. a temple of Dionysus) Th. Ar. Is. D.
2 (prob. ref. to a place in Laconia, w. a temple of Artemis) Call.

—Λιμναῖος ου *masc.adj.* (epith. of Dionysus) **of the Marshes** Call.

λιμναῖος ᾱ ον *adj.* (of birds, frogs, crocodiles) belonging to lakes or marshes, **lake-dwelling** or **marsh-dwelling** Hdt. Ar.

λιμνάς άδος *fem.adj.* (of nymphs) **of the lakes** Theoc.

λιμνᾶτις ιδος *dial.fem.adj.* (of a leech) **of the marshes** Theoc.

λίμνη ης, dial. **λίμνα** ᾱς *f.* [reltd. λειμών] **1** area of standing water, **pond, lake, marsh** Hom. +
2 lake, reservoir (ref. to a man-made construction) Hdt.
3 (gener.) area of open water, **sea** Hom. Hes. Thgn. Simon. Trag.

—λίμνηθεν *adv.* **from a lake** (to the sea) AR.

λιμνουργός όν *adj.* [ἔργον] (of an old man) **working** or **making a living in the marshes** Plu.

λιμνώδης ες *adj.* **1** (of terrain, part of a river) **marshy** Th. Plb.
2 (of a sea, river) **lake-like** (in its shape or the quality of its water) Plb. Plu.

λῑμο-θνής ῆτος *masc.fem.adj.* [λῑμός, θνῄσκω] **dying of hunger, starving** A.

λῑμοκτονέω *contr.vb.* [κτείνω] **starve to death** —*a person* Pl.

λῑμοκτονίᾱ ᾱς *f.* **starvation diet** (as a medical treatment) Pl.

λῑμός οῦ *m.* (*also f.*) **1** hunger or threat of hunger (fr. lack of food, for an individual or community), **hunger, starvation, famine** Hom. +; (personif., as a deity) **Hunger** Hes. Semon.
2 state of feeling hungry, **hunger** Hom. +
3 (fig.) **dearth, poverty** (in a rich man's mind) E.
4 (ref. to a person) **starving wretch** Men.

λῑμό-ψωρος ου *m.* [ψώρᾱ] skin disease caused by lack of appropriate food, **scurvy** Plb.

λῑμώττω *Att.vb.* (of an army) **starve** Plb.

λῖν (acc.sg.): see λίς¹

Λίνδος ου *f.* **1** Lindos (city of Rhodes) Il. Simon. Hdt. +
2 (masc.) Lindos (as the name of the eponymous hero) Pi.

—Λίνδιος ᾱ ον *adj.* (of a man) of Lindos, **Lindian** Pl. ‖ MASC.PL.SB. people of Lindos, Lindians Hdt.

—Λινδόθεν *adv.* **from Lindos** (the city) —*ref. to a city tracing its origin* Call.

λίνεος ᾱ (Ion. η) ον, Att. **λινοῦς** ῆ οῦν *adj.* [λίνον] **1** made from flax; (of ropes) **of flax** Hdt.
2 (of garments) **linen** Hdt. Th. Pl. Plb.; (of a cuirass) Hdt. X. Plu.; (of a sack) X.; (of a net) Call.

λινό-δεσμος ον *adj.* [δεσμός] (of a bridge of boats) **bound with flax** (i.e. ropes made fr. it) A.

λινό-δετος ον *adj.* [δέω¹] **1** (of a flying insect) **tied** (W.GEN. by its foot) **with flax** (i.e. a cord made fr. it) Ar.; (of a fetter, meton. for a bridge of boats) **bound with flax** Tim.
2 (of tethers, ref. to mooring-lines) providing a flaxen fastening, **of ropes of flax** E.

λινό-ζωστος ον *adj.* [ζωστός] (of the sides of ships) **bound with flax** (ref. to reinforcing ropes) Tim.

λινο-θώρηξ ηκος *Ion.masc.fem.adj.* [θώρᾱξ] (of a warrior) **wearing a linen cuirass** Il.

λινό-κροκος ον *adj.* [κρόκη] (of a robe, also envisaged as a sail) woven with threads of flax, **linen** E.

λίνον ου *n.* **1** flax plant, **flax** Hdt.
2 seed of the flax plant, **linseed** Alcm.; (also) λίνου σπέρμα Th.
3 (collectv.sg.) unspun fibres of the flax plant, **flax fibres, flax** Alcm. Sapph.(or Alc.) Hdt. E. Ar. X.
4 (sg. and pl.) yarn spun from flax, **flax thread, linen thread** (used for making cloth, ropes or nets) A. E. Ar. Pl. X.
5 thread, string (guiding Theseus through the labyrinth) Plu.; (of a necklace, W.ADJ. *golden*, ref. either to gold wire or to linen thread gilded or entwined w. gold) hHom.
6 (specif.) **thread** (of destiny, spun by the Fates) Hom. Call. Theoc.
7 device made of linen thread; **line** (for fishing) Il.; **net** (for fishing or hunting) Il. Theoc. Plb. Plu.; **lamp-wick** NT.
8 cloth woven from linen thread, **linen** (as a material) Il. Alc. Hdt.
9 (ref. to a specific item) **linen cloth, sheet** Od. ‖ PL. sail AR.
10 (provbl.) λίνον λίνῳ συνάπτειν *link thread with thread* (*i.e. like with like*) Pl.

λινο-πόρος ον *adj.* (of winds) **conveying the linen sail** (of a ship) E.

λῑνοπτάομαι *mid.contr.vb.* [reltd. ὀπτήρ, ὀπτεύω] | ῑ *metri grat.* | **watch over one's hunting net** (fig.ref. to maintaining one's post) Ar.(dub.)

λινό-πτερος ον *adj.* [πτερόν] (of a ship) **with linen wings** (fig.ref. to sails) A.

λινο-ρραφής ές *adj.* [ῥάπτω] (app. of a ship's awning) **of stitched linen** A.

Λίνος ου *m.* **1** Linos (mythol. musician, subject of songs of lament) Hes.*fr.* Pi.*fr.* Carm.Pop. Hdt. Theoc.
2 Linos-song (sung at the grape-harvest) Il.; (as a lament) Hdt. | see also αἴλινον

λινο-σινής ές *adj.* [λίνον, σίνος] (of the tearing of a veil) **linen-destroying** A.

λινό-στολος ον *adj.* [στολή] (of the Egyptians) **linen-clad** B.

λινουργός οῦ *m.* [ἔργον] **flax-worker** Plu.

λινοῦς *Att.adj.*: see λίνεος

λινο-φθόρος ον *adj.* [φθείρω] (of tearing) **destroying the linen** (W.GEN. of garments) A.

λίπα *adv.* **richly, liberally** —*ref. to anointing one's body w. oil* (usu. after bathing) Hom. Hes. Th. Plu. —*ref. to anointing a gravestone* Plu.

λιπαίνω *vb.* [λίπα] (of a river) **enrich** —*a land* E.

Λιπάρᾱ ᾱς, Ion. **Λιπάρη** ης *f.* Lipara (largest of the volcanic Aeolian islands N. of Sicily) Th. Call. Plb.

—Λιπαραῖος ᾱ ον *adj.* (of the islands) **of Lipara, Liparaean** Plb.; (epith. of Hephaistos) Theoc. ‖ MASC.PL.SB. people of Lipara Th. Plb.

λιπαρ-άμπυξ υκος *masc.fem.adj.* [λιπαρός] (of Mnemosyne, Delphian maidens) **wearing a gleaming headband** Pi.; (fig., of a sauce, ref. to the oil on its surface) Ar.

λιπαρ-αυγής ές *adj.* [αὐγή] (of trays of food) **brightly gleaming** Philox.Leuc.

λῑπαρέω *contr.vb.* [reltd. λίπτω] **1 persevere, hold out** (in war, famine) Hdt.
2 persist —W.PTCPL. *in holding one's ground* Hdt. —*in inquiring* Hdt. —W.DAT. *in drinking* Hdt.
3 be persistent or insistent in making a request; **entreat, implore, plead** A. Hdt. S. Ar. Isoc. Pl. + —W.INF. *to be granted*

sthg. S. —to be instructed in sthg., not to be put to death X.; **earnestly ask to be informed** —W.INDIR.Q. *what someone means* Pl.; **earnestly ask a favour** —W.PREP.PHR. *fr. someone* D.
4 (tr.) **entreat, implore, plead with** —*someone* Pl. Plb. Plu. —(W.INF. *to do sthg.*) A. Plb. —(W.INF. *that one may be granted sthg.*) S. ‖ PASS. **be earnestly entreated** X.
5 plead at, supplicate at —*altars and offertory tables* Plb.
λιπαρής ές *adj.* **1 persistent, persevering, earnest** (W.PREP.PHR. on a particular topic, in asking questions) Pl.; (W.PTCPL. in making a request) Plu. ‖ NEUT.SB. **earnestness** Plu.
2 (of handiwork) **assiduous** Ar.
3 (of a statesman) **eagerly solicitous** (of popular favour) Plu.
4 (of a hand) **suppliant, making supplication** S.; (of a lock of hair) **offered in supplication** S.(dub.)
5 (prep.phr.) πρὸς τὸ λιπαρές **insistently, earnestly** —*ref. to speaking* S.
—**λιπαρῶς** *adv.* **insistently, earnestly** —*ref. to calling upon the gods* Pl.; (w. ἔχειν) **be eager** —W.INF. or ACC. + INF. *to do sthg., for sthg. to happen* Pl.
λιπαρίη ης *Ion.f.* **perseverance, tenacity** (against an enemy) Hdt.
λιπαρό-ζωνος ον *adj.* [λιπαρός, ζώνη] (of mythol. heroines) **bright-girdled** B.; (app. of Helios) **bright-belted** E.
λιπαρό-θρονος ον *adj.* [θρόνος] **1** (of Selene) having a gleaming throne, **bright-throned** Theoc.; (of Justice and Peace) Lyr.adesp.
2 (of altar-hearths) app. **with gleaming thrones** (for Erinyes) A.
λιπαρο-κρήδεμνος ον *adj.* [κρήδεμνον] (of goddesses) **with gleaming head-dress** Il. hHom.
λιπαρ-όμματος ον *adj.* [ὄμμα] (of a goddess) **bright-eyed** Licymn.
λιπαρο-πλόκαμος ον *adj.* (of a goddess, her head) **with gleaming tresses** Il. Pi.*fr.*
λιπαρός ά (Ion. ή) όν *adj.* [λίπα] **1 gleaming from the application of oil**; (of persons, parts of their body, esp. hair, feet) **gleaming, shiny, sleek** Od. E.*Cyc.* Ar. X. Call. Theoc. Plu.; (of an athlete, in the gymnasium) Ar.; (of persons, after washing in a particular spring, as if in olive oil) Hdt.
2 (of foodstuffs) **gleaming with oil** Ar.
3 (of a woman's head-dress) **glossy, shiny** (fr. treatment w. oil, to produce a sheen) Hom. AR.; (fig., of a city's head-dress, ref. to its battlements) **gleaming, bright** Od.
4 (of stones by the roadside) **shiny** (fr. being anointed w. oil, as a mark of sanctity) Thphr.
5 (of a wrestling school) **gleaming** (fr. the use of oil by wrestlers) Theoc.; (of dancing-places or groups of dancers, perh. fr. their use of oil) Hes.
6 (of a liquid) **oily, slippery** Pl. Arist. Plu.; (fig., of an argument) Pl.; (of a liquid) **shiny, glossy** Pl.; (of a kind of soil) **with oil-like properties** Plu.
7 (gener.) having a smart or healthy appearance; (of persons) **freshly groomed, sleek** X.; (of animals) **sleek-coated** X.
8 (fig., of old age) **comfortable, prosperous, rich** Od. Pi. Plu.(quot.com.); (of royal ordinances) perh. **bringing prosperity** Il.
9 (fig., of light fr. a person's eyes) **shining brightly** Theoc.; (of persons) **with a bright** or **cheerful look** (W.ACC. on their faces) Plu.
10 (of a calm sea, as reflecting the light) **bright, glittering** Theoc.; (of Calm, as a goddess) Call.*epigr.*; (of an anchorage) Call.
11 (as an epith. of general commendation, of Themis, the goddess Day) **bright, radiant** Hes. B.; (of a wife) B.
12 (of a city or region) **shining, gleaming, glorious** (in appearance; or fig., fr. prosperity or fame) Hes.*fr.* Thgn. Lyr. Ar. AR.; (of Athens) Pi. Hdt.(oracle) E. Ar.; (of an island) hHom. Pi. Call.; (of the house of Herakles) B.; (wkr.sens., of thrones) AR.
13 (of victory in athletic contests, victory-garlands) **glittering, glorious** Pi. B.
14 having or imparting a quality of richness; (of soil, ploughland) **rich, fertile** Sol. AR.; (of Egypt) Pi.*fr.*; (of rivers) fertilising (the soil), **enriching** A.; (of river-nymphs) perh. **bringing fertility** Call.
15 (of animal sacrifices) **rich** Call.
—**λιπαρῶς** *adv.* **prosperously, in comfort** —*ref. to growing old* Od.
λιπαρότης ητος *f.* **1** oil-like quality, **oiliness** (of a liquid) Plu.
2 splendid condition, **sleekness** (of a mule) Plu.
λιπαρό-τροφος ον *adj.* [τρέφω] (of sheep) **richly fed** Pi.*fr.*
λιπαρό-χρως ωτος *masc.fem.adj.* [χρώς] | acc. λιπαρόχρων | (of a young man) **sleek-skinned** Theoc.
λιπαρ-ώψ ῶπος *masc.fem.adj.* (of a table laden w. food) **shiny-looking** Philox.Leuc.
λιπάω *contr.vb.* [λίπα, λιπαρός] | ep.ptcpl. (w.diect.) λιπόων | (of the hands of the Graces) **gleam, be shiny** (w. oil or perfume) Call.; (of a gymnasium, fr. the oil used by wrestlers) Call.
λιπεῖν (aor.2 inf.): see λείπω
λιπερνής ῆτος *masc.fem.adj.* [perh. λείπω, ἔρνος] perh., deprived of the fruits of one's land; **deprived, destitute, poor** Archil. A.(cj.)
—**λιπερνῆτις** ιδος *f.* **destitute woman** Call.
λιπεσ-άνωρ ορος *dial.fem.adj.* [λείπω, ἀνήρ] (of the daughters of Tyndareos) **husband-deserting** Stesich.
λιπο-γάμετος ον *adj.* [γαμέτης] (of Helen) **husband-deserting** E.(cj.) [or perh. λιπόγαμος *marriage-deserting*]
λιποθυμέω *contr.vb.* [θυμός] **lose consciousness, faint** Plu.
λιποθυμία ᾱς *f.* **loss of consciousness, fainting** Plu.
λιπο-μαρτύριον ου *n.* (leg.) **charge of failing to appear as witness** D.
λίπον (ep.aor.2): see λείπω
λιπό-ναυς νᾱος, Att. **λιπόνεως** νεω *m.* [ναῦς] | Att.acc.pl. λιπόνεως | (ref. to a commander) **deserter from the fleet** A.; (ref. to a sailor) **deserter from one's ship** D.
λιπο-ναύτᾱς ᾱ *dial.m.* [ναύτης] **deserter of one's fellow sailors** Theoc.
λιπό-ξυλος ον *adj.* [ξύλον] **lacking wood**; (fig., of an argument) **lacking in concreteness** or **material illustration** Emp.
λιπο-πάτωρ ορος *masc.fem.adj.* [πατήρ] (of Helen) **father-deserting** E.
λιπο-πνόη ης *f.* [πνοή] **failure of breath** (ref. to death) Tim.
λίπος εος (ους) *n.* [λίπα] **1** app. **glistening fat** (W.GEN. of blood, ref. to the bloody flesh of a corpse) S.
2 oil (used to anoint hair) Call.
λιποστρατίᾱ ᾱς, Ion. **λιποστρατίη** ης *f.* [λείπω, στρατός] **desertion from the army** or **refusal to perform military service, desertion** Hdt. Th.
λιποστράτιον ου *n.* (leg.) **crime of desertion** or **refusal to perform military service** Th.
λιπο-τάξιον ου *n.* [τάξις] (leg.) **crime of deserting the ranks, desertion** Att.orats. Pl.

λιπό-τεκνος ον *adj.* [τέκνον] (of a house) lacking children, **childless** Pi.*fr.*

λίπ-ουρος ον *adj.* [οὐρᾰ́] (of animals) lacking a tail, **tailless** Call.

λιποψῡχέω *contr.vb.* [ψῡχή] **1 lose consciousness, faint** Th. X.
2 app. **be faint-hearted** Hdt.

λιποψῡχίᾱ ᾱς *f.* **faintness** (fr. loss of blood) Plu.

λιπών (ep.ptcpl.): see λιπάω

λίπτω *vb.* [reltd. λιπαρέω] | pf.mid. λέλιμμαι | **desire, want** —W.GEN. *sthg.* AR. —W.INF. *to do sthg.* Call.; (pf.mid.) —W.GEN. *battle* A. —W.NEUT.ACC. *neither a less nor an equal share* (*of plunder*) A.

λιπών (aor.2 ptcpl.): see λείπω

λῑρός ᾱ́ όν *adj.* (of a person) **shameless** Call.

λῖς[1] *m.* | only nom., and acc. λῖν | **lion** Il. Hes. Call. Theoc.

λῖς[2] *fem.adj.* [reltd. λισσός] | only nom. | (of a rock) **smooth** Od.

–λῖς *m.* | only acc. λῖτα, dat. λῖτί | **smooth** or **plain cloth** Hom.

λίσαι (aor.mid.imperatv.), **λίσῃ** (2sg.aor.mid.subj.): see λίσσομαι

λίσπος η ον *adj.* app., smooth or flat; (fig., of Euripides' tongue) **smooth** Ar.

–λίσπαι ῶν *f.pl.* **half-dice** (ref. to split knucklebones, used as matching tokens) Pl.

λισσᾱ́νιε Lacon.voc. (in an address) perh. **my good man** Ar.

λισσάς, Boeot. **λιττάς**, άδος *fem.adj.* [λισσός] (of a rock or cliff) **smooth, bare, sheer** A. E. Corinn. AR. Theoc.; (of an island) **rugged** AR. ‖ SB. **cliff** Plu.

λίσσομαι (also **λίτομαι** hHom. Ar.) *mid.vb.* | ep.3sg.impf. ἐλλίσσετο, 3pl. ἐλλίσσοντο | 3sg.iteratv.impf. λισσέσκετο | aor.1 ἐλισάμην, ep. ἐλλισάμην, imperatv. λίσαι, 2sg.subj. λίσῃ | aor.2 inf. λιτέσθαι, opt. λιτοίμην |
1 make a prayer or entreaty (to a god or person), **pray, beg** Hom. Thgn. Pi. B. Hdt. Trag. + —W.INF. *that one may do sthg.* AR.
2 (tr.) **pray to, beg, implore** —*a god or person* Hom. hHom. Lyr. S. E. Ar. + —(W.INF. *to do sthg.*) Hom. Pi. Hdt. E. Ar. AR. —(*that one may do sthg.*) Pi. —(W. μή + INF. *that one shd. not suffer sthg.*) Hippon. —W.ACC. + INF. *that someone shd. do sthg.* B.
3 pray for, beg for —*sthg.* Il. E. —W.DBL.ACC. *sthg. fr. someone* Od. —W.ACC. + INF. *someone to do sthg., sthg. to happen* Hom. S. Call.

λισσός ή όν *adj.* [reltd. λῖς[2]] (of a rock or cliff) **smooth, bare, sheer** Od. AR.; (of an island) **rugged** AR.

λιστός ή όν *adj.* [λίσσομαι] (of gods) **able to be moved by prayers** Pl.(quot.)

λιστρεύω *vb.* [λίστρον] **dig round, dress** —*a plant* Od.

λίστρον ου *n.* implement for working soil; app. **spade** or **hoe** Od. Mosch.

λῖτα (acc.sg.): see under λῖς[2]

λιταί ῶν (dial. ᾰ̓ν, ep. ᾰ́ων) *f.pl.* [λίσσομαι] | Ion.dat. λιτῆσι |
1 prayers, entreaties (to gods or persons) Od. Pi. Hdt. Trag. AR. Plu.
2 (personif.) **Prayers** (as daughters of Zeus) Il.; (name given to an episode in Book 9 of the *Iliad*) Pl.

λιταίνω *vb.* **entreat, implore** (someone) E.

λιτανεύω *vb.* | ep.impf. ἐλλιτάνευον | ep.aor. ἐλλιτάνευσα |
1 make a prayer or entreaty (to a god or person), **pray, beg** Pl. X. Plu. —W.INF. *that one may do sthg.* Pi.
2 (tr.) **pray to, beg, implore** —*a god or person* Hom. Pi. —(W.INF. *to do sthg.*) Il. Hes. Theoc.

λιτανός ή όν *adj.* (of songs) **of prayer** A.

λιταργίζω *vb.* [perh. ἀργός 2] | fut. λιταργιῶ | app. **run quickly, hurry** Ar.

λιτέσθαι (aor.2 mid.inf.): see λίσσομαι

λιτί (dat.sg.): see under λῖς[2]

λιτοίμην (aor.2 mid.opt.), **λίτομαι** *mid.vb.*: see λίσσομαι

λιτουργός όν Ion.*adj.* [1st el.uncert., 2nd app. ἔργον] (pejor., of a woman) perh. **sluttish** or **vicious** Semon.

λιτός ᾱ́ όν dial.*adj.* [λίσσομαι] **1** (of sacrifices, incantations) **supplicatory** Pi.(dub.) [or perh. *f.pl.* λιταί *prayers*]
2 (of Dawn) **prayed for** Pi.*fr.*(dub.)

λῑτός ή όν *adj.* [reltd. λῖς[2]] **1** (of clothing, a helmet) **plain, simple** Men. Plb. Plu.; (of a meal, food, lifestyle) Plb.; (of a house) Plu.; (of salt, symbolising a frugal lifestyle) Call.*epigr.*; (of unguents, ref. to being unscented) Call.; (of a statue) Call.(cj.); (of a speech, ref. to its style) Arist.
‖ NEUT.SB. **simplicity, plainness** (of a dwelling, lifestyle) Plu.
2 (of a person) **simple, modest, frugal** (in lifestyle or dress) Plb. Plu.; **lowly, insignificant** (opp. great) Call.; (of a personif. river) Call.; (of towns) Plb.; (pejor., of a person) **niggardly** Plu.

–λῑτῶς *adv.* **simply, frugally** —*ref. to living* Plu.

λῑτότης ητος *f.* **simplicity, plainness** (of a person's lifestyle) Plu.; (of a garland) Plu.

λίτρᾱ ᾱς *f.* [Lat. *libra*] **pound weight** Plb. NT. Plu.

λίτρον, also **νίτρον** (Theoc., v.l. Hdt. Pl.), ου *n.* [loanwd.] **sodium carbonate, soda, washing-soda** Hdt. Pl. Theoc.

λιτρώδης ες *adj.* (of substances) having the quality of soda, **soda-like** Pl.(v.l. νιτρώδης)

λιττάς Boeot.*fem.adj.*: see λισσάς

Λιτυέρσης ου, dial. **Λιτυέρσᾱς** ᾱ *m.* **Lityerses** (son of Midas, assoc.w. a reaping song) Theoc.; (as the name of the song) Men.

λιχμάζω *vb.* [reltd. λείχω] | iteratv.impf. λιχμάζεσκον | **1** (of snakes) make a licking or flickering movement with the tongue, **flick the tongue** Hes.
2 (of Zeus, as a bull) **lick** —*Europa's neck* Mosch.

λιχμάω *contr.vb.* | masc.nom.pl.pf.ptcpl. λελιχμότες | **1** (of snakes) **lick** —*a person's cheek* E.
2 ‖ PF.PTCPL.ADJ. (of snakes) **licking, flickering** (W.DAT. w. their tongues) Hes.
3 ‖ MID. (of snakes) make a licking or flickering movement with the tongue, **flick the tongue** Theoc.; (fig., of the heads of flatterers, envisaged as snakes) —W.PREP.PHR. *around the head of a politician* (*envisaged as a mythical monster*) Ar.

λιχνείᾱ ᾱς *f.* [λιχνεύω] (sg. and pl.) **gluttony** Pl. X.

λιχνεύω *vb.* [λίχνος] **be greedy for, crave** —*acclaim* Plu.

λίχνος η ον *adj.* [reltd. λείχω] **1 gluttonous** Pl. X. Plb. Plu.; (fig.) **greedy** (W.ACC. in one's mind, i.e. mental appetites) Pl.
2 (of a lover's eyes) **lustful** Call.; (hyperbol., of a person) **lusting** (W.INF. to know about sthg.) E. Call.

λίψ[1] λιβός *m.* [λείβω] **1 south-west wind** Hdt. Theoc. Plb. Plu.
2 (ref. to the region or direction) **South West** Plb. NT.

λίψ[2] λιβός *f.* [λείβω] | only acc. λίβα, and gen. | **outpouring, stream** (ref. to a libation) A.; **trickle, drip** (of blood, fr. the eyes) A.; (W.GEN. of honey) AR.

λιψ-ουρίᾱ ᾱς *f.* [λίπτω, οὖρον[1]] **desire to urinate** A.

λοβός οῦ *m.* **1 ear-lobe** Il. hHom. Plu.
2 lobe (of the liver) A. E. Pl. Plu.; (gener.) **liver** A.

λογάδες[1] ων *m.pl.* [λέγω] (usu.ref. to troops, sts. appos.w. ἄνδρες, ὁπλῖται) **picked** or **select men** Hdt. E. Th. Plu.

λογάδες[2] ων *f.pl.* **whites of the eyes**; (gener.) **eyes** Call.

λογάδην *adv.* [λέγω] **by a process of picking out**; (quasi-adjl., of stones, used in constructing a wall) **collected,**

picked up (fr. the ground, opp. quarried and hewn) Th.; (of horsemen) **picked, select** Plu.

λογάριον ου *n.* [dimin. λόγος] (pejor.) **little speech** D.

λογεῖον ου *n.* [λόγος] place from which speeches are delivered, **stage** (in a theatre) Plu.

λογεύω *vb.* collect (revenue) ‖ PASS. (of a sum of money) be raised (by a sale) Plb.

λογίδιον ου *n.* [dimin. λόγος] **1 little story, tale** (ref. to the plot of a comedy) Ar.
2 (pejor.) **wretched discourse** (of a sophist) Isoc.

λογίζομαι *mid.vb.* | fut. λογιοῦμαι | aor. ἐλογισάμην | pf. λελόγισμαι ‖ PASS.: aor. ἐλογίσθην ‖ neut.impers. vbl.adj. λογιστέον | **1** make an arithmetical calculation, **calculate, count** Hdt. Th. Lys. Ar. Pl. X. + —W.DAT. *w. counters* (*on the abacus*) Hdt. Ar. Thphr.
2 (tr.) **count** —*items* Ar.; **calculate** —*interest* Ar. —W.INDIR.Q. *how much money is available* X. ‖ PASS. (of persons or things) be counted —W.PREDIC.ADJ. or SB. *as being such and such* (*in number or value*) Hdt. X.; (of a calculation) be made Pl.
3 reckon up the finances (of oneself or another); **do one's accounts** Lys.; (of officials) **audit accounts** —W.DAT. *for magistrates* D. Arist.
4 enter (a sum) in one's accounts (as a charge to another); **debit, charge** —*a sum* Ar. D. —(W.DAT. *to someone*) Lys.; **reckon up an account** —w. πρός + ACC. w. someone (*i.e. present an account of money owed*) Thphr.; **claim in one's accounts** —W.INF. *to have paid sthg. to someone* D.
5 employ rational calculation, **think, reflect, reason** (sts. W.PREP.PHR. about sthg.) Hdt. S. Ar. Att.orats. Pl. X. +; **make a plan** —W.INF. *to do sthg.* E.
6 (tr.) **take into account, bear in mind, consider** —*sthg.* Hdt. S. E. Th. Att.orats. Pl. +
7 **reckon, consider** —W.ACC. + INF. or COMPL.CL. *that sthg. is the case* Hdt. Th. Att.orats. Pl. X. + —W.ACC. + PTCPL. Hdt. And. —W.ACC. + PREDIC.SB. or ADJ. *sthg.* (*to be*) *such and such* E. Ar. X. —W.INDIR.Q. *what is the case* Hdt. And. X. Aeschin.
8 **count on, expect** —*sthg.* (*in the future*) S.; **reckon** —W.FUT.INF. *that one will do sthg.* Hdt. Th. X. —W.ACC. + INF. *that someone will do sthg., that sthg. will be the case* Hdt. Ar. Isoc. X.
9 ‖ PASS. (of an argument) be reasoned through or formulated Pl. ‖ NEUT.PF.PASS.PTCPL.SB. rational thought or reasoned behaviour E.

—**λελογισμένως** *pf.pass.ptcpl.adv.* **1** in a calculated manner, **by calculating** —w. ὅπως + FUT. *in order to ensure that sthg. will happen* Hdt.
2 in a reasoned manner, **rationally** E. Plu.

λογικός ή όν *adj.* **1** (of organs of the body) of or relating to speech, **vocal** Plu.
2 (of virtues) relating to reason, **intellectual** (opp. moral) Arist.(dub.)
3 (of syllogisms, a topic for discussion) relating to logic, **logical** Arist.
4 (of arguments, objections, proofs) **purely logical, theoretical, abstract** Arist. Plu.
5 (of a branch of medicine, doctors) **theoretical** (opp. practical) Plb.

—**λογικῶς** *adv.* **in purely logical** or **abstract terms, theoretically** Arist.

λόγιμος η ον (also ος ον) *adj.* (of a person, city, nation, shrine) **notable, important** Hdt.

λόγιον ου *n.* **1 oracular statement, prophecy** Hdt. Th. Ar. Arist. Plb. Plu. ‖ PL. utterances (of God, received by Moses) NT.
2 **story, tale** Corinn.

λόγιος ᾱ ον *adj.* **1** (of persons) **versed in historical tales** Hdt. ‖ MASC.PL.SB. storytellers Pi. Ion Hdt.; (opp. poets) Pi.
2 (gener.) **learned, erudite** Hdt. Arist. Plb. Plu.
3 skilled in speaking, **eloquent** NT. Plu.

λογιότης ητος *f.* **eloquence** Plu.

λογισμός οῦ *m.* [λογίζομαι] **1** arithmetical calculation; (ref. to the process) **calculating, counting** Th. Pl. Aeschin.; (ref. to the result) **calculation, count** Th. X. ‖ PL. numerical calculations, arithmetic Isoc. Pl. X.
2 financial calculation (of money spent or claimed), **account** D. Thphr.
3 **audit** (of a magistrate's accounts) Arist.; (fig., of a person's actions) D.
4 (sg. and pl.) mental calculation, **calculation, evaluation, assessment** (of a situation) Th. Att.orats. +
5 (sg. and pl.) **rational thought, reasoning, reflection** Th. Ar. Att.orats. Pl. +
6 calculation as grounds for belief or action, **reasoning, reason** (for doing sthg.) Isoc. Pl. X. +
7 **reasoning power, faculty of reason** Pl. X. Arist. Plb. Plu.

λογιστήριον ου *n.* [λογιστής] (sg. and pl.) **building of the auditors** (at Athens) And.(decree) Lys.

λογιστής οῦ *m.* [λογίζομαι] **1** one who calculates; **calculator** (W.GEN. of blessings fr. the gods) D.; one who is skilled in calculation, **arithmetician** or **mathematician** Pl.
2 (at Athens) one who examines the accounts (of outgoing magistrates), **auditor** Aeschin. D. Arist.; (fig., of a person's actions) D.
3 one who thinks rationally, **reasoner, thinker** Ar.

λογιστικός ή όν *adj.* **1** (of persons) **good at calculation, skilled at arithmetic** Pl. X. ‖ MASC.SB. arithmetician Pl.
2 (of the science or discipline) **of calculating, of arithmetic** Pl. ‖ FEM.SB. calculation or arithmetic Pl.; (also neut.sg.pl.sb.) Pl.
3 (of persons) possessing reason, **rational, reasoned, reflective** X. Men.; (of a desire for sthg.) **rational** Arist.
4 (of a mental faculty) **reasoning, calculative** (opp. ἐπιστημονικός *knowing, scientific*) Arist. ‖ NEUT.SB. reasoning part (of the soul), power or faculty of reasoning Pl. Arist.
5 ‖ NEUT.SB. that which is knowable or intelligible Pl.

λογιστός ή όν *adj.* (of a cost) **able to be calculated** Call.

λογογραφέω *contr.vb.* [λογογράφος] **write a speech** or **speeches** Plu.

λογογραφίᾱ ᾱς *f.* **speech-writing** Pl.

λογογραφικός ή όν *adj.* (of an inescapable rule) **of speech-writing** Pl.

λογο-γράφος ου *m.* [λόγος, γράφω] **1 prose-writer** (opp. poet, usu.ref. to a historian) Th. Arist. Plb.
2 (freq. pejor.) **speech-writer** (usu.ref. to one who is hired to write speeches for others, and therefore may be accused of menial employment or indifference to the truth) Att.orats. Pl. Arist. Plb.

λογο-δαίδαλος ον *adj.* using elaborate language; (iron., of a sophist) **expert in elaborate phrasing** Pl.

λογοποιέω *contr.vb.* [λογοποιός] **1 compose tales** or **narratives** Pl.
2 **compose speeches** Isoc. Pl.
3 (pejor., of a politician, populace) **make speeches** (opp. take action) Din. Plu.

λογοποιικός

4 (pejor.) **make up stories** Lys. D. Plb. —w.COMPL.CL. *that sthg. is the case* And. D. —W.ACC. *of untruths, lawless acts, calamities, or sim.* Th. Att.orats. X.

λογοποιικός ή όν *adj.* (of the art) **of speech-writing** Pl.

λογο-ποιός οῦ *m.* [ποιέω] **1 prose-writer** (ref. to a chronicler) Hdt. Isoc.; (ref. to Aesop) Hdt. Plu.; (opp. poet) Isoc. Pl.
2 speech-writer Pl. Din.
3 one who makes up stories, **rumour-monger** D. Thphr. Plu.

λόγος ου *m.* [λέγω] | The sections are grouped as: (1–5) calculation, reckoning, (6–12) explanation, argument, reasoning, (13–27) expression in words. |
1 financial calculation, **reckoning, account** (of money spent, received or owed) Hdt. Att.orats. Pl. Arist. +; (fig.) **price** (put on sthg.) S.
2 account, reckoning (of a person's actions or sim.) Hdt. S. Ar. Att.orats. Pl. Arist. +; (prep.phr.) εἰς λόγον *when it comes to an assessment* (W.GEN. *of sthg., i.e. w. regard to it*) Th. D. Plb.
3 reckoned total, **total, tally** (of ships, troops, years) A. Hdt. Th.
4 proportionate amount; **proportion** (of natural elements) Heraclit.; (math.) **proportion, ratio** Arist.; (prep.phrs.) κατὰ λόγον *in proportion, proportionately* Hdt.; (W.GEN. to sthg.) Hdt. X.; (also) ἀνὰ λόγον Pl.
5 evaluation or assessment (of persons or things); **esteem, consideration, regard** (freq. W.GEN. for someone or sthg.) Hdt. Trag. Pl. +; (phrs.) ποιεῖσθαι (or sim.) ἐν (οὐδενὶ) λόγῳ *treat as of some (no) account* Tyrt. Hdt.; ἐν ἀνδραπόδων λόγῳ *as slaves* Hdt.
6 explanation, reason, ground, motive (for sthg.) Hdt. Trag. Att.orats. Pl. +
7 (philos.) **argument, theory, proposition, hypothesis** Heraclit. Parm. Democr. Pl. Arist.
8 (gener.) **argument, plea** Trag. Ar. Pl. +; (wkr.sens.) **point of view, hypothesis** Hdt.
9 reflection, deliberation, reasoning Hdt. S. Pl. D. Arist.; (specif.) **abstract reasoning, theory** (opp. outward experience) Pl. Arist.
10 reasoned definition, **formula, term** (for sthg.) Pl. Arist.
11 reason (as a faculty) Pl. Arist.
12 (prep.phr.) κατὰ λόγον *in accordance with reason, rationally* Pl.; *in accordance with logic, as expected, naturally* Hdt. Arist.
13 that which is spoken, **utterance, word, statement, remark, expression** (w. neutral connot., or ref. to advice, command, stipulation, or sim., as indicated by ctxt.) Archil. +
14 talk (sts. W.GEN. about someone or sthg.) Thgn. + || Pl. **words, talk** Hom. +
15 (sg. and pl., pejor.) **speech, word, talk** (opp. deed, fact, or sim.) Hes. +; (phr.) λόγους λέγειν *talk idle talk, speak futile words* E. D.
16 (phrs.) λόγῳ ... ἔργῳ (or sim.) *in word or theory ... in action or fact* Hdt. Trag. Th. +; (τῷ) λόγῳ *supposedly, by pretence* Hdt.; λόγου χάριν *in name only* (opp. truly) Arist.; (also) *for instance* Arist. Plb.; λόγου ἕνεκα *for the sake of saying sthg.* (opp. w. useful purpose) Pl.; (also) *for the sake of argument* Pl.
17 spoken account, **account, report, story** Alc. +
18 spoken or written narrative, **narrative, story, tale** (sts. ref. to a specific legend or fable) Hes. +; (ref. to a historical work) Hdt.; (opp. myth or legend) Pl. Arist.
19 speech (ref. to a formal utterance on a specific subject) Trag. +; (ref. to an oration delivered in public or in a court) Pl. Aeschin. Arist. Thphr.
20 saying, proverb, maxim Pi. Trag. Pl. +
21 (sg. and pl.) use of words for the purpose of discussion, **discussion, debate, deliberation** Hdt. E. Th. Ar. Pl. Aeschin. Arist.; **dialogue** (as a form of philosophical debate) Pl.; (as a form of literature) Arist.
22 right of discussion or **speech** Hdt. S. Th. X. D. Arist. Plb.
23 that which provides the material (for talk or writing), **subject, matter, topic, theme** Thgn. Pi. Hdt. +; **plot** (of a narrative or drama) Arist.; (prep.phr.) πρὸς λόγον *to the point* Pl.
24 message, word (of God, esp.ref. to Christian teaching) NT.
25 Word, Logos (co-eternal w. God, incarnate in Jesus Christ) NT.
26 speech (opp. song) Pl. X.; **prose** (opp. poetry) Pl. Arist.
27 (gramm.) unit of meaning (in language), **word** Arist. NT.; **phrase** Arist.; **sentence** Pl.

λόγχη ης, dial. **λόγχα** ᾶς *f.* **1 spear-head** Hdt. S. E. X.; app. **sword-blade** E.
2 (gener.) **spear** Pi. Hdt. Trag. Ar. Pl. X. +
3 (meton.) **body of spearmen** S. E.

λογχ-ήρης ες *adj.* [ἀραρίσκω] **equipped with a spear** E.

λογχίς ίδος *f.* **spear** Lycophronid.

λογχόομαι *pass.contr.vb.* [λόγχη] (of a spear) **be fitted with a sharp point** Arist.

λογχο-ποιός οῦ *m.* [ποιέω] **spear-maker** E.

λογχο-φόρος ον *adj.* [φέρω] (of a people) **spear-bearing** E. || MASC.SB. **spearman** Ar. X. Plb. Plu.

λογχωτός ή όν *adj.* [λογχόομαι] (of a spear) **sharp-pointed** B. E.

λόε (ep.3sg.impf.), **λόεον** (ep.1sg.impf.), **λόεσθαι** (ep.mid.inf.), **λόεσσα** (ep.aor.), **λόεσσᾶ** (dial.2sg.aor. mid.), **λοέσσατο** (ep.3sg.aor.mid.), **λοέσσομαι** (ep.fut.mid. or aor.subj.): see λούω

λοετρόν *ep.n.*: see λουτρόν

λοετροχόος *ep.adj.*: see λουτροχόος

λοέω *ep.contr.vb.*: see λούω

λοιβεῖον ου *n.* [λοιβή] **libation-vessel** Plu.

λοιβή ῆς, dial. **λοιβά** ᾶς *f.* [λείβω] **libation, drink-offering** (to deities or the dead) Il. Pi. S. E. AR. Plu.; (ref. to wine, offered by Odysseus to the Cyclops) Od.

λοίγιος ον *adj.* [λοιγός] (of deeds) **destructive, ruinous, disastrous** Il.; (of suffering) AR. || NEUT.PL.SB. **disasters** Il.

λοιγός οῦ *m.* **destruction, ruin, disaster** Il. Hes. A. Pi.

λοιδορέω *contr.vb.* | aor.pass. (sts. w.mid.sens.) ἐλοιδορήθην | **1** speak abusively or insultingly; **abuse, insult, revile, disparage** —*persons, gods, things* A. Pi. Hdt. E. Th. Ar. +; (intr.) **be abusive** or **insulting** E. Lys. Isoc. Pl. +; (wkr.sens.) **reproach** —*oneself* E.; **say by way of reproach** (to oneself) —W.DIR.SP. *sthg.* E. || PASS. (of persons) **be abused** or **insulted** Isoc. Pl. X.
2 || MID. and AOR.PASS. **be abusive** or **insulting** (freq. W.DAT. towards someone or sthg.) Ar. Att.orats. Pl. + —(W.INTERN. or COGN.ACC. w. *insults, foul language*) Hdt. Aeschin. D.
3 || MID. (of two or more persons) **be abusive to one another, trade insults** Ar. Att.orats.

λοιδόρημα ατος *n.* instance of insulting speech, **abuse, insult** Arist.

—**λοιδορημάτιον** ου *n.* [dimin.] **mild insult** Arist.(quot. Ar.)

λοιδόρησις εως *f.* use of insulting speech || PL. **insults** Pl.

λοιδορησμός οῦ *m.* use of insulting speech, **abusiveness, trading of insults** Ar.

λοιδορητικός ή όν *adj.* given to being abusive Arist.
λοιδορίᾱ ᾱς *f.* use of insulting or abusive speech, **insulting language, abuse** Th. Ar. Att.orats. Pl. + ‖ PL. insults Att.orats. Pl. +
λοίδορος ον *adj.* (of quarrelling, ribaldry) **abusive, insulting** E.*Cyc.* Men.
λοιμικός ή όν *adj.* [λοιμός] of or relating to plague; (of outbreaks or conditions) **of plague** Plb.; (fig., of a state of war) **pestilential** Plb.
λοιμός οῦ *m.* **plague, pestilence** Il. Hes. A. Hdt. S. Th. +; (fig., ref. to a person) D. NT.
λοιμώδης ες *adj.* (of a sickness) having the characteristics of plague, **pestilential** Th. Plu.
λοιπός ή όν *adj.* [λείπω] **1** (of persons or things) **left behind, remaining, surviving** (after others have been killed, lost, or sim.) Trag. Th. Ar. +; (of a person) **last remaining** (W.GEN. of a family) E. And. ‖ MASC.PL.SB. (w.art.) persons remaining, survivors A. Hdt. Th. + ‖ NEUT.SB. (sg. and pl.) what is left (W.GEN. of sthg.) A.
2 ‖ W.ART. the remainder of, the rest of (persons or things, after others have been accounted for) Hdt. + • ἡ λοιπὴ στρατιά *the rest or remainder of the army* Th. • οἱ λοιποὶ Λυδοί *the rest of the Lydians* Hdt. ‖ SG.SB. (w.art., in same gender as GEN.) rest (W.GEN. of sthg.) Hdt. + • ἡ λοιπὴ τῆς Λιβύης *the rest of Libya* Hdt. ‖ PL.SB. (w.art.) rest, remainder (sts. W.GEN. of persons or things) Hdt. + ‖ NEUT.SB. (sg. and pl.) rest (sts. W.GEN. of sthg.) A. Hdt. +
3 left over (for the future); (of sufferings, tasks, or sim.) **remaining** A. E. Isoc. + ‖ NEUT.IMPERS. (w. ἐστί, sts. understd.) it remains (sts. W.DAT. for someone) —W.INF. *to do sthg.* Isoc. Pl. X. Plb.
4 left to come (within a specific period); (of time, life, months, part of a day, or sim.) **still left, remaining** Pi. Hdt. S. E. Isoc.; (advbl.phr.) τὸ λοιπόν *for the remainder* (W.GEN. *of one's life, a day, winter*) Hdt. Th. X.
5 left to come (in the future); (of time) **yet to come, future** Pi. Hdt. S. Th. +; (of a generation, happiness, prayers) Pi.; (of friendship) D.(dub.) ‖ MASC.PL.SB. men to come, future generations Pi. E. ‖ NEUT.PL.SB. future events E.
6 (advbl. and prep.phrs.) τὸ λοιπόν *for the future, henceforward, hereafter* Pi. Hdt. Trag. Th. +; (also) ὃ ... λοιπόν A.; τὰ λοιπά Trag. Th. +; τοῦ λοιποῦ Hdt. Th. Ar. +; ἐς (εἰς) τὸ λοιπόν A. E. Th. +; ἐκ τοῦ λοιποῦ X.; ἐκ τῶν λοιπῶν Pl.
—**λοιπόν** *neut.adv.* **1** for the future, hereafter Pi.
2 (wkr.sens., as 1st wd. in cl., expressing consequence) **as a result, so** Plb.
λοισθήιος ον *Ion.adj.* [λοῖσθος¹] (of a prize) awarded for the last place, **last** Il. ‖ NEUT.PL.SB. last prize Il.
λοίσθιος ᾱ ον (also ος ον A.) *adj.* **1** (of persons or things) last in a series, **last, final** Trag. AR.; (advbl.phr.) τὸ λοίσθιον *finally, last of all* E.
2 (of things done or experienced) last before death, **last, final** A. B. E. AR. Theoc.
3 (of a calamity, labour) last and worst, **crowning** E.
4 at the final point spatially; λοίσθιον τύμβευμα *furthest point of a burial chamber* S.
—**λοίσθιον** *neut.sg.adv.* at last, finally, in the end Pi. S. Theoc.
—**λοίσθια** *neut.pl.adv.* at the last, for the last time (before death) AR.
λοῖσθος¹ ον *adj.* | superl. λοισθότατος | **1** (of a person) in last place (in a race), **last** Il.
2 (of a person) **last** (in a sequence) Hes.*fr.* ‖ SUPERL. very last Hes.

λοῖσθος² ου *m.* piece of timber (fr. a ship), **spar** E.
Λοκροί ῶν *m.pl.* **1** men of Locris, **Locrians** (as a population or military force of three regions in central Greece, distinguished as Opountian, Epiknemidian and Ozolian Locrians, or ref. to the inhabitants of the Opountian colony in S. Italy, known as Zephyrian or Epizephyrian Locrians) Il. +
2 Lokroi (name of the Locrian colony in S. Italy) Arist. Plb.
3 ‖ SG. (as pers. name) Lokros Hes.*fr.* Pi.
—**Λοκρός** ᾱ́ όν *adj.* (of a man) belonging to the Locrians, **Locrian** Alc. X. Arist. Plu.; (of ships) E.
—**Λοκρίς** ίδος *fem.adj.* **1** (of a woman) **Locrian** Pi. Call. Plu.; (of a city) Hdt. Pl. Call.; (of dogs) X.
2 ‖ SB. Locris (name of one of the territories occupied by Locrians) Th. Ar. X. +
Λοξίᾱς ου, Ion. **Λοξίης** εω *m.* [perh. λοξός] (name of Apollo, esp. as god of prophecy) **Loxias** Pi. B. Hdt. Trag. Ar. Men.
λοξόομαι *pass.contr.vb.* [λοξός] ‖ PF.PTCPL.ADJ. (of the orbits of heavenly bodies) slanting, oblique Arist.
λοξός ή όν *adj.* **1** slanting (opp. straight); (of the neck of a person or god) **aslant, turned away** (app. fr. lack of concern) Tyrt. Thgn.; (of the heads of sailors, to avoid an oncoming wave) AR.
2 (of eyes) turned sideways, **sidelong, askance** (fr. anger or disdain) Call. AR.; (fr. shyness) AR.
3 (of a phalanx) **deployed at an angle** Plu.
4 (of the sun's orbit) **oblique, on the ecliptic** Arist. Plu.
5 (of a snake) **coiled** Call.*epigr.*
—**λοξόν** *neut.sg.adv.* with sidelong glance, askance (i.e. w. anger, disdain or mistrust) —*ref. to looking at someone* Sol. Anacr. Call.
—**λοξά** *neut.pl.adv.* askance (i.e. w. disdain) Theoc.
—**λοξότερον** *compar.adv.* (w. ἔχειν) be more mistrustful (w. πρός + ACC. *towards someone*) Plb.
λόον (ep.3pl.impf.): see λούω
λοπάς άδος *m.* [λέπω] shallow earthenware dish (for boiling or stewing fish or meat), **cooking-pan** Ar. Thphr. Men.
—**λοπάδιον** ου *n.* [dimin.] **little cooking-pan** Ar. Men.
λοπίς ίδος *f.* [reltd. λοπός] ‖ PL. scales (of a fish) Ar.
λοπός οῦ *m.* [λέπω] peelable outer layer, **skin** (W.GEN. of an onion) Od.
λορδόω *contr.vb.* [λορδός *bent backwards*] bend oneself backwards; (of a person suffering fr. back trouble or attempting to remedy it) **arch one's back** Men. ‖ MID.PASS. (of women's bodies) be arched (in sexual intercourse) Ar.
λούμενος (Att.mid.ptcpl.), **λοῦσα** (ep.aor.), **λοῦσθαι** (mid.inf.), **λοῦται** (3sg.mid.): see λούω
λούτριον ου *n.* [λουτρόν] dirty water from washing, **bathwater** Ar.
λουτρο-δάϊκτος ον *adj.* [δαΐζω] **murdered in one's bath** A.
λουτρόν, ep. **λοετρόν**, οῦ *n.* **1** water for washing or bathing, **washing-water, bathing-water** Hes. Call.; (collectv.pl.) Hom. hHom. Trag. Men. Call. AR.; (periphr., W.GEN. ὑδάτων) S.
2 act of bathing (oneself or another), **bathing, bath** Hdt. Ar. Pl. X. Plu.; (also pl.) Hdt. E. Ar. Pl. X. +; (pl. for sg.) Trag. Call.
3 (specif., ref. to a ritual act) **bathing, washing** (of a corpse) S.; (pl. for sg.) S. E. ‖ PL. bathing, bath (of bride or groom before their wedding) A. E. Men.
4 ‖ PL. bathing places (ref. to springs, streams, or sim.) Pi. Hdt. S. E. Ar. Theoc.; (fig.) baths (W.GEN. of Okeanos, ref. to the places where the constellations dip below the horizon) Hom.

λουτροφόρος

5 ‖ PL. baths or bathrooms (in the houses of wealthy individuals) X. Plu.
6 public bath, **bath-house, baths** Call.
7 vessel for bathing, **bath, bath-tub** Plu.
8 ‖ PL. libations (poured for a dead person) S.

λουτρο-φόρος ον *adj.* [φέρω] **1** (of the delight) **of bearing water for bathing** (for the ritual bath of bride or groom before marriage) E.
2 ‖ SB. (masc., ref. to a boy) bearer of bathing-water (for the groom's ritual bath) Men.; (fem., ref. to an urn, or perh. a figure carrying one, placed on the tombs of unmarried persons) D.

λουτρο-χόος, ep. **λοετροχόος**, dial. **λωτροχόος**, ον *adj.* [χέω] **1** (of a cauldron) **holding water to be poured for bathing** Hom.
2 ‖ MASC.FEM.SB. pourer of bathing-water, bath-pourer Od. X. Call.

λουτρών ῶνος *m.* public bath, **bath-house, baths** X. Plu.

λούω *vb.* —also **λόω** *contr.vb.* —also **λοέω** *ep.contr.vb.* | 3sg. λούει (Hdt. Bion), also λόει (Scol.), inf. λούειν' (Pl.), ptcpl. λούων (Plu.) | IMPF.: 1pl. ἐλούμεν (Ar.), ep.1sg. λόεον, 3sg. λόε, 3pl. λόον, also ἐλόεον | FUT.: λούσω, dial. λουσῶ (Theoc.) | AOR.: ἔλουσα, ep. λοῦσα, also λόεσσα ‖ MID.: 3sg. λοῦται, 3pl. λοῦνται, also λούονται (Call.) | inf. λοῦσθαι (Od. +), λούεσθαι (Il.), ep. λόεσθαι | ptcpl. λούομενος (Hdt. Call.), Att. λούμενος (Ar. +) | IMPF.: ἐλούμην, perh. also ἐλουόμην (Plb. Plu.), dial.3pl. λῶντο, λώοντο (Call.) | FUT.: λούσομαι, ep. λοέσσομαι (unless aor.subj.) | AOR.: ἐλουσάμην, ep.3pl. λούσαντο | dial.2sg. λοέσσᾱ (Call.), ep.3sg. λοέσσατο, ep.ptcpl. λοεσσάμενος | PF.: λέλουμαι, ptcpl. λελουμένος |
1 wash by pouring water over (esp. in ritual ctxts., as a duty to a guest or as a purificatory rite); **wash, bathe** —*a person, part of the body* Hom. + —*a corpse* Il. Hdt. S. E. Pl. —*horses* Il. —*goats* (*in a lake*) Theoc. ‖ PASS. be washed or bathed (by Zeus, i.e. by rain) Hdt.
2 ‖ MID. **wash oneself, take a bath** Hom. + —W.GEN. *in a river* Il. AR.; (tr.) **wash, bathe** —*one's body* Hes. hHom. Hdt. E. AR.
3 ‖ MID. (of a star, dipping below the horizon) **bathe** —W.GEN. *in Okeanos* Il.
4 (fig.) **bathe** —*one's weapons* (W.DAT. *in blood*) Call. Theoc.

λοφάω *contr.vb.* [λόφος] (mock-medic., of an armourer with a stock of unsold helmet crests) **suffer from a crest complaint** Ar.

λοφεῖον ου *n.* box for storing helmet crests, **crest-case** Ar.

λοφιά ᾶς, Ion. **λοφιή** ῆς *f.* ridge of hair or bristles on the back and neck (of an animal); **mane** (of a horse) Hdt.; (of a wild boar) Od. Hes.; (fig., of Aeschylus, envisaged as a wild boar) Ar.

λοφίδιον ου *n.* [dimin. λόφος] small ridge, **hillock** Men.

λοφο-ποιός οῦ *m.* [ποιέω] **maker of helmet-crests** Ar.

λόφος ου *m.* **1** neck and upper back (of an animal); **neck** (of a horse or ox) Il. S. Call.
2 back of the neck, **neck** (of a man) Il.; (in fig.ctxt., as bearing the yoke of submission to a despot) S.
3 crest (of a lark) Simon.; **comb** (of a cock) Ar.
4 crest (of a helmet, usu. made of horsehair) Hom. Tyrt. Alc. A. Hdt. Ar. +
5 crest (as the hairstyle of a Libyan tribe, ref. to a central strip of hair, remaining after the rest of the head has been shaved) Hdt.
6 crest, **summit** (of a hill) Od.
7 (gener.) **hill** Od. hHom. Pi. Hdt. Th. Ar. +

λόφωσις εως *f.* **cresting** (ref. to birds having crests, w. further connot. of occupying high ground) Ar.

λοχ-ᾱγέται *dial.m.pl.* [λόχος, ἡγέομαι] | only nom., and acc. λοχᾱγέτᾱς | commanders of companies of troops, **captains** A. E.

λοχᾱγέω, Ion. **λοχηγέω** *contr.vb.* [λοχᾱγός] be captain —W.GEN. *of a specific Spartan company, of select troops* Hdt. —*of 120 men* (*in a Roman army*) Plu.; **be captain of a company of troops** X. Is. Arist.

λοχᾱγίᾱ ᾱς *f.* office of company-commander, **captaincy** X. Arist.

λοχ-ᾱγός οῦ *dial.m.* [λόχος, ἄγω] **1** (specif., in the Spartan army) commander of a company, **company-commander** Th.; (in other armies) **captain** (of units of varying or indeterminate size) Isoc. X. Arist. Plu.
2 (gener.) **captain, commander** S. E. Isoc.

λοχαῖος ᾱ ον *adj.* [λόχος] (of a place) **of ambush** E.

λοχάω *contr.vb.* [reltd. λέχομαι] | ep.3pl. (w.diect.) λοχόωσι, masc.nom.pl.ptcpl. (w.diect.) λοχόωντες ‖ pf.mid.ptcpl. λελοχημένος | **1 lie in wait for, set an ambush for** —*persons, troops, ships, a sea-creature* Od. Hdt. S. Th. AR.; (also mid.) Od. AR.
2 (intr.) **wait in ambush** Il. Hdt. E. ‖ STATV.PF.MID.PTCPL. waiting in ambush AR.
3 set an ambush on —*a road* Hdt.
4 (fig.) **lay a trap** —W.ACC. *of friendship w. someone* (*i.e. entrap him by pretending to be friendly*) Plb.

λοχείᾱ ᾱς, Ion. **λοχείη** ης *f.* [λοχεύω] **childbirth** E. Pl. Call. Plu.

λόχεια ων *n.pl.* place of giving birth (for Leto, ref. to Delos) E.

λόχεος οιο *ep.m.* [λόχος] **place of ambush** Hes.

λόχευμα ατος *n.* [λοχεύω] **1** act of giving birth, **childbirth** E.
2 ‖ PL. (fig.) birth-pangs (W.GEN. of a sheath of corn, when bringing forth the ear) A.
3 offspring, child E.

λοχεύω *vb.* [λόχος] **1** (of a woman) **give birth to** —*a child* hHom.; (mid.) Emp.(cj.) E. Call. AR.
2 (of a midwife, god) help to give birth, **deliver** —*a woman* (*of a child*) E.; (intr., of a woman in labour) **give birth** E. ‖ PASS. (of a woman) be delivered (of a child) E. Plu.; (of Semele) —W.DAT. *by lightning fire* E.
3 ‖ PASS. be brought to birth; (of Athena) be delivered (fr. the head of Zeus) —W.DAT. *by Prometheus* E.; (of a child) be born S.(dub.)
4 ‖ MID. (of an eel, w. play on λόχος *ambush*) **lie embedded** —W.PREP.PHR. *among beetroots* Ar.(mock-trag.)

λοχηγέω *Ion.contr.vb.*: see λοχᾱγέω

λοχίζω *vb.* [λόχος] **1** place (W.ACC. troops) **in ambush** Th. Plu.
2 ‖ PASS. be ambushed Th.
3 divide (W.ACC. troops) **into companies** Hdt. Plu.

λόχιος ᾱ (Ion. η) ον *adj.* **1** of or relating to childbirth; (of pains, ailments) **of childbirth** E.; (of secret recesses, ref. to Zeus' thigh, fr. which Dionysus was born) E.; (of the axe of Hephaistos, used to deliver Athena fr. Zeus' head) Call.
2 (epith. of Artemis) **presiding over childbirth** E.; (of the Fates) E.
3 (of a woman) **having just given birth** Call.; (of a sow's womb) AR.

λοχισμός οῦ *m.* [λοχίζω] **1 setting of ambushes** Plu.
2 marshalling of companies A.(cj.) [unless sense 1]

λοχίτης ου *m.* [λόχος] **1** (milit.) **member of the same company** X. Plu.

2 (gener.) **comrade in arms** A.
3 (ref. to a member of a bodyguard) **armed attendant** A. S.
λοχμαῖος ᾱ ον *adj.* [λόχμη] (of a Muse, fig.ref. to the nightingale) **of the thickets** Ar.
λόχμη ης, dial. **λόχμᾱ** ᾱς *f.* [λέχομαι] **thicket, bush** (esp. as a place of concealment for persons or animals) Od. Pi. S.*Ichn.* E. Ar. Plu.; (fig., ref. to pubic hair) Ar.
λοχμώδης ες *adj.* (of a path) **full of dense undergrowth, overgrown with bushes** Th.
λόχος ου *m.* [λέχομαι] **1** body of men lying in wait or ambush (or detailed for such a purpose), **group of ambushers** Hom. Hdt. E. Plu.
2 place of concealment or **ambush** Il. Hes. E. AR.; (ref. to the Trojan Horse) Od.
3 deployment of an ambush, **ambush** Hom. Pi. S. E.
4 (gener.) **underhand methods, secret designs** Plb.
5 group of armed men, band, troop Od. E.
6 (milit., as a division of an army) **company** Hdt. Trag. Th. Ar. X. +; (fig., of birds, envisaged as troops) Ar.
7 (gener.) **band, throng** (of Erinyes, maenads, suppliants, women and children) A. E.
8 (in certain cities, as a formal grouping within a populace) **company, division** X. Arist.
9 process of giving birth (for humans or animals), **birth** A.
—**λόχονδε** *adv.* **to** or **for an ambush** Hom.
λοχόωντες (ep.masc.nom.pl.ptcpl.), **λοχόωσι** (ep.3pl.): see λοχάω
λόω *contr.vb.*: see λούω
λύᾱ ᾱς *dial.f.* [λύω] **dissension, strife, quarrel** Alc. Pi.
λυαία ᾱς *dial.f.* **deliverance** (w.GEN. fr. troubles) Tim. [or perh. fem.adj. *bringing deliverance*, as epith. of Cybele]
λυάω *contr.vb.* [λύᾱ] | only aor. ἐλύησα | (of persons) **quarrel** —w.DAT. w. *one another* Call.
λυγαῖος ᾱ (Ion. η) ον *adj.* [reltd. ἠλύγη] (of night, clouds) **dark, murky** E. AR.
λύγδην *adv.* [λύζω] **with sobs** S.
λυγίζω *vb.* [λύγος] | dial.fut.inf. λυγιξεῖν ‖ dial.aor.pass. ἐλυγίχθην | **1 bend, twist** —*one's sides* (*in a vigorous dance*) Ar.
2 ‖ PASS. (of the ankle joint) **turn in the socket** S.
3 ‖ MID. **twist about** (in an evasive movement, as in wrestling) Pl.; (fig.) **twist, dodge** —w.DAT. w. *one's tales* S.*Ichn.*
4 (app., in wrestling) get (an opponent) at a disadvantage by twisting; (fig., of a lover) **wrestle down, throw** —*Eros* Theoc. [or perh. *twist one's arms around*, in an inescapable hold] ‖ PASS. perh., be thrown —w.PREP.PHR. *by Eros* Theoc.; (of a person) be dashed or overcome —w.ACC. *in one's feelings* Theoc.
λυγισμοί ῶν *m.pl.* acts of bending or twisting; (fig.) **twists, dodges** (by a speaker) Ar.
λύγξ[1] λυγκός *f.* **lynx** hHom. E. X. Call.
λύγξ[2] λυγγός *f.* [λύζω] **1 hiccuping, hiccups** Pl.
2 (medic., w.ADJ. *empty*) **retching** Th.
λύγοι ων *f.pl.* **pliant twigs of willow** (used for binding or plaiting), **osiers, withies** Hom. hHom. E.*Cyc.* Plu.
‖ COLLECTV.SG. willow (used for a garland) Anacr.
λυγρός ᾱ́ (Ion. ή) όν *adj.* [reltd. λευγαλέος] **1** suffering grief or pain; (of a person) **wretched, miserable, pitiable** S. AR.; (of halcyons) **gloomy, mournful** AR.
2 (of death, old age, adverse circumstances) accompanied by grief or pain, **wretched, pitiable, grim, painful** Hom. Hes. hHom. Sapph. Trag. AR.
3 (pejor., of persons) **wretched, pitiful** Hom.; (of a person's belly, ref. to appetite) Od.; (of garments) Od.

4 bringing grief or pain; (of monsters) **grim, baneful** Hes. A.
5 (of poisons, diseases, wounds, war, strife, or sim.) **grievous, painful** Hom. +
6 (predic., of a feast, marriage) turning out painfully (for someone), **disastrous** Pi. E.
7 ‖ NEUT.PL.SB. **grim sufferings** (endured or inflicted) Hom. Hes. Sol. Hdt. AR. ‖ SUPERL. **most grievous troubles** Theoc.*epigr.*
—**λυγρόν** neut.adv. **pitifully** —*ref. to animals gnashing their teeth fr. cold* Hes.
—**λυγρῶς** *adv.* **painfully** —*ref. to striking someone* Il.
Λυδίᾱ *f.*: see under Λῡδοί
Λῡδι-εργής ές *adj.* [Λῡδοί, ἔργον] (of an object) **of Lydian workmanship** Call.
Λῡδίζω *vb.* **speak in the Lydian language** Hippon.; (of an actor, as author of a comedy called Λῡδοί) **play a Lydian role** (either linguistically or musically) Ar.
Λυδίη Ion.*f.*, **Λῡδικός** *adj.*, **Λῡδιος** *adj.*: see under Λῡδοί
Λῡδιστί *adv.* [Λῡδίζω] (mus., sts. quasi-adjl., w. ἁρμονίᾳ) **in the Lydian mode** Pl. Arist.
Λῡδοί ῶν *m.pl.* **Lydians** (a people of western Asia Minor, whose kingdom was famed for its wealth and cultural achievements) Mimn. Hippon. Xenoph. Lyr. Hdt. Trag. + ‖ SG. Lydian man, Lydian Hdt. E. +
—**Λῡδαί** ῶν *f.pl.* **Lydian women** E.
—**Λῡδός** οῦ *m.* **Lydos** (king after whom the Lydian people were reputedly named) Hdt.; (as the name of a slave) Men.
—**Λῡδη** ης, dial. **Λῡδᾱ** ᾱς *f.* **Lyde** (as a woman's name) Call. Mosch.
—**Λῡδός** ή όν *adj.* (of a man or woman) **Lydian** Sapph. Pi. Hdt. S. +; (of a musical mode) Pi.
—**Λῡδιος** ᾱ (Ion. η) ον *adj.* **1** of or belonging to the Lydians; (of the people, land, cities, or sim.) **Lydian** A. Hdt. E. Tim. + ‖ FEM.SB. Lydian woman S.
2 of or characteristic of Lydia or the Lydians; (of goods) **Lydian** Alcm. Sapph. X. Call.; (of music, a musical mode; of an aulos, ref. to the mode being played on it) Pi. B.*fr.* Telest.; (of a victor's headband, fig.ref. to a victory-song in the Lydian mode) Pi.; (of a stone, ref. to a touchstone) B.*fr.* Theoc.; (of behaviour) Hdt.
—**Λῡδίᾱ** ᾱς, Ion. **Λῡδίη** ης *f.* [Λῡδοί] **land of the Lydians, Lydia** Sapph. B. Hdt. E. Isoc. +
—**Λῡδικός** ή όν *adj.* (of the kingdom) **Lydian** Hdt.
λύζω *vb.* **hiccup**; app. **sob gaspingly** Ar.(v.l. ἀλύω)
λύθεν (ep.3pl.aor.pass): see λύω
λύθρος ου *m.* —or **λύθρον** ου *n.* [reltd. λῦμα] | only dat. λύθρῳ | **spilled blood, gore** Hom. Call.
λυκάβᾱς αντος *m.* **period of time** (of uncert. duration, perh. month or year) Od.; **year** AR. Bion
Λυκαβηττός οῦ *m.* **Lykabettos** (hill in Athens, NE. of the Acropolis) Ar. Pl. X.
λύκαινα ης *f.* [λύκος] **she-wolf** Plu.
Λύκαιον ου *n.* [reltd. Λυκᾱ́ων] **Lykaion** (mt. in SW. Arcadia) Pi. Th. Theoc. Plb. Plu.
—**Λυκαῖος** ᾱ ον *adj.* (epith. of Zeus) belonging to Mt. Lykaion, **Lykaios** Pi. Hdt. Call. Plb.; (of his sanctuary) **Lykaian** E.
—**Λύκαια** ων *n.pl.* **Lykaia** (festival of Zeus Lykaios) X. Plu.; (as transl. of Lat. *Lupercalia*) Plu.
Λυκάων ονος *m.* **Lykaon** (mythol. king of Arcadia) Hes.*fr.* AR.
—**Λυκαονίδᾱς** ᾱο *dial.m.* **descendant of Lykaon** (ref. to Arkas) Theoc.
—**Λυκαονίη** ης *Ion.fem.adj.* (of a bear, ref. to the metamorphosed Kallisto) **born of Lykaon** Call.
λυκέη ης *Ion.f.* [λύκος] **wolf-skin** (worn by a warrior) Il.

λύκειος ᾱ ον (also ος ον E.) *adj.* **1** of or relating to a wolf; (of a hide) **of wolf-skin** E. ‖ FEM.SB. wolf-skin (as the covering of a helmet) Plb.
2 (of Apollo) **wolf-like** (w. play on his epith. Λύκειος) A.
Λύκειος, dial. **Λύκηος** (Alcm.), ον *adj.* [λύκειος or Λύκιος, by pop.etym.] (epith. of Apollo) **Lykeios** (app. either *wolf-like* or *Lycian*) Alcm. A. S. Call. Plu.; (of the market-place at Argos, in which his temple stood) S.
—**Λύκειον** ου *n.* **Lykeion, Lyceum** (gymnasium in Athens, named after a temple of Apollo Lykeios, later site of the Peripatetic school founded by Aristotle) Ar. Isoc. Pl. X. D. Arist. +
Λυκη-γενής ές *adj.* [perh. Λύκιος; γένος, γίγνομαι] (epith. of Apollo) perh. **Lycian-born** Il.
Λυκίᾱ *f.*: see under Λύκιοι
λυκιδεύς έως *m.* [λύκος] **wolf-cub** Theoc. Plu.
Λύκιοι ων *m.pl.* **Lycians** (a people of SW. Asia Minor) Il. A. Pi. B. Hdt. E. +
—**Λύκιος** ᾱ ον *adj.* **1** of or relating to Lycia or the Lycians; (of men) **Lycian** Il. Pi. Hdt. E. Call. +; (of the mountains, springs) S.
2 (of bows) of Lycian workmanship, **Lycian** Hdt.
3 (epith. of Apollo) **Lykios** Simon. Pi. Ar.(quot. E.) Call. | see also Λύκειος
—**Λυκίᾱ** ᾱς, Ion. **Λυκίη** ης *f.* land of the Lycians, **Lycia** Il. hHom. Pi. Hdt. E. Th. +
—**Λυκίηθεν** *Ion.adv.* **from Lycia** Il. AR.
—**Λυκίηνδε** *Ion.adv.* **to Lycia** Il.
Λυκιουργής, Ion. **Λυκιοεργής**, ές *adj.* [ἔργον] (of spears, goblets) **of Lycian workmanship** Hdt. D.
λυκο-δίωκτος ον *adj.* [λύκος, διωκτός] (of a heifer) **pursued by wolves** A.
λυκο-κτόνος ον *adj.* [κτείνω] (of Apollo, w. allusion to his epith. Λύκειος) **wolf-killing** S.
λυκόομαι *pass.contr.vb.* (of sheep) **be mangled by wolves** X.
λύκος ου *m.* **wolf** (freq. as exemplifying a savage predator) Hom. +; (believed to strike a person dumb, if it sees him before being seen) Pl. Theoc.; (provbl.) λύκον τῶν ὤτων λαβεῖν *take a wolf by the ears* (i.e. *be foolhardy*) Plb.; λύκου βίον ζῆν *live a wolf's life* (i.e. *by banditry and rapine*) Plb.; λύκος χανών *open-mouthed wolf* (*ref. to a person cheated of his hopes*) Men.
Λυκοῦργος, ep. **Λυκόοργος**, ου *m.* **1 Lykourgos** (mythol. ruler of Thrace, punished for opposing Dionysus) Il.
2 Lykourgos (traditional founder of the institutions and lawcode of Sparta) Hdt. Isoc. Pl. X. +
3 Lycurgus (Athenian statesman and orator, c.390–325 BC) Hyp. D. Din. Plu.
—**Λυκούργεια** ᾱς *f.* **Lykourgeia** (tetralogy of plays by Aeschylus concerning the mythol. Lykourgos) Ar.
Λυκωρεύς έος, also **Λυκωρεῖος** οιο *ep.masc.adj.* [Λυκώρεια *Lykoreia* (*name of the summit of Parnassos, also of a village on the mt.*)] (epith. of Apollo at Delphi) **Lykoreian** Call. AR.
λῦμᾱ *dial.f.*: see λύμη
λῡμαίνομαι *mid.vb.* [λύμη] | fut. λυμανοῦμαι | aor. ἐλυμηνάμην ‖ PASS.: aor. ἐλυμάνθην | **1 inflict gross insult** or **outrage upon, maltreat** —*a person, hands* Hdt. E. Ar. D. —W.DAT. *a person or corpse* Hdt. E.; (fig.) **defile** —W.ACC. *one's tongue* (W.DAT. *w. obscene pleasures*) Ar. ‖ PASS. (of a person or body) **be maltreated** A. Antipho Lys.
2 (of troops, commanders, or sim.) **inflict damage on** —*the enemy, a country, ships, buildings* Isoc. X. Plb. Plu.; (of a novice) —*a musical instrument* X.; (of boars) —*fields, plants* Call.; (of ships) —W.DAT. *the enemy* Hdt.; (of ground) —*horses' hooves* X.
3 (fig.) **mutilate, ruin** —*speeches* (*by delivering them badly*) Isoc. D.
4 (gener., of persons, things, circumstances) **harm, damage, ruin** —*persons, their families, happiness or interests* S. Att.orats. X. Arist. + —*a city, institutions, the public interest, laws, or sim.* Att.orats. X. + —*the truth* Isoc. Plu. —W.DAT. *a state of affairs* Isoc. X. D. —*one's reputation* D.; (of a god) —*someone's life* Lys.; (intr., of persons, circumstances) **cause harm** Th. Isoc. Men. ‖ PASS. (of a city's honour) **be ruined** D.
5 (w. moral connot.) **corrupt** —*persons* Isoc. X. —W.DAT. Ar.; (of Dionysus, by causing promiscuity) —W.ACC. *marriage beds* E.
λῡμαντήρ ῆρος *m.* (ref. to an adulterer) **destroyer, corrupter** (of a husband's and wife's relationship) X.
λῡμαντήριος ᾱ ον *adj.* **1** (of Prometheus' fetters) **tormenting** A.
2 (of a person) **ruinous** (W.GEN. to a house) A. ‖ MASC.SB. **abuser** (W.GEN. of a woman) A.
λῡμαντής οῦ *m.* (ref. to a marriage) **destroyer, bane** (W.GEN. of a person's life) S.
λύματα των *n.pl.* [reltd. λύμη] **1 impurities** (such as are removed by cleansing); (collectv.) **pollution** (ref. to dirt, or traces of childbirth, washed by a goddess fr. her body) Il. Call.; (ref. to off-scourings fr. washed bodies) Il.; (ref. to blood on a killer's hands) S.
2 impure waste, waste, refuse (fr. an animal sacrifice) E. AR.; (W.GEN. of earth, carried away by a river) Call.; (W.GEN. of a feast) Call.; (ref. to dung) Call.
3 app. **brutal outrages** A.(dub.)
4 ‖ SG. (ref. to a person) **bane, destroyer** (W.GEN. of one's enemies) E.; **disgrace** (W.DAT. to one's old age) S.
λῡμεών ῶνος *m.* [λύμη] **1** (ref. to a person) **destroyer** (of others, their interests) S. Isoc. Plu.; (of a drowning person's body, ref. to the sea) Tim.; (of pleasures, ref. to fear) X.
2 corrupter, seducer (of another's wife) E.
λῡμεωνεύομαι *mid.vb.* **behave perniciously** Plb.
λύμη ης, dial. **λύμᾱ** ᾱς *f.* [reltd. λύματα] **1** act of **gross insult** or **outrage**; (sg. and pl.) **maltreatment, brutal outrage, indignity** (inflicted upon others) Hdt. Trag. AR.; (sg.) **ruining** (W.GEN. of a person's life) S.; **destruction, ruin** (of a family) A.
2 injury, damage (to crops and livestock, by insects or wild animals) Ar. X.; (to a city, fr. malpractices within it) Pl.
3 source of damage or **harm** (W.DAT. to metal and wood, ref. to rust and woodworm) Plb.; (to human beings, ref. to base pleasures or sim.) Arist.; **source of disfigurement** (to the body, ref. to the aulos, which distorted the player's features) Melanipp.
4 ‖ PL. **filth, waste** (ref. to sewage, carried by a river) Plb.
λύμην, λύντο (ep.1sg. and 3pl.athem.aor.mid.): see λύω
λῡπέω *contr.vb.* [λύπη] | fut.pass. λυπήσομαι ‖ neut.impers. vbl.adj. λυπητέον | **1** (of persons, things, events, circumstances) **cause annoyance, trouble, distress** or **pain** (freq. W.ACC. to persons) Hes. Hdt. S. E. Th. Ar. +
2 (of troops, cavalry) **harass** —*the enemy* Hdt. Th. X.; (of pirates) —*persons, a country* Th. Ar.
3 ‖ PASS. **be annoyed** or **distressed, feel pain** or **sorrow** (sts. W.DAT. or PREP.PHR. over sthg.) Hdt. S. E. Th. Ar. Att.orats. + —W.NEUT.ACC. *over sthg.* S. ‖ NEUT.IMPERS.VBL.ADJ. **it is necessary to be distressed** X.
λύπη ης, dial. **λύπᾱ** ᾱς *f.* (sg. and pl.) **annoyance, distress, anguish, pain** Hdt. Trag. Th. Ar. Att.orats. +; (opp. ἡδονή *pleasure*) Isoc. Pl. Arist.

λύπημα ατος n. [λῡπέω] painful act or experience, **pain** S.(dub.)

λυπηρός ά όν adj. [λύπη] **1** (of persons) causing pain, trouble or annoyance, **troublesome, annoying, offensive** (sts. W.DAT. to others) S. E. Th. Ar.(mock-trag.) Plu.
2 (of communities, ref. to their capacity for military action) **troublesome, threatening** (W.DAT. to others) Th. X.
3 (of persons, because of their own sufferings) causing pain or sorrow, **painful, distressing** (W.DAT. to others) E. Th.
4 (of behaviour, speech, events or circumstances) causing pain, distress or annoyance, **painful, distressing, annoying, upsetting** (to oneself or others) Hdt. S. E. Th. Att.orats. Pl. + ‖ NEUT.SB. pain or distress Th. Pl. D. Arist. Men.
—**λυπηρῶς** adv. in a manner or circumstances causing pain, **painfully, distressingly** S. Isoc. X. Arist.; (w. ἔχειν, of a circumstance) *be painful or distressing* S. E.

λυπρός ά (Ion. ή) όν adj. **1** in a distressed condition; (of land) **poor, unfertile** Od. Hdt.; (gener., of places) **in a sorry state** (through poverty or sim.) Plb. Plu.
2 (of news, events, circumstances) **painful, distressing** (to oneself or others) A. E. Plu.
3 (of persons) causing pain, trouble or annoyance, **troublesome, annoying, offensive** (to others) A. E.
‖ NEUT.SB. annoyance, distress (W.GEN. caused by someone) E.
—**λυπρά** neut.pl.adv. **wretchedly, badly** —*ref. to faring* Plu.
—**λυπρῶς** adv. **1** with pain or distress (to oneself), **painfully, sorrowfully** E.
2 poorly, badly —*ref. to faring* Plu.

λύρα ας, Ion. **λύρη** ης f. stringed musical instrument, **lyre** (orig.ref. either to a bowl lyre, βάρβιτος or χέλυς, or to a box lyre, κιθάρα or φόρμιγξ, but later specif. to the former) hHom. Archil. Thgn. Scol. Lyr. Trag. +

λυρικός ή όν adj. (of poems) composed for singing to the accompaniment of the lyre, **lyric** Plu. ‖ MASC.PL.SB. lyric poets Plu.

λύριον ου n. [dimin. λύρᾱ] **lyre** Ar.

λυροποιική ῆς f. [λυροποιός] **art of lyre-making** Pl.

λυρο-ποιός οῦ m. [ποιέω] **lyre-maker** And. Pl. Aeschin. Arist.

λυρ-ῳδός οῦ m.f. [ἀοιδή] one who sings to the accompaniment of the lyre, **lyre-singer** Plu.

λυσ-ανίας ου m. [λύω, ἀνία] (ref. to a son) **reliever of the pain** (W.GEN. of his father's troubles) Ar.

Λυσίας ου m. **Lysias** (Athenian orator, c.458–380 BC) Pl. Plu.

λυσί-ζωνος ον adj. [λύω, ζώνη] (epith. of Eileithuia) **loosing the girdle** (ref. to assisting women in childbirth) Theoc.

λυσί-κακος ον adj. [κακός] (of sleep) **bringing release from troubles** Thgn.

Λυσι-μάχη ης f. **Lysimakhe** (Athenian female pers. name, applied to the goddess Peace and in pl. to Lysistrata and her companions, w.connot. *Ender of fighting*) Ar.

λυσι-μελής ές adj. [μέλος] (of sleep) **loosening** or **weakening the limbs** Od. Mosch.; (of love, desire) Hes. Alcm. Archil. Sapph. Carm.Pop.; (of thirst) Thgn.; (of death, numbness caused by poison) E. AR.

λύσιμος ον adj. [λύσις] **1** (of prayers) **bringing release** (fr. trouble) A.(dub.)
2 (of financial pledges) **able to be redeemed** Pl.

λύσιος ᾱ ον adj. [λύω] (of gods) **bringing release** or **absolution** (fr. curses, pollution, or sim.) Pl.

λυσί-πονος ον adj. [πόνος] (of attendants, rites) **bringing release from labours** or **troubles** Pi.

λύσις εως (Ion. ιος) f. **1 release, freeing** (of a person, W.GEN. or ἀπό + GEN. fr. fetters) Pl.; (of the soul, fr. the body, in death) Pl.
2 release, ransoming (of a corpse or captive) Il. Lys. D.
3 deliverance, escape (W.GEN. fr. death) Od. Thgn.
4 deliverance, release (W.GEN. fr. conflict, debts, poverty, sorrows, fears, or sim.) Hes. Thgn. Pi. Hdt. S. E. +; (w. ἐκ + GEN. fr. troubles) Anacr. Thgn.
5 release (fr. a difficult situation) S.; (W.PREP.PHR. towards a destination, W.DAT. for an army constrained to remain in a place) S.
6 (specif.) **release, absolution** (fr. pollution or the effects of wrongdoing, by expiatory rites) Pl. Arist. Plu.
7 resolution, settlement, solution (of a problem, impasse, dispute or conflict) D. Arist. Plb. Plu.
8 resolution, dénouement (of a dramatic plot, opp. δέσις *complication*) Arist.
9 (leg.) **release, redemption** (of mortgaged property) D.
10 dissolution, destruction (of a city-state, time and space, the natural order) Pl.
11 dissolution, annulment (of laws) Arist.; (of a marriage) Plu.
12 breaking, breach (of laws) Arist.
13 refutation, rejection (of an argument) Arist.
14 resting-place (W.GEN. for dining) Pi.

λυσιτέλεια ας f. [λυσιτελής] **advantage, benefit** Plb.

λυσιτελέω contr.vb. **1** (of things, situations) **be profitable** or **advantageous** (freq. W.DAT. for someone) Ar. Att.orats. Pl. X. +; (of a person) **be beneficial** or **useful** —W.DAT. *to someone* X. ‖ NEUT.PTCPL.SB. profit, advantage Th. Att.orats. Pl. +
2 ‖ IMPERS. it is profitable or advantageous (freq. W.DAT. for someone) —W.INF. *to do sthg.* Hdt. Att.orats. Pl. X. +
—W.ACC. + INF. *that someone shd. do sthg., that sthg. shd. be done* Att.orats. + —W.DAT. + PTCPL. *for someone to be doing or to have done sthg.* Lys. Pl.
—**λυσιτελούντως** ptcpl.adv. **profitably, advantageously** X. D.

λυσι-τελής ές adj. [λύω, τέλος] **1** paying expenses or dues; (of things, events, circumstances) **profitable, beneficial, advantageous** (sts. W.DAT. to someone) Isoc. Pl. X. D. Arist. +
2 (of merchandise) **cost-effective** X.
3 (of a person) **beneficial, useful** Pl.
—**λυσιτελῶς** adv. **profitably, advantageously** Plb. Plu.

λυσι-ῳδός οῦ m. [pers. name Λῦσις, ἀοιδή] **performer of bawdy songs** (in a style assoc.w. a poet named Lysis) Plu.

λύσσα, Att. **λύττα**, ης (dial. ᾱς) f. **1 frenzy, fury, lust for battle** (of a warrior) Il. Alc.
2 mad frenzy (esp. as inflicted by gods or Erinyes) A. B. E. Ar. Plu.; (ref. to love) S.fr. Pl. Theoc.; (personif., as a goddess) **Frenzy** E.
3 rabies (in dogs) X.

λυσσαίνω vb. be in a frenzy, **rage** —W.DAT. *at someone* S.

λυσσαλέος η ον Ion.adj. (of dogs) **frenzied, rabid** AR.

λυσσάς άδος fem.adj. **1** (of Spirits of Vengeance) **frenzied, raging mad** E.; (of a woman or goddess) Tim.
2 (of a fate allotted to Herakles) **of frenzied madness** E.

λυσσάω, Att. **λυττάω** contr.vb. | dial.inf. λυσσῆν (Theoc.) |
1 (of persons, their minds or feelings, a lover's soul) **be in a mad frenzy, be frantic** S. Pl. Plb.; (of a soldier, in battle) **go berserk** Hdt. ‖ PTCPL.ADJ. (of desires) frenzied, frantic Pl.
2 (of dogs, wolves) **be rabid** Ar. Theoc.

λύσσημα ατος n. **fit of frenzy** (sent by Erinyes) E.

λυσσητήρ ῆρος m. one who rages madly; (pejor., appos.w. κύων) **mad dog** (fig.ref. *to an enemy warrior*) Il.

λυσσώδης ες adj. (of persons) **frenzied, maddened, frantic** Il. E.; (of an affliction sent by a deity) **of frenzied madness** S.

λυτέος ᾱ ον *vbl.adj.* [λύω] (of a law) **to be annulled** D.
λυτήρ ῆρος *m.* **1 deliverer, rescuer** (W.GEN. fr. troubles) E.; (fr. marriage, ref. to a path of escape) A.
2 resolver, ender (W.GEN. of conflicts, ref. to personif. Iron) A.
λυτήριον ου *n.* **1** (sg. and pl.) **means of release** or **deliverance** E.*fr.*; (W.GEN. fr. one's fate, troubles) Stesich. S.
2 means of absolution or **expiation** (W.GEN. for a murder) S. AR.
3 (ref. to a victory-song) **means of providing payment** (in return), **recompense** (W.GEN. for one's expenses) Pi.
—λυτήριος ον *adj.* (of deities, prayers, remedies, stratagems) **bringing release** or **deliverance** (sts. W.GEN. or ἐκ + GEN. fr. sthg.) Trag.
λυτικός ή όν *adj.* [λυτός] (philos., of types of arguments) providing refutation, **refutative** Arist.
λύτο and **λῦτο** (ep.3sg.athem.aor.mid.): see λύω
λυτός ή όν *adj.* [λύω] **1** (of things tied up or joined together) **able to be released** or **untied** Pl.
2 (of substances) able to be dissolved, **soluble** Pl.
3 (of arguments) able to be refuted, **refutable** Arist.
λύτρον ου *n.* **1 recompense** (W.GEN. for efforts, sufferings) Pi.
2 amends, expiation, atonement (W.GEN. for spilt blood) A.
3 ‖ PL. **price of release, ransom** (usu. for captives or corpses) Hdt. Th. Att.orats. Pl. X. +; (sg., ref. to a person, W.GEN. for baggage) Plu.; (ref. to the life of Jesus, w. ἀντί + GEN. **in exchange for many**) NT.
λυτρόω *contr.vb.* **1 hold** (someone) **to ransom** Pl. ‖ MID. **free by paying a ransom, ransom** —*someone* Arist. Men. Plu. ‖ PASS. **be ransomed** Aeschin. D. Arist.
2 ‖ MID. **redeem** —*a mortgaged plot of land* Plb.
3 ‖ MID. (fig., of Christ) **redeem, set free, rescue** —*Israel* NT.
λύτρωσις εως *f.* **1 ransoming** (W.GEN. of captives) Plu.
2 (fig.) **redemption, liberation** (of Jerusalem, God's people) NT.
λυτρωτής οῦ *m.* (ref. to Moses) **redeemer** (of his people) NT.
λύττα *Att.f.*, **λυττάω** *Att.contr.vb.*: see λύσσα, λυσσάω
λυχνεῖον ου *n.* [λύχνος] **ballot-stand** (app.ref. to a device resembling a lamp-holder, w. two pans, holding the two kinds of voting-token to be used by jurors) Arist.
λυχνίᾱ ᾱς *f.* **lamp-stand** NT. Plu.
λύχνιον ου *n.* **lamp** Theoc.
—λυχνίον ου *n.* **lamp-stand** Plu.
λυχνο-καΐη ης *Ion.f.* [καίω] **lighting of the lamps** (as the name of an Egyptian festival) Hdt.
λύχνον *n.*: see λύχνος
λυχνο-ποιός οῦ *m.* [ποιέω] **lamp-maker** Ar.
λυχνο-πώλης ου *m.* [πωλέω] **lamp-seller** Ar.
λύχνος ου *m.* —also **λύχνον** ου (Hippon.) *n.* ǀ nom.acc.pl. λύχνα, also nom. λύχνοι (Ar. NT.) ǀ **lamp** (usu. of terracotta, w. oil feeding a wick) Od. Alc. Hippon. Emp. Hdt. E.*Cyc.* +
λυχνοῦχος ου *m.* [ἔχω] **lamp-holder** (into which a lamp was placed for outdoor use), **lantern** Ar.
λυχνοφορίω *Lacon.vb.* [λυχνοφόρος] **carry a lamp** Ar.
λυχνο-φόρος ου *m.* [φέρω] **lamp-bearer** (ref. to a person) Plu.
λύω *vb.* ǀ ep.pres. usu. λύω ǀ impf. ἔλυον, ep. λύον ǀ fut. λύσω ǀ aor. ἔλυσα ǀ pf. λέλυκα ‖ MID.: impf. ἐλυόμην, ep. λυόμην ǀ aor. ἐλυσάμην ǀ ep.athem.aor. (w.pass.sens.) λύμην, 3sg. λύτο, also λῦτο, 3pl. λύντο ‖ PASS.: fut. λυθήσομαι ǀ aor. ἐλύθην, ep.3pl. λύθεν ǀ pf. λέλυμαι, ep.3sg.opt. λελῦτο ǀ fut.pf. λελύσομαι ‖ neut.impers.vbl.adj. λυτέον ‖ The sections are grouped as: (1–8) **set loose** (fr. another's control, a physical constraint or an unwelcome condition), (9–18) **loosen a fastening** or sthg. fastened, (19) **make loose** or **slack**, (20–22) **break up** or **weaken**, (23–29) **bring to an end**, (30–35) **discharge, fulfil** or **pay off**. ǀ
1 set loose (a person, fr. restraint or captivity); **release, free** —*a person, hands* (sts. W.GEN. or PREP.PHR. *fr. bonds or sim.*) Hom. Hes. Alc. Pi. Hdt. Trag. + ‖ MID. **free oneself** Od. ‖ PASS. **be freed** Od. Hes.*fr.* A. Pi.*fr.* Hdt. E. +; (of a people) **be given liberty** —W.INF. *to speak freely* A.
2 set loose (an animal); **unyoke** —*horses, mules* (freq. W.PREP.PHR. *fr. a chariot or wagon, or fr. beneath the yoke*) Hom.(sts.mid.) —*oxen* Hes.; **untether** —*horses* Il.; **unleash** —*a dog* X. —*a sow* Ar.
3 set free (fr. sthg. unwelcome); **set free, release** —*a person* (W.GEN. or PREP.PHR. *fr. troubles, pain, fear, ruin, or sim.*) Od. Sapph. Pi. B. Trag. +; (mid.) Hes. A. ‖ PASS. **be freed** —W.GEN. *fr. pain, despondency* Sapph. Pi.*fr.*
4 (of a pillaging warrior) app. **free, strip** —*houses* (W.GEN. *of their valuables*) Pi.
5 (usu. in military ctxt.) **release in return for payment**; **release, ransom** —*a captive* (sts. W.DAT. *to someone, sts.* W.GEN. *for a price*) Il.; **restore** —*a corpse, a slain man's armour* (*to the enemy*) Il. ‖ MID. **purchase the release of**, **ransom** —*a captive or corpse* Il. Hdt. Att.orats. +; (gener., without notion of payment) **secure the release of, rescue** —*someone* Od. Pi. ‖ PASS. (of a captive or corpse) **be released** or **ransomed** Il. +
6 ‖ MID. **buy the freedom of** —*a slave-girl* Hdt. Ar. D. ‖ PASS. (of a slave-girl) **be freed** —W.GEN. *for a large sum of money* Hdt.
7 ‖ MID. **buy back** —*a horse* (fr. its new owner) X.; **redeem** —*a piece of land* (fr. the mortgagers) D.
8 (wkr.sens.) **release** (fr. one's control), **relinquish, give up** —*royal power* Pi.
9 loosen (a fastening); **loosen, undo, unfasten, untie** —*bonds or sim.* A. E. Ar. —*a noose* (W.GEN. *fr. a neck*) A. E. —*a ship's mooring-cables* Od. E. —*its tackle, sail* Od. hHom. Archil. ‖ PASS. (of ropes) **be undone** hHom.; (of stitches, fastenings) **come undone** Od. E.
10 loosen or **unfasten** (fr. the body); **loosen, undo, unfasten** —*someone's belt or cuirass* Il. —*a dead man's armour* (as plunder) Il.(mid.) —*someone's shoes* A. —*one's clothing* S. —*a head-dress* (W.PREP.PHR. *fr. oneself*) Od. ‖ MID. **undo, take off** —*one's breast-band* Il. Ar. —*one's belt* Hdt. ‖ PASS. (fig., of the yoke of despotism) **be loosened** or **removed** A.
11 (specif., of a man) **loosen, untie** —*a woman's girdle* (as a prelude to sexual intercourse) Od. hHom. Alc. Mosch.; (of a woman) —*her girdle* Pi. AR. —(fig.) *her maidenhood* E.; (mid., of a woman) —*her girdle* (*in childbirth*) Call.
12 ‖ MID. **let loose** or **down** —*one's hair* Bion
13 unloose (fr. moorings), **release, unmoor** —*a ship's stern* E.; (periphr.) —*a ship's course* (*i.e. unmoor it and set it on course*) E.
14 (of a bird) **release** (fr. its throat), **let out** —*its song* Ar.
15 untie, undo —*a knot* Hdt. Plu. —(fig.) *a knot of words* E.; (intr., fig.) **untie a knot** (i.e. resolve a difficulty) S.; (of a dramatist) **unravel a plot** Arist.
16 undo, unfasten —*door-bolts* E. ‖ PASS. (of bolts) **be undone** A. E.
17 undo the fastenings of, undo, untie, open —*a wineskin, chest, or sim.* Od. Hdt. E.; **unseal** —*a writing-tablet, letter* E. Th.; **open up** —*stables* E.
18 unseal, open —*one's mouth* (*to break silence*) E. Isoc. —*one's eyes* E.

19 make loose (opp. taut), **loosen, slacken** —*a horse's rein* S.(dub.); **relax** —*one's brow* E. —*(fig.) one's thoughts* E.
20 resolve into component parts (so as to disintegrate or destroy), **break up, dismantle, destroy** —*a bridge, barricade, city's battlements* Hom. B.*fr.* Hdt. Th. X. ‖ PASS. (of a bridge) be broken up Hdt. X.; (gener., of living things) be dissolved (in death) Emp.; (fig., of civic order) D. ‖ PF.PASS. (of cables) be decayed Il.
21 cause (a person's body or strength) to be weakened or collapse (esp. through death, unconsciousness or exhaustion); (usu. of warriors) **weaken, undo** —*someone's limbs, knees, strength* Hom.; —*an ox's strength* (*by slaughtering it*) Od.; (fig., of a commander, by deceptive tactics) —*the enemy's mental readiness for battle* X. ‖ PASS. (of a person's limbs, life or strength; fig., of a heart) be undone, give way Hom. hHom. A. E.; (of a woman) —W.ACC. *in the fastenings of her limbs* E.; (wkr.sens., of a person's joints) be relaxed —W.DAT. *in sleep* Od.
22 app. **relax** —*one's eyes* (W.PREDIC.ADJ. *in darkness, i.e. close them in death*) S.
23 put an end to, **dissolve, dismiss** —*an assembly* Hom. ‖ PASS. (of an assembly) be dissolved Il. Ar.; (of an army) be disbanded X.; (of a market, dinner-party) break up X. Plb.
24 break off —*a siege* X. Plb. —*a military campaign* (*by disbanding*) Hdt.
25 break —*a truce, an agreement, or sim.* Hdt. Th. Lys. X. +; **rescind, annul** —*a law, decision, penalty, or sim.* Hdt. Th. D. Arist. +; **revoke** —*a will* Is.; **disregard, set at naught** —*an oracular command* E. —*the holiness of suppliants' boughs* (*i.e. deny their sacred right to sanctuary*) E. ‖ PASS. (of a truce, an agreement) be broken Th. +; (of a law or sim.) be annulled Aeschin. D.
26 bring to an end, **resolve, settle** —*quarrels, grievances, enmity, censure, war, or sim.* Hom. A. Pi. E. Th. Ar. +; (of gods) —*blood-guilt, pollution* A.(mid.) —*a spirit of competition* (*in a city*) S. ‖ PASS. (of disagreements) be resolved Th.
27 dissolve, dispel —*anxieties, fear, grief* Hom. Trag.; **relieve** —*hardships, the weight of pain* S. ‖ MID. **relieve** —*one's pain* Sol.
28 end —*one's life* B. E.(cj.); (periphr.) **close** —*the end of one's life* S.
29 (philos.) **undo** —*an earlier conclusion* Pl.; **solve** —*a problem* Arist.; **refute** —*an argument* Arist. ‖ PASS. (of a problem) be solved Pl.
30 settle or discharge (a debt or obligation); **pay** —*wages* (*that are owing*) X.
31 discharge, fulfil —*an oath, oracular command* S. Plb. —*an obligation to suppliants* E.
32 make amends for, atone for —*wrongdoings* Sapph. S. Ar.
33 pay back —*murder* (W.DAT. *w. murder*) S. E.
34 (impers.phr.) τέλη λύει *it pays expenses or dues* (*i.e. it pays, it is profitable or worthwhile*) —W.DAT. *for one who is wise* (*i.e. for him to be wise*) S. | see also λυσιτελέω
35 (intr., of marriage, suffering) **be beneficial** or **worthwhile** (sts. W.DAT. for someone) E. ‖ IMPERS. it is beneficial or worthwhile —W.DAT. + INF. (sts. understd.) *for someone* (*to do sthg.*) E. —W.ACC. + INF. *that someone shd. do sthg.* S. E.*fr.*

λῶ *dial.contr.vb.* | indic. and subj., w. identical forms: 2sg. λῇς, 3sg. λῇ, 1pl. λῶμες, 2pl. λῆτε, 3pl. λῶντι | inf. λῆν (Th., cj.) | **wish, want, be willing** (freq. W.INF. to do sthg.) Thgn. Carm.Pop. Th.(treaty, cj.) Ar. Hellenist.poet.

λωβάομαι *mid.contr.vb.* [λώβη] | fut. λωβήσομαι | aor. ἐλωβησάμην, dial.subj. λωβάσωμαι ‖ PASS.: aor. ἐλωβήθην | pf. λελώβημαι | **1 inflict gross insult** or **outrage upon, maltreat** —*a person* Il. —W.DAT. Ar.; (intr.) **behave outrageously** Il. Semon.
2 inflict gross physical injury on, **maim, mutilate** —*a person or body* Hdt. Pl.; (of a sickness) **ravage, torment** —*a person* S. ‖ PASS. (of a person or body) be maimed or mutilated Hdt. Pl.
3 inflict serious damage on, **ravage, devastate** —*a city* Lys. Theoc. Plb. —*a populace* X. Plb.; (of locusts) —*vines* Theoc.; (of a person) **destroy** —*one's own life* (W.DAT. *w. a noose*) S.
4 (gener.) inflict harm on, **harm, injure, damage** —*persons, their body or appearance, other attributes* Pl. Arist.; (of injustice) —W.DAT. *a person* Pl. ‖ PASS. (of persons) be harmed or impaired (in some capacity) Arist.; (of the soul) be marred —W.PREP.PHR. *by association w. the body* Pl.
5 (w. moral connot., esp. of sophists) **corrupt** —*persons, the young* Pl.; (of seducers) —*men's wives* E. ‖ PASS. (of a person) be corrupted Pl.

λωβατός *dial.adj.*: see λωβητός

λωβεύω *vb.* shamefully mock, **torment** —*a person* (*w. words of false hope*) Od.

λώβη ης, dial. **λώβᾱ** ᾱς *f.* **1** violent or insulting act or behaviour, **outrage** Hom. Hes. S. E. AR.; (ref. to maiming or mutilation) Hdt. E. Pl.
2 (ref. to a circumstance) cause of shame, **disgrace, dishonour** (sts. W.DAT. for someone) Hom.; (ref. to a person) Il. Call.
3 (gener.) harm, injury, damage (to persons, cities) Pl.; **ruin** (W.GEN. of a household) E.; (ref. to Paris) source of ruin, **bane** (of Troy) E.
4 (w. moral connot., ref. to sophists, poetry) **source of corruption, noxious influence** Pl.

λωβήεις εσσα εν *adj.* (of actions) **outrageous, disgraceful** AR.

λωβητήρ ῆρος *m.f.* **1** (as a term of abuse) one who behaves insultingly or disgracefully, **shameful wretch** Il. AR.
2 ‖ PL. tormentors, destroyers (ref. to Erinyes) S.; (W.GEN. of songs, ref. to bad poets) Tim.

λωβητής οῦ *m.* ‖ PL. (ref. to bad tragic poets) destroyers, corrupters (W.GEN. of their craft) Ar.

λωβητός, dial. **λωβᾱτός**, ή (dial. ά) όν *adj.* [λωβάομαι]
1 treated outrageously or dishonourably; (of a person, allotted unmixed ill-fortune by Zeus) **downtrodden** Il.; (of a person or body) **maimed, ravaged** (by physical sufferings) S.; (of Ares) **shamed, dishonoured** (by being stripped of his armour in battle) Hes.; (of an unburied corpse) S.(dub.)
2 creating outrage or dishonour; (of words, spoken against a person) **dishonouring, shaming, abusive** S.; (of cargo, fig.ref. to a mistress whom a wife is forced to take into her house) **that does outrage** (W.GEN. to her feelings) S.

λωίτερος *Ion.compar.adj.*: see under λῴων
λωίων *dial.compar.adj.*: see λῴων
λῶντι (dial.3pl.indic. and subj.): see λῶ
λῶντο, λώοντο (dial.3pl.impf.mid.): see λούω
λώπη ης *f.* [reltd. λέπω, λοπός] app., that which provides outer covering; (specif.) **cloak** (worn by men and women) Od. AR. Theoc.

λώπιον ου *n.* [dimin. λώπη or λῶπος] **cloak** Arist.

λωποδυτέω *contr.vb.* [λωποδύτης] **1 be a cloak-thief** Ar. Pl. X. D. Arist.
2 (tr.) **steal a cloak from** —*a person* Ar. Men.
3 (fig., of a ruler) **strip, rob, plunder** (neighbouring peoples) D.

λωποδύτης ου *m*. [λώπη, δύω¹] app., one who puts on a cloak (belonging to another); (specif.) one who steals a cloak by force from its wearer (a crime punishable by death in Athenian law), **cloak-thief** S.*eleg*. Ar. Att.orats. Pl. Arist. Plb.

λῶπος εος *dial.n*. **cloak** Anacr. Hippon. Theoc.

λῷστος *superl.adj*.: see under λῴων

λωτίζομαι *mid.vb*. [λωτός] (fig.) cull (as if a flower), **pick, select** —*what is most pleasing* (*of choices offered*) A.

λώτινος η ον *adj*. **1** (of a neck-garland) **made of lotus flowers** Anacr.
2 (of an aulos, a scabbard) **made of lotus wood** Pi.*fr*. Theoc.
3 (of the banks of Acheron) lotus-covered, **rich in clover** Sapph.

λωτίσματα των *n.pl*. [λωτίζομαι] picked flowers; (fig., ref. to soldiers) **choicest and best ones, flower** (W.GEN. of Greece) A.*fr*. E.

λωτόεις εσσα εν *adj*. [λωτός] | only contr.neut.acc.pl. λωτοῦντα | (of plains) **rich in clover** Il.

λωτός οῦ *m*. **1** a kind of plant (which provides good pasture), **trefoil, clover** Hom. hHom.; (used in making a garland) Theoc.
2 a kind of water-lily (which grows in the Nile), **Egyptian lotus** Hdt.
3 a kind of tree or shrub (which grows in N. Africa), **lotus tree** Hdt. Plb.
4 lotus-pipe (sts. described as *Libyan*, ref. to the aulos, made fr. the wood of a tree growing in N. Africa, perh. the nettle tree) E.
5 a kind of mythical fruit, **lotus** (which when eaten causes travellers to wish to remain for ever in the land where it grows, forgetting their home) Od. E.; (identified as the fruit of the N. African lotus tree) Hdt.

λωτο-τρόφος ον *adj*. [τρέφω] (of a meadow) producing clover, **rich in clover** E.

Λωτο-φάγοι ων *m.pl*. [φαγεῖν] **Lotus-eaters** (a mythical people) Od. Pl. X.; (name of the inhabitants of a headland or island off the coast of N. Africa) Hdt. Plb.

λωτροχόος *dial.adj*.: see λουτροχόος

λωφάω, ep. **λωφέω** (AR.) *contr.vb*. | ep.impf. ἐλώφεον |
1 come to a state of rest or cessation; (of a swollen river, wind, storm) **abate, subside, let up** Il. AR. Plu.; (of divine anger, misfortunes, sickness, physical symptoms, ambition) Th. Isoc. Pl. Plu.

2 (of stones, being showered on troops by attackers) **let up, stop** X.
3 rest or cease (fr. an effort or emotion); (of persons and gods) **rest, cease** —W.GEN. *fr. toil, talk, wrongdoing, ambition* S. Pl. AR.; (of the eye of Zeus) **be relieved** —W.GEN. *of passionate desire* (*by its being satisfied*) A.; (of the mind of Zeus) **relent** —W.GEN. *fr. anger* A.; (of Hephaistos) **rest or cease from** —W.PREDIC.PTCPL. *using his bellows* AR.
4 be relieved (of what is unwelcome); **find relief** or **respite** —W.GEN. *fr. pain, troubles* Od. Pl. AR. —W. ἀπό + GEN. *fr. plague and war* Th.
5 (causatv.) **bring relief** (to someone in torment) A.

λωφήιος η ον *Ion.adj*. (of sacrificial rites) bringing relief (fr. divine anger), **of expiation** AR.

λώφησις εως *f*. **reduction of the pressure** (W.GEN. of war, w. ἀπό + GEN. on a territory) Th.

λῴων λῷον, dial. **λωίων** λώιον *compar.adj*. | masc.fem.acc. sg. λῴω (S.), pl. λῴους (S.) | neut.nom.acc.pl. λῴω (Pl.), dial. λώια (Theoc.) |
1 (of a circumstance, course of action) **preferable, better** (than another) Od. Hes. Thgn. Hdt.(oracle) Trag. Call. +; (of a wife) Semon. || NEUT.SB. (without art.) better portion (of sthg.) Od. Hes.; (w.art.) better part (of things to come) Theoc.; (prep.phr.) ἐς τὸ λῷον *for the better* E. || NEUT.PL.SB. (w.art.) better circumstances Theoc.
2 || NEUT.IMPERS. (w. ἐστί, sts. understd.) it is better —W.ADV. *thus* (*i.e. for sthg. to be so*) Il. Hes. —W.INF. or DAT. + INF. (*for someone*) *to do sthg.* Il. Thgn. X. Hellenist.poet. —W.DAT. + PTCPL. *for someone to be doing sthg*. Pl. X. Theoc.*epigr*. Plb. Plu.

—**λῷον**, Ion. **λώιον** *compar.adv*. **better** Od. Hes. Thgn. S. Theoc.

—**λωίτερος** η ον *Ion.compar.adj*. (of circumstances) **preferable, better** Od. Call.; (of a person) **superior** AR.
|| NEUT.IMPERS. (w. ἐστί understd.) it is better —W.INF. *to do sthg*. AR.

—**λῷστος** η ον *superl.adj*. (of a circumstance, course of action) **best** S. E.; (of a person) **most excellent, best** Timocr. S. E.*Cyc*. Pl. Theoc. || MASC.VOC. **dear fellow** Pl. X. Call.*epigr*.
|| NEUT.SB. (sg. and pl., w.art.) what is best Trag.
|| NEUT.IMPERS. (w. ἐστί understd.) it is best —W.INF. *to do sthg*. Thgn.

—**λῷστα** *superl.adv*. (phr.) ὡς λῷστα *as well as possible* Theoc.

Μ μ

μά *pcl.* **1** (in solemn oaths or vehement statements, appealing to gods, divine powers, their attributes, sacred objects, or sim., freq. preceded by ναί, νή or οὐ) **by** (followed by the name, title, etc.) Hom. hHom. Eleg. Lyr. Trag. Ar. Att.orats. + • μὰ τὸν Ποσειδῶ *by Poseidon* E.*Cyc.* • μὰ τοὺς θεοὺς Ὀλυμπίους *by the Olympian gods* Is. • μὰ τὴν πατρῷαν ἑστίαν *by the paternal hearth* S. • ναὶ μὰ τόδε σκῆπτρον *certainly, by the power of this sceptre* Il. • οὐ μὰ Ζῆνα *certainly not, by Zeus* Od. | see also ναί 4 and νή
2 (w. name of the deity suppressed, to avoid religious disrespect or ill omen) • μὰ τόν Ar. Pl. Call. • μὰ τήν Men.
3 (used by writers in rejecting the opinion of others on a certain topic) • οὐ μὰ Δία *certainly not* Plb. Plu.

μᾶ *interj.* [reltd. dial.voc. μᾶτερ] **1** μᾶ Γᾶ *mother Earth* A.
2 (as exclam., expressing indignation, used by a woman, app. as an appeal to the Mother Goddess) *holy Mother!* Theoc.

μάγαδις ιδος *f.* [perh.reltd. μαγάς *bridge of a lyre*] | acc. μάγαδιν | dat. μαγάδῖ X.(dub.) | app., concord of two notes an octave apart, **octave concord** (played on a stringed instrument) Alcm. Anacr.(dub.) Telest.; (on trumpets) X.

μαγγανεία ᾶς *f.* [μαγγανεύω] **magic, trickery, sorcery** Pl.

μαγγανεύματα των *n.pl.* **magic rituals, spells** (of seers or miracle-workers) Pl.; (fig.ref. to techniques of persuasion or seduction) Pl. Plu.

μαγγανεύω *vb.* **1** (of Circe) **practise sorcery** Ar.; (of a false healer) **perform sham rituals** D.
2 (of a female worshipper) **utter incantations** —W.PREP.PHR. *to Demeter and Persephone* Plb.

μαγεία ᾶς *f.* [μαγεύω] **magian doctrine** or **arts** (W.GEN. of Zoroaster) Pl. ‖ PL. **magic arts** NT. Plu.

μαγειρεῖα ων *n.pl.* [μαγειρεύω] **butchers' shops** or **stalls** Thphr.

μαγειρεύω *vb.* [μάγειρος] **work as a hired cook** Thphr.

μαγειρικός ή όν *adj.* **1** (of a man) **skilled as a cook** Pl.; (of the practice or art) **of the cook** Pl. ‖ FEM.SB. **art of cookery** Pl.
2 (of a knife) **of a butcher** Plu.
3 (fig., of little sayings) as though from a cook, **tasty** Ar.
—**μαγειρικῶς** *adv.* **like a good butcher** or **cook** Ar.

μάγειρος ου *m.* **1** slaughterer and preparer of meat for cooking (freq. specially hired, e.g. for a sacrifice); **butcher, meat-cook** Ar. Pl. Call.; (derog., ref. to the man-eating Cyclops) E.*Cyc.*
2 (gener.) preparer of food, **cook** Hdt. Ar. Pl. Aeschin. D. Arist. +

μαγεύματα των *n.pl.* [μαγεύω] **magic arts** (to prolong life) E.

μαγευτικός ή όν *adj.* (of the art) **of magic** Pl.

μαγεύω *vb.* [μάγος] **1 practise magic** E. NT. Plu.
2 (specif., of a Persian) **practise** or **be skilled in magian arts** Plu.

μαγικός ή όν *adj.* (of doctrines) of or relating to the magi, **magian** Plu.

Μαγνησίᾱ ᾱς, Ion. **Μαγνησίη** ης *f.* [Μάγνητες¹] **1** land of the Magnesians, **Magnesia** (region on the E. coast of Thessaly) Simon. Hdt. Aeschin. D. Plb. Plu.
2 [Μάγνητες²] city of the Magnesians, **Magnesia** (in Asia Minor) Hdt. Th. Plu.

Μάγνητες¹ ων *m.pl.* men of Magnesia (in Thessaly), **Magnesians** (as a population or military force) Il. Pi. Hdt. Th. +
—**Μάγνης** ητος *masc.adj.* **1** (of a man) from Magnesia, **Magnesian** S. Plb. Plu.; (of a centaur, ref. to Chiron) Pi.; (of a donkey) Call.
2 ‖ SB. Magnes (eponymous founder of the people) Hes.*fr.*
—**Μάγνησσα** ης *fem.adj.* (of a girl) **Magnesian** Lyr.adesp.; (of the coast) AR.; (of a ship, ref. to the Argo) Theoc.
—**Μαγνῆτις** ιδος *fem.adj.* (of horses) **Magnesian** Pi.; (of a city) AR.
—**Μαγνήσιος** η ον *Ion.adj.* (of the land) **Magnesian** Hdt.
—**Μαγνητικός** ή όν *adj.* (of the land) **Magnesian** A.

Μάγνητες² ων *m.pl.* men of Magnesia (in Asia Minor), **Magnesians** Archil. Thgn. Hdt. Plb. Plu.
—**Μάγνης** ητος *masc.adj.* (of a man) **from Magnesia** Hdt. Plu.
—**Μαγνῆτις** ιδος *fem.adj.* (of a stone, ref. to a magnet) **Magnesian** Pl.(quot. E.)

μάγος ου *m.* **1 magus** (member of a Median or Persian class of priests and diviners) Hdt. X. Arist. Plb. NT. Plu. ‖ PL. **Magians** (as name of a Median tribe) Hdt.
2 (gener., usu.pejor.) **magician, wizard, sorcerer** S. E. Pl. Aeschin. NT.

μαγο-φόνια ων *n.pl.* [φόνος] **commemoration of the massacre of the magi** (a Persian holy day) Hdt.

μαδάω *contr.vb.* app., be moist or drip; (of a person) shed one's hair, **be** or **become bald** Ar.

μᾶζα ης, Megar. **μάδδα** ᾱς (Ar.) *f.* [μάσσω] kneaded cake (made of roasted barley-meal, mixed w. water, milk, wine or oil, worked into a solid paste and eaten unbaked, esp. by the poor; freq. opp. ἄρτος, oven-baked wheaten bread); **barley-cake** Hes. Archil. Hippon. A. Hdt. Lys. +
—**μαζίσκη** ης *f.* [dimin.] **little barley-cake** Ar.

μαζός *Ion.m.*: see μαστός

μαθεῖν (aor.2 inf.), **μαθεῦμαι** (dial.fut.): see μανθάνω

μάθη ης *f.* [μανθάνω] process of acquiring knowledge, **learning** Emp.

μάθημα ατος *n.* **1** that which is learned (through instruction or experience), **knowledge, learning, understanding** Th. Ar. Isoc. Pl. X. + ‖ PL. lessons (given by a schoolteacher) Thphr.; (ref. to understanding gained fr. sufferings) Hdt.
2 (freq.pl.) **branch of knowledge, subject of study** E. Isoc. Pl. X. +; (specif., ref. to the mathematical sciences) Pl. Arist.
3 (gener.) **information** (acquired fr. another) S.

μαθηματικός ή όν *adj.* **1** (of a category of activity) **relating to learning** Pl.
2 (specif.) relating to mathematics; (of the science, practice, diagrams, numbers, or sim.) **of mathematics, mathematical** Arist. Plu. || MASC.SB. **mathematician** Pl. Arist. Plb. Plu. || FEM.SB. **science of mathematics** Arist. || NEUT.PL.SB. **mathematics** Arist.; **mathematical entities** (such as numbers and lines) Arist.
—**μαθηματικῶς** *adv.* **in a mathematical** or **scientific way** Arist.
μαθηματο-πωλικός ή όν *adj.* [πωλέω] (of a skill, a category of activity) **relating to the sale of knowledge** Pl.
μάθησις εως (dial. ιος) *f.* **1** process of acquiring knowledge, **learning, understanding** Alcm. S. E. Th. Pl. X. +
2 capacity to learn or understand, **understanding, comprehension** S. E. Pl.
3 result of learning, **knowledge, understanding** (W.GEN. of sthg.) S. E.*fr.* Pl. X. +
4 pursuit of knowledge, **study** (sts. W.GEN. of a particular subject) Pl. X. Arist. Plb. Plu.
μαθήσομαι (fut.): see μανθάνω
μαθητέος ᾱ ον *vbl.adj.* [μανθάνω] (of things) **to be learned** Pl.
μαθητεύω *vb.* [μαθητής] **make (someone) a pupil; teach** or **make a disciple of** —*persons* NT. || PASS. **become a disciple** —W.DAT. *of Jesus* NT.; **be trained** —W.DAT. *for the Kingdom of Heaven* NT.
μαθητής οῦ *m.* [μανθάνω] **1 learner, student** (sts. of a particular subject) Hdt. Ar. Isoc. Pl. Aeschin.
2 student, pupil, follower (of a particular teacher, philosopher, orator, or sim.) Ar. Att.orats. Pl. X. Arist. +
3 follower, disciple (of Jesus) NT.
4 adherent (of the Christian faith), **follower, believer** NT.
—**μαθήτρια** ᾱς *f.* female adherent, **believer** NT.
μαθητιάω *contr.vb.* [desideratv. μανθάνω] **long to be a student** or **pupil** Ar.
μαθητικός ή όν *adj.* **1** (of persons) **disposed to learning** (W.GEN. about certain things) Pl.
2 (of animals) **capable of learning** Arist.
μαθητός ή όν *adj.* (of things) **learnable** Pl. X. Arist.
μαθήτρια *f.*: see under μαθητής
μάθον (ep.aor.2): see μανθάνω
μάθος εος (ους) *n.* **learning, knowledge** Alc. A.
μαῖα ᾱς *f.* [reltd. μᾶ] **1 mother** (as an affectionate or respectful term, used by a child) E.
2 || VOC. (as an affectionate or respectful address to a woman older than the speaker) **mother** Od. hHom. E. Ar. Call.; (as an address to Earth) A.
3 older woman who assists with children, **nurse** A.*satyr.fr.* Men.
4 older woman who assists at a birth, **midwife** Ar. Pl.
Μαῖα ᾱς, Ion. **Μαίη** ης, Boeot. **Μῆα** ᾱς *f.* **Maia** (daughter of Atlas, mother of Hermes by Zeus) Hes. hHom. Hippon. Lyr. Trag. +
—**Μαιάς** άδος *f.* **Maia** Od. Hes.*fr.* hHom. Iamb. Simon. E.
—**Μαιανδεύς** έος Ion.*m.* **son of Maia** (ref. to Hermes) Hippon.
Μαίανδρος ου *m.* **Maeander** (river in SW. Asia Minor) Il. Hes. Hdt. Th. X. +; (noted for its winding course) Hdt.
—**Μαιάνδριος** ᾱ (Ion. η) ον *adj.* (of a goose, an eel) **of** or **from the Maeander** Semon.
μαιεία ᾱς *f.* [μαιεύομαι] **midwife's skill** Pl.
μαίευμα ατος *n.* **act of midwifery** (fig.ref. to bringing an idea to birth) Pl.

μαιεύομαι *mid.vb.* [μαῖα] **1 act as a midwife** Pl. —W.ACC. *to a woman in labour* Pl.; (of a dung-beetle, in an Aesopic fable) —*to an eagle* Ar.
2 (fig., of Socrates) **act as a midwife** (in bringing ideas to birth) Pl. —W.ACC. *to a man* (*giving birth to an idea*) Pl. || PASS. (of offspring, fig.ref. to ideas) **be brought to birth** —W.PREP.PHR. *by Socrates* Pl.
μαίευσις εως *f.* **midwifery** Pl.
μαιευτικός ή όν *adj.* **1** (of a person) **skilled in midwifery** Pl.
2 (of the art) **of midwifery** Pl. || FEM.SB. **art of midwifery** Pl.
Μαίη Ion.*f.*: see Μαῖα
Μαιήτης Ion.masc.adj.: see under Μαιῶται
Μαιῆτις Ion.fem.adj.: see Μαιῶτις, under Μαιῶται
Μαιμακτηριών ῶνος *m.* **Maimakterion** (fifth month of the Athenian year, in early winter) Is. D. Plu.
μαιμάω *contr.vb.* | (w.diect.) ep.3pl. μαιμώωσι, ptcpl. μαιμώων, fem. μαιμώωσα | ep.aor. μαίμησα | **1 act in an eager** or **excited manner**; (of a warrior, his heart, hands and feet) **be eager** (for action) Il. AR.; (perh. W.GEN. for slaughter) S.
2 (of Harpies) **be eager** —W.GEN. *for food* AR.; (of a lion) —W.INF. *to gorge on flesh* Theoc.
3 (of a person, compared to a bull stung by a gadfly) **rage** AR.; (of a serpent) A. AR.; (of Excess) Hdt.(oracle)
4 (of a spear-point) **speed relentlessly** Il.
Μαίναλον ου *n.* **Mainalon** (mt. in Arcadia, sacred to Pan, assoc.w. Atalanta) E. AR. Theoc.
—**Μαινάλιος** ᾱ (Ion. η) ον *adj.* **of** or **from Mainalon**; (of glens, heights) **Mainalian** Pi. Call.; (of wild animals) Call. AR. || FEM.SB. **region of Mainalon, Mainalia** Th. || MASC.PL.SB. **men of Mainalia, Mainalians** (as a population or military force) Th.
μαινάς άδος *fem.adj.* [μαίνομαι] **1** (of Cassandra) **maddened, raving** E.; (of a woman or goddess) Tim. || SB. **mad** or **raving woman** Il.; (ref. to Cassandra) E.; (pl., ref. to Erinyes) A.
2 || SB. (specif.) **maenad** (ref. to a woman in an ecstatic state of possession by Dionysus) hHom.; (appos.w. βάκχη *Bacchant*) E.; (pl.) S. E. Ar.
3 (of a love-spell) maddening, **inspiring mad passion** Pi.
μαινίς ίδος *f.* a kind of small fish; **sprat** Ar. Plu.
μαινόλης ου, dial. **μαινόλᾱς** ᾱ *masc.adj.* [μαίνομαι] (of a lover's heart) **maddened, frenzied** Sapph.; (of a boar) Lyr.adesp.
—**μαινόλις** ιδος *fem.adj.* | acc. μαινόλιν | (of a woman) **mad, crazy** Archil.; (of an intention) A.
μαίνομαι *mid.vb.* [reltd. μέμονα, μένος] | impf. ἐμαινόμην, ep.3sg. μαίνετο | Ion.fut. μανέομαι | aor. ἐμηνάμην, ep.2sg. ἐμήναο, 3sg. μήνατο | statv.pf. μεμάνημαι || PASS.: aor.2 ἐμάνην, ptcpl. μανείς, inf. μανῆναι || also ACT.: causatv.aor.1 ἔμηνα | statv.pf. μέμηνα, dial. μέμᾱνα (Alcm.) |
1 act with unreasoning rage or **fury**; (of persons, gods) **rage, rave** Hom. Semon. Thgn. E.*Cyc.* Call. —W.COGN.ACC. *w. fits of rage* Ar.
2 act with martial frenzy; (of Ares, a warrior, his hand or spear) **rage** Hom. A. B. E. || STATV.PF.ACT. (of Ajax) Alcm.
3 (mid., also statv.pf.act. and aor.pass., esp. of the followers of Dionysus) **be possessed by divinely inspired frenzy, be frenzied** or **maddened** Hdt. S. E. Pl. Theoc. || PRES.PTCPL.ADJ. (of Dionysus) **frenzied, wild** Il.
4 be or **behave as if out of one's mind** (freq. w.connot. of being stupid); (of persons, their heart) **be mad** or **crazy** Hom. Thgn. Hdt. Trag. Ar. Att.orats. +; (also statv.pf.act.) Trag.; (statv.pf.mid.) Men.; **be madly eager** —W.INF. *to do sthg.*

Bion ‖ AOR.PASS. (of persons, their mind) become or be driven mad Hdt. S. E. Att.orats. +; be driven to an act of madness E.
5 ‖ PRES.PTCPL.ADJ. (of a person) **mad, crazy** Hdt. E. Ar. +; (of a heart or mind) Il. Pi.; (of Quarrel) Emp.; (of Eris) E.*fr.*; (of feet) **frenzied** Mosch. ‖ MASC. and FEM.PTCPL.SB. (sg. and pl.) **madman** or **madwoman** Il. Ar. Pl. + ‖ NEUT.PTCPL.SB. **madness** E.
6 (of a person or mind) **be maddened** or **frenzied** —W.DAT. *w. lamentations, sufferings* A.
7 be mad with love Anacr. S.(statv.pf.act.) —w. ἐπί + DAT. *for a person, the goddess Ambition* E. Theoc.(also statv.pf.mid.); (of horses) **be mad with desire** —w. ἐπί + DAT. *for a plant* Theoc. ‖ AOR.PASS. be maddened (by love) Pl. Theoc.
8 be wildly enthusiastic, be crazy (about sthg.) Ar. —W.DAT. *about sthg.* E.*Cyc.*
9 (of inanimate things) **be violent** or **uncontrolled**; (of a forest fire) **rage** Il.; (of the sea) Semon. ‖ STATV.PF.ACT. (of waves) Mosch.; (of a desire) E.(dub.) ‖ PRES.PTCPL.ADJ. (of a shaking movement) **mad, frenzied** E.; (of sufferings, stings of passion, an onslaught) S. E.; (of a hope) Hdt.(oracle); (quasi-advbl., of unmixed wine seething as it is poured into a mixing-bowl) **in a frenzy** or **ferment** Pl.
10 (causatv., aor.act., of a god, a person using drugs) **drive mad, madden** —*a person, oneself* E. Ar.; (of circumstances) **infuriate** —*a person* X.

μαίομαι, Aeol. **μάομαι** mid.vb. | fut. μάσσομαι | **1 search** Od. hHom. Pi.; (tr.) **search for, seek** —*hiding-places, shelter, flowers, sea-channels* Od. Hes. AR.; (of wolves) —*prey* AR.
2 seek out —*a wife* (W.DAT. *for someone*) Il.
3 seek after —*power* Alc. —*what is possible* Pi.
4 (perh.intr.) **yearn** Sapph.; (tr.) **yearn** or **long for** —*a person* Sapph. —*the voice of a goddess* (*i.e. to hear it*) Pi.
5 be eager (for sthg. to happen) Pi.*fr.* —W.INF. *to see or do sthg.* A. Pi. S. AR. —W.GEN. *for sthg.* AR.

μαιόομαι mid.contr.vb. [reltd. μαιεύομαι] | ep.3pl.aor. μαιώσαντο | (of nymphs) **act as midwives for** —*a goddess* Call.

μαίωσις εως f. **assistance with birth**; **delivery** (W.GEN. of a child) Plu.

Μαιῶται ῶν, Ion. **Μαιῆται** έων m.pl. **Maeotians** or **Maeetians** (a Scythian tribe, N. of the Black Sea) Hdt. X.
—**Μαιήτης** εω *Ion.masc.adj.* (of the R. Tanais) **Maeetian** Hdt.
—**Μαιῶτις**, Ion. **Μαιῆτις**, ιδος *fem.adj.* | acc. Μαιῶτιν, Ion. Μαιῆτιν | (of the λίμνη *lake*) **Maeotian** or **Maeetian** (ref. to the Sea of Azov, NE. of the Black Sea) A. Hdt. Ar. Plb. Plu. ‖ SB. Lake Maeotis E. Plb. Plu.
—**Μαιωτικός** ή όν *adj.* (of a strait, ref. to the Cimmerian Bosporos) **Maeotic** A.
—**Μαιωτιστί** *adv.* **in the style of the Maeotians** (i.e. Scythians) —*ref. to a bow being curved* Theoc.

μάκαρ μάκαιρα *masc.fem.adj.* | nom.masc. also μάκᾱρ (Sol. Hippon.), dial. μάκαρς (Alcm.) | fem.nom. also μάκαρ (E.), Boeot. μάκηρα | masc.acc. μάκαρα, fem. μάκαιραν | masc.gen. μάκαρος (also fem. E.) | fem.dat. μάκαρι (Ar.) ‖ compar. μακάρτερος, superl. μακάρτατος |
1 (of gods) **blessed, happy** Hom. Hes. Hippon. Eleg. Lyr. A. +; (of a haunt of divinities) **favoured** E. ‖ MASC.PL.SB. blessed gods Od. Hes. Thgn. Lyr. A. E. +
2 (of persons) blessed with happiness (in terms of material prosperity, divine favour, victory, marriage, or sim.; freq. nom. or voc. w. ὦ, in acclamations), **blessed, happy, fortunate** Hom. Alcm. Hippon. Thgn. Pi. E. +; (of a region, stream, hearth) Pi. E. ‖ MASC.PL.SB. fortunate men Hes. | see also τρίσμακαρ
3 (of a daimon, ref. to a person worshipped after death) **blessed** E. ‖ MASC.PL.SB. blessed ones (ref. to respected dead persons, in the underworld) Hes.; (enjoying an afterlife on remote islands) Hes. Pi. E. Ar. Pl. +
4 (of fortune) conducive to happiness, **happy** E. Ar.

μακαρίᾱ ᾱς *f.* [μακάριος] **state of blessedness**; (in an imprecation) ἐς μακαρίαν (*go*) *to heaven!* (euphem. for ἐς κόρακας *to hell!*) Ar. Pl. Men.

μακαρίζω *vb.* [μάκαρ] | fut. μακαριῶ | aor. ἐμακάρισα ‖ neut.impers.vbl.adj. μακαριστέον | **1 call** or **consider** (W.ACC. a person, community, the gods) **blessed, happy** or **fortunate** Od. Pi. Hdt. S. E. Democr. + ‖ PASS. be considered fortunate Democr. Pl. X. Arist. Plb.; (of a death) be counted as happy Plu.; (of beauty) be counted as a blessing Aeschin.
2 consider (someone or sthg.) **fortunate** (because of a specific circumstance); **consider** (W.ACC. tortoises) **fortunate** —W.GEN. *because of their shells* Ar.; **congratulate** —*a person* (sts. W.GEN. *on sthg.*) Hdt. Ar. Att.orats. Pl. +; **offer congratulations on** —*a person's strength or capacities* Hdt. Aeschin. —(*iron.*) *a people's naivety* Th. ‖ PASS. (of plague survivors) be congratulated Th.; (of persons, on specific occasions) Plu.
3 ‖ NEUT.PL.PRES.PTCPL.SB. fortunate experiences (of a person) Plu.

μακάριος ᾱ ον (also ος ον Pl.) *adj.* **1** (of persons or communities) blessed with happiness (in terms of material circumstances, status, esteem, marriage, or sim.), **blessed, happy, fortunate** Pi. E. Ar. Tim. Isoc. Pl. +; (of the dead) Pl. X.; (w. sarcasm, of a queen's hand) E.
2 (of persons) blessed with divine favour, **blessed** NT.; (of eyes, a womb) NT.
3 (specif.) **prosperous, well-to-do** Arist. Men.; (of a city) Plb.
4 (nom. or voc. w. ὤ or ὦ, in acclamations, freq. W.GEN.) E. Ar. X. • ὦ μακάριε τῆς τύχης *happy man for your good fortune!* (*i.e. congratulations on it*) Ar. • ὦ μακάριος ... δῆμος *oh what a happy populace!* Ar. • ὦ μακαρία μοι φασμάτων ἥδ᾽ ἡμέρα *oh how lucky this day for me in its revelations!* E.
5 (in voc. address, usu. friendly, occas. condescending; sts. w. proper name) ὦ μακάριε *my dear* (*friend*) Pl. Men. Plu.
6 (of things or circumstances) **conducive to** or **attended by happiness**; (of a fortune, marriage, life, death, sight, or sim.) **blessed, happy** E. Pl. X. Arist. Plb. +; (of songs and shouts) **of blessing** (for a bride or groom) E.; (of pleasure) **blissful** E. ‖ NEUT.SB. state of blessedness, felicity Arist. ‖ NEUT.PL.SB. blessings Pl.
—**μακαρίως** *adv.* | compar. μακαριώτερον, superl. μακαριώτατα | **happily, fortunately** Ar. Pl. X. Arist. Plu.

μακαριότης ητος *f.* **happiness, bliss** Pl. Arist.

μακαρισμός οῦ *m.* [μακαρίζω] **1 declaring happy** or **blessed**, **felicitation, congratulation** (of a person) Pl. Arist. Plu.
2 acclamation (of a dead person) Plu.

μακαριστός ή όν *adj.* **accounted** or **to be accounted blessed** or **happy**; (of persons) **blessed, enviable** Hdt. Ar. Isoc. X. Hyp. Theoc.; (of things or circumstances) Lyr.adesp. Ar. Pl. X. Plb.

μακαρίτης ου, dial. **μακαρίτᾱς** ᾱ *m.*—also **μακαρῖτις** ιδος *f.* [μάκαρ] **1** (ref. to a dead person) **blessed man** A.; **blessed woman** Theoc.
2 ‖ MASC.ADJ. (iron., of the life of a man too poor to pay for his funeral) blessed Ar.

μακεδνός ή όν *adj.* [perh.reltd. μακρός] **1** (of a poplar) **tall** Od.
2 (of a city) **at a height, high** Hes.*fr.*

Μακεδόνες ων *m.pl.* Macedonian men, **Macedonians** (ref. to occupants of a region in the N. of Greece, or its military forces) A. Hdt. Th. +; (appos.w. ἱππῆς *cavalrymen*) Th.
—**Μακεδών** όνος *masc.adj.* —also **Μακηδών** όνος (Hes.*fr.* Call.) *m.* **1** (of a man) **Macedonian** Hdt. D. Plb. NT. Plu. ‖ SB. Macedonian Hdt. Plb.; (ref. to the king, i.e. Philip) D. Call. Plb. Plu.
2 Makedon (son of Zeus, after whom the people were named) Hes.*fr.*
—**Μακεδονίς** ίδος *fem.adj.* (of the land) **Macedonian** Hdt.
—**Μακεδονίᾱ** ᾱς, Ion. **Μακεδονίη** ης *f.* land of the Macedonians, **Macedonia** Hdt. Th. Att.orats. +
—**Μακεδονικός** ή όν *adj.* of or relating to Macedonia or the Macedonians; (of a mountain) **Macedonian** Hdt.; (of an army, cities, power, style of military equipment, or sim.) X. D. Plb. Plu.; (as a Roman cognomen) Plu.
—**Μακεδονικῶς** *adv.* in the Macedonian manner Plu.
Μακεδονίζω *vb.* [Μακεδών] **1 act in the interests of Macedon, side with the Macedonians** Plb. Plu.
2 speak Macedonian Plu.
Μακεδονιστί *adv.* in Macedonian speech Plu.
μάκελλα ης *f.* —also **μακέλη** ης, dial. **μακέλᾱ** ᾱς *f.* [app.reltd. δίκελλα] implement for breaking up ground, **mattock** Il. Hes. Hellenist.poet.; (fig., as an instrument of Zeus, for causing destruction) A. Ar.(mock-trag.)
μᾱκιστήρ ῆρος *dial.masc.adj.* [reltd. μήκιστος] (of a speech) **long** A.
μάκιστος *dial.superl.adj.:* see μήκιστος
μακκοάω *contr.vb.* [Μακκώ *Makko*, a proverbially stupid woman] | pf.ptcpl. μεμακκοᾱκώς | (of a person, a face) **gawp stupidly** Ar.
μᾶκος *dial.n.:* see μῆκος
μάκρα *f.:* see μάκτρᾱ
μακρᾱγορίᾱ ᾱς *dial.f.* [reltd. μακρηγορέω] **long tale** Pi.
μακρ-αίων ωνος *masc.fem.adj.* [μακρός, αἰών¹] **1** (of persons) **long-lived** A.*fr.* S. Tim.; (of the Fates) S.; (of a nymph) AR. ‖ FEM.PL.SB. long-lived ones (ref. to nymphs) S.
2 (of inactivity) **long-lasting** S.; (of a life) **long** Emp. S.
μακράν *fem.acc.sg.adv.:* see under μακρός
μακραυχενό-πλους ουν *contr.adj.* [μακραύχην, πλόος] (of a line of ships) **sailing the long neck of the sea** (i.e. a strait) Tim.
μακρ-αύχην ενος *masc.fem.adj.* [αὐχήν] (fig., of a scaling-ladder) **long-necked** E.
μακρηγορέω *contr.vb.* [ἀγορεύω] (pejor.) **talk at length, make a long speech** A. E. Th.
μακρημερίη ης *Ion.f.* [ἡμέρᾱ] **time when days are long** (i.e. summertime) Hdt.
μακρήν *Ion.fem.acc.sg.adv.:* see under μακρός
μακρό-βιος ον *adj.* [βίος] **with a long life, long-lived** Hdt. Isoc. Arist.
μακροβιότης ητος *f.* **longevity** Arist.
μακρο-βίοτος ον *adj.* (of a span of life) **long-lived, long** A.
μακρό-δρομος ον *adj.* [δρόμος] (of hares) **running a long distance** X.
μακρόθεν *adv.:* see under μακρός
μακροθῡμέω *contr.vb.* [θῡμός] be long-suffering, **be patient** —w. ἐπί + DAT. w. someone NT.
μακροθῡμίᾱ ᾱς *f.* **patience** Plu.
μακροθύμως *adv.* **patiently** NT.
μακρό-κωλος ον *adj.* [κῶλον] (of a periodic sentence) **with long clauses** Arist.
μακρολογέω *contr.vb.* [μακρολόγος] (sts.pejor.) **speak at length** or **be verbose** Att.orats. Pl. X. Plb.

μακρολογίᾱ ᾱς *f.* **1 speaking at length** (opp. brevity of speech) Pl.
2 lengthy discussion (of a topic) Pl.
3 (pejor.) **verbosity, prolixity** Isoc. Pl. Arist.
μακρο-λόγος ον *adj.* giving speeches in a lengthy style, **verbose** Pl.
μακρό-πνους ουν *Att.adj.* [πνοή] (of a life) having breath for a long time, **long-lasting** E.
μακροποιέω *contr.vb.* **elaborate** (W.ACC. hypotheses) **at length** Arist.
μακρο-πόλος ον *adj.* [πέλω] (of oar-beats) **long-sweeping** E.*fr.*
μακρός ᾱ́ (Ion. ή) όν *adj.* [reltd. μῆκος] | compar. μακρότερος, superl. μακρότατος | see also μάσσων, μήκιστος | **1** long in extent; (of objects, weapons, structures, parts of the body, clothing, stretches of land or sea, or sim.) **long** Hom. +; (specif., of ships, usu.ref. to warships) A. Hdt. Th. Ar. Att.orats. +; (of the walls of Athens, see τεῖχος 5) Th. Att.orats. X. + ‖ FEM.SB. long line (drawn in wax by jurors favouring the harsher of two proposed penalties) Ar.
2 extending a long way high or low; (of mountains, waves, trees, columns, or sim.) **tall** Hom. Hes. hHom. Hellenist.poet.; (of persons) Od. hHom.; (of a well) **deep** Il. ‖ NEUT.SB. height Call.
3 extending far in distance; (of roads, journeys, or sim.) **long** Il. Hes. hHom. Thgn. Hdt. Trag. +; (of an athlete's jump) Pi. ‖ NEUT.PL.IMPERS. (w. ἐστί understd.) it is a long way —W.INF. *to travel* Pi.
4 at or to a far distance; (of a place) **far away, remote** A. NT.; (of fetching water) **from a distance** Th.; (of trading enterprises, reinforcements) **going far afield** S.*fr.* X. ‖ COMPAR. (of an achievement) going further (than a specified limit) Pi. ‖ SUPERL. (of a limit) furthest E. ‖ NEUT.PL.SB. distant things Pi.; (compar., fig.) things beyond (W.COMPAR.GEN. one's capabilities) Th.; (superl.) remotest regions Hdt.
5 extensive in amount; (of wealth, a favour) **great** S.; (of property) **large** Arist.; (of property ratings) **high** Arist.; (of interest charges) Plu.
6 long in duration (sts. w.connot. of undesirable length); (of a period of time, esp. a lifetime) **long** Od. Hes. Ibyc. Hdt. Trag. Th. +; (of old age) **advanced** S. ‖ NEUT.IMPERS. (w. ἐστί, sts.understd.) it takes a long time —W.INF. *to do sthg.* Pi. And. Pl. X.
7 (of events and circumstances, such as a war, siege, prosperity, sickness, suffering, or sim.) **long-lasting, long** Pi. Hdt. Trag. Th. Isoc. +; (of death) **lingering** Pl.; (of a wish) **long-held** Od.
8 (of a speech, song, story, or sim., sts. w.connot. of undesirable length) **long, lengthy** Pi. Trag. Th. Ar. Att.orats. + ‖ NEUT.PL.SB. long stories Pi.
9 (of vowels or syllables) long in quantity, **long** Arist.
10 (prep.phrs.) διὰ μακροῦ *at a long distance* Pl.; *after a long time* E. Th.; *for a long time* E.; διὰ μακρῶν (μακροτέρων) *at (greater) length* (*in speech*) Isoc. Pl. D. Arist. Plu.; ἐκ μακροῦ *over a long distance* Plb.; *for a long time* Plu.; ἐπὶ μακρόν *for a long distance* X. AR.; ἐπὶ μακρότερον (μακρότατον) *to a further* (*the furthest*) *extent or degree* Hdt. Th.; ἐς μακρόν *for a long time or distance* Pi.; ἐς τὰ μακρότατα *to the utmost* Th.
—**μακρόν** *neut.sg.adv.* | compar. μακρότερον | **1** over a long distance, **far** Call. Bion ‖ COMPAR. further X. Plu.
2 so as to be heard afar, **loudly** —*ref. to shouting or sim.* Hom. Pl. Hellenist.poet.
3 ‖ COMPAR. at greater length —*ref. to speaking* Th. Lys.

4 ‖ COMPAR. longer (W.GEN. than sixty years) —*ref. to living* Plu.

—**μακρά** *neut.pl.adv.* **1** over a long distance, **far** Pi. Mosch.; with long strides Hom.; **in long bounds** —*ref. to a rock tumbling* Hes.
2 loudly Il. hHom. Thgn.; (in threats) **loud and long** —*ref. to being made to wail* Ar. Men.
3 (in a formula of dismissal) **heartily** —*ref. to bidding farewell* Plu. | see χαίρω 8
4 for a long time —*ref. to delaying* S.

—**μακρᾱ́ν**, Ion. **μακρήν** *fem.acc.sg.adv.* | compar. μακροτέρᾱν, superl. μακροτάτην | **1 at a long distance, far off** (sts. W.GEN. or ἀπό + GEN. fr. somewhere or someone) Trag. Th. Ar. Att.orats. Pl. +
2 to or **over a long distance, far** B. Trag. Ar. Pl. X. + ‖ COMPAR. **further** Th. Pl. X. ‖ SUPERL. **furthest** X.
3 at length (in speech) Trag. Ar.
4 for a long time S. Men.
5 far into the past S.
6 far in the future; (neg.phr.) οὐ μακράν *without delay, soon* E.
7 (prep.phr.) εἰς μακράν *in the future* NT.; (w.neg.) οὐκ εἰς (ἐς) μακράν (μακρήν) *soon* A. Hdt. Ar. X. +

—**μακρῷ** *neut.dat.sg.adv.* (w.compar. or superl.adj. or adv., also w. wds. implying comparison) **by far** Hdt. Trag. Ar. Pl.

—**μακρῶς** *adv.* **1 at length** (in speech or writing) Arist. Plb. Plu.
2 taking a long time, **slowly** Plb.

—**μακροτέρως** *compar.adv.* **1 at greater length** Arist.
2 to a greater extent or **degree** Pl.

—**μακροτέρω** *compar.adv.* **further away** (in location) E.*Cyc.*(cj.)

—**μακρόθεν** *adv.* **1 from** or **at a distance** Plb. NT.; (also) ἀπὸ μακρόθεν NT.
2 at some distance prior in time, **long before** Plb.

μάκρος ους *n.* **length** (of a wall) Ar.

μακρό-χειρ χειρος *masc.adj.* [μακρός, χείρ] **long-armed** (as a nickname) Plu.

μάκτρᾱ ᾱς *f.* [μάσσω] **1 kneading-trough** Ar. X.
2 bath-tub Plb. [perhaps to be written μάκρᾱ]

μᾱκύ́νω *dial.vb.*: see μηκύνω

μακών (aor.2 ptcpl.): see μηκάομαι

μάκων *dial.f.*, **μᾱκωνίᾱς** *dial.masc.adj.*: see μήκων

μάλα *adv.* **1** (intensv., w.vbs.) **very much, extremely, greatly** Hom. + • μάλα λίσσοντο *they strongly pleaded* Il. • μάλα μαίνομαι *I am quite mad* Thgn.
2 (w.adjs. and advs.) Hom. + • μάλα καρτερός *very powerful* Hom. • μάλ' ὦκα *very quickly* Hom. hHom. • μάλ' αὖθις *yet again* Trag. Ar.
3 (strengthening an assertion) **indeed, certainly** Hom. +
• σοὶ δὲ μάλ' ἕψομ' ἐγώ *I shall certainly follow you* Il.
4 (in affirmative answers, freq. μάλα γε, καὶ μάλα) **certainly, yes indeed** Pl. X.

—**μᾶλλον**, Ion. **μάλιον** (Tyrt. Call.) *compar.adv.* **1** (w.vbs., adjs. or advs.) to a greater extent or higher degree, **more, rather** (oft. w. ἤ *than* or compar.gen.) Hom. +; (pleon., w.compar.adj. or adv.) Il. + • μᾶλλον εὐτυχέστερος *more fortunate* E.
2 (correcting a statement) μᾶλλον δέ *or rather* Ar. + • ἄκουε δή, μᾶλλον δὲ ἀποκρίνου *listen, or rather reply* Pl.

—**μάλιστα** *superl.adv.* **1 most, most of all, above all, especially** Hom. +; (pleon., w.superl.adj. or adv.) Hdt. +
2 (w.art.) τὰ μάλιστα, (also) εἰς (ἐς) τὰ μάλιστα *to the highest degree* A.(dub.) Hdt. +; ἐν τοῖς μάλιστα *especially* Th. Pl. Plb. Plu.

3 (in affirmative answers) most certainly, **yes indeed** S. +
4 (in specifying number, time, or sim.) **approximately, about** Hdt. +

μάλαγμα ατος *n.* [μαλάσσω] **padding** (to soften a blow) Pl.(dub.)

μαλακ-αύγητος ον *adj.* [μαλακός, αὐγή] (of sleep) perh. **gentle on the eyes** Arist.*lyr.*

μαλακίᾱ ᾱς, Ion. **μαλακίη** ης *f.* **1 softness** (of temperament or manner) Pl.; (pejor., of lifestyle) X. Arist. Plu.; (specif.) **effeminacy, unmanliness** Arist. Plb. Plu.
2 feebleness, faint-heartedness Hdt. Th. Isoc. Pl. X. D. +
3 lack of vigour or effort, **torpor, inertness** Lys. X.
4 infirmity, sickness NT.

μαλακίζομαι *mid.vb.* | aor. ἐμαλακισάμην ‖ aor.pass. ἐμαλακίσθην ‖ neut.impers.vbl.adj. μαλακιστέον | **1** be weak in purpose, **be faint-hearted** Th. X. Men. ‖ AOR.PASS. become weak or faint-hearted Th. | see also μαλκίω 2
2 be lenient or **indulgent** (towards an accused person) Th.
‖ AOR.PASS. become lenient D.
3 ‖ AOR.PASS. (of a disputant) become easy-going, give up the effort (of pursuing an argument) Pl.
4 be weak in health, **be unwell** Thphr. ‖ AOR.PASS. become unwell Thphr.

μαλακίων ωνος *m.* (pejor., in an address to a faint-hearted lover) **softie** Ar.

μαλακο-γνώμων ονος *masc.adj.* (of Zeus) soft in judgement, **lenient, indulgent** A.

μαλακ-όμματος ον *adj.* [ὄμμα] (of sleep) **gentle on the eyes** Lyr.adesp.

μαλακο-πτυχής ές *adj.* [πτύσσω] (of loaves) **softly-folded** Philox.Leuc.

μαλακός ή (dial. ᾱ́) όν *adj.* [reltd. μαλθακός] **1** (gener., of things) having the quality of softness (opp. hardness), **soft** Pl. X. + ‖ NEUT.SB. **softness** (as an abstract quality) Pl.
2 soft to the touch or yielding to pressure; (of meadows, grass, flowers) **soft** (esp. to lie or walk on) Hom. Hes. hHom. Sapph.(or Alc.) Theoc.; (of beds and bedding) Hom. hHom. Thgn. Pl. X. +; (of garments) Hom. Hes. Pi. Ar. Aeschin. +; (of wool, hair, fleeces) Od. X. AR. Theoc. Plu.; (of sheep) **soft-fleeced** D. Plb.
3 (of parts of a person's or horse's body) lacking firmness, **soft** Pl. X.; (of the Horai, W.ACC. on their feet) Theoc.
‖ COMPAR. (w. sarcasm, of a dead warrior) softer (W.INF. to handle, i.e. than when alive) Il.
4 (of soil) **soft** Il. Pl. X.; (of foam) hHom.
5 (of skin or flesh) **soft, delicate** S. E. Pl.
6 having the quality of mildness or gentleness; (of deities) **mild, gentle** Pl. Theoc.; (of hands) Pi.; (of sleep, its fetters) Hom. Mosch.; (of a death) Od.; (of love, desires) Pl. Theoc.
‖ NEUT.SB. gentle treatment (fr. a person) X.; (pl.) gentle or kindly thoughts Pi.
7 (of weather, breezes) **mild, calm** Pi.*fr.* X. Plu.; (of a night) Plu.
8 (of a voice, words, blandishments, incantations) **soft, gentle, soothing** Hom. Hes. A. Pi. Parm. Ar. Plu.
9 (of a kiss, a look) **soft, tender** Ar. X.; (of intimacy) hHom.
10 (of streams) **gentle** (in flow) hHom.; (of terrain, in slope) X. Plu.
11 (pejor., of a region) **soft, enervating** Hdt.
12 (of actions, behaviour, sentiments, punishment, sickness, a form of government) **mild** Th. Pl. Arist. Plu.; (of perspiration) **light, faint** Plu.
13 ‖ NEUT.SB. luxury, self-indulgence Ar.; (pl.) comforts, luxuries X.

μαλακότης

14 (colloq., of goods) **light, easy to handle, movable** or **portable** Men.
15 lacking in robustness or vigour; (of a person's physique) **weak** Isoc. || NEUT.PL.COMPAR.SB. weaker capabilities Sol.
16 (of persons, their disposition) **soft, sensitive, impressionable** Pl. Arist.
17 (pejor.) **soft, weak, effete** Hdt. Isoc. Pl. X. Arist. +; (specif.) **effeminate, unmanly** Arist.
18 (of persons, their conduct) lacking in firmness of purpose, **weak, feeble, faint-hearted** Hdt. Th. Ar. Pl. X. +
19 (of persons) softened, **mollified** (by persuasion) D.
20 (of a speech) **lacking in vigour** Isoc.; (of an argument) **weak** Arist.
21 (of a musical mode) **soft, languid** Pl.
—**μαλακῶς** adv. | compar. μαλακώτερον, also μαλακωτέρως (Th. Arist.) | superl. μαλακώτατα | **1 softly, comfortably** —ref. to sitting Od. Ar. X. Theoc.; **luxuriously** —ref. to entertaining guests, bathing Thphr. Men.
2 softly, gently Pl. X. Arist. Plu.; **tenderly** X.
3 with lack of vigour, half-heartedly Th. Plu.
4 in a relaxed state Arist.; **in a lax manner, leniently** Plu.
5 loosely —ref. to reasoning Arist.
6 (w. ἔχειν) **be feeble or faint-hearted** Plu.; **be ill or infirm** Plu.
μαλακότης ητος f. **1 softness** (as an abstr. quality) Pl. Arist.; (of flesh, wool) Pl.
2 (pejor.) **weakness, feebleness** (of a person) Plu.
μαλακο-φλοΐς ίδος fem.adj. [φλοιός] (of almonds) **soft-shelled** Philox.Leuc.
μαλακό-χειρ χειρος masc.fem.adj. [χείρ] (of the application of medicines) **gentle-handed** Pi.
μαλακτήρ ῆρος m. [μαλάσσω] **moulder** or **fashioner** (W.GEN. of gold and ivory) Plu.
μαλακύνομαι mid.pass.vb. [μαλακός] (of troops) **be weak** or **faint-hearted** X.
μαλάσσω, Att. **μαλάττω** vb. | fut. μαλάξω | aor. ἐμάλαξα || aor.pass. ἐμαλάχθην | **1 soften, temper** —one's high-spirited nature (compared to iron) Pl. —hardness of character Plb. || PASS. (of iron) be softened —W.PREP.PHR. in fire Plu.; (of tyranny, compared to iron) Plu.
2 (of moisture) **soften** —vapours Plu.
3 soften up, weaken —a person (by assaulting him) Ar. || PASS. (of a pancratiast) be weakened or crushed Pi.; (of a person) be softened —W.DAT. or PREP.PHR. by love, pleasures Plu.
4 (of the Dioscuri) **calm** —the sea and winds Pi.fr.
5 (of time) **soothe** —a person, his distress E. || PASS. be relieved —W.GEN. of a sickness S.
6 soften, calm —one's own or another's anger E.; **mollify, appease** —a person, a city Plu. || PASS. be softened, relent (in one's anger) S. Plu.; be weakened (in one's resolution) Plu.; (of a juror) be made soft-hearted Ar.
μαλάχη ης f. **a kind of plant** (w. an edible root), **mallow** Mosch.; (as food for the poor) Hes. Ar.
μαλερός ά (Ion. ή) όν adj. **1** (of fire) app. **fierce** or **ravening** Il. Hes. Hdt.(oracle) AR.; (of the jaws of fire) A.; (of a torch) **blazing** AR.; (of buildings, W.DAT. w. fire) E.(dub.)
2 (fig., of Ares) **blazing, fiery** S.; (of songs, w. which a poet sets alight a city) Pi.; (of a longing) A.
3 (of lions) perh. **ravenous** A.; (of hands) **greedy** Philox.Leuc.; (of toils) **consuming** Arist.lyr.
μάλευρον ου n. [perh.reltd. ἄλευρα] **wheat-flour** Call. Theoc.
μάλη ης f. [app.reltd. μασχάλη] **1 armpit**; (only in phr.) ὑπὸ μάλης **under the armpit** (as a place for the concealment of a dagger) Pl. X. Plu.; (of an erect penis, envisaged as a spear)

Ar.; (w. wider application, ref. to concealment under the arm and in the hand) **about one's person** Pl.
2 (fig., ref. to making a legal challenge) **in an underhand manner, furtively** (opp. before witnesses in the agora) D.
μάλθα ης f. [perh.reltd. μαλθακός] **a kind of malleable wax; wax** (used for caulking ships) Hippon.; (for writing-tablets) D.; (fig., as the material fr. which the bodies of cowards are made) S.Ichn.
μαλθακίᾱ ᾱς f. [μαλθακός] (pejor.) **feebleness** (of a person) Pl.
μαλθακίζομαι mid.pass.vb. | aor.pass. ἐμαλθακίσθην || neut.impers.vbl.adj. μαλθακιστέον, also pl. μαλθακιστέα |
1 be weak in purpose, be faint-hearted Ar. Pl. || AOR.PASS. become faint-hearted Pl.
2 be soft or **lenient** (in attitude) A. || PASS. be softened —W.DAT. by threats A.; (aor.) become lenient E.
μαλθακός ή (dial. ᾱ) όν, Aeol. **μόλθακος** ᾱ ον, Lacon. **μαλσακός** ᾱ όν adj. [reltd. μαλακός] **1 soft to the touch** or **yielding to pressure;** (of a bed, cushion, cloak) **soft** Archil. Sapph. Alc. Ar.; (of flowery ground) hHom.
2 (of timber) **soft, pliable** Plu.; (fig., of a soul) **pliant, malleable** Pl.
3 (of terrain) **soft** (i.e. not stony) A.fr. E. Plu. || NEUT.SB. soft surface Pl.
4 (of flesh) **soft, delicate** E.; (of youthfulness) Pi.fr.
5 having the quality of gentleness or mildness; (of a voice, words, utterances) **soft, gentle, mild, soothing** Alcm. Thgn. Pi. S. E.; (of song and its effects; of dew, fig.ref. to song) Pi.; (of bird-song) Ar.; (of sleep) Hes.fr. Thgn.; (of a glance fr. the eyes) A. || NEUT.SB. gentleness, mildness Pi.
6 (of birth-pains) lacking severity, **mild** Pl.
7 (of athletes' limbs, after exertion) **soothed, relieved** (by a hot bath) Pi.
8 || NEUT.SB. ease, comfort (W.GEN. in life) E.; (pl.) comforts, luxuries Plu. || COMPAR. greater comfort Ar.
9 (of a disposition, behaviour, interaction) **kindly** Pi. E.(dub.)
10 (fig., of a person overpowered by Eros) **soft** (instead of hard as iron) Theoc.
11 (of a person) **softened, submissive** A.
12 (of a lawmaker) **soft-hearted, lenient** Pl.
13 (pejor., of persons, their disposition) **soft, weak, effete** Pl.; **delicate** or **effeminate** Theoc.
14 (of persons, their conduct) **feeble, faint-hearted** Il. A. Ar. Pl.
15 (of hesitation) **feeble, faltering** Alc.
—**μαλθακῶς** adv. | compar. μαλθακωτέρως (Pl.) | **1 on a soft bed, comfortably** —ref. to lying down Ar.
2 gently, mildly —ref. to ruling, speaking A. S. Pl.
3 tenderly —ref. to kissing Ar.
μαλθακό-φωνος ον adj. [φωνή] (of songs) **gentle-voiced** Pi.
μαλθάσσω vb. **1 soften, mollify** —the heart (of an enemy) A. —an enemy (W.DAT. w. one's words) E. —one's attitude E.fr. || PASS. be softened —W.DAT. by sleep A. —by entreaties A.
2 soothe —a person (w. a false report) S.
μᾱλίᾱ Aeol.f.: see μηλέᾱ
Μᾱλιεῖς m.pl., **Μᾱλιεύς** masc.adj.: see under Μηλίς
μάλινος ᾱ ον dial.adj. [μῆλον²] (of branches) **of apple trees** Sapph.
μᾶλλον Ion.compar.adv., **μάλιστα** superl.adv.: see under μάλα
μᾱλίς dial.f.: see μηλίς
μαλκίω vb. [reltd. μάλκη numbness from cold] **1** (of hounds) **be numb with cold** —W.ACC. in their noses X. | see also μυλιάω

2 (fig., of a populace) **freeze, be inert** (in the face of an enemy) D.(dub., v.l. μαλακίζομαι)

μᾶλλον *compar.adv.*: see under μάλα

μαλλός οῦ *m.* **tuft of wool** (used to garland a suppliant's branch, a cup used in a religious ceremony) A. S.; (to fringe a Bacchant's fawnskin) E.; (as a swab for applying an ointment) S. ‖ PL. **wool** (of the fleeces of live sheep) Hes.

μαλο-γενής ές *dial.adj.* [μῆλα; γένος, γίγνομαι] (of a flock) **sheep-born** Philox.Leuc. [perh. to be written μηλο-]

μαλο-δροπῆες ων *Aeol.m.pl.* [μῆλον², δρέπω] **apple-pickers** Sapph.

μᾶλον *dial.n.*: see μῆλον²

μαλο-πάραυος ον *Aeol.adj.* [παρειά] perh., with cheeks like apples, **rosy-cheeked** Alc.(cj.) Theoc. [or perh. 1st el. μᾱλός, *white-cheeked*]

μᾱλός ή όν *adj.* (of a goat) **white** Theoc.*epigr.*

μάλουρις ιος *dial.f.* [οὐρά̄] **white-tailed creature** (ref. to a cat) Call.

μᾱλοφορέω *dial.contr.vb.* [μηλοφόρος] **carry apples** Theoc.*epigr.*

μαλσακός *Lacon.adj.*: see μαλθακός

μαμμᾶ *interj.* [reltd. μάμμη] ‖ acc. (as though declinable *f.*) μαμμᾶν ‖ **mamma** (a baby's cry for food) Ar.

μαμμά-κυθος ου *m.* [μάμμη, perh. κεύθω] (derog.) perh., one who hides in his mother's skirts, **infantile person, mummy's boy** Ar.

μάμμη ης *f.* **1 mamma, mummy** (as a family term for mother) Thphr. Men.
2 grandmother Plu.

μαμμία ᾱς *f.* **mummy** (term used by a baby) Ar.

μαμωνᾶς ᾶ *m.* [Semit.loanwd.] **mammon, wealth** NT.

μᾶν *dial.pcl.*: see μήν¹

μανδαλωτός ή όν *adj.* [μανδαλός *bolt or pin* (*for fastening a door*)] (of a song) **with a bolt** (fig.ref. to the tongue) inserted, **like a French kiss** (i.e. lascivious, saucy) Ar.

μάνδρᾱ ᾱς *f.* **pen, enclosure** (for horses or farm animals) S.*fr.* Call. Theoc.

μανδραγόρᾱς ου *m.* [perh.loanwd.] **mandrake** (a plant used to make a sleep-inducing drug) Pl. X. D.

μανθάνω *vb.* ‖ fut. μαθήσομαι, dial. μαθεῦμαι (Theoc., dub.) ‖ aor.2 ἔμαθον, ep. μάθον, also ἔμμαθον, inf. μαθεῖν ‖ pf. μεμάθηκα ‖ *neut.impers.vbl.adj.* μαθητέον ‖
1 acquire knowledge (by inquiry, observation, experience, example, or sim.); **learn, get to know, discover, find out** —*facts, information* Hdt. Trag. +—W.INDIR.Q. or COMPL.CL. *what* (or *that sthg.*) *is the case* Pi. Hdt. Trag. +—W.NOM. or ACC. + PTCPL. *that one is so and so, or is doing such and such, that sthg. is the case* Hdt. Trag. Th. +; (w.ptcpl.understd.) Anacr.; (intr.) **learn** (sthg.) Thgn. Pi. Hdt. Trag. +
2 learn (a way of behaviour, by experience or instruction); **learn** —*bad ways* Od. Eleg. —*foreign customs* Hdt. —W.INF. *to do* (or *how to do*) *sthg.* Il. Pi. Emp. Hdt. Trag. +; (intr.) Hdt. +
3 learn by study, learn —*a particular subject or skill* A.*satyr.fr.* Hdt. Ar. Isoc. Pl. +; (intr.) Hdt. +
4 learn by heart, memorise —*poems* X. Thphr.
5 be aware of the true nature or meaning of, understand —*sthg.* Pi. Hdt. Trag. +; (intr.) Hdt. Trag. +
6 (colloq., in qs., w. a note of indignation) τί μαθών ...; *on the basis of what knowledge* (i.e. *why ever*)? Ar. D. Men.; (in indir.cl.) ὅτι μαθών *just because* Pl. • τί ἄξιός εἰμι παθεῖν ἢ ἀποτεῖσαι, ὅτι μαθὼν ἐν τῷ βίῳ οὐχ ἡσυχίαν ἦγον; *What do I deserve to suffer or pay, just because I did not lead a quiet life?* Pl.

μανίᾱ ᾱς, Ion. **μανίη** ης *f.* [μαίνομαι] **1** (sg. and pl.) state or fit of irrational or mentally impaired behaviour, **madness, insanity, craziness** Eleg. Pi. B. Hdt. Trag. Ar. +; (hyperbol., ref. to stupid or objectionable actions or beliefs) Ar. Att.orats.; (personif.) **Madness** Thgn.
2 altered state of mind (caused by the gods), **madness, frenzy** Pi.*fr.* Trag. Ar.; **inspiration** (fr. the gods, esp. the Muses) Pl.
3 madness (assoc.w. love) Anacr. Ibyc. S.*fr.* Pl. Theoc.; **frenzy, thrill** (assoc.w. philosophy) Pl.
4 madness, fury (W.GEN. of a wind) Scol.

μανιάκης ου *m.* [loanwd.] a kind of neckband (sts. made of gold, usu. twisted, typically worn by Persians and Gauls), **necklet, torque** Plb. Plu.

μανιάς άδος *fem.adj.* [μανίᾱ] **1** (of frenzy) **mad, deranged** S.*fr.* E.
2 (of sickness) causing madness, **maddening, deranging** S. E.

μανικός ή όν *adj.* **1** (of persons, their characters) disposed to irrational or mentally impaired behaviour, **mad, insane, crazy** Pl. Arist. Plu.
2 (of behaviour, activities, statements, circumstances) characteristic of one who is mad or irrational, **mad, crazy, manic** Ar. Isoc. Pl. X. + ‖ NEUT.SB. frenzied nature (of barbarian tribes) Plu.
3 ‖ FEM.SB. manic art (ref. to prophecy, w. supposed link to μαντική *prophetic art*) Pl.
4 (wkr.sens., of persons) **passionate, over-emotional** Arist.
5 (of drugs) **inducing madness** Plu.

—**μανικῶς** *adv.* in the manner or condition of one who is mad or irrational, **madly, crazily** Isoc. Pl. X. Plu. ‖ see also νεανικῶς 2

μᾶνις *dial.f.*, **μᾱνίω** *dial.vb.*: see μῆνις, μηνίω

μανιώδης ες *adj.* [μανίᾱ] **1** characterised by madness or irrationality; (of a person) **mad, insane** Plb.; (of untrained hounds) X.; (of human nature, in a crisis) Plu.
2 (of Bacchus) **manic, frenzied** Theoc. ‖ NEUT.SB. manic state (of Bacchus or his devotees) E.
3 (of a promise) characteristic of one who is mad, **mad, crazy** Th.; (of behaviour) Plu.

μάννα *indecl.n.* unidentified foodstuff (eaten by the Israelites in the desert), **manna** NT.

μαννο-φόρος ον *adj.* [app. reltd. μανιάκης; φέρω] (of fawns) **wearing collars** Theoc. [or perh. *with neck-markings*]

μᾰνός ή όν *adj.* ‖ compar. μᾰνότερος, superl. μᾰνότατος ‖
1 thin in texture; (of a layer of bone) **thin** Pl.; (of flesh, the body) **porous** Pl. Plu.; (of chaff) **rare** (opp. dense) Pl. ‖ NEUT.SB. thin texture (opp. density, as a quality of matter) Arist.
2 thinly dispersed; (of a hare's scent) **diffuse** X.; (of spoken words) **rare, infrequent** X.; (of pleasures and pains) Pl.

—**μᾰνότερον** *compar.adv.* **at less frequent intervals** —*ref. to troops wheeling round* X.

μᾰνότης ητος *f.* **1 loose texture** (of the spleen) Pl.; (of flesh) Arist.; **porousness** (of bones) Pl.
2 loose spacing (of notes in a melody) Pl.

μαντείᾱ ᾱς, ep. **μαντείη**, Ion. **μαντηίη**, ης *f.* [μαντεύομαι]
1 prophetic utterance (spoken or inspired by a god), **prophecy, oracle** hHom. Tyrt. Hdt. S. E. Att.orats. +; (fig.) **oracular language** (of an interlocutor, ref. to its puzzling nature) Pl.
2 art or power of prophetic utterance, **prophetic skill** hHom.

μαντεῖον

3 skill or activity of a seer or diviner, **divination** S. E. Ar. Pl. Aeschin.; **mode of divination** Hdt.
4 (gener.) **prediction, conjecture** Pl.

μαντεῖον, Ion. **μαντήιον**, ου *n*. [μαντεῖος] **1** prophetic utterance (of a god, delivered through an oracle or seer), **prophecy, oracle** Od. Hes.*fr*. Hdt. S. E. Th. +
2 seat of an oracular god, **oracle** Hdt. Trag. Th. Ar. Isoc. Pl. Plu.

μαντεῖος ᾱ ον (also ος ον E.), Ion. **μαντήιος** η ον *adj*. [μάντις] **1** (of Apollo) endowed with the gift of prophecy, **prophetic** E. Ar. AR.
2 of or relating to prophecy; (of an altar, a shrine) **prophetic** Pi. E.; (of ash fr. burnt offerings) S.
3 (of fillets) of a prophetic priestess, **priestly** A.

μάντευμα ατος *n*. [μαντεύομαι] prophetic utterance (of a god, delivered through an oracle or seer), **prophecy, oracle** Pi. Trag. Ar. Plu.

μαντεύομαι *mid.vb*. —also **μαντεύω** (Plu.) *act.vb*. [μάντις] | aor. ἐμαντευσάμην, dial. μαντευσάμην ‖ pf.mid.pass. μεμάντευμαι ‖ aor.pass. ἐμαντεύθην ‖ neut.impers.vbl.adj. μαντευτέον | **1** utter divinely inspired predictions or interpret signs and omens, **prophesy** or **practise divination** (sts. W.DAT. for someone) Hom. Hdt. Trag. Pl. Arist. NT. Plu.(also act.); prophesy in regard to, **interpret** —W.INTERN.ACC. *sthg*. Od. A.; (tr.) **prophesy, foretell** —*sthg*. Il.
2 (of a god) **deliver an oracular response, prophesy** A. E. Call. —W.INTERN.ACC. *about sthg*. E.; (tr.) **declare, pronounce** —*sthg*. (*to be the case*) D. —W.ACC. + INF. *someone to be such and such* Hdt.(oracle) ‖ PASS. (of a command) be delivered by an oracle E. ‖ IMPERS.AOR.PASS. an oracular command was given —W.DAT. + INF. *to someone to do sthg*. Hdt. ‖ NEUT.PL.PF.PASS.PTCPL.SB. oracular commands Hdt.
3 (fig., of a Muse) **give an oracle** (to a poet, envisaged as her prophet) Pi.*fr*.
4 consult an oracle (sts. W.PREP.PHR. about sthg.) Pi. Hdt. E. Th.(treaty) Ar. Plu. —W.INTERN.ACC. *about sthg*. E. Pl. —W.COGN.ACC. *for a prophecy* Aeschin.
5 seek a sign or **omen** Hdt.; **consult a seer** or **diviner** Ar. Pl. X.
6 (gener.) **make a prediction** Od.; (of a rumour) —W.PREP.PHR. *about sthg*. Aeschin.; (tr.) **predict, foretell** —*sthg*. Il. Pl. Men. —W.ACC. + FUT.INF. *that sthg. will be the case* Plu.
7 (wkr.sens.) **divine, intuit, surmise** (sts. W.ADV. truly or sim.) Pl. Theoc. —*sthg*. Pl. Arist. —W.INDIR.Q., COMPL.CL. or ACC. + INF. *what* (or *that sthg.*) *is the case* Emp. Pl. Arist. —W.GEN. and ὡς + PTCPL. *that someone is dead* A.; app. **imagine** —*sthg*. (*in a dream*) Theoc.(dub.)

μαντευτός ή όν *adj*. (of a person, god, sacrifices) **named by an oracle** E. X. Arist.

μαντηίη Ion.*f*., **μαντήιον** Ion.n., **μαντήιος** Ion.*adj*.: see μαντεία, μαντεῖον, μαντεῖος

μαντικός ή όν *adj*. [μάντις] **1** of or relating to a prophet or seer; (of the race or breed) **of seers** S. E.(dub.); (of the life) **of a seer** Pl.; (of a person's fame) **as a seer** A.
2 (in Roman ctxt., of the staff) **of an augur** Plu.
3 (of skill, inspiration) of or relating to prophecy, **prophetic** Trag. Pl. Arist. Plu.; (of an inner sanctum, the seat of an oracular priestess) A.; (of utterances) S. Pl. Plu.; (of birds' wings) Ar.
4 ‖ FEM.SB. art or practice of prophecy or divination Hdt. Trag. Th. Isoc. Pl. X. +; power of insight (of Socrates' divine guiding spirit) Pl.
5 (of persons, their nature or soul; of swans, as sacred to Apollo) **skilled in prophecy** or **divination** Pl. Plu.; (of a person) **occupied in divination** Plu. ‖ MASC.FEM.SB. seer or diviner Plu.

—**μαντικῶς** *adv*. **1 in the manner of a seer** Ar.
2 with prescience or insight, **prophetically** Pl.

μαντιπολέω *contr.vb*. [μαντιπόλος] (fig., of a song) act as a prophet, **be prophetic** (of future events) A.

μαντι-πόλος ου *f*. [πέλω] woman who is occupied in prophecy, **prophetess** (appos.w. Βάκχη *frantic woman*, ref. to Cassandra) E.

μάντις εως (Ion. ιος, ep. ηος) *m.f*. **1** one who foretells the future (either as mouthpiece of a god or as interpreter of signs and omens); **oracular priest** or **priestess, prophet, seer, diviner** Hom. +; (ref. to Apollo, as prophetic god) A. E.; (ref. to Dionysus) E.
2 (in Roman ctxt.) **augur** Plu.
3 (gener. or fig., ref. to a person) **prophet, predictor, forecaster** (sts. W.GEN. of future events) Trag.; (ref. to a person's heart) Mosch.; (ref. to a person's folly, a terrifying dream) A.; (ref. to good judgement) E.(dub.)
4 a kind of insect, **praying mantis** Theoc.

μαντοσύνη ης, dial. **μαντοσύνᾱ** ᾱς *f*. (sg. and pl.) **art** or **practice of prophecy** or **divination** Hom. Hes.*fr*. Pi. Emp. AR.

μαντόσυνος η ον (also ος ον E.), Boeot. **μαντόσουνος** ᾱ ον *adj*. (of a command, a tripod) of or relating to a prophetic god, **prophetic, oracular** E. Corinn.; (of inspiration, forced upon a priestess) E.

μᾱνύω *dial.vb*.: see μηνύω

μάομαι Aeol.*mid.vb*.: see μαίομαι

μαπέειν *ep.aor.2 inf*. [app.reltd. μάρπτω] | 3pl.redupl.opt. μεμάποιεν | (of Gorgons, Fates, hunting dogs) **seize, snatch, catch** —*a victim* Hes.

μάραγνα ης *f*. [Iran.loanwd.] **whip, lash** (used for punishment) A. E.

μάραθον ου *n*. **fennel** (used in garlands) D.

Μαραθών ῶνος *m*. (*also f*. Pi.) **Marathon** (deme on the E. coast of Attica, site of a victory over the Persians in 490 BC) Od. A. Pi. Hdt. +

—**Μαραθῶνάδε** *adv*. **to Marathon** And. D. Arist.(quot.poet.)

—**Μαραθώνιος** ᾱ ον *adj*. **1** (of a citizen) of the deme of Marathon, **Marathonian** Plu.
2 (of a bull captured by Theseus, the battle) **of Marathon, Marathonian** Plu.

Μαραθωνο-μάχαι ῶν *m.pl*. [μάχομαι] **men who fought at Marathon** Ar.

μαραίνω *vb*. | aor. ἐμάρᾱνα ‖ PASS.: aor. ἐμαράνθην | pf. μεμάραμ(μ)αι or μεμάρασμαι (Plu.) | **1 extinguish, put out** —*embers* hHom.; (fig.) —*one's sight* (*by blinding*) S. ‖ PASS. (of a fire, flame, pyre) die down or be extinguished Il. Plu.; (fig., of military strength, compared to a flame) Plu.
2 ‖ PASS. (of a wind) die down Plu.
3 ‖ PASS. (of rivers) dry up Hdt.
4 cause (sthg.) to lose freshness; (of time) **wither** —*a rose* Theoc. ‖ PASS. (of flowers or plants) wither, fade Mosch. Bion Plu.; (fig., of achievements, envisaged as flowers) Plu.
5 (gener.) cause (someone or sthg.) to waste away or weaken; (of Erinyes, sickness) **waste away, weaken, wither** —*a person* A.; (of a commander) —*an enemy's strength* Plu.; (of time) —*strength, perfection* Plu. —*all things* S.; (of injustice and wickedness) —*the soul* Pl.; (of sickness) —*beauty* Isoc.; (of squalor) —*a body* S.
6 ‖ PASS. (of persons, their bodies) waste away Th. Pl. Plu. —W.DAT. *w. sickness* E.; (of the thigh of a dying person)

weaken Bion; (of anger) die down Plu.; (of luxury) die out Plu.; (of blood-pollution) fade A.; (of military or political strength) Plu.

μαργαίνω vb. [μάργος] (of a warrior) **rage furiously** —W.PREP.PHR. *against an enemy* Il. A.*fr.*

μαργαρίτης ου *m*. [Iran.loanwd.] **pearl** NT. Plu.

μαργάω contr.vb. [μάργος] ‖ PRES.PTCPL. (of a warrior, a hand) raging furiously, frenzied A. E.; (of horses) E. Call.; (quasi-adjl., of murder) E.; (of opponents) lusting —W.INF. *to attack one another* E.

μαργόομαι mid.pass.contr.vb. ‖ PRES.PTCPL. in a frenzy of eagerness (for war) Pi. ‖ PF.PTCPL. maddened —W.DAT. *by unholy passion* A.

μάργος η ον (also ος ον) *adj*. **1** wild and uncontrolled (in thought, behaviour, appetites or passions); (of persons) **raving mad, crazy** Od. Pi. E. Call.; (of Erinyes) **rabid** A.; (of Ares) **wild, reckless** A.*fr.*; (of Eros) Alcm. AR.
2 (of the snorting of war-horses, a blast of frenzy, a surge of air) **wild, furious** A. Emp.
3 (of a person's heart) **reckless, uncontrolled** Thgn.; (of the mouth of Strife) Ibyc.; (of pleasures) Pl.
4 (of wine) **causing wild behaviour** Hes.*fr.*(dub.)
5 (of a beggar's belly) **ravenous, gluttonous, insatiable** Od. ‖ NEUT.SB. **ravenous greed** (W.GEN. of the Cyclops' jaws) E.*Cyc.*
6 (of a man or woman) **wanton, lustful, lecherous** Thgn. A. E.

μαργοσύνη ης *f*. (sg. and pl.) **wild, wanton** or **lustful behaviour** Anacr. Thgn. AR.

μαργότης ητος *f*. **1 lustfulness** E.
2 greed, gluttony Pl.

Μαριανδυνοί ῶν *m.pl*. **Mariandyni** (Bithynian tribe, celebrated for their ritual laments) Hdt. Pl. X. AR. ‖ SG.ADJ. (of a dirge-singer) **Mariandynian** A.

μαρίλη ης *f*. **charcoal dust** Hippon. Ar.

μαρίλο-καύτης ου *m*. [καίω] **burner of charcoal dust** S.*Ichn.*

μαρμαίρω vb. ‖ only pres. and impf. ‖ (of warriors, their bronze weapons and armour) **gleam, glitter, glint, flash** Il. Theoc. Plu.; (of the Dioscuri, riding to war) E.; (of houses or objects, crafted w. gold) Il. E.(cj.) Mosch. Plu.; (of a house) —W.DAT. w. *bronze* (fr. *weapons stored there*) Alc. —w. *gold and ivory* B.*fr.*; (of Apollo) —w. *gold* (ref. *to his hair*) E.; (of night) —w. *stars* A.; (of the glare of a lightning-bolt) Hes.; (of the eyes of a goddess) Il.; (of a white spot on a bull's brow) Mosch.

μαρμάρεος ᾱ (Ion. η) ον *adj*. (of Zeus' aigis, a shield-rim) **gleaming, glittering** Il.; (of the gates of Tartaros) Hes.; (of the sea) Il.; (of rays of sunlight) Ar.; (of the lustre of Apollo's bow) AR.

μαρμαρίζω vb.: see μαρμαρύζω

μαρμάρινος η ον *adj*. [μάρμαρος] (of a monument) **of stone** or **marble** Theoc.*epigr.*

μαρμαρόεις εσσα εν *adj*. [μαρμαίρω] (of the radiance of Olympos) **gleaming, glittering** S.

μάρμαρον *n*.: see μάρμαρος

μαρμαρό-πτυχος ον *adj*. [μαρμαίρω, πτύξ] (of the bosom of Amphitrite, meton. for the sea) **with gleaming folds** (ref. to her dress and the waves) Tim.(cj.)

μάρμαρος ου *m*. (also *f*. Theoc.) —also **μάρμαρον** ου (Call.) *n*.
1 piece of rock (used as a missile); **stone, rock** Hom. E. Ar.; (appos.w. πέτρος) Il. E.; (W.ADJ. *wrought*, ref. to a piece torn fr. a funeral monument, so perh. of marble) Theoc.
2 rock (appos.w. μύλακρος *millstone*) Alcm.
3 rock (ref. to the metamorphosed Niobe) Call.

μαρμαρο-φεγγής ές *adj*. [μαρμαίρω, φέγγος] (of teeth) **bright-gleaming** Tim.

μαρμαρυγή ῆς *f*. **1** (freq.pl.) **gleam, sparkle, radiance** (of precious metals, armour) B. Pl. Plu.; (of daylight, the sun's rays, fire, a shooting star) Pl. AR. Plu.; (of the Golden Fleece) AR.; (of eyes) AR.
2 ‖ PL. **flashing movements, flash** (of a dancer's feet or tunic) Od. hHom.

μαρμαρύζω vb. (of rays) **flash** —W.PREP.PHR. fr. *a person's eyes* Pi.*fr.*(v.l. μαρμαρίζω)

μαρμαρ-ωπός όν *adj*. [ὤψ] (of Lyssa, described as a Gorgon) **with flashing eyes** E. [or perh. *whose look turns to stone*, w.connot. of μάρμαρος]

μάρναμαι mid.vb. ‖ only pres. and impf. ‖ ep.imperatv. μάρναο ‖ impf. ἐμαρνάμην, ep.2sg. ἐμάρναο, 3sg. ἐμάρνατο, ep. μάρνατο, ep.1pl. μαρνάμεθα, ep.3pl. μάρναντο, 3du. ἐμαρνάσθην, ep. μαρνάσθην ‖
1 fight (w. weapons), **fight, do battle** (sts. W.DAT. or PREP.PHR. against an enemy) Hom. Hes. Eleg. Pi. B. E. AR.; (hyperbol., against a woman) E.; (of a huntress, against wild beasts) Pi.
2 fight with the hands, **brawl, come to blows** Od. Hes.*fr.*
3 fight with words, **wrangle, quarrel** Il.
4 (wkr.sens., of persons, toil and expense) **strive, contend** (sts. W.PREP.PHR. for sthg.) Pi.

μάρπτις εως *m*. [μάρπτω] **one who seizes, grasper, robber** A.

μάρπτω vb. ‖ ep.3sg.subj. μάρπτῃσι ‖ impf. ἔμαρπτον, ep. μάρπτον ‖ fut. μάρψω ‖ aor. ἔμαρψα, ep. ἔμμαρψα (Hes.*fr.*) ‖ pf. μέμαρπα ‖ see also ep.aor.2 inf. μαπέειν ‖
1 lay hold of, **seize, clasp** or **grasp** —*a person, part of the body* Hom. S. E. AR. —*snakes, a bird* Pi. AR. —*weapons, reins, other objects* Hes.*fr.* Emp. S. E. AR.; (of a bird of prey) —*a bird, an animal, food* Hes. Ar.
2 catch up or **overtake** —*a fugitive* Il. Hes.*fr.* Archil.; **chase down** —*wild animals* A.*satyr.fr.*; (fig., of a legal vote) **catch** —*a defendant* (envisaged as being hunted down) A. ‖ PASS. (of a nymph) **be caught** (by a pursuing lover) Call.
3 catch, capture —*a wild animal* E.; **bring down** —*a bird* (W.DAT. w. *an arrow*) E.
4 (of sleep, old age) **take hold of** —*a person* Hom. Hes. Sapph.; (of the nether world, i.e. death) **seize, carry off** —*a person* S.
5 (fig., of fields lying fallow) **wrest back, gather** —*strength* Pi.
6 (of a goddess flying through the air, in neg.phr.) **come into contact with, touch** —*the ground* (W.DAT. w. *her feet*) Il.
7 (of a lightning-bolt) **inflict** (W.ACC. *wounds*) **by striking** (a person) Il.

μάρσιππος ου *m*. **bag, sack** X.

μαρτυρέω contr.vb. [μάρτυς] ‖ pf. μεμαρτύρηκα ‖ PASS.: fut. μαρτυρηθήσομαι, also μαρτυρήσομαι ‖ pf. μεμαρτύρημαι ‖
1 provide attestation or evidence (in support of facts, statements, or sim.); (of persons, sts. writers or their works; also of inanimate objects and circumstances) **bear witness, testify** (freq. W.NEUT.ACC., sts. W.DAT., to sthg., also W.DAT. for someone) Simon. Pi. Hdt. Trag. Ar. Isoc. + —W.COMPL.CL. or ACC. + INF. *that sthg. is the case* A. E. Isoc. Pl. + —W.NOM.AOR.PTCPL. *to having experienced sthg*. Pi. —W.AOR.INF. *to having heard sthg*. S. —W.DAT. + PTCPL. *that someone is doing sthg*. A. ‖ IMPERS.PASS. **it is attested** Pl. —W.COMPL.CL. *that sthg. is the case* X.
2 (in legal ctxt.) **be a witness, testify** or **give evidence** (in court or in a deposition, sts. W.DAT. for someone) A. E. Ar.

μαρτύρημα

Att.orats. Pl. + —w.acc. *concerning a matter* Att.orats. —w.compl.cl. or acc. + inf. *that sthg. is the case* A. Att.orats. —w.inf. *that one has done sthg.* Is.; **state in evidence** —w.intern. or cogn.acc. *the truth, falsehood, hearsay, or sim.* Att.orats. Pl.
3 ‖ pass. (of a person) be attested —w.nom.ptcpl. *as doing sthg.* Is.; (of facts) be stated in evidence Att.orats.; (of testimony) be given Is. D. ‖ neut.pl.pres. or pf.ptcpl.sb. things stated in evidence Att.orats. ‖ impers.pf.pass. it has been stated in evidence —w.compl.cl. or acc. + inf. *that sthg. is the case* Att.orats.

μαρτύρημα ατος *n.* **testimony** (to an oath-taking, ref. to a tripod inscribed w. the oath) E.

μαρτυρίᾱ ᾱς, Ion. **μαρτυρίη** ης *f.* **1 attestation** or **evidence** (in support of facts, statements, or sim.), **testimony** or **evidence** Pl. Arist. Call.*epigr.* Plb. NT. Plu.; (of Christian truth) NT.; act of giving testimony, **testifying** NT.
2 ‖ pl. (w. quasi-legal connot.) formal assertion, **testimony** (of a person or god) Od. Hes.; (of a snake, ref. to Kekrops) Call.
3 (in legal ctxt.) **witness-statement** Ar. Att.orats. Pl. Arist. NT. Plu.

μαρτύριον ου *n.* **1 piece of evidence** (in support of facts, statements, or sim.), **evidence, testimony** A. Pi. Hdt. Th. Att.orats. Pl. +
2 testimony (of God, revealed through His law) NT. | see σκηνή 7

μαρτύρομαι *mid.vb.* | aor. ἐμαρτυράμην | **1 call upon** (w.acc. gods) **to witness** (a statement, an injustice, or sim.) A.*satyr.fr.* E. Pl. D. Men. Plu. —w.indir.q. or compl.cl. *what (or that sthg.) is the case* Hdt. E. Din. —w.nom.ptcpl. *that one is doing sthg.* E. —w.inf. Plu.
2 call upon (w.acc. persons) **to witness** (an injustice) Antipho Plu. —w.indir.q. *what is the case* S. —w.nom.ptcpl. *that one is in a certain state* Plu.
3 call for witnesses (usu. to an injustice or injury that one is suffering, esp. in anticipation of an eventual trial) Lys. Ar. —w.neut.acc. *to sthg.* (*an injustice or injury*) Ar. Men. —w.nom.ptcpl. *to the fact that one is being beaten* Ar. —w.compl.cl. *to the fact that someone said sthg.* Ar.; (gener.) **make protestations** (against an alleged injustice) Plu.
4 cite (w.acc. Homer) **as a witness** —w.gen. *to sthg.* Pl.; (of an interlocutor) **call on witnesses** (against the truth of an argument) Pl.
5 cite evidence (against someone) Th.; **cite in evidence, invoke** —*an oath* E.
6 call upon, appeal to —*the sun* (w.inf. *to shine*) Alcm. —*a person* (sts.understd., *to do sthg.*) Plb. Plu.
7 call upon (w.acc. persons) **to attest** or **acknowledge** —w.inf. *that they hear sthg.* A. —w.compl.cl. *that sthg. is the case* Plb.
8 solemnly assert, claim —*sthg.* Pl. —w.compl.cl. *that sthg. is the case* Th. Plu. —w.acc. + inf. Plu.
9 provide attestation or **supporting evidence; testify** (to a fact) Plu.; **attest** —*sthg.* Plu.
10 bear witness, testify (to divine truth) NT. —w.dat. *to someone* NT. —(w.compl.cl. *that sthg. is the case*) NT.

μάρτυρος ου *m.* **1 witness** (ref. to a god, invoked to validate an oath or vow) Hom. Hes.; (ref. to Zeus, who protects suppliants) Od.
2 witness, eyewitness (to an event) Il.

μάρτυς υρος *m.f.* | acc. μάρτυρα, also μάρτυν (Simon. Plu.) | dat.pl. μάρτυσι, perh. also μάρτυρσι (Hippon., cj.) |
1 witness (ref. to a deity, invoked to validate an oath or vow, or to affirm the truth of sthg.) Pi. S. E. Th. Pl. +
2 witness (present at an event or utterance) hHom. Hippon. Hdt. Trag. Th. Ar. +; (ref. to eyes) X. Plb.; (ref. to an inanimate object invoked as being present at the scene, or as being a permanent reminder) Simon. Pi. E. Att.orats.; (ref. to days or time, as observers of events) Pi. Plu.
3 (leg.) one who provides testimony (to support a speaker's case), **witness** A. E. Ar. Att.orats. Pl. +
4 (without legal connot.) **expert witness, authority** (ref. to one who has knowledge and experience to affirm the truth of sthg.) Thgn. Pi. S. E. Ar. X. +; (ref. to a person or thing, invoked as having qualities which demonstrate one's point) **witness, example** Pl. X. Arist. +
5 (ref. to a poet or writer, quoted as testimony) **witness, authority** Pi. Pl. Arist. Plb. Plu.
6 witness (to Jesus, the Christian truth) NT.; (specif.) one who dies bearing witness, **martyr** NT.

μᾰρύομαι *dial.mid.vb.*: see μηρύομαι

μάρψω (fut.): see μάρπτω

Μάρων ωνος *m.* **Maron** (a priest of Apollo, who gave wine to Odysseus, w. which he made the Cyclops drunk) Od. E.*Cyc.*; (meton. for the wine) E.*Cyc.*

μασάομαι *mid.contr.vb.* **chew** —*food* Ar.; (intr.) Ar.; (to make the food digestible for a baby) Ar. Thphr.

μάσασθαι (aor.inf.): see ἐπιμαίομαι

μασδός *dial.m.*: see μαστός

μάσθλης, Aeol. **μάσλης**, ητος *m.* **1 leather whip**; (fig.) **slippery rogue** Ar.
2 app., **leather strap; leather sandal** Sapph.

μασθός *m.*: see μαστός

Μασσαλίᾱ ᾱς, Ion. **Μασσιλίη** ης *f.* **Massalia** (mod. Marseille, city founded by Greek settlers c.600 BC) Hdt. Th. +
—**Μασσαλιῶται**, also **Μασσαλιῆται**, ῶν *m.pl.* **Massaliots** (as a population or military force) D. Arist. Plb. Plu.
—**Μασσαλιωτικός**, also **Μασσιλιητικός**, ή όν *adj.*
1 relating to Massalia; (of one of the two mouths of the Rhône) **Massaliot** Plb.
2 (of ships) belonging to Massalia or its people, **Massaliot** Plb.

μάσσομαι (fut.mid.): see μαίομαι

μάσσω, Att. **μάττω** *vb.* [reltd. μᾶζα] | fut. μάξω | aor. ἔμαξα | pf. μέμαχα ‖ pf.pass.ptcpl. μεμαγμένος | **1 mould into shape** (w. the hands), **knead** —*a barley-cake* Ar. Arist. Call. —*a honey-cake* Ar. —*barley-groats* Ar.(mid.) Pl. Plu. —*powdered fish* (to make a kind of bread) Hdt.(mid.) —*magic herbs* Theoc.; (intr.) **knead dough** or **barley-cakes** Ar. X. Arist. Men. Plu. ‖ pass. (of foodstuffs) be kneaded Ar.
‖ pf.pass.ptcpl. (of barley-cakes, corn) kneaded Archil. Th. Ar. X.; (of dung) Ar.
2 (fig.) **knead, shape** —*ideas* Ar.

μάσσων ον, gen. ονος *compar.adj.* [μακρός] | masc.acc.sg. μάσσω | neut.nom.acc.pl. μάσσονα, also μάσσω | for superl. see μήκιστος |
1 (of a statue) **taller** Call.
2 (of animals) **larger** Call.
3 (of a route, walk, run) **longer, further** X.
4 (of a life) **longer** A.; (of prosperity) **more long-lasting** Pi.
5 (of a narrative) **lengthier** A.
6 (of victories) **more numerous** Pi.
7 (of sufferings, when put in the scales) **heavier** A.
—**μᾶσσον** *neut.adv.* **1 further** (in distance) Od. Call.
2 more (in extent or time) A.

μάσταξ ακος f. [reltd. μασάομαι] **1 mouth** (of a person) Od. **2 mouthful, morsel** (of food, fed to chicks by a bird) Il. Theoc.; (of olive-cake) Call.

μασταρύζω vb. **purse one's lips** (in consternation) Ar.

μάστειρα fem.adj.: see under μαστήρ

μαστευτής οῦ m. [μαστεύω] **searcher** (for an object) X.

μαστεύω vb. [μαστήρ, reltd. ματεύω] | dial.inf. μαστευέμεν (Pi.) | ep.iteratv.impf. μαστεύεσκον | aor. ἐμάστευσα, dial. μάστευσα (Pi.) | **1 search for, seek** —someone or sthg. Hes.fr. A.(dub., cj. ματ-) E. X. AR.; (intr.) **search** AR. | see also μνηστεύω 3
2 strive for —sthg. Pi. E.
3 seek, strive —W.INF. to do sthg. Pi. E. X.

μαστήρ ῆρος m. [μαίομαι] **searcher, seeker** (usu. W.GEN. after someone) S. E. AR.

—**μάστειρα** ᾱς fem.adj. (of divine anger) **searching** (W.GEN. after Io) A.

μαστήριος ᾱ ον adj. (epith. of Hermes) **good at searching** A.

μαστιάω contr.vb. [reltd. μαστίω] | ep.pres.ptcpl. (w.diect.) μαστιόων | (of a lion) **lash** —its sides and shoulders (W.DAT. w. its tail) Hes.

μαστιγίᾱς ου m. [μάστιξ] **one who has been much whipped or deserves a whipping** (usu. ref. to a slave, freq. voc. as a term of abuse); **rogue, villain** Ar. Pl. D. Men. Plu.

μαστιγο-φόροι ων m.pl. [φέρω] **whip-bearers** (escorting prisoners, the Persian king) Th. X.; (for disciplining Spartan boys) X. ‖ ADJ. (of attendants of the Thirty Tyrants at Athens) **whip-bearing** Arist.

μαστιγόω contr.vb. | fut.pass. μαστιγώσομαι | **1 beat with a whip, flog** —persons (esp. slaves or prisoners) Hdt. Isoc. X. +; (of Xerxes) —the Hellespont Hdt.; (intr.) **use a whip** Ar. D. ‖ PASS. **be flogged** Hdt. Lys. Ar. Pl. +
2 use a whip on —a horse X.

μαστιγωτέος ᾱ ον vbl.adj. (of a person) **to be whipped** Ar.

μαστίζω vb. | aor. ἐμάστιξα, ep. μάστιξα | **1 apply the whip**; (of a charioteer, rider, groom) **whip on** —horses Hom. Plu.
2 flog (as a punishment) —a person NT. —a statue of Pan (W.DAT. w. squills, app. as part of a ritual) Theoc.

μαστικτήρ ῆρος m. **one who uses a whip**; (fig., ref. to a speech) **scourge** (W.GEN. of the heart) A.

μαστίκτωρ ορος m. **whipper, flogger** (of criminals) A.

μάστιξ ῑγος f. **1 whip** or **goad** (used to spur on horses or mules) Hom. hHom. Hdt. S. Pl. X. Plu.; (to control other animals) hHom. S. Pl. Plu. [in ep. the whip was prob. a form of goad, i.e. a pointed stick; cf. κέντρον]
2 whip, lash (used to control persons, sts. soldiers) Hdt. Ar. X. Plu.; (specif., for punitive flogging or torture) Anacr. Hdt. S. E.Cyc. Ar. Pl. +
3 (fig.) **whip, lash** (of Zeus, w. which he controls human warriors) Il.; (of Pan, causing panic) E.; (of a god, striking the impious) A.; (of Ares) A.; (of Persuasion) Pi.; (W.ADJ. from the gods, ref. to the gadfly which pursued Io) A.
4 physical affliction, illness, suffering NT.

μαστιόων (ep.pres.ptcpl.): see μαστιάω

μάστις ιος Ion.f. [reltd. μάστιξ] | only acc. μάστιν and dat. μάστῑ | **whip** (used to spur on horses) Hom.

μαστιχάω contr.vb. [μάσταξ] | ep.pres.ptcpl. (w.diect.) μαστιχόων | (of a boar) **gnash one's teeth** Hes.

μαστίω vb. [reltd. μάστις] | ep.3du.impf. μαστιέτην | **1 apply a whip** (to horses) Il. —W.ACC. to horses Hes.
2 ‖ MID. (of a lion) **lash** —its sides and haunches (W.DAT. w. its tail) Il.

μαστο-ειδής ές adj. [μαστός, εἶδος¹] (of a hill) **breast-shaped, rounded** Plb.

μαστός, Ion. **μαζός**, dial. **μασδός** (Alcm.), perh. also **μασθός** (Plb. Plu.), οῦ m. **1 breast** (of a woman or goddess) Hom. Archil. Lyr. Hdt. Trag. Hellenist.poet. +; (sg. for pl.) E.
2 breast or **nipple** (of a man or god) Hom. X. AR. Plb. Bion Plu.
3 udder or **teat** (of female animals) E. Hellenist.poet. Plu.
4 breast (of the personif. island of Delos, envisaged as nurse of Apollo) Call.; (fig., of an island, w.connot. of nurture or fruitfulness) Call.; (of land, ref. to a hill on which a colony is founded) Pi.
5 (gener., ref. to a round or breast-shaped object) **hill, knoll** X. Plb.
6 loop or **eyelet** (of cord, at the top of a hunting net) X.

μαστροπεία ᾱς f. [μαστροπεύω] **procuring** (of persons, for sex) X.

μαστροπεύω vb. [μαστροπός] **act as go-between** or **procurer for** —a person X. —(fig., w. πρός + ACC. in relation to a city, i.e. introduce him into public life) X.

μαστροπός οῦ m.f. [perh.reltd. μαστήρ] **one who finds a sexual partner for another** (or commends one to another), **go-between** or **procurer** Ar. X.

μαστύς ύος f. [μαστεύω] **activity of searching, search** Call.; (W.GEN. for food) S.(cj.)

μασχάλη ης f. **armpit** hHom. Ar. X. Thphr.

μασχαλίζομαι pass.vb. | aor. ἐμασχαλίσθην | (of a murdered man) **have one's extremities cut off and strung round the neck and under the armpits, be mutilated** A. S.

μασχαλιστήρ ῆρος m. **band passing under the armpits, chest-band** Hdt.; (fettering Prometheus) A.

μάτᾱ dial.f.: see μάτη

ματάζω vb. [μάταιος] **1 engage in useless** or **misguided activities** E.fr.
2 (of a person's inner feelings) **be vain** or **deluded** A.
3 be reckless S.

ματαιο-λόγος ον adj. (of poets) **idly talking** Telest.

ματαιοπονέω contr.vb. **labour in vain** Plb.

μάταιος ᾱ ον (also ος ον) adj. [μάτη] **1 achieving no result**; (of a remedy, prayer, labour, or sim.) **vain, ineffective, fruitless, futile** A. E. Pl. X. D. Arist. +; (of a person) **ineffectual** E.
2 having no real substance or useful purpose; (of thoughts, emotions, arguments, activities, or sim.) **vain, empty, idle, useless** Thgn. A. S. Isoc. Pl. X. +
3 (of persons, their speech, thoughts, emotions, actions) **foolish, rash, irresponsible** Thgn. Pi. B. Hdt. Trag. Pl. +; (of untrained hounds) X.
4 (w. some sexual connot., of persons) **reckless, wanton** E.; (of an assailant's hands) S.; (of animals) A. ‖ NEUT.SB. (sg. and pl.) **wantonness** A.
5 (of actions) **violent, injurious** A. E.Cyc.; (of speech) **offensive** Hdt.
6 (of a person) **deluded, mistaken** S.; (wkr.sens.) **light-hearted, carefree** Hdt. ‖ VOC. (w. ὦ, sts. w. note of pity) **poor fool** Hdt. Trag. Ar. D.

—**ματαίως** adv. **1 vainly, to no useful purpose** Arist. Plb.
2 rashly (i.e. falsely) —ref. to making an accusation S.

μάτᾱν dial.acc.adv.: see μάτην

ματάω contr.vb. | ep.3du.aor.subj. ματήσετον | usu. in neg.phr. | **1** (of persons) **be ineffective, fail** (in a task) Il. AR.; (of scouts) —W.DAT. in their mission A.; (of panicking horses) **falter** Il.
2 (of a task, a divine decree) **be fruitless** or **ineffectual** A. S.; (of a forecast) **be mistaken** A.

μᾱτέρος (dial.gen.): see μήτηρ

ματεύω vb. [reltd. μαστεύω] **1 search for, seek** —*someone or sthg.* Lyr. Trag. Theoc.; (intr.) **search** Il. A.(cj., for μαστ-) Pi. S. Ar.
2 seek, strive —W.INF. *to do sthg.* Pi. S.
ματέω contr.vb. | dial.fem.nom.pl.ptcpl. ματεῦσαι | **search for, seek** —*sthg.* Melanipp.
μάτη ης, dial. **μάτᾱ** ᾱς *f.* —also **ματίη** ης (Od. AR.) *Ion.f.*
1 misguided behaviour, **stupidity, folly** Od.
2 (w. sexual connot.) irresponsible behaviour, **recklessness, intemperance** or **lust** A.(pl.) AR.
μάτημι[1] *Aeol.vb.* | 2sg. μάτης, fem.nom.ptcpl. ματεῖσα (Pi,*fr.*) | **seek** —*sthg.* Theoc. —W.INF. *to do sthg.* Pi,*fr.*
μάτημι[2] *Aeol.vb.* [app.reltd. πατέω] | fem.nom.pl.ptcpl. μάτεισαι | **tread upon** —*flowery grass* Sapph.(or Alc.)
μάτην, dial. **μάτᾱν** *acc.adv.* [μάτη] **1** without achieving a result, **ineffectually, fruitlessly, to no avail, in vain** hHom. Alcm. Pi. Hdt. Trag. +
2 without reason or purpose, **idly, at random, pointlessly, uselessly** Eleg. Hdt. Trag. +
3 falsely, wrongly, deceptively or **mistakenly** Trag.
4 (quasi-adj.) • τὸ μάταν ... φροντίδος ἄχθος *the futile burden of anxiety* A. • κόμποι μάτην *idle boasting* E.
μάτηρ *dial.f.*: see μήτηρ
ματίη *Ion.f.*: see μάτη
μᾱτιο-λοιχός οῦ *m.* [μάτιον *scrap, trifle*; λείχω] (ref. to a legal opponent) **trifle-licker, feeder on quibbles** Ar. [cj. ματτυολοιχός *greedy parasite*, reltd. ματτύη *a kind of rich food*]
μᾱτρ-αδελφεός οῦ *dial.m.* [μήτηρ, ἀδελφός] **brother of one's mother, maternal uncle** Pi.
μᾱτρό-δοκος ον *dial.adj.* [δέχομαι] (of generative seed) **received by a mother** Pi.
μᾱτρόθε(ν) *dial.adv.*: see μητρόθεν
μᾱτρο-κασιγνήτᾱ ᾱς *dial.f.* [κασιγνήτη] **sister by the same mother** A.
μᾱτροκτόνος *dial.adj.*: see μητροκτόνος
μᾱτρο-μάτωρ ορος *dial.f.* [μήτηρ] **mother of one's mother, maternal grandmother** Pi.
μᾱτρόπολις *dial.f.*: see μητρόπολις
μᾱτρο-πόλος ον *dial.adj.* [πέλω] (epith. of Eileithuia) **attendant upon mothers** Pi.
μᾱτροφόνος *dial.m.,* **μᾱτροφόντᾱς** *dial.m.*: see μητροφόνος, μητροφόντης
μᾱτρυιά *dial.f.*: see μητρυιά
μᾱτρυλεῖον ου *n.* **tavern** or **tavern-cum-brothel** Men.
μᾱτρῷος *dial.adj.,* **μάτρως** *dial.m.*: see μητρῷος, μήτρως
ματτυολοιχός *m.*: see μᾱτιολοιχός
μάττω *Att.vb.*: see μάσσω
μαῦλις ιος *dial.f.* **knife** Call.
μαυρόω contr.vb. [reltd. ἀμαυρόω] **1** (of the gods) **weaken, enfeeble** or **bring low** —*a person* Hes. || PASS. (of a citizen-stock) be weakened or diluted (by unsuitable marriages) Thgn.
2 || PASS. (of cargo) be ruined Hes.
3 || PASS. (of a beacon-fire) be dimmed A.; (of unwelcome things) be obscured —W.DAT. *in darkness* A.(cj., for ἀμαυρόω)
μάχᾱ *dial.f.*: see μάχη
μάχαιρα ᾱς (Ion. ης) *f.* **1 knife** (used for cutting hair fr. a sacrificial animal, an embedded arrow-head fr. flesh) Il.; (for killing sacrificial animals, carving meat, or sim.) hHom. Hippon. Pi. Hdt. E. Ar. +
2 (as a weapon) **knife** or **dagger** Il. Hes,*fr.* Pi. Hdt. Antipho Lys. +

3 short sword or **sabre, sword, sabre** X. Plb. NT. Plu.; (opp. ξίφος *long straight sword*) X.
4 blade or **razor** (for cutting a person's hair) Ar. || PL. scissors Plu.
5 (meton.) **war** (opp. peace) NT.
μαχαίριον ου *n.* [dimin.] **1 small knife** Plu.; (used by a barber for cutting nails) Plu.; (specif.) **scalpel** (used by a surgeon) Arist.
2 dagger X.
μαχαιρίς ίδος *f.* [dimin.] **knife** Ar. Plu.
μαχαιρομαχέω contr.vb. [μάχομαι] **practise sword-fighting** —W.DAT. w. *wooden swords* Plb.
μαχαιροποιεῖον ου *n.* [μαχαιροποιός] **knife-making workshop, cutler's factory** D.
μαχαιρο-ποιός οῦ *m.* [ποιέω] **1 knife-maker, cutler** Ar. Aeschin. D. Plu.
2 sword-maker Plu.
μαχαιρο-πώλιον ου *n.* [πωλέω] **cutlery shop** Plu.
μαχαιρο-φόρος ον *adj.* [φέρω] (of Asian troops) **sword-bearing** or **sabre-bearing** A. || MASC.PL.SB. **swordsmen** or **knife-men** (ref. to non-Greek troops) Hdt. Th. X. Plu.; (as bodyguards) Plb. Plu.
μαχαίτᾱς *Aeol.m.*: see μαχητής
μᾱχανά *dial.f.,* **μᾱχάνᾱ** *Aeol.f.*: see μηχανή
μαχατᾱς *dial.m.*: see μαχητής
μάχη ης, dial. **μάχᾱ** ᾱς *f.* [μάχομαι] **1** state or activity of fighting under arms, **fighting, warfare, battle** Hom. +
2 specific instance of fighting, **battle, fight** (betw. opposing armies or individuals) Hom. +; (betw. ships) Pi.; (specif., on land, opp. at sea) Lys. Ar.
3 mode of fighting (adopted by a particular people) Archil. Hdt. X.
4 (in non-military ctxt., freq.fig.) **fighting, fight, battle, combat** Archil. Semon. Alc. Pi. Hdt. Trag. +; (specif., ref. to the pankration, boxing) Pi. Pl. Theoc.
—**μάχηνδε** *adv.* **to combat** Theoc.
μαχήμων ον, gen. ονος *adj.* (of a person's heart) **warlike** Il.
μαχητής οῦ, dial. **μαχᾱτᾱς** ᾶ, Aeol. **μαχαίτᾱς** ᾱ *m.* **1 fighter, warrior** Hom. Alc. Pi. Plu.
2 || ADJ. (of a person's spirit) **warlike** Pi.
μαχητικός ή όν *adj.* **1** (of persons) of the fighting kind, **pugnacious, belligerent** Arist.; **disposed to fight** (W.PREP.PHR. over sthg.) Arist.; (of horses) **bellicose** Pl. || FEM.SB. art of fighting Pl. || NEUT.SB. fighting spirit Plu.
2 (of games) of the physically competitive kind, **combative** (opp. of the disputatious kind) Arist. || NEUT.SB. fighting part (of the combative art, opp. the competitive part) Pl.
—**μαχητικῶς** *adv.* **pugnaciously, belligerently** Pl.
μαχητός ή όν *adj.* (of an evil, ref. to Charybdis, in neg.phr.) **able to be fought against** Od.
μάχιμος η ον (also ος ον) *adj.* | compar. μαχιμώτερος, superl. μαχιμώτατος | **1** (of men, armies, ships) able and ready to fight, **fighting, battle-ready** Hdt. Th. Ar. Pl. X. +; (of women) Ar.; (of elephants) Plu. || NEUT.SB. fighting force (available or in the field) Hdt. Th. Pl. X. Plu.; (superl.) best fighting force Plu. || MASC.PL.SB. persons fit for military service Isoc.
2 (of a class in society) **fighting, military** Pl. Plu.; (of persons) **belonging to the military class** Hdt. || NEUT.SB. military class Pl. Arist.; military way of life Hdt. || MASC.PL.SB. fighting men Arist.
3 (gener., of men, peoples, in their nature or culture) **warlike, skilled in fighting** A. Hdt. Th. Lys. Ar. Pl. +; (of animals) **pugnacious, belligerent** Plu. || NEUT.SB. warlike spirit Plu.
4 (of quails) **trained to fight, fighting** Plu.

μάχλος ον *adj.* (of women) **lustful, lecherous** Hes. E.*fr.*; (of Ares) A.; (transf.epith., of the ears of a lover) Call.

μαχλοσύνη ης *f.* **lust, lechery** (of a man) Il.(dub.); (of women) Hes.*fr.* Hdt.

μάχομαι *mid.vb.* | PRES.: ep.opt. μαχεοίμην | 2du.imperatv. μάχεσθον | ep.ptcpl. μαχειόμενος, also μαχεούμενος | impf. ἐμαχόμην, ep. μαχόμην, ep.3du. μαχέσθην, 3sg.iteratv. μαχέσκετο | fut. μαχοῦμαι, Ion. μαχήσομαι, ep.3pl. μαχέονται | AOR.: ἐμαχεσάμην, ep.3sg. μαχέσσατο, 1pl. μαχεσσάμεθα | ep.ptcpl. μαχεσσάμενος | inf. μαχέσασθαι, ep. μαχέσσασθαι | pf. μεμάχημαι || neut.impers.vbl.adj. μαχετέον, also μαχητέον || freq. W.DAT. or PREP.PHR. against someone or sthg., also W.INSTR.DAT. w. weapons, hands, or sim. |
1 (of gods, men, armies, commanders) **fight** (in war or battle) Hom. + —W.COGN.ACC. *a battle* Hom. Hdt. +; (of individuals, in single combat) Il. +
2 (in non-military ctxt., of individuals or groups) engage in combat, **fight** Hom. +; (w. wild beasts or monsters) Il. +; (of animals, w. humans) Hom. +; (of animals or birds, w. one another) Il. +
3 engage in contention; **fight, contend** (in athletic or other competitions) Il. + —W.COGN.ACC. *in the pankration* Ar.
4 quarrel, wrangle, dispute (w. a person or god) Il. +
5 put up resistance (against divine, physical, natural or emotional forces); (of the gods, in neg.phr.) **fight** (against Necessity) Simon.; (of persons, against disease, poverty, famine, thirst, or sim.) Att.orats. Pl. X. Men.; (against pleasure, grief, one's nature, or sim.) Heraclit. Pl. X. D. Arist. +; (of a young horse, against the reins) A.; (of a ship, against rain) Alc.
6 (of arguments) **contend** (w. each other, in one's mind) Pl.; (of material or non-material things) **conflict** (w. others) Pl. Arist. Plb.

μάχος *dial.n.*: see μῆχος

μάψ *adv.* **1** without reason or purpose, **vainly, fruitlessly, pointlessly** Il. hHom.
2 recklessly, rashly, irresponsibly Hom.
3 without consideration, **idly, casually, heedlessly** Hom. hHom.
4 randomly —*ref. to breezes blowing* Hes.

μαψ-αῦραι ῶν *f.pl.* [αὔρᾱ] **random breezes** Call.

μαψίδιος ον (Ion. η ον) *adj.* **1** (of love) perh. **fruitless** or **reckless** Hes.*fr.*
2 (of repute) **unfounded** E.; (of talk) **idle** Theoc.

—**μαψιδίως** *adv.* **1** without consideration, **idly, casually, heedlessly** Hom. Alcm.
2 haphazardly, randomly Od. hHom.

μαψι-λόγος ον *adj.* (of birds of omen) **vain-talking** hHom.

μαψ-υλάκᾱς ᾱ *dial.m.f.* [ὑλακτέω] **1 idle yapper** Pi.
2 || FEM.ADJ. (of a tongue) idly yapping Sapph.

με (acc.1sg.enclit.pers.pron.): see ἐγώ

μεγα-βρόντης ου *m.* [μέγας, βροντή] (epith. of Zeus) **loud-thunderer** Ar.

μεγα-θαρσής ές *adj.* [θάρσος] (of Herakles) **mightily courageous** Hes.*fr.*

μέγαθος *Ion.n.*: see μέγεθος

μεγά-θυμος ον *adj.* [θῡμός] (of persons and peoples) **great-spirited, stout-hearted** Hom. Hes. Mosch.; (of Athena) Od. Sol. B.; (of a giant) Hes.; (of a bull, a lion) Il. Plu.(oracle)

μεγ-αίνητος ον *adj.* [αἰνητός] (of persons) **highly praised, renowned** B.

μεγαίρω *vb.* [app. μέγας] | aor. ἐμέγηρα, ep. μέγηρα |
1 regard (sthg.) as excessive (and so be unwilling to grant or allow it); **be grudging** or **niggardly** AR. —W.DAT. *to someone* Il. Hdt.(oracle) —W.ACC. *to a place* Call.
2 begrudge —W.ACC. or GEN. *sthg.* (usu. W.DAT. *to someone*) Il. A. AR.
3 (in neg.phr.) **begrudge** —W.DAT. or ACC. + INF. *someone doing sthg.* Od. hHom. Call. Theoc. —(W.INF. alone) Il. Archil. —W.COMPL.CL. Sol.
4 (in neg.phr.) **mind, care** (in a choice betw. options) Od.; (if someone does sthg.) AR.
5 app. **cast a spell on, bewitch** —*someone's eyes* AR.

μεγα-κήτης ες *adj.* [κῆτος; or perh.reltd. κητώεις] **1** (of a ship) with a great hollow, **great-bellied, capacious** Il. [or perh. *having the appearance of a great sea-creature*]
2 (of the sea) **teeming with great sea-creatures** Od. AR. [or perh. *with great hollows or depths*]
3 (of a dolphin) being a great sea-creature, **monstrous** Il. [or perh. *great-bellied*]

μεγαλᾱγορίᾱ *dial.f.*: see μεγαληγορίᾱ

μεγαλ-άδικος ον *adj.* **unjust on a grand scale** Arist.

μεγαλᾱνορίᾱ ᾱς *dial.f.* [μεγαλάνωρ] **great manly deed, proud exploit** Pi.

μεγαλ-άνωρ ορος *dial.masc.fem.adj.* [ἀνήρ] **1** (of a person) **proud, haughty** Pi.
2 (of Hesychia) **grand, august** Pi.*fr.*
3 (of wealth) associated with manly greatness, **man-exalting, lordly, noble** B.*fr.*

μεγάλ-ατος ον *adj.* [ἄτη] (of a king) **victim** or **bringer of great ruin** A.; (of Erinyes) A.(dub.)

μεγαλαυχέω *contr.vb.* [μεγάλαυχος] **1** (act. and mid.) **be proud** or **self-satisfied** A. Pl. Plb. || MID. **express self-satisfaction** or **boast** Pl. Plu.
2 (act. and mid.) **pride oneself** —w. ἐπί + DAT. *on sthg.* Isoc. Plb. —W.DAT. Plu.

μεγαλαυχίᾱ ᾱς *f.* **1 pride, self-confidence** Pl. Plu. || PL. displays of pride Pl. Plu.
2 boastfulness Plu. || PL. boasts Plu.

μεγάλ-αυχος ον *adj.* [αὔχη] (usu.pejor., of persons) **proud, self-confident** Lyr.adesp. A. Pi. Pl. Plu.; (of Erinyes) A.; (of a person's might) B.; (of a country) Plu.(oracle) || NEUT.SB. pride, arrogance X.

μεγαλεῖος ᾱ ον *adj.* **1** (of achievements, possessions, words) **grand, magnificent, impressive** X. Men. Plb.; (pejor., of persons) **grandiose** Plb.
2 || NEUT.SB. grand scale (W.GEN. of activities) Plb.; (pl.) mighty deeds (W.GEN. of God) NT.

—**μεγαλείως** *adv.* | compar. μεγαλειότερον, also μεγαλειοτέρως | **1 grandly, magnificently, impressively** Pl. X. Plb.
2 severely —*ref. to punishing* X.
3 seriously —*ref. to being slighted or mistaken* Plb.
4 enormously —*ref. to being delighted* Plb.

μεγαλειότης ητος *f.* **grandeur, majesty** (W.GEN. of God, Artemis) NT.

μεγαλ-επήβολος ον *adj.* **intent on achieving great things, ambitious on a grand scale** Plb.(v.l. μεγαλεπίβολος)

μεγάλ-ευκτος ον *adj.* [εὐκτός] **earnestly prayed for** Plu.(quot.poet.)

μεγαληγορέω *contr.vb.* [μεγαλήγορος] **speak boastfully** X. Plu.

μεγαληγορίᾱ, dial. **μεγαλᾱγορίᾱ**, ᾱς *f.* **boastful speech** E. X.

μεγαλ-ήγορος ον *adj.* [ἀγορεύω] **boastful** A. X.

μεγαλ-ήτωρ ορος *masc.fem.adj.* [ἦτορ] **1** (of persons and peoples) **great-hearted, stout-hearted** Hom. Hes.
2 (of a spirit) **mighty, proud** Hom. Hes.; (of impulses) Pi.

μεγαλίζομαι *mid.vb.* think highly of oneself, **be proud** or **haughty** Hom.

μεγαλογκίη ης *Ion.f.* [ὄγκος²] **great bulk** Democr.

μεγαλογνωμοσύνη ης *f.* [μεγαλογνώμων] **high-mindedness, high-principled behaviour** X.

μεγαλο-γνώμων ον, *gen.* ονος *adj.* (of persons, their behaviour) **high-minded, high-principled** X.

μεγαλό-δοξος ον *adj.* [δόξα] (of Eunomia) **of great repute, glorious** Pi.; (of Rome) Plu.

μεγαλοδωρία ᾱς *f.* [μεγαλόδωρος] **great generosity, munificence** Plb.

μεγαλό-δωρος ον *adj.* [δῶρον] (of a person or god) bestowing gifts on a large scale, **munificent** Ar. Plb. Plu. ‖ NEUT.SB. **munificence, lavish giving** Plu.

μεγαλό-θῡμος ον *adj.* [θῡμός] (of a temperament) **high-spirited** Pl.

μεγάλ-οιτος ον *adj.* [οἶτος] (of a rejected lover) **utterly ruined** Theoc.

μεγαλο-κευθής ές *adj.* [κεῦθος] (of chambers) **with great inner depths, capacious** Pi.

μεγαλο-κίνδυνος ον *adj.* **braving danger for great causes** Arist.

μεγαλο-κλεής ές *adj.* [κλέος] (of an athlete's prayers) **for great glory** B.

μεγαλό-κολπος ον *adj.* [κόλπος] (of Night) **great-bosomed** B.*fr.* [cj. μελανόκολπος *black-bosomed*]

μεγαλο-κόρυφος ον *adj.* [κορυφή] (of the earth) **with great mountain peaks** Arist.(quot.)

μεγαλομέρεια (also **μεγαλομερίᾱ** Plb.) ᾱς *f.* [μεγαλομερής] **1 large size of particles** Arist. **2 great scale** (of a state) Plb.

μεγαλο-μερής ές *adj.* [μέρος] **1** (of liquids) **consisting of large particles** Pl. **2** on a great scale; (of a country, a work of art) **magnificent, splendid, impressive** Plb.; (of a person's circumstances) Plb. **3** (of hospitality, entertainment) **lavish** Plb.

—**μεγαλομερῶς** *adv.* | *compar.* μεγαλομερέστερον, *superl.* μεγαλομερέστατα | **magnificently, splendidly, impressively** Plb.

μεγαλό-μητις ιδος *fem.adj.* [μῆτις] (of a woman) **of great scheming** A.

μεγαλόνοια ᾱς *f.* [νόος] **high-mindedness, high-principled attitude** Pl.

μεγαλό-πετρος ον *adj.* [πέτρᾱ] (of the Acropolis) **on a great rock** Ar.

μεγαλό-πολις ιος *dial.f.* [πόλις] (appos.w. name of the city) **mighty city** Pi. E.

μεγαλο-πόνηρος ον *adj.* [πονηρός] **wicked on a grand scale** Arist.

μεγαλοπρᾱγμοσύνη ης *f.* [μεγαλοπράγμων] **high ambition** Plu.

μεγαλο-πράγμων ον, *gen.* ονος *adj.* [πρᾶγμα] **intent on achieving great things, highly ambitious** X. Plu.

μεγαλοπρέπεια ᾱς, Ion. **μεγαλοπρεπείη** ης *f.* [μεγαλοπρεπής] **1 magnificence** (of buildings, lifestyle, behaviour) Isoc. Plu. **2 grandeur** (of style, in epic poetry or oratory) Arist. Plu. **3 impressiveness, prestige** (of a person) Hdt. **4** (w. moral connot.) **loftiness of mind, great-mindedness** Pl. **5** (as a cardinal virtue) **magnificence** or **munificence** (ref. to expenditure on an appropriately grand scale in a good cause, the mean betw. μικροπρέπεια *paltriness* and βαναυσία or δαπανηρία *vulgar extravagance*) Arist.

μεγαλο-πρεπής ές *adj.* [πρέπω] **1 standing out as great;** (of achievements, actions, stories, material things, abstract qualities) **magnificent, splendid, impressive** Hdt. Ar. Pl. X. Hyp. D. +; (of a horse) X. **2** (of persons) **grand, impressive** Isoc. X.; (of an orator) Plu. **3** (w. moral connot.) **lofty-minded, great-minded** Pl. **4 magnificent** or **munificent** (ref. to one who spends on an appropriately grand scale in a good cause) Arist.

—**μεγαλοπρεπῶς**, Ion. **μεγαλοπρεπέως** *adv.* | *compar.* μεγαλοπρεπέστερον, *superl.* μεγαλοπρεπέστατα | **magnificently, splendidly, impressively** Hdt. Isoc. Pl. X. D. Arist. +

μεγαλο-σθενής ές *adj.* [σθένος] (of a deity or person) **of great strength, mighty** Lyr.

μεγαλο-σπλαγχνος ον *adj.* [σπλάγχνον] (of a person's spirit) **in high passion** E.

μεγαλό-στονος ον *adj.* [στόνος] (of sufferings) **bringing great lamentation** A.

μεγαλο-σχήμων ον, *gen.* ονος *adj.* [σχῆμα] (of a position of honour) **mighty in form, magnificent, imposing** A.

μεγαλουργία ᾱς *f.* [μεγαλουργός] **1 undertaking** or **achievement of great things** Plu. **2 great workmanship** Plu.

μεγαλουργός όν *adj.* [ἔργον] **achieving great things** ‖ NEUT.SB. **enterprising spirit** Plu.

μεγαλοφρονέω *contr.vb.* [μεγαλόφρων] **1 have confidence** —w. ἐπί + DAT. **in oneself** X.; **be self-confident** Plb. Plu. **2** ‖ MID. (pejor.) **have a high opinion of oneself** Pl.

μεγαλοφροσύνη ης *f.* **1 high-mindedness** or **magnanimity** Hdt. D. Plu. **2 self-confidence** Isoc. Pl. Plu. **3** (pejor.) **arrogance** Hdt. Antipho

μεγαλό-φρων ον, *gen.* ονος *adj.* [φρήν] **1 high-minded, proud-spirited** or **self-confident** Isoc. Pl. X. Aeschin. Plb. Plu.; (of Hesychia) Ar.(dub., cj. ἀγανό-) ‖ NEUT.SB. **self-confidence** (of a person) X. **2** (of a horse's temperament) **high-spirited** X. **3** (of an agreement) **confidently formulated** Isoc.

—**μεγαλοφρόνως** *adv.* (pejor.) **arrogantly** Pl. X.

μεγαλο-φυής ές *adj.* [φυή] | *compar.* μεγαλοφυέστερος | ‖ COMPAR. (of a person) **of nobler nature** Plb.

μεγαλό-φωνος ον *adj.* [φωνή] **loud-voiced** Plu.; (pejor.) D.

μεγαλοψῡχίᾱ ᾱς, Ion. **μεγαλοψῡχίη** ης *f.* [μεγαλόψυχος] **greatness of soul, nobility of spirit** (embracing such qualities as self-esteem, courage, ambition, generosity) Att.orats. X. Arist. Plb. Plu.

μεγαλό-ψῡχος ον *adj.* [ψῡχή] (of a person) **noble-spirited** Att.orats. Arist. Plb. Plu.; (of character or conduct) Plb. Plu.

—**μεγαλοψύχως** *adv.* **in a noble-spirited manner** Aeschin. D. Plb. Plu.

μεγαλύνω *vb.* | Aeol.mid.imperatv. μεγαλύννεο | **1 make large or larger** (in size or degree), **enlarge** —*an item of dress* NT.; **enhance** —*the dignity of an office* Plu. **2** (of God) **give a large amount of, bestow generously** —*compassion* NT. **3** (of a god) **make great** or **powerful** —*a people* Plu. **4 give strength or confidence to, boost** —*one's enemies* Th.; (of sumptuous armour) —*one's spirits* Plu. ‖ MID.PASS. **be elated** X. Plu. —W.DAT. *by a victory* Plu. **5 extol, exalt, acclaim** —*persons, their deeds, a name, a country, God* E. NT. Plu. ‖ PASS. (of a name) **be acclaimed** NT. **6 exalt** or **magnify** —*oneself* X. Plu. ‖ MID. **pride oneself** —W.DAT. or ἐπί + DAT. *on an action or circumstance* A. X. —w. περί + GEN. *on a possession* Sapph.(or Alc.)

7 exaggerate —*one's power, a circumstance* Th. Plu.; (intr.) Th.

μεγαλ-ώνυμος ον *adj.* [ὄνομα] (of deities, mythol. figures) with a mighty name, **renowned, glorious** Sapph.(or Alc.) B.(cj.) S. Ar.

μεγαλωστί *adv.*: see under μέγας

μεγ-άνωρ ορος *dial.masc.adj.* [ἀνήρ] (of wealth) associated with manly greatness, **man-exalting, lordly, noble** Pi.

Μεγάρα ᾶς, Ion. **Μεγάρη** ης *f.* Megara (wife of Herakles, killed by him in a fit of madness) Od. Pi. E.

Μέγαρα¹ ων *n.pl.* Megara (a city on the Saronic Gulf, betw. Athens and Corinth, opposite Salamis) Hes.*fr.* +

—**Μεγαρεύς** έως *m.* | nom.pl. Μεγαρεῖς, Att. Μεγαρῆς, Ion. Μεγαρέες, ep. Μεγαρῆες | gen.pl. Μεγαρέων (ep. ήων) | citizen of Megara, **Megarian** Thgn. Hdt. Th. + ‖ PL. Megarians (as a population or military force) Eleg.adesp. Hdt. +

—**Μεγαρίς** ίδος *f.* Megarid (region around Megara) Th. Plb. Plu.; (appos.w. χώρη *region*) Hdt. ‖ ADJ. (of ships) Megarian Th.

—**Μεγαρικός** ή (dial. ᾱ́) όν *adj.* of or relating to Megara or the Megarians; (of a person) **Megarian** Ar. Plu.; (of walls, produce, manufactured items) Ar.; (of a decree of Perikles concerning the city) Ar. Plu.; (pejor., of a plan, w.connot. of deceitfulness, allegedly a characteristic of the people) Ar. ‖ FEM.SB. Megarian territory Lys. X. Plu. ‖ MASC.PL.SB. Megarian school (of philosophers, founded by Eukleides of Megara, an associate of Socrates) Arist.

—**Μεγαράδε** *adv.* to Megara Ar. Att.orats. Pl. Arist.

—**Μεγαρόθεν** *adv.* from Megara And. Ar. Pl. Plu.

—**Μεγαροῖ** *adv.* at Megara Ar. Pl. Arist.

Μέγαρα² ων *n.pl.* Megara (Greek city in Sicily) Th.

—**Μεγαρεῖς**, Att. **Μεγαρῆς**, Ion. **Μεγαρέες**, έων *m.pl.* people of Megara, **Megarians** Hdt. Th. Pl. Plu.

Μεγαρίζω *vb.* [Μέγαρα¹] | fut. Μεγαριῶ | **play the Megarian** (w.connot. of being deceitful) Ar.

μέγαρον ου *n.* **1** (sg. and pl.) chief room or general living-room (in a palace, a humble dwelling, the abode of a god), **hall** Hom. hHom. AR.

2 (esp.pl.) building or set of buildings, **house, home** (of persons or gods) Hom. Hes. Lyr. Emp. AR. Theoc.

3 (sg. and pl.) room or rooms reserved for women, **women's quarters** Hom.

4 (sg.) temple-building (or its inner chamber), **temple, sanctuary, shrine** Hdt. Plu.

—**μεγαρόνδε** *adv.* to the hall Od.

μέγας μεγάλη μέγα *adj.* | masc.voc. μέγας, also μεγάλε (A., dub.) | acc. μέγαν μεγάλην μέγα | gen. μεγάλου (Aeol. ω) ης ου | dat. μεγάλῳ η ῳ | PL: nom. μεγάλοι αι α | du.masc.nom.acc. μεγάλω ‖ compar. μείζων, dial. μέζων | superl. μέγιστος |

1 great in size; (of persons, parts of the body) **large, big** or **well-built** Hom. +; (of persons) **tall** Hom. +; (of a warrior) tall and mighty, **great** Hom. +

2 (of persons) **full-grown, adult** Od. +

3 (of animals) **large, big, great** or **full-grown** Hom. +

4 (of natural expanses or features of the landscape, such as sky, sea, a tract of water or land, a mountain) **large, great, extensive, vast** Hom. +

5 (of man-made things) **large, big, great, extensive, vast** Hom. +; (w.connot. of lavishness or impressiveness) **great, grand** Hom. +

6 great in strength; (of natural elements or phenomena, such as wind, storm, fire, water) **great, strong, powerful** or **violent** Hom. +

7 (of sounds, voices) **great, mighty, loud** Hom. +

8 (of deities and divine agencies, their will) **great, powerful, mighty** Hom. +; (of an oath, under divine sanction) Hom. +

9 great in power, achievement or fame; (of persons) **great, mighty, powerful** Hom. +; (esp. of Persian, Hellenistic or Macedonian rulers) **great** A. +; (of a people, family, city, state, or sim.) A. +

10 (w.art., of a person, opp. a less important namesake) **the great** Il. +; (of the Panathenaia) Th. +; (perh., of a person) **the elder** Plb.

11 great in skill or attainment; (of persons) **great, distinguished** Hom. +

12 great in degree; (of personal qualities or attributes, states of mind, sufferings, or sim.) **great** or **intense** Hom. +

13 great in importance, consequence or difficulty; (of things, circumstances, events, actions, tasks) **great, important, mighty** or **weighty** Hom. +

14 (pejor., of words, plans or deeds, w.connot. of infamy or boastfulness) **violent, outrageous, audacious** Hom. +

15 great in number; (of herds, flocks, a race, an army) **large, great, huge** Hom. +

16 great in price or value; (of things) **great, costly** Hom. +

17 (of a favour or kindness, a friend or ally) **great, valuable** Thgn. Trag. +; (of gratitude or thanks) **great, sincere** Hdt. Th. +

—**μέγα**, **μεγάλα** *neut.sg.pl.adv.* **1** to a great degree or extent, **greatly** Hom. +

2 powerfully, strongly Hom. +

3 (strengthening an adj. or adv.) **very** Hom. +; (strengthening a compar. or superl.) **by far** Hom. +

4 loudly Hom. +

—**μεγάλως** *adv.* **greatly** or **mightily** (in extent, degree, power, or sim.) Hom. Hes. A. Hdt. E. Ar. +

—**μεγαλωστί** *adv.* **1** (strengthening μέγας) **mightily** —*ref. to a mighty person having fallen* Hom.; (without μέγας) AR.

2 to a great degree or on a large scale, **greatly** or **grandly** Sapph. Hdt. Pl. AR. Plb.

—**μεῖζον**, dial. **μέζον** *neut.compar.adv.* **more greatly** or **mightily** (in extent, degree, power, or sim.) Thgn. Trag. +

—**μειζόνως**, Ion. **μεζόνως** *compar.adv.* **more greatly** or **mightily** Hdt. E. Th. Isoc. +

—**μέγιστον**, **μέγιστα** *neut.sg.pl.superl.adv.* **most greatly** or **mightily** Hdt. S. E. Th. +

μεγα-σθενής ές *adj.* [σθένος] (of a person or deity) of great strength, **mighty** Hes.*fr.* Lyr. A. Ar. AR.; (of a prophecy, curse, divinely inspired desire) Simon. A.; (of gold) Pi.

μεγ-αυχής ές *adj.* [αὔχη] **1** (of the spirit of a dead king) great in self-confidence, **proud** A.

2 (of the pankration) worthy of great pride, **glorious** Pi.

μέγεθος ους, Ion. **μέγαθος** εος *n.* **1** largeness (as a measurable property, freq. opp. πλῆθος *amount*, a countable property); **magnitude, size** Hdt. +

2 magnitude, size, dimensions (of objects, buildings, places, or sim.) Hdt. Th. Ar. +; (specif.) **tallness, height** Hdt. +

3 bodily size (esp. in terms of height); **stature, build, tallness** (of persons, deities, animals, mythol. beings) Hom. Hes. Tyrt. A. Hdt. Pl. +

4 (gener.) largeness (opp. smallness); **large size** or **expanse** (of things, places, or sim.) Th. Ar. +

5 magnitude (in terms of a calculable sum); **amount** (of money) Hdt.; **value** (of stolen objects) Isoc.; **size** or **large**

μέγηρα

size (of a population, military force, crowd, or sim.) Th. Pl. +
6 greatness (in scale or degree); **magnitude, scale, extent** (of trouble, danger, wrongdoing, victory, happiness, or sim.) Hdt. E. Th. Att.orats. Pl. +
7 (specif.) **strength, violence** (of a storm) Th. X. +; (of a fire) Plb.; (of anger, passion) Isoc. Pl. Aeschin.; **loudness** (of shouting) Th. Plu.; intensity, **volume** (of a voice, speaking or singing) Arist.
8 gravity, seriousness (of a crime, accusation, event, or sim.) Hdt. Isoc. X. +; **severity** (of a penalty or punishment) Att.orats. Pl. Arist. Plu.; **importance** (of an action or event) Hdt. Isoc. +; (of a literary theme) Isoc.; **grandeur** (of a literary composition, in its scope or style) Isoc. Arist.
9 greatness (in power or influence); **greatness** (of a city, a people, an empire, or sim.) E. Th. Isoc. Pl. +; (of a god) E. X.
10 (gener.) **greatness** or **loftiness** (of a person, his behaviour or character) Plu.

μέγηρα (ep.aor.): see μεγαίρω

μεγ-ήριτος ον adj. [app.reltd. νήριτος, ἀριθμός] (of the children of Nereus) **numerous** Hes.

μεγιστᾶνες ων m.pl. [μέγιστος, see μέγας] **men of power and influence, grandees** (at court) NT.

μεγιστο-άνασσα ᾱς dial.f. (epith. of Hera) **most mighty queen** B.

μεγιστο-πάτωρ ορος m. [πατήρ] (epith. of Zeus) **most mighty father** B.

μεγιστό-πολις εως fem.adj. [πόλις] (epith. of Hesychia) **maker of most mighty cities** Pi.

μέγιστος (superl.adj.): see μέγας

μεγιστό-τῑμος ον adj. [τῑμή] (of Justice) **most greatly honoured** A.

μεδέων ουσα (dial. οισα), gen. οντος ούσης masc.fem.ptcpl. adj. [reltd. μέδω] | Aeol.masc.nom. μέδεις (as if fr. μέδημι) | Ion.masc.dat. μεδεῦντι |
1 (of Zeus) **ruling, holding sway** (W.ADV. fr. Ida) Il.; (of Zeus, another deity or a deified person, W.GEN. over a place) Il. Hes. hHom. Scol. Lyr. E. +; (over dolphins) Ar.; (over arrows) E.; (over song) Call.; (over the soul) Melanipp.; (over everything) B.fr.(cj.) E.fr.; (W.DAT. at a place) Pi.; (of an island, W.DAT. in a sea) Pi.fr.
2 ‖ MASC.SB. (ref. to a king) **ruler** Call.

μέδιμνος ου m. **medimnos** (a dry measure, esp. for grain, equiv. to 48 Attic khoinikes, approx. 52 litres, but varying in other Greek states) Hes.fr. Hippon. Hdt. Ar. Att.orats. X. +

Μέδουσα ης, dial. **Μέδοισα** ᾱς f. **Medusa** (a Gorgon) Hes. Pi.

μέδω vb. [reltd. μεδέων] **1** (of a god) **rule, hold sway** —W.PREP.PHR. in a place S. —W.GEN. over a place, the sea Ar.(quot. S.)
2 (of an element in the natural world) **have charge** —W.GEN. of a prerogative Emp.

—μέδων οντος masc.ptcpl.adj. (of Zeus) **ruling, holding sway** (W.ADV. on high) Hes.; (of Poseidon, a sea god, W.GEN. over the sea) Od. Corinn. ‖ PL.SB. **leaders, commanders, chiefs** (W.GEN. of a people) Hom.

—μέδομαι mid.vb.| ep.3du.impf. μεδέσθην | fut. μεδήσομαι |
1 (of gods) **devise, plan** —trouble (W.DAT. for someone) Il.
2 (of persons) **take thought, prepare** —W.GEN. for fighting, departure, food, sleep Hom.

μέζεα dial.n.pl.: see μήδεα²

μεζόνως Ion.compar.adv., **μέζων** dial.compar.adj.: see μέγας

μεθ-αιρέω contr.vb. [μετά] | iteratv.aor.2 μεθέλεσκον | **catch in one's turn** —a ball Od.

μεθ-άλλομαι mid.vb. | only ep.athem.aor.ptcpl. μετάλμενος | **1** leap or rush after (someone or sthg.); (of a warrior, a lion) **spring forth in attack** (against an enemy, a prey) Il.; (of a runner) **dash in pursuit** (of a competitor) Il.
2 (of Eros, as a bird) **jump from place to place** Bion

μεθ-ᾱμέριος ον dial.adj. [ἡμέριος] (of mixing-bowls, ref. to their use) **during the day, by day** E.

μεθ-αρμόζω vb. **1 set in new order; rearrange** —a troop-formation Plu.; **reshape** —geometrical lines Plu. [or perh. adapt mesolabes] | see μεσόγραφος
2 put right, correct —a person (who is in error) S.
3 ‖ MID. **change, convert** —persons (W.PREP.PHR. to a particular way of life) Plu.; **transfer** —a marriage alliance (W.PREP.PHR. to a different person) Plu.; (intr.) **change** —W.PREP.PHR. to a different kind of behaviour Plu.
4 ‖ MID. **adapt oneself to, adopt** —new habits A. —a better life E.

μεθάρμοσις εως f. **rearrangement, reshuffle** (W.GEN. of political masters) Plb.

μεθέηκα (ep.aor.): see μεθίημι

μεθείην (athem.aor.opt.), **μεθεῖμεν**¹ (1pl.), **μεθείμην**, **μεθεῖο** (1 and 2sg. mid.): see μεθίημι

μεθεῖμεν², **μεθεῖτε**, **μεθεῖσαν** (1, 2 and 3pl. athem.aor.), **μεθεῖναι** (inf.), **μεθείς** (ptcpl.), **μεθείω** (ep.aor.subj.): see μεθίημι

μεθειμένος (pf.pass.ptcpl.), **μεθεῖται, μεθεῖνται** (3sg. and pl. pf.pass.): see μεθίημι

μεθείσθω (3sg.aor.pass.imperatv.), **μεθεῖτο** (3sg.athem.aor.mid.): see μεθίημι

μεθεκτέον (neut.impers.vbl.adj.): see μετέχω

μεθεκτός ή όν adj. (of Platonic Forms) **able to be participated in** Arist.

μεθέλεσκον (iteratv.aor.2): see μεθαιρέω

μεθέμεν (ep.athem.aor.inf.), **μεθέμενος** (athem.aor.mid. ptcpl.): see μεθίημι

μέθεξις εως f. [μετέχω] **sharing, partaking** or **participation** (freq. W.GEN. in sthg.) Pl. Arist.

μεθέξω (fut.): see μετέχω

μεθ-έπομαι mid.vb. | 3sg.impf. (tm.) μετὰ ... εἵπετο | fut. μεθέψομαι | ep.aor.2 ptcpl. μετασπόμενος | **1** (of troops) **come after, follow** (others) Il.(tm.); (tr., of a warrior) **follow up** —a retreating enemy Il.
2 follow (w. further connot. **comply with**) —W.DAT. a person S.(dub.)

μεθ-έπω vb. [ἕπω] | ep.impf. μέθεπον, Aeol.1pl. πεδήπομεν | ep.aor.2 ptcpl. μετασπών | **1 be concerned about, care for** —a person Il.(tm.) Sapph.; (of a poet) **attend to** —a burden (fig.ref. to a responsibility) Pi.
2 direct or **drive** (W.ACC. one's horses) **in pursuit of** —a person Il.; **drive in search of** —a person Il.
3 pursue —a deer Pi.; (fig.) —a dispensation fr. Zeus (ref. to an athletic victory) Pi. —a sweet lie (ref. to a phantom) Pi.
4 go after, seek out —persons AR.; (of a lion) —its mate AR.
5 pursue or **follow** —W.DAT. on swift feet Hom.
6 pay a visit (to a place) Od.

μεθ-ερμηνεύομαι pass.vb. (of words or writings) **be translated** Plb. NT. Plu.

μέθες (athem.aor.imperatv.), **μεθέσθαι, μέθεσθε** (athem.aor.mid.inf. and 2pl.athem.aor.mid.imperatv.): see μεθίημι

μεθέστηκα (pf.): see μεθίστημι

μέθετε (2pl.athem.aor.imperatv.), **μεθετέον** (neut.impers.vbl.adj.), **μέθετον** (2du.athem.aor.imperatv.): see μεθίημι

μέθη ης *f.* [μεθύω] **1 strong drink** (i.e. wine) Hdt. S. E. Antipho Pl. X. +

2 drunkenness, intoxication Att.orats. Pl. X. +

3 ‖ PL. **bouts of drinking** Pl. Plb. Plu.

4 (fig.) **tipsy state** (W.GEN. of terror) Pl.

μεθῆκα (aor.): see μεθίημι

μεθ-ήκω *vb.* [μετά] **come to fetch** —*someone* E. Ar.; **come to get** —*sthg.* E.(dub.)

μέθ-ημαι mid.vb. [ἧμαι] **sit among** —W.DAT. *people* Od.

μεθ-ημερινός ή όν *adj.* (of activities or circumstances) **during the day, daytime** Pl. X. D. Plu.

μεθημοσύνη ης *f.* [μεθήμων] **slowness or reluctance to take action, slackness** Il.

μεθήμων ον, gen. ονος *adj.* [μεθίημι] **slow or reluctant to take action, slack, remiss, lazy** Hom.

μεθησέμεν, μεθησέμεναι (ep.fut.infs.), **μεθήσω** (fut.): see μεθίημι

μεθ-ιδρύω *vb.* (of a soul) **change the location of** —*its life* Pl. ‖ MID. **change one's location, migrate** —W.ADV. *to a place* Arist. Plu.

μεθ-ίημι, Ion. **μετίημι** *vb.* | PRES. (ῑ usu. in Att., sts. in Hom.): 2sg. μεθίης, ep. μεθίεις, 3sg. μεθίησι, ep. μεθίει, Ion. μετίει, 3pl. μεθιᾶσι, Ion. μετιεῖσι | imperatv.: 2sg. μεθίει, 3sg. μεθιέτω, 2pl. μεθίετε, 3pl. μεθιέντων | ptcpl. μεθιείς, Ion. μετιείς | inf. μεθιέναι, ep. μεθιέμεν, also μεθιέμεναι | subj. μεθιῶ, ep.3sg. μεθίησι ‖ IMPF.: 3sg. μεθίει, Ion.3pl. μετίεσαν, ep.3pl. μέθιεν | iteratv. μεθίεσκον | FUT.: μεθήσω, Ion. μετήσω, ep.inf. μεθησέμεν, also μεθησέμεναι ‖ AOR.: μεθῆκα, Ion. μετῆκα, ep. μεθέηκα ‖ ATHEM.AOR.: 1pl. μεθεῖμεν, 2pl. μεθεῖτε, 3pl. μεθεῖσαν | 2sg.imperatv. μέθες, pl. μέθετε, du. μέθετον | ptcpl. μεθείς, Ion. μετείς | inf. μεθεῖναι, Ion. μετεῖναι, ep. μεθέμεν | subj. μεθῶ, ep. μεθείω | opt. μεθείην, 1pl. μεθεῖμεν ‖ MID.: impf. μεθιέμην | fut. μεθήσομαι | athem.aor.: 3sg. μεθεῖτο, 2pl.imperatv. μέθεσθε, ptcpl. μεθέμενος, inf. μεθέσθαι, opt. μεθείμην, 2sg. μεθεῖο ‖ PASS.: 3sg.impf. μεθίετο (Tim.), Ion. ἐμετίετο | Ion.fut. μετήσομαι | aor.: Ion.3sg. μετείθη, 3sg.imperatv. μεθείσθω, Ion. μετείσθω, 3pl. μεθείσθων | pf.: 3sg. μεθεῖται, 3pl. μεθεῖνται, ptcpl. μεθειμένος, Ion. μεμετιμένος ‖ neut.impers.vbl.adj. μεθετέον ‖ The sections are grouped as: (1–10) release (fr. contact, detention or constraint), (11–14) give up, abandon, (15–17) let go (in downward or forward motion), (18–20) let out, (21–26) set aside, (27–29) slacken off. |

1 let go (fr. one's grasp), **let go of, release** —*a person, hand or embrace, an object* Il. S. E. Ar. AR.; (intr.) **let go** Emp. E. Ar. ‖ MID. **release one's grip, let go** S. E. Ar. —W.GEN. *of a person, part of the body, clothing, an object* E. Ar. Plu. ‖ PASS. (of an object) **be released** (fr. one's grasp) Ar.

2 (fig., of cold, fatigue, sleep) **let go of** —*a person* Od. AR.

3 let go (fr. detention or other constraint on movement); **let go, release** —*a person* (esp. *a captive*) Il. Hes. A. Hdt. E. Pl. + —*captive birds* Ar. —*a visitor* (*i.e. not detain him*) Od. E.; (wkr.sens.) **let** (W.ACC. persons) **go** (on their way) AR. ‖ PASS. (of an army) **be let loose** A.; (of a person) **be allowed to go** Hdt. Plu. —W.PREP.PHR. *to a place* Hdt.

4 release, free —*a person* (W.PREP.PHR. *fr. slaughter, i.e. the threat of it*) E.; **relieve** —*one's heart* (W.GEN. *of grief*) Il. ‖ PASS. **be relieved** —W.GEN. *of an activity* Pl.; **be deprived** —W.GEN. *of the faculties of sight and perception* Pl.

5 allow to get away, **let off** —*an enemy* (W.PREDIC.ADJ. *unwounded, unpunished*) S. E.

6 let off, release —*an interlocutor* (fr. *questioning or discussion*) Pl.

7 release (fr. marriage), **divorce** —*a wife* Hdt.

8 leave —*persons or things* (W.PREDIC.ADJ. *in a certain state*) Hdt. E. Pl.

9 leave free (for action or movement); **leave, allow** —W.ACC. + INF. *someone to do sthg. or go somewhere* Hdt. S.(dub., v.l. παρίημι) E. ‖ MID. (of a channel) **become free** —W.INF. *to flow* (*into the sea*) Pl. ‖ PF.PASS. (of springs) **be free** —W.INF. *to flow* Pl.

10 (fig.) **release, let loose** —*pleasures, kinds of knowledge* (*envisaged as streams*) Pl. —(W.INF. *to flow towards a certain goal*) Pl. ‖ PASS. (fig., of pleasures, kinds of knowledge) **be let loose** Pl.

11 give up, hand over, surrender (sts. W.DAT. to someone) —*persons, a corpse, bones, weapons, a tiller* Il. S. E.(also mid.) Plu.; **yield** —*victory, primacy* (*to someone*) Il. Plu.; (wkr.sens.) **give over, dedicate** —*a sanctuary* (*to a god*) E.

12 (intr., of rowers) app. **surrender control** —W.DAT. *to a ship* (*i.e. let it go where it wishes*) S. [perh. also w.connot. *ease off* (fr. *one's exertions*), as 27 below]

13 abandon, forsake —*a person, his friendship* Il. Thgn.; (of gods) —*a city* E.; **leave alone, ignore, neglect** —*a person* AR.

14 abandon (to the elements or chance); **cast** —*fillets* (W.DAT. *to the winds*) E.; **leave, commit** —*one's cause* (W.PREP.PHR. *to fortune*) Plu.

15 release (in downward motion); **let** (W.ACC. an object) **fall** —W.PREP.PHR. *into a river* Od.; **let down** —*an anchor* A.; **let** (W.ACC. one's limbs, body) **sink** (to the ground) A. E.; **cast** —*one's body, a corpse* (W.PREP.PHR. *into the sea*) E. —*a hook* (*into a river*) Hdt.

16 release (in forward motion); **discharge, let fly** —*arrows, spears* Il.(tm.) E. X.; **launch** —*a sword* (*envisaged as a missile*) E.; **set in flight** —*winged chariot-horses* E.fr. ‖ PASS. (of a missile) **be discharged** Tim.

17 (gener.) cause (sthg.) to go (W.PREP.PHR. into or towards a place); **set** —*one's foot* (*inside a building*) E. —*a sword* (*in a scabbard*) E.; **introduce** —*an object* (*into the mouth*) Pl. —*a notion* (*into a city*) Pl.; **turn** —*one's eyes* (*towards the sky*) E.; (of a god) **send** —*hostile dream-visions* (W.ADV. + DAT. *back against one's enemies*) S.

18 let out, **utter** —*speech, song* Hdt. Trag.; app. **cause** —*an uproar* Od.(v.l. μετατίθημι); (of a subterranean noise) **give forth** —*a deep rumble* E. | see μετατίθημι 12

19 let fall, **shed** —*tears* Hdt. E.Cyc.; **let** (W.ACC. blood) **drip** —W.PREP.PHR. *into a pool* A.fr.

20 (of the lungs) **let out, discharge** —*breath* Pl.; (of Erinyes) —*poison* (W.GEN. fr. *their hearts*) A.; (of statues) **exude** —*drops of blood* Plu.; (of a tree) **put forth** —*shoots* Hdt.

21 lay aside, put down —*weapons* Hdt.; **set aside, abandon** —*offerings* S.

22 lay aside, give up, abandon —*power* Hdt. —*a quarrel, anger, pride, awe, obduracy, decorum, or sim.* Hom. Trag. —*one's life, breath, pleasure in living* E. ‖ MID. **let go** —W.GEN. *of power* E. —*of life* Plu.

23 cast off —*a fit of madness* E. —*sleep* Theoc.epigr.

24 put aside, avert —*a danger* E.

25 leave aside, abandon, dismiss —*a matter, discussion, plan, form of government, or sim.* Hdt. Trag. Ar. Pl. AR.; **disregard, neglect, ignore** —*issues or considerations* Hdt. S. E. ‖ PASS. (of a plan or topic) **be dropped** Hdt. Pl.

26 remit, cancel —*tribute payments* Hdt.; **overlook, forgive** —*offences* Hdt.

27 (intr.) relax one's efforts, **slacken, ease off, let up** Hom. Callin. —W.GEN. *in fighting, toil, endeavour, or sim.* Hom. Tyrt. AR. —fr. *one's usual colour* Ar.(cj., see μεθίστημι 12) —W.INF. *in doing sthg.* Il. —W.PTCPL. AR.

μεθίστημι

28 cease (lamenting) Il. —W.INF. *doing sthg.* Hdt. —W.GEN. *fr. anger* Od. —*fr. making a request* Hdt.; (mid.) —*fr. shouting* A.(cj.) —*fr. making a noise* E.
29 be remiss about, be neglectful of —W.GEN. *a person* Il.; **neglect** —W.INF. *to do sthg.* X.

μεθ-ίστημι, Ion. **μετίστημι** *vb.* | impf. μεθίστην | fut. μεταστήσω | aor.1 μετέστησα ‖ MID.: aor.1 μετεστησάμην ‖ PASS.: aor. μετεστάθην ‖ neut.impers.vbl.adj. μεταστατέον ‖ The act. and aor.1 mid. (sts. also impf.mid.) are tr. For the intr.mid. see μεθίσταμαι below. The act. athem.aor., pf. and plpf. are also intr. |
1 change the location (of persons or things); **move** —*people* (sts. W.ADV. *elsewhere*) Th. —*a troop-formation* Hdt. —*a market* (W.PREP.PHR. *to a place*) Th. —*one's possessions* Plb. —*stones* (fr. *a place*) Plu. —*one's foot* (i.e. *move on foot*, W.PREP.PHR. *to another land*) E. —*a war* (W.ADV. + PREP.PHR. *fr. one country to another*) Plu. —*a month* (W.PREP.PHR. *fr. its place in the calendar*) Plu.
2 (aor.1 mid.) **cause** (persons) **to withdraw** (fr. one's presence); **dismiss** —*persons* Hdt. Th. And. X. Aeschin. Plb.
3 (aor.1 mid.) **remove** —*a person* (fr. *a place of asylum*) Plu. —*garrisons* (fr. *towns*) Plb.
4 remove —*oneself* (W.PREP.PHR. *fr. a country*) Plu.; (specif.) **banish, exile** —*persons* (sts. W.PREP.PHR. *fr. a city*) Arist. Plu.; (aor.1 mid.) Th. Aeschin.; (impf.mid.) Arist. ‖ PASS. **be banished** D.
5 remove from power or office; depose, overthrow —*political leaders* Th.; (aor.1 mid.) Plb.; (of God) **remove** —*a king* (fr. *his throne*) NT. ‖ PASS. **be removed** —W.PREP.PHR. fr. *an office* NT.
6 relieve, free —*a person* (W.GEN. fr. *sickness, troubles, an unwelcome duty*) S. E. —*a statue* (fr. *blood pollution*) E.; **wake** —*a person* (W.GEN. fr. *sleep*) E.
7 get rid of —*foolishness, envy, hatred, slander* Men. Plu.
8 change (one thing for another); **change** —*a gift* Od. —*a name* E.; (of a god) —*a person's fortune* E.
9 change (sts. by revolution) —*an existing form of government* (sts. W.PREP.PHR. *to another*) Hdt. Th. Att.orats. Pl. X. Arist. + —*a city or people* (*to or fr. a form of government*) Th. X. —*laws* X.
10 create by change, change to —*a new form of government* (W.PREP.PHR. fr. *an existing one*) Arist.
11 (intr., of circumstances) **cause change** (in a city, its fortunes) Th.
12 change —*one's habits, a person's thinking or character* E. Antipho Ar. Isoc. Pl. Arist. +; (of trouble) —*a person's appearance* E.; (of passions and emotions) —*the body* Arist.; (intr., of a person) —W.GEN. fr. *one's usual colour* Ar.(dub., cj. μεθέστηκα, also μεθίημι) | see μεθίημι 27
13 cause a change of allegiance; bring over —*a person, a country* (sts. W.DAT. or PREP.PHR. *to a certain side*) Th. X. Plb. Plu.
14 change the mind of, convert —*a person* (*to one's point of view*) Th. NT. Plu.

—**μεθίσταμαι** *mid.vb.*| imperatv. μεθίστασο | impf. μεθιστάμην, Ion. μετιστάμην | fut. μεταστήσομαι ‖ also ACT.: athem.aor. μετέστην, dial. μετέσταν, imperatv. μετάστηθι, dial. μετάστᾱθι, 3sg. μεταστήτω, 2pl. μεταστήτε | pf. μεθέστηκα, ptcpl. μεθεστηκώς, also μεθεστώς, Ion. μετεστεώς | 3sg.plpf. μεθειστήκει, Ion. μετεστήκεε ‖ aor.pass. (w.mid.sens.) μετεστάθην |
1 go and stand with —W.DAT. *one's companions* Il.
2 change one's location, move (usu. W.ADV., GEN. or PREP.PHR. *to or fr. a place*) Hdt. Trag. Att.orats. Pl. Plb.; (of rivers) —W.PREP.PHR. fr. *their beds* (*during an earthquake*) Plu.; (of a war) —*to another country* Plu.
3 move aside, retire, withdraw Hdt. E. Th. X. Aeschin. D. +; **leave, depart** —W.DAT. *in flight* E.
4 (specif.) **go into exile, be banished** And. Plu.
5 depart —W.GEN. or PREP.PHR. fr. *life* (i.e. *die*) E. Plb.; **die** Plu.
6 give up —W.GEN. *a throne* E.; **abandon** —W.GEN. *one's weapons* Plu.
7 let go of —W.GEN. *anger, grief* A. E.; **be freed** —W.GEN. fr. *troubles, fear* E.
8 (of a wind, the wind of fortune) **change direction, shift** E. Plu.; (of a person's fortune, its course, a situation, sts. W.ADV. or PREP.PHR. *for the better, to sthg. different*) A. Hdt. E. Antipho Plu.
9 (of a city, a form of government) **undergo change** (sts. by revolution) Att.orats. X. Arist. Plb.
10 (gener., of things, situations) **undergo change** Pl.; (of a god, in neg.phr.) Pl.; (of a city's prestige) D.
11 come into existence by change; (of a particular type of person, a form of government) **develop, arise** —W.PREP.PHR. fr. *another* Pl.
12 (of a person) **change** —W.PREP.PHR. *to a different lifestyle* Th. —W.GEN. fr. *a former way of life* Ar. —W.PREP.PHR. fr. *an old man* (W.PREDIC.ADJ. *to being young*) E.
13 change —W.GEN. fr. *a former state of mind* E.(also aor.pass.); **change one's mind** Hdt. Ar.
14 change one's allegiance; secede (fr. an alliance) Th.; **defect** (sts. W.PREP.PHR. *to the enemy*) Th. X. Plu.
15 (of a person's feelings) **change** —W.PREP.PHR. fr. *joy, for the better* E.; (of a person's thinking) E.(aor.pass.); (of anger) **subside** E.

μεθοδεύομαι *mid.vb.* [μέθοδος] **behave craftily** Plb.
μεθοδικός ή όν *adj.* (of logic, knowledge) **systematic** Plb.; (of experience) **systematically acquired** Plb. ‖ NEUT.SB. **systematic method** Plb.; (pl., title of a lost treatise) Arist.
—**μεθοδικῶς** *adv.* **systematically** Plb.
μέθ-οδος ου *f.* [ὁδός] **1 pursuit** (of knowledge); **inquiry, investigation** (into a subject) Pl. Arist. Plu.
2 mode of prosecuting such an inquiry, line of inquiry, method, system Pl. Arist.
3 technique (used in an art or science) Plu.
μεθ-ομῑλέω *contr.vb.* **keep company** —W.DAT. w. *people* Il.
μεθ-όριος ᾱ ον *adj.* (of a region, city, mountain) **forming a border** or **lying on the border** (W.GEN. betw. two territories) Th. ‖ FEM.SB. **borderland** Th. Plu. ‖ NEUT.SB. (sg. and pl.) **border region** Th. X. Plu.; (fig., betw. two concepts) Pl.; (fig.ref. to a type of person, W.GEN. betw. two other types) Pl.
μεθ-ορμάομαι *pass.contr.vb.* | only aor.ptcpl. (w.mid.sens.) μεθορμηθείς | **mount an expedition in pursuit** (of a person) Il.; (of a swimmer) **strike out in pursuit** (of a boat) Od.
μεθ-ορμίζω, Ion. **μετορμίζω** *vb.* | fut. μεθορμιῶ | aor.mid.inf. μεθορμίσασθαι | **1 move** (W.ACC. naval forces) **to a new mooring** —W.PREP.PHR. *at a place* Plu.; (intr.) **shift one's mooring** —W.PREP.PHR. *to a place* X.; (mid.) —W.PREP.PHRS. fr. *one place to another* Hdt. Th.
2 ‖ MID. **find a haven** —W.GEN. fr. *disaster, distress* E.
3 (fig.) **dislodge** —*a lock of hair* (W.PREP.PHR. fr. *its place*) E.; (of wine-drinking) —*a person* (W.GEN. fr. *a sullen state of mind*) E.

μέθυ *n.* | only nom.acc. | **1 intoxicating drink, wine** Hom. Archil. Xenoph. S. E. AR.
2 beer (W.PREP.PHR. fr. *barley*) A.

μεθ-υποδέομαι mid.contr.vb. [μετά] **change one's footwear** Ar.

μεθύση f.: see μέθυσος

μέθυσις εως f. [μεθύω] **drunkenness** Thgn.

μεθύσκομαι pass.vb. | aor.pass. ἐμεθύσθην, Aeol.inf. μεθύσθην | **become intoxicated, get drunk** Alc. Heraclit. Hdt. E.*Cyc.* Ar. Att.orats. + —W.GEN. *on nectar* Pl. —(fig.) *on undiluted freedom* Pl. —W.DAT. *on the fumes (fr. a burning narcotic plant)* Hdt.

—**μεθύσκω** act.vb. (fig., of wealth, beauty, or sim.) **intoxicate** —*persons* Pl.

μεθυσο-κότταβος ον adj. [μέθυσος] (of youths) **drunk from playing kottabos** Ar.

μέθυσος ου m. —also **μεθύση** ης f. [μεθύω] **1** (appos.w. γραῦς *old woman*, κύων *bitch*) **drunkard, alcoholic** Ar. **2** || MASC.VOC. (as an insult) sot Plu.

μεθ-ύστερος ᾱ ον adj. [μετά] **coming later** || MASC.PL.SB. **future generations** A.

—**μεθύστερον** neut.adv. **1 later, afterwards** hHom. A. AR.; (phr.) τὸ μεθύστερον *in the future* S. **2 after the event, too late, belatedly** A. S.

μεθυστικός ή όν adj. [μεθύω] **1** (of a person) **prone to get drunk, drunken** Pl. Plu. **2** (of certain musical modes) **having the effect of intoxication** (i.e. enervating) Arist.

μεθύω vb. [μέθυ] | only pres. and impf. | **1 be drunk** (on wine) Od. Thgn. Lyr. E.*Cyc.* Ar. Att.orats. + **2** (fig.) **be drunk** —W.DAT. *w. love* Anacr. —W.PREP.PHR. *w. sexual passion* X. —*w. luxury* Pl. —*under the influence of an argument* Pl.; (of a boxer) **be groggy** —W.DAT. *fr. blows* Theoc. **3** (of a bull's hide) **be drenched** —W.DAT. *w. fat* Il.

μεθῶ (athem.aor.subj.): see μεθίημι

μειαγωγέω contr.vb. [μεῖον app. *small sacrificial lamb*; ἀγωγός] (of a father) **bring in a small lamb** (app. weighed before sacrifice) when presenting his son to his phratry at the Apatouria; (fig.) **offer** (W.ACC. *tragedy*) **for weighing** Ar.

μεῖγμα (also **μῖγμα** or **μίγμα**) ατος n. [μείγνυμι] **1 mixture, compound** Arist.; (W.GEN. of myrrh and aloe, ref. to an ointment) NT. **2 mixture** (of speech and barking) Plu.

μείγνυμι (sts. written **μίγνυμι**) vb. —also (pres. and impf.) **μειγνύω** (Pi. Plu.), also **μίσγω** (Hom. +) | dial.inf. μειγνύμεν (Pi.), ep. μισγέμεναι | impf. ἔμισγον, ep. μίσγον, dial.3pl. μείγνυον (Pi.) | fut. μείξω, ep.inf. μειξέμεναι | aor. ἔμειξα || PASS.: impf. ἐμειγνύμην, also ἐμισγόμην, ep. μισγόμην, 3sg.iterat v. μισγέσκετο, 3pl. μισγέσκοντο | fut.inf. μείξεσθαι (Od.) | fut.2 μιγήσομαι (Il.) | aor.1 ἐμίχθην, also ἐμείχθην, ep. μίχθην, ep.3pl. ἔμιχθεν, ep.inf. μιχθήμεναι | aor.2 ἐμίγην, ep. μίγην, ep.3pl. μίγεν, ptcpl. μιγείς, Boeot. μιγίς, inf. μιγῆναι, ep. μιγήμεναι, also μιγήν (Parm.), ep.2sg.subj. μιγήῃς | also ep.athem.aor.: 3sg. ἔμικτο, also μίκτο | pf. μέμιγμαι, also μέμειγμαι | ep.3sg.plpf. ἐμέμικτο | stat v.fut.pf. μεμείξομαι (Hes. A.) || neut.impers.vbl.adj. μεικτέον |

1 mix together, mingle, blend —*different things* Od. Emp. Pl. Arist. Plu.; (mid.) —*elements of a discourse* (W. πρός + ACC. *w. each other*) Isoc. **2 mix** (one thing w. another); **mix or mix in, mingle, combine** —*sthg.* (usu. W.DAT. *w. sthg. else*) Il. hHom. A. Ar. Pl. X. + —(W. μετά + GEN.) Pl. NT. || PASS. (of things) **be mingled, mixed or combined** (usu. W.DAT. *w. others*) Hom. Hes. Simon. A. Pi. Emp. + —(W. σύν + DAT.) Pi. —(W. μετά + GEN.) NT.; (of persons) —W. ἐν + DAT. *among others* E. **3 mix together** (in confusion or without distinction); **mix up, jumble together** —*stones* (*of different colours*) Pl.; (of dead soldiers, fr. opposing armies) —*their limbs* E.; (of wealth) **confound, confuse** —*birth or pedigree* (*by promoting undesirable unions*) Thgn. || PASS. (of goats) be mixed or jumbled together Il.; (of different languages) Hom.; (of shouts) E. **4 form by combination, put together, blend** —*sthg.* (w. ἐκ + GEN. *out of two or more elements*) Pi.; (mid.) —*a political framework* (*out of democracy and monarchy*) Plu. **5** (of a man and woman) **join together in, contract** —*marriage* Pi.; (of two animals) —*friendship* Archil.; (of persons) **join** or **engage in** —*dancing* Pi.fr. || PASS. (of a marriage) be contracted Pi. **6** || PF.PASS. (esp. PTCPL.) **constitute a mixture or compound**; (of primeval creatures) be compounded (of male and female elements) Emp.; (of the Minotaur) —W.DAT. *w. the twofold nature of man and bull* E.fr. —W. ἐκ + GEN. *fr. man and bull* Isoc.; (of things) —*fr. two or more elements* Pl. Arist.; (of a council) consist of a mixed group —W.GEN. *of old and young men* Pl.; (of an army) be made up —W.DAT. *fr. Greeks and barbarians* Plu.; (of a jar of milk) be a mixture (of that of cows and sheep) E.*Cyc.*; (of wines) Arist. **7** || MID.PASS. (of persons) **join company** (usu. W.DAT. or PREP.PHR. w. others) Hom. AR. **8** || MID.PASS. **reach, come to** —W.DAT. *a place* Il. Pi. —w. ἐν + DAT. Pi. **9** || MID.PASS. (of a spear) **make contact** —W.DAT. *w. vital organs* Il.; (of a storm-wind) —W.DAT. *w. the sea* Il.; (of a severed head) —*w. dust* Hom.; (of a fallen warrior) —w. ἐν + DAT. Il. **10** || MID.PASS. (of persons or deities) **keep company, associate, consort** —W.DAT. *w. others* Od. hHom. A. Pl.; (of things, w. other things) Emp. Pl. **11** || MID.PASS. (of persons) be joined in sexual union, **have sexual intercourse** Il. Pi. AR.; (of an individual) Hom. Hes. hHom. Hdt. E.fr. —W.DAT. *w. someone* Hom. Hes. Lyr. Parm. Hdt. Trag. +; (of animals) **mate** —W.DAT. *w. others* hHom. Pi. —*w. humans* Pi.fr. Hdt. **12 bring together in conflict; join, clash, match** —*hands, might, weapons, battle* (sts. W.DAT. *w. an enemy*) Il. Alc. Pi. S. AR. —*hands* (*w. hands*) AR. || PASS. (of war) be joined Callin.; (of warriors, their might) come together, meet, clash (sts. W.DAT. *w. an enemy*) Il.; (of winds) Od. **13 bring into physical contact; join, touch** —*one's lips* (W.DAT. *to another's*) Bion **14** (wkr.sens.) **bring into association; involve** —*persons* (W.DAT. *in hardship and pain*) Od.; **endow** —*a person* (W.DAT. *w. garlands*) Pi.; **inflict** —*death* (W.DAT. *on someone*) Pi. || PASS. be endowed —W.DAT. *w. garlands, praises* Pi.; be struck —W.DAT. *w. wonder* Pi. || PF.PASS. (of a person, in his tomb) perh., be a participant —w. ἐν + DAT. *in blood sacrifices, honours* Pi.; (of persons) be involved —w. σύν + DAT. *in troubles* S.(dub.)

μειδάω contr.vb. | only ep.aor. μείδησα, ptcpl. μειδήσᾱς, inf. μειδῆσαι | (of persons or deities) **smile** Hom. Hes. hHom. AR.; (of the earth) hHom.

μειδήματα των n.pl. **smiles** Hes.

μειδίᾱμα ατος n. [μειδιάω] **smile** Plu.

μειδιάω contr.vb. | ep.3sg. μειδιάει, Aeol. μειδίαι (Theoc.), ep.ptcpl. (w.diect.) μειδιόων (fem. μειδιόωσα), also μειδιάων | aor. ἐμειδίᾱσα, Aeol.fem.ptcpl. μειδιαίσαισα | **smile** Il. hHom. Sapph. Anacr. Ar. Pl. +

μείζων (compar.adj.), **μειζόνως** compar.adv.: see μέγας

μεικτός (also written **μικτός**) ή όν adj. [μείγνυμι] **1** (of things) **capable of mixing** or **being mixed** Arist.; (W.DAT. w. other things) Pl.
2 consisting of a mixture; (of things) **compounded, blended** (sts. w. ἐκ + GEN. fr. certain elements) Pl. Arist.; (of unguents, i.e. combining oil w. perfume) Call.
3 (of persons, speeches, achievements, abstr. qualities) **of a mixed nature** (i.e. containing different or contrasting elements) Isoc. Pl. Arist. Plu.; (of the limbs of unnatural beasts, i.e. partly human, partly bestial) AR.

μείλανι (ep.masc.dat.adj.): see μέλᾱς

μείλιγμα ατος n. [μειλίσσω] **1** that which soothes; **soothing power** (W.GEN. of a person's tongue) A. || PL. soothing morsels (W.GEN. for the fierce temper of dogs) Od.; soothing strains (W.GEN. of the Muses) Theoc.
2 appeasement (W.GEN. of a person's anger) Plu. || PL. appeasements, propitiatory offerings (ref. to libations, for Erinyes, the dead or powers below) A.
3 (pejor.ref. to a person) **smooth charmer** (W.GEN. of concubines) A.

μειλικτήρια ων n.pl. **propitiatory offerings** (ref. to libations, W.DAT. for the dead) A.

μείλικτρα ων n.pl. **propitiatory offerings** (for Erinyes) AR.

μείλινος Ion.adj.: see μέλινος

μείλιον ου n. [reltd. μείλιχος] **1** that which soothes; **propitiatory gift, goodwill offering** (to a person) Il.(pl.); (to gods) AR.(pl.); (sg., ref. to an object offered to a goddess, W.GEN. against unfavourable weather at sea) Call.
2 || PL. **requital, recompense** (for wrong done) AR.
3 (sg. and pl.) **plaything, toy** (for a child) AR.
4 || PL. (wkr.sens.) **gifts** AR.

μειλίσσω vb. [μείλιχος] | ep.inf. μειλισσέμεν | fut. μειλίξω | ep.3sg.aor.mid. μειλίξατο | **1** (of Zeus) **soothe, appease** —the anger of a goddess E. || PASS. (of the feelings of a child) be soothed or comforted hHom.
2 propitiate or **console** —corpses (W.GEN. w. fire, i.e. by cremation and funeral rites) Il.
3 make propitiatory offerings (in order to avert anger or win favour) AR. || MID. **appease, propitiate** —deities, the dead AR.
4 || MID. **attempt to win over** —a person AR.
5 || MID. **induce, persuade** —a person (W.INF. to do sthg.) AR.(also act.)
6 || MID. **implore, beseech** —a person AR. —(W.INF. to do sthg.) AR.
7 || MID. (of a sorceress) **charm, tame, subdue** —the blast of fire AR.
8 treat kindly —a guest Theoc.
9 || MID. **use soft** or **comforting words** (to gloss over the truth) Od.
10 (of rivers) **soften** or **treat gently** —the soil A. [or perh. make (the soil) amenable (for agriculture)]

μειλιχίη ης Ion.f. [μειλίχιος] **1 gentleness, tenderness** (as a gift of Aphrodite) Hes.
2 courtesy, graciousness (of a guest, a suppliant) AR.; (W.GEN. in battle, as inappropriate behaviour) Il.

μειλίχιος ᾱ (Ion. η) ον adj. [μείλιχος] **1** (of words) **gentle, soothing, kindly** or **conciliatory** Hom. Pi. B. AR. || NEUT.PL.SB. gentle or kindly words Hom. Hes.fr. AR.
2 (of play) **genial, happy** AR.
3 (of respect) **gracious** Od. Hes.
4 (of drink-offerings) **propitiatory** S. [also interpr. as sweetened with honey, as if reltd. μέλι] || NEUT.PL.SB. propitiatory sacrifices Plu.
5 (cult epith. of Zeus) **the Kindly** or **Compassionate** Th. X.; (of Dionysus) Plu.

—**μειλίχιον** neut.adv. **gently, softly** —ref. to a bull lowing Mosch.

—**μειλιχίως** adv. **in a gentle** or **kindly manner** —ref. to speaking AR.

μειλιχό-γηρυς υ, gen. υος adj. [γῆρυς] (of a tongue) **with gently persuasive speech** Tyrt.

μείλιχος, Aeol. **μέλλιχος**, ον adj. **1** (of persons or deities) **mild, gentle, kindly** Il. Hes. Anacr. Plu.; (of words) Od. Hes. || NEUT.SB. mildness (of speech) Thgn.
2 (of the gifts of Aphrodite) **gentle, tender** hHom. Mimn.; (of an amorous feeling) Pi. || NEUT.PL.SB. gentle gifts (bestowed by Grace) Pi.
3 (of a wind) **mild, gentle** AR.; (of a bird) AR.; (of a bull) **tame** Mosch.; (of a life) **calm, untroubled** Pi.
4 (of eyes) **gentle, soft** Sapph.
5 (of wine) **mellow** Xenoph.

—**μείλιχον** neut.sg.adv. **in a kindly manner** —ref. to offering a welcome AR.

—**μέλλιχα** Aeol.neut.pl.adv. **gently** —ref. to winds blowing Sapph.

—**μειλίχως** adv. **gently** —ref. to speaking Semon.

μειξ-έλληνες (also **μῑξ-**) ων m.pl. [μείγνυμι, Ἕλλην] **men with a mixture of Greek and foreign ancestry, mixed-race Greeks** Plb. Plu.

μειξ-εριφ-αρνο-γενής (also written **μῑξ-**) ές adj. [ἔριφος, ἀρήν; γένος, γίγνομαι] (of a sausage) **made of a mixture of kid and lamb, kid-and-lamb** Philox.Leuc.

μεῖξις (also **μῖξις**) εως (Ion. ιος) f. **1 mingling** (of natural elements, w. each other) Parm. Emp.
2 process of mixing or **state of being mixed, mixing, mixture, combination** (of concr. or abstr. things) Pl. Arist. Plu.
3 blending (W.GEN. of children, through the union of parents w. different characteristics) Pl.
4 mixing in, admixture (of credibility, in a story) Plu.
5 sexual intercourse Hdt. Pl. Plu.; (specif.) **incest** Isoc.
6 mating (of asses w. horses) Anacr.; (gener.) **coupling** (of animals) Plu.

μειξο-βάρβαρος (also **μῑξ-**) ον adj. (of people) **of mixed Greek and barbarian race, half-barbarian** (by birth) Pl. X.; (of a warrior, fr. the style of his armour) E.

μειξό-θηρ ηρος masc.adj. [θήρ] (of men) **half-beast** E.

μειξό-θροος ον adj. [θρόος] (of plunder, ref. to women) **with mingled cries** (i.e. fr. young and old) A.

μειξο-λῡδιστί (also **μῑξ-**) adv. (mus.) **in the Mixolydian mode** Pl. Arist.

μειξό-μβροτος ον adj. [βροτός] (of an animal, ref. to Io) **half-human** A.

μειξο-πάρθενος (also **μῑξ-**) ον adj. [παρθένος] (of a plunderer, ref. to the Sphinx) **half-girl** E.; (of a viper) Hdt.

μείξω (fut.): see μείγνυμι

μεῖον neut.compar.adj. and adv.: see μείων

μειονεκτέω contr.vb. [μείων, ἔχω; cf. πλεονεκτέω] **1 have** or **be satisfied with less** (rather than more) X.
2 have or **get less** —W.GEN. of sthg. X. —W.COMPAR.GEN. than others X.
3 have or **get less** (than the norm or than expected); **be short** X. —W.GEN. of sthg. X.
4 fall short (in giving) X.

5 (gener.) **be at a disadvantage** X.
6 be shorter (in height) —w.COMPAR.GEN. *than sthg.* Call.

μειονεξίᾱ ᾱς *f.* state of having less (than others or one's due), **disadvantage** X.

μειόνως *adv.*: see under μείων

μειότερος ᾱ ον *compar.adj.* [reltd. μείων] (of a river) **smaller** AR.

μειόω *contr.vb.* **1 make less** (in size), **lessen, reduce, decrease** —*a space* Plb. ‖ MID.PASS. (of territory) be decreased X.; (of μείς *month*, in a supposed etymology) grow less Pl.
2 make less (in amount, degree or strength); **reduce, diminish** —*one's resources* Plu.; **cut down on** —*an activity* X. ‖ MID.PASS. (of a swollen river) be reduced, decrease (in volume) Plu.; (of cavalry, in numbers) X.; (of an enemy, in strength or numbers) X.; (of a person's power) Plu.; (of friendship, goodwill) X.; (of households) deteriorate X.; (of old people) —w.ACC. *in their intellectual faculties* X.
3 lessen (in status or honour), **humiliate** —*persons* X.
4 underrate, underestimate —*an enemy's strength* X.; **understate, play down** —*an achievement* X.
5 (intr.) **understate** or **depreciate** (as a rhetorical technique) Arist.
6 ‖ MID. **fall short** —w.GEN. *of others* (*in the performance of an activity*) X.; **be inferior, be wanting** —w.GEN. *in physical strength* X.

μειρακιεύομαι *mid.vb.* [μειράκιον] **behave boyishly, lark about** Plu.

μειράκιον ου *n.* [dimin. μεῖραξ] (colloq.) **young man, lad, boy** Ar. Att.orats. Pl. X. Arist. Thphr. +; (derog., ref. to a grown man) **mere boy** Plb. Plu.

μειρακιόομαι *mid.contr.vb.* **become a young man** X.

μειρακίσκη ης *f.* [dimin. μεῖραξ] **girl** Ar.

μειρακίσκος ου *m.* **lad, boy** Pl. Men. Plu.

μειρακιώδης ες *adj.* [μειράκιον] **1** (of an education) **suitable for boys** Pl.
2 (usu. pejor., of a writer, his technique, a speech, opinion, state of mind, action, or sim.) **youthful, boyish** or **childish** Isoc. Pl. Arist. Plb. Plu.

—**μειρακιωδῶς** *adv.* **boyishly, childishly** Plb. Plu.

μειρακύλλιον ου *n.* [dimin. μειράκιον] **youngster, lad** or **mere lad** Ar. D. Men.

μεῖραξ ακος *f.* (colloq.) **girl** Ar. Men.

μείρομαι *mid.vb.* ‖ ep.imperatv. μείρεο ‖ PASS.: 3sg.pf. ἔμμαρται, also μεμόρηται, 3sg.plpf. ἔμμαρτο, also μεμόρητο (AR.) ‖ pf.ptcpl. εἱμαρμένος, Aeol. ἐμμόρμενος, also μεμορμένος (AR. Plu.) ‖ pf.inf. εἱμάρθαι (B.) ‖ also ep.3sg.pf.act. ἔμμορε, 2sg. (inflected as aor.2) ἔμμορες (AR.) ‖ **1 receive as one's portion** or **due, be allotted, take as one's share** —*half of a man's honour* (ref. to his dominion) Il.
2 ‖ STATV.PF.ACT. **have one's allotted portion** or **share** —w.GEN. *of honour* Il. Hes. hHom.; have allotted to one —w.ACC. *a share* (*of sthg.*) AR.
3 ‖ STATV.PF.ACT. (wkr.sens.) **get** —w.GEN. *honour* or *respect* Od. Thgn. —*good value, a good neighbour* Hes. —*a prize* Call. —*a mad passion* AR.
4 ‖ STATV.PF.ACT. (of glory) **have been allotted** or **have fallen to** —w.ACC. *a person* AR.
5 ‖ IMPERS.PF. and PLPF.PASS. **it is (was) fated** —w.ADV. *for the good* B. —w.ACC. + INF. *that sthg. shd. be the case* Hom. Hes. Callin. Pl. —w.DAT. + INF. *for someone to do sthg.* Isoc. Pl. D. Arist. Plu.
6 ‖ PF. and PLPF.PASS. (of a person) **be fated** —w.PTCPL. *to be doing sthg.* AR.

—**εἱμαρμένος**, Aeol. **ἐμμόρμενος**, also **μεμορμένος**, η (dial. ᾱ) ον *pf.pass.ptcpl.adj.* (of persons or things) **allotted, appointed, destined** (by fate or the gods) Alc. Thgn. A. S. Pl. Men. + ‖ NEUT.SB. **destiny** Plu.

—**εἱμαρμένη** ης *f.* **1 fate, destiny, appointed span of life** or **time of death** Att.orats. Pl. Arist. Plb. Plu.
2 natural span (w.GEN. of time, for an illness) Pl.

μείς *dial.m.*: see μήν²

μείωμα ατος *n.* [μειόω] **loss, shortfall** (in monetary terms) X.

μείων ον, gen. ονος *compar.adj.* ‖ PL.: masc.nom. μείονες, also μείους ‖ masc.acc. μείους ‖ neut.nom.acc. μείονα, also μείω ‖ **1** (of a person) **less** (in size or stature), **smaller** Il.; (of a fish) Plb.
2 lesser (in status or wealth), **humbler** or **poorer** B. E. X.
3 lesser (w.DAT. in age, i.e. younger) S.
4 (of a city) **less great** (in power or reputation) E. Plu.
5 (of things) **less, lesser** (in amount, extent, degree, value or importance) Pi. Trag. X. Arist. Call. Bion ‖ NEUT.SB. **lesser amount** A. S. X. Plu.
6 (phr.) μεῖον ἔχειν *be at a disadvantage, come off worse* X. ‖ cf. μειονεκτέω
7 ‖ PL. (of persons or things) **fewer** (in number) Hes. Xenoph. X. Plu.

—**μεῖον** *neut.adv.* **to a lesser degree** or **extent, less** A. X. Call. Plu.

—**μειόνως** *adv.* (of a person, w. ἔχειν) **be too lowly** S.

μείωσις εως *f.* [μειόω] **1 shortening** (of days and nights) Plb.
2 decrease (in the volume of water in a river) Plb.

μελάγ-γαιος (also **μελάγγειος** Plu.) ον *adj.* [μέλᾱς, γῆ] (of land) **black-soiled** Hdt. Plu.

μελάγ-κερως ων, gen. ω *adj.* [κέρας] **black-horned** A.

μελάγ-κευθής ές *adj.* [κεῦθος] (of a cloud) **bringing dark concealment** B.(cj.)

μελάγ-κορυφος ου *m.* [κορυφή] a kind of black-headed bird; perh. **coal tit** or **sombre tit** Ar.

μελάγ-κουρος ον *adj.* [κουρά] (of Obscurity) **black-haired** Emp.

μελάγ-κροκος ον *adj.* [κρόκη] (of the journey across Acheron) for which black woven cloth is worn, **black-clothed** A.

μελαγ-χαίτης ου, dial. **μελαγχαίτᾱς** ᾱ *masc.adj.* [χαίτη] (of a centaur) **black-haired** Hes. S.; (of Hades) E.

μελάγ-χιμος ον *adj.* [prob. χεῖμα] (of night, clothes, earth, poison) **black, dark** A. E. AR.; (of persons, their limbs) **dark-skinned** A.; (of a sheep) **black-fleeced** E. ‖ NEUT.PL.SB. dark spots (of ground, not covered by snow) X.

μελαγ-χίτων ωνος *masc.fem.adj.* [χιτών] (of the mind) **clothed in a black tunic, gloom-enveloped** A.

μελάγ-χλαινος ον *adj.* [χλαῖνα] **wearing a black cloak** (in mourning) Mosch.

μελαγχολάω *contr.vb.* [μελάγχολος] **suffer from an excess of black bile** (a symptom of bodily and mental disturbance), **be mad, crazy** or (specif.) **depressive, melancholic** Ar. Pl. D. Men.

μελαγχολίᾱ ᾱς *f.* emotion caused by an excess of black bile, **madness** or **depression** Plu.

μελαγχολικός ή όν *adj.* (of persons, their natures) **prone to madness** or **depression** Pl. Arist. Men.

μελάγ-χολος ον *adj.* [χολή] (of a poison) **of black gall** S. [or perh., of an arrow *dipped in black gall*]

μελάγ-χροιής οῦ *Ion.masc.adj.* [χροιά] **dark-skinned, swarthy** Od.

μελάγ-χρους ουν *Att.adj.* [χρώς] **dark-skinned, swarthy** Plu.

μελάγ-χρως ωτος (dial. οος) *masc.fem.adj.* **1** (of people) **dark-skinned** Hdt.; (of a horse) **black-coated** Pl. **2** (of Acheron, Erinyes) **black-hued** E.

μέλαθρον ου *n.* | ep.gen.dat.sg.pl. μελαθρόφιν | **1 roof-beam** Od. hHom. Sapph. AR. **2** (meton.) **roof** (under which guests are entertained) Hom.; (strengthened against storms) AR. **3 roof** (brought down by an enemy, meton. for the whole house) Il. **4** (gener., freq.pl. for sg.) **hall** or **halls, dwelling, abode** (ref. to a house or palace) B. Trag. Ar. Men. Hellenist.poet.; (ref. to a temple) Pi. E. Call.; (ref. to a cave) S. E.*Cyc.*; (W.ADJ. *of heaven*, ref. to the vault of the sky) E.; (W.ADJ. *of night*, ref. to the underworld) E.

μέλαινα (fem.adj.): see μέλᾱς

μελαίνομαι *mid.pass.vb.* [μέλᾱς] | aor.pass. ἐμελάνθην | **1** (mid.) **blacken one's hair** —W.DAT. *w. a dye* Ar. **2** (mid.pass., of soil) **turn black** or **dark** (behind the plough) Il.; (of the white hair of rejuvenated old men) Pl.; (of the moon, in an eclipse) Plu.; (of the gloom of night) AR.; (of a wounded goddess) —W.ACC. *in her fair skin* (*fr. blood*) Il. **3** (mid.pass., of an island) **be black** —W.DAT. *w. dark forests* AR. **4** || AOR.PASS. (of grapes, serpents' jaws) **be made black** (by an artist) Hes. || AOR.PASS.PTCPL.ADJ. (of blood) **black** S.(dub.); (of a metal) Pl.
—**μελαίνω** *act.vb.* (intr., of flesh) **turn black** —W.PREP.PHR. *fr. burning* Pl.

μέλαις (Aeol.masc.nom.adj.): see μέλᾱς

μελαμ-βαθής ές *adj.* [βάθος] (of the abyss of Tartaros) **with black depths** A.; (of a dragon's lair) E.; (of a river) AR.

μελάμ-βροτος ον *adj.* [βροτός] (of a race) consisting of black persons, **black** E.*fr.*

μελαμ-πᾱγής ές *dial.adj.* [πήγνῡμι] **1** (of blood) **black-clotted** A. **2** (of an evil-doer, compared to bronze adulterated w. lead) **with ingrained blackness** A.

μελάμ-πεπλος ον *adj.* [πέπλος] (of a mourner, a costume) **black-robed** E.; (of Night) E.

μελαμ-πεταλο-χίτων ωνος *masc.fem.adj.* [πέταλον, χιτών] (of the knees of Cybele) **robed in black leaves** Tim.

μελάμ-πτερος ον *adj.* [πτερόν] (of Death) **black-winged** E.

μελάμ-πῡγος ον *adj.* [πῡγή] (of an eagle) **black-rumped** Archil.; (of a person) **with a black-haired arse** (regarded as a sign of tough masculinity) Ar.

μελαμ-φαής ές *adj.* [φάος] (of Erebos) **black-lit** E.

μελαμ-φᾱρής ές *adj.* [φᾶρος] (of darkness) **black-robed** B.

μελάμ-φυλλος ον *adj.* [φύλλον] (of trees, land, mountains) **black-leaved, dark with foliage** Pi. B. S. Ar. Theoc.*epigr.*

μελαμ-ψήφις ῑδος *masc.adj.* [ψῆφος] (of rivers) **black-pebbled** Call.

μέλαν ανος *n.* **carbon black** (ref. to a substance ground to make ink) D.; **black ink** Pl. Thphr.(cj.) Plu.

μελάν-αιγις ῐδος *masc.fem.adj.* [αἰγίς²] (of an Erinys) **storm-black** A.

μελαν-αυγής ές *adj.* [αὐγή] (of a stream of blood) **dark-gleaming** E.

μελάν-δετος ον *adj.* [δέω¹] **1** (of swords) **black-bound** (prob. w. leather round their hilts) Il. Hes. **2** (wkr.sens., of a shield) **black, dark** A.; (of a sword, sts. W.DAT. w. blood) E.

μελαν-είμων ον, gen. ονος *adj.* [εἷμα] (of persons) **clothed in black** Plb. Plu.; (transf.epith., of the attacks of Erinyes) A.

μελανέω *contr.vb.*: see under μελάνω

μελ-ανθής ές *adj.* [ἄνθος] (of the Egyptian race) **black-complexioned** A.

μελανίᾱ ᾱς *f.* **1 blackness** (as a quality, opp. whiteness) Arist. **2 blackness** (covering a plain, ref. to the impression created by a huge army) X. **3** || PL. **patches of blackness, lividities** (on the flesh) Plb.

Μελανιππίδης ου *m.* **Melanippides** (5th-C. BC dithyrambic poet fr. Melos) X. Arist.

μελανό-ζυξ ζυγος *masc.fem.adj.* [ζεύγνῡμι, or perh. ζυγόν] (of ruin, ref. to a ship bringing ruin) **black-built** (i.e. coated in pitch) A. [or perh. *black-benched*, i.e. inflicted by sailors occupying the benches of a black ship]

μελανο-κάρδιος ον *adj.* [καρδίᾱ] (of a rock, in the Styx) **black-hearted** Ar.

μελανόκολπος *adj.*: see μεγαλόκολπος

μελαν-όμματος ον *adj.* [ὄμμα] **black-eyed** Pl. Arist.

μελαν-νεκυο-είμων ον, gen. ονος *adj.* [νέκυς, εἷμα] **clothed in cadaverous black** Ar.

μελανό-πτερος ον *adj.* [πτερόν] (of Night) **black-winged** Ar.; (of a dream-vision) E.

μελανο-πτέρυξ ῠγος *masc.fem.adj.* (of dreams) **black-winged** E.

μελανο-συρμαῖος ον *adj.* [συρμαία] (of a people, ref. to Egyptians) **black and fond of purgatives, black laxative-taking** Ar.

μελανό-χροος ον *adj.* [χρώς] (of a man) **dark-skinned, swarthy** Od.

μελανό-χρως χροος *dial.masc.fem.adj.* **1** (of beans) **black-skinned** Il. **2** (of a woman) **dark-skinned, swarthy** Theoc.

μελαν-τειχής ές *adj.* [τεῖχος] (of the house of Persephone, in the underworld) **black-walled** Pi.

μελάντερος (compar.adj.): see μέλᾱς

μελάν-υδρος ον *adj.* [ὕδωρ] (of a spring) **of dark water** Hom. hHom. Thgn.

μελάνω *vb.* (of the sea) **grow black, darken** —W.PREP.PHR. *under a storm-wind* Il.
—**μελανέω** *contr.vb.* | Ion.masc.acc.sg.ptcpl. μελανεῦντα (Call.) | **1** (of deep water) **be dark** AR. **2** (of a young man) **darken** —W.ADV. *handsomely* (perh. w. a *growth of beard*) Call.*epigr.*

μέλᾱς μέλαινα μέλᾰν *adj.* | Aeol.masc.nom. μέλαις | gen. μέλᾰνος μελαίνης (dial. ᾱς) μέλᾰνος | ep.masc.dat. μέλανι || compar. μελάντερος (Il. X. Thphr.), superl. μελάντατος (Arist. AR.) | **1** (of a colour) **black** Pl. || NEUT.SB. **black** (as a colour) Pl. Arist.; (as a pigment) Pl. || NEUT.PL.SB. **black colours** Pl. Plu. | see also μέλαν **2** having a naturally black or very dark colour; (of rock, dust, ash, iron, enamel, rust) **black, dark** Hom. Hes. Anacr. Thgn. E. Ar. +; (of smoke) A. E.*fr.*; (of plants, foliage, vegetables, fruits, juices, oil) Od. hHom. Hippon. Hdt. Ar. Theoc.; (of grapes) Il. Hes. E.; (of wine) Od. Ar. Tim.; (of bile) Pl. Thphr. Men. || NEUT.SB. **dark part** (W.GEN. of an oak, ref. to either its bark or its inner core) Od. **3** (of hair, freq. opp. white, as a sign of youth) **black, dark** Sapph. Anacr. S. Ar. Pl. Thphr. +; (of a bearded chin, as a sign of maturity) Alc. Pi. **4** (of animals, birds, their eyes, hair, coat, feathers, colouring) **black, dark** Hom. hHom. Hdt. Ar. Pl. X. + || NEUT.PL.SB. **dark patches** (on a hare's coat) X. **5** (of persons) having a naturally black or dark skin, **black-skinned** Hdt.; (of their semen) **black** Hdt. || MASC.PL.SB. **Black Men** (as the name of a tribe) Hes.*fr.* Call.

6 having a dark complexion (through exposure to the sun, a mark of manliness), **dark, swarthy, tanned** S. Ar. Pl. D. Arist. Men.; (of brows) Theoc.; (of a complexion) X.
7 (of earth, land, fields, the ground) **black, dark** Hom. Hes. Archil. Semon. Eleg. Lyr. E.
8 (of sea, waves, water) **black, dark** Hom. Pi.*fr.* E. AR.; (of the rippling surface of the sea) Od.; (of fresh water) Hom. AR. Theoc.; (of a rainstorm) AR.
9 (of blood, usu. shed or spilt) **black** Hom. Hes. Thgn. Hdt.(oracle) Trag. Hellenist.poet.; (of gore, bloodshed) Od. Pi.; (of poisonous blood) S.; (of a haemorrhaging vein) S.
10 marked with a black or dark colour; (of ships) **black, dark** (fr. a coating of pitch) Hom. Hes. hHom. Alc. E.*Cyc.*; (of ramparts, fr. painting) Hdt.; (of clothing or fabrics, fr. dyeing) Il. Hdt. X. Plu.; (of a Spartan soup, fr. the colour of its ingredients) Plu.
11 (of a ballot) **black** (opp. white, for casting one of two possible votes) Arist. Plu.
12 black from discolouration; (of a cooking-pot) **black** (fr. scorching) Ar.; (of hands, fr. dirt, or perh. sores) Theoc.; (of teeth, fr. decay) Thphr.; (of fingernails, fr. illness) Thphr.(cj.)
13 dark from the absence of light; (of night, evening, gloom) **black, dark, murky** Hom. Hes. Alcm. Pi. Trag. Ar. AR.; (of subterranean gloom) E.; (of a cloud) Il. E.; (of a cloud of death, grief) Hom. Thgn. E.; (of silence, as representing obscurity and oblivion) Pi.*fr.*
14 black (as the colour assoc.w. death and things which are sinister or ill-omened); (of death, the fate of death) **black** Hom. Hes. Tyrt. Pi. E.; (of Hades, his house, his inescapable power) Thgn. S. E.; (of Erebos) Ar.; (of the Keres *Fates*, Erinyes, Ares, Ate) Hes. Mimn. A.
15 (of garments worn by mourners) **black** Il. E. Lys. X. Is. Plu.; (of a sail, signalling bad news) Plu.; (of a cup for sacrificial blood) Ar.; (of a mourner's blow to the head) **funereal** A. [or perh. *causing black bruises*] ‖ COLLECTV.NEUT.SG.SB. black (ref. to mourning dress) Call.
16 (of a curse) **dark, deadly** A.; (of a sword, perh. w. further connot. *bloodstained*) E.
17 (of pain) **grim, dire** Il.; (of a dream) **gloomy, sinister** A.; (of fortune) A.(dub.)
18 (in Roman ctxt., of a day assoc.w. a past disaster) **black, ill-omened** Plu.
19 (of a person's mind or heart, under strong emotion) **gloomy, grim** Hom. Thgn. Pi.*fr.*; (of an eye) perh. **grim** or **pained** B. | see also ἀμφιμέλᾱς

μέλδω *vb.* soften (by boiling), **make tender** —*the flesh or entrails of oxen* Call. ‖ MID. (of a boiling cauldron) **melt down** —*a hog's fat* Il. [unless PASS. (of the fat) *be melted down*, or (of the hog) *be made tender*]

μέλε Att.interj. [perh.reltd. μέλεος] | only in phr. ὦ μέλε | **my dear** (as an address to a man or woman, w. tone ranging fr. friendly sarcasm or mild reproach to indignation and exasperation) Ar. Pl.

μελεδαίνω *vb.* [μελεδῶναι] **1 care for** —*the sick* Hdt.
2 (freq. in neg.phr.) be concerned or care about, **mind** —*public censure* Archil. —*parental advice* Theoc.(dub.) —W.GEN. poverty and abusive enemies Thgn. —scorching heat Theoc. —W.INF. doing sthg. Thgn. —W.ACC. + PTCPL. someone doing sthg. Theoc.

μελέδημα ατος *n.* **1** (pl.) **care, concern, anxiety** Hom.; (W.GEN. about someone) Od.; (brought on by love) AR.
2 (pl.) **care, concern** (W.GEN. of the gods, towards humans) E.
3 interest (in a particular pursuit) Thgn.; (W.GEN. in shameful deeds) E.*fr.*(cj.) | see μελέτημα 1

4 (ref. to a person) object of care, **darling** (prob. W.GEN. of certain deities) Ibyc.

μελεδήμων ονος *masc.fem.adj.* (of persons) **concerned** (W.GEN. for good deeds) Emp.

μελεδῶναι, Aeol. **μελέδωναι**, ῶν (Ion. έων) *f.pl.* —also **μελεδῶνες** ων (AR., and freq. v.l.) *f.pl.* **cares, anxieties** Od. hHom. Mimn. Thgn. AR. Theoc.; (brought on by love) Hes. Sapph.

μελεδωνεύς έως *m.* **guardian, tutor** (of a child) Theoc.

μελεδωνός οῦ *m.f.* **overseer, supervisor, manager** (W.GEN. of a person and his possessions, a king's household, animals and their feeding) Hdt.

μελέεσσι (ep.dat.pl.): see μέλος

μελεϊστί *adv.*: see under μέλος

μελεο-παθής ές *adj.* [μέλεος, πάθος] **suffering pitifully** A.

μελεο-πόνος ον *adj.* **toiling pitifully** A.

μέλεος ᾱ (Ion. η) ον (also ος ον) *adj.* **1** (of speech, an effort) **ineffectual, unavailing, vain** Od.; (of a shout, a hope) AR.; (of glory) **empty** Il.
2 (of persons, sufferings, circumstances, sts. w. note of remonstrance) **unhappy, wretched, miserable, pitiful** Stesich.(cj.) Hdt.(oracle) Trag. Ar.(oracle and mock-trag.) Men.(mock-trag.) AR.
3 (of a goatskin cloak) **miserable, pitiful** E.*Cyc.*; (of tendons which give out, perh. w. hint of sense 1) Call.
—**μέλεον** neut.adv. **idly, uselessly, to no effect** Il.

μελεό-φρων ονος *masc.fem.adj.* [φρήν] **wretched at heart** E.

μελετάω *contr.vb.* [μελέτη] | neut.impers.vbl.adj. μελετητέον | **1** have care or concern for, **take thought for, attend to** —W.GEN. one's work or livelihood Hes.
2 think carefully about, **study** —*a topic, subject, problem, or sim.* Hdt. Isoc. Pl. Hyp. Plu.
3 consider carefully —W.COMPL.CL. how to do sthg. Isoc.; **take care to ensure** —W.COMPL.CL. that sthg. is done Isoc.
4 take trouble over, practise, cultivate —*a skill, activity, habit* hHom. Anacr. Hdt. S. Antipho Ar. +; (intr.) **behave, act** —W.ADV. in a certain way E. ‖ PASS. (of an activity or form of behaviour) be cultivated Th. Isoc. Pl.
5 take trouble to acquire or promote, cultivate —*a reputation for military prowess* Th.
6 make it one's concern or **practice** —W.INF. to do sthg. Isoc. Pl. X. Plu.
7 train oneself (to do sthg.); **practise** Antipho Ar. X. Arist. Plu. —*a skill or activity* Th. Isoc. Pl. X. Plu. —W.INF. doing sthg. Ar. Att.orats. Pl. X. Thphr. Plu. —W.PTCPL. doing sthg. X. —w. ὡς + FUT.PTCPL. w. a view to doing sthg. X. ‖ PASS. (of skills) be practised Th. X. Plu.
8 (specif.) **train** (for battle) Th. X. —W.DAT. w. the body (i.e. undergo physical training) X.
9 (causatv.) **train** (persons) —W.COMPL.CL. to ensure that they do sthg. X.
10 practise, rehearse (a speech) Pl. D. —*a speech or poem* D. Men. Plu.
11 (intr.) be a practitioner (of the art of oratory), **practise oratory** Isoc.; **be practised** or **adept** —W.INF. at speaking Aeschin.
12 deliver a speech (as an exercise), **perform, declaim** Plu.
13 (of a musician) **practise** or **perform** Arist. Plu.
14 plan or **plot** —*vain things* NT.
—**μεμελετημένως** *pf.pass.ptcpl.adv.* **in a trained manner** Plu.

μελέτη ης, dial. **μελέτᾱ** ᾱς *f.* **1 care, attention** (given to an activity) Hes. Archil. Thgn. Pi. Emp.; (paid by a trainer to an

μελέτημα

athlete, by parents to children) B. E. ‖ PL. attentions, assiduities (W.GEN. of the κερκίς *pin-beater*, in weaving) Ar.(quot. E.)
2 effort, discipline (in repressing anger) Pi.
3 concern (W.GEN. for an objective, i.e. effort to ensure it) S.; (for an activity, i.e. interest in it) E.
4 concern, interest, theme (of a poet, ref. to his subject matter) Pi.
5 habitual performance, practice Even.; (W.GEN. of hard work) Th.; (of kindness) Plu. ‖ PL. **practices** Th.
6 practice, training (as a means of acquiring a skill) Th. Critias Isoc. Pl. X. D. +; (W.GEN. for sthg.) Pl. X.
7 (in military or naval ctxt., freq.pl.) **exercise, drill, training** Th. Isoc. X. Plb. Plu.
8 (sg. and pl.) **intellectual exercise, study** Isoc. Pl.
9 subject of study, discipline Isoc. Pl.
10 rhetorical exercise, practice-speech Plu.

μελέτημα ατος *n.* **1 form of behaviour, practice** Critias; (W.GEN. of shameful deeds) E.*fr.*(dub., cj. μελέδημα)
2 preparation (for a later performance) Pl.
3 ‖ PL. **exercises, training** (for men or horses, in preparation for war) X.

μελετηρός ά όν *adj.* **assiduous in practice** (of military skills) X.

μελετητήριον ου *n.* **practice room** (for an orator) Plu.

μελετητός ή όν *adj.* (of an expertise) **acquired by practice or training** Pl.

μελέτωρ ορος *m.* [μέλω] **one who takes care, protector, avenger** (w. ἀμφί + ACC. for a murdered man) S.

μεληδόνες ων *f.pl.* **cares, anxieties** Simon. AR.

μεληθείς (aor.pass.ptcpl.): see μέλω

μέλημα ατος *n.* **1 matter for one's concern, concern, duty** A. S.
2 source of concern, anxiety A. Theoc.
3 (ref. to a man or woman) **object of affectionate concern, beloved one, darling** Ar. Men.; (W.DAT. of the people, unmarried girls, a household) Alcm. A. Pi.; (derog., of Death) Ar.; (W.GEN. of the Graces, ref. to Pan) Pi.*fr.*

μελησίμ-βροτος ον *adj.* [βροτός] (of cities) **cared about by mortals, celebrated** Pi.

μελήσω (fut.), **μελητέον** (neut.impers.vbl.adj.): see μέλω

Μελητίδης *m.*: see Μελιτίδης

μέλι ιτος *n.* **1 honey** Hom. +; (in comparisons, as an exemplar of sweetness) Il. Ar. Pl. Theoc. Mosch.; (fig., ref. to song or poetry) Pi. Lyr.adesp. Mosch.; (W.ADJ. *wild*, perh.ref. to a kind of sap or gum) NT. ‖ PL. **drops of honey** Emp.
2 sweet liquid, syrup (made fr. fruits and cereals) Hdt.

μελία ᾱς, Ion. **μελίη** ης *f.* | dial.gen.pl. μελιᾶν (Hes.) | **1 ash tree** Il. Hes. Ar.
2 object made of ash, ash-wood spear Hom. Hes. Tyrt. AR.

μελιάδής dial.adj., **μελιάδης** Aeol.adj.: see μελιηδής

Μελίαι ῶν *f.pl.* [perh.reltd. μελία] **Meliai** (a race of tree-nymphs) Hes. Call.

μελι-βόας ᾱ dial.masc.adj. [μέλι, βοή] (of a hymn) **with honeyed tones** Lasus (dub.); (of a swan) E.*fr.*

μελι-γαθής ές dial.adj. [γηθέω] (of water) **as delightful as honey** Pi.*fr.*

μελί-γδουπος ον dial.adj. [δοῦπος] (of songs) **with honeyed sound** Pi.

μελί-γηρυς, dial. **μελίγαρυς**, υος masc.fem.adj. [γῆρυς] (of singers, their voices or songs) **honey-toned** Od. hHom. Alcm. Pi.; (of the voices or songs of birds) hHom. Theoc.*epigr.*; (of an orator) Pl.

μελί-γλωσσος ον *adj.* [γλῶσσα] (of a nightingale, fig.ref. to a poet) **honey-tongued** B.; (of songs, spells, poems) A. B.*fr.* Ar.

μελίζω, dial. **μελίσδω** *vb.* [μέλος] | dial.inf. μελίζεν | dial. fut.mid. μελίξομαι | **1 sing of** —*sufferings* A. —*a festival* Pi.*fr.*; **celebrate** —*a person* (W.DAT. w. *songs*) Pi.
2 (of swans) **sing** —*a song of grief* Mosch. ‖ MID. (of persons) **sing** Alcm.
3 (act. and mid.) **make music** Hellenist.poet.; (fig., of a pine tree, in the wind) Theoc.; **play** —W.DAT. *on a panpipe* Theoc. Mosch. —(W.ACC. *a tune*) AR.

μελίη Ion.*f.*: see μελία

μελιη-γενής ές Ion.adj. [μελία, Μελίαι; γένος, γίγνομαι] (of an early race of men) **born from ash trees** or **ash-tree nymphs** AR.

μελι-ηδής, dial. **μελιαδής**, ές, Aeol. **μελιάδης** ες *adj.* [μέλι; ἡδύς, ἥδομαι] **1** (of wine) **honey-sweet** Hom. hHom. Thgn. Lyr.; (of fruit, corn, cakes) Hom. Hes. hHom. Call.; (of grass) Od. Theoc.; (fig.ref. to a woman's virginity) Pi.; (of beeswax, ref. to its fragrance) Pl.
2 (fig., of a person's life or soul) **honey-sweet** Hom.; (of sleep) Od.; (of a voice) Simon.; (of a homecoming) Od. AR.

μελι-καρίδες ων dial.*f.pl.* [κηρίον] **honeycomb cakes** Philox.Leuc.(dub.)

μελί-κομπος ον *adj.* [κόμπος] (of songs) **with honey-sweet praise** Pi.

μελί-κρατον, Ion. **μελίκρητον**, ου *n.* [κεράννυμι] **mixture of honey** (w. milk, as a libation), **honey-mixture** Od.; (W.GEN. w. milk) E.(pl.); (w. water, as a medicine) Arist.

μελικτάς ᾶ dial.*m.* [μελίζω] **musician** Theoc. Mosch.

μελί-λωτος ου *m.* [μέλι, λωτός] **a kind of sweet clover, melilot** Sapph.

μελίνη ης *f.* **1 millet** (ref. to the seed or crop) Hdt. X.; (pl., ref. to the stored grain) D.
2 ‖ PL. **millet fields** X.

μέλινος, Ion. **μείλινος**, η ον *adj.* [μελία] (of a spear) **made of ash, ashen, ash-wood** Il.; (of a threshold) Od.

μελί-πηκτον, dial. **μελίπακτον**, ου *n.* [μέλι, πηκτός] **honey-curdled confection, honey-cake** Philox.Leuc. Men.

μελί-πνους ουν contr.adj. [πνοή] (of a panpipe) **with honeyed breath** (fr. the wax used in its construction) Theoc.

μελι-πτέρωτος ον *adj.* [πτερωτός] (of the songs of the Muses) **honey-winged** Lyr.adesp.

μελί-ρρυτος ον *adj.* [ῥυτός] (of springs) **flowing with honey** Philox.Leuc.(cj.) Pl.

μελίσδω dial.vb.: see μελίζω

μέλισμα ατος *n.* [μελίζω] **1 song** Theoc.
2 melody, music Theoc. Mosch.
3 (meton.) **a kind of musical instrument, pipe** Mosch.

μέλισσα, Att. **μέλιττα**, ης (dial. ᾱς) *f.* [μέλι] **1 bee** Hom. +
2 (meton.) **honey** S.
3 (meton. or fig.) **bee** (ref. to the priestess at Delphi) Pi.; (perh.ref. to priestesses of Demeter) Call.
4 (fig.) **bee** (ref. to a poet) B.; (as object of comparison for a poet, envisaged as gathering honeyed songs) Ar. Pl.; (for a victory-song, flitting fr. one theme to another) Pi.; (as an affectionate address to a female singer) **honey-bee** (W.GEN. of the Muse) Ar.

μελισσο-κόμος ου *m.* [κομέω] **bee-keeper** AR.

μελισσο-νόμοι ων *f.pl.* [νέμω] **bee-guardians** (ref. to priestesses of Artemis) Ar.(quot. A.)

μελισσό-τευκτος ον *adj.* [τεύχω] (of honeycombs) **bee-built** Pi.*fr.*

μελισσο-τρόφος ον *adj.* [τρέφω] (of an island) **bee-nurturing** E.

μελι-σταγής ές *adj.* [μέλι, στάζω] (of a libation) **of dripping honey** AR.

Μελιταῖος *adj.*: see under Μελίτη²

μελίτεια ᾱς *f.* a kind of herb; perh. **balm** Theoc.

μελίτειον ου *n.* [μέλι] drink made from honey, **mead** Plu.

Μελίτη¹ ης *f.* **Melite** (Attic deme) Ar. Pl. Is. D. Plu.

—Μελιτεύς έως *m.* **man from Melite** D.

Μελίτη² ης *f.* **Malta** (island betw. Sicily and Africa) NT.

—Μελιταῖος ᾱ ον *adj.* (of a breed of small dog) from Malta, **Maltese** Thphr.

Μελιτίδης (or **Μελητίδης**) ου *m.* **Melitides** or **Meletides** (name of a proverbial blockhead) Ar. Men.

μελιτόεις εσσα εν, Att. **μελιτοῦς** οῦττα οῦν *adj.* [μέλι] **1** (of calm) **honeyed, honey-sweet** Pi.
2 (of stuffed loaves, as an offering to a god) **honeyed** Ar. ‖ FEM.SB. **honey-cake** (as an offering) Hdt. Ar.

μελιτόομαι *pass.contr.vb.* | pf.ptcpl. μεμελιτωμένος | (of poppy-seed) **be sweetened with honey** Th.

μελιτο-πώλης ου *m.* [πωλέω] **honey-seller** Ar.

μέλιττα *Att.f.*: see μέλισσα

μελίττιον ου *Att.n.* [dimin. μέλισσα] (fig., in voc. address to a person) **little bee** Ar.

μελιττουργίᾱ ᾱς *Att.f.* [μελιττουργός] **bee-keeping** Arist.

μελιττουργός οῦ *Att.m.* [ἔργον] one whose work is concerned with bees, **bee-keeper** Pl.

μελί-φθογγος ον *adj.* [μέλι, φθόγγος] (of Muses, songs) **honey-voiced** Pi.

μελί-φρων ον, gen. ονος *adj.* [φρήν] with a honeyed mind or sweet as honey to the mind; (gener., of wine, food, fruits) **honey-sweet** Hom. hHom. AR.; (of sleep) Il. B.; (of life) Hes.; (of feelings) A.*fr.*; (of a poetic theme, song, voice, words) Pi. AR.

μελί-χλωρος ον *adj.* [χλωρός] (of persons) **honey-yellow** (in complexion, as a lover's euphemism for pale or sallow) Pl.; (app. for dark) Theoc.

μελιχρός ᾱ́ όν, Aeol. **μέλιχρος** ᾱ ον *adj.* (of wine) **honey-sweet** Alc. Anacr.; (of apples) Theoc.; (of poetry) Call.; (of a lover's promises) AR.

—μελιχρῶς *adv.* **with honey-sweet sound** Lyr.adesp.

μελλ-είρην ενος *m.* [μέλλω] (at Sparta) youth about to become an eiren, **eiren-to-be** Plu.

μελλήματα των *n.pl.* **delays, procrastinations** E. Aeschin. Plu.

μέλλησις εως *f.* **1 intention** (to act) Arist.; (in military ctxt.) **threat of action** Th.; **prospect** (W.GEN. of aggression) Th.
2 delay in taking action, delay, procrastination, hesitation Th. Pl. Plu.

μελλητέον (neut.impers.vbl.adj.): see μέλλω

μελλητής οῦ *m.* **delayer, procrastinator** Th. Arist. Plu.

μελλιχό-μειδος ον (or **μελλιχομείδης** ες) Aeol.*adj.* [μείλιχος, μειδάω] **sweetly smiling** Alc.

μέλλιχος Aeol.*adj.*: see μείλιχος

μελλό-γαμος ον *adj.* [μέλλω, γάμος] **about to marry, betrothed** S.(dub.) Theoc.

μελλο-δειπνικός όν *adj.* [δεῖπνον] (of a song) performed for those about to dine, **pre-dinner** Ar.

μελλο-νῑκιάω *contr.vb.* [Νικίας *Nikias*, Athenian commander, reputedly dilatory] (pseudo-medic.) **get the Nikian dithers** Ar.

μελλό-νυμφος ον *adj.* [νύμφη] **1** ‖ FEM.SB. **bride-to-be** S.
2 (of a house) **ready for a marriage** S.(dub.)

μελλώ οῦς *f.* **delay** A.

μέλλω *vb.* | impf. ἔμελλον, also ἤμελλον, ep. μέλλον, iterатv. μελλεσκον | fut. μελλήσω | aor. ἐμέλλησα, also ἠμέλλησα ‖ neut.impers.vbl.adj. μελλητέον |

1 be likely, destined or **bound** —W.INF. to be or do sthg. Hom. + • (w.pres.inf.) ὅτι που μέλλουσιν ἄριστοι βουλὰς βουλεύειν *where the leading men are likely to be deliberating* Il. • (aor.) μέλλω ἀθανάτους ἀλιτέσθαι *I am likely to have offended the immortal gods* Od. • (fut.) ἡ Διὸς κλεινὴ δάμαρ μέλλουσ' ἔσεσθαι *she who is destined to be the famous wife of Zeus* A. ‖ IMPERS. **it is likely** or **bound** —W.PRES. or FUT.INF. *to happen or sim.* Hom. +

2 (in rhetorical qs., esp. impers., w.inf. understd.) • Ἐριχθόνιον οἶσθ' ἢ οὔ; τί δ' οὐ μέλλεις, γέρον; *Do you know Erikhthonios or not? Why should you not, old man?* E. • πῶς γὰρ οὐ μέλλει; *how could it not be so?* Pl.

3 be about, going or **intending** —W.INF. (usu. FUT., sts. PRES. or AOR.) *to do sthg.* Hom. +

4 delay, put off —W.INF. or w. μή or μὴ οὐ + INF. (usu. PRES., sts. AOR.) *doing sthg.* Trag. Th. Ar. +

5 delay, hesitate, procrastinate Trag. Ar. Pl. + ‖ PASS. (of actions) **be delayed** X. D. ‖ IMPERS.PASS. **there is delay** S.(cj.)

6 ‖ PASS. (of a position of strength, based on hope) **be in the future** Th.

—μέλλων ουσα ον *pres.ptcpl.adj.* (of time, life, sufferings, events, situations) **to come, future** Lyr. Hdt. Trag. Th. Isoc. + ‖ NEUT.SB. (sg. and pl.) **what is to come, the future** Pi. B. Trag. Th. Isoc. +

μέλον (ep.impf.): see μέλω

μελοποιέω *contr.vb.* [μελοποιός] **compose lyric poetry** Ar.

μελοποιΐᾱ ᾱς *f.* **1 creation of melody** (opp. rhythm, as a constituent of musical composition) Arist.
2 composition of music Pl.; (specif.) **composition of music and lyrics** (for tragic drama) Arist.
3 product of musical composition, music Arist.

μελο-ποιός όν *adj.* [μέλος, ποιέω] **1** (of the cares of the nightingale) **music-making, melodious** E.
2 ‖ MASC.SB. **composer of lyric poetry** Ar. Pl. Plu.

μέλος εος (ους) *n.* | dat.pl. μέλεσι, ep. μέλεσσι, also μελέεσσι |
1 ‖ PL. **limbs** (of the body, human or animal) Hom. +
2 articulated melody; tune, melody, strain hHom. Hippon. Thgn. Lyr. A.*fr.* E. +; (gener.) **music** Pl. Arist.
3 song (freq.ref. to a lyric poem) Archil. Lyr. A. Hdt. E. Ar. +
4 (gener.) **sound** (W.GEN. of weeping, shouting) E.; **cry, shout** S. Call.
5 (fig.phrs.) ἐν μέλει *in tune* (i.e. correctly, properly) Pl.; παρὰ (πὰρ) μέλος *out of tune* (i.e. incorrectly, unsuitably) Pi. Pl. Arist.

—μελεϊστί *adv.* **limb from limb** —*ref. to tearing a person apart* Hom. AR.

μελοτυπέω *contr.vb.* [τύπτω] beat out in melody, **chant out** —*terrifying things* A.

μέλπηθρα ων *n.pl.* [μέλπω] (ref. to an unburied corpse) **plaything** (W.GEN. or DAT. for dogs) Il.

Μελπομένη ης *f.* **Melpomene** (one of the nine Muses) Hes.

μέλπω *vb.* | impf. ἔμελπον, ep. μέλπον | fut. μέλψω | aor. ἔμελψα | **1 celebrate with song and dance** —*a god* Il. ‖ MID. **sing and dance** Il. hHom.; (fig., of a warrior) **dance** —W.DAT. *for Ares* (i.e. fight in battle) Il.
2 sing A. E. Bion; (mid.) Od. Hes. hHom. Pi. AR. Theoc.
3 (tr.) **sing** —*a song, lament, hymn, or sim.* A. E. Corinn. Mosch.; (of a nightingale) —*a melody* E.*fr.* —*a honeyed song* Theoc.*epigr.*; (mid., of persons) —(*app.*) *a song* Sapph.; (of a god) —*a musical strain* E.; (of a lyre) —*commands to rowers* E.*fr.* ‖ PASS. (of laments) be sung E.
4 celebrate with song, sing of —*a deity, person, victory, or sim.* Hes.*fr.*(dub.) Lyr. E. Ar. Hellenist.poet. Plu.(quot.); (mid.) —*a deity* Pi. E. AR.

μελύδριον

5 (causatv.) **sound** —*the shrill voice of a lyre* E.
6 **make music** Mosch.; (mid.) —W.DAT. *on a panpipe* Theoc.*epigr.*
7 (gener.) **utter** —*a cry* E.
8 ‖ MID. **play games** AR.

μελύδριον ου *n.* [dimin. μέλος] **little song, ditty** Ar. Theoc. Bion

μέλω *vb.* | ep.inf. μελέμεν | impf. ἔμελον, ep. μέλον | fut. μελήσω, ep.inf. μελησέμεν | aor. ἐμέλησα | pf. (w.pres.sens.) μεμέληκα, ep. μέμηλα | 3sg.plpf. (w.impf.sens.) ἐμεμελήκει, ep. μεμήλει ‖ MID.: fut. μελήσομαι | pf.ptcpl. (w.pres.sens.) μεμελημένος (Call. Theoc.) | 3sg.plpf. (w.impf.sens.) μεμέλητο (Theoc.) | also ep.pf. (w.pres.sens.): 3sg. μέμβλεται, 2pl. μέμβλεσθε (AR.) | ep.plpf. (w.impf.sens.): 3sg. μέμβλετο (Hom. +) ‖ PASS.: aor.ptcpl. (w.mid.sens.) μεληθείς (S.) ‖ neut.impers.vbl.adj. μελητέον |

1 (usu. of things, sts. of persons) **be an object of care, concern** or **interest** —W.DAT. *to someone* Hom. +; (also mid.) Hom. Hes. Trag. Call. AR.
2 (of persons, gods) **be concerned** —W.GEN. *about someone or sthg.* Il. Trag. AR. —W.INF. *to do sthg.* E.; (of a heart) **be full of concern** E.
3 ‖ PF. (w.pf.sens.) **contrive** —*sthg.* hHom.(dub., cj. μέμηδα) | see μήδομαι
4 ‖ MID. and AOR.PASS. **concern oneself** —W.GEN. *w. someone or sthg.* Trag. AR. —w. ἀμφί + ACC. or GEN. AR. —W.INF. *w. doing sthg.* A. E.
5 ‖ IMPERS. (freq.neg.) **there is a concern** (usu. W.DAT. *for someone, i.e. one is concerned*) Od. + —W.GEN. *about someone or sthg.* Archil. Lyr. Trag. Ar. —w. περί + GEN. A. Hdt. E. Ar. Isoc. + —w. ὑπέρ + GEN. D. —W.INF. *to do sthg.* Od. Hdt. Trag. Th. —W.COMPL.CL. or INDIR.Q. *that sthg. is* (or *shd. be*) *the case, what* (or *if sthg.*) *is the case* Hdt. S. E. Att.orats. X. NT.
6 ‖ NEUT.ACC.PRES.PTCPL. (in same constrs. as section 5) **there being a concern** Lys. Ar. Pl. X.; (also pf.ptcpl.) Plu.
7 ‖ NEUT.PRES.PTCPL. (quasi-adjl., in periphr. w. ἔσται *will be*, ἦν *was*) **of concern** S. Pl.
8 ‖ IMPERS.MID. **there is a concern** —W.DAT. *for someone* (*i.e. one is concerned*, W.GEN. *for sthg.*) Theoc. —(W.INF. *to do sthg.*) S. AR.

—**μελόμενος** η (dial. ᾱ) ον *mid.ptcpl.adj.* (of a person) **of concern** (W.DAT. to bloody lustral water, i.e. destined for sacrifice) E.; (of a cry, W.DAT. to the dead, i.e. assoc.w. them) E.

—**μεμελημένος** η ον *pf.mid.ptcpl.adj.* (of persons) **of concern** (W.DAT. to others) Theoc.; **concerned** (W.DAT. w. the truth) Call.

—**μεμελημένως** *pf.mid.ptcpl.adv.* **carefully** Pl.

μελῳδέω *contr.vb.* [μελῳδός] **sing a song** Ar. ‖ PASS. (of parts of a choral performance) **be sung to musical accompaniment** Pl.

μελῳδίᾱ ᾱς *f.* 1 **singing** E. Arist.; (opp. dancing) Pl.
2 **melody, tune, music** Pl. Plb.
3 **lyric poem** Pl.

μελ-ῳδός όν *adj.* [μέλος, ἀοιδή] 1 (of a Muse, a singer) **tuneful** E.; (of a swan, a nightingale) E.; (of sounds) E.
2 ‖ MASC.SB. **singer** Pl.

μεμάᾱσι (3pl.pf.): see μέμονα
μεμάθηκα (pf.): see μανθάνω
μεμακυῖαι (ep.fem.nom.pl.pf.ptcpl.): see μηκάομαι
μέμαμεν (1pl.pf.): see μέμονα
μέμᾱνα (dial.pf.), **μεμάνημαι** (pf.mid.): see μαίνομαι
μεμάποιεν (ep.3pl.aor.2 redupl.opt.): see μαπέειν

μέμαρπα (pf.): see μάρπτω
μέμασαν (3pl.plpf.), **μέματε** (2pl.pf.), **μέματον** (2du.pf.), **μεμάτω** (3sg.pf.imperatv.): see μέμονα
μέμαχα (pf.): see μάσσω
μεμαώς (pf.ptcpl.): see μέμονα
μέμβλεσθε (ep.2pl.pf.mid.), **μέμβλεται** (3sg.), **μέμβλετο** (3sg.plpf.): see μέλω
μέμβλωκα (pf.): see βλώσκω
μεμβράς άδος *f.* **sprat** or **anchovy** Ar.
μέμειγμαι (pf.pass.): see μείγνῡμι
μεμελετημένως *pf.pass.ptcpl.adv.*: see under μελετάω
μεμέληκα (pf.), **μεμελημένος** (pf.mid.ptcpl.), **μεμελημένως** (pf.mid.ptcpl.adv.), **μεμέλητο** (3sg.plpf.mid.): see μέλω
μεμελιτωμένος (pf.pass.ptcpl.): see μελιτόομαι
μεμένηκα (pf.): see μένω
μεμεριμνημένος (pf.pass.ptcpl.): see μεριμνάω
μεμετιμένος (Ion.pf.pass.ptcpl.): see μεθίημι
μέμηδα (pf.): see μήδομαι
μεμηκώς (pf.ptcpl.): see μηκάομαι
μέμηλα (ep.pf.), **μεμήλει** (ep.3sg.plpf.): see μέλω
μέμηνα (pf.): see μαίνομαι
μεμηχανημένως *pf.pass.ptcpl.adv.*: see under μηχανάομαι
μεμίαγκα (pf.), **μεμίασμαι** (pf.pass.): see μιαίνω
μέμιγμαι (pf.pass.): see μείγνῡμι
μέμνᾱμαι (dial.pf.mid.), **μέμνημαι** (pf.mid.), **μέμνητο** (ep.3sg.plpf.): see μιμνήσκομαι, under μιμνήσκω

Μέμνων ονος *m.* **Memnon** (son of Tithonos and Eos, king of Aithiopia, ally of the Trojans, slain by Achilles) Od. Hes. Alcm. Pi. Hdt. S.*fr.* +

—**Μεμνόνειος** η ον *Ion.adj.* (of a city, a palace) **of Memnon** Hdt.

μέμονα *statv.pf.vb.* [reltd. μένος, μαίνομαι] | 2sg. μέμονας, 3sg. μέμονε, 1pl. μέμαμεν, 2pl. μέματε, 3pl. μεμάᾱσι | 2du. μέματον | ptcpl. μεμαώς (gen. μεμαῶτος), also μεμᾱώς (gen. μεμᾱότος) | 3sg.imperatv. μεμάτω | inf. μεμονέναι (Hdt.) ‖ PLPF.: 3sg. μεμόνει (Theoc., cj.), 3pl. μέμασαν |

1 **be full of intense feeling, be eager** or **keen** Il. A. AR. —W.INF. *to do sthg.* Hom. Hes. hHom. Pi. Hdt. Hellenist.poet.; (of warships in harbour) **be impatient** (to sail) E.
2 **be eager** —W.GEN. *for a fight, task,* or *sim.* Il. AR.; (of calves) —*for milk* Theoc.
3 **hasten, speed, rush** —W.ADV. *in some direction* Il.
4 ‖ PTCPL.ADJ. **eager, keen, intent, vehement** Hom. hHom. Pi. AR.; (of a stomach) **ravenous** Od.; (quasi-advbl., w.vb. of motion) **with eager haste** Hom. Stesich.; (w.vb. of speech) **with passion** or **vehemence** AR.
5 (wkr.sens.) **have in mind, intend** —*evil deeds* hHom. —W.INF. *to do sthg.* Hom.
6 (of a person's spirit) **incline, be pulled** —W.ADV. *in two directions* Il.; **ponder** —W.ACC. *alternative courses of action* E.

μεμόρηται (3sg.pf.pass.), **μεμόρητο** (3sg.plpf.pass.), **μεμορμένος** (pf.pass.ptcpl.): see μείρομαι
μεμορυγμένος (pf.pass.ptcpl.): see μορύσσω
μεμούσωμαι (pf.pass.): see μουσόομαι

μεμπτός ή όν (also ός όν S.) *adj.* [μέμφομαι] 1 **deserving blame**; (of persons, their conduct, things or circumstances, esp. in neg.phr.) **blameworthy, open to criticism, to be found fault with** (sts. W.PREP.PHR. in some respect) Pi.*fr.* Hdt. S. E. Th. Pl. +
2 (of punishment, in neg.phr.) **undeserved** Plu.
3 *according blame*; **critical, disapproving** (W.DAT. of a person) S.

—**μεμπτῶς** *adv.* **discreditably** —*ref. to fighting* Plu.

μέμῡκα (pf.), **μεμῡ́κει** (ep.3sg.plpf.): see μῡκάομαι
μεμυρισμένος (pf.pass.ptcpl.): see μυρίζω
Μέμφις ιδος (also εως Plb., Ion. ιος) *f.* | acc. Μέμφιν | dat. Μέμφει (Plb.), Ion. Μέμφῖ | **Memphis** (city in Egypt) A. B.*fr.* Hdt. Plb. Plu.
—**Μεμφίτης** εω *Ion.m.* (appos.w. ἀνήρ) **citizen of Memphis** Hdt.
μέμφομαι *mid.vb.* | Boeot.1sg. μέμφομη | fut. μέμψομαι | aor. ἐμεμψάμην ‖ aor.pass. (usu. w.mid.sens.) ἐμέμφθην |
1 blame, find fault with, criticise —*someone or sthg.* Hes. Eleg. Pi. Hdt. Trag. Th. + —(w. πρός + ACC. *to someone*) E. X. —(w. εἰς + ACC. *for sthg.*) X. —(W.COMPL.CL. *for doing sthg.*) Isoc. ‖ PASS. (of a person) be blamed Plu.
2 blame, find fault with, criticise —W.DAT. *someone* Hdt. Trag. Lys. Ar. Isoc. + —(W.ACC. *for sthg.*) Hdt. Th. Ar. Pl. + —(W.GEN.) A. X. —(W.COMPL.CL. *for doing sthg., because sthg. is the case*) Hdt. Pl. X. +
3 complain Pi. Trag. Th. Ar. Isoc. Pl. + —W.GEN. *about sthg.* E. Th. —W.COMPL.CL. *that sthg. is the case* Sapph. Hdt. E. Th. Ar. + —w. τοῦ + μή W.INF. (after neg.) *about doing sthg.* A.*fr.* —w. μή + INF. *that one ought not to do sthg.* Th.
μεμψιμοιρέω *contr.vb.* [μεμψίμοιρος] **be dissatisfied** or **discontented, find fault** —W.DAT. or πρός + ACC. *w. someone* Plb. Plu.
μεμψιμοιρίᾱ ᾱς *f.* **dissatisfaction, discontent** Arist.
μεμψί-μοιρος ον *adj.* [μοῖρα] **1 finding fault with one's lot** or **share** ‖ MASC.SB. **ungrateful grumbler, malcontent** Thphr.
2 (of old age, i.e. aged persons) **prone to discontent** Isoc.
μέμψις εως *f.* **blame, complaint, criticism** Trag. Ar. Att.orats. Pl. +
μέν *pcl.* [reltd. μήν¹] | The pcl. (usu. 2nd wd. in cl.) lends emphasis, affirming an idea or concentrating attention upon it, freq. in preparation for a contrasting idea. |
1 (ep. and Ion., emph., equiv. to μήν) • ὄμοσσον ἦ μέν μοι πρόφρων ἔπεσιν καὶ χερσὶν ἀρήξειν *swear that you will indeed be ready to help me in word and action* Il. • κάρτιστοι μὲν ἔσαν ... καὶ τοῖσιν ἐγὼ μεθομίλεον ... καὶ μέν μεο βουλέων ξύνιεν *they were indeed the mightiest ... and with them I kept company ... and to my advice they listened* Il. • οὐ μὲν γάρ τι κακὸν βασιλευέμεν *for it is certainly not a bad thing to be a king* Od.
2 (introductory, without an expressed or implied antithesis) • ἀκτὴ μὲν ἥδε τῆς περιρρύτου χθονὸς Λήμνου *this is the shore of sea-washed Lemnos* S.
3 (marking a q. as preliminary to any further discussion) E. + • ἐλπὶς μὲν οὐκέτ' ἐστὶ σῴζεσθαι βίον; (*first let me ask*) *is there no longer hope of her life being saved?* E.
4 (w. an antithesis implied) • τἂν δόμοισι μὲν καλῶς *well, as for the situation in the house* (*at least*) S. • τίνος; ἐμὸς μὲν οὐχί *whose? not mine* E. • ἐγὼ μὲν οὐκ οἶδα *I for my part don't know* Pl. X. D. Plu.
5 (most freq., introducing an expressed contrast, answered by δέ or οὐδέ) • χεῖρες μὲν ἁγναί, φρὴν δ' ἔχει μίασμά τι *my hands are pure, but my mind is tainted* E. • παῖδες δύο, πρεσβύτερος μὲν Ἀρταξέρξης, νεώτερος δὲ Κῦρος *two sons, the elder Artaxerxes, the younger Cyrus* X. • ὣς οἱ μὲν τὰ πένοντο κατὰ στρατόν· οὐδ' Ἀγαμέμνων λῆγ' ἔριδος *so the men went about their business in the camp, but Agamemnon would not relent in his quarrel* Il.
6 (answered by δέ, in anaphoric cls.) • χαῖρε μὲν χθών, χαῖρε δ' ἡλίου φάος *greetings, land, greetings, light of day* A.
7 (answered by other conjs. or advs.) • σμικρὸς μὲν ἔην δέμας, ἀλλὰ μαχητής *he was small in stature, but a fighter* Il.

• Πέρσας μὲν αὐτοὺς λέληθε, ἡμέας μέντοι οὔ *it has escaped the notice of the Persians, but not of us* Hdt. • πρῶτον (or πρῶτα) μὲν ... εἶτα (or ἔπειτα or sim.) *first ... then* S. +
8 (combined w. another pcl., each usu. retaining its original force) esp. γε μέν (equiv. to γε μήν), μέν γε, μὲν δή, μέν τοι | see also μέντοι
9 (combined to form a new sense) μὲν οὖν (contradictory) A. + • περιβλέπεσθαι τίμιον; κενὸν μὲν οὖν *Is it an honour to be widely admired? No, it is an empty thing* E.; (assentient) • πάνυ μὲν οὖν *yes, very much so* Pl. +; μενοῦν (beginning a cl.) *on the contrary* NT.
μεν-αίχμης ου *m.* [μένω, αἰχμή] app., **one who stands firm in battle, stalwart fighter** Anacr.
Μένανδρος ου *m.* **Menander** (comic poet, 4th-3rd C. BC) Plu.
μενεαίνω *vb.* [μένος, reltd. μενοινάω] | ep.aor. μενέηνα |
1 (of persons) **be filled with a strong desire, be eager** (for sthg.) Hom. —W.INF. *to do sthg.* Hom. AR. —W.GEN. *for battle* Hes.; (of an arrow) —W.INF. *to fly* (*at an enemy*) Il.
2 be filled with anger, be furious Il. AR.; **vent one's fury** —W.DAT. *against someone* Hom. hHom. AR.
3 be filled with martial fervour or frenzy, rage Il. —W.DAT. *against the enemy* Il.
μενε-δήιος ον *Ion.adj.* [μένω] (of a warrior, his heart) **steadfast against the enemy** Il. AR.
μενέ-κτυπος ον *adj.* [κτύπος] **steadfast in the din of battle** B.
Μενέλᾱος ου, Att. **Μενέλεως** ω, dial. **Μενέλᾱς** ᾱ *m.* **Menelaos** (brother of Agamemnon, husband of Helen) Hom. +
μενε-πτόλεμος ον *ep.adj.* [πόλεμος] **steadfast in battle** Hom. B.
μενετέον (neut.impers.vbl.adj.): see μένω
μενετός ή όν *adj.* **able or willing to wait**; (of gods) **patient** Ar.; (of opportunities in war, in neg.phr.) **lasting** Th.
μενε-χάρμης, also **μενέχαρμος**, ου *masc.adj.* [χάρμη] **steadfast in fighting** Il. Hes.*fr.* Stesich.
μενέω (Ion.fut.): see μένω
μενο-εικής ές *adj.* [μένος, ἔοικα] app., **suited to one's desires**; (of food, drink, gifts, booty, or sim.) **sufficient, satisfying** Hom. hHom. AR. Plu.(quot.)
μενοινάω *contr.vb.* [μένος, reltd. μενεαίνω] | (w.diect.) ep.1sg. μενοινώω, 3sg. μενοινάᾳ, 3sg.subj. μενοινήῃσι (dub.), masc.acc.pl.ptcpl. μενοινώοντας (AR.) | impf.: ep.3sg. μενοίνᾱ, 3pl. μενοίνεον | ep.3sg.aor. μενοίνησε |
1 have a strong desire, be eager (for sthg.) Hom. Thgn. —W.INF. *to do sthg.* Hom. Hes. hHom. Pi. E.*Cyc.* Ar.
2 be eager for, be intent upon —*sthg.* Hom. hHom. Pi. S. AR.
3 be preoccupied with, ponder —*sthg.* Il. Theoc.
4 wonder —W.INDIR.Q. *whether one will accomplish sthg.* Il.
μενοινή ῆς *f.* **eager desire, intention** or **plan** Call. AR.
μένος εος (ους) *n.* [reltd. μέμονα] **1 strong emotional energy** (in persons, gods or animals, assoc.w. aggression, anger, fear, or sim.), **passion, excitement, vehemence, fury, rage** Hom. Hes. Mimn. Hdt.(oracle) Trag. Ar. +
2 (assoc.w. persistence or determination) **spirit, resolve, courage** Hom. Hes. hHom. Pi. X.
3 vital energy, life force, life Hom. Emp.
4 physical energy (of persons, gods or animals), **might, vigour, strength** Hom. Hes. A. Pi.*fr.* Hellenist.poet.; (ref. to semen) Archil.; (ref. to blood) S.
5 energy or strength (in things); **force, strength, might** (of the earth) Emp.; (of a spear) Il.; (of a pillar) Simon.; (of fire,

the sun, rivers, winds, storms, snow, hail, air) Hom. Hes. Sol. Lyr. A. Emp. +; (of a bridle) A.; (of Ruin) A.; (of a stench) AR.
6 (periphr., w.gen. of pers. name) Hom. Hes.*fr*. • μένος Ἀλκινόοιο *mighty Alkinoos* Od.

μέντοι *postpos.adv. and conj.* [μέν, τοι¹] **1** (affirmative) **to be sure, indeed, in truth** Thgn.(dub.) Hdt. Trag. Ar. Pl. + • τοιοῦτον μέντοι ... ἔστι τὸ τῇ ἀληθείᾳ σοφόν τε καὶ τέλειον ἄνδρα εἶναι *this is indeed how it is, to be a truly wise and accomplished man* Pl. • εὖ μέντοι λέγεις *you certainly make a good point* Ar.
2 (adversative) **all the same, however, nevertheless** Hdt. S. E. Th. Att.orats. + • τὸ μέντοι μέλλον οὐκ ἔχω μαθεῖν *what is to come, however, I cannot guess* E. • οὐ μέντοι γε ὑμᾶς, ὦ ἄνδρες, ἀξιῶ ὧν ὀμωμόκατε παραβῆναι οὐδέν *nevertheless, comrades, I will not ask you to violate any oath that you have sworn* X.
3 (progressive or connective) **well, now, then** Hdt. Trag. Th. + • οἱ μέντοι Λακεδαιμόνιοι ἄσμενοι ἔλαβον πρόφασιν στρατεύειν ἐπὶ τοὺς Θηβαίους *now the Spartans were keen to grasp a pretext for going on campaign against the Thebans* X. • ταύτας μέντοι σὺ θεὰς οὔσας οὐκ ᾔδεις οὐδ᾽ ἐνόμιζες; *so you didn't realise that they were goddesses, or believe in them?* Ar.

μένω *vb.* | ep.inf. μενέμεν | ep.impf. μένον, iteratv. μένεσκον | fut. μενῶ, Ion. μενέω | aor. ἔμεινα, ep. μεῖνα | pf. μεμένηκα ‖ neut.impers.vbl.adj. μενετέον | **1** (of persons or things) remain (in a place or position); **remain, stay** Hom. +
2 remain inactive; **wait, linger** Hom. +
3 remain unchanged; **remain, continue** (usu. W.ADV., PREP.PHR., PREDIC.ADJ. or SB. in a certain condition) Hom. Pi. Parm. Hdt. Trag. Th. +; (of wine) **keep** Plb.; (of spiritual food) **last** NT.
4 remain in existence; (of walls) **last, endure, survive** Hdt.; (of a city) NT.; (of an oath, treaty, agreement, custom, or sim.) **continue, hold good** A. Hdt. E. Th. Ar. Pl. +; (of a person) **remain alive** NT.
5 (of persons) stand one's ground, **stand fast** or **firm** (in the face of an enemy) Hom. Tyrt. Hdt.(oracle) S. E. Th. +
6 (tr.) await the attack of, **stand up to, face** —*an enemy, his weapons, a wild animal* Hom. Hes.*fr*.(cj.) A. Hdt.(oracle) E. Th. +; (of a wild animal) —*hunters* Il.; (of a cliff) **withstand** —*winds and waves* Il.
7 (wkr.sens.) **face, endure** —*a contest* Pi.; **put up with** —*indecision* E. —*the smell and noise of elephants* Plb.
8 (tr.) **wait for, await** —*persons, ships, an event or circumstance* Hom. Hes. Hdt. Trag. Th. Pl. + —W.ACC. + INF. *a person or particular time to arrive, sthg. to happen* Hom. Semon. Pi. Hdt. E.
9 (of death, a fate, honour, disgrace, or sim.) **await, be in store** A. E. —W.DAT. *for someone* A. —W.ACC. Pi. Hdt.(oracle) Trag. + ‖ IMPERS. it remains —W.ACC. + INF. *for someone to do sthg.* S.
10 wait —W.INF. *to do sthg.* (*at a future time*) A.; **delay** —W.INF. *doing sthg.* Thgn. S.

μεο (Ion.enclit.gen.1sg.pers.pron.): see ἐγώ

μερίζω, dial. **μερίσδω** (Bion) *vb.* [μέρος] | fut. μεριῶ | aor. ἐμέρισα ‖ PASS.: aor. ἐμερίσθην, pf. μεμέρισμαι | **1** divide into parts; **divide up** —*an entity* Pl. —*spheres of government, a community* Arist. —*one magistracy* (w. εἰς + ACC. *into several*) Arist.; (of two rulers) **partition** —*a kingdom* Plb. ‖ MID. **divide** —*a whole* (w. εἰς + ACC. *into two*) Pl. ‖ PASS. (of an entity) be divided into parts Pl.; (of water) —W.PREP.PHR. *by fire* (*i.e. be evaporated*) Pl.; (of authority) be divided (betw.

two people) Plu.; (of a triumph) —W.PREP.PHR. *betw. two days* Plu.
2 (intr.) **make a division** (of a citizen-body) —W.PREP.PHR. *on certain lines* Arist.; **make divisions** (of things into categories) Pl. Arist.; (math.) **divide** (a number) Arist.
3 divide up, apportion —*interest on a loan* (w. πρός + ACC. *in relation to a voyage, i.e. make it proportionate to a voyage's length*) D.
4 divide up —*one's troops* (*for different duties*) Plb.(also mid.) Plu.; **separate off, detach** —*persons, troops* (*fr. a main body or group*) Plb. Plu.; **separate** —*two groups of people* Arist. —*a person* (w. ἀπό + GEN. *fr. someone else*) Bion
5 apportion, distribute —*money, booty, food* (W.DAT. *to persons*) Arist. Plb. NT. —*obligations, letters* (*to cities*) Plb. ‖ PASS. (of money, grants) be apportioned D. Plu.; (of property, land, revenues) —W.DAT. or PREP.PHR. *to people* Arist. Plu.
6 assign —*an island* (W.DAT. *to someone*) Plb. ‖ PASS. (of troops) be assigned —W.PREP.PHR. *to a place* Plb.
7 ‖ MID. be party to a division (of things); **divide up, share out** —*money, an inheritance, profits* (sts. w. μετά + GEN. w. *someone*) D. Din. Plb. NT.; **get a share** —W.GEN. *of property, ill-gotten gains* Is. Arist.
8 ‖ MID. (of a fisherman) **share** —*a catch, his dreams* (w. *another*) Theoc.
9 ‖ PASS. (of people) be divided (against each another, i.e. into factions) Plb.; (of a kingdom, city, house) —W.PREP.PHR. *against itself* NT.; (of Satan) —*against himself* (*i.e. have divided interests*) NT.
10 ‖ PF.PASS. (of a people) count as part (of a total population) D.

μέριμνα ης (dial. ᾱς) *f*. **1** (sg. and pl.) anxious or attentive thought, **care, concern, anxiety** Hes. Eleg. Lyr. Trag. Ar. Call. +; (W.GEN. for someone or sthg.) Trag.; (w. ἐς + ACC. *for someone*) E.
2 (gener.) **thought** hHom.
3 object of concern; (ref. to dead children) **concern** (W.DAT. *to their mother*) E.; (ref. to a god) **worry, trouble** (for gods and mortals) hHom.
4 (w. intellectual connot.) **thought, idea** Emp. Ar.
5 thought focused on an objective; **design, endeavour, aspiration, ambition** Pi. B. E.
6 mind or **inspiration** (W.ADJ. *Kean, i.e. of Bacchylides*) B.

μεριμνάω *contr.vb.* | pf.pass.ptcpl. μεμεριμνημένος | **1 be concerned** or **anxious** NT. —W.ACC. *about many things* X. —W.GEN. or PREP.PHR. *about sthg.* NT. —W.INDIR.Q. *how one is to do sthg., what one is to do* NT.
2 have as one's concern, **pursue** —*an occupation, a way of life* S.
3 (w. intellectual connot.) **think** X. —W.ADV. *subtly* Pl.(quot.poet.) —W.ACC. or PREP.PHR. *about sthg.* X. ‖ PF.PASS.PTCPL.ADJ. (of a saying) carefully thought out Men.
4 give careful thought —W.INF. *to doing sthg.* D. —w. ὅπως μή + SUBJ. *to ensuring that sthg. does not happen* X.

μεριμνήματα, dial. **μεριμνάματα**, των *n.pl.* **cares, concerns** Pi.*fr*. S.(dub., see ἀμερίμνητος)

μεριμνητής οῦ *m*. **meditator** (W.GEN. *of arguments*) E.

μεριμνο-φροντιστής οῦ *m*. **reflective thinker, careful cogitator** Ar.

μερίς ίδος *f*. [reltd. μέρος] **1** allotted portion, **portion, share** (of property, power, or sim.) Isoc. Pl. D. Men. Plb. +; (in the ownership of a mine) D.

2 (specif.) **portion** (of food or meat) D. Din. Thphr. Men. Plu.
3 portion into which a whole is divided, **section, part** Antipho Pl. Arist. Plu.
4 division, grouping, class Arist. Men. Plb. Plu.; (W.GEN. of citizens) E.
5 one of two opposing classes, **side, party** D. Plb. Plu.
6 category (W.GEN. of what is beneficial, virtuous, or sim.) Plb. Plu.
7 element or constituent (contributing to an outcome), **factor, contribution** D. Plb.
8 part, role (which a person performs in a given situation) NT.
9 part (of a larger territory), **region, district** NT.

μερίσδω *dial.vb.*: see μερίζω

μερισμός οῦ *m.* [μερίζω] **1** (gener.) breaking down into parts, **division** (of things) Pl.
2 (specif.) **partition** (of a country, kingdom, military forces) Plb.
3 branching (of a river, into several channels) Plb.
4 (log.) **arrangement of the parts** (W.GEN. of a contradiction) Arist.
5 arrangement, scheme (of the subject matter of a historical work) Plb.
6 division (for the purpose of distribution); **division** (of spoils) Plb.; **apportionment, allocation** (of funds) Arist.; **going shares** (in discovered goods) Men.

μεριστής οῦ *m.* one who makes a division and apportionment, **divider, distributor** (of property) NT.

μεριστός ή όν *adj.* **1** (of things) **divided into parts** Pl. Arist.
2 divisible into parts Pl. Arist.
3 apportionable (W.DAT. to people) Arist.

μερίτης ου *m.* [μέρος] one who receives a share, **sharer** (W.GEN. in sthg., sts. also W.DAT. w. someone) D. Plb.

μέρμερος ον *adj.* [perh.reltd. μέριμνα] perh., such as to cause anxiety; (of actions, by warriors) **grievous, grim** Il.; (by women) Hes.; (of a trouble or evil) E.; (of a person) **troublesome, irksome** Pl. ‖ NEUT.PL.SB. grim deeds Il.

μέρμηραι ῶν (ep. ἄων) *f.pl.* [μερμηρίζω] **cares, concerns, anxieties** Hes. Thgn.

μερμηρίζω *vb.* [reltd. μέρμερος] | fut. μερμηρίξω | ep.aor. μερμήριξα | **1** be anxious or thoughtful; **ponder, consider, deliberate** Hom. —W.INDIR.Q. *what to do, how* (or *whether*) *to do sthg.* Hom. —W.INF. *whether to do sthg.* Hom.
2 (tr.) **think about, brood on** —*many things* Od.; **have in mind, contemplate, plan** —*sthg.* Hom. Call.*epigr.*
3 think of or **discover** —*someone to help* Od.

μερμίς ῖθος *f.* **cord, string** (used for tying a bag) Od.

μέρμνος ου *m.* **hawk** or **buzzard** Call.

μέροπες ων *masc.pl.adj.* | ep.dat. μερόπεσσι | (of persons) perh. **human** or **mortal** Hom. Hes. hHom. A. ‖ SB. humans, mortals A. E. Call. AR.

μέρος εος (ους) *n.* [μείρομαι] **1** allotted portion, **portion, share** (freq. W.GEN. of sthg.) Thgn. Lyr. Emp. Hdt. Trag. Th. +
2 lot, portion (W.PREP.PHR. in life, ref. to one's circumstances) E.
3 personal share, interest or involvement; **part, share** (W.GEN. in an activity) E.; (W.PREP.PHR. w. specif. persons) NT.; **role, function** (W.GEN. of a messenger) A.
4 turn, time (for a person to do sthg.) Pl.; (W.INF. to do sthg.) Pl. X.; (W.GEN. for an activity) A. Hdt.
5 (gener.) contributory element (in a situation); **role, importance, significance** (attributed to sthg.) E. Th. Isoc. +
6 (periphr.) τοὐμὸν μέρος *my part* (*i.e. me*) S.; (advbl.acc.) τοὐμόν (τὸ σόν, τὸ σφέτερον) *for my* (*your, their*) *part, so far as concerns me* (*you, them*) S. E. Th. Pl.; τοὐκείνου μέρος *as far as he is concerned* E.; (also) κατὰ τὸ τούτου μέρος Isoc.; τὸ μέρος *for one's own part, to the best of one's ability* Th.
7 (prep.phrs.) ἐν (τῷ) μέρει *in turn, in return* (*w. a single action answering another*) A. Hdt. E. Ar. +; *taking turns, in succession* (*w. one or more actions following others*) A. Hdt. E. Th. Ar. +; *by turns* (*w. implication of indefinite repetition*) Emp. E. Pl.; (also, in these senses) ἀνὰ μέρος E. Arist. Plb. Plu.; κατὰ μέρος Th. Pl. X. D. +; παρὰ μέρος Plu.; ἀπὸ μέρους *by turns, by rotation* (*of offices*) Th.; παρὰ τὸ μέρος *beyond one's turn* (*i.e. to excess*) X.
8 portion into which a whole is divided, **section, part** hHom. Pi. Emp. Hdt. E. Th. +
9 (specif.) part facing in a particular direction, **side** (of a building, mountain, or sim.) Hdt. Th. ‖ PL. side (W.GEN. of a boat) NT.
10 division (of an army) X.
11 division of a population, **race** or **tribe** Th.
12 (gramm.) **part** (W.GEN. of speech) Arist.
13 (gener.) branch of activity, **matter, business** Men. Plb. NT.
14 (prep.phr., w.vb. τιθέναι, ποιεῖσθαι *place, treat*, or sim.) ἐν μέρει *in the class or category* (W.GEN. *of someone or sthg.*) Isoc. Pl. D. Men.
15 (advbl. and prep.phrs.) μέρος τι *in part, partly* Th. Isoc. X. D.; (also) τὸ μέρος Hdt. Th.; κατὰ τι μέρος Pl.; κατὰ τὸ πολὺ μέρος *for the greater part* Pl.; πρὸς μέρος *proportionately* Th. Pl. D.; κατὰ μέρος *part by part* (*opp. as a whole*) Pl.; (also) ἀνὰ μέρος Arist.; (quasi-adj.) ἐπὶ μέρους *concentrated on a part* Arist. Plb. • αἱ ἐπὶ μέρους συντάξεις *specialised treatises* Plb.

μέσαβον (or **μεσάβουν**) *n.* [perh. μέσος, βοῦς] | only dat. μεσάβῳ (v.l. μεσάβων) | app. **leather strap** (bound around the pole and peg of a yoke) Hes.

—**μέσσαβα** ων *ep.n.pl.* **yoke-ends** (fastened to the necks of oxen) Call.

μεσ-άγκυλον ου *n.* [ἀγκύλη] javelin with a thong in the middle (enabling the thrower to impart spin), **thonged javelin** E. Men. Plb. Plu.

μεσαι-πόλιος ον *adj.* [πολιός] (of a person, ref. to his hair) half-grey, **greying** Il.

μεσαίτατος (superl.adj.), **μεσαίτερος** (compar.): see μέσος

μέσ-ακτος ον *adj.* [ἀκτή¹] (of islands in the Aegean) **midway between the shores** (of Europe and Asia) A.

μεσαμβρίη Ion.*f.*: see μεσημβρία

μεσαμβρινός dial.*adj.*: see μεσημβρινός

μεσᾱμέριον dial.*adv.* [ἡμέρα] **at midday** Theoc.

μέσατος, ep. **μέσσατος**, also **μεσσάτιος** (Call.), η (dial. ᾱ) ον superl.*adj.* [μέσος] **1** (of a day, a journey) **midmost** (i.e. at its midmost point) Thgn. Theoc.; (of part of a person's chest) Call.; (phr.) ἐν μεσσάτῳ *at the midmost point* (*betw. two locations*) Il.
2 (of a son) **middle** (of three, i.e. second) Ar.

μεσ-εγγυάομαι *mid.contr.vb.* **deposit as a security with a third party** —*a sum of money* D.; (intr.) **deposit a security** Antipho ‖ PASS. (of money) be deposited as security Lys.

μεσεγγύημα ατος *n.* **security deposit** Isoc.(v.l. μεσεγγύωμα) Aeschin.

μεσ-εγγυόομαι *mid.contr.vb.* [ἔγγυος] (of teachers) **have** (W.ACC. their pupils' fees) **deposited as security** (for their subsequent payment) —W.GEN. *w. certain persons* Isoc. ‖ PASS. (of an object) be deposited as security Pl.(v.l. μεσεγγυάομαι)

μεσεύω *vb.* **1** (of the Greek people) **occupy a middle location** (relative to Europe and Asia) Arist.
2 (of a form of government) **be midway** —W.GEN. *betw. monarchy and democracy* Pl.

μέση 916

3 (of political leaders) **maintain a position of neutrality** (in relation to warring states) X.
μέση *f.*: see under μέσος
μεσηγύ, also ep. **μεσσηγύ** and **μεσσηγύς** *adv. and prep.* [2nd el.perh.reltd. ἐγγύς] | also μεσσηγῦς (Od.) | **1** in the space separating two things or places, **in the middle, midway, between** Il. AR. || NEUT.SB. (w.art.) mid-point (W.GEN. of the day) Theoc.
2 (ref. to the full distance intervening betw. two things or places) **between** AR. || NEUT.SB. (w.art.) intervening space hHom. Thgn.
3 in the middle of a journey or process, **in mid-course, on the way** Hom. AR.
4 (gener.) **in the meantime** (while other things are happening) AR.; **in the middle** (of doing sthg.) AR.; **in the course of** —W.PTCPL.PHR. *sthg. happening* AR.
5 (as prep., ref. to location) **between** —W.GEN. *two things, places, groups of people* Hom. Hes. AR. Theoc.
6 (ref. to reciprocal relationship) **between** —W.GEN. *two peoples* Il.
μεσήεις εσσα εν *adj.* (of warriors) **of middle rank** (in fighting ability) Il.
μεσ-ημβρίᾱ ᾱς, Ion. **μεσαμβρίη** ης *f.* [ἦμαρ] **1** time around the middle of the day, **midday, noon** Archil. A. Hdt. Th. Ar. Pl. +
2 direction of the sun in the middle of the day, **south** Hdt. X. Plb. NT. Plu.
μεσημβριάζω *vb.* **pass the middle of the day** (in sleep) Pl.
μεσημβριάω *contr.vb.* | ep.ptcpl. (w.diect.) μεσημβριόων | || PRES.PTCPL.ADJ. (of the sun) midday AR.
μεσημβρινός ή όν, dial. **μεσαμβρινός** ά όν *adj.* | also μεσαμβρῑνός (Call.) | **1** (of the heat of the sun) **at midday, at noon** A. Ar.; (of the hissing of a snake) A.; (of rest, quiet, a meal) A. Call. Plu.; (of the time) **around midday** Call. AR.; (advbl.phr.) τὸ μεσαμβρινόν *at midday* Theoc.
2 (quasi-advbl., of a person arriving, waking up) **at midday** Ar.
3 (of a route) towards the south, **southerly** A. || NEUT.PL.SB. southern parts (of a country) Th.
μεσίδιος ᾱ ον *adj.* (of a magistrate or judge) **in the middle** (betw. two parties), **intermediary, mediatory** Arist.
μεσῑτεύω *vb.* [μεσίτης] **mediate** (betw. opponents) Plb.; (tr.) —*a cessation of hostilities* Plb.
μεσίτης ου *m.* **mediator** Plb.
μεσοβασιλεία ᾱς *f.* [μεσοβασιλεύς] **interregnum** (period for which an interrex is appointed) Plu.
μεσο-βασιλεύς έως *m.* (at Rome) **interrex** (a temporary magistrate) Plu.
μεσό-γαιος (also **μεσόγειος**) ον, Att. **μεσόγεως** (Pl.), ep. **μεσσόγεως** (Call.), ων *adj.* [γῆ, γαῖα] (of persons) in the middle of a country, **inland** Hdt. Plb.; (of cities, regions) Call. Plb. Plu. || FEM.SB. interior (of a region or country) Arist. Plb. Plu. || NEUT.SB. interior (of a city) Plb. || MASC.PL.SB. inlanders Pl.
—**μεσόγαια**, also **μεσόγεια**, ᾱς *f.* inland region, **interior** (of a country) Hdt. Th. Pl. X. D. Plb.; **land** or **continent** (opp. island) Call. || ACC.ADV. in an inland direction or by an inland route Hdt.
μεσό-γραφος ον *adj.* [γράφω] (geom., of a line) **of mean proportion** Plu. [cj. μεσόλαβος *mesolabe, instrument for finding mean proportional lines*]
μεσό-δμη ης *f.* [δέμω] **1** perh. **cross-beam** (of a roof) Od.
2 app., notched beam in which a ship's mast rested, **mast-socket** Od. | cf. ἱστοπέδη

μεσό-κοιλος ον *adj.* [κοῖλος] (of a city) **low in the centre** (of a peninsula, due to surrounding hills) Plb.
μεσολαβέω *contr.vb.* [μεσολαβής] stop (someone) in the middle (of speech, a narrative); **interrupt** Plb. —*a speaker* Plb. —*oneself* (*i.e. one's narrative*) Plb. || PASS. (of a person, a narrative) be interrupted Plb.
μεσο-λαβής ές *adj.* [λαμβάνω] (of a goad) **gripped in the middle** A.
μεσόλαβος *m.*: see μεσόγραφος
μεσό-λευκος ον *adj.* [λευκός] (of a purple tunic) with a mixture of white, **shot with white** X.
μεσ-όμφαλος ον *adj.* [ὀμφαλός] **1** (of Apollo's Delphic temple, altar, oracles) **at the central navel** A. E.; (W.GEN. of the earth) S. E.
2 (of an altar) **at the very centre** (of a house) A.
μεσο-νύκτιος ον *adj.* [νύξ] (quasi-advbl., of a god being welcomed) **in the middle of the night, at midnight** Pi.; (of a woman meeting her doom) E. || NEUT.SB. midnight NT. Plu. || NEUT.ACC.ADV. at midnight Theoc. NT.; (also GEN.) NT.
μεσοπορέω *contr.vb.* [μεσόπορος] **be at the half-way point of a voyage** Thphr.
μεσό-πορος ον *adj.* [πόρος] (of the upper air) at the midmost point of passage (for a constellation), **mid** E.
μεσο-πόρφυρος ον *adj.* [πορφύρᾱ] (of a white headband) with a mixture of purple, **shot with purple** Plu.
μεσο-ποτάμιος ᾱ ον *adj.* (of an island) **in the middle of a river** Plu.
—**Μεσοποταμίᾱ** ᾱς *f.* region between two rivers (Tigris and Euphrates), **Mesopotamia** Plb. NT. Plu.
μεσο-πύργιον ου *n.* [πύργος] **space between towers** (in a wall) Plb. Plu.
μέσος, ep. and dial. **μέσσος**, η (dial. ᾱ) ον *adj.* | compar. μεσαίτερος (Pl.), superl. μεσαίτατος (Hdt. AR.), ep. μεσσότατος (AR.) | see also μέσ(σ)ατος | **1** (of persons, things, activities) at their middle point or part, **in the middle** Hom. + • μέσ(σ)ον σάκος *a shield at its middle* (i.e. *middle of a shield*) Il. A. E. • ἐν αἰθέρι μέσῳ *in mid-air* S. • κατὰ μέσην τὴν χώραν *in the middle of the country* Pl. • ἐν μέσαις ταῖς εὐφροσύναις *in the midst of good cheer* X. • μέσῃσι μετὰ δμωῇσι *in the midst of the female slaves* Od. || SUPERL. (of a country) at its midmost point (i.e. at the very middle of it) AR.
2 (of a period of time) at its mid-point Hom. + • μέσ(σ)ον ἦμαρ (ἆμαρ) *midday* Hom. hHom. Pi. S.*fr.* AR. Theoc. • μέσαι νύκτες *midnight* Anan. Hdt. Th. Ar. Pl. + • θέρεος ἔτι μέσσου ἐόντος *while it is still midsummer* Hes.
3 (quasi-advbl., of a person being seized or held) **by the middle** (i.e. around the waist) Thgn. Pi. Hdt. E. Ar. D.; (of a warrior being pierced by a spear) **through the middle** Il.
4 situated in the middle (betw. or surrounded by other things); (of a brother) **middle** (of three, i.e. second) Hdt.; (of persons or things) **midmost, middle, central** Hes. +; **midway between** (W.GEN. two others) Pl.; (W. ἀπό + GEN.) S. || COMPAR. (of positions) more in the middle (W.GEN. than the middle) Pl. || SUPERL. (of a place, a river-mouth) most central Hdt. AR.
5 intermediate (betw. extremes); (of a person) **middle-ranking** (in status or wealth) Hdt. Th. Arist. Plu.; (of conduct, a disposition, path in life, form of government) **middling, moderate** Thgn. A. X. Arist.; (gener., of persons or things) **ordinary, average** Hdt. Pl. Plu.; (of a voice) **medium** (in volume) Arist. || MASC.PL.SB. middle-class persons Arist. || NEUT.PL.SB. moderate elements (W.GEN. in a city's affairs) Pi.; neutral elements (W.GEN. among citizens) Th.

6 (of a judge) acting as intermediary and committed to neither side, **mediating, impartial, neutral** Th.

—**μέσ(σ)η** ης f. **1** (mus.) **middle string** (of a lyre) Arist.; **middle note** (in pitch, perh. ref. to the tonic of a scale) Pl. **2** (geom.) **mean proportional line** Arist. Plu. **3** direction of the sun at the mid-point of its course, **south** Call. | cf. μεσημβρία

—**μέσ(σ)ον** ου n. **1** middle part, **middle, centre** (freq. W.GEN. of sthg.) Il. +; (prep.phrs.) ἐν μέσ(σ)ῳ *in the middle* Hes. +; (also) μέσσῳ Od.; κατὰ μέσ(σ)ον Il. Hdt. +; κατὰ τὸ μέσον Th. X.; ἐς μέσον *into the middle* hHom. + ‖ PL. central areas (of a country, empire, city) Th. Plu.
2 middle or intervening space, **space between, middle** Hom. +; (prep.phrs.) ἐν μέσ(σ)ῳ (also ἐν τῷ μέσῳ) *in the middle* (sts. W.GEN. betw. persons or things) Hom. +; (also) μέσ(σ)ῳ Hom. AR.; εἰς μέσ(σ)ον (sts. τὸ μέσον) *into the middle* (sts. W.GEN. betw. two groups) Hom. +; ἀνὰ μέσ(σ)ον *midway* (sts. W.GEN. betw. two things or places) Theoc. Plb.; (also) διὰ μέσου Pl.; (advbl.phr.) τὸ μέσον *in the space between* (W.GEN. buildings or sim.) Hdt.
3 middle space (as an arena of openness or accessibility); (prep.phrs.) εἰς (τὸ) μέσον *into the open, into the public sphere, openly, for all to see or hear* Sol. Thgn. Pi.fr. Hdt. S. E. +; ἐκ μέσου *openly* E.; (esp.ref. to prizes set out for competition) ἐν μέσ(σ)ῳ *in the open, on display or on offer* Thgn. B. Ar. X. +; (also, in this sense) ἐς μέσσον Il.
4 (prep. and advbl.phrs.) ἂν τὸ μέσον (ὂν τὸ μέσσον) *in the middle or midst* Alc. Xenoph.; ἀνὰ μέσον *in the midst* (W.GEN. of things) E.; ἐν μέσῳ *in between* Trag. +; ἐν (τῷ) μέσῳ *in the way* (as an obstacle) X.; (w. τοῦ + INF. or W.ACC. + INF. *to doing sthg., to someone doing sthg.*) X. D.; ἐκ (τοῦ) μέσου *out of the way, aside* X. D. Thphr. Men.; *on the sides, uninvolved, neutral* Hdt.
5 (w. temporal connot.) ἐν μέσῳ *in the interval or meantime* Trag. Aeschin.; (also) διὰ μέσου Hdt. Th. Plu.
6 intervening amount or degree, **difference** E.; (W.GEN. betw. things) Hdt.
7 middle (as common ground); (prep.phrs.) ἐς (τὸ) μέσον *in the common interest, impartially* Il. Thgn.; ἐν μέσῳ *in common* E.
8 middle (as lying betw. extremes); **average** (of two numbers) Th.; middle state, **mean** Arist.; middle-of-the-road behaviour, **moderation** E.fr. Th.; (in neg.phr.) **middle course** (W.GEN. for enmity) Hdt.; (phrs.) ἂν τὸ μέσον *on a middle course* (W.GEN. betw. two things) Thgn.; οἱ διὰ μέσου *persons uncommitted to either party, moderates or neutrals* Th. X. Plu.; ἀνὰ μέσον *with moderation* Men.
9 middle class (in a city) Arist.; (also) οἱ διὰ μέσου Men.; τὸ διὰ μέσου Arist.
10 (phr.) ἔτος ἔνατον ἐκ μέσου *the ninth year to the extent of half* (i.e. *half the ninth year*) Th.
11 (gramm.) letter between a vowel and a consonant, **semivowel** Pl.; accent between an acute and a grave, **circumflex** Arist.

—**μέσ(σ)ον** neut.sg.adv. **1** app. **through the middle** (of the sea) Od.
2 between (W.GEN. one place and another) Il. Hdt. E.

—**μέσα** neut.pl.adv. **in the middle** (W.GEN. of heaven) E.

—**μέσως** adv. **1 in a middle way** (betw. two extremes) Pl. Arist.; (specif., w. ἔχειν) *maintain a mean* Arist.
2 to a middling degree, **moderately** E. Th. Isoc. Pl. Arist. Men.

—**μεσσόθεν** ep.adv. **from the middle** Parm.; **in the middle** AR.

—**μεσσόθι** ep.adv. **in the middle** Hes. AR.; (W.GEN. of a ship) AR.

μεσότης ητος f. **1 middle** or **central position, centrality** Pl.
2 mean (betw. two extremes) Arist.; (math., betw. two numbers or proportions) Pl.

μεσοτομέω contr.vb. [τέμνω] **1** make a cut in the middle; **cut** (a stalk) **half-way up** X.
2 make a division in the middle (of a topic) Pl.

μεσόω contr.vb. **1** (of a day, night, year, month, season) **be at the mid-point, be half over** Hdt. Th. X. Men. Plu.; (of a drama, speech, event) Ar. Pl. NT. Plu.; (in neg.phr., of trouble) A. E.
2 (of circumstances) **be intermediate** —W.GEN. betw. extremes Pl.
3 (of persons) **be in the middle** (of a term of office) Th. —W.GEN. of an activity Hdt. —W.PTCPL. of doing sthg. Pl.

μέσσαβα ep.n.pl.: see under μέσαβον

μέσσατος, also **μεσσάτιος** ep.superl.adjs.: see μέσατος

μέσσ-αυλος ου ep.m.f. [αὐλή] **1** (m.) **inner courtyard** (where cattle are stalled), **cattle-fold** Il.; (ref. to the cave of the Cyclops) Od.
2 (f.) **central door** (betw. a courtyard and the main building) AR. | cf. μέταυλος

μεσσηγύ(ς) ep.adv. and prep.: see μεσηγύ

μεσσ-ήρης ες dial.adj. [ἀραρίσκω] **1** (of Apollo's seat at Delphi) **at the centre** (W.GEN. of the earth) E.
2 (of Sirius) **in mid-heaven** E.

μεσσόγεως ep.adj.: see μεσόγαιος

μεσσόθεν, μεσσόθι ep.advs.: see under μέσος

μεσσο-παγής ές ep.adj. [πήγνῡμι] (of a spear) **planted up to the middle** (in the ground) Il.

μέσσος ep. and dial.adj.: see μέσος

μέστα dial.prep., conj. and adv.: see μέσφα

μεστός ή όν adj. **1 filled to capacity**; (of a drinking-vessel) **full** Anacr. X. Men.; (of a prison) X.; (of a house, compared to an inn) Thphr.
2 filled to capacity or extensively occupied (by specified contents); (of places, buildings, containers, or sim.) **full, filled** (W.GEN. w. persons or things) Hdt. Ar. Att.orats. Pl. X. +; (of a crocodile's mouth, w. leeches) Hdt.; (of a person's jaws, w. coins) Ar.; (of eyes, w. dust, ash) E.Cyc.
3 (of a specified measure of a commodity) **full, complete** Hdt.
4 (of a person) full of food, **full, replete** Ar. X.; **sated** (W.GEN. w. food) Plu.
5 having had one's fill, **sated, surfeited** (W.PTCPL. w. being angry, resentful) S. D.; (W.GEN. w. vengeance, killing, viewing) Plu.; (in neg.phr., w. wealth) Ar.; **weary** (W.GEN. of persons or things) D. Plu.
6 having an abundance (of material things); (of buildings, places) **full, filled** (W.GEN. w. statues, trees, animals, produce, or sim.) Hdt. Isoc. X. D. Plu.; (of a mattress, w. bedbugs) Ar.; (of a beard, w. grey hairs) Thphr.; (of persons, w. sperm, wind) Pl. X.; (of a garment) **covered** (W.GEN. w. decorations, stains) Pl. Thphr.; (of a body, w. wounds) Plu.; (of a soul, w. scars) Pl.; (of persons) **laden, with pockets filled** (W.GEN. w. money) X.
7 having an abundance (of non-material things); (of persons, a life) **full, filled** (W.GEN. w. hope, suspicion, anger, folly, or sim.) Att.orats. Pl. X. +; (of wild animals, w. savagery) Isoc.; (of a mixing-bowl, w. good cheer) Xenoph.; (of places, events, circumstances, w. wars, calamities, confusion, joy, lamentation, or sim.) Ar. Isoc. Pl. X. +; (of speeches, w. falsehood, contradictions, or sim.) Isoc. D.; (of a law, w. injustice and inhumanity) D.; (of letters, w. lamentation) Plu.; (of a drama, w. martial spirit) Ar.; (of a soul, W.DAT. w. wickedness) Pl.

μεστόω

8 (fig., of a person) **obsessed** (W.GEN. w. the theatre) Pl.
9 (of a city) **full** (W.GEN. of a person, i.e., app., much frequented by him) E.
μεστόω contr.vb. cause to be full, **fill** —*a person* (W.GEN. w. *anger*) S. ‖ PASS. (of persons) be filled —W.GEN. w. *arrogance, wrongdoing, or sim.* Pl.; (pf.) be full —W.GEN. *of wine* NT.
μέσφα, dial. **μέστα** prep., conj. and adv. [reltd. μέχρι]
1 (prep.) **until** —W.GEN. *dawn* Il. —W.ACC. *yesterday* Theoc.
2 (prep.) **as far as, up to** —W.ACC. *a place* Call. —W.GEN. AR.; (adv.) **all the way** —w. ἐπί, ἐς, ποτί + ACC. *to a place* Call. AR.
3 (conj.) **as long as, while** Call.; **until** Call. AR.; (phr.) μέσφ' ὅτε *until the time when* Call.
4 (adv.) **meanwhile** Call.
μετά, dial. **πεδά** prep. | W.ACC., GEN. and DAT. | sts. following its noun (w. anastrophe of the accent), e.g. ἀνδρῶν μέτα *with men* Pi. |
—A | movt. or direction |
1 **towards, to, into** or **amongst** —W.ACC. *gods, people, animals, places, things* Hom. +
2 **in search** or **pursuit of, after** —W.ACC. *persons or things* Hom. Hes. Thgn. Pi. S. E. +
3 (advbl.phr.) μετὰ νῆάδε *to a ship* AR.
—B | location |
1 **amid, among** —W.DAT. *people, places, things* Hom. Hes. Archil. Eleg. A. Pi. +; (as adv.) **in the midst** (of a group) Il. AR.
2 **throughout** —W.ACC. *a group of people* Hom.
3 (ref. to holding, gripping, or sim.) **between, in** —W.DAT. *the hands or arms* Hom. Hes. Hdt. S. Call. Theoc. —W.ACC. Hdt. Th. X. Aeschin. Plb. —W.DAT. *the jaws* Il. | see also χείρ 7
4 (ref. to a baby falling, during birth) **between** —W.DAT. *its mother's feet* Il.
5 **in** —W.DAT. *the heart* Hom. Hes. hHom. AR.
—C | spatial sequence or succession |
1 **following behind** or **to the rear of, after, behind** —W.ACC. *someone or sthg.* Hom. +; (as adv.) Hom. Call. AR.
2 **next in location** (fr. the viewpoint of a traveller), **next after, beyond** —W.ACC. *a place or people* Hdt.; (as adv.) **next, further on** AR.
3 **following the path of, in** —W.ACC. *a person's tracks, the swathe* (*during reaping*) Hom. Call.*epigr*.
4 **following along with, in conformity with** —W.ACC. *another's will* Il.
—D | comparison |
next (in respect of some quality or criterion); **next to, next after, after** —W.ACC. *someone or sthg.* Hom. Alcm. Alc. A. Theoc.
—E | accompaniment |
1 **in company with, together with, along with** or **among** —W.GEN. *persons or things* Hom. +; (as adv.) **alongside, together** (w. others) Il. AR.
2 (ref. to sleeping) **with** —W.GEN. *someone* Hdt. Ar. Plu.
3 **in support of** or **association with, with** —W.GEN. *persons* (*esp. allies or sim.*) Il. Hes. S. Th. +
4 **with the aid of** —W.GEN. *gods or persons* hHom. +; **with the support of** —W.GEN. *the law* Antipho Pl.
5 **in addition to, along with, as well as** —W.GEN. *sthg.* S. E. Th. +
6 (ref. to being equipped) **with** —W.GEN. *weapons* E. Th. NT.
7 **to the accompaniment of** —W.GEN. *a musical instrument* E. Plb. Plu.
—F | manner or attendant circumstances |
1 **in association with** (emotions, abstr. qualities, circumstances, or sim.); **with, in** —W.GEN. *hope, fear, virtue, truth, or sim.* S. E. Th. Pl. + —*tears* S. Isoc. Pl. Plb. + | see also δίκη 2, καιρός 3
2 (ref. to marching, dancing, or sim.) **in** —W.GEN. *time* Th. Pl. X. Plu. | see ῥυθμός 7
3 **by means of, with** —W.GEN. *speed, haste, force, design, or sim.* E. Isoc. Pl. D. Plb. + | see also βία 14, δρόμος 1, ἐπιβουλή 3, σπουδή 1, τάχος 5
—G | time |
1 **at a time subsequent to, after** —W.ACC. *a point in time, an event, someone* (*existing, being born, doing sthg., or sim.*) Hom. +; (as adv.) **afterwards** Hom. A. Pi. Hdt. Call. AR. | for μετὰ δήν, μετὰ δηρόν *after a long time* (Call. AR.) see δήν 2, δηρόν (under δηρός); see also βραχύς 17, δηθά, μικρός 11, χρόνος 6
2 **at the same time as** —W.GEN. *an event or activity* Th.
3 **throughout the course of, during** —W.ACC. *day, night* Pi. Hdt. E. Att.orats. +
μέτα prep. | The wd. is used as equiv. to 3sg. μέτεστι (see μέτειμι¹). | 1 **be present in company** —w. ἐν + DAT. *among certain people* Od.
2 ‖ IMPERS. **there is a share** —W.DAT. + GEN. *for someone in sthg.* (i.e. one has a share of, part in or claim on sthg.) Hdt. E. Ar.
3 (of nothing, in neg.phr.) **belong** —W.DAT. *to sthg.* Parm.
4 ‖ IMPERS. **there is a right** —W.DAT. + INF. *for someone, to do sthg.* S. E.
μετα-βαίνω vb. | fut. μεταβήσομαι | also dial.act.fut. (causatv.) μεταβάσω (Pi., cj.) | athem.aor. μετέβην | also dial.aor.1 (causatv.) μετέβασα (E., cj.), inf. μεταβάσαι (Pi.) ‖ ep.3sg.aor.2 mid. μετεβήσετο (AR.) | 1 **go into a different location;** (of persons or things) **pass, cross, move** (freq. W.PREP.PHR. to or fr. a place) A. Hdt. Pl. Plb. NT. Plu.; **transfer** —W.PREP.PHR. *to a new ship* Antipho (dub., cj. μετεκβαίνω); (of a commander) **change position** Plb.; (of a spectator in a theatre) **change seats** Plu.; (of a rider) **change horses** Plu.; (of stars) **cross over** (to the other side of the sky), **pass the zenith** Od.(tm.); (wkr.sens., of a person) **depart** (sts. W.ADV. or PREP.PHR. fr. a place) NT.; (aor.2 mid.) app. **come out** (of a house) AR.
2 **pass on** (to a new subject, in speech or writing); **change one's theme** or **subject** Od. Arist.; **change over, move on** —W.ADV. or PREP.PHR. *to a different song, a particular topic* hHom. Pl. Arist. Plb. —*fr. one metre to another* Arist.
3 **pass, change** (freq. W.PREP.PHR. to or fr. a particular state) Pl. Arist. NT. Plu. —W.ACC. *to a new mode of life* E. ‖ IMPERS. **there is a change** —W.PREP.PHRS. *fr. one state to another* Arist.
4 **change course** or **shift ground** (in one's policy or standpoint) Hdt. Pl. Arist. Plu.
5 (fut. and aor.1, causatv.) **transfer, convey** —*a person* (W.ADV. or PREP.PHR. *to or fr. a place*) Pi.; (of Zeus) **change, reverse** —*the courses of the stars, the sunrise* (i.e. its *location*) E.
μετα-βάλλω vb. | aor.2 μετέβαλον | 1 **cast into a different position; turn over** —*soil* X.; **shift** —*one's body* E.; (fig.) —*oneself* (W.ADVS. *up and down*, i.e. continually change one's *ground*) Pl.; (mid.) —*a carrying-pole* (fr. *one shoulder to the other*) Ar.
2 **cast into a reverse position or state; turn** —*one's back* (*in flight*) Il.(tm.); (of a god) **turn round, reverse** —*the Sun's chariot, the courses of the stars* (i.e. their direction) E. —*a fortunate person* (i.e. *his fortune*) E. —*persons* (W.INF. *so that they experience misfortune and then good fortune again*) E.; (of a person) —*one's cloak* (i.e. re-drape it, W.ADV. *fr. left to*

right) Ar.; (mid.) —*one's weapons* X. —*one's horse-riding* (*i.e. its direction*) X.

3 (gener.) **change, alter** —*a name, way of life, style of dress, form of government, or sim.* Hdt. E. Th. Ar. Isoc. Pl. +; (of captured cities) —*their inhabitants* (*by causing them to relocate*) Th.; (mid.) —*one's clothes* X. Thphr. Plu. —*one's ways* E. Ar. Isoc. —*one's occupation* Isoc.

4 take up instead, change to, adopt —*other ways, another message* E. —*a new kind of music* Pl. —*a different ruler* Th. Pl. Plu.; **move to** —*a place* Pl.; **substitute** —*one letter* (W.PREP.PHR. *for another*) Pl. ‖ MID. adopt instead, **prefer** —*silence* (W.GEN. *to speech*) S.

5 (intr., of persons or things) **change** (in condition, sts. W.PREP.PHR. to or fr. sthg.) Hdt. Isoc. Pl. X. +; (act. and mid., of fortune, sts. envisaged as a wind) E. Antipho Ar. Din. Plb. ‖ IMPERS.MID. there is a change (in a situation) Th.

6 ‖ PTCPL. (pres. or aor., quasi-advbl., modifying a vb.) changing round, instead Hdt. Pl. + • μεταβαλὼν πρὸς τὸν Λύσιν ἐποιούμην τοὺς λόγους *instead I directed my words to Lysis* Pl.

7 (of herds of cattle) **change location** Arist.; (of sailors, a helmsman) turn (one's vessel), **change course** Plu. ‖ MID. (of things) **shift about** Pl.; (of troops, a commander) **wheel round** X. Plb. Plu.

8 change one's strategy; **turn instead** —W.PREP.PHR. *to someone* Hdt.

9 change, switch round (in one's attitude or opinion) Th.; (mid.) Hdt. Att.orats. Pl. +

10 (intr.) change one's allegiance, **change sides** Hdt.; (mid.) Th. Att.orats. X. Plu.

11 ‖ MID. engage in commercial exchange; **do business in** —*the produce of others, the sale of food and wine* Pl.; (intr.) **do business, trade** X.

μετάβασις εως *f.* [μεταβαίνω] **1** process of change, **change, transformation** Pl. Arist.; (specif.) **change of fortune** (in tragedy) Arist.

2 change of location Plb. Plu.

3 transfer, transition (to a different subject) Plb.

μετα-βιβάζω *vb.* | fut. μεταβιβάσω | aor. μετεβίβασα |
1 cause (someone or sthg.) to change place or direction; **transfer** —*persons, an army, a war* (W.PREP.PHR. *to a place*) X. Plb. —*a narrative* (*to a scene of action*) Plb. —*a public practice* (*to private use*) D.; (of Fortune) —*persons* (fr. one place and activity to another) Plb.; **divert** —*desires* Pl.

2 (of a wrestler or boxer) **cause** (W.ACC. an opponent) **to change posture** —W.PREP.PHR. *to the other side* (*i.e. use this side for offence or defence*) Pl.

3 (of a god) **shift** —*the wind of fortune* (W.PREP.PHR. *towards the good*) Ar.

4 effect a transition step by step (in a state of affairs or a person's convictions) Pl. ‖ PASS. be led to a change (in one's convictions) Arist.

μετα-βλέπω *vb.* **look towards** or **at** —*sthg.* AR.

μεταβλητικός ή όν *adj.* [μεταβάλλω] **1** (of a form of acquisition) **through exchange** Pl.; (of the use of an item) **for the purpose of exchange** Arist. ‖ FEM.SB. art of exchange Pl. Arist.

2 (of potentiality, as a primary cause) **productive of change** (in things) Arist.

μεταβλητός ή όν *adj.* (of a substance) **liable to change** Arist.

μεταβολεύς έως *m.* **trafficker, haggler** (W.GEN. in vice) D.

μεταβολή ῆς, dial. **μεταβολά** ᾶς *f.* **1 changing** (of one thing for another) Pi.; **change** (W.GEN. of sails) Pi.; (of clothing) X.; (of a letter in a word) Pl.; (of inhabitants, a ruler, a form of government) Th. Isoc. Pl. X. +

2 exchange (of goods for money); **exchange, barter** Th.; (W.GEN. of goods) Arist.

3 change (fr. one condition to another); (gener.) **change** (esp. of circumstances) Hdt. E. Th. Att.orats. Pl. +; (specif.) **reversal** (W.GEN. of troubles, good fortune) E. Pl. Din. Plb. ‖ PL. varied tones (W.GEN. of lamentation) E.

4 (specif.) **counter-revolution** Th. | cf. μετάστασις 11

5 change (in climate, movement of heavenly bodies, appearance of the sky, or sim.) Hdt. E. Th. Pl. +; (fr. daylight to darkness, ref. to an eclipse) Hdt.

6 reversal (of direction); **turning around, wheeling about** (of a person) Plb. Plu.; (by troops or ships, esp. for renewed attack or flight) Plb.

7 change (in feelings, intentions, or sim.) Att.orats. Pl. +; (W.GEN. to inactivity) Th.; (esp., prep.phr.) ἐκ μεταβολῆς *in an about-turn, with a change of heart* Aeschin. Plb. Plu.

8 change of sides, defection Plu.; (W.PREP.PHR. to a particular side) Plb.

9 (prep.phr., wkr.sens.) ἐκ μεταβολῆς *contrarily, conversely* Plb.; *in turn, afresh or anew* Plb. Plu.

μεταβολικός ή όν *adj.* (of a manner) **changeable, variable** Plb.

μετα-βουλεύω *vb.* **1** (of gods) **decide upon a different plan** —W.PREP.PHR. *for someone* Od. ‖ MID. (of a person) **change one's mind** or **plan** Hdt. E. D.

2 ‖ MID. **decide instead** —w. ὥστε + INF. or μή + INF. *to do* (or not do) *sthg.* Hdt.(sts.tm.)

μεταβουλίᾱ ᾱς *f.* **change of heart** (by a god) Simon.

μετά-βουλος ον *adj.* [βουλή] **prone to change one's mind, fickle** Ar.

μετ-άγγελος ου *m.f.* conveyor of messages (betw. gods or humans), **messenger** Il. Hes.*fr.* hHom.

Μεταγειτνιών ῶνος *m.* **Metageitnion** (second month of the Athenian year) Att.orats. Plu.

μετα-γίγνομαι *mid.vb.* (of the lot of marriage) **fall as a share** —W.DAT. *to a man* Hes.(tm.)

μετα-γιγνώσκω, Ion. and dial. **μεταγῑνώσκω** *vb.* | athem.aor. μετέγνων | **1 decide differently, change one's mind** Hdt. S. Th. Att.orats. Pl. X. +

2 change one's mind about —W.ACC. *sthg.* E. Th.; **reverse** —*a previous decision* Th.; **regret** —*one's former words or actions* E. Is.

3 decide instead —W.INF. *to do sthg.* A. Th. —W.COMPL.CL. *that sthg. is the case* X.

μετάγνοια ᾱς *f.* change of mind, **regret** S.

μετάγνωσις εως *f.* **1 change of mind** Hdt.; (W.GEN. about sthg.) Plu.

2 regret, remorse Plu.

μετα-γράφω *vb.* **1** make changes in writing; **rewrite, revise, alter** —*a statement, document, law* E. Th. Isoc. X. Din. Plu.; **write instead** —*a word* (w. ἀντί + GEN. *in place of another*) X.; (intr., of an official) **alter the written record** D. ‖ PASS. (of statements) be rewritten Isoc.; be written instead (of others) Is.

2 ‖ MID. **have** (W.ACC. a letter) **translated** —w. ἐκ + GEN. *fr. another language* Th.

μετ-άγω *vb.* **1** cause (someone or sthg.) to move from one place to another; **bring** or **take** —*a person* (W.PREP.PHR. *to someone*) Men.; **transfer** —*people, troops, an assembly, court, money* (usu. W.ADV. or PREP.PHR. *to or fr. a place*) Plb. Plu. —*money, control of affairs* (*to persons*) Plb. Plu. —*a narrative*

μεταδαίνυμαι

(fr. one theme to another) Plu. —the practice of a skill (fr. one field to another) Plu.
2 (of a commander) **draw on** —an opponent (W.ADV. or PREP.PHR. *this way and that, fr. one encounter into another*) Plu.
3 **win over** —a person, a crowd Plu. || PASS. (of a man) be led on or seduced (by a woman) Plu.
4 (intr., of a commander) lead one's troops after (a colleague), **march in pursuit** X.

μετα-δαίνυμαι *mid.vb.* | 3sg.fut. μεταδαίσεται | ep.aor.subj. μεταδαίσομαι | **1 dine with** or **among** —W.DAT. *other persons* Hom.
2 join (w. others) in eating, **partake of** —W.GEN. *sacrificial offerings* Il.

μεταδετέον *neut.impers.vbl.adj.* [δέω¹] **one must tether** (W.ACC. a horse) **in a different place** —W.PREP.PHR. *away fr. the manger* (after it has fed) X.

μετα-δήμιος *ον adj.* **1** (of harm) **among the people** Od.
2 among one's own people; (of a god) **at home** (opp. abroad) Od.

μετα-διδάσκω *vb.* teach new ideas to, **re-educate** —a person Plu.

μετα-δίδωμι *vb.* | dial.athem.aor.inf. μεταδοῦν (Thgn.) | neut.impers.vbl.adj. μεταδοτέον | **1** give a share (of or in sthg., to someone); **share** —W.GEN. (sts.understd.) *food, land, power, money, one's happiness, thoughts, or sim.* (freq. W.DAT. w. someone) Thgn. Hdt. E.(sts.tm.) Th. Ar. Att.orats. +
2 **share** —W.ACC. *a specified part of sthg.* (W.DAT. w. someone) Hdt. Ar. Att.orats. Pl. X.; **attribute, give credit for** —a specified part of sthg. (W.DAT. to Fortune, experience, or sim.) Isoc.; (gener.) **give out** —provisions or sim. X. Plu.
3 (intr.) share information, **communicate** —W.PREP.PHR. *about sthg.* (usu. W.DAT. w. someone) Plb.

μετα-δίομαι *mid.vb.* [δίομαι¹] **pursue** —a person A.(tm.)

μεταδίωκτος *ον adj.* [μεταδιώκω] (of a person) **chased after, tracked down** Hdt.

μετα-διώκω *vb.* **1 pursue, chase after** —persons Hdt. X.; (intr.) **go in pursuit** X.
2 (wkr.sens.) **follow on** (after persons who have gone ahead) X.; (in the footsteps of a predecessor) Pl.
3 **seek out** (esp. by intellectual inquiry), **go looking for** —a certain kind of person, causes, facts, or sim. Pl. || PASS. (of persons or things) be looked for Pl.
4 seek to obtain or achieve, **pursue** —vengeance, pleasures, or sim. Pl. || PASS. (of a goal) be pursued Pl.

μετα-δοκεῖ *impers.contr.vb.* [δοκέω] | aor.: μετέδοξε, neut.ptcpl. μεταδόξαν | **1** it is decided differently, **there is a change of mind** (sts. W.DAT. by someone) Hdt. Hyp. D. Plu.
2 it is decided instead —W.DAT. + INF. *by someone, to do sthg.* D.; (also pf.pass.) Hdt.

μετα-δοξάζω *vb.* **change one's opinion** Pl.

μετα-δόρπιος *ον adj.* [δόρπον] **1** (quasi-advbl., of a person weeping) **during supper** Od.
2 (of a song, sent as a gift) **for after supper** Pi.fr.
|| NEUT.PL.SB. after-supper fruits, dessert Pl.

μετάδοσις *εως f.* [μεταδίδωμι] **1** giving a share, **sharing** (usu. W.GEN. of sthg.) X. Arist. Plu.
2 reciprocal giving, **exchange** Arist.
3 || PL. acts of generosity Plu.; (W.GEN. towards people) Plu.

μεταδοῦν (dial.athem.aor.inf.): see μεταδίδωμι

μετά-δουπος *ον adj.* [δοῦπος] (of days) perh. **of changeable thunder** (i.e. of uncertain omen) Hes.

μεταδρομάδην *adv.* [μετάδρομος] **running** or **racing in pursuit** Il. AR.

μεταδρομή *ῆς f.* (pl.) **pursuit, chase** (by hounds) X.; (W.GEN. by Erinyes) E.

μετά-δρομος *ον adj.* [δραμεῖν] (of hounds, fig.ref. to Erinyes) **running in pursuit** (W.GEN. of crimes) S.

μέταζε *adv.* [μετά] afterwards; (phr.) τὰ μέταζε *in the future* Hes.

μετα-ζεύγνυμι *vb.* **yoke** (W.ACC. horses) **afresh** (i.e. yoke a new team of chariot-horses) X.

μετάθεσις *εως f.* [μετατίθημι] **1 change of position** (of an object) Arist.; change (W.GEN. of an orator's posture) Plu.
2 change (W.GEN. in a state of affairs) Plb.; (W.PREP.PHR. for the better, the worse) Plb.
3 change, alteration (of what has been written) Plb.; (W.GEN. of words, statements) D. Plb.; (specif.) **change of wording, amendment** (to a treaty) Th.
4 amendment (W.GEN. of errors) Plb.
5 change of subject (in speech) Plb.
6 change of heart Plb.
7 change of sides Plb. Plu.; **defection** (W.PREP.PHR. to a particular side) Plb.
8 exchange (of merchandise) Plb.

μετα-θέω *contr.vb.* [θέω¹] | fut. μεταθεύσομαι | **1** (of hounds, hunters) **run in pursuit** (of a quarry) Pl. X.; (of a dog) **run after** (a wolf) X. || PASS. (of a hare) be chased after X.
2 (of troops) **go in pursuit** (of a retreating enemy) X.
3 (of a person) **hasten after** —others (to catch up w. them) Plu.
4 (fig., of a person, sts. compared to a hound) **chase after, pursue, follow** —an argument Pl. —the tracks (W.GEN. of a person, envisaged as a wild animal; of the truest form of government) Pl.
5 (of a commander) **hurry about** —W.ADV. *this way and that* (amid the fighting) Plu.

μεταΐγδην *ep.adv.* [μεταΐσσω] **with a lunge forwards** AR.

μετα-ΐζω *vb.* **sit in company** (w. others) Od.

μετ-αίρω, dial. **πεδαίρω** (E.) *vb.* **1** move (to a different place) by lifting; **remove** —a statue (W.PREP.PHR. fr. its base) E.; (euphem., of the Sphinx) —youths (fr. a region, i.e. kill them) E.
2 (periphr.) **lift, shift** —a leg, foot (i.e. remove oneself) E.; (intr.) **depart** —W.ADV. or PREP.PHR. fr. a place NT. || PASS. (of a sick person) be lifted up and moved Plu.
3 (wkr.sens.) **raise** —one's shield E.
4 **revoke** —a decree D.

μετ-αΐσσω *ep.vb.* [ᾄσσω] | aor.ptcpl. μεταΐξας, Aeol. μεταΐξαις | **1** (of a warrior or assailant) **rush at** (an opponent), **charge in** Hom.; rush after, **charge in pursuit** Il. Theoc.; (of a person) **rush after** (a cry) AR.
2 eagerly **follow after** —a person (i.e. the example set by him) Pi.

μετ-αιτέω *contr.vb.* **1 ask for a share** Hdt. D. —W.GEN. *of sthg.* Hdt.
2 **ask for** —a share (W.GEN. of sthg.) Ar.
3 ask (W.ACC. someone) **for a share** Ar.

μετ-αίτιος *ᾱ ον* (also *ος ον*) *adj.* **1** being jointly a cause (of sthg.); (of persons or gods) **jointly responsible, sharing responsibility** (W.GEN. for an action, decision, outcome, sts. also W.DAT. w. someone) A. E.
2 sharing culpable responsibility (for sthg.); **equally to blame** Hdt.; (W.GEN. for a murder, calamity, war, or sim.) A. Hdt. S. Pl. X.; (W.DAT. + INF. for someone's death) S. X.

μετ-αίχμιον *ον n.* [αἰχμή] **1** (sg. and pl.) **space between two armies, no-man's-land** Hdt. E. Plu.; (fig., betw. two political factions) Sol.

2 (fig.) **intervening space** (betw. lands, ref. to a sea) Iamb.adesp.; **borderland** (W.GEN. of darkness, i.e. time betw. darkness and light) A.

—**μεταίχμιος**, dial. **πεδαίχμιος**, ον adj. **1** (of a class of being) **intermediate** (W.GEN. betw. man and woman) A.
2 (of celestial phenomena) **between heaven and earth** A.

μετα-καθοπλίζω vb. **arm** (W.ACC. troops) **in a different way** Plb.

μετα-καλέω contr.vb. **1** go after with a call, **summon** —persons (sts. W.PREP.PHRS. fr. one place to another) Plu.; (specif.) **summon back, recall** —ships, persons Th. Men. Plb. Plu. ‖ MID. call to oneself, **summon** —persons NT.
2 win over —persons (sts. w. πρός + ACC. to oneself) Plu.
3 turn away, divert —a person (w. ἀπό + GEN. fr. an alliance, a plan) Plb.; (of danger) —a person's mind (fr. anger) Aeschin.

μετά-κειμαι mid.pass.vb. [κεῖμαι] (of a letter in a word) **be transposed** Pl.

μετά-κερας ατος n. [κεράννῡμι] mixture of hot and cold water, **warm water** Call.(tm.)

μετα-κῑνέω contr.vb. **1** move from one position to another; **dislodge** —a person Hdt.; **shift** —part of the body X.; **change the position of** —troops Plu. ‖ PASS. (of persons) change location Hdt.; (of objects) be relocated Hdt.
2 change, alter —a habit, form of government, laws, or sim. X. D. Arist. Plu. ‖ PASS. (of things) be changed Pl. X. Arist.

μετακίνησις εως f. **change of position** (of troops) Plu.

μετακῑνητός ή όν adj. (of an agreement) **able to be changed, alterable** Th.

μετα-κλαίομαι mid.vb. **1 weep afterwards** (when it is too late) Il.
2 weep for, bewail —one's life and sufferings E.(dub.)

μετα-κλείω ep.vb. [κλέω] **rename** —islands AR.

μετα-κλίνομαι pass.vb. (of a battle, i.e. its fortune) **be altered, shift** Il.

μετα-κοιμίζομαι pass.vb. (of the power of Ruin) be changed to a state of sleep, **be put to sleep** A.

μετακοίμιος ον adj. (of a god) **bringing respite** (W.GEN. fr. disaster) E.(cj., for μετακύμιος amid the waves)

μετά-κοινος ον adj. [κοινός] **sharing** or **acting in common** (sts. W.DAT. w. someone) A.

μετα-κομίζω vb. **1 transport, transfer** —sthg. (sts. W.PREP.PHR. to or fr. a place) Plb. Plu. ‖ MID. **have** (W.ACC. sthg.) **transported to oneself** Lycurg. ‖ PASS. (of persons or things) be transported or transferred —W.PREP.PHR. to a place Pl. Plb. Plu.
2 transfer —a city (W.PREP.PHR. to a confederacy, i.e. make it a member) Plu.

μετα-κοσμέω contr.vb. (of a ruler) **reorder, reshape, remould** —a people's habits Plu. —a people (W.PREP.PHR. in the direction of peace) Plu.; (of madness) —a person Plu. ‖ PASS. (of a people) be reshaped —W.PREP.PHR. by a ruler Plu.

μετακόσμησις εως f. **reordering, rearrangement** Pl. Plu.

μετα-κυλίνδω vb. **roll** (W.ACC. oneself) **over** —W.PREP.PHR. to the safer side of a ship (fig.ref. to joining the winning side) Ar.

μετακύμιος adj.: see μετακοίμιος

μετα-λαγχάνω vb. **1 have a share allotted to oneself; partake of, gain** —W.GEN. knowledge, justice Pl. Plu.; **incur** —W.GEN. disgrace Pl.; **get a part, participate** —W.GEN. in a battle Pl.
2 receive, get —W.ACC. a share (W.GEN. of someone's misfortune) E.

μετα-λαμβάνω vb. **1 receive a share** (after division or distribution); **receive a share** Ar. D. Plu. —W.GEN. of spoils, money, property, or sim. Hdt. Ar. X. Is. Men.; **receive** —W.GEN. an apportionment Pl.
2 receive a share or specified amount (of sthg.); **receive** —W.ACC. a share (W.GEN. of property, martial spirit, misfortunes, virtue) E. Isoc. Pl. D. —half (of sthg.) Hdt. —half of an inheritance Is. —a specified portion (of the votes) Att.orats. Pl. —none (of the votes) Is. —no, few, two hundred votes Att.orats.
3 (gener.) **share in** or **partake of** —W.GEN. toil, power, citizenship, benefits, immortality, blood-guilt, or sim. Pi. Th. Att.orats. Pl. +; (of physical entities) —the Forms Pl.
4 get some time with —W.GEN. a person X.
5 ‖ MID. **lay claim to** —W.GEN. a name Hdt.
6 take afterwards (in succession to sthg. else); **take next** —a lance (after a javelin) X.; (of a horse) —a smooth bit (after a rough one) X.
7 take over (in succession to another); **take over** —an enemy's encampment Plb.; **succeed to** —royal power Plb.; **take up** —the discourse (i.e. reply) Plb. —one argument (w. ἐκ + GEN. after another) Pl.; (intr.) **reply** Plb.
8 (of two persons) **exchange** —tools Pl.; **alternate** —command Plb.; (of two sets of troops) —front position (w. rear position) Plb.
9 (intr., of night) **come on** Plb.
10 take in exchange (for sthg. else); **get a change of, change** —clothing, practices, attitude, a form of government, or sim. Th. Isoc. Pl. X. +
11 substitute —war (w. ἀντί + GEN. for peace) Th. —one form of government (for another) Isoc. —a different opinion (for one's present one) Isoc. —a different name (for pleasure) Pl. —one person (W.GEN. for another) Pl.; **get instead** —leisure and inaction (after forfeiting the opportunity for action) D.; **choose instead** —W.INF. to do sthg. (w. ἀντί + GEN. instead of doing sthg. else) Th.; (of troops) **take up** —rear position (w. ἀντί + GEN. instead of front position) Plb.
12 (gener.) **get, find** —an appropriate time Plb. NT.

μετ-αλγέω contr.vb. **feel pain afterwards, feel remorse, repent** A.(dub.) E.

μετ-αλδήσκω vb. (of a dragon's teeth) **change while growing** (into armed men) AR.

μετάληψις εως f. [μεταλαμβάνω] **1 participation, sharing** (sts. W.GEN. in sthg.) Pl. Arist.
2 alternation, succession (W.GEN. of arguments) Pl.
3 taking over (W.GEN. of command) Plb.
4 alteration, change (W.GEN. of the layout of a camp, a topic of study) Plb.; (prep.phr.) ἐκ μεταλήψεως **by way of a change, as an alternative** Plb.
5 receiving in exchange, acceptance (W.GEN. and ἀντί + GEN. of one thing in place of another) Arist.

μεταλλαγή ῆς, dial. **μεταλλαγά** ᾶς f. [μεταλλάσσω]
1 change, transformation (of things) Pl.; (W.GEN. of daylight, ref. to an eclipse) Hdt.
2 change, reversal (in a person's circumstances) Men.; (W.GEN. of fortune) E.; (of tears of sadness, to tears of joy) E.
3 change, exchange (perh. of ownership) S.; (W.GEN. of war, i.e. of one enemy for another) X.
4 exchange, interchange (W.GEN. of kinds of knowledge) Pl.
5 taking in exchange, adoption (W.GEN. and ἀντί + GEN. of one letter of the alphabet in place of another) Pl.

μεταλλακτός όν adj. **1** (of a divine power) **changed** or **changeable** A.
2 (of things) **to be changed** Pi.fr.

μετάλλαξις εως *f.* change (W.GEN. of posture) X.

μετ-αλλάσσω, Att. **μεταλλάττω** *vb.* **1** make a change (in the appearance or nature of things); **change, alter** —*laws, an administrative system, a name* Hdt. Th. Pl. —*one's appearance, character, habits* Pl. Aeschin. Plu. —*a legal case and a hearer's perception of it* Aeschin.; (of ruinous errors) —*human life* S.*fr.*; (of a person's fate) —*its nature* S.*fr.* ‖ MID. **cause a change in** —*one's fortunes* Din.
2 (intr.) **undergo a change**; (of a climate) **change** Hdt.; (of a person) **adapt** —W.PREP.PHR. *in the face of difficulty* E.*satyr.fr.*; **undergo** —W.COGN.ACC. *a change* (W.GEN. *in one's life*) Pl.
3 make an exchange (of one thing for another); **change** —*one's friends* Isoc. —*one's clothes* Plu. —*the paths of one's life* (*i.e. keep changing one for another*) Emp.
4 exchange, interchange —*two people's fortunes* Isoc.; (of creatures) —*their forms and capacities* (w. each other) Pl.; (of two sets of persons) —*their level of understanding* (*relative to each other*) Isoc. ‖ PASS. (of crafts and tools) be exchanged or interchanged (betw. different professions) Pl.
5 get in exchange; take on, assume —*the physical nature of birds* (*in exchange for that of humans*) Ar.
6 change or exchange places; change, alter —*one's position* Aeschin. Lycurg.; **move, switch** —*persons* (W.PREP.PHR. *to a place vacated by others*) Pl. —*troops* (*to different places*) Plb.; **move to** —*another place* Pl. Lycurg. —*one place* (W.PREP.PHR. *after another*) Pl.
7 exchange —*life* (w. εἰς + ACC. *for immortality*) Hyp.; **give up, quit** —*life* (*in exchange for immortality*) Isoc. —(*in exchange for death*) Lycurg. Plb.; (intr.) **die** Plb.; (of a person translated to heaven) **depart from the earth** Plu.

μετάλλατος ον *dial.adj.* [μεταλλάω] (of an objective) **to be sought after** Pi.

μεταλλάω *contr.vb.* [perh.reltd. μέταλλον] ǀ aor. μετάλλησα, dial. μετάλλᾱσα ǀ **1 make inquiries, ask, inquire** (sts. W.PREP.PHR. about someone) Hom. AR.
2 (tr.) **ask** or **inquire about** —*someone or sthg.* Hom.
3 inquire of, question —*a person* Hom.; **ask** —*persons* (W.INDIR.Q. *who they are*) Od.
4 ask —W.DBL.ACC. *someone about sthg.* Hom.
5 (of a god's voice) **seek out** —*a person* Pi.

μεταλλείᾱ ᾱς *f.* [μεταλλεύω] **1 extraction of minerals from the earth, mining** Pl. ‖ PL. **mining operations** Pl.
2 ‖ PL. **excavations** (for channelling water), **channels** Pl.; **mines** Plu.

μεταλλεῖα ων *n.pl.* **substances obtained by mining, minerals** Pl.

μεταλλεύς έως *m.* **one who extracts minerals from the earth, miner** Pl. Plu.

μεταλλευτικός ή όν *adj.* (of an item) **for use in mining** Pl. ‖ FEM.SB. **art of mining** Arist.

μεταλλεύω *vb.* [μέταλλον] **1 dig a mine** or **tunnel** (under an enemy wall, in siege-operations) Plb.
2 ‖ PASS. (of substances, i.e. minerals) **be obtained by mining, be mined** Pl. Arist.

μετα-λλήγω *ep.vb.* [λήγω] ǀ iteratv.impf. μεταλλήγεσκον ǀ **cease, desist** (fr. doing sthg.) AR. —W.GEN.*fr. anger, toil* Il. hHom. AR.

μεταλλικός ή όν *adj.* [μέταλλον] (of a law, an action at law) **relating to mines** D. Arist.

μέταλλον ου *n.* **1** (freq.pl.) **mine** (for extraction of minerals, esp. gold, silver, salt) Hdt. Th. Ar. X. Hyp. D. +
2 (milit.) **mine, tunnel** (in siege-operations) Plb.

μετάλμενος (ep.athem.aor.mid.ptcpl.): see μεθάλλομαι

μετα-λωφέω *ep.contr.vb.* [λωφάω] **cease, rest** (fr. rowing) AR.

μετα-μάζιος ον *Ion.adj.* [μαστός] (quasi-advbl., of a chest that is struck) **between the breasts** Il.

μετα-μαίομαι *mid.vb.* (of an eagle) **search after** —*its prey* Pi.

μετα-μανθάνω *vb.* **1** (intr.) **learn afresh, relearn** (opp. *learn fr. the beginning*) Arist.
2 (tr.) **relearn** or **learn instead** —*a song, a language* (*i.e. learn a new song or language in place of an old one*) A. Hdt.
3 come to a new understanding or **point of view** Ar. Pl.
4 (tr.) **come to a new understanding of, learn to appreciate** —*freedom* (*when one has lost it*) Aeschin. [or perh. **unlearn, learn to forget**]

μετ-αμείβω, dial. **πεδαμείβω** *vb.* ǀ dial.aor. πεδάμειψα (Pi.) ǀ **1 change** (one thing into another); **change, transform** —*someone* (W.ADV. + PREP.PHR. *back fr. a cow*, W.PREDIC.SB. *into a woman*) Mosch.
2 exchange (one thing for another); **receive** (W.ACC. *great good*) **in exchange** —W.GEN. *for pain* Pi.
3 ‖ MID. **undergo a change to a different condition, recover** —w. ἐκ + GEN. *fr. hardships* Pi.
4 give or receive in succession; bequeath (W.ACC. *a land*) **in succession** —W.DAT. *to one's children's children* E. ‖ MID. **receive** (W.ACC. *countless blessings*) **in succession** —W.DAT. *to others* E.
5 ‖ MID. **take turns** (at doing sthg.) Pi.

μετα-μείγνῡμι, also **μεταμίσγω** *vb.* ǀ impf. μετέμισγον ǀ fut. μεταμείξω ǀ **1 mix together** —*firebrands* (w. *firewood*) Od.
2 combine —*someone's possessions* (W.DAT. w. *another's*) Od.

μεταμειπτός όν *adj.* [μεταμείβω] (of an item) **able to be exchanged** Hes.*fr.*

μετα-μέλει *3sg.impers.vb.* [μέλω] ǀ neut.ptcpl. μεταμέλον ǀ impf. μετέμελε ǀ fut. μεταμελήσει ǀ aor. μετεμέλησε ǀ **1 there is a feeling of regret** or **remorse** —W.DAT. *for someone* (*i.e. one is regretful, remorseful, sorry*) Hdt. Th. Ar. Att.orats. Pl. X. + —(W.GEN. *about sthg.*) Att.orats. Pl. X. Men. Plu. —(W.NEUT.ACC.) Hdt. Ar. Men. —(W.DAT.PTCPL. *for doing or having done sthg.*) Hdt. Antipho Pl. X. D. —(w. ὅτι + CL.) X.
2 (app.pers., of πόνος *effort*) **be a matter of regret** A.(dub.)

μεταμέλεια ᾱς *f.* **1 regret, remorse** (over an action) Th. Pl. X. Arist. Plb. Plu.
2 change of heart, second thoughts (over a decision) Th. Plb.

μεταμελητικός ή όν *adj.* **inclined to feel regret** or **remorse** Arist.

μετα-μέλομαι *mid.vb.* ǀ also perh. contr.pres. μεταμελέομαι (Plu.) ǀ fut. μεταμελήσομαι ǀ aor.pass. (w.mid.sens.) μετεμελήθην (Plb. +) ǀ **1 experience a change of feeling, feel regret** or **remorse** Hdt. X. Arist. NT. Plu. —W.DAT. or PREP.PHR. *over sthg.* Plb. Plu. —W.PTCPL. *at having* (or *not having*) *done sthg.* Th. Plu. —w. ὅτι + CL. Th. NT. Plu. ‖ NEUT.FUT.PTCPL.SB. **later feeling of regret** X.
2 change one's mind, have second thoughts Th. Plb. Plu.

μετάμελος ου *m.* **regret** (W.GEN. over an action) Th.

μετα-μέλπομαι *mid.vb.* **sing** or **dance among** —W.DAT. *others* hHom.

μεταμίσγω *vb.*: see μεταμείγνυμι

μετα-μορφόομαι *pass.contr.vb.* [μορφή] (of Jesus) **be changed in appearance, be transfigured** NT.

μετ-αμπίσχομαι *mid.vb.* (fig.) **put on a new garb** —W.ACC. *of slavery* (w. ἀντί + GEN. *in place of freedom*) Plu.

μετ-αμφιέννυμαι *mid.vb.* **change one's dress** Plu.; (tr.) **change into** —*a garment* (w. ἀντί + GEN. *in place of another*) Plu.

μεταμώνιος ον *adj.* [2nd el.app.reltd. ἄνεμος] **1** (quasi-advbl., of dust rising) **on the wind or high in the air, airborne** Simon.; (of a person, envisaged as having taken wing) Ar.
2 (of words, weaving, falsehoods, aspirations, a prophecy) perh., carried away on the wind, **vain, idle, empty, futile** Hom. Pi. AR. Theoc.
3 (combining both connots., of an object disappearing, like a dream) **turned to nothing, gone with the wind** AR.
—**μεταμώνια** *neut.pl.adv.* **vainly, to no effect** AR.
μετ-αναγιγνώσκομαι *pass.vb.* | only 3sg.aor. μετανεγνώσθη | **be persuaded to repent** —W.GEN. *of anger and quarrels* S.
μετα-ναιετάω *contr.vb.* **dwell with** —W.DAT. *persons* hHom.
μεταναιέτης ου *m.* **dweller together** (W.GEN. w. someone) Hes.
μετανάστασις εως *f.* [μετανίστημι] **1 relocation** (to another country, fr. countryside to city) Th. X.
2 change of position (by troops) Plu.
μετανάστης ου *m.* **migrant** Il. Hdt.
μετα-νιπτρίς ίδος *f.* [reltd. νίπτρα] cup drunk from after washing the hands at the end of a meal, **after-washing cup** Philox.Leuc.
μετα-νίσομαι (also **μετανίσσομαι** AR.) *mid.vb.* **1** (of the sun) **cross over** —W.ADV. *in the direction of the end of the day* (i.e. *the west*) Hom.
2 (of a river) **pass** or **flow on** —w. εἰς + ACC. *into another* AR.
3 (of a god) **make for, travel to** —*a place* AR.(tm.)
4 (of ships) **go in pursuit of** —*a person* E.; (of a wild animal) —*flocks* AR.; (of a person) **seek after** —*wealth* Pi.
μετ-ανίστημι *vb.* | aor.1 μετανέστησα | **cause** (persons) to **get up and move; remove** —*people* (W.PREP.PHR. *to other cities*) Plb.; **relocate** —*a populace* Plb.
—**μετανίσταμαι** *mid.vb.* | also athem.aor.act. μετανέστην |
1 (of a country) **be in a state of upheaval** Th.
2 (of a person, a populace, troops) **uproot oneself, change location** (sts. W.ADV. or PREP.PHR. to or fr. a place) Hdt. S. Th.
3 (of a person) **get up and change seats** Pl.
μετα-νοέω *contr.vb.* **1 think again** (in hindsight), **reconsider** Pl.
2 consider on further reflection —w. μή + SUBJ. *whether sthg. is the case* X.
3 have second thoughts or **change one's mind** (sts. w. further connot. of feeling regret or remorse) Antipho X. D. Men. Plb. Plu.
4 repent (of sins or wickedness) NT.
μετάνοια ᾱς *f.* **1 second thoughts** or **change of mind** (sts. w. further connot. of regret or remorse) Antipho Th. Plb. Plu.
2 repentance NT.
μετα-ξύ *adv.* and *prep.* [μετά, perh. ξύν] **1** (adv.) in the space separating two things or places, **between, in between, midway** Il. A. Hdt. Th. + ‖ NEUT.SB. (w.art.) space between (sts. W.GEN. things or places) Hdt. Th. Ar. +; (quasi-adj.) Hdt. + • ὁ μεταξὺ χῶρος *the intervening territory* Hdt.
2 in the interval separating two concepts or types of thing, **midway between** S.*Ichn.* Pl. Arist. • φίλος ἢ ἐχθρὸς ἢ μεταξὺ *friend or enemy or neutral* Arist. ‖ NEUT.SB. (w.art.) word of neutral gender Arist.; (pl.) things midway (betw. two concepts or types) Pl. Arist.; middle course or policy D.
3 between two points of time; **in the meantime** (while sthg. is happening) Pl. X. Thphr.; (w. focus on the mid-point) **in the middle, half-way through, before the end** Hdt. Isoc. Pl. X. D. +; (w.ptcpl., doing sthg.) Hdt. Ar. Att.orats. Pl. X. • μεταξὺ θύων *in the middle of sacrificing* Ar.; (quasi-adj.) • ὁ μεταξὺ χρόνος *the intervening time* Hdt. Att.orats. Pl. Plb. Plu. ‖ NEUT.SB. (w.art.) the intervening time Hdt. Isoc.; (prep.phr.) ἐν τῷ μεταξύ *in the meantime* D. NT.; (pl.) intervening events Isoc.
4 afterwards; (phr.) τὸ μεταξὺ σάββατον *the next Sabbath* NT.
5 (prep., sts. following its noun) **between** —W.GEN. *two persons, things or places* Archil. Hippon. Hdt. Th. + —*two concepts or types of thing* Hdt. Th. Pl. X. + —*two occurrences or points of time* Th. D. +; (ref. to a reciprocal relationship) —*two persons* NT.
6 (w. only the more distant extreme expressed) **between** (here or now and) —W.GEN. *a place or time* S. E. Th. Ar. + • τὸ μεταξὺ τῆς νήσου *the area up to the island* Th. • τὰ μεταξὺ τούτου *the time until this point* S.
μετα-παιφάσσομαι *mid.vb.* (of lightning) **flash in different directions** AR.
μετα-παύομαι *mid.vb.* (of warriors) **rest at intervals** Il.
μετα-παυσωλή ῆς *f.* **interval of rest, pause** (W.GEN. in fighting) Il.
μετα-πείθω *vb.* **persuade** (someone) **to change an opinion or belief; change the mind of** —*persons, a populace* Ar. Att.orats. Pl. Arist. + —(W.ACC. *about sthg.*) Men.; **persuade** —*someone* (w. μή + INF. *not to fear death*) Pl. ‖ PASS. be persuaded to change one's mind Isoc. Pl. X. D. Arist.
μετα-πειράομαι *mid.contr.vb.* **try something new** Ar.
μεταπειστός όν *adj.* [μεταπείθω] (of a belief) **able to be changed by persuasion** Pl.
μεταπεμπτέος ᾱ ον *vbl.adj.* [μεταπέμπω] (of ships) **to be sent for** Th.
μετάπεμπτος ον *adj.* (of a person) **sent for, summoned** Hdt. Th. X. Plu.
μετα-πέμπω *vb.* **send for** or **summon** —*persons* E.(tm., dub.) Th. —*troops, ships* Th. —*garlic* Ar.; (mid.) —*persons, troops, ships, commodities, help* Hdt. Th. Ar. Att.orats. Pl. + ‖ PASS. (of persons) be sent for or summoned Th. Att.orats. +
μετάπεμψις εως *f.* **summoning** (of a person) Plu.
μετα-πίπτω *vb.* **1 fall differently;** (of a sherd, tossed in a game) **fall the other way up** Pl.; (of votes) **be cast differently** (i.e. for a different verdict) Pl. Aeschin.
2 (of fortune) **fall out differently, change** E. Att.orats. Men. Plu.; (of a person) —W.PREP.PHRS. *fr. good fortune to bad* Arist.
3 (of persons) **change** (in mind or feelings, sts. W.PREP.PHR. to or fr. a state) E. Ar. Isoc. Arist. Plb. Plu.; (in their physical state) Plu.; (of the appetitive part of the soul) **shift about** —W.ADVBL.PHR. *in opposite directions* Pl.
4 (gener., of things, circumstances) **change** or **shift** (sts. W.PREP.PHR. to or fr. a state) Heraclit. Democr. Th. Pl. Lycurg. Arist. + —W.GEN. *fr. a state* Pl. —W.PREDIC.ADJ. *for the better* E.; (of a person's appearance) Hdt.
μετα-πλάττω *Att.vb.* **remould, refashion** —*gold figures* Pl.; (of creator gods) —*living creatures* Pl.
μετα-ποιέω *contr.vb.* **1 compose differently, rework** or **alter** —*a verse* Sol. —*laws* D. —*a political decision* Plu. ‖ PASS. (of a law) be altered D.; (of abstract qualities) Arist.
2 ‖ MID. represent oneself as sharing in, **lay claim to** —W.GEN. *a trading-centre* Hdt. —*virtue, intelligence, a skill* Th. Pl. Plu.
μετα-πορεύομαι *mid.vb.* **1 move to a different place** Pl.
2 follow up, pursue —*a private feud* Lys.
3 seek to punish —*persons, crimes* Plb.; (intr.) **seek punishment** Plb.
4 seek after —*an office* Plb.

μεταπρεπής ἐς *adj.* [μεταπρέπω] (of a house) **standing out** or **conspicuous among** (W.DAT. the gods, i.e. their houses) Il.

μετα-πρέπω *vb.* (of gods, persons, animals) **stand out, be pre-eminent** or **conspicuous** (usu. W.DAT. among others) Hom.(sts.tm.) Hes.(sts.tm.) Eleg. B. AR. Theoc.; (w. 2ND DAT. through some quality or attribute) Il. Hes. AR.; (W.INF. at doing sthg.) Hom.(sts.tm.)

μετα-πτοέω *contr.vb.* **scare into migrating** A.(dub.cj.)

μετάπτωσις εως *f.* [μεταπίπτω] **1 change of position** Pl. **2 change** (W.GEN. + PREP.PHR. of an existing state to the opposite) Plu. **3 change of mind** or **feelings** Plb. **4 change of sides, defection** (w. πρός + ACC. to someone) Plb.

μετα-πύργιον ου *n.* [πύργος] **space between towers** (in a wall) Th.

μετ-αρίθμιος ον *adj.* (of Dionysus) **numbered among** (W.DAT. the immortals) hHom.; (of a person, W.DAT. a group of heroes) AR.

μετα-ρρέω *contr.vb.* [ῥέω] (fig., of sight, envisaged as a stream, when reflected by a mirror) **change in flow** —W.PREP.PHR. *to the opposite direction* Pl.; (of wishes, compared to the Euripos) **ebb and flow** Arist.

μετα-ρρίπτω *vb.* [ῥίπτω] **1 throw out of place**; (of a god) **reshuffle** —*everything* Simon.; (of a person) **dislodge** —*someone's deep-rooted feelings* D. **2 bring** (W.ACC. persons) **over** —W.PREP.PHR. *to someone (as an ally), to or fr. an alliance* Plb. **3 transfer** —*kingship* (W.PREP.PHR. *to someone*) Plb.

μετα-ρρυθμίζω *vb.* [ῥυθμίζω] **1 change the shape of** —*letters* Hdt. ‖ PASS. (of a fire) **be changed in form** Pl.; (of the class of birds) **arise by a process of transformation** (fr. other beings) Pl. **2 change the nature of** —*a sea-crossing (by bridging it)* A. **3** (fig.) **reshape** (by instruction), **reform, rectify, improve** —*a person* X. Arist. —*methods of agriculture* X.

μεταρσιολεσχίᾱ ᾱς *f.* [μετάρσιος, λέσχη] **elevated talk** (on philosophical matters) Plu.

μεταρσιόομαι *pass.contr.vb.* (of a cloud) **rise high into the air** Hdt.

μετάρσιος, *dial.* **πεδάρσιος** (A. Ar.), ον (also ᾱ ον) *adj.* [μεταίρω] **1 raised high in the air**; (of a person's step) **lifted high** AR.; (of hanging by a noose) **high in the air** E.(dub.); (perh., of a ship's tackle) **aloft** Theoc.; (of crags) **lofty** A.; (fig., of boasts) E. **2** (of a god, claps of thunder) **high in the sky** A. Ar. ‖ NEUT.PL.SB. **celestial phenomena** (as the subject of philosophical speculation) Plu. **3** (quasi-advbl., of a person leaping, flying, being held) **high in the air** S. E. Ar.; (of gall fr. a sacrifice, being sprayed) S.; (fig., of a person soaring, i.e. in the realms of philosophical speculation) E.; (of words leaping, perh. envisaged as sparks) A. **4** (quasi-advbl., of persons living) **off the ground** (i.e. in wagons) A.; (of a person's flanks and head being raised) E. **5** (of ships) **on the open sea, offshore** (opp. beached) Hdt. —**μετάρσιον** *neut.sg.adv.* **high up** or **in suspense** Emp. —**μετάρσια** *neut.pl.adv.* **shallowly** —*ref. to drawing breath fr. the throat (opp. the lungs)* E.

μετα-σεύομαι *mid.vb.* | *ep.3pl.impf.* μετεσσεύοντο | *ep.3sg.athem.aor.* μετέσσυτο | *ep.3sg.pf.* μετέσσυται | **1 hasten to follow** (someone) Il.; **hasten in pursuit** (of someone) Il.; **hasten to find** —*someone* Il.

2 (of a tide) **rush back** —W.ADV. *to the open sea* AR.

μετα-σκευάζω *vb.* **1 reclothe** —*oneself (in one's former costume)* Ar. **2 redesign** —*chariots* X.; **redraft** —*a law* Din.

μετα-σκευωρέομαι *mid.contr.vb.* **remodel** —*a name* Pl.

μετα-σπάω *contr.vb.* (hyperbol.) **tear away** —*a person (fr. a place)* S.

μετασπόμενος (ep.aor.2 mid.ptcpl.): see μεθέπομαι

μετασπών (ep.aor.2 ptcpl.): see μεθέπω

μέτασσος η ον *adj.* (of lambs) **born later** (i.e. after the first-born) Od.; (advbl.phr.) τὰ μέτασσα *afterwards* hHom.

μετάστασις εως *f.* [μεθίστημι] **1 change of location, move, shift, transfer** (sts. W.PREP.PHR. to or fr. a place) Pl. Plu.; **relocation** (of an ostracised person) Plu. **2 change of course** (W.GEN. of the sun) E. **3 removal, deposition, overthrow** (W.GEN. of a person) Plb. **4 release, relief** (W.GEN. fr. labours) S.*Ichn.*; (fr. trouble) And. **5 departure** (w. ἐκ + GEN. fr. life) Plb.; **death** Plb. **6 change of condition, transformation** (of people into stones) Pi.*fr.*; (W.GEN. of a person's form) E. **7 change of formation** (by troops) Plb. **8 change** (of attitude) S. D.; (W.GEN. of mind) E. **9 change, shift** (in human fortune, compared for swiftness to the movement of a dragonfly) Simon. **10 change** (in circumstances) Th. Isoc. Plb. Plu. **11 change** (W.GEN. in the form of government) Pl. Arist. Plu.; **change of government** Th.; (specif.) **revolution** Lys. Isoc. X.; **counter-revolution** (opp. στάσις *revolution*) Th.

μετα-στείχω *vb.* | ep.aor.2 μετέστιχον | **1 go in search of, seek** —*a person* E. **2 follow** —*someone's tracks* Call. **3** (intr.) **go after** (someone), **follow** AR.

μετα-στένω *vb.* **1 lament afterwards** (or w. a change of attitude), **look back upon with grief, later regret** —*one's reckless folly* Od. —*one's labours* A.; (intr.) **feel regret** (for one's actions) E. **2** ‖ MID. **share in lamenting, grieve in sympathy for** —*someone's pain* E.

μετα-στοιχεί *adv.* [στοῖχος] **in a row** —*ref. to contestants taking up position (at the start of a race)* Il.

μετα-στοναχίζομαι *mid.vb.* **utter groans of anguish later** Hes.

μετα-στρατοπεδεύω *vb.* **move camp** X.(mid.) Plb. Plu.

μεταστρεπτικός ή όν *adj.* [μεταστρέφω] (of a study) **capable of giving redirection** (W.PREP.PHR. towards a goal) Pl.

μετα-στρέφω *vb.* | PASS.: fut.2 μεταστραφήσομαι | aor. (freq. w.mid.sens.) μετεστρέφθην, aor.2 μετεστράφην | **1 turn** (sthg.) **in a reverse direction**; (of a god) **turn round, reverse** —*a part of the human body (so that it faces the opposite way)* Pl.; (of sailors) —*oars (so that the blades face into the ship)* AR. **2** app. **bend back** —*someone's fingers* Hippon. **3** (fig.) **turn round** —*an argument (in order to examine it fr. all sides)* Pl. **4** ‖ MID. and AOR.PASS. (of persons, gods, things) **turn around** hHom. Hdt. Ar. Pl. X. D. +; (specif., of warriors or troops, in flight or to face the enemy) Il. Hdt. X. **5** ‖ MID. (of a disputant) **turn back, revert, return** —W.PREP.PHR. *to previous statements* Pl. **6 turn round, reverse** —*accusations (i.e. make accusations to counter them)* D. —*a saying (i.e. make it mean the opposite)* Arist.

7 reverse or interchange —*two concepts* (*i.e. their meanings*) Pl. —*hand and foot* (*i.e. use the one in place of the other*) Arist.
8 change, alter —*justice* Arist. —*a word* (*i.e. its meaning*) Arist.
9 change —*one's mind or feelings* Il. AR.; (intr.) Hom.
10 redirect —*someone's feelings* (W.PREP.PHR. *towards a certain goal*) Plu.
11 ‖ PASS. (of a person's fortunes) be reversed or changed E.; (of a decree) Ar.; (of a way of life) Call.; (of the sun) change, turn —W.PREP.PHR. *to darkness* NT.
12 introduce by change, substitute —*one letter* (w. ἀντί + GEN. *for another*) Pl.
13 ‖ AOR.PTCPL. (intr., quasi-advbl.) taking the opposite approach, looking at things the other way Pl.
14 (intr.) app., turn round (so as to take notice of sthg.); (of chariot-horses, in neg.phr.) take notice of, heed —W.GEN. *their driver, harness or chariot* E.

μεταστροφή ῆς *f.* redirection, conversion (of the soul or the understanding, towards a higher goal) Pl.

μετασχεῖν (aor.2 inf.): see μετέχω

μετάσχεσις εως *f.* [μετέχω] (philos.) participation (W.GEN. in sthg., i.e. partaking of its essence) Pl.

μετα-σχηματίζω *vb.* alter the form or arrangement (of persons or things); transform —*elements in nature* (*into others*) Pl. —*oneself* (*in appearance and manner, as required by a change of circumstances*) Plu. ‖ PASS. (of a concept) be transformed —W.DAT. *in wording* (*i.e. be given a different name*) Pl.

μετάταξις εως *f.* [μετατάσσω] change in formation (of troops) Plb.

μετα-τάσσω *vb.* **1** change the order of, transpose —*definitions* Arist.
2 ‖ MID. (of troops) change formation X.
3 ‖ MID. (of a people) change allegiance, go over —W.PREP.PHR. *to a particular side* Th. Plu.

μετα-τίθημι *vb.* **1** change the position (of things); move, shift, transfer —*sthg.* (sts. W.PREP.PHR. *to a place*) Pl. Plb. Plu. —*an honour* (*fr. a hero to a god*) Plu.; rearrange —*a lock of hair* Call. ‖ MID. transfer —*a war* (*to another country*) Plu. ‖ PASS. (of things) be moved or transferred (sts. W.ADV. or PREP.PHR. *to a place*) Pl. Arist. NT. Plu.
2 change the nature or condition (of things); change, alter —*names, institutions, words, statements, situations, or sim.* Hdt. Th. Isoc. Pl. X. D. +; (intr.) make amendments (to a treaty) Th.(treaty) ‖ MID. (intr.) make a change (in government) Th.; (in wording) Pl.; (in costume) Plb. ‖ PASS. (of statements) be changed —W.DAT. *in expression* Arist.
3 ‖ MID. change (usu. sthg. of one's own); change, alter —*one's statement, plan, manner, name, or sim.* Isoc. Pl. X. D. Plu. —*one's coinage* Arist. —*laws* (*which one has made*) X.; (of advice, circumstances) —*someone's nature* Plb.
4 put (sthg.) in place (of sthg. else); substitute —*one thing* (w. ἀντί + GEN. *for another*) D. Arist.; (mid.) —*a name* (W.DAT. *for another one*) D. ‖ PASS. (of things) be substituted —w. ἀντί + GEN. *for other things* Pl.
5 ‖ MID. get (sthg.) in place (of sthg. else); adopt —*a different name* Pl. D.
6 ‖ MID. change to —*madness* E. —*good sense* E.(cj.)
7 change —*someone's opinion* Plu.; change the mind of, convert, win over —*someone* Plu. ‖ PASS. be won over or converted —W.PREP.PHR. *by someone* Plu.
8 ‖ MID. change —*one's opinion* Hdt. D. Plu.; (intr.) change one's mind or adopt a different standpoint E. Pl. D. Arist. Men. + —W.INF. *so as to do one thing instead of another* Pl.; change to the view —W.ACC. + INF. *that sthg. is the case* Pl.
9 ‖ MID. adapt oneself —W.DAT. *to circumstances* Plb.; (pejor.) be shifty Aeschin.
10 change (by way of correction); rectify —*people in error* Plb.; (mid.) —*one's error* Plb.
11 cause a change of allegiance; shift —*one's country* (W.PREP.PHRS. *fr. one affiliation to another*) Plb. ‖ MID. change sides, go over (usu. W.PREP.PHR. *to someone*) Plb. Plu.
12 create (W.ACC. *an uproar*) among (people) Od.(dub.) | see μεθίημι 18

μετα-τίκτω *vb.* (fig., of an impious deed) later beget —*more such deeds* A.(tm.)

μετα-τρέπω *vb.* | aor.2 μετέτραπον, Aeol.3sg. πεδέτροπε ‖ aor.2 mid. μετετραπόμην | **1** overturn, overthrow —*a tyrant* Alc. [or perh. *a city*]
2 (of fate) turn round, turn back —*departing persons* AR.(tm.) ‖ MID. (of a person) turn round Il.(tm.) AR.(tm.)
3 ‖ MID. turn round (so as to take notice of sthg.); (in neg.phr.) have regard, feel concern —W.GEN. *for friendship, birds of omen, promises, or sim.* Il. AR.
4 ‖ MID. (of human skin) change in complexion (in response to the seasons) Hes.(tm.)

μετα-τρέφομαι *pass.vb.* be brought up among —W.DAT. *certain people* AR.

μετα-τρέχω *vb.* | fut. μεταθρέξομαι | run to get —*sthg.* Ar.

μετατροπά ᾶς *dial.f.* [μετατρέπω] reversal (of a state of affairs); (specif.) retribution (W.GEN. *for actions*) E.

μετα-τροπαλίζομαι *mid.vb.* [reltd. τροπέω] turn round (to look behind) Il.

μετατροπία ᾶς *f.* [μετατρέπω] reversal of fortune Pi.

μετάτροπος ον *adj.* **1** reversing in direction; (of a deity) turning round Call.; (of the wind of fortune) veering round E.; (W.GEN. *away fr. war*) Ar.; (of a god, i.e. fortune, w. ἐπί + DAT. *against someone*) A.
2 (of a person) reversing one's intentions, with a change of mind AR.
3 (of acts) bringing a reversal, giving redress, making amends Hes.

μετα-τρωπάομαι *mid.contr.vb.* (of a woman) turn —W.PREP.PHR. *to pallor* (W.ACC. *in her cheeks*) AR.

μετ-αυδάω *contr.vb.* **1** (of persons, gods) speak among or to, address —W.DAT. *others* Hom. hHom. AR. —(W.COGN.ACC. *in words*) Hom. AR.; speak (among others, addressing all or one of them) Hom.
2 (tr.) address —*a person* (W.DAT. *w. words*) AR. Mosch.

μεταῦθις Att.adv.: see μεταῦτις

μέτ-αυλος ον *adj.* [αὐλή] **1** (of a door) from courtyard to house, inner (opp. αὔλειος *outer, fr. courtyard to outside*) E. Lys. ‖ FEM.SB. inner door Plu.
2 (predic., of a murderess who is refused admittance) as an alien within the hall E.(cj.) | cf. μέτοικος

μετ-αυτίκα *adv.* straight afterwards, immediately Hdt. Theoc.

μετ-αῦτις, Att. **μεταῦθις** *adv.* afterwards A. Hdt. AR.

μετα-φέρω *vb.* **1** take (someone or sthg.) to a different place; transfer, move, carry —*persons or things* (sts. W.ADV. or PREP.PHR. *to or fr. a place*) Th. Att.orats. Pl. Thphr. Men. +; (mid.) Plu. ‖ PASS. (of things) be transferred or moved Plb. Plu.
2 ‖ MID.PASS. (of hounds) move in a different direction X.; (of substances) Pl.

μετάφημι

3 transfer —*persons* (W.PREP.PHRS. *fr. one class to another*) Arist.
4 transfer (non-material things) to a different place; **transfer, import** —*foreign laws and customs* (W.ADV. or PREP.PHR. *to one's own country*) Plu.
5 borrow, derive —*an inappropriate demand* (W. ἐκ + GEN. *fr. a particular source*) Aeschin.; (pejor., of a poet) **lift material** —w. ἀπό + GEN. *fr. other sources* Ar.(cj.)
6 transfer (sthg.) to a different person; **transfer** —*public duties* (W.PREP.PHRS. *fr. the poor to the rich*) D. —*an office, responsibility, or sim.* (*to someone*) Plu. ‖ PASS. (of jurisdiction) be transferred —w. εἰς + ACC. *to certain people* Plu.
7 transfer (sthg.) to a different usage; **transfer** —*practices, words, concepts, or sim.* (W.PREP.PHR. *to different contexts or applications*) Att.orats. Pl. X. Arist. Plb. ‖ PASS. (of an inquiry, a remark, or sim.) be transferred —w. ἐπί + ACC. *to a different context* Pl. Plb. Plu.
8 transform —*a system of government* (W.PREP.PHRS. *fr. one type to another*) Plu.
9 change, alter —*one's mind* S. —*facts, a location* (*for a meeting*) Aeschin.; **redirect** —*one's thinking* D.; **shift, transpose** —*dates* (i.e. confuse them) Aeschin. D. ‖ PASS. (of a legal system) be turned upside down Aeschin.
10 translate —*words* (w. εἰς + ACC. *into one's own language*) Pl. ‖ PASS. (of a remark) be translated Plu.
11 transfer (a word) to a new sense; **transfer, apply** —*a term* (w. ἐπί + ACC. *to one thing,* w. ἀντί + GEN. *in place of another*) Arist.; (intr.) **apply a transferred sense, use metaphor** Arist. ‖ PASS. (of a word) be applied in a transferred or metaphorical sense Arist.

μετά-φημι *vb.* | only 3sg.athem.aor. μετέφη | (of persons, gods) **speak among** or **to** —W.DAT. *others* (*in addressing one or all of them*) Hom.; (of a person, in addressing a prayer to a god) Il.

μεταφορά ᾶς *f.* [μεταφέρω] **1 transference** (of the sense of words), **metaphor** Isoc. Arist. Plu.
2 (pejor.) **change** (of application or sense), **distortion** (W.GEN. of meaning) Plu.

μετα-φορέω *contr.vb.* **transfer, move** —*corpses, objects* (W.PREP.PHR. *to a different place*) Hdt.

μεταφορικός ή όν *adj.* [μεταφέρω] (of a person) **good at using metaphor** Arist.

μετα-φράζω *vb.* **1** ‖ MID. **consider** or **discuss** (W.ACC. sthg.) later Il.
2 translate —*a literary work, an inscription* Plu. ‖ PASS. (of an inscription) be translated Plu.

μετάφρασις εως *f.* **change of wording, paraphrase** Plu.

μετά-φρενον ου *n.* [φρήν] part of the body behind the chest, **back** Hom. Hes. Tyrt. Pl. Men. AR. Plu.; (pl. for sg.) Il. Archil.

μετα-φροντίζω *vb.* **reconsider, rethink** —*sthg.* Ar.(cj.)

μετα-φύομαι *pass.vb.* | also 3pl.athem.aor.act. μετέφυν | **change one's nature**; (of persons) **become** —W.PREDIC.ADJ. *different* Arist.(quot. Emp.); (of men, in a later incarnation) —W.PREDIC.SB. *women* Pl.

μετα-φωνέω *contr.vb.* **1 speak among** or **to** —W.DAT. *others* (*in addressing all or one of them*) Hom. AR.; **speak** (amid a company) Od. AR. —W.COGN.ACC. *a word* AR.
2 (tr.) **address** —*a person* AR.

μετα-χάζομαι *mid.vb.* | ep.2sg.fut. (or perh. aor.subj.) μεταχάσσεαι | **shrink back** —W.GEN. *fr. a task* AR.

μετα-χειρίζω *vb.* | aor. μετεχείρισα ‖ MID.: fut. μεταχειριοῦμαι | aor. μετεχειρισάμην | pf. μετακεχείρισμαι ‖ PASS.: aor. μετεχειρίσθην | **1 have in one's hand, handle, wield** —*a sceptre* E.*fr.* ‖ MID. **handle** —*a cup* Antipho —*gold and silver* Pl.
2 take in hand, handle —*money* Hdt. ‖ MID. **handle, deal with** —*a stone* (*blocking an entrance*) Hdt.
3 ‖ MID. (of the mind) **manage, control** —*the body* X.; (of a rider) —*his horse* Plu. ‖ PASS. (of speech) be controlled —W.DAT. *by art* Pl.
4 (gener.) **handle, manage** —*shipbuilding, public affairs, war, an enterprise* Th.; (mid.) —*an activity, responsibility, calamity, or sim.* Lys. Ar. Pl. X. D. +
5 ‖ MID. **handle, deal with** —*persons* (sts. W.ADV. *in a certain way*) Th. Pl. D. Men. Plb. Plu.; (of doctors) **attend to, treat** —*persons* Pl.
6 ‖ MID. **engage in, practise** —*an activity, occupation, art, or sim.* Isoc. Pl. Arist.
7 ‖ MID. **commit** —*an act of treachery* Plb.

μετα-χρόνιος ᾱ (Ion. η) ον *adj.* **coming afterwards**; (app. through misapplication, of the Harpies, their feet) **high in the air** Hes.; (of Iris) AR.; (quasi-advbl., of the Argo, lifted by a wave) AR.; (fig., of an ecstatic soul) AR.

μετα-χωρέω *contr.vb.* **1 go to a different place; move away** —W.ADV. or PREP.PHR. *to or fr. a place* A.(tm.) Th. X.; (of a crane) **migrate** —W.PREP.PHR. *to a country* Ar.
2 withdraw —w. ἐκ + GEN. *fr. a debate* Th.
3 change allegiance, go over —w. πρός + ACC. *to someone* Plu.

μετα-ψαίρω *vb.* **brush aside** —*a stone* (W.DAT. w. *one's foot*) E.

μετεάσι (ep.3pl.): see μέτειμι[1]

μετ-εγγράφομαι *pass.vb.* | fut. μετεγγραφήσομαι | (of a person) **be included in a different list** Ar.

μετέγνων (athem.aor.): see μεταγιγνώσκω

μετέειπον (ep.aor.2): see μετεῖπον

μετέησι (ep.3sg.pres.subj.): see μέτειμι[1]

μετείθη (Ion.3sg.aor.pass.): see μεθίημι

μετ-εικάς άδος *f.* **twenty-first day** (of a month) Hes.

μέτ-ειμι[1] *vb.* [εἰμί] | neut.acc.ptcpl. μετόν, Ion. μετεόν | ep.3pl. μετέασι | ep.pres.subj. μετέω, also μετείω, 3sg. μετέῃσι | inf. μετεῖναι, ep. μετέμμεναι | ep.fut. μετέσσομαι ‖ see also μέτα (used for 3sg. μέτεστι) |
1 be among or **in the company of** —W.DAT. *persons, gods, the living, the dead* Hom. Hes. hHom. Tyrt. Xenoph. Theoc.; **be in the midst** —W.DAT. *of all delights* AR.
2 (of a respite) **come between** (activities), **intervene** Il.
3 ‖ IMPERS. **there is a share** —W.DAT. + GEN. *for someone in sthg.* (i.e. one has a share of, part in or a claim on sthg.) Hdt. Trag. Ar. Att.orats. Pl. X. + ‖ NEUT.ACC.PTCPL. **when there is a share, or sim.** Hdt. Th. Ar. Att.orats. Pl.
4 (of a share, an equal amount, half, nothing, or sim., freq. W.GEN. of sthg.) **belong** —W.DAT. *to someone* Hdt. E. Th. Ar. Att.orats. Pl. +
5 ‖ IMPERS. **there is a right** —W.DAT. + INF. *for someone, to do sthg.* S.
6 ‖ IMPERS. **it is in the nature or within the capacity** —W.DAT. + INF. *of someone or sthg., to do sthg.* Pl.

μέτ-ειμι[2] *vb.* [εἶμι] | Only pres. and impf. (other tenses are supplied by μετέρχομαι). The pres.indic. usu. has fut.sens. |
1 go after or **behind, follow** Il. X.
2 follow —*a track* (fig.ref. *to an intellectual interest*) Pl.; **follow up** —*an argument* Pl.
3 (intr.) **proceed** (in an argument, inquiry or task) Pl. Arist. Plu. —W.ADV. *to a point in an argument* Ar.

4 proceed with the aim of achieving or mastering, **pursue** —*a goal, skill, subject of study, or sim.* Isoc. Pl. X. Arist. Plu. —*a murder* E.
5 seek after, go to find or **fetch** —*persons or things* Hdt. S.(dub.) Ar. X. Thphr. Men. +
6 go after (w. intent to punish), **pursue** —*a person* A. E. Pl. —(W.INTERN.ACC. *in vengeance*) A. E. —(W.DAT. *w. vengeance*) Th.; (of retribution) —*someone's successes* Plu.; (intr., of Justice) **come in pursuit** S.
7 go after (w. intent to influence), **approach, petition, appeal to** —*a person* Th. AR. —(w. μή + INF. *not to do sthg.*) Th.; **propitiate** —*deities* (W.DAT. *w. sacrifices*) Hdt.
8 seek, be a candidate or **canvass for** —*an office* Plu.
9 (gener., of a person or god) **come** or **go** AR. —W.ACC. *to a place* AR.
10 (w.pres.sens.) **make one's way** —W.ADV. *to war* Il.

μετεῖναι[1] (inf.): see μέτειμι[1]
μετεῖναι[2] (Ion.athem.aor.inf.): see μεθίημι
μετ-εῖπον, ep. **μετέειπον** aor.2 vb. **1** (of persons, gods) **speak among** or **to** —W.DAT. *others* (*in addressing all or one of them*) Hom. Hes. AR. —(W.COGN.ACC. *w. a speech*) AR.(sts.tm.); **speak** (*amid a company*) Hom. AR. Theoc.
2 (tr.) **recount** —*someone's advice* (W.DAT. *to persons*) AR.
μετείς (Ion.athem.aor.ptcpl.), **μετείσθω** (Ion.3sg.aor.pass.imperatv.): see μεθίημι
μετ-είσομαι ep.fut.mid.vb. [εἴσομαι[2]] | only aor.ptcpl. μετεισάμενος | **hurry about** Il.
μετείω (ep.subj.): see μέτειμι[1]
μετ-εκβαίνω vb. | iterativ.impf. μετεκβαίνεσκον | **1 get out** (of one vehicle) and **change** (to another); **change one's mode of transport** —w. ἐκ + GEN. *fr. a chariot* (w. ἐς + ACC. *to a ship, a carriage*) Hdt.; **transfer** —w. εἰς + ACC. *to a different vessel* Antipho
2 (gener.) **change over, pass on** —w. εἰς + ACC. *to a particular topic, a form of behaviour* Pl.
μετέκβασις εως f. **transfer** (w. εἰς + ACC. to a different vessel) Antipho
μετ-εκδίδομαι mid.vb. (of a Roman husband) **lend out** (one's wife) **again** (for childbearing) Plu.
μετ-εκδύομαι mid.vb. take off one's clothes and put on others; (fig., of a demigod) **divest oneself of** —*one's own nature* Plu.
μετ-εκίαθον aor.2 (or impf.) vb. [reltd. κίω] **1** go after, **pursue** —*an enemy, an animal* Il.; (intr.) **go in pursuit** Il.
2 go after, seek out —*an object* AR.
3 go to visit —*persons* Od. Call. AR.
4 make for —*a place* AR.; **arrive at** —*a place* AR.
5 arrive next or afterwards Il. AR.
6 go over or overrun —*a plain* Il.
μετ-εμβαίνω vb. embark on a different ship; **transfer** Plu. —w. εἰς + ACC. *to a vessel* Plu.
μετ-εμβιβάζω vb. **transfer** —*troops* (w. ἐς + ACC. *to a different vessel*) Th.
μετέμισγον (impf.): see μεταμείγνῡμι
μετέμμεναι (ep.inf.): see μέτειμι[1]
μετ-εννέπω vb. **recount, relate** —*sthg.* (W.DAT. *to persons*) AR.; **say** —W.DIR.SP. *sthg.* (W.DAT. *to persons*) Mosch.
μετ-εντίθημι vb. || MID. **transfer** (W.ACC. a cargo) **to another ship** D.
μετ-εξαιρέομαι mid.contr.vb. **remove** (W.ACC. a cargo) **for transfer to another ship** D.
μετ-εξέτεροι αι α pl.pron.adj. [ἐκ, ἕτερος] **some among others, some** (freq. W.GEN.PL. of the full number) Hdt.

μετ-έπειτα adv. **1 afterwards, later** Hom. Parm. Hdt. Arist. +
2 then, next (in sequence) Od. Hellenist.poet.
μετ-έρχομαι, Aeol. **πεδέρχομαι** mid.vb. | fut. μετελεύσομαι (Il. AR.) | aor.2 μετῆλθον, ep. μετήλυθον (AR.), Aeol.3sg.imperatv. πεδελθέτω | Impf. (and usu. fut.) are supplied by μέτειμι[2]. |
1 go among —W.DAT. *persons, gods* Hom.; (of a lion, w. hostile connot.) —W.DAT. or μετά + ACC. *animals* Hom.; (gener., of a person or god) **come on the scene** Hom. AR.(tm.)
2 go on one's way Il. AR. Plb. —W.ADV. *to a place, to war* Il. —w. εἰς + ACC. *to a place* Plb. Plu.; **go to, visit** —*a place* Od. AR.
3 go after or behind; (of delight) **follow** (hard work) Pi.
4 follow —*a track* (fig.ref. to an argument) Pl.; **follow up** —*an argument* Pl.; (intr.) **proceed** (in argument) Pl.
5 follow up, **attend to, deal with** —*business* Il. —*an issue, an activity* E. Ar. Pl.
6 go after, seek out, go to find or **fetch** —*persons or things* Il. Archil. Pi. E. Lys. Ar. +; **go in search of** —*news* (*of someone*) Od. —*the Golden Fleece* E. —*dead persons* (*in the underworld*) Pl.; **go to recover** —*one's home, a share in a land* E.
7 seek to achieve —*manliness* Th. —*someone's freedom* Th. —*someone's death* A. —*a catch* (*of fish, fig.ref. to entrapping a person*) E.
8 (of avenging spirits) **pursue** —*a person* Alc. —W.DBL.ACC. *a person, for a crime* E.; (intr.) **go in pursuit** Hdt.(oracle); (of retribution, prosecution) **catch up with** or **overtake** —*a person* Hdt. Pl. Plu.
9 pursue, prosecute —*complaints* Th.; (of persons) **avenge** —*a crime* E. Plb.; **take vengeance on, punish** —*persons, a city* Aeschin. Lycurg. Plb. Plu. —W.DBL.ACC. *a city, for a crime* E.Cyc.; (leg.) **prosecute** —*a person* Antipho
10 (wkr.sens., of Aphrodite) **pursue** —*a person* (W.ADV. *gently*) E.
11 assail verbally, **rebuke** —*a person* Hdt.
12 appeal to, petition —*a person* AR. —(W.INF. *to do sthg.*) Hdt. Theoc. —*a god* (W.DAT. *w. prayers*) E. —*a hallowed object* (*w. sacrifices*) Hdt.
13 be a candidate or **canvass for, seek** —*an office* Plu.
14 change places, move —W.PREP.PHR. *to or fr. a location* Plu.; **change over** —W.PREP.PHR. *to a different boat, to a chariot drawn by horses* (*instead of elephants*) Plu. —W.INTERN.ACC. *to paths of fresh sorrows* E.
μετέσσυνται (ep.3sg.pf.mid.), **μετέσσυτο** (ep.3sg.athem.aor.mid.): see μετασεύομαι
μετ-εύχομαι mid.vb. | aor.imperatv. μέτευξαι | **change one's prayer** E.
μετ-έχω, Aeol. **πεδέχω** vb. | Aeol.inf. πεδέχην | fut. μεθέξω | aor.2 μετέσχον, inf. μετασχεῖν || neut.impers.vbl.adj. μεθεκτέον | **1 partake of, have a share of, share in** —W.GEN. *things, activities, conditions or circumstances* (sts. W.DAT. *w. someone*) Thgn. Lyr. Hdt. Trag. Th. + —(w. ξύν + DAT.) S.
2 (specif.) **share in, be a member of** —W.GEN. *a city or state* (*i.e. have citizenship*) Att.orats. X. Arist. Plu. —*the Assembly, the Senate, other councils* Arist. Plb. Plu.
3 (without GEN.) **be a partner** or **participant** Hdt. Th. Ar. Att.orats. X. + —w. περί + GEN. *in sthg.* Arist.; (specif.) **be a shareholder** (in a financial enterprise, sts. W.DAT. *w. someone*) And.
4 share feelings, **sympathise** or **concur** —W.DAT. *w. someone* E.
5 have —W.INTERN.ACC. μέρος, μοῖραν or μόριον (usu. specified by ADJ.) + GEN. *a* (*specified*) *share of sthg.* A. Pi.fr. Hdt. Th. Ar. Att.orats. +

μετέω

6 have as one's share —W.ACC. *an equal amount* (W.GEN. *of sthg.*) *or things equal in number* Ar. X. Is. —*profitless recompense* S.
7 (philos., of things) **participate** —W.GEN. *in sthg. universal, esp. a Form* (*i.e. share its essence*) Pl. Arist. ‖ PASS. (of a Form) be participated in Arist.

μετέω (ep.subj.): see μέτειμι¹

μετεωρίζω *vb.* [μετέωρος] | aor. ἐμετεώρισα | **1** raise to a height (fr. the ground), **raise high** —*a fortification* Th.
2 lift high in the air (off or above the ground); **lift** or **raise up** —*persons, parts of the body, objects* Pl. X. Plu. ‖ MID. **hoist aloft** —*dolphin-bombs* (on a warship) Ar. ‖ PASS. (of wind, smoke, dust, or sim.) be raised up Ar. Pl. X.
3 (fig.) **elevate** —*the dignity of someone's character* Plu.
4 ‖ PASS. (of a commander of a fleet) be on the open sea Th.
5 (fig.) **buoy up** —*a populace* (W.DAT. *w. hopes*) Plu.; **excite** or **raise the hopes of** —*persons* D. Plb. ‖ PASS. (of persons) be buoyed up, elated or excited Plb.; (of a mind) —W.PREP.PHR. *by words* Ar.
6 ‖ PASS. be anxious or in suspense NT.

μετεωροκοπέω *contr.vb.* [κόπτω] (of a person, flying on a dung-beetle) app. **beat the air** Ar.

μετεωρο-λέσχης ου *m.* [λέσχη] (pejor.) one who talks about celestial matters, **high-talker** Pl. Plu.

μετεωρολογέω *contr.vb.* [μετεωρολόγος] be a student of celestial matters Pl.

μετεωρολογίᾱ ᾶς *f.* study of celestial matters; (pejor.) **high-flown speculation** (assoc.w. Anaxagoras) Pl. Plu.

μετεωρολογικός ή όν *adj.* (of persons) **devoted to the study of celestial matters** Pl.

μετεωρο-λόγος ου *m.* **student of celestial matters** Pl.; (pejor.) **high-thinker** Pl.

μετεωροπορέω *contr.vb.* [πόρος, πορεύω] **travel through the heavens** Pl.

μετέωρος, ep. **μετήορος**, dial. **πεδάορος** (A.), ον *adj.* [μεταίρω] **1** raised up (above the ground); (of a person) **off the ground** (opp. lying flat on it) X.; (of things) **raised up in the air** Hdt. Plu.; (of drain-pipes) **overhead** Arist.
2 (predic. or quasi-advbl., of persons, animals or things being lifted, thrown or flying) **up in the air, aloft** Il. hHom. Hdt. Ar. Pl. X. +
3 rising or raised (above a base level); (of ground) **high** Th. Plu.; (of a road) **raised** D.; (of a river) **swollen** Plu.; (of a commander) **on high ground** Plu. ‖ NEUT.SB. elevated position Th.; (sg. and pl.) high ground Th. Plb. Plu.
4 (of rooms) **above ground** (opp. underground) Hdt.
5 (of a horse) **high-stepping, prancing** X.; **high** (W.ACC. as to its neck, i.e. w. neck held high) AR.
6 (of a hound's eyes) **prominent** X.
7 (of musical sounds) perh. **high-pitched** or **discordant** hHom.
8 high in the air; (of persons or things) **in mid-air** Il. Hdt. Ar. Pl.; (of the earth) **suspended in space** Ar.
9 (of deities, regions, celestial bodies or natural phenomena) **high in the sky** or **heavens** A. Ar. X. Plu.
10 (of matters) relating to the upper regions or heavens, **celestial, heavenly** Ar. X. ‖ NEUT.PL.SB. celestial matters Ar. Pl. X. Plu.
11 (fig., of a spectacle) **lofty, dignified** Plu.
12 (of ships, sailors) **on the open sea, out at sea** Th. D. Plb. Plu.
13 (of persons, cities, countries) **buoyed up, excited** or **in suspense** (w. hope, anticipation, anxiety, uncertainty or similar states and feelings) Th. Plb. Plu.; (of a person) **eager** (W.INF. to do sthg.) Plb.
14 (of a city) **in a precarious situation** Th. Plu.; (of a situation) **uncertain** D. Plu.
—**μετεώρως** *adv.* **in a state of uncertainty** or **suspense** Plu.

μετεωρο-σκόπος ου *m.* [σκοπέω] (pejor.) one who looks at celestial phenomena, **stargazer** Pl.

μετεωρο-σοφιστής οῦ *m.* (pejor.) **celestial expert** Ar.

μετεωρο-φένᾱξ ᾱκος *m.* **celestial quack** Ar.

μετῆκα (Ion.aor.): see μεθίημι

μετήορος *ep.adj.*: see μετέωρος

μετήσω (Ion.fut.): see μεθίημι

μετίημι, μετίστημι *Ion.vbs.*: see μεθίημι, μεθίστημι

μετ-ίσχω *vb.* [μετά] **1 participate** or **share in** —W.GEN. *a murder* Hdt. —*discussion, cultural activity* Pl.
2 (of things) **partake of** —W.GEN. *accuracy, motion* Pl.

μετοικεσίᾱ ᾱς *f.* [μετοικέω] removal to a foreign country, **resettlement, deportation** (of a population) NT.

μετ-οικέω *contr.vb.* **1** change one's place of residence; **go to dwell** —W.DAT. *in a city* Pi. —W.ACC. *in the darkness beneath the earth* E. —w. πρός + ACC. *w. foreigners* Plu.
2 reside as an immigrant, be a foreign resident (sts. W.ADV. or PREP.PHR. in a city or land, or among certain people) E. Ar. Att.orats. Pl. Plu. —W.GEN. *in a land* A.
3 (of a citizen in an oligarchy) **be no better than an alien** Isoc.
4 move house Plu.

μετοίκησις εως *f.* **1** change of residence; **migration** (of a person or the soul, on death, W.ADV. or PREP.PHR. fr. one place to another) Pl.
2 residence as an immigrant (in a city) Pl.

μετοικίᾱ ᾱς *f.* **1** change of residence, **migration** (of a population) Th.
2 status or fact of being a resident immigrant, **immigrant status, residence as foreigner** A. Lys. Pl. X.
3 residence (W.ADV. above the ground, i.e. w. the living) S.

μετ-οικίζω *vb.* **1** cause (someone) to reside in a different place; **move, relocate** —*a person or population* (W.ADV. or PREP.PHR. *to another city or country*) NT. Plu. ‖ MID. (of the population of a city) **move** (to a new location) Plu.; (of persons) —W.ADV. *to a particular city* Plu.
2 (of a lawgiver) **cause** (W.ACC. a person) **to change household** (by forcing him to remarry) Plu. ‖ MID. (of a person) **move to a new household** (on marriage) Plu.
3 ‖ MID. **move house** Ar.

μετοικικός ή όν *adj.* [μέτοικος] (of a man) **belonging to the class of resident immigrants** Plu.

μετοίκιον ου *n.* **1** tax for resident immigrants, **metic tax** Lys. Pl. X. D. Plu.
2 ‖ PL. Metoikia, Resettlement (name of an Athenian festival, usu. called Synoikia) Plu.

μετοικισμός οῦ *m.* [μετοικίζω] change of residence (to another city), **emigration** Plu.

μετοικιστής οῦ *m.* **resettler** (of a population) Plu.

μετ-οικοδομέω *contr.vb.* **1 build a house in a different place** Men.
2 rebuild —*an existing house* (*in a grander style*) Plu.

μέτ-οικος ου *m.f.* [οἶκος] **1** one who changes residence (to another city or country); **immigrant, settler** Hdt. Trag. Plu.
2 (specif., in a Greek city-state, esp. Athens) **resident immigrant, metic** (ref. to a non-citizen, w. a legal or recognised status and some of the privileges of citizenship) Th. Ar. Att.orats. Pl. X. +
3 immigrant (iron.ref. to one who is buried abroad, sts. W.GEN. in a specified land) Trag.; (ref. to birds, envisaged as living in the realm of the gods) A.; (in the underworld, ref. to a woman on her way to death) S.; (ref. to such a person)

resident (W.DAT. among neither the living nor the dead) S.

μετοικο-φύλαξ ακος *m.* **guardian of metics** (ref. to a state official at Athens) X.

μετ-οίχομαι *mid.vb.* **1 go on one's way** Od.
2 go after, seek out —*someone or sthg.* Hom. AR.
3 seek to perform —*a purification* E.

μετ-οιωνίζομαι *mid.vb.* procure a change of omens; **effect an improvement in** —*a city's activities, one's fortune* Din.

μετ-οκλάζω *vb.* change one's crouching position (by squatting now on one leg, now on the other), **shift about, be restive** Il.

μετ-ονομάζω *vb.* **1** call by a new name, **rename** —*sthg.* Hdt. —(W.PREDIC.SB. *as such and such*) Plu.; **adopt a new name** —W.PREDIC.ACC.SB. *of such and such* Hdt. ‖ PASS. (of persons or things) be renamed —W.PREDIC.SB. *such and such* Hdt. Th. —w. ἐπί + GEN. *after someone* Hdt.
2 ‖ PASS. (of a verbal expression) be reformulated —W.ADV. *in a novel way* Pl.

μετόπιν *adv.* [reltd. μετόπισθε] **1** afterwards; (quasi-adjl., of a life) **future, later** S.
2 (as prep.) **after the death** —W.GEN. *of someone* AR.

μετ-όπισθε(ν) *adv.* **1** (ref. to location) in a position behind, **behind, at the back, in the rear** Il. Hellenist.poet.
2 behind (relative to the east, i.e. towards the west) Od.
3 (as prep.) at the back or to the rear of, **behind** —W.GEN. *someone or sthg.* Hom. Theoc.
4 (ref. to remaining or being left, when others have departed) **behind** Il.
5 (ref. to turning to face rearwards) **back round** Il.
6 (ref. to time) in the future, **hereafter, thereafter, afterwards, later** Hom. Hes. hHom. Hdt.(oracle) AR.
7 (as prep.) **after the death** —W.GEN. *of someone* AR.

μετοπωρινός ή όν *adj.* (of the season) **of autumn** X. Plu.; (of nights) **autumnal** Th.

—μετοπώρινον *neut.adv.* **in autumn** Hes. Call.

μετ-όπωρον ου *n.* [ὀπώρᾱ] time after the harvest season, **autumn** Th. X. Plu.

μετορμίζω *Ion.vb.*: see μεθορμίζω

μετ-όρχιον ου *n.* [ὄρχος] **space between rows** (of vines or fruit trees) Ar. [or perh. *space between individual vines or fruit trees in a row*]

μετουσίᾱ ᾱς *f.* [μέτειμι¹] **1** state or right of sharing (in sthg.); **participation** (W.GEN. in an event, forms of behaviour) Ar.; **right of participation** (W.GEN. by persons, in an event) D.
2 right, entitlement (W.GEN. to property, an inheritance, family tombs, privileges, liberty, office, or sim.) Att.orats. Plu.
3 possession or **use** (W.GEN. of a stretch of land) X.
4 possession or **claim to possession** (W.GEN. of moral qualities) D. Plu.

μετοχή ῆς *f.* [μετέχω] **1 right of communal use** (of a sanctuary) Hdt.
2 sharing, participation (W.GEN. in good things) Arist.; (philos., in the nature of sthg.) Arist.

μετ-οχλίζω *vb.* **heave aside, dislodge** —*a door-bar, a bed* (*fixed to the ground*) Hom.

μέτοχος ον *adj.* [μετέχω] **1** having a part or share (of sthg. material); **sharing** (W.GEN. in a wealthy household) E.; (in produce) Pl.
2 sharing (w. others, in sthg. abstract); **sharing** (W.GEN. in a calamity) Hdt.; (in someone's hopes) E.; (in responsibility) Lys.
3 having a part (in sthg.); **partaking, participating** (W.GEN. in activities) Pl.; (in a city, i.e. civic life) Pl ‖ MASC.SB. **participant** (in government) Th.; **partner** (in work) NT.
4 sharing culpability, **complicit** (W.GEN. in murder) E. Antipho
5 having possession, **possessed** (W.GEN. of certain qualities) Pl.
6 (of things) **partaking** (W.GEN. of certain attributes) Pl.

μετρέω *contr.vb.* [μέτρον] **1** take measurements (to ascertain length, size, or sim.); **measure** —*land, buildings, areas, objects* (sts. W.DAT. OR PREP.PHR. *by a specific unit of measurement*) Hdt. Ar. X. AR.(mid.) Plb. Plu. —*length, depth, breadth, speed* Pl. X. —*a lifespan* (W.DAT. *by periods of seven years*) Arist.; (fig.) —*a goddess* (W.INDIR.Q. *how great she is*) E.fr.; (intr.) **take measurements** Pl. X. Arist. ‖ PASS. (of things) be measured A. Hdt. S. Pl. X. +; (of a unit of measurement) —W.PREDIC.ADJ. *as having a particular dimension* Hdt.
2 (fig.) **measure, gauge, evaluate** —*persons, abstract qualities* (usu. W.DAT. or πρός + ACC. *by some criterion*) Pl. D. Arist. Plb. Plu.; (of money) **be a measure of** (i.e. a criterion by which to evaluate) —*all things* Arist. ‖ PASS. (of things) be measured (sts. W.DAT. or πρός + ACC. *by some criterion*) Pl. Arist. Plu.
3 measure with the eye, **scan** —*walls* (*to estimate their height*) E. ‖ MID. **look over, examine** —*footprints* (*to discover someone's whereabouts*) S.
4 calculate —*a number or total* Pl.; ascertain the number of, **count** —*waves* (*provbl. for a futile endeavour*) Theoc. ‖ PASS. (of a number) be calculated Theoc.*epigr.* Plu.; (of an amount of work) Hdt.
5 (of a singer) **measure out** (into metrical units) —*the pattern of a tune* Theoc.
6 apportion by measure, **measure out** —*grain, other commodities* (*for sale or loan*), *rations* (*for a household or troops*), *fodder* (*for horses*) E. Ar. Thphr. Plb. Plu. —(fig.) *a bit of peace* Ar.; (gener.) **provide** —*maintenance* (W.DAT. *for a mother*) D.; (intr.) **give a measure** (of sthg.) NT. ‖ MID. **have** (W.ACC. a commodity, rations) **measured out to one** D. Theoc. Plu.; (intr.) **ensure that one receives a measure** —W.ADV. *favourably* (w. παρά + GEN. *fr. a neighbour, i.e. get a good measure of a commodity borrowed fr. him*) Hes. ‖ PASS. (of rations) be measured out Ar. ‖ IMPERS.PASS. a measure is given NT.
7 travel the length of, **traverse** —*a sea* Od. AR. Mosch.(mid.); (intr.) **cross the sea** AR.

μέτρημα ατος *n.* **1** measured extent, **dimensions** (of an area) E.
2 measured amount, **measure** (W.GEN. of wine) E.; (of grain) Plb.
3 (specif.) measured amount of provisions, **rations** (for troops) Plb.

μέτρησις εως *f.* process of measuring, **measurement** Pl. X. Arist. Plu.; (W.GEN. of a country) Hdt.; (of the sky) S.*satyr.fr.*

μετρητής οῦ *m.* **metretes** (a liquid measure, approx. 40 litres) D. Plb. NT.

μετρητικός ή όν *adj.* (of an art) related to measuring, **of measurement** Pl. ‖ FEM.SB. art of measurement Pl.

μετρητός ή όν *adj.* (of things) **measurable** Pl. Arist.; (of grief, in neg.phr.) E.(dub.)

μετριάζω *vb.* [μέτριος] **1** (of persons) be moderate (in behaviour), **show moderation** or **restraint** S. Th. Isoc. Pl. D. Arist. +
2 (of a political system) **be moderate** (opp. extreme) Arist.; (of a story) —W.DAT. *in length* Arist.
3 (tr.) **moderate, regulate, restrain** —*a youthful spirit, ruling powers, an office* Pl. Arist.

μετρικός ή όν *adj.* [μέτρον] (of certain speech rhythms) conforming to certain units of verse, **metrical** Arist. || FEM.SB. metrical theory, metrics Arist. || MASC.PL.SB. writers on metre, metricians Arist.

μετριο-πότης ου *m.* [μέτριος] **moderate drinker** (of wine) X.

μέτριος ᾱ ον (also ος ον Pl., perh. E.) *adj.* **1** of normal measurement; (of men) **of normal height** Hdt.; (of a belly) **of normal size** X.; (of a cubit) **of normal length, standard** Hdt.; (of the time for a person to reach maturity) **normal** Pl.
2 sufficient or appropriate in number or amount (for specific circumstances); (of tasks) **appropriate** (for requirements) Hes.; (of cavalrymen, for a task) X.; (of a period of time, for an activity) Pl. X.; (of payment, W.DAT. for a particular kind of person) Pl.; (of a quantity of poison, W.INF. to drink, so as to cause death) Pl.; (of the length of a speech) Pl.; (of a speech, in length) Isoc. Pl.
3 || NEUT.IMPERS. (w. ἐστί, sts.understd.) it is appropriate or reasonable (sts. W.INF. to do sthg.) Pl. X.
4 moderate in amount, degree or quality; (of money, property, lifestyle, dress, or sim.) **moderate, modest** E. Th. Att.orats. Pl. X. +; (of a portion or fortune in life) S. || NEUT.PL.SB. moderate means, resources or possessions E. Isoc. +
5 (of people) **moderate** (in number) Pl. Arist.; (perh.iron., of a two-word sentence) **of moderate length** Pl.
6 (of abstr. things, such as friendship, delight, trouble, fear, anger, punishment) not excessive in degree, **moderate** E. Th. Att.orats. Pl. +
7 (of a storm or breeze) **moderate** E. Pl.; (of summer) **temperate** Ar.; (of certain times of the day) X.
8 (of a prayer, request, statement, or sim.) **moderate, reasonable** A. Hdt. E. Ar. Att.orats. Pl. +; (of the terms of an agreement) Th. D.; (of speech) **measured** (in content or delivery) X.
9 (of gods, individuals or communities) **moderate, reasonable** (in desires, demands, the exercise of power, dealings w. others, or general conduct) Thgn. E. Th. Ar. Att.orats. Pl. +
10 (of laws, political systems) **balanced, fair** Th. Pl. Arist.
11 (gener., sts. w. depreciatory connot., of commodities, things said and done, circumstances, or sim.) **middling, unexceptional, average, ordinary** Hippon. + || NEUT.PL.SB. relatively minor matters Th.
12 || NEUT.SB. (sg. and pl.) mean (betw. extremes), moderation, or what is reasonable or appropriate Sol. S. E. Att.orats. Pl. +
—**μέτριον** *neut.sg.adv.* **for an appropriate amount of time** X.; (also) τὸ μέτριον X.
—**μέτρια** *neut.pl.adv.* **to a moderate** or **reasonable extent** or **degree** E. Pl. X. +; (also) τὰ μέτρια Th.
—**μετρίως** *adv.* | compar. μετριώτερον, superl. μετριώτατα |
1 moderately, reasonably, appropriately (or sim.) Hdt. E. Th. Ar. Att.orats. Pl. +
2 (qualifying an adj.) not excessively, **moderately** Pl. D. Theoc.

μετριότης ητος *f.* **1** quality of conforming to a measure, **measuredness** Pl.
2 regularity of measurement, **correct proportions** Arist.
3 middle course, mean (betw. extremes) Isoc. Pl. Arist.
4 moderateness (W.GEN. of Athenian speech, ref. to its avoidance of extremes of dialect) Isoc.
5 moderateness, relative smallness (of property ratings, interest payments) Arist. Plu.; (of a change) Plu.
6 moderation (in conduct or attitude) Th. Att.orats. Pl. X. Men. +

μέτρον ου *n.* **1** act of measuring, **measurement** Pl. X. +
2 || PL. measurements, measures (as an invention or discovery contributing to the development of civilisation) E.
3 (specif.) standard unit of measurement (of a solid or liquid commodity), **measure** Hes.*fr.* Hdt. And. Ar. Pl. + || PL. weights and measures (ref. to a system invented by Pheidon) Hdt.
4 quantity represented by such a unit, **measure** (sts. W.GEN. of the commodity) Hom. Hes. Thgn. Th.(treaty) Tim. X. +; (fig., W.GEN. of wisdom) Thgn.; (of young manhood) Hom. Hes. hHom. Thgn. E.
5 measuring-scoop (for dealing out such a quantity) Hes.; **measuring-vessel** (fr. which the quantity is dealt out) Thphr.
6 device for taking measurements, **measuring-rod** Il. Call.
7 standard of judgement (against which things may be assessed); **measure, criterion, test** (freq. W.GEN. of sthg.) Pl. X. D. Arist. Plu.
8 (gener.) **rules** (W.GEN. of poetry, understanding) Sol. || PL. techniques (of carpentry) Stesich.
9 magnitude, quantity or extent ascertained by measuring; **size** (of a hoofprint) S.*Ichn.*; **length** (of a pin) Hdt.; **span** (of time) Pi.; (of a song) Pi. || PL. (W.GEN.) dimensions (of a structure) Hdt. Plu.; (of a person's form, i.e. bodily proportions) E.; lengths, extent (of a journey, the sea) Od. Hes. Hdt.(oracle) AR.; span (of time) E.; amount (of a crop yield) Hdt.
10 length, extent (W.GEN. of sea, as a measurable distance, i.e. distance by sea) Th.
11 distance (separating one thing fr. another), **spacing** Pl. X. Plu. || PL. distances, co-ordinates (of a stone or river, measured relative to other things) Hdt.
12 || PL. measured or appropriate lengths (of reed) hHom.
13 (sg. and pl.) **prescribed** or **appropriate measure** (of distance, time or quantity) Od. Sol. Heraclit. Pi. E. Pl. + || PL. full complement (W.GEN. of benches and oars) E.
14 || PL. prescribed limits or boundaries (demarcating an individual's holding in a mine) Hyp. D.
15 (sg. and pl.) **due measure, moderation** Hes. Thgn. Pi. E. Critias Pl. +
16 limit, end (W.GEN. to sufferings) S. E.
17 || PL. app., restraints, curbs (ref. to a horse's bridle or bit) Pi.
18 (in versification) **measure, metron** (ref. to one of a series of identical or equivalent units constituting a section of verse) Ar. Tim. Isoc. Pl.; (gener., also collectv.pl.) use of such units, **metre, verse** (opp. prose) Isoc. Pl. X. Aeschin. Arist.
19 metre (ref. to a specific metrical form, e.g. dactylic or iambic) Arist.

μετρο-νόμοι ων *m.pl.* [νέμω] **controllers of weights and measures** Arist.

μετωπηδόν *adv.* [μέτωπον] with a front line, **in line abreast** (opp. in column) —*ref. to troops or ships assuming a formation or attacking* Hdt. Th. Plb. Plu.

μετώπιος ον *adj.* (quasi-advbl., of a warrior being struck) **on the forehead** Il.

μέτ-ωπον ου *n.* [μετά, ὤψ] **1** space between the eyes, **brow, forehead** (of persons, deities, animals) Hom. Hes. Stesich. Emp. Hdt. S. +
2 (fig.) **brow** (of a land, ref. to a mountain) Pi.

3 front (of a helmet) Il.
4 front, face or **side** (of a wall, building, city, or sim.) Hdt. Th.
5 front (ref. to the aspect of an attacking force) A.
6 line or **front line** (of troops or ships, opp. column) X. Plb. Plu.; (esp. prep.phrs.) ἐν μετώπῳ, εἰς μέτωπον in or into line X. Plb.

μευ (Ion.enclit.gen.1sg.pers.pron.): see ἐγώ

μέχρι, also **μέχρις** adv., prep. and conj. [reltd. ἄχρι]
1 (modifying a prep.phr.) as far as, **right up** —w. εἰς, ἐπί, πρός + ACC. to a location or point in time Hdt. Pl. X. Arist. Call. Theoc. +
2 (modifying an adv. of time or place) as far as, **up to** —w.ADV. now, then, here, where, or sim. Hdt. Th. Ar. Att.orats. Pl. X. +; (also) μέχρι οὗ Hdt.
3 far enough, **sufficiently** —w. ἵνα + OPT. to do sthg. Call.
4 (prep.) as far as, **up to** —w.GEN. a point in time, location, consideration, degree, number Il. Eleg. Hdt. Th. Ar. Att.orats. + —a person (i.e. his lifetime) Hdt. Th. Isoc. Pl. + —persons of a certain age or family relationship (in terms of descent or inheritance) Pl. X. Is. D.; (also) μέχρι οὗ (or ὅτευ) Hdt.
5 for the duration —w.GEN. of someone's lifetime Hdt. —of a certain number of days Hdt. X. —of a voyage of a certain number of days Hdt.
6 (conj., freq. μέχρι(ς) οὗ) up to a point in time when, **until** —w.INDIC. sthg. happened Hdt. Th. Pl. X. + —w. ἄν (sts. omitted) + SUBJ. (usu. AOR.) or OPT. sthg. shd. happen Hdt. Th. X. D. +
7 as long as, **while** —w.PRES. or IMPF.INDIC. sthg. is or was happening Hdt. Th. X. D. +; (also) μέχρι ὅσου Hdt. —w. ἄν (or κε) + PRES.SUBJ. Pl. Call.(dub.) Plb. Plu.

μέχρι-περ (or **μέχρι περ**) adv. [περ¹] **1 until** —w. ἄν + AOR. or PRES.SUBJ. or OPT. sthg. shd. happen Pl. Arist.
2 while —w.IMPF.INDIC. sthg. was happening Pl. —w. ἄν + PRES.SUBJ. sthg. is happening Pl.
3 (as prep.) **as far as, up to** (i.e. up to the limits prescribed by) —w.GEN. a certain consideration Pl.

μέχρις adv., prep. and conj.: see μέχρι

μή neg.adv. | In gener., μή is used in expressing a neg. opinion, wish or command, by contrast w. οὐ, which is used to negate a fact or statement. The difference betw. the simple negs. holds true for their cpds. (οὐδέ, μηδέ, οὐδείς, μηδείς, etc.), and several of the cpds. in μη- are treated in the corresponding entries for οὐ-. | For μή οὐ see below; for οὐ μή see under οὐ. |
—A | w. individual words |
(negating a noun or adj., esp. w.art., in generalising phrs.) **not** Trag. + • τὰ μὴ δίκαια what is not just A. E. Plu. • ὁ μὴ ἰατρός the man who is not a doctor Pl.
—B | in independent clauses |
1 (in a prohibition, 2sg.pl., usu. w.pres.imperatv. or aor.subj.) **not** Hom. + • μὴ βοηθήσητε τῷ πεπονθότι δεινά, μὴ εὐορκεῖτε do not support the victim of maltreatment, do not keep your oath D.; (w. pres. or aor.inf. for imperatv.) • οἷς μὴ πελάζειν do not go near them A.
2 (in an exhortation, 1 or 3sg.pl., w. pres. or aor.imperatv. or subj.) Hom. + • μὴ λαθέτω let it not escape notice Pi. X. • μὴ διώκωμεν let us not pursue Hdt.
3 (in a wish, w.opt.) Hom. + • ὃ μὴ τελέσειε Κρονίων may the son of Kronos not bring this about Od.
4 (in an unfulfilled wish, w. past tenses of indic.) Hom. + • μὴ ὄφελον νικᾶν I wish I had not been victorious Od. • εἴθ' ἐξ ἀγῶνος τήνδε μὴ 'λαβές ποτε I wish you had never won her in the competition E.
5 (in an oath or asseveration, w.indic.) Hom. + • μὰ τὴν Ἀφροδίτην … μὴ 'γώ σ' ἀφήσω by Aphrodite … I shall not let you go Ar.
6 (in a cautious statement, as if w. ellipse of an introductory vb. expressing apprehension) Pl. + • μὴ ἀγροικότερον ᾖ τὸ ἀληθὲς εἰπεῖν (I fear that) it may be too uncivil to speak the truth Pl.
7 (in a q., usu. expecting a neg. answer, freq. after ἆρα or ἦ, w.indic.) Hom. + • μή τί σοι δοκῶ ταρβεῖν; do I seem to you to be afraid (i.e. I don't, do I)? A.
8 (in a deliberative q., w.subj.) • τί μὴ ποήσω; what should I not do? S.
9 (colloq., w. ellipse of imperatv.) • μὴ σύ γε don't do that! S. E. Pl. + • μή μοι πρόφασιν no excuses! Ar.
10 (contradictory) μὴ ἀλλά (μἀλλά) no (don't say that) but (rather) A. E.(cj.) Ar. Pl. • ἄπελθε νύν μοι. —μἀλλά μοι δὸς ἓν μόνον Please go away. —No, but give me just one thing Ar.
—C | in dependent constructions |
1 (in final cls., w.subj. or opt., usu. after conj. ἵνα, ὅπως, ὄφρα, or sim.) **not** Hom. + • ὡς μὴ πάντες ὄλωνται in order that all may not die Il. • (without conj.) ἀπόστιχε, μή τι νοήσῃ Ἥρη go away, so that Hera does not notice anything Il.
2 (in protasis of conditional cls., and in temporal cls. w. conditional sense) Hom. + • κάκιστ' ἀπολοίμην, Ξανθίαν εἰ μὴ φιλῶ may I die in utter misery, if I don't love Xanthias Ar. • οὐκ ἔστι λαθεῖν ὅτε μὴ χρῄζων θεὸς ἐκκλέπτει it is not possible to hide, unless a willing god spirits one away E.
3 (in relatv.cls. expressing a condition or generality) Hom. + • ὃς δὲ μὴ εἶδέ κω τὴν καννάβιδα anyone who has not yet seen the hemp-plant Hdt.
4 (in ptcpl.cls. expressing a condition, cause, generality, characteristic, or sim.) • οὐδείς, σάφ' οἶδα, μὴ μάτην φλύσαι θέλων no one, I am sure, unless wishing to talk empty nonsense A. • καὶ τίς πρὸς ἀνδρὸς μὴ βλέποντος ἄρκεσις; and what help (can there be) from a man who cannot see? S.
5 (w.inf., as the regular neg.) Hom. + | for οὐ w.inf. see οὐ C 5
6 (in indir.q. introduced by εἰ or εἴτε) • ἤρετό με … εἰ μὴ μέμνημαι he asked me if I did not remember Aeschin.
7 (after vbs. of fear or apprehension, w.subj., opt. or indic.) **lest, that, in case** Hom. + • δείδω μὴ δὴ πάντα θεὰ νημερτέα εἴπῃ I fear that everything the goddess said may be true Od.
8 (in indir.q., where fear or apprehension is implied) • περισκοπῶ μή πού τις ἡμῖν ἐγγὺς ἐγχρίμπτει βροτῶν I look around to see whether anyone is coming near me S.
—D | w. duplication or as pleonasm |
1 (followed by cpd.neg.) Hom. + • ὁμολογία γίγνεται ὥστε … μὴ ἀποθανεῖν μηδένα an agreement is made that no one should be killed Th.
2 (pleon., w.inf., after vbs. of denying, doubting, disputing) Hom. + • ἠρνοῦντο μὴ πεπτωκέναι they denied that they had fallen Ar.
—μὴ οὐ neg.advs. **1** (w. separate force, after vbs. of fear or apprehension) Hom. + • δείδω μὴ οὔ τίς τοι ὑπόσχηται τόδε ἔργον I fear that no one will undertake this task for you Il. | see μή C 7
2 (without introductory vb.) • μή νύ τοι οὐ χραίσμωσιν ὅσσοι θεοί εἰσ' ἐν Ὀλύμπῳ (I fear that) all the gods on Olympos will not protect you Il. • (in a cautious statement) ἀλλὰ μὴ οὐ τοῦτ' ᾖ χαλεπόν but (I suspect that) this may not be difficult Pl. | see μή B 6
3 (w. single neg. force, after a neg. expressed or implied, w.inf.) • οὐκέτι ἀνεβάλλοντο μὴ οὐ τὸ πᾶν μηχανήσασθαι they no longer hesitated to try every measure Hdt. • τί δῆτα

Μῆα

μέλλει μὴ οὐ παρουσίαν ἔχειν; *then why does he hesitate to show his presence?* S.; (occas. w.ptcpl.) • δυσάλγητος γὰρ ἂν εἴην τοιάνδε μὴ οὐ κατοικτίρων ἕδραν *I would be unfeeling if I did not pity such a supplication* S.; (exceptionally, w.sb.) πόλεις ... χαλεπαὶ λαβεῖν ... μὴ οὐ χρόνῳ καὶ πολιορκίᾳ *cities difficult (i.e. not easy) to capture, except by a lengthy siege* D.

Μῆα *Boeot.f.*: see Μαῖα

μηδαμά, μηδαμῇ, μηδαμόθεν *neg.advs.*: see οὐ-

μηδαμοί *neg.pl.pron.adj.*: see οὐδαμοί

μηδαμοῖ, μηδαμόσε, μηδαμοῦ, μηδαμῶς *neg.advs.*: see οὐ-

μηδέ *neg.pcl.*: see οὐδέ

μήδεα¹ έων *n.pl.* [μήδομαι] **thoughts, plans, designs, schemes** Hom. Hes. hHom. A. Pi. AR.

μήδεα², dial. **μέζεα** (Hes.), έων *n.pl.* **genitals** (of men or gods) Od. Hes. Emp. Call. AR.; (of animals) Hes.

Μήδεια ᾱς, Ion. **Μηδείη** ης *f.* **Medea** (daughter of Aietes, wife of Jason, murderess of their children) Hes. Pi. Hdt. E. +; (title of a drama, esp. that by Euripides) Ar. Arist.

Μήδειοι *m.pl.*: see Μῆδοι

μηδείς *neg.pron.adj.*, **μηδέν** *neg.neut.adv.*: see οὐδείς

μηδέποτε, μηδέπω, μηδεπώποτε *neg.advs.*: see οὐ-

μηδέτερος *neg.adj.*: see οὐδέτερος

μηδετέρωθεν, μηδετέρως, μηδετέρωσε *neg.advs.*: see οὐδ' ἑτέρωθεν, οὐδετέρως, οὐδετέρωσε, under οὐδέτερος

Μηδίᾱ *f.*: see under Μῆδοι

μηδίζω *vb.* [Μῆδοι] | aor. ἐμήδισα | **collaborate with the Persians, medize** Hdt. Th. X. D. Plu.

Μηδικός *adj.*, **Μηδίς** *f.*: see under Μῆδοι

μηδισμός οῦ *m.* **collaboration with the Persians, medism** Hdt. Th. Isoc. D. Arist. Plu.

Μῆδοι, also **Μήδειοι** (Ibyc. Pi. Call.), ων *m.pl.* **Medes** or **Persians** (orig.ref. to inhabitants of Media, a region SW. of the Caspian Sea, conquered by Cyrus the Great of Persia in 550–49 BC; gener.ref. to inhabitants of the Persian Empire, usu. in connection w. the Persian wars of 490 and 480–79 BC) Thgn. Lyr. A. Hdt. E. Th. +

—**Μῆδος** ου *m.* (sts. appos.w. ἀνήρ) **Mede** or **Persian** Hdt. Th. Ar. X. Call.(cj.) +; (appos.w. ὕπνος *sleep*, envisaged as a hostile invader) Ar.; (collectv., w.art.) **the Persians** (as a military force) Hdt. Th. Plu.

—**Μηδίᾱ** ᾱς *f.* **country of the Medes, Media** X. Plb. Plu.

—**Μηδίς** ίδος *f.* **Median woman** Hdt.

—**Μηδικός** ή όν *adj.* **1** (of a land, empire, nation, customs, dress, or sim.) **of or relating to the Medes, Median** Hdt. Pl. X. Plu.; (of a kind of grass, ref. to lucerne) Ar. ‖ FEM.SB. **Median land** Hdt. X. Plu.

2 (of an army) **Median, Persian** A.; (of dress, spoils, tapestries, rule, or sim.) Th. Ar. Plu.; (of a war, a military achievement) **against the Persians** Th. Arist. Plu. ‖ NEUT.PL.SB. **Persian Wars** Hdt. Th. And. Ar. X. Arist. +

—**μηδικώτερον** *compar.adv.* **in a rather Median or Persian manner** —*ref. to being dressed* Plu.

μήδομαι *mid.vb.* [prob.reltd. μέδω] | 3sg.impf. ἐμήδετο, ep. μήδετο | fut. μήσομαι, ep.2sg. μήσεαι | aor. ἐμησάμην, ep.2sg. μήσαο, 3sg. ἐμήσατο, ep. μήσατο | pf.act. μέμηδα (hHom., cj.) |

1 (intr., of a person or god) **take thought, plan** Il. Pi.

2 (tr.) **devise, contrive, plan** —*sthg.* (more freq. bad than good, sts. W.DAT. *for someone*) Hom. Hes. Lyr. Trag. Ar. Hellenist.poet. —W.DBL.ACC. *sthg. bad for someone* Hom. AR. —W.ACC. + INF. *that sthg. shd. be the case* Pi.

Μῆδος *m.*: see under Μῆδοι

μηθαμῶς *Att.neg.adv.*: see οὐδαμῶς

μηθείς *Att.neg.pron.adj.*: see οὐδείς

μηθέτερος *Att.neg.adj.*: see οὐδέτερος

μηκάδες ων *fem.pl.adj.* [μηκάομαι] (of goats) **bleating** Hom.; (of sheep) E.*Cyc.* ‖ SB. **bleating goats** Theoc.

μηκάομαι *mid.contr.vb.* | impf. (fr. pf. stem) μέμηκον (v.l. ἐμέμηκον) | aor.2 ptcpl. μακών | pf.ptcpl. μεμηκώς, fem.pl. μεμακυῖαι | **1** (of sheep and goats) **bleat** Hom.

2 (of a hunted or wounded animal) **bellow** or **scream** Hom.; (of a person, felled by a blow) Od.

μηκασμός οῦ *m.* **bleating** (of goats) Plu.

μηκέτι *neg.adv.*: see οὐκέτι

μήκιστος η ον, dial. **μάκιστος**, ᾱ ον *superl.adj.* [μῆκος, μακρός] | for compar. see μάσσων | **1** (of a man) **tallest** Hom.

2 ‖ NEUT.SG.SB. **furthest limit** (W.GEN. of a person's life) X. ‖ NEUT.PL.SB. **longest distance** S.

3 (of wealth of understanding) **greatest** Emp.; (of troubles) E.; (of a portent) AR.

4 (of a war) **longest** Plu.

—**μήκιστον**, dial. **μάκιστον** *neut.sg.superl.adv.* **furthest** (in distance) S. X.

—**μήκιστα** *neut.pl.superl.adv.* **in the end, finally** Od.

μῆκος, dial. **μᾶκος**, εος (ους) *n.* [reltd. μακρός] **1 quality of being long, length** Pl. Arist.

2 spatial extent, length (of an object, structure, stretch of land or water, or sim.) Od. Pi. Hdt. E. Th. Pl. +

3 height, tallness (of a person) Od. Ar. X. Plu.; (of a wall) Ar.; (of a tree) AR.

4 length, distance (of a throw) Pi. Plu.; (of a ship, fr. shore) E.; (W.GEN. of a journey, voyage, or sim.) Hdt. Th. Pl. X. +; (of one's sight, i.e. distance that one can see) X.

5 durational extent, length (usu. W.GEN., e.g. of time, a life, year-long watch, night) Trag. Att.orats. Pl. X. Arist. +; (of a war, campaign, siege) Th. D. Plb. Plu.

6 length (of a speech, story, or sim.) A. S. Th. Isoc. Pl. D. + ‖ ADVBL.ACC. **at length** (opp. concisely) S.

7 length (of a vowel or syllable, in pronunciation) Pl. Arist.

8 greatness (in scale or degree); **greatness, magnitude** (of prosperity) Emp.; **intensity** (of pleasure) S.

μήκοτε (and **μή κοτε**) *Ion.neg.adv.*: see οὔποτε

μηκύνω, dial. **μακύνω** *vb.* | fut. μηκυνῶ, Ion. μηκυνέω | aor. ἐμήκυνα | **1 make long or longer** (in spatial extent), **lengthen, extend** —*the front of a military formation* X.; (of a dragon) **stretch out** —*its coils* AR. ‖ PASS. (of carded wool) **be lengthened out** Pl.; (of a sea-monster's tail) **be stretched out** AR.; (of sprouting grain) **grow long** NT.

2 make longer (in duration), **prolong** —*time* (*before death*), *one's life* E. —*a journey* X. —*a war* Plu. ‖ PASS. (of a war) **be prolonged** Th.; (of a journey) —W.DAT. *by a certain number of days* Hdt.; (of a day, daylight) Call. AR.

3 prolong (the time before), **postpone, delay** —*the achievement of a goal* Pi.

4 prolong, protract, spin out —*a speech, narrative, or sim.* Hdt. S. Th. Isoc. Pl. Plu. ‖ PASS. (of an argument) **be treated at length** Pl.; (of epic poetry) **be drawn out** —W.DAT. *by episodes* Arist.

5 speak at length E.*fr.*(dub.) Ar. Pl. Arist. —W.ACC. *about sthg.* Th. Isoc. Pl. —W.PREP.PHR. Hdt.

6 utter loudly, raise —*a cry* S.

μήκων, dial. **μάκων**, ωνος *f.* **1 poppy** Il. Stesich. Iamb.adesp. Call. Theoc.

2 (collectv.sg.) **poppy-seed** Hdt. Th. Ar.

—**μᾱκωνίᾱς** ᾱ *dial.masc.adj.* (of loaves of bread) **made with poppy-seed** Alcm.

μή κως *Ion.neg.adv.*: see οὔπως

μῆλα ων *n.pl.* **sheep, goats** or **flocks** (of sheep or goats) Hom. Hes. Iamb.adesp. Pi. B. Trag. Hellenist.poet.

—**μῆλον**¹ ου *n.sg.* **sheep** or **goat** Od.

μηλέα, Aeol. **μᾱλίᾱ**, ᾶς, Ion. **μηλέη** ης *f.* [μῆλον²] **apple tree** Od. Sapph.

μήλειος¹, Ion. **μήλεος**, ον *adj.* [μῆλα] **1** (of the sacrificial killing) **of a sheep** E. **2** (of meat) **of sheep** (i.e. mutton) Hdt.; (of milk) **of sheep** or **goats** E.*Cyc.*

μήλειος² ον *adj.* [μῆλον²] (of the trunk) **of an apple tree** AR.

Μηλιακός *adj.*, **Μηλιάς** *fem.adj.*, **Μηλιεῖς** *m.pl.*, **Μηλιεύς** *masc.adj.*: see under Μηλίς

Μήλιοι *m.pl.*, **Μήλιος** *adj.*: see under Μῆλος

μηλίς, dial. **μᾱλίς**, ίδος *f.* [μῆλον²] **apple tree** Ibyc. Theoc.

Μηλίς ίδος *f.* **1 Malis** (region on the NE. coast of Greece) Hdt. **2** ‖ ADJ. of or relating to Malis; (of the land) of Malis Hdt. Call.; (of the sea, ref. to the Gulf) Malian S.

—**Μηλιεῖς**, Ion. **Μηλιέες**, Att. **Μηλιῆς** (Th.), also **Μᾱλιεῖς** (Aeschin. D. Arist.), ῶν (Ion. έων) *m.pl.* | acc. Μηλιέας, also Μᾱλιέας, Att. Μηλιᾶς (Th.) | **men of Malis, Malians** (as a population or military force) Hdt. Th. X. Aeschin. D. Arist.

—**Μηλιεύς**, also **Μᾱλιεύς** (Plu.), έως (also Att. ὡς Th.) *masc.adj.* | acc. Μηλιέα, also Μᾱλιέα, contr. Μηλιᾶ (A. Ar.) | (of the people, a man) of Malis, **Malian** Hdt. S.; (of the Gulf) A. Hdt. Th. Ar. Plb. Plu.

—**Μηλιάς** άδος *fem.adj.* **1** (of nymphs) from Malis, **Malian** S. **2** (of the coast) **of Malis** E.(cj.)

—**Μηλιακός** ή όν *adj.* (of the Gulf) **Malian** Th.

μηλο-βοσκός όν *adj.* [μῆλα, βόσκω] (of a house) associated with the pasturing of flocks, **pastoral** E.*fr.*

μηλο-βότᾱς ᾱ *dial.m.* pasturer of flocks, **shepherd** Pi. E.*Cyc.*

μηλο-βοτήρ ῆρος *m.* pasturer of flocks, **shepherd** Il. hHom. AR.

μηλό-βοτος ον *adj.* **1** (of a region) **grazed by flocks** Hes.*fr.* A. Pi. B. **2** (predic., of a region abandoned, as a consequence of war) **to be grazed by flocks, for pasturage** Isoc. Lycurg. Plu.

μηλογενής *adj.*: see μαλογενής

μηλο-δαΐκτᾱς ᾱ *dial.masc.adj.* [δαΐζω] (of a lion) **flock-killing** B.

μηλο-δόκος ον *adj.* [δέχομαι] (of Pytho, i.e. Delphi) **that receives animals from the flock** (i.e. sheep or goats, for sacrifice) Pi.

μηλο-θύτᾱς ᾱ *dial.masc.adj.* [θύω¹] (of Pytho, an altar) **where animals from the flock are sacrificed** B. E.

μηλολόνθη ης *f.* a kind of flying beetle, **cockchafer** Ar.

μῆλον¹ *n.sg.*: see under μῆλα

μῆλον², dial. **μᾶλον**, ου *n.* **apple** (sts. gener.ref. to other tree-fruits) Hom. Hes. Lyr. Hdt. Ar. +; (specif., ref. to the golden apples of the Hesperides) Hes. Pi.*fr.* S. Isoc. Hellenist.poet.; (ref. to an ornament or design on a staff or spear) Hdt.; (pl., fig.ref. to a woman's breasts) Ar. Theoc.; (ref. to large tears) Theoc.

μηλο-νόμᾱς ᾱ *dial.m.* [μῆλα, νέμω] pasturer of flocks, **shepherd** E.

μηλο-νόμος ου *m.* pasturer of flocks, **shepherd** E.*Cyc.*

Μῆλος ου *f.* **Melos** (island in the SW. Cyclades) Th. Isoc. X.

—**Μήλιοι** ων *m.pl.* inhabitants of Melos, **Melians** (as a population or military force) Hdt. Th. Att.orats. X. Plu.

—**Μήλιος** ᾱ ον *adj.* **1** of or relating to Melos; (of a man or woman) **Melian** Lys. Ar. Plu.; (of the sea to its south) Thgn. **2** (of famine) **of the Melian kind** (ref. to that suffered during the Athenian siege of 416 BC) Ar.

μηλο-σκόπος ον *adj.* [μῆλα, σκοπέω] (of a mountain peak) **with a view over flocks** hHom.

μηλό-σπορος ον *adj.* [μῆλον², σπόρος] (of a place) **where apples are planted** E.

μηλοσφαγέω *contr.vb.* [μῆλα, σφάζω] **perform ritual slaughter of sheep** or goats Ar. —W.INTERN.ACC. *as monthly offerings* S.; **perform ritual slaughter** —W.INTERN.ACC. *of a jar of wine* Ar.

μηλο-τρόφος ον *adj.* [τρέφω] (of a land) that nurtures flocks, **sheep-rearing** Archil. A. B. Hdt.(oracle)

μηλο-φόνος ον *adj.* [θείνω] (of ruin) consisting in the slaughter of flocks, **flock-slaughtering** A.

μηλο-φόρος ον *adj.* [μῆλον², φέρω] (of leaves, meton. for leafy branches) **apple-bearing** E.

μῆλ-οψ οπος *masc.fem.adj.* [μῆλον², ὤψ] having the appearance of an apple; (of grain) **apple-hued** (i.e. yellow or golden) Od.

μήν¹, dial. **μάν** *pcl.* [reltd. μέν] | Hom. has both μήν and μάν, as well as emph. Ion. μέν (see μέν 1). The wd. usu. stands in second position. | **1** (emph., in statements and commands) **indeed, truly** Hom. + • οὐ μὰν ἀκλεῖς Λυκίην κάτα κοιρανέουσιν ἡμέτεροι βασιλῆες *not without glory, indeed, do our kings rule in Lycia* Il. • ἴστε μὰν Αἴαντος ἀλκάν *you know, for sure, of Ajax's might* Pi. • ἴτε μάν *now go!* A. **2** (adversative, freq. w.neg.) **yet, however** • ἐπὶ μὰν βαίνει τι καὶ λάθας ἀτέκμαρτα νέφος *but without warning some cloud of forgetfulness comes upon them* Pi. • οὐ μὴν ἄτιμοί γ' ἐκ θεῶν τεθνήξομεν *but we shall certainly not die unavenged by the gods* A. • λελάθοντο δὲ μαλοδρόπηες, οὐ μὰν ἐκλελάθοντ', ἀλλ' οὐκ ἐδύναντ' ἐπίκεσθαι *the apple-pickers have forgotten it —no, they have not forgotten it, but could not reach it* Sapph. **3** (emph., w. interrog.) • τί μὴν ἔμελλον; *why ever did I delay?* E. • (ellipt.phrs.) ποῦ μήν; *well, where then?* Pl. • ἀλλὰ πότε μήν; *well, when then?* X. • (strongly affirmative) τί μήν (μάν); *how else?* (i.e. naturally, certainly, of course) Trag. Pl. Theoc.*epigr.*; (also) ἀλλὰ τί μήν Pl. **4** (w. ἀλλά, adversative or affirmative, or adding a new point) A. + • ἀλλὰ μὴν ἵμειρ' ἐμὸς παῖς τήνδε θηρᾶσαι πόλιν; *and yet my son desired to conquer this city?* A. • ἀλλὰ μὴν ἐπιθυμῶ γε εἰδέναι *I do indeed want to know* Pl. • ἀλλ' οὐδὲ μὴν ναῦς ἔστιν *but there is not even a ship* E. | for οὐ μὴν ἀλλά see ἀλλά 11 **5** (w. γε, adversative, or adding a new point) A. + • νῦν δ' ἔλπομαι μέν, ἐν θεῷ γε μὰν τέλος *now I am hopeful, yet the outcome lies with the god* Pi. • (in a list) Κριτόβουλός γε μήν ... *Kritoboulos too* ... X. **6** (w. ἦ, introducing a confident assertion, promise or threat) Il. + • ἦ μὴν ἔτι Ζεὺς ... ἔσται ταπεινός *for sure, Zeus will be humbled* A. • Πέλοπα κατόμνυμι ... ἦ μὴν ἐρεῖν σοι *I swear by Pelops that I will tell you* E. **7** (w. καί, affirmative, or modifying what has been said, introducing a new fact, or moving on to a new topic, freq. reinforced by γε) Hom. + • ὧδε γὰρ ἐξερέω, καὶ μὴν τετελεσμένον ἔσται *for so I shall declare, and indeed it will be fulfilled* Hom. • φιλοκαλωτέρους ἐν τοῖς κινδύνοις, καὶ μὴν αἰδημονεστέρους *more heroic amidst dangers, and yet also more modest* X. • (in dialogue) ἔχ' ἐλπίδας. —καὶ μὴν τοσοῦτόν γ' ἐστί μοι τῆς ἐλπίδος *Have hope. —Yes, indeed, I have just this much hope* S. • καὶ μήν, ἔφη, οὐκ ἄλλο τί γε ποιοῦσιν *'Why, certainly', he said, 'that is exactly what they are doing'* Pl. • (moving on in a list) καὶ μὴν Τάνταλον εἰσεῖδον *and next I saw Tantalos* Od. • (moving on to the next argument) καὶ μὴν ἴστε γε *furthermore, you are well aware* D.

μήν

8 (w. καί, in drama, introducing a new arrival) Trag. Ar. • καὶ μὴν Ὀδυσσεὺς ἔρχεται *look, here comes Odysseus* E.

μήν², dial. **μείς**, μηνός *m.* **1** moon as visible during any one lunar month (affording a measurement of time within the month, waxing or waning, or within the year, through its position in a numbered sequence); **moon** Od. Hes. hHom.
2 time between successive moons, **month** Hom. +
3 moon-shaped or crescent-shaped disc (protecting a statue's head), **disc** Ar. | see μηνίσκος 1

μηνάς άδος *f.* [μήνη] **moon** E.

μήνατο (ep.3sg.aor.mid.): see μαίνομαι

μήνη ης, dial. **μήνᾱ** ᾱς *f.* [μήν²] **moon** Il. A. AR. Bion; (as a goddess) **Moon** hHom. Pi.

μηνιαῖος ᾱ ον *adj.* (of a year) **consisting of a single month** Plu.

μηνιάω contr.vb. [μηνίω] | ep.3pl. (w.diect.) μηνιόωσι | **be angry** —W.DAT. w. someone AR.

μήνιγξ ιγγος *f.* **membrane** (of the eye) Emp.

μηνιθμός οῦ *m.* [μῆνις] **anger, wrath** Il.

μήνιμα ατος *n.* **1 anger** (of a god or avenging spirit) A.(cj.) E. Antipho Pl. Plu.
2 (ref. to an unburied person) **cause of anger** (W.GEN. + DAT. for the gods, against someone) Hom.

μῆνις, dial. **μᾶνις**, ιος *f.* resentful or vengeful anger, **anger, wrath** (of persons, gods, the spirits of the dead, or sim.) Hom. Hes. Thgn. Lyr. Hdt. Trag. +; (pl.) AR.; (personif.) **Wrath** A.

μηνίσκος ου *m.* [dimin. μήν²] **1** small convex moon-shaped or (as viewed frontally) crescent-shaped disc (fixed over the head of a statue, for protection against bird-droppings), **disc** or **crescent** Ar.
2 convex battle-line, **crescent** Plb.

μηνίω, dial. **μᾱνίω** vb. [μῆνις] | pres. also ῑ (A.) | 3sg.impf. ἐμήνιε, ep. μήνιε, also μήνῑε | aor. ἐμήνῑσα | (of persons or gods) feel resentful or vengeful anger, **be angry** (sts. W.DAT. w. someone) Hom. Simon. Pi.fr. Hdt. S. E. Arist.; (also mid.) A. —(W.GEN. over sthg.) Il. S. Theoc.

μηνο-ειδής ές *adj.* [μήν², εἶδος¹] in the form of a crescent moon; (of a partially eclipsed sun) **crescent-shaped** Th. X. Plu.; (of a structure or a feature of the landscape) Hdt. Th. Plu.; (of a battle-formation) X. Plb. Plu. || NEUT.SB. crescent-shaped formation (W.GEN. of ships) Hdt.

μήνυμα ατος *n.* [μηνύω] **1** (sg. and pl.) information (laid against a person by an informant), **information, denunciation** Th.
2 (gener.) disclosure of information || PL. disclosures, revelations Men.

μήνυσις εως *f.* **1** laying of information (against a person, about a crime, or sim.), **information, revelation, disclosure** And. Lys. Pl. Plu.
2 (gener.) **disclosure of information** Men.

μηνυτήρ ῆρος *m.* **informant** (W.ADJ. voiceless, fig.ref. to the scent of a murderer) A.

μηνυτής οῦ *m.* **1** one who lays information (against a person, about a crime, or sim.), **informer** Th. Att.orats. Pl. Plb. Plu.
2 (gener.) one who discloses information, **informant** Pl.; (appos.w. χρόνος time) E.

μήνυτρον ου *n.* **reward for information** hHom. Hippon.; (pl.) Th. And. Lys. Plu.

μηνύω, dial. **μᾱνύω** vb. | also pres. and impf. ῠ (Pi., sts. hHom. B.) | fut. μηνύσω | aor. ἐμήνυσα || PASS.: aor. ἐμηνύθην | 3sg.plpf. ἐμεμήνυτο | **1** give information (about sthg.); **disclose, reveal, indicate** (freq. W.DAT. to someone) —sthg. hHom. Pi. B. Hdt. S. E. + —W.ACC. + PTCPL. or INF. that sthg. is the case Antipho Pl. Plu. —W.COMPL.CL. or INDIR.Q. that (what, or sim.) is the case Pl. Arist. || PASS. (of things) be disclosed E. Plb.
2 (of a touchstone) **indicate** —gold B.fr.
3 (intr.) **give information** hHom. Pi. Ar. Pl.; **give an indication** —w. ὡς + GEN.PTCPL. of sthg. happening Pl.
4 (specif.) **be an informer, lay information** (sts. W.DAT. to someone) Th. Att.orats. Pl. Plu. —(W.PREP.PHR. against someone) Att.orats. —(W.ACC. or PREP.PHR. about sthg.) Th. And. —W.COMPL.CL. or ACC. + INF. that sthg. is the case Att.orats.
5 inform against, denounce, expose —someone Att.orats. X. Arist. —(W.PTCPL. as doing or being such and such) Hdt. Antipho; (fig., of the facts) —a person (W.PREDIC.ADJ. as evil) E. || PASS. (of persons) be informed against or denounced Th. And. Lys. X. Plu.; (of wrongdoing, plotting, or sim.) be exposed S. Th. Pl. Plu. || IMPERS.PASS. information is laid Th. And. Lys. || NEUT.PL.PF.PASS.PTCPL.SB. denunciations Lys.

μὴ ὅπως, μὴ ὅτι neg.advbl.phrs.: see ὅπως 6, ὅτι¹ 4

μὴ οὐ neg.advs.: see under μή

μήποτε (and **μή ποτε**, also **μή ποκα**) neg.adv.: see οὔποτε

μήπω (and **μή πω**) neg.adv.: see πω

μηπώποτε (and **μή πώποτε**) neg.adv.: see οὐπώποτε

μή πως neg.adv.: see οὔπως

μῆρα ων n.pl. [μῆρος] | du. μῆρε | **thigh-bones** (of sacrificial victims, wrapped in fat and burned on the altar as the gods' portion) Hom. Ar. AR.

μηρία ων n.pl. **1 thigh-bones** (of sacrificial victims) Hom. Hes. Callin. Thgn. B.fr. Hdt. + | see μῆρα
2 [dimin.] **poor thighs** (of wounded Adonis) Bion

μηριαῖαι ῶν f.pl. **upper thighs** (of a horse or hound) X.

μήρινθος, also **σμήρινθος** (Pl.), ου *f.* **cord, string** Pl.; (for tethering a bird) Il.; (for fishing) Ar. Theoc.

μηρός οῦ *m.* | du. μηρώ | **1 thigh** (of a person or god) Hom. +; (of an animal) Hdt. X.
2 || PL. and DU. thighs or thigh-bones (of sacrificial victims) Hom. S. Ar. | see μῆρα

μηρυκάομαι mid.contr.vb. (of animals) **chew the cud, ruminate** Plu.

μηρύματα των n.pl. [μηρύομαι] **brailing rings** (on a ship's yard-arm, which guide the ropes used to furl the sail) Plu.

μηρύομαι, dial. **μαρύομαι** mid.vb. **1 draw up, furl** —sails Od.
2 wind up —a ship's rope AR. [or perh. stow away the tackle]
3 (of a weaver) **weave, wind, thread** —the weft Carm.Pop. —(w. ἐν + DAT. into the warp) Hes.
4 (intr., of an ivy decoration) **wind** —W.PREP.PHR. towards the lip of a cup Theoc.

μήσαο, μήσατο (ep.2sg. and 3sg.aor.mid.), **μήσεαι** (ep.2sg.fut.): see μήδομαι

μήστωρ ωρος *m.* [μήδομαι] | dat. μήστορι (Tim., dub.) | **1** (ref. to a person) **counsellor, adviser** Hom. Hes.fr.; (ref. to Zeus) Il.
2 one who devises or contrives; (ref. to a warrior) **rouser** (W.GEN. of the battle-cry) Il.; **creator** (W.GEN. of panic) Il. Hes.fr.; (ref. to horses) Il.
3 planner or **agent** (W.ADJ. λαιμότομος throat-cutting, ref. to a sword) Tim.

μήτε neg.conj.: see οὔτε

μήτηρ μητρός (also poet. μητέρος), dial. **μάτηρ** μᾱτρός (also μᾱτέρος) *f.* | voc. μῆτερ, dial. μᾶτερ | acc. μητέρα, dial. μᾱτέρα | dat. μητρί, dial. μᾱτρί, also μητέρι, dial. μᾱτέρι || PL.: nom. μητέρες, dial. μᾱτέρες | acc. μητέρας, dial. μᾱτέρας | gen. μητέρων, dial. μᾱτέρων | dat. μητράσι |

1 mother (ref. to a woman or goddess) Hom. +; (ref. to a bird or animal) Hom. Anacr. Hdt. E. Ar.; (of a poet, fig.ref. to his Muse) Pi. ‖ PL. mothers (ref. to a mother and grandmother) Plu.

2 (voc., as respectful term of address to a woman senior in status or years) **mother** A. Theoc.

3 Mother (as name of Demeter) Hdt.; (as name of Cybele, sts. w.epith. μεγάλη *great* or ὀρεία *mountain*, or W.GEN. θεῶν *of the gods*; sts. identified w. Rhea or Demeter) hHom. Lyr. Hdt. E. Ar.

4 (ref. to Earth) **mother** (W.GEN. of all things) Hes. E.*fr.*; (of the gods) Sol.; (as epith. of Earth or earth, without GEN.) Pi. S. E.; **mother earth** Pi. E.*fr.*

5 (fig., ref. to a region) **mother** (W.GEN. of flocks, wild animals) Hom. Hes. hHom.; (of mountains) E.

6 (fig., ref. to a land or city) **mother** (of persons or a populace) Pi. Trag. Att.orats. Pl.; (W.GEN. of brave men) S.

7 (fig.) **mother** (W.GEN. of a city, ref. to Athena) E.; (of contests, ref. to Olympia) Pi.; (of a region, ref. to a city) Pi.

8 (fig., ref. to a lake) **source** (W.GEN. of a river or sea) Hdt.

9 (fig., ref. to deities or to concrete or abstract entities, acting as causes or sources); **mother** (W.GEN. of passions, ref. to Aphrodite) Pi.*fr.* B.; (of dreams, ref. to Earth) E.; (of sight, ref. to sunlight) Pi.*fr.*; (of grape-blossom, ref. to fruitfulness) E.; (of victories, ref. to a shield) E.; (of songs, ref. to the lyre) Ar.; (of helplessness, ref. to poverty) Thgn.; (of success, ref. to obedience) A.; (of evil deeds, ref. to the mind) S.; (of a feeling of shame, ref. to a rumour) S.; (of all other arts, ref. to agriculture) X.; (of all other forms of government, ref. to monarchy and democracy) Pl.

10 (without GEN., ref. to the vine) **mother** (of wine) A. E.; (ref. to night, of day) A.

11 (fig., ref. to a day) **mother** (opp. μητρυιά *stepmother*, i.e. a good day opp. a bad one) Hes.

μήτι (and **μή τι**) *neg.neut.adv.*: see οὔτι, under οὔτις

μητιάω *ep.contr.vb.* [μῆτις] | all forms w.diect. | 3pl. μητιόωσι | ptcpl.: fem.nom. μητιόωσα, masc.dat. μητιόωντι, masc.pl.nom. μητιόωντες, dat. μητιόωσι | iteratv.impf. μητιάασκον (AR.) ‖ MID.: 2pl.imperatv. μητιάασθε | inf. μητιάασθαι | 3pl.impf. μητιόωντο |

1 (of persons or gods) **take thought, deliberate** Il. AR.

2 think over, consider —*plans or sim.* Il. AR.

3 ‖ MID. **consider** —W.INDIR.Q. *what to do, whether to do one thing or another* Il. AR.

4 (tr.) **have in mind, plan, devise, contrive** —*sthg.* (*good or bad*) Hom. AR.; (mid.) AR.

5 ‖ MID. **plan** —W.INF. *to do sthg.* Il.

μητίετα *ep.nom. and voc.m.* (epith. of Zeus) **counsellor, planner** Hom. Hes. hHom.

μητιόεις εσσα εν *adj.* **1** (of Zeus) **wise in counsel, resourceful** Hes. hHom.

2 (of drugs) perh. **clever** Od.

μητίομαι *mid.vb.* | fut. μητίσομαι | aor.inf. μητίσασθαι | **1** (of charioteers) **be skilful** Il.

2 (of Zeus) **plan, scheme** Od.

3 (tr., of persons or gods) **plan, devise, contrive** —*sthg.* (*usu. bad*) Hom. hHom. Pi. Emp. AR. —(W.ACC. *against someone*) Od.

4 (of a divine agent) **invent** or **create** —*Love* Pl.(quot. Parm.)

μῆτις ιδος (dial. ιος) *f.* | acc. μῆτιν | dat. μήτιδι (Hdt., oracle), ep. μήτι ‖ PL.: acc. μήτιδας (A.), ep. μήτιας (hHom.) | dial.dat. μητίεσσι (Pi.) | **1 skill, cleverness, shrewdness** (of a person or god) Hom. Pi. Emp. AR.; (specif., of a poet) Pi.; (of a fox) Pi.

2 thoughts, counsel, planning, advice Hom. A. Pi. Hdt.(oracle) AR.

3 scheme, design, plan Hom. Hes. A. Pi. B. S. AR.

4 (personif., as wife of Zeus, mother of Athena) **Metis** Hes. Pl.

μῆτις (and **μή τις**) *neg.pron.adj.*: see οὔτις

μήτοι (and **μή τοι**) *neg.pcl.*: see οὔτοι

μήτρᾱ ᾱς, Ion. **μήτρη** ης *f.* [μήτηρ] **womb** (of women or animals) Hdt. Pl. NT.

μητρ-αγύρτης ου *m.* (pejor., as nickname of a person) **begging priest of the Great Mother** (i.e. Cybele) Arist. Plu.

μητρ-αλοίᾱς ου *m.* [ἀλοάω] **one who strikes his mother, mother-beater** Lys. Pl.; (ref. to a matricide) A.

μητρίδιον ου *n.* [dimin. μήτηρ] **mummy** Ar.

μητρικός ή όν *adj.* (of respect) **due to a mother** Arist.

μητρίς ίδος *f.* **motherland** (said to be a Cretan wd.) Pl.

μητρόθεν, dial. **μᾱτρόθε(ν)** *adv.* **1 from one's mother** —*ref. to inheriting physical features, the right of free speech* Pi. E.

2 from a mother —*ref. to a baby coming forth, being received by a nurse* A. —*ref. to acquiring a herb* Ar.(mock-trag.)

3 on a mother —*ref. to fathering a child* E.

4 on one's mother's side —*ref. to tracing one's descent* Pi. Hdt. Plu.

5 by one's mother's name —*ref. to identifying oneself* Hdt.

6 with one's mother —*ref. to fulfilling or consummating an incestuous marriage* S.

μητρο-κοίτης εω Ion.*m.* [κοίτη] **man who sleeps with his mother, mother-fucker** Hippon.

μητροκτονέω *contr.vb.* [μητροκτόνος] **kill one's mother** A. E. Arist.

μητρο-κτόνος, dial. **μᾱτροκτόνος**, ον *adj.* [κτείνω] **1** (of a son, his hands) **mother-killing, matricidal** A. ‖ MASC.SB. **killer of one's mother, matricide** A. E. Pl.

2 (of the blood, pollution, ordeal) **of matricide** A. E.

μητρο-πάτωρ ορος *m.* [πατήρ] **father of one's mother, maternal grandfather** Il. Hdt. Plu.

μητρό-πολις εως, dial. **μᾱτρόπολις** ιος *f.* [πόλις] **1 mother-city** (of those born and living there) Pi. S.

2 mother-city (of colonies) Hdt. Th. Plu.; (W.GEN. of a particular city) A. Pi.

3 city of origin, original home (of a family line) Plu.

4 (ref. to a region) **mother-country, original homeland** (W.GEN. of a populace) Hdt. Th.

5 capital city (of a country) Hdt. Pl. X. Plu.

μητρο-φόνος, dial. **μᾱτροφόνος**, ου *m.* [θείνω] **murderer of one's mother, matricide** A. Plu.

μητρο-φόντης ου, dial. **μᾱτροφόντᾱς** ᾱ *m.* **matricide** E. Arist. ‖ ADJ. (of a serpent, fig.ref. to a man) **matricidal** E.; (of the pain of punishment) **for matricide** A.(dub.cj.)

μητρυιά (also **μητρυᾱ́** Pl.), dial. **μᾱτρυιᾱ́**, ᾶς, Ion. **μητρυιή** ῆς *f.* **1 stepmother** (traditionally regarded as hostile to stepchildren) Il. Pi. Hdt. E. Att.orats. Pl. +

2 (fig.) **stepmother** (ref. to a day, opp. μήτηρ *mother*, i.e. a bad day opp. a good one) Hes.; (W.GEN. of ships, ref. to a dangerous cape) A.; (ref. to a foreign land, opp. motherland) Pl.

μητρῷος, dial. **μᾱτρῷος**, ᾱ ον, Ion. **μητρώϊος** η ον *adj.* **1 associated with one's mother and her family**; (of a house) **maternal** Od.; (of gods, i.e. traditionally worshipped by her family) X.; (of lineage) Plu.

2 of or belonging to a mother (one's own or another's); (of the body, blood, hand, strong will, faults, or sim.) **of a**

μήτρως

mother Trag.; (of a kingdom, dwelling) Isoc. Pl. ‖ NEUT.PL.SB. inheritance from one's mother, mother's estate D.; a mother's side (in a dispute w. a father) Hdt.
3 relating to a mother; (of the murder) **of a mother** E.; (of a murder) **committed by a mother** E.; (of marriage) **to one's mother** S. E.; (of sufferings) **inherited from one's mother** S.; (transf.epith., of a sacrifice offering purification) **for one's mother** (i.e. for her murder) A.
4 (of the dignity of the name) **of mother** S.
—**Μητρῷον** ου *n.* **Metroön** (at Athens, sanctuary of the Mother Goddess, Cybele, used as a repository of public records) Att.orats.

μήτρως, dial. **μάτρως**, ωος *m.* | acc. μήτρωα | dial.dat. μάτρῳ, also μάτρωι | **1** mother's brother, **maternal uncle** Il. Pi. B. Hdt. AR.
2 mother's father, **maternal grandfather** Pi.
3 mother's ancestor Pi. ‖ PL. mother's ancestors Pi. S.*Ichn.*; (gener.) mother's relatives E.

μηχανάομαι *mid.contr.vb.* [μηχανή] | ep.pres. (w.diect.): 2pl. μηχανάασθε, 3pl. μηχανόωνται, inf. μηχανάασθαι, 3sg.subj. μηχανάāται, 3sg.opt. μηχανόῳτο, Ion.3pl.opt. μηχανῴατο | impf. ἐμηχανώμην, ep.3pl. (w.diect.) μηχανόωντο, Ion. ἐμηχανέοντο | fut. μηχανήσομαι | aor. ἐμηχανησάμην | pf. μεμηχάνημαι ‖ neut.impers.vbl.adj. μηχανητέον |
1 contrive to create —*a wall* Il. —*a voice* (W.DAT. *for a dead creature*) S.*Ichn.* —*the human eye* Ar. —*laughter, good sense, fear, happiness, or sim.* (*for others*) X. Plu.
2 contrive to procure (for oneself) —*ships, a hare* Hdt. X. —*cooks, money, food, luxuries* X.
3 rustle up, manage to provide —*a boat* (*as part of a plan*) Th.
4 (gener.) **contrive, devise, plan** or **effect** —*an action* (*good or bad*), *stratagem, technique, argument, or sim.* Hom. Hes. Hdt. Trag. Th. Ar. +
5 (intr.) **lay plans, scheme, plot** Od. Hdt. E. Isoc. X.
6 contrive —W.INF. *to do sthg.* Ar. Pl. X. Plu. —w. ὡς or ὅπως (ὅκως) + CL. *that sthg. shd. happen* Hdt. Pl. X. Plu. —W.ACC. + INF. (sts.w. ὥστε) Hdt. Pl. X. Plu.
7 contrive to render —*a person* (W.PREDIC.ADJ. *such and such*) Plu.

—**μηχανάω** *act.contr.vb.* | ep.nom.pl.ptcpl. (w.diect.) μηχανόωντες ‖ PASS.: pf. μεμηχάνημαι | 3sg.plpf. ἐμεμηχάνητο | **1 contrive, devise** —*evil things* Od. AR.; (of a god) —*all things* S.*satyr.fr.*
2 ‖ PF. and PLPF.PASS. (of a stronghold) **have been designed** —W.ADV. *in a certain way* (w. ὥστε + CL. *so as to achieve a particular result*) Hdt.; (of things) **have or had been contrived or devised** Hdt. S. Att.orats. Pl. X. Plu. —w. ὅκως + CL. *to ensure that sthg. happens* Hdt. —W.ACC. + INF. X.
‖ IMPERS.PLPF.PASS. a plan had been formed Antipho

—**μεμηχανημένως** *pf.pass.ptcpl.adv.* **designedly, premeditatedly** —*ref. to being mistreated* E.

μηχανή ῆς, dial. **μᾱχᾱνά**, also **μηχανά**, ᾶς, Aeol. **μᾱχάνᾱ** ᾱς *f.* [reltd. μῆχος] **1** (concr.) **device** (ref. to a hoist, for raising building-stones) Hdt.; (ref. to an automaton) Plb.; (ref. to a bridge of boats) A.(pl.); (W.ADJ. *fish-spearing*, ref. to Poseidon's trident) A.
2 (specif.) **siege-engine** Th. X. Arist. Plb. Plu.; **defensive machinery** Plb.
3 crane (enabling gods and others to appear in the air in tragedy, sts. in fig.ctxt.) Pl. D. Arist. Men. Plb. Plu.
4 (abstr., sg. and pl., sts. pejor.) **device, contrivance, stratagem, scheme** Hes. Alc. Iamb. Pi. Hdt. Trag. +

5 (gener.) **means** (of effecting sthg.); **means, way, possibility** (W.GEN. of safety or sim.) A. E. Ar. Pl. X.; (W.INF. to do sthg.) E.; (w. ὥστε + INF.) Pl.; (W.ACC. + INF. for sthg. to happen) Pl.; (w. ὅπως + CL.) Pl.; (after neg. or quasi-neg., w. μὴ οὐ + INF. or ACC. + INF. to avoid doing sthg., for sthg. not to happen) Hdt. Pl.; (also w. τὸ μὴ οὐ) Hdt.; (w. ὅπως (ὅκως) οὐ + CL. that sthg. will not happen) Hdt. Pl.
6 remedy (W.GEN. for misfortunes) E.
7 (advbl.phrs.) μηχανῇ οὐδεμιᾷ (or sim.) *on no account, under no circumstances* Hdt. Th.(treaty) Lys. D.; πάσῃ μηχανῇ *on every count, thoroughly* Ar.; (gener.) *by every possible means* Lys. Pl. X. Plu.; μηχανῇ ἡτινιοῦν *by any means whatever* D.(law)

μηχάνημα ατος *n.* **1 device, contrivance** (ref. to a robe used as a snare) A.; **invention** (ref. to a recipe) Pl. X. ‖ PL. devices or inventions (ref. to practical skills given to mortals by Prometheus) A.
2 (specif.) **siege-engine** X. D. Plb. Plu. ‖ PL. mechanical devices (for raising a portcullis, for defensive use in war) Plb.; (gener.) equipment (on ships, for defence against enemy ships) X.; military machinery Plu.
3 (abstr., freq.pl., usu. pejor.) **contrivance, stratagem, scheme** Trag. Antipho Ar. Pl. X. Plu.

μηχάνησις εως *f.* **device** (for grinding corn) Plb.

μηχανητικός ή όν *adj.* (of a commander) **resourceful, inventive** X.; (W.GEN. in a particular capacity) X.

μηχανικός ή όν *adj.* **1** (of persons) **resourceful, inventive** X.; (W.GEN. over provisions, i.e. in acquiring them) X.
2 (of medical appliances) **mechanical** Arist. ‖ FEM.SB. mechanics (as a science) Arist. Plu.
3 (specif., of siege apparatus) **mechanical** Plu.; (of skill) **in siege mechanics** Plu. ‖ MASC.SB. siege-engineer Plu. ‖ NEUT.PL.SB. siege-engineering Plu.

μηχανιώτης ου *m.* | ep.voc. μηχανιῶτα | **schemer** (ref. to Hermes) hHom.

μηχανο-δίφης ου *m.* [δῑφάω] (pejor.) **invention-seeker** Ar.

μηχανόεις εσσα εν *adj.* full of contrivance or invention ‖ NEUT.SB. (periphr.) inventiveness (W.GEN. of skill, i.e. skill in invention) S.

μηχανο-ποιός οῦ *m.* [ποιέω] **1** maker of military machinery (for attack or defence), **engineer** Pl. X. Plu.
2 machinist, crane-operator Ar. | see μηχανή 3

μηχανορραφέω *contr.vb.* [μηχανορράφος] stitch schemes together, **scheme, plot** A.

μηχανο-ρράφος ου *m.* [ῥάπτω] one who stitches schemes together; **contriver, plotter** S.; (W.GEN. of evil deeds) E.

μηχανο-φόρος ον *adj.* [φέρω] (of wagons) **for transporting siege-engines** Plu.

μῆχαρ *n.* [reltd. μῆχος] | only nom.acc.sg. | **1 resource, help** (ref. to Zeus) A.
2 remedy (W.GEN. against marriage, a storm, an affliction) A.

μῆχος, dial. **μᾶχος**, εος (ους) *n.* [reltd. μηχανή] **1 means, way, possibility** (W.INF. of doing sthg.) Hom.
2 means (of remedying a situation); **remedy** Hom. AR.; (W.GEN. for troubles, sickness) Hdt. E. Theoc.

μία *fem.num.adj. and sb.*: see εἷς

μιαίνω *vb.* | fut. μιανῶ | aor. ἐμίᾱνα, ep.3sg.subj. μιήνῃ | pf. μεμίαγκα (Plu.) ‖ PASS.: fut. μιανθήσομαι | aor. ἐμιάνθην, ep. μιάνθην | pf. μεμίασμαι | **1 stain, colour** —*ivory* (W.DAT. w. *crimson dye*) Il.
2 stain (so as to disfigure); **stain, sully, soil** —*clothes* (w. *dirt*) Theoc.; (of an arrow) —*parts of the body* (W.DAT. w. *blood*) Stesich.; **befoul, pollute** —*clear water* (W.DAT. w. *mud*)

A. ‖ PASS. (of persons, parts of the body, a helmet) be soiled Il. —W.DAT. *w. blood, dust* Il.; (of horses' manes, w. dust) Il.; (of gold) be tarnished Simon.

3 (specif.) pollute (by an action entailing ritual impurity); **stain, pollute** —*one's hands, limbs, an altar or temple* (W.DAT. *w. bloodshed*) A. Emp. Pl. Plu. —*one's clothes* (W.PREP.PHR. *by contact w. a corpse*) Theoc.; (of death) —*persons who have contact w. corpses or graves* Plu. ‖ PASS. (of a person) be polluted —W.DAT. *by bloodshed* S.; (of kindred blood, by the murder of a parent) Pl.; (of cleavers, used in murder) A.; (of a person, by contact w. birth or death) Thphr.; (by entering a forbidden place during Passover) NT.; (of a house) —W.DAT. *by a funeral* Plu. ‖ PF.PASS. have (W.ACC. one's hands) polluted —W.DAT. *by bloodshed* AR.

4 (of a ritually impure person, esp. a murderer) **pollute** —*a city, shrines, or sim.* E. Antipho Lys. Pl. —*the light of day* E. ‖ PASS. (of a city or land) be polluted (by a murderer) Antipho Th.; (of a person) —W.DAT. *by the voice of a murderer* E.

5 pollute (by an act of profanation); **pollute** —*the gods* (*by denying burial, rejecting suppliants*) S. E. ‖ PASS. (of a god) be polluted (by murder in his shrine) E.; (of shrines, by denial of burial) Lys.; (of a city, by failure to protect suppliants) A.; (of suppliant branches, by the maltreatment of their bearers) E.; (of fire, as a sacred element) —W.PREP.PHR. *by barbarians* Plu.

6 (gener.) **pollute, defile** —*justice, laws, piety* A. E. —*the divine part of the soul* (*by contact w. the mortal part*) Pl. —*divine gold in the soul* (*by the admixture of earthly gold*) Pl.; (of hawks) —*kinship* (*by killing other birds*) A. ‖ PASS. (of persons) be polluted —W.ACC. *in their souls* Pl.; (of the soul, by the body) Pl.

7 (gener. or fig.) **soil, taint, tarnish** —*one's own or another's reputation* Sol. E. —*a place* (W.DAT. *w. one's dishonour*) Pi. —*a joyful day* (*w. bad news*) A. ‖ PASS. (fig., of persons) be tainted (by bathing w. traitors) Plb.

μιαιφονέω *contr.vb.* [μιαιφόνος] shed blood that pollutes, **stain one's hands with blood, commit murder** E. Pl. Plu.; (tr.) **murder** —*relatives, fellow-citizens, slaves* Isoc. D.

μιαιφονία ᾱς *f.* **bloodthirstiness, murderousness** D. Plu.

μιαι-φόνος, perh. also **μιηφόνος** (Archil.), ον *adj.* [reltd. μιαίνω, μιαρός; θείνω] **1** shedding blood that pollutes; (of Ares) **bloodthirsty, murderous** Il. Archil.; (of a man or woman, a woman's mind, the Sphinx) B.*fr.* Hdt. E. Arist. Plu.; (of tyranny) Hdt.; (of deeds) E.*fr.* ‖ NEUT.SB. murderousness E.

2 ‖ MASC.FEM.SB. **murderer or murderess** A. X. Arist.; (W.GEN. of one's children) E.

3 (of the pollution) **of murder** E.; (of a marriage) **polluted by murder** S.; (of an ancestral crime) **blood-tainted** E.

4 (of a murderer's hands) **bloodstained** E.; (transf.epith., of the hair of a woman who has caused deaths in war) E.

μιαρίᾱ ᾱς *f.* [μιαρός] **1 blood-guilt, pollution** (of a murderer) Antipho

2 (gener.) **vileness, depravity** X. Is. D.

μιαρός ά όν *adj.* [μιαίνω] ‖ compar. μιαρώτερος, superl. μιαρώτατος ‖ **1** (of a dead warrior) **stained, sullied** (w. blood) Il.

2 (of a person) ritually impure, **polluted** Antipho Pl.; (of a place, by bloodshed) E.

3 (of an animal) **impure, unclean** Hdt.; (of the sea, as being undrinkable) Heraclit.

4 (strongly pejor., of persons) **filthy, vile, foul, abominable,** **damnable** E.*Cyc.* Ar. Att.orats. Pl. X. +; (of a person's character, a part of one's nature) S.; (of an animal, sts. meton. for a person) Ar.; (of a throat, meton. for a greedy eater) Ar.; (of a physical affliction, quasi-personif.) S.; (periphr., ref. to a person, sts. as voc. address) μιαρὰ κεφαλή *vile creature* Ar. Aeschin. D.

5 (voc. or exclam.nom., sts.superl., as a strong insult) ὦ μιαρέ, ὦ μιαρός (or sim.) **vile creature!, damnable villain!** S.*Ichn.* Ar. D. Din. Men. Plu.; (iron.) **you devil!** Pl.

6 (of a voice, an ill-smelling cloak) **loathsome, repulsive** Ar.; (of actions, circumstances, words, or sim.) **abominable, disgusting** Aeschin. D. Arist. Call. Plu.

7 (app. wkr.sens., of women, perh. w. sexual connot.) **indecent** Alc.

—**μιαρῶς** *adv.* **by foul means** Ar.; **in a foul** or **disgusting manner** D.

μίασμα ατος *n.* **1 pollution** (a state of ritual impurity, incurred fr. the shedding of blood, breaking of certain religious taboos, or contact w. certain aspects of birth and death, carrying a threat of contagion for individuals, communities and locations) Trag. Antipho Pl. D. Plu.

2 (concr., ref. to a murderer) **source** or **carrier of pollution** A. S.

3 (wkr.sens.) **taint, blight, blemish** (marring a situation) Plu.

μιασμός οῦ *m.* ritual impurity, **pollution** Plu.

μιάστωρ ορος *m.f.* **1** (ref. to a murderer) **source or carrier of pollution; polluted killer** Trag.; **polluter** (W.GEN. of a land) S. E.

2 one who kills a murderer (and so takes on that person's pollution); **blood-avenger** Trag.

μίγα *adv.* [reltd. μείγνῡμι] (as prep.) **mingled with, amidst** —W.DAT. *wailing* Pi. —*women* AR.

μιγάζομαι *mid.vb.* (of a god and goddess) **have sexual intercourse** Od.

μιγάς άδος *masc.fem.adj.* **1** consisting of a mixture of elements; (of an army of barbarians) **mixed** E.; (of a libation of milk and honey) AR.(pl.) ‖ PL. (of people, troops) of **mixed kinds or origins** Isoc. Plb. Plu.

2 ‖ PL. (of groups of people) **mixed up together** E. Plu.; (of people of one nationality) mingling or mingled (W.DAT. w. those of another) AR.

μίγδα *adv.* **1** (ref. to the bones of two dead persons) **mixed together** Od.; (ref. to different flowers) hHom.

2 (as prep.) **amidst, in company with** —W.DAT. *other gods* Il.; **mixed** —W.DAT. *w. sthg. else* Call.

μίγδην, dial. **μίγδᾱν** *adv.* **1** with a mixture (of two types), **both together** hHom.

2 (as prep.) mixed together, **in company** —W.DAT. *w. the Graces* Pi.*fr.*

3 indiscriminately AR.

μιγείς (aor.2 pass.ptcpl.), **μιγῄς** (Boeot.), **μιγῆναι** (aor.2 pass.inf.), **μιγήσομαι** (fut.2 pass.): see μείγνῡμι

μίγην (ep.aor.2 pass.), **μίγεν** (3pl.), **μιγῇς** (2sg.subj.), **μιγήμεναι** and **μιγῆν** (infs.): see μείγνῡμι

μῖγμα (or **μίγμα**) *n.*: see μεῖγμα

μίγνῡμι *vb.*: see μείγνῡμι

Μίδᾱς ου (also ᾱ), Ion. **Μίδης** εω *m.* **Midas** (king of Phrygia, provbl. for his wealth) Tyrt. Pi. Hdt. Pl. X. +

μιῇ, μιῆς (Ion.dat. and gen. fem.num.adj. and sb.): see εἷς

μιήνῃ (ep.3sg.aor.subj.): see μιαίνω

μιηφόνος *adj.*: see μιαιφόνος

μικκός *dial.adj.*: see μικρός

μίκκῠλος ᾱ ον *dial.adj.* [dimin. μικκός] (of a baby's hands) **tiny** Mosch.

μῑκρ-αδικητής οῦ *m.* [μῑκρός, ἀδικέω] one who commits injustice on a small scale, **petty wrongdoer** Arist.

μίκρ-ασπις ιδος *masc.adj.* [ἀσπίς¹] **with a small shield** Pl.

μῑκροδοσίᾱ ᾶς *f.* [δίδωμι] giving of small amounts, **niggardliness** Plb.

μῑκρο-κίνδῡνος ον *adj.* **braving danger for minor causes** Arist.

μῑκροληψίᾱ ᾶς *f.* [λαμβάνω] **ready acceptance of small amounts** (of money) Plb.

μῑκρολογέομαι *mid.contr.vb.* [μῑκρολόγος] **1** be preoccupied with trivial matters, **fuss over details** Lys. X. **2** be concerned over petty expenditure, **be mean** or **penny-pinching** Plu. **3** be mean-spirited —W.PREP.PHR. *towards someone* Plu.

μῑκρολογίᾱ (also **σμῑκρολογίᾱ**) ᾶς *f.* **1** preoccupation with trivial matters, **fussing over details** Pl. Arist. **2** petty thinking, pursuit of the trivial Isoc. Pl. Plu. **3** use of depreciatory language, **belittlement, disparagement** Isoc. **4** concern over petty expenditure, **meanness, penny-pinching** Plb. Plu.

μῑκρο-λόγος (also **σμῑκρολόγος**) ον *adj.* **1 preoccupied with trivial detail** Pl.; (of old age) **fussy, pernickety** Isoc. **2** concerned over petty expenditure, **mean, penny-pinching** D. Men. Plu. || MASC.SB. penny-pincher Thphr.

μῑκρό-λῡπος ον *adj.* [λύπη] (of a temperament) pained by trivialities, **easily upset, irritable** Plu.

μῑκρο-μερής (also **σμῑκρομερής**) ές *adj.* [μέρος] **consisting of small parts** Pl. Arist.

μῑκρο-πολίτης ου *m.* **citizen of a minor state** Ar. X. Aeschin. Plu.

μῑκρο-πόνηρος ον *adj.* [πονηρός] **wicked on a small scale** Arist.

μῑκροπρέπεια ᾶς *f.* [μῑκροπρεπής] **1 paltriness** (in expenditure) Arist. | see μεγαλοπρέπεια 5 **2 petty ostentation, tawdriness** Plu.

μῑκρο-πρεπής ές *adj.* [πρέπω] **1** (of a person) **shabby, mean** (in expenditure) Arist.; (of over-exact counting of costs) Arist. **2** (of literary rivalry) **undignified** Plu.

μῑκρός (also **σμῑκρός**, Aeol. **σμῑκρος**), dial. **μικκός** (A.*satyr.fr.* Ar. Call. Theoc.), ᾱ (Ion. ή) όν *adj.* | compar. (σ)μῑκρότερος, superl. (σ)μῑκρότατος || σμ- is the older form and is generally preferred in verse. Freq. w.neg., in litotes, *not small*, i.e. *great, considerable*. |
1 small in size or stature; (of persons, sts.pejor.) **small, little, short** Il. Archil. Hdt. Ar. Pl. X. +
2 (of a child) **small, little** hHom. Sapph. Alc. Eleg. E. Ar. + || MASC.SB. (w.art.) the baby A.*satyr.fr.* Men. Theoc.
3 (of animals, birds, reptiles, fish) **small, little** Il. Thgn. Hdt. +; (of the young of an animal) E.*Cyc.*
4 small in size or extent; (of concr. things, such as buildings, cities, ships, objects) **small** Od. Hes.*fr.* Archil. Hdt. Trag. Th. +; (of spears, daggers, arrows) **short** Hdt.
5 small in amount; (of food, wine, money) **little** E. Ar. X.; (of a total number of persons) **small** Hdt. E. || NEUT.SB. small amount, little (sts. W.GEN. of sthg.) Hes. Anacr. Hdt. S. E. Ar. +; (advbl.gen.) for a small amount (of money), cheaply X.; (phr.) (σ)μῑκροῦ ἄξιος *worth little* Pl. X. || NEUT.PL.SB. small amounts (of money) Lys. Isoc.; small resources or humble circumstances Pi. E. X.
6 small in degree, intensity or importance; (of abstr. things, such as misfortune, hope, an accusation, offence, tasks, situations in general) **small, slight, trivial** Thgn. Xenoph. Pi. Hdt. Trag. + || NEUT.SB. (sg. and pl.) small or trivial matter Hdt. S. E. Th. Ar. Att.orats. +
7 (of the Panathenaia) **lesser** (opp. μεγάλα *greater*) Lys.; (of the Mysteries, held at Agrai, opp. *greater*, held at Eleusis) Pl. Plu. | see μυστήρια 2
8 (of a person) of small account, **humble, lowly** Pi. S. X. Call.; (of a goddess, in neg.phr.) E.; (of ancestry) S.; (of a helper) **puny** E.
9 (of time, life) **short** Thgn. Pi. E. Ar. Isoc. Pl. +
10 (of speech) **short, brief** S. E. Pl.; (of a journey) E.
11 (prep.phrs.) ἐν (σ)μῑκρῷ *in a short space* X. Arist.; *in a short time* E. X.; *of little account* S. Plb.; ἐπὶ (σ)μῑκρόν *to a small extent or degree* Hdt. S. X. +; *for a short distance* Pl.; *in detail* Antipho; κατὰ (σ)μῑκρόν *little by little, gradually* Th. Ar. Att.orats. Pl. +; *to a small extent or degree* Att.orats. Pl. +; *in detail* Ar. Pl.; *in small pieces* X.; μετὰ μικρόν *after a short time* Arist. NT. Plu.; παρὰ (σ)μῑκρόν *to a small extent or degree* Isoc. Plb. Plu.; *all but, almost* Isoc. D. Plb. Plu.; *by a narrow margin* D. Arist. Plu.; *little by little, gradually* Arist.
12 (vbl.phrs.) παρὰ μικρὸν ἐλθεῖν *come within an inch* (W.INF. *of doing sthg.*) E. Isoc. Plb. Plu.; παρὰ μικρὸν ἡγεῖσθαι *regard as of little importance* Isoc. Plu.; (also) περὶ σμῑκροῦ ποιεῖσθαι Pl. | For μῑκροῦ δεῖν (in various phrs.) see δέω² 2, 3 and δεῖ 7 (under δέω²).

—**μῑκρόν** (**σμῑκρόν**), dial. **μικκόν** (Theoc.), also **μῑκρά** (**σμῑκρά**) *neut.sg.pl.adv.* **little, a little** (in degree, distance or time) Trag. Ar. Att.orats. Pl. +

—**μῑκροῦ** (**σμῑκροῦ**) *neut.gen.sg.adv.* **all but, almost** X. D. Men.

—**μῑκρῷ** (**σμῑκρῷ**) *neut.dat.sg.adv.* **by a small amount** (W.COMPAR.ADJ. or ADV.) Att.orats. Pl. +

—**σμῑκρῶς** *adv.* | compar. σμῑκρότερον, superl. (σ)μῑκρότατα | **1 to a small degree** Pl. || SUPERL. to the smallest degree Pl. X. **2** || COMPAR. for a shorter time Pl. **3** || SUPERL. in the smallest pieces Pl.

μῑκρότης (also **σμῑκρότης**) ητος *f.* **1 smallness** (in size or amount) Isoc. Pl. Arist. Plu. **2 smallness, insignificance** (of a city) Isoc. Plu. **3 slightness, unimportance** (of an action, event or topic) Arist. **4 inferiority** (relative to other persons) Arist. **5 pettiness** (W.GEN. of character) Plu.

μῑκρο-φιλότῑμος ου *m.* **man of petty ambition** Thphr.

μῑκροψῡχίᾱ ᾶς *f.* [μῑκρόψυχος] **meanness of spirit** (embracing such qualities as low self-esteem, lack of courage or ambition, selfishness) Isoc. D. Arist. Men.

μῑκρό-ψῡχος ον *adj.* [ψυχή] **mean-spirited** Isoc. D. Arist. Men.

μίκτο (ep.3sg.athem.aor.pass.): see μείγνῡμι

μικτός *adj.*: see μεικτός

μῖλαξ (also **σμῖλαξ**) ακος *f.* a kind of plant; perh. **bryony** E. Ar. Pl. X.

Μίλητος, dial. **Μίλᾱτος** (Theoc.), Aeol. **Μίλλᾱτος** (Theoc.), ου *f.* **Miletos** (city on the coast of Asia Minor) Il. hHom. Hippon. Hdt. +

—**Μῑλήσιος** ᾱ (Ion. η) ον *adj.* (of persons or things) of or from Miletos, **Milesian** Carm.Pop. Hdt. Th. Ar. + || FEM.SB. Milesian territory Hdt. Th. Plb. Plu. || MASC.PL.SB. Milesians (as a population or military force) Anacr. Demod. Hdt. +

—**Μῑλησιακά** ῶν *n.pl.* **Milesian tales** (a notorious work of erotic fiction, composed c.100 BC) Plu.

μίλιον ου *n.* [Lat. *mille*] distance of a thousand paces; (Roman) **mile** NT. Plu.

μιλτ-ηλιφής ές Ion.adj. [μίλτος, ἀλείφω] (of ships) **painted red** Hdt.

μιλτο-πάρῃος ον Ion.adj. [παρήιον] (of ships) **red-cheeked** (ref. to their painted prows) Hom.

μιλτό-πρεπτος ον adj. [πρεπτός] (prob. of a phallus) **conspicuously red** A.satyr.fr.

μίλτος ου f. **red ochre** (a mineral pigment, used as a body paint, cosmetic and dye) Hdt. Ar. X.

μιλτόω contr.vb. **1** ‖ MID. **smear oneself with red ochre** Hdt. **2** ‖ PASS. (of a rope, used to herd persons into the Assembly) be smeared with red ochre Ar.

μίμαρκυς υος f. dish consisting of the entrails and blood of a hare, **hare stew** Ar.

μιμέομαι mid.contr.vb. [μῖμος] | aor. ἐμιμησάμην | pf.mid.pass.ptcpl. μεμιμημένος | **1 have as one's model or follow the example of, imitate, emulate, copy** —persons, behaviour, institutions, or sim. Thgn. Hdt. E. Th. Ar. Att.orats. + **2** assume or create the features or effect of, **imitate, mimic, simulate, represent, portray** —persons, voices, sounds, appearance, behaviour, or sim. hHom. A. Pi. E. Ar. Pl. +; (specif., of poets, dramatists, artists, or sim.) Pl. Arist. Plb. Plu. **3** ‖ STAT.V.PF.MID.PASS.PTCPL. (of figures in wood or metal) serving as an imitation (of real things) Hdt.; (of columns) —W.ACC. of palm trees Hdt. **4** ‖ FUT., AOR. and PF.PASS.PTCPL. (of things) reproduced (or about to be reproduced) by imitation Pl. Arist. ‖ NEUT.PL.SB. imitations (opp. real things) Ar.

μιμηλός ή (dial. ᾱ) όν adj. (of a portrait) **giving a likeness** (of a person) Plu.(quot.)

μίμημα ατος n. (concr. or abstr., ref. to an artefact, action, process, or sim.) result or product of imitating or copying, **imitation, copy, likeness, representation** (sts. W.GEN. of someone or sthg.) A.satyr.fr. E. Pl. Aeschin. Arist. Plu.

μίμησις εως f. act or process of imitation or copying, **imitation** (sts. W.GEN. of sthg.) Hdt. Th. Ar. Pl. Arist. +; (specif., ref. to the way in which language and the arts represent their objects) Pl. Arist.

μιμητέος ᾱ ον vbl.adj. (of a person's expression) **to be imitated** or **portrayed** (in art) X.

μιμητής οῦ m. **1 imitator, emulator** (W.GEN. of exemplary people or things) Isoc. X. Plb. Plu. **2 creator of imitations** (of reality, ref. to an artist, poet or actor) Pl. Arist. **3** (pejor.) **mere imitator** (sts. W.GEN. of someone or sthg.) Pl.

μιμητικός ή όν adj. **1** (of persons, esp. poets; of speech, an art) concerned with imitation, **imitative** Pl. Arist.; (of a tragic plot, W.GEN. of things arousing pity and fear) Arist. ‖ FEM.SB. art of imitation Pl. Arist. **2** (of eagerness) **for imitation** or **emulation** (of an achievement) Plu.

μιμητός ή όν adj. (of things) **able to be imitated** or **portrayed** (in art) X.

μιμνάζω vb. [μίμνω] **1 stay, remain** (in a place) Il. AR. **2** (tr.) **wait for, await** —someone hHom.

Μίμνερμος ου m. Mimnermus (elegiac poet, fr. Smyrna, late 7th C. BC) Call. Plu.

μιμνήσκω vb. | fut. μνήσω, dial. μνάσω | aor. ἔμνησα, dial. ἔμνᾱσα, dial.2sg.subj. μνᾴσῃς | **1 cause (someone) to remember; remind** —a person Od. —(W.GEN. of sthg.) Hom. Thgn. Pi.fr. **2 remind** (someone) Theoc. —W.ACC. of sthg. E. **3 bring to the attention** (of all), **make famous** —one's ancestral home Pi.

—μιμνήσκομαι mid.vb.| pres. perh. also μνήσκομαι (Anacr., cj. μνῆσαι) | ep.3sg.impf. μιμνήσκετο, dial. μιμνάσκετο | fut. μνήσομαι, dial. μνάσομαι ‖ AOR.: ἐμνησάμην, ep.3sg. μνήσατο, dial. ἐμνάσατο | imperatv. μνῆσαι, pl. μνήσασθε | inf. μνήσασθαι, dial. μνάσασθαι | subj. μνήσωμαι, ep.1pl. μνησόμεθα | opt. μνησαίμην, ep.3pl. μνησαίατο ‖ ep.3sg.iteratv.aor. μνήσασκετο ‖ PF. (w.pres.sens.): μέμνημαι, dial. μέμνᾱμαι, 2sg. μέμνησαι, dial. μέμνᾱσαι, ep. μέμνηαι, also μέμνῃ | imperatv. μέμνησο, dial. μέμνᾱσο, Aeol. μέμναισο, Ion. μέμνεο, 2pl. μέμνησθε | inf. μεμνῆσθαι, dial. μεμνᾶσθαι | subj. μέμνωμαι, Ion.1pl. μεμνεώμεθα | opt. μεμνήμην, 3sg. μεμνῇτο ‖ PLPF. (w.impf.sens.): ἐμεμνήμην, ep.3sg. μέμνητο, ep.3pl. μέμνηντο, dial. ἐμέμνᾱντο, Ion. ἐμεμνέατο ‖ FUT.PF. (w.fut.sens.): μεμνήσομαι ‖ PASS.: fut. (w.mid.sens.) μνησθήσομαι | AOR. (usu. w.mid.sens.): ἐμνήσθην, dial. ἐμνάσθην, imperatv. μνήσθητι, dial. μνάσθητι, pl. μνήσθητε, dial. μνάσθητε |

1 recall to or retain in one's memory, remember —W.GEN. someone or sthg. Hom. + —W.ACC. Hom. hHom. Pi. Hdt. S. Att.orats. + —W.COMPL.CL. or INDIR.Q. (freq. w. preceding acc.) that (how, when, or sim.) sthg. is the case Hom. +; (w. preceding gen.) S. —W.PTCPL. (usu. aor.) doing sthg. A. E. Pl. X. + —W.PRES. or STAT.V.PF.PTCPL. that one is doing sthg. or is such and such Pi. E. —W.ACC. + PTCPL. someone doing sthg., sthg. happening E. Th. Pl. + ‖ AOR.PASS. (of things) be remembered NT.

2 (intr.) **remember** Hom. + ‖ PF.PTCPL. (quasi-advbl., esp. w.imperatv.) **without forgetting, without fail** Il. Hes. hHom. Semon. A.

3 remember, be sure —W.INF. to do sthg. Il. hHom. A. E. Ar. Pl. —w. ὅπως + FUT. Ar.

4 be mindful of, think of, pay heed to, attend to —W.GEN. activities, duties or concerns (such as food, drink, fighting, work, song, marriage) Hom. Hes. hHom. Eleg. B. Hdt.

5 (most freq. aor. or fut., esp.pass.) recall (to the memory of others, in speech or writing); **make mention of, tell of** —W.GEN. someone or sthg. Od. Pi. Hdt. Trag. Th. Ar. + —W.ACC. Od. Tyrt. Hdt. —W. περί + GEN. Hdt. Th. Att.orats. Pl. + —W. ὑπέρ + GEN. D. —W. ἀμφί + ACC. hHom.; (intr.) **mention** (sthg.) Pi. Hdt. S. +

μίμνω vb. [reltd. μένω] | only pres. and impf. | ep.dat.pl.masc.ptcpl. μιμνόντεσσι | impf. ἔμιμνον, ep. μίμνον | **1 remain, stay, wait** (in a place) Hom. Hes. hHom. B. Trag. Hellenist.poet. **2 remain** (in an unchanged condition); (of treasures) **remain** —W.PREDIC.ADJ. safe Hom. ‖ IMPERS. it remains (as a divine ordinance) —W.ACC. + INF. that the doer must suffer A. **3** (of a warrior, his heart) **hold fast** or **firm** (in the face of the enemy) Il. A.; (of a personif. river, in a threatening situation) Call.; (of a person, in testing circumstances) Thgn. **4** (tr.) await the attack of, **stand up to, face** —an enemy Il.; (of trees) **withstand** —wind and rain Il.; (of a rock) —waves AR. **5** (tr.) **wait for, await** —persons, a particular circumstance or time Hom. Hes. Thgn. B. Ion S.; (intr.) **wait** —W.CL. until sthg. happens Od. —W.ACC. + INF. for sthg. to happen AR. **6** (of sufferings) **await, be in store** AR.; (of murder) —W.DAT. for someone A.

μῖμος ου m. (also f. Plu.) **1 imitator** (of the sound of bulls, ref. to a bull-roarer) A.fr. [or perh. imitation, as 2] **2** act of imitating, **imitation** (of an animal's posture) E. **3 mime** (a dramatic sketch mimicking scenes of everyday life) Arist.

μῖμῳδός

4 (pejor.) **performer** (W.GEN. of comic routines) D.
5 (usu. in Roman ctxt.) **actor** (or perh.specif. *mime-actor*; oft. seen as a person of ill-repute) Plu.; (fem., appos.w. γυνή *woman*) Plu.

μῑμ-ῳδός οῦ *m*. [ἀοιδή] **mime-singer** Plu.

μιν dial.3sg.enclit.acc.pers.pron. [reltd. νιν] **1 him, her, it** Hom. Hes. Iamb. Eleg. Lyr. Hdt. +; (ref. to pl. δώματα *house*) Od.
2 (reflexv., in subordinate cl., ref. to subject of main cl.) **himself, herself** Hdt.; (also w. αὐτόν, αὐτήν) Hdt.; (w. αὐτόν, in main cl.) Od.

μίνθη ης Ion.*f*. a kind of plant, **mint** Hippon.

μινθόω contr.vb. [μίνθος *excrement*] **befoul with excrement, shit on** —*a rower on the bench below* Ar.; **rub** (W.ACC. someone's nose) **in shit** Ar.

Μινύαι ῶν (Ion. έων, dial. ᾶν) *m.pl*. **Minyans** (ancient inhabitants of Orkhomenos in Boeotia, also of Iolkos in Thessaly) Pi. Hdt. E.; (ref. to the Argonauts) Pi. Call. AR.
—**Μινύᾱς** ᾱ dial.*m*. —also **Μινύης** ᾱο ep.Ion.*m*. **Minyas** (eponymous king, assoc.w. both places) Pi. AR.
—**Μινύειος** ᾱ (dial. ᾰ) ον, Ion. **Μινυήιος** η ον adj. (of Orkhomenos) **Minyan** Hom. Hes.*fr*. Th. Theoc.; (of a person) AR. ∥ FEM.SB. land of the Minyans Pi.
—**Μινυηιάδης** ᾱο ep.Ion.*m*. Ion.*f*. **son of Minyas** Hes.*fr*.
—**Μινυηίς** ίδος Ion.*f*. **daughter of Minyas** AR.

μινύθω vb. [reltd. μείων] | also μινύθω (B.) | only pres., except for dial.impf. μίνυθον (B., cj.), ep.iteratv.impf. μινύθεσκον | **1 make less or smaller**; (of gods, esp. Zeus) **diminish, weaken, humble** —*people, strength, valour, households* Il. Hes.
2 **make fewer, deplete** —*pigs* (by eating them) Od.
3 (intr., of houses, farmlands, the fruits of the earth) **be ruined** Il. Hes.*fr*.; (of households, cultivation) **decline** Hes.
4 (of springs) **fail** S.
5 (of summer nights) **grow short** Theoc.
6 (of a person or deity) **waste away** —W.DAT. w. *longing or despair* hHom. AR.; (of the heart or spirit) **grow weak** (in adversity) Od. Thgn. A.
7 (of life) **fade away, dwindle** B.(cj.); (of the light of excellence) B.; (of self-conceit) A.; (of hostile speech) B.

μίνυνθα adv. **for a short time** Hom. Mimn. AR.

μινυνθάδιος ᾱ (Ion. η) ον adj. **1** (of life, sorrow, sickness, sleep) lasting for a short time, **short, brief** Il. AR.
2 (of persons) **short-lived** Hom.

μινυρίγματα των *n.pl*. [app. μινυρίζω] (ref. to a dish, served hot) app. **warblings** (perh.ref. to birds) Philox.Leuc.

μινυρίζω vb. **1 whimper, whine** (in grief or complaint) Hom.
2 **make melodic sounds, sing, hum, warble** Ar. Pl. Plu. —W.ACC. *tunes* Ar.

μινυρίσματα των *n.pl*. **warblings** (of birds) Lyr.adesp. Theoc.*epigr*.

μινύρομαι mid.vb. **1** (of a person) **hum** (opp. *sing*) A. —*a tune* Ar.
2 (of a nightingale) **sing, warble** S.
3 **lament, sob** Call.

μινυρός ά όν adj. **1** (of young birds) **twittering, cheeping** Theoc.
2 ∥ NEUT.PL.SB. **whimperings** (of a person) A.

Μίνως ω (ep. ωος) *m*. | acc. Μίνω, also Μίνων, Μίνωα | dat. Μίνῳ, ep. Μίνωι | **Minos** (legendary king of Crete, husband of Pasiphae, judge in the underworld) Hom. +
—**Μῑνωίς** ίδος fem.adj. **of or relating to Minos**; (of a girl, ref. to his daughter Ariadne) **Minoan** Call. AR.; (of Crete; of other islands under his rule, ref. to the Cyclades) AR.; (of Athena, as worshipped on Crete) AR.
—**Μῑνώιος** ον adj. (of Knossos) **Minoan** hHom.; (of the sea around Crete) AR.

Μῑνώ-ταυρος ου *m*. [ταῦρος] **Minotaur** (monster, half-bull, half-man, offspring of the union of a bull w. Pasiphae) Plu.

μιξέλληνες *m.pl*., **μιξεριφαρνογενής** adj.: see μειξ-
μίξις *f*.: see μεῖξις
μιξοβάρβαρος adj.: see μειξοβάρβαρος
μιξ-οδίη ης Ion.*f*. [μείγνυμι, ὁδός] **place where ways meet, cross-roads, meeting-point** (W.GEN. of the sea, ref. to the Strait of Messina) AR.(pl.)
μιξολῡδιστί adv., **μιξοπάρθενος** adj.: see μειξ-
μῑσαγαθίᾱ ᾱς *f*. [μισέω, ἀγαθός] **disdain for morality** Plu.
μῖσ-αθήναιος ον adj. [Ἀθῆναι] **Athens-hating** Lycurg. D.
μῖσ-αλέξανδρος ον adj. **Alexander-hating** Aeschin.
μῑσανθρωπίᾱ ᾱς *f*. [μισάνθρωπος] **hatred of mankind, misanthropy** Isoc. Pl. D.
μῖσ-άνθρωπος ον adj. **hating mankind, misanthropic** Isoc. Pl. Plu.

μισγ-άγκεια ᾱς (Ion. ης) *f*. [μίσγω, ἄγκος] **place where valleys meet** Il.; (fig., where different kinds of knowledge meet) Pl.

μίσγω vb.: see μείγνυμι

μῖσ-έλλην ηνος masc.adj. [μισέω, Ἕλλην] (of foreigners) **having a hatred of Greeks, anti-Greek** X. Plu.

μῑσέω contr.vb. | aor. ἐμίσησα | pf. μεμίσηκα ∥ PASS.: fut. μισήσομαι | aor. ἐμισήθην | pf. μεμίσημαι | **1 hate, detest, loathe, resent** —*persons or things* Lyr. Trag. Th. Ar. Att.orats. + ∥ STATV.PF. **have come to hate** —*someone* Ar. Pl. Thphr. ∥ PASS. **be hated** Hdt. Trag. Th. Ar. Att.orats. + ∥ STATV.PF.PASS. **have come to be hated** Isoc.
2 **hate, be appalled by** —W.ACC. + INF. (the thought) that sthg. shd. happen Il. —W.INF. (someone) doing sthg. E.
3 (in neg.phr.) **hate, spite** —*a city* (w. τὸ μὴ οὐ + INF. so as to deny that it is such and such) Ar.

μίσημα ατος *n*. (ref. to women, Erinyes) **object of hatred or loathing** (sts. W.GEN. or DAT. to someone) Trag.

μισητέος ᾱ ον vbl.adj. **to be hated** X.

μισητίᾱ ᾱς *f*. **immoderate desire** (for possessions), **avarice, greed** Ar.

μισητός ή όν adj. (of persons, their characters, behaviour, activities) **hateful, detestable, loathsome** Archil. A. Pl. X. Arist. Thphr. Plb.

μισθάριον ου *n*. [dimin. μισθός] **miserable fee** (for jury service) Ar.

μισθαρνέω contr.vb. [μισθός, ἄρνυμαι] **1 earn a fee** or **wage** Pl. Arist.
2 (pejor.) **work for hire** (w.connot. of receiving underhand payment or sim.) S. Att.orats. Plu.; (ref. to prostitution) Aeschin. D.

μισθαρνητικός ή όν adj. (of an activity) **of the kind that earns a fee or wage, paid** Pl. ∥ FEM.SB. **art of wage-earning** Pl.

μισθαρνίᾱ ᾱς *f*. **1 wage-earning** (of a labourer) Arist.; **fee-earning** (of a legal specialist) Plu.
2 (pejor.) **working for hire** D.
3 **mercenariness** (ref. to marrying a rich wife) Plu.

μισθαρνικός ή όν adj. (of crafts or occupations) **wage-earning** Arist.

μισθ-αρχίδης ου *m*. [ἄρχω] **one who holds a paid public office, paid officer** Ar.

μίσθιος ᾱ ον adj. (of persons, carriages) **hired** Plu. ∥ MASC.SB. **hired workman** NT.

μισθοδοσίᾱ ᾱς *f.* [μισθοδότης] **payment of wages** (to troops or mercenaries) Th. X. Plb.

μισθοδοτέω *contr.vb.* **provide pay** (for troops or mercenaries) X. D. Plb. Plu. —W.DAT. *for mercenaries* X. D.; (tr.) **pay** —*troops* Plb. Plu.; (pejor.) **have in one's pay** —*politicians* D. ‖ PASS. (of public officials, troops or mercenaries) **be paid** Plb.

μισθο-δότης ου, dial. **μισθοδότᾱς** ᾱ *m.* [δίδωμι] **one who provides pay, paymaster** (of employees) Pl.; (of troops, esp. mercenaries) X. Theoc. Plb. Plu.; (pejor., ref. to a person who buys the loyalty or military support of others) Aeschin. Plb. Plu.

μισθός οῦ *m.* **1 hired service** Il.
2 wage, pay (for hired service) Hom. Hes.(dub.) Pi. Hdt. Ar. Pl. +
3 pay (for troops, sailors, mercenaries) Th. Ar. Att.orats. Pl. +; (for public officials, jurymen, or sim.) Th. Ar. Att.orats. Pl. +; **payment, grant** (to disabled citizens) Aeschin.
4 payment (for a specific task or purchase) Hom. Pi. Hdt. S. E. Th. +
5 fee (for one who performs a professional service, such as a doctor, poet, diviner, teacher, craftsman, prostitute) Thgn. Pi. Hdt. E. Ar. Isoc. +
6 non-material return, reward Pi. E. Isoc. Pl. +; (iron., esp.ref. to punishment or death) A. Hdt. S. Pl.

μισθοφορᾱ́ ᾶς *f.* [μισθοφόρος] **receipt of pay or pay received; payment, pay** (esp. for military or public service) Th. Ar. Att.orats. X. Arist. Plu.

μισθοφορέω *contr.vb.* **1 earn or receive a wage, fee or payment**; (of an estate-manager) **earn a wage** X.; (of a doctor) **receive fees** Ar.; (of public officials, jurymen, or sim.) **be paid** Th. Ar. D. Arist. —W.ACC. *a sum of money* Arist. —*w. public money* Ar. —*w. the money of corrupt politicians* Lys.; (of a disabled citizen) **receive a grant** Aeschin.
2 (of troops or sailors) **draw pay, be paid** Ar. Arist. —W.ACC. *at a certain rate* Ar. —*groats* (i.e. rations) Ar.
3 (specif.) **serve for pay, be a mercenary** X. D. Plb. Plu.
4 (pejor., of a politician) **receive pay** —w. παρά + GEN. *fr. a foreign ruler* D.
5 (of houses, draught animals, slaves) **bring in income** (fr. being let or hired out) X. Is. ‖ PASS. (of money) **be raised through rental or hire** X.

μισθοφορίᾱ ᾱς *f.* **receipt of pay, payment** (for military or public service) Pl. X. D.

μισθοφορικός ή όν *adj.* (of military forces) **serving for pay, hired, mercenary** Plb. ‖ NEUT.SB. **mercenary force** Plb.

μισθο-φόρος ον *adj.* [φέρω] **1** (of public service) **earning pay, paid, remunerated** Arist.; (of warships) perh. **pay-earning** (i.e. collecting tribute, used to pay troops or public officials) Ar.
2 (of troops) **serving for pay, hired, mercenary** Th. X. D. Plu.; (of a peltast, fig.ref. to a disputant) Pl. ‖ MASC.PL.SB. **mercenaries** Th. Isoc. Pl. X. D. Arist. +; (also sg.) X. Plu.
3 (pejor., of persons) **for hire, paid** Isoc. D. ‖ MASC.PL.SB. **paid henchmen, hirelings** Aeschin. D.
4 (of a marriage) **made for financial gain, mercenary** Plu.

μισθόω *contr.vb.* **1 let out (for rent), let, lease** —*land, property, a house, a business* (sts. W.DAT. *to someone*) Att.orats. Arist. ‖ MID. **have let out to oneself, rent, take out a lease on** —*land, a house, or sim.* Hdt. Att.orats. X. Arist. Plu. ‖ PASS. (of property) **be leased or rented out** Is. D. Plu.
2 hire out —*ships, slaves, troops, or sim.* (sts. W.DAT. *to someone*) Ar. Hyp. D. Arist. Thphr. —(pejor.) **oneself** (i.e. sell one's loyalty) D. Din. ‖ MID. **hire for oneself, hire**

—*mercenaries, workmen, slaves, ships, equipment, or sim.* Hdt. Th. Ar. Att.orats. Pl. X. + —*a person* (W.INF. *to do sthg.*) Hdt. Aeschin. D. ‖ PASS. (of persons) **be hired** Hdt. Att.orats. Pl. +
3 contract out, farm out —W.INF. *the building of a temple* Hdt. —W.ACC. *a trierarchy* (i.e. pay someone to perform it) D. —W.COGN.ACC. *contracts* Arist. ‖ MID. **contract for** —W.INF. *the building of a temple* Hdt. —W.ACC. *a trierarchy* D.

μίσθωμα ατος *n.* **1 financial arrangement** (for the performance of work), **contract** Isoc. D. Arist.
2 price agreed on for a contract, cost (of building a temple) Hdt.
3 cost of hiring, fee (of a prostitute) Plu.
4 (concr.) **rented house** NT.

μίσθωσις εως *f.* **1 hiring** or **letting** (as a transaction) Pl. Arist.
2 hire (of a male prostitute) Aeschin.; (W.GEN. of ships) D.
3 lease, rental (of land, property, or sim.) Is. D. Arist. Plu.
4 rental payment, rent Ar. Att.orats. Pl. Arist.; **income** (fr. the lease or property or sim.) Is. D.
5 hire-cost (of slaves) D.; (W.GEN. of soldiers) Lys.
6 contract (for building projects or sim.) Plu.

μισθωτής οῦ *m.* **one who takes a lease** (on property), **lessee, tenant** Is. D.

μισθωτικός ή όν *adj.* (of the art) **of wage-earning** Pl. ‖ FEM.SB. **art of wage-earning** Pl.

μισθωτός ή όν *adj.* **1** (of troops) **hired, mercenary** Hdt. Th. Isoc. Pl.
2 (of a house) **rented** X. Thphr.
3 ‖ MASC.SB. (usu.pl., sts.pejor.) **wage-earner, employee, hired worker** Ar. Att.orats. Pl. Thphr. Men. +
4 ‖ MASC.SB. (pejor.) **hireling** (ref. to one who sells his loyalty) D. Din.; (W.GEN. of a person) D.

μισο-βάρβαρος ον *adj.* [μισέω] (of the character of a city) **hating foreigners, anti-barbarian** Pl.

μισοδημίᾱ ᾱς *f.* [μισόδημος] **hatred of democracy** And. Lys.

μισό-δημος ον *adj.* [δῆμος] **hating the people, anti-democratic** Att.orats. Pl. X. Plu.; (in Roman ctxt., of a leader) **hostile to the common people** Plu. ‖ MASC.SB. **enemy of the people, anti-democrat** Ar.

μισό-θεος ον *adj.* [θεός] (of a house) **god-hating** A.

μισό-θηρος ον *adj.* [θήρᾱ] ‖ NEUT.SB. **hatred of hunting** X.

μισο-καῖσαρ αρος *masc.adj.* **hating Caesar, anti-Caesar** Plu.

μισο-λάκων ωνος *masc.adj.* **hating Laconians, anti-Spartan** Ar.

μισο-λάμαχος ον *adj.* (of a day) **hating Lamakhos, anti-Lamakhos** Ar.

μισολογίᾱ ᾱς *f.* [μισόλογος] **hatred of argument** Pl.

μισό-λογος ον *adj.* [λόγος] **hating argument** or **discussion** Pl.

μισο-πέρσης ου *m.* [Πέρσαι] **hater of Persians** X.

μισό-πολις εως *masc.fem.adj.* [πόλις] **hating the city** (of Athens) Ar.

μισοπονέω *contr.vb.* [πόνος] **hate work** Pl.

μισοπονηρέω *contr.vb.* [μισοπόνηρος] **be a hater of wrongdoers** or **wrongdoing** Lys. Plb.

μισοπονηρίᾱ ᾱς *f.* **hatred of wrongdoing** Plu.

μισο-πόνηρος ον *adj.* [πονηρός] **hating wrongdoers** or **wrongdoing** Aeschin. D. Men. Plu. ‖ NEUT.SB. **hatred of wrongdoing** Plb.

—**μισοπονήρως** *adv.* **with severity towards wrongdoing** Plb.

μισο-πορπᾱκίστατος η ον *superl.adj.* [πόρπᾱξ] (of Eirene) **with bitterest hatred of the shield-band** Ar.

μισο-ρρώμαιος ον *adj.* [Ῥωμαῖοι, Ῥώμη] (of an action) **showing hatred of Rome** or **the Romans** Plu.

μῖσος εος (ους) n. [μῑσέω] **1 hate, hatred, loathing, detestation** (freq. W.GEN. or PREP.PHR. for persons or things) Hdt. Trag. Th. Ar. Att.orats. Pl. + ‖ PL. **feelings of hatred** Pl. D. Plu.
2 (ref. to a person, freq.voc.) **object of hatred, hateful creature** Alc. Trag.
μῑσό-σοφος ον adj. [σοφός] **hating wisdom, anti-philosophical** Pl.
μῑσο-σύλλας ου masc.adj. **hating Sulla, anti-Sulla** Plu.
μῑσοτεκνίᾱ ᾱς f. [μῑσότεκνος] **hatred of one's children** Plu.
μῑσό-τεκνος ον adj. [τέκνον] **child-hating** Aeschin.
μῑσο-τύραννος ον adj. (of a person or city) **tyrant-hating** Hdt. Aeschin. Plu. ‖ NEUT.SB. **hatred of tyrants** Plu.
μῑσο-φίλιππος ον adj. (of Demosthenes) **Philip-hating** Aeschin.
μῑσό-χρηστος ον adj. [χρηστός] **hating the better class of person** X.
μιστύλλω vb. | ep.impf. μίστυλλον | aor. ἐμίστῡλα (Semon.) | **cut up** —meat (for roasting) Hom. Semon.
μίτος ου m. **1 warp-thread** (on the loom) Il.
2 thread (spun by a spider) E.fr.
3 (fig.phr.) κατὰ μίτον **thread by thread, one thread after another** (ref. to the forty books of a historical work, envisaged as warp-threads, being woven together to form a connected whole) Plb.
μίτρᾱ ᾱς, Ion. **μίτρη** ης f. **1 metal covering** (protecting the lower part of a warrior's body, perh. hung fr. a belt), **metal waist-guard** Il.
2 waist-band (of a woman or goddess, equiv. to ζώνη) Hes.fr. hHom. Hellenist.poet.
3 headband (worn by women) Alcm. E. Ar. Men. Plu.; (worn by oriental men) Hdt.; (worn by victorious athletes) Pi. B. E.; (W.ADJ. Lydian, fig.ref. to a victory-song in the Lydian mode) Pi.
4 app. **diadem** (of an Egyptian king) Call.
5 fillet (worn by sacrificial oxen) Plu.
6 breast-band (worn by a woman) AR.
7 belt (of bronze, worn in ritual dances by priests of Mars) Plu.
8 (gener.) **band** (used to strap on a quiver) AR.
μιτράνᾱ ᾱς dial.f. **headband** (worn by a woman) Sapph.
μιτρη-φόρος ον Ion.adj. [φέρω] (of an oriental man) **wearing a headband** Hdt.
μιτροφορέω contr.vb. **wear a headband** Ar.
Μιτυλήνη f., **Μιτυληναῖος** adj.: see Μυτιλήνη
μίτυλος ᾱ ον dial.adj. (of a goat) perh. **with small horns** Theoc.
μιτώδης ες adj. [μίτος] (of a noose of cloth) **made from woven threads, woven** S.
μιχθήμεναι (ep.aor.pass.inf.), **μίχθην** (ep.aor.pass.): see μείγνῡμι
μνᾶ ᾶς f. [Semit.loanwd.] | PL.: nom. μναῖ, Ion. μνέαι | acc. μνᾶς, Ion. μνέᾱς | gen. μνῶν, Ion. μνέων ‖ du.gen.dat. μναῖν | **mna, mina** (unit of weight, also the same weight of silver as a unit of currency, equiv. to 100 drachmas, approx. 430g or one sixtieth of a talent) Hippon. Hdt. Th. +
μναῖος (also perh. **μνιαῖος**) ᾱ ον adj. **1** (of a stone) **weighing a mina** X.
2 (of a salary) **of one mina** Plb.
μνάμᾱ dial.f., **μνᾶμα** dial.n., **μναμήιον** dial.n.: see μνήμη, μνῆμα, μνημεῖον
Μναμόνᾱ Lacon.f.: see under μνημοσύνη
μναμοσύνᾱ dial.f.: see μνημοσύνη
μνάμων dial.adj.: see μνήμων

μνάομαι mid.contr.vb. [reltd. μιμνήσκω] | ep.2sg. (w.diect.) μνάᾳ, 3sg. μνᾶται, 1pl. μνώμεθα, 3pl. μνῶνται | ptcpl. μνώμενος, ep. (w.diect.) μνωόμενος | imperatv. μνώεο (AR.), 3sg. μνάσθω | inf. μνᾶσθαι, ep. (w.diect.) μνάασθαι ‖ IMPF.: 3sg. ἐμνᾶτο, ep. μνᾶτο, 3pl. ἐμνῶντο, ep. (w.diect.) ἐμνώοντο, also μνώοντο | 3sg.iteratv.impf. μνάσκετο |
1 recall to one's memory, remember —W.GEN. a person or event Hellenist.poet. —W.ACC. a name AR.; (intr.) Od.
2 think of, have a mind for —W.GEN. war, flight, sleep, work, food and drink Il. AR.; **turn one's thoughts** —W.ADV. to flight Il.
3 think over —W.COMPL.CL. what has happened AR.(v.l. μύρομαι)
4 seek (as a wife), **woo** —a woman Od. hHom. Hdt. Hellenist.poet. Plu.; (intr.) **be a wooer, go wooing** Od. Hes.fr. Anacr.
5 solicit —a husband (W.DAT. for one's daughter) Plu.; (fig.) —a kind master Plu.; **propose** —marriage Plu.
6 seek eagerly, court, sue for, solicit —public distinction Pi.fr. —power, kingship, an office, a triumph, a war (i.e. charge of it) Hdt. Plu. —reconciliation and friendship Plu.
μνάσασθαι (dial.aor.mid.inf.), **μνάσθητε, μνάσθητι** (dial.2pl. and 2sg.aor.pass.imperatv.): see μιμνήσκομαι, under μιμνήσκω
μνᾱσιδωρέω dial.contr.vb. [μιμνήσκω, δῶρον] **remember to bring gifts** (for the gods) D.(oracle)
μνάσομαι (dial.fut.mid.): see μιμνήσκομαι, under μιμνήσκω
μνάστειρα dial.f., **μναστήρ** dial.m.: see μνηστήρ
μναστεύω dial.vb.: see μνηστεύω
μνᾶστις dial.f.: see μνῆστις
μνάσω (dial.fut.), **μνάσῃς** (dial.2sg.aor.subj.): see μιμνήσκω
μνέαι (Ion.nom.fem.pl.): see μνᾶ
μνείᾱ ᾱς f. [μιμνήσκομαι, under μιμνήσκω] **1 faculty of remembering, memory** Isoc.
2 action or fact of remembering or thinking about (sthg.); **recollection, memory** (W.GEN. of persons or things) E. Ar. Isoc. Pl. Arist.; (W.COMPL.CL. of how sthg. is done) Men.; **consideration** (W.GEN. for one's present life) S.
3 act of recalling (in speech or writing); **mention** (usu. W.GEN. or περί + GEN. of someone or sthg.) E. Att.orats. Pl. Arist. Plb.
μνέων (Ion.fem.gen.pl.): see μνᾶ
μνῆμα, dial. **μνᾶμα**, ατος n. **1** (ref. to a physical object or place) **that which reminds, reminder, record, memorial** (usu. W.GEN. of persons, things, events) Hom. Sapph. Thgn. Pi. S. E. Th.(quot.epigr.); (ref. to a place-name) A.; (ref. to a song of praise) Pi.; (ref. to circumstances) S.
2 (specif.) **monument** or **tomb** (of a dead person) Hippon. Hdt. E. Att.orats. Pl. X. +
3 (abstr.) **remembrance, memory** (W.GEN. of sthg.) Thgn.
μνημεῖον, Ion. **μνημήιον**, dial. **μνᾱμήιον**, ου n. **1** (ref. to a physical object) **that which reminds, reminder, record, memorial** (usu. W.GEN. of persons or things) Hdt. Trag. Th. Ar. Att.orats. Pl. +; (ref. to a song of praise) Pi.; (ref. to an event, achievement or circumstance) E. Lys. Isoc. Pl. X.
2 (specif.) **monument** or **tomb** (of a dead person) Th. Pl. X. Lycurg. NT. Plu.
3 record (imprinted on the mind) Pl.
μνήμη ης, dial. **μνᾶμᾱ** ᾱς f. **1 power** or **faculty of remembering, memory** A. S. Th. Pl. X. +
2 (personif., as mother of the Muses) **Memory** Lyr.adesp.
3 action or fact of remembering or thinking about (sthg.); **recollection, memory** (of persons or things) Thgn. Hdt. S. E. Th. Ar.; (specif.) **affectionate remembrance** (of absent friends) X.

4 perpetuated knowledge or recollection, **remembrance, memory** (esp. of the dead, their virtues or achievements) A. Hdt. E. Th. Att.orats. Pl. +
5 collective memory of the past, **memory, record, tradition** Hdt. Th. X.
6 that which perpetuates a memory, **reminder, record, memorial** (in written form) Pl. Arist. Call.
7 act of recalling (in speech or writing), **mention** (freq. W.GEN. of persons or things) Hdt. E. Th. Pl. +; (w. περί or ὑπέρ + GEN.) Plb.; (W.INDIR.Q. of what is the case) Hdt.

μνημόνευμα ατος *n.* [μνημονεύω] means of remembering, **reminder, record** (W.GEN. of a place) Men.

μνημονευτός ή όν *adj.* (of dead persons, things) **remembered** or **worthy of being remembered** Hyp. ‖ NEUT.PL.SB. things remembered, recollections Arist.

μνημονεύω *vb.* [μνήμη] | fut.pass. μνημονευθήσομαι, also μνημονεύσομαι (E.) ‖ neut.impers.vbl.adj. μνημονευτέον |
1 recall to or retain in one's memory, **remember** —*someone or sthg.* Hdt. Trag. Att.orats. Pl. + —W.GEN. Isoc. X. Hyp. Arist. Plb. NT. —W.COMPL.CL. or INDIR.Q. *when sthg. happened, what* (*that sthg., or sim.*) *is the case* S. Att.orats. Pl. + —W.ACC. + PTCPL. Att.orats. + ‖ PASS. (of persons or things) be remembered E. Th. Att.orats. Pl. + ‖ NEUT.PTCPL.SB. (w.art.) long remembered or celebrated remark Plu.
2 (intr.) **remember** Isoc. Pl. Arist. +
3 remember —W.INF. *to do sthg.* Ar.
4 give a reminder of —*sthg.* Pl.
5 perpetuate knowledge or recollection of, **record** —*events* Hyp. —W.ACC. + PTCPL. *sthg. as being the case* X. Plu. ‖ PASS. (of persons) be recorded Arist.; (of an event) —W.INF. *as having happened* Th.; (of a war) —W.PTCPL. *as having been well fought* Pl.
6 repeat from memory —*someone's words* Isoc.
7 recall (to the memory of others, in speech or writing), **make mention of, tell of** —W.GEN. *someone or sthg.* Plu. —w. περί or ὑπέρ + GEN. Plb.

μνημονικός ή όν *adj.* [μνήμων] **1** (of persons) **having a good memory, good at memorising** Ar. Pl. X. Aeschin. D. Plu.; (of the mind) **retentive** Pl. ‖ NEUT.SB. good memory X.
2 (of a technique) **for memorising** Pl. ‖ NEUT.SB. art of memorising, memory technique Pl. X.

—**μνημονικῶς** *adv.* with a good memory, accurately from memory Pl. X. Aeschin. D.

μνημοσύνη ης, dial. **μναμοσύνα** ᾶς *f.* **1** act of bearing in mind, **mindfulness, thought** (W.GEN. of sthg.) Il.
2 act of recalling to the mind, **remembering, recollection, memory** Xenoph. Pi. Critias; (W.GEN. of a person) Sapph.; (of a place) E.*fr.*

—**Μνημοσύνη** ης, dial. **Μναμοσύνα**, Lacon. **Μναμόνα** (Ar.), ᾶς *f.* **Mnemosyne, Memory** (mother of the Muses) Hes. hHom. Sol. Lyr. E. Ar. Pl.

μνημόσυνον ου *n.* **1** that which acts as a permanent reminder (of persons or their actions); (ref. to a physical object) **memorial, record** (sts. W.GEN. of a person or event) Hdt. Th.; (ref. to prayers, offerings) NT.; (ref. to a building) **monument** Hdt. Th.
2 (ref. to a situation or circumstance) **record, reminder** Hdt.
3 written record (of speech), **memorandum** Ar.
4 state of remembering, **memory, remembrance** NT.

μνήμων, dial. **μνάμων**, ον, gen. ονος *adj.* [μιμνήσκομαι, under μιμνήσκω] **1** (of a person) **possessing a good memory** Ar. Pl. Plb.
2 clear in recollection (of sthg.) Od.

3 not forgetful, mindful (of services rendered) Ar. X.; (W.GEN. of agreements) Plu.
4 (of a ship's captain) **mindful, heedful** (W.GEN. of his cargo) Od.
5 (of Wrath) **unforgetting** A.; (of Erinyes) **ever-mindful** A. S.; (W.GEN. of wrongs) A.
6 (of the writing-tablets of the mind) preserving a memory or record, **recording** A.
7 ‖ MASC.SB. (as the title of an official) **recorder, registrar** Arist.

μνῆσαι (aor.mid.imperatv.), **μνήσασθαι** (aor.mid.inf.), **μνησάσκετο** (3sg.iteratv.aor.mid.), **μνήσατο** (ep.3sg.aor.mid.), **μνησθήσομαι** (fut.pass.), **μνήσθητι** (aor.pass.imperatv.): see μιμνήσκομαι, under μιμνήσκω

μνησικακέω *contr.vb.* [μνησίκακος] **1** remember past injuries, **harbour a grudge** or **grievance, bear malice** Hdt. Th. Ar. Att.orats. X. Arist. + —W.DAT. *against someone* Th. Att.orats. + —w. πρός + ACC. Aeschin. D. —W.GEN. *over sthg.* Antipho Lys. —w. περί + GEN. Isoc. —W.ACC. Ar.(dub.) —W.DAT. (or πρός + ACC.) + GEN. *against someone, over sthg.* And. X. Arist.
2 recall past sufferings —W.DAT. *to someone* Pl.

μνησικακίᾱ ᾱς *f.* memory of past injuries, **feeling of grievance, resentment** Plu.

μνησί-κακος ον *adj.* [κακός] **remembering past injuries, harbouring a grudge** or **grievance, bearing malice, resentful** Arist.

μνησι-πήμων ον, gen. ονος *adj.* [πῆμα] (of pain) **bringing a reminder of past suffering** A.

μνήσκομαι *mid.vb.*, **μνήσομαι** (fut.mid.): see μιμνήσκομαι, under μιμνήσκω

μνηστείᾱ ᾱς *f.* [μνηστεύω] **proposal of marriage** (W.GEN. to a woman) Plu.

μνηστεύματα των *n.pl.* **wooing, courtship** E.; (W.GEN. of a woman) E.

μνηστεύω, dial. **μναστεύω** *vb.* [μιμνήσκομαι, μνάομαι] | pf.pass.ptcpl. ἐμνηστευμένος (v.l. μεμν-) (NT.) | **1** (of a man) seek marriage with, **woo, court** —*a woman* Od. Hes.*fr.* E. Isoc. Theoc. Plu.(mid.) —(W.INF. *to take in marriage*) X.; (intr.) **be a suitor** Od. Thgn. ‖ PASS. be wooed E. Isoc.; be betrothed —W.DAT. *to someone* NT.
2 solicit —*a marriage* Pl. Call.
3 (of a mother) **woo, seek** —*a wife* (*for her son*) Stesich.; **solicit** —*a marriage* (*for her daughter*) E.(dub., cj. μαστεύω); (of the Muses, for a son of Apollo) AR.
4 (fig.) **sue for, solicit** —*votes* Isoc.; (mid.) —*sole rule, a war* (i.e. *command of it*) Plu.
5 ‖ MID. seek, be eager —W.INF. *to rule* Plu.

μνηστήρ, dial. **μναστήρ**, ῆρος *m.* **1 wooer, suitor** (of a woman) Od. Hes.*fr.* Thgn. Pi. Hdt. S. +; (W.GEN. for marriage) A.; (fig., ref. to a people) **lover** (W.GEN. of war) Pi.
2 (ref. to a tune) **reminder, prompter of thoughts** (W.GEN. of contests) Pi.

—**μνάστειρα** ᾱς *dial.f.* (ref. to the ripeness of youth) **prompter of thoughts** (W.GEN. of Aphrodite) Pi.

μνῆστις εως, dial. **μνᾶστις** ιος *f.* [μιμνήσκομαι, under μιμνήσκω] **1** act of bearing in mind, **thought** (sts. W.GEN. of someone or sthg.) Od. Hdt. AR.
2 action or fact of remembering, **recollection, memory** (usu. W.GEN. of someone or sthg.) Alcm. Simon. S. AR.
3 power or faculty of remembering, **memory** (W.GEN. of all things) AR.
4 act of recalling (to another), **reminder** (W.GEN. of someone) Theoc.

μνηστός ή όν *adj.* [μνάομαι] (of a wife) won by wooing, **wedded** Hom. ‖ FEM.SB. wedded wife AR. ‖ FEM.PL.SB. women wooed (by a god) hHom.

μνηστύς ύος *f.* | *acc.* μνηστύν | **wooing** Od.

μνήστωρ ορος *masc.adj.* [μιμνήσκομαι, under μιμνήσκω] (of gods) **mindful, heedful** (W.GEN. of sacrificial rites) A.

μνήσω (fut.): see μιμνήσκω

μνιόεις εσσα εν *adj.* [μνίον *a kind of seaweed*] (of clumps) **of seaweed** AR.

μνοΐα ᾱς *dial.f.* [reltd. δμώς] (collectv.sg.) **public slaves** or **serfs** (on Crete) Scol.

μνωόμενος (ep.ptcpl.), **μνώοντο** (ep.3pl.impf.): see μνάομαι

μογερός ά όν *adj.* [μόγος] **1** afflicted with pain and toil; (of Prometheus) **suffering, careworn** AR.; (gener., of persons) **wretched, miserable** A. E. Ar.; (of a house) S.; (of a pregnant hare, about to be killed) A.
2 bringing or entailing pain and toil; (of Fate, sorrows) **grievous, painful** A. E.; (of labour) **wearying** AR.

μογέω *contr.vb.* | Lacon.1pl. μογίομες (Ar.), dial. μογεῦμες (Bion) | iteratv.impf. μογέεσκον | ep.aor. μόγησα | **1 toil, labour** Il. Hellenist.poet. —W.NEUT.ACC.PL. *much or sim.* Hom. Hes. Thgn. AR. Theoc.
2 endure —W.COGN.ACC. *sufferings, struggles, pain, or sim.* Od. AR. Theoc.
3 be weary Od. AR.
4 (gener.) **suffer pain** or **be in distress** A. E. Ar. Theoc.

μογι-λάλος ου *m.* [μόγις, λαλέω] **man with a speech impediment** NT. [or perh. specif. *mute man*]

μόγις, Aeol. **μύγις** *adv.* [μόγος] **1 with difficulty** or **only with difficulty, only just, barely, scarcely** Hom. Sapph. Semon.(cj.) A. Hdt. E.*Cyc.* +
2 only after some time or difficulty, at last Hdt. Pl. Plb. Plu.
3 only with reluctance, reluctantly Semon. Pl. D. Arist. NT.

μόγος ου *m.* **1 physical effort, toil** Il.
2 mental strain, suffering, distress S.

μογοσ-τόκος ον *adj.* (epith. of Eileithuia) **overseeing the pains of childbirth** Il. hHom.; (of Artemis) Theoc.

μόδιος ου *m.* [Lat.loanwd.] **1** *modius* (a Roman dry measure, esp. for grain, one sixth of a medimnus, approx. 9 litres) Plb. Plu.(dub.)
2 measuring-vessel (of this capacity) NT.

μόθαξ ακος *m.* [reltd. μόθων] son of a helot brought up as foster-brother of a Spartan, **adopted helot child** Plu.

μόθος ου *m.* **battle** or **turmoil of battle** Il. Hes.

μόθων ωνος *m.* [app.reltd. μόθος] **1 a vulgar and obscene dance, cancan** Ar.
2 shameless scoundrel Ar.; (as a deity) **Impudence** Ar.

μοθωνικός ή όν *adj.* (of a manner of conversation) **presumptuous** Plu.(quot.)

μοι (enclit.dat.1sg.pers.pron.): see ἐγώ

μοιμνάω *contr.vb.* [reltd. μῦω] **purse one's lips** (in disgust) Ar.

μοῖρα ᾱς (Ion. ης) *f.* [μείρομαι] **1 portion, share** (of material or non-material things) Hom. Hes. Semon. Sol. Lyr. Trag. +
2 apportioned fortune, lot, destiny, fate Hom. Hes. Semon. Lyr. Hdt. Trag. +; (W.INF. to do or suffer sthg.) Hom. Thgn. S. E. AR.; (prep.phrs.) ὑπὲρ μοῖραν *beyond what is fated* Il.; πρὸ μοίρας *before one's fated day* (*i.e. prematurely*) Isoc.
3 fate (W.GEN. of death) Od. Hes.*fr.* hHom. Eleg. A. E.; (without GEN.) **fate, doom** Hom. Hes. Pi. B. Hdt. Trag. +
4 destiny (as the agent responsible for apportioning fortune) Pi. Trag. Pl. +
5 destiny as dispensed by the gods; dispensation (W.GEN. of a god or the gods) Od. Semon. Alc. Sol. Pi. AR.; (W.ADV. fr. the gods) E.; (W.ADJ. *divine*) Pl. X. Arist.
6 dispensation (W.GEN. of good or bad things) Thgn. Pi. B.; **allotted span** (W.GEN. of life) Il. Simon. S.
7 (gener.) **piece of good fortune** E.
8 natural apportionment (of things); **appropriateness, propriety, fitness** (of a state of affairs) E.; (prep.phrs.) κατὰ μοῖραν *in proper order or manner* (*i.e. in ordered sequence*) Hom.; *properly, appropriately* Hom. Hes. AR.; (also) ἐν μοίρᾳ (μοίρῃ) Hom. Pl.; παρὰ μοῖραν *inappropriately* Od.
9 role or **function** (allotted to a god, demigod, person, things in general) Od. Hes. A.; **proper** or **natural role** (W.GEN. of a man) Th.
10 due share of consideration (accorded to a person), **respect, esteem, estimation** A. Hdt. S. Pl. Theoc.
11 portion into which a whole is divided, part (sts. W.GEN. of sthg.) Hom. Hes. Pi. Hdt. Th. Ar. +
12 portion of land (in one's possession), **territory** Hdt.
13 portion (of a populace); **group** (of people) Hdt.; **class** (of citizens) E.
14 group (of supporters), **faction, party, side** Hdt.
15 division, detachment (of an army) Hdt.
16 class, category (for the purpose of evaluation) Thgn.; (prep.phr.) ἐν μοίρᾳ *in a class or category* (W.ADJ. *of a particular kind*) Pl.; (W.GEN. *of a particular person or thing*) Pl. D.

—**Μοῖρα** ᾱς *f.* **Moira, Fate** (as apportioner of destinies, sg. and pl.) Il. Hes. Eleg. Lyr. Parm. Hdt. +

μοιραῖος ᾱ ον *adj.* (of wounds) ordained by fate, **fated** Bion

μοιράομαι *mid.contr.vb.* **1 divide among one another** —*possessions* A.
2 (of mourners) **tear** —*their hair* AR. [or perh. *cut off locks of hair*]

μοιρη-γενής ές *Ion.adj.* [γένος, γίγνομαι] **born with a favourable destiny** Il.

μοιρ-ηγέται ῶν *m.pl.* [ἡγέομαι] **guiders of destiny** (epith. of assistants of Cretan Cybele) AR.

μοιρίδιος ᾱ ον (also ος ον) *adj.* **1** (of the power) **of destiny** S.
2 (of a skill) **granted by destiny** Pi.; (of an event, a day, vengeance) **determined by destiny, destined** Pi. S.; (of a guest-friend) Pi.

μοιρό-κραντος ον *adj.* [κραίνω] (of a day, an ordinance) **decreed by destiny** A.

Μοῖσα *Aeol.f.*: see Μοῦσα

Μοισᾱγέτᾱς *Aeol.m.*: see Μουσηγέτης

Μοισαῖος *Aeol.adj.*: see Μουσεῖος

μοισόπολος *Aeol.m.f.*: see μουσοπόλος

μοιχ-άγρια ων *n.pl.* [μοιχός, ἀγρέω] **penalty for adultery** Od.

μοιχαλίς ίδος *fem.adj.* (of a generation) **adulterous** NT.

μοιχάω *contr.vb.* **1** (fig., of a naval commander) **commit adultery with, debauch** —*the sea* (envisaged as the wife of an enemy commander) X.
2 ‖ PASS. (of a man or woman) **commit adultery** NT.

μοιχείᾱ ᾱς *f.* [μοιχεύω] **adultery** or **seduction** Att.orats. Pl. Arist. NT. Plu.

μοιχεύτρια ᾱς *f.* **adulteress** Pl.

μοιχεύω *vb.* [μοιχός] **seduce another man's wife** (or, in Athenian law, any of his female dependants, incl. daughter, sister, concubine); **be a seducer** or **adulterer** Xenoph. Ar. X. Hyp. Arist. +; (tr.) **seduce** or **commit adultery with** —*a woman* Lys. Ar. Pl. Arist. Men. + ‖ PASS. (of a woman) **commit adultery, be an adulteress** Ar. D. NT. Plu.

μοιχίδιος ᾱ (Ion. η) ον *adj.* relating to an adulterer; (of crimes against parents) **committed by bastard sons** Hdt.

μοιχός οῦ *m.* **illicit lover, seducer** or **adulterer** Hippon. Ar. Att.orats. Pl. X. Arist. +

μοιχο-τρόφος ον *adj.* [τρέφω] (of women) **harbouring adulterers** Ar.(cj., for μοιχότροπος *with adulterous habits*)

μοιχώδης ες *adj.* **looking like a seducer** or **adulterer** Men.

μοκλός *Ion.m.*: see μοχλός

μολγός οῦ *dial.m.* **leather flask** Ar.

μολεῖν (aor.2 inf.): see βλώσκω

μόλθακος *Aeol.adj.*: see μαλθακός

μολίβδινος *adj.*, **μολιβδοῦς** *adj.*: see μολύβδινος, μολυβδοῦς

μόλιβδος *m.*, **μόλιβος** *ep.m.*: see μόλυβδος

μόλις *adv.* **1 with difficulty** or **only with difficulty, only just, barely, scarcely** S. E. Th. Ar. Att.orats. Pl. +; (neg.phr.) οὐ μόλις *without difficulty, readily* A. E.(dub.)
2 only after some time or difficulty, **at last** S. E. Th. Ar. Att.orats. Pl. +
3 only with reluctance, **reluctantly** S. D. Men. Plb. Plu.

μολοβρίτης εω *Ion.m.* [μολοβρός] (appos.w. σῦς *swine*) **wild boar** Hippon.

μολοβρός οῦ *m.* (ref. to a beggar, as a term of abuse) **greedy swine** Od.

μόλον (ep.aor.2): see βλώσκω

Μολοσσοί, Att. **Μολοττοί**, ῶν *m.pl.* **Molossians** (occupants of a region in Epeiros; as a population or military force) Hdt. E. Th. Aeschin. Arist. + ‖ SG. Molossian man Plu.

—**Μολοσσός** ή όν *adj.* of or belonging to the Molossians; (of territory) **Molossian** A.; (of a musical instrument) Pi.*fr.*

—**Μολοσσίᾱ**, Att. **Μολοττίᾱ**, ᾶς *f.* **land of the Molossians, Molossia** Pi. E. And. Hyp.; (appos.w. γῆ) E.

—**Μολοσσίς**, Att. **Μολοττίς**, ίδος *fem.adj.* (of the land) **Molossian** Pi.*fr.* ‖ SB. Molossian land Plu.

—**Μολοττικός** ή όν *Att.adj.* (of dogs, notoriously fierce) **Molossian** Ar.

μολοῦμαι (fut.mid.): see βλώσκω

μολπάζω *vb.* [μολπή] **sing** Ar. —a song A.*satyr.fr.*

μολπή ῆς, *dial.* **μολπά̄** ᾶς, Aeol. **μόλπᾱ** ᾱς *f.* [μέλπω] **1 song accompanied by dance** (sts. w. focus on song, sts. on dance), **singing, dancing** or **song and dance** Hom. hHom.
2 (specif., sg. and pl.) **singing, song** Hes. hHom. Xenoph. Lyr. A. E. +
3 subject for song E.
4 music (W.GEN. of panpipes, the lyre) S. E.
5 (gener.) **play, games** AR.

μολπηδόν *adv.* **in a song-like manner** A.

μολύβδαινα ης *f.* [μόλυβδος] **leaden weight** (used to sink a fishing-line) Il.

μολύβδινος (also written **μολίβδινος**) η ον *adj.* (of objects) made of lead, **leaden** Arist. Plb.

μολυβδίς ίδος *f.* **1 leaden weight** Pl.; (specif.) **plumb** (of a mason's line) Call.
2 lead pellet (discharged fr. a sling) Plb. ‖ PL. lead shot X. Plu.

μόλυβδος (also written **μόλιβδος**), ep. **μόλιβος**, ου *m.* **lead** Il. Thgn. Simon. Hdt. E. Th. +

μολυβδοῦς (also written **μολιβδοῦς**) ῆ οῦν *adj.* (of weights) **leaden** Plb.

μολυβδοχοέω *contr.vb.* [χέω] **pour molten lead over** —*the feet of a person* (*envisaged as a statue to be fixed on a pedestal*) Ar.

μολυβρός ά όν *adj.* (of a coin) **lead-coloured** Thphr.(cj.)

μολῡνοπρᾱγμονέομαι *pass.contr.vb.* [μολύνω, πρᾶγμα] **be mired in dirty business** Ar.

μολύ̄νω *vb.* **1 make dirty, befoul** —*a person* Theoc. —*one's beard* Ar.; (of Circe) —*men* (*by turning them into pigs*) Ar. ‖ PASS. (fig., of a person, compared to a pig) be mired, wallow —W.PREP.PHR. in ignorance Pl.; (of an orator) be smirched (w. abuse), be the object of mud-slinging Isoc.
2 bugger —*a boy* Theoc.

μομφή ῆς, *dial.* **μομφά̄** ᾶς *f.* [μέμφομαι] **blame, complaint** or **criticism** Pi. Trag. Ar.

μοναδικός ή όν *adj.* [μονάς] (of number) **consisting of abstract units** Arist.

μοναμπυκίᾱ ᾱς *f.* [μονάμπυξ] **single racehorse** Pi. [or perh. *racing with single horses*]

μον-άμπυξ υκος *masc.fem.adj.* [μόνος, ἄμπυξ] (of a horse) wearing individual headgear (i.e. bridled for riding, opp. harnessed in a chariot team), **single bridled** E. ‖ SB. bridled horse E.; (specif.) cavalry horse E.

μοναρχέω, Ion. **μουναρχέω** *contr.vb.* [μόναρχος] **exercise sole rule, be a monarch** (as king or tyrant) Pi. Hdt. Pl. Arist. Plu. —W.DAT. *over people* B.*fr.* —W.GEN. Arist.; (at Rome, as dictator) Plu. ‖ PASS. (of a household, city, army) be under the control of a single man Arist. Plu.

μοναρχίᾱ ᾱς, Ion. **μουναρχίη** ης *f.* **1 rule by a single man, sole rule, monarchy, autocracy** (ref. to kingship or tyranny) Alc. Hdt. Trag. Ar. Isoc. Pl. +; (at Rome, ref. to dictatorship) Plu.
2 sovereignty (of the people) E.
3 sole command (of an army) X. Plu.

μοναρχικός ή όν *adj.* **1** relating to or characteristic of a sole ruler; (of a system or element of government; of power, orders, conduct) **monarchical** Pl. Arist. Plb. Plu.; (of an acropolis) **suited to a monarchical system** Arist. ‖ NEUT.SB. monarchical system Pl.; autocratic element (W.GEN. of kingship) Plu.
2 (of a person) of an imperious or domineering kind, **autocratic** Plu.

—**μοναρχικώτερον** *compar.adv.* **more autocratically** Plu.

μόν-αρχος, Ion. **μούναρχος**, ου *m.* [μόνος, ἄρχω] **1 sole ruler, monarch** or **despot** (ref. to a king or tyrant) Eleg. Pi.*fr.* Hdt. Th. Ar. Isoc. +; (ref. to Zeus) A.; (at Rome, ref. to a dictator) Plu.; (fig., ref. to Passion) Pl.
2 ‖ ADJ. (of the people) sovereign Arist.; (of a sceptre) Pi.
3 commander (W.GEN. of light-armed troops) E.

μονάς άδος *f.* **1 the number one, one** Pl.
2 quality of being one, **oneness, unity** Pl.
3 that which has oneness, **unit** Pl. Arist.; (ref. to fire, in Pythagorean philosophy) Plu.
4 ‖ MASC.FEM.ADJ. (of a person) **alone, solitary** A. E.; (of desolation, a life) **lonely** E.

μοναυλέω *contr.vb.* [μόναυλος *single aulos*] **play a single aulos** Plu.

μοναυλίᾱ ᾱς *f.* [αὐλή] state of being housed alone, **living alone** (without a wife) Pl.

μοναυλικός ή όν *adj.* (of a creature) **living alone, solitary** Arist.(cj.)

μοναχός ή όν *adj.* (of an entity) **unique** Arist.

—**μοναχῇ** *adv.* **by one route only** X.; **in one way only** Pl. Arist.

—**μοναχοῦ** *adv.* **in one place only** Pl. Arist.

—**μοναχῶς** *adv.* **in one way** or **sense only** Arist.

μονή ῆς *f.* [μένω] **1 act of staying, remaining, stay** (in a place) Hdt. E. Th. Ar. Pl. X.
2 waiting, wait E. Th. X.
3 state of rest, **rest** (opp. motion) Pl. Arist. Plb.
4 place to reside, residence NT.

μονίη ης *Ion.f.* [μόνος] **solitude** Emp.

μόνιμος ον *adj.* [μονή, μένω] **1** (of persons) remaining in the same condition as before, **steadfast, constant** S. Men.; (of a lover or friend) **lasting** Pl. Arist. || NEUT.SB. **constancy, reliability** Plu.
2 remaining constant (in an activity), **persevering** (W.PREP.PHR. in study, war, duties) Pl.
3 (of troops) standing firm (in the face of an enemy), **steady, steadfast** Pl. X. Plu. || NEUT.SB. **steadfastness** Plu.
4 (of physical objects, cities, institutions, laws, conditions or circumstances) **lasting, abiding, permanent** E. Th. Pl. Arist. Plb. Plu.
5 (of things) **at rest** (opp. in motion) Pl.
6 (of a military formation) **slow-moving, sluggish** Plu.

μονιός ά όν *adj.* [μόνος] (of a wild animal) **alone, solitary** Call.

μόν-ιππος ου *m.* [ἵππος] single horse (for riding, opp. member of a chariot team), **riding horse** Pl. X.

μονο-βάμων ον, gen. ονος *dial.adj.* [βῆμα, βαίνω] (of horses) **treading singly** (i.e. for riding, opp. member of a chariot team) E.*fr.*

μονο-γενής, Ion. **μουνογενής**, ές *adj.* [γένος, γίγνομαι]
1 alone in birth; (of a son or daughter) **only-born, only** Hes. A. Hdt. Pl. AR. NT. Plu.
2 (of a royal line) **from a single family** Pl.
3 alone in kind; (of being, heaven) **unique** Parm. Pl.
—**μουνογένεια** ᾶς *Ion.fem.adj.* (of a daughter) **only-born** AR.

μονο-δέρκτᾱς ᾱ *dial.masc.adj.* [δέρκομαι] (of the Cyclops) **single-eyed** E.*Cyc.*

μον-όδους οντος *masc.fem.adj.* [ὀδούς] (of the Graiai) possessing only one tooth (betw. them), **single-toothed** A.

μονό-δροπος ον *adj.* [δρέπω] (of timber for a statue) **hewn as a single whole** Pi.

μονο-ειδής ές *adj.* [εἶδος¹] **1** (of things) **single in form, uniform** Pl. Plb. || NEUT.SB. **uniform nature** (W.GEN. of a historical work) Plb.
2 (of a kind of matter) **unique in form** Pl.

μονό-ζυξ ζυγος *masc.fem.adj.* [ζεύγνῡμι] (of a wife, in the absence of her husband) yoked alone, **unpartnered** A.

μον-οίκητος ον *adj.* [οἰκητός] (of a region) **with solitary dwellings** E.*fr.* [or perh. *dwelling alone, isolated*]

μονό-κερως ων, gen. ω *adj.* [κέρας] (of a ram) **single-horned** Plu.

μονό-κλαυτος ον *adj.* [κλαυτός] (of a lament) **wailed by a solitary mourner** A.

μονοκοιτέω *contr.vb.* [κοίτη] (of women, whose husbands are at war) **sleep alone** Ar.

μονο-κρηπῑς ῑδος *masc.fem.adj.* [κρηπίς] (of a man) **with a single sandal** Pi.

μονό-κροτος ον *adj.* [κρότος] (of ships) **manned by a single bank of rowers** X.

μονό-κωλος, Ion. **μουνόκωλος**, ον *adj.* [κῶλον] **1** (of rooms, built along the top of a wall) **with a single frontage** (i.e. in a row, contiguous) Hdt.
2 (fig., of national characteristics) **one-sided** (i.e. lacking variety) Arist.
3 (of a sentence) **consisting of a single clause** Arist.

μονό-κωπος ον *adj.* [κώπη] **on one's own using oars, rowing alone** E.

μονό-λυκος ου *m.* [λύκος] (as the name applied by Demosthenes to Alexander of Macedon) **lone wolf** (regarded as particularly savage) Plu.

μονο-μάτωρ ορος *dial.masc.fem.adj.* [μήτηρ] (of the lamentations) **of a bereft mother** (ref. to the nightingale) E.

μονομαχέω, Ion. **μουνομαχέω** *contr.vb.* [μονομάχος]
1 fight in single combat, fight a duel Hdt. E. Men. Plb. Plu. —W.DAT. *w. someone* Hdt. Pl. Plu. —W. πρός + ACC. Plb.
2 (in Roman ctxt.) **fight as a gladiator** Plu.
3 (of the Athenian troops at Marathon) **fight single-handed** —W.DAT. *against the Persians* (i.e. without support fr. other Greeks) Hdt.

μονομαχίᾱ ᾱς, Ion. **μουνομαχίη** ης *f.* **1 single combat, duel** Hdt. Plu.
2 || PL. (in Roman ctxt.) **gladiatorial show** Plb.

μονομαχικός ή όν *adj.* (of a fighting spirit) **of the kind found in single combat** Plb.

μονο-μάχος ον *adj.* [μάχομαι] **1** (of champions) **fighting in single combat** A.
2 (of fighting) **in single combat** E.
3 (of a desire) **for single combat** E.
4 || MASC.SB. (in Roman ctxt.) **gladiator** Plb. Plu.

μονονού(κ), **μονονουχί** *neg.advs.*: see μόνον, under μόνος

μονό-ξυλος ον *adj.* [ξύλον] **1** (of a votive offering) **made from a single block of wood** Pl.
2 (of a boat, ref. to a canoe) made from a single tree trunk, **dug-out** X. Aeschin. Plb. || NEUT.PL.SB. **dug-outs, canoes** Plb.

μονό-παις παιδος *masc.fem.adj.* [παῖς¹] (of a son) **who is an only child** E.

μονό-πεπλος ον *adj.* [πέπλος] (of a woman) **clad in a single garment** E.

μονοπρᾱγματέω *contr.vb.* [πρᾶγμα] (of a person's attention) **be directed to a single task** Arist.

μονοπωλίᾱ ᾱς *f.* [πωλέω] exclusive right of sale, **monopoly** Arist.

μονό-πωλος ον *adj.* [πῶλος] (of Dawn) **with a single horse** or **riding alone** E.(dub.)

μονό-ρρυθμος ον *adj.* [ῥυθμός] (of dwellings) perh., **arranged individually, separate** A.

μόνος, Ion. and dial. **μοῦνος**, also dial. **μῶνος** (Hellenist.poet.), η (dial. ᾱ) ον *adj.* | *superl.* μονώτατος |
1 alone (without the presence of others), **alone, on one's own** Hom. +; (W.GEN. without someone) S. E.; **separated** (w. ἀπό + GEN. fr. others) Il. hHom. S. Call. AR.
2 alone (without help), **alone, on one's own, unaided, single-handed** Hom. +
3 alone (to the exclusion of all others), **alone, only, sole** Hom. +; (W.PARTITV.GEN.) Semon. + • μοῦνος ποταμῶν *alone of rivers* (i.e. the only river) Hdt.
4 (in numerations) **only one, a single** Il. + • μοῦνος ὀφθαλμός *a single eye* Hes.; (w. numeral added) **only** Od. + • τρεῖς μόναι ψῆφοι *only three votes* D.
5 (w. rhetorical exaggeration) alone (above all others), **alone, unique** Pi. S. E. Lys. Ar. +
6 || SUPERL. **very much alone, wholly unique or exclusively qualified** Ar. Lycurg. Theoc.
7 (prep.phr.) κατὰ μόνας *on one's own, by oneself* Th. Pl. X. Is. Arist. Men. +

—**μόνον**, Ion. and dial. **μοῦνον** *neut.adv.* **1 no more than, only, solely, merely, just** (usu. following the wd. or phr. which it limits) Sol. Lyr. Hdt. Trag. Th. +
2 (w. a command or wish) **only, just** Thgn. Trag. Ar. + • πιθοῦ μόνον *just do as I say* E.
3 (in conditional cl.) εἰ (ἐάν, ἄν, ἤν) μόνον *if only, only provided that* S. Pl. X. D. Arist. +
4 οὐ μόνον ... ἀλλὰ (καί) *not only ... but (also)* S. Th. Att.orats. +
5 μόνον οὐ (οὐκ, οὐχί) *all but, very nearly, almost* Ar. Att.orats. Pl. X. Thphr. + [sts. written μονονού(κ), μονονουχί]

—**μόνως** *adv.* **in one way only** Pl. Plb. Plu.; (w. οὕτως) *only in this way* Pl. X. Aeschin. Arist. +; μόνως ... εἰ *only ... if* Th.

μονοσιτέω *contr.vb.* [σῖτος] **eat only one meal a day** X.

μονό-σκηπτρος ον *adj.* [σκῆπτρον] (of a throne) single-sceptred, **of sole sovereignty** A.

μονο-στιβής ές *adj.* [στείβω] **travelling alone** A.

μονό-στιχον ου *n.* [στίχος] **single line of verse** Plu.

μονό-στολος ον *adj.* [στέλλω] **1** despatched alone; (of weapons) **for a solitary mission** (i.e. for a duel) E. **2** (of an orphaned child) **companionless, forlorn** E.

μονό-τεκνος ον *adj.* [τέκνον] (of the murder) **of one's only child** E.

μονο-τράπεζος ον *adj.* [τράπεζα] (of hospitality) **at a separate table** (fr. one's hosts) E.

μονό-τροπος ον *adj.* [τρόπος] having or consisting of an isolated way of life; (of a person) **solitary** E. Men.; (of a lifestyle) Plu.

μονοτροφία ᾱς *f.* [τρέφω] **individual rearing** (of animals, opp. communally in herds) Pl.

μονο-φάγος ον *adj.* [φαγεῖν] | superl. μονοφαγίστατος | **habitually eating alone** (i.e. reluctant to share one's food) Ar.

μον-όφθαλμος, Ion. **μουνόφθαλμος**, ον *adj.* [ὀφθαλμός] (of a fabled people) **one-eyed** Hdt.; (of a person who has lost the use of the other eye) NT.; (as nickname of a Macedonian noble) Plb.

μονό-φρουρος ον *adj.* [φρουρός] (of the bulwark of a land, ref. either to a group of elders or to a queen) **keeping sole guard** (in the ruler's absence) A.

μονό-φρων ονος *masc.fem.adj.* [φρήν] alone in one's thinking, **of independent mind** A.

μονό-χαλος ον *dial.adj.* [χηλή] (of horses' ankles) with a single hoof, **solid-hoofed** E. | see μῶνυξ

μονο-χίτων ωνος *masc.fem.adj.* [χιτών] **wearing only a tunic** (i.e. without an overgarment) Arist. Plb. Plu.

μονό-ψηφος, dial. **μονόψᾱφος**, ον *adj.* [ψῆφος] **1** (of a ruler's nod) casting the sole vote, **sole-deciding** A. **2** (transf.epith., of the sword of Hypermnestra, who alone of her sisters refused to kill her husband) casting an independent vote, **sole-dissenting** Pi.

μονόω, Ion. **μουνόω** *contr.vb.* **1** (of Zeus) **make single** —*a family line* (*i.e. allow only one son in each generation*) Od. **2 isolate** —*a person* (*i.e. leave him without supporters*) Plb. || PASS. (of persons seeking election) be isolated (in the voting, i.e. receive only a single vote) Hdt. **3** || PASS. be left alone or on one's own Hom. Archil. A. Hdt. Pl. X. + —W.GEN. by others Hdt.; be separated —w. ἀπό + GEN. *fr. someone* E.; be bereft or deprived —W.GEN. *of someone* (*by death*) E. **4** || PASS. (of troops or sailors, while on service) be left isolated (i.e. without support) Hdt. Th. Plu.; (of a people or city at war) be left to stand alone (i.e. without allies or other support) Hdt. Th. Pl.; be left deprived —W.GEN. *of allies* Hdt. **5** || PASS. (of water) be separated (fr. air and fire) Pl.; (of abstract things) stand alone, be independent (of other things) Pl. Arist.; be deprived or devoid —W.GEN. *of certain attributes* Pl.

μονῳδέω *contr.vb.* [ἀοιδή] **sing a solo** (fr. a tragic drama) Ar.

μονῳδία ᾱς *f.* **1 solo song, solo, aria** Ar. Pl. **2** singing of solos, **solo singing** Pl.

μόνως *adv.*: see under μόνος

μόνωσις εως *f.* [μονόω] **1** state of being the only one, **uniqueness** Pl. **2** state of being left on one's own, **abandonment** Plu.

μονώτης ου *masc.adj.* (of a man, a life) of a solitary kind, **solitary** Arist.

μονωτικός ή όν *adj.* (of the behaviour of a city) **isolationist** Arist.(dub.)

μον-ώψ, Ion. **μουνώψ**, ῶπος *masc.fem.adj.* **one-eyed** A. E.*Cyc.* Call.

μόρᾱ ᾱς *f.* [μείρομαι] **division** (of troops in the Spartan army) X. Aeschin. D. Din. Plu.

μορία ᾱς *f.* [perh.reltd. μόρος, μόριον] (freq.pl.) **sacred olive tree** (belonging to the Athenian state, perh. regarded as apportioned to a deity) Lys. Ar. Arist. Plu.; (appos.w. ἐλαία, esp. when contrasted w. ἰδία *private*) Lys. Arist.

μόριμος *adj.*: see μόρσιμος

μόριον ου *n.* [dimin. μόρος] **1 part** (opp. whole); **part, portion, section** (of land, an army, navy, soul, other material and non-material things, freq. W.GEN.) Hdt. E. Th. Pl. X. Arist. Plu.; (of a month, day, hour, or sim.) Th. Plu.; **branch** (of knowledge, an art, or sim.) Pl. Arist.; (specif., without GEN.) **period** (of time) Th. **2** constituent or component part, **part, member** (of a whole) Hdt. Pl. Arist. Plu. • τρία μόρια εἶναι γῆν πᾶσαν, Εὐρώπην τε καὶ Ἀσίην καὶ Λιβύην *the whole earth consists of three parts: Europe, Asia and Libya* Hdt.

Μόριος ου *masc.adj.* [app.reltd. μορία] (epith. of Zeus) **Morios** (app. as protector of olive trees) S.

μορμολυκεῖον ου *n.* [μορμολύττομαι] scary creature, **bogey** Ar. Pl.

μορμολύττομαι *Att.mid.vb.* [Μορμώ] frighten with a bogey-woman, **scare** —*a person* Ar. Pl. —(w. ἀπό + GEN. *away fr. sthg.*) X.; (intr.) **be scary** Pl.

μορμορ-ωπός όν *adj.* [ὤψ] (fig., of words) **bogey-faced, scary** Ar.

μορμύρω *vb.* [perh.reltd. μύρομαι] (of waters) **surge, seethe** or **roar** Il. AR.

μορμύσσομαι *mid.vb.* [reltd. μορμολύττομαι] frighten with a bogey-woman, **scare** —*a girl* Call.; (of a wedding song) —*the living quarters of marriageable girls* Call. [or perh. *disrupt their customary ways*]

Μορμώ όος (οῦς) *f.* **Mormo** (shape-changing female monster, invoked to frighten children) Ar. Theoc.

—**μορμών** όνος *f.* (as a generic term, sts.pl.) **bogey-woman** Ar. X.

μορόεις εσσα εν *adj.* [μόρον mulberry] (of earrings) **like mulberries** (in shape) Hom.

μόρος ου *m.* [μείρομαι] **1** apportioned fortune, **destiny, fate** Hom. hHom. Alc. Pi.*fr.* Hdt.(oracle) AR.; (W.INF. to do or suffer sthg.) Il. AR.; (prep.phr.) ὑπὲρ μόρον *beyond what is fated* Hom. AR.; *beyond the normal limit, to excess* Od. **2 doom, death** (esp. violent) Hom. hHom. Semon. Pi. Hdt. Trag. +; (of ships, meton. for their crews) A. **3** (as a deity) **Doom** Hes.

μόρσιμος, also **μόριμος** (Il. A. Pi.), ον *adj.* **1** (of events or circumstances) determined by destiny, **destined, fated** Hom. Stesich. A. Pi. E. AR. Mosch.; (of a marriage) **hallowed by destiny** A. **2** (of a person) **destined, fated** (to do or suffer sthg.) Hom. Pi. **3** || NEUT.IMPERS. (w. ἐστί) it is fated AR. —W.DAT. + INF. *for someone to do or suffer sthg.* Hom. Thgn. A. E. —*for a city to be captured* Hdt. || NEUT.SB. (sg. and pl.) what is fated, destiny Sol. Pi. Trag.

μορύσσω *vb.* | pf.pass.ptcpl. μεμορυγμένος | || PF.PASS.PTCPL.ADJ. (of clothes) **stained or made dirty** (W.DAT. by smoke) Od.

μορυχώτερον *compar.adv.* in a rather vague or obscure way —*ref. to explaining sthg.* Arist.(dub.)

μορφάεις εσσα εν *dial.adj.* [μορφή] (of an athlete) handsome (W.INF. to behold) Pi.

μορφάζω *vb.* make shapes; (of a speaker, compared to an aulos-player) posture or make faces (to match his words) X.

μορφή ῆς, *dial.* **μορφά** ᾶς, *Aeol.* **μόρφα** ᾱς *f.* 1 physical or visible form; form or appearance (of persons, deities, animals, things) Eleg. Lyr. Parm. Emp. Hdt. Trag. +; (specif.) shape or form (opp. εἶδος *appearance*) Arist.
2 attractive form or appearance, beauty (of persons or deities) Pi. E. X. Bion; (of speech) Od.
3 kind, sort or aspect (of non-physical or abstract things, such as calamities, activities, changes, life) E. Pl. Plu.

μόρφνος ου *masc.adj.* (of an eagle) perh. dark-coloured (ref. to the golden eagle) Il. ǁ SB. perh., golden eagle Hes.

μόρφωμα ατος *n.* [μορφόω *create a shape*] shape, form (of a person, monster, bird) A. E. Pl.(quot. E.)

μορφώτρια ᾱς *f.* (ref. to Circe) form-creator (W.GEN. of swine, by transforming humans) E.

μόσσῡν ῠνος *m.* [prob. Iran.loanwd.] | dat.pl. μοσσῠ́νοις (cj. μοσσῠ́νοιν) | tower-like building of wood (assoc.w. the Mossynoikoi), wooden tower X. AR. ǁ PL. wooden walls or fortifications (of a city) Call.

—**Μοσσῠ́νοικοι** ων *m.pl.* Mossynoikoi (tribe on the S. coast of the Black Sea) Hdt. X. AR.

μόσχειος ᾱ ον *adj.* [μόσχος] 1 (of hair) of a calf E.; (of meat, i.e. veal) X.; (of the skin) Plb.
2 (of a sack) made of calf-skin X. ǁ NEUT.SB. calf-skin X.

μοσχεύω *vb.* plant a shoot; (fig.) plant, propagate —*certain kinds of persons* (W.PREP.PHR. *in lawcourts*) D.

μοσχίδια ων *n.pl.* [dimin. μόσχος 3] shoots (W.GEN. of fig-slips) Ar.

μοσχίον ου *n.* [dimin. μόσχος 1] young calf Theoc.

μοσχοποιέω *contr.vb.* [μόσχος 1] make a calf (as an idol) NT.

μόσχος ου *m.f.* 1 young of a bull or cow, calf or heifer Hdt. E. Pl. Theoc. NT. Plu.; (ref. to the deity Apis) Hdt.
2 (*f.*) heifer (fig.ref. to a woman) E.; (ref. to a daughter) girl E.
3 (*m.*) offshoot (of a tree or plant), shoot (appos.w. λύγος *willow*) Il.

μου (enclit.gen.1sg.pers.pron.): see ἐγώ

μουνάξ *Ion.adv.* [μόνος] alone, by oneself —*ref. to dancing* Od.; in single combat —*ref. to being killed* Od.

μουναρχέω *Ion.contr.vb.*, **μουναρχίη** *Ion.f.*, **μούναρχος** *Ion.m.*: see μοναρχέω, μοναρχίᾱ, μόναρχος

Μουνιχίᾱ[1] (also **Μουνυχίᾱ** Plu.) ᾱς, Ion. **Μουνιχίη**[1] ης *f.* Mounichia (steep hill and harbour on the E. coast of the Peiraieus peninsula) Hdt. Th. And. X. Arist. Din. Plu.

—**Μουνιχίαζε** *adv.* to Mounichia Lys.

—**Μουνιχίᾱσι** *adv.* at Mounichia Th. Lys. Is.

—**Μουνιχίᾱ**[2] ᾱς, Ion. **Μουνιχίη**[2] ης *fem.adj.* Mounichia (epith. of Artemis, as having a temple there) X. D. Call.

—**Μούνιχος** ου *m.* Mounichos (eponymous hero) E.

Μουνιχιών (also **Μουνυχιών** Plu.) ῶνος *m.* Mounichion (tenth month of the Athenian year) Ar. Aeschin. D. Plu.

μουνογενής *Ion.adj.*: see μονογενής

μουνό-γληνος ον *Ion.adj.* [γλήνη] (of eyes) with a single eyeball (periphr. for the single eyes of the Cyclopes) Call.

μουνόκωλος *Ion.adj.*: see μονόκωλος

μουνό-λιθος ον *Ion.adj.* [λίθος] (of a structure) made of a single block of stone Hdt.

μουνομαχέω *Ion.contr.vb.*, **μουνομαχίη** *Ion.f.*: see μονομαχέω, μονομαχίᾱ

μοῦνον *Ion. and dial.neut.adv.*: see μόνον, under μόνος

μουνο-πάλᾱ ᾱς *dial.f.* [πάλη] simple wrestling match (opp. the pankration or wrestling in the pentathlon) B.

μοῦνος *Ion. and dial.adj.*: see μόνος

μουνο-τόκος ον *Ion.adj.* (of sheep, goats) that bear or have borne a single offspring Call.

μουνόφθαλμος *Ion.adj.*: see μονόφθαλμος

μουνο-φυής ές *Ion.adj.* [φυή] (of a row of teeth) growing as one, formed of a single piece (of bone) Hdt.

μουνόω *Ion.contr.vb.*: see μονόω

Μουνῠχίᾱ *f.*, **Μουνυχιών** *m.*: see Μουνιχίᾱ[1], Μουνιχιών

μουνώψ *Ion.masc.fem.adj.*: see μονώψ

μουριάς *Boeot.f.*: see μῡριάς

Μοῦσα ης, *Aeol.* **Μοῖσα**, *dial.* **Μῶσα** (Alcm.), ᾱς, Lacon. **Μῶά** ᾱς (Ar.) *f.* 1 Muse (one of a number of goddesses, most commonly nine, daughters of Zeus and Mnemosyne, sources of poetical, musical and intellectual inspiration and presiding over the arts in general) Hom. +
2 (meton., written μοῦσα, μοῖσα, sg. and pl.) music, song or poetry hHom. Lyr. Ion Trag. Ar. Pl. +

Μουσαῖος ου *m.* Mousaios (legendary early poet and author of oracular verses, freq. assoc.w. Orpheus) Hdt. E. Ar. Arist. Plu.

Μοῦσ-αρχος ου *m.* [Μοῦσα, ἄρχω] (epith. of Apollo) leader of the Muses Lyr.adesp.

Μουσεῖος ον, *Aeol.* **Μοισαῖος** ᾱ ον *adj.* of or relating to the Muses or the arts over which they preside; (of the seat, ref. to Pieria) of the Muses E.; (of a mountain, app.ref. to Parnassos) E.*fr.*; (of songs, arts) Pi.; (of the chariot, fig.ref. to poetry) Pi.; (of a stone, fig.ref. to a poetical monument) Pi.

—**μουσεῖον** ου *n.* 1 perh. sanctuary of the Muses Pl. Arist.; (as the name of a specific building, in Athens and elsewhere) Museum Plb. Plu. ǁ PL. poetical monuments (W.GEN. of words, iron.ref. to complex names for rhetorical techniques) Pl.
2 ǁ PL. musical haunts (of birds, ref. to branches) E.; music-halls (W.GEN. of swallows, derog.ref. to bad poets) Ar.; app., singers E.

—**Μουσεῖα** ων *n.pl.* festival of the Muses (an event for schoolchildren) Aeschin. Thphr.

Μουσ-ηγέτης ου, *Aeol.* **Μοισᾱγέτᾱς** ᾱ *m.* [ἡγέομαι] (epith. of Apollo) leader of the Muses Pi.*fr.* Pl.

μουσίζω, *dial.* **μουσίσδω** *vb.* sing Theoc.; (mid.) —*a charmless racket* E.*Cyc.*

μουσικός, *dial.* **μωσικός**, ή (dial. ά) όν *adj.* 1 relating to music; (of the art) of music Pl.; (of contests, shows) musical Th. Ar. Pl. Plu.; (of an instrument) Plu.; (of a blending of rhythms and harmonies) Plu.; (of poems set to music, in neg.phr.) melodious Pl. ǁ NEUT.PL.SB. music Pl. Plb. Plu.
2 (of persons, Apollo, birds) engaged or skilled in music, musical Pl. X. Lyr.adesp.; (of birds' wings, meton. for the birds themselves) Ar.; (of a lyric opp. epic poet) Pl. ǁ MASC.SB. musician Pl. Arist. Theoc. Plu.
3 (gener., of persons) devoted to the arts associated with the Muses (esp. music and poetry), cultured, sophisticated Ar. Pl. Arist. Plu.; (of a city, noted for its lyric poets) Isoc. ǁ MASC.SB. cultured man Arist. ǁ NEUT.SB. culture Arist.
4 ǁ NEUT.PL.SB. musical or poetic compositions X.; liberal arts (i.e. music and poetry, as a subject of study) Pl.
5 (of persons) attuned (W.INF. to speaking in public) E.
6 (of a particular degree of wealth) suitable (for a particular type of person) Pl.

—**μουσική** ῆς, *dial.* **μουσικά** ᾶς *f.* 1 music (incl. singing to music) Pi. Hdt. S.*satyr.fr.* E.*fr.* Th. Ar. +

2 (specif., w. no connot. of music) **poetry** Ar. Pl.
3 (gener.) music and poetry (as essential components of a proper education), **liberal arts, culture** Ar. Isoc. Pl. X. Plu.
—**μουσικῶς** *adv.* | compar. μουσικωτέρως (Arist.), superl. μουσικώτατα | **1 in terms of music** —*ref. to designating an art* Pl.
2 harmoniously (w. one another) —*ref. to arguments being formulated* Pl.
3 skilfully, intelligently, with taste —*ref. to speaking, judging, or sim.* Ar. Isoc. Pl. Arist.
μουσίσδω *dial.vb.*: see μουσίζω
μουσό-ληπτος ον *adj.* [ληπτός] **inspired by the Muses** Plu.
μουσό-μαντις εως *m.* [μάντις] **musical prophet** (ref. to a bird) Ar.(quot. A.)
μουσο-μήτωρ ορος *f.* [μήτηρ] (ref. to memory) **mother of the Muses, creator of the arts** A.
μουσόομαι *pass.contr.vb.* | pf. μεμούσωμαι | **be trained in the liberal arts, be educated** Ar. ǁ NEUT.PF.PASS.PTCPL.SB. **sophistication** (of a person) Plu.
μουσο-παλαιο-λύμᾱς ᾱ *dial.m.* [παλαιός, λύμη] (ref. to an inferior poetic innovator) **corrupter of the old Muse** Tim.
μουσοποιέω *contr.vb.* [μουσοποιός] **write poetry about** —*sthg.* Ar.
μουσο-ποιός όν *adj.* [ποιέω] (of the practised skill) **of poetry-making** E. ǁ MASC.FEM.SB. **poet** Hdt. E. Theoc.*epigr.*
μουσο-πόλος, Aeol. **μοισόπολος**, ου *m.f.* [πέλω] **1 one who is concerned with the Muses, poet** or **singer** Sapph. E. Telest.
2 ǁ FEM.ADJ. (of a lament) **poetical or tuneful** E.(dub.)
μουσουργός οῦ *m.f.* [ἔργον] **maker of music, musician** X. Plu.
μοχθέω *contr.vb.* [μόχθος] | Aeol.masc.pl.nom.ptcpl. μόχθεντες ǁ neut.impers.vbl.adj. μοχθητέον | **1 work hard, toil, labour** Alc. E. Th. Ar. X. Hellenist.poet. —W.COGN.ACC. *w. toils or hardships* E. X. —W.NEUT.PL.ACC. *over this, much, more, or sim.* S. E. Th. Ar. X. + —W.ACC. *over learning, one's children* E. —*over sleep* (i.e. toss and turn) Bion
2 suffer hardship or **distress** E.; **be afflicted** —W.DAT. *by a storm* Alc. —*by rain and sun* S. —*by cares* Il.
μοχθήματα τῶν *n.pl.* **toils, labours** Trag.
μοχθηρίᾱ ᾱς *f.* [μοχθηρός] **1 badness** (in quality); **incompetence** (W.GEN. of a doctor, a helmsman and crew) Antipho Pl.
2 badness (in condition); **poor condition** (W.GEN. of a body) Pl.; **poor state of affairs** D.
3 badness (of conduct or character); **wickedness, depravity, vice** Ar. Pl. X. D. Arist. Plu.; **cowardice** (of soldiers) Plu. ǁ PL. **acts of depravity** Arist.
μοχθηρός ά (Ion. ή) όν *adj.* [μόχθος] | perh. accented μόχθηρος in sense 1 | **1 enduring toil or suffering**; (of persons, esp. in voc. address, sts. iron.) **wretched, poor, pitiable** A. S. Ar. Pl. Call.*epigr.*
2 causing toil or trouble; (of tasks) **burdensome, troublesome** A. Ar.; (of a letter, ref. to carving it) Ar.; (of life) Hdt. S. Arist.; (of a route) Plu.
3 bad in quality; (of a doctor, teacher) **bad, poor, incompetent** Antipho (v.l. πονηρός) Pl. Plb.; (of speech, a voice, a tragic drama) **poor, unimpressive** Pl. X. Arist.; (of an ox) **of poor quality** Ar.
4 bad in condition; (of a body, flesh, clothes, or sim.) **in poor condition** Pl. Plu.; (of a situation, state of affairs, or sim.) **unfavourable** D. Plu.; (of hopes) **slender** Din. Plb. Plu.
5 morally bad; (of persons, their characters, actions, words, or sim.) **bad, wicked, depraved, evil** Ar. Isoc. Pl. X. D. Arist. +; (of laws) Plu.; (of a person, W.ACC. in appearance) And.

6 (gener., of persons or things) **worthless, no-good, disreputable** Th. Ar. Pl. Arist. +
—**μοχθηρῶς** *adv.* | compar. μοχθηροτέρως (Pl.) | **1 in a poor condition, wretchedly** Pl. D. Arist. Plu.
2 with trouble, effort or **hardship** Plu.
3 in an unsatisfactory manner, badly, poorly Plu.
μοχθίζω *vb.* **1 work hard, toil, labour** Thgn. Pi.*fr.* AR. Theoc. —W.COGN.ACC. *w. toils* Mosch.
2 be afflicted —W.DAT. *by a wound* Il. —*by lice* Archil. —*w. thirst and pain* AR. —*w. sorrows* Mosch.
μόχθος ου *m.* **1 hard work, toil, labour** Hes. Pi. Hdt. Trag. Ar. X. +; (specif., of Herakles, Sisyphos) Alc. S. E. Theoc. Mosch.; (W.GEN. over one's children, i.e. that involved in their birth and upbringing) E.
2 (ref. to a war) **cause of toil, labour** (W.DAT. for troops, a country) Pi.
3 (concr.) result of hard work, **work, product** (W.GEN. of Hephaistos' anvils, ref. to armour) E.; **fruit of labour** (ref. to a child) E.
4 hardship, suffering, distress, trouble Alc. Thgn. Pi. Lyr.adesp. Trag. X.
μοχλευτής οῦ *m.* [μοχλεύω] **upheaver** (W.GEN. of land and sea, ref. to Poseidon) Ar.; (fig.) perh. **engineer** (W.GEN. of new-fangled words) Ar.
μοχλεύω *vb.* [μοχλός] **raise or move by force of leverage; lever up** —*a stone, structure, rocks* Hdt. E.*Cyc.*; **prise open** —*doors* E. ǁ PASS. (of a siege-engine) **be levered forward** Plu.
μοχλέω *contr.vb.* **prise up** —*supports* (*of a fortification*) Il.
μοχλός, Ion. **μοκλός** (Anacr.), οῦ *m.* **1 lever, crowbar** (for forcing doors, prising up heavy objects or structures) E. Ar.; (pl., for moving a ship to the sea) Od. [or perh. *rollers*]
2 stake (used for blinding) Od. E.*Cyc.*
3 bar (of wood or iron, placed across a door or gate on the inside and secured w. a bolt-pin) Anacr. A. E. Th. Ar. X. + | see βάλανος 3
μῦ *interj.*: see μῦμῦ
μῦ-γαλῆ ῆς *f.* [μῦς] **shrewmouse** Hdt.
μύγις Aeol.*adv.*: see μόγις
μυγμός οῦ *m.* [μύζω¹] **sound of moaning** or **whining** Plu.; (as a stage-direction, for the moan or whine of a chorus of Erinyes) A.
μυδαίνω *vb.* [reltd. μυδάω] | aor.ptcpl. μῡδήνᾱς | **make wet, moisten, soak** —*a drug* AR.
μυδαλέος ᾱ (Ion. η) ον *adj.* **1** (of persons, their skin) **wet, soaked** (w. rain) Hes. AR.; (of dust, a person, W.DAT. w. tears) Hes. S.; (of raindrops) **dripping** (W.DAT. w. blood) Il.
2 (of a stench) **dank, putrid** AR.
μυδάω *contr.vb.* | only ptcpl. μυδῶν ῶσα ῶν, ep.fem. (w.diect.) μυδόωσα | **1 be in a state of dampness**; (of the juice of burning meat) **be damp** S.; (of drops of blood) S.(dub.)
2 (of hair on the corpse of a poisoned man) **be clammy** AR.
3 be in a state of decay through dampness; (of a corpse) **be dank, putrid** or **rot** S.; (of leather shields, fr. rain) Plb.
μυδροκτυπέω *contr.vb.* [μυδροκτύπος] (of Hephaistos) **forge iron** A.
μυδρο-κτύπος ον *adj.* [μύδρος, κτυπέω] **making molten metal resound**; (of the likeness) of one forging iron, **of a smith** E.
μύδρος ου *m.* [perh.reltd. μυδάω] **1 lump of molten metal** (thrown into the sea in an oath-taking, to affirm that the oath will last as long as the metal does not surface) Hdt. Arist. Call. Plu.; (also W.ADJ. *of iron*) Hdt.

μυελόεις

2 **lump of red-hot iron** (handled as an ordeal, to affirm an oath) S.
3 **mass of molten iron** (in Hephaistos' forge) Call.

μυελόεις εσσα εν *ep.adj.* [μυελός] (of bones) **full of marrow, marrowy** Od.

μυελός, ep. and dial. **μῡελός,** οῦ *m.* **1 marrow** (in human bones) Plu.; (specif., in the spine) Il.; (in the brain) S.; (in animal bones, as a food) Il.; (incl. semen, as a fundamental life-giving substance) Pl.
2 (gener.) **sap** (as the source of vitality) A.
3 (fig.) **marrow** (of a person, ref. to the inmost part of one's being, as seat of the emotions) Theoc.; (W.GEN. of the soul) E.
4 (fig.) **marrow** (W.GEN. of men, ref. to groats, as a staple food) Od.
5 (fig.) **marrow** (W.GEN. of Sicily, ref. to Syracuse, as an essential part of it) Theoc.
6 **a kind of milky dessert** (made fr. beestings), **custard** Philox.Leuc.

μυελο-τρεφής ές *adj.* [τρέφω] (of wild marjoram, perh. spread beneath a corpse) **marrow-bred** Tim.

μυέω *contr.vb.* [reltd. μύω] **carry out initiations** (into mysteries or rites); **initiate** —*a person* And. D. ‖ PASS. **be initiated** Hdt. Ar. Att.orats. Pl. Thphr. Plu. —W.ACC. *into secret rites* Hdt. —*into visions* (*of the divine*) Pl. —(*fig.*) *into philosophical matters* Pl.

μύζω[1] *vb.* [reltd. μῦ, see μῦμῦ] **1 moan, whine** A.
2 (specif.) **say 'mumu'** Ar.

μύζω[2] *vb.* [app.reltd. μῦ, see μῦμῦ] app., position the lips as for saying 'mu'; (of non-Greeks) **suck** (barley-wine, w. a straw) X. —*beer* (W.DAT. *w. a straw*) Archil.(cj.)

μύησις εως *f.* [μυέω] **initiation** (into mysteries or rites) Plu.

μυθέομαι *mid.contr.vb.* [μῦθος] | Ion. μυθεῦμαι (Theoc.) | ep.2sg. μυθέαι, also μυθεῖαι | Ion.imperatv. μυθεῦ | ep.impf. ἐμυθεόμην, also μυθεόμην, ep.Ion.3pl. μυθεῦντο, ep.3pl.du. μυθείσθην | 3pl.iteratv.impf. μυθέσκοντο | ep.3sg.aor. μυθήσατο |
1 **speak** (sts. W.ADV. thus, truthfully, gently, boastfully, or sim.) Hom. hHom. Semon. A. AR. Theoc.; **converse** Thgn. —W.DAT. *w. one another* AR.
2 **utter, say, speak** —*the truth, abuse, a prophecy, or sim.* Hom. Hes. Eleg. A. S. Theoc. —W.DIR.SP. *sthg.* Hom. S. AR. Theoc.
3 **say** —W.ACC. + INF. or COMPL.CL. *that sthg. is the case* Hom. AR. —W.INDIR.Q. *what is the case* Od. Pi. Theoc.; **give** —W.COGN.ACC. *an explanation* (W.INDIR.Q. *of why one has done sthg.*) Od.
4 **speak of, tell of, mention** or **describe** —*someone or sthg.* Hom. AR. Theoc. —*a city* (W.PREDIC.ADJ. *as being such and such*) Il.; **give an account** Od. hHom. Call.
5 (of an oracle) **give instructions** —W.INF. *to do sthg.* A.

—**μυθέω** *act.contr.vb.* | Ion.nom.fem.pl.ptcpl. μυθεῦσαι (cj. μυθεύουσαι) | **say** —*sthg.* E.(dub.)

μύθευμα ατος *n.* [μυθεύω] **plot** (of a drama) Arist.; **story-line** (in epic) Plu. ‖ PL. (pejor.) **fables, fictions** Plu.

μυθεύω *vb.* [μῦθος] **tell stories, spin a yarn** E. ‖ PASS. (of a legendary warrior) **be told of in stories** E. ‖ IMPERS.PASS. **a story is told** E. Arist.

μυθίζω, dial. **μυθίσδω,** Lacon. **μυσίδδω** *vb.* | dial.inf. μυθίσδεν, Lacon. μυσίδδην | Lacon.aor.inf. μυσίξαι | **1 say** —*sthg.* Ar. Theoc.
2 **speak of, tell of** —*sthg.* Ar. Theoc.

μυθιῆται ὧν *m.pl.* **talkers** (app. euphem., ref. to plotters or conspirators) Anacr.

μυθικός ή όν *adj.* **1** (of a hymn, a digression) **dealing with myth, with a mythical theme** Pl. Plb.
2 (of a giant or monster) **belonging to myth, mythical, fabled** Plu.

—**μυθικῶς** *adv.* **in terms of myth** Arist.

μυθίσδω *dial.vb.*: see μυθίζω

μυθο-γράφος ου *m.* [γράφω] **one who writes about myths and legends, mythographer, fabulist** Plb. Plu.

μυθολογεύω *vb.* [reltd. μυθολογέω] **speak of, recount** —*sthg.* Od.

μυθολογέω *contr.vb.* [μυθολόγος] **1 tell a story, legend** or **myth** Isoc. Pl. Arist. Plu. —W.ACC. *about someone or sthg.* Isoc. Pl. Arist. Plu. —W.PREP.PHR. Pl.
2 **tell in a story** or **by way of a myth** —W.ACC. + INF., COMPL.CL. or INDIR.Q. *that* (or *how*) *sthg. happened* Pl. X. Arist. Plu.
3 ‖ PASS. (of persons or things) **be recorded in stories, legends** or **myths** Pl. D. Arist. —W.INF. or COMPL.CL. *as existing or doing sthg.* Pl. D. Plu. ‖ IMPERS.PASS. **legend has it** —W.ACC. + INF. *that someone did sthg.* Arist.
4 ‖ PRES.PASS.PTCPL.ADJ. (of a state of affairs) **legendary, fabled** Plu. ‖ PRES. or PF.PASS.PTCPL.NEUT.SB. (sg. and pl.) **legend** or **fable** Arist. Plu.
5 **describe** or **invent** (as if a myth), **fictionalise** —*a form of government* Pl.

μυθολόγημα ατος *n.* **piece of story-telling, tale, fable** Pl. Plu.

μυθολογία ᾱς *f.* **1 story-telling** (sts. opp. poetry) Pl.
2 **legendary narrative** Pl. Plu.

μυθολογικός ή όν *adj.* **skilled in story-telling** or **myth-making** Pl.

μυθο-λόγος ου *m.* **1 story-teller, fabulist** (opp. poet) Pl.
2 ‖ ADJ. (of a record) **mythological** Call. [or perh. *in narrative prose,* opp. in poetry]

μυθο-ποιός οῦ *m.* [ποιέω] **story-maker** Pl.

μῦθος ου *m.* **1 that which is spoken, utterance, word, statement, speech** (w. neutral connot., or ref. to advice, a command, proposal, plea, or sim., as indicated by ctxt.) Hom. Hes. Eleg. B. Trag. Hellenist.poet. ‖ PL. **words, talk, speech** Hom. Hes. Thgn. B. Emp. Trag. +
2 **word** (opp. fact or reality) A.; (sg. and pl.) **speech** (opp. action) Hom.
3 **saying, maxim** A.
4 **that which is in one's mind** (but not yet spoken), **purpose, plan, design** Hom.; **matter, issue** Od.
5 **spoken narrative, account, story, tale** Od. hHom. B. Parm. Emp. Trag. +; (W.GEN. *about someone or sthg.*) Od. Parm. S.; (pejor.) **talk, rumour** S.
6 **fictional narrative, story, tale** or **fable** A.*fr.* Ar. Pl. Arist. Call. Theoc.; (opp. reality) E.*Cyc.*
7 **inherited story** (about the gods, the distant past, or sim.), **story, legend, myth** Xenoph. Hdt. E. Ar. Att.orats. Pl. +
8 **incredible** or **deceptive story, tale, fiction, yarn** Pi. Ar. Pl. D. Call.*epigr.*
9 **form in which a story is adapted for representation in epic** or **drama, story-line, plot** Arist.

μυθώδης ες *adj.* (of stories) **characterised by mythical, legendary** or **fabulous elements, mythical, legendary** or **fabulous** Att.orats. Pl. Plu.; (pejor., of stories, events, explanations) **fictitious, fanciful** Plu.; (of a writer) **prone to fiction** Plu. ‖ NEUT.SB. (pejor.) **element of fabulousness** (in a narrative) Th.; **fiction** Plu.; (pl.) **fanciful traditions** Arist.

μυῖα ᾱς (Ion. ης) *f.* **two-winged insect, fly** Il. Hippon. Simon. Ar. X. Thphr. +; (W.ADJ. *bronze,* ref. to a horsefly) Carm.Pop.

Μυκαναι *dial.f.pl.*: see Μυκῆναι

μῡκάομαι *mid.contr.vb.* | *aor.* ἐμῡκησάμην ‖ also act.: *ep.aor.2* μύκον | *pf.* (w.pres.sens.) μέμῡκα | *ep.3sg.plpf.* (w.impf.sens.) μεμύκει | **1** (of a bull) **bellow** Il. Pl. Mosch.; (of a warrior or deranged man, compared to a bull) Il. E.; (of an angry man) Ar.; (of the mouth of a chasm, refusing admission) Pl.
2 (of calves or heifers) **low, moo** Od. A. E. Theoc.; (of the meat of slaughtered cattle) Od.
3 (of a woman, compared to a lioness) **roar** Theoc.
4 (of a conch-blower) **blare** Theoc.; (of thunder) **peal** Ar.
5 (of gates, while opening) **groan** Il.; (of earth and woodland, in a storm) Hes.
6 (of the nostrils of a person engaged in vigorous exertion) **snort** Ar.
μῡκή ῆς *f.* **bellow** (of a phantom) AR.(pl.)
μῡκηθμός οῦ *m.* **1 bellowing** (of a bull) AR. Plb.; (of the earth, in pain) AR.
2 lowing (of cattle) Hom. AR. Theoc.
μύκημα ατος *n.* **1 bellow** (of a bull) AR.; (of the Minotaur) Call.
2 lowing (w.GEN. of cattle) E.(pl.)
3 roar (w.GEN. of a lioness) Theoc.
4 peal (w.GEN. of thunder) A.
Μυκῆναι ῶν (dial. ᾶν, ep. ἄων), dial. **Μυκᾶναι** ᾶν (Simon.) *f.pl.* —also **Μυκήνη** ης, dial. **Μυκήνᾱ** ᾶς *f.* **Mycenae, Mycene** (city in the Peloponnese, nr. Argos, ruled by Agamemnon) Hom. Simon. Pi. S. E. Th. +
—**Μυκήνηθεν** *adv.* **from Mycenae** Il.
—**Μυκηναῖος** ᾱ ον *adj.* (of men) **of** or **from Mycenae, Mycenaean** Il. E.; (of the people, an army, altars, a dwelling) E. ‖ MASC.PL.SB. **Mycenaeans** (as a population or military force) Il. Pi.*fr.* Hdt. S. E. Th. +
—**Μυκηνίς** ίδος *fem.adj.* (of women, military strength, footwear) **Mycenaean** E. ‖ PL.SB. **women of Mycenae** E.
μύκης ητος *m.* | also Ion.gen. μύκεω (disyllab., Archil.) |
1 fungus or **fungus-like excrescence** ‖ PL. **fungus** (forming on a lamp-wick in damp air, taken as a portent of rain) Ar. Call.
2 cap (of a scabbard, covering the sword point) Hdt.
3 penis Archil.
μῡκητάς ᾶ *dial.masc.adj.* [μῡκάομαι] (of oxen) **lowing** Theoc.
μύκον (ep.aor.2): see μῡκάομαι
Μύκονος ου *f.* **Mykonos** (island in the Cyclades) A. Hdt. E. Th.
μυκτήρ ῆρος *m.* [μύσσομαι *blow one's nose*] **1** (sg. and pl.) **nostril** (of a person) S.*satyr.fr.* Ar. Pl. X. Arist. Plu.; (pl., of a horse) Hdt. E. Ar. X.; (of a hare) X.
2 (fig.) **nozzle** (of a lamp, through which the wick protrudes) Ar.
μυκτηρό-κομπος ον *adj.* [κόμπος] (of horses' breath) **from proudly snorting nostrils** A.
μύλακρος ου *m.* [reltd. μύλαξ] **millstone** or **rock as heavy as a millstone** (used as a missile) Alcm.
μύλαξ ακος *m.* [μύλη] **millstone** or **rock as heavy as a millstone** (used as a missile) Il.
μύλη ης, dial. **μύλᾱ** ᾱς *f.* **1 handmill, quern** (for grinding grain, w. a fixed flat lower stone and a smaller hand-held upper one) Od. Alcm. Semon. Carm.Pop. AR. Theoc.
2 millstone Ar.
μυλή-φατος ον *adj.* [reltd. θείνω] **1** (of barley) **mill-ground** Od.
2 (of the task) **of mill-grinding** AR.
μυλίᾱς ου *masc.adj.* (of a stone) **for a mill** (i.e. millstone) Pl.

μυλιάω *contr.vb.* | only masc.nom.pl.ptcpl. (w.diect.) μυλιόωντες | (of animals) **grind** or **gnash the teeth** Hes.(cj. μαλκιόωντες)
μυλικός ή όν *adj.* (of a stone) **for a mill** (i.e. millstone) NT.
μύλλω *vb.* (fig., w. sexual connot.) **grind** —*a woman* Theoc.
μυλο-ειδής ές *adj.* [εἶδος¹] (of a rock) **like a millstone** Il.
μύλος ου *m.* **1 handmill, mill** NT.
2 millstone NT.
μυλωθρέω *contr.vb.* [μυλωθρός] **be a mill-keeper** or **miller** Men.
μυλωθρός οῦ *m.* [reltd. μυλών] **mill-keeper** or **miller** D. Arist. Din.
μυλών ῶνος *m.* [μύλη] **millhouse, mill** (freq. as a place of hard labour, suitable for the punishment of slaves) E.*Cyc.* Th. Att.orats. Men.; (fig.ref. to a trireme) Arist.(quot.)
μῦμῦ (or **μῦ μῦ**) *interj.* [reltd. μύζω¹] **mumu** (representing the sound of sobbing, also of inarticulate protest) Ar.
μύνη ης *f.* app. **pretext, excuse** Od.
μύξα ης *f.* [reltd. μυκτήρ] **1 discharge from the nose, mucus** Hes. Hippon.
2 nozzle (of a lamp, through which the wick protrudes) Call.*epigr.*
μυξωτῆρες ων *m.pl.* **nostrils** Hdt.
μυομαχία ᾱς *f.* [μῦς, μάχη] **battle of mice** (fig.ref. to a minor conflict) Plu.
μυο-πάρων ωνος *m.* [perh. μῦς; πάρων *light ship*] **light swift ship, galley** (used esp. by pirates) Plu.
μύ-ουρος ον *adj.* [μῦς, οὐρά] **1 like a mouse's tail** (app. regarded as forming a slim or insubstantial appendage into which the body tapers; (of satyrs' phalluses, when not erect) **like mouse-tails** A.*satyr.fr.*
2 (of clauses and periodic sentences) **tailing off** or **slender, short** (opp. long) Arist.; (of a plot, when narrated too briefly) **insubstantial, inadequate** Arist.
μύραινα ης *f.* **moray eel** (as exemplar of a dangerous sea-creature) A. Ar.
μυρεψικός ή όν *adj.* [μυρεψός] **1** (of the art) **of perfumery** Arist.
2 (of a reed plant) **used in perfumery** Plb.
μυρ-εψός οῦ *m.* [μύρον, ἕψω] **one who decocts perfume, perfumer** Plu.
μυριάκις *adv.* [μυρίος] **ten thousand times, countless times** Ar. Pl. Aeschin. D. Arist. Men. Plu.
μυρι-άμφορος ον *adj.* [ἀμφορεύς] (of a verbal expression) **with the capacity of countless amphoras** (i.e. infinitely impressive) Ar.
μυρί-ανδρος ον *adj.* [ἀνήρ] **1** (of a city) **with a myriad of men, very populous** Isoc. Arist. Plu.
2 (of a bodyguard) **of a myriad of men** Plu.
μυρι-άρχης εω Ion.*m.* —also **μυρίαρχος** ου *m.* [ἄρχω] **commander of ten thousand men** Hdt. X.
μυριάς, Boeot. **μουριάς**, άδος *f.* **1 ten thousand** (usu. W.GEN. of persons or things) Hdt. E. Th. Ar. Att.orats. Pl. +; (gener., as a very large incalculable number) **multitude, myriad** A. E. Lys. Ar. Isoc. Pl. +
2 ‖ ADJ. (of men, cities, stones) **innumerable** Hdt. E. Corinn.(cj.)
μυρι-έτης ες *adj.* [ἔτος] (of a period of time) **of ten thousand years, incalculable** A.
μυρίζω, dial. **σμυρίζω** *vb.* [μύρον] | *aor.* ἐμύρισα ‖ *pf.pass. ptcpl.* μεμυρισμένος, dial. ἐσμυριχμένος (Archil.) | **anoint with perfumed oil** —*a person* Ar. —*a corpse* NT. ‖ MID. **put on perfume** Men. ‖ STATV.PF.PASS. **have** (W.ACC. one's hair, head, body) **perfumed** Archil. Hdt. Ar.

μυρίκη ης *f.* | nom.pl. μυρῖκαι (*metri grat.*) | **tamarisk** Il. hHom. Hdt. Theoc.

μυρίκινος η ον *adj.* (of the shoot) **of a tamarisk** Il.

μυριό-καρπος ον *adj.* [μῦρίος, καρπός¹] (of foliage) **with innumerable fruits** S.

μυριό-κρᾱνος ον *adj.* [κρᾱνίον¹] (of the Hydra) **with innumerable heads, myriad-headed** E.

μῡριό-λεκτος ον *adj.* [λεκτός] (of a remark) **spoken ten thousand times, endlessly repeated** X.

μῡριό-νεκρος ον *adj.* [νεκρός] (of battles) **with incalculable numbers of dead** Plu.

μῡριόντ-αρχος ου *m.* [ἄρχω] **commander of ten thousand men** A.

μῡριοπλάσιος ον *adj.* (of things) **ten thousand times more** (W.COMPAR.GEN. than persons, i.e. than they have) X.; (of harmful things, than an animal, i.e. than it can do) Arist.

μῡριό-πλεθρος ον *adj.* [πλέθρον] (of land) **measuring ten thousand plethra** Plb.

μῡριο-πληθής ές *adj.* [πλῆθος] (of good order) **creating an abundant population** E.(dub.)

μῡρίος ᾱ (Ion. η) ον *adj.* **1** incalculable in number; (of persons, animals, things) **innumerable, countless** Hom. +; (collectv.sg., of a crowd, race, military force, or sim.) E. AR.; (sg. for pl., of a path) Pi. B.; (of a report) B.; (of a hand) E.
2 (of material things) incalculable in magnitude, amount or extent; (of shingle) **unlimited, boundless** Il.; (of wealth) hHom.; (of bronze, gold, a weight of gold) Pi. E. Theoc.; (of blood) E.; (of rain, sea) AR.
3 (of non-material things, such as grief, amazement, happiness, time) **measureless, immense, endless, infinite** Hom. +
4 [pl., accented μύριοι] (of persons or things) **ten thousand** Hes. Emp. Hdt. Th. +; (collectv.sg., of cavalry, infantry) A. Hdt. X. ‖ MASC.PL.SB. (as the title of an assembly of Arcadians) **Ten Thousand** X. D.

—**μῡρίον** neut.sg.adv. **to an immeasurable degree, immeasurably, infinitely** Pl.

—**μῡρίῳ** neut.dat.sg.adv. (in expressions of comparison or difference) **by an immeasurable amount, immeasurably, infinitely** E. Pl.

—**μῡρία** neut.pl.adv. **1 times without number** —*ref. to complaining* Call.*epigr.*
2 [μύρια] **by the ten thousands** —*ref. to counting* A.

μῡριοστός ή όν *num.adj.* **1** (of a year) **ten thousandth** Pl. Arist.; (of a person, in ranking) X.
2 (of a part) **ten thousandth, tiniest** Ar.

μῡριοστύς ύος *f.* (milit.) **division of ten thousand men** X.

μῡριο-ταγός οῦ (or **μῡριόταγος** ου) *m.* **commander of ten thousand men** A.(cj.)

μῡριο-τεύχης ες *adj.* [τεύχεα] (of a commander, or perh. his fleet) **with countless armed men** E.

μῡριο-φόρος ον *adj.* [φέρω] **with a capacity of ten thousand** (perh. talents); (of a ship) **of large tonnage** Th.

μῡρι-ωπός όν *adj.* [ὤψ] (of a herdsman, ref. to Argus) **myriad-eyed** A.

μύρμηξ ηκος, dial. **μύρμᾱξ** ᾱκος *m.* **ant** Hes.*fr.* Archil. A. Hdt. Ar. Pl. +; (ref. to fabled giant creatures in India, which dig up gold) Hdt. Call.; (fig.ref. to people in a crowd) Theoc.

Μυρμιδόνες ων *m.pl.* **Myrmidons** (members of a warlike Thessalian people, ruled by Peleus, who fought under Achilles at Troy) Hom. Hes. Stesich. Pi.*fr.* E. Call.; (early inhabitants of Aegina, who migrated w. Peleus to Thessaly) Pi. AR.

—**Μυρμιδών** όνος *masc.adj.* (of an army) **Myrmidon** E.

μύρομαι *mid.vb.* [perh.reltd. μορμύρω] | ep.2sg.subj. μύρηαι (Theoc.) | ep.3sg.impf. μύρετο | aor.: ep.3sg. μύρατο, inf. μύρασθαι (Mosch.) | **1 shed tears, weep** or **lament** Hom. Hes. Thgn. B. Hellenist.poet. —W.ACC. **for someone** Hellenist.poet. | see also μνάομαι 3
2 (of a river) **flow** AR.; (of buildings) **drip** —W.DAT. *w. blood* AR.

—**μύρω** *act.vb.* | ep.impf. μῦρον | (fig., of arrows, meton. for deadly poison) **drip** —W.DAT. *w. tears* Hes.

μύρον ου *n.* **perfumed unguent** (a compound of oil and aromatic fragrance), **perfume** Archil. +

μυρο-ποιός οῦ *m.* [ποιέω] **maker of perfumes, perfumer** Anacr.

μυρο-πώλης ου *m.* [πωλέω] **perfume-seller** X. Hyp.

—**μυρόπωλις** ιδος *f.* **female perfume-seller, perfume-woman** Ar.

μυροπώλιον ου *n.* **perfume shop** Att.orats. Thphr. Plu.

μυρό-χριστος ον *adj.* [χριστός] **anointed with perfume** E.*Cyc.*

μύρρᾱ ᾱς Aeol.*f.* [reltd. σμύρνα] **myrrh** Sapph.

μύρρινος Att.*adj.*: see μύρσινος

μυρρινών ῶνος Att.*m.* [μυρσίνη] **myrtle grove** Ar.

μυρσίνη, Att. **μυρρίνη**, ης, dial. **μυρσίνα** ᾱς *f.* [μύρτος]
1 myrtle shrub, myrtle Archil. Pi. E. Men. Plu.
2 myrtle branch or **sprig** Hdt. E. Ar. Pl. Plu.
3 myrtle garland Ar. Thphr. Plu.

μυρσινο-ειδής ές *adj.* [μύρσινος, εἶδος¹] (of branches) **having the form of myrtle, of myrtle** hHom.

μύρσινος, Att. **μύρρινος**, η ον *adj.* **1** (of leaves, a branch) **of myrtle** Stesich. Call.
2 ‖ NEUT.SB. **myrtle bush** (fig.ref. to male pubic hair) Ar.

μυρτίς ίδος *f.* [μύρτος] **myrtle shrub, myrtle** Philox.Leuc. Plb.

μύρτον ου *n.* **1 myrtle shrub, myrtle** Ibyc. Plu.
2 ‖ PL. **myrtle berries** Ar. Pl. Thphr.
3 myrtle bush (fig.ref. to the female pubic area) Archil. Ar.

μύρτος ου *f.* **1 myrtle shrub, myrtle** Scol. Simon. Ar. Call. Theoc.*epigr.*
2 ‖ PL. **sprig of myrtles** (for a garland) Pi. Ar.

μύρω *vb.*: see under μύρομαι

μύρωμα ατος *n.* [μύρον] **application of perfume** Ar.

μῦς μυός *m.* | acc.sg. μῦν, pl. μῦς | **1** small rodent; (esp.) **mouse** or **rat** Hdt. Ar. Arist. Thphr. Plu. | see also ἀρουραῖος 1
2 (provbs.) μῦς πίττης γεύεται (or sim.) *he is like a mouse tasting pitch* (ref. to embarking on an action w. a risky outcome, i.e. playing w. fire) D. Theoc.; ὠδίνειν ὄρος, εἶτα μῦν ἀποτεκεῖν (the saying that) *the mountain goes into labour, then gives birth to a mouse* (ref. to an outcome falling short of expectation) Plu.
3 [reltd. μυών] **muscle** X. Theoc.

μύσαγμα ατος *n.* [μυσάττομαι] **feeling of revulsion, disgust, distaste** A.

μύσαν (ep.3pl.aor.): see μύω

μυσαρός ά όν *adj.* [μύσος] **1** (of circumstances or material things) **causing defilement** or **pollution, defiling, polluting** Hdt. E.
2 (specif., of actions assoc.w. the killing of kin) **polluted** or **polluting** E.
3 (of killers of kin) **polluted, defiled** E.; (W.DAT. by bloodshed) E.
4 (gener., of persons) **loathsome, abominable, vile** E. Ar. Theoc.; (of a cannibal's teeth) **revolting** or **polluted** E.*Cyc.*

μυσάττομαι Att.*mid.vb.* [μύσος] | aor.pass. (w.mid.sens.) ἐμυσάχθην | **be disgusted by** —*an event, foodstuffs* E. X.

μυσίδδω Lacon.*vb.*: see μυθίζω

Μῡσοί ῶν m.pl. **Mysians** (occupants of a region in NW. Asia Minor; as a population or military force) Il. Hes.fr. Anacr. A. Hdt. E. +; (provbl. for weakness or cowardice) Pl. D. Arist.; (title of a play by Aeschylus or Sophocles) Arist. ‖ SG. Mysian man S.fr. Pl. X.

—**Μῡσός**[1] οῦ m. **Mysos** (king after whom the people were reputedly named) Hdt.

—**Μῡσός**[2] ή όν adj. (of men) **Mysian** A. E.fr. Ar. X. AR.; (of a city) A.(dub.); (of a mountain) Call.

—**Μῡσίᾱ** ᾱς, Ion. **Μῡσίη** ης f. land of the Mysians, **Mysia** Hdt. E.fr. X. Arist. +

—**Μῡσιος** ᾱ (Ion. η) ον adj. of or relating to the Mysians; (of a man) **Mysian** A.; (of the land, mountains, a city, artefacts, or sim.) Pi. Hdt. S. E.fr. Ar. Tim. +; (advbl.phr.) τὸ Μύσιον *in the Mysian manner* (ref. to lamenting loudly) A.

—**Μῡσίς** ίδος fem.adj. (of the land) **Mysian** AR. ‖ SB. land of Mysia AR.

μύσος εος (ους) n. **1 defilement, pollution** (usu. fr. the murder of kin) Emp. Trag. Plu.

2 perh., object of loathing, **abomination** (ref. to Erinyes) A.

μυσο-πολέω contr.vb. [μῦς] (of a person) **scurry about like a mouse** or **rat** Ar.

μυσσωτός, Att. **μυττωτός**, οῦ m. a kind of spicy sauce (of crushed garlic, w. cheese, honey, oil, vinegar, or sim.), **savoury sauce** Hippon. Anan. Ar.

μυσταγωγίᾱ ᾱς f. [μυσταγωγός] **initiate-guidance** Plu.; (fig.ref. to the escorting of the procession of initiates fr. Athens to Eleusis) Plu.

μυστ-αγωγός οῦ m. [μύστης] **1** one who instructs or sponsors a candidate for initiation into the mysteries, **initiation-guide** Plu.

2 (fig.ref. to a kindly daimon) **guide to the mysteries** (W.GEN. of life) Men.

μύσταξ ακος dial.m. [perh.reltd. μάσταξ] **moustache** Theoc. Plu.

μυστήρια ων n.pl. [μύστης] **1** mystery or secret rites, **mysteries** Heraclit.; (of an Egyptian god, the Kabeiroi on Samothrace) Hdt.; (at Rome) Plu.

2 Mysteries (esp. of Demeter and Kore at Eleusis) E. Th. Ar. Att.orats. X. Arist. +; (defined as μεγάλα *greater*, opp. (σ)μικρά *lesser*, held at Agrai nr. Athens) Ar. Pl. Plu.; (concr., ref. to the place or buildings where the rites were conducted) E.

3 (fig., ref. to arcane teachings or philosophical doctrines) **mysteries** Ar. Pl.

4 mysteries, secrets (W.GEN. of the Kingdom of Heaven) NT.(also sg.)

μυστηρικός ή όν adj. (of pigs, for sacrifice) **at the Mysteries** Ar.

μυστηριῶτις ιδος fem.adj. (of a truce) **for the Mysteries** Aeschin.

μύστης ου m. [μύω, μυέω] **1** app., one who closes his eyes (during initiation) or his lips (to keep a secret), **initiate** E. Lys. Ar. X. Aeschin. +; (W.GEN. of a god) E.fr.

2 ‖ ADJ. (of dances) of initiates Ar.

μυστικός ή όν adj. relating to the mysteries; (of Iacchus or the Iacchic song) **mystic** Hdt. Plu.; (of visions and voices) Plu.; (of torches, their aroma) Ar. Plu.; (of baskets carried in procession) Plu.; (of sacrificial pigs) Ar. ‖ NEUT.PL.SB. mysteries Th. Arist. Plu.

μυστιλάομαι mid.contr.vb. [μυστίλη] **1 spoon up soup with bread** Ar.; (fig.) **spoon up** —W.PARTITV.GEN. *public money* Ar.

2 ‖ PASS. (of a bread-spoon) be scooped into shape —W.DAT. *by hand* Ar.

μυστίλη ης f. piece of bread scooped out in the form of a spoon, **bread-spoon** Ar.

μυστο-δόκος ον adj. [μύστης, δέχομαι] (of a temple) **receiving initiates** Ar.

μυσώδης ες adj. [μύσος] (of an act of impiety) **abominable** Plu.

Μυτιλήνη, also **Μιτυλήνη** (NT. Plu.), ης, dial. **Μυτιλήνᾱ** (Carm.Pop.), also **Μιτυλήνᾱ** (Theoc. Mosch.), ᾱς f. **Mytilene** (chief city of Lesbos) Hdt. +

—**Μυτιληναῖος**, also **Μιτυληναῖος** (Call. Plu.), Aeol. **Μυτιλήναος**, ᾱ (Ion. η) ον adj. of or from Mytilene; (of a man) **Mytilenean** Sapph. Hdt. Pl. Call.epigr. Plu.; (of a ship) Hdt. ‖ MASC.PL.SB. Mytileneans (as a population or military force) Hdt. Th. Att.orats. Pl. +

μυττωτεύω Att.vb. [μυσσωτός] pound into a savoury sauce; (fig.) **beat to a pulp** —*a person* Ar.

μυττωτός Att.m.: see μυσσωτός

μύχατος (superl.adj.): see μύχιος

μυχθίζω vb. [reltd. μύζω[1]] | ep.3pl.aor.opt. μυχθίσσειαν | **1** exhale loudly; (of the Cyclopes, labouring in a forge) **snort** Call.

2 sneer —W.DAT. *w. the lips* Theoc.

3 mutter contemptuously Plb.

μυχθισμός οῦ m. laboured breathing, **gasping** (W.GEN. of dying men) E.

μύχιος ᾱ (Ion. η) ον adj. [μύχος] | irreg.superl. μυχοίτατος (Od.), μύχατος (Call. AR.) | **1** (of a temple-servant) **of the inner chamber** Hes.; (quasi-advbl., of a person lying down) **in the inner chamber** (of a house) Hes.; (of Eros mating w. Khaos) **in a secluded recess** (of the earth) Ar.(cj.)

2 (of breezes) **from the depths** (of the earth) AR.

3 (of the Propontis) having recesses or bays, **formed into bays** A.

4 ‖ SUPERL. (of a building, the earth, a coast, river, sea, its depths) at or from the innermost, remotest or deepest part Call. AR.; (quasi-advbl., of a person sitting) in the furthest corner Od.

μυχμός οῦ m. [μύζω[1]] **groaning, moaning** Od.

μυχόθεν adv.: see under μυχός

μυχοίτατος (irreg.superl.adj.): see μύχιος

μυχός οῦ m. | also neut.pl. μυχά (Call.) | **1** (sg. and pl.) innermost or secluded part (of a dwelling or structure); **innermost part, recess** or **corner** (usu. W.GEN. of a house, room, cave, tomb, or sim.) Hom. hHom. Semon. Sol. Pi. Hdt. Trag. +

2 (sg. and pl.) **inner sanctum** (of a temple or oracle) A. Pi. E. Call.

3 ‖ PL. inner rooms (W.GEN. of a city, ref. to its storerooms or coffers) Xenoph.

4 innermost part (W.GEN. of a harbour) Th. ‖ PL. recesses, nooks (W.GEN. of a harbour, as a refuge for fish fleeing a dolphin) Il.; (of the thighs) Ar.

5 innermost part, **head** (of a gulf or lake) Hdt. Plb.

6 inner part, **interior** (W.GEN. of a country) Pi.

7 remote corner (W.GEN. of a region) Hom.; (of islands) Hes.; (of a sea) AR. ‖ PL. far reaches (W.GEN. of a country, the sea) E.

8 hollow recess (W.GEN. of a rock, ref. to a cave) E.; (of an island, ref. to a cavern) AR.

9 (sg. and pl.) remote subterranean recess, **depths** (W.GEN. of the earth) Hes. E. Aeschin.(quot. E.); (of Hades) Anacr. A. E. ‖ PL. inner depths (of Mt. Aetna) Pi. Call.

10 (sg. and pl.) **depths** (of the sea) Pi. Ar.

11 recess or hollow (betw. mountains), **valley, glen** A. Pi. B. X. ‖ PL. (gener., ref. to glens or sim.) haunts (W.GEN. of the Muses) Pi.
12 indentation of the sea (into land), **bay or gulf** A. E. AR.
13 ‖ PL. recesses, upper reaches (W.GEN. of the air) E.; (of the stars, i.e. depths of heaven) E.
14 (sg., fig.) **recesses, depths** (W.GEN. of the mind) Theoc.
15 (fig., prep.phr.) διὰ μυχῶν in a hole-and-corner way (i.e. covertly) S.
—**μυχόθεν** adv. **from the innermost part** (of a house) A.
—**μυχόνδε** adv. **1 to the innermost part** (W.GEN. of a hall) Od.
2 into a recess or **cavern** (in the ground) AR.
μυχώδης ες adj. (of cliffs) full of recesses, **cavernous** E.
μύω vb. | aor. ἔμυσα, ep.3pl. μύσαν | **1** (pres.) **have one's eyes closed** Pl. X. Arist. Call.; (aor.) **close one's eyes** S. Ar. Pl.; (fig.) —W.DAT. **to reasoning** Plu.
2 (aor., of eyes) **close** Il. E.; (fig., of pain) **be lulled to rest, abate** S.
3 (aor.) **close one's mouth** Plu.; (of mouths of passageways) **close** Pl.
μυών ῶνος m. [reltd. μῦς 3] **muscle** Il. AR. Theoc.
μυωπίζω vb. [μύωψ¹] **1** ‖ PASS. (of a horse) **be troubled by flies** X.
2 spur on —a horse X.; (fig.) —**oneself** Plb.
μύωψ¹ ωπος m. **1** insect which torments horses and cattle, **gadfly, horsefly** A. E.fr. Call. AR.
2 spur (attached to a rider's heel) X.; (pl.) Thphr. Plb. Plu.
3 (fig., ref. to a person) **spur** (W.GEN. to action) Plu.; (ref. to Socrates) Pl. [unless gadfly]
μύ-ωψ² ωπος masc.fem.adj. —also **μυωπός** όν (X.) adj. [μύω, ὤψ] (of persons, hounds) closing the eyes (i.e. squinting, through short-sightedness), **short-sighted** X. Arist.
Μωᾶ Lacon.f.: see Μοῦσα
μῶλος ου m. **1 struggle, battle** (in war) Il. Hes. Archil. AR.
2 fight, brawl (betw. individuals) Od.
μῶλυ n. | only acc. | **moly** (a magical plant) Od.
μώλωψ ωπος m. **bruise** Plu.
μώμαι dial.mid.vb. [perh.reltd. μαίομαι, μαιμάω] | only ptcpl. μώμενος, imperatv. μῶσο, inf. μῶσθαι | **seek after, be intent on** —sthg. Thgn. A. S. X.(quot.com.) —W.INF. doing sthg. A.; (reltd. Μοῦσα in a fanciful etymology) Pl.
μωμάομαι, Ion. **μωμέομαι** mid.contr.vb. [μῶμος] | Ion.3pl. μωμεῦνται, Ion.ptcpl. μωμεύμενος, Lacon.inf. μωμῆσθαι | fut. μωμήσομαι | ep.3sg.aor. μωμήσατο, dial. μωμάσατο | **find fault with, blame, criticise** —someone or sthg. Il. Alcm. Semon. Thgn. Simon. A. Hellenist.poet.; (intr.) **find fault** Thgn. Ar.
μωμεύω vb. **find fault** Od. Hes.
μωμητός ή όν adj. [μωμάομαι] (of a person) **able to be faulted, reproachable** A.

μῶμος ου m. **1 blame, reproach, censure** Od. Semon. Thgn. Lyr.
2 (personif., son of Night) **Censure** Hes. Pl. Call.
μῶν interrog.pcl. [μή, οὖν] | The pcl. freq. implies that the questioner is reluctant to accept that the suggestion posed by his question is true (fr. certainty that it is not true, hope that it may not be true, apprehension or surprise at the possibility that it is true). It may also convey genuine uncertainty, and even expectation of a positive answer. |
1 it is not the case that ... ? Hippon. Trag. Ar. Pl. • μῶν βεβούλευμαι κακῶς; I have not made a bad decision, have I? E. • μῶν καὶ θεός περ ἱμέρῳ πεπληγμένος; not smitten with passion, even though a god? A.
2 (uncertainty) **is it the case that ... ?** • μῶν ἐκ θεῶν του καινὸν ἀγγέλλεις ἔπος; are you bringing news from one of the gods? E. • μῶν ἀπολώλεκε τὰς ἐμβάδας; did he lose his shoes? Ar.
3 (expecting a positive answer) **so may I assume that ... ?** • μῶν τὸν λάρυγγα διεκάναξέ σου καλῶς; so it (the wine) gurgled nicely down your throat? E.Cyc.
μῶνος dial.adj.: see μόνος
μῶνυξ υχος masc.fem.adj. —also **μώνυχος** ον (E.) adj. [perh.reltd. εἷς; ὄνυξ] (of horses) with single hoof (opp. the cloven hoof of sheep and cattle), **solid-hoofed** Hom. Hes.fr. Sol. Thgn. E.; (of a class of animals) Pl.
μωραίνω vb. [μωρός] | fut. μωρανῶ | aor. ἐμώρᾱνα ‖ aor.pass. ἐμωράνθην | **1 be foolish** or **stupid** E. X. Arist. —W.INTERN.ACC. in an undertaking (i.e. foolishly undertake sthg.) A.
2 (w. sexual connot., of a woman) **be wayward** or **irresponsible** E.(dub.)
3 ‖ PASS. (of salt) **become insipid** or **tasteless** NT.
μωρίᾱ ᾱς, Ion. **μωρίη** ης f. **1 folly, stupidity** Hdt. Trag. Th. Ar. Isoc. Pl. +
2 (euphem., w. sexual connot.) **waywardness, irresponsibility** (of a man or woman) E.
μωροποιέομαι mid.contr.vb. (of avarice) **cause foolish behaviour** Plb.
μωρός ά όν, Att. **μῶρος** ᾱ ον (also ος ον E.) adj. **1** (pejor., of persons) lacking in intelligence, **foolish, stupid** Simon. S. E. Ar. Isoc. Pl. +; (of speech, thoughts, behaviour) S. E. Ar. Isoc. X.
2 (euphem., w. sexual connot., of a man or woman) **wayward, irresponsible** E. ‖ NEUT.SB. wantonness, sexual irresponsibility E.
—**μώρως** adv. **foolishly** X.
Μῶσα dial.f.: see Μοῦσα
μῶσθαι (dial.mid.inf.): see μῶμαι
μωσικός dial.adj.: see μουσικός
μῶσο (dial.mid.imperatv.): see μῶμαι
Μωσο-φίλειτος ον dial.adj. [Μοῦσα, φιλητός] (of a place) **loved by the Muses** Corinn.

N ν

ναα (dial.acc.sg.), **ναας** (dial.acc.pl.), **ναες** (dial.nom.pl.), **νάεσσι** (Aeol.dat.pl.): see ναῦς

ναέτᾱς ᾱ *dial.m.* [ναιετάω] **inhabitant** (W.GEN. of a place) Simon.

—**ναιέτις** ιδος *f.* (ref. to a goddess) **resident** (W.GEN. of a place) Call.

νᾱέω *dial.contr.vb.*: see νηέω

ναί *adv.* [reltd. νή] **1 yes indeed** (expressing strong affirmation in response to another person's words; standing alone or introducing a reply) Hom. +; (reinforced by repetition) ναὶ ναί A. S. Ar. Call. Theoc. NT.; (w. another pcl.) ναὶ δή Hom. AR.; ναὶ μάν Theoc.
2 (introducing an emph. repetition of one's own statement or q.) • σέ τοι, σὲ κρίνω, ναὶ σέ *you, I mean you, yes you* S. • προφήτην; ναί, λέγω ὑμῖν, καὶ περισσότερον προφήτου *a prophet? Yes, I tell you, and more than a prophet* NT.
3 (indicating assent, w. some reservation conveyed by an adversative conj.) • ναί, ἀλλά *yes, but* Att.orats. Pl. Arist.
4 (affirmative, in an oath, w. μά + ACC.) • ναὶ μὰ Δία, μὰ τόδε σκῆπτρον *yes by Zeus, by this staff* (or sim.) Il. hHom. Thgn. Pi. + • (also W.ACC. without μά) E. Ar. X.
5 (in supplication or strong request) **yes, I implore you** (w. πρός + GEN. by the gods, my right hand, or sim.) E. Ar. Men.

—**ναίχι** (also **ναιχί**) *adv.* [ναί, w. intensv. suffix, cf. οὐχί] (expressing strong affirmation) **yes indeed** S. Ar. Men. Call.*epigr.*; (also introducing an oath, w. πρός + GEN. by Ganymede) Call.*epigr.*

ναῖ (dial.dat.), **ναι** (Aeol.dat.): see ναῦς

ναιάς, Ion. **νηιάς**, άδος (also **N-**) *f.* —also **ναΐς**, Ion. **νηΐς**, ΐδος (also **N-**) *f.* [νάω] **nymph of flowing water, naiad, Naiad** (sts. appos.w. νύμφη) Hom. Lyr. A.*satyr.fr.* E. X. +

ναΐδιον ου *n.* [dimin. ναός¹] **small shrine** (in a house) Plb.

ναιετάω *contr.vb.* [app.intensv. ναίω] | always uncontr., except in S. | ptcpl. ναιετῶν (S., cj.), ep.fem.ptcpl. ναιετάωσα, perh. also ναιετόωσα | iteratv.impf. (w.diect.) ναιετάασκον |
1 (of persons, deities) **live habitually or permanently** (in a place); **live, dwell, have a home** —W.ADV., DAT. or PREP.PHR. *in or near a place, w. someone, or sim.* Hom. Hes. hHom. Pi. Call. AR.
2 (tr.) **inhabit** —*a place* Hom. hHom. Simon. S. AR.; **live in, have** —*a house* (W.DAT. or PREP.PHR. *in a certain place*) Il. Hes. hHom.
3 (of cities, islands) **be situated, be found** —W.PREP.PHR. *in a certain place* Hom. Hes.*fr.* AR.

—**ναιετάων** ωσα ον *ptcpl.adj.* (of an island) app., having inhabitants, **inhabited** Od.; (w. εὖ well, of a city, house) **well-peopled, thriving, prosperous** Hom. Hes.*fr.* hHom.

ναιέτις *f.*: see under ναέτᾱς

ναῖον¹ (ep.impf.): see ναίω

ναῖον² (ep.impf.): see νάω

νάϊος¹ ᾱ ον *adj.* [ναός¹] (of the navel of the earth) **of** or **in the temple** (at Delphi) Pi.(cj.)

νάϊος² *dial.adj.*: see νήιος

ναΐς *f.*: see ναιάς

ναιχί (also **ναιχί**) *adv.*: see under ναί

ναίω *vb.* | ep.impf. ναῖον, iteratv.impf. ναίεσκον | aor. ἔνασσα, ep. νάσσα || MID.: fut. νάσσομαι (AR.) | ep.aor. νασσάμην || PASS.: aor. ἐνάσθην, ep. νάσθην | **1** (of persons, gods, spirits) **dwell, live** —W.ADV., DAT. or PREP.PHR. *in a place* Hom. Hes. Thgn. Lyr. Trag. Ar. +; (of Inferiority, Virtue) —W.ADV. or PREP.PHR. *nearby, in an inaccessible place* Hes. Simon.; (wkr.sens., of an island) **lie, be situated** (in a place) Hom. S.; (of anger) **be present, exist** (in or w. someone) S.
2 (tr.) **live in, inhabit** —*a place, house* Hom. Hes. Sol. Lyr. Trag. + || PASS. (of a city) **be inhabited** or **settled in** —W.DAT. *by people* Hellenist.poet.
3 || AOR. **build** —*a temple* hHom.; **establish** —*a city* (W.DAT. *for someone, i.e. to live in*) Od. || AOR.MID. **establish** —*cities* AR.
4 || AOR. **settle** —*someone* (W.PREP.PHR. or ADV. *in a place*) Pi. AR.(mid.) || AOR. and FUT.MID. (of persons, gods) **settle** —W.ACC. or PREP.PHR. *in a place* Hes. AR. || AOR.PASS. **be settled, settle** (in a place) Il. Call. AR.

—**ναιόμενος** η ον *pass.ptcpl.adj.* (w. εὖ, of islands, cities) **well-peopled, thriving, prosperous** Hom.

νάκη ης *f.* **skin** or **fleece** (of a goat, used to sleep on) Od.

νάκος εος (ους) *n.* **skin** or **fleece** (esp. of a ram or goat) Pi. Hdt. Theoc.

νακτός ή όν *adj.* [νάσσω] (of builders' sand) **close-packed** Plu.

νᾶμα ατος *n.* [νάω] **1 that which flows; water** (of a river) Theoc.; (for drinking) E.*Cyc.*; (for agriculture, bathing) Pl.; (fig., of the grape, ref. to wine) Ar.; (of the nymphs, ref. to water opp. wine) Men.
2 stream, waters (of a river or spring) E. Pl. X. Arist.; (of a named deity) Trag. Pl. Theoc. || PL. **source** or **supply** (of water or other liquid) Pl.
3 flowing stream (usu. of liquid); **stream, flood** (of tears) S. E.; (of nourishment, in the veins) Pl.; (of fire) E.; (of speech) Pl.

ναματιαῖος ᾱ ον *adj.* (of water) **of** or **from streams, flowing** Aeschin.

νᾱμέρτεια ᾱς *dial.f.* [νημερτής] **truth** or **fulfilment** (of a prophecy) S.

νᾱμερτής *dial.adj.*: see νημερτής

νᾱνο-φυής ές *adj.* [νᾶνος *dwarf*, φυή] (pejor., of dancers) of dwarf-like stature or appearance, **dwarfish** Ar.

Ναξιουργής ές *adj.* [Νάξος, ἔργον] (of a kind of boat) **made in Naxos** Ar.

Νάξος ου *f.* **Naxos** (Aegean island) hHom. Archil. Anan. A. +

—**Νάξιος** ᾱ ον *adj.* (of a man) **of** or **from Naxos, Naxian** Hdt.

ναον

Arist. Call.*epigr.*; (of a whetstone) Pi. || MASC.PL.SB. Naxians (as a population or military force) Archil. Hdt. Th. Arist. Plu.
—**Ναξόθεν** *adv.* from Naxos Pi.*fr.*
ναον (ep.impf.): see νάω
ναο-ποιός οῦ *m.* [νᾱός¹, ποιέω] temple-builder Arist.
ναο-πόλος, Ion. **νηοπόλος**, ου *m.* [πέλω] temple-servant Hes. Pi.*fr.*
ναός¹, Ion. **νηός**, οῦ, Att. **νεώς** νεώ, Aeol. **ναυος** ναύω *m.* [app.reltd. ναίω] | Att.acc. νεών, dat. νεῷ | **1** temple (consecrated to the worship of a divinity) Hom. +; (fig., ref. to Christ's body) NT.
2 representation of a temple (in wood, used to carry a god's image in procession), **shrine** Hdt.
ναός² (dial.gen.), **ναος** (Aeol.gen.): see ναῦς
ναο-φύλαξ ακος *m.* [ναός¹] temple custodian E. Arist.
ναπαῖος ᾱ ον *adj.* [νάπη] (of winding terrain, plains) among valleys S. E.
νάπη ης *f.* mountain valley, glen Il. Lyr. Hdt. S. E. Ar. +
νάποινος *dial.adj.*: see νήποινος
νάπος εος (ους) *n.* **1** mountain valley, glen Pi. S. E. Theoc. Bion
2 gorge, ravine X.
νᾶπυ υος *n.* [reltd. σίνᾱπι] mustard; (fig.phr.) βλέπειν νᾶπυ *give a look as sharp as mustard* Ar.
νάρδινος η ον *adj.* [νάρδος] (of a kind of perfumed oil) made from nard Plb.
νάρδος ου *f.* [loanwd.] a kind of aromatic plant (or the oil derived fr. it); **spikenard, nard** (appos.w. μύρον *oil*) NT.
ναρθηκο-πλήρωτος ον *adj.* [νάρθηξ, πληρόω] (of the source of fire given to mortals) **placed in a fennel-stalk** A.
ναρθηκο-φόρος ου *m.* [φέρω] fennel-rod bearer (ref. to a Bacchic worshipper) Pl.; (iron., ref. to a fighter in a mock battle) X.
νάρθηξ ηκος *m.* **1** giant fennel plant or stem, **fennel-stalk** (in which Prometheus concealed fire) Hes.
2 fennel rod (used for beating someone) X. Plu.; (ref. to the Bacchic thyrsos) E.
3 a kind of container (for a manuscript, perh. made fr. the plant or named fr. its cylindrical shape), **canister, casket** Plu.
ναρκάω *contr.vb.* [νάρκη] **1** (of a person, part of the body) **become numb** (fr. a wound, the shock of a sting-ray) Il. Pl.; (of eyes) **grow dim** Bion
2 (of a person, fr. strong emotion or state of confusion) **grow weak** or **faint** Theoc. —W.ACC. *in one's mind and speech* Pl.
νάρκη ης *f.* **1** a kind of fish, **sting-ray, torpedo** Pl.
2 torpor, numbness (in the body) Ar. Theoc.
—**ναρκίον** ου *n.* [dimin.] ray or skate (as a culinary delicacy) Philox.Leuc.
νάρκισσος ου *m.f.* a kind of flower, **narcissus** (ref. to various species) hHom. S. Theoc. Mosch.
ναρκώδης ες *adj.* [νάρκη] (of a distressing sensation) **of widespread numbness** (in the feet) Plu.
νάσθην (ep.aor.pass.): see ναίω
νᾱσιώτᾱς *dial.m.*, **νᾱσιῶτις** *dial.fem.adj.*: see νησιώτης
νασμός οῦ *m.* [νάω] **1** flowing waters (of a river or spring, esp. to drink or for purification) A.*fr.* E.
2 stream of water (poured for washing) E.
3 gushing (of blood) E.
νᾶσος *dial.f.*: see νῆσος
νάσσα (ep.aor.): see ναίω
νᾶσσα *dial.f.*: see νῆσσα
νασσάμην (ep.aor.), **νάσσομαι** (fut.mid.): see ναίω
νάσσω, Att. **νάττω** *vb.* | aor. ἔναξα || pf.pass. νένασμαι | **pile up densely, pack** —*earth* (*around an object planted in the ground*) Od. || PASS. (of animal skins) **be piled high** (as a bed) Theoc.
ναστός οῦ *m.* large baked cake, **stuffed loaf** or **cake** (sts. assoc.w. sacrifices) Ar.
ναυᾱγέω, Ion. **ναυηγέω** *contr.vb.* [ναυᾱγός] (of ships, sailors) **be shipwrecked** Hdt. D. Plb.
ναυᾱγίᾱ ᾱς, Ion. **ναυηγίη** ης *f.* **shipwreck** Pi. Hdt. E. Ar. D. Plb.
ναυάγιον, Ion. **ναυήγιον**, ου *n.* **1** piece of wreckage Men. Plu.; (fig., ref. to a person) Plu. || PL. wrecked ships or pieces of wreckage A. Hdt. E. Th. Lys. X. +
2 (collectv.sg. and pl.) **shipwreck** E. Plu.; (fig., of a chariot team, in a race) S.; (of a city, envisaged as a ship) Plu.
ναυ-ᾱγός, Ion. **ναυηγός**, όν *adj.* [ναῦς, ἄγνυμι] (of persons) **shipwrecked** Hdt. E. X. Call.*epigr.*
ναυαρχέω *contr.vb.* [ναύαρχος] **be a naval commander** (sts. W.GEN. of ships) Hdt. X. D. Plb. Plu.
ναυαρχίᾱ ᾱς *f.* **1** office of naval commander, **naval command** Th. X. Arist. Plu.
2 period of naval command X.
3 naval supremacy or victory Arist.
ναυαρχίς ίδος *f.* commander's ship, **flagship** Plb. Plu.
ναύ-αρχος ου *m.* [ἄρχω] **1** commander of a ship, **captain** A. Hdt.
2 commander of a fleet, **admiral** (esp. in Sparta) Hdt. S. Th. Att.orats. +; (appos.w. *body of a king*) A.
ναυ-βάτης ου, dial. **ναυβάτᾱς** ᾱ *m.* [βαίνω] **1** one who goes by ship, **seafarer, mariner** B. Hdt. Trag. Th. Plu.; (appos.w. ἀνήρ) A. E.
2 || ADJ. (of an armed force, a host of men) going by ship, **seaborne** A. E.
ναύ-δετον ου *n.* [δέω¹] mooring rope for a ship, **hawser** E.
ναυηγέω *Ion.vb.*, **ναυηγίη** *Ion.f.*, **ναυηγός** *Ion.m.*: see ναυᾱγέω, ναυᾱγίᾱ, ναυᾱγός
ναυκληρέω *contr.vb.* [ναύκληρος] **1 be a ship-owner** Lys. Ar. X.
2 be in charge of a ship, be a ship's commander D. Plu.; (fig.) **captain, govern** —*a city* A. S.
3 (of a woman) **be manager of, manage** —*a boarding-house* Is.
ναυκληρίᾱ ᾱς *f.* **1** occupation of a ship-owner; (sts.pl.) **ship-owning** Att.orats. Pl. X. Arist. Plu.
2 (specif.) seafaring enterprise or expedition, **voyage** E.
3 (concr.) **vessel** (used for a particular voyage) E.
ναυκλήρια ων *n.pl.* **1** fleet of ships (owned by someone), **shipping** (for trading) D.
2 assembly of ships (drawn up in one place), **ships** E.
ναυκληρικός ή όν *adj.* of or relating to a ship-owner || NEUT.PL.SB. ship-owning Pl.
ναύκληρος ου *m.* [ναύκρᾱρος; 2nd el. κλῆρος, app. by pop.etym.] **1** one who owns a ship, **ship-owner** Hdt. S. Th. Ar. X. D. +
2 one who commands a ship, **captain** A.; (fig., ref. to a charioteer) E.
ναυκρᾱρίᾱ ᾱς *f.* [ναύκρᾱρος] (in the early Athenian constitution) administrative district (into which the city was subdivided for the purpose of collecting revenue, esp. for financing warships), **naucrary** Arist.
ναυκρᾱρικός ή όν *adj.* (of revenue) **from a naucrary** or **the naucraries** Arist.
ναύ-κρᾱρος ου *m.* [ναῦς, κάρᾱ] (at Athens) chief official of a naucrary, **naukraros** Hdt. Arist.
ναυ-κρατέες έων *Ion.masc.pl.adj.* [κρατέω] (of a people) **ruling by naval power** (W.GEN. over the sea) Hdt.

ναυκρατέω contr.vb. (of commanders, their forces) rule by naval power, **have control of the sea** Th. Plu. ‖ PASS. (of peoples) be defeated at sea X.

Ναύκρατις ιος f. Naucratis (earliest Greek settlement in Egypt) Hdt. Pl. Plb.

—**Ναυκρατίτης** ου m. **1 man of Naucratis** Call.epigr. **2** ‖ ADJ. (of a garland) of Naucratian style Anacr.

—**Ναυκρατιτικός** ή όν adj. (of goods) **from Naucratis** D.

ναυ-κράτωρ ορος m. [ναῦς, κράτος] **1 ship's captain** S. **2** ‖ PL. rulers of the sea Hdt. Th.; (W.GEN. over other peoples) Th.

ναῦλον ου n. —also **ναῦλος** ου (Ar.) m. **1** price of transport by ship or ferry, **fare, freight charge** (sts. W.GEN. or ὑπέρ + GEN. for persons or goods) Ar. X. D. Din. Plb. Plu. **2 freight, cargo** D.

ναυλόομαι mid.contr.vb. hire for oneself for sea-transport, **charter** —a ship Plb.

ναυλοχέω contr.vb. [ναύλοχος] (of commanders, warships) **lie in wait at sea** (usu. in a sheltered place) Hdt. E. Plu.; (tr., of a flotilla) **lie in wait for** —enemy ships Th.

ναυλόχια ων n.pl. **anchorages** or **harbours** Th.

ναύ-λοχος ον adj. [λόχος] **1** (of a bay) **affording safe harbour** Od.; (of a place) **where ships are beached** S. E. ‖ NEUT.PL.SB. anchorages or harbours Plu. **2** (of hot springs) **near sheltered waters** S.

ναυμαχέω contr.vb. [ναύμαχος] **1** (of a people, city-state, commander) **engage in naval warfare** or **take part in a sea-battle** (sts. W.DAT. or PREP.PHR. against an enemy, their ships) Hdt. Th. Ar. Att.orats. Pl. X. +; **fight** —W.COGN.ACC. a sea-battle Lys. Ar. D. **2** (fig.) **fight, battle** —W.DAT. against troubles Ar.; ram —W.DAT. a cunt Ar.

ναυμαχησείω vb. [desideratv. ναυμαχέω] (of troops) **be eager for a sea-battle** Th.

ναυμαχίᾱ ᾱς, Ion. **ναυμαχίη** ης f. **naval engagement, sea-battle** (oft. W.PREP.PHR. near a place or against someone) Hdt. Th. Att.orats. Pl. +; (opp. μάχη land battle) Th. Att.orats. Pl. Plb.

ναύ-μαχος ον adj. [ναῦς, μάχομαι] **1** (of weapons) **for sea-fighting** Il. Hdt. **2** (of persons) participating in sea-fights, **sea-fighting** Plu.; (in theatre shows) Plu.

ναῦος Aeol.m.: see ναός[1]

ναυπηγέω contr.vb. [ναυπηγός] **1** be a builder of ships or boats, **build ships** Ar. ‖ PASS. (of ships) be built Th. X. Arist. **2** ‖ MID. **build boats** Hdt. **3** ‖ MID. (of a city, a people) have (ships) built (for military purposes); **build** —ships, a fleet Hdt. Th. Att.orats. +; (intr.) Th. Pl. X. + **4** ‖ MID. **make repairs** (to an old ship) Ar.

ναυπηγήσιμος ον (also η ον Pl.) adj. (of timber) used for building ships, **for shipbuilding** Hdt. Th. Pl. X. +

ναυπηγίᾱ ᾱς, Ion. **ναυπηγίη** ης f. **1** process or business of building ships, **shipbuilding** Hdt. Th. Pl. Plb. Plu.; building (W.GEN. of warships) Th. Plu. **2 art of shipbuilding** Pl. Arist. **3 shipbuilding material** (ref. to wood) E.Cyc.

ναυπηγικός ή όν adj. of or relating to shipbuilding ‖ FEM.SB. art of shipbuilding Arist.

ναυπήγιον ου n. **shipyard** Ar.

ναυ-πηγός οῦ m. [ναῦς, πήγνῡμι] **shipbuilder, shipwright** Th. Pl. X. Arist. +

Ναυπλίᾱ ᾱς, Ion. **Ναυπλίη** ης f. **Nauplia** (coastal town nr. Argos) Hdt. E. X. Plu.

—**Ναύπλιος** ᾱ ον adj. (of the harbour, shore, land) of **Nauplia, Nauplian** E.

—**Ναυπλίειος** ᾱ ον adj. (of the harbour) **Nauplian** E.

ναυ-πόρος ον adj. [ναῦς, πορεύω] (of an oar, meton. for a ship or voyage) **seafaring** E.

—**ναύπορος** ον adj. [πόρος] **1** (of shores) **ship-frequented** A. **2** (of a channel) **navigable** AR.

ναυ-πρύτανις ιος masc.adj. (of an island's good fortune) **ship-ruling** Pi.fr.

ναῦς νεώς (ep. νηός, dial. νᾱός, Aeol. νᾶος), Ion. **νηῦς** νεός f. | acc.sg. ναῦν, dial. νᾶα, ep. νῆα (also νηῦν AR.), Ion. νέα | dat.sg. νηί, dial. νᾱί, Aeol. νᾶι | DU.: gen.dat. νεοῖν ‖ PL.: nom. νῆες, dial. νᾶες, Ion. νέες | acc. ναῦς, dial. νᾶας, ep. νῆας, Ion. νέας | gen. νεῶν, dial. νᾱῶν, ep. νηῶν, Aeol. νάων | dat. ναυσί, ep. νηυσί (also νήεσσι, νέεσσι), Aeol. νάεσσι | ep.gen.dat.sg.pl. ναῦφι | sea-going vessel (for travelling, trading, fighting), **ship** Hom. +; (W.ADJ. μακρά long, ref. to a warship) Hdt. Th. Ar. Plb. Plu.; (w. στρογγύλη round-hulled, ref. to a merchant ship) Hdt. Th. Plb. Plu.

—**νῆάδε** ep.adv. (w.vb. of movt.) **to a ship** Od.; (also) μετὰ νῆάδε AR.

ναυσθλόω contr.vb. [ναῦλον] **1** transport (someone or sthg.) by ship (as passenger or cargo); **carry by ship** —a person, a dead body E. ‖ PASS. (of a captive) be transported (to another land) E. **2** (of winds) **carry over the sea** —a person E. ‖ MID. take oneself as a passenger on a voyage, **go by sea, sail** E. Ar.

ναυσίη Ion.f.: see ναυτίᾱ

ναυσι-κλειτός ή όν adj. [ναῦς] (of a man, an island) **famed for ships** or **seafaring** Od. hHom.

ναυσι-κλυτός όν (also dial. ᾱ́ όν) adj. (of a people, an island) **famed for ships** or **seafaring** Od. Pi.

ναυσι-πομπός όν adj. (of a breeze) **ship-escorting** E.

ναυσι-πόρος ον adj. [πορεύω] (of an army; of oars, meton. for ships) **seafaring** E.

—**ναυσίπορος** ον adj. [πόρος] (of a river) giving passage to ships, **navigable** X.

ναυσί-στονος ον adj. [στόνος] (of insolent aggression) **bringing woe to ships** (through defeat in battle) Pi.

ναυσι-φθόρος ον adj. [φθείρω] (of winds) **ship-wrecking** Tim.

ναυσι-φόρητος ον adj. [φορητός] (of men) habitually travelling by ship, **seafaring** Pi.

ναύ-σταθμον ου n. [σταθμός] —also **ναύσταθμος** ου m. **1** harbour or anchorage used by warships, **naval station** or **base** Th. Plb. Plu.; (used by pirates) Plu. **2 moored fleet** Plu. **3** beached fleet of warships (as a defensive position), **naval encampment** E.

ναυστολέω contr.vb. [στόλος, στέλλω] ‖ fut.pass. ναυστολήσομαι | **1** convey (someone or sthg.) on a sea voyage; (of persons, a ship, the sea) **convey by ship** —persons, goods E.; (fig., of persons) —victory songs Pi. —misfortunes E. ‖ PASS. (of a prisoner) be conveyed by ship E. ‖ NEUT.PL.PASS.PTCPL.SB. goods carried by sea E.fr. **2** (of a ruler, envisaged as a helmsman) **guide, steer** —a city E. **3** (intr., of persons) go by ship, **sail** S. E.; (fig.) —W.PREP.PHR. through troubles E.fr.; travel through the air (as if sailing), **sail along** Ar. —W.ACC. on wings Ar.

ναυστολήματα των n.pl. **sailing in ships** (W.GEN. over the sea) E.

ναυστολίᾱ ᾱς f. **nautical expedition** E.

ναύτης ου, dial. **ναύτας** ᾱ m. [ναῦς] one who sails on a ship (on a specific occasion or as a way of making a living), **seaman, sailor** Hom. Hes. Semon. Lyr. Hdt. Trag. +; (fig., W.GEN. of the symposium, i.e. a participant in it) Dionys.Eleg. ‖ ADJ. (of an armed company) of sailors E.

ναυτίᾱ ᾱς, Ion. **ναυσίη** ης f. **1** sea-sickness Plu.
2 feeling of revulsion, **nausea** Semon.

ναυτιάω contr.vb. (of persons) **suffer from sea-sickness** Ar. Pl. Arist. Plu.

ναυτικός ή όν adj. **1** of or relating to a sailor or sailors; (of men, a people) **seafaring, maritime** Th. Pl.; (of a particular class, at Athens) **serving in the navy** Arist.
2 for the use of sailors; (of instruments) **navigational** Pl.; (of money or loans, a contract) **maritime** Att.orats.
3 typical of sailors; (of lawlessness, gossip) **among sailors** E. Plu.
4 (of a fighting force) composed of sailors or a fleet, **naval** Hdt. Trag. Th. Att.orats. +; (of a war, landing or encampment) S. Th. Att.orats. Pl.; (of rule or power, an alliance or assistance in war) Th. Arist. Plb. Plu.
5 of or relating to ships; (of cables, timbers, decks, hulls) **of a ship** or **ships, of a fleet** Trag.; (of wreckage) A. E.
—**ναυτικόν** οὗ n. **1** that which relates to sailors or a navy; **naval strength** or **power** Th.; (pl.) **naval experience** or **skill** Th. Pl. X. Arist.
2 fighting force of men and ships, **company of ships, fleet** or **navy** Hdt. Th. Ar. Att.orats. X. Arist. +
3 maritime loan Att.orats. X.
—**ναυτική** ῆς f. **1** naval force or power Hdt. Th. D. Arist.
2 naval art or skill, **seamanship** Hdt.

ναυτιλίᾱ ᾱς, Ion. **ναυτιλίη** ης f. [ναυτίλος] **1** occupation or custom of going to sea, **seafaring** Hes. Arist. Call. Theoc.
2 skill in sailing, **seamanship, navigation** Od. Pl. AR.
3 journey by ship, **voyage** Thgn. Pi. Hdt. Pl. X. AR. +
4 traffic of ships (at a port), **shipping** Plu.

ναυτίλλομαι mid.vb. ‖ only pres. and impf., and ep.3sg.aor.subj. ναυτίλεται ‖ (of persons) make a voyage or voyages, **sail** Od. Hdt. S. Pl. AR. —W.ACC. over a sea Hdt.

ναυτίλος ου m. [ναύτης] **1** seafarer, sailor Hdt. Trag. Hellenist.poet.
2 a kind of octopus, **nautilus** Call.epigr.
—**ναυτίλος** ον adj. (of rowing-benches, an oar) **of a sailor** or **sailors** A. S. Ar.(quot. E.)

ναυτιώδης ες adj. [ναυτίᾱ] (of boredom) **nauseating** Plu.

ναυτο-δίκαι ῶν m.pl. [ναύτης, δίκη] **judges of the nautical court** (at Athens) Lys.

ναύ-φαρκτος ον adj. [ναῦς, φράσσω] **1** (of a military force) **ship-fenced, equipped with ships, naval** A. E. Ar.; (of Ares, meton. for war) A.
2 (fig.phr.) ναύφαρκτον βλέπειν **give a look like a warship** (i.e. aggressive) Ar.

ναύ-φθορος ον adj. [φθορά] **from the destruction of a ship**; (of clothes) **tattered from shipwreck** E.

ναύφι (ep.gen.dat.sg.pl.): see ναῦς

νάω ep.contr.vb. ‖ only pres. and impf. ‖ 3sg. νάει ‖ impf. ναῖον (Od.), νᾶον (Call. AR.) ‖ **1** (of water) **flow, run** Pl.(quot.epigr.); (of rivers, springs, wells, seas) Hom. —W.DAT. w. water, wine, milk, oil AR.; (of a hill) —w. blood (fr. boar-hunting) Call.
2 (of buckets) **overflow** —W.DAT. w. whey Od.

ναῶν (dial.gen.pl.), **νάων** (Aeol.), **νέα** (Ion.acc.sg.): see ναῦς

νε-άγγελτος ον adj. [νέος, ἀγγέλλω] (of a message) **newly reported** A.

νεάζω vb. [νέος] ‖ only pres. ‖ **1** (of a person) **be young** or **youthful** (w.connot. of immaturity or impetuosity) S. E.; (w.connot. of vigour) E. —W.DAT. in emotion Plu.
‖ NEUT.SG.PTCPL.SB. **young life-force** (envisaged as a plant) S.
2 (of hubris) **flourish anew** A.

νε-αίρετος ον adj. [αἱρετός] (of a wild animal) **newly caught** A.; (of a city) **newly captured** A.

νε-ακόνητος ον adj. [ἀκονάω] **newly sharpened** (on the whetstone); (fig., of bloodshed) **keen-edged** S.

νε-αλής ές adj. [perh.reltd. ἀλδαίνω] **1** (of messengers and their horses, of soldiers) **full of energy, fresh** (opp. tired) X. Plb. Plu.; (of disputants, envisaged as on a journey) Pl.
2 (fig., of a newly imprisoned man, envisaged as a newly caught fish) **fresh** D.

νε-άλωτος ον adj. [ἁλωτός] (of fish) **newly caught** Hdt.(v.l. νεοάλωτος)

νεᾱνίᾱς ου, Ion. **νεηνίης** εω m. [νέος] **1 young man** Od. hHom. Lyr. Hdt. S. E. +; (appos.w. ἀνήρ, φίλος, γαμβρός, τέκνων, or sim.) Od. hHom. Alcm. Pi. Hdt. E. Ar.; (w.connot. **active, energetic**) E. Ar. X. D.; (w.connot. **immature, impetuous**) E. Pl. D.
2 ‖ ADJ. (of persons) **youthful** Lys.; (of a man's shoulders, chest and arms) **young, strong** E.; (fig., of a loaf of bread) **hearty, substantial** Ar.
3 ‖ ADJ. (of taunting words) **brash, wilful** E.

νεανίευμα ατος n. [νεανιεύομαι] **1 spirited act** Plu.
2 rash word or **act, impertinence** Pl. Plu.

νεανιεύομαι mid.vb. [νεανίᾱς] **1** behave like a young man; **behave high-spiritedly** D.; **be emboldened** —W.DAT. by sthg. Plu. —W.INF. to do sthg. Plu.
2 (pejor.) **act** or **speak wilfully, behave conceitedly** Att.orats. Pl.; **exult** —W.PREP.PHR. in unkindness to others Plu.
3 boast, brag —W.COMPL.CL. that sthg. is the case D.; **promise boastfully** —W.INF. to say or do sthg. Plu.

νεανικός ή όν adj. **1** (of a man, in terms of physical or mental attributes, ability in argument, his nature, spirit, conduct, physique) of the kind that is vigorous or energetic, **vital, dynamic, powerful** Ar. Pl. D. Plb. Plu.; (of a family) Pl.; (of strength, in an old man) Ar.
2 (of a strategy, action, words, a beginning or outcome) full of force or effectiveness, **forceful, effective, dynamic, powerful** Pl. D. Plu.; (w. a note of sarcasm) **smart, clever** Ar. D.; (of a political system, w. some pejor.connot.) **extreme, radical** Arist. ‖ NEUT.SB. **forcefulness** (of words) Pl.
3 full or overfull of vigour or energy; (of a pursuit or task) **strenuous, gruelling** or **zealous** Ar. Plu.; (of a military skirmish, a debate or dispute) **brisk, fierce** Plb. Plu.; (of a drinking-session) **boisterous** Plu.
4 overfull of intensity; (of wounds, pain) **severe** Plu.; (of a fear, a desire) **extreme** E. Arist.
5 (of a share of meat) **for a big appetite, hearty** Ar.
—**νεανικῶς** adv. **1 vigorously, forcefully, strenuously** Ar. Pl. Plb. Plu.
2 acutely, intensely —ref. to running a fever Plu.(cj., for μανικῶς)

νεᾶνις, Ion. **νεῆνις** (contr. **νῆνις** Anacr.), ιδος f. ‖ acc. νεάνιδα (A. E.), also νεᾶνιν (E.Cyc.) ‖ Ion.contr.dat. νήνῑ ‖ **1 young woman** Hom. Lyr. Trag. Ar. AR.
2 ‖ ADJ. (of vigour) **youthful** E.

νεανισκεύομαι mid.vb. [νεανίσκος] **pass one's youth** X.

νεανίσκος, Ion. **νεηνίσκος**, ου m. [dimin. νεανίᾱς] **1 young man, youth, lad** Hdt. Th. Ar. Att.orats. Pl. X. +
2 ‖ PL. **soldiers** Plb. Plu.

νεαρός ᾱ όν adj. [νέος] **1** (of persons, animals, their bodies) **youthful, young** Il. Pi. Trag. X. Plu.; (of the sap of life, virtue) A. Pi. ‖ NEUT.SB. **youthful looks** or **character** X. Plu.

2 (pejor., of a man) **immature** (W.ACC. in character) Arist.
3 (of hymns, songs) **new** Hes.fr. Pi.; (of the colour of a dye) as if new, **fresh** Plu.
4 (of events, circumstances) **new, recent** S. Plu.
—**νεαρωτέρως** compar.adv. **more vigorously** (than expected) —ref. to speaking Isoc.
νέας (Ion.acc.pl.): see ναῦς
νεάτη f.: see under νέατος¹
νεατός οῦ m. [νεάω] working of uncultivated land, **tilling** or **ploughing** X.
νέατος¹, ep. **νείατος** (also **νειάτιος** Call.), η ον superl.adj. [app.reltd. νειός] **1** (of the belly, chin, flank) **at the lowest part** Il.; (of a vertebra) **at the base** Il. AR.; (of a tree) AR.
2 (of an object or position) which is very low down; (of foundations, tree roots, depths of the sea) **furthest down, very deep** Sol. AR.; (of a foothill) **lowest** Il.; (of feet) **underneath** (the body) Hdt.(oracle); (of an item, amongst others stored in a chest) **in the lowest position, bottom** (W.GEN. of all) Hom. ‖ NEUT.PL.SB. **foundations** (of the earth, a mountain) Il. Call.
3 (of a chin, shoulder) at its furthest extremity, **at the very edge** Il.
4 (esp. of a geographical feature) which is furthest away (fr. the centre) or at the edge; (of a vine-row, mountain peaks) **outermost, last** Od. AR.; (of a branch of the Nile Delta) **furthest** (app. the easternmost) Call.; (of a river channel, app. the southernmost) AR.; (of cities) **at the far edge** (W.GEN. of a place) Il.
—**νεάτη**, also contr. **νήτη**, ης f. (mus.) **bottom string** (of a lyre, the furthest fr. the player's body in position and highest in pitch) Arist.; **highest note** (in a scale) Pl.
νέατος² η ον superl.adj. [νέος] (of events or actions in a series) newest or latest in time; (of a day, number of years, journey, person's offspring) **last** S.
—**νέατον** neut.adv. **for the last time** —ref. to looking at one's homeland E.
νεάω contr.vb. [νειός; perh.reltd. νέος by pop.etym.] **plough** —fields Ar. —the middle of a field (fig.ref. to moderation in musical style) Pratin. ‖ PASS. (of land) **be ploughed** Hes.
νέβρειος ον adj. [νεβρός] (of bones) **of fawns** (used as musical instruments) Call.
νεβρίζω vb. **dress** (W.ACC. Dionysian initiates) **in fawnskins** D.
νέβρινος η ον adj. (of the skin) **of a fawn** (worn as a garment) S.Ichn.
νέβριον ου n. [dimin. νεβρός] **young fawn** Sapph.
νεβρίς ίδος f. **fawnskin** (as a Dionysian garment) E.; (as a dedication to Pan) Theoc.epigr.
νεβρός οῦ m.f. **young deer, fawn** Hom. Anacr. Thgn. A. B. Hdt. +; **fawnskin** Hdt.
νεβρο-φόνος ον adj. [θείνω] **fawn-killing** A.satyr.fr.
νέες (Ion.nom.pl.), **νέεσσι** (ep.dat.pl.): see ναῦς
νεηγενής ep.adj.: see νεογενής
νεη-θαλής ές dial.adj. [νέος, θάλλω] (transf.epith., of a broom of laurel) **fresh-grown** E.
νε-ήκης ες adj. [reltd. ἀκίς, ἀκωκή] (of axes) with a new edge, **newly sharpened** Il.
νε-ηκονής ές adj. [ἀκόνη] (of a sword) **newly sharpened** S.
νεήλατα των n.pl. [app. ἐλαύνω] perh. **flat cakes** or **rolls** (prepared for a cult ritual) D.
νέ-ηλυς υδος m.f. [νέος; ἐλεύσομαι, ἤλυθον, see ἔρχομαι] one who has recently arrived (esp. in a country); (ref. to a person, a horse) **newcomer** Il. Hdt. Pl.
νεηνίης Ion.m., **νεῆνις** Ion.f., **νεηνίσκος** Ion.m.: see νεανίας, νεᾶνις, νεανίσκος

νεή-φατος ον ep.adj. [φατός] (of a voice, ref. to the sound of the newly invented lyre) **new-speaking** hHom.
νεί Boeot.adv.: see νή
νεῖαι (ep.2sg.mid.): see νέομαι
νείαιρα ep.Ion.fem.adj.: see νεῖρα
νειάτιος, νείατος superl.ep.adjs.: see νέατος¹
νεικεστήρ ῆρος m. [νεικέω] **reviler** (W.GEN. of good people) Hes.
νεικέω contr.vb. —also **νεικείω** ep.vb. [νεῖκος] | ep.3sg.subj. νεικείῃσι, also νεικείῃ | ep.impf. νείκειον, Ion. ἐνείκεον, iteratv. νεικείεσκον | aor. ἐνείκεσα, ep. νείκεσα, also νείκεσσα |
1 engage in a dispute, **quarrel** (oft. W.DAT. w. someone) Hom. Hdt. Theoc.
2 speak reproachfully Il. —W.DAT. to someone Hom.
3 (tr.) **taunt, revile, abuse** —a person (sts. W.DAT. w. words which are angry, shameful, or sim.) Hom. Hes. Hdt. Pl. AR.
νεῖκος εος (ους) n. **1 personal dispute** or **quarrel** (not usu. involving physical force) Hom. +
2 military strife (betw. peoples), **strife, struggle** (sts. W.GEN. of war) Hom. Pi. Hdt. X.
3 dispute concerning justice (before an arbiter or court), **legal dispute** Hom. Hes. A. E. Ar.
4 (philos.) separating or repelling principle in the cosmos (opp. φιλία attraction), **strife** Emp. Isoc. Pl. Arist. Plu.
5 (personif., as a figure depicted in art) **Quarrel** D.
Νειλοθερής adj.: see εἰλοθερής
Νεῖλος ου m. **Nile** (Egyptian river) Hes. Sol. A. Pi. B. Hdt. +
—**Νειλῶτις** ιδος fem.adj. (of the land) **of the Nile** A.
νεῖμα (ep.aor.): see νέμω
νειόθεν adv. [νειός, reltd. νέατος¹] **1 down below** or **from down below** AR.
2 from deep down (in one's heart or feelings) Il. Archil. AR.
νειόθι adv. **1 at the bottom** (W.GEN. of a lake) Il.
2 (ref. to location or movt.) **down below** AR.; (W.GEN. the earth) AR.
3 deep down (in one's heart) Hes.
νεῖον ep.neut.adv.: see under νέος
νειοποιέω contr.vb. (of farmers) **work fallow** or **uncultivated land** X.
νειός, also **νεός** (X.), οῦ f. **fallow** or **uncultivated land** Hom. Hes. X. Hellenist.poet.; (appos.w. ἄρουρα) Hes.
νεῖρα ᾶς Att.fem.adj. —also **νείαιρα** ης ep.Ion.fem.adj. [reltd. νειός, νέατος¹] **1** (of the belly or side of the body, as the location of a spear-thrust or sword-thrust) **in the lower part, lower** Il. E.
2 ‖ SB. abdomen or belly A. Call.
νεῖσθε (2pl.mid.), **νεῖται** (3sg.): see νέομαι
νείφω (also **νίφω**) vb. [νίφα] | ep.inf. νειφέμεν | **1** (of Zeus) **snow, bring on a snowstorm** Il. X.; (fig.) **descend like a snowstorm** —W.DAT. w. gold Pi. ‖ IMPERS. **it is snowing** Ar.
2 ‖ MID. (fig., of stones) **rain down** (upon city gates) A.
3 ‖ PASS. (of a region, statue) **be snowed on** Hdt. Plb.; (of troops) **be in snowy weather** Ar. X. Plu.
νεκάδες ων f.pl. [νέκυς] | dat. νεκάδεσσι | **heaps of corpses** (on a battlefield) Il. Call.
νεκρο-δέγμων ονος m. [νεκρός, δέχομαι] (epith. of Hades) **receiver of the dead** A.
νεκρο-θήκη ης f. **place where the dead are kept, tomb** or **graveyard** E.fr.
νεκρο-πομπός οῦ m. (appos.w. γέρων, ref. to Charon) **ferryman of the dead** E.
νεκρός οῦ m. [reltd. νέκυς] **1 dead body, corpse** Hom. Thgn. Pi. Hdt. Trag. Th. +; (of an animal) S.; (periphr.) νεκροῦ σῶμα body of a dead person E. Pl. Plu.

νεκροσῡλίᾱ

2 one who is on the point of death, **dying man** E. Antipho Th.(dub.)
3 (hyperbol.) one who is as good as dead (through isolation or deprivation), **living corpse** S. Men.
4 spirit of a dead man (conceived as departing fr. the body), **spirit** Il. || PL. spirits or shades of the dead (in the underworld or afterlife) Od. Hippon. Trag. Ar. NT.; (also sg.) E.
—**νεκρός** ά όν *adj.* 1 (of a person, horse, body) **dead** Pi.*fr.* NT. Plu.
2 (of armies) **nothing but corpses** Plu.
νεκροσῡλίᾱ ᾱς *f.* [σῡλάω] **plundering from corpses** Pl.
νεκρο-φόρος ου *m.* [φέρω] one who bears the dead to their graves, **undertaker** Plb. Plu.
νεκρόω *contr.vb.* (of poison) **kill** (someone) Plu.
νεκρώδης ες *adj.* (of a colour) corpse-like, **deathly** Plu.
νέκταρ αρος *n.* 1 drink of the gods, **nectar** (sts. described as red and sweet) Hom. +; (given for its restorative or preservative power to a warrior or corpse) Il.; (as the exemplar of delicious taste and smell) Od. Ar.
2 (fig.) liquid having an attribute of nectar; **nectar** (ref. to wine) Ion Call.*epigr.* Theoc.; (ref. to poetry, song) Pi. Theoc.; (W.GEN. of bees, ref. to honey) E.
3 app. **food of the gods** Alcm. | cf. ἀμβροσία
νεκτάρεος ᾱ (Ion. η) ον *adj.* like nectar (in smell or sweetness); (of libations, a draught of wine, flowers) **divinely fragrant** Pi. Philox.Leuc.; (of a goddess's robe, hero's tunic, perh. anointed w. oil) Il.; (of oil) AR.
—**νεκτάρεον** *neut.adv.* **with divine sweetness** —*ref. to a woman smiling* AR.
νέκυια ᾱς *f.* [νέκυς] **Evocation of the Dead** (as title of *Odyssey* 11) Plu.
νεκυο-μαντεῖον, Ion. **νεκυομαντήιον**, ου *n.* **oracle of the dead** (sanctuary where spirits of the dead are called up fr. the underworld; on the R. Acheron in Thesprotia in NW. Greece) Hdt.; (at Herakleia on the Black Sea) Plu.
νέκυς υος *m.* [reltd. νεκρός] | also ep.nom. νέκῡς | acc. νέκυν, ep. νέκῡν | Ion.dat. νέκυϊ, ep. νέκυι (disyllab.) || PL.: acc. νέκυας, ep. νέκῡς | dat. νέκυσι, ep. νέκυσσι, also νεκύεσσι |
1 **dead body**, **corpse** (of a person) Hom. Pi.*fr.* Hdt. S. E. Hellenist.poet.; (periphr.) νεκύων σώματα *bodies of the dead* E.
2 || PL. **spirits of the dead** (in the underworld) Hom. Sapph. S. E. Ar. +; (also sg.) E.
νεκύσια ων *n.pl.* (in Roman ctxt.) **offerings to the dead** (as a ceremonial rite) Plu.
Νεμέᾱ ᾱς, Ion. **Νεμέη**, ep.Ion. **Νεμείη**, ης *f.* **Nemea** (wooded region betw. Argos and Corinth, home of a mythol. lion killed by Herakles, and location of a sanctuary of Zeus where Panhellenic games were held) Hes. Pi. B. S. E.*fr.* Th. +
—**Νεμεαῖος**, ep. **Νεμειαῖος**, ᾱ ον *adj.* (epith. of Zeus) **Nemean** Pi. B.; (of the lion) Hes.; (of glory, in the games) Pi.
—**Νεμεάς** άδος *fem.adj.* (of the sacred month) of the Nemean games, **Nemean** Pi.; (of the land, a ravine) E.*fr.* Aeschin.
—**Νέμειος** ᾱ ον *adj.* (epith. of Zeus) **Nemean** Th. D.; (of the lion) E.; (of the meadow) E.*fr.* || NEUT.PL.SB. **Nemean games** Pi. Plu.
—**Νέμεος** ᾱ ον *adj.* (epith. of Zeus) **Nemean** Theoc.; (of the lion) Theoc. || NEUT.PL.SB. **Nemean games** Pi. Arist. Plb.
—**Νεμέηθε** *Ion.adv.* **from Nemea** Call.
νεμέθομαι *mid.vb.* [νέμω] | ep.3pl.impf. νεμέθοντο | (of doves, represented on a cup) **be feeding** Il.
νεμεσάω, ep. **νεμεσσάω** *contr.vb.* [νέμεσις] | impf. ἐνεμέσων (Plu.), ep.3sg. ἐνεμέσσᾱ, also νεμέσσᾱ | aor. ἐνεμέσησα, ep. νεμέσησα, 3sg.aor.opt. νεμεσῆσαι (D.), dial. νεμεσᾶσαι (Pi.) || MID.: fut. νεμεσήσομαι | ep.3sg.aor.opt. νεμεσσήσαιτο || PASS.: aor. (usu. w.mid.sens.) ἐνεμεσήθην (Plu.), ep. νεμεσσήθην, ep.3pl. νεμέσσηθεν || Mid. and aor.pass. (w.mid.sens.) are confined to Hom. |
1 (act., mid. and aor.pass., of persons or gods) **feel indignant** or **resentful** Hom. Thgn. Arist. Call. Plu. —W.DAT. *against someone* Hom. Hes. Pi. Pl. D. Arist. + —(+ PTCPL. *for doing sthg.*) Il. —(+ INF. *for doing sthg.*) Il. —W.ACC. *over sthg.* Od. Hes. —W.DAT. D. —W.ACC. + INF. *that sthg. shd. be the case* Od. || PASS. (of a person) **be resented** Plu.
2 || MID. **be dissatisfied with oneself**, **be ashamed** Hom. —W.INF. *to do sthg.* Od.
Νεμέσεια ων *n.pl.* **festival of Nemesis** (at Athens), **Nemeseia** D.
νεμεσήμων ον, gen. ονος *adj.* [νεμεσάω] (of gods) **liable to feel resentment** (W.DAT. against the boastful) Call.
νεμεσητικός ή όν *adj.* [νεμεσητός] (of persons) **disposed to feel resentment** (at the undeserved good or bad fortune of others) Arist.
νεμεσητός, ep. **νεμεσσητός**, ή όν *adj.* —also **νεμεσσᾱτός** ά όν *dial.adj.* 1 (of an action or circumstance, freq. expressed as INF.SB.) **worthy of indignation, resentment or shame**, **disgraceful, shameful** or **to be resented** Hom. Tyrt. S. Pl. Arist. Call. +
2 (of falsehood) **repugnant** (W.DAT. to honour and justice) Pl.
3 (of an experience) resulting from the displeasure or resentment of the gods, **bringing justified retribution** Plu.
4 (of a person or goddess) **prone to vengeful anger** Il. Theoc.
νεμεσίζομαι *mid.vb.* [νέμεσις] | only pres. and impf. | 1 **feel indignation** or **resentment** Il. —W.DAT. *against someone* Hom. —(W.ACC. *over sthg.*) Il. —W.ACC. + INF. *that sthg. shd. be the case* Il.
2 **feel shame** Od. —W.ACC. + INF. *that sthg. shd. be the case* Il.
3 **feel the anger of, stand in awe of** —*the gods* Od.
νέμεσις εως *f.* [νέμω] | ep.dat. νεμέσσῑ | 1 feeling of disapproval or resentment (by persons, at another's conduct), **indignation, resentment, resentful anger** Il. Hes.*fr.* Thgn. A. Pi. Plu.; (W.GEN. against someone) Il.; (W.GEN. or PREP.PHR. of or fr. someone) Hom. Hes.*fr.*
2 **indignation, resentment** (at the undeserved good or bad fortune of others, as the mean betw. φθόνος *envy* and ἐπιχαιρεκακία *malice*) Arist.
3 matter of justified indignation, reproach or shame; (in neg.phr., w. ἐστί, usu. understd.) *it is discreditable or to be resented* Call. —W.INF. or DAT. + INF. (*for someone*) *to do sthg.* Hom. —W.ACC. + INF. *that someone shd. do sthg.* Il.
4 divine disapproval or resentment (leading to retribution); **displeasure, resentment** (freq. W.GEN. or PREP.PHR. of or fr. the gods) Hes.*fr.* Thgn. Hdt. S. E. AR. Plu.; (W.GEN. over sthg.) Plu.; (personif., as a goddess) **Nemesis, Displeasure, Resentment** Hes. Pi. E. Isoc. Pl. Call. Plu.; (W.GEN. of a dead man, i.e. his personal avenging deity) S.
νεμεσσάω *ep.contr.vb.*, **νεμεσσᾱτός** *dial.adj.*, **νεμεσσητός** *ep.adj.*: see νεμεσάω, νεμεσητός
νεμέτωρ ορος *m.* [νέμω] **dispenser of justice**, **avenger** (ref. to Zeus) A.
νέμησις εως *f.* **distribution** (of land, property, spoils, political power) Is. Plu.
νέμος εος *n.* 1 **grove, thicket** Il.
2 **pasture** S.

νέμω vb. | fut. νεμῶ | aor. ἔνειμα, ep. νεῖμα ‖ MID.: fut. νεμοῦμαι, also νεμήσομαι (Plu.) | aor. ἐνειμάμην ‖ PASS.: fut. νεμηθήσομαι (Plu.) | aor. ἐνεμήθην | pf.mid.pass. νενέμημαι ‖ The sections are grouped as: (1–2) pasture, graze (animals, land), (3–4) be at pasture, graze, feed, (5–9) inhabit, possess, manage, (10–16) distribute, dispense, assign. |

1 put (animals) to pasture; (of herdsmen) **pasture, graze** —*horses, oxen, sheep* Hdt. E. +; (intr.) **pasture one's flocks** Od.

2 use (land) for pasture; **pasture, graze** —*land, hills* (w. *herds*) Th. Pl. X.

3 ‖ MID. (of cattle, horses, pigs) **be at pasture, graze** Hom. Hdt.; (of birds, animals) **range over** —*land* Pi. E.; (fig., of ulcers on the body) **spread** Hdt.

4 ‖ MID. (of animals) have as food, **feed on** —*plants, foliage, pasture* Hom. Hdt. E. Ar.; (of humans) —*crops* S.; (fig., of humans, envisaged as birds) **browse on** —*laws* Ar.; (of fire) **devour** —*corpses, parts of a city* Il. Hdt. ‖ PASS. (of land, a military phalanx) be consumed —W.DAT. *by fire* Il. Plu.

5 ‖ MID. (of persons) **occupy, inhabit** —*cities, places, fields* Hom. A. Pi. Hdt. E. Th. +; (of nymphs, Erinyes) —*groves, Tartaros* Il. hHom. A.; (of fish) —*a region* Ibyc.; (of towns) **be situated in** —*a region* Hdt.

6 ‖ MID. enjoy (a resource) for profit; **exploit, enjoy** —*land, an inheritance, money* Hom. Hes. Hdt. Th. D. —*mineral resources* Hdt. Th. —*gifts, privileges, power* Hdt. S.

7 ‖ MID. **pass, spend** —*a day* (w. *Zeus*), *a tearless life* Pi.; (intr.) **live** —W.PREP.PHR. *outside a city* (*like deer*) Thgn. —W.ADV. or PREP.PHR. *peacefully, under someone's control* Pi.

8 have management or control (of persons, places, things); (of deities) **possess, hold** —*a city, region, mountain* A. Pi. S.; (of Zeus) **rule over** —*lightning, a people, everything* A. Pi. S.; (of goddesses) **maintain** —*their honours and privileges* A.; (of persons) **rule, manage** —*a city, a people* Hdt. —*hoarded wealth* Pi.; (of women) —*the home* E.*fr.*; (intr.) **rule** —W.DAT. *in a city* Pi. ‖ PASS. (of a city, a land) be maintained (in a specified way) A. Th.; be ruled —w. ὑπό + DAT. *by barbarians* Hdt.

9 direct, guide —*one's tongue* (*in prophesying accurately*), *one's footsteps* (*in following a family tradition*) A. Pi. —(fig.) *the rudder of one's mind* A.; (of old men) **support** —*their feeble strength* (*on staffs*) A.

10 distribute, deal out, dispense —*food and drink, sacrificial offerings* (sts. W.DAT. *to someone*) Hom. —*true justice* Hes. —*a portion, inheritance, rule, or sim.* Od. Pi. B. Trag. Th. ‖ MID. (of persons) distribute —*property* (*amongst themselves*) Plu.; (intr.) distribute property (among beneficiaries) Lys. D. ‖ PASS. (of property, a grain supply) be distributed D. Plu.; (of a wise saying, honest behaviour) be maintained (as a custom) Simon. Hdt.

11 (of Zeus, the gods) **allocate, dispense** —*good or bad fortune* Od. Pi. Hdt. Trag. +; (of Apollo) —*prophecies* (*to mortals*) E.; (of a person or god) **grant** —*confidence, pleasures* (*to persons*), *passage* (*to sailors*) Trag.; (fig., of a day in the Olympic games) —*a prize* (*to a runner*) B.

12 (of persons) assign or attribute (sthg., to someone); **assign, give** (to a person or god) —*one's anger, respect, thanks* S. Antipho Ar. Pl. —*responsibility* (*for a crime*), *a choice, a difficult problem* S. Antipho.; (of Philoktetes' bow) —*honour* (*to Odysseus*) S.

13 give —*the greater share* (W.DAT. *to someone, i.e. favour him*) A. E. —(*to feelings, injustice, or sim.*) E. Th. —*the lesser share* (*to injustice, i.e. disfavour it*) E.; **assign** —*second place* (*in happiness*, W.DAT. *to someone*) Hdt.; **dispense, tell** —*the truth* S.

14 (of lawgivers) **distribute, divide** (usu. by lot) —*councils, juries, or sim.* (*into groups*) Arist. ‖ PASS. (of councils, jurors) be divided (into groups) Arist.; (of meat) be cut up (into pieces) X.; (of unity) be divided —W.ACC. *into many parts* Pl.

15 (of a commander, an army) **assign, detail** —*soldiers* (*to their posts*) E.; **consign** —*towns* (*to flames*) Hdt.; (of a resident alien) **designate** —*a legal protector* (fr. among the citizens) Isoc. Arist. ‖ PASS. (of athletes) be enrolled Plb.; (of barley and wheat supplies) be assigned —W.PREP.PHR. *for flour-making* Pl.

16 include (someone or sthg., in a certain category); **count** —*someone or sthg.* (W.PREDIC.SB. or ADJ. *as a god, friend, error, or sim.*) S.

νένασμαι (pf.pass.): see νάσσω
νενίηλος ον *adj.* (of persons) app. **foolish** Call.
νένιμμαι (pf.mid.): see νίζω
νεοάλωτος *adj.*: see νεάλωτος
νεο-αρδής ές *adj.* [νέος, ἄρδω] (of a garden) **newly watered** Il.
νεό-γαμος ον *adj.* [γάμος] (of a man or woman) **newly married** A. Hdt. E. X. Plb. Plu.
νεο-γενής, ep. **νεηγενής**, ές *adj.* [γένος, γίγνομαι] (of children, animals) **newborn** Od. A. Pl. X.
νεογιλλός (v.l. **νεογῑλός**) ή όν *adj.* (of a puppy, baby) **newborn, very young** Od. Theoc.
νεο-γνός ή όν *adj.* [γίγνομαι] **1** (of a child) **newborn** hHom. A. Hdt. E. X. Plu.; (of animals) E. X.
2 (of childbirth) **recent** E.
νεό-γονος ον *adj.* [γόνος] (of a child) **newborn** E.; (of lambs) E.*Cyc.*
νεό-γραπτος ον *adj.* [γραπτός] (of a bridal chamber) **newly painted** Theoc.
νεό-γυιος ον *adj.* [γυῖα] (of men fallen in war) **young-limbed** Pi.; (of the youthful prime of boys) Pi.*fr.*
νεο-δᾱμώδεις ων *Lacon.m.pl.* [δημώδης] newly made members of the populace (of Sparta), **ex-helots** Th. X. Plu.
νεό-δαρτος ον *adj.* [δείρω] (of oxen) **newly skinned** or **flayed** X.; (of animal-skins) **newly stripped** Od.
νεό-δμᾱτος ον *dial.adj.* [δέμω] (of altars) **newly built** Pi.
νεο-δμής ῆτος *masc.fem.adj.* [δάμνημι] (of a colt) **newly tamed** or **broken** hHom.; (of a marriage) **newly won** E.
νεό-δμητος ον *adj.* (of a girl) **newly won** (as a bride) E.
νεό-δρεπτος ον *adj.* [δρέπω] (of boughs, carried by suppliants) **freshly gathered** A.; (of altars, made fr. greenery) Theoc.
νεό-δροπος ον *adj.* (of boughs) **freshly gathered** A.
νεό-ζυγής ές *adj.* [ζεύγνῡμι] (of a colt) **newly harnessed** A.
νεό-ζυγος ον *adj.* (of a bride) **newly married** E.
νεό-ζυξ ζυγος *masc.fem.adj.* **1** (of a colt) **newly harnessed** E.*fr.*
2 (of a young man) **newly married** E.*fr.* ‖ FEM.PL.SB. newly married brides AR.
νεοθᾱλής *dial.adj.*: see νεοθηλής¹
νεόθεν *adv.* **just now, recently** —ref. to troubles coming S.
νεο-θηγής ές *adj.* [θήγω] (of a sickle) **newly sharpened** AR.
νεό-θηκτος ον *adj.* [θηκτός] (of knives) **newly sharpened** Plu.
νεο-θηλής¹, dial. **νεοθᾱλής**, ές *adj.* [θάλλω] (of grass, vegetation) newly sprouting or flourishing, **fresh** Il. hHom.; (fig., of victory) Pi.; (of enthusiasm, modesty) hHom. E.
νεο-θηλής² ές *adj.* —also **νεόθηλος** ον (A.) *adj.* [θηλή] (of an animal) new to the teat, **suckling** Anacr. A.

νεο-θνής ῆτος *masc.fem.adj.* [θνήσκω] (of a person) **newly dead** Pl.

νεό-θρεπτος ον *adj.* [τρέφω] (of vine-shoots) **newly planted** AR.

νεοίη ης *ep.f.* **youthful impetuosity** Il.

νέ-οικος ον *adj.* [οἶκος] (of an abode, ref. to a city-state) being a new settlement, **newly founded** Pi.

νεοῖν (gen.dat.du.): see ναῦς

νεο-κατάστατος ον *adj.* [καθίστημι] (of people) **newly settled** (in a land) Th.

νεο-κηδής ές *adj.* [κῆδος] (of a person's spirit) **newly mourning, recently bereaved** Hes.

νεό-κλωστος ον *adj.* [κλωστός] (of a sword-belt) **newly woven** Theoc.

νεό-κμητος ον *adj.* [κάμνω] (of a corpse) **newly dead** E.

νεό-κοπτος ον *adj.* [κόπτω] (of a millstone) **freshly sharpened** Ar.

νεό-κοτος ον *adj.* [κότος] (of troubles, an event) **bringing new distress** A.

νεο-κρᾶς ᾶτος *m.* [κεράννυμι] **newly mixed bowl** (of wine) A.

νεό-κροτος ον *adj.* [κρότος] (of victory in a chariot-race) **bringing fresh applause** B.

νεό-κτιστος ον (also dial. ᾱ ον Pi.) *adj.* [κτιστός] (of a city) **newly founded** Pi. Hdt. Th.; (of part of an altar) **newly built** Pi.

νεό-κτιτος ον *adj.* [κτίζω] (of playthings) **newly made** A.*satyr.fr.*; (of joy) **newly found** B.

νεό-κτονος ον *adj.* [κτείνω] (of a warrior) **recently killed** Pi.

νεο-λαίᾱ ᾱς *dial.f.* [λᾱός] **young people, youth** (of a country) A.; **young group** (of women) Theoc.

νεό-λεκτρος ον *adj.* [λέκτρον] (of women) **newly married** A.*fr.*

νεό-λλουτος ον *ep.adj.* [λούω] (of a baby) **freshly bathed** hHom.

νέομαι *mid.contr.vb.* [reltd. νόστος] | only pres. and impf.; pres.indic. oft. has fut.sens. *shall return* ‖ PRES.: ep.1sg. νέομαι (once disyllab., v.l. νεῦμαι Il.) | ep.2sg. νεῖαι | 3sg. νεῖται (Od. Call.) | ep.1pl. νεόμεσθα (AR.), dial. νεύμεθα (AR. Theoc.) | 2pl. νεῖσθε (E. +), ep. νέεσθε (AR.) | ep.3pl. νέονται (disyllab. Pi.) | ep.imperatv.: 3sg. νεέσθω, 3pl. νεέσθων | ep.subj.: 2sg. νέηαι, 3sg. νέηται | ep.3sg.opt. νέοιτο (Call. AR.) | ep.ptcpl. νεόμενος (E.), dial. νεύμενος (Call.) | inf. νεῖσθαι (Od. +), ep. νέεσθαι ‖ EP.IMPF.: νεόμην, 3pl. νέοντο, also ἐνέοντο (AR.) |

1 (of persons) **go** or **come back** (to one's home or native land); **return home** Hom. Hes. Pi. Call. Theoc. —W.ADV. *homewards* Hom. Hes.

2 set out, leave, get away (fr. a place or person) Hom.

3 (w. focus on the destination) **arrive** (at a place, sts. after having been sent or summoned); **come** or **arrive** Hom. Pi. Call.; **come** —W.ADV. or PREP.PHR. *to a place* S. E.; (of rich and poor) —*to the grave* Pi.

4 go on one's way, travel Hom. Pi. S. Hellenist.poet. —W.ACC. *on a road* Parm.; (fig., of a poet, in his song) Pi.

5 (of things) **start out, travel** or **arrive**; (of rivers) **flow** Il.; (of a constellation) **move** Pi.; (of nectar and ambrosia) **pass** —W.PREP.PHR. *across the tongue* Call.; (of a basket of ritual offerings) **arrive** Call.; (of the sun, blame) **be gone** Il. Call.; (of a family name) **arise** Call.

νεομηνίᾱ *dial.f.*, **νεομηνίη** *Ion.f.*: see νουμηνίᾱ

νεο-παθής ές *adj.* [νέος, πάθος] (of a bereaved parent) suffering recent sorrow, **newly stricken** A.

νεο-πενθής ές *adj.* [πένθος] (of the hearts of young women) **freshly sorrowing** Od. [or perh. *enduring sorrow in youth, i.e. dying young*]

νεό-πλουτος ον *adj.* [πλοῦτος] (pejor., of persons) **newly rich** Ar. D. Arist.; (of meals, behaviour) typical of the newly rich, **ostentatious** Plu.

νεό-πλυτος ον *adj.* [πλύνω] (of clothing) **newly washed** Od. Hdt.

νεό-ποκος ον *adj.* [πόκος] (of wool) **newly shorn** S.

νεό-πολις, ep. **νεόπτολις** (A.), εως *masc.fem.adj.* [πόλις]
1 (of a citizen) **of a newly founded city** Pi.*fr.*
2 (of a city) **newly founded** A.

νεο-πολίτης ου *m.* **newly enfranchised citizen** Arist.

νεο-πρεπής ές *adj.* [πρέπω] **1** (of a person) **youthful in appearance** Plu.
2 immature (in character) Plu.; (fig., of an argument) Pl.

νεό-πριστος ον *adj.* [πρίστος] (of ivory) **newly sawn** or **carved** Od.

Νεοπτόλεμος ου *m.* **Neoptolemos** (also called Pyrrhos, son of Achilles) Hom. Pi. S. E. Pl. Arist. Plu.

νεόπτολις *ep.masc.fem.adj.*: see νεόπολις

νεό-ρραντος ον *adj.* [ῥαίνω] (of a sword) **newly spattered** (w. blood) S.

νεό-ρρυτος ον *adj.* [ῥυτός] **1** (of liquids) **freshly flowing** S. Tim.
2 (of a sword) **newly streaming** (w. blood) A.

νέ-ορτος ον *adj.* [ὄρνυμι] **1** (of an event) **newly arisen, new** S.
2 (of a woman) perh. **young** Plu.(quot. S.)

νεός[1] *f.*: see νειός

νεός[2] (Ion.gen.): see ναῦς

νέος ᾱ (Ion. η) ον *adj.* | For compar. and superl. see νεώτερος, νεώτατος. | **1** (of persons) **young in age** (freq. opp. old), **young, youthful** Hom. + ‖ MASC.FEM.SB. (sg. and pl.) young man or woman Hom. + ‖ NEUT.SG.SB. youthfulness S. E.; (collectv.) young persons Arist.; (gener.) young creatures (embracing all living things) Pl.

2 (of animals) newly born, **young** E. X. AR. Theoc.; (of shoots, plants, vegetables) newly grown or sprouted, **young, fresh** Hom. Ar. Pl.

3 belonging to a young person; (of the body, arms, hair, flesh, stomach, soul, mind) **young, youthful** Pi. Trag. Lys. Pl. +; (of spears, meton. for the persons carrying them) E.; (of a time of life) E.

4 appropriate to or associated with young persons; (of contests, nurture) **of** or **for the young, youthful** Pi. S.

5 (pejor., of persons) having the characteristics of youth (such as immaturity, impetuosity or irresponsibility), **childish** S. E. Pl. +; (of rashness, thinking) A.

6 (of gods) **young, new** (relative to those of an earlier generation) A.; **new and unfamiliar, novel** E. Ar.

7 (of things) made or brought into existence for the first time, **new** Hom. +

8 (of actions, events, circumstances) having occurred, come to notice or been experienced recently, **new, fresh, recent** Hom. hHom. Pi. Trag. Th. Ar. +; (of blood) **freshly shed** A. E.; (of fish) recently caught, **fresh** Ar.; (of the harvest season) **just begun** S.*fr.*

9 having recently come into a particular state or relationship; (of a wife) **new, young** Od. Pi.; (of a son) **new-found** E.

10 succeeding or replacing what went before; (of a race of men, generation of people) **new** A. Pi.*fr.* S.; (of a wife, marriage) Il. S. E.; (of a master, commander, children) E.; (of

the ruler of the gods, i.e. Zeus A.; (of a moon) S.fr.; (of a season) Ar.; (of behaviour) A.
11 (specif., of a day of the month) **first** Pl. AR. | for ἔνη (τε) καὶ νέα *last day of the month*, see ἔνος 2
12 additional to what went before; (of pain, suffering, or sim.) **new, fresh, further** Il. Trag.; (of a sacrifice) E.; (of a bowl of wine) E.
13 (of things, esp. information or news) not known before, **new** Trag. Ar. +
14 (w. mildly or strongly sinister connot., of events, actions, news, plans) **unforeseen, untoward, disturbing** Trag. Th. +
15 (prep.phr.) ἐκ νέης **anew, afresh** Hdt.
—**νέον**, ep. **νεῖον** (Call. AR.) *neut.adv.* **1 lately, recently, freshly** Hom. Hes. Pi. B. Trag. Call. AR.; (also) τὸ νέον Hdt.
2 once again, anew Il. Hes.
νεο-σίγαλος ον *adj.* [reltd. σιγαλόεις] (of a poetic technique) **sparkling new** Pi.
νεό-σμηκτος ον *adj.* [σμήχω] (of armour) **newly polished or burnished** Il. Plu.; (of knucklebones) Call.
νεο-σπαδής ές *adj.* [σπάω] (of a sword) **freshly drawn** A.
νεο-σπάς άδος *masc.fem.adj.* (of branches) **freshly plucked** S.
νεό-σπορος ον *adj.* [σπόρος] (of an embryo) **newly implanted** (in a mother's womb) A.
νεοσσεύω (also **νοσσεύω** Hdt.), Att. **νεοττεύω** *vb.* [νεοσσός] | pf.mid.ptcpl. νενοσσευμένος | **1** (of birds) make one's nest, **nest** Plu.; (mid., of certain kinds of birds) Hdt.
2 (tr., of Eros) produce as nestlings, **hatch out** —*the race of birds* Ar.
νεοσσιά (also **νοσσιά** NT.), Att. **νεοττιά**, ᾶς, Ion. **νεοσσιή** ῆς *f.* **1 nest** (built by birds) Archil. Hdt. Ar. X. Men. Plu.; (fig.) **retreat** (for persons) Pl.
2 brood of nestlings, brood Lycurg. Men. NT.
νεοσσός (also **νοσσός** NT.), Att. **νεοττός**, οῦ *m.* [reltd. νέος] **1 young bird, nestling, fledgling, chick** (sts. W.GEN. of a sparrow, cock, or sim.) Il. Trag. Ar. Philox.Leuc. AR. Theoc. +; (fig.ref. to a child) A. E. Pl.
2 (ref. to a crocodile, bee) **young hatchling** Hdt. X.
3 (fig.) **young cockerel** (ref. to a military leader) Plu.; **offspring, scion** (W.GEN. of Ares, ref. to the Persian king) Ar.
4 (fig., collectv.sg.) **brood** (W.GEN. of the Trojan Horse, ref. to Argive warriors) A.
νεό-στροφος ον *adj.* [στρέφω] (of a bowstring, app. made of separate strands) **newly twisted** (in preparation for use) Il.
νεο-σύλλεκτος ον *adj.* [συλλέγω] (of troops) **newly enlisted** Plu.
νεο-σύλλογος ον *adj.* **1** (of payments) **recently collected** Hyp.
2 (of troops) **newly enlisted** Plb.
νεο-σφαγής ές *adj.* [σφάζω] (of a bull, a person) **newly slain** Trag.; (of blood) **newly spilt** S.; (of a head) **newly severed** Plu.
νεότᾱς *dial.f.*: see νεότης
νεο-τελής ές *adj.* [τέλος] (of persons) **newly initiated** (into love) Pl.
νεό-τευκτος ον *adj.* [τεύχω] (of metal) **newly wrought** Il.
νεο-τευχής ές *adj.* (of chariots, a cup) **newly made** Il. Theoc.; (of music) **new-styled, innovative** Tim.
νεότης ητος, dial. **νεότᾱς** ᾱτος *f.* **1 youth, youthfulness** (as a time or state of life) Il. Hes.fr. Anacr. Thgn. Pi. E. +
2 youthful spirit, impetuosity, rashness Thgn. Hdt. And. Pl. Men. +
3 (collectv.sg.) young people (of a city or country), **youth** Pi. Hdt. Th. Arist. Plu.

νεό-τμητος, dial. **νεότμᾱτος**, ον *adj.* [τμητός] **1** (of flesh) **freshly cut** AR.; (of vine-leaves) Theoc.
2 (of particles of food) **freshly broken down** (in the digestive system) Pl.
νεο-τόκος ον *adj.* **1** (of a mother, doe, mare) **having recently given birth** E. Plu.
2 (of a bed) **of recent childbirth** Pi.fr.
νεό-τομος ον *adj.* [τέμνω] (of a tendril of ivy) **newly cut** E.; (of wounds on the body) **newly inflicted** A. S.
νεο-τρεφής ές *adj.* [τρέφω] (of boys) newly reared, **young** E.
νεό-τροφος ον *adj.* (of a child) newly reared, **young** A.
νεοττεύω Att.vb., **νεοττιά** Att.f., **νεοττός** Att.m.: see νεοσσεύω, νεοσσιά, νεοσσός
νεόττιον ου Att.n. —also **νοσσίον** ου (NT.) *n.* [dimin. νεοσσός] **young bird, nestling, chick** Ar. NT. Plu.; (fig.ref. to a child) Thphr.
νεοττοτροφέομαι Att.pass.contr.vb. [τρέφω] (fig., of a son) **be looked after as a fledgling** Ar.
νεουργής ές *adj.* [νέος, ἔργον] (of a shoe) **newly made** Plu.
νεουργός όν *adj.* (of garments) **newly made** Pl. Plu.; (of works of art) **modern, up-to-date** Plu.
νε-ούτατος ον *adj.* [οὐτάζω] (of a warrior, a part of his body) **recently wounded** Il. Hes.
νεό-φονος ον *adj.* [φόνος] (of blood) **from a recent killing, newly shed** E.
νεο-χάρακτος ον *adj.* [χαράσσω] (of footprints) **newly imprinted, fresh** S.
νεοχμός όν *adj.* [reltd. νέος] **1** (of a song) **new, novel** Alcm.; (of playthings) A.satyr.fr.; (of a marvel) Ar.; (w.pejor.connot., of laws, a ruler) A. S.
2 (pejor.) new and so provoking alarm; (of news, an event, a misfortune) **new, strange** Trag. Theoc.; (of an action) **unexpected, startling** Hdt. E.
νεοχμόω contr.vb. **1** perform unexpected or harmful acts; (in military ctxt.) **do harm** or **act rashly** —w. κατά + ACC. *towards someone* Hdt.
2 (of an event) **cause** (W.NEUT.PL.ADJ. many) **political disturbances** Th.
νεόω contr.vb. [νέος] | aor.imperatv. νέωσον | **renew, re-enact** —*a traditional story* A.
νέποδες ων *m.f.pl.* | dat.pl. νεπόδεσσι | also nom.sg. νέπους (Call.) | **1** app. **offspring, progeny** (of the sea, ref. to seals, fish) Od. Call.
2 app. **descendants, children** (of a god or person) Hellenist.poet.+ (sg.) Call.
νέρθε(ν) *adv. and prep.*: see ἔνερθε(ν)
νέρτερος ᾱ ον (also ος ον) *compar.adj.* [reltd. ἐνέρτερος] **1** in a lower position; (of an oar, fig.ref. to the rank of oarsman) **lower down** (than a person on the helmsman's bench) A. || NEUT.PL.SB. what is below (opp. above) Ar.(mock-oracle)
2 (of deities, daimons) of or in the underworld (opp. the world above, or Olympos), **infernal** Trag.; (of the light) Lyr.adesp.; (of plains, land, dwelling places) S. E.; (of a sound like thunder, of the ferryman's oar) E.
3 || MASC.PL.SB. those of the underworld (ref. to deities or the dead) Trag.
4 (of a funeral pyre) **for the dead** E.
νέρτος ου *m.* app. **vulture** Ar.
Νέστωρ ορος *m.* **Nestor** (king of Pylos, an Achaean commander at Troy, noted for his longevity and wisdom) Hom. +
—**Νεστόρειος** ᾱ ον, ep.Ion. **Νεστόρεος** η ον *adj.* (of the ship, chariot, horses, shield) **of Nestor** Il. Pi.

νεῦμα ατος *n.* [νεύω] **1** inclining of the head (as a command, esp. by a person in authority), **nod** Th. Ar. Plb. Plu. **2 intent, will** (of a ruler) A. **3** involuntary inclining of the head, **nod** (by a tired person) X.

νεύμεθα (dial.1pl.mid.), **νεύμενος** (dial.mid.ptcpl.): see νέομαι

νευρά ᾶς, Ion. **νευρή** (also **νευρειή** Theoc.) ῆς *f.* | ep.gen.dat.sg.pl. νευρῆφι | cord made of sinew, **bowstring** Hom. Hes. Lyr. E. X. +; (gener.) **bow** S.

νεῦρα ων *n.pl.* **1 tendons, sinews** (of humans or animals) Pl. Arist. Call. Theoc. Plu.; (sg.) Il. **2** treated animal sinews (used for parts of weapons, sewing leather, moving puppets, or sim.), **sinews, cords** Pl. X. Plb.; (sg.) Il. Hes. ‖ COLLECTV.PL. bowstring Il. **3 cords** (derived fr. plants) Pl. **4** (fig.) sinews as the seat of vitality (esp. as cut or diseased); **sinews, vital elements** or **power** (of a city-state, a people) Aeschin. D. Plu.; (of a person) Plu.; (of the soul) Pl.; (of a tragedy) Ar.; (of politics, ref. to money) Plu. **5** ‖ SG. (colloq.) **penis** Call.

νευρειή Ion.*f.*: see νευρά

νεύρινος η ον *adj.* (of clothes, a mesh) **made of sinews** or **fibres** (fr. plants) Pl. Plu.

νευροκοπέω contr.*vb.* [κόπτω] cut the Achilles tendon of, **hamstring** —*animals* Plb.

νεῦρον *n.sg.*: see νεῦρα

νευρόομαι pass.contr.*vb.* (of a situation, w. sexual double entendre) **become tense** Ar.

νευρορραφέω contr.*vb.* [νευρορράφος] (of a shoemaker) **stitch with cord, stitch** Pl. X.

νευρο-ρράφος ου *m.* [ῥάπτω] cord-stitcher, **shoemaker, cobbler** Ar. Pl.

νευρο-σπαδής ές *adj.* [σπάω] (of an arrow-shaft) **drawn back with the bowstring** S.

νευρό-σπαστος ον *adj.* (of puppets) **moved by strings** Hdt. ‖ NEUT.PL.SB. (pejor.ref. to performing slaves) **marionettes** X.

νευρώδης ες *adj.* (of parts of the body) **full of sinews, sinewy** Pl.

νευστάζων οντος *masc.ptcpl.adj.* [νεύω] **1** (of a warrior, striding forward) repeatedly inclining the head, **nodding, bobbing** (W.DAT. w. his helmet plume) Il. **2** (of a person) **signalling** (W.DAT. w. his eyebrows) Od. **3** (of a person, when sad, thinking, bashful or drunk) **with head kept bowed** or **hanging down** Od. Bion **4** (of a lion, after receiving a violent blow) **with faltering** or **unsteady head** Theoc.

νευστέον (neut.impers.vbl.adj.): see νέω[1]

νευστικός ή όν *adj.* [νέω[1]] (of certain animals, opp. those that walk) of the kind that swim, **swimming** Pl. ‖ NEUT.PL.SB. **swimming creatures** Pl.

νεύω *vb.* | aor. ἔνευσα, ep. νεῦσα | pf. νένευκα | **1** make a signal by nodding, **nod, signal** (sts. W.DAT. w. one's head, sts. W.DAT. to someone, sts. W.INF. to do sthg.) Hom. hHom. Lyr.adesp. E. Ar. Pl. + **2** (of a god, esp. Zeus, of a person in authority) assent by inclining the head, **nod, agree** (to a request) Il. Pi. S. Theoc. —W.NEUT.ACC. w. sthg. E. —W.INTERN.ACC. *to a favour* (*for someone*) Alc. S. —W.FUT.INF. *that one will do sthg.* AR. —W.ACC. + INF. *that sthg. shd. be the case* Il. hHom. Pi. **3** (of warriors advancing in close formation) move the head back and forth, **nod** Il.; (of helmet plumes) **bob up and down** Hom. AR.; (of a puppet) —W.ACC. w. *its penis* Hdt.

4 (of a person) incline the head towards the ground, **bow one's head** (in a stupor) Od.; (in fear, dejection, to avoid contact w. another) S. AR. Plb.; (to examine sthg.) E.; (of jurors, perh. sitting forwards on backless seats) Ar. ‖ PF.PTCPL.ADJ. (of a boxer) with head lowered Theoc.; (of a person mortally wounded) with head collapsed Theoc. **5** (of the plumes of helmets hung on a wall) **droop down** Alc.; (of a nozzle hanging fr. a beam) Th.; (of ears of corn) —W.ADV. *towards the ground* Hes. **6** (of a person) **defer, submit** —W.PREP.PHR. *to one who is more powerful* Plb. **7 devote oneself** —W.PREP.PHR. *to the Muses* Call. —*to a task* Plb. **8** (of aspects of government, events) **incline** —W.PREP.PHR. *towards the same goal* Pl. Plb.; (of features of a constitution) **be out of balance** (w. others) Plb. **9** (of geographical features, ships, objects) **face** —W.ADV. or PREP.PHR. *in a particular direction* Plb.

νεφέλη ης, dial. **νεφέλα** ᾱς *f.* [νέφος] **1 cloud** (usu.pl.) Hom. Hes. Sol. Lyr. S. E. +; (pl., personif. as deities) Ar. **2** (ref. to an image of Helen, created by Hera) **cloud-phantom** E. **3** mass of cloud (providing cover or concealment), **cloud, mist** Hom. Hes.; (fig.ref. to death, envisaged as enfolding a warrior) Hom.; (ref. to sleep) Pi. **4** (ref. to sorrow or troubles, coming upon persons) **cloud, storm** Hom. Trag.; (W.GEN. or ADJ. of slaughter, blood) Pi. S. **5** fine-mesh net for catching birds, **bird-net** Ar. Call.

νεφελ-ηγερέτα ᾱο *ep.m.* [ἀγείρω] **cloud-gatherer** (epith. of Zeus) Hom. Hes. hHom.

Νεφελο-κοκκυγία ᾱς *f.* [κόκκυξ] **Cloudcuckoo City** (built by birds) Ar.

—**Νεφελοκοκκυγιεύς** έως *m.* **citizen of Cloudcuckoo City** Ar.

νέφος εος (ους) *n.* **1 cloud** (oft.pl.) Hom. + **2** cloud or mist (providing cover or concealment); **cloud** Il. E. Ar. Pl.; (of gold, on Olympos) Il.; (fig., of death) Hom. Thgn. B.; (of darkness, ref. to blindness) S.; (of forgetfulness) Pi.; (of sadness, mourning) E. **3** (fig.) **storm-cloud** (W.GEN. of war) Il. Ar.; (ref. to a single warrior) Pi. **4** very large number (of persons, animals, things); **cloud, flock, swarm** (of birds) Il. Ar.; (of warriors, their shields) Il. Hdt. E.

νεφρῖτις ιδος *fem.adj.* [νεφρός] (of a disease) **in the kidneys** Th. Plu.

νεφρός οῦ *m.* **kidney** (in the human body, usu.pl. or du.) Ar. Pl.; (perh.euphem., ref. to the testicles) Ar.

νεώ (Att.gen.), **νεῷ** (Att.dat.): see ναός[1]

νέω[1] contr.*vb.* | inf. νεῖν, Ion. νέειν, ptcpl. νέων | fut. νεύσομαι | impf. ἔνεον, ep. ἔννεον ‖ neut.impers.vbl.adj. νευστέον | (of persons) **swim** Hom. Pi.*fr.* Hdt. Th. Pl. X. +; (fig., of a person) **drown** (in oversize shoes) Ar.

νέω[2] contr.*vb.* | ep.3sg. νῇ | fut. νήσω | neut.pl.aor.pass.ptcpl. νηθέντα | (of a spider) **spin** —*a web* Hes.; (of persons) —*thread* Ar. ‖ NEUT.PL.AOR.PASS.PTCPL.SB. **products of spinning** (ref. to thread) Pl.

νέω[3] contr.*vb.* [νηέω] | aor. ἔνησα | **pile up** —*a funeral pyre, wood* (*on an altar*) Hdt. E. Th. Ar. Plu.

—**νενημένος** η ον *pf.pass.ptcpl.adj.* (of food) **stored** or **piled up** X.; (of amphoras, pejor.ref. to a theatre audience) Ar.

νεωκορέω contr.*vb.* [νεωκόρος] (iron., of a scoundrel) **be a temple custodian** —W.ACC. w. *respect to some sanctuary, i.e. by robbing it* Pl.

νεω-κόρος ου *m.f.* [ναός¹, perh. κορέω¹] **1 guardian of a temple** (sts. W.GEN. of a deity or hero) Pl. X. Plu.
2 (ref. to a city) **custodian of the temple** (W.GEN. of Artemis) NT.

νεωλκέω *contr.vb.* [ναῦς, ἕλκω] **haul ships onto land, beach ships** Plb. Plu.; (tr.) **beach** —*ships* Plu.; (fig.) **haul** (a reluctant animal, as if it were a ship) —W.ACC. *on a road* Men.

νεών (Att.acc.): see ναός¹

νεῶν (gen.pl.): see ναῦς

νε-ώνητος ον *adj.* [νέος, ὠνητός] (of a slave) **newly bought** Ar.; (fig., pejor.ref. to an orator) **newly hired** (W.DAT. by the populace) Plu.

νε-ώρης ες *adj.* [reltd. ὄρνυμι] **1** (of a sound, fear) **new or strange** S.
2 (of blood) **newly shed** E.*fr.*; (quasi-advbl., of a lock of hair having been cut) **newly, recently** S.

νεώριον ου *n.* [ναῦς, οὖρος²] **enclosure for ships** (being built or repaired), **shipyard** E. Th. Ar. Att.orats. +

νεώς¹ *Att.m.*: see ναός¹

νεώς² (gen.sg.): see ναῦς

νεώσ-οικος ου *m.* [οἶκος] (usu.pl.) **ship-shed** (for construction and repair) Hdt. Th. Ar. Att.orats. +

νεωστί *adv.* [νέος] **in recent times, lately, recently** Hdt. S. E. Th. Att.orats. +

νέωτα *adv.* [app. νέος, ἔτος] (usu. w. εἰς or ἐς) **in the following year, next year** Semon. X. Thphr. Theoc.

νεώτατος η ον *superl.adj.* [νέος] **1** (of persons) **youngest** (in age) Hom. +; (of animals) Hdt. Ar.
2 (of certain gods) **coming into existence most recently, youngest** Hdt. Pl. X.
3 (of a race) **youngest** (of all races) Hdt.; (of a country) **very new** Plu.
4 (of a song, an obligation, achievement) **newest, latest, most recent** Od. Pi. Plu.
5 (of a democracy) **of the newest sort** Arist.

—**νεώτατα** *neut.pl.superl.adv.* **most** or **very recently** Th.

νεωτερίζω *vb.* [νεώτερος] | *fut.* νεωτεριῶ | **1** (of persons) **make innovations** or **changes** (in the established social or political order, in an alliance) Th. Pl. Arist.; (of persons, states) **take extreme** or **violent actions** (against others) Th. X. D.; (of cold nights, after hot days) **cause a change** (in people) —W.PREP.PHR. *to sickness* (*fr. health*) Th.
2 (specif.) **attempt political change, organise an insurrection, revolt** Th. Att.orats. Plb. Plu.; (tr.) **change, overturn** —*a government* Th. ‖ PASS. (w.indef. or gener. subject, ref. to a situation or event) **change for the worse** Th.

νεωτερικός ή όν *adj.* **1** (of education) **in one's youth** Plb.
2 (of behaviour, ambitions) **youthful** Plb. Plu.

—**νεωτερικῶς** *adv.* **with the impetuosity** or **naivety of youth** Plu.

νεωτερισμός οῦ *m.* **desire** or **concerted movement for social change, innovation, sedition, conspiracy** Pl. D. Plu.

νεωτεριστής οῦ *m.* **revolutionary, conspirator** Plu.

νεωτεροποιΐα ᾱς *f.* [νεωτεροποιός] **innovative** or **revolutionary character** (of a people) Th.

νεωτερο-ποιός όν *adj.* [ποιέω] (of a people) **habitually making innovations, innovative** Th.; (of a section of society) **inclined to make political changes, revolutionary** Arist.

νεώτερος ᾱ (Ion. η) ον *compar.adj.* [νέος] **1** (of persons) **younger** (in age, than others) Hom. Hes. Sapph. Hdt. Trag. Th. +; (than previously, through rejuvenation or sim.) Od. Ar.; (than one is now) Pl.
2 belonging to the younger generation (opp. the older), **younger** Hom. Hdt. S. E. Th. + ‖ MASC.PL.SB. **younger persons, the younger generation** Hom. A.*satyr.fr.* Hdt. E. Th. Ar. +
3 (of gods) **coming into existence later than others, younger** A. Pl.
4 (in neg.phr., of the soul) **younger** (than the body) Pl.
5 (of a person) **too young** (for an office) Th.; (W.GEN. for past events, i.e. to remember them) D.
6 (of things, actions, events, news) **newer, fresher, more recent** Thgn. Pi. Hdt. E. Ar. +; (advbl.acc.) τὰ νεώτερα *more recently* Hdt.
7 (w. mildly or strongly sinister connot., of events, actions, decisions, or sim.) **strange, untoward, disturbing, drastic** Pi. Hdt. E. Th. Ar. Pl. +; (specif., of actions or events) entailing political or social change, **revolutionary** Hdt. Th. Isoc. +

—**νεωτέρως** *compar.adv.* **rather vigorously** —*ref. to expressing oneself* Pl.

νή, Boeot. **νεί** (Ar.) *adv.* [reltd. ναί] | For usages 1–3, see also μά. | **1** (w. the name of Zeus in acc., as an oath used to affirm or emphasise) νὴ (τὸν) Δία *yes by Zeus* Ar. Att.orats. Pl. X. +; (introducing an answer, followed by explanatory cl. w. γάρ) Ar. Pl. X. D.; (making an objection, following ἀλλά) Ar. Att.orats. Pl. X.; (w.imperatv., to urge a course of action) Ar.
2 (w. other named gods or heroes) Ar. Att.orats. Pl. +; (w.du.) νὴ τὼ θεώ (ref. to Demeter and Persephone) Ar. Men.; (w.pl.) νὴ τοὺς θεούς Ar. Pl. X. +; νὴ τὸν οὐρανόν *by heaven* Ar.
3 (as a mock-oath) νὴ τοὺς κονδύλους, νὴ τὴν προεδρίαν *by these fists, by this seat* Ar.; νὴ τὸν κύνα *by the dog* Pl. | see κύων 2
4 (without acc., introducing an assenting statement, in dialogue) **yes** Men.

νῆα (ep.acc.sg.), **νῆας** (pl.): see ναῦς

νῆάδε *ep.adv.*: see under ναῦς

νηγάτεος η ον *ep.Ion.adj.* (of garments, sts. also described as beautiful or white) perh. **spotless** or **unsullied** Il. hHom. AR.; (of a bedchamber) AR. [or perh. *newly made*]

νήγρετος ον *adj.* [privatv.prfx., ἐγείρω] (of sleep) **without waking, deep, sound** Od. hHom.; (of the sleep of death) Mosch.

—**νήγρετον** *neut.adv.* **without waking, soundly** Od.

νη-δεής ές *adj.* [privatv.prfx., δέος] (of a heart) **fearless** Alcm.(cj.)

νήδυια ων *n.pl.* [νηδύς] **internal organs** (of persons, as vulnerable to wounding), **vital parts** Il. AR.

νήδυμος ον *adj.* [perh. fr. false division of ἔχεν ἥδυμος (ὕπνος)] (of sleep) **sweet** Hom. hHom. Mosch.; (of music) hHom.

νηδύς ύος *f.* **1 stomach** (as organ of digestion) Od. Hes. Trag. Call.
2 belly, abdomen (of a person) Il.; **intestines, guts** (of a person or animal) A. Hdt.
3 womb, belly (of a woman or goddess) Il. Hes. A. E.; (fig.ref. to the belly of Zeus, in which he hid the unborn Athena) Hes.; (ref. to the thigh in which he hid Dionysus) E.

νῆες (nom.pl.), **νήεσσι** (ep.dat.pl.): see ναῦς

νηέω, dial. **νᾱέω** *contr.vb.* [reltd. νέω³] | ep.impf. νήεον | ep.aor. νήησα | aor.mid.: dial.3sg. νᾱήσατο, inf. νηήσασθαι | **1 heap** or **pile up** —*wood* (*for a fire or pyre*) Hom. AR. —*a fire, pyre, altar* Od. B.(mid.) AR. —*objects* (*on a cart*) Il. | see also ἀπονέομαι, περινέω
2 (act. and mid.) **load up** —*a ship* (sts. W.GEN. w. *goods*) Il.

νήθω *vb.* [reltd. νέω²] (of persons) **spin** (thread) Pl. Call.; (in neg.phr., of lilies) NT.

νήϊος η ον *Ion.adj.* —also **νάϊος** ᾱ ον (also ος ον) *dial.adj.* [ναῦς] | Trag. uses the dial. form | **1** (of a piece of timber) **for a ship** Hom. Hes. AR.; (of the timbers, stern, bench, keel, tackle) **of a ship** hHom. Lyr.adesp. E. AR.; (of ramming, in battle) **of** or **by ships** A. ‖ NEUT.SG.SB. ship's timber Il.
2 (gener.) related to ships; (of a skill) **maritime** S.; (of persons, an army) **nautical, sea-going** A. E. Tim.; (of an expedition, flight, a mode of transport) **by ship** A. E.
3 (of drops of blood) **of sailors** Tim.(dub.)

νηιάς, also **νηίς** *Ion.f.*: see νᾱιάς

νή-ις ιδος *masc.fem.adj.* [privatv.prfx.; 2nd el.reltd. οἶδα, εἰδέναι] | acc. νήιδα, also νῆιν | (of persons, a life) **ignorant, unaware** (sts. W.GEN. of sthg.) Hom. hHom. B. Call. AR.

Νήϊσται ὧν *fem.pl.adj.* (of one of the gates of Thebes) **Neistan** A. E.(dub.)

νηΐτης ου *masc.adj.* [ναῦς] (of a military force, an expedition) consisting of ships, **naval** Th. AR. Plb.

νη-κερδής ές *adj.* [privatv.prfx., κέρδος] **1** (of a plan, words) bringing no gain, **profitless, useless, pointless** Hom.
2 (of a person's fate) **joyless** AR.

νή-κεροι *masc.pl.adj.* [κέρας] | only nom. | (of forest creatures) not horned, **hornless** Hes.

νήκεστον *neut.adv.* [ἀκέομαι] **incurably** —*ref. to being harmed* Hes. hHom.(cj.)

νηκουστέω *contr.vb.* [νήκουστος] (of a god) **fail to listen, be deaf** —W.GEN. *to a goddess* Il.

νήκουστος ον *adj.* [ἀκουστός] not listening, **deaf** (W.GEN. to protestations) Emp.

νηλεής, also **νηλής**, ep. **νηλειής**, ές *adj.* [ἔλεος] **1** (of persons, their spirit, mind, heart) not feeling pity, **pitiless, ruthless** Il. Hes. Thgn. A. Pi. AR.; (of Cerberus, the Cyclops, an Erinys) Hes. E.*Cyc.* AR.
2 (of bronze as a weapon, fetters) **pitiless, cruel** Hom. Hes.; (of the day of one's death, a fate, murder) Hom. Emp. AR.; (of a theft, old age) hHom.; (of sleep, ref. to an instance w. unfortunate consequences) Od.
3 not receiving pity; (of corpses left exposed) **unpitied** S.
—**νηλεῶς**, Ion. **νηλέως**, ep. **νηλειῶς** *adv.* **pitilessly, mercilessly** Anacr. A. AR.

νηλείτιες (or perh. **νηλείτιδες**) *fem.pl.adj.* [ἀλείτης] | only nom. | (of female slaves) **guiltless** Od.

νηλεό-ποινος ον *adj.* [νηλεής, ποινή] (of Erinyes) punishing mercilessly Hes.

Νηλεύς¹ έως (ep. ῆος) *m.* **Neleus** (son of Poseidon and Tyro, father of Nestor) Hom. Hes.*fr.* E. Isoc. Men. AR.
—**Νηλείδης** εω *Ion.m.* —also **Νηλεΐδης** ᾱο *ep.m.* **son of Neleus** (ref. to Nestor) Il. ‖ PL. descendants of Neleus Hdt. AR.
—**Νηληιάδης** ᾱο (also εω) *ep.m.* **son of Neleus** (ref. to Nestor) Hom. Hes.*fr.*
—**Νηλήϊος** η ον *ep.Ion.adj.* (of Nestor) **son of Neleus** Il.; (of a son) **of Neleus** Il. AR.; (of a grandson) Il.; (of the mares) Il.; (of the city of Pylos) Hom. Mimn.
—**Νηληΐς**¹ ίδος *f.* (of a daughter) **of Neleus** AR.

Νηλεύς² έως (ep. ῆος) *m.* **Neleus** (son of Kodros and founder of Miletos) Call. Plb.
—**Νηληΐς**² ίδος *fem.adj.* (epith. of Artemis on Miletos) **Neleid** Call.

νηλής *adj.*: see νηλεής

νήλιπος ον *adj.* [privatv.prfx., perh. ἦλιψ *a kind of shoe*] —also **νηλίπους** ουν, gen. ποδος *adj.* [app. πούς by pop.etym.] (of a person) **unshod, barefoot** S. AR. Theoc.

νῆμα ατος *n.* [νέω²] that which is spun; **yarn, thread** (sg. and pl.) Od. E. Pl. AR. Theoc.; (spun by a spider) Hes.

νημερτής, dial. **νᾱμερτής**, ές *adj.* [privatv.prfx., ἁμαρτάνω]
1 (of a prophet) **unerring, infallible** Od. Hes. AR.; (of nymphs) A.*fr.*
2 (of Hermes, a person's mind) **lacking deceit, truthful** Od. hHom.
3 (of the will of the gods) **sure, absolute** Od. hHom.
4 (of a report, story) **true, reliable** Hom. hHom. A. AR.
‖ NEUT.PL.SB. true things, the truth Hom. hHom.
—**νημερτές** *neut.adv.* **truly** —*ref. to speaking, promising, thinking, or sim.* Hom. hHom. AR.
—**νημερτέως** *Ion.adv.* **truly** —*ref. to speaking* Od. hHom.

νηνεμία ᾱς, Ion. **νηνεμίη** ης *f.* [νήνεμος] absence of wind (esp. in the mountains or at sea), **windless weather** Hom. Hdt. Pl. AR. Plu.; **windlessness** (as a state) Arist.

νήνεμος ον *adj.* [privatv.prfx., ἄνεμος] **1** (of the sky) without wind, **windless** Il. Ar. AR.; (of the sea, swell, ref. to midday) A. E.; (of a shore, night) AR.
2 (of a crowd of people) **still, silent** E.; (of calmness, as an emotional state) A.

νῆνις *Ion.f.*: see νεᾶνις

νηοπόλος *Ion.m.*: see νᾱοπόλος

νηός¹ *Ion.m.*: see νᾱός¹

νηός² (ep.gen.): see ναῦς

νηο-σσόος ον *ep.adj.* [ναῦς; σόος, see σῶς] (epith. of Apollo, Artemis) **ship-protecting** AR.

νη-πενθής ές *adj.* [privatv.prfx., πένθος] (of a drug) **banishing sorrow** Od.

νηπιαχεύω *vb.* [νηπίαχος] (of a boy) engage in childish amusements, **play** Il.

νηπίαχος ον *adj.* [dimin. νήπιος] (of boys) **young** Il.; (pejor.) **childish, silly** Il.; (of a child) **infant** Il. AR.

νηπιάχω *vb.* (of a person, nestlings) **be young** AR. Mosch.

νηπιέη ης *ep.f.* [νήπιος] | acc.pl. νηπιάᾱς, dat.pl. νηπιέῃσι | behaviour of a child, **childishness** Il. ‖ COLLECTV.PL. childlike ways or behaviour Il.; (pejor., in adults) childish folly Hom.

νήπιος ᾱ (Ion. η) ον *adj.* **1** (of persons, esp. infants) **young in years, young** Hom. Sol. Hdt. E. Antipho Lys. +; (of the offspring of a bird or animal) Il. ‖ NEUT.PL.SB. offspring or cubs (of a lion) Il.
2 (of children's physical strength) **weak, puny** Il.
3 (of persons) childish (in thought, speech or behaviour), **thoughtless, foolish** Hom. Hes. Archil. Eleg. Pi. Hdt.(oracle) Trag. +; (of speech) A. Ar. ‖ MASC.SB. fool Il. Hes.
‖ NEUT.PL.SB. foolish words, behaviour or thoughts Od. Pi.*fr.* E. AR.

νηπιότης ητος *f.* **childishness, immaturity** (of children's minds) Pl.

νή-πλεκτος ον *adj.* [privatv.prfx., πλεκτός] (of grieving Aphrodite) **with unbraided hair** Bion

νή-πλυτος ον *adj.* [πλύνω] (of a shield-covering) **unwashed** Anacr.

νή-ποινος, dial. **νάποινος**, ον *adj.* [ποινή] **1** (of persons justifiably killed) with no compensation exacted, **unavenged** Od.
2 (of a plot of land) not yielding recompense, **without reward** (W.GEN. fr. fruit trees) Pi.
—**νήποινον** *neut.adv.* **without payment** or **recompense** Od.
—**νηποινεί** *adv.* without paying a penalty, **with impunity** And.(law) Pl. X. D.(law)

νήπτης ου *m.* [νήφω] man of sober behaviour, **level-headed man** Plb.

νηπυτίη ης *Ion.f.* [νηπύτιος] period of being a young child, **infancy** AR.

νηπύτιος η ον *Ion.adj.* [dimin. νήπιος] 1 (of a person) **in babyhood** AR.
2 (of words) **childish, foolish** Il.
3 ‖ MASC.SB. (ref. to an adult) **foolish child** Il. Ar.

Νηρεύς έως (ep. ῆος, dial. έος) *m.* **Nereus** (son of Pontos and Gaia, father of the Nereids) Hes. hHom. Lyr. E. Ar. +; (meton., ref. to the sea) Call.

—**Νηρηΐδες**, also **Νηρεΐδες**, contr. **Νηρῇδες** (E.), ὧν *f.pl.* daughters of Nereus, **Nereids** Il. Lyr. Hdt. S. E. Pl. +

—**Νηρηΐς** ΐδος, contr. **Νηρῇς** ῇδος (E.) *f.* **Nereid** (ref. to Thetis) B. E.

—**Νηρέιος** ᾱ ον *adj.* (of the plain) **of Nereus** (i.e. the sea) Lyr.adesp.

νήριθμος ον *adj.* [privatv.prfx., ἀριθμός] (of possessions) **countless** Theoc.

νήριτος ον *adj.* 1 (of animal tracks) **countless** AR.
2 (of a forest) with countless trees, **immense** Hes.
3 (of a scent) immensely powerful, **overwhelming** AR.

νησαῖος ᾱ ον *adj.* [νῆσος] (of a land, cities, mountains) belonging to an island, **insular** E.; (perh. of a person) A.*satyr.fr.*

νησίδιον ου *n.* [dimin. νῆσος] **small island, islet** Th.

νησίζω *vb.* (of a place) **be an island** Plb.

νησίον ου *n.* [dimin. νῆσος] **small island** NT.

νησίς ῖδος *f.* **small island** Hippon. Hdt. Th. Call. Plb. Plu.

νῆσις εως *f.* [νέω²] action of spinning thread, **spinning** Pl.

νησιώτης ου, dial. **νᾱσιώτᾱς** ᾱ *m.* [νῆσος] 1 one who lives on an island, **island-dweller, islander** E.; (app.ref. to a mainlander in danger of drowning) Tim. ‖ PL. islanders Pi. Hdt. Th. Ar. Att.orats. +
2 ‖ ADJ. (of a people) **island-dwelling** Pi.; (of a life) spent on an island E.

—**νησιῶτις**, dial. **νᾱσιῶτις**, ιδος *fem.adj.* of or belonging to an island; (of a bee, fig.ref. to a poet) **island-dwelling** B.; (of a crag, an altar) **on an island** A. S.; (of cities) Hdt.

νησιωτικός ή όν *adj.* 1 of or relating to islanders; (of tribes, persons) being islanders, **insular** Hdt. Men.; (of tribute) **from islanders** Plu.; (of a server of legal summonses) **dealing with islanders** Ar. ‖ NEUT.SB. island status (of certain Athenian allies) Th.
2 of or relating to islands; (of a name) **of an island** E.; (of a home) **on an island** E.

νῆσος, dial. **νᾶσος**, ου *f.* **island** Hom. +; (phr.) Πέλοπος νῆσος (νᾶσος) *island of Pelops* (ref. to the Peloponnese) Tyrt. Alc. B. S.

νῆσσα, Att. **νῆττα**, ης, dial. **νᾶσσα** ᾱς *f.* **duck** (esp. as food) Hdt. Ar. Plu.

νηστείᾱ ᾱς, Ion. **νηστείη** ης *f.* [νηστεύω] (sg. and pl.) period of abstinence from food (for religious reasons), **fasting, fast** Hdt. NT.

νηστεύω *vb.* [νῆστις] abstain from food (for religious reasons), **fast** Ar. NT. Plu.; (of the followers of Pythagoras) **abstain** —W.GEN. *fr. living things* Call.

νηστική ῆς *f.* [νέω²] process of spinning yarn, **spinning** Pl.

νῆστις ιδος (ep. ιος) *masc.fem.adj.* [privatv.prfx., ἔδω, ἐσθίω] | acc. νῆστιν (A.) ‖ PL.: nom. νήστιδες, ep. νήστιες | acc. νήστεις (A. Plb. NT.), ep. νήστιας | 1 (of persons) going without food, **hungry, famished** Hom. A. Plb. NT.; **starved** (W.GEN. of food) E.; **fasting** (for religious reasons) Call.; (medic.) **dieting** Plu.
2 (of the pains, sickness) **of hunger** A.; (of hunger) **starving** A.
3 (of winds that strand a fleet) **causing hunger** A.
4 ‖ FEM.SB. intestine or belly (of a pig) Philox.Leuc.

νησύδριον ου *n.* [dimin. νῆσος] (derog.) **little island** Isoc. X.

νήτη *f.*: see νεάτη, under νέατος¹

νητός ή όν *adj.* [νέω³] (of treasure) **heaped up** Od.

νῆττα Att.*f.*: see νῆσσα

νηττάριον ου Att.*n.* [dimin. νῆττα] **little duck, duckie** (as a term of endearment to a lover) Ar.

νηῦς Ion.*f.*: see ναῦς

νηυσι-πέρητος ον *Ion.adj.* [ναῦς, περατός] (of rivers) allowing the passage of ships, **navigable** Hdt.

νήυτμος ον *adj.* [privatv.prfx., ἀυτμή] **breathless** Hes.

νηφάλιος ᾱ (Ion. η) ον *adj.* [νήφω] (of propitiatory offerings) **sober** (i.e. without wine) A. AR.

νηφαντικός ή όν *adj.* (fig., of the fountains of wisdom) **sobering** Pl.

νήφω, dial. **νάφω** *vb.* | dial.inf. νηφέμεν | impf. ἔνηφον (Plu.) | 1 **be** or **stay sober** Archil. Thgn. Plb. Plu.
2 be sober in one's thoughts or behaviour, **be level-headed** or **self-controlled** Pl. X. Plb.(quot.com.)

—**νήφων** οντος *masc.ptcpl.adj.* not drunk, **sober** Hdt. S. Ar. Att.orats. +; (of a god, fig.ref. to water) Pl.

νήφων ονος *m.* **sober man** Thgn.; (pl., appos.w. ἄνδρες) Thgn.

νή-χυτος ον *adj.* [perh. intensv.prfx., χυτός] (of water, sea-spray) **flowing, abundant** AR.; (of sea-foam, moisture) Call. AR.

νήχω *vb.* [νέω¹] | only pres., fut. and impf. | ep.inf. νηχέμεναι | ep.impf. νῆχον | fut.mid. νήξομαι | (act. and mid.) **swim** Od. AR. Plb. Mosch. Plu.; (of dolphins, swans) Hes.; (fig., of olives in brine) Call.

νῆψις εως *f.* [νήφω] **sobriety** (in behaviour or character) Plb.

νηῶν (ep.gen.pl.): see ναῦς

νίγλαρος ου *m.* specialised effect produced by a musical instrument; perh. **trill** Ar.

νίζω, also (pres.) **νίπτω** (NT. Plu.) *vb.* | fut. νίψω | aor. ἔνιψα, ep. νίψα ‖ MID.: aor. ἐνιψάμην | pf. νένιμμαι | 1 (usu. of a servant or inferior) wash (feet); **wash** —*a person's feet, a person* (i.e. *his feet*) Od. Hdt.(oracle) NT. Plu. —W.DBL.ACC. *a person, his feet* Od. ‖ MID. have (W.ACC. one's feet) **washed** NT.
2 ‖ MID. wash one's hands (for purpose of purification, before a meal, prayer or religious occasion); **wash** —*one's hands* Hom. Hes. NT. Plu.; (intr.) **wash** (one's hands) Hom. Theoc.
3 wash (an object, to purify it); **wash clean** —*a wine-cup* (before a libation) Il. —*sacrificial implements, a holy statue* E.; (fig., of a river, in neg.phr.) —*a polluted house* S.
4 **wash away** —*blood* (w. ἀπό + GEN. *fr. a wound*) Il. —*bloodshed* (i.e. its pollution, fr. a person) E. AR. ‖ MID. **wash oneself clean of** —*blood* E. —*bloodshed* (i.e. its pollution) AR.
5 **wash clean** —*a table* Od. —*one's body* (W.DAT. *in spring-water*) E. —*cattle* (*in seawater*) E. —*the wounds of dead warriors* E. ‖ MID. **wash** —*one's foot* (*in a lake*) Hes.*fr.* —*one's body* (*in a stream*) B. —*one's eyes* (W.DAT. *w. urine, to cure blindness*) Hdt. —*one's face* NT.; **wash** (W.ACC. *one's body*) **clean** —W.ACC. *of brine* Od.; (intr.) **wash** (in a bathing-pool) NT.
6 (of seawater) **wash away** —*sweat* (w. ἀπό + GEN. *fr. a person's skin*) Il.
7 (provb., ref. to a futile endeavour) **wash** —*a mud-brick* Theoc.

νίκᾱ dial.*f.*: see νίκη

νῑκαῖος ᾱ ον *adj.* [νίκη] (of a refrain) **in celebration of victory** Call.

νῑκάτωρ ορος dial.*m.* [νῑκάω] **conqueror** (as a ruler's title) Plu.

νῑκᾱφορίᾱ ᾱς *dial.f.* [νῑκηφόρος] winning of a victory (in an athletic contest); (sg. and pl.) **win, victory** Pi.
νῑκᾱφόρος *dial.adj.*: see νῑκηφόρος
νῑκάω *contr.vb.* —also **νίκημι** (Theoc.) *Aeol.vb.* [νίκη] | dial.3sg.impf. νίκη (Pi. Theoc.) | iteratv.impf. νῑκάσκον | fut. νῑκήσω, dial.2sg. νῑκάσεις (Theoc.), dial.inf. νῑκάσειν, Aeol. νῑκάσην (Theoc.) | aor. ἐνίκησα, ep. νίκησα, dial. ἐνίκᾱσα, also νίκᾱσα | pf. νενίκηκα ‖ PASS.: dial.3pl.pf. νενίκᾱνται (Pi.) ‖ neut.impers.vbl.adj. νῑκητέον |
1 be victorious (in a military, athletic or other conflict or contest, freq. W.DAT. or INTERN.ACC. specifying its nature) Hom. +; **win** —W.COGN.ACC. *a victory* E. Att.orats. +
2 (tr.) gain victory over, **vanquish, defeat** —*someone* (freq. W.DAT. *specifying the nature of the conflict or contest*) Hom. +; (of shamelessness and insolence) —*justice* Thgn.; **win** —W.COGN.ACC. *a victory* (W. 2ND ACC. *over someone*) Od. ‖ PASS. be defeated Il. +
3 win (a legal case) A. Arist. —W.INTERN.ACC. *a case* Ar. Thphr.
4 (of circumstances, emotions, or sim.) **get the better of, overpower, overcome** —*persons, their mind, judgement, or sim.* Il. + ‖ PASS. be overcome —W.DAT. OR PREP.PHR. *by circumstances, emotions, or sim.* Trag. Th. +
5 ‖ PASS. (of persons) be overcome —W.GEN. *by desire* A.; yield or submit —W.GEN. *to someone* S. E. Ar. —*to a verdict, the truth* Antipho; (fig., of doors) be overwhelmed —W.GEN. *by guests* Pi.
6 surpass, outdo —*others* (usu. W.DAT. *in sthg.*) Il. +; (of non-existence) **exceed** —*all possible reckoning* (i.e. *be best*) S.
7 (intr.) **excel, be pre-eminent** —W.DAT. *in a particular skill or attribute* Hom. + —W.ACC. Pl. —W.PTCPL. *in doing sthg.* X.
8 (of a point of view, a proposed law, or sim.) **win the day, be carried** Hom. Hdt. S. E. +; (of a speaker) **prevail** E. —W.DAT. *w. his view* Hdt. ‖ IMPERS. the prevailing view is —W.INF. *to do sthg.* Hdt. S. —W.ACC. + INF. *that sthg. is the case* Th.; it is preferable —W.INF. *to do sthg.* Pl.
νίκη ης, dial. **νίκᾱ** ᾱς *f.* **1** occasion or fact of being victorious (in war, athletic or other contests, disputes or conflicts of all kinds), **victory** Hom. +; (W.GEN. of someone, i.e. the victor) Il. +; (over someone or sthg.) Ar. +; (in a battle, contest, or sim.) Il. +
2 (personif., as a deity, sts. identified w. Athena) **Victory** Hes. Pi. B. Hdt.(oracle) S. E. +
νίκημα ατος *n.* specific instance of victory (in battle), **victory** Plb. Plu.
νῑκητήριος ᾱ ον *adj.* **1** relating to victory (in a contest); (of a prize, kiss) **for victory** Pl. X.
2 ‖ NEUT.SB. (freq. pl. for sg.) prize or reward for victory (in war, athletic or other contests) E. Ar. Pl. X. D. Plu.
3 ‖ NEUT.SB. thank-offering for victory (ref. to a sacrifice to the gods) Plu.; (pl.) victory celebrations (ref. to a banquet) X. Plu.
νῑκητικός ή όν *adj.* **1** (of military resources) **conducive to victory** X. Plu.
2 (of a point of view) **likely to prevail** Plb.
νῑκηφορέω *contr.vb.* [νῑκηφόρος] (iron.) **carry off** (W.ACC. tears) **as a victory prize** E.
νίκη-φόρος, dial. **νῑκᾱφόρος**, ον *adj.* [φέρω] **1** (of persons, their hand, might) winning victory, **victorious** Pi. S. E. Pl. X. Plu.; (transf.epith., of a person's head) E.; (of a chariot-team) Pi.; (of a person, W.GEN. in a contest or activity) X.
‖ MASC.PL.SB. winners, victors Pi. Pl. X.
2 (of contests, deeds) bringing or resulting in victory, **victorious** Pi.; (of the spear, meton. for war) E.; (of the outcome of a trial) A.; (of a struggle) **bringing victory** (W.GEN. in war) A.
3 (epith. of Justice) **bringing victory** A. E.(dub.); (as a cult title of Venus) Plu.
4 (of oracles) **predicting victory** Plu.
5 (of a chariot) **carrying Victory** (i.e. an effigy of the goddess) Plu.
6 (of garlands, splendour) associated with the winning of victory, **of victory** Pi.; (of safety, a prey) **won by victory** (in war, hunting) E.
7 (fig., of a kind of life) **winning first place** Pl.
νῖκος ους *n.* **victory** NT.
νιν *dial.3sg.enclit.acc.pers.pron.* [reltd. μιν] **1** (masc.fem.) **him, her** Lyr. Trag. Ar. Hellenist.poet.; (neut.) **it** Pi. B. Trag. Theoc. Bion
2 (pl., masc.fem.neut.) **them** Pi. B. Trag.
νιπτήρ ῆρος *m.* [νίζω] portable washing-bowl, **basin** NT.
νίπτρα ων *n.pl.* **1** (collectv.) **washing water** (for the hands) E. Philox.Leuc.; (gener., for the body) E.
2 Washing Episode (as title of *Odyssey* 19) Arist.
νίπτω *vb.*: see νίζω
νίσομαι (sts. written **νίσσ-** or **νείσ-**) *mid.vb.* [νέομαι] | only pres. and impf. | ep.3sg.impf. νίσ(σ)ετο (Call. AR.), 3pl. νίσοντο | **1** (of persons) go or come back, **return** (freq. W.PREP.PHR. OR ADV. to or fr. a place) Hom. hHom. E. Call.; (pres., w.fut.sens.) Il.
2 (gener.) proceed on one's way, **come, go, travel** (freq. W.PREP.PHR. OR ADV. to or fr. a place) Hom. Hes. Stesich. Pi. Hellenist.poet.; (of an animal or bird) E.; (of a rock) **move** (by magic) AR.
νίτρον *n.*, **νιτρώδης** *adj.*: see λίτρον, λιτρώδης
νίφα *acc.f.* [reltd. νείφω] **snow** Hes.
νιφάς άδος *f.* **1 snow** (lying or falling) Il. A. Pi. ‖ PL. snowflakes Il. Simon. Call.; (W.ADJ. *golden*, fig.ref. to wealth, as a gift of Zeus) Pi.
2 ‖ ADJ. (of a mountain) **snow-covered** S.
3 (fig.) **shower, hail** (of missiles) E.; (W.GEN. of stones) A.*fr.*; **storm** (W.GEN. of war) Pi.
νιφετός οῦ *m.* **snowstorm, snowfall** Hom. Pi.*fr.* Hdt. Call. AR. +
νιφετώδης ες *adj.* (of a day, night) **snowy** Plb. Plu.
νιφό-βολος ον *adj.* [βάλλω] (of mountains, valleys, plains) **snow-beaten** E. Ar.(mock-dithyramb) Plu.; (of dithyrambic preludes, perh. w. implication of being artistically frigid) Ar.
νιφόεις εσσα εν *adj.* (of mountains) **snowy** Hom. Hes. Pi. S. Ar. Hellenist.poet.; (of the sky) Alc.; (of the Black Sea) Theoc.
νιφο-στιβής ές *adj.* [στείβω] (of winter storms) in which one treads on snow, **with snow underfoot** S.
νίφω *vb.*: see νείφω
νίψα (ep.aor.): see νίζω
νίψις εως *f.* [νίζω] **washing** (of one's master's feet) Plu.
νίψω (fut.): see νίζω
νοέω *contr.vb.* [νόος] | aor. ἐνόησα, ep. νόησα | pf. νενόηκα ‖ MID.: aor.ptcpl. νοησάμενος, Ion. νωσάμενος | Ion.pf. νένωμαι | Ion.3sg.plpf. ἐνένωτο ‖ PASS.: aor. ἐνοήθην |
1 perceive visually, **observe, notice** —*persons or things* (sts. W.PTCPL. OR ADJ. *doing sthg., in a certain state*) Hom. Hes. hHom.
2 perceive mentally, **identify, recognise** —*someone* (fr. a description) S. ‖ MID. **visualise, imagine** —*the future* S.
3 be aware of, understand, know —*someone's intentions, the facts of a situation, or sim.* Hom. Hes. Alc.(mid.) Sol. S. E. + —W.COMPL.CL. *that sthg. is the case* Hom. Hes.; (intr.) **understand** Hom.

4 have in mind, **consider, contemplate** —*thoughts, ideas, or sim.* Hom. Anacr.(mid.) Eleg. Pi. + —W.INDIR.Q. *whether to do sthg.* Il.; (intr.) **think** Parm. E. Ar. +
5 hold a certain opinion or view (about sthg.); **think, believe** —*sthg.* Il. + —W.COMPL.CL. *that sthg. is or will be the case* Il. Sol.; **deem, judge** —W. ὡς + PTCPL. or PREDIC.ADJ. *someone as being dead, sthg. as best* S.; **be inclined** or **disposed** —W.ADV. *well, badly* (W.DAT. *towards someone*) Hes. Hdt. X.; (phr.) δύο νοεῖν *have two (different) states of mind or mood* Semon.
6 think out, devise —*a thought, plan, or sim.* Hom. Hdt. E. Ar. +; (intr.) **plan** —W.PREP.PHR. *for two possible options* Hdt.; **judge matters** —W.ADV. *correctly* Hdt. || PASS. (of plans) be devised Pl.
7 intend or **plan** —W.INF. *to do sthg.* Hom. Pi. S.; (mid.) Il. Hdt.
8 (of a person, an oracle, a law) intend to say, **mean** —*sthg.* S. Ar. Pl.; (of a name, an event) stand for, **signify** —*sthg.* Pl.
—**νοέων** ουσα ον *ptcpl.adj.* with understanding, **of good sense, wise** Hom.

νόημα, Aeol. **νόημμα**, Ion. **νῶμα** (Emp.), ατος *n.* **1** that which is thought, **thought, idea, notion** Hom. Ar. Plu.; (in comparisons, as the exemplar of swiftness) Hes. hHom. Thgn. X. Plu.; (philos.) **concept** (opp. sense-perception) Parm. Pl. X. Arist.
2 that which is planned, **purpose, intention** Hom. hHom. Lyr. Hdt. Ar. Pl.; (specif.) **plan** Od. Alc.
3 way of thinking (of a person), **cast of mind** Od. Hes. Pi. Ar. Theoc.*epigr.*
4 capacity for thought, **understanding, mind, intelligence** (as a human faculty) Od. Hes. Emp. Ar. Pl.
5 good sense, wisdom Il. hHom. Thgn.

νοήμων ον, gen. ονος *adj.* **1** (of persons, their minds) thinking correctly, **thoughtful, wise** Od. Theoc.
2 in one's right mind, **sane** Hdt.

νόησις εως *f.* mental perception, **intelligence, thinking, reason** Lyr.adesp. Pl. Arist. Plu.

νοητικός ή όν *adj.* (of parts of the soul) **intellectual** Arist. || NEUT.SB. power of thinking Arist.

νοητός ή όν *adj.* **1** capable of being thought about; (of a world, Forms, creatures, objects, or sim.) **intelligible** (opp. visible) Pl. Arist. Plu. || NEUT.IMPERS. (w. ἐστί) it is thinkable or conceivable —W.COMPL.CL. *that sthg. is the case* Parm.
2 || NEUT.SB. object of thought Pl. Arist. || NEUT.PL.SB. intelligible things, concepts Pl. Arist. Plu.

νοθᾱ-γενής ές *adj.* [νόθος; γένος, γίγνομαι] (of persons) born out of wedlock, **illegitimate** E.

νοθείᾱ ᾱς *f.* illegitimate birth (of a person) Plu.

νόθος η ον *adj.* **1** (of persons) born out of wedlock, **illegitimate** Il. Pi. Hdt. S. E. Th. +; (gener.) **base-born** Pl. || MASC.FEM.SB. bastard Hdt. E. Ar. Pl. Is. +
2 || MASC.SB. (at Athens) child of an alien mother D. Plu.
3 (of a sexual relationship) **irregular, illicit** E.; (of reasoning, education, pleasures) **spurious, illegitimate** Pl.; (of persons) **counterfeit, bogus** Pl.

νοίδιον ου *n.* [dimin. νόος] **little idea** Ar.

νομαδικός *adj.*: see under νομάς

νόμαιος η ον *Ion.adj.* [νόμος] (of a cry to a god) **customary** Call. || NEUT.SB. (usu.pl.) custom or practice (of a particular country) Hdt.

νομ-άρχης ου *m.* [νομός, ἄρχω] **governor of a province** or **district** (esp. in Egypt) Hdt.

νομάς άδος *masc.fem.adj.* [νέμω] **1** (of horses, seamen) **wandering, roaming** S. Tim. || MASC.SB. wanderer or shepherd S.(cj.)
2 (of streams) app. **wandering** S. [or perh. *distributors,* W.GEN. *of waters*]
—**νομάδες** ων *m.f.pl.* people who wander for pasture (sts. appos.w. ethnic name), **nomads** A. Pi.*fr.* Hdt. X. Arist.
—**νομαδικός** ή όν *adj.* (of a way of life, a kind of clothing) of a shepherd or herdsman, **pastoral** Arist. Plb.
—**Νομάδες** ων *m.pl.* **1 Nomads** (a people of NE. Africa) Pi.
2 Numidians (a people of NW. Africa) Plb. Plu. || SG. Numidian man Plb. Plu.
—**Νομαδικός** ή όν *adj.* (of persons or things) of or associated with the Numidians, **Numidian** Plb. Plu. || FEM.SB. Numidian land, Numidia Plu.

νόμευμα ατος *n.* [νομεύω] **flock** (of sheep) A.

νομεύς έως (Ion. έος, ep. ῆος) *m.* [νέμω] **1 herdsman** or **shepherd** Hom. hHom. Hdt. S. Pl. +
2 distributor, apportioner (sts. W.GEN. of sthg.) Pl.
3 || PL. supporting ribs or frames (of ships) Hdt.

νομευτικός ή όν *adj.* (of the art or science) **of herding** Pl.

νομεύω *vb.* **1** put out to pasture, **herd, pasture** —*flocks, cattle* Od. hHom. Pl. Theoc. Mosch.; (of a ruler) —*cattle without horns (fig.ref. to citizens)* Pl.; (intr.) **herd animals** Theoc. || PASS. (fig., of citizens, envisaged as cattle) be herded —W.PREP.PHR. *according to laws* Pl.
2 graze —*pastures* (W.DAT. *w. cattle*) hHom.

νομή ῆς *f.* [νέμω] **1** (pl.) land used for grazing (of animals), **pasture** Hdt. S. Pl. +; (sg.) **feeding ground** (of hares) X.
2 herd (of grazing animals) X.
3 pasturing of animals (as an occupation), **pasturing, grazing** X. Arist. Plb.
4 grass or other herbage for animal food; **provender, forage** Pl.; (fig., ref. to blood) **sustenance, food** (of the body) Pl.
5 spreading (of fire) Plb. Plu.; (of ulcers) Plb.
6 distribution, allocation (of resources, money, land, or sim.) Hdt. Pl. Aeschin. D. Arist. Plu.

νομίζω, Aeol. **νομίσδω** *vb.* [νόμος] | fut. νομιῶ | aor. ἐνόμισα || PASS.: fut. νομισθήσομαι | aor. ἐνομίσθην | pf. νενόμισμαι || neut.impers.vbl.adj. νομιστέον |
1 (of persons, esp. a people) have a customary practice; **use, have** —*a certain language, certain weapons, practices* Hdt.; **practise** —*a way of life, horse-breeding* A. Pi.; **observe** —W.COGN.ACC. *a city's practices* E.; **customarily hold** —*an assembly* Arist.
2 be habitual (in a certain practice); **use** —W.DAT. *a certain language* Hdt. —*pigs (in sacrifices), heroes (in cults)* Hdt.; **observe** —W.DAT. *certain customs, practices, constraints* Th.
3 (wkr.sens., of persons) **observe, cherish** —W.ACC. *a common enmity* A.
4 have as a custom, **be accustomed** —W.INF. *to do sthg.* Hdt. E.
5 establish as a custom; (of a ruler, legislator, the common people) **make** (W.ACC. sthg.) **customary** E. X.; **make it customary** —W.INF. *to do sthg.* X.
6 || PASS. (of things) be customary Alc. Xenoph. Heraclit. Trag. Antipho Th. + || IMPERS. it is customary (freq. W.INF. or ACC. + INF. to do sthg., for sthg. to be the case) Hdt. Trag. Th. Ar. + || NEUT.PL.PTCPL.SB. (pres.) customary practices, rites or offerings Hdt. Ar. Att.orats.; (aor.) established or customary songs (in honour of a god) E.
7 deem, judge, consider —*someone or sthg.* (W.PREDIC.SB. or ADJ., sts. w. ὡς (*as being*) *such and such*) Scol. Pi. Hdt. Trag. Th. + —W.ADV. *nowhere* (i.e. *of no account*) A. || PASS. (of persons or things) be considered —W.PREDIC.SB. or ADJ. *such and such* Hdt. + —W.GEN. *as belonging to someone* S. E.*fr.*

νομικός

8 regard, accept —*Eros, Reverence, or sim.* (W.PREDIC.SB. *as a god*) Pl. X.; **recognise, believe in** —*certain gods* Hdt. Pl. X. —(*esp. in neg.phr.*) *gods* E. Lys. Pl.
9 recognise, have —*the same friends and enemies* (*as someone else*) E. Th.
10 think —W.INTERN.ACC. *vain thoughts* Thgn. —*about justice* (W.ADV. *in the wrong way, i.e. have wrong ideas about it*) Thgn.
11 (gener.) **think, consider, believe** (sthg.) Hdt. Th. + —W.INF. or ACC. + INF. *that sthg. is the case* Hdt. S. E. Th. + —W.ACC. + PTCPL. Th. Pl. —W.COMPL.CL. Th. —W.NOM.PTCPL. *that one is doing sthg.* X. ‖ PASS. (of things) be believed (to be the case) Hdt. ‖ NEUT.SG.PF.PASS.PTCPL.SB. that which is believed (W.PREP.PHR. by people) Hdt.

νομικός ή όν *adj.* **1** relating to laws or conventions; (of modes of behaviour) **based on law** Pl.; (of justice) **legal** (opp. natural) Arist.; (of a kind of friendship, opp. one based on moral obligations) Arist.
2 (of persons) **with legal experience** or **expertise** NT. Plu.
3 ‖ NEUT.PL.SB. legal matters Plu.

—**νομικῶς** *adv.* **1 in conformity with legal principles** (opp. feelings) —*ref. to having personal relationships* Arist.
2 on conventional principles, in a general way —*ref. to making distinctions* Arist.

νόμιμος η ον (also ος ον) *adj.* **1** conforming to custom, usage or law; (of power, actions, or sim.) **lawful, legitimate** E. Th. Ar. Att.orats. +; (of an oath, a contract) **legally binding** And. Isoc.; (of gods, invoked in a legal oath) **appropriate, customary** Pl.
2 (of persons) **law-abiding** Antipho And. Pl.

—**νόμιμα** ων *neut.pl.sb.* **1 natural laws** (sanctioned by the gods) S.
2 ancestral or **traditional rules** or **customs** (relating to marriage, burial, or sim.) A. Hdt. E. Th. Att.orats. +; (sg.) Emp. Lys. X.
3 enacted laws Hdt. Antipho Th.
4 activities and places specified by the laws; (phr., of persons accused of murder) εἴργεσθαι τῶν νομίμων *be excluded fr. the legally specified things* (*such as religious ceremonies, lawcourts, the agora*) Antipho Pl. Arist.

—**νομίμως** *adv.* **justly, equitably** —*ref. to performing actions* Th. Att.orats. Pl. +

νόμιος ᾱ ον *adj.* [νομός] **1** (epith. of Pan) **of the pastures** hHom.; (of Apollo) Pi. Hellenist.poet.; (of Hermes) Ar.
2 (of a melody) **of a shepherd, pastoral** AR.

νόμισις εως *f.* [νομίζω] **customary belief** (about the gods) Th.

νόμισμα ατος *n.* **1** that which is customary, **custom, ritual** (*ref. to collective behaviour, in sacrificing, voting, or sim.*) Alc. A. E.
2 standard or **legal measure** (of wine) Ar.
3 money as standard measure of value (within a city or country), **coinage, currency** Xenoph. Hdt. S. E.*Cyc.* Ar. Att.orats. +; (fig.) **standard currency** (*ref. to the gods, as invoked in oaths*) Ar. ‖ PL. **coins** or **coinage** Ar. Pl. X. Arist. Plb. Plu.

νομισματο-πωλικός ή όν *adj.* [πωλέω] (pejor., of a skill) app. **comparable in kind to money-selling** (i.e. money-changing) Pl.

νομιστέος ᾱ ον *vbl.adj.* [νομίζω] (of arguments) **to be believed** Pl.

νομιστεύομαι *pass.vb.* (fig., of the practice of bribery) **be common currency** —W.PREP.PHR. *among a people* Plb.

νομο-γράφος ου *m.* [νόμος, γράφω] **one who drafts laws, legal draughtsman** Pl. Plb.

νομο-δείκτης ου *m.* [δείκνυμι] **one who explains laws, legal adviser, jurist** Plu.

νομο-διδάκτης ου *m.* [διδάσκω] **tutor in law** Plu.

νομο-διδάσκαλος ου *m.* **teacher of the law** (of Moses) NT.

νομοθεσίᾱ ᾱς *f.* [νομοθετέω] **1** (sts. collectv.pl.) **action of giving** or **making laws, lawmaking, legislation** Pl. Arist. Plu.
2 system of laws, legal code, legislation Lys. Arist.; (of Lykourgos, Solon) Plb. Plu.

νομοθετέω *contr.vb.* [νομοθέτης] **1 be a lawgiver, make laws, legislate** (sts. W.PREP.PHR. or NEUT.ACC. about sthg.) Att.orats. Pl. X. Arist. ‖ MID. (of the state, lawgivers) **make laws** Pl. ‖ PASS. (of persons, the state) **be given laws** Pl.
2 make it a legal requirement —W.INF. *to do sthg.* Isoc. ‖ MID. (of the state) **decree, prescribe** —*sthg.* Pl. ‖ PASS. (of rules) **be prescribed by law** Pl. ‖ IMPERS.PF.PASS. **it has been prescribed by law** (*that a particular practice is proper or prohibited*) Hdt. Pl. Arist.
3 lay down principles (of conduct) —W.DAT. *for kings* Isoc. ‖ MID. **prescribe** —*models* (*for poetic composition*) Pl.

νομοθέτημα ατος *n.* **that which is prescribed by law, law, ordinance** Pl. Arist. Plb.

νομο-θέτης ου *m.* [νόμος, τίθημι] **1 lawgiver, legislator** (in a Greek city-state, freq.ref. to a historical figure, such as Solon or Themistokles) Att.orats. Pl. X. Arist. Plb. Plu.; (iron., ref. to a prosecutor) Antipho
2 ‖ PL. (at Athens) **legal commissioners** (members of a council regularly appointed to consider proposed changes in the laws) Th. Att.orats.

νομοθετητέος ᾱ ον *vbl.adj.* [νομοθετέω] (of festivals) **to be established by law** Pl.

νομοθετικός ή όν *adj.* [νομοθέτης] **1** (of actions) **worthy of a lawgiver** Pl. Arist.
2 (of persons) **skilled in legislation** Arist. ‖ FEM.SB. **art of legislation** Pl. Arist.

νομός οῦ *m.* [νέμω] **1 grazing ground, pasture** (for animals) Hom. Hes. Pi. S. E. Hellenist.poet.; (for birds) Ar.
2 (fig.) **feeding ground** or **customary dwelling-place, pasture** (of persons, animals or dolphins, i.e. land or sea, imagined as inverted) Archil. Hdt.
3 (fig.) **field** (W.GEN. for words, song, ref. to their range or scope) Il. Hes. hHom.
4 administrative division of a country (esp. in Scythia, Egypt, Persia), **province** Hdt. Pl.

—**νομόνδε** *adv.* **to pasture** Hom.

νόμος ου *m.* **1 generally accepted standard of social behaviour, custom, convention** (sts. divinely ordained) Hes. +; (personif.) **Custom** Pi.*fr.* E.; (prep. and advbl.phrs.) κατὰ (κὰν) νόμον **according to custom, in the prescribed manner** Hes. Pi. Hdt. S.*Ichn.* E. Th. +; νόμῳ **by custom** or **convention** Hdt. Th. Ar. Pl. +; (opp. φύσει *by nature, according to the natural order*) Isoc. Pl. X. Arist. Plu.
2 body of rules imposed by authority (divine or human), **law** Archil. Heraclit. Hdt. +
3 specific instance of such a rule, law Hes. Thgn. Heraclit. Pi. Trag. +; (opp. ψήφισμα *special decree*) Pl. Arist.
4 (gener., in phrs.) ἐν χειρῶν νόμῳ (also ἐς χειρῶν νόμον Hdt.) **in** (**to**) **the use of hands, in** (**to**) **hand-to-hand fighting** Hdt. Plb.; (in political ctxt.) **by the use of force, by direct action** Aeschin.; ἐν χερὸς νόμῳ **by force of authority** or **under martial law** (*ref. to the right of a king on campaign to execute an offender*) Arist.
5 nomos, nome (specific nameable melody, for kithara or aulos, played or sung in a formal setting for which it was conventionally appropriate) Pi. Hdt. Ar. Pl. Arist.

6 (gener.) **melody, tune, strain, song** A. Pi. E. Th. Ar. Telest. Pl.; (of birds) Alcm.

νομοφυλακέω contr.vb. [νομοφύλαξ] (of the Areopagus) **be guardian of the laws** Arist.

νομοφυλακίᾱ ᾱς f. **1 safeguarding of the laws** Pl.
2 office of law-guardian Arist.

νομο-φύλαξ ακος m. **guardian of the laws** (as the title of an official in a city-state) Pl. X. Arist.; (W.GEN. relating to household matters, fig.ref. to a wife) X.

νόος ου, contr. **νοῦς** νοῦ m. | Aeol.acc. νῶν | dat. νόῳ, contr. νῷ | **1 mind** (of gods or humans, as the seat of thought and perception) Hom. + | cf. ἔχω 15, προσέχω 3
2 (w. wider application) **nature, disposition, temper, feelings** Hom. +
3 good sense, intelligence, understanding Hom. +
4 state of mind (embracing thoughts, intentions, wishes, expectations) Hom. +
5 purpose, plan, design, scheme Hom. +
6 (philos.) **mind, reason** (as a creative principle in the universe) Pl. Arist.
7 sense, point, meaning (W.GEN. of a word) Ar.; (of a ritual, gift) Hdt.; **tenor** (W.GEN. of a speech) Plb.

νοσακερός ά όν adj. [νόσος] liable to illness, **sickly** Arist.

νοσερός ά όν adj. **1** (of persons, their bodies) **sick** E. Plu. || NEUT.SB. sickness or disease Arist. Plu.
2 (of a bed) **of sickness** E.
3 (of air, excrement, places) causing sickness, **unhealthy** Plu.

—**νοσερῶς** adv. **in a state of ill health** Arist.

νοσέω contr.vb. **1** (of persons, their body or mind) **be diseased, ill, sick** (sts. W.COGN.ACC. or DAT. w. a sickness) Hdt. Trag. Th. +; (fig., of an unjust argument) E.
2 (of a land) **be unhealthy** or **afflicted** (by a crop failure) X.; (of a city) **fall sick** (w. an epidemic) S. Th.
3 (of persons, their temperament) **be disordered** or **afflicted** (w. mental or emotional sickness) Trag. Pl.
4 (of persons) **be distressed, suffer** (due to their own actions, fate, a misfortune) S. E. X.
5 (of soldiers, their defensive position) **be weak** E.
6 (of cities, states, the people, their affairs) **be weak, suffer** (fr. factional strife, war) Hdt. S. E. Pl. X. +; (of a marriage, home, family) **be in disorder** E. Arist.; (of worship of the gods) **fall into disuse, decay** E.

νοσηλείᾱ ᾱς f. **1 infection** S.
2 care of the sick, nursing Plu.

νοσηλεύω vb. care for during sickness, **nurse** —a person Isoc.

νόσημα, Ion. **νούσημα**, ατος n. **1 instance of illness, disease, sickness** (of the body) S. E. Th. Ar. Att.orats. +; (ref. to an epidemic) S. Th. || PL. **pangs of childbirth**) E.
2 disordered state of affairs, disorder (in a city) Isoc. Pl. D. Plu.
3 emotional or mental disorder, sickness (ref. to love, passion, anguish) S. E. Ar. Pl. Plu.
4 defect of character or behaviour; disease (ref. to false speaking, unsound thinking) A.; (ref. to mistrust, as inherent in tyranny) A.; (ref. to unjust behaviour or moral standards) Pl. Aeschin.

νοσημάτιον ου n. [dimin.] **diseaselet** (as an example of a diminutive word-form) Arist.(quot. Ar.).

νοσηματώδης ες adj. (of vices, madness) **due to sickness** Arist.

—**νοσηματωδῶς** adv. (w. ἔχειν) be in a state of sickness Arist.

νοσηρός ά όν adj. [νόσος] (of places) **unhealthy** X.

νόσος, Ion. **νοῦσος**, ου f. **1 sickness, disease** (in an individual person, or as an epidemic) Hom. +; (fig., ref. to disorder in the state) S.
2 madness, frenzy (esp. as sent by the gods) A. S.; (ref. to sexual desire) S. E.
3 (ref. to discord, foolish speech or behaviour) **sickness, fault** E. Pl.
4 instance of suffering (inflicted or endured), **suffering, pain** Hes. Pi. S.
5 (concr., ref. to an unjust person) **pest, plague** Pl.; (ref. to a whirlwind) S.

νοσοτροφίᾱ ᾱς f. [τρέφω] concern for one's ill-health, **valetudinarianism** Pl.

νοσσεύω vb., **νοσσιά** f., **νοσσός** m.: see νεοσσεύω, νεοσσιά, νεοσσός

νοσσίον n.: see νεόττιον

νοστέω contr.vb. [νόστος] **1 go** or **come home** (esp. safely) Hom. Pi. Hdt. AR. —W.ADV., PREP.PHR. or ACC. **homewards, to one's home or homeland** Hom. Hdt. S. E. Hellenist.poet.
2 go or come back (to a place), **return** Hom. S. E. Ar. —W.ADV. **back** Hdt. Ar.
3 (gener.) **make one's way, go, come** (usu. W.ADV. or PREP.PHR. or ACC. **to a place**) Od. E. Ar.

νόστιμος ον adj. **1** (of a day, esp. as eagerly awaited) **of homecoming** Od. A. AR.; (of the safety) **of a return home** (i.e. safe return) A.; (of a voyage) **homeward** E.
2 (of persons) **able** or **destined to return home** Od.; **safely returned home** A. AR.
3 (of animals and crops) giving a good return, **productive, abundant** Call.

νόστος ου m. [νέομαι] **1 journey home, return home, homecoming** Hom. hHom. Archil. Sol. Pi. Hdt. +; (W.GEN. or PREP.PHR. to one's land) Od. S. E.; (sg. for pl.) A. S.
2 returning, return (to a place) Il.; (fr. a place) Il. Theoc.
3 arrival (W.GEN. at a place) Od.; **journey, expedition** (W.PREP.PHR. to a place) E.

νόσφι(ν) adv. and prep. **1 in a far-off place, away, absent, far away** Hom. hHom. AR. —W.PREP.PHR. fr. persons, places, pleasures Il. Hes. Theoc.; (prep.) **far away** —W.GEN. fr. persons, places, situations Hom. AR.
2 away in private, apart, separately, by oneself Hom. AR.; (prep.) **apart, without help** —W.GEN. fr. others Hom. Thgn. A. AR. —fr. hounds (in hunting) Call.
3 (prep.) **away, free** —W.GEN. fr. troubles Hes. Thgn. B.; **without** —W.GEN. justice (i.e. unjustly) Simon.
4 (ref. to movt.) **away** Hom. —W.GEN. fr. persons, places Il. hHom. AR.
5 in a hidden manner, secretly —ref. to plotting, hearing news, criticising, or sim. Il. Ibyc. AR.
6 (prep.) **leaving out of account** (in a statement), **except, not including** —W.GEN. someone or sthg. Hom. Hes. AR. Mosch.; (introducing a cl. qualifying a statement) νόσφιν ἤ **except for, other than** (sthg.) Theoc.
7 (introducing a further consideration) **in addition, moreover** AR.

νοσφίζω vb. | fut. νοσφιῶ | aor. ἐνόσφισα || MID.: ep.fut. νοσφίσσομαι (AR.) | aor. ἐνοσφισάμην, ep. νοσφισάμην, ep.ptcpl. νοσφισσάμενος || PASS.: aor. (usu. w.mid.sens.) ἐνοσφίσθην |
1 (act. and mid.) **deprive, rob** —a person (W.GEN. of sthg.) A. E. AR. —(W.ACC.) Pi. S. —a father (W.PREDIC.ADJ. so as to leave him childless) E.; **separate, remove** —a person (W.GEN. or PREP.PHR. fr. someone) E. AR.
2 rob —someone (W.GEN. of life) S.; **kill** —someone A. || PASS. **be killed** A.

νοσφισμός

3 ‖ MID. and AOR.PASS. (of persons) **turn away** (sts. W.GEN. fr. someone) Od. Thgn.
4 ‖ MID. and AOR.PASS. **forsake, abandon, leave** —*one's family and marriage, one's home or homeland* Od. hHom. AR. —W.GEN. *one's family home* Thgn.; (fig.) **turn one's back on, spurn** —W.ACC. *a false dream, sworn agreement* Il. Archil. —*the ruler of one's country* S.
5 ‖ MID. **keep back for oneself, appropriate** —*treasure, loot, profit* X. Plb. Plu.; (intr.) **make an appropriation** —w. ἀπό + GEN. *fr. a purchase price* NT.

νοσφισμός οῦ *m.* **appropriation, stealing** Plb.

νοσώδης ες *adj.* [νόσος] 1 (of persons, their bodies) **full of disease, diseased, sick** Pl. Arist. Plu. ‖ NEUT.SB. **diseased condition** Pl.
2 (of a life) spent in sickness, **sickly** Pl.; (of a place, winter) spreading disease, **unhealthy** Isoc. Plu.
3 (of a medical treatment, an error) causing sickness, **harmful** Pl.; (of acting contrary to a doctor's orders) Pl.; (of certain substances, pleasures) Arist.
4 (of a sick person's glances) **unhealthy** (for others) E.; (of a state of affairs, W.DAT. for persons) E.

νοτερός ά (Ion. ή) όν (also ός όν E.) *adj.* [νότος, reltd. to νοτίς]
1 (of spring-water, the ground, breezes, a garment) **damp, moist** E. Plu.; (of eyes, substances in the body) E. Pl.; (of a storm, night) **wet, rainy** Th. Plu.; (of an inlet) **sea-washed** E. ‖ NEUT.SB. **moisture** Pl. Plu.
2 (of kingfishers) **living by water** Call.*epigr.*

νοτέω *contr.vb.* **be wet**; (hyperbol., of a woman) **be soaked** —W.DAT. *in perfume* Call.*epigr.*

νοτίζω *vb.* (of tears and lamentation) **make wet** —*one's eye* E.; (of the Nile) **moisten, fertilise** —*the earth* Ar.; (intr., of the union betw. Earth and Heaven) A.*fr.* ‖ PASS. (of felled timber) become damp or moist AR.; (of skin, w. sweat) Pl.

νοτίη ης *Ion.f.* **rain shower** Il.

νότιος ᾱ (Ion. η) ον (also ος ον A. E.) *adj.* 1 [νοτίς] (of sweat, tears, perfume, dew) **moist, damp** Il. Alcm. A. Call. Theoc.; (of sea-eddies, drops of seawater or rain, a spring) **of water, watery** E. Ar.(quot. E.) Call.; (of a summer, night) **wet, rainy** Pi.*fr.* Plu. ‖ MASC. or NEUT.SB. app., **water or sea** Od.
2 [νότος] of or in the south; (of a sea, esp. the Indian Ocean) **southern** Hdt.; (of a city wall, the side of a town) And. Plb. Plu.
3 (of winds) from the south, **southerly** E. Arist. Plu. ‖ NEUT.SB. **south wind** X.
4 (of a bird's flight) **to the south** Ar.

νοτίς ίδος *f.* [νότος] **moisture, water** (of a river or spring, the sea) E. AR.; (of rain) E.*fr.*; (of tears) E.; (as present in certain substances) Pl. Plu.; **humidity** (of weather) Plb.

νότος ου *m.* 1 **south** or **south-west wind** (sts. personif.) Hom. Hes. Lyr. Hdt. S. E.*fr.* +
2 (phrs.) πρὸς νότον (sts. w. ἄνεμον) *to the south* Hdt. Th. Pl. Plu.; πρὸς νότου *on the south side* Od. Hdt. Pl.; ἀπὸ νότου *from the south* NT.; βασίλισσα νότου *Queen of the South (i.e. of Sheba)* NT.

νουβυστικός ή όν *adj.* [νόος, βύω] (of a person) **crammed full of intelligence, very brainy** Ar.

—**νουβυστικῶς** *adv.* **intelligently** Ar.

νουθεσίᾱ ᾱς *f.* [νουθετέω] **instruction in right thinking, admonition, advice** Ar. Plu.(sts.pl.)

νουθετέω *contr.vb.* [νόος, τίθημι] 1 **create good sense; admonish** or **advise** —*persons* Hdt. Trag. Ar. Att.*orats.* Pl. + —*the thinking of others* E. —(W.NEUT.PL.INTERN.ACC. *in such and such terms*) E. —(W.COMPL.CL. *that sthg. will be the case*) X.; (intr.) **give admonishment** or **advice** Ar. Att.*orats.* Pl. + —W.NEUT.PL.INTERN.ACC. *in such and such terms* S. Ar. X. ‖ PASS. **be admonished** or **advised** S. E. Ar.(quot. E.) Pl. +
2 **give advice concerning, warn against** —*someone's plans* E.
3 **deliver admonishment** (by physical means); **admonish** —*someone* (W.DAT. *w. fists, blows*) Ar. Pl.

νουθέτημα ατος *n.* (pl.) **warning given, warning, admonition** Trag. Pl. Plu.

νουθέτησις εως *f.* (sg. and pl.) **giving of a warning, warning, admonition** E. Pl. Arist.

νουθετητέος ᾱ ον *vbl.adj.* (of a person, a god) **to be warned** or **admonished** E.

νουθετητικός ή όν *adj.* (of words, a kind of teaching or education) **advisory, admonitory** Pl.

νουθετικός ή όν *adj.* (of words) **of advice** X.

νουμηνίᾱ, dial. **νεομηνίᾱ** (Pi., quadrisyllab.), ᾱς, Ion. **νεομηνίη** ης *f.* [νέος, μήν²] **day of the new moon, new moon, first day of the month** Th. Ar. Arist. Thphr. Plu.; (W.GEN. of a particular month) Plu.; (as a festival) Pi. Hdt. Ar. D.; (as a market-day) Ar.; (fr. which bills were calculated) Ar. X.

νουνέχεια ᾱς *f.* [νουνεχής] **good sense** Plb.

νουν-εχής ές *adj.* [νόος, ἔχω] (of persons, their thinking) possessing good sense, **sensible** Plb.

—**νουνεχῶς** *adv.* ‖ compar. νουνεχέστερον ‖ **sensibly** Plb. NT. ‖ for νοῦν ἐχόντως (or νουνεχόντως) see ἐχόντως, under ἔχω

νοῦς *contr.m.*: see νόος

νούσημα *Ion.n.*: see νόσημα

νοῦσος *Ion.f.*: see νόσος

νυ *ep.enclit.adv.*: see νυν

νῦ *indecl.n.* [Semit.loanwd.] **nu** (letter of the Greek alphabet) Pl.

νυγμή ῆς *f.* [νύσσω] **puncture, prick** (fr. a snakebite) Plu.

νυγμός οῦ *m.* **pricking** (as a bodily sensation) Plu.

νυκτεγερτέω *contr.vb.* [νύξ, ἐγείρω] (of soldiers) **be on night-watch** Plu.

νυκτερείᾱ ᾱς *f.* [νυκτερεύω] **night-work** (ref. to hunting) Pl.

νυκτερεύματα των *n.pl.* **night-quarters** (for pigs) Plb.

νυκτερευτής οῦ *m.* **night-worker** (ref. to a hunter) Pl.

νυκτερευτικός ή όν *adj.* (of hounds) **trained for night-work** X.

νυκτερεύω *vb.* [νύκτερος] 1 (of soldiers) **pass the night in the open, bivouac** X. Plb. Plu.
2 (of persons) **spend the night** (in a place or an activity) X. Aeschin. Plu.

νυκτερήσιος ον *adj.* (of the charms of love, amorous activities) **nocturnal** E.(dub.) Ar.

νυκτερινός ή όν *adj.* 1 (of activities, events, experiences, circumstances) happening at night, **night-time, nocturnal** Th. Ar. Pl. X. Arist. +
2 (of a messenger) **travelling by night** X.; (of a letter) **delivered at night** Aeschin.
3 (of a day) having the quality of night, **night-like, dark as night** Pl.

νυκτερίς ίδος *f.* **creature of the night, bat** Od. Hdt. Pl. X. Arist.; (as a nickname of a person) Ar.

νύκτερος ον *adj.* [νύξ] 1 (of the moon and stars, activities, events, circumstances) in or of the night, **night-time, nocturnal** Trag. Ar.; (quasi-advbl., of persons arriving, being possessed by madness) **in the night** S. E.
2 (of the doom of Hades) **dark as night** E.

νυκτερ-ωπός όν *adj.* [ὤψ] (of dream-visions) **appearing at night** E.

νυκτηγορέω *contr.vb.* [ἀγορεύω] (of guards) **give a night report** E. ‖ PASS. (of an attack) **be discussed at a night-council** A.

νυκτηγορίᾱ ᾱς *f.* military report of the night's activities, night report E.

νυκτ-ηρεφής ές *adj.* [ἐρέφω] (of a circumstance) roofed over by night, **shrouded in darkness** A.

νυκτι-βάτᾱς ᾱ *dial.masc.adj.* [βαίνω] (of a scout) **night-prowling** Scol.

νυκτί-βρομος ον *adj.* [βρόμος] (of panpipes) **sounding at night** E.

νυκτι-κρυφής ές *adj.* [κρύπτω] (of the sun) **hidden at night** Arist.

νυκτι-λαμπής ές *adj.* [λάμπω] (of a makeshift boat) **gleaming in the night** Simon.(dub.cj.)

νυκτι-παγής ές *adj.* [πήγνῡμι] (of the north wind) **night-freezing** Tim.

νυκτί-πλαγκτος ον *adj.* [πλαγκτός] **1** (of terrors) **that come wandering through the night** A.; (of a baby's cries) **that cause wandering in the night** (for its nurse) A.
2 (of weariness) **from roaming at night** A.
3 (of a bed) in which there is tossing and turning in the night, **restless, uneasy** A.

νυκτι-πόλος ον *adj.* [πέλω] **1** (of Dionysus, his followers, Brimo, Hekate) going about by night, **of the night, nocturnal** E. AR.; (of assaults, assoc.w. Hekate) **in the night** E.
2 (of the mouth of the Styx) **shrouded in night** A.*fr.*

νυκτί-σεμνος ον *adj.* [σεμνός] (of food for chthonic deities) **offered in the solemnity of night** A.

νυκτι-φαής ές *adj.* [φάος] (of the light of the moon) **night-shining** Parm.

νυκτί-φαντος ον *adj.* [φαίνομαι] (of an attendant of Hekate) **appearing by night** E. | see also νυκτίφοιτος

νυκτί-φοιτος ον *adj.* [φοιτάω] (of dreams) **visiting by night** A.(v.l. νυκτίφαντος)

νυκτι-φρούρητος ον *adj.* [φρουρέω] (of audacity) **alert at night** A.

νυκτογραφίᾱ ᾱς *f.* [γράφω] **nocturnal writing** (of speeches) Plu.

νυκτο-θήρᾱς ου *m.* [θηράω] **night hunter** X.

νυκτομαχέω *contr.vb.* [μάχομαι] **fight a night battle** Plu.

νυκτομαχίᾱ ᾱς, Ion. **νυκτομαχίη** ης *f.* **night battle** Hdt. Th. Plu.

νυκτο-περιπλάνητος ον *adj.* [περιπλανάομαι] (of a phallic deity) **roaming about by night** Ar.

νυκτοπορέω *contr.vb.* [πόρος] **make a night march** X. Plb.

νυκτοπορίᾱ (perh. also **νυκτοπορείᾱ**) ᾱς *f.* **night march** Plb. Plu.

νυκτοφυλακέω *contr.vb.* [νυκτοφύλαξ] **keep watch at night, be a night-sentry** X.

νυκτο-φύλαξ ακος *m.* **night-sentry** X.

νυκτ-ωπός όν *adj.* [ὤψ] (of the truth of prophetic dreams) **appearing by night** E.

νύκτωρ *adv.* **by night, at night** (sts. w.connot. of secrecy or stealth) Hes. Archil. S. E. Ar. Att.orats. +

νύμφα (ep.voc.), **νύμφα** *dial.f.*: see νύμφη

νυμφᾱ-γενής ές *dial.adj.* [νύμφη; γένος, γίγνομαι] (of a satyr) **nymph-born** Telest.

νυμφ-ᾱγέτᾱς ᾱ *dial.m.* [ἡγέομαι] **leader of the nymphs** (ref. to Pan) Lyr.adesp.

νυμφαγωγέω *contr.vb.* [νυμφαγωγός] **1** (of sailors) **escort** (W.ACC. a woman) **as bride** —W.DAT. *to the bridegroom* Plb.
2 (of a bride's relative) **promote** or **negotiate** —*a marriage* Plu.

νυμφαγωγίᾱ ᾱς *f.* **escorting of a bride** (to the bridegroom), **bridal escort** Plb.

νυμφ-αγωγός οῦ *m.f.* [νύμφη] **person who escorts a bride, bridal escort** E.

νυμφαῖος ᾱ ον *adj.* (of hilltops) **of the nymphs** E. || NEUT.SB. **sanctuary of the nymphs, Nymphaeum** Men. Plu.

νυμφεῖον, ep. **νυμφήιον**, ου *n.* **1 bridal chamber** S.; (fig., ref. to a place where a baby was conceived) Call.; (iron., ref. to a tomb for a young woman) S.
2 || PL. **nuptials** (i.e. bridal rites or wedding) S. E. Mosch.; (concr.) **bride** (W.GEN. of someone) S.

νυμφεῖος ᾱ ον (also ος ον) *adj.* (of a bed) **bridal, nuptial** Pi. E.

νυμφεύματα των *n.pl.* [νυμφεύω] **1 nuptials, marriage** (sts. W.GEN. of or w. someone) S. E.; (W.ADJ. *unholy*, ref. to rape) E.
2 || SG. (concr.) **bride** (W.DAT. for someone) E.
3 || SG. **bridal chamber** E.*fr.*

νυμφευτήρια ων *n.pl.* [νυμφευτής] **nuptials**; (concr.) **bride** (W.GEN. for a man's bed) E.

νυμφευτής οῦ, dial. **νυμφευτᾱς** ᾱ *m.* [νυμφεύω] **1 one who is married, husband** E.
2 one who arranges marriages; (fig., ref. to a herdsman) **matchmaker** (of animals) Pl.

νυμφεύτρια ᾱς *f.* **woman who accompanies the bride** (to the bridal chamber), **bride's attendant** Ar. Plu.

νυμφεύω *vb.* [νύμφη] **1** (of a parent or guardian) **give as bride, betroth** —*a woman* (*to her future husband*) Pi. E. Plu.; (intr., of a father and the bridal pair) **proceed with a marriage** E. || MID. (of Kypris) **give in marriage** —*a man* (*to his bride*) E.*fr.*; **give as bride** —*Semele* (W.DAT. *to Zeus' lightning*) E. || PASS. (of a woman) **be given in marriage** E.
2 (of a man) **marry** E. —W.ACC. *a woman* E.(also mid.); (of a woman) **marry** —W.DAT. *a man* S.
3 || PASS. and FUT.MID. (of a woman) **be taken in marriage** E.; **be married** —W.DAT. or παρά + DAT. *to someone* E.
4 (of a god) **rape** —*a woman* Isoc. || PASS. (of a woman) **be raped** (by a god or mortal) E.

νύμφη ης, dial. **νύμφᾱ** ᾱς *f.* | ep.voc. νύμφᾰ | **1 bride, young wife** Hom. Lyr. Hdt. Trag. +; (as a term of address, by an older woman to a younger) Hom. E.; (ref. to a daughter-in-law) NT.
2 young unmarried woman (esp. as a potential bride), **young woman, maiden** Il. Hes.
3 (usu.pl.) semi-divine female spirit of nature, **nymph** (oft. assoc.w. a specific place) Hom. +; (of the mountains) Hom. +; (of fresh water, meadows, trees, rocks) Hom. +; (of the sea) Alc. S.; (ref. to Calypso, Circe, Maia) Od. hHom.

νυμφήιον *ep.n.*: see νυμφεῖον

νυμφίδιος ᾱ ον (also ος ον E. Ar.) *adj.* **1** of a bride or her marriage; (of songs, the torch, entrance to the bedroom) **bridal, nuptial** Ar. AR.
2 of a young wife; (of the bed, bedroom, home) **marital** E. AR.
3 (of a contest betw. women for a man) **to be bride** E.

νυμφικός ή όν *adj.* **1** (of a bed, chamber, house) **bridal** Trag.; (of rites, intimacies) S. E.; (of a ritual bath) Ar. || NEUT.PL.SB. **nuptials** Pl.
2 (of dwelling-places) **of the nymphs** S.*Ichn.*

νυμφίος ου *m.* **1 bridegroom** Pi. Trag. Ar. Pl. +; (ref. to Hades, for a woman about to be murdered) E.
2 recently married man, young husband Hom. || PL. **newly-weds** A. E. AR.

νύμφιος ᾱ ον *adj.* (of a feast) **bridal, marriage** Pi.; (of a bed) Call.

νυμφο-γέννητος ον *adj.* [γεννητός] (of satyrs) **born from nymphs** S.*Ichn.*

νυμφό-κλαυτος ον *adj.* [κλαυτός] (of an Erinys) **bringing tears to brides** A.

νυμφοκομέω *contr.vb.* [νυμφοκόμος] (of a woman) **wear one's bridal apparel** E.

νυμφο-κόμος ου *f.* [κομέω] (ref. to modesty) **adorner of a bride** A.*fr.* || ADJ. (of a woman) decked out as a bride E.(dub.) [or perh., of a mother *tending the bride*]

νυμφό-ληπτος ον *adj.* [ληπτός] (of persons) **possessed by nymphs, frenzied, enraptured** Pl. Arist. Plu.

νυμφό-τῑμος ον *adj.* [τῑμή] (of a song) **honouring the bride, bridal** A.

νυμφών ῶνος *m.* **bridal chamber** NT.

νῦν *temporal adv.* **1** at this moment, **now** Hom. +; (quasi-adjl.) • ἡ νῦν ὁδός *the present journey* S.; (advbl.phrs.) τὸ νῦν, τὰ νῦν *now* Thgn. Pi. Hdt. S. +; τὰ νῦν τάδε *at this moment* Hdt. E. Ar.; τὸ νῦν εἶναι *for the present, for the time being* Isoc. Pl. X. Arist. +
2 at the present time (opp. in the past), **now, currently** Hom. +; (quasi-adjl.) • ὁ νῦν τρόπος *the current fashion* Th.; (quasi-sb.) τὸ νῦν *the present* Pl.; οἱ νῦν *those of the present age* Pi. +
3 (less commonly, w. past vb.) in the immediate past, **just now** Hom. +
4 (w. fut.vb.) in the immediate future, **now, presently** Hom. E.
5 (usu. w. δέ *but*, expressing what is the case, opp. what might have been) **as it is, in fact** Hom. +

—νῡνί *temporal adv.* **1** (w. stronger force) **right now** Th. Ar. Att.orats. +
2 as it is, in fact Att.orats. Arist.

—νῡνδί *conj.* [νῡνὶ δέ] **but right now** Ar.

—νῡνμενί *adv.* [νῡνὶ μέν] **right now** (w. contrasted cl. linked by δέ) Ar.

—νῦνδή *adv.* [νῦν δή] (w. past vb.) a moment ago, **just now** Ar.(cj.) Pl.

νυν (also **νῦν**), ep. **νυ** *enclit.adv.* **1** (temporal) **now** Il. Sapph. Pi. Parm.
2 (affirmative or weakly inferential, freq. in commands or qs.) **then, therefore** Hom. +

νύξ νυκτός *f.* **1** period of time from evening to morning, **night, night-time** (opp. day) Hom. +; (advbl.gen.) νυκτός *at night, by night* Od. Hdt. +; (also pl.) τῶν νυκτῶν Ar.; (advbl.acc.) (τὴν) νύκτα, (τὰς) νύκτας *during or through the night* Hom. +; (prep.phrs.) ἅμα νυκτί *at night, by night* Hdt.; (also) ἀνὰ νύκτα Il. Theoc. Bion; ἐν νυκτί Trag. Th. +; ἐπὶ νυκτί Il. Hes. Alc. AR.; διὰ νύκτα *during the night* Hom.; (also) διὰ νυκτός Th.; μετὰ νύκτας Pi.; ὑπὸ νύκτα Hdt. Th. +; ἐκ νυκτῶν *after nightfall, at night* Od. Thgn. A. E. X.; (also sg.) ἐκ νυκτός X. | see also μέσος 2
2 (personif., as a deity, mother of Day, Sun, Sleep) **Night** Il. Hes. B. Parm. Trag. Ar. +
3 period of night-time (spent on watch, in activity, sleep), **night** Hom. +
4 a particular night (esp. in a sequence), **night** Hom. +
5 darkness (app.ref. to the western part of the sky, where the sun sets) Hes.
6 darkness (sent by a god as protection) Hom.
7 night, darkness (as the state of death or insensibility, or as a symbol of what is dire or death-like) Hom. Trag.

νύξα (ep.aor.): see νύσσω

νυός οῦ *f.* **1 daughter-in-law** Hom. hHom. AR. Mosch. Plu.
2 (gener.) **bride** or **wife** Theoc.

Νῦσα ης (dial. ᾱς), Ion. **Νύση** ης *f.* **Nysa** (mt. sacred to Dionysus, of varying location) hHom. Hdt. E. X.

—Νῡσαῖος ᾱ ον *adj.* (of the heights) of Nysa, **Nysaian** S.

—Νῡσήιος η ον *Ion.adj.* **1** (epith. of Dionysus) **Nysean** Ar. AR.; (of a mountain and plain) AR.
2 || NEUT.SB. Nysean mountain Il.

—Νῡσιος ᾱ ον *adj.* (epith. of Dionysus) **Nysian** Ar.; (of a plain) hHom.

νύσσα ης *f.* [perh.reltd. νύσσω] **turning-post** (at each end of a race-course) Il. Call. Theoc.; (used as the starting-line) Hom.; (as the finishing-line) AR.

νύσσω, Att. **νύττω** *vb.* | aor. ἔνυξα, ep. νύξα | **1** touch with a sharp point; **stab** (freq. W.DAT. w. a sword or spear) Il. —*a person, part of the body, a shield* Il. Theoc. NT. Plu.; (of a god) **stab at, strike** —*a shield* (W.DAT. w. *his hands*) Il.; (fig., of a rhetorician) **puncture** —*an argument* (W.DAT. w. *another argument*) Ar. || MID. (of combatants) **stab one another** —W.DAT. w. *swords and spears* Il.
2 prick —*a fish* Theoc. —*a bull* (W.DAT. w. *a spear, as if w. a goad*) AR. —*a person* (w. *a sword, to see if he is alive*) Plu.
3 (of horses) **scratch, scrape** —*the ground* (W.DAT. w. *their hooves*) Hes.
4 jab, nudge (a person) Ar. —*a person* (W.DAT. w. *one's elbow*) Od.

νυστάζω *vb.* [perh.reltd. νεύω] | aor. ἐνύστασα (Thphr.), also ἐνύσταξα (NT.) | be half asleep, **be drowsy, doze, nod off** Ar. Pl. X. Arist. Thphr. +

νυστακτής οῦ *masc.adj.* (of sleep) **drowsy** Ar.

νύττω *Att.vb.*: see νύσσω

νυχεύω *vb.* [νύξ] **pass the night** E.

νύχιος ᾱ ον (also ος ον E.) *adj.* **1** belonging to night; (of darkness) **of night** E.
2 happening at night; (of a beacon-fire, wind, dream, lament, or sim.) **at night** Trag. AR.
3 (of the sea, a cave, the halls of Persephone) **dark as night** A. E.
4 (quasi-advbl., of a person meeting another) **at night** E.; (of a person lying asleep) **in darkness** S.
5 (epith. of Hermes) **nocturnal** A.(dub.)

νώ, ep. **νῶι** *nom.acc.1du.pers.pron.* | also ep.nom. νῶιν | gen.dat. νῷν, ep. νῶιν | **the two of us, we both** Hom. +

νῷ (contr.dat.): see νόος

νωδός ή όν *adj.* [privatv.prfx., ὁδούς] (of persons, esp. in old age) **toothless** Ar. Theoc.; (as an example of a privatv.wd.) Arist.

νωδυνίᾱ ᾱς *f.* [νώδυνος] **relief from pain** Pi. Theoc.

νώδυνος ον *adj.* [privatv.prfx., ὀδύνη] **1** (of toil) **painless** Pi.
2 (of a herb) **pain-relieving** S.

νώθεια ᾱς *f.* [νωθής] **1 slowness, sluggishness** (of the mind) Pl.
2 idleness, slothfulness Plu.

νωθής ές *adj.* [prob. privatv.prfx.; perh. ὄθομαι or ὠθέω] | compar. νωθέστερος, superl. νωθέστατος | **1** (of a donkey, horse, dog, snake) **slow, sluggish** Il. Pl. AR. Plu.; (of an old man's legs) E.; (of a soul) Pl.; (of water as an element, opp. air and fire) Pl.
2 (of a person) **slow-witted, stupid** A. Hdt.

νωθρός ά όν *adj.* | compar. νωθρότερος | **1** (of a bull, being led) **slow, stubborn** Call.
2 (of persons) **slow, sluggish** (in mind, disposition, behaviour) Pl. Plb. Plu.

—νωθρῶς *adv.* **slowly, sluggishly** Plb. Plu.

νωθρότης ητος *f.* **sluggishness** (of mind) Arist. Plu.

νῶι *ep.nom.acc.1du.pers.pron.*, **νῶιν** (ep.nom.gen.dat.): see νώ

νωίτερος η ον *ep.Ion.adj.* [νώ] of us two; (of the bed of Zeus and Hera, the voice of the Siren pair) **our** Hom.

νωλεμές neut.adv. **1 unceasingly** (sts. w. αἰεί *always*) Hom. AR. **2 steadfastly, firmly** Od. AR. Theoc.

—**νωλεμέως** adv. **1 unceasingly** Il. Tyrt.; **in constant succession** Od. **2 steadfastly, firmly** Hom. Tyrt.

νῶμα Ion.n.: see νόημα

νωμάω contr.vb. [νέμω] | iteratv.impf. νωμᾱσκον (Mosch.) | dial.fut. νωμᾱσω | ep.aor. νώμησα, dial.ptcpl. νωμᾱσᾱς | **1 distribute** —*food, wine* Hom. Pi. **2 move or control** (w. the hands); **move** —*a staff, shield, bow* (W.ADVS. *this way and that*) Hom.; **wield, brandish** —*a spear, sword, shield* Il. A. Pi. E. AR. —*a club* Pi.fr. —*a mattock* Mosch.; (fig.) **deal out** —*painful fighting* AR. **3** (gener.) **handle** —*a bow* Od. AR.; **lift** —*a cup* Od.; **deploy** —*firesticks* Theoc. **4 manipulate, manage, control** —*a steering-oar, sail-sheet, reins, chariots* Od. Pi.; (fig.) —*the tiller* (*of the ship of state*) A. **5** (of Justice) **guide, direct** —*everything* (W.PREP.PHR. *to its end*) A.; (fig., of a ruler) **steer** —*a people* (W.DAT. w. *a just rudder*) Pi. **6 put in motion, ply** —*one's legs, feet* Il. S.; (of a boxer) —*his fists* Theoc.; (of a bird) —*its wings* B.; (of Pan) —*his body* (*in the dance*) Lyr.adesp. **7 deploy** —*astuteness, an astute mind* Od. —*one's eye, ear, tongue* Simon. Parm.; (of god) —*his supreme mind* Diagor. **8** perh. **peer** —W.PREP.PHR. *around oneself* hHom. **9 observe** (adduced as a synonym of σκοπέω) Pl. —*someone* (W.PTCPL. *doing sthg.*) Hdt.; (of seers) —*birds of omen, tell-tale signs in sacrificial victims* A. E.; **understand through observation, grasp** —*all things* S.

νώμησις εως f. **study** or **contemplation** Pl.

νῶν (gen.dat.1du.pers.pron.): see νώ

νώνυμος, ep. **νώνυμνος**, ον adj. [privatv.prfx., ὄνομα] **1 not having a name**; (of a place, river) **nameless, unnamed** Pi. AR. **2 leaving no name behind**; (of dead persons) **nameless, unremembered** Hom. Hes. A. AR. **3 having no fame**; (of a land) **little known** Od.; (of a person, family) **undistinguished, inglorious** Od. S.

—**νωνυμνί** adv. **without being named, anonymously** Call.

νῶροψ οπος masc.fem.adj. (of bronze armour) app. **flashing, gleaming** Hom.

νωσάμενος (Ion.aor.mid.ptcpl.): see νοέω

νώτια ων n.pl. [dimin. νῶτον] **back** (of a pig, as a dish at a banquet) Philox.Leuc.

νωτιαῖος ᾱ ον adj. (of veins) **of the back** Pl.; (of the vertebrae, marrow) **spinal** E. Pl.

νωτίζω vb. | only aor. ἐνώτισα | **1 turn one's back** (in flight) E.; (of Ares) —W.INTERN.ACC. *in rapid retreat* (W.GEN. fr. *a land*) S. **2** (of a beacon-flame) **cross the back of** —*the sea* A. **3** (of ivy) **cover the back of** —*the baby Dionysus* E.

νῶτον ου n. —also sg. **νῶτος** ου m. | freq. pl. for sg. | **1 back of the body** (of a person); **back** Hom. +; (prep.phr.) κατὰ νώτου *behind the back* (W.GEN. *of a person*) Hdt.; *in the rear* (*of troops*) Hdt. Th. Plb. Plu. **2 back of the body** (of an animal or reptile), **back** Hom. +; (fig., of a branch, on which a person is sitting, as if on a horse) E. **3** (specif.) back of an animal that is cut off for meat, **chine** Hom. hHom. Hdt. **4** (fig., usu. pl. for sg.) upper part or surface (of things); **back, surface** (of the sea) Hom. Hes. hHom. Thgn. E. Call.; (of the earth) Pi.(also sg.) E. AR.; **expanse** (of the sky) E. Ar.(quot. E.) Pl.(sg.); **topmost ridge** (of a mountain) Pi.; **face** (of a rock) E.; **top** (of a tomb, wagon) E.

νωτο-φόρος ου m. [φέρω] **animal that carries** (luggage) on its back, **pack-animal** X.

νωχελής ές adj. (of persons) **sluggish** E.fr.; (of a person's body, W.DAT. through sickness) E.

νωχελίη ης Ion.f. **sluggishness, inertia** (of a person) Il.

Ξ ξ

ξαίνω vb. | fut. ξανῶ | aor. ἔξηνα | **1** prepare wool by combing with a card (in order to remove impurities and separate and straighten the fibres); **card** (wool) Ar. Pl. Arist. —*wool* Od. E.
2 card wool for, **prepare** —*the sacred robe* (*presented to Athena at the Panathenaia*) Ar.
3 rake or lacerate (the skin, by flogging); **thrash** (a person) —W.INTERN.ACC. *w. many lashes* (W.PREP.PHR. *on the back*) D. ‖ PASS. be thrashed —W.DAT. *w. rods* Plu.
4 ‖ PASS. (of the loose surface of the ground) be raked up —W.DAT. *by the charging of troops* Plu.; (of seawater) be broken up (in waves or foam, on the beach) AR.
5 ‖ PASS. (of a crop) be threshed S.*fr.*(dub.)
Ξανθίας ου *m.* [ξανθός] **Xanthias** (common slave-name, fr. hair colour, indicating northern origin) Ar. Pl. Aeschin. Men.
—**Ξανθίδιον** ου *n.* [dimin.] **dear old Xanthias** Ar.
ξανθίζω *vb.* make brown (by cooking), **brown** —*meat* Ar.
Ξάνθιος *adj.*: see under Ξάνθος³
ξανθο-δερκής ές *adj.* [δέρκομαι] (of a serpent) **fiery-eyed** B.
ξανθό-θριξ τριχος *masc.fem.adj.* [θρίξ] **1 fair-haired** or **golden-haired** Sol. Simon. Theoc. | see also πυρσόθριξ
2 (of a horse) with brown hair or mane, **bay** or **chestnut** B.
ξανθο-κόμης ου, dial. **ξανθοκόμᾱς** ᾱ *masc.adj.* [κόμη] **fair-haired** or **golden-haired** Pi. Theoc.
ξανθός ή (dial. ᾱ́) όν *adj.* **1** (of hair) blonde or light brown in colour (w.connots. of beauty, nobility, or northern and foreign origin), **light, fair, golden** Hom. hHom. Archil. Thgn. Lyr. E. +; (of a beard) Lyr.adesp. Theoc.
2 (of persons or a people, heroes, heroines and divinities, their heads) with fair hair (sts. w.connot. of fair skin), **fair, golden-haired** Hom. Hes. Thgn. Lyr. E. +
3 (of cheeks, brows) with light complexion, **fair** AR.
4 (of horses) **bay** or **chestnut** Il. Hes.*fr.* Alc. B. S. E.*fr.*; (of cattle, a lion) **tawny** Pi.*fr.*
5 (of things) of a golden, yellow or light brown colour; (of the ripening olive, olive oil) **yellow, golden, golden-brown** A. E.; (of honey) Simon. Emp. Philox.Leuc.; (of drops of incense, ointments) Pi.*fr.* Call.; (of flowers, saffron) Pi. Theoc. Mosch.; (of gold, fire, or things assoc.w. them) Pi. B. Arist.; (of the R. Akragas) Emp.; (of loaves, roasted meat) Xenoph. Ar.; (of an altar-coping, stained w. blood) E.
6 (of a colour) **yellow** Pl. ‖ NEUT.SB. **yellow colour** Pl.
Ξάνθος¹ ου *m.* **Xanthos** (horse of Achilles) Il.; (of Castor) Stesich.
Ξάνθος² ου *m.* **Xanthos** (divine name of Scamander, river nr. Troy) Il. Pl.
Ξάνθος³ ου (dial. ω) *m.f.* **Xanthos** (name of a city and river in Lycia) Il. Alcm. Pi. Hdt. Men. Call. +
—**Ξάνθιος** ᾱ ον *adj.* (of the plain) **of Xanthos** Hdt.
‖ MASC.PL.SB. men of Xanthos, **Xanthians** (as a population or military force) Hdt. Plb. Plu.

ξανθό-χροος ον *adj.* [ξανθός, χρώς] (of the body of Zeus, in the guise of a bull) **of golden hue** Mosch.
ξάντης ου *m.* [ξαίνω] one who cards wool, **wool-carder** Pl.
ξαντικός ή όν *adj.* of or relating to carding wool ‖ FEM. or NEUT.SB. wool-carding Pl.
Ξάντριαι ῶν *f.pl.* **Women carders** A.(title)
ξειν- (Ion.): see ξεν-
ξεινά dial.*f.*, **ξείνη** Ion.*f.*: see under ξένος²
ξεινήϊον Ion.*n.*: see ξένιον, under ξένιος
ξεινοσύνη ης Ion.*f.* [ξένος²] **guest-friendship** Od.
ξεν-άγέται ᾶν dial.*m.pl.* [ξενᾱγέω] (ref. to the Delphians) **guides for visitors** Pi.
ξενᾱγέω contr.*vb.* [ξενᾱγός] **1** be a commander of mercenaries D.; be in command —W.GEN. *of mercenaries* X.
2 ‖ PASS. be guided as a stranger or visitor Pl.
‖ IMPERS.PF.PASS. guidance has been given —W.DAT. *by someone* Pl.
ξεν-ᾱγός οῦ dial.*m.* [ξένος², ἄγω] **1** (at Sparta) officer in charge of allied contingents Th.
2 (elsewhere) commander of foreign mercenaries X. Plu.
ξεν-απάτης, Ion. **ξειναπάτης** (E.), ου, dial. **ξεναπάτᾱς** (Pi.), also **ξειναπάτᾱς** (Ibyc.), Aeol. perh. **ξενναπάτᾱς** (Alc.), ᾱ *m.* [ἀπατάω] **1** (ref. to Paris) **deceiver of one's host** Alc. Ibyc. E.; (ref. to Jason) E.
2 (ref. to Augeas) **deceiver of one's guest** Pi.
ξεν-αρκής ές *adj.* [ἀρκέω] (of justice) **protecting guests** Pi.
ξένη *f.*: see under ξένος²
ξενηλασία ᾱς *f.* [ξενηλατέω] **1** (usu.pl.) **alien expulsion** or **exclusion** (fr. a city-state, esp. as practised by the Spartans) Th. Pl. X. Arist. Plu.; (at meals and sacrifices, as practised by Egyptians) Pl.
2 outlawing (W.GEN. of luxury crafts, at Sparta) Plu.
ξενηλατέω contr.*vb.* [ξένος², ἐλαύνω] **expel** or **exclude foreigners** (fr. a city-state) Ar. ‖ PASS. (of foreigners) be expelled or excluded —w. ἐκ + GEN. *fr. all Greece* Plb.
ξενία ᾱς, Ion. **ξεινίη**, ep.Ion. **ξενίη**, ης *f.* **1** offering of hospitality to a stranger, visitor or guest (traditionally involving ritual obligations); **hospitality, welcome** Od. Thgn. Pi. B. E. Pl. + ‖ PL. acts of hospitality Pi.
2 tie of guest-friendship (betw. men fr. different families or communities, involving sacred responsibilities as though to one's own kin; also betw. an individual and another state, or betw. two states); **guest-friendship** Pi. Hdt. E. Th. Att.orats. X. +
3 welcome or right of residence for a foreigner (esp. for an exile or religiously unclean person); **welcome, asylum** S. E. Antipho
4 (leg.) alien status (opp. that of citizen or metic); γραφή ξενίας *alien status prosecution* (*against one who has usurped citizen rights*) Ar. Att.orats. Arist.
5 room and material provision for a guest or visitor, **accommodation** NT. Plu.

ξενίζω, Ion. **ξεινίζω** vb. | fut. ξενιῶ | ep.aor. ἐξείνισσα, also ξείνισσα, ξείνισα | **1** give hospitality; **welcome, entertain, be hospitable to** —*a person* Hom. Hdt. S. E. Att.orats. +; (intr.) **entertain guests** Thphr. ‖ PASS. **be welcomed or entertained** Hdt. Ar. X. +
2 speak like a foreigner D. Men.
3 (of a sight, report) **be strange** or **unusual** Plb. NT.
4 ‖ PASS. **be surprised or bewildered** (freq. W.DAT. or PREP.PHR. by or at sthg.) S.*Ichn*. Plb. —(W.ACC.) Plb.

ξενικός, Ion. **ξεινικός**, ή όν (also ός όν E.) adj. **1** of or relating to a host, guest or guest-friend; (of a god, the dinner-table, duties) **of hospitality** Pl. Aeschin. Arist.; (of violation of obligations and the resulting pollution) **relating to guests** A. Pl.; (of flesh, eaten by the Cyclops) **of guests** E.*Cyc*.; (of a bond) **of guest-friendship** Arist.; (of an item entrusted for safe-keeping) **belonging to a guest-friend** Hdt.
2 (of persons or a class of people) in the category of foreigners (in a city-state, opp. citizen or metic), **foreign, alien** Pl. Arist. Men. Plu.; (of a court) dealing with matters relating to residents who are alien, **for aliens** Arist. ‖ NEUT.PL.SB. legal cases involving aliens Arist.; alien tax D.; alien affairs Arist.
3 of or relating to foreigners or foreign things (either abroad or coming fr. abroad); (of envoys) **foreign** Aeschin.; (of gods, religious rites, customs, coinage, goods, or sim.) **foreign** or **imported** Hdt. Pl. Aeschin. Arist. Plb.; (pejor., of crowns, favours) **awarded by** or **to foreigners** Aeschin. Plb.; (of flattering words) **of foreigners** Ar. ‖ NEUT.PL.SB. foreign affairs D.; foreign merchandise Plu.
4 of or relating to foreign enemies; (of a war, invasion, troops) **foreign** E. Arist. Plb.; (of a cart carrying captives, a journey to the captors' land) E.
5 of or relating to troops who are hired or from allied states; (of a contingent or sim.) **of foreign allies, foreign** or **mercenary** Hdt. Th. Isoc. Pl. + ‖ NEUT.SB. mercenary force Ar. Att.orats. X. Plb.; foreign bodyguard Arist.
6 (of a road) **used by persons coming from abroad** Plu.
7 (of words, language, literature) of or in another dialect, **dialectal, foreign** Pl. Arist.; not in everyday speech, **strange, unfamiliar** Arist.
—**ξενικῶς** adv. **in dialect** Pl.

ξένιος ᾱ (Ion. η) ον (also ος ον), Ion. **ξείνιος** η ον adj. **1** of or relating to a guest or host; (of the dinner-table, a guardian spirit or god) **of hospitality** Od. A. Pi. Pl. Plu.; (of a city, hearth) **hospitable, welcoming** Pi.
2 of or relating to a foreigner; (of an illicit affair) **with a foreigner** Pi.
3 of or relating to guest-friends; (of persons) **in a guest-friend relationship** Hdt.
—**Ξένιος**, Ion. **Ξείνιος**, ου m. (cult title of Zeus) God of host or guest (in terms of watching over sacred obligations), **God of hospitality** Hom. A. Pi. E.*Cyc*. Pl. +
—**ξένιον**, Ion. **ξείνιον**, ου n. —also **ξεινήιον** ου (Hom. AR. Theoc.) *Ion.n*. (freq.pl.) **gift** or **provision of hospitality** (ref. to food and drink, entertainment, presents, provisions for the road, or sim.) Hom. Archil. Thgn. A. Pi. Hdt. +; (appos.w. δῶρα *gifts*) Od.

ξένισις εως f. [ξενίζω] **provision of hospitality; entertainment** (W.GEN. of persons) Th.

ξενισμός οῦ m. **1 provision of hospitality; entertainment** (sts. W.GEN. of persons) Pl. Plu.
2 strangeness, unfamiliarity (of certain food, excess in expression of emotions) Plb.

ξενῑτεύω vb. **1 live abroad in exile** Plb.
2 ‖ MID. **serve abroad as a mercenary** Isoc.

ξέννος Aeol.adj. and m.: see ξένος¹ and ξένος²

ξενο-δαΐκτᾱς, also **ξεινοδαΐκτᾱς** (E.), ᾱ dial.m. [ξένος², δαΐζω] **murderer of one's guests** (ref. to Laomedon, king of Troy) Pi.*fr*.; (ref. to Cycnus 2) E.

ξενο-δαίτᾱς ᾱ dial.m. [δαίνῡμι] **devourer of guests, guest-eater** (ref. to Polyphemos) E.*Cyc*.

ξενο-δαιτυμών όνος m. **one who dines on guests, guest-eater** (ref. to Polyphemos) E.*Cyc*.

ξενοδοκέω, Ion. **ξεινοδοκέω** contr.vb. [ξενοδόκος] **welcome guests, act as host** E. Pl.; (tr.) **welcome with hospitality** —*all men* Hdt.

ξενοδοκίᾱ ᾱς f. **entertainment of guests** X. Thphr.

ξενο-δόκος, Ion. **ξεινοδόκος**, ου m. [δέχομαι] **one who welcomes guests, host** Hom. Hes. Simon. Call. Theoc.

ξενόεις εσσα εν adj. (of the oracular throne of Apollo) **frequented by visitors** E.

ξενοκτονέω, Ion. **ξεινοκτονέω** contr.vb. [ξενοκτόνος] **kill visitors** or **guests** Hdt. E.

ξενοκτονίᾱ ᾱς f. **killing of a guest-friend** Plu.

ξενο-κτόνος ον adj. [κτείνω] of or relating to the killing of a stranger or guest-friend; (of the function of a priestess) **of killing foreigners** E.; (of an avenging spirit) **for the killing of a guest-friend** Plu. ‖ MASC.SB. **murderer of a host** Aeschin.

ξενολογέω contr.vb. [ξενολόγος] **recruit mercenaries** Isoc. D. Plb. Plu.; (tr.) **recruit as mercenaries** —*a certain number or kind of troops* Plb. ‖ PASS. (of men) **be recruited as mercenaries** Plb.

ξενολογίᾱ ᾱς f. **recruitment of mercenaries** Plb.

ξενολόγιον ου n. **contingent of mercenaries** Plb.

ξενο-λόγος ου m. [λέγω] **recruiter of foreign soldiers** or **mercenaries** Men.(title) Plb. Plu.

ξενόομαι, Ion. **ξεινόομαι** mid.pass.contr.vb. | fut. ξενώσομαι | aor. ἐξενώθην | pf. ἐξένωμαι | **1 be welcomed as a stranger, visitor or guest** (in another city or land, at a festival, in someone's home); **be a guest, find a welcome** Pi. Trag. Pl. X. AR.
2 be a traveller, visitor or alien abroad (esp. as a result of rejection by one's own people); **be away** or **live in another land** S. E.
3 (of individuals, city-states or peoples) **be guest-friends, have a special relationship** (sts. W.DAT. w. someone, w. one another) Hdt. Lys. Pl. X.
4 (tr., in neg.phr.) **welcome, be hospitable to** —*those who steal fr. the gods* A.

ξενοπαθέω contr.vb. [πάθος] (of horses, w. new riders) **feel strange** or **uncomfortable** Plu.; (of people) —w. πρός + ACC. *towards a change in government* Plu.

ξένος¹, Ion. **ξεῖνος**, η (dial. ᾱ) ον, Aeol. perh. **ξέννος** ᾱ ον (Theoc.) adj. **1** (of a land, city, house, peoples, gods) **foreign, alien, distant, strange** or **unfamiliar** Pi. S. E. Att.orats. +; (of hands, a foot) **of a stranger** S. E.; (of marriage) **with a foreigner** E. ‖ FEM.SB. **foreign land** S. E. X.
2 (of things) not typical of one's ordinary experience, **strange, unfamiliar, extraordinary** A. B. E. Arist. Plb. +
3 (of a person) **unfamiliar, unacquainted** (W.GEN. w. a report, w. what has been done) S.; (w. painful love-affairs) Theoc.
—**ξένως** adv. (w. ἔχειν) **be unfamiliar** —W.GEN. w. *a style of speech* Pl.

ξένος², Ion. **ξεῖνος**, Aeol. perh. **ξέννος** (Theoc.), ου m. [ξένος¹] **1 man who is a stranger or unknown person** (to oneself, one's family, associates, people, city, or sim.;

traditionally held to be under Zeus' protection and thus owed duties of hospitality; freq. appos.w. ἄνθρωπος, ἀνήρ, or a pers. name; also freq. voc., as a term of address); **stranger, visitor, foreigner** Hom. +; (ref. to an enemy) **foreigner, alien** A. Hdt. E.
2 man giving or receiving hospitality (whether in a formal ongoing relationship or through recent acquaintance); **host, guest, friend** Hom. +
3 man in a formal relationship of friendship (w. another fr. a different family, Greek or non-Greek, involving reciprocal and ritualised obligations); **guest-friend, friend** Hom. +; (pl., ref. to two states or peoples in such a relationship) Hdt.
4 resident foreigner (in a city-state, without the rights of a metic), **foreigner, alien** Th. +
5 hired foreigner (for military enterprises), **mercenary** Th. +
—**ξένη**, Ion. **ξείνη**, ης, dial. **ξένᾱ** (also **ξείνᾱ**) ᾱς f. girl or woman not from one's own family or community (sts. appos.w. γυνή or sim.; freq. voc., as a term of address); **foreigner, stranger, guest** or **friend** hHom. Pi. Trag. +
ξενό-στασις εως f. [στάσις] place of rest for a foreigner, **hospitable lodging** S.
ξενό-τῑμος ον adj. [τῑμή] (of conduct) **guest-honouring** A.
ξενοτροφέω contr.vb. [τρέφω] (of a people, city-state) **maintain foreign soldiers** or **mercenaries** Th. Isoc. D. Plu.
Ξενοφάνης ους m. **Xenophanes** (6th-C. BC poet and philosopher fr. Colophon) Pl. Arist.
ξενοφονέω contr.vb. [ξενοφόνος] **murder one's host** E.
ξενοφονίᾱ ᾱς f. **murder of strangers** Isoc.
ξενο-φόνος ον adj. [ξένος², θείνω] (of the function of a priestess) **of murdering foreigners** E.
Ξενοφῶν ῶντος m. **Xenophon** (c.430–354 BC, soldier, historian and follower of Socrates) X. Plb. Plu.
ξενύδριον ου n. [ξένος²] **guest-room** Men.
ξενών ῶνος m. **guest-room** E. Pl.
ξένωσις εως f. strangeness of behaviour, **aberration** E.
Ξέρξης ου (Ion. εω), dial. **Ξέρξᾱς** ᾱ m. **Xerxes** (king of Persia 486–465 BC, son of Darius I) A. Hdt. Th. +
ξερόν οῦ n. [perh.reltd. ξηρός] **dry land** Od. AR.
ξέσσα (ep.aor.): see ξέω
ξέστης ου m. [app.reltd. Lat. sextarius] a kind of container for liquids, **jug** NT.
ξεστός ή (dial. ᾱ́) όν adj. [ξέω] (of wood, stone, or things crafted fr. them) shaped and made smooth, **hewn, carved** or **polished** Hom. Hes. Tyrt. Pi. B. Hdt. +; (of horn) Od.
ξέω vb. | impf. ἔξεον | aor. ἔξεσα, ep. ξέσσα | **1** shape and smooth the surface (of wood); **shape, plane** —timbers Od. || MASC.PL.PTCPL.SB. men who plane wood Pl.
2 shape (a wooden object) by carving; **carve out, carve** —a bed, doorpost, threshold Od. —a cult image AR.
ξηραίνω vb. [ξηρός] | fut. ξηρᾰνῶ | aor. ἐξήρᾱνα || PASS.: aor. ἐξηράνθην | 3sg.pf. ἐξήρανται (NT.) | **1 dry up** —a channel (by diverting water) Th.
2 || PASS. (of measures of soaked grain) be dried out D.
3 || PASS. (of blood) be staunched NT.
4 remove natural moisture in order to preserve, **dry, desiccate** —fruits X.
5 (of the god of wine) **dry out, parch** —a person (who leaves wine undrunk) E.Cyc. || PASS. (of a part of the body) be made dry (by lack of moisture) Pl.
6 (of the sun) **dry up, parch** —vegetation X. || PASS. (of a plain) be dried up (by fire) Il.; (of the earth) be parched (through lack of rain) Arist.; (of vegetation) wither NT. (fig., of a person, compared to a branch) NT.; (of a person possessed by a spirit) NT.
—**ἐξηραμμένος** η ον pf.pass.ptcpl.adj. (of a fig tree) **withered** NT.; (of a limb, through paralysis) NT.
ξηραλοιφέω contr.vb. [ἀλοιφή] app. **rub oneself dry with oil** Aeschin.(law) Plu.
ξηροβατικός ή όν adj. [βαίνω] (of a category of animal husbandry) **concerned with animals that walk on land** Pl.
ξηρός ᾱ́ (Ion. ή) όν adj. **1** (of land, earth) **dry** (opp. covered by water) Pl. X.; (opp. wet w. blood) E.; (of a person's foot) **on dry land** E. || NEUT.SB. dry ground Hdt. Th. Pl. Plb. || FEM.SB. dry land (opp. sea) AR. NT.
2 (of substances or materials, as a physical property) **dry** (opp. liquid) Pl. X. Arist. || NEUT.SB. dryness Pl.
3 (of food, esp. bread, opp. drink) **dry, solid** Pl. Arist. Plb. Plu. || NEUT.PL.SB. dry or solid food E. Arist. Theoc.
4 not subject to excess dampness || NEUT.PL.SB. dry places (for storage) X. || FEM.SB. dry soil X.
5 (of eyes) without tears, **dry** A. E.
6 (of fruit or other foodstuffs, suitable for storage) **dried, dry** Pl. X. Plu.; (of an animal skin) Plu.; (of wood or other material suitable for burning) Pl. Plu.; (phr.) ξηρὸς χῑλός dry fodder (i.e. hay) X.
7 (of measures of capacity for non-liquid foodstuffs, esp. grain) **dry, solid** Pl. Arist. Plu.
8 dried up (fr. heat or lack of rain); (of soil, land, vegetation) **dry, parched** E. X. Plb. NT. Plu.; (of air) Hdt.; (of a wind) Ar.; (of a river) Hdt. || NEUT.SB. dry bed (of a river) X.
9 (of a milking-flock, its flow of milk) **dried up, dry** Philox.Leuc.
10 (of a person, lips) **dry, parched** AR. Theoc.
11 (of thirst or heat) causing dryness, **parching** AR. Plu.; (of sweating fr. exertion) perh., causing thirst, **draining** Pl.
12 (of persons, their body, limbs) lacking vigour or vitality (because of deformity, hunger, illness, grief or fear), **drained, wasted** or **withered** Hippon. E. Theoc. NT.
13 (fig.) dry (w. respect to the senses or emotions); (of an inglorious victory) **joyless** (W.DAT. w. the passage of time) E.; (of an old man's habits) **austere** Ar.
ξηρότης ητος f. **1 dryness** (as a condition) Pl. Arist. Plu.
2 dryness (of air) Plu.; **aridity** (of soil, causing plants to wither) X.
3 absence of excess dampness, **dryness** (of ships, achieved through periodic removal fr. the water) Th.
ξηροτροφικός ή όν adj. [τρέφω] (of a category of animal husbandry) **concerned with the rearing of land animals** Pl.
ξιπο-μάκαιρα ᾱς f. [ξίφος, μάχαιρα] | pidgin Gk. | **sword** Ar.
ξιφ-ήρης ες adj. [ἀραρίσκω] equipped with a sword; (of men, a hand, an ambush) **sworded** E. Plu.; (of the constellation Orion) E.; (of a lion in an emblem) Plu.
ξιφη-φόρος ον adj. [φέρω] **1** (of men, Justice) **sword-bearing** E.
2 (of combat, a snare) **of sword-bearers** A. E.
ξιφίδιον ου n. [dimin. ξίφος] small sword, **dagger** Th. Ar. X. Plu.
ξιφιστήρ ῆρος m. **sword-belt** Plu.
ξιφο-δήλητος ον adj. [δηλέομαι] destroying with the sword; (of death) **dealt by the sword** A.; (of a struggle) **dealing death by the sword** A.
ξιφο-κτόνος ον adj. [κτείνω] (of hands, a thrust) **dealing death by the sword** S. E.
ξίφος εος (ους) n. | ep.dat. ξίφεϊ, pl. ξιφέεσσι | **sword** Hom. +
ξιφουλκίᾱ ᾱς f. [ξιφουλκός] **drawing of a sword** (fr. the sheath) Plu.

ξιφουλκός όν *adj.* [ἕλκω] (of a hand) **drawing a sword** A.
ξιφουργός οῦ *m.* [ἔργον] **sword-maker** Ar.
ξόανον ου *n.* [ξέω] image (usu. of a god) carved in wood; **image, statue** E. X. AR. Theoc.*epigr.* Plu.; (ref. to the Trojan Horse, as a dedication to Athena) E.
ξουθό-πτερος ον *adj.* [ξουθός, πτερόν] (of a bee) **with humming** or **vibrating wings** E.
ξουθός ή (dial. ἅ) όν *adj.* moving rapidly or vibrating with resonance (also app. w.connot. of bright colour, perh. influenced by ξανθός); (of the wings of the Dioscuri) **reverberating, vibrant** or **golden, tawny** hHom.; (of the wings of an eagle) B.; (of bees) E. Theoc.; (of birds, esp. the nightingale, its throat) A. E. Ar. Theoc.*epigr.*; (of the mythol. horse-cock) Ar.(quot. A.)
Ξοῦθος ου *m.* **Xouthos** (son of Hellen, father or putative father of Ion, ancestor of the Ionians) Hes.*fr.* Hdt. E.
ξυγγ-, ξυγκ-, ξυγχ-: see συγγ-, συγκ-, συγχ-
ξυήλη ης *f.* [ξύω] small knife or tool for whittling or scraping (esp. assoc.w. Sparta); **knife** or **rasp** X.
ξυλεία ᾶς *f.* [ξύλον] **1 timber** (as a material used in construction) Plb.
2 collecting of wood (by soldiers) Plb.
ξυληγέω *contr.vb.* [ἄγω] **import timber** D.
ξυλήφιον ου *n.* [dimin. ξύλον] **small wooden writing-tablet** Plb.
ξυλίζομαι *mid.vb.* **gather wood** (for fuel) X. Plu.
ξύλινος η ον *adj.* **1** (of ships, buildings, objects) **made of wood, wooden** Lyr. Hdt. Th. Ar. Pl. +; (of a building or wall, fig.ref. to a pyre) Pi. B.; (of a wall, an ambush, fig.ref. to a navy) Hdt.(oracle) Arist.(oracle) ‖ NEUT.PL.SB. wood fittings or woodwork Ar.; wooden objects Arist.
2 (of the produce) **of trees** Pl.
ξυλλ-: see συλλ-
ξυλοκοπέω *contr.vb.* [ξύλον 9, κόπτω] (as a Roman military punishment) **club to death** —*soldiers* Plb. ‖ PASS. (of soldiers) be clubbed to death Plb.
ξυλοκοπία ᾶς *f.* **punishment of being clubbed to death** (in the Roman army) Plb.
ξυλο-κόπος ον *adj.* [ξύλον, κόπτω] (of an axe) **for chopping wood** X.
ξύλον ου *n.* **1 wood** (as a substance) Hdt. Pl. Arist. Men. Plb.
2 living wood, tree Call. NT. ‖ PL. (collectv.) timber-trees (as a resource) Th. X. +
3 wood (W.GEN. or ADJ., specifying a particular kind of tree, as the source fr. which particular things are made) Hdt. Pl.; (W.GEN. of the vine, as the source of wine) E.*Cyc.*; εἴρια ἀπὸ ξύλου *wool from wood* (i.e. cotton) Hdt.; εἵματα ἀπὸ ξύλων *cotton clothing* Hdt.
4 wood (for burning); **stick, log** Alc. S.; (collectv.) **wood** Ar. ‖ PL. (collectv.) firewood Hom. hHom. S. E.*Cyc.* Ar. X. +
5 piece of wood (used in carpentry, building); **log, plank, beam, post** or **pole** Il. Hdt. S. E.*fr.* Ar. Att.orats. +; (phr.) κορμοὶ ξύλων *wooden logs* Hdt.
6 ‖ PL. (collectv.) timber Hes. Hdt. Th. Ar. Att.orats. +
7 wooden part (of a manufactured object, e.g. a writing-tablet, instrument, animal trap, siege-engine) Hdt. Th. Pl. X.; (ref. to the shaft of a weapon) X. Plb. Plu.
8 wooden object (oft. w.connot. of relatively simple or cheap construction); **seat, bench** Ar. D.; **counter** (in a banker's premises) D.; **beam, perch** (for roosting cockerels) Ar.; **piece of wood** (for cleaning a horse) X.
9 piece of wood (carried for beating, killing or protection; sts. as a symbol of authority or for punishment of criminals); **stick, cudgel, club** Hdt. E.*Cyc.* Ar. Att.orats. +; (of Herakles) E.; (phr.) ξύλων κορύναι (or ῥόπαλα) *wooden clubs* Hdt.
10 wooden shackle or **collar, stocks** Hdt. Ar. Att.orats. +
11 cross (for crucifixion) NT.
ξυλοργέω *Ion.contr.vb.* [ἔργον] **work in wood** Hdt.
ξυλουργία ᾶς *f.* **woodworking, carpentry** (as a craft) A.
ξυλουργικός ή όν *adj.* of or relating to working in wood ‖ FEM.SB. art of woodwork or carpentry Pl.
ξυλοφορέω *contr.vb.* **carry wood** Men.
ξυλοχίζομαι *mid.vb.* [ξύλοχος] app., gather brushwood; **gather** —*heath-shrubs* Theoc.
ξύλοχος ου *f.* [perh. ξύλον, λόχος] app., brushwood or undergrowth providing cover (for animals), **thicket** Hom. AR.
ξύλωσις εως *f.* (collectv.) **woodwork** (of houses, ref. to beams, doors, or sim.) Th.
ξυμβ-, ξυμμ-, ξυμπ-, ξυμφ-: see συμβ-, συμμ-, συμπ-, συμφ-
ξυν-: see συν-
ξύν *prep.* and *adv.*: see σύν
ξυνάν, ξυνάων *dial.m.f.*: see ξυνήων
ξυνδείπνιον *n.*: see σύνδειπνον
ξυν-εείκοσι *ep.indecl.num.adj.* [εἴκοσι] **twenty altogether** Od.
ξυνεωνίη ης *Ion.f.* [reltd. ξυνήων] **companionship** Archil.
ξυνήιος η ον *ep.Ion.adj.* [ξυνός] (of weapons) held in common, **shared** Il. ‖ NEUT.PL.SB. common store (of valuable possessions) Il.
ξυνήων ονος *Ion.m.f.* —also **ξυνάων** ονος, contr. **ξυνάν** ᾶνος *dial.m.f.* **1** one who shares (w. someone, in sthg.); **accomplice** (in a plot) Pi.; (W.GEN. in evil or troublesome activities) Hes.; **joint parent** (W.GEN. of children, ref. to a father) A.*fr.*
2 one who has a share (of sthg.); **sufferer** (W.GEN. fr. sores) Pi.
ξυνν-: see συνν-
ξυνός ή (dial. ἅ) όν, Aeol. **ξῦνος** ᾱ ον *adj.* [ξύν] **1** (of events, enterprises, circumstances, emotions, values, or sim.) participated in or shared alike (sts. W.DAT. w. someone or by both or all); **common, shared** Hes.*fr.* Heraclit. Pi. S. Aeschin.(quot.*epigr.*) Hellenist.*poet.*
2 (of women) shared (by men, i.e. as prostitutes) Pi.*fr.*
3 (of places, territory, a seat, or sim.) possessed or used alike (by two or more), **shared** Hes.*fr.* Alc. Call.; (of the domains of earth and Olympos, W.GEN. amongst all the gods) Il.
4 (of that which is a glory, benefit, cure, or sim.; also, conversely, a nuisance, harm, or sim.) affecting all alike (sts. W.DAT. specifying those affected); **common, shared** Il. Archil. Eleg. Pi. B. Hdt. + ‖ NEUT.SB. something for sharing (W.DAT. by all mankind, ref. to a piece of advice) Thgn.; (pl.) common interest (of men and gods) A.; (prep.phr.) ἐν ξυνῷ *in the common interest* Pi.
5 (of Ares) affecting (both sides in battle) in the same way, **impartial** Il. Archil.
6 (of a result) common (to two rivals), **equal, even** Call.
7 (of the history of a family) **common** (to all its members) Pi.; (of a story, W.GEN. to two peoples) Hdt. ‖ NEUT.SB. that which is common (W.GEN. to all things in the same category) Heraclit.
8 (of the beginning and end of a circle) **common, one and the same** Heraclit.
—**ξυνά** *neut.pl.adv.* in common (w. others), **jointly** Pi.

—**ξῠνῇ** *adv.* **1** in common (w. others), **jointly** Democr. Call. AR. **2 all together, jointly** A.

ξυρέω, Ion. **ξυράω** *contr.vb.* —also **ξύρω** (Plb. Plu.) *vb.* [ξυρόν] | pf.pass.ptcpl. ἐξυρημένος | **1 shave** —*a person's head, cheeks, beard* Hdt. Plu.; —W.DBL.ACC. *a person, his hair* (*i.e. a person's hair*) Hdt.
2 ‖ MID. **shave** (one's hair, beard or body) Hdt. Plb. Plu. —*one's head, beard, eyebrows, whole body* Hdt. NT. Plu.
3 ‖ PF.PASS.PTCPL.ADJ. **shaved** (in respect of one's head and beard) Hdt.; **clean-shaven** (as a sign of effeminacy) Ar. Men.; having (W.ACC. one's head or arse) shaved Ar. Plb.
4 (fig., of a circumstance) ξυρεῖν ἐν χρῷ *shave close to the skin* (*i.e. bring one close to some outcome*) S.; (provbl.) ξυρεῖν λέοντα *shave a lion* (*i.e. attempt sthg. risky*) Pl.

ξυρ-ήκης ες *adj.* [reltd. ἀκίς, ἀκωκή] **1** subject to the sharp edge of a razor; (of a head, cropped hair) **razor-shorn** E.
2 (of javelin-heads) **razor-sharp** X.

ξυρο-δόκη ης *f.* [δέχομαι] **razor-case** Ar.

ξυρόν οῦ *n.* [ξύω] **razor** E. Ar. Plu.; (fig.) ἐπὶ ξυροῦ (ἀκμῆς) *on a razor's edge* (*i.e. in a critical or precarious position*) Il. Thgn. Hdt. Trag. Theoc.

ξυροφορέω *contr.vb.* **carry a razor** Ar.

ξυρρ-, **ξυσ(σ)-**: see συρρ-, συσ(σ)-

ξυστίς ίδος *f.* [ξυστός; cf. ξύω 1] long upper garment of refined appearance (worn by men and women), **fine robe** Ar. Pl. Theoc. Plu.

ξυστόν οῦ *n.* **1** smoothed shaft (of a thrusting weapon), **shaft** Hdt. Plu.; (ref. to the whole weapon) **spear** Il. Tyrt. E. Plu.; **lance** (of a horseman) X. Plu.; (w. extra length, used in sea-fighting) **pike** Il.
2 area of smoothed or polished paving-stones, **paved walkway** X.

ξυστός όν *adj.* [ξύω] (of a spear) smoothed down, **polished** Alcm. Hdt.(dub.) AR.

ξυστοφορέω *contr.vb.* [ξυστοφόρος] be a lance-carrier ‖ PASS. be escorted or protected by lancers Alc.

ξυστο-φόρος ον *adj.* [ξυστόν, φέρω] (of cavalry) **lance-carrying** Plb. ‖ MASC.PL.SB. lancers X. Plu.

ξύω *vb.* | ep.impf. ξῦον | aor. ἔξῦσα | **1** scrape to remove roughness, irregularities or debris (fr. a surface); **rake clean** —*an earth floor* Od.; comb out the rough nap of, **give a fine finish to** —*a garment* Il.
2 ‖ MID. (of a soldier) smooth down, **polish** —*a light spear* X.
3 scrape or scratch —*the ground* (W.DAT. w. a stick, to draw geometrical figures) Call.

O o

ὁ (also demonstr. ὅ), fem. ἡ (also demonstr. ἥ), neut. τό, τοῦ τῆς τοῦ demonstr. and pers.pron., also def.art. | Aeol.masc.nom. ὀ | dial.fem.nom. ἁ (Aeol. ἀ), acc. τάν, gen. τᾶς, Aeol. τάς | ep.masc.neut.gen.sg. τοῖο, dial. τῶ, Aeol. τώ ‖ PL.: nom. οἱ αἱ τά, dial. τοί ταί τά, also as demonstr.pron. οἵ αἵ τά | dial.masc.acc. τώς, Aeol. τοίς | Aeol.fem.acc. ταίς | ep.fem.gen. τάων, dial. τᾶν, Aeol. τᾶν | masc.neut.dat. τοῖς, also τοῖσι, Aeol. τοίς, fem. ταῖς, also ταῖσι, Aeol. ταίς, Ion. τῇσι, ep. τῇς ‖ DU.: masc.fem.neut.nom.acc. τώ, also fem.nom.acc. τά (S.dub., Ar.dub.), masc.fem.neut.gen.dat. τοῖν, also fem. ταῖν, ep.masc.fem.neut. τοῖιν ‖ As a demonstr.pron., ὁ in prose is used chiefly in advbl.phrs. in conjunction w. καί or δέ (A 2), or w. μέν ... δέ (A 3). ‖ The demonstr.pron. is sts. used as a relatv.pron. (A 6). The pron. (either as a relatv. or as a demonstr.) is sts. reinforced either by τε (Hom. Hes.) or by περ[1] (Hom. Hdt.). These are sts. combined in a single wd. (e.g. ὅσπερ, ὅστε). The forms τῇ, τό and τῷ are also used as advs. | The development fr. the earlier demonstr.pron. (A) to the def.art. (B) is gradual, and it is not always possible to distinguish betw. the two. | —also ὅς[3] masc.nom.demonstr.pron. | Examples of this pron. are included in A 1 and 2. It is to be distinguished fr. the relatv.pron. ὅς[1], which is unrelated. |
—A | 3sg.pl. demonstr. and anaphoric pers.pron. |
1 this, that, those, he, she, it, they Hom. + • ὃ γὰρ ἦλθε *for he came* Il. • ἀλλὰ καὶ ὃς δείδοικε *but even he is fearful* Il. • τὴν δ' ἐγὼ οὐ λύσω *but I shall not let her go* Il. • ἀλλὰ τὸ θαυμάζω *but I marvel at this* Od. • ὃ γὰρ γέρας ἐστὶ θανόντων *for this is the honour due for the dead* Hom. • τὰς βασιληΐας ἱστίας ἐπιώρκηκε ὅς καὶ ὅς *this or that man has sworn falsely over the king's sacred hearth* Hdt. • (emph., w. explanatory relatv.cl.) κείνοισι δ' ἂν οὔ τις τῶν οἳ νῦν βροτοί εἰσιν ἐπιχθόνιοι μαχέοιτο *with them not one of those who are now mortals upon the earth could fight* Il. • μηδ' ὅν τινα γαστέρι μήτηρ κοῦρον ἐόντα φέροι, μηδ' ὃς φύγοι *no, even a male child whom a mother carries in her womb, even he is not to escape* Il.
2 (in prose, after καί) Hdt. + • καὶ οἳ εἶπον *and they said* X. • (w. δέ) ἦ δ' ὅς *he said* Ar. Pl. • ἦ δ' ἥ *she said* Pl.
3 (freq. w. μέν and δέ, denoting an opposition); ὁ μὲν ... ὁ δέ *the former ... the latter, the one ... the other* Hom. + • οἱ μὲν ἐπορεύοντο, οἱ δ' εἵποντο *the men on one side continued to march, and those on the other followed* X. • (w. a prep.) ἐν μὲν ἄρα τοῖς συμφωνοῦμεν, ἐν δὲ τοῖς οὔ *in some things we agree and in others we do not* Pl.
4 (prep.phrs.) ἐκ τοῦ (also ep. ἐκ τοῖο) *after this (time), from this man* Hom. • πρὸ τοῦ (sts. written προτοῦ) *before this (time)* A. Hdt. + • ἐν τοῖς *in or amongst these (ref. to men, gods, times, circumstances)* Hom. + • Πηλεύς τε καὶ Κάδμος ἐν τοῖσιν ἀλέγονται *Peleus and Kadmos are counted amongst these* Pi. • (w.superl.adj. or adv.) τοῦτό μοι ἐν τοῖσι θειότατον φαίνεται γενέσθαι *this seems to me in these circumstances to be a particularly wondrous happening* Hdt.
5 (w. a noun or pers. name in poetry, freq. w. note of commendation) **this** or **that famous, the great** (or sim.) Hom. + • βέβληται μὲν ὁ Τυδεΐδης κρατερὸς Διομήδης *that famous son of Tydeus, mighty Diomedes, has been struck* Il. • φθίσει σε τὸ σὸν μένος *this great spirit of yours will destroy you* Il.; (also derog.) **this** or **that infamous, the terrible** (or sim.) Hom. + • τὸν λωβητῆρα ἐπεσβόλον ἔσχ' ἀγοράων *he stopped this terrible bad-mouth from speaking in the assembly* Il.
6 (as relatv.) **who, which** Hom. + • Ἀπόλλωνι ἄνακτι, τὸν ἠΰκομος τέκε Λητώ *to lord Apollo, whom lovely-haired Leto bore* Il. • τῇ περ δώδεκα παῖδες ἐνὶ μεγάροισιν ὄλοντο *whose twelve children perished in her halls* Il. • εἴ περ εἶδες τό περ ἐγώ, κάρτα ἂν ἐθώμαζες *if you had seen what I saw, you would be really amazed* Hdt. • ὁ μὲν δή οἱ ἔλεγε τά περ ὀπώπεε *he was telling him what he had seen* Hdt. • τά τε στυγέουσι θεοί περ *which even the gods generally detest* Il. Hes. • τοῖσίν τε κοτέσσεται *with whom typically she is angry* Hom.
—B | as def.art. |
1 the Hom. + • (marking a person, thing or group, as distinguished fr. others, called to one's attention, or well-known) ὁ ποιητής *the poet* (ref. to one already mentioned, or who is famous) Pl. • ἐρωτώντων τινῶν διὰ τί ἀπέθανεν ὁ ἄνθρωπος *some asking why the man in question had been put to death* X. • ἀλλὰ μέρος τι αὐτῶν, οἷον οἱ στρατιῶται *but a proportion of them, for example the soldiers* And. • (freq. where English would use a possessv.pers.pron.) τὴν κεφαλὴν κατεάγην *I fractured my skull* And. • (freq. w.abstr. nouns) ἥ τε ἐλπὶς καὶ ὁ ἔρως *hope and desire* Th. • (w.pron., giving it emph.) δεινὸν μὲν τοίνυν ἔτι προσδοκᾶν οὐδὲν δεῖ τὸν ἐμέ *I for my part do not need any longer to anticipate anything terrible* Pl. • (sim., w.num.) τῶν λόχων δώδεκα ὄντων οἱ τρεῖς *three out of the twelve companies that there were* X.
2 (marking persons or things as representative of their class, or usual in a particular circumstance) • μάτην ἄρ' οἱ γέροντες εὔχονται θανεῖν *not with sincerity do old men pray to die* E. • πονηρὸν ὁ συκοφάντης *what a wicked thing is the slanderer* D. • τί σοι δοκεῖ ὁ τοιοῦτος; *what do you think of a man of this sort?* X. • τὸ μέρος τῶν ψήφων *the share of the votes (required to win)* D.
3 (marking a proper name, as distinguished fr. others, called to one's attention, or well-known) ὥσπερ ἐν τῇ Πολιτείᾳ τῇ Πλάτωνος· ἐκεῖ γὰρ ὁ Σωκράτης φησί ... *as in Plato's Republic; for there Socrates says ...* Arist. • Ζεὺς δ', ὅστις ὁ Ζεύς *and Zeus, whoever this Zeus may be* E. • ὡς ὁ Λάϊος κατασφαγείη πρὸς τριπλαῖς ἁμαξιτοῖς (*I thought I*

heard fr. you) that this Laios was killed where three roads meet S. • ἡ Εὐρώπη *Europe* (esp. opp. ἡ Ἀσία *Asia*) Th. + **4** (w. attributive wd. or phr., giving it emph.) • ὁ ἀγαθὸς ἀνήρ *the good man* Pl. • αἱ ἐκ τῆς Ζακύνθου νῆες *the ships from Zakynthos* Th. • περιημεκτήσας τῇ ἁπάσῃ συμφορῇ *incensed by the whole disaster* Hdt. • (w. a postpos. attributive, giving more emph. to the noun) ὁ δῆμος ὁ Ἀθηναίων *the Athenian people* X. • τοὺς κύνας τοὺς χαλεποὺς *the dogs, that is the fierce ones* X.
5 (w.adj., adv., ptcpl. or inf., creating a substantival use) • τὸ δίκαιον *that which is just* Thgn. + • τοὐμόν (τὸ ἐμόν) *my interests* S. • ἡ Ἀττική (w. γῆ understd.) *Attica* Th. • οἱ τότε *men of that time* Th. • προβήσομαι ἐς τὸ πρόσω τοῦ λόγου *I shall go on further in the account* Hdt. • οἱ λογοποιοῦντες *rumour-mongers* Isoc. D. • τὸ φρονεῖν *wise thinking* S. +
6 (singly, w. more than one noun, combining the whole into one notion) • οἱ στρατηγοὶ καὶ λοχαγοὶ τῶν Ἑλλήνων *the Greek generals and commanders* X.
7 (neut., specifying a wd., num., phr. or sentence) • τὸ ἄνθρωπος *the word 'man'* Arist. • ἔστιν τὰ δώδεκα δὶς ἕξ *twelve is twice six* Pl. • τὸ μηδὲν ἄγαν *the maxim 'nothing to excess'* Pi.*fr*. + • ἐν τοῖς Περὶ τοῦ Ἡρακλέους *in the work 'On Herakles'* Plu. • (w.interrog., ref. to a question which needs to be asked about sthg. mentioned) πάσχει δὲ θαυμαστόν. —τὸ τί; *but he's experiencing a most extraordinary thing. —What's that then?* Ar.
8 (ellipt., w.gen. or prep.phr., expressing an association of some kind) • Θουκυδίδην τὸν Ὀλόρου *Thucydides son of Oloros* Th. • Μένων καὶ οἱ σὺν αὐτῷ *Menon and the men with him* X. • τὸ τῶν Ἑρμῶν *the affair of the Herms* Th. • τὸ τοῦ Ὁμήρου (introducing a quotation) *the words of Homer* Pl. • ἐγγὺς τῶν Πυθοδώρου *near Pythodoros' property* D. • τὴν ἔξω τείχους (w. ὁδόν understd.) *the road outside the town wall* Pl.
9 (ellipt., w. a deity's name left out, to avoid the full force of an oath) • μὰ τόν *by ...* Ar. +
—**τῇ**, dial. **τᾷ**, also **τῇπερ** (or **τῇ περ**) *fem.adv*. **1** *in* (or *to*) *this or that place*, **here, there** Hom. +; (most freq. in advbl.phrs.) • τῇ καὶ τῇ *in this direction and that* Hes.—*on this side and that* Hdt. • τὸ μὲν τῇ, τὸ δὲ τῇ *one thing here and another there* X. • τῇ μὲν ... τῇ δέ *in one place ... in the other, in some places ... in others, partly ... partly* Hdt. Th. +
2 (w. περ¹, as relatv.) *in the place where*, **where** Hom. Hdt.
3 (w. περ¹, as relatv.) **by the way that** Hdt.
4 (w. περ¹, as relatv.) *in the way in which*, **how** Hdt.
5 in this or **that respect** or **way** Od. Emp.; τῇ μὲν ... τῇ δέ *in one way ... in another* Emp. E. Pl. X. + | τῇ is also *fem.dat.def.art*.; see also τῇ
—**τό** *neut.adv*. (introducing a cl. expressing a consequence or inference fr. what has just been stated; freq. w. καί) **therefore, so** Hom. + • ἀλλὰ τά γ' οὐκ ἐγένοντο· τὸ καὶ κλαίουσα τέτηκα *but these things did not happen; and so I pine away weeping* Il.; (in coming to a conclusion about what is certainly known, w. δέ) Th. Pl. + • τὸ δὲ κινδυνεύει, ὦ ἄνδρες, τῷ ὄντι ὁ θεὸς σοφὸς εἶναι *but the fact is, gentlemen, it is likely that in reality the god is wise* Pl. • τὸ δέ τι καί *and moreover, besides* Th.; τὸ μὲν ... τὸ δέ (also freq.pl., τὰ μὲν ... τὰ δέ) *partly ... partly, on one hand ... on the other* Hom. + • τὰ μὲν οὖν ἤειδε, τὰ δὲ φρεσὶν ἄλλα μενοίνα *he was singing of those things, but in his mind he was planning these others* hHom.
—**τῷ** (also written **τώ, τώ**) *neut.adv*. *for this* (or *that*) *reason* or *in this* (or *that*) *circumstance*, **therefore, then** Hom. + | τῷ is also *masc.neut.dat.def.art*.

ὅ¹ (neut.relatv.pron.): see ὅς¹
ὅ² *neut.relatv.adv*.: see under ὅς¹
ὅ³ (masc.demonstr.pron.): see ὁ
ὄ *interj*.: see ὂ ὂ ὂ
ὀᾶ *interj*. (as a cry of anguish or foreboding) **ah, alas!** A.
ὄαρες ων *f.pl*. | contr.dat.pl. ὤρεσσι | **close women relatives, womenfolk** (of warriors) Il.
ὀαρίζω *vb*. | only pres. and impf. | contr.iteratv.impf. ὠρίζεσκον | **keep close company, engage in intimate talk** hHom. Pi.*fr*. —W.COGN.ACC. hHom. —W.DAT. *w. someone* Il. hHom.
ὀαρισμοί ῶν *m.pl*. **sweet** or **intimate talk** Hes. Call.
ὀαριστής οῦ *m*. **intimate friend** (of Zeus, ref. to Minos) Od. Plu.; (of pompous talk, ref. to Pythagoras) Plu.(quot.philos.)
ὀαριστύς ύος *f*. **1 intimate talk, dalliance** (of lovers) Il.
2 (fig.) **dalliance** (w.GEN. of warriors in the front line, ref. to their meeting in conflict) Il.; (of war) Il.
ὄαροι ων *m.pl*. [ὄαρες] **1 intimate company and talk, discourse** Hes. hHom. Ariphron Call. AR.; (in philosophy) Emp.; (fig., betw. voices and musical accompaniment) Pi.
2 ‖ SG. **gentle speech** Pi.
ὀβελισκο-λύχνιον ου *n*. [ὀβελίσκος] **spit-lamp** (app. a tool which could be used as either a lamp-stand or a cooking-spit, to which is likened a magistracy w. more than one duty) Arist.
ὀβελίσκος ου *m*. [dimin. ὀβελός] **1 skewer** Ar. X. Plu.; (made of copper or iron, used as a form of currency) Plu.
2 spit-like blade (as a feature of an Iberian sword), **blade** Plb.
3 spit-like object (used to mark an Iberian warrior's grave); perh. **sword** Arist. [also interpr. as *pointed stone*]
ὀβελός, dial. **ὀδελός**, οῦ *m*. **1 spit** (for roasting meat) Hom. Hdt. E.*Cyc*. Ar.
2 tapering monumental column (made of stone, characteristic of Egypt), **obelisk** Hdt.
ὀβολός οῦ *m*. | du. (sts. used after numeral δύο, δυοῖν *two*) ὀβολώ, ὀβολοῖν | silver coin worth one-sixth of a drachma, **obol** Th. Ar. Att.orats. Pl. +
ὀβολο-στάτης ου *m*. [ἵστημι] app., weigher of obols, **money-lender** Ar.
ὀβολοστατική ῆς *f*. trade of the money-lender, **money-lending, usury** Arist.
Ὀβριάρεως *m*.: see Βριάρεως
ὀβρίκαλα (also **ὄβριχα**) ων *n.pl*. **young** (of wild animals) A.
ὀβριμο-δερκής ές *adj*. [ὄβριμος, δέρκομαι] (of Athena) **with might in the glance** B.
ὀβριμο-εργός όν *adj*. [ἔργον] (of warriors) **committing brutal acts** Il. Hes.; (of the Cimmerians) Callin.
ὀβριμό-θυμος ον *adj*. [θυμός] (of Ares) **with violent spirit** hHom.; (of one of the Cyclopes) Hes.
ὀβριμο-πάτρᾱ ᾱς, Ion. **ὀβριμοπάτρη** ης *f*. [πατήρ] (epith. of Athena) **goddess with the mighty father** Hom. Hes. Sol. Ar.
ὄβριμος ον (also dial.fem. ᾱ E.) *adj*. [app.reltd. βρίμη, βριαρός] **1** formidable in combat or attack; (of Ares, warriors, their spears and deeds) **mighty, violent, brutal** Hom. Hes. Tyrt. A. AR.; (of an enemy, a lion) A. Pi.
2 possessing natural might or power; (of giants and the race of bronze) **mighty, powerful** Hes. Pi.; (of a Mother goddess) E.; (of Orion, who brings gales) Hes.; (of Zeus' thunderbolt) E.; (of floodwater) Il.; (of the water of Styx) hHom.; (of a boy, in terms of his attractiveness) Thgn.
3 of huge proportions; (of a stone, a bundle of wood) **mighty, weighty** Od.; (fig., of an object of hatred) A.

—ὄβριμον neut.adv. **mightily** —ref. to Zeus thundering Hes.
ὀβριμό-σπορος ον adj. [σπορᾴ] (of Earth) **with mighty offspring** B.
ὄβριχα n.pl.: see ὀβρίκαλα
ὀγδοαῖος ᾱ ον num.adj. [ὀγδόη, see ὄγδοος] (of travellers) **taking eight days, arriving on the eighth day** Plb. Plu.
ὀγδόατος η ον num.adj. [ὄγδοος] **eighth** Hom. Hes. Emp. Call. ‖ FEM.SB. **eighth day** (of the month) Hes.
ὀγδοήκοντα, dial. **ὀγδώκοντα** indecl.num.adj. **eighty** Il. +
ὀγδοηκοντα-τάλαντος ον adj. [τάλαντον] (of an estate) **valued at eighty talents** Lys.
ὀγδοηκοστός ή όν num.adj. **eightieth** Th. Plu.
ὄγδοος η ον num.adj. [ὀκτώ] **eighth** Hom. + ‖ FEM.SB. **eighth day** (of a month) Att.orats. Plu.
ὀγδώκοντα dial.indecl.num.adj.: see ὀγδοήκοντα
ὀγδωκοντα-έτης ες dial.adj. [ὀγδοήκοντα, ἔτος] **eighty years old** Sol. Simon.
ὄγε demonstr.pron.: see γε A4
Ὄγκᾱ ᾱς dial.f. **Onka** (name of Athena at Thebes) A.
ὀγκάομαι mid.contr.vb. (of a donkey) **bray** Arist. Call.
ὀγκηρός ά όν adj. [ὄγκος²] **swollen to beyond normal size** ‖ NEUT.SB. **pomposity** Arist.
—**ὀγκηρότερον** neut.compar.adv. **more pompously** X.
ὄγκιον ου n. [perh.reltd. ὄγκος²] a kind of storage box (for armour and weapons), **chest** Od.
ὄγκος¹ ου m. **barb** (of an arrow) Il.
ὄγκος² ου m. **1 total of a large or dense collection** (of things or people); **pile** (of wood) Hdt.; **mass** (of a population) Pl.; (of a battle-line) X.; (of wealth or possessions) Pl.; (of stories) Pl.
2 total weight (of things); **weight** (of ashes, a corpse, w.connot. of relative lightness) S. Pl. Men.; **heavy weight, bulk** (of iron coinage, fighting ships) Plu.
3 dead weight of a thing (which must be carried, physically or mentally); **weight, burden** (ref. to a child in the womb) E.; (ref. to an impediment to running) X.; (ref. to sthg. which demands responsibility or causes trouble) S. Pl.
4 sum of matter (constituting an object); **mass** (of a body, an element or substance) Parm. Emp. Pl.; (of the human body) Pl.
5 sum (of an abstr. quality); **mass, accumulation** (of virtue, enmity, or sim.) Pl. Arist.
6 weight, dignity, importance (of a family, city-state, leader or office) E. Pl. Plu.; (of the name of mother) S.; (accorded to the distinguished, the dead) Pl. Plu.
7 (pejor.) **pride** S. E. Isoc.; **pomposity** Plu.
8 weight, consequence (of sthg. said) S.
9 weight, fullness (of a poem, rhetorical or literary style) Arist.
ὀγκόω contr.vb. ‖ aor. ὤγκωσα ‖ **1 inflate the importance of, aggrandise, exalt** —a city, a man's life E. —one's ideas Ar.
2 ‖ PASS. **be exalted** —W.DAT. through family reputation E.; (of a dead man) **be dignified** —W.DAT. w. a tomb E.
3 ‖ MID. **swell with pride, be full of pride** or **boastful** (because of wealth, fame, noble birth) E. Ar. X.
ὀγκύλλομαι mid.vb. **puff oneself up** (w. haughtiness), **be full of oneself** Ar.
ὀγκώδης ες adj. **1** (of parts of an animal's body) **full, fleshy** X.; (pejor., of a person) **overweight** Plu.
2 (of a man) **puffed up, pretentious** Pl.
3 (of ideas, expressed in speeches) **weighty** Isoc.; (of the epic hexameter) Arist.
ὀγμεύω vb. [ὄγμος] ‖ only pres. and impf. ‖ **1 move forward as though cutting swathes or ploughing a furrow;** (of soldiers, on a hunt) **move slowly forward in a line** (to flush out game-animals) —W.DAT. for their commander X.
2 (of Philoktetes) **move laboriously forward** —W.ACC. on his path S.
ὄγμος ου m. **1 line followed** (when working in a field); **furrow** (made by a ploughman) Il.; **swathe** (cut by a reaper) Il. Theoc.
2 (fig.) **furrow** (in the skin of an ageing person), **wrinkle** Archil.
3 line of movement (in the sky); **course** (of the moon) hHom.
4 ‖ PL. **swathes** (of cornland) hHom.; **tracts** (in the sky) Call.
ὄγχνη ης f. —also **ὄχνα** ᾱς dial.f. **1 pear tree** Od. Call.
2 fruit of the pear tree, pear Od. Praxill. Theoc.
ὀδαγμός οῦ m. [ὀδάξω] **persistent biting pain** S.(v.l. ἀδαγμός)
ὀδαῖα ων n.pl. [ὀδάω, ὀδός] **goods** or **provisions for a voyage** Od.
ὀδακτάζω vb. [ὀδάξ] **bite firmly on** —a sacred tree-trunk (in a ritual) Call.; (of a horse) **champ** —the bit AR.
ὀδάξ adv. [ὀδούς, ὀδών] **1 with teeth tightly clenched** (on hitting the ground in a violent death) Il. E. AR.; (whilst pressing on the lips in silent rage) Od.
2 with sharp teeth —ref. to gnawing through sthg., holding onto or biting someone Pi.fr. Ar.
3 as though with sharp teeth, with biting pain —ref. to smoke stinging the eyes Ar.
ὀδάξω vb. —also **ἀδαξάομαι** mid.contr.vb. **1 feel an irritating pain, itch** X.
2 ‖ MID. **scratch an itch** Thphr.
ὀδάω contr.vb. [ὀδαῖα] **sell** (sthg., to someone) **for the road; sell** —provisions (to travellers) E.Cyc. ‖ PASS. (of a person) **be sold** (to pirates) E.Cyc.
ὅδε (Aeol. **ὅδε**), fem. **ἥδε** (dial. **ἅδε**, Aeol. **ἅδε**), neut. **τόδε**, τοῦδε τῆσδε (dial. τᾶσδε) τοῦδε demonstr.pron. and adj. [reltd. ὁ] ‖ PL.: Aeol.masc.gen. τωνδέων ‖ dat.: Ion. and poet. masc.neut. τοισίδε, ep. τοίσδεσι, also τοίσδεσσι, poet.fem. ταισίδε, Ion. τῃσίδε ‖
1 (of persons or things, w. strong deictic force) **the one here** (in a place indicated by the speaker) Hom. + • Ἕκτορος ἥδε γυνή here is the wife of Hector Il.; (marking the arrival of a person) • ἀλλ' εἰσορῶ γὰρ τόνδε τὸν Διὸς τρόχιν but I see Zeus' errand-runner here A.; (setting the scene of a play) • τάσδε Θήβας ἔσχον I took as my home this city of Thebes E.
2 (in self-reference) • ὅδ' ἐγὼ … ἤλυθον here (as you see) I have come Od. • τῇδέ γε ζώσης ἔτι while I am still alive S.
3 (gener.) **the one which is immediately present in place or time** or **is the current object of attention, he, she, this** Hom. + • ἀλλ' ὅδ' ἀνὴρ ἐθέλει περὶ πάντων ἔμμεναι ἄλλων but this man wishes to be above all others Il. • τί κακὸν τόδε πάσχετε; what is this evil you are suffering? Od. • προσεῖδον νυκτὶ τῇδε φάσματα I saw visions this night S. ‖ NEUT.PL. (as predic., ref. to a present situation) • οὐ γάρ ἐσθ' Ἕκτωρ τάδε for Hector is not here now E.
4 the one present in one's thoughts • τοῦδ' ἀνδρὸς Ὀδυσσῆος φίλος υἱός the dear son of this man Odysseus (of whom we were talking) Od.
5 the particular one (defined by what follows) • τόδε μοι κρήηνον ἐέλδωρ grant me the following wish Il.; (contrasted w. οὗτος) • ταῦτα μὲν Λακεδαιμόνιοι λέγουσι … τάδε δὲ ἐγὼ … γράφω this is what the Lacedaemonians say, but my account is as follows Hdt.
6 (responding to a relatv.pron.) • ἀλλ' ὃν πόλις στήσειε, τοῦδε χρὴ κλύειν the man whom the city appoints is the one to whom one must listen S.

ὀδελός

—**ὁδί** ἡδί τοδί *demonstr.pron. and adj.* (w. stronger force) **he, she, this** Ar. Is. D. Arist. Men.; (w. contrastv. δέ interposed) ἐμοὶ μὲν ὄνομα Πεισέταιρος, τῳδεδὶ Εὐελπίδης *my name is Peisetairos, his is Euelpides* Ar.

—**τῇδε**, dial. **τᾷδε** *fem.dat.adv.* **1 in this place, here** Hom. Hdt. S. E. Pl. +
2 by this way or **in this direction** Thgn. S. E. Ar.
3 in this way, by this means Hdt. Trag. Ar. Pl. +

ὀδελός *dial.m.*: see ὀβελός

ὁδεύω *vb.* [ὁδός] **1** (of troops on the battlefield) **find a way, advance** —W.PREP.PHR. *to a place* Il.
2 make a journey (by land or sea), **journey, travel** X. AR. NT. Plu. —W.COGN.ACC. *along a road, over land* AR. Plu.; (of a river) Call. Mosch.; (of a personif. island, envisaged as leading a procession) Call.
3 (of Fate) **move ever onwards** —W.PREP.PHR. *to the end of men's lives* Lyr.adesp.

ὁδηγέω *contr.vb.* [ὁδηγός] **1** be a guide on a journey; **guide** —*a person* A.
2 be a guide (for someone who cannot move or walk w. ease); **lead the way** E.; (tr.) **lead** —*a blind person* NT.; (fig., ref. to giving spiritual instruction) NT.

ὁδ-ηγός οῦ *m.* [ὁδός, ἄγω] **one who leads the way, guide** (for travellers or an army, over unfamiliar territory) Plb. Plu.; (for those in search of a person, or of spiritual truth) NT.

ὁδί *masc.demonstr.pron. and adj.*: see under ὅδε

ὅδιος ον *adj.* [ὁδός] of the road or journey; (of birds of omen, which have been sighted) **on the road** A.; (of the command, meton. for the commanders) **of the expedition** (to Troy) A.

ὅδισμα ατος *n.* constructed road, **roadway** (ref. to Xerxes' bridge of boats) A.

ὁδίτης ου, dial. **ὁδίτᾱς** ᾱ *m.* **traveller** or **passer-by** Od. hHom. S. Hellenist.poet.; (appos.w. ἄνθρωπος) Il.

ὀδμάομαι *mid.contr.vb.* [ὀδμή] **have the sense of smell** Democr.

ὀδμή, Att. **ὀσμή**, ῆς, dial. **ὀδμᾶ** ᾶς *f.* **1 smell, odour** Pl. X. Arist.; (of sthg. unpleasant, such as animals, raw minerals, leather, burning) Hom. Hdt. Ar. +; (fr. dung, corpses, infection, rotting food, Harpies) Hippon. Hdt. S. Th. AR.
2 smell, fragrance (of sthg. pleasant, such as incense, perfumes, flowers, trees) Od. hHom. Xenoph. Hdt. E.*fr.* Pl. +; (of wine) hHom. E. Ar.; (of sacrifices, cooking) hHom. Pi.*fr.* Hdt.(oracle) Pl. +; (of deities or things assoc.w. them) hHom. Thgn. E. Ar. +
3 scent (of someone approaching) A.; (of humans, animals, blood, meat, esp. as attracting predators) A. Hdt. X. +
4 sense of smell Democr.

ὁδοι-δόκος ου *m.* [ὁδός, δέχομαι] one who lies in wait on the road, **highwayman** Plb.

ὁδοιπλανέω *contr.vb.* [reltd. πλάνος¹] **make one's wandering way** Ar.

ὁδοιπορέω *contr.vb.* [ὁδοιπόρος] | impf. ὡδοιπόρουν | **1 be on one's way, walk** S.
2 be on the road, be on a journey or **march** (sts. W.COGN.ACC. ὁδόν) A.*satyr.fr.* Hdt. S. X. Bion +

ὁδοιπορίᾱ ᾱς, Ion. **ὁδοιπορίη** ης *f.* **journey, expedition** or **march** (esp. a long or difficult one) hHom. Hdt. X. NT. Plu.

ὁδοιπορικός ή όν *adj.* (of clothes) **suitable for travelling** Plb.

—**ὁδοιπορικῶς** *adv.* **in the manner of travellers** —*ref. to wearing certain clothes* Plu.

ὁδοιπόριον ου *n.* **gift for a journey** Od.

ὁδοι-πόρος ου *m.* **one who makes a journey** (esp. a long or difficult one, on land or sea), **traveller** Il. Sapph. Trag. Ar. D. +

ὀδοντοφυέω *contr.vb.* [ὀδοντοφυής] be at the stage of growing teeth, **teethe** Pl.

ὀδοντο-φυής ές *adj.* [ὀδούς, φύω] (of the Theban race) **sprung from teeth** (of the dragon killed by Kadmos) E.

ὁδοποιέω *contr.vb.* [ὁδοποιός] | impf. ὡδοποίουν || pf.pass.ptcpl. ὡδοποιημένος | **1** make or clear a way for passage (over difficult ground); **make** or **clear a road** (sts. W.DAT. for people) X. —W.COGN.ACC. *a road* X. || PASS. (of a road, an exit) be created X.
2 (of an army) **make one's way** (along a road beset by an enemy) Plu.; (of a commander) —W.ACC. *by a specified route* Plu.
3 (of water) **form a channel** D.
4 || IMPERS.PF.PASS. a way has been made (by underground streams, to their outlets) Pl.
5 (fig.) **pave the way** (in argument, speech) —W.DAT. *for others, for a statement to follow* Arist.

ὁδοποίησις εως *f.* **paving the way, preparation** (for sthg. that follows, ref. to a prologue or prelude) Arist.

ὁδοποιΐᾱ ᾱς *f.* **clearing** or **building of roads** X. Plu.

ὁδο-ποιός οῦ *m.* [ποιέω] **clearer** or **builder of roads** X. Plu.; (as a public official in city-states) Aeschin. Arist.

ὁδός, Ion. **οὐδός** (Od.) *f.* | also once οὐδός (Od.) | **1** fact or instance of travelling (on land or water); **journey** (freq. w. measurement in time or distance) Hom. +; (w. focus on the purpose) **mission, foray, march, race** (or sim.) Hom. +; (w. focus on the beginning, end or duration) **setting out, going, coming, progress, being on the road, roaming** Hes. +
2 direction or route of travel, **way, path, road** Hom. +
3 means of access, passage or travel; **way in, out** or **through, way to leave** Hom. +
4 (concr.) **path, track** Hom. +; public road (cleared and constructed, sts.w. prefixed proper name), **road** or **street** Hom. +; **passage** (to another part of a building) Od.; (fig., in the soul) Heraclit.
5 course (of things in motion); **path** (of heavenly bodies, day and night) Hes. Hdt. E.; (of a river) Hdt. X.; (of birds of omen) Pi. S.; (of a weapon) Antipho
6 course of change or development (in physical substances); **course, process** Hdt. Pl.
7 course in life or course of action (good or bad); **way, path, course** Hes. Thgn. Pi. Trag. Th. Ar. +
8 path (of Justice, silence, truth, wisdom or moderation) Pi. E.
9 route or means (for doing or achieving sthg.); **path, way** (towards a goal) Thgn. Pi. E. Th. +; **way through** (a difficulty) Ar.; **manner** (of divination) S.; **right way, system, procedure** (for investigating sthg.) Parm. Pl. +
10 path (of one's thoughts) or system (of thought); **way** Thgn. S. E.; (in philosophy or science) Parm. +; (in spiritual terms) NT.
11 path or direct path (of words); **path, course** or **version** (of speech or song, divine prophecy) A. Pi. E. Ar.; (of a poem, story, play) Lyr. Hdt. E. Ar.; (of letters in a word) Pl.
12 (prep.phr.) πρὸ ὁδοῦ **ahead** or **well on** (*in a journey*) Il.; (*in a physical process, in progress in a task, in an argument or discussion*) Pl. D. Arist. | see also φροῦδος

ὀδός, Ion. **οὐδός**, οῦ *m.* **1** sill of a doorway or raised floor of an outside gallery or entrance-way; **threshold, entrance, step** (of a building or house) Hom. hHom. B.*fr.* Arist. Theoc. +; (of a temple) Il. hHom. Hdt. E.; (of the Roman Senate) Plb.;

(of a bride's new home) Plu.; (of Hades or Tartaros, of the place where Night dwells) Il. Hes. Parm. S.; (of a cave) hHom. **2** (fig.) **threshold** (W.GEN. consisting of old age, ref. to the last period of life, as a time of transition) Hom. Hes. Hdt. Att.orats. +

ὀδ-ουρός οῦ *m.f.* [ὁδός, οὖρος²] **guardian on the road, escort** E.

ὀδούς, Ion. ὀδών, όντος *m*. **1 tooth** (human or animal, usu.pl.) Hom. +; **tooth, fang** (of a fierce animal, a monstrous being) Od. Hes. E. AR. Theoc. +; **tusk** (of a wild boar) Hom. +; (cut into plates and arranged in rows on a warrior's helmet) Il. AR.; (of an elephant, also ref. to ivory) Hdt. Plb. Plu. **2 tooth** (assoc.w. various attributes or emotions, usu.pl.); (as white, esp. through cleaning) Ar. Thphr.; (loose or lost in old age) Anacr. Hdt. Ar. +; (loosened or knocked out in violence) Hom. Semon. E.*Cyc.* Men. NT. Plu.; (in ctxt. of eating, esp. greedily) E.*Cyc.* Ar. Call.; (w.vbs. of sharpening, chattering, grinding, biting, in expressions of aggression, fear, grief, determination) Hom. Tyrt. Hippon. E. Ar. Lycurg. +; (as an attribute of personif. Time) Simon.

ὁδο-φύλακες ων *m.pl*. [ὁδός, φύλαξ] **guards of the roads** (who inspect or intercept persons and letters) Hdt.

ὁδόω *contr.vb*. | aor. ὥδωσα | **guide** (someone or sthg.) along the right way; (of the Nile) **guide, lead** —*a person* (W.PREP.PHR. *to a place*) A.; (of a divinity) —*mortals* (*to an art*) A. —(W.INF. *to understanding*) A.; **direct** —*a cup of poison* (*against a person*) E. ‖ PASS. (of affairs) **be set afoot or initiated** (by someone) Hdt.

ὀδυνάω *contr.vb*. [ὀδύνη] | aor.pass. ὠδυνήθην | **1 cause pain, hurt** —*someone* Ar. Men.; (intr., of a state of mind) **cause pain** E.

2 ‖ PASS. **be hurt, feel pain** Ar. Pl. NT.; **be distressed** (by events, misfortune) S. Ar. Aeschin. Men. NT.

ὀδύνη ης, dial. ὀδύνᾱ ᾱς *f*. **1** physical pain (fr. a wound or illness), **pain** Hom. +

2 mental pain (fr. ill-treatment, misfortune, poverty, or sim.), **pain, distress, anguish** Hom. +; (fr. love) Archil. AR.

ὀδυνηρός, dial. ὀδυνᾱρός, ά όν *adj*. full of pain (affecting body or mind); (of physical wounds, life, experiences) **painful, distressing** Mimn. Thgn. Pi. E. Ar. Pl. +

ὀδυνή-φατος ον *adj*. [θείνω] (of drugs, a medicinal root) **pain-killing** Il.

ὄδυρμα ατος *n*. [ὀδύρομαι] **cry of lamentation** Trag.

ὀδυρμός οῦ *m*. (sg. and pl.) **lamentation** A. E. Tim. Isoc. Pl. Men. +; **complaint, moaning** Pl. Plu.

ὀδύρομαι, also δύρομαι (A. B. E. Mosch.) *mid.vb*. | ep.3sg.impf. ὀδύρετο, Ion.3sg.iteratv.impf. ὀδυρέσκετο (Hdt.) | fut. ὀδυροῦμαι | aor. ὠδυράμην, ptcpl. ὀδυράμενος | **1** utter cries of lamentation or expressions of grief (over the dead); **wail, lament** Hom. + —W.ACC. *over persons, their death* Hom. S. E. Aeschin. +

2 lament (in circumstances of misfortune, impending death, setback, defeat); **wail, lament** Hom. + —W.ACC. *over misfortunes* A. E. And. Pl. + —W.DAT. *to others* Hom.

3 lament (for what is lost, far away or unattainable); **weep, lament** —W.ACC. *over an unfaithful husband* E.; **weep with longing** —W.ACC. *for one's homeland, a homecoming* Od. —W.GEN. *for a loved one* (*who has died or is far away*) Hom.

4 express one's grief or displeasure in a complaining way (oft.pejor., in order to impress those listening); **lament, moan** Att.orats. + —W.ACC. *over misfortunes, mistakes, injuries, poverty, old age* Att.orats. + —W.COMPL.CL. *that sthg. is the case* D. Men. +

ὀδυρτά *neut.pl.adv*. **woefully, painfully** —*ref. to being pierced by a spear* Ar.

ὀδυρτικός ή όν *adj*. of the type to lament or complain; (of old men) **querulous** Arist. ‖ NEUT.SB. **complaining nature** Arist.

—ὀδυρτικωτέρως *compar.adv*. **in a relatively mournful mood** Arist.

ὀδύσασθαι *ep.aor.mid.inf.* | only 2sg. ὠδύσαο, 3sg. ὠδύσατο, also ὠδύσσατο, 3pl. ὀδύσαντο, ptcpl. ὀδυσσάμενος | 3sg.pf. ὀδώδυσται | **1** (of the gods) **be full of hatred** Il. —W.DAT. *towards a mortal* Hom.

2 (of a father) **be full of resentment** —W.DAT. *towards his offspring* Hes.; (of a man, w. play on the name Odysseus) **be at odds** —W.DAT. w. *one's fellow men* Od.

Ὀδυσσεύς έως (ep. ἦος, Ion. έος Il. Pi.), also ep. Ὀδυσεύς ἦος (also εὖς Od.) *m*. | acc. Ὀδυσσέα, also Ὀδυσσῆ (Pi. E.), ep. Ὀδυσσῆα, Ὀδυσῆα | **Odysseus** (king of Ithaca, hero of the *Odyssey*) Hom. +

—Ὀδύσειος, ep. Ὀδυσήιος, ον *adj*. (of the palace) **of Odysseus** Od.; (of the son, ref. to Telemachus) Stesich.

—Ὀδύσσεια ας (Ion. ης) *f. **Odyssey*** (of Homer) Hdt. Pl. Arist.

ὄδωδα (pf.), ὀδώδει (ep.3sg.plpf.): see ὄζω

ὀδώδυσται (3sg.pf.mid.): see ὀδύσασθαι

ὀδών *Ion.m*.: see ὀδούς

ὀδωτός ή όν *adj*. [ὀδόω] (of things) **able to be got underway, practicable, feasible** (W.DAT. *for someone*) S.

ὀείγω *Aeol.vb*.: see οἴγω

ὄεσσι (ep.dat.pl.): see οἶς

Ὀζόλαι ῶν *m.pl*. **Ozolians** (inhabitants of a region in Lokris) Hdt. Th. X. D.

ὄζος, Aeol. ὔσδος, ου *m*. **1 branch from a main stem** (of a tree), **branch** Hom. Hes. Sapph. Pi. E. +

2 node, knot (on a stem) Ar. Theoc.

3 (fig.) **branching out** (in a narrative) Arist.(quot.)

4 (fig.) **offshoot, scion, son** (of Ares, ref. to a warrior) Il. Hes. E.; (du., of Athens, ref. to the two sons of Theseus) E.; (of gold, ref. to adamant) Pl.

ὄζω, dial. ὄσδω (Theoc.) *vb*. [reltd. ὀδμή] | impf. ὦζον, dial. ὦσδον | fut. ὀζήσω | pf. ὄδωδα | 3sg.pf.plpf. ὀδώδει, ep. ὀδώδει | **1 give off a smell** (good or bad); (of persons, places, things) **smell** (usu. W.NEUT.ADV. ἡδύ *sweetly*, κακόν *foully*, or sim.) Hippon. Ar. Pl. X. Arist. + —W.GEN. *of sthg.* Alcm. A. Ar. X. Theoc. Plu.; (mid.) —W.GEN. Alc. Xenoph. Thphr.(cj.)

2 be distinguishable as though by smell; smack —W.GEN. *of sthg.* Ar. X. Plu.

3 ‖ IMPERS. **there is a smell or scent** —W.NEUT.ADV. or GEN. *of a certain kind, of sthg.* Hdt. Lys. Ar. X. Thphr.

4 ‖ STATV.PF. and PLPF. (of a scent or fragrance) **pervade the air** Od.; (of a person, place or thing) **have a smell** —W.NEUT.ADV. or GEN. *of a certain kind, of sthg.* Plb. Plu.

ὅθεν *relatv.adv*. [ὅ, under ὅς¹; correlatvs. τόθεν, πόθεν] from which place, person, source or situation; **whence, from whom, from which, from whatever source, wherefore** Hom. +; (intensified w. περ¹) Pi. Hdt. S. E. Th. +

ὅθι *relatv.adv*. [correlatvs. τόθι, πόθι] in which place, **where, in which** Hom. Hes. Pi.*fr.* B. S. E. Hellenist.poet.; (intensified w. περ¹) Hom. hHom. Pl. AR.

ὄθμα *dial.n*.: see ὄμμα

ὀθνεῖος ᾱ (Ion. η) ον (also ος ον E.) *adj*. [reltd. ἔθνος] **1** of or relating to another family, community or race; (of persons) **unrelated** E. Pl. Is. Arist.; **foreign** Pl. Arist. AR. Plb. Plu.; (of sacred family images, uprooted to another community) **alien** (W.DAT. *to a land and its traditions*) Lycurg.

ὄθομαι

2 (of blood, money) **of a foreigner** AR. Theoc.*epigr.*; (of a land) **foreign** Theoc.*epigr.*; (of a war, opp. civil) Pl.; (of a prize, to be won in another country) AR.

ὄθομαι *ep.mid.vb.* | only pres. and impf. | **be troubled** or **concerned** —W.GEN. *over someone or sthg.* Il. AR.; **have scruples** —W.INF. *about saying sthg.* Il. —W.PTCPL. *about doing sthg.* Il.

ὀθόνη ης *f.* **linen cloth** Od. NT.; (as a screen) Plu.; (pl., as a female garment or wrap) Hom. Emp. AR.

—ὀθόνιον ου *n.* [dimin.] (freq.pl.) **piece of linen cloth, linen** (for dressing a wound) Ar.; (for sail-making) D. Plb.; (as a layer on a shield) Plb.; (as a shroud) NT.

ὀθούνεκα (also **ὀθούνεκεν** AR. Theoc.), Ion. **ὀτεύνεκεν** *conj.* [ὅτου, see ὅστις; ἕνεκα] **1** (introducing an explanation) **in that, because** Iamb.adesp. Trag. Theoc.
2 (introducing a compl.cl., after a vb. of saying, knowing, or sim.) **that** S. E. AR.

ὄθριξ *adj.*: see ὄτριχες

Ὄθρυς υος *f.* **Othrys** (mt. peak and range in southern Thessaly) Hes. Hdt. E. Hellenist.poet.

οἱ (masc.nom.pl.def.art.): see ὁ
οἵ[1] (masc.nom.pl.demonstr.pron.): see ὁ
οἵ[2] (masc.nom.pl.relatv.pron.): see ὅς[1]
οἷ[1], also encl. **οἱ** (3sg.dat.pers.pron.): see ἕ
οἷ[2] *relatv.adv.*: see under ὅς[1]

οἴ *interj.* **oh, alas, woe!** (exclam. of anguish or foreboding; sts.w. nom. or dat. 1st pers.pron.) Trag.; (sts. repeated) οἰοῖ or οἰοιοῖ A. S.*fr.* | see also οἴμοι

οἵ *Ion.interj.* **yow!** (exclam. of disapproval and fear, w. play on Ion.dat. of οἷς *sheep*) Ar.

οἷα (and Aeol. **οἷα**) *neut.pl.adv. and conj.*: see οἷον, under οἷος

οἰακίζω, Ion. **οἰηκίζω** *vb.* [οἴαξ] **1 guide as though with the tiller**; **handle, manoeuvre** —*shields* (W.DAT. *w. straps*) Hdt. —*a beam* (*of a grappling device*) Plb.; **guide, steer** —*horses swimming* (W.DAT. *w. leading reins*) Plb.; (fig.) —*the young* (w. *reward or punishment*) Arist.
2 (of the thunderbolt, w. its eternal fire) **control** —*all things* Heraclit.

οἰακο-νόμοι ων *m.pl.* [νέμω] **controllers of the tiller, steerers** (of mortal affairs, ref. to the gods) A.

οἰακοστροφέω *contr.vb.* [οἰακοστρόφος] (of good sense) **steer** —*someone's heart* A.

οἰακο-στρόφος ου *m.* [στρέφω] **1 one who turns the tiller, helmsman** (W.GEN. *of a ship*) A. E.
2 (fig.) **controller** (W.GEN. of necessity, ref. to one of the Fates or Erinyes) A.; (appos.w. κυβερνατήρ *helmsman*, ref. to a trainer of athletes) Pi.

οἴαξ ἄκος, Ion. **οἴηξ** ηκος *m.* **1** (sg. and pl.) **steering-oar, tiller** (of a ship) A. E. Pl. Arist. AR. Plu.; (of the ship of state) A. Plu.; (fig., of a chariot) E.; (W.GEN. of one's mind) A.; (of one's step, ref. to a person) E.
2 ‖ PL. **guiding rings** (for the yoke of a horse or mule, to which the driving reins are attached) Il.

οἴγω, Aeol. **ὀείγω** (or **ὀΐγω**) *vb.* | fut. οἴξω | aor. ᾦξα, ep. ᾦιξα, ptcpl. οἴξας ‖ ep.3pl.impf.pass. ὠείγοντο (Il.) | —also perh. **οἴγνυμι** *vb.* | ep.3pl.impf.pass. ὠίγνυντο (Il., dub.) |
1 open —*doors, gates* Hom. S. E. AR. Theoc.; (intr.) **open the door** Il. ‖ PASS. (of doors, gates) **be opened** Il. Alc. Pi.
2 make (the interior of a building) **accessible**; **open** —*rooms* Sapph.(or Alc.) E. —*a temple* Ar.(quot. A.) ‖ PASS. (of rooms) **be opened** Pi.*fr.*
3 make (the interior of a receptacle or its contents) **accessible**; **open** —*a jar* Hes. —*wine* (*i.e. a jar of it*) Od.; (fig.) —*a treasury* (*of the Muses*) Tim.

4 open —*one's mouth* (*i.e. speak openly*) A.
5 ‖ MID. (of the Clashing Rocks) **open** AR.

οἶδα *pf.vb.* [reltd. aor.2 εἶδον] | 2sg. οἶσθα, also οἶσθας, οἶδας, 1pl. ἴσμεν, also οἴδαμεν, dial. ἴδμεν, 2pl. ἴστε, also οἴδατε, 3pl. ἴσασι (also sts. in Hom. ἴσᾶσι), also οἴδᾱσι, dial. ἴσαντι (Theoc.), 2du. ἴστον ‖ IMPERATV.: ἴσθι, 3sg. ἴστω, Boeot. ἴττω (Ar.), 2du. ἴστον ‖ SUBJ.: εἰδῶ, ep. εἴδω, 1pl. εἰδῶμεν, ep. εἴδομεν, 2pl. εἰδῆτε, ep. εἴδετε ‖ OPT.: εἰδείην, 1pl. εἰδεῖμεν, also εἰδείημεν, 2pl. εἰδεῖτε, also εἰδείητε, 3pl. εἰδεῖεν, also εἰδείησαν ‖ INF.: εἰδέναι, ep. ἴδμεναι, ἴδμεν ‖ PTCPL.: masc. εἰδώς, fem. εἰδυῖα, ep. ἰδυῖα ‖ PLPF.: ᾔδη, also ᾔδειν, Ion. ᾔδεα, ep. ἠείδειν, 2sg. ᾔδησθα, ᾔδεις, ep. ἠείδης, 3sg. ᾔδει(ν), Ion. ᾔδεε, ep. ἠείδει, ᾔδη, 1pl. ᾖσμεν, also ᾔδεμεν, ᾔδειμεν, 2pl. ᾖστε, also ᾔδετε, ᾔδειτε, 3pl. ᾖσαν, also ᾔδεσαν, ᾔδεισαν, ep. ἴσαν, also ᾔδειν, ἠείδειν, 3du. ᾔστην ‖ FUT.: εἴσομαι, ep. εἰδήσω (also Isoc.), ep.fut.inf. εἰδησέμεν ‖ aor.inf. εἰδῆσαι (Arist.) ‖ neut.impers.vbl.adj. ἰστέον ‖ see also dial.vb. ἴσᾱμι |
1 have seen or been made aware (of sthg.); **know** (tr. or intr., freq. w.adv., εὖ *well*, εὖ μάλα *very well*, σάφα or σαφῶς *clearly*, βεβαίως *certainly*, or sim.) Hom. +; (intr., freq. w.compl.cl.) —W.NOM.PTCPL. *that one is doing sthg. or is in a certain state* Hom. + —W.ACC. + PTCPL. *that someone or sthg. is doing sthg., or is in a certain state* Hom. + —W.COMPL.CL. *that sthg. is the case* Hdt. + —W.INDIR.Q. *what is the case* Hom. +; (neg.phr., expressing disbelief or doubt) οὐκ οἶδ' εἰ ... *I am unsure whether, I doubt that* ... Il. +; οὐκ οἶδα ὅπως ... *I don't know how* ... Pl.
2 (specif.) **be aware of** (an event, circumstance, item of information, fr. report or one's own observation); **know, know about** —*sthg.* Hom. +; **have information** —W.INF. *to report* A.; (pejor., of a woman, as a busybody) **know** —*everything* Semon. ‖ NEG.PHR. οἶδα οὐδέν not know anything (sts. W.GEN. about a matter or event) Hdt. +; (w.connot. of limitations to one's thinking, or of stupidity) Archil. Anacr. Eleg. S. Men.
3 be aware of (sthg.) intuitively or through divine revelation; **know** —*a fate or fortune, the future, truth* Hom. +
4 be aware of (someone or sthg.) as existing (esp. under a certain name); **know of** or **about** —*a person, god, thing* Hom. + —*a place, geographical feature* Hdt. + —*a path, route* Hdt. + —*a method or plan, a means* Pi. E. Pl.; (in neg.phr., of an inland people) —*the sea* Od.
5 be familiar with (the nature or character of someone or sthg.) through experience or acquaintance; **have experience of, know about, know** —*certain emotions, troubles, or sim.* Il. + —*a person or god, their character, feelings, actions, or sim.* Hom. + —*a place, its character* Od. +; **have experience** —W.GEN. *of childbirth, battles, work, councils* Hom.
6 recognise (someone or sthg.) as having authority or requiring obligation; **acknowledge** —*a god* Hdt. —*gratitude, a debt* Il. + —*justice, laws* Eleg. +
7 recognise (sthg.) as very important or certain (freq. imperatv.); **know** or **understand for sure** —*sthg.* Od. +; (freq. parenth.) • καὶ Ζηνὶ τῶν σῶν, οἶδ' ἐγώ, μέλει πόνων *and Zeus, I am sure, is concerned about your sufferings* E.; (parenth. and ellipt.) • οὔτ' ἂν ὑμεῖς οἶδ' ὅτι ἐπαύσασθε πολεμοῦντες *and you, I am sure, would not have stopped fighting* D. • μὰ τὸν Δί' οὔκουν τῷ γε σῷ, σάφ' ἴσθ' ὅτι *no by Zeus, not in your case, be completely clear about that* Ar.
8 have understanding or insight; (of a person or god, their mind) **know** —*sthg. wise, many things, everything, the minds of others* Hom. + —W.INF. *to do sthg. in a situation* Il. +
9 hold in one's mind (thoughts which are typical of one's

character or disposition); **think** —*thoughts which are fierce, lawless, gentle, clever, or sim.* Hom. hHom.
10 have practical knowledge or skill (through study or practice); **be skilled in** —*crafts, songs, prophecies, deeds of war, athletic contests, medicines* Hom. Alcm.; **be skilled** —W.GEN. *in crafts, use of a weapon, a style of fighting, portents, or sim.* Hom.; (of hounds) —*in the hunt* Il.; **have the skill** or **knowledge** —W.INF. *to do or say sthg.* Hom. +; **understand** —*a subject or topic* Att.orats.
—**εἰδότως** pf.ptcpl.adv. **in a well-informed way** Aeschin.

οἰδαίνω vb. [reltd. οἰδέω] | iteratv.impf. οἰδαίνεσκον | (of angry feelings) **swell up** AR.

οἰδαλέος η ον Ion.adj. (of the lungs of persons grieving) **swollen, bursting** (W.PREP.PHR. w. pain) Archil.

οἰδάνω vb. **1** (of anger, wine) **swell** —*the heart or mind* Il. AR. || PASS. (of the heart) **be swollen** —W.DAT. w. anger Il.
2 (intr., of a ripening fruit) **swell** Ar.

οἰδέω contr.vb. | ep.impf. ᾤδεον | aor. ᾤδησα | pf. ᾤδηκα, dial.3pl. ᾠδήκαντι (Theoc.) | **1** (of a quill of a feather) **swell** (in growth) Pl.; (of a material, through the agency of fire) **swell up** Plu. || PF. (of muscles) **stand out** (through exertion) Theoc.
2 (of parts of the body) **swell, swell up, be swollen** (through injury) Od. Theoc.; (of a person) —W.ACC. *in the feet, stomach* Ar. Men.
3 || PF. (of a corpse) **be swollen** Men.
4 (fig., of political affairs) **be unsettled, be liable to erupt** Hdt.; (of a city, a populace) Pl. Plu.
5 (fig., of a person) **be swollen** (w. pride) Plu.; (of a poet's art, w. bombast) Ar.; (of an orator) **be turgid** Plu.

οἴδημα ατος n. **swelling** (in the body, fr. injury or inflammation) D. Plu.

οἴδησις εως f. **swelling, tumescence** (of passionate feelings, seen as a physical reaction in the body) Pl.

Οἰδίπους ου m. | gen. also Οἰδίποδος, ep. Οἰδιπόδαο, Ion. Οἰδιπόδεω, dial. Οἰδιπόδᾱ | acc. Οἰδίπουν, dial. Οἰδιπόδᾱν | voc. Οἰδίπου, also Οἰδίπους, dial. Οἰδιπόδᾱ | dat. Οἰδίποδι | **Oedipus** (king of Thebes, who killed his father Laios and married his mother Jocasta, and solved the riddle of the Sphinx) Hom. +; (as the title of a drama) Arist. Plu.; (as the character in drama) Ar. Pl.; (as the type of a man who marries a woman old enough to be his mother) Ar.

—**Οἰδιπόδειος** ον adj. (of a fountain, in Thebes) **of Oedipus** Plu.

οἶδμα ατος n. [reltd. οἰδέω] **1** (sg. and pl.) **swell, surge** (of the sea, a river) Il. Hes. Pi.fr. B. S. E. +; **inrush** (of air into the body) Emp.
2 (gener.) **sea** E. AR.

οἰ-έανος ον adj. [οἶος¹, ἑανός] **wearing only a single garment** AR.

οἴεος η ον Ion.adj. [οἶς] (of skins, to be made into parchment) **from sheep** Hdt.

οἶες (nom.pl.), **ὄϊες** (Ion.nom.pl.), **οἴεσι** and **ὀίεσσι** (ep.dat.pl.): see οἶς

οἰ-έτης ες adj. [copul.prfx., ἔτος] | acc.pl. οἰέτεας | (of horses, girls) **of the same age** Il. Mosch.

οἰζυρός (also **οἰζῡρός** Theoc.) ᾱ́ όν, Ion. **οἰζῡρός** ή όν adj. [οἰζύς] **1** suffering sorrow or hardship; (of persons) **woeful, wretched, miserable, pitiable** Hom. Call. Mosch.; (of a village) Hes.; (of ploughmen) **long-suffering** AR.
2 (of circumstances) accompanied by sorrow or hardship; (of war) **woeful, wretched, painful** Il.; (of distress at sea) hHom.; (of a way of life) Hdt.; (of lamentation, days and nights spent in tears) **sorrowful** Od.; (of an utterance) Call.
3 (pejor., of persons) **wretched, pitiful, pathetic** Hes. Thgn.; (of women) Semon.
4 || VOC. (as colloq. term of address, w.connot. of indignation or impatience; w. ὦ in crasis) ᾠζυρέ (ᾠζῠρέ Theoc.) **wretched man** Ar. Theoc.; ᾠζῠρά́ **wretched woman** Ar.

οἰζύς, ep. **ὀϊζῡς**, ύος f. [reltd. οἶ] | ep.dat. ὀϊζυῑ̈ | ῡ in nom.acc., ῠ in other cases | **misery, sorrow, hardship** Hom. Hes. Archil. A. E. AR.; (personif.) **Misery** Hes.

ὀϊζύω (also **ὀϊζῡ́ω** AR.) ep.vb. | aor.ptcpl. ὀϊζῡ́σᾱς | **1 be distressed** Il. AR.
2 suffer misery or **hardship** Od.; **suffer** —W.COGN.ACC. *much misery* Il.; (of a ship, envisaged as a pregnant woman) **labour** AR.
3 || PTCPL.ADJ. (of music) **distressing, dismal** Theoc.

οἴη ης ep.f. **village** AR.

οἰηθῆναι (aor.pass.inf.): see οἴομαι

οἰήϊον ου n. [reltd. οἴαξ] (sg. and pl.) **steering-oar** (of a ship) Hom. AR.

οἰηκίζω Ion.vb., **οἴηξ** Ion.m.: see οἰακίζω, οἴαξ

οἴησις εως f. [οἴομαι] **supposition, opinion** Pl. Arist. Men.

οἰήσομαι (fut.mid.), **οἰητέον** (neut.impers.vbl.adj.): see οἴομαι

οἶδα (dial.acc.), **ὄϊες** (ep.nom.pl.): see οἶς

οἶκα Ion.pf.vb.: see ἔοικα

οἴκαδε adv., **οἴκαδις** dial.adv.: see under οἶκος

οἰκειοπρᾱγία ᾱς f. [οἰκεῖος, πρᾱ́σσω] **performance of one's own particular duties** (by a class in the state) Pl.

οἰκεῖος ᾱ ον (also ος ον E.), Ion. **οἰκήϊος** η ον adj. [οἶκος]
1 of or relating to one's house; (of buildings, goods and chattels) **of the house, at home** Hes. A. Hdt. E. +
2 of or relating to one's home; (of persons) **of one's family** or **household** Hdt. Trag. +; (of events and circumstances) **of** or **in one's own home, domestic** S. E. Antipho Ar. +
3 of or relating to one's family's means; (of land, property and wealth) **one's own, at home, from home** Lyr. A. Hdt. E. +; (of profit, expense) **personal** Archil. Thgn. Hdt. Th. +
4 of or relating to one's homeland; (of the land, a city) **one's own, native** Hdt. S. Th. +; (of events and circumstances) affecting the homeland, **domestic, internal** Th. Lys. +; (of territory, resources) under the possession or influence of the homeland, **one's own** Th. +; **friendly, with close ties** D.
5 of or relating to one's people; (of persons) **of one's own community** Hes. Pl. +; **close, intimate** E. Lys. +; (of military forces, battle territory) **one's own** Hdt. Th.; (of a war) **civil** Hdt. E. Th. +; (of events and circumstances) affecting the community, **in common** Th. +
6 of or relating to one's person or inner self; (of possessions) **personal, under one's control** A. E. Th. +; (of a hand which is responsible for sthg.) **one's own** A. S. Antipho; (of suicide, troubles) **self-inflicted** S. Th. +; (of troubles fr. outside, circumstances and states of mind) affecting oneself, **personal** Pi. Hdt. S. +; (of qualities and attributes) **inner, innate** Hdt. Th. Ar. +
7 (of a thing in relation to another, of qualities and attributes in relation to a person, their character or actions) **fitting, pertinent, proper** (freq. W.GEN. to sthg. or for someone) Hdt. +; (of writing or words, in relation to the rest of what is said, or to the occasion and intention) Pl. Men. + || NEUT.IMPERS. (w. ἐστί) **it is proper or appropriate** —W.INF. *to do sthg.* Arist.
8 (of qualities or attributes) **intrinsic** Arist.; (of words) **in proper literal sense** (opp. metaphorical) Arist.

—**οἰκείως** adv. | compar. οἰκειότερον, superl. οἰκειότατα |
1 on friendly terms, familiarly, intimately Th. +

οἰκειότης

2 **patriotically** Th. +
3 **personally, privately** Ar. +
4 **appropriately** Pl. +
5 **innately** Plb. Plu.

οἰκειότης, Ion. **οἰκηιότης**, ητος *f.* 1 **relationship** (betw. peoples), **close ties** Th. +; **closeness, intimacy** (betw. individuals) Att.orats. +
2 relationship through descent or intermarriage (betw. peoples), **kinship tie** Hdt. Arist.; relationship through descent or marriage (betw. individuals), **marriage** or **family connection, close ties** Att.orats. Pl. X. Men. +
3 relationship in dealings (betw. individuals in the same state), **relations, dealings** Isoc.
4 relationship (betw. abstr. concepts, persons and things), **affinity** Pl. D. Arist.
5 proper or inherent quality (of an object); **property** Plb.; **proper literal sense** (of a word, opp. metaphor) Plu.
6 **fittingness** (of a subject for an audience) D.

οἰκειόω, Ion. **οἰκηιόω** *contr.vb.* 1 ‖ MID. **make one's own, win over** —*people* (*as friends, allies, followers*) Pl. Plu. ‖ PASS. find a place of intimacy —W.DAT. *in someone's friendship, his writing* Pl.; (of audiences) be drawn —W.DAT. *to what they hear first* Arist.
2 **organise** (people) according to kinship; **reconnect** —*persons in a community* (w. εἰς + ACC. *w. their natural ties of kinship*) Th. ‖ MID. **claim as one's own kin** —*an individual, a people* Hdt. Plu.
3 ‖ MID. **appropriate** (power and property) for oneself; (of an authority) **appropriate** —*everything in a city* Pl. —*territories, peoples* D. Plu.; (of an individual) —*someone else's property* Pl. Plu. ‖ PASS. (of a place) be brought under one's influence Th.
4 ‖ MID. (of a race) claim as one's own possession, **claim** —*lands, peoples, inventions, foreign customs* Hdt. Plu.
5 **fit, harmonise** —*a piece of discourse* (W.DAT. *w. what is said before or after*) Isoc. Plb. ‖ PASS. (of a physical body) find a place to settle Pl.; (of rhythm and harmony) find a place —W.DAT. *in the souls of the young* Pl.; (of a piece of writing) appeal —w. πρός + ACC. *to a certain kind of readership* Plb.

οἰκείω *ep.vb.*: see οἰκέω
οἰκείωσις εως *f.* **appropriation** (W.GEN. of goods) Th.
οἰκειωτικός ή όν *adj.* (of a skill) **appropriative, acquisitive** Pl.
οἰκετεία ᾱς *f.* [οἰκετεύω] (collectv.) **slaves of a household** NT.
οἰκετεύω *vb.* [οἰκέτης] 1 **be a member of a household; live in** —*the house of Hades* E.
2 be a member of a community Ar.(cj.)
οἰκέτης ου, dial. **οἰκέτας** ᾱ *m.* [οἰκέω] 1 **one who lives in a person's home, member of a household** (ref. to a woman, child, servant or slave) Hdt. +; (fig., ref. to glory) **inhabitant** (in a god's precinct) Simon.
2 **household servant** or **slave** Hdt. Trag. +
—**οἰκέτις** ιδος *f.* **female servant** or **slave** E. Call.; **housewife** (confined to the home) Theoc.
οἰκετικός ή όν *adj.* 1 (of the persons, duties or dress) **of household slaves** Aeschin. Arist. Plu.; (of names of activities) **relating to household slaves** Pl. ‖ NEUT.SG.SB. (collectv.) slaves Plu.
2 (of a young pig) **hand-reared at home** Philox.Leuc.
οἰκεύς έως (Ion. ἦος) *m.* [οἶκος] **member of one's household** Il.; **household servant** or **slave** Od. Hes.*fr.* S. Lys.(law) Theocr.
οἰκέω *contr.vb.* —also **οἰκείω** *ep.vb.* —**οἴκημμι** Aeol.*vb.* ‖ impf. ᾤκουν, ep. ᾤκεον, Ion. οἴκεον ‖ fut. οἰκήσω ‖ aor.

ᾤκησα, Aeol. ἐοίκησα ‖ pf. ᾤκηκα ‖ aor.pass. (sts. w.mid.sens.) ᾠκήθην ‖ pf.mid.pass. ᾤκημαι, Ion.3pl. οἰκέαται ‖
1 (of a people or race) **live, have houses** or **settlements** (freq. W.PREP.PHR. in, around or nr. a place) Hom. +; (tr.) **live in, inhabit** —*a land or city* Il. + ‖ PASS. (of a land or city) be inhabited or civilised (esp. opp. be wild or deserted) Hdt. +
2 (of a people or race) come to live in (a place) for the first time; **settle** —*land* hHom. +; **found** —*a city* Hdt. + ‖ PASS. (of a land, city or state) be settled or founded Hdt. +
‖ STATV.PF.PASS. (of a city) stand Hdt. Pl.
3 (of individuals or families) **live, have one's home** (in a place, house, alone or w. others) Il. +; (tr.) **live in, inhabit** —*a land, city, house, home* Pi. + —*a cave* A.; (of a dead person) —*a tomb* E.
4 (of individuals or families) come to stay (in a place) permanently or temporarily; **settle, seek shelter** E. +; **live** (in another community, as guest, exile or metic) Hdt. +; (tr.) **settle in, take over** —*a land, city, home* A. +
5 ‖ MID. and AOR.PASS. (of a people, an individual) settle oneself, **settle** Il. Hdt.; (tr.) **settle in** —*lands* Hdt.
‖ STATV.PF.MID. be an inhabitant Hdt.
6 (of divine or mythological beings) **live, have a temple** or **dwelling** (on earth, in heaven or beneath the earth) hHom. +; (tr.) **live in, inhabit** —*a place* Pi. E.
7 (of a people, an individual) settle or live (under certain conditions); **make a home, live** (w. a certain style of house, w. family or spouse, w. or without wealth, order, peace, or sim.) Thgn. +; (tr.) **live in** —*a place* (*under certain conditions*) E. Th.; **inhabit** —*another life* (*after death*) E.
8 (of a city or district) **be situated** (in a place) Hdt. +; (of a city or constitution, a house) **exist, flourish** —W.ADV. *in a well-ordered way, in isolation, or sim.* Th. +; (of the soul, spirit, thought, abstr. qualities) **dwell, go to dwell** (in a certain place or under certain conditions) Hdt. S. +
9 cause (a place) to be lived in with order or government; **order, govern** (esp. W.ADV. w. moderation, well, badly, or sim.) —*a land, city, family home or estate* S. E. Th. + —*a person's mind* Ar.(quot. E.) ‖ PASS. (of a city or home) be ordered or governed E. Th. +

—**οἰκουμένη** ης *fem.pass.ptcpl.sb.* **inhabited land, civilised** or **known world** Att.orats. X. Arist. +
οἴκηιος Ion.*adj.*, **οἰκηιότης** Ion.*f.*, **οἰκηιόω** Ion.*contr.vb.*: see οἰκεῖος, οἰκειότης, οἰκειόω
οἴκημα ατος *n.* [οἰκέω] 1 **place of habitation, house, dwelling** A. Pi. Hdt. Plu.
2 single-room building or chamber, **building, house, chamber** Hdt. Th. +; (used for a workshop, agricultural or military purposes, an official meeting, or sim.) Hdt. Th. +; (ref. to a sanctuary or Egyptian tomb) Hdt. Th. +
3 separate room (in a public building or private residence); **room, apartment, chamber** Hdt. Att.orats. +; (for sleeping, dining, or sim.) Hdt. Th. +
4 room used as a place of confinement; **house** (for captive birds) Hdt.; (for prisoners) Hdt. Th. NT. Plu.; (euphem., ref. to a specific prison) D. Plu.
5 (euphem.) **house** (ref. to a brothel) Hdt. Att.orats. Pl.
6 **storey** (of a siege-engine) X.
οἴκημμι Aeol.*vb.*: see οἰκέω
οἰκήσιμος η ον *adj.* (of terrain) **habitable** Plb.
οἴκησις εως *f.* 1 **dwelling-place** (of individuals or family, ref. to land or buildings); **dwelling, residence** Hdt. Th. Ar. Pl. +; (of gods, ref. to temples) Arist.; (of that which is good) Pl.

2 settlement, territory (of a people and their ruler) Th. +; (of animals) Pl. X.; **dwelling** (of Zeus, ref. to the aither) Ar.(quot. E.)
3 (gener.) place to inhabit or occupy, **habitable place, dwelling** A. +; (for ants) Hdt.; (for a dead person) S. X.; (for the soul, Love) Pl.
4 place to stay (for refugees or visitors), **house, lodging** Th. Plu.; **quarters, stronghold** (for troops) X.
5 act of moving in to live (on a plot of land), **occupation** Th.
6 right of residence (in a city, for foreigners, metics or slaves), **residence** Pl. X. Arist.
7 inhabited or **habitable land** (in the world) Plb.; **region** (distinguished by climate or sim.) Plb. Plu.

οἰκητήρ ῆρος *m.* **inhabitant** Lyr.adesp. A. S.

οἰκητήριον ου *n.* [οἰκητής] **place to live in, residence** E. Plu.; (for a king, ref. to a power-base) Plb.

οἰκητής οῦ *m.* [οἰκέω] **inhabitant** S. Pl.

οἰκητός ή όν *adj.* (of a place) **inhabited** S. || NEUT.IMPERS. (w. ἐστί) it is possible to live (in a place) Thphr.

οἰκήτωρ ορος *m.* **settler, colonist** Hdt. Th. +; **inhabitant, dweller** Hdt. Trag. Th. Tim. +

οἰκία ων *n.pl.* [οἶκος] **1 dwelling** or **dwellings, house** or **houses** (of gods or humans) Hom. Hes. Hippon. Hdt. Call. AR.; (sg.) Call.
2 dwellings (of octopuses and seals) hHom.; (of bees, wasps, an eagle, ref. to their nests) Il.

οἰκία ᾱς, Ion. **οἰκίη** ης *f.* **1 dwelling, residence, house** Archil. Semon. Hdt. Th. +
2 domestic establishment, household, home Hdt. Th. +
3 family (fr. which one is descended) Hdt. Th. +

οἰκιακός ή όν *adj.* of or belonging to a residence || MASC.PL.SB. members of a household NT. || NEUT.PL.SB. domestic matters Plu.

οἰκίδιον ου *n.* [dimin. οἶκος] **small house** or **building, humble dwelling** Ar. Att.orats. Plu.; (derog.) Men.

οἰκίζω *vb.* | fut. οἰκιῶ | aor. ᾤκισα, Ion. οἴκισα, dial. ᾤκισσα || MID.: fut. οἰκιοῦμαι | aor. ᾠκισάμην | pf. ᾤκισμαι || PASS.: fut. οἰκισθήσομαι | aor. ᾠκίσθην | Ion.3sg.pf. οἴκισται |
1 found as a new settlement, found, establish —a city, colony Hdt. E.*fr.* Th. Ar. + || PASS. (of a city or colony) be founded Hdt. Th. +
2 resettle with one's own people, refound, repopulate —a captured or abandoned city Th. D. Plu. || PASS. (of a city) be refounded or repopulated D. Plu.
3 make a new home or settlement in, settle, colonise — a place, a land Hdt. Antipho Th. Ar. +
4 establish (a person or a people) in a new settlement or home; **settle** —an individual, a population Pi. +; (fig., of fate) —a person (W.PREDIC.ADJ. in low estate) E. || MID. **take up residence, settle** (in a place) Pl. Call. || PF.MID. be settled, reside E. || PASS. be settled as a colonist (by a state) X.; (of the soul) be settled (in a place, by a god) Pl.
5 || MID. **establish for oneself** —a stronghold (in a place) E.

οἰκίη Ion.*f.*: see οἰκία

οἰκίον *n.sg.*: see οἰκία

οἴκισις εως *f.* [οἰκίζω] **founding** (of a colony) Th.

οἰκίσκη ης *f.* [dimin. οἶκος] **small house** or **workshop** D.

οἰκίσκος ου *m.* **small room, chamber** D. Plu.

οἰκισμός οῦ *m.* [οἰκίζω] **foundation** (of a city) Sol. Plu.

οἰκιστήρ ῆρος *m.* **founder** (of a homeland or colony) Pi. Hdt.(oracle) Call.

οἰκιστής οῦ *m.* **founder** (of a homeland, state or colony) Hdt. Th. Isoc. Pl. Arist. Men. +; (fr. the perspective of the colony, ref. to a citizen of the motherland) Th. Isoc. Plu.

οἰκο-γενής ές *adj.* [οἶκος; γένος, γίγνομαι] (of a slave) **born in the household** Pl.; (of quails) **home-bred** Ar. || MASC.SB. home-born slave Plb.

οἰκο-δεσπότης ου *m.* **master of a house** or **estate** NT.

οἰκοδομέω contr.*vb.* [οἰκοδόμος] | aor. ᾠκοδόμησα, Ion. οἰκοδόμησα | **1 build** —a house, wall or other large structure Hdt. Th. Ar. Att.orats. + —a city Plb.; (intr.) **build a house** Pl. X. D. + || PASS. (of houses, walls, or sim.) be built Hdt. Th. +
2 || MID. **build for oneself** or **have built** —a house or other large structure Hdt. Th. And. Pl. +; (intr.) **build a house for oneself** X.
3 (fig.) **build up** —an art (W.DAT. w. great words and deeds) Ar.
4 build (sthg.) on a foundation; (fig.) **build** —friendly acts (w. ἐπί + ACC. onto existing ties of friendship) X. —one's successes (w. ἐπί + DAT. on foundations laid by others) Hyp.

οἰκοδομή ῆς *f.* || PL. (concr.) buildings NT. Plu.

οἰκοδόμημα ατος *n.* that which is built, **building, edifice, structure** Hdt. Th. Att.orats. +

οἰκοδόμησις εως *f.* **1 building, construction** (as a process) Th. Pl. Arist.; (pl., on more than one site) Pl.
2 || PL. (concr.) buildings Pl.

οἰκοδομητός ή όν *adj.* (of a potential structure) **buildable** Arist.

οἰκοδομία ᾱς *f.* **1 building, construction** (as a process) Th. Att.orats. Pl. +; (pl., on more than one site) Plb.
2 || PL. (concr.) buildings Th. Pl.

οἰκοδομικός ή όν *adj.* [οἰκοδόμος] of or relating to building; (of the art) **of building** Pl. || MASC.SB. man skilled in building Pl. || FEM.SB. building art or technique Pl. Arist. || NEUT.SB. building (as a process) Pl.(sts.pl.) Arist.

οἰκο-δόμος ου *m.* [δέμω] **builder** (of a house or other structure) Hdt. Pl. X. Arist. +

οἴκοθεν, οἴκοθι, οἴκοι, οἴκόνδε *advs.*: see under οἶκος

οἰκό-θετος ον *adj.* [θετός] (of a resource) **stored up at home** Pi.*fr.*

οἰκονομέω contr.*vb.* [οἰκονόμος] | pf. ᾠκονόμηκα || pf.pass.ptcpl. ᾠκονομημένος | **1** (of a man) **manage** —one's house or household Pl. X. —an estate (for another) X.; (intr.) **be a manager** or **steward** (of one's own or a landowner's estate) X. NT.
2 (of a woman, in the role of servant) be an attendant for, **attend to** —a house S.; (intr., of a wife) **manage a household** Arist.
3 (gener.) **manage** —one's life or affairs Isoc. X. || MID. (intr.) **manage, cope** —W.DAT. in matters of the greatest importance Men.(dub.)
4 (of a god) **control, order** —matters X.; (of a poet) —aspects of his art Arist.
5 manage public or military affairs; **arrange** —matters Plb.; **be a manager of finance** (for a state) Plu.; (fig., of a certain kind of friendship) **dispense** —few benefits Pl. || PASS. (of a constitution, military or financial matters) be managed or governed Arist. Plb. Plu. || NEUT.PL.PF.PASS.PTCPL.SB. arrangements made Plb. Plu.

οἰκονομία ᾱς *f.* **1 headship of a household** Pl. Arist.; **household** or **estate management** Pl. X. Arist. NT. Plu.; management of household affairs (by a woman), **housekeeping** Arist.
2 financial or **economic management** (of a home or state, an army or a war) Pl. X. Arist. Plb. Plu. || PL. business (relating to buying and selling) Plb. Plu.
3 management or conduct of public affairs (political, military or naval; sts.pl.), **administration, organisation,**

οἰκονομικός

operation Din. Plb. Plu.; **administrative office** Plu. ‖ PL. (collectv.) body of administrative officers Plb.
4 ordering (by nature, of the way things are), **ordinance, direction** Plb.
5 ordering of a layout or theme; **arrangement** (of a military camp, battle-line) Plb.; (of signs of the Zodiac) Plb.; (of an account of historical events) Plb.

οἰκονομικός ή όν *adj.* **1** (of a man) practised in household, administrative or financial management, **good at management** Pl. X. Arist.; (specif.) **careful with money, astute in business** X. ‖ MASC.SB. manager or businessman Pl. X. Arist.; good household manager X.; (as the title of a work) X.
2 (of the nature, function or role) **of a householder** or **manager** X. Arist.; (of the public office) **of an administrative** or **financial manager** X. Arist. ‖ FEM.SB. practice of household, administrative or economic management Pl. X. Arist. Plu. ‖ NEUT.PL.SB. administrative affairs Pl. X.
3 (of man as a being, of one of the kinds of justice) relating to governing a family, **domestic** Arist.

οἰκο-νόμος ου *m.f.* [νέμω] **1** (*m.*) one who manages a house or estate, **householder** or **estate manager** (ref. to the owner, or someone who works for him, esp. in respect of finances) Pl. X. Arist. NT.; (ref. to a kind of ruler, seen as in an equivalent position) Arist.
2 manager, steward (of a public treasury) Plu.
3 one acting in the manner of a manager, **dispenser** (of enjoyment, to listeners) Arist.(quot.)
4 (fig., ref. to pottery) **housekeeper** Critias
5 (*f.*) housekeeper (ref. to a wife) Lys.; (fig., ref. to Wrath, which presides over the house of Atreus) A.

οἰκό-πεδον ου *n.* [πέδον] plot of land for a building (or on which a building stands), **site** Th. Pl. X. Aeschin. Arist. Plu.; (gener.) location (of a deserted city) Plb.

οἰκο-ποιός όν *adj.* [ποιέω] (of a means of sustenance) **making a building habitable** S.

οἶκος ου *m.* **1 house, home** (as a dwelling, sts. incl. the surrounding land) Hom. + ‖ COLLECTV.PL. house, palace or estate Od. Pi. Hdt. Trag.
2 part of a house, **room, chamber, quarters** (for specific persons) Od. Hes. S. Philox.Leuc. Plu.
3 house and its occupants (sts. incl. servants), **house, household** Hom. +
4 house, family, dynasty (ref. to successive generations) Pi. +
5 house as an asset; **house, living, estate** Hom. +; **estate** (as a legal term) Att.orats. +
6 place of one's home or upbringing (freq. w.connots. of attachment and emotion), **home** Od. +
7 temporary place to live (esp. on a military campaign), **lodging, quarters** Il. S. E.; (for Spartan boys) Plu.
8 building or structure (for a specific purpose); **building, room** (used as a mill) Od.; (for storing grain, ship's tackle) Hes.; (for exercising, dining) X. Plu.
9 house, home (where a divinity dwells, in the natural world) Il. hHom. A. E. Pl. +; **temple** (built for a divinity) Pi. Hdt. E. Ar.; (for God) NT.; (gener.) abode (W.GEN. of the winds, i.e. the sky) Lyr.adesp.

—**οἴκαδε**, dial. **οἴκαδις** (Ar.) *adv.* to one's house or homeland, **homeward, home** Hom. +

—**οἴκοθεν** (also **οἴκοθε** Call.) *adv.* **1** (ref. to movt. or direction) from one's house or homeland, **from home** Il. Pi. S. E. Th. +; (quasi-adj., of persons) **from home** X.
2 (ref. to location) in one's house or homeland, **at home** Pi. S. E. +

3 (quasi-adj., of laws, customs, friends, or sim.) of one's homeland, **at home** A. E. Pl. +; (of a city) **one's own, native** Pi.*fr.*; (of circumstances, calamities) of one's house, **domestic** E.
4 (ref. to source) from one's own home resources, **from one's store** Il.
5 (fig.) from one's own mental or physical resources, **from within oneself** Pi. E. Lys. Ar. +
6 in one's own person, **in oneself** (opp. in relation to others) E.; (quasi-adj., of pleasures) **one's own, personal** E.
7 (ref. to time) **from one's early years** Arist. Plu.
8 from the start, from the outset Is. Aeschin.

—**οἴκοθι** *adv.* at one's house or in one's homeland, **at home** Hom.

—**οἴκοι** *adv.* in one's house or homeland, **at home** Hom. +

—**οἴκόνδε** *adv.* to one's house or homeland, **homeward, home** Od. Hes. AR.; **to one's own room** Od.

οἰκό-σιτος ον *adj.* [σῖτος] **1** (of a hired worker) **supplying one's own food** Thphr.
2 (of soldiers) **maintained at the expense of one's king** (although fighting for an ally) Plu.
3 (of a lyre-player's audience) perh. **paying for oneself** (opp. paid by him to attend) Men.

οἰκο-τριβής ές *adj.* [τρίβω] (of expense) **ruinous for a house** Critias

οἰκό-τριψ τριβος *m.* slave born and bred in the house, **family slave** Men. Plu.; (ref. to a free person, as a term of abuse) **menial wretch** Ar. D.

οἰκότως *Ion.pf.ptcpl.adv.*: see εἰκότως

οἰκουμένη *fem.pass.ptcpl.sb.*: see under οἰκέω

οἰκουρέω *contr.vb.* [οἰκουρός] **1** (of a woman, men behaving like women) stay at home (performing domestic tasks), **look after the house** S. D.
2 (wkr.sens., of a man in mourning or wanting privacy) **stay indoors** Plu.; (of female dogs, while breeding) Pl.
3 (of a man) **stay at home** (opp. be away on military service) Plu. —W.ACC. in a city A.; (fig., of a bridegroom's penis) Ar.; (pejor., of troops conducting a fruitless siege) **sit at home** Plu.
4 (of initiates) **stay indoors** (in a temple) Arist.; (of a snake) **be resident** (in a temple) S.

οἰκούρημα ατος *n.* **1** act of stewardship, **housekeeping** (by a wife, in her husband's absence) E.
2 (pejor.) **sitting at home** (by men, instead of going to war) E.
3 staying and watching, **vigil** (over a sick person) S.

οἰκουρία ᾱς *f.* **1 housekeeping** (as the role of a wife) Plu.
2 waiting and watching at home (by a wife, when her husband is away) E. Plu.
3 (pejor.) **stay-at-home habits** (of a man) Plu.

οἰκούρια ων *n.pl.* **reward for looking after the house** (during a husband's absence) S.

οἰκουρός οῦ *m.f.* [οὖρος²] **1** one who has charge of the house (while the master is away), **housekeeper** (ref. to a wife or other woman) E. D.; (pejor., ref. to an old man left by his son to look after his family) E.; (fig., app.ref. to a κερκίς *pin-beater*) Lyr.adesp.
2 (pejor., ref. to a womanish man) **stay-at-home** A.; (ref. to a man who avoids military service) Din.; (ref. to a dog, alluding to a man) Ar. ‖ FEM.ADJ. (of a way of life) stay-at-home Plu.
3 (ref. to a snake) **resident** or **guardian** (of a temple) Ar.

οἰκοφθορέω *contr.vb.* [οἰκοφθόρος] **squander one's resources** Pl. ‖ PASS. have one's livelihood ruined Hdt.

οἰκοφθορίᾱ ᾱς *f.* **destruction of livelihood** Pl.

οἰκο-φθόρος ον *adj.* [φθείρω] **destructive of livelihood or property;** (of a man, an attribute in a man) **ruinous** Pl. Plu.

οἰκο-φύλαξ ακος *m.* (ref. to Zeus) **guardian of homes** (W.GEN. of pious men) A.

οἰκτείρω *vb.*: see οἰκτίρω

οἰκτίζω *vb.* [οἶκτος] | fut. οἰκτιῶ | aor. ᾤκτισα | 1 **express or feel pity for**, **pity** —*a person* (*who has suffered misfortune*) Trag. Plu. —*a person's suffering* S. —*a wrongdoer* (*when moved by his plea*) X.; **pity, cry for** —*oneself* A.; (intr.) **feel or express pity** A. S. Call. || MID. **take pity on** —*suppliants* E.; (of plague survivors) —*persons suffering or dying* (*fr. the plague*) Th.; (intr.) **feel pity** (for sufferers) A.
2 **lament** —*dead persons* E.(also mid.) || MID. **wail** —W.COGN.ACC. **in lamentation** A. E.
3 || MID. feel or express pity for oneself (in an unjustified or unmanly way), **pity oneself, cry** Din. Plb.; **bewail** —*one's approaching death* E.

οἰκτιρμός οῦ *m.* [οἰκτίρω] **pity, compassion** Pi.

οἰκτίρμων ονος *masc.adj.* **compassionate** NT.; (wkr.sens.) **sympathetic, considerate** Theoc.

οἰκτίρω (also written **οἰκτείρω**) *vb.* [οἰκτρός] | fut. οἰκτῐρῶ | aor. ᾤκτῑρα (ᾤκτειρα), Ion. οἴκτῑρα | 1 **be filled with pity and compassion for**, **pity** —*persons* (*who have suffered misfortune*), *their fate, suffering or death* Il. hHom. Anacr. Simon. B. Trag. + || PASS. **be pitied** Hdt. S. X.
2 (of gods, esp. Zeus) **have compassion for, take pity on** —*persons, their suffering or supplication* Trag. Ar. Pl. + —*a donkey* (*bearing burdens*) Stesich.
3 (of military or political authorities) **show mercy to** or **be sympathetic with** —*people defeated or in difficulties* X. Plu.
4 **feel sorry for** —*a person* Il. Ar. Pl. +; **forgive** —*a weakness* Plu.
5 **pity** (w. some condemnatory moral judgement) —*persons, their bad qualities* X. Plu.
6 **feel regret, be sorry** —W.INF. at doing sthg. S.; (mid.) —W.PTCPL. Plu.

οἰκτίσματα των *n.pl.* [οἰκτίζω] **laments** (of suppliants) E.

οἰκτισμός οῦ *m.* **lamentation** (in agony, fr. torture) A.; (when complaining) X.

οἴκτιστος η ον *superl.adj.* [reltd. οἶκτος] (of a violent or painful death) **most pitiful, most wretched** Od. AR.; (of the sight of such a death) Hom.; (of songs of lament) AR.; (of a woman who hanged herself) Call.
—**οἴκτιστα** *neut.pl.adv.* **most pitifully** Od.

οἶκτος ου *m.* 1 **feeling or expression of pity; compassion, pity** (esp. for those about to die, those bereaved or without family, captives or suppliants) Od. Simon. Hdt. S. E. Th. +; (for victims of political injustice) Th. Isoc. Plu.
2 **compassion, pity** (of divine beings, for mortals) A. E. Th.; (of Artemis, for animals) A.
3 pity which is too lenient or sentimental; **pity, emotion** S. E. Th. Pl. Plu.; (evoked by music) Pl.
4 pity for oneself or a demand for pity which is unjustified and unmanly; **self-pity, pleading, grovelling** A. E. Th. Att.orats. +
5 (freq.pl.) vocal expression of pity or sorrow, **lament** Trag. Pl.

οἰκτρό-γοος ον *adj.* [οἰκτρός, γόος] (of speeches) **of piteous lamentation** Pl.

οἰκτρός ά όν *adj.* [οἶκτος] 1 **full of distress which arouses pity;** (of persons) **pitiful, piteous** (in circumstances of great misfortune) Il. Trag. Tim. Pl. +; (of things relating to such circumstances) **miserable, heart-rending** Od. Lyr. Hdt. Trag. Att.orats. +; (of a cry, words, pleading, tears) Od. S. E. Plu.; (of the nightingale, w. her song) S.; (of stories) Pl.
|| NEUT.IMPERS. (w. ἐστί understd.) **it is a pitiful thing** —W.INF. **to do or suffer sthg.** A. Isoc. Aeschin.
2 involving pity for oneself; (of the female sex) **prone to lamenting** E.; (of an experience) **miserable, humiliating** X.; (wkr.sens., of persons or their experience, through failing in an argument) **pitiable** Pl. X.
3 arousing pity in a deliberate or shallow way; (of persons) **looking pitiful** Plu.; (of things said to win over people) **full of sentiment** X.
—**οἰκτρόν** *neut.adv.* **with a pitiful cry** E. Bion; (pl.) Od.
—**οἰκτρῶς**, Boeot. **ὐκτρῶς** *adv.* | superl. οἰκτρότατα | **pitifully, piteously** Trag. Att.orats. Corinn. Plu.; **miserably, in a grovelling** or **humiliating manner** And. Plu.

οἰκτροχοέω *contr.vb.* [χέω] **pour out pitifully** —*a plea* Ar.

οἰκώς (Ion.pf.ptcpl.): see ἔοικα

οἰκωφελίᾱ ᾱς, Ion. **οἰκωφελίη** ης *f.* [οἶκος, ὀφέλλω²] **betterment** or **enrichment of a family** Od. Theoc.

οἶμα ατος *n.* **swoop, pounce** (of an eagle, a lion) Il.

οἶμαι *mid.vb.*: see οἴομαι

οἰμάω *contr.vb.* [reltd. οἶμα] | ep.aor. οἴμησα | (of a bird of prey) **swoop down** Il.; (of a warrior, likened to an eagle) **swoop, charge** Hom.; (of fish) **leap up** Hdt.(oracle)

οἴμη ης *f.* [perh.reltd. οἶμος] narrative song, **song, ballad** Od. Call. AR.

οἴμοι *interj.* [οἴ; μοι, see ἐγώ] (as exclam. of extreme dismay or alarm) **woe is me, alas, oh!** Emp. Trag. Ar. D. Men. Theoc. Plu.; (w. elision) οἴμ' ὡς *oh how* ... ! S. Ar.

οἶμος ου *m.* (sts. *f.*) [perh.reltd. οἴμη] 1 way available for going (fr. place to place), **path, track** Trag. AR.
2 course being taken (on land, sea or through the air), **course, track, path** A. Pi. E. Call. AR.
3 **path** (to Hades) Pl.(quot. A.) AR.; (towards virtue) Hes.
4 continuing theme (in music or speech), **path, thread** or **strain** hHom. Pi. Pl. Call.
5 continuous pattern (on a cuirass), **band** Il.

οἰμωγή ῆς, dial. **οἰμωγά** ᾶς, Aeol. **οἰμώγᾱ** ᾱς *f.* [οἰμώζω] (sg. and pl.) crying out in distress, **crying, wailing, lamentation** Hom. Alc. Hdt. Trag. Th. Ar. +

οἰμώγματα των *n.pl.* **cries, wails** or **laments** A. E.

οἰμωγμός οῦ *m.* **crying** (fr. the pain of love) S.fr.

οἰμώζω *vb.* [οἴμοι] | fut. οἰμώξομαι | aor. ᾤμωξα | 1 utter a cry of distress (in dismay, shock or grief), **cry out** Hom. Hdt. Trag.; (in agony fr. a wound) Hom.
2 (tr.) express sorrow for, **cry for, lament** —*persons, their actions or fate, the dead* Tyrt. Trag. || PASS. (of a person) be lamented Thgn.
3 (colloq., freq. as an imprecation) have reason to cry, **be sorry** Ar. X. D. Men. Plu.

οἷν (gen.dat.du.relatv.pron.): see ὅς¹

οἴνᾱ *dial.f.*: see οἴνη

οἰν-άνθη ης, dial. **οἰνάνθᾱ** ᾱς *f.* [οἴνη, ἄνθος] **vine-cluster** (of flowers or ripening fruit) Pi. S.fr. E. Ar. Call.

οἰνανθίς ίδος *f.* **young vine-cluster** Ibyc.

οἰνάρεος ᾱ ον *adj.* [οἴναρον] (of shoots) **of vine leaves** Ibyc.
|| NEUT.PL.SB. **vine leaves** Theoc.

οἰναρίζω *vb.* **strip vine leaves** (enabling the fruit to ripen) Ar.

οἰνάριον ου *n.* [dimin. οἶνος] **wine** (perh. w.connot. of poor quality) D. Thphr.; **drink of wine** Plu.

οἴναρον ου *n.* [οἴνη] **vine leaf** X.

οἰνάς άδος *f.* **vine** Ion

οἴνη ης, dial. **οἴνᾱ** ᾱς *f.* [reltd. οἶνος] **vine** Hes. E.

οἰνηρός ᾱ (Ion. ή) όν adj. [οἶνος] **1** relating to wine; (of libations) **of wine** E.; (of an island) **wine-producing** Call. **2** (of vessels) holding wine, **for wine** Pi. Hdt. E. **3** (of standard measures) **of wine** Arist.

οἰν-ήρυσις εως f. [ἀρύω] cup for drawing off wine (fr. a storage jar), **dipping vessel, ladle** Ar.

οἰνίζομαι mid.vb. **supply oneself with wine** Il. —W.COGN.ACC. w. wine Il.

οἰνοβαρέω contr.vb. [οἰνοβαρής] | ep.ptcpl. οἰνοβαρείων | be heavy with wine, **be drunk** or **befuddled** Od. Thgn.

οἰνο-βαρής ές adj. [βαρύς] heavy with wine; (as an insult) **drunk, befuddled** Il.

οἰνο-δόκος ον adj. [δέχομαι] (of a goblet) holding wine, **for wine** Pi.

οἰνο-δότᾱς ᾱ dial.m. [δίδωμι] (epith. of Dionysus) **bestower of wine** E.

οἰνό-μελι ιτος n. [μέλι] drink made from wine and honey, **oenomel** Plb.

οἰνόομαι pass.contr.vb. | aor.ptcpl. οἰνωθείς | pf.ptcpl. ᾠνωμένος, Ion. οἰνωμένος | **1** get drunk on wine, **become intoxicated** Od.
2 ‖ STATV.PF. be intoxicated Hdt. S. Arist.; (fig.) —W.DAT. w. the wine bowl and music E.
3 ‖ STATV.PF. (of a person's eyes) be clouded by wine A.
—**οἰνόω** act.contr.vb. **intoxicate** —the body (W.DAT. w. immoderate drinking) Critias

οἰνό-πεδος ον adj. [πέδον] (of a plot of land) with soil fit for producing wine, **wine-bearing** Od. hHom. ‖ NEUT.SB. **vineyard** Il. Thgn. Theoc.

οἰν-οπίπης ου m.f. [ὀπιπεύω] (ref. to a woman) **ogler of wine** Ar.

οἰνο-πλάνητος ον adj. [πλανητός] (of drinking-contests) **where wine goes around** E.

οἰνο-πληθής ές adj. [πλῆθος] (of an island) **with wine in abundance** Od.

οἰνο-ποιός όν adj. [ποιέω] (of the vine) **wine-producing** E.fr.

οἰνο-ποτάζω vb. [ποτόν] **drink wine** Od. Anacr.

οἰνοποτέω contr.vb. **be a wine-drinker** Call.(v.l. ζωροποτέω)

οἰνο-ποτήρ ῆρος m. [πίνω] **wine-drinker** Od.

οἰνο-πότης ου m. (sts.pejor.) **wine-drinker** Anacr. Call. Plb. NT.
—**οἰνοπότις** ιδος fem.adj. (of a woman) **wine-drinking** Anacr.

οἰνοπωλέω contr.vb. **offer wine for sale** Thphr.

οἶνος ου m. **1 wine** (made fr. grapes) Hom. +; (as a libation to the gods or in honour of the dead) Hom. +; (at an occasion of hospitality or celebration, usu. mixed w. water) Hom. +; (as restorative or relieving anxiety) Hom. +; (assoc.w. Dionysus, w. love) hHom. Anacr. Thgn. E. Pl.; (bringing excessive intoxication) Hom. +; (used medicinally) Arist. + ‖ PL. **varieties of wine** X. Arist.
2 (provbl., as a divulger of the truth) Lyr. Pl. Theoc. +
3 (ref. to the grape juice, in the ripening fruit or the wine-press) Od. Lyr. A. Ar. NT.
4 (prep.phrs.) ἐν οἴνῳ, ἐν τοῖς οἴνοις **in a drinking session** Th. Ar. Pl. +
5 wine (made fr. lotus, barley) Hdt. Plb.; (fr. palm, also used as a preservative) Hdt.

οἰνοῦττα ης Att.f. a kind of bread or cake made with wine, **wine cake** Ar.

οἰνοφλυγίᾱ ᾱς f. [οἰνόφλυξ] **drunkenness** X. Arist. Plb. Plu.

οἰνό-φλυξ υγος m. [φλύω] app., one who makes no sense because of wine, **drunkard** X. Arist.

οἰνο-φόρος ον adj. [φέρω] (of a cup) **holding wine** Critias; (of a piece of land) **wine-producing** Mosch.

οἰνοχοέω contr.vb. —also **οἰνοχοεύω** ep.vb. [οἰνοχόος] | ep.3sg.impf. οἰνοχόει, ἐῳνοχόει | fut. οἰνοχοήσω | AOR.: inf. οἰνοχοῆσαι, Aeol.3sg. ᾠνοχόαισε, imperatv. οἰνοχόαισον |
1 be the pourer of wine (drawn fr. the krater, into drinking-cups); **pour out wine, be a cup-bearer** (sts. W.DAT. for someone) Hom. Eleg.adesp. Scol. X. Plb. ‖ IMPERS. wine is poured Od.; (imperatv.) let wine be poured Thgn.
2 (tr.) **pour out, pour** —wine Od. Anacr.; (fig.) —songs Dionys.Eleg.; (of a leader) —undiluted freedom (W.DAT. for citizens) Plu.
3 (of Hebe, Hephaistos, Hermes) **pour out, pour** —nectar (for the gods) Il. Sapph.; (of Aphrodite, at human festivities) —nectar (fig.ref. to delights) Sapph.; (of Ganymede) **be cup-bearer** (for Zeus) Il.

οἰνοχόη ης f. utensil for drawing wine (fr. the krater, and for pouring it into drinking-cups), **jug, cup, ladle** Hes. E. Th.

οἰνοχόημα ατος n. **distribution of wine** (at a festival) Plu.

οἰνο-χόος ου m. [χέω] **wine-pourer, cup-bearer** (at feasts, freq. a position of honour) Hom. Pl. X. Thphr. Call. AR.; (appos.w. θέραψ attendant) Ion; (ref. to Ganymede, for Zeus) Theoc.; (ref. to Silenos and Odysseus, for the Cyclops) E.Cyc.; (ref. to an officer of a king's household, in Thrace, Persia or Hellenistic kingdoms) Hdt. X. Plb.; (fig., ref. to a leader, envisaged as pouring undiluted freedom for citizens) Pl.

οἰνό-χυτος ον adj. [χυτός] (of a drink) consisting of poured wine, **of wine** S.

οἶν-οψ οπος masc.adj. [reltd. ὤψ] app., having the appearance of wine; (of the sea) **wine-coloured, wine-dark** Hom. Hes. hHom. Alc.; (of oxen, ref. to their coats) Hom.

οἰνόω contr.vb.: see under οἰνόομαι

οἰνών ῶνος m. storage place for wine, **wine-cellar** X.

οἰν-ωπός όν adj. [ὤψ] having the appearance of wine; (of a serpent) **wine-coloured, wine-dark** E.; (of a man, the cheek of a man or bull) E. Theoc.; (of ivy, a bunch of grapes, the froth on a libation) S. E.; (of the colour of spring water) Plu.

οἰν-ώψ ῶπος m. **wine-faced one** (epith. of Bacchus, ref. to his complexion) S.

οἶξας (aor.ptcpl.): see οἴγω

οἷο (ep.masc.gen.possessv.pron.adj.): see ὅς²

οἰο-βουκόλος ου m. [οἶος¹] **herdsman of a single creature** (epith. of Argus, as Io's guardian) A.

οἰο-βώτᾱς ᾱ dial.m. [βόσκω] (fig., ref. to Ajax) **solitary herdsman** (W.GEN. of his thoughts) S.

οἰό-ζωνος ον adj. [ζώνη] alone and girt for travelling, **travelling alone** S.

οἰόθεν, οἰόθι advs.: see under οἶος¹

οἰό-κερως ων, gen. ω adj. [οἶος¹, κέρας] (of a bull) **with a single horn** Call.(cj.)

οἴομαι, also contr. **οἶμαι**, ep. **ὀΐομαι** mid.vb. | impf. ᾠόμην, contr. ᾤμην, ep.3sg. ὠΐετο, also οἴετο (hHom.), Ion. οἴετο | fut. οἰήσομαι ‖ AOR.PASS. (w.mid.sens.): ᾠήθην, ep. ὠΐσθην, ep.ptcpl. ὀϊσθείς, inf. οἰηθῆναι ‖ EP.AOR.MID.: ὠϊσάμην (AR.), 3sg. ὀΐσατο (Od.), also ὠΐσατο (Mosch.), ὀΐσσατο (AR.), ptcpl. ὀϊσάμενος (Od.), also ὀϊσσάμενος (AR.) ‖ —also ep.act.pres. (only 1sg.) ὀΐω, ὀΐω, οἴω, Lacon. οἰῶ ‖ neut.impers.vbl.adj. οἰητέον |
1 think in a concentrated or prolonged way (esp. about a present or imminent misfortune), **think only of, be fixed on** —death Il. —lamentation Od.; **think all the time about** —a person (who is absent) Od.

2 think in a way which is suspicious or fearful; **suspect, fear, sense** —*sthg., some trick* Od. —W.ACC. + PRES. or FUT.INF. *that sthg. is or will be the case* Od. Hdt. +; **be suspicious, have a fear** Hom. ‖ IMPERS. there is a fear —W.DAT. *in someone* (i.e. felt by him) Od.
3 think in a way which calculates probabilities or comes to a conclusion; **calculate, suppose, conclude, be sure** Hom. + —W.ACC. + PRES. or FUT.INF. *that sthg. is or will be the case* Hom. Trag. Th. Ar. + —W.ACC. + AOR.INF. *that someone did sthg.* Hom. S. + —W. ὡς + CL. *how sthg. might be or might have happened* Od.; **have an opinion** (opp. know) Pl. Arist.
4 (as a summation of one's own rhetorical point, or as a reply to another) οἶμαι *I think so, probably* E. Ar. Pl. +; (parenth., in modifying one's assertion) *I think, probably* Hom. +; (in modifying an assertion which is too difficult or awful to believe) πῶς οἴει *can you imagine?* Ar. Att.orats. Pl. + | cf. πῶς 11, δοκέω 2

οἶον, οἷον neut.adv. and conj.: see under οἷος, ὅς¹
οἷον-εί adv. [εἰ] (parenth.) as if (sthg. were the case), **as it were, so to speak** Men. Plb.
οἷόνπερ relatv.adv. and conj.: see under οἷόσπερ
οἷονπερεί adv. [οἰονεί, περ¹] (parenth.) **as it were, so to speak** Pl.
οἴομαι pass.contr.vb. [οἷος¹] | ep.aor. οἰώθην | (of a person) **be left on one's own** Il.; (of a battle) **be left alone** (for the human participants, without intervention fr. the gods) Il.
οἰο-πέδιλος ον adj. [πέδιλον] **with only one sandal** AR.
οἰοπολέω contr.vb. [οἰοπόλος] **wander alone** E.Cyc.
οἰο-πόλος ον adj. [πέλω] **1** (of places) **remote, lonely, isolated** Hom.
2 (of Hermes, Triton, nymphs) alone or haunting lonely places, **solitary, alone** hHom. Pi. AR.
—**οἰοπολάς** άδος f. **goddess of the wilds** (title of Artemis) Pi.fr.
οἰός (gen.sg.), **ὄιος** (Ion.gen.sg.): see οἶς
οἷος (Aeol. **οἶος**) ᾱ (Ion. η) ον relatv.adj. [reltd. ὅς¹] **1** (of a person, in terms of character or behaviour) of which sort or nature, **such as, as, like** Hom. + • πρὸς ἄνδρας τολμηρούς, οἵους καὶ Ἀθηναίους *to daring men such as the Athenians* Th.
2 (of a thing) of which sort, quality or condition, **such as, as, like** Hom. + • οὐ γὰρ ἐμὴ ἲς ἔσθ' οἵη πάρος ἔσκεν ἐνὶ γναμπτοῖσι μέλεσσιν *my strength is not what it used to be in my supple limbs* Il. • (w.superlatv.) ὁρῶντες τὰ πράγματα οὐχ οἷα βέλτιστα ἐν τῇ πόλει ὄντα *seeing that affairs in the city are not the same as the very best possible* Lys.
3 (of a person or thing, in exclam., or in indir.exclam. or q.; eulogistic or derog.) **how great, how strong, how bad, how terrible** (or sim.) Hom. + • θαύμαζ' Ἀχιλῆα ὅσσος ἔην οἷός τε *he marvelled at Achilles, how tall he was and how noble* Il. • οἷον τὸ πῦρ *how dreadful the fire* A.
4 (of a person or thing) of such a sort as, **proper, fit, suitable** (W.INF. to do sthg.) Hom. + • οὐ γὰρ ἦν ὥρα οἷα τὸ πεδίον ἄρδειν *for it was not the proper time to irrigate the plain* X. • τοιοῦτος οἷος τῶν ἐμῶν (λόγων) μηδενὶ ἄλλῳ πείθεσθαι *not the sort of man to be persuaded by any other of my arguments* Pl.
5 (esp. w.pcl. τε) • περὶ τίνων τῇ πόλει συμβουλεύειν οἷοί τε ἐσόμεθα; *on what matters shall we be qualified to give advice to the city?* Pl. ‖ NEUT.IMPERS.PHR. οἷόν τέ ἐστι (also pl. οἷά) it is possible (freq. W.INF. to do sthg.) Hdt. +
—**οἷον** (also pl. **οἷα**, Aeol. **οἶα**) neut.adv. and conj. **1** (in exclam.) **how** Hom. • οἷον δή νυ θεοὺς βροτοὶ αἰτιόωνται *how indeed then mortals blame the gods* Od. • οἷον ἐερσήεις *how fresh* Il.

2 (in a comparison) **just as, as, like** Hom. + • σιγαλόεντα, οἷόν τε κρομύοιο λοπὸν κάτα ἰσχαλέοιο *shining, as the sheen on the skin of a dried onion* Od. • (parenth.) δεῖ τοὺς τοιούτους λόγους αὐτοῦ λέγεσθαι οἷον ὑεῖς γνησίους εἶναι *such discourses should be spoken of, as it were, as his legitimate children* Pl.
3 (w. numerals) **approximately, about** Th. + • ἀπὸ τοῦ Δηλίου οἷον δέκα σταδίους *from Delium about ten stades* Th.
4 (conj., introducing an explanation or reason) **since, seeing that, as** Hom. + • ὦ γέρον, οὔ νύ τι σοί γε μέλει κακόν, οἷον ἔθ' εὕδεις *old man, no trouble concerns you, since you are still asleep* Il. • (w.ptcpl.) οἷα ἀπροσδοκήτου κακοῦ ἐν εἰρήνῃ γενομένου *as trouble occurred unexpectedly in peacetime* Th.
5 (conj., introducing an illustration of what has been said) **as for instance, as for example** Pl. + • οἷον καὶ Ἡσίοδος περὶ ἁμάξης λέγει *as for example Hesiod says about a wagon* Pl.
6 ‖ NEG.PHR. οὐχ οἷον ... ἀλλὰ ... *not only not ... but ...* Arist. Plu.
—**οἵως** adv. (in exclam.) **how, in what condition ... !** S.
οἷος¹ ᾱ (Ion. η) ον adj. **1** (of a person) alone (without those w. whom one usu. keeps company); **on one's own** (sts. W.GEN. or PREP.PHR. away fr. or without certain other people) Hom. hHom. S. AR.; (of a mountain) Od.
2 alone (in a far-off place, in the darkness or in a difficult predicament); **on one's own, alone, solitary** Hom. Alc. Pi. S. AR.
3 (of a person or thing) alone (w. no one else or no similar thing besides, sts. w.connot. of pre-eminence); **alone, unique, sole** Hom. hHom. Archil. Semon. Pi. Hdt.(oracle) AR.
4 (w. a cardinal number) **only** (one, two, etc.) Hom. AR.
—**οἷον** neut.adv. and conj. **1** amounting to nothing else besides, **only, merely** Hes. AR.
2 (conj.) except for one thing (ref. to a restriction, drawback or exception); **only** AR.; (w. μή + SUBJ. *let sthg. not happen* A.
—**οἰόθεν** adv. **on one's own, alone** AR.; (w. οἷος) Il. AR.
—**οἰόθι** adv. **1 on one's own, alone** AR.
2 with everyone or everything else excluded, **only, exclusively** AR.
οἷος² Aeol.relatv.adj.: see οἷος
οἰοσ-δήποτε οἰαδήποτε οἰονδήποτε relatv.adj. [οἷος, δή ποτε] (of an end) **of whatever kind** (it may be) Arist.
οἷόσ-περ (or **οἷός περ**) relatv.adj. [περ¹] **such as** Hom. +
—**οἷόνπερ** (or **οἷόν περ**) relatv.adv. and conj. **just as** Hdt. +
οἰό-φρων ονος fem.adj. [οἷος¹, φρήν] (fig., of a crag) with solitary thoughts, **lonely** A.
οἰο-χίτων ωνος masc.adj. [χιτών] **with only a tunic, lightly clad** Od.
οἷπερ relatv.adv.: see under ὅσπερ
οἶς οἰός, Ion. **ὄις** ὄιος m.f. | acc. οἶν, Ion. ὄιν, dial. οἴδα (Theoc.) | Ion.dat. ὀΐ (Ar.) ‖ PL.: nom. οἶες, Ion. ὄιες, ep. ὄιες (Call.), perh. (metri grat.) ὄιες (Od.) | acc. οἶς, Ion. ὄϊς, dial. ὄϊς (Theoc.) | gen. οἰῶν, Ion. ὀΐων | ep.dat. ὀΐεσσι, also ὄεσσι, οἴεσι | **sheep** (male or female; sts. w.adj. denoting gender, sts. opp. αἶγες *goats*) Hom. +; (as a sacrificial animal, as providing a certain kind of fleece, wool, meat, milk) Hom. +; (as providing gut to string a bow) Od.; (pl., as a symbol of wealth and prosperity) Hom. +; (provbl., alluding to defencelessness amongst wild animals, esp. wolves) Hom. +
ὀισάμενος (ep.aor.mid.ptcpl.), **ὀίσατο** (3sg.): see οἴομαι
οἶσε, οἰσέτω (2 and 3sg.fut.imperatv.), **οἴσειν** (fut.inf.), **οἰσέμεν, οἰσέμεναι** (ep.fut.infs.), **οἰσεῦμες** (dial.1pl.fut.): see φέρω

οἶσθα, **οἶσθας** (2sg.pf.): see οἶδα
οἰσθείς (ep.aor.pass.ptcpl.): see οἴομαι
οἰσθήσομαι (fut.pass.), **οἴσομαι** (fut.mid.): see φέρω
οἴσπη (v.l. **οἰσύπη**) ης *f.* [app.reltd. οἶς] **wool grease, lanolin** Hdt.
οἰσπώτη ης *f.* **sheep-dung** (caught up in wool) Ar.
οἰσσάμενος (ep.aor.mid.ptcpl.), **οἴσσατο** (3sg.): see οἴομαι
οἰστέος ᾱ ον *vbl.adj.* [φέρω] **1** (of misfortunes) **to be borne** S.
2 (of similes and metaphors) **to be brought in** or **applied** Arist.
ὀιστευτής οῦ *Ion.m.* [ὀιστεύω] **archer** Call.
ὀιστεύω *Ion.vb.* [ὀιστός¹] **shoot an arrow** or **arrows** (sts. W.GEN. at someone) Hom. Call. AR.; (of Eros) AR.
ὀιστο-δέγμων ονος *Ion.masc.adj.* [δέχομαι] (of a repository for missiles, ref. to a quiver) **arrow-containing** A.
ὀιστο-δόκη ης *Ion.f.* **arrow container** (appos.w. φαρέτρη *quiver*) AR.
ὀιστός¹, Ion. **ὀιστός**, οῦ *m.* **arrow** Hom. Hes. Lyr. Hdt. E. Th. +; (fig., of Aphrodite, inspiring desire) E.; (delivering fame or praise, ref. to poetry) Pi.
οἰστός² ή όν *adj.* [φέρω] (of difficulties) **tolerable** Th.
οἰστράω (also **οἰστρέω** Theocr.) *contr.vb.* [οἶστρος] | aor. ᾤστρησα || aor.pass.ptcpl. οἰστρηθείς | **1** (of Io) **be driven in frenzy by a gadfly** —W.ACC. (gener., of persons) **rush in frenzy** —W.PREP.PHR. *through a country* E.; **be frenzied** (w. madness or desire) Pl. Theoc.
2 (of the soul, as though affected by physical pain) **smart, sting** Pl.
3 (tr., of Dionysus) **drive in frenzy** —*women* (W.PREP.PHR. *fr. their homes*) E. || PASS. (of women) be driven in frenzy —W.PREP.PHR. *fr. their looms* (*by Dionysus*) E.; (of Ares) be stung to frenzy S.
οἰστρ-ήλατος ον *adj.* [ἐλαύνω] (of Io's fear) **gadfly-driven** A.
οἴστρημα ατος *n.* [οἰστράω] **sting** (of mental pain) S.
οἰστρο-δίνητος ον *adj.* [οἶστρος, δινέω] (of Io) **driven about by the gadfly** A.
οἰστρο-δόνητος ον *adj.* [δονέω] (of Io) **hounded by the gadfly** A.; (of the sea) **whipped into a frenzy** Ar.
οἰστρο-δόνος ον *adj.* (of Io) **hounded by the gadfly** A.
οἰστρο-μανής ές *adj.* [μαίνομαι] (of the sea) **tumultuously raging** Tim.
οἰστρο-πλήξ ῆγος *masc.fem.adj.* [πλήσσω] (of Io) **stung by the gadfly** A. S.; (of maenads) **smitten with frenzy** E.
οἶστρος ου *m.* **1 gadfly** (an insect which harasses cattle) Od. AR.; (sent by Hera to torment Io) A. E.
2 (fig.) that which stings, torments or maddens; **sting, stabbing pain** (fr. poison, a thunderbolt) S. E.; **maddening sting** (of Erinyes) E.; (of Aphrodite, ref. to sexual desire) Simon.
3 wild passion, mad frenzy (esp.ref. to sexual desire) Hdt. S. E. Pl. Plu.
οἰστρώδης ες *adj.* (of desires) **frenzied** Pl.
οἴσυα ων *n.pl.* [οἰσύα *osier*] app. **wickerwork goods** (in a market) Lycurg.
οἰσύινος η ον *adj.* (of a defensive screen) **wicker** Od.; (of shields) Th. X.
οἰσύπη *f.*: see οἴσπη
οἰσυπηρός ά όν *adj.* (of raw wool) **full of grease** Ar.
οἴσω (fut.), **οἰσῶ** (dial.): see φέρω
Οἴτη ης, dial. **Οἴτα** ᾱς *f.* **Oita** (mt. in Thessaly, site of Herakles' death) Hdt. S.
—Οἰταῖος ᾱ ον *adj.* **belonging to the region of Oita**; (of a valley, the land) **of Oita** S.; (of a person) X.; (of Poias, Philoktetes' father) S. || MASC.PL.SB. **men** or **people of Oita** Hdt. Th. +
οἶτος ου *m.* **unfortunate fate** (oft. W.ADJ. κακός), **fate, doom** Hom. Hippon. S. E. Hellenist.poet.
οἴφω *vb.* **fuck** —*a woman* Plu.
Οἰχαλιᾱ ᾱς, Ion. **Οἰχαλίη** ης *f.* **Oikhalia** (city of Eurytos and his daughter Iole, location uncertain, sacked by Herakles) Il. Hes.*fr.* B. S. E. AR.
—Οἰχαλιεύς έως (ep. ῆος) *m.* **man of Oikhalia, Oikhalian** (ref. to Eurytos) Il. Plu.
—Οἰχαλίηθεν *Ion.adv.* **from Oikhalia** Il.
οἰχνέω *contr.vb.* [reltd. οἴχομαι] | ep.3pl. οἰχνεῦσι | iteratv.impf. οἴχνεσκον | **1** (of gods, persons, birds) **go, make one's way, travel** Hom. Pi.*fr.* S.; **go to, visit** —*persons, places* Pi.
2 (of a person) **go about** (in one's daily life) S.
3 (of a fire) perh. **go** or **have gone** —W.PREP.PHR. *to ashes* (i.e. subside) Call.
οἴχομαι *mid.vb.* | impf. ᾠχόμην, Ion. οἰχόμην | fut. οἰχήσομαι || pf.act. οἴχωκα (A. S., v.l. ᾤχωκα), Ion.ptcpl. οἰχωκώς (Hdt.) | Ion.3sg.plpf. οἰχώκεε | **1 venture out** (on a mission or campaign, to take a message or visit a sacred place), **set out, go, be gone, be away** Hom. +
2 go off (for a relatively short time, to do sthg., to fetch someone or sthg.), **go, go off, be away** Hom. +; (of persons, rumour) **go around** (to various people or places) Hom. +; (of arrows) **rain down** (on an army) Il.
3 go away (fr. a place where one has stayed for a time), **leave, depart, be gone** Hom. +; (of enemies, moving to fight elsewhere, giving up or changing sides) Il. +
4 leave (after a disagreement or when sent away), **depart, go, be gone** Il. +; **go off** (on one's own, suddenly or without proper notice) Hom. +
5 leave (avoiding or abandoning someone or sthg.), **go, get away, vanish, be gone** Hom. +; (of those who take what they want, criminals and fugitives) Hom. +
6 (of the sun, objects, phantoms, vaporous substances or liquids, music or words) **disappear, vanish, be gone** Hom. +; (of a theory, a sight of sthg.) Pl. Arist.; (of life and its blessings, qualities such as trust, courage; less freq. of bad things) Il. +; (of a wind, a current or other force) —W.PTCPL.PHR. *sweeping someone or sthg. away* Hom. Thgn. Hdt. Ar.
7 (of a person) **be lost, disappear** (fr. the face of the earth) Od.; **depart** (to the next world) Il. Mimn.; **be departed** Trag. +; (of persons, a family line, a nation or city, sts. hyperbol.) **perish, be done for** Trag. +; (colloq.) **go** —W.PREP.PHR. *to the crows* (i.e. to death w. no burial) Ar.
ὀΐω, **ὀίω**, **οἴω** *ep.vbs.*, **οἰῶ** *Lacon.vb.*: see οἴομαι
οἰωνίζομαι *mid.vb.* [οἰωνός] | impf. οἰωνιζόμην | aor. οἰωνισάμην | **1 take omens from the behaviour of birds, practise augury** Plu.; (gener.) **interpret omens** or **auspices** X.
2 regard (W.ACC. sthg. or someone) **as an omen** (esp. a bad one) D. Arist. Plu.
3 divine (fr. an omen) —W.ACC. + INF. *that sthg. is the case* X.
οἰωνίσματα των *n.pl.* **omens** (W.GEN. fr. birds) E.
οἰωνισμός οῦ *m.* **ominous sign** (of a favourable event) Plu.
οἰωνιστήριον ου *n.* [οἰωνιστής] **ominous event, omen** (ref. to thunder) X.
οἰωνιστής οῦ *m.* **interpreter of bird omens, diviner, augur** Il. Hes.; (appos.w. θεοπρόπος *seer*) Il.
οἰωνιστικός ή όν *adj.* **relating to a diviner** || FEM.SB. **art of the diviner** Pl.

οἰωνο-θέτᾱς ᾱ *dial.m.* [θέτης] one who gives an interpretation of omens from birds, **diviner, augur** S.
οἰωνό-θροος ον *adj.* [θρόος] (of lamentation) **of clamorous birds** A.
οἰωνο-κτόνος ον *adj.* [κτείνω] (of winter's cold) **killing birds** A.
οἰωνό-μαντις εως *m.* [μάντις] diviner from bird omens, augur E.
οἰωνο-πόλος ου *m.* [πέλω] interpreter of bird omens, **diviner, augur** Il. A.
—**οἰωνοπόλος** ον *adj.* (of the office) **of diviner** Pi.*fr.*
οἰωνός οῦ *m.* **1 bird** Od. Hes. hHom. Alcm. Pi. Trag. +; (as a scavenger) Hom. Trag. AR.; (ref. to a griffin) A.
2 bird of omen (whose behaviour is seen as portending the will of the gods or the future) Hom. Hes. Trag. X. Call. AR.
3 omen from birds Il. Sol. Thgn. E. X. AR.
4 (gener., ref. to an occurrence) **omen, portent** hHom. Hdt. E. Th. Ar. Pl. +
οἰωνοσκοπέω *contr.vb.* [οἰωνοσκόπος] **observe birds of omen** E.; (gener.) **practise divination** E.
οἰωνο-σκόπος ου *m.* [σκοπέω] one who observes birds of omen, **diviner, augur** E.
οἴως *adv.*: see under οἶος
ὄκα, ὄκκα, ὄκκᾱ *dial.relatv.advs.*: see ὅταν and ὅτε[1]
ὀκέλλω *vb.* [reltd. κέλλω] | *impf.* ὤκελλον | *aor.* ὤκειλα |
1 drive ashore, **run aground** —*ships* Hdt. Th.; (of a wave) E.
2 (intr., of ships) **run aground** Th. X.; (fig., of a cooked squid) **be beached** (i.e. placed before a diner) Ar.
ὄκη *Ion.adv. and conj.*: see ὅπη
ὀκλαδίᾱς ου *m.* [ὀκλάζω] portable seat with bent or crossed legs (perh. foldable), **stool** Ar.
ὀκλαδόν *adv.* **cross-legged** or **squatting** AR.
ὀκλάζω *vb.* | *aor.* ὤκλασα | **1** (of a person) **crouch down, squat** (to look for tracks on the ground) S.*Ichn.*; (to rest) S.; (as a movement in a dance) X.; (of a bull) Mosch.
2 (tr., of a horse) **bend** —*its hind legs* X.
ὀκλάξ *adv.* **with knees bent** or **buckling** AR.
ὀκνέω *contr.vb.* —*ep.* **ὀκνείω** *vb.* [ὄκνος] | *impf.* ὤκνουν, *ep.* ὤκνεον | *fut.* ὀκνήσω | *aor.* ὤκνησα || *neut.impers.vbl.adj.* ὀκνητέον | **1** hesitate (due to moral qualms); **hesitate, be reluctant, averse** or **disinclined** S. E. Th. Att.orats. Pl. + —W.INF. *to do sthg.* Il. Trag. Th. Att.orats. Pl. +; (of nobles) **be averse** —W.INF. *to sharing power* (w. the people) X.
2 hesitate (due to fear); **be afraid** (to do sthg.) Isoc. —W.INF. *to do sthg.* S. E. X.
3 hesitate (due to calculation); **be cautious** Hdt. S. X.
4 hesitate, be slow (to do sthg.) S. E. —W.INF. *to do sthg.* D. Men. Theoc. NT.
5 be afraid S. —W.ACC. *of persons* S. X. —*of sthg. prophesied* S. —*of enmity, danger* D. —W.COMPL.CL. *that sthg. may happen* X. D.
6 (wkr.sens.) **suspect** —W.COMPL.CL. *that sthg. may be the case* Pi. X. D. Call.*epigr.* Plb.
ὀκνηρός ά (Ion. ή) όν *adj.* | *compar.* ὀκνηρότερος |
1 hesitant (due to fear or caution); (of a deer) **timid** Call.(cj.); (of a person, troops) **cautious** Antipho Th.; (of hopes) Pi.
2 hesitant (due to modesty or lack of ambition); (of persons) **diffident, retiring** Arist.; (of a character trait) D.
3 (of a slave) **sluggish, lazy** NT.
4 (of personif. poems, which have not found favour) **abashed, downcast** Theoc.
5 (of a turn of events) **frightening** S.; (of fear) **numbing** Theoc.

—**ὀκνηρῶς** *adv.* **hesitantly, reluctantly, diffidently** Isoc. X. D. Men. Plu.
ὄκνος ου *m.* **1** hesitation (in the face of danger or crisis, hostile people or adverse circumstances), **hesitation, fear** Il. S. E. Plu.; (in a storm) Alc. | see also ὄτλος
2 hesitation (in the face of an undertaking, a duty, or sim.), **reluctance, disinclination** Trag. Th. Isoc. Pl. +
3 slowness (due to thoughtfulness or calculation), **caution** A. Th.
4 hesitation (in telling what is on one's mind, bad news, or sim.), **hesitation, qualms** S. E. Theoc.; (in pursuing an argument or stating one's case) Pl.
5 sluggishness, laziness Bion
6 (personif.) **Oknos** (app.provbl. for one whose labour is wasted in ineffectiveness) Ar.
ὀκοδαπός, ὀκόθεν, ὀκοῖος, ὀκόσος, ὀκότε, ὀκότερος, ὄκου (Ion. forms): see ὁποδαπός etc.
ὀκριάομαι *mid.contr.vb.* [ὀκρίς] | *ep.3pl.impf.* (w.diect.) ὀκριόωντο | (of two men) grow sharp with each other, **exchange sharp words** Od.
ὀκρί-βας αντος *m.* [βαίνω] **platform** (in the Odeion at Athens) Pl.
ὀκριόεις εσσα εν (also ειν Call.) *adj.* with sharp point or points; (of a stone or boulder, usu. as a missile) **jagged, sharp** Hom. A. B.*fr.*; (of an arrow) **pointed** Theoc.; (of ground, a landscape) **rugged** Hes.*fr.* A. Call.(cj.) AR.
ὀκρίς ίδος *fem.adj.* (of a ravine) **jagged, rugged** A.
ὀκρυόεις εσσα εν *ep.adj.* [reltd. κρυόεις] | The form prob. arose fr. misinterpretation of gen. -οο κρ- as -ου ὀκρ-. | (of a person, war) **chilling** Il.(dub., cj. κρ-); (of fear) AR.; (of a cave) AR.
ὀκτά-βλωμος ον *adj.* [ὀκτώ; βλωμός *piece of bread*] (of a loaf) **of eight portions** (prob. marked in the dough) Hes.
ὀκτακισ-μύριοι αι α *pl.num.adj.* [ὀκτάκις *eight times*, μυρίος] **eighty thousand** Plb.
ὀκτακισ-χίλιοι αι α *pl.num.adj.* | also Ion.fem.sg. ὀκτακισχιλίη | **eight thousand** Hdt. +; (sg., w.collectv.fem. ἀσπίς *infantry*, ἵππος *cavalry*) Hdt.
ὀκτά-κνημος ον *adj.* [ὀκτώ, κνήμη] (of wheels) **eight-spoked** Il.
ὀκτακόσιοι αι α *pl.num.adj.* **eight hundred** Hdt. +
ὀκτά-μηνος ον *adj.* [μήν[2]] **eight months old** X.
ὀκτά-πηχυς υ, *gen.* ους *adj.* [πῆχυς] **eight cubits long** Plb.
ὀκταπλάσιος ᾱ ον *adj.* (of a portion) **eight times as great** Pl.
—**ὀκταπλάσιον** *neut.adv.* **eight times as much** Ar.
ὀκτά-πλεθρος ον *adj.* [πλέθρον] (of a length) **of eight plethra** Plu.
ὀκτα-πόδης ες *adj.* [πούς] **eight feet long** Hes.
ὀκτα-ρρῡμος ον *adj.* [ῥυμός] (of a heavy vehicle) **with eight shafts** (i.e. pulled by eight pairs of oxen) X.
ὀκτάς άδος *f.* **the number eight** Arist.
ὀκτ-ήρης ους *f.* [ἐρέσσω] **eight-rowed ship** (w. three banks of oars, and rowers seated in groups of eight, so that one level of oars had two men per oar and two levels had three) Plb. Plu.
ὀκτώ *indecl.num.adj.* **eight** Hom. +
ὀκτω-δάκτυλος ον *adj.* **eight fingers long** Ar.
ὀκτω-καί-δεκα *indecl.num.adj.* [δέκα] **eight and ten, eighteen** Hdt. +
ὀκτωκαιδεκά-δραχμος ον *adj.* [δραχμή] (of barley) **at the price of eighteen drachmas** (per medimnos) D.
ὀκτωκαιδέκατος η ον *num.adj.* (of a year, a day) **eighteenth** Plb. Plu. ǁ FEM.SB. eighteenth day (of a month) Od.
ὀκτωκαιδεκ-έτης ες (or **ὀκτωκαιδεκετής** ές) *adj.* [ἔτος] **eighteen years old** D. Theoc.

ὀκτώ-πους πουν, gen. ποδος *adj.* [πούς] (of an area) **of eight square feet** Pl.

ὀκχέω *dial.contr.vb.*: see ὀχέω

ὀκχή ῆς *f.* [reltd. ὀχέω] **support** (W.GEN. of old age, ref. to a walking-stick) Call.

ὄκχος *dial.m.*: see ὄχος

ὅκως, ὅκωσπερ *Ion.relatv.adv.*: see ὅπως, ὅπωσπερ

ὀλαί, Ion. **οὐλαί,** ῶν *f.pl.* **barley grains** (thrown during a sacrifice over the victim's head) Od. Hdt. Ar. Thphr.; (made into a cake) Ar.

ὀλβίζω *vb.* [ὄλβιος] | fut. ὀλβιῶ | aor. ὤλβισα | PASS.: aor. ὠλβίσθην | pf.ptcpl. ὠλβισμένος | **1** acclaim (someone) as blessed and happy; **bless, congratulate** —*a bride, a groom* E. —*a mother* (*for her fine son*) E. || PASS. (of the winner of a contest) be acclaimed S.; (of persons) be blessed or favoured (in respect of birth or status) E.
2 bless (someone or sthg.) with one's presence (by bringing joy, happiness, prosperity); (of a husband) **bless** —*a home, a place* E.; (of a day) —*a person* E.; (of a river) —*a land* E.; (fig., of ivy tendrils, w. their shady shoots) —*newborn Dionysus* E.
3 deem as happy —*a person* (*after death*) A. S.(dub.)
4 make happy, give joy to —*a god* (W.DAT. w. song) Ar.

ὀλβιο-δαίμων ονος *masc.adj.* (of a king) **favoured by fortune** Il.

ὀλβιό-δωρος ον *adj.* [δῶρον] (of earth) **with gifts of prosperity** E.

ὀλβιό-πλουτος ον *adj.* [πλοῦτος] (of a feast) **blessed with opulence** Philox.Leuc.

ὄλβιος ᾱ ον *adj.* [ὄλβος] | compar. ὀλβιώτερος, superl. ὀλβιώτατος | also dial.superl. ὄλβιστος (Call.) | **1** (of a person, a people, their home) blessed with prosperity (in terms of wealth, peace, children, fame, or sim.), **prosperous, happy** Hom. Thgn. Lyr. Hdt. Trag. Pl. +; (of persons) **wealthy** (in terms of possessions or personal accomplishments) Od. +; (of gods and their home, a person in the afterlife) **blessed** hHom. +
2 (of a person in a named circumstance, in love or friendship, avoiding life's pain, as having knowledge, or sim.) **blessed, happy, fortunate** Hes. hHom. Sol. Lyr. +; (in wishes or acclamations; of gods, persons, esp. a child, one getting married, a guest or friend; freq. voc.) Od. +
3 (of gifts) bringing blessings, **fortunate, happy** Od.; (of a task, circumstances, attitudes) Ion Hdt. E.; (of treasures, herds) **rich, abundant** Hdt. E. || NEUT.PL.SB. prosperity Od. hHom. Theoc.
—**ὀλβίως** *adv.* **in a blessed manner** —*ref. to dying* S.

ὀλβο-δότᾱς ᾱ *dial.m.* —also **ὀλβοδότειρα** ᾱς *f.* [δοτήρ] **bestower of prosperity** (ref. to Peace, a river) E.

ὄλβος ου *m.* **1 prosperity** (of persons or lands, esp. assoc.w. peace, family, homeland; freq. as bestowed by the gods, but sts. divorced fr. virtue, attracting envy or short-lived) Hom. Hes. Eleg. Lyr. Hdt. Trag. +; (wished for others, esp. at birth and marriage) Od.
2 material prosperity, **wealth, riches, abundance** Hom. Hes. Eleg. Trag. +; (fr. Mother Earth, the harvest) hHom. Theoc.

ὀλβο-φόρος ον *adj.* [φέρω] (of rulers) **winning prosperity, prosperous** E.

ὀλέεσθαι (ep.fut.mid.inf.): see ὄλλυμαι, under ὄλλυμι

ὀλέθριος ᾱ (Ion. η) ον (also ος ον E. Plb. Plu.) *adj.* [ὄλεθρος]
1 bringing violent or untimely death; (of a day, destiny, judicial sentence) **of death** Il. A.; (of night, fig.ref. to misfortune) as though of death, **deathly** S.
2 (of persons, things, actions, circumstances) with death or destruction as the likely or inevitable consequence, **fatal, deadly, destructive** Heraclit. Hdt. Trag. Call. Plb. Plu.; (W.GEN. to someone or sthg.) A. Pl.

ὄλεθρος ου *m.* [ὄλλῡμι] **1** violent or unnatural destruction of life (in war, through murder, as a punishment, in a shipwreck, or sim.); **violent death, death, destruction** Hom. +
2 (gener.) **ruin** (of an army, a people or city, a person) Hom. +; (of livelihood) Men.; (of things which exist) Parm. Pl.
3 (hyperbol.) **perdition, hell** Timocr. S. Ar. Men.
4 source of destruction (ref. to a situation) Pl. X. Plb.; (hyperbol., ref. to a person) **pest, devil** Hdt. Ar. D. +

ὀλείζων *compar.adj.*: see under ὀλίγος

ὀλέ-κρᾱνον ου *n.* [ὠλένη, κρᾱνίον¹] **point of the elbow, elbow bone** Ar.

ὀλέκω *vb.* [reltd. ὄλλῡμι] | ep.impf. ὄλεκον, iteratv. ὀλέκεσκον || dial.mid.pass.impf. ὠλεκόμᾱν (S.) | **destroy** or **kill** —*persons, animals* Hom. hHom. S. AR. Theoc. —*creation* Emp. || MID.PASS. **perish, be killed** Il. A.; **be ruined** (by one's exertions) S.

ὄλεσα (ep.aor.): see ὄλλῡμι

ὀλεσ-ήνωρ, dial. **ὀλεσᾱ́νωρ,** ορος *masc.fem.adj.* [ὄλλῡμι, ἀνήρ] (of the Hydra) **man-destroying** Stesich.; (of false oaths) Thgn.

ὀλέσθαι (aor.2 mid.inf.): see ὄλλυμαι, under ὄλλῡμι

ὀλεσί-θηρ ηρος *masc.fem.adj.* [θήρ] (of an arm) **monster-slaying** E.

ὀλεσι-σιαλο-κάλαμος ου *m.* [σίαλον] (pejor., ref. to the aulos) **spittle-wasting reed** Pratin.

ὄλεσσα (ep.aor.), **ὀλέσω** and **ὀλέσσω** (ep.fut.): see ὄλλῡμι

ὀλετήρ ῆρος *m.* **destroyer** (of a man) Il.; (of vines, ref. to an insect) Alcm.

ὀλιγάκις *adv.* [ὀλίγος] **only a few times, seldom, rarely** E. Th. Pl. X. D. +

ὀλιγανδρέω *contr.vb.* [ἀνήρ] (of the Senate) **have too few men, be undermanned** Plu.

ὀλιγανδρίᾱ ᾱς *f.* **shortage of men** Plu.

ὀλιγανθρωπίᾱ ᾱς *f.* [ὀλιγάνθρωπος] **1 smallness of population** Th. X. Arist. Plb.
2 shortage of men (for a fighting force) Th. Pl.; (for public offices) Arist.

ὀλιγ-άνθρωπος ον *adj.* (of a land, a city) with a small number of inhabitants, **thinly populated** X.

ὀλιγᾱριστίᾱ ᾱς *f.* [ἄριστον] **light breakfast** Plu.

ὀλιγαρχέομαι *pass.contr.vb.* [ἄρχω] (of people, a state) **be ruled by an oligarchy, have an oligarchic system** Th. Isoc. Pl. X. D. Arist. +; (of a constitution) **be oligarchic** Arist. || ACT. be an oligarchic ruler or an adherent of oligarchy Arist.

ὀλιγαρχίᾱ ᾱς, Ion. **ὀλιγαρχίη** ης *f.* **oligarchy** Hdt. Th. Att.orats. Pl. +

ὀλιγαρχικός ή όν *adj.* **1** (of persons, a conspiracy or faction) supporting or advocating oligarchy, **oligarchic** Th. Att.orats. Pl. + || MASC.SB. oligarch (ref. to a ruler or supporter) Att.orats. Pl. +
2 (of a state) governed by an oligarchic system, **oligarchic** Arist. +; (of a constitution and its features, a law) characteristic of an oligarchic system (esp. opp. democratic), **oligarchic** Th. Pl. D. Arist. +
3 (of a person's behaviour or demeanour) **elitist** Plu.

—**ὀλιγαρχικῶς** *adv.* **in a manner typical of an oligarch** or **an oligarchy** Pl. D. Arist. Plu.

ὀλιγαχόθεν *adv.* **from a few sources** (of revenue or gain) Hdt. Arist.

ὀλιγαχοῦ *adv.* **in few places or instances, rarely** Pl. Arist.

ὀλιγηπελέων ουσα *ep.masc.fem.ptcpl.adj.* [πέλω] | only nom.sg. | app., having little power of movement; (of a person or god) **with little strength, feeble, helpless** Hom.

ὀλιγηπελίη ης *Ion.f.* **feebleness** Od.

ὀλίγιστος *superl.adj.*: see under ὀλίγος

ὀλιγογονίᾱ ᾱς *f.* [ὀλιγόγονος] **production of few offspring** Pl.

ὀλιγό-γονος ον *adj.* [γονή] (of certain animals) **producing few offspring** Hdt.

ὀλιγοδρανέω *contr.vb.* [δραίνω] | *ep.masc.nom.sg.ptcpl.* ὀλιγοδρανέων | (of a person) be able to do little, **be powerless** or **helpless** Iamb.adesp.; (of a warrior) Il.; (of a cockerel, in a fight) Ion

ὀλιγοδρανής ές *adj.* (of the race of humans, opp. birds) **powerless, helpless** Ar.

ὀλιγοδρανίᾱ ᾱς *f.* **helplessness** (of the human race) A.

ὀλιγοετίᾱ ᾱς *f.* [ἔτος] **fewness of years** (of adolescents) X.

ὀλιγό-παις παιδος *masc.fem.adj.* [παῖς¹] **with few children** Pl.

ὀλιγό-πιστος ον *adj.* [πιστός] **of little faith** NT.

ὀλιγοπονίᾱ ᾱς *f.* [πόνος] **lack of effort** Plb.

ὀλίγος η (dial. ᾱ) ον *adj.* | For compar. ὀλείζων (ep. ὀλίζων) and superl. ὀλίγιστος see below. The compar. is more commonly supplied by ἐλάσσων, ἥσσων, μείων. |
1 little in size or weight; (of a man, a boy) **little, small** Hom. hHom. Theoc.; (of fish) Od.; (of a shield, drinking-cup, table) Hom.; (of a ship) Hes.
2 of little consequence; (of a man) **little, small, insignificant** Od. hHom. Callin. Alc. S. Th. +; (of the strength of a mortal) Simon.; (of Strife, when not in full spate) Il.; (of a pain) Sol.
3 little in value or worth (estimated in monetary terms or by other standards); (of money, a gift, quality or attribute) **only little, little** Hom. Thgn. Scol. Pi. Hdt. Att.orats. +
4 (of a stretch of land, distance or space) little in extent or area, **only little, little, scant** Il. hHom. Hdt. Th. +; (of scope or opportunity) Thgn.
5 (of a period of time) little in duration, **only little, short** Il. Hes. Simon. Pi. Hdt. Th. +; (of a respite, life, or sim.) Od. +
6 little in intensity; (of a voice, cry, outcry) **small, low** Od. Th.
7 little in amount, quantity or size; (of a commodity or foodstuff) **little, not much, meagre** or **slight** Il. +; (of a spring, a wave) Hom.; (of a number of things or persons, a fighting force, line of troops, or sim.) Hdt. E. Th. +
8 ‖ PL. (of persons, animals or things) few in number (freq. opp. a majority grouping) Hes. Alc. Thgn. Simon. Hdt. Th. +; (esp. of troops or ships, against opponents) Hdt. Th. Att.orats. +; (of money, resources, goods, buildings, or sim.) Thgn. Th. Att.orats. +; (of periods of time) Th. Att.orats. +; (of words or things said) E. Th. Att.orats. +; (of actions, events, circumstances) Thgn. A. Th. +
9 ‖ MASC.PL.SB. few men or a small group (esp. opp. a larger group) Simon. +; (ref. to men w. power in a city or community, esp. aristocrats or oligarchs) Th. Att.orats. +
10 ‖ NEUT.SB. (sg. and pl.) only a little (of sthg., esp. in terms of space, distance, time, value; freq. in prep.phrs.) hHom. Sapph. Eleg. Pi. Hdt. E. Th. +
— **ὀλίγον** *neut.sg.adv.* **1** in terms of only a little degree, amount, distance or time; **a little way, a short time, only a little** or **only just** Hom. Hes. Pi. Hdt. E.Cyc. Th. +
2 only a little, hardly (W.COMPAR.ADJ. **braver, older, more powerful, or sim.**) Hom. Hdt. +
— **ὀλίγου** *neut.gen.adv.* **1** within only a little degree, amount, distance or time; **almost, nearly** Od. Th. Ar.; (w. expressions of number) • ὀλίγου ἅπαντες **almost all** Pl. • ὀλίγου ἐς χιλίους **close on a thousand** Th. | see also δέω² 2, δεῖ 7
2 for a little, at a cheap price Hdt. Att.orats. +
— **ὀλίγῳ** *neut.dat.adv.* by only a little degree, amount, distance or time; **a little, only a little** or **hardly** A. Hdt. +; (W.COMPAR.ADJ. **larger, more, worse, or sim.**) Hdt. Th. +; (*earlier* or *later*, esp. in a discussion, narrative, or sim.) Hdt. +
— **ὀλίγα** *neut.pl.adv.* **in a few cases only, hardly at all** Hippon. E. Th.
— **ὀλίγως** *adv.* (in neg.phr.) **in a small amount** Call.; **in an insignificant way** Call.(dub.cj.)
— **ὀλείζων**, ep. **ὀλίζων**, ον, gen. ονος *masc.fem.compar.adj.* (of troops) **fewer** (than the enemy) X.; (of mortals, depicted on a shield) **smaller** (than gods) Il.; (of certain gods) **lesser** (in importance) Call.
— **ὀλίγιστος** η ον *superl.adj.* **1** least in amount or quantity, **least** Il. Hes. S.(cj.) Ar. Pl. +
2 fewest in number, **fewest** Ar. Pl. +
3 shortest in size or extent, **shortest, smallest** Arist.
— **ὀλίγιστον** *neut.sg.superl.adv.* in the least degree, **least** Pl.
— **ὀλιγίστου** *neut.superl.gen.adv.* **at the least cost** D.
— **ὀλίγιστα** *neut.pl.superl.adv.* **in the fewest cases** Pl.

ὀλιγοσθενέω *contr.vb.* [σθένος] **have little strength** B.

ὀλιγοσιτίᾱ ᾱς *f.* [σῖτος] **moderate** or **meagre diet** Arist. Plu.

ὀλιγό-στιχος ον *adj.* [στίχος] (of a poem or poet) **employing few lines** Call.

ὀλιγοστός ή όν *adj.* **accompanied by few other persons** Plu.

ὀλιγότης ητος *f.* fewness in number or scantiness in amount; **small number** or **quantity** Pl. Arist. Plu.; **shortness** (of time) Pl.

ὀλιγοφιλίᾱ ᾱς *f.* [φίλος] **shortage of friends** Arist.

ὀλιγο-χρόνιος ον (also ᾱ ον Arist.) *adj.* (of youth, compared to a dream) lasting only a short time, **fleeting** Mimn. Thgn.; (of a person, possessions, conditions) **short-lived** Hdt. Pl. X. Arist.; (of a period of rule or pre-eminence) Arist. Plb.

ὀλιγοψῡχέω *contr.vb.* [ψῡχή] (of a wounded man) **be faint** Isoc.

ὀλιγωρέω *contr.vb.* [ὀλίγωρος] | aor. ὠλιγώρησα ‖ pf.pass. ὠλιγώρημαι | **1** have little care (in military or political duties), **be neglectful** or **negligent** Th. Att.orats. Pl. +; **neglect** —W.GEN. *one's forces or territory, one's people, allies or emissaries, duties towards these* Att.orats. Plb.
2 have little care (in duties towards family and society, upholding the law and religious values); **have no respect** Arist. —W.GEN. *for authorities and public opinion, law and justice, customs and rituals* Att.orats. + —*teachers or instruction* Pl. Arist. NT.
3 have little care (in duties towards oneself), **neglect** —W.GEN. *one's life, interests, reputation, conduct* Att.orats. Arist. +
4 pay little attention (to someone or sthg., in order to pursue someone or sthg. else); **neglect** —W.GEN. *persons (in favour of others, or for gain)* Att.orats. X. Plb.; **sacrifice** —W.GEN. *sthg. (for what is seen as more advantageous)* Pl. D. Plb.
5 judge (someone or sthg.) of little worth or importance; **be contemptuous** or **indifferent** Th. D. +; **think little** —W.GEN. *of other people, their actions and ideas* Att.orats. + —*of possessions and honours* Th. Arist.; **not take seriously** —W.GEN. *bad qualities* Isoc. Arist. —*portents* Pl.; **scorn** —W.GEN. *death and danger* Pl.; **think it not worthwhile** —W.INF. *to do sthg.* Plb.

ὀλιγωρίᾱ

6 ‖ PASS. (of persons) be neglected or slighted Arist. Plb.; (of things) receive little attention or be held in contempt Att.orats. +

ὀλιγωρίᾱ ᾱς, Ion. **ὀλιγωρίη** ης *f.* **1** slackness (in military, political or religious matters); **indifference, neglect** or **contempt** Th. Att.orats. +
2 lack of care (in personal behaviour); **lack of concern, indifference** Isoc. Arist. Plu.
3 indifference (towards others); **lack of respect, disdain** Hdt. Th. D. Arist. Plu.

ὀλίγ-ωρος ον *adj.* [ὥρᾱ] **1** having little concern or respect; (of persons, their character or conduct) **disdainful, contemptuous** Hdt. D. Arist. Plb. Plu.; (W.GEN. of propriety, the laws) Isoc. Plu.; (of a peace-treaty w. Persia) **demeaning** (W.GEN. to the Greeks) Isoc. ‖ NEUT.SB. disdain Arist.
2 (of a person) **unconcerned, indifferent, negligent** D.; (of state policies) **careless** Plu.

—**ὀλιγώρως** *adv.* **1** disdainfully, contemptuously Att.orats. Plb. Plu.
2 unconcernedly, indifferently, negligently Att.orats. X. Plb. Plu.
3 dispassionately Pl.

ὀλίζων *ep.compar.adj.*: see under ὀλίγος

ὄλισβος ου *m.* dildo Ar.

ὀλισθάνω (also **ὀλισθαίνω** AR.) *vb.* | aor.2 ὤλισθον, ep. ὄλισθον | **1** lose one's foothold, slip Il. S. X. Men. Plu.
2 slip (in wrestling, fig.ref. to making a mistake) Ar.; (of a person's tongue) **make a slip** (in pronouncing a name) Plu.
3 (of things) slip out of place; (of land) slide Plu.; (of a house) **fall down** Call.; (of words, which shd. not be uttered) slip —W.PREP.PHR. *through the teeth* Call.
4 slide (as a result of deliberate action); **slide** (over snow) Plb.; (of a ship, on rollers) AR.; (of an arrow) **glide** (through flesh) Theoc.; (of the tongue, in pronouncing a sound) Pl.

ὀλίσθημα ατος *n.* **1** slip, fall (of a person, fr. a ladder) Plu.; (of a bird, fr. the sky) Plu.; (of a heavenly body, fr. its normal position) Plu.
2 smooth flow, gliding (of water) Pl.
3 slippery surface (on a mountainside) Plu.
4 (fig.) moral slip, **lapse, failing** Plu.

ὀλισθηρός ά όν *adj.* **1** liable to cause one to slip; (of a path, terrain, stones) **slippery** Pi. X. Plu.
2 liable to slip from one's grasp or control; (of reins) **slippery** X.; (fig., of a particular kind of topic) Pl.
3 (of a person) easily moved (w. πρός + ACC. to anger) Plu.

ὀλίσθησις εως *f.* slipping (of persons, on difficult terrain) Plu.

ὄλισθος ου *m.* slipperiness (of bloody corpses) Plb.

ὁλκαίη ης *Ion.f.* [ὁλκή] tail (of a sea-monster) AR.(v.l. ἀλκαίη)

ὁλκαῖον ου *n.* stern-post (of a ship) AR.

ὁλκάς άδος *f.* [ἕλκω] hauler of cargo; **cargo ship** Pi. B.(cj.) Hdt. E.*Cyc.* Th. +

ὁλκεῖον (also **ὁλκίον**), Ion. **ὁλκήιον**, ου *n.* [ὁλκή] **1** a kind of container, **jar** Plb. Plu.
2 stern-post (of a ship) AR. [or perh. *aft cross-beam*]

ὁλκή ῆς *f.* [ἕλκω] **1** pulling, dragging (of a person, by the hair) A.; **drawing out, stretching** (of cloth, in the process of dressing it) Pl.
2 drawing (W.GEN. of children, towards established principles, as an educational process) Pl.
3 (fig.) stretching, straining (W.GEN. of arguments) Pl.
4 force of attraction, **attraction** (created by a magnet) Pl.; (of a flame, to a volatile substance) Pl.; (fig., of like to like) Pl.

5 downward pull (in the scales); **weight** (of an object) Men. Plb. Plu.
6 app. **pressure** (affecting the flow of water) Plu.

ὁλκίον *n.*: see ὁλκεῖον

ὁλκός οῦ *m.* **1** (sg. and pl.) trace made by drawing (sthg. through or over sthg. else); **groove, track, trace** (made by a piece of wood being dragged along) X.; (W.GEN. of a knife, in carving letters on wood) Ar.; **furrow** (in the earth) AR.; (in the sea, made by an oar) AR.; (in the sky, made by a fiery object) AR.
2 (sg. and pl.) **slipway** (of stone blocks, for launching ships and hauling them ashore) Hdt. E. Th.; (of logs) AR.
3 (pl.) dragging movement, **sweep** (of a laurel branch, used as a broom) E.
4 (pl.) dragging (of a person tied to a bull) E.*fr.*; (of a fallen charioteer, by the reins, meton. for the reins themselves) S.

—**ὁλκός** ή όν *adj.* (of a subject of study or sim.) **conducive to the drawing or attracting** (W.GEN. of the soul, W.PREP.PHR. *towards or away fr. sthg.*) Pl.

ὄλλῡμι *vb.* | pres.ptcpl. ὀλλύς, fem.pl. ὀλλῦσαι | 3pl.impf. ὤλλυσαν (A. S.) | fut. ὀλῶ, ep. ὀλέσω, ὀλέσσω | aor. ὤλεσα, ep. ὄλεσα, ὄλεσσα | —also (pres.) **ὀλλύω** (Archil.) | For mid. and pf.act. see below. |

1 destroy (people) in fighting; **kill, destroy** —*men, an army, ships, a people, their city or land* Hom. Hes. Eleg. A. E. +
2 destroy (individuals); **kill, destroy** —*persons* Od. Archil. Thgn. Lyr. Trag. + —*a monstrous beast* E. Theoc.
3 ruin (people) through misfortune or wrongdoing; **ruin, destroy** —*a race, city, persons, their life or family* Hom. Hes. Thgn. Pi. Trag. +
4 ruin (sthg. good) in terms of health, quality or integrity; **ruin, take away** —*livelihood, youthful appearance, strength* Od. —*good sense* Il.; **wipe out** —*a drawing* A.
5 lose (someone or sthg.) through ruin, destruction or death; **lose** —*one's men, one's people* Hom. E. + —*a person who is dear* (esp. *offspring*) Hom. A. E. + —*youth, beauty, strength, possessions, hopes, life* Hom. Anacr. Eleg. E. +, —*prey, a prize* AR.

—**ὄλλυμαι** *mid.vb.* | impf. ὠλλύμην | fut. ὀλοῦμαι, ep.2pl. ὀλέεσθε, ep.inf. ὀλέεσθαι | aor.2 ὠλόμην, ep. ὀλόμην, dial. ὀλόμᾱν, inf. ὀλέσθαι ‖ pf.act. ὄλωλα | ep.3sg.plpf. ὀλώλει |

1 lose one's life, **be destroyed, perish** Hom. Hippon. Eleg. Trag. Ar. +; lose reason for living, **be ruined** S. E.; (aor.opt., as an imprecation, upon others or oneself) Od. Trag.
2 (of creation) **cease to exist** Parm.; (of a dead body) **be destroyed** S.; (of homeland, livelihood or possessions, the opportunity to return home) **be ruined** or **lost** Hom. Lyr.adesp. E.; (of youth, fame, rumour) **fade, die** Il. hHom. Alcm. Thgn. A. S.; (of a rose, perfumes, song) Hellenist.poet.
3 ‖ PF.ACT. have perished, be dead Hom. Trag.; be as good as dead, be done for Trag.; (of an army, a family) be destroyed A. E.; (of things) be lost or gone Hom. Thgn. Trag.

—**ὀλόμενος**, ep. **οὐλόμενος**, Aeol. **ὠλόμενος**, η (dial. ᾱ) ον aor.2 mid.ptcpl.adj. **1** (of persons or things) deserving the curse ὄλοιο (*go to perdition*, usu. because they themselves bring death or destruction); (of a person, a goddess) **accursed, deadly** Hom. E.; (of death, Fate, other such agents) Il. Tyrt. A. B.*fr.* Emp. AR.; (of anger, strife, insolence, a task, a threat) Il. Thgn. Pi.*fr.* Emp. AR.; (of Achilles' armour, Paris' ship) Od. E.; (of snakes) Theoc.; (of a storm) AR.
2 accursed (for being destructive of the body); (of hunger, poverty, old age, misery) **accursed, ruinous** Od. Hes. hHom. Alc. Thgn. Pi.; (of a drug) Od.; (of the affliction of exile) Pi.; (of a sleep) E.; (of wounds) E.; (of fear) AR.

ὁλμο-ποιός οῦ *m.* [ὅλμος, ποιέω] **maker of mortars** Arist.

ὅλμος, Ion. **οὖλμος**, ου *m.* [reltd. εἰλέω²] **mortar** (utensil, made of stone or wood, in which foodstuffs are pounded) Il. Hes. Hdt. Ar. Men.

ὀλόεις εσσα εν *adj.* [reltd. ὀλοός] (of blows) **deadly** S.

ὀλοιός (also **ὀλοίιος**) *ep.adj.*: see ὀλοός

ὀλοί-τροχος, Ion. **ὀλοίτροχος**, ep. **ὀλοοίτροχος**, ου *m.* [εἰλέω², τρέχω] movable stone, **boulder** Il. Hdt. X. Theoc.

ὁλοκαυτέω *contr.vb.* [ὁλόκαυτος] | *aor.* ὡλοκαύτησα | **make a whole burnt offering** X. —w.ACC. *of certain animals* X.

ὁλό-καυτος ον *adj.* [ὅλος, καυτός] (of a city) **entirely on fire** Call.

ὁλοκαύτωμα ατος *n.* **whole burnt offering** NT.

ὁλοκληρία ᾶς *f.* [ὁλόκληρος] **perfect health** NT.

ὁλό-κληρος ον *adj.* [κλῆρος] **1** having a complete allocation; (of persons, their body or soul) **complete, perfect** Pl. Arist.; (of celebrants of the mysteries, their visions) Pl.

2 (of objects) **complete, perfect** Plu.; (of meanness, generosity) **entire, unqualified** Arist. Plu.; (of renown) **universal** Plb.; (of an individual's service to the state, both political and military) **comprehensive** Plu.

ὀλολυγή ῆς, dial. **ὀλολυγά** ᾶς *f.* [ὀλολύζω] **loud emotional cry** (by women); **shout, yell** (at sacrifices) Hdt.; (during other rituals) Il. hHom. Alc. Ar. Call.; (at the epiphany of a god) E.; (at the birth of a god) Call.; (in triumph or at a victory) Ar.; (during an attack on men) Th.; (by triumphant barbarian men) Plu.

ὀλολύγματα των *n.pl.* **cries, shouts** (of girls performing ritual dances) E.

ὀλολυγμός οῦ *m.* loud emotional cry (by women); **shout, scream, yell** (at a sacrifice) A.; (after the killing of a person) A. E.; (at a moment of triumph) A.; (by men, at a sacrifice, w.DAT. in the manner of women) A.

ὀλολυγών όνος *f.* **screecher** (name of a kind of bird or animal) Theoc.

ὀλολύζω *vb.* | *fut.* ὀλολύξομαι | *aor.* ὠλόλυξα, ep. ὀλόλυξα | (of women) utter a loud cry (in reaction or accompaniment to an emotionally or ritually powerful event); **shout, yell** (when a sacrificial victim is struck down) Od.; (after a human killing) Od.; (at a moment of victory or triumph) A. E.; (after a prayer for help) Od.; (at the epiphany of a god) hHom. B. AR.; (at the birth of a god or person) hHom. Theoc.; (performing a magic rite) S.*fr.*(mid., cj., for ἀλαλάζομαι); (of men, at a moment of religious significance) Ar.; (of Bacchants) E.(cj., for ἀλαλάζω); (pejor., of a man, in oriental cult worship) NT.

ὀλόμενος *aor.2 mid.ptcpl.adj.*: see under ὄλλῡμι

ὀλόμην (ep.aor.2 mid.): see ὄλλυμαι, under ὄλλῡμι

ὄλον¹ *n.*, **ὄλον²** *neut.adv.*: see under ὅλος

ὄλονθος *m.*: see ὄλυνθος

ὀλοοίτροχος *ep.m.*: see ὀλοίτροχος

ὀλοός, ep. **ὀλοιός**, also **οὐλοός** (Call. AR.), ᾱ (Ion. ἡ) όν, also **ὀλοίιος** η ον (Hes.) *adj.* [reltd. ὄλλῡμι] | *voc.* ὀλέ (Alcm.) | *compar.* ὀλοώτερος, *superl.* ὀλοώτατος ‖ see also οὔλιος², οὖλος³ | **1** bringing destruction or death; (of gods or monstrous beings, animals, persons, their attributes, states of mind, or sim.) **destructive, deadly** Hom. Hes. Alcm. S. Hellenist.poet.; (of war, strife, anger, words, tasks) Hom. A. AR.; (of a sword, ships) Call.; (of supernatural agents, forces of nature) Hom. Hes. A. B. AR. Mosch.

2 weakening or destroying (the body); (of old age, illness, lack of breath, fear, anguish, or sim.) **destructive, dreadful** Hom. Hes. hHom. Call. AR.; (of shackles) Od. Hes.

3 affected or pervaded by destruction or death; (of persons) **doomed** A. Ar.; (of lamentation, suffering, or sim.) **dreadful, dire** Il. Pi.*fr.* E. AR.; (of daylight, over sacked Troy) E.; (of the stench of animals) Od.; (of a raven's black plumage) Call.

—**ὀλοά** *neut.pl.adv.* **despairingly** —*ref. to lamenting* S.

ὀλοό-φρων ον, *gen.* ονος *adj.* [φρήν] with deadly or destructive intent; (of animals) **dread, deadly** Il.; (of Atlas, Aietes, Minos) Od.; (of Scylla) AR.

ὁλο-πόρφυρος ον *adj.* [ὅλος, πορφύρᾱ] (of a Persian royal garment) **entirely purple** X.

ὁλόπτω *vb.* [perh.reltd. λοπός] | *aor.* ὥλοψα | **strip, pluck** (hair, fr. a Cyclops' chest) Call.

ὅλος, Ion. **οὖλος** (Od. Parm.), η (dial. ᾱ) ον *adj.* | The adj. is sts. reinforced w. πᾶς. For ep. οὖλε see below. |

1 the complete amount or extent of (a thing, opp. a part or some parts); **the whole of, whole, entire** Pi. Parm. Ar. Att.orats. + • ὅλος ὀφθαλμός *the full eye (of the moon)* Pi. • ὅλος ὁ στίχος *the whole line (of verse)* Ar. ‖ PL. the whole number of (things under consideration) Att.orats. + • ὅλα τὰ πράγματα *matters in general* Isoc.

2 the entirety of (someone or sthg.; emphasising that no part of a person or thing is excluded fr. the action of the vb.); **every part of, the whole of** Hdt. E. Th. Ar. Att.orats. + • πόλιν ὅλην διαφθεῖραι *destroy a city in its entirety* Th. • ἐκπιεῖν ὅλον πίθον *drink dry a whole jar* E.*Cyc.*

3 (w. the name of a measurement) **whole, complete, all of** Hdt. • ὅλον καὶ ἥμισυ πλέθρον *a whole plethron and a half* Hdt.

4 (of an object, a human or animal body) complete or whole in every way; (of a loaf, a roasted animal, a fish) **whole, entire** Od. Hdt. Ar. Philox.Leuc. • βοῦν ἀπηνθράκιζ᾿ ὅλον *she roasted a whole ox on the coals* Ar.; (of a chariot, a Herm) **undamaged** Pi. Lys.; (fig., of a concept being discussed) Pl.

5 completely applying to every part or aspect, **all, every bit** (of a person or thing, w. noun or adj. playing an attributive role) Ar. Att.orats. X. • παιπάλημ᾿ ὅλον *complete piece of trickery (ref. to a person)* Ar. • ὅλον ἁμάρτημα *a complete mistake (ref. to an action)* X. • τὸ τίμημα ἐποίησεν ὅλον δημόσιον *he made the fine payable in its entirety to the state* D.

6 (of a person or thing) completely involved or affected (in an action or state), **all, all over, all out** Xenoph. Ar. Att.orats. X. + • ὅλος πρὸς τῷ λήμματι καὶ τῷ δωροδοκήματι *wholly devoted to moneymaking and bribery* D.

7 (in temporal phrs.) the whole period of, **whole, all of** (w. noun referring to a length of time, or w. a specified number of days, weeks, or sim.) Od. Pi. S. Th. Att.orats. + • ὅλην τὴν ἡμέραν *throughout the whole day* Th. +

—**ὅλον¹** ου *n.* **1** sum of all parts or elements, **whole** Pl. X. +; **generality** Pl.

2 (sg. or pl.) sum of all existing things, **universe, all that is** Pl. X.

3 ‖ PL. everything (in one's life or circumstances) D.; everything summed up or in general (ref. to subjects under consideration) D.

—**ὅλον²** (also τὸ ὅλον) *neut.adv.* **generally speaking, generally, on the whole** Att.orats. +; in every possible way, **completely** Att.orats. +; (also dat.adv.) ὅλῳ **completely** Pl.

—**ὅλως** *adv.* **1** in a way which is complete or to the full extent, **wholly, completely, altogether, in all respects** Att.orats. +

2 in a way in which a thing, person or group is considered as a whole, **on the whole, generally, generally speaking** Att.orats. +

ὁλοσίδηρος

3 in any way, **at all** Men. +; (w.NEG. *not*) Thgn. Att.orats. + • τίς ἀνθρώπων ὅλως; *who at all on earth?* Men.

—**οὖλε** *ep.voc.adj.* (quasi-imperatv., as a greeting) **be well!, hail!** Od. hHom.

ὁλο-σίδηρος ον *adj.* (of a helmet, a spear) **of solid iron** Plu.

ὁλο-σχερής ές *adj.* [reltd. σχέσθαι, see ἔχω; cf. σχερός] | *compar.* ὁλοσχερέστερος | **1** (of a tree, torn up) with all the parts holding together, **whole, entire** Theoc.
2 (of a circumstance, state or event) complete in extent or effect, **full, general** Plb.; (of an emotion, intent, thought, or sim.) Plb.

—**ὁλοσχερῶς** *adv.* **completely, totally, utterly** Plb.

ὁλό-σχιστος ον *adj.* [σχιστός] (of cloth, leather) **cut out of one piece, one-piece** Pl.

ὁλό-σχοινος ου *m.* [σχοῖνος] **a kind of large rush** (which can be soaked to make a tough fibre); (provbl.) ἀπορράπτειν τὸ στόμα ὁλοσχοίνῳ ἀβρόχῳ *sew up* (*a person's*) *mouth with an unsoaked rush* (to stop him talking, i.e. unceremoniously) Aeschin.

ὁλότης ητος *f.* **wholeness** (as a quality) Arist.

ὁλοφυγγών όνος *f.* [app.reltd. φλύκταινα] **blister** or **pimple** (on the tongue) Theoc.

ὁλοφυδνός ή όν *adj.* [reltd. ὁλοφύρομαι] (of words) **evoking tears, piteous** Hom.

ὀλοφυρμός οῦ *m.* (sg. and pl.) **lamentation, cries of despair** or **distress** Th. Ar. Plu.

ὀλοφύρομαι *mid.vb.* | *aor.* ὠλοφυράμην, ep.2sg. ὀλοφύραο, ep.3sg. ὀλοφύρατο | *aor.pass.ptcpl.* ὀλοφυρθείς | **1 express or feel intense despair, pity** or **regret**; **lament, cry** Hom. hHom. Pi.*fr.* Hdt. Th. Lys. + —w.ACC. *over a person* Hom. Tyrt. Hdt. S. E. Th. + —*for oneself* Lys. —*for one's youth, one's fate* Thgn. AR. —w.GEN. *on account of a person* Il. || PASS. (of a person) **be lamented** —w.DAT. *because of his misfortunes* Th.
2 deplore the need for —w.INF. *being resolute* (*in facing an enemy*) Od. —w.PTCPL. *doing sthg.* (*involving expense*) Lys.

ὁλόφυρσις εως *f.* **1 crying** (w.GEN. over persons, homes and land, i.e. their loss) Th.
2 crying out (of the dying) Th.

ὄλπᾱ ᾱς *dial.f.* **a kind of container** (for oil), **flask, jar** Theoc.

ὄλπις ιδος *f.* | *acc.* ὄλπιν | **a kind of container, flask, jar** (w. a narrow spout, for oil or wine) Sapph. Call. Theoc.

Ὀλυμπίᾱ (also **Οὐλυμπίᾱ** Pi.) ᾱς, Ion. **Ὀλυμπίη** ης *f.* [Ὀλύμπιος] **Olympia** (grove and sanctuary of Olympian Zeus in Elis, where the Olympic games were held every four years) Xenoph. Pi. B. Hdt. S. Th. +

—'**Ὀλυμπίαζε** *adv.* **to** or **at Olympia** Th. And. Pl. Arist. Plu.

—'**Ὀλυμπίᾱσι(ν)** *adv.* **at Olympia** Th. Ar. Att.orats. Pl. +

Ὀλύμπια ων *n.pl.* **festival of Olympian Zeus** (in Elis), **Olympic games** Hdt. Th. Pl. X. +; (in Cyrene, Macedonia) Pi. D.

Ὀλυμπιακός ή όν *adj.* [Ὀλυμπιάς] **of** or **relating to the celebration of the Olympic festival**; (of the road to it, the hill at the site) **Olympic** X.; (of the truce proclaimed during the festival, the law pertaining to it) Th. Aeschin. Plu.; (of the year) X.; (of contests, victories) Pl. Plu.

Ὀλυμπιάς άδος *fem.adj.* [Ὀλύμπιος] | *dat.pl.* Ὀλυμπιάσι, ep. Ὀλυμπιάδεσσι | **1** (of the Muses, as daughters of Zeus) **Olympian** Il. Hes. hHom. Alcm. Sol.; (of the Graces) Ar.; (of goddesses assoc.w. Mt. Olympos in Mysia) S. || PL.SB. Olympian goddesses Hes.*fr.* Pi.
2 (of the olive, ref. to its foliage, as a victory-garland) **at the Olympian festival** Pi.; (of a victory) Pl.
3 || SB. **Olympian festival** Pi. Hdt. Th. Isoc. Pl.
4 || SB. **victory at the Olympian festival** Hdt.
5 || SB. **Olympiad** (period of four years betw. Olympian festivals, used as a dating system, the first festival being in 776 BC) Plb. Plu.

Ὀλυμπιεῖον (also perh. **Ὀλύμπιον** Pl. Arist.) ου *n.* **temple of Olympian Zeus** Th. And. Pl. Arist. Plb. Plu.

Ὀλυμπικός ή όν *adj.* **1** [Ὀλύμπια] **of** or **relating to the Olympic festival**; (of the games, a contest or victory) **Olympic** Th. Ar. Plu.; (title of a speech by Gorgias) Arist.
2 [Ὄλυμπος] (of the pass, the foothills) **of Mount Olympos** Hdt. Plu.

—'**Ὀλυμπικῶς** *adv.* **in Olympic fashion** —*ref. to a victor drinking a toast to Olympian Zeus* Pl.

Ὀλυμπιο-δρόμος ον *adj.* [δραμεῖν] (of horses) **racing at the Olympic games** B.

Ὀλυμπιο-νίκης ου, *dial.* **Ὀλυμπιονίκᾱς** (also **Οὐλ-** Pi.) ᾱ *m.* [νίκη] **Olympic victor** Pi. Hdt. Th. And. Pl. + || ADJ. (of a hymn) **for an Olympic victor** Pi.

Ὀλυμπιονῑκίᾱ ᾱς *f.* **Olympic victory** B.

Ὀλυμπιό-νῑκος ον *adj.* **victorious in the Olympic games** Pi.

Ὀλύμπιος ᾱ (Ion. η) ον *adj.* [Ὄλυμπος] **of** or **relating to Mt. Olympos**; (of the gods, their homes) **Olympian** Hom. +; (as cult title of deities, esp. Zeus) Hom. +; (of the altar of Zeus) Pi.; (of Perikles, as a nickname) Ar. Plu. || MASC.SB. **Olympian** (ref. to Zeus) Hom. +; (pl., ref. to the gods) Il. +

Ὄλυμπος, ep. **Οὔλυμπος**, ου *m.* **1 Olympos** (mt. on borders of Thessaly and Macedonia, home of the gods, under the rule of Zeus) Hom. +
2 Olympos (name of mts. in Mysia, Laconia) Hdt. X. Plb.

—**Οὔλυμπόνδε** *adv.* **to Olympos** Od. Hes. Thgn. Pi. AR.
—**Οὐλυμπόθεν** *adv.* **from Olympos** Pi.

ὄλυνθος (also **ὄλονθος** Hdt.) ου *m.* **fruit of the wild fig tree, wild fig** Hes.*fr.* Hdt.

Ὄλυνθος ου *f.* **Olynthos** (city of Chalcidice, destroyed by Philip of Macedon in 348 BC) Hdt. Th. X. Aeschin. D.

—**Ὀλύνθιοι** ων *m.pl.* **inhabitants of Olynthos, Olynthians** Hdt. Th. Att.orats. X. +

—**Ὀλύνθιος** ᾱ ον *adj.* (of a person) **of** or **from Olynthos, Olynthian** Th. Att.orats. Plu. || FEM.SB. **Olynthian territory** X. Is.

—**Ὀλυνθιακός** ή όν *adj.* (of a war) **against Olynthos, Olynthian** Arist. || MASC.SB. *Olynthiac* (title of a speech) D.

ὄλυραι ῶν (Ion. έων) *f.pl.* **a kind of grain, spelt** Hdt. D.; (used as food for horses) Il.

ὄλωλα (pf.): see ὄλλυμαι, under ὄλλυμι

ὅλως *adv.*: see under ὅλος

ὁμᾱγερής *dial.adj.*, **ὁμάγυρις** *dial.f.*: see ὁμηγερής, ὁμήγυρις

ὁμαδέω *contr.vb.* [ὅμαδος] **1** (of a group of people) **make a din, shout, clamour** Od. AR.; **mutter together** —w.ADV. *in low tones* AR.
2 (of bronze bulls, breathing fire) **roar** AR.
3 (of trees, in a wind) **rustle** AR.

ὅμαδος ου *m.* **1 loud** or **confused noise; hubbub, din** (of a group of people, esp. warriors) Hom. Hes. Pi. AR.; (of a tempest) Il.; (of a lament) E.; (w.GEN. of the Graces, ref. to people singing boisterously in celebration of a victorious athlete) Pi.; (fig. and pejor., w.GEN. of books, containing incantations or sim.) Pl.; (personif.) **Hubbub** Hes.
2 (concr.) **noisy** or **bustling crowd, throng** (of people, warriors) Il. AR.

ὁμαίμιος ον *adj.* [ὅμαιμος] (of a grandfather) **of the same blood** (as oneself), **one's very own** Pi.

ὅμ-αιμος, Boeot. ὅμημος, ον adj. [ὁμός, αἷμα] 1 (of persons) of the same blood, **related by blood, kindred** A. S.; (W.GEN. to someone) A. Plu.; (of murder, blood that is shed) **of kin** A. 2 (of peoples) sharing the same ancestry, **related** Hdt. ‖ NEUT.SB. consanguinity (of the Greeks) Hdt. 3 ‖ MASC.FEM.SB. blood-relative, kinsman or kinswoman (ref. to a brother or sister) S. E. Corinn. Theoc. ‖ PL. (gener.) kin A. E.

ὁμαίμων ον, gen. ονος adj. | compar. ὁμαιμονέστερος | 1 of the same blood, **related by blood, kin** (W.GEN. to someone) S.fr. ‖ COMPAR. more closely related by blood (W.GEN. than others) S. ‖ MASC.FEM.SB. blood-relation, kinsman or kinswoman (ref. to a brother or sister) S. ‖ PL. blood-relatives, kin S. E. 2 (epith. of Zeus, Justice) **who looks after blood-relations** A. 3 (fig., of plundering) **closely akin, related** (W.GEN. to rampage) A. 4 (of Ionians) having the same ancestry, **related** (to mainland Greeks) Hdt.

ὁμαιχμία ᾱς, Ion. ὁμαιχμίη ης f. [ὅμαιχμοι] **military alliance** Hdt. Th.

ὅμ-αιχμοι ων m.pl. [αἰχμή] **military allies** Th.

ὁμαλής ές adj. [ὁμαλός] 1 (of ground) **level** Pl. X. ‖ NEUT.SB. level ground X. Plu. 2 (of men in a community) on equal terms (in position or wealth), **equal** Plu. 3 (of troops) **equal** (in number, to the enemy) Plu.; (of heaps of grain, in size) Plu. —ὁμαλές neut.adv. **on the level** (opp. uphill) X.

ὁμαλίζω vb. | PASS.: fut. ὁμαλιοῦμαι | aor. ὡμαλίσθην | pf. ὡμάλισμαι | 1 **make uniform** —the threshing-floor (i.e. the supply of grain under the animals' feet) X. ‖ PASS. (of the threshing process) be made uniform X. 2 make equal (in scope or value), **equalise, level** —ambitions, property (in a society) Arist. ‖ PASS. (of estates, property) be brought to the same level (in value) Arist. 3 ‖ PASS. (of persons, city-states) be brought down to the same level (of misery, by unfortunate events) Isoc. 4 **be consistent** (in one's behaviour) Plb.

ὁμᾶλιξ dial.m.f.: see ὁμῆλιξ

ὁμαλός ή όν adj. [ὁμός] 1 (of a physical body) presenting no variation (in terms of its parts), **even, uniform** Pl.; (of a whittled stake) **smooth** Od. 2 (of a physical state, quality or action) **even, uniform, steady** or **consistent** Pl. Arist. Plu. 3 (of a length of time) **unbroken, lasting** Pi.fr. 4 (of ground or earth, esp. as advantageous for travel or fighting) **level** Plb. Plu.; (of a route) **over level ground** X. Plb. ‖ NEUT.SB. level ground Th. X. Plb. ‖ FEM.SB. route over level ground X. 5 (of persons or a city-state, status, property, wealth) on equal terms, **equal, egalitarian** Pl. Arist. Plu.; (of a marriage) **of equals** A. ‖ NEUT.SB. equality Pl. 6 (of a group of people) alike in character, **like** (W.DAT. one another) Theoc.; (of a person) like anyone else (in the same occupation), **no better or worse** Theoc.; (of loves, inspiring two people) **equal** Theoc. 7 (of the ideal dramatic character) **consistent** Arist. —ὁμαλῶς adv. 1 **evenly, uniformly, consistently** Th. Critias X. + 2 in a way that applies to both or all, **equally, generally** Plu. 3 **on equal terms, in a state of equality** Isoc.

ὁμαλότης ητος f. 1 **evenness, consistency, uniformity** (of physical states and qualities, of form) Pl. Arist. 2 **levelness, evenness** (of ground, a calm sea) Arist. 3 **equality** (betw. children in a family) Pl.; (of wealth) Arist.

ὁμαλύνω vb. | aor.inf. ὁμαλῦναι ‖ aor.pass.inf. ὁμαλυνθῆναι | 1 make a uniform height, **level** —a field of grain Arist. 2 **smooth** or **even out** —motions Pl. ‖ PASS. (of motions) be evened out Pl. 3 ‖ PASS. (of physical conditions) be made uniform Arist.

ὁμαρτέω, ep. ἁμαρτέω (Hom. cj., B.) contr.vb. [app. ὁμός, ἅμα; ἀραρίσκω] | Aeol.imperatv. ὑμάρτη (Theocr.) | impf. ὡμάρτουν, Ion. ὡμάρτευν (AR. Theocr.) | fut. ὁμαρτήσω | aor. ὡμάρτησα | 1 (of two people) act together or at the same time, **act in concert, join together** Hom. 2 (of a person or deity) **accompany, attend** or **follow closely** (freq. W.DAT. someone) Il. Hes. B. Trag. Hellenist.poet.; (of hounds) —W.DAT. a huntsman E.; (of a person) **consort** —W.DAT. w. evil persons Thgn. 3 (of a wind) **accompany** or **follow** —W.DAT. rain Hes.; (of the stars) —Night (on her journey across the heavens) E.; (of rocks) —Orpheus E.; (of a distaff, as a present) —its giver Theoc.; (of an olive-branch) attend (a corpse, on its way to the grave) Call. 4 (of Envy, Erinyes) **follow after, pursue, hound** —W.DAT. people Hes. A.; (of Argus) **follow** —W.PREP.PHR. in Io's footsteps A. 5 (of a herdsman) **look after, tend** —W.DAT. flocks E. Theoc. 6 (of a falcon, fishes) **keep pace** (w. a ship) Od. AR.

ὁμαρτῇ, ὁμαρτήδην advs.: see ἁμαρτῇ, ἁμαρτήδην

ὁμαυλία ᾱς f. [ὅμαυλος] living together (in marriage), **union** A.

ὅμ-αυλος ον adj. [αὐλή] 1 having a shared residence ‖ MASC.PL.SB. (of satyrs) neighbours or companions (W.GEN. of gods) S.satyr.fr. 2 [αὐλός] (of the sound of lamentation) **in harmony** (w. a paean) S.

ὀμβρέω contr.vb. [ὄμβρος] (of Zeus) **send down rain** Hes. AR.

ὀμβρηρός ά όν adj. (of winter) **rainy** Hes.

ὄμβριος ᾱ ον adj. 1 (of water) **from rain** Hdt. Ar. Arist. 2 (of a cloud) **rainy** Ar.; (of the offspring of a cloud, fig.ref. to raindrops) Pi.; (of hail) **showering** S.

ὀμβρο-κτύπος ον adj. (of a squall) **of driving rain** A.

ὄμβρος ου m. 1 (sg. and pl.) **rain** (esp.ref. to heavy rain or a rainstorm) Hom. +; (fig., ref. to a time of slaughter) A. Pi.; **shower** (of blood) S.(dub.) 2 (gener.) **water** Emp.; (of a river) S.; (of the sea) Tim.

ὀμβρο-φόρος ον adj. [φέρω] (of winds, clouds, thunder) **rain-bringing** A. Ar.

ὀμείρομαι mid.vb. **desire** or **care for** —W.GEN. someone NT.

ὀμείχω vb. | aor. ὤμειξα | **urinate** Hes.; **piss** —blood Hippon.

ὁμ-ευνέτης ου, dial. ὁμευνέτᾱς ᾱ m. [ὁμός] one who shares the same bed (w. a woman), **bed-mate** E.; (appos.w. θεός god) E.

ὁμευνέτις ιδος f. | acc. ὁμευνέτιν | **bed-mate** (ref. to a concubine) S.

ὅμ-ευνος ου masc.fem.adj. [εὐνή] sharing the same bed ‖ FEM.SB. bed-mate (ref. to a wife) Call.

ὁμ-ηγερής, dial. ὁμᾱγερής, ές adj. [ἀγείρω] 1 (of gods or men) **gathered together** (usu. for a council) Hom. AR.; (around a funeral pyre) Il.; (of a group of women, for a festival) Pi. 2 (of a tribe) **settled together** (in a city) AR.

ὁμηγυρίζομαι mid.vb. [ὁμήγυρις] **bring together** —one's troops (w. εἰς + ACC. for a public meeting) Od.

ὀμ-ήγυρις εως, dial. **ὀμάγυρις** ιος *f.* [ἄγυρις] **1** gathering together; **gathering, assembly** (of the gods, for a council) hHom.; **crowd** (of women, in mourning) A.; (of a person's friends) E.
2 community, company (of the gods, presided over by Zeus, on Olympos) Il. hHom. Pi.; (of the stars, at night) A.
ὀμήθης *adj.*: see ὁμοήθης
ὀμηλικίη ης *Ion.f.* [ὁμῆλιξ] **1** state of being in the same age group, **similar age** Il.
2 (concr.) person, pair or group of the same age (male or female); **one** or **two of similar age** Hom.; **peer group, friends, one's generation** Hom. Mimn.(or Thgn.) AR.
ὀμ-ῆλιξ, dial. **ὀμᾶλιξ**, Aeol. **ὑμᾶλιξ**, ικος *m.f.* **1** (usu.pl.) person of the same age and social group, **peer, friend, contemporary** Hom. Hes. Alcm. Sapph. Thgn. Hdt. +
2 ‖ FEM.ADJ. (of traditions) coeval with, as old as (W.DAT. time) E.
ὄμημος *Boeot.adj.*: see ὄμαιμος
ὄμηρα *n.pl.*: see under ὄμηρος
ὁμηρείᾱ ᾱς *f.* [ὁμηρεύω] **1** giving of a guarantee of good faith, **pledge, security** Th. Pl.
2 condition of being given as a hostage, **hostage status** Plb. Plu.
Ὁμήρειος *adj.*: see under Ὅμηρος
ὁμηρεύματα των *n.pl.* **pledges, securities** (ref. to women held as hostages) Plu.
ὁμηρεύω *vb.* [ὅμηρος] | aor. ὡμήρευσα | **1 be a hostage** E. Is. Aeschin. Plb. Plu.
2 take as hostages —*children* E.
3 ‖ MID. app. **give as hostages** or **securities** —*women* Plu.
ὁμηρέω *contr.vb.* [reltd. ὅμηρος, ὁμαρτέω] | Ion.fem.pl. ptcpl. ὁμηρεῦσαι | aor. ὡμήρησα | **1 come together with, meet** or **accompany** —W.DAT. *someone* Od.
2 (of the Muses) **be in unison** —W.DAT. w. *their voices* Hes.
Ὅμηρος ου *m.* **Homer** (epic poet, also meton. for his poetry) Xenoph. Simon. +
—**Ὁμηρίδαι** ῶν *m.pl.* **Homeridae** (ref. to reciters of his poetry) Pi. Isoc. Pl.
—**Ὁμήρειος** ᾱ ον *adj.* (of the poetry) **of Homer** Hdt. Call.*epigr.* ‖ MASC.PL.SB. **Homerists** (ref. to persons who claim to be experts in his poetry) Pl.
—**Ὁμηρικός** ή όν *adj.* of or associated with Homer or his poetry; (of a book) **of Homer's poetry** Plu.; (of Odysseus, a way of life, a saying) **Homeric** Pl. Call. Plu. ‖ MASC.PL.SB. **Homeric scholars** Arist. ‖ NEUT.SG.SB. **line from Homer** Plu. ‖ PL. **Homeric poems** Plu.
—**Ὁμηρικῶς** *adv.* **in Homeric manner** Pl.
ὅμηρος ου *m.f.* [ὁμός, ἀραρίσκω] **1 hostage** (ref. to a person, esp. as taken to ensure fulfilment of treaty obligations in war) Hdt. E. Th. Ar. +
2 hostage (ref. to a piece of territory) Th.; (fig., ref. to an example offered by a disputant) Pl.
—**ὄμηρα** ων *n.pl.* **securities** (ref. to hostages) Lys. Plb. Plu.
ὁμιλαδόν (also **ὁμιληδόν** Hes.) *adv.* [ὅμιλος] **in a crowd, in a massed throng** —*ref. to people or animals gathering, fighting, or sim.* Il. Hes. AR. Mosch.
ὁμιλέω *contr.vb.* | Aeol.3sg. ὁμίλλει | aor. ὡμίλησα | pf. ὡμίληκα | **1** form a gathering or crowd, **crowd** —W. περί + ACC. *around someone* Hom.
2 gather (for an occasion, esp. for drinking or a feast); **join, be amongst** —W.DAT. *others* Od. Pi.; **meet, congregate** Od.
3 gather or join in battle; **meet, be in the fray** (sts. W.DAT. or PREP.PHR. w. or amongst the enemy, alongside comrades or allies, in the frontline) Hom. E.
4 make contact (w. another territory or land); **visit** —W.DAT. *a land, a city* Hdt.; (w. hostile intent) **enter** —W.DAT. *a land* A. Hdt.
5 spend time in company (w. another or others) or (more formally) have social or political dealings (in one's own or w. another community); **keep company** (sts. W.DAT. or PREP.PHR. w. others, esp. friends or peers) Hom. +; **have dealings, associate, communicate** (w. others, freq. W.ADV. or PREP.PHR. *properly, on an equal basis, kindly, harshly, or sim.*) Hom. + ‖ MASC.PL.PTCPL.SB. **friends** or **associates** Hdt. E.
6 (specif.) **converse, talk, speak** (sts. W.DAT. or PREP.PHR. w. another or others, freq. W.ADV. *kindly, haughtily, or sim.*) Plb. NT.
7 associate (w. a great man or teacher); **be a follower** or **associate** —W.DAT. or PREP.PHR. *of someone* Hdt. X. Plu.
8 have a sexual association, **consort** —W.DAT. w. *someone* Alc. S. Att.orats. +
9 have an encounter (w. things which arise in life); **meet, deal** —W.DAT. w. *good or bad fortune, events, circumstances* Pi. E. Ar. Isoc. Plu.
10 have dealings or involve oneself, **be involved** or **familiar** —W.DAT. w. *power* Th. —*domestic work* AR. — *a subject of study, philosophy, gymnastics, or sim.* Pl. +; **live** —W.PREP.PHR. *outside one's character (i.e. be untrue to it)* S.
11 (of abstr. qualities or states) come upon (persons or places); (of fame) **visit** —W.DAT. *cities* Pi.; (of wealth, prosperity, delight) **be in attendance** (sts. W.DAT. upon someone) Pi. B. S. E.; (of strife) Pi.
ὁμιληδόν *adv.*: see ὁμιλαδόν
ὁμιλήματα των *n.pl.* **relations** (w. people in or outside one's community) Pl.
ὁμιλητής οῦ *m.* **close associate** (of Socrates) X.
ὁμιλητικός ή όν *adj.* (of a man) **sociable, affable** Isoc. Arist.
ὁμιλητός ή όν *adj.* (in neg.phr., of a woman's audacity) **able to be lived with** A.
ὁμιλίᾱ ᾱς, Ion. **ὁμιλίη** ης *f.* **1 fellowship** (amongst peers, friends or relatives, those embarked on a common enterprise); **company, friendship, comradeship** A. Hdt. E. Th. Ar. Att.orats. +
2 relationship (w. other people and their affairs), **association, dealings, relations** Pl. +
3 relationship (of one thing to another) Pl. D.
4 relationship and meetings (w. a philosopher or teacher), **company, society, discussion** Pl. X. D.; **association** (of a historian, w. previous writers) Plu.
5 relationship (outside one's community, w. other peoples or lands); **contact, connection** Hdt. E. Plb.; (of gods w. mortals) A. E. Ar. Pl.; (of enemy w. enemy, in time of war) Pl.
6 keeping company (amongst friends, relatives, betw. husband and wife); **company, closeness, friendliness** or **conversation** S. E. Att.orats. Pl. +
7 sexual intimacy or **intercourse** Hdt. E. Pl. X. Arist. Plu.
8 conversation, discussion Isoc. Plb. Plu.
9 social gathering (for a festive or religious occasion), **gathering** S. E.
10 association of individuals (linked by birth or common interests, or temporarily brought together by circumstance); **band, group** (of men, brothers, sailors, Erinyes) Hdt. Trag.
ὅμιλος ου *m.* [perh.reltd. ὁμός] **1** men gathered together as a force (in one place or on the move, esp. for a military purpose), **mass, force** Hom. A. Pi. B. Hdt. E. Th. +; (W.ADJ. ψιλός *light-armed*, opp. hoplite troops) Th.

2 mass of men in the thick of battle, **press, fray** Hom. Pi. Hdt. Th. AR. Theoc.; fighting force out of control, **mob, affray** Il. Hdt.
3 crowd gathered (around an important person or in response to an event), **crowd** Il. Hes.*fr.* A. Hdt. AR.
4 group standing or sitting together; **assembly** (of gods) A.; **group, company** (of satyrs, persons) E.*Cyc.* AR.
5 gathering (for games, a festive or religious occasion or other event), **crowd** Hom. Pi. B. Hdt. E. Th. +
6 party of men; **band, group** (of hunters) Hom. AR.; (of people travelling together) A.
7 company (as a collectv. unity, opp. an individual singled out), **multitude, group** Il. hHom. Hdt. AR.; **crowd, mass** (of objects) Od.
8 population living in a place; **company** (of gods or the Blessed, mortals in the world) Pi. Lyr.adesp. E.; **tribe, people** A. Hdt.; mass of the population, **populace** Pi. Hdt. Th. Ar.
9 (pejor.) **mob, rabble** (in a military or civil ctxt.) Il. Hdt. Plu.; (ref. to the common people) Hdt. Th.

ὀμίχλη ης, dial. **ὀμίχλᾱ** ᾱς *f.* **1** cloud of vapour (esp. fr. the sea or water, over mountains, under a dense sky, at dawn), **mist** Il. hHom. Ar. Pl. X. +; (fig., ref. to an unclear situation, obscuring wrongdoing) Ar.; (personif., as a deity) **Mist** Ar.
2 mist (in the eyes, fr. tears) A.
3 cloud (W.GEN. of dust, whipped up by wind) Il.

ὀμιχλώδης ες *adj.* (of a region, a morning) **misty, hazy** Plb. Plu.; (of a rising vapour) Plu.

ὄμμα, dial. **ὄθμα**, Aeol. **ὄππα**, ατος *n.* [reltd. ὄπωπα, see ὁράω] | Aeol.dat.pl. ὀππάτεσσι | **1** (sg. and pl.) act of looking (at someone or sthg., or in a certain direction), **look, glance, gaze** Il. +; (sg., as INTERN.ACC. w.vb. of looking) A. E.
2 visual appearance (of persons or things), **sight, aspect, image** Trag. Pl. +
3 (concr.) **eye** (in its function of seeing and looking) Hom. +
4 eye or face (as revealing a person's emotions or character, described as calm, bold, or sim., or used in ctxts. implying such features) Hom. +
5 (fig.) **eye** (of the heavens, ref. to the sun) Ar.; (of the sun, dawn) S. E.; (of night, ref. to darkness) A. E.; (of a lamp, ref. to its light) Ar.(mock-trag.)
6 (fig., as the principal or most precious part of a place) **eye, glory** (W.GEN. of a palace, ref. to the king's presence) A.; (of Athens, ref. to the populace or perh. to the Acropolis) A.
7 (fig.) source of comfort or joy, **light, comfort** (ref. to a beloved person) S.; (W.GEN. of a message) S.; (of safety) E.; **delight** (W.DAT. for foreigners, ref. to a city's prosperity) Pi.; (W.GEN. of a goddess, ref. to a mountain) E.

ὀμματο-στερής ές *adj.* [στερέω] **1** (of Oedipus) deprived of eyes, **sightless** S. E.
2 (of hot weather) stripping the eyes (fig.ref. to plant-shoots), **bud-destroying** A.

ὀμματόω *contr.vb.* | aor. ὤμμάτωσα | (fig.) **open the eyes** (of a person, by clarifying an issue) A. || PF.PASS.PTCPL.ADJ. (of a mind) furnished with eyes, clear-sighted A.

ὀμμεμείχμενος (Aeol.pf.pass.ptcpl.): see ἀναμείγνυμι

ὀμμένω Aeol.vb.: see ἀναμένω

ὀμμιμνᾱσκόμενος (Aeol.mid.pass.ptcpl.), **ὄμναισαι** (Aeol.aor.inf.), **ὀμνάσθην** (Aeol.aor.pass.inf.): see ἀναμιμνήσκω

ὄμνυμι *vb.* | imperatv. ὄμνῡθι, ὄμνῡ, 3pl. ὀμνύντων | impf. ὤμνῡν | fut. ὀμοῦμαι (also ὀμόσω Plu.), Lacon.1pl. ὀμιώμεθα (Ar., dub.) | aor. ὤμοσα, ep. ὤμοσσα, ὄμοσα, ὄμοσσα | pf. ὀμώμοκα | plpf. ὠμωμόκειν || PASS.: fut. ὀμοσθήσομαι | aor. ὠμόσθην, ὠμόθην | 3sg.pf. ὀμώμοται, also perh. ὀμώμοσται (Arist.), ptcpl. ὀμωμο(σ)μένος | —also (pres. and impf.) **ὀμνύω** | 3sg.imperatv. ὀμνυέτω | impf. ὤμνυον |
1 make a solemn declaration (w. an appeal to a divinity or sthg. sacred; esp. in the enactment of a new law, when taking office or embarking on a campaign, or when declaring loyalty or cementing an agreement); **swear** Hom. +; (in a court of law, to uphold duties in judgement or the truth of statements) Hes. +; **swear allegiance** —w. εἰς + ACC. *to someone* Plu.
2 (less formally) promise or give an undertaking (that sthg. is so, or about the future, what one will or will not do); **swear** Thgn. +
3 (in conversation) assert or declare (that one's statement is true, that one will or will not do sthg., w. a serious tone, or more casually, as when expressing anger or irritation); **swear** Thgn. +
4 (tr.) **swear** —W.INTERN.ACC. ὅρκον *an oath*, ἐπίορκον *a false oath* Hom. + —*certain things* Il. S. E. + —*a treaty, a peace* Th. D. || PASS. (of an oath) be sworn A. Att.orats. Arist.
5 swear —W.ACC. *by a deity, or sthg. held sacred or precious* Hom. +; (of gods) —*by the water of Styx* Il. AR. || PASS. (of Zeus) be sworn by, be witness to an oath E. Ar.
6 swear (w. ἦ μήν, Ion. ἦ μέν, *in very truth*, strengthening the assertion of the oath) Hom. S. Th. Ar. +
7 swear —W.INF. (ref. to present, past or future) *that sthg. is so, that one is doing, will do or has done sthg.* Hom. + —W.DIR.SP. *sthg.* X. Arist. Theoc. —w. ὅτι + DIR.SP. NT.

ὁμο-βώμιος ον *adj.* [ὁμός] (of gods) **of the common altars** (i.e. worshipped by all Greeks) Th.

ὁμο-γάλακτες ων *m.pl.* [γάλα] **those of the same mothers' milk** (ref. to people of a household or village) Arist.

ὁμό-γαμος ον *adj.* [γάμος] **1** (of Zeus) equal in marriage, **sharing a wife** (i.e. Alkmene, w. Amphitryon) E.
2 united in marriage (W.DAT. to someone) E.

ὁμο-γάστριος ον *adj.* [γαστήρ] (of brothers) from the same womb, **with the same mother** Il.

ὁμο-γενέτωρ ορος *m.* one who is of the same father, **brother** E.

ὁμο-γενής ές *adj.* [γένος, γίγνομαι] **1** (of persons) **of the same family, related by birth** E. Pl.; (of the neck, the life) **of a kinsman** E.; (of a city) **linked by kinship** (W.GEN. to the inhabitants of another city) E.; (of blood pollution) incurred by kinship, **kindred** E. || MASC.SB. relative, kinsman E.
2 || NEUT.SB. common ancestry, community of race (shared by two groups of people) Plb.
3 (of animals) **of the same species** Democr.
4 || MASC. and NEUT.PL.SB. persons or things of the same kind or class Arist.
5 (of Oedipus) **jointly engendering children** (w. his own mother) S.

ὁμό-γλωσσος, Att. **ὁμόγλωττος**, ον *adj.* [γλῶσσα] (of a people) **having the same language** (sts. W.DAT. as another) Hdt. X. Plb.; (of the Greeks as a whole) **having a common language** Hdt.

ὁμόγνιος ον *adj.* [reltd. ὁμογενής] **1** (epith. of Zeus, of the gods in general) **overseeing kinship** S. E. Ar. Pl.
2 (of a person) of the same family, **related** (W.GEN. to someone) AR.

ὁμογνωμονέω *contr.vb.* [ὁμογνώμων] (of persons) **be of one mind, be in agreement** (freq. W.DAT. w. others) Th. X. Aeschin. D. Arist. +; (of an individual) —W.DAT. *w. oneself* Arist.

ὁμο-γνώμων ον, gen. ονος *adj.* **1** (of persons, esp. in political ctxt.) **of like mind, in agreement** (among one another or w. others) Th. X. D. Plb.; (W.DAT. w. others) Th. Lys. X. Aeschin.
2 in favour (W.DAT. of sthg.) D.
—**ὁμογνωμόνως** *adv.* **unanimously** Lycurg.
ὁμό-γονος ον *adj.* [γόνος] **1** ‖ MASC.SB. (sg. and pl.) **relative, kinsman** Pi. Pl. X.
2 (of a class of things) **akin, similar** (W.DAT. to other things) Pl.
ὁμό-δᾱμος ον *dial.adj.* [δῆμος] **1** (of offspring of stone, ref. to the race created by Deukalion and Pyrrha) **forming a common people** Pi.
2 (of a man) **belonging to the same land** (W.DAT. as a people) Pi.
ὁμο-δέμνιος ον *adj.* [δέμνιον] (of a husband) **sharing the same bed** (as his wife) A.
ὁμοδοξέω *contr.vb.* [reltd. ὁμοδοξία] **1 have the same opinion** (as another) Plb.
2 (of the soul) **be in agreement** —W.DAT. *w. the body* Pl.; (of one part of an individual, w. another part) —W.ACC. + INF. *that sthg. shd. be so* Pl.
ὁμοδοξία ᾱς *f.* [δόξα] **agreement in opinion, unanimity** Pl. Arist.
ὁμό-δουλος ου *m.f.* [δοῦλος] **fellow slave** E. Pl. Plu.; (W.GEN. or DAT. along w. others) Pl. X.
ὁμο-εθνής ές *adj.* [ἔθνος] **1** (of persons) **of the same people or race** Hdt. Arist. Plb.
2 (of people or animals) **of the same species** Arist.
ὁμο-ειδής ές *adj.* [εἶδος¹] (of things) **alike in form** or **kind** Arist. Plb. Plu.
ὁμό-ζυξ ζυγος *m.* [ζεύγνῡμι] **one who is under the same yoke, mate** (ref. to a horse in a pair) Pl.
ὁμο-ήθης (also **ὁμήθης** Call. AR.) ες *adj.* [ἦθος] | *compar.* ὁμοηθέστερος | (of a person) **similar in habits** or **character** (to another) Pl. Arist. ‖ MASC.PL.SB. **friends** or **associates** Call.; (appos.w. κοῦροι, ἄνδρες) AR.
ὁμο-θάλαμος ου *f.* **sharer of the abode** (W.GEN. of the Nereids, ref. to a sea goddess) Pi.
ὁμόθεν *adv.*: see under ὁμός
ὁμό-θηρος ου *f.* [θήρᾱ] **partner in the hunt** (w. Artemis) Call.
ὁμό-θρονος ου *f.* [θρόνος] **sharer of the throne** (of Zeus, ref. to Hera) Pi.
ὁμοθῡμαδόν *adv.* [θῡμός] **with a common spirit** or **purpose, with one accord** Ar. Pl. X. D. +
ὁμοίιος ον *ep.adj.* [perh.reltd. ὁμοῖος, or assoc. by pop.etym.] | *gen.* ὁμοιίου (or ὁμοιίοο) | **1** (of war, strife, old age, death) perh., **the same for all, impartial, levelling** Hom. hHom.
2 (of day) **equal** (in duration, w. night) Bion
3 (in neg.phr., of a father) **having characteristics in common** (W.DAT. w. his children) Hes.; (of a god, w. mortals) Xenoph.
ὁμοιο-ειδής ές *adj.* [ὁμοῖος, εἶδος¹] (of an art) **of a similar kind, similar** (W.DAT. to another) Isoc.
ὁμοιομέρεια ᾱς *f.* [ὁμοιομερής] **likeness of parts** (in the teaching of Anaxagoras) Plu.
ὁμοιο-μερής ές *adj.* [μέρος] (of a physical thing) **having** or **consisting of similar parts** (both in relation to each other and to the whole, esp. in the teaching of Anaxagoras) Arist.
ὁμοιοπαθέω *contr.vb.* [ὁμοιοπαθής] (of persons) **have similar experience** or **feelings** —W.DAT. *to someone else* Arist.

ὁμοιο-παθής ές *adj.* [πάθος] **1** (of persons) **similar in experience** or **feelings** (W.DAT. to others) NT.; (of standards of behaviour) Pl.
2 (of substances) **similarly affected** (in a process) Pl.
ὁμοιο-πρεπής ές *adj.* [πρέπω] (of persons) **looking** or **seeming like** (W.DAT. others) A.
ὁμοιό-πτωτος ον *adj.* [πίπτω] (gramm., of a word) **with a similar ending** or **inflection** Plu.
ὁμοῖος, Att. **ὅμοιος**, Aeol. **ὔμοιος**, ᾱ (Ion. η) ον *adj.* [ὁμός] | *compar.* ὁμοιότερος, *superl.* ὁμοιότατος | **1** (of persons or things) **being the same, similar** or **a match** (in appearance, character, attributes, or sim., sts. W.ACC. in a certain respect, or W.INF. in doing sthg.); **alike** (i.e. similar to one another) Hom. +; **similar** (W.DAT. to one another, or to someone or sthg. else) Hom. + ‖ MASC.SB. (usu.pl.) **equal** or **peer** Hdt. X. Arist.; (appos.w. ἀνήρ) Il.
2 (ellipt.) Hom. + • κόμαις Χαρίτεσσιν ὁμοῖαι *hair like (that of) the Graces* Il. • (w.relatv.adj.) ὅμοιον εἶναι τὸ τῶν Λακεδαιμονίων πρᾶγμα οἷόνπερ τὸ τῶν ποταμῶν *the situation with the Spartans is much the same as that of rivers* X. | see also καί 2
3 (implying a judgement betw. qualities, whether good or bad, esp. in neg.phrs.) Hom. + • ἐπεὶ οὔ πω πάντες ὁμοῖοι ἀνέρες ἐν πολέμῳ *for in no way are all men equal in war* Il. • ἀσπάλαθοι δὲ τάπησιν ὁμοῖον στρῶμα θανόντι *thorns are as good a bed as rugs for a dead man* Thgn. • θεὸν οὐ θεοῖς ὁμοίαν *a goddess unlike the gods* A.
4 being or **remaining the same** (as in another time, place or circumstance), **the same** Hom. + • (w.relatv.adj.) εἴ τοι ὁμοίη ἐγὼν ἰνδάλλομαι εἶναι, οἵην δή με τὸ πρῶτον ἐν ὀφθαλμοῖσι νόησας *whether I appear to you to be the same as (I was when) you first saw me* hHom.
5 ‖ NEUT.IMPERS. (w. ἐστί, sts.understd.) **it is all the same, it makes no difference** A. +; (also pl.) E.; **it is like** —W.INF. *doing sthg.* E.
—**ὁμοῖον** *neut.sg.adv.* **in a similar way to, like** (W.DAT. sthg.) Theoc.
—**ὁμοῖα** *neut.pl.adv.* **in similar ways, alike, equally** A.; **like** (W.DAT. someone or sthg.) Hdt. +
—**ὁμοίως** *adv.* **1 in the same** or **a similar manner** (for both in a pairing of persons or things, or all in a group); **similarly, alike, equally, all the same** Hdt. Trag. Th. +; (W.DAT. for someone, both, all) Sol. +
2 in the same or **a similar manner as, like** (W.DAT. someone or sthg.) Hdt. E. Att.orats. +
3 in the same or **a similar manner** (as in another time, place or circumstance, or as on all occasions), **similarly, alike, equally** Pi. Hdt. Trag. Th. +; (w. ὡς, ὥσπερ, *as if*) Hdt. +; (w. καί *as in fact*) Hdt. +
ὁμοιοσχημόνως *adv.* [σχῆμα] **as similar in kind** —*ref. to things being categorised* Arist.
ὁμοιο-τέλευτον ου *n.* [τελευτή] (rhet.) **ending** (of successive words or phrases) **with the same sound, homoioteleuton** Arist.
ὁμοιότης ητος *f.* **1 state of having characteristics in common, likeness, similarity, resemblance** (betw. two things; sts. W.GEN. + DAT. of one thing to another; sts. W.GEN. in some respect) Pl. Arist. Plb.; (betw. individual things in a group or class) Pl. +; (betw. persons, in appearance or attributes) Isoc. Pl. +
2 likeness or **equivalence** (betw. cases examined in a study), **similarity, analogy** Pl. Arist.; (betw. words) Arist.; (betw. historical events) Plb.

3 similarity of condition, **comparability, balance** Pl.; (amongst citizens, in their privileges) Isoc. Arist.
4 sameness of composition or properties, **homogeneity, uniformity** (of the heavens) Pl.; (in building, town plans) Pl. Plb.

ὁμοιό-τροπος ον *adj*. [τρόπος] **1** (of different persons, peoples or city-states) **of similar character** or **conduct** Th. **2** (of practices) of a similar nature, **similar** (W.DAT. to a people, i.e. to their practices) Th.; (of certain duties, to others) Arist.

—ὁμοιοτρόπως *adv*. **in a similar manner** (W.DAT. to sthg. else) Th.; **likewise** Arist.

ὁμοιόω *contr.vb*. [ὁμοῖος] | impf. ὡμοίουν | fut. ὁμοιώσω | aor. ὡμοίωσα ‖ PASS.: fut. ὁμοιωθήσομαι | aor. ὡμοιώθην, ep.inf. ὁμοιωθήμεναι ‖ PF.MID.PASS.: ὡμοίωμαι |
1 create a likeness; **make** (W.ACC. someone or sthg.) **similar** —W.DAT. *to someone or sthg. else* (*in appearance or nature*) Isoc. Pl.; **make** (W.ACC. an image) **as a likeness** —W.DAT. *to a person* E. ‖ PASS. (of things) be made alike Emp.; (of persons or things) be made to resemble —W.DAT. *others* Pl. Arist.
2 create uniformity; **level** —*excavated earth* (W.DAT. *w. the surrounding ground*) Hdt.; (of war) **assimilate, adapt** —*people's temperaments* (W.PREP.PHR. *to circumstances*) Th.
3 ‖ PRES.MID.PASS. (of persons or things) be like (others, in appearance, nature, behaviour, or sim.); **be like, be comparable** (usu. W.DAT. to someone or sthg. else) Hdt. E. Th. Isoc. Pl. +
4 ‖ AOR.PASS. (of the Dioscuri) take on the appearance of —W.DAT. *stars* E.; (of Zeus) —*a swan* Isoc.; (of gods) —*men* NT.; (of people) come to be like —W.DAT. *certain people* (*in nature or behaviour*) Th. NT.; (of dogs) —*wolves* Pl.; (of the Kingdom of Heaven, in a parable) be like —W.DAT. *sthg. else* NT.
5 ‖ AOR.PASS. be considered or treated as equal (to another) Hom.; become equal to, live up to —W.DAT. *one's own or another's achievements or aspirations* Th. Isoc.
6 ‖ PF.MID.PASS. (of persons or things) be in a similar state —W.DAT. *to others* Pl. Arist.; (of a situation) be the same (as before) Plb.
7 **liken, compare** —*persons or things* (W.DAT. *to others*) Isoc. Pl. NT. Plu. —*someone's misfortunes* (*to one's own*) Hdt.(mid.) ‖ PASS. (of a city-state) be likened —W.DAT. *to a wise man's head and senses* Pl.

ὁμοίωμα ατος *n*. **1** that which resembles or is made to resemble (sthg. else); **similar** or **comparable thing** Pl. Arist.; **likeness, image** Pl. Arist. NT.; **representation** (of sthg., in music) Pl.
2 point or points of resemblance, **similarity** (to sthg. else, or betw. different forms of the same thing) Arist.; (of a name, to what it represents) Pl.; (of numbers, to certain qualities) Arist.

ὁμοίως *adv*.: see under ὁμοῖος

ὁμοίωσις εως *f*. **1** process of becoming alike, **becoming similar** (W.DAT. to a god) Pl.
2 condition of being alike, **likeness** (betw. things) Pl.

ὁμό-καποι ων *m.pl*. [ὁμός, κάπη] **those who share the same manger** (fig.ref. to members of a household) Arist.(quot.)

ὁμο-κέλευθος ου *m*. **companion on the road** Pl.

ὁμόκλαρος *dial.adj*.: see ὁμόκληρος

ὁμοκλάω (or **ὁμοκλάω**), also **ὁμοκλέω** (or **ὁμοκλέω**) ep.contr.vb. [ὁμοκλή] | impf. ὁμόκλεον, 3sg. ὁμόκλᾱ | aor. ὁμόκλησα, 3sg.iterat.v. ὁμοκλήσασκε | **shout, cry out** (esp. in encouragement or rebuke, or threateningly) Hom. AR. —W.DAT. *to people* Il. —W.ACC. + INF. *that people shd. do sthg.* Il. —W. μή + INF. *not to do sthg.* Od. —W.FUT.INF. *that one will do sthg.* AR.; (of charioteers) —W.DAT. *to their horses* S.

ὁμοκλή (or **ὁμοκλή**) ῆς *f*. [reltd. καλέω] **1 shout, cry** (esp. as an encouragement, order, rebuke or threat) Hom. Hes. hHom. Emp. Call. AR.
2 cry, baying (of hounds) AR.
3 stirring call (of the aulos) A.*fr*. Pi.

ὁμό-κληρος, dial. **ὁμόκλᾱρος**, ον *adj*. [ὁμός, κλῆρος] (of Apollo and Artemis) **sharing an equal heritage** (as tutelary deities of a place) Pi.; (of a brother, w. his brother, both being victorious in the games) Pi.; (of a country, W.GEN. w. another country, both having the same founders) Plu.

ὁμοκλητήρ ῆρος *m*. [ὁμοκλάω] **one shouting encouragement** (to men in battle, to horses in a race) Il.

ὁμό-κλῑνος ου *m*. [κλίνη] **companion of the dining couch** (ref. to an honoured guest) Hdt.

ὁμό-κοιτις ιος *f*. [κοίτη] **woman who shares a bed, wife** Pl.

ὁμό-λεκτρος ον *adj*. [λέκτρον] (of a wife) **sharing the marriage bed** E.; (of a man) **sharing one's wife** (W.GEN. w. Zeus) E.

ὁμο-λεχής ές *adj*. [λέχος] **sharing the same bed** Lyr.adesp.

ὁμολογέω *contr.vb*. [ὁμόλογος] | aor. ὡμολόγησα | pf. ὡμολόγηκα ‖ PASS.: aor. ὡμολογήθην | pf. ὡμολόγημαι ‖ neut.impers.vbl.adj. ὁμολογητέον | **1** make an agreement (informally or in law); **make an agreement** or **contract** Att.orats. —W.DAT. *w. someone* Pl. + —W.DAT. *on a price* Hdt. —W.INF. *to be such and such* Hdt.
2 (in war) make an agreement (about a truce, peace or surrender); **come to terms** (sts. W.DAT. w. a foreign leader or state, an enemy) Hdt. Th. +
3 give one's agreement (to sthg. said, esp. to a proposition in philosophical dialogue); **assent, concede, agree** Hdt. + —W.DAT. *w. someone* Ar. + —W.ACC. *about sthg.* Pl. —W.ACC. + INF. or COMPL.CL. *that sthg. is so, that someone is such and such* Heraclit. Att.orats. Pl. + ‖ MID. **reach a conclusion jointly** Pl.
4 assent (to a request); **agree** —W.FUT.INF. *to do sthg.* Att.orats. +
5 assent (to an allegation of wrongdoing, lack of openness, failure); **make an admission, confess** Hdt. E. Th. + —*sthg.* S. Antipho + —W.INF. or COMPL.CL. *to doing or being sthg.* Th. Ar. +
6 agree by common consensus; **agree** —W.COMPL.CL. *that sthg. is so, that someone is such and such* Th. Ar. +
7 be in agreement (about the past); (of a people) **tell the same story** Hdt.; **agree** —W.DAT. *amongst themselves, w. others* Hdt. —W.COMPL.CL. *that sthg. was so* Hdt. Th.
8 correspond (in beliefs, customs, identity, purpose); (of a people) **be similar** —W.DAT. *to others* (sts. W.PREP.PHR. *in relation to practices*) Hdt.; (of persons) **have a connection** (through kinship) —*w. someone* Hdt.; (of two characters) **be similar** (to each other) Lys.; **agree on the same policy** Hdt.
9 openly acknowledge (beliefs, customs, an identity); **profess** —W.INF. *to honouring sthg.* Hdt. —*to following an occupation* Isoc.; **affirm one's belief** NT.
10 (of persons, their speech or actions) be consistent (w. the evidence); (of witnesses, at a trial) **be consistent** —W.DAT. *w. the argument presented* Antipho; (of an argument) —*w. the witnesses* Antipho; (of a person's actions) —*w. his words* Th.; (of words) —*w. actions* Th. Pl. ‖ MID. (of a person, in his way of life) **have the characteristic of consistency** Plb.
11 (of things) be consistent (w. other things); (of an endeavour) **match** —W.DAT. *other people's* Isoc.; (of events) **have links** —W.DAT. *w. others* And.

ὁμολόγημα

12 ‖ MID. (of laws, stories, statements) **be consistent** (sts. W.DAT. w. one another) Att.orats. +
13 ‖ PASS. (of persons or things) **be agreed, acknowledged** or **admitted** (freq. W.INF. to be such and such) Th. + ‖ IMPERS. **it is agreed** or **acknowledged** Hdt. Th. +
—**ὁμολογούμενος** η ον *pass.ptcpl.adj.* (of things) **admitted** or **acknowledged generally, agreed upon, undisputed** Th. + ‖ NEUT.SB. **congruity** (betw. things) Pl.; (pl.) **agreed facts** Att.orats. +; (prep.phr.) ἐξ ὁμολογουμένου **beyond dispute** Plb.
—**ὁμολογουμένως** *pass.ptcpl.adv.* **1 admittedly, by common consent** or **unquestionably** Th. Att.orats. +
2 consistently, coherently X.; **in a manner consistent** (W.DAT. w. one's words) X.

ὁμολόγημα ατος *n.* **admission, agreement** Pl. Hyp.

ὁμολογίᾱ ᾱς, Ion. **ὁμολογίη** ης *f.* **1 terms of agreement; agreement, contract** Hdt. Att.orats. Pl. +
2 (in war) **terms** (for a truce, peace or surrender; freq.pl.); **accord, agreement, capitulation** Hdt. Th. +
3 state of assent (to an argument or proposition); **agreement** (esp. in philosophical dialogue) Pl.; (betw. judges) Pl.
4 admission of guilt Att.orats.
5 general agreement (about the usage of words) Pl.
6 correspondence (betw. rhythms in music, words) Pl.

ὁμό-λογος ον *adj.* [λόγος] **1** (of persons) **agreeing** X.; (of things) **corresponding** (W.DAT. w. others) Arist.
2 (prep.phr.) ἐξ ὁμολόγου **as agreed** Plb.; **beyond dispute** Plb.
—**ὁμολόγως** *adv.* **in a corresponding manner** Arist.

ὁμολογουμένως *pass.ptcpl.adv.*: see under ὁμολογέω

Ὁμολωΐδες ων *fem.pl.adj.* (of a gate of Thebes) **Homoloid** A. E.

ὁμο-μαστῑγίᾱς ου *m.* [ὁμός] **fellow floggee** (com.epith. of Zeus, as patron of slaves) Ar.

ὁμο-μήτριος, dial. **ὁμομάτριος**, ᾱ ον *adj.* [μήτηρ] (of a brother or sister) **with the same mother** (by the same or a different father) Hdt. Ar. Att.orats. +

ὁμο-μήτωρ ορος *masc.fem.adj.* **with the same mother** Pl.(quot.poet.)

ὁμονοέω *contr.vb.* | aor. ὡμονόησα | **1** (of citizens, political factions, allies, Greek peoples) **be of one mind** (in peace, friendship or agreed purpose), **be united, agree** Th. Att.orats. +—W.DAT. w. **one another** And. Arist. —W.PREP.PHR. **about sthg.** Isoc.
2 (of persons, esp. friends or family) **concur in feeling and opinion, be of one mind, agree** Isoc. Pl. X. Arist. —W.DAT. w. **others** Pl.
3 (of persons) **have the same opinion** (in a particular instance), **agree** Isoc. —W.ACC. **on sthg.** X. —W.DAT. w. **another**, w. **what has been said** Isoc. Pl. —w. **oneself** (i.e. **be sure**) Pl. —W.PREP.PHR. **about sthg.** Pl. Arist. —W.COMPL.CL. **that they shd. do sthg. together** Pl.
4 (of a person, in his life) **be in harmony** Isoc. —W.DAT. w. **himself** Pl.
5 (of things which are usu. opposed to each other) **be in accord**; (of success) **be commensurate** —W.DAT. w. **risks taken** Lys.; (of judgement and desire) **be in harmony** Pl.

ὁμονοητικός ή όν *adj.* (of a circumstance) **of agreement** or **unity** Arist.; (of a way of life, the soul) **in a state of harmony** Pl.
—**ὁμονοητικῶς** *adv.* **in unity, harmoniously** Pl.

ὁμόνοια ᾱς, Ion. **ὁμονοίη** ης *f.* **1 unanimity, concord** (betw. citizens or states) Th. +; (in a household) Isoc. +
2 agreement (betw. individuals) Pl. X.
3 harmony (in the elements of one's life) Men.; (betw. opposing qualities, in an art or science) Pl.
4 Concord (as a goddess) AR. Plu.

ὁμό-νομος ον *adj.* [νόμος] **sharing the same laws** Pl.

ὁμό-νόως (also contr. **ὁμόνως**) *adv.* [νόος] **of one mind, in unity** X.

ὁμόομαι *pass.contr.vb.* | aor.inf. ὁμωθῆναι | (of husband and wife) **be united** —W.DAT. **in lovemaking** Il.

ὁμοπαθέω *contr.vb.* [ὁμοπαθής] (of an army) **be of like mind** (w. its commander) Plu.

ὁμο-παθής ές *adj.* [πάθος] **of similar attitudes** Arist.; **having the same experience** (W.GEN. of sthg.) Pl.

ὁμο-πάτριος ᾱ ον (also ος ον Hes.*fr.* A.) *adj.* [πατήρ] (of sisters or brothers) **from the same father** (w. the same or a different mother) Hes.*fr.* A. Hdt. Lys. Pl. Men.; (specif., w. a different mother) Att.orats. Pl.

ὁμο-πάτωρ ορος *masc.adj.* (of a brother) **from the same father** Pl. Is. D.; (of a nephew) **on the father's side** Is.

ὁμοπλοέω *contr.vb.* [πλόος] (of ships) **sail in company** Plb.

ὁμο-πολέω *contr.vb.* (of Apollo, w. play on his name) **move** (W.ACC. all things) **in unison** Pl.

ὁμό-πτερος ον *adj.* [πτερόν] **1 of the same plumage**; (of different kinds of birds) **of the same feathered tribe** A. Ar.; (of winged souls) Pl.
2 (of hair) **similar** (to another's) A. E.; (of a pair of brothers) **kindred** E.

ὁμό-πτολις εως *ep.masc.fem.adj.* [πόλις] (of a people) **sharing the same city** S.

ὁμοργάζω *vb.* [reltd. ὁμόργνυμαι] | impf. ὡμόργαζον | **keep rubbing** —one's eyes (as if on waking *fr.* sleep) hHom.

ὁμόργνυμαι *mid.vb.* | 3pl.impf. ὡμόργνυντο | aor.ptcpl. ὁμορξάμενος | **wipe away** —one's tears Hom. AR.

ὁμορέω, Ion. **ὁμουρέω** *contr.vb.* [ὅμορος] **share a border**; (of a country, a people, an estate) **be adjacent** —W.DAT. **to another** Hdt. Plu.; (of cities) **border** —W.DAT. **on a gulf** Hdt.

ὄμ-ορος, Ion. **ὄμουρος**, ον *adj.* [ὁμός, ὅρος] **1** (of a land, a people) **sharing a border** (sts. W.DAT. w. another) Hdt. Th. D. Plu. ‖ MASC.SB. **neighbour** (ref. to a ruler) Th.; (ref. to an enemy force) Isoc. X.; (pl.) **neighbouring people** Hdt. Th. Att.orats. + ‖ FEM.SB. **neighbouring city** or **land** Th. Plu. ‖ NEUT.SB. **fact of being neighbours** Th.
2 (of a mountain) **of** or **on the border** Plb.; (of a war) D. Plu.; (of marauders) Plu.
3 (of an estate) **bordering, adjacent** (to another) D.
4 (of persons) **having a close resemblance** Arist.

—**ὁμούριος** ον *Ion.adj.* (of a place, a people) **bordering** (W.DAT. on another place or people) Call. AR.

ὁμορροθέω *contr.vb.* [ὁμόρροθος] **be in complete agreement, concur** S. Ar.(quot. S.); (of a fact) **completely support** —W.DAT. **a person's words** E.

ὁμό-ρροθος ον *adj.* [ῥόθος] **making a concordant sound**; (gener., of persons, their minds) **in unison, with similar intent** Simon. Theoc.*epigr.*

ὁμός ή όν *adj.* [reltd. ὁμαλός] **1 shared amongst all**; (of fighting) **all together, in a mass** Il.; (of a journey) **same** (as undertaken by others) Od.; (of tracks, as used by others) Call. ‖ NEG.PHR. (of shouting, fr. a huge crowd) **discordant** Il.
2 shared between two; (of the parentage of brothers) **shared by both, common, in common** Il.; (of a marriage bed) Il. Hes.; (of a fate or misfortune) Hom.; (of an urn) Il.; (of honour) Il.; (of thoughts) Hes. ‖ NEG.PHR. (of the appearance of fabulous beasts) **having nothing in common** (W.DAT. w. men) AR. ‖ NEUT.SB. **that which is like** (sthg. else) Parm.
3 (prep.phr.) εἰς ὁμά **together** (W.DAT. w. someone, ref. to sleeping) Theoc.

—**ὁμόθεν** *adv.* **1 from the same place** or **direction** AR. Plu. **2 from the same stock** —*ref. to being born* Hes. hHom. S. E. X.; (prep.phr.) ἐξ ὁμόθεν *from the same root or stem* —*ref. to things growing* Od. **3 at close quarters** —*ref. to fighting, pursuing, or sim.* X.

—**ὁμόσε** *adv.* **1 together to the same place** or **point**; **together into one place** Il. Plb.; **together towards an agreed conclusion** —*ref. to deliberating* D. Plb. **2 together along with, alongside** (W.DAT. things or persons) Plb. **3 together to a place** or **point of confrontation**; **into close quarters, to full engagement** Il.; (w.vbs. of movt.; W.DAT. w. an enemy, or fig., w. a difficult challenge) Th. Ar. X. Arist. +; (w. an argument or opinion) E. Pl. +

—**ὁμοῦ**, Aeol. **ὔμοι** *adv.* and *prep.* **1 together** (in the same place or company), **together, side by side, all together** Hom. +; (prep.) **together with, along with, alongside** —W.DAT. *persons or things* Hom. Hdt. S. Th. +; **among** —W.DAT. *the clouds* Il.; (ref. to living) **within** —W.DAT. *a city* S. **2 together** (at the same time), **at the same time, both at once** or **all together** Il. + **3 together** (in united purpose or effort), **together, all together, side by side, in unity** Il. Hdt. Ar. +; **in unison** —*ref. to singing* A. S.; (prep.) **together** —W.DAT. *w. the gods* S. **4 close at hand, nearby** S. Ar. Pl. X.; (prep., ref. to lying) **close by** —W.DAT. *someone's side* S. **5** (in reckoning, w. numeral or sim.) **altogether, in all, in total** S. Th. D. Plu.; (phr.) ὁμοῦ τι *nearly, approximately* D. Plu.; (gener., ref. to saying sthg.) *more or less* Men. **6** (reinforcing a connection or antithesis betw. two nouns or cls.) **both, alike** (or sim.) Hom. + • εἰ δὴ ὁμοῦ πόλεμός τε δαμᾷ καὶ λοιμὸς Ἀχαιούς *if war and pestilence alike will destroy the Achaeans* Il. • πόλις δ' ὁμοῦ μὲν θυμιαμάτων γέμει, ὁμοῦ δὲ παιάνων τε καὶ στεναγμάτων *the city is full not only of incense but also of paeans and groaning* S.

—**ὁμῶς** *adv.* **1 in a way that applies equally** (to two persons, things or situations), **equally, in the same way, similarly, likewise** Hom. Hes. Iamb. Eleg. A. Pi. + **2 in a way that applies equally** (to all persons, things or situations, considered collectively; freq. w. πάντες, πάντα *all*, or sim.), **alike, together** Hom. Hes. Eleg. Simon. A. Pi. + **3 in the same way** (W.DAT. as someone or sthg. else) Il. hHom. Tyrt.(cj.) E.fr.(cj.) **4** (ref. to location) **together, side by side** Theoc.

ὤμοσα (ep.aor.), **ὀμοσθήσομαι** (fut.pass.): see ὄμνυμι

ὀμόσε *adv.*: see under ὁμός

ὁμο-σίπυοι ων *m.pl.* [σιπύη] **those who share the same grain-tub** (ref. to members of a household) Arist.(quot.)

ὁμοσῑτέω *contr.vb.* [ὁμόσῑτοι] (of wives) **share meals** —W.DAT. *w. their husbands* Hdt.

ὁμό-σῑτοι ων *m.pl.* [σῖτος] **persons dining together** (w. μετά + GEN. w. a king) Hdt.

ὁμό-σκευος ον *adj.* [σκευή] (of a tribe) **with the same military equipment** (as another) Th.

ὁμό-σπλαγχνος ον *adj.* [σπλάγχνον] (of siblings, their bodies) **from the same womb** A. S.

ὁμό-σπονδος ον *adj.* [σπονδή] **sharing in libations** Hdt. Att.orats.

ὁμό-σπορος ον *adj.* [σπορά] **1 of the same sowing**; (of a brother or sister) **born of the same father** Trag.; (of hands, blood, a race) **of the same male line, kindred** A. Pi. ‖ MASC.FEM.SB. **brother or sister** hHom. Trag. **2** (of Oedipus) **fathering children with the same woman** (as his father) S.; (of his wife) **bearing children to both** (husband and son) S.

ὄμοσσα (ep.aor.): see ὄμνυμι

ὁμο-στῐχάω *contr.vb.* (of a herdsman) **walk along with** —W.DAT. *his cattle* Il.

ὁμό-στολος ον *adj.* [στόλος] **1 travelling in company** (W.DAT. w. someone) AR.; (of Bacchus, W.GEN. w. Maenads) S. **2 similarly equipped** or **attired**; (gener., of a person's physical appearance) **similar** (to another's) A.

ὁμο-σύζυγος ον *adj.* (of honey and cheese) **equally partnering** (other food) Philox.Leuc.

ὁμόσω (fut.): see ὄμνυμι

ὁμό-ταφος ον *adj.* [τάφος¹] (of heroes) **sharing a grave** Aeschin.

ὁμο-τέρμων ονος *m.* **one who shares a property boundary, close neighbour** Pl.

ὁμό-τεχνος ου *m.f.* [τέχνη] **fellow craftsman** or **practitioner** Hdt. Pl. D. NT.; (W.DAT. w. someone) Pl.

ὁμό-τῑμος ον *adj.* [τῑμή] **of equal high honour** or **rank** Il. Simon. Plu.; **honoured as highly** (W.DAT. as the gods) Theoc.; **sharing the privilege** (W.GEN. of military command) Plu. ‖ MASC.PL.SB. **equals in honour, peers** (as a Persian rank) X.; (at Rome, ref. to patricians) Plu.

ὁμό-τοιχος ον *adj.* [τοῖχος] **with a boundary wall in common**; (of a neighbour) **next-door** A. Pl.; (of a property) **adjoining** Is. ‖ MASC.SB. **next-door neighbour** Call.

ὁμό-τονον ου *n.* [τόνος] (mus.) **even pitch** or **tone** (equiv. to that of the speaking voice, opp. high or low) Pl.

ὁμό-τράπεζος ον *adj.* [τράπεζα] **sharing the same table** (usu. W.DAT. w. someone, as a mark of honour or friendship) Hdt. Pl. X. Din. ‖ MASC.PL.SB. **table companions** (of the Persian king, as a title of honour) X.

ὁμό-τροπος ον *adj.* [τρόπος] (of a person) **of similar character** (sts. W.DAT. to oneself) Men.; (of the soul, to the body) Pl.; (of customs or rites, to those of others) Hdt. ‖ MASC.PL.SB. **equals in character** or **way of life** (W.GEN. to a certain person) Aeschin.

—**ὁμοτρόπως** *adv.* **with the same meaning** —*ref. to using different words* Arist.

ὁμό-τροφος ον *adj.* [τρέφω] **1** (of a deity) **sharing the same upbringing** or **nurture** (sts. W.DAT. or GEN. as another) hHom. Pi.; (of the soul, as the body) Pl.; (of domestic animals) **raised and living together** (W.DAT. w. humans) Hdt. **2** (of fields) **providing the same nurture** (for someone, W.DAT. as for oneself) Ar.

ὁμοῦ *adv.* and *prep.*: see under ὁμός

ὁμοῦμαι (fut.mid.): see ὄμνυμι

ὁμουρέω *Ion.contr.vb.*: see ὁμορέω

ὁμούριος, ὅμουρος *Ion.adjs.*: see ὅμορος

ὁμό-φοιτος ον *adj.* [ὁμός, φοιτάω] (of deception) **always attendant** (W.GEN. upon flattering stories) Pi.

ὁμο-φράδμων ονος *masc.fem.adj.* (of the understanding of good men) **thinking unanimously** Lyr.adesp.

ὁμοφρονέω *contr.vb.* [ὁμόφρων] (of a husband and wife, friends, comrades) **be of one heart** or **mind** Od. Hdt.; (of a people, allies, a war) **be of one purpose, be united** Hdt. X. Arist. Plb. Plu.

ὁμοφροσύνη ης *f.* **oneness of mind, concord** Od. AR. Plu.

ὁμό-φρων ονος *masc.fem.adj.* [φρήν] **1** (of the Muses) **alike in thought** Hes.; (of the spirit, amongst friends in an enterprise; of hounds, in pursuit) **of one purpose, united**

ὁμοφυής hHom. Thgn.; (in neg.phr., of the spirit of wolves and lambs) alike Il.
2 (of a marriage) **harmonious** Pi.; (of words, binding an alliance) **united** Ar.
ὁμο-φυής ές adj. [φυή] (of a condition or quality) **of the same nature** (as sthg. else) Pl.; (of persons) **of the same temperament** Pl.
ὁμό-φυλος ον adj. [φυλή] **1** (of a people or an individual) **of kindred tribe** or **stock** Th. Isoc. +; (of friendship) **based on kinship** E. Pl. || MASC.PL.SB. people of the same tribe, countrymen X. + || NEUT.SB. kinship E. +
2 (of birds, fish) **of the same kind** or **species** X. Plb. || NEUT.SB. one's own kind (amongst animals) Plb. Plu.; matching kind (amongst physical elements) Pl. X.
3 (epith. of Zeus) **god of kinship** Pl.
ὁμοφωνέω contr.vb. [ὁμόφωνος] **1** (of Ionian cities) **share a common dialect** —W.DAT. w. one another Hdt.
2 (of elements of a man's soul) **be in unison** —W.DAT. w. reason Arist.
ὁμοφωνίᾱ ᾱς f. (mus.) **unison** (of note or pitch) Arist.
ὁμό-φωνος ον adj. [φωνή] **1 having a language** or **dialect in common** Pl.; (W.DAT. w. another people) Hdt. Th. || MASC.PL.SB. people speaking the same language Th. Pl. X.
2 (of a song) **sounding in accompaniment** Call.; (of a lament) **in unison** (W.DAT. w. prophecies of doom) A.
—**ὁμοφώνως** adv. **with one voice, in unison** Plu.
ὁμό-χροια ᾱς, Ion. **ὁμοχροίη** ης f. [χροιᾱ́] **1 surface of the flesh, skin** (cut in a blood pact betw. two men) Hdt.
2 similar colour (of an animal, to the landscape) X.
ὁμό-χρως ων, gen. ωτος adj. [χρώς] | acc. ὁμόχρων | (of a staff, used as a token, to match a juror w. a court) **of a matching colour** (W.DAT. to the court) Arist.; (of the court, to the staff) Arist.
ὁμό-ψηφος ον adj. [ψῆφος] **1** (of an official) **having a vote of equal weight** (W.DAT. to other persons) Hdt.; (w. μετά + GEN. w. others) Hdt.
2 voting alongside (W.DAT. others, for a policy) And. Lys.
3 (of the Senate) **unanimous** (on an issue) Plu.
ὀμπετάννῡμι Aeol.vb.: see ἀναπετάννῡμι
ὄμπη ης f. a kind of sacrificial cake Call.
ὄμπνιος ᾱ ον adj. (epith. of Demeter) **nourishing, bounteous** Call.; (of a grain crop) AR.; (of agriculture, water) Call.
ὀμφᾱ́ dial.f.: see ὀμφή
ὀμφακίᾱς ου m. [ὄμφαξ] **wine made from unripe grapes** || ADJ. (of emotion) of the sour-grape type Ar.
ὀμφαλητομίᾱ ᾱς f. [ὀμφαλητόμος] **cutting of the umbilical cord** Pl.
ὀμφαλη-τόμος ου f. [ὀμφαλός, τέμνω] **cutter of the umbilical cord** (ref. to a midwife) Hippon.
ὀμφαλόεις εσσα εν adj. **1** (of a shield) with a central boss, **bossed** Hom. Tyrt. Ar.; (com., of warriors' groans) Ar.
2 (of a wooden yoke) with a central knob, **knobbed** Il.
ὀμφαλός οῦ m. **1 navel** (of a human being) Il. E. Ar. Pl. Theoc.; (as a measure of the height of sthg.) Hdt. X.
2 umbilical cord Call.
3 (fig.) **central point** (or that which occupies it); **navel** (of the sea, where Circe's island was located) Od.; (of the earth, ref. to a stone at Delphi, or the sanctuary itself) Pi. B. Trag. Pl.; (ref. to an altar at Athens) Pi.fr.
4 boss (ref. to a metal protuberance at the centre of a shield) Il.; (pl., ref. to raised decorations around the edges) Il.
5 knob (in the middle of a wooden yoke) Il. Hes.fr.

6 (fig.) **navel** (of a feast, ref. to a kind of large cake) Philox.Leuc.
ὀμφαλωτός ή όν adj. (of a cake, to which a shield is likened) **in the shape of a boss** Plb.
ὄμφαξ ακος f. **unripe grape** (usu.pl. or collectv.sg.) Od. Hes. Archil. Alc. A. S.fr.; (to which a girl is likened) Theoc.
ὀμφή ῆς, dial. **ὀμφᾱ́** ᾱς f. **1 divine voice** (of authority or prophecy) Hom. hHom. Thgn. Pi.fr. E. +; (pl.) S.; (speaking through a bird) AR.
2 voice (of humans, spoken or sung) Pi. Trag. Melanipp. AR.
3 voice (of musical instruments) Pi.fr. B. S.Ichn. Corinn.
ὀμωθῆναι (aor.pass.inf.): see ὄμομαι
ὀμ-ῶλαξ ακος dial.masc.fem.adj. [ὁμός, αὖλαξ] having adjoining furrows; (of fields) **adjacent, neighbouring** AR.; (of people) Call. AR.
ὀμώμοκα (pf.), **ὀμωμόκεν** (plpf.), **ὀμώμοται** (3sg.pf.pass.): see ὄμνῡμι
ὁμωνυμίᾱ ᾱς f. [ὁμώνυμος] **1 identity of personal name** Plu.; **same title** (of office, as that borne by another person) Plu.
2 (rhet.) **use of the same word for different things, homonymy** Arist.; (ref. to the misunderstanding which can be caused by such use) **equivocation, ambiguity** Arist.
ὁμ-ώνυμος ον adj. [ὄνομα] **1** (of persons, places, things) **sharing the same** or **a similar name** (freq. W.DAT. or GEN. w. someone or sthg.) Il. Pi. Lamprocl. E.fr. Th. Ar. + || MASC.SB. **namesake** (sts. W.DAT. or GEN. of someone) Hdt. Pl. Aeschin. D.
2 (of a word) **sounding the same** (W.DAT. as one meaning sthg. else) Pl.
3 (of things) with the same name (but not entirely the same in reality), **equivocal** Arist.
—**ὁμωνύμως** adv. **1 by the same name** Plu.
2 equivocally Arist.
ὀμ-ωρόφιος ον adj. [ὄροφος] (of a person) **under the same roof** (as another, as a sign of friendship) D.; (W.DAT. as a murderer, in neg.phr., to avoid pollution) Antipho
ὁμῶς adv.: see under ὁμός
ὅμως, Aeol. **ὔμως** conj. [reltd. ὁμῶς] **1** (limiting a previous statement or making a contrary assertion, freq. w. following δέ) **all the same, even so, nevertheless, anyway** Hom. + • ὅμως δ' οὐ λήθετο χάρμης but even so (in spite of what has happened) he did not forget the fight Il.
2 (after ἀλλά) Archil. + • ἀλλ' ὅμως ... μὴ παρίει καλά but nevertheless do not forgo fine deeds Pi.; (ellipt.) E. Ar.
• ἤκουσα κἀγώ, τηλόθεν μὲν ἀλλ' ὅμως I too heard it, from far away but (I heard it) nonetheless E.
3 (w. following μήν, dial. μᾱ́ν) Pi. Pl. • ὅμως μὴν πειρώμεθα λαβεῖν αὐτό but let's try to grasp it anyway Pl.; (w. γε μήν) Ar.; (w. μέντοι) Hdt. + • ὅμως μέντοι ἀντεῖχε καὶ οὐκ εἶκε but nevertheless he held out and did not yield Hdt.; (w. γε μέντοι) Ar.
4 (after concessive ptcpl. or conditional protasis) Hdt. Trag. + • οἱ δὲ ἄτε Περιάνδρου ἐόντα παῖδα, καίπερ δειμαίνοντες, ὅμως ἐδέκοντο because he was Periander's son, even though they were afraid, they nevertheless took him in Hdt. • κεἰ τὸ μηδὲν ἐξερῶ, φράσω δ' ὅμως even if I shall relate nothing consequential, I shall tell it just the same S.; (attached to the protasis itself) Trag. • μέμνησ' Ὀρέστου, κεἰ θυραῖός ἐσθ' ὅμως remember Orestes, even if he is abroad A.; (w.ptcpl. replacing protasis) Hdt. + • κλῡθί μου νοσῶν ὅμως hear me even though you are sick S.
ὁμωχέται ῶν dial.m.pl. [ὁμοῦ, ἔχω] **joint holders** (ref. to deities worshipped in a Boeotian temple) Th.
ὄν[1] (Att.neut.ptcpl.): see εἰμί

ὄν² *Aeol.prep.*: see ἀνά
ὀναίμην (aor.2 mid.opt.): see ὀνίνημι
ὄναρ *n.* [reltd. ὄνειρος] | only nom.acc.sg. | **1 vision seen in sleep, dream** Il. Trag. Ar. Pl. X. +
2 (as a symbol of what is short-lived, lacking in substance or illusory) **dream** Od. Mimn. A. Pi. Pl. Theoc. +
3 threatening apparition (in the real world, ref. to a person or creature), **nightmare** Il. A.
4 ‖ ADVBL.ACC. **in a dream** Sapph. A. E. Pl. Plu.; (w. οὐδέ) *not even in a dream* (*much less in reality*) E. Pl. D. Call.*epigr*. Mosch. Plu.
5 ‖ ADVBL.ACC. **in dreaming** (i.e. in imagination or a state of unreality, sts.opp. ὕπαρ *in a waking state or in reality*) Pl. Men. Plb.
6 (provbl.) τὸ ἐμόν γε ... ἐμοὶ λέγεις ὄναρ *you are telling me my own dream* (*i.e. nothing new*) Pl. | see ὄνειρος 5
ὀνάριον ου *n.* [dimin. ὄνος] **young donkey** NT.
ὀνάρταις (Aeol.masc.sg.pres.ptcpl.): see ἀναρτάω
ὄνασει *dial.*3sg.fut.), **ὄνασθαι** (aor.2 mid.inf.): see ὀνίνημι
ὄνασις *dial.f.*: see ὄνησις
ὄνδε (masc.acc.possessv.pron.adj.): see ὅς² 4
ὄνδειξαι (Aeol.aor.inf.): see ἀναδείκνυμι
ὄνειαρ¹ (also disyllab. **ὄνεαρ** hHom.) ατος *n.* [ὀνίνημι]
1 good thing, blessing or **help** (ref. to food, a supply of foliage for bedding) Od. Hes. Theoc.; (ref. to a remedy, a strategy) Od. AR.; (ref. to favourable winds or days) Hes.
2 blessing (ref. to a person, in time of danger) Il. AR.; (ref. to a good neighbour) Hes.; (ref. to Demeter) hHom.
3 ‖ PL. **food, provisions** Hom.; **goods, valuables** Il. AR.
ὄνειαρ² ατος *n.* [reltd. ὄναρ] **dream** Call.*epigr*.
ὀνείδειος ον *adj.* [ὄνειδος] (of words) **taunting, reproachful, abusive** Hom. ‖ NEUT.PL.SB. **abusive words** Il.
ὀνειδίζω *vb.* | fut. ὀνειδιῶ | aor. ὠνείδισα, ep. ὀνείδισα | pf. ὠνείδικα ‖ 2pl.fut.mid. (w.pass.sens.) ὀνειδιεῖσθε (S.) ‖ aor.pass. ὠνειδίσθην ‖ neut.impers.vbl.adj. ὀνειδιστέον |
1 speak tauntingly, reproachfully or **in criticism** (sts. W.DAT. to or against someone) Hom. + —W.ACC. *on account of sthg.* Hom. + —W.INF. *for being such and such* Pl.; **say accusingly** —W.COMPL.CL. *that sthg. is the case* Il. Lys. + ‖ PASS. (of a thing) **be a matter for reproach** Th. Pl. +
2 cause (someone or sthg.) **to become the object of reproach; expose to criticism, hold up for blame** or **scrutiny** —*persons, their circumstances or actions* (sts. w. 2ND ACC. *on account of sthg.*) Thgn. S. E. Att.orats. + ‖ PASS. (of persons) **be criticised** S. E. Pl. +
ὀνείδισμα ατος *n.* **reproach, criticism** Hdt.
ὀνειδισμός οῦ *m.* **statement intending reproach, taunt, insult** Plu.
ὀνειδιστήρ ῆρος *masc.adj.* (of words) **of reproach** E.
ὀνειδιστής οῦ *m.* **one who is critical** (W.GEN. of sthg.) Arist.
ὄνειδος εος (ους) *n.* **1 expression of reproach, reproach, taunt, insult** Hom. Alc. Pi. Hdt. Trag. +
2 matter or **cause of reproach, disgrace, shame** Il. Hes. hHom. Stesich. Thgn. Pi. +
ὄνειος ᾱ ον *adj.* [ὄνος] (of meat, milk, skin) **of an ass** Ar. Plb. Plu.
ὀνείρατα *n.pl.*: see ὄνειρος
ὀνείρειος η ον *Ion.adj.* [ὄνειρος] (of the gates) **of dreams** Od.
ὀνειρο-κρίτης ου, dial. **ὀνειροκρίτᾱς** ᾱ *m.* [κριτής] **interpreter of dreams** Thphr. Theoc.
ὀνειροκριτικός ή όν *adj.* (of a board) **for interpreting dreams** Plu.
ὀνειρό-μαντις εως *m.* [μάντις] **dream-diviner** A.

ὄνειρον *n.*: see ὄνειρος
ὀνειροπολέω *contr.vb.* [ὀνειροπόλος] **1 deal in thoughts which are dream-like** (opp. rational); **indulge in imaginings, fantasise** Ar. Pl. Plu.; **dream about** —*horses and riding* Ar. —*ambitions, conquests or riches* D. Plu.
2 have a foreboding of —*danger* Plu.
ὀνειρο-πόλος ου *m.* [πέλω] **one who deals in dreams, dream interpreter** Il. Hdt.
ὄνειρος ου, Aeol. **ὄνοιρος** ω *m.* [reltd. ὄναρ] —also **ὄνειρον** ου *n.* —also **ὀνείρατα** των *n.pl.* | dat. ὀνείρασι | also gen.sg. ὀνείρατος (Pl. AR.), dat. ὀνείρατι (A.) |
1 vision seen in sleep, dream (freq. regarded as sent by the gods and as an interpretable portent, sts. deceptive) Hom. +; (personif.) **Dream** Il.; (pl., as a tribe) Od. Mosch.; (as children of Night) Hes.
2 dream (as a symbol of what is short-lived, lacking in substance or illusory) Od. A. E. AR. Plu. ‖ PL. **faint vestiges** (of a great empire) Pl.
3 dream, vision (in the waking mind, of future realities) S. Pl.
4 dream, aspiration (of conquests) Plu.
5 (provbl.) μὴ λέγε ... τοὐμὸν ὄνειρον ἐμοί *don't tell me my own dream* Call.*epigr*. | see ὄναρ 6
ὀνειρό-φαντος ον *adj.* [φαίνομαι] (of fanciful visions) **appearing in dreams** A.
ὀνειρό-φρων ονος *masc.fem.adj.* [φρήν] **knowledgeable about dreams** (and their interpretation) E.
ὀνείρωξις εως *f.* [ὀνειρώσσω] **dreaming state** Pl.
ὀνειρώσσω, Att. **ὀνειρώττω** *vb.* [ὄνειρος] **be in a dreaming state** (whether asleep or awake) Pl. Plb.; **dream** —W.ACC. *about sthg.* Pl. Plb. Plu.
ὄνεκτος *Aeol.adj.*: see ἀνεκτός
ὀνέλων (Aeol.aor.2 ptcpl.): see ἀναιρέω
ὀνεμείχνυτο and **ὀνεμίγνυτο** (Aeol.3sg.impf.pass.): see ἀναμείγνῡμι
ὀνέμναισα (Aeol.aor.): see ἀναμιμνήσκω
ὀνέτροπον (Aeol.aor.2): see ἀνατρέπω
ὀνεύω *vb.* [ὄνος] | impf. ὤνευον | **draw up with a windlass; haul** or **wrench up** —*stakes or piles* Th.
ὀν-ηλάτης ου *m.* [ἐλαύνω] **donkey-driver** D. Men. Plu.
ὀνήμενος (aor.2 mid.ptcpl.), **ὄνησα** (ep.aor.): see ὀνίνημι
ὀνήσιμος ον *adj.* [ὀνίνημι] **1** (of a portent) **bringing blessings** hHom.; (of blessings) **beneficial** (W.GEN. to life) A.; (of gifts fr. enemies, in neg.phr.) S. ‖ NEUT.PL.SB. **beneficial things** S.
2 (of a weapon, which ends suffering) **bringing relief** S.
—ὀνησίμως *adv.* **in a beneficial way** Pl.
ὀνησί-πολις εως *masc.fem.adj.* [πόλις] (of justice) **beneficial to the state** Simon.
ὄνησις εως (Ion. ιος), dial. **ὄνᾱσις** ιος *f.* **1 benefit arising from circumstances or material things; benefit, advantage, good, enjoyment** Od. S. E. Pl. X. +; (W.GEN. of or fr. one's children, wealth, lifestyle, or sim.) Trag. Tim. Pl. Aeschin. +
2 benefit deliberately bestowed, benefit, help (sts. W.DAT. for someone) S. E. Pl. D.
ὄνησο (aor.2 mid.imperatv.), **ὀνήσω** (fut.): see ὀνίνημι
ὀνθία ων *n.pl.* [dimin. ὄνθος] **pieces of dung** (pejor.ref. to satyrs) S.*Ichn.*
ὄνθος ου *m.* **animal dung** Il. Plb.
ὀνθύλευσις εως *f.* [ὀνθυλεύω] **stuffing** (for a fish dish) Men.
ὀνθυλεύω *vb.* | pf.pass.ptcpl. ὠνθυλευμένος | **stuff** (food, in cooking) ‖ PF.PASS.PTCPL.ADJ. **stuffed** (W.DAT. w. fat) Plu.(quot.com.)
ὀνῑᾱ *Aeol.f.*, **ὀνῑᾱτος** *Aeol.adj.*: see ἀνῑᾱ, ἀνῑᾱτος

ὀνίδες ων f.pl. [ὄνος] donkey dung Ar.
ὀνίδιον ου n. [dimin. ὄνος] (pejor.) **useless donkey** Ar.
ὀνικός ή όν adj. (of a millstone) of the type pulled by a donkey (opp. belonging to a handmill), **heavy** NT.
ὀνίνημι vb. | ptcpl. ὀνινᾶς | fut. ὀνήσω, dial.3sg. ὀνᾱσεῖ (Theoc.) | aor. ὤνησα, ep. ὄνησα, dial. ὤνᾱσα (Theoc.) || MID.: ὀνίναμαι | impf. ὠνινάμην | fut. ὀνήσομαι | aor.2 ὠνήμην, imperatv. ὄνησο, ptcpl. ὀνήμενος | also aor.2 ὠνάμην, dial.2sg. ὤναο (Call.), perh. 2pl. ὤνασθε (E., cj. ὤνησθε) | inf. ὄνασθαι | opt. ὀναίμην, dial. ὀναίμᾱν || aor.pass. ὠνήθην, dial. ὠνάθην (Theoc.) |
1 bring blessings or favour; (of gods, reverence, justice) **bless** —persons Il. Hes. hHom. Antipho +; (of songs) —heroes (w. fame) Theoc.
2 (of persons or things, such as children, possessions); **bring advantage** or **happiness to, delight** —a person Il. hHom. X. Theoc.
3 bring help (in danger or distress); (of a person, medicine) **help, aid** —a person Pl.; (of a weapon, a protected place) —a warrior, a besieged population, fugitives Od. Hdt.(oracle) E. Plb.; (of a leader) —men under his protection, a suppliant Hom. Hdt. +
4 bring benefit through a favour; **perform a kindness** or **service for** —a person, a people Hes. Thgn. Ar. X. +
5 bring benefit or advancement (through advice, example, education, argument); (of persons) **benefit** —a person, a people Il. Isoc. Pl. —one's children, land or home E. X.; (of education, training, an art, debate, or sim.) **benefit, profit** —a person, a people Pl.
6 (of an action, situation or circumstance) **benefit, profit** —a person, a people hHom. E. Plu.; **be a good thing** Plu.; (of old age, as saving someone fr. punishment) Od.
7 (of a person, thing, circumstance, in neg.phr.) **be of avail** (sts. W.ACC. to someone) Il. E. Arist. +
8 || MID. (intr.) receive benefit or enjoyment (freq. W.GEN. or PREP.PHR. in or fr. sthg.); **be blessed, take delight** (in children, marriage, possessions, good fortune) E. Men.; (in food and drink) Hom. E.; **be content** (w. a meal) Od.; **be happy** (in escape fr. danger, release fr. a situation) Il. Thgn. E. Men. Plu.; **benefit, profit** (fr. circumstances, kind deeds, chastisement, advice, study, or sim.) S. E. Pl. +; (fr. medicine) E.
9 (aor.mid.opt.) ὀναίμην, ὄναιο (or sim.) **may I** (you) **be blessed with happiness** Trag. + —W.GEN. in someone or sthg. S. +
—**ὀνήμενος** η ον aor.2 mid.ptcpl.adj. (of a man) of whom one may say ὄναιο (may you be blessed), **worthy of blessings** Od.
ὀνκαλέω Aeol.contr.vb.: see ἀνακαλέω
ὀννέλην (Aeol.aor.2 inf.): see ἀναιρέω
ὀνοβατέω contr.vb. [ὄνος, reltd. βαίνω] **mate** (W.ACC. mares) **with a donkey** X.
ὄνοιρος Aeol.m.: see ὄνειρος
ὄνομα, ep. **οὔνομα**, dial. **ὄνυμα**, ατος n. **1 personal name** (of a divinity, person or animal), **name** Od. +
2 ethnic or **geographical name** (of a people, place or landscape feature), **name** Hdt. +
3 proper name used to single out or specify (individual persons or places in a group), **name** Il. +; (as written in a list or document, on a monument) Att.orats. +
4 proper name (of a person or place) as talked about (in good or bad terms); **name, reputation** S. +; (esp.) famous and honoured name, **name, repute** Thgn. +; (as remembered after a person's death or lapse into obscurity) Od. +
5 proper name as representing the essential characteristics (of a person or place, esp. as loved or hated), **name** Trag. +
6 common noun used for designation (of a person or thing, reflecting associated attributes; freq. evoking strong positive or negative emotion); **word, name, title** Hdt. +
7 name or **word** (without proper correspondence in actual fact, opp. real or true thing); **name, mere name, word** Hdt. +; **professed reason** Hdt. +
8 name or **word** used for a distinct class or type (of persons, animals or things), **name** Hdt. +
9 name or **word** used in a precise and limited sense (esp. in politics, law, philosophy, a science or art); **name, expression, term, technical term** E. + || PL. terminology Pl. X.
10 (gramm.) **word, noun** or **proper name** Ar. Pl. Arist.
ὀνομάζω, dial. **ὀνυμάζω** vb. | impf. ὠνόμαζον, ep. ὀνόμαζον, dial. ὀνύμαζον (Pi.) | fut. ὀνομάσω | aor. ὠνόμασα, dial. ὠνύμασα (Pi.), ὠνύμασσα (Alc.), also ὀνύμαξα (Pi.) | pf. ὠνόμακα || PASS.: fut. ὀνομασθήσομαι, dial. ὀνυμάξομαι (Pi.) | aor. ὠνομάσθην, dial.3pl. ὀνύμασθεν (Pi.) | pf. ὠνόμασμαι || neut.impers.vbl.adj. ὀνομαστέον |
1 give a name or **title** (for the first time); **name, call** —a deity, person, animal, place, invention (W.PREDIC.SB. or ADJ. such and such) Hes.fr. Alc. A. Pi. Hdt. E. + —(W. ἀπό + GEN. after sthg.) Th. || PASS. (of persons, places, things) be given the name —W.PREDIC.SB. such and such Pi. Hdt. E. Th. + —(W. ἐκ + GEN. after a certain circumstance) S.; (of a saying, about someone) be derived —w. ἀπό + GEN. fr. a particular person Hdt.
2 name —W.ACC. + PF.PASS.INF. a goddess as having been established (W.PREP.PHR. w. a particular title, i.e. give her or her temple such a title) E.
3 use an existing or **current name; call** —a person, deity, populace, place, or sim. (W.PREDIC.SB. such and such) Hdt. E. Th. + —(W. εἶναι + PREDIC.SB.) Hdt. Pl. X. —(W.COGN.ACC. by a name) E. || PASS. be called, be known as —W.PREDIC.SB. or ADJ. such and such Hdt. S. E. Th. + —W. εἶναι + PREDIC.SB. Pl.
4 || MID. **call** —someone (W.PREDIC.SB. one's son) S.
5 || PF.PASS. (of persons, places, or sim.) **have been given the name, have the name** —W.PREDIC.SB. such and such Th. Pl. +; (of a person) **be referred to, be known** —W.GEN. (as son) of a particular person S. E. || PTCPL. (of people, places, or sim.) called —W.PREDIC.SB. or ADJ. such and such E.fr. Th. + —W.COGN.ACC. by a certain name S.
6 || PASS. **have one's name widely mentioned, be** or **become celebrated** Pi. —W.DAT. through an event Th.
7 address or **call upon by name** —a person Hom. Hes.; **call out the name** —W.DIR.SP. Solon Hdt.
8 mention by name, name —a person, people, deity Od. Hdt. E. +; **mention, utter** —W.COGN.ACC. a name Hdt. || PASS. be mentioned by name Hdt.; (of a name) be mentioned Hdt.
9 identify by naming || PASS. (of rivers) be identified by name Hdt.; (of symptoms) —W.PREP.PHR. by doctors Th.
10 name, nominate, appoint —a surety Plu. —someone (W.PREDIC.SB. as dictator) Plu.
11 go through by name, specify, enumerate —gifts Il. —varieties of tree Od. || PASS. (of ancestors) be enumerated or traced X.
12 make explicit mention of, mention, refer to —someone's sickness A. —an event Th. —items, activities D.
13 express in words, describe —W.INDIR.Q. how sthg. is the case E. || PASS. (of thoughts) be expressed —W.DAT. in not a few words S.

14 devise, coin —*a word or term* (*for sthg.*) Hdt. Pl. +; **use the expression** —W.CL. '*whoever wishes the people to rule*' Th. ‖ PASS. (of a term) be used to describe, be the name for —W.PREDIC.SB. *sthg.* Th.; be used —W. ἐπί + DAT. *for sthg.* (*i.e. to describe it*) Th.
—**ὠνομασμένως** *pf.pass.ptcpl.adv.* **by giving names** Arist.
ὄνομαι *mid.vb.* | 2sg. ὄνοσαι, 3pl. ὄνονται | 3sg.opt. ὄνοιτο | ep.fut. ὀνόσσομαι | aor. ὠνοσάμην, 3sg. ὤνατο (dub., cj. ὤνοτο), 3sg.opt. ὀνόσαιτο, ep.ptcpl. ὀνοσσάμενος |
1 make light of, scorn, disparage —*persons, their attributes, actions, words* Hom. —*craftsmen* Hdt. —*one's master* A.(cj.)
2 (iron.) **be dissatisfied** —W.GEN. *w. one's sufferings* (*i.e. think them insufficient*) Od. —*w.* ὅτι + CL. *that sthg. is happening* Od.
ὀνομαίνω *vb.* [ὄνομα] | Ion.fut. ὀνομανέω | aor. ὠνόμηνα, ep. ὀνόμηνα, Boeot. ὠνούμηνα | **1** give a name (for the first time); **name, call** —*a person, place, river* (W.PREDIC.SB. *such and such*) Hes. Is. Call. AR. —*a country* (w. ἀπό + GEN. *after oneself*) Corinn.; **devise** —*a name* (W.INF. + DAT. *to be someone's*) Hes.*fr.*
2 address or **call upon by name** —*a person* Il. —*certain gods* Il.
3 tell the names of, enumerate by name —*a group of people, rivers* Hom. hHom. Hdt.
4 mention by name, name —*a person* AR.; **reveal the name of** —*a god* Od.; **mention the name** (of a god) Od. hHom.
5 name, nominate, appoint —*someone* (W.PREDIC.SB. *as another's attendant*) Il.
6 specify, enumerate —*gifts, exploits* Hom. Hes.*fr.*
7 promise —W.FUT.INF. *to give sthg.* Od.
ὀνομακλήδην *adv.*: see ἐξονομακλήδην
ὀνομά-κλυτος ον (dial. ᾱ ον) *adj.* [κλυτός] **with famous name**; (of a person) **renowned** Il. Ibyc.; (of a lineage, a family) hHom. Semon.; (of the island of Aigina) Pi.*fr.*
ὀνομασίᾱ ᾱς *f.* [ὀνομάζω] **1 naming, system of names** Pl. Plb.
2 use of words, verbalisation Arist.
ὀνόμασις εως *f.* **naming** Pl.(dub.)
ὀνομαστικός ή όν *adj.* **of or relating to giving names**; (of the art) **of naming** Pl. ‖ MASC.SB. **name-giver** Pl.
ὀνομαστός ή όν, dial. **ὀνυμαστός** ά όν *adj.* **1 mentioned or worthy of mention by name**; (of a person, family, place) **notable, famous** Thgn. Pi. Hdt. Isoc. Pl. +; (of deeds or events) E. Th. Isoc. Pl. +; (of a way of life) Plu.; (of Homer's *Iliad*) Isoc.
2 (of geographical features) **worthy of record, noteworthy** Hdt.
3 (pejor., of a leader after defeat) **infamous** Isoc.; (of a disastrous event) Plu.; (of the hundred-handed giants) Hes.; (of gifts) Hes.*fr.*; (of dishonourable conduct) AR.
‖ ADVBL.NEUT. οὐκ ὀνομαστόν **unspeakably** hHom.(cj.)
4 (w.neg. οὐκ, of Ilios) **that one hardly dares to name** (*because of ill-omen or fear*) Od.
—**ὀνομαστί** *adv.* **with use of a name or names, by name** Hdt. Th. Critias Att.orats. +
ὀνοματο-λόγος ου *m.* [ὄνομα] (at Rome) one who tells (his master) the names (of approaching persons), **nomenclator** Plu.
ὀνοματοποιέω *contr.vb.* **invent** or **coin names** (for things) Arist.
ὀνοματουργός οῦ *m.* [ἔργον] **name-maker** Pl.
ὀνόμηνα (ep.aor.): see ὀνομαίνω
ὄνος ου *m./f.* **1 ass, donkey** (esp. as a beast of burden, also as exemplifying ugliness, clumsiness, stupidity) Il. +
2 (provbl.) ὄνου σκιά *donkey's shadow* (*ref. to what is trivial or worthless*) Ar. Pl.

3 donkey-jug (*ref. to a vessel w. two large handles, as if ears*) Ar.
4 ‖ PL. **Asses** (two stars in the constellation Cancer) Theoc.
5 ὄνος ἄγριος **wild ass, onager** (*Asian animal, noted for speed, hunted for meat*) X.; (*used for drawing war-chariots*) Hdt.
6 (fig.) ὄνος ἀλέτης **grinder-donkey** (*ref. to the upper of two millstones, which turns upon the lower*) X.
7 ὄνος ξύλινος **wooden ass, windlass** Hdt.
ὀνόσαιτο (3sg.aor.mid.opt.), **ὀνοσσάμενος** (ep.aor.mid.ptcpl.), **ὀνόσσομαι** (ep.fut.mid.): see ὄνομαι
ὀνοστός *adj.*: see ὀνοτός
ὀνοσφαγίη ης Ion.*f.* [ὄνος, σφάζω] **sacrifice of asses** Call.
ὀνοτάζω *vb.* [reltd. ὄνομαι] **1 scorn** —*Justice* Hes.; (mid., of girls) —*a marriage* A.
2 (in neg.phr.) **treat lightly** —*an omen* hHom.
ὀνοτός, also **ὀνοστός** (Il.), ή όν *adj.* [ὄνομαι] **1** (of a woman) **to be treated with scorn, despicable** AR.
2 (in neg.phr., of gifts) **to be scorned** Il.; (of an island) Call.
3 (of a man) **not to be commended, unimpressive** (W.INF. *to look at*) Pi.
ὀνο-φορβός οῦ *m.* [ὄνος, φέρβω] **one who provides fodder for donkeys, donkey-keeper** Hdt.
ὀντρέπω Aeol.*vb.*: see ἀνατρέπω
ὄντων (3pl.imperatv.): see εἰμί
ὄντως *ptcpl.adv.*: see under εἰμί
ὄνυμα *dial.n.*, **ὀνυμάζω** *dial.vb.*, **ὀνυμαστός** *dial.adj.*: see ὄνομα, ὀνομάζω, ὀνομαστός
ὄνυξ υχος *m.* | dat.pl. ὄνυξι, ep. ὀνύχεσσι | **1 nail** (of the hand or foot) Pl. Arist.
2 (specif.) **fingernail** (esp. in ctxt. of cheek-tearing by mourners) Hdt. Trag. Ar. Tim. +; (meton. for a finger-tip) Call.
3 toenail Ar. Plu.; (pl., meton. for tips of the toes) E.
4 talon or **claw** (of an eagle or other bird of prey) Hom. Hes. Ar. Plu.; (of a lion or other animal) Pi. Hdt. Theoc. Plu.; (of the Fates or other fearsome beings) Hes. E. Ar.
5 hoof (of a horse) X.
ὀνύχινος η ον *adj.* (of writing-tablets) **made of onyx** Plu.
ὀνύψυχω Aeol.*vb.*: see ἀναψύχω
ὀξ-άλμη ης *f.* [ὄξος] **vinegar and salt-water** (used as a condiment), **brine-vinegar** Ar.
ὀξέα Ion.fem.adj. and neut.pl.advs., **ὀξέως** *adv.*: see ὀξύς
ὀξίνης ου *m.* [ὄξος] **sour wine** Plu. ‖ ADJ. (fig., of a politician, a warrior's spirit) **sharp, bitter** Ar.
ὀξίς ίδος *f.* **1 vinegar cruet** Ar.
2 app., a kind of stinging creature; perh. **scorpion** Ar.
ὄξος εος (ους) *n.* [ὀξύς] **1 vinegar** (esp. used as a condiment) Sol. Ar. Arist. Thphr. Men. Plu.; (fig., ref. to a man's temper) Theoc.
2 sour or **poor-quality wine** Theoc. NT. Plu.; (ref. to a kind of wine made fr. dates) X.; (fr. the African lotus-fruit) Plb.
ὀξύ-βαφον ου *n.* [βάπτω] **small vinegar-dish for dipping food into, vinegar-dish** Ar. Philox.Leuc.; (fig., pejor.ref. to Sicily) Plb.
ὀξυ-βελής ές *adj.* [βέλος] (of an arrow) **sharp-pointed** Il.; (of a hedgehog's spines) Emp. ‖ MASC.SB. **missile** (fr. a military catapult) Plu.
ὀξύ-βόας ᾱ *dial.masc.adj.* [βοή] (of a lament) **that screams out shrilly, piercing** A.
ὀξύ-γαλα ακτος *n.* [γάλα] **sour milk** (as a drink) Plu.
ὀξύ-γοος ον *adj.* [γόος] (of entreaties) **with shrill-wailing lamentation** A.
ὀξυ-δερκής ές *adj.* [δέρκομαι] (of the crocodile, when out of the water) **sharp-sighted** Hdt.

ὀξύη ης *f.* beech tree; (meton.) **beechwood spear** Archil. E.

ὀξυ-ήκοος ον *adj.* [ὀξύς, ἀκούω] (of physical sensibility) **keenly responsive** Pl.

ὀξύ-θηκτος ον *adj.* [θηκτός] (of a weapon) sharply whetted, **keen-edged** E.

ὀξυθυμέομαι *mid.pass.contr.vb.* [ὀξύθυμος] | *aor.* ὠξυθυμήθην | **be sharp-tempered** E. —W.DAT. *w. someone* Ar.

ὀξυθυμίᾱ ᾱς *f.* **sharp temper, irascibility** (of old men) E.

ὀξύ-θυμος ον *adj.* [θῡμός] (of persons, their state of mind) **sharp-tempered, irascible** E. Ar. Arist.; (of the Areopagus) A. || NEUT.SB. **sharp temper** E. Ar. Men.

ὀξυ-κάρδιος ον *adj.* [καρδίᾱ] **sharp-spirited** A. Ar.

ὀξύ-κώκῡτος ον *adj.* [κωκῡτός] (of a death) **bewailed with piercing cries** S.

ὀξυλαβέω *contr.vb.* [λαμβάνω] **seize an opportunity** X. Men.

ὀξύ-λαλος ον *adj.* [λάλος] (of a poet's tooth) **sharp-talking** Ar.

ὀξυ-μέριμνος ον *adj.* [μέριμνα] (of disputants) **sharp-thinking** Ar.

ὀξυ-μήνῑτος ον *adj.* [μηνίω] (of a murder, or perh. a trial for it) **arousing violent anger** A.

ὀξύ-μολπος ον *adj.* [μολπή] (of laments) **shrilly sung** A.

ὀξύνω *vb.* | *aor.* ὤξυνα || *aor.pass.* ὠξύνθην | **provoke to anger** —*someone's tongue* S. || PASS. **be provoked to anger** Hdt.

ὀξυόεις εσσα εν *adj.* [ὀξύη; pop.etym. ὀξύς] (of a spear) **of beechwood** Hom. Hes.*fr.* [also interpr. as *sharp*]

ὀξυ-παραύδητος ον *adj.* [ὀξύς, παραυδάω] (of the voice of a drowning man) **with a shrill and distorted sound** Tim.

ὀξυπείνως *adv.* [πείνη] **ravenously** Men.

ὀξυ-πευκής ές *adj.* [πεύκη] (of a sword) **sharp, piercing** A.

ὀξύ-πους ποδος *masc.adj.* [πούς] | *acc.* ὀξύπουν | (of a person) **keen of step, hastening** E.

ὀξύ-πρωρος ον *adj.* [πρῷρα] (of spears) **sharp-pointed** A.

ὀξυ-ρεπής ές *adj.* [ῥέπω] (of a feint in wrestling) **with a quick shift of balance** Pi.

ὀξύ-ρροπος ον *adj.* (of persons, their temper) **quickly shifting, flaring up** Pl. Plu.

ὀξύς εῖα (Ion. έα) ύ *adj.* | Ion.fem.dat.sg. ὀξείῃ, pl. ὀξείῃσ(ι) | *compar.* ὀξύτερος, *superl.* ὀξύτατος | **1 made sharp** (for piercing or cutting); (of stakes) **sharp, pointed** Hom.; (of a weapon, tool, or sim., ref. to the point or edge) **sharp, keen** Hom. +

2 naturally sharp; (of a stone, rock or peak) **sharp, pointed** Hom. +; (of sedge) Theoc.; (of claws) Pi. Hdt.; (of personif. Time, W.ACC. in respect of its teeth) Simon.

3 with a sharp corner or tapering at one extremity; (of the turn of the coast around a promontory) **sharply curved** Th.; (of an egg) **elongated at one end** (opp. spherical) Plu.; (geom., of an angle) **acute** Pl. || SUPERL.ADJ. (fig., of the acme of a man's life) **highest possible** Pl. || NEUT.SB. **apex** (of the Nile Delta) Hdt.; **point** (of a tall hat) Hdt.

4 sharp as perceived by the ear; (of sounds, esp. cries or shouts) **shrill, piercing** Il. +; (of musical sounds) **high-pitched, high** A. Ar. Pl. +; (of the speaking voice) Arist.; (pejor.) Aeschin.

5 (gramm., of an accent) **acute** Pl.; (of a syllable) **with an acute accent** Pl.

6 (of sight, hearing) **sharp of perception, keen** Pi. S. +; (of an Erinys, a dragon) **keen-eyed** Pi. AR.

7 (of what is perceived by the senses) **sharp or of sharp intensity**; (of the sun, its rays, heat, wind or snow) **keen, piercing** Il. +; (of torches, purple colour) **dazzling** Ar. Plu.; (of flavour, food or wine, bile) **sharp, acidic** Alc. Pl. X.; (of a wasp's sting) **sharp** Ar.; (fig., of blame, slander) **cutting** Pi. Plb.; (of old age) **bitter** B.*fr.* E.; (of discipline) **harsh** Pi.

8 (of feelings, unstable or dangerous events and circumstances) **rapid in onset or acute in intensity**; (of Ares or war, a contest or attack) **keen, violent** Il. Tyrt. B. Hdt. E. +; (of pain, illness, distress) **sharp, acute** Hom. +; (of a poison) **fast-acting** Plu.; (of erotic pleasure) **intense** Pl.; (of flight) **precipitate** Plu.; (of a change or crisis) **acute, rapid, sudden** Pl. X. D. Men. +

9 (of persons or natural forces) **moving with intense speed or force**; (of men, esp. troops, of horses) **rapid, swift** Hdt. S. Pl. X. +; (of a stream of blood) A. S.; (of a strait) Call.; (of a blast of fire) AR.; (of a rumour) S. || NEUT.SUPERL.SB. **extreme agility** Pl.

10 (of persons, their mind, temperament, reactions, or sim., sts. pejor.) **sharp, keen, rapid, precipitate** Archil. Thgn. +

—**ὀξύ** *neut.sg.adv.* | *superl.* ὀξύτατον (Il.) | **1 with sharp vision or perception** Hom. +; **with sharp ear or attention** Il. +

2 with piercing sound Il. +

3 with pungent smell Ar.

4 with dazzling brightness Plu.

5 with zeal or vigour Th. +; **with impetuosity** Plu.

—**ὀξέα** (also **ὀξεῖα** Hes.) *neut.pl.adv.* **1 with keen sight** hHom. AR.

2 with shrill cries or sounds Il. Hes. S.

3 with acute pains AR.

—**ὀξέως** *adv.* **1 sharply, keenly** Pl. Plu.

2 acutely, violently Pl. Plu.

3 rapidly, suddenly Plb. Plu.

4 expeditiously, energetically Th. Pl. +

5 in a very agile manner, rapidly Th. Pl. +

6 impetuously Th. Pl. +

ὀξύ-στομος ον *adj.* [στόμα] **1** (of a griffin) **sharp-beaked** A.; (of a gadfly, a gnat) **with sharp-stinging mouth** A. Ar.

2 (of a knife) **sharp-edged** E.

ὀξύτης ητος *f.* **1 sharpness, acuteness** (of angles) Pl.

2 high pitch or tone (in music or speech) Pl.

3 (gramm.) **acute accent** Pl. Arist.

4 sharpness, acidity (as a quality of a substance) Pl.

5 crisis, urgency (of a situation) D. Plu.; **abruptness** (of events, fortune) Plb. Plu.

6 rapidity (of a current) Plb.; **violence** (of fire) Pl.; (of a battle or attack, of a painful death) Plu.

7 acuteness, keenness, speediness (as a characteristic of persons, their bodies, minds or other attributes) Pl. Arist. Plu.; (pejor.) **rashness, violence** Arist. Plb. Plu.

8 sharp-edged quality (of speeches) Plu.

ὀξυ-τόμος ον *adj.* [τέμνω] (of an axe) **sharp-cutting** Pi.

ὀξύ-τονος ον *adj.* [τόνος] (of laments) **shrill-toned, high-pitched** S.; (of the wind) S.

ὀξύ-τορος ον *adj.* [τορεῖν] (of a bridle) **sharp-biting** S.(dub.)

ὀξύ-φρων ον, *gen.* ονος *adj.* [φρήν] **having keen intelligence** E.

ὀξυφωνίᾱ ᾱς *f.* [ὀξύφωνος] **high-pitched speaking voice** Arist.

ὀξύ-φωνος ον *adj.* [φωνή] (of the nightingale) **shrill-voiced** S.; (of the plucking of lyre-strings) Telest.

ὀξύ-χειρ χειρος *masc.fem.adj.* [χείρ] **1** (of a drunken man, Herakles) **with quick or violent hand, quick to strike** Lys. Theoc.*epigr.*

2 (of head-beating, by a mourner) **quick-handed** A.

ὀξύ-χολος ον *adj.* [χόλος] **with a sharp temper** Sol. S.

ὄον ου *n.* **fruit of the service tree, sorb-apple** Pl.

ὄ ὄ ὄ (accentuation and aspiration uncert.) *interj.* (expressing strong emotion) A. Ar.

ὅου (ep.gen.sg.relatv.pron.): see ὅς[1]

ὅπα, ὅπᾳ *dial.adv. and conj.*: see ὅπη

ὀπᾱδέω *dial.contr.vb.*, **ὀπᾱδός** *dial.m.*: see ὀπηδέω, ὀπηδός

ὀπάζω, Aeol. **ὀπάσδω** *vb.* [reltd. ἕπομαι] | impf. ὤπαζον, ep. ὄπαζον | fut. ὀπάσω, ep. ὀπάσσω | aor. ὤπασα, ep. ὄπασσα, dial. ὤπασσα (Alc.) || MID.: aor. ὠπασάμην, ep.3sg. ὀπάσσατο, ep.2sg.subj. ὀπάσσεαι, ep.ptcpl. ὀπασσάμενος |
1 follow closely after (someone); (of a warrior) **pursue, press hard** Il. —*an enemy* Il.; (fig., of old age) —*a person* Il.; (of dangers, the anger of a goddess) AR. || PASS. (of a river) **be driven on** —W.DAT. *by rain fr. Zeus* Il.
2 cause (someone) **to attend upon, follow or go with** (another or others); **provide** —*an escort, guide, companion or servant, company of men* (sts. W.DAT. *for someone*) Hom.; **appoint** —*a leader* (W.PREP.PHR. *amongst a band of men*) Od.; **hand over** —*a bride* (W.DAT. *to a husband*) AR. —*a person* (*to an enemy*) AR.
3 || MID. **cause** (someone) **to follow one**; (of a warrior or ruler) **take** (W.ACC. someone) **as an attendant** or **companion** Hom.
4 cause (good things) **to come to** (people); (of the gods) **give, present** —*glory, victory, gifts, blessings* (sts. W.DAT. *to someone*) Hom. Hes. Eleg. Lyr. A. E. +; (of a person) —*gifts, honours, goodwill offerings* (*esp. to a host, guest or friend*) Hom. AR. Theoc. —*an offering* (*to a divinity*) E. Theoc.; (of a relative, esp. a parent) —*endowments or gifts* (*to a family member*) Il. Pi. Hellenist.poet.+; (of a son) **bring** —*glory* (*to his parents*) Hes.
5 cause (unwelcome things) **to come to** (people); (of the gods) **send** —*misery, a bad fate, the race of women* Od. Semon. Thgn. A. E. Call.; **impose** —*an oracular command* A.; (of Helen) **bring** —*ill-repute* (W.DAT. *upon women*) Od.
6 contribute (sthg. additional); **add** —*deed* (W.DAT. *to deed*) hHom. —*effort* (*to one's deeds*) Pi. —*a piece of craftsmanship* (W.PREP.PHR. *to a shield*) A.

ὀπαῖον ου *n.* [ὀπή] **1 opened-up area in the roof of a building, skylight** Plu.
2 (prep.phr.) ἀν' ὀπαῖα (perh.) **through the smoke-hole** Od.(v.l. ἀνοπαῖα or ἄνοπαια, interpr. as *upwards*)

ὀπᾱνίκα *dial.adv.*: see ὀπηνίκα

ὄ-πατρος ον *adj.* [copul.prfx., πατήρ] (of a brother) **by the same father** Il.

ὀπάων ονος, Ion. **ὀπέων** ωνος *m.f.* [perh.reltd. ὀπάζω]
1 (*m.*) **attendant** (to a warrior, commander or ruler) Il. Hdt. Trag. AR.; (to a visitor, stranger or traveller) A. B.; (to flocks) Pi.; (to a queen) E.
2 (*f.*) **attendant** (to a goddess, a woman) hHom.

ὄπεας, Ion. **ὕπεας**, ατος *n.* [reltd. ὀπή] **incising tool, awl** Hippon. Hdt.

ὅπερ (neut.relatv.pron.): see ὅσπερ

ὀπή ῆς *f.* [perh.reltd. ὤψ] **hole** (in a cloak, wall, or sim.) Ar.

ὅ-πη (also **ὅπῃ**), ep. **ὅππῃ**, Ion. **ὅκη**, dial. **ὅπα** (also **ὅπᾱ**), Aeol. **ὅππα** (also perh. **ὅππᾱ**), also dial. **ὅπᾳ** (Pi. Ar.) *adv. and conj.* (relatv., indef.relatv., indir.interrog.) [ὅς[1], πῆ] **1 in which region or place, where** Od. Lyr. Pl. +; **in which precise spot, where** Hom. Semon. A. B. Th. Ar.; (indef.) **wherever** Od. +
2 to which place or in which direction, to where, where Hom. Hes. A. Hdt. +; (indef.) **wherever** Hom. +
3 by which route, path or means, in which way Hom. A. Pi. Hdt. +; (indef.) **by whichever means** Il. +

ὀπηδέω, dial. **ὀπᾱδέω** *contr.vb.* [ὀπηδός] | only pres. and impf. | 3sg.impf. ὀπηδεῖ | **1 follow closely or keep company** (w. someone or sthg.); (of a person) **follow, accompany, attend** —W.DAT. *a person* Il. —w. ἅμα + DAT. *cattle* hHom.; (of a personif. island) **follow** (others, in a procession) Call.
2 (of a dream-vision) **follow** —W.DAT. *the paths of sleep* A.
3 (of a divinity) **attend upon, favour** —W.DAT. *persons* Od. Hes. Theoc.
4 (fig., of Persuasion) **wait upon, serve** —W.DAT. *Truth* Parm.; (of a bow) —*a warrior* Il.; (of a wise man) —*opportunity* Pi.
5 (of a land's resources) **minister to, support** —W.DAT. *a people* hHom.
6 (of wealth, honour, prowess, beauty, or sim.) **keep company** —W.DAT. *w. people* Hom. Hes. hHom. Thgn. Theoc.; (of rank and fame) —*w. wealth* Hes.; (of famine, calamity, in neg.phr.) —w. μετά + DAT. *w. just people* Hes.

—ὀπηδεύω *vb.* (of an oxherd) **follow** (after oxen) AR.; (of sheep) —W.DAT. *a shepherd* AR.

ὀπη-δή *relatv.adv.* [ὅπη] **in any way whatever** Pl.

ὀπηδός, dial. **ὀπᾱδός**, οῦ *m.* [reltd. ὀπάων] **1 attendant, companion** (W.DAT. to the Muses, ref. to Apollo) hHom.; (to the Nymphs, ref. to Pan) Scol.; (W.GEN. of the Great Mother, ref. to Pan) Pi.*fr.*; (of deer, ref. to Artemis) S.; (of Night, ref. to stars) Theoc.; (of victories in the games, ref. to song) Pi.; (of virtue, envisaged as a god, ref. to certain pleasures) Pl.
2 (ref. to a person) **attendant** (sts. W.GEN. or DAT. to another, of higher status) Trag. Plu.; **follower** (W.GEN. of a god) Pl.; (W.DAT. of wrongdoers) AR.; **guardian** (of one's soul) Simon.

ὁ-πηλίκος η ον *indir.interrog.adj.* [ὅς[1]] **of what size, how large** Pl.

ὁ-πηνίκα, dial. **ὀπᾱνίκα** *indir.interrog. and relatv.adv.* **1** (as relatv. or correlatv.conj.) **at the time** or **on the day when** S. D. Theoc. Plu.; **in the year when** (one reaches a certain age) Pl.; (indef.) **on any day** or **occasion when** D. Plu.
2 (as indir.interrog.) **when precisely** Th. Pl. X.; (in a reply, repeating the q.) **what time, did you ask?** Ar.

ὀπη-οῦν *relatv.adv.* [ὅπη] **in any way whatever** Pl.

ὅπη-περ *relatv.adv.* [περ[1]] **wherever** or **in whichever way** Pl.

ὀπη-τι-οῦν *relatv.adv.* **in any way whatever** Pl.

ὀπίας ου *m.* [ὀπός[1]] **1 fig-juice variety** (of cheese, made w. fig rennet) E.*Cyc.*
2 (w. play on ὀπή *hole*) **man as thin as whey** Ar.

ὀπιδνοτάτη ης *fem.superl.adj.* [ὀπίζομαι] (epith. of Styx) **most awe-inspiring** AR.

ὀπίζομαι *mid.vb.* [ὄπις] | ep.2sg.impf. ὀπίζεο, 3sg. ὀπίζετο |
1 have fear and reverence (for the gods); **stand in awe of** —*gods, their anger or ordinances* Od. Hes. hHom. AR. —W.GEN. *gods, Zeus* Thgn. AR.; (intr.) **show reverence** Pi.; **be overawed** (by a person resembling a god) Pi. || PTCPL.ADJ. (of gratitude) **reverent** Pi.
2 have regard for, take heed of —*a person* Il. —*a mother's request* Il. —W.GEN. *someone's words* Call.

ὄπιθε(ν) *ep.adv.*: see ὄπισθε(ν)

ὀπιθό-μβροτος ον *ep.adj.* [ὄπισθε, βροτός] (of acclaim) **coming after the mortal man, posthumous** Pi.

Ὀπικοί ῶν *m.pl.* **Oscans** (people of S. Italy) Th. Arist.

—Ὀπικίᾱ ᾱς *f.* **Oscan territory** Th.

ὀπιπεύω (also perh. **ὀπιπτεύω** AR.) *vb.* **1 look intently; watch closely** (during the threshing process) Hes.; (tr., of the dragon) —*the Golden Fleece* AR.
2 watch surreptitiously or **for a sinister purpose; keep an eye on** —*an enemy* Il. AR.; **ogle, leer at** —*women* Od. AR.

ὄπις

3 observe as a mere bystander; **gawk at** —*a battlefield* Il. —*public disputes* Hes.
4 (gener.) **glance** (at people) AR.

ὄπις ιδος *f.* [app.reltd. ὄψομαι, ὄπωπα; see ὁράω] | acc. ὄπιδα, also ὄπιν | dial.dat. ὀπῖ (Pi.) | **1** watchfulness (of the gods, w. regard to human wrongdoing); (specif.) **vengeance, punishment** (W.GEN. of the gods or a god) Hom. Hes. Theoc.; (without gen.) Od. Hes.
2 favour (W.GEN. of the gods) Pi.
3 reverence, respect, regard (W.GEN. for the gods) Hdt.; (for guests) Pi.; (for an old man) Mosch.

ὄπισθε(ν), ep. **ὄπιθεν** (also perh. **ὄπιθε** AR.) *adv. and prep.*
1 (ref. to location) in a position behind, **behind, at the back, in the rear** Hom. +; (quasi-adjl., of a door, wheels) **at the rear, back** Semon. Hdt. || MASC.PL.SB. (w.art.) troops in the rear X. Plu. || NEUT.PL.SB. hind parts, back (of a person) Il.; rear (of an army) X.
2 (prep.) at the back or to the rear of, **behind** —W.GEN. *persons, things, places* Il. Hippon. Pi. Hdt. E.*Cyc.* Ar. +; (fig.) **second to** —W.GEN. *someone's will* S.
3 to a position or in the direction behind, **behind** Il.
4 (prep.phrs.) εἰς τὸ ὄπισθεν (or τοὔπισθεν) *to the back, backwards* E. Lys. Ar. Pl. +; (also) πρὸς τὸ ὄπισθεν X.; ἐκ τοῦ ὄπισθεν *from behind* Th. Ar. X.; ἐν τῷ ὄπισθεν *behind* Pl.
5 (ref. to remaining or being left, when others have departed) **behind** Hom. Aeschin.
6 (ref. to time) in the future, **hereafter, thereafter, afterwards, later** Hom. Hes. Pi. Theoc.*epigr.*; (quasi-adjl., of a narrative) **future, later** Hdt.

ὀπίσθιος (also **ὀπισθίδιος** Call.) ᾱ (Ion. η) ον *adj.* (of an animal's foot or leg) **back, hind** Semon. Hdt. X. Call. Plu.

ὀπισθό-δομος ου *m.* [δόμος] **rear** or **inner chamber** (of a temple, esp. of Athena on the Acropolis, used as a treasury) Ar. D. Plu. || ADJ. (of inscribed pillars) in inner chambers Plb.

ὀπισθο-νόμος ον *adj.* [νέμω] (of a certain kind of cattle) **walking backwards while grazing** Hdt.

ὀπισθό-πους ποδος *masc.adj.* [πούς] (of a group of persons) **walking behind, following** E. || SB. follower, attendant A.

ὀπισθό-τονος ου *m.* [τόνος] (medic.) **opisthotonos** (convulsive muscular tension, causing the body to arch backwards) Pl.

ὀπισθο-φύλακες ων *m.pl.* [φύλαξ] **rearguard** (of an army) X.

ὀπισθοφυλακέω *contr.vb.* **1** (of troops) **form the rearguard** X. Plu.
2 (of a commander) **be in charge of the rearguard** X.

ὀπισθοφυλακίᾱ ᾱς *f.* **post of rearguard** X.

ὀπισσο-πόρευτος ον *dial.adj.* [ὀπίσω, πορευτός] **travelling back** (the way one came) Tim.

ὀπίστατος η ον *superl.adj.* [ὄπισθεν] (of one among fleeing troops) **last, hindmost** Il.

ὀπίσω, ep. **ὀπίσσω**, Aeol. **ὑπίσσω** *adv. and prep.* [reltd. ὄπισθεν] **1** (ref. to movt.) in a backwards direction (opp. forwards), **backwards, back** Hom. Hes. Pi. Pl. +; (also) εἰς τοὐπίσω Lys. Pl.; *to the back* —*ref. to being moved fr. the front* S.*Ichn.*
2 back to the place or in the direction from which one has come, back, back again Od. Pi. Hdt. E.*fr.* AR. Theoc. +; (quasi-adjl., of a route, a journey) **back** Hdt.; τὸ ὀπίσω *back* Hdt.; ἐς (εἰς) τὸ ὀπίσω (τοὐπίσω) Hdt. Plb.; (fig., in an argument) Pl.
3 (ref. to a reversal of circumstances) **back, back again** (to a former state) Od. Hdt. E.
4 (ref. to location) in a position behind, **behind, at the back, in the rear** Il. Tyrt. Plb. Plu.; (quasi-adjl., of a side of a camp) **rear** Plb. || MASC.SB. (w.art.) man behind (oneself) Plu.; (pl.) troops in the rear Plb. || NEUT.SB. (w.art.) area behind (oneself) Plu.; rear (W.GEN. of an army) Plb.; (pl.) back (W.GEN. of a person's head) Hdt.
5 (specif.) **behind the back** —*ref. to tying someone's hands* Il. Hdt. Ar. X. D. +; ἐς τοὐπίσω —*ref. to clasping one's own hands* Th.
6 (as prep., ref. to location) **behind, to the rear of** —W.GEN. *persons, a building* Plb. Plu.; (ref. to following) **behind, after** —W.GEN. *a person* (*esp. a teacher or leader*) NT.
7 (ref. to remaining or being left, when persons have departed or died) **behind** Hom. Hes.
8 (ref. to time) in the future, **hereafter, thereafter, later** Hom. Hes. Stesich. Eleg. AR.; (quasi-adjl., of a narrative) **future, later** Hdt.; ἐς ὀπίσσω *for the future* Od.; (as prep.) **after** —W.GEN. *a person* (*i.e. his time*) NT.
9 into the future —*ref. to seeing* (w. prophetic vision) S.
10 (phr.) πρόσσω καὶ ὀπίσσω (sts. preceded by ἅμα) *at the same time*) *forwards and backwards* —*ref. to looking or directing one's thoughts* (i.e. *using experience of the past to anticipate the future*) Hom.

ὅπλα ων *n.pl.* [reltd. ἕπω] **1** implements or items of equipment (for seafaring or other purposes); **rigging, tackle** (of a ship) Od. Hes. hHom. Archil. AR. Theoc.; **ropes, cables** (for building Xerxes' bridge across the Hellespont) Hdt.; **tools** (of a blacksmith) Hom. || SG. rope Od. AR.; implement (ref. to an old man's staff) Call.*epigr.*
2 (esp.) implements for fighting, **weapons, arms, armour** Il. Pi. B. Hdt. Trag. +; (of Zeus, ref. to thunder and lightning) Hes. || SG. weapon or piece of armour Hdt. E. Pl. X. +; (fig., ref. to the body itself) Plu.
3 (specif.) heavy spear and shield (of a hoplite); **heavy armour, arms** A. Hdt. E. Th. Ar. +; (of an athlete in a race) Pi.
4 (w. various meton. senses) **armed men, infantry, military arts, force** or **aggression** S. E. Th. +

ὁπλάρια ων *n.pl.* **weaponry** Plu.

ὁπλέω *contr.vb.* **equip, make ready** —*a mule cart* Od. | see also ὅπλομαι

ὁπλή ῆς *f.* **hoof** (of an animal) Il. Hes. hHom. Semon. Pi. Hdt. +

Ὅπλης ητος *m.* **Hoples** (son of Ion, eponymous founder of one of the four Ionic tribes) Hdt. || PL. Hopletes (members of the tribe) E. Plu.

ὁπλίζω *vb.* [ὅπλα] | aor. ὥπλισα, ep. ὥπλισσα || MID.: aor. ὡπλισάμην, ep. ὡπλισσάμην (also perh. ὁπλισ(σ)άμην) || PASS.: aor. ὡπλίσθην, ep.3pl. ὥπλισθεν (or ὅπλισθεν) | PF.MID.PASS.: ὥπλισμαι |
1 make ready (food or drink); **prepare** —*a potion* Il. —*a feast* E. || MID. **prepare** or **cause to be prepared** —*one's meal* Hom. —*a sacrificial feast* E.
2 make ready (things needed for a journey or undertaking); **prepare** —*a mule cart* Il. —*food supplies* Od. || MID. **prepare for oneself, get ready** —*one's horses* (by harnessing them) Il. Hes.*fr.* —*a lantern* Emp. || PASS. (of ships) be made ready (for sailing or to go to war) Od.
3 make ready or **equip** (persons); **equip** —*persons* (w. *certain attributes or powers*) Pl. || MID. **make preparations, get ready** Od. —W.INF. *to do sthg.* Il. E. || AOR.PASS. (of women) get ready, dress up Od. || PF.MID.PASS.PTCPL. equipped —W.ACC. w. *a lyre* (W.PREP.PHR. *in one's hands*) E.*fr.*
4 equip (persons, w. weapons or armour); **arm** —*individuals, troops, or sim.* (W.DAT. w. *a certain kind of*

weaponry or armour) Hdt. E. Th. X. + —*persons* (*w. axes*) Call. —*one's hand* E.(also mid.) —(*w. a sword*) E.(mid.); (specif.) **arm** (W.ACC. men) **as hoplites** Th. Lys. ‖ PF.MID.PASS.PTCPL. (of women) armed —W.DAT. *w. thyrsoi* E.; (of Athena's breastplate) —*w. coiling snakes* E.

5 ‖ MID. **arm oneself** Hom. E. X. Call. AR. Plu. —W.ACC. *w. anything to hand* Men.; (fig.) —*w. rashness* S.; (of the heart) **take up arms** E.

6 ‖ PASS. (esp. pf.ptcpl.) **be armed** (freq. opp. be unarmed or unprepared) Hdt. S. E. Th. + —W.DAT. or ADV. *w. a certain kind of weaponry or armour, well, poorly, or sim.* E. Th. +; (of a hoplite, for a race; of Athena's statue) be in full armour Pl. ‖ NEUT.PL.PF.PASS.PTCPL.SB. protected side (of a body of hoplites, i.e. the left, as covered by their shields) X.

7 ‖ PF.PASS.PTCPL.ADJ. (of a torch) ready as a weapon (W.PREP.PHR. in a warrior's hand) A.

ὅπλισις εως *f.* **military equipment, weaponry** Th. Ar. Pl. X. +

ὅπλισμα ατος *n.* **1** item of weaponry, **weapon** E. ‖ COLLECTV.PL. equipment for war Pl.

2 armed naval force, **fleet** E.

ὁπλισμός οῦ *m.* **1 weaponry, armour** Plu.

2 (pl.) **arming** (of troops) A.

ὁπλῖτ-αγωγός όν *adj.* [ὁπλίτης] (of a ship) **for transporting troops** Th.

ὁπλῖτείᾱ ᾱς *f.* [ὁπλῑτεύω] **military service** Pl.

ὁπλῑτεύω *vb.* [ὁπλίτης] **serve** or **be ready to serve as a hoplite** Th. Lys. X. Arist.

ὁπλίτης ου *m.* [ὅπλα] **1** fighter of the type who is heavy-armed (typically w. a spear and round shield); **armed man** (sts. appos.w. ἀνήρ) A. Hdt. E. +; (in the army of a city-state, fighting in phalanx formation) **hoplite, infantryman** Hdt. +; (opp. other kinds of fighter, e.g. light-armed, cavalry, bowman, slinger) Hdt. +; (in a Macedonian phalanx or Roman legion) Plb. Plu.

2 hoplite (ref. to a man listed by the city-state as ready for service) Ar. Pl. + ‖ PL. hoplite class (fr. which such men were drawn) Th. Lys. Arist.

3 hoplite (as a competitor in a race for fully-armoured men) Pl.

4 ‖ ADJ. (of equipment) for a warrior E.; (of an army) under arms E.; heavily armed Plu.; (of a race) run in full armour Pi.

ὁπλῑτικός ή όν *adj.* **1** of or relating to a hoplite; (of a force, ranks, a division or phalanx) **of hoplites** or **heavy infantry** X. Arist. Plu.; (of a battle) **with hoplite-style fighting** Pl. Plu.; (of weapons) **for hoplites** X. ‖ NEUT.SB. hoplite force or heavy infantry Th. Pl. X. Arist.; armed or hoplite class (in a city-state) Arist.

2 ‖ FEM. and NEUT.SB. art of fighting as a hoplite Pl.

ὁπλῑτο-πάλᾱς ᾱ *dial.m.* [πάλη] **fighter in hoplite arms** Plu.(quot. A.)

ὁπλο-θήκη ης *f.* **arms store, armoury** Plu.

ὁπλό-κτυπος ον *adj.* [ὁπλή, κτύπος] (of the ground) **resounding with hoof-beats** A.

ὅπλομαι *mid.vb.* [reltd. ὁπλέω] **get things ready for, prepare** —*one's meal* Il.(cj. ὁπλέομαι)

ὁπλομαχέω *contr.vb.* [ὁπλομάχος] **fight in heavy armour** (as a skill acquired by training) Isoc. Arist. Plu.

ὁπλο-μάχης ου *m.* **skilled heavy-armed fighter** Pl.

ὁπλομαχίᾱ ᾱς *f.* **fighting in heavy armour** (as a skill) Pl. X.

ὁπλο-μάχος ου *m.* [μάχομαι] **1** instructor in the skill of fighting in heavy armour, **armed-combat teacher** (ref. to an itinerant professional, who also gave public displays of his technique) X. Thphr.

2 ‖ PL. heavy-armed troops Plb.

ὅπλον *n.sg.*: see ὅπλα

ὁπλοποιική ῆς *f.* [ποιέω] **art of making weapons** Pl.

ὁπλότερος ᾱ (Ion. η) ον *compar.adj.* [app. ὅπλα] **1** app., more capable of bearing arms (because younger and more vigorous); (gener., of men and women) born relatively recently, **young, youthful** (opp. old) Hom. hHom. Pi. Ar. AR.; **younger** (sts. W.GEN. than someone else) Hom. hHom. AR.; (than a sibling) Hom. B. Theoc.

2 of later generations Simon. AR. Theoc.

—**ὁπλότατος** η ον *superl.adj.* (of a sibling) **youngest** Hom. Hes. hHom. Pi. AR.

ὁπλοφορέω *contr.vb.* [ὁπλοφόρος] **bear weapons** X. ‖ PASS. (of kings) be given military protection —W.DAT. **by infantry and cavalry** Plu.

ὁπλο-φόρος ον *adj.* [ὅπλα, φέρω] **1** (of wagons) **conveying armour** or **weapons** Plu.

2 (of an encampment) **armed** E.; (of duties) **under arms** X.

3 ‖ MASC.PL.SB. armed men, soldiers E. X.; (as an escort) X. Plu.

ὁ-ποδαπός, Ion. **ὁκοδαπός**, ή όν *indir.interrog.adj.* [ὅς[1]] of or from what country, **from where** Hdt. Pl.

Ὀπόεις *ep.f.*: see Ὀποῦς

ὁ-πόθεν, ep. **ὁππόθεν**, Aeol. **ὅπποθεν**, Ion. **ὁκόθεν** *indir.interrog. and relatv.adv.* **1** (indir.interrog., ref. to movt.) from which place, **from where** Od. +

2 (relatv., ref. to location) **from where** Sapph. +

3 (indir.interrog.) from what source or origin, **from where** Od. +; (relatv.) Antipho +

4 (indef.adv.) **from wherever it may be** Pl.; ὁπόθεν δήποτε *from whatever source, somehow or other* D.

5 (indir.interrog.) from which starting-point (in a narrative or sim.), **from which point, where** Parm. +; (indef.adv.) **from whatever point it may be** Arist.

6 (indir.interrog.) from what cause (it comes about that), **how** or **why** Hdt. Ar. Att.orats. +

ὁποθεν-οῦν *indef.relatv.adv.* [ὁπόθεν] **from any place whatsoever** Pl.

ὁ-πόθι, ep. **ὁππόθι** *indir.interrog. and relatv.adv.*
1 (indir.interrog.) at what place, **where** Od. AR.

2 (relatv.) at the place where, **where** Il.

3 (relatv.) in a situation where, **where, when** A.

ὅ-ποι, Aeol. **ὅππυι** (Theoc., cj.) *indir.interrog. and relatv.adv.* [ποῖ] **1** (indir.interrog.) to what place or in what direction, **where, to where** Trag. +; at what place, **where** —*ref. to arriving, remaining, or sim.* Trag. +

2 (ref. to spending money) **on what** Att.orats.

3 (in response to the q. ποῖ *where?*) **do you ask 'where'?** Ar.

4 (relatv.) to the place or in the direction where, **where** Trag. +

ὁ-ποῖος, ep. **ὁπποῖος**, Ion. **ὁκοῖος**, ᾱ (Ion. η) ον *indir.interrog. and relatv.adj.* **1** (indir.interrog., of persons or things) **of what kind, what sort of** Od. +

2 (in making a selection or distinction betw. two or more) **which** Hdt. +

3 (relatv.) **of the kind which** Archil. +; (indef.) **whatever kind of** Hom. +; (in response to the q. ποῖος *of what kind?*) **of whatever kind** E.

—**ὁποῖα** *neut.pl.conj.* in ways such as would suit, **like** (a certain kind of person) S.

ὁποιοσ-δήποτε ὁποιᾱδήποτε ὁποιονδήποτε *indef.relatv.adj.* [δή ποτε] (pejor.) **of whatever kind it may be, of some kind or other** D.

ὁποιοσ-οῦν ὁποιᾱοῦν ὁποιονοῦν *indef.relatv.adj.* **of any kind whatsoever, of whatever kind** Pl. Arist. Din.

ὁποῖοσ-περ ὁποίαπερ ὁποῖόνπερ *relatv.adj.* [περ¹] **of the kind which** A.

ὁποιοστισοῦν (or **ὁποῖός τις οὖν**) ὁποιᾱτισοῦν ὁποιοντιοῦν *indef.relatv.adj.* **of any kind whatsoever, of whatever kind** Lys. X. D.

ὅποι-περ (or **ὅποι περ**) *relatv.adv.* [περ¹] **where** S. X. Arist.

ὁποί-ποτε *indef.relatv.adv.* [ὅποι, ποτέ] **wherever it may be, wheresoever** —*ref. to living* Plu.

ὀπός¹ οῦ *m*. **plant juice** (w. acidic properties) Pl.; (fr. herbs used in magic) S.*fr*.; (app.fr. the fig tree, used as rennet to curdle milk for cheese) Il.; (used in making an ointment) Ar.; (fig.phr.) βλέπειν ὀπόν *give a sour look* Ar.

ὀπός² (gen.sg.): see ὄψ

ὁ-ποσάκις, Aeol. **ὁππόσσακιν** *indir.interrog. and relatv.adv.* [ὅς¹] **1 how many times** —*ref. to multiplying* Theoc.
2 (relatv.) **as many times as, as often as** Pl. X.

ὁποσαχῇ *relatv.adv.* [ὁπόσος] **in as many ways as** X.

ὁ-πόσος, ep. **ὁππόσος** (also **ὁπόσσος**), Ion. **ὁκόσος**, η ον *indir.interrog. and relatv.adj.* **1** (indir.interrog.; sg., of things) of what size, amount or quantity, **how large, how great, how much** Thgn. Hdt. + ‖ PL. (of persons or things) of what number, how many Hom. Pi. Hdt. +
2 (relatv., sg.) **as great** or **as large as, as much as** Xenoph. A. Hdt. + ‖ PL. **as many as** Od. +
3 (indef.) **however great, however much** Hdt. Att.orats. +

—**ὁπόσον**, ep. **ὁπόσσον** *neut.sg.adv.* **to the extent that, as far as** Il. E. Ar. X.

—**ὁπόσῳ** *neut.dat.sg.adv.* **by how much** Pl.

ὁποσοσ-δή ὁποσηδή ὁποσονδή —also Ion. **ὁκόσος (η ον) δή** *indef.relatv.adj.* **of any amount whatever** Hdt. Pl.

ὁποσοσ-οῦν ὁποσηοῦν ὁποσονοῦν —also Ion. **ὁκόσος (η ον) ὦν** *indef.relatv.adj.* **of any size** or **amount whatever** Pl. X. Arist. ‖ PL. **in any number** Hdt. Th. +; (as relatv., w.cl.) **however many** Hdt.(dub.)

—**ὁποσονοῦν** *indef.neut.sg.adv.* **to any extent whatever** Th.; (as relatv., w.cl.) καθ' ὁποσονοῦν *to the extent or amount that* D.

ὁπόσοσ-περ ὁπόσηπερ ὁπόσονπερ *relatv.adj.* [περ¹] ‖ PL. **as many as** Pl. X.

ὁποσου-τινοσ-οῦν *indef.neut.gen.sg.adv.* [ὁπόσος, τις] **at any price whatever** Lys.

ὁπόσσος *ep.adj.*: see ὁπόσος

ὁ-πόστος η ον *indir.interrog.adj.* (of an individual) how far on in a numerical series, **in what number** or **place** Pl. X. Arist.

ὁποστοσ-οῦν ὁποστηοῦν ὁποστονοῦν *indef.relatv.adj.* **in whichever place** Plu.; (w.neg.) **in any place at all** D.

ὁ-πότε, ep. **ὁππότε**, Aeol. **ὅππότα**, Ion. **ὁκότε**, dial. **ὁππόκα** *indir.interrog. and relatv.adv.* **1** (indir.interrog.) **at what time, when** Od. Th. Ar. +
2 (relatv., as conj., ref. to pres. or past time, w.indic.) **at the time or on the occasion that, when** Hom. Hes. Pi. B. S. E. +
3 (ref. to fut. time, usu. after fut. main vb., w.subj.) **when** Hom.; (w.fut.indic.) Pi. Ar. +; (in indir.sp., after past main vb., w.opt.) S. Th. +
4 (ref. to a repeated action, usu. after pres. main vb., w.subj.) **on each occasion that, when, whenever** Hom. Hes. Sapph. Sol. Thgn.; (after past main vb., w.opt.) Hom. +; (introducing a simile, w.subj.) ὡς ὁπότε *as when* Hom. Hes. hHom.; (w.indic.) Il. Call. AR.
5 (after vb. of waiting, or in ctxt. of expectancy, usu. w.opt.) **for the time** or **moment when** Hom. Th. AR.; (w.fut.indic.) Hdt. Ar. • δέγμενος ὁππότε ναῦφιν ἀφορμηθεῖεν Ἀχαιοί *waiting for the time when the Achaeans would move out from their ships* Il.
6 in circumstances in which, when Thgn. Hdt. S. +; (causal) **when it is the case that, because, since** Hdt. E. Th. +

—**ὁπόταν** (also **ὁπότ' ἄν**), ep. **ὁππόταν** (also **ὁππότ' ἄν** and **ὁππότε κεν**) *conj.* [ἄν¹] **1** (w.subj., ref. to an occurrence in fut. time, usu. w.fut. main vb.) **when** Hom. +
2 (w.subj., ref. to a repeated action, or in a general statement) **when, whenever** Hom. +

ὁποτε-οῦν *indef.relatv.adv.* **at any time whatever, at any and every time** Arist.

ὁ-πότερος ᾱ ον, ep. **ὁππότερος**, Ion. **ὁκότερος**, η ον *indir.interrog. and relatv.adj.* **1** (indir.interrog.) **which** (of two persons or things) Hom. +; (pl., ref. to a team of horses, a defined group of people) Il. Hes. Th. + ‖ NEUT.PL.SB. **which** (of alternatives) Hdt.
2 (relatv.) **who** or **which** (of two) Il. Hes. Hdt. +; (pl., ref. to a defined group) Il. Hdt. Th. +
3 (indef.relatv., w.subj., usu. w. ἄν or κε) **whoever** or **whichever, no matter who** or **which** (of two) Hom. +; (pl., ref. to a defined group) Il. Hdt. ‖ NEUT.PL.SB. **whichever** (of alternatives) A. Hdt. +
4 (indef.adj.) **one** or **other, either** (of two) And. Pl.; (pl., ref. to a defined group) X. D.

—**ὁπότερον** *neut.sg.indir.interrog.adv.* (introducing alternative propositions, linked by εἴτε ... εἴτε *either ... or*) **whether** Isoc.

—**ὁπότερα**, Ion. **ὁκότερα** *neut.pl.indir.interrog.adv.* (introducing alternative propositions, linked by ἤ ... ἤ *either ... or*) **whether** Hdt. Pl.; (linked by εἴτε ... εἴτε) X.; (the second only linked by ἤ) Ar. X.

—**ὁποτέρως** *adv.* (indir.interrog.) **in which way** (of two) Th.; (indef.relatv.) **in whichever way** (of two) Att.orats. Pl. Arist. Plu.

—**ὁπποτέρωθεν** *ep.adv.* (indir.interrog., ref. to movt.) **from which direction** (of two) Il.

—**ὁποτέρωθι** *adv.* (indef.relatv.) **on whichever side** (of an army) X.

—**ὁποτέρωσε** *adv.* **1** (indir.interrog.) **in which direction** (of two) Th. Plu.
2 (indef.relatv.) **in whichever direction** (of two) Th. Pl.

ὁποτεροσ-οῦν ὁποτεραοῦν ὁποτερονοῦν *indef.relatv.adj.* **whichever one, one or the other** Pl. X. Arist.; (pl., ref. to a defined group) Th. Arist.; (neut.pl.) ἐφ' ὁποτεραοῦν *in one direction or the other* Arist.

ὅ-που, Ion. **ὅκου** *indir.interrog. and relatv.adv.* [reltd. ὅς¹, ποῦ] **1** (indir.interrog.) **in or to what place, where** Od. +
2 (in response to the q. ποῦ *where?*) **do you ask 'where'?** Ar.; (indef.relatv.) **wherever** A. E.
3 in what circumstances, where Od.(dub.) Hdt. +
4 (relatv.) **in or to the place where, where** Semon. Hippon. Hdt. S. E. +
5 in circumstances where, where, when Thgn. Trag. +; (causal) **in that, inasmuch as, since** Hdt. Antipho +

Ὀπούντιος *adj.*: see under Ὀποῦς

ὁπου-οῦν *indef.relatv.adv.* [ὅπου] **in any place whatsoever, no matter where** Pl. X. Arist.

ὅπου-περ (or **ὅπου περ**) *relatv.adv.* [περ¹] **in the place where** E. Ar. X. Is.; **in circumstances where, where, when** Pl.

Ὀποῦς οῦντος, ep. **Ὀπόεις** εντος *f*. **Opous** (city in Lokris) Il. Pi. Th. Aeschin. +

—**Ὀπούντιος** ᾱ (Ion. η) ον *adj.* **1** (of Lokrians) **from or belonging to Opous** (opp. other regions of Lokris),

Opountian Hdt. Th. X.; (sg.) Ar. Arist.; (of cities belonging to them) AR.

2 ‖ MASC.PL.SB. citizens or inhabitants of Opous Ar. Plu.

ὄππα Aeol.n.: see ὄμμα

ὄππᾳ Aeol.adv., **ὄππῃ** ep.adv.: see ὅπῃ

ὁππόθεν ep.adv., **ὄππoθεν** Aeol.adv.: see ὁπόθεν

ὁππόθι ep.adv.: see ὁπόθι

ὁπποῖος ep.adj.: see ὁποῖος

ὁππόκα dial.adv.: see ὁπότε

ὀπποποῖ interj. [reltd. πόποι] (expressing annoyance) **hey!** S.Ichn.

ὁ-ππόσε ep.indir.relatv.adv. [ὅς¹, πόσε] to whatever place, **wherever** Od.

ὁππόσος ep.adj.: see ὁπόσος

ὁππόσσακιν Aeol.adv.: see ὁποσάκις

ὁππόταν ep.conj.: see under ὁπότε

ὁππότε ep.adv., **ὄπποτα** Aeol.adv.: see ὁπότε

ὁππότερος ep.adj., **ὁπποτέρωθεν** ep.adv.: see ὁπότερος

ὄππυι Aeol.adv.: see ὅποι

ὅππως ep.adv., **ὄππως** Aeol.adv.: see ὅπως

ὀπταλέος η ον Ion.adj. [ὀπτός] (of meat) **roasted** Hom.

ὀπτάνιον (also **ὀπτανεῖον** Plu.) ου n. room or space for cooking, **kitchen** Ar. Men. Plu.

ὀπτάνομαι mid.vb. [reltd. ὀπτήρ] (of the risen Christ) be visible, **appear** —W.DAT. *to people* NT.

ὀπτασίᾱ ᾱς f. **apparition** (of a heavenly being) NT.

ὀπτάω contr.vb. | PASS.: dial.pres.ptcpl. ὀπτεύμενος | aor.inf. ὀπτηθῆναι | pf. ὤπτημαι | **1** roast over the fire (on a spit) or in an oven; **roast** —*meat, a whole animal* Hom. hHom. Hdt. Ar. Pl. X. + —*fish* Hdt. Ar. —*human flesh* Hdt. Plu.; (intr.) **do the roasting, cook** Ar. ‖ MID. have (W.ACC. birds) **roasted** Ar. ‖ PASS. (of meat, birds, fish) be roasted Od. Ar.

2 cook (grain products, on a griddle or in an oven); **bake** —*bread, cakes* Hdt. Ar. X. Men.; (intr.) **bake bread** Hdt.

3 bake (clay products, in kilns); **fire, bake** —*bricks* Hdt. ‖ PASS. (of a pot) be fired Pl.

4 ‖ PASS. (of a person) be roasted (to death) Men.

5 (of the sun) **bake, burn** —*a person* Bion ‖ PASS. (of the earth) be baked (by the sun) X.

6 (fig.) inflame with love, **roast** —*a person* Ar. ‖ PASS. be roasted (by love) Call.epigr. Theoc.

ὀπτέον (neut.impers.vbl.adj.): see ὁράω

ὀπτεύω vb. [reltd. ὀπτήρ] (of birds) **survey, scrutinise** —*the whole earth* Ar.

ὀπτήρ ῆρος m. [ὄπωπα, see ὁράω] **1** one who observes (for others); **watchman, lookout** Od.

2 one who observes (on his own account); **observer** A. X.

3 one who happens to see (sthg. which occurs); **observer, eyewitness** S. Antipho

ὀπτήρια ων n.pl. offerings on seeing (a newborn or newly found child) for the first time; **first-sight offerings** E. Call.

ὀπτήτειρα ης Ion.fem.adj. [ὀπτάω] (of a kiln) **for baking** Call.

ὀπτικός ή όν adj. [reltd. ὀπτήρ] relating to sight ‖ FEM.SB. theory of sight Arist. ‖ NEUT.PL.SB. optics Arist.

ὀπτός ή όν adj. [ὀπτάω] **1** (of meat, fish, human flesh) roasted Od. A. Hdt. E.Cyc. Ar. +

2 (of bread) **baked** Hdt.

3 (of bricks) **fired, baked** Hdt. Ar. X.

4 (of land or soil) **baked dry** (by the sun) X.; (of figs) Call.epigr.

5 (of iron, in the hardening process) baked (w. ἐκ + GEN. in fire) S.

ὀπυίω, Att. **ὀπύω** vb. | ep.inf. ὀπυιέμεν, ὀπυιέμεναι | ep.impf. ὤπυιον, also ὄπυιον | Att.fut. ὀπύσω | **1** (of a man) take or have as a wife, **marry or be married to** —*a woman* Hom. Hes. Pi. Ar. AR. Theoc.; (intr.) have a wife, **be married** Il. ‖ PASS. (of a woman) be taken in marriage, be married Il. Plu.

2 (of women, in neg.phr.) **play the active role in sex** Arist. ‖ PASS. play the passive role Arist.

ὄπφις m.: see ὄφις

ὄπωπα (pf.), **ὀπώπει** (ep.3sg.plpf.): see ὁράω

ὀπωπή ῆς f. [ὄπωπα, see ὁράω] **1** seeing or view (of someone, on the first occasion), **sight** Od. hHom.

2 casting of a look (in someone's direction), **glance** AR.

3 faculty of vision, **sight** Od.

4 (concr.) **eye** AR.; **eyeball** AR.

ὀπωπητήρ ῆρος m. **watcher, spy** (at night, ref. to Hermes) hHom.

ὀπώρᾱ ᾱς, Ion. **ὀπώρη** ης f. **1** time of the ripening and gathering in of fruits (esp. grapes or orchard produce, opp. corn), **fruitful season, time of the fruit harvest** (ref. to late summer or autumn) Il. Alc. Pi.fr. Hdt. S.fr. Pl.; (opp. summer) Od. Theoc. Plu.; (opp. summer, winter, spring) Alcm.; (opp. winter and spring, i.e. incl. summer) Ar.; (following spring) X.; (personif., as a goddess) **Harvest Time** Ar.

2 (fig., ref. to a man's or woman's coming to maturity) **youthful ripeness** A. Pi.

3 (concr.) fruit gathered at the harvest, **harvest fruit** A. S. Pl. X. D. Arist. +; (pl.) Is.

4 (gener.) **fruit** Alcm. X.

ὀπωρίζω vb. | Ion.masc.pl.fut.ptcpl. ὀπωριεῦντες | **1 pick, harvest** —*fruits* Pl.; (intr.) **gather fruit** Plu.

2 pick the ripe fruit from —*date-palms* Hdt.

ὀπωρινός ή όν adj. | ῑ in Hom. | of the time of the fruit harvest; (of the star, ref. to Sirius) **of harvest time, autumnal** Il.; (of the North Wind, a breeze) Hom. hHom.; (of rain, a stormy day) Il. Hes.

ὀπωρ-ώνης ου m. [ὠνέομαι] buyer of fruit (for resale); (derog. w.connot. of being a petty tradesman) **fruiterer** D.

ὅπως, ep. **ὅππως**, Aeol. **ὄππως**, Ion. **ὅκως** relatv.adv. [ὅς¹, πῶς] **1** (sts. w.correlatv. ὥς or οὕτως) in such a manner as, **as, just as** Hom. + • ἔρξον ὅπως ἐθέλεις *do as you wish* Hom.; (w.indef.cl.) • οὕτως ὅπως ἂν αὐτοὶ βούλωνται *in whatever way they themselves wish* X.; (w. a noun) **like** (someone or sthg.) Trag. • ὅπως ἁ πάνδυρτος ἀηδών *like the mournful nightingale* S.

2 (w.superl.adv.) **as much as** A. + • ὅπως ἀνωτάτω *as high as possible* Ar.

3 (temporal) **when** Hom. + • ὅπως ἴδον αἷμα *when they saw the blood* Il.; (w.indef.cl.) • ἑώθεε ... ὅκως ἡ βασιλεία καλέοι φοιτᾶν *he was accustomed to go whenever the queen called him* Hdt.

4 (conj., introducing a statement, after a vb. of thinking or speaking) **that** Hdt. + • ἐρῶ μὲν οὐχ ὅπως τάχους ὕπο δύσπνους ἱκάνω *I will not say that I come breathless from haste* S.

5 οὐκ ἔστιν ὅπως (or sim.) there is no way that, **it is not possible that** —W.INDIC. *sthg. is the case* Hdt. +

6 οὐχ (or μὴ) ὅπως (followed by ἀλλά or sim.) **not to say that ... but** (i.e. not only ... but) Th. + • οὐχ ὅπως ὑμῖν τῶν αὑτοῦ τι ἐπέδωκεν ἀλλὰ τῶν ὑμετέρων πολλὰ ὑφῄρηται *so far from giving you something of his own, he has stolen much of what is yours* Lys.

7 (introducing an indir.q.) in what manner, **how** Hom. + • ἔσπετε νῦν μοι ... ὅππως δὴ πρῶτον πῦρ ἔμπεσε νηυσὶν

ὁπωσδήποτε

Ἀχαιῶν *now tell me how fire first fell on the ships of the Achaeans* Il.
8 (in response to the q. πῶς *how?*) **do you ask 'how'?** Ar.
9 (after a vb. of taking care, deliberating, or sim., w.fut.indic. or deliberative subj.) • ἔπρασσον ὅπως τις βοήθεια ἥξει *they tried to arrange for some help to come* Th.
• φραζώμεθ' ὅπως ὄχ' ἄριστα γένηται *let us consider how it may turn out for the very best* Od.; (w.opt., after a past tense)
• ἐπεμελήθημεν ὅπως ἐξαλειφθείη αὐτῷ τὰ ἁμαρτήματα *we took care that his offences should be expunged* Lys.
10 (after a vb. of fearing, w.fut.indic. or aor.subj.) • φόβος οὖν ἐστιν ... ὅπως μὴ καὶ αὖθις διασχισθησόμεθα *so there is a fear that we may be split in two again* Pl. • τὴν θεὸν ... ὅπως λάθω δέδοικα *I am worried how I may escape the notice of the goddess* (i.e. *that I may not*) E.
11 (in warnings or commands, after a vb. of cautioning or sim.) • ὅρα ὅκως μή σευ ἀποστήσονται Πέρσαι *watch out that the Persians don't revolt from you* Hdt.; (w. leading vb. omitted) • ὅπως οὖν ἔσεσθε ἄνδρες ἄξιοι τῆς ἐλευθερίας ἧς κέκτησθε *so be sure to prove you are men worthy of the freedom you possess* X.
12 (after a vb. of asking, w.subj., sts.w. ἄν) • ὅπως μὴ ἀποθάνῃ ἠντεβόλει *he pleaded that he should not be put to death* Lys.
13 (introducing a purpose cl.) **so that, in order that** (w.subj., sts.w. ἄν, or opt.) Hom. + • γέγωνέ μοι πᾶν τοῦθ', ὅπως εἰδῶ τίς εἶ *tell me all this, so that I may know who you are* S. • πὰρ δέ οἱ αὐτὸς ἔστη, ὅπως θανάτοιο βαρείας χεῖρας ἀλάλκοι *he himself stood by him, to keep away the heavy hands of death* Il.; (w.fut.indic.) • ἐμισθώσατο τοῦτον εὐθέως, ὅπως συνερεῖ *he immediately hired this man, to speak in support* D.; (w. past tense of indic., expressing an unfulfilled obligation) • φράσαι πρὸς ὑμᾶς ἅ καὶ τῇ βουλῇ ἐν ἀπορρήτῳ εἰσήγγειλα, ὅπως αὐτόθεν προῄδετε (*I would have dearly wished*) *to tell you what I also reported in secret to the Council, so that you might have known it at once* And.

ὁπωσ-δήποτε *indef.relatv.adv.* [δή ποτε] **in whatever way it might be, in some way or other** D. Arist.

ὁπωσ-οῦν *indef.relatv.adv.* **in any way whatever** Th. Att.orats. Pl. X. Arist. Plu.

ὅπωσ-περ, Ion. **ὅκωσπερ** (or **ὅκως περ**) *relatv.adv.* [περ¹]
1 **in such a manner as, just as** Heraclit. S.
2 (modifying a noun) **just like** Heraclit. Hdt.

ὁπωσ-τι-οῦν *indef.relatv.adv.* [τις] **1 somehow or other** Pl. D.
2 οὐδ' (or μηδ') ὁπωστιοῦν *in no way whatever* Th. X. D.

ὅραμα ατος *n.* [ὁράω] **1 that which is seen, sight, spectacle** (sts. horrific or impressive) X. D. Arist. Plu.
2 **prophetic or mystical sight, vision** NT.
3 **thing which is perceived or understood, discovery** (w.GEN. by Thales) Arist.(dub.)

ὅρανος *Aeol.m.*: see οὐρανός

ὅρασις εως *f.* [ὁράω] **1 faculty of seeing, sight** (as one of the senses) Plb.
2 **act of seeing, seeing** Arist. Plb.
3 **ability to see, vision** (as being impeded at night) Plb.
4 **way of looking** (at sthg.) **with the intellect, view** Men.
5 **prophetic or mystical sight, vision** NT.

ὁρατικός ή όν *adj.* || NEUT.SB. **that which relates to seeing** Arist.

ὁρατός ή όν *adj.* (of things) **able to be seen, visible** Pl. X. Arist. Theoc. Plu. || NEUT.SB. **that which is able to be seen** Pl. X. Arist.

ὁράω, Ion. **ὁρέω** *contr.vb.* | ep. (w.diect.) ὁρόω, 2sg. ὁράᾳς, 2pl.opt. ὁρόῳτε, ptcpl. ὁρόων, fem.ptcpl. ὁρόωσα, masc.pl.ptcpl. ὁρόωντες | dial. 2sg. ὁρῇς, 3sg. ὁρῇ, 3pl. ὁρεῦντι, also ὁρέοντι, imperatv. ὅρη, pl. ὁρῆτε | inf. ὁρᾶν, dial. ὁρῆν (Ar.) | impf.: Att. ἑώρων, ep.3sg. ὅρα | fut. ὄψομαι | pf. ὄπωπα, Att. ἑόρακα (later ἑώρακα) | plpf.: ep.3sg. ὀπώπει, Ion. ὠπώπεε, 3pl. ὀπώπεσαν, Att.3pl. ἑοράκεσαν || MID.: ep.inf. (w.diect.) ὁράασθαι | ep.3sg.impf. ὁρᾶτο || PASS.: Att.impf. ἑωρώμην | fut. ὀφθήσομαι | aor. ὤφθην, ptcpl. ὀφθείς, also ὁραθείς (Plu.) | Att.pf. ἑώραμαι, also 2sg. ὦψαι, 3sg. ὦπται || neut.impers.vbl.adj. ὀπτέον || The aor.act. is supplied by ἰδεῖν. | The mid. is used in poetry in the same senses as the act. | —also **ὄρημμι** *Aeol.vb.* | 3sg. ὄραι (Theoc., cj.) | mid.2sg. ὄρηαι (Od.) |
1 have the faculty of sight, be able to see, see S. E. Pl. +; (fig., of the words of a blind man) S.
2 (specif.) **be in a condition to see, see** —*the light* (*of the sun*, i.e. *be alive*) Hom. hHom. Alc. Thgn. S. E. || MASC.PL.PTCPL.SB. **the living** E.
3 direct one's eyes (towards someone or sthg.); **look** Hom. + —W.ADV. or PREP.PHR. *in a certain direction, towards or at persons or things* Hom. +; (tr.) **look at** —*persons or things* Hom. +
4 discern with the eyes, see, perceive —*persons, things* (sts. *doing sthg., or in a certain state*) Hom. + || PASS. (of persons or things) **be seen** Hdt. Trag. Th. +
5 perceive with the mind, become aware, understand, realise —W.INDIR.Q. or COMPL.CL. *what* (or *that sthg.*) *is the case* Hom. + —W.NOM.PTCPL. *that one is acting wrongly or sim.* E. Th. —W.ACC. + INF. *that sthg. is impossible* Th.
6 look with attention or concern, look, pay heed —w. εἰς (ἐς) + ACC. *to one's business* Od. —*to someone's appearance, lineage, speech* Hom. Sol.
7 pay attention to, take thought for —*a situation or goal* Semon. S. E.; **see to, provide** —*a chair* (W.DAT. *for someone*) Theoc.; **see to it, take care** —W.COMPL.CL. *that sthg. shd.* (or *shd. not*) *be the case* Hdt. S. E. Th. +
8 (interrog., drawing attention, sts. reproachfully) **ὁρᾷς;** *do you see* (i.e. *that sthg. is the case*)? S. E. Ar. Pl. Thphr. Men.
9 go to see, visit —*someone* Hom.; **meet with** —*someone* E. Thphr. Men.; **admit to one's presence, see** —*someone* Od.
10 have an expression (of a certain kind); **have a look of** —*determination* Pi. —*springtime* Theoc.; **glare** —W.ADV. *alarmingly* Hes.
11 (of a place) **be situated facing, look** —W.PREP.PHR. *towards another place* Th.

ὀργά *dial.f.*, **ὄργᾱ** *Aeol.f.*: see ὀργή

ὀργάζω *vb.* [reltd. ὀργάω] **work by continually pressing, knead, make supple** —*a scalp* Hdt. —*clay* Ar. || PASS. (of wax) **be kneaded** Pl.

ὀργαίνω *vb.* [ὀργή] | aor.opt. ὀργάναιμι | **1 be angry** S. —W.DAT. *w. someone* E.
2 (hyperbol.) **provoke to anger** —*a stone* S.

ὀργανικός ή όν *adj.* [ὄργανον] **1 having the nature of an instrument or tool;** (of the human body) **equipped with organs** or **faculties** Plu.; (of parts of the body) **useful, instrumental** (to the act of motion) Arist.; (of merits of slaves, in accomplishing tasks) Arist.
2 (of a kind of rhetoric) **effective** (w. εἰς + ACC. *on crowds*) Plu.
3 (of illustrations, equipment) **mechanical** Plu. || FEM.SB. **art of mechanics** Plu.

—**ὀργανικῶς** *adv.* **instrumentally** —*ref. to good things being useful* Arist.

ὄργανον ου n. [reltd. ἔργον] **1** piece of equipment, **instrument, implement, tool** (for making sthg., or for use in an activity) S. Pl. X. Aeschin. Arist. +
2 (specif.) **musical instrument** Pi.fr. E. Melanipp. Telest. Pl. X. +
3 surgical instrument Pl. X. Arist.
4 (fig., ref. to a person) **instrument** (W.GEN. of evil deeds) S.; (gener., ref. to a friend, assistant, slave, as helping a person to accomplish a task) Arist.
5 sensory organ (esp.ref. to the eye) Pl.
6 product of workmanship (ref. to an ornament, weapon, city-walls), **work, product** E.

ὀργάς άδος f. [ὀργάω] **1** app., area of fertile but uncultivated land; (specif.) **mountain glade** E. X.
2 (ref. to a region betw. Athens and Megara, dedicated to the deities of Eleusis) **sacred land** D. Call. Plu.

ὀργάω contr.vb. [app.reltd. ὀργή] **1** (of crops, fruits) **be ripe** Hdt. X. —W.PASS.INF. *for being reaped, picked, gathered* Hdt.; (of a girl) **be ready** (for marriage) Plu.
2 be full of enthusiasm or passion, **be eager** Th. Ar. Plu. —W.INF. *to do sthg.* A. Th.; (of men, w. sexual connot.) Ar.; (of a horse) —w. πρός + ACC. *for a run* Plu.

ὀργεών ῶνος, ep. **ὀργήων** (or **ὀργείων**) ονος m. [reltd. ὄργια] **performer of rites, minister** hHom.; (at Athens, ref. to a member of a religious fraternity) Is.

ὀργή ῆς, dial. **ὀργά** ᾶς, Aeol. **ὄργᾱ** ᾱς f. | freq. collectv.pl. |
1 emotional constitution; **temper, temperament, disposition** Hes. Semon. Thgn. Lyr. Hdt. Trag. +
2 heightened emotional state (gentle, harsh or violent, esp. in reaction to a circumstance, a person, sthg. done or said); **emotion, feeling, mood, passion** hHom. Sapph. Thgn. Pi. Trag. Th. +; (inspired by a god, esp. Bacchus, Pan) Pi.fr. E.
3 (specif.) **indignation, anger, fury** Pi. Hdt. Trag. Th. Ar. +; (of the gods, Erinyes, Retribution) Trag. +; (of a dead man's spirit) A. S.; (of battle, troops) Tyrt. Th. Ar.

ὄργια ων n.pl. [perh.reltd. ἔρδω, ἔργον] **1** acts of religious ritual, **rites** A. S. Arist.; (celebrated in honour of a particular god, esp. in a mystery cult) hHom. A.fr. Hdt. E. Ar. Call. +; (of Dionysus) Hdt. E.; (of Aphrodite or the Muses, fig.ref. to erotic love, music and poetry) Lyr.adesp. Ar.
2 (concr.) **secret cult objects** (of Dionysus) Theoc.

ὀργιάζω vb. | aor. ὠργίασα | **1 celebrate rites** Isoc.; (for Dionysus) E.; **celebrate** —W.COGN.ACC. *rites, sacrifices, or sim.* Pl. Plu. || MID. **celebrate rites** —W.DAT. *for divine beings* Pl. || PASS. (of the rites of a goddess) be celebrated Plu.
2 celebrate with rites —*a person* (as if a god) Pl. —*a goddess* Plu.
3 honour with rites —*sacred objects* Plu. || PASS. (of the private shrines of ancestral gods) be honoured with rites Pl.
4 (of Dionysus) **celebrate one's rites** AR.

ὀργιασμοί ῶν m.pl. **secret rites** (of Dionysus) Plu.; (of a mystery cult) Lyr.adesp.(cj.)

ὀργιαστής οῦ m. **celebrant** (of a mystery cult) Plu.

ὀργιαστικός ή όν adj. of the kind associated with religious rites; (of the aulos and its music) **producing religious excitement** Arist.

ὀργίζω vb. [ὀργή] | aor. ὤργισα || MID.: fut. ὀργιοῦμαι | pf. ὤργισμαι || PASS.: fut. ὀργισθήσομαι | aor. ὠργίσθην || neut.impers.vbl.adj. ὀργιστέον |
1 make (someone) impassioned or angry (by one's words or actions); **provoke, anger** —*a person* Ar. X. Arist. —*a colony of wasps* Ar.; (of a speaker) **move to anger** —*listeners* Pl. Arist.
2 || MID. (also FUT. and AOR.PASS.) **be** or **become angry** (sts. W.DAT. w. someone or sthg.) S. E. Ar. Att.orats. +; (esp. in political or military ctxts., w. leaders or envoys, w. fellow citizens or a foreign people) Th. Att.orats. +; (in lawcourts or other gatherings, w. persons or their wrongdoing, esp. when one is swayed by oratory) Att.orats.; (in a way which prevents sound judgement) Th. Att.orats. + || NEUT.PTCPL.SB. angry state (W.GEN. of mind) Th.
3 || MID. (of gods) **be angry** (at human actions) And. || AOR.PASS. **become angry** —W.DAT. w. *persons, a family* E. Ar.

ὀργίλος η ον adj. **1** prone to strong emotion (as a character trait); **emotional, quick-tempered** or **angry** Pl. Arist. Men.
2 full of strong emotion (on a particular occasion); **angry, impassioned, heated** X. D. Men.
—**ὀργίλως** adv. **emotionally, angrily, ill-humouredly** D. Arist. Men.

ὀργιλότης ητος f. **quick-temperedness** Arist.

ὄργυια, dial. **ὀρόγυια** (Pi.), ᾶς (Ion. ῆς), Att. **ὀργυιά** ᾶς f. [reltd. ὀρέγω] | acc. ὄργυιαν, Att. ὀργυιάν || PL.: nom. ὀργυιαί | gen. ὀργυιῶν, Ion. ὀργυιέων | dat. ὀργυιαῖς, Ion. ὀργυιῇσι | distance between the tips of both sets of fingers (w. the arms outstretched sideways); **fathom** (as a measure of length, height or depth, approx. six feet) Hom. Pi. Hdt. X. Plb. NT.

ὀργυιαῖος ᾱ ον adj. (of statues) measuring a fathom (in height), **six feet tall** Call.

ὄρεα (nom.acc.pl.): see ὄρος

ὄρεγμα ατος n. [ὀρέγω] **1** action of stretching or straining (of a part of the body); **outstretching** (of one's arms, in mourning) A.; (of one's cheeks and hair, in embracing someone) E.
2 stride, pace (to reach the safety of an altar) E.; (of a horse's steps) A.

ὀρέγνῡμι vb. | ptcpl. ὀρεγνύς | **stretch out** (in prayer or pleading) —*one's hands* Il.; (mid.) Mosch.

ὀρέγω vb. | impf. ὤρεγον | fut. ὀρέξω | aor. ὤρεξα, ep. ὄρεξα |
1 stretch out, hold up —*one's hands* (in prayer, sts. W.PREP.PHR. *to heaven*) Hom. Plu. —(*in greeting or recognition, in offering or receiving help, in pleading or begging, sts. W.DAT. to someone*) Hom. Pi. Hdt. S. E. Ar. +
2 (of a juror) **hold up** (to view) —*a token* (which assigns him to a particular court) Arist.
3 hand over or **hand out** —*a cup, weapon, food, drink, or sim.* Hom. hHom. Critias Ar. Pl. X. +
4 (esp. of a god) **grant** —*victory, fulfilment, prosperity, or sim.* Hom. Hes. Pi. B. S.
—**ὀρέγομαι** mid.vb. | fut. ὀρέξομαι | aor. ὠρεξάμην, ep.3sg. ὀρέξατο | ep.3pl.redupl.pf. ὀρωρέχαται, 3pl.plpf. ὀρωρέχατο || PASS.: aor. (w.mid.sens.) ὠρέχθην | **1** reach out or up (towards sthg.); **reach up** (to lift down an object) Od.; (of a fish, for the bait) Theoc.; (of a person) **reach out** —W.GEN. *for food* E.
2 reach out with one's hands or arms (towards someone); **stretch out one's hands** or **arms** (in pleading, desperation, grief, love or longing) Hom. —W.GEN. *to a person* Il. E. —*for another's hand* AR. —W.INF. *to take sthg.* hHom.; **reach out** —W.DAT. or INTERN.ACC. w. *one's hand or hands* Il. hHom. A.
3 reach out with one's arms and body (to attack an enemy, to get a grip on sthg.); **lunge** or **make a thrust** (sts. W.DAT. w. a weapon, w. the hand) Il. Hes. —W.GEN. *at the enemy, at prey* Il. Tyrt. AR. Theoc.; **grab hold of** —W.GEN. *sthg.* AR.
4 extend one's step; take a long step or **stride** Il.; (of horses) **gallop** —W.INF. *to go into battle* Il.
5 (of a person committing suicide by hanging) **stretch one's body** —W.PREP.PHR. *by the neck* E.; (of a snake) **extend one's coils** Il.

ὀρειάς

6 stretch oneself in exertion or determination (to get somewhere or accomplish sthg.); **press forward** Plb. —W.GEN. *towards a place* X. Plb.; **set one's hand** —W.GEN. *to a terrible deed* E.; (of things) **strive towards** —W.GEN. *a certain goal* Pl.
7 reach out (for sthg., w. the mind); **reach out** (so as to understand) Emp.; **have a desire** or **ambition** Arist. —W.GEN. *for sthg.* E. Th. Att.orats. + —W.INF. *to do or become sthg.* E. Pl. X.; **covet** —W.GEN. *things which do not belong to one* Antipho Th. X.

ὀρειάς *fem.adj.*: see under ὄρειος

ὀρειβατέω *contr.vb.* [ὀρειβάτης] **walk over** or **climb mountains** Plu.

ὀρει-βάτης (also **ὀριβάτης** Ar., cj.) ου, dial. **οὐριβάτᾱς** ᾱ *m.* [ὄρος, βαίνω] one who walks or dwells in the mountains, **mountain dweller** (esp. as a herdsman or shepherd) E.; (ref. to the Cyclops) E.; (appos.w. ὄρνις bird, θήρ beast) S. Ar.

ὀρει-δρόμος ον *adj.* [δραμεῖν] (of a god or human) **running on the mountains** Pi.*fr.*; (of Artemis) Simon.; (of maenads) E.

ὀρεικός *adj.*: see ὀρικός

ὀρει-λεχής ές *adj.* [λέχος] (of lions) **with mountain lairs** Emp.

ὀρει-νόμος ον *adj.* [νέμω] (of Centaurs) **mountain-dwelling** E.

ὀρεινός ή όν *adj.* **1** (of places) **mountainous** Hdt. X. Arist. Plb. Plu. || FEM.SB. mountainous country Plb. Plu. || NEUT.SB. (fig.) rugged nature (of Orestes, in explanation of his name) Pl.; (pl.) mountainous country Plu.
2 (of a road or route) **over mountains** X. Plu. || FEM.SB. mountain route X.
3 (of a Thracian tribe) **of the hills** or **mountains** Th. X.

ὄρειος ᾱ (Ion. η) ον (also ος ον), dial. **οὔρειος** ᾱ (Ion. η) ον *adj.* **1** (of divine or semi-divine beings, esp. nymphs, Cybele) **of the mountains** Hes.*fr.* hHom. Lyr. E. Ar. Men. +; (of people, wild animals, flocks) S. E. Pl. X. Plb.; (of rocks, trees, peaks, or sim.) Hippon. A. E. Ar. Tim. Telest.; (of mist) Plu.; (of the lyre, as first made fr. the shell of a tortoise on Mt. Cyllene) E.
2 (of headlands) **mountainous** S.
3 (of the casting out of an unburied body) **in the mountains** E.
—**ὀρειάς** άδος *fem.adj.* (of nymphs) **of the mountains** Bion

ὀρείπλαγκτος *adj.*: see ὀρίπλαγκτος

ὀρεῖται (ep.3sg.fut.mid.): see ὄρνυμαι, under ὄρνῡμι

ὀρεί-τροφος ον *adj.* [ὄρος, τρέφω] (of cattle) **pastured on the hills** S.*Ichn.*

ὀρειχάλκινος η ον *adj.* [ὀρείχαλκος] (of a stele) **made of orichalc** Pl.

ὀρεί-χαλκος ου *m.* [χαλκός] **mountain copper** (a legendary precious metal); **orichalc** Hes. hHom. Ibyc. Pl. Call. AR.

ὀρεκτικός ή όν *adj.* [ὀρεκτός] (of a part of the soul, the mind) **characterised by appetite** or **desire** Arist.; (of a man) **naturally inclined** (W.GEN. towards sthg.) Arist.

ὀρεκτός ή όν *adj.* [ὀρέγω] **1** (of spears) **outstretched** (for action) Il.
2 (of a pleasure or good) reached for, **desired** Arist.; (of a person) **desirable** Arist.

ὄρεξις εως *f.* **1 appetite** (W.GEN. of the stomach) Plu.
2 desire (sts. W.GEN. for sthg.) Arist.

ὀρεοκόμος *m.*: see ὀρεωκόμος

ὀρέοντι (dial.3pl.): see ὁράω

ὀρέοντο (ep.3pl.aor.2 mid.): see ὄρνυμαι, under ὄρνῡμι

ὀρεσί-τροφος ον *adj.* [ὄρος, τρέφω] (of a lion) **mountain-bred** Hom.

ὀρεσ-κόος, ep. **ὀρεσκῷος**, ον *adj.* [κεῖμαι] **1** (of wild animals) **with mountain lair** Hom. hHom. Alcm. E.; (of nymphs, the Centaurs, Atalanta) **mountain-dwelling** Hes.*fr.* hHom. A.
2 (of the Cyclops' diet) **of mountain creatures** E.*Cyc.*

ὄρεσσι (ep.dat.pl.): see ὄρος

ὀρεσσι-βάτᾱς ᾱ *dial.masc.adj.* [βαίνω] (of Pan, a wild animal) **mountain-roaming** S.

ὀρεσσί-γονος ον *ep.adj.* [γόνος] (of nymphs) **mountain-born** Ar.

ὀρεσσι-νόμος ον *ep.adj.* [νέμω] (of a goat) **mountain-ranging** Hes.

ὀρέστερος ᾱ ον *compar.adj.* (contrastv., of wild animals) **of the mountains** (opp. the countryside) Hom. E.; (epith. of Earth, Artemis) S. E.

Ὀρέστης ου (Ion. εω), dial. **Ὀρέστᾱς** ᾱ *m.* | voc. Ὀρέστα | **Orestes** (son of Agamemnon and Clytemnestra, who killed his mother to avenge his father's murder and was then pursued by Erinyes and brought to trial in Athens) Hom. Hes.*fr.* Pi. Hdt. Trag. +
—**Ὀρέστειος** ᾱ ον *adj.* (of the misfortunes) **of Orestes** S.; (of his hand, as slayer of Neoptolemos) E.; (of pitchers, ref. to a competition at the Χόες festival, when wine-drinkers drank in silence, as Orestes was obliged to do when he came unpurified to Athens) Call.
—**Ὀρέστεια** ᾱς *f.* **Oresteia** (title of a trilogy of tragedies by Aeschylus) Ar.

ὀρεστιάδες ων *fem.pl.adj.* [ὄρος] (of nymphs) **of the mountains** Il. hHom.

ὄρεσφι (ep.gen.dat.sg.pl.): see ὄρος

ὀρεῦντι (dial.3pl.): see ὁράω

ὀρεύς έως, Ion. **οὐρεύς** έος (ep. ῆος) *m.* [reltd. ὄρος] **mule** Il. Hes. hHom. Ar. Arist. Call.

ὄρευς (dial.gen.): see ὄρος

ὀρεχθέω *contr.vb.* [app.reltd. ῥοχθέω, or perh. ὀρέγω] | ep.3pl.impf. ὀρέχθεον | aor. ὠρέχθησα (Men.) | **1** (of oxen) **bellow** —W.PREP.PHR. *over the slaughterer's knife* Il. [or perh. *be stretched out*]
2 (of the sea) app. **roar** or **beat** —W.PREP.PHR. *against the shore* Theoc.
3 (of persons in a crowd) app. **roar, cry out** —W.DIR.SP. *sthg.* Men.
4 (of a person or heart) app. **swell** or **throb** (w. a strong emotion) Ar. AR.

ὀρέω Ion.*contr.vb.*: see ὁράω

ὀρεω-κόμος (also **ὀρεοκόμος**) ου *m.* [ὀρεύς, κομέω] one who takes care of mules, **muleteer** Ar. Pl. X. Hyp. Plb.

ὄρη (Att.nom.acc.pl.): see ὄρος

ὄρη (dial.imperatv.), **ὀρῇ** (dial.3sg.), **ὄρηαι** (Aeol.2sg.mid.), **ὄρημμι** *Aeol.vb.*, **ὀρῆν**, **ὀρῆτε** (dial.inf. and pl.imperatv.): see ὁράω

ὄρηται (ep.3sg.aor.2 mid.subj.), **ὄρθαι** (ep.aor.2 mid.inf.): see ὄρνυμαι, under ὄρνῡμι

ὀρθεύω *vb.* [ὀρθός] **keep upright, support** —*a person's body* E.

Ὀρθίᾱ ᾱς *f.* **Orthia** (cult title of Artemis in Laconia and Arcadia) X. Plu.
—**Ὀρθωσίᾱ** ᾱς, Ion. **Ὀρθωσίη** ης *f.* **Orthosia** (cult title of Artemis) Pi. Hdt.

ὀρθιάδε *adv.*: see under ὄρθιος

ὀρθιάζω *vb.* [ὄρθιος] (of mourners) **raise a shrill** or **loud cry** A.

ὀρθιάσματα των *n.pl.* **loud cries** Ar.

ὄρθιος ᾱ ον (also ος ον) *adj.* [ὀρθός] **1** extending upwards; (of a hill) **steep, sheer** X. Plu.; (of fortifications) E.; (of a tree-trunk) **straight** Plu.
2 leading up to higher ground; (of a path, route, ascent) **steep** Hes. E. Th.(dub., v.l. ὄρθριον) X. ‖ NEUT.SB. **uphill slope** X.; (prep.phr.) πρὸς (τὸ) ὄρθιον **uphill** X.
3 in a vertical position; (of shields, as a line of defence) **vertical, upright** Hdt.; (of hair on the head) **on end** (out of strong emotion or fear) Trag.
4 ‖ NEUT.PL.SB. **upwards or inland extent** (of a country, i.e. N.–S., opp. E.–W.) Hdt.
5 in a direct line; (of a bird's flight) **direct, straight** Plu.
6 (of a phalanx, cohort, or other company of soldiers) in a long extended line (for marching), **in a column** X. Plb. Plu.
7 (of persons or a people, their character, judgement, speech, or sim.) direct in nature, **straight, upright, strict** Plu.
8 with a loud, commanding or penetrating sound; (of wailing) **loud** or **piercing** Pi.*fr.* S.; (of a baby's demands) A.; (of a proclamation, the blare of a trumpet) S. E.
9 (of a well-known melody, sung to the accompaniment of the lyre, said to have been invented by Terpander) **high-pitched** or **rousing, orthian** Hdt. Ar.; (pl., fig.ref. to Cassandra's prophetic singing) A. ‖ MASC.SB. (specif.) **orthian melody** Sapph. Ar.
10 (of the impudence of donkeys, ref. to braying) **noisy** Pi. [also interpr. w. sexual connot. as *excited, rampant*]
—**ὄρθιον** *neut.sg.adv.* **1** (ref. to movt.) **uphill** X.
2 loudly A. Pi. E.
—**ὄρθια** *neut.pl.adv.* **1** (ref. to movt.) **uphill** X.
2 loudly Il. hHom. AR.
—**ὀρθιάδε** *adv.* **uphill** X.
ὀρθό-βουλος ον *adj.* [βουλή] (of Themis) of right counsel, **prudent, wise** A.; (of a policy, plans) Pi.
ὀρθο-γώνιος ον *adj.* [γωνίᾱ] (of a triangle) **right-angled** Plu.
ὀρθο-δαής ές *adj.* [δαῆναι] **having the right knowledge** (W.INF. to do sthg.) A.
ὀρθο-δίκαιος ον *adj.* (of a city-state) **straight and just** A.
ὀρθο-δίκᾱς ᾱ *dial.masc.adj.* [δίκη] (of the navel of the earth, ref. to the Delphic oracle) **straight-judging** Pi.
ὀρθό-δικος ον *adj.* (of a person, the goddess Styx) **straight-judging** B.
ὀρθοδοξέω *contr.vb.* [δόξα] **be of the right opinion** Arist.
ὀρθοδρομέω *contr.vb.* [δρόμος] (of a horse) **be on a straight course** X.
ὀρθοέπεια ᾱς *f.* [ἔπος] **correctness of diction** Pl.
ὀρθό-θριξ τριχος *masc.fem.adj.* [θρίξ] (of a prophetic dream) **causing the hair to stand on end** A.
ὀρθό-κραιραι ᾱων *ep.fem.pl.adj.* [reltd. κέρας] (of cattle) **straight-horned** Hom. hHom.; (fig., of ships, app.ref. to their curved stem-post and stern-post) Il.
ὀρθό-κρᾱνος ον *adj.* [κρᾱνίον¹] **with head erect**; (of a funeral mound) **tall** S.
ὀρθολογίᾱ ᾱς *f.* [λέγω] **correctness of speech** Pl.
ὀρθομαντείᾱ ᾱς *f.* [ὀρθόμαντις] **true prophecy** A.
ὀρθό-μαντις εως *m.* [μάντις] **true prophet** (ref. to Teiresias) Pi.
ὀρθο-νόμος ον *adj.* [νέμω] (of the Fates) **dispensing justly** A.
ὀρθό-πολις ιος *dial.masc.fem.adj.* [πόλις] (fig., of a ruler) **keeping the city upright** Pi.
ὀρθό-πους πουν, gen. ποδος *adj.* [πούς] **erect upon the feet**; (of a hill) **steep** or **high** S.

ὀρθοπρᾱγέω *contr.vb.* [reltd. πρᾱ́σσω] **act rightly** Arist.
ὀρθός, Lacon. **ὀρσός**, ή (dial. ᾱ́) όν *adj.* **1** (of a person or animal) **upright, on one's feet, up** (as a position of the body, opp. bending, lying, or sim., esp. when rising fr. sleep, restless, ready to act or speak) Hom. +
2 remaining upright or on one's feet again; **on one's feet** (opp. falling) Od. +; (as a sign of restored health) Pi. +
3 (of a person or animal, the body or part of it) straight and not crooked (as a sign of health, beauty, youth, good breeding), **upright, straight, erect** or **tall** E. Pl. X. Arist.; (of a soul) Pl. D.; (of an ankle, fig.ref. to a good foundation) Pi. Call.
4 raised to a position which is relatively high; (of the head, body, arms, or sim.) **up** or **upright** A. +; (of the head or ears, esp. of an animal, w.connot. of alertness) **raised** Hdt. +; (of hair) **on end** (fr. fear, cold, aggression) Il. +; (of a phallus) **erect** E.*Cyc.* Ar.; (of a god, a person) **with phallus erect** Carm.Pop. Ar.; (of a foot) **standing firm** (ready for action or the road ahead, sts.fig.) A. +; (of a horse) **rearing** Hdt. Theoc.; (of fish, leaping) **straight up** Simon.
5 (fig., of a city, people, army) **aroused, excited** Att.orats. Plb. Plu.; (w. play on sense 4, *with erect phallus*) Ar.
6 in a position which is upright or extending outwards (when held, placed, planted, bound or propped up); (of things) **vertical, upright, pointing upwards** Od. Pi. Hdt. S. E. +; (of objects, esp. weapons, carried on the shoulder or held ready for action) **upright** or **straight out** X. Plb. Plu.
7 (w. emphasis on length or height) stretching outwards or upwards; (of a knife) **long and straight** E.; (of a cloud, the aither) **rising high** or **tall** Archil. E.; (of a grave mound) E.; (of a kind of head-dress) Hdt. Ar. Plb. Plu.; (of plants) X.
8 remaining standing or set upright again (opp. fallen or ruined); (of buildings) **standing** Hdt. Th. Plu.; (of a chariot, siege-engine) **upright** (opp. overturned) S. Plu.; (of a city-state, public or private affairs, opp. in danger or ruin) S. Att.orats. +; (of one's heart, a hope) Pi. S.
9 extending in a straight line; (of a row of trees) **straight** X.; (of an object) **rising perpendicular** Plb.; (of the rule of a builder, carpenter, mathematician) **exact, true** Thgn. E. Ar.; (of a piece of land) **with straight boundaries** Pl.; (geom., of an angle) **right** Pl. ‖ FEM.SB. **straight line** or **line at right angles** Pl. Arist. Plb.; **right angle** Pl. Arist. Plb.; **vertical plane** Plb.
10 (of a road, path or course; also, of a course taken in thought, speech or action) without bends or diversion, **direct, straight** Pi. S. E. Ar. Pl. D. +; (of a furrow or crop row) Pi. Theoc.; (of a ray of light) Ar. ‖ FEM.SB. **straight road** or **course** S. Ar. D.
11 (quasi-advbl., of a person, animal or ship moving) on a straight course, **straight, straight ahead, direct** S. E. Ar. D. Plb.
12 (of the eyes or gaze) **straight ahead** (w.connot. of honesty, opp. lowered) S. E. X. Theoc.
13 (of things) right in terms of a standard or principle, **right, proper, true** (opp. inferior, incorrect, false, or sim.) Pl. D. +
14 (specif., of things relating to authority) upright in terms of standards or principles; (of a city, leadership, laws, education) **proper, good, right** Pi. B. S. Pl. +; (of an exchange, contract, currency) **valid** Pl. Arist.; (of a guiding hand) **straight** Pi.
15 (of a person, words or thinking) upright or correct in terms of truth, **upright, proper, true, correct** Pi. Hdt. Trag. Ar. Pl. +; (of a name, term or definition) Hdt. Pl.
16 (prep.phrs.) εἰς (ἐς) ὀρθόν *to an upright position, upright* S. E. Plu.; *in a straight direction, straight* Pl.; κατ᾽ ὀρθόν *on a*

straight path S.; *rightly, correctly* S. Pl.; ἐν ὀρθῷ *on a correct footing, soundly* Plb.
—**ὀρθόν** *neut.sg.adv.* **straight ahead** X.
—**ὀρθά** *neut.pl.adv.* **1 straight ahead** Ar.
2 in the right way, correctly S. E. Pl.
—**ὀρθῶς** *adv.* **1 in the right direction** (on a road) S.; **straight ahead** (in terms of achievement), **successfully** S.
2 in a mathematically precise manner, **accurately** A. Hdt. E. +
3 in a manner which is right or appropriate in terms of the facts and truth, **correctly, rightly, truly** B. Hdt. Trag. Th. +; (as an assent to another's statement) E. Pl. +
4 in a manner which is right in terms of a standard or principle, **correctly, rightly, properly** or **appropriately** Hdt. Trag. Th. +
—**ὀρθότατα** *neut.pl.superl.adv.* **1 in the straightest line** Pl.
2 most accurately or **precisely** Antipho Pl.
3 most correctly, rightly or **properly** Hdt. Antipho Pl. +
ὀρθο-στάδην *adv.* [reltd. στάδιος, ἵστημι] **in an upright position** A.
ὀρθο-στάδιον ου *n.* [στάδιος] a kind of woman's garment which falls straight, **straight-line dress** Ar.
ὀρθο-σταδόν *adv.* **standing up straight** E.*fr.*; **rising up tall** —*ref. to shoots growing* AR.
ὀρθο-στάται ῶν *m.pl.* [ἵστημι] upright vertical structures (acting as a support); **uprights** (W.GEN. of a ladder) E.; **props, poles** (of a tent) E.; **supports** (of an altar or tomb, ref. to upright blocks of masonry) E.
ὀρθότης ητος *f.* **1 upright posture** (of humans) X.
2 quality of conforming to a standard, **rightness, appropriateness, correctness** or **excellence** Ar. Pl. Arist.
3 uprightness, rectitude (in law, justice, government, religion, personal conduct) Pl. Arist. Plu.
ὀρθόω *contr.vb.* | *aor.* ὤρθωσα ‖ *aor.pass.* (sts. w.mid.sens.) ὠρθώθην, dial.3pl. ὤρθεν (Corinn.) | **1** raise to an upright or higher position, **lift up** —*a person, the head* Il. S. E.; (of a god) **hold upright** —*the human body* Pl.; (w.connot. of restoring fortune) **raise** —*a person* Archil.
2 ‖ MID. and AOR.PASS. lift oneself up, **sit up, get up, rise** Il. A. Corinn. AR. Theoc.; (of the body) **be upright** (opp. bent) X.
3 ‖ MID. remain standing (as a sign of being healthy, not wounded or intoxicated); **stand up, stand up straight** or **tall** S. E. X.; (of plants, in good conditions) X.
4 set upright, **raise** —*a trophy, a fort* E. Th.; (fig.) —*a hymn of praise* Pi.
5 raise again, **restore, build again** —*a city, wall* Hdt. E. X. Din.
6 lift (out of trouble or misfortune), **raise up, restore** —*a people, city or land, a person, family* Trag. Th. Plu. ‖ PASS. be sustained or set right Pi. Plu.
7 make straight, **straighten** —*a corpse* E. —*warped parts* (*of timbers*) Arist. ‖ PASS. (of a crooked message) be made (to seem) straight (by the messenger) A.
8 set or keep on a straight road or path, **guide, support** —*an old person* E. ‖ MID. (of a charioteer) **keep a straight course** S. ‖ AOR.PASS. (of a discharged arrow) fly straight S.
9 set on a straight, successful or prosperous course, **guide to success, promote, exalt** —*persons, a city or land, public or private affairs, family or friends* Scol. Pi. +; **advance** —*oneself* Hdt.; (of a god) **make** (W.ACC. of a contest) **go right** A. ‖ MID. **keep on a straight course, be successful** S. Antipho Th. +; (of a marriage) **prosper** E. ‖ AOR.PASS. (of schemes, undertakings) be successful Hdt. E.

10 guide correctly —*the mind, judgement, tongue, speech* Thgn. A. S. ‖ MID. (of a statement) **be true** Hdt.; (of one's thinking) **go right, be sound** E.
11 ‖ PASS. (of an oath) be properly maintained, be honoured A.
ὀρθρεύω *vb.* [ὄρθρος] **be awake before daybreak** E.(sts.mid.) Theoc.
ὀρθρίζω *vb.* **come before daybreak** —W.PREP.PHR. *to someone* NT.
ὀρθρινός ή όν *adj.* (quasi-advbl., of persons arriving) **before daybreak** NT.
ὄρθριος ᾱ (Ion. η) ον *adj.* (quasi-advbl., of persons arriving or sim.) **at** or **before daybreak** hHom. Thgn. Ar. Pl. Men.; (of the cockerel, ref. to its crowing) Theoc.; (of a song) Ar.; (of a meeting) Pl.
—**ὄρθριον** *neut.adv.* **at** or **before daybreak** Th.(v.l. ὄρθιον) Ar.; τὸ ὄρθριον *in the early hours* Hdt.
—**Ὀρθρία** ᾱς *f.* **Orthria** (goddess of Daybreak) Alcm.(dub.)
ὀρθρο-γόη ης Ion.*fem.adj.* [γόος] (of the swallow) **lamenting before daybreak** Hes.
ὄρθρος ου *m.* [app.reltd. ὀρθός] period of time before dawn (when people rise to go about their tasks); (gener.) **first light, daybreak, early morning** Hes. hHom. Hdt. E. Th. Ar. +; (when birds begin to sing) Ibyc.; (W.ADJ. βαθύς *deep*) *very first light, imminent daybreak* Ar. Pl. Theoc. NT.; (w. ἔσχατος *furthest*) Theoc.
ὀρθρο-φοιτο-συκοφαντο-δικο-ταλαίπωρος ον *adj.* [φοιτάω, συκοφάντης, δίκη] (of habits) **of crack-of-dawn-wandering trumped-up-lawsuit wretchedness** Ar.
ὀρθ-ώνυμος ον *adj.* [ὀρθός, ὄνομα] **rightly named** A.
Ὀρθωσία *f.*: see under Ὀρθία
ὀρθωτήρ ῆρος *m.* [ὀρθόω] **sustainer** (of a ruler, ref. to a god) Pi.
ὅρια ων *n.pl.* [ὅρος] **1 boundary lines** or **markers** (of a property or piece of land) Th. Pl. Arist.
2 boundary areas, borders, frontiers (of a country or state) B. E. Th. Att.orats. Pl. X. +
3 (gener.) **region, district** NT.
ὀριβάτης *m.*: see ὀρειβάτης
ὀρίγανος ου *f.* (*also m.*) —also **ὀρίγανον** ου *n.* a kind of herb, **wild marjoram** (used for seasoning) Ion Ar. Tim. Thphr. Men.; (fig.phr.) βλέπειν ὀρίγανον *have a look as pungent as marjoram* Ar.
ὀριγνάομαι *mid.contr.vb.* [reltd. ὀρέγω] | *aor.pass.* (w.mid.sens.) ὠριγνήθην | **1** stretch out one's hand for, **reach for** —W.GEN. *an object* Theoc.; (fig.) —*a kind of glory* Isoc.
2 hunt for —W.GEN. *animals* E.
3 (of fighters) aim at one another (w. their weapons) Hes.
ὀρί-γονος ον *adj.* [ὄρος, γόνος] (of pines, meton. for ships) **mountain-born** Tim.
ὁρίζω, Ion. **οὐρίζω** *vb.* [ὅρος] | *aor.* ὥρισα, Ion. οὔρισα | *pf.* ὥρικα ‖ MID.: *fut.* ὁριοῦμαι | *aor.* ὡρισάμην ‖ PASS.: *fut.* ὁρισθήσομαι | *aor.* ὡρίσθην | *pf.* ὥρισμαι ‖ *neut.impers.vbl.adj.* ὁριστέον ‖ The sections are grouped as: (1–2, of places) form a boundary, (3–8, of persons) create or have a boundary, (9) separate (persons or things), (10–11) limit or restrict, (12) determine or decide, (13–15) define or distinguish. |
1 (of places, geographical features) form a boundary (for peoples or places); (of a strip of land or a mountain, of a river, lake or sea) **be the boundary of** —*a country, a kingdom* E.*fr.* X. Plb. Plu.; **mark the boundary between**

—W.DBL.ACC. (linked w. καί) *one land or people and another* Hdt. Th. X. Plb. Plu. —W.ACC. + DAT. Hdt.; **mark** —*the midpoint* (W.DAT. *for two peoples, i.e. be the boundary betw. them*) Hdt.; (of tribes, i.e. their location) **mark the borders** (of a kingdom) Th. ‖ PASS. (of an island, a kingdom) be bounded (by certain geographical features) E. Th. X.
2 (of a country) **border** —w. πρός + ACC. *on another* Hdt.
3 (of persons) **mark** or **fix the boundaries of** —*a country* (W.DAT. *by cities located on them*) Isoc.; (of Io, by giving her name to the Bosporos) **mark** or **define the boundary of** —*the continent on one side of it* A.
4 ‖ MID. (of a ruler) **have as one's boundaries** (and include within one's realm) —*certain regions* A.; **extend the boundaries of** —*one's empire* (W.PREP.PHR. *as far as a certain region*) Pl.; mark out within boundaries, **count as one's own** —*a country* E.*fr.*
5 (of persons) trace the boundaries of, **mark out, demarcate** —*a territory, a sacred enclosure, altars, or sim.* Hdt. S.(sts.mid.) Plu. ‖ MID. (of deities) **mark out** (for themselves) —*a sanctuary* E.
6 ‖ MID. **set up** (W.ACC. pillars) **as boundary markers** X.
7 ‖ MID. (specif.) **place mortgage markers on** —*a house* D. ‖ PASS. (of property) be mortgaged D.
8 (of a traveller) trace a boundary between, **pass between** —*two opposite coasts* E.
9 make a boundary (betw. persons or things, so as to separate them); (of a wide stretch of sea) **separate** —*persons* (W.GEN. *fr. a ship*) S.; (of a storm) —*the courses of ships* E.; (of a ship) **part** —*a person* (w. ἀπό + GEN. *fr. a country*) E. ‖ PASS. (of a baby) be parted —w. ἐκ + GEN. *fr. its mother's arms* E.; (of a room) be separated (by a door) —w. ἀπό + GEN. *fr. another* X.
10 impose a limit or restriction; **limit, restrict, curtail** —*vengeful behaviour* Th. —*an enemy's empire* Isoc. ‖ PASS. (of procrastination) be given a limit (beyond which it must not go) Th.
11 impose a fixed limit on, **determine, fix** —*an amount, a time, or sim.* Att.orats. Pl. + ‖ MID. **decide upon** —*a period of time* (*for doing sthg.*) X.; (of a claimant) **set as a limit** (W.DAT. *for himself*) —*a certain proportion* (*of a property*) Lys. ‖ PASS. (of an amount) be determined D.; (of a time) be fixed —W.DAT. *for an event* E.*fr.*
12 impose a definite regulation or decision; **determine, decide** —*a penalty, a person's fate, a plan, or sim.* A. E. Att.orats. + —W.ACC. + INF. *that sthg. shd. be the case* E. Lycurg. D. ‖ MID. determine for oneself, **decide upon** —*a remedy* (*consisting of flight*) A. ‖ PASS. (of a penalty or sim.) be determined Att.orats. +
13 (act. and mid.) formulate in a definite way, **establish, determine, define** —*laws, justice, principles of conduct* S. Att.orats. + —W.INDIR.Q. *what is the case* Isoc. X. ‖ PASS. (of laws, principles, or sim.) be established or defined Att.orats. +
14 draw boundaries (betw. similar things); **separate, specify, distinguish** —*one thing or group of things* (*fr. another*) Pl. ‖ MID. **distinguish between** —*right and wrong* E. ‖ PASS. (of things) be distinguished Pl. Arist.
15 (act. and mid.) define (by making distinctions or using some other criterion); **define** —*a person or thing* Att.orats. Pl. + —(W.INF. + PREDIC.SB. *as being such and such*) Att.orats. Pl. + ‖ PASS. (of persons or things) be defined (sts. W.PREDIC.ADJ. *as such and such*) Pl. +
—**ὡρισμένος** η ον *pf.pass.ptcpl.adj.* (of things) **definite, precise** Arist. Plb. NT. Plu.

—**ὡρισμένως** *pf.pass.ptcpl.adv.* **in a definite** or **precise manner** Arist. Plb.
ὀρι-κοίτᾱς ᾱ *dial.masc.adj.* [ὄρος, κοίτη] (of a centaur) **whose bed is in the mountains** Lyr.adesp.
ὀρικός (also **ὀρεικός**) ή όν *adj.* [ὀρεύς] (of a draught pair) **of mules** Pl. Is. Aeschin. Plu.
ὀρίνω *vb.* [reltd. ὄρνυμι] | aor. ὤρινα, ep. ὄρινα ‖ PASS.: aor. ὠρίνθην, ep. ὀρίνθην | **1** stir up (natural elements); (of winds, Poseidon) **stir** or **whip up** —*the sea* Hom. Hes.; (of a river god) —*his streams* Il. ‖ PASS. (of sea, winds) be stirred up Il. AR.
2 stir up (w. emotions, esp. through one's words); **stir, move** —*a person's heart* Hom. Archil. Thgn. ‖ MID. **stir up** (in one's heart) —*anger* B. ‖ PASS. (of the heart) be stirred up Hom. hHom. AR.
3 stir up to action; (of Dionysus) **incite** —*maenads* Theoc. ‖ MID. (of warriors) **surge forth** (fr. ploughed furrows) AR. ‖ PASS. (of a boxer) be incited Theoc.
4 stir up (w. shock or confusion); **confound** —*opponents* Od. ‖ PASS. (of men) be in confusion, be panicked Hom.
5 produce or call forth (sounds); (of a river in spate) **stir up** —*a din* (*of logs and stones*) Il.; (of a person, by one's words) —*sounds of lamentation* Il. ‖ PASS. (of frenzied cries) be aroused Pi.*fr.*
ὅριος ου *masc.adj.* [ὅρος] **1** (epith. of Zeus) **protecting boundaries** Pl. D.
2 (of a god, ref. to Roman *Terminus*) **of boundaries** Plu.
ὀρι-πλάγκτος ον *adj.* [ὄρος, πλαγκτός] (of nymphs) **mountain-roaming** Ar.(cj., for ὀρεί-)
ὅρισμα, Ion. **οὔρισμα**, ατος *n.* [ὁρίζω] **1 line of demarcation, natural boundary** (betw. territories) Hdt.
2 ‖ PL. **borders** (of a land) E.; (gener.) **confines** or **territory** E.
ὁρισμός οῦ *m.* **1** setting of a limit, **limitation** (sts. W.GEN. of behaviour, emotion, or sim.) Hyp. Arist.
2 giving of an exact verbal description (of a thing, being, concept, or sim.), **definition** Arist.
3 means of determination (of a difference of opinion, involving a sum of money as a forfeit for being wrong), **wager** Plu.
ὁριστής οῦ *m.* **1** one who determines boundaries, **boundary magistrate** Hyp. Plu.
2 definer, determiner (W.GEN. of justice betw. states) D.
ὁριστικός ή όν *adj.* (of a verbal description) **defining** Arist.
ὁριστός ή όν *adj.* ‖ NEUT.PL.SB. definable things Arist.
ὀρι-τρεφής ές *adj.* [ὄρος, τρέφω] (of a wild olive) **grown on a mountain** AR.
ὀρκάνη ης, dial. **ὀρκάνᾱ** ᾱς *f.* [reltd. ἕρκος] **dungeon** E.; (fig.) **encircling wall** (ref. to an enemy surrounding a city) A.
ὀρκιᾱτομέω *dial.contr.vb.* [ὅρκιον, τέμνω] **swear a solemn agreement** —W.DAT. w. *someone* Timocr.
ὁρκίζω *vb.* [ὅρκος] | aor. ὥρκισα | **1** administer an oath; **make** (W.ACC. someone) **swear an oath** X. D. Plb. Plu. —w. ἦ μήν + FUT.INF. *that one will do sthg.* Plb. ‖ PASS. be made to swear an oath Plb.
2 formulate —W.COGN.ACC. *an oath* (w. εἰς + ACC. *to oneself, i.e. one promising allegiance to oneself*) Plu.
3 adjure, implore —*a person* (w. 2ND ACC. *by God, Jesus*) NT.
ὅρκιον ου *n.* [ὅρκιος] **1** (freq.pl.) that which is sworn or sworn to, **oath, pledge, promise, agreement** Hom. +; (concr., ref. to a bride, a hymn) **pledge** Pi.
2 ‖ PL. sacrificial victims or other offerings in the solemnising of an oath, **oath-offerings** Il.

ὅρκιος ᾱ ον *adj.* [ὅρκος] **1** (of persons) **bound by oath** S. **2** (of gods) **invoked in** or **witnessing oaths** E. Th. Aeschin. AR. Plu.; (of Poseidon, W.DAT. by certain people) Call.; (epith. of Zeus) S. E.; (of Themis) E.
3 (of a sword) **witnessing an oath** E.
ὁρκισμός οῦ *m.* [ὁρκίζω] **administering of an oath** Plb.
ὅρκος ου *m.* **1 solemn and binding promise with an invocation to a deity or thing held sacred** (framed in a particular form of words, sts. accompanied by a blood sacrifice or ceremony); **oath** Hom. +
2 (wkr.sens.) **oath** (uttered more casually to support an assertion in conversation) Hom. +
3 oath (sworn easily and later broken, by false friends, women or lovers) Od. Hes. Thgn. Pl.
4 (leg.) **oath** (in a city-state; sworn by two peoples, armies, or political factions, in ratification of an agreement) Hdt. +; (sworn by troops, in allegiance to a leader and comrades, or concerning distribution of booty) Hdt. +; (by leaders or magistrates on entering upon a term of office) Att.orats. +; (by a judge or jurors, by both parties in a legal dispute and their witnesses) A. Att.orats. +
5 divinity or thing held sacred invoked in an oath; oath (ref. to water of the Styx, as invoked by the gods) Hom. Hes. Arist.; (ref. to Zeus, as invoked by mortals) Pi.; (ref. to salt and table, witnesses of the bonds of guest-friendship) Archil.
—**Ὅρκος** ου *m.* (personif.) **Horkos** (son of Eris) Hes. Pi. Hdt.(oracle) S.
ὁρκόω *contr.vb.* | aor. ὥρκωσα | **1 administer an oath** Lys. Ar. D.; **make** (W.ACC. someone) **swear** (sts. W.COGN.ACC. an oath) Th. Ar. X. D. Plu. —W.FUT.INF. or ἦ μήν + FUT.INF. *to do (or not to do) sthg.* Th. Is. Plu.
2 administer an oath of allegiance —w. εἰς + ACC. *to an emperor* Plu.
ὁρκώματα των *n.pl.* **sworn oaths** A.
ὁρκωμόσια ων *n.pl.* [ὁρκωμοτέω] **1 victims sacrificed at an oath-taking** Pl.
2 assertions on oath Pl.
—**Ὁρκωμόσιον** ου *n.* **place of the oath-taking** (nr. the temple of Theseus in Athens) Plu.
ὁρκωμοτέω *contr.vb.* [ὅρκος, ὄμνῡμι] | aor. ὡρκωμότησα | **swear an oath** (sts. W.ACC. by gods) E. Plu. —W.FUT.INF. *that one will do sthg.* A. Plu. —W.ACC. and μή + FUT.INF. *that someone will not do sthg.* A. —w. τὸ μή + AOR. or PF.INF. *that one has not done sthg., does not know sthg.* S.
ὁρκωτής οῦ *m.* **administrator of oaths** Antipho X.
ὁρμά *dial.f.*: see ὁρμή
ὁρμαθός οῦ *m.* [reltd. ὅρμος¹] **1 series** (of similar things) interlinked or in a line; **chain** (of metal pieces, hanging fr. a magnet) Pl.; **row** (of bats, hanging fr. a rock) Od.; **line** (of wagons, pack-animals) X.
2 garland (of dried fruits, worn in a religious procession) Ar.; (of sweet confections, as a gift) Ar.
3 sequence (of choral lyrics) Ar.
4 string (of legal documents, perh. threaded, or fig.ref. to an interminable succession of them) Thphr.
ὁρμαίνω *vb.* [ὁρμή] | aor. ὥρμηνα | **1 turn over** (one thought after another); (of a person or mind) **think over, consider, deliberate** —*things* (esp. *problems*) Hom. hHom. AR.; (intr.) **think, ponder** Il. B. —W.INDIR.Q. *what will happen, how one might do sthg., or sim.* Hom. AR. —W.DIR.SP. *sthg.* Od.
2 think over, assess —*an omen* Pi.
3 think over (a precise plan); **contemplate** —*war, murder, deception, a particular action* Hom. hHom. AR. —*a voyage, a journey* Od. —*the impracticable* Semon.

4 be intent (on doing sthg.); (of a horse) **be ready to go** A.; (of a person) **be eager** Pi. —W.INF. *to do sthg.* B. AR. Theoc.
5 hasten on —*a marriage* A.*satyr.fr.*; (of a man dying violently) **hasten away** —*his life* A.(dub.)
ὁρμάω *contr.vb.* | fut. ὁρμήσω | aor. ὥρμησα, Ion. ὥρμησα, dial. ὥρμᾱσα, Lacon.imperatv. ὁρμᾶον (Ar.) | pf. ὥρμηκα || MID.: Ion.3sg.impf. ὁρμᾶτο | fut. ὁρμήσομαι | aor.: only subj. ὁρμήσωμαι (Il.) | pf. ὥρμημαι, Ion. ὅρμημαι, 3pl. ὁρμέαται | plpf. ὡρμήμην, Ion. ὁρμήμην, 3pl. ὁρμέατο || PASS.: aor. (w.mid.sens.) ὡρμήθην, Ion. ὁρμήθην, dial. ὡρμᾱθην || The act. can be tr. (**A**), or intr. like the mid. or aor.pass. (**B**). |
—**A 1** (act.) **cause** (someone or sthg.) **to move or start out; hurry away** —*someone* (W.PREP.PHR. *fr. another's hands*) E.; **direct, speed** —*one's foot* Ar.(mock-trag.); **urge on** —*a horse* X.; **send, despatch** —*an army* Hdt. E. +; (of the goddess Memory) —*the Muse* (to a singer) Ar.; (of a lamp) —*a flame-signal* Ar.(mock-trag.); (of a circumstance) **speed** —*a ship* (W.ADV. *homeward*) E. || PASS. **be despatched or sent on one's way** (by a god) A. S.
2 (of a person or god) **cause** (someone) **to embark** (on an undertaking or in pursuit of a goal); **urge, impel, incite, stir on** —*persons* (sts. W.PREP.PHR. *towards sthg.*) Il. Pi. B. S. E. Th. + —W.INF. *to do sthg.* Hdt. || PASS. **be stirred on** (by love) Pl.
3 cause (sthg.) **to arise**; (of a god) **stir up, bring about** —*war* Od.; **stimulate, incite** —W.ACC. + INF. *sthg. to happen* Pl.
—**B** | intr., act. and mid. or aor.pass. (w.mid.sens.) |
1 stir oneself (fr. a state of inaction); **get going** Od. S. Ar. Pl. +; **start** —W.INF. *to go, run, walk* Pl. +; (of a chariot team) **spring forward** Od.
2 go quickly, run, rush, hasten Il. hHom. A. Hdt. E. Th. + —W.INF. *to do sthg.* Il. Hdt. +; (of ships) **speed onwards** Th.; (of torchlight, fire, water) A. Hdt. Pl. +.
3 (w.connot. of aggression) **advance, rush, launch an attack** Hom. Hes. Hdt. S. E. Th. + —W.GEN. *at an enemy* Il.; (of a blow) **be launched** S. E.
4 set out (to or fr. a place, esp. fr. home or homewards) Hom. Hes. Hdt. Trag. +; (fr. home or a base, for daily duties) Hdt. Th. Att.orats. +
5 set out (on a military campaign, march, ride or voyage, mission or undertaking); **set out** Il. Hdt. S. E. Th. + —W.INF. *to make war or sim.* Hdt. +
6 set out (on a plan of action, a course in life); **be intent** (sts. W.PREP.PHR. on sthg.) Hdt. Th. Att.orats. + —W.INF. *on doing sthg.* Il. Pi. Hdt. S. Th. +
7 (of things) **arise or proceed**; (of a city-state) **rise up** Isoc. Pl.; (of a plant-shoot, a person) **grow** Pl. X.; (of a lineage) **originate** Hdt.; (of a river, fire, wind) **arise** Hdt. Pl.; (of song, a tear) **issue forth** Pi. E.; (of violence, divine vengeance, grief, or sim.) **be stirred up** or **come about** S. E. Pl. +
8 (of persons, in ctxts. relating to rhetoric, dialogue, literature) **set out** (on an argument, investigation, style of writing) Att.orats. +; **begin** —W.INF. *to speak, tell a story, write* Hdt. Att.orats. +; **proceed, move quickly** (to another point) Att.orats. +; (of a story, narrative, dialogue) **arise, begin** Hdt. Pl. + —W.PASS.INF. *to be told* Hdt.
ὅρμενος (ep.aor.2 mid.ptcpl.): see ὄρνυμαι, under ὄρνῡμι
ὁρμέω *contr.vb.* [ὅρμος²] | impf. ὥρμουν, Ion. ὅρμεον | (of a ship or those on board) **be moored** or **lie at anchor** (alongside or nr. land) Hdt. E. Antipho Th. X. D. +; (fig., of a person) **be reliant** —w. ἐπί + GEN. *on two anchors* (i.e. be doubly secure) D. —*on the same anchor as others* (i.e. be in the same condition) D. —w. ἐπί + DAT. *on small resources* S.;

(of a city) —*on two councils* (compared to anchors) Plu.

ὁρμή ῆς, dial. **ὁρμά** ᾶς *f.* [reltd. ὄρνῡμι] **1** sudden rush or expenditure of physical force; **huge effort, exertion** (to save oneself, in a dangerous situation) Hom.; **vigour, briskness** (in athletics, walking, running or fleeing) B. E. Pl. +; **spring** (in the knees of a jumper) Pi.; (of a bent rod recoiling) Theoc.
2 swift advance over land or sea (by travellers, an army); **march, rush, impetuous course** Pl. X. +
3 swift hostile advance; **rush, assault, attack** (of a murderer, a warrior, an army or navy) Il. B. Hdt. S.(dub.) Th. Ar. +
4 swift advance (of animals, forces of nature); **onrush, rush** (of attacking animals, galloping horses) Il. hHom. Thgn. D. +; (of fire, water, winds) Hom. E. Ar. AR. Plu.; (of land, colliding) Pl.
5 impetus (of a weapon or other object); **flight, thrust** (of a spear) Il. Hes.; **onrush** (of sthg. in motion towards a mark) Pl.; (of a ship, ramming another) Plb.
6 first impetus (of divine origin, bringing sthg. about); **impulse, compulsion** Emp. Hdt. Pl. +
7 first or continuing impetus (of persons, on a journey or in an undertaking); **lead, initiative, enterprise** Hom.; **first steps, start** X. +; **course embarked on, direction** (in life) Pl.; **starting-point** or **direction** (of an argument) Pl.
8 special effort (for a war campaign or other project); **war-effort, effort, enterprise** S. E. Th. Pl.
9 impetus (in the mind); **impulse, compulsion, ardour, motivation** Hes.*fr.* S. Pl. +; (W.INF. to do sthg.) Th. D. +
10 strong emotion (roused amongst a people, a crowd or an army; sts. translated into simultaneous action); **wave of feeling, feeling, ardour, impulse** Th. X. +; (W.INF. to do sthg.) NT.
11 inclination due to innate character (towards a direction in life, good or bad values, a talent, a field of study); **drive, inclination, motivation** Pl. +

ὅρμημα ατος *n.* [ὁρμάω] ‖ PL. impulses or desires (of Helen, in eloping w. Paris) Il. [or perh. *struggles* for others, caused by her]

ὁρμητήριον ου *n.* **1** location used as a starting-place (for going to war); **military base, base of operations** Isoc. D. Plb. Plu.
2 (fig.) base (for a political career, ref. to a magistracy, a capacity for public speaking) Plu.
3 ‖ PL. words of command (for a horse) X.

ὁρμιά ᾶς *f.* [reltd. ὅρμος¹] | ῑ Theoc. | **fishing-line** Theoc. Plu.

ὁρμιᾱ-τόνος ου *m.* [τείνω] one who extends a line, **fisherman** E.

ὁρμίζω *vb.* [ὅρμος²] | aor. ὥρμισα, ep. ὅρμισα, ep.subj. ὁρμίσσω ‖ MID.: fut. ὁρμιοῦμαι | aor. ὡρμισάμην ‖ PASS.: aor. (w.mid.sens.) ὡρμίσθην | pf. ὥρμισμαι |
1 bring to a mooring (and secure w. ropes or anchor), **moor** or **anchor** —*a ship or boat* Hom. Hdt. Th. Plb. Plu. ‖ PF.PASS. (of a ship) be moored E.
2 (fig.) moor —*one's foot* (i.e. halt) E.(cj.); **settle** —*a baby* (W.PREP.PHR. in swaddling-clothes) A.; (of a god) —*a person* (on land, after taking her through the air) E.(cj.) ‖ PF.PASS. (of a person, compared to a ship) be anchored —W.DAT. w. bonds Ar.(mock-trag.); (of a soldier) —w. ἐκ + GEN. *to chance* (i.e. be dependent on it) E.
3 ‖ MID. and AOR.PASS. (of a ship or those on board) come to a mooring or anchorage, **moor** Hdt. S. Antipho Th. X. D. +; (fig., of earth, when it unites w. other natural elements) —W.PREP.PHR. *in the harbours of Kypris* (i.e. love) Emp.
4 secure as though with an anchor, **anchor** —*an inflated skin* (in water, w. stones) X.

ὅρμος¹ ου *m.* [εἴρω¹] **chain, necklace** Hom. Hes. Alcm. A. E. Ar. +; **garland** (made of flowers or leaves) Pi.

ὅρμος² ου *m.* [perh.reltd. εἴρω¹] **1** place or state of being moored; **mooring** or **anchorage** Hom. Hdt. Trag. Th. +
2 place of refuge, hiding-place (of wild animals) X. [or perh. *fixing-points* for hunting nets]

ὀρνᾱπέτιον ου *dial.n.* [reltd. ὄρνις] **little bird** Ar.

ὄρνεον ου *n.* **bird** Il. Hdt. Th. Ar. Pl. +

ὀρνίθ-αρχος ου *m.* [ἄρχω] officer in the bird community, **bird-official** Ar.

ὀρνῑθείᾱ ᾱς *f.* divination from birds, **augury** Plb.

ὀρνίθειος ᾱ ον (also ος ον) *adj.* **1** (of meat) from birds Ar. X. ‖ NEUT.PL.SB. poultry Ar. Arist.
2 (com.epith. of Hestia) of the birds Ar.

ὀρνῑθευτής οῦ *m.* [ὀρνιθεύω] **bird-snarer, fowler** Ar. Pl.

ὀρνῑθευτικός ή όν *adj.* of or relating to snaring birds ‖ FEM.SB. art of snaring birds, fowling Pl.

ὀρνῑθεύω *vb.* **catch** or **snare birds** X.

ὀρνῑθίᾱς ου *m.* [ὄρνις] wind which brings migratory birds, **bird wind** Ar.

ὀρνίθιον ου *n.* [dimin. ὄρνις] **little bird** Hdt. Ar. Plu.

ὀρνῑθό-γονος ον *adj.* [γόνος] (of Helen) of bird stock, **bird-born** (as sired by Zeus as a swan) E.

ὀρνῑθο-θήρᾱς ου *m.* [θηράω] **hunter of birds, bird-catcher** Ar.

ὀρνῑθομανέω *contr.vb.* [μαίνομαι] **be crazy about birds** Ar.

ὀρνῑθο-σκόπος ον *adj.* [σκοπέω] **1** observing birds; (of a seer's seat) **for bird-divination** S.
2 ‖ MASC.SB. observer of omens from birds, **bird-diviner** Thphr.

ὀρνῑθοτροφίᾱ ᾱς *f.* [τρέφω] **rearing of birds** Plu.

ὄρνις (also **ὄρνῑς**) ῑθος (dial. ῑχος) *m.f.* | acc. ὄρνῑθα, also ὄρνιν, ὄρνῑν, dial. ὄρνῑχα ‖ PL.: acc. ὄρνῑθας, also ὄρνῑς (v.l. ὄρνεις) | dat. ὄρνῑσι, dial. ὄρνιξι, ὀρνίχεσσι |
1 bird (wild or domesticated) Hom. +; (appos.w. noun indicating the species, e.g. αἰγυπιός *vulture*) Hom. +; (as exemplifying the devoted parent, who grieves for loss) Il. Pl. +; (as exemplifying one who has a small mind) Thgn.; (fig.ref. to a poet, as a sweet or raucous singer, according to the species compared) Theoc.; (provb.) ὀρνίθων γάλα *birds' milk* (ref. to an extreme or improbable luxury) Ar.
2 (specif., *m.*) **cock-bird** (of various species, esp. as set to fight) A. Pl. +; **cockerel** (esp. as crowing in the morning) S. Ar. + ‖ PL. domestic fowl or poultry X.
3 bird (as a divine messenger, or god in disguise) Hom. Hes. Pi. Trag. Hellenist.poet.; (as sacred in Egypt) Hdt.
4 bird of omen (whose flight or cries are observed) Hom. +; (gener., without ref. to birds) **omen** (good or bad, ref. to a person, thing or event) Il. Pi. Trag. Ar. +

ὀρνῑχο-λόχος ου *dial.m.* [λοχάω] **bird-trapper** Pi.

ὄρνῡμι *ep.vb.* —also (pres. and impf.) **ὀρνύω** | 3sg. ὀρνύει (Pi.) | imperatv. ὄρνυθι, 2pl. ὄρνυτε | inf. ὀρνύμεναι, ὀρνύμεν | impf. ὤρνυον | fut. ὄρσω | aor. ὦρσα | 3sg.iterataor. ὄρσασκε | 3sg.redupl.aor.2 ὤρορε ‖ For the intr.mid. (and intr.act.pf. and plpf.) see ὄρνυμαι below. |
1 cause to rise up (esp. fr. a position of rest or fr. sleep); **raise, rouse** —*a person* Hom. AR.; **stir up** —*wild animals* Hom.; (of a god) **rouse, bring on** —*Dawn* Od. —*daylight* (W.PREP.PHR. *after darkness*) Pi.*fr.*
2 cause to move into action; **rouse, urge, impel, send** —*a person* (esp. a messenger, sts. W.INF. to do sthg.) Hom. hHom. Pi. AR. —*snakes* (W.PREP.PHR. *to a place*) Theoc.

ὄροβοι

3 rouse into hostile action; **urge on, incite** —*warriors, their might, an army* (sts. W.INF. *to fight*) Il. E.
4 **urge, prompt, drive** —*a person* (W.INF. *to say or do sthg.*) Od. S. AR.; (of Zeus, confidence) —*a poet, his tongue* (*to speak or sing of sthg.*) Pi.; (of insolence) —*a person* (W.PREP.PHR. *to ruin*) Pi.
5 (fig., of a poet) **despatch** —*his utterance* (*compared to a javelin*) Pi.
6 **stir up** (feelings); **rouse** —*a desire or urge, fear, anger, grief, joy* Hom. Pi. B. AR.
7 **cause** (natural elements) to rise up; (of horses' hooves) **stir up** —*dust* Il.; (of a divine force) **rouse** —*winds, the sea, fire* Hom. hHom. AR. —*wintry weather* A.
8 **rouse up** (sthg. destructive or unwelcome); **rouse, stir up** —*a plague, strife, battle, war, outrage* Hom. E.
9 **cause** (a sound) to rise up; **raise** —*a din, cry, lamentation, laughter* Hom. AR.
10 **cause** (sthg.) to happen or come into existence; **raise up, institute** —*an honour* (W.DAT. *for a dead person, ref. to an athletic festival*) Pi.*fr.*; **bring** —*glory* (*to a place*) Pi.; **prompt** —*sthg.* (*to come into being*) Parm.

—**ὄρνυμαι** *ep.mid.vb.*| imperatv. ὄρνυο, 2pl. ὄρνυσθε | impf.: 3sg. ὤρνυτο, 3pl. ὤρνυντο | fut.: 3sg. ὀρεῖται ‖ AOR.2: 3sg. ὦρτο, also ὤρετο, 3pl. ὀρέοντο | imperatv. ὄρσο, ὄρσεο | 3sg.subj. ὄρηται, 3sg.opt. ὄροιτο | inf. ὄρθαι | ptcpl. ὄρμενος, also ὀρόμενος (A. E.) ‖ PF.: 3sg. ὀρώρεται, 3sg.subj. ὀρώρηται ‖ also ACT. (w.mid.sens.): 3sg.pf. ὄρωρε, also ὤρορε, 3sg.subj. ὀρώρῃ | 3sg.plpf. ὠρώρει, also ὀρώρει ‖ AOR.PASS. (w.mid.sens.): dial.3pl. ὦρθεν (Corinn.) |
1 **rise up** (esp. fr. a position of rest or fr. sleep); (of a person) **rise up, get up** or **come forward** Hom. hHom. Corinn. AR.; (of a person returning fr. the underworld) —W.PREP.PHR. *into the light of day* Ar.(mock-ep.); (of a bird) **take flight** Il.
2 (of Dawn) **rise** —W.PREP.PHR. *fr. her bed, fr. Okeanos* Hom. hHom.; (of night) **come on, arrive** Od.; (of midday) Theoc.; (of the swallow, in spring) **appear** Hes.
3 move into action; (of a person, god or animal) **rouse oneself, set out, act** or **move quickly, speed** (sts. W.PREP.PHR. *to* or *fr. a place*) Hom. Hes. Lyr. A. E. AR.; **hasten** —W.INF. *to do sthg.* Hom. AR.; (of a horse, ship, missile) **speed on** Hom. Pi. B.; (of a dead person, compared to a bird) —W.PREP.PHR. *to the underworld* S.; (of a person) **cast oneself, plunge** —W.PREP.PHR. *into the sea* B.
4 move into hostile action; (of troops, their might) **rise up, rush on** Il. A. Pi. S. AR.
5 (of a person's limbs) **have strength of movement, be vigorous** Hom.
6 **stir oneself, be moved** (to speak or sing) Hom.
7 (of the mind, heart or emotions) **be stirred** Hom. Thgn. AR.; (of thought) Emp.
8 (of waves, wind, fire, dust) **be set in motion, be stirred, rise up** Hom. Simon. A. Emp. AR.
9 (of war, conflict, evil) **arise** Hom. Hes. A. Pi. AR.
10 (of sounds, laughter, lamentation) **rise up** Hom. Hes. Alc.(cj.) S. AR.
11 (of things) **arise, originate** (sts. W.PREP.PHR. fr. a certain source) Il. Hes. hHom. Alc. A. AR.
12 ‖ PF. and PLPF.ACT. (wkr.sens., of persons or things) be, exist AR.

ὄροβοι ων *m.pl.* **wild pulses** (fr. a kind of vetch, as a cheap food) D.
ὀρόγυια *dial.f.*: see ὄργυια
ὀροδαμνίς ίδος *f.* [ὀρόδαμνος] **branch** (of a tree) Theoc.
ὀρόδαμνος ου *m.* **cutting** (fr. a tree) Call.

ὀροθεσίᾱ ᾱς *f.* [ὅρος, τίθημι] **fixing of boundaries** NT.
ὀροθύ̄νω *vb.* [perh.reltd. ἐρέθω] | ep.3sg.impf. ὀρόθῡνε | aor.imperatv. ὀρόθῡνον | **1 stir, rouse up** —*men* (*to action*) Il. AR. —W.INF. *to do sthg.* Od.
2 (of a river) **let loose** —*torrents* Il.; (of Poseidon) —*blasts* (*of wind*) Od.
3 **upset** —*women* (*by talking of sorrows*) Mosch.; (of a god) **incite** —*men* (*to madness*) Od.
4 ‖ PASS. (of dissension) **be stirred up** (amongst the gods) A.
ὄροιτο (ep.3sg.aor.2 mid.opt.): see ὄρνυμαι, under ὄρνῡμι
ὀροιτύπος *ep.m.*: see under ὀροτύπος
ὄρομαι *ep.mid.vb.*: see ἐπιόρομαι
ὀρο-μᾱλίδες ων *dial.f.pl.* [ὅρος; μῆλον², μηλίς] app. **wild apples** Theoc.
ὀρόμενος (ep.aor.2 mid.ptcpl.): see ὄρνυμαι, under ὄρνῡμι
ὅρος, Ion. **οὖρος**, ου *m.* **1 boundary** (of a geographical, political or ethnic territory, sts. marked by stones or a natural feature, such as a river, sea or mountains; freq.pl.); **border, frontier** Hdt. Trag. Th. +; (gener., ref. to the whole country) Hdt.(oracle) E.
2 **boundary, edge** (of a continent, empire, the world) A. E. Pl. +
3 **border, frontier** (of one's homeland, esp. w. emotional, ritual or political significance as a crossing point) Hdt. E. Th. +; (fr. which a criminal is expelled or an enemy turned away) Hdt. S. E. Th. +
4 **boundary** or **boundary marker** (of land or property) Il. E. Th. +; (of a tomb) Hdt.; (of a market, a trading stall) Ar. Pl.; (keeping people apart, fig.ref. to a person) Sol.
5 (leg.) **boundary marker** or **notice** (of mortgaged land); **marker, mortgage** or **debt notice** Eleg. Att.orats.
6 **defined limit** (for movement or activity); **limit, boundary** (for a path or territory, travelled or roamed over) A. Hdt. Call. ‖ PL. **bounds** (for a javelin to be thrown within) Antipho; (for hounds chasing a scent) X.; (for an expedition) Plu.
7 **defined limit** (for size or quantity, what is permitted or reasonable, what one might do, say or ask); **rule, standard, proper limit** or **restriction** A. Att.orats. Pl. +; (for the action in a drama) Arist.
8 **period of time** (within certain limits); **range** (within which an eclipse is predicted) Hdt.; (in age, which is ideal for marriage) Pl.; **period** (of the moon's orbit, ref. to a month) Plb.
9 **limit** (of a period of time); **end limit** (of human life) B. Hdt.
10 **defining point** or **line** (for judging or deciding sthg., for separating one concept fr. another); **distinguishing characteristic, determining principle, criterion** or **standard** E. Pl. D. Arist. +
11 **defining statement** (which distinguishes one thing fr. another), **definition** (sts. W.GEN. of sthg.) Pl. Arist.
12 (log.) **term** (of a proposition) Arist.
13 (math., ref. to a number) **term** (within a ratio or proportion) Pl. Arist.
14 (mus.) **boundary** of an interval (in a scale), **note** Pl.
ὀρός οῦ *m.* **watery part** (of curdled milk), **whey** Od.; **serum** (of blood) Pl.
ὄρος εος (ους) *n.* | ep.gen. οὔρεος, dial. ὤρεος (Alc. Theoc.), also ὄρευς (Call. Theoc.) | dat. ὄρει, Ion. ὀρέϊ, ep. οὔρεϊ ‖ PL.: nom.acc. ὄρεα, Att. ὄρη, ep. οὔρεα, dial. ὤρεα (Theoc. Mosch. Bion) | gen. ὀρέων, Att. ὀρῶν, ep. οὐρέων (disyllab., AR.) | dat. ὄρεσι, ep. ὄρεσσι, also οὔρεσι ‖ ep.gen.dat.sg.pl. ὄρεσφι |

1 high and rugged ground, **mountain** or **mountainous area** Hom. +

2 (gener.) **high ground, hill, height** hHom. +

ὀρο-τύπος ον *adj.* [τύπτω] (of water) **crashing down a mountain** A.

—ὀροιτύπος ου *ep.m.* **mountain worker** (app. ref. to a woodcutter) Call.

ὀρούω *vb.* [reltd. ὄρνῡμι] | impf. ὤρουον | fut. ὀρούσω | aor. ὤρουσα, ep. ὄρουσα | **1** **start up and move swiftly**; (of persons) **rush, spring, dart** (usu. W.PREP.PHR. to or fr. a place) Hom. hHom. A. Pi. B. E. +; (of a warrior or fighter, against or into the enemy) Il. Hes. E. Theoc. Plu. —W.COGN.ACC. *w. a leap* A.; (of Hades) **rush forth** (in his chariot, to seize Persephone) hHom.

2 (of a wild animal, a snake) **dart, rush** (towards or upon prey) Il. Plu.; (of a person, compared to a lion) E.; (of a dog, at a person, in order to bite) Theoc.

3 (of a goddess, compared to a lead weight) **plunge** —W.PREP.PHR. *to the depths of the sea* Il.; (of a boulder) *—fr. a cliff* Hes.; (of insolence, fr. its height) —*towards the inevitable* S.; (fig., of a guilty man) —*into a struggle w. justice* S.

4 (of a spear) **speed** —W.PREP.PHR. *fr. the hand* Il.

5 **go all out, strive** —W.GEN. *towards a goal* Pi. —W.INF. *to achieve glory* Pi.

ὀροφή ῆς *f.* [ἐρέφω] **1 roof, roofing** (of a building or temple, made of timbers, reed, tiles, or a single stone slab) Od. Hdt. Th. Ar. X. Lycurg. +

2 (fr. the interior perspective) **ceiling** Ar. Pl. Plu.

ὀροφίας ου *m.* one who lives in the roof, **roof dweller** (ref. to a person, envisaged as a mouse) Ar.

ὄροφος ου *m.* **1** (app.collectv.) **reed** or **thatch** (as a roof covering) Il.

2 roof (as the covering or open top floor of a building; sts. collectv.pl.); **roofing, roof** A. Th. Ar. Pl. X. Plu.; (of a temple, a tent) Hdt.(oracle) E.; (as marking the direction above one's head) Ar.; (ref. to persons associating) ὑπὸ τὸν αὐτὸν ὄροφον *under the same roof* Pl.

ὀρόω (ep.1sg.), **ὀρόων** (ep.ptcpl.): see ὁράω

ὄρπετον *Aeol.n.*: see ἑρπετόν

ὄρπηξ ηκος, dial. **ὄρπαξ** ᾱκος *m.* **young stem** (of a tree); **shoot, sprig, sapling** Hellenist.poet.; (cut to make the rim of a chariot frame or wheel) Il. Theoc.; (to make garlands) Sapph. Pi.*fr.*; (as a whip for oxen) Hes.; (to which a man is compared) Sapph.; (fig., ref. to the first men or women) Emp.; (ref. to a light javelin) E.

ὀρρο-πύγιον ου *n.* [ὄρρος, πῡγή] **rear end around the tail bone; rump, tail** (of wasps, gnats) Ar.

ὄρρος ου *m.* [reltd. οὐρά] area of the tail bone (animal or human); **rump, arse** Ar.

ὀρρωδέω, Ion. **ἀρρωδέω** *contr.vb.* | aor. ὠρρώδησα | **be afraid** Hdt. Isoc. Pl. Plu. —W.GEN. *about sthg.* Hdt. —W.PREP.PHR. *for oneself or another* Th. And. Lys. Plu. —W.ACC. *of death, treachery, war, someone's behaviour or power, or sim.* Hdt. E. Ar. Isoc. Pl. + —*of someone* Ar. X. Plu. —W.INF. *to do sthg.* Plu. —w. τό + INF. Th. —W.ACC. + INF. *that someone may die* E. —w. μή + SUBJ. *that sthg. may happen* Hdt. Antipho Th. Pl. Plu. —w. ὅτι + CL. *that sthg. is the case* Hdt.

ὀρρωδία ᾱς, Ion. **ἀρρωδίη** ης *f.* **fear, dread** Hdt. E. Th.

ὄρσασκε (ep.3sg.iteratv.aor.): see ὄρνῡμι

ὄρσεο (ep.aor.2 mid.imperatv.): see ὄρνυμαι, under ὄρνῡμι

ὀρσί-αλος ου *masc.adj.* [ὄρνῡμι, ἅλς] (epith. of Poseidon) **rousing the sea** B.

ὀρσι-βάκχας ᾱ *dial.masc.adj.* [βάκχη] (epith. of Dionysus) **rousing Bacchants** B.

ὀρσι-γύναιξ αικος *dial.masc.adj.* [γυνή] (epith. of Dionysus) **rousing women** (i.e. Bacchants) Lyr.adesp.

ὀρσί-κτυπος ου *masc.adj.* [κτύπος] (epith. of Zeus) **rousing the crash of thunder** Pi.

ὀρσι-νεφής οῦ *masc.adj.* [νέφος] (epith. of Zeus) **rousing clouds** Pi.

ὄρσο (ep.aor.2 mid.imperatv.): see ὄρνυμαι, under ὄρνῡμι

ὀρσο-θύρη ης *Ion.f.* [ὄρρος, θύρᾱ] app. **rear door** Od.

ὀρσολοπέομαι *pass.contr.vb.* [ὀρσολόπος] (of the heart) **be harassed** or **tormented** A.

ὀρσολοπεύω *vb.* **give a hard time to** —*a thief* hHom.

ὀρσο-λόπος ου *masc.adj.* [ὄρρος, λέπω] app., arse-flaying or tearing from behind; (epith. of Ares) **harassing the enemy from behind** (i.e. in a rout) Anacr.

ὀρσός *Lacon.adj.*: see ὀρθός

ὀρσο-τρίαινα ᾱ *dial.masc.adj.* [ὄρνῡμι] | acc. ὀρσοτρίαιναν | (epith. of Poseidon) **who wields the trident** Pi. || SB. **Wielder of the trident** Pi.

ὄρσω (ep.fut.): see ὄρνῡμι

ὀρτάζω *Ion.vb.*: see ἑορτάζω

ὀρτάλιχος ου *m.* **young bird, chick** A. Theoc.; (for eating) Ar.

ὀρτή *Ion.f.*: see ἑορτή

Ὀρτυγίᾱ ᾱς, Ion. **Ὀρτυγίη** ης *f.* **1** Ortygia (island of uncertain location, assoc.w. Artemis) Od.; (birthplace of Artemis, perh. Rheneia, nr. Delos) hHom.; (ref. to Delos) Pi.*fr.* Call. AR.; (island at Syracuse's port entrance, also sacred to Artemis) Pi.

2 (cult title of Artemis) Ortygia S.

ὀρτυγο-θήρᾱς ου *m.* [ὄρτυξ, θηράω] **quail-hunter** Pl.

ὀρτυγο-κόπος ου *m.* [κόπτω] **quail-tapper** (ref. to a contestant in a gambling game, who must dislodge an opponent's quail by hitting it on the head) Pl.

ὀρτυγο-μήτρᾱ ᾱς *f.* [app. μήτηρ] **a kind of bird** (perh. corncrake); **quail-mother** (com.epith. of Leto, as mother of Artemis, born on Ortygia) Ar.

ὀρτυγο-τρόφος ου *m.* [τρέφω] **quail-breeder** Pl.

ὄρτυξ υγος *m.* **quail** Hdt. Ar. Pl. X. +

ὄρυγμα ατος *n.* [ὀρύσσω] **1** **action or process of digging, digging work, excavation** Hdt.

2 that which is excavated; **bed, channel, ditch** (esp. for control of water) Hdt. Th. Plu.; **trench, tunnel** (as siege or defensive work) Hdt. X. Plb. Plu.; (dug in metalworking, extracting material for bricks) Th. Plb.

3 pit (for burning things, catching wild animals) Hdt. X. Plu.; **execution pit** (for criminals) Lycurg. Din.

ὀρυκτός ή όν *adj.* (of a defensive ditch) **dug, excavated** Il. X.; (of a lake, water channels, opp. existing naturally) Hdt.; (of a grave) E.; (of entrances to an underground dwelling) X.

ὀρυμαγδός οῦ *m.* **loud or echoing noise; din, crashing** (of weapons and armour, battle) Hom. Hes.; (of woodcutters at work, a pile of wood thrown down) Hom.; (of tree-trunks and stones carried in a torrent) Il.; (of the sea, rowers) Simon. AR.; **noise** (of men shouting, dogs yelping) Hom.

ὄρυξις εως *f.* [ὀρύσσω] **excavation** (of a defensive military trench) Plu.

ὄρυς υος *m.* app., **a kind of antelope, oryx** Hdt.

ὀρύσσω, Att. **ὀρύττω** *vb.* | fut. ὀρύξω | aor. ὤρυξα, ep. ὄρυξα || MID.: aor. ὠρυξάμην || PASS.: aor. ὠρύχθην, aor.2 ὠρύγην (Plu.) | pf. ὀρώρυγμαι | plpf. ὀρωρύγμην |

1 excavate a hollow in the ground (esp. for water or other liquids); **dig** Hdt. X. Plu.; (tr.) **dig, dig out** —*a trench, pit, tunnel, well, canal, or sim.* Hom. Hdt. Th. X. +; (also mid.) Hdt. AR. || PASS. (of a trench or sim.) **be dug** Hdt. +

ὀρφάνευμα

2 (of horses) **hollow out** —*a bed* (*in sand*, W.DAT. *w. their hooves*) Ar.
3 **dig** (to bury, plant or hide sthg.) X. NT. —*a grave* X. —*a hole or trench* (*for planting*) X. —W.PARTITV.GEN. *a place in the ground* S. || PASS. (of a hole) be dug Hdt. +
4 **clear away** (earth) by digging (in order to construct sthg.); **dig out** —*earth* Hdt. —*a strip of land* (*to make a sea channel*) Hdt. —*an area of ground* (*before building*) Plu. || PASS. (of earth, an area) be dug out Hdt.
5 **dig up the ground** (looking for sthg.); **dig** (for water, gold, treasure) Pl. X. Plu.; **dig up** —*ground* Plu. —*graves* (*to steal from*) Plu. || PASS. (of land) be excavated (for metals) X.
6 **dig up** (sthg. which is of value or use); **dig up** —*roots* (*to eat, to use in magic*) Il. Hdt. Theoc. —*stones* (*to make mills*) X. —(*for building*) Hdt.(mid.) || PASS. (of alabaster, precious metals, salt) be mined Hdt. X.
7 **dig into, gouge, poke** —*someone's eyes, their arsehole* Ar.; (intr., w. sexual connot.) Ar.

ὀρφάνευμα ατος *n.* [ὀρφανεύω] **orphanhood** E.

ὀρφανεύω *vb.* [ὀρφανός] **1** (of a father, a deity) **care for in orphanhood** —*children* (*who have lost their mother*) E.
2 || MID.PASS. (of children, who have lost a parent) **be orphaned** or **live in orphanhood** E.

ὀρφανίᾱ ᾱς *f.* **1** state of being orphaned, **orphanhood** Att.orats. Pl. Plb. Plu.
2 **lack, dearth** (W.GEN. of victory-garlands) Pi.
3 **bereavement** (of households, in time of war) Pl.

ὀρφανίζω *vb.* | fut. ὀρφανιῶ | aor. ὠρφάνισα | **1** (of a mother, by her death) bring to a state of orphanhood, **orphan** —*children, their lives* E. || PASS. be orphaned or bereft —W.GEN. *of father and mother* S.
2 || MID.PASS. **live as though orphaned** (i.e. away fr. one's parents) Pi.
3 **deprive, rob** —*an evil tongue* (W.GEN. *of its voice*) Pi. —*Pan* (*of his sleep*) Theoc.*epigr.*

ὀρφανικός ή όν *adj.* **1** (of a child) **orphaned** Il.
2 (of a particular day, a fate) of the kind which makes an orphan, **of orphanhood** Il. Pl.
3 (of business) **relating to an orphan** Pl.; (of an estate) **belonging to an orphan** Arist. || NEUT.PL.SB. affairs relating to orphans Arist.

ὀρφανιστής οῦ *m.* [ὀρφανίζω] one who cares for orphans, **guardian** S.

ὀρφανός ή όν (also ός όν E.) *adj.* **1** (of a child, through the death of parents or abandonment) in a state of orphanhood, **orphan** Od. Hes. S. E. Att.orats. Pl. +; (of a young bird) Ar.; (of a child) **orphaned, bereft** (W.GEN. of a parent or parents, of kin) E. Pl. D. Plu. || MASC.FEM.SB. orphan Att.orats. Pl. +; (fig., ref. to an argument whose author is dead) Pl. || NEUT.PL.SB. orphanhood Pl.
2 (of a home) **bereft** (through the death of a child or the childlessness of its master) E.; (of a parent, W.GEN. of a child, through its death) E.; (of a person's fate, W.GEN. of progeny, through failure to have children) Pi.; (of a bird's nest, W.GEN. of chicks, through their abduction) S.; (of men, women, a country, in time of war, W.GEN. of comrades, husbands, or sim.) Pi. E. Lys.
3 (of people, a city) **bereft** (of a father-like leader) NT. Plu.
4 (gener., of persons) **bereft** (of valued possessions) Pl.; **devoid** (W.GEN. of insolence) Pi.; (of a place, W.GEN. of dancing) Pi.*fr.*; (of a captured fighter) perh. **finished** (W.GEN. w. battles) Tim.; (of a person's life) **desolate** Pl.

ὀρφανο-φύλαξ ακος *m.* **guardian of orphans** (ref. to a state official at Athens) X.

Ὀρφεο-τελεστής οῦ *m.* [Ὀρφεύς, τελέω] one who conducts Orphic rituals, **Orphic priest** Thphr.

Ὀρφεύς έως *m.* **Orpheus** (legendary Thracian singer and musician, to whom were attributed the sacred hymns of a mystery religion) A. Pi. E. Ar. Tim. Isoc. +; (husband of Eurydike, whom he tried to bring back fr. Hades) Pl. Mosch.; (as an Argonaut) AR.; (killed by Thracian women) Pl.

—**Ὀρφεῖος** ᾱ (Ion. η) ον *adj.* (of the voice, lyre, hymns) **of Orpheus** E. Pl. AR.

—**Ὀρφικός** ή όν *adj.* (of rites) **Orphic** Hdt. Plu.; (of a way of life) Pl.

ὀρφναῖος ᾱ (Ion. η) ον *adj.* [ὄρφνη] **1** of or relating to darkness; (of night) **dark** Hom. hHom. E. AR.; (quasi-advbl., of a beacon-fire appearing) **in the darkness** A.
2 (of a building, ref. to its interior) **dark** AR.
3 (of the garments of an underworld goddess) **dark** AR.

ὄρφνη ης, dial. **ὄρφνᾱ** ᾱς *f.* **1 darkness** (of night) Pi. E. Ar. X. AR. Theoc. Plb.; (of a divine mist or cloud) E.; (of the underworld) E.
2 (fig.) **darkness** (concealing the future) Thgn.

ὄρφνινος η ον *adj.* (of a colour) app. **dark violet** or **black** Pl.; (of a garment of this colour) X.

ὀρφώς (or **ὀρφῶς**) ῶ *m.* **sea-perch** Ar.

ὄρχαμος ου *m.* **leader, chief** (W.GEN. of men, in terms of military command or of nobility or good character) Hom. Hes.*fr.*; (of an army) A.; (of robbers, ref. to Hermes) hHom.; (of the Argonauts) AR.

ὄρχατος ου *m.* [ὄρχος] **orchard, garden** (of fruit trees, vines or other plants) Hom.

ὀρχέομαι *mid.contr.vb.* | ep.3pl. ὀρχέονται (trisyllab.), or perh. ὀρχεῦνται | impf. ὠρχούμην, ep.3pl. perh. ὠρχέοντο (trisyllab.), dial. ὠρχεῦντο (Theoc.) | fut. ὀρχήσομαι | aor. ὠρχησάμην |
1 dance Hom. Hes. Anacr. Ion Hdt. Ar. + —W.COGN.ACC. *a certain style of dance* Hdt. X. Call.
2 (of calves) **skip, frisk** Theoc.
3 (fig., of the ground) **be set dancing** —W.DAT. *by an earthquake* E.*fr.*; (of a person's heart, a land) —*w. fear* A. Call.; (of the soul, by the recitation of poetry) Pl.

—**ὀρχέω** *act.contr.vb.* **cause dancing** Pl.

ὀρχηδόν *adv.* [ὄρχος] (w. ἕκαστος *each man*) perh., **row after row, without exception** —*ref. to receiving a handout* Hdt.

ὀρχηθμός οῦ *m.* [ὀρχέομαι] **dancing** Hom. Hes. hHom.(v.l. ὀρχηστύς) Thgn.

ὄρχημα ατος *n.* **dance step** or **dancing** A.*satyr.fr.* Pi.*fr.* S. X.

ὄρχησις εως (Ion. ιος) *f.* **dancing** Hdt. S.*satyr.fr.* Pl. X. Arist. Plu.; (performed w. armour and weapons by men of military age) Pl. X. Plb. Plu.

ὀρχησμοί ῶν Att.m.pl. **dances** or **dancing** (of Erinyes) A.

ὀρχηστήρ ῆρος *m.* **dancer** Il. Hes.*fr.*

ὀρχηστής οῦ (Ion. έω), dial. **ὀρχηστᾱς** ᾶ *m.* **dancer** (performing on a particular occasion, or ref. to a professional) Il. Scol. Pi.*fr.* Ar. Pl. X. +

ὀρχηστικός ή όν *adj.* (of the art) **of dancing** Pl.; (of a particular metre and type of composition) **suited to dancing** Arist. || FEM.SB. art of dance Plb.

ὀρχηστο-διδάσκαλος ου *m.* **dancing-master** X.

ὀρχήστρα ᾱς *f.* [reltd. ὀρχηστήρ] **1 orchestra** (ref. to the area in a theatre in front of the stage, where the chorus danced and sang) Att.orats. Plb.; (W.GEN. of Ares, fig.ref. to the Boeotian plain) Plu.
2 orchestra (ref. to a part of the Agora) Pl.

ὀρχηστρίς ίδος *f.* **dancing-girl** Ar. Pl. X. Arist. Plu.

ὀρχηστύς ύος *f.* | ep.acc. ὀρχηστύν | ep.dat. ὀρχηστυῖ | **dancing** (as an art) Hom.; (as performed on a specific occasion) **dance** Od. hHom.(v.l. ὀρχηθμός) E.*Cyc.*

ὀρχίλος ου *m.* perh. **wren** Ar.

ὀρχί-πεδα ων *n.pl.* [ὄρχις, πέδον] **testicles** Ar.

ὀρχιπεδίζω *vb.* | aor. ὠρχιπέδισα | **fondle the testicles** (of a man) Ar.

ὄρχις εως (Ion. ιος) *m.* | Ion.nom.pl. ὄρχιες | (usu.pl.) **testicle** Hippon. Hdt. S.*satyr.fr.* Ar. X. D.

Ὀρχομενός, dial. **Ἐρχομενός**, οῦ *m.* (*also f.*)
1 Orkhomenos (city in Boeotia, ancestral home of the Minyans) Hom. Hes.*fr.* Pi. Hdt. Th. +
2 Orkhomenos (city in Arcadia) Il. Hdt. Th. +

—Ὀρχομένιος ᾱ ον *adj.* (of a person) **from Orkhomenos** (in Boeotia or Arcadia) Hdt. Th. + ‖ MASC.PL.SB. **men from Orkhomenos** Hdt. Th. +

ὄρχος ου *m.* **row** (of vines or fruit trees) Od. Hes. B. Ar. X. Theoc.

ὄρωρε, ὀρώρει (ep.3sg.pf. and plpf.), **ὀρώρεται** (ep.3sg.pf.mid.): see ὄρνυμαι, under ὄρνῡμι

ὀρωρέχαται, ὀρωρέχατο (ep.3pl.redupl.pf. and plpf.mid.): see ὀρέγομαι, under ὀρέγω

ὀρώρῃ (ep.3sg.pf.subj.), **ὀρώρηται** (ep.3sg.pf.mid.subj.): see ὄρνυμαι, under ὄρνῡμι

ὀρώρυγμαι (pf.pass.), **ὀρωρύγμην** (plpf.pass.): see ὀρύσσω

ὅς[1] ἥ (dial. ἅ, Aeol. ἀ) *ὅ relatv.pron.* | GEN.: masc.neut. οὗ, fem. ὅου, dial. ἅ, fem. ἧς, dial. ἆς, ep. ἕης | DU.: masc.fem.neut. nom.acc. ὥ, masc.fem.neut.gen.dat. οἷν, fem. αἶν (S., dub.) ‖ PL.: οἵ αἵ ἅ, ep.fem.dat. ᾗς, ᾗσι ‖ Only the most common uses are illustrated here. | See also ὅσπερ, ὅστε (ὅς τε), ὅστις. For ὅς γε, see γε B 3. |

1 (as relatv., introducing a cl. which defines the antecedent and is necessary to complete the sense) **who, which, that** Hom. + • ἕνεκ᾿ ἀρητῆρος ὃν ἠτίμησ᾿ Ἀγαμέμνων *because of the priest whom Agamemnon dishonoured* Il.

2 (adding further information about the antecedent, the sense being already complete) • Πολύφημον, ὅου κράτος ἐστὶ μέγιστον πᾶσιν Κυκλώπεσσι *Polyphemos, whose power is greatest among all the Cyclopes* Od. • τὸ ναυτικὸν τὸ τῶν βαρβάρων, ὃ τίς οὐκ ἂν ἰδὼν ἐφοβήθη; *the fleet of the barbarian, by the sight of which who would not have been terrified?* Lys.

3 (w. causal sense) • νήπιοι, οἳ κατὰ βοῦς Ὑπερίονος Ἠελίοιο ἤσθιον *fools, because they ate the cattle of Helios Hyperion* Od. • θαυμαστὸν ποιεῖς, ὃς ἡμῖν ... οὐδὲν δίδως *you do a surprising thing in giving us nothing* X.

4 (w. final force) • ἄγγελον ἧκαν, ὃς ἀγγείλειε γυναικί *they sent a messenger to report to the woman* Od. • τριάκοντα ἄνδρας ἑλέσθαι, οἳ τοὺς πατρίους νόμους συγγράψουσι *to choose thirty men to codify the ancestral laws* X.

5 (in general statements) • οὐ δηναιὸς ὃς ἀθανάτοισι μάχηται *he who fights against the immortals does not live long* Il.

6 (as indir.interrog.) • μήποτε γνοίης ὅς εἶ *may you never discover who you are* S.

7 ‖ NEUT.SB. (in prep.phrs., esp. of time) • ἐς ὅ *until* Hom. Hdt. • ἐν ᾧ *while* Hdt. + • ἐξ οὗ *from the time when, since* Hom. +; (also) ἀφ᾿ (ἀπ᾿) οὗ Hdt. +

—ὅ *neut.sg.relatv.adv.* **1** (introducing a compl.cl., after a vb. of knowing, seeing, or speaking) **that** Hom. Hes. AR.
2 (as conj.) in that, **because, since** Hom. AR.
3 (as demonstr.) in view of which, **for that reason** E. Ar. D.; **whereas** Th.

—ἅ *neut.pl.relatv.adv.* in view of which, **for that reason** S. Isoc.

—ᾗ, dial. **ᾆ** (also **ἇ**) (Ar.) *fem.relatv.adv.* **1** in the place in which, **where** Hom. +; (as demonstr.) ᾗ μὲν ... ᾗ δὲ ... ᾗ δέ *in one place ... in another ... in another* E.
2 to the place or in the direction where, **where, to where** Hom. +
3 in the situation in which, **where** E.; in cases in which, **where, when** Pl. Arist.
4 in the way that, **as** Trag. Th. +; (as indir.interrog.) in what way, **how** Hdt. Trag.
5 (w. τις + SB.) **as, like** (an animal) Ar.
6 (causal) because of which, **for which reason** Th.
7 **in so far as** Pl. X.; to the extent that, **as far as** Pl.; (as indir.interrog.) **to what extent** Pl.
8 (qualifying a noun) in so far as being, **as being** (sthg.) Arist.
9 (w.superl.adv.) • ᾗ ἐδύνατο τάχιστα *as quickly as he could* X. • ᾗ δυνατὸν μάλιστα *as much as possible* X. • ᾗ τάχιστα *as quickly as possible* Pi.; (also) ᾆ τάχος Pi.

—οἷ *relatv.adv.* **1** to the place or in the direction where, **where, to where** S. E. Th. Ar. +
2 (as indir.interrog.) to what place, **where** E. Pl. +; to what degree or extent, **how far** E. Ar.; (W.PARTITV.GEN. in trouble, dishonour, disgraceful behaviour) S. E. D.

—οὗ *relatv.adv.* **1** in the place where, **where** Anacr. Trag. Th. +
2 in the circumstances where, **where, when** S. E. +
3 (as indir.interrog.) in what place, **where** S.; (fig., W.GEN. in fortune) E.

—ὧ *dial.relatv.adv.* **from where** Theoc.

ὅς[2] ἥ ὅν *possessv.pron.adj.* [reltd. ἑός] | ep.masc.gen. οἷο | ep.fem.gen.dat.sg.pl. ᾗφι | **1** (as 3sg.) **his, her, its** Hom. Hes. Lyr. Hdt. Trag. Call. Theoc.; (as 3pl.) **their** Call. AR.
2 (as 1sg.) **my** Hom.(dub.) AR. Mosch.; (as 1pl.) **our** Od.(dub.)
3 (as 2sg.) **your** Od.(dub.) Hes. Call.; (as 2pl.) AR.
4 (w. suffix -δε) ὅνδε δόμονδε *to his own house* Od. Hes.

ὅς[3] *demonstr.pron.*: see ὁ

ὅσα *neut.pl.relatv.adv.*: see under ὅσος

ὁσάκις, ep. **ὁσσάκι** (also **ὁσάκις**) *relatv.adv.* [ὅσος] **1 as many times as, as often as** Hom. Hdt. Th. Pl. X. D. +
2 (as indir.interrog.) **how many times** Lys. Call.*epigr.*

ὁσαχῇ-περ *relatv.adv.* [ὅσος, περ[1]] **in just as many ways as** Pl.

ὁσαχοῦ *relatv.adv.* **in as many places** or **circumstances as** D.

ὁσαχῶς *relatv.adv.* **in as many ways as, as often as** Arist.

ὁσαχῶσ-περ *relatv.adv.* [περ[1]] **in just as many ways as** Arist.

ὄσδω *dial.vb.*: see ὄζω

ὀσ-έτη *adv.* [ὅσος, ἔτος] **as many years as there are, every year** Ar.

ὀσ-ημέραι *adv.* [ἡμέρᾱ] **as many days as there are, every day, daily** Th. Ar. Hyp. D. Thphr. Men. Plu.; **any day** Pl.

ὁσίᾱ ᾱς, Ion. **ὁσίη** ης *f.* [ὅσιος] **1** conduct that is appropriate in relation to the gods, **right behaviour, rightness, holiness** hHom. E. Ar. D.
2 (w. ἐστί, sts.understd., freq. in neg.phr.) it is (not) right (W.INF. to do sthg.) Od. Pi. Hdt.; (w.inf.understd.) Call.
3 (personif., as a goddess) **Righteousness, Holiness** E.
4 (specif.) religious rite or observance, **rite** hHom.
5 perh. **proper share** (for a god, W.GEN. of sacrificial meat) hHom.

ὅσιος ᾱ (Ion. η) ον (also ος ον) *adj.* **1** right or righteous in terms of divine law (in relations w. other persons or peoples, or w. the gods; sts.ref. to being without bloodguilt; freq. in neg.phr.); (of persons, their actions, thoughts, speech, way of life, or sim.) **upright, principled, pure, holy** Simon. B. Hdt. Trag. Th. Ar. +

ὁσιότης

2 (of Athens, the Areopagus court) **upright, holy** E.; (of a place for giving birth) as required by religious law, **not taboo** Ar.; (of ritual or ceremonial actions, esp. those assoc.w. cleansing, sacrifices, marriage, death) **pure** Trag. Ar. +; (of Justice) **holy** Thgn.
3 ‖ NEUT.IMPERS. (w. ἐστί, sts.understd., freq. in neg.phr.) it is (not) right (in terms of divine law or morality) —W.INF. to do sthg. Hdt. S. E. Th. Att.orats. +
4 ‖ NEUT.SB. uprightness, morality or holiness E. Th. Pl. X.; religious duty Pl. Plb. ‖ PL. right, principled or holy things Hdt. Trag. Ar. Att.orats. +; religious duties or rituals E. Th. +; holy places Isoc.
—**ὁσίως** adv. | compar. ὁσιώτερον, superl. ὁσιώτατα | in a divinely sanctioned, right or principled way, **rightly, uprightly** —esp.ref. to conducting oneself in a legal ctxt., performing a public office, acting towards others, living one's life Th. Att.orats. +; **in a pure** or **holy way** —ref. to conducting oneself in a religious ctxt. E. Antipho Pl. X. Aeschin.

ὁσιότης ητος f. **uprightness** (of a person, people or ruler) Isoc. Pl. X.; **holiness** (in religious observance) Isoc. Pl. X. NT. Plu.

ὁσιόω contr.vb. | aor.pass. ὡσιώθην | **1** make (someone) free from pollution; **purify** (fr. bloodguilt) —a murderer (returning fr. exile) D. —(W.DAT. through exile) E. ‖ PASS. (of souls, at death) be purified or sanctified Plu.
2 make pure or holy (for a religious function) ‖ MID. (of Bacchants) **purify** or **sanctify** —their fennel rods E. ‖ PASS. (of a cult initiate) be consecrated (into the service of a deity) E.fr.
3 ‖ PASS. (of days of mourning) be religiously observed X.

ὀσμή Att.f.: see ὀδμή

ὅσος, ep. **ὅσσος**, Aeol. **ὄσσος**, η (dial. ᾱ) ον relatv. and indir.interrog.adj. [reltd. ὅς¹] **1** (freq. correlatv.w. τόσος, τοσόσδε, τοσοῦτος) such in magnitude or number as, **as great, as much** or **as many as** Hom. + • οὔ τι τόσος γε ὅσος Τελαμώνιος Αἴας not as large as Ajax son of Telamon Il. • πάντας ὅσοι Τρωσὶν πολέμιζον all who fought against the Trojans Od.; (w. ellipse of vb. εἶναι) • ἀσπίδες ὅσσαι ἄρισται all the best shields Il.
2 (as indir.interrog., sts.w. τις) **how great, how much** or **how many** Hom. + • τὴν δύναμιν τῶν Βαβυλωνίων … δηλώσω ὅση τις ἐστί I shall show how great is the strength of the Babylonians Hdt.
3 (after exclam. or vb. of emotion) **how great, how much** or **how many** Hom. • κεχολωμένοι ὅσσοι ὄλοντο angry at how many (i.e. that so many) died Il. • ὦ Ζεῦ βασιλεῦ, τὸ χρῆμα τῶν νυκτῶν ὅσον Lord Zeus, what a great length of night-time! Ar.
4 (reinforcing an adj. of quantity) Hdt. + • ἄφθονοι ὅσοι γίνονται they (monkeys) exist in huge numbers Hdt. • ὄχλος ὑπερφυὴς ὅσος such an enormous crowd Ar. • μετὰ ἱδρῶτος θαυμαστοῦ ὅσον with a remarkable amount of sweat Pl.; (in advbl. constructions) • θαυμαστὸν ὅσον διαφέρει it differs to a remarkable extent Pl.
5 ‖ NEUT.SB. sufficient amount (W.INF. to do sthg.) Od. + • ἐλείπετο τῆς νυκτὸς ὅσον σκοταίους διελθεῖν τὸ πεδίον there was enough of the night left for them to cross the plain under cover of darkness X.
6 (ellipt., w. δή or δή κοτε) **of whatever size** or **quantity** Hdt. • ἐπὶ μισθῷ ὅσῳ δή for some fee or other Hdt.

—**ὅσον**, ep. **ὅσσον** neut.sg.relatv.adv. **1** to such a degree or extent as, **as much** or **as far as** Hom. + • οὐ μέν τοι ἐγὼ τόσον αἴτιός εἰμι ὅσσον οἱ ἄλλοι πάντες I am not so much to blame as all the others Il.; (w.inf.) S. + • ὅσον γ' ἔμ' εἰδέναι as far as I know Ar.; (w.superl.adv.) • ὅσον τάχιστα as quickly as possible Trag.
2 to such a distance as, **as far as** Hom. +
3 (as indir.interrog.) to what extent, **how much, how far** Hom. +
4 (limitative, ref. to distance or degree) **only as far as** or **only in so far as** Hom. + • ὅσον ἐς Σκαιάς τε πύλας καὶ φηγὸν ἵκανε he came only as far as the Skaian gates and the oak tree Il. • ἐγὼ μέν μιν οὐκ εἶδον εἰ μὴ ὅσον γραφῇ I have not seen it except only in a painting Hdt.
5 (ref. to measurement) **approximately** Th. + • ὅσον δύ' ἢ τρία στάδια about two or three stades Pl.; (also) ὅσον τε Hom. Hdt.
6 (w.neg.) ὅσον οὐ just not, all but, almost E. Th. +; οὐδ' ὅσον (ὅσσον) not even a little, not at all Call. AR.
7 (prep.phrs.) εἰς ὅσον, ἐφ' ὅσον, καθ' ὅσον to the extent that, so far as Hdt. +; ἐν ὅσῳ while Hdt. +; up to the time that, until Th.

—**ὅσα** neut.pl.relatv.adv. to such a degree or extent as, **as far as** Hdt. + • ὅσα ἐγὼ μέμνημαι as far as I recall X.; (w.superl.adv.) • ὅσα ἐδύνατο μάλιστα as much as she was able Hdt.

—**ὅσῳ** dat.neut.sg.relatv.adv. (usu. w. compar. or superl. adv. or adj.) **by as much as** Hdt. E. Th. +; (as indir.interrog.) **by how much** Hes. Hdt. S. E. +

ὁσοσ-οῦν ὁσηοῦν ὁσονοῦν, Ion. **ὅσος (η ον) ὦν** indef. relatv.adj. however great in magnitude or number; (of a sum of money) **however much it might be** (i.e. of no specific amount) Hdt.; (of people) **however many** Arist.
—**ὅσον ὦν** indef.relatv.adv. **to any extent whatever** Hdt.

ὁσοσ-περ (also **ὅσος περ**, ep. **ὅσσος περ**, Aeol. ὄσσοσπερ), ὅσηπερ ὅσονπερ (etc.) relatv.adj. [περ¹] **as great** or **as many as** Hes. Hdt. Trag. Th. +
—**ὅσονπερ** (also **ὅσον περ**, ep. **ὅσσον περ**) neut.sg.relatv. adv. **just as much** S. E. Isoc. +; (ref. to measurement) **about, approximately** Hdt.
—**ὅσῳπερ** dat.neut.sg.relatv.adv. (w. compar. or superl. adv. or adj.) **by just as much as** S. Ar. Isoc. +

ὁσ-περ (also **ὅς περ**) ἥπερ (dial. ἅπερ) ὅπερ relatv.pron. [ὅς¹, περ¹] **the very one who, which** or **that** (but freq. not distinguishable fr. ὅς¹ who) Hom. +
—**ἅπερ** neut.pl.relatv.adv. in the way that, **as** A. X.; (W.SB.) **like** (someone or sthg.) A. S.
—**ᾗπερ** (also **ᾗ περ**), dial. **ἅπερ** (also **ἄπερ**) relatv.adv. **1** in the very place in which, **where** Th. +
2 to the very place or in the very direction where, **where, to where** Il.
3 by the very route by which, **by the way that** Il. Emp. E. Th. +
4 through the very circumstances or means by which, **whereby** Th.
5 in the very manner in which, **in the way that, as** Il. Ibyc. Emp. E. +; (W.SB.) **like** (someone or sthg.) Ar.
6 in so far as Emp.
—**οἷπερ** relatv.adv. to the place or in the direction where, **where, to where** S. E. Th. +
—**οὗπερ** relatv.adv. in the very place in which, **where** Trag. Th. +
—**ὧπερ** dial.relatv.adv. **from where** Theoc.

ὄσπριον ου n. (usu.pl.) edible seed of a leguminous plant (such as pea, bean, lentil), **pulse** Hdt. Pl. X. Plu.

ὄσσα, Att. **ὄττα** (Pl.), ης f. [reltd. ὄψ] | only nom. and acc. ὄσσαν, Att. ὄτταν | **1 rumour** or **report** (W.PREP.PHR. fr. Zeus, i.e. fr. an untraceable source, opp. fr. specific persons) Od.; (opp. one conveyed by a bird of omen) AR.; (personif., as a messenger of Zeus) **Rumour** Hom.

2 voice (of the Muses) Hes.; (of Apollo, addressing a mortal) Pi.; **cry** (of a bird of omen) AR.; **utterance** (by a person, of ill-omened words) Pl.
3 voice, sound (of the lyre) hHom.; **noise** (of a bellowing bull) Hes.; (of battle) Hes.

ὁσσάκι, ὁσσάκις ep.relatv.advs.: see ὁσάκις

ὁσσάτιος η ον ep.relatv.adj. [ὅσος] (of an army) **how great** Il.

—ὁσσάτιον neut.adv. to the extent, amount or distance that, **as much as** AR.

ὄσσε ep.n.du. [reltd. ὄπωπα, see ὁράω] | also NEUT.PL.: gen. ὄσσων, dat. ὄσσοισι | **eyes** (of a god, human, wild animal) Hom. Hes. Sapph. Pi.fr. Licymn. Trag. Hellenist.poet.

ὁσσίχος ᾱ ον dial.relatv.adj. [dimin. ὅσος] (of a wound) **how small** Theoc.

ὄσσομαι ep.mid.vb. [ὄσσε] | only pres. and impf. | 3sg.impf. ὄσσετο, 3pl. ὄσσοντο | **1** give a signal (w. one's look), **have a look of** —malice Il.; (of eagles) —destruction Od.
2 direct one's gaze (in a certain way); **look** —W.ADVBL.PHR. grimly askance Call.
3 see or **imagine that one is seeing** —W.ACC. + PTCPL. sthg. happening AR.
4 see (in the imagination); **imagine, picture** —an absent person (sts. W.PREP.PHR. in one's mind) Od.
5 foresee, anticipate —pain, trouble Hom.
6 (of a god or human) **bode, threaten** —evil (W.DAT. for someone) Il. Hes.; (of a turbulent sea) **presage, give warning of** —a coming wind Il.

ὅσσος ep.relatv.adj., **ὅσσος** Aeol.relatv.adj.: see ὅσος

ὅσ-τε (also **ὅς τε**) ἥτε (dial. ἅτε) ὅτε relatv.pron. [ὅς¹, τε¹] | τε sts. has a generalising force; but the cpd. freq. cannot be distinguished fr. ὅς¹. | **1 who, which, that** Hom. Hes. Eleg. Lyr. Emp. Trag. +
2 (neut., in prep.phrs.) ἐξ οὗτε (or ἐξ οὗ τε) since the time when Semon. A.; ἐφ' ᾧτε (or ἐφ' ᾧ τε, also ἐπ' ᾧ τε Hdt.) **on condition that** —W.FUT.INDIC. sthg. will be the case Hdt. Arist. —W.INF. or ACC. + INF. one (or someone else) does sthg. Hdt. Ar. Att.orats. Pl. X. +

—ἆτε, also **ἅτε** dial.fem.adv. **as, like** Ar.

ὅ τε ep.neut.adv. **1** (as conj., introducing a compl.cl., after a vb. of knowing or sim.) **that** Hom.
2 in that, because, since Hom. hHom.

ὀστέϊνος η ον adj. [ὀστέον] (of a pipe for blowing air) **made of bone** Hdt.; (of parts of the body) Pl.

—ὄστινα ων neut.pl.sb. **bone-pipes** (ref. to auloi) Ar.

ὀστέον, dial. **ὀστίον**, ου, Att. **ὀστοῦν** οῦ n. | ep.gen.dat.sg.pl. ὀστεόφι(ν) | **1 bone** (pl., as the framework of the body; sg., as a distinct part of it) Hom. +
2 bone (as reached by a missile, or crushed in injury) Hom. +; (afflicted by illness or pain) Hdt. S. Pl.; (by love) Archil. Theoc.; (showing through the skin in hunger) Od. Call. AR.; (exposed when flesh is burned away) E.
3 || PL. **bones** (as remaining after death, to be collected and ritually disposed of, esp. fr. the battlefield) Hom. +; (in a mummy, when flesh is dissolved) Hdt.; (scattered or disposed of without proper rites) Od. Call. +; (as scattered remains of animals) Hdt.; (of fawns, made into wind instruments) Call.
4 || PL. **bones** (as revered sacred relics) Hdt. Plu.
5 || PL. **bones** (fr. sacrificial animals, as part of the gods' portion) Hes. Men.; (sg. and pl., as an animal eaten by others, or butchered for eating by humans) Pi.fr. Hdt. Thphr.; (fr. a person being devoured) E.
6 (sg.) **material or substance of bone, bone** Pl. Arist.

ὅστις (ep. **ὅτις**, Aeol. **ὄττις**) ἥτις (dial. ἅτις) ὅτι (ep. ὅττι, Aeol. ὄττι) relatv.pron.adj. [ὅς¹, τις] | ὅστις and other forms are sts. written as two words, esp. the neut. ὅτι (written as ὅ τι, sts. ὅ, τι), to distinguish it fr. the conj. ὅτι that. For neut.adv. ὅτι, ὅττι, see below. | This relatv. either describes a person or thing in general, or emphasises its particular identity or category. ‖ w. inflection of both 1st and 2nd el.: acc. ὅντινα, fem. ἥντινα (dial. ἅντινα), neut. ὅτι (ep. ὅττι, Aeol. ὄττι) | gen.masc. and neut. οὕτινος, fem. ἧστινος | dat.masc. and neut. ᾧτινι, fem. ᾗτινι ‖ PL.: nom. οἵτινες αἵτινες ἅτινα (Ion. ἅσσα, Att. ἅττα), etc. ‖ also w. only 2nd el. inflected: ep.acc.masc. ὅτινα | gen.masc.neut. ὅτου, Ion. ὅτευ, ep. ὅττεο, ὅττευ, Aeol. ὄττω | dat.masc.neut. ὅτῳ, Ion. ὅτεῳ (sts. disyllab. in ep.), also masc. ὅτινι (Theoc.) ‖ PL.: Aeol.nom.masc. ὄττινες, ep.neut. ὅτινα | ep.acc.masc. ὅτινας, Aeol. ὄττινας, Aeol.neut. ὄττινα | gen.masc.neut. ὅτων, Ion. ὅτεων | dat. ὅτοις, also ὅτοισι, Ion. ὀτέοισι (trisyllab. in ep.) |
1 (introducing an indir.q.) **who, which, what** Hom. + • εἴπ' ἄγε μοι καὶ τόνδε, φίλον τέκος, ὅς τις ὅδ' ἐστί come tell me, dear child, who this man is Il. • κρίσις γίνεται μεγάλη τῶν γυναικῶν καὶ φίλων σπουδαὶ ἰσχυραὶ περὶ τοῦδε, ἥτις αὐτέων ἐφιλέετο μάλιστα ὑπὸ τοῦ ἀνδρός great rivalry arises amongst the wives and strong contention amongst their friends on this point: which of them was loved most by her husband Hdt. • ὅ τι μὲν νυν τὰ λοιπὰ τῶν χρηστηρίων ἐθέσπισε, οὐ λέγεται as to what the rest of the oracles prophesied, there is no account Hdt. • (w. deliberative subj.) οὐ γὰρ εἶχον ὅ τι ποιέωσι ἄλλο for they did not know what else to do Hdt.
2 (identifying a person or thing, as though in reply to a q.) **the one who** or **which, who, which** Hdt. + • ὡς Πολυκράτεα πάντως ἀπολέσαι, δι' ὅντινα κακῶς ἤκουσε so as to completely destroy Polykrates, thanks to whom he heard ill of himself Hdt. • Ἀπόλλωνος Ἀρχηγέτου βωμὸν ὅστις νῦν ἔξω τῆς πόλεώς ἐστιν ἱδρύσαντο they set up the altar of Apollo Arkhegetos, the one which is now outside the city Th. • (in response to an actual q.) οὗτος, τί ποιεῖς; —ὅ τι ποιῶ; You there, what are you doing?—What am I doing? Ar.
3 (w.vb. εἶναι, freq.neg.) • ἔστιν οὖν ὅστις βούλεται ἄθλιος καὶ κακοδαίμων εἶναι; is there anyone who wants to be wretched and unfortunate? Pl. • τοιούτοις χρώμεθα συμβούλοις ὧν οὐκ ἔστιν ὅστις οὐκ ἂν καταφρονήσειεν we employ the kind of advisers whom no one would fail to look down on Isoc.
4 (indef.relatv.) **whoever, whichever, whatever** Hom. + • πέμψει δέ τοι οὖρον ὄπισθεν ἀθανάτων ὅς τίς σε φυλάσσει whichever of the immortals looks after you will send a fair wind at your back Od. • (w.subj.) χαίρει δέ μιν ὅς τις ἐθείρῃ whoever happens to cultivate it is glad Il. • (+ ἄν) ἅσσα δ' ἂν ἕκαστα τῶν χρηστηρίων θεσπίσῃ συγγραψαμένους collecting in writing whatever each of the oracles prophesied Hdt. • (w.opt.) Λυδοῖσί τε πᾶσι προεῖπε θύειν πάντα τινὰ αὐτῶν τοῦτο ὅ τι ἔχοι ἕκαστος and he instructed all the Lydians, each and every one, to sacrifice whatever he had Hdt.
5 (ellipt., as indef.adj.) **whoever** or **whichever it is** Pl. + • ἀφ' ἧστινος τέχνης from whatever craft Pl. • μηδὲ οἵτινες none whatever X.
6 (prep.phrs.) ἐξ ὅτου (ὅτευ) **from what cause or source** S. +; **from the time when** Hdt. + • μέχρι ὅτου (ὅτευ) until Hdt. + • ἕως ὅτου until Plb. NT. • καθ' ὅτι **on what terms** or **by what means** Th. + • κατ' ὅ τι **because** Hdt.

—ὅτι, ep. **ὅττι**, Aeol. **ὄττι** neut.adv. **1** (introducing an indir.q.) **for what reason or purpose, why** Hom. + • ὅς κ' εἴποι ὅ τι τόσσον ἐχώσατο Φοῖβος Ἀπόλλων who might say why Phoibos Apollo was so greatly angered Il.

ὁστισδή

2 (after neg.cl.) ὅτι μή *except* Hdt. + • οὐ γὰρ ἦν κρήνη ὅτι μὴ μία *for there was no spring except one* Th.
3 (strengthening superl.adj. or adv.) • ὅτι μεγίστη πρόφασις *the strongest possible excuse* Th. • ὅτι (ὅττι) τάχιστα *as quickly as possible* Hom. +; (also) ὅτι τάχος Hdt. Th.

ὅστισ-δή (also **ὅστις δή**) ἥτισδή ὅτιδή *indef.relatv.adj.* **whoever** or **whichever it is, some or other** Hdt. + • ἥτινιδὴ γνώμῃ *with whatever motive* Th. • θεῶν ὅτεῳ δή *to some god or other* Hdt.

ὅστισ-δήποτε (also **ὅστις δήποτε**), Ion. **ὅστις δή κοτε**, ἥτισδήποτε ὅτιδήποτε *indef.relatv.adj.* [δή ποτε] **whoever** or **whichever it is** Hdt. + • ὅ τι δή κοτε πρήξων *whatever it was that he was intending to do* Hdt. • ἀπετύγχανεν ὁτουδήποτε *he had no success with anyone at all* D.

ὅστισ-δηποτ-οὖν (or **ὅστις δή ποτ' οὖν**) *masc.indef. relatv.adj.* **whoever** or **whichever it is** Aeschin. D.

ὅστισ-οὖν, Ion. **ὅστις ὦν**, ἥτισοῦν ὁτιοῦν *indef.relatv.adj.* **whoever** or **whichever it is** Hdt. + • πρὸς ἄλλον ὁντινοῦν ἀγωνιζόμενος *in a contest with any other person whatever* Isoc.

ὅστισ-περ ἥτισπερ ὅτιπερ *relatv.pron.adj.* [περ¹] **whoever, whichever, whatever** Th. +

ὅστλιγγες ων *f.pl.* 1 **curled locks** (of hair) Call.
2 **curling flames** (of fire) AR.

ὀστολογέω *contr.vb.* [ὀστολόγοι] | aor. ὠστολόγησα | **gather up bones** (after cremation) Is.; (fr. the battlefield) Men.

Ὀστο-λόγοι ων *m.pl.* [ὀστέον, λέγω] **Bone-gatherers** (who bring home dead loved ones) A.(title)

ὀστοῦν *Att.n.*: see ὀστέον

ὀστρακίζω *vb.* [ὄστρακον] | aor. ὠστράκισα | **banish** (a leading Athenian citizen, for a period of time) by voting with a potsherd (on which his name would be written); **practise ostracism** Arist.; **ostracise** —*a man* Arist. ‖ PASS. be ostracised Th. And. Arist.

ὀστρακίνδα *adv.* (w. play on ὄστρακον 3 and 5) ὀστρακίνδα βλέπειν *have a look as though about to play the ostraka game* Ar.

ὀστράκινος η ον *adj.* (of containers) **earthenware** NT.

ὀστρακισμός οῦ *m.* [ὀστρακίζω] **temporary banishment** (fr. Athens) by an ostrakon vote, **ostracism** Arist. Plu.

ὄστρακον ου *n.* 1 **clay pot** (used for water) Ar.; (for planting) X.; (in which to expose a baby) Ar.
2 **fragment of a broken pot, sherd, potsherd** Men.; (as a makeshift weapon) Lys. ‖ PL. sherds (as a percussion instrument, derog.ref. to castanets) Ar.
3 (specif.) **potsherd, ostrakon** (used to register a vote for banishment) Plu.; **ostrakon vote** (ref. to the process) Plu.
4 **shell** (of a tortoise) hHom.; (of a conch, used as a trumpet) Theoc.
5 ostrakon (in a game, thrown to see which way up it lands); perh. **shell** or **potsherd** Pl.

ὀστρακοφορίᾱ ᾱς *f.* [φέρω] **holding of an ostrakon vote** Arist. Plu.

ὀστρέϊνος η ον *adj.* [ὄστρεον] (of bodies) **of the mollusc kind, of shellfish** Pl.

ὀστρειο-γραφής ές *adj.* [γραφή] (of shields) **painted in purple** Plu.(quot.epigr.)

ὄστρεον (also **ὄστρειον**) ου *n.* 1 **mollusc, shellfish** (app.incl. the oyster) S.*Ichn.* Pl.
2 **pigment from a kind of shellfish** (app. the murex, used to make a luxury dye), **purple** Pl.

ὀστώδης ες *adj.* [ὀστέον] (of the head of a good horse) **rich in bone, bony** X.

ὀσφραίνομαι *mid.vb.* | fut. ὀσφρήσομαι | aor.2 ὠσφρόμην |
1 **have perception through the sense of smell, smell** Pl. X. Arist.
2 **deliberately sniff or inhale; smell a fragrance** (fr. wine) E.*Cyc.*; **smell** —W.GEN. *pleasant fragrances* X.; **inhale fumes** —W.GEN. *fr. a burning fruit* Hdt.
3 **catch a smell accidentally or unwillingly; inhale a bad smell** Ar.; **catch a smell** or **whiff** (as of sthg. cooking, garlic, fish, excrement, a fart) Ar. —W.GEN. *of onions* Ar. —*of wine, sthg. cooking* X. Plb.
4 **perceive as though by smell**; (fig.) **get a whiff** (of sthg. dangerous or unwelcome) Ar. —W.GEN. *of sthg. bad* Ar.
5 (of animals) **catch a scent** X. —W.GEN. *of prey, a feared animal, disturbed earth* Hdt. X.; **smell** —W.ACC. *the scent (of an animal)* Hdt.

ὀσφραντήριος ᾱ ον *adj.* **serving as an instrument of smell**; (of nostrils) **olfactory** Ar.(mock-trag.)

ὄσφρησις εως *f.* **sense of smell, smell** Pl. Arist. NT.

ὀσφῦς ύος *f.* 1 **lower part of the trunk of the body; lower back** (wrenched in hard physical work) Men.; **crotch, loins** (as the part of the body usu. clothed, or assoc.w. sexual potency) Ar. NT.
2 **loins** (of a horse, a dog) X.; (of a wasp) Ar.
3 **loin** or **loins** (ref. to a portion of meat fr. a sacrificed or cooked animal) A. Hdt. Ar. Philox.Leuc. Men.

ὅσῳ *dat.neut.sg.relatv.adv.*: see under ὅσος

ὅτα Aeol.*relatv.adv.*: see ὅτε¹

ὅτ-αν, ep. **ὅτ' ἄν** (also **ὅτε κεν**), dial. **ὅκκα** (also **ὅκκᾱ** Theoc.) *relatv. temporal adv.* [ὅτε¹, ἄν¹] 1 (as conj., ref. to an occurrence at an indef. fut. time, w.subj.) **at whatever time, when** Hom. +; (w.fut.indic.) NT.
2 (ref. to a repeated occurrence, w.subj.) **when, whenever** Hom. +; (w.pres. or impf.indic.) Plb. NT.
3 (ref. to a single occurrence in the past, w.aor.indic.) **when, after** Plb. NT.
4 (causal, w.subj.) **when it is the case that, when, as, given that** E. + • καὶ τοῦτο τυφλόν, ὅταν ἐγὼ βλέπω βραχύ *this (my staff) is also blind, given that I see poorly* E.

ὅταν-περ (also **ὅταν περ**) *relatv. temporal adv.* [περ¹] **when** or **whenever** S.*fr.* Isoc. Pl. X.

ὅ-τε¹, Aeol. **ὅτα**, dial. **ὅκα** (also **ὅκκα**) *relatv. temporal adv.* [ὅς¹, τε¹] 1 (as conj., w.indic.) **at the time** or **on the occasion that, when** Hom. +; **from the time when, since** Hom.
2 (ref. to an occurrence prior to that of the main vb., w.aor.indic.) **when, after, as soon as** Hom. +
3 (ref. to an occurrence at an indef. fut. time, w.subj. or opt.) **when** Hom. +
4 (ref. to a repeated action, w.subj. or opt.) **on each occasion that, when, whenever** Hom. +
5 (introducing a simile, w.indic. or subj.) ὡς ὅτε *as when* Hom. Hes. Hellenist.poet.; (w. ellipse of vb.) Hom. hHom. Lyr. • ἤσπαιρ', ὡς ὅτε βοῦς *he struggled, as an ox does* Il.
6 (ellipt.) ἔστιν ὅτε (ἔσθ' ὅτε) *there is a time (there are times) when, at some time, sometimes* Pi. +
7 (causal) **when it is the case that** (usu. w.pres.indic.), **when, as, since** Hom. +

—**ὁτέ**, dial. **ὅκα** *indef.adv.* (in contrastv.cls.) **sometimes, now and then** Hom. + • ὁτὲ μέν ... ὁτὲ δέ (or ἄλλοτε δέ or sim.) *at one time ... at another* Hom. +; (without 1st el.) ὁτὲ δέ *but sometimes* Il. X.

ὅτε² (neut.relatv.pron.): see ὅστε

ὅ τε *ep.neut.adv.*: see under ὅστε

ὅτε-περ (also **ὅτε περ**) *relatv. temporal adv.* [ὅτε¹, περ¹] (w.indic.) **when** Il. +; (w.subj.) **whenever** Il.; (w.opt.) Is.

ὅτευ, ὅτεῳ, ὅτεων, ὁτέοισι (Ion.gen.dat.sg. and pl.relatv.pron.): see ὅστις

ὅτι¹, ep. ὅττι *conj.* [ὅστις] **1** (introducing a compl.cl., esp. after vbs. of thinking or speaking) the fact that, **that** (sthg. is the case) Hom. +; (after impers. δῆλον *it is clear*) Th. Ar. Att.orats. Pl. +
2 (pleon., introducing dir.sp.) Hdt. + • λέγων ὅτι Ἐγὼ εἰ μὴ περὶ πολλοῦ ἡγεύμην … *saying 'If I didn't regard it as very important …'* Hdt.
3 (confirming a previous cl.) S. + • οἶδ' ὅτι *I know this* S. • δῆλον δὴ ὅτι *this is clear, clearly* Pl.
4 οὐχ (or μή) ὅτι (followed by ἀλλά or sim.) *not to say that … but* (i.e. *not only … but*) Th. + • μὴ ὅτι κατὰ τὸ σῶμα ἀλλὰ καὶ κατὰ τὴν ψυχήν *not only in the body but also in the soul* Pl.; (not followed by 2nd cl.) *regardless of the fact that, although in fact* Pl.
5 (causal) **in that, because, since** Hom. +
6 (pleon., w. τί; *why?*) ὅτι τί δή; (or ὅτι δὴ τί; or sim.) *because why?* Ar. Pl. D.

ὅτι² (neut.relatv.pron.adj. and adv.): see ὅστις

ὁτιή *conj.* [reltd. ὅτι¹] **1** the fact that, **that** Ar. Pl.
2 because A.*satyr.fr.* E.*Cyc.* Ar.; (pleon.) ὁτιὴ τί (δή); *because why?* Ar.

ὅτι-περ *conj.* [ὅτι¹, περ¹] **because** Th.

ὅτις, ὅτινα, ὅτινι, ὅτινας (ep.masc.nom.acc.dat.sg., acc.pl.): see ὅστις

ὀτλεύω *vb.* [ὄτλος] (of miners) **bear, endure** —*heavy labour* AR.

ὀτλέω *contr.vb.* | ep.fut.inf. ὀτλησέμεν | **bear, endure** —*toil, calamity, punishment* Call. AR.

ὄτλος ου *m.* **burden, labour** (of bringing up children) A.; **trouble** (in relation to a marriage) S.(dub., v.l. ὄκνος)

ὀτοβέω *contr.vb.* [ὄτοβος] **make a crashing sound** —w.DAT. w. *cymbals* A.*fr.*

ὄτοβος ου *m.* **1 din, crash** (of battle) Hes.; (of thunder) S.
2 clatter (of war-chariots) A.
3 sound, music (of the aulos) S.

ὅτοις, ὅτοισι (masc.neut.dat.pl.relatv.pron.): see ὅστις

ὀτοτοῖ *interj.* —also ὀτοτοτοῖ, ὀτοτοτοτοῖ, ὀτοτοτοτοτοῖ —also ὀτοτοῖ, ὀττοτοῖ (exclam. of extreme pain or grief) **ototoi** (or sim.) Trag.

ὀτοτύζω *vb.* | fut.mid. ὀτοτύξομαι | **wail** Ar.; (mid.) —w.ACC. *for one's head* (which has been beaten) Ar. || PASS. (of a dead man) *be bewailed* A.

Ὀτοτύξιοι ων *m.pl.* **Otoтуxians** (i.e. *Wailers*, coined w. play on Ὀλοφύξιοι *Olophyxians*, a people on the Athos peninsula) Ar.

ὅτου (masc.neut.gen.sg.): see ὅστις

ὀτραλέως *adv.* [reltd. ὀτρύνω] **readily, eagerly** Hom. Hes. Sapph. AR.

ὀτρηρός ά (Ion. ή) όν *adj.* (of servants) **ready, eager** or **busy** Hom. Ar.

—ὀτρηρῶς *adv.* **quickly** Od.

ὄ-τριχες ων *masc.fem.pl.adj.* [copul.prfx., θρίξ] (of mares) **with similar coats** Il.

ὀτρυγη-φάγος ον *adj.* [app. ὀτρύγη *straw*; φαγεῖν] (of a donkey) app. **straw-eating** Archil.

ὀτρυντύς ύος *f.* [ὀτρύνω] **summons** (to an army) Il.

ὀτρύνω *vb.* | ep.inf. ὀτρυνέμεν | impf. ὤτρυνον, iteratv. ὀτρύνεσκον | ep.fut. ὀτρυνέω | aor. ὤτρυνα |
1 rouse (fr. a sitting position, inactivity or sleep) —*a person* Hom.
2 urge (someone) to action; **urge** —*persons* (sts. W.INF. *to do sthg.*) Hom. Hes. Pi. S. AR.; **order, send** —*a messenger, spy,* *servant,* or sim. (sts. W.INF. *to perform a task*) Hom. Pi. E. AR.; **urge on** —*dogs* (against wild animals) Il.
3 (specif.) urge (warriors) to action; **order, drive on** —*men, their strength or spirit, battle formations, chariots* Il. B. S. —W.INF. *to fight, take up the spear* Il. E.
4 (of persons) give impulse to (an activity, by persuasion or command); **press for, urge** —*a journey, a departure* Od.; **send** —*a message* Od.; **rouse** —*the battle, the battle-cry* Il. B.; (of a poet) **set afoot, start** —*a story* Pi.
5 (of things) provide the impulse (for an activity); (of rumour, sthg. said, the heart, stomach, desire) **urge, drive on** —*a person* (sts. W.INF. *to do sthg.*) Il. Pi. AR.; (of strife) —*an Erinys* A.; (of an athletic contest) —*people* (W.PREP.PHR. *to a sacrifice*) Pi.; (of light, fr. a beacon) **spur on** —*the duty of lighting the next* A.
6 ‖ MID. hurry oneself, **hasten** (sts. W.INF. *to do sthg.*) Hom.

ὅττα *Att.f.*: see ὅσσα

ὅττεο, ὅττευ (ep.masc.neut.gen.sg.): see ὅστις

ὀττεύομαι *Att.mid.vb.* [ὄσσα] **hope for a sound** or **voice** (conveying an omen) Ar.

ὅττι¹ *ep.conj.*: see ὅτι¹

ὅττι², ὅττι (ep. and Aeol.neut.sg.relatv.pron.adj. and adv.): see ὅστις

ὅττις, ὅττω, ὅττινες (Aeol.masc.nom.gen.sg., nom.pl.): see ὅστις

ὀττοτοῖ, ὀττοτοτοῖ *interj.*: see ὀτοτοῖ

ὅτῳ, ὅτων (masc.neut.dat.sg., gen.pl.): see ὅστις

οὗ¹ *relatv.adv.*: see under ὅς¹

οὗ² (masc.neut.gen.relatv.pron.): see ὅς¹

οὗ³ (masc.neut.gen.possessv.pron.adj.): see ὅς²

οὗ⁴ (3sg.gen.pers.pron.): see ἕ

οὐ, also (before a vowel) οὐκ, οὐχ *neg.adv.* | In gener., οὐ is used to negate a fact or statement, by contrast w. μή, which is used in expressing a neg. opinion, wish or command. The difference betw. the simple negs. holds true for their cpds. (οὐδέ, μηδέ, οὐδείς, μηδείς, etc.), and cpds. in μη- are treated in the corresponding entries for οὐ-. | For οὐ μή see below; for μὴ οὐ see under μή. |

—A | w. individual wds. |

1 (forming a quasi-cpd. w. the wd. which follows, so as not merely to negate it, but to give it an opposite meaning) **not** Hom. + • οὔ φημι *I do not say* (i.e. *I deny* or *refuse*) Hom. + • οὐκ ἐῶ *I do not allow* (i.e. *I prevent*) Hom. + • οὐκ ὀλίγος, οὐκ ὀλίγοι *not small, not few* (i.e. *great, many*) Hom. + • οὐχ ἥκιστα *not least* (i.e. *most of all*) A. +
2 (negating a noun, usu. w.art.) • τὴν τῶν χωρίων ἀλλήλοις οὐκ ἀπόδοσιν *the failure to restore the territories to each other* Th. • οὐ πάλης ὕπο *through not wrestling* E.

—B | in independent cls. |

1 (w.indic., also w.opt. except in wishes) **not** Hom. +; (w.subj. used in fut. sense) Hom.
2 (in a q., usu. expecting a positive answer) Hom. + • οὔ νυ καὶ ἄλλοι ἔασι; *are there not others?* Il.; (w. 2nd pers. fut.indic., as a command) • οὐκ ἀπαλλάξῃ; *won't you go away?* E.
3 οὔ (so accented, standing alone, w. ellipse of vb.) • οὔκ, ἄν γε ἐμοὶ πείθῃ *not if you listen to me* Pl.

—C | in dependent constrs. |

1 (in cls. introduced by ὅτι, ὡς, after vbs. of saying, knowing, or sim.) **not** Hom. + • λέξω δέ σοι ὡς οὐ δίκῃ γ' ἔκτεινας *I will tell you how you killed unjustly* S.
2 (in causal cls., and in temporal or relatv.cls. except where there is a conditional or final sense) Hom. + • μή με κτεῖν', ἐπεὶ οὐχ ὁμογάστριος Ἕκτορός εἰμι *do not kill me, since I*

οὐά

am not from the same womb as Hector Il. • οὐκ ἔστ' ἐραστὴς ὅστις οὐκ ἀεὶ φιλεῖ *there is no lover who is not always in love* E.
3 (in consecutive cls., after ὥστε, w.indic. or opt.) • ὥστ' οὐ δέδοικα *so that I am not afraid* Isoc.
4 (in conditional cls., w. εἰ and indic., when protasis precedes apodosis) Hom. • εἰ δέ μοι οὐ τίσουσι βοῶν ἐπιεικέ' ἀμοιβήν, δύσομαι εἰς Ἀΐδαο *but if they will not pay me suitable compensation for the cattle, I shall go down to Hades* Od.; (when the sense is causal or the neg. coheres w. an individual wd.) Hom. + μὴ θαυμάσῃς εἰ πολλὰ τῶν εἰρημένων οὐ πρέπει σοι *do not be surprised if much of what has been said does not apply to you* Isoc. • εἰ τοὺς θανόντας οὐκ ἐᾷς θάπτειν *if you forbid burial of the dead* S.
5 (w.inf. in indir.sp., when inf. represents indic. of dir.sp.) Hom. + λέγοντες οὐκ εἶναι αὐτόνομοι *saying that they are not autonomous* Th.
6 (w.ptcpl., stating a fact, opp. a condition) Hom. +
—D | w. duplication or as pleonasm |
1 (followed by cpd.neg.) Hom. + οὐ μιν οἴομαι οὐδὲ πεπύσθαι λυγρῆς ἀγγελίης *I do not think that he has even heard the sad news* Il.
2 (pleon., after vbs. of denying, doubting, disputing) • ἀμφισβητεῖν ὡς οὐχὶ ... δοτέον δίκην *to dispute that it is necessary to be punished* Pl.; (in 2nd part of a compar.phr., usually w.neg. in 1st part) • ἥκει γὰρ ὁ Πέρσης οὐδέν τι μᾶλλον ἐπ' ἡμέας ἢ οὐ καὶ ἐπ' ὑμέας *for the Persian king is coming no more against us than against you* Hdt.
—οὐκί neg.adv. (as last wd. in cl., in phr. ἦε καὶ οὐκί or sim.) not Hom. Theoc.; (as strengthened form of οὐ) Hdt.
—οὐχί neg.adv. (as strengthened form of οὐ) not Parm. Trag. Th. Ar. Att.orats. Pl. +
—οὐ μή emph.neg.adv. **1** (prohibiting, in q., w. 2nd pers.fut.indic.) • οὐ μὴ προσοίσεις χεῖρα μηδ' ἅψῃ πέπλων; *will you not (i.e. do not) lay a hand on me or touch my robes?* E. | cf. οὐ B 2
2 (denying, w.subj., usu.aor.) • οὐ μὴ πίθηται *he will not obey* S.; (rarely w.fut.indic.) • οὔ σοι μὴ μεθέψομαι *I shall not follow you* S.

οὐά interj. [Lat. *uah*] (exclam. of scornful wonder) **aha!** NT.
οὐαί interj. [Lat. *uae*] (exclam. of pain or displeasure) **woe!, alas!** NT.
οὖας ep.n.: see οὖς
οὐατόεις (also **ὠτώεις** Il. Hes.) εσσα εν adj. [οὖς] **1** (of a donkey) **long-eared** Call.
2 (of a tripod-cauldron) **with handles** (envisaged as ears) Il. Hes.; (of a cup) Simon.
οὐ γὰρ ἀλλά (neg. w.pcl. and conj.): see γάρ F
οὐδ-άλλος ου neg.masc.adj. [οὐδέ] **neither** (of two men) Theoc.
οὐδαμά (Aeol. **οὐδάμα**), also **μηδαμά** (Aeol. **μηδάμα**) neg.adv. [οὐδαμοί] **never** Hippon. Thgn. Lyr. A. Emp. Hdt. +
οὐδαμῇ, also **μηδαμῇ** neg.adv. **1 in no place, nowhere** Hes. A. Hdt. Pl. +
2 to no place or in no direction, nowhere Hdt. S. Ar.
3 in no way, by no means, not at all A. Att.orats. +
οὐδαμόθεν, also **μηδαμόθεν** neg.adv. **1 not from any place or source, from nowhere** Th. Isoc. Pl. +; (derog., ref. to a person's ancestry) D.
2 from no side (in a dispute) Is.; (in terms of family connection) Is.
3 (gener.) **not from any source, in no way, not at all** And. D.
οὐδαμόθι neg.adv. not in any place, **nowhere** Hdt.

οὐδ-αμοί, also **μηδαμοί**, αἱ ά neg.pl.pron.adj. [οὐδέ, μηδέ; ἀμός any, reltd. ἀμόθι] **1** (as pron.) **not any, none** Hdt.
2 persons of no consequence, nobodies Hdt.
3 (as adj., of men) **not any, no** Hdt.
οὐδαμοῖ, also **μηδαμοῖ** neg.adv. **not to any place, nowhere** Ar. X. Is. D. Thphr.
οὐδαμόσε, also **μηδαμόσε** neg.adv. **not to any place or not in any direction, nowhere** Th. Pl. D.
οὐδαμοῦ, also **μηδαμοῦ** neg.adv. **1 not in any place, nowhere** Hdt. Trag. Th. +; (w.PARTITV.GEN. in one's right mind, i.e. out of it) E.
2 to no place, nowhere S. E.
3 nowhere (in terms of value, rank or achievement), **nowhere, of no account** Trag. Pl. D.
οὐδαμῶς (dial. **οὐδ' ἀμῶς** Alcm.), also **μηδαμῶς** (Att. **μηθαμῶς** Men.) neg.adv. **not by any means, in no way, not at all** Hdt. Trag. Ar. Att.orats. +
οὖδας εος n. **1 surface of the earth, ground, earth** Hom. Hes. Thgn. Emp. Trag. Hellenist.poet.
2 floor (of a room or house) Hom. hHom. E.; (of a chasm) Hes.
—οὔδασδε adv. **to the ground** Hom.
οὐ-δέ, also **μηδέ** neg.pcl. **1** (as conj., adversative, without a preceding neg.cl., sts. answering μέν) **but not** Hom. + • ἔνθ' ἄλλοις μὲν πᾶσιν ἑήνδανεν, οὐδέ ποθ' Ἥρῃ οὐδὲ Ποσειδάωνι *then it found favour with all the other gods, but never with Hera or Poseidon* Il. • δαινύμενοι τερπώμεθα, μηδὲ βοητὺς ἔστω *let us take pleasure in feasting, but let there be no shouting* Od. • δόλῳ οὐδὲ βίηφι *by trickery, not force* Od.
2 (continuative, without a preceding neg.cl.) **and not** Hom. + • ἂψ δ' ἐς κουλεὸν ὦσε μέγα ξίφος, οὐδ' ἀπίθησεν μύθῳ Ἀθηναίης *he quickly thrust his great sword back into the scabbard and did not disobey Athena's words* Il. • δεινὸν γὰρ οὐδὲ ῥητόν *for it is dreadful and not able to be described* S.
3 (w. a neg.cl. preceding) **and not, nor** Hom. + • οὐ γάρ πω τοίους ἴδον ἀνέρας οὐδὲ ἴδωμαι *for I have not yet seen such men, nor shall I see them* Il. • ἀπὸ τῶν Ἀθηναίων οὐδεμία ἐλπὶς ἦν τιμωρίας οὐδὲ ἄλλη σωτηρία ἐφαίνετο *there was no hope of support from the Athenians, and no other prospect of rescue appeared* Th. | for οὔτε ... οὐδέ see οὔτε 3
4 (w. preceding neg. omitted, but to be understd.) Hdt. + • γῆ δ' οὐδ' ἀὴρ οὐδ' οὐρανὸς ἦν *there was no earth or air or heaven* Ar.
5 (as adv.) **also not, not ... either** S. + • ὕβριν γὰρ οὐ στέργουσιν οὐδὲ δαίμονες *for the gods do not like insolence either (any more than mortals)* S. • ὥσπερ οὖν οὐκ οἶδα, οὐδὲ οἴομαι *just as I don't in fact know, I also don't think I know* Pl.
6 (w. a sense of climax) **not even** Hom. + • οὐδέ με τυτθὸν ἔτισε *he honoured me not even a little* Il. • τότε μὲν εὖ ζῶντες νῦν δὲ οὐδὲ ζῶντες *at that time living well, but now not even living* Pl.
οὐδ-είς (also **μηδείς**) οὐδεμία (μηδεμία) οὐδέν (μηδέν) neg.pron.adj. [εἷς] | also Aeol.fem. οὐδ' ἴα | gen. masc.neut. οὐδενός (μηδενός), fem. οὐδεμιᾶς (Ion. οὐδεμίης, μηδεμίης) || MASC.PL.: nom. οὐδένες (μηδένες), gen. οὐδένων (μηδένων), dat. οὐδέσι | —also **οὐθείς** (**μηθείς**) οὐθέν (μηθέν) Att.adj.
1 (adj., of a person or thing) **not one, no** Hom. +
2 (pron.) **no one, nobody, nothing** Hom. + || MASC.PL. none Hdt. Ar.(cj.) Att.orats. Pl. X.
3 not one, none (w.PARTITV.GEN.PL. of persons or things) Thgn. +

4 (ellipt.phr.) οὐδεὶς ὅστις οὐ *no one who (does) not ... (i.e. everyone does)* Semon. + • οὐδὲν ὅ τι οὐκ ὑπίσχετο *there was nothing that he did not promise* Hdt. • οὐδενὶ ὅτῳ οὐκ ἀποκρινόμενος *replying to everyone* Pl.
5 (both οὐδείς and μηδείς, w. specific or generic ref.) one who is non-existent, worthless or ineffective, **nobody, nonentity, non-person** S. Ar. Pl.; (also w.art.) S. ‖ PL. nobodies, nonentities Hdt. E.; (also w.art.) S. E.
6 ‖ NEUT.SG. (both οὐδέν and μηδέν, as predic. w. εἶναι or ptcpl. ὤν, or w. these understd., ref. to a person or group of persons, a thing or things, either specific or generic) thing of nothingness, nothing (i.e. of no account, worthless, ineffective, ruined, non-existent or virtually so) Pi. Emp. Trag. Ar. Pl. X. +; (also) τὸ μηδέν Hdt. S. E. Ar.; (w.masc.fem. art.) ὁ μηδέν, ἡ μηδέν S.
7 ‖ NEUT.SG. (gener.) nothing (in terms of value) • οὐδενὸς ἄξιος εἶ *you are worthless* Thgn. + • ἐς οὐδὲν ἀνήκει *it amounts to nothing* Hdt. • ἐς τὸ μηδὲν ἥκομεν *we have come to nothing (i.e. to ruin)* E. • λέγοντες οὐδέν *talking nonsense* Hdt. • ταρβῶ μὴ ... θῆται παρ' οὐδὲν τὰς ἐμὰς ἐπιστολάς *I fear that he may treat my letter as of no account* E.
8 ‖ NEUT.SG. (colloq., in answers) it is nothing, no matter, never mind E. Ar.
—**οὐδέν**, also **μηδέν** *neg.neut.adv.* **not at all, in no way, by no means** Hom. +
οὐδέκοτε, οὐδέκω *Ion.neg.advs.*: see οὐδέποτε, οὐδέπω
οὐδενίᾱ ᾱς *f.* [οὐδείς] **worthlessness, uselessness** (of a person) Pl.
οὐδέ-ποτε (also **μηδέποτε**), Ion. **οὐδέκοτε**, Aeol. **οὐδέποκα** *neg.adv.* **never** Thgn. Hdt. S. E. Th. Ar. +
οὐδέ-πω (also **μηδέπω**), Ion. **οὐδέκω** *neg.adv.* **not yet** Alc. A. Hdt. E. Th. Ar. +
οὐδε-πώποτε, also **μηδεπώποτε** *neg.adv.* never at any time at all, **never at all, never ever** S. Th. Ar. Att.orats. +
οὐδ-έτερος, also **μηδέτερος**, ᾱ (Ion. η) ον *neg.adj.* —also **οὐθέτερος** (**μηθέτερος**) ᾱ ον *Att.neg.adj.* not the one nor the other, **neither one, neither** (of two persons or things, sts. W.PARTITV.GEN.PL.) Parm. Hdt. E. Th. Ar. +
—**οὐδέτεροι**, also **μηδέτεροι**, ων *neg.masc.pl.sb.* neither group of men or people; **neither side, party, class** or **group** Hes. +; (in a battle, war or confrontation) Hes. Hdt. Th. Att.orats. +; (in a political or class conflict) Sol. Th. Isoc.; (in a commercial transaction) Hdt.
—**οὐδέτερον**, also **μηδέτερον** *neg.neut.sg.adv.* according to neither one nor the other (of alternatives, sts. W.PARTITV.GEN.PL. τούτων), **neither** Hdt. Att.orats. Pl. +
—**οὐδέτερα**, also **μηδέτερα** *neg.neut.pl.adv.* according to neither one nor the other (of alternatives, sts. W.PARTITV.GEN.PL. τούτων), **neither** Hdt. Att.orats. Pl. +; (in a q. presenting alternatives, or as a response to such a q.) E. Pl.
—**οὐδ' ἑτέρωθεν**, also **μηδετέρωθεν** *neg.adv.* **1 not even from the other side** (in a dispute) Lys.
2 from neither side (of a family line) D.(law)
—**οὐδετέρως**, also **μηδετέρως** *neg.adv.* **in neither way** Pl. Arist.
—**οὐδετέρωσε** (or **οὐδ' ἑτέρωσε**), also **μηδετέρωσε** *neg.adv.* **neither this way nor that, neither to one side nor the other** Il. Thgn. Th.
οὐδός[1] *ep.f.*: see ὁδός
οὐδός[2] *Ion.m.*: see ὀδός
οὖθαρ ατος *n.* **1 udder** (of a female animal, esp. one kept for milk) Od. Hdt. Theoc.; (fig., W.GEN. ἀρούρης *of ploughland*, ref. to richly productive land) Il. hHom.
2 teat (of a woman) A.

οὐθείς *Att.neg.pron.adj.*: see οὐδείς
οὐθέτερος *Att.neg.adj.*: see οὐδέτερος
οὐκ *neg.adv.*: see οὐ
οὐκ-έτι, also **μηκέτι** *neg.adv.* [οὐ, also μή, ἔτι; μηκέτι w. -κ-, by analogy w. οὐκέτι] **1** (temporal) **no longer, no more** (after a point in the past or present) Hom. + • τὸν μὲν δὴ παῖδα εὗρον οἱ μετιόντες οὐκέτι περιεόντα *those who went after him found that the boy was no longer alive* Hdt.
2 (ref. to a time period up to the present, w. possible expectation of future change) **thus far not, not yet** Od. + • εἰ δ' ἀληθέσι κέχρηται τοῖς λόγοις, οὐκέτι τοῦτο τοῖς κρίνουσι γνῶναι ῥᾴδιον ἐξ ὧν ὁ πρότερος εἴρηκεν *it is not yet easy for the jury to decide, from what the first speaker has said, whether he has used arguments which are true* Isoc.
3 (ref. to movt. or spatial extent) **no longer, no further** Hdt. + • τὸ ὦν δὴ ἀπὸ Ἡλίου πόλιος οὐκέτι πολλὸν χωρίον *then beyond Heliopolis there is no longer a large amount of land* Hdt.
4 (ref. to proceeding further in action) **no more, no further** Hom. + • τῷ δ' οὐκέτι δῶρ' ἐτέλεσσαν *they did not go on to give him the gifts* Il. • ἐν δὲ Γέλᾳ ἀντιστάντος αὐτῷ τοῦ πράγματος οὐκέτι ἐπὶ τοὺς ἄλλους ἔρχεται *with fortune going against him at Gela, he did not continue his approach to the other people* Th.
5 no more, never again Hdt. + • κατακοιμηθέντες ἐν αὐτῷ τῷ ἱρῷ οἱ νεηνίαι οὐκέτι ἀνέστησαν *after lying down to sleep in the temple itself, the young men did not get up again* Hdt. • πρὸς οἶκον οὐκέθ' ἵκετο *he never came home again* S.
6 (following on fr. a previous point in an argument) **again not** Att.orats. + • οὐκέτι μοι δοκεῖ, ὦ Σώκρατες, οὗτος θεοῦ νόμος εἶναι *again I do not think, Socrates, that this is a god's law* X.
7 (modifying another adv., esp. temporal, in various senses) Hom. + • οὐκέτ' ἀνεκτῶς *in a way no longer bearable* Hom. • οὐκέτι δηρόν *not for much longer* Hom. hHom. Thgn. • οὐκέτι (μηκέτι) δήν *not any longer* A. AR. • οὐκέτι ὕστερον *not again afterwards* Th. • μηκέτι νῦν *no longer now* Hom. Pl. AR. • οὐκέτ' (μηκέτ') ἔπειτα *then no longer, never hereafter or thereafter* Hom. Hes. AR.
οὐκί *neg.adv.*: see under οὐ
οὐκ-ουν (also **οὐκοῦν**), Ion. **οὐκ ὦν** *neg.pcl.* [οὐ, οὖν] | In general, in οὔκουν the neg. element predominates, in οὐκοῦν the pcl. But accentuation in particular uses is freq. uncertain. Only the most common are illustrated below. |
—**οὔκουν** *neg.pcl.* **1** (introducing a neg. statement) **therefore not** Trag. + • οὔκουν ἀπιστεῖν εἰκός *so it is not reasonable to be sceptical* Th.
2 (introducing an emph. neg. statement, usu. w. γε, as the neg. counterpart of γοῦν) **certainly not** Trag. + • ἐμνήσατ' οὖν ἐμοῦ τι τῷ τότ' ἐν χρόνῳ; —οὔκουν ἐμοῦ γ' ἑστῶτος οὐδαμοῦ πέλας *Did he make any mention of me at that time? —No, at least not when I was standing anywhere nearby* S.
3 (introducing a neg.q., inviting assent) **not therefore, not then** Trag. + • οὔκουν σὺ ταῦτ' ἄριστος εὑρίσκειν ἔφυς; *well, weren't you the best person to discover this?* S.
—**οὐκοῦν** *pcl.* **1** (introducing a strongly affirmative inference or response) **so then, yes indeed** Trag. + • οὐκοῦν ἐπειδὰν πνεῦμα τοὐκ πρῴρας ἀνῇ, τότε στελοῦμεν *so, when the headwind lets up, we shall sail* S. • οὐκοῦν χρή *one surely must* Pl.
2 (introducing a q.) • οὐκοῦν ἐπὶ τούτοις εἰσίω; *so may I come in on these terms?* Ar. • οὐκοῦν σοι δοκεῖ ... ; *so don't you think ... ?* X.
οὔκω, οὔ κως *Ion.neg.advs.*: see πω, οὔπως
οὖλα[1] ων *n.pl.* **gums** (around the teeth) A. Pl.

οὖλα² *neut.pl.adv.*: see under οὖλος²

οὐλαί *Ion.f.pl.*: see ὀλαί

οὐλαμός οῦ *m.* [εἰλέω¹] **1 press, throng** (of warriors) Il. **2 troop** (of cavalry) Plb. Plu.

οὐλάς άδος *f.* [οὖλος²] **knapsack** Call.

οὐλαφη-φόρος ου *m.* [οὖλαφος *corpse*, φέρω] **corpse-bearer, undertaker** Call.

οὖλε *ep.voc.adj.*: see under ὅλος

οὐλή ῆς *f.* **mark of an old wound, scar** Od. E. Pl. X. D. Arist. +

οὔλιος¹ ον *adj.* [οὖλος²] (of a cloak) **woollen** B.

οὔλιος² ᾱ ον *adj.* [reltd. ὀλοός, οὖλος³] **1 associated with destruction or death;** (of a star as a portent) **destructive, deadly** Il.; (of Ares, spears) Hes. Pi.; (of a passion, ref. to Ajax's madness) S. **2** (of the Gorgons' song of lament for Medusa) **full of death** Pi.

οὐλό-θριξ τριχος *masc.fem.adj.* [οὖλος², θρίξ] (of a people) **with thick curly hair** Hdt.

οὐλο-κάρηνος¹ ον *Ion.adj.* [ὅλος, κάρηνον] (of animals being consumed in a fire) **heads and all** hHom.

οὐλο-κάρηνος² ον *adj.* [οὖλος²] (of a person) **with a head of thick curly hair** Od.

οὐλο-κόμης ου *masc.fem.adj.* [κόμη] (of a person) **with thick curly hair** Plu.

οὐλόμενος *ep.aor.2 mid.ptcpl.adj.*: see ὀλόμενος, under ὄλλῡμι

οὖλον *neut.adv.*: see under οὖλος³

οὐλοός *ep.adj.*: see ὀλοός

οὐλό-πους ποδος *Ion.adj.* [ὅλος, πούς] (of animals being consumed in a fire) **feet and all** hHom.

οὖλος¹ *Ion.adj.*: see ὅλος

οὖλος² η ον *adj.* **1** (of garments, rugs, cloth) **woolly, fleecy, thick** Hom. B. Ar. Theoc. **2** (of the hair of a god, a person or a people) **thick and curly or wavy** Od. Hdt. Call. **3** (of the plant anise) **curly** Mosch.; (of garlands) **thickly twined, twisted** Stesich. **4** (quasi-advbl., of the nautilus, envisaged as rowing) **with vigour** Call.*epigr.*
—**οὖλα** *neut.pl.adv.* **1 thickly** —*ref. to smoke surging* Call. **2 vigorously** —*ref. to dancing* Call.

οὖλος³ η ον *adj.* [reltd. ὀλοός] (of Ares, Achilles) **destructive, deadly** Il.; (of Eros) Mosch.; (of passion) AR.; (of a misleading dream) Il.; (of winter) Bion
—**οὖλον** *neut.adv.* **direly, dreadfully** —*ref. to shrieking* (*by birds or warriors under attack*) Il. [also interpr. as reltd. οὖλος², *in dense confusion*]

οὖλος⁴ ου *m.* **sheaf** (of corn) Carm.Pop. [or perh. *bale* (*of wool*)] | cf. ἴουλος 2

οὐλό-φρων ονος *masc.fem.adj.* [οὖλος³, φρήν] (of persons) **of murderous intent** A.

οὐλο-φυής ές *Ion.adj.* [ὅλος, φυή] (of primeval forms) **whole-natured** (i.e. complete and organic) Emp.

οὐλο-χύται ῶν *Ion.f.pl.* [ὀλαί, χυτός] **barley grains for sprinkling** (over a victim at the altar), **sacrificial barley grains** Hom. AR.

Οὐλυμπίᾱ *f.*, **Οὔλυμπος** *ep.m.*: see Ὀλυμπίᾱ, Ὄλυμπος

οὐ μά (pcl. w.neg.): see μά

οὐ μάν (dial.pcl. w.neg.): see μήν¹

οὐμές *Boeot.2pl.pers.pron.*: see ὑμεῖς

οὐ μή *emph.neg.adv.*: see under οὐ

οὐ μήν (pcl. w.neg.), **οὐ μὴν ἀλλά** (pcl., w.neg. and adversative): see μήν¹, ἀλλά 11

οὖν, dial. **ὦν** *pcl.* **1** (as affirmative pcl.) **really, indeed, in fact, with certainty** (attached closely to another wd., esp. another pcl., but reinforcing the whole statement about sthg. which is already mentioned or known) Hom. + • φημὶ γὰρ οὖν κατανεῦσαι ὑπερμενέα Κρονίωνα *for I say with certainty that the supremely mighty son of Kronos gave his promise* Il. **2** (providing emph. to one of opposing or alternative cls.) • εἰ δ᾽ ἔτ᾽ ἐστὶν ἔμψυχος γυνὴ εἴτ᾽ οὖν ὄλωλεν εἰδέναι βουλοίμεθ᾽ ἄν *if the lady is still alive, or whether she is indeed dead, we would like to know* E. • μίαν δὴ σωτηρίαν συνενόουν, λεπτὴν μὲν καὶ ἄπορον, μόνην δ᾽ οὖν *they saw one hope of salvation, a thin and desperate one, but really the only one* Pl. **3** (in question or answer, esp. spoken w. vehemence, impatience, or sim.) • εὖ γὰρ οὖν λέγεις *you are very right in what you say* S. • ἀλλ᾽ οὖν τοσοῦτόν γ᾽ ἴσθι *well then, know this much at least* S. • πῶς οὖν διέζης ἢ πόθεν μηδὲν ποιῶν; *how then have you lived, or on what, since you do nothing?* Ar. • τίς οὖν ἔσται ἡμῶν ὁ πόλεμος; *what then is to be our war?* Th. **4** (strengthening a relatv.adv. or pron.) • δόλοις ὀλούμεθ᾽ ὥσπερ οὖν ἐκτείναμεν *we shall perish by trickery in exactly the same way as we killed* A. • οἱόνπερ οὖν μεμίμηται τῷ ὀνόματι *something of the very sort that has been reproduced in the name* Pl. **5** (appended to relatv.pron. or adv., strengthening an indef. or generalised force) • ἄλλος ὁστισοῦν *anyone else at all* Pl. | see also ὁπηοῦν, ὁποθενοῦν, ὁποιοσοῦν, ὁποιοστισοῦν, ὁποσοσοῦν, ὁποστοσοῦν, ὁποτεοῦν, etc. **6** (in continuing a narrative, esp. after a digression) **so, then** Hom. + • καὶ τὰ μὲν οὖν παρὰ πυθμέν᾽ ἐλαίης ἀθρόα θῆκαν *then they set these things together by the trunk of the olive tree* Od. • ἐπειδὴ οὖν αὐτῷ ... οὐκ ἀπήντησαν, πεῖραν ἐποιεῖτο *so when they did not come out to meet him, he took a gamble* Th. • (sts. in tm. position in Hdt., w.aor.vb., ref. to recurrent events) ἐπὰν ἀποδείρωσι τὸν βοῦν, κατευξάμενοι κοιλίην μὲν κείνην πᾶσαν ἐξ ὧν εἷλον *whenever they skin the bull, after praying they then take out the whole stomach* Hdt. **7** (w. inferential sense) **so, then, therefore, hence** Hdt. + • ἤλθομεν σοὶ χαριζόμενοι μακρὰν ὁδόν· καὶ σὺ οὖν ἡμῖν δίκαιος εἶ ἀντιχαρίζεσθαι *we came on a long journey to render a favour to you; so you too are right to return a favour to us* X. **8** | for μὲν οὖν, μενοῦν see μέν 9

οὕνεκα¹ (also **οὕνεκεν**), dial. **ὤνεκα** *relatv.adv. and conj.* [οὗ², ἕνεκα] **1** (relatv.) **on account of which, for which reason, why** Od. Parm. **2** (as demonstr.) **for that reason, therefore, so** Il. Pi. Parm. **3** (conj.) for the reason that, **seeing that, in that, because, since** Hom. Hes. Thgn. Pi. Trag. Hellenist.poet. **4** (conj., introducing compl.cl. after vbs. of knowing, saying, or sim.) **that** Hom. Hes. Thgn. S. E. Hellenist.poet.

οὕνεκα² *prep.* **by reason, because** —W.GEN. *of someone or sthg.* Eleg. Trag. Ar. D.(quot.epigr.) Hellenist.poet. Plu.

οὔνομα *ep.n.*: see ὄνομα

οὔπερ *relatv.adv.*: see under ὅσπερ

οὔ πη, dial. **οὔπᾱ** *neg.adv.* **in no way** Hom. Ar. Pl.

οὔ-ποτε (and **οὔ ποτε**), dial. **οὔποκα** (and **οὔ ποκα**), also **μήποτε** (and **μή ποτε**), Ion. **μήκοτε** (and **μή κοτε**), dial. **μή ποκα** *neg.adv.* **1 not ever, never** Hom. + **2** (as conj., μή ποτε, κοτε, ποκα) **in case ever** Hom. +

οὔ που *neg.adv.*: see που, under ποῦ

οὔπω (and **οὔ πω**), also **μήπω** (and **μή πω**) *neg.advs.*: see πω

οὐ-πώποτε (and **οὐ πώποτε**), also **μηπώποτε** (and **μή πώποτε**) *neg.adv.* [πώποτε] **never yet** A. E. Th. Ar. Pl. X. +

οὔ-πως (also **οὔ πως**), Ion. **οὔ κως**, also **μή πως**, Ion. **μή κως** *neg.adv.* **1 not in any way, not at all** Hom. Hes.*fr.* hHom. Hdt. Th.(dub., v.l. οὔπω) Call.
2 (as conj., μή πως, μή κως) **in case in any way, in case perhaps** Hom. Hes. Thgn. Hdt. Ar. Pl. +

οὐρά ᾶς, Ion. **οὐρή** ῆς *f.* [reltd. ὄρρος] **1 tail** (of an animal or mythical creature) Hom. Hes. Hdt. E. X. Plu.
2 rearguard, rear (of an army) X. Thphr. Plb. Plu.

οὐρᾱγέω *contr.vb.* [οὐρᾱγός] (of an armed force or its leader) **be the rearguard** (of an army) Plb. Plu.

οὐρᾱγίᾱ ᾱς *f.* armed force protecting the rear (of an army) or the duty of doing so; **rearguard** Plb. Plu.

οὐρ-ᾱγός οῦ *m.* [οὐρά, ἄγω] **rearguard officer** X.; (ref. to a rank in the Roman army, Lat. *optio*) Plb.

οὐραῖος ᾱ (Ion. η) ον *adj.* **1** (of horsehair) **of the tail** Il.; (of a dove's feathers) AR.
2 (of feet) of the hind part (of an animal), **hind** Theoc.
3 ‖ NEUT.SB. tail (of a fish) Men.; (pl., of the constellation Bear) E.

Οὐρανίᾱ ᾱς, Ion. **Οὐρανίη** ης *f.* [οὐρανός] **1 Ourania** (one of the nine Muses, daughter of Ouranos) Hes. B. Pl.
2 Ourania (daughter of Okeanos and Tethys) Hes.; (attending upon Persephone) hHom.
3 Ourania (title of Aphrodite) Hdt. Pl. X. Theoc.*epigr.*; (title of other eastern goddesses identified w. her) Hdt.

Οὐρανίδης *m.*: see under Οὐρανός

οὐράνιος ᾱ (Ion. η) ον (also ος ον) *adj.* **1 of or relating to heaven**; (of gods and things relating to them) **heavenly, celestial** hHom. S. E. +; (opp. chthonic) Lyr.adesp. Pl. Plu.; (as epith. of particular deities) Pi.*fr.* Hdt. S. E. +; (of God) NT. ‖ NEUT.PL.SB. heavenly things (opp. earthly or human) Pl.
2 of or relating to the sky; (of the vault or mansion, the light, air) **of the heavens** Trag. Tim.; (of stars and other bodies) **in the sky** Simon. A. Pi. Pl. +; (of weather phenomena) **in** or **from the sky** Pi. S. E. Ar. Plb.; (of a portent or vision) X. AR. NT. Plu.; (of a divine statue fallen to earth) E. ‖ NEUT.PL.SB. heavenly bodies or phenomena (esp. as a subject for study) Pl. X. Arist. Plu.
3 (hyperbol.) as high or wide as the sky; (of a mountain, tree branch, walls) **towering sky-high** Pi. E.; (of shouting in supplication, laments, flames of disaster) **reaching to high heaven** A. S.
4 in the direction of the sky; (of the leap of a fawn; quasi-advbl., of a leg flung by a dancer) **skyward, high in the air** E. Ar.; (of a noose) **on high** E.
5 (advbl.phr.) οὐράνιον ὅσον **as high or great as heaven** —*ref. to shouting, making a mistake* Ar.
—**οὐρανίᾱν** *fem.acc.adv.* **skyward, high in the air** —*ref. to a dancer kicking out* Ar.
—**οὐράνια** *neut.pl.adv.* **to high heaven** —*ref. to a noise sounding* E.

Οὐράνιος ᾱ ον *adj.* [Οὐρανός] (of the offspring) **of Ouranos** (ref. to Kronos and the Titans) A.

οὐρανίσκος ου *m.* [dimin. οὐρανός] **canopy** (over a throne) Plu.

οὐρανίωνες ων *m.pl.* **1 heavenly ones** (ref. to the gods, sts. appos.w. θεοί) Hom. Hes. hHom. Theoc.
2 sons of Ouranos (ref. to the Titans) Il.

οὐρανό-δεικτος ον *adj.* [δείκνῡμι] (of the moon's gleam) **displayed in heaven** hHom.

οὐρανόθεν, **οὐρανόθι** *advs.*: see under οὐρανός

οὐρανο-μήκης ες *adj.* [μῆκος] (usu. hyperbol.) in length or height as great as the sky or heaven; (of the sound of thunder) **spanning the sky** Ar.; (of the light fr. sacrificial fire) **reaching up to heaven** A.; (of trees) **towering sky-high** Od. Hdt.; (of fame, renown, evil) Simon. Ar. Isoc. Arist.

οὐρανό-νῑκος ον *adj.* [νίκη] (of Hera's anger) **prevailing in heaven** A.

οὐρανός οῦ, dial. **ὠρανός** ῶ, Aeol. **ὤρανος** (also **ὄρανος**) ω *m.* **1 sky, heaven** or **heavens** (above the earth and sea) Hom. +; (held up by Atlas) Od. Hes. A. Pi. Hdt. E. +; (described as of bronze or iron) Hom. Pi. Ar. +; (as the place of the sun, moon or stars, dawn, day or night) Hom. +
2 sky (as the abode of immortal beings); **heaven** Hom. Hes. Archil. Lyr. Trag. +; (situated around Olympos) Il. Hes.; (reached by sacrificial fire, prayer, an oath, a boast) Hom. +
3 sky (as the place where portents appear, fr. which objects of divine origin fall) Il. B. Hdt. E. Ar. +
4 (philos.) **heavens, universe** Pl. Arist.
5 sky (as the place of air or weather phenomena, clouds, rain, thunder and lightning) Od. +; (as the place of such phenomena over a region) **climate** Hdt.
6 sky (as the place of the utmost height or breadth, esp. in hyperbol. statements) Hom. Hes. Lyr. Hdt. E.*fr.* Ar. +; (reached or pervaded by sthg. vast: a mountain peak or an edifice, a wave, cloud of dust or arrows, fire or smoke, extraordinary fragrance or brightness) Hom. Hes. Hdt. E. Ar.; (by the noise of masses on the move, fighting, shouting) Hom. Hes. E. Ar.; (by someone's fame, misfortune, wickedness, or sim.) Hom. Trag. Ar.
7 ‖ DAT. (or ACC. in prep.phr.) **skywards, into the air** (as a direction towards which one looks, listens, stretches out arms, leaps, throws, is tossed, or sim.) Hom. S. E. Ar. +
—**οὐρανόθεν**, dial. **ὠρανόθεν** *adv.* **from heaven** or **the sky** Hom. Hes. Stesich. Call. AR. NT.; (also) ἀπ' οὐρανόθεν Hom. Hes.; ἐξ οὐρανόθεν Il.
—**οὐρανόθι** *adv.* **in the sky** Il.

Οὐρανός οῦ *m.* **Ouranos** (son of Erebos and Gaia) Hes. +; (of Khaos and Eros) Ar. +; (husband of Gaia, father of Kronos, the Titans, Mnemosyne and others) Hes. hHom. A. Pi. E.; (invoked as witness to an oath) Il. AR.
—**Οὐρανίδης** ου, dial. **Οὐρανίδᾱς** ᾱ *m.* **son of Ouranos** (ref. to Kronos) Hes. Pi. AR. ‖ PL. sons of Ouranos (ref. to the Titans) Hes. Call.; (gener.) heavenly ones (sts. appos.w. θεοί) Pi. E. AR. Theoc.

οὐρανοῦχος ον *adj.* [ἔχω] (of the rule of the gods) **occupying heaven** A.

οὔρεα (ep.nom.acc.pl.), **οὔρεϊ** (ep.dat.sg.): see ὄρος

οὔρειος *dial.adj.*: see ὄρειος

οὔρεος (ep.gen.): see ὄρος

οὐρεσι-βώτᾱς ᾱ *dial.masc.adj.* [ὄρος, βόσκω] (of wild animals) **mountain-grazing** S.

οὐρεύς Ion.*m.*: see ὀρεύς

οὐρέω *contr.vb.* [οὖρον¹] | fut. οὐρήσω, also οὐρήσομαι | **urinate** Hes. Hdt. Ar. X.

οὐρή Ion.*f.*: see οὐρά

οὐρητιάω *contr.vb.* [desideratv. οὐρέω] **want to urinate** Ar.

οὐρίαχος ου *m.* [reltd. οὐρά] **lower end, butt** (of a spear-shaft) Il. AR.

οὐριβάτᾱς *dial.m.*: see ὀρειβάτης

οὐρίζω¹ *Ion.vb.*: see ὁρίζω

οὐρίζω² *vb.* [οὖρος¹] | fut. οὐριῶ | aor. οὔρισα | **1** (fig.) **send with a fair wind** —*a message (to the underworld)* A.

οὐρίθρεπτος

2 (of a ruler) **give a fair wind to** —*a land* (*struggling in a sea of troubles*) S.
3 (intr., of the wind of fortune) **blow favourably** A.

οὐρί-θρεπτος ᾱ ον *dial.adj.* [ὄρος, τρέφω] (of a heifer) **mountain-bred** E.

οὔριος (also perh. dial. **ὤριος** Theoc.) ᾱ (Ion. η) ον (also ος ον) *adj.* [οὖρος¹] **1** (of a wind) **fair, favourable** (for sailing) E. Th. X. Plb. Plu.; (of an oar, sail or wave, meton. for a voyage or the wind) S. E. Ar.; (of a voyage, course or enterprise, sts. fig.ref. to one's fortune) Trag.; (of circumstances) Theoc.(v.l. ὥριος) ‖ FEM.SB. fair or following wind Archil. B. Pl. Plb. ‖ NEUT.PL.SB. (in prep.phr.) ἐξ οὐρίων *with fair winds* S.
2 (of Zeus) **sending a fair wind, favourable** A.
3 (fig., of a fan, for raising fire) **producing a fair wind** Ar.
4 (of sacrificial blood) **flowing strong, propitious** E.
—**οὔρια** *neut.pl.adv.* **with a favourable wind** Ar.

οὐριο-στάτᾱς ᾱ *dial.masc.adj.* [ἵστημι] (fig., of a song) **setting the wind fair** or **with wind set fair** (i.e. causing or assoc.w. good fortune) A.

οὔρισμα *Ion.n.*: see ὅρισμα

οὖρον¹ ου *n.* **urine** Hdt.

οὖρον² ου *n.* [perh.reltd. οὖρος³] **1** (sg. and pl.) app. **limit, range** (W.GEN. of mules, ref. to the amount of land which they can plough in a given time) Hom.
2 ‖ PL. limits, range (W.GEN. of a discus, when thrown) Il.
3 ‖ PL. boundaries (of a territory) AR.

οὐρός οῦ *m.* app., **trench in the ground** ‖ PL. **slipways** (for boats to be hauled in or out of the water) Il.

οὖρος¹ ου *m.* **1 good wind** (for sailing); **favourable, fair** or **brisk wind** Hom. hHom. Pi. B. Hdt.(oracle) Trag. +
2 (fig.) **fair wind** (W.GEN. of a poet's song) Pi.; (ref. to a time which is good for action) S.; (as an agent which speeds a person on a fortunate course or out of trouble, or a bad person or circumstance away fr. one) Pi. Trag.

οὖρος² ου *m.* [reltd. ὁράω] **overseer, protector** (of property, during one's absence) Od.; (W.GEN. of a people, ref. to Nestor, Achilles) Hom. Pi.; (of Crete, ref. to Talos) AR.

οὖρος³ *Ion.m.*: see ὅρος

οὖς, dial. **ὦς**, ὠτός *n.* ‖ PL.: nom.acc. ὦτα, dial. ὤατα, gen. ὤτων, dat. ὠσί ‖ —also **οὖας** οὔατος *ep.n.* **1 ear** (freq.pl.) Hom. +; (of animals, esp. a dog or horse, sts. as indicating mood or behaviour) Od. Hes. Hdt. S. E. Ar. +; (as torn or scarred, the characteristic of a boxer, esp. as freq. amongst the Spartans) Pl. Theoc.; (provb.) τὸν λύκον τῶν ὤτων ἔλαβον *they caught hold of the wolf by the ears* (i.e. *did sthg. dangerous or fatal*) Plb.
2 ear (as the organ of hearing, paying attention and understanding) Hom. +; (as not leading to understanding, or not to be trusted) Heraclit. Hdt. +; (as receiving whispered or confidential words) S. E. Pl. +
3 person who acts as an **ear** (for another); **ear** (ref. to an officer under a ruler, esp. the Persian king) X. Arist.
4 ear, handle (of a cup or cauldron) Il.

οὖσα (Att.fem.ptcpl.): see εἰμί

οὐσίᾱ ᾱς, Ion. **οὐσίη** ης *f.* [εἰμί] **1** that which exists as a possession or is owned (by a man, family, men of a city-state); **property, means** Hdt. E. Th. Ar. Att.orats. +; (pl.) Att.orats. +; φανερὰ οὐσία *real estate* Att.orats.; ἀφανὴς οὐσία *personal or movable property* Att.orats.
2 (philos.) quality of being real or existing, **being, existing, existence** Pl. Arist. ‖ PL. realities or existences Pl. Arist.
3 that which makes a thing what it is, **underlying** or **essential nature, essence, substance** Pl. Arist.; (opp. πάθος *attribute* or *property*) Pl. Arist.; (as that which defines a being) Pl. Arist.; (considered in terms of a being's form, opp. matter) Arist.

οὐτάζω *vb.* ‖ fut. οὐτάσω ‖ aor. οὔτασα ‖ pf.pass. οὔτασμαι ‖ —also **οὐτάω** *contr.vb.* ‖ ep.imperatv. οὔταε ‖ aor. οὔτησα ‖ 3sg.iteratv.aor. οὐτήσασκε ‖ aor.pass.ptcpl. οὐτηθείς ‖ also (as if fr. οὔτημι) ep.athem.aor.: 3sg. οὖτα, inf. οὐτάμεναι, οὐτάμεν, ptcpl. (w.pass.sens.) οὐτάμενος ‖ also 3sg.iteratv.impf. οὔτασκε ‖

1 strike (w. a weapon, usu. a spear or sword, sts. a missile) so as to wound or cause damage; **strike** —*a person* (esp. an enemy warrior), *part of the body, horse, shield* Hom. Hes. Tyrt. E. —*a person* (W.ACC. in a part of the body) Hom. —*a wild boar, bulls' flanks* AR.; (of Zeus) —*a person* (W.DAT. *w. a thunderbolt*) E. ‖ PASS. (of persons) **be struck or wounded** Hom. A. AR.; (of a shield) **be struck** Hes.
2 (intr.) **strike a blow** Hes. AR. ‖ MID. (of two warriors) **exchange blows** Il.
3 inflict —*a wound* (W.ACC. on someone) Il. ‖ PASS. (of a wound) **be inflicted** Il.
4 (of a sword) **strike** —W.INTERN.ACC. *a blow* A.

οὖτᾱν (Boeot.fem.acc.): see οὗτος

οὔ-τε, also **μήτε** *neg.conj.* ‖ The conj. corresponds to μή, as οὔτε to οὐ. ‖ **1 and not, neither, nor** Hom. +; (most freq., repeated in order to join two wds. or cls.) οὔτε ... οὔτε, μήτε ... μήτε *neither ... nor* Hom. + • οὔτ' ἐς δαῖτ' ἰέναι οὔτ' ἐν μεγάροισι πάσασθαι *neither to go to the feast nor to dine in the hall* Il. • μήτε σύ γ' Ἄρηα τό γε δείδιθι μήτε τιν' ἄλλον ἀθανάτων *do not fear Ares as regards this nor any other of the immortals* Il. • (repeated twice) ἄλγος ... οὔτ' αὐτῆς Ἑκάβης οὔτε Πριάμοιο ἄνακτος οὔτε κασιγνήτων *grief neither for Hecuba herself nor for king Priam nor for my brothers* Il. • (after a neg.) ὡς δὲ οὐκ ἔπειθεν οὔτε τοὺς στρατηγοὺς οὔτε τοὺς στρατιώτας *and when he failed to persuade either the generals or the soldiers* Th. • (w. the first neg.conj. omitted) ναυσὶ δ' οὔτε πεζὸς ἰών *travelling neither by ship nor on foot* Pi.
2 οὔτε ... τε *not ... but, not only not ... but also* Hom. + • τῷ νῦν μήτ' ἀπόληγε κέλευέ τε φωτὶ ἑκάστῳ *now do not stop, but call to each man* Il. • καὶ μήτε κινδύνευε σωθήτω τέ μοι τέκνα *and do not put yourself in danger, and let my children be saved as well* E. • ἰδὼν δὲ οὔτε ἐξεπλάγη ἐντός τε ἑωυτοῦ γίνεται *at this sight he was not only not astounded but also kept his composure* Hdt.
3 οὔτε ... οὐδέ *not ... but not* Od. + • νῦν δ' οὔτ' ἄρ πη θέσθαι ἐπίσταμαι, οὐδὲ μὲν αὐτοῦ καλλείψω *as things are I do not know of anywhere to put this, but I will not leave it here* Od.; (w. οὐδέ introducing a third neg. item) οὔτε πόλις οὔτε πολιτεία οὐδέ γ' ἀνήρ *neither a city-state nor a constitution nor yet a man* Pl.
4 οὔτε ... δέ (w. the second cl. introducing some opposition) *not ... and furthermore, not ... but* Il. + • οὔτ' αὐτός νέος ἐσσί, γέρων δέ τοι οὗτος ὀπηδεῖ *you are not young yourself and furthermore this old man is your companion* Il. • ἀλλὰ δὴ ἐκεῖ μὲν οὔτε πλοῖά ἐστιν οἷς ἀποπλευσούμεθα, μένουσι δὲ αὐτοῦ οὐδὲ μιᾶς ἡμέρας ἔστι τὰ ἐπιτήδεια *but there we have no ships in which to sail away, but if we remain here we have provisions for not so much as a single day* X.
5 (preceded or followed by οὐ) οὐ ... οὔτε *not ... nor*, οὔτε ... οὐ *neither ... nor* Hom. + • οὔ τις ἀνὴρ προπάροιθε μακάρτατος οὔτ' ἄρ' ὀπίσσω *no man in the past was so blessed nor indeed shall ever be hereafter* Od. • οὔτε γὰρ τότε λόγοις ἐτέγγεθ' ἥδε νῦν τ' οὐ πείθεται *she was not softened by my words then and she is not listening to me now* E. • τοὺς οὔτε νιφετός, οὐκ ὄμβρος, οὐ καῦμα, οὐ νὺξ ἔργει μὴ οὐ

καταινύσαι τὸν προκείμενον αὐτῷ δρόμον *these men are stopped neither by snow nor rain nor heat nor darkness from accomplishing their appointed course* Hdt. • (w. οὐ preceding οὔτε ... οὔτε) οὐ νιφετός, οὔτ' ἄρ χειμὼν πολὺς οὔτε ποτ' ὄμβρος *there is no snow, nor heavy storm, nor ever rain* Od. **6** (paired w. μήτε, according to their respective normal usage) Hdt. + • ἐγὼ δὲ θρασὺς μὲν καὶ βδελυρὸς καὶ ἀναιδὴς οὔτ' εἰμὶ μήτε γενοίμην *I am not reckless, loathsome and shameless, nor may I ever be* D.

οὕτερος (Ion.masc.nom.): see ἕτερος

οὐτιδανός ή όν neg.adj. [οὖτις] **1** (derog., of men) **of no account, worthless** (esp. in terms of strength or honour) Hom. Mosch.; (of the Satyrs) Hes.*fr.* ‖ MASC.PL.SB. good-for-nothings Il. **2** (of surging waves, fig.ref. to devastation) **bringing all to nothing** A.

οὖτις (and **οὔ τις**) οὔτι (and οὔ τι), also **μήτις** (and **μή τις**), μήτι (and μή τι) *neg.pron.adj.* | gen. οὔτινος (οὔ τινος), μήτινος (μή τινος) | **1** (as adj., of persons or things) **not any, no** Hom. Hes. Archil. Thgn. Pi. Trag. + **2** (as pron.) **no one, nobody, nothing** Hom. + **3 not any, none** (W.PARTITV.GEN.PL. of persons or things) Hom. Hes. Pi. B. Trag. + **4** (as conj., μή τις) **in case anyone** Hom. +

—**οὔτι** (and **οὔ τι**), also **μήτι** (and **μή τι**) *neg.neut.adv.* **1 by no means, not at all** Hom. Hes. Archil. Ibyc. Eleg. Hdt. + | for οὔ τί που see που 3, under ποῦ **2** μή τι γε *let alone, much less* D. Plu.; (also) μή τι γε δή D.; μή τι δή Plb.; μή τι δὴ ... γε Pl.

Οὖτις m. | only nom., and acc. Οὖτιν | **No One** (name assumed by Odysseus to deceive Polyphemos) Od. E.*Cyc.* Ar.

οὔ-τοι (and **οὔ τοι**), also **μήτοι** (and **μή τοι**) *neg.pcl.* [τοι[1]] **assuredly not, not at all** Hom. Hes. Archil. Thgn. Lyr. Hdt. Trag. +

οὗτος, fem. **αὕτη** (dial. **αὕτᾱ**), neut. **τοῦτο**, gen. τούτου ταύτης (dial. ταύτᾱς) τούτου *demonstr.pron. and adj.* | Boeot.fem.acc. οὕτᾱν | Ion.fem.gen.pl. τουτέων | neut.pl. ταῦτα | **1** (adj., of persons or things) **the one which is immediately present in place or time or is the current object of attention, this** Hom. + **2** (pron.) **this person or thing, he, she, this** Hom. + **3** (specif., contrasted w. ὅδε, to designate that which is more remote) • Φόρκυνος μὲν ὅδ' ἐστὶ λιμήν ... τοῦτο δέ τοι σπέος *this is the harbour of Phorkys, and that is the cave* Od.; (to designate what precedes, opp. what follows) • οὐκ ἔστι σοι ταῦτ', ἀλλὰ σοὶ τάδ' ἐστί *that is not for you, but this is* S. **4** (contrasted w. ἐκεῖνος, to designate that which is the closer in time, place or thought) • οὗτος μὲν ... ἐκεῖνος δέ *the latter ... the former* Pl. • (designating the more important, not the grammatically closer) τοῦτο παρέντες ἐκεῖνο ποιοῦσι *overlooking this* (the better course of action) *they do that* (the worse) D. | For the phr. οὗτος ἐκεῖνος, see ἐκεῖνος 6. **5** (defined by what follows) • ὀνομαστὸς ἐπὶ τούτῳ γέγονε *he has become famous for the following reason* X. • (antecedent to a relatv.pron.) τοῦτο δέ τοι ἐρέω, ὅ μ' ἀνείρεαι *I will tell you what you ask me* Hom. • (responding to relatv.) καὶ μεῖζον' ὅστις ἀντὶ τῆς αὑτοῦ πάτρας φίλον νομίζει, τοῦτον οὐδαμοῦ λέγω *and the man who considers a friend more important than his own country, him I put nowhere* S. **6** (the one which is known to the hearer or to people in general) • οἱ τὰς τελετάς ... οὗτοι καταστήσαντες *those people who established the rituals* Pl. **7** (calling attention) • οὗτος, τί ποιεῖς; *you there, what are you doing?* A.

8 (contemptuous) • ὁ πάντ' ἄναλκις οὗτος *this utterly feeble person* S. **9** (heightening the effect of an added phr.) καὶ οὗτος *and that moreover* Hdt. + • δι' ἑνὸς αὐλῶνος καὶ τούτου στεινοῦ *through a single gorge, and a narrow one at that* Hdt. • ναυτικῷ ἀγῶνι καὶ τούτῳ πρὸς Ἀθηναίους *in a naval conflict, and that against Athenians* Th. **10** (neut.pl., colloq., acquiescing in a request or command) *I will do that* Ar. Men. **11** (prep.phrs.) πρὸς ταῦτα *in view of that, therefore* Hdt. Trag. +; ἐν τούτῳ *in the meantime* Hdt. S. Th. +; πρὸς τούτοις (τούτοισι) *on top of that, in addition* A. Hdt. +

—**οὑτοσί** αὑτηί τουτί *demonstr.pron. and adj.* **1** (w. stronger force) **he, she, this** A.*satyr.fr.*(cj.) S.*Ichn.* E.*Cyc.* Ar. Att.orats. Pl. + **2** (w. a pcl. interposed before suffix) αὑτηγί, ταυταγί, τουτογί, τουτονγί (for -ί γε) Ar. Men.; ταυτηνδί, τουτοδί (for -ί δέ) Ar.; τουτουμενί (for -ί μέν) Ar.

—**ταύτῃ**, dial. **ταύτᾱ** *fem.dat.adv.* **1 in this place, here** Hdt. S. E. Th. + **2 to this place, here** E. **3 by this way** or **in this direction** Hdt. Th. + **4 in this way, thus** Hdt. Trag. +; **in this respect** Hdt. **5 on this side** (in a matter of judgement or dispute) Hdt. S. E.(cj.) Lys. Ar.(cj.) +

—**ταῦτα** *neut.pl.adv.* **1 for that reason, that is why** Il. +; (also sg. τοῦτο) S. + **2** καὶ ταῦτα (adding a circumstance which heightens the effect of what has been said) *and that moreover* A. + • ἥτις τοιαῦτα τὴν τεκοῦσαν ὕβρισεν, καὶ ταῦτα τηλικοῦτος *who has abused her mother in this way, and that at her age* S.

οὕτω(ς) *adv.* | also strengthened form οὑτωσί (Ar. Att.orats. +) | **1 in this manner** or **way, thus, so** Hom. +; (in expressing similarity or a comparison, freq. in correlation w. ὡς, ὥσπερ) • οὕτω ῥᾷον ἢ 'κείνως *easier in this way than in that way* Pl. • ὥσπερ δὲ κύων γενναῖος ἄπειρος ἀπρονοήτως φέρεται πρὸς κάπρον, οὕτω καὶ ὁ Κῦρος ἐφέρετο *as a well-bred untrained hound rushes recklessly upon a boar, so too Cyrus rushed on* X. **2** (ref. forward to a following dir. or indir. statement, freq. in correlation w. ὡς, ὥσπερ, ὥστε) **in the manner about to be indicated, as follows, thus, so** Hom. + • ἀλλ' οὕτω χρὴ ποιεῖν *but we must do as follows* X. • ἔστιν γὰρ οὕτως ὥσπερ οὗτος ἐννέπει *for it is like this, just as this man says* S. • συντεθεὶς δ' ὁ πᾶς λόγος κτενεῖ νιν οὕτως ὥστε μηδαμοῦ φυγεῖν *the whole case put together will so surely cause her death that there will be no escape* E. **3** (in beginning a story) • οὕτως ἦν νεανίσκος Μελανίων τις *once upon a time there was a young man called Melanion* Ar. **4** (after a preceding statement, freq. w. emph. inferential sense) **in the manner previously indicated, in this way, thus, so, therefore** Hom. + • οὕτω ὦν, ὦ Κροῖσε, πᾶσά ἐστι ἄνθρωπος συμφορή *so, Croesus, a human being is altogether a thing of chance* Hdt. • τούτων μὲν οὕτω *so much then for these things* A. **5** (after a preceding ptcpl. or temporal cl.) • ὑπὲρ μεγίστων καὶ καλλίστων κινδυνεύσαντες οὕτως τὸν βίον ἐτελεύτησαν *after undergoing danger in the cause of what is greatest and finest they thus came to the end of their lives* Lys. • ἐπειδὴ περιελήλυθε ὁ πόλεμος καὶ ἀπίκται ἐς ὑμέας, οὕτω δὴ Γέλωνος μνῆστις γέγονε *since war has come round and reached you, now there is thought of Gelon* Hdt. **6** (ref. to a preceding description) • ἀλλὰ ταῦτα μὲν θεῶν τις ἐξέπραξεν ὥσθ' οὕτως ἔχειν *but some god brought it about that these things should be so* E. • οὐ μέντοι τοσοῦτός γε

λοιμὸς οὐδὲ φθορὰ οὕτως ἀνθρώπων οὐδαμοῦ ἐμνημονεύετο γενέσθαι *but such a great plague and death on this scale was nowhere remembered to have occurred* Th. • οὕτως οὐδέποτε εἴδομεν *we have never seen the like* NT.
7 (introducing an imprecation backing up a strong statement) • οὕτως ὀναίμην τῶν τέκνων, μισῶ τὸν ἄνδρ' ἐκεῖνον *as surely as I would wish to have the benefit of my children, I hate the man* Ar.
8 (in confirming a statement or answering a q.) • ἔσσεται οὕτως *so shall it be* Od. • οὕτως *as you say, quite so* Pl. +
9 (w.adj. or adv.) **so, so very, so excessively** Hom. + • καλὸν δ' οὕτω ἐγὼν οὔ πω ἴδον *I have never seen so fine a man* Il. • οὕτως εὐπετέως *so easily* Hdt.
10 (ref. to the situation underlying an indignant q. or command) **just like that, without further ado** Hom. + • εἰπεῖν τι δώσεις ἢ στραφεὶς οὕτως ἴω; *will you allow me to speak or shall I turn and just go?* S. • ἔρρ' οὕτως *just get away* Il.
11 (w. a limiting function) • μὴ διὰ μέθης ... ἀλλ' οὕτω πίνοντας πρὸς ἡδονήν *not in a state of drunkenness, but drinking only enough for pleasure* Pl. • νῦν μὲν οὕτως οὐκ ἔχω εἰπεῖν *just right now I have nothing to say* Pl.

οὐχ *neg.adv.*: see οὐ
οὐχί *neg.adv.*: see under οὐ
οὐψι-βίας āo *Boeot.masc.adj.* [ὕψι, βίᾱ] (of the sons of Orion) **tall and powerful** Corinn.
οὐψόθεν *Boeot.adv.*: see ὑψόθεν, under ὕψι
ὀφειλέτης ου *m.* — also **ὀφειλέτις** ιδος (E.) *f.* [ὀφείλω] **1 one who is indebted** (to another, for benefits received) Pl. Plu.
2 one who is under an obligation (W.DAT. + INF. to someone, to do sthg.) S. E.
3 (specif., in financial ctxt.) **debtor** Plb. NT.
4 one who is guilty of an offence (against another, against God), **offender** NT.
ὀφειλή ῆς *f.* financial obligation, **debt** NT.
ὀφείλημα ατος *n.* **1** obligation owed (to the gods, family, friends, for benefits received), **obligation** Th. Pl.
2 financial obligation (freq. in ctxts. where there is failure to pay), **debt** D. Arist. Plb.
3 offence, wrong (done to another) NT.
ὀφείλω, ep. **ὀφέλλω** *vb.* | impf. ὤφειλον, ep. ὤφελλον, also ὄφειλον, ὄφελλον | fut. ὀφειλήσω | aor.1 ὠφείλησα | aor.2 ὤφελον, ep. ὄφελον | plpf. ὠφειλήκειν ‖ PASS.: aor.1 ptcpl. ὀφειληθείς |
1 be under obligation to pay or repay (a debt or favour, w. goods, money, a service, or sim.); **owe** —*recompense, gratitude, a contribution, or sim.* (sts. W.DAT. *to a person or god*) Hom. + —*a song* (*to an athletic victor*) Pi.; (intr.) **be indebted** —W.DAT. *to someone* (W.GEN. *for sthg.*) A.*satyr.fr.* ‖ PASS. (of a debt of obligation or sim.) be owed Hom. + ‖ IMPERS.PASS. it is owed or due —W.DAT. + INF. *to someone to receive gratitude* Lys.
2 ‖ PASS. (of harm, enmity, or sim.) be due in requital Pl. +
3 be under obligation to pay (a penalty); **be liable for** —*a penalty, fine, damages, or sim.* Od. + ‖ PASS. (of a penalty or sim.) be owed Att.orats.
4 owe (money, to a state treasury or an individual); **owe, be liable for** —*a sum of money, a debt, wage, or sim.* Hdt. +; (intr.) owe money, be a debtor Hdt. + ‖ PASS. (of money or sim.) be owed Th. +
5 (gener.) **be bound by obligation** (to do sthg. that is appropriate or necessary); **be obliged, be duty-bound, ought** —W.INF. *to do or not do sthg.* Il. +; (impf. or aor.2, w.connot. of failure, regret, or sim.) Hom. • ὤφελεν ἀθανάτοισιν εὔχεσθαι *he ought to have prayed to the immortals* Il. ‖ IMPERS. there is a binding duty —W.ACC. + INF. *for someone to do sthg.* Pi.
6 behave in a predictable way (as if bound by fate or necessity); (of persons or things) **be bound** or **certain** —W.INF. *to do or be sthg.* Hdt. + ‖ IMPERS.PASS. it is certain or fated —W.DAT. + INF. *for someone to do or experience sthg.* (esp. *to die*) S. E. Plb.
7 ‖ IMPF. or AOR.2 (introducing a wish that is unfulfilled, W.PRES. or AOR.INF., freq. strengthened by ὡς, εἰ γάρ, εἴθε, ep. αἴθε) Hom. + • ἀνδρὸς ... ὤφελλον ἀμείνονος εἶναι ἄκοιτις *I could wish that I were the wife of a better man* Il. • ὡς ὄφελον θανέειν *I wish I had died* Od. • εἰ γὰρ ὤφελον *if only I had* (done sthg.) E. • αἴθ' ὄφελον μεῖναι παρὰ Φαιήκεσσι *I really ought to have remained among the Phaeacians* Od. ‖ IMPERS. one wishes that, if only —W.ACC. + INF. *sthg. were the case* Timocr. AR. —W.INDIC. Call.*epigr.*

ὀφέλλω¹ *ep.vb.*: see ὀφείλω
ὀφέλλω² *ep.vb.* [reltd. ὄφελος] | 3pl.subj. (pres. or aor.) ὀφέλλωσι | 3sg.impf. (or aor.) ὤφελλε, also ὄφελλε | 3sg.aor.opt. ὀφέλλειε ‖ 3sg.impf.pass. ὀφέλλετο |
1 cause (sthg.) **to increase** (in size, amount, strength, intensity or duration); (of gods or humans) **increase, enhance, intensify, add to** —*a man's stature and youthful vigour, his valour* Hom. —*hardship, conflict, violence, or sim.* Hom. Hes.; (of an axe) —*its user's power* Il.; (of industry) —*productivity* Hes.; (of a wind) **swell, raise high** —*waves* Il.; (of persons) **prolong** —*talk* (opp. *taking action*) Il.; **promote, advance** —*the cause of the enemy* A. ‖ PASS. (of a horse's strength) be increased Il.; (of a crashing noise) grow louder A.
2 cause (persons, animals, places) **to increase** (in wealth or well-being); **enrich, make prosperous** —*an estate, a land* Od. Hes. Pi. Call.; **cause** (W.ACC. *herds*) **to thrive** Theoc. ‖ PASS. (of an estate) be increased, grow richer Od.; (of places and people) be enriched —W.DAT. *by the rain of Zeus* Theoc.
3 exalt, raise —*a person* (W.DAT. *in honour*) Il.
4 (of Zeus, a spear) **add strength to** —*a person* AR.; (intr., of persons) **give support** (to others) AR.

ὀφέλλω³ *vb.* **sweep** —*a room* Hippon.
ὄφελμα ατος *n.* **broom** Hippon.
ὄφελον (ep.aor.2): see ὀφείλω
ὄφελος *indecl.n.* [reltd. ὀφέλλω²] **1 that which can be turned to some profitable purpose**; (ref. to a person or group of persons) **advantage, use, benefit** (sts. W.DAT. to others, esp. friends, comrades or one's city) Il. Thgn. S. Ar. Pl. +; (ref. to a thing or circumstance) Il. hHom. Hdt. Ar. +
2 advantage, use, benefit (W.GEN. in someone or sthg.) Thgn. A. Hdt. Ar. Att.orats. +; (W.INF. or ACC. + INF. in doing sthg., or sthg. being the case) Att.orats. Pl. +

ὀφέλσιμα ων *n.pl.* advantageous circumstances, **prosperity** (given by a god to a city) Call.
ὀφεώδης (also **ὀφιώδης** Pi.) ες *adj.* [ὄφις] **1** (of the Gorgon) teeming with snakes, **snaky** Pi.
2 ‖ NEUT.SB. snake-like element (in human nature) Pl.
ὀφθαλμία ᾱς *f.* [ὀφθαλμός] inflammation of the eyes, **ophthalmia** Ar. P. X.
ὀφθαλμιάω *contr.vb.* **1 suffer from ophthalmia** Hdt. Ar. X. +
2 (fig.) **look with envious eyes** —W.ACC. or περί + ACC. *on sthg.* Plb.
ὀφθαλμίδιον ου *n.* [dimin. ὀφθαλμός] **dear little eye** Ar.(du.)
ὀφθαλμός οῦ *m.* **1 eye** (as the organ of sight; usu.pl., sts.du.) Hom. +; (as full of emotion or tears, affected by sleep, old

age or blindness, closed in death) Hom. +; (flashing fire, light or glances, looking in a certain direction, watchful or full of longing) Hom. +; (displaying honesty, shame, brazenness) Thgn. +; (as the agent of a person's mental view, judgement or appreciation) Hom. +; (pleon.dat. *with the eyes*, w.vbs. of seeing) Hom. +

2 ‖ PL. **eyes** (as representing the range of vision, and thus attention or thought; freq. in prep.phrs., ref. to someone or sthg. being in front or present, out in the open, watched closely, or sim.) Hom. +

3 (specif.) **eye** (which is all-seeing or watchful); **eye** (of Zeus, a god or master) Hes. X. Call.; (of Justice) Plb.(quot.provb.); (fig.ref. to a master, leader or guide) A. E.; (ref. to an officer who reports back to a ruler, esp. the Persian king) A. Hdt. Ar. X. +

4 (fig., as the principal or most precious part of sthg.) **eye, light, glory** (w.GEN. of a land, ref. to its young men; of an army, ref. to a warrior and seer) Pi.

5 (fig.) source of comfort or joy, **light, comfort** (ref. to an event) S.; (w.GEN. of one's life, ref. to a son) E.

6 (fig.) **eye** (of the moon) Pi.; (w.GEN. of night, ref. to the moon) A.

7 bud (of a plant) which resembles an eye; **eye, bud** X.; (on vines) Alcm. Ion

8 app. **oar-port** (of a trireme, perh. also w. play on the anatomical sense) Ar.

ὀφθαλμό-τεγκτος ον *adj.* [τέγγω] (of a flood of tears) **drenching the eyes** E.

ὀφθαλμ-ωρύχος ον *adj.* [ὀρύσσω] (of a punishment) consisting of the gouging out of eyes, **eye-gouging** A.

ὀφθείς (aor.pass.ptcpl.), **ὀφθήσομαι** (fut.pass.): see ὁράω

ὄφις εως (also εος E., dial. ιος) *m.* | also **ὄφῐς** (AR.), **ὄπφῐς** (Il. Hippon.) | **1** snake-like monster (esp. in mythol. or fabulous stories), **snake, serpent** Il. Hes. Pi. Hdt. Trag. Ar. +

2 snake (as a reptile, esp. assoc.w. a god or portent) Hdt. E. Ar. D. Thphr. +; (as a creature which may be charmed) Pl.

3 snake (exemplifying a person who is cold, devious or odious) Thgn. Carm.Pop. A. Theoc. NT. Plu.; (who is astute) NT.; (ref. to a thing which has a coiling shape or movement) Pl.; (fig.ref. to Apollo's arrow, fr. its darting movement or bite) A.

4 snake (as a representation in art) Hippon. A. Hdt. Call.*epigr.*; (ref. to a kind of bracelet) Men.

ὀφιώδης *adj.*: see ὀφεώδης

ὄφλημα ατος *n.* [ὀφλισκάνω] that which is incurred as a legal penalty, **fine, penalty** Att.orats. Arist. Plu.

ὀφλισκάνω *vb.* [reltd. ὀφείλω] | fut. ὀφλήσω | aor.2 ὦφλον | pf. ὤφληκα | **1** (leg.) incur a penalty by losing a lawsuit (sts. W.DAT. to someone); **lose one's case** Th. And. Ar. Pl. D. Plu. —W.INTERN.ACC. δίκην (or sim.) *one's case* S.*fr.* Ar. Att.orats. Pl. + ‖ PASS. (of a case) be lost D.

2 be convicted —W.GEN. or δίκην + GEN. *of a particular crime* A. Att.orats. Pl. Plu. —W.PTCPL. *of committing a particular crime* Pl.

3 incur —w. δίκην + GEN. *the penalty of death* Pl. —*a penalty consisting in the sum claimed by the plaintiff* Is. —*forfeiture of a security deposit* Thphr.

4 incur a penalty of, **be fined** —*a certain sum* Ar. Att.orats. Pl. X.

5 (fig. or gener.) **be guilty of** —*lawlessness, cowardice, shameful conduct, foolishness,* or sim. Hdt. S. E. Th. Pl. +

6 incur —*a penalty, harm* E. —*ridicule* E. Ar. Pl. Plb.

ὄφρα *ep.conj.* [reltd. τόφρα] **1** (as temporal conj., ref. to actual occurrence in pres. or past time, sts. correlatv. w. τόφρα *all that time*) **as long as, while** —W.PRES. or IMPF.INDIC. *sthg. is or was the case* Hom. hHom. Eleg. A. Call. AR.

2 (ref. to fut. time) **as long as, while** —w. ἄν or κε (sts. omitted) + PRES.SUBJ. *sthg. is the case* Hom. Tyrt. Thgn. S. AR.

3 (ref. to an actual occurrence in past time, sts. correlatv. w. τόφρα) up to the time when, **until** —W.AOR.INDIC. *sthg. was the case* Hom. Thgn. AR.

4 (ref. to fut. time) **until** —w. ἄν or κε (sts. omitted) + AOR.SUBJ. or (after a historic tense) OPT. *sthg. is the case* Hom. Mimn. A. AR.

5 (as final conj., introducing cl. of purpose) **so that, in order that** —w. ἄν or κε (sts. omitted) + SUBJ. or (after a historic tense, or by attraction to a preceding potential opt.) OPT. *sthg. may be the case* Hom. Hes. Archil. Thgn. Lyr. Hellenist.poet. —W.FUT.INDIC. *sthg. will be the case* Hom. AR. —W.AOR.INDIC. *sthg. might have been the case* AR.

6 (as demonstr.adv.) **for a while** Il.

ὀφρύη ης *f.* [reltd. ὀφρῦς] **ridge** (of high ground) E.; **belt** (of dunes, across Libya) Hdt.

ὀφρυόεις εσσα εν (ειν Call.) *adj.* (of Ilion, as the citadel of Troy) **set on the brow of a steep rock** Il. Call.; (of Corinth, ref. to its acropolis) Hes.*fr.* Hdt.(oracle)

ὀφρῡ́ς (or **ὀφρῦς**) ύος *f.* | acc. ὀφρῦν (or ὀφρύν) ‖ PL.: nom. ὀφρύες | acc. ὀφρῦς, also ὀφρύας | dat. ὀφρύσι |

1 (sg.) **eyebrow** Il. A.(dub.) E. Ar. Call. Theoc.

2 (specif.) **eye** (of the Cyclops) E.*Cyc.*

3 ‖ PL. **eyebrows, brows** or **brow** (freq. assoc.w. a particular facial expression or strong emotion) Hom. +; (assoc.w. a nod of command) Hom. hHom.; (as the seat of grief or distress) S. E.; (knitted in a frown, relaxed as a sign of calmness or cheerfulness) E. Ar. Men. Plu.; (raised in arrogance or self-importance) Ar. D. Men.; (assoc.w. proud looks) Call.; (meton., ref. to proud or frowning looks) Ar. Plu. ‖ SG. **brow** (as the location of a frown) E.

4 ‖ PL. (gener.) **eyelashes, eyelids** or **eyes** (fr. which tears fall) Hom. S.; (stung by soap) Ar.; (fr. which a look is cast) Theoc.; (assoc.w. a smile) hHom. Pi.(sg.) AR.

5 (sg. and pl.) prominent stretch of high ground, **brow, ridge** Il. Pi. AR. Plb. Mosch. +

6 (sg. and pl.) **bank** (of a river) AR. Plb.

ὄχα *ep.adv.* [reltd. ἔξοχος] (strengthening ἄριστος *best*) **by far** Hom.

ὀχάνη ης *f.* [reltd. ὄχανον] **handle** (of a shield) Plu.

ὄχανον ου *n.* [ἔχω] **handle** (of a shield) Anacr. Hdt.

ὄχεα *n.pl.*: see under ὄχος

ὀχείᾱ ᾱς *f.* [ὀχεύω] **mating** (w. the female, by the male) X. Arist.

ὀχεῖον ου *n.* male breeding animal (selected for good characteristics), **stud** Plu.

ὄχεσφι(ν) (ep.gen.dat.pl.): see ὄχεα, under ὄχος

ὀχεταγωγίᾱ ᾱς *f.* [ὀχετός, ἀγωγός] **construction of water-supply channels** Pl.

ὀχετεύω *vb.* | 3sg.impf.pass. ὠχετεύετο | **1** carry (water) along a channel; **divert** —*a river* Hdt. ‖ PASS. (of water) be channelled (along pipes) Hdt.; (fig., of rumour, into a house) A.

2 channel, pour —*fire* (fig.ref. to wine, W.PREP.PHR. *into the body and soul*) Pl.

ὀχετ-ηγός οῦ *m.* [ἄγω] one who constructs a water channel (for plants), **irrigator** Il.

ὀχετός οῦ *m.* [reltd. ὄχος] **1** channel for conveyance of water (to settlements, fields for irrigation); **water channel, conduit** Hdt. Th. Pl. X. Arist. Plu.; natural channel underground, **channel** Pl.

ὀχεύς

2 channel, drain (for removal of waste fr. a city) Arist.
3 channel (in the body, for conveyance of air, fluids or waste products); **channel, canal, duct** Pl. X.
4 ‖ PL. **channels** or **streams** (of a river) Pi. E.
5 (fig.) **channel, course** (of a person's life) E.
6 (fig.) **channel, pit** (W.GEN. of ruin, into which a city sinks) Pi.

ὀχεύς έως (Ion. ῆος) *m.* [ἔχω] **1** that which holds or fixes (an object) in place; **fastener** (of a belt) Il.; (of a helmet) Il.; (of a Roman shield, to the shoulder) Plb.
2 bolt or **bar** (of a door) Hom. Parm. Theoc.

ὀχεύω *vb.* **1** (of a male animal) **mount** —*the female* Pl. Theoc.
2 (intr., of male animals, men envisaged as animals) **mate, copulate** Hdt. Pl.; (mid., of animals and birds, ref. to both sexes) Hdt.

ὀχέω, dial. **ὀκχέω** (Pi. Call.) *contr.vb.* [reltd. ὄχος] | dial.3pl. ὀκχέοντι (Pi.) | 3sg.impf. ὤχει | iterat v.impf. ὀχέεσκον | fut. ὀχήσω | dial.aor. ὤκχησα (Pi.) ‖ MID.: fut. ὀχήσομαι | ep.3sg.aor. ὀχήσατο ‖ MID.PASS.: Aeol.ptcpl. ὀχήμενος | 3sg.impf. ὠχεῖτο, ep. ὀχεῖτο, Ion. ὠχέετο |
1 cause (a person) to be conveyed or carried; **allow** (W.ACC. someone) **to ride** (on a horse or donkey) Ar. X.
‖ PRES.MID.PASS. have oneself carried, **be conveyed** or **ride** (usu. W.DAT. or PREP.PHR. on an animal, in a vehicle, on a ship) Il. hHom. Sapph.(or Alc.) Hdt. Lys. Ar. + ‖ AOR.MID. (of a god) convey oneself, ride —W.DAT. *on the waves* Od.
2 carry or convey (w. additional connot. of offering support); **carry** or **support** —*a sick person* (*on his way to a place*) E.; (of a dry river-bed) —*wagons* Call.; (fig., of the body) **be a vehicle for** —*the soul* Pl.
3 offer support (without connot. of conveyance); **support** —*a goblet* (W.DAT. *on three fingers*) X.; **carry, hold** —*a lyre, a laurel branch* Thgn. Pi.*fr.*
4 (of an anchor, fig.ref. to a hope) **sustain, hold fast** —*one's fortunes* E. ‖ MID.PASS. (fig., of a person) **be buoyed up** —w. ἐπί + GEN. *by a theory* (*compared to a raft*) Pl. —*by a hope* Pl. —*by faint strength, a slender hope* E. Ar.
5 bear, sustain, endure —*a burden* (*of suffering*) S. —*misery, pain, one's lot* Od. Hes. Pi. —*guard duty* (*fig.ref. to being shackled to a cliff*) A.
6 keep on with, maintain —*one's childish ways* Od.

ὄχημα ατος *n.* **1** that which provides carriage or conveyance (freq. specified by ADJ. or GEN.); **carriage, conveyance, vehicle** Pl.; (ref. to a chariot, wagon, or sim.) Pi.*fr.* Hdt. Trag. Tim. Pl. X. +; (ref. to a ship) Trag. Pl. +; (ref. to a riding animal) Ar.; (fig., for the soul, ref. to the body) Pl.; (W.GEN. for songs, ref. to a victory-ode) Pi.*fr.*
2 support (W.GEN. for the earth, ref. to Zeus) E.; (for the foot-soldier, ref. to the ground, opp. a horse, w. play on sense 1) X.

ὄχησις εως *f.* **1 riding** (of horses) Pl.
2 mode of transport Pl.

ὄχθαι ὦν *f.pl.* [reltd. ὄχθος] **1 banks** (of a river) Hom. Hes.*fr.* Xenoph. Lyr. Trag. X. +; (sg.) Il. hHom. Plu.
2 edges, shore (of the sea) Od.
3 rock faces, cliffs (beside the sea) Pi.; (sg.) AR.
4 slopes (of a high mountain) Pi. S.
5 sides, banks (of a military defensive trench) Il. X.

ὀχθέω *contr.vb.* [app.reltd. ἔχθω] | aor. ὤχθησα | **be agitated** or **troubled** Hom.

ὄχθος ου *m.* **high ground** (rising fr. a plain or beside water; freq.pl.); **height, hill, slope, rock** hHom. Lyr. Hdt. Trag. Ar. +; **mound** (of a tomb) A. Ar.(quot. A.)

ὀχλαγωγέω *contr.vb.* [ὄχλος, ἀγωγός] **draw crowds, attract the mob** Plb.
ὀχλαγωγία ᾶς *f.* **fooling of the mob** Plu.
ὀχλέω *contr.vb.* **annoy, bother** —*a person* A. Hdt.; (intr.) **cause trouble, be a nuisance** S. ‖ PASS. be troubled (by other people) Arist.; (by unclean spirits) NT.
ὀχληρός ά όν *adj.* causing trouble (sts. W.DAT. for others); (of persons) **troublesome, annoying** E. Ar.(mock-trag.) Att.orats. Pl. Arist. Men.; (of mice) Call.; (of situations, things said) Hdt. Ar. Isoc. X. D.
ὄχλησις εως *f.* [ὀχλέω] causing of trouble, **annoyance** Plb.
ὀχλίζω *vb.* [ὄχλος] | ep.aor. ὤχλισσα | move (sthg. heavy) with great effort; **heave up** —*a boulder, rocks* Hom. AR.; (of a god) —*islands* Call.
ὀχλικός ή όν *adj.* (of political arrangements or behaviour) **appealing to the crowd, popularist** Plu.
ὀχλο-κόπος ου *m.* [κόπτω] one who incites the mob, **firebrand** Plb.
ὀχλοκρατία ᾶς *f.* [κράτος] **mob rule** Plb.
ὀχλοποιέω *contr.vb.* **form a mob** NT.
ὄχλος ου *m.* **1** crowd of people (going about their business, assembled around a sight or person, attending a public event, or sim.); **people, crowd** Pi. S. E. Th. Ar. +
2 people or citizenry (of a state, as collectively exercising political or judicial power); **people** E. Th.
3 ordinary people (opp. the rulers, elite, educated, or sim.); **people, common people** E. Th. Pl. X. +
4 (derog.) common people or crowd (as easily persuaded or roused to strong feeling, to be avoided as vulgar or unpleasant, or sim.); **people, crowd, mob, rabble** E. Th. Pl. +; (ref. to an individual) common person, **riff-raff, pleb** Men.
5 general population (of a city or region, of a race or tribe, of humankind); **population, people** E. Isoc. +
6 group (of the same type or class, or of persons engaged in the same activity); **crowd, throng, company** Sapph. S.*Ichn.* E. Pl. +; (W.ADJ. *old, foreign, female*, or sim.) E. Th. Ar. +
7 (specif.) group (of persons attendant upon a person of authority); **crowd, retinue** A. E. Ar. Pl. +; (in an army) **camp followers** X. Plb.
8 large force (of troops, chariots, cavalry, ships); **mass, multitude, host** A. E. Th. X. +; (ref. to a savage or untrained force) **horde, rabble** Th. Plb.
9 body of ordinary men or soldiery (in an army, opp. the commanders); **main body, troops, men** E. Th. X. +; **crew** (manning triremes) Th.; **force, contingent** (W.ADJ. *cavalry, naval, mercenary*, or sim.) E. Th. Arist.
10 body of troops or ships hard pressed or out of control; **disorderly mass, crush** Th. X.
11 large number (of things) considered all together; **mass, host** (of troubles) A.; (of spoils) E.; (of things which could be said) A. Isoc.; (of elements in a whole) Pl.
12 number of troublesome things considered collectively; **trouble, annoyance, nuisance** (caused by demands, arguments, tedious repetition, or sim.) Hdt. E. Th. Ar. +
ὀχλώδης ες *adj.* **1** (of a wild animal) **unruly, uncontrolled** Pl.
2 (of a Roman triumph) **tumultuous** Plu.
3 (of an opinion) **common, vulgar** Plu.
4 ‖ NEUT.SB. troublesomeness, complexity (of an undertaking) Th.
ὀχμάζω *vb.* [reltd. ὄχος, ὄχανον] | aor. ὤχμασα | **1 hold fast, grip** —*the handle of a torch* E.*Cyc.* —*a shield* AR. —*a person* (*round the waist*) E.; **fasten, bind** —*a prisoner* (*to a rock*) A.
2 fit a bridle to, break in —*horses* E.; (mid.) S.(cj.)

ὄχνᾱ *dial.f.*: see ὄγχνη

ὄχοι ων *m.pl.* [ἔχω] places of holding, **safe havens** (W.GEN. for ships, ref. to harbours) Od.

ὄχος, dial. **ὄκχος** (Pi.), ου *m.* [reltd. ὀχέω] **1** means of conveyance (on land, sea or through the air); **carriage, vehicle** A. E.
2 (specif.) chariot (for a god, a warrior or person of authority, used esp. in war or racing; sts.pl. for a single vehicle) hHom. Pi. Hdt. Trag. Critias
3 (meton.) **team** (of deer) Call.

—ὄχεα ων *n.pl.* | ep.gen.dat. ὄχεσφι(ν) | **chariot** (collectv., ref. to a single vehicle; sts. as true pl.) Hom. hHom. Mimn. Ibyc. Pi.

ὀχυροποιέομαι *mid.contr.vb.* [ὀχυρός, ποιέω] strengthen against attack, **fortify** —*military positions* Plb.

ὀχυρός ά όν *adj.* [reltd. ἐχυρός] **1** (of a plough-tree, made fr. a certain kind of wood) **solid, sturdy** Hes.
2 secure from collapse or being broken into; (of stonework, for a house) **strong, secure** X.; (of living quarters for girls) E. ‖ NEUT.SB. secure place (for valuables) X. Plu.
3 affording resistance to enemy attack; (of a city or military position) **strong, secure, impregnable** X. Men. Plb. Plu.; (of a defensive barrier) A.(v.l. ἐχυρός); (of a mountainous area) **impassable** X. ‖ NEUT.SB. secure place or stronghold X.
4 (of commanders, their qualities) having the power to resist (an enemy), **strong, solid, stalwart** A.(v.l. ἐχυρός) Plu.; (of a yoked pair, ref. to the Atreidai) A.

—ὀχυρῶς *adv.* **in security** —*ref. to growing old* E.; **securely** —*ref. to a door being bolted* Plu.

ὀχυρότης ητος *f.* **security, strength, impregnability** (of a location) Plb. ‖ PL. security advantages (of a location) Plb. Plu.

ὀχυρόω *contr.vb.* | aor.mid. ὠχυρωσάμην | (act. and mid.) strengthen against attack, **fortify, garrison** —*a position* X. Plb. Plu.

ὀχύρωμα ατος *n.* fortified position, **stronghold, entrenchment** X. Plb.

ὄψ ὀπός *f.* [reltd. ἔπος] | only acc.gen.dat.sg. | **1 voice, word** (human or divine) Hom. hHom. S. E. Ar. AR.; **sound** (of the monster Typhon) Il.
2 voice (of animals); **call, cry** (of newborn lambs) Il.; (of a bird) Alcm. E. AR.
3 voice as an instrument of song; **voice, song** Hom. Hes. Lyr. Ar. AR.; (of cicadas) Il.; (of a nightingale) A. Theoc.*epigr.*; (fig., of auloi) Thgn.

ὀψ-ᾱμάτᾱς ᾱ *dial.m.* [ὀψέ, ἀμητήρ] **one who reaps till late in the day** Theoc.

ὄψανον ου *n.* [ὄψομαι, see ὁράω] **vision** (in a dream) A.

ὀψάριον ου *n.* [dimin. ὄψον] **fish** Men. NT.

ὀψ-αρότης ου *m.* **late plougher** (in the season) Hes.

ὀψαρτῡτής οῦ *m.* [ὀψαρτύω] **gourmand** Plb.

ὀψ-αρτύω *vb.* [ὄψον] season food; (fig., of a writer) **describe food dishes** Plb.

ὀψέ, Aeol. **ὄψι** *adv.* **1** at an advanced hour in the day (when darkness is about to fall or has already fallen, or after the usual time for sleep); **late** Hom. Th. +
2 relatively late in the course of the day (in terms of starting sthg., esp. a military action); **late** Th. Ar. X. Plb.
3 late in the season; **late** (for ploughing) Hes.; (for grapes to ripen) Alc.(cj.)
4 (phr. W.GEN.) ὀψὲ τῆς ἡμέρας *late in the course of the day* Th. X.; ὀψὲ τῆς ὥρας *at a late hour* D. Plb. Plu.; *late in the season* Plu.
5 at a relatively late stage or very late (in the course of events); **late** Hom. Th. +; (in a period of history, in the development of sthg.) Arist. +; (in one's life) Pl. +
6 after a deferred period or delay (longer than one might expect); **in the fullness of time** Il. A. Pi. S.; **at length, finally** Hom. AR. Mosch. Plu.
7 late and therefore not long since, **recently** Pl. D. Arist.
8 later than the right time (to realise the facts; esp. to prevent a terrible event); **late** or **too late** S. E. X. AR. +
9 (as prep.) later than, **after** —W.GEN. *the Sabbath* NT.

ὀψείω *vb.* [desideratv. ὄψομαι, see ὁράω] **wish to see** —W.GEN. *sthg.* Il.

ὀψαίτερος, ὀψαίτατος (compar. and superl.adj.): see ὄψιος

ὀψι-γάμιον ου *n.* [ὀψέ, γάμος] (leg.) **late marriage** (as a crime at Sparta) Plu.

ὀψί-γονος ον *adj.* [γόνος] **1** (of persons) **of a later generation** or **age** (than one's own) Il. Call. AR. ‖ MASC.PL.SB. future generations or posterity Od. AR.
2 (of a child) **born late** (to a relatively old parent, or after a father's death) hHom. Stesich. Plu.
3 (of a child) born relatively late (after other children in a family), **younger** A.; **born more recently** Hdt.
4 born only recently, **very young** Theoc.

ὀψίζω *vb.* **1** (act. and mid.) **be late** (in the day, when one starts sthg.) X.
2 arrive late (in the day, at a camp or back home) X. Plu. ‖ PASS. be kept out late (by hunting) X.

ὀψί-κοιτος ον *adj.* [κοίτη] (of a person's eyes) resting only at a very late hour, **wakeful** A.

ὀψι-μαθής ές *adj.* [μανθάνω] **1** (of a people) learning only late in one's history, **slow to learn** (W.GEN. about sthg.) Isoc.
2 (of persons) acquiring knowledge late in life, **learning late** (W.GEN. about sthg.) Pl. Plu.
3 learning only recently, **late in learning, novice** (sts. W.GEN. in respect of sthg.) Isoc. X.
4 (pejor.) learning late in life (and inclined to show off one's erudition, in a pretentious or pedantic way); (of a philosopher or historian) **late-learning** Plb. Plu. ‖ MASC.SB. late-learner Thphr.

ὀψιμαθίᾱ ᾱς *f.* late-learning, **pedantic irrelevance** (of a historian) Plb.

ὄψιμος η ον *adj.* | superl. ὀψιμώτατος | **1** (of a portent fr. Zeus) late in time, **late** Il.
2 (of sowing) late in the season, **late** X.

ὀψί-νοος ον *adj.* [νόος] (of Epimetheus) **slow to understand** Pi.

ὄψιος ᾱ (Ion. η) ον *adj.* | compar. ὀψιαίτερος, also ὀψίτερος (Pi.) | superl. ὀψιαίτατος | (of the afternoon) **at an advanced hour, late** Hdt. Th. Lycurg. D. +; (of night) Pi.; (of the time of day) NT. ‖ COMPAR. (of the sack of Troy) achieved late in time, delayed Pi.*fr.* ‖ SUPERL. latest (in arriving back fr. work) X. ‖ FEM.SB. evening or late hour NT.

—ὀψιαίτερον *compar.adv.* **later** (W.GEN. than appropriate) Pl.

—ὀψιαίτατα *superl.adv.* **very late** (in the day) X. D.; (in the season) X.; **latest** (in age) —*ref. to ending attendance at school* Pl.

ὄψις εως (Ion. ιος) *f.* [ὄψομαι, see ὁράω] **1** faculty or function of seeing; **vision, sight** Il. Heraclit. Hdt. S. E. Th. +; (fig., in the mind) Arist. Plb.
2 fact of seeing or action of looking; **sight, look, glance** or **gaze** Od. Trag. Th. +
3 looking with close attention; **watchful eye, scrutiny, inspection** S. Th. Pl.
4 looking with one's own eyes (opp. theorising or learning by report); **eyewitnessing, looking, observation** Hdt. S. Th. +

ὀψιτέλεστος

5 vision over a certain distance; **range of vision, sight** (esp. in phrs. *within sight, in front of the eyes*, or sim.) E. Th. X. +; **view** (fr. a certain position) Plu.
6 immediate sight or proximity (of a person, esp. one of authority); **sight, presence** Hdt. Trag. +
7 impression on one's sight (of a person, as handsome, fearsome, or sim., freq. evoking emotion); **appearance, look, face** Il. hHom. S. E. Th. Att.orats. +; (changing according to mood or situation) Th. Pl. +
8 characteristic features (of an individual); **figure, form** or **face** S. Pl. +; (taken on as a disguise) Pi.; (in a painting) Plu.
9 appearance or characteristic features (of a thing); **look, form, shape** Hdt. S.*fr.* Philox.Leuc. Pl. +
10 indistinct appearance, **impression** (in the dark or at a distance) Th. Pl.; outward appearance (not necessarily corresponding to reality), **look, outward show** Th. Lys. Pl. +
11 thing seen (esp. of a striking or remarkable nature); **sight, spectacle** Trag. Th. Ar. +; (in the arts, in drama) Hdt. Pl. X. Arist. Plu.
12 seeing as part of a ritual; **observation, sight** (of sacred objects or ceremony) E. Ar. Plu.
13 thing seen which is supernatural (usu. in a dream); **vision** Hdt. Trag. Ar. Isoc. +

ὀψι-τέλεστος ον *adj.* [ὀψέ, τελέω] (of a portent fr. Zeus, relating to the sack of Troy) **to be fulfilled late in time** Il.

ὀψίτερος (compar.adj.): see ὄψιος

ὄψομαι (fut.mid.): see ὁράω

ὄψον ου *n.* **1** supply of a meat, fish or vegetable foodstuff (opp. staple grains or wine); **fresh food, fish** or **meat** Th. X. Thphr. +; (for those travelling or on campaign) Od. Lys. X. Plu.
2 main food dish at dinner (made fr. meat, fish or vegetable, dipped into w. bread and eaten w. the fingers); **dish, meat** Ar. Pl. X.
3 expensive or elaborate dinner dish (as prepared and cooked in an expert way, w.connots. of variety, taste, luxury or overindulgence, opp. staple foods); **dish, fine dish, fine food** Ar. Pl. X. Arist. Thphr. Plu.
4 small quantity of savoury food as an accompaniment (to bread or wine, such as olives, onion, cress, cheese); **relish, savoury** Il. Pl. +
5 small quantity of a dinner dish; **tasty morsel** (offered to a child) Il.; (fig., as the price for winning someone over) X.; (pl., ref. to words, for the envious to chew on) Pi.

ὀψοποιέομαι *mid.contr.vb.* [ὀψοποιός] prepare food dishes, **prepare dinner** X. D. —W.COGN.ACC. X.

ὀψοποιητικός ή όν *adj.* (of an art) relating to the skilled preparation of food dishes, **of cookery** Arist. ‖ FEM.SB. art of cookery Arist.

ὀψοποιΐα ᾶς *f.* **cookery, cuisine** Pl. X.

ὀψοποικός ή όν *adj.* (of matters) **relating to a cook** or **chef** Pl.; (of utensils) **for food preparation** X.; (of the art) **of the cook** or **chef** Pl. ‖ FEM.SB. art of the cook or chef Pl. Arist.

ὀψο-ποιός οῦ *m.* [ποιέω] preparer of the main dishes for dinner (esp. of meat or fish, oft. for an important man or on an important occasion); **cook, chef** Hdt. Pl. X. Arist. Plu.

ὀψο-πώλιον ου *n.* [πωλέω] **food-market** or **fish-market** Plu.

ὀψοφαγέω *contr.vb.* [ὀψοφάγος] be one who likes to eat the fancy dishes (at dinner), **dine luxuriously** Ar.

ὀψοφαγία ᾶς *f.* **luxurious eating, gluttony** Aeschin. Arist.

ὀψο-φάγος ον *adj.* [φαγεῖν] | superl. ὀψοφαγίστατος | eating the main dishes (which are expensive or fancily prepared, rather than the bread), **dining luxuriously, gluttonous** Ar. X. ‖ MASC.SB. gourmet or glutton X. Arist. Plb.

ὀψ-ωνέω *contr.vb.* [ὠνέομαι] | pf. ὠψώνηκα | **buy food for dinner, buy fish** or **meat** Ar. X. Thphr. Plu.
‖ NEUT.PL.PF.PASS.PTCPL.SB. fish or meat purchases Thphr.

ὀψωνία ᾶς *f.* **purchase of fish** or **meat** Plu.

ὀψωνιάζω *vb.* [ὀψώνιον] | aor. ὠψωνίασα | provide money for purchase of food; (specif.) **pay** —*troops* Plb. ‖ PASS. (of a council) be paid (by a ruler, as a bribe) Plb.

ὀψωνιασμός οῦ *m.* (sg. and pl.) **payment** (of troops) Plb.

ὀψώνιον ου *n.* [ὄψον, ὠνέομαι] (collectv.sg. or pl.) **pay, wages** (esp. for soldiers or mercenaries) Plb. NT.; (for craftsmen) Plb.

Π π

πᾳ *dial.enclit.adv.*: see πῃ
πᾷ *dial.interrog.adv.*: see πῇ
πᾶἀ *Lacon.fem.adj.*: see πᾶς
πᾱγά *dial.f.*: see πηγή
Παγασαί ῶν (Ion. έων) *f.pl.* Pagasai (port in Thessaly) Hdt. X. D. Call. AR. Plu.
—**Παγασαῖος** ᾱ (Ion. η) ον *adj.* (of Apollo) of Pagasai Hes.
—**Παγασήιος** η ον *ep.Ion.adj.* —also **Παγασηίς** ίδος *fem.adj.* (of the harbour, the coast) of Pagasai AR.
—**Παγασίτης** ου *masc.adj.* (of the bay) of Pagasai D.
Πᾱγασίς *dial.fem.adj.*, **Πᾱγασος** *dial.m.*: see Πήγασος
παγ-γέλοιος ον *adj.* [πᾶς] (of a person, a situation) thoroughly ridiculous Pl.
παγ-γλυκερός ά όν *adj.* (of a woman) utterly delicious Ar.
παγγλωσσίᾱ ᾱς *f.* [γλῶσσα] indiscriminate speech, **chatter, gabble** (of inferior poets, likened to crows) Pi.
παγείς (aor.2 pass.ptcpl.), **πάγεν** (ep.3pl.aor.2 pass.): see πήγνῡμι
παγετός οῦ *m.* [reltd. πάγος 2] **freezing** (W.GEN. of the ground) Pi.*fr.*; **frost** X.
παγετώδης ες *adj.* (of a cave) full of frost, **ice-cold** S.; (of water) Plu.
πάγη ης *f.* [πήγνῡμι] that which fixes or fastens; **snare, trap** (for animals, birds, persons) Hdt. Pl. X. Plu.
πάγην (ep.aor.2 pass.), **παγήσομαι** (fut.pass.): see πήγνῡμι
παγιδεύω *vb.* [παγίς] (fig.) **lay a trap for, ensnare** —*someone* (W.PREP.PHR. in speech) NT.
παγίς ίδος *f.* **snare, trap** (for birds, mice) Ar. Call.; (fig., for persons) NT.
παγίως *adv.* [πήγνῡμι] **fixedly, positively, definitely** —*ref. to stating or envisaging sthg., to sthg. existing* Pl. Arist.
παγ-καίνιστος ον *adj.* [πᾶς, καινίζω] (of a dye fr. a sea-creature) **ever-renewable** A.
πάγ-κακος η ον *adj.* [κακός] | superl. παγκάκιστος | **1** (of persons) **thoroughly bad** or **evil** Thgn. Pl. Arist. Plu.(quot.) || SUPERL. (usu.voc.) **vilest of villains** S. E.
2 (of a day) **wholly bad** (for people) Hes.; (of oil, for plants) Pl.
—**παγκάκως** *adv.* **in utter misery, in agony** —*ref. to perishing or sim.* A. E.; **very badly** —*ref. to imitating sthg.* Pl.
πάγ-καλος η ον *adj.* [καλός] (of persons, their hands) **extremely beautiful** Ar. Pl. X.; (of Eros) Pl.; (of animals, fish) Pl. X. Plu.; (of things) **extremely fine, excellent** Pl. X. Plu.
—**παγκάλως** *adv.* **quite splendidly** or **excellently** E.*fr.* Pl. X. D. Plu.
παγκάρπεια ᾱς *f.* [πάγκαρπος] **offering consisting of all kinds of fruit** E.*fr.*
πάγ-καρπος ον *adj.* [καρπός¹] **1** (of an offering) **of fruit of all kinds** S.
2 (of earth, plants, an orchard) **rich in every fruit** Pi. AR.; (of the bay tree) **fruitful, rich in berries** S.

παγ-καταπύγων ον, gen. ονος *adj.* (of the female sex) **utterly debauched** Ar.
παγ-κατάρατος ον *adj.* (of a person) **utterly damnable, diabolical** Ar.
παγ-κευθής ές *adj.* [κεῦθος] (of the plains of Hades) **all-enshrouding** S.
πάγ-κλαυτος ον *adj.* [κλαυτός] (of a person) **ever-weeping** S.; (of eyes) **ever wet with tears** S.; (of sorrows, a harvest of ruin, a lifetime) **ever bringing tears** A. S.
παγκληρίᾱ ᾱς *f.* [πάγκληρος] entire estate, **inheritance, patrimony** A. E.
πάγ-κληρος ον *adj.* [κλῆρος] (of a house) **acquired by inheritance** E.
πάγ-κοινος ον *adj.* [κοινός] **1** (of Olympia, Eleusis, Hades) **common to all, open to all, all-receptive** Pi. S.; (of an omen, a truth, an object of hatred) **universal** Pi.*fr.* S. E.; (of Zeus' scourge, which destroys men in battle) **impartial** A.; (of a poet's voice) **heard by all** Pi.*fr.*
2 (of a group of people) **with common voice** or **purpose, united** A.
παγ-κοίτης ου, dial. **παγκοίτᾱς** ᾱ *masc.adj.* [κοίτη] (of a chamber, ref. to the underworld) **where all are laid to rest** S.; (of Hades) **who puts all to rest** S.
παγ-κόνιτος ον *adj.* [κονίω] (of a wrestling contest) **enveloped in dust** S.
παγ-κρατής ές *adj.* [κράτος] **1** (of gods, esp. Zeus) **all-powerful** B. Trag. Ar.; (of Zeus' throne) A.; (of his thunderbolt) Pi.; (of fire) Pi. S.; (of sleep, time) S.; (of truth) Simon. B.*fr.*
2 (of a person) **all-victorious, triumphant** A.
παγκρατιάζω *vb.* [παγκράτιον] **compete in the pankration, be a pancratiast** Isoc. Pl.; (fig., of a speaker gesticulating inappropriately) **do a prize-fighting routine** Aeschin.
παγκρατιαστής οῦ *m.* **competitor in the pankration, pancratiast, prize-fighter** Pl. X. D. Plb.
παγκρατιαστικός ή όν *adj.* (of a person, a skill) **pancratiastic** Pl. Arist.
παγκράτιον ου *n.* [παγκρατής] **all-in fight, pankration** (a combat sport, in which boxing and wrestling were combined w. kicking and strangling, w. nothing barred except biting and gouging) Xenoph. Pi. B. Hdt. Th. Ar. +; (fig., ref. to a speaker's inappropriate gesticulations) **prize-fighting routine** Aeschin.
παγ-κρότως *adv.* [κρότος] **with all oars splashing** —*ref. to a ship being rowed* A.
πάγ-ξενος, Ion. **πάγξεινος**, ον *adj.* [ξένος²] (of Aigina) **all-welcoming, hospitable** B.; (of the Olympic olive in a garland, as a prize) **for all comers** B.
πάγος ου *m.* [πήγνῡμι] **1** that which is fixed or firmly set, **rocky hill, hill, crag** Hes. Archil. Pi. Trag. Call. AR. + || PL. rocks

πᾱγός

or crags (on a shoreline) Od. | For Ἄρειος or Ἄρειος (Ion. Ἀρήιος) πάγος see Ἄρης 2, and Ἄρειος πάγος, under Ἄρειος. **2 frost** Alc. A. S. Pl. Plb. Plu. | cf. παγετός

πᾱγός dial.adj.: see πηγός

πᾶγος ου m. [Lat. pagus] **district** Plu.

πάγουρος ου m. **crab** Ar.

παγ-χάλεπος ον adj. [πᾶς, χαλεπός] (of a task or sim.) **thoroughly difficult** Pl. Arist.; (of a word, to explain) Pl.; (of the typical sophist, w.INF. to form an image of, to distinguish fr. others) Pl. ‖ NEUT.IMPERS. (w. ἐστί, sts.understd.) **it is very difficult** —W.INF. to do sthg. Antipho Pl. Arist. Plu.

—παγχαλέπως adv. **1 with extreme difficulty** X. **2 with hard feelings** (W.PREP.PHR. towards someone) X.

παγ-χάλκεος ον adj. (of a sword, a club) **all of bronze** Od.; (of the body of the giant Talos) AR.; (fig., of a warrior, ref. to his invulnerability) Il.

πάγ-χαλκος ον adj. [χαλκός] (of a helmet) **all of bronze** Od.; (of a shield, armour, an axe) Trag.; (of dedications, ref. to armour) S.; (of a body of spearmen) **clad all in bronze** E.

πάγ-χρηστος ον adj. [χρηστός] (of a vessel) **all-purpose** Ar.; (of a possession) **thoroughly useful** X.

πάγ-χριστος ον adj. [χριστός] (app. of a poisoned robe) **well-anointed** S.

παγ-χρύσεος, Lacon. **παγχρύσιος**, ον adj. (of tassels on Athena's aigis, her comb) **all-gold, of pure gold** Il. Call.; (of Artemis' bow, her chariot) hHom.; (of a snake ornament, assoc.w. Artemis) Alcm.; (of the apples of the Hesperides) Hes. AR.; (of their abode) Stesich.; (of the fleece sought by the Argonauts) AR.

πάγ-χρῡσος ον adj. [χρῡσός] (of the fleece sought by the Argonauts) **all-gold, of pure gold** Pi. E.; (of spoils, as an offering to Athena; of Pelops' chariot, as a gift fr. Poseidon) S.; (of the cheek of an ornamental snake, as a gift fr. Athena) E.; (of a temple of Artemis) Ar.; (of Aphrodite's bed) Bion; (of a cup) Pi. E.

πάγχυ dial.adv. [reltd. πάνυ] (in strong asseverations or negations, sts. intensv. w. individual wds.) **wholly, altogether, certainly** Hom. Hes. Eleg. Lyr. A. Hdt. +

πάδη (Lacon.imperatv.): see πηδάω

παθαίνομαι mid.vb. [πάθος] (pejor., of a woman) **be in an emotional state** Men.

παθέειν (ep.aor.2 inf.), **παθεῖν** (aor.2 inf.): see πάσχω

πάθη ης, dial. **πάθᾱ** ᾱς f. [παθεῖν, see πάσχω] **1 passive experience** (opp. activity) Pl.; **experience, sensation** (of heat, sound) Pl.
2 what is done or happens (to someone), **happening, event** S.
3 suffering, affliction Pi. Hdt. S.

πάθημα ατος n. **1 passive experience or state of feeling, feeling, sensation, emotion** Pl. X. Arist. Plu.
2 happening, event, experience Pl. Arist.
3 suffering, misfortune, calamity Hdt. S. E. Antipho Th. Ar. +
4 (philos.) **attribute, property** (of things) Pl. | cf. πάθος 7

παθητικός ή όν adj. **1** (of the relationship of one person, quality or thing to another) **passive** (opp. active) Arist.
2 (of persons) **capable of feeling** (sts. W.GEN. emotions) Arist.; (of the human capacity) **of feeling** Arist. Plu.
‖ NEUT.SB. **undergoing pain, suffering** Plu.
3 (of a type of poetry) that has to do with feeling or suffering, **emotional** Arist.; (of the effect of a particular musical mode or instrument) **evoking emotions** Arist.; (of style) **expressive of emotion, impassioned** Arist.; (of a writer) Plu.

—παθητικῶς adv. **with emotion** —ref. to speaking Arist.

παθητός ή όν adj. (of Christ) **subject to suffering** NT.
‖ NEUT.SB. **suffering or feeling** (as a human faculty) Plu.

πάθον (ep.aor.2): see πάσχω

πάθος εος (ους) n. **1 that which happens** (or is done) **to one, happening, event, experience** Antipho Pl. Arist.; (opp. activity) Pl. Arist.
2 (freq.pl.) **adverse experience, suffering, misfortune** Hdt. Trag. Ar. Att.orats. Pl. +
3 (ref. to a specific event) **calamity, disaster** Hdt. Trag. Th. X. +
4 that which one experiences passively, experience, sensation Pl. Arist.
5 feeling, emotion, passion Pl. Arist.; (in style or language) Arist.
6 passive state (of a person), **state, condition** (W.GEN. of ignorance or sim.) Pl.
7 (philos.) **non-essential attribute** (of things, as being subject to change, opp. οὐσία essence), **attribute, property** Pl. Arist.

πάθω (aor.2 subj.), **παθών** (aor.2 ptcpl.): see πάσχω

Παιάν (also **παιάν**) dial.m.: see Παιών

παιανίζω dial.vb., **παιανισμός** dial.m.: see παιωνίζω, παιωνισμός

παιᾶνις ιδος dial.fem.adj. [Παιών] (of songs) **in the form of a paean** Pi.fr.

παῖγμα ατος n. [παίζω] **that which is played** (on the aulos), **tune** E.

παιγμοσύνᾱ ᾱς dial.f. **playfulness, merriment** (assoc.w. Apollo) Stesich.

παιγνίᾱ ᾱς, Ion. **παιγνίη** ης f. **1 playfulness, play** Hdt.; **game, sport** Hdt.
2 (concr.) **entertainment, party** Ar.

παιγνιήμων ονος Ion.masc.fem.adj. (of a person) **playful** Hdt.

παίγνιον, Ion. **παίχνιον**, ου n. **1 plaything, toy** A.satyr.fr. Call.epigr.; (fig., W.GEN. of god, ref. to man) Pl.
2 playmate (ref. to a girl's lover) Ar.; (ref. to a man's catamite) Plu.
3 game, sport, amusement Pl. Call.; (as generic name for a class of arts or crafts more pleasing than useful) Pl.
4 humorous song (about a person) Plb.
5 (ref. to a person) **trickster** Theoc.

παιγνιώδης ες adj. | compar. παιγνιωδέστερος |
‖ NEUT.SB. **playful manner or behaviour** X.(compar.) Plu.

παιδαγωγεῖον ου n. [παιδαγωγός] **1 attendants' waiting room** (in a school) D.
2 (gener.) **school** Plu.

παιδαγωγέω contr.vb. | fut.pass. παιδαγωγήσομαι | **1** (of a slave) **escort a child** (to school); (fig., of a person) **lead like a child** —an old man E. ‖ PASS. **be led like a child, be made a fool of** (by someone) Hyp.
2 (fig., of the disciple of a philosopher or poet) **follow about like a child's attendant, attend on, shadow** —someone Pl.
‖ PASS. **be shadowed** (by a disciple) Pl.
3 (gener., of educators or sim.) **guide, train** —someone Pl.; **control, regulate** —diseases Pl. ‖ PASS. **be schooled or trained** (in sthg.) Pl. —W.INF. to do sthg. Plu.; (of people, a city, a symposium) **be regulated** Pl.

παιδαγωγίᾱ ᾱς f. **1 escorting of a child** (to school); (fig.) **attendance, guidance, help** (for a sick person, by a friend) E.
2 tuition, education, schooling (of children) Plu.; (gener.) **guidance, training, schooling** (of people) Pl.

παιδαγωγικός ή όν *adj.* (of a system of medicine) monitorial, supervisory (W.GEN. over diseases) Pl.

παιδ-αγωγός οῦ *m.* [παῖς¹, ἀγωγός] **1 child-attendant, tutor** (slave who escorted a boy to and fr. school and had general charge of him while out of doors) Hdt. Att.orats. Pl. +; **childhood servant, tutor** (of a royal child) E. Pl.
2 (pejor. title applied to Fabius Maximus 'Cunctator') **lackey, shadow** (of Hannibal, whom he followed rather than engaged in battle) Plu.
3 guide, mentor (of kings, tyrants) Plu.

παιδάριον ου *n.* [dimin. παῖς¹] **1 young child** (ref. to a boy) Ar. Pl. X. D. Men. Plb.; (ref. to a girl) D. Men.; **baby** (of either sex) Men.; **boy** (ref. to Eros) Call.*epigr.*; (pejor., ref. to a young man) **mere child** Ar. ‖ PL. **children** (opp. adults) Ar. Att.orats. +
2 young slave (male) Ar. Thphr. Men. Plb. Plu.; (female) Thphr.

παιδαριώδης ες *adj.* (pejor., of activities, topics) **childish, puerile** Pl. Arist. Plb. Plu.; (of persons, ref. to their behaviour or competence) Plb.
—**παιδαριωδῶς** *adv.* **childishly** Plb.

παιδδῶαν (Lacon.fem.gen.pl.ptcpl.): see παίζω

παιδεία ᾱς, Ion. **παιδείη** ης *f.* [παῖς¹] **1 childhood, boyhood** Simon.; (ref. to appearance) **youthfulness** Thgn.
2 process or manner of rearing a child, **upbringing** A. E. Lys.
3 process of training and teaching, **education** Th. Ar. Att.orats. Pl. +
4 product of training and teaching, **culture, learning, education** Att.orats. Pl. +

παίδειος ον *adj.* **1** of or relating to children; (of prizes, activities, or sim.) **for the young** Pl.; (of the upbringing) **of children** S.; (of the flesh) **of one's own children** A.
2 (of songs) **addressed to boys** (by poets) Pi.

παιδεραστέω *contr.vb.* [παιδεραστής] **be a lover of boys** Pl. Plu.

παιδ-εραστής οῦ *m.* [παῖς¹, ἐραστής] (ref. to a man) **lover of boys** (i.e. adolescents) Pl. X.; (pejor.) **pederast** Ar.

παιδεραστίᾱ ᾱς *f.* **love of boys** Pl.

παίδευμα ατος *n.* [παιδεύω] **1** one who is brought up; (sg. and poet.pl., ref. to a person) **nursling, foster-child** (W.GEN. of a father or surrogate) E.; (of Misfortune, ref. uncert.) Lyr.adesp. ‖ PL. **nurslings** (W.GEN. of gods, ref. to humans) Pl.; (of the foliage of Parnassos, fig.ref. to sheep) E.
2 that which is taught, **subject of learning** or **instruction** Isoc. Pl. X. Arist. Plu. ‖ PL. **instruction, education** D. Plu.
3 that which provides instruction; (ref. to Eros) **living lesson** (W.GEN. in Wisdom) E.*fr.*

παίδευσις εως *f.* **1** process or system of training or teaching, **training, instruction, education** Hdt. Ar. Isoc. Pl. X. Plu.; (ref. to Athens) **lesson, example** (W.GEN. to Greece) Th. ‖ PL. **subjects of instruction** Pl. X. Plu.
2 result of teaching, **learning, culture, education** Ar. Isoc. Arist. Plu.

παιδευτέος ᾱ ον *vbl.adj.* (of people) **to be educated** Pl. Arist.

παιδευτής οῦ *m.* **teacher, instructor** or **educator** (of the young) Pl. Plb. NT. Plu.

παιδευτικός ή όν *adj.* relating to teaching ‖ FEM.SB. **educative art, education** Pl. ‖ NEUT.SB. **educative capability** or **capacity** (of a person, Homer's poetry) Plu.

παιδευτός ή όν *adj.* (of virtue) **acquired by training** Pl.

παιδεύω *vb.* [παῖς¹] **1 bring up** (a child) ‖ PASS. (of a person, a god) **be brought up**, be reared, grow up S. E. Call.
2 teach, train, educate —*children, pupils, ignorant persons, or sim.* Hdt. S. E. Ar. + —W.DAT. or PREP.PHR. *in some skill or branch of learning* Th. Att.orats. Pl. +; **train** —W.DBL.ACC. *someone, in sthg.* Hdt. Antipho Pl. + —W.ACC. + INF. *a person or animal, to do sthg.* Hdt. X. —W.ACC. + PREDIC.ADJ. *someone, to be such and such* S. E.; (intr.) **teach, give instruction** Isoc.
3 ‖ MID. **have** (W.ACC. the young, one's son) **taught** or **trained** Pl. Theoc.
4 ‖ PF.PASS. (esp. ptcpl.) **have received teaching, be well educated** or **cultured** X. Arist.; **be trained** or **expert** Pl. Arist. Thphr.
5 educate, school —*someone's character* S. —*one's soul and body* X.
6 punish —*someone* NT.
—**πεπαιδευμένως** *pf.pass.ptcpl.adv.* **informedly** —*ref. to criticising someone* Isoc.

παιδιά ᾶς *f.* [παίζω] (sg. and pl.) **childish play, amusement, fun, game** S.*Ichn.* E. Th. Ar. Att.orats. Pl. +; (fig., ref. to present hardships) **mere child's play** (compared to those to come) A.

παιδίᾱ ᾱς *f.* [παῖς¹] condition like that of a child, **childishness** (assoc.w. incapacity, lack of sense) Pl.

παιδικά ῶν *n.pl.* [παιδικός] **1** (w.sg.ref.) object of affection, **beloved, sweetheart, darling boy** (sts. W.GEN. of someone) S.*satyr.fr.* Th. Ar. Pl. X. Arist.; (w.pl.ref.) Pl. X.; (w.gener.ref.) **boys** (as objects of sexual attraction, opp. women) E.*Cyc.*
2 (fig., ref. to philosophy) object of passion, **favourite pursuit** (of a person) Pl.

παιδικός ή όν *adj.* [παῖς¹] **1** of or relating to a child or boy; (of faults, friendships, subjects of study, or sim.) **childish, of childhood** Arist. Plb. Plu.; (of a gift) **for a child** Arist.; (of a chorus) **of boys** Lys. Is.; (derog., of a penis) **a mere boy's** Ar.
2 (pejor., of emotions, behaviour, or sim.) **childish** Pl. Arist. Plb.
3 of or relating to a youth as an object of homosexual love; (of songs) **in praise of boys** B.*fr.*; (of sexual relations) **with boys** X.; (of beauty) **of boyhood** Theoc.; (of a kind of story) **about boys** (i.e. a love-story) X.
4 (of an explanation, conversation) **playful** (opp. σπουδαῖος serious) Pl. X.
—**παιδικῶς** *adv.* **1 childishly** Arist. Plb. Plu.
2 playfully Pl.

παιδίον ου *n.* [dimin. παῖς¹] **1 male or female child, child** or **baby** Hdt. Ar. Att.orats. Pl. +; (phr.) ἐκ παιδίον *from childhood* Ar. X. Is. Plb. Plu. ‖ PL. **children** (opp. adults) Carm.Pop. Hdt. +
2 male slave, boy Ar. Men.
—**παιδιόθεν** *adv.* (prep.phr.) ἐκ παιδιόθεν *from childhood* NT.

παιδισκάριον ου *n.* [dimin. παιδίσκη] **young slave-girl** Men.

παιδίσκη ης *f.* [dimin. παῖς¹] **1 young girl** Ar. X. Men. Plb. Plu.
2 slave-girl Att.orats. Men. NT. Plu.; (ref. to a prostitute) Hdt. Att.orats. Plu.

παιδίσκος ου *m.* **1 young boy** Ar. X.
2 young slave-boy Philox.Leuc.

παιδιώδης ες *adj.* [παιδιά] **fond of amusement** Arist.

παιδνός όν *adj.* [παῖς¹] **1** (of a person, a god) **having the age of a child, infant** Od. Call.; (of a hand) E.
2 (pejor.) **childish, infantile** A.

παιδο-βόρος ον *adj.* [βορά, βιβρώσκω] (of anguish) **from eating one's children** A.

παιδογονίᾱ ᾱς *f.* [παιδογόνος] **begetting of children** Pl.

παιδο-γόνος ον *adj.* **1 begetting children**; (of Zeus) **fathering a child** Call.; (W.GEN. w. Io) Pl.
2 (of a penis) **procreative** Theoc.*epigr.*

παιδοκτονέω *contr.vb.* [παιδοκτόνος] **murder one's children** E.

παιδο-κτόνος ον *adj.* [κτείνω] (of madness) **prompting child-murder** E. ‖ MASC.SB. **child-murderer** S.; (ref. to weapons) E.

παιδ-ολέτειρα ᾱς *f.* [ὀλετήρ] **child-murderess** (ref. to Medea) E.

παιδολέτωρ ορος *masc.fem.adj.* (of strife, caused by Oedipus' curse on his sons; of the nightingale, ref to Prokne) **child-murdering** A. E. ‖ FEM.SB. **child-murderess** (ref. to Medea) E.

παιδο-λῡμάς άδος *fem.adj.* [λύμη] (of Althaia, mother of Meleager) **who destroyed her son** A.

παιδο-μαθής ές *adj.* [μανθάνω] **trained from boyhood** (W.PREP.PHR. in some activity) Plb.

παιδονομίᾱ ᾱς *f.* [παιδονόμος] **1 office of superintendent of children** Arist.
2 supervision of children Arist.

παιδο-νόμος ου *m.* [νέμω] **superintendent of children** (title of an official at Sparta and elsewhere) X. Arist. Plu.

παιδοποιέω *contr.vb.* [παιδοποιός] **1** (of a man) **father children** E.; (mid.) E. Att.orats. Pl. X. Men. Plu.
2 (of a woman) **bear children** S. Ar.; (mid.) D.
3 ‖ MID. (of both parents) **produce children** Pl.

παιδοποίησις εως *f.* **child-bearing** (as a period of a woman's life) Pl.

παιδοποιΐᾱ ᾱς *f.* **1 production of children** (by either parent, or jointly) Isoc. Pl. Aeschin. Plb. Plu.
2 making (someone) one's own child, **creation of a family** (by adoption) Arist.

παιδο-ποιός όν *adj.* [ποιέω] **1** (of a woman) **child-bearing** E. Plu.; (of troubles) **from bearing children** E.; (of pleasure) **of child-begetting** E.
2 (of sperm) **fertile** Hdt.

παιδοσπορέω *contr.vb.* [σπορά, σπείρω] **beget children** (seen as an animal pleasure) Pl.

παιδοτριβέω *contr.vb.* [παιδοτρίβης] **train up, coach** —*a potential malefactor* D.; (fig.) **foster** —*a tyranny* Plu.

παιδο-τρίβης ου *m.* [τρίβω] **one who exercises children, physical training instructor, trainer, coach** Ar. Att.orats. Pl. Arist.

παιδοτριβικός ή όν *adj.* ‖ FEM.SB. **physical training** Isoc. Arist.

παιδοτριβικῶς *adv.* **like a physical trainer** —*ref. to using a kind of vocabulary* Ar.

παιδοτροφέω *contr.vb.* **rear children**; (fig.) **feed the infant needs of** —*one's penis (envisaged as a child deprived of its nurse)* Ar.

παιδοτροφίᾱ ᾱς *f.* [παιδοτρόφος] **rearing of children** Pl. X. D. Men. Plu.

παιδο-τρόφος ον *adj.* [τρέφω] (of hands) **child-nursing** A.*satyr.fr.*; (of the olive) **child-nourishing** S.; (of a season) **for rearing chicks** (by a bird) Simon. ‖ FEM.SB. (ref. to a mother) **rearer of children** E.

παιδό-τρωτος ον *adj.* [τρωτός] **wounded by children**; (of sufferings) **from child-inflicted wounds** A.

παιδουργέω *contr.vb.* [παῖς¹, ἔργον] (of a bird) **produce young, propagate** E.

παιδουργίᾱ ᾱς *f.* **1 production of children** (by parents) Pl.
2 (perh.concr.) **children produced** (by a mother), **progeny** S.

παιδοφιλέω *contr.vb.* (of men) **love a boy** or **boys** Sol. Thgn. Call.

παιδοφίλης ου *m.* **lover of boys** Thgn.

παιδοφονίᾱ ᾱς *f.* [παιδοφόνος] **killing of one's children** Plu.

παιδο-φόνος ον *adj.* [θείνω] **1 murdering a child or children** (one's own or another's); (of a man) **who has murdered a child** (of another) Il.; (of a lioness, fig.ref. to Medea) **child-murdering** E.
2 (of a calamity) **consisting of child-murder** Hdt.; (of blood) **of murdered children** E.

παίζω, *dial.* **παίσδω** *vb.* [παῖς¹] | Lacon.fem.gen.pl.ptcpl. παιδδωᾶν | dial.fut. παιξοῦμαι | aor. ἔπαισα, later ἔπαιξα (Theoc. Plu.) | pf. πέπαιχα (Plu.) ‖ PF.PASS.: 3sg. πέπαισται, 3sg.imperatv. πεπαίσθω |
1 (of children or adults) **act like a child, have fun, play** (sts. w. a specific object, such as a toy, ball or weapon) Od. +
2 (specif., of a dancer) **play, frolic** Od. Hes. hHom. Ar. Pl.; (of a woman, envisaged as a horse) **gambol** Anacr.
3 (of persons) **take recreation, enjoy oneself** (in hunting) Od. S. Plu.
4 (euphem., w. sexual connot.) **have fun** —w. πρός + ACC. w. someone Ar. X.
5 (gener.) **fool about, jest, joke** (opp. behave or speak seriously) Thgn. Hdt. E. Ar. Att.orats. Pl. +—w. πρός + ACC. w. someone or at someone's expense E. Pl. X. Men.; **have fun** —w. εἰς + ACC. w. someone's hair (by playing w. it and joking about it) Pl.; (euphem., w. criminal connot.) **play dirty tricks** Theoc. ‖ PF.PASS. (of a story) **have been made up in jest** Hdt.(v.l. πέπλασται) ‖ IMPERS.PF.PASS. **fun has been had** Ar.; (imperatv.) **let the fun stop** Pl.
6 (of a musician) **play** (an instrument) Pi. Ar.

παιήσω (fut.): see παίω

παιητέος ᾱ ον *vbl.adj.* [παίω] (of a door) **to be knocked on** Men.

Παιήων *ep.m.*: see Παιών

παιξοῦμαι (dial.fut.): see παίζω

Παίονες ων *m.pl.* **Paeonians** (a people living in Macedonia and Thrace) Il. Mimn. A. Pi.*fr.* Hdt. E. + ‖ SG.ADJ. (of an army) **Paeonian** E.

—**Παιονίᾱ** ᾱς, Ion. **Παιονίη** ης *f.* **Paeonia** Il. Hdt. Th. +
—**Παιονικός** ή όν *adj.* (of a town, tribes) **Paeonian** Th. ‖ FEM.SB. **Paeonian land** Hdt.
—**Παιονίς** ίδος *fem.adj.* (of women) **Paeonian** Hdt.

παίπαλα ων *n.pl.* **rocky ground** Call.

παιπάλη ης *f.* **1 sieved meal, fine flour** Ar.
2 (fig., pejor.ref. to a person) **smooth talker, sly rogue** Ar.

παιπάλημα ατος *n.* (pejor.ref. to a person) **smooth talker** Ar. Aeschin.

παιπαλόεις εσσα εν *adj.* (of a mountain, a hilltop) *app.* **rugged, rocky** Hom. Hes.*fr.* hHom.; (of an island) Hom. hHom. AR.; (of a road or path) Hom.; (perh. of vales) Hes.(dub.)

παῖς¹ παιδός (Aeol. πάιδος), Boeot. **πῆς** πηδός *m.f.* | voc. παῖ | acc. παῖδα, dial. πάιδα | PL.: dial.acc. παίδας | gen. παίδων, dial. παιδῶν | dat. παισί, ep. παίδεσσι ‖ also disyllab. in ep. and lyr.: nom. πάις, also πάϊς | voc. πάϊ | acc. πάιν (AR.) |
1 male or female offspring (by birth or adoption, regardless of age), **son** or **daughter** Hom. + ‖ PL. **children** Hom. +; **young** (of birds) A.
2 (fig.) **offspring** (W.GEN. of the sea, ref. to fishes) A.; (of the vine, ref. to wine) Pi.; (of a mountain rock, ref. to Echo) E.
3 ‖ PL. (gener.) **descendants** (of someone) A. Hdt.; (W.GEN. of Greeks, Lydians, periphr.ref. to the nations) A. Pi. Hdt.; **sons** (of Asklepios, periphr.ref. to the medical profession) Pl.; (of painters, periphr.ref. to professional artists) Pl.
4 (ref. to a person's age, w. no parental relationship implied) **male or female child, boy** or **girl, child** Hom. + ‖ VOC. (as a familiar address by an older person) **my child** Il. + ‖ MASC.PL. (as familiar address to equals) **my boys, lads** Ar. Theoc.

5 male or female slave, **boy, girl, slave** (oft. in voc. address) Anacr. Hippon. A. Ar. +
6 [perh. reltd. παπαῖ] ‖ VOC. (exclam., w. no specific addressee) **oh boy!** Men.
παῖς² *Aeol.adj*.: see πᾶς
παίσδω *dial.vb*.: see παίζω
παιφάσσω *vb*. | only pres. and impf. | (of a goddess, a hero) app. **rush** or **dart about** Il. AR.
παίχνιον *Ion.n*.: see παίγνιον
παίω *vb*. | fut. παίσω, also παιήσω (Ar.) | aor. ἔπαισα | pf. (in cpds.) -πέπαικα ‖ aor.pass. ἐπαίσθην |
1 hit with an aimed blow; (of persons) **strike, hit** (w. a weapon, stick, missile, the hand, or sim.) —*a person, a part of the body, an animal, an object* Pratin. Hdt. Trag. Ar. X. + —(fig., W.DAT. w. *phrases, envisaged as missiles*) Ar. —*a person* (W. 2ND ACC. or PREP.PHR. *on a part of the body*) Hdt. S. Ar. X.; (of a weapon or sim.) —*a person, a part of the body* Hdt. S. E.; (of a person) **strike** —W.COGN.ACC. *a blow* S. —W.ACC. + COGN.ACC. *a person, w. a blow* S. X. ‖ PASS. **be struck** (by a weapon, someone's hand) A. Antipho Th. Lys. X.; (fig.) **be struck with anguish** (as if by a sword) A.
2 (intr.) **deliver a blow** (w. a weapon, one's hand) Trag. Ar. X. + —W.PREP.PHR. *to a part of the body* S. E.; (fig., ref. to a futile action) —*against a tormenting goad* A.
3 (of a warship) **dash, drive** —*its ram* (W.PREP.PHR. *against another ship*) A.; (intr., of sailors) **strike** —W.DAT. w. *rams* (W.PREP.PHR. *against enemy rams*) Th. ‖ PASS. (of sailors, i.e. their ships) **be struck** (by rams) A.
4 (colloq.) **bang, fuck** —*a woman* Ar.
5 beat away —*wasps* (W. ἀπό + GEN. *fr. a house*) Ar.
6 cause (sthg.) to strike (sthg. else); strike —*a thyrsos, a person* (W.PREP.PHR. *against a rock*) E. —*a sword* (*into someone's throat*) E.; (of a heavy sea) **dash** —*ships* (W.PREP.PHR. *against a coast*) Plu.
7 hit (sthg.) non-aggressively (w. a hand or implement); **strike** —*the sea* (w. oars) A. E. —(W.DAT. w. *hands and feet, while trying to keep afloat*) Tim. —*one's head* (w. *one's hand, in grief*) S. —*a door* (i.e. *knock on it*) E.; (mid.) —*one's thigh* (w. *one's hand*) X. Plu.
8 hit (an obstacle) accidentally; **strike** —*one's skull* (*against sthg. hard*) E.*Cyc.*; (of a charioteer) —*a turning-post* S.; (fig., of a person's destiny, envisaged as a ship) —*a hidden reef* A.; (intr., of stones thrown as missiles) **crash** —W.PREP.PHR. *against rocks* X.; (fig., of a person) —*against a reef* A.*fr*.; (of frenzied words, seen as a muddy torrent) —*against waves of ruin* A.

Παιών ῶνος, dial. **Παιάν** ᾶνος, ep. **Παιήων** ονος, Aeol. **Πάων** ονος *m*. **Paion, Paian, Paieon, Paon** (god of healing; in Hom. and Hes.*fr*. a separate god, in later authors usu. equated w. Apollo) Hom. Hes.*fr*. Sapph. Sol. Pi. Trag. +; (epith. of Asklepios) Ar.(quot. S.)
—**παιών** ῶνος, dial. **παιάν** ᾶνος, ep. **παιήων** ονος *m*. **1** (fig., ref. to a person) **healer** (W.GEN. of *troubles*) A. S.; (epith. of death) A.*fr*. E.; (epith. of sleep) S.
2 song of petition, thanksgiving or celebration (addressed esp. to Apollo, but also to other gods, in various ctxts., e.g. before a battle, after victory, at a wedding, accompanying libations at a symposium), **paean** Il. hHom. Alcm. Archil. Thgn. B. +; (ref. to a dirge or sim.) A. E.
3 (exclam.) ἰὴ παιών, ἰὴ παιήον (or sim., ritual cry assoc.w. such songs, also separately as an appeal for good fortune) Lyr.adesp. Carm.Pop. Pi.*fr*. Ar. Call.
4 metrical foot consisting of one long and three short syllables, **paeon** Arist.

Παίων *masc.adj*.: see Παίονες
παιωνίζω, dial. **παιανίζω** *vb*. [Παιών] | aor. ἐπαιώνισα, dial. παιάνιξα (B.) ‖ 3sg.plpf.pass. ἐπεπαιώνιστο | **1** (of victorious soldiers and others) **sing a paean** (in thanksgiving or celebration) B. Hdt. Th. Ar. +; (of soldiers, before an attack, petitioning for victory) Th. X.; (of symposiasts) X. ‖ IMPERS.PLPF.PASS. a paean had been sung (before an attack) Th.
2 (of women, petitioning for victory) **sing** (W.COGN.ACC. *a ritual cry*) **as if a paean** A.
3 ‖ PASS. (of Death) **be honoured with paeans** A.*fr*.
παιώνιος ᾱ ον *adj*. related to Paion and his art; (of hands, remedies) **healing** A. S. Ar.; (fig., of an oath) **bringing a cure** (to a problem) A.; (of a sound) **soothing** A. ‖ MASC.SB. **healer** (ref. to Apollo) A.; (W.GEN. of *sufferings*, ref. to a person) S. ‖ NEUT.PL.SB. festival of Paion Ar.
παιωνισμός (sts. written as dial. **παιανισμός**) οῦ *m*. **singing of a paean** (by attacking troops) Th.
πᾱκτίς *dial.f*., **πᾶκτις** *Aeol.f*.: see πηκτίς
πᾱκτός *dial.adj*.: see πηκτός
πακτόω *contr.vb*. [reltd. πήγνυμι] **1 make fast, fasten up** (w. bars or sim.) —*a door, house, gateway* Hippon. S. Ar.
2 make tight, seal up —*cracks in a wall* (by *plugging them w. rags*) Ar.
πάλα *dial.f*.: see πάλη
παλάθη ης, dial. **παλάθα** ᾱς *f*. **pressed cake of dried fruit** (esp. figs), **fruit-cake** Carm.Pop. Hdt. Plu.
πάλαι *temporal adv*. **1** (ref. to the distant past) **long ago, formerly, originally** Hom. +; (w.art.) τὸ πάλαι Hdt. Th. Pl. D.; (quasi-adj.) of *long ago* • οἱ πάλαι φωτές **men of old** Pi.
2 (ref. to past time, incl. the recent past) **formerly, once, recently** Hom. + • νῦν τε καὶ πάλαι **now as formerly** S. • εἶπον πάλαι *I said a moment ago* S. • (quasi-adjl.) οἱ πάλαι λόγοι *earlier words* A.
3 (w.pres. or impf.vb.) **for a long time** (ref. to a period lasting until the present or some past time) Hom. + • ἰχνεύω πάλαι *I have long been tracking* (*someone*) S. • ἔχεν πάλαι *he had long been holding* (*sthg.*) Il.
παλαι-γενής ές *adj*. [γένος, γίγνομαι] **1** (of living persons or gods) **born long ago, ancient, aged** Hom. hHom. Thgn.(v.l. χαμαιγενής) A.; (of olive-wood) AR.
2 coming into being or existing earlier; (of an enemy) **long-standing** A.; (of a transgression) **ancient, old** A.; (of singers, heroes) **of old** E. AR.
παλαί-γονος ον *adj*. [γόνος] (of persons of an earlier generation) **born long ago, ancient, of older times** Pi. ‖ MASC.PL.SB. **men of old** Pi.
παλαί-θετος ον *adj*. [θετός] (of logs) **stored up some time ago** Call.
παλαιμονέω *contr.vb*. [reltd. παλαίω] (fig., of a person making an incorrect assertion) **flail around** Pi.
παλαιμοσύνη (also **παλαισμοσύνη**) ης *f*. [πάλαισμα] **wrestling** (as a sport) Hom. Tyrt. Ibyc. Xenoph.
Παλαίμων ονος *m*. **Palaimon** (sea god, the deified Melikertes) E. Call. ‖ PL. app., sea gods Call.
παλαιο-γενής ές *adj*. [παλαιός; γένος, γίγνομαι] (of an old man) **born long ago, ancient** Ar.
παλαιο-μάτωρ ορος *dial.f*. [μήτηρ] **mother in ancient times, ancestress** (of a race, ref. to Io) E.
παλαιόμισημα *n*.: see παλεομίσημα
παλαιόομαι *pass.contr.vb*. (of things) **grow old** or **antiquated** Pl.
παλαιό-πλουτος ον *adj*. [πλοῦτος] (of a city) **wealthy from ancient times** Th.; (of persons) **with inherited wealth** Arist.

παλαιός ᾱ (Ion. ή) όν *adj.* [πάλαι] | compar. παλαίτερος, also παλαιότερος | superl. παλαίτατος, also παλαιότατος |
1 having existed for a long time; (of living persons, their bodies, or sim.) **aged, old** Hom. Tyrt. Trag. Ar.; (of wine) Od. Pi.; (of ships) Od. Lys. Ar.; (of objects) Od. Trag. Ar. Pl.; (of places) **of early origin, ancient** Pi. Hdt. Trag. Th. || COMPAR.MASC.PL.SB. **the older generation, elders** Tyrt. Thgn. Pi. E.
2 unchanging over a long time; (of a friend, ref. to the period of friendship) **long-standing, old** Il. S. E. Lys.; (of laws, practices) A. E. Antipho Lys.; (of hatred, anger) S. E.
3 (of a period of time) **long** S. E. Th. || NEUT.IMPERS. (w. ἐστί understd.) **it is a long time** S.
4 belonging to an earlier time; (of persons) **ancient, of old** Hom. hHom. Pi. Th. Ar. +; (of things, events, pronouncements, feelings) **old, former, earlier** Od. Pi. Hdt. Trag. Th. +; (pejor., of rumours) **outdated** S. || MASC.PL.SB. **men of old** Ar. Isoc. || NEUT.PL.SB. **old times, the past** Th. Isoc. D.
5 (advbl.acc.) τὸ παλαιόν **in old times, formerly, originally** A. Hdt. Ar. +; (prep.phr.) ἐκ (or ἀπὸ) παλαιοῦ (or sim.) **from an early time, from the beginning** Hdt. Antipho Th. +
παλαιότης ητος *f.* **1 longevity** (of a person) Aeschin.; **oldness, antiquity** (of sthg.) Pl.
2 (pejor.) **outdatedness, staleness** (of food, written law) Pl. NT.; **lack of originality, fustiness** (in a suggested plan) E.
παλαιό-φρων ον, gen. ονος *adj.* [φρήν] (of deities) **with ancient wisdom, old and wise** A.
πάλαισμα ατος *n.* [παλαίω] | dial.dat.pl. παλαισμάτεσσι (Pi.) |
1 wrestling match Pi. Pl. X. Plu.
2 (gener.) **contest** (betw. soldiers) A. *S.fr.* Plu.; **struggle** (of a man, to escape fr. his burning clothes) E.; **tussle** (betw. negotiators) Plb.; **competition** (betw. citizens) S. || PL. **series of struggles** (ref. to life, w. its successes and failures) E.
3 (specif., in wrestling) **fall, throw** (of which three were needed for victory) A. Hdt. Pl.; (fig., W.GEN. by one's own hand, ref. to suicide) E.
4 wrestling trick Theoc. Plu.; (fig.) **trick, ploy** (of a politician, speaker, commander) Ar. X. Aeschin. Plu.
5 (fig.) prob. **hold** (on an enemy) A.
παλαισμοσύνη *f.*: see παλαιμοσύνη
παλαιστή *f.*, **παλαιστιαῖος** *adj.*: see παλαστή, παλαστιαῖος
παλαιστής οῦ (Ion. έω) *m.* [παλαίω] **1 wrestler** Od. Hdt. Ar. Pl. +; (fig., ref. to a god forcing himself on a woman) A.
2 (fig.) **rival, adversary, opponent** Trag.
παλαιστικός ή όν *adj.* (of a person) **skilled in wrestling** Arist.
παλαίστρα ᾱς, Ion. **παλαίστρη** ης *f.* **1 palaestra, wrestling school** (a public or private establishment, usu. an enclosed courtyard w. surrounding rooms, comparable to a gymnasium but smaller) Hdt. E. Ar. Pl. +; (hired out for public performances by sophists, musicians, or sim.) Thphr.; (mythol., ref. to the place where Kerkyon forced passers-by to wrestle w. him) B.
2 training school (of a military leader) Plu.
παλαιστρίδιον ου *n.* [dimin.] **little palaestra** (owned by an individual) Thphr.
παλαίτερος (compar.adj.), **παλαίτατος** (superl.): see παλαιός
παλαί-φατος ον *adj.* [πάλαι, φατός] **1** (of a prophecy, curse, saying) **spoken long ago** Od. A. Pi. S.; (of oracular foreknowledge) **revealed long ago** S.
2 spoken of since ancient times; (of a family, a place) **long-famed, legendary** A. Pi.; (of Justice) A.; (of an oak, assoc.w. the origins of mankind) perh. **legendary, proverbial** Od.
—παλαίφατον *neut.adv.* according to ancient story, **in legend** Pi.
παλαί-χθων ον, gen. ονος *adj.* [χθών] (of Theban Ares) **long dwelling in the land** A.; (of the Athenian people) Aeschin.(quot.epigr.)
παλαίω *vb.* [πάλη] **1 wrestle** Il. Xenoph. *S.fr.* *E.satyr.fr.* Ar. Isoc. + —W.DAT. *w. someone* Od. Thphr. —*w. a lion, a boar* Pi. Bion
2 (fig.) **wrestle, come to grips, contend** —W.DAT. *w. calamities, losses, or sim.* Hes. E. X. Plb.; (of Ajax, ref. to his suicide) —*w. a bloody death* Pi. || PASS. (of a person, ref. to a violent death) **be thrown** E.; (of wine, i.e. its effects) **be grappled with** E.*Cyc.*
παλαμάομαι *mid.contr.vb.* [παλάμη] | dial.fut. παλαμάσομαι | **1** put in hand, **contrive, devise** —*sthg.* Ar.; (intr.) **plan, scheme** Alc. Ar.
2 grasp, secure —*the necessities of life* (W.DAT. *w. one's hands*) X.
παλάμη ης, dial. **παλάμᾱ** ᾱς *f.* | ep.gen.dat.sg.pl. παλάμηφι(ν) | **1** palm of the hand, **hand** (as used in grasping sthg.) Hom. *Hes.fr.* hHom. Lyr. AR.
2 hand (used in acts of violence) Il. Simon. E. Mosch.; **act of violence** S.; instrument of violence, **weapon** (ref. to a sword) E.
3 hand (used in creating works of art, in construction, or sim.) Il. Hes. Ibyc. Pi. Emp.
4 (usu.pl.) act of skill or cunning, **device, stratagem** (of a god) Alc. A. Pi. S.; (of a human) Pi. Hdt. Ar.
5 (gener.) **method, means** (of achieving sthg.) Alc. Emp.; (W.GEN. of achieving a livelihood, success) Thgn.
Παλαμήδης ους *m.* | acc. Παλαμήδη, also Παλαμήδην, dial. Παλαμήδεα | **Palamedes** (celebrated for his inventions, esp. of writing, falsely accused of treason by Odysseus and stoned to death by the Greeks at Troy) E. Ar. Pl. X. Arist.(quot.com.)
παλαμναῖος ου *m.* [παλάμη] **1** one polluted by committing an act of violence; **man with blood on his hands** A. S. AR. Plu. || ADJ. **with blood on one's hands** Plu.(quot.com.)
2 daimon which takes vengeance on a polluted killer, avenger E.(dub.) X. || ADJ. (of a daimon) **avenging** Plu.
παλάσιον ου *n.* [dimin. παλάθη] **little fig-cake** Ar.
παλάσσομαι *ep.mid.vb.* [app.reltd. πάλος, πάλλω] | only pf.inf. πεπαλάχθαι, 2pl.pf.imperatv. πεπάλαχθε (in Hom. oft. emended to forms of πάλλω) | **cast lots** Hom.(dub.) —W.ACC. *for sthg.* AR.
παλάσσω *vb.* | ep.fut.inf. παλαξέμεν || pf.pass. πεπάλαγμαι | **1** (of a person being killed) **spatter, befoul** —*the floor* (W.DAT. *w. his blood and brains*) Od. || PASS. (esp. pf. and plpf., of persons or things) **be spattered** (usu. W.DAT. w. blood or sim.) Hom. Hellenist.poet. —W.ACC. *on one's hands, feet* Hom. —*on one's genitals* (W.DAT. *w. semen, as an example of ritual impurity*) Hes.
2 || PF.PASS. (wkr.sens., of nymphs) **be sprinkled or covered** —W.ACC. *w. barley meal* hHom.
3 || PASS. (of brains) **be spattered about** Il.; (of a river) —W.DAT. *by a thunderbolt* Call.
παλαστή (or **παλαιστή**) ῆς, Aeol. **παλάστᾱ** ᾱς *f.* [reltd. παλάμη] (as a measure) **palm, palm's breadth** Alc. X. Plb.
παλαστιαῖος (or **παλαιστιαῖος**) ον *adj.* (of objects) **measuring a palm's breadth** Hdt. Plb.
παλεο-μίσημα (or perh. **παλαιομίσημα**) ατος *n.* [παλαιός] (ref. to the sea) **object of long-standing hatred** (to Persians) Tim.

παλεύω *vb.* **1** (of a captured bird or person) **act as a decoy** Ar. **2** (fig., of a commander) **decoy, ensnare** —*the enemy* Plu.

παλέω *contr.vb.* | only 3sg.aor.opt. παλήσειε, ep.3sg.athem. aor.mid. πάλτο | **1** (of a fleet) app. **be disabled** or **wrecked** Hdt. **2** ‖ MID. (of a soldier) **come to harm, trip** (on his shield) Il.

πάλη ης, dial. **πάλᾱ** ᾱς *f.* **1 wrestling** (as a form of exercise or training and as a competitive sport) Hom. Pi. B. S.*satyr.fr.* E. Th. + **2 wrestling trick** Ar. **3 struggle, contest, fight** A.; (W.GEN. w. the spear) E.

πάλι *dial.adv.*: see πάλιν

παλιγγενεσίᾱ ᾱς *f.* [πάλιν, γίγνομαι] **regeneration** (of the world, in the time of the Messiah) NT.

παλίγ-γλωσσος ον *adj.* [γλῶσσα] **1** with speech that is the converse (of some norm); (of a city) **foreign-speaking** Pi.; (of a report) **untrue** Pi. **2** (of rivalry, in neg.phr.) app., with reversed voice, **relenting** Pi.*fr.*

παλιγκαπηλεύω *vb.* [παλιγκάπηλος] **buy goods for resale** D.

παλιγ-κάπηλος ου *m.* (pejor.) one who sells goods for a second time (i.e. which he has bought fr. an importer or other middleman), **resale tradesman** Ar.; (fig.) **second-hand peddler** (W.GEN. of vice, contrasted w. simple κάπηλος) D.

παλίγ-κοτος ον *adj.* [κότος] **1** with recurring rancour; (of a person) **spiteful** Sapph. Theoc.; (of rumours) **malicious** A.; (of fortune, a dream) **malign** A. Mosch. **2** (gener., of persons) **adverse, hostile** (W.DAT. to someone) Ar. ‖ MASC.PL.SB. **adversaries, enemies** A. Pi. **3** (of pain or suffering) **injurious, malignant** Pi. **4** (of a crag) **hostile, formidable** Archil.

—παλιγκότως *adv.* **adversely, with adverse effects** (for someone) Hdt.

παλιλλογέω *contr.vb.* [λόγος] | aor. ἐπαλιλλόγησα | **go over again in speech, relate** —*a narrative* Hdt. ‖ PASS. (of an event) **be retold** Hdt.

παλίλ-λογος ον *adj.* [λέγω] (of items) **collected together again, reassembled** Il.

παλίμ-βᾱμος ον *dial.adj.* [βῆμα, βαίνω] (of the steps of a woman working at the loom) **pacing back and forth** Pi.

παλίμ-βλαστής ές *adj.* [βλαστάνω] (of the Hydra) **regenerating** (w. new heads) E.

παλίμ-βολος ον *adj.* [βάλλω] **1 thrown in the reverse direction**; (of persons, their character) **unstable, unreliable, shifty** Pl. Plu.; (of an action) **duplicitous** Plu. ‖ NEUT.SB. (ref. to a person) **backslider** Aeschin. **2** (pejor., of a slave who has often changed hands, **good-for-nothing** Men.

παλιμ-μήκης ες *adj.* [μῆκος] (of a period of time) with the same length again, **doubled** A.

παλιμ-πετές *neut.adv.* [πίπτω] **falling backwards; back** —*ref. to moving in a reverse direction* (to the one desired) Il. AR.; **back again** —*ref. to returning to a place* Od. Call. AR.

παλίμ-πηξις εως *f.* [πῆξις] **refixing** (of soles on shoes, by stitching, as a sign of stinginess) Thphr.

παλίμ-πλαγκτος ον *adj.* [πλαγκτός] (of a person's course) **backward-wandering, returning** A.

παλιμ-πλάζομαι *pass.vb.* | only aor.ptcpl. παλιμπλαγχθείς (perh. better written πάλιν πλαγχθείς) | (of a person) **be driven back, be repulsed** Hom.

παλίμ-πνοια ης *ep.f.* [πνοή] **contrary blast** (of wind) AR.

παλίμ-ποινα ων *n.pl.* [ποινή] **repayment, recompense** A.

παλιμ-πόρευτος ον *adj.* [πορευτός] (of an army's flight) **backward-travelling** Tim.

παλίμ-πορος ον *adj.* [πόρος] (of an army's flight) **backward-moving** Tim.

παλίμ-πρητος ον *Ion.adj.* [πρᾱτός] (of a slave) **resold, good-for-nothing** Call.

παλιμ-προδοσίᾱ ᾱς *f.* **counter-treachery** Plb.

παλίμ-φᾱμος ον *dial.adj.* [φήμη] (of a song) with a reverse message, **of contrary meaning** (to a preceding song) E.

πάλιν (also dial. **πάλι** Call.*epigr.*) *adv.* **1** (w.vb. of movt.) in a backwards direction, **backwards, back** Il. +; **away** (fr. sthg.) —*ref. to averting one's eyes* Il.; (as prep.) **back** —W.GEN. **away fr. someone** Hom. **2** (w.vb. of movt., esp. of returning) **back to a starting-point, back, back again** Hom. + **3** (ref. to being restored to a former state) **back, back again** Od. + **4** (w.vb. of giving, receiving, or sim.) **back again, in return** Hom. + **5** in a reverse way; (w.vb. of speaking) **in contradiction** Il.; (w.vb. of thinking) **to the contrary, differently** A. ‖ NEUT.SB. (w.art.) **the reverse** (W.GEN. of youth, i.e. old age) Pi. **6** (ref. to a reciprocal action, in response to another) **in turn** Hdt. S. E. Ar. Pl. Men. **7** (ref. to a repeated action, as if going back to the beginning) **again, once again** Il. + **8** (adding a further detail to a narrative or argument) **then again, next, after that** X. Arist. Call.

παλιν-άγρετος ον *adj.* [ἀγρέω] (in neg.phrs.) **able to be taken back**; (of speech, an action) **revocable** Il. Hes. Call. AR.; (of youth) **recoverable** Theoc.

παλιν-αίρετος ον *adj.* [αἱρετός] (of decomposing matter in the blood) produced by reversal (of the healthy order), **back-product** Pl.

παλιν-αυτόμολος ου *m.* man who deserts back (to his original side), **double deserter** X.

παλινδικίᾱ ᾱς *f.* [δίκη] going to law again, **new trial** Plu.

παλινδρομέω *contr.vb.* [δρόμος] (of a sailor) **retrace one's course** (because of contrary winds) Plu.; (fig., w. nautical ref.) **reverse one's course** (of action) Plb.

παλίν-ορσος ον *Ion.adj.* [ὄρρος] **1** (quasi-advbl., of persons moving) in a backwards direction, **backwards** Il. **2** (quasi-advbl., of a person, blood) **back to a starting-point, back, back again** Emp.; (of a wave caused by disturbed water) AR.

—παλίνορσον, Att. **παλίνορρον** *neut.adv.* **1** in a reverse direction, **backwards** Ar. **2 back to a starting-point, back again** AR. **3** perh. **back, in return** —*ref. to giving* Call.

παλίν-ορτος ον *adj.* [ὄρνυμι] (of Wrath) **rising again, resurgent** A.

παλίν-σκιος (also **παλίσκιος**) ον *adj.* [σκιά] doubly (i.e. thickly) shaded; (of a cave, the side of a hill) **darkly shaded** hHom. Plu.; (prep.phrs.) ἐν παλινσκίῳ *in the shadow (of a wall)* Archil.; *in a dark place* Plu.; ἐκ τοῦ παλισκίου *out of the shadows* Plu. ‖ NEUT.PL.SB. **shady places** X.

παλινστομέω *contr.vb.* [στόμα] **speak contrary** (to what is right), **speak words of ill omen** A.

παλιν-στραφής ές *adj.* [στρέφω] (of hoofprints) **turned back to front, reversed** S.*Ichn.*

παλίν-τιτος ον *adj.* [τίνω] **1** (of actions) **done in requital, retributive** Od. **2** (of breezes) **bringing recompense** (for damaging winds) Emp.

παλίν-τονος ον *adj.* [τόνος] **1** (of a bow) **bent back, curved** (ref. to the reflex curve of a composite bow in its unstrung state) Hom. hHom. Hdt. S. AR.

παλιντράπελος

2 (of reins) **drawn tight, taut** Ar.
3 (of a physical connection or concord) **caused by opposite tensions** (as in the bow, where the tension of the string is balanced by the tension exerted by the arms) Heraclit.(v.l. παλίντροπος)

παλιν-τράπελος ον *adj.* [τρέπω] (of a sorrow) that turns back (to its opposite), **reversed** (i.e. to joy) Pi.

παλιν-τριβής ές *adj.* [τρίβω] 1 (of a stubborn ass) **beaten again and again** Semon.
2 perh., rubbed again and again (w.connot. of being thoroughly tested or experienced) ‖ NEUT.PL.SB. (fig., w. personal ref.) **hardened criminals** S.

παλιντροπάομαι *mid.contr.vb.* [παλίντροπος] | only (w.diect.): 3pl.impf. παλιντροπόωντο, aor.inf. παλιντροπάασθαι | (of persons, a ship) **turn back** AR.

παλιντροπίη ης *Ion.f.* **reversal** ‖ PL. **fluctuating emotions** AR.

παλίν-τροπος ον *adj.* [τρέπω] 1 (of eyes, sight) **turned away, averted** A.
2 (of a person) **turning back, returning** (on a journey) S.; **reverting** (to a former state) E.; (of a path, fig.ref. to a way of thinking) turning back (on itself), **contradictory** Parm. | see also παλίντονος 3
3 (of thinking) turned away or back (i.e. off course), **deranged** B.
4 (of progress) in the reverse direction, **contrary** (W.DAT. to expectation) Plb.; (of expectation) **frustrated** Plb.; (of victory) **shifting to the other side** Plu.; (of plans) **changing, contradictory** Plu. ‖ NEUT.PL.SB. reversals of fortune Plb.
5 (of Vengeance) **coming in return** (for wrongdoing) Call.

παλιντυπές *neut.adv.* [τύπτω] beaten back, **back** —*ref. to a sword and hammer rebounding* AR.

παλιν-τυχής ές *adj.* [τύχη] (of the destruction of a person's life) **in a reversal of fortune** A.

παλινῳδέω *contr.vb.* [ἀοιδή] **recant** (ref. to changing a wish) Pl.

παλινῳδία ᾶς *f.* 1 singing of a reverse song, **recantation, palinode** (ref. to an ode by Stesichorus, in which he recanted his attack on Helen) Isoc. Pl.; (ref. to a speech recanting an earlier one) Pl. Plu.
2 (fig., ref. to a change of mind) **change of tune** Plb.

Πάλιον *dial.m.*: see Πήλιον

παλίουρος ου *m.* a kind of spiky shrub, **thorn-bush** E.*Cyc.* Theoc.

παλι-ρρόθιος ον *adj.* [πάλιν, ῥόθιος] (of a wave) **surging backwards** (i.e. out to sea) Od. ‖ COLLECTV.NEUT.PL.SB. waves surging backwards, backwash AR.

παλί-ρροια ᾶς, Ion. **παλιρροίη** ης *f.* [ῥοή] 1 backwards flow, **counter-current** (in a stream) Hdt.; **tide** or **current** (of the sea) Call.
2 (fig., ref. to events) **turn of the tide** Plb. Plu.; (ref. to the changed direction of an invading horde) Plu.

παλί-ρροπος ον *adj.* [ῥέπω] (of an old man's knee or leg) inclining in a contrary direction (to what it should), **bent** or **tottering** E.

παλί-ρρους ουν Att.*adj.* [ῥόος] 1 (of surf, seen fr. a ship heading seawards) flowing back (towards land), **inrushing** E.
2 (fig., of justice, divine favour, envisaged as a returning tide) **streaming back** E.

παλί-ρροχθος ον *adj.* [ροχθέω] (of a place beside a channel) **where the waters roar in their ebb and flow** A.

παλι-ρρύμη ης *f.* [ῥύμη] **backwards thrust** (of sea-swell) Plu.; (fig.) **ebb-tide** (of Fortune) Plb.

παλί-ρρυτος ον *adj.* [ῥυτός] (of the blood of murderers) flowing in turn, **shed in retribution** S.

παλίσκιος *adj.*: see παλίνσκιος

παλί-σσυτος ον *adj.* [σεύω] 1 (of persons, animals) **rushing back** (to where they came from) E. AR. Plb.; (of the running of defeated troops) **in hasty retreat** S.; (wkr.sens., of persons) **returning** AR. Mosch.
2 (quasi-advbl., of an arrow rebounding) **backwards** Theoc.
3 (of a person) app., returning (to a normal state), **recovering** AR.

παλ-ίωξις εως *f.* [reltd. ἰωκή, ἰωχμός] **pursuit in turn, counter-attack** Il. Hes.

Παλλάδιον ου *n.* [Παλλάς] 1 **statue of Pallas** Hdt. Plu.; (placed in the stern of Athenian warships) Ar.
2 **Palladion** (name of a homicide court at Athens) Att.orats. Arist.

παλλακεύομαι *mid.vb.* [παλλακή] 1 **keep** (W.ACC. a woman) **as a concubine** Hdt.
2 ‖ PASS. be a concubine (sts. W.DAT. to someone) Plu.

παλλακή ῆς *f.* **concubine** (female, slave or free, supported by a male in a semi-permanent sexual relationship other than marriage) Hdt. Ar. Att.orats. Pl. +

παλλακίᾱ ᾱς *f.* state of being a concubine, **concubinage** Is.

παλλακίς ίδος *f.* **concubine** Hom. X. Plu.

Παλλάς άδος *f.* **Pallas** (epith. of Athena) Hom. +; (more freq., as name of Athena) hHom. +

πάλ-λευκος ον *adj.* [πᾶς, λευκός] 1 (of clothes) **all of white** (as a sign of celebration, opp. funereal black) A. E.*fr.*
2 (of a woman's foot or neck) **pure white, snow-white** E.; (of an old woman's head, ref. to her hair) E.

Παλλήνη ης *f.* 1 **Pallene** (westernmost peninsula of Chalcidice) Hdt. Th. X. D.
2 **Pallene** (name of an Athenian deme) | see Βαλληνάδε

—**Παλληνεύς** έως (Ion. έος) *masc.adj.* (of a man) **from the deme Pallene** Hdt. Hyp. D. Call. Plu.

—**Παλληνίς** ίδος *fem.adj.* (epith. of Athena) **of Pallene** (where she had a temple) Hdt. E. Arist.

πάλλω *vb.* | ep.impf. πάλλον | aor. ἔπηλα, ep. πῆλα, dial. ἔπᾱλα, dial.imperatv. πᾶλον ‖ MID.: aor.inf. πήλασθαι | ep.pf.inf. πεπαλάσθαι, ep.2pl.pf.imperatv. πεπάλασθε (dub.: better redupl.aor.2 πεπαλέσθαι, πεπάλεσθε) ‖ PASS.: pf. πέπαλμαι ‖ see also παλάσσομαι |
1 **poise** —*a spear or other missile* (*before throwing it*) Hom. Hes. Pi. E. Ar. +
2 **brandish, wield** —*a shield* Hes. E. Ar. —*a spear* Carm.Pop. —*a bow* S. —*an axe, a staff* AR.
3 (of a parent) **dandle** —*a baby* Il. E.
4 (in making decisions or choices) **shake** —*lots* (*in a container*) Hom. Alcm.; (intr.) **shake the lots** Il.; **sort** —*horses* (W.DAT. by lot) S.(dub.) ‖ MID. **cast lots** Il. Hdt. Call. ‖ PASS. (of a lot) be cast S.
5 (gener.) set in vigorous or agitated motion; (of a dancer) **sway, swing** —*one's foot* E.; (of a boxer limbering up) —*his arms* AR.; (of an eagle) **ply** —*its wings* AR.; (periphr., of a warrior) **move** —*his swift legs* (i.e. *rush*) AR. —**high steps** (i.e. *leap*) AR.; (of Night) **drive on, hurry along** —*her chariot team* E.; (intr., of horses) **prance, gallop** E.; (of a dolphin) **gambol** E.; (of a dancer) **leap** Ar.
6 ‖ PASS. (of a dancer's knee) shake, sway Ar.; (of netted fish) quiver or thrash about Hdt.; (of eagles) swoop (across the sea) Pi.; (of a sunbeam reflected by water) dance or quiver AR.
7 ‖ PASS. be physically affected by emotion; (of a person, a heart) be shaken, quake or quiver (usu. w. fear) Il. hHom. A.

Hdt.(oracle) AR. Plu.; suffer palpitations (of the heart) Plu. || ACT. (intr.) quake —W.DAT. w. fear S.

πάλμυς υδος *m.* [Lydian loanwd.] | acc. πάλμυν | **king** (in Lydia) Hippon.; (of Thrace, ref. to Rhesos) Hippon.; (com.ref. to Zeus, Apollo, W.GEN. of the gods, of Mt. Cyllene) Hippon.

πάλος ου *m.* [πάλλω 4] **1 lot** (cast fr. a shaken container) Alcm. A. Call.
2 process or result of casting lots, **casting of lots, lottery** Hdt. Trag. Call. AR.
3 role or duty assigned by lot (to someone), **allotment, lot** A.
4 fortune assigned by the gods, **lot** Sapph. A.
5 vote (cast fr. an urn) A.

πάλτο (ep.3sg.athem.aor.mid.): see παλέω

παλτός ή όν *adj.* [πάλλω] **1** (of Zeus' thunderbolt) **brandished** S.
2 || NEUT.SB. **lance** (used by foreign soldiers and horsemen) X. Plu.

παλῡ́νω *vb.* | aor. ἐπάλῡνα | **1 sprinkle, scatter, strew** —*barley meal* (over or into sthg.) Hom. —*dust* (over a corpse) S.
2 cover by sprinkling (w. grain, liquid); **sprinkle** —*meat* (W.DAT. w. barley meal) Od. || MID. **sprinkle oneself** (w. a liquid) AR.
3 (of snow) **cover with flakes, fleck** —*fields* Il. || PASS. (of mountains) **be flecked** —W.DAT. w. *snow* AR.; (of a panpipe) —w. *mildew* Theoc.

παμ-βασιλείᾱ ᾱς *f.* [πᾶς] **absolute monarchy** Arist.

παμ-βασίλεια ᾱς (Ion. ης) *f.* **almighty queen** (ref. to a deity) Ar. AR.

παμ-βασιλεύς ῆος *ep.m.* —**παμβασίλευς** ηος *Aeol.m.* **almighty king** (ref. to Zeus) Alc. Stesich.

παμ-βδελυρός ά όν (or **παμβδέλυρος** ᾱ ον) *adj.* (of a person) **utterly loathsome** Ar.

παμ-βίᾱς ᾱ *dial.masc.adj.* [βίᾱ] (of Zeus' thunderbolt) **almighty** Pi.

πάμ-βοτος ον *adj.* [βόσκω] (of a region, a meadow) **all-nourishing, very fertile** A.

παμ-βῶτις ιδος *fem.adj.* (of the goddess Earth) **all-nourishing** S.

παμμαχίᾱ ᾱς *f.* [πάμμαχος] **all-in fight** (ref. to the pankration) B.

πάμ-μαχος ον *adj.* [μάχη] (of the boldness of a god) **shown in every fight** or **in the all-in fight** (ref. to the pankration) A. || MASC.SB. **all-round fighter, prize-fighter** (ref. to a pancratiast) Theoc.; (fig.ref. to a sophist) Pl.

—**παμμάχος** ον *adj.* [μάχομαι] (epith. of Athena) **all-conquering, victorious** Ar.

πάμ-μεγας μεγάλη μεγα *adj.* [μέγας] (of a fact or circumstance) **all-important** Pl.

παμ-μεγέθης ες *adj.* [μέγεθος] (of physical entities) **very large** Pl. Arist. Plb. Plu.; (of a task, penalty, wrong, or sim.) **very great, very heavy** X. D. Men. Plb.; (of evidence, circumstances, or sim.) **all-important** Pl. D. Arist. Plb.

—**παμμέγεθες** *neut.adv.* **very loudly, at the top of one's voice** Aeschin. Men.

πάμ-μεικτος ον *adj.* [μεικτός] (of a military horde, ref. to the Persian army; of allied soldiers in that army) **drawn from all nations, mixed** A.

παμ-μέλᾱς αινα αν *adj.* (of a bull, a sheep) **completely black** Od.; (of a bird) Plu.(oracle)

παμ-μήκης ες *adj.* [μῆκος] (of a speech) **very lengthy** Pl.; (of lamentations) **prolonged** S.

πάμ-μηνος ον *adj.* [μήν²] (quasi-advbl., of a life beset by troubles) **in every month, month by month** S.

παμ-μήτειρα ης *Ion.f.* [μήτηρ] **mother of all, universal mother** (ref. to the goddess Earth) hHom.

πάμ-μητις ιος *dial.masc.fem.adj.* [μῆτις] (of god) **contriving all things, all-wise** Simon.

παμ-μήτωρ ορος *f.* [μήτηρ] **1 mother of all** (ref. to Earth) A.
2 mother in all respects, **devoted mother** (of a dead man) S.

παμ-μίαρος ον *adj.* [μιαρός] (of a person) **utterly vile** Ar.

παμ-μιγής ές *adj.* [μείγνῡμι] **1 with a mixture of all kinds**; (of weapons) **varied** A.; (of the Persian army) **in all the diversity** (of its contingents) Tim.; (pejor., of an assembly) **motley** Plu.
2 (of shouting) **mingled all together** (W.DAT. w. screaming) Tim.(dub.)

παμ-μῑ́κρος ον *adj.* [μῑκρός] (of a thing) **very small** Arist.

πάμ-μορος ον *adj.* [μόρος] (of a person) **thoroughly ill-fated, long-suffering** S.

παμ-μῡσαρός ά όν (or **παμμῡ́σαρος** ᾱ ον) *adj.* (of a person) **utterly disgusting** Ar.

παμ-πάλαιος ον *adj.* [παλαιός] **1** (of a person) **from times long past** Pl. Arist.; (of a prophecy, a festival) **of great antiquity** Plu.
2 (of a living person) **old beyond one's years, extremely mature** Plu.

πάμ-παν *adv.* [redupl. πᾶς] (in strong asseverations or negations, sts. intensv. w. individual wds.) **wholly, altogether, entirely** Hom. +; (also w.art.) τὸ πάμπαν E. Pl. Plu.

παμ-πειθής ές *adj.* [πείθω] (of a longing) **all-persuasive, compulsive** Pi.

παμπήδην *adv.* **wholly, completely** Thgn. A. S.

παμπησίᾱ ᾱς *f.* [2nd el. πέπᾱμαι] **entire property, worldly goods** (of a person) A. E. Ar.

παμ-πληθής ές *adj.* [πλῆθος] **1** (of soldiers) **in great numbers, en masse** X.
2 (of persons, things) **very numerous** Isoc. Pl. D.; (of property) **very substantial** Isoc.

—**παμπληθές** *neut.adv.* **a long way, by a mile** —*ref. to being far fr. doing sthg.* D.

—**παμπληθεί** *adv.* **en masse, all together** —*ref. to shouting* NT.

παμ-πληκτός όν *adj.* [πλήσσω] (of a contest) **thick with blows** S.

παμ-πλούσιος ον *adj.* (of persons) **very rich** Pl.

παμ-ποίκιλος ον (also η ον Pl.) *adj.* [ποικίλος] **1** (of robes) **richly decorated** Hom. hHom.; (of jars) **richly painted** Pi.; (of fawnskin garments) **dappled** E.
2 (of physical changes) **of every variety, manifold** Pl.; (of a populace) with a variety of trades, **diverse** Plu.

πάμ-πολυς πόλλη πολυ *adj.* [πολύς] **1** (pl., of people or things) **very many** Ar. Pl. X. D. Men. Plb.
2 (sg. or collectv.pl.) very great in number or extent; (of an army, a crowd, an area, or sim.) **very large, enormous, huge** Pl. X.; (of an amount of money) X. D.; (of an amount of wine) Pl.; (perh. of wealth) **very great** S.(dub.); (of laughter, confusion, anger, or sim.) Ar. Pl. D.; (of toil) **hard** or **interminable** Pl.; (of a period of time) **very long** Pl. D. Men.; (neut.gen.sg.) παμπόλλου **at a very high price** X.

—**πάμπολυ** *neut.adv.* **to a very large degree, very much** Pl. X. Is. D. Arist. Plb.

παμ-πόνηρος ον *adj.* [πονηρός] (of persons) **thoroughly bad, rotten** S.*Ichn.* Ar. Pl. X. D. Plu.; (of an argument, a kind of poetry) Ar.

παμ-πορθής ές *adj.* [πορθέω] (of a life) **completely ruined** A.(cj.)

παμ-πόρφυρος ον *adj.* [πορφύρᾱ] (of the radiance of violets) **dark purple** Pi.

πάμ-πρεπτος ον *adj.* [πρεπτός] (of places where birds sit) **in full view** A.

πάμ-πρωτος ον *adj.* [πρῶτος] (quasi-advbl., of a person doing sthg.) **first of all** (before another) Il.; (of an activity) Pi.

—**πάμπρωτον** *neut.sg.adv.* **first of all** (before sthg. else) —*ref. to doing sthg.* Od. AR.; **for the very first time** Pi.

—**πάμπρωτα** *neut.pl.adv.* | *superl.* παμπρώτιστα (AR.) | **first of all** (before sthg. else) Il. AR.

παμ-φάγος ον *adj.* [φαγεῖν] **1** (of animals) eating all kinds of food, **omnivorous** Arist.; (of a person) **gluttonous** Alcm.; (of animals' jaws) **all-devouring, voracious** Ar.
2 (of fire) **all-consuming** E.

παμ-φαής ές *adj.* [app. πᾶς, φάος, but cf. παμφαίνω] **1** (of firelight, the sun's rays, a star) **shining brightly, gleaming, brilliant** E. Ar.; (of honey) **glistening** A.
2 (of Herakles, at his apotheosis) **resplendent** (W.DAT. w. divine fire) S.

παμφαίνω *ep.vb.* [redupl. φαίνω] | only pres. (usu.ptcpl.) and impf. | **1** (of a star) **shine brightly, gleam** Il. Hes.; (of golden studs on a sword) Il.; (of a shield) —W.DAT. w. *bronze* Il.; (of a lightning-bolt, depicted on a cloak) AR.
2 (of a warrior) **be resplendent** (usu. W.DAT. in his armour) Il.; (of a dead warrior stripped of his armour) —W.DAT. w. *bared breast* Il.; (of Athena, emerging fr. the head of Zeus) AR.

—**παμφανόων** ωσα ων, *gen.* ωντος ώσης ωντος *ep.ptcpl.adj.* [as if fr. παμφανάω, w.diect.] **1** (of the sun, a flame, the flash of bronze) **shining brightly, gleaming, brilliant** Hom.; (of stars) Ibyc.; (of the aither) Emp.
2 (of a spear, helmet, armour) shining with reflected light, **gleaming, radiant** Il. hHom. AR.; (of a chariot, a cauldron, the walls of a building) Hom.; (of a couch) AR.

παμ-φάρμακος ον *adj.* [φάρμακον] (of Medea) **skilled in all medicines** Pi.

παμ-φεγγής ές *adj.* [φέγγος] (of rays of starlight) **gleaming, brilliant** S.

πάμ-φθαρτος ον *adj.* [φθαρτός] (of a person's fate) **bringing total extinction** A.

πάμ-φθερσις εως *fem.adj.* [φθείρω] (of civil strife) **all-destructive** B.*fr.*

πάμ-φλεκτος ον *adj.* [φλέγω] (of fire, sacrificial altars) **fiercely blazing** S.

πάμ-φορος ον *adj.* [φέρω] **1** (of Earth) **all-productive, very fruitful** or **fertile** A.; (of land, sea) Hdt. Pl. X. Plb. Plu.; (of a possession, fig.ref. to a friend) **productive** X.
2 (of flood-debris) **carrying everything along** (w. itself) Pi.

παμ-φυής ές *adj.* [φυή] (of the body of Pan) **comprising all natures** Lyr.adesp. [or perh. *multiform*]

Πάμφυλοι ων *m.pl.* **Pamphylians** (descendants of one of the three original Dorian tribes, named after its mythical founder Pamphylos) Tyrt. A. Hdt. Theoc.

—**Παμφυλίᾱ** ᾱς *f.* country of the Pamphylians, **Pamphylia** (on the S. coast of Asia Minor) Th. Pl. +

πάμ-φυλος ον *adj.* [φῦλή, φῦλον] of every race or tribe; (of animals) **of every species** Ar.; (of a class of people) **of all sorts, heterogeneous** Pl.

πάμ-φωνος ον *adj.* [φωνή] (of marriage-songs) **full-voiced** Pi.; (of auloi, their music) **full-toned** Pi.; (of a lyre) Men.; (fig., of wine) **which loosens the tongue** Philox.Cyth.

πάμ-ψυχος ον *adj.* [ψυχή] (of the prophet Amphiaraos, in the underworld) **with full powers of mind** S.

Πάν Πανός *m.* **1 Pan** (rustic god, esp. assoc.w. Arcadia, usu. son of Hermes and a nymph, in appearance half man and half goat) hHom. +; (as responsible for mental disturbances, incl. panic among soldiers) E.
2 || PL. **Pans** (rustic deities, akin to satyrs) Ar. Pl. Theoc.

παν-αγής ές *adj.* [πᾶς, ἄγος] **1** (perh. of the sea) **all-hallowing, all-purifying** Call.
2 (of Vestal Virgins) **all-hallowed, sacrosanct** Plu.

πάν-αγρος ον *adj.* [ἄγρᾱ] (of a fishing-net) **that catches all** Il.

πανάγυρις *dial.f.*: see πανήγυρις

Παν-αθήναια ων *n.pl.* [Ἀθηναῖος, under Ἀθῆναι] **Panathenaia** (annual festival at Athens, in honour of Athena, marked by a procession to the Acropolis; every fourth year it was celebrated as τὰ μεγάλα Παναθήναια, *the great Panathenaia*, w. athletic and musical competitions open to all Greece) Hdt. Th. Ar. +

—**Παναθηναϊκός** ή όν *adj.* (of the procession) **Panathenaic, at the Panathenaia** Th. || MASC.SB. (w. λόγος understd.) *Panathenaicus* Isoc.(title)

παν-άθλιος ᾱ ον *adj.* (of a person) **wholly wretched, in utter misery** Trag. Ar.(quot. E.); (of a mourner's head) **anguished** A.

πάν-αιθος η ον *adj.* [αἰθός] (of helmets) **blazing, gleaming** Il.

παν-αίολος ον *adj.* [αἰόλος] **1** (of a warrior's belt, cuirass, shield) **glittering, flashing** Il. Hes.; (of a woman's girdle) **highly coloured** AR.
2 (of cries of grief) **ever-changing, varied** A.

παν-αίσχης ές *adj.* [αἶσχος] (of persons) **very ugly** Arist.

παναίσχρως *adv.* [αἰσχρός] **quite disgracefully** —*ref. to abandoning one's weapons* Plb.

παν-αίτιος ον *adj.* **1** (of Zeus) **who is the cause of all** A.
2 (of a god) **wholly responsible** (for someone's death, opp. μεταίτιος *jointly responsible*) A.

παν-ακής ές *adj.* [ἄκος] (of a medicine) **all-healing** Call.*epigr.*

—**Πανάκεια** ᾱς *f.* **Panakeia, All-healer** (minor deity, usu. daughter of Asklepios) Ar. Lyr.adesp.; (also w. allusion to a medicinal plant so named) Call.

παν-αληθής ές *adj.* **1** (of an Erinys, envisaged as a prophet) **wholly true** or **reliable** A.; (of a warning) Call.*epigr.*
2 (of a pleasure) **wholly true** or **real** Pl.

—**παναληθῶς** *adv.* **in all truth, really and truly** A.

παν-αλκής ές *adj.* [ἀλκή] (of gods) **all-powerful** A.(v.l. παναρκής)

παν-αλουργής ές *adj.* (of robes) **dyed all purple** Xenoph.

παν-άλωτος ον *adj.* [ἁλωτός] (of Ruin) that catches everyone (in her net), **all-catching** A.

παν-ᾱμερεύω *dial.vb.* [ἡμερεύω] (of a city) **devote the whole day** —W.ACC. *to bands of revellers* E.

πανᾱμέριος, πανᾱμερος *dial.adjs.*: see πανημέριος, πανήμερος

παν-άμωμος ον *adj.* (of a person) **completely blameless** Simon.

πᾶν-άπαλος ον *adj.* [ἀπαλός] | πᾱν- *metri grat.* | (of a young man) **most delicate** (in looks) Od.

παν-απευθής ές *adj.* (of a path of inquiry) **wholly impossible to learn** Parm.

παν-απήμων ον, *gen.* ονος *adj.* (of a particular day, in terms of luck) **entirely harmless** Hes.

παν-απηρής ές *adj.* (of the head and feet of participants in the Mysteries) **completely unharmed** (by sickness) Call.

παν-άποτμος ον *adj.* (of a person) **utterly ill-fated** Il.

παν-άργυρος ον *adj.* (of a bowl) **all-silver** Od.

παν-άριστος ον *adj.* (of a type of person) **best of all** Hes.

παν-αρκής ές *adj.* [ἀρκέω] (of the sun) sufficient for all, that shines on all alike Call. | see also παναλκής

παν-αρμόνιος ον *adj.* [ἁρμονίᾱ] containing all the musical modes; (fig., of speeches) with wide harmonic range, **varying in tone** Pl. ‖ NEUT.SB. music with wide harmonic range Pl.

πάν-αρχος ον *adj.* [ἀρχή] (of a ruler) **with supreme power** S.

πανατρεκές *neut.adv.* [ἀτρεκής] **very truly** or **precisely** AR.

παν-αφῆλιξ, gen. ικος *masc.adj.* [ἀπό, ἧλιξ] (of an orphan child) **entirely cut off from one's contemporaries** Il.

παν-άφυλλος ον *adj.* (of ploughland) **completely leafless** hHom.

Παν-αχαιοί ῶν *m.pl.* [Ἀχαιός] **all the Achaeans together** Hom.

—**Παναχαΐς** ίδος *fem.adj.* (of the land, sts. understd.) **of all Achaea** AR.

παν-αώριος ον *adj.* [ἄωρος¹] (of a child) app. **doomed to an all-too-early death** Il.

παν-δαίδαλος ον *adj.* (of a market-place) **richly adorned** Pi.*fr.*

παν-δαισίᾱ ᾱς, Ion. **πανδαισίη** ης *f.* [δαίς] **full-scale feast, banquet** Hdt. Ar.

παν-δακέτης ου *m.* [δάκνω] **biter of all, snappy dog** (ref. to Cato as a vindictive prosecutor) Plu.(quot.epigr.)

παν-δάκρῡτος ον *adj.* [δακρυτός] **1** (of a family, a life, mankind, persons) thoroughly wept over, **lamentable, pitiable** Trag. Lyr.adesp.

2 (of lamentations) **very tearful** S.

παν-δαμάτωρ ορος *m.* [δαμάζω] (appos.w. sleep) **subduer of all** Hom.; (appos.w. time) Simon. B.; (appos.w. a god, an Erinys) S. AR.

πανδᾱμεί *dial.adv.*, **πάνδᾱμος** *dial.adj.*: see πανδημεί, πάνδημος

παν-δείματος ον *adj.* [δεῖμα] (of deities) **inspiring utter fear** Lyr.adesp.

πάν-δεινος ον *adj.* [δεινός] **1** (of actions, circumstances) **quite terrible, utterly dreadful, outrageous** Pl. D. Men.

2 (of persons) **supremely clever** D.; (w.INF. at doing sthg.) Pl.

παν-δερκέτᾱς ᾱ *dial.m.* [δέρκομαι] one who sees all, **all-seer** (W.GEN. over mortals, ref. to Zeus) E.

παν-δερκής ές *adj.* (of a mark of honour) **seen by all** B.

παν-δεχής ές *adj.* [δέχομαι] (of a substance) **all-receptive** Pl.

πανδημεί, dial. **πανδᾱμεί** *adv.* [πάνδημος] with the participation of the whole people, **in a body, en masse, to a man** A. Hdt. Th. Isoc. X. Plb.; (milit.) **in full force** A. Hdt. Th. Att.orats. X. +

πανδημίᾱ ᾱς *f.* **all the people, whole community** Pl. Plu.

—**πανδημίᾳ** *dat.adv.* with all the people, **unanimously** —*ref. to voting* A.

παν-δήμιος ον *adj.* [δῆμος] (of a beggar) who goes around all the people, **public, professional** Od.

πάν-δημος, dial. **πάνδᾱμος**, ον *adj.* **1** for or belonging to all the people; (of cattle) **public** S.; (of a contest, a prison) E.; (of a sacrifice) Plb.; (of a mill) AR.; (of an assembly) Plu.

2 extending among all the people; (of goodwill) **popular, widespread, general** Arist.(quot.); (of gossip, a fault, a reputation) Plb.

3 (cult-title of Aphrodite, as daughter of Zeus and Dione) **of the People, Popular, Common** (opp. *Heavenly*, cult-title of Aphrodite, as daughter of Ouranos) Pl. X. Theoc.*epigr.*; (epith. of Eros) Pl.; (of the love and lovers assoc.w. these deities) **common** Pl.

4 consisting of all the people; (of a city, an army) assembled, **entire** S.; (of a military force) **complete** Plb.

πάν-δικος ον *adj.* [δίκη] (of feelings) **thoroughly justified** S.; (of an object of reverence, ref. to a country) **justifiable** (i.e. rightly so regarded) or **righteous** A.

—**πανδίκως** *adv.* in a way that is right and proper, **as in duty bound, duly** —*ref. to acceding to a request or doing what the circumstances require* A. S.; **rightly, justifiably** —*ref. to being hated or killed* A. E.; (intensv., w.adj.) **truly, entirely** A.

Πανδῑονίς ίδος, Aeol. **Πανδίονις** ιδος *f.* **1 daughter of Pandion** (Prokne, who was metamorphosed into a swallow or nightingale) Hes. Sapph.

2 ‖ ADJ. (of an Athenian tribe) **Pandionid** Aeschin. D. ‖ SB. (w. φυλή understd.) **Pandionid tribe** Aeschin. D.

πανδοκείᾱ ᾱς *f.* [πανδοκεύω] **innkeeping** (as a disreputable profession) Pl.

πανδοκεῖον (also **πανδοχεῖον** NT.) ου *n.* [πανδοκεύς] **place which takes in all, inn, tavern** Ar. D. Thphr. Men. Plb. +

πανδοκεύς (also **πανδοχεύς** NT.) έως *m.* [πάνδοκος]
1 innkeeper, landlord Pl. Plb. NT.; (fig., ref. to a person) **host** (W.GEN. to every vice) Pl.

2 ‖ ADJ. (of Hades) **all-welcoming** Lyr.adesp.

—**πανδοκεύτρια** ᾱς *f.* **1 female innkeeper, landlady** Ar.

2 ‖ ADJ. (fig., of a whale) receptive of everything, **voracious** Ar.

πανδόκευσις εως *f.* [πανδοκεύω] **innkeeping** Pl.

πανδοκεύω *vb.* [πανδοκεύς] **1 entertain en masse**
—*distinguished persons* Hdt.

2 be an innkeeper (as an example of a disreputable profession) Pl. Thphr.; (of a mean host) **play the innkeeper** Timocr.

πανδοκέω *contr.vb.* [πάνδοκος] (fig., of a land, as mother and nurse) be hospitable to, **welcome, accept** —*the trouble of rearing its inhabitants* A.

πάν-δοκος (or **πανδόκος**) ον *adj.* [δέχομαι] **1** (of Hades) welcoming all, **hospitable** A.; (of a house, W.GEN. to strangers) A.; (of a temple, a sacred precinct) Pi.

2 (of a person's hospitality) **all-welcoming** Pi.

πανδοξίᾱ ᾱς *f.* [πάνδοξος] **absolute renown, perfect glory** Pi.

πάν-δοξος ον *adj.* [δόξα] (of a house) **all-glorious** Pi.*fr.*

πανδοχεῖον *n.*, **πανδοχεύς** *m.*: see πανδοκεῖον, πανδοκεύς

πάν-δυρτος ον *adj.* [δύρομαι] **1** (of a person) **all-lamented, keenly mourned** A.

2 (of the nightingale) **ever-mourning** S.

3 (of a voice, a lament) **all-sorrowful, plaintive** A. E.

Παν-δώρᾱ ᾱς, Ion. **Πανδώρη** ης *f.* [δῶρον] **1 Pandora, Giver of All Gifts** (chthonic goddess) Hippon. Ar.

2 Pandora (the first human female) Hes. [Created by Zeus to punish mortals, she released evils into the world fr. a jar. The name was interpr. as *given a gift*, or *given as a gift, by all the gods*]

πάν-δωρος ον *adj.* (of Destiny) **who dispenses all** B.*fr.*

παν-είκελον *neut.adv.* [εἴκελος] **in just the same way** Call.

Παν-ελλάς άδος *f.* [Ἑλλάς] **the whole of Greece** Pi.*fr.* Call.

Παν-έλληνες, dial. **Πανέλλᾱνες**, ων *m.pl.* [Ἕλλην] **all the Greeks** Il. Hes. Archil. Pi. B. Ion +

Πᾱνελόπᾱ *dial.f.*: see Πηνελόπη

πᾱνέλοψ *dial.m.*: see πηνέλοψ

παν-εργέτᾱς ᾱ *dial.m.* [ἔργον] **accomplisher of all** (ref. to Zeus) A.

παν-έστιος ον *adj.* [ἑστίᾱ] (quasi-advbl., of persons migrating) **with the whole household** Plu.

παν-έσχατος ον *adj.* (of a gulf) **last of all, furthest** AR.

πάν-ετες neut.adv. [ἔτος] all year long Pi.
παν-ευέφοδος ον adj. (of a place) very easy of access Plb.
παν-εύκηλος ον adj. (of the air) perfectly still AR.
πάν-εφθος ον adj. [ἐφθός] (of tin) fully smelted, refined Hes.
πανηγυρίζω vb. [πανήγυρις] 1 (of the Egyptians) hold a religious gathering (sts. W.COGN.ACC.) Hdt.; (of a country) hold a public festival Plu.; (of a person) take part in a public festival Plu.
2 (pejor., of soldiers) make merry Plu.; (fig., of prodigality) run riot Plu.
3 (of an orator) make a speech at a public festival Isoc.
πανηγυρικός ή όν adj. 1 (of a crowd, a show) at a public festival Isoc. Plu.
2 (of a speech) composed for a public festival or national gathering Isoc. Plu.; Panegyricus (title of a speech by Isocrates, composed for a Panhellenic gathering at Olympia) Isoc.; (w. λόγος understd.) Arist.
3 (of decoration, a procession) festal Plu.
4 (of persons, their behaviour) ostentatious Plu.
—**πανηγυρικῶς** adv. | compar. πανηγυρικώτερον | ostentatiously, sumptuously —ref. to being equipped or decorated Plu. || COMPAR. rather ostentatiously, with pomp and ceremony —ref. to behaving Plb. Plu.
παν-ήγυρις εως (Ion. ιος), dial. **πανάγυρις** ιος f. [ἀγείρω] 1 full gathering, general assembly (of citizens, for deliberation) A.
2 (in Egypt) religious assembly, festival Hdt.
3 national festival (ref. to a public, esp. Panhellenic, festival, such as the games at Olympia, the great Panathenaia and City Dionysia at Athens) Pi. Hdt. Ar. Att.orats. Pl. +
4 (concr., collectv.) persons attending a festival, assembled people Hdt. Th.
5 (fig., ref. to enjoyment of the fruits of victory) festival, party X.; (ref. to life) Men.
6 (gener.) assembly, gathering, group (of gods, ref. to their statues) A.; (of children, friends) E.; entourage (of the Persian king) Tim.
πανηγυρισμός οῦ m. (sts. pejor.) festive behaviour, revelry Plu.
παν-ῆμαρ neut.adv. all day long —ref. to ploughing Od.
παν-ημέριος, dial. **πανᾱμέριος**, ον adj. [ἡμέρᾱ] 1 (quasi-advbl., of persons or animals fighting, carousing, or sim.) all day long Hom. Hes. Thgn. E. AR.; (of the wind blowing or sim.) AR.; (of a ship, ref. to distance travelled) in a whole day Od.
2 (of a period of time) a whole day long E.
παν-ήμερος, dial. **πανάμερος**, ον adj. (quasi-advbl., of persons or animals doing sthg.) all day long A. Ar. Call. AR.; (of a ship speeding, rocks clashing) AR.
—**πανημερόν** neut.adv. all day long Hdt.
παν-θαλής ές adj. [θάλλω] (of Clio) giver of all bloom (to the flowers of song) B.
παν-θαλής ές dial.adj. [θηλέω] (of flowers) all-blooming, luxuriant B.
πάνθηρ ηρος m. panther or leopard (or sim.) Hdt. X.
πανθυμαδόν adv. [πᾶς, θῡμός] with great passion —ref. to exchanging angry words Od.
πάν-θυτος ον adj. [θύω¹] (of rites) with full sacrifices S.
πᾱνίκα dial.adv.: see πηνίκα
πᾱνικός ή όν adj. [Πάν] inspired by Pan; (of confusion among soldiers) striking without warning, panicked Plu. || NEUT.SB. panic (among soldiers) Plb.

παν-ίμερος ον adj. [πᾶς] (of a person) full of desire S.(cj.)
πᾱνίσδομαι dial.mid.vb. [πήνη] wind off from the spool —spun yarn Theoc.
Πᾱνιστής οῦ m. [Πάν] Pan-worshipper Men.(cj.)
Παν-ιώνιον ου n. [πᾶς, Ἴωνες] Panionium (temple and meeting-place of the cities of the Ionian league at Mykale) Hdt.
—**Πανιώνια** ων n.pl. Panionia (festival of the Ionian league) Hdt.
πάν-νῑκος ον adj. [νίκη] (of a feat of wrestling) all-victorious, triumphant B.
παννυχίζω, Aeol. **παννυχίσδω** vb. [παννυχίς] | fut. παννυχιῶ | 1 (of women) celebrate an all-night festival, revel all night Sapph. Ar. Men.
2 (of men, w. sexual connot.) make a whole night of it Ar. Men.
3 (of a flame) blaze all night long Pi.
παννύχιος ον (Ion. η ον) adj. 1 (quasi-advbl., of persons or gods doing sthg.) all night long Hom. Hes. hHom. AR. Mosch.; (of winds blowing, a ship sailing, lamps burning) Hom. Hdt.
2 (of dancing) lasting all night, all-night E.; (of the moon) that shines all night E.
παν-νυχίς ίδος f. [νύξ] 1 all-night festival, night-long revel (in honour of a god, celebrated by women, usu. w. dancing) Hdt. E. Ar. Pl. Men. Plu.
2 night-long vigil (of a woman lamenting) S.
πάννυχος ον adj. 1 (quasi-advbl., of persons or gods doing sthg.) all night long Hom. Anacr. Thgn. A. S.; (of a lamp burning, the moon shining, stars moving) Hdt. E. AR.
2 (of sleep) lasting all night, night-long Il. Sapph.; (of dancing, sounds of anguish) S.
πάν-οιζυς υ adj. [οἰζύς] (of a household) in utter misery A.
πανοικεσίᾱ, Ion. **πανοικίη** fem.dat.adv. —also **πανοικεί** (NT.) adv. [οἶκος, οἰκίᾱ] 1 with one's whole household —ref. to doing or suffering sthg. Hdt. Th. NT.
2 with every household, completely —ref. to obliterating a city Th.
παν-οίμοι interj. utter woe! A.
παν-όλβιος (also **πάνολβος** A.) ον adj. (of persons) wholly fortunate, truly happy hHom. Thgn. A.
παν-ομῑλεί adv. [ὅμῑλος] in full company —ref. to an army advancing A.
παν-ομφαῖος ον adj. [ὀμφή] (epith. of Zeus) lord of all omens Il. Hes.fr.
πανοπλίᾱ ᾱς, Ion. **πανοπλίη** ης f. [πάνοπλος] complete armour of a hoplite (i.e. shield, helmet, cuirass, greaves, sword, spear), full armour, full suit of arms Hdt. Th. Ar. Isoc. Pl. +
πάν-οπλος ον adj. [ὅπλα] 1 (of soldiers, an army) in full armour, fully armed Tyrt. A. E.; (of Athena, the Sown Men) E.
2 (of a soldier's equipment) of full armour E.
παν-οπλότατος η ον superl.adj. (of a daughter) very youngest AR.
παν-όπτης ου, dial. **πανόπτᾱς** ᾱ masc.adj. [ὅπωπα, see ὁράω] (of Zeus, Helios, Argus) all-seeing A. || SB. (as pers. name) All-seer (ref. to Argus) E. Ar.
πάν-ορμος ον adj. [ὅρμος²] (of harbours) where all may moor Od.
πᾱνός οῦ m. [perh.reltd. φᾱνός²] torch Trag. Men.
πανουργέω contr.vb. [πανοῦργος] be ready to do anything, stop at nothing, act unscrupulously, be a criminal (sts. W.INTERN. or COGN.ACC. in some action) S. E. Ar. Att.orats. Plu.

πανούργημα ατος *n.* criminal act, evil crime S.
πανουργίᾱ ᾱς *f.* (oft.pl.) criminal behaviour, villainy, wickedness A. S. Ar. Att.orats. Pl. +
πανοῦργος ον *adj.* [πᾶς, ἔργον] (of persons) ready to do anything, **unscrupulous, villainous, criminal** E. Lys. Ar. Pl. +; (of a person's hand) A.; (of acts, behaviour) Ar. Plu. ‖ NEUT.SG.SB. villainy S. ‖ NEUT.PL.SB. (w.pers.ref.) villains S.
—**πανούργως** *adv.* unscrupulously, villainously Ar. Pl. Men. Plb. Plu.
παν-όψιος ον *adj.* [ὄψις] (quasi-advbl., of a spear, ref. to how it is being wielded) **visible to all, in full view** Il.
πανσαγίᾱ ᾱς, Ion. **πασσαγίη** ης *f.* [σαγή] **full equipment** (uncert. of what kind) Call.
—**πανσαγίᾳ** *dat.adv.* in full armour S.
παν-σέληνος (sts. written **πασσέληνος**) ον *adj.* [σελήνη] **1** (of the orb) **of the full moon** E.
2 ‖ FEM.SB. (w. ὥρα understd.) time of the full moon Hdt. S. Th. And. Ar. X. +; (concr.) full moon A.
πάν-σμῑκρος ον *adj.* [σμῑκρός] (of a quantity) **very small** Pl.
πάν-σοφος (sts. written **πάσσοφος**) ον *adj.* [σοφός] **1** (of persons) wise in all things, **all-wise, very wise** Pl.; (of a person's name, as honorific epith.) A.; (of thinking) Pl.
2 (of an invention) **very clever** E.
πανσπερμεί *adv.* [σπέρμα] with all seeds sown together —*ref. to a variety of crops growing* Lyr.adesp.
πανσπερμίᾱ ᾱς *f.* universal seed-supply (ref. to the mixture of elements fr. which humans and perh. also animals are created) Pl.
παν-στρατιᾱ́ ᾱς *f.* **whole army, full force** (W.GEN. of citizens and foreigners) Th.
—**πανστρατιᾷ**, Ion. **πανστρατιῇ** *dat.adv.* **with the whole army, in full force** Hdt. Th. Lys. Plu.
πανσυδί (sts. written **πασσυδί**) *adv.* [reltd. πανσυδία] **1** (in military ctxt.) **with all speed** X.
2 utterly —*ref. to an army being destroyed* Th.
παν-συδίᾱ (sts. written **πασσυδίᾱ**), Ion. **πανσυδίη** (also **πασσυδίη**) *fem.dat.adv.* [σύδην] **with all speed, in eager haste** Il. B. E. X. Call. AR.
πάν-συρτος ον *adj.* [σύρω] (fig., of a life of troubles, envisaged as a torrent) **swept along** S.
πάντᾱ, πάντα, παντᾷ *dial.advs.*: see πάντῃ
παν-τάλᾱς αινα αν *adj.* **1** (of a woman) **utterly wretched** E.
2 (of sorrows) **grievous** A.
παντ-ανάμικτος ον *adj.* [ἀναμείγνῡμι] (of a food dish) **of all things mixed up together** Philox.Leuc.
παντάπᾱσι(ν) *adv.* [redupl. πᾶς] **1** (intensv., w.vb., adv. or adj.) **altogether, completely, entirely** Anacr. A.*satyr.fr.* Hdt. Th. Att.orats. Pl. +; (also) τὸ παντάπασι Th.
2 (in affirmative answers) **by all means, absolutely so** Pl. X.
παντ-αρκής ές *adj.* [ἀρκέω] (of a king) **all-sufficient** (i.e. equal to every responsibility) A. [or perh. *all-powerful*]
παντ-άρχᾱς ᾱ *dial.masc.adj.* [ἀρχή] (of birds, envisaged as gods) **ruling over all** Ar.
πάντ-αρχος ον *adj.* [ἄρχω] (of Zeus) **ruling in sovereignty** (W.GEN. over the gods) S.
πανταχῇ, dial. **πανταχᾷ** *adv.* **1 in every place, everywhere** Hdt. Th. Lys. Ar. Pl.; **in every part** (W.GEN. of a place) Hdt. E.
2 on every side (of a central position or building) Hdt. E. Th. Pl. X.
3 to every place Hdt. Ar. X. +; **in every direction** S. E. Th. Ar. Pl. +
4 in every way, in all respects, completely A. Hdt. E. Isoc. Pl. +; in each and any way, **in whatever way** S.; **in any case, at all events** S.

πανταχόθεν *adv.* **1 from every direction, from all sides** Hdt. Th. Att.orats. Pl. +
2 from all sides, by all parties —*ref. to agreements being reached among people* And. Ar.
3 from every source —*ref. to getting sthg.* Isoc. Pl. X. Arist.
4 in every way, entirely —*ref. to factors contributing to a situation* Th. D.
πανταχοῖ *adv.* **in every direction, everywhere** Ar. D.
πανταχόσε *adv.* **1 in every direction, everywhere** Th. Pl. D. Plu.; **to every part** (W.GEN. of a place) Plu.
2 in every place Plu.
πανταχοῦ *adv.* **1 in every place, everywhere** E. Th. Ar. Att.orats. Pl. +; (W.GEN. in a country, on earth) E. Ar. Pl.
2 (w.vb. of motion) **in every direction, everywhere** NT.
3 in all circumstances, in every case, always S. E. Th. Att.orats. Pl. +; in all respects, **completely** Pl.
πανταχῶς *adv.* **in every way, in all respects, entirely** Isoc. Pl. D. Men.
παντέλεια ᾱς *f.* [παντελής] **completion** (of a temple) Plb.; **completeness** (W.GEN. of destruction) Plb.
παν-τελής ές *adj.* [τέλος] **1 fully complete in amount**; (of a traveller's baggage) **complete, entire** A.; (of freedom, a system of training, a suit of armour) Pl.; (of destruction) Plb.; (of sacrificial altars and hearths in a city) **every single one, one and all** S.
2 fully complete in quality; (of a living creature) **complete** Pl.; (of virtue, pleasure) **perfect, consummate** Isoc. Pl. Arist.; (of a guardian in a proposed state) Pl.
3 bringing all to completion or fulfilment; (of Zeus, time) **all-fulfilling** A.(dub.); (of personif. Year) perh. **bringing all to fruition** Pi.*fr.*; (of a benefactor) **all-effective** S.*Ichn.*(cj.)
4 (of a wife) having the fulfilment of marriage, **legally wedded** S.
5 having complete authority; (of monarchy) **absolute** S.; (of a vote, a proclamation) **authoritative** A. S.*Ichn.*
6 (prep.phr., w.neg.) εἰς τὸ παντελές **at all** NT.
—**παντελῶς**, Ion. **παντελέως** *adv.* **1 completely, thoroughly, totally** A. Hdt. Th. Att.orats. Pl. +; **outright** —*ref. to being put to death* S.
2 (neg.phr.) οὐδὲν (or οὐδὲ εἷς) παντελῶς **nothing (no one) at all** Isoc. Men.
3 (in affirmative answers) **entirely so, certainly, decidedly** Pl.
παν-τερπής ές *adj.* [τέρπω] (of a Muse, aulos music) **giving every delight, utterly delightful** Lyr.adesp.
παντευχίᾱ ᾱς *f.* [τεύχεα] **1 full armour, full suit of arms** A. E.; (fig., ref. to a bird's plumage) **full panoply** S.*fr.*
2 army in full array E.
πάν-τεχνος ον *adj.* [τέχνη] (of fire) **that enables every craft or technology** A.; (of the hands or skills of Hephaistos and Athena) **that encompass every craft, all-fashioning** Pi.*fr.*
πάντῃ (sts. written **πάντη**), Aeol. **πάντα** (also dial., sts. written **πάντα**), dial. **παντᾷ** *adv.* **1** (w.vb. of motion) **in all directions, every way, everywhere** Hom. Hes. Pi. B. Hdt. +
2 in every place, on all sides, everywhere Hom. Hes. Semon. Eleg. Lyr. Hdt. +
3 by every possible means Ar. Pl.
4 (ref. to degree) **in every way, altogether, completely** Emp. E. Ar. Pl. AR. NT.; (phr.) πάντῃ (πάντα) πάντως **in every possible way, completely and utterly** E. Pl. Arist.
πάν-τῑμος ον *adj.* [τῑμή] (of a prize of victory) **bringing all honour, glorious** S.
παν-τλήμων, dial. **παντλᾱ́μων**, ον *adj.* **all-suffering, utterly wretched** S. E.

παντοδαπός ή (dial. ἄ) όν *adj.* **1** (of persons, places, material or abstr. things) **of every kind, of all sorts** hHom. Lyr. A. Ion Hdt. E. +
2 (of the monster Empousa) taking on every kind of shape, **shape-shifting** Ar.; (fig., of a person, compared to Proteus) **changeable, versatile** Pl.
—**παντοδαπῶς** *adv.* **in all kinds of ways** Eleg.adesp. Pl. Arist.
πάντοθεν (also **πάντοθε** Theoc.) *adv.* **1 from all directions, from every side** Hom. Hdt. S. E. And. Pl. +
2 on all sides, all about Hom. Hes. Sol. Pi. B. Parm. +
3 from all sides, **by all parties, universally** —*ref. to agreements being reached among people* A. Is.
4 from all possible sources —*ref. to getting sthg.* X. Arist. Men.
πάντοθι *adv.* **all around** —*ref. to entwining sthg.* (*around sthg. else*) Theoc.
παντοῖος ᾱ (Ion. η) ον *adj.* **1** (of material or abstr. things) **of every kind, of all sorts** Hom. Hes. Eleg. Lyr. Hdt. S. +
2 (of gods) **taking all forms** Od.; (fig., of a person) adopting every shape, **trying every means** (to achieve sthg.) Hdt. Plu.
—**παντοίως** *adv.* **in all kinds of ways** Hdt. Pl.
πάν-τολμος ον *adj.* [τόλμα] **1** (of the strength of Herakles) **all-daring, bold** Pi.*fr.*
2 (of persons) **reckless, relentless** A.; (of sexual passion, destructive actions) A. E.
παντο-μισής ές *adj.* [μῖσος] (of beasts, ref. to Erinyes) **utterly loathsome** A.
παντο-πόρος ον *adj.* (of a person) **all-resourceful** S.
παντ-όπτης ου, dial. **παντόπτᾱς** ᾱ *masc.adj.* [ὄπωπα, see ὁράω] (epith. of Zeus, Helios) **all-seeing** A. S.; (of birds, envisaged as gods) Ar.
παντοπωλέω *contr.vb.* be a seller of everything, **run a general store** Men.
παντοπώλιον ου *n.* (fig., ref. to a democratic city) **bazaar, supermarket** (W.GEN. for the sale of constitutions) Pl.
πάντοσε *adv.* **1 in every direction, everywhere** Hom. hHom. Parm. Emp. X. AR. Theoc.*epigr.*
2 on every side —*ref. to a shield being well-balanced* Il. —*ref. to a grove encircling a fountain* Od.; **on every part** (of the body) —*ref. to being wounded* X.
παντό-σεμνος ον *adj.* [σεμνός] (of a ruler) **absolute in majesty** A.
πάντοτε *adv.* [τότε] **at all times, always** Arist. NT.
παντό-τολμος ον *adj.* [τόλμα] (of a person, an action) **of utter audacity, utterly reckless** A.
παντουργός όν *adj.* [ἔργον] (of a person) **ready to do anything, villainous** S.
παντο-φόρος ον *adj.* [φέρω] (of a land) **bearing every sort of produce** Arist.
παντό-φυρτος ον *adj.* [φύρω] (of goods) **all jumbled together** A.
παντό-φωνος ον *adj.* [φωνή] (of musical instruments) with every voice, **with wide melodic range** Lyr.adesp.
πάν-τρομος ον *adj.* [τρόμος] (of a dove) **trembling, timorous** A.
πάν-τροπος ον *adj.* [τροπή] (of flight) **involving utter rout** A.
πάντως *adv.* **1 in every manner, in all possible ways** —*ref. to moving* Parm. Pl.
2 (intensv., w.vb., adv. or adj.) **in every way, altogether, completely** hHom. A. Th. Ar. Pl. +; (w.vb. expressing necessity) **absolutely** A. Hdt. E., (w.imperatv., or vb. of entreating, wishing, or sim.) **at all costs, urgently** A. Pi. Hdt. E. Th. X. | see also πάντη 4

3 (in strong affirmations) **at all events, certainly, assuredly** Sol. Thgn. Hdt. Trag. Pl. +
4 (in strong negations, followed by neg.) *by no means, certainly not* Hom. A. Hdt. E. Pl.; οὐδὲν (or οὐδέν τι) πάντως *not at all* Hdt.
5 (in affirmative answers) **by all means, absolutely so, certainly** And. Pl.
6 under all possible circumstances, **at all events, in any case, anyway** Sol. Hdt. Trag. Ar. Pl. +
7 (phr.) ἄλλως τε πάντως καί *in all other circumstances and ... (i.e. above all, especially)* A. Pl.
πάνυ *adv.* **1** (intensv., w.vbs.) **wholly, greatly, really** A. S. Th. Ar. Att.orats. Pl. +; (also) καὶ πάνυ Th. +
2 (w.adjs., advs., advbl.phrs., oft. placed after them) **very, extremely** Xenoph. A. E.*Cyc.* Th. Ar. Att.orats. +
3 οὐ πάνυ (w.vbs. or adjs.) *not quite, not really* or *not at all* S. Th. Ar. Isoc. Pl. +
4 (in affirmative answers, esp. in phrs. πάνυ γε, πάνυ μὲν οὖν) **by all means, certainly** Ar. Pl. X. D. Men.
5 (quasi-adjl.) ὁ πάνυ Περικλῆς *actual Pericles (i.e. the very man, opp. his son)* X.
παν-υπέρτατος η ον *superl.adj.* **1** (of Ithaca, relative to neighbouring islands) in the very furthest position, **furthest of all** (W.PREP.PHR. towards the west) Od.
2 (of oaks on a mountain) in the very highest position, **very highest** (W.GEN. of all the trees) AR.
3 (of Zeus) highest of all (gods), **supreme** Call.
παν-ύστατος η ον *adj.* —also **πανυστάτιος** ᾱ ον (Call.) *dial.adj.* **1** (quasi-advbl., of a person or animal doing sthg.) **last of all** (after others) Hom. AR.
2 last of all before death; (of a bath, for a person) **last of all, final** E.; (of a person's smile) E.; (of the act of seeing) E. Call.; (of a military campaign, disastrous for its participants) Aeschin.
3 last of all (for a person, at death); (fig., of a journey, i.e. to the underworld) **last of all, final** S.; (of a bath for a dead girl before burial, w. further allusion to last ritual bath before marriage) E.
4 (of sufferings) **latest** (in a series) E.
—**πανύστατον** *neut.adv.* **for the very last time** (before death) E.(also pl.) Ar. Theoc. Bion
παν-ῳδός όν *adj.* [πᾶς, perh. also Πάν; ἀοιδή] (of a sound) **very tuneful** (app. also w.connot. *of the music of Pan*) Lyr.adesp.
πανωλεθρίᾱ ᾱς *f.* [πανώλεθρος] **utter destruction** (of a city, in war) Plu.
—**πανωλεθρίᾳ**, Ion. **πανωλεθρίη** *dat.adv.* **with utter destruction, catastrophically** Hdt. Th.
παν-ώλεθρος ον *adj.* [ὄλεθρος] **1** (of persons, a race, a city) suffering utter destruction, **utterly destroyed** Trag. Ar. Plb.; (of a tree) Hdt.
2 (of persons) utterly destructive (in their actions or intentions), **deadly, murderous** S. E.; (pejor., of women in general) Ar.
3 (of ramming of ships) **utterly destructive** A.; (of a vengeful daimon, a calamity) A. Hdt.
παν-ώλης ες *adj.* [ὄλλυμι] **1** (of persons) **utterly destroyed** or **ruined** Trag.
2 (of persons) utterly destructive (in their actions or intentions), **deadly, murderous** S. E.; (of a person's misfortunes) bringing ruin, **ruinous** S.
πάν-ωρος ον *adj.* [ὥρᾱ] (of crops) **produced in every season** A.
πάξ *interj.* [reltd. πήγνυμι] (putting an end to a discussion) **enough!, shush!** Men.

πᾶξα (dial.aor.), **πάξω** (dial.fut.): see πήγνῡμι

πάομαι *mid.vb.* | pres. not used | fut. πάσομαι (A.), dial. πᾱσεῦμαι (Call.) | aor. ἐπᾱσάμην, ptcpl. πᾱσάμενος | pf. πέπᾱμαι, inf. πεπᾶσθαι |
1 get, acquire —*wealth* Thgn. Call.; (*of a wrongdoer*) —*an avenger* A.; **become master** (*of slaves*) Theoc.
2 ‖ PF. **have got, have, possess** —*wealth, other desirable acquisitions* Sol. Thgn. Pi. E. Ar. X. Theoc. —*a sickness* A. —*a godless mind, servile speech* A. E. —*someone* (*as a relative or friend*) E.

πᾱόομαι *dial.pass.contr.vb.* [πηός] | Aeol.aor.ptcpl. πᾱώθεις | **become a kinsman by marriage** —W.DAT. *to someone* Alc.

παπαῖ (sts. written **παπᾶ**) *interj.* **1** (sts. repeated, expressing grief or distress) **oh oh!, ah ah!** Trag. Ar.; (expressing alarm or disgust) A.; (physical pain) S. Ar.
2 (wkr.sens., expressing astonishment) **oh dear!, good heavens!** Hdt. E.*Cyc.* Ar. Pl. X. Plu.
—**παπαπαῖ**, also **παπαπαπαῖ** (Ar.) *interj.* (expressing astonishment and pleasure) **wow!** E.*Cyc.* Ar.
—**παππαπαππαπαῖ** *interj.* (expressing pain) **aah!** S.

παπαιάξ *interj.* **1** (expressing astonishment and pleasure) **wow!** E.*Cyc.* Ar.
2 (expressing mild grief or regret) **oh my!** Ar.

παππάζω, also **παππίζω** (Ar.) *vb.* [πάππας] (of children) **cry out 'daddy'** Ar. —W.ACC. *to one's father* Il.

παππάξ, also **παπαπαππάξ** *interj.* (expressing the sound of farting) Ar.

πάππας (less correctly written **πάπᾱς**) ου *m.* [reltd. πατήρ, πάππος] | voc. πάππᾰ | (child's word for *father*, esp. in voc. address) **daddy** Od. A.*satyr.fr.* Ar. Thphr. Men. Theoc.

παππίας ου *m.* [dimin.] | voc. παππίᾱ | (in address to a father by his child) **dad** Ar. Men.; (in address to an older man who is not one's father) Men.

παππίδιον ου *n.* [dimin. πάππας] (in address to a father by his child) **daddy dear** Ar.; (in address to an older man who is not one's father) **dad** Ar.

παππίζω *vb.*: see παππάζω

πάππος ου *m.* [reltd. πάππᾱς] **1 grandfather** Hdt. Ar. +
2 ‖ PL. forefathers, ancestors Ar. Pl. Arist. Men. Call.; forefeathers (w. pun on sense 3, perh. *downy feathers*) Ar.
3 down (on a thistle) S.*fr.*

παππῷος ᾱ ον *adj.* **1** (of a name, a reputation, property) **belonging to or inherited from one's grandfather, grandfather's** Pl. Is. D.; (of a public fund) **inherited from one's grandfathers** Ar.
2 (of a way of life) **inherited from one's forefathers, ancestral, hereditary** Ar.

πάπραξ ακος *m.* a kind of fish (found in a Thracian lake); perh. **perch** Hdt.

παπταίνω *vb.* | ep.aor. πάπτηνα, Aeol.aor.ptcpl. παπτάναις |
1 (of persons, their eyes) **give a sharp, searching or anxious look, look sharply, peer, gaze** Hom. Hes. Semon. Pi. S. Hellenist.poet. Plu. —W.COMPL.CL. *to see whether or how sthg. may happen* Hom.; (of the moon) —W.PREP.PHR. *towards the rays of the sun* Parm.; (of a person) **look warily, beware** A. —W.COMPL.CL. *in case sthg. shd. happen* A.
2 (tr.) **look out for, try to spot** —*someone* Il. AR.; **catch sight of** —*sthg.* Pi. AR.; **look at, stare at** —*someone or sthg.* S. AR. —*distant things* (fig.ref. to being over-ambitious) Pi.

παρά, dial. **πάρ**, ep. **παραί** *prep.* | W.ACC., GEN. and DAT. | sts. following its noun (w. anastrophe of the accent), e.g. θεοῦ πάρα *from a god* Il. + |
—**A** | space or location |
1 by the side of, beside, by —W.ACC. or DAT. *someone or sthg.* Hom. +; (as adv.) **alongside** Hom. E.
2 (phrs.) παρ' ὄμμα *in one's sight* E.; παρὰ δόρυ *on the spear-side* (i.e. right) X. | for παρὰ (πὰρ) ποδί, πόδα, ποδός, πόδας *by the foot* (fig.ref. to closeness in space or time) see πούς 5, 7, 8, 11
3 along the side of, along —W.ACC. *a river bank, shore, road, or sim.* Il. +
4 in the company or house of, with —W.DAT. *someone* Hom. +
5 in the presence of, before —W.DAT. *a king, judge, jury, audience, or sim.* Od. +
6 among or belonging to the community of, among —W.DAT. *people* Pl. X. D. —W.ACC. (dial.) Ar.
7 in the judgement of —W.DAT. *someone, oneself* Hdt. S. E. +
8 (ref. to having influence) **with** —W.DAT. *someone* Pl.
9 in —W.DAT. *an author* (i.e. *his writings*) Plb.
—**B** | movt. or direction |
1 along the length of, along —W.ACC. *a field, road, wall, stream, or sim.* Hom. +; (fig.phr.) παρὰ στάθμην *along the chalk-line* (see στάθμη 5) | see also γνώμων 2
2 to a position at the side of, beside —W.ACC. *a person, place, object* Hom. +
3 into the presence or protection of, to —W.ACC. *someone* Hdt. Th. +
4 to the room or house of, to —W.ACC. *someone* Hom. +
5 alongside and past, past, beyond —W.ACC. *a place* Hom. +
—**C** | time |
1 on the occasion of, during —W.ACC. *drinks or a drinking-party* Hdt. X. Aeschin. + —W.DAT. *drinks, a feast* S. AR. | see also πότος
2 during the course of, during —W.ACC. *a period of time* Pi. Hdt. D.
3 during the whole of, throughout —W.ACC. *a period of time* B. Pl.
—**D** | alternation |
(ref. to one thing alternating) **with** —W.ACC. *another* E. +
• παρὰ ... ἄλλαν ἄλλα μοῖρα *one fate after another* E. • (ref. to flogging two persons) πληγὴν παρὰ πληγήν *stroke for stroke* Ar. • ἡμέραν παρ' ἡμέραν *on alternate days, every second day* D. • (also) παρὰ μίαν Plb.
—**E** | separation |
1 away from, from —W.GEN. *a place* Hom. +
2 from the presence or company of, from —W.GEN. *someone* Hom. +
—**F** | source or origin |
1 (ref. to asking, taking, receiving, learning, or sim.) **from** —W.GEN. *someone or sthg.* Od. +
2 (ref. to things originating) **from** or **through the agency of** —W.GEN. *someone or sthg.* Il. + | for παρὰ (πὰρ) ποδός *from one's foot*, πὰρ χειρός *from one's hand* (fig.ref. to the immediate vicinity) see πούς 8, χείρ 7
—**G** | comparison or value |
1 (ref. to comparing one thing) **alongside, with** —W.ACC. *another* Pl. D.
2 (without a vb. expressing comparison) **compared with** —W.ACC. *sthg.* Antipho Th. Pl. +
3 (ref. to accounting sthg.) **at a level of, as worth** —W.ACC. *little, nothing* Hdt. Trag. Isoc. + | see also ἐλάσσων 7, μικρός 12, οὐδείς 7
—**H** | extent, degree or margin |
1 to an extent or degree further than, beyond —W.ACC. *another, another's performance, one's strength, hope, or sim.* Il. +
2 beyond (and therefore in violation of or contrary to), **beyond** or **contrary to** —W.ACC. *sthg.* Od. +; (phrs.) παρὰ

πάρα

δίκην *contrary to justice*; παρὰ καιρόν *beyond the appropriate measure*; παρὰ μέλος *out of tune*; παρὰ φύσιν *contrary to nature*; παρὰ τὸ εἰκός *unreasonably* (see δίκη 2, καιρός 1, 3, μέλος 5, φύσις 8, ἔοικα 9) | see also αἶσα 4, 7, μέρος 7, προσδοκία 2, μοῖρα 8
3 within —W.ACC. *a certain margin (freq.* W.INF. *of achieving sthg.)* Hdt. E. Th. Isoc. + • τὴν Ἠιόνα παρὰ νύκτα ἐγένετο λαβεῖν *he was within a night of capturing Eion* Th.; (phrs.) παρὰ μικρόν *within a short distance*; παρὰ πολύ *by a wide margin* (see μικρός 12, πολύς 5) | see also βραχύς 17, ἐλάχιστος 4, 5, ἔρχομαι 6, μικρός 11, τοσοῦτος 4
4 all but, but for —W.ACC. *a certain number* Plu.
—**I** | *cause or purpose* |
for reason of, **because of** —W.ACC. *sthg.* Th. Att.orats. Pl. +; (ref. to toiling) **for the sake of** —W.ACC. *a meagre livelihood* Pi.

πάρα, also **πάρ** (Il.) *prep.* | The wd. is used as equiv. to 3sg. πάρεστι and 3pl. πάρεισι, also 3pl.subj. παρέωσι (Od.) | see παρείμι[1] | **1** (of persons or things) **be present, be at hand** Hom. Hes. Sol. Lyr. Hdt. Trag. +
2 || IMPERS. the opportunity is present, it is possible —W.INF. or DAT. + INF. (*for someone*) *to do sthg.* Od. Thgn. Trag. Ar. +

παρα-βαίνω, ep. **παρβαίνω** *vb.* | fut. παραβήσομαι | athem.aor. παρέβην | pf. παραβέβηκα, ep.pf.ptcpl. παρβεβαώς || PASS.: aor. παρεβάθην | pf. παραβέβασμαι || see also παραβάσκω |
1 go past; (of an apparition) **pass by unnoticed, escape** —*someone* E.; (of persons) **pass over, omit** (in speech) —*a topic* S. D.; **let pass** —*an opportunity* Din.
2 (of a comic chorus) **come forward** (to address the audience, oft. in the poet's name) Ar.
3 || STATV.PF. and PLPF. (of two warriors) **stand beside** —W.DAT. *each other* Il.; (of a warrior in a chariot) —*the charioteer* Il.; (of the charioteer) —*his passenger* Hdt.
4 (w. moral connot.) go beyond (what is right, legal or proper); **overstep, transgress, break** —*a law, an oath, a treaty, justice, or sim.* A. Hdt. E. Th. Ar. Att.orats. +; **transgress against, offend** —*a god* Hdt.; (intr.) **be a transgressor** A. Arist. || PASS. (of a law, an oath, or sim.) be transgressed against or broken Th. D.

παρά-βακτρος ον *adj.* [βάκτρον] (of a wife's attendance) **beside the staff** (of her blind husband) E.

παρά-βακχος ον *adj.* [Βάκχος or Βάκχη] (of Demosthenes, described as a frenzied orator) **in the company of Bacchus** Plu.(quot.) [or perh. *Bacchant-like*]

παρα-βάλλω *vb.* | fut. παραβαλῶ | aor.2 παρέβαλον | pf. παραβέβληκα | **1** throw (sthg.) alongside; **throw down** —*fodder (beside horses)* Hom.(tm.) Pl. —*wood, stones (beside a wall or along a route)* Th. —*brushwood (beside an altar)* Ar. —*poison (for animals)* X.; **place along the sides** (of ships) —*protective screens* X. || MID. **have set beside one** —*items of food* Pl. || PASS. (of stones) be laid alongside —W.DAT. *a wall* Th.; (of manure) be applied —W.DAT. *to roots* Pl.
2 (fig., of a speaker) **throw in** —*a topic* D. Arist.; throw in as a reproach, **cast** (W.ACC. *sthg.*) **in the teeth** —W.DAT. *of someone* Aeschin.
3 put (someone) into another's hands; **hand over, give as prey** —*a person (to a mob)* D. Plb. —*birds (as a race, to humans)* Ar.; **entrust** —*children (to someone, for education)* Hdt. || PASS. be given up or abandoned —W.DAT. *to prostitutes and dicing* (perh. w. play on 4, *stake oneself on*) Ar.
4 || MID. set down (sthg. of value) as a guarantee; **deposit,**
stake —*a sum of money* Plu.; **wager, risk** —*one's life* Il. —*one's children* Hdt. Th.; (in ctxt. of war, games) —*more, most, an equal amount (compared to one's opponents)* Th. X.; put at risk, **endanger** —*someone* Hdt. Th.; **run** —W.INTERN.ACC. *a risk to one's person* Th.; **risk** —W.INF. *doing sthg.* Plu.; (intr.) **take risks** Plb.
5 set (one thing) beside (another) for comparison; **compare** —*two things* Ar. Isoc. Arist. —*sthg.* (W.DAT. or PREP.PHR. w. *another*) Att.orats. Pl. X. Arist.; **match** (competitively) —*a horse* (W.DAT. w. *another*) X. || MID. **match** —*one's laments* (W.DAT. *to a halcyon, i.e. to its laments*) E.; (of goddesses) **vie with one another** E. || PASS. (of persons or things) be matched or compared —W.DAT. or PREP.PHR. w. *someone or sthg.* Hdt. S. Pl. X.
6 (of sailors) **haul** or **bring alongside** (their ship) —*a small boat* Ar.(mid.) Plu.; (intr., of sailors, a ship) **come alongside** —W.DAT. *another ship (in battle)* Plb. || MID. (of sailors) **bring** (W.ACC. one's ship) **alongside** (another ship) AR.(tm.); **throw ashore** —*mooring-ropes* AR.(tm.); (of a helmsman) **come alongside** (a landing-place) Ar.
7 (of persons) come alongside, **join** (sts. W.DAT. w. a group of people) Pl.; (intr.) put in (at a place), **enter** Arist. Men.; **arrive** (at pleasures) Arist.
8 (intr., of persons, ships) go across (the sea), **cross over** Hdt. Th. D.
9 move or turn (one's head or sim.) to the side; **turn** —*one's head (to listen to a new speaker)* Pl. —*one's eyes (to see sthg.)* Ar.; **bend** —*one's ears (to the direction of a sound)* Pl.; (of a hare) **throw aslant** —*its ear (towards a danger)* X.; (of an animal when eating) **move sideways, grind** —*its molars* Ar.

παρα-βάπτομαι *pass.vb.* (of items) **be dyed alongside** (other items) Plu.

παράβασις, ep. **παραίβασις**, εως *f.* [παραβαίνω] **1** going aside; **means of escape** (W.GEN. fr. death, ref. to a narrow sea-channel) AR.
2 forward movement (of a person or his legs) Plu.
3 overstepping, transgression (W.GEN. of a law, justice) NT. Plu.; **offence** NT.

παρα-βάσκω *ep.vb.* | only 3sg.impf. παρέβασκε | (of a warrior, conveyed in a chariot) **go beside** (the charioteer) Il.; (of a warrior on a ship) **have one's place beside** —W.DAT. *the helmsman* AR.

παραβάτης ου, ep. **παραιβάτης** εω *m.* [παραβαίνω]
1 fighter who stands beside the driver of a chariot, **chariot-fighter** Il. E. X.
2 (in a foreign contingent hired by a Macedonian king) app. **foot-soldier** (accompanying the cavalry) Plu.
3 transgressor (W.GEN. of the law) NT.

—**παραιβάτις** ιδος *ep.f.* **1 passenger** (in a chariot) AR.
2 partner (ref. to a woman working beside another) Theoc. [or perh. better taken as pers. name]

—**παραιβατέω** *dial.contr.vb.* (of a woman masquerading as Athena) **ride alongside** (the tyrant Peisistratos, in his chariot) Arist.(dub.)

παραβατός, dial. **παρβατός** (A.), όν *adj.* (of Zeus' mind, a ruler's authority, in neg.phrs.) **to be thwarted** A. S.

παραβέβασμαι (pf.pass.): see παραβαίνω

παρα-βιάζομαι *mid.vb.* **1** (of soldiers) **break through, force** —*a palisade* Plb.
2 (of persons) **use abnormal force** (in gaining compliance w. their requests) Plb.; **force** (W.ACC. people) **into compliance** Plu.; (wkr.sens.) **prevail upon** —*someone (to do sthg.)* NT.
3 do violence to, pervert —*the sense of a proposal* Plu.

παρα-βλαστάνω vb. (fig., of passions) **spring up alongside** (Eros, the master-passion) Pl.

παρα-βλέπω vb. **1 steal a sideways glance** (furtively, at someone) Ar.; **glance furtively round** Ar.; **look askance** (at someone) Ar.
2 (of historians) **overlook, fail to see** —sthg. Plb.

παραβλήδην adv. [παραβάλλω] **1 riskily** —ref. to Zeus attempting to provoke Hera Il. [or perh. *deceitfully, deviously*]
2 in reply —ref. to speaking or sim. AR. [or perh.sts. *deceitfully*]

παραβλήματα των n.pl. **awnings of cloth or hide stretched along the sides of a warship** (for protection against spray or missiles), **side-screens** X.

παραβλητέος ᾱ ον vbl.adj. (of a person) **to be compared** (W.DAT. w. someone) Plu.

παραβλητός όν adj. (of a person) **comparable** (W.DAT. w. someone) Plu.

παρα-βλώσκω vb. | only ep.pf. παρμέμβλωκα | ‖ PF. (of Aphrodite, Thetis) **have come beside, stand by** —W.DAT. *Paris, Achilles* (to protect him) Il.

παραβλώψ ῶπος masc.fem.adj. [παραβλέπω] (of Prayers) **looking sideways**, **looking askance** (W.ACC. w. their eyes) Il.

παρα-βοάω contr.vb. (of members of a claque, beside a speaker's platform) **shout from the sidelines** D.

παραβοήθεια ᾱς f. [παραβοηθέω] (in military ctxt.) **assistance, support, help** Plb.; (gener., W.GEN. in tasks) Pl.

παρα-βοηθέω contr.vb. **1** (usu. of troops, commanders) **come to the rescue, bring help** (oft. W.DAT. to someone) Th. Ar. X. Plb. Plu.
2 (gener.) **give help of a contrary kind** (to that given by others) Pl.

παραβολή ῆς f. [παραβάλλω] **1 placing side by side** (for purpose of comparison), **juxtaposition, comparison** (sts. W.GEN. of things) Pl. Arist. Plb.
2 comparison, analogy, illustration (of one thing by ref. to another) Isoc.; (as a technique used in argument, w. examples drawn fr. real life, opp. fables) Arist.
3 parable (short discourse making a comparison, characteristic of the teaching of Jesus) NT.; **proverb** NT.
4 state of being side by side; **broadside position** (of ships in battle) Plb.
5 (astron.) app. **conjunction** (of stars) Pl.
6 sideways direction, oblique turning (of a path) Plu.

παράβολος ον adj. **1** (of a person) **risk-taking, reckless, foolhardy** Ar.; (of an attempted proof) **risky** Arist.; (of a statement) Men.
2 (of actions, behaviour, circumstances) **risky, hazardous, perilous** Hdt. Isoc. Plb. Plu.; (of rugged terrain) Plb.

—**παραβόλως** adv. **riskily, recklessly, perilously** Men. Plb. Plu.

—**παραιβόλα** ep.neut.pl.adv. **riskily, boldly** —ref. to jesting hHom. [or perh. *by way of interjection*]

παρα-βραβεύομαι pass.vb. (of a person) **be a victim of a miscarriage of justice** Plb.

παρά-βυστος ον adj. [βύω] **stuffed aside or crammed into a corner**; (phr.) ἐν παραβύστῳ **in a hole-and-corner way, on the sly** D.

παραγγελίᾱ ᾱς f. [παραγγέλλω] **1 issuing of orders** (by a commander) Plb.
2 public announcement (by a commander) X.; **command, order** (by a magistrate) NT.
3 system of instruction (governing behaviour) Arist.; (governing historical writing) Plb.
4 communication for the purpose of soliciting support, canvassing (by litigants) D.; (by candidates for public office) Plu.; (gener.) **candidature** Plu. ‖ PL. **proceedings involving candidates, elections** Plu.

παρ-αγγέλλω vb. | fut. παραγγελῶ | aor. παρήγγειλα | **1** (of beacon-signallers) **pass on a message** A.; (of the person who arranges for the beacons) **send a message** A.; (of a beacon) **pass on** (as a message), **transmit** —*its light* A.
2 (of persons) **pass on, hand down** (to successive generations) —*the memory of sthg.* E.; (of gods) —*a clear message* (to humans) E.
3 (of persons in authority, esp. commanders) **pass word, transmit** or **give orders** (oft. W.DAT. to someone, usu. also W.INF. to do sthg.) Hdt. Trag. Th. Ar. Pl. +; **give** —W.INTERN. or COGN.ACC. *an order or sim.* E. Lys. Pl. Hyp. Thphr.; **give orders for, order** —*provisions* Hdt. Th. ‖ PASS. (of a military campaign) **be announced or levied** Aeschin. ‖ IMPERS. **an order is (was) given** (usu. W.INF. to do sthg.) Lys. Pl. X. Aeschin. ‖ NEUT.PRES. or PF.PASS.PTCPL.SB. (usu.pl.) **order or command** Th. Isoc. Pl. +
4 (wkr.sens.) **pass on a request** (to friends) Lys.
5 communicate (w. someone) **for the purpose of soliciting support**; (of a litigant) **canvass support** (sts. W.DAT. fr. someone) D.; (of a politician) **canvass, be a candidate** —W.ACC. or εἰς + ACC. *for an office* Plu.

παράγγελμα ατος n. **1 transmitted message** (W.GEN. fr. a beacon) A.
2 order (fr. persons in authority, esp. commanders) Th. Lys. Plb. Plu.; (ref. to a legal provision) Hyp.
3 instruction, precept, lesson (fr. a father or teacher) Isoc. X.

παραγγελματικῶς adv. **according to the rules** (governing historical writing) Plb.

παράγγελσις εως f. (in military ctxt.) **transmission of orders** (as a process) Th. Pl. X.; **giving of an order** (in specific circumstances) X.

παρα-γεύω vb. (fig., of Lykourgos) **cause** (W.ACC. Spartan women) **to have a taste** —W.GEN. *of honourable ambition* Plu.

παρα-γηράω contr.vb. (fig., of a populace) **be in extreme old age, be in one's dotage** Aeschin.

παρα-γίγνομαι, Ion. **παραγίνομαι** mid.vb. | aor.pass. (w.mid.sens.) παρεγενήθην (Plb.) | **1 be beside, near** or **with** —W.DAT. *someone* (who is doing or experiencing sthg.) Hdt. +; **be present** (usu. W.DAT. or PREP.PHR. at some event, as witness or participant) Hdt. +
2 (specif., of a chamberlain) **be in attendance** —W.DBL.DAT. *on persons, at meals* Od.
3 (of gods and humans) **stand by in support** or **come as a helper** —W.DAT. *for someone* Hes. A. Hdt. +; (of troops) **come to help** (oft. W.DAT. someone) Hdt. Th. Ar. + —W.DBL.DAT. *someone, in a battle* Th.
4 (of persons, ships, or sim.) **arrive** (usu. W.PREP.PHR. at a place) Hdt. +; (of the seasons) Hdt.
5 (of wealth, power, virtue, or sim.) **come, accrue** (oft. W.DAT. to someone) Sol. Thgn. Hdt. Th. +
6 (of grain, oxen's horns) **come on** (in growth), **grow to maturity** Hdt.

παρα-γιγνώσκω vb. (of jurors) **make a misjudgement** X.

παρ-αγκάλισμα ατος n. **object of embraces** (ref. to one's wife) S.

παρᾱγορέω dial.contr.vb., **παράγορος** dial.adj.: see παρηγορέω, παρήγορος

παράγραμμα ατος n. [παραγράφω] **additional detail** (in a document) D.

παραγραφή ῆς *f.* 1 that which is written at the side (of a text), **marginal note** or **sign** (as an aid to finding a passage) Isoc.; (marking the end of a metrical sequence) Arist. 2 (in Athenian law) **counter-prosecution** (in which the defendant charged the plaintiff w. bringing an inadmissible prosecution) Isoc. D.; (in Roman law, ref. to the *exceptio*) **counterplea** or **objection** Plu.

παρα-γράφω *vb.* 1 **write words in addition** (to graffiti on a door) Ar. ‖ PASS. (of information) be additionally inscribed (in a notice) Pl. 2 (in legal ctxts.) **add, subjoin, append** (further details, in laws, contracts, or sim.) Ar. Hyp. D. 3 **cancel** (information in a document) by a marginal sign ‖ PASS. (fig., of friendly relations betw. states) be cancelled Plb. 4 ‖ MID. **arrange to have** (W.ACC. laws) **transcribed** (on a notice-board) **for comparison** (w. a proposed law) D. ‖ PASS. (of laws) be transcribed for comparison Aeschin. D. 5 ‖ MID. **have** (W.ACC. someone, i.e. his name) **inserted** or **appended** (in a legal document) D. ‖ PASS. (of persons, i.e. their names) be appended Plb. 6 **write, sign** (W.ACC. oneself, i.e. one's name) **with an additional detail** —W.GEN. *of a father* (*i.e. w. his name*) D. 7 ‖ MID. **bring a counter-prosecution** (against an allegedly inadmissible prosecution) Isoc. D. —W.ACC. *against someone* D.; **claim by way of counter-argument** —W.COMPL.CL. *that a prosecution is inadmissible* D.

παρα-γυμνόω *contr.vb.* (fig.) **lay bare, disclose** —*plans, information* Hdt. Plb. ‖ IMPERS.PASS. **it is disclosed** —W.COMPL.CL. *that sthg. is the case* Plb.

παρ-άγω *vb.* | impf. παρῆγον, dial. πάραγον (Pi.) | aor.2 παρήγαγον, dial. πάραγον (Sapph.) | 1 (of guides) **lead** (W.ACC. someone) **past** —*a place* Hdt.; (intr., of troops) **pass by** (a city) Plb. ‖ PASS. (of a captive) be led past (in a triumphal procession) Plu. 2 (of a commander) **move** (W.ACC. troops) **along** (fr. one part of a battle formation to another, past those betw. them) Hdt.; (specif., ref. to moving up troops fr. a rear column into the front line) X. ‖ PASS. (of sacrificial victims) be brought up (in front of an army) E. 3 **let** (W.ACC. time) **go past** (i.e. procrastinate, delay) Plu.; (intr.) **delay** Plu. [or perh. *be evasive*] | cf. παραγωγή 8 4 **lead in a different direction, divert** —*lake water* Plu.; (of a bird) —*its wings* (*i.e. fly away*) E.; (intr., of sailors) **take an indirect course** Plb. 5 **divert, deflect** —*the Fates* Hdt. —*someone* (*fr. mourning*) S. ‖ PASS. (of gods) be deflected (fr. their purposes, by sacrifices or sim.) Pl. 6 (w. moral connot.) **lead on** (into an undesirable situation); (of a god, poverty) **lead astray** —*someone, his heart* (W.PREP.PHR. *into wrongdoing*) Thgn.; (of one's belly) —*one's mind* (*into shamelessness*) Archil.; (of Ruin) —*mortals* (*into her net*) A.; (of Fortune) —*people* (*into uncertainty*) E. 7 (gener., app. of Aphrodite) **lead astray** —*Helen* Sapph.; (of lovemaking) —*Clytemnestra* Pi.; (of Homer's poetic skill) **mislead, delude** —*people* Pi.; (of gods and humans) —*people, their thinking* Th. Att.orats. Pl. ‖ PASS. be led astray (by persons, fear, argument, bribery, or sim.) S. E. Th. Pl. X. D. 8 (of unscrupulous persons) **pervert, put to improper use, distort the meaning of** —*a law* Pl. Is. 9 (gramm.) **alter** —*a word, letters in a word* (*to create another word*) Pl. ‖ PASS. (of a word) be altered Pl.; (of a noun) become by alteration —W.PREDIC.ADJ. *a particular adjective* Arist.

10 **conduct into a house or room; take** (W.ACC. someone) **inside** Hdt. E. Men.; **take** —*someone* (W.ADV. *inside*) Hdt. ‖ PASS. (of a person, envisaged as an avenging spirit) be introduced or ushered —W.PREP.PHR. *inside a house* S. 11 (intr., usu. imperatv.) **get moving** or **go inside** Men.; (imperatv.) perh. **get along** Ar. 12 **bring before an audience; bring forward, introduce, present** —*someone* (*before a public assembly or sim.*) Hdt. Th. Att.orats. X.; (lit. and fig.) **bring** (W.ACC. someone) **into court** Att.orats.; (of comic poets) **bring on stage** —*immoral behaviour, a certain type of character* Ar. Arist. ‖ PASS. (of a lawsuit) be brought into court Antipho 13 **bring forward, introduce** —*a topic* (*into a discussion*) Pl. —*music* (*into education*) Arist.; (of gods) —*compulsion* (*into their relations w. humans*) Plu.

παραγωγή ῆς *f.* 1 **carrying across, transportation** (of things, by ship) X. 2 **moving up** (of troops, fr. a rear column into the front line) X. Plb.; (of ships, closer to a city under siege) Plb. 3 **changing the angle of one's oar-blade at the end of a stroke** (so that it leaves the water silently), **feathering** (W.GEN. of oars) X. 4 **leading astray, deception** (W.GEN. by a ruse) Hdt.; **misleading argument, half-truth** D. Plu.; **perversion, travesty** (W.GEN. of the truth) D. 5 **deflecting, diverting** (of the gods, by prayers) Pl. 6 **divergence, variation** (in language, ref. to a dialect) Hdt. 7 **breach** (of a rule) Pl. 8 **evasive** or **delaying behaviour** Plu. | cf. παράγω 3

παραγωγιάζω *vb.* [παραγώγιον] **levy a toll on** —*sailors entering the Black Sea* Plb.

παραγώγιον ου *n.* [παράγω 10] **entry-toll** (levied on ships) Plb.

παρα-δαρθάνω *ep.vb.* | only aor.2 παρέδραθον, inf. παραδραθέειν | (of a man) **sleep beside** —W.DAT. *a woman* Hom.

παράδειγμα ατος *n.* [παραδείκνῡμι] 1 **example for copying, model** (used by a painter or sculptor) Pl.; **pattern, exemplar** (existing in heaven, after which earthly things are made) Pl.; (ref. to Platonic Forms) Arist.; **specification, plan** (of a temple) Hdt. [or perh. *model*] 2 **product of copying, small-scale copy, model** (W.GEN. of an embalmed corpse) Hdt. 3 **example, sample** (W.GEN. of gold) S.*Ichn.* 4 (ref. to events, activities, behaviour) **example, illustration** (of sthg.) Att.orats. Pl.; (ref. to persons) Th. Pl.; (w. moral connot., ref. to persons, their behaviour) **good example, model** (for imitation) Th. Att.orats. + 5 **example from the past** (as a warning for the future); **example, lesson, warning** Th. Att.orats. +; (ref. to persons, their fate) S. Th. Ar. D. + 6 **example in illustration or proof** (of an argument); **example, illustration, demonstration** (sts. W.GEN. of sthg.) Th. Ar. Att.orats. Pl. + 7 **proof based on factual examples, evidence, proof** (of an assertion) Th.; (log.) **inductive proof** Arist. 8 **standard of comparison, standard** (provided by vice, by which to assess virtue) E.

παραδειγματίζω *vb.* **make an example of** —*someone, a revolt* (*by punitive action*) Plb.; **expose to public view, make a spectacle of** —*someone's misfortune* Plb.; **expose** (W.ACC. someone) **to public shame** Plb.

παραδειγματικῶς *adv.* **with the use of examples** —*ref. to formulating an argument* Arist.

παραδειγματισμός οῦ *m*. **exemplary punishment** Plb.; (less formally) **public shaming** Plb.

παραδειγματώδης ες *adj*. (of orators, their speeches) **characterised by the use of examples** Arist.; (log., of a kind of argument) **based on examples** Arist.

παρα-δείκνῡμι *vb*. —also (pres. and impf.) **παραδεικνύω** (Isoc. Plb.) **1 exhibit** (W.ACC. objects) **side by side** (w. others, for comparison) Isoc.
2 ‖ MID. **exhibit, display** —*one's achievements* D.
3 (intr.) app. **use examples** (in argument) Pl.
4 point out, indicate —*sthg*. Plb. —W.INDIR.Q. or COMPL.CL. *what is the case, that sthg. is the case* Plb. Plu.
5 formally make over, **assign** —*tribute money* (W.DAT. *to someone, to spend for a specific purpose*) X.

παράδεισος ου *m*. [Iran.loanwd.] **1 walled park** or **pleasure-ground** (of Persian kings and nobles) X. Plu.
2 paradise (as the abode of God and the redeemed) NT.

παραδεκτέος ᾱ ον *vbl.adj*. [παραδέχομαι] **to be admitted** (into a city) Pl.

παρα-δέχομαι, Ion. **παραδέκομαι** *mid.vb*. **1 receive from another; receive, take over** —*persons, a city, a horse* Hdt. Ar. X. —*letters or sim.* Il. X. —*goods* Pl. X.; (of earth) —*drops of rain fr. heaven* E.*fr.*
2 (specif.) **receive from one's parents or ancestors, inherit** —*a war, an empire, a custom* Hdt. —*wise thinking* Pi. —*an art, a story* Pl.
3 (of pupils) **take in knowledge** (fr. teachers) Plu.
4 (of soldiers) **take over** (a fight, fr. others) Hdt.
5 take upon oneself, undertake —W.INF. *to do sthg.* D.
6 allow to enter, **admit, allow, accept** —*someone or sthg.* (usu. W.PREP.PHR. *into the ideal city*) Pl. —*someone* (W.PREP.PHR. *into a region, city, house*) Aeschin. D. Plb. —*a custom* (*into court, trials*) Aeschin.; (of a city) —*a garrison and governor* Aeschin. —*neighbouring people* (*as citizens*) Arist.; (of a teacher) **accept** —*someone* (*as a pupil*) Pl. ‖ PASS. (of visitors) be received or welcomed NT.
7 accept as admissible; (of magistrates) **permit, allow** —*someone's arrest* Lys.; (of a disputant) —*points in an argument* Pl.; (of an allegation) **justify** —*a procedural delay, an excuse* Hyp.; (of a person's lifestyle) —*an allegation* Hyp.

παρα-δηλόω *contr.vb*. **1 reveal obliquely, allude to, make an insinuation about** —*someone* D. —*sthg*. Plu.
2 insinuate —W.COMPL.CL. *that sthg. is the case* Plu.

παρα-διᾱκονέω *contr.vb*. **serve on the side, do odd jobs** —W.DAT. *for someone* Ar.

παρα-δίδωμι *vb*. | neut.impers.vbl.adj. παραδοτέον, also pl. παραδοτέα (Th.) | **1 hand over** (what is in one's charge or possession) to another; **hand over, entrust** —*someone or sthg.* (oft. W.DAT. *to someone*) Pi. Hdt. + ‖ PASS. (of persons or things) be handed over or entrusted (to another) Hdt. Ar. +
2 hand on to the next person in a series; (of couriers, intermediaries) **hand on, pass on** —*instructions, letters* Hdt. X.; (of a sentry) —*a bell* (*to the next sentry*), *his own watch* (*to the next*) Th. Plu.; (of parents) —*life* (*compared to a relay-torch*) Pl.; (of a disputant) —*the task of speaking next* Pl.; (of a councillor, magistrate) —*a prosecution, an office* (*to a successor*) Antipho Ar. ‖ PASS. (of a baby) be passed on (fr. one person to another) Hdt.; (of instructions) Hdt.
3 hand down to one's descendants; (of parents, ancestors) **bequeath** —*possessions, places, privileges, or sim.* Hdt. Th. Ar. + ‖ PASS. be handed down or bequeathed Th. Is. +
4 hand down (by word of mouth) —*a story or tradition* Pl. —*an account of events witnessed at first hand* NT.; (of a virtuous person) **transmit** (by teaching) —*virtue* Pl. ‖ PASS. (of writings, customs, or sim.) be handed down Att.orats. +; (of a family celebrated by poets) be handed down in legend Pl. ‖ PASS.PTCPL.ADJ. (of stories) **traditional** D. Arist.; (of one kind of tyrannical rule) Arist.; (of gods) Din.
5 give up (to someone), **hand over, surrender** —*a land, city, ships, or sim.* Hdt. Th. + —*one's weapons* Th. X. —*leadership, freedom* Hdt. —*oneself* Hdt. Th.; (wkr.sens.) **risk** —*one's life* (W.PREP.PHR. *for Christ's name*) NT.; (intr.) **surrender** Th. ‖ PASS. (of persons or things) be handed over or surrendered Hdt. Th. +
6 give up, surrender —*oneself* (W.DAT. *to fortune*) Th. —(*to pleasures, desires*) Pl.; (intr.) **surrender, give oneself up** —W.DAT. *to pleasure* Pl.
7 (in legal ctxts.) **hand over** —*someone* (*for trial, punishment, imprisonment, usu.* W.DAT. or PREP.PHR. *to a court, magistrates, the popular assembly, prison*) Ar. Att.orats. + —*a slave* (*for examination by torture*) Att.orats. ‖ PASS. (of a person) be handed over Att.orats. +
8 (of a god) **give, grant** —*glory, a choice* (W.DAT. *to someone*) Pi.; (of destiny) **bestow** —*wealth* Pi.; (of excessive sexual passions, in neg.phr.) —*good repute* E.
9 grant a possibility or opportunity; (of a god) **allow** (sthg. to happen) Hdt. X. D.; (of opportunities, circumstances) Isoc. Plb. NT.; (of persons) —W.DAT. + INF. *someone to do sthg.* Hdt.; (of a god) —W.ACC. *an action* (*by someone*) Hdt.
10 (of a wrestler) **allow, grant** (unwillingly) —*a hold* (*to his opponent*) Ar. ‖ PASS. (of a blow, i.e. the opportunity to deal one) be presented E.

παρα-διηγέομαι *mid.contr.vb*. **relate incidentally** —*a piece of information* Arist.

παραδοξολογίᾱ ᾱς *f*. [παραδοξολόγος] **1 narration of the unexpected or unbelievable, fairy-tale, make-believe, romantic nonsense** Aeschin. Plb.
2 absurd or illogical manner of argument, **use of paradox** Plb.

παραδοξο-λόγος ον *adj*. [παράδοξος] (of a historian) **using absurd** or **illogical arguments** Plb.

παραδοξο-νίκης ου *m*. [νίκη] **victor-extraordinary** (ref. to a winner in wrestling and the pankration on the same day) Plu.

παρά-δοξος ον *adj*. [δόξα] (of a statement, situation, or sim.) contrary to expectation or belief, **surprising, incredible** Att.orats. Pl. X. +; (of an argument) **self-contradictory, paradoxical** Pl. Arist.

—**παραδόξως** *adv*. **surprisingly, unexpectedly** Aeschin. Plb.

παραδόσιμος ον *adj*. [παράδοσις] **1** (of the renown of one's ancestors) **handed down as an inheritance** Plb.; (of an event, a story, a person's fame) **handed down by tradition** Plb.
2 (of a monument) **commemorative** Plb.

παράδοσις εως *f*. [παραδίδωμι] **1 handing over** (by one person to another), **transfer** (of goods, money) Arist.; (of kingship) Plu.
2 handing over to an enemy, surrender (of a city) Th. Plb.; (of persons, oneself) Plu.
3 handing over, surrender (of a criminal, to magistrates) D.; (of a slave for torture) Isoc.
4 handing down (to succeeding generations), **bequeathing** (of a sceptre) Th.; (gener.) handing on, **transmission** (of knowledge, instructions) Pl. Plu.
5 knowledge handed down from earlier generations, tradition Plb.; **traditional teaching** or **doctrine** NT.

παραδοτέος ᾱ ον *vbl.adj*. (of a city) **to be entrusted** (W.DAT. *to persons*) Pl.

παραδοτός ή όν *adj.* (of virtue) **capable of being transmitted** (to persons, by teaching) Pl.

παραδοχή ῆς *f.* [παραδέχομαι] **1** that which has been received by inheritance from earlier generations ‖ PL. **traditions** E.
2 welcome, acceptance, approval (of a person, a historical composition) Plb.

παραδραθέειν (ep.aor.2 inf.): see παραδαρθάνω

παρα-δραμεῖν *aor.2 inf.* | aor.2 παρέδραμον, ep.3du. παραδραμέτην | pf. παραδεδράμηκα | The pres. and impf. are supplied by παρατρέχω. |
1 (of a person, an animal) **run past** (a place, person, net) Il. Ar. X. Thphr. Plu.; **hurry past** —*someone* Theoc.; (fig., of a missile) **fly past** (someone) Plu.; (of a remark, i.e. its significance) **pass by** —*someone* Plb. | see also περιδραμεῖν 5
2 (of persons herding cattle) **run alongside** (the animals) Plb.
3 (of a runner) **outrun** —*someone* Il.; (fig., of a commander) —*enemy ships* Plb.
4 (fig., of a speaker) **outstrip, surpass** —*another speaker* (*in argument*) Ar.; (of a person) —*others* (*in moral qualities, in reputation*) Ar. Plb.; (of a bird) —*a piper* (*w. its music*) hHom.; (of evils) —*former evils* E.
5 (fig., of a writer) **hurry past** (and ignore a topic) Plb.; (of a speaker) rush over a topic, **speak cursorily** Isoc.
6 run across —*a piece of ground* X.; (intr.) **run across** (somewhere) —W.PREP.PHR. *to a place* X.; (of soldiers) **move rapidly across** —W.PREP.PHR. *to the wings* (*of an army*) X.

παρα-δράω *contr.vb.* | ep.3pl.pres.subj. (w.diect.) παραδρώωσι | (of subordinates) **be at hand to perform** —*services* (W.DAT. *for superiors*) Od.

παράδρομα ων *n.pl.* [παραδραμεῖν] spaces between nets through which hunted animals may run, **gaps** X.

παραδρομή ῆς *f.* **1 rapid passage** (W.GEN. through a country, by a commander) Plu.
2 (fig.) **cursory treatment** (of a topic) Arist. Plb.

παρα-δυναστεύω *vb.* **rule beside** (another), **be a fellow prince** Th.

παρα-δύομαι *mid.vb.* [δύω¹] | athem.aor.act. παρέδῡν, ep.inf. παραδύμεναι | pf.act. παραδέδυκα | **1** (of persons) **slip past, steal past** (someone) Il. Plu.; **go covertly, slip along** (somewhere) Ar. Plu.
2 (fig., of a commander, a politician) **edge** or **worm one's way** —W.PREP.PHR. *into a country* D. Plu. —*into an office* D. —*towards succession to imperial office* Plu.; (of lawbreaking, wealth and poverty) **slip in, steal in** (sts. W.PREP.PHR. *to a city*) Pl. Arist.; (of a custom) —W.PREP.PHR. *to government* Aeschin.

παράδυσις εως *f.* slipping in (to a territory), **encroachment** (by a warship) D.

παραδωσείω *vb.* [desideratv. παραδίδωμι] (of a general) **wish to hand over** (command) Th.

παρ-αείδω *vb.* (of a minstrel) sing in the presence of, **sing before** —W.DAT. *someone* Od.

παρ-αείρω *vb.* | aor. παρήειρα ‖ aor.pass. παρηέρθην | lift aside or detach; (of a deity) **unhinge** —*someone's mind* Archil. ‖ PASS. (of a person's partially severed head) hang to one side Il.

παρα-ζεύγνῡμι *vb.* (of a goddess) **set** (W.ACC. two guardian snakes) **beside** —W.DAT. *a baby* E.

παράζυγες ων *m.pl.* additional members of a group (beyond a certain quota), **extra persons** Arist.

παρα-ζώννῡμι *vb.* fasten at the waist, **put on** —*a sword* Pl.; (mid.) Plu.

παρα-θαλάσσιος, Att. **παραθαλάττιος**, ᾱ (Ion. η) ον (also ος ον) *adj.* (of cities, peoples, or sim.) **beside the sea, coastal** Hdt. Th. X. Plb. NT. Plu. ‖ FEM.SB. **coastal area, seaboard** Th. X. ‖ NEUT.PL.SB. **coastal areas** Hdt.
—**παραθαλασσίδιος** ον *adj.* (of a town) **coastal** Th.

παρα-θάλπομαι *pass.vb.* **be soothed** or **comforted** —W.ACC. *in one's heart* (W.DAT. *by words*) E.

παρα-θαρσύνω, Att. **παραθαρρύνω** *vb.* **embolden, encourage** —*someone* Th. Pl. X. Hermoloch. Plu. —(W.INF. *to do sthg.*) Plu.

παρα-θέλγω *vb.* **soothe away, assuage** —*anger* A.

παρα-θερίζω *vb.* | dial.aor. παρέθρισα | (of the Clashing Rocks) **cut off, sever** —*the tip of a ship's stern-post* AR.

παρα-θερμαίνομαι *pass.vb.* (fig.) **become overheated** or **inflamed** (through drunkenness) Aeschin.

παρά-θερμος ον *adj.* [θερμός] (fig., of a commander) **overheated, overexcited** (by the prospect of fighting) Plu.

παράθεσις εως *f.* [παρατίθημι] **1 juxtaposition, proximity** (of peoples) Plb.
2 comparison (of things) Plb.
3 provision or **administration** (of liquids, to a sick person) Plb.
4 setting aside, storage (of supplies) Plb. ‖ PL. (concr.) **supplies, provisions** Plb.
5 setting before (a reader), **citation, mention** (of names) Plb.
6 laying of advice (before someone), **advice, suggestion** Plb.

παρα-θέω *contr.vb.* [θέω¹] **1 run along** (a ship's deck) Pl.; **run alongside** (a group of soldiers) Plu. —W.DAT. *someone on horseback* Plu.; (of cavalry) **speed alongside** (the enemy line) X.; (of a deified soul) —W.DAT. *the moon* Call.
2 (of persons, animals) **run past** X. —*someone* X.
3 (fig.) **run beyond, overrun** —*the right limit* Pl.; (of righteousness) **outstrip** —*gold* Call.

παρα-θεωρέω *contr.vb.* **1** view (sthg.) beside (sthg. else) for comparison; **compare** —*oneself* (W.PREP.PHR. *w. others*) X.
2 ‖ PASS. (of people) **be overlooked** NT.

παραθήκη ης *f.* [παρατίθημι] that which is entrusted to another, **deposit** (ref. to money) Plb.; **item held as security** (ref. to hostages) Hdt.; **pledge of good faith** (ref. to a message) Hdt.

παρα-θραύω *vb.* break off ‖ PF.PASS. (of fairness) constitute a breach —W.GEN. *of the strict criterion for justice* Pl.

παραί *ep.prep.*: see παρά

παραιβασίη ης *ep.f.* [παραβαίνω] **transgression, crime** Hes. | cf. παρβασία

παραίβασις *ep.f.*: see παράβασις

παραιβατέω *dial.contr.vb.*: see under παραβάτης

παραιβάτης *ep.m.*, **παραιβάτις** *ep.f.*: see παραβάτης

παραιβόλα *ep.neut.pl.adv.*: see under παράβολος

παραϜιδών (Lacon.aor.2 ptcpl.): see παροράω

παρ-αιθύσσω *vb.* | dial.aor. παραίθυξα | **1** make (sthg.) move rapidly past or along; (fig., of spectators) **let fly** —*a cheer* Pi.
2 (intr., of a bird) **speed past** (a ship) AR.; (fig., of a casual comment, likened to a spark fr. an anvil) **shoot forth** Pi.

παραίνεσις εως (Ion. ιος) *f.* [παραινέω] **1 exhortation** (to troops, a populace, or sim.) A. Hdt. Th. X. Plb. Plu.
2 advice Hdt. E. Th. X. Plb. Plu.; **recommendation, encouragement** (W.GEN. towards sthg.) Th.
3 (specif.) **advisory discourse** (ref. to a literary composition, opp. πάρκλησις *hortatory discourse*) Isoc.

παρ-αινέω *contr.vb.* | fut. παραινέσω, also mid. παραινέσομαι | aor. παρῄνεσα, Ion. παραίνεσα ‖ pf.pass.inf. παρῃνῆσθαι |
1 (of private persons, public speakers, commanders) **give**

advice, make a recommendation or deliver an exhortation (oft. w.DAT. to someone) Pi. Hdt. Trag. Th. Ar. + —w.INF. *to do sthg.* Hdt. S. E. Th. Ar. +
2 advise, recommend —*sthg.* (*oft.* w.DAT. *to someone*) Pi. Hdt. Trag. Th. Ar. + ‖ PASS. (of words or sentiments) be offered in advice or exhortation Th.
παραιπεπίθησι (dial.3sg.redupl.aor.2 subj.),
παραιπεπιθών (ptcpl.): see παραπείθω
παραίρεσις εως *f.* [παραιρέω] **1** act of taking away (fr. someone); **removal** (w.GEN. of revenues, armour) Th. Arist.
2 taking away (fr. sthg.); **encroachment** (w.GEN. on one's wealth) Pl.
παρ-αιρέω contr.vb. | aor.2 παρεῖλον | aor.2 mid. παρειλόμην, later aor.1 παρειλάμην (Plb.) | **1** take (sthg.) away (fr. someone or sthg.); **take away, remove** —*strongholds* (*fr. an enemy*) X. —*an excess of grief, of honours* (*fr. someone*) E. Plb. —*one curse* (w.GEN. *fr. an allotted three, i.e. use it up*) E.
2 ‖ MID. take away (usu. w.GEN. fr. someone); **remove, take away** —*a daughter, wife, companions* E. X. Arist. —*weapons* X. Arist. Plu. —*territory, possessions, or sim.* Hdt. X. D. Arist. Men. + —*fears, freedom, power, hope, or sim.* Hyp. D. Plb. Plu. ‖ PASS. have (w.ACC. one's weapons, resources) taken away D. Arist.(quot.)
3 take away a part (w.PARTITV.GEN. of sthg.); (of a tsunami) **destroy a part** —*of a fort* Th.; (of a god) **diminish the power or force** —*of someone's pride* E.; (of thoughts about the gods) —*of someone's pain* E.; (of persons) **lessen the intensity** —*of their grief* Hyp.
4 ‖ MID. (of a state) exclude from citizenship, **disfranchise** —*the children of slaves* Arist.
παραίρημα ατος *n.* that which has been removed (fr. sthg.); **strip** (of clothing, used as a noose) Th.
παρ-αισθάνομαι mid.vb. **1** perceive an additional fact; **notice** —w.GEN. *people* (*who are overtaking one*) X.; (intr.) **realise** (*that someone is getting angry*) Theoc.
2 be subject to illusory sights, sounds or feelings; **misperceive** (things) Pl.
παρ-αίσιος ον *adj.* (of signs fr. heaven or sim.) **of ill omen** Il. Call.
παραΐσσω ep.vb.: see παράσσω
παρ-αιτέομαι mid.contr.vb. **1** make a request (for sthg., fr. someone); **make a request, plead, beg** A. Hdt. Pl. D. Arist.; **make** —w.COGN.ACC. *a request* Pl.; **request, ask for, plead for** —*sthg.* (sts. w.ACC. *fr. someone*) Pi. Hdt. E. Pl.; **ask** (sts. w.ACC. someone) **for permission** Hdt. —w.INF. *to do sthg.* Hdt. Pl.
2 ask, beg, entreat —w.INF. or ACC. + INF. (*someone*) *to do sthg., or that sthg. may happen* A. Hdt. Th. And. Ar. Pl. + —w.GEN. + INF. *someone to do sthg.* E.
3 beg for the life or welfare of a person; **intercede for** —*someone* Hdt. Plb.; **plead to save** —*someone* (w.GEN. *fr. punishment*) Plu.; (intr.) **plead, intercede** —w.PREP.PHR. *for someone* X.
4 plead (w. someone) in order to avert an action; **appeal to, plead with** —*someone* Hdt. E. Ar. Aeschin.; (intr.) appeal (against being killed), **ask to be spared** E. And.; **ask to be excused** (fr. an examination) D.
5 avert by pleading; **beg for the remission of** —*a penalty* Aeschin. Plb. NT.; **beg for the cooling of** —*anger, hatred* Aeschin. Plu.; **beg to be spared** —*a sophistic argument* Pl.
6 beg to be excused, **beg pardon** (of someone) And. Plb. —w.DBL.ACC. *of someone, for sthg.* E.
7 beg to be excused an invitation; **decline, turn down** —*drinking parties* Plu. —*a person* Plb.; (intr.) **decline an invitation** NT.
παραίτησις εως *f.* **1** request, plea (sts. w.GEN. for sthg.) Pl. Plu.
2 excuse or apology (for sthg.) Th. Plb.
παραιτητής οῦ *m.* one who delivers a plea (for another), intercessor Plu.
παραιτητός ή όν *adj.* **1** (of the gods) capable of being won over by entreaty Pl.
2 ‖ MASC.SB. one who intercedes, mediator Plu.
παρ-αίτιος ον (also ᾱ ον) *adj.* **1** (of Fate, Aphrodite) being a cause or partial cause, **responsible** or **sharing responsibility** (w.GEN. for sthg.) A.
2 (gener., of persons, wealth, circumstances) **responsible** (w.GEN. for sthg.) Plb. Plu.
παραιφάμενος (ep.pres. or athem.aor.mid.ptcpl.): see παράφημι
παραιφασίη ης ep.Ion.*f.* [παράφημι] (collectv.pl.) advice AR.
παραίφασις, also **πάρφασις**, ιος ep.*f.* **1** persuasion, advice Il.
2 seductiveness, allurement (by means of a love-charm) Il.
3 deceitful speaking Pi.
παρ-αιωρέω contr.vb. **1** suspend (sthg.) at one's side ‖ PASS. (of a dagger) be hung at one's side Hdt.
2 (gener.) suspend —*sthg.* (*by ropes*) Plu. ‖ PASS. (of a person) be suspended, dangle (fr. a rope) Plu.
παρακάββαλον (ep.aor.2): see παρακαταβάλλω
παρα-καθέζομαι mid.vb. | aor.2 παρεκαθεζόμην ‖ aor.pass.ptcpl. (w.mid.sens.) παρακαθεσθείς (NT.) | **sit down beside** (oft. w.DAT. someone) Ar. Pl. X. Thphr. NT. Plu.
παρα-κάθημαι, Ion. **παρακάτημαι** mid.vb. **1** sit or be seated nearby or alongside (someone) Ar. Att.orats. Pl. + —w.DAT. *someone* Th. Ar. Pl. +; be seated at —w.DAT. *a table* Hdt.(cj.); (fig., of a populace) sit idly by Plu.
2 (of an official) sit with, attend the sittings of —w.DAT. *an assembly* Arist.
3 (of an army) be encamped nearby Plb.; (fig., of a person, w. military connot.) be encamped or stationed near —w.DAT. *a city* Plu.
παρα-καθιδρύομαι pass.vb. (of an image of a serpent) be set up beside —w.DAT. *a statue of a goddess* Plu.
παρα-καθίζω vb. | aor. παρεκάθισα ‖ MID.: fut. παρακαθιζήσομαι | aor. παρεκαθισάμην | **1** make (a person) sit down next to another; (fig.) make (w.ACC. certain character traits) **squat down close by** (beneath the ruling character trait, as if servile oriental courtiers) Pl.
2 ‖ MID. (of jurors) invite (w.ACC. their wives and children) to sit down beside —w.DAT. *themselves* Lycurg.; appoint (w.ACC. one's own arbitrator) to sit alongside (a neutral arbitrator) D.
3 (intr.) sit down beside —w.DAT. *someone* Plu. ‖ MID. sit down beside (someone) Pl. X.
παρα-καθίημι vb. | 3sg.impf.pass. παρακαθίετο | let down (sthg.) at the side; (fig., of nations at war) drop (w.ACC. their hands) to the side (i.e. relax their combative stance) Plu.; (intr., of combatants) flag, droop, sink (through fatigue) Plb. ‖ PASS. (of steering-oars) be lowered on either side (of a ship) E.
παρα-καθίστημι vb. place (someone) beside (another); attach, assign —*a person* (*to another, to keep watch on him*) D. —*guards* (*to a property*) Plu.; set up side by side —*conflicting governments* Isoc.
παρα-καίομαι pass.vb. (of a lamp) be kept burning nearby Hdt.

παρα-καίριος ον *adj.* (of behaviour) **out of place, wrong** Hes.

παρακαίρως *adv.* [καιρός] **beyond the proper limit, inordinately** —*ref. to loving wealth* Isoc.

παρα-καλέω *contr.vb.* | The sections are grouped as: (1–3) summon, (4–5) encourage, (6–7) entreat or require. |
1 call (someone) **to come; call over, summon, invite** —*someone* (*usu.* W.PREP.PHR. *to a place, an activity*) E. Th. Lys. Ar. Pl. +; (fig., of one sorrow in a sequence) **beckon** —*someone* (W.ADV. *away fr. a previous sorrow*) E.
2 summon (someone) to give help or advice; **call on, summon** —*persons, friends, allies, or sim.* Hdt. E. Th. + —*someone* (W.PREDIC.ACC. *as an ally or adviser*) Hdt. Pl. X. —*a populace* (W.PREP.PHR. *to war*) Hdt. D.; **call on** (for support), **invoke** —*a god or gods* X. Aeschin. D.; (of the soul) **summon** (to its aid) —*calculation and thought* Pl. ǁ PASS. (of a god) be called on (for support in war) Th.; (of a populace) be summoned —W.PREP.PHR. *to* (*join*) *an alliance* Th. —W.INF. *to resist the enemy* Pl.
3 (in legal ctxts.) **call on, summon** —*persons* (*as supporters, witnesses*) Att.orats. ǁ PASS. be invited (to a court) Aeschin.
4 call to (someone) encouragingly; **encourage, incite** —*troops* A. X. Plb. —W.PREP.PHR. *to battle, glorious deeds* E. X.; **exhort** —*someone* (W.PREP.PHR. *to virtue, recollection, or sim.*) Isoc.; **deliver** —W.COGN.ACC. *an exhortation* (*to virtue*) Aeschin. ǁ PASS. be cheered or comforted NT.
5 encourage, invite —W.ACC. + INF. *someone to do sthg.* E.*Cyc.* Lys. X.; **provoke, prompt** —*someone* (W.PREP.PHR. *to tears, alarm*) E.; (fig., of incendiary materials) **encourage, excite** —*a flame* X.; (of perceptions) **stimulate** —*the intellect* (W.PREP.PHR. *to reflection*) Pl. ǁ PASS. (of persons, their intellect) be stimulated Isoc. Arist.
6 call upon (someone) with a request; **appeal to, entreat, implore** —*someone* Plb. NT. ǁ NEUT.PL.PASS.PTCPL.SB. demands, proposals (of a negotiator) Plb.
7 (fig., of storage rooms) **call for, require** —*the contents appropriate to them* X.

παρα-καλπάζω *vb.* [app. κάλπη *trotting* (*of a horse*)] (of a person) **trot alongside** —W.DAT. *a horse* Plu.

παρακάλυμμα ατος *n.* [παρακαλύπτω] **1 covering, curtain** Plu.
2 (fig., ref. to behaviour) **screen, veil** (to disguise the truth) Plu.

παρα-καλύπτω *vb.* **1 hide** (someone or sthg.) **away from view; veil** (someone, by placing a cloak before his eyes) Plu. ǁ MID. **veil one's eyes** (to avoid seeing sthg.) Pl.; (fig., to avoid seeing a danger) Plu.; (of a woman) **veil one's face** (out of modesty) Men.; (of a goddess, to avoid visual contact w. someone) Plu.; (fig., of a personified argument, as if timid) Pl. ǁ PASS. (of a remark, i.e. its meaning) be hidden (fr. someone) NT.
2 (fig., of circumstances) **veil, disguise** —*true feelings* Plu. ǁ MID. (of a person) **blank out** —*one's thoughts* (W.DAT. *in drunkenness*) Plu.

παρα-καταβαίνω *vb.* (of a cavalryman) **dismount** Plb.

παρα-καταβάλλω *vb.* | aor.2 παρακατέβαλον, ep. παρακάββαλον | **1 throw down** (W.ACC. *timber*) **by the side** (of a pyre) Il.; **put** (W.ACC. *a fighter's waist-cloth*) **down near** (him) Il.
2 (leg.) **pay a deposit** (to a court) Is. D. —W.GEN. *in an inheritance case* D.
3 ǁ MID. **subjoin, annex** —*a decree* (W.PREP.PHR. *to a decision*) Plb.

παρακαταβολή ῆς *f.* (leg.) **deposit paid by a litigant in advance of the hearing** (forfeited in case of failure to win); **court deposit, caution money** (in claims against the state for confiscated property and in certain inheritance claims) D.; (ref. to the παράστασις, πρυτανεῖα and other types of deposits levied by the courts) Isoc. D.

παρα-καταθήκη ης *f.* **1 that which is entrusted to another for safekeeping, deposit** (of money or property) Hdt. Th. Att.orats. +; (ref. to money deposited in a bank) Isoc. D.; (fig., ref. to a favour, as being repayable) X.
2 one whose care is entrusted to another, charge, trust, responsibility (ref. to children or sim., as entrusted to guardians) Hdt. X. D. Plb.; (ref. to the laws, protection of the citizens, as entrusted to juries or sim.) Att.orats.
3 guarantee of good faith (ref. to statements, as if pledges of good behaviour) Lys.; (ref. to a family left at home by a traveller, as if hostages) Aeschin.

παρα-κατάκειμαι *mid.vb.* (of a diner) **lie** or **sit beside** —W.DAT. *someone* X.

παρα-κατακλίνω *vb.* make (someone) **lie down beside** another; **put** (W.ACC. *one's wife*) **to bed** —W.DAT. *w. another man* (i.e. prostitute her) Aeschin.

παρα-καταλείπω *vb.* (of an army) **leave** (W.ACC. *soldiers*) **behind in company** —W.DAT. *w. settlers* Th.

παρα-καταλέχομαι *mid.vb.* | only ep.3sg.athem.aor. παρκατέλεκτο | (of a man or woman, w. sexual connot.) **lie down beside** —W.DAT. *their partner* Il.

παρα-καταπήγνῡμι *vb.* **fix** (W.ACC. *stakes*) **in the ground alongside** (earthworks) Th.

παρα-κατατίθεμαι *mid.vb.* [κατατίθημι] | ep.3sg.athem.aor. παρακάτθετο, 2sg.imperatv. παρακάτθεο (AR.) | **1 entrust** (someone or sthg.) **for safekeeping** (usu. W.DAT. to someone); **entrust** —*an island, a city, property, persons* (*to someone*) Hdt. Att.orats. Pl. X. AR. + —*children* (*to teachers*) Aeschin. Din. —*the laws* (*to citizens*) Aeschin. —*the government* (*to consuls*) Plu. —*one's life* (*to a horse, one's armour*) X. Plu. —*one's safety, power, prosperity* (*to persons, their goodwill*) Isoc.
2 deposit —*money* (w. someone) Isoc. Pl.; (fig.) —*terms agreed on* (W.DAT. *w. the populace,* W.PREDIC.SB. *as witness to them*) Plu.; **give** —*guarantees of good faith* (*to a city, ref. to having family and property there*) Din.

παρα-κατέχω *vb.* **1 keep back with oneself, keep back, detain** —*someone* Plb. Plu.
2 restrain —*others* (fr. *a common purpose*) Th.
3 restrain, check —*one's anger, someone's behaviour, or sim.* Plb.
4 retain in one's possession —*a territory* Plb.

παρακάτημαι Ion.*mid.vb.*: see παρακάθημαι

παρα-κατοικίζω *vb.* **settle** (W.ACC. *people*) **nearby** —W.PREDIC.ACC. *as neighbours* Isoc.; (fig.) **establish** (W.ACC. *a cause of fear,* ref. *to a garrison*) **near** —W.DAT. *to one's allies* Plu. ǁ MID. **allow** (W.ACC. *a people*) **to settle nearby** Isoc.

παρα-καττύομαι Att.*mid.vb.* (fig.) **cobble together for oneself** (W.ACC. *a pallet-bed*) **alongside** (another person's bed) Ar.

παρά-κειμαι, ep. **πάρκειμαι** *mid.pass.vb.* [κεῖμαι] | 3sg.iteratv.impf. παρεκέσκετο | **1** (of objects) **be placed nearby, lie at hand** (sts. W.DAT. for someone, i.e. ready to use) Hom. Xenoph. Pi. Hdt. Ar. Pl. +
2 (gener., of things) **be available, be at hand** (sts. W.DAT. for someone) Pl. Aeschin.; (of helplessness) **be ever-present for,**

beset —W.DAT. *someone* Thgn. ‖ PRES.PTCPL.ADJ. (of troubles) **present, current** Ar. ‖ NEUT.SG.PTCPL.SB. **the present** Pi. ‖ IMPERS. **the choice lies** —w. ἐναντίον + DAT. *facing someone* (W.INF. *to fight or flee*) Od.
3 (of a diner) **lie** or **sit beside** (someone) Thphr.(cj.)
4 (of a gate, city, mountain, a people, or sim.) **lie nearby, be adjacent** (sts. W.DAT. to a place) Plb.
5 (of sensations) **exist side by side** Pl.; (of opposing notions) **be present simultaneously** (in one's memory) Pl.
6 (w. aggressive connot., of rulers) **press upon, exert influence over** —W.DAT. *foreign rulers* Plb.

παρακεκινδυνευμένως *pf.pass.ptcpl.adv.*: see under παρακινδυνεύω

παρα-κελεύομαι *mid.vb.* **1 recommend, prescribe** —*a course of action* (oft. W.DAT. *to someone*) Hdt. Lys. Ar. Pl. X.; **urge, exhort, encourage** —W.DAT. *someone* (W.INF. or COMPL.CL. *to do sthg.*) Th. Att.orats. Pl. +; (of persons) **say to encourage each other** —W.COMPL.CL. *that sthg. is the case* Th. ‖ ACT. **instruct** —W.ACC. + INF. *someone to do sthg.* Plb.(dub.) Plu.
2 (in military ctxt., of a commander) **offer exhortation** or **encouragement** (sts. W.DAT. to troops) Th. X. Plu.; **exhort, encourage** —W.DAT. + INF. *troops, to do sthg.* X. Plb.; (of troops) **exhort** or **encourage one another** Hdt. Th. X. Plu. ‖ IMPERS.PLPF.PASS. **instructions had been given** —W.DAT. *to someone* Hdt.

παρακέλευσις εως *f.* **1** (in military ctxt.) **encouragement, exhortation** (by a commander, by soldiers to each other) Th. Isoc. X. Plu.
2 (gener.) **encouragement** Pl. Arist. Plu.; **injunction, advice** Pl.

παρακέλευσμα (also **παρακέλευμα**) ατος *n.* **1** (in military or political ctxt.) **exhortation** E. Pl.
2 (gener.) **encouragement** (given by a father's words) E.
3 maxim, precept (of a gnomic poet) Pl.

παρακελευσμός οῦ *m.* (in military ctxt.) **encouragement, exhortation** (of each other, by troops) Th. Lys. X. Plb.

παρακελευστικός ή όν *adj.* (of an argument) **designed to give encouragement** (W.PREP.PHR. towards virtue) Pl.

παρακελευστός ή όν *adj.* (of persons) **encouraged, appealed to** (by a politician, to support him) Th.

παρα-κελητίζω *vb.* | fut. παρακελητιῶ | (of a racehorse, w. fig. sexual ref. to a person) **outride** —*another horse* Ar.

παρα-κέλομαι *mid.vb.* | ep.3sg.aor.2 παρακέκλετο | **call upon, invoke** —*deities* AR.

παρακινδῡ́νευσις εως *f.* [παρακινδυνεύω] **risk-taking** Th.
παρακινδῡνευτικός ή όν *adj.* (of an argument) **risky, venturesome, dangerous** Pl. D.
—**παρακινδῡνευτικῶς** *adv.* **riskily, adventurously** —*ref. to speaking* Pl.
παρα-κινδῡνεύω *vb.* **undergo abnormal risk or danger, take a great risk** Th. And. Ar. Pl. +; **run** —W.COGN.ACC. *a particular risk* Ar. Pl.; **venture, risk going** —W.PREP.PHR. *to a place* Th.; **take the risk** —W.INF. *of doing sthg.* Ar. X.; **run the risk** —W.INF. *of suffering sthg.* Plu.
—**παρακεκινδῡνευμένος** η ον *pf.pass.ptcpl.adj.* (of an action, an illicit meeting) **risky, perilous** Plu.; (of a poetic metaphor) **daring** Ar.
—**παρακεκινδῡνευμένως** *pf.pass.ptcpl.adv.* **riskily** Pl.
παρα-κῑνέω *contr.vb.* **1** (tr.) **move aside** (fr. a settled position), **disturb** —*an element in one's soul* Pl.; (intr., of a country, a person) **cause a disturbance, cause trouble** D. Men.
2 (of a person) **shift one's ground** (opp. stay resolute) Pl.

3 be disturbed in one's mind, be out of one's senses Pl.; **have one's head turned** (by physical beauty) X.
4 (of troops) **be in a state of unrest, be mutinous** Plu.
5 (tr.) app. **stir up, excite** —*someone* (i.e. his hopes) Plu.; (intr.) **be stirred** or **drawn** —W.PREP.PHR. *to someone's discourse* Plu.

παρακῑνητικῶς *adv.* **in a deranged manner** Plu.
παρα-κιών *ep.aor.2 ptcpl.* [κίω] | only nom. | (of a traveller) **passing by** Il.(tm.)
παρα-κλείω, Ion. **παρακληίω** *vb.* [κλείω¹] **shut out, exclude** —*someone* (fr. a profession, by displacing him) Hdt.
παρα-κλέπτω *vb.* **steal, filch, pilfer** —*sthg.* Ar. ‖ NEUT.PL.PASS.PTCPL.SB. **sums pilfered** Is.
παράκλησις εως *f.* [παρακαλέω] **1 invitation, summons** (to a meeting) Att.orats.
2 appeal (for help, by a nation) Th.
3 exhortation (to a populace, troops, individuals) Th. Isoc. Arist. Plb. Plu.; **encouragement** (W.GEN. or PREP.PHR. to virtue) Aeschin.; **appeal** (of an argument) Hyp.
4 (specif.) **hortatory discourse** (ref. to a literary composition, opp. παραίνεσις *advisory discourse*) Isoc.
5 comforting, consolation (of persons, by a message, circumstances, or sim.) NT.

παρακλητικός ή όν *adj.* **1** (of sensory perceptions or their objects) **stimulating, provoking** (W.GEN. thought) Pl.
2 (of speeches) **exhortatory, encouraging** Plb.

παράκλητος ου *m.* **1 one who is called in** (to help), **supporter** (in a lawcourt) D.
2 (ref. to the Holy Spirit) **counsellor, advocate** NT.

παρακλιδόν *adv.* [παρακλίνω] **1 aside** —*ref. to turning one's eyes* hHom.; **sideways** —*ref. to a person falling* AR.; **on one side** (of a road), **by the wayside** —*ref. to being left behind* AR.
2 app. **into a horizontal position** —*ref. to lowering a mast* AR.
3 evasively —*ref. to giving an answer* Od.

παρα-κλῑ́νω, ep. **παρκλῑ́νω** *vb.* | aor. παρέκλῑνα ‖ PASS.: 3sg.pf. παρακέκλιται | **1 bend** or **turn aside** —*one's head* Od. AR. Theoc.; (of a girl) **turn aside** —*her cheeks* (i.e. face) AR.; (of an animal) —*its nostrils* (towards a smell) Ar.; (of a charioteer, a horseman) —*his horses* Il. Plu.
2 (fig., of an Erinys) **divert** (W.ACC. a marriage) **from the right course** A.; (of rulers) **pervert** —*judgements* Hes.; (wkr.sens.) **alter** —*a small part* (*of a word*) Pl.
3 turn at an angle, set (W.ACC. a gate) **ajar** Hdt.; **open** (W.PARTITV.GEN. a door) **a little** Ar.
4 ‖ PF.PASS. (of a region) **lie adjacent** —W.DAT. *to another* Call.; (of a desert) **stretch out** AR.; (of a coast) —W.DAT. *before a traveller* AR.; (of a person, w. sexual connot.) **lie beside** —W.DAT. *someone* Theoc.

παρακλίτης ου *m.* **one who reclines beside another, neighbour at dinner** X.

παρ-ακμάζω *vb.* | pf. παρήκμακα | **1** (of persons, fruits) **pass one's prime** Plu.; (of a person's beauty) X.; (of a city, ref. to its power) Plb. ‖ STATV.PF. (of persons) **be past one's prime** (in age, strength, or sim.) X. Arist. Plu.
2 (of anger) **abate** Men. Plu.; (of courage, power) **wane** Plu.

παρακμή ῆς *f.* **passing of the peak point, abatement** (W.GEN. of a sickness) Plu.

παρα-κοινάομαι *dial.mid.contr.vb.* [κοινόω] **communicate** —*a story* (W.DAT. *to someone*) Pi.

παρα-κοιτέω *contr.vb.* [κοίτη] (of soldiers on guard) **occupy a station alongside** (sts. W.DAT. *someone*) Plb.

παρ-ακοίτης ου *m.* **bedfellow, husband** Il. Hes. Theoc.
—**παράκοιτις** ιος *f.* | acc. παράκοιτιν | ep.dat. παρακοίτῑ | **wife** Hom. Hes. hHom. Stesich. AR.

παρ-ακολουθέω *contr.vb.* **1 attend closely, follow close behind** (usu. W.DAT. someone, sts. w.connot. of unwelcome closeness or importunity) Ar. Att.orats. X. Men. Plb. Plu. **2** (fig.) **follow attentively** —W.DAT. *a disease* (*i.e. its progress*), *actions, events* Pl. Aeschin. D. Plb. NT.; **follow** (w. understanding) —W.DAT. *an argument* Aeschin. D.; **understand** —W.DAT. *the answer to a question* Plb. —W.COMPL.CL. *that sthg. is the case* Plb. **3** (of misfortune, hostility, physical ailments, or sim.) **attend, dog** —W.DAT. *someone* Att.orats. Plb.; (of dissension) —*an army* Aeschin.; (of a principle) **hold good** X. **4** (of a reflected image) **correspond** —W.DAT. *to its original* Pl.; (of things, to each other) Pl.; (philos., of an abstr. entity or notion) **be inseparably associated** (w. another) Arist.; (of theoretical studies, in neg.phr.) **be linked, be relevant** —W.DAT. *to real life* Isoc.

παρακομιδή ἧς *f.* [παρακομίζω] **1 transportation, conveyance** (of things, fr. one place to another) Th. Plb. **2 transit, crossing** (of a sea or river) Th. Plb.

παρα-κομίζω *vb.* **1 convey along, help along, escort** —*an old man* E. Plu. —*ambassadors* X. **2 convey across** (sea or land), **transport** —*persons, provisions, or sim.* Hdt. Plb. Plu.; (of trierarchs) **bring** (W.ACC. their ships) **across** (to a pier) D.; (of individuals) **carry with one** —*a stake* (*for a palisade*) Plb. ‖ MID. **have** (W.ACC. soldiers, grain) **transported** Th. X. ‖ PASS. (of persons, provisions, or sim.) **be transported** X. D. Plb. Plu.; (of objects) **be carried along** (in a procession) Plu. **3** ‖ PASS. **be conveyed along** (a coast); (of sailors) **coast along** Th. —W.ACC. *a country* Th. —W.PREP.PHR. *to a place, into a harbour* Th. Plb.

παρ-ακονάω *contr.vb.* (fig., of a soldier) **whet, sharpen, hone** (W.ACC. his courage) **at the same time** (as his spear) X. ‖ PASS. (fig., of a clever person's nature) **be honed sharp** Ar.

παρακοπή ἧς, dial. **παρακοπά** ᾶς *f.* [παρακόπτω] **derangement, madness** A. Plb. Plu.

παράκοπος ον *adj.* (of persons, their minds, their thinking) **deranged, maddened, crazed** A. E. Ar. Tim.; **driven out** (W.GEN. of one's mind) E.

παρα-κόπτω *vb.* **1 knock aside** (fr. a straight course); (fig., of a god) **send awry, derange, madden** —*the mind* E. ‖ PASS. **be knocked off the track**; (fig., of a person) **lose track** (W.GEN. of someone's prophecies, by failing to follow them) A. **2** ‖ MID. (fig.) **swindle, cheat** —*someone* (sts. W.GEN. *out of sthg.*) Ar. ‖ PASS. **be cheated** Ar. **3 strike** (coins) **falsely** ‖ PF.PASS.PTCPL.ADJ. (fig., of persons) **mis-struck, mis-minted** (perh. also w.connot. *deranged*) Ar. **4** ‖ PASS. (of limbs) **be chopped off** Plb.

παράκουσμα ατος *n.* [παρακούω] **that which is misheard; misunderstanding** (W.GEN. of Plato's teaching) Plu.

παρ-ακούω *vb.* **1 hear incidentally, happen to hear of** —*someone's skill* Hdt. **2 overhear** —*sthg.* (sts. W.GEN. or παρά + GEN. *said by someone*) Ar. Pl. NT. —W.ACC. + PTCPL. *that sthg. is the case* Thphr. **3 mishear, misunderstand** —*sthg.* Pl. Arist. **4 refuse to listen, pay no heed, turn a deaf ear** Plb. —W.GEN. *to persons, orders, advice, or sim.* Plb. NT.; (of a political leader) **pretend not to hear** —W.GEN. *of his colleagues' offences* Plu. ‖ PASS. **have a deaf ear turned to one** Plb.

παρα-κρεμάννυμι *vb.* | aor.ptcpl. παρακρεμάσας ‖ PASS.: παρακρέμαμαι | **1** (of a wounded warrior) **let** (W.ACC. one's hand) **hang by one's side** Il. **2** ‖ PASS.PTCPL.ADJ. (of parts of a kingdom) **dependent** Plb.

παρά-κρημνος ον *adj.* [κρημνός] (of a river) **with steep banks** Plu.; (of terrain) **precipitous** Plu.

παρα-κρίνομαι *pass.vb.* **be sorted into rows**; (of soldiers; of sailors, i.e. their ships) **be drawn up in line** Hdt. Plu.; (of troops) **be drawn up in line opposite** or **nearby** Plu.; (of people) **be lined up** (by the roadside) Plu.

παράκρουσις εως *f.* [παρακρούω] **1 cheating, deception** D. **2 error, fallacy** (in logic) Arist.

παρα-κρούω *vb.* **1 knock off course** ‖ MID. **turn aside, parry** —*a spear* (w. *a sword*) Plu. **2** (fig., of a misfortune) **derange** —*someone* Pl. **3** ‖ MID. **mislead, deceive, cheat** Isoc. D. —*someone* Att.orats. Pl. Arist. Men. Plu.; (of an argument) **be fallacious** Arist. ‖ PASS. **be misled or deceived** Att.orats. Pl.

παρα-κτάομαι *mid.contr.vb.* **acquire in addition, adopt** —*foreign customs* Hdt.

παρ-άκτιος ᾱ ον *adj.* [ἀκτή¹] (of a path, meadows, sand) **by the shore** Trag.; (quasi-advbl., of persons riding) **along the shore** E.

παρα-κύπτω (also dial. **παρκύπτω** Theoc.) *vb.* **1 bend over or stoop forward; poke one's head out, peep out** (fr. a window, door, cave) Ar. Theoc.; (fig., of Salvation, i.e. allow one a glimpse of her) Ar.; **stoop to look** (into a tomb) NT. **2** (fig., of mercenary forces, as not fighting for a cause) **cast a sideways** or **casual glance** —w. ἐπί + ACC. *at a war* D. **3** (of a lyre-player) perh. **slouch** or **shamble out** (onto the stage) Ar.

παρα-λαλέω *contr.vb.* **chatter idly** Men.

παρα-λαμβάνω *vb.* | fut. παραλήψομαι, Ion. παραλάμψομαι | aor.2 παρέλαβον | **1 take over** (sthg. in another's possession, either by consent or by force); **take over** —*places, property, ships, or sim.* Hdt. E. Th. + —*sovereignty, political control, or sim.* Hdt. Ar. Isoc. Plu.; **acquire** —*writing, customs, names* (fr. *other nations*) Hdt. Pl. —*a skill* (fr. *a teacher*) Pl. **2 take over** (sthg.) **from an immediate predecessor; take over** —*a command, an office* Th. Att.orats.; (of Euripides) —*an art* (i.e. *tragedy, fr. Aeschylus*) Ar.; **take up** —*a speech* (fr. *the previous speaker*) Plb. **3 take over from a parent; inherit** —*kingship, property, or sim.* Hdt. Th. Att.orats. + —*a curse* E. **4 receive from one's forebears; inherit** —*a city, laws, traditions, or sim.* Th. Att.orats. —*a story* Th. Isoc. —*knowledge* Isoc.; (fig., of a lawgiver, a city) **inherit** (an existing state of affairs), **find** —W.ACC. + PTCPL. *sthg. to be the case* Isoc. X. ‖ PASS. (of details) **be handed down and accepted** (as true) Plb. ‖ PF.PASS.PTCPL.ADJ. (of stories) **received, accepted, traditional** Arist. **5** (of a litigant) **take over** (for torture) —*a slave* (*belonging to the opposing party*) Att.orats. **6 receive by hearing or report; ascertain, learn** —*facts, the truth* (sts. W.GEN. fr. *someone*) Hdt. **7 hear and exploit** (the words of a previous speaker); **seize on** —*a remark, a name* Hdt. **8** (of a historian) **resume, pick up** (a narrative) —W.GEN. fr. *a certain point* Plb. **9 take in hand, take on** —*a task* Ar.; (of an arbitrator) —*a case* Aeschin. ‖ NEUT.PL.PASS.PTCPL.SB. **undertakings** Hdt. **10 take on** (someone) **as a pupil**; (of tutors, officials) **take on** —*children* (*to educate or influence them*) Pl.

11 take on (someone) as an associate; (in military ctxt.) **pick up** —*troops, allies* Hdt. Th. +; (gener.) —*a person* (*as helper, adviser, witness*) Att.orats. Pl. +; **take along** (w. one) —*a guest* (*to dinner*) Hdt. X. ‖ PASS. be admitted —W.PREP.PHR. *to a communal dining-hall* Plu.
12 ‖ PASS. be captured alongside (someone else) Plb.

παρα-λανθάνω vb. (of facts, assertions) **escape the notice of** —*someone* Isoc. Pl. D.

παρα-λέγω vb. **1** pluck out (superfluous hair) ‖ PASS. (of a woman) app., have one's eyebrows plucked Ar.
2 ‖ MID. (of sailors) choose a parallel course; **coast along** —*a country* NT.

παρα-λείπω vb. | fut. παραλείψω | aor.2 παρέλιπον | pf. παραλέλοιπα ‖ pf.pass. παραλέλειμμαι | **1** leave untouched, **leave aside** or **alone** —*someone's land* Th. X. —*people* Lys. ‖ PASS. (of land) be left untouched Th.
2 leave (sthg.) for another (to do); **leave** —*an opportunity for speaking, the right to speak first* (W.DAT. *to another*) Aeschin. ‖ PASS. (of topics) be left (for other speakers to deal with) Isoc.; (of an action) be left or reserved —W.DAT. *for someone* (*to perform*) D.
3 leave —W.DAT. + INF. *someone to do sthg.* Isoc.; leave an opportunity for, **allow** —W.DAT. + INF. *someone to do sthg.* Plu.
4 leave out, omit —*a person* (*in an invitation, a will*) Lys. Ar.
5 leave out, pass over, omit (in speech or writing) —W.NEUT.ACC. *sthg., nothing, or sim.* E. Th. Att.orats. Pl. + —*facts, things, places* Att.orats. Pl. +; (intr., of a lawgiver) **make an omission, leave a loophole** (in a law) Arist. ‖ PASS. (of things) be omitted (in speech) Att.orats. X.
6 neglect, disregard —*religious constraints* E. —*important features of a craft* Ar. —*a duty, a consideration* Isoc. X. Is.; omit to perform, **avoid, sidestep** —*the performance of an action* D. —*an examination* (*of a witness*) Lys.; **leave aside, ignore** —*someone or sthg.* Arist. ‖ PASS. (of things) be overlooked or neglected Th. Ar. Isoc. Pl. +
7 leave (sthg.) undone; **leave** —W.ACC. + PREDIC.ADJ. *a speech uncriticised* Isoc. —*sthg. unexamined* X. Arist. —*a pass unguarded, a person uncared for* X.
8 fail to exploit (a situation); **miss** —*a time, an opportunity* Aeschin. D. —*a source of profit* Isoc.; (of hounds) —*a hare* (*by running past it*) X.

παρ-αλείφω vb. **smear** —*one's eyelids* (w. *an ointment*) Ar.; (of a nurse) **wet** —*a baby's lips* (w. *her spittle*) Arist.

παρα-λέχομαι mid.vb. | fut. παραλέξομαι | 3sg.aor.1 παρελέξατο, 3sg.athem.aor. παρέλεκτο | (of a man or woman, w. sexual connot.) **lie beside** (usu. W.DAT. *their partner*) Hom.(sts.tm.) Hes. hHom. Ibyc. Pi. AR.

παραληπτός όν adj. [παραλαμβάνω] (of virtue) **capable of being received** (fr. others, through teaching) Pl.

παρα-ληρέω contr.vb. **talk** or **behave nonsensically, blather** Ar. Isoc. Pl. Arist.

παράληψις εως f. [παραλαμβάνω] **1** taking over (of sthg. in another's possession); **appropriation** (of cities) Plb.
2 taking over (fr. an immediate predecessor); **succession** (W.GEN. to an office, royal power) Plb. Plu.

παρ-άλιος ᾱ ον (also ος ον NT. Plu.) adj. **1** (of sand) **of the seashore** A.
2 (of a land, city, region) **by the sea** E. NT. Plu.; (of birds) **coastal** S. ‖ NEUT.PL.SB. coastal regions Plu.
—**παραλίᾱ** ᾱς, Ion. **παραλίη** (also ep.Ion. **παρραλίη** AR.) ης f. **seacoast, seaboard** Hdt. Isoc. Arist. AR. Plb. Plu.; (ref. to the W. coast of Attica, fr. Phaleron to Sounion; cf. Πάραλος²) Hdt. Th. Arist.

—**παράλιοι** ων m.pl. **people living by the sea** Plu.; (ref. to inhabitants of the παραλία of Attica, as a political faction in the 6th C. BC) Arist. | cf. πάραλος 2

παρ-αλιταίνω vb. | aor.2 παρήλιτον | **do wrong, offend, sin** AR. —W.ACC. *against the gods* AR.

παραλλαγή ῆς f. [παραλλάσσω] **1** exchange, **transmission** (of beacon-signals) A.
2 interchange (of one means of knowledge for another); **substitution** (of thought for perception) Pl.
3 variation, distinction, difference (betw. personal behaviour, intentions) Plb.
4 change, alteration (in a situation) Plb.

παράλλαγμα ατος n. **variation, difference** (betw. the lengths of the solar and lunar year) Plu.

παραλλάξ adv. **1** by turns —*ref. to things occurring* S.
2 skewed (opp. in a straight line) —*ref. to how islands are situated* Th.

παράλλαξις εως f. **1** alteration, deviation (fr. an existing state) Pl. X.
2 alternating movement (of a person's legs) Plu.; perh. back-and-forth movement (of dancers) Plu.

παρ-αλλάσσω, Att. **παραλλάττω** vb. **1** (intr.) change position or direction away (fr. some point); (of two adjacent gulfs) **diverge** (fr. each other) Hdt.; (of an archer) **deviate** —W.GEN. *fr. a target* Pl.; (fig., of a person's words) **be astray** (i.e. off the mark, mistaken) E.
2 (of an illusory vision of happiness) **turn aside, slip away** A.
3 change position away (fr. some state); (of a person) be astray in one's mind, **be deranged** Pl. Plu.
4 be divergent or different (fr. someone or sthg., sts. W.NEUT.ACC. *a little,* or sim.); (of a nation) **diverge, differ** (fr. another, in dress) Hdt.; (of soldiers, fr. others, i.e. be superior) —W.DAT. *by virtue of some quality* Plb.; (of social conventions) —W.GEN. *fr. others customary elsewhere* Pl.; (of the comparative usefulness of slaves and animals) Arist. ‖ IMPERS. it makes a difference (whether this or that is the case) Pl. Arist.
5 (of an opinion, an existing state) **be liable to change, be subject to variation** Isoc. Pl.; (of a leader) **change** —W.PREP.PHR. *to the ways of an autocrat* Plu.
6 (tr.) change (one state of affairs, for another); **change, alter** —*a few details, a syllable* Hdt. Aeschin.; (intr., of a reformer) **make** (W.NEUT.ACC. a little) **change** Arist. ‖ PASS. (of things) be changed or altered (fr. what is normal or customary) Plb.
7 (of a commander) **divert, deflect** —*his army's sufferings* (*by providing entertainment*) Plu.; (fig., of money) **warp, pervert** —*honest minds* S.
8 mistakenly interchange or transpose —*two sensory perceptions* Pl.
9 change direction so as to avoid (a place, persons); (of troops on the march) **bypass** —*a city* Plb.; (of a stream) —*someone's land* D.; (of persons) **evade, elude** —*enemy troops, an ambush, sentinels* X. Plu.; (of a young man) **pass beyond** —*boyhood* Plu.

—**παρηλλαγμένος** η ον pf.pass.ptcpl.adj. (of behaviour, circumstances, or sim.) **extraordinary, unusual** Plb. Plu.
—**παρηλλαγμένως** pf.pass.ptcpl.adv. in a deranged manner, maniacally —*ref. to fighting* Plb.

παρ-άλληλος ον adj. **1** (of ships) beside one another, **side by side** Plb.; (of objects, hills) Plb. Plu.; (of troops) **in parallel columns** Plb.

παραλογίζομαι

2 (of a palisade, a trench, or sim.) running alongside, **parallel** (W.DAT. to sthg. else) Plb. Plu.
3 (of Plutarch's *Lives*, in which the biography of a Greek is given alongside that of a Roman) **parallel** Plu.; (prep.phr.) ἐκ παραλλήλου *alongside each other, in parallel* (ref. to examining such lives) Plu.
4 (of persons, their characteristics, circumstances) **matching, comparable** Plu.

παρα-λογίζομαι *mid.vb.* 1 **falsify accounts** (in a business transaction) Isoc. D.; **defraud** —W.DBL.ACC. *someone, of a sum of money* Arist.
2 (of a person, a mind) **make a false inference, draw a wrong conclusion** Arist.; (of a philosopher) **reason falsely, use fallacies** Arist.
3 **mislead by false reasoning, deceive, outwit** —*someone, oneself* Isoc. Aeschin. Plb. Plu. ‖ PASS. (of persons, their intellect) be misled Arist. Plb. Plu.

παραλογισμός οῦ *m.* 1 **false inference** or **reasoning, fallacy** Arist.
2 (in legal ctxt.) **misleading argument, quibble** Lycurg.
3 (gener.) **deception, cheating** Plb.

παραλογιστής οῦ *m.* one who defrauds by false accounting, **fraudster** Arist.

παραλογιστικός ή όν *adj.* (of an argument) **fallacious** Arist.

παρά-λογος[1] ου *m.* [λόγος] (sg. and pl.) incalculable element, **unexpectedness, unpredictability, surprise** Th. Plu.

παράλογος[2] ον *adj.* 1 (of events, circumstances, or sim.) contrary to reasonable expectation, **unexpected, unpredictable, surprising** D. Arist. Plb. Plu.
2 ‖ NEUT.PL.SB. unscheduled items of food, **extras** X.

—**παραλόγως** *adv.* 1 **unexpectedly, unpredictably** D. Arist. Men. Plb. Plu.
2 **unreasonably** Lys. Plb. Plu.

πάρ-αλος ον *adj.* [ἅλς] 1 (of caves, regions) **beside the sea, maritime** S. E.
2 (of inhabitants of Attica, as a political faction in the 6th C. BC) **inhabiting the Coastal Region** Hdt. ‖ MASC.PL.SB. inhabitants of the Coastal Region Plu. | cf. παράλιοι, Πάραλος[2]
3 (of a military force) **sea-going, naval** Hdt.
4 (of a squid, w. pun on Πάραλος[3]) **salted and ship-shape** Ar.

—**Πάραλος**[1] ου *m.* **Paralos** (commander of troops fr. the Coastal Region, of which he was later eponymous hero) E.
—**Πάραλος**[2] ου *f.* (appos.w. γῆ) **Coastal Region** (ref. to the W. coast of Attica, fr. Phaleron to Sounion) Th. | cf. παραλία
—**Πάραλος**[3] ου *f.* (sts. appos.w. ναῦς) **Paralos** (name of one of two Athenian triremes, fast ships w. elite crews, used for state business as well as fighting) Th. Ar. X. Is. D. + | cf. Σαλαμινία, under Σαλαμίς[1]
—**Πάραλοι** ων *m.pl.* **crew of the Paralos** Th. Ar. Aeschin.

παρ-άλπιος ον *adj.* [Ἄλπεις] (of a people) **living near the Alps** Plu.

παρα-λῡπέω *contr.vb.* 1 (of ordinary sicknesses) **cause trouble as well** (as the plague) Th.; (of a commander) **harm** (W.ACC. the enemy) **as well** (as achieving sthg. else) Plu.
2 **cause incidental trouble**; (of a commander) **create a diversion** Th.; (tr., of emotions) **annoy** —*the soul* Pl.; (of circumstances) **irk, irritate** —*someone* Plu.; (of a combination of scents) **cause trouble** (for hunting hounds) X.
3 **cause trouble against** (someone); **harm the interests of** —*someone* X.; (intr.) **be a troublemaker** X.

παράλυσις εως *f.* [παραλύω] **paralysis** (W.GEN. of spirit, fig.ref. to feeling helpless) Plb.

παραλυτικός οῦ *m.* **paralysed** or **lame person** NT.

παρα-λύω (also **παραλύω**) *vb.* 1 **loose from physical attachment; unfasten, take off** —*a rudder* (fr. *a ship*) Hdt. X.(mid.) —*one's cuirass* Plu.; (of death) **separate, part** —*husbands* (W.GEN. fr. *wives*) E. ‖ PASS. (of trace-camels) be cut loose Hdt.; (of ships) have (W.ACC. their oars) removed Plb.; (of a city) be detached or removed —W.GEN. fr. *a confederacy* Hdt.
2 (wkr.sens.) **loosen** —W.PARTITV.GEN. *one's cloak* Plu. ‖ MID. app. **tear** —W.ACC. *the seam of one's tunic* (to give more freedom of movement) Plu.
3 **remove** —*hardships* (W.GEN. fr. *a country*, i.e. release it fr. them) E.; **rescind, cancel** —*a claim* Is.
4 **release** (someone, fr. a situation); **release, discharge** —*someone* (W.GEN. fr. *military service*) Hdt.; **relieve** —*someone* (W.GEN. *of command, office*) Hdt. Th. Arist. —(*of anger, debts, suffering, or sim.*) Th. Plb.; (of success) —*a competitor* (*of anxieties*) Pi.; (of a person) **release** —*oneself* (W.GEN. fr. *life*) Plu.; **rescue** (fr. imminent death) —*someone's life* E.; (fig., of a comic poet) **get rid of, pension off** —*a type of comic character* Ar. ‖ PASS. be exempted (sts. W.GEN. fr. active service or sim.) Hdt. Plb.; be relieved —W.GEN. *of command* Hdt. —*of fear, expense* Plb.; be released —W.GEN. fr. *custody* Plu.
5 **set loose** (W.ACC. another hound) **as well** X.
6 **deprive of strength or firmness; weaken** —*one's body* (by fasting or sim.) Plu.; **damage** —*a wall, an enemy's oars, or sim.* Plb.; (fig., of a sight) **shatter** —*someone's spirits* Plu.; (of old age) **sap** —W.PARTITV.GEN. *one's courage* Plu.; (of a person) **allay** —*someone's anger* Plu.
7 ‖ PASS. (of persons, parts of the body) be **paralysed** or **crippled** Arist. NT. Plu.; (of persons, an army) be weakened or lose strength Plb. Plu.; (of persons) be rendered powerless —W.DAT. *in body and mind* Plb.; (of a city's strength) be crippled Lys. ‖ PF.PASS.PTCPL.SB. paralysed person, cripple NT.

παρ-αμείβω *vb.* | aor. παρήμειψα | 1 **change position so as to go past** (a fixed point); **pass by** —*places, animals* AR.; (of troops) **march past** —*a camp* Plu.(dub.) ‖ MID. (of persons, a river) **go past, pass by** —*people, places* Od. hHom. Hdt. S. E. AR.(tm.) +; (of a ship) —*another ship* Pl.; (of troops) **march past** —*a place* X. Plu.; (of a dead person) **pass through** —*gates* (to the underworld) Thgn.
2 ‖ MID. (intr., of a time for doing sthg., of youth) **pass by** Hes. Mimn.; (of the sun) **pass the highest point** AR.
3 ‖ MID. (of a writer) **pass over, omit to mention** —*persons* Hdt.
4 (of a person) **surpass, outdo** —*one person's kind of wisdom* (W.DAT. w. *one's own*) S. ‖ MID. (of a god) **outstrip** (in speed) —*a dolphin* Pi.
5 ‖ MID. **turn aside, divert** —*a voyage* (fig.ref. to the course of a poem) Pi.
6 ‖ MID. (intr., of a commander) **change** —W.PREP.PHR. *to a particular formation* (of troops) X.

παρα-μείγνῡμι (sts. written **παραμίγνυμι**) *vb.* —also (pres.) **παραμίσγω** Ion.vb. **mix in** (sthg.) as an additional element; **admix, mix in** —*water* Hdt. —*grass* (to a fodder of seaweed) Plu.; (fig.) **blend in** —*a little honey* (W.DAT. *in someone's heart*) Ar. —*outspokenness* (W.DAT. *to flattery*) Plu. ‖ PF.PASS. (of metals, fig.ref. to temperaments) be an element or constituent —W.DAT. *in people* Pl.; (of pleasure) —*in happiness* Arist.

παρ-αμελέω contr.vb. **be past caring, pay no heed** Hdt. Pl. X. Plu.; **disregard, be neglectful of** —W.GEN. *someone or sthg.* Th. Lys. Isoc. X. Arist. Plu. ‖ PASS. (esp.pf., of persons or things) **be disregarded, neglected or overlooked** A. Isoc. Pl. Plu. ‖ PF.PASS.PTCPL.ADJ. (of a particular state of activity) **remiss and inattentive** Arist.

παρα-μελο-ρυθμο-βάτᾱς ᾱ *dial.masc.adj.* [μέλος, ῥυθμός, βαίνω] (of a reed-pipe) **going against melody and rhythm** Pratin.

παρα-μένω, ep. **παρμένω** vb. **1 remain beside, stay with, stand by** —W.DAT. *someone (as helper or supporter)* Il. E. Ar. Isoc. X. +
2 stay where one is, **stay behind** (opp. depart) Hdt. Th. Att.orats. Pl. + —W.DAT. w. *someone (to keep him company or listen to him)* Pl.; (of slaves, opp. run away) Pl. X.
3 (of warriors, persons facing danger, or sim.) **stand one's ground, stand fast** Il. Pi. Hdt. S.*Ichn.* Ar.; **stand firm** (to continue a war) Th.; (fig., of a person's nature or character) E.
4 (wkr.sens.) **stay constant, remain** —W.PREP.PHR. *in a flourishing condition* Pi.; (of a commander) **remain in one's post** Th.
5 (of beliefs, success, health, or sim.) **stay, last, endure** Hdt. Isoc. Pl. X. Men. Plu.; (of a constitution) **be permanent** Lys.
6 (of children) **remain alive, survive** Hdt.

παρ-άμερος ον *dial.adj.* [ἡμέρᾱ] (of a blessing) **coming day by day, daily** Pi.

παρα-μετρέω contr.vb. **1 measure** (one thing) **against** (another) ‖ MID. **compare oneself in size** (sts. W.DAT. to sthg.) Pl.
2 (of sailors) cover a distance in going past, **pass by** —*a place* AR.(sts.tm.)

παρ-αμεύσασθαι *dial.aor.mid.inf.* ‖ only 3sg.subj. παραμεύσεται ‖ **surpass** —*someone* (W.DAT. *in beauty*) Pi.

παρα-μήκης ες *adj.* [μῆκος] **with sides of unequal length**; (of a shape, a hole) **oblong** Plb.

παρα-μηρίδια ων *n.pl.* [μηρός] **thigh-pieces** (as protective armour for cavalrymen, also for horses) X.

παραμίγνῡμι vb.: see παραμείγνῡμι

παρ-αμιλλάομαι mid.contr.vb. (of a writer) **out-rival, surpass** —*others* Plb.

παρα-μιμνήσκομαι mid.vb. ‖ aor. παρεμνησάμην ‖ pf. (w.pres.sens.) παραμέμνημαι ‖ **mention incidentally or in passing, mention, give the name of** —W.GEN. *someone* Hdt. S.

παρα-μίμνω vb. **stay behind** (in a place), **remain, linger** Od.

παραμίσγω Ion.vb.: see παραμείγνῡμι

παραμόνιμος ον, also dial. **παρμόνιμος** ᾱ ον *adj.* [παραμένω] ‖ see also πάρμονος ‖ **1** (of a possession, an advantage, happiness) **lasting, permanent** Thgn. Pi. Pl.
2 (of a slave, subordinate, friend) **constant, steadfast, trusty** X.

παρά-μουσος ον *adj.* [μοῦσα] (of the stroke of Ruin, ref. to murder of kin) **out of tune, discordant** A.; (of Ares, W.DAT. w. the festivities of Dionysus) E.

παρ-αμπίσχω vb. **1 wrap around with a garment, cloak, cover** —*one's body, its shame* Arist.(quot.)
2 (fig.) **cloak deceptively, disguise** —*one's words (i.e. prevaricate)* E.

παρ-αμπυκίδδω Lacon.vb. [ἄμπυξ] (of a woman dancer) **bind up** —*her hair* (W.DAT. w. *her hand*) Ar.

παρα-μῡθέομαι mid.contr.vb. **1 talk** (someone) **round; encourage, exhort** —*a person, a hound* Ar. Pl. X.; (of philosophy) —*the soul* Pl.
2 offer encouragement —W.INF. *to do sthg.* S. —W.DAT. + INF. *to someone, to do sthg.* Il.; **encourage, exhort, urge** —W.ACC. *someone* (W.INF. *to do sthg.*) Pl. —(w. 2ND ACC. *to a course of action*) A.
3 speak soothingly or comfortingly; **reassure** —*someone (who is afraid or sim.)* Th. Isoc. Pl. D. Men. —W.ACC. + COMPL.CL. *someone, that sthg. is the case* X.; **comfort, console** —*someone* Hdt. E. Att.orats. Pl. +; **soothe, pacify** —*a person, an animal* Pl. X.
4 assuage, allay, relieve —*one's envy, fear* Plu.; (of a ruler) **palliate, soften** —*the name of monarchy (by sharing it)* Plu.

παραμῡθητικός ή όν *adj.* (of a friend) **able to give consolation** Arist.

παραμῡθίᾱ ᾱς *f.* **1 provision of encouragement, encouragement, reassurance** Pl. X. Plu.
2 provision of comfort, comfort, consolation, solace (sts. W.GEN. for sthg.) Plu.; (provided by music or sim.) Pl.
3 soothing, pacifying (W.GEN. of jurors, crowds, or sim., effected by the speech-writer's art) Pl.
4 assuaging, alleviation (W.GEN. of envy, by denigrating other people's achievements) Plu.

παραμῡθιον ου *n.* **1 act of providing encouragement, encouragement, reassurance** Pl. Plu.
2 act of providing comfort, comfort, consolation, solace (sts. W.GEN. for suffering, troubles, or sim.) S. E.*fr.* Pl. Theoc. Plu.; (W.DAT. for danger) Th.
3 assuaging, alleviation (W.GEN. of harsh behaviour) Plu.

παρα-μῡκάομαι mid.contr.vb. (of the sound of thunder underground) **bellow in response** (to an earthquake) A.

παρ-αναγιγνώσκω vb. **1 read** (sthg., silently or aloud) **alongside** (sthg. else, for purpose of comparison); **read and compare** —*two documents* Isoc. —*a document or sim. (usu. W.DAT. or* παρά + DAT. w. *another)* Att.orats. ‖ PASS. (of documents, recorded dates) **be read out for comparison** Pl. Aeschin.
2 read publicly, read out —*a document* Plb.

παρ-αναδύομαι mid.vb. (of snakes) **emerge** —W.PREP.PHR. *out of their baskets* Plu.

παρα-ναιετάω contr.vb. **live beside** —*a place* S.

παρα-ναίομαι mid.vb. ‖ aor. παρενασσάμην ‖ (aor.) **take up residence beside** —W.DAT. *someone* Call.

παρ-αναλίσκω vb. —also **παραναλόω** contr.vb. ‖ aor.pass. παρανᾱλώθην ‖ **1 spend beyond need, waste, squander** —*financial resources* D.
2 (of a commander) ruin incidentally, **needlessly destroy** —*a city* Plu.; **needlessly sacrifice** —*soldiers* Plu.; (of a soldier) —*oneself* Plu. ‖ PASS. (of a soldier) **be sacrificed needlessly, throw away one's life** Plu.

παρ-ανάλωμα ατος *n.* **1 unnecessary waste** (of money) Plu.
2 additional or **needless loss** (of soldiers) Plu.

παρα-νέομαι mid.contr.vb. (of sailors) **go past** —*a landmark* AR.

παρα-νηνέω ep.contr.vb. [reltd. νέω³, νηέω] ‖ only impf. παρενήνεον ‖ **heap up by the side** (of someone or sthg.) —*food, an altar of stones* Od. AR.

παρα-νήχομαι mid.vb. ‖ ep.aor.subj. παρανήξομαι ‖ **swim along** (a coastline) Od.; (of a dog, a horse) **swim alongside** —W.DAT. *or* παρά + ACC. *a ship* Plu.

παρα-νῑκάω contr.vb. (of female passion) **pervert and conquer, selfishly subvert** —*wedded unions* A.

παρα-νίσομαι (also **παρανίσσομαι** AR.) mid.vb. (of a ship, sailors) **go past** —*an island, a people* hHom. AR.

παρ-ανίστημι vb. ‖ athem.aor. παρανέστην ‖ (aor., of one about to speak) **rise and come forward** Plu.

παρ-ανίσχω vb. **1** raise (W.ACC. fire-signals) **in response** (to the enemy's) Th.
2 (intr., of weapons displayed in a triumphal procession) **project forth** —W.PREP.PHR. *through piles of armour* Plu.

παρα-νοέω contr.vb. **1** be out of one's mind, **be deranged** E. Ar. Is. Arist.
2 think amiss, **misunderstand** Pl.

παράνοια ᾱς f. **derangement, madness, insanity** A. E. Ar. Att.orats. Pl. +

παρ-ανοίγνῡμι vb. open with extra force, **force open** —*gates and doors* D.

παρανομέω contr.vb. [παράνομος] | aor. παρενόμησα, later παρηνόμησα (Plu.) | **1** behave contrary to law, **act illegally** Th. Att.orats. Pl. +; **commit a crime** or **illegal action** —W.NEUT. or COGN.ACC. *of a particular kind* Th. Att.orats. X. +; **act in violation of** —W.ACC. *a law* D.
2 act contrary to conventional ideas of right and wrong, **act outrageously** X. Aeschin. D.; **commit an offence** or **outrage** —W.NEUT.ACC. *of a particular kind* Hdt. Lys. X.
3 ‖ PASS. (of a person) be treated illegally or be wronged D. Plu.; suffer outrageous treatment (physically) Plu.
4 ‖ PASS. (of return fr. exile) be achieved illegally Th.

παρανόμημα ατος n. **illegal act, crime** Th. Plb. Plu.; **wrong, outrage** Plb.

παρανομίᾱ ᾱς f. **1** illegal behaviour, **lawlessness** Th. Att.orats. Pl. Arist. Plb. Plu.
2 flouting of convention (W.GEN. by someone) Th. Plu.; **unconventional** or **outrageous nature** (W.GEN. of a person's lifestyle and aspirations) Th.

παρά-νομος ον adj. [νόμος] **1** acting contrary to law or conventional ideas of right and wrong; **rebellious against law and convention** Pl.; (gener.) **lawless, criminal** Att.orats. Pl. Arist. Men.; (of a beast, fig.ref. to a person) E.
2 (of actions, behaviour) **illegal** Th. Ar. Att.orats. Pl. +; (of rage) **lawless** E. ‖ NEUT.SB. **illegality, lawlessness** Pl. Aeschin. D. Arist.
3 (of a proposal) **illegal, unconstitutional** Aeschin. D. ‖ NEUT.PL.SB. illegal or unconstitutional proposal Th. Att.orats. X. Arist.
—**παρανόμως** adv. | compar. παρανομωτέρως (And.) | **illegally, lawlessly** Th. Att.orats. Pl. Plb. Plu.

παρά-νους ουν adj. [νόος] **out of one's mind, demented, mad** A.

πάρ-αντα adv. [ἄντα] **on a level path** (opp. uphill, downhill) —*ref. to mules moving* Il. —*ref. to Helios driving his chariot at midday* Thgn.(cj.)

παρα-νυκτερεύω vb. (of soldiers, sentries) **pass the night nearby** Plu.

παράξᾱς (aor.ptcpl.), **παράξον** (imperatv.): see παράσσω

παρά-ξενος ον adj. [ξένος²] (fig., of persons, envisaged as coins) **illegally foreign** (i.e. not qualified as Athenian citizens) Ar.

παρα-ξιφίς ίδος f. [ξίφος] knife worn beside the sword, **dagger** Plu.

παρ-αξόνιον ου n. [ἄξων] pin inserted in the axle, **linchpin** Ar.

παράορος, Ion. **παρήορος**, dial. **πάρᾱρος** (Theoc.), ον adj. —also **παρηόριος** η ον (AR.) *Ion.adj.* [παραείρω]
1 harnessed or linked at the side ‖ MASC.SB. chariot-horse harnessed to the side of the yoked pair, **trace-horse** Il. | cf. συνάορος
2 (of a slain warrior) app., on one's side, **sprawling** Il.; (of the body of Typhon, struck by a thunderbolt) A.
3 (of a person) app. **deranged, unhinged** Il.; (W.GEN. in one's mind) Archil. ‖ MASC.SB. crazy fool Theoc.
4 (quasi-advbl., of a ship being knocked by the waves) **off course** AR. [or perh. *from side to side*]

—**παρηορίαι** ῶν *Ion.f.pl.* **traces** (reins attaching the trace-horse to the yoked pair) Il.

παρα-παίω vb. **1** (fig., of a prayer) **hit the wrong note** A.
2 (fig., of a person) **be demented, be crazy** Ar. Pl. Plb. ‖ PF.PASS.PTCPL.ADJ. (perh. of words) crazy S.*Ichn.*
3 (wkr.sens.) **go astray, be mistaken** Plb.; **deviate** —W.GEN. *fr. the truth, fr. customary behaviour* Plb.; **fail in, fall short of** —W.GEN. *one's duty* Plb.

παρα-πάλλομαι mid.vb. (of a runner) **bound along beside** —W.DAT. *a chariot* E.

παρά-παν adv. [πᾶς] | usu. w.art. τὸ παράπαν | **1** (in strong affirmations) **altogether, absolutely, completely** Hdt. Th. Ar. Att.orats. Pl. +; (w.neg.) *absolutely not, not at all* Hdt. Ar. Att.orats. Pl. +
2 (in reckoning a sum of money) **in total, in all** D.; (in reckoning a grain-yield) **generally, usually** Hdt. [or perh. *in total*]

παρ-απατάω contr.vb. **trick, distract** —someone (W.DAT. w. wine) A.(dub.) | see παραπαφίσκω

παρ-απαφίσκω vb. | ep.aor.2 παρήπαφον, aor.1 παρηπάφησα (A., cj. for παρηπάτησα) | **mislead, beguile, trick** —someone Od.(tm.) A.(dub.) Theoc. —W.ACC. + INF. someone into doing sthg. Il. AR.

παρα-πείθω vb. | aor. παρέπεισα | dial.redupl.aor.2 ptcpl. παρπεπιθών, also παραιπεπιθών, 3sg.subj. παραιπεπίθῃσι | win over by persuasion, **persuade, prevail upon** —someone, the mind or heart Hom. Pl. —W.ACC. + INF. someone to do sthg. Od. E.

παρα-πειράομαι mid.contr.vb. (of seers) **make trial of, test the will of** —W.GEN. *Zeus* Pi.

παρα-πέμπω vb. **1** (of Hera) **send** (W.ACC. the Argo) **past** —the Clashing Rocks Od.
2 send (W.ACC. ships, foot-soldiers) **along the coast** Th. ‖ PASS. (of a commander) be despatched along the coast Th.
3 (of the captain of a warship) **provide a convoy for, escort** —troops (on troop-ships), grain-ships, a grain-shipment D.; (of a commander) **provide** —W.COGN.ACC. *a convoy* (for supplies to an army) X. ‖ PASS. (of merchant ships) be escorted (by a warship) D.
4 (gener.) **escort** —someone (on his way, or to a place) Plb. Plu. ‖ PASS. (fig., of a person) be attended —W.PREP.PHR. *by good repute* Hyp.
5 (of a commander) **send** (W.ACC. troops) **along the line** or **flanks** (in support) X.
6 (of a mountain) **send on, echo** —*a sound* S.; (of spectators) **convey** —*a noise of approval* (to a playwright) Ar.
7 (fig.) app. **entertain** —oneself (W.DAT. w. amusements, drink and music) Plu.; (intr.) app. **conduct oneself** —W.DAT. w. unshowy graciousness Plu.
8 put aside (as not deserving of attention or respect), **set aside, dismiss, ignore** —someone or sthg. Plb. Plu. ‖ PASS. (of an issue) be shelved Plb.

παρα-πετάννῡμι vb. | pf.pass.ptcpl. παραπεπετασμένος | **spread alongside** ‖ NEUT.PL.PF.PASS.PTCPL.SB. hangings (ref. to curtains) Plb.

παρα-πεπληγμένος η ον pf.pass.ptcpl.adj. [πλήσσω] (of a person) struck awry, **deranged, demented, mad** Ar. Plu.; (of laughter, decisions) E. Ar.

παραπέτασμα ατος n. [παραπετάννῡμι] **1** that which is spread alongside; **hanging, drape, tapestry** (as a wall decoration) Hdt. Ar. Men.; **awning** (for a boat) Plu.; **curtain** (for a carriage window) Plu.; **drapery** (used to conceal a light) Plu.

2 curtain, screen, cover (as providing concealment or protection) Pl.; (fig., ref. to an art, a legal challenge, as disguising one's true interest or intent) Pl. D.; (ref. to rustic isolation, as disguising one's poverty) Men.

παρα-πέτομαι, dial. **παρπέταμαι** (Call.) *mid.vb.* | aor.1 παρεπτάμην, aor.2 παρεπτόμην, athem.aor.act. παρέπτην (Call.) | **1** (of Eros, Perseus) **fly past, fly by** (someone) Anacr. Ar.; (of flies) Arist.; (of the Muses, past brawling poets) Call.; (fig., of a person's love) —W.ACC. *what lies at hand* Call.*epigr.*; (of an oar, meton. for a ship) **fly along** S. **2** (of a beetle) **fly up** —W.DAT. *to someone* Semon.

παρα-πήγνῡμι *vb.* | aor. παρέπηξα | pf. παραπέπηγα | **1 fix or plant** (W.ACC. a spear) **nearby** (in the ground) Hdt. AR.(tm.) **2** ‖ STATV.PF. (of the spears of warriors at rest) **stand fixed** (in the ground) nearby Il.(tm.); (of pikes) **be planted alongside** (other weapons, in a pile of booty) Plu.; (fig., of pains) **be affixed or attached** —W.DAT. *to pleasures* Isoc.

παρα-πηδάω *contr.vb.* **1** (of hounds) **leap side by side** X. **2** (fig., of a person) **leap over, transgress** —*laws* Aeschin. **3** (fig., of an adult) **spring forth** —W.PREP.PHR. *fr. school (i.e. leave it prematurely, be insufficiently trained)* Plu.

παρα-πίμπραμαι *pass.vb.* [πίμπρημι] (of a horse's legs) **be liable to become inflamed** X.

παρα-πίπτω *vb.* **1** (of the body of a slain soldier) **fall nearby** Plu. **2** (of a ship, a person or animal) **come along, turn up** Hdt. Lys. X. Plu.; (of allies, to give help) Plb.; (of a lawgiver) **appear opportunely** —W.DAT. *for a city (which is in need of one)* Pl. **3** (of an opportunity) **come one's way, be offered** Th. Isoc. D. Plb. Plu.; (of a means of safety) E.; (of a pleasure, an argument) Pl.; (of a critical moment) **arrive** X. ‖ IMPERS. an opportunity is offered Pl. —W.DAT. and ὥστε + INF. *for someone, to do sthg.* X. **4** (of a person) **come up against, fall foul of** —W.DAT. *someone's anger* Plu.; (of a hindrance or obstacle) **fall in one's path** Pl. Plb. Plu. **5** (of fortuitous or lucky outcomes) **fall out**; (of a particular horse) **fall to one's lot** X.; (of a happy result) **turn out** —W.DAT. *for someone* Pl. **6** (of soldiers) **rush past** Plb.; **rush on** —W.PREP.PHR. *into a place* Plb. **7 deviate** —W.GEN. *fr. a path* Plb.; (of a historian) —*fr. the truth, fr. propriety* Plb.; (gener.) **go astray, make a mistake** X. Plb. **8 fall down or humble oneself before someone, fawn, cringe** D.

παρα-πλάζω *vb.* **1** (of winds, waves) **drive** (W.ACC. someone) **off course** —W.GEN. *fr. a place* Od. ‖ PASS. (of an arrow) **be deflected** Il. **2** (of a god) **lead astray** —*someone's mind* Od.; (of mental confusion) —*a person* Pi. ‖ PASS. **go astray, err** Pi.; **be deflected, stray** —W.GEN. *fr. right thinking* E.

παρα-πλευρίδια ων *n.pl.* [πλευρᾱ́] **side-pieces** (as armour for the flanks of chariot-horses) X.

παρα-πλέω *contr.vb.* [πλέω¹] —also **παραπλώω** *Ion.vb.* | aor. παρέπλευσα, ep.3sg.athem.aor. παρέπλω | Ion.pf. παραπέπλωκα | **1** (of sailors) **sail past** —*people, places* Hdt. Pl. X. NT. Plu. —w. παρά + ACC. Hdt.; (intr., of ships) Od. Th. X. Plb. **2** (of sailors, ships) **sail along the coast, coast along** —*a region* Hdt. Th. Plu. —w. παρά + ACC. X. Plu.; (intr.) Hdt. Th. X. D. +

παρα-πληκτός όν *adj.* [πλήσσω] (of a killer's hand) **stricken with madness, frenzied** S.; (of cries) Melanipp.

παραπλήξ ῆγος *masc.fem.adj.* **1** (of shores which are accessible to a swimmer) **struck obliquely** (by waves) Od. **2** (of a person) **deranged, demented, mad** Hdt. Ar. X. D. Plu. **3** (of divine compulsion, acting on a person's mind) **deranging, maddening** B.

παρα-πλήσιος ᾱ (Ion. η) ον (also ος ον) *adj.* **1 close alongside**; (of persons, things, events) **similar in nature or quality, similar, comparable** (oft. W.DAT. to someone or sthg.) Hdt. +; (of combatants) **evenly matched** Hdt. **2** (of persons or things) **similar in number, size or extent, similar, comparable, almost equal** (oft. W.DAT. to someone or sthg., sts. W.ADVBL.ACC. τὸν ἀριθμόν, τὸ μέγεθος *in number, size*, or sim.) Hdt. +

—**παραπλήσιον** *neut.adv.* **a comparable distance** —*ref. to being apart* Th.

—**παραπλησίως** *adv.* **in a similar way, comparably** Hdt. Isoc. +; **in an evenly balanced way** —*ref. to fighting* Hdt.

—**παραπλησιαίτερον** *compar.adv.* **in a more comparable way, more closely** Pl.

παρά-πλους ου *Att.m.* [πλόος] **1 voyage along the coast** Th. X. Plb. Plu.; (W.GEN. towards a place) Th. **2 sailing past** (a place), **passage** (W.GEN. of an enemy fleet) Th.

παραπλώω *Ion.vb.*: see παραπλέω

παρα-πνέω *contr.vb.* (of a gust fr. the winds imprisoned in a bag by Aiolos) **blow past** (the fastenings), **escape** Od.

παρα-ποδίζω *vb.* **tether the feet**; (fig., of terrain) **impede, hamper** —*a military formation, the use of weapons* Plb. ‖ PASS. (of a person) **be tripped up** (by an argument) Pl.; (of the functioning of rowers and helmsmen) **be impeded** Plb.; (of a purpose) **be thwarted** Plb.

παρ-αποδύομαι *mid.vb.* (of a visitor to a wrestling school) **strip off as well** (along w. the wrestlers) Pl.

παρα-ποιέω *contr.vb.* (of Homer) **introduce** (W.ACC. a story) **incidentally** or **mistakenly** Hdt.(cj.)

—**παραπεποιημένα** ων *neut.pl.pf.pass.ptcpl.sb.* **things created by a change from the normal, word changes, quirky expressions** (as a source of humour) Arist.

παρ-απόλλῡμι *vb.* **1** (of a person) app. **ruin undeservedly** —*one who loves him* Plu. **2** ‖ MID. or PF.ACT. **perish pointlessly, come to an unhappy end** Ar. Men. ‖ STATV.PF. **be ruined undeservedly** D.

παραπομπή ῆς *f.* [παραπέμπω] **1 military escort** (for a person, an embassy) Plb.; **convoy** (for supplies to an army) X. Aeschin.; (for grain-ships) D. **2 transportation, conveyance** (of produce, to or fr. a city) Arist.

παραπομπός όν *adj.* (of ships) **acting as escort, providing a convoy** Plb.

παρα-πορεύομαι *mid.vb.* | aor.pass. (w.mid.sens.) παρεπορεύθην | **1** (of troops, animals) **proceed alongside** (someone or sthg.) Plb. **2** (of troops, persons) **go past, pass by** Plb. NT. Plu. —*a place* Plb.

παρα-ποτάμιος ᾱ (Ion. η) ον (also ος ον Plu.) *adj.* (of a city, a plain) **beside a river, riverside** Hdt. E.; (of a battle) Plu.

παρα-πράσσω, Att. **παραπράττω**, Ion. **παραπρήσσω** *vb.* **1 act alongside** (someone), **lend a hand** S. **2 do** (sthg.) **beside** (one's chief aim); **do** (W.ACC. nothing) **more** Hdt. **3 exact additional** or **unfair taxes** Plu.

παρα-πρεσβείᾱ ᾱς *f.* **misconduct as an ambassador** D.; (title of a speech by Aeschines, usu. given as *False Embassy*) Plu.

παρα-πρεσβεύω *vb.* **be guilty of misconduct as an ambassador** Aeschin. D.; (mid.) Isoc. Pl. D.

παρα-πρίσματα των *n.pl.* [πρίω] (fig.) **sawn-off pieces** (W.GEN. of words or verses, ref. to carefully honed expressions) Ar.

παρ-άπτομαι *mid.vb.* touch lightly, **tap** (a gong) Men.; **prick** (bodies, w. a sword, to check for signs of life) Plu.

παράπτωμα ατος *n.* [παραπίπτω] **slip, blunder** Plb.; **offence, sin** NT.

παράπτωσις εως *f.* **1** rushing past or onward, **impetuosity** (W.GEN. of a pursuit) Plb.; **impetuous pursuit** (W.PREP.PHR. after someone) Plb.
2 going astray, **deviation** (W.GEN. fr. propriety) Plb.; **blunder, mistake** (by a writer) Plb.
3 state of being aside (fr. sthg.); **aloofness, separation** (W.GEN. of a place, fr. a war-zone) Plb.

παρ-άρθρησις εως *f.* [ἄρθρον] (medic.) **dislocation** (of a limb) Plu.

πάραρος *dial.adj.*: see παράορος

παρα-ρράπτομαι *pass.vb.* [ῥάπτω] (of animal skins) **be sewn as a fringe** —W.PREP.PHR. *along the edges of cloaks* Hdt.

παρα-ρρέω *contr.vb.* [ῥέω] | pf. παρερρύηκα | aor.2 pass. (w.act.sens.) παρερρύην | **1** (of rivers or sim.) **flow past** —*a place* Hdt. —w. παρά + ACC. Hdt. X. Plu.; (intr.) Hdt. X. Plb. Plu.
2 (of an arrow) fall aside, **slip out** (fr. a quiver) S.; (fig., of considerations) **be overlooked** Pl. || AOR.2 PASS. (of snow) slip off (people) X.
3 (of misleading expressions) **slip in** (to common usage) D.; (of an eagerness for philosophy) —W.PREP.PHR. *to a city* Plu.

παρα-ρρήγνῡμι, also **παραρρηγνύω** (Plu.) *vb.* [ῥήγνῡμι] | pf. παρέρρωγα | **1** break (a line of battle) apart; (of a commander, troops) **cause a breach** Th. —W.ACC. *in a formation* Plu. || PASS. (of an army) be broken or cut in two Th. Plu.
2 || AOR.PASS. or PF.ACT. (of a haemorrhaging vein) have burst open S.; (of a dress) be torn open Ar. Plu.; (of mountainsides) be torn away (by earthquakes or sim.) Plu.
3 || PASS. (fig., of a commander, ref. to his military strength) be broken Plu.; (of a speaker, ref. to his voice, through excessive passion) Plu.

παρα-ρρητός όν *adj.* [ῥητός] (of persons) open to persuasion, **persuadable** (W.DAT. by words) Il. || NEUT.PL.SB. persuasive words, persuasion Il.

παρα-ρρίπτω *vb.* [ῥίπτω] make a risky throw at dice; (fig.) **risk** —W.PTCPL. *incurring reproaches* S.; (of sailors) —W.ACC. *trading-enterprises* S.fr.

παρα-ρρύματα (sts. written **παραρύματα**) των *n.pl.* [ῥῦμα²] awnings of cloth or hide stretched along the sides of a warship (for protection against spray or missiles), **side-screens** (also serving to conceal troops) X.

παρα-ρρύσεις εων *f.pl.* [reltd. ῥύομαι] **side-screens** (W.GEN. of a ship) A.

παρ-αρτάομαι *pass.contr.vb.* | 3sg.plpf. παρήρτητο | (of a sword) **be hung by one's side** Plu.

παρ-αρτέομαι *mid.contr.vb.* | 3sg.plpf. παρήρτητο | **make ready, prepare** —*a military force, ships* Hdt.; (intr.) —w. ὡς + PREP.PHR. or + FUT.PTCPL. *for sthg., for doing sthg.* Hdt.

παρ-αρτίζομαι *mid.vb.* | aor.ptcpl. παραρτισάμενος | **fit out, equip** —*ships* Plu.(v.l. παραρτυσάμενος)

παρά-ρυθμος ον *adj.* [ῥυθμός] against the rhythm; (of the notes of a lyre) **out of time** (W.DAT. w. dance-steps) Ar.

παραρύματα *n.pl.*: see παραρρύματα

παρασάγγης ου *m.* [loanwd.] **parasang** (Persian measure of distance, equiv. to 30 stades) Hdt. X.

παρα-σάσσω *vb.* **stuff** (W.ACC. gold-dust) **beside** —w. παρά + ACC. *one's legs* (i.e. in one's boots) Hdt.

παρά-σειρος ον *adj.* [σειρά] harnessed at the side by a trace; (fig., of a friend offering support) **like a trace-horse** E.
—**παράσειρον** *neut.adv.* **on the side** (of a hare's tail) X.

παρα-σείω *vb.* (of a person fleeing) swing one's arms by one's sides, **run with all haste** Arist.

παρα-σημαίνομαι *mid.vb.* **1** set one's seal beside another's; **counterseal** —*property* Pl.
2 set one's seal on —*documents* (to validate them) D. —*rooms, bags of gold* (to close them for security) D. Plu.
3 counterfeit —*a seal* Th.
4 mark in passing, **take note of** —*topics, behaviour* Arist. Plb. Plu.

παρασημασίᾱ ᾱς *f.* taking note (of sthg.) in passing; **mention, commendation** (as deserved by a person) Plb.

παράσημος ον *adj.* **1** falsely marked; (of debased coinage, stamped as if true metal) **counterfeit** D.
2 (fig., of the power of wealth) **falsely stamped** (W.DAT. w. praise, i.e. undeservedly approved) A.; (of persons who are not what they seem) **counterfeit, sham** Ar. D.; (of a person's thoughts) E. || NEUT.SB. behaviour that rings false Plu.
3 (of a writer, his letters) **striking, distinctive** (in style) Plu.; (of a person's name) **indicative, symbolic** (W.GEN. of sthg.) Plu.
—**παράσημον** ου *n.* **distinguishing mark, symbol** (of status or sim.) Plu.; **figurehead, emblem** (on a ship) NT. Plu. || PL. insignia (of office) Plu.

παρα-σῑτέω *contr.vb.* **1 take meals alongside** —W.DAT. *someone* Pl.
2 (as the term coined by Solon to describe the privilege of dining in a public building at public expense) **dine out** Plu.

παράσῑτος ου *m.* one who dines at another's table (and repays him w. flattery), **parasite** Thphr.

παρα-σιωπάω *contr.vb.* **pass over** (W.ACC. sthg.) **in silence** Plb.; (intr.) **remain silent** (about sthg.) Plb.

παρα-σκευάζω *vb.* | Ion.3pl.plpf.pass. παρεσκευάδατο |
1 make ready, prepare —*a meal or sim.* (for someone) Hdt. —*items* (for use) Ar. —*ships, military forces* Lys. X. —*a campaign* Th.
2 || MID. cause to be made ready for oneself, **have prepared, get ready** —*ships or sim.* Hdt. Th. + —*a meal, equipment* Hdt.; **prepare for** —*a sea-battle* Hdt. —*a military campaign, a voyage, war* Th.
3 || MID. (intr.) **make preparations, prepare** (for sthg.) Hdt. Th. + —w. εἰς (ἐς) + ACC. *for sthg.* Hdt. Th. —W.INF. (sts. w. ὥστε) *to do sthg.* A. Hdt. + —W.COMPL.CL. Th. Pl. + —W.FUT.PTCPL. (oft. w. ὡς) *for doing sthg.* Hdt. Th. +
4 || PF. and PLPF.PASS. (of persons, things) be ready, be prepared Hdt. E. + —W.INF. *to do sthg.* A. Hdt. + —w. ὥστε + INF. E. —w. ὡς + FUT.PTCPL. *for doing sthg.* Hdt. X. —W.ACC. + INF. *for someone to do sthg.* A. || IMPERS. preparations have or had been made Th. Pl.
5 provide, furnish (oft. W.DAT. for someone) —*commodities, benefits* E. Th. And. —*speeches* Isoc. —*access to a country* Hdt. —*immunity, support, happiness, or sim.* Lys. Isoc. Pl.; **foment** —*anger* (W.DAT. against someone) Lys.; (pejor.) **contrive, arrange** —*someone's death* Antipho; **cook up** —*a legal case* Lys. D. || MID. provide for oneself, **arrange** —*safety* Lys.; **organise** (unwittingly) —*a formidable adversary* A. || PASS. (of a meal) be provided Hdt.
6 (act. and mid., pejor., in legal ctxts.) **procure by inducement, suborn** —*supporters, witnesses, or sim.* Att.orats. X. —*a court* (i.e. a jury) Lys.; (intr.) **procure an**

underhand advantage Is. D. Arist. ‖ PASS. (of persons) be suborned Att.orats.
7 ‖ PF. and PLPF.PASS. (of persons) be provided, furnished or equipped —W.DAT. *w. sthg.* A. Hdt. Th. —W.ACC. Pl. Thphr.; (of an army, a fleet, or sim.) be equipped —W.ADV. or PREP.PHR. *in some way* Hdt. Th. +
8 make, render —*someone or sthg.* (W.PREDIC.ADJ. or PTCPL. *such and such*) Isoc. Pl. +; (of god) **design** —*the nature of women* (W.PREP.PHR. *for particular activities*) X.
9 put (W.ACC. *someone or sthg.*) **in a position** —W.INF. (sts. w. ὡς) *to do sthg.* Isoc. Pl. X. —W.COMPL.CL. Lys. Pl. X.; (act. and mid.) **arrange, contrive** —W.ACC. + INF. or W.COMPL.CL. *that sthg. shd. happen* Hdt. Lys. Isoc. +
παρασκεύασμα ατος *n.* **technique** (for promoting health, ref. to exercise or sim.) X.
παρασκευαστής οῦ *m.* **provider** (of food) Pl.
παρασκευαστικός ή όν *adj.* **skilled at provision** (W.GEN. of military supplies) X.
παρασκευαστός όν *adj.* (of virtue) **acquirable** Pl.
παρασκευή ῆς *f.* **1** process of making ready, **equipping, preparation** (of ships, for war) Th. Ar.
2 process of making oneself ready, **preparation** (esp. for war) Hdt. Th. +; **preparatory training** (by a speaker or politician) Isoc. X.
3 state of being ready, **readiness, preparedness** (esp. for war) Th. X. +
4 (prep.phrs.) ἐκ (also ἀπό) παρασκευῆς *by prior arrangement* or *deliberately* E. Th. Att.orats.; δι' ὀλίγης παρασκευῆς *at short notice* Th.; ἀπὸ ἴσης παρασκευῆς *on an equal footing* Lys.
5 process of making available (essential or desirable things); **provision** (of food or sim.) Hdt. Pl.; **procuring, ensuring** (of health or sim.) Pl.; **availability** (of friends and resources) Pl.; **technique, contrivance** (for ensuring sthg.) Pl.
6 way of presenting, **presentation, style** (of a meal) Hdt.
7 (concr., ref. to material benefits) **trappings** Pl. X.; **provisions, spread** (ref. to a meal) X.
8 (pejor., in legal ctxts.) underhand or dishonest plotting, **machination, intrigue** Att.orats.
9 (milit.) **armed force** Th. And. Isoc. +; **equipment** Hdt. Th.
10 preparatory section (of a literary work), **preface** Plb. | cf. προκατασκευή
11 preparation for the Jewish Sabbath, **day before the Sabbath** NT.
παρα-σκηνέω contr.vb. **pitch one's tent beside** —W.DAT. *someone* X.
παρα-σκήνια ων *n.pl.* [σκηνή] **side-buildings** (on each side of the orchestra in the Athenian theatre, app. where the chorus prepared for performances) D.
παρα-σκιρτάω contr.vb. (of a donkey) **run friskily past** Plu.
παρα-σκοπέω contr.vb. **take a sideways look at** —*someone* Pl.
παρα-σκώπτω *vb.* **make a casual jest** hHom. Plu.; **jest at, mock** —*someone or sthg.* Men. Plu.
παρα-σοβέω contr.vb. (of a woman) **strut past** Plu.
παρα-σοφίζομαι mid.vb. (provbl.) **outsmart** —*a doctor* Arist.
παρα-σπάω contr.vb. **1** draw or pull aside; (of a soldier) **tear aside** —*an enemy's shield* Plu.; (intr., of a charioteer) **pull aside** (i.e. one's horses, to avoid an accident) S.; **wrest** or **wrench** (W.ACC. *someone*) **aside** —W.GEN. *fr. his purpose* S.; (fig., of Eros) **warp** —*a person's mind* S. ‖ MID. (fig.) **wrench oneself away** —W.GEN. *fr. a powerful argument* Pl.
2 ‖ MID. **wrest away** (fr. another) for one's own use; (of a commander) **wrest away, forcibly appropriate** —*cities or sim.* (usu. W.GEN. *fr. someone*) X. Plb. —*part of someone's sphere of influence* D.

παρ-ασπίζω *vb.* [ἀσπίς¹] **1** carry a shield beside someone (w.connot. of offering support or protection, as in the hoplite phalanx, where the man on the left is protected by the shield of the man on his right); (of Athena, in battle) **carry a shield beside** —W.DAT. *Zeus* E.; (of Iolaos) **fight alongside** (Herakles) Plu.; (fig., of a woman) **stand by in support** (of her mother, who is on the battlefield lamenting her slain sons) E.
2 (fig., of a bow and arrows) **hang as a protection** —W.DAT. *on one's arm* E.
παρασπιστής οῦ *m.* **1** one who carries a shield beside another (as in the hoplite phalanx), **comrade-in-arms** E.; (gener., of a loyal friend) **right-hand man** E.
2 aide-de-camp (of a commander) Plb.(cj.)
παρασπονδέω contr.vb. [παράσπονδος] **break a truce** or **treaty** D. Plb. Plu.; (tr.) **wrong by breaking a treaty** or **agreement, break faith with** —*someone* Plb. Plu. ‖ PASS. be betrayed Plb.
παρασπόνδημα ατος *n.* **violation of a truce** Plu.; (gener.) **act of treachery, breach of faith** Plb. Plu.
παρασπόνδησις εως *f.* **breaking of faith, treacherous behaviour** Plb.
παρά-σπονδος ον *adj.* [σπονδή] **1** (of a military action) **in breach of a truce** or **treaty** Th. Isoc. X. Plu.; **in breach of good faith** Plb.
2 (of persons) **guilty of breaking a truce** Lys. Plu.
—**παρασπόνδως** *adv.* **treacherously** Plb.
παρ-ᾶσσον *adv.* [ἆσσον] **1 next, at once, immediately** AR.
2 perh. **side by side** —*ref. to trees being planted* AR.
παρ-άσσω, ep. **παραΐσσω** *vb.* | iteratv.impf. παραΐσσεσκον | ep.aor. παρήϊξα | aor.ptcpl. παράξας, imperatv. παράξον |
1 (of warriors) **hurry past** Il.; (of horses) **speed past** —*a person* Il.; (of a person, a dog) **dash along** —W.PREP.PHR. *to or into a place* Ar.
2 (of Harpies) **outstrip** (in speed) —*winds* AR.
παράστᾱ (athem.aor.imperatv.): see παρίσταμαι, under παρίστημι
παρασταδόν *adv.* [παρίσταμαι] **standing nearby, close at hand** Hom. Thgn. A.
παραστάς άδος *f.* **1** ‖ PL. **doorposts or pillars**; (collectv.) **portico, vestibule** (of a palace) E.; (of a house) Men.(dub.)
2 perh. **side pillar** (of a temple) E. [or perh. *side wall* of its porch]
παράστασις εως *f.* [παρίστημι] **1** action of putting aside; (sg. and pl.) app. **expulsion, banishment** (of persons, fr. their city to a more distant region) Pl. Arist.
2 putting forward (to people's notice); **promotion, marketing** (of goods for sale) Arist.
3 standing nearby (someone); **post, position** (of courtiers standing, opp. sitting, in a king's presence, in order of precedence) X.
4 being beside oneself (as a mental or emotional state); **distraction, derangement** Plb.; **perverse belief, propensity** or **plan** Men. Plb.; **ecstatic emotion, fervour, excitement** Plb.; **desperate courage** Plb. Plu.
5 (leg.) that which is put forward as a pledge, **court fee, deposit** (payable by a prosecutor in certain cases) And. Is. Arist. Men. | cf. παρακαταβολή
παραστατέω contr.vb. [παραστάτης] **1** (of a god, a person; fig., of fear) **stand nearby, be at hand, be in attendance** A.; (of a person) **stand alongside** or **nearby** —W.DAT. *someone, a ruler's throne* S. E.; (of a lamp) —*someone* Ar.

παραστάτης

2 stand alongside as a helper or supporter; (of Justice, fortune, gods) **stand by, attend on** —W.DAT. *someone* Trag. Ar.

παραστάτης ου, dial. **παραστάτᾱς** ᾱ m. [παρίσταμαι]
1 person standing nearby, **bystander** Hdt.
2 (milit.) **next man** (in the line of battle) Hdt.; (opp. ἐπιστάτης *soldier behind one*) X. Plb.; (gener.) **comrade-in-arms** Trag. X. Arist. Plu.; (w.GEN. *of someone*) E.; (W.DAT.) Pi.
3 **guard** stationed by (a place); **guard** or **defender** (W.GEN. *of a gate*) E.
4 (ref. to a god) **helper, supporter** Pl. X.; (ref. to a person) Plb. Plu.
5 **member of** or **colleague in** a chorus (opp. its leader) Arist.

παραστατικός ή όν adj. 1 (of persons, their state of mind) **deranged** Plb.; (of a soldier) **fiery** Plb.; (of eagerness) **frenzied** Plb.
2 (of an event, a stimulus) **such as to incite** (W.GEN. a feeling, an attitude) Plb. Plu.
—**παραστατικῶς** adv. **frenziedly** Plb.

παραστάτις ιδος f. 1 woman standing by (as an eyewitness), **bystander** S.
2 **companion, attendant** (of a blind old man, ref. to his daughter) S.; (ref. to Virtue) **supporter, protector** (W.DAT. *for servants*) X.

παρα-στείχω vb. | ep.aor.2 παρέστιχον | 1 **go past** —*a palace, a chariot* A. S.; **pass by** —*a region* hHom.
2 **go into, enter** —*a palace* S.

παρα-στενάχομαι mid.vb. **lament beside** or **with** —W.DAT. *someone* AR.

παρα-στρατηγέω contr.vb. (of civilians) **interfere in military matters** Plu. ‖ PASS. (fig., of a politician) be **outgeneralled** or **outmanoeuvred** Arist.

παρα-στρατοπεδεύω vb. (of troops) **encamp nearby** or **opposite** Plb. Plu. —W.DAT. *enemy troops, a city, or sim.* Plb. Plu.

παρα-στρέφω vb. 1 **turn aside** ‖ PASS. (fig., of a soul) be **warped** —W.GEN. *fr. its natural state* (by music) Arist.
2 **make** (W.ACC. small) **changes** (in words) Pl.
3 (of a stingy person, sitting down) **turn up** —*his tunic* (to avoid wear and tear) Thphr.

παρα-στρωφάομαι mid.pass.contr.vb. (of the eyes of ploughing oxen) **turn sideways, roll** (app. fr. exhaustion) AR.

παρα-συγγραφέω contr.vb. [συγγραφή] **break a contract** —W.ACC. *w. someone* D.; (intr.) D.

παρα-συλλέγομαι pass.vb. | aor.2 ptcpl. παρασυλλεγείς | (of people) **assemble together** —W.DAT. *w. someone* And.

παρα-σύνθημα ατος n. (milit.) pre-arranged signal in response to another, **counter-signal** Plb.

παρα-σύρω vb. 1 (of sailors) **shear off** —*the oars of enemy ships* (by brushing past them) Tim. Plb.; (fig., of a person, envisaged as a torrent) **sweep away** —*trees and persons* (W.GEN. *fr. their sites*) Ar.
2 (fig., of a speaker) perh. **sweep along, bulldoze** —*an intolerable proposal* (i.e. in a torrent of words) A.

παρα-σφάλλω vb. | aor. παρέσφηλα, dial. παρέσφαλα | **cause** (someone) **to go astray and miss the goal**; (of a god) **thwart, foil** (an archer) Il.; (fig., of a person's timid disposition) **cheat** —*him* (W.GEN. *of his deserts*) Pi. ‖ PASS. (of a drunken person's mind) be **fuddled** Critias

παρα-σχεδόν adv. 1 **alongside** (someone) AR.
2 **at once, straightaway** AR.

παρασχεθεῖν (ep.aor.2 inf.), **παρασχεῖν** (aor.2 inf.), **παρασχέμεν** (ep.aor.2 inf.), **παράσχες** (aor.2 imperatv.), **παρασχήσω** (fut.): see παρέχω

παρα-σχίζω vb. (intr., of embalmers) **cut lengthways** —w. παρά + ACC. *along the side of a corpse* Hdt.

παρασχίστης ου m. criminal who mutilates the body of his victim by cutting it, **ripper, slasher** Plb.

παρα-τανύω vb. **set out** (W.ACC. a table) **by the side** (of someone) Od.(tm.)

παράταξις εως f. [παρατάσσω] 1 **formation of a battle-line** Aeschin.; (phr.) ἐκ παρατάξεως μάχη (or sim.) **pitched battle** Th. Aeschin. D. Plb. Plu.
2 engagement between troops in battle formation, **pitched battle** Plb.; (gener.) **engagement, clash** (betw. gods taking opposite sides in the Trojan War) Isoc.
3 (concr.) body of troops in battle formation, **formation, battle-line** Din. Plb. Plu.
4 **coterie, cabal** (of political or legal opponents) Aeschin. D.
5 (wkr.sens.) **partisanship** (of spectators at a dramatic contest) Plu.

παρα-τάσσω, Att. **παρατάττω** vb. 1 (of a commander) **arrange** (W.ACC. troops) **in battle-lines** Hdt. Th. +; **post, station** —W.ACC. + INF. *soldiers, to do sthg.* X. ‖ MID. arrange one's troops in battle-lines, **get into battle formation** X. Thphr. Plb. Plu.; (gener.) **engage in battle** Plb.
2 ‖ MID. (of troops) **form in line, take up battle stations** (sts. W.DAT. or πρός + ACC. against an enemy) Th. Att.orats. +
3 ‖ PF.MID. or PASS. (usu. PTCPL.) (of troops) **be in battle-lines** Hdt. Th. +; **be posted** —w. παρά + ACC. *along a shore* Hdt.; (of a soldier) **be stationed in line** Ar.; (gener.) **be ready for a fight** —W.DAT. *w. someone* Men.; (fig., of a person) be **resolutely opposed** —W.PREP.PHR. *to doing sthg.* Pl.
4 ‖ MID. (of sailors) **form** (W.ACC. their ships) **in line** Th.; (intr.) Th.
5 ‖ MID. (of a commander, a soldier) **station** (W.ACC. a son or lover) **alongside** (sts. W.DAT. oneself) Isoc. X. ‖ PASS. (of a soldier) be **stationed next in line** Th. —W.DAT. *to someone* Pl.; (of troops) be **stationed alongside** —W.DAT. *others* Th.; (fig., of a politician) **stand shoulder to shoulder** —w. μετά + GEN. *w. a political ally* Aeschin.
6 **set alongside** (for comparison), **compare** —W.ACC. + DAT. *someone, w. sthg.* Isoc.

—**παρατεταγμένως** pf.mid.pass.ptcpl.adv. **at battle stations**; (fig.) **resolutely** —*ref. to confronting misfortune* Pl.

παρα-τείνω vb. | fut. παρατενῶ | aor. παρέτεινα ‖ pf.pass. παρατέταμαι | 1 **cause** (sthg.) **to be extended**; (of soldiers, a commander) **extend, stretch** —*a phalanx, flank, or sim.* (sts. w. παρά + ACC. *alongside a place*) Th. X. Plb.; (of a queen) —*a reservoir* (alongside a river) Hdt.; **stretch out** —*oneself* (on the ground) Plu. ‖ PASS. (of a trench) be **extended** X.
2 ‖ PASS. (fig., of an island, envisaged as a person) be **stretched out** or **knocked flat** (by aggressors) Ar.; (of a person) be **laid out flat** or **worn out** (by a long journey) X.; (fr. laughing and clapping too much) Pl. ‖ 2SG.FUT.ACT. (colloq., said of a tiresome person) perh. *you'll wear me out* Men.
3 (intr., of a mountain range, island, wall, or sim.) **extend, stretch** (sts. w. παρά + ACC. alongside a place) Hdt. Th. Plb. ‖ PF.PASS. (of a mountain range, a peninsula) **extend, stretch out** (in a given direction) Hdt.; (of an island) Ar.
4 ‖ MID. (fig.) **stretch oneself, exert oneself** (to achieve sthg.) Th.
5 (of a waiter) **extend, hold out, offer** —*a bowl of perfume* Xenoph.
6 **stretch** (someone) **on the rack**; (fig.) **torment, annoy** —*someone* X. ‖ PASS. (fig.) be **racked** —W.DAT. *w. hunger* Pl.; be **tormented** or **annoyed** (by someone's behaviour) Pl.

7 (of tragic poets) **expand, protract** —*a narrative, a plot* Arist.; (of a speaker) **prolong** —*his talk* NT.
8 (geom.) place alongside, **apply** (a plane figure, or part of it, to another) Pl. —*a figure* (w. παρά + ACC. *to a line*) Pl. || PASS. (of a figure) be applied (to a line) Pl.

παρα-τείχισμα ατος *n.* (milit.) **counter-wall** (defensive rampart built to prevent besiegers completing an encircling wall) Th.

παρα-τεκταίνομαι *mid.vb.* **1** construct or fashion (sthg.) differently; (of Zeus) **remake, rearrange, change** —*an outcome* Il.; (of a liar) **fabricate** —*a story* Od.
2 have (W.ACC. a house) **built close by** (another building) Plu.

παρα-τέμνω *vb.* | aor.2 παρέτεμον | cut lengthways, **slice off, fillet** —*half one's body* (comically envisaged as a fish) Ar.

παρατεταγμένως *pf.mid.pass.ptcpl.adv.*: see under παρατάσσω

παρα-τηρέω *contr.vb.* **1 keep a close watch on** —*persons, places, activities* Arist. Plb. NT.(also mid.); **examine carefully** —W.INDIR.Q. *whether sthg. is the case* X. || PASS. (of persons) be kept under observation Men.
2 observe closely, wait and see —W.INDIR.Q. *whether someone will do sthg.* X. Thphr. NT.(also mid.); **watch out for, wait for** —*a time, a person* Plb.; (intr.) **be on the lookout** (for an opportunity) Arist. Plb. || PASS. (of envoys) be awaited Plb.
3 watch out for, be on guard against —*people, plots* Aeschin. —*an attack* Plb. —*faults* (*in historians*) Plb.; **be on the watch** —W.COMPL.CL. *to ensure that sthg. does or does not happen* Isoc. D.
4 maintain, observe —*the proper limit* (*in doing sthg.*) Arist.

παρατήρησις εως *f.* **1 close attention** (to someone or sthg.) Plb.
2 watching out (for the coming of God's kingdom) NT.

παρα-τίθημι, ep. **παρτίθημι** *vb.* | dial.contr.pres. (as if fr. παρατιθέω) 2sg. παρατιθεῖς, 3sg. παρτιθεῖ | **1 place** (W.ACC. a chair, table, cup, or sim.) **close by** (sts. W.DAT. someone or sthg.) Od.(sts.tm.) Stesich. Hdt. Ar. || MID. have (W.ACC. torches) **placed close by** Od.; **place close by** (for one's own use) —*a cup, a jar, an implement* E.*Cyc.* Ar. Pl. || PASS. (of tables) be placed close by —W.DAT. *guests* Hdt.
2 set out (food) beside (someone); **serve** —*a meal, food, drink, or sim.* (oft. W.DAT. *to someone*) Hom.(sts.tm.) Ar. Philox.Leuc. Pl. + —W.PARTITV.GEN. *a share of everything* Hdt.; (fig., of a philosopher) **serve up, offer** —*philosophical theories* (W.INF. *for people to taste*) Pl. || MASC.PL.PTCPL.SB. those serving (a meal), waiters X. || MID. have (W.ACC. a meal) **served** —W.DAT. *to someone* Od.; **have oneself served** —*Persian cuisine* Th. —*items of food* Ar. X. || PASS. (of food) be served Lys. X. Arist.
3 (of teachers or sim.) **offer, present** —*poems* (W.DAT. + INF. *for pupils to read*) Pl. —*a parable* (W.DAT. *to listeners*) NT.; **set out** —*each point* (*in an explanation*) X. || PASS. (of pictures) be presented —W.DAT. *to viewers* Pl.
4 place (one thing) beside (another, for comparison); **compare** —*one's family relationship* (w. someone else's) Is. —*someone* (W.DAT. w. someone else) Plu. —W.COMPL.CL. *how someone did sthg.* D.; (gener.) **juxtapose** —*pains* (W.DAT. w. *pleasures*) Pl.
5 || MID. place (sthg.) in another's hands for safekeeping; **deposit** —*money* (w. someone) Hdt. —*people* (as hostages, w. ἐς + ACC. w. someone) Hdt.; **entrust, commit** —*one's property* (W.DAT. *to an island, i.e. transfer it there for safety*) X. —*a person* (*to someone, for protection*) AR. NT. —*one's spirit* (W.PREP.PHR. *into the hands of God*) NT.
6 || MID. (fig., of a founder) **establish** —*a god* (i.e. his worship, W.DAT. *in a land*) Call.
7 || MID. **set aside** —*money taken as booty* (W.PREP.PHR. *for one's own use*) Plb.
8 || MID. **endanger, risk, lay on the line** —*one's life* Od. hHom. Tyrt. Aeschin.
9 || MID. **bring forward, introduce** —*an argument* Pl.; **adduce** (in evidence or as authority) —*a myth, an example* Pl. —*the sense of sight* (opp. *reasoning*) Pl.

παρα-τίλλω *vb.* | fut. παρατιλῶ || pf.mid.pass.ptcpl. παρατετιλμένος | **1** remove body-hairs || MID. (of an idle man) **pluck out hairs** (perh. fr. his head or beard) Ar. || PF.MID. or PASS.PTCPL. (of women) with pubic hair partially plucked (for cosmetic purposes), plucked, trimmed Ar.
2 (w.connot. of violence) **pluck out** —*someone's eyelashes* Ar. || PASS. (of an adulterer) be plucked (i.e. have one's pubic hair plucked out, as a punishment, perh. merely ref. to a token procedure) Ar.

παρά-τολμος ον *adj.* [τόλμα] (of a woman) **abnormally bold** Plu.

παράτονος ον *adj.* [παρατείνω] (of a dead woman's arms) stretched alongside, **hanging limp by one's sides** E.

παρα-τρέπω *vb.* | aor.1 παρέτρεψα, aor.2 παρέτραπον (Hes.) || aor.mid.1 (tr.) παρετρεψάμην, aor.mid.2 (intr.) παρετραπόμην |
1 turn (someone or sthg.) aside (fr. a course); (of a charioteer) **turn aside, wheel** —*his horses* Il.; (of a person) **divert** —*a river or sim.* Hdt. Th. Plu.; (of a commander) —*his opponent* (fr. places) Plu. || MID. **change course** (at sea) X.; **turn aside** —W.GEN. fr. *a topic under discussion* X.
2 turn aside an evil; (of a god) **turn aside, deflect** (W.DAT. away fr. someone) —*the stone of Tantalos* (fig.ref. to a military threat) Pi.(tm.); (of music) —*sorrows* Hes.
3 turn (someone) aside (fr. a purpose); **deflect, sway** —*someone's decision* Hdt. —*the mind of the gods* B. —*a person* (W.DAT. w. *words, bribes*) AR. Theoc.(mid.) || PASS. (of gods) be deflected —W.DAT. *by offerings* Pl.
4 turn aside (fr. the truth), **pervert, distort, falsify** —*a story* Hdt.
5 turn aside (fr. good sense); **drive** —*someone* (by drugs, W.PREP.PHR. *to perverse impulses*) Plu.; (of a person's bodily condition) **derange** —*his mind* Plu.

παρα-τρέφω *vb.* (of Athenian archons) **support in addition** (to themselves) —*a herald and aulos-player* (i.e. w. their food allowance) Arist.; (of a wealthy man) **keep** (W.ACC. dogs and horses) **as well** Men.(dub.) || PASS. (of concubines) be kept as well (as a wife, by a king) Plu.; (of military forces) receive maintenance Plu.; (derog., of a person) D.; (fig., of a warlike spirit) be maintained or cultivated Plu.

παρα-τρέχω *vb.* | aor. παρέθρεξα (AR.) | The aor. is usu. supplied by παραδραμεῖν. | **1 run past** —*a place, a person* X. Plu.; **run alongside** (a horse, cattle) X. Plb.; (of sailors) **speed past** —*land* X.; (of the sound of a wind) **hurry past** (someone) AR.
2 (fig., of a difference in behaviour) **pass by** (W.ACC. someone) unnoticed Plb.
3 hurry off —W.PREP.PHR. *to somewhere* Ar.

παρα-τρέω *contr.vb.* | ep.3pl.aor. παρέτρεσσαν | (of horses) **rush aside in fear, swerve** Il.

παρατριβή ῆς *f.* [παρατρίβω] (fig.) **friction, strained relations** (betw. people, cities) Plb.

παρα-τρίβω *vb.* **1** rub (a precious metal) alongside (another) for comparison (on a touchstone); rub (w.ACC. pure gold) **alongside** —w.DAT. *other gold* Hdt. ‖ PASS. (fig., of a person, envisaged as pure gold alongside gold adulterated w. lead) be rubbed (i.e. have one's purity tested) in comparison (w. others) Thgn.
2 ‖ MID. or PASS. (fig., of people) be the cause or object of friction, **have strained** or **antagonistic relations** (usu. w.PREP.PHR. w. others) Plb.

παρατροπά ᾶς *dial.f.* [παρατρέπω] turning aside, **averting** (w.GEN. of death) E.

παρα-τροπέω *ep.contr.vb.* turn aside, **deflect, sway** —*someone* (fr. a purpose, w. speech) Od. AR.

παράτροπος ον *adj.* **1** (of sexual unions) deviating, (fr. propriety), **aberrant, illicit** Pi.
2 (of a song) **able to avert** (w.GEN. death) E.

παράτροφοι ων *m.pl.* [παρατρέφω] those brought up alongside (the children of the household), **home-bred slaves** Plb.

παρα-τρώγω *vb.* | *aor.2* παρέτραγον | **nibble off a bit** —w.PARTITV.GEN. *of an olive* Ar.; (fig.) —*of the year's cycle* (ref. to suppression of calendar days) Ar.

παρα-τρωπάω *ep.contr.vb.* turn aside, **deflect, sway** —*the gods* (fr. their purpose, w.DAT. w. offerings) Il.

παρα-τυγχάνω *vb.* | *aor.2* παρέτυχον | **1 happen to be present** (oft. w. no notion of coincidence); (of the goddess Eris) **be present** —w.DAT. *among soldiers in combat* Il.; (of a person) —*among persons engaged in debate* Pl. —*at a discussion, a disaster* Hdt.; (intr.) Hdt. Th. X. Plb. NT. Plu.; (of a person, a lion) **come one's way** X. Plb.
2 (of a person) **be present at, take part in** —w.DAT. *a battle, dangerous ventures, or sim.* Plb. Plu.
3 (of troops) **happen to be at hand** or **available** X.; (of a weapon) —w.DAT. *for someone* Pl.; (of an opportunity, a way of escape, a means of safety) Th. ‖ AOR.2 NEUT.ACC.PTCPL. there being an opportunity available —w.INF. *to do sthg.* Th.
—**παρατυγχάνων** οντος *masc.ptcpl.sb.* —also **παρατυχών** όντος *aor.2 masc.ptcpl.sb.* person who happens to be at hand or available, **any casual person, man in the street** Th. Men.
—**παρατύγχανον** οντος *neut.ptcpl.sb.* —also **παρατυχόν** όντος *aor.2 ptcpl.sb.* whatever turns up, **immediate circumstances** Th.

παραυά *Aeol.f.*: see παρειά

παρ-αυδάω *contr.vb.* **1** talk round, **coax** (someone) —w.ACC. *into sthg.* Od.; **dissuade** (someone, fr. doing sthg.) Od.
2 encourage, cheer (someone) Od.
3 speak comfortingly —w.ACC. *about death* Od.

παραυιδών (Lacon.aor.2 ptcpl.): see παροράω

παραυλίζω *vb.* [πάραυλος] (of a rock) be adjacent to, **abut** —w.DAT. *a cliff* E.

πάρ-αυλος ον *adj.* [αὐλή] having a dwelling nearby; (of a person) **living close by** (a city) S.; (fig., of a cry) **nearby, from close at hand** S.

πάραυτα (or **παραυτά**) *adv.* [παρά, αὐτά] **1** near the time of events themselves; **immediately afterwards** A. D.; **immediately after** —w.NOM.AOR.PTCPL. *doing sthg.* Plb.
2 for the immediate present, **at first** (opp. later) Plb.
3 (quasi-adj., of an advantage) **immediate, instant** Plb.

παρ-αυτίκα *adv.* **1** (sts.w. τό) **immediately, instantly, at once** A. Hdt. E. Th. Ar. Plb. Plu.
2 (sts.w. τό) **for the immediate present, at first** (opp. later) Hdt. Th. Isoc. Plb. Plu.

3 ‖ NEUT.SB. (w. τό) the immediate present Arist.; (prep.phrs.) ἐν τῷ παραυτίκα *in the immediate present* Th. Pl. X. Plu.; (also) ἐς τὸ παραυτίκα νῦν Hdt.; ἐκ τοῦ παραυτίκα *instantly* Plu.
4 (quasi-adj., of death, splendour, hope, pleasure, or sim.) **immediate, instant** E. Th. Pl. X. D. Plb.

παρα-φαίνω, dial. **παρφαίνω** (Ar.) *vb.* **1** allow (a part of the body) to be visible beyond (the edge of a garment); (of a man) **reveal, expose** —*his genitals* Hes.; (of a woman) —*no part of her body* Ar.; (of a soldier) —*battle scars* Plu. ‖ PASS. (of a woman's breast) be exposed Call.; (fig., of a weak spot in the mind of a commander) Plb.; (of the similarity of a statue's features to those of a person) be visible only from certain angles Plu.
2 ‖ PASS. (of foot-soldiers hidden behind cavalry) become visible X.; (of the sun) Plu.; (of a person, an animal) show up, appear Men. Plu.
3 ‖ PASS. (of gold) come into circulation (as currency) X.; (of tragedy and comedy) emerge, come on the scene Arist.; (of a war) break out Plu.
4 make (sthg.) manifest; **unveil, set out** —*an oath* (i.e. the procedure for swearing it) Ar. ‖ PASS. (of a new argument in a discussion) be disclosed Pl.; (of a calamity) come into sight Pl.
5 (intr., of a torchbearer) **go beside** (someone) **and light the way** Ar. —w.DAT. *for someone* Plu.

παρα-φέρω, dial. **παρφέρω** *vb.* **1** bring forward, **produce, exhibit** —*skulls* (as trophies) Hdt. —*goads and whips* (as threats) Hdt.
2 present, serve —*items of food* (sts. w.DAT. *to someone*) Hdt. Philox.Leuc. X. ‖ PASS. (of food) be served Hdt. Pl.
3 bring forward in speech, **advance, present** —*a tale of woe* E.; **adduce, cite** (in support of an argument) —*one's achievements* Hdt. —*a law* Antipho —*a person, a name* Aeschin. Hyp.; **tell of** —*one's sufferings* S.(dub.)
4 bring to the next person in a series; **take along** —*a watchword* (w.DAT. *to company-commanders*) E. ‖ PASS. (of a sentry's bell) be taken along (to the next sentry) Th.
5 carry (w.ACC. torches) **beside** —w.DAT. *a chariot* E.
6 carry (objects) **past** (a screen) Pl. ‖ PASS. (of objects) be carried past Pl.; (of horsemen) ride past Plu.; (of hares) rush past X.; (fig., of an argument, envisaged as a river) Pl.; (of a storm) pass by Plu.
7 let pass, ignore, overlook —*the time for a sacrifice* D.(oracle) —*a remark* Plu.
8 (intr., of days) be past (a total), **be additional** (to a number of years, in the calculation of a period of time) Th.
9 (of a river) **carry** (w.ACC. *someone*) **along** Plu. ‖ PASS. (of sailors) make one's way along (w. punt-poles) Plu.
10 move (sthg.) to the side; (of an orator) **wave** —*his hand* (w.ADV. *in this or that direction*) D.; (of soldiers) **turn aside, deflect** —*a spear* (w. their hands) Plu.; (of bodyguards) **carry** (w.ACC. a person) **out of the way** Plu.; (of God) **take away, remove** —*a cup of sorrows* NT.
11 move (sthg.) in the wrong direction ‖ PASS. (of paralysed limbs) move awry Arist.; (fig., of persons) be led astray (in their perceptions) Pl.; stray (fr. the truth) Pl.

παρα-φεύγω, ep. **παρφεύγω** *vb.* | *ep.aor.2 inf.* παρφυγέειν | (of sailors) **pass safely by** (a place) Od.; (of elephants) **flee past** Plb.

παρά-φημι, ep. **παραίφημι**, dial. **πάρφᾱμι** *vb.* [φημί] | *dial.pres.* or *athem.aor.inf.* παρφάμεν ‖ MID.: *dial.pres.* or *athem.aor.inf.* παρφάσθαι, *ptcpl.* παρφάμενος, ep. παραιφάμενος |

1 talk (someone) round; **advise** —W.DAT. + INF. *someone to do sthg.* Il.
2 ‖ MID. **win over, persuade, coax** —*someone* Hom. hHom. Parm. AR.; **speak persuasively** Hes. —W.INTERN.ACC. *certain words* AR.
3 **utter deceptively** —*a speech, an oath* Pi. ‖ MID. **beguile, deceive** —*someone* Pi.; **say** (W.ACC. *certain things*) **deceitfully** AR.

παρα-φθάνω *vb.* | ep.athem.aor.: 3sg.opt. παραφθαίησι (dub.), ptcpl. παραφθάς, mid.ptcpl. παραφθάμενος | (act. and mid., of a runner, a charioteer) **get past and ahead of, outstrip** —*someone* Il.

παρα-φθέγγομαι *mid.vb.* 1 **say** (sthg.) **aside from the point at issue; add a superfluous remark** (as an answer to a q.) Pl.
2 **remark casually** —W.COMPL.CL. *that sthg. is the case* Is. Hyp.; **remark privately** (sts. W.COMPL.CL.) Plb. Plu.

παρά-φθεγμα ατος *n.* **superfluous remark** (as an answer to a q.) Pl.

παρα-φορά ᾶς *f.* **distraction, derangement** (of the mind) A. Plu.

παρα-φορέω *contr.vb.* 1 **present, serve up** —*food* (W.DAT. *to someone*) Ar. ‖ PASS. (of food) **be served** Hdt.
2 **bring along** —*rubble* (as material for wall-building) Ar. ‖ MID. **gather materials together** Pl.

παράφορος ον *adj.* [παραφέρω] 1 (of a blinded person's step) **carried astray, reeling** E.; (of movement) **erratic, lurching** Plu.; (fig., of a drunken person) **awkward, clumsy** (W.INF. at sowing seed, ref. to procreation) Pl.
2 (of moving things) **carried aside from, missing** (W.GEN. a target) Pl.; (of a soul aiming for truth, W.GEN. understanding) Pl.
3 (fig., of a person) **carried away** (by ambition) Plu.
4 (of a person) **deranged** Plu.; (of stories) **crazy** Plu.

παραφορότης ητος *f.* **awkward movement** (of an ill-proportioned body) Pl.

παρα-φράγματα τῶν *n.pl.* 1 (milit.) **defensive fortifications, parapets** (of wood) Th.; **bulwarks** or **screens** (on a ship) Th.
2 (gener.) **screen** (for concealment) Pl.

παρα-φράσσομαι *pass.vb.* (of an area) **be provided with screens** Plb.

παραφρονέω *contr.vb.* [παράφρων] 1 **be out of one's mind, deranged** or **mad** Hdt. Ar. Att.orats. +
2 (pejor.) **be crazy** (in the eyes of a person disapproving of one's speech or behaviour) Hdt. Ar. Att.orats. +
3 **act like a madman** (fr. intoxication) Hdt.; **be frantic** (fr. fear, pain) A. S.
4 **be senseless, be dazed** (fr. a blow) Theoc.

παραφρόνιμος ον *adj.* (of a person) **out of one's senses, mad** S.

παραφροσύνη ης *f.* **mental aberration, derangement** Pl. Plu.

παρα-φρυκτωρεύομαι *mid.vb.* [φρυκτωρός] **make secret beacon-signals** —W.DAT. *to the enemy* Lys.

παρά-φρων (also dial. **πάρφρων**) ον, gen. ονος *adj.* [φρήν] 1 (of persons) **out of one's mind, senseless, deranged, mad** E. Plu.; (wkr.sens.) **lacking in sense** or **judgement** S. Pl.
2 (of frenzy) **maddening** B.

παραφυάς άδος *f.* [παραφύομαι] **side-growth**; (fig., ref. to the category of Relation) **offshoot** (W.GEN. of the category of Being) Arist.

παραφυής ές *adj.* ‖ NEUT.SB. (ref. to rhetoric) **offshoot** (W.GEN. of dialectic) Arist.

παραφυλακή ῆς *f.* [παραφυλάσσω] **garrison** (in a city) Plb.

παρα-φυλάσσω, Att. **παραφυλάττω** *vb.* 1 (of soldiers, commanders) **guard closely** —*a place* Plb. Plu.; **garrison** —*a city, a region* Plb. Plu.; (intr., of a cohort) **be on guard-duty** Plu.; (fig., of a garrison) **stand guard over** —*the liberty and safety* (*of a populace*) Plb. ‖ MID. (of a commander) **have** (W.ACC. *places*) **garrisoned** Plb. ‖ PASS. (of persons) **be under guard** Plb. Plu.
2 (of soldiers) **guard against, be on the watch for** —*an attack* Plb. ‖ MID. **be on watch** Plb.
3 (gener., of persons) **keep a close eye on** —*someone or sthg.* Ar.(cj.) Pl. X. Plu.; **watch out for** —*an opportunity* Hyp. Plu.; **be careful to ensure** —W.COMPL.CL. *that sthg. shd. be the case* Pl. Hyp. D. ‖ MID. (of a historian) **be on one's guard** (against making biased judgements) Plb. ‖ PASS. (of Odysseus) **be watched closely, be dogged** —W.PREP.PHR. *by Poseidon* Arist.

παρα-φύομαι *pass.vb.* | statv.pf.act. παραπέφυκα | 1 (of a pod) **grow at the side** (of a plant) Hdt.
2 (of a tree) **grow nearby** Plu.

παρα-χαλάω *contr.vb.* (of a part of a boat) **become slack, spring a leak** Ar.

παρα-χειμάζω *vb.* (of persons) **spend the winter** (usu. W.ADV. or PREP.PHR. *somewhere*) D. Plb. NT. Plu.; (of a ship) NT.

παραχειμασία ᾶς *f.* **wintering, winter stay** (in a place) Plb. NT.; (concr.) **winter quarters** Plb.

παρα-χέω *contr.vb.* 1 **pour in besides, add** (to a paste) —*water* Hdt.
2 **heap up** (W.ACC. *soil*) **along** —w. παρά + ACC. *the banks of a river* Hdt.

παρα-χορδίζω *vb.* [χορδή] | fut. παραχορδιῶ | (fig., ref. to behaviour) **strike a wrong note** Ar.

παρα-χόω *contr.vb.* **heap up** (W.ACC. *an embankment*) **along** —w. παρά + ACC. *the banks of a river* Hdt.

παρα-χράομαι *mid.contr.vb.* | Ion.ptcpl. παραχρεώμενος | 1 **misuse, abuse** —W.DAT. *one's wealth* (by prodigal behaviour) Plu.(quot. Arist.) —*one's body, oneself* (in prostitution) Plu.
2 **deal casually or perversely** (w. persons or things); **treat casually, take lightly, have no regard for** —W.ACC. *an oracle, a warrior class* Hdt.; **mishandle** —*a task* Hdt.
3 (intr.) **behave casually, be indifferent** —w. ἐς + ACC. *to someone* Hdt.; (of soldiers) **fight with reckless disregard for one's life** Hdt.; **underestimate the enemy** Hdt.

παρα-χρῆμα *adv.* 1 (sts.w. τό) **on the spot, immediately, instantly, at once** Hdt. Th. Ar. Att.orats. +
2 (sts.w. τό) **for the immediate present, at first** (opp. later) Hdt. Th. Critias Plu.
3 (prep.phrs.) εἰς (ἐς) τὸ παραχρῆμα *for the immediate present, for a moment* Antipho Th. Pl.; ἐκ τοῦ παραχρῆμα *on the spur of the moment* Th. Pl. X. D.; (also) ἀπὸ τοῦ παραχρῆμα X.; ἐν τῷ παραχρῆμα *instantly* Antipho And. Pl.
4 (quasi-adjl., of necessity, fear, pleasure) **immediate** Th. Pl. ‖ NEUT.PL.SB. (w. τά) **immediate issues** (opp. future eventualities) Th.

παρα-χρώζομαι *pass.vb.* | pf.ptcpl. παρακεχρωσμένος | (of harmonies and melodies) **be irregular in colouring** (perh.ref. to being highly ornamented) Arist.

παρα-χωρέω *contr.vb.* | fut. παραχωρήσομαι (D.) | 1 **move over, step aside, give way** Ar. Pl. —W.DAT. *to someone* X.; (gener.) **retire, withdraw** Plb. Plu.
2 (of a speaker) **yield the floor** And. Pl. D. —W.DAT. *to someone* Isoc.
3 **give up, withdraw from** —W.GEN. *occupied territory or sim.* Plb.; **step aside from, give up** —W.GEN. *kingship* D. Arist. —*a line of legal defence* Aeschin. —(fig.) *honourable behaviour* (envisaged as a military post) D.

παραχώρησις

4 step aside from and yield (to another); **yield, surrender** —W.GEN. *a road* (W.DAT. *to an elder or superior, i.e. make way for him*) X.; (of a speaker) —*a platform* (*to someone*) Aeschin.; (fig., of a channelled-off river) —*a route* (*to troops*) X.; (of people) —*one's country, city, freedom* (*to an enemy*) Isoc. D. —*one's property* (*to a slave*) D. —*political power, military command, the right to honours, or sim.* (*to someone*) Aeschin. D. Plb. Plu. —*the task of punishment* (*to the state*) D.
5 give way, yield —W.DAT. *to someone* Pl. —(W.GEN. *in respect of some ability*) Pl. —*to someone's esteem* (*i.e. to someone in esteem*) Arist.
6 leave an opportunity —W.DAT. + INF. *for someone to do sthg.* Pl. Plu.

παραχώρησις εως *f.* **withdrawal** (by a person, W.GEN. fr. a military command) Plu.

παρα-ψάλλω *vb.* **lightly twang** —*bowstrings* Plu.

παρα-ψαύω *vb.* (of a breastplate) **touch with the edge, touch** —W.GEN. *the wearer's groin* Plu.

παρα-ψιδάζω *vb.* [ψιάς] **spatter** (someone) —W.DAT. *w. shit* Hippon.

παρά-ψογοι ων *m.pl.* **indirect censures** (ref. to examples of a rhetorical technique which were composed by the sophistic poet Evenus of Paros) Pl.

παρα-ψυκτήριον ου *n.* (ref. to a musical instrument) **refreshment, comfort, consolation** (W.GEN. for grief) S.*Ichn.*

παραψυχή ῆς *f.* [παραψύχω] cooling or refreshment; (fig., ref. to a person) **comfort, consolation** E.; (W.GEN. for one's sorrows) E.; (W.GEN. in life) Is.; (ref. to seeing a defendant reduced to silence) D.; (ref. to the glory of one's dead sons) D.

παρα-ψύχω *vb.* [ψύχω¹] **cool down, calm, soothe** —*a hot-tempered person* Call. ‖ MID. **comfort, console** —*a person grieving* Theoc.

παρβάδᾱν *dial.adv.* [παραβαίνω, βάδην] **by transgression, lawlessly** A.

παρβαίνω *ep.vb.*: see παραβαίνω

παρβασίᾱ ᾱς *dial.f.* **transgression, crime** A. | cf. παραιβασίη

παρβατός *dial.adj.*: see παραβατός

παρβεβαώς (ep.pf.ptcpl.): see παραβαίνω

παρβολάδην *ep.adv.* [παράβολος] **alongside** (a ship) —*ref. to dolphins appearing* AR.

παρδακός όν *adj.* (of clothes) **wet** Semon.; (of ground) **sodden** Ar.

παρδαλέᾱ ᾱς (also contr. **παρδαλῆ** ῆς), Ion. **παρδαλέη** ης *f.* [πάρδαλις] **leopard-skin, panther-skin** (as a garment) Il. Pi. Hdt. Ar.

πάρδαλις (also **πόρδαλις**) εως (Ion. ιος) *f.* [loanwd.] **leopard** or **panther** Hom. hHom. Semon. S.*Ichn.* Ar. Pl. +

παρέᾱσι (ep.3pl.): see πάρειμι¹

παρέγγραπτος ον *adj.* [παρεγγράφω] (of a man) **illegally registered** (as a citizen) Aeschin.

παρ-εγγράφω *vb.* [παρά] **1** (leg.) **inscribe** (W.ACC. one's name) **by the side** (of others) Pl.
2 write in additionally (w.connot. of dishonesty), **insert, interpolate** —*a clause, name, verse, or sim.* (W.DAT. or PREP.PHR. *in a document or sim.*) Aeschin. Plu.
3 ‖ PASS. be illegally enrolled (as a citizen) Aeschin.

παρ-εγγυάω *contr.vb.* **1 entrust, commend, recommend** —*someone* (W.DAT. *to one's friends*) Hdt.; **entrust** —*one's daughter* (W.DAT. *to a guardian*) Men.; (of Chance) **assign** —*a slave* (W.DAT. *to a master*) Men.; (of a consul) —*his office, troops* (*to someone*) Plu.
2 (of soldiers, commanders) **pass on** (down the line) —*an exhortation, a watchword* (sts. W.DAT. *to someone*) E. X. Plu.; **pass on an order** (sts. W.DAT. *to someone*) X. Plb. Plu. —W.INF. or ACC. + INF. *to do sthg., that sthg. shd. be done* X. Plu. ‖ IMPERS.PASS. the order is given X.
3 (of a god, through his oracle) **pass on an assurance, promise** —W.DAT. *to someone* (W.ACC. + FUT.INF. *that sthg. will happen*) S.
4 ‖ MID. (of one about to die) **make a request** —W.DAT. + INF. *to someone to do sthg.* Plu.

παρεγγύη ης *f.* (milit.) **order which is passed on, order** X.

παρεγγύησις εως *f.* (milit.) **passing on of orders** X.

πάρ-εγγυς *adv. and prep.* [ἐγγύς] **1** (quasi-adjl., ref. to persons) **near, close** (in age) Arist.
2 (quasi-adjl., ref. to a constitution) **close** (in resemblance) —W.GEN. *to another* Arist. ‖ NEUT.PL.SB. (w. τά) closely related parts (W.GEN. of the soul) Arist.

παρ-εγείρω *vb.* **partly lift up** —*horses* (i.e. raise their forelegs fr. the ground w. ropes, for exercise in a confined space) Plu.

παρ-εγκλίνω *vb.* (of a constitution) **diverge** —W.GEN. *fr. an earlier one* Arist. ‖ PF.PASS.PTCPL.ADJ. (of the sun's course) having a slight inclination (to the plane of the ecliptic) Plu.

παρέγκλισις εως *f.* **shift** (W.GEN. of posture, by a speaker changing the direction in which he faces) Plu.

παρ-εγχειρέω *contr.vb.* **argue to the contrary** (in reply to an assertion) —W.COMPL.CL. *that sthg. is the case* Plu.

παρ-εγχέω *contr.vb.* **pour in additionally, add** —*vinegar* Arist.

παρέδραθον (ep.aor.2): see παραδαρθάνω

παρέδραμον (aor.2): see παραδραμεῖν

παρεδρεύω *vb.* [πάρεδρος] **1** (of a dead person, as a mark of honour) **sit beside** —W.DAT. *Persephone, Pluto* E. Isoc.; (of a ship's commander) —*the steering-oar or tiller* E.*fr.*
2 (at Athens) **act as assessor** or **assistant** (to an archon) D. Arist. —W.DAT. Aeschin. D.
3 (of envoys, a commander) **remain on the spot** (to watch or wait for sthg.) Plb.

παρεδριάω *contr.vb.* | pres.ptcpl. (w.diect.) παρεδριόων | (of a rower) **sit beside** (someone) AR.

πάρ-εδρος ον *adj.* [ἕδρᾱ] **1** (of a person) **sitting alongside** (sts. W.DAT. someone or sthg.) Hdt. E.; (of a debate among the gods) **in session beside** (W.DAT. Zeus) E.
2 (of Themis, Eileithuia, other deities, ref. to their status or function) **enthroned beside** (W.GEN. or DAT. Zeus, other deities) Pi. S.(dub.) E. Ar.; (of the Pythian priestess) **whose seat is close by** (W.GEN. the eagles of Zeus) Pi.

—**πάρεδρος** ον *m.f.* **1** (ref. to Hera) sharer of the throne, **consort** (W.GEN. of Zeus) B.; (ref. to Menelaos, alongside the deified Helen) Isoc.; (ref. to Rhadamanthys) **assistant, counsellor** (W.DAT. to Kronos) Pi.; (ref. to a god, a human acolyte) **companion** (usu. W.GEN. of a deity) Pi. E. AR.; (ref. to Victory) **attendant** (W.GEN. at dramatic contests) Men.; (gener., ref. to a god or mortal) **associate, adviser** E.
2 (ref. to an official) **counsellor** (W.GEN. of the Persian king) Hdt.; (at Athens) **assessor, assistant** (to an archon) Is. D. Arist.; (to a public examiner) And.(decree) Arist.
3 (at Rome) **associate** (W.GEN. in office) Plu.
4 (*f.*) **attendant** (to a woman in labour) Plu.

παρ-έζομαι *mid.vb.* | impf. (or aor.2) παρεζόμην | **sit alongside** (usu. W.DAT. someone) Hom. —w. παρά + ACC. *someone* Thgn.

παρεθῆναι (aor.pass.inf.): see παρίημι

παρέθρεξα (aor.): see παρατρέχω

παρέθρισα (dial.aor.): see παραθερίζω

παρειά ᾶς, Ion. **παρειή** ῆς, Aeol. **παραύα** ᾶς (Theoc.) *f.* [παρά, οὖς] **cheek** (esp. in ctxt. of weeping or tearing in grief) Hom. Hes. Simon. Hdt. Trag. Pl. +; (of an eagle) Od.

παρείας ου *m.* (sts. appos.w. ὄφις) a kind of snake (assoc.w. the worship of Asklepios and Sabazios), **sacred snake** Ar. D. Thphr.

παρείατο (3sg. and 3pl. impf.mid.): see πάρημαι

παρεῖδον (aor.2): see παροράω

παρείθην (aor.pass.), **παρεῖκα** (pf.act.): see παρίημι

παρ-εικάζω *vb.* **1 make up** (W.ACC. a name for a category) **in an analogous way** (to names for other categories) Pl.
2 liken, compare —*one person or thing* (W.DAT. *to another*) Arist. Plu.

παρ-είκω *vb.* | aor.2 παρείκαθον | **1 give way, yield** (to persons) S. Plu. —W.DAT. *to circumstances* Plu.
2 (of a person's ability, terrain, laws) **allow** (sthg.) Th. Pl. Plu.; (of a god) —W.DAT. or DAT. + INF. *someone* (*to do sthg.*) Pl.
3 ‖ IMPERS. **it is practicable or possible** (sts. W.DAT. for someone) S. Th. Pl. —W.INF. *to do sthg.* Pl.

παρείμαι (pf.mid.pass.), **παρείμην** (athem.aor.mid.): see παρίημι

πάρ-ειμι[1] *vb.* [εἰμί] | ep.3pl. παρέᾱσι | inf. παρεῖναι, ep. παρέμμεναι | Ion.ptcpl. παρεών | Ion.subj. παρέω | impf. παρῆν, also παρῇ, ep. παρέην (Call.), 3sg. παρῆν, ep. παρῆεν, (tm.) πάρ ... ἔην, ep.3pl. πάρεσαν | ep.fut. παρέσσομαι ‖ see also πάρα (used for 3sg. πάρεστι, 3pl. πάρεισι) |
1 (of persons) **be present** (opp. absent) Hom. + —W.DAT. or PREP.PHR. *at some event* Hom. +
2 be in company with (a person, esp. habitually); **be with** —W.DAT. *someone* Hom. +
3 (esp. in military or legal ctxts.) **be with or beside someone as helper**; **stand by** (usu. W.DAT. someone) Hom. Trag. +
4 (impf. and fut.) **come** or (pres.) **have come** Hdt. + —W.PREP.PHR. or ADV. *to a place* Hdt. + —W.ACC. E. —W.DAT. or PREP.PHR. *to a person* (*e.g. to their house*) Hdt. +
5 (of desirable things) **be at hand, be available** (oft. W.DAT. for someone) Hom. +
6 (of circumstances or feelings, such as war, trouble, fear, wonder) **be present** or **arise** (oft. W.DAT. for someone) Hdt. Trag.
7 ‖ PRES.PTCPL.ADJ. (of circumstances, events, time) **present, current** A. + ‖ NEUT.PTCPL.SB. (sg. and pl., w.art.) **present state of affairs, present circumstances** Hdt. +; (acc.sg.adv.) **just now** Pl.
8 ‖ IMPERS. **the opportunity is present, it is possible** —W.INF. or DAT. + INF. (*for someone*) *to do sthg.* Anacr. Hdt. Trag. + ‖ NEUT.PTCPL. **it being possible** (for sthg. to be the case) Hdt. +

πάρ-ειμι[2] *vb.* [εἶμι] | impf. παρῄειν, Ion. παρήια, 3pl. παρήισαν | neut.pl.impers.vbl.adj. παριτητέα (Th.) ‖ Only pres. and impf. (other tenses are supplied by παρέρχομαι). The pres.indic. has fut. sense. |
1 (of persons or things) **go past, pass by** (someone or somewhere) Od. Eleg. Simon. Hdt. E.*Cyc.* + —W.ACC. or παρά + ACC. *a person, a place* Hdt. And. Pl. X.
2 pass by, overtake, surpass —*someone* X.
3 (of guards) **walk alongside** (prisoners) Th.
4 (of troops) **go along the coast** Th. X.
5 (of a speaker) **pass on, go on** (fr. one point to another) Ar. Pl.
6 (of a military watchword) **pass on, be passed along** X.
7 (of soldiers, groups of people) **go on, go forward, advance** Hdt. Ar. Pl. X. +; (fig., of an individual, in repute or influence) Hdt.
8 (of persons) **approach** (a building, w. a view to entering); **go on** —W.ADV. *inside* E. —W.PREP.PHR. *into a building* Hdt. E. X.; **pass inside** Hdt. Pl.
9 (of a speaker) **come forward** Th. Att.orats. Pl. —W.PREP.PHR. *to the rostrum* Isoc. Aeschin.

παρεῖναι[1] (inf.): see πάρειμι[1]

παρεῖναι[2] (athem.aor.inf.): see παρίημι

παρ-εῖπον aor.2 *vb.* | ep.sts. πᾰρ- | **1 talk round, win over, persuade** —*someone, his mind* Il. A.; **speak persuasively** Il.
2 urge, advise —*a fair course of action* Il.

παρ-ειρύω *Ion.vb.* [ἐρύω] | aor. παρείρυσα | **stretch out** (a structure) **alongside**; **run** (W.ACC. a fence) **along the side** (of a bridge) Hdt.

παρ-είρω *vb.* [εἴρω[1]] | aor. παρεῖρα | **1 thread in or insert** (sthg.); **insert** —*one's hand* (*into a cluster of intertwining branches*) Plb.; (in neg.phr., illustrating shortage of space) —*not even a hair, not even a word* (*during the course of others' conversation, i.e. not get a word in edgeways*) X.
2 (fig.) **weave in** —*laws and justice* (*to the texture of life*) S.(dub.)

παρείς (athem.aor.ptcpl.): see παρίημι

παρεῖσα (aor.): see παρίζω

παρ-εισάγω *vb.* **1 lead in by one's side, bring forward, introduce** —*persons* (*before an audience or sim.*) Isoc. Plb. Plu.
2 bring in, introduce —*troops* (sts. W.PREP.PHR. *into a city*) Plb. Plu. ‖ PASS. (of troops, supplies) **be brought in** Plb.
3 appoint (to an office, fr. an inferior rank), **promote** —*someone* Plb.; **put forward** (for an office), **propose** —*someone* Plu.
4 introduce —*customs, practices* Plb.
5 (of writers) **introduce into a narrative, introduce, represent** —*persons, things* Plb.

παρεῖσαν (3pl.athem.aor.): see παρίημι

παρ-εισδέχομαι (or -εσδέχομαι) *mid.vb.* **take in** (someone) **incidentally or additionally**; (of a wife) **take in** (to her house) —*her husband's mistress* (*envisaged as excess freight*) S.

παρ-εισδύομαι *mid.vb.* | athem.aor.act. παρεισέδῡν | (fig., of a vice) **creep, slip** —W.PREP.PHR. *into a city* Plu.; (perh. of a lover) **ingratiate oneself** Call.*epigr.*

παρ-είσειμι *vb.* **go in** (sts. W.PREP.PHR. *to a city*) Plb.

παρ-εισέρχομαι *mid.vb.* | aor.2 παρεισῆλθον | **go in** (to a place, sts. w.connot. of stealth) Plb. Plu. —W.PREP.PHR. *to a place* Plb. Plu.

παρείσθω (3sg.pf.pass.imperatv.): see παρίημι

παρ-εισπίπτω *vb.* (of soldiers) **rush in** (sts. W.PREP.PHR. to a city) Plb. Plu.; (of a mule) **happen to come** (to a place, opp. be driven) Plu.

παρ-εισρέω *contr.vb.* (of people) **stream in** —W.PREP.PHR. *to a city* Plu.; **slip or creep in** —W.PREP.PHR. *to a building* Plu.

παρ-εισφέρω *vb.* **bring in** (sthg.) **besides**; **introduce** (W.ACC. a law) **as an alternative** (to an existing law) D. ‖ PASS. (of a law) **be introduced as an alternative** D.

παρ-έκ (or **πάρεκ**), also (only before a vowel in Att., but always in Ion.) **παρέξ** (or **πάρεξ**) *prep. and adv.*
—**A** *prep.* **1** (ref. to position) **along and out of, alongside** —W.ACC. *the sea* Il. Hes.*fr.*; **across the mouth** —W.GEN. *of a harbour* Od.
2 aside from, off —W.GEN. *a path* Il. hHom.; **away from** —W.GEN. *somewhere* AR.

παρεκβαίνω

3 past and away from, **past, beyond** —W.ACC. *someone, somewhere* Hom. hHom. AR. —W.GEN. AR.
4 (fig.phr.) παρὲξ ὀλίγον *within an inch* —W.GEN. *of death* AR.
5 (abstr., oppositional) **contrary to, in defiance of** —W.ACC. *good sense* Il. hHom. —*right, expectation* Call. —*someone's knowledge, wishes, oracular advice* AR. —W.GEN. *an omen* AR.; **without the knowledge of** —W.ACC. *someone* Il. —W.GEN. AR.; **differently** —W.GEN. *fr. someone* Hdt.
6 (additional) **aside from, apart from, besides** —W.ACC. *sthg.* Archil. —W.GEN. *someone or sthg.* Parm. Hdt. Plb. Plu.
—**B** *adv.* **1** (ref. to movt. or position) **along** (a shore) **outside** (the breakers) —*ref. to swimming* Od.; **along the edge** (of a court) **outside** (a palace) —*ref. to a colonnade extending* AR.
2 forwards and beside, **forth beside** (someone) —*ref. to a warrior coming to take a stand* Il.
3 (ref. to movt.) **away past** (a place) Od.; **away** (fr. a place) Od. AR.; **out of the way, aside** Hes.
4 (ref. to speaking) **away from the point, inappropriately** Hom.; **obliquely** Od.; **on a different subject** Od.
5 (quasi-adjl., in phr. w. ἄλλο *another thing*, μηδέν *nothing*) **besides, more** AR. Plb. Mosch.
6 (marking an exception to a period of time) πάρεξ ἢ ὅσον *except for as long as* Hdt.

παρεκ-βαίνω *vb.* **1** move aside and out; (of soldiers) **step out** —w. ἐκ + GEN. *fr. their ranks* Plb.
2 (of persons) **deviate from** —W.GEN. *justice, virtue, duty, or sim.* Hes. Arist. Plb. Plu.; (of a form of government) **diverge from** —W.GEN. *another* Arist. ‖ PF.PTCPL.ADJ. (of a form of government, a nose) deviant, divergent (fr. an approved or perfect form) Arist.
3 overstep, **transgress, offend against** —W.ACC. *the majesty of Zeus* A. —*prophecies* AR.(tm.); (intr.) **commit offences or transgressions** Arist.; (of a law) **be faulty** Arist.
4 forsake, abandon —W.ACC. *customary practices* Arist. Plb. Plu.
5 (of a writer) **digress** Plb. —W.GEN. *fr. a subject* Plb. —W.ADV. or ἀπό + GEN. *at a certain point* Arist. Plb.

παρέκβασις εως *f.* **1** deviation (W.GEN. fr. justice) Arist.; (fr. customary behaviour) Plu.; (of a form of government, sts. W.GEN. fr. another form) Arist.; (in harmony or melody) Arist.
2 digression (by a speaker or writer) Is. Plb. Plu.

παρεκ-δέχομαι *mid.vb.* take in a wrong way, **misrepresent** —*arguments* Plb.

παρεκ-δραμεῖν *aor.2 inf.* (of soldiers) **rush out from the flanks** (of an army, against the enemy's flanks) Plu.

παρεκέσκετο (3sg.iteratv.impf.): see παράκειμαι

παρεκ-θέω *contr.vb.* [θέω¹] (of sailors) **speed past** —*a place* AR.

παρεκ-κλίνω *vb.* (intr.) turn aside, **deviate** (fr. the proper line of conduct) Aeschin.; (of a word) **diverge** —W.GEN. *fr. another* (*in form*) Arist.

παρεκ-λέγω *vb.* collect underhandedly, **embezzle** —*public funds* D.

παρεκ-νέομαι *mid.contr.vb.* (of sailors) **go past** —*a place, a people* AR.

παρεκ-προφεύγω *vb.* (of prizes) **slip away past, elude** —*someone* Il.

παρεκ-τείνω *vb.* **1** (of a military or naval commander) **extend one's battle-line** Plb.; (tr.) **extend** —*one's siegeworks* Plb.
2 stretch out (W.ACC. *a corpse*) **alongside** —W.DAT. *another* Plu. ‖ PASS. (of a snake) be stretched out alongside —W.DAT. *the body of a sleeping person* Plu.; (of a camp) —w. παρά + ACC. *a river* Plu.

παρ-εκτός *prep.* apart from, except for —W.GEN. *sthg.* NT.

παρεκ-τρέπω *vb.* (fig.) turn aside, divert —*the stream* (*of one's life*) E.

παρ-ελαύνω *vb.* —also **παρελάω** *dial.contr.vb.* | dial.acc.sg. pres.ptcpl. παρελᾶντα (Theoc.) | aor. παρήλασα, ep. παρέλασσα |
1 (of a charioteer) **drive past, overtake** —*another* Il. Hes.; (fig., of a poet) —*his rivals* Ar.; (of two charioteers) **drive** (W.ACC. *their chariots*) **past** (each other, in opposite directions) Ar.
2 (of a charioteer) **outrun, outstrip** —*another* Il.; (fig., of a notion) **leave behind** —*persons* (*i.e. elude their comprehension*) Parm.
3 (of horsemen) **ride along** (sts. W.PREP.PHR. *to a person*) X. Plu.; **ride past** (someone) X. Plu.; (specif.) ride past troops marching or stationed ahead, **ride up** (sts. W.PREP.PHR. *to the front*) X.; (of a commander) **ride** (W.ACC. *a horse*) **up** —W.PREP.PHR. *to the front* X.
4 (of a commander in a chariot or on horseback, inspecting or addressing troops) **ride past** X. —W.ACC. *troops* X.; (of a horseman) **ride along** —W.PREP.PHR. *beside a ditch* Plb.
5 (of a herdsman) **drive** (W.ACC. *goats, heifers*) **past** (someone) Theoc.
6 (of sailors) **row past** (a place) Od. —W.ACC. *persons* Od.

παρ-έλκω *vb.* | aor. παρείλκυσα | **1** (fig., of forgetfulness) draw aside, **displace, wrest** —*the straight path of action* (W.PREP.PHR. *fr. the mind*) Pi.
2 drag along —*a wounded person, a weapon embedded in one's flesh* Plu.
3 (fig. and pejor., of a philosopher) **drag in** —*mind* (*as an agent*) Arist.; (of a playwright) **drag on** (i.e. on stage) —*a play* Ar. ‖ PASS. (of a type of knowledge) be dragged along beside, be a mere appendage —W.DAT. *to a profession* Plb.
4 (of camels harnessed one on each side of another, like trace-horses) **pull at the side** Hdt. ‖ PASS. (of a boat) be towed from the side (i.e. fr. the bank) Hdt.
5 drag (sthg.) in a pointless or dishonest way; (of lazy rowers) perh. **pull idly** or **pretend to pull** —*their oars* Ar. ‖ MID. draw to oneself by false pretences, **beguile, extract** —*gifts* (*fr. people*) Od.
6 (intr.) **drag things out, procrastinate** (or perh. *evade the issue*) Od.; **delay** Plb.; (tr.) **defer** —*a military engagement* Plb. ‖ PASS. (of things) be deferred or delayed Plb.

παρ-εμβάλλω *vb.* **1** throw in additionally or incidentally; (of a speaker) **throw in, interject, introduce** —*a turn of phrase, irrelevant arguments, abuse, or sim.* Ar. D. Arist. Thphr.
2 (of citizens) **introduce** —*unqualified persons* (*into a city, to make up numbers in times of emergency*) Pl.
3 (of a commander) insert in a battle-line, **position** —*troops* Plb. Plu.; (gener.) **draw up, arrange** —*troops* Plb.; (intr.) **position one's troops** Plb. Plu.
4 (intr., of troops) **take up a position, station oneself** (either in battle formation or in an encampment) Plb. Plu.
5 (of a commander, troops) **advance** Plb.; (specif.) **make an incursion** (into a region) Plb. Plu.

παρ-εμβλέπω *vb.* (of a bull being manhandled) **cast a sideways look, squint** —W.PREP.PHR. *towards its horns* E.

παρεμβολή ῆς *f.* [παρεμβάλλω] **1** insertion (in a speech), **introduction, intrusion** (W.GEN. *of arguments, irrelevant matters*) Aeschin.
2 (milit.) **position** (ref. to battle formation or encampment) Plb.; (concr.) **encampment, camp** Plb. Plu.; **quarters** (in a camp) Plb.(pl.) Plu.; **barracks** (in a city) NT.

παρέμμεναι (ep.inf.): see πάρειμι¹

παρ-εμπίμπλημι *vb.* surreptitiously fill —*a place* (w.GEN. *w. soldiers*) Plu.

παρ-εμπίπτω *vb.* 1 (of water) force a way in (to a drowning animal's mouth) Plu.; (of unsuitable persons) intrude, infiltrate —W.PREP.PHR. *into the citizen body* Aeschin.; (of ignorance) creep in Pl.
2 (of a commander, troops) make an incursion Plu.

παρ-εμπολάω *contr.vb.* (fig., of a husband) smuggle in —*another marriage* (i.e. marry again in an underhand way) E.(dub.)

παρ-εμφαίνω *vb.* 1 (of a template which copies material forms) impose —*its visible features* (*upon them*) Pl.
2 (of a speaker or writer) indicate, suggest —W.ACC. or COMPL.CL. *sthg., that sthg. is the case* Plb. Plu.

παρενήνεον (ep.impf.): see παρανηνέω

παρ-ενήνοθε *ep.3sg.pf.* (of a person's planning) app. have reached (a certain stage) AR.

παρενθεῖν (dial.aor.2 inf.): see παρέρχομαι

παρ-ενθήκη ης *f.* [ἐντίθημι] 1 that which is put in besides, addition (to building works) Hdt.; appendix (to an oracular utterance) Hdt.; (W.GEN. to a speech, a narrative) Hdt.
2 activity filling an interval (W.GEN. in a war) Plu.

παρ-εννέπω *vb.* win (someone) over by speaking —*certain words* AR.

παρ-ενοχλέω *contr.vb.* 1 cause incidental annoyance, cause trouble, be annoying Hyp. Arist. Men. Plu.; trouble, annoy —*someone* Plu. ‖ PASS. be annoyed, feel annoyance D.
2 (specif., of troops, states, or sim.) cause trouble Plu. —W.DAT. *for someone* Plb.; trouble, harass —*the enemy, a populace* Plb. Plu. ‖ PASS. (of a commander) be harassed Plb.

παρ-ενσαλεύω *vb.* [ἐν, σαλεύω] (of a dancer imitating the Cyclops) perh. sway along —W.DAT. *on his feet* Ar.

παρ-εντείνω *vb.* stretch (a musical string) into (a lyre) in addition; (fig.) add as an extra string (to one's discourse) —*a philosopher* (i.e. his doctrines) Plu.

παρέξ, **πάρεξ** *prep. and adv.*: see παρέκ

παρεξ-άγω *vb.* (of Aphrodite) lead astray —*the mind of Zeus* hHom.(tm.)

παρεξ-αλλάσσω *vb.* change (sthg.) by comparison (w. what went before); (intr.) change one's tone of voice Men.

παρεξ-αμείβω *vb.* (of sailors) go past —*a place* AR.; (of a fighter) perh. get (W.ACC. his knee) past —W.GEN. *an opponent's knee* AR.(tm.)

παρεξ-αυλέομαι *pass.contr.vb.* | pf.ptcpl. παρεξηυλημένος | ‖ PF.PTCPL.ADJ. (fig., of an old man) played out like an aulos beyond (his natural life), played out Ar.

παρέξ-ειμι *vb.* [εἶμι] | ep.inf. παρεξίμεν ‖ Only pres. and impf. (other tenses are supplied by παρεξέρχομαι). The pres.indic. has fut. sense. |
1 go past, pass by Hdt. E. Plu. —*a place, a person* Hdt. Plu.; (fig., of a personif. argument wishing to escape notice) slip past Pl.
2 overstep, transgress, offend against —*the mysteries* hHom. —*a king's authority* S.; (of the plans of mortals) —*the governance of Zeus* A.

παρεξ-ειρεσίᾱ ᾶς *f.* (concr.) outrigger (structure built out fr. the sides of a trireme to support the thole-pins for the highest bank of oars) Th.

παρεξ-ελαύνω *vb.* | ep.2sg.aor.subj. παρεξελάσησθα | 1 (of a charioteer) drive past, overtake (competitors in a race) Il.; (of a horseman) ride past (someone) Plu.; (of two horsemen) ride in parallel —W.DAT. *to each other* Plu.; (gener., of horsemen) ride up, out or along Plu.

2 (of a commander) march past (a place) Hdt.
3 (of a ship, its captain) sail past —W.ACC. *a place* AR. Plu. —w. παρά + ACC. *enemy prows* Plu.

παρεξ-ερέομαι *mid.contr.vb.* inquire casually —W.ACC. *about sthg.* AR.(dub.)

παρεξ-έρχομαι *mid.vb.* | aor.2 παρεξῆλθον ‖ Impf. and fut. are supplied by παρέξειμι. | 1 go past, pass by (someone) Hom. Plu. —*a person* Hdt. —w. παρά + ACC. *a place* Plu.
2 go along the coast —w. ἐκ + GEN. *fr. a place* Th.
3 overstep, transgress —*a divine law* S.; override —*the mind of Zeus* Od.
4 deviate —W.GEN. *fr. the truth* Pl.

παρεξ-ετάζω *vb.* examine or scrutinise (W.ACC. people) by comparison —w. παρά + ACC. *w. others* D.

παρεξ-ευρίσκω *vb.* find in addition or by contrast (to an existing law) —*another law* Hdt.

παρεξ-ίστημι *vb.* | athem.aor. παρεξέστην | (intr.) change by comparison (w. what went before), be distracted or demented —W.DAT. *in one's mind* Plb.

παρ-έπαινοι ων *m.pl.* indirect praises (ref. to examples of a rhetorical technique which were composed by the sophistic poet Evenus of Paros) Pl.

παρεπιδημέω *contr.vb.* [παρεπίδημος] be a foreign resident (in a city or country) Plb.; pay a visit (to a country) Plb.

παρεπιδημίᾱ ᾶς *f.* residence or visit (by a foreigner) Plb.

παρ-επίδημος ον *adj.* (of a foreigner) residing abroad Plb.

παρ-επισκοπέω *contr.vb.* watch (W.ACC. events) from the sidelines Plu.

παρ-επιστροφή ῆς *f.* turning sideways (W.GEN. of one's face) towards (someone) Plu.

παρ-έπομαι *mid.vb.* 1 (of persons) follow close beside, accompany, attend (sts. W.DAT. someone or sthg.) X. Plb. Plu.
2 (of a listener) follow attentively Pl.
3 (of an event) follow in sequence, follow X.
4 (of existence) follow by natural association, be associated (w. all that is perceived) Pl.; (of gratification) —W.DAT. *w. food and drink* Pl.; (of behaviour) —*w. someone* Plb.

παρεπτάμην (aor.mid.), **παρέπτην** (athem.aor.act.), **παρεπτόμην** (aor.2 mid.): see παραπέτομαι

παρ-εργάτης ου *m.* one who produces what is superfluous to the main task; (pejor., ref. to a herald who adds his own commentary) meddler (W.GEN. w. words) E.

πάρ-εργον ου *n.* [ἔργον] 1 that which is beside the main task; side-issue, matter of secondary importance Th. Att.orats. Pl. Theoc. +; (opp. ἔργον) Pl. Arist.; (w. πρός + ACC. compared w. sthg.) D.; issue which is irrelevant (W.GEN. to someone's misfortunes) E.
2 adjunct (W.GEN. to someone's efforts) E.; additional act (W.GEN. of justice) E.; detour (W.GEN. on a journey) E.
3 (ref. to a person) supernumerary member (W.GEN. of a house) E.; (ref. to a statue) minor work (W.GEN. of a famous craftsman) Call.
4 (prep.phrs.) ἐν παρέργῳ (also ἐν παρέργου μέρει Pl.) as a side-issue, secondary consideration or afterthought S. Th. Pl. Plb.; as a distraction (W.GEN. *fr. someone's misfortunes*) E.; ἐκ παρέργου as a side-line, casually, perfunctorily Th. Plb.

πάρ-εργος ον *adj.* (of an explanation) subsidiary, incidental, accessory (to another) Pl.

—παρέργως *adv.* casually, perfunctorily Pl. D. Arist. Din. Men. +

παρ-έρπω *vb.* | aor. παρείρπυσα | 1 (of a speaker w. bad eyesight) shuffle forward (to the rostrum) Ar.
2 creep furtively, sneak —W.ADV. *inside (a house)* Ar.; (of a robber) sneak up (on a passer-by) Theoc.
3 (gener.) go past, pass by —*a tomb* Call.epigr.

παρ-έρχομαι *mid.vb.* | fut. παρελεύσομαι (Il. Thgn.) | aor.2 παρῆλθον, ep. παρήλυθον (Theoc.), dial.inf. παρενθεῖν, dial.2sg.subj. παρένθῃς (Theoc.) | pf. παρελήλυθα ‖ Impf. (and usu. fut.) are supplied by πάρειμι². |
1 (of persons or things) **go past, pass by** (sts. W.ACC. a person, a place) Hom. Hes. A. Hdt. S. X. +
2 (of a cross-wall, those building it) **pass, overlap** *—a besieger's wall* Th.
3 (of events, circumstances) pass by and be gone; (of youth, things happening) **pass by** (sts. W.ACC. someone) Thgn. Theoc.; (of war) Th.; (of heat) Pl.; (of a danger, compared to a cloud) D.; (of the deadly effects of a curse) **pass away** A.
4 (of a period of time) **pass, pass by** Hdt. Lys. X. D. ‖ AOR. or PF.PTCPL.ADJ. (of time, events, or sim.) **past** Hdt. S. E. Att.orats. Pl. +
5 (of persons or things) surpass (others, in competitive or moral sense); (of a charioteer) **pass by, overtake** *—another* Il.; (of a runner) **outstrip** *—another* Od.; (of a person) **outdo, surpass** *—someone* (*in trickery, wealth, brazenness, or sim.*) Od. Thgn. E. Ar. Theoc.; (of a shrine) *—another* (*in splendour*) Call.; (of a person, ref. to his repeated misconduct) **go beyond** *—a provbl. expression* (*which describes such conduct*) D.; (of actions) **transcend, signify more than** *—words* D.
6 go past (to a further degree than is proper); **outwit, override** *—a superior, the mind of Zeus* Il. Hes.; **go beyond, overstep** *—one's allotted fate* E.
7 bypass, disregard *—the gods* E. *—laws or sim.* Att.orats.; (wkr.sens.) **pass over, omit, overlook** *—someone or sthg.* E. Ar. Pl.
8 pass by unnoticed, **elude** *—sentries, a watch* Hdt. X. *—accusations and slanders* D.; (of a sight) *—someone's vigilance* S.; (of the need to mention sthg.) **escape** *—someone* D.
9 go on —W.PREP.PHR. *into a building* Hdt. S. X. *—into a city* X. —W.ADV. *inside* A. S. Ar. Men.; **go on inside, enter** Hdt. E. Men. Theoc. —W.ACC. *a building* E.; (fig., of the technique of verbal delivery) **enter** —W.PREP.PHR. *into an art-form* Arist.
10 (of a speaker) **come forward** Hdt. Th. Ar. Att.orats. + —W. ἐπί + ACC. *to the rostrum* Aeschin. —W. εἰς + ACC. *before the people, the Council, the Assembly* Th. And. X. Aeschin.
11 (of troops, a commander) **go on, advance** (sts. W.PREP.PHR. to a place, into a region) Th. Aeschin. D. Arist.; (of a nation) —W.PREP.PHR. *to a position of supremacy* D.
12 (gener., of a person) **come on, come along, arrive** E. Th. Pl. X.; (of love, opp. depart) Thgn.
13 (of a watchword) **pass on, be passed along** X.
πάρες (athem.aor.imperatv.): see παρίημι
πάρεσαν (ep.3pl.impf.): see πάρειμι¹
παρ-εσθίω *vb.* (fig., of a person envisaged as a dog) **gnaw at bits** —W.PARTITV.GEN. *of someone's oracles* (*which he is interpreting to his own advantage*) Ar.
πάρεσις εως *f.* [παρίημι] letting go (unpunished), **release** (W.GEN. of a person) Plu.
παρέσσομαι (ep.fut.mid.): see πάρειμι¹
παρ-έστιος ον *adj.* [ἑστία] **1** (of libations) **at the hearth** S.; (quasi-advbl., of a person being killed) E.; (of a person making offerings) AR.
2 (of a person) **beside the same hearth** (W.DAT. as someone else, i.e. sharing the same house) S.
παρέστιχον (ep.aor.2): see παραστείχω
παρέσχεθον (ep.aor.2), **παρέσχον** (aor.2): see παρέχω
παρετέον (neut.impers.vbl.adj.): see παρίημι
παρέτραγον (aor.2): see παρατρώγω

παρ-ευδιάζομαι *mid.vb.* [εὐδία] (of a nation) **live alongside** (one's neighbours) **in tranquillity** Plb.
παρ-ευδοκιμέω *contr.vb.* **surpass** (W.ACC. someone) **in fame** Plu. ‖ PASS. be surpassed in fame Plu.
παρ-ευθύνω *vb.* (fig.) **keep in line, control** *—someone* (W.DAT. *w. one's hands, i.e. by physical force*) S.
παρ-ευκηλέω *contr.vb.* [εὔκηλος] **soothe away cares; comfort, reassure, beguile** *—children* (W.DAT. *w. one's words*) E.
παρ-ευνάζομαι *mid.vb.* (of a man) **go to bed** —W.DAT. *w. a woman* Od.
πάρ-ευνος ον *adj.* [εὐνή] **1** in bed beside (someone); (fig., of a sorrow, ref. to dead sons) **sleeping beside** (W.DAT. their dead father) A.
2 ‖ FEM.SB. **bedfellow** Ion
παρ-ευρίσκω *vb.* find additionally, **discover** *—causes for blame* Hdt. ‖ PASS. (of an injustice) be detected Hdt.
παρ-ευτακτέω *contr.vb.* (of troops, a king's courtiers) **be available to take orders, be on duty** Plb.
παρ-ευτρεπίζω *vb.* **help to make ready** or **arrange** *—the preliminaries to a sacrifice* E. ‖ MID. (of a king) **organise** *—matters* (*in a particular country*) Plb. ‖ PASS. (of a weapon) be made ready (for use) E.*Cyc.*
παρ-εφεδρεύω *vb.* (of an army) **be stationed in reserve** (in a place) Plb.; (of a commander) **provide on-the-spot cover** —W.DAT. *for foraging parties* Plb.
παρ-έχω *vb.* | πᾰρέχ- once in Od. | fut. παρέξω, also παρασχήσω | aor.2 παρέσχον, inf. παρασχεῖν, ep.inf. παρασχέμεν, imperatv. παράσχες | ep.aor.2 παρέσχεθον, inf. παρασχεθεῖν ‖ pf.mid. παρέσχημαι ‖ neut.impers.vbl.adj. παρεκτέον |
1 (of persons) **present, provide, supply** (oft. W.DAT. to or for someone) *—gifts, food, ships, money, or sim.* Hom. +; (also mid.) Hdt. +
2 (of persons or things) **produce, afford, cause** (sts. W.DAT. for someone) *—trouble, laughter, happiness, grief, fear, or sim.* Hom. +
3 (of persons) **afford, show** (sts. W.DAT. to someone) *—friendship, thanks, goodwill, a submissive manner* Hom. S. E. ‖ MID. **display, show** *—enthusiasm, goodwill, daring, or sim.* Hdt. E. Th. Att.orats. +
4 (of a racehorse) **offer, present, display** *—a body needing no goad* Pi.; (of a person) **show** *—oneself* (*in public*) X.
5 (gener., esp. of places) provide or present (products or sim.); (of the sea) **supply, yield** *—fish* Od. ‖ MID. (of places) **give rise to, bring forth** *—races of men, crocodiles* Hdt.; **display** *—natural features, monuments, or sim.* Hdt.; (of a nation) **provide** *—a commander* Hdt.; (of the souls of the dead) **present** *—apparitions* Pl.
6 ‖ MID. (of a year) make a total of, **make** *—a certain number of days* Hdt.; (of three hundred chariots) *—three hundred drivers* X.
7 (leg.) present before an official body, **produce** *—someone* (w. εἰς + ACC. *before a council, an assembly, for trial*) Lys. X. Aeschin. ‖ MID. **produce** *—witnesses, testimony, proofs* Att.orats. Pl.
8 ‖ MID. **present** (also perh. w.connot. of providing fr. one's own resources) *—one's own armour* (*as a qualification for citizenship*) Th. Arist. *—rated property* (*as a qualification for jury service*) Arist.
9 ‖ MID. (of envoys, citizens) **have to offer, have to show for oneself** *—a great or important city* Th.; (gener., of a person) **offer** or **promise** *—sthg.* Th.

10 offer, present, show —*oneself* (W.PREDIC.ADJ. or SB. *as such and such*) Th. Att.orats. Pl. X. + —*Zeus* (*as one's guarantor*) Thgn.
11 make, render —*someone or sthg.* (W.PREDIC.ADJ. or PTCPL. *as such and such, e.g. a gate secure, people better, allies ready to accept a treaty*) Hdt. E. Th. And. Pl.(also mid.) +; (mid.) —*a god* (*well-disposed to one*) E. —*people* (*more hostile to one*) Pl.
12 offer (one's person, to another); (of a bird) **present, offer** —*its body* (*to a predator*) A.; (of a person) —*one's body, neck, hands* (*to an executioner or captor*) E. —*one's body* (W.DAT. + INF. *to someone, to strike*) Ar. —*oneself* (*to someone, to practise on, question, make use of*) Pl. X. —*one's soul* (*to someone, to care for*) Pl.
13 (intr.) offer one's person in submission (to someone); **allow** —W.INF. or DAT. + INF. (*someone*) *to trample on one, to treat one in such and such a way* S. Ar. —*a doctor, to cut and cauterise one* Pl. X.; **submit** —W.DAT. *to an argument* (*as if to a doctor*) Pl.; **make oneself available** —W.DAT. *to an interlocutor* (*to answer questions*) Pl.; (of a woman) **comply** (w. a demand for sex) Ar.; (of a soldier) **give up the fight** (and resign himself to death) Hdt.
14 present an opportunity or make it possible (for sthg. to be the case); **allow** —W.INF. or DAT. + INF. (*someone*) *to do sthg.* S. E. Th. Theoc. —W.ACC. + INF. *that someone shd. be such and such* E. Th.
15 ‖ IMPERS. it is in the power (of someone), it is possible (usu. W.DAT. + INF. for someone to do sthg.) Pi. Hdt. E. Th. ‖ NEUT.PTCPL. it being possible Hdt. Th.
16 ‖ IMPERATV. (as a formulaic address to bystanders by the leader of a procession) give way!, make way! E. Ar.

παρέω (Ion.subj.), **παρεών** (Ion.ptcpl.): see πάρειμι¹
παρ-ηβάω *contr.vb.* (of a person) **be past one's youth** or **prime** Th. Plu.; (fig., of time) A.(dub.)
παρηγορέω, dial. **παρᾱγορέω** *contr.vb.* [παρήγορος] | iteratv.impf. παρηγορέεσκον (AR.) | **1** urge to a course of action; **exhort, encourage, urge** —*someone* A. Hdt. AR. —W.INF. *to do sthg.* Pi.(mid.) Hdt.(mid.) AR.; **offer encouragement** AR.; **say** (W.ACC. sthg.) **by way of encouragement** AR. Plu.
2 persuade (someone) —W.COMPL.CL. *that sthg. is the case* E. ‖ PASS. be won over (to a course of action) Plu.
3 mollify, assuage —*an angry city* E.; **comfort, console** —*someone* A. AR. Plu.; **offer comfort** or **consolation** A.(dub.); **say** (W.ACC. sthg.) **by way of consolation** —W.DAT. *to someone* AR.
4 assuage —*one's grief* Plu.; **offer consolation for** —*an injury* Plu.
παρηγορίᾱ ᾱς, Ion. **παρηγορίη** ης *f.* **1 exhortation, encouragement, persuasion** AR.; (fig.) **inducement, blandishment** (W.GEN. of personif. oil, which is feeding a flame) A.
2 comfort, consolation (sts. W.GEN. of persons, their grief) Plu.
παρ-ήγορος, dial. **παρᾱ́γορος**, ον *adj.* [ἀγορεύω] (of words) **encouraging** AR. ‖ FEM.SB. (ref. to a person) **comforter** S.
παρήειν (impf.): see πάρειμι²
παρῆεν (ep.3pl.impf.): see πάρειμι¹
παρήϊα (Ion.impf.): see πάρειμι²
παρήϊξα (ep.aor.): see παράσσω
παρήϊον *ep.n.* [reltd. παρειά] **1 cheek** (of a person, a wild animal) Hom. AR. Theoc.
2 cheek-piece (for a horse) Il.

παρηΐς ίδος, also contr. **παρῇς** ῇδος (E.) *f.* [reltd. παρήϊον] (sg. and pl.) **cheek** (oft. described as white or stained w. blood) A. B. Hdt. E. AR. Bion
παρήϊσαν (Ion.3pl.impf.): see πάρειμι²
παρῆκα (aor.): see παρίημι
παρήκμακα (pf.): see παρακμάζω
παρ-ήκω *vb.* [παρά, ἥκω] (of a region, sea, populace, army) **extend along, extend, stretch** (oft. W.PREP.PHR. along somewhere, to somewhere, or sim.) Hdt. Th. Plb.; (of a hound's ribs) —W.PREP.PHR. *obliquely* X.; (of a poetical composition) —*to a certain length* Arist.
παρ-ῆλιξ ικος *masc.fem.adj.* [ἧλιξ] (of a horse) **past the prime of life** Plu.
παρήλιτον (aor.2): see παραλιταίνω
παρηλλαγμένως *pf.pass.ptcpl.adv.*: see under παραλλάσσω
πάρ-ημαι *mid.vb.* [ἧμαι] | only ptcpl. παρήμενος and 3sg. and pl. impf. παρείατο (Hes.fr. Call.) | **be seated beside** or **nearby** —W.DAT. *a person, animals, ships* Hom. —*an altar* E.; **be seated at** —W.DAT. *a meal* Od.; (intr.) **be seated beside** (someone) or **nearby** Hom. Hes.fr. Hdt. Call. AR.; (of vultures) **squat** or **perch nearby** Od.
πάρηξις εως *f.* [perh. παρήκω] app. **walkway** or **decking** (on a warship) A.
παρηορίαι Ion.*f.pl.*, **παρηόριος**, **παρήορος** Ion.*adjs.*: see παράορος
παρηπαφον (ep.aor.2), **παρηπάφησα** (aor.1): see παραπαφίσκω
παρῇς *f.*: see παρηΐς
παρήσω (fut.): see παρίημι
παρθενείᾱ *f.*: see παρθενίᾱ
παρθένειος, also dial. **παρθενήϊος** (Archil. Pi.), ον *adj.* [παρθένος] **1** of or belonging to an unmarried girl; (of eyelids, bloom, a life) **maiden, maidenly** Archil. A. Pi.; (of a bed, ref. to marriage) E. ‖ NEUT.PL.SB. maidenly thoughts Pi.fr.
2 of or relating to the state of virginity; (of girlhood) **virgin** E.; (of pleasure, for a man) **in being a virgin, in virginity** E.
—**παρθένεια** ων *n.pl.* songs sung by a chorus of unmarried girls (such as were composed by Alcman, Pindar and others), **maiden-songs** Ar.
παρθένευμα ατος *n.* [παρθενεύω] state of being a maiden, **girlhood, maidenhood** E.; (concr.) **girlish work** (W.GEN. fr. the loom, ref. to a piece of weaving) E. ‖ PL. girlish pursuits E.
παρθενεύω *vb.* [παρθένος] **1** (of a father) **bring up** (W.ACC. children) **before marriage** E.
2 ‖ MID. (of a woman) **remain** or **live unmarried** A. Hdt. E. Plu.; (of a Vestal Virgin, w.connot. of living in chastity) Plu.
παρθενίᾱ (also **παρθενείᾱ** E.) ᾱς, Ion. **παρθενίη** ης *f.* state of being an unmarried girl, **unwedded state, girlhood, maidenhood** Sapph. A. Pi. E. Telest. Pl. +
παρθενική ῆς, dial. **παρθενικᾱ́** ᾶς, Aeol. **παρθενίκᾱ** ᾱς, Lacon. **παρσενικᾱ́** ᾶς *f.* unmarried girl, **girl, maiden** Hom. Hes. Lyr. E. Hellenist.poet.; (appos.w. νεῆνις *young woman*) Od.
παρθενικός ή όν *adj.* (of a style of tunic at Sparta) **for a girl** Plu.
παρθένιον ου *n.* a kind of medicinal plant, **feverfew** Plu.
παρθένιος ᾱ (Ion. η) ον (also ος ον) *adj.* **1** of or belonging to an unmarried girl; (of a girdle) **maiden, maidenly** Od. Call. Mosch.; (of blood, hair, a head, soul, foot) A. Pi.fr. B. E.; (of whispers, dances, modesty) Hes. E. AR.; (of the heads of the Graiai) Pi.; (of the Sphinx's wing) E.; (of the voice of the Sirens) AR.
2 relating to a maiden; (of a man) **born of an unmarried girl** Il.; (of an unborn child) **conceived by a maiden** Pi.; (of a

παρθενοπίπης

child's swaddling-clothes) **woven by a maiden** E.; (of a husband) **whom one married as a girl** Plu.
3 (epith. of Hera, Artemis) **Maiden** Pi. Call.
4 (fig., of myrtle-berries) **young, untouched, virginal** Ar.
—**παρθένιον** neut.adv. **girlishly** —ref. to an attractive boy casting a glance Anacr.
παρθεν-οπίπης ου m. [ὀπιπεύω] **ogler of girls** (ref. to Paris) Il.
παρθένος, Aeol. **πάρθενος**, Lacon. **παρσένος**, ου f. | The wd. is used of an unmarried woman who has reached the age of puberty. It normally reflects a social distinction (betw. unmarried and married) and not a biological one (betw. virgin and non-virgin: see section 4). |
1 unmarried girl, **girl, maiden** Hom. +; (opp. γυνή married woman, wife) S. E.; (fig., ref. to an inexperienced playwright) Ar.
2 (specif.) maiden daughter, **daughter** (W.GEN. of a named father or mother) B. E. Ar. AR.; (W.ADJ. my, your) S. E.; (ref. to Persephone, as daughter of Demeter) E.; (appos.w. θυγάτηρ) X.
3 (ref. to deities) **maiden** (ref. to Artemis, Athena) A. Pi. B. E. Ar. Call.; (ref. to a Taurian goddess, identified w. Iphigeneia) Hdt. ‖ PL. (ref. to nymphs, Muses) **maidens** Lyr. E. Ar.; Ἑστιάδες (also ἱεραί) παρθένοι **Vestal Virgins** Plu.
4 virgin (opp. a woman who has had sexual experience) A.fr. D. Theoc.; (ref. to a wife whose marriage is unconsummated) E. NT.
5 ‖ ADJ. (of the hand of an unmarried daughter, the hand of Athena) **of a maiden** E.
6 ‖ ADJ. (of a man's soul) **virgin** E.; (of a spring) **pure** A.
παρθενό-σφαγος ον adj. [σφαγή] (of streams of blood) **from the slaughter of a maiden** A.
Παρθενών ῶνος m. **Parthenon** (temple of Athena on the Acropolis) D. Plu.
παρθενῶνες ων m.pl. **living quarters of an unmarried girl or girls, girls' apartments** A. E. Plu.
παρθεν-ωπός όν adj. [ὤψ] (pejor., of a man) **with girlish looks** E.
Πάρθοι ων m.pl. **Parthians** (nomadic Iranian people living SE. of the Caspian Sea, founders of a kingdom eventually covering a much wider area) Hdt. NT. Plu. ‖ SG.ADJ. **Parthian** Plu.
—**Παρθικός** ή όν adj. **1** (of an army) of Parthians, **Parthian** Plu.
2 (of a war, a commander-in-chief) in Parthia, **Parthian** Plu.; (of exploits, defeats) **in the Parthian wars** (fought by Rome in 1st C. BC) Plu. ‖ NEUT.PL.SB. **Parthian wars** Plu.
3 ‖ FEM.SB. **Parthian land**, Parthia Plu.
—**Παρθιστί** adv. **in the Parthian language** Plu.
—**Παρθυαῖα** ᾶς f. —also **Παρθυηνή** ῆς f. **Parthia** Plb.
παρ-ιαύω vb. (of guards, dogs) **sleep close by** (someone) Hom.(tm.); (w. sexual connot., of a man) **sleep beside** —W.DAT. a woman Il. AR.
παρ-ίζω, Aeol. **παρίσδω** vb. | impf. παρῖζον | aor. παρεῖσα |
1 sit alongside (usu. W.DAT. someone) Od. Alc. Hdt. Call.; (mid.) Hdt. Bion; (of a ruler) **sit in attendance** —W.PREP.PHR. at a council Hdt. —W.DAT. alongside councillors Hdt.
2 (causatv.) **make** (W.ACC. someone) **sit nearby** or **alongside** (somewhere, someone) Il.(sts.tm.) AR. —W.DAT. someone Hdt.
παρ-ίημι vb. | pres.: ῑ in Att. | Aeol.3pl. (tm.) πὰρ ... ἵεισι | inf. παριέναι | 3pl.impf. παρίεσαν | fut. παρήσω | aor.1 παρῆκα, 3pl. παρῆκαν | athem.aor.: 3pl. παρεῖσαν, inf. παρεῖναι, ptcpl. παρείς, imperatv. πάρες | pf. παρεῖκα ‖ MID.: athem.aor. παρείμην ‖ PASS.: aor. παρείθην, inf. παρεῖναι | pf. παρεῖμαι, 3sg.imperatv. παρείσθω ‖ neut.impers.vbl.adj. παρετέον |

1 (of guards, defenders, or sim.) **let** (W.ACC. someone) **go past** Hdt.; **admit** —someone or sthg. (oft. W.PREP.PHR. into a country, a city, or sim.) Hdt. E. Pl. X. ‖ MID. **admit** —slaves and barbarians (W.PREP.PHR. into one's citadels) D.; (of innkeepers) —guests Plb.
2 let (time) **go past; let** (W.ACC. winter, a period of time, or sim.) **pass** Hdt. Antipho; **see** (W.ACC. one's youth, one's prime of life) **pass by** S. Pl.; **let slip** —an opportunity Th. D.
3 (of a charioteer) **leave aside, bypass** —a mêlée of chariots S.; (of persons) **avoid** —old age B. —one's expected fate E.
4 leave aside, disregard, ignore —persons, places Hdt. E. Ar. —instructions, duties, a tradition Trag. Th. Ar. Att.orats. +; **let** (W.ACC. someone) **off** (unpunished) Aeschin. D.; **neglect, omit** —W.INF. to do sthg. Pl. ‖ MID. **neglect** —lawful behaviour E. ‖ PASS. (of a person) **be let off** D.; (of punishment) **be unprescribed or overlooked** (in a legal code) Lycurg.
5 leave aside (in a narrative), **pass over, omit** —a topic, details Pi. Hdt. Trag. Th. Att.orats. +
‖ IMPERS.PF.PASS.IMPERATV. **let no more be said** Plb.
6 let (sthg.) **go loose or free** (so that it collapses or falls); **let** (W.ACC. oneself, one's body) **sink** (to the ground) S.; (of birds) **let** (W.ACC. their wings) **drop** (to their sides) Sapph.(tm.); (of a dying bird) **let** (W.ACC. its claws) **go limp** E.; (of a person) **let** (W.ACC. a cloak, held as a veil) **fall** (fr. before one's eyes) E.; (of surrendering soldiers) **lower** or **drop** —their shields Th. ‖ PASS. (of a cord tethered at one end) **fall loose** —W.PREP.PHR. towards the ground Il.; (of the body of someone jumping fr. a height) **plunge** E. ‖ PF.PASS. (of a person) **be limp or collapsed** (through fatigue, disease, sleep, old age) E. Pl.
7 (in nautical ctxts.) **slacken** —ropes Ar. —W.PARTITV.GEN. a sheet Ar.
8 let go of, leave off, give up —lamentation, anger, a desire, gluttony E. —one's former practices Th. ‖ PASS. (of desire for sthg.) **be given up** S.
9 hand over or yield (sthg., to someone); **give up, yield, resign** —victory, kingship, command, responsibilities Hdt. E. Th. Arist.; **hand over** —a task S.; **surrender** —a person E. Ar.; (of sailors) —themselves (W.DAT. to the motion of the waves) E.; (intr., of an old man) **give up, give in** —W.DAT. through fatigue E.
10 leave, allow —W.DAT. + INF. someone to do sthg. Hdt. +; **give permission** (for sthg.) Hdt. + | see also μεθίημι 9
11 ‖ MID. **ask** (W.ACC. someone) **for permission** Pl.
12 ‖ MID. **ask for pardon** E.; **ask a favour** —W.GEN. of someone S. Pl.
παρ-ίκω vb. (of events) **be in the past** Pi.
Πάριος adj.: see under Πάρος
παρ-ιππεύω vb. **1** (of the Dioscuri) **ride over** (W.ACC. the sea) **alongside** (a ship) E.
2 (of horsemen) **ride past** or **along** (one's own or the enemy's lines) Th. Plb. Plu.
πάρ-ιππος ον adj. [ἵππος] **riding alongside** (someone) ‖ MASC.SB. **accompanying rider** Plb.
Πάρις ιος (Il. Pi.), also ιδος (A. Plu.) m. | acc. Πάριν | **Paris** (alternative name of Alexandros, son of Priam and Hecuba, abductor of Helen) Il. Ibyc. Pi. Trag. Theoc. Plu.
παρίσδω Aeol.vb.: see παρίζω
πάρ-ισος ον adj. [ἴσος] **1** (of military forces, a contest, or sim.) **nearly equal, evenly balanced** Plb.
2 ‖ NEUT.SB. (rhet.) **even balance** (of clauses) Arist.

παρ-ισόω *contr.vb.* **1** make equal ‖ MID. or PASS. (of a person) **put oneself on a par, claim equal status** —W.DAT. *w. someone* Hdt. ‖ PASS. be matched or compared —W.DAT. *w. someone* Theoc.
2 ‖ PASS. (of a person, w. iron.ref. to the rhetorical technique of παρίσωσις) be evenly balanced —W.DAT. *in virtue* Pl.
παρ-ίστημι *vb.* —also (pres. and impf.) **παριστάνω** (Plb.) | impf. παρίστην, also παρίστανον (Plb.) | fut. παραστήσω | aor.1 παρέστησα, dial. παρέστᾱσα | later pf. παρέστακα (Plb.) ‖ MID.: aor.1 παρεστησάμην ‖ The act. (incl. later pf.) and aor.1 mid. (sts. also pres. and fut. mid.) are tr. For the intr.mid. see παρίσταμαι below. The act. athem.aor., pf. and plpf. are also intr. |
1 station (W.ACC. troops) **nearby** or **alongside** (somewhere, other troops) D. Plb.
2 (of a god) send (W.ACC. the goddess of childbirth) **as a helper** —W.DAT. *to a woman in labour* Pi.
3 set beside for comparison, **compare** —*one thing* (W.DAT. *w. another*) Isoc.
4 ‖ MID. (in legal ctxt.) set by one's side or nearby, **bring forward, produce** —*one's children* (*in court*) Lys. D. —*witnesses* Is. D. —*someone* (W.PREP.PHR. *for judgement*) Pl.; (in non-legal ctxt.) —*sacrificial victims* X.
5 (of the risen Christ) present —*himself* (W.DAT. *to the Apostles*) NT.; (mid., of a person) —*oneself* (W.PREP.PHR. and ADV. *for battle, in a certain frame of mind*) Plb.
6 bring (sthg.) before someone's mind, sight or feelings; **put across, bring home** —*arguments, considerations* (W.DAT. *to someone*) Lys. X. D. —W.COMPL.CL. *that sthg. is the case* Pl.; **present** —*a topic for deliberation* (W.DAT. *to someone*) D.; (of persons, events) **arouse** —*hopes, anger, reflection, fear, or sim.* (W.DAT. *for someone*) Aeschin. D. Plb.; (of the gods) **inspire** —W.DAT. + INF. *someone to do sthg.* D.
7 ‖ MID. bring (someone) over to one's side; **bring** (W.ACC. persons, places) **into line, force** (them) **to submit** or **capitulate** Hdt. S. Th.; **force** —*someone* (W.PREP.PHR. *into paying tribute*) Pl.; (wkr.sens.) **induce, prompt** —*someone* (W.PREP.PHR. *to a course of action*) Plb. —(W.INF. *to do sthg.*) Plu.(act.)
—**παρίσταμαι** *mid.vb.*| fut. παραστήσομαι | also ACT.: athem.aor. παρέστην, ep. πάρστην, imperatv. παραστῆθι, also παράστᾱ (Men.) | pf. παρέστηκα, inf. παρεστάναι, ep. παρεστάμεναι, also παρεστάμεν | plpf. παρειστήκειν, ep.3pl. παρέστασαν | fut.pf. παρεστήξω (Men.) ‖ aor.pass. (w.mid.sens.) παρεστάθην |
1 come and stand by or near, come up close (oft. W.DAT. *to someone or sthg.*) Hom. hHom. Pi. B. Hdt. Trag. + ‖ PF., PLPF. and FUT.PF.ACT. stand by, beside or near (oft. W.DAT. *someone or sthg.*) Hom. +
2 come and stand by as a helper or supporter; **support, help** (oft. W.DAT. *someone*) Hom. Archil. Pi. Hdt. Trag. + ‖ PF.ACT. stand by (oft. W.DAT. *someone*) in support Hom. Hes. Trag.
3 (of fate, death, old age) **be at hand** (usu. W.DAT. *for someone*) Od. hHom.; (of a marvellous event) **happen** —W.DAT. *for someone* Hdt.; (of circumstances, panic, an opportunity, a need) **arise** E. Th. X. D. ‖ PF.ACT. (of death or sim.) be close (sts. W.DAT. *for someone*) Il. hHom. Mimn.; (of a contest) E.; (of perplexity, fear) hang over —W.DAT. *someone* And. Pl. ‖ PF.ACT.PTCPL.ADJ. (of circumstances, sufferings, or sim.) at hand, present, current S. E. Ar. Pl. + ‖ NEUT.PF.ACT.PTCPL.SB. (sg. or pl.) present circumstances A. Ar. Pl.

4 (of a thought, an opinion, or sim.) be presented, **occur** —W.DAT. *to someone* S. E. Att.orats. Pl. ‖ IMPERS. (sts. PF.ACT.) it occurs —W.DAT. + INF. *to someone to do sthg.* Hdt. Lys. —W.DAT. or ACC. + INF. or W.COMPL.CL. *to someone, that sthg. is the case* Th. Lys. Pl.
5 come over —W.PREP.PHR. *to someone's opinion* Hdt.; **come to terms, surrender, submit** Hdt. D.
6 be moved (by a speech) Plb. ‖ PF. and PLPF.ACT. be distracted —W.DAT. *in one's mind* Plb.; have lost —W.GEN. *one's wits* Plb. | cf. παρεξίστημι
παρ-ίσχω *vb.* | ep.inf. παρισχέμεν | **1** (of an assistant) **keep at hand, hold ready** (for someone) —*horses* Il.
2 offer —*gifts* (W.DAT. *to someone*) Il.; (of a god) **be the giver** (of human fortunes) Pi.; (of an innkeeper) **provide, serve** —*meat* Timocr.
παρίσωσις εως *f.* [παρισόω] (rhet.) **equal balance** (of clauses) Arist. ‖ PL. balanced clauses Isoc. | cf. πάρισος 2
παριτητέα (neut.pf.impers.vbl.adj.): see πάρειμι²
παριτός ή όν *adj.* [πάρειμι²] (in neg.phr., of a mountain) **to be traversed** or **trodden** (by someone) Call.
παρκατέλεκτο (ep.3sg.athem.aor.mid.): see παρακαταλέχομαι
πάρκειμαι, παρκλίνω *ep.vbs.*: see παράκειμαι, παρακλίνω
παρκύπτω *dial.vb.*: see παρακύπτω
παρμέμβλωκα (ep.pf.): see παραβλώσκω
Παρμενίδης ου *m.* **Parmenides** (Presocratic philosopher, late 6th and early 5th C. BC) Isoc. Pl. Arist. Plu.
παρμένω *ep.vb.*: see παραμένω
παρμόνιμος *dial.adj.*: see παραμόνιμος
πάρμονος ον *dial.adj.* [παρμένω, reltd. παραμόνιμος] | compar. παρμονώτερος | (of prosperity) **lasting** Pi.
Παρνασσός (also **Παρνᾱσός**), Ion. **Παρνησσός** (also **Παρνησός**), οῦ *m.* **Parnassos** (mt. range in Phocis, overlooking Delphi, traditional home of the Muses) Od. hHom. Pi. Trag. Th. +
—**Παρνάσσιος** (**Παρνάσιος**) ᾱ ον (also ος ον) *adj.* of or belonging to Parnassos; (of rocks, slopes, greenery, or sim.) **Parnassian** Pi. Trag. Ar. Theoc.; (of a person) **from Parnassos** E.
—**Παρνασσιάς** (**Παρνασιάς**) άδος *fem.adj.* (of the peaks) **of Parnassos** E.
—**Παρνησσίς** (**Παρνησίς**) ίδος *fem.adj.* (of an accent) **Parnassian** A.
πάρνοψ οπος *m.* **locust** Ar.
παρ-οδεύω *vb.* (of a traveller) **pass by, disregard** (a tomb) Theoc.
πάρ-οδος ου *f.* [ὁδός] **1** means of passing (fr. one place to another), **passage, access, route** Th. X. +
2 (concr.) **passage, route** (esp. through difficult terrain) Lys. X. +; **pass** (through mountains, esp. ref. to Thermopylae) Att.orats. X. +
3 walkway or decking (on a warship) Plu.
4 process of passing (by an army), **passage** Th. D. +
5 passage by the dramatic chorus into the orchestra, **entry of the chorus** Arist.; **entrance-song** (of the chorus, opp. stasimon) Arist.; (fig.) **entrance** (W.PREP.PHR. *into public life, by a politician*) Plu.
6 (as a later term for eisodos) **side entrance** (to the stage or orchestra, for actors or chorus) Plu.
παρ-οίγνυμι *vb.* | aor.ptcpl. παροίξας | **partially open** —W.ACC. or PARTITV.GEN. *a door* E. Ar.
πάροιθε(ν), Aeol. **πάροιθα** *adv.* and *prep.* [πάρος] **1** (ref. to position) **before, in front** Hom. E. AR.; (as prep.) **in front** —W.GEN. *of someone or sthg.* Hom. Alc. A. B. E. AR.

2 (ref. to time) before something happens; **before then, beforehand, first** Hom. S. E. Call. AR. —w. πρίν + INF. *before doing sthg.* S. —w. πρίν + ACC. and INF. *before someone does sthg.* Call.; (as prep.) **earlier than, before** —W.GEN. *someone* A. S. —*an event* E.; (as conj.) **before** —W.INF. *doing sthg.* Theoc.
3 in time past, **before, formerly** Hom. Lyr. Trag. AR.; (also) τὸ πάροιθε(ν) Od. Hes. Pi.*fr.* E. Hellenist.poet.; (quasi-adjl., of misfortunes, persons, or sim.) **earlier, former** Alc. A. Pi. E.; (of night, day) **previous** A. E.

παροικέω contr.vb. [πάροικος] **1** (of a populace, individuals, cities) **live nearby, be neighbours** (sts. W.DAT. to persons, places) Th. X. Men. Plb. Plu.
2 (of a people) **live alongside** (a place); **dwell along the coast of** —*Asia* Isoc.; **live alongside** —*a river* Plb.
3 live as an alien in —*a city* NT.

παροίκησις εως *f.* state of living nearby, **neighbourship, proximity** Th.

παροικίᾱ ᾶς *f.* **temporary residence in a foreign land** NT.

παρ-οικίζω vb. settle (someone) nearby ‖ MID. **locate** (W.ACC. a statue) **beside one's house** Call.*epigr.* ‖ PASS. (of a populace) settle nearby —W.DAT. *someone* Hdt.

παρ-οικοδομέω contr.vb. **1** build (a structure) **along the side** (of a ramp) Th.; build (a wall) **along the side** (of a flooded road) D. ‖ PASS. (of a wall) be built along —w. παρά + ACC. *the side of a road* Pl.
2 build (a counter-wall) past (the path of a besieger's wall, to cut it off before it can encircle the city); (of occupants of a besieged city) **build past** (the enemy wall) Th. Plu.; **build** (W.ACC. a wall) **past** —W.DAT. *the enemy (i.e. their wall)* Th. ‖ PASS. (of a counter-wall) be built past (the enemy's wall) Th.

πάρ-οικος ον adj. [οἶκος] **1** (of persons, places) **dwelling or situated nearby, neighbouring** (usu. W.GEN. on a place) Trag.; (of war) **against one's neighbours** Hdt. ‖ MASC.SB. neighbour (of an adjacent country) Th. Arist. Plu.; (fig., of virtue, ref. to wealth) Sapph.
2 ‖ MASC.SB. **resident foreigner** NT.

παρ-οιμίᾱ ᾱς *f.* [οἶμος] byword, **saying, maxim, proverb** Trag. Ar. Pl. +; (ref. to a kind of parable not easily understood) NT.

παροιμιάζομαι mid.vb. **1** (of persons) **use proverbial language, cite proverbs** Pl. Arist.; (of an expression) **be proverbial** Pl.
2 (tr.) **make a proverb about, proverbialise** —*god* Pl.

παροιμιώδης ες adj. (of an expression) **proverbial** Plu.

παροινέω contr.vb. [πάροινος] | impf. ἐπαρᾠνουν | aor. ἐπαρᾠνησα | pf. πεπαρᾠνηκα | aor.pass. ἐπαρῳνήθην |
1 misbehave when drunk, behave violently or **abusively when drunk** Att.orats. Pl. X. Men.; **commit a drunken assault** —w. εἰς + ACC. *on someone* Att.orats. Men. ‖ PASS. be subjected to drunken violence or abuse Antipho D. Plu.
2 misbehave as if drunk, **behave violently** or **abusively** Ar. Men. Plu. —w. εἰς + ACC. *towards someone* Men. ‖ PASS. be abused or mocked Plu.; (fig.) —W.PREP.PHR. *by fortune* Plu.

παροινίᾱ ᾱς *f.* **drunken violence** or **abuse** Att.orats. X. Plu.

παροίνια ων n.pl. **drinking songs** Plu.

παροινικός ή όν adj. (of a person) **inclined to drunken misbehaviour** Ar.

πάρ-οινος ον adj. [οἶνος] (of a person) **drunk and disorderly** Pratin. Lys. D. ‖ NEUT.SB. **outrageous behaviour** Men.

παροίτατος η ον ep.superl.adj. [πάροιθε] (quasi-advbl., of a person acting or speaking) **first of all** (before others) AR.

παροίτερος η ον ep.compar.adj. **1** (of horses) **further forward** (than others), **in front, ahead** Il.; (of an island) **at the head** (W.GEN. of a strait) AR.
2 (quasi-advbl., of a person speaking) **first** (before another) AR.

—**παροίτερον** neut.compar.adv. (ref. to time) **before anything else happens, first** AR.; in earlier times, **formerly, previously** AR.

—**παροιτέρω** compar.adv. (ref. to movt.) **further on** AR.

παρ-οίχομαι mid.vb. | impf. παρῳχόμην | pf. παρῴχημαι | ep.3sg.pf. παροίχωκε, Ion.3sg.plpf. παροιχώκεε |
1 (of love, trouble, fear, pleasure, or sim.) **be past, be gone** Thgn. A. Pi. Arist. Plu.(quot.com.) ‖ PF. and PLPF. (of a night, festival, time) **have gone past, be past** Il. Hdt. Plu.
2 (impf., of a person) go past, **pass on, go on one's way** Il.
3 ‖ PRES.PTCPL.ADJ. (of a night, a year, troubles, or sim.) past Hdt. X. AR. Plu.; (also pf.ptcpl., of generations, a night) NT. Plu. ‖ NEUT.PTCPL.SB. (pl., usu. w.art.) past things or events Hdt. X. Arist.; (sg., w.art.) the past Arist.
4 (of persons) **be dead and gone** Pi.; (fig.) **be beside oneself** —W.DAT. *w. fear* A.
5 (fig.) have gone astray or aside; **have lost track** —W.GEN. *of one's destiny (i.e. failed to understand it)* E.; perh. **have stepped aside** —W.GEN. *fr. a dispute* A.

παροκωχή ῆς *f.* [παρέχω] act of providing, **provision** (W.GEN. of ships, for allies) Th.

παρ-ολιγωρέω contr.vb. **pay no heed** (to a request, a situation) X. Plb.; **neglect, overlook** —W.GEN. *an aspect of historical narrative* Plb. ‖ PASS. (of persons) be slighted Plb.

παρ-ολισθάνω vb. | aor.2 παρώλισθον | (fig., of a nation) **slip** (fr. its former standard of conduct) Plb.

παρ-ομαρτέω contr.vb. (of a crowd on either side of a river) **walk alongside, accompany** (a boat) Plu.

παρομοιάζω vb. [παρόμοιος] (of persons) **be like, resemble** —W.DAT. *sthg.* NT.

παρ-όμοιος ον (also Ion. η ον) adj. (of persons or things) **closely comparable, similar, equivalent** (sts. W.DAT. to someone or sthg.) Hdt. Th. D. + —W.ACC. *in number* X.

παρ-ομοίωσις εως *f.* similarity (of the sound of syllables at the beginning or end of successive phrs. or cls., as a rhetorical technique), **paromoiosis, assonance** Arist.

παρ-ομολογέω contr.vb. **agree** —W.INF. *to do sthg.* Plb. —W.COMPL.CL. *that sthg. is the case* Plb.

παρ-ονομάζω vb. give (someone) a derived name ‖ PASS. be given a cognomen —w. ἐκ + GEN. *derived fr. some word* Plu.

παροξυντικός ή όν adj. [παροξύνω] **1** (of a circumstance, a speech) **offering an incentive** (W.PREP.PHR. to an action) X. Plu.; (of arguments) **provocative, inflammatory** (W.PREP.PHR. w. a view to urging a course of action) D.
2 (of behaviour) **exasperating** Isoc.

παρ-οξύνω vb. | fut. παροξυνῶ | aor. παρώξυνα | pf. παρώξυκα ‖ PASS.: aor. παρωξύνθην | pf. παρώξυμμαι |
1 (of persons, circumstances) **incite, stimulate, spur on** —*someone* Th. X. D. + —(W.PREP.PHR. *to some act*) Isoc. X. + —(W.INF. *to do sthg.*) Att.orats. X. —(W.PREP.PHR. *against someone*) Plu. ‖ PASS. be spurred on Att.orats. X. —W.PREP.PHR. *to some act* Isoc. X. Men. —W.INF. *to do sthg.* Isoc. Plb.; (of a man) be inflamed —W.PREP.PHR. *by a woman (to do sthg.)* Lys.
2 provoke, **irritate, exasperate** —*someone, the mind* E. Th. Men. ‖ PASS. be provoked, irritated or exasperated Th. Att.orats. +

παροξυσμός οῦ *m.* **1 exasperation, irritation** D.
2 sharp disagreement (betw. persons) NT.

παρ-οπλίζω vb. disarm —someone Plb. ‖ PASS. be left without weapons Plu.

παρ-οπτάομαι pass.contr.vb. (of a person, in the bronze bull of Phalaris) **be half-roasted** Plb.

παρόρᾱσις εως f. [παροράω] **overlooking** (of faults) Plu.

παρ-οράω contr.vb. ǀ impf. παρεώρων ǀ fut. παρόψομαι ǀ aor.2 παρεῖδον ǀ Lacon.aor.2 ptcpl. παραυιδών (παραγιδών) Ar. ‖ aor.pass. παρώφθην ‖ neut.impers.vbl.adj. παροπτέον ǀ
1 see or **detect** (W.ACC. a good or bad quality) **in** —W.DAT. someone Hdt. Ar.
2 look sideways; (of troops on the march) **cast a sideways glance** —W.PREP.PHR. at each other, at the standard X.; (of a person) **cast a furtive look** —W.PREP.PHR. at someone X.; **catch a glimpse of** —W.ACC. a woman's breasts Ar.
3 overlook, disregard —persons, situations, laws, mistakes, or sim. Att.orats. X. + ‖ PASS. (of persons or things) be overlooked or disregarded Aeschin. D. Arist. Plb. Plu.
4 see incorrectly, have faulty vision Pl.; (fig., ref. to faulty understanding) Pl.

παρ-οργίζω vb. **make** (someone) **angry** Arist. ‖ PASS. be made angry D.(dub.)

παρ-ορμάω contr.vb. **urge on, incite** —someone X. Plb. Plu. —(W.PREP.PHR. to some act) X. Plb. Plu. —(W.INF. to do sthg.) X. Arist. Plb. Plu.; (intr.) **rush** —W.PREP.PHR. in pursuit of some objective Plb. ‖ PASS. be excited, be stimulated, become eager Plb. —W.PREP.PHR. for sthg. Plb. —W.INF. to do sthg. Plb.

παρ-ορμέω contr.vb. (of a naval commander, sailors, ships) **lie at anchor nearby** Plu.; (aor., of a person) **come to anchor nearby** Men.(dub.)

παρόρμησις εως f. [παρορμάω] **incitement, inducement** Plb.; (W.GEN. + PREP.PHR. of someone, to some action) X. Plb.

παρορμητικός ή όν adj. (of a circumstance) **offering an incentive** (W.PREP.PHR. to marriage) Plu.

παρ-ορμίζω vb. **bring** (W.ACC. a ship) **to anchor alongside** (a place) Lys.

πάρ-ορνις ιθος masc.fem.adj. [ὄρνις] **with contrary bird-signs**; (of a journey) **ill-omened** A.

παρ-όρνῡμι vb. **stir** (W.ACC. someone) **to action** AR.(tm.)

παρ-ορύσσω vb. **dig** (W.ACC. a trench) **alongside** (a palisade) Th.

πάρος adv. and prep. [reltd. παρά, πάροιθε] ǀ sts. w.art. τὸ πάρος ǀ **1 in time past, before, formerly, previously** Hom. Hes. B. Hdt. Trag. Ar. +; (quasi-adjl., of persons, events, time, or sim.) **earlier, former** Carm.Pop. Pi. Trag.
2 (w.pres.vb., ref. to a period lasting until the present) **from of old, always** Hom. AR. • οἷος πάρος εὔχεαι εἶναι such as you have always claimed to be Il.; **up to now, hitherto** Hom.
• πάρος ... οὔ τι θαμίζεις you have not been a frequent visitor before now Od.
3 before something happens; before then, beforehand, first Hom. Trag. AR.; **first** (before another person) AR.; (w.neg., as antecedent to πρίν) **not until** —W.ACC. + INF. someone does sthg. Hom.; (as conj.) **before** —W.INF. or ACC. + INF. doing sthg., someone does sthg., sthg. happens Hom. AR. Theoc.; (also) πάρος ἤ Call.
4 (ref. to position) **in front, ahead** S. AR.
5 (ref. to choice) **sooner, rather, for preference** A. E.
6 (prep., ref. to position) **in front** —W.GEN. of someone or sthg. Il. S. E. AR. Theoc.
7 (prep., ref. to time) **earlier than, before** —W.GEN. someone E.
8 (prep., ref. to choice) **in preference; ahead** —W.GEN. of sthg. S. E.; **instead** —W.GEN. of someone E.

Πάρος ου f. **Paros** (island in the Cyclades, birthplace of Archilochus) hHom. Archil. A. Pi. Hdt. +
—**Πάριοι** ων m.pl. **inhabitants of Paros, Parians** Hdt. Th. +
—**Πάριος** ᾱ (Ion. η) ον adj. (as ethnic adj., of a man or woman) **from Paros, Parian** Hdt. Pl. +; (of stone, i.e. marble) Pi. Hdt. Theoc.

παρ-οτρύνω vb. **stir up, incite** —people (against someone) NT.

παρουαῖος η ον Ion.adj. [παρῶας chestnut-coloured] (of hounds) **red-brown, chestnut** Call.(cj.)

παρουσίᾱ ᾱς f. [πάρειμι¹] **1 presence** (oft. W.GEN. of a person or persons, sts. w.connot. of support or assistance) Trag. Th. Isoc. X. +; (W.GEN., periphr., ref. to the persons present) E.; (ref. to military presence, i.e. troops) Th.; (of good or bad things, abstr. qualities) E. Ar. Pl. D. Arist.
2 arrival S. E. Th. D. Plb. Plu.
3 advent (of Christ, ref. to his second coming) NT.

παροχέομαι mid.pass.contr.vb. [πάροχος] ǀ fut. παροχήσομαι ǀ **1** (of a charioteer) **ride beside** —W.DAT. someone X.
2 (of a relative or friend of the bridegroom) **ride beside bride and groom** (in the carriage that conveyed them fr. the bride's parental home to her husband's), **be groomsman** Men.

παρ-οχετεύω vb. **turn from the present course, divert** —a water-supply Plu.; (fig., of a respondent) **say** (W.NEUT.ACC. sthg.) **by way of deflecting the question** E.; (w. play on both senses) **tamper with** —laws about water-supplies (W.DAT. w. verbal arguments) Pl.

παροχή ῆς f. [παρέχω] **1 provision** (W.GEN. of hospitality) Plb.
2 (concr.) **provisions, sustenance** Plb.

πάρ-οχος ου m. [ὀχέω] one who rides beside bride and groom, **groomsman** Ar.

παρ-οψίς ίδος f. [ὄψον] **1 side-dish, appetiser** Philox.Leuc. X.
2 dish or **plate** (for food) NT.

παρόψομαι (fut.mid.): see παροράω

παρ-οψωνέω contr.vb. (of women) **buy food additionally** or **secretly, buy extra dishes** —W.DAT. for themselves Ar.

παροψώνημα ατος n. (fig., in dub.ctxt.) **added relish** (ref. to pleasure) A.

παρπεπιθών (dial.redupl.aor.2 ptcpl.): see παραπείθω

παρπέταμαι dial.mid.vb.: see παραπέτομαι

παρ-πόδιος ον dial.adj. [παρά, πούς] (of bloodshed) **before one's feet, imminent** Pi.

παρραλίη ep.Ion.f.: see παράλιος

παρρησίᾱ ᾱς, Ion. **παρρησίη** ης f. [πᾶς, ῥῆσις]
1 outspokenness, frankness, freedom of speech (as praiseworthy, desirable, a mark of liberty) E. Ar. Att.orats. Pl. +; (euphem. for slander) Thphr.
2 (pejor.) **uncontrolled language** E. Isoc. Pl.

παρρησιάζομαι mid.vb. ǀ fut. παρρησιάσομαι ǀ aor. ἐπαρρησιασάμην ǀ mid.pass.pf. πεπαρρησίασμαι ǀ **speak freely** or **openly** Att.orats. Pl. X. + —W.NEUT.ACC. all that one feels, many things D. Plb. Plu. ‖ PASS. (of things) be said freely Isoc.

παρρησιαστής οῦ m. **free speaker** Arist.

παρρησιαστικός ή όν adj. (of a type of person) **free-spoken, outspoken** Arist.

παρσενικά Lacon.f., **παρσένος** Lacon.f.: see παρθενική, παρθένος

πάρστην (ep.athem.aor.): see παρίσταμαι

παρτίθημι ep.vb.: see παρατίθημι

παρ-υπομιμνήσκω vb. (of a historian) **record side by side** —two kinds of information Plb.

παρ-υφαίνω vb. weave as a border or fringe || PASS. (fig., of armed men extended in a long line) form a cordon (behind which unarmed persons are hidden) X.

παρφαίνω dial.vb.: see παραφαίνω

παρφάμεν (dial.pres. or athem.aor.inf.), **παρφάμενος** (mid.ptcpl.), **παρφάσθαι** (mid.inf.): see πάραφημι

πάρφασις ep.f.: see παραίφασις

παρφέρω dial.vb.: see παραφέρω

παρφεύγω ep.vb.: see παραφεύγω

πάρφρων dial.adj.: see παράφρων

παρφυκτός όν dial.adj. [παραφεύγω] (of fate, in neg.phr.) **to be escaped** or **avoided** Pi.

παρῳδίᾱ ᾱς f. [παρῳδός] composition in verse which distorts another work or genre, **parody**, **burlesque** (assoc.w. Hegemon of Thasos, prob. 5th C. BC, perh. because he was first to enter such compositions into public contests) Arist.

παρ-ῳδός όν adj. [ἀοιδή] **singing discordantly**; (of riddles) **distorting**, **oblique** E.

παρ-ωθέω contr.vb. | aor.ptcpl. παρώσας || pf.pass.inf. παρεῶσθαι | **1** (of an elephant) **push aside** —an opposing elephant's trunk Plb.; (of a person) **eject** —someone (W.PREP.PHR. fr. his inheritance) Plu. || PASS. (of material objects) **be pushed aside** or **displaced** Plb.
2 cast or **brush aside, reject, spurn** —persons E. D. —marriage w. a slave E.; **dismiss out of hand** —a god, a person (as responsible for sthg.) S. Plu.; **put out of mind** —a dead husband E. || MID. **brush aside, reject** —persons, arguments E. Aeschin. Plu. || PASS. (of persons) **be brushed aside, spurned** or **slighted** X. D.
3 || MID. **put aside, put off, defer** —a topic for discussion Pl.

παρ-ωκεάνιος ον adj. [Ὠκεανός] (of certain Gaulish tribes) **living beside the ocean** (i.e. the Atlantic) Plu.

παρωνυμιάζομαι pass.vb. [παρωνύμιος] (of a word) **be derived** (fr. another) Arist.

παρ-ωνύμιος ον adj. [ὄνομα] (of a word) **with a change of meaning, with a secondary sense** Pl. || NEUT.SB. **description that is derived** (W.GEN. fr. sthg.) Pl.; **surname** (derived fr. a place) Arist.; (as transl. of Lat. cognomen) Plu.; **nickname** (derived fr. a characteristic) Plu.

—παρώνυμος ον adj. (of a person's name, borne by another) **as a secondary name** A.

—παρωνύμως adv. **by way of derivation** —ref. to words being related Arist.

παρωνυχίᾱ ᾱς f. [ὄνυξ] (medic.) **inflammation about the fingernail**; (fig.) **minor blemish** (in a writer) Plb.

παρ-ώρεια ᾱς f. [ὄρος] (sg. and pl.) **region beside a mountain, foothills** Plb.

παρ-ωροφίς ίδος f. [ὄροφος] **cornice** (projecting outwards fr. the top of a temple wall, just below the roof) Hdt.

πᾶς (Aeol. **παῖς**) πᾶσα (Aeol. παῖσα, Lacon. πάά) πᾶν (dial. πᾶν) adj. and collectv.pron. | gen. παντός πάσης παντός | fem.gen.pl. πᾱσῶν, Ion. πᾱσέων (disyllab.), ep. πᾱσάων | masc.neut.dat.pl. πᾶσι, Aeol. πάντεσσι || cf. ἅπᾱς, σύμπᾱς | The wd., when used of one item (and sts. of collectv.pls.), denotes *all* (*the whole*) of it; when used of many, *all* (*every one*) of them. In gener., the art. is present only if the sb., standing alone, would have it. |
1 (sg.) **the entirety of, all** (of), **the whole** (of) Hom. + • πᾶν ἦμαρ *a whole day* Il. • πᾶσα ἡ σκευή *all the equipment* Hdt.; (quasi-advbl.) ἦν ἡ μάχη ἐν χερσὶ πᾶσα *the battle was all hand-to-hand* Th.; (preceded by the art.) ὁ πᾶς ἀριθμός *the full total* A. || NEUT.SB. (w.art.) **the whole** A. +; (philos.) **the whole universe** Emp. Pl.
2 (sg.) **each single, every** Hom. + • πᾶν ἔργον *every task* Il.

• πᾶς ἀνήρ *every man* Hdt. || COLLECTV.PRON. **everyone, everything** Hom. + • πᾶς τις *every single one* Thgn. +
3 || PL. **all** Hom. + • πᾶσαι ἀγυιαί *all the streets* Od. • πάντες οἱ φιλόσοφοι *all the philosophers* Pl.; (preceded by the art., to stress totality) οἱ πάντες ἄνθρωποι *all of mankind* X.
|| PL.COLLECTV.PRON. **everyone, everything** Hom. +
|| MASC.NEUT.PL.SB. (freq. w.art.) **the full number, the whole** A. +; **everything one could wish for** Hdt. + • πάντ' ἐκεῖνος ἦν αὐτοῖς *he was everything to them* D.
4 (sg. and pl.) **every possible, every sort of, all manner of** Hom. + • πάντας δὲ δόλους καὶ μῆτιν ὕφαινον *I wove every kind of trick and device* Od. • πᾶσαν σπουδὴν ποιεύμενος *making every possible effort* Hdt.
5 || PL. (w. numbers, sts. w.art.) **altogether, in total** Hom. +
• ἐννέα πάντ' ἔτεα *nine years in all* Hes. • ἑξακοσίους καὶ χιλίους τοὺς πάντας ὁπλίτας *sixteen hundred hoplites in total* Th.
6 (sg., hyperbol.) **complete and utter, extreme** Hdt. + • ἐν πάσῃ ἀναρχίᾳ καὶ ἀνομίᾳ *in utter anarchy and lawlessness* Pl.; (neut., W.PARTITV.GEN.) • ἐς πᾶν ἤδη κακοῦ ἀπιγμένοι ἦσαν *they had now reached an extremely critical situation* Hdt. • ἐν παντὶ δὴ ἀθυμίας ἦσαν *they were in utter despair* Th.; (without GEN.) • ἐν παντὶ εἶναι *be in desperate straits* Pl.
• εἰς πᾶν ἐλθεῖν *come into grave danger* D.
7 (sg. and pl.) **any out of the whole range of possibilities, any whatever, any** Hdt. + • ἀμήχανον δὲ παντὸς ἀνδρὸς ἐκμαθεῖν ψυχήν *it is impossible to understand any man's heart* S. || MASC.SB. **anyone** Pl. +; (w.neg.) *not anyone* (i.e. *none*) NT. || NEUT.SB. πᾶν, πάντα **anything** Pi. + • πᾶν μᾶλλον ἢ στρατιή *anything rather than an army* Hdt. • παντὸς μᾶλλον *more than anything, above all* Pl.
8 || NEUT.ACC.ADV. πᾶν, τὸ πᾶν **altogether, completely** A. Hdt. +; (w.neg.) *not at all* A.; (dat.sg.) τῷ παντί *altogether* X.
|| PL. πάντα, τὰ πάντα *in all respects, entirely* Hom. +
9 (prep.phrs.) διὰ παντός *through all time, for ever* S. Th.; *completely* Pl.; ἐς τὰ πάντα, κατὰ πάντα *altogether, completely* Th. Pl.; πρὸ παντός *above all* Pl.; περὶ παντός (w. ποιεῖσθαι *esteem*) *above all* X.; ἐπὶ πᾶν *on the whole, in general* Pl.

πᾱσάμενος (aor.mid.ptcpl.): see πάομαι

πᾱσάμην (ep.aor.mid.), **πάσασθαι** (aor.mid.inf.): see πατέομαι

πᾱσεῦμαι (dial.fut.mid.): see πάομαι

πᾱσι-μέλουσα fem.ptcpl.adj. [πᾶς, μέλω, perh. better written as two wds.] | only nom. | (of the Argo) **that is of interest to all, celebrated** Od.

πᾱσι-φανής ές adj. [φαίνομαι] (of Virtue) **shining for all to see** B.

πάσομαι (fut.mid.): see πατέομαι

πᾱ́σομαι (fut.mid.): see πάομαι

πάσον (Lacon.aor.2): see πάσχω

πασπάλη ης f. [perh.reltd. παιπάλη] app., **millet-seed** or **barley-meal**; (fig., ref. to a tiny amount) **grain, crumb** (W.GEN. of sleep) Ar.

πασπαλη-φάγος ον adj. [φαγεῖν] (of a sow) **meal-eating** Hippon.

πασσαγίη Ion.f.: see πανσαγίᾱ

πασσαλεύω, Att. **πατταλεύω** vb. [πάσσαλος] **1 fix with pegs** or **pins, peg, pin, nail** —someone (w. πρός + DAT. *to a cliff*) A. —spoils of war or hunting (W.DAT. or πρός + DAT. *to a house, its triglyphs*) A. E. || PASS. (of a person) **be pinned** or **nailed fast** —W.DAT. *w. fetters* A.
2 fix, nail —a wedge (W.PREP.PHR. *through someone's chest*) A.

πάσσαλος, Att. **πάτταλος**, ου, Megar. **πάσσᾱξ** ᾱκος *m.* [πήγνῡμι] | ep.gen.dat.sg.pl. πασσαλόφι | **1 peg** (on which arms, clothes, a lyre, or sim. are hung) Hom. hHom. Lyr. E. Ar. Theoc.; (as attachment-points for ropes) Hdt.; (w. which soldiers dig up bulbs, perh. ref. to tent-pegs) Ar.
2 peg (used to prop an animal's mouth open while inspecting its tongue for disease; also, in a threat, as a gag for a person) Ar.
3 (fig., ref. to a penis) **peg, knob** Ar.
4 (fig., ref. to sthg. small or trifling) **clothes-peg** or **pin** Ar. Call.

πάσσασθαι (ep.aor.mid.inf.): see πατέομαι

πασσέληνος, **πάσσοφος** adjs.: see πανσέληνος, πάνσοφος

πασσυδί, **πασσυδίᾳ** advs., **πασσυδίη** Ion.adv.: see πανσυδί, πανσυδίᾳ

πάσσω, Att. **πάττω** vb. | aor. ἔπασα, ep. πάσσα || pf.pass. πέπασμαι | **1 scatter, sprinkle** —W.PARTITV.GEN. *some salt* (*on meat*) Il. —W.ACC. *barley groats* (*on a sacrificial fire*) Theoc. —*drugs* (*in the air*) AR.
2 cover by sprinkling, sprinkle —*meat* (W.DAT. *w. salt*) Thphr. || PASS. (of a mulberry) **be sprinkled** —W.DAT. *w. flour* Plu.(quot.com.)
3 shower —*someone* (W.DAT. *w. roses, gold-dust*) Ar.
4 || PASS. (of woven decorations) **be sprinkled, be scattered here and there** —w. ἐν + DAT. *in the border of a robe* AR. | cf. ἐμπάσσω 2

πάσσων ep.compar.adj.: see παχύς

παστάς άδος *f.* [reltd. παραστάς] **1 external gallery** or **corridor supported by pillars** (beside a temple or sim.), **portico, colonnade** Hdt. X. Plu.
2 porch, vestibule (providing entry to a palace) AR. Plu.
3 (gener.) **chamber** (in a palace, occupied by a woman) E.; (ref. to a bedchamber) Theoc.; (ref. to the cave in which Antigone is immured) S.

παστέος ᾱ ον vbl.adj. [πάσσω] (of meat) **to be sprinkled** (W.DAT. *w. salt*) Ar.

παστήρια ων *n.pl.* [πατέομαι] **edible parts of sacrificial victims, innards** E.

πάσχα indecl.n. [Semit.loanwd.] **1 Passover** (festival) NT.
2 Passover meal NT.
3 Paschal lamb NT.

πάσχω vb. | dial.inf. πασχέμεν | fut. πείσομαι | aor.2 ἔπαθον, ep. πάθον, Lacon. πάσον (Alcm.), ptcpl. παθών, inf. παθεῖν, ep. παθέειν, subj. πάθω | pf. πέπονθα, ep.2pl. πέπασθε, also πέποσθε | ep.fem.pf.ptcpl. πεπαθυῖα | plpf. ἐπεπόνθη |
1 (gener.) **undergo, experience** —*sthg.* Od. Hdt. Trag. +; (intr.) **be passive, be the sufferer** (opp. the doer) Thgn. E. Th. Arist.
2 (w. adverse or unpleasant connots.) **undergo, experience** —*troubles, evils, harm, or sim.* Hom. +; (specif.) **suffer** —W.NEUT.ACC. *these things, many things, or sim.* Hom. +; (intr.) Trag. Th.; (leg.) ὁ παθών *the injured party* Ar. Att.orats. Pl.
3 (intr., provbl.) **suffer** (in retribution for one's actions) A. Pi.; (as a learning experience) Hes. A. S.
4 (leg.) **suffer, incur** —W.NEUT.ACC. *some penalty* E. And. Pl. X.
5 (euphem., ref. to a harmful experience) ἤν τι πάθω (or sim.) *if anything happens to me* (*i.e. if I die*) Callin. Hdt. Ar. Att.orats. Theoc.; (in other constructions, of persons or things, sts. euphem.) παθεῖν τι *come to some harm* Hom. +; (wkr.sens.) πάσχειν τι *be upset* Men.
6 (w. favourable connots.) **experience** —*things which are good, pleasant, amusing, or sim.* Eleg. Pi. Hdt. S. E. Ar. +
7 (intr., w. the nature of the experience defined by an adv.) **be treated** or **fare** —w. εὖ, κακῶς *well, badly* Od. Thgn. Pi. Hdt. Trag. Th. +—w. ἀδίκως, δικαίως *unjustly, justly* E. Th.; εὖ πάσχειν *be well off*—W.GEN. *for possessions* Thgn. Pi.
8 (gener., of persons or things) **have** (sthg.) **happen to one, be affected** —W.NEUT.ACC. or ADV. *in some respect, in the same way, or sim.* Pi. Hdt. E. Th. Ar. Att.orats. +
9 (in qs.) τί πάσχω, τί πάσχεις *what is the matter with me, with you?* E. Ar.; τί παθών ... ; *as a result of what experience* (*i.e. why ever*) ... ? Hom. Ar.; τί πάθω; *what am I to undergo* (*i.e. what is to become of me*)? Hom. Trag. Ar. Men. Theoc.; τί γὰρ πάθω; *what is to become of me* (*if I don't do sthg., i.e. how can I do otherwise*)? Hdt. +

παταγέω contr.vb. [πάταγος] | iteratv.impf. πατάγεσκον (Alc.) | **1 make a loud or sharp sound** (esp. by striking sthg.); (of a Bacchant) **make an uproar** (w. drum or clappers) Pratin.; (of hostile persons, compared to flocks of birds) **chatter, squawk** S.; (provbl., said to someone making a welcome response) καλὰ δὴ παταγεῖς *you chime nicely* Pl. || PASS. (of drums and clappers) **be sounded** (by Cybele's votaries) Lyr.adesp.
2 emit a loud or resounding noise (usu. as a result of being struck); (of a wine-jar) **ring** Alc.; (of thunder-clouds, after colliding) **crash, rumble** Ar.; (of soup, in someone's stomach, compared to thunder) Ar.; (of the sea, struck by wind and rain) **roar** Theoc.

πάταγος ου *m.* **1 loud or sharp noise** (usu. made by things striking or being struck); **crash** (of warriors meeting, battle, shields, fists) Il. S. E. Ar. Call.; (of falling rocks) Hdt.; **splash** (of bodies and rocks falling into water) Il. Pi.; **rumble** (of thunder-clouds) Ar.; **crack** (of breaking timbers) Il. Plu.; **ringing** (of horses' hooves) Call.; **clatter** (of spears, arrows in a quiver) A. S.; (of pots) Ar.; **rattle** (of metallic bridle-bits) Ar.; **clashing** (of bronze utensils, weapons) Plu.; **chattering** (of teeth) Il.
2 (gener.) **din, hubbub** (of persons carousing, soldiers on the attack, or sim.) Anacr. A. Hdt. Plu.

πατάξ interj. (addressed to birds) **shoo!** Ar.

πατάσσω vb. [reltd. πάταγος] | ep.impf. πάτασσον | fut. πατάξω | aor. ἐπάταξα | In Hom. only pres. and impf., in later writers only fut. and aor. | **1** (intr., of the heart) **knock, beat fast, thump** (fr. fear or excitement) Il.
2 deliver a blow (to a person); (intr.) **strike** (w. a weapon, hand, or sim.) S. E. Th. Ar. Att.orats. + —W.INTERN.ACC. *a blow* Pl.; (tr.) **strike** —*a person, part of the body* Lys. Ar. Pl. X. D. + | see also ἀλοάω 5
3 (fig., of a circumstance, an emotion) **affect deeply, strike** —*someone's heart* Thgn. Ar.; (of a person) —*one's spirit* (W.DAT. *w. ruin*) S.(dub.)
4 knock forcefully against (an object); **strike** —*a door* Ar. —*the ground* (w. one's foot, i.e. *stamp on it*) Theoc.; (of a person falling) —*one's back* (W.PREP.PHR. *against a pillar*) E.; (of a falling object) —*someone* D.
5 (of a thorn) **prick** —*someone* Theoc.

πατέομαι mid.contr.vb. | fut. πάσομαι | aor. ἐπασάμην, ep. ἐπασάμην, πασάμην | aor.inf. πάσασθαι, ep. πάσσασθαι | ep.plpf. πεπάσμην | **1 partake of** (food or drink); **taste, consume** —W.ACC. or GEN. *a meal, entrails, grain, wine, nectar, or sim.* Hom. Hes. A. Hdt. Ar.(mock-ep.) Call. AR. —*drugs* AR.; (intr.) **eat, dine** Il. Hdt.; (of a killer) **taste, drink** —W.GEN. *his victim's blood* S.
2 (fig., of a person) **have a taste of, engage in** —W.GEN. *talk* Call.

πατερίζω vb. [πατήρ] (of a son) **cry out 'dear father'** Ar.

πατέω contr.vb. | dial.1pl. πατεῦμες, 3pl. πατεῦσι (Call.) |
1 **tread, walk** A. Pi. NT.; (fig.) —W.GEN. *on high* (i.e. *enjoy greatness*) Pi.
2 (tr.) **tread on, walk on** or **over** —*ground, an island, mud* S. Ar. Theoc. —*fabrics, fleeces* (as a sign of luxury) A. Theoc.; **step through** —*palace gates* A.(dub.); **walk through** —*a city* (in procession) Call.; **tread** —*a path* Call.; (of carriages) **travel** —*roads* Call. ‖ PASS. (of hills) be trodden Call.
3 **crush with the foot, tread** —*grapes* Scol.; (of draught animals) **trample, thresh** —*corn* X. Call.; (wkr.sens.) **press down** (w. one's foot) —*an object on the ground* Plu.
4 (of a person or animal) **tread on injuriously, trample on** —*someone* S. Pl. X. Theoc. Plu. —*vines, laurel* Ar. Call. ‖ PASS. (of persons) be trampled on Ar. X. Plu.
5 (fig.) tread on contemptuously, **trample under foot** —*a council, a person* Ar. Plu. —*justice, regulations, honours due to the gods* S. Ar. AR.; **desecrate, defile** —*someone's bed* (by adultery w. a spouse) A. Call. ‖ PASS. (of holiness) be trampled on A.; (of a city, a country's pride) be crushed under foot NT. Plu.
6 (phr.) πέδον (or perh. πέδοι) πατεῖν *trample under foot, grind into the ground* —W.ACC. *a reputation* A. —*a command* Call.; (pass., of Justice, honours) *be trampled under foot* A.
7 **go through, study carefully** —*an author* (i.e. *his work*) Ar. Pl.

πατήρ πατρός (also poet. πατέρος) m. | voc. πάτερ | acc. πατέρα | dat. πατρί (also πατέρι) ‖ PL.: nom. πατέρες | acc. πατέρας | gen. πατέρων, ep. πατρῶν (Od.) | dat. πατράσι |
1 **father** Hom. +; πατρὸς πατήρ **grandfather** Hom. +
2 (fig., ref. to a king) **father** (of his people) Hdt.; (ref. to a brother, who holds for a sister the place of their dead father) S.; (respectful ref. to Parmenides, as a teacher) Pl.; (voc., as respectful term of address to an elder) Hom. Ar. Men.
3 (epith. of Zeus) **father** (sts. W.GEN. of gods, men, all) Hom. +
4 (ref. to God) **Father** (of men or Jesus Christ) NT.
5 ‖ PL. **forefathers, ancestors** Hom. +; (ref. to the parent nation of colonists) Hdt. Plu.
6 (fig.) **father** (W.GEN. of all things, ref. to Time) Pi.; (ref. to the creator god) Pl.; (of songs, ref. to Orpheus) Pi.; (of sunbeams, ref. to Helios) Pi.; (of laws, ref. to Olympos, i.e. the gods) S.; **author, initiator** (W.GEN. of a debate or sim.) Pl.
7 (fig.) original sum of money, **principal** (w. play on τόκος as *offspring* and *interest*) Pl.

πατησμός οῦ m. [πατέω] **treading, walking** (W.GEN. on fabrics, as a sign of luxury) A.

πάτος[1] ου m. **trodden path, path, track** (esp. as a sign of human habitation) Hom. Hes.fr. Parm. AR.

πάτος[2] εος n. **robe** (woven for Hera) Call.

πάτρα ᾱς, Ion. **πάτρη** ης f. [πατήρ] 1 **fatherland, homeland, native land** Hom. Hes.fr. Thgn. Pi. Hdt. Trag. +
2 **descent from a father, parentage, lineage** Il.
3 **body of persons descended from a common ancestor, house, clan** Pi.

—**πάτρᾱθε**, Ion. **πάτρηθεν** adv. 1 **from one's fatherland** —*ref. to travelling* AR.
2 (ref. to one's descent) **from a** (specified) **clan** Pi.

πατρ-άδελφος ου, dial. **πατραδελφεός** οῦ m. [ἀδελφός] **father's brother, uncle** Pi. Is. D.

—**πατραδελφείᾱ** (or perh. **πατραδέλφεια**) ᾱς f. (app. collectv., ref. to female cousins) **cousinhood, one's uncle's children** A.

πατρ-αλοίᾱς ου m. [ἀλοάω] **one who strikes his father, father-beater** Lys. Ar. Pl. D.

πάτρη Ion.f., **πάτρηθεν** Ion.adv.: see πάτρᾱ

πατριά ᾶς, Ion. **πατριή** ῆς f. 1 **ancestry, lineage** Hdt. NT.
2 **clan, tribe** Hdt.; **nation** NT.

πατρι-άρχης ου m. [ἄρχω] **progenitor of a race, patriarch** NT.

πατρίδιον ου n. [dimin. πατήρ] ‖ VOC. (in address to a father by his child) **daddy** Ar.; (in familiar address to an older man who is not one's father) **dad** Men.

πατρίκιος ου m. [Lat. *patricius*] (usu.pl.) **person of patrician rank, patrician** Plb. Plu.

πατρικός ή όν adj. | compar. πατρικώτερος (Isoc.) |
1 **associated with one's father or forefathers**; (of a friend) **ancestral, family** Th. Ar. Att.orats. Pl. +; (of an enemy) **hereditary** Lys. Isoc.; (of friendship, hostility, or sim.) Att.orats. Plb. Plu.; (of monarchy) Th. Isoc.; (of virtues, reputation) Th. Arist. Din.; (of an obligation) Plu.
2 **of or belonging to a** (specific) **father**; (of the voice) **of one's father** S.Ichn.; (of a loan) **made by one's father** D.; (of a pronouncement by Parmenides: cf. πατήρ 2) Pl.
3 (gener., of a model for behaviour, authority, affection, or sim.) **of a father, paternal** Arist. Plb.; (of the branch of household management dealing w. discipline over children) Arist.; (of respect) **due to a father** Arist.
4 **of a fatherly kind**; (of government or sim.) **fatherly, paternal** Arist. Plu.

—**πατρικῶς** adv. **like a father, in a paternal manner** —*ref. to political leaders dealing w. others* Arist. Plu.

πάτριος ᾱ ον (also ος ον) adj. 1 **associated with one's father or forefathers**; (of a friend) **family** E.; (of a land, city, house, or sim.) **ancestral, native** Pi. Trag. Ar. Tim.; (of monarchy) **hereditary** X. Arist.; (of gods, practices, laws, or sim.) **ancestral, hereditary** A. Hdt. E. Att.orats. +; (of a form of government) Att.orats. X. Arist.; (of a path of conduct) **traditional** Pi. ‖ NEUT.PL.SB. **inherited or traditional customs** Hdt. Th. Ar. Att.orats. Pl. + ‖ NEUT.SG.SB. **tradition** Th.
2 ‖ NEUT.IMPERS. (w. ἐστί, sts.understd.) **it is traditional** (usu. W.DAT. + INF. for someone to do sthg.) Carm.Pop. Th. Att.orats. Pl. X. Call.
3 **of or belonging to a** (specific) **father**; (of the voice, virtues, armour) **of one's father** Pi. B. S.

πατρίς ίδος fem.adj. (of a land, city, or sim.) **of one's forefathers, ancestral, native** Hom. Hes. hHom. Sol. Trag. ‖ SB. **native land, homeland** Hom. +

πατριώτης ου, dial. **πατριώτᾱς** ᾱ m. 1 **one who comes from the same country as another, fellow countryman, compatriot** (ref. to a slave, W.GEN. of another slave) Pl.; (fig., ref. to Mt. Kithairon, W.GEN. of Oedipus) S.
2 ‖ ADJ. (of a horse) **from one's own country, native** X.

—**πατριῶτις** ιδος fem.adj. (of one's land, ref. to Athens) **native** E.

πατρόθεν adv. [πατήρ] 1 **on one's father's side** —*ref. to tracing one's descent* Pi. S. Call.
2 **by one's father's name** —*ref. to addressing or identifying someone* Il. Hdt. Th. Pl. +
3 (ref. to compulsion, a curse, an avenging spirit) **originating from a father** A. Pi.
4 **through the father** (of another) —*ref. to a relationship existing* Pl.
5 **from the time of one's father** or **forefathers** —*ref. to a connection existing* Plu.

πατρο-κασίγνητος ου m. **father's brother, uncle** Hom. Hes. hHom.

πατροκτονέω contr.vb. [πατροκτόνος] kill (another's) father, **be a father-killer** A.

πατροκτονίᾱ ᾱς f. killing of one's father, **patricide** Plu.

πατρο-κτόνος ον adj. [κτείνω] **1** ‖ MASC.SB. killer of one's father, patricide A. S. Plu.
2 (of a person; of a robe, as instrument of death) **that killed a father** (of another) A.
3 (of the hand) **of a murderous father** E.

πατρο-νομέομαι pass.contr.vb. [νέμω, νόμος] (of a people) **be governed with paternal authority** (by a ruler) Pl. Plu.

πατρονομική ῆς f. (perh. w. τροφή understd.) **upbringing under parental guidance** (opp. state of being an orphan) Pl.

πατρο-πάτωρ ορος m. [πατήρ] father of one's father, **paternal grandfather** Pi. AR.

πατρο-στερής ές adj. [στερέω] (of children) **deprived of a father, fatherless** A.

πατροῦχος f.: see πατρωιοῦχος

πατρο-φονεύς ῆος ep.m. murderer of one's father, **patricide** Od.

πατρο-φόνος ον adj. [θείνω] **1** (of a hand) of one who murdered his own father, **patricidal** A. ‖ MASC.SB. patricide Pl.
2 (of a person) **who murdered a father** (of another) E.

πατρο-φόντης ου m. **1** murderer of one's father, **patricide** S.
2 murderer of a father (of another) S.

πατρωιοῦχος ου f. [πατρῷος, ἔχω] (appos.w. παρθένος unmarried girl) one who has inherited a deceased father's property, **heiress** Hdt.(cj., for πατροῦχος)

πατρῷος ᾱ ον (also ος ον), dial. **πατρώιος** ᾱ (Ion. η) ον adj. **1** associated with one's father or forefathers; (of friends) **family** Hom. E.; (of a house, home, tombs, or sim.) Hom. +; (of a land, city, or sim.) **ancestral, native** Hom. +; (of customs, courage, reputation, or sim.) **ancestral** Trag. X.; (of a skill, a responsibility) **hereditary, inherited** Pi. Hdt. S. ‖ NEUT.PL.SB. native land Hdt.
2 (of gods) traditionally worshipped by one's race or family, **ancestral** or **familial** Hdt. Trag. Th. Ar. Pl. +; (epith. of Zeus, Apollo, Hermes, Hestia; esp. as patron of one's race, family, or person) Trag. Lys. Pl. X. Arist.; (of God) NT.; (of altars, shrines, or sim.) A. Att.orats. Pl.
3 (cult title of Zeus) protector of fathers' rights, **paternal** Ar. Pl.
4 associated with a father (opp. a mother); (of lineage) **on the father's side, paternal** Plu.
5 associated with a (specific) father; (of possessions or sim.) **one's father's** Hom. +; (of sufferings, hatred for someone) **inherited from one's father** S. E. ‖ NEUT.PL.SB. patrimony, inheritance Od. Hdt. E. Ar. Att.orats. +
6 of or belonging to a father (one's own or another's); (of a tomb, throne, wife, possessions, or sim.) **of a father, a father's** Od. Pi. Trag. +; (of hands, knees, the mind, a decision) Trag.; (of blood, murder, sufferings) Trag. Ar.; (of courage, virtue, reputation, hatred for someone) Il. Pi. E. Isoc. Pl. D.
7 of or relating to a father; (of an appeal, an oath) **made to a father** A. S.; (of a standard of devotion) **due to a father** Pi.; (of grief, vengeance) **for a father** E.; (of trials, a curse) **inflicted by a father** Pi. E.

πάτρως ωος m. | acc. πάτρωα, also πάτρων (Hdt.) | dat. πάτρῳ | **1 father's brother, uncle** Hes.fr. Pi. Hdt.
2 ancestor on the father's side Stesich.

πατταλεῖον ου Att.n. [dimin. πάσσαλος] (fig., ref. to avarice) **peg** (W.GEN. of every vice, i.e. as offering support or encouragement to it) Plb.

πατταλεύω Att.vb., **πάτταλος** Att.m.: see πασσαλεύω, πάσσαλος

πάττω Att.vb.: see πάσσω

παῦ (imperatv.): see παύω

παῦλα ης f. [παύω] **cessation, end** (of a state of affairs) S. Th. Arist. Plb.; (W.GEN. of sickness, troubles, activities) B.(dub.) S. Ar. Pl. +

παυράκι adv. [παῦρος] **rarely, seldom** Thgn.

παυρίδιος η ον Ion.adj. [dimin. παῦρος] (of a period of time) **very short** Hes.

παῦρος ον adj. | compar. παυρότερος | **1** ‖ PL. **few in number**; (of persons or things) few Hom. Hes. Eleg. Lyr. Trag. Call. AR.
2 (sg., of a people, a group) **small in number** Il. E.
3 small in size or extent; (of a warp thread) **thin** Hes. [or perh. thinly spaced] ‖ NEUT.SB. small part (opp. whole, W.GEN. of a ship's keel) AR.
4 short in duration; (of a time, a life) **short, brief** Hes. Simon. Emp. Mosch.; (of a sleep) Pi.; (of a speech) Pi.
—παῦρα neut.pl.adv. **1 seldom** Hes.
2 (ref. to doing good, causing pain) **little** hHom. Ar.

παυσ-άνεμος ον adj. [παύω] (of a sacrifice) **calming the winds** A.

παυσί-λῡπος ον adj. [λύπη] (of the vine, meton. for wine) **putting an end to suffering** E.

παυσί-πονος ον adj. [πόνος] (of a rescuer) **bringing an end to the toils** (W.GEN. of slavery) E.; (of a grape tendril) toil-ending Ar.(mock-trag.)

παυστήρ ῆρος m. (ref. to a god, a rescuer) one who brings to an end, **terminator** (W.GEN. of sickness, troubles) S.

παυστήριος ᾱ ον adj. (of a god) **bringing an end** (W.GEN. to a sickness) S.

παυσωλή ῆς f. **cessation, respite** (fr. fighting) Il.

παύω vb. | colloq. imperatv. παῦ (for παῦε) Men. | iteratv.impf. παύεσκον | fut. παύσω | aor. ἔπαυσα, ep. παῦσα | pf. πέπαυκα ‖ MID.: pf. πέπαυμαι | fut.pf. πεπαύσομαι (S.) ‖ PASS.: fut. παυσθήσομαι | aor. ἐπαύσθην, also ἐπαύθην, ep. παύθην ‖ neut.impers.vbl.adj. παυστέον |
1 cause (someone or sthg.) to cease from an action; **check, restrain, stop** —someone or sthg. Hom. +—(W.GEN. fr. sthg.) Hom. +—(W.PTCPL. fr. doing sthg.) Il. +—(W.INF. fr. doing sthg.) Il. Hdt. —(w. μή or τὸ μή + INF.) A. Th. Ar.; (euphem.) **put a stop to, silence** (i.e. kill) —someone Od. S.
2 cause (sthg.) to cease; **bring to an end, stop, end** —an activity, a condition, an emotion Hom. + ‖ PASS. (of war) be stopped Th.; (of an empire) be brought to an end Th.
3 cause (someone) to be released (fr. sthg.); **relieve, free** —someone (W.GEN. fr. suffering, other unwelcome conditions) Hom. +; (w. ἐκ or ἀπό + GEN.) S. X.
4 cause (someone) to be removed (fr. sthg.); **remove** —someone (W.GEN. fr. kingship, an office) Hdt. Th. X.; **depose** —an official Th.; **detach** —someone (W.GEN. fr. an alliance) Th. ‖ PASS. be removed —W.GEN. fr. an office Hdt.
5 ‖ MID. cease from an action; **cease, desist** Hom. + —W.GEN. fr. sthg. Hom. + —w. ἐκ + GEN. E. —W.PTCPL. fr. doing sthg. Hom. +; take one's rest Il.; (of conditions or inanimate things) **cease, abate, come to an end** Hom. + ‖ PASS. cease —W.GEN. fr. anger Hes.
6 ‖ MID. **find relief** or **deliverance** —W.GEN. fr. war, troubles, or sim. Hom. + —w. ἐκ + GEN. E. Ar.
7 ‖ PRES.SG.IMPERATV. (intr.) stop, leave off, desist S. E. Ar. Pl. Men. —W.GEN. fr. sthg. Hes. Ar. —W.PTCPL. fr. doing sthg. Ar.

Πάφιος adj.: see under Πάφος

παφλάζω, Aeol. **παφλάσδω** vb. **1** (of waves) **seethe, bubble** Il.; (perh. of wine) Alc.; (of air) Emp.
2 (fig., of a person) **splutter, bluster** Ar.
παφλάσματα των n.pl. **splutterings, blusterings** (ref. to declamation of paratragic verses) Ar.
Πάφος ου f. **Paphos** (town on SW. coast of Cyprus, assoc.w. Aphrodite) Od. +
—**Πάφιος** ᾱ ον adj. (of a person) from Paphos, **Paphian** Hdt.; (epith. of Aphrodite) Ar. ‖ FEM.SB. Paphian goddess Theoc. Bion
πάχετος ον adj. [παχύς] (of a discus, the trunk of an olive tree) **thick, stout** Od.
πάχιστος ep.superl.adj.: see παχύς
πάχνη ης, dial. **πάχνᾱ** ᾱς f. [πήγνῡμι] **1** frozen dew or mist (coating the ground or skin), **hoar-frost, rime** Od. A. Pl. X. Call. AR. Plu.
2 (fig.) **clotted blood** A.
παχνόω contr.vb. (fig., of theft) **freeze, chill** —the heart (of the victim) Hes. ‖ PASS. (of a person or heart, through grief or despair) be chilled, go cold A. E. AR.; (of the heart of a hunted lion) Il.
πάχος εος (ους) n. [παχύς] **1** (as a dimension) **thickness** (of an object, a serpent; sts. opp. length) Od. Pi. Hdt. Th. +
2 (as a quality) **thickness** (opp. thinness) Pl.; **plumpness, fatness** (W.GEN. of a person's flesh) E.Cyc.
παχύ-δερμος ον adj. [δέρμα] thick-skinned; (fig., of a person) **thick-witted, insensitive** Men.
παχύ-κνημος ον adj. [κνήμη] (of unhealthy persons) **thick-calved** Ar.
παχυλῶς adv. **in a rough and ready way** —ref. to demonstrating sthg. Arist.
παχύνω vb. ‖ aor. ἐπάχῡνα ‖ **1** impart thickness ‖ MID. (of a runner or boxer) **build oneself up** (by exercising) —W.ACC. in one's shoulders or legs X. ‖ PASS. (of a skull) become thicker and stronger Hdt.; (of a horse's legs) X.; (of runners, boxers) —W.ACC. in their legs, shoulders X.
2 fatten up —human bodies, animals Pl. X. ‖ PASS. get fattened up Ar.
3 (fig.) fatten, **build up, increase** —wrath A. ‖ PASS. (of wealth) become fat or bloated A.; (of a person) become spoilt Plu.
4 ‖ PASS. (fig., of understanding) be made dull, be blunted NT.
παχύς εῖα ύ adj. ‖ compar. παχύτερος, ep. πάσσων ‖ superl. παχύτατος, ep. πάχιστος ‖
1 (of things) thick in dimension (opp. thin); (of a muscle, human skin, animal hide) **thick** Il. Hdt. Ar.; (of lips, bone) X.; (of a staff, spear, or sim.) Il. Hdt. X. Plb.; (of a tree, ref. to its trunk) Hes. X.; (of a stone, at the base, opp. pointed, at the top) Il.; (of a wall, timbers) Th.; (of gold plating) Hdt.; (of a wick, a rope) Ar.; (of fetters) Ar. D.; (of clothing) Pl. X. Thphr.
2 (of a person) solid or well-built, **sturdy** Od.; (of the hand of a warrior, Hera or Penelope) Hom. hHom. Theoc.; (of a warrior's thigh, the Cyclops' neck) Hom.
3 (of a person) **fat** (opp. thin) Pl.; (W.PREP.PHR. around the ankles) Archil.; (of a foot) **swollen** Hes.; (of a pig, a sacrificial animal) **plump** Ar. Men. Call.; (of an erect penis) **thick, big** Ar.; (w. sexual double entendre, of gratitude, a topic) Ar.
4 (of persons) **fat, plump** (as a sign of prosperity) Ar. Men.; **prosperous, wealthy** Hdt. Ar.
5 (pejor., of a poem) **fat, bloated** Call.
6 (of liquids or sim.) thick in consistency; (of a jet of blood) **thick** Od.; (of blood) **clotted** Il.; (of juice, paste) **thick, dense** Hdt.; (of fog) Men.; (of soil) **rich, heavy** X.
7 (of a person) thick-witted, **thick, dense, stupid** Ar.

—**παχέως** adv. ‖ compar. παχύτερον, also παχυτέρως ‖
1 broadly, roughly, crudely —ref. to defining or prescribing sthg. Pl. Arist.(cj.)
2 thick-wittedly, **dimly** —ref. to understanding sthg. Pl.
πᾶχυς dial.m.: see πῆχυς
παχύτης ητος f. **1 thickness** (of stalks, ropes, skin) Hdt.; (of timbers) Th.; (of embossed metalwork) Plu.
2 thickness, density (of lees) Hdt.
παχύ-φρων ονος masc.fem.adj. [φρήν] **thick-witted** Arist.
Πάων Aeol.m.: see Παιών
πεδά dial.prep.: see μετά
πέδαι ῶν (dial. ᾱν) f.pl. —also **πέδη** ης, dial. **πέδᾱ** ᾱς f.sg. [πούς] **1** fetters for the legs; **hobbles** (for horses' legs) Il.; (gener.) **fetters, shackles** (usu. for humans) Il. Eleg. A. Parm. Hdt. Ar. +; (fig., ref. to a robe impeding movt.) A.; (w.epith. of Greece, said by Philip of Greek cities in Macedonian hands) Plb.; (fig., ref. to fishing nets) **traps** E.fr. ‖ SG. fetter Semon. S.; (fig., ref. to a poisoned robe which adheres to its wearer) S.
2 ‖ SG. a kind of exercise for horses (involving turning) X.
πεδαίρω, **πεδαίχμιος**, **πεδαμείβω**, **πεδάορος**, **πεδάρσιος** (dial. forms): see μεταίρω, μεταίχμιος, μεταμείβω, μετέωρος, μετάρσιος
πεδ-αυγάζω dial.vb. [πεδά, see μετά] **watch out** (for someone) Pi.
πεδάω contr.vb. [πέδαι] ‖ ep.3sg. (w.diect.) πεδάᾳ ‖ iteratv.impf. (w.diect.) πεδάασκον ‖ aor. ἐπέδησα, ep. πέδησα, dial. πέδᾱσα ‖
1 fetter, shackle —a person Hdt.; (fig., of sleep) Od. S.
2 secure —doors (w. a rope) Od.(dub.) ‖ see ἐπιδέω[1] 2
3 (of gods, fate) constrain as if with fetters; **shackle, fetter, hold in check** —a warrior, his limbs Hom. AR. —a warrior (W.DAT. w. slaughter, i.e. kill him) Pi.fr. —a ship (by turning it into stone) Od. —a spear Pi.; **constrain, force** —someone (W.INF. to remain on the spot) Il. —(to succumb to persuasion, death) Od.; (of Fate, Necessity) —existence (to remain changeless), heaven (to hold the stars in place) Parm.
4 (fig., of persons) **fetter, entrap** —someone (W.DAT. by trickery) Pi. —(in a robe) A.; (of a charioteer) **hold back, obstruct** —a rival's chariot Il.; (of a wounded horse) —its chariot Pi.; (of a sorceress) —motions of heavenly bodies AR.; (of sensations) —motions of the soul (ref. to the power of reasoning) Pl. ‖ PASS. (of a person) be checked (by an opponent) Pi.fr.; be constrained —W.ACC. in strength (by sickness) Pi.fr. —in capacity for reasoning (by sleep) Pl.; (of a ship) be held fast (by currents) AR.
πεδεινός adj.: see πεδιεινός
πεδέρχομαι, **πεδέχω** Aeol.vbs.: see μετέρχομαι, μετέχω
πεδέτροπε (Aeol.3sg.aor.2): see μετατρέπω
πέδη f.: see πέδαι
πεδήπομεν (Aeol.1pl.impf.): see μεθέπω
πεδιακοί ῶν m.pl. [πεδίον] inhabitants of the plain, **plainsmen** (ref. to an Athenian political faction in 6th C. BC) Arist.
πεδιάς άδος fem.adj. **1** (of ground, a region) **flat, level** Hdt. Pl. Plb. Plu.; (of a highway) Pi. E.
2 (of a wood) **on a plain** S.; (of a battle) Plu.
3 (of spearmen) **on a battlefield** S.
πεδιεινός, also **πεδεινός**, **πεδῑνός**, ή όν adj. ‖ compar. πεδιεινότερος (Pl.), πεδιεώτερος (X., dub. for πεδῑνότερος) ‖
1 (of ground, a region) **flat, level** Hdt. Pl. X. Plb. NT. Plu.; (of a route, a military retreat) **over level ground** X. Plb. Plu.
2 (of hares) **found on the plains** (opp. mountains) X.
πεδιεῖς έων m.pl. **plainsmen** Plu. ‖ see πεδιακοί
πεδι-ήρης ες adj. [ἀραρίσκω] (of regions) consisting of plains, **plain-filled** A.

πέδῐλον ου *n.* [πούς] **1** (usu.pl.) **sandal** (worn by gods and humans, male and female) Hom. Hes. Pi. E. Ar. Lycophronid. +; (sg., in fig.ctxt., ref. to a situation into which one puts one's foot, i.e. enters) Pi.
2 shoe (made of hide) Od. Hes.; **boot** (covering half or all of the calf, as worn by barbarian races) Hdt.; (made of fawnskins) Hdt.
3 (meton., ref. to a dancer's sandal) **measure, rhythm** (of a choral ode) Pi.

πεδῐνός *adj.*: see πεδιεινός

πεδίον ου *n.* [πέδον] **1 stretch of low-lying and level ground, plain** Hom. +; (ref. to a specific plain, w. name given by GEN. or ADJ.) Hom. +; (w.art., ref. to the plain of Attica) Hdt. Th. Is. D.
2 (in provbl. ctxt.) **field of battle** Pl.
3 expanse (of sea) E. Tim.
4 (fig., ref. to the female pubic area) **nether regions** Ar.

—**πεδίονδε** *adv.* (ref. to movt.) **to the plain** Hom. Hes. hHom. AR.; (w. sexual connot.) **to the nether regions** Ar.

πεδιο-νόμος ον *adj.* [νέμω] (of deities) **inhabiting the plains, rural** A.

πεδο-βάμων ον, gen. ονος *dial.adj.* [πέδον; βῆμα, βαίνω] (of creatures) **ground-walking** (opp. winged) A.

πεδόθεν, πέδοι *advs.*: see under πέδον

πεδ-οιχνέω *dial.contr.vb.* [πεδά, see μετά] **go in search of, seek** —*sthg.* B.

πέδον ου *n.* [πούς] **1 surface of the earth, ground, earth** Pi. Trag. Ar. AR. || DAT. **on the ground** hHom. Pi. E. Theoc.*epigr.*; **to or onto the ground** S. E. Call. | For πέδον (or πέδοι) πατεῖν *trample under foot* see πατέω 6.
2 (ref. to a specific region or sacred site, oft. w. its name or that of its inhabitants or patron deity given by GEN. or ADJ.) **ground, place, region** B. Trag. Ar. Call. AR.
3 expanse, region (w.GEN. of heaven) E.*fr.*

—**πεδόθεν** *adv.* **1** (ref. to movt., by persons or things) **from the ground** E. AR.; **from the sea-floor** Pi.
2 from the foundations —*ref. to a mountain being shaken* Hes.; (fig.) —*ref. to love (likened to a storm-wind) affecting the mind* Ibyc.
3 app., from the bottom of one's heart, **fundamentally, deeply** —*ref. to being fond of deceitful stories* Od.; perh. **comprehensively** —*ref. to composing a narrative* Pi.

—**πέδοι** *adv.* (ref. to movt., by persons or things) **to or towards the ground** A. | see also πατέω 6

—**πέδονδε** *adv.* (ref. to movt.) **to or towards the ground or the level ground** Hom. hHom. S.

—**πεδόσε** *adv.* (ref. to movt.) **to the ground** E.

πέδ-ορτος ον *adj.* [ὄρνυμι] (of the sound of stamping feet) **arising from the ground** S.*Ichn.*

πεδο-στιβής ές *adj.* [στείβω] **1** (of creatures) **ground-treading** (opp. winged) A.; (of a foot, opp. wings) E.; (of soldiers) **marching** (opp. mounted on horses) A.; (of a carriage, opp. ship) **travelling by land** E.
2 (of fatigue) **from marching** E.

πεζᾷ *dial.fem.dat.adv.*: see πεζῇ, under πεζός

πέζα ης *f.* [πούς] **1 foot, extremity, end** (of a chariot-pole, where the yoke was attached) Il.
2 edge, border, hem (of a tunic) AR.
3 coastline AR.

πεζ-ακοντιστής οῦ *m.* [πεζός] **foot-soldier armed with a javelin, foot-javelineer** (Roman *ueles*) Plb.

πέζ-αρχος ου *m.* [ἄρχω] **infantry-commander** X.

πεζ-έταιροι ων *m.pl.* [ἑταῖρος] **footguards** (name of a detachment in the Macedonian army) D. Plu.

πεζεύω *vb.* **1** (of persons, esp. soldiers) **go on foot** (opp. by sea or on horseback) Isoc. X. Plb. NT. Plu.; **be a foot-soldier** Arist.
2 (gener.) **walk about** —w.ACC. **on foot** E.

πεζῇ *fem.dat.adv.*: see under πεζός

πεζῐκός ή όν *adj.* **1 of or relating to a foot-soldier** (opp. cavalryman); (of armour) **of a foot-soldier** or **infantryman** Pl. || NEUT.PL.SB. **infantry skills** X.
2 of or relating to the infantry (opp. the navy); (of military strength, troops, or sim.) **infantry, land-based** X. Arist. Plb. Plu.

πεζο-βόᾱς ᾱ *dial.m.* [βοή] **infantryman who raises the battle-cry, fighting foot-soldier** Pi.

πεζο-θηρικός ή όν *adj.* [θήρᾱ] (of one of two kinds of hunting) **concerned with hunting land-animals** (opp. water-animals) Pl.

πεζομάχᾱς ᾱ *dial.m.* [μάχη] (appos.w. ἀνήρ) **foot-soldier, infantryman** Pi.

πεζομαχέω *contr.vb.* | Aeol.masc.acc.pl.ptcpl. πεσδομάχεντας (cj.) | **1** (of soldiers) **fight on foot** (opp. fr. horse or chariot) Sapph.(cj.); (of a cavalryman who has lost his horse) Plb.
2 fight on land (opp. at sea) Hdt. Ar. Att.orats. X. Plu. —W.DAT. **against someone** Th.; **fight a land-battle** —W.PREP.PHR. *fr. one's ships* Th.

πεζομαχίᾱ ᾱς, Ion. **πεζομαχίη** ης *f.* **1 land-battle** (opp. sea-battle) Hdt. Th. Aeschin. Plb. Plu.
2 infantry-fight (opp. cavalry-fight) Plb.

πεζο-μάχος ον *adj.* [μάχομαι] (of a commander, a soldier) **who fights on land** (opp. at sea) Plu.

πεζονομικός ή όν *adj.* [πεζονόμος] (of the art) **of tending creatures that go on foot** (opp. birds) Pl. || FEM.SB. **art of tending creatures that go on foot** Pl.

πεζο-νόμος ον *adj.* [νέμω] (of commanders) **governing land-forces** A.

πεζοπορέω *contr.vb.* [πόρος] **1** (of a cavalryman) **go on foot** (opp. on horseback) X.
2 (of soldiers) **travel on foot, march** Plb.

πεζός ή όν, Aeol. **πέσδος** ᾱ ον *adj.* [πούς] **1** (of warriors) **on foot** (opp. in a chariot) Hom.; (of a god) hHom.; (of persons, opp. in a carriage) Od. || MASC.PL.SB. **foot-soldiers** (opp. those in chariots) Hom. Sapph.; **runners in a foot-race** (opp. charioteers) AR.
2 (of soldiers) **on foot** (opp. on horseback) Hdt. Call.*epigr.*; (of a military force) **infantry** (opp. cavalry) Hdt. X. || MASC.SG.SB. **infantry** Hdt. || NEUT.SG.SB. **infantry** X. Thphr. || MASC.PL.SB. **infantrymen, infantry** Th. X. D.
3 (of a military force) **land-based, land** (opp. naval) A. Hdt. Th. Att.orats. + || MASC.SG.SB. **land-army, land-forces** Hdt. Th. || NEUT.SG.SB. **land-forces** Th. Isoc. || MASC.PL.SB. **land-troops** A. Ar.
4 (of a battle or sim.) **on land** Ar. Isoc. Pl. D. || NEUT.PL.SB. **land-based fighting** Th.
5 (of animals, opp. birds and fishes) **land** Pl. Arist.; (of hunting) **of land-animals** Pl. || NEUT.SG. and PL.SB. **land-animals** Pl.
6 (quasi-advbl., of persons travelling) **by land** (opp. by sea) Hom. A. Pi. E. Th. AR. Theoc.; (opp. by swimming) Call.
7 (fig., of a type of writing) **pedestrian** (i.e. not elevated, prob.ref. to iambic verse) Call.

—**πεζῇ**, dial. **πεζᾷ** (Theoc.) *fem.dat.adv.* **1 on foot** (opp. in a chariot or on horseback) Hdt. Pl. X. D.; (opp. by swimming or sailing) X.
2 on or **by land** (opp. sea, esp.ref. to an army travelling) Hdt. Th. Pl. +
3 (fig.) **in prose** (opp. verse) Pl.

πεῖ¹ *indecl.n.* [Semit.loanwd.] **pi** (letter of the Greek alphabet, later πῖ) Pl.

πεῖ² *dial.interrog.adv.*: see πῇ

πειθ-ανάγκη ης *f.* [πείθω] **compulsion under the guise of persuasion** Plb.

πειθ-άνωρ ορος *dial.masc.fem.adj.* [ἀνήρ] (of a person, envisaged as a horse) obeying men, **obedient** A.

πειθαρχέω *contr.vb.* [πείθαρχος] **obey authority; be obedient** —W.DAT. *to persons, laws, instructions* S. E. Ar. Isoc. Pl. +; (intr.) Isoc. X. Arist. Men. Plu.; (mid.) Hdt.

πειθαρχία ᾱς *f.* **obedience** A. S. Isoc. Pl. X. Plu.

πειθαρχικός ή όν *adj.* (of a person, a part of the soul) **disposed to be obedient** (sts. W.DAT. *to sthg.*) Arist. Plu.; (of the virtue) **of obedience** Plu.

πείθ-αρχος ον *adj.* [πείθω, ἀρχή] (of a mind) **obeying authority, obedient** A.

πειθ-ήνιος ον *adj.* [ἡνίαι] (of a horse) **obedient to the reins** Plu.; (fig., of people) **obedient** (sts. W.DAT. *to someone, to laws*) Plu.

πειθώ οῦς *f.* **1** exercise of persuasion or capacity to persuade, **persuasiveness, persuasion** (by language or rhetoric) Trag. Th. Pl. X. +
2 means of persuading, **inducement** E. Ar.; means of inducing belief, **assurance, proof** (of sthg.) E.
3 obedience X.; app. **confidence, trust** (placed in someone) E.*fr.*
—**Πειθώ** οῦς (Lacon. ῶς), Aeol. **Πείθω** ως *f.* **Persuasion** (deity assoc.w. both sexual and verbal allurement) Hes. Lyr. Parm. Hdt. Trag. Ar. +

πείθω *vb.* | dial.inf. πειθέμεν (Pi.) | Aeol.inf. πίθην, ptcpl. πίθεις | impf. ἔπειθον, ep. πεῖθον | fut. πείσω, ep.inf. πεισέμεν | ep.redupl.fut. πεπιθήσω | ep.fut. (w.mid.pass.sens.) πιθήσω | aor.1 ἔπεισα | ep.redupl.aor.2 πέπιθον, inf. πεπιθεῖν, ptcpl. πεπιθών (also w.mid.pass.sens. Pi.), subj. πεπίθω, opt. πεπίθοιμι | dial.aor.2 πίθον (Pi.), 3du. πιθέτᾱν, (more freq.) inf. πιθεῖν, ptcpl. πιθών, opt. πίθοιμι | also ep.aor.ptcpl. (w.mid.pass.sens.) πιθήσᾱς | pf.1 πέπεικα | pf.2 (w.mid.pass.sens.) πέποιθα, imperatv. πέπισθι (A.), subj. πεποίθω, opt. πεποιθοίην | 3sg.plpf.1 ἐπεπείκει | ep.plpf.2 (w.mid.pass.sens.) 1sg. πεποίθεα, 3sg. πεποίθει, 1pl. ἐπέπιθμεν, Ion.3pl. ἐπεποίθεσαν ǁ MID.: fut. πείσομαι | aor.2 ἐπιθόμην, ep. πιθόμην | aor.2 opt. πιθοίμην, ep.redupl. πεπιθοίμην ǁ PASS.: fut. πεισθήσομαι | aor. ἐπείσθην | mid.pass.pf. πέπεισμαι ǁ neut.impers.vbl.adj. (in both act. and pass.sens.) πειστέον |
1 win over (someone) to an act or course of action (esp. by speech or entreaty, oft. opp. compulsion or deception); **win over, prevail upon, persuade** —*persons, their heart or mind* Hom. + —(W.INF. *to do sthg.*) Il. + —(w. ὥστε + INF.) Thgn. Hdt. S. E. Th. —(W.PREP.PHR. *to a course of action*) Th. —(W.NEUT.ACC. *about sthg., i.e. to do it*) Hdt. Trag. Pl.
2 (oft. pejor.) win over by financial inducement, **induce, suborn** —*someone* (usu. W.DAT. or PREP.PHR. w. *money or sim.*) Hdt. Th. Lys. X. —(W.INF. *to do sthg.*) Hdt.
3 convince (someone) of the truth of something; **convince, persuade** —*persons, their heart or mind* Od. —*one's own mind* Pi. —*someone* (w. 2ND ACC. *of sthg.*) Pi.*fr.* Trag. —(W.COMPL.CL. *that sthg. is the case*) Hdt. S. Pl. —(W.ACC. + INF.) Hdt. —(W.ACC. + PTCPL.) Th.; **convince** —*oneself (i.e. believe, be confident*) And. Pl. —W.ACC. + INF. *that sthg. is the case* Th.
4 ǁ MID.PASS. (also ep.fut.) let oneself be won over (so as to obey); **be persuaded, comply** Hom. +; **comply with, obey** —W.DAT. *someone or sthg.* Hom. + —W.GEN. *someone* Il. Hdt.

E. Th.; **be persuaded, obey a request** (oft. W.DAT. by someone) —W.INF. or ὥστε + INF. *to do sthg.* Pi. Trag. Th. Pl.
5 ǁ MID.PASS. yield to something about to occur; **resign oneself** —W.DAT. *to old age, an unwelcome meal, night* Hom.
6 ǁ MID.PASS. let oneself be won over (so as to believe); **be persuaded, be convinced** Hdt. E. + —W.NEUT.ACC. *about sthg.* A. Hdt. E. —W.COMPL.CL. or ACC. + INF. *that sthg. is the case* Hom. Hdt. S.*Ichn.* E. +; **be convinced by, believe** —W.DAT. *a person, message, version of events* Od. Hdt. E. —*a person* (i.e. *his statement*, W.ACC. *about sthg.*) Ar. Pl. —(W.INF. *that sthg. is the case*) X.
7 ǁ STATV.PF.2 and PLPF.2 ACT. (also, less freq., mid. and pass.) feel assurance or confidence (that sthg. is true) Hom. Trag.; put one's trust in, rely on, have confidence in —W.DAT. *persons, things, abstract or personal qualities* Hom. Hes. Thgn. Pi. Trag. —*oneself* Pl.; have confidence (sts. W.DAT. in someone or sthg.) —W.INF. *to do sthg., that one* (or *someone*) *will do sthg., or sim.* Hom. Pi. Hdt. Trag.
8 ǁ EP.AOR.PTCPL. trusting in, relying on —W.DAT. *persons, things, abstract or personal qualities* Hom. Hes. hHom.; giving way —W.DAT. *to a state of mind* Il. Pi.; persuaded —W.DAT. *by a gift* A.

πείκω *ep.vb.*: see πέκω

πεῖν (aor.2 inf.): see πίνω

πεῖνα *f.*: see πείνη

πεινάω *contr.vb.* [πείνη] | 2sg. πεινῇς, 3sg. πεινῇ, dial.3pl. πεινῶντι | ep.ptcpl. πεινάων, dial.masc.dat.sg. πεινάντι | inf. πεινῆν, ep.Ion. πεινήμεναι | fut. πεινήσω, later πεινάσω (NT.) | aor. ἐπείνησα, later ἐπείνασα (NT.) |
1 (of persons, animals) **be hungry** Il. Hdt. Ar. Pl. X. + —W.GEN. *for food* Od.
2 (fig.) **be hungry for, crave after** —W.GEN. *money, praise* X. —W.ACC. *righteousness* NT.
3 be in want —W.GEN. *of good things, allies* Pl. X.

πείνη (also **πεῖνα**) ης *f.* **1** extreme scarcity of food, **famine** Od.; **hunger** (as a bodily sensation, sts. opp. thirst) Pl. Arist. Call.
2 (fig.) **craving** (W.GEN. *for sthg.*) Pl.

πεινητικός ή όν *adj.* (of a person) **who deliberately goes hungry** Arist.

πειρά ᾶς *f.* [πείρω] **cutting-edge** (of a cleaver) A.

πεῖρα ᾱς (Ion. ης), Lacon. **πῆρα** ᾱς (Alcm.) *f.* **1** process of testing (so as to gain knowledge); **trial, experimentation** Alcm. Thgn. Pi. S.
2 experiment, trial, test (sts. W.GEN. *of someone or sthg.*) Pi. E. Th. Ar. Pl. AR.; (phr.) πεῖραν λαμβάνειν **make a test** (oft. W.GEN. *of someone or sthg.*) Att.orats. Pl. X. Arist. +
3 result of testing; **experience** (sts. W.GEN. *of someone or sthg.*) Thgn. Th. Pl. X. +; result of experience, **acquaintance** (W.GEN. w. *someone*) X.; (phr.) πεῖραν διδόναι **give evidence** (oft. W.GEN. *of sthg.*) Th. Att.orats. Pl. X. +
4 (gener.) process of trying (to do sthg.), **trying, endeavour** Hdt. Pl. Theoc.
5 (sg. and pl.) **attempt, undertaking, venture, enterprise** A. S. Th. Ar. D. +; **attack, assault** (W.GEN. by someone) A.; (W.GEN. on someone) S.; **attempt** (on someone's life) Plu.; **overture, approach** (by an unwelcome suitor) Plu.

πειράζω *vb.* **1** make trial of (someone's views, by questioning), **test, sound out** —W.GEN. *someone* Od. Plb. —W.ACC. NT.; (intr.) Od. AR.
2 (of the Devil) **test, tempt** (someone) NT.
3 (gener.) **attempt** —W.INF. *to do sthg.* Plb. NT.; (of soldiers) **make an attempt on** —W.ACC. *a ridge* Plb.
4 begin —W.GEN. *a song* AR.

Πειραιεύς, later **Πειραεύς**, έως (Att. ῶς) *m.* | acc. Πειραιέα, Att. Πειραιᾶ | αι sts. scans as short (Ar. Men.) | **Peiraieus** (main harbour of Athens) Hdt. Th. Ar. Att.orats. +

—**Πειραιοῖ** *loc.dat.adv.* **at Peiraieus** Lys. X.

—**Πειραϊκός** ή όν *adj.* (of a gate at Athens) **Peiraic** Plu.

πειραίνω *dial.vb.* [πεῖραρ] | aor.ptcpl. πειρήνᾱς ‖ 3sg.pf.pass. πεπείρανται ‖ cf. περαίνω | **1** (of a judge) **bring to an end, settle** —*legal disputes* Pi. ‖ PASS. (of actions) be completed Od. S.

2 fasten —*a rope* (W.PREP.PHR. *around someone*) Od. | cf. πεῖραρ 6

3 [cf. πείρω] app. **pierce** (w. an awl) —w. διά + ACC. *through a shell* hHom. [unless tm. διά ... πειραίνω]

πειράομαι *mid.contr.vb.* [πεῖρα] | fut. πειρᾱ́σομαι, Ion. πειρήσομαι | aor. ἐπειρᾱσάμην, Ion. ἐπειρησάμην, ep. πειρησάμην | pf. πεπείρᾱμαι, Ion. πεπείρημαι | Ion.3pl.plpf. ἐπεπειρέατο ‖ PASS.: aor. (usu. w.mid.sens.) ἐπειρᾱ́θην, Ion. ἐπειρήθην, ep. πειρήθην ‖ neut.sg.impers.vbl.adj. πειρᾱτέον, also pl. πειρᾱτέα |

1 make a test, trial or experiment (by words or actions, usu. w. the purpose of learning sthg.); **make a test, try an experiment** Hom. +; **try one's fortune** (in a fight, contest, or sim.) Hom.; **test** —W.INDIR.Q. *whether sthg. is the case* Il. Thgn. A. Pl. —*sthg.* (W.INDIR.Q. *to see whether it does sthg.*) Il.

2 test (by questioning) for veracity or reliability; **test, sound out** —W.GEN. *someone* Hom. A. Hdt. —*a god* Hdt.

3 test (by action or combat) for ability or quality; **test** —W.GEN. *an opponent, his weapons* Il. Hes. A. —*someone's mind, one's resolve* Thgn. Pi. —*someone* (W.ACC. *in a contest*) Od.; **try out** —W.GEN. *one's strength or sim.* Hom. —*one's fortune* (i.e. chance one's luck) A. —*sexual manoeuvres* Ar.

4 get experience (of sthg.); **experience** —W.GEN. *freedom, slavery, misfortunes, good things, or sim.* Hdt. E. Th. Att.orats. + —*words and deeds* Heraclit.; **become acquainted** —W.GEN. *w. someone* Th. Att.orats. Pl. —*w. arrows* (by being struck by them) Od.; **discover through experience** —W.COMPL.CL. *that sthg. is the case* Lys. —W.GEN. *someone* (W.COMPL.CL. or PREDIC.ADJ. *as being such and such*) Lys. Plu.; (intr.) **learn through experience** S. ‖ PF. have experience —W.GEN. *of ships* Hes. —*of a nation* Hdt.; be experienced X. —W.DAT. *in sthg.* Od.

5 make an attempt (to accomplish sthg.); **attempt, endeavour, try** Hom. + —W.INF. *to do sthg.* Il. + —w. ὅπως + SUBJ. *to ensure that sthg. happens* X. —W.PTCPL. *doing sthg.* Hdt. Pl. —W.ACC. *a stratagem or sim.* S. X.

6 attempt, undertake, engage in —W.GEN. *a contest, a task* Hom. Pi. S. —*a fight, a sea-battle* Pi. Th.; **try one's hand** —W.GEN. *w. a bow* (i.e. to string it) Od.

7 make an aggressive attempt (on someone or sthg.); **make an attempt** or **attack** —W.GEN. *on opponents, a city, a wall, or sim.* Hom. Hdt. Th.; (intr.) Il. Hdt. Th.; (w. sexual connot., of Ixion) —W.ACC. *on Hera* Pi.

—**πειράω** *act.contr.vb.* | Lacon.3sg.imperatv. πηρήτω (Alcm.) | fut. πειρᾱ́σω, Ion. πειρήσω | aor. ἐπείρᾱσα, ep.Ion. πείρησα (AR.) | **1 test, sound out** —W.GEN. *someone* Il.; **try out** —W.GEN. *weapons* AR.; **test** —W.INDIR.Q. *whether sthg. is possible* Th.; **make a test** (of gold) Pi.

2 attempt, try (to do sthg.) Th. —W.INF. *to do sthg.* Il. hHom. Alcm. S. Th. —W.ACC. *many things, every device* Th. —w. ὡς or ὅπως + SUBJ. or OPT. *to ensure that sthg. happens* Hom.

3 attempt to gain, strive after —W.GEN. *wealth* Pi.*fr.*

4 (of troops) **make an attempt** or **attack** Hdt. Th. —W.GEN. *on opponents, places* Hdt. Th. —(of a lion) —*on flocks* Hom.

5 make a sexual attempt (on someone); **make advances to, proposition** —W.ACC. *a woman* Lys. Ar. X. —*a man or boy* E.*Cyc.* Th. Ar.; (intr.) Th. Ar.; **make an attempt at** —W.GEN. *union w. another's wife* Pi. ‖ PASS. (of a man or boy) be propositioned (by a man) Th. Pl.

πεῖραρ ατος *dial.n.* [prob.reltd. πείρω, πέρᾱ², πόρος] | usu. pl., sts. for sg. | cf. πέρας | **1 end, limit, boundary** (oft. W.GEN. of the earth or sim.) Hom. Hes. hHom. Alc. Parm. AR.; (of the soul) Heraclit.; (of helplessness) Thgn.; perh. **extreme** (W.GEN. of misery) Od.; **compass** (of one's words) Emp.

2 (w. temporal connot.) **end, completion** (W.GEN. of labours, a journey, or sim.) Od. AR.

3 (w. causal connot.) **power of determining an outcome, determination** (of a dispute, by an arbitrator) Il.; **power** (over), **key** (W.GEN. to life and death, as held by Zeus, by a vein in the body) Lyr.adesp. AR.

4 means of accomplishing (W.GEN. an art, a contest, or sim.) Hom. Pi.; **means of achieving** (W.GEN. victory, virtue, or sim.) Il. Archil. Sol. Thgn.

5 (periphr.) **final limit, end, finality** (W.GEN. of destruction, ref. to death in battle) Il.

6 (concr.) **boundary as physical link, rope, cord** (to restrain someone) Od. hHom.; (fig., W.GEN. of destruction) Hom.; (of strife and war, fig.ref. to a rope stretched over opposing armies) Il.; (fig.) **strand** (of a narrative) Pi.

πεῖρας *dial.n.*: see πέρας

πείρᾱσις εως *f.* [πειράομαι] **overture, approach, proposition** (by a would-be lover) Th.

πειρασμός οῦ *m.* [πειράζω] **temptation** (to sin) NT.; (by the Devil) NT.

πειραστικός ή όν *adj.* (of dialectic) **experimental** (opp. cognitive) Arist.

πειρᾱτήρια ων *n.pl.* [πειράομαι] **1 trial** (for murder) E.

2 [πειρᾱτής] **pirate-bands** Plu.

πειρᾱτής οῦ *m.* **1 brigand** Plb.

2 pirate Plb. Plu.

πειρᾱτικός ή όν *adj.* of or relating to pirates; (of ships, goods, or sim.) belonging to pirates, **pirate** Plu.; (of crimes) **by pirates** Plu.; (of war) **with pirates** Plu. ‖ NEUT.SG.SB. **piracy** Plu. ‖ NEUT.PL.SB. **pirate-ships** Plu.

πειράω *contr.vb.*: see under πειράομαι

πειρήνᾱς (aor.ptcpl.): see περαίνω

πειρητίζω *vb.* | only pres. and impf. | **1 test, sound out** —W.GEN. *someone* Hom.; (intr.) **inquire** Od.

2 test —W.GEN. *one's strength* Od.; **try out** (a lyre) —W.DAT. *w. a plectrum* hHom.

3 try —W.INF. *to do sthg.* Il.; **try one's hand** —W.GEN. *w. a bow* (i.e. to string it) Od.

4 (of a warrior) **make an attack** Il.; (of a lion or boar) —W.ACC. *on hunters* Il.

πείρινθα (acc.) ινθος *f.* app. **luggage-basket** (for attaching to a carriage) Hom. AR.

πείρω *vb.* | aor. ἔπειρα, ep. πεῖρα ‖ pf.pass.ptcpl. πεπαρμένος | **1 pass through** (sthg.) with a pointed object; **pierce, spit** —*meat* (usu. W.DAT. or ἀμφί + DAT. *on skewers*) Hom. ‖ PF.PASS.PTCPL. (of meat) spitted hHom.

2 pierce —*someone* (W.DAT. + PREP.PHR. *w. a spear, through the hand*) Il.; (intr.) —W.PREP.PHR. *through someone's teeth* (*w. a spear*) Il.; **spear, harpoon** —*swimmers* (*like fish*) Od. ‖ PASS. (usu. pf.ptcpl., of a leopard) be impaled —w. περί + DAT. *on a spear* Il.; (of a nightingale) —w. ἀμφί + DAT. *on a hawk's claws* Hes.; (of a staff, a cup) be pierced or studded —W.DAT. *w. golden nails or rivets* Il.; (fig., of a person, the

πεῖσα heart) be pierced —w.DAT. w. pain Il. hHom. Archil. —w. ἀμφί + DAT. AR.

3 (of a ship) **cleave** —a path (through waves) Od.; (of sailors) **cross** —the sea AR.; (fig., of a person) **cleave through** —wars and waves Hom.; (intr.) **cross** (the sea) AR. —w.INTERN.ACC. on a voyage AR.

πεῖσα ης f. [πείθω] **obedience** Od.

πεισθήσομαι (fut.pass.): see πείθω

πεισί-βροτος (also **πεισίμβροτος**) ον adj. [βροτός] (of an athlete's fame, as conveyed by a poet) **that convinces men** (that it is deserved) B.; (of a ruler's sceptre) **that gains men's obedience** A.

πεισι-χάλινος ον adj. [χαλινός] (of a chariot-team) **obedient to the bit** Pi.

πεῖσμα ατος n. **1 mooring-line** (by which a ship is tethered to land, opp. anchor-cable); **mooring-cable, stern-cable** Od. A. E. Call. AR.; (in fig.ctxts., ref. to sthg. providing security) Thgn. Pl.

2 (gener.) **rope** (used to bind an animal's feet) Od.

πείσομαι[1] (fut.mid.): see πάσχω

πείσομαι[2] (fut.mid.), **πειστέον** (neut.impers.vbl.adj.): see πείθω

πειστήριος ᾱ ον adj. [πείθω] (of arguments) **persuasive** E.

πειστικός ή όν adj. (of a person, a skill, words, or sim.) **persuasive** Pl. X. Arist. Men. Plb. || FEM.SB. **art of persuasion** Pl. || NEUT.SB. **capacity to persuade** Pl.

πεκτέω contr.vb. [πέκω] **shear** —a fleece Ar. || PASS. (fig., of a person) **be plucked bare** (prob. by having one's hair torn out) Ar.

πέκω, ep. **πείκω** vb. | aor. ἔπεξα || aor.pass. ἐπέχθην | **1 pluck** or **comb** (wool or sim.); **comb, card** —wool Od. || MID. **comb** —one's hair Il.

2 shear —sheep Hes. Theoc. || MID. (of a sheep) **be shorn** —w.ACC. of its fleece Theoc.; (fig., of a wrestler called Krios Ram) **get oneself shorn** (i.e. defeated) Simon. || PASS. (fig., of Krios) **be shorn** Ar.

πελαγίζω vb. [πέλαγος] **1** (of an overflowing river) **create a sea or lake, flood** —w.PREP.PHR. over a plain Hdt.

2 (of a plain) **become a lake, be flooded** Hdt.

3 (of sailors) **cross the open sea** X.

πελάγιος ᾱ ον (also ος ον) adj. **1 of or relating to the open sea**; (of the surge, expanse, embrace) **of the sea** E. Ar.; (of creatures) E.; (periphr.) ἅλς πελαγία **open sea** A.

2 out at sea; (of a person) **at sea** S.; (of breezes, waves, opp. coastal) Plb. Plu.; (of a voyage) **on the open sea** (opp. along the coast) D. Plb.; (of ships or sailors, quasi-advbl., ref. to sailing) Th. X. Plb. Plu.; (of a promontory, quasi-advbl., ref. to stretching) **out to sea** Plb.

πέλαγος εος (ους) n. | dat.pl. πελάγεσι, ep. πελάγεσσι |
1 (sts.pl. for sg.) **open sea, high sea, sea** Hom. Hes. Pi. B. Hdt. Th. +; (periphr. w.GEN. ἁλός) **expanse of the sea** Od. hHom. Archil. E. Men. AR.; (w. πόντου, θαλάσσης) Pi.fr. AR.; (w.ADJ. πόντιον, ἅλιον) Pi. E.; (ref. to a specific sea, w. name given by GEN. or ADJ.) Pi. B. Hdt. Trag. Th. +

2 (fig., ref. to flooded land) **open sea** Hdt.

3 (fig., ref. to vastness in quantity or extent) **sea, ocean** (w.GEN. of words, opp. brief and precise discussion) Pl.; (of troubles, pain, ruin) A. E. Men.; (app. of troubles) S.; (of wealth) Pi.fr.; (gener., ref. to a distance to be covered) S.

—**πελαγόσδε** adv. (ref. to movt.) **to the open sea** AR.

πελάζω vb. [πέλας] | fut. πελάσω, Att. πελῶ, inf. πελᾶν | aor. ἐπέλασα, poet. ἐπέλασσα, ep. πέλασα, πέλασσα || MID.: ep.3pl.aor.opt. πελασαίατο | ep.athem.aor.: 3sg. ἔπλητο, also πλῆτο, 3pl. ἔπληντο, also πλῆντο | pf.ptcpl. πεπλημένος

|| PASS.: aor. ἐπελάσθην, ep. πελάσθην, 3pl. πέλασθεν | also aor. ἐπλάθην, poet.3sg. πλάθη S.(cj.) |

1 (intr., act., mid. and pass.) **come near, approach** Hom. Trag. Th. X. + —w.DAT. persons, places, or sim. Hom. + —w.GEN. S. Plb. —w.PREP.PHR. Hes. S. E. —w.ACC. a place S.(dub.) E.

2 meet with —w.DAT. death, ruin E. AR.

3 (of natural phenomena, ref. to their duration) **continue** —w.PREP.PHR. to a specified time Hdt.

4 (specif.) **come to** (someone, for sexual intercourse); **couple** —w.DAT. w. a woman Pi.; (of Zeus) —w. a cow A. || PASS. (of a woman, sts. w.connot. of reluctance) **be coupled** —w.DAT. w. a god or man A. B. E. —w.GEN. S.; **come** or **be forced to** —w.DAT. or GEN. a man's bed E.

5 (tr.) **bring** (a person or thing) **near** (to another); (of a person, god, wind) **bring** (w.ACC. someone or sthg.) **close** (to a person or place) Il. —w.DAT. or PREP.PHR. or ADV. to a person, place, or sim. Hom.(also mid.) E. Ar. || MID. **bring** (sthg.) **close** (to oneself) Emp. —w.DAT. to a place Il.

6 bring (a person or thing) **into contact** (W.DAT. w. someone or sthg.); **place** —someone (on the ground) Il.; **cast** —someone or sthg. (to the ground) Hom. Theoc.; **draw** —a bowstring (to one's breast) Il.; **bring** (for attachment) —a mast (to the mast-holder) Il. —a plough (to the pole) Hes. —oxen (to the yoke) Pi. AR. —a string (to a bow's tip) Theoc.; **put** —someone (in fetters) A. —one's neck (in a noose) E.; **bring** (W.ACC. one's chest) **into contact** —W.DAT. w. the sea (i.e. let it come up to one's chest) Od. || MID. (of a person collapsing) **meet, strike** —W.DAT. the ground Il.; (of opposing shields) —each other Il.; (of a spear-point) —a corslet Il.; (tr., of a warrior) **press** —one's breast (W.DAT. against an opponent's) Tyrt.

7 (gener.) **bring** —someone (W.DAT. to victory) Pi.; **subject** —someone (W.DAT. to pain) Il.; **invest** —a promise (W.DAT. w. adamant, i.e. make it unbreakable) Hdt.(oracle)

πελάθω vb. [reltd. πελάζω] | only pres. | **come close, draw near** E. Ar.(quot. A.) —W.DAT. to a place Ar.

πελᾶν (Att.fut.inf.): see πελάζω

πελανός οῦ m. **1 mixture of meal, honey and oil** (poured as a libation or burnt on the altar), **liquid offering, sacrificial mixture** A. E. Ar. Pl.

2 (ref. to blood or clotted blood, in ctxts. of sacrifice or slaughter) **offering** A. E.; (ref. to a crazed person's spittle) **mixture** (W.ADJ. foam-like) E.

3 meal-cake (as an offering) AR. Plb.

πελαργιδεύς έως m. [πελαργός] **young stork** Ar.

Πελαργικόν οῦ n. **1 Pelargikon** (enclosed area beneath the Acropolis) Th.

2 (appos.w. τεῖχος) **Pelargikon** (name of the ancient wall of the Acropolis) Hdt. Arist.

3 [πελαργός] **Storkade** (wall of Cloudcuckoo City, w. play on 2) Ar.

—**Πελαργικός** ή όν adj. (epith. of Poseidon) **of the Storkade** (w. play on πελάργιος of the sea) Ar.

πελαργός οῦ m. **stork** Ar. Pl. Call. Plu.

πέλας adv. and prep. **1** (ref. to location) **near, close by** Od. Trag. AR.; (as prep.) —W.GEN. someone or sthg. Od. Hdt. Trag. Call. AR. —W.DAT. Pi. Trag. Mosch.; (ref. to circumstances) **close** —W.GEN. to hanging (i.e. suicide) E.

2 || MASC.SB. (sg. and pl., w.art.) **neighbour or neighbours** Alc. Trag. Plat. Hdt. Trag. +

Πελασγοί ῶν m.pl. **1 Pelasgians** (name of supposedly pre-Hellenic inhabitants of Greece and neighbouring regions) Hom. Alc. A. Hdt.; (assoc.w. Dodona) Hes.fr. Call.; (assoc.w. Thessaly) Hellenist.poet.

2 Pelasgians (ref. to Argives, named after Pelasgos as founder of their race) A. E. Call.*epigr.* ‖ SG. Pelasgian man Call. [The association of the name w. Peloponnesian Argos prob. derives fr. its earlier association w. Thessalian Argos: see Πελασγικός below.]

—**Πελασγός** οῦ *m.* **1 Pelasgos** (mythical ancestor of the Arcadians) Hes.*fr.* Lyr.adesp.
2 Pelasgos (mythical king of Peloponnesian Argos) A.

—**Πελασγίᾱ** ᾱς, Ion. **Πελασγίη** ης *f.* **Pelasgia** (ref. to early Greece) Hdt.; (ref. to Peloponnesian Argos) A. E.

—**Πελασγιάς** άδος *f.* **Pelasgian** (i.e. Argive) **woman** Call.

—**Πελασγικός** ή όν *adj.* (of the pre-Hellenic race) **Pelasgian** Hdt. Th.; (of a place, an army) Hdt. Call. AR.; (of Zeus of Dodona) Il.; (of Thessalian Argos) Il.; (of Peloponnesian Argos, its people or army) E.

—**Πελασγίς** ίδος, also **Πελασγιῶτις** ιδος *fem.adj.* (of a woman) **Pelasgian** (i.e. pre-Hellenic) Hdt.; (of Thessaly, Thessalian things) AR.

—**Πελασγιῶται** ῶν *m.pl.* **Pelasgiots** (earlier name for the Danaans) E.*fr.*

—**Πελασγός** ή όν *adj.* (of a Thessalian horse) **Pelasgian** Pi.*fr.*; (of Argos) E.

πελατεύω *vb.* [πελάτης] **be a dependant** A.*satyr.fr.*

πελάτης ου, dial. **πελάτᾱς** ᾱ *m.* [πελάζω] **1** one who comes near or approaches; **visitor** (to a person or place) S. E.*fr.*; (W.GEN. to Hera's bed, ref. to Ixion) S.
2 one who comes for protection or employment; **dependant** (ref. to a labourer on another's land) Pl. Arist.; (in Spartan ctxt.) **retainer** (of a queen mother) Plu.; (at Rome) **cliens, client** Plu.
3 one who lives nearby; **neighbour** (W.GEN. of a place) A.

—**πελάτις** ιδος *f.* (in Roman ctxt., ref. to a woman) **dependant** (of someone) Plu.

πελάω *contr.vb.* [reltd. πελάζω] | only inf. (w.diect.) πελάᾱν | (of a helmsman) **bring** (W.ACC. a ship) **close** —W.DAT. *to land* hHom.

πέλεθος ου *m.* (sg. and pl.) human excrement, **shit** Ar.

πέλεθρον *ep.n.*: see πλέθρον

πέλεια ᾱς (Ion. ης) *f.* **pigeon** or **dove** Hom. Trag. AR. | see also τρήρων

Πελειάδες *f.pl.*: see Πλειάδες

πελειάς άδος *f.* **1 pigeon** or **dove** Il. hHom. Lamprocl. Hdt. Trag. AR.
2 dove (name of prophetic priestesses at Dodona) Hdt. S.

πελειο-θρέμμων ον, gen. ονος *adj.* [τρέφω] (of an island) **dove-nurturing** A.

πελεκᾶς ᾶντος *m.* a kind of bird; prob. **pelican** Ar.

πελεκάω *contr.vb.* [πέλεκυς] | ep.aor. πελέκκησα | **hew** or **shape** (W.ACC. timbers) **with an axe** Od.; (fig., for the sake of word-play, of pelicans) **use the beak as an axe, peck** Ar.

πελεκίζω *vb.* **kill with an axe, behead** —*someone* Plb. Plu.

πελεκίνος ου *m.* **pelican** Ar.

πέλεκκον ου *n.* (or **πέλεκκος** *m.*) **haft of an axe, axe-handle** Il.

πέλεκυς εως (Ion. εος) *m.* | acc. πέλεκυν | dat.pl. πελέκεσι, ep. πελέκεσσι ‖ sts. ῠς and ῠν *metri grat.* in ep. | **1** tool or instrument for hewing, cleaving or chopping (sts. two-edged); **axe** (for cutting timber) Hom. Pi. E.*fr.* Th. X. +; (used for killing sacrificial animals) Hom. E.*Cyc.* AR.; (for killing persons) Hdt. Trag. Ar.; (used by Hephaistos to split open Zeus' head for the birth of Athena) Pi. Call.; (as a prize at games) Il.; (as a target in an archery contest) Od.; (ref. to a toy axe) Men.; (app. ref. to a kitchen cleaver) Men.
2 axe (ref. to an executioner's axe, Lat. *securis*, carried by lictors in the *fasces* of Roman magistrates) Plb. Plu.; (meton., ref. to a lictor) Plb.
3 (specif.) **two-edged battle-axe** Il. Hdt. Call. AR.
4 hammer (of a smith) Anacr.

πελέμ-αιγις ιδος *fem.adj.* [πελεμίζω, αἰγίς¹] (epith. of Athena) **aigis-shaking** B.

πελεμίζω *vb.* [reltd. πάλλω] | ep.inf. πελεμιζέμεν | aor. πελέμιξα ‖ aor.pass. πελεμίχθην | **1 cause** (someone or sthg.) **to shake, quiver** or **tremble; make** (W.ACC. a spear, a bow) **quiver** Hom.; **shake, dislodge** —*an opponent's shield* Il.; (of winds) **shake** —*a wood* Il.
2 ‖ PASS. (of a warrior) **be sent reeling** or **staggering** Il. Pi.; (of limbs) **tremble** Emp.; (of the earth) **be shaken** (by thunder) Hes.; (of Olympos) **quake** (beneath Zeus' feet) Il. Hes.; (of a spear-butt) **quiver** Il.

Πεληάδες *dial.f.pl.*: see Πελειάδες

Πελιᾱο-φόνος ου *dial.f.* [θείνω] (ref. to Medea) **killer of Pelias** Pi.

Πελίᾱς ου (dial. ᾱ), ep.Ion. **Πελίης** ᾱο *m.* | acc. Πελίᾱν, ep.Ion. Πελίην | dat. Πελίᾳ, ep.Ion. Πελίῃ | **Pelias** (son of Poseidon and Tyro, king of Iolkos, father of Alkestis, deviser of the expedition for the Golden Fleece, killed by his daughters at the prompting of Medea) Hom. Hes. Mimn. Pi. E. Pl. +

πελιδνόομαι *dial.pass.contr.vb.* [πελιτνός] | aor.ptcpl. πελιδνωθείς | (of Athena) **turn livid** (w. anger) Alc.; (prob. of Athena) Call.

πελιός ά όν *adj.* [reltd. πολιός, πελιτνός] (of part of a body) **black and blue** (w. bruising) D.

πελιτνός ή όν *Att.adj.* [reltd. πελιός] (of the body of a plague victim) **livid** Th.

πελίχνᾱ ᾱς *dial.f.* [reltd. πέλλα] **food-bowl** Alcm.

πέλλα, Ion. **πέλλη**, ης *f.* **1** wooden bowl for milk, **milk-pail** Il. Lyr.adesp. Theoc.
2 pail (used to drink from) Hippon.

πελλίς ίδος *f.* **pail** (used to drink from, through want of a cup) Hippon.

πέλλος (or **πελλός**) η (dial. ᾱ) ον *adj.* [reltd. πελιός] **dark-coloured**; (of a goat) **grey** or **black** Theoc.

πέλμα ατος *n.* **sole** (of a shoe) Plb.

πέλομαι *mid.vb.*: see πέλω

Πελοπόν-νησος ου *f.* [Πέλοψ, νῆσος] **island of Pelops, Peloponnese** (the peninsula of southern Greece) hHom. +

—**Πελοποννήσιος** ᾱ ον *adj.* **from** or **belonging to the Peloponnese** (of an army, a person, or sim.) **Peloponnesian** Hdt. Th. Plu. ‖ MASC.PL.SB. **Peloponnesians** (as a population or military force) Hdt. Th. Ar. +

—**Πελοποννᾱσιστί** *dial.adv.* **in the dialect of the Peloponnese** (i.e. Doric) —*ref. to speaking* Theoc.

Πέλοψ οπος *m.* **Pelops** (eponymous hero of the Peloponnese, son of Tantalos, father of Atreus and Thyestes) Il. +

—**Πελοπίδης** ου *m.* | pl. Πελοπίδαι, dial. Πελοπιᾱδαι | **descendant of Pelops** (ref. to Agamemnon) Hdt.; (ref. to Theseus) Plu.; (pl.) Pi. Trag. Th. +

—**Πελόπιος**, also **Πελοπήιος** (AR.), ᾱ ον *adj.* (of the land, the back) **of Pelops** E. AR.; (of a tribe) **descended from Pelops** AR.

—**Πελοπηίς** ίδος *fem.adj.* (of the land) **of Pelops** AR. ‖ SB. **land of Pelops** Call.

πέλτᾱ *dial.f.*: see πέλτη

πελτάζω *vb.* [πέλτη] **carry a light shield, serve as a peltast** X.

πελτάριον ου *n.* [dimin. πέλτη] **light shield** (of Macedonian soldiers) Plu.

πελταστής οῦ *m.* (usu.pl.) infantryman carrying a light shield (and one or more javelins), **peltast** E. Th. Lys. Isoc. X. + [The term was orig. used of Thracian mercenaries, but was later applied to any light infantry similarly armed.]

πελταστικός ή όν *adj.* (of a soldier, weapons, a fight) **of the peltast kind** Pl. Plb. Plu.; (of a section of an army) **consisting of peltasts** X. || FEM.SB. technique of a peltast Pl. || NEUT.SB. (concr.) force of peltasts X. Plu.

—**πελταστικώτατα** *superl.adv.* **with all the skill of a peltast** —*ref. to fighting* X.

πέλτη ης, *dial.* **πέλτα** ᾱς *f.* small wooden or wicker shield with covering of skin (esp. assoc.w. Thracians), **light shield** Hdt. E. Ar. Pl. X. Plu.

—**πελτίον** ου *n.* [dimin.] **little shield** Men.

πελτο-φόρος ον *adj.* [φέρω] (of cavalrymen) carrying a light shield, **light-armed** Plb. || MASC.PL.SB. light infantry, peltasts X. Plb.

πελῶ (Att.fut.): see πελάζω

πέλω *vb.* —also **πέλομαι** *mid.vb.* | inf. πέλειν, Aeol. πέλην (Theoc.), ep. πελέναι (Parm.) | impf. ἔπελον, ep. πέλον | ep.3sg.aor.2 ἔπλε || MID.: Ion.imperatv. πέλευ | ep.impf. πελόμην | iteratv.impf.: 2sg. πελέσκεο, 3sg. πελέσκετο | ep.aor.2 (sts. w.pres.sens.) 2sg. ἔπλεο, perh. also ἔπλευ, 3sg. ἔπλετο |

1 (act. and mid., of circumstances, activities) **come into existence, exist, be** Hom. +

2 (act. and mid., of persons, things) **turn out to be, become, be** —W.PREDIC.ADJ. or SB. *such and such* Hom. +

πέλωρ, also **πέλωρον** *ep.n.* [perh.reltd. τέρας] | pl. πέλωρα || only nom.acc. sg. and pl. | living being of unusual or frightening size or appearance; **monster, prodigy** (ref. to Hephaistos, the Gorgon, the Cyclops, Scylla, Typhon, other mythical creatures) Hom. Hes. AR.; (ref. to persons turned into animals by Circe) Od.; (ref. to a large stag, Apollo in the guise of a dolphin, a serpent, a lion) Od. hHom. Hellenist.poet.; (ref. to a portent of a snake devouring nine birds) Il.

πελώριος ον (η ον AR.), sts. also **πέλωρος** ον (η ον Hes.) *adj.* **1** (of living beings) of unusual or frightening size or strength (w. both positive and negative connots.); (of Ares, Hades, Orion, the Cyclops) **monstrous, prodigious, awesome** Hom. Theoc.; (of the goddess Earth) Hes. Thgn.; (of the serpent Pytho) E. AR.; (of chief warriors, mythol. heroes) **mighty** Il. AR.; (of a boxer, his chest) Pi. Theoc.; (of Xerxes, cited as an example of exaggerated description) Arist.; (of wild or mythical creatures) Hellenist.poet.; (of a snake or goose in an eagle's talons) perh. **portentous** Hom.

2 (of armour, a god's spear, the sickle w. which Kronos castrated Ouranos) **mighty, awesome** Il. Hes.; (of the earth) Hes.; (of Sisyphos' boulder, storm-waves) Od.; (of a tree, spear, plank, wind) AR.; (of the rule of the older gods overthrown by Zeus) A.; (of strange footprints or hoofmarks) **portentous** hHom.

3 (of fame, a heroic act) **prodigious, awesome** Pi.; (of a scheme) Ar.; (of a noise, an oath) AR.; (of evil, cited as an example of exaggerated description) Arist.

—**πελώριον** *neut.adv.* **awesomely** —*ref. to a dragon hissing* AR.

—**πελώριστος** ᾱ ον *dial.superl.adj.* (of the city of Syracuse) **stupendous** Theoc.*epigr.*

πέμμα ατος *n.* [πέσσω] baked pastry, **cake** Sol. Stesich. Hdt. Philox.Leuc. Pl. Plu.

πεμπάδ-αρχος ου *m.* [πεμπάς, ἄρχω] **commander of five soldiers** X.

πεμπάζω *vb.* | ep.3sg.aor.mid. πεμπάσσατο, 3sg.subj. πεμπάσσεται | **1** count on five fingers or by fives; (gener.) **count** —*things* Od.(mid.) A. AR.

2 (act. and mid.) reckon up in one's mind, **ponder, think over** —*prophecies, considerations* AR.

πεμπ-ἅμερος ον *dial.adj.* [πέμπε, ἡμέρᾱ] (of athletic contests) **lasting five days** Pi.

πεμπάς (also **πεμπτάς**) ᾰδος *f.* **1** group of five; (specif.) **squad of five soldiers** X.

2 (abstr.) the number five, **five** Pl.

πεμπαστάς ᾶ *dial.m.* [πεμπάζω] one who counts; **counter** (W.ACC. of multitudes of troops) A.

πέμπε, gen.pl. ων *Aeol.num.adj.* [πέντε] (of cubits) **five** Alc.

πεμπε-βόησος ον *Aeol.adj.* [βόειος] (hyperbol., of sandals) **made of five oxhides** Sapph.

πεμπταῖος ᾱ ον *adj.* [πέμπτη, under πέμπτος] **1** (quasi-advbl., of persons doing sthg.) **on the fifth day** (after departure or sim.) Od. Plb. Plu.

2 (reckoning backwards in time; quasi-advbl., of a child being born) **five days ago** Pi.; (of sthg. happening) D.; (of a person lying unburied) **for five days** Ar.; (of a corpse) **five days old** X.

πεμπτάς *f.*: see πεμπάς

πεμπτη-μόριον ου *n.* [πέμπτος] **fifth part, fifth** (of sthg.) Pl.

πεμπτήρ ῆρος *m.* [πέμπω] **guide** (W.GEN. of ships, ref. to a pilot) E.*fr.*

πεμπτός ή όν *adj.* [πέμπω] (of ambassadors) **sent** (by someone) Th.(dub.)

πέμπτος η ον *num.adj.* [πέντε] **1** (of persons or things) **fifth** (in a list or sequence) Hom. +

2 (phrs.) πέμπτον μέρος *fifth part, i.e. one fifth* (*of an item, quantity or distance*) Hdt. Att.orats. Pl. Plb. Plu.; πέμπτη σπιθαμή *span coming fifth* (*after four cubits, i.e. four cubits and a span*) Hdt.

3 || NEUT.SG.ADV. (w.art.) **for the fifth time** Plu.

—**πέμπτη** ης *f.* **1 fifth day** (of a month) Hes. Ar.

2 fifth street (in a Roman camp, separating the fifth and sixth maniples, Lat. *quintana*) Plb.

—**πέμπτα** *neut.pl.adv.* **fifthly** (in order of importance) Hdt.

πέμπω *vb.* | ep.inf. πεμπέμεν, πεμπέμεναι, Aeol. πέμπην | iteratv.impf. πέμπεσκον | fut. πέμψω, dial. πεμψῶ, ep.inf. πεμψέμεναι | aor. ἔπεμψα, ep. πέμψα | pf. πέπομφα || PASS.: fut. πεμφθήσομαι | aor. ἐπέμφθην | 3sg.pf. πέπεμπται | pf.ptcpl. πεπεμμένος || neut.impers.vbl.adj. πεμπτέον |

1 cause (someone) to go (on a journey or mission); **send, send forth, despatch** —*someone* Hom. + —(W.INF. *to do sthg.*) Hom. Hes. Trag.; (of a country) —*troops* (*to war*) A. || MID. **have** (W.ACC. someone) **brought** (fr. a place) S. E.; **have** (W.ACC. someone) **sent** (to fetch someone) S. || PASS. be sent or despatched Pi. Hdt. Trag. +

2 enable (someone) to go on a journey (by organising the means, or acting as escort); **send on one's way, send off** —*someone* Hom. S.; (of a bird of omen) —*an army* A.; (of gods or humans) **conduct, convey, escort** —*someone* Hom. +; (of ships, breezes) **convey, carry** —*someone* Od. A.; (of ships) **accompany** —*the dances of Nereids* E. || PASS. (of persons on a ship) be conveyed Pi. E.

3 cause (sthg.) to be conveyed; **send, despatch** —*a gift, offering, letter, entreaties, or sim.* Hom. +

4 (intr.) **send a message** (to someone) S. E. Th. X. —W.INF. *to do sthg.* E. X. —W.NOM.PTCPL. *ordering, inquiring* (*sthg.*) Th. X.

5 propel (a missile) forwards; **launch** —*rocks* Hes.; **despatch, discharge** —*arrows* hHom.; (fig.) —*an arrow fr.*

one's eye (i.e. a glance) A. —aggressive words A.; **send** (by knocking) —a noise (inside a building) E.; **utter** —speech, lamentation A. S.

6 (of a god or non-human agent) **cause** (sthg.) **to come** (to someone); **send** —evil, a wind, dream, omen, vengeance, help, or sim. Hom. +; (of a breeze) —sleep S.; (of the earth) **give forth** —produce (for people) S.

7 (phrs.) πομπὴν πέμπειν **set in motion a procession** (i.e. arrange or take part in it) Hdt. Th. Lys. Ar. +; Βοηδρόμια πέμπειν **celebrate the festival of Boedromia with a procession** D.

8 ‖ PASS. (of a sacred or ritual object) **be carried in a procession** Hdt. Plu.; (in Roman ctxt., of a triumphal procession) **be held** Plu.

πεμπ-ώβολον ου ep.n. [πέμπε, ὀβελός] **five-pronged fork** (used to hold sacrificial meat over a fire) Hom.

πέμφῑξ ῑγος f. **1 blast** (of wind) A.fr.
2 drop (perh. of rain) Ibyc.

πέμψις εως (Ion. ιος) f. [πέμπω] **sending, despatch** (of someone or sthg.) Hdt. Th. Arist.

πενεστείᾱ ᾱς f. [πενέστης] **serf class** Arist.

πενέστερος, **πενέστατος** compar. and superl.adjs.: see πένης

πενέστης ου m. [πένομαι] **1** ‖ PL. **paupers, serfs, labourers** (ref. to a class of persons without citizen's rights in Thessaly) Ar. X. D. Theoc.
2 (gener.) **vassal, slave** (W.GEN. of someone) E.; (ref. to an ambassador to Thessaly, w. play on 1) **pauper** Ar.

πενεστικός ή όν adj. (of the Thessalian class) **of serfs** Pl.

πένης ητος masc.adj. (also neut. E.) | compar. πενέστερος, superl. πενέστατος | **1** (of persons) **poor, needy** Hdt. S. Ar. Att.orats. +; (of a person's body, a house) E.; (of a horse, as having no possessions) X. ‖ MASC.SB. **poor or needy person** E. Ar. +
2 (of a person) **wanting** (W.GEN. in money) E.

πενθαλέος ᾱ ον adj. [πένθος] (of a goddess) **grief-stricken, in mourning** Bion

πενθάς άδος fem.adj. (of birds) **in mourning** Mosch.

πένθεια ᾱς f. **mourning** or **mourning woman** A.(dub.)

πενθερός οῦ m. **1 father-in-law** Hom. Hdt. S. E. Call. Theoc. + ‖ PL. **parents-in-law** E.
2 brother-in-law E.

—πενθερά ᾱς, Ion. **πενθερή** ῆς f. **mother-in-law** D. Call. Plb. NT. Plu.

πενθέω contr.vb. [πένθος] | ep.3du. πενθείετον | ep.inf. πενθήμεναι | aor. ἐπένθησα | **1 express one's grief, lament, mourn** Od. Hdt. Trag. Pl. + —a dead person Il. A. Hdt. E. Ar. + —one's country Isoc. —sthg. one has lost Thgn. S.fr. ‖ PASS. **be mourned** Lys. Isoc.
2 bewail, bemoan —sufferings, misfortunes B.fr. Trag. Att.orats.

πένθημα ατος n. **lamentation, mourning** A. E. Theoc.

πενθ-ήμερον ου n. [πέντε, ἡμέρᾱ] **period of five days** (counting inclusively, i.e. four days); (phr.) κατὰ πενθήμερον for four days at a time X.; every four days Arist.

πενθ-ημιπόδιος ον adj. [ἡμιπόδιον] (of a trench) measuring five half-feet, **two and a half feet** (in depth) X.

πενθήμων ον, gen. ονος adj. [πενθέω] (of dream-visions) **full of sorrow** (for the dreamer) A.

πενθ-ήρης ες adj. [πένθος, ἀραρίσκω] (of a woman's head, ref. to its being shaven or beaten) **in mourning** E.

πενθητήρ ῆρος m. [πενθέω] **mourner** A.

—πενθήτρια ᾱς f. (ref. to a woman) **mourner** (W.GEN. of someone's misfortunes) E.

πενθητήριος ᾱ ον adj. (of a lock of hair placed on a tomb) **as a token of mourning** A.

πενθικῶς adv. [πένθος] **mournfully** X.

πένθιμος ον adj. **1** (of a woman, ref. to her appearance) **in mourning** E.; (of a person's old age) **spent in mourning** (for a dead son) E.; (of hair that is shorn) **as a sign of mourning** E.; (of a song) **of mourning** Mosch.; (of the attire) **of a mourner** Plu. ‖ NEUT.PL.SB. **tokens of mourning** (ref. to garments, offerings) Mosch. Plu.
2 (gener., of tears of shame, cries) **sorrowful** A. E.

πένθος εος (ους) n. [reltd. πάθος] **1** (sg. and pl.) **feeling of sadness or distress; sorrow, grief, distress** (sts. W.GEN. for someone) Hom. +; (W.GEN. for sthg. one has lost) S.fr.
2 (sg. and pl.) **feeling or expression of sorrow for the dead; mourning, lamentation** (sts. W.GEN. for someone) Hom. +

πενίᾱ ᾱς, Ion. **πενίη** ης f. [πένομαι] **poverty, want, need** Od. +; (personif.) **Poverty** Alc. Thgn. Ar. Pl. Men.

πενιχρός ά (Ion. ή) όν, Aeol. **πένιχρος** ᾱ ον adj. | superl. πενιχρότατος (Plb.) | (of persons) **poor, needy** Od. Alc. Eleg. Pi. Ar. Call. +; (fig., of a tyrant's soul) Pl.

—πενιχρῶς adv. **in a niggardly** or **cost-cutting way** —ref. to manufacturing an object Arist.

πένομαι mid.vb. [reltd. πόνος] | only pres. and impf. | **1 busy oneself, work, toil** Hom.; (tr.) **busy oneself with, work at** —tasks Hom. Hes.; **get ready** —a meal (for someone) Hom. Call. Theoc. —baths AR.
2 have to work for one's living; be poor, be needy Eleg. E. Th. Ar. Att.orats. Pl. +; (of a house, a city) **be impoverished** A. Lys.
3 be in need, be short —W.GEN. of sthg. A. E.

πεντά-δραχμος ον adj. [πέντε, δραχμή] (of an item that is sold) **for a sum of five drachmas** Hdt.; (of a transaction) Arist.

πεντάεθλον Ion. and dial.n., **πεντάεθλος** Ion. and dial.m.: see πένταθλον, πένταθλος

πενταετηρίς, also **πεντετηρίς**, ίδος f. [πενταετής] **1 festival held every fifth year** (counting inclusively, i.e. every four years), **quadrennial festival** Pi. Hdt. Th. Arist.; (appos.w. ἑορτά festival) Pi.; **quadrennial celebration** (W.GEN. of the Panathenaia) Lycurg.
2 period of five years (counting inclusively) Hdt. D. Plb.; (prep.phr.) διὰ πενταετηρίδος every four years Hdt. Arist.

—πενταέτηρος ον adj. (of an animal) **five years old** Hom.

—πενταετηρικός ή όν adj. (of an athletic contest) **held every fifth year, quadrennial** Plu.

πεντα-ετής ές (or **πενταέτης** ες), Att. **πεντέτης** ες adj. [πέντε, ἔτος] **1** (of a child) **five years old** Hdt. Pl. Plu.; (of a peace-treaty, w. play on sense libation, ref. to wine) Ar.
2 (of a peace-treaty) **lasting five years** Th.

—πεντάετες neut.adv. **for five years** Od.

πενταετίᾱ ᾱς f. **period of five years** Plu.

πενταθλεύω vb. —also **πενταθλέω** contr.vb. [πένταθλον] **compete in the pentathlon** Xenoph.

πένταθλον, Ion. and dial. **πεντάεθλον**, also dial. **πενταέθλιον** (Pi.), ου n. [ἆθλος] **athletic contest consisting of five events held on the same day** (discus, long jump, javelin, running, wrestling), **pentathlon** Pi. B. Hdt. X. Plu.

πένταθλος, Ion. and dial. **πεντάεθλος**, ου m. **competitor or victor in the pentathlon, pentathlete** Pi. B. Hdt. X. Arist. Plu.

πεντάκις num.adv. **1 five times** Pi. Ar. Att.orats. +
2 (in multiplication) πεντήκοντα πεντάκις five times fifty A.; πεντάκις ... χίλιοι five thousand Pl. Plb.

πεντακισ-μύριοι αι α pl.num.adj. [μυρίος] **fifty thousand** Hdt. Plb. Plu.

πεντακισ-χίλιοι αι α *pl.num.adj.* **five thousand** Hdt. Th. Att.orats. Pl. +

πεντακοσί-αρχος ου *m.* [πεντακόσιοι, ἄρχω] **commander of five hundred soldiers** Plu.

πεντακόσιοι, ep. **πεντηκόσιοι**, αι α *pl.num.adj.* [πέντε] **1 five hundred** Od. Hdt. +
2 ǁ MASC.SB. **the Five Hundred** (ref. to members of the Council) Th. Att.orats. Arist. Plu.

πεντακοσιο-μέδιμνος ου *m.* **person who possesses land yielding five hundred dry measures annually, five-hundred-measure man** (ref. to a member of the highest of four census-ratings used by Solon to define eligibility for political office) Th. D. Arist. Plu.

πεντακοσιοστός ή όν *num.adj.* **1 five-hundredth**; (of a member of the Council) **being one of the five hundred** Lys. **2** ǁ FEM.SB. (w. μοῖρα understd.) **five-hundredth part**; (specif.) **tax of one-fifth of a percent** Ar.

πεντά-μετρον ου *n.* [πέντε, μέτρον] **line of verse consisting of five metrical units, pentameter** Call. ǁ PL. (meton.) **elegiac couplets** Call.

πεντά-μηνος ον *adj.* [μήν²] (of babies) **five months old** (fr. conception), **four months premature** Men.

πενταξός ή όν *adj.* [πένταχα] (math., of points) **fivefold, in five sets** Arist.

πεντά-πηχυς υ, gen. ους (Ion. εος) *adj.* [πῆχυς] (of a man) **measuring five cubits** (in height) Hdt.

πενταπλάσιος ᾱ ον, Ion. **πενταπλήσιος** η ον *adj.* (of a fleet, property) **fivefold, five times as great** (as a certain size or value) Hdt. Arist.; (of property) **five times greater** (W.GEN. than another) Arist.; (of enemies) **five times more numerous** Plb.

πεντά-πολις εως (Ion. ιος) *f.* [πόλις] **Pentapolis, Five Cities** (a confederacy of Dorian cities in the SE. Aegean, comprising Lindos, Ialysos, Kamiros, Kos, Knidos) Hdt.

πεντά-ρραβδος ον *adj.* [ῥάβδος] (of the joining of strings on a musical instrument) perh., **resembling or consisting of five rods, five-rodded** Telest.

πενταρχίᾱ ᾱς *f.* [ἀρχή] **board of five officials** (at Carthage) Arist.

πεντάς άδος *f.* **the number five, five** Arist.

πεντά-στομος ον *adj.* [στόμα] (of the Nile, the Istros) **with five mouths** Hdt.

πένταχα, also **πενταχοῦ** (Hdt.) *adv.* **in five ways, in five divisions** —ref. to troops being marshalled Il.; **into five channels** —ref. to a river dividing Hdt.

πεντά-χους ουν *Att.adj.* [χοῦς¹] (of a water-clock) **holding five khoes** (approx. sixteen litres) Arist.

πέντε *indecl.num.adj.* **five** Hom. + | see also **πέμπε**

πεντεδραχμίᾱ ᾱς *f.* [δραχμή] **sum of five drachmas** X. Din.

πεντείκοντα *Boeot.num.adj.*: see **πεντήκοντα**

πεντε-καί-δεκα *indecl.num.adj.* [δέκα] **five and ten, fifteen** Hdt. +

πεντεκαιδεκα-ναΐᾱ ᾱς *f.* [ναῦς] **squadron of fifteen ships** D.

πεντεκαιδεκα-τάλαντος ον *adj.* [τάλαντον] (of property) **worth fifteen talents** D.

πεντεκαιδέκατος η ον *num.adj.* **fifteenth** NT. Plu.

πεντεκαιδεκ-ήρης ους *f.* [ἐρέσσω] (sts. appos.w. ναῦς) **fifteen-rowed ship** (app. w. three banks of oars, and rowers seated in groups of fifteen, so that every oar had five men) Plb. Plu.

πεντεκαιδεχ-ήμερος ον *adj.* [ἡμέρᾱ] (of an armistice) **lasting fifteen days** Plb.

πεντε-και-εικοστός ή όν *num.adj.* **twenty-fifth** Pl.

πεντε-και-πεντηκοντούτης (less correctly written **-πεντηκοντέτης, -πεντηκονταετής**) ες *adj.* (of a person) **fifty-five years old** Pl.

πεντε-και-τριᾱκοντούτης ες *adj.* (of a person) **thirty-five years old** Pl.

πεντε-πάλαστος (or **-πάλαιστος**) ον *adj.* [παλαστή or παλαιστή] (of a spear-blade, a hole) **measuring four palms** (in length, depth) X.

πεντέ-πους πουν, gen. ποδος *adj.* [πούς] (of the square root of a number, measured in foot-lengths) **of five feet** Pl.

πεντε-σπίθαμος ον *adj.* [σπιθαμή] (of nets, stakes) **measuring five spans** (in length, i.e. just over a metre) X.

πεντε-σύριγγος ον *adj.* [σῦριγξ] (of a pillory) **with five holes** (for hands, feet and head) Ar.; (fig., of a disease, ref. to paralysis, as restricting the sufferer's movement) Arist.(quot.)

πεντε-τάλαντος ον *adj.* [τάλαντον] (of property) **worth five talents** Is. D.; (of a lawsuit) **for the recovery of five talents** Ar.

πεντετηρίς *f.*: see **πενταετηρίς**

πεντετής *Att.adj.*: see **πενταετής**

πεντήκοντα, Boeot. **πεντείκοντα** *indecl.num.adj.* **fifty** Hom. +

πεντηκοντά-δραχμος ον *adj.* [δραχμή] (of a course of instruction) **costing fifty drachmas** Pl.

πεντηκονταετής *adj.*, **πεντηκονταέτις** *fem.adj.*: see **πεντηκοντούτης**

πεντηκοντα-και-τριετής ές *adj.* (of a period of time) **lasting fifty-three years** Plb.

πεντηκοντα-κέφαλος (perh. also **πεντηκοντο-** Pi.) ον *adj.* [κεφαλή, w. ᾱ *metri grat.*] (of Cerberus, Typhon) **hundred-headed** Hes. Pi.*fr.*

πεντηκοντά-παις (v.l. **πεντηκοντό-**) παιδος *masc.fem.adj.* [παῖς¹] (of a father) **having fifty children** A.; (of one generation of a family) **consisting of fifty children** A.

πεντηκονταρχέω *contr.vb.* [πεντηκόνταρχος] **serve as pentecontarch** D.

πεντηκονταρχίᾱ ᾱς *f.* **office of pentecontarch** Pl.

πεντηκόντ-αρχος ου *m.* [ἄρχω] (title of an officer on a trireme, subordinate to the trierarch; perh. orig. title of commander of a pentéconter) **pentecontarch** X. D.

πεντηκόντ-ερος (also **πεντηκόντορος**) ου *f.* [ἐρέσσω] (sts. appos.w. ναῦς) **fifty-oared ship, penteconter** (w. twenty-five rowers' seats on each side of the hull) Pi. Hdt. E. Th. Pl. +

—πεντηκοντηρικός ή όν *adj.* (of ships) **fifty-oared** Plb.

πεντηκοντήρ (v.l. **πεντηκοστήρ**) ῆρος *m.* (title of an officer in the Spartan army) **commander of a fiftieth-part unit, platoon commander** Th. X.; (in a Greek army, app. as a temporary arrangement) X.

πεντηκοντό-γυος ον *adj.* [γύης] (of an estate) **of fifty measures, fifty-acre** Il.

πεντηκοντ-όργυιος ον *adj.* [ὄργυια] (of a lake) **measuring fifty fathoms** (in depth) Hdt.

πεντηκόντορος *f.*: see **πεντηκόντερος**

πεντηκοντούτης ες (v.l. **πεντηκονταετής** ές) *adj.* —also **πεντηκοντοῦτις** (v.l. **πεντηκονταέτις**) ιδος *fem.adj.* [ἔτος] (of a person) **fifty years old** Pl.; (of a truce) **lasting fifty years** Th. Aeschin.; (of exile) Plu.

πεντηκόσιοι *ep.pl.num.adj.*: see **πεντακόσιοι**

πεντηκοστεύομαι *mid.vb.* [πεντηκοστός] **pay duty of two percent** (on imports) D. ǁ PASS. (of imports) **be liable to a two-percent duty** D.

πεντηκοστή ῆς *f.* **1** tax of one fiftieth, **two-percent tax** D.; (specif., at Athens) two-percent duty (on imports and exports), **customs duties** Att.orats.; (fig. and sarcastic, ref. to a donation) **two-percent buy-out** (W.GEN. fr. cavalry service) D.
2 fiftieth day (after the Passover), **Pentecost** NT.

πεντηκοστήρ *m.*: see πεντηκοντήρ

πεντηκοστο-λόγος ου *m.* [πεντηκοστός, λέγω] collector of two-percent duty (on imports and exports), **customs officer** D.

πεντηκοστός ή όν *num.adj.* [πεντήκοντα] (of a year) **fiftieth** Th. Arist. Plb. Plu.; (of a person, in a series) Pl.

πεντηκοστύς ύος *f.* (in the Spartan army) unit consisting of one fiftieth part of the whole, **fiftieth-part unit, platoon** Th.; (in a Greek army, app. as a temporary arrangement) X. [less plausibly interpr. as *unit of fifty men*]

πεντ-ήρης ου *f.* [ἐρέσσω] **five-rowed ship, quinquereme** (w. three banks of oars, and rowers seated in groups of five, so that the oars on two levels were operated by two men) Plb. Plu.

—πεντηρικός ή όν *adj.* (of a ship) **five-rowed** Plb.

πέντ-οζος οιο *ep.f.* [ὄζος] **five-brancher** (ref. to the human hand) Hes.

πεντ-ώβολον ου *n.* [ὀβολός] **sum of five obols** Ar.

πεντ-ώρυγος ον *adj.* [ὄργυια] (of hunting nets) **measuring five fathoms** (in length) X.

πέος ους *n.* **prick, dick, cock** (colloq. term for penis) Ar.

πέπαγα (dial.pf.): see πήγνυμι

πεπαθυῖα (ep.fem.pf.ptcpl.): see πάσχω

πεπαιδευμένως *pf.pass.ptcpl.adv.*: see under παιδεύω

πεπαίνω *vb.* [πέπων] | aor. ἐπεπάνθην | **1** (of a gall-fly) cause to become ripe, **ripen** —*a date* Hdt.; (of a cultivator) —*the fruit of the vine* X.; (intr., of vines) bring (their fruit) to ripeness, **ripen** Ar. || PASS. (of crops, a fruit) become ripe, ripen Hdt. Plb.
2 (fig.) **soften, assuage** —*someone's anger* Ar. || PASS. (of a person) be mellowed, turn soft E.; (of anger) be assuaged X.
3 || PASS. (fig., of a lover's flesh) melt Theoc.

πεπαίτερος (compar.adj.): see πέπων

πεπάλαγμαι (pf.pass.): see παλάσσω

πεπαλάχθαι (pf.mid.inf.), **πεπάλαχθε** (2pl.pf.mid.imperatv.): see παλάσσομαι

πεπαλέσθαι (ep.redupl.aor.2 mid.inf., unless ep.pf. **πεπαλάσθαι**), **πεπάλεσθε** (ep.2pl.redupl.aor.2 mid.imperatv., unless ep.pf. **πεπάλασθε**), **πέπαλμαι** (pf.pass.): see πάλλω

πέπαμαι (pf.mid.): see πάομαι

πεπαρεῖν *redupl.aor.2 inf.* **display** —*sthg.* Pi.

πεπαρμένος (pf.pass.ptcpl.): see πείρω

πεπᾶσθαι (pf.mid.inf.): see πάομαι

πέπασθε (ep.2pl.pf.): see πάσχω

πεπάσμην (ep.plpf.mid.): see πατέομαι

πέπεικα (pf.): see πείθω

πέπειρα *fem.adj.*, **πέπειρος** *adj.*: see πέπων

πεπείρανται (3sg.pf.pass.): see πειραίνω

πέπεισμαι (pf.mid.pass.): see πείθω

πεπέρανται (3sg.pf.pass.): see περαίνω

πεπερημένος (ep.redupl.pf.pass.ptcpl.): see πέρνημι

πέπερι *n.* [loanwd.] | gen. πεπέρεως (Plu.) | **pepper** Arist. Plu.

πέπηγα (pf.), **πεπήγειν** (ep.plpf.): see πήγνυμι

πεπιθήσω (ep.redupl.fut.), **πεπιθοίμην** (ep.redupl.aor.2 mid.opt.), **πέπιθον** (ep.redupl.aor.2), **πέπιθι** (2sg.pf.2 imperatv.): see πείθω

πεπλανημένως *pf.mid.pass.ptcpl.adv.*: see under πλανάω

πεπλασμένως *pf.pass.ptcpl.adv.*: see under πλάσσω

πέπλευκα (pf.), **πέπλευσμαι** (pf.pass.): see πλέω¹

πέπληγα (pf.), **πεπληγέμεν** (ep.redupl.aor.2 inf.), **πεπλήγετο** (ep.3sg.redupl.aor.2 mid.), **πέπληγον** (ep.redupl.aor.2), **πεπληγών** (ep.pf.ptcpl.), **πεπλήξομαι** (fut.pf.pass.), **πέπληχα** (pf.): see πλήσσω

πεπλημένος (pf.mid.ptcpl.): see πελάζω

πέπλος ου *m.* **1** woven cloth, **cloth, sheet** (used to cover chariots when not in use, to drape over chairs, to wrap bones before burial) Hom.
2 (oft. pl. for sg.) outer garment, **robe** (worn by women and goddesses) Hom. hHom. Pi. Trag. Ar. X. +
3 (specif., ref. to a robe embroidered w. mythol. scenes, carried in procession and presented to Athena at the Panathenaia) **peplos** E. Ar. Pl. Arist. Plu.
4 robe (worn by oriental men, sts.pl.) A. X.; (sg., ref. to any outer garment worn by a Greek male) **robe, cloak, tunic** S. E. AR. Theoc. || PL. (gener.) robes, garments, clothing (of a man or men) A. E. Ar.(mock-trag.) Philox.Leuc. AR. Theoc.

πέπλωκα (Ion.pf.): see πλέω¹

πέπλωμα ατος *n.* **robe, garment** (of men or women) Trag. Ar.(mock-trag.)

πέπνῡμαι *ep.pf.pass.* [perh.reltd. πινύσκω, πινυτός] | w.pres.sens. | most freq. ptcpl. πεπνῡμένος | imperatv. πέπνυσο (Thgn.) | 2sg.plpf. πέπνῡσο |
1 have intelligence; (of persons) **have good sense, be wise** Hom. Thgn.; (of a dead person in the underworld) be **conscious, be in full mental vigour** Od. Call. || PTCPL.ADJ. (of persons, speech, advice, or sim.) wise, sensible, sound Hom. Hes. Thgn. Plu.
2 [as if reltd. πνέω *breathe*] (adjl., of persons) ζῶντες καὶ πεπνυμένοι *living and breathing* Plb.

πέποιθα (pf.2), **πεποίθεα** (ep.plpf.2): see πείθω

πέπομφα (pf.): see πέμπω

πέπονθα (pf.): see πάσχω

πέπορδα (pf.): see πέρδομαι

πεπόσθαι (pf.pass.inf.): see πίνω

πέποσθε (ep.2pl.pf.): see πάσχω

πέπρᾱγα (pf.2), **πέπρᾱγμαι** (pf.pass.), **πεπράξομαι** (fut.pf.pass.), **πέπρᾱχα** (pf.1): see πράσσω

πέπρᾱκα (pf.), **πέπρᾱμαι** (pf.pass.), **πεπράσομαι** (fut.pf.pass.), **πέπρημαι** (Ion.pf.pass.): see πέρνημι

πέπρηγα (Ion.pf.2), **πέπρηγμαι** (Ion.pf.pass.), **πέπρηχα** (Ion.pf.1): see πράσσω

πεπρωμένος (pf.pass.ptcpl.), **πέπρωται** (3sg.pf.pass.), **πέπρωτο** (3sg.plpf.pass.): see πορεῖν

πέπταμαι (pf.pass.): see πετάννυμι

πεπτεώς (ep.pf.ptcpl.), **πέπτωκα** (pf.), **πεπτώς** (pf.ptcpl.): see πίπτω

πεπτηώς¹ (ep.pf.ptcpl.): see πίπτω

πεπτηώς² (ep.pf.ptcpl.): see πτήσσω

πεπύθοιτο (ep.3sg.redupl.mid.opt.), **πέπυσμαι** (pf.mid.), **πέπυστο** (ep.3sg.plpf.): see πυνθάνομαι

πέπωκα (pf.): see πίνω

πέπων πέπειρα πέπον *adj.* [πέσσω] | gen.masc.neut. πέπονος | voc.masc. πέπον || compar. πεπαίτερος | **1** (of fruit) **ripe** Hdt. Ar. X.
2 (fig., of a person envisaged as fruit) **ripe** (i.e. ready to be made use of) Ar.; (pejor., of a woman) **over-ripe** (i.e. spoiled by excess of sexual activity) Archil. Anacr. || COMPAR. (pejor., of a man) riper (W.GEN. than a pear, i.e. past his prime) Theoc.

3 (fig., of a person) **mellow, soft, mild** (W.DAT. to one's enemies) A.; (of anger, anguish) **softened, assuaged** S. || COMPAR. (of a fate) **milder** (W.GEN. than tyranny) A.
4 || VOC. (in a courteous or familiar address to a person) **dear** Hom. Hes. hHom. AR.; (to a favourite ram) Od. || PL. (to persons, in reproach) **weaklings** Il.

—**πέπειρος** ον *adj.* (fig., of a woman) **ripe** (for sexual activity) Ar.(dub., v.l. πέπειρα); (for marriage) Plu.

περ¹ *enclit.pcl.* [reltd. περί] | The pcl. adds emphasis of various kinds. In sections 1-4 it is mainly confined to Hom.; in section 5 it is used more widely in poetry and by Hdt.; with conjs. (section 6) it is sts. used in prose authors. |
1 (intensv.) **very much** Hom. Thgn. • ἐλεεινότερός περ *more pitiable by far* Il. • πρῶτόν περ *the very first time* Il.; (w.neg.) οὔ περ *not at all* Hom. hHom.
2 (determinative, concentrating attention on one thing to the exclusion of an alternative) Hom. Hes. Theoc. • οἴκαδέ περ *homewards (and nowhere else)* Il. • ἀμφότεροί περ *both (opp. one only)* Il.
3 (limitative) **at least** Hom. • τόδε πέρ μοι ἐπικρήηνον ἐέλδωρ *grant me this request at least* Il. • νῦν δή πέρ *now at any rate* Od.
4 (contrastive, appearing in 1st or 2nd cl.) Hom. • ἄλλοτέ περ ... νῦν δέ *at one time ... but now* Il. • κεῖνον μὲν ... ἡμεῖς δ' αὐτοί περ *him ... but we ourselves* Il.
5 (concessive, esp. w.ptcpl.) **however much, even though** Hom. + • φράδμων περ *however shrewd* Il. • πέμπω ... ὀψέ περ *I send ... however late* Pi. • γυνή περ οὖσα *although a woman* A. • ἀσκευής περ ἐών *although being unequipped* Hdt.; (also καὶ ... περ) • καὶ ἀχνύμενοί περ *although grieving* Il. • καὶ θεός περ *although a god* A.; (neg., w. οὐδέ) • οὐ τέθνηκας οὐδέ περ θανών *although dead, you have not died* A. | see also καίπερ
6 (reinforcing, w. conditional, compar., relatv. and temporal conjs., sts. w. other wds. intervening) εἴ περ, ἤ περ, ὅς περ, οἷός περ, ὥς περ, ἔνθα περ, ὅτε περ (or sim.) Hom. + | see also εἴπερ, ἤπερ, ὅσπερ

περ² *Aeol.prep.*: see ὑπέρ

πέρᾱ¹ ᾱς *f.* **land beyond** (a stretch of water); **coast opposite** (sts. W.GEN. to a town) A.

πέρᾱ² *adv. and prep.* | The prep. sts. stands after the gen. || see also περαίτερος, πέρᾱν | 1 (ref. to movt. or increase) **to a more advanced point, beyond, further** Pl. —W.GEN. *than some limit* Arist.; **beyond the reach** —W.GEN. *of one's enemies* S.
2 (ref. to position) **at a more advanced point, beyond** —W.GEN. *a frontier* D.(law)
3 (ref. to continuing an activity, esp. speaking) **further, longer, more** S. E. Ar. Pl. X. Plb.; (w.art.) τὸ πέρα Pl.; **beyond** —W.GEN. *what has already been said* S. E.
4 (ref. to time) **beyond, past** —W.GEN. *midday* X.
5 (ref. to extent or degree) **further, more** S. E. Ar. —W.GEN. *than a certain quantity* Is. —*than what was expected* Th. —*than marvels, words* E. —*than the greatest possible fear, an outrage, expectation* Pl. D. Plu.; πέρα ἤ *more than* —W.PHR. or CL. S.
6 (ref. to transgression) **beyond** —W.GEN. *what is right or proper, prudence, the laws, or sim.* Trag. Antipho Pl. D. Plb. Plu.

περάᾱν¹ (ep.inf.), **περάασκον** (iteratv.impf.): see περάω
περάᾱν² (ep.fut.inf.): see πέρνημι
περάγείς ἐς *Boeot.adj.* [περί, reltd. ἅγιος] (of a prophet) **very reverend** Corinn.

πέραθεν, Ion. **πέρηθε** *adv.* [πέρᾱ²] **from beyond** (a stretch of water), **from across the sea** Hdt. E. X.

περαιᾱ́ *f.*, **περαίη** Ion.f.: see under περαῖος

περαίνω *vb.* [πέρας] | fut. περανῶ | aor. ἐπέρᾱνα || aor.pass. ἐπεράνθην | 3sg.pf.pass. πεπέρανται | cf. πειραίνω |
1 **follow through to the end, complete, accomplish** —*a task, an order, or sim.* Trag. Pl. X. + —*a journey* Ar. —*a voyage* (W.PREP.PHR. *to the furthest point*) Pi.; (intr.) **complete one's business, get on with the job** X. D. Men. || PASS. (of a task or sim.) **be completed or accomplished** A. Th. Philox.Leuc. Isoc. Pl. +; (of an alliance) **be cemented** X.
2 **effect, achieve** —*sthg., nothing, everything* E. Th. Att.orats. Pl. Plb. || PASS. (of an oracle) **be fulfilled** E. Ar.
3 **go through with, act on** —*a hope, an impression* E.
4 (specif., of a speaker) **complete** or **proceed with** —*a speech or sim.* A. E. Ar. Isoc. Pl.; **recount** —*every detail* A. Pl.; **deliver** —*a funeral oration* Pl.; **recite** —*lines of verse* Ar. D.; (intr.) **go on to the end, go on, proceed** E. Ar. Isoc. Pl. || PASS. (of a speech, an argument) **be completed or concluded** Ar.(quot. E.) Pl.
5 (intr., of a geometrical figure) **end** —w. εἰς + ACC. *at some point* Pl.; (of a path, a poison) **lead in the end** —W.PREP.PHR. *to a place, to a certain state of health* Plu.; (of actions) —*to a goal* Arist.
6 || PASS. (of things, places) **be limited** —W.DAT. *by sthg.* Arist. || PF.PASS. (of an entity) **be finite** Arist.
7 (intr., of reverence for someone) **permeate** —w. διά + GEN. *through people's ears and minds* A.

περαιόθεν *adv.* [περαῖος] **from beyond** (a river), **from the further bank** AR.

περαῖος (or **πέραιος**) ᾱ (Ion. η) ον *adj.* [πέρᾱ²] (of a mainland, an island) **beyond** (a stretch of water), **on the other side, opposite** AR.; (of the land where the sun rises) **across the sea, beyond the horizon** AR. || NEUT.PL.SB. **regions opposite** (W.GEN. an island) Call.

—**περαιᾱ́** ᾱς, Ion. **περαίη** ης *f.* **opposite coast** Hdt. AR. Plb. Plu.; (specif.) **Peraia** (territory on the mainland opposite Rhodes) Plb.

περαιόω *contr.vb.* | fut.mid.inf. (w.pass.sens.) περαιώσεσθαι (Th. AR.) | **cause** (someone or sthg.) **to go to the other side** (of sthg.); (of a commander) **take** or **send** (W.ACC. troops or sim.) **across** (a sea, river, ditch) Th. Plb. Plu.; **send** (W.ACC. troops) **across** —*a river* Plb. || PASS. (of persons, ships, or sim.) **be taken across, go across, cross over** Od. Hdt. Th. Ar. X. AR. + —*a sea, a river* Hdt. Th. Plb.; (also act.) Th.(dub.)

περαίτερος ᾱ ον *compar.adj.* [πέρᾱ²] (of roads) **leading further** (W.GEN. than others) Pi.

—**περαίτερον** *neut.compar.adv.* **to a further degree, better** (W.GEN. than other people) —*ref. to telling things* Pi.

—**περαιτέρω** *compar.adv.* 1 (ref. to distance) **to a more advanced point, further** Isoc. Pl. Plb.; (W.GEN. than a place or sim.) Th. Pl. X. Aeschin.; (than a moderate distance) X.; (fig., than present behaviour) A.; **further ahead** (in forethought) Th.; (as sb., w.art.) οἱ περαιτέρω *those further back, remoter ancestors* Is.
2 (ref. to extent or degree) **further, more** S. E. Th. Ar. Att.orats. +; (W.GEN. than one should, than is suitable, or sim.) Pl. +; **too far** S.; **to a higher degree** (W.GEN. of boldness) Plu.
3 (quasi-adjl., of an activity) **more far-reaching** (W.GEN. than another) Pl.; (of sthg. dangerous, ref. to women) **worse** (W.GEN. than fire or a viper) E.

περαίωσις εως *f.* [περαιόω] **passage across** (a sea, by troops) Plu.

Πέραμος *Aeol.m.*: see Πρίαμος

πέρᾱν, Ion. **πέρην** *adv. and prep.* [acc. of πέρᾱ¹] 1 (prep., ref. to movt.) **to land beyond** (usu. a stretch of water); **to the**

further side of, beyond, across —W.GEN. *a sea, a river* Il. Pi. S. E. Th. Theoc. —*a ravine* X.; **past** —W.GEN. *persons (by overtaking them)* E.; **out of** —W.GEN. *a wood* E.; (adv.) **across** (the sea) Hdt. Th. X.; (a border) S.
2 (prep., ref. to location) **on the far side of, beyond** —W.GEN. *a sea, a river* Il. Hes. A. Pi. Hdt. Th. + —*an island, a chasm* Il. Hes. —*a temple, a road* Hdt.; (adv.) **across the sea** Hdt. Th. AR.; **on the other side** (of a river) Th. X. Plb.
3 (w.art.) εἰς τὸ πέραν *to the opposite shore* X.; *to the opposite bank* (W.GEN. *of a river*) X.; **beyond** (W.GEN. *a certain time*) Pl.; ἐν τῷ πέραν *on the opposite bank* X.; τὰ (or οἱ) πέραν *events (or people) on the opposite bank* X. Plu.
4 (adv., in fig.ctxt.) **beyond what is appropriate, too high** Pi.
5 (phr., quasi-sb., qualified by acc.adj.) πέραν δυσεκπέρατον βίον *across in a difficult crossing to the other side of life (i.e. to death)* E.

περαντικός ή όν *adj*. [περαίνω] (of a politician) good at bringing things to a conclusion, **conclusive, effective** Ar.

περάπτω *Aeol.vb*.: see περιάπτω

πέρας, dial. **πεῖρας** (Alc. Pi.), ατος *n*. [πεῖραρ] **1 boundary, limit** (ref. to a door) Men. ‖ PL. ends, boundaries (W.GEN. of the earth) Alc. Th. X. NT.; ends of the earth or sky (where the sun rises), **far horizon** AR.; boundaries (W.GEN. of a country) Plb.
2 (abstr.) **limit, termination, end** (oft. W.GEN. of sthg.) A. E. Att.orats. Pl. +; (periphr.) **final end, finality** (W.GEN. of death) Pi.; (w. τοῦ + INF. consisting in being released fr. danger, in being reconciled, i.e. *final release, final reconciliation*) Th. D.
3 (ref. to a numerical series or to entities, esp. as envisaged by certain philosophical schools) **that which limits** or **has limits** (opp. τὸ ἄπειρον *that which is without limits*) Pl. Arist.
4 (leg.) **final decision** (W.GEN. on matters of right and wrong) Din.

—**πέρας** *acc.adv.* as the final act or point in a sequence, **finally** Aeschin. D. Plb.; (also w.art.) τὸ πέρας Lys. Men. Plb.

πέρασα (ep.aor.): see πέρνημι

περάσιμος η ον *adj*. [περάω] (of a river) able to be crossed, **passable** Plu.

πέρασις εως *f*. **passage to the end** (W.GEN. of life) S.

περάτη ης *f*. [perh. πεῖραρ, πέρα²] app. **end** or **furthest point** (of either the earth or sky, i.e. the horizon, or of Night's course) Od.; **far horizon** (where the sun rises) AR.; (where it sets) Call.

—**περάτηθεν** *adv*. **from the horizon** (where the moon is rising) AR.

περατο-ειδής ές *adj*. [πέρας, εἶδος¹] (of a class of things) **finite in form** Pl.

περατός ή όν *adj*. [περάω] (in neg.phrs., of a sea, river, ditch) able to be crossed, **passable** Pi. Plu.

περάω *contr.vb*. [πέρα²] | (w.diect.): ep.3pl. περόωσι, ep.inf. περάαν | iteratv.impf. περάασκον | fut. περάσω, Ion. περήσω, inf. περήσειν, also περησέμεναι | aor. ἐπέρασα, Ion. ἐπέρησα, ep.Ion. πέρησα, Aeol. ἐπέραισα | pf. πεπέρᾱκα |
1 (of persons, ships, or sim.) go to the other side (of a stretch of water or land); **cross, traverse** —*a sea, a river* Od. Hes. Thgn. Lyr. Hdt. Trag. + —*a ditch* Il. —*a region* A. E. —*a path* Call.
2 go beyond, **go past, pass** —*the gates of Hades* Il. Thgn. —*guards* Hdt. —*a place, a border* A. E.; **get through** —*a crowd* Theoc.
3 (of rain) **go through, penetrate** —*bushes* Od.; (of a weapon) —*someone's teeth* Il.; (intr., sts. W.PREP.PHR. through a part of the body) Il.
4 (intr., of persons) **pass, cross** (oft. W.PREP.PHR. to, from, through a place, or sim.) Hom. Hes. Thgn. Lyr. Trag. Ar. +; (of a thought) —W.PREP.PHR. *through one's mind* hHom.; (of an animal's tracks) **lead** (fr. a place) X.
5 cross a threshold; **enter** —*a house* E.; **emerge from, leave** —*a house* E.
6 cross an intervening space; **arrive** —W.PREP.PHR. *at a place* E.; (tr.) **arrive at, reach** —*a place* E.
7 (w. temporal connot.) **pass** —W.PREP.PHR. *through old age* X.; **pass through life** X.(oracle)
8 (tr.) pass through completely, **go through, complete** —*a dangerous enterprise* A. —*a period of office* Pi. —*the last day of one's life* E. —*life's end* S.(dub.) —*the time of youth* X. —*a voyage* X.; (wkr.sens.) **have** —*one's bath* A.
9 (lit. and fig.) **go too far** S.; (tr.) **go beyond, transgress** —*an oath* A.(dub.)

περβέβαται (Aeol.3sg.pf.pass.): see ὑπερβαίνω

Πέργαμος ου *f*. —also **Πέργαμον** ου (Hdt.) *n*. Pergamos, Pergamon (citadel of Troy, or ref. to Troy itself) Il. Ibyc. Pi. Hdt. E.

—**Πέργαμα** ων *n.pl*. **citadel** (of Troy, or ref. to Troy itself) Stesich. S. E.; (of Thebes) E.; (ref. to Olympos) A.

—**Περγαμίᾱ** ᾱς *f*. **land of Pergamos** (ref. to Troy) Pi.

πέρδιξ ικος *m.f*. | acc. πέρδικα (Archil.) | **partridge** Archil. Ar. Philox.Leuc. X. Plu.

πέρδομαι *mid.vb*. | act.aor.2 (in cpds.) -έπαρδον | pf. (w.pres.sens.) πέπορδα | 3sg.plpf. (w.impf.sens.) ἐπεπόρδει | **fart** Ar.

περεσκήνωσε (3sg.aor.): see περισκηνόω

πέρηθε Ion.adv., **πέρην** Ion.adv. and prep.: see πέρᾱθεν, πέρᾱν

πέρθεσθαι (Aeol.athem.aor.mid.inf.), **περθέτω** (Aeol.3sg.athem.aor.imperatv.): see περιτίθημι

πέρθω *vb*. | iteratv.impf. πέρθεσκον | fut. πέρσω | aor.1 ἔπερσα, ep. πέρσα | aor.2 ἔπραθον, ep. πράθον, ep.inf. πραθέειν ‖ PASS.: 3sg.fut. πέρσεται | athem.aor.inf. πέρθαι |
1 ravage, sack, lay waste to —*a city or sim*. Hom. Hes. Lyr. S. E. + —*a ruler* (meton. for his city) Pi. ‖ PASS. (of a city or sim.) be sacked or ravaged Il. hHom. A. Hdt.(oracle) AR.
2 ravage, destroy —*an army, enemies* Pi. E. —*monstrous beasts* E.; (of a mourner) —*one's beard* (by plucking it) A.; **cut off** —*someone's head* Pi.
3 (gener., of the inventor of weapons) **destroy** —*mankind* S.; (of Eros) —*mortals* E.; (of persons) —*the leaf of the olive* S.; (of sickness or sim.) —*a person* S. ‖ PASS. (of persons) be racked —W.DAT. *by heat or cold* Pi.
4 take as booty (by sacking a city), **plunder** —*slave women* E.

περί *prep*. | W.ACC., GEN. and DAT. | sts. following its noun (w. anastrophe of the accent), e.g. ἄστυ πέρι *around the town* Il. | for Aeol. περί see ὑπέρ |

—**A** | space or location |

1 on all sides of, **around, all around** —W.ACC. *places, things* Hom. + —W.GEN. *a cave* (ref. to a vine growing) Od.
2 (ref. to placing or wearing weapons, clothing, or sim.) **around, over** —W.ACC. or DAT. *a part of the body* Hom. + —W.GEN. AR.
3 (ref. to a snake coiling) app. **around in** —W.DAT. *its lair* Il.
4 (ref. to blood spurting) **around** —W.DAT. *a spear (i.e. its point)* Il.
5 (ref. to standing as a protector) **over** —W.DAT. *a fallen warrior, young animal* Il. Ar.(mock-oracle)
6 (ref. to falling or lying) **on top of** —W.DAT. *a corpse* S. E.; (ref. to falling and striking one's head) **on** —W.DAT. *a stone* Ar.; (ref. to falling or being impaled) **upon** —W.DAT. *a weapon* Il. Pi. S.

περιαγγέλλω

7 in the vicinity of, **round about, near, beside, by** —W.ACC. *places, things* Hom. +; (as adv.) **all around, round about** Il.
8 in —W.ACC. *a country* Hdt. —*one's soul (ref. to rejoicing)* Pi.
9 | for pleon. combinations ἀμφὶ περί, περί τ' ἀμφί τε, περὶ ... ἀμφί see ἀμφί A 10
—B | movt. |
1 (ref. to circling) **around** or **all around** —W.ACC. *persons, places, things* Hom. +
2 around (within the confines of) —W.ACC. *an island* Od.
—C | accompaniment |
grouped about, **in the company of, with, following** —W.ACC. *a leader, teacher, or sim.* Th. Pl. X. + | freq. *those in the company of* is equiv. to *someone and his company*, e.g. οἱ περὶ Ἀρχίαν πολέμαρχοι *Archias and his fellow polemarchs* X.
—D | time |
approximately at, **around** —W.ACC. *a point in time* Hdt. Th. X. +
—E | purpose |
(ref. to fighting, competing, running risks) on account of, **for the sake of, over, for** —W.GEN. *someone or sthg.* Hom. +
—F | cause |
1 (ref. to being afraid, concerned, confident, or sim.) **on account of, because of, over** —W.GEN. or DAT. *someone or sthg.* Hom. +
2 (ref. to collapsing or failing) **on account of** —W.DAT. *someone* Hdt. Th. | see πταίω 2
3 through, out of —W.DAT. *fear* A. Pi. —*delight* hHom. —*pain* AR.; **by reason of** —W.DAT. *one's honoured status* Pi.
—G | value or worth |
(ref. to reckoning someone or sthg., in terms of esteem or importance, esp.w. ποιεῖσθαι) **worth** —W.GEN. *much, little, nothing, or sim.* Hdt. Th. Att.orats. + | see ἐλάσσων 7, ἐλάχιστος 4, μικρός 12, πᾶς 9, πλεῖστος 6, πολύς 8
—H | superiority |
above, beyond —W.GEN. *all or others* Hom. Hes. Pi. AR. Theoc.; (as adv.) **surpassingly, exceedingly** Hom. AR.
—I | approximation |
approximately, **about, around** —W.ACC. *a certain number* Th. X.
—J | specification |
1 (ref. to hearing, speaking, knowing, or sim.) **about** —W.GEN. *someone or sthg.* Od. +
2 in the matter of, **in respect of, with regard to, concerning** —W.ACC. or GEN. *someone or sthg.* Pi. Hdt. Antipho Th. +
3 (ref. to being occupied) **with** —W.ACC. *an activity* Hom. +

περι-αγγέλλω *vb.* **1** carry round news; **announce** Hdt. —*an event* Hdt. Th.
2 send or **take round orders** —W.INF. or DAT. + INF. (*to people*) *to do sthg.* Th. X. —W.ACC. *for a commodity* Th. ‖ PASS. (of a request for help) be sent round Hdt. Th.

περι-αγείρω *vb.* ‖ MID. (of an athlete) **travel about collecting for oneself** —*prizes* Pl.

περι-άγνυμαι *pass.vb.* **1** (of the turbulent waters of a river) **break all around** —W.ACC. *a people (who live by its shores)* AR.
2 (fig., of a voice) **burst out all around** Il.; (of an echo) Hes.(tm.)

περι-άγω *vb.* **1** (of a guide or sim.) **take** or **lead** (W.ACC. a person, an animal) **around** (a place) Hdt. Th. Ar. X. Plb. Plu. —w. 2ND ACC. *a place* Hdt.(dub.) Pl. D. Men.; **bring round** —*ships* (W.ADV. *to a place*) Plu. —*a river* (W.PREP.PHR. *to a place, by redirecting its course*) Plu.; **cause** (W.ACC. the wing of an army) **to move round** (an enemy's wing) Plu. ‖ PASS. (of persons) be led around Hdt. X. Plb.

2 carry around (on a wagon, a boat) —*corpses, cargo, or sim.* Hdt. —*a person (in a litter)* Plu.; (of a ship, its commander) —*a passenger* Hdt. D.; (of sophists) **hawk** or **peddle** (W.ACC. their teaching) **around** Pl.
3 (act. and mid.) **take** (W.ACC. someone) **around with one** (as a companion) X. D. Men. Plu.
4 cause (W.ACC. the stars) **to go round** Pl.; (of circular motion) **carry round** —*celestial circles, winged souls* Pl.; **make** (W.ACC. an object) **rotate** Pl. ‖ PASS. (of a wheel) rotate Pl.
5 (fig.) lead in a circuitous argument, **confuse** —*someone* And.(dub.) Pl. ‖ PASS. be led along circuitously, be confused —W.DAT. *by an argument* Pl.
6 turn round, swivel —*one's head, neck* Ar. Pl. —*one's gaze* Plu.; **reverse** —*an object* Pl. ‖ MID. or PASS. (of persons or things) turn round E.*Cyc.* Pl.
7 reorient —*someone's mental vision* Pl.; **bring round** (by argument) —*the people* Plu.; **change** —*one form of constitution* (W.PREP.PHR. *to an alternative one*) Arist.
8 twist —*a stick (in a noose, to tighten it)* Hdt.; **wrench** —*someone's hands* (W.PREP.PHR. *behind his back*) Lys. —(W.ADV.) Plu.
9 (intr.) **travel round, go round** NT. —W.ACC. *a place* NT.

περι-αγωγή ῆς *f.* **1** turning round (in a different direction); **wheeling round** (of a horseman) Plu.; **reversal of course** (by a ship) Plu.
2 reorientation (of mental processes) Pl.
3 turning round (in a circle), **rotation, revolution** (of the universe) Pl.; **whirling round** (of a sling) Plb.
4 transportation around (the Peloponnese, W.GEN. of supplies) Plu.

περιαιρετός ή όν *adj.* [περιαιρέω] (of gold plate on a statue) **removable** Th.

περι-αιρέω *contr.vb.* | aor.2 περιεῖλον | **1** remove (sthg. that surrounds or covers); **strip off** —*a clay mould* Hdt. —*skins* (W.GEN. *fr. animals*) Pl. —*brasses (fr. a horse's neck)* X. —*gold plate (fr. a statue)* Plu.
2 demolish, destroy —*a wall (around a city)* Hdt. Th. Lys. X. D. Plu.; **remove** —*hilly regions (surrounding a city, as an impossible task)* Arist. ‖ PASS. (of walls) be demolished D. Plb. Plu.
3 separate —*hangers-on (fr. a ruler)* Pl.
4 (act. and mid.) **strip away, remove** —*property, power, insolence, metre, or sim.* (usu. W.GEN. *fr. someone or sthg.*) Att.orats. Pl. X. Arist. ‖ PASS. (of things) be stripped away Th. Pl. D.
5 ‖ MID. remove from oneself, **strip off, take off, remove** —*one's helmet, ring, ribbons, crown* Hdt. Pl. Arist.; perh. **divest oneself** —W.ACC. *of documents (carried on one's person, and handed over to another)* Hdt.; (fig.) **strip away** —*military resources, an opportunity* (W.GEN. *fr. oneself*) Lys. Lycurg.
6 ‖ PASS. (of a person) be stripped —W.ACC. *of possessions* D.

περι-ακοντίζω *vb.* **pelt** (W.ACC. a carriage) **with javelins from all sides** Plu.

περίακτος ον *adj.* [περιάγω] ‖ NEUT.SB. remark that does the rounds, old proverb Plu.

περι-αλγέω *contr.vb.* **be greatly distressed** Th. —W.DAT. *by a calamity, an indignity* Th. Pl.

περι-αλγής ές *adj.* [ἄλγος] **in great distress** Pl. Plu.; **in great physical pain** Plu.

περι-αλείφω *vb.* **anoint (sthg.) all round**; **put ointment on** —*sores* Ar. —*one's body (after bathing)* Plu.; (fig.) **overlay, coat** —*a temple* (W.DAT. *w. silver*) Pl.

περί-αλλα *neut.pl.adv.* [ἄλλος] above all others, especially, pre-eminently hHom. Pi. S. Ar.(quot. E.) AR. Theoc.; **more than any other** (W.GEN. of the gods) AR.

περι-αλουργός όν *adj.* [ἁλουργής] (fig., of a person) thoroughly purple-dyed, **deep-stained** (W.DAT. w. troubles) Ar.

περί-αμμα ατος *n.* [ἅμμα] charm (for effecting a cure) worn about the body, **amulet** Plb.

περι-αμπέχω *vb.* | aor.2 περιήμπεσχον | **1** put (W.ACC. a garment) **around** or **on** —W.ACC. *someone* Ar. || PASS. (fig., of a speech) be clothed in —W.ACC. *certain kinds of words and phrases* Pl.
2 (of sinews) **enfold** —*flesh and bones* Pl.

περι-αμύ̄νω *vb.* (of a soldier) **offer protection on every side** (for a comrade) Pl.

περι-αμφιέννῡμι *vb.* (of skin) **envelop** —*the head* Pl.

περίαπτον ου *n.* [περιάπτω] charm (for effecting a cure) worn about the body, **amulet** Pl. Plu.; (ref. to pleasure, as merely ornamental) Arist.

περι-άπτω, Aeol. **περάπτω** (Pi.) *vb.* **1** fasten (sthg.) around (a part of the body); **fasten** (W.ACC. a noose) **around** —W.DAT. *one's neck* Plu.; **fasten** (W.ACC. a necklace) **on** —W.DAT. *someone* Plu.; (of a judge in the afterlife) **attach** —*a notice of a verdict* (*to a soul*) Pl.; (of a doctor) **apply** —*remedies* (*i.e. poultices or sim.*, W.DAT. *to an invalid's limbs*) Pi.
2 || MID. attach to oneself, **wear** —*gold and silver* (*as jewellery*) Pl.; (fig., of a city, envisaged as a woman) **ornament oneself with** —*precious stones, statues and temples* Plu.
3 attach (sthg. to someone) as an amulet; (fig.) **attach** —*one's reputation* (W.DAT. *to someone*) Plu. || MID. **adopt** —*a name* Plu.; **take up with** —*a person* Plu.
4 (fig.) **fasten, pin** —*a reproach or sim.* (W.DAT. *on someone*) Lys. Ar. Pl. —*a speech* (*on someone, i.e. attribute it to him*) Plb.; **bring** —*disgrace or sim.* (*to someone*) Pl. X. D.; **secure** —*wealth, happiness, honour, or sim.* (*for someone*) Ar. X.
5 ignite, **light** —*a fire* NT.

περι-αρμόζω *vb.* **fit** (W.ACC. a metal rim) **around** —W.DAT. *a shield* Plu.; **attach** —*spoils* (*to a trophy*) Plu. || PF.PASS. (of women) have had (W.ACC. false beards) fitted Ar.

περι-αρτάομαι *pass.contr.vb.* (of an amulet) **be hung around** —W.DAT. *someone's neck* Plu.

περι-αστράπτω *contr.vb.* (of light fr. heaven) **shine around** —W.ACC. or περί + ACC. *someone* NT.

περιαυτολογίᾱ ᾱς *f.* [αὐτός, λόγος] excess of self-reference, **immoderate boasting** (by a speaker) Plu.

περι-αυχένιος ον *adj.* (of a torque) **that goes round the neck** Hdt.

περίαχε (ep.3sg.impf.): see περιιάχω

περι-βάδην *adv.* **astride** —*ref. to sitting on someone's shoulders* Plu.

περι-βαίνω *vb.* | aor.1 (causatv., tm.) περὶ … ἔβησα |
1 go round; (of a warrior) plant one's feet on each side of, **bestride** —W.GEN. or DAT. (sts. understd.) *a fallen comrade* (*to protect him*) Il.; (of a mother dog) —W.DAT. *her puppies* Od.(tm.).
2 (of a rider) **bestride** —W.ACC. *a horse* Plu.; (of a swimmer) —W.GEN. *a floating keel* Od.(tm.); (of a woman) **straddle** —W.ACC. *an altar* Plu.; (of a woman) —W. περί + ACC. *a penis* Ar.; (of a hole in a plank) **encircle** —W. περί + ACC. *a pole* Plb.
3 (of sounds) go round, **surround** —W.DAT. *someone* S.; (of sthg. bad) —W.ACC. *someone* Ar.
4 (causatv., aor.1) **place** (W.ACC. an arrow) **on** (a bow-string) Theoc.(tm.)

περι-βάλλω *vb.* | The sections are grouped as: (1–5) place (sthg.) around, (6–13) surround or go round (someone or sthg.), (14) turn (sthg.) round, (15) be superior. |
1 throw or place (W.ACC. sthg.) around (sthg.); **put** (a rim) **around** (a shield) Il.; **put** (a canopy of cloth) **over** —W.DAT. *a roof* E.; (fig.) **throw** (a yoke) **over** —W.DAT. *a city* A.; **fasten** (ropes) **around** (objects) Hdt.(also mid.) Th.; (of carrion birds) **fold** or **flap** (their wings) **over** (a corpse) Il.(tm.); (of a sick person) **drape** (his limbs) **over** —W.DAT. *another's* E.; **run** —*a ship* (w. περί + ACC. *onto a submerged obstacle*) Th.
2 put (sthg.) around (a person or part of the body); **throw, place** (W.ACC. one's hands or arms) **around** —W.DAT. (sts. understd.) *someone, a part of the body* Od.(tm.) E.(sts.tm.) Ar. Pl.; **throw** (W.ACC. bonds) **around** —W.DAT. *someone* A. E.; **put** —*a breastplate* (w. περί + ACC. *around a horse's chest*) Hdt. —*a shroud* (w. ἀμφί + DAT. *over one's head*) E.; (of the gods) **put, confer** —*a winged body* (W.DAT. *on a person*) A.
3 (fig.) bestow (sthg., on someone); **confer** —*a benefit, kingship* (W.DAT. *on someone*) Hdt. E.; **prompt** —*unmanly behaviour* (W.DAT. *in someone*) E.; **procure** —*someone's safety* E.; **show** —*pity* (*for someone*) E.
4 || MID. put around oneself, **put on** —*armour, garments* Od. Hdt. E. —*a girdle* (W.DAT. *around one's waist*) Od.(tm.) —*a sword* (W.DAT. *over one's shoulders*) Il.(tm.); (fig.) —*an outward appearance* Pl.
5 (act. and mid.) put (W.ACC. a wall or barrier) **around** —W.DAT. or περί + ACC. (sts. understd.) *a city or sim.* Hdt. Lys. Isoc. + —W.ACC. *a city* Hdt. || MID. put round oneself, **encompass oneself with** —*a wall or barrier* Hdt. Th. Isoc. Pl. Arist.; **surround** —*an island* (W.DAT. *w. a wall*) Pl. || PF.PASS.PTCPL. (of a place) encircled or enclosed (by a wall) Hdt. Pl. D.
6 encompass (someone or sthg., usu. W.DAT. w. sthg.); **embrace** —*someone* (w. one's hands) E. Pl. X. Thphr. Men. Plu.; (mid.) Theoc.; **encircle** —*a neck* (w. a noose) Hdt.(tm.) —*prey, fish* (w. a net) Sol. Hdt.; (fig.) **entrap** —*someone* (*inside a house*) E.; (of a killer) perh. **catch** —*a victim* (W.DAT. *w. a sword*) A.; (of a gaping hole) **engulf** —*a chariot* E.
7 envelop, wrap —*someone, the body* (*in a garment*) E. Ar. Plu.; **clothe** —*someone* NT.
8 (fig.) **encompass** —*a channel* (w. fetters, i.e. bridge it by boats tied together) A.; **bind** —*someone* (w. an oath) E.
9 (of persons) **encircle, surround** —*someone* E.; (of a river) —*a city* E.; (of darkness, a cloud of lamentation, fear) —*a person* E.; (of sleep) —*the limbs* Lyr.adesp.(tm.) || MID. (of troops) **encircle** —*an encampment* X.; **round up** —*animals* Hdt. X.; (fig.) perh. **take a roundabout route** (*in an argument*) Pl.
10 (fig.) **involve** —*someone* (W.DAT. *in trouble, calamity, disgrace, or sim.*) E. Att.orats. X. +
11 || MID. invest oneself with or embrace as one's own, **acquire, gain** —*possessions, a city, or sim.* Hdt. —*booty* Plb. —*power, territory* Isoc. —*a reputation* X. —*one's objectives* D.
12 || MID. encompass (things) mentally; **encompass** —*related items* (*by including them together in the same class*) Pl.; **embrace** —*a course of action* (W.DAT. *in one's mind*) Isoc.
13 (of horses) go round —*a turning-post* Il.(tm.); (of ships, sailors) —*a promontory* Hdt.; (intr., of a hare) **double back** X.
14 (of gods) **turn round, reverse** —*human fortunes* E.
15 be superior (to others); (of horses) **be outstanding** —W.DAT. *in quality* Il.; (tr., of a person) **surpass, outdo** —*everyone* (W.DAT. *in gifts*) Od.

περι-βᾱρίδες ων f.pl. [βᾶρις] **paddle-boats** (ref. to a kind of fancy female shoe, prob. broad and flat in style) Ar.

περί-βαρυς υ adj. [βαρύς] (of a chill of terror) **extremely painful, grievous** A.

περι-βιβάζω vb. (of grooms) **put** (W.ACC. a rider) **astride** (a horse, i.e. help him to mount) Plu.

περι-βιόω contr.vb. | fut.inf. περιβιώσεσθαι | athem.aor.inf. περιβιῶναι | (of persons) live on, **survive** Plu.

περίβλεπτος ον adj. [περιβλέπω] (of persons, their life, achievements, or sim.) **admired by observers on all sides, admired** E. Att.orats. X. Plu.; (of a horse) X.; (of kingship) Plb.

περι-βλέπω vb. **1 look round about, gaze around** Ar. X. Plb. Plu.; (mid.) NT. Plu.
2 look around at —people X. Plu.; (mid.) —people, things NT.
3 (of the masses) look at from all sides, **admire** —a ruler X. || PASS. (of a person) be widely admired E. Plb.
4 (act. and mid.) **look around for, look out for** —a person, place, solution, pretext Plb.
5 consider, question —the rightness (of an action) S.; **watch out, take care** —W.COMPL.CL. to ensure sthg. Plb.

περίβλεψις εως f. **careful attention** (to detail) Plu.

περιβλήματα των n.pl. [περιβάλλω] **encirclements** (of earth or stone, ref. to walls) Pl.

περι-βληχρόν neut.adv. [βληχρός] **in a state of great physical weakness** AR.

περι-βλύω vb. [reltd. βλύζω] (of waves) **seethe around** —W.DAT. rocks AR.

περι-βοάω contr.vb. shout all around, **widely proclaim** —a person's fate AR.(tm.)

περιβόητος ον adj. **1** (of persons or things) shouted all around, **much talked of, celebrated** Th. D. Men. Plb. Plu.; **notorious** Att.orats. Pl. Plu.
2 (of Ares) **surrounded by cries of battle** S.

—**περιβοήτως** adv. **notoriously** Aeschin. D.

περίβολα ων n.pl. [περιβάλλω] perh. **wrappings or coverings** (for arrows, set alight as fire-darts) Tim.

περιβόλαιον ου n. that which is cast around (persons or things); **garment** (W.GEN. of death, ref. to funeral clothes) E.; **coverlet, rug** (for keeping warm) Plu.; **awning** (of a carriage) Plu. || PL. (fig.) clothing (W.GEN. of flesh, ref. to the human body) E.

περιβολή ῆς f. **1 placing around** (opp. ὑποβολή placing underneath, W.GEN. of coverings) Pl.; (concr.) **robe** Plu.
2 || PL. throwing around (W.GEN. of hands), **embraces** E.; (without GEN.) Men. Plu.; **caresses** (of puppies by their mother) X.
3 (fig.) **attempted seizure** (W.GEN. of power) X.
4 || PL. (concr.) enclosing sides (W.GEN. of a tent) E.; encircling walls (of a city) E.; coverings (W.GEN. of earth, ref. to burials) E.; wrappings (W.GEN. serving as a seal, ref. to strings around a writing-tablet) E.; garlands (W.GEN. for one's hair) E.; encasement (for a sword, ref. to a scabbard) E.
5 bend, turn (round a promontory) Th.; journey round (a place), **circuit** X. Plu.
6 compass, size (W.GEN. of a house, ref. to its spatial extent) Hdt.; **scope** (W.GEN. of a speech) Isoc.; **coverage, comprehensive treatment** (W.GEN. of events, by a historian) Plb.

περίβολος ου m. **1** that which encircles or encloses; **perimeter, circumference** (of a city) Th. Plb. Plu.; perh. **continuous line, fringe** (W.GEN. of dockyards, ref. to their location around a bay) E.; area round about, **periphery** (W.GEN. of a cave) E.fr.
2 || PL. coils (of a serpent) E.
3 (concr.) **enclosing wall** (of a palace, city, house, or sim.) Hdt. Th. Pl. Plb.; (of a tomb) E.; **enclosure, cage** (ref. to an aviary) Pl.; (for the soul, ref. to the body) Pl.
4 that which is enclosed, **enclosed area, enclosure** Pl.

—**περίβολος** ον adj. (of garlands) **encircling** (one's head) E.

περι-βόσκομαι mid.vb. (of ash) **feed around** —the embers of a fire Call.

περί-βουνος ον adj. [βουνός] (of a place) **surrounded by hills** Plu.

περι-βραχεῖν aor.2 inf. | 3sg. (tm.) περὶ ... ἔβραχε | (of water) **gurgle all round** AR.(tm.)

περι-βραχιόνιος ον adj. [βραχίων¹] **1** (of an ornament) **for the arm** Plu.
2 || NEUT.SB. armlet (app. ref. to protective armour) X.

περι-βρέμω vb. (of a shout) **ring all around** Alc.(tm.); (of a shore, the sky) re-echo (a noise), **resound** AR.(tm.)

περι-βρομέω contr.vb. | iteratv.impf. περιβρομέεσκον | (of bees) **buzz around** —lilies AR.; (of a person's ears) **be filled with a roaring** or buzzing AR.

περι-βρύχιος ον adj. (of stormy seas) opening up troughs around (a mariner), **enfolding, engulfing** S.

περι-γηθής ές adj. [γηθέω] (of persons) **very joyful, overjoyed** AR.; (of solitude) **joyous** Emp.(v.l. περιηγής)

περι-γίγνομαι, Ion. **περιγίνομαι** mid.vb. **1** (usu. of persons, esp. in military ctxts.) be superior, **get the upper hand, prevail, win** (sts. W.DAT. in sthg.) Hdt. Th. Lys. Isoc. Pl. X.; be superior to, **get the better of, prevail over** —W.GEN. someone or sthg. (sts. W.DAT. in sthg.) Hom. Hdt. Th. Ar. Att.orats. Pl. + —W.ACC. Hdt.
2 (of a military resource) **be an advantage** —W.DAT. for someone Th.; (of a development) **turn out advantageously** —W.DAT. for someone Th. || IMPERS. it is an advantage —W.DAT. + INF. for someone, to do sthg. Th.
3 live on; (usu. of persons) **survive, escape** (death or danger) Hdt. Th. Att.orats. Pl. —W.GEN. a calamity Hdt. —justice Pl. —w. ἐκ + GEN. the worst (of a disease) Th.
4 (of a quantity, usu. of money) **be left over, be in surplus** Heraclit. Lys. Ar. Isoc. Pl. X.
5 be a result or consequence; (of wealth, honours, experience, or sim.) **result, accrue** (usu. W.PREP.PHR. fr. sthg.) Th. Lys. D. Plb.; (of a virtue) **be the product** —w. ἐκ + GEN. of sthg. Arist.; (of aims) **be attained** —W.DAT. by someone Th. || IMPERS. it follows, the upshot is —w. ὥστε + INF. that sthg. is the case X.

περι-γλαγής ές adj. [γλάγος] (of pails) **overflowing with milk** Il.

περι-γληνάομαι mid.contr.vb. [γλήνη] (of a lion) roll the eyeballs, **glare about** Theoc.

περί-γλωσσος ον adj. [γλῶσσα] (of people) very gifted in speech, **very eloquent** Pi.

περι-γνάμπτω vb. (of sailors) steer a course around, **round** —a headland or sim. Od. AR.

περιγραπτός όν adj. [περιγράφω] (prep.phr.) ἐκ περιγραπτοῦ from a circumscribed position (i.e. w. limited room for manoeuvre) Th.

περιγραφή ῆς f. **1** line or lines defining the contour (of sthg.); **outline, contour** (W.GEN. of a foot) A.; **rough sketch** (opp. detailed representation) Pl. Arist.
2 perimeter, circumference (of a place or object) Arist. Plb.
3 compass, scope (of a historical narrative) Plb.

περι-γράφω vb. **1 draw a circle round** —someone or sthg. (on the ground) Hdt. Plb.; **draw** (W.ACC. a circle) **round** (sthg.) Hdt.; **create** (W.ACC. an illusion of virtue) **round** —w. περί + ACC. oneself Pl.; (fig.) **cordon off, hem in** —someone Aeschin.

2 trace the perimeter —w.ACC. *of sthg.* Plb. Plu.; (intr., ref. to feeling someone's body) Ar.
3 draw a preliminary outline ‖ MID. **have** (w.ACC. a design for sthg.) **sketched in outline** Plu. ‖ PASS. (of a topic) be drawn in outline, be sketched Arist.
4 (act. and mid.) **mark off, single out** —*items of relevance or importance* Arist.
5 circumscribe, fix a limit to —*an empire* Plb.; **define, determine, prescribe** —*a period of time* X.; (of a historian) **encompass** —*events* (*in defined time-periods*) Plb. ‖ PASS. (of a limit) be prescribed (by a deity) X.

περι-δαίω *vb.* (of a goddess) **burn, singe** —*someone's flesh* AR.(tm.) ‖ PASS. (fig., of a lover) **burn** —w.DAT. *for someone* AR.

περιδεδράμηκα (pf.), **περιδέδρομα** (pf.2): see περιδραμεῖν

περι-δεής ές *adj.* [δέος] **very fearful, terrified** Hdt. Th. And. Isoc. Plb. Plu. ‖ NEUT.SB. **terror, panic** Th. Plu.

—περιδεῶς *adv.* **in great fear** Th. Isoc. D. Plu.

περι-δείδω *vb.* | only aor. and pf. | ep.aor.1 περίδδεισα | ep.3sg.aor.2 (tm.) περὶ ... δίε | pf. (w.pres.sens.) περιδείδια | **be very fearful, be terrified** Hom. AR.(sts.tm.) —w.GEN. or DAT. *for someone or sthg.* Il. —w.INF. *to do sthg.* AR.

περί-δειπνον ου *n.* [δεῖπνον] **funeral banquet** D. Men.

περι-δέξιος ον *adj.* [δεξιός] **1** (of a person) **dextrous on both sides, ambidextrous** Il. Call.
2 (fig., of arguments) **very dextrous, ultra-clever** Ar.

περι-δέραιος ον *adj.* [δέρη] **1** (of a piece of jewellery) **going around the neck** Plu.
2 ‖ NEUT.SB. **necklace** Arist. Plu.

περι-δεύω *vb.* [δεύω¹] **wet, moisten** —*one's lips* (w.DAT. w. *honey*) AR.(tm.)

περι-δέω *contr.vb.* [δέω¹] **1 fasten** (w.ACC. fruit) **on** —w.DAT. *a tree* Hdt.; **tie** —*a beard* (w.DAT. *on sthg.*) Ar.
2 ‖ MID. **fasten around oneself, put on** —*an anklet, a helmet, a false beard* Hdt. Ar.
3 bind up, garland —*an ox's skull* (w.DAT. *w. ribbons*) Thphr. ‖ PASS. (of a corpse's face) **be wrapped** —w.DAT. *in a cloth* NT.

περι-δίδομαι *mid.vb.* [δίδωμι] **wager, stake, bet** —w.GEN. *an object, oneself* (i.e. one's life) Hom.; **make a bet** (w. περί + GEN. for a certain stake, or w.DAT. w. someone) —w.COMPL.CL. *that sthg. is the case* Ar.

περι-δινεύω *vb.* **circle round** —*a place* AR.(tm.)

περι-δινέω *contr.vb.* (of an orator) **whirl** (w.ACC. oneself) **round** (as an extravagant gesture) Aeschin. ‖ PASS. (of persons) **circle round** AR.(tm.); (of a wheel) **spin round** X.

περιδίνησις εως *f.* **whirling motion** (w.GEN. of air) Plu.

περίδινοι ων *m.pl.* **rovers** (name for brigands or pirates operating around Italy) Pl.

περι-δραμεῖν aor.2 inf. | aor.2 περιέδραμον, ep. περίδραμον | fut. περιδραμοῦμαι | pf. περιδεδράμηκα | pf.2 περιδέδρομα | Pres. and impf. are supplied by περιτρέχω. |
1 (of a person) **run around** (inspecting a house, chasing an animal) Thphr. Plu. —w.ACC. *a city* (*looking for someone*) Men.; **run round** (the side of a house) Ar.; (gener.) **hurry around** —*a region* NT.
2 (of people) **run up and stand round** (a fallen warrior) Il. —*a wounded man* Hdt.; **flock around** (to see sthg.) X.
3 (of an argument) **come around** (to its starting-point, i.e. full circle) Pl.
4 run over (in one's mind) —*arguments* Plu.
5 (fig.) **give the run-around** —w.ACC. *to someone* (*i.e. deceive him*) Ar.(dub., v.l. παρα-)

6 ‖ PF.2 (of a sickness) **have come over** —*someone's limbs* AR.; (w.pres.sens., of water) **flow round** —*a rock* Call.; (statv., of a precinct) **surround** —*a statue* Theoc.epigr.

περι-δράττομαι Att.mid.vb. [δράσσομαι] (of a person's hand) **grasp** —w.GEN. **six obols** (i.e. one drachma, in explanation of its sense 'handful') Plu.; (of a climber) **get a hand-hold** Plu.

περιδρομή ῆς *f.* [περιδραμεῖν] **1 running around** (a city, by priests, as a ritual) Plu.
2 wheeling round (of an animal, to face a hunter) X.; **flanking movement** (to get around or behind enemy troops) Plu.
3 revolution, cycle (w.GEN. of a year) E.

περίδρομος¹ ον *adj.* **1** (of a fugitive) **running around, roaming** A.; (of hell-hounds) Ar.; (fig., of a woman) **roving, promiscuous** Thgn.
2 (of a wheel-hub) **revolving, rotating** Il.
3 (of chariot-rails) **running round, surrounding** (the bodywork) Il.; (of a perimeter fence) Od.; (of the rim of a shield) A. E.
4 (of a land) **surrounded** (w.DAT. by mountains) AR.
5 (of a hill) **that one may go round, standing apart, detached** Il.

περίδρομος² ου *m.* **1 that which runs round** (sthg.); **edge, rim** (of a shield) E.; **circuit, circumference** (formed by a surrounding wall) Pl.
2 string running round (the top of a hunting net), **string, cord** X.
3 gallery running round (a building), **gallery, colonnade** X.

περι-δρύπτομαι *pass.vb.* | ep.aor. περιδρύφθην | (of a charioteer) **have the skin all torn off** —w.ACC. *parts of his body* Il.

περι-δύω *vb.* [δύω¹] **1 strip from around one, strip off** —*one's tunic* Il.
2 strip —*someone* (*of his clothes*) Antipho

περι-ειδον (aor.2): see περιοράω

περι-ειλέω *contr.vb.* —also **περιίλλω** *vb.* [εἰλέω²] | aor.mid.ptcpl. περιιλάμενος ‖ pf.pass. περιείλημαι | **wrap** (w.ACC. sacking) **around** —w. περί + ACC. *animals' feet* X. ‖ MID. **wrap oneself up** —w.DAT. *in rags* Ar. ‖ PASS. (of a shield) **be covered** —w.DAT. *w. canvas and calf-skin* Plb.

περιειλίσσω Ion.vb.: see περιελίσσω

περιεῖλον (aor.2): see περιαιρέω

περί-ειμι¹ *vb.* [εἰμί] | ep.2sg. περίεσσι, Ion. περίεις | ptcpl. περιών, Ion. περιεών | **1** (of a wall) **be around** (a place) Th.
2 (usu. of persons) **be superior to, surpass, excel** —w.GEN. *someone or sthg.* (sts. + ACC. or DAT. *in sthg.*) Hom.(sts.tm.) Emp. Hdt. Th. Pl. +—(+ INF. *at doing sthg.*) Il. AR.; (intr.) **be superior** (in numbers, courage, or sim.) Hdt. Th. X.; (gener.) **win through, prevail, be successful** Th.; (prep.phr.) ἐκ περιόντος *from a position of superiority, with the odds in one's favour* Th.
3 (of persons, ships, places) **continue to exist, survive** (death or danger) Hdt. Th. Hyp. D. +; (of noteworthy objects) **be still in existence, be extant** Hdt. ‖ NEUT.PTCPL.SB. **surviving part, remainder** (of an army) Th.
4 (of a quantity, esp. of money) **be left over, be in surplus** Att.orats. Pl. X. Arist.; (of good or bad qualities) **be in abundance** or **excess** Isoc. Pl. D. ‖ NEUT.PTCPL.SB. (in ctxt. of doing sthg. easily) **generous margin** (w.GEN. of safety) Th.
5 be a result or **consequence**; (of success, shame, a state of affairs, or sim.) **be left, ensue** —w.DAT. *for someone* Th. Aeschin. D. Arist. ‖ IMPERS. **the upshot is, it is left** —w.DAT. + INF. *for someone to do sthg.* D.

περί-ειμι² *vb.* [εἶμι] | ptcpl. περιών, also περιών | impf. περιῄειν, Ion. περιήια ‖ neut.impers.vbl.adj. περιτέον ‖ Only pres. and impf. (other tenses are supplied by περιέρχομαι). The pres.indic. has fut. sense. |
1 make a circular or circuitous movement; (tr., of persons) **make a circuit of, go around** —*a mountain, building, region* Hdt. —*an altar* Ar.; (of the sun) —*the moon* Pl.; (of a trench) **encircle** —*a city* Plu.; (of aulos-music) **waft round** —*someone* Ar.
2 (intr., of persons) **circle round** (a place) Hdt. Th.; (of a crowd, following someone) Pl.; (of heavenly bodies) Pl.; (wkr.sens.) **walk round** (to a place) Pl.; (of a commander) **take a roundabout route** X.; (fig., of an orator) D.; (of a person engaged in philosophical inquiry) Pl.
3 go around (within a place), **go around and about** Hdt. Ar. Att.orats. Pl. +; (tr.) **make the rounds of** —*sentries* Hdt.
4 (of events, states) come round (by cyclical progression); (of summer) **come round** Th.; (of the seasonal cycle) —W.PREP.PHR. *to the same point* Hdt.; (of a year, happenings) **come full circle** Pl. X. Plu.; (of time) **elapse** Hdt. Plu.
5 come round (in turn or by inheritance); (of sovereignty) **devolve** —W.PREP.PHR. *on someone* Hdt.

περι-είργω, Ion. **περιέργω** *vb.* | aor. περιείρξα ‖ pf.pass.ptcpl. περιειργμένος | **1** enclose all around, **fence off** —*a funeral monument* Th.; (of an exterior wall) **surround** —*courtyards* Hdt.; (of a reaper) enclose (in one's hand), **grasp** —*a small amount of corn* Hes.(tm.)
2 ‖ PTCPL.ADJ. (of a trench) surrounding (a field) Th. ‖ PF.PASS.PTCPL. (of a park) enclosed X.; (fig., of a person) with (W.ACC. one's face) hemmed round —W.DAT. *w. briers* (ref. to a beard) Ar.

περι-είρω *vb.* [εἴρω¹] (of Egyptian boatbuilders) **fix** (W.ACC. planks) **in rows around** (the hull) —w. περί + ACC. *over pegs* Hdt.

περίεις (Ion.2sg.): see περίειμι¹

περιέλασις εως *f.* [περιελαύνω] space (on top of a city wall) for driving around (in a chariot), **circuit** Hdt.

περι-ελαύνω *vb.* | fut. περιελῶ | aor. περιήλασα, ep.aor. (tm.) περὶ ... ἔλασσα | pf. περιελήλακα | **1** (of horsemen or charioteers) drive or ride in a circuit, **ride around** X. Plu. —*a city, camp, or sim.* Hdt. X. Plu.
2 (gener.) ride around (hither and thither), **ride about** Hdt. X. —*a country* X.
3 (of cavalry) **ride round** (enemy troops, to outflank or encircle them) Plu. —W.PREP.PHR. *to the enemy's rear* X.; (tr.) **encircle, outflank, cut off** —*enemy troops* Th. ‖ PASS. (of a commander) be encircled or outflanked Plu.
4 (fig.) **outflank, beset, harass** —*someone* (W.DAT. *w. claptrap, trickery*) Ar. ‖ PASS. (fig., of a person) be beset or harassed —W.DAT. *by factional strife* Hdt. Arist. —w. ὑπό + GEN. *by opponents at law* D.
5 (tr.) cause (sthg.) to go round; (fig., of wine-waiters, compared to charioteers) **speed round** —*the cups* X. ‖ PASS. (of air in the body) be driven round, circulate Pl.
6 ‖ MID. **round up** —*slaves and cattle* (as booty) Plb.; **carry off** —*booty* Plb. ‖ PASS. (of booty) be carried off Plb.
7 drive or extend (sthg.) around (an area, so as to enclose it); (of a craftsman) **extend** (W.ACC. a fence) **around** (a vineyard, depicted on a shield) Il.(tm.); (of a town-planner) **drive** (W.ACC. a furrow) **round** —W.DAT. *boundary lines* Plu. ‖ PASS. (of a fence) be extended round (an orchard) Od.(tm.); (of a city) be enclosed —W.ACC. *by a wall* A.(tm.)

περι-ελίσσω, Att. **περιελίττω**, Ion. **περιειλίσσω** *vb.*
1 wind (sthg.) around; **wind** (W.ACC. a letter) **around** (an arrow) Hdt. —w. 2ND ACC. *a staff* Plu.; **wind** —*bark* (W.DAT. *around a stone*) Plu. —*one's cloak* (W.DAT. or περί + ACC. *around one arm, to leave the other free*) X. Plu.; (ref. to landscaping an estate) **make** (W.ACC. streams) **wind around** —W.DAT. *houses* Plu. ‖ MID. **wrap** (W.ACC. thongs) **around** (one's hands) Pl. ‖ PASS. (of serpents) be coiled around (sts. W.DAT. objects) Plu.; (of rivers, likened to serpents) —w. περί + ACC. *the earth* Pl.; (gener., of a river) wind Pl.
2 entwine —*a diadem* (W.DAT. w. *a laurel wreath*), *an ox's horns* (w. hay), *chests* (w. ribbons), *a person* (w. one's hair) Plu.
3 (intr., of a guide) **take a circuitous route** Plu.

περι-έλκω *vb.* **1** (pejor., of a commander) **drag around** —*his troops* (on a difficult campaign) X.
2 drag around, manhandle —*knowledge* (likened to a slave) Arist.; (of a disputant) **lead round** (W.DAT. in a circle) —*an auditor* (i.e. mislead him) Pl. ‖ PASS. (of knowledge) be dragged around (like a slave) Pl.
3 (in military ctxt.) **distract, divert** —*an enemy* Plu.

περι-έννυμι *ep.vb.* | only aor. (tm.) περί ... ἔσσα, aor.mid.inf. περιέσσασθαι | **put** (W.ACC. garments, one's armour) **around** or **on** —*someone* Il.(tm.) ‖ MID. put round oneself, **put on** —*a garment* Hes.

περιέπλεο (ep.2sg.aor.2 mid.): see περιπέλομαι

περι-έπω *vb.* | impf. περιεῖπον | fut. περιέψω | aor.2 περιέσπον, inf. περισπεῖν ‖ fut.mid.inf. (prob. w.pass.sens.) περιέψεσθαι | aor.pass. περιέφθην |
1 behave towards (someone or sthg., in a specified way); **treat, handle** —*someone or sthg.* (W.ADV. or DAT.PHR. *harshly, well, w. indignity, respect, or sim.*) Il.(tm.) Hdt. X. Plu. —(W.PREDIC.PHR. *as a friend, enemy, slave*) Hdt. X. ‖ PASS. be treated —W.ADV. or PREDIC.PHR. *harshly, as an enemy* Hdt. X.
2 (in positive sense) **treat well** or **respectfully, be attentive to** —*someone* X. Plu.
3 (intr.) **be attentive** or **vigilant** Plb.

περιεργάζομαι *mid.vb.* [περίεργος] **1** take excessive trouble, **waste one's labours, waste time** —W.NOM.PTCPL. *doing sthg.* Hdt. Pl. D. —W.ACC. *on sthg.* Ar. —W.COMPL.CL. *to ensure sthg.* Antipho; (of a speaker) **overdo things** —W.DAT. *w. a word* (i.e. use a redundant word) Hdt.; (of a performer) —w. *gestures* (i.e. overact) Arist.
2 take inappropriate trouble, **meddle, interfere** Isoc. D. Men. —W.ACC. *in sthg.* D. Plb.

περιεργία ᾱς *f.* overdoing things, **overzealousness, officiousness** Isoc. Plu.; **inquisitiveness, meddlesomeness** Plu.

περί-εργος ον *adj.* [ἔργον] **1** (of a person) taking excessive trouble, **over-zealous, over-conscientious** Lys. Thphr. Plu.
2 interfering in others' concerns, **over-officious, meddlesome** Att.orats. X. Men.; **over-inquisitive, nosy** Men.
3 (of words) **over-elaborate** Aeschin.; (of arguments or sim.) **superfluous** Pl. Arist.; (of an expense) Arist.; (of friends) Arist.; (of a war) **pointless** Isoc. ‖ NEUT.SB. something superfluous or unnecessary, a waste of time And.; over-elaboration (in dress) Isoc. ‖ NEUT.IMPERS. (w. ἐστί) it is superfluous, unnecessary, a waste of time —W.INF. *to do or say sthg.* Att.orats. Arist.
4 (of rituals) **exotic, magic** Plu. ‖ NEUT.PL.SB. magic arts NT.

—**περιεργότερον** *compar.adv.* **too fussily** —*ref. to being dressed* Arist.

περιέργω *Ion.vb.*: see περιείργω

περι-έρρω vb. (of an old man) **wander around** Ar.

περι-έρχομαι mid.vb. | impf. περιηρχόμην (Ar.) | aor.2 περιῆλθον ‖ Fut. (and usu. impf.) are supplied by περίειμι². |
1 make a circular or circuitous movement; (of persons) **circle round** (a place) Hdt. Th. Ar. X. Plb. —*a city, a hill* Plb.; **surround** —*an enemy* Plu.
2 (of sounds) **encompass, flood round** —*persons, their senses* Hom.(tm.) hHom.(tm.); (of wine, i.e. its effects) Od.(tm.)
3 (of things) **go round in a complete circle**; (of the sun, the moon) **go round** —W.INTERN.ACC. *its orbit (i.e. complete it)* Pl.; (of a year) **come full circle** X.; (fig., of an argument, by returning to its starting-point) Pl.; (of a discussion, by reaching its conclusion) X.
4 (gener., of persons) **go around** (within a place); **go round and about** Ar. Att.orats. Pl. X. Men.; (tr.) **go around** —*a city, a region, the agora* Att.orats. X. Men.; **make the rounds of, visit in turn** —*people, temples, altars* Hdt. Th. Ar. Arist.; (of a transmigrating soul) —*various creatures* Hdt.
5 (of events, states, or sim.) **come round** (by cyclical progression, in turn, or by inheritance); (of a period of time) **come round** Hdt.; (of war) Hdt.; (of sovereignty or sim.) —W.PREP.PHR. *to someone* Hdt. Plu.; (of pollution) Pl.; (of a people) —W.PREP.PHR. + ADV. *to a state of tyranny again* Hdt.; (of a sickness) **turn** —W.PREP.PHR. *to consumption* Hdt.; (of vengeance) come round to, **catch up with** —W.ACC. *someone* Hdt.
6 (fig., of a disputant) **go around** —W.PREP.PHR. *in a circle (i.e. beat about the bush)* Pl.; **take a circuitous route** (in argument) Pl.
7 (fig., of persons) **get round, circumvent, trick** —*someone* Hdt. Ar. Plu.

περιέσπον (aor.2): see περιέπω

περίεσσι (ep.2sg.): see περίειμι¹

περι-έσχατα των *n.pl.* [ἔσχατος] **extremities, edges** (of a pyre) Hdt.; **outskirts** (of a city) Hdt.

περιέτραγον (aor.2): see περιτρώγω

περι-έχω, also **περιίσχω** (Th.) vb. | fut. περιέξω, also περισχήσω (Th.) | aor.2 περιέσχον, inf. περισχεῖν, ep.aor.2 (tm.) περὶ ... ἔσχεθον ‖ aor.2 mid. περιεσχόμην, ep. περισχόμην, ep.imperatv. περίσχεο |
1 (of things) **be around** (persons or things); (of a ditch, road, river, or sim.) **surround, encompass, enclose** —*people or places* Il.(tm.) Th. Att.orats. Pl. X.; (of lines) —*a space* Pl.; (of the universe) —*all living things* Pl. ‖ NEUT.PTCPL.SB. **the heavens** Plb.; **atmosphere** Plb. Plu.
2 (of persons) **surround, crowd round** —*someone* Plu. ‖ PASS. (of troops) **be surrounded** Hdt. X.; (fig.) **be beset** (by some difficulty) Men. —W.DAT. *by misery* AR.
3 **surround** —*someone* (W.DAT. *w. one's hands, i.e. embrace him*) Plu. ‖ MID. hold one's hands round, **cling to, clasp, embrace** —W.ACC. or GEN. *someone's knees (in emotion or supplication)* AR.; throw one's arms round in protection, **protect, defend** —W.ACC. or GEN. *someone* Hom.
4 (fig.) cling to (what one is fond of); **be strongly attached to, be reluctant to let go of** —W.GEN. *someone, some possession or goal* Hdt. Plu.; **cling to a resolution, persist in a desire** —W.ACC. + INF. *that someone shd. do sthg.* Hdt.
5 (of troops in battle formation) extend beyond, **outflank** (sts. W.GEN. the enemy) Th.; (fig., of a commander) **gain the advantage, come out on top** Th.
6 (philos., of concepts) **encompass, embrace, include** —*particular things* Pl. Arist. ‖ PASS. (of parts) be embraced —W.PREP.PHR. *by the whole* Pl.
7 ‖ PTCPL.ADJ. (log., of terms) **generic** (opp. specific) Arist. ‖ NEUT.SG.PTCPL.SB. **the universal** (opp. particulars) Arist. ‖ NEUT.PL.PASS.PTCPL.SB. **particulars** (opp. the universal) Arist.

περιεώρων (impf.): see περιοράω

περι-ζαμενές *neut.adv.* [ζαμενής] **violently** —*ref. to a wind blowing* Hes.fr.

περιζαμενῶς adv. **furiously** —*ref. to being angry* hHom.

περί-ζυξ ζυγος *masc.fem.adj.* [ζεύγνυμι] **over and above a pair**; (of straps for harness, packs, or sim.) **spare, extra** X.

περί-ζωμα ατος *n.* [ζῶμα] **waist-cloth** (worn by men) Plb. Plu.

περι-ζώννυμαι mid.vb. **1** fasten one's clothing with a belt around the waist (to leave one's lower limbs, or sts. upper limbs, unencumbered, in readiness for physical activity); **hitch up, belt up** —*one's cloak or robe* Plb. Plu.; (fig., of the populace, described as naked) belt up with, **wrap oneself up in** —*a politician (as its protector)* Ar. ‖ PF.MID.PASS. wear as a belt —*a horse's halter* Arist.
2 (intr.) secure one's clothing at the waist (to be ready for action), **belt up** Arist. Plu. ‖ PF.MID.PASS. be belted for action Ar.

περι-ηγέομαι mid.contr.vb. **1** guide or lead (W.DAT. someone) **around** —*a mountain* Hdt. —*trees* Men.
2 ‖ PASS. (of a scheme) be described in outline Pl.

περιηγής ές *adj.* (of a ball, a rock) **circular, round** AR.; (of a pit, the lake on Delos) Call. AR.; (of a shore, a fastening) **curved** AR.; (of villagers) **surrounding** Call.; (of the Cyclades, which lie around Delos) Call. | see also περιγηθής

περιήγησις εως (Ion. ιος) *f.* **contour, profile, shape** (of a bird) Hdt.

περιηγητής οῦ *m.* **guide-book writer** Plu.

περιήδη (3sg.plpf.): see περίοιδα

περι-ήκω vb. **1** (of an opportunity) **have come round** Plu.; (of sovereignty) —W. εἰς + ACC. *to someone* X.
2 (of a person) have come round to, **have achieved** or **attained** —*a status, an ability* Hdt.

περι-ήλυσις εως *f.* **1** going around, **cycle** (of a soul transmigrating) Hdt.
2 skirting round (a mountain) Plu.

περιημεκτέω Ion.contr.vb. [perh.reltd. ἐμέω] **be very upset, aggrieved** or **angered** Hdt. —W.DAT. *by a calamity, deception, delay, the prospect of slavery* Hdt.

περι-ηχέω contr.vb. (of a bronze shield, struck by a stone) **ring all around** Il.

περιήχησις εως *f.* **echo from all sides** (of a valley) Plu.

περι-θαμβής ές *adj.* [θάμβος] **1** (of persons) **marvelling greatly** AR.
2 greatly alarmed (W.DAT. at someone's fate) AR. ‖ NEUT.SB. **panic** Plu.

περι-θαρσής ές *adj.* [θάρσος] (of persons) **valiant, bold** AR.; **confident** (W.DAT. in one's strength) AR.

περι-θειόω contr.vb. [θειόω¹] | 3pl.aor.imperatv. περιθεωσάτωσαν (ε for ει *metri grat.*) | (of quack healers) fumigate by ritual encirclement (w. sulphur), **ritually fumigate** —*someone* Men.

περι-θείωσις εως *f.* **ritual fumigation** Pl.

περίθετος ον (also **περιθετός** ή όν Plb.) *adj.* [περιτίθημι] (of a head-dress or wig) **for putting on** Ar.; (of hair, ref. to a wig) **false** Plb.

περι-θέω contr.vb. [θέω¹] **1** (of animals) **run round** —*a barrier* X.
2 (of outbuildings or sim.) extend round, **run round** (a house) Od.(tm.); (of a wall, a moat) —W.ACC. *a city or sim.*

περιθρεκτέον

Hdt. Pl.; (of a metal ring) **encircle** (a spear) Il.(tm.); (fig., of a style of behaviour) **clothe, pervade** —*one's relations w. other people* Plu.
3 (of persons) **run hither and thither, run around** Pl. X. Plu. —W.ACC. *household slaves (making threats to them)* Ar.; **rush around** —*a country (levying troops)* Plu.
4 (of a warrior's shield) **move to and fro** Hdt.

περιθρεκτέον (neut.impers.vbl.adj.), **περιθρέξαι** (aor.inf.), **περιθρέξομαι** (fut.mid.): see περιτρέχω

περι-θρηνέομαι mid.contr.vb. (of the world) **be completely filled with lamentation** Plu.

περι-θριγκόω contr.vb. **fence round** —*vineyards* (W.DAT. w. *the bones of corpses*) Plu.

περί-θυμος ον adj. [θυμός] (of curses) **very full of passion or anger, impassioned, furious** A.
—περίθυμον neut.adv. **with rage** —*ref. to shrieking* Plu.
—περιθύμως adv. **passionately, furiously** —*ref. to uttering reproaches* A.; (w. ἔχειν) **be very angry** Hdt. Pl.

περι-ιάχω ep.vb. | 3sg.impf. περὶ ... ἴαχε (tm.), also περίαχε | (of the earth, sea, a cave) **ring all around** (w. an echo) Od. Hes.

περιίδμεναι (ep.pf.inf.): see περίοιδα

περι-ίζομαι mid.vb. (of people) **sit round** (a fire) Hdt. —W.ACC. *a person* Hdt.; (of soldiers) **take up a position around** —*fugitives* Hdt.

περιϊλάμενος (aor.mid.ptcpl.): see περιειλέω

περι-ιππεύω vb. **1** (of cavalry) **ride around** (to an enemy's rear) Plb. —W.ACC. *an enemy's wing* Plu.
2 (of a horseman) **ride around** (hither and thither) Plu.

περι-ίστημι vb. | aor.1 περιέστησα | MID.: aor.1 περιεστησάμην ‖ For the act. athem.aor., pf. and plpf. see περιίσταμαι below. |
1 place around; station (W.ACC. persons, soldiers) **around** (a place) Hdt. Th. D.; **station** —*an army* (w. περί + ACC. *around a city*) X.; **place** (W.ACC. a container) **around** —W.DAT. *sthg.* Hdt. Pl.; (fig.) **impose, inflict** —*troubles, dangers, trials* (W.DAT. *on persons*) D. Plb. Plu.
2 (aor.1 mid.) **place round oneself** —*persons, bodyguards, symbols of authority* X. Plu.
3 (aor.1 mid.) app. **place** (hunting nets) **around** (traces of game) X.
4 bring round —*political power* (W.PREP.PHR. *to oneself*) Arist. —*a form of government* (*to monarchy*) Plb.; (of persons, fortune) —*a situation* (*to a certain state*) Att.orats.; **transfer** —*one's misfortunes* (W.PREP.PHR. *to someone*) D.

—περιίσταμαι mid.vb.| fut. περιστήσομαι | ep.3pl.aor.1 περιστήσαντο | ACT.: athem.aor. περιέστην, ep. περίστην, ep.3pl.subj. περιστήωσι | pf. περιέστηκα | 3sg.plpf. περιεστήκει ‖ AOR.PASS. (w.mid.sens.): περιεστάθην, ep.3sg. περιστάθη |
1 (of persons) **stand around** (someone) Il. Hdt. E. X. + —W.ACC. *someone or sthg.* Hom. Hdt. S. Th. + —W.DAT. *someone or sthg.* Lys. Pl.; (fig., of a mountainous wave) **rise and stand around** (lovers, to shield them) Od.
2 (of a commander) **surround** —*a city* Th. —*a hill* (W.DAT. w. *an army*) X.; (of air, cold) —W.ACC. or περί + ACC. *sthg.* Pl.
3 ‖ MASC.PL.PF.PTCPL.SB. **bystanders, spectators** (standing around the edges of a lawcourt) Att.orats. Thphr.; (in the theatre, at performances by sophists) Ar. Isoc.
4 (fig., of fear, danger, turmoil, war, disgrace) **surround, beset** —W.ACC. or DAT. *persons, a city, or sim.* Th. Att.orats.; (intr., of danger, troubles, crises) Th. Lys. Plb.
5 (of circumstances, situations) **come round in the course of events**; (of suspicion) **come round** —w. εἰς + ACC. *to someone* Th.; (of praise, disrepute, slavery, a duty) —W.DAT. *to someone* Th. Lys. D.; (of events) **develop, shift** —w. εἰς + ACC. *to such and such a state* Isoc. D.; (of fortune) **shift round, change, be reversed** Th.; (of an argument) —W.PREP.PHR. *to the opposite* Pl.; (of an offence) **be shifted** —w. εἰς + ACC. *onto someone* Th.; (of war) **be changed** —W.PREP.PHR. *to a matter of chance* Th.; (of good sense) **change** —W.PTCPL.PHR. *to appearing as sthg. different* Th.; (of the opposite result) **turn out** (sts. W.DAT. for someone) Th. Lys. Isoc. Pl. ‖ IMPERS. **circumstances change** —W.ACC. or DAT. + INF. (sts. ὥστε + INF.) w. *the result that someone does sthg., or that sthg. happens* Pl. Lycurg. D.

περιίσχω vb.: see περιέχω

περιιτέον (neut.impers.vbl.adj.): see περίειμι²

περικάββαλον (ep.aor.2): see περικαταβάλλω

περικάδομαι dial.mid.vb.: see περικήδομαι

περι-καθαίρω vb. **purify by ritual encirclement, ritually purify** —*someone or sthg.* Pl. Thphr.

περι-καθάπτω vb. **fasten** (W.ACC. a fish) **onto** —W.DAT. *a hook* Plu.

περι-καθέζομαι mid.vb. **be encamped around, besiege** —*a city wall* D.

περι-κάθημαι, Ion. **περικάτημαι** mid.vb. | Ion.3pl.impf. περικατέατο | **1 sit around** —*someone* Hdt. Plu. —W.ACC. *a fire* Plu.
2 (of a commander, his troops) **be encamped around, besiege** —*a city or sim.* Hdt. D.; **blockade** —*an island* Hdt.; (fig., of a woman) **lay siege** (to a man, w. further sexual connot. **straddle**) Men.

περι-καίω, Att. **περικάω** vb. (of fire) **burn all around, consume** —*a forest* Plu.; (of a barber) **burn the edges of, singe** —*someone's hair* Plu. ‖ PASS. (of animals) **be singed** Hdt.; (fig., of a person) —W.DAT. *by the fire of war* Plu.; (gener.) **be inflamed, be excited** And.

περι-κακέω contr.vb. [κακός] **be in great distress** Plb.

περικάκησις εως f. **extreme distress** (of a person) Plb.

περι-καλλής ές adj. [κάλλος] **1** (of women, goddesses, the children of gods) **very beautiful** Hom. Hes.fr. hHom. Ar. AR. Mosch.; (of a goddess's neck, a man's eyes) Hom.; (of the voice of the Muses) Hes.
2 (of things) **very beautiful** Hom. hHom. Hdt.(quot.epigr.) D.(quot.epigr.) AR. Theoc.; (of an island, a country) Stesich. Thgn. Hdt.

περι-κάλυμμα ατος n. **garment which covers one all around, wrap, covering** Pl.

περι-καλύπτω vb. **1 cover** (persons or things) **all round**; (of a deity) **cover, envelop** —*a person* (W.DAT. *in clouds*) AR.(tm.); (of heaven) —*earth* Hes.(tm.); (of a lionskin) —*a person's sides* Theoc.(tm.); (of a hand) —*a stone* Il.(tm.); (fig., of a cloud of war) —*everything* Il.(tm.); (of sleep) —*a person* Od.(tm.) AR.(tm.); (of the Soul of the Cosmos) —*heaven* Pl.; (intr., of night) Il.(tm.)
2 (specif., of persons, earth) **cover, shroud** —*a corpse* X. Plu.
3 cover all round (w. a specified covering); **cover, envelop, shroud** —*a tree* (W.DAT. w. *felt*) Hdt. —*an object* (W.DAT. w. *one's cloak*) Plu.; (of a god) —*a corpse* (w. *his aigis*) Il.(tm.) —*a person* (w. *clouds*) AR.(tm.)
4 (specif.) **cover** —*a person's face* (i.e. **blindfold** him) NT.; **blindfold** —*a person* NT.
5 give protective cover to —*people* (W.DAT. w. *a ring of armed men*) Plu.
6 (fig.) **wrap up, include** —*the politician* (W.PREP.PHR. *along w. other types of person*) Pl.; (of ancestral customs) **invest, endow** —*laws* (W.DAT. w. *security*) Pl.

7 put (sthg.) around as a covering; (of Sleep) **shed** (w.ACC. slumber) **around** —w.DAT. *someone* Il.(tm.); (of the creator god) **place** (w.ACC. *the body*) **around** —w.DAT. *the soul* Pl.; (fig.) **draw** (w.ACC. *darkness*) **as a veil over** —w.DAT. *events* E.

—**περικαλυπτέα** *neut.pl.impers.vbl.adj.* **one must cover oneself up** Ar.

περικαλυφή ῆς *f.* **wrapping, covering** (as a process) Pl.

περι-κάμπτω *vb.* (intr.) **bend round** (sthg.), **turn a corner** Pl.

περι-κάππεσον (ep.aor.2): see περικαταπίπτω

περι-κάρδιος ον *adj.* [καρδίᾱ] (of blood) **around the heart** Emp.

περι-καταβάλλω *vb.* | ep.aor.2 περικάββαλον | (of a suppliant) **drop** (w.ACC. *one's head*) **into** —w.DAT. *someone's lap* AR.(dub.)

περι-κατάγνῡμι *vb.* | aor.inf. περικατᾶξαι | **break** (w.ACC. *a stick*) **over** —w.DAT. *people* (*while beating them*) Ar.

περι-καταλαμβάνομαι *pass.vb.* **1** (of troops) **be overtaken** (by the enemy) Plb. —w.PREP.PHR. *by flames* Plb.; (fig., of a commander) —w.DAT. *by circumstances* Plb.

2 (of corn) **be captured from all around** Plb.

περι-καταπίπτω *vb.* | ep.aor.2 περικάππεσον | **fall down around** (sthg.); (of a boar) **impale oneself on** —w.DAT. *a spear* AR.; (of a hawk) —*a ship's stern-post* AR.

περι-καταρρέω *contr.vb.* (of city walls) **fall completely into ruin** Lys.

περι-καταρρήγνῡμι *vb.* ∥ MID. (of a woman) **tear from top to bottom** —*her dress* X.

περι-κατασφάζω *vb.* **slaughter** (w.ACC. *captives*) **around** —*someone's corpse* Plb.

περι-κατατίθημι *vb.* | ep.3sg.athem.aor.mid. περικάτθετο | ∥ MID. **fasten on** —*one's quiver* (w.DAT. *by a strap*) AR.

περι-κάτημαι *Ion.mid.vb.*: see περικάθημαι

περι-κάω *Att.vb.*: see περικαίω

περικαῶς *adv.* [reltd. περικαίω] **very ardently** —*ref. to being in love* Plu.

περί-κειμαι *mid.pass.vb.* [κεῖμαι] **1 lie embracing** —w.DAT. *a dead comrade* Il.

2 (of a weapon-case) **be placed around** —w.DAT. *a bow* Od.; (of a garland) —*a person* (i.e. *his head*) Pi.; (of a muzzle) —*a horse's mouth* X.; (fig., of a millstone) —w. περί + ACC. *around someone's neck* NT.; (of gold plates) **be overlaid** (on a statue) Th.; (fig., of a stain) **be placed on** —w.DAT. *someone* Plu. ∥ PTCPL.ADJ. (of land, cities) **surrounding** Plb.

3 (of greaves) **be hanging** (on pegs) Alc.

4 (usu. ptcpl.) **have** (sthg.) **placed around one**; (of persons) **wear** (a shield-strap) —w. περί + DAT. *around one's neck and left shoulder* Hdt. —w.ACC. *garments, garlands* Plu. —(fig.) *a chain* NT.; (fig.) **be clad in** —w.ACC. *insolence* Theoc. —*military power* Plu.; (of hunting nets) **have** (w.ACC. *cords*) **running around** (them) X.

5 be stored up as a surplus ∥ IMPERS. (in neg.phr.) οὐδέ τί μοι περίκειται *and it is no benefit to me* (*to have done sthg.*) Il.

περι-κείρω *vb.* (act. and mid.) **cut short all round, shear off** —*one's hair* Hdt.; (act.) **shear** —*someone's head* Plu. ∥ FEM.PASS.PTCPL.SB. **Woman with Shorn Hair** Men.(title)

περι-κεράω *contr.vb.* [κέρας] **outflank** —*the enemy* Plb.; (also intr.) Plb.

περι-κεφαλαίᾱ ᾱς *f.* —also **περικεφάλαιον** ου *n.* [κεφαλή] **that which goes around the head; helmet** Plb.

περι-κήδομαι, dial. **περικάδομαι** *mid.vb.* **show great concern** or **care** —w.GEN. *for someone or sthg.* Od. Pi.

περί-κηλος ον *adj.* [reltd. κήλεος] (of timber) **well dried** Od.

περι-κίων ον, gen. ονος *adj.* (of a temple) **surrounded by columns** E.

περι-κλαδής ές *adj.* [κλάδος] (of a forest) **with branches all around, dense** AR.

περι-κλαίω *vb.* **1 weep over** —*a corpse* Plu.

2 ∥ MID. **weep for** —w.GEN. *a land* Call.

περίκλασις εως *f.* [περικλάω] **1 breaking around, cleaving** (w.GEN. *of the aither, by the moving stars*) Plu.

2 wheeling round (of troops) Plb. Plu.

3 brokenness, irregularity (of ground) Plb.

περι-κλάω *contr.vb.* | aor. περιέκλασα | **1 break** (w.ACC. *one's sword*) **on** —w.DAT. *someone's helmet* Plu. ∥ PASS. (of siege-engines) **bend and break** —w.DAT. *under their own weight* Plu.; (of a person) **bend over** Theoc.

2 wheel round —*troops* Plb.

3 divert —*a river* Plu.

—**περικεκλασμένος** η ον *pf.pass.ptcpl.adj.* (of terrain) **broken, rough, uneven** Plb.; (of houses) **on uneven ground** Plb.

περι-κλεής ές *adj.* [κλέος] (of a city) **very famous, famed, renowned** Ibyc. AR.; (of a name) AR.

Περικλέης, Att. **Περικλῆς**, έους *m.* | voc. Περίκλεις | acc. Περικλέα | dat. Περικλέϊ | **Perikles** (Athenian statesman, c.495–429 BC) Hdt. Th. Ar. Att.orats. +

περι-κλειτός όν (also ή όν Theoc.) *adj.* (of heroes, a queen) **very famous, famed, renowned** B. Theoc.; (of a palace, a contest) B.

περι-κλείω, Att. **περικλῄω**, Ion. **περικληΐω** *vb.* [κλείω¹] **1** (of lands, mountains) **shut in all around, enclose** —*a region* Hdt.; (of headlands) —*a harbour* Plb. ∥ PASS. (of a region) **be shut in** or **enclosed** —w.DAT. *by mountains* Hdt.

2 (of ships) **hem in** —*enemy ships* Th.; (mid., of an admiral) Th. ∥ PASS. (of troops) **be hemmed in** Th. Plb.

περι-κλινής ές *adj.* [κλίνω] (of hills or sim.) **sloping on all sides, sloping, steep** Plu.; (of the roof of the Odeion) **convex** Plu.

περι-κλύζω *vb.* (of a river) **surge around** (people fording it) Plu. ∥ PASS. (of a city on an island) **be washed all around, be sea-girt** Th.; (of a ship) **be struck by a surging sea** Plu.

περίκλυστος ον (also ᾱ ον A.) *adj.* (of an island) **washed all around, sea-girt** Hes. hHom. A.; (of a city) **sea-washed** E.; (of belvederes) Plu.

περι-κλυτός όν *adj.* **1** (of men) **very famous, famed, renowned** Hom. hHom.; (of Hephaistos, as a craftsman) Hom. Hes.; (of cities) Od.

2 (of gifts, handiwork) **fine, splendid, glorious** Il. Hes.*fr.* Mosch.

περι-κνημῖδες ων *f.pl.* [κνημίς] **greaves** Plu.

περι-κοκκάζω *vb.* [app.reltd. κοκκύζω] | aor. περιεκόκκασα (v.l. περιεκόκκυσα) | **crow around** or **over** (someone), **crow in contempt** Ar.

περι-κομίζω *vb.* (of a commander) **bring** (w.ACC. *ships*) **round** (to a place) Th. ∥ PASS. (of sailors) **proceed round** (to a place) Th.

περικόμματα των *n.pl.* [περικόπτω] **chopped up scraps** (of meat), **mincemeat** Ar. Men.

—**περικομμάτια** ων *n.pl.* [dimin.] **mincemeat** Ar.

περί-κομψος ον *adj.* [κομψός] (of conjectures) **very subtle, all too clever** Plu.

περικοπή ῆς *f.* [περικόπτω] **1 mutilation** (of statues) Th. And. Plu.

2 trepanning (of a skull) Plu.

3 (fig.) **trimming down, curtailment** (w.GEN. *of extravagance*) Plu.

4 outline or outward form, **general appearance** or **bearing** (of a person) Plb.

περι-κόπτω *vb.* **1** cut all around, **mutilate** —*statues* And. Lys. D.; **cut off** —*a ship's figurehead* Plu. ‖ PASS. (fig., of human nature) be cut free —W.ACC. *of leaden weights* Pl.
2 devastate, ravage —*a region, its inhabitants* D. Plu.; (fig.) **plunder, rob** —*people* D. ‖ PASS. (of persons, cities) be robbed or stripped —W.GEN. *of military strength, possessions* Plu.
3 cut off —*troops, ships, supplies, access* Plu. —*people* (W.GEN. *fr. a place*) Plu. ‖ PASS. (of a fortress) be cut off —W.DAT. *by cliffs* Plu.; (of a person) —W.ACC. *fr. supplies, one's fleet* Plu.
4 (fig.) **cut down, trim, curtail** —*someone's troops, extravagance, meddlesomeness* Plu. ‖ PASS. (of honour and power) be curtailed Plu.; (of a person) —W.ACC. *in authority* Plu.

περι-κράνιος ον *adj.* [κρᾱνίον¹] (of a cap) **fitting the skull** Plu.

περι-κρατής ές *adj.* [κράτος] (of sailors) **in full control** (W.GEN. of a ship's boat) NT.

περί-κρημνος ον *adj.* [κρημνός] (of a ridge) **with cliffs on all sides** Plu.

περι-κρούω *vb.* **1** hammer (W.ACC. fetters) **around** —W.DAT. *a person* Men.
2 (fig.) **strike on all sides** —*desirable qualities* (*as if they were physical objects, to test their soundness*) Pl.
3 ‖ PASS. (fig., of a soul) be knocked free —W.ACC. *of accretions* (*acquired fr. the physical world*) Pl.

περι-κρύβω *vb.* [κρύπτω] **seclude** (W.ACC. oneself) **completely** NT.

περι-κτίονες ων *masc.pl.adj.* [κτίζω] | ep.dat. περικτιόνεσσι | (of people) **dwelling round about, neighbouring** Hom. Hes.*fr.* hHom. Th. ‖ SB. dwellers round about, neighbours Il. Simon. Pi. Hdt.(oracle) AR.

περικτίται *ep.m.pl.* | only nom. | **neighbours** Od.

περι-κυκλόω *contr.vb.* (of enemies) **encircle, surround** —*a city* NT.; (mid.) —*persons* Hdt. Ar.(tm.) X.

περι-κύκλωσις εως *f.* **encirclement** (by enemy soldiers) Th.

περι-κυλινδέομαι *pass.contr.vb.* (of things) **roll forward while spinning** Pl.

περι-κυλίω *vb.* | aor.ptcpl. περικυλίσᾱς | (of a dung-beetle) **roll around** —*a ball of dung* (*w. its feet*) Ar.

περι-κύμων ον, gen. ονος *adj.* [κῦμα] (of an island) **surrounded by waves** E.

περι-κωμάζω *vb.* go round on an amorous excursion, **cruise around** —*wrestling schools* Ar.

περι-κωνέω *contr.vb.* [κῶνος] smear with pitch, **black** —*shoes* Ar.

περι-λαλέω *contr.vb.* **chatter too much** Ar.

περι-λαμβάνω *vb.* **1** catch hold of (by placing one's arms or hands around), **embrace** —*someone* X. Plu. —*a tree trunk* AR.(tm.); (of persons, likened to gods or giants) **clasp** —*rocks and trees* Pl.
2 catch by encirclement, **surround, trap** —*troops, ships* Hdt. Th. Plb. Plu.; **catch** —*an animal* (W.DAT. *in a net*) Pl.; (fig.) —*a person* Ar.; (gener.) **surround** —*a place* (W.DAT. *w. a trench, a stockade, or sim.*) Plb. Plu. ‖ PASS. be trapped or caught Ar. X.; (fig.) —W.DAT. *by circumstances* Plb.; (of ambition) be confined —W.DAT. *by territorial boundaries* Plb.
3 get in one's grasp, **get one's hands on, get control of** —*someone* Hdt. —*someone's property* Is. —*territories* Plb.
4 (of the sides of an oblong figure) **enclose** —*sth.* Pl.; (of the spherical universe) **contain, embrace** —*all living things* Pl.

5 (of persons) cover all around, **coat, overlay** —*walls or sim.* (W.DAT. *w. precious metals*) Pl.; (of water, fire) **cover** —*an area* Plb. ‖ PASS. (of a head) be encased or covered —W.DAT. *by sinews* Pl.; (of pillars) —*w. metal plates* Plb.
6 incorporate (sth., esp. within sth. else); **include, encompass** —*many persons or things* (W.DAT. *under a single name or idea*) Pl. Aeschin. D. Arist. —*various things, everything* (sts. W.DAT. *in one's discourse or sim.*) Isoc. Pl.; (of a single name, a general term) —*many things* Pl. Arist. Plb.; **include** —*someone* (W.DAT. *in a treaty*) Plb.; (of a law) **cover** —*specific offences* Lycurg.; (of a historian) —*a subject* (W.DAT. *in his writing*) Plu. ‖ PASS. (of things) be encompassed or covered —W.DAT. *by a single name or sim.* Pl. Arist.; (of offences) —*by laws* Arist.; (of a period of time) —W.PREP.PHR. *by a historical work* Plb.
7 (specif.) **define** —*sth.* (W.PREP.PHR. or ADV. *in general terms or sim.*) Isoc. Pl. Arist.
8 grasp, comprehend (W.DAT. in one's mind) —*a likely outcome* Plu.

περιλαμπής ές *adj.* [περιλάμπω] (fig., of a person's capacity for action) **dazzling** Plu.

—**περιλαμπές** *neut.adv.* **very brightly** —*ref. to steel gleaming* Plu.

περι-λάμπω *vb.* (of light, the glory of God) **shine around** —*a person* NT.; (of armour) **flash all around** —*a place* Plu.; (intr., of lights, armour) shine all around or very brightly, **flash, gleam** Plu. ‖ PASS. (of persons or places) be illuminated (by light, fire) Plu.

περι-λείμματα των *n.pl.* things left over, **residue** Pl.

περι-λείπομαι *pass.vb.* (of persons) **be left over, remain, survive** (after a disaster or sim.) Hdt. E. Pl. Lycurg. Plb. Plu. —W.GEN. *after a war* Il.(tm.); (of things) And. Ar. Pl. Is. Plb.

περι-λείχω *vb.* (of snakes) **lick all around** —*someone's eyelids* Ar.

περί-λεξις εως *f.* [λέξις] **circumlocution** Ar.

περι-λέπω *vb.* **strip off** —*bark* (W.GEN. *fr. trees*) Hdt.; (of an axe) —W.DBL.ACC. *bark and leaves, fr. timber* Il.(tm.)

περι-λεσχήνευτος ον *adj.* [λεσχηνεύομαι] (of a courtesan) talked of everywhere, **notorious** Hdt.

περι-ληπτός όν *adj.* **1** (of things) able to be grasped or comprehended, **apprehensible** (W.DAT. by the mind, by thought) Emp. Pl.
2 (of a multitude of people, in neg.phr.) **imaginable, calculable** (W.DAT. in numerical terms) Plu.

περι-λιμνάζω *vb.* (of a river) **form a lake around** —*a city* Th.

περιλιπής ές *adj.* [περιλείπομαι] (of boats) **left over, remaining, surviving** Plb. ‖ MASC.PL.SB. survivors (W.GEN. of a catastrophe) Pl.

περι-λιχμάομαι *mid.contr.vb.* **1** (of a lion) **lick all around** —*its jaws* Theoc.
2 (of the heads of decapitated cattle) **lick up** —*their own gore* Plu.

περί-λοιπος ον *adj.* [λοιπός] (of persons or things) **left over, remaining, surviving** Th. X. Plu.

περι-λούω *vb.* **wash thoroughly** —*a child, a corpse* Plu.

περί-λυπος ον *adj.* [λύπη] (of persons) **very distressed, in deep grief** Isoc. Arist. NT. Plu.

περι-μαιμάω *contr.vb.* | fem.pres.ptcpl. (w.diect.) περιμαιμώωσα | (of Scylla) **search eagerly around** —*a rock* Od.

περι-μαίνομαι *mid.vb.* (of Ares) **rage around** —*a grove* Hes.

περιμανής ές *adj.* (of a desire) **thoroughly mad, furious** Plu.

περι-μάσσω, Att. **περιμάττω** *vb.* | 3pl.aor.imperatv. περιμαξάτωσαν | (of quack healers) wipe while encircling, **ritually wipe clean** —*someone* Men.

περι-μάχητος ον *adj.* [μαχητός] **1** (of Athens) **fought over** (by Athena and Poseidon) Ar.; (of domination, W.PREP.PHR. by Athens and Sparta) Isoc.; (of water, W.DAT. by thirsty soldiers) Th.; (of a chorus-trainer, by rival choruses) Ar.; (of handsome boys, by rival lovers) Aeschin.
2 (fig., of things) **fought over** or **worth fighting for, highly desirable** Isoc. Pl. X. Aeschin. Arist. Plu.
3 (of Helen's beauty) **worth fighting over** Isoc.
περι-μάχομαι *mid.vb.* (of troops) fight around, **encircle** (a defensive ring of soldiers) X.
περι-μενεαίνω *vb.* **be very eager** —W.INF. *to do sthg.* AR.(tm.)
περι-μένω *vb.* **1 wait around for, await** —*persons, troops, ships* Hdt. Th. Ar. Att.orats. Pl. + —*an event, opportunity, or sim.* Th. Isoc. Pl. D. +; (of a present need, in neg.phr.) **afford to wait for** —*some later action* Plu.
2 wait for —W.ACC. + INF. *someone to do sthg., sthg. to happen* E. Th. Pl. D. Men.; (of an argument) **wait** —W.PASS.INF. *to be completed* Pl.
3 (intr.) **wait, stay** (for some time, or in some place) Hdt. Th. Ar. Isoc. Pl. +
4 (of a fate, a penalty) **await, be in store for** —*someone* S. Pl.
5 endure, put up with —W.ACC. + PTCPL. *someone speaking at length* Pl.
περί-μεστος ον *adj.* [μεστός] **1** (of a hoop) **closely set round** (W.GEN. w. swords) X.
2 (of a person) **very full** (W.GEN. of good feeling) Plu.
περί-μετρον ου *n.* [μέτρον] **measurement around** (an area), **perimeter, circumference** Hdt.
περί-μετρος ον *adj.* **1** (of the web on a loom) **very large** Od.
2 ‖ FEM.SB. (w. γραμμή *line* understd.) **perimeter, circumference** Plb. Plu.
περι-μήκετος ον *adj.* [μῆκος] (of a tree, a mountain) **very tall** Hom.
περιμήκης ες *adj.* **1** (of a pole, timbers, or sim.) **very long** Od. Hes.; (of a monster's neck) Od. AR.
2 (of a mountain, peak, mast, or sim.) **very tall** or **high** Hom. AR.
3 (gener., of statues, anchors, blocks of stone) **very large, massive** Hdt.; (of a torch) AR.; (of an underground chamber, farm buildings) **extensive** Hdt. Theoc.
περι-μηχανάομαι *mid.contr.vb.* **craftily plan** —*a scheme* Od. —*slavery* (W.DAT. *for someone*) Od.
περι-μινύθω *vb.* (of the skin of corpses) **decay around** (their bones) Od.(tm.)
περι-μυκάομαι *mid.contr.vb.* (of war-drums) **bellow around** —*an army* Plu.
περι-μύρομαι *mid.vb.* **lament for** —W.GEN. *someone* Mosch.
περιναιετάει *m.pl.* [περιναιετάω] | only nom. | **dwellers round about, neighbours** Il. AR.
περι-ναιετάω *ep.contr.vb.* | 3pl. περιναιετάουσι | masc.pl.ptcpl. περιναιετάοντες | (of persons) **dwell round about** Od. Hes. Pi. AR.; (of cities) **lie round about** Od.
περι-ναίω *vb.* (of a people) **dwell around** —*a river* A.
περι-νέμομαι *mid.vb.* (of fire) **spread around** Plu. —*houses* Plu.
περι-νέφελος ον *adj.* [νεφέλη] (of the sky) **cloud-girt** Ar.
περινέω, ep. **περινηέω** *contr.vb.* [νέω³, νηέω] **1 pile up** (W.ACC. sacrificial victims, wood) **around** (a corpse, a building) Il.(tm.) Hdt.
2 make a pile (W.DAT. of wood) **around** —*a house, a grove* Hdt.
περί-νεως εω *m.* [ναῦς] | acc.pl. περίνεως | **supernumerary sailor** (i.e. one who is not a member of the crew), **passenger** Th.

περι-νίζομαι *pass.vb.* (of a corpse) **be washed completely clean** —W.ACC. *of blood* Il.(tm.)
περι-νίσομαι *mid.vb.* (of the time of a festival) **come round** E.
περι-νοέω *contr.vb.* **think around** or **devote excessively clever thought to** —*everything* Ar.; **ponder, contemplate, have in mind** —*great projects, a dangerous situation* Plu.
περίνοια ᾱς *f.* **excessive cleverness** Th.
περι-νοστέω *contr.vb.* **1** (of a person looking for someone) **go around, make the rounds of** —W.ACC. *wrestling schools* Ar. —W. περί + ACC. *couches* Ar.
2 (gener.) **walk around** Ar. Pl. D. Plu.
πέριξ *prep. and adv.* [περί] **1** (ref. to position) **around** —W.GEN. *a place* Hdt. X. Plb. —W.ACC. (and sts. placed following it) *a person or place* A. Hdt. E.
2 (adv., ref. to position) **around, round about** A. Hdt. E. Th. Pl. X. +; (phr.) πέριξ λαβεῖν **surround** —W.ACC. *someone* Hdt.
3 in a roundabout way, deviously —*ref. to thinking* E.
περιξεστός ή όν *adj.* [περιξέω] (of a rock) **highly polished** Od.
περι-ξέω *contr.vb.* (of a torrent) **polish** (W.ACC. boulders) **all round** Theoc.
περι-οδεύω *vb.* **go around, make a circuit of** —*a place* Plu.; (fig.) —*a person* (*whom one is trying to corrupt, likened to an impregnable fortress*) Plu.
περί-οδος, dial. **πέροδος** (Pi.), ου *f.* [ὁδός] **1 journey** or **march round** (a place); **circuit** (sts. W.GEN. made by someone) Hdt. Plu.; (W.GEN. of a place) Hdt.; (fig., ref. to philosophical inquiry) **roundabout route** Pl.
2 encircling, outflanking (W.GEN. of enemy troops) Th.
3 circumference (of a building or place) Hdt. X.
4 map (W.GEN. of the world) Hdt. Ar.; (fig., ref. to the world itself) D.; **narrative of travels** (W.GEN. around the world) Arist.
5 movement (of an object, heavenly body, celestial sphere) in a circle back to a starting-point, **circuit, orbit** Pl. X. Arist. Plu.
6 recurring length of time, cycle, period (sts. W.GEN. of years, time) Pi. Pl. Arist. Plu.; (prep.phr.) ἐκ περιόδου (also ἐν περιόδῳ) *for a period at a time, in rotation* Plb. Plu.
7 periodic recurrence, cycle (of events) Isoc. Pl. Arist.; **recurrence** (of a fever) D.
8 way of going about (one's daily business), **routine** Pl.
9 passing round (of food at a meal), **course** X.; **round** (of speeches at a symposium) X.
10 (rhet.) **period** (a sentence so constructed that its ending completes the syntax of its beginning) Arist.; (gener.) **sentence** Plu.
περί-οιδα *pf.vb.* [οἶδα] | ep.inf. περιίδμεναι | 3sg.plpf. περιῄδη | **1 have great skill** —W.DAT. or INF. *in sthg., at doing sthg.* Hom.
2 have greater skill —W.GEN. + ACC. or DAT. *than someone at sthg.* Hom.
περι-οικέω *contr.vb.* **live around** —*people or places* Hdt. Ar. Isoc. X. NT. Plu.; (intr.) **live round about** Hdt. Lys. Plb. Plu.
‖ PASS. (of a country) **be surrounded** —W.DAT. *by cities* Plb.
περιοικίς ίδος *fem.adj.* [περίοικος] (of cities, villages, islands, or sim.) **lying around, outlying** Hdt. Th. X. Arist. Plb. Plu. ‖ SB. **surrounding territory** Th.; **outlying city** X. Arist.
περι-οικοδομέω *contr.vb.* **build** (a wall) **around** —*a piece of land* D.; **build** (W.ACC. a wall) **around** (a piece of land) D.
‖ PASS. (of a piece of land) **be walled round** Hdt. D.; (of captives) **be walled up** Th.; (of animals) **be penned up** X.
περί-οικος ον *adj.* [οἶκος] (of people) **dwelling round about** (a place), **neighbouring** Hdt.

—**περίοικοι** ων *m.pl.* **1** (gener.) **neighbours** Hdt.
2 (specif.) **free-born inhabitants of towns around (and subject to) Sparta**, **subject neighbours** Hdt. Th.; (ref. to comparable actual or imagined subject populations) Pl. Arist.; (W.GEN. of Greece, ref. to barbarians) Isoc.
περιοιστέος ᾱ ον *vbl.adj.* [περιφέρω] (of a key) **to be carried around** (W.DAT. by someone) Men.
περι-ολισθάνω *vb.* (of a ship lifted out of the water by a machine) **slip out** (fr. its grip) Plu.
περιολίσθησις εως *f.* **slippage, displacement** (W.GEN. of soil) Plu.
περιοπτέος ᾱ (Ion. η) ον *vbl.adj.* [περιοράω] (of an event) **to be allowed** (to happen) Hdt.; (of a country) —W.PTCPL. **to perish** Hdt.
περίοπτος ον *adj.* **1** (of a location) **visible or with a view all round, conspicuous, commanding** Plu. ‖ NEUT.PL.SB. **belvederes** Plu.
2 (of a soldier) **conspicuous** (W.DAT. in his armour) Plu.; (of acts of bravery) Plu.
—**περιόπτως** *adv.* **gloriously** —*ref. to fighting or falling in battle* Plu.
περι-οράω *contr.vb.* [ὁράω] | impf. περιεώρων, Ion. περιώρων | fut. περιόψομαι | aor.2 περιεῖδον ‖ neut.impers.vbl.adj. περιοπτέον | **1 watch from the sidelines, wait to see** —*an outcome* Th. —W.COMPL.CL. *what will happen, whether sthg. will happen* Th.(mid.) Isoc. Aeschin.; (intr.) **wait and see** Th.(mid.) Thphr. ‖ MID. **stand aloof from** —W.ACC. *dangers* Th.
2 ‖ MID. (fig.) **watch out for** —W.GEN. + COMPL.CL. *a place, in case it comes to harm* Th. ‖ PASS. (of people) **be watched carefully** Th. ‖ NEUT.IMPERS.VBL.ADJ. *one must watch out for* —*sthg.* (W.COMPL.CL. *to ensure that it does not happen*) Th.
3 overlook (so as to tolerate or allow sthg., freq. w.neg.); **disregard, overlook, take no notice of** —W.ACC. + PTCPL. *someone doing sthg., sthg. happening* Hdt. Th. Ar. Att.orats. Pl. + —W.ACC. *someone* (i.e. ignore what he is doing) Th. Ar. Hyp. D. Men.; **overlook, tolerate** —W.ACC. *sthg.* X.; (intr.) **turn a blind eye** (to sthg.) Th. Isoc. D.
4 (freq. w.neg.) **allow** —W.ACC. + INF. *someone to do sthg., sthg. to happen* Hdt. Th. —W.ACC. *someone* (*to do sthg.*) Hdt.; (intr.) Hdt.
περι-οργής ές *adj.* [ὀργή] (of a populace) **very angry** Th.
περι-οργίζομαι *pass.vb.* **be made very angry** Plb.
περίοργος ον *adj.* (of passion) **intense** A.(dub.)
περί-ορθρον ου *n.* [ὄρθρος] **time towards dawn** Th.
περι-ορίζομαι *pass.vb.* (of an empire) **be bounded all around** —W.DAT. *by the ocean* Plu.; **have boundaries determined** —W.PREP.PHR. *by nature* Plb.
περιορισμός οῦ *m.* **boundary** (of a field) Plu.
περι-ορμέω *contr.vb.* (of a blockading fleet) **anchor around** (an island) Th.
περι-ορμίζω *vb.* **bring** (W.ACC. a ship, a fleet) **round** (to a place) **to anchor** D. Plu. ‖ MID. **bring one's fleet round to anchor** Th.
περι-ορύσσω, Att. **περιορύττω** *vb.* **1 form by digging in a circle, dig** —*a lake* Hdt.
2 dig (a trench) **around** (a tent) Plu. ‖ PASS. (of a trench) **be dug around** (a place) Pl.
3 dig up (W.ACC. ground) **round about** Plu.
4 dig around —*rocks* (*in the ground*) Plu.
περι-ορχέομαι *mid.contr.vb.* **dance** (W.INTERN.ACC. a war-dance) **around** (a statue) Call.(tm.)
περιουσίᾱ ᾱς *f.* [περίειμι¹] **1** that which is left over or is in surplus; **surplus, abundance** (W.GEN. of ships, money, provisions, or sim.) Th. D. Plb. Plu.; **sufficient residue** (of troops) Th.; (W.GEN. of water in a water-clock) D.; **excess** (W.GEN. of shame, wickedness, or sim.) Pl. D. Plu.
2 (gener.) **affluence, luxury, excess, profit** Th. Ar. Pl. X. D. Arist. + ‖ PL. **sufficient resources** Th.; **luxuries** (opp. necessities) Isoc.
3 (prep.phr.) ἐκ περιουσίας *from a position of affluence or advantage* Th. Pl. D. Arist. Plu.; (also) ἀπὸ περιουσίας Th.
4 survival, continued independence (of a territory) D.
περιοχή ῆς *f.* [περιέχω] **1 compass, scope** (of a person's undertakings) Plb.
2 mass, body (of a meteorite) Plu.
3 content or **section** (of a written work) NT.
περιόψομαι (fut.mid.): see περιοράω
περιπαθέω *contr.vb.* [περιπαθής] **be deeply moved** Plu.
περι-παθής ές *adj.* [πάθος] **1** (of persons) **deeply moved** or **distressed** (sts. W.DAT. by an event) Plb. Plu.
2 (of a narrative, a style of speaking) **deeply moving, passionate** Plu.
—**περιπαθῶς** *adv.* (w. ἔχειν) **be deeply moved** Plu.
περι-παπταίνω *vb.* **peer all around** Mosch.(tm.)
περι-πατέω *contr.vb.* **1 walk about, stroll around** Ar. Att.orats. Pl. X. Arist. Thphr. +
2 (fig.) **conduct oneself, behave** NT.
περιπατητικός ή όν *adj.* (of a philosopher) **Peripatetic** (i.e. belonging to the school of Aristotle) Plu.
περί-πατος ου *m.* [πάτος¹] **1 walking around, walk, stroll** Ar. Pl. X. Thphr. +
2 (fig.) **perambulation** (w. περί + GEN. around a topic, i.e. discussion of it) Ar.
3 place in which to walk around (esp. a colonnade or sim.), **walking-place, walk** X. Plu.
4 philosophical school (fr. the custom of teaching while walking in colonnades or sim.) Plb.(cj.); (specif.) **Peripatetic school** (ref. to the followers of Aristotle) Plb.
περι-πείρω *vb.* **1 impale** —*a head* (w. περί + ACC. *on a spear*) Plu. —*a fish* (W.DAT. *on a hook*) Plu.
2 (fig.) **pierce** —*oneself* (W.DAT. w. *sorrows*) NT.
περι-πέλομαι *ep.mid.vb.* | only aor.2: 2sg. περιέπλεο (AR.) and ptcpl. περιπλόμενος | **1** (of enemies) **be around, surround** —*a city* Il.; (of maidservants) **gather round** (someone) AR.
2 (of months, a year, years) **circle round, revolve, pass** Hom. Hes. hHom. Emp. Theoc.
3 (fig., of Eros) **get the better of, overpower** —*someone* AR.
περίπεμπτος ον *adj.* [περιπέμπω] (of orders to make sacrifices) **sent round** (a city) A.
περι-πέμπω *vb.* **1 send** (W.ACC. ships) **round** (an island or sim.) Hdt. Th. Plu.; **send** —*supplies* (*round the Peloponnese*) Th. —*cavalry* (w. περί + ACC. *round a hill*) Th. —*troops* (*round the enemy's flank*) Plu.; **send** (W.ACC. someone) **by a roundabout route** Plu.
2 send around (to various places) —*messengers or sim.* Hdt. Th. Plu.; (intr.) **send around messages** Th. Plu.
περι-πέσσω, Att. **περιπέττω** *vb.* | PASS.: aor.ptcpl. περιπεφθείς | pf. περιπέπεμμαι | **bake** (a crust) **round** (sthg.); (fig.) **cover up, disguise** —*one's wickedness* (W.DAT. w. *misleading words*) Ar.; (of reeds) **provide protective cover for** —*someone in hiding* Plu. ‖ PASS. (of pains) **have one's true nature concealed** —W.DAT. *by pleasures* (i.e. *be disguised as pleasures*) X.; (of heavenly bodies) —*by verbal accounts* (*so as to be taken for divinities*) Pl.; (of a person) **be taken in** —W.DAT. *by catchphrases* Ar.

περι-πετάννῡμι vb. —also (pres.) **περιπεταννύω** (X.) | aor. περιεπέτασα ‖ pf.pass. περιπέπταμαι | **spread** (w.ACC. one's arms) **around** (someone) E.(tm.); (of a vine) —*its leaves* (*around grapes*) X.; **spread out** —*rugs* Aeschin. ‖ PF.PASS. (of carved acanthus-leaf) be spread around —w. ἀμφί + ACC. *a cup* Theoc.; (fig., of a net, around people) AR.(tm.)

περιπεταστός όν adj. spread around; (of a kiss) **with lips spread wide** Ar.

περιπέτεια ᾱς f. [περιπετής] **1 sudden change** (of fortune, usu. fr. good to bad) Arist. Plb.; (gener.) **accident, calamity** Plb. Plu.
2 (specif., in a tragic drama, ref. to an unexpected change of circumstances) **sudden reversal** Arist.

περιπετής ές adj. [περιπίπτω] **1** (of a person) **falling around, with arms flung around** (W.DAT. someone's robes, in supplication) A.; (w. ἀμφί + DAT. around someone) S.; (of a person committing suicide) **falling on** (one's sword) S.
2 falling victim to (W.DAT. some obstacle or misfortune); (of soldiers) **impeded by** (stakes and ditches, one another) Plu.; (fig., of a person) **meeting with** (trouble) Men.; **implicated in** (a criminal charge) Plu.; (of a city) **plunged into** (civil war) Plu.; **at odds with** (itself) Plu.
3 (of a situation, a person's fortunes) **suddenly reversed, ruined** Hdt. E.

περι-πέτομαι mid.vb. (of birds) **fly around** Ar. —*someone* Ar.

περιπέττω Att.vb.: see περιπέσσω

περιπευκής ές adj. [πεύκη] (of an arrow) **very sharp, piercing** Il.

περι-πήγνῡμι vb. | Aeol.aor.ptcpl. (tm.) περὶ ... πάξαις |
1 fix (W.ACC. bark) **around** —W.DAT. *a javelin* Plu.
2 ‖ PASS. (of shoes) become stiff around (feet, through cold) X.
3 fence round —*a sacred precinct* Pi.(tm.)

περι-πίμπλαμαι pass.vb. (of a house) **be completely filled** (w. people) X.; (of an object of vision) —W.GEN. *w. whiteness* Pl.

περι-πίμπρημι vb. **set on fire** (W.ACC. a forest) **around** (people inside it) Th.; **singe** (W.ACC. hair) **around** (an animal's body) X.

περι-πίπτω vb. **1 fall around, embrace** —W.DAT. or εἰς + ACC. *a person, a funeral urn* X. Plu.; (of a headband) **fall around** —W.DAT. *someone's head* Plu.
2 fall over —w. ἐπί + DAT. *someone* Plu.; (of a person comitting suicide) **fall on** —W.DAT. *one's sword* Ar. Plu.
3 (of ships) **become entangled with, fall foul of** —W.DAT. or περί + ACC. *each other* Hdt.; **be wrecked on** —w. περί + ACC. *a cape* Hdt.
4 (of particles circulating in the body) **interact** (w. others) Pl.
5 (of persons) **fall in with** (by accident), **meet, encounter** —W.DAT. *someone* Hdt. X. D. Arist. NT. Plu.; (of ships, sailors) Hdt. Th. Plb. Plu.; (fig., of disputants) **light upon** —W.DAT. *topics* Pl.
6 (fig., of persons) **be tripped up** —W.DAT. or ἐν + DAT. *by oneself* (i.e. one's own actions) Hdt. Th. —W.DAT. *by one's own words* Aeschin.; (intr.) **come to grief, be ruined** Plb.
7 (gener.) **meet with, encounter, fall victim to** —W.DAT. *misfortunes, slavery, illness, penalties, or sim.* Hdt. E. Th. Ar. Att.orats. Pl. + —*a javelin* Antipho; (of a person's hair) —*a knife* Anacr.
8 (of a misfortune) **befall** —W.DAT. *someone* Ar.
9 (of a calamitous situation) **be reversed** —W.PREP.PHR. *to a position of advantage* Plb.

περι-πίτνω vb. (of a chill of despair) **fall around, envelop** —*someone's heart* A.

περι-πλανάομαι mid.contr.vb. **1 wander around** —*an island* Hdt.; (fig.) **take a roundabout route** (to achieve a goal) X.
2 (of a lionskin) **envelop** —*someone* Pi.

περι-πλάσσω, Att. **περιπλάττω** vb. **mould** (W.ACC. the likeness of the human form) **around** —W.DAT. *a body* Pl.; (W.ACC. congealed blood) —w. περί + ACC. *around someone's toe* Plu. ‖ PASS. (of a likeness) be moulded around Pl.

περίπλεκτος ον adj. [περιπλέκω] (of dancers' feet) **intertwined, weaving this way and that** Theoc.

περι-πλέκω vb. | PASS.: ep.aor. περιπλέχθην | aor.2 inf. περιπλακῆναι (Plu.), ptcpl. περιπλακείς (Plu.), περιπλεκείς (Tim.) | **1 weave** (one's arms) **around, embrace** —*someone* Call.epigr.; **join** (W.ACC. one's hands) **around** —W.DAT. *one's back* Plu. ‖ MID. **twine one's hands about, clasp** —W.DAT. *someone's beard* (in supplication) Call. ‖ PASS. be entwined around, embrace —W.DAT. *someone* Od. Plu. —*a mast* Od. —w. ἀμφί + DAT. *someone's knees* (in supplication) Tim.; (of a snake) be coiled around —W.DAT. *someone* Plu.
2 ‖ PASS. (of a net, fig.ref. to the human body) be woven or folded around (a person) X.
3 ‖ PASS. (of a diadem) be intertwined —W.DAT. w. *a wreath* Plu.; (of floating debris) become entangled Plu.; (fig., of a topic) be made intricate or complicated Pl.
4 (fig.) weave (euphemistic language) around (sthg.); **gloss over** (someone's behaviour) Aeschin.

περιπλευμονίᾱ ᾱς f. [πλεύμων] **inflammation of the lungs** Pl.

περί-πλευρος ον adj. [πλευρά] (of a breastplate) **encasing the flanks** E.

περι-πλέω contr.vb. —also **περιπλώω** Ion.vb. [πλέω¹] **1** (of persons, ships) **sail round** —*a promontory, an island, or sim.* Hdt. Th. Att.orats. X. + —w. περί + ACC. Hdt.; (intr.) **sail round** (fr. or to a place) Th. X. D. Plu.
2 sail up and down or here and there (within a locality or betw. places), **sail around** Th. Isoc. X. D. Plu. —*islands* Hdt. —*a sea, river, coast* Plu.; (fig., ref. to gaining experience of the ways of the world) —W.ACC.ADV. *a lot* Ar.
3 sail round (enemy ships, to attack them in the side or rear) Th.; **sail round and round** —*enemy ships* (*formed in a defensive circle*) Th.; (fig., of a person envisaged as a dog, also ref. to travelling round collecting money) —*a food-bowl* Ar.

περί-πλεως ων Att.adj. —also **περίπλεος** ον (AR.) Ion.adj. [πλέως] **1** (of a place) very fully occupied, **very full** (W.GEN. of soldiers) Th. Plu.; (of a shore) **covered** (W.GEN. w. wrecks) Plu.
2 (of soil) having a great abundance, **very full** (W.GEN. of putrefied matter) Plu.; (of a person, a cloth) **covered all over** (W.GEN. w. blood) Plu.; (of a person, w. swellings) Plu.; (fig., of a soul) **burdened** (W.GEN. w. a body) Plu.
3 (of a city) **filled** (W.DAT. w. smoke fr. sacrifices) AR.
4 (of spare timber) **in plentiful supply** X.

περι-πληθής ές adj. [πλῆθος] **1** (of an island) having a very great number (of inhabitants), **populous** Od.
2 (of a person's physique) of a great size, **corpulent** Plu.

περι-πλήθω vb. (of herds) **abound, teem** (w. cattle) Theoc.

περιπλοκή ῆς f. [περιπλέκω] **1 clinging embrace** (W.GEN. by a woman, in supplicating a man, or perh. a statue or altar) Plb.
2 (pejor.) tortuous weaving (of language) ‖ PL. deceitful turns (W.GEN. of phrase) E.; evasive expressions Plu.

περιπλόμενος (ep.aor.2 mid.ptcpl.): see περιπέλομαι

περί-πλοος, Att. **περίπλους**, ου m. [πλόος] **1 voyage round** (sts. W.GEN. or περί + ACC. a promontory, an island, the Peloponnese) Hdt. Th. Isoc. X. Aeschin.

περιπλύνω

2 (as a naval manoeuvre, opp. διέκπλους) **sailing round** (a line of enemy ships, to attack them in the side or rear) Th. X.

περι-πλύνω vb. **wash** (W.ACC. a wounded man) **thoroughly clean** D.

περιπλώω Ion.vb.: see περιπλέω

περι-πνέω contr.vb. (of breezes) **blow around** —an island Pi.

περι-ποιέω contr.vb. **1 cause** (persons or things) to survive (the threat of death or sim.); **preserve, save** —persons Hdt. Th. Att.orats. Plu. —(W.PREP.PHR. fr. trouble and war) Lys. —a city, buildings, or sim. Hdt. Th. Lys.; (mid.) —one's life X. Arist. NT. —one's hopes D.

2 procure, secure —property, safety, happiness, or sim. (W.DAT. for someone) Is. D. Plb. Plu.; **bring about** —disgrace (W.DAT. for someone) Isoc. Plb.; **obtain, get** —management of public affairs, property (w. ἐς + ACC.PERS. into one's own hands) Th. Is. —a laugh (W.PREP.PHR. out of someone) X. || MID. procure for oneself, **acquire, gain** —power, reputation, money, or sim. Th. Att.orats. X. Arist. + —a friend Men.

3 (act. and mid.) accumulate a surplus, **save money** X.; (act.) **save** —W.PARTITV.GEN. some of one's income Is.; (mid.) —W.ACC. money X. Is. Aeschin.

περι-ποίκιλος ον adj. [ποικίλος] (of an animal's tail) **spotted all round** X.

περιπόλ-αρχος ου m. [περίπολοι, ἄρχω] **commander of frontier guards** Th.

περι-πολέω contr.vb. **1** (of persons or gods) **go around, range about** S. E. Pl.; (of an army) Isoc.; (tr., of intruders) —an enemy camp E.; (of a soul, evils) —a place Pl.

2 (at Athens, of frontier guards) **patrol** —the country X. Arist.

περιπόλιον ου n. [περίπολοι] station for frontier guards (in Attica or elsewhere), **frontier post, garrison, fort** Th.

περι-πολλόν neut.adv. [πολύς] **very much, very greatly** AR.

περίπολοι ων m.pl. (also f.pl.) [περιπολέω] **1** (at Athens) **patrolmen, frontier guards** (ref. to a mobile force patrolling Attica) Th. Ar. X. Plu.; (sg.) Aeschin.

2 (at Rome) **patrols** (assigned to parts of the city) Plu.

3 (f.) **attendants** (of Dionysus, ref. to nymphs) S.

περι-πόνηρος ον adj. [πονηρός] (of a person) **very wicked** Ar.

περι-πορεύομαι mid.vb. | aor.pass.ptcpl. (w.mid.sens.) περιπορευθείς | **1 travel around, go around** Pl. Din. —a city Plb.

2 (of messengers) **make the rounds of** —cities Plb.; (of women) —shrines Plb.

3 (of troops) **march round** —a city (i.e. its perimeter) Plb.; **circle round** (an enemy's flank) Plb.

περι-πόρφυρος ον adj. [πορφύρα] (of a tunic) **with purple border** Plb.; (of a robe, ref. to the Roman toga) Plb. Plu.; (of a boy) **toga-wearing** Plu. || FEM.SB. (w. τήβεννα or τήβεννος understd.) **toga** Plu.

περι-ποτάομαι mid.contr.vb. (of prophecies of doom) **hover around** —someone S.

περι-πρό (or **πέριπρο**) adv. **extremely, especially** Il. Call. AR.

περι-προχέομαι pass.contr.vb. | aor.ptcpl. περιπροχυθείς | (of sexual passion) be poured forth around, **flood over** (someone's heart) Il.

περι-πταίω vb. **fall victim to** —W.DAT. a criminal charge Plu.

περι-πτίσσω vb. | pf.pass.ptcpl. περιεπτισμένος | **strip** (grain) of its husk || PASS. (fig., of residents of Athens present at the Lenaian festival) be husked (i.e. be free of foreigners, who were absent) Ar.

περίπτυγμα ατος n. [περιπτύσσω] that which is folded around, **covering** (of a cradle) E.

περίπτυξις εως f. **embracing** (W.GEN. of a corpse) Plu.

περι-πτύσσω vb. **1 enfold, enclose** —someone (W.DAT. in a tomb) S.; (of robes) **enshroud** —a corpse E.

2 wrap (W.ACC. one's hands) **around** (someone, in an embrace) E.; **enfold** —someone (W.DAT. in one's arms) Plb.; **embrace** —someone Plb. Bion Plu.; (of a suppliant) —someone's knees E.; (of a dragon) **envelop** —someone (W.DAT. in its jaws) AR. || MID. wrap oneself around; (of Eros) **envelop, engulf** (a person) Pl.; (of a person) **embrace** —someone Plu.

3 (milit.) **envelop, outflank** —enemy troops X. Plu. || MID. **outflank the enemy** X.

περιπτυχαί ῶν f.pl. **1 embraces** (w. the arms) E.

2 (periphr.) **envelopments** (W.GEN. of walls, i.e. enveloping or encircling walls) E.; (W.GEN. of a house, i.e. an enveloping house) Ar.(mock-trag.); (W.GEN. of the sun, i.e. places which the sun's light envelops, ref. to the whole world) E.; (W.ADJ. where ships lie anchored, i.e. a harbour enclosing ships) E.

περιπτυχής ές adj. **1** (of a shroud) **enfolding** (a corpse) S.

2 (of a person committing suicide) **wrapped around, impaled on** (W.DAT. his sword) S.

περίπτωμα ατος n. [περιπίπτω] **accident, mischance** Pl.

περί-πυστος ον adj. [πυνθάνομαι] (of a person's behaviour) **fully** or **widely known** (W.DAT. to people) AR.

περι-ρραίνω vb. [ῥαίνω] **sprinkle by ritual encirclement with lustral water, ritually sprinkle** —altars Ar. || MID. ritually sprinkle oneself, **purify oneself with water** Thphr. Men. Plu.

περίρρανσις εως f. **ritual sprinkling of water** Pl.

περιρραντήριον ου n. basin for lustral water (placed in the entrance to a temple or sim.), **font** Hdt. Plu.; (placed around the perimeter of the Athenian agora) Aeschin.

περι-ρρέω contr.vb. [ῥέω] | aor.inf. περιρρεῦσαι (Lycurg.) | pf. περιερρύηκα || aor.2 pass. (w.act.sens.) περιερρύην |

1 (of a river or sim.) **flow around** Hdt. Th. —a place Hdt. Pl.; (of blood) —a stake Od.; (of air) —a place Pl.; (of fire) **surge around** —a place Lycurg.; (fig., of people) —a person Pl.; (intr., of winds) **waft around** Plu. || PRES.PASS. (of a place) be surrounded —W.DAT. or PREP.PHR. by a river X. Plu.; (of horses) be drenched —W.DAT. w. sweat Plu.

2 (of a person's life) be overflowing, **abound in luxuries** S.; (of a commodity) **be in surplus** Plu.

3 (pres. and pf., of soil on a mountainside) **slip away** (into the sea) Pl. || AOR.2 PASS. (of a shield) slip (off someone's arm) Th.; (of a rider, off an elephant) Plu.; (of fetters) —W.DAT. off someone X.; (of a cover) —W.GEN. off a horse Plu.

περι-ρρήγνυμι vb. —also (impf.) περιρρηγνύω (Plu.) [ῥήγνυμι] **1 tear off** —someone's clothes D. Plb. NT. Plu. —someone's breastplate Plu.; (mid.) —one's clothes Plu. || PASS. (of clothes) be torn off A.

2 (of a god) **break off** (W.ACC. a hill) **on all sides** (to separate it fr. surrounding land) Pl. || PASS. (of earth) be torn away (by floodwater) Plu.

3 (causativ., of a mythol. king) **make** (W.ACC. the Nile) **break into branches** —w. περί + ACC. around a place Isoc. || PASS. (of the Nile) break into branches (at the Delta) Hdt.

4 || PASS. (of thunder) crash around —W.DAT. someone Plu.

περι-ρρηδής ες adj. [perh.reltd. ῥαδινός] (of a person or an ox, falling wounded) perh. **crumpled, limp** or **sprawling** Od. AR.

—περιρρήδην adv. perh. **with a bend** or **slope** —ref. to a coast curving AR.

περι-ρροή ῆς *f.* [ῥοή] **circling flow** (of underground rivers) Pl.

περι-ρρομβέω *contr.vb.* [ῥόμβος] **spin round** —*a ship* (*by ramming it*) Plu.

περί-ρροος ον *adj.* [ῥόος] (of a country) **surrounded by water** Hdt.

περί-ρρυτος η (dial. ᾱ) ον (also ος ον) *adj.* [ῥυτός] **1** (of an island, a country, or sim.) **surrounded by water, sea-girt** Od. Hes. Alcm. Lyr.adesp. Trag. Th. X.
2 (of waters) flowing round, **encircling** (an island) E.

περιρρώξ ῶγος *masc.fem.adj.* [περιρρήγνῡμι] (of a crag, serving as a fortress) **broken off all round, precipitous** Plb.

περί-σᾱμος ον *dial.adj.* [σῆμα] | superl. περισᾱμότατος |
1 (of a coast) **famous, renowned** Call.; (of a murder) **infamous** E.
2 (of Eros) **distinctive, notable** (in appearance) Mosch.

περι-σάττω *Att.vb.* [σάσσω] **block up the space around** —*an object* Plb.

περί-σεμνος ον *adj.* [σεμνός] (of a person's authority) **very grand** Ar.

περί-σεπτος ον *adj.* [σεπτός] ‖ NEUT.PL.SB. **great reverence** (paid to deities) A.

περι-σθενέω *contr.vb.* [σθένος] **be very strong** Od.

περι-σθενής ές *adj.* **1** (of men) having great strength, **powerful** AR.
2 (of the pankration) requiring great strength, **mighty** Pi.
3 (of death) **overpowering** Pi.*fr.*

περι-σκελής ές *adj.* [σκέλλω] **1** (of iron) **very hard** S.
2 (fig., of a person's will) **unyielding, resolute** S.

περι-σκεπής ές *adj.* [σκέπας] **1** (of a mountain) **sheltered all round** (W.DAT. w. bushes) Call.
2 (of towers) **giving shelter all round** (an island) Call.

περι-σκέπτομαι *mid.vb.* | aor. περιεσκεψάμην | **consider carefully** —W.INDIR.Q. whether sthg. is the case Hdt. Pl. Plu. —W.ACC. a situation Plb. Plu.

περίσκεπτος ον *adj.* (of a farm, a bedroom) **visible from all round** Od. [or perh. **with a view all round**]

περι-σκέπω *vb.* (of a shield) **completely shelter** —*a soldier* Plb.; (of an embroidered peacock) **cover** (W.ACC. the edges of a basket) **all the way round** —W.DAT. w. its tail-feathers Mosch.

περι-σκηνόω *contr.vb.* | 3sg.aor. περεσκήνωσε | **throw** (W.ACC. a garment) **like a tent around** (someone) A.

περι-σκιάζομαι *pass.vb.* (of the moon, a path) **be obscured** Plu.

περι-σκοπέω *contr.vb.* | aor. περιεσκόπησα (Plu.) | **1 look round** or **all around** (in search, inquiry, or anxiety) S. Ar.(mid.) Pl. AR. Plu.
2 (tr.) **survey, examine** —*a beach, birds of omen* Plu.; **look around for** —*a person, a place* Plu.
3 examine carefully —*immediate prospects* Th. —W.INDIR.Q. which side will prevail Th. ‖ MID. **anxiously consider** —*the future* Plu.

περι-σκυλακισμός οῦ *m.* [σκύλαξ] **ritual purification with a puppy's blood** Plu.

περι-σοβέω *contr.vb.* **1 strut around** —*cities* Ar.
2 pass round —*a wine-cup* Men.

περι-σοφίζομαι *mid.vb.* **outdo in cleverness, hoodwink** —*someone* Ar.

περι-σπασμός οῦ *m.* [περισπάω] **1 wheeling round** (by a body of troops) Plb. Plu.
2 ‖ PL. **distractions, preoccupations, other calls on one's time** Plb.

περι-σπάω *contr.vb.* **1 strip off** —*someone's clothing, helmet* Isoc. Plu.; (mid.) —*one's headgear, cloak* X. Plu.(also act.)
‖ PASS. **be stripped** or **robbed** —W.ACC. *of sthg.* Men.
2 strip away —*someone's power* Plu. ‖ MID. **strip oneself of, dismiss** —*one's bodyguard* Plb.
3 (of a commander) **wheel round** —*a body of troops* Plb.
4 turn round —*a system of government* (W.PREP.PHR. *to its opposite*) Arist.
5 divert —*a war* (*to a place*) Plb. Plu.; **deflect** —*power* (W.PREP.PHR. *to someone*) Plu.; **draw off, divert** —*a commander, enemy troops* Plb. Plu.; (gener.) **distract, preoccupy** —*someone* Plb. Plu. ‖ PASS. **be distracted** or **preoccupied** Plb. NT.
6 mislead —*someone* Men.
7 pronounce (W.ACC. a syllable) **with a circumflex accent** Plu.

περισπεῖν (aor.2 inf.): see περιέπω

περι-σπειράω *contr.vb.* [σπεῖρα] **1 wind** (W.ACC. a garment) **around** —W.DAT. *one's head* Plu.
2 ‖ MID. **cordon** —*parts of a city* (W.DAT. w. troops) Plu. ‖ PASS. (of persons) **be formed into a cordon round** (someone) Plu.

περι-σπερχής ές *adj.* [σπέρχω] (of sufferings) **brought on by a reckless act** (i.e. by someone's suicide) S.

περι-σπέρχομαι *pass.vb.* | aor.ptcpl. περισπερχθείς | **be made very angry, be incensed** —W.DAT. *by a decision* Hdt.

περί-σπλαγχνος ον *adj.* [σπλάγχνον] (of a person) **great-hearted** Theoc.

περι-σπογγίζω *vb.* **sponge all over** —*a wounded man* Thphr.

περι-σπούδαστος ον *adj.* [σπουδαστός] (of a goal) **much sought after** Plu.

περι-σσαίνω *ep.vb.* [σαίνω] (of dogs) **crowd around and fawn upon** —*someone* Od. Theoc.

περι-σσείομαι *ep.pass.vb.* [σείω] (of helmet plumes) **wave around** Il.

περίσσευμα ατος *n.* [περισσεύω] **1 remainder** (of sthg.) NT.
2 abundance, plenty NT.

περισσεύω, Att. **περιττεύω** *vb.* [περισσός] **1 be over and above** (a specified total); (of a number or quantity) **be left over** Hes.*fr.* Plb.; (of troops, ref. to a battle-line) **outnumber** —W.GEN. *the enemy* (*and so outflank them*) X.
2 be more than enough; (of a sum, commodity, provisions, or sim.) **be in surplus** Pl. X. Plb. NT.; (of resources) **be surplus to, exceed** —W.GEN. *expenses* X.; (of food) **be left over** NT.; (of grounds for confidence) **be ample** Th.; (of things) **be abundant** NT.
3 (of persons) **have more than enough, abound** —W.DAT. *in resources* Plb. —W. ἐν + DAT. *in sthg.* NT.; (mid.) —W.GEN. *in sthg.* NT. ‖ PASS. (of a person) **be made to abound** (in sthg.) NT.
4 (pejor., of words) **be superfluous** S.

περισσός, Att. **περιττός**, ή (dial. ᾱ) όν *adj.* [reltd. περί, πέριξ] | compar. περισσότερος, περιττότερος |
1 (of things) **beyond what is normal in number or size**; (of gifts) **exceptional** Hes.; (of a measuring line) **unusually long** Pi.
2 beyond what is normally expected; (of knowledge, ability) **out of the ordinary, extraordinary, exceptional** Thgn. Arist. Call.; (of a detail in a narrative) S.; (of actions, schemes, speech, suffering, or sim.) Hdt. E. Isoc. D. Arist. AR. +; (of prey) E. ‖ NEUT.SB. **exceptional quality** (of someone's speech) Arist.
3 (of persons) **out of the ordinary** E. Arist.; **superior to, surpassing** (W.GEN. *others*, W.PREP.PHR. *in grief*) S.; **outstanding** (oft. W.DAT. *in sthg.*) Plu.
4 (pejor., of persons) **above oneself, superior, arrogant** E.; (iron.) **eminent** Aeschin.; **over-zealous** Plb. Plu.

περισσόφρων

5 beyond what is proper; (of a body, fig.ref. to a person) **grown to excess** S.; (of an amount, expenditure, attention paid to sthg.) **excessive** Pl. X.; (of exploits) **extravagant** Isoc.; (of speech or action) going beyond one's rights, **out of line** Trag.
6 beyond what is needed or suffices; (of matter) **excessive, superfluous** Emp.; (of words) E.; (of extra equipment) **unneeded** Theoc. ‖ NEUT.PL.SB. further or needless talk Call.; parts left over (fr. a dismembered body) Theoc.
7 (of provisions, equipment, or sim., w. positive connot.) **spare, surplus** X.; (W.GEN. to what suffices) X.; (of cavalry) **reserve** X. ‖ MASC.PL.SB. extra men (in a line, compared w. the enemy's) X.; spare members (W.GEN. of a guard) X. ‖ NEUT.SB. surplus (of money) Lys. X.(inscription); (of troops) X.
8 (gener., w.neg.connot.) beyond what is useful; (of effort) **wasted** A. S. X.; (of a burden on the earth, ref. to women) **useless** S.
9 (math., of a number) **uneven, odd** Pl. Arist.; (of persons or things) **odd in number** Pl. X. ‖ NEUT.SB. (as a concept) odd (opp. even) Pl. Arist.
10 ‖ COMPAR. (of misfortunes, an achievement) more or greater (W.GEN. than other people, i.e. than they suffered or achieved) Antipho Isoc.; (of punishment) more severe NT.; (of a person) more eminent (W.GEN. than others) Call.; more or greater (W.GEN. than a prophet) NT.
11 (prep.phr.) ἐκ περιττοῦ *exceedingly* Pl.; *superfluously, pointlessly* Pl. Plb.
—**περιττόν** Att.neut.sg.adv. **to excess** —*ref. to being bold* Plb.
—**περισσά** neut.pl.adv. **exceedingly** —*ref. to being aggrieved, honoured* Pi. E.; (qualifying an adj.) E.
—**περισσῶς**, Att. **περιττῶς** adv.| compar. περισσότερον, περιττότερον, also περισσοτέρως (Isoc.) |
1 (sts. qualifying an adj.) beyond the normal manner or degree, **extraordinarily, exceedingly, exceptionally** Pi,*fr.* Hdt. E. Arist. NT. Plu.
2 elaborately, extravagantly Plb. Plu.; **over-zealously** Plu.
3 even more —*ref. to shouting, being surprised* NT.
4 ‖ COMPAR. more lavishly Hdt.; to a far greater degree Isoc.; even more NT.; (w. οὐδέν) *to no greater extent* Antipho(cj.) Plb.; *no more unusually* Pl.

περισσό-φρων ον, gen. ονος adj. [φρήν] (iron.) **exceptionally intelligent** A.

περίσσωμα, Att. **περίττωμα**, ατος *n.* unwanted excess; **waste, excrement** (of a bird, a person) Arist. Plu.; (fig., ref. to undesirable elements in a city) Plu.

περισταδόν adv. [περιίσταμαι] **1** standing round, **on all sides, all around** —*ref. to people stationing themselves* Il. Hdt. E. Call. AR.
2 from all sides —*ref. to being pelted w. missiles* Th.; **all around** —*ref. to animals parading* Theoc.; **tightly round** (one's feet) —*ref. to fitting sandals* Theoc.

περιστάθη (ep.3sg.aor.pass.): see περιίσταμαι

περίστασις εως *f.* **1 space surrounding** (W.GEN. or περί + ACC. sthg.) Plb.
2 circumstance, situation, state of affairs Plb.
3 (specif.) **critical situation, crisis, danger** Plb.
4 personal circumstances (of someone's life or behaviour) Plb.
5 condition (of the atmosphere, ref. to climatic events) Plb.

περίστατος ον *adj.* (of a person, a conjuring show) **surrounded, thronged** (w. ὑπό + GEN. by people) Isoc.

περι-σταυρόω contr.vb. (of troops) **build a stockade round** —*a city, hill* Th. X. ‖ MID. **build a stockade around one's camp** X. ‖ PASS. (of houses) be stockaded X.

περι-στείχω vb. | ep.aor. περίστειξα | **1 walk around** —*the Trojan Horse* Od.
2 (of a wine-cup) **go round** Call.

περι-στέλλω vb. **1** arrange (clothing) around, **clothe** —*one's limbs* Pi. —*oneself* (W.DAT. *in a hat and cloak*) Plu.; (of a deity) —*human souls* (*in a garment of flesh*) Emp.; (of a person) **wrap up** —*someone* (*for warmth*) Thphr. —*a severed head* (W.DAT. *in the folds of one's dress*) Plb.; (fig.) **drape** —*one's song* (W.DAT. *over a deity and region, i.e. honour them w. it*) Pi.
2 (specif.) **dress, shroud** (for burial) —*a corpse* Od. Hdt. E. Men. Call. Plu. —*a head* Plu.; (gener.) **solemnly bury** or **honour with funeral rites** —*a corpse, the dead* S. Pl.; **adorn, honour** —*a tomb* S. ‖ PASS. (of the dead) be shrouded E.
3 (fig.) **cloak, cover up** —*injustice* (W.DAT. *w. one's speech*) E. —*offences* Plb.
4 secure all around (w. earth) —*a sword* (*fixed in the ground*) S.
5 protect, defend, look after —*someone, a city* Hdt. S. Theoc. Plb.; **maintain, preserve** —*a system of government, laws, customs, traditions* A. Hdt. D.; **cherish** —*a privilege* D.; (wkr.sens.) **attend to, ply** —*one's business* Theoc. ‖ MID. **attend to** —*one's troubles* E. ‖ PASS. (of a person) be protected Plb.

περι-στενάζομαι mid.vb. (of the world) **be completely filled with mourning** Plu.

περι-στεναχέω ep.contr.vb. [στενάχω, στοναχέω] (of the earth) **groan all around** (under horses' hooves) Hes.

περι-στένω vb. (of the echo of a song) **moan round** —*a mountain top* hHom. ‖ MID. (of a wolf's belly) **groan, growl** (fr. being glutted) Il.

περίστεπτος ον adj. [περιστέφω] (of an honoured guest) **crowned** (W.DAT. *w. ribbons and garlands*) Emp.

περιστερά ᾶς *f.* **pigeon** or **dove** Hdt. Ar. Pl. X. Thphr. NT.

περιστερεών ῶνος *m.* **dovecote** or **aviary** Pl.

περι-στεφανόω contr.vb. (of a crowd of admirers) **form a ring around, encircle** —*someone* Ar. ‖ PASS. (of a region) be surrounded —W.DAT. *w. mountains* Hdt.; (of a hat) —*w. feathers* Hdt.; (of a city) be ringed or crowned —W.DAT. *w. trophies or sim.* Plu.

περιστεφής ές adj. [περιστέφω] **1** (of a tomb) **garlanded, crowned** (W.GEN. *w. flowers*) S.; (of a region) **encircled** (W.DAT. *by mountains*) Plu.
2 (of ivy) **encircling** (someone) E.

περι-στέφω vb. (of Zeus) **wreathe** —*the sky* (W.DAT. *w. clouds*) Od.; (of a serpent) —*a mountain* (w. *its coils*) Call.; (of a commander) **encircle, ring** —*an island* (w. *soldiers*) Plu. | see also ἀμφιπεριστέφομαι

περι-στίζω vb. **1** (of a commander) **mark** or **dot** (W.ACC. a city wall) **all round** —W.DAT. *w. severed breasts* Hdt.
2 place (W.ACC. people) **at intervals around** (sthg.) Hdt.(dub.)

περι-στιχίζω vb. [στίχος] **place** (W.ACC. a net) **around** (someone) A.(dub.)

περι-στοιχίζομαι mid.vb. **set in a row around**; (fig.) **cast a net around, ensnare** —*someone* D.

περί-στοιχος ον adj. [στοῖχος] (of olive trees) **set round about in rows** D.

περι-στόμιον ου *n.* **mouth** (of a jar) Plb.

περι-στοναχίζομαι (v.l. -στεναχίζομαι) mid.vb. | sts.tm. | (of a house) **resound** or **echo all round** (w. weeping, carousing) Od. —W.DAT. *w. dancers' feet* Od.

περι-στρατοπεδεύω vb. (of a commander, troops) **encamp around, besiege** —*a city or sim.* X.(mid.) Plb. Plu.; **mount**

guard round (a building) Lycurg. ‖ PASS. (of occupants of a city) be besieged X.

περι-στρέφω vb. **1** (of Zeus) **whirl round** —Ate (before throwing her fr. heaven) Il.; (of a person) —a discus Od. **2 turn** (W.ACC. oneself) **round** (to face in the reverse direction) Pl.; (of a rider) **wheel round** —a horse Plu. ‖ PASS. (of a person, a body) turn or be turned round Ar. Pl.; (of human nature) —W.PREP.PHR. *to face the truth* Pl.; (of an epithet) come round —W.PREP.PHR. *to someone* (i.e. become applicable to him) Pl.; (fig., of philosophers) turn round and round (in a dizzying quest) Pl. **3 twist** (W.ACC. someone's hands) **round** (behind his back) Lys.; (W.ACC. a piece of clothing, round someone's neck, to throttle him) Plu. **4 twist together, plait** —bonds of osier hHom.

περιστροφή ῆς f. **1 revolution, spinning** (of a shell, in a game) Pl. **2 turning round** (to face in the reverse direction) Plu.

περι-στρωφάομαι mid.contr.vb. **do the rounds of** —all the oracles Hdt.

περί-στῡλος ον adj. [στῦλος] **1** (of a courtyard, a building) surrounded with pillars, **colonnaded** Hdt. E. Plb. **2** ‖ NEUT.SB. (or perh. MASC.) **colonnade** Plb. Plu.

περι-σῡλάομαι pass.contr.vb. **be stripped** —W.ACC. *of one's property* Pl.

περι-σύρω vb. | fut.inf. περισυρεῖν | **carry off** —booty or sim. (sts. W.GEN. fr. someone) Plb.

περι-σφαλής ές adj. [σφάλλω] (of ground) **precarious** (fr. being muddy) Plu.

περι-σφύριον ου n. [σφυρόν] **anklet** Hdt.

περισχεῖν (aor.2 inf.), **περίσχεο** (ep.aor.2 mid.imperatv.): see περιέχω

περι-σχίζω vb. **1 tear off** —someone's clothes Plu. **2** ‖ PASS. (of a river) be divided into branches around —a place Hdt. —w. περί + ACC. Plb.; (of people, following in someone's wake) divide into two branches Pl.; (of winds) be split in two (by a mountain peak) AR.

περι-σχοινίζομαι mid.vb. [σχοῖνος] (of the council of the Areopagus, when in private session) **rope oneself off** D.

περισχόμην (ep.aor.2 mid.): see περιέχω

περι-σῴζω vb. **ensure** (someone's) **safety and survival; save, preserve** —people, a city X. Plu. ‖ PASS. save one's life X. Men. Plu.; (of troops, ships) survive X.; (of beliefs) be preserved Arist.

περι-σωρεύω vb. **pile up** (W.ACC. combustible material) **around** —W.DAT. *a corpse* Plu. ‖ PASS. (of a tent) be heaped up all around —W.DAT. w. spoils Plu.

περιτάμνω dial.vb.: see περιτέμνω

περι-ταφρεύω vb. (of besiegers) **dig a trench around** —a city Plb.; (of enemy troops) **hem in** —a commander Plu. ‖ PASS. (of a commander) be hemmed in Plu. ‖ PF.PASS.NEUT.PTCPL.SB. place surrounded by a trench X.

περι-τείνω vb. **1 stretch** (W.ACC. hides, nets, or sim.) **around** —W.DAT. or περί + ACC. sthg. Hdt. X. Plu. **2** ‖ PASS. (of membranes) extend around —W.DAT. particles Pl.; (of moisture) —w. περί + ACC. *around air* Pl.

περι-τειχίζω vb. **1 build a wall around** —a place (to create a city) Ar. ‖ PASS. (of a place) be walled round Plb. **2** (of besiegers) build a wall around, **wall in, circumvallate, blockade** —a place, its occupants Th. X. D. Plu.; (of troops) **build a defensive wall around** —a camp Plu. ‖ PASS. (of a city, its occupants) be walled in, be blockaded Th. Plu.; (of a commander) be blockaded or hemmed in —W.PREP.PHR. *by land and sea* Plb.

3 ‖ PASS. (of a blockading wall) be built round (a city) X.

περιτείχισις εως f. **blockade, circumvallation** Th.

περιτείχισμα ατος n. **blockading wall** Th. X. D. Plu.; **circuit wall** (for defence) Th.

περιτειχισμός οῦ m. **blockade, circumvallation** Th. Plu.

περι-τελέομαι ep.pass.contr.vb. | only 3sg.aor. (tm.) περὶ … ἐτελέσθη | (of days) **complete a cycle** Od. Hes.

περι-τέλλομαι pass.vb. (of years) **revolve, come round** Hom. hHom.; (of seasons) S. Ar.; (of a star, ref. to its seasonal rising) **come round, return** Alc.

περι-τέμνω, dial. **περιτάμνω** vb. | ep.inf. περιταμνέμεν | **1 make a cut around** (a scalp) —w. περί + ACC. *in the region of the ears* Hdt.; **prune** —vines Hes. ‖ MID. **cut oneself around** —one's arms Hdt. **2** (specif.) **circumcise** —persons, their genitals Hdt.(also mid.) NT. ‖ MID. (of a nation) **practise circumcision** Hdt. **3 cut off** —someone's ears and nose Hdt. ‖ PASS. (fig.) be docked (i.e. deprived) —W.ACC. *of land* Hdt. —of one's kingdom Plb. **4** ‖ MID. (of raiders) **cut off, round up, rustle** —cattle Od. ‖ PASS. (of chariots) be cut off, be intercepted —W.PREP.PHR. *by cavalry* X.

περι-τέχνησις εως f. [τεχνάομαι] **extreme ingenuity** (W.GEN. of military enterprises) Th.

περι-τήκω vb. **1** (of rain) **dissolve, wash away** —earth Pl. **2 coat** (W.ACC. an encircling wall) **all round** —W.DAT. *w. tin* Pl.

περι-τίθημι, Aeol. **περτίθημι** vb. | Aeol.3sg.athem.aor. imperatv. περθέτω ‖ Aeol.athem.aor.mid.inf. πέρθεσθαι | **1 place** (W.ACC. logs) **around** or **on** (fires) Od.(tm.); **place** (wood) **around** (an altar) Men.; **twist** (W.ACC. inflammable cord) **around** —w. περί + ACC. *arrows* Hdt. **2 place** (sthg.) around (part of the body); **place** (W.ACC. a necklace) **around** —w. περί + DAT. *someone's neck* Alc.; **place** (W.ACC. a garland, helmet, or sim.) **on** —W.DAT. or περί + ACC. *someone, a head* Hdt. Ar. Pl. Plb. Plu.; (W.ACC. a muzzle) —W.DAT. *on a horse* X. ‖ MID. **place** —a helmet (W.DAT. *on one's head*) Il.(tm.); **hang** —a sword (W.DAT. *around one's shoulder*) Od.(tm.); **put on** —a necklace, garland Sapph. E. Ar. X. —a cloak, veil, costume Sapph. Ar. Pl. Plb. Plu. —a ring Pl. **3 attach, add** —letters (W.DAT. *to vowels and consonants*) Pl. **4 bestow, confer** —strength, kingship, freedom, honour (W.DAT. *on someone or sthg.*) Od. Hdt. Th. Isoc. +; **inflict, impose** —disaster, dishonour, or sim. (W.DAT. *on someone*) Th. Att.orats.; **prescribe** —a style of fighting (W.DAT. *for someone*) Arist.; **associate** —a skill (W.DAT. *w. a god*) Arist.

περι-τίλλω vb. pluck the outside leaves off, **strip** —a lettuce Hdt.

περι-τῑμήεις εσσα εν adj. (of Delos) **highly honoured** hHom.

περί-τῑμος ον adj. [τῑμή] (of a family) **highly honoured** Call.

περι-τῑω (also **περιτίω** AR.) vb. | ep.impf. (tm.) περὶ … τίον ‖ 3sg.iteratv.impf.pass. (tm.) περὶ … τιέσκετο | **highly honour** —someone Il.(tm.) ‖ PASS. (of a person, a place) be highly honoured Il.(tm.) AR.

περιτμήματα των n.pl. [περιτέμνω] (fig.) **trimmings, shavings** (W.GEN. of speeches, opp. fully fashioned speeches) Pl.

περιτομή ῆς f. **circumcision** NT.

περίτομος ον adj. (of a hill) cut off all round, **isolated** Plb.

περιτοξεύω vb.: see ὑπερτοξεύω

περι-τορνεύω vb. create as if on a lathe; (fig., of a god) **turn out** (W.ACC. a body) **around** —W.DAT. *a soul* Pl.; (W.ACC. a sphere of bone) —w. περί + ACC. *around a brain* Pl.

περι-τραχήλιον ου *n.* [dimin. τράχηλος] piece of protective armour for the throat, **gorget** Plu.

περι-τρέπω *vb.* | Aeol.inf. περτρόπην | ep.aor.2 (tm.) περὶ ... ἔτραπον | **1 turn round** —*an accusation* (W.PREP.PHR. *against oneself, i.e. cause it to rebound against one*) Lys.
2 turn round (a person's fortunes); (of a god) **turn** —*a person* (w. ἐκ + GEN. *fr. trouble*) Sapph.
3 turn round, distort —*a word* (W.INF. *to signify the opposite*) Pl.
4 (intr., of seasons) **go round, pass** Od.(tm.)
5 turn upside down, topple —*someone* Plu.; (fig.) —*an argument* Pl. ‖ PASS. (of a spring) **be violently disturbed** (by some natural cause) Plu.; (of a country) **be overthrown** Plu.
6 turn aside, baulk at —*uncongenial work* Semon.(dub.)
7 (of much learning) **reduce, drive** —*someone* (W.PREP.PHR. *to madness*) NT.

περι-τρέφω *vb.* | pf. περιτέτροφα | ‖ PF. (causatv., of an icy vapour) **make** (W.ACC. hoar-frost) **congeal around** (a cave) AR. ‖ PASS. (of ice) **grow thick** or **congeal around** —W.DAT. *shields* Od.; (of milk being stirred) **curdle all round** Il.

περι-τρέχω *vb.* | fut. περιθρέξομαι | aor.inf. περιθρέξαι ‖ neut.impers.vbl.adj. περιθρεκτέον ‖ The aor. is usu. supplied by περιδραμεῖν. |
1 run around —*a lake* Ar. —*a place* (*looking for someone*) Ar.; (intr.) **run around, run about** Lys. Ar. Pl. X. Men. Plu.
2 (of puppies) **run around in circles** X.; (of a person) —W.PREP.PHR. *to the same point* (*fig.ref. to being unable to make progress in argument*) Pl.; **make a ritual circuit** —W.DAT. w. *a new argument* (*fig.ref. to carrying a newborn child round the altar*) Pl.
3 (of a room, as perceived by a drunken man) **go round and round, spin** Thgn.
4 (of words or concepts) **be in circulation** Pl.; (of an association betw. persons) **be ongoing** or **recurrent** Plu.

περι-τρέω *contr.vb.* (of people) **flee in every direction** Il.

περι-τριβής ές *adj.* [τρίβω] (of a workman's hands) **thoroughly worn** AR.

περί-τριμμα ατος *n.* that which is well worn; (fig., pejor.ref. to a person) **old hand** (W.GEN. *at lawsuits*) Ar.; **smooth customer** (W.GEN. *in the agora*) D.

περι-τρομέομαι *mid.contr.vb.* (of flesh) **tremble all over** —W.DAT. *one's limbs* Od.

περιτροπάδην *adv.* [περιτροπέω] **by rounding up** (sheep) AR.

περι-τροπέω *contr.vb.* **1** (of a year) **come round** Il.
2 round up —*sheep* Od.; (of Hermes) **shepherd around, lead this way and that** —*the races of men* hHom.

περιτροπή ῆς *f.* [περιτρέπω] **1 revolution, passing** (W.GEN. *of a year*) Semon.; **cycle** (*in the life of plants and animals*) Pl.
2 turning around, rotation (W.GEN. *of a baton, a pestle*) Pl.
3 (prep.phr.) ἐν περιτροπῇ **in rotation, in turn, one after another** Hdt.
4 danger of toppling over Plu.

περίτροπος ον *adj.* (of motion) **rotatory, circular** Plu.(cj.)

περιτρόχαλα *neut.pl.adv.* [τροχαλός] **running round in a circle** —*ref. to a style of hair-cutting* Hdt.

περι-τροχάω *ep.contr.vb.* | 3pl. (w.diect.) περιτροχόωσι | (of songs, envisaged as a garland) **circle around** —*an island* Call.

περίτροχος ον *adj.* [περιτρέχω] (of a mark on a horse's forehead, likened to the moon) **circular** Il.; (of the sun's orb) AR.; (of a hat) Call.

περι-τρώγω *vb.* | aor.2 περιέτραγον | (fig., of the Athenian populace) **gnaw round, nibble** —*the scrag-end of empire* (i.e. *have little benefit fr. it*) Ar.; (of a politician) —*jurors* (i.e. *reduce their pay*) Ar.; **steal, snaffle** —*someone's jewellery* Ar.

περιττάκις *Att.adv.* [περισσός] **an odd number of times, by an odd number** —*ref. to multiplying* Pl.

περιττεύω *Att.vb.*: see περισσεύω

περιττολογίᾱ ᾱς *Att.f.* [λόγος] **1 excessive talk, prolixity** Isoc.
2 discursiveness, detailed argumentation (involved in certain subjects of study) Isoc.

περιττός *Att.adj.*: see περισσός

περιττότης ητος *Att.f.* **1 excess, extravagance** (of sophistic techniques) Isoc.; (of a populace) Plb.
2 (math.) **oddness** (of number) Pl. Arist.

περίττωμα *Att.n.*, **περιττῶς** *Att.adv.*: see περίσσωμα, περισσῶς

περι-τυγχάνω *vb.* **1 happen to encounter, meet** —W.DAT. *persons, ships* Th. Att.orats. Pl. +
2 happen to see —W.DAT. *an event* And. Aeschin.; **light upon, find** —W.DAT. *medicines, arguments, excellence* Pl.
3 fall victim to —W.DAT. *misfortunes* Plb.
4 (of a disaster) **befall** —W.DAT. *someone* Th.

περι-υβρίζω *vb.* **treat** (W.ACC. someone) **outrageously** Hdt. Ar.; **show contempt for** —*religion* Plu. ‖ PASS. **be treated outrageously** Hdt. Ar. Plu.

περι-φαιδρύνω *vb.* **cleanse, purify** —*one's head* (W.DAT. *in seawater*) AR.(v.l. ἐπι-) —*one's skin* (w. *oil*) AR.(tm.)

περι-φαίνομαι *pass.vb.* **1** (of a mountain, a place) **be seen from all round, be conspicuous** Il. hHom.; (of a commander's tent) Plu.; (of a commander, meton. for his army) Plu. ‖ NEUT.PTCPL.SB. **place open to view** Od.
2 (of a commander) **be seen all around** (a region, i.e. in one place after another) Plu.

περιφάνεια ᾱς, Ion. **περιφανείη** ης *f.* [περιφανής] **1 clear information** (W.GEN. *about a region, a situation*, or sim.) Hdt. Is. D.
2 glaring nature, notoriety (W.GEN. *of someone's crimes*) D.

περιφανής ές *adj.* [περιφαίνομαι] | compar. περιφανέστερος, superl. περιφανέστατος | **1** (of a city, statue, structure) **seen from all round, conspicuous** Th. Plu.; (of a sickness) **clearly visible, in full view** S.
2 (of circumstances, facts) **clear, obvious** Lys. Ar. Pl. X. D.; (of a person) **manifest** (*as being such and such*) X.; (of proof) **clear, signal** Lys. D.
3 (of crimes) **glaring, notorious** Att.orats.; (of effrontery) **barefaced** D.; (of achievements) **conspicuous** Plu.

—**περιφανῶς** *adv.* **1 clearly, visibly, for all to see** Ar. Att.orats. Pl. +
2 obviously, certainly, clearly S. Th. Ar. Att.orats. Pl. +

περίφαντος ον *adj.* (of a person) **in full view** S.; (of Salamis) **conspicuous** or **famous** (W.DAT. *in the sight of all*) S.

περίφασις εως *f.* **clear view** (W.GEN. *of a place*) Plb.

περι-φείδομαι *mid.vb.* **spare the life** —W.GEN. *of someone* AR. Plu.

περιφέρεια ᾱς *f.* [περιφερής] **1 circumference** (of a circle) Plu.; (of a shield, a cave) Plu.
2 (geom.) **curve** Arist.
3 surface (of a helmet) Plu.

περιφερής ές *adj.* [περιφέρω] **1** (of a shape) **rounded, curved** Pl.; (of bodily features of a hound or hare) X.; (of a hole) **round** X.; (of a country, a shield) **of circular shape** Plb. ‖ NEUT.PL.SB. **circles** Plu.
2 (of the earth, primordial beings, or sim.) **spherical** Pl.
3 ‖ NEUT.SB. (geom.) **circumference** Pl.

περιφύω

4 (of a path) **curving, winding** E.; (of an animal's tracks) X.
5 (of a palace) **encircled, surrounded** (W.DAT. by cornices) E.

περι-φέρω vb. **1** carry round (in a circle); **carry round** —*a weasel, a sacrificial victim* (*in a purificatory ritual*) Ar. Plb.; **transport** (W.ACC. a lion) **round** (a city wall) Hdt. ‖ PASS. (of a purificatory sacrifice) be carried round Aeschin.; (of a lion) —W.ACC. *a city wall* Hdt.
2 (of circular motion) **bring** (W.ACC. sthg.) **round** —W.PREP.PHR. *to the starting-point* Pl. ‖ PASS. (fig., of disputants) be brought back round, return —W.PREP.PHR. *to the starting-point, to an earlier statement* Pl.
3 carry around (fr. place to place); **carry around** —*a baby* E. Men. —*a pet animal* Plu. —*portable objects* Hdt. Ar. Pl. X. Men.; (pejor., of a commander) **drag around** —*troops* Plu. ‖ PASS. (of a person, an object) be carried around Lys. Pl. Arist.; (of hounds, soldiers) rush around X. Arist.
4 pass around, distribute —*food, wine* X. —*items* (*for inspection*) Aeschin.
5 move round (part of the body); **bring round** —*one's foot* (*over a horse's back, in mounting it*) X.; (of acrobats performing somersaults) —*one's legs* (W.PREP.PHR. *into an upright position*) Pl.(mid.); **turn** —*one's head* Plu. —*one's gaze* (W.PREP.PHR. *towards someone*) Plu.
6 ‖ PASS. (of a wheel, objects) revolve Hdt. Pl.; (of a year) go round, pass Hdt.; (of fate) circle round Plu.
7 bring (W.ACC. a city, management of affairs) **round** —W.PREP.PHR. *to oneself* (*i.e. within one's control*) Plu.
8 ‖ PASS. (of a saying, poem, or sim.) circulate, do the rounds Pl. Plb. Plu.; (of letters, in words) appear repeatedly, recur Pl.; (of concepts) Pl.
9 ‖ PASS. (fig., of a person) be whirled round, be made dizzy —W.DAT. *w. the magnitude of one's undertakings* Plu.; (of a mind) be giddy —W.DAT. *w. power* Plu.
10 (of a recollection of sthg.) **take** (W.ACC. someone) **back** (in time) Pl.; (of a circumstance) —*someone* (W.INF. *to knowing sthg., i.e. jog his memory of it*) Hdt.
11 (intr., of a nation at war) **hold out, survive** Th.

περι-φεύγω vb. **1 escape, survive** —*a war* Il.(tm.) —*destruction* Pl.; (intr.) **survive** (an injury) D.; (a curse) Plu.
2 (of a person concealing his identity) **avoid** —*lights* (*in a house*) Plu.
3 (of grains of sand) **escape, elude** —*counting* Pi.

περί-φημος ον adj. [φήμη] (of a person) **very famous** Archil.

περι-φθείρομαι pass.vb. **wander about wretchedly** Isoc. Lycurg. Men.

περι-φλεγής ές adj. [φλέγω] (of a fever) **burning** X.
—**περιφλεγῶς** adv. **with a burning thirst** —*ref. to being parched* Plu.

περι-φλέγομαι pass.vb. (of a person) **be scorched all over** Plb.

περι-φλεύω vb. [reltd. φλέω, φλύω] (of lightning) **singe** —*someone* Ar. ‖ PASS. (of walls) be scorched —W.DAT. *by fire* Hdt.

περί-φλοιος ον adj. [φλοιός] (of a wooden stick) **with bark intact** X.

περί-φοβος ον adj. [φόβος] **1** (of persons, animals) **very fearful, terrified** Th. Att.orats. X. +; (W.GEN. of sthg.) Pl.
2 (of fear) entailing great terror, **intense** A.
—**περιφόβως** adv. **in a state of great fear** Plu.

περι-φοίτησις εως f. **travelling about** Plu.

περί-φοιτος ον adj. [φοιτάω] **1** (of the moon) **travelling around** Parm.
2 (of a lover) **inconstant** Call.epigr.

περιφορά ᾶς f. [περιφέρω] **1 bringing round, serving** (of food) X.
2 circular movement, revolution, rotation Pl.; (of a wheel) E.; (of the heavens or heavenly bodies) Ar. Pl. X. Plu.; (concr.) **revolving heaven** or **universe** Pl. Plu.
3 circumference (of a spindle) Pl.
4 cycle, period (in the natural world) Pl.
5 reversal (W.GEN. of circumstances) Plu.
6 ‖ PL. **movements around** (by someone, within a society), **social contacts** Plu.

περι-φορέω contr.vb. **carry around** —*figurines* (*in a religious ritual*) Hdt.

περιφόρητος ον (or **περιφορητός** όν) adj. **1** (of reed-houses) **portable** Hdt.; (of a person, prob. by misinterpretation of Anacreon in 2) **carried about** (by servants) Plu.
2 (of a person, app. known for a luxurious lifestyle) prob. **much talked of, notorious** Anacr.

περίφραγμα ατος n. [περιφράσσω] **barricade** Plu.

περιφραδής ές adj. [περιφράζομαι] (of a god or human) **very clever** or **skilful** hHom. S.
—**περιφραδέως** Ion.adv. **1 very skilfully** or **carefully** Hom. AR.
2 very sensibly —*ref. to speaking* AR.

περι-φράζομαι mid.vb. **give thought to, devise** —W.GEN. sthg. Od.

περίφρακτον ου n. [περιφράσσω] **place which is fenced around, enclosure** Plu.

περι-φράσσω, Att. **περιφράττω** vb. **1 fence round** —*baggage* (*in a camp*) Plb. ‖ MID. **build** (W.ACC. a wall) **for oneself as a barricade** Plu. ‖ PASS. (of a place) be fenced in —W.DAT. *w. railings* Plu.; (of persons) be enclosed on all sides —W.PREP.PHR. *under awnings* Plu.
2 hedge in, hem in —*enemy troops* Plb.; (fig., of a person) **fence in, barricade, isolate** —*oneself* Pl.; (of Fortune) **hedge about, encompass** —*someone* (W.DAT. *w. good things*) Plu.

περι-φρονέω contr.vb. **1 speculate about, scrutinise** —*the sun, a problem* Ar.
2 think of contemptuously, **disdain, despise, scorn** —*someone* Th. Aeschin. —*sthg.* Plu. —W.GEN. *someone* Plu.; (of fabulousness in narrative) **disdain, defy** —W.GEN. *credibility* Plu.; (intr., of a person) **be arrogant** Plu.

περιφρόνησις εως f. **contempt, scorn** (W.GEN. or PREP.PHR. for someone or sthg.) Plu.

περιφροσύνη ης f. **contempt, scorn** Plu.

περι-φρουρέομαι pass.contr.vb. (of occupants of a city) **be blockaded all round** —W.DAT. *by a siege-wall* Th.

περί-φρων ον, gen. ονος adj. [φρήν] | voc. περίφρον, also περίφρων (*metri grat.*) | **1** (of women, esp. Penelope) with great good sense, **prudent, shrewd, wise** Hom. Theoc.; (of Persephone) hHom.; (of children of Zeus and Metis) **very clever** Hes.; (of Hephaistos) **very skilled** Hes.; (of Aristaios) AR.
2 (of persons, their speech) **haughty, arrogant** A.

περιφυγή ῆς f. [περιφεύγω] **place affording a means of escape, refuge, bolt-hole** Plu.

περι-φυσητός όν adj. [φυσάω] (of persons, envisaged as flames) **blown on** or **fanned from all sides** (W.PREP.PHR. by winds) Ar.

περι-φυτεύω vb. **plant** (W.ACC. elms) **round** (a grave-mound) Il.(tm.)

περι-φύω vb. | athem.aor. περιέφῡν | pf. περιπέφῡκα, ep.3pl. (tm.) περὶ ... πεφύᾱσι | **1** (of the creator god) **make** (W.ACC. a covering) **grow around** —w. περί + ACC. *the body* Pl.

2 ‖ PF. (of trees, shrubs) grow round about Od.(tm.) Plu.; (of incrustations) grow around —W.DAT. sthg. Pl.; (of rocky ground) be all around (a hill) Plu.; (of sthg. that can be perceived only by the mind) exist on the periphery of —W.DAT. *the senses* Pl. ‖ PRES.PASS. (of a rumour) become attached —W.DAT. *to someone* Isoc.

3 ‖ ATHEM.AOR. cling round, embrace (someone) Od. —W.DAT. *someone* Od.; (of an object) cling, stick —W.DAT. *to sthg.* Ar.

περι-φωνέω contr.vb. (of sounds) **echo around** —*hills and valleys* Plu.

περι-χαρακόω contr.vb. (of defenders) **build a palisade round** —*a city wall* Aeschin. —*places affording access by sea* Plb.; (of besiegers) —*a city or sim.* Plb. Plu. ‖ PASS. (fig., of a country) be palisaded, be made secure —W.DAT. *by someone's diplomacy* Din.

περι-χάρεια ᾱς f. [περιχαρής] **extreme joy, rapture** Pl.

περι-χαρής ές adj. [χαίρω] **extremely glad, overjoyed** (sts. W.DAT. or PREP.PHR. at sthg.) Hdt. S. Ar. Isoc. Pl. + ‖ NEUT.SB. extreme joy Th. Plu.; (W.GEN. at sthg.) Th.

περι-χειλόω contr.vb. [χεῖλος] **edge round** —*an equestrian exercise-area* (W.DAT. *w. an iron border*) X.

περί-χειρον ου n. [χείρ] **armlet** or **bracelet** Plb.

περι-χέω contr.vb. | aor. περιέχεα, ep. περίχευα | ep.3sg.aor.mid.subj. περιχεύεται | **1** (of a river) **pour** (W.ACC. a great amount of shingle) **over** —W.DAT. *someone* Il. ‖ PASS. (of a river) overflow Plu.

2 (of a goddess) **cast, shed** (W.ACC. mist, beauty) **over** —W.DAT. *someone* Hom.(sts.tm.); (fig., of an orator) **shed** (W.ACC. darkness) **around** —W.DAT. *a court* (*i.e. blind it to the facts*) Plu. ‖ PASS. (of sleep) be spread over (someone) Il.(tm.)

3 spread (W.ACC. gold or gold leaf) **around** —W.DAT. *silver* Od.(mid.) —*the horns of a sacrificial animal* Hom.; **pile** (W.ACC. twigs) **around** —W.DAT. *a burning brand* AR.(mid., tm.)

4 ‖ MID. (of a commander) **spread** (W.ACC. his troops) **around** —W.DAT. *a place* Plu.

5 ‖ PASS. (of persons) be gathered round Hdt. Plu. —W.DAT. *someone or sthg.* Pl. Plu. —W.ACC. *someone* X.; (of troops, ships) surround —W.DAT. *someone* Plb. Plu.

περι-χορεύω vb. **dance round** (someone, in joy) E.

περι-χώομαι mid.contr.vb. **be enraged** (sts. W.DAT. w. someone) **over** —W.GEN. *someone* Il.

περι-χωρέω contr.vb. **1 go round** (an altar) Ar.

2 (of a commander) **surround** (someone) —W.DAT. *w. an army* Plu.

3 (of kingship) **come round, come in turn** —W.PREP.PHR. *to someone* Hdt.

περί-χωρος ον adj. [χώρᾱ] **1** ‖ MASC.PL.SB. people in places round about, neighbours D. Plu. ‖ NEUT.PL.SB. regions bordering (W.DAT. on a country) Plu.

2 ‖ FEM.SB. neighbouring region NT.

περι-ψάω contr.vb. | inf. περιψῆν | aor. περιέψησα | **wipe all round, wipe clean** —*feet* Hippon. —*one's eyes* Ar.

περι-ψιλόομαι pass.contr.vb. (of corpses) **be completely stripped** —W.ACC. *of flesh* Hdt.

περί-ψυκτος ον adj. [ψύχω¹] (of places) **chilly** Plu.

περί-ψυξις εως f. **chilling** (of body heat) Plu.

περιωδυνίᾱ ᾱς f. [περιώδυνος] **severe pain** Pl. Arist.

περι-ώδυνος ον adj. [ὀδύνη] **1** (of a person) **in extreme pain** D.

2 (of a fate, i.e. death) **very painful** A.

περι-ωθέω contr.vb. **1** (of natural processes) **push** or **propel** (W.ACC. sthg.) **round** (in the body or sim.) Pl.

2 (fig.) **push around, harass** —*someone* D.

3 ‖ PASS. (of a commander) be driven —W.PREP.PHR. *out of a country* Plu.; (fig., of people) be pushed aside or rejected Th. Arist. Plu.

περιών (ptcpl.): see περίειμι¹

περιών (ptcpl.): see περίειμι²

περι-ώνυμος ον adj. [ὄνομα] (of a person) **far-famed** S.lyr.fr.

περι-ωπή ῆς f. [ὤψ] **1 place commanding a view all round, lookout place, vantage-point** Hom. Pl. AR.

2 circumspection, **careful consideration** (W.GEN. of sthg.) Th.

περιώρων (Ion.impf.): see περιοράω

περιώσιος ον adj. [περί, reltd. περισσός] (of material and non-material things) **extraordinary, prodigious** (in terms of number, size, extent or degree) Sol. Emp. Lyr.adesp. AR.

—**περιώσιον** neut.sg.adv. **very much** or **too much, extremely, exceedingly** Hom. AR. Theoc.; **much more** (W.GEN. than other persons or things) hHom. Pi. AR.

—**περιώσια** neut.pl.adv. **very much, extremely, exceedingly** hHom. AR. Theoc.

περκάζω vb. [περκνός] (of fruit, usu. grapes) **change from light to dark on reaching maturity**; (fig., of a young man, ref. to his beard) **darken like a ripening grape** Call.

περκαίνω vb. [reltd. περκάζω] (fig., of the Minotaur, ref. to his cheek, described as *wine-coloured*) **darken like a ripening grape** E.fr.

πέρκη ης f. [app.reltd. περκνός] a kind of fish; **perch** Call.

περκνός ή όν adj. **1** (of a kind of eagle) **dusky, dark** (or perh. *with dark patches, dappled*) Il. [sts. taken as πέρκνος *dark eagle*]

2 (of grape-clusters) **darkening** Theoc.(cj.)

πέρνημι vb. | 3pl. πέρνᾱσι, ptcpl. περνάς | iteratv.impf. πέρνασκον | ep.fut.inf. (w.diect.) περάαν | aor. ἐπέρασα, ep. ἐπέρασσα, also πέρασα | pf. πέπρᾱκα, plpf. ἐπεπράκειν ‖ PASS.: pres. πέρναμαι | impf. ἐπερνάμην | fut.pf. (w.fut.sens.) πεπράσομαι | aor. ἐπράθην, Ion. ἐπρήθην | pf. πέπρᾱμαι, Ion. πέπρημαι | pf.ptcpl. πεπρᾱμένος, ep. πεπερημένος | plpf. ἐπεπράμην | —also **πιπράσκω**, Ion. **πιπρήσκω** (Call.) | impf. ἐπίπρᾱσκον (Plu.) ‖ pass. πιπράσκομαι (Lys. X., perh. Pl.) ‖ In Att. the pres.act. is usu. supplied by πωλέω, fut. and aor. by ἀποδίδομαι. |

1 sell or **trade** (to foreign buyers) —*persons* (*as slaves*) Hom. Hippon. Thgn. X. —*goods* Hippon. E.Cyc. ‖ PASS. (of persons) be sold Il. Sol. Hdt. S. E. Lys. +; (of songs, envisaged as prostitutes) Pi.; (of goods) Il. Ar. Pl.

2 ‖ PASS. (hyperbol., when speaking of oneself) be sold into slavery, be sold off (i.e. ruined) Trag.

3 (gener.) **sell** —*goods, property, or sim.* Att.orats. X. + ‖ PASS. (of things) be sold Th. Ar. Att.orats. Pl. +; (of women, to husbands) Hdt.

4 (of politicians) sell for a bribe, **sell** —*oneself* D. —*the city's interests, or sim.* D. —*one's country* Din.

πέροδος dial.f.: see περίοδος

περόνᾱμα ατος dial.n. —also **περονᾱτρίς** ίδος dial.f. [περονάω] garment pinned at the shoulders, **dress** Theoc.

περονάω contr.vb. [περόνη] **1 pierce** —*someone* (W.DAT. *w. a spear*) Il.

2 ‖ MID. **fasten about oneself with a pin or brooch, pin fast** —*one's cloak or dress* Il. AR. Theoc.

περόνη ης f. —also **περονίς** ίδος (S.) f. [πείρω] **1** object that pierces (ref. to a long pin, sts. a safety-pin or brooch, used

to fasten clothes, usu. at each shoulder); **pin, brooch** Hom. Ibyc. Hdt. S. E. Call. AR.; (used for wounding oneself or others) Hdt. S.
2 cleat, pin (on a ship, for securing ropes) AR.
3 rivet or **nail** (in a metal door) Parm.; (in a Roman javelin) Plu.
4 ligament (at the back of a horse's leg) X.

πέροχος Boeot.adj.: see ὑπέροχος

πέρπερος ου masc.adj. [reltd. Lat. *perperam*] (of a person) **braggart** Plb.

πέρρ Aeol.prep.: see ὑπέρ

Πέρραμος Aeol.m.: see Πρίαμος

περρέχω Aeol.vb., **πέρροχος** Aeol.adj.: see ὑπερέχω, ὑπέροχος

πέρρυσιν Aeol.adv.: see πέρυσι

πέρσα (ep.aor.): see πέρθω

Πέρσαι ὧν (Ion. ἐων, dial. ἆν) m.pl. [loanwd.] **Persians** (an Iranian people) Simon. A. +

—**Πέρσης** ου (Ion. εω) m. | voc. Πέρσα | (oft. appos.w. ἀνήρ) **Persian** Hdt. +; (appos.w. στρατός *army*) Tim.; (ref. to the king) Hdt. X.; (collectv.sg., ref. to the army or nation) **Persians** Hdt. Aeschin. Lycurg.

—**Περσικός** ή όν adj. of or relating to Persia or the Persians; (of an army, the race, dress, or sim.) **Persian** A. Hdt. Th. Ar. +; (of a war) Hdt. + ‖ FEM.SB. Persian land, Persia Hdt. ‖ FEM.PL.SB. (w. ἐμβάδες understd.) Persian shoes (a type of female footwear) Ar. ‖ NEUT.PL.SB. Persian wars Isoc. Pl.

—**Περσίς** ίδος fem.adj. (of the land) **Persian** A. Hdt. Tim. X.; (of the language) A. Hdt. Th.; (of a woman) Hdt. Isoc.; (of clothing) Tim.; (of a standard of measurement, ref. to the schoinos) Call. ‖ SB. Persia Pl. X.; (w. χλαῖνα understd.) a kind of Persian cloak Ar. ‖ PL.SB. Persian women A. X.

περσέ-πολις, also **περσέπτολις**, εως masc.fem.adj. [πέρθω, πόλις] (epith. of Athena) **sacker of cities** Ar.(quot.lyr.) Call.; (of the Persian army, w. play on Πέρσαι) A.

πέρσεται (3sg.fut.pass.): see πέρθω

Περσεύς έως (ep. ῆος, dial. έος) m. **Perseus** (son of Zeus and Danae, rescuer of Andromeda, decapitator of the Gorgon Medusa) Il. +

—**Περσεῖος**, also **Περσήιος** (Theoc.), ᾱ ον adj. (of an abode, a descendant) **of Perseus** E. Theoc.

—**Περσείδης** ου, dial. **Περσείδᾱς** ᾱ, ep. **Περσηϊάδης** ᾱο m. **son** or **descendant of Perseus** Il. B. Ion Hdt. Th. +

—**Περσηίς** ίδος fem.adj. (of Alkmene) **descendant of Perseus** E.

Περσεφόνη ης (Hes. +), dial. **Περσεφόνᾱ** ᾱς (E.), also **Φερσεφόνη** ης (E.), dial. **Φερσεφόνᾱ** ᾱς (Pi.) f. —also ep. **Περσεφόνεια** ης (dial. ᾱς E.), **Φερσεφόνεια** ης (Hes.fr.) f. —also dial. **Περσέφασσα** ᾱς (A. E.), **Φερσέφασσα** ᾱς (S. E.), Att. **Φερρέφαττα** ης (Ar. Pl.) f. **Persephone** (daughter of Zeus and Demeter, abducted by Hades to become queen of the underworld) Hom. +

Περσηίς fem.adj.: see under Περσεύς

Πέρσης m.: see under Πέρσαι

Περσίζω vb. [Πέρσαι] **speak Persian** X.

Περσικός adj., **Περσίς** fem.adj.: see under Πέρσαι

πέρσις ιδος f. [πέρθω] | acc. πέρσιν | **sack, destruction** (W.GEN. of Troy, as the subject matter of tragic drama) Arist.

Περσιστί adv. [Πέρσαι] **in the Persian language** Hdt. X. Plu.

περσκέθοισα (Aeol.fem.aor.2 ptcpl.): see ὑπερέχω

περσονομέομαι pass.contr.vb. [Πέρσαι, νέμω] (of people) **be under Persian rule** A.

περσονόμος ον adj. (of the honour) **of Persian rule** A.

πέρσω (fut.): see πέρθω

περτίθημι Aeol.vb.: see περιτίθημι

περτρόπην (Aeol.inf.): see περιτρέπω

πέρυσι(ν), Aeol. **πέρρυσιν** (Theoc.) adv. **a year ago, last year** Simon. Ar. Pl. +

περυσινός ή όν adj. (of officials, ref. to the time of their appointment) **of last year, last year's** Pl.; (of an object, of food, ref. to its age) Ar. X.

πεσδομάχεντας (Aeol.masc.acc.pl.ptcpl.): see πεζομαχέω

πέσδος Aeol.adj.: see πεζός

πέσεα ων n.pl. [πεσεῖν, see πίπτω] **falls** (of opponents in battle) E.

πεσεῖν (aor.2 inf.), **πεσέομαι** (Ion.fut.mid.): see πίπτω

πέσημα ατος n. **1 falling down, fall** (of a person, usu. in battle or through violent death) Trag.; (fr. a chariot) E.; (of a building) E.; (hyperbol., of an animal lying down to rest) E.
2 (concr.) that which has fallen; **fallen body** (ref. to a corpse) E.; **victim** (W.GEN. of a spear) E.; **thing fallen** (W.GEN. fr. heaven, ref. to a divine statue) E.

πέσον (ep.aor.2), **πεσοῦμαι** (fut.mid.): see πίπτω

πεσσεύω, Att. **πεττεύω** vb. [πεσσοί] **play draughts** Pl. X.

πεσσοί, Att. **πεττοί**, ῶν m.pl. **1 counters used in a board-game, counters, pieces** E.fr. Pl.
2 game involving the placing of counters on a board (sts. determined by dice-throws), **draughts** or **backgammon** Od. Pi.fr. Hdt. E. Ar. Arist.; (ref. to an outdoor area where the game was played) **draughts boards** E.

πεσσονομέω contr.vb. [νέμω] arrange the counters; (fig., of a leader) **make a move, adjust one's plans** A.

πέσσω, Att. **πέττω** vb. [reltd. πέπων] | aor. ἔπεψα | pf.pass. πέπεμμαι | **1 cook by dry heat, bake** —*bread, cakes, or sim.* Hdt.(mid.) Ar. Pl. X. Arist. Men.
2 (of the west wind) **ripen** —*fruit* Od.
3 digest (food); (fig.) **cherish, keep warm** —*one's anger* Il.; **brood on, dwell on** —*one's troubles* Il.; **nurse, carry** —*a wound* Il.; **enjoy** —*one's privileges* Il. —*a life without danger* Pi. —*rewards due for rearing a child* AR.
4 (fig.) **digest, assuage** —*one's anger* Arist.

πεσών (aor.2 ptcpl.): see πίπτω

πέταλον, also **πέτηλον** (Hes.), ου n. [πετάννῡμι] **1** (usu.pl.) **leaf** (of a tree, plant or flower) Hom. +
2 sheaf (of corn) Hes.
3 (fig.) **leaf** (W.GEN. of strife, w. allusion to the use of olive leaves for voting; cf. ἐκφυλλοφορέω) Pi.; (collectv.sg.) **leaves** (W.GEN. of good fortune, ref. to a victor's olive wreath) B.

πέταμαι dial.mid.vb.: see πέτομαι

πετάννῡμι vb. [reltd. πίτνημι] | fut. -πετάσω, Att. -πετῶ | aor. -επέτασα, ep. πέτασα, πέτασσα ‖ PASS.: aor. -επετάσθην, ep. πετάσθην | pf. πέπταμαι, also -πεπέτασμαι | ep.3sg.plpf. πέπτατο ‖ The simple vb. is rare, except in aor. act. and pass. and in pf.pass. |
1 spread out —*sails* (W.DAT. *to the wind*) Od. —*clothes* (W.PREP.PHR. *along a shore*) Od. ‖ PASS. (of chariot covers) be spread out Il.; (of sails) AR.; (of a fleece) Ar. AR.
2 ‖ PASS. (of a clear sky, the sun's light) be spread wide Hom. Call.; (of a series of lakes) extend —W.PREP.PHR. *throughout a land* AR.; (of ground) stretch out openly Plb.
3 stretch out —*one's hands* (*in despair*) Il. —(*in swimming, greeting, searching*) Od. —*a hand* (*in entreaty*) B.
4 (of a host, when receiving guests) **open up** (his house) Theoc.; (fig., of a person) app. **lift up** —*someone's heart* Od. ‖ PASS. (of doors) be spread wide, be opened Hom.; (of eyes) Mosch.

πετάσματα των n.pl. **fabrics spread out** (on the ground) A.

πετεινός, also **πετηνός**, ep. **πετενός**, ή όν adj. [πέτομαι, reltd. πτηνός] (of young birds) **able to fly, fledged** Od.; (gener., of birds) **winged** Il. Hes. A. E. Ar.; (of Perseus, a

πέτευρον

horse) Men. ‖ NEUT.SB. winged creature, bird Hom. Thgn. Hdt. E.*fr.* Ar. +

πέτευρον ου *n.* **1** pole or beam for birds to roost on, **perch** Theoc.
2 platform (on top of a siege-engine) Plb.
3 inscribed tablet Call.

πέτηλον *n.*, **πετηνός** *adj.*: see πέταλον, πετεινός

πετοῖσα, πετόντεσσι (Aeol.fem.sg. and masc.dat.pl. aor.2 ptcpl.): see πίπτω

πέτομαι, dial. **πέταμαι** (Sapph. Pi.) *mid.vb.* ǀ impf. ἐπετόμην, ep. πετόμην, dial. πετόμᾱν ǀ fut. πετήσομαι, also (in cpd.) -πτήσομαι ǀ athem.aor. ἐπτάμην, 3sg. ἔπτατο, ep. πτᾶτο, inf. -πτάσθαι, ptcpl. πτάμενος, ep.3sg.subj. πτῆται ǀ also aor.2 -επτόμην, inf. πτέσθαι, ptcpl. -πτόμενος ǀ also athem.aor.act. -έπτην, dial. -έπτᾶν ǀ pf. -έπτηκα (Men.) ǀ
1 (of birds and other winged creatures) **fly** Hom. +; (of gods, their horses) Il. hHom. E. Ar.; (fig., of young children, envisaged as fledgling birds) S.; (of a soul) —W.PREP.PHR. *fr. someone's body* Il.; (of smoke) **fly upwards** E.
2 (of an arrow, a spear, a missile) move fast through the air, **speed, fly** Il.; (of Zeus' lightning) E.; (of snow and hail) —W.PREP.PHR. *fr. the clouds* Il.; (of an oar, a weapon) **spring** —W.PREP.PHR. *away fr. the user's hands* Od.
3 (of persons) **wing one's way, speed on** Hom. E.*Cyc.* Ar. Pl.; (of horses, chariots) Hom. Hes.; (of a hound) Pi.*fr.*; (of a ship of an oar, meton. for a ship) E.; (of love) **take wing** (in pursuit of someone) E.; (of a people's name, ref. to its reputation) **fly far and wide** Pi.
4 (fig., of persons) **take flight, soar aloft** —W.DAT. or PREP.PHR. *in one's thoughts, w. ambition* Pi.; **be agitated** —W.DAT. *w. foreboding* S.; (provbl., of an argument) be impossible to catch, **be elusive** Pl. ‖ NEUT.PL.PTCPL.SB. (provbl.) what takes flight, what always eludes the grasp Arist.
5 (pejor., of persons) **be all of a flutter** Anacr.; **be flighty** (i.e. fickle) Ar.; (of persons, their minds) **be all in the air** (i.e. lacking in sense) Thgn. E.

πέτρᾱ ᾱς, Ion. **πέτρη** ης *f.* **1** mass of rock (on land, or in or bordering on the sea), **rock** or **cliff** Hom. +
2 detached mass of stone, **rock, boulder** Od. Hes. Hippon. A. Pi. E. +
3 rock (as a symbol of immovability) Od. NT.; (of hard-heartedness) A. E.

πετραῖος ᾱ (Ion. η) ον *adj.* **1** associated with rocks or cliffs; (of Scylla) **who lives on a rocky cliff** Od.; (of the octopus) **that clings to rocks** Pi.*fr.*; (of Nymphs) **of the crags** (i.e. mountains) E.; (of a bird) S.*fr.*; (of a spring) **issuing from a rock** AR.; (of shade) **thrown by a rock** Hes.; (of a fall) **from a cliff** E.; (quasi-advbl., of a person wandering like an animal) **over rocks** S.
2 consisting of rock or rocks; (of a crag, an island, or sim.) **rocky** A. AR.; (of a tomb, a cave) S. E.; (periphr., of a stone) E.*Cyc.*; (of an avalanche) **of rocks** hHom.; (of a sharp edge) **of a rock** AR.
3 (epith. of Poseidon) **of the Rocks** (so called for splitting the mountains to create the valley of Tempe) Pi. B.

πετρήεις, dial. **πετράεις,** εσσα εν *adj.* (of a region, an island, a mountain top) **rocky** Hom. hHom. Pi.; (of a cavern) **in a rock** Hes.

πετρ-ηρεφής ές *adj.* [ἐρέφω] **1** (of a cave) **rock-roofed** A. E.*Cyc.*
2 (of cliffs) **providing a roof of rock** (for a cave) E.

πετρ-ήρης ες *adj.* [ἀραρίσκω] (of a dwelling, ref. to a cave) **rocky** S.

πέτρινος η (dial. ᾱ) ον *adj.* **1** consisting of rock; (of a mountain, crag, or sim.) **rocky** Hdt. E.; (of a bed, a dwelling) S. E.*Cyc.*; (of a pillow, fig.ref. to the ground) E.; (of a heavy burden) **of rock** E.; (of a herald's platform) E.
2 (of the throwing) **of rocks** E.
3 (fig., of a person, ref. to stupidity) **made of rock** Men.
4 associated with rocks; (of Prometheus' fetters) **fixed to rocks** A.; (of a spring) **issuing from a rock** E.

πετροβολίᾱ ᾱς *f.* [πετροβόλος] **throwing of stones** (at a person) X.

πετροβολικός ή όν *adj.* (of military engines) **for throwing rocks** Plb.

πετρο-βόλος ου *m.* [πέτρος, βάλλω] **1** ‖ PL. (milit., ref. to a unit of men) stone-throwers X.
2 engine for throwing rocks (sts. distinguished fr. a catapult), **mangonel** Plb.

πετρόομαι *pass.contr.vb.* **1 be stoned** (to death) E.
2 (of a warrior) **be pelted with stones** E.

πετρο-ρριφής ές *adj.* [ῥίπτω] (of a person) **pelted with stones** (as a punishment) E.

πέτρος ου *m.* **1** detached piece of rock, **stone** or **boulder** Hdt. Trag. Pl. X. AR. Theoc.
2 stone (used as a missile, by warriors or sim.) Il. A. Pi. E. X.; (used in stoning someone to death) Trag.
3 object made of stone; **stone** (ref. to a discus) Pi.; (ref. to a grave-column) Pi.; (ref. to a fountain) Call.; (ref. to a person petrified by the Gorgon) E.; (ref. to the petrified Niobe) Call.
4 (as a symbol of hard-heartedness or insensibility) **stone** S. E.
5 (provbl.) πάντα κινῆσαι πέτρον *leave no stone unturned* E.

πετρώδης ες *adj.* (of ground) **rocky** Th. Plb. NT. Plu.; (of a cavern, a prison) S.; (of glens) Ar.; (of accretions to the soul, compared to incrustations on a sea-god) Pl.

πέτρωμα ατος *n.* [πετρόομαι] **stoning** (of a person, to death) E.

πεττείᾱ ᾱς Att.*f.* [πεσσοί] **game of draughts, draught-playing** Pl. Arist.

πεττευτής οῦ Att.*m.* **draught-player** Pl. Plb.

πεττευτικός ή όν Att.*adj.* (of a person) **expert at draughts** Pl.; (of the art) **of playing draughts** Pl. ‖ NEUT.SB. (sg. and pl.) draught-playing Pl.

πεττεύω, πέττω Att.*vbs.*: see πεσσεύω, πέσσω

πεύθομαι *mid.vb.*: see πυνθάνομαι

πευθώ οῦς *f.* [πεύθομαι, see πυνθάνομαι] **information, news** A.

πευκάεις εσσα εν *dial.adj.* [πεύκη] **1** (of a ship) **made of pinewood** E.
2 (of Hephaistos, meton. for fire) fed by pine torches, **pine-fed** S.
3 (of a cry) **piercing, shrill** A.(dub.)

πευκάλιμος η ον *Ion.adj.* sharp or piercing; (fig., of a person's wits) **sharp, shrewd** Il. Hes.*fr.* Mosch.

πευκεδανός ή όν *adj.* (of war) **sharp, piercing, biting** Il.

πεύκη ης, dial. **πεύκᾱ** ᾱς *f.* **1 pine tree, pine** Il. Hes. Pi.*fr.* E. Ar. +
2 (collectv.sg., ref. to timber) **pinewood** E. Pl. Plu.
3 pine torch Trag. Ar. Call. AR.
4 pinewood (meton., ref. to a writing-tablet) E.; (ref. to the Trojan Horse) E.; (ref. to a ship or oar) Tim.

πεύκινος η ον *adj.* **1** (of branches) **of a pine tree, pine** E.*fr.*
2 (of a torch, logs, planks) **of pine** S. E. Plb.
3 (of dripping resin) **from a pine torch** E.

πεύσομαι (fut.mid.), **πευσοῦμαι** (dial.fut.mid.), **πευστέον** (neut.impers.vbl.adj.): see πυνθάνομαι

πεφάνθαι (pf.mid.pass.inf.), **πέφανται**[1] (3sg.pf.mid.pass.): see φαίνομαι, under φαίνω
πέφανται[2] (3pl.pf.pass.), **πεφάσθαι** (pf.pass.inf.): see θείνω
πέφαργμαι (pf.pass.): see φράζω
πεφάσθω (3sg.pf.pass.imperatv.): see φημί
πέφασμαι (pf.mid.pass.): see φαίνομαι, under φαίνω
πεφασμένως *pf.pass.ptcpl.adv.*: see under φαίνω
πέφαται (3sg.pf.pass.): see θείνω
πέφηνα (pf.), **πεφήσομαι**[1] (fut.pf.mid.pass.): see φαίνομαι, under φαίνω
πεφήσομαι[2] (fut.pass.): see θείνω
πεφιδήσομαι (ep.redupl.fut.mid.), **πεφιδόμην** (ep.redupl.aor.2 mid.): see φείδομαι
πέφνον (ep.redupl.aor.2), **πεφνέμεν** (inf.), **πεφνών** (ptcpl.): see θείνω
πεφοβημένως *pf.mid.pass.ptcpl.adv.*: see under φοβέω
πέφραδε (ep.3sg.redupl.aor.2, also 2sg.imperatv.), **πεφραδέειν**, **πεφραδέμεν** (inf.), **πέφρακα** (pf.): see φράζω
πέφρῑκα (pf.): see φρίσσω
πεφροντισμένως *pf.pass.ptcpl.adv.*: see under φροντίζω
πεφυζότες (ep.masc.nom.pl.pf.ptcpl.): see φεύγω
πέφῡκα (pf.), **πεφύᾱσι** (ep.3pl.pf.): see φύομαι, under φύω
πεφῡκότως *pf.ptcpl.adv.*: see under φύω
πεφυλαγμένως *pf.mid.ptcpl.adv.*: see under φυλάσσω
πεφυυῖα, **πεφυῶτας** (fem.nom.sg. and masc.acc.pl. ep.pf.ptcpl.): see φύομαι, under φύω

πη, Ion. **κη**, dial. **πα** *enclit.adv.* **1** (adding a note of indefiniteness) in some way, **by some means, somehow, at all** Hom. Hes. A.(dub.) Pi. Hdt. Th. +; μάλιστά κη *somewhere about, approximately* Hdt.
2 in some place, **somewhere, anywhere** Hom. Th. Ar. X. Theocr.; πῇ μὲν ... πῇ δέ *in some places ... in others* Plu.
3 in some direction, **somewhere, anywhere** Hom.

πῆ, Ion. **κῆ**, dial. **πᾷ**, also **πεῖ** *interrog.adv.* | used in dir. and indir.qs. | **1** in what way, **how?** Od. Archil. Sol. B. Hdt. E. +; (freq.) πῇ; *how so?* Pl.
2 for what purpose, **why?** Hom.
3 in what place, **where?** Il. Hdt. S. E. Ar. +
4 by which route, **by which way?** Hom. Trag. Ar. Plb.
5 in which direction, **whither?, where?** Hom. hHom. AR. Theocr.

πηγαῖος ᾱ ον (also ος ον E.) *adj.* [πηγή] (of a stream, a bowl, a burden) **of spring water** A. E.; (of water) **from springs** Pl. Plb. Plu.; (of nymphs) **of the springs** E.

πήγανον ου *n.* a kind of herb; **rue** Ar. NT.

πηγάς άδος *f.* [πήγνυμι] **frost** Hes.

Πήγασος, dial. **Πάγασος**, ου *m.* Pegasos (winged horse of Bellerophon) Hes. Lyr. Ar.; (pl., ref. to chimaeric creatures) Pl.

—Πηγάσιον ου *n.* [dimin.] **dear little Pegasos** (ref. to a young horse) Ar.

—Παγασίς ίδος *dial.fem.adj.* (of a fountain) **of Pegasos** (ref. to Hippokrene on Mt. Helikon, created by the stamp of his hoof) Mosch.

πηγεσί-μαλλος ον *ep.adj.* [πηγός, μαλλός] (of a ram) **thick-fleeced** Il.

πηγή ῆς, dial. **πᾱγά** ᾶς *f.* **1 spring, source** (of a river or stream) Il. Hdt. X. AR. Plb.; (ref. to a natural water-source, opp. κρήνη *fountain*) Th.
2 (gener., usu.pl.) water flowing from a source, **spring, stream** Hom. Hes. Lyr. A. E. Pl. +
3 stream (of water or sim., poured fr. a bowl) S. E.; (of milk) S. E. Pl.; (of wine) E.*Cyc.* ‖ PL. (gener.) waters (of the sea, or fr. a stream) E.
4 (fig.) **stream, spring** (of tears) Trag.; (of volcanic fire) Pi.; (of verses) Pi.; **channel** (of hearing, i.e. through the ears) S.
5 place of origin, **root** (of the physical universe, ref. to Tartaros) Hes.(pl.); **source** (of sunlight, ref. to the east) A.(pl.); (of fire; of silver, ref. to a mine) A.; **life-source** (ref. to a motherland) A.
6 originating cause, **fountainhead, source** (of misfortunes, pleasures, sicknesses, motion, or sim.) A. Pl. X. Arist. Plb.

πῆγμα ατος *n.* [πήγνυμι] **1** that which is fixed; (periphr.) **security, bond** (W.GEN. of an oath) A.
2 congealed nature, **frozenness** (W.GEN. of snow) Plb.

πήγνῡμι *vb.* —also (pres.) **πηγνύω** (X. Plb.) | fut. πήξω, dial. πᾱ́ξω | aor. ἔπηξα, ep. πῆξα, dial. πᾶξα, dial.inf. πᾶξαι | pf. πέπηγα, dial. πέπᾱγα | plpf. ἐπεπήγειν, ep. πεπήγειν ‖ MID.: 2sg.dial.aor. ἐπᾶ́ξᾱ (Theoc.) ‖ PASS.: fut. παγήσομαι | aor.1 ἐπήχθην, ep.3pl. πήχθεν, ptcpl. πηχθείς | aor.2 ἐπάγην, ep. πάγην, ep.3pl. πάγεν, ptcpl. παγείς |

1 fix firmly in the ground (or other place); **plant** —*an oar* (W.DAT. or PREP.PHR. *in the ground, on a tomb*) Od. —*a winnowing-shovel* (W.PREP.PHR. *on a heap of grain*) Theoc. —*a sword* (W.PREP.PHR. *in the ground*) AR.; **plant in the ground** —*a sword, sceptre, spear, military standard, or sim.* S. Plb. Plu. —*a palisade* Th. —*stakes* (for nets) X.
‖ STATV.PF.PLPF. (of a sword) be fixed or planted (in the ground) S.; (of a palisade) Th.; (of boundary-stones) Sol.; (of a pillar, military standards) Plu. ‖ PASS. (of spear-heads) be planted or fixed —W.PREP.PHR. *in the ground* Plu.
2 fix to the ground, **pitch** —*a tent* Hdt.(mid.) And. Pl. Plu.; **build** —*winter accommodation* Plu. ‖ STATV.PF.PLPF. (of a tent) stand pitched Hdt. Plb.
3 set (an object) firmly onto (another); **fix** —*a plough-tree* (w. ἐν + DAT. *in a stock*) Hes. —*a pole* (w. ἐς + ACC. *into a socket*) Hdt. —*reed slats (in a lyre)* hHom.; **impale** —*a head, a body* (W.DAT. or PREP.PHR. *on a stake or sim.*) Il. E. ‖ PASS. (of persons) be impaled A. —W.PREP.PHR. *on spits* E.*Cyc.*; (of a peg) be fixed —w. ἐν + DAT. *in wood* E.*fr.*
4 stick, plunge, plant —*a spear, sword, arrow, axe* (W.DAT. or PREP.PHR. *into someone, a part of the body*) Hom. Pi. B. Call. Theoc. ‖ PASS. and PLPF. (of a spear, an arrow) be stuck —W.PREP.PHR. *in someone, a part of the body, a shield, the ground* Il. Theoc.
5 fix (different parts) together; **construct, build** —*ships, a ship's deck* Hom. —*rafts* Plb. —*a palace* Pi. —*an altar* (W.PREP.PHR. *fr. horns*), *a city's foundations* Call. —*seating (for a theatre)* Plu.(mid.) ‖ MID. **build for oneself** —*a wagon* Hes. —*ships* Hes. Hdt. Plu.; **make for oneself** —*a panpipe* Theoc. ‖ PASS. (of a body and soul) be fixed together Pl.; (of a ship) be built —W.PREP.PHR. *fr. pinewood* Ar.; (of shields) be constructed Plu. ‖ STATV.PF. (of a poet's skill) be designed (i.e. be suited) —W.INF. *to do sthg.* Pl.
6 make (circumstances) fixed or immovable; **fix, establish** —*boundaries* Lycurg. ‖ MID. **keep fixed** (W.PREP.PHR. *in one's mind*) —W.COMPL.CL. *that sthg. is the case* Pi. ‖ PASS. (of a boundary) be fixed Th.; (of an oath) be struck (betw. persons) A. E. ‖ STATV.PF. (of circumstances) be fixed —W.DAT. *by a god* D.; (of feelings) be deeply rooted —W.DAT. *in one's nature and habits* D.; (of a person) —W.PREP.PHR. *in good health* Plu.
7 fix, set, hold firm —*one's eyes* (W.PREP.PHR. *on the ground*) Il. Theoc.; (*before one's feet*) AR. ‖ STATV.PF. (of eyes) stay fixed —W.PREP.PHR. *on sthg.* Pl.; (of items of headgear) be formed or stiffened (into a certain shape) Hdt.
8 make solid or stiff; (of a god, the weather) **freeze** —*a river* A. Ar.; (of the north wind) **numb** —*people* X. ‖ PASS. and STATV.PF.PLPF. (of streams, the sea) become or be frozen

πηγός Alc. Hdt. Plu.; (of wine) X.; (of snow) Theoc.; (of ice) become strong Th.
9 ‖ PASS. and STATV.PF.PLPF. (of persons, their limbs) become or be frozen, stiff or numb (fr. cold) Hippon. Pl.; (fr. fear or some strong emotion) Il. Ibyc. E. Men. AR. Theoc.
10 (tr.) **solidify, set** —*cheese* (w. rennet) Theoc. ‖ PASS. (of salt) **crystallise** Hdt.; (of foam on a horse's mouth) **become congealed** Call.; (of blood) Plu. ‖ STATV.PF. (of spilt blood) **be congealed** A.

πηγός ή όν, dial. **πᾱγός** ά όν *adj*. **1** (of horses) **solid, sturdy, strong** Il. Alcm.; (of a wave) **mighty** Od.
2 (of hounds, app. fr. a misunderstanding of 1) **black** Call. [or perh. *white*]

πηγυλίς ίδος *fem.adj*. (of a night, a mist) **frosty, icy, freezing-cold** Od. AR.

πηδάλιον ου *n*. [πηδόν] **1 steering-oar** or **tiller** (of a boat or ship, sts. gener. **helm**) Od. Hes. Thgn. Hdt. E. Ar. +; (pl., ref. to a pair, as used on a single ship) hHom. Hdt. E. Ar. Pl. +
2 (fig.) **rudder** (w. which a ruler guides his people) Pi.; **steering-gear** (for horses, ref. to harness or reins) A. ‖ PL. **steerage, control** (W.GEN. of someone's thinking) Pl.

πηδάω *contr.vb*. [πούς] | Lacon.imperatv. **πᾴδη** | fut. πηδήσομαι | **1** (of persons, their legs; of gods, animals) **leap, spring, bound** Il. hHom. S. E. Ar. Pl. +
2 (fig., of a spear) **leap** (fr. someone's hand) Il. E.; (of a lot, fr. a helmet) A.; (of a spasm, through the brain) E.; (of the wheel or hub of a crashed chariot) **hurtle through the air** E.; (of crimes) **dart** (to heaven, on wings) E.*fr*.; (of the flame of a reveller's torch) **dance** E.
3 (of the heart, the soul) **race, throb, palpitate** (w. excitement or emotion) Ar. Pl.
4 make a sudden or rapid change (of mind or in behaviour); (of a person) **jump** (to another idea) Ar.; (of a herald, to the side of a successful person) E.(dub.); (of gods, their behaviour, a person's fortunes) **jump about, shift rapidly** E.

πήδημα ατος *n*. **1 leap, bound** (of a person, an animal) Trag.; (ref. to throwing oneself on one's sword in suicide) S.
2 throbbing, palpitation (of the heart, in anxiety) E.

πήδησις εως *f*. **1 leaping, cavorting** (by revellers) Plu.
2 throbbing, palpitation (of the heart, in anxiety) Pl.

πηδόν οῦ *n*. [πούς] **oar-blade**; (gener.) **oar** Od. AR.

πηκτίς, dial. **πᾱκτίς**, ίδος, Aeol. **πᾱκτις** ιδος *f*. [πήγνυμι] **1** a kind of **harp** (prob. of Lydian origin); **harp** Lyr. Hdt. Ar. Pl. Arist.
2 lyre Theoc.*epigr*.

πηκτός ή όν, dial. **πᾱκτός** ά όν *adj*. **1** (of a sword) **stuck, fixed** (W.PREP.PHR. in the ground) S.
2 (of woodwork) **fixed together** (by a joiner); (of a plough) **jointed** (opp. one-piece) Hom. Hes.; (of a stool) hHom.; (of ladders) E.
3 ‖ FEM.SB. **device for catching birds, trap** Ar.
4 ‖ NEUT.PL.SB. **close joinings, fastenings** (W.GEN. of a house, ref. to doors) Ar.(mock-trag.)
5 (of milk) **curdled** E.*Cyc*.; (of water, sea) **frozen** Lyr.adesp. Pl.; (of beeswax) **compacted** Theoc. ‖ FEM.SB. **curds or cream cheese** Theoc.

πῆλα (ep.aor.), **πήλασθαι** (aor.mid.inf.): see πάλλω

Πηλεύς έως (ep. έος, ῆος) *m*. **Peleus** (mythol. husband of Thetis, father of Achilles) Hom. +

—**Πήλειος** ᾱ ον, ep. **Πηλήιος** η ον *adj*. (of the home, the offspring) **of Peleus** Il. E.

—**Πηλεΐδης** (also **Πηληιάδης**) εω (also ᾱο) *ep.m*. —also **Πηλεΐδᾱς** ᾱ *dial.m*. **son of Peleus** (ref. to Achilles) Hom. Hes.*fr*. Pi. B. E. AR.

—**Πηλεΐων** ωνος *m*. **son of Peleus** Hom.

—**Πηλειωνάδε** *adv*. **to Peleus' son** (i.e. to his abode) Il.

πηλεφανής Aeol.*adj*.: see τηλεφανής

πήληξ ηκος *f*. **helmet** Hom. Ar. AR.

Πηλιάς *fem.adj*.: see under Πήλιον

πηλίκος η ον *interrog.adj*. [reltd. ἡλίκος, τηλίκος] **1** (in dir. and indir.qs., of things) **how large, how great** Ar. Isoc. Pl. D. +; (of persons) **how tall** Arist.
2 (of a person) **how old** Xenoph. Men.
3 (indef., of a child) **of such and such an age** Arist.

—**πηλίκον** *neut.adv*. **how loudly** D.

πήλινος η ον *adj*. [πηλός] (of sculpted figures) **made of clay, clay** D. Arist.; (of walls) Plu.

Πήλιον, dial. **Πάλιον**, ου *n*. **Pelion** (mountain in Thessaly) Hom. +

—**Πηλιάς** άδος *fem.adj*. (of Achilles' spear of ash) **from Pelion** Il.; (of pines, ref. to torches made fr. them) E.; (of the woods, crags, nymphs, or sim.) **of Pelion** E. AR.; (epith. of the Argo, ref. to the source of its timber) AR.

—**Πηλιῶτις** ιδος *fem.adj*. (of Iolkos) **at the foot of Pelion** E.

πήλοθεν, πήλοι Aeol.*advs*.: see τηλόθεν, τηλοῦ

πηλός οῦ *m*. **1 clay** (used by masons and potters) Hdt. Th. Ar. Pl. +; (as the material fr. which man was made) Ar. Call.
2 mud Heraclit. A. Hdt. Th. Ar. +; (fig.) **mire** (of destruction) A.

πηλοφορέω *contr.vb*. [φέρω] **carry clay** (to a bricklayer, for making bricks or using as mortar) Ar.

πηλώδης ες *adj*. (of ground) **muddy** Th.; (of a river) Pl.

πῆμα ατος *n*. **1 misery, calamity, affliction** Hom. +
2 (ref. to a person, deity, action, or sim.) **cause of misery, bane, plague, trouble** (usu. W.DAT. to someone) Hom. Hes. Thgn. Pi. Trag. AR.

πημαίνω *vb*. | fut. πημανῶ, Ion. πημανέω | aor. ἐπήμηνα ‖ PASS.: fut. πημανοῦμαι | aor. ἐπημάνθην ‖ neut.impers. vbl.adj. πημαντέον | (of gods, humans, circumstances) **afflict, trouble, harm** —someone Il. Hes. Archil. S. E. Ar. Pl. —*a country* Hdt.; (intr.) **cause harm** Il. Thgn. S. ‖ PASS. (of a person) **suffer harm** Od. A. S. Pl. AR.; (of a ship) Od.

πημονή ῆς, dial. **πημονά** ᾶς *f*. **misery, calamity, affliction** Archil. Trag.; (prep.phr.) ἐπὶ πημονῇ *with intent to do harm* Th.(treaty)

πημοσύνη ης *f*. **misery, affliction, trouble** A. E.*fr*.

Πηνελόπη ης, dial. **Πᾱνελόπᾱ** ᾱς (Stesich.), ep. **Πηνελόπεια** ης *f*. **Penelope** (wife of Odysseus) Od. +; (mother of Pan) Hdt.

πηνέλοψ, dial. **πᾱνέλοψ**, οπος *m*. a kind of duck; perh. **widgeon** Alc. Ibyc. E.

πήνη ης, dial. **πήνᾱ** ᾱς *f*. **thread on the spool or bobbin** (which will form the weft), **spool-thread, weft-thread** E.*fr*. ‖ PL. **weaving** (ref. to a woven garment) E.; (meton.ref. to a loom) E.

πηνίκα, dial. **πᾱνίκα** *interrog.adv*. [reltd. ἡνίκα, τηνίκα] | used in dir. and indir.qs. | **1 at what time** (of day) Ar. Pl. Aeschin.
2 (gener.) **when** D. Men. Call. Plb. Plu.; (phr.) πηνίκ' ἄττα *when roughly* Ar.

πηνίον ου *n*. [πήνη] **spool, bobbin** (on which the weft-thread was wound, and passed betw. the warp-threads) Il.

πηνίσματα των *n.pl*. [reltd. πᾱνίσδομαι] **spool-threads, weft-threads** Ar.(mock-trag.)

πῆξα (ep.aor.): see πήγνυμι

πῆξις εως *f*. [πήγνυμι] **1 fixing** (by joinery), **construction** (W.GEN. of doors) Pl.
2 coagulation (of moisture in the body, caused by cold) Pl.; **coalescence** (of particles of matter) Plu.

πήξω (fut.): see πήγνυμι
πηός οῦ *m.* **1 kinsman by marriage, in-law** Hom.
   2 (gener.) **kinsman, relative** Od. Hes. Call. Theoc.
πηοσύνη ης *f.* **kinship by marriage** AR.
πήποκα *dial. temporal adv.* [πώποτε] **at any time, ever** Theoc.
πήρᾱ ᾱς, Ion. **πήρη** ης *f.* **bag, pouch, knapsack** (for provisions or sim., oft. assoc.w. beggars or rustics) Od. Ar. Philox.Cyth. Men. Theoc. +
πήρα *Lacon.f.*: see πεῖρα
πηρήτω (Lacon.3sg.imperatv.): see πειράω, under πειράομαι
πηρίδιον ου *n.* [dimin. πήρᾱ] **little bag** Ar. Men.
πηρός όν *adj.* **physically damaged or mutilated**; (of a musician) **crippled, paralysed** (i.e. unable to sing or play) Il.; (fig., of a woman) **stunted** (in ability or intellect) Semon.
πηρόω *contr.vb.* **1 cause physical damage; maim, disable** —*someone* Ar. ‖ PASS. (usu. PF.) **be maimed, disabled or incapacitated** (freq. W.ACC. in some part of one's body) D. Arist. Plu.; **be blind** Plu.; (of a child) **be deformed** Arist.; (of growth) **be stunted** Arist.
   2 damage, stunt —*someone's skill* Pl. ‖ PASS. (of persons) **be stunted** —W.PREP.PHR. *in the capacity to achieve excellence* Ar.; (of a political career) **be blighted** (by poverty) Plu.
πήρωμα ατος *n.* **deformed creature** Arist.
πήρωσις εως *f.* **physical injury, maiming, disablement** Pl. Arist.
πῆς *Boeot.m.f.*: see παῖς¹
πηχθείς (aor.pass.ptcpl.), **πῆχθεν** (ep.3pl.aor.pass.): see πήγνυμι
πηχυαῖος ᾱ (Ion. η) ον *adj.* [πῆχυς] (of things) **a cubit long or tall** Hdt. Plb. Plu. ‖ NEUT.SB. **length of one cubit** Pl.
πήχυιος η ον *Ion.adj.* (of a ditch) **a cubit long** AR.; (fig., of a period of time) no longer than a cubit, **of short span** Mimn.
—**πήχυιον** *neut.adv.* **by a cubit** (in length) AR.; (in height) AR.
πηχύνω *vb.* **hold with one's arm; hold** —*a shepherd's crook* (W.PREP.PHR. *in one's hand*) AR.
πῆχυς, dial. **πᾶχυς**, εος (also εως) *m.* | acc.pl. πήχεις, Ion. πήχεας, ep. πήχῡς | ep.nom.acc.du. πήχεε | gen.pl. πήχεων, later πηχῶν | **1 forearm** (fr. wrist to elbow, opp. βραχίων *upper arm*) Pl. X.; (gener.) **forearm** or **arm** Hom. hHom. Lyr. E. Call. AR.; (of a personif. vine, fig.ref. to a tendril) Ion
   2 ‖ PL. **arms** (of a lyre) hHom. Hdt.
   3 (as measure of length, distance fr. elbow to tip of middle finger, 24 finger-widths, approx. one and a half feet) **cubit** Hdt. E.*Cyc.* Th. Pl. X. +
   4 rod (or sim.) for measuring a cubit, **cubit-rule** Ar. Arist.
   5 small span of time (opp. a lifetime), **hour** NT.
   6 centre-piece, grip (of a bow) Hom.
πιάζω *vb.*: see πιέζω
πιαίνω, also **πῑαίνω** (Pi.) *vb.* [πίων, πῖαρ] | fut. πῑανῶ | aor. ἐπίᾱνα, poet. πίᾱνα ‖ aor.pass. ἐπιάνθην | **1** (of a person, the earth) **fatten** —*a flock, a herd* E.*Cyc.* Pl. Theoc.; (of a buried prophet) **enrich** —*a land* (by his presence) A.; (of persons being cremated) **feed** —*smoke* (W.DAT. *w. their bodies*) Pi. ‖ PASS. (of persons, likened to animals) **be fattened** or **grow fat** Semon. Pl. Plu.; (of oxen's thighs, an ear of corn) Theoc.; (of ground) **be enriched** (by dead bodies) Plu.
   2 (gener., of an activity) **fatten, enrich** —*a city's coffers* Xenoph.; (of a person) **increase, enlarge** —*one's wealth* Pi.; (of a rumour) **bolster, encourage, cheer** —*someone* A. ‖ PASS. (fig., of persons) **get fat** A.; **feed** —W.DAT. *on spiteful talk, envy* Pi. B.
πῖαρ *n.* | only nom. and acc. | **1 fat** (of sacrificial animals) hHom.
   2 richness (of soil) Od. hHom.
   3 rich part (of milk), **cream** Sol.; **rich juice** (W.GEN. of the olive) AR.; (prob. fig.) **cream** (i.e. fattest or choicest animal, W.GEN. of a herd of oxen) Il.
πίασμα ατος *n.* [πιαίνω] **enrichment** (W.DAT. for a land, ref. to its being watered by a river) A.
πιδακόεις εσσα εν *adj.* [πῖδαξ] (of water) **gushing from a spring** E.
πιδακώδης ες *adj.* (of places) **rich in springs** Plu.
πῖδαξ ακος *f.* **spring** (of water) Il. Hdt. E. Hellenist.poet.
πιδάω *contr.vb.* (of udders) **gush** —W.GEN. *w. milk* Theoc.
πιδήεις εσσα εν *ep.adj.* (of a mountain) **rich in springs** Il.
πιδυλίς ίδος *f.* **rock from which water springs** Call.
πιδύω *vb.* (of water) **gush from a spring** Plu.
πιέ (aor.2 imperatv.), **πιέειν** (ep.inf.): see πίνω
πιέζω *vb.* | aor. ἐπίεσα ‖ aor.pass. ἐπιέσθην | —also (pres. and impf.) **πιεζέω** (Plb. Plu., perh. Hdt.) *contr.vb.* —also **πιάζω** *vb.* | aor. ἐπίαξα (Theoc.), ἐπίασα (NT.) |
1 exert pressure by physical contact; press tight, squeeze, pinch —*a part of someone's* or *one's own body* Il. Hes. Ar. Pl. —*a ball of wax* Od.; **press** —*someone's hand* (fr. affection) Plb.; (intr., of persons or things) **exert pressure** X. Arist.; (fig.) **squeeze** —*officials* (envisaged as figs, to test them for ripeness) Ar.
   2 (of a captor, a wrestler) **hold tight, grip** —*someone* Od. Plu.; **secure** (W.ACC. someone) **tightly** —W.PREP.PHR. *in fetters* Od.
   3 grasp firmly —*a bull* (W.GEN. *by its hoof*) Theoc.; (wkr.sens.) **take hold of** —*someone* (W.GEN. *by the hand*) NT.; **seize, arrest** —*someone* NT.; **catch** —*fish* NT.
   4 press with a weight or burden; (of a region) **press upon, lie heavily on** —*the chest of Typhon* Pi. ‖ PASS. (of a person, a part of the body, a tree) **be weighed down** Ar. X.
   5 exert force against; (of a person) **press against** —*a door* (to prevent it being opened) Ar.; (of troops) **press hard** —*enemy troops* Hdt. Th. Plb. ‖ PASS. (of troops or sim.) **be hard pressed** Hdt. Th. X. Plb.
   6 (of persons, unfavourable circumstances) **press hard on, oppress, crush** —*someone* A. Pi. Hdt. E. Th. Ar. +; (of unfavourable weather) **damage** —*crops and vines* Ar.; (in logic, of a name for sthg.) **put** (W.ACC. a philosopher) **in a difficult position** Pl. ‖ PASS. (of persons) **be oppressed, be hard hit** (oft. W.DAT. or PREP.PHR. by sthg.) Sol. Hdt. Th. Lys. X. Plb.; (of a river, ref. to its volume) **be adversely affected** (by the time of year) Hdt.
   7 repress, stifle —*one's anger* Pi. —*someone's pride* Plu.; **check, control** —*someone* (W.DAT. *by one's speech*) Plu.; **counteract** —*misfortune* (W.DAT. *w. some blessing*) E.
   8 press, put weight on, insist on —*a principle or factor* (in an argument) Pl. Plb.
πιεῖν (aor.2 inf.): see πίνω
πίειρα *fem.adj.*, **πιείρη** *Ion.fem.adj.*: see πίων
πιέμεν (ep.aor.2): see πίνω
Πιερίᾱ ᾱς, Ion. **Πιερίη** ης *f.* **Pieria** (mountainous region N. of Olympos, assoc.w. the Muses) Hom. Hes. Hdt. E. Th. +; (appos.w. γῆ *land*) Simon.
—**Πιερίᾱθεν**, Ion. **Πιερίηθεν** *adv.* (ref. to motion or origin) **from Pieria** Hes. hHom. B. Tim.(cj.) AR.
—**Πιερίδες** ων *fem.pl.adj.* (of the Muses) **from Pieria, Pierian** Hes. Sapph. Sol. B. E. Theoc.; (sg., of a single Muse) E.; (of writing-tablets, meton. for poetry) **inspired by the Muses** E. ‖ SB. **Pierides, Muses of Pieria** Pi. B. E. AR. Theoc.
—**Πιερικός** ή όν *adj.* **from** or **relating to Pieria**; (of pitch) **Pierian** Hdt.; (of a gulf) Th.

πίησθα (ep.2sg.aor.2 subj.): see πίνω
πιθάκνη, Att. **φιδάκνη**, ης *f.* [πίθος] **storage-jar** Ar. D.
πίθᾱκος *dial.m.*: see πίθηκος
πιθανολογέω *contr.vb.* [πιθανός, λόγος] (of a mathematician) **argue from plausibility** (opp. offer proof) Arist.
πιθανολογίᾱ ᾱς *f.* **argument from plausibility** (opp. geometric proof) Pl.
πιθανός ή όν *adj.* [πείθω] **1** (of persons, esp. public speakers) **persuasive, convincing, plausible** Th. Pl. D. Arist. Men.; (W.INF. in speaking) Pl.; **persuasive enough** (W.INF. to cause trouble) E.(dub.)
2 (of arguments, speech) **persuasive, convincing** A. Ar. Pl. X. D. Arist. || NEUT.SB. **persuasiveness** Pl. Arist.
3 (of a verbal account or sim.) **convincing, credible, plausible** Hdt. Pl. Men. Plb. || NEUT.IMPERS. (w. ἐστί) **it is believable** —W.ACC. + INF. *that someone did sthg.* Men. || NEUT.SB. **plausibility** (opp. truth) Plb.
4 (of a person's manners, the character of a soul) **winning** X. Pl.
5 (of statues) **convincing, lifelike** X.
6 (of persons) easily persuaded, **obedient, submissive** X.
—**πιθανῶς** *adv.* **persuasively, convincingly, plausibly** —*ref. to speaking, arguing* Ar. Pl. X. Arist. +
πιθανότης ητος *f.* **persuasiveness, plausibility** (of persons, their speech or manner) Men. Plb. Plu.; (of an argument, a narrative) Pl. Arist. Plb. Plu. || PL. **plausible arguments** Plb.
πιθανουργικός ή όν *adj.* [ἔργον] (of the art) **of effecting persuasion** Pl.
πιθανόω *contr.vb.* (of an appropriate style of speech) **give credibility to** —*a fact* Arist.
πιθεῖν (aor.2 inf.), **πίθεις** (Aeol.pres.ptcpl.): see πείθω
πιθηκίζω *vb.* [πίθηκος] | aor. ἐπιθήκισα | **behave like a mischievous or thieving monkey**; (of a person) **monkey around** Ar.; **play monkey tricks** —W.DAT. *on someone* Ar.
πιθηκισμοί ῶν *m.pl.* **monkey tricks, dirty tricks** Ar.
πίθηκος, *dial.* **πίθᾱκος**, ου *m.* **ape, monkey** (usu.ref. to the Barbary ape, oft. as a symbol of ugliness, or assoc.w. trickery) Iamb. S.*Ichn.* Ar. Pl. +; (kept as a pet) Thphr. Plu.; (pejor.ref. to a person) **jackanapes** Ar. D. Arist.(quot.)
πιθηκοφαγέω *contr.vb.* [φαγεῖν] (of a people) **eat apes** Hdt.
πίθην (Aeol.pres.inf.), **πιθήσᾱς** (ep.aor.ptcpl.), **πιθήσω** (ep.fut.): see πείθω
πίθι (aor.imperatv.): see πίνω
πιθ-οιγίς ίδος *fem.adj.* [πίθος, οἴγνυμι] (of the dawn) **of the Opening of the Jars** (ref. to the Pithoigia, first day of the Athenian festival of the Anthesteria) Call.
πιθοίμην (aor.2 mid.opt.), **πίθοιμι** (aor.2 opt.), **πιθόμην** (ep.aor.2 mid.), **πίθον** (dial.aor.2): see πείθω
πίθος ου *m.* **1 large jar** (used for storage, usu. of wine), **storage-jar, jar** Hom. Hes. Lyr. Hdt. E.*Cyc.* +; (as a symbol of plentiful resources) Theoc.
2 (provb.) ἐν τῷ πίθῳ τὴν κεραμείαν ἐπιχειρεῖν μανθάνειν **try to learn pottery on the big jar** (i.e. try to run before one can walk) Pl. | For provbl. πίθος τετρημένος *leaking jar*, see τετραίνω 2.
πιθών¹ ῶνος *m.* **store-room** (for storage-jars) S.*fr.*
πιθών² (aor.2 ptcpl.): see πείθω
πίθων ωνος *m.* [πίθηκος] **ape** (as a symbol of ugliness) Pi.
πικραίνομαι *mid.pass.vb.* [πικρός] **be embittered or exasperated, lose one's temper** Pl. Theoc.
πικρίᾱ ᾱς *f.* **1 bitterness** (of taste) NT.
2 bitterness, malevolence, spitefulness (of a person's feelings or behaviour) D. Plb. Plu.

3 asperity, acerbity (of speech) Plu.
πικρό-γαμος ον *adj.* [γάμος] (of suitors) **finding a bitter kind of marriage, seeing one's wooing end in pain** Od.
πικρό-γλωσσος ον *adj.* [γλῶσσα] (of curses) **from a bitter tongue** A.
πικρό-καρπος ον *adj.* [καρπός¹] (of homicide) **bearing a bitter fruit** (i.e. w. bitter consequences) A.
πικρός ᾱ́ (Ion. ή) όν (perh. also ός όν Od. in section 2) *adj.*
1 sharp to the touch; (of arrows, missiles) **pointed, sharp, stinging** Hom. Mimn. Theoc.; (of an arrow-head, a sword) S.; (of barbs of the tongue, fig.ref. to gossip) **sharp, painful** E.
2 sharp in taste or odour; (of a medicinal root) **bitter** (to the taste) Il.; (of food and drink) Pl.; (of low-quality salt) Men.; (of seawater, a spring) **brackish** Od. Hdt. Pl. Call.; (of a grape) **sour** (i.e. unripe) A.; (of the smell of seals) **pungent** Od.(dub., sts. taken as neut.adv. πικρόν *pungently*)
|| NEUT.SB. **bitterness** (opp. sweetness) Pl.
3 (of pain) **sharp, piercing** Il.; (of anguish) A. S.
4 (of an actor's voice) **shrill, piercing** Ar.; (of sounds of lamentation, w. further connot. of pain and anguish) **painful, bitter** S. E.
5 causing or associated with pain or distress; (of experiences, happenings, activities) **bitter, painful** Stesich. Pi. Trag. Pl. +; (of grief) S. E.; (of places or things) **baneful, hateful** S. E.
6 (of words, speech, curses) **bitter, stinging, cruel** S. E. Pl. D. Call.*epigr.* Theoc.
7 (predic., freq. in threats, of persons or things) **turning out bitter or painful** (for someone), **bitterly regretted, disastrous** Od. Trag. Ar.
8 (of persons) feeling or expressing hostility or harshness, **bitter** (opp. sweet, W.DAT. to someone) Sol. Thgn.; (of persons, their conduct or disposition) **harsh, hostile** (sts. W.DAT. or PREP.PHR. to someone) Hdt. Trag. D. +; (of a god) Sapph. A. Theoc.; (of necessity) **cruel, relentless** Antipho
9 (of a person) **hateful, uncongenial** (W.DAT. to someone) S. E.
—**πικρῶς** *adv.* **1 bitterly, harshly, vindictively** A. S. Att.orats. Men. Plb.
2 bitterly —*ref. to lamenting, weeping* S.(cj.) NT.
3 with bitter resentment, grudgingly E.
4 painfully, disastrously, to one's cost E.; **to one's discomfort** E.
πικρότης ητος *f.* **1 bitterness** (of food, to the taste) Pl. Arist.
2 bitterness (of feeling or speech) E. Isoc.
3 harshness, cruelty (of behaviour) Hdt.
πικτίς ίδος *f.* (*or perh. m.*) **name of an unknown animal**; perh. **badger** Ar.
πιλέω *contr.vb.* [πῖλος] **compress** (wool or other animal hair) **into felt**; (fig., of people) **mat** (W.ACC. themselves) **together** (into political factions) Ar. || PASS. (of the primordial earth) **be solidified** AR.
πίλημα ατος *n.* **felt hat** or **cap** Call.
πίλησις εως *f.* **1 process or product of felt-making**; **felting** or **felt** Pl.
2 compression (of things, into a tighter compass) Pl.
πιλητικός ή όν *adj.* (of the art) **of felting** Pl.
πιλητός ή όν *adj.* (of things) **made of felt, felted** Pl.
πιλίδιον ου *n.* [dimin. πῖλος] **felt cap** Ar. Pl. D. Plu.
πιλίον ου *n.* [dimin. πῖλος] **felt cap** Plb. Plu.
πιλνάω *ep.contr.vb.* [πέλας] | athem.mid. πίλναμαι, 3sg.impf. πίλνατο | **1 cause** (sthg.) **to make contact** (w. sthg.); (of the north wind) **bring down** —*trees* (W.DAT. *to the ground*) Hes.
2 || MID. (of chariots bouncing up and down, of a ball) **strike, touch** —W.DAT. *the ground* Il. AR.; (of earth and

heaven) **meet** (each other) Hes.; (of a person) **come close, come up** —w.dat. *to houses* hHom.

πῖλος ου *m.* **1 wool or other animal hair compressed into felt**; **felt** (as lining of a helmet) Il.; (as lining of boots) Hes. Pl. **2 felt cap** Hes. Hdt. Th. Theoc. Plu.; (derog.) **hat** (of brass, i.e. helmet) Ar.; (ref. to a human head of hair) Pl. **3 felt cloth or mat** Hdt. X. Plu.

πιμελή ῆς *f.* [πίων, πῖαρ] animal fat, **fat, lard** Hdt. S. Plu.
πιμελώδης ες *adj.* (of a liquid) **fatty** Plu.
πιμπλάνομαι *pass.vb.* [πίμπλημι] **be filled** —w.gen. *w. rage* Il.
πιμπλάω *contr.vb.* **fill** —*jars* Lyr.adesp.(dub.)
πίμπλημι *vb.* | Aeol.3pl. πίμπλεισι | ep.3sg.subj. πιμπλῇσι | ptcpl. πιμπλάς, ep.fem.nom.pl. πιμπλεῖσαι | 3pl.impf. ἐπίμπλασαν, dial. πίμπλων | fut. πλήσω | aor. ἔπλησα, ep. πλῆσα | pf. (in cpds.) -πέπληκα ‖ mid.: aor. ἐπλησάμην | ep.athem.aor. (w.pass.sens.) 3sg. πλῆτο, 3pl. πλῆντο ‖ pass.: fut. πλησθήσομαι | aor. ἐπλήσθην, ep.3pl. πλῆσθεν | 3pl.pf. (unless pres.) πλῆνται (Parm.) |
1 (act. and mid.) **fill a receptacle** (usu. w.gen. w. sthg.); **fill** —*a vessel* (w. wine, water, or sim.) Hom. hHom. Alc. A. Hdt. S. + —*a table, a knapsack* (w. food) Od. —*a chest* (w. garments) Il. —*a barn* (w. foodstuffs) Hes. —*a boat, a wagon* (w. cargo, a load) Od. Hdt. —*the folds of one's tunic* (w. gold) Hdt. —*a hat* (w. silver) Plu. —*someone, a mouth or belly* (w. food or drink) E.Cyc.; (of ewes) —*their udders* (w. milk) Theoc. ‖ pass. (of buckets and jars) **be filled** Lyr.adesp.
2 fill up the whole extent of a space (usu. w.gen. w. someone or sthg.); (of warriors, a god) **fill** —*a place* (w. corpses) Il. E. —*a shore* (w. ships) Il. —*plains* (w. chariots) E.; (of Zeus) —*fields* (w. crops) Mosch.; (of a goddess) —*a doorway* (w. light) hHom.; (of winds) —*fields, a plain* (w. dust) Hes. S.; (of fish) —*a harbour's recesses* Il.; (of persons) —*the surface of a bowl* (w. pictures) Hdt. —*tablets* (w. writing) E. —*paths* (w.dat. w. cries and flight) Il. —*a land* (w.gen. w. ugly talk) E. —(w.dat. w. tears) E. —*the sea* (w.gen. w. one's voice) Mosch.
3 ‖ pass. (of rooms, a cave, or sim.) **be filled** —w.gen. w. *people* Hom. Plu.; (of a plain, a river) —w. *men and horses* Hom.; (of a plain) —w. *water* Il. Plu.; (of pools) —w. *fish* Hdt.; (of a land) —w. *snakes* Hdt.; (of pens) —w. *cattle* Theoc.; (of ground) —w. *chariot wreckage* S.; (of places) —w. *signs of someone's power* Hdt. —w. *a fragrance* Thgn. —w. *the flash of armour, w. light* Od. hHom. —w. *fire, darkness* Parm. —w. *shouting* E. AR.; (of the mouth of Fear) —w. *teeth* Hes.; (of gateways) —w.dat. *by doors* Parm.; (of persons) **be covered** —w.gen. w. *blood* Plu.
4 fill (someone) with an emotion (or sim.); (of a deity) **fill** —*someone, the mind* (w.gen. w. might, boldness) Il. ‖ pass. (of a person, the mind) **be filled** —w.gen. w. *fury, anger* Hom. Hes. Hdt. Plu. —w. *forgetfulness and vice* Pl.; (of a person, limbs) —w. *strength* Il.; (of a torrent) **be swollen** Plu.
5 fill —*someone, one's own eyes* (w.gen. w. tears) S. E. ‖ pass. (of eyes) **be filled** —w.gen. w. *tears* Hom. —w. *fire* AR.; (of marriage beds, an army) —w.dat. w. *tears* A. Th.
6 ‖ mid. **satisfy** —*one's appetite* (sts. w.gen. w. food and drink) Od. ‖ pass. (of an aspect of human nature) **be satisfied** —w.prep.phr. *by poets* Pl.; (of persons) **have one's fill** (sts. w.gen. of food, drink) Hdt. E. Pl. X.; (of an eagle) **be sated** —w.gen. w. *bloodshed* S.; (of persons) —w. *pleasures* Pl.; **be wearied** —w.gen. *of someone's sickness* S.
7 complete, perform —*a tune* (on the aulos) A.*fr.*; **complete** —*the rungs of a ladder* (i.e. finish climbing it) E.
8 ‖ mid. perh. **fulfil** (in accordance w. prediction) —*an incestuous marriage* S. [or perh. **consummate**]

πίμπρημι *vb.* —also perh. **πρήθω** *vb.* | imperatv. πίμπρη | ptcpl. πιμπράς | inf. πιμπράναι | fut. πρήσω | aor. ἔπρησα, ep. πρῆσα, also ep.3sg. ἔπρεσε (Hes.), inf. πρῆσαι |
1 (of a wounded man) **blow, spout** —*blood* (out of his mouth and nose) Il.; (of wind) **blow out, swell out** —*a sail* Od.
2 blow up (a fire); (usu. of hostile agents) **burn** —*gates* (w.gen. w. fire) Il. —*ships* E. —*cornfields* Th. —*corpses* Il. S.; **burn down** —*a city, temples, houses, tents, a palace* A. E. Tim. Plu.; **destroy with fire** —*a land and its gods* S.(dub.); **burn, scorch** —*a monster's heads* Hes.; **burn to death** —*a person* E. ‖ pass. (of persons) **be burnt to death** Ar.
3 (of bellows) **make** (w.acc. fire) **burn** AR.
4 ‖ pass. (of a person bitten by a snake) **become inflamed or swollen** NT.

πινακηδόν *adv.* [πίναξ] **plank by plank** —*ref. to demolishing sthg.* Ar.
πινακίδιον ου *n.* [dimin. πίναξ] **writing-tablet** NT. Plu.
πινάκιον ου *n.* **1 tablet** (for registering a juror's vote for a preferred penalty) Ar. Arist.; (for registering a charge against a magistrate) D. Arist.; (for registering a vote for a preferred candidate in an election) Pl.; (ref. to a bronze ticket w. a candidate's name, used in choosing magistrates by lot) D.; (ref. to a boxwood ticket, used in choosing jurors by lot) Arist.
2 notice-board (for decrees, official announcements) Ar. Plu.; (derog., opp. work of art) Isoc.
3 writing-tablet Plb. Plu.
4 board, tablet (of a dream-interpreter) Plu.
πινακίς ίδος *f.* **writing-tablet** Plu.(pl.)
πινακίσκος ου *m.* [dimin. πίναξ] **board, platter** (for preparing fish) Ar.
πινακο-πώλης ου *m.* [πωλέω] **one who sells goods from a tray** (opp. a stall or shop), **tray-vendor** Ar.
πίναξ ακος *m.* **1 board, plank** (of a ship) Od.
2 platter, plate Od. NT.; **tray** (w. food on it) Ar.
3 writing-tablet (consisting of two folding wooden boards) Il. ‖ pl. **boards** (of a writing-tablet) Ar.; (collectv., unless a true pl.) **writing-tablet** A.
4 tablet presented in a temple (or sim.), **votive tablet** A. Arist. Call.*epigr.* Plu.
5 board (for writing a list of names on) D.; **board containing a list of names, register, list** D. Arist.; **catalogue** (of a writer's works) Plu.
6 board (for drawing or painting on) Pl.; **painting** Plu.; (ref. to a map) Plu.
7 tablet, plate (of bronze, w. an engraved map) Hdt.; (of gold, w. an inscription) Pl.
8 board, table (ref. to an astrological chart, used for casting nativities or telling fortunes) Plu.
πιναρός ά όν *adj.* [πίνος] (of hair) **dirty, filthy** E.
Πίνδαρος ου *m.* **Pindar** (lyric poet, 1st half of 5th C. BC) Hdt. Isoc. Pl. +
—**Πινδάρειος** α ον *adj.* (of a saying) **of Pindar** Ar.
Πίνδος ου *f.* **Pindos** (mountain range in northern Greece) A. Pi. Hdt. +
—**Πινδόθεν** *adv.* (ref. to motion) **from Pindos** Pi.
πινόεις εσσα εν *adj.* [πίνος] (of a person's skin) **dirty, filthy** AR.
πινόομαι *pass.contr.vb.* | pf.ptcpl. πεπινωμένος | ‖ pf. (of a person's complexion, in a painting) **be made swarthy** Plu.
πίνος ου *m.* **dirt, filth** (on a person's body or clothes) S. AR.; (fig.) **uncleanliness** (w.gen. of hands, ref. to moral impurity) A.

πῑνο-τήρης ου *m.* [πίνη *fan mussel*, τηρέω] mussel-guard (a tiny crab that lives in the fan mussel's shell, and warns it of approaching danger); (fig., ref. to a small son of the poet Καρκίνος *Crab*, envisaged as performing a warning dance) **baby crab, pea crab** Ar.

πινύσκω, also perh. ep. **πινύσσω** *vb.* [πινυτός, perh.reltd. πέπνῡμαι] | ep.3sg.impf. or aor. ἐπίνυσσε (but perh. fr. ἐπινύσσω) | **1 admonish, instruct** —*someone* (W.DAT. *w. advice, cunning speech*) A. Call.; (*of a command*) —*someone* Il.(dub.)

2 (*of Zeus*) app. **moderate, calm** —*a period of days* (ref. to the windless halcyon days) Simon.

πινυτή ῆς *f.* **wisdom, understanding, good sense** Hom.

πινυτός ή (dial. ἅ) όν *adj.* **1** (*of persons*) **wise, sensible, prudent** Od. Thgn. Pi. AR. Theoc.; (*of Themis*) B.

2 (*of circumstances under the rule of Good Law*) **rational, correct** Sol.

πίνω, Aeol. **πώνω** *vb.* | ep.inf. πῑνέμεν, πῑνέμεναι, Aeol. πώνην | iteratv.impf. πίνεσκον | fut. πίομαι, also πιοῦμαι (X. Arist.) | AOR.2: ἔπιον, ep. πίον, ep.2sg.subj. πίῃσθα, imperatv. πίε, also πῖθι, inf. πιεῖν, ep. πιέειν, πιέμεν, also πίεμεν (*metri grat.*), later πεῖν (NT.) | pf. πέπωκα || PASS.: πίνομαι | (only cpds.) fut. -ποθήσομαι | aor.ptcpl. -ποθείς | pf.inf. πεπόσθαι (Thgn.) || neut.impers.vbl.adj. ποτέον |

1 drink (*a liquid*); **drink** —*wine, water, or sim.* Hom. + —*cups or bowls of wine* Il. —W.GEN. *wine, blood* Od. Thgn. —W.GEN. *fr. a spring or river* Thgn. Hdt.; (*intr., opp. eat*) Hom. + || PASS. (*of wine, water, a river*) **be drunk** Hom. Thgn. Hdt. +

2 (*intr., specif.*) **drink wine, drink** (for the purpose of enjoyment or intoxication) Thgn. Lyr. Hdt. E. Ar. + || STATV.PF. **be drunk** E.*Cyc.* Ar.

3 (*of the earth*) **drink up, soak up** —*water, rain* Hdt.; (*of plants*) X.; (*of earth, dust, or sim.*) —*blood* (*of a slain person*) Trag.

πινώδης ες *adj.* [πίνος] (*of a head of hair*) **dirty, filthy** E.

πίομαι, πιοῦμαι (fut.mid.), **πίον** (ep.aor.2): see **πίνω**

πῖος *adj.*, **πιότερος** (compar.), **πίοτατος** (superl.): see **πίων**

πιπάλλω *vb.* **brandish** —*a bow* A.(cj. ἐπιπάλλω)

πιπίσκω *vb.* [πίνω] | fut. πίσω | aor. ἔπισα | **cause** (W.ACC. *someone*) **to drink** —*sacred waters* Pi.; **give** (*someone*) **a drink** (to save his life) Arist.(cj.)

πιππίζω *vb.* (*of birds*) **tweet, cheep, chirrup** Ar.

πιπράσκω, Ion. **πιπρήσκω** *vb.*: see **πέρνημι**

πίπτω *vb.* | ep.impf. πίπτον | fut. πεσοῦμαι, Ion. πεσέομαι | AOR.2: ἔπεσον, ep. πέσον, dial. ἔπετον, ptcpl. πεσών, Aeol.ptcpl.fem.sg. πετοῖσα, masc.dat.pl. πετόντεσσι, inf. πεσεῖν, Ion. πεσέειν | also aor.1 ἔπεσα, 3pl. ἔπεσαν (NT.) | pf. πέπτωκα, ptcpl. πεπτωκώς, also poet. πεπτώς, ep. πεπτεώς (disyllab.), also πεπτηώς (AR.) |

1 (*of persons or things*) **fall to or towards the earth** (sts. W.ADV. or DAT. or PREP.PHR. *to earth or sim.*); (*of persons*) **fall** (fr. a ship, chariot, roof, or sim.) Hom. +; (*of material objects*) Hom. +; (*of snow, spray, rain*) Hom. A. Hdt.

2 (gener.) **fall downwards**; (*of a baby, at birth*) **fall, drop** —W.PREP.PHR. *betw. its mother's feet* Il.; (*of tears*) Od. A. E. —W.PREP.PHR. *onto someone's cheeks* E.; (*of sleep, darkness*) —*onto someone's eyes* Od. Hes.*fr.* A.; (*of strife, fear*) —*on persons, their minds* Hom.; (*of stars*) **sink** —W.PREP.PHR. *into the sea* Hes.; (*of a river*) **flow down, issue** —W.PREP.PHR. *into the sea* Hes.; (*of blood*) **be spilt** —W.PREP.PHR. *on the ground* A. E.*fr.*

3 fall from an upright position (fr. wounding, infirmity, or sim.); (*of persons*) **fall over, fall down, collapse** Hom. +; (*of trees*) Il. E.; (*of a mast*) Od.

4 (*of persons*) **fall deliberately**; **fall, throw oneself** —W.PREP.PHR. *into someone's arms* Hes.*fr.* E. —*upon a corpse* (to embrace it) A. E.; (*of suppliants*) —*at someone's knees, before a statue or sim.* Il. Trag.; (*of a person committing suicide*) —*on a sword* S.; (*of persons in flight*) **duck for cover** —W.PREP.PHR. *into their wives' arms, their ships* Il.

5 fall or hurl oneself aggressively (on someone or sthg.); **fall** —W.PREP.PHR. *on ships, opponents* Il. Hes. —*on cattle* S.; (*of boars*) —*on dogs* Il.; (*of chariot-horses*) —*on city-gates* A.; (*of winds*) —*on a pyre, land, sea* Il. Hes.; (fig., of tearing, as if personif.) —*on clothes* A.

6 (*of persons killed by violence, esp. soldiers*) **fall dead, fall** Hom. +; (*of sacrificial animals*) A. E.

7 (*of walls, houses*) **collapse** or **be levelled to the ground** Hdt. E. Th.

8 (*of cities*) **fall** (to an enemy) Hdt. E. Pl.

9 (*of persons, military forces, empires*) **come to grief, meet with disaster** Alc. Hdt. Trag. Th.; (*of inflexible wills*) **collapse** S.; (*of boasts*) **come to nothing** A.; (*of an argument*) **be overthrown** Pl.

10 (*of wind*) **be reduced in force, fall, drop, subside** Od.; (*of the sea*) A.

11 fail in one's endeavours; (*of persons*) **fall down, be dashed, be disappointed** Ar. Pl. —W.DAT. *in one's hopes* Plb.; **fall short** —W.PREP.PHR. *of one's expectations* Hdt.; (*of thinking*) **fall** —W.ADV. *to the ground* (i.e. be frustrated) Pi.

12 fall into a (usu. worse) **state**; (*of persons*) **fall** —W.PREP.PHR. *into fetters, a trap, enemy hands* Pi. S. E. —*into one's grave* (i.e. be killed) S. —*into disaster, slavery, difficulties, or sim.* Sol. Pi. E. Th. Ar. —*into vice, boldness, cowardice, drunken revelry* Thgn. S.*Ichn.* E. —*into illness* (i.e. fall ill) A. Hdt. —*into sleep* (i.e. fall asleep) Pi. Trag. —*out of favour* (w. someone) Il.; **be reduced** —W.PREP.PHR. *to tears, anger, fear* Hdt. E.; (fig., of a city) **plunge** —W.PREP.PHR. *to the depths* S.

13 escape from a worse state; (*of prey*) **slip, escape** —W.PREP.PHR. *fr. a net* A.; (*of a person*) —*out of trouble* Ar.; **change** —W.PREP.PHRS. *fr. fear to confidence* E.

14 (*of a dice-throw*) **fall out** (in a certain way) A. Pl.; (*of a situation, war, words*) **turn out** (oft. W.ADV. or PREP.PHR. or PREDIC.ADJ. *well, against expectation, or sim.*) Pi. Hdt. S. E. Pl.

15 (*of a lot*) **fall** (out of an urn) Pl.; (ref. to an allotted duty) **devolve** —W.PREP.PHR. *on someone* NT.

16 come into someone's possession; (*of sovereignty*) **fall, pass** —W.PREP.PHR. *to someone* Hdt.; (*of revenue or sim.*) **accrue** —W.DAT. *to someone* Plb.

17 come within stated limits (of time or scope); (*of an event*) **fall** —W.PREP.PHR. *within a period of time* Plb.; (*of a period of time, of circumstances*) —*within the scope of a historical work* Plb.; (*of things*) —*within a category, under a heading* Arist.

πίρωμις ιος *m.* [Egyptian loanwd.] (in Egypt) **man of standing** (equiv. to καλὸς κἀγαθός) Hdt.

Πῖσα ης, dial. **Πίσᾱ** ᾱς *f.* **Pisa** (name of a district around Olympia, used to designate Olympia itself) Lyr. Hdt. E. Hellenist.poet.

—**Πῑσαῖος** η ον *Ion.adj.* (epith. of Zeus) **of Pisa** Call.

—**Πῑσάτης** ου, dial. **Πῑσάτᾱς** ᾱ *masc.adj.* (of a man, ref. to Oinomaos) **from Pisa** Pi. || PL.SB. **men from Pisa** Pi. X.

—**Πῑσᾶτις**, dial. **Πῑσᾶτις**, ιδος *fem.adj.* (of the olive, ref. to a victor's garland) **from Pisa** Pi.; (of a girl, ref. to Hippodameia) E.

πίσεα (also **πίση**) *n.pl.* | only nom. and acc. | **meadows** or **water-meadows** Hom. Call. AR.

πισῆες ων *ep.m.pl.* **dwellers in meadowlands** Theoc.
πίσινος η ον *adj.* [πίσος *pea*] (of soup) **made of peas, pea** Ar.
πίσσα, Att. **πίττα**, ης *f.* **pitch** (used for fuelling fire, caulking ships and jars, flavouring wine) Hes.*fr.* Hdt. Th. Ar. +; (as a symbol for blackness) Il. Call. | see also μῦς 2
πισσήρης ες *adj.* (of the bubbling of a flame) **pitchy** (fr. burning alive someone coated in pitch) A.
πίσσυγγος (or **πίσυγγος**) ου *m.* **cobbler, shoemaker** Sapph.
πιστευτικός ή όν *adj.* [πιστεύω] **1** (of persons) inclined to trust, **trusting, trustful** Arist.
2 (of persuasion) **creating belief** Pl.
—**πιστευτικῶς** *adv.* (w. ἔχειν) *have confidence* —W.DAT. *in sthg.* Pl.
πιστεύω *vb.* [πιστός] **1** have belief or confidence (in someone or sthg.); **trust, have faith, have confidence** —W.DAT. *in persons, their words, gods* Hdt. S. E. Th. Att.orats. + —*in prophecies* A. —*in evidence, the truth, the justice of one's case, hope, reason, or sim.* Th. Att.orats. + ‖ PASS. (of persons, reports, evidence) **be trusted or believed** Th. Att.orats. +
2 (intr.) be convinced (about sthg.); **be confident, believe** Hdt. S. Th. +; **be convinced** (sts. W.DAT. by persons or their words) —W.NEUT.ACC. *about sthg.* (*i.e. believe it*) S. E. Th. X. Thphr.
3 trust —W.DAT. + PRES. or FUT.INF. *someone to do sthg.* Hdt. X.; **be confident, be convinced, believe** —W.ACC. + INF. *that someone will do sthg., that sthg. is the case* Hdt. E. Th. Att.orats. +; (w. ὅτι or ὡς + COMPL.CL.) Ar. X.; **be confident** —W.INF. *of doing sthg.* S. Th. +; **have the confidence** —W.INF. *to do sthg.* D. ‖ PASS. (of persons) be trusted or thought certain —W.FUT.INF. *to do sthg.* X.; (of things) be believed —W.INF. *to be the case* Pl.
4 have confidence —W.DAT. *in someone* (W.ACC. *in matters of leadership, agreements, or sim.*) X.
5 ‖ PASS. be entrusted —W.ACC. or GEN. w. *sthg.* Plb.
6 (of persons, ref. to religious faith or belief) **trust, have faith** —w. ἐν + DAT. or εἰς + ACC. *in God, the Gospel, or sim.* NT.; (intr.) NT.
πιστικός ή όν *adj.* [perh.reltd. πιστός] (of a balm made fr. nard) perh. **genuine, pure** NT.
πίστις εως (Ion. ιος) *f.* [πιστός] | Ion.dat.sg. πίστῑ, acc.pl. πίστῑς, dat.pl. πίστισι | **1** feeling of trust or confidence (in someone or sthg.); **trust** Hes.(pl.) Thgn.; (in a god) S.; **confidence** (sts. W.GEN. in sthg.) Th. D. Plu.; **assurance** (W.GEN. for fears, i.e. for persons in fear, ref. to an appeal to the gods) E.
2 religious faith, **faith, belief** NT.
3 quality of being trustworthy; **trustworthiness, honesty, loyalty** Thgn. A. Hdt. S.; (as a deity) **Trust** Thgn. Plu.
4 claim to be trusted or believed; **credence, credibility** (possessed by a person, an account, an argument) Parm. Emp. S. E. Arist. Plb.
5 financial reliability, **creditworthiness, credit** D.; (W.GEN. for a certain sum) D.
6 that which gives confidence; **guarantee of good faith, assurance, pledge** (freq.pl., oft. described as given, received or made) Hdt. Trag. Th. Ar. Att.orats. +
7 that which gives ground for belief or produces conviction; **evidence, proof, confirmation** S. E. Plu.; (given to the mind by the senses) Democr.; (in oratory or philosophy) **proof, argument** Att.orats. Pl. Arist.
8 position of trust, **trusteeship, guardianship** (of an estate) Plu.
9 (concr.) that which is entrusted to someone; **trust** (ref. to a regency, guardianship) Plb.
10 (in Roman ctxts.) **protection** (offered to another nation by the state) Plb. Plu.(quot.poet.); (offered by the Senate to citizens) Plb.
πιστός ή όν *adj.* [πείθω] | compar. πιστότερος, superl. πιστότατος | **1** (of persons) to be habitually trusted or relied on; (of a spouse, friend, servant, or sim.) **trustworthy, faithful, reliable, loyal** (sts. W.DAT. to someone) Hom. +; (of a person's mind, eye, tongue, thoughts, or sim.) Thgn. Pi. Trag.; (of a conquered country) **obedient** X. ‖ MASC.PL.SB. trusted counsellors (of the Persian king) X.
‖ NEUT.PL.COLLECTV.SB. trusted council (of Persian elders) A.
2 (of things) in which one may feel confidence; (of oaths, pledges, or sim.) **trustworthy, reliable, sure** Hom. Hes.*fr.* hHom. Thgn. A. Pi. NT.; (of advice) A.; (of evidence, signs, prophecies, or sim.) Pi. Hdt. Trag. Th. Hermoloch.; (of hope, friendship) Th.; (of a show of divine strength) **to be counted on, unfailing** E. ‖ NEUT.SB. reliability (periphr. W.GEN. of truth, i.e. honest truth) S.; confidence (that sthg. will happen) Th.; (W.GEN. derived fr. skill) Th.; spirit of trust Th.
3 ‖ NEUT.SB. that which offers a basis for trust or belief, pledge, guarantee S.; evidence, proof A.(dub.); (W.GEN. for a statement) E. ‖ NEUT.PL.SB. pledges, guarantees (sts. W.GEN. of sthg.) A. Hdt. Th. X.
4 (of a speaker, a messenger, on specific occasions) worthy of belief, **believable, credible** E. Antipho Th.; (of speech, a message, an argument, or sim.) Parm. Hdt. E. Att.orats. Pl. +; (of happenings, sights, circumstances) Archil. Pi. E. Ar.
5 having trust or confidence, **trusting** (W.DAT. in someone or sthg.) Thgn. A. S. Pl.; (phr.) οὐκέτι πιστὰ γυναιξί *there is no longer any trusting in women* Od.
6 (of persons) having faith, **believing** (in God, Christ) NT. ‖ MASC.SB. believer NT.
—**πιστῶς** *adv.* **1 faithfully, reliably, loyally** Th. Att.orats. +
2 plausibly (opp. truly) Antipho
3 trustingly D.
πιστός ή όν *adj.* [ἔπῑσα, see πιπίσκω] (of a medicine) **for drinking** A.
πιστότης ητος *f.* [πιστός] **1 trustworthiness, faithfulness, loyalty** Hdt. Pl. X.
2 trustfulness, belief And.
πιστόω *contr.vb.* **1 make** (W.ACC. someone) **pledge fidelity** —W.DAT. *to oaths* Th. ‖ MID. **make** (W.ACC. someone) **pledge good faith** —W.PREP.PHR. *under oath* S.; **secure the confidence** or **loyalty** —W.ACC. *of someone* Plb. ‖ PASS. (of a person) be bound by a pledge or pledge oneself hHom. E. —W.DAT. + FUT.INF. *to someone, to do sthg.* Od.
2 ‖ MID. **give confidence** or **reassurance** (to someone) Il.; (of two parties) give pledges (to one another), **exchange pledges** Il. Plb. ‖ PASS. be assured (of sthg.) Od.; be given a pledge or assurance S. —W.COMPL.CL. *that sthg. will be the case* S.
3 ‖ MID. make (a promise, an argument) credible; **confirm, guarantee** —*promised gifts* Plb.; **prove** —W.ACC. or COMPL.CL. *sthg., that sthg. is the case* Plu.
πίστρᾱ ᾱς *f.* —also **πίστρον** ου *n.* [ἔπῑσα, see πιπίσκω] **drinking-trough** (for animals) E.*Cyc.*
πιστώματα των *n.pl.* [πιστόω] **1** assurances of faithfulness, **pledges** (betw. husband and wife, betw. conspirators) A.
2 (concr., ref. to Persian elders) **trusty counsellors** A. | cf. πιστός 1
3 assurances (W.GEN. of a Muse) Emp.
4 (in legal ctxt.) **confirmation, corroboration** (of an argument or evidence) Arist.

πίστωσις εως *f.* **corroboration** (of a claim) Pl.; (as a rhetorical technique) **confirmation** (of an argument) Pl.

πίσυγγος *m.*: see πίσυγγος

πίσυνος ον *adj.* [πείθω] **trusting** (W.DAT. in someone or sthg.) Hom. +

πίσυρες *ep.pl.num.adj.*: see τέσσαρες

πίσω (fut.): see πιπίσκω

Πιτάνη ης, dial. **Πιτάνα** ᾱς *f.* **Pitane** (district of the city of Sparta) Pi. Hdt. E. Call.

—**Πιτανάτης** ου, Ion. **Πιτανήτης** εω *masc.adj.* (of a military division) from Pitane, **Pitanate** Hdt. Th.

πίτνημι *ep.vb.* [reltd. πετάννῡμι] | ptcpl. πιτνᾱ́ς | impf.3sg. πίτνᾱ, 3pl. πίτνᾱν, also ἔπιτνον (Hes., dub.) ‖ 3pl.impf.pass. ἐπίτναντο, also πίτναντο | **1** (of a goddess) **spread out** —*a mist* (*in front of warriors*) Il.; (of harvesters) —*sheaves* (W.DAT. *on a threshing-floor*) Hes.(dub.) ‖ PASS. (of hair) **stream out** Il.
2 stretch out —*one's hands* Od. Pi.; (of a satyr) —(*prob.*) *his phallus* S.*Ichn.*
3 ‖ PASS. (of braziers) **be set out** E. [or perh. of altars, *be strewn* (w. *offerings*)]

πίτνω *vb.* [πίπτω] | only pres. and impf. | impf. ἔπιτνον, also πίτνον | 1st syllab. scans short in Trag. | **1 fall from a height**; (of persons) **fall** (fr. a chariot) E.; (of a cornice, fr. a roof) E.
2 (of persons) **fall from an upright position**; **fall down, collapse** —W.PREP.PHR. *to the ground* E.
3 (of confusion) **fall** —W.PREP.PHR. *upon someone's mind* A.; (of noise, sufferings) —*on a house* E.
4 (of persons) **fall deliberately**; **fall, throw oneself** —W.PREP.PHR. *into the sea* E.; (of a victor) —*into the arms or at the knees of Victory* Pi.; (of suppliants) **fall down** (sts. W.PREP.PHR. or ADJ. at someone's knees, before an altar) E.; (wkr.sens., of a wife) **come** —W.PREP.PHR. *to her husband's bed* E.
5 (of persons, things) **fall forcefully** (on someone or sthg.); (of a person) **make an assault** —W.PREP.PHR. *on cattle* S.; (wkr.sens., of breezes) **fall** —W.PREP.PHR. *upon a sail* B.; (of a wave) —W.ADV. *onto the land* Alcm.
6 (of a wave) **fall** (opp. rise) A.; (of sorrow) **subside** Pi.
7 (of persons) **fall dead, fall** Trag.
8 (of persons, houses) **be ruined, come to grief, meet with disaster** A. E.; (of honours due to the gods) **be overthrown** E.; (of delight) **fall** —W.ADV. *to the ground* Pi.
9 come to a state or activity; (of a house) **fall, plunge** —W.PREP.PHR. *into an ordeal* E.; (of persons) **resort** —W.PREP.PHR. *to questioning* E.
10 (of fortunes) **fall out, turn out** —W.ADV. *badly* E.

πίττα Att.*f.*: see πίσσα

πιττάκιον ου *n.* **written note, memo** Plb.

πιτυλεύω *vb.* [πίτυλος] prob. **ply the oar, row** Ar.

πίτυλος ου *m.* **1 beating of oars, oar-beat** E.*fr.*; **beating oars** E.; (W.GEN. of a ship, periphr. for oared ship) E.; (fig., ref. to sailors dying together) ἐνὶ πιτύλῳ *at a stroke* A.
2 repeated blows with the hands; **beat** (of mourners' hands on their heads, imagined as oar-beats) A. E.; **rain of blows** (by a boxer) Theoc.
3 onslaught (ref. to a military attack) E.; (W.GEN. of spearmen) E.; **onset, attack** (W.GEN. of fear, madness, also W.PTCPL.ADJ. mad) E.; **rush** (W.GEN. of tears) E.; (fig.) **impetus** (W.GEN. of a wine-cup, ref. to the effects of wine) E.

πιτυο-κάμπτης ου *m.* [πίτυς, κάμπτω] **pine-bender** (ref. to Sinis, who killed travellers by tying them betw. two pine-trees bent to the ground and then released) Plu.

πίτῡρα ων *n.pl.* **husks of corn, bran** (used in purificatory and magic rituals) D. Theoc.

πίτυρις ιδος *f.* [perh. πίτυρα] | acc. πίτυριν | **a kind of olive**; perh. **bran-coloured olive** Call.

πίτυς υος *f.*; | ep.dat.pl. πίτυσσι | **pine tree, pine** Hom. Simon. A.*satyr.fr.* Hdt. Pl. +; (phr.) πίτυος τρόπον *like a pine* (i.e. utterly, root and branch, supposedly because the pine, once cut down, does not grow again) Hdt.

πιτυώδης ες *adj.* (of a region) **abounding in pines** B.

πιφαύσκω *vb.* [reltd. φάος, w. reduplication] | sts. -ῑ- *metri grat.* in ep. | only pres. and impf. | **1 make visible or display** (an impressive object or phenomenon); (of the Persian king) **show forth, reveal, display** —*his tiara* A.; (of a beacon) —*a light* A.; (mid., of a god) —*a great fire* Il. —*a snowstorm, flames* (envisaged as arrows) Il. hHom.
2 reveal in words (what is not yet visible); (act. and mid.) **tell of, mention** —*a person, horses* Hom.
3 make (sthg.) **known**; (act. and mid.) **reveal, disclose, divulge** —*a story, news, divine decrees, one's plans* Hom. Hes. hHom. Emp. AR.; **talk of, propose** —*a ransom* Il. —*evil actions* Il.; (act.) **warn of, predict** —*punishments* A.; **tell of, proclaim** —*a victory* B.
4 speak —*words* Hom.; (intr.) **make a declaration, speak out, speak** Hom. B. AR.; (mid.) Od.
5 give a signal —W.DAT. *to someone* (by whistling) Il.; (of a beacon) **be the signal for** —W.ACC. *the start of dancing* A.
6 tell, order —W.DAT. + INF. *someone to do sthg.* A.

πίων πῖον, gen. πίονος *adj.* —also irreg.fem. **πίειρα**, Ion. **πιείρη** —also perh. **πῖος** ᾱ ον (Philox.Leuc.) *adj.* [πῖαρ] | ep.compar. πιότερος, superl. πιότατος | **1** (of sheep, goats, pigs, cattle, their thigh-bones) **rich in fat, fat, fatty** Hom. Hes. Xenoph. Pl. Theoc.; **rich** (W.DAT. in fat) Hom. Hes. hHom.; (of squid) **fat** Philox.Leuc.(dub.)
2 (pejor., of persons) **fat** Ar. Pl. X.
3 (of places) **rich in natural products**; (of land, fields) **rich, fertile** Hom. hHom. Tyrt. Pl. AR. Theoc.; (of a country, an island, a region) Hom. Hes. Sol. Pi. Call. AR. +; (of a god's domain) Pi.; (of a grain-harvest) **fruitful, abundant** Theoc.; (of a quantity or measure of grain) Theoc.
4 (of a goat's teat) **rich** (in milk) Call.; (of a tree) perh., **rich in resin, resinous** S.
5 (of natural products and food) **thick or rich in consistency**; (of fat) **rich, thick** Hom.; (of oil) Hdt. Call.; (of cheese, honey) Xenoph. Theoc.; (of grape-juice) S.; (of a cake) Ar.; (of food, fruit) Call.; (of bread) Plu.(quot.poet.); (of a meal) Il.
6 (of smoke rising fr. a burning city) **rich, thick** Call.; (of puffs of wealth, fig.ref. to smoke fr. a burning city) A.
7 (fig., of a city, house, temple) **rich, wealthy** Hom. hHom. Thgn. Carm.Pop. Theoc.
8 (of a spun thread) **generous in width, thick** Pl.

πλᾱγά dial.*f.*: see πληγή

πλαγγών όνος *m.* **wax doll** Call.

πλαγείς, πλάγεις (dial. and Aeol. aor.2 pass.ptcpl.): see πλήσσω

πλαγιάζω *vb.* [πλάγιος] **turn** (sthg.) **sideways**; (intr., fig.) **be devious** —W.ACC. *in speech or action* Plu.

πλαγί-αυλος ου *m.* [αὐλός] **transverse pipe, flute** Theoc. Bion

πλάγιος ᾱ ον *adj.* [πλάζω] **1 in a sideways direction or position**; (quasi-advbl., of persons, ref. to the direction of their approach) **from the side** Ar.; (ref. to being knocked down) **sideways** Pl.; (of a root being planted, i.e. horizontally, opp. vertically) X.; (of a ship) **broadside on** (to a harbour mouth, to block it) Th.; (to another ship, in an engagement) Plb. Plu.; (of motion) **transverse, oblique, sideways** (opp. directly ahead) Pl.

2 ‖ NEUT.SB. slope X.; (pl.) sides, slopes (of an acropolis) Pl.; borders (of a country) Hdt.
3 (milit., of troops, sts. predic. w.vb. *attack* or sim.) **on the flank** or **flanks** X. Plb. Plu. ‖ NEUT.PL.SB. flanks (of an army) Th. X. Plb.; (of a fleet) Th.; (prep.phrs.) ἐκ πλαγίου *on the flank or flanks* Th. X. Plb. Plu.; ἐκ (τῶν) πλαγίων *on the flanks* Plb. Plu.; **broadside on** (*in a naval engagement*) Plb.
4 (prep.phrs., in non-military ctxts.) εἰς (τὰ) πλάγια (also τὸ πλάγιον) *sideways* Pl. X.; ἐκ πλαγίου *from the side* Pl. X.
5 (fig., of persons) not straightforward, **unreliable** Plb.; (of a mind, effrontery) **crooked, devious** Pi.; (of thoughts) E.

—**πλάγια** *neut.pl.adv.* **across a slope** (opp. up or down hill) —*ref. to riding* X.

—**πλαγίως** *adv.* **obliquely** —*ref. to speaking* Plu.

πλαγιόω *contr.vb.* (of a rider) **cause** (W.ACC. a horse) **to lean** (fr. the vertical, in a turn) X. ‖ PASS. (of a rider) **lean** X.

πλαγκτός (perh. also **πλακτός** Parm.) ή όν (also ός όν A.) *adj.* [πλάζω] **1** (of a cloud) **wandering** E.; (of Delos) Call.; (of the cloaks of drowned sailors) **carried about** (by the waves) A.(dub.)
2 (fig., of a person) astray (in one's mind), **deranged, crazy** Od. A.; (of a person's mind) **erring, deluded** Parm.

—**Πλαγκταί** ῶν *f.pl.* (usu. w. πέτραι understd.) **Wandering** (or perh. *Clashing*) **Rocks** (near Scylla and Charybdis) Od.; (ref. to the Κυάνεαι *Dark Rocks* or to the *Symplegades*) Hdt. AR.; (ref. to the Aeolian islands) AR.; (sg., ref. to one of these islands) AR.

πλαγκτοσύνη ης *f.* **wandering, roaming** Od.

πλαγκτύς ύος *f.* **wandering, roaming** Call.

πλαδαρός ή όν *Ion.adj.* (of the heads of emerging earth-born men) perh. **soft, weak** AR.

πλαδάω *contr.vb.* | fem.ptcpl. (w.diect.) πλαδόωσα | (of soil) **be moist** AR.

πλαδδιάω *Lacon.contr.vb.* [perh.reltd. πλάζω] | inf. πλαδδιῆν, imperatv. πλαδδίη | **be crazy, talk nonsense** Ar.

πλάζω *vb.* [reltd. πλήσσω] | ep.impf. πλάζον | ep.aor. πλάγξα ‖ MID.PASS.: ep.impf. πλαζόμην | fut. πλάγξομαι | aor.mid.inf. πλάγξασθαι (AR.) | aor.pass. ἐπλάγχθην, ep. πλάγχθην ‖ also pres.mid.pass. πλάττομαι (Parm.), but prob. to be corrected to πλάζομαι | see also παλιμπλάζομαι |
1 (of a wave) **strike, beat upon** —*someone's shoulders* Il. ‖ PASS. (of a shipwrecked sailor) **be beaten or driven** —W.DAT. *by waves* Od. Hippon.
2 (of a god) **drive** (W.ACC. someone) **off course** —W.PREP.PHR. *fr. a place* Od.; (of a ridge) **turn back, divert** —*a stream* Il. ‖ PASS. (of persons) be driven off course Pi. Hdt. E.; be driven away, be forced to flee (a place) Hom.; stray —W.PREP.PHR. *fr. one's ship* Od. —W.GEN. *fr. a path* E.; (of a missile) be deflected, glance —W.PREP.PHR. *off a helmet* Il.; (of things) be separated (fr. each other) Parm.
3 ‖ MID.PASS. (wkr.sens.) travel without fixed direction; (of persons, animals, winds, sounds, an island) **wander, roam** Hom. hHom. Tyrt. Parm. Emp. S. +; (of women) —W.ACC. *over mountains* Call.
4 divert (persons, fr. their goal); **foil, baffle, thwart** —*someone* Il. ‖ PASS. be thwarted Plu.
5 drive (persons, out of their minds); (of a goddess) **daze, befuddle** —*drinkers* Od. ‖ PASS. (of drinkers) become befuddled Pi.*fr.*; (of a person) be deranged —W.DAT. *by an attack of madness* E.

πλαθανίτᾱς ᾱ *dial.masc.adj.* [πλάθανον] (of a cake) **kneaded on a board** Philox.Leuc.

πλάθανον ου (dial. ω) *n.* [πλάσσω] **kneading-board** (for making bread, cakes, or sim.) Theoc.

πλάθη (poet.3sg.aor.pass.): see πελάζω

πλάθω *vb.* [reltd. πελάζω] (of persons, death) **come close, approach** E.; (of persons) —W.ACC. *a place* E. ‖ MID. (of a person's fame) **reach** —W.DAT. *a place* Plu.(quot.epigr.)

πλαίσιον ου *n.* **1** rectangular wooden frame or box (used for making bricks), **brick-frame** Ar.
2 framework, frame (enclosing the wooden tablets on which Solon's laws were inscribed) Plu.; (of a siege-engine, a support for a dais) Plu.
3 hollow rectangular formation of troops, **square** Th. X. Plu.
4 rectangular formation, **rectangle** (of lamps) Plu.

πλακερός ά όν *adj.* [πλάξ] (of a belt) **broad** Theoc.(v.l. πλοκερός *woven, plaited*)

πλακοῦς οῦντος *m.* flat (i.e. unleavened) cake, **cake** Ar. Men.

πλακτός *adj.*: see πλαγκτός

πλᾶκτρον *dial.n.*: see πλῆκτρον

πλανάτᾱς *dial.m.*: see πλανήτης

πλανάω *contr.vb.* | aor. ἐπλάνησα, dial.3sg.subj. πλανάσῃ ‖ MID.PASS.: ep.3pl. (w.diect.) πλανόωνται | fut. πλανήσομαι | aor. ἐπλανήθην, dial.ptcpl. πλανᾱθείς | pf. πεπλάνημαι ‖ neut.impers.vbl.adj. πλανητέον |
1 cause (someone) to wander; (of a gadfly) **drive** (W.ACC. someone) **hither and thither** A.; (of an enemy) **lead** or **entice** (W.ACC. one's opponents) **this way and that** Hdt.
2 ‖ MID.PASS. travel without fixed course or intention; (of persons) **wander, roam** Archil. Semon. Sol. Hdt. Trag. Th. + —W.ACC. *over a country* E. Plu.; (of horses, animals) Hdt. X. Theoc.; (of heavenly bodies, in a popular belief) Pl.; (of racehorses) leave a fixed course, **veer off course** Il.; (fig., of a person) **stray** —W.GEN. *fr. what is appropriate* Pi.; (of a speaker) **digress** —W.ADV. or PREP.PHR. *fr. a subject* Isoc. Pl.
3 ‖ MID.PASS. (of misery) **roam around** A.; (of reports by travellers, a rumour) **go around** S. Aeschin.; (of dreams) **wander about** (among humans) Hdt.
4 lead (someone) astray (by speech or sim.); (of a speaker) **distract** (someone) **from the main point** D.; (of a person's judgement) **mislead, deceive** (him) S.; (of persons, Eros, circumstances) —*someone* Pl. Arist. Men. Mosch. NT. ‖ MID.PASS. (of persons) **go astray, be misled** Parm. NT. —W.DAT. *by a word, a name* Plb. —W.DAT. *in one's judgement* Isoc.; (of a person's judgement) be astray Isoc.
5 ‖ MID.PASS. be unsettled in one's purpose; **behave unpredictably** Hdt.; **prevaricate, be shifty** (in speech) Hdt.; **keep changing one's mind** —W.INDIR.Q. *as to what sthg. means* Hdt.
6 ‖ MID.PASS. be in a state of mental confusion, **ramble, be at a loss** A. Pl. Men. NT.

—**πεπλανημένως** *pf.mid.pass.ptcpl.adv.* **mistakenly** Isoc.

πλάνη ης *f.* **1 wandering, roaming** (by persons) A. Hdt. Pl. Arist. Plb. Plu.; (of a sickness, ref. to its periodic visitations) S.(dub.)
2 discursiveness (in philosophical inquiry) Pl.; **digression** (in speech) Pl.
3 going astray, **error, confusion** Pl. Arist. NT.

πλάνημα ατος *n.* **1 wandering** A.
2 (fig.) **restlessness, wavering** (W.GEN. of feelings) S.

πλάνης ητος *m.* **1 wanderer** S. E. Isoc. Plu.
2 ‖ ADJ. (of a style of life) **itinerant** Plu.
3 (appos.w. ἀστήρ *star*, sts. understd.) **planet** X. Arist.

πλάνησις εως *f.* **dispersal** (of ships, in bad weather) Th.

πλανήτης ου, dial. **πλανάτᾱς** ᾱ *m.* **1 wanderer** S. E.; **straggler** E.; **roamer** (W.PREP.PHR. fr. city to city, ref. to a merchant) Pl.; (over all terrains, ref. to a hare) X.
2 ‖ ADJ. (of a life) **of wandering** E.

πλανητός ἡ όν adj. 1 (of the sophists) **itinerant** Pl.
2 ‖ NEUT.PL.SB. **planets** (ref. to the sun, moon, other heavenly bodies) Pl.
3 ‖ NEUT.SG.SB. **fluctuating area** (betw. knowledge and opinion) Pl.

πλᾶν-όδιος η ον ep.Ion.adj. [app. πλανάομαι w. ᾱ metri grat.; ὁδός] (of cattle) **on a wandering route** (unless fem.sb. wandering route) hHom. [or perh. πληνόδιος off road, reltd. πλήν]

πλάνος[1] ου m. 1 **wandering, roaming** S. E. Ar. Isoc. Pl. +; **straggling** (by troops) Plu.
2 **to and fro motion** (W.GEN. of a κερκίς pin-beater) E.
3 (fig.) **ranging, roving** (W.GEN. of one's anxious thoughts) S.
4 **wandering, aberration** (W.GEN. of the mind, ref. to mental disorder) E. Plu.
5 (gener.) **confusion, perplexity** Isoc. Plu.

πλάνος[2] ον adj. 1 (of fishing-bait) **leading astray, deceptive** Theoc.; (of Eros' gifts) Mosch.; (of a fisherman's prey) **elusive, slippery** Mosch.
2 (of Fortune) **fickle** Men.
3 ‖ MASC.SB. **deceiver, impostor** NT.

πλανο-στιβής ές adj. [στείβω] (of land) **trodden in one's wanderings** A.

πλανύττω Att.vb. **wander about** Ar.

πλάξ πλακός f. 1 **flat and broad area; expanse** (W.GEN. of a continent) A.; **plain** A. E.; (W.GEN. of the dead, ref. to Hades) S.
2 **expanse** (of the sea) A. Pi. Ar. Lyr.adesp.; (of the sky) E.
3 **flat hilltop, tableland, plateau** S. E.
4 **top** or **platform** (of a wall or tower) S.

πλᾶξα (dial.aor.), **πλάξιππος** dial.adj.: see πλήσσω, πλήξιππος

πλᾶσιον Aeol.adv.: see πλησίον, under πλησίος

πλάσις εως f. [πλάσσω] 1 **modelling, moulding** (of a mask, prob. in wax) Pl.; (of a person's character) Plu.; **modulation** (of an orator's voice) Plu.
2 **artificiality, fancifulness** (of a theory) Arist.

πλάσμα ατος n. 1 **object formed or moulded; artefact, figure** (W.GEN. fr. clay) Ar.; (ref. to a waxwork or sim.) Pl.
2 **figment, fiction, invention** (ref. to a narrative) Xenoph. Plu.; **fabrication** (ref. to a will) D.
3 **deceptive conduct, deception, pretence** Hyp. Plu.
4 **studied tone, modulation** (of an orator's voice) Plu.

πλασματίας ου masc.adj. (of an argument) **fanciful** Arist.; (of a writer) Plu.

πλασματώδης ες adj. (of a theory) **artificial, fanciful** Arist.; (of a narrative) **fictional** Plu.

πλάσσω, Att. **πλάττω** vb. | aor. ἔπλασα, dial. ἔπλασσα (Theoc.), ep. πλάσσα | aor.mid. ἐπλασάμην ‖ PASS.: aor. ἐπλάσθην | pf. πέπλασμαι | 1 **mould into shape** (fr. soft substances, such as earth, clay, wax); (of deities) **mould, form** —a human being (fr. earth or clay) Hes. Semon. Men. Call. —human bodies Pl. —a woman's image (fr. aither) E. —mice Call.; (of persons) —animal figurines (fr. dough) Hdt. —human figurines (fr. clay) D. —figures (fr. gold) Pl.; (of a child) —toy houses Ar.; (of a legislator) —an imaginary city and citizens (fr. wax) Pl.; (of a bird) —an egg (fr. myrrh) Hdt.; (of a person) **model, sculpt** (opp. draw) —sthg. Pl. ‖ PASS. (of wax images) **be moulded** Pl.; (of a cake, fr. dung) Ar.; (of objects) **be sculpted** (opp. be drawn) Isoc. Pl.
2 **mould back into shape, patch up, mend** —a water-jar Ar.
3 ‖ PASS. (gener., of the reeds of a panpipe) **be fashioned** —W.PREP.PHR. w. an auger Pratin.

4 (fig., of teachers or sim.) **mould, form, shape** —souls (W.DAT. w. stories, opp. bodies w. hands) Pl. —oneself, one's body Pl. —a lyre-player's hands Theoc. ‖ PASS. (of a hare's unborn young) **be moulded** —W.PREP.PHR. in the womb Hdt.
5 **create in the imagination, invent, devise** —an immortal being Pl. —a happy city, happiness, laws Pl.
6 **put into a certain shape or style; shape, configure** —one's mouth (to pronounce sthg.) Pl.; (of an orator) **style** —one's mode of delivery Plu. ‖ MID. **compose oneself** —W.ADV. inscrutably (in one's appearance) Th.
7 (fig.) **fashion for the purpose of deception;** (act. and mid.) **fabricate, invent, make up** —slanders, accusations, excuses, arguments S. Att.orats. Pl. X.; (act., of a writer) **invent** —a god Call.; **forge** —a letter Plb.; (intr.) **make things up** Hdt. ‖ MID. **falsely assume, put on, affect** —a mode of behaviour Lys. —an air of benevolence D.; (intr.) **dissemble** Arist.
8 ‖ PASS. (of a boast, story, name, argument) **be made up, be invented** A. Hdt. E. Att.orats. Pl.; (of an adoption) **be fictitious** Is.; (of a will) **be forged** Is.; (of a lawsuit) **be fabricated** D.; (of a mode of behaviour) **be assumed** or **put on** Men. | see also παίζω 5

—**πεπλασμένως** pf.pass.ptcpl.adv. 1 **pretendedly, falsely** (opp. truly) Pl. X.
2 **artificially** (opp. naturally) Arist.

πλάστης ου m. 1 **moulder, modeller, sculptor** (in clay or wax) Pl. Plu.; (app. ref. to a hairdresser) Plu.
2 **sculptor** (in stone) Plu.

πλάστιγξ ιγγος f. 1 **pan used in weighing, scale-pan** Ar. Pl.
2 (fig.) **scale, balance** (of Fortune) S.fr.(cj.) Lyr.adesp.
3 **collar, poitrel** (tied around a horse's neck and breast and attached to each end of a yoke beam) E.; prob. **collar** (of metal, for a human captive undergoing humiliation) A.

πλαστικός ή όν adj. [πλάσσω] 1 (of earth) **able to be moulded, plastic** Pl.
2 (of arts) **related to moulding or sculpting, plastic** Pl.
3 (of a person) **skilled in the plastic arts** (opp. painting) X.

πλαστός ή (dial. ᾱ) όν adj. 1 (of a woman, ref. to Pandora) **moulded** (fr. earth) Hes.; (of a likeness of a person or god) **sculpted** (opp. painted) Plu.; (of an art) **related to moulding or sculpting, plastic** Pl.
2 (fig.) **fashioned for the purpose of deception;** (of an argument, an insinuation) **made up, fabricated, false** Hdt. D.; (of religious rites) **sham, fake** E.; (of friendship) X.; (of a will, a letter) **forged** Is. Plu.; (of a son) **pretended, supposed** S.

—**πλαστῶς** adv. **feignedly** (opp. truly or naturally) Pl.

πλάτα dial.f.: see πλάτη

πλαταγέω contr.vb. **make a noise by striking; clap one's hands** Theoc.; (tr.) **loudly beat** —one's breast Bion

πλαταγή ῆς f. **rattle** (as a child's toy) Arist.; (for scaring birds) AR.

πλατάγημα ατος n. **smack** (of a leaf or sim., slapped against the arm, in a game of divination) Theoc.

πλαταγώνιον ου n. **poppy petal** (as used in a game of divination) Theoc.

Πλάταια, Boeot. **Πλάτηα**, ᾱς f. **Plataia** (city in Boeotia) Il. Hdt. Th. Corinn.

—**Πλαταιαί** ῶν f.pl. **Plataia** Hdt. Th. Att.orats. Pl. +

—**Πλαταιᾶσι(ν)** adv. **at Plataia** Th. D. Plu.

—**Πλαταιεύς** έως m. | PL.: nom. Πλαταιεῖς, Att. Πλαταιῆς, Ion. Πλαταιέες || acc. Πλαταιέας, Att. Πλαταιᾶς | gen. Πλαταιέων, Att. Πλαταιῶν | **man from Plataia, Plataian** Hdt. Lys. D. Plu. ‖ PL. **Plataians** (as a population or military force) A. Hdt. Th. Ar. +

—**Πλαταιικός** ή όν *adj.* (of territory) **Plataian** Hdt.
‖ NEUT.PL.SB. events at Plataia Hdt.

—**Πλαταιίς** ίδος *fem.adj.* (of the territory) **of Plataia** Hdt. Th. Plu. ‖ SB. territory of Plataia Hdt. Plu.

πλαταμών ῶνος *m.* [πλατύς] broad flat object or area; **slab** (of stone or rock) hHom. AR. Plb.

πλατάνιστος ου *f.* **plane tree** Il. Hdt. AR. Theoc.

πλάτανος ου *f.* **plane tree** Ar. Pl. X. Theoc. Mosch. Plu.

πλατειάσδω *dial.vb.* [πλατύς] (of a person speaking in the Doric dialect) **pronounce** (w.ACC. everything) **with broad vowels** Theoc.

πλατεῖον ου *n.* **tablet** (of wood, for writing) Plb.

πλάτη ης, dial. **πλάτᾱ** ᾱς *f.* broad flat blade of an oar; **oar-blade, oar** Trag. Ar. Plu.; (meton. for ship, fleet or voyage) S. E.

Πλάτηα *Boeot.f.*: see Πλάταια

πλᾱτίον *dial.adv.*: see πλησίον, under πλησίος

πλᾶτις ιδος *f.* [reltd. πελάτης] **consort, wife** Ar.

πλατόομαι *pass.contr.vb.* [πλάτη] (of oar-shafts) **be fitted with blades** A.

πλᾱτός ή όν *adj.* [πέλας] (of the breath of Erinyes, in neg.phr.) **approachable** A.

πλάτος εος (ους) *n.* [πλατύς] **breadth, width** (of an object or area) Ar. Pl. X. Arist.; (math., as a dimension, opp. length, depth) Pl. Arist. ‖ ADVBL.ACC. in breath or width Emp. Hdt. Pl. X.

πλάττομαι (pres.mid.pass.): see πλάζω

πλάττω *Att.vb.*: see πλάσσω

πλατυγίζω *vb.* [πλατύς] strike the sea with the flat of one's oar; (fig.) **make a useless splash** (i.e. waste one's energy in ranting) Ar.

πλατύνω *vb.* **broaden, extend, enlarge** —*the front of a column of cavalry* X. —*phylacteries* (as a sign of ostentatious piety) NT. ‖ PASS. (of cakes) perh., be made broad and flat (i.e. like pancakes) Philox.Leuc.; (of a territory) be extended or enlarged X.; (of a family, by additional births) Plu.

πλατύ-ρρους ουν *adj.* [ῥόος] (of the Nile) **broad-flowing** A.

πλατύς εῖα (Ion. έα) ύ *adj.* **1** large in measurement from side to side; (of a shoulder-strap, a winnowing-fan) **broad, wide** Il.; (of the Hellespont) Il. A.; (of a region, sea, ditch, or sim.) Hdt. Pl. X. +; (of a road) Pi. E. X. Call.; (of a hearth) E.*Cyc.*; (of planks) Th.; (of a threshold) Theoc.; (of parts of animals' bodies) Hdt. X.; (of the Cyclops' nose) Theoc.; (of a boar-spear, a sword) **broad-bladed** E.*fr.* Theoc. ‖ FEM.SB. (w. ὁδός understd.) highway or street Plb. NT. Plu.
2 broad (w. further connot. of flatness); (of land) **broad and flat** Hdt. X.; (of a kind of nut) X.; (of the earth, opp. round) Pl.; (of a kneading-trough) Pl.; (of the ray-fish) Pl. ‖ FEM.SB. (w. χείρ understd.) flat of the hand Ar. ‖ NEUT.SB. broad and level ground, plain X.
3 (of persons) broad in stature (w.connot. of strength or sturdiness), **broad, burly** S. Theoc.; (of a shoulder, back, fist) **mighty, sturdy** AR. Theoc.; (of an ox's neck) AR. Theoc.
4 extending over a large area; (of herds of goats) **wide-ranging** Hom. Hes.; (of an attack) **on a broad front** E.
5 (fig.) having a wide scope; (of an oath) **comprehensive, binding** Emp.; (of mockery) **flat, gross, downright** Ar.
6 (of water fr. a well) app. **brackish** Hdt.

—**πλατύ** *neut.adv.* **profusely** —*ref. to spitting at someone* Ar.

πλατύτης ητος *f.* broadness of body, **bulk** (of a boar) X.

Πλάτων ωνος *m.* **Plato** (Athenian philosopher, c.429–347 BC) Pl. +

—**Πλατωνικός** ή όν *adj.* **by Plato, Platonic** Plu.

πλέᾱ (fem.sg. and neut.pl.adj.): see πλέως

πλέγμα ατος *n.* [πλέκω] **1** plaited work, **wickerwork** (of a cradle) E.; (fig.) **network** (of ducts or airways in the body, compared to a weel, i.e. wicker trap for catching fish) Pl.
2 woven work, **web** Pl.; **mesh, net** (for catching animals) X.
3 plaiting (of a wicker cage, by a child) Theoc.; (fig.) **interweaving** (by a statesman, of different types of character in the state) Pl.; **combination** (of nouns w. verbs) Pl.

πλέες, πλέας (ep.nom. and acc.pl.): see πλείων

πλεθριαῖος ᾱ ον *adj.* [πλέθρον] (of a river, a bridge) measuring a plethron, **one hundred feet** (in breadth) Pl. X.; (of a date-palm, in height) X.

πλεθρίζω *vb.* (fig.) perh., extend to the length of a plethron, **exaggerate** —*a verbal account of sthg.* Thphr.

πλέθρον, ep. **πέλεθρον**, ου *n.* **1 plethron** (measure of great but unknown distance) Hom.; (specif.) **one hundred feet** Hdt. E. Th. Pl. X. Plb.
2 (as a square measure of land) **ten thousand square feet** (approx. a quarter of an acre) Att.orats. Pl. Plu.; (app. equiv. to Lat. *iugerum*, approx. two thirds of an acre) Plu.

Πλειάδες (Ion. **Πληιάδες**), also **Πελειάδες** (dial. **Πελῃάδες**), ων *f.pl.* [pop.etym. πελειάς] **Pleiades** (seven daughters of Atlas, transformed into a cluster of stars in the constellation Taurus, sts. envisaged as doves fleeing before the hunter Orion; the times of their rising and setting were noted as markers of the seasons) Hom. Hes. Lyr. A. E. D. +

—**Πλειάς** άδος *f.* (collectv.sg.) **Pleiad** E. Arist. Theoc.*epigr.* Plb.

πλεῖν[1] *Att.compar.adv.*: see under πλείων

πλεῖν[2] (Att.inf.): see πλέω[1]

πλεῖος *ep.adj.*, **πλειότερος** *ep.compar.adj.*: see πλέως

πλειστάκις *superl.adv.* [πλεῖστος] the greatest number of times, **most often, very often** Isoc. Pl. X. Arist. Thphr.; (phr.) ὡς (or ὅτι) πλειστάκις *as often as possible* Antipho Pl. X.

πλεῖστ-αρχος ον *adj.* [ἄρχω] (of the privilege) **of ruling over the greatest number** (w.GEN. of people) B.

πλειστ-ήρης ες *adj.* [ἀραρίσκω] (of a period of time) greatest, **longest imaginable** A.

πλειστηρίζομαι *mid.vb.* **count** (w.ACC. someone) **as most important** —w.PREDIC.SB. *as an inducement* (to sthg.) A.

πλειστό-μβροτος ον *dial.adj.* [βροτός] (of a festival) **crowded with people** Pi.

πλεῖστος η (dial. ᾱ) ον *superl.adj.* [πολύς] **1** (ref. to amount, degree or intensity; of material or abstr. things, such as dust, wealth, gold, trouble, pleasure, punishment) **most** or **very much, greatest** or **very great** Hom. +; (of the practice of philosophy) **strongest** (in a particular place) Pl.; (of a person, their judgement) **most strongly inclined** (in a certain direction) Hdt.
2 (ref. to size; of a crowd, race, army, or sim.) **largest** or **very large** Hom. + ‖ PL. (ref. to number; of persons, things) most or very many Hom. +; (w.art.) the largest number Hdt. +
3 ‖ SB. (in same gender as GEN.) greatest part (w.GEN. of sthg.) Th. ‖ NEUT.SB. greatest part (of sthg.) Hdt. +; πλεῖστον ἔχειν *have the greatest advantage* Th.
4 (prep.phrs.) εἰς πλεῖστον *to the highest degree, most* S.; ἐπὶ πλεῖστον *to the highest degree, to the greatest extent* (sts. w.GEN. *of sthg.*) Hdt. +; ὡς ἐπὶ (τὸ) πλεῖστον *for the most part* Th. Pl.; κατὰ τὸ πλεῖστον *for the most part* Plb.
5 (ref. to distance) διὰ πλείστου *furthest off* Th.
6 (ref. to value or worth) πλείστου ἄξιος (or sim.) *most highly valued* Hdt. +; περὶ πλείστου ποιεῖσθαι (or sim.) *regard most highly* Hdt. +

πλείω

7 (of time) **longest** or **very long** Hdt. +; (prep.phrs.) διὰ πλείστου *for the longest time* Th.; ἐπὶ πλεῖστον *for a very long time* Th. ‖ ADVBL.ACC. (w.art.) **at most** Ar.

—**πλεῖστον** *neut.sg.superl.adv.* **1 to the greatest extent** or **in the highest degree**, **most** or **very much** Il. +; (intensv., w.superl.adj.) S. E.

2 (ref. to distance) **furthest off** Th. Pl. X.

—**πλεῖστα** *neut.pl.superl.adv.* **1 to the greatest extent** or **in the highest degree**, **most** or **very much** S. E.

2 **most often, very many times** Pi. S. Th.

3 **for the most part** A.; (w.art.) τὰ πλεῖστα *for the most part* Pl.; **for the greatest part** (W.GEN. of one's life) S.

πλείω *ep.vb.*: see πλέω¹

πλειών ῶνος *m.* [perh.reltd. πλέως] **1** perh. **seed** (which fills the earth or multiplies) Hes. [interpr. by later writers as *full year*]

2 year Call.

πλείων πλεῖον, also **πλέων** πλέον *compar.adj.* [πολύς] | acc.masc.fem. πλείονα, πλέονα, also πλείω, πλέω, Ion. πλεῦνα | Ion.neut. πλεῦν, Att. πλεῖν (as adv.) | gen. πλείονος, πλέονος, Ion. πλεῦνος ‖ PL.: nom.masc.fem. πλείονες, πλέονες, also πλείους, πλέους, ep. πλέες, Ion. πλεῦνες | acc.masc.fem. πλείονας, πλέονας, also πλείους, πλέους, ep. πλέας, Ion. πλεῦνας | neut.nom.acc. πλείονα, πλέονα, also πλείω, πλέω |

1 (ref. to amount, degree or intensity; of material or abstr. things, such as wine, wealth, good fortune, time, trouble) **more, greater, longer, further** Hom. + ‖ NEUT.SG.SB. (w. or without art.) **greater part, more** (of sthg.) Il. +

2 ‖ PL. (ref. to number; of persons or things) **more** Hom. + ‖ MASC.SB. (w.art.) **the larger number, the majority** Hom. +; (ref. to the common people, opp. their leaders) Hdt. Th.; (euphem., ref. to the dead) Ar. Plb.

3 (neut.sg., in phrs.) πλέον ἔχειν (or φέρεσθαι) **have an advantage** (W.GEN. *over someone*) Hdt. +; οὐδὲν πλέον ποιεῖν (or sim.) *achieve nothing special, do no good* E. And. Pl.; (w. ἐς πλέον) S.; οὐδὲν πλέον (ἐστί or sim.) *there is no advantage or benefit* S. Att.orats. Pl.; τί πλέον (ἐστί or sim.) *what benefit is there?* E. Antipho Ar.

4 (prep.phrs.) ἐπὶ πλέον *to a greater extent, more, further* Hdt. Th. Pl. +; (also) ἐς πλέον S.; ἐκ πλέονος *for a long time* Th.; *a long time earlier* Th.; *from a greater distance* Th.

—**πλεῖον, πλέον**, also (in sense 2) Att. **πλεῖν** *neut.sg.compar.adv.* **1 to a greater extent, more, rather** (oft. w. ἤ *than* or COMPAR.GEN.) hHom. +; (also) τὸ πλέον Th.

2 (in counting) **more** (w. ἤ *than* + numeral or sim.) Ar. Att.orats. X.; (without ἤ) Ar.; (W.COMPAR.GEN.) Semon. X.

3 (w.art.) τὸ πλέον **for the greater part** Hdt. Th.; **to a greater extent, more particularly** Th.; **what is more, furthermore** E.

—**πλείω** *neut.pl.compar.adv.* **to a greater extent, more** Th. Pl. D.; (w.art.) τὰ πλείω *for the greater part* A. Th.

—**πλεόνως** *compar.adv.* **excessively** —*ref. to liking wine, being drunk* Hdt.

πλέκος ους *n.* [πλέκω] **wicker basket** or **pouch** Ar.

πλεκτανάομαι *pass.contr.vb.* [πλεκτάνη] (of Erinyes) **be wreathed** —W.DAT. *w. serpents* A.

πλεκτάνη ης *f.* [πλεκτή] **1** ‖ PL. **coils** (of snakes) A.

2 **coil, wreath** (of incense-smoke) Ar.

πλεκτή ῆς *f.* [πλεκτός] **1 twisted** or **twined cords, rope** E.

2 **mesh, net** (for catching animals) Pl.

3 ‖ PL. **coils** (of a viper, fig.ref. to Clytemnestra) A.

πλεκτικός ή όν *adj.* (of the art) **of plaiting** Pl.; **of wickerwork** Pl.; (of the art of weaving) **concerned with intertwining** (W.GEN. of warp and weft) Pl.

πλεκτός ή (dial. ά) όν, Aeol. **πλέκτος** ᾱ ον *adj.* [πλέκω] **1 made by plaiting** or **twining**; (of a woman's headband) **plaited** Il.

2 (of a garland) **woven** Xenoph. Lyr. E.

3 (of a basket, a cradle) **of wicker** Hom. E.; (of chariots, ref. to their superstructure) Hes.; (of a helmet) **woven** or **plaited** (perh. of wickerwork, or ref. to a decorative pattern) Hdt.; (of a caravan, a hut) **wattled** A. Theoc.

4 (of a rope, noose, thong) **plaited, twisted, twined** Od. S. E.; (of items of a ship's gear) **corded** (opp. wooden, ref. to rigging, perh. also to sails) X.

5 (of material) **used for plaiting** or **twining**; (of flowers, leaves) **plaited, twined, woven** (into a garland) A. E.

6 (of serpents' coils) **twisting** S.*fr.*

πλέκω *vb.* | fut. πλέξω | aor. ἔπλεξα ‖ PASS.: aor. ἐπλέχθην | pf. πέπλεγμαι | **1 intertwine** (strands of pliable material); **plait, braid** —*one's hair* Il. AR.(mid.); **weave** —*rushes* Call.

2 ‖ PASS. (of a person) **be twined** —W.DAT. *around a statue* (i.e. embrace it) A.

3 **form by plaiting** or **twining**; **plait, twine, weave** —*a garland* Pi. Ar. Theoc. NT. Plu. —*a sling* X. —*a cage for a cicada* (fr. rushes and asphodel), *a basket* Theoc. —*a belt* Pl.; (of a god) —*an altar* (fr. horns) Call. ‖ MID. **make for oneself** (by plaiting or sim.) —*a rope* Od. —*hunting nets* Ar.; **have** (W.ACC. a rope) **made** Hdt. ‖ PASS. (of garlands, fabric) **be woven** Ar. Pl. ‖ PF.PASS.PTCPL.ADJ. (of ropes) **plaited** (W.PREP.PHR. fr. cords) Hdt.; (of a noose, a snare) X.; (of helmets) **woven** or **plaited** (perh. of wickerwork, or ref. to a decorative pattern) Hdt.

4 (fig., of a poet) **weave** —*words, a song* Pi.; **interweave** —*a theme* (W.DAT. *in one's song*) Scol.

5 (pejor., of persons) **devise, contrive** —*trickery, plots* A. E. Ar. Pl. —W.COGN.ACC. *wiles* E.; (of a speaker) **weave** —*words* (i.e. make up intricate or deceptive arguments) E. Pl. —*words of encouragement* (to troops) Plu.

6 ‖ PASS. (of things, concepts) **be combined** or **compounded** (fr. other things) Pl.; **be intricate** or **complex** Pl.

7 **create a complex plot** (for a tragedy) Arist.

‖ PF.PASS.PTCPL.ADJ. (of a type of tragedy, a plot or narrative) **complex** Arist.

πλέξις εως *f.* **art of weaving** Pl.

πλέον¹ *neut.compar.adj.* and *adv.*: see πλείων

πλέον² (ep.impf.): see πλέω¹

πλεονάζω *vb.* [πλέον¹] **1 do more** (than is sufficient or appropriate), **overreach oneself** Th. Isoc. D.; **go on too long** (in praising someone) Isoc. Plu.

2 ‖ PASS. (of assertions) **be exaggerated** Th.

3 (of things) **be in surplus** Arist.; (of an amount of sthg.) **be too much** Arist.; (of criticism, honours, fear, or sim.) **be excessive** Plb. Plu.

4 (of persons) **have a surplus** —W.GEN. *of sthg.* Arist.

5 **be more** (in number, frequency, amount); (of troops, ships) **be more numerous** (than a given number) Plb.; (of slanders, the arrival of embassies) **become more frequent** (than before) Plb.; (of a definition) **be fuller** (than another) Arist.; (of a cause of motion) **be multiple** (opp. single) Arist.

πλεονάκις *compar.adv.* **1 more frequently, more often** Lys. Isoc. Pl. X. +

2 (not contrastv.) **several times, frequently** Arist. Plb.

3 **by a larger number** —*ref. to multiplying a smaller number* Pl.

πλεονασμός οῦ *m.* [πλεονάζω] **repeated** or **excessive treatment** (of a topic, by a writer) Plb.

πλεοναχῇ *adv.* [πλείων] **in many ways, from many points of view** Pl.

πλεοναχῶς adv. in various ways or senses Arist.
πλεονεκτέω contr.vb. [πλεονέκτης] **1** have or claim more than one's due, **be greedy, be grasping** Hdt.
2 (sts. pejor.) have or **claim a larger share** Pl. X. Arist. —W.GEN. *of sthg.* Th. Pl. X. Arist.
3 (sts. pejor.) have or gain an **advantage** (in money, strength, or sim.) Th. Att.orats. Pl. X. + —W.GEN. *over someone* Att.orats. Pl. X. Men. —W.ACC. *over someone* Plu. —W. παρά + GEN. *fr. someone* Arist.; **get the better of** —W.GEN. *the laws* Pl.; **take advantage of** —W.GEN. *someone's simplicity* D. || PASS. be taken advantage of Th. X.; be defrauded —W.DAT. *by a certain sum* D.
πλεονέκτημα ατος *n.* (sts. pejor.) **advantage, gain** Pl. X. D. Arist. Plb. Plu.
πλεον-έκτης ου *masc.adj.* [πλέον¹, ἔχω] | superl. πλεονεκτίστατος (X.) | **1** having or claiming more than one's due; (of persons) **greedy, grasping, rapacious** Th. Att.orats. X. Arist. Plb. Plu.; (of an argument) **selfish, self-seeking** Hdt.
2 (of a ruler) **getting the better** (W.GEN. of his enemies) X.
πλεονεκτικός ή όν *adj.* **1** (of persons) **greedy, grasping, self-seeking** Isoc. Arist. Plb.; (of vice) D.; (of behaviour, a lifestyle) **selfish** D. Plb.
2 (of reconciliations) **advantageous** Arist.
—πλεονεκτικῶς adv. **selfishly** Pl. D.
πλεονεξίᾱ ᾶς, Ion. **πλεονεξίη** ης *f.* **1 greed, selfishness, self-interest** Hdt. E. Th. Att.orats. Pl. +
2 (sg. and pl., sts. pejor.) **advantage, gain** Isoc. X. D. Arist. +
3 larger share (W.GEN. of sthg.) Arist.
4 excess (opp. deficiency, both seen as undesirable) Pl.
πλεόνως compar.adv.: see under πλείων
πλέος Ion.adj.: see πλέως
πλεύμων (also **πνεύμων**) ονος *m.* | variant form app. fr. πνέω by pop.etym. | **1** (sg.) **lungs** Il. S. Ar. Pl. Theoc.; (pl.) Alc. Archil. Trag. Ar.
2 sea-lungs, jellyfish Pl.
πλεῦν (Ion.neut.sg.), **πλεῦνος** (gen.sg.), **πλεῦνες** (masc.fem.nom.pl.): see πλείων
πλευρά ᾶς, Ion. **πλευρή** ῆς *f.* **1 rib** (of an ox) Hdt.
2 || PL. **ribs, sides** or **side** (of a person or animal) Hom. +; (sg.) S. E. Ar.
3 side (of a ship) Thgn.; (of a mountain) Simon.; (of a jar) Ar.; (of a square of soldiers) X. Plb. Plu.
4 (geom.) **side** (of a shape) Pl. Arist.
πλευρῖτις ιδος *fem.adj.* **1** (of a sickness) affecting the sides (i.e. the chest, in breathing), **pleuritic** Plu.
2 || SB. **pleurisy** Ar. Arist. Men. Plb.
πλευρόθεν adv.: see under πλευρόν
πλευροκοπέω contr.vb. [κόπτω] (of a frenzied person) **hew the sides** (of cattle) S.
πλευρόν οῦ *n.* **1 side** (of a person) S. Plu. || PL. **side** or **sides** (of a person or animal) Il. Hdt. Trag. Hellenist.poet.
2 side, flank (of an army) X.; (of a naval camp) S.
—πλευρόθεν adv. **by the side** (of a person) S.
πλευρώματα των *n.pl.* **sides** (of a person, an urn) A.
πλευστικός ή όν *adj.* [πλέω¹] (of a breeze) **favourable for sailing, fair** Theoc.
πλέω¹ contr.vb. —also **πλείω** ep.vb. —**πλώω** Ion.vb. | Att.inf. πλεῖν | Att.imperatv. πλεῖ | impf. ἔπλεον, ep. πλέον, Ion. πλῶον | fut. πλεύσομαι, also πλευσοῦμαι, later πλεύσω (Plb.) | aor. ἔπλευσα, Ion. ἔπλωσα | pf. πέπλευκα, Ion. πέπλωκα || pf.pass. πέπλευσμαι || neut.sg.impers.vbl.adj. πλευστέον, also pl. πλευστέα || Only εε and εει contract. |
1 (of persons or ships) **travel by** or **on the sea, sail** (oft. W.PREP.PHR. to or fr. a place) Hom. +; **sail on** or **over**
—W.COGN.ACC. *a sea or sim.* Od. hHom. Hdt. Att.orats.; **make, undertake** —W.INTERN.ACC. *a voyage* S.; (of goods) **go by sea** Th. D. || PF.PASS. (of a voyage) **be completed** D. || NEUT.PF.PASS.PTCPL.SB. **amount of water covered in sailing** X.
2 (of armour, corpses, timbers) **float freely** Hom.; (of an island) Hdt.
3 (fig., of a city envisaged as a ship) **sail** —W.PREDIC.ADJ. *upright* S. D.; (of circumstances) —W.PREP.PHR. *on an even keel* Pl. | for provb. ἐπὶ ῥιπὸς πλεῖν sail on wicker see ῥίψ
πλέω² (masc.fem.acc.sg., neut.nom.acc.pl.): see πλείων
πλέων¹ compar.adj.: see πλείων
πλέων² (neut.adj.): see πλέως
πλέως πλέα πλέων Att.adj. | pl. πλέῳ, fem. πλέᾳ, neut. πλέᾱ | —**πλέος** πλέη πλέον Ion.adj. —**πλεῖος** πλείη πλεῖον ep.adj. | compar. πλειότερος | —**πλῆος** πλῆα πλῆον Aeol.adj. [πίμπλημι]
1 (of a cup or bowl) filled to capacity, **full** Il. Alc. Anacr. E. AR.
2 (of buildings, places, vessels, or sim.) **fully** or **extensively occupied, full** (usu. W.GEN. of persons or things) Hom. Hes. Alcm. Sapph. Hdt. S. +
3 (of persons) **full, sated** (w. food and drink) Ar.; (W.GEN. w. wine) E.*Cyc.* || COMPAR. (of a person's hand) **fuller** (fr. having received more gifts) Od.
4 having an abundance (of non-material things); (of persons) **full** (W.GEN. of fear, courage, impudence, forgetfulness, or sim.) Archil. Hdt. Trag. Ar. Pl.
5 (of words, prophecies, circumstances) **full** (W.GEN. of folly, lies, surprise, or sim.) Trag. Ar.
6 (of things) filled (w. sthg. unwelcome); (of infected rags) **full** (W.GEN. of disease) S.; (of a monster's teeth, W.GEN. of death) Od.; (of a hand) **soiled, contaminated** (w. ἀπό + GEN. by sthg.) X.
7 (of a year) **full, complete** Hes.; (of a day) **at its fullest** (ref. to midday) Hes.
πληγείς (aor.2 pass.ptcpl.), **πλήγη** (ep.3sg.aor.2 pass.): see πλήσσω
πληγή ῆς, dial. **πλᾱγά** ᾶς *f.* [πλήσσω] | The noun is freq. used as intern.acc. (w.vb. *strike* or sim.). It is sts. understd. w.fem.adj., as τρίτην ἐπενδίδωμι I deliver a third blow (A.), τυπτόμενος πολλάς being struck many blows (Ar.). |
1 blow, stroke (of a fist, stick, missile) Hom. Pi. Ar. Att.orats. +; (of a sword or other sharp weapon) Pi. Trag. Ar. Pl. X.; (of a warship's ram) Tim.; (of a shipwright's iron tools) Pi.; (of a weaver's batten, used for striking the weft into place) A.
2 stroke, lash (of a whip, in controlling animals) Hom. Pl.; (in flogging persons) Hom. Hdt. Th. Ar. Att.orats. +; (for a spinning top) Call.*epigr.*
3 blow (of a mourner's hand, to the breast or head) Trag.; **beat** (of a dancer's foot) E.
4 coming to blows, use of blows (ref. to a fight w. fists or clubs) Hdt. Antipho
5 stroke (of lightning) Il. Hes. E.; **buffeting** (of waves) A.; **lashing** (of wind) S.
6 impact, impression (transmitted through the ears, ref. to sound) Pl.
7 (fig.) **blow, stroke** (of calamity) A. S. Arist. Plb.; (fr. a god, esp. Zeus) Il. Trag.
πληγήσομαι (fut.pass.): see πλήσσω
πλῆγμα ατος *n.* **blow** (of a fist) S. E.; (of a mourner's hand, to the head) E.; **stroke** (of a sword, a pickaxe) S.
πλῆθος εος (ους) *n.* [πίμπλημι] **1 great number, multitude, mass** (of persons or things) Tyrt. Thgn. Pi. Hdt. Trag. Th. +

πληθύνομαι

2 (w.art.) **greater part, majority** (of an army, a populace, a group) Hdt. Th. X.; **largest part** (of the soul, ref. to sensations and emotions opp. reason) Pl.
3 (w.art.) common people, **people, populace** Hdt. S. E. Th. Ar. Att.orats. +; (ref. to the popular assembly) Th. Att.orats. +; (equiv. to Lat. *plebs*) Plb. ‖ PL. masses, populace Pl. D.
4 numerical strength, **superior numbers** (of persons) Il.
5 (gener.) **large amount** (of money, food, trouble, or sim.) Trag. Th. Pl. +; **great volume** (of water) Hdt. Plb.; (oxymor., W.ADJ. *small*) **mass, amount** (of dust) E.
6 great length (W.GEN. of time) Th. Isoc. Pl.; **great number** (of years) Ar.; **lapse** (of many months) S.
7 (in calculations, ref. to a specific total) **quantity, number** (of people or things) A. Hdt. E. Th. Ar. Pl. + ‖ ACC.ADV. (sts. w.art.) in number A. Hdt. +
8 (in measurement, esp. at large scale) **size, magnitude, extent** (of an area of land, of a river) Hdt.
9 (prep.phrs.) ἐς πλῆθος *in great numbers* Th.; ὡς ἐπὶ τὸ πλῆθος *for the most part* Pl.

πληθύνομαι *pass.vb.* **1** (fig., of a person) app. **have full support** —W.INF. *for doing sthg.* A.; (of voters' hands) app. **be in the majority** A.
2 (of a population, a group) **increase in number** NT.(also act.); (of teaching, godlessness) **be increased** NT.

πληθύς ύος *f.* | acc. πληθύν | dat. πληθυῖ | **1 great number, multitude, body** (of a populace) Il.
2 general mass, throng (of troops, sts. opp. their leaders) Hom. AR.; **crowd** (of people) AR.
3 numerical strength, **superior numbers** (of troops) Hom. Tyrt.
4 greater part, majority (of people) Plb.; **larger part, bulk** (W.GEN. of an army) Plu.
5 number (of troops, ref. to a specific total) Plb.

πληθύω *vb.* | impf. ἐπλήθυον | aor. ἐπλήθυσα | **1** be or become great in number or amount; (of reports) **be numerous** A.; (of Erinyes) **come in swarms** A. [or perh. *increase in number*]
2 have a great number or amount (of sthg.); (of a city, a country) **be full** (usu. W.GEN. of people) Arist. Plb. Plu.; (of places) —W.GEN. *of corpses* A. E.; (of a person) **abound, be rich** —W.DAT. *in children* S.; (of plains) —*in cities* Plb.; (of a diet) —W.GEN. *in milk* Arist.
3 (as indicating time) ἀγορῆς πληθυούσης *when the agora is full* (i.e. at mid-morning) Hdt.
4 be or become great in size or extent; (of a river) **be swollen, be in flood** Hdt.(also pass.); (of a story) **be most widespread, prevail** S.
5 be greater in number or extent; (of a population, of indiscipline and sicknesses) **increase** Pl.; (of time) **advance** S.; (of blood) **be replenished** (as a natural process) Pl.; (of human sperm) **increase, grow** (during youth) Arist.

πλήθω *vb.* [reltd. πίμπλημι] | pf. πέπληθα | 3sg.plpf. ἐπεπλήθει ‖ ep.3pl.impf.pass. πλήθοντο | **1** (of receptacles or sim.) be or become full to capacity; (of jars) **be full** AR.; (of barns) —W.GEN. *of foodstuffs* Hes.; (of tables, sts. W.GEN. of food) Od.; (of a person) —W.GEN. + ACC. *of meat, in one's hands* (i.e. have one's hands full of meat) A. ‖ PASS. (of irrigation channels) be filled up —W.DAT. *w. streams of water* AR.
2 (of spaces) be occupied fully or extensively (by persons or things); (of rivers, sea, shores) **be filled** —W.GEN. *w. corpses, wreckage* Il. A. —*w. monsters* A.(dub.); (of a place) —*w. noise* AR. ‖ STATV.PF. (of wrestling floors) be covered —W.DAT. *w. blood* Call. ‖ PASS. (of islands) be occupied —W.DAT. *by people* AR.
3 (as indicating time) πληθούσης (τῆς) ἀγορᾶς, ἐν (τῇ) ἀγορᾷ πληθούσῃ *when the agora is full* (i.e. at mid-morning) Th. Pl. X. Thphr.
4 (of a crowd) become numerous, **gather, throng** Pi.
5 (of a river) **be full, be swollen** Hom. Hes. Call. AR. —W.DAT. *fr. rain* Hes.
6 (of the moon) **be full** Il. Sapph.; (of the moon's orbit) **be complete** hHom.
7 have in abundance; (of fields) **be full** (w. crops) Hes.; (of a stream) **abound, be rich** —W.DAT. *in reeds* Call.; (fig., of marriages) **be full** —W.GEN. *of pain* Theoc. ‖ STATV.PF. (of a spring) be brimful —W.DAT. *of water* Theoc.

πληθώρη ης *Ion.f.* **1** time of fullness (W.GEN. of the market-place, i.e. mid-morning) Hdt.
2 satiety, enough (W.GEN. of success) Hdt.

Πληιάδες *Ion.f.pl.*: see Πλειάδες

πλήκτης ου *masc.adj.* [πλήσσω] **1** (of a kind of person) liable to come to blows, **aggressive, violent** Arist.
2 (of soldiers) capable of delivering a powerful blow, **hard-hitting** Plu.; (of a commander) **strong-armed** Plu.

πληκτίζομαι *mid.vb.* **1 come to blows** —W.DAT. *w. someone* Il.
2 (w. sexual connot.) **exchange blows** —W.PREP.PHR. *w. a woman's buttocks* Ar.

πληκτικός ή όν *adj.* (of the catching of fish) by striking, **by spearing** Pl. ‖ FEM.SB. art of spearing Pl.

πλῆκτρον, dial. **πλάκτρον**, ου *n.* **1** instrument for striking (the strings of a lyre), **plectrum** hHom. Pi. E. Pl. Arist. Plu.
2 bolt, fork (W.GEN. of lightning) E.; **whip** or **goad** (for a horse) E.
3 spur (of a fighting-cock) Ar.
4 paddle (of a boat) Hdt.

πλήμη (or **πλήσμη**) ης *f.* [πίμπλημι] **flood-tide** Hes.*fr.* Plb.

πλημμέλεια ᾱς *f.* [πλημμελής] **1** (fig.) being out of tune (w. a standard of conduct), **dissonant behaviour** Pl. Plu.
2 misjudgement, mistake, error Isoc. Pl. Plu.; **transgression, vice** Pl. Plu.

πλημμελέω *contr.vb.* | aor. ἐπλημμέλησα | **1** act discordantly or inappropriately, **do wrong, offend** E. Att.orats. Pl. X. Plb. Plu.
2 ‖ PASS. (of a person, a god) be wronged Pl. X. D. ‖ NEUT.PL.PASS.PTCPL.SB. wrongs committed Isoc. Plu.

πλημμελήματα των *n.pl.* **offences, wrongs** Aeschin.

πλημ-μελής ές *adj.* [πλήν, μέλος; cf. ἐμμελής] **1** out of tune, off-key; (fig., of a person) **at fault** Pl.
2 (of actions, suffering) **inappropriate, harmful, outrageous** E. Pl. ‖ NEUT.IMPERS. (w. ἐστί or sim.) it is wrong —W.INF. *to do sthg.* Pl. Arist.

—**πλημμελῶς** *adv.* **wrongly** —*ref. to making an assertion, answering a question* Pl. Plu.; **faultily, awkwardly** —*ref. to moving* Pl.; **carelessly** —*ref. to overturning sthg.* Plu.

πλημμυρίς *f.*: see πλημυρίς

πλήμνη ης *f.* [app. πέλω] **nave, hub** (of a wheel) Il. Hes. AR.

πλήμυρα (or **πλήμμυρα**) ᾱς (ης NT.) *f.* [πλημυρίς] **overflowing** (of a river or sea), **flood** NT. Plu.

πλημυρέω *contr.vb.* (of a river) **overflow, flood** Plu.

πλημυρίς (or **πλημμυρίς**) ίδος *f.* [πλήμη] | acc. πλήμυριν (B.) | ῠ Od. B., ῡ A. E.; both AR. | **1 flood-tide** Hdt. B.*fr.* AR.; (fig.) **flood** (of tears) A. E.
2 shoreward swell (created by a boulder thrown into the sea) Od.; **swell** (created by rocks crashing together) AR.

πλημύρω *vb.* **1** (of a river) **overflow** —W.DAT. *w. gold* Call.; (hyperbol., of a penis) **spurt out a flood** Archil.

2 (of a sow's teats) **overflow, swell** (w. milk) AR.; (fig., of a boar) —W.DAT. w. *strength* B.

πλήν *prep. and conj.* [reltd. πέλας] **1** (prep.) setting aside, **with the exception of, except for** —W.GEN. *someone or sthg.* Od. +

2 (conj., linking wds. or phrs.) **except** A. + • τί οὖν μ' ἄνωγας ἄλλο πλὴν ψευδῆ λέγειν; *so what else are you ordering me to do except tell lies?* S. • παντὶ δῆλον πλὴν ἐμοί *clear to everyone except me* Pl. • (also) πλὴν ἤ Hdt. Ar. Pl. X.

3 (followed by another conj.) except in a specified case; πλὴν εἰ (ἐάν), ὅταν, ὅτι (or sim.) *except if* (*when, that, i.e. unless*) A. + [In a conditional cl., the vb. is sts. omitted, as οὐδεὶς οἶδεν ... πλὴν εἴ τις ἄρ' ὄρνις *nobody knows, except if some bird* (knows) Ar.]

4 (introducing an independent cl., which adds a qualification to a previous statement) **except that, however** Hdt. + • πέπεισμαι· πλὴν σμικρόν τί μοι ἐμποδῶν *I am convinced – only I have a slight difficulty* Pl.

5 (in breaking off and passing to a new subject) **however** Plb. Plu.; (also) πλὴν ἀλλά Plu.

πληνόδιος *adj.*: see πλᾱνόδιος

πλῆντο¹ (ep.3pl.athem.aor.mid.): see πελάζω

πλῆντο² (ep.3pl.athem.aor.mid.): see πίμπλημι

πλῆξα (ep.aor.): see πλήσσω

πλήξ-ιππος, dial. **πλάξιππος**, ον *adj.* [πλήσσω] striking a horse (w. whip or goad); (of individuals, a populace, a city, its eponymous nymph) **horse-driving** Il. Hes. Pi. B. Call.

πλῆος Aeol.adj.: see πλέως

πλήρης ες *adj.* [πίμπλημι] **1** (of receptacles or areas) full to capacity; (of a cup, bowl, basket, storeroom, or sim.) **full** (sts. W.GEN. of sthg.) Hdt. E. Ar. Philox.Leuc. Pl.; (of a person's mouth, W.GEN. of honey) Theoc.; (of a basin excavated for a lake) **filled** (w. water) Hdt.; (of an open space, w. brushwood) Th.; (of a river) full to overflowing, **swollen** Hdt. || NEUT.SB. fullness (opp. emptiness) Pl.

2 (of a person) full of food, **full, replete** X.

3 having an abundance (of people or things, usu. W.GEN.); (of a bath-house, a theatre) **full, crowded** Ar. Isoc.; (of cities) **filled** (W.DAT. w. people) E.; (of buildings, places, or sim., W.GEN. w. persons or things) Hdt. E. Ar. X.; (of altars, w. carrion) S.; (of a mist covering the eyes, w. tears) A.; (of a table) **loaded** E.; (of a person, W.GEN. w. money) Pl.

4 having an abundance (of non-material things); (of persons, a soul) **full, filled** (W.GEN. w. empty notions, modesty, arrogance, or sim.) S. E. Pl. D.; (of a building, w. destruction, someone's pain) S.; (of a city, w. commotion) D.; (of a struggle, w. lamentations) E.; (of a narrative, w. illogicality) Plb.

5 having had one's fill; (of a person's heart) **sated, satisfied** (W.GEN. w. what he desires) S.

6 (of the moon, its orb) completely illuminated, **full** Sapph. Hdt.

7 complete in number; (of a military assembly) **full, complete** E.; (of the Assembly) Ar. X.; (of the Council) And.; (of courts) Arist.; (of ships) **fully manned** Th. X. D.

8 (of a voting-token) complete, **solid** (opp. perforated) Aeschin. Arist. | see τετρυπωμένος, under τρυπάω

9 given in full measure; (of offerings, sacrifices) **full, complete** Hdt. E.; (of a favour, payment, contribution) E. X. D.

10 (of a period of time) **full, whole** Hdt.

πληροφορέομαι *pass.contr.vb.* (of things) **be fulfilled** or **accomplished** NT.

πληρόω *contr.vb.* **1** fill (a receptacle); **fill** —*a chest* (W.GEN. w. *stones*) Hdt. —*ships* (W.GEN. w. *goods*) Hdt. —*baskets* (W.GEN. w. *cheese*) Theoc. —*a bowl, drinking-troughs* (w. *wine, water*) E.; (of bees) —*hives* (w. *honey*) Theoc.; (of water) —*subterranean channels* Pl.; (gener., of Centaurs) —*their hands* (W.DAT. w. *pine trunks*) E. || PASS. (of a treasury) be filled —W.GEN. w. *gold* Pl.; (of a voting-urn, w. ballots) A.; (of a trumpet) —W.GEN. w. *breath* A.; (of horses' muzzles) —W.DAT. w. *their breath* A.

2 fully occupy (a space, area or building); **fill** —*a room* (w. *tables*) Philox.Leuc.; (of a commander) **fill up** —*a gap* (w. *troops*) Th.; (of soldiers) **man** —*parapets* A. || PASS. (of a council-chamber, tent, theatre) be filled A. E. D. —W.DAT. *by people* E.(cj.); (of the sky) —W.GEN. w. *rain* E.fr.

3 fill (w. non-material things) || PASS. (of persons) be filled —W.GEN. w. *fear, hope, knowledge, or sim.* Isoc. Pl.; (of a land) —w. *a sound* E.

4 fill to satiety; **fill, satisfy** —*a person, one's appetite* (W.GEN. w. *food*) E. —*a stomach* Arist. || PASS. (of persons) be filled or satisfied —W.GEN. w. *food and drink* Hdt.

5 sate, satisfy —*one's anger* S. E. Pl. —*one's desires or sim.* Pl. Arist. || MID. satisfy one's desires Pl. || PASS. (of persons, desires) be satisfied Pl.

6 (specif.) equip (a ship) with a full complement of crew; (of a state or sim.) **man** —*ships* Hdt. Th. Ar. Att.orats. X. Plb.; (of sailors) Hdt.; (mid., of an admiral or trierarch) X. Is. D. || PASS. (of ships) be manned or equipped Hdt. +

7 fill (a court) with a full complement of jurors; **fill up, empanel** —*a court* D. Arist. || PASS. (of a court) be filled or empanelled Att.orats. Arist. || ACT. (fig., of cupidity) **fill up** —*robber bands* (i.e. w. *recruits*) Aeschin.

8 || PASS. (of the Assembly) fill up Ar.; (of people) assemble in numbers E.

9 (gener.) make complete; **build up** —*a pyre* E.; **fit out, equip** —*horses' necks* (w. *trappings*) E.; **fill out** —*a discourse* (W.DAT. w. *certain topics*) Arist.

10 supply, make good —*a deficiency* Th. || PASS. (fig., of a beacon-signaller, envisaged as a torch-bearer in a relay race) be supplied (by the person before) A.

11 fill up a period of time; (of a woman) **complete** —*ten months* (*of pregnancy*) Hdt.; (of time) **bring to completion** —*a year* Pl. || PASS. (of a period of time) be completed Th. NT.

12 fully make up a number; (of a journey) **make up the full total of** —*one thousand five hundred stades* Hdt. || PASS. (of a sum of money) be made up to the full Hdt.

13 || PASS. (of the moon) come to fullness S.fr.

14 do (sthg.) fully; **render in full** —*repayment for nurture* (W.DAT. *to one's motherland*) A.; **pour out in full** —*a measure of wine* E.; **fulfil** —*one's destiny* Plu. || PASS. (of a prophecy) be fulfilled NT.

15 (fig., of a person) traverse fully, **cover** —*a whole city* E.fr.

16 (of a male) **impregnate** —*a female* Arist. || PASS. (of a female) be impregnated Arist.

πλήρωμα ατος *n.* **1** that which fills (a receptacle); **contents** (of mixing-bowls, baskets, or sim.) E. NT.

2 (periphr., W.GEN.) **abundance** (of a feast, i.e. a feast that fills) E.; (of cheese, i.e. cheese which fills baskets) E.Cyc.; **complement** (of mortals, as filling the earth to capacity) E.

3 (collectv.) body of men filling a ship, **crew** Th. Att.orats. Pl. X. Plb. Plu.

4 completed whole, **full complement** (of a state, ref. to the citizen body) Arist.; (ref. to the classes which constitute the state) Pl. Arist.; (gener.) **large group** (of friends) E.

5 full complement, **total** (of ships) Hdt.; (of money) Ar.

πλήρωσις

6 that which fills a gap; **patch** (W.GEN. for a garment) NT.
7 full period of time; **span** (of a person's life, ref. to eighty years) Hdt.
8 action of filling, **filling up** (of cups, ref. to a task) E.; **heaping up** (of a pyre) S.
9 filling of an auditorium; **performance, show** Thphr.
10 fullness (of God or Christ, i.e. perfection or bountifulness) NT.

πλήρωσις εως (Ion. ιος) *f*. **1** process of filling; **filling** (opp. emptying) Pl.
2 process or state of being filled; **fullness** (opp. emptiness) Pl.
3 (specif.) filling, **empanelling** (W.GEN. of courts) Pl.; **manning** (of ships) D.
4 satisfying, **satisfaction, gratification** (of a want or desire) Pl.; (of anger) Plu.; **state of satisfaction** Arist.
5 completion (of a period of time) Hdt.

πληρωτής οῦ *m*. one who makes up a sum, **contributor** (W.GEN. to a joint loan) Hyp. D.

πλῆσα (ep.aor.), **πλῆσθεν** (ep.3pl.aor.pass.), **πλησθήσομαι** (fut.pass.): see πίμπλημι

πλησιάζω vb. [πλησίος] | fut. πλησιάσω | aor. ἐπλησίασα | pf. πεπλησίακα | **1** (of persons) **be near, be present** S.
2 come near, approach (usu. W.DAT. someone, sthg., a place) Isoc. Pl. X. Arist. Plb. Plu. —W.GEN. *a place* X.
3 (of the acquisition of intelligence by youths) come close (in time), **be associated** —W.DAT. *w. the arrival of a beard* Pl.
4 (fig.) **make an approach to, embark on** —W.DAT. *education* Pl.; **aspire to, court** —W.DAT. *political office* Thphr.
5 (of persons) **associate, keep company** —W.DAT. w. *someone* S. Att.orats. Pl.
6 (specif.) **be a follower** or **pupil** (oft. W.DAT. of someone) Isoc. Plu.
7 (euphem., w. sexual connot.) **have relations, be intimate** —W.DAT. w. *someone* Att.orats. Plu. —w. πρός + ACC. Arist.; (fig.) **have intimate contact** —W.DAT. w. *reality* Pl. —w. *pleasures* Arist.
8 (tr.) **bring** (W.ACC. a horse under training) **close** —W.DAT. *to sights and sounds* X. ‖ PASS. (of a person) be brought close, be given access —W.DAT. *to someone* E.

πλησιαίτερος, πλησιαίτατος compar. and superl.adjs.: see πλησίος

πλησιασμός οῦ *m*. [πλησιάζω] **approach** (W.GEN. of sthg. frightening) Arist.

πλησίος ᾱ ον adj. [πέλας] | compar. πλησιαίτερος (X.), superl. πλησιαίτατος (X.) | **1** (of persons sitting) **close together** Hom. Ar.; (of persons or things) **nearby** Tyrt. S. E. X.; **near** (W.GEN. someone or sthg.) Od. A.; (W.DAT.) Hom. S.; (w. παρά + ACC.) Il.; (w. πρός + DAT.) E.*fr*.
2 ‖ MASC.SG.SB. person nearby, **neighbour** Hom. Thgn. Hdt. ‖ PL. neighbours A. Hdt. Ar.

—πλησίον, Aeol. **πλάσιον**, dial. **πλατίον** (Theoc.) adv. | compar. πλησιαιτέρω (Hdt.), πλησιαίτερον (X.) | superl. πλησιαίτατα (X.) |
1 nearby, near Hom. +; (as prep.) **near** —W.GEN. *someone* or *sthg*. Hom. + —W.DAT. Od. Tyrt. E. Pl. D.
2 ‖ MASC.SB. (w.art.) neighbour Ar. Att.orats. Pl. X. Arist. Men. + ‖ NEUT.PL.SB. things belonging to one's neighbour E.

πλησιό-χωρος ον adj. [χώρᾱ] (of people, cities) **situated nearby, neighbouring** Hdt. Th.; **adjacent** (W.DAT. to another people) Hdt. Th.; ‖ MASC.SB. neighbour (W.GEN. of someone) Ar.; (pl.) Hdt. Th. Pl.

πλησ-ίστιος ον adj. [πίμπλημι, ἱστίον] **1** (of a breeze) **that fills the sails** Od. E.

2 (fig., of a person, quasi-advbl. w.vb. of motion) **with wind in one's sails** Plu.

πλήσμη *f*.: see πλήμη

πλήσμιος ᾱ ον adj. [πίμπλημι] (of kinds of food) **filling, cloying** Plu. ‖ NEUT.SB. (fig.) cloying nature (of flattery) Plu.; glut, surfeit (of pleasure) Plu.

πλησμονή ῆς, dial. **πλησμονᾱ́** ᾶς *f*. **1** filling (opp. emptying) Pl.
2 satiety, surfeit (sts. W.GEN. of sthg.) A. Ar. Isoc. Pl. X. Plu.
3 (specif.) being full of food, **gorging, overeating** Pl. X. Plb. Plu.

πλήσσω vb. | aor.1 ἔπληξα, ep. πλῆξα, dial. πλᾶξα | ep.redupl.aor.2 πέπληγον, also ἐπέπληγον, inf. πεπληγέμεν | pf. πέπληγα, ptcpl. πεπληγώς (also w.pass.sens. Plu.), ep. πεπλήγων (also w.pres.sens. Call.) | later pf. πέπληχα (Men.) ‖ MID.: aor.1 ἐπληξάμην, ep.3sg. πλήξατο | ep.3sg.redupl. aor.2 πεπλήγετο, 3pl. πεπλήγοντο ‖ PASS.: fut. πληγήσομαι, also (in cpds.) -πλαγήσομαι | fut.pf. πεπλήξομαι | aor.1 ptcpl. -πληχθείς | aor.2 ἐπλήγην, ep.3sg.aor.2 πλήγη, ptcpl. πληγείς, dial. πλᾱγείς, Aeol. πλᾱ́γεις | also aor.2 -ἐπλάγην | pf. πέπληγμαι ‖ The act. is uncommon in Att. except in cpds. |
1 deliver a blow with a hand, fist, foot, stick, or sim.; (of persons) **strike, beat** —someone, part of the body Hom. Ar. AR. Theoc.; **kick** —a table, a person Od. AR.; (of horses) —a corpse (w. their hooves) Il. ‖ PASS. (of persons) be struck or beaten Il. Ar. Att.orats. Pl. X.; (fig.) be knocked down —W.PREP.PHR. by an argument Pl.
2 deliver a stroke with a weapon; (of persons) **strike** —someone, a part of the body or armour (usu. w. a sword) Il. Hdt. X. AR. —W.DBL.ACC. someone, on a part of the body Hom. AR. —a bird (w. an arrow) AR.; (of a goddess) —a mountain (w. a sceptre, to cleave it apart) Call. ‖ PASS. (of persons) be struck (by a weapon) Il. Hdt. Trag. Th. Ar. + —W.COGN.ACC. by a fatal blow A.; (by a javelin) Antipho; (of a bird, by an arrow) A.*fr*.; (of a tree, by an axe) Call.
3 (of Zeus) **strike** —someone (w. his lightning) Hes. ‖ PASS. (of persons or things) be struck (by lightning, usu. fr. Zeus) Hom. Hes. E. X.
4 (of a rider) **strike, lash** —horses (w. a whip) Il. ‖ PASS. (fig., of a person) be struck —W.DAT. by a god's lash A.
5 ‖ PASS. (of persons) be wounded or stricken —W.DAT. by a bite (of a serpent or beast) A. S.; be bitten (by a serpent) Arist.
6 strike a part of one's body with one's hands (in grief or other emotion); (of a man) **beat** —his breast Od. ‖ MID. (of women) **beat** —their breasts Il.; (of persons) **strike** —their thighs (in alarm) Hom. hHom. —their head (in grief) Hdt.
7 strike a material object; (of dancers) **strike, beat** —the ground (w. their feet) Od. Call. —one's armour (to make a noise) Call.; (of sailors) —the sea (w. their oars) AR.; (of a person) **bang, slam** —a door Men. ‖ PASS. (of bronze vessels) be struck (so as to make a noise) Pl.; (of a door) —W.DAT. by a key Od.; (fig., of a person's appearance) be beaten out or struck (on a die or sim.) A.(dub.)
8 (of things) deliver a blow; (of a wave, a mast) **strike** —someone, a head Od. ‖ PASS. (of a person) be struck —W.DAT. by timber fr. a ship E.; (of a ship) —by a wave Alc.
9 propel (sthg.) forcefully towards a place; (of horses' hooves) **kick** —dust (W.PREP.PHR. up to heaven) Il. ‖ PASS. (of birds) be dashed (by the wind) —W.PREP.PHR. into nets Call.
10 cause (sthg.) to strike (someone); (of Zeus) **strike, dash** —his lightning (W.PREP.PHR. against someone) Pi.
11 ‖ PASS. (of persons) be stricken or afflicted —W.DAT. by sickness S. —by a calamity, a fate, or sim. A. Hdt. E. AR. D.; (of

a country) —by fire Pi.fr.; (of mourners' clothing, fig.ref. to their persons) be struck —W.DAT. by a calamity (i.e. that for which the clothing is torn) A.

12 ‖ PASS. (of troops) take a battering, suffer a blow Hdt. Th. Plu.

13 affect (someone) emotionally; (of a thought) **strike** —someone B. ‖ PASS. (of persons) be smitten —W.DAT. by desire A. E. —by grief E. Men. Plu.; have one's head turned —W.DAT. by bribes Hdt.

πλήσω (fut.): see πίμπλημι

πλῆτο[1] (ep.3sg.athem.aor.mid.): see πελάζω

πλῆτο[2] (ep.3sg.athem.aor.mid.): see πίμπλημι

πλινθεύω vb. [πλίνθος] **1** make bricks Ar.; (mid.) Th.
  2 make (W.ACC. earth) into bricks Hdt.
  3 build (W.ACC. walls) of brick Th.

πλινθηδόν adv. **brick-fashion** —ref. to constructing a hull fr. planks laid in courses w. alternating vertical joints Hdt.

πλίνθινος η ον adj. (of buildings) **made of bricks, brick** Hdt. X. Arist.

πλινθίον ου n. [dimin. πλίνθος] **1 brick** Th. X.
  2 square (of troops) Plu. | cf. πλαίσιον 3
  3 quarter, region (of the sky, in divination) Plu.

πλινθοβολέω contr.vb. [βάλλω] **lay bricks** Ar.(cj.)

πλίνθος ου f. **1 brick** (of mud or clay, usu. sun-dried) Alc. Hdt. Th. Ar. +; (kiln-baked, a non-Greek technique) Hdt. Ar. X.; (used in torture, to press a victim) Ar. | see also νίζω 7
  2 (ref. to the material) **brick** Hdt.
  3 ingot (of gold or silver) Plb.

πλινθουργέω contr.vb. [πλινθουργός] **make bricks** Ar.

πλινθουργός οῦ m. [ἔργον] **brick-maker** Pl.

πλινθοφορέω contr.vb. [πλινθοφόρος] **carry bricks** Ar.(dub.)

πλινθο-φόρος ου n. [φέρω] **brick-carrier** Ar.

πλινθ-υφής ές adj. [ὑφαίνω] (of houses) **brick-built** A.

πλίσσομαι mid.vb. | ep.3pl.impf. πλίσσοντο | (of mules) perh., stride along, **trot** Od.

πλοιάριον ου n. [dimin. πλοῖον] **boat** Ar. X. Men. NT.

πλοΐζομαι mid.vb.: see πλῴζω

πλόιμος adj.: see πλώιμος

πλοῖον ου n. [πλέω[1]] **boat** or **ship** (ref. to any kind of vessel, other than a trireme) A. +; (w. μακρόν long, ref. to a warship) Hdt. Th. Isoc. Pl. D.; (w. στρογγύλον round, ref. to a merchant ship) X. D.; (opp. trireme) Th. Pl. X. D.

πλοκαμίς ίδος f. [πλόκαμος] **braided lock of hair** Bion; (collectv.sg.) **braided locks** Theoc.

πλόκαμος ου m. [πλέκω] **1** (freq.pl.) braided lock of hair (of a man or woman), **braid** or (gener.) **lock** Il. hHom. A. Pi. Hdt. E. +; (collectv.sg.) **hair, locks** A. E. Call.
  2 strand of wool E.

πλόκανον ου n. **1 web, network** (ref. to the respiratory system) Pl.
  2 sieve (for winnowing corn) Pl.
  3 plaited work (ref. to part of an animal trap) X.

πλοκερός adj.: see πλακερός

πλοκή ῆς f. **1** process or product of weaving, **weaving** Pl. ‖ PL. woven threads, **tapestry** E.
  2 (fig., pejor.) **contrivance, device, trick** E.
  3 wickerwork Plb.
  4 process of making complex; **complication** (of a tragic plot, opp. its resolution) Arist.

πλόκιον ου n. [dimin. πλόκος] **Necklace** Men.(title)

πλόκος ου m. **1.** (sg. and pl.) braided lock of hair (of a man or woman), **braid** or (gener.) **lock** Trag. AR.
  2 plaited garland (of greenery or flowers), **garland, wreath** Pi. B. E.; **diadem, crown** (of intricate gold-work) E.

πλόος ου, Att. **πλοῦς** οῦ m. [πλέω[1]] | Att.dat. πλῷ | Att.nom.pl. πλοῖ, dat.pl. πλοῖς | **1** action or instance of sailing (to a place), **voyage** Od. +; (as a measure of distance, defined in terms of days) Hdt. Th. Lycurg. D.; **course, direction** (of a voyage) Pi.; (fig., W.GEN. through life) Pl.
  2 (provbl.) δεύτερος πλοῦς **second voyage, next best course** (perh. ref. to the use of oars, if the wind fails) Pl. Arist. Men. Plb.
  3 time or opportunity for sailing; **sailing season** Hes.; **sailing weather** or **fair wind** Alc. S. E. Antipho Th. X. +
  4 pathway on land, road Call.

πλουθ-υγίεια ας f. [πλοῦτος, ὑγίεια] **health and wealth** (as blessings fr. the gods) Ar.

πλοῦς Att.m.: see πλόος

πλούσιος ᾱ ον adj. [πλοῦτος] **1** (of persons) possessing an abundance of wealth, **wealthy, rich, opulent** Hes. +; (of a treasury, shrine, house) Hdt. E.; (sarcastically, of a family) **rich and noble** S.; (of ploughland) abounding in natural resources, **rich** E.fr.
  2 (fig., of a person) **rich** (W.GEN. in wisdom, in a good and rational life) Pl.; (W.DAT. in useless possessions) Plu.; (of a person's fortune, W.GEN. in troubles) E.; (of a person's character) **richly endowed** E.
  3 (of a table) richly furnished (w. food), **rich, sumptuous** S. E.; (of funeral offerings) **lavish** E.; (of a lamp) abundantly equipped, **enriched** (W.DAT. w. twenty nozzles) Call.epigr.
  —**πλουσίως** adv. **richly, sumptuously, lavishly** —ref. to being equipped or sim. Hdt. E. Plu.; **in an opulent manner, like the wealthy** —ref. to swaggering Ar.

πλούταξ ακος m. (pejor.) **person used to rich living** Men.

Πλουτεύς m.: see under Πλούτων

πλουτέω contr.vb. [πλοῦτος] **1** (pres.) **be wealthy, be rich** Hes. + —W.GEN. in money Arist.; (fig., ref. to having many friends) X.
  2 (fut., aor., pf.) **become rich** Thgn. +; (fig.) —w. ὄναρ in a dream (i.e. illusorily) Pl.
  3 abound in a natural resource; (of a city) **be rich** —W.DAT. in timber, iron, or sim. X.

πλουτηρός ά όν adj. (of a method) **for creating wealth** X.

πλουτίζω vb. | fut. πλουτιῶ | aor. ἐπλούτισα | **1** make wealthy, **enrich** —someone (w. goods, gifts, or sim.) X. Plu. ‖ PASS. (of persons) **be enriched, become wealthy** X.
  2 (of circumstances) **benefit, profit** —someone A.; (fig., of a doomed priestess's insignia) **enrich** —someone else (W.GEN. w. ruin) A.; (of the maxims of the wise) —their possessors (W.DAT. w. virtue) X. ‖ PASS. (of Hades, w. allusion to his name Πλούτων) **be enriched** —W.DAT. by lamentations (for the dead) S.

πλουτίνδην adv. **according to wealth** —ref. to choosing officials Arist. Plb. Plu.

πλουτο-γᾱθής ές dial.adj. [γηθέω] (fig., of a storeroom) **rejoicing in wealth** A.

πλουτο-δότης ου m. —also **πλουτοδότειρα** ᾱς f. [δοτήρ] (ref. to a deity) **giver of riches** Hes. Lyr.adesp.

πλουτοκρατίᾱ ᾱς f. [κρατέω] **rule by the wealthy, plutocracy** X.

πλουτο-ποιός όν adj. [ποιέω] (of an art) **wealth-creating** Plu.

πλοῦτος ου m. [πλέω[1]] **1** (sts.pl.) **riches, wealth** Hom. +; (W.GEN. of silver) Hdt.
  2 (fig.) **wealth** (W.GEN. of clothing) A.; (W.GEN. of earth, as a possession for the dead) A.; (of a person's intellect or wisdom) Emp. Pl.; (in a person's soul) X.

—Πλοῦτος ου *m.* **Ploutos** (god of wealth, son of Demeter) Hes. +; (described as blind, because he lavishes his favours indiscriminately) Hippon. Timocr. Ar. Theoc.

πλουτό-χθων ονος *masc.fem.adj.* [χθών] (prob. of a populace) **enriched by the soil** (ref. to the silver mines of Laureion) A.

Πλούτων ωνος *m.* [Πλοῦτος] **1 Plouton, Pluto** (euphem. name for Hades) S. E. Ar. Isoc. Pl. Call.*epigr.* **2** (name of a mythol. river which flows w. gold) A.

—Πλουτεύς έος *dial.m.* | dat. Πλουτέι, also Πλουτῆι | **Plouteus, Pluto** (god of the underworld, alternative name for Πλούτων) Mosch.

πλοχμός οῦ *m.* [πλέκω] (pl.) **braid, lock** (of hair) Il. AR.

πλυνός οῦ *m.* [πλύνω] **trough for washing clothes** (by trampling them underfoot in water), **washing-trough** Hom.

πλύνος ου *m.* item to be washed, **dirty washing** (pejor.ref. to a person) Ar.

Πλυντήρια ων *n.pl.* **Plynteria** (festival at Athens, in which the ancient statue of Athena, and perh. her clothes, were washed) X. Plu.

πλυντικός ή όν *adj.* of or relating to washing || FEM.SB. **art of washing** (clothes) Pl.

πλύνω *vb.* [reltd. πλέω¹] | iteratv.impf. πλύνεσκον | fut. πλυνῶ, Ion. πλυνέω | aor. ἔπλῡνα, ep. πλῦνα || pf.pass. πέπλυμαι | **1 clean** (linen or sim.) by washing; **wash** —*clothes* Hom. Pl. Thphr. —*a woven fabric* Od. —*fleeces* Ar. —*fishing nets* NT.; (intr.) **wash clothes, do the laundry** Od. Ar. **2** (gener.) **wash** —*offal* Ar. Men. —*a horse's tail and mane* X. —*someone's arse* Ar.; (fig.) —*a person* (envisaged as a metal, to see whether he is unstained) Thgn.; **wipe** —*one's mouth* (after an unwelcome kiss) Theoc.; (of women) **clean** —*temple floors* (w. their hair) Plb. || PASS. (of a cup) be washed Theoc. **3 treat** (someone) **like dirty washing** (by soaking him in verbal abuse, perh. w. further connot. of trampling on him); **give** (W.ACC. someone) **a lathering** A.*satyr.fr.* Ar. D. Men.

πλύσις εως *f.* **washing** (of fabrics) Pl.

πλωάς άδος *fem.adj.* [πλώω, see πλέω¹] (of birds) **floating** (on a lake) AR.

πλώζω, Ion. **πλωίζω** *vb.* —also **πλοΐζομαι** (Plb.) *mid.vb.* | iteratv.impf. πλωΐζεσκον | **1** (of a person) **go to sea, sail** (as a way of life) Hes.; (mid.) Plb.; (of a nation) **take to the sea, practise navigation** Th. **2** (of the Homeric Achilles) perh. **wade about** (in grief) Pl. [in a misquotation for δινεύεσκε *toss about*]

πλώϊμος (later **πλόϊμος**) ον *adj.* | compar. πλωΐτερος | **1** (of ships) **fit for sailing, seaworthy** Th. Aeschin. D. **2** (of a river, a sea) allowing the passage of ships, **navigable** Tim. Plu.; (of the sea) **easily navigable** (in the sailing season) Thphr. || NEUT.PL.COMPAR.SB. circumstances more favourable for navigation Th.

πλώσιμος ον *adj.* (of a sea, fig.ref. to an undertaking) **easy to sail** S.

πλωτεύομαι *pass.vb.* (of a sea-channel) **be crossed by sailing** (opp. by a bridge) Plb.

πλωτήρ ῆρος *m.* one who sails on a ship (as crew or passenger), **sailor** E. Ar. Pl. Arist.

πλωτικός ή όν *adj.* (of persons) **engaged in shipping** (as owners) Plu.

πλωτός ή όν *adj.* [πλώω, see πλέω¹] **1** (of mythol. islands) **floating** Od. Hdt.; (as the name of certain islands) AR.; (of wagons, fig.ref. to ships) Lyr.adesp. **2** (of the race of fishes) whose nature it is to swim, **swimming** S.*fr.*; (of beasts, ref. to dolphins) Lyr.adesp.; (of creatures, opp. flying) Arist.

3 (of a sea, a river) **navigable** Hdt. Plb.; (of the sea) **open** AR.
4 (of a place) **accessible by sea** Plb.
5 (of a time) **suitable for sailing** Plb.

πλώω *Ion.vb.*: see πλέω¹

πνείω *ep.vb.*: see πνέω

πνεῦμα ατος *n.* [πνέω] **1** natural movement of air (whether gentle or strong), **breath** or **blast** (W.GEN. of wind) Archil. A. Emp. Hdt. E.; (gener.) **breeze** or **wind** Hdt. Trag. Th. Ar. Pl. +; (fig.) **wind** (ref. to a fart) Ar.
2 (fig.) **favouring wind, breeze** (of fortune or sim.) A. E.; **blast, attack** (of frenzy) A.; (gener., as emanating fr. humans) **spirit, emotion** A. S.
3 air exhaled from the lungs or (gener.) respiration, **breath** or **breathing** (of persons or animals) A. E. Th. Telest. Pl. Men. +; (W.GEN. of life, i.e. the state of being alive) A.; (meton., as essential to life) **breath, life-spirit** A. E. Plb. NT. Plu.
4 breath, **breathed melody** (of the aulos or panpipe) E. Theoc.*epigr.*
5 breath (W.GEN. of heaven, ref. to air) E.; **scent, fragrance** (of a goddess, a child's skin) E.
6 non-corporeal nature, **spirit** (of God or Christ) NT.
7 non-corporeal being, **evil spirit** NT.

πνευματικός ή όν *adj.* associated with air; (of the dryness of certain substances) app. **porous** Plu.

πνευμάτιον ου *n.* [dimin. πνεῦμα] **wretched little life** Plb.

πνευματό-ρρους ου Att.m. [ῥόος] **wind-flow** (as an example of a compound word) Pl.

πνευματώδης ες *adj.* (of letters, ref. to ζ, σ, φ, ψ) **pronounced with an audible release of breath** Pl.

πνεύμων *m.*: see πλεύμων

πνευστιάω *contr.vb.* [πνέω] **breathe hard, pant** Arist.

πνέω *contr.vb.* —also **πνείω** *ep.vb.* | fut. (in cpds.) -πνεύσομαι, also πνευσοῦμαι (Ar.) | aor. ἔπνευσα | **1** (of winds or breezes) **blow** Od. +; (of Zephyros) **blow** or **breathe forth** —*dew* Call.
2 (fig., of Ares, Bacchus, a person, an object, envisaged as a wind) **blow, bluster** (usu. W.PREDIC.ADJ. μέγας, πολύς *strongly*) E. Even. Ar. D. Plb.(quot.); (of a person) **blow** or **breathe forth** —*the changing wind of one's mind* A.
3 (of persons) **breathe, draw breath** A. E. Ar. —W.ADV. *for the last time* B.; **draw the breath of life** Hom. Pi. S. Call.*epigr.*
4 (of persons or animals) **breathe hard, pant** Il. E. Ar.; (fig., of a runner) **gasp out** —*the river Alpheios* (w. iron. allusion to races held at Olympia, beside this river) Ar.
5 (fig. or mythol.; of monsters, horses, Erinyes) **exhale, breathe** —*fire* Hes. Pi. E.; (of the player of an aulos or panpipe) **breathe forth** —*music* E.; (of Zeus) **breathe down** —*a wind* E.
6 (of persons, gods, animals) express through one's breathing (an emotion or state of mind); **breathe out** —*fury, wrath, war* Hom. Trag. —*fire* X. —*murder, love* Theoc. —*one's favour* (W.DAT. on someone) A. —*weapons and armour* Ar.(mock-trag.)
7 (fig., of persons) breathe (in a specified way, envisaged as matching one's behaviour or state of mind); **breathe** —W.NEUT.ADV. *strongly, too strongly* (i.e. huff and puff, be high and mighty) A. E. —w. ever-changing purposes (i.e. behave ineffectually) Pi. —*humbly* (i.e. have low aspirations) Pi. —*emptily* (i.e. strive in vain) Pi. —*w. the Spartan spirit* Ar. —W.DAT. *w. a bold heart* (i.e. show courage) Pi.; (of soldiers, their spirits) **pant eagerly** Hes. A.
8 (of prophetic inspiration) **breathe down** (on someone) E.; (of a deity) **breathe favourably** —W.DAT. or PREP.PHR. *on someone* Call.*epigr.* Theoc.

9 (of natural phenomena) breathe forth (an effect); (of lightning, the stars) give off —*fire* Pi.*fr.* S.; (of a burning stake) —*smoke* E.*Cyc.*(cj.); (of lightning) —*pain* E.
10 (of persons or things) give off an odour, **smell** —W.ADV. *sweetly, foully, or sim.* Od. Ar. AR. Theoc.; (fig., of a house) **breathe out, reek of** —W.ACC. *bloodshed* A.

πνιγεύς έως *m.* [πνίγω] that which chokes off the air; **baking-cover** (hemispherical vessel used as an oven for baking bread) Ar.

πνῑγηρός ά όν *adj.* 1 (of huts) **stifling** (fr. heat) Th. Plu.
2 (fig., of a route to Hades, ref. to hanging) **choking, suffocating** Ar.

πνῖγμα ατος *n.* **throttling** Arist.(quot.)

πνιγμός οῦ *m.* 1 **fit of choking** (as a physical affliction) Men.; **suffocation** (of a person, by a crowd) Plb.
2 **choking** (of grain by weeds) X.

πνῖγος ους *n.* **stifling heat** Th. Ar. Pl. X. Arist. Plu.

πνίγω *vb.* | aor. ἔπνῑξα ‖ PASS.: aor.2 ἐπνίγην | pf. πέπνῑγμαι |
1 **throttle, strangle** —*someone* Antipho NT. Plu. ‖ PASS. be throttled Hyp.
2 (of water) **cause** (someone) **to choke** Arist.; (of weeds) **choke** —*grain* X.; (of a doctor) —*someone* (w. *medicine*) Pl. ‖ PASS. (of persons) **choke to death** Plu.; **drown** X. NT.
3 (fig.) cause to be choked (i.e. annoyed), **plague the life out of** —*someone* S.*Ichn.* ‖ PASS. (fig.) be choked —W.PREP.PHR. *in one's insides* (fr. *eagerness to do sthg.*) Ar.
4 **cook** (food) in an enclosed vessel; **bake** —*a plant* (*in an oven*) Hdt. ‖ PASS. (fig., of a lawsuit, envisaged as a tasty delicacy) be cooked (in a casserole) Ar.

πνῑγώδης ες *adj.* 1 (of places) **stifling** (fr. heat) Plu.
2 (of breathing) **choked** (by dust-filled air) Plu.

πνῑκτός ή όν *adj.* (of an animal) **killed by strangulation** (to preserve its blood) Philox.Leuc. NT.

πνοή ῆς, dial. **πνοά** ᾶς, Aeol. **πνόᾱ** ᾱς, ep. **πνοιή** ῆς, dial. **πνοιά** ᾶς *f.* [πνέω] 1 **blast, gust** (W.GEN. of *wind*) Hom. +; (gener.) **breeze, wind** Hom. +; (fig., W.GEN. fr. *Aphrodite*, directing a lover towards someone) E.
2 **blast** (fr. *bellows*) Th.; (W.GEN. fr. *Ares*) A.; (W.GEN. of *Hephaistos*, i.e. of *flame*) Il.; (of *fire*) E.; **air** (passing through a gnat's intestine) Ar.
3 **puff of breath** (fr. a goddess, diverting a spear) Il.; **breath, inspiration** (of a god) E.; (fig.) **puff** (W.GEN. of *wealth*, ref. to the smoke of a burning city) A.
4 **breath** (of persons, horses) Il. Pi. S. E. Call.; **panting** (W.GEN. of *an angry spirit*, i.e. angry panting) E.
5 **breath of life, life** A. E.
6 **breath, breathed melody** (of the aulos or panpipe) Pratin. Pi. B. E. Ar.

Πνύξ Πυκνός (later Πυνκός) *f.* **Pnyx** (hill at Athens where the Assembly met, nr. the Acropolis) Th. Ar. Pl. Aeschin. D. Plu.

πόα *f.*: see ποία

ποδ-αβρός όν *adj.* [πούς, ἁβρός] (of Croesus) **tender-footed** Hdt.(oracle)

ποδ-ᾱγός οῦ *dial.m.f.* [ἄγω] 1 one who guides on foot, **guide** (to a place) S.
2 one who guides a person's steps, **support, prop** E.

ποδ-άγρα ᾱς *f.* 1 **foot-trap** (for an animal) X.
2 a kind of incapacitating foot-disease, **gout** Plu.

ποδαγράω *contr.vb.* **suffer from gout, be gouty** Ar.

ποδαγρικός ή όν *adj.* **suffering from gout, gouty** Plb. Plu.

ποδάνεμος *dial.adj.*: see ποδήνεμος

ποδα-νιπτήρ ῆρος *m.* [νίζω] vessel for washing the feet, **foot-bath** Stesich. Hdt. Arist. Plu.

ποδάνιπτρα ων *n.pl.* **water for a foot-bath** Od.

ποδαπός (later **ποταπός**) ή όν *interrog.adj.* 1 (of persons or things, esp. in an inquiry about national or civic identity) **of what origin, where from?** Hdt. Trag. Ar. Pl. +
2 (wkr.sens., of persons or things) **of what kind?** NT.

ποδ-άρκης ες *adj.* [πούς, ἀρκέω] 1 app., helping with the feet (i.e. running to the rescue); (of Achilles) **swift-footed** (i.e. equiv. to ποδώκης) Il.; (of Hermes) B.
2 (of a racecourse) **for swift feet** Pi.; (of a day) **of swift foot-races** Pi.

ποδ-ένδυτος ον *adj.* [ἐνδύνω] (of a capacious robe) **put on to cover the feet** (of a corpse) A.

ποδεών ῶνος *m.* 1 leg of an animal-skin (used as a container for wine); **nozzle, spout, neck** (of a wineskin) Hdt.
2 ‖ PL. **paw-ends** (of a lionskin) Theoc.
3 **strip, tongue** (of land) Hdt.

ποδηγέω *contr.vb.* [ποδᾱγός] (of the soul) **act as a guide** (to the body) Pl.

ποδ-ηνεκής ές *adj.* [ἐνεγκεῖν, see φέρω] (of an animal-skin, as a garment) **reaching to the feet** Il. AR.; (of a tunic) Hdt.; (of a shield) Il.

ποδ-ήνεμος, dial. **ποδάνεμος**, ον *adj.* [ἄνεμος] (of Iris) **with feet as swift as the wind** Il. hHom.; (of a runner) B.

ποδ-ήρης ες *adj.* [ἀραρίσκω] 1 (of a garment) **reaching to the feet** E. X.; (of a shield) X. Plu. ‖ NEUT.SB. **foot-length robe** Call.
2 (of a pillar) **sure-footed, firmly based** A.
3 ‖ NEUT.PL.SB. **foot-parts** (of dismembered bodies) A.

ποδιαῖος ᾱ ον *adj.* (of a trench) **measuring one foot** (in depth) X.; (of a line, in length) Pl. Arist.

ποδίζομαι *pass.vb.* (of horses) **have the feet bound, be hobbled** X.

ποδιστήρ ῆρος *masc.adj.* (of a robe) **foot-length** (perh. w. further connot. of entangling the feet, i.e. hobbling) A.

ποδοκάκκη ης *f.* device for securing the feet, **stocks** Lys.(law)

ποδό-ρρωρος η ον *ep.Ion.adj.* [ῥώννῡμι] (of Atalanta) **strong-footed, swift-footed** Call.

ποδο-στράβη ης *f.* [reltd. στρεβλός] trap for the feet (of animals), **snare, gin-trap** X.; (in fig.ctxt.) Hyp.

ποδότης ητος *f.* **footedness** (as an attribute of certain animals) Arist.

ποδουχέω *contr.vb.* [ἔχω] | poet.3sg.impf. ποδούχει | control the sheets (of a sailing-ship); (fig., of a king) **control, direct** —*his army* A.(cj.)

ποδό-ψηστρον ου *n.* [ψάω] **foot-wiper, doormat** (as a squalid object) A.

ποδώκεια ᾱς (Ion. ης) *f.* [ποδώκης] **swiftness of foot** Il.(pl.) E. Plu.; (gener.) **swiftness** (W.GEN. of *legs*) A.

ποδ-ώκης ες *adj.* [ὠκύς] | superl. ποδωκέστατος, ep. ποδωκηέστατος (AR.) | 1 (of Achilles) **swift-footed** Hom. Scol.; (of other individuals) Il. Hes. Alcm. AR. Plu.; (of soldiers) Th. Plu.; (of horses) Il. Hes. Pl. X. Plu.; (of the Chimaira) Hes.; (of hares and hounds) X.
2 (fig., of Punishments fr. the gods, app. ref. to Erinyes) **prompt** S.; (gener., of an eye, a sword) **swift, quick** A.

ποέω Att.*contr.vb.*, **πόημμι** Aeol.*vb.*: see ποιέω

ποθεινός ή όν (also ός όν E.), Aeol. **πόθεννος** ᾱ ον *adj.* [ποθέω] 1 **longed for** (sts. W.DAT. by someone); (of persons, deities) **longed for, desired, desirable** E. Ar. Men. Theoc. Plu.; (of a baby) Pi.; (of a person's voice or presence) S.; (of love, life, fame, a country) Lyr.; (of a day) E. Ar.; (of vengeance) Th.; (of death) Lys.; (of an occupation, a character trait) X.

πόθεν

2 (of a dead or absent person) **longed for, missed** (sts. W.DAT. by someone) Callin. E. Ar. Pl. X.; (of things absent or lost) X. Aeschin.
3 (of tears) **filled with longing** E.(dub.) [or perh. *caused by longing*]
—**ποθεινοτέρως** *compar.adv.* (w. ἔχειν) **be more desirous** —W.GEN. *of someone* X.

πόθεν, Ion. **κόθεν**, dial. **πῶ** *interrog.adv.* **1** (ref. to place) **from where, whence?** Hom. + • (W.GEN.) πόθεν ... ἀνδρῶν *from what people?* Hom. • πόθεν γῆς *from what land?* E.
2 (ref. to origin or race) **from what stock?** Od.
3 (ref. to acquisition) **from where?** hHom. +
4 (ref. to a beginning) **from what point?** A. +
5 (ref. to cause) **for what reason, why?** hHom. +
6 (ellipt.) πόθεν; *how so, how could that be?* E. Ar. D.; (also) πῶ; A.
—**ποθέν**, Ion. **κοθέν** *enclit.adv.* (ref. to origin) **from somewhere** or **anywhere** Hom. + • (W.PREP.PHR. or ADV.) ἐκ βιβλίου ποθέν *from some book or other* Pl. • ἐνθένδε ποθέν *from hereabouts* Pl.

πόθεννος *Aeol.adj.*: see ποθεινός
ποθέρπω *dial.vb.*: see προσέρπω
ποθ-έσπερος ον *dial.adj.* [πρός, ἑσπέρᾱ] || NEUT.PL.ADV. (sts. w.art.) **in the evening** Theoc.
ποθέω, Aeol. **ποθήω** *contr.vb.* | *ep.inf.* ποθήμεναι | *ep.impf.* πόθεον | *iteratv.impf.* ποθέεσκον | *fut.* ποθήσω, also ποθέσομαι | *aor.* ἐπόθησα, also ἐπόθεσα, ep. πόθεσα |
1 feel longing (for that which is absent or lost); **long for, yearn after, miss** —*a loved person, land, or sim.* Hom. + —*a person or thing on which life depends* Hom.; (intr.) **be full of longing** Sapph. S.(also mid.) Pl. + || PASS. (of persons or things) **be longed for** S. E. Ar. Pl. +
2 (wkr.sens.) **feel with regret** —W.ACC. + μή and PASS.INF. *that sthg. has not been done* Pl.
3 (of a person or thing) **stand in need of, want, require** —*sthg.* Isoc. Pl. || PASS. (of an account) **need** —W.PASS.INF. *to be stated* Arist.
4 **want, desire, be eager** —W.INF. *to do sthg.* Pi. Emp. Trag. Antipho +

ποθή ῆς *f.* **1 longing** (for that which is absent, dead or lost); **longing, yearning, desire** (oft. W.GEN. for someone or sthg.) Hom. AR.
2 **want, lack, shortage** (W.GEN. of sthg.) Od.
3 **desire** (W.INF. to do sthg.) Call.

πόθι *dial.interrog.adv.* | equiv. to ποῦ | **1 in what place, where?** Od. S. E.; (W.GEN. on a particular mountain) E.; (in someone's mind) Pi.
2 **to what place, whither?, where?** AR.
—**ποθί** *dial.enclit.adv.* | equiv. to που | **1 somewhere, anywhere** Hom. S. Call. AR.
2 (adding a note of uncertainty) **perhaps, probably** Hom.

ποθ-ίκω *dial.vb.* [πρός, ἵκω] **1 come to, visit** —W.DAT. *someone* Theoc.
2 || MASC.PL.PTCPL.SB. (w.art.) **relatives** (of someone) D.(oracle)

ποθοράω, ποθορέω *dial.contr.vbs.*, **ποθόρημι** *Aeol.vb.*: see προσοράω

πόθος, Lacon. **πόσος** (Alcm.), ου *m.* [ποθέω] **1 longing** (usu. for that which is absent, dead or lost); **longing, yearning, desire** (oft. W.GEN. for someone, sthg., a place) Hom. +
2 **sexual longing, longing, desire** (sts. W.GEN. for someone) Hes. +; (as a deity) **Desire** A. Ar.
3 (gener.) **longing, desire** (W.INF. to do sthg.) E.

ποῖ[1] *interrog.adv.* **1 to what place, whither?, where?** Trag. +; (W.GEN. in a particular country, on earth) Trag. Ar.; (in thought, speech) S.
2 (in ctxt. of finishing sthg., fulfilling a promise, or sim.) **at what point** or **with what outcome, where?, how?** Trag. Pl. +; (in ctxt. of waiting) **for what end, to what purpose?** Ar. [or perh. *to what point of time?, how long?*]
3 (w.wd. or phr. used by previous speaker repeated indignantly or incredulously) **why do you say, what do you mean by** (such and such)? Ar. | cf. ποῖος 4, τί (under τίς)
—**ποι**[1] *enclit.adv.* **to some** or **any place, somewhere** or **anywhere** Trag. +; (W.GEN. in a particular country) Th. X.

ποῖ[2], **ποι**[2] *Aeol.advs.*: see ποῦ, που

ποία (also **πόα**) ᾱς, Ion. **ποίη** ης *f.* **1 grass, pasturage** (for grazing animals, also assoc.w. flowering meadowland) Hom. Hes. Sapph. Hdt. E.*Cyc.* Pl. +; (W.ADJ. *Median*, ref. to lucerne) Ar.
2 **grassy place** (in which to rest) Pl. X. Plu.
3 (gener.) **foliage, leaves** Pi.; (W.ADJ. *Parnassian*, ref. to laurel) Pi.; (fig.) **flower** (ref. to a woman's virginity) Pi.
4 **hay-time** (as a marker of the season, i.e. summer) Call.

ποιάεις, Ion. **ποιήεις**, εσσα εν *adj.* **1** (of meadows, vales, or sim.) **covered with grass, grassy** Hom. hHom. S. AR.; (of regions) **rich in grassy meadows** Hom. Hes. hHom.
2 (of garlands) **leafy, verdant** Pi.

ποιέω, Att. **ποέω** *contr.vb.* —also **πόημμι** *Aeol.vb.* | *ep.impf.* ποίεον, 3sg. ποίει | *iteratv.impf.* ποιέεσκον | *fut.* ποιήσω | *aor.* ἐποίησα, ep. ποίησα, Aeol. ἐπόησα | *pf.* πεποίηκα || *neut.impers.vbl.adj.* ποιητέον || In Att., πο- sts. replaces ποι- before ει and η, but not before οι, ου, ω. || The sections are grouped as: (1-4) create (material things), (5-8) create (abstr. states), (9-12) put or place (things or persons) in a certain state, (13-14) reckon (persons or things) to be in a certain state, (15-22) do or perform (certain actions). |
1 create (a material object); **make, create, construct** —*a building, shield, work of art, or sim.* Hom. + —(W.GEN. or W. ἀπό or ἐκ + GEN. *fr. a specified material*) Hdt. Th. X. || MID. **make** (W.ACC. sthg.) **for oneself** Hom. +; **have** (W.ACC. sthg.) **made** (for oneself) Hdt. + || PASS. (of a bed) **be made up** (for someone) Od.
2 **bring** (persons) **into existence**; (of gods) **create** —*the race of men* Hes.; ὁ ποιῶν *the creator* Pl.; (fig., of the Athenians) **raise up** —*a second Philip* (as enemy) D. || MID. (of a man) **beget, father** —*a child* And. Pl. X. D.; (of a woman) **conceive** —*a child* Pl.
3 (of poets) **compose** —*an epic, a drama, or sim.* Hdt. +; **put into verse** —*a narrative* Pl. Lycurg.; **create** —*characters* (in drama) Ar.; **portray** —*someone* (sts. W.PREDIC.ADJ. or PTCPL. *as being or doing such and such*) Pl. Arist.; **invent** —*gods, names* Hdt. Pl. Arist.; **coin** —*new words* Arist.; (intr.) **write, compose** Hdt. Ar. Pl.
4 **bring into existence** (rain, crops); (of Zeus) **create** —*rain* Ar. Thphr.; (of humans) **grow, produce** —*barley* Ar. —*measures of grain* D.; (of trees) —*fruit* NT.
5 **bring about** (a benefit, for oneself or others); **procure, secure** —*immunity* (for someone) Th.; (of a law) —*the right of inheritance* Is.; (of a speech) —*money* D. || MID. **procure for oneself, gain** —*fame* Od. —*immunity, support* Th. —*a livelihood* (fr. some activity) Th. X.
6 (act. and mid.) **bring about** (a specified effect or result); **cause, produce** —*an end* (to sthg.), *a rout, clear sky, silence, shame, war, or sim.* Hom. +; **make, establish** —*an agreement, alliance, truce, friendly relations, or sim.* Od. +

7 bring about (a time); **bring on** —*midnight (i.e. continue talking until then)* Pl.; **fix, set** —*a time for sthg.* (W.PREP.PHR. *after midnight*) D.; **allow, cause** —*no time (to elapse)* D.(dub.); **pass, spend** —*three months (in a place)* NT.
8 bring about, ensure —W.ACC. + INF. (sts. w. ὥστε) *that someone does sthg.* Od. Hdt. + —w. ὅκως + FUT.INDIC. *that sthg. will happen* Hdt. —w. ὡς or ὡς ἄν + OPT. X.(also mid.)
9 (act. and mid.) **render, make** (W.ACC. *someone or sthg.*) —W.PREDIC.ADJ. or SB. *such and such* (e.g. *senseless, subservient, ready, a king, one's friend, wife, adopted son*) Hom. + ‖ MID. **treat** —*someone's achievement* (W.GEN. *as that of oneself, i.e. appropriate it as one's own*) Hdt. S. ‖ ACT. **create, appoint** —*officials* Hdt. —*disciples* NT. ‖ PASS. (of a heart) be made —W.PREDIC.ADJ. *heavy* Sapph.
10 ‖ MID. (specif.) **make one's own, adopt** —*a child* Hdt. Pl. D.
11 cause (someone or sthg.) to be (W.PREP.PHR. in a certain place or condition); **place, put** —*ships (on dry land)* Th. —*troops (out of range)* X. —*offices (into the hands of a few)* Th. —*a country (under someone's control)* D. —*a city (in disgrace, i.e. to shame)* D. —*oneself (far fr. suspicion)* Isoc. ‖ MID. **place** —*troops, ships (somewhere)* Th. —*a river (behind one, i.e. place one's army so as to ensure that this is the case)* X.; **bring** —*a nation or sim. (under one's control)* Hdt. X.; **admit** —*people (into an alliance)* Hdt.; **take** —*people (into custody)* Th.
12 (of a god) **put** (W.PREP.PHR. in someone's mind) —*a thought* Od. Hdt. —W.INF. *the idea to do sthg.* Il. Hdt.
13 ‖ MID. **treat** (sthg.) in a certain way; **take, regard, reckon** —*a circumstance* (W.PREDIC.SB. *as a misfortune, a godsend*) Hdt. Pl.; **reckon it to be** —W.NEUT.ADJ. *a dreadful thing, a serious matter, or sim.* (sts. + INF. or COMPL.CL. *to do sthg., that sthg. is the case*) Hdt. Th.; **treat** (W.ACC. *someone or sthg.*) —W.PREP.PHR. *as of no account* S. —*lightly* Hdt. Th. —*as lawful, safe* Hdt. —*as important, more important, less important* Lys. Isoc. Pl. +
14 suppose (for the purpose of argument), **assume, imagine** —W.ACC. + INF. or COMPL.CL. *that sthg. is the case* Hdt. Pl. X. ‖ PASS. (of persons or things) be assumed to be, be regarded as —W.PREDIC.ADJ. *such and such* Pl. ‖ 3SG.PASS.IMPERATV. let it be assumed (that sthg. is the case) Pl.
15 perform (a specified action); **do** —*sthg., nothing, good, evil, or sim.* Hom. + ‖ PASS. (of things) be done, be accomplished Il. +
16 bestow or **render** (benefits, injuries, to persons or things); **perform, do** —W.DBL.ACC. *good, harm, or sim., to someone or sthg.* Hdt. + —(W.DAT. *to someone*) Ar. D.; **behave** or **act towards, treat** —*someone or sthg.* (W.ADV. *well, badly, or sim.*) A. Hdt. +
17 ‖ MID. (periphr.) perform an action stated or implied (in the ACC. object); **make, undertake** —*a journey, departure, contest, decision, or sim.* Hdt. + —*the offering of an excuse (i.e. offer an excuse)* Od.; **perform, carry out** —*talking, fighting, or sim.* Hdt. S. +; **express** —*anger, forgetfulness, mourning, or sim. (i.e. be angry, forget, mourn)* Hdt.
18 (act. and mid.) **perform** (rites or ceremonies); **perform, offer** —*sacrifices* Hdt. X.; **celebrate** —*a festival, funeral, or sim.* Hdt. Th. Pl. X.
19 (of the Athenians) **call** or **hold** —*an Assembly* Th. Ar. + ‖ MID. (of Zeus, a commander) **call, convene** —*an assembly* Il.
20 perform an action as described (i.e. by another vb.); **do so** A. Hdt. Is. D.

21 (intr.) **be active, act** (opp. be inactive) Hdt.; **be the doer** (opp. the sufferer) Hdt.; **act** —W.ADV. *in a specified way* Hdt. S. Pl. X.
22 (of actions, circumstances) **achieve** —*a certain effect* Th.; (intr., of a feeling, a reputation) **be widespread** Th.; (of poison) **act, be effective** Pl.

ποίη *Ion.f.*: see ποία
ποιήεις *Ion.adj.*: see ποιάεις
ποίημα ατος *f.* [ποιέω] **1** thing made, **work, artefact** (sts. W.GEN. of a specified craftsman) Hdt. Pl.; (gener.) **object** (ref. to a plough, battle-axe, or sim.) Hdt.
2 invention (W.GEN. of a lover, ref. to a flattering epithet) Pl.
3 literary production (ref. to a letter, opp. spoken word) Isoc.
4 metrical composition, **poem** Att.orats. Pl. Arist. Call.*epigr.* +
5 production of an effect, **action** (opp. passive experience) Pl. Arist.
—**ποιημάτιον** ου *n.* [dimin.] **short** or **slight poem** Plu.
ποιηρός ά όν *adj.* [ποία] (of pastureland, a valley) **grassy** E.
ποίησις εως *f.* (Ion. ιος) *f.* [ποιέω] **1** process of creating; **creation, production** (W.GEN. of perfume, ships, tunes, or sim.) Hdt. Th. Pl. D. Arist.; art of creating (knowledge), **productive art** (as claimed by sophists) Pl.; **making** (opp. πρᾶξις *doing*) Pl. Arist.
2 (specif.) process of creating poetry; **composition** (W.GEN. of dithyrambs, tragedies, or sim.) Pl. X. Arist.; art of poetic composition, **poetry** Hdt. Pl. Aeschin. Arist.
3 product of poetic composition, **poetry** Dionys.Eleg. Hdt. Th. Ar. Isoc. Pl. +
4 (leg.) **adoption** (of a child) Is. D.
ποιητέος ᾱ ον *vbl.adj.* **1** (of hymns) **to be composed** Pl.
2 (of an agreement) **to be made** Th.; (of lots) **to be arranged** Pl.
3 (of a person) **to be represented as** (W.PTCPL. *being such and such*) Pl.
4 (of things) **to be done** Hdt. Th. Ar. Att.orats. +
5 (of persons) **to be treated** (W.ADV. *well*) X.
6 (of care) **to be taken** Antipho
ποιητής οῦ *m.* **1 maker** (of material objects); **creator, maker** (W.GEN. of certain categories of object, ref. to a god, carpenter, artist) Pl.; **deviser** (of stratagems) X.; (pejor.) **inventor** (of gods) Pl.
2 creator of a poetical composition; **composer, author** (W.GEN. of a comedy or sim.) Pl.; (of stories or plots) Arist.; **poet** Hdt. Th. Ar. Isoc. Pl. +; (as composer of the accompanying music) Pl.; ὁ ποιητής *the poet* (*usu.ref. to Homer*) Pl. Arist. Plb.
3 author (W.GEN. of a speech) Isoc.; (opp. deliverer of it) Pl.
ποιητικός ή όν *adj.* **1** relating to creation; (of an activity, ref. to literary composition) **creative** Isoc.; (of an art) **productive** (opp. acquisitive arts like money-making, hunting) Pl.; (of implements, sciences, qualities, opp. those relating to thinking or doing) Arist.
2 producing a specific effect; (of opposites) **productive** (W.GEN. of opposites) Arist.; (of an art, W.GEN. of wealth) Arist.
3 (of persons) occupied with or skilled in poetry, **poetic, poetical** Pl. Arist. Plb. ‖ MASC.SB. poet Pl.
4 (of a style, word, metaphor, or sim.) associated with poetry, **poetic** Isoc. Pl. Arist. Plb.; (of imitation, i.e. representation) **by means of poetry, poetic** Pl.; (fig., of the doors) **of poetry** (as welcoming the newcomer) Pl.
5 ‖ FEM.SB. art of poetry, **poetry** Pl. Arist. Plu.
—**ποιητικῶς** *adv.* **in a poetic manner, poetically** Pl. Arist.

ποιητός ή όν *adj.* **1** created by workmanship; (of a shield, chamber, roof, house) **constructed** (W.ADV. solidly) Hom. hHom.; (of houses, gates, objects) **crafted, well-made** Hom. **2** created artificially (opp. existing naturally); (of a well, opp. a spring) **constructed** Plu.; (of good sense) **created, crafted** Thgn.
3 (of a child) **adopted** Pl. Is. D. Men.; (of a father) **adoptive** Lys. Lycurg.
4 (of citizens) **adopted** (i.e. not such by birth) D. Arist.
5 (of a story) **invented, fabricated** (i.e. false) Pi. E.; (of a manner of behaviour) **feigned, assumed** E.
ποιηφαγέω Ion.contr.vb. [ποίᾱ, φαγεῖν] (of persons) **eat grass** or **live on grass** Hdt.
ποικιλ-άνιος ον *dial.adj.* [ποικίλος, ἡνία] (of horses) **with richly decorated reins** Pi.
ποικιλ-είμων ον, gen. ονος *adj.* [εἶμα] (of night) **in spangled garb** (i.e. dotted w. stars) A.
ποικιλίᾱ ᾱς *f.* **1** process of creating variegated colours (as on tapestries, by weaving or embroidery), **ornamentation, decorative work** Pl. ‖ PL. (concr.) richly patterned tapestries X.
2 quality or condition of being varied in colour; **variegation, variety, diversity** (W.GEN. of colours, on the surface of the earth) Pl.; (W.PREP.PHR. in the heavens) Pl.
3 (gener.) condition of being varied, **variety, diversity** Pl. Arist. Plb.; (specif.) **elaborate variety** (W.GEN. of food) Pl.
4 quality of being complex (opp. simple); **variety, complexity** (in literary style) Isoc.; (in musical sounds) Pl.; **complicated nature** (W.GEN. of a constitution, circumstances) Plb.
5 versatility, ingenuity, subtlety D.
ποικίλλω *vb.* | aor. ἐποίκιλα ‖ pf.pass. πεποίκιλμαι ‖ neut.impers.vbl.adj. ποικιλτέον | **1** introduce a variety of colours or patterning; **weave** or **embroider** —*figures* (*on a tapestry*) E. Pl.; (of painters) **decorate** —*votive tablets* Emp. ‖ PASS. (of a roof) **be embellished** —W.DAT. *w. precious metals* Pl.; (of a headband worn by a victor, fig.ref. to the ode sung in his honour) **be embroidered** or **embellished** —W.ADV. *w. ringing tones* Pi.; (of a garment) **be variously patterned** —W.DAT. *w. all kinds of colours* Pl.; (fig., of a city) —*w. all kinds of characters* Pl.; (of the earth, prob. by flowers) Lyr.adesp.
2 (of Hephaistos) create with elaborate workmanship, **elaborately depict** —*a dance-floor* (*on a shield*) Il.
3 introduce variety into (activities or sim.); (of a commander) **vary** —*a cavalry march* (*w. changes of formation*) X.; (of Fortune) **diversify** —*human life* (*w. a blend of good and bad*) Plu.; (of bodily humours) **give rise to a variety of** —*disorders of every kind* Pl.; (of lawgivers) **distinguish, differentiate** —*the life of orphans* (fr. that of others, by separate rules) Pl.; (pejor.) **complicate** —*people's lives* E.Cyc.; (intr.) **introduce variety** (in words, by changing syllables) Pl. ‖ PASS. (pejor., of a country) **be devious or shifty** —W.ACC. *in its ways* E.
4 (of a writer, poet, speaker) **embroider, embellish, elaborate** —*a narrative* Pi. Pl. Plu.
5 (pejor.) speak in a subtle or complicated way (opp. plainly); **say** (W.ACC. sthg.) **in riddles** S.; (intr.) **equivocate** or **complicate matters, beat about the bush** Pl.
ποικίλματα τῶν *n.pl.* **1 woven** or **embroidered designs** (on a garment) Hom. Pl. Men.(cj.) Plu.; (fig.) **spangled tapestry** (W.GEN. of stars) E.; **spangles** (W.PREP.PHR. in the heavens, ref. to stars) Pl.; (gener.) **elaborate decorations** (for a house, a ceiling) Pl. X. ‖ SG. richly patterned fabric A.
2 (gener.) **variations** (in number, rhythm, or sim.) Pl.

ποικιλό-βουλος ον *adj.* [βουλή] (of Prometheus) of varied counsel, **crafty, cunning** Hes.
ποικιλό-γᾱρυς υ, gen. υος *dial.adj.* [γῆρυς] (of the lyre) **with changeful voice, many-toned** Pi.
ποικιλό-δειρος ον *dial.adj.* [δέρη] (of a nightingale, a widgeon) **with speckled neck** Hes. Alc.
ποικιλό-δέρμων ον, gen. ονος *adj.* [δέρμα] (of horses) with dappled skin, **piebald** E.
ποικιλό-θριξ τριχος *masc.fem.adj.* [θρίξ] (of a fawn) **dapple-coated** E.; (of birds) **dapple-feathered** Lyr.adesp.
ποικιλό-θρονος ον *adj.* [θρόνος] (of Aphrodite) **ornately enthroned** Sapph. [unless reltd. θρόνα, *with woven flowers* (*on her robe*)]
ποικιλο-μήτης ου *masc.adj.* [μῆτις] (of Odysseus) full of varied skills or schemes, **resourceful, cunning** Hom.; (of Zeus, Hermes) hHom.
—**ποικιλόμητις** ιδος *fem.adj.* (of ruinous calamities, as if personif.) **with cunning plans** S.*fr.*
ποικιλό-μορφος ον *adj.* [μορφή] (of dyed garments) having variegated appearance, **elaborately coloured** Ar.
ποικιλό-μουσος ον *adj.* [μοῦσα] (of Orpheus, or perh. of his lyre) **with highly ornamented music** Tim.
ποικιλό-νωτος ον *adj.* [νῶτον] (of a serpent, a deer) **with dappled back** Pi. E.
ποικιλό-πτερος ον *adj.* [πτερόν] (of Eros) **with wings of varied hue** E.; (fig., of a song, whose singer is envisaged as a swan) Pratin.
ποικίλος η (dial. ᾱ) ον *adj.* **1** having a natural intricacy (of colour, shade, texture); (of wild beasts, animal-skins, a tortoise-shell) **dappled, spotted, mottled** Hom. S.*Ichn.* E. Ar. Theoc.; (of birds, their wings) Thgn. Lyr. Ar.; (of snakes) Hdt.; (of a snake concealed in the bosom, w. further connot. *cunning* or *changeable*, ref. to a person's character) Thgn.; (of a serpent pictured on a shield, perh. w. further connot. *elaborately wrought*) Pi.; (of a toad or its breath, fig.ref. to the sound of the aulos, w. further connot. *intricate*) Pratin.; (of a liver-lobe, as used in divination) A.; (of the earth, flowers) **with varied hues** Pi. Pl. Call.; (of granite) **variegated** Hdt.; (of the Gorgon's head, W.DAT. w. locks of serpents) Pi.
2 (of fabrics, garments, or sim.) having an intricacy of colour or pattern (fr. dyeing, weaving or embroidery), **richly patterned** Hom. Lyr. A. Hdt. E. Pl. +; (of woven decorations) **elaborate, intricate** Il.; (of tattooed or painted bodies) **multi-coloured** X. ‖ NEUT.PL.SB. rich fabrics or tapestries A. Ar. Men. Theoc.
3 στοὰ Ποικίλη *Stoa Poikile, Painted Portico* (*in the Athenian agora, decorated w. painted panels*) Aeschin. D.
4 (of armour, chariots, furniture, or sim.) **elaborately** or **intricately wrought** Hom. Hes. Mimn. Sapph. Pi.*fr.* E.; (of a golden serpent as a bangle, also w.connot. *dappled*) Alcm.
5 having a structural intricacy (in respect of music or language); (of a song) **intricate, elaborate** Pi.; (of a nightingale's voice) Ar.; (of a bow aimed by a lover at his beloved, fig.ref. to song) **subtly tuned** B.; (of a rhetorical style) **varied, ornate** Isoc.
6 having a complexity of forms; (of a mythical beast, of the good) **diverse, multiform** Pl.; (of pleasures) **varied** Pl.; (of a meal, a menu) **elaborate** Men.
7 having complexity (opp. simplicity); (of a knot) **intricate, complex, complicated** Od.; (of winding passageways) Hdt.; (of a law, sickness, activity, situation) Pl. X. Plb.; (of speech, thought, or sim.) **abstruse, recondite** Hdt. E. Pl. Arist. Plb.
8 changeable or variable over time; (of a person's disposition) **versatile, adaptable** Thgn.; (of divine power)

complex, changeable E.; (of a person, a disposition) variable, unstable Pl. Arist.; (of hopes) shifting Plb.

9 (pejor., of persons) **cunning, crafty** Hes. A. E. Ar. Plb.; (of a fox) Pl.; (of schemes, falsehoods, arguments, or sim.) Thgn. Pi. B. S. E. Ar.

—**ποικίλον** *neut.adv.* **with an elaborate melody** —*ref. to playing on the lyre* Pi.

—**ποικίλως** *adv.* **1 craftily, cunningly** S. E. Ar. Plb.; **riddlingly** Ar.

2 (of a situation, w. ἔχειν) **be complex** X.

ποικιλο-σάμβαλος ον *dial.adj.* [σάνδαλον] (of a girl) **with fancy sandals** Anacr.

ποικιλό-στολος ον *adj.* [στόλος] (of a ship) **with richly decorated prow** (perh. w. garlands) S.

ποικιλό-τραυλος ον *adj.* [τραυλός] (of the song of blackbirds) **intricately twittering** Theoc.*epigr.*

ποικιλο-φόρμιγξ ιγγος *masc.fem.adj.* (of singing) **to the intricate notes of the lyre** Pi.

ποικιλό-φρων ον, gen. ονος *adj.* [φρήν] (of a fox, Odysseus) **sly-witted, cunning** Alc. E.

ποικιλόω *contr.vb.* | pf. πεποικίλωκα | (of a god) **adorn** (w.ACC. the hoopoe) **with varied colours** S.*fr.*

ποίκιλσις εως *f.* [ποικίλλω] **varying, variation** (of numbers) Pl.(pl.)

ποικιλτής οῦ *m.* **pattern-weaver** (as an occupation) Aeschin. Plu.

ποικιλ-ῳδός όν *adj.* [ἀοιδή] (of the Sphinx) **with riddling song** S.

ποιμαίνω *vb.* [ποιμήν] | iteratv.impf. ποιμαίνεσκον || 3sg.pf.pass. πεποίμανται | **1** (of persons) **shepherd, herd, tend** —*sheep, flocks* Od. Hes. E.*Cyc.* Pl. AR.; (intr.) **shepherd flocks** (on a particular occasion) Il. Men. AR.; **be a shepherd** (as an occupation) Lys. Pl. Theoc. Plb. NT. || PASS. (of flocks) **be shepherded** Il. D.; (of a place) **be ranged over** (by Erinyes, envisaged as a flock) A.; (of dreams) **range or roam afield** Mosch.

2 (fig.) **look after like a shepherd** (either w. solicitude or to assert control); (of a deity) **shepherd, look after** —*a person, a populace* Anacr. A.; (of a lover) **cherish** —*someone* E.; (of a poet's tongue) **nurture** —*someone's praise* Pi.; (of success and praise) —*life's bloom* Pi.; (of Jesus, Christian leaders) —*God's people* NT.; (of a parent or guardian) **manage, control** —*a child* Pl.; (of the shepherd Polyphemos) **keep under control** —*his love* (*by singing*) Theoc.

ποιμάν *dial.m.*: see ποιμήν

ποιμανόριον ου *n.* [ποιμάνωρ] (fig.) **flock** (ref. to a king's army) A.

ποιμάνωρ ορος *m.* [ποιμήν, ποιμαίνω; ἀνήρ] (fig.) **shepherd of the people** (ref. to a country's ruler) A.

ποιμενικός ή όν *adj.* [ποιμήν] **of or relating to a shepherd;** (of a seat, a felt hat) **shepherd's** Theoc. || FEM.SB. **art of shepherding** Pl.

ποιμήν, dial. **ποιμάν** (Theoc.), ένος *m.* **1 shepherd** Hom. +; **herdsman** (of oxen) Od.

2 (fig.) **shepherd** (W.GEN. of people, ref. to rulers and chieftains, esp. Agamemnon) Hom. Hes.; **commander, leader** A.*fr.*; **king, ruler** E.; **master** (of a property) Pi. || PL. **commanders or captains** (W.GEN. of ships) A.; (of companies of soldiers) E.; **drivers** (of chariots) E.; (ref. to the Erotes) **dispensers or managers** (of the gifts of Aphrodite) Pi.; (ref. to soldiers) **guardians or protectors** S.(dub.)

ποίμνη ης, dial. **ποίμνα** ᾱς *f.* **1 flock** (of sheep, sts. extended to include other animals accompanying them) Od. Hes. Hdt. Trag. Pl. +; (of boars and lions) Pi.*fr.*; (fig., of suppliant women, Erinyes) A.; (fig.ref. to the human race) Pl.; (ref. to followers of Jesus) NT.

2 (ref. to a single animal) **sheep** E.

—**ποίμνηθεν** *adv.* **from a flock** —*ref. to taking sheep* AR.

ποιμνήιος η ον *Ion.adj.* (of a farmstead, a pen) **for sheep** Il. Hes.

ποίμνιον ου *n.* **1 flock** (usu. of sheep) Hdt. S. E. Pl. +

2 (fig.) **flock** (ref. to Jesus' followers) NT.

ποιμνίτης ου *masc.adj.* (of mating-songs, played on the panpipe) **for the flocks** E.

ποινάομαι *mid.contr.vb.* [ποινή] | fut. ποινάσομαι || aor.pass.ptcpl. ποιναθείς | **take revenge on** —*someone* E. || PASS. **be punished** E.

ποινάτωρ ορος *m.* **one who exacts retribution** (for another's death), **avenger** (sts. W.GEN. of someone) A. E.

ποινή ῆς, dial. **ποινά** ᾶς *f.* **1 compensation** (for a murdered person, paid to his family); **blood-price, recompense** (W.GEN. for someone) Il. Hdt.

2 compensation (ref. to a gift or other recompense paid in requital for loss or damage) Il.

3 (gener.) **requital** (for a person killed in war or murdered); **retribution, vengeance, revenge** (oft. W.GEN. for someone) Hom. A. Hdt. E. AR.

4 (leg.) **retribution** (imposed for a crime); **penalty, punishment** (oft. W.GEN. for sthg.) Hes. Pi. Trag. Antipho X.

5 (w. positive connot.) **recompense, reward** (W.GEN. for sthg.) A. Pi.

6 (personif., usu.pl.) **Spirit of Vengeance, Avenging Fury** E. Aeschin. Plb. Plu.

ποίνιμος ον *adj.* (of Erinyes, Justice) **avenging** S.; (of sufferings inflicted by Zeus) **punitive** S.

ποιολογέω *contr.vb.* [ποία, λέγω] **gather grass or hay** Theoc. [or perh. *magic herbs*]

ποιο-νόμος ον *adj.* [νέμω] (of cattle) **feeding on grass, grazing** A.

—**ποιόνομος** ον *adj.* (of places) **where grass is grazed** A.

ποῖος ᾱ ον, Ion. **κοῖος** η ον *interrog.adj.* | used in both dir. and indir.qs. | sts. w.art. (ὁ ποῖος or sim.) when the q. refers to sthg. already mentioned | **1** (of persons or things) **of what kind, what sort of?** Od. Simon. Pi. Hdt. Trag. +

2 (esp. of place or time) **which, what?** Od. Pi. Hdt. Trag. +

3 (exclam., of sthg. said or done, expressing surprise or anger) **what ever, what!** Hom. Archil. Hdt. || NEUT.ACC.SB. **what on earth** (w.2sg.vb. have you said or done)! Hom.

4 (w. wd. used by previous speaker repeated in same case, expressing indignation or incredulity) **why, what do you mean by** (such and such)? S. E. Ar. Pl. Men. Theoc.

5 of whom, whose? NT.

—**κοίη** *Ion.fem.dat.adv.* **in what way, how?** Hdt.

—**ποιός** ά όν *indef.adj.* **1** (oft. followed by τις, of things) **of a certain kind** Pl. Arist.

2 || NEUT.SB. **quality** (of things, opp. τὸ ποσόν *quantity*) Arist.

ποιότης ητος *f.* **quality** (of things, opp. ποσότης *quantity*) Pl. Arist.

ποιό-φυτος ον *adj.* [ποία, φύω] (of an enclosure) **planted with grass, grassy** A.*fr.*

ποιπνύω *vb.* [reltd. πνέω] | pres.ptcpl. ποιπνύων, also ποιπνύων (Pi.) | 3pl.impf. ἐποίπνυον, ep. ποίπνυον | aor.ptcpl. ποιπνῡσᾱς | app., **pant from effort;** (of servants or attendants) **bustle about, be busy** Hom. AR.; (of a god, a commander) Il.; (of a friend) **be eager** (on someone's behalf) Pi.

ποιφύγματα των *n.pl.* [perh. ποιφύσσω *blow, snort*] (pejor.) perh. **panting, bellowing** (ref. to sounds made by terrified women) A.

ποιώδης ες *adj.* [ποίᾱ] (of land) **grassy** Hdt.

πόκα, ποκά *dial.advs.*: see πότε, ποτέ

ποκάδες ων *f.pl.* [πόκος] **tufts** (of pubic hair) Ar.

ποκίζομαι *dial.mid.vb.* | 3sg.aor. ἐποκίξατο | **shear** —*goat's hair* (instead of wool, i.e. act perversely) Theoc.

πόκος ου *m.* [πέκω] **shorn wool** (or wool that may be shorn), **fleece** Il. E. Ar. Theoc.; **tuft of wool** (fr. a fleece) S.

πολέα (dial.neut.pl.), **πολέας** (acc.pl.), **πολέες** (nom.pl.), **πολέεσσι** (dat.pl.), **πολεῖ** (dat.sg.), **πολεῖς** (nom.pl.): see πολύς

πόλει (dat.): see πόλις

πολεμᾱ-δόκος ον *dial.adj.* [πόλεμος, δέχομαι] (of Athena) **war-sustaining, bearing the brunt of war** Alc.(cj.) Lamprocl.; (of armour) Pi.

πολεμ-αίνετος ον *adj.* [αἰνετός] (of Herakles) **famed in war** B.*fr.*

πολεμάρχειον, also **πολεμάρχιον**, ου *n.* [πολέμαρχος] **residence of a polemarch** or **military commander** X. Arist. Plb.

πολεμαρχέω *contr.vb.* **be a polemarch** or **military commander** Hdt. X. D. Arist. Plb. Plu.

πολεμαρχίᾱ ᾱς *f.* (at Athens) **office of polemarch** Arist.

πολέμ-αρχος ου *m.* [πόλεμος, ἄρχω] **1 leader in war, warlord** (sts. W.GEN. of a people) A. B.

2 (at Athens) **polemarch** (one of the nine archons, appointed annually, originally w. military command, later w. mainly legal and religious functions) Hdt. Ar. Att.orats. Arist.

3 (in other states) **military commander** Hdt. Th. X. D. Plb. Plu.

πολεμέω *contr.vb.* | fut. πολεμήσω | aor. ἐπολέμησα | pf. πεπολέμηκα ‖ PASS.: fut. πολεμήσομαι, also πολεμηθήσομαι (Plb.) | aor. ἐπολεμήθην ‖ neut.impers.vbl.adj. πολεμητέον, also pl. πολεμητέα |

1 (of nations, their leaders, or sim.) **be at war, go to war, fight a war** Hdt. Th. Ar. + —W.DAT. or πρός + ACC. w. *someone* Hdt. Th. Ar. + ‖ PASS. **be fought against** Th. Isoc. X. D. Plb.

2 fight —W.COGN.ACC. *a war* Lys. Pl. Arist. Plb. ‖ PASS. (of a war) **be fought** Th. Pl. X.; (of hostilities) **take place** Th. X.

3 (wkr.sens., of Herakles) **fight, do battle** (w. a monster) Stesich.; (of soldiers) —w. ἀπό + GEN. *fr. a horse, a camel* Pl. X.

4 (fig.) **wrangle, quarrel** —W.DAT. w. *someone* Hippon. X. Is. D. —w. *necessity, a god's will* S. E.; (of certain practices) **militate** —W.DAT. *against health* E.

πολεμήιος η (dial. ᾱ) ον *adj.* **of or relating to war**; (of deeds) **warlike** Hom. hHom. AR.; (of armour, weapons) **borne in war** Il. Hes. hHom. B. AR.; (of a horse) **trained for war, military** Call.; (of a trumpet-call) **to war** B.

πολεμησείω *vb.* [desideratv. πολεμέω] (of a people) **be eager for war** Th.

πολεμητήριον ου *n.* (ref. to a town) **war-base** Plb.

πολεμίζω, ep. **πτολεμίζω** *vb.* | ep.inf. πολεμιζέμεν, πολεμιζέμεναι | ep.impf. πολέμιζον | fut. π(τ)ολεμίξω | ep.3sg.aor. πτολέμιξε (AR.) | **1** (of persons) **engage in war** or **fighting, do battle, fight** (sts. W.DAT. w. *someone*) Hom. Hes. Tyrt. Anacr. Pi. Ar. + —W.COGN.ACC. Il.; (of horses) **go into battle** Il.

2 (fig.) **wage war** —W.DAT. w. *one's tongue* (i.e. engage in verbal disputation) Ar.

πολεμικός ή όν *adj.* **1 of or relating to war**; (of activities, equipment, regulations, experience, or sim.) **military** Th. Isoc. Pl. X. + ‖ FEM.SB. **art of war** Pl. ‖ NEUT.PL.SB. **military matters** or **warfare** Th. Ar. Pl. +

2 ‖ NEUT.SB. **signal for battle** X. Thphr.

3 (of persons) **occupied in the business of war, military** Pl. ‖ NEUT.SB. **fighting part of the populace, military class** (opp. civilians) Arist.

4 (of persons, a populace) **skilled in** or **disposed to war, warlike** Th. Isoc. X. Aeschin.; (of horses) **suited to war** X.; (fig., of persons) **acting in a warlike manner, belligerent** Hyp. Men.; (of actions, feelings) **warlike, hostile** X. ‖ NEUT.SB. **warlike spirit** Plu.

—**πολεμικῶς** *adv.* | superl. πολεμικώτατα | **1 in a military manner** Arist.

2 in a warlike manner, belligerently Isoc. X. Aeschin.

πολέμιος ᾱ (Ion. η) ον (also ος ον) *adj.* | compar. πολεμιώτερος, superl. πολεμιώτατος | **1** (of events, situations) **of** or **relating to war**; (of the troubles) **of war** Pi.; (of a wave, fig.ref. to turmoil) E. ‖ NEUT.PL.SB. **military matters, warfare** Hdt. Th. X. Arist.

2 (of persons or things) **warlike, enemy, hostile** (sts. W.DAT. **to someone** or **sthg.**) Pi. Hdt. Trag. Th. + ‖ MASC.SB. **enemy** (sts. W.GEN. of someone) Pi. Hdt. E. Th. +; (pl., more freq.) Hdt. Trag. Th. + ‖ NEUT.SB. **hostility** (sts. W.GEN. towards an enemy) Th.

3 of or relating to an enemy; (of fear) **directed towards an enemy** A.(dub.); (of shipwrecks) **of enemy vessels** Lys.; (of fire-signals) **warning of an enemy approach** Th.

4 of or belonging to an enemy; (of weapons) **enemy** Trag. Ar.; (of ships) Hdt. Th. X.; (of spoils) E.; (of a land) Hdt. Trag. Th. X. ‖ FEM.SB. **enemy country** Th. Ar. Isoc. X. ‖ NEUT.PL.SB. **enemy goods** Ar.

—**πολεμίως** *adv.* **in a hostile manner** or **spirit** Th. X.

πολεμιστήριος ᾱ ον (also ος ον) *adj.* [πολεμιστής] **of or relating to war** or **warriors**; (of horses) **for use in war, military** Hdt. X. D. Plu.; (of chariots) Hdt. Pl. X.; (of weapons, opp. those of gladiators) Plu.; (of equipment, a cuirass) Ar. Plu.; (of a mixing-bowl) Ar.; (of a battle-cry, courage) Ar. Plu. ‖ NEUT.SB. **war-chariot** Pl. X.; (used for racing) Ar.

πολεμιστής οῦ, ep. **πτολεμιστής** έω, dial. **πολεμιστάς** ᾶ *m.* [πολεμίζω] **1 warrior, fighter** Hom. Hes.*fr.* Pi. Theoc. Plu.

2 ‖ ADJ. (of a person) **experienced in war** Plu.; (of a horse) **military** Plb. Plu.; (used for racing) Theoc.

πολεμο-κέλαδος ον *adj.* [πόλεμος] (of Bromios) **raising the battle-cry** Lyr.adesp.

πολεμό-κραντος ον *adj.* [κραίνω] (of an outcome, ref. to victory or defeat) **that decides a war** A.

πολεμο-λᾱμαχαϊκός ή όν *adj.* [Λάμαχος, perh. also Ἀχαϊκός] **of or relating to war and Lamachos** (an Athenian general) **and Achaeans**; (of an expeditionary force) **for the Lamachaean war** Ar.

πολεμόνδε, ep. **πτολεμόνδε** *adv.* **to war** or **battle** Hom. Lyr.adesp. AR.

πολεμόομαι *mid.contr.vb.* (of a state) **make** (W.ACC. a people) **one's enemy** Th. ‖ PASS. (of a ruler, a country) **be made one's enemy** Th.

πολεμοποιέω *contr.vb.* [πολεμοποιός] (of a person) **be belligerent** X. Plu.

πολεμο-ποιός όν *adj.* [ποιέω] (of persons) **stirring up war, belligerent** Arist. Plu.

πόλεμος, ep. **πτόλεμος**, ου *m.* [perh.reltd. πελεμίζω] **1** (sts.pl.) **armed conflict** (oft. betw. individual warriors or groups), **battle, fight, fighting** Hom.

2 war (betw. nations or cities, ref. either to a state of conflict, opp. peace, or to a specific conflict) Hom. +

3 (personif.) **War** Heraclit. Pi.*fr.* Ar.

πολεμο-φθόρος ον *adj.* [φθείρω] (of disasters or deluded plans) **involving destruction by war** A.

πολέοιν (Att.gen.du.), **πόλεος** (dial.gen.), **πόλεσι** (dat.pl.), **πόλεως** (Ion.gen.): see πόλις

πολέος (dial.gen.), **πόλεσι** and **πολέσσι** (dial.dat.pl.): see πολύς

πολεύω *vb.* [reltd. πέλω, πόλος] **1** (of a woman) **go about, roam** —w.PREP.PHR. *in a city* Od.; (of satyrs) **tramp around** S.*Ichn*.(cj.)
2 (of a ploughman) **work over (the soil), plough** (land) S.

πολέω *contr.vb.* **1 go about**; (of persons) **loiter** —w.ADV. or PREP.PHR. *in a place* E.; (of celestial phenomena, w. word-play on πόλος *firmament*) **move about** or **around** Pl.; (tr., of a corpse) **drift around** —*an island* A.(dub.) ‖ PASS. (of the sky, w. word-play on πόλος) perh., **be frequented** (by birds) Ar.
2 (of a ploughman) **work over (the soil), plough** (land) Hes.

πολέων (ep.gen.pl.): see πολύς

πόλεων (gen.pl.), **πόλη** (Att.nom.acc.du.), **πόλη** (Att.dat.sg.), **πόληες**, **πόληος** and **πόληι** (ep. nom.pl., gen. and dat.sg.): see πόλις

πόλησις εως *f.* [πολέω] **movement** (around the heavens) Pl.

πολιά ᾶς *f.* [πολιός] **greyness** (of hair, in old age) Arist.

πολιαίνομαι *pass.vb.* (of the sea) **be whitened** (by strong wind) A.

πολιάοχος *dial.adj.*: see πολιοῦχος

πολί-αρχος, ep. **πτολίαρχος**, ου *m.* [πόλις, ἄρχω] **ruler of cities** (ref. to a king) Pi. E. Call.

Πολιάς άδος *fem.adj.* (of Athena, as her chief cult-title on the Acropolis) **Guarding the City** Hdt. S. Ar. Aeschin. Din. ‖ SB. **Guardian of the City** Pi.*fr.* Plu.

πολιάτᾱς *dial.m.*: see πολίτης

πολίζω *vb.* [πόλις] | ep.aor. ἐπόλισσα, also πόλισσα ‖ pf.pass. πεπόλισμαι | **1 create a city; found** —*a city* AR.; **build** —*a city wall* Il. ‖ MID. **build for oneself** —*a city* AR.
‖ STATV.PF.PLPF.PASS. (of a city) **have been built, stand** Il. Hes.*fr.* Hdt.
2 make (a place) **into a city; build a city in** —w.ACC. *a place* X. Plu. ‖ PF.PASS. (of a country) **have cities** (by a specific river) Hdt.

πολιήοχος *ep.adj.*: see πολιοῦχος

πολιήτης, **πολιῆτις** *Ion.m.f.*: see πολίτης

πόλινδε *adv.*: see under πόλις

πολιο-κρόταφος ον *adj.* [πολιός] (of persons) **with grey hair on one's temples, grey-templed** Il. Hes.; (fig., of old age) B.*fr.*

πολιορκέω *contr.vb.* [πόλις, ἕρκος] | aor. ἐπολιόρκησα ‖ fut.pass. πολιορκήσομαι, also πολιορκηθήσομαι | **1** (of an army, a commander) **besiege, blockade** —*a city, its occupants, or sim.* Hdt. + ‖ PL.PTCPL.SB. **besiegers** (opp. besieged) Isoc. ‖ PASS. **be besieged** Hdt. +; (of a fleet) **be blockaded** (by another fleet, i.e. be penned into harbour) Isoc.; (hyperbol., of the personif. river Scamander) **be attacked** or **be under siege** (by Achilles) Pl.
2 (fig., of persons) **harass** —*the weak* X. ‖ PASS. **be harassed** (by informers) Pl.; (of a person's body) **be oppressed** (by sufferings) X.; (of an argument) **be challenged** Pl.

πολιορκητέος ᾱ ον *vbl.adj.* (of an army) **to be put under siege** X.

πολιορκητικός ή όν *adj.* (of strategies) **appropriate to a siege** Plb.

πολιορκίᾱ ᾱς, Ion. **πολιορκίη** ης *f.* **1 siege** (of a town or sim.) Hdt. +
2 (fig.) **harassment** (of persons, by informers) Pl.; (by billeted soldiers) Plu.(dub.)

πολιός ά (Ion. ή) όν (also ός όν E.) *adj.* **1 of an indeterminate lightish hue**; (of iron or steel) **grey** Hom. Hes. hHom. E.; (of χαλκός *bronze*, meton. for iron) Pi.
2 (of a wolf) **grey** Il. hHom. AR. Theoc.; (of a crow) Ar.; (of a swan) **grey** or **white** E.
3 (of the sea) **white-flecked** Hom. Archil. Alc. Thgn. Pi. S. +; (of a wave) Anacr.; (of a shore, a harbour, when waves are breaking) S. AR.
4 grey or **white from age**; (of persons) **grey-haired** or **white-haired** Od. Hes. S. E. Ar. Pl. +; (of hair, a beard) **grey, white** Il. hHom. S. E. Ar. +; (of the head, temples, chin, or sim., ref. to their hair) Hom. Tyrt. Anacr. E.; (of old age) **grey-haired, hoary** Thgn. Pi. B. E. ‖ FEM.PL.SB. **grey hairs** Pi. Ar. Isoc. Aeschin. Thphr. Call.; (collectv.sg.) Call.
5 (of a womb, flesh) **aged, old woman's** Pi. E.; (of tears) **of an old man** E.
6 (of wine) **well-aged, vintage** E. Men.; (of a law, stories, knowledge) **age-old, time-honoured** A. E. Pl.
7 (of spring) app. **bright** Hes.; (of aither, air) **clear** E. AR.
—**πολιά** *neut.pl.adv.* **in grey old age** —*ref. to living as a spinster* E.

πολιοῦχος, ep. **πολιήοχος**, dial. **πολιάοχος**, also **πολίοχος**, ον *adj.* [πόλις, ἔχω] (epith. of a god or goddess) **who guards the city** A. Pi. Hdt. Ar. Pl. Call. +; (of royal power) **city-guarding** E.

πολιοφυλακέω *contr.vb.* [πόλις, φύλαξ] (of a commander) **garrison a city** (rather than take the field) Plb.

πολιό-χρως ωτος *masc.fem.adj.* [πολιός, χρώς] | acc. πολιόχρων | (fig., of an old man, compared to a swan) **with white complexion, white-plumed** E.

πόλις, ep. **πτόλις**, εως (dial. ιος, also εος, ep. ηος, Ion. ευς) *f.* | voc. πόλι | acc. π(τ)όλιν, ep. πόληα | dat. πόλει, Att. πόλη, ep. πόληι, πτόλεϊ, dial. πόλῑ ‖ PL.: nom. πόλεις, dial. πόλιες, ep. πόληες | acc. πόλεις, Ion. πόλῑς, dial. πόλιας, ep. πόληας | gen. πόλεων, dial. πολίων | dat. πόλεσι, dial. πόλισι, also πόλεσι (Pi.), ep. πολίεσσι ‖ ATT.DU.: nom.acc. πόλη, gen. πολέοιν |
1 city, settlement or **fort** (built on high ground); (at Troy) **citadel, acropolis** (ref. to Pergamos; oft. specified as πόλις ἄκρη or ἀκροτάτη *topmost part of the city*) Il.; (at Athens) **Acropolis** (usu. in prep.phrs. εἰς (τὴν) πόλιν, ἐν (τῇ) πόλει, or sim.) Th. Ar. Att.orats. X. Arist. Plu.; (at Thebes, ref. to the Kadmeia) Plu.
2 city or **town** Hom. +; (w. name in appos. or GEN.) Hom. +
3 city as a political entity (characterised in the classical period by political and legal autonomy, oft. w. some degree of citizen participation in government), **city-state, state** (usu. also including the surrounding country) Hom. +
4 (ref. to a person's origins or domicile) **native city** or **home city** Od. +
5 (gener.) **inhabited region, territory, land** (ref. to an island) Il. A. Pi. E. Lys. Ar.; (ref. to a country) E. Lys.
6 (collectv., ref. to the occupants of a city) **community, citizen body** Il. +
—**πόλινδε** *adv.* **to** or **towards a city** Hom. AR.

πόλισμα ατος *n.* [πολίζω] **1 foundation, settlement, town** Hdt. Th. X. Plb. Plu.
2 city (not distinguishable fr. πόλις 2) Hdt. Trag. Ar. Men.(quot.trag.) Call.; (collectv., ref. to its occupants) Trag.
—**πολισμάτιον** ου *n.* [dimin.] **small town** Plb. Plu.

πολισσο-νόμος ον *adj.* [νέμω] (of the authority) **of governing a city** A.; (of a life, w. positive connots.) prob. **under a city's government** A.

πολισσοῦχος ον *adj.* [reltd. πολιοῦχος] **1** (of a deity) **who guards the city** A.; (of a ruler, a dead hero) Call. AR.
2 (of a populace) **occupying a city** A.

πολῑτ-άρχης ου *m*. [πολίτης, ἄρχω] (in Thessalonike) **civic magistrate** NT.

πολῑτείᾱ ᾱς, Ion. **πολῑτηίη** ης *f*. [πολῑτεύω] **1** status and rights of a citizen, **citizenship** Hdt. Th. X. Arist. ǁ PL. grants of citizenship (to foreigners) Arist.
2 daily life of a citizen, **civic life, public life** Att.orats. Plb.
3 activity of governing a city, **political life, politics, government** Th. Ar. Att.orats. +
4 (specif.) political programme or course of action, **policy** Aeschin. D.
5 particular form of government, **political system, constitution** Th. Att.orats. Pl. +
6 (specif.) **constitutional government, free democratic government** (opp. tyranny, aristocracy, or sim.) Isoc. D. Arist.
7 (concr.) community of citizens, **citizen body** Arist.

πολίτευμα ατος *n*. **1** (sg. and pl.) political decision or course of action, **policy** Aeschin. D. Plu. ǁ PL. political practices or institutions Isoc. Pl.
2 (concr.) **government** Aeschin. Arist. Plb. Plu.

πολῑτεύω *vb*. [πολίτης] | aor.mid. ἐπολῑτευσάμην ǁ aor.pass. (sts. w.mid.sens.) ἐπολῑτεύθην | **1** be a citizen (of a place); **live as a citizen, enjoy civic rights** Th. X.; (mid.) And. ǁ MID. and PASS. **behave publicly** —W.ADV. *in a certain way* Lys.
ǁ PASS. be given citizen rights or exercise one's rights as a citizen Th.
2 engage in public or political activities; **conduct one's political life** —W.ADV. or PREP.PHR. *in a certain way* Th. X.; (of a community) —W.ADJ. *on one's own* Th. ǁ MID. **take part in public life, engage in politics, be a politician** E.*fr*. Att.orats. Pl.
3 ǁ MID. (of politicians or a populace) **adopt** or **follow a policy** —W.ADV. or PREP.PHR. or ACC. *of a certain kind* Ar. Aeschin. D. —W.ACC. *regarding sthg.* Ar. D. ǁ PASS. (of a city) be run —W.ADV. *well, badly* Isoc. Pl. X. Arist.
ǁ NEUT.PL.PF.PASS.PTCPL.SB. political measures or policies Isoc. D.
4 have a specified form of constitution; (of a populace) **be governed, live** —W.ADV. or PREP.PHR. or COGN.ACC. *under a certain type of government, under certain conditions* Th. X. Plb.; (mid.) Att.orats. Pl. X.
5 ǁ MID. (wkr.sens., of persons) **conduct oneself, live** —W.ADVBL.PHR. *in a certain way* NT.

πολῑτηίη *Ion.f*.: see πολῑτείᾱ

πολίτης ου, dial. **πολίτᾱς** ᾱ, Ion. **πολιήτης** εω, dial. **πολιᾱ́τᾱς** ᾱ (Alc. Pi.) *m*. [πόλις] **1** ǁ COLLECTV.PL. inhabitants of a (particular) city, **townspeople, citizens** Hom. +
2 (sg. and pl.) male inhabitant of a city (esp. as participating in its government through some kind of assembly), **citizen** Hdt. +; one who lives in the same city (as another previously mentioned), **fellow citizen, countryman** Hdt. E. +
3 ǁ ADJ. (of gods, in an invocation) of one's own city A.; (of the populace) Ar.

—**πολῖτις** ιδος *f*. | acc. πολῖτιν | **1** (sg. and pl.) **free woman of a city, female citizen** Att.orats. Pl. Arist. Men. Plu.
2 (pl.) **fellow townswoman** S. E.

—**πολιῆτις** ιδος *Ion.f*. **1 woman of one's city** AR.
2 ǁ ADJ. (of a shore, as a boundary) of one's city E.

πολῑτικός ή όν *adj*. **1** of or relating to citizens (of a particular city); (of households) **belonging to citizens** Isoc.; (of public services) **performed by citizens** (opp. resident aliens) D.
2 consisting of citizens; (of military forces) **composed of citizens** (opp. allies or sim.) Att.orats. X. Plb. ǁ NEUT.SB. citizen force X.
3 used by the citizens as a whole; (of a carriage) **communal, public** X.; (of words) **in common use** Isoc.
4 exhibiting the behaviour of a citizen; (of assistance given by an individual) **public-spirited** D.; (of a person) **civil, urbane** Plb.
5 (of activities, relationships) in the sphere of the city or state (opp. individual affairs); (of equality under the laws) **civil, political** Th.; (of cooperation, rivalry, virtue, or sim.) X. Arist.; (phr.) ὁ ἄνθρωπος φύσει πολιτικὸν ζῷον *man is by nature a political animal* Arist.; (of honours) **public, civic** Isoc. X.; (of speeches) **on public themes** Isoc.; (of a legal issue) **public** (opp. private) D.; (in Sparta, of land as a type of property) Plb.; (of the office of Roman praetor) **urban** Plu.
ǁ NEUT.SB. political community Hdt. Th.
6 (of activities, skills) relating to civic politics; (of affairs, activities, an assembly) **political** Att.orats. Pl. +; (of a person, a mind) **suited for politics, statesmanlike** Isoc. Pl. X.; (of the skill) **of a statesman, political** Pl. ǁ MASC.SB. politician, statesman Pl. X. Arist. ǁ FEM.SB. art of statesmanship, political science Pl. Arist. ǁ NEUT.PL.SB. state business, political activities, politics Th. Att.orats. Pl. +
7 (specif.) relating to constitutional government; (of rule) **constitutional** (opp. despotic or sim.) Arist.

—**πολῑτικῶς** *adv*. | superl. πολιτικώτατα | **1** in a way which relates to the city or its citizens; **for the public benefit** Att.orats. Plb.; **in the public sphere** Arist.; (w. ἔχειν) *be public-spirited* Isoc.
2 in the style of civic discourse (opp. that of rhetoricians) —*ref. to speaking* Arist.
3 in a statesmanlike manner Arist.; **constitutionally** (opp. monarchically or sim.) Arist.
4 (gener.) **in ordinary** or **everyday terms** —*ref. to defining a word* Arist.
5 urbanely, diplomatically —*ref. to criticising someone* Plb.

πολῖτις *f*.: see under πολίτης

πολῑτογραφέομαι *pass.contr.vb*. [γράφω] (of an immigrant) **be enrolled as a citizen** Plb.

πολῑτο-φθόρος ον *adj*. [φθείρω] (of impious acts) **harmful to the citizen-body** Pl.

πολῑτο-φύλαξ ακος *m*. **civic guard** (as the title of a police magistrate) Arist.

πολίχνη ης *f*. [dimin. πόλις] **little town, village** Th. Call. Plu.

πολίχνιον ου *n*. [dimin. πολίχνη] **village, hamlet** Isoc. Pl. Plu.

πολλάκις, also poet. **πολλάκι** *adv*. [πολύς] **1 many times, often** Hom. +; (also) τὸ πολλάκις Pi.
2 (in multiplication) πολλάκις μύριοι *many tens of thousands* Pl.; πολλάκις τοσοῦτος *many times as great* Pl. Plu.
3 (after εἰ, μή *if, in case*, or sim.) as often happens, **as may well happen, possibly** Th. Ar. Pl. D.

πολλαπλασιάζω *vb*. [πολλαπλάσιος] (fig.) **multiply, exaggerate** —*a country's services* Plb.

πολλαπλάσιος ᾱ ον (also ος ον), Ion. **πολλαπλήσιος** η ον *adj*. [reltd. πολύς] (of persons or things) **many times as great** or **as many** Hdt. Th. Att.orats. +; **many times greater** or **more** (W.GEN. than sthg.) Hdt. Antipho Th. Isoc. Pl. +; (w. ἤ) Hdt. Th. Pl.

—**πολλαπλάσια** *neut.pl.adv*. **to a much greater extent** or **degree** X.

—**πολλαπλασίως** *adv*. **to a much greater extent** or **degree** Plb.

πολλαπλασιόω *contr.vb*. **multiply** —*a number* Pl.

πολλαπλασίων ον, gen. ονος *adj.* (of persons or things) **many times as much** or **as many** Plb.(dub.) NT. Plu.

πολλαπλασίωσις εως *f.* **1 multiplication** (of numbers) Pl. Arist.
2 proportional increase (in the value of one thing relative to another) Arist.

πολλαπλοῦς ῆ οῦν *Att.adj.* **1** (of a life) **many times as long** (as a given life) Pl.; (of a compound word) **multiple** Arist.
2 (of a person) playing multiple roles, **versatile** Pl.

πολλαχῇ *adv.* **1 in many places** Sol. Th. Pl. X. +
2 in many ways A.(dub.) Hdt. Democr. Th. Isoc. Pl. +
3 perh. **from many sides** —*ref. to a god calling someone* S.
4 from many angles —*ref. to examining sthg.* Ar.
5 for many reasons —*ref. to doing sthg.* Hdt.

πολλαχόθεν *adv.* **1 from many places** or **sides** Th. Lycurg. Hyp. Plu.
2 from many sources —*ref. to acquiring sthg.* Th. Pl.
3 on many grounds —*ref. to deducing or demonstrating sthg.* Lys. D.
4 on many sides —*ref. to sthg. being agreed* Pl. D.
5 for many reasons Th.

πολλαχόθι *adv.* **in many places** Plu.; **in many parts** (W.GEN. of a city, a country) Plu.

πολλαχόσε *adv.* **1 to** or **into many places** Th. Pl. D.; **into many parts** (W.GEN. of a country) X.
2 in many directions Plu.
3 in many places —*ref. to selling one's services* D.

πολλαχοῦ *adv.* **1 in many places** E. Th. Lys. Pl. X. +
2 on many occasions (within a speech or poem) Pl. Aeschin. Arist.; (W.GEN. in one's poetry) Plb.
3 in many cases —*ref. to sthg. happening or being demonstrated* X.
4 in many respects —*ref. to being at a disadvantage* D.

πολλαχῶς *adv.* **1 in many ways** Isoc. D. Arist. Plb.
2 in many senses —*ref. to using a word* Arist.

πολλή *fem.adj.*: see πολύς

πολλο-δεκάκις *adv.* (hyperbol.) **many tens of times over** —*ref. to being wretched* Ar.

πολλός, πολλόν *Ion.masc. and neut.adj.*: see πολύς

πολλοστη-μόριος ον *adj.* [πολλοστός, μόριον] (of a quantity) **many times smaller** (sts. W.GEN. than another) Arist. ‖ NEUT.SB. quantity (of troops) **much smaller** (W.GEN. than an opponent's, i.e. a mere fraction of them) Plu.

πολλοστός ή όν *adj.* **1 far down in a numerical listing**; (of persons) **low on the list, relatively insignificant** Isoc. D.; (of a thing) **lesser, minor** Pl.
2 (w. μόριον) **very small part, small fraction** (of sthg.) Th.; (w. μέρος) Att.orats. X. Arist. Plb. Plu.
3 (phr.) πολλοστῷ χρόνῳ **on a very late occasion** (i.e. after a very long time) Ar. D.

—**πολλοστῶς** *adv.* **in a lower degree** —*ref. to sthg. being the case* Arist.

πόλος ου *m.* [πέλω] **1 pivot** or **axis** (around which sthg. moves); **axis** (of the celestial sphere) Pl.
2 one of the points on the celestial sphere around which the stars appear to revolve, pole E. Pl. Arist.
3 vault (of heaven), **firmament, celestial sphere** A. E.*fr.* Ar. Tim.; (W.GEN. of stars) Pl.
4 sundial (ref. to a dish-shaped dial) Hdt.
5 centre (of a circular threshing-floor) X.

πολουσπερίες (Boeot.nom.pl.adj.): see πολυσπερής

πολτός οῦ *m.* **porridge** (made fr. beans) Alcm.

πολυ-αίμων ον, gen. ονος *adj.* [πολύς, αἷμα] (of decapitation) **very bloody** A.

πολυ-αίνετος ον *adj.* [αἰνετός] (of a city) **much praised, famed** E.

πολύ-αινος ον *adj.* [αἶνος] (of Odysseus) **much praised, famed** Hom. Lyr.adesp.

πολυ-άϊξ ϊκος *ep.masc.fem.adj.* [ἄσσω] **with a great rush**; (of war or battle) **furious, seething** Hom.; (of weariness) **from furious fighting** Il.

πολυ-άμπελος ον *adj.* (prob. of a person) **rich in vines** B.

πολυανδρέω *contr.vb.* [πολύανδρος] **be full of men**; (of cities) **be packed** —W.DAT. *w. mobs* Th.

πολυάνδριον ου *n.* **common grave** (for soldiers, on a battlefield) Plu.

πολύ-ανδρος ον *adj.* [ἀνήρ] **1** (of a country, a city) **full of men, populous** A.
2 (of persons) **many in number, numerous** A. Tim.

πολυ-άνθεμος ον *adj.* [ἄνθεμον] (of fields) **rich in flowers, flowery** Sapph.; (of spring) Mimn.; (of the Seasons) Pi.

πολυ-ανθής ές *adj.* [ἄνθος] (of woodland) **flowering, flowery** Od.; (of spring) hHom.; (fig., of the hue of a bird's wings) Mosch.

πολυανθρωπίᾱ ᾱς *f.* [πολυάνθρωπος] **large population** X. Arist.

πολυ-άνθρωπος ον *adj.* **1** (of a city, region, or sim.) **with a large population, populous** Th. X. D. Arist. Plu.
2 (of political power, democratic government) **based on a large population** Th. Arist.
3 (of tribes) consisting of a large number of people, **populous** Plb. Plu.

πολυ-άνωρ ορος *dial.masc.fem.adj.* [ἀνήρ] **1 associated with many men**; (of a city) **well-populated** Ar.; (of the Delphic oracle) **well-frequented** E.; (of good order) perh. **maintained among a crowd of people** Lyr.adesp.
2 (of a woman, ref. to Helen) **with many men** (as husbands or lovers) A.

πολυ-άρατος, ep. **πολυάρητος**, ον *adj.* [ἀράομαι] **1** (of a god) **much prayed to, as the object of many prayers** Od.
2 (of a child) **much prayed for, as the answer to many prayers** Od. hHom.; (iron., of someone's wisdom) **earnestly desired** Pl.
3 (of a trouble) **much prayed against** (in the hope of averting it) Thgn. [or perh. *accursed*]

πολυ-άργυρος ον *adj.* **1** (of a nation) **rich in silver** Hdt.
2 (of an estate) **wealthy** Plu.

πολυ-αρκής ές *adj.* [ἀρκέω] **providing much help** or **support** (to people); (of a river) **life-sustaining** Hdt.; (of a city, ref. to its natural advantages and resources) Plu.

πολυ-άρματος ον *adj.* [ἅρμα] (of Thebes) **with many war-chariots** S.

πολυ-αρμόνιος ον *adj.* [ἁρμονία] (of musical instruments) **with a wide harmonic range** Pl.

πολύαρνι (dat.adj.): see πολύρρην

πολυαρχίᾱ ᾱς *f.* [ἄρχω] **multiplicity of command, divided leadership** (in an army, as a disadvantage) Th. X. Plu.

πολύ-αστρος ον *adj.* [ἄστρον] (of heaven) **starry** E.

πολυ-άχητος ον *dial.adj.* [ἠχέω] (of a throng of singers) **rich in sound, full-voiced** E.

πολύ-βατος ον *adj.* [βατός] (of a meeting-place in a city) **much-trodden** A. Pi.*fr.*

πολυ-βενθής ές *adj.* [βένθος] (of the sea, a harbour, a lake) **very deep** Hom. AR.

Πολύβιος ου *m.* **Polybius** (historian, c.200–c.120 BC) Plu.

πολύ-βορος ον *adj.* [βορός] | superl. πολυβορώτατος | (of an animal, ref. to the elephant) **voracious** Pl.

πολύ-βοσκος ον *adj.* [βόσκω] (of a land) **nourishing, bountiful** Pi.

πολύ-βοτος ον *adj.* [βοτόν] (of a people) **with many herds** Tim.

πολύ-βοτρυς υ, gen. υος *adj.* [βότρυς] (of places) **rich in grapes** Hes.*fr.* Simon. Theoc.; (of the vine) E.

πολύ-βουλος ον *adj.* [βουλή] (of Athena) **rich in counsel, resourceful** Hom.; (of a person's judgement) Pi.

πολύ-βούτης εω *Ion.masc.adj.* [βοῦς] (of persons) **with many oxen** Il. Hes.*fr.*

πολύ-βροχος ον *adj.* [βρόχος] (of fastenings) **with many encircling ropes** E.

πολύ-βωμος ον *adj.* [βωμός] (of places) **with many altars** Call.

πολυ-γηθής, dial. **πολυγᾱθής**, ές *adj.* [γηθέω] (of the seasons) bringing much gladness (by a change in the year), **gladdening** Il.; (of Dionysus) **bringer of joy** Hes. Pi.*fr.*; (of marriage w. Zeus) Pi.

πολυ-γήραος ον *adj.* [γῆρας] (of a person) **very aged** Asius

πολύ-γλωσσος ον *adj.* [γλῶσσα] **1** (of the oracular oak at Dodona) speaking with many tongues (perh. ref. to the rustling of its leaves), **many-voiced, conveying many messages** S.; (of threats) **in many languages** Plu.
2 (of a person's shouting) **loud-voiced, clamorous** S.

πολύ-γναμπτος ον *adj.* [γναμπτός] (of glens) **with many bends, winding** Pi.; (of celery, ref. to its leaves) **curling, curly** Theoc.

πολυ-γνώμων ον, gen. ονος *adj.* (of persons) **very knowledgeable** Pl.

πολύ-γνωτος ον *adj.* [γνωτός] (of a family, a victory) **well-known, famous** Pi.

πολύ-γομφος ον *adj.* [γόμφος] (of ships) **with many dowels** Hes. Ibyc.; (of a floating bridge) A.

πολυγονίᾱ ᾱς *f.* [πολύγονος] **fecundity** (of certain kinds of animal) Pl.

πολύ-γονος ον *adj.* [γόνος] (of animals) producing many offspring, **prolific** A. Hdt. X.

πολυ-δαίδαλος ον *adj.* **1** (of weapons, jewellery, furniture, or sim.) **richly or skilfully wrought** Hom. Hes. hHom.; (of weaving) **richly worked, finely decorated** Hes.
2 (of persons) **very skilled in one's craft** Il.

πολυ-δάκρυος ον *adj.* [δάκρυον] **1** (of battle) that causes many tears, **fraught with tears, woeful, grievous** Il.; (of Ares) Tyrt.; (of Hades) E.; (of slavery) B.
2 (of a dead person's shade) full of tears, **tearful** AR.

πολύ-δακρυς υ, gen. υος *adj.* [δάκρυ] **1** (of war, battle, Ares) that causes many tears, **fraught with tears, woeful, grievous** Il. Thgn.; (of a plan) B.
2 (of Itys) **much lamented** Ar.
3 (of a person) full of tears, **tearful** E.
4 (of lamentation) accompanied by many tears, **tearful** A. E.

πολυ-δάκρῡτος ον *adj.* [δακρυτός] **1** (of a dead person) much wept over, **much lamented** Il.
2 (of a person) full of tears, **tearful** E.
3 (of lamentation) accompanied by much weeping, **tearful** Od. A. Ar.

πολυ-δάπανος ον *adj.* [δαπάνη] **1** indulging in great expense; (of a person) **extravagant** X.
2 causing great expense; (of a temple) **costly, sumptuous** Hdt.; (of cuisine) **expensive** X.

πολυ-δέγμων ονος *masc.adj.* [δέχομαι] (euphem.epith. of Hades) who welcomes many, **all-welcoming, hospitable** hHom.

πολυ-δειράς άδος *masc.fem.adj.* (of Olympos) **many-ridged** Il.

πολυ-δέκτης ου *masc.adj.* [δέχομαι] (euphem.epith. of Hades) who welcomes many, **all-welcoming, hospitable** hHom.

πολυ-δένδρεος ον *adj.* [δένδρεον] (of an estate or sim.) **with many trees** Od. Sol.; (of a region, a mountain) **wooded** hHom. Theoc.

πολύ-δενδρος ον *adj.* (of a mountain or sim.) **wooded** Simon. E. Theoc.

πολυ-δερκής ές *adj.* [δέρκομαι] (of Dawn, the light of day) **far-seeing** Hes.

πολύ-δεσμος ον *adj.* [δεσμός] (of an improvised sailing-vessel) having many bonds, **strongly bound together** Od.

Πολυδεύκης, dial. **Πωλυδεύκης** (Alcm. Call.), εος (ους) *m.* Polydeukes (son of Leda by Tyndareos or Zeus, brother of Helen and Kastor) Hom. + | see also Διόσκοροι

—**Πολυδεύκειος** η ον *Ion.adj.* (of the hand) **of Polydeukes** Call.

πολύ-δηρις ι, gen. ιος *adj.* [δῆρις] (of a refutative argument) strife-encompassed, **contentious** Parm.

πολυδικέω *contr.vb.* [δίκη] engage in many lawsuits, **be litigious** Pl.

πολύ-δίψιος ον *adj.* (of a region) very thirsty, **waterless, arid** Il.

πολύ-δονος ον *adj.* [δονέω] (of Io's wanderings) **much-driven, hounded, harassed, persecuted** A.; (of drowned bodies) **driven to and fro** (by the waves) A.

πολύ-δρομος ον *adj.* [δρόμος] (of flight) with much running (i.e. covering a long distance), **far-running** A.

πολυδωρίᾱ ᾱς *f.* [πολύδωρος] **lavish giving, open-handedness** X.

πολύ-δωρος ον *adj.* [δῶρον] (of a wife) prob. **bringing many gifts** (to her parents, as a bride-price) Hom.

πολύ-εδρος ον *adj.* [ἕδρᾱ] (of a public building) **with many seats** Plu.

πολυ-ειδής ές *adj.* [εἶδος¹] (of shouts in battle) **of many kinds** Th.; (of the nature of the soul, a class of things, or sim.) **multiform, manifold** Pl. Arist. Plb.

πολυειδίᾱ ᾱς *f.* multiformity (of part of the soul) Pl.

πολύ-ελαιος ον *adj.* [ἐλαίᾱ] (of persons) **rich in olives** X. [or perh.reltd. ἔλαιον, i.e. *rich in oil*]

πολύ-ἑλικτος ον *adj.* [ἑλικτός] (of the pleasure of the dance) **with many twists and turns** E.

πολύ-επαίνετος ον *adj.* [ἐπαινετός] (of a person) **much praised** X.

πολυ-επής ές *adj.* [ἔπος] (of the art of prophets) **wordy** A.

πολύ-εραστος ον *adj.* [ἐραστός] (of a person) **much loved** (by his friends) X.

πολύ-εργος ον *adj.* [ἔργον] (of labourers) **with many tasks, busy** Theoc.

πολυ-ετής ές *adj.* [ἔτος] (quasi-advbl., of a person returning) **after many years** E.

πολύ-ευκτος ον *adj.* [εὐκτός] (of prosperity, wealth, the sound of a person's voice) much prayed for, **longed for** A. Hdt.(oracle) X.

πολύ-εύχετος ον *adj.* [εὔχομαι] (of a child) much prayed for, **being the answer to many prayers** hHom.

πολύ-ζηλος ον *adj.* [ζῆλος] (of a person, a life) **much envied** B. S.

πολύ-ζήλωτος ον *adj.* [ζηλωτός] **1** (of a person) **much envied** B.; (of the river Asopos, by other rivers) B.
2 (of posthumous fame) **enviable** B.
3 (of a goddess, dispensing favours) **causing much envy** (towards the person who receives them) E.

πολύ-ζυγος ον *adj.* [ζυγόν] (of a ship) **with many rowing-benches** Il.; (of a ship's hull) Hippon.

πολυ-ηγερής ές *ep.adj.* [ἀγείρω] (of allied troops) **gathered from many places** Il.

πολυ-ήκοος ον *adj.* [ἀκούω] (of pupils) **constantly listening** (to things read aloud) Pl.

πολυ-ήμερος ον *adj.* [ἡμέρᾱ] (of a journey, a feast) **lasting many days** Plu.

πολυ-ήρατος ον *adj.* [ἐρατός] **1 much desired or to be desired**; (of marriage, the bed of love) **longed for** Od. Hes. **2** (of youth, its bloom) **lovely, delightful** Od. Hes.*fr.* hHom. Thgn. Simon.; (of a child, a woman's form) Hes.; (of a city, land, grove) Od. hHom. Sol. B. Hdt.(oracle) Ar.; (of river water) Hes.; (of a couch) Mimn.

πολυ-ηχής ές *adj.* [ἠχή] creating much noise; (of a shore, rocks) **resounding, roaring, booming** (w. crashing waves) Il. AR.; (of wind) **howling** AR.; (of the nightingale's voice) **resonant, full-throated** Od.

πολυ-θαρσής ές *adj.* [θάρσος] showing great boldness; (of martial spirit) **courageous, valiant** Hom.; (of warfare) **adventurous** AR.

πολυ-θεάμων ον, gen. ονος *adj.* [θεάομαι] (of a person) **very observant** (W.GEN. of sthg.) Pl.

πολύ-θεος ον *adj.* [θεός] (of the altars) **of many gods** A.

πολύ-θερμος ον *adj.* [θερμός] (of a person's natural body temperature) **very warm** Plu.

πολύ-θεστος ον *adj.* [θέσσασθαι] (of a child) much prayed for, **being the answer to many prayers** (W.DAT. for its parents) Call.

πολύ-θηρος ον *adj.* [θήρ] (of a glade) **haunted by wild beasts** E.; (epith. of Diktynna) **goddess of wild beasts** E.

πολυ-θρέμμων ον, gen. ονος *adj.* [τρέφω] (of the Nile) that nourishes many, **nurturing** A.

πολύ-θρηνος ον *adj.* [θρῆνος] **1** (of a song) **full of lamentation, mournful** A.; (of a life) A.(dub.) **2** (of Itys) **much lamented** E.*fr.*

πολύ-θριγκος ον *adj.* [θριγκός] (of chambers) **with many cornices** Lyr.adesp.

πολύ-θροος ον *adj.* [θρόος] (of lustful pursuit of women) accompanied by much shouting, **clamorous, vociferous** A.

πολυ-θρύλητος ον *adj.* [θρυλέω] (of a saying) **much repeated, celebrated** Pl. Plu.; (of a subject) much mentioned, **familiar** Pl.; (of liberty at Sparta) **much vaunted** Plb.

πολύ-θυρος ον *adj.* [θύρᾱ] **with many doors**; (of folding writing-tablets) **many-leaved** E.

πολύ-θυτος ον *adj.* [θύω¹] **1** (of a banquet, a procession) **with many sacrifices** Pi.; (of the honour) **of receiving many sacrifices** E.; (of slaughter) **of many sacrificial animals** S. **2** (of a grove) where many sacrifices are performed, **sacrificial** E.

πολυϊδρείη, also **πολυϊδρίη**, ης *Ion.f.* [πολύιδρις] **1** (pl.) **great cleverness** Thgn.; **shrewdness** (W.GEN. of mind) Od. **2 much knowledge** Call.

πολυϊδρίδᾱς ᾱ *dial.masc.adj.* (of a person) **very clever** S.*satyr.fr.*

πολύ-ιδρις ιος *Ion.masc.fem.adj.* [ἴδρις] | dat. πολυῐ̈δριδι (Sapph.) | (of a person) **very knowing, astute, clever** Od. Hes. Sapph. Alc. Ar. Theoc.

πολύ-ιππος ον *adj.* [ἵππος] (of a person) **rich in horses** Il.

πολύ-ιχθυος ον *adj.* [ἰχθύς] (of the sea) **teeming with fish** hHom.

πολυ-καγκής ές *adj.* [reltd. κάγκανος] (of thirst) **parching** Il.

πολυκαισαρίη ης *Ion.f.* [Καῖσαρ, w. play on πολυκοιρανίη] **plurality of Caesars** Plu.

πολυ-κανής ές *adj.* [καίνω] (of sacrifices) **prodigal in slaughter** (W.GEN. of cattle) A.

πολύ-καπνος ον *adj.* [καπνός] (of a house) **very smoky** E.

πολυκαρπίᾱ ᾱς *f.* [πολύκαρπος] **abundance of fruit, plentiful crops, good harvest** X.

πολύ-καρπος ον *adj.* [καρπός¹] **1 abundant in fruit**; (of a vineyard, land, tree, myrtle garland) **fruitful, fruit-laden** Od. Pi. Ar. Pl.; (of Demeter) Theoc. **2** (of a grape-cluster) **full-fruited** E. **3** (of a nation) **enjoying abundant harvests** Hdt.

πολυκερδείη ης *ep.Ion.f.* [πολυκερδής] (pl.) **great cunning or astuteness** (sts. W.GEN. of mind) Od.

πολυ-κερδής ές *adj.* [κέρδος] (of Odysseus' mind) **very cunning, astute, calculating** Od.

πολύ-κερως ων, gen. ω *adj.* [κέρας] (of slaughter) **of many horned cattle** S.

πολύ-κεστος ον *adj.* [κεστός] (of a helmet strap) with much stitching, **well-made** or **richly decorated** Il.

πολυ-κέφαλος ον *adj.* [κεφαλή] (of a beast) **many-headed** Pl.; (fig., of a person using intricate arguments) Pl.

πολυ-κήδης ες *adj.* [κῆδος] (of a journey) **care-laden, troubled** Od.; (of a person) **anguished** AR.

πολυ-κήτης ες *adj.* [κῆτος] (of the Nile) **abounding in big fish** Theoc.

πολύ-κλαυτος ον (perh. η ον A.) *adj.* [κλαυτός] **1** (of a dead person) **much lamented** A.; (of human beings) **pitiable** Emp.; (perh. of a country) Archil.; (of a birth) **lamentable, woeful** E.; (of a tomb) **tear-stained** Pl.(quot.poet.) **2** (of persons, a personif. river) full of tears, **tearful** E. Mosch.; (of grief) AR.

πολύ-κλειτος ᾱ ον *dial.adj.* [κλειτός] (of a family, a city) **far-famed** Pi.

Πολύκλειτος ου *m.* **Polykleitos** (of Argos, late 5th C. BC, celebrated Greek sculptor) Pl. X. Arist. Plu.

πολυ-κληΐς ῑδος *Ion.fem.adj.* [κλείς] (of ships) **with many thole-pins, many-oared** Hom. Hes.

πολύ-κληρος ον *adj.* [κλῆρος] (of a person) owning a large portion of land, **propertied, wealthy** Od. Theoc.

πολύ-κλητος ον *adj.* [κλητός] (of allied troops) **called from many lands** Il.

πολύ-κλυστος ον *adj.* [κλύζω] **1** (of the sea) **surging** Od. **2** (of an island, cliffs) buffeted by many waves, **sea-washed** Hes. AR.

πολύ-κμητος ον *adj.* [κάμνω] (of iron) **wrought with much labour** Hom.; (of a chamber) **finely built** Od.; (of fabrics) **elaborately worked** AR.; (of the olive, meton. for its oil) **gained with much labour** AR.

πολύ-κνημος ον *adj.* [κνημός] (of a place) with many mountain spurs, **many-spurred, mountainous** Il.

πολύ-κνῑσος ον *adj.* [κνῖσα] (of a sacrificial offering) **richly smoking** AR.

πολύ-κοινος ον *adj.* [κοινός] (of Hades) **which all must share** S.; (of a warning message) **for the world at large** Pi.; (of happiness, as the reward of virtue) **universally attainable** Arist.

πολυκοιρανίη ης *Ion.f.* [πολυκοίρανος] **plurality of rulers** (as a bad thing) Il.

πολυ-κοίρανος ον *adj.* (of a king) ruling over many, **with wide dominions** Ar.(quot. A.)

πολυ-κόλυμβος ον *adj.* [κολυμβάω] accompanied by much diving; (transf.epith., of the music of frogs) **busily diving** Ar.

πολύ-κρᾱνος ον *adj.* [κρᾱνίον¹] (of a serpent) **many-headed** E.

πολυ-κρατής ές *adj.* [κράτος] (of Curses, fate) **powerful, mighty** A. B.

Πολυκράτης εος (ους) *m.* **Polykrates** (tyrant of Samos, late 6th C. BC) Anacr. Ibyc. Hdt. +

—**Πολυκράτειος** ᾱ ον *adj.* (of building works) **of Polykrates** Arist.

πολύ-κρημνος ον *adj.* [κρημνός] (of a land) **with many cliffs, craggy** B.

πολύ-κρῑθος ον *adj.* [κρῑθαί] (of a land) **rich in barley** B.

πολύ-κριμνος ον *adj.* [κρῖμνον] (of a region) **rich in barley** Call.(v.l. πολύκρημνος)

πολύ-κροτος ον (also η ον Anacr.) *adj.* [κρότος] **1** (of Pan) **noisy, rowdy** hHom.
2 (of schemes) perh., highly contrived, **subtle, cunning** Hes.*fr.*; (of a person) **canny** Anacr. Call.

πολυ-κτέανος, ep. **πουλυκτέανος**, ον *adj.* [κτέανα] (of a land) **with many possessions, richly endowed, wealthy** Pi.; (of Apollo at Delphi, fr. dedications and treasuries there) Call.

πολυ-κτήμων ον, gen. ονος *adj.* [κτῆμα] (of persons) **with many possessions, rich** Il. S.; (W.GEN. in lifestyle) E.

πολύ-κτητος ον *adj.* [κτητός] (of a house) **possessing many things, wealthy** E.

πολύ-κτονος ον *adj.* [κτείνω] (of a person or god) **who kills many or causes many deaths, murderous** A. E.; (of the girdle of the Amazon Hippolyte) **that caused many deaths** (when sought by Herakles) E.; (of a calamity) **with much killing** A.

πολυ-κύμων ον, gen. ονος *adj.* [κῦμα] (of the sea) **with many waves, billowing** Sol. Emp.

πολυ-κώκυτος ον *adj.* [κωκυτός] (of the underworld) **full of wailing** Thgn.

πολύ-κωπος ον *adj.* [κώπη] (of a ship) **many-oared** S. E.

πολυ-κώτιλος ον *adj.* [κωτίλος] (of nightingales) **warbling** Simon.

πολύ-λᾱις ιδος *dial.fem.adj.* [ληίς] (of Athena) **generously giving booty** Alc.

πολυ-λήιος, dial. **πολυλάϊος**, ον *adj.* [λήιον] (of persons) **rich in cornfields** Il. hHom. AR.; (of places) Hes.*fr.* B. AR.

πολύ-λλιστος ον *ep.adj.* [λίσσομαι] **1** (of a deity) **sought after with many prayers** Od.; (of holy water) Simon.(dub.)
2 (of a temple, an altar) **where many prayers are made** hHom. B.

πολύ-λλιτος ον *ep.adj.* [λιταί, λίσσομαι] **1** (of a god) **to whom many prayers are made** Call.
2 (of an island) **where many prayers are made** Call.

πολυλογίᾱ ᾱς *f.* [πολύλογος] **1 talkativeness, loquacity** (of a person) X.; **wordiness, verbosity** (as a characteristic of a social group) Pl. NT.
2 much to say (about a topic, for a writer) Arist.

πολύ-λογος ον *adj.* [λόγος] (of persons) **of many words, talkative, loquacious, verbose** Pl. X.

πολυ-μαθής ές *adj.* [μανθάνω] (of persons) **knowledgeable, well-informed, learned** Ar. Isoc. Pl. X. Plu.

πολυμαθίᾱ ᾱς, Ion. **πολυμαθίη** ης *f.* **knowledge of many things, much learning** Heraclit. Pl.

πολυ-μελής ές *adj.* [μέλος] (of hubris) **with many limbs, many-faceted** Pl.(dub., v.l. πολυμερής)

—**πολυμμελής** ές *dial.adj.* (of a Muse) **full of melodies** Alcm.

πολυ-μερής ές *adj.* [μέρος] (of an action) **with many parts, multipartite** Arist. | see also πολυμελής

πολύ-μετρος ον *adj.* [μέτρον] (of a harvest) **giving large measure, plenteous, abundant** Ar.(quot. E.)

πολυ-μηκάς άδος *masc.fem.adj.* (of goats) **bleating** Hdt.(oracle)

πολύ-μηλος ον *adj.* [μῆλα] (of a person) **rich in flocks** Il. Hes.; (of a place) Il. Hes.*fr.* hHom. Pi. E.

πολύ-μητις ιος *masc.fem.adj.* [μῆτις] **having much capacity for planning or scheming**; (of Odysseus) **resourceful, astute, crafty** Hom. Ar.; (of Hephaistos) Il. AR.; (of Hermes, Athena) hHom.

πολυμηχανίη ης *Ion.f.* [πολυμήχανος] **inventiveness, resourcefulness** Od.

πολυ-μήχανος ον *adj.* [μηχανή] (of Odysseus) **having many devices, inventive, resourceful, crafty** Hom. S.; (of Apollo) hHom.; (of Hera) Theoc.

πολύ-μιτος ον *adj.* [μίτος] (of garments) **having many warp-threads, close-woven** A.

πολυμμελής *dial.adj.*: see under πολυμελής

Πολυμνήστεια ων *n.pl.* **songs of Polymnestos** (7th-C. BC musician fr. Colophon) Ar.

πολυ-μνήστη ης *fem.adj.* [μνηστός] (of a woman) **wooed by many suitors** Od.

πολύ-μνηστος, dial. **πολύμναστος**, ον *adj.* [μιμνήσκομαι] **1** (of gratitude) perh. **deeply mindful** (of the debt incurred) A.
2 (app. of an adornment) **long remembered** A.

πολυ-μνήστωρ ορος *masc.fem.adj.* (of a god) **long remembering, mindful** (of sthg.) A.

Πολύμνια ᾱς *f.* [ὕμνος] **Polyhymnia** (one of the nine Muses) Hes. Pl. Lyr.adesp.

πολύ-μορφος ον *adj.* [μορφή] (of badness) **multiform** Arist.

πολύ-μοχθος ον *adj.* [μόχθος] **1 suffering much labour or hardship**; (of a person, the human race) **trouble-laden, long-suffering** E.; (of a wanderer) **toil-worn, wearied** S.
2 causing much labour or hardship; (of Ares) **who causes much suffering** E.; (of Virtue) **causing much labour** (W.DAT. for the human race) Arist.*lyr.*; (of a blow, ref. to misfortune) **painful, wearying** S.
3 (of ivory) **much laboured over, highly wrought** Theoc.

πολύ-μυθος, dial. **πουλύμῡθος** (Call.), ον *adj.* [μῦθος] **1** (of a person) of many words, **talkative, loquacious, verbose** Hom. Call. Theoc.
2 (of great achievements) **inspiring many stories** Pi. [or perh. *deserving many words*, i.e. of praise]
3 (of epic poems) **containing many stories** Arist.

πολύ-ναος ον *adj.* [ναός¹] (of a goddess) **with many temples** Theoc.

πολυ-ναύτᾱς ᾱ *dial.masc.adj.* [ναῦς] (of a commander) **with many ships** A. [or perh.reltd. ναύτης, i.e. *with many sailors*]

πολυ-νεικής ές *adj.* [νεῖκος] **1** (of Eteokles and Polyneikes, w. play on the latter name) **full of strife** A.
2 (of Helen) **causing much strife** Lyr.adesp.

πολυ-νεφέλᾱς ᾱ *dial.masc.adj.* [νεφέλη] (of the sky) **cloud-filled** Pi.

πολυ-νιφής ές *adj.* [νιφάς] (of mountain thickets) **deep in snow** E.

πολύνοια ᾱς *f.* [νόος] **braininess** (opp. πολυλογία *wordiness*) Pl.

πολύ-ξενος, Ion. **πολύξεινος**, ον (also ᾱ ον Pi.) *adj.* [ξένος²] **1** (of a person, a house) **entertaining many guests, hospitable** Hes. Pi.*fr.* E.; (euphem., of the god of the underworld, of its gates) A. S. Call.
2 (of a dinner) **with many guests** Hes.; (of an island, an altar) **thronged by visitors** Pi.

πολυοινέω *contr.vb.* [πολύοινος] (of a vine-grower) **be rich in wine** hHom.

πολυοινίᾱ ᾱς *f.* **hard drinking** Pl.

πολύ-οινος ον *adj.* [οἶνος] (of a region, vine-growers) **rich in wine** Th. X.

πολύ-ολβος ον *adj.* [ὄλβος] **1** (of Aphrodite) **rich in blessings, bountiful** Sapph.
2 (of persons) **richly blessed** Sapph.; (of a city) **richly prosperous** Lyr.adesp.

πολυ-όρνῑθος ον *adj.* [ὄρνις] (of an island) **of many birds, bird-thronged** E.

πολυοχλίᾱ ᾱς *f.* [πολύοχλος] **over-crowding, congestion** Plb.

πολύ-οχλος ον *adj.* [ὄχλος] (of a region) **densely populated** Plb.; (of a social class) containing a large number of people, **numerous** Arist.

πολυοψίᾱ ᾱς *f.* [ὄψον] (fig.) **good crop of savoury food** (w. play on πολυκαρπία *good harvest*) X.

πολυπαιδίᾱ ᾱς *f.* [παῖς¹] **abundance of children** (born to a father) Isoc.

πολυ-παίπαλος ον *adj.* [παιπάλη] (of persons) perh. **full of guile, devious, crafty** Od.

πολυ-πάλακτος ον *adj.* [παλάσσω] (of hands) **much bespattered** (w. blood) A.

πολύ-παλτος ον *adj.* [παλτός] (prob. of a weapon) **much-brandished** Call.

πολυ-πάμων ον, *gen.* ονος *adj.* [πάομαι] (of a person) with many possessions, **wealthy** Il.

πολυ-πάταξ αγος *masc.fem.adj.* [πάταγος] (of an altar) **noisy** (fr. music and dancing) Pratin.

πολυπειρίᾱ ᾱς *f.* [πολύπειρος] **great** or **long experience** (of events, education, or sim.) Th. Pl. Plb. Plu.

πολύ-πειρος ον *adj.* [πεῖρα] (of a woman) **widely experienced, worldly-wise** Ar.; (of a habit) **resulting from much experience** Parm.

πολυ-πείρων ον, *gen.* ονος *adj.* [πεῖραρ] (of a people) with many boundaries, **widely dispersed** hHom.

πολυ-πενθής ές *adj.* [πένθος] (of a person, a heart) **grief-laden, sorrowful** Od.; (of the halcyon) Il.; (of a person's fate) A.

πολυ-πήμων ον, *gen.* ονος *adj.* [πῆμα] **1** (of a person) prob. **hurtful** (to others) Alcm.; (of magic or sim.) **harmful** hHom.
2 (of exertions, maltreatment, distress) **very painful** AR.; (of sicknesses, W.DAT. for people) Pi.

πολύ-πηνος ον *adj.* [πήνη] (of high-quality garments) having many weft-threads, **close-woven** E.

πολυ-πίδαξ ακος *masc.fem.adj.* (of Mt. Ida) **with many springs** Il. hHom.; (of mountain heights) AR.; (of a region) hHom. Simon. Theoc.

πολύ-πικρα *neut.pl.adv.* [πικρός] **with very bitter consequences** (for oneself), **disastrously** —*ref. to taking vengeance* Od.

πολυ-πινής ές *adj.* [πίνος] (of a vagrant's head) **dirty, filthy, squalid** E.

πολύ-πλαγκτος ον *adj.* [πλαγκτός] **1** (of persons) **much-travelled** Od.; (of pirates) **roaming** Od.; (fig., of perils) Thgn.(dub.); (of Io, Herakles) **driven far afield** A. E.
2 (of years) **drifting on and on** S.; (of judgement, hope) **often going astray** B. S.; (of limbs) app. **changeable** (in nature) Parm.
3 (of the wind, the sea) **that drives many off course** Il. B.

πολυ-πλανής ές *adj.* [πλανάω] (of a person, a vehicle) **roaming far and wide** E. Pl.; (of a journey) **circuitous** Plu.

πολυ-πλάνητος ον *adj.* [πλανητός] (of a nomadic people) **roaming far and wide** Hdt.; (of a fruitless search for someone) E.; (of people's lives, ref. to their fortune) **ever shifting to and fro** E.

πολύ-πλανος ον *adj.* [πλάνος¹] (of a serpent's watchful eyes) **darting about** E.; (of wanderings) **far-flung** A.

πολύ-πλεθρος ον *adj.* [πλέθρον] (of land) **of many acres** E.

πολυπλήθεια ᾱς *f.* [πλῆθος] **great size, vastness** (W.GEN. of a crowd) Men.

πολυπλοκίαι ῶν *f.pl.* [πολύπλοκος] **subtleties, chicaneries, trickeries** Thgn.

πολύ-πλοκος ον *adj.* [πλέκω] **1** (of a serpent's coils) **twisting, sinuous, entwining** E.; (fig., of a mythical creature) **convoluted, complex** Pl.
2 (of an infantry formation) **complicated, intricate** X.; (of patterns of counters on the draughts board) E.; (of the movements of a meteorite) Plu.
3 (of a woman, her thinking) **subtle** Ar.; (pejor., of the octopus) **wily, cunning** (w. further connot. *entwining*) Thgn.

πολυ-ποίκιλος ον *adj.* [ποικίλος] (of garments) **richly patterned** E.

πολύ-ποινος ον *adj.* [ποινή] (of Justice) **who punishes severely** Parm.

πολύ-πονος ον *adj.* [πόνος] **1** full of trouble or suffering; (of mankind in general) **toil-worn, trouble-laden** Pi. E.; (of persons, in specific circumstances) Trag. Ar.; (of a person's life, compared to a sea) **troubled** S.
2 (specif., of a body of soldiers) experienced in the hardships of war, **battle-hardened** S. E.; (of a spear, fig.ref. to the one who wields it) A.
3 (w. positive connot., of persons) **hard-working, energetic** Arist.; (of the bee) **industrious, busy** E.*fr*.
4 causing much trouble; (of Helen's name, liaisons w. women) **troublesome, baneful** E.; (of the chariot-race of Pelops) S.; (of a bow, for its possessor) S.
5 (gener., of things) accompanied by pain or effort; (of cruelty, fate, lamentation, sufferings) **woeful, grievous, painful** S. E.; (of activities) **gruelling** Pl. Plu.
—**πολυπόνως** *adv.* **with great effort, laboriously** Plu.

πολύ-πορος ον *adj.* [πόρος] (of plains) **with many paths** (fig.ref. to the sky) Ar.

πολυποσίᾱ ᾱς *f.* [πόσις²] **hard drinking** Plb.

πολυ-πόταμος ον *adj.* (of a lake) **fed by many rivers** E.

πολυ-πότης ου *masc.adj.* (of a person) **hard-drinking** Plb. Plu.

πολυ-πότνια ᾱς *fem.adj.* (of Demeter) **most sovereign** hHom.; (of Demeter and Persephone) Ar.; (of Cybele, Rhea, a queen) AR.

πολύ-πους¹ πουν, *gen.* ποδος *adj.* [πούς] (of certain living creatures) **many-footed** Pl. Arist.; (of an Erinys, w.connot. of swiftness or untiring effort) S.

πολύπους² *m.*: see πώλυπος

πολυπρᾱγματέω *contr.vb.* [πρᾶγμα] (of a person's attention) **be directed to many tasks** (opp. one) Arist.

πολυπρᾱγμονέω, Ion. **πολυπρηγμονέω** *contr.vb.* [πολυπράγμων] | *aor.* ἐπολυπρᾱγμόνησα ‖ *neut.impers. vbl.adj.* πολυπρᾱγμονητέον |
1 (pejor.) take trouble over many things (which do not concern oneself), **be meddlesome, meddle, interfere** Hdt. Ar. Isoc. Pl. X. Aeschin. +
2 take much or **too much trouble** (over sthg.) Pl.
3 (in positive sense) **take trouble to learn, be curious** (about sthg.) Plb.; (tr.) **be curious about, investigate, study** —*sthg.* Plb. ‖ PASS. (of topics) be investigated or studied Plb.

πολυπρᾱγμοσύνη ης *f.* **1** tendency to interfere in many things, **meddlesomeness** Lys. Ar. Isoc. Pl. X. +; (as a typically Athenian characteristic) Th.
2 trouble taken in gaining knowledge, **curiosity, study, research** Plb.

πολυ-πράγμων ον, gen. ονος *adj.* [πρᾶγμα] **1** (pejor., of persons) **meddlesome, interfering** Lys. Isoc. Arist. Plu. **2** restless for knowledge, **inquisitive** Ar. **3** taking trouble to gain knowledge, **scholarly** Plb.

πολύ-πρεμνος ον *adj.* [πρέμνον] (of a wood) with many tree trunks, **well-timbered, dense** AR.

πολυπρηγμονέω Ion.contr.vb.: see πολυπρᾱγμονέω

πολυ-πρόβατος ον *adj.* [πρόβατον] (of people) **rich in cattle** or **sheep** Hdt. X.

πολυ-πρόσωπος ον *adj.* [πρόσωπον] (fig., of the sky) **many-faced** Arist.(quot.)

πολύ-πτολις ιος *ep.masc.fem.adj.* [πόλις] (of a goddess, the earth) **with many cities** Call.

πολύ-πτυχος ον *adj.* [πτύξ] having many folds; (of Olympos, Ida) **with many glens** Il. Hes.; (of a mountainous region) E.

πολύ-πυργος ον *adj.* [πύργος] (of Troy) **many-towered** B.(cj.)

πολύ-πῡρος ον *adj.* [πῡρός] (of places) **rich in wheat** Hom. hHom. A.

πολύ-ρραπτος ον *adj.* [ῥάπτω] (of a quiver) with much stitching, **finely stitched** Theoc.

πολύ-ρραφος ον *adj.* [ῥαφή] (of a shield-band) **well-stitched** S. | see πόρπαξ

πολύ-ρρην ηνος *masc.fem.adj.* [ῥήν] | only dat.sg. πολύαρνι, nom.pl. πολύρρηνες | (of persons) having many sheep, **rich in sheep** Il. Hes.fr. AR. Theoc.

—**πολύρρηνος** ον *adj.* (of a person) **rich in sheep** Od.

πολύ-ρρῑνος ον *adj.* [ῥῑνός] (of a shield) **of many hides** AR.

πολύ-ρροδος ον *adj.* [ῥόδον] (of meadows) **full of roses** Ar.

πολύ-ρροθος ον *adj.* [ῥόθος] (of shouts) creating a great hubbub, **tumultuous, rowdy** A.

πολύ-ρυτος ον *adj.* [ῥυτός] (of the sea) **full-flowing** A.(cj.)

πολύς πολλή (dial. ᾱ́) πολύ *adj.* | acc. πολύν πολλήν (dial. ᾱ́ν) πολύ | gen. πολλοῦ ἧς (dial. ᾱ̀ς) οὗ || For compar. and superl. see πλείων, πλεῖστος. | —also **πολλός** ή όν *Ion.adj.* | acc. πολλόν ήν όν (also S.) || also ep. (and lyr.) forms: nom. πουλύς ύ, acc. πουλύν ύ | gen. πολέος | dat. πολεῖ (A.) | nom.pl. πολέες, πολεῖς | acc.pl. πολέας (trisyllab.), πολέας (disyllab.) or πολῡ́ς, neut. πολέα (A.) | gen.pl. (trisyllab. or disyllab.) πολέων | dat.pl. πολέσι, πολέσσι, πολέεσσι |
1 (ref. to size; of a group of people, a country, sea, or sim.) **large, great** Hom. +; (w.art.) **greater part** (of sthg.) Hdt. Th.
2 (ref. to number) || PL. (of persons or things) **many** Hom. +; (w.art.) the majority of, **most** Il. + || PL.SB. (in same gender as GEN.) **many** (W.GEN. of persons or things) Hom. +
|| MASC.PL.SB. (w.art.) **people at large, ordinary people** Th. Pl. +
3 (ref. to amount, degree or intensity; of material or abstr. things, such as rain, noise, laughter, talk, necessity, shame) **much, great** Hom. +; (of things repeated, such as talk or sim.) **frequent** Hdt. +; (w.art.) **greater part** (of a life) S.
4 || SG.SB. (in same gender as GEN.) **much** (W.GEN. of sthg.) Th. +; (w.art.) **greater part** (W.GEN. of sthg.) Hdt. +
|| NEUT.SG.SB. **much** (W.GEN. of sthg.) Od.; (w.art., sg. and pl.) **greater part** (W.GEN. of sthg.) Hdt. +
5 (advbl. and prep.phrs.) (ὡς) τὸ πολύ or τὰ πολλά *for the most part, generally* E. Th. Pl. +; ὡς ἐπὶ (τὸ) πολύ Th. Isoc. Pl. +; ἐπὶ πολύ *to a large degree* Th. Pl. +; ἐς πολλά *to a great extent, greatly* E.; παρὰ πολύ *by a wide margin* Th. Ar. Isoc. Pl. +
6 (of a person or god) **great, powerful, important** Hdt. E. Ar.; **violent, overbearing** D.; **in full physical strength** Call. AR.
7 (quasi-advbl., of gods or persons moving, behaving, or sim.) **with great strength** Hdt. E. Th. Ar. +; (wkr.sens., of persons doing or saying sthg.) **at length** or **often** A. Hdt. E. +
8 (phrs., ref. to value or worth; of persons or things) πολλοῦ (πολέος) ἄξιος (or sim.) *highly valued* Hom. +; περὶ πολλοῦ ποιεῖσθαι (or sim.) *regard highly* or *as important* Hdt. +; ἐπὶ πολλῷ *at a high price* D.
9 (ref. to distance or extent; of a journey) **long** Od. A. +; (quasi-advbl., of persons or things extending) **far** Il.; (prep.phrs.) διὰ πολλοῦ *at a great distance* Th. X.; ἐκ πολλοῦ *from a great distance* Th. +; ἐπὶ πολύ *for a great distance* Hdt. Th. +; **over a large extent** (W.GEN. of land, sea) Th.
10 (of a time or interval) **long** Hom. +; (of an hour) **late** Plb. NT.; (of night) **deep** (perh.ref. to the darkest time) Th.; (prep.phrs.) ἐκ πολλοῦ *for a long time* (past) Antipho Th. +; ἐπὶ πολύ *for a long time* (in the future) Th.; *for a large part* (W.GEN. of the day) Th.
—**πολύ**, Ion. **πολλόν** *neut.sg.adv.* **1 a long way, far** or **far away** —*ref. to travelling, being in a certain position* Hom. Hdt. Th.
2 for a long time Hdt.
3 to a great extent or **degree, much, greatly** (sts. emphasised by μάλα, πάνυ, or sim.) —*ref. to excelling, rivalling, preferring, or sim.* Hom. +
4 (w.compar. or superl.adj. or adv., also w. wds. implying comparison) **much, by far** Hom. +
—**πολλοῦ** *neut.gen.sg.adv.* (intensv., w. πολύς or other adj.) **very** Ar.
—**πολλῷ** *neut.dat.sg.adv.* (w.compar. or superl.adj. or adv., or w. wds. implying comparison) **much, by far** A. +
—**πολλά** *neut.pl.adv.* **1 to a great extent** or **degree, much, greatly** —*ref. to toiling, lamenting, thinking, or sim.* Hom. +
2 (intensv., w.adj.) **very** A.; (w. πολλάκις *possibly*) Ar.
3 many times, often Hom. Lyr. Trag.

πολυσαρκίᾱ ᾱς *f.* [σάρξ] **fleshiness, plumpness** (of a person) X.

πολυ-σημάντωρ ορος *m.* (epith. of Hades) **commander of many, major general** hHom.

πολυ-σῑνής ές *adj.* [σίνος] (of a dog) causing much harm, **dangerous** A.

πολυσῑτίᾱ ᾱς *f.* [πολύσῑτος] **plentiful supply of grain** X.

πολύ-σῑτος ον *adj.* [σῖτος] **1** (of persons) **rich in grain** X.
2 overfed Theoc.

πολύ-σκαρθμος ον *adj.* [σκαρθμός] (of an Amazon) perh., with a long leap, **light of foot** Il.; (subject uncert.) Call.

πολυ-σκεδής ές *adj.* [σκεδάννῡμι] (of opponents) **widely scattered, routed** A.fr.

πολύ-σκιος ον *adj.* [σκιά] (of a grove) **very shady** AR.

πολύ-σκοπος ον *adj.* [σκοπέω] (of a personif. sunbeam) **far-seeing** Pi.fr.

πολύ-σπαστον ου *n.* [σπάω] **compound pulley** (devised by Archimedes) Plu.

πολυ-σπερής ές *adj.* [σπείρω] | Boeot.nom.pl. πολουσπερίες | **1** (of people) **scattered far and wide** (over the earth) Hom. Hes.
2 (of women) **fruitful, fertile** Corinn.

πολύ-σπορος ον *adj.* [σπορά] (of Asia) **rich in crops, fruitful, fertile** E. [or perh. *populous*]

πολυ-στάφυλος ον *adj.* [σταφυλή] (of places) **rich in grape-clusters** Il. S.; (of Dionysus) hHom.

πολύ-σταχυς υ, gen. υος *adj.* [στάχυς] (of Demeter) **rich in corn-ears** Theoc.

πολυ-στέφανος ον *adj.* (of the earth) **with many garlands** (i.e. foliage or flowers) Lyr.adesp.

πολυ-στεφής ές *adj.* [στέφω] (of a person) **richly crowned** (W.GEN. w. laurel) S.; (of a shrine) **richly garlanded** (w. wreaths and fillets) A.

πολύ-στῐος ον *adj.* [στῐᾰ́] (of a river) **many-pebbled** Call.
πολυστομέω *contr.vb.* [στόμα] **talk much, be talkative** A.
πολύ-στονος ον *adj.* [στόνος] **1** (of a person, soul, fortune) **full of sorrow, grief-laden** Od. Hippon. E.; (of a voice, a cry) **sorrowful** A. E. AR.; (of Acheron) where there is sorrowing, **doleful** Theoc.; (of pain) **full of tears** AR.
2 (of persons) **much lamented** A.; (of a tomb) **much wept over** Pi.*fr.*
3 causing sorrow; (of troubles, Strife, a curse, an Erinys) **grievous, woeful** Il. E.; (of Troy) S.; (of battle) Archil.; (of hubristic behaviour) B.; (of Frenzy, the Sphinx) causing injury, **baneful** E.; (of an arrow) Il. AR.
πολύ-στροφος ον *adj.* [στρέφω] (of the minds of mortals) **changeable** Pi.*fr.*
πολύ-στῡλος ον *adj.* [στῦλος] (of the Odeion) **with many columns** Plu.
πολύ-σχιστος ον *adj.* [σχιστός] (of paths) **branching many ways** S.
πολυτεκνέω *contr.vb.* [πολύτεκνος] (of women) **bear many children** Arist.
πολυτεκνίᾱ ᾱς *f.* **abundance of children** (as a source of happiness) Arist.
πολύ-τεκνος ον *adj.* [τέκνον] **1** (of a woman) **with many children, prolific** A.
2 (of an eager desire) **to father many children** E.
3 (of rivers) **promoting fertility** (in people and animals) A.
πολυτελείᾱ ᾱς, Ion. **πολυτελείη** ης *f.* [πολυτελής] **1 great expenditure, extravagance** Hdt. Th. Isoc. X. D. Men. +
2 costliness, extravagance (W.GEN. of clothing, feasts, buildings) X. Aeschin. Plb.
πολυ-τελής ές *adj.* [τέλος] | *superl.* πολυτελέστατος | **1** (of material things, activities) **expensive, costly** Hdt. Th. Att.orats. Pl. X. +; (of a corpse) **expensively buried** Men.; (of a mistress, a wife) **expensive to maintain** Aeschin. D. Men.
|| ADVBL.NEUT.PL.ACC. (superl., w.art.) **in the most expensive way** Hdt.
2 (of a person) spending lavishly, **extravagant** Men.
—**πολυτελῶς** *adv.* **expensively, extravagantly, sumptuously** Att.orats. X. Plb. Plu.
πολυ-τέχνης ες *Ion.adj.* [τέχνη] (of Hephaistos) **skilled in many crafts** Sol.
πολύ-τεχνος ον *adj.* (of building projects) **calling for many crafts** Plu.
πολυ-τῑμᾱτος, dial. **πολυτῑμᾱτος**, ον (also η ον Ar.) *adj.* [τῑμητός] **1** (of deities, in invocations or exclamations) **highly honoured, revered** Ar. Men.; (of persons, in addresses) Ar. Pl.
2 (of grain, ref. to its price, w. play on 1) **very dear** Ar.; (sarcastic, of a drug-store) **precious** Plb.(quot.); (of land) **very valuable** Plu.
πολύ-τῑμος ον *adj.* [τῑμή] (of things) **very valuable, precious** NT. Plu.
πολύ-τῐτος ον *adj.* [τίω] (of a person) **worthy of great honour** Hdt.(oracle)
πολύ-τλᾱς *masc.adj.* [τλῆναι] | only *nom.* | (of Odysseus) having to endure or capable of enduring much, **long-suffering, stalwart, tireless** Hom.; (iron.) S.
πολυ-τλήμων ον, *gen.* ονος *adj.* (of Odysseus) **tireless** Od.; (of a warrior's spirit) Il.; (of mortals) **long-suffering** Ar.
πολύ-τλητος ον *adj.* [τλητός] (of old men) **who have suffered much** Od.
πολυ-τρήρων ον, *gen.* ωνος *adj.* (of a place) **where pigeons abound** Il.
πολύ-τρητος ον *adj.* [τρητός] (of a sponge) **full of holes, porous** Od.

πολυτροπίη ης *Ion.f.* [πολύτροπος] **ingenuity, cunning** Hdt.
πολύ-τροπος ον *adj.* [τροπή, τρέπω] **1** (of Odysseus) of many ways, **ingenious, versatile, resourceful** (less plausibly interpr. as *wandering far and wide*) Od.; (of Hermes) hHom.; (of a person's mind) Plu.; (pejor., of Odysseus) **shifty, cunning** Pl.; (of certain animals) Pl.
|| NEUT.SB. **versatility** (of a person) Plu.; (W.GEN. of someone's mind) Th.
2 changing in manner; (of fortunes) **varied, changeable** Th. Plu.; (of a war, W.DAT. in its fortunes) Plu.; (of an illness) **complicated** Plu.; (of destruction) **coming in many guises** AR.; (of nations) **with many different customs** Plu.
πολυ-τρόφος ον *adj.* [τρέφω] (of Demeter) **who gives nourishment to many** Call.
—**πολύτροφος** ον *adj.* (of physiques) **overfed** Plu.
πολύ-ῠδρος ον *adj.* [ὕδωρ] (of places) **with a plentiful supply of water** Pl.
πολύ-ῠμνητος ον *adj.* [ὑμνητός] (of a sanctuary of Zeus) **much famed in song, much hymned** Pi.
πολύ-ῠμνος ον *adj.* [ὕμνος] **1** (of Dionysus) **much celebrated in song, much hymned** hHom. E.; (of Athens) Ar.; (of strife over Helen) Ibyc.
2 (of the Muses' treasure-chamber) **rich in song** Tim.
πολύφᾱμος *dial.adj.*, **Πολύφᾱμος** *dial.m.*: see πολύφημος, Πολύφημος
πολύ-φᾰνος ον *adj.* [φᾰνός²] (of a festival) **with many torches** Alcm.
πολύ-φαντος ον *adj.* [φαίνομαι] (of great renown) **conspicuous** B.
πολυ-φάρμᾰκος ον *adj.* [φάρμᾰκον] (of doctors, Paion) **skilled with medicines** Il. Sol.; (of Circe, Medea) **skilled with drugs** or **spells** Od. AR.
πολύ-φᾰτος ον *adj.* [φᾰτός] (of the Olympic games) **much spoken of, celebrated, famous** Pi.; (of a song, its sound) **voiced by many** Pi. D. [or perh. *glorious*]
πολύ-φημος, dial. **πολύφᾱμος**, ον *adj.* [φήμη] **1** (of a singer, w. play on his name Φήμιος) **with a rich store of tales** Od. [or perh. *renowned*]
2 (of a place of assembly) **where many voices are heard** Od.; (*prep.phr.*) ἐς πολύφημον *to the public assembly* Hdt.(oracle)
3 (of a dirge) **sung by many voices** Pi.
4 (of a road or journey, ref. to a philosophical method) **far-famed** Parm. [or perh. *of much discourse*]
Πολύφημος, dial. **Πολύφᾱμος**, ου *m.* **Polyphemos** (one-eyed Cyclops, son of Poseidon, blinded by Odysseus) Od. E.*Cyc.*; (as wooer of Galateia) Hellenist.poet.
πολύ-φθορος ον *adj.* [φθείρω] (of the Sphinx) **destroying many, murderous, deadly** E.; (of days of fighting) Pi.; (of Zeus' rain, fig.ref. to a massacre) **devastating** Pi.
—**πολύφθορος** ον *adj.* **1** (of persons) **destroyed in great numbers** A.; (of a house) **desolated by many deaths** S.; (of a country) **ruined** S.
2 (of sailors) **ruinously wandering far and wide** S.*fr.*; (of Io's misfortunes) **of wretched far-flung wanderings** A.; (of her wanderings) **wretched far-flung** A. | cf. φθείρω 6
πολυφιλίᾱ ᾱς *f.* [πολύφιλος] **large number of friends** Arist. Plu.
πολύ-φιλος ον *adj.* [φίλος] (of persons) **with many friends** Lys. Arist. Plu.; (of a companion, fig.ref. to wealth) Pi.
πολύ-φιλτρος ον *adj.* [φίλτρον] (of a lover) **feeling much passion, passionate** Theoc.
πολύ-φλοισβος ον *adj.* [φλοῖσβος] (of the sea) **loudly roaring** Hom. Hes. hHom. Archil.

πολυ-φόνος ον *adj.* [θείνω] (of the Hydra, a warrior's hand) **murderous** E.

πολύ-φορβος ον (also η ον) *adj.* [φέρβω] (of the earth) providing nourishment for many, **nourishing, bountiful** Il. hHom.; (of Demeter) Hes.

πολυφορίᾱ ᾱς *f.* [πολυφόρος] **productiveness** (of the vine) X.

πολυ-φόρος ον *adj.* [φέρω] **1** (of land) **very productive** Pl. **2** (of wine) capable of bearing a large admixture of water; (fig., of a person's misfortune) **undiluted, potent, overwhelming** Ar.

πολύ-φορτος ον *adj.* [φόρτος] (of a wagon) **heavily freighted** Mosch.

πολυ-φραδής ές *adj.* [φράζω] (of a suggestion) **very clever** Hes.; (of a woman) **very sensible** Semon.

πολυ-φράδμων ον, gen. ονος *adj.* (of a divine prophet) **wise** AR.

πολύ-φραστος ον *adj.* (of divine horses) **wise** Parm.

πολυφροσύνη ης *f.* [πολύφρων] **cleverness, ingenuity** Thgn. Hdt.

πολύ-φρων ον, gen. ονος *adj.* [φρήν] (of a person) **sensible** Hom.; (of Hephaistos, Odysseus) **clever, ingenious, resourceful** Hom.; (perh. of Sisyphos) Hes.*fr.*

πολύ-χαλκος ον *adj.* [χαλκός] **1** (of a person, a city) **rich in bronze** Hom. **2** (of heaven, envisaged as a solid firmament or vault) made of bronze, **brazen** Hom.; (of door pivots) Parm.

πολυ-χανδής ές *adj.* [χανδάνω] (of a pitcher) capable of holding much (water), **capacious** Theoc.

πολυ-χαρείδᾱ *Lacon.m.voc.* [reltd. χάρις] (as a courteous address by a Spartan) **gracious sir** Ar.

πολύ-χειρ χειρος *masc.fem.adj.* [χείρ] **1** (of an Erinys) **many-handed** S.; (of a composite being) Arist. **2** (of a commander) **with great armed strength** (of soldiers) A.

πολυχειρίᾱ ᾱς *f.* **large number of hands** (engaged in or available for a task) Th. X. Plb. Plu.

πολυχορδίᾱ ᾱς *f.* [πολύχορδος] use of many notes, **complexity** or **ornamentation** (in a certain style of music) Pl.

πολύ-χορδος ον *adj.* [χορδή] **1** (of musical instruments, a lyre) capable of producing many notes, **many-stringed** Pl. Theoc.; (of pipes) **with many notes, many-toned** Pl. Lyr.adesp.; (of the nightingale's voice) E. **2** (of songs) **accompanied by many strings** (i.e. the lyre) E.

πολύ-χους ουν *Att.adj.* [χέω] **1** pouring forth much; (of argumentation) **copious and varied** Arist. **2** (of virtue) **widely disseminated** (among related families) Plu.

πολυχρηματίᾱ ᾱς *f.* [πολυχρήμων] **accumulation of wealth** X.

πολυ-χρήμων ον, gen. ονος *adj.* [χρῆμα] (of a city) possessing much wealth, **wealthy** Plb.

πολύ-χρηστος ον *adj.* [χρηστός] (of certain educational subjects) **very serviceable, very valuable** Arist.

πολυ-χρόνιος ον *adj.* **1** of long duration; (of animal-hides) **long-lasting** hHom.; (of impressions on wax) Pl.; (of a person's kingship) Hdt.; (of institutions, magistracies, honours, or sim.) X. Arist. Plb.; (of horse-rides) **protracted, lengthy** X.; (of war, peace) Plb.; (of a practice) **long-standing** Even. **2** (of a person, the soul, the human race, a nation) living a long time, **long-lived** Pl. Arist. Call. Plb.; (of a dead person) **who has lived a long life** Call. **3** (of death) coming at the end of a long life, **long-delayed** Call.

πολύ-χροος ον *adj.* [χρώς] (of pigments) **of various colours** Emp.

πολύ-χρῡσος ον *adj.* [χρῡσός] **1** possessing much gold; (of persons, a nation, a land) **rich in gold** Il. Archil. E. X.; (of an army) A.; (of cities) Hom. A. S.; (of a fortress) Plu.; (of Olympos, the home of Zeus) B. E.; (of palaces, chambers) A. Pi. E.; (of Delphi, its shrine and valley) Pi. S.; (of Delphic Apollo) Call. **2** consisting of much gold; (of religious offerings at Delphi) **of abundant gold** E.; (of a dowry) E.; (of wealth) Pi.*fr.* **3** (epith. of Aphrodite) **golden, radiant** Hes. hHom.

πολύ-χωστος ον *adj.* [χωστός] (of a burial mound) **heaped high** A.

πολύ-ψαμμος ον *adj.* [ψάμμος] (of a bank) **of sand piled high** A.

πολυψηφίᾱ ᾱς *f.* [ψῆφος] **large number of votes** Th.

πολυ-ψηφίς ῖδος *masc.fem.adj.* [ψηφίς] (of a river) **many-pebbled** Hdt.(oracle) Pl.(oracle)

πολυ-ώδῡνος ον *adj.* [ὀδύνη] (of an arrow) **bringing much pain** Theoc.

πολυωνυμίη ης *Ion.f.* [πολυώνυμος] **multitude of names** (borne by Artemis) Call.

πολυ-ώνυμος ον *adj.* [ὄνομα] **1** (of deities) known by or worshipped under many names; (of Hades, Apollo) **of many names** hHom.; (of the mother of Helios) Pi.; (of Dionysus) S.; (of Artemis) Ar.; (of Aphrodite) Theoc. **2** (of hubris) possessing many names, **described by many different words** Pl. **3** (of the water of Styx) **widely famed, renowned** Hes.; (of a cave) Pi.

πολυ-ωπός όν *adj.* [ὀπή] (of a fishing-net) with many holes, **fine-meshed** Od.

πολυωρέομαι *pass.contr.vb.* [ὤρᾱ] (of persons) **be treated with great respect** —W.PREP.PHR. *by those inferior in birth* Arist.

πολυ-ωφελής ές *adj.* [ὄφελος] (of a particular knowledge) **very beneficial** or **advantageous** (W.DAT. for someone) Arist. —**πολυωφελῶς** *adv.* | *superl.* πολυωφελέστατα | **very advantageously** (W.DAT. for someone) Ar. X.

πόμα *n.*: see πῶμα²

πομπαῖος ᾱ ον *adj.* [πομπή] **1** (epith. of Hermes, as protector of travellers and conductor of souls to Hades) **who gives escort** Trag. **2** (of a wind for sailors) **escorting, favourable** Pi.

πομπείᾱ ᾱς *f.* [πομπεύω] **1 holding of a procession** Plb. **2** processional behaviour (ref. to ritual insulting of bystanders by men conveyed in wagons during the procession at the Anthesteria); **ribaldry, abuse** D. Men.

πομπεῖα ων *n.pl.* **1** objects conveyed in a sacred procession, **processional objects** And. D. Plu. **2** ‖ sg. processional hall (in which such objects were stored) D.

πομπεύς έως (ep. ῆος) *m.* **1** (ref. to a person or god) **escort** (for someone) Od. AR.; (ref. to a favourable wind, W.GEN. for a ship) Od. **2 participant in a procession** Th.

πόμπευσις εως *f.* **participation in processions** Pl.(pl.)

πομπεύω *vb.* [πομπή] | *ep.impf.* πόμπευον, *iterat*v. πομπεύεσκον | **1** (of a goddess) **escort, guide** —*someone* (*on a journey*) Od.; (of a herald) **ply** —*the craft of Hermes* (i.e. the herald's trade, of which he was patron, ref. to his title πομπαῖος) S.

2 take part in a procession (on a religious or ceremonial occasion) Aeschin. D. Arist. Thphr. Plb. Plu. —w.COGN.ACC. Plb.; process in celebration —w.ACC. *of a sacrifice* Plb.; (of wild animals) go in a procession Theoc. ‖ PASS. (of a corpse) be carried in procession Plu.
3 (of a Roman general) hold a triumphal procession Plu. ‖ PASS. (of captives, spoils) be led in a triumphal procession Plu.
4 engage in ribald processional behaviour, be scurrilously abusive (opp. make a formal accusation) D. | cf. πομπεία 2

πομπή ῆς, dial. **πομπά** ᾶς *f.* [πέμπω] **1** safe escort (of a person to a destination); escort (oft. w.GEN. by gods or humans) Hom. A. Hdt. E.; guidance (w.GEN. by an animal) AR.; conveyance (by ship) Pi.; (of a ship, by a wind) Pi. E.
2 (gener.) sending of persons on their way, sending off, despatch Od. E.
3 sending of a person or troops on a mission; despatch (w.GEN. or PREP.PHR. by someone) hHom. A. E.; mission (on which one is sent) A. E.
4 sending of things; sending (of timber for shipbuilding, by a city) Th.; (of signs or dreams, by gods) Hdt. Pl.
5 procession (religious or ceremonial) Heraclit. Pi. Hdt. Th. Ar. Att.orats. +; (w.GEN. of sacrificial animals) Pi.
6 (at Rome) triumphal procession (of a general) Plb. Plu.

πομπικός ή όν *adj.* **1** (of a horse) of the kind used in processions, processional X.; (of trumpet-music) Plu.
2 (of the appearance of spoils) suited to a triumphal procession, grand Plu.

πόμπιμος ον (also dial. ᾱ ον E.) *adj.* **1** sending or helping on one's way; (of a god) acting as escort or guide E.; (of a person, compared to a favouring wind) E.; (of a land) that gives safe passage (w.GEN. to friends) E.; (of oars, winds) that speed on the way (a ship or its passengers) S. E.; (of the beat of mourners' hands, imagined as an oar-beat) accompanying (the journey of the dead across the Acheron) A.; (of the goal or geographical limit of a journey) that sends one (w.GEN. on the journey home) Pi.
2 (of a gift) sent (w.DAT. to someone) S.; (of a message) conveyed, transmitted E.; (fig., of the joints of a messenger's feet) despatched on a mission A.

πομπός οῦ *m.* (*also f.* Od.) [πέμπω] **1** one who sends or helps on one's way; (ref. to a person, god or goddess) escort (for someone) Hom. Hdt. S. E. Plu.; (w.GEN. in an activity) A. E. ‖ PL. (ref. to ships) convoy Plu.
2 (ref. to Hermes and other underworld gods) conductor (w.GEN. of the dead, either to the underworld or back to the upper world as ghosts) A.; (ref. to Hermes alone) A.*fr.* S.; (ref. to a bird of good omen, w.GEN. for a military leader) A.
3 sender, despatcher (w.GEN. of commodities) Plu.; (ref. to a dead person, w.GEN. of blessings, i.e. fr. the underworld to mourners on earth) A.
4 one who conveys messages, messenger S.; (appos.w. πῦρ *fire*, ref. to a beacon) A.

πομφολυγο-παφλάσματα των *n.pl.* [πομφόλυξ] (ref. to the songs of frogs) bubbly splutterings Ar.

πομφολύζω *vb.* [πομφόλυξ] | dial.aor. πομφόλυξα | (of tears) bubble up, burst forth Pi.

πομφόλυξ υγος *f.* [reltd. πέμφιξ] bubble Pl.

πονέω *contr.vb.* —also **πόνημ(μ)ι** *Aeol.vb.* —also **πονάω** (Pi. Theoc.) *dial.contr.vb.* [πόνος] | fut. πονήσω | aor. ἐπόνησα, dial. πόνησα (Pi.) ‖ MID.PASS.: Ion.ptcpl. πονεόμενος or πονεύμενος, Aeol. πονήμενος | Ion.3pl.pf. πεπονέαται | ep.3sg.plpf. πεπόνητο, 3pl. πεπονήατο ‖ PASS.: dial.3sg.aor.subj. πονάθῇ | dial.pf.ptcpl. πεπονᾱμένος ‖ neut.impers.vbl.adj. πονητέον |
1 ‖ MID. work hard, exert oneself, be busy Hom. Archil. Semon. Alc. Thgn. Ar. + ‖ MID.STATV.PF. and PLPF. be in a busy state or be busy (w. a task) Il. Hdt. Pl.
2 ‖ MID. (of warriors) toil in combat, take part in a battle Il.; (act.) Pi. E.
3 ‖ MID. (tr.) busy oneself with —*a task, a ship's tackle* Hom.; labour to create, construct —*a tomb* Il. —*a plough* Hes. —*a fence* Mosch.; (of the Cyclopes) —*a thunderbolt (for Zeus)* AR.; prepare —*food, a meal* AR. Theoc. ‖ PASS. (of objects) be made AR. Theoc.
4 (act.) work hard, labour Alc. Thgn. Pi. Hdt. Trag. Th. + —w.COGN. or INTERN.ACC. *at a task* Trag. + —w.ACC. *in a foot-race* E. ‖ IMPERS.PF.PASS. hard work has been done Pl.
5 (tr.) toil to achieve —w.NEUT.ACC. *sthg.* Pi.*fr.* E.; gain by hard work —*material things* X. ‖ PASS. (of sthg. noble) be achieved by toil Pi.
6 ‖ STATV.PF.PASS. (of a person) be trained or expert —w.PREP.PHR. *in sthg.* Arist.; (of an athlete's physique) be trained —w.PREP.PHR. *for sthg.* Arist.; (of a pupil) be trained or fashioned —w.PREP.PHR. *to a teacher's will* Theoc.
7 (act., intr.) suffer hardship or distress Trag. —w.DAT. *fr. thirst* A. —w.PREP.PHR. *fr. a storm* Antipho; suffer pain —w.ACC. *in one's side* (w.DAT. *fr. an arrow*) S.; (of living creatures) feel pain Arist. ‖ STATV.PF.ACT. be in pain —w.ACC. *in one's legs* Ar.; (of a person, a horse) be fatigued X.
8 (of troops) be hard pressed, suffer, be in trouble Th. X.
9 (of ships) suffer damage Th.; (of a ship's tackle) be under strain (in a storm) D. ‖ STATV.PF.ACT. (of weapons) be worn out Plb.
10 (tr., of circumstances) distress, irk —*someone* Pi. ‖ PASS. (of persons) be afflicted (w. plague) Th.; (of a city) be troubled —w.DAT. *by a war* Th. ‖ STATV.PF.PASS. (of a person) be racked —w.DAT. *w. pains* S.

πόνημα ατος *n.* thing made by toil; (ref. to honey) product, work (w.GEN. of bees) E.

πονηρεύματα των *n.pl.* [πονηρεύομαι] wicked actions, wrongs D. Plu.

πονηρεύομαι *mid.vb.* [πονηρός] behave wickedly or scandalously Hyp. D. Arist. Men. Plu.

πονηρίᾱ ᾱς, Ion. **πονηρίη** ης *f.* **1** badness (in quality); adverse state or condition (of a person or health) Hippon.; (of the soul, parts of the body, or sim.) Pl.; poor quality (of food) Pl.
2 badness (of persons, in respect of their moral, social or political conduct); worthlessness, depravity, disgraceful behaviour S.*Ichn.* E.*Cyc.* Th. Ar. Att.orats. Pl. +; (of a populace, in the eyes of disaffected politicians) Th. X. ‖ PL. (concr.) depravities, evil-doings Isoc. D. Arist. NT.

πονηροκρατέομαι *pass.contr.vb.* (of a city) be governed by the worse sort of people (opp. the virtuous) Arist.

πονηρός ά όν *adj.* [πόνος] | perh. accented πόνηρος in 1 | superl. πονηρότατος ‖ The wd. is freq. contrasted w. χρηστός *good.* |
1 enduring toil or suffering; (superl., of Herakles) enduring toil, tough Hes.*fr.*; (of persons, in voc. address) poor, pitiable Ar. Plu.; (of a situation or state of affairs) wretched, dire Th.; (of a circumstance) grievous Thgn.
2 bad in quality or condition; (of people, animals, an army, a person's body, or sim.) in a sorry state, good for nothing Sol. E.*Cyc.* Ar. Pl. X.; (of medicine, navigation, education, diet, a constitution, or sim.) bad, poor Pl. Aeschin. Arist.; (of jokes, a decision) Ar.; (of a judge, a criterion) unreliable E.; (of an utterance) faulty, misguided A.; (of merchandise) shady, dodgy Ar.; (concr., of a peg in a piece of wood) ill-

πονηρόφιλος

fitting E.fr.; (of coinage) **poorly minted** Ar. | see also μοχθηρός 3
3 morally bad; (of persons or their behaviour, activities, emotions, or sim.) **bad, wicked, base, evil** Anacr. Timocr. S. E. Th. Ar. + || MASC.SB. (w.art.) **the evil one** (i.e. the Devil) NT.
4 (of persons, w.connot. of political or social disapproval) **worthless, no-good** E. Th. Ar. Att.orats. Pl. X. Thphr.
—**πονήρως** adv. **laboriously, with difficulty** —ref. to soldiers marching X.; **poorly** —ref. to living, seeding fields Plu.; (of persons or things, w. ἔχειν) **be in a poor state** Th. Att.orats. X. Plu.; (w. διακεῖσθαι) Isoc.; (w. διατεθῆναι) D.
—**πονηρῶς** adv. **basely, dishonourably** —ref. to giving favours Pl.; **badly, poorly** —ref. to teaching X.; **unfavourably** —ref. to being regarded by people X.
πονηρό-φιλος ον adj. [φίλος] (of tyranny) **friendly to the wicked** Arist.
πόνος ου m. [πένομαι] | freq.pl. | **1** (gener.) **hard work, labour, toil, effort** (by workers, athletes, travellers, students, or sim.) Hom. +; (ref. to specific instances) Hom. +
2 (in military ctxts.) **toil of war, burden of battle** Hom. Pi. S.; (pl., periphr. W.GEN. of the war-god, i.e. fighting) Pi.; **struggle** (sts. W.GEN. of men, ref. to the field of battle) Il. Thgn.; (ref. to a battle or war) Hdt.
3 hardship, suffering, distress, trouble Hom. +; (specif.) **calamity** (ref. to a storm at sea) Hdt.; **affliction** (ref. to a disease) Th.
4 (concr.) result of hard work, **labour, work, product** (W.GEN. of bees, ref. to a honeycomb) Pi.; (of masons, ref. to a parapet) E.; (of persons, ref. to the fruits of their labours, as being appropriated by another) E.; (of labour pains, ref. to a baby) E.; (of a poet, ref. to an epic) Call.epigr.; (periphr., of wealth, i.e. wealth gained by hard work) A. || PL. **fruits of** (W.POSSESSV.ADJ. someone's) **labours** X.
5 scene of toils, place of exercise (W.GEN. of young men, ref. to race-tracks and gymnasia) E.
6 (personif., as son of Eris) **Toil** Hes.
ποντιάς άδος fem.adj. [πόντος] (of the brine) **of the sea** Pi.; (of a breeze) **on the sea** E.; (of a bridge, fig.ref. to an isthmus) **across the sea** Pi.
ποντίζω vb. | aor. ἐπόντισα | **put** (Danae) **out to sea** (in a chest) A.satyr.fr.; (of an excess of cargo) **capsize** —a ship A. [unless intr., of a ship, capsize] || PASS. (of a person) **be thrown into the sea** S.
Ποντικός adj.: see under Πόντος
πόντιος ᾱ ον (also ος ον E.) adj. **1** (epith. of Poseidon) **of the sea** hHom. Pi.fr. B. Trag. Ar.; (of Thetis, other demigoddesses) Pi. E.; (of Aphrodite, ref. to her birth fr. the sea) E.; (of the trident) **of the sea god** (i.e. Poseidon) E.
2 from or belonging to the sea; (of waves, water, or sim.) **of the sea** Lyr. Trag. Ar.; (of creatures) A. Pi.fr. AR.; (of pebbles) Pi. | see also ἔρση 2
3 sailing on the sea; (of persons) **sea-faring** Pi.; (of ships) **sea-going** A. E.; (of an armed force) **sea-borne** E.; (of ropes) **used at sea** E.
4 happening at sea; (of calamities) **at sea** A.; (of purifications, ref. to a labour of Herakles) E.; (of death by drowning) A.; (quasi-advbl., of a storm-wind springing up) S.
5 in or beside the sea; sea-girt Pi. S. E.; (of the Clashing Rocks) E.; (of the Isthmos of Corinth) Pi.; (of a shore, a cliff) **by the sea** A. E.
6 (quasi-advbl., of persons shipwrecked) **at sea** E.Cyc.; (of a person killed by drowning) **in the sea** E.fr.; (of a corpse thrown) **into the sea** E.
7 (of a visitor, fig.ref. to iron) **from across the sea** A.

Πόντιος adj.: see under Πόντος
ποντίσματα των n.pl. [ποντίζω] **offerings thrown into the sea, sea-gifts** (W.DAT. for a drowned man) E.
ποντόθεν adv.: see under πόντος
ποντο-μέδων οντος masc.ptcpl.adj. [πόντος, μέδω] (epith. of Poseidon) **ruler of the sea** A. Pi. Ar. || SB. (ref. to a lesser sea god) **sea lord** (W.GEN. of a stretch of sea) E.
ποντο-ναύτης ου m. **seafarer** S.fr.
πόντονδε, Πόντονδε advs.: see under πόντος, Πόντος
ποντοπορεύω vb. [ποντοπόρος] (of sailors, ships) **cross the sea** Od. Plu.(oracle)
ποντοπορέω contr.vb. (of sailors, ships) **cross the sea** Od. Plu.
ποντο-πόρος ον adj. (of ships) **crossing the sea, sea-going** Hom. Hes. hHom. S. E.; (of a cow, ref. to Io) Mosch.
Ποντο-πόσειδον voc.m. [Ποσειδῶν] **Poseidon of the Sea** Ar.
πόντος ου m. [reltd. πάτος¹] | ep.gen.dat. ποντόφι | **1 open or deep sea, sea** Hom. +; (periphr. W.GEN. ἁλός of the sea) **deep** Il. Thgn.; (prep.phr.) ἐκ πόντου from the sea (ref. to a wind blowing) Th.; (fig.) **ocean** (W.GEN. of diversity) Pl.
2 (ref. to a specific sea, defined by ADJ., as Aegean, Black, Ionian) Hom. +
3 (personif.) **Pontos** (son of Earth) Hes.; (father of Galateia) E.
—**ποντόθεν** adv. (ref. to movt.) **from the sea** (i.e. towards the shore) Il.
—**πόντονδε** adv. (ref. to movt.) **towards the open sea, seawards** Od. A. AR.; **into the sea** Od. B. Emp. AR.
Πόντος ου m. **1 Pontos** (the Black Sea) A. Hdt. E. Th. Ar. Att.orats. +
2 Pontus (region bordering the SE. coast of the Pontos) Plu.
—**Πόντιος** ᾱ ον adj. (of the mouth) **of the Pontos** (ref. to the Bosporos) E.; (of the channels) S.(dub.)
—**Ποντικός** ή όν adj. **1** (of trading-centres) **on the Pontos** Hdt.; (of salt fish) **from the Pontos** Plb. Plu.; (of the sea) **Pontic** Plb. Plu.
2 (of kings) **of Pontus** Plu.; (of persons) **from Pontus** NT. Plu.; (of spoils) Plu.; (of wars) **in Pontus** Plu.
—**Πόντονδε** adv. (ref. to movt.) **to the Pontos** AR.
ποντο-χάρυβδις εως f. (fig.ref. to a glutton) **whirlpool** Hippon.
πονωπόνηρος ᾱ ον adj. [intensv. πονηρός] (of persons) **wickedly wicked** Ar.
πόπανον ου n. [πέσσω] **round flat cake** (used in ceremonies of worship or sacrifice), **cake** Ar. Pl. Thphr. Men. Plb.
ποπάξ interj. (expressing horrified astonishment) **ah ah!** A.
πόποι (also **ποποῖ**) interj. **1** (after ὤ or ὦ at the start of a sentence, expressing surprise, anger, grief or other strong emotion, or drawing attention to sthg.) **ah!, oh!, alas!, oh shame!, look!** Hom. A. Pi.fr. Emp. S. AR. Theoc.; (in mid-sentence) A. S.
2 (in various positions in a sentence, sts. combined w. other interjs., expressing grief, distress or alarm) **ah ah!** A.
ποππύζω vb. | dial.inf. ποππύσδεν (Theoc.) | aor. ἐπόππυσα |
1 make an explosive sound with the lips, go 'pop-pop' (to attract the attention of an animal or child) Ar. Thphr.; (as a reaction to lightning) Ar.
2 (derog., of an aulos-player) **tootle** Theoc.
ποππυλιάσδω dial.vb. (of a woman attracting a goatherd) **make a kissing sound** Theoc.
ποππυσμός οῦ m. **kissing sound** (or sim., made to soothe a horse) X.
ποπώζω vb. | 3sg.impf. ἐπόπωζε | (of the ἔποψ hoopoe) **cry 'popoi'** Ar.(cj.)

πόρδαλις *f.*: see πάρδαλις

πορδή ῆς *f.* [πέρδομαι] **fart** Ar.

πορείᾱ ᾱς *f.* [πορεύω] **1** act of travelling, **travel, journey** A. Ar. Att.orats. Pl. X. +
2 (milit.) **march** Th. Isoc. Pl. X. Hyp. Men. +
3 course taken (by someone or sthg.); **path, direction** (of a javelin, a person) Antipho Pl.; **course, progress** (of the universe) Pl.
4 capacity for travelling, **locomotion** Pl.
5 (fig.) **journey, progress** (in discussion or sim.) Pl.

πορεῖν *aor.2 inf.* [reltd. πόρος, πείρω] | *aor.2* ἔπορον, ep. πόρον | *ptcpl.* πορών ‖ PASS.: 3sg.pf. πέπρωται, ep.3sg.plpf. πέπρωτο | *pf.ptcpl.* πεπρωμένος |
1 confer or bestow (material things, on someone); (of gods or humans) **furnish, supply, offer, give** (oft. W.DAT. to someone) —*a gift, weapon, food, clothing, or sim.* Hom. Hes. A. Pi. S. AR.
2 present (a person to another); **give** —*a woman (to someone, as wife or concubine)* Hom. —*a child* (W.DAT. + INF. *to someone, to teach*) Pi. —*a person (to someone, to take away)* AR. —*a son (to a woman, by impregnating her)* Il.; (of a god) **set in the way** (of a warrior) —*an enemy* Il.; (of a person) **consign** —*someone* (W.DAT. *to death*) Pi.; **deliver, bring** —*someone* (W.ADV. *to a place*) S.
3 supply (abstr. things); **bestow, grant, give** (oft. W.DAT. to someone) —*prophetic ability, honour, prosperity, grief, death, or sim.* Hom. Hes. A. Pi. B. S. AR.; **take** —*an oath* AR.; **leave** —*a good name (for one's descendants)* Pi.
4 grant, **allow, ensure** —W.ACC. + INF. *that sthg. happens* Il. —W.DAT. + INF. *that someone does sthg.* Pi. S.
5 ‖ PF.PASS. (of an act) **be allowed, destined or ordained** (by fate) A.; (of Fate) —W.INF. *to do sthg.* A. ‖ IMPERS. **it is destined, ordained or fated** —W.ACC. + INF. *that someone shd. do sthg., that sthg. shd. happen* Il. Hes. A.*fr.* E. AR. Plu. —W.DAT. + INF. Hes. A. AR. Plu.; (also) πεπρωμένον ἐστί —W.ACC. + INF. Pi. Hdt.(oracle) X. —W.DAT. + INF. A. Theoc. Plu. ‖ NEUT.ACC.PF.PTCPL. **it being fated** (that sthg. shd. happen) E.(cj.)

—**πεπρωμένος** η ον *pf.pass.ptcpl.adj.* **1** (of a god) **endowed** (W.DAT. w. a share of sthg.) Il.; (of a person) **doomed** (W.DAT. by a fate) Il. AR.; (of a king) **destined** (W.DAT. for a city) Pi.; (of a husband, W.DAT. for someone's marriage bed) E.
2 (of fate or destiny) **ordained** A. Pi. B. Hdt. E. AR.; (of death, the day of death) Il. E. X. Call.; (of strife, misfortune, time, a decision, marriage, or sim.) Pi. B. S. E. ‖ FEM.SB. **appointed lot, fate, destiny** A. Hdt. E. Isoc. D. Plu.; (also neut.sb.) A. Pi.*fr.* E. Plu.; (pl.) E.

πορεῖον ου *n.* [πορεύω] (concr.) **means of conveyance, carriage** (for people) Pl.; (ref. to a trolley for conveying ships across land) Plb.

πορεύματα των *n.pl.* **journeys, travels** (W.GEN. of people, ref. to travelling in company w. others) A.

πορεύσιμος ον *adj.* **1** (of a sea) able to be crossed, **navigable** Pl.; (of a river-bed, a route along it) **traversable on foot** X.
2 ‖ NEUT.IMPERS. (w. ἐστί) **it is possible to travel** (by a certain route) E.

πορευτέος ᾱ ον *vbl.adj.* **1** (of a journey) **to be made** S.
2 (of mountains) **to be crossed** X.

πορευτικός ή όν *adj.* (of an arrangement of troops, intervals betw. them) **suitable for a march** Plb.

πορευτός ή όν (ός όν A.) *adj.* **1** (of a beacon-signal) **travelling, journeying** A.
2 (of a place) **accessible on foot** (opp. by sea) Plb.
3 (of a time) **suitable for marching** Plb.

πορεύω *vb.* [πόρος] | dial.inf. πορεύεν (Pi.) | impf. ἐπόρευον, ep. πόρευον | aor. ἐπόρευσα, ep. πόρευσα ‖ MID.: fut. πορεύσομαι ‖ PASS.: aor. (w.mid.sens.) ἐπορεύθην | pf. πεπόρευμαι ‖ neut.impers.vbl.adj. πορευτέον |
1 convey or transport (someone, to or fr. a place); (of a person, ship, wind, dolphin) **convey, take, carry** —*someone (somewhere, by sea)* Pi. S. E. Lyr.adesp.; (of Herakles) —*someone (back to earth fr. the underworld)* E.; (of a winged horse) —*someone (to heaven)* Ar.; (of a ferryman) —W.DBL.ACC. *someone, over a river or lake* S. E.
2 cause (someone) to go (to or fr. a place); (of a god, a dolphin) **speed** (someone) **on one's way** (on a chariot, a ship) Pi. E.; (of a person's heart) **prompt** (W.ACC. him) **to travel** (somewhere) Pi.; (of a host) **despatch, send** —*a guest (to someone)* S.; (of parents) —*a son (to war)* E.; (of a killer) —*a victim (to the underworld)* Pi. E.; (of a commander) **launch** —*an expedition* E.; **take** —*an army (somewhere)* Th.; (of a person) **bring** —*someone (to another person, fr. somewhere)* S. E.; (of a god) **lead** —*someone (into trouble)* E.
3 convey or transport (sthg., to or fr. a place); **bring** —*things requested, a message (to someone)* S. E.; **take, carry** —*a shield (to a place)* E. —*gifts (fr. a carriage)* E.
4 cause (sthg.) to be conveyed (to or fr. a place); **despatch, send** —*gold (to someone)* E.; (of a god) **bring forth, produce** —*a golden lamb* E.; (of oracular priestesses) **transmit** —*the thoughts of Zeus (to inquirers)* E.*fr.*; (of motion) **convey** —*speed and slowness* Pl.
5 ‖ MID. and AOR.PASS. (intr., of persons or animals) **go on one's way, proceed, travel** (on foot, by sea, or other means) Hdt. Trag. Th. Ar. + —W.ADV. or PREP.PHR. *to or fr. a place* Pi. Hdt. S. E. + —W.ACC. *to a place* S. E. —W.COGN. or INTERN.ACC. *on a route, in flight, or sim.* E. Pl. X.; (of ships) **travel** Hdt.
6 ‖ MID. and AOR.PASS. (of troops) **march** Hdt. Th. X. Plb. Plu.
7 ‖ MID. and AOR.PASS. (gener. or fig.) **walk** —W.PREP.PHR. *into a trap* E.; **conduct oneself** —W.ADV. *arrogantly* S.; (of disputants) **proceed** (in argument) Pl. X.; (of a speaker) **come** —W.PREP.PHR. *to a topic* D.; (of vice) **advance** —W.PREP.PHR. *in a certain way* X.

πορθέω *contr.vb.* [reltd. πέρθω] | ep.impf. ἐπόρθεον, also πόρθεον | aor. ἐπόρθησα | **1 sack, plunder** —*a city or sim.* Il. Pi. Hdt. Trag. Th. Isoc. +; **ravage, lay waste to** —*land, a country, or sim.* Od. Hdt. S. E. Th. Att.orats. +; **ransack, despoil** —*a house, a temple* E. Th. Isoc. X. ‖ PASS. (of places) **be plundered or laid waste** A. E. Th. Att.orats. Pl. X. +; (of a house) **be ransacked** D.; (of cattle) **be massacred** E.
2 ‖ PASS. (of people) **be plundered or have one's land ravaged** Th.; (hyperbol., of a person) **be ransacked** —W.ACC. *of some garlic* Ar.; (fig., of occupants of a besieged city) **be sacked or ruined** —W.PREP.PHR. *by themselves (i.e. through panic)* A.; (of a person) **be ruined** (by someone's death) A.
3 take as plunder, **plunder** —*objects* hHom. ‖ PASS. (of women, property, cattle) **be plundered** A. E.

πορθήματα των *n.pl.* **acts of plunder, looting** Plu.

πόρθησις εως *f.* **sacking, plundering** (of a city, a camp) D. Plu.

πορθητάς ᾶ *dial.m.* **sacker** (of a city, ref. to a commander) E.

πορθήτωρ ορος *m.* **sacker** (of a city) A.; **ransacker, despoiler** (of a house) A.

πορθμείᾱ ᾱς *f.* [πορθμεύω] **business of ferrying, ferrying** Plu.

πορθμεῖον, Ion. **πορθμήιον**, ου *n.* **1 ferry-boat, ferry** Hdt. X. Plb. Plu.
2 ferryman's fee Call.

πόρθμευμα

3 ‖ PL. Ferry, Straits (as name of a specific stretch of water) Hdt.

πόρθμευμα ατος *n.* (ref. to Acheron) **ferry-crossing** (W.GEN. ἀχέων *of sorrows*) A.

πορθμεύς έως (Ion. ῆος) *m.* **1 ferryman** Od. Ar. Aeschin. Din. Theoc.; (W.GEN. of the dead, ref. to Charon) E. Call. Theoc.
2 ‖ PL. boatmen, seamen (on a passenger ship) Hdt.

πορθμευτικός ή όν *adj.* (of a class of maritime workers) engaged in carrying passengers Arist.

πορθμεύω *vb.* [πορθμός] **1** act as a ferryman, **ferry people** (across a river or strait) —W.PREP.PHR. *to a place* Aeschin. ‖ PASS. be ferried Hdt.
2 (of a commander) **ferry, transport** —*an army* (*over a sea*) E.; (of a person) **convey** —*a person, an object* (*by sea*) S. E.; **sail** (W.ACC. a ship) **across** (the sea) E.
3 **transport, convey** (over land) —*a person* E. —*instructions* A.; **have** (W.ACC. someone) **transported** (somewhere) E.; (periphr.) **move** —*one's steps* (*i.e. walk*) E.; **take** —*one's foot* (*somewhere, i.e. travel there*) E. ‖ PASS. be conveyed (in a carriage) E.; (of a god) travel —W.ACC. *through the sky* E.
4 (fig.) **direct** —*a pursuit* (*somewhere*) E.; **bring** —*someone* (W.PREP.PHR. *to tears*) E.
5 (intr., of a planet or star) **cross the sky** E.

πορθμήιον *Ion.n.*: see πορθμεῖον

πορθμίς ίδος *f.* **1 ferry-boat**; (gener.) **ship** (used to convey someone) E.
2 (fig., ref. to the belly) **freighter** E.*Cyc.*; (ref. to a portable table) Philox.Leuc.

πορθμός οῦ *m.* [πείρω, πόρος] **1** strip of water traversable by ferry, **strait, channel** Od. Pi.*fr.* Hdt. Trag. Th. AR. +
2 sea as a route for travel, **sea-route** Pi. E.; (W.GEN. to a country) E.*Cyc.*
3 **sea-crossing** E.; (W.GEN. by ships) E.; **opportunity to make a sea-crossing** (dependent on the wind) Th.
4 service as ferryman, **ferrying** (by an individual) S.
5 (fig.phr.) κατὰ πορθμόν (w. πλεῖν *sail*) **with the current in the strait** (*i.e. adapt oneself to circumstances*) E.
6 **passageway** (for water, through a pipe or sim.) Emp.

πορίζω *vb.* [πόρος] ‖ fut. ποριῶ ‖ aor. ἐπόρισα ‖ pf. πεπόρικα ‖ MID.: fut. ποριοῦμαι ‖ aor. ἐπορισάμην ‖ pf. πεπόρισμαι ‖ PASS.: fut. πορισθήσομαι ‖ aor. ἐπορίσθην ‖
1 provide, furnish, supply (freq. W.DAT. to someone) —*money, pay, food, or sim.* Th. Ar. Isoc. X. + —*an excuse, a reply, salvation, truth, or sim.* Th. Pl.; **supply, devise** —*a solution, schemes, delays* E. Ar. Pl.; **make up, concoct** —*a charge* (*against someone*) Th.; (of a god) **bestow** —*victory* Ar.; (of a ewe) **offer** —*her teats* (*to her young*) E.*Cyc.*(cj.); (perh. of a tortoise-shell, ref. to the lyre) **produce** —*a voice* S.*Ichn.* ‖ PASS. (of material or non-material things) be provided or supplied Th. Ar. +; (of punishment) be in store —W.DAT. *for someone* S.*Ichn.*
2 (intr., of gods) **provide** —W.ADV. handsomely (*for someone's well-being*) E.
3 ‖ MID. **furnish oneself with, procure, acquire** —*money, weapons, provisions, a livelihood, or sim.* Th. Att.orats. Pl. X. —*recreations, pleasures, or sim.* Th. Isoc. Pl. —*witnesses* Att.orats.; **devise** —*an excuse* Lys. D. —*arguments or sim.* Ar. Is. D. Thphr.
4 (of a god) **bring, send** —*someone* (*to a place*) S.

πόριμος ον *adj.* **1** (of people) **resourceful, able to provide** (W.PREP.PHR. for all eventualities) Th.; (of a person, W.DAT. for himself) Ar.
2 (of a war that cannot be won) **dealing** (W.ACC. what cannot be dealt with) A.

3 (of boldness) **resourceful, inventive** Ar.; (of work) **effective** Ar.; (of Love) **productive** (W.GEN. of wisdom) Pl.

πόρις ιος *f.* [reltd. πόρτις] **calf, heifer** Od. E.; (of Inakhos, ref. to Io) E.

πορισμός οῦ *m.* [πορίζω] **1 supplying** or **procuring** (W.GEN. of provisions, money) Plb. Plu.
2 **money-making** Plu.; **way of making money** Plu.

ποριστής οῦ *m.* **1 provider, supplier** (W.GEN. of funds) D.
2 ‖ PL. (at Athens, title of officials app. assigned to devise emergency sources of revenue) **dispensing officers** Antipho Ar.
3 ‖ PL. (ref. to oligarchs, as instigators of evil actions by others) **facilitators** (W.GEN. + DAT. of crimes by the populace) Th.
4 **procurer, moneymaker** (euphem. for pirate or bandit) Arist.

ποριστικός ή όν *adj.* **1** (of a tradesman or manufacturer) **capable of maintaining a supply** (W.GEN. of commodities) Pl.; (of a commander, W.GEN. + DAT. of provisions for his men) X.
2 (of virtue) **productive** (W.GEN. of good) Arist.

πόρκης ου *m.* **band, ring, hoop** (securing a spear-head to its shaft) Il.

πόρκος ου *m.* **wicker fish-trap, creel** Pl.

πορνεία ᾶς *f.* [πόρνη] **1 prostitution** (practised by a man) Aeschin. D.
2 sexual intercourse outside marriage (by a man or woman), **fornication** NT.; (specif.) **adultery** (by a married woman) NT.

πορνεῖον ου *n.* **brothel** Antipho Ar. Aeschin.

πορνεύομαι *mid.vb.* ‖ pf. πεπόρνευμαι ‖ (of a woman) **prostitute oneself, be a prostitute** Hdt. D.; (of a man) Aeschin. D.

πόρνη ης, dial. **πόρνα** ᾶς *f.* [πέρνημι] woman who sells herself for sex, **prostitute, whore** Alc. Hippon. Scol. Ar. X. Aeschin. +; (appos.w. *f.* ἄνθρωπος) Lys. D.

—πορνίδιον ου *n.* [dimin.] **prostitute, tart** Ar. Men.

πορνικός ή όν *adj.* (of a tax) **on prostitutes** Aeschin.

πορνοβοσκέω *contr.vb.* [πορνοβοσκός] (of a man) **keep prostitutes, run a brothel** Ar. D. Thphr.; (of a woman) Hyp.

πορνοβοσκία ᾶς *f.* **brothel-keeping** Aeschin.

πορνο-βοσκός οῦ *m.f.* [βόσκω] one who keeps prostitutes; (ref. to a man) **pimp** or **brothel-keeper** Aeschin. D. Arist. Thphr. Men. Plu.; (ref. to a woman) **procuress** Plu.

πόρνος ου *m.* **male prostitute, rent-boy** Ar. X. Aeschin. D. Plb.

πορν-ῳδίαι ῶν *f.pl.* [ἀοιδή] performances of songs by prostitutes, **whore-songs, dirty ditties** Ar.

πόρον (ep.aor.): see πορεῖν

πόρος ου *m.* [πείρω, πορεῖν] **1** place where a river may be crossed; **crossing-place, ford** (sts. W.GEN. of a river) Il. hHom. A. Th.
2 stretch of flowing water which may be crossed or forded; **stream** or **channel** (of a river) Hes. Pi. B. Trag.
3 stretch of sea which may be crossed; **strait** (ref. to a narrows, such as the Hellespont, or a comparatively narrow passage in a larger sea, as betw. Sicily and Africa) A. Pi.*fr.* Hdt. Ar. Aeschin. Plb. +
4 (ref. to a broader expanse of water, such as the Adriatic, Aegean, Black Sea) **sea** Pi. E.
5 (gener.) route across the sea, **path** (pl., W.GEN. or ADJ. *of the sea*) Od. A. S.; (sg.) Lyr.adesp.; **course** E.*fr.*; (phr.) ἐν πόρῳ (w. εἶναι or sim., of a reef, a city) **be on a sea-route** Hdt. Th.; (of an island) **be in the path** (W.GEN. *of a naval battle*) Hdt.; **voyage** E.

6 artificial passage over a river or strait, **pontoon, bridge** A. Hdt.; (W.GEN. for a crossing) Hdt.
7 (gener.) **passageway** (betw. two rivers, ref. to a strip of land) E.
8 pathway, route (over the ground) A. E.; (W.GEN. of wild animals) X.; (W.GEN. of birds, ref. to the sky) A.; (W.GEN. of escape) A.; (fig.) **course, path** (W.GEN. of Zeus' thinking) A.; (of life) Pi.; (of songs) Emp.; **journey** A.
9 (pl.) **passageway, channel** (through which ἀπορροαί *effluences* pass fr. material objects into the sensory organs, in the doctrine of Empedocles) Pl.
10 way or means of accomplishing; **way, means** (W.GEN. of capture, safety, travel, inquiry, or sim.) Hdt. E. Ar. Pl.; (W.INF. of doing sthg.) Emp. E. And.; (W. πρός + ACC. for doing sthg.) X.; **device, scheme** A. E. Ar.
11 means of escaping, **way** (W.PREP.PHR. out of difficulties) A. Ar.; **way out** (W.GEN. of misfortune, difficulties) E. Lyr.adesp.
12 resource (for mortals, ref. to the gift of fire) A.; (ref. to ships) Ar.; (ref. to fishing-tackle) Theoc.
13 procurement, provision, supply (of sthg.) S. Ar. Pl.; (W.GEN. of money) E.
14 (in public ctxts.) **supply** or **provision** (W.GEN. of money, revenue) X. D. ‖ PL. revenues or funds Hyp. D. Arist.
15 (personif., in a cosmogony) **Means** (assoc.w. Τέκμωρ *End*) Alcm.; (son of Metis, father of Eros) **Resource** Pl.

πορπᾰκίζομαι *mid.vb.* [πόρπαξ] | aor.ptcpl. πορπακισάμενος | **fasten on a shield-band** (to a shield, to make it ready for carrying, or perh. fasten it to one's arm, i.e. carry the shield) Ar.

πορπάματα των *n.pl.* [πόρπη] garment pinned at the shoulders, **cloak** E.

πόρπαξ ᾰκος *m.* **1** arm-grip of a hoplite shield, **arm-grip, shield-band** (a bronze bar w. a loop at the centre through which the holder passed his left forearm, to grasp a leather thong near the shield rim, so that the shield was supported at both points) B.*fr.* S. E. Ar. Plu.; (app. made of leather) S.; (ref. to being detachable when the shield was not in use) Ar.
2 ‖ PL. shield-thongs (as in 1, but extending around the whole rim) E.

πορπᾱ-φόρος ον *adj.* [φέρω] **wearing a brooch** (as a fastening) S.*satyr.fr.*

πορπάω *contr.vb.* | dial.aor.imperatv. πόρπᾱσον | **pin, fasten** —*someone's arm* (*to a rock*) A.

πόρπη ης *f.* [πείρω; cf. περόνη] safety-pin or brooch (used to fasten clothes, usu. at each shoulder), **pin, brooch** Il. hHom. E.; (used to blind oneself or another) E.; (used to incise letters on bark) Plu.

πόρρω *Att.adv.*, **πορρωτέρω** *Att.compar.adv.*, **πορρωτάτω** *Att.superl.adv.*: see πρόσω

πόρρωθεν *Att.adv.*, **πορρωτέρωθεν** *Att.compar.adv.*: see under πρόσωθεν

πορσαίνω *ep.vb.*: see πορσύνω

πόρσιον, **πόρσιστα** *compar. and superl.advs.*: see under πρόσω

πορσύνω *vb.* [πόρσω, see πρόσω] | fut. πορσυνῶ | aor. ἐπόρσῡνα, ep. πόρσῡνα | —also **πορσαίνω** *ep.vb.* | fut. πορσανέω | iteratv.impf. πορσαίνεσκον |
1 bring forth, **provide, prepare** —*a feast, drink, sacrifice, or sim.* Pi. E. AR. —*subsistence, hospitality, or sim.* S. E. ‖ MID. **prepare for oneself** —*a meal* A.
2 (of a wife) **provide** —*the bed* (*for a husband, i.e. sleep w. him, w. sexual connot.*) Hom. AR.
3 (of persons, Fate) **bring about, cause** —*hostilities, death, good and evil* A. E. X.; (of painters) **produce, create**

—*likenesses* Emp. ‖ PASS. (of troubles) be caused (for someone) A. E.
4 look after, see to, attend to —*religious rites* Hdt. —*a task, plan, instructions, or sim.* Trag. X. AR.; **perform** —*a service* (*for someone*) E.; (of Fate) **arrange** —*a course* (*for a ship*) B.; (intr., of wives) **arrange** or **manage things** —W.PREP.PHR. *in their houses* hHom. ‖ PASS. (of a crime, task, plan) be carried out A. X. AR.; (of an expedition) be set under way —W.ADV. *towards some goal* S.
5 look after, care for —*a father, child, injured person* Hes.*fr.* Pi. E. AR.; **honour** —*a god* AR. —*a person* (*like a god*) AR.; (of women) perh. **attend to** (i.e. prepare for burial) —*a dead man* Hes.*fr.* ‖ PASS. (of parents) be cared for AR.
6 esteem, cherish —*a saying* Pi.; (of possessions) **enhance, enrich** —*a house* Pi.

πόρσω *dial.adv.*: see πρόσω

πόρταξ ακος *m.f.* [reltd. πόρτις] **calf** Il.

πόρτις ιος *m.f.* **1** (*f.*) **calf, heifer** Il. hHom. S. Hellenist.poet.
2 (*m.*) **calf** (ref. to Epaphos, son of Io) E.

πορτι-τρόφος ον *adj.* [τρέφω] (of a region) heifer-nourishing, **calf-breeding** hHom. B.

πορφύρᾱ ᾱς, Ion. **πορφύρη** ης *f.* **1 purple shellfish, murex** S.*fr.*
2 purple dye (obtained fr. the murex) Alcm. Sapph. A. Hdt. Isoc. Pl. +
3 purple-dyed fabric A. Plu.
4 purple cloak Plb. NT. Plu.; (collectv.) **purple clothing** Arist.

πορφύρεος ᾱ (Ion. η) ον, contr. **πορφυροῦς** ᾶ (Ion. ῆ) οῦν, Aeol. **πορφύριος** (also **πόρφυρος**) ᾱ ον *adj.* | neut.pl. πορφύρᾱ (i.e. εα) Sapph. | **1** purple-dyed; (of fabrics, esp. garments, oft. w.connot. of wealth or luxury) **purple, crimson** Hom. hHom. Lyr. Hdt. E. X. +; (of a ball) Anacr.
2 purple-coloured; (of wings) **purple, crimson** Pi.; (of a garland) Thgn. Pi.; (of a kind of rock-salt) Hdt.
3 (of Aphrodite) **rosy** (perh. ref. to complexion) Anacr.; (of a girl's mouth) Simon.
4 (of blood) **dark, red, crimson** Il. Stesich.; (of dye, fig.ref. to blood) A.; (of death in battle) **dark** or **bloody** Il.
5 (of dizziness) **dark** (ref. to blacking out) AR.
6 (of a rainbow) **purple, lurid** Il.; (of a supernatural cloud) Il. hHom.
7 (of waves, the sea) **dark-blue** or **dark** Hom. hHom. Semon. Thgn. Lyr. E. AR.; (of river-water) E. [In ep. perh. rather to be interpr. as *seething, heaving, surging*, by assoc.w. πορφύρω]

πορφυρεύς έως *m.* **murex-fisher** Hdt. E.*fr.*

πορφυρευτικός ή όν *adj.* (of a shelter, ref. to a cave) **for murex-fishers** Il.

πορφυρίς[1] ίδος *f.* **purple cloak** X. Plb. Plu.

πορφυρίς[2] ίδος *f.* perh. **blue rock-thrush** Ibyc. Ar.

πορφυρίων ωνος *m.* a kind of swamp-hen, **purple gallinule** Ar.

πορφυρο-δίνᾱς ᾱ *dial.masc.adj.* [δίνη] (of a river) **with dark eddies** B.

πορφυρο-ειδής ές *adj.* [εἶδος[1]] (of the sea) **dark** or **dark-blue in appearance** A. E.

πορφυρό-ζωνος ον *adj.* [ζώνη] (of Aphrodite) **with purple girdle** B.

πορφυρό-πωλις ιδος *f.* [πωλέω] **seller of purple fabrics** NT.

πορφυρό-στρωτος ον *adj.* [στρωτός] (of a pathway) **strewn with crimson** or **purple fabrics** A.

πορφυροῦς *contr.adj.*: see πορφύρεος

πορφύρω *ep.vb.* [redupl. φύρω] | impf. πόρφυρον | **1** (of the sea) **heave, surge** (or perh. *darken*) Hom. AR.; (of flames) **rage** AR. [or perh. as 3, *become dark red or lurid*]

πορών

2 (fig., of a person's heart) **be restless, be in turmoil** Hom.; (wkr.sens., of a person or heart) **think, ponder** AR.; **consider** —*everything, alternative courses of action* AR. —W.INDIR.Q. *how to do sthg.* AR.
3 [app. influenced by πορφύρα] (of the river Krathis, whose waters had the property of dyeing things red or gold) **become red, redden** —W.DAT. *w. wine (i.e. turn into wine)* Theoc.; (of a person's cheeks) Bion; (mid., of a mourner's breasts, fr. being beaten) Bion

πορών (aor.2 ptcpl.): see πορεῖν

ποσάκις, dial. **ποσσάκι** *interrog.adv.* [πόσος] **1 how many times, how often?** Call. NT.
2 (math., in multiplication) so many times, **times** (a certain number) Arist.

ποσαπλάσιος ᾱ ον *interrog.adj.* (math., of a space) **how many fold, how many times as great** (as another)? Pl.; **how many times greater** (w.GEN. than another)? Pl.

ποσά-πους ουν, gen. ποδος *interrog.adj.* [πούς] (math.) **how many feet** (in length)? Pl.

ποσαχῶς *interrog.adv.* **1 in how many ways?** —*ref. to things being combined* Arist.
2 **in how many senses?** —*ref. to using a word* Arist.

πόσε *ep.adv.* [reltd. ποῦ] to what place, **whither?** Hom. Stesich.

Ποσειδῶν ῶνος, ep. **Ποσειδάων** ωνος, Ion. **Ποσειδέων** ωνος, dial. **Ποσειδάν** ᾶνος (Lyr. Trag.), Aeol. **Ποσείδᾱν** ᾱνος *m.* —also dial. **Ποτειδάν** ᾶνος (Pi. X.), **Ποτειδάων** ωνος (Call.), Boeot. **Ποτῑδάων** ωνος *m.* | voc. Πόσειδον, ep. Ποσείδᾱον | acc. Ποσειδῶ, ep. Ποσειδάωνα, Megar. Ποτειδᾶ (Ar.) | **Poseidon** (son of Kronos, god of the sea, also assoc.w. earthquakes and horses) Hom. +

—**Ποσειδάνιος** (also **Ποσειδαώνιος** B.) ᾱ ον *dial.adj.* (of a son, the horses, the trident) **of Poseidon** Pi. B.*fr.*; (of a precinct, a spring) **sacred to Poseidon** Pi. E.(dub.); (periphr., w. ἐνάλιος θεός) *Poseidonian sea god* S.

—**Ποσειδώνιον** (also **Ποσείδιον** Plb.) ου *n.* **temple of Poseidon** Th. Plb.

—**Ποσιδήιος** η ον *ep.Ion.adj.* (of a grove) **sacred to Poseidon** Il. hHom. ‖ NEUT.SB. *temple of Poseidon* Od.

πόσθη ης *f.* [perh.reltd. πέος] (colloq. term for penis) **dick, cock** Ar.

—**ποσθίον** ου *n.* [dimin.] **little dick** Ar.

—**πόσθων** ωνος *m.* [dimin.] (as a boy's nickname) **Dickie boy** Ar.

ποσί (dat.pl.): see πούς

ποσί-δεσμος ου *m.* [πούς, δέω¹] **foot-shackler** (ref. to the sea, which hampers walking; fanciful etymology of Poseidon) Pl.

Ποσιδεών ῶνος, Ion. **Ποσιδηιών** ῶνος *m.* [Ποσειδῶν] **Posideon** (sixth month of the Athenian year, roughly December) Anacr. D. Arist. Thphr.

ποσίνδα *interrog.adv.* [πόσος] ‖ INDECL.SB. (as name of a game, w. παίζειν *play*) how many times? (i.e. guess the number) X.

πόσις¹ ιος *m.* [reltd. δεσπότης, πότνια] **husband** Hom. +; (specif.) **lawful husband** (opp. ἀνήρ *lover*) S.

πόσις² εως (Ion. ιος) *f.* [πίνω] **1 drinking** (opp. eating) Hom. hHom. Thgn. Pl. X. Plb.; **carousing** (in a drinking-bout) Anacr. Thgn. Hdt. Th. Critias +
2 (concr.) **drink** (opp. food) Hom. Hes. Thgn. Pl. X.
3 (specif.) **drink, draught** A. Antipho Pl.

πόσος¹, Ion. **κόσος**, η ον *interrog.adj.* | Used in both dir. and indir.qs. Also used w. exclamatory rather than interrog. force. |

1 (sg., of things) of what magnitude, **how large, how great, how much?** Trag. Att.orats. Pl. +
2 ‖ PL. (of persons or things) of what number, **how many?** Hdt. E. Ar. Att.orats. Pl. +
3 (of abstr. things, such as desire, reputation, wickedness, folly) of what degree, **how great?** Ar. Isoc. Pl. D.
4 (of a route or journey) of what distance, **how long?** E. X.
5 (of time) of what duration, **how long?** S. E. Ar. Isoc. +; (prep.phr.) μέχρι κόσου *how long?* Hdt.
6 (of sound) of what intensity, **how loud?** E.
7 (ref. to value or worth) ‖ NEUT.SB. how much (i.e. what sum of money)? Ar. X.; (advbl.gen.) πόσου *for how much, at what price?* Ar. Pl. X. Thphr.; (also) ἐπὶ πόσῳ Pl. X.

—**πόσον** *neut.acc.sg.adv.* **1 what distance, how far?** E. X.
2 **how loudly?** Ar. Pl.

—**πόσῳ** *neut.dat.sg.adv.* (w.compar.adv. or adj., or w.vb. implying comparison) **by how much?** E. D. Plb. NT.

—**πόσα** *neut.acc.pl.adv.* to what amount or degree, **how much?** X.

—**ποσός** ή όν *indef.adj.* **1** (of things) **of a certain quantity** or **magnitude** Pl. Arist. Plb.; (prep.phrs.) ἐπὶ ποσόν *for some time* Plb.; κατὰ ποσόν *to some extent* Plb.
2 ‖ NEUT.SB. quantity Pl. Arist.; (ref. to being equal) κατὰ ποσόν *in quantity* Arist.

πόσος² Lacon.*m.*: see πόθος

ποσότης ητος *f.* [πόσος¹] (sg. and pl.) **quantity** Arist. Plb.

ποσόω *contr.vb.* calculate the quantity (of sthg.); **quantify, add up** —*counters on an abacus* Thphr.

ποσσάκι dial.*interrog.adv.*: see ποσάκις

ποσσ-ῆμαρ *ep.interrog.adv.* [πόσος¹, ἦμαρ] **for how many days?** Il.

ποσσί (ep.dat.pl.): see πούς

ποσσί-κροτος ον *ep.adj.* [πούς, κρότος] (of a country) **to be tapped or trodden down by the feet** (of conquerors, envisaged as dancers) Hdt.(oracle)

ποσταῖος ᾱ ον *interrog.adj.* [πόσος¹] (quasi-advbl., of a person arriving) **in how many days?** X.

πόστος η ον *interrog.adj.* [cf. πολλοστός] how far on in a numerical series; (of a number of years, since sthg. happened) **how many?** Od.; (of a fraction of sthg.) **how small?** X.

πότ *dial.prep.*: see πρός

πότα, ποτά Aeol.*advs.*: see πότε, ποτέ

ποτάγω *dial.vb.*, **ποταγωγίδες** *dial.f.pl.*, **ποταείδω** *dial.vb.*: see προσάγω, προσαγωγίδες, προσάδω

ποταίνιος ᾱ ον (also ος ον S.*fr.*) *adj.* [reltd. προταινί] **1** of recent origin; (of blood) newly shed, **fresh** A.; (of a garland, as a prize) not previously offered, **new** Pi.
2 new and surprising; (of a suffering) **unexpected** A.; (of a din) A.(dub.); (of a tomb, for a living person) **strange, unheard of** S.; (of a plan) **novel** B.; (of pleasures) not previously experienced, **new** S.*fr.*

ποτ-αμείβομαι *dial.mid.vb.* [πρός] **answer** —*someone* Theoc.

ποτ-αμέλγομαι *dial.pass.vb.* (of a goat) be milked in addition (to suckling her young), **yield milk as well** Theoc.

ποταμηίς ίδος *fem.adj.* [ποταμός] (of a nymph) **of a river** AR.

ποτάμιον ου *n.* [dimin. ποταμός] **small river, stream** Plu.

ποτάμιος ᾱ ον (also ος ον E.) *adj.* **1** (of banks, streams, water) **of or from a river** A. E.; (of a drink) **of river-water** S.*fr.*
2 (of birds) **frequenting a river** Ar.; (of a swan) E.; ἵππος ποτάμιος *river-horse, hippopotamus* Hdt.
3 (of boats) **used on a river** Plb. Plu.; (of Charon's oar) **plied on the river** (of the underworld) E.

4 (of a city) **on a river** Pi.
5 (epith. of Artemis) **of the river** (i.e. the Alpheios) Pi.
6 like a river; (of melted snow on a mountainside) **flowing in streams** E.

ποταμός οῦ *m*. **1 river** or **stream** Hom. +; (w. name of a specific river) Hom. +; (personif., as a river god) Hom.
2 (fig.) **river** (of volcanic fire) A.; (of lava) Pi.

—**ποταμόνδε** *adv*. 1 (ref. to movt.) **to** or **towards a river, riverwards** Hom.
2 **into a river** —*ref. to pouring sthg.* AR.

ποτανός ά όν *dial.adj*. —also **ποτηνός** ή όν (Pl.) *Ion.adj*. [ποτάομαι] 1 (of birds, a flock of birds) **in flight, on the wing** A. E.; (of a chariot-ride w. winged horses) **flying** E.; (of doves) **winged** Lamprocl.; (of Eros) Pl.(quot.poet.); (of Perseus' sandals) E. ‖ NEUT.PL.SB. **winged creatures** (ref. to birds) Pi.
2 (fig., of persons, in a wish to escape) **taking wing** E.; (of the dead departing to Hades) E.; (of a person compared to an eagle) **soaring** (W.PREP.PHR. among the Muses, i.e. in poetical achievements) Pi.; (of a poet's art, his subject matter) Pi.

ποτάομαι, also **πωτάομαι**, Ion. **ποτέομαι** *mid.contr.vb*. —also **πότᾱμαι** *Aeol.mid.vb*. [reltd. πέτομαι] | Aeol.2sg. πότα (Sapph., dub.) | Lacon.3sg. ποτήται, 3sg.imperatv. ποτήσθω (Alcm.) | Ion.2sg.imperatv. ποτεῦ (Call.) | Aeol.ptcpl. ποτήμενος (Theoc.) | ep.3pl.impf. πωτῶντο | pf. πεπότημαι, dial. πεπότᾱμαι |
1 (of birds and other winged creatures) **move through the air** or **soar aloft, fly, fly about** Hom. hHom. Alcm. Simon. E. Ar. +; (of deities) hHom. E. Call.; (of Perseus) Hes.; (of the souls of poets) Ar.
2 ‖ PF. **have taken wing** or **be on the wing**; (of a bird, bees) **be in flight** AR.; (of a person's mind) **be in the clouds** Ar. AR.
3 (of a dead person's soul) **remain suspended in the air, hover** (above someone) E.; (of terror, before someone's heart) A.; (of a thought, in someone's mind) A.; (of Tantalos) **hang** (in mid-air, as a punishment) E.
4 ‖ PF. and PLPF. (of birds, bees) **hover** Il.; (of Aphrodite, likened to a bee) E.; (of a soul which has left the body) Od.; (of Strife, depicted on a shield) Hes.; (fig., of a person's mind) **be all of a flutter** Ar.
5 (of stones as missiles, a spear, thunderbolt, sparks) **move quickly through the air, speed, fly** Il. Hes. hHom. Archil.; (of wine-drops, shaken fr. cups) Alc.
6 (fig., of a person) **fly, soar** —W.PREP.PHR. *to heaven* (i.e. *aspire too high*) Alcm. —*over the sea* (on the wings of fame) Thgn.
7 (of a person) **fly off** (in pursuit of someone) Sapph.; (of a messenger) **wing one's way, speed on** Ar.; (of a noise, a prayer, speech) A. AR.

ποταπός *interrog.adj*.: see ποδαπός
ποτᾰτός (dial.gen.): see ποτής
ποταρχέω *contr.vb*. [ποτόν, ἀρχή] **be in charge of the drinking** (at a symposium), **be toast-master** Eleg.adesp.
ποταυλέω *dial.contr.vb*.: see προσαυλέω
ποτᾱῷος *dial.adj*.: see προσηῷος

πότε, Ion. **κότε**, dial. **πόκα**, Aeol. **πότα** *interrog. temporal adv*. | used in both dir. and indir.qs. | **at what time, when?** Hom. +; (also) ἐς πότε S.

—**ποτέ**, Ion. **κοτέ**, dial. **ποκά**, Aeol. **ποτά** *indef. temporal adv*. | enclit., except in 5 | 1 (ref. to past time) **once upon a time, once, formerly** Hom. +
2 (ref. to future time) **at some time, some day** Hom. +
3 (in conditional, relative or neg. cls.) **at any time, ever** Hom. +
4 (intensv., w.interrog., e.g. τίς who) **ever** A. +
5 (in first position, in contrastv. cls.) ποτὲ μέν ... ποτὲ δέ (or αὖθις δέ, τοτὲ δέ or sim.) **at one time ... at another** Pl. X. +; ποτὲ μέν ... εἶτα E.; (without first element) ποτὲ δέ *but sometimes* E. Thphr. Plb.
6 | See also δή ποτε, μήποτε, μηδέποτε, μηπώποτε, οὔποτε, οὐδέποτε, οὐπώποτε

ποτέθηκα (dial.aor.): see προστίθημι
Ποτείδαια ας, Ion. **Ποτειδαίη** ης *f*. **Poteidaia** (city on the isthmus of the western peninsula of Chalcidice) Hdt. Th. Ar. +
—**Ποτειδεᾶται** ῶν, Ion. **Ποτειδαιῆται** έων *m.pl*. **people of Poteidaia, Poteidaians** Hdt. Th.; (sg.) Hdt.
—**Ποτειδαιατικός** ή όν *adj*. ‖ NEUT.PL.SB. **events at Poteidaia** Th.
Ποτειδάν, Ποτειδάων *dial.m*.: see Ποσειδῶν
ποτεῖδον (dial.aor.2): see προσοράω
ποτελέξατο, ποτεμάξατο (dial.3sg.aor.mid.): see προσλέγομαι, προσμάσσω
ποτένθῃς (dial.2sg.aor.2 subj.): see προσέρχομαι
ποτέοικα *dial.pf.vb*.: see προσέοικα
ποτέομαι *Ion.mid.contr.vb*.: see ποτάομαι
ποτέος ᾱ ον *vbl.adj*. [πίνω] (of wine, in neg.phr.) **to be drunk** Pl.
ποτεπλάσθην (dial.aor.pass.): see προσπλάσσομαι
ποτερίσδω *dial.vb*. [πρός, ἐρίζω] (of a singer) **compete** —W.DAT. *w. someone* Theoc.
πότερος ᾱ ον, Ion. **κότερος** η ον *interrog. and indef.adj*.
1 (in dir. and indir.qs.) **which** (of two)? Il. +
2 (indef.) **one or other, either** (of two) Pl.
—**πότερον, πότερα**, Ion. **κότερον, κότερα** *neut.sg.pl.adv*. (in qs., introducing alternative propositions, the second linked by ἤ *or*) **is it the case that ... ?** A. +; (w. alternative implied but not expressed) A. +; (w. third or fourth option added) Hdt. Trag.
—**ποτέρωθι** *interrog.adv*. **on which side** (i.e. in which of two categories or situations)? Pl. X.
—**ποτέρως** *interrog.adv*. (in dir. and indir.qs.) **in which way** (of two)? Pl. X. Arist.
—**ποτέρωσε** *interrog.adv*. (in dir. and indir.qs.) **in which direction** (of two)?; **in which category?** —*ref. to placing* (i.e. *classifying*) *sthg*. X.; **to which side** (i.e. to which of two people)? —*ref. to turning for support* Plu.
ποτερρίπτουν (dial.impf.): see προσρίπτω
ποτέρχομαι *dial.mid.vb*., **ποτέχω** *dial.vb*.: see προσέρχομαι, προσέχω
ποτεῦ (Ion.mid.imperatv.): see ποτάομαι
ποτέφᾱ (dial.3sg.aor.): see πρόσφημι
ποτή ῆς *f*. [πέτομαι] **flight** (of a bird) Od. hHom.
πότημα ατος *n*. **flight** (of Erinyes) A.
ποτήμενος (Aeol.mid.ptcpl.): see ποτάομαι
ποτήνεπε (dial.3sg.impf.): see προσεννέπω
ποτηνός *Ion.adj*.: see ποτανός
ποτήρ ῆρος *m*. [ποτόν] **drinking-cup** E.
ποτήριον ου *n*. **drinking-cup** Sapph. Alc. Hdt. Ar. X. Thphr. +
ποτής ῆτος (dial. ᾰτος) *f*. **drink** (opp. food) Hom. hHom. S.Ichn. Philox.Leuc. AR.
πότης ου *m*. **1 drinker** (of wine), **tippler** Call.
2 ‖ ADJ. (fig., of a lamp, ref. to its consumption of oil) **thirsty** Ar.
—**ποτίστατος** η ον *superl.adj*. (of women) **very hard-drinking** Ar.
ποτήσθω (Lacon.3sg.mid.imperatv.), **πότηται** (3sg.): see ποτάομαι
ποτητόν οῦ *n*. [ποτάομαι] **winged creature, bird** Od. AR.

ποτί *dial.prep.*: see πρός
ποτιβλέπω *dial.vb.*, **ποτιγλέπω** *Lacon.vb.*: see προσβλέπω
Ποτῑδάων *Boeot.m.*: see Ποσειδῶν
ποτιδέγμενος (ep.athem.pres.mid.ptcpl.): see προσδέχομαι
ποτιδεῖν (dial.aor.2 inf.): see προσοράω
ποτιδέρκομαι *dial.midvb.*: see προσδέρκομαι
ποτιδεύομαι *dial.mid.vb.*: see under προσδέω²
ποτι-δόρπιος ον *ep.adj.* [πρός, δόρπον] contributing to the evening meal; (of firewood, milk, water) **for use at supper-time** Od. AR.
ποτιδραμεῖν (dial.aor.2 inf.): see προσδραμεῖν
ποτίζω, dial. **ποτίσδω** (Theocr.) *vb.* [ποτόν] | aor. ἐπότισα | **1** cause (someone) to drink; **give** (W.ACC. someone) **a drink** Arist.(cj.) Thphr. NT.; **water** —cattle Theoc. NT.; **give** (W.DBL.ACC. nectar, to horses) **to drink** Pl.; (a cup of water, to someone) NT.
2 (of a god) **water** —plants (w. rain) X.
ποτίθες (dial.athem.aor.imperatv.): see προστίθημι
ποτιθιγγάνω *dial.vb.*: see προσθιγγάνω
ποτι-κάρδιος ον *dial.adj.* [καρδία] (of Eros' arrows, a lover's wound) **about the heart** Theoc. Bion
ποτικέκλιται (ep.3sg.pf.pass.): see προσκλίνω
ποτι-κιγκλίζομαι *dial.mid.vb.* | 2sg.impf. ποτεκιγκλίζευ | (fig., of a person submitting to anal intercourse) **wag one's rump about in response** Theoc.
ποτικός ή όν *adj.* [ποτόν] (of persons) **fond of drink** (i.e. wine) Plu.
—**ποτικῶς** *adv.* (of a person's body, w. ἔχειν) *be in a condition to take drink* Plu.
ποτί-κρανον ου *dial.n.* [πρός, κρᾱνίον¹] support for the head (i.e. pillow); (gener.) **cushion** (for a seat) Theoc.
ποτι-κρίμνημι *dial.vb.* | ptcpl. (tm.) ποτί ... κριμνᾱ́ς | **hang** (W.ACC. an anchor) **against** —W.DAT. *a ship* (i.e. raise it) Pi.(tm.)
πότιμος ου *adj.* [ποτός, πίνω] | compar. ποτιμώτερος | **1** (of water) **drinkable** Hdt. X. Plb. Plu.; (of a river) Plu.; (of seawater, W.DAT. by fishes) Heraclit.
2 (fig., of speech) **palatable, wholesome** (opp. salty, brackish) Pl.
3 (fig., of a person) **agreeable, kind** Theoc.
4 (of stone) permeable by water, **porous** Pl.
ποτι-νίσομαι *ep.mid.vb.* —also **προσνίσομαι** (S.) *mid.vb.*
1 come to (someone or somewhere); (of a band of people) **come** —W.ADV. *home* (i.e. to their home city) Pi.; (of worshippers) **approach** —the gods (w. offerings) A.; (of riches) **come, be brought** —W.PREP.PHR. *to a city* Il.
2 (of troops) **come on, advance** S.
ποτι-πεπτηυῖαι *ep.fem.pl.pf.ptcpl.* [app. πρός, πτήσσω] | only nom. | (fig., of headlands) app. **crouching forwards** Od. [prob. better written πότι πεπτηυῖαι, see πτήσσω 4]
ποτιπέσω (dial.aor.2 subj.): see προσπίπτω
ποτιπτύσσομαι *ep.mid.vb.*: see προσπτύσσομαι
ποτισαίνω *dial.vb.*: see προσσαίνω
ποτίσδω *dial.vb.*: see ποτίζω
ποτι-στάζω *dial.vb.* [πρός] drip (sthg.) on (someone); (fig., of Grace) **shed, cast** —a glorious appearance (W.DAT. *on someone*) Pi.; (of a person) **let fall, pour gently forth** —soothing speech Pi.
ποτίστατος *superl.adj.*: see πότης
ποτίστρη ης *Ion.f.* [ποτίζω] **drinking-trough** (for horses) Call.
ποτίσχω *ep.vb.*: see προσίσχω
ποτι-τέρπω *ep.vb.* [πρός] perh. **entertain** (W.ACC. someone) **further** Il.
ποτιτρόπαιος *dial.adj.*: see προστρόπαιος

ποτίφορος *dial.adj.*: see πρόσφορος
ποτι-φωνήεις εσσα εν *ep.adj.* (of an animal) capable of addressing (someone), **able to speak** Od.
ποτιψαύω *dial.vb.*: see προσψαύω
πότμος ου *m.* [πίπτω] **1** what befalls one; (in adverse sense) **lot, fate, ill fate** Hom. Pi. Emp. Trag. Men. Call.
2 (specif.) **fated end, doom, death** Hom. Lyr. E. AR. Theoc.*epigr.*
3 (in neutral or positive sense) **lot, fortune, destiny** Pi. Trag.
4 (personif., as giver of good fortune) **Destiny** Pi.
πότνα *f.* [reltd. πότνια] | usu. voc., twice nom. (hHom. Call.) | **1** (in address to a goddess, appos.w. θεά) **lady** Od. AR.; (w. Σελάνα *Moon*) Theocr.; (in nom., w. no noun) Call.; (W.PARTITV.GEN. θεάων, θεᾶν) *queen among goddesses* hHom. E. Theoc.
2 (in address to a queen) **lady, majesty** AR.
πότνια ᾱς *f.* [reltd. πόσις¹] | acc. πότνιαν | Ion.gen.pl. ποτνιέων | **1** (epith. of goddesses or demigoddesses, also of personif. natural elements, such as Night, Earth) **lady, queen** Hom. Hes. Thgn. Lyr. Trag. Ar. +; (w. a personif. abstraction, such as Reverence, Forgetfulness, Fate) E.; **mistress** (W.GEN. of wild beasts, ref. to Artemis) Il.; (of love's arrows, of passions, ref. to Aphrodite) Pi. E.*fr.* || PL. (ref. to Erinyes) revered ladies S.; (ref. to Demeter and Persephone) Hdt. S. Ar.
2 lady (ref. to a queen, or to a mistress as addressed or referred to by her servant) E.; (ref. to a person's mother, appos.w. μήτηρ) Hom.
3 (in invocations to places or things) || ADJ. (of the shade of Oedipus) august or revered A.; (of a tomb) hallowed A.; (of the shore of a sacred lake) E.; (of a breeze) blessed E.*fr.*
4 || ADJ. (of a mother bird) app., distraught Mosch. | cf. ποτνιάομαι
—**ποτνιάς** άδος *fem.adj.* (of goddesses, ref. to Erinyes) **august, revered** E.; (of Bacchants) **hallowed, holy** E.
Ποτνιαί ῶν *f.pl.* **Potniai** (town in Boeotia) X.
—**Ποτνιάς** άδος *fem.adj.* (of horses) **of Potniai** (ref. to the mad flesh-eating horses of Glaukos) E.
ποτνιάομαι *mid.contr.vb.* perh., invoke (a goddess) with the cry ὦ πότνια; (gener., of women in distress) **shriek** Plu.
ποτόδδω *Lacon.vb.*: see προσόζω
ποτόν οῦ *n.* [ποτός] **1** (gener., sg. and pl.) that which is drunk, **drink** (opp. food) Hdt. E. Pl. X. D. Arist. +
2 (specif.) **drink** (ref. to wine) Hom. Hdt. Trag. Ar. Theoc. Plu.; (ref. to the blood of a sacrificial animal) A.*fr.*
3 drink (of water) S. E. Th. Call.; (specif.) **drinking-water** or **water** (fr. a drinkable source) A. S. AR. Theoc. Plu.
4 (fig.) **draught** or **sip** (W.GEN. of freedom) Plu.
πότ-ορθρος ον *dial.adj.* [πρός, ὄρθρος] || NEUT.ADV. (w.art.) **around dawn** Theoc.
ποτός ή όν *adj.* [πίνω] (of a drug) **to be drunk, for drinking** A. E.; (of water) Th.
πότος ου *m.* (oft.pl.) **drinking bout, drinks party** Critias Ar. Att.orats. Pl. X. Arist. +; (prep.phr.) παρὰ πότον *during drinks* X. Aeschin. Thphr. Plb. Plu.
ποτόσδω *dial.vb.*: see προσόζω
ποῦ, Ion. **κοῦ**, Aeol. **ποῖ** *interrog.adv.* | used occas. in indir.qs. | **1** in what place, **where?** Hom. Carm.Pop. B. Trag. Ar. +; (W.GEN. on earth, w. emph. force) Hdt. Trag. Ar. Men.; (W.GEN. in a particular region, in a city) S. E. X.; (in a task, in a chorus, ref. to being assigned a role or position) E. Pl.
2 to what place, **whither, where to?** Il. Sapph. NT.
3 (w.vb. *be* or *stand*) **where** (W.GEN. in thought, speech, fortune, a business, i.e. what is someone thinking or saying, what is someone's situation)? S. E.

4 where (in value, ranking or effectiveness)? Trag.
5 by what means, **how?** A. E.; (in a neg.q.) **how can it be** (that sthg. is not the case)? Hdt.; (expressing indignation and incredulity) **by what right, on what grounds, in what sense** (is sthg. the case)? S. E. D.

—**που**, Ion. **κου**, Aeol. **ποι** *indef.enclit.adv.* **1** in some place, **somewhere, anywhere** Hom. +; (w.GEN. in the fields) Od.; (w.GEN. in a country) X. D.; (w. other advs. of place, e.g. *near, far off, elsewhere*) S. +
2 (conveying indefiniteness, uncertainty or diffidence) **somehow, possibly, perhaps, I suppose, I think** Hom. +; (w. numerical expressions) **around, approximately** Hdt.
3 (in neg.q., expressing incredulity) οὔ που, οὔ τί που *surely not* Pi. S. E. Ar. Pl.
4 | for ἦ που see ἦπου

πουκτεύω *Boeot.vb.*: see πυκτεύω
πουλυ-βότειρα ης *ep.fem.adj.* [πολύς, βοτήρ] (of the earth) **that feeds many, nourishing, nurturing, bounteous** Hom. Hes. hHom.; (of a region) Il.
πουλυκτέανος *ep.adj.*: see πολυκτέανος
πουλυ-μέδιμνος ον *ep.adj.* (epith. of Demeter) **giver of many measures** (of grain) Call.
πουλυ-μέλαθρος ον *ep.adj.* [μέλαθρον] (of a goddess) **with many shrines** Call.
πουλύμυθος *dial.adj.*: see πολύμυθος
πούλυπος, πουλύπους *m.*: see πώλυπος
πουλύς *dial.adj.*: see πολύς
πούς ποδός *m.* | dat.pl. ποσί, ep. ποσσί, also πόδεσσι | gen.dat.du. ποδοῖν, ep. ποδοῖιν | **1 foot** (of a person) Hom. +; (of a horse, ox, other quadruped, a bird) Hom. +; app. **arm, tentacle** (of an octopus) Hes.
2 foot (in ctxts. of walking, travelling, trampling, dancing, or sim.) Hom. +; (freq. advbl.dat.) ποδί, ποσί *on foot* Hom. +; (also advbl.acc.) πόδα Thgn. E. Ar.
3 (in ctxts. of running or racing, esp. w.connot. of speed) Hom. +; ὡς ποδῶν ἔχει (or sim.) *as he is off for feet (i.e. as quickly as he can)* Hdt. Pl.
4 foot (as standing for the whole person, w.epith. *sacker of a city*) A.; (w.epith. *heaven-blessed*) Pi.; (periphr., W.GEN. of a person, who is coming or going) E.
5 (fig., as belonging to inanimate things which move) **foot** (W.GEN. of time, as if personif.) E.; (of a ship, ref. to an oar) Tim.; νόστιμον κινεῖν πόδα (*of a ship*) *set off on a return journey* E.; (prep.phr.) πὰρ ποδὶ ναός *close by a ship* Pi.
6 (as a reference-point for measurement or direction) ἐς πόδας ἐκ κεφαλῆς *from head to foot* (or sim.) Il. Ar.; (hyperbol., ref. to a person's spirit sinking) παραὶ ποσί *to his feet* Il.
7 (prep.phrs., ref. to relative position) πὰρ ποδί *close to a person's foot* (*i.e. close by*) Pi.; πρὸ (πρόσθε, προπάροιθε) ποδός (or ποδῶν) *at one's feet, in front of one* Il. E. Pl. X.
8 (fig., quasi-adjl., of a matter) πρὸ ποδός *at one's feet, of immediate concern* Pi.; (also) πὰρ ποδός Thgn. Pi.; παρὰ πόδας Pl.; πρὸς ποσί S.
9 (in fig. and provbl. ctxts., as the part of the body in contact w. danger); **foot** (burnt in an unnoticed fire by a complacent sinner) S.; (plunged into bilge-water) E.; (kept out of the mire of destruction) A.; (out of trouble, suffering, or sim.) Alc. Trag.; (W.ADV. *out*, i.e. out of harm) Pi.
10 (in advbl. and prep.phrs., ref. to speed, strength, or sim.) ποσὶν καὶ χερσίν (or sim.) *with hands and feet (i.e. w. all one's might)* Il. Aeschin.; ἀμφοῖν ποδοῖν *with both feet (i.e. quickly or energetically)* Ar.; οὐ (οὐδὲ) τὸν πόδα τὸν ἕτερον (or sim.) *not (even) with one foot (i.e. not a single step)* Ar. Din.; ὅλῳ ποδί *totally* Ar.; ἀφ' ἡσύχου ποδός *relaxedly* E.

11 (ref. to time) παρὰ πόδα *before one's feet* (*i.e. then and there, immediately*) S. Pl.; παρὰ πόδας *immediately afterwards* Plb.
12 (prep.phrs.) ἐν ποσί *in one's path* (*ref. to encountering someone*) Hdt.; (quasi-adjl., of a village) Th.; (of a business, a trouble) *of immediate concern* Pi. S. E.; (of matters) *common, everyday* Pl. Arist.; ἐκ ποδός *out of one's path* (*ref. to removing obstacles*) Pi.
13 (ref. to close accompaniment or pursuit) κατὰ πόδας *at the heels* (sts. W.GEN. *of someone*) Hdt. Th. X.; (also) ἐκ ποδός Plb. Bion; ἐκ ποδῶν Plu.; (ref. to time) κατὰ πόδα *at once* Pl.; (quasi-adjl.) κατὰ πόδας *immediately following* (sts. W.GEN. *sthg.*) Plb.
14 (ref. to soldiers retreating but still facing the enemy) ἐπὶ πόδα *step by step, gradually* X. Plb. | cf. σκέλος 2
15 (ref. to location, quasi-adjl., of a place) ὑπὸ πόδα *below, lower down* (*a hillside*) Plb.
16 foot (as a measure of length) Hdt. E. Th. +
17 foot (as a unit or component of metre or rhythm) Ar. Pl.
18 lowest part, **foot** (W.GEN. of a couch) X.
19 foot, foothill (W.GEN. of a mountain) Il. Pi.
20 extremity (W.GEN. of the Peloponnese, ref. to the Isthmos of Corinth) Call.; **mouth** (W.GEN. of the Nile) Call.
21 (in oracular language) **neck** (W.GEN. of a wineskin) E. | cf. ποδεών
22 (naut.) **sheet** (rope by which each lower corner of a sail was made fast to the ship) Od. +; (slackened for safety in high wind) S. E. Ar.

ποῶ (Att.1sg.): see ποιέω
πρᾶγμα, Ion. **πρῆγμα**, ατος *n.* [πράσσω] **1** (sg. and pl.) that which is done (by someone), **deed, action, act** Thgn. Pi. Trag. D.; (opp. speech, words) E. D.; (sg., gener.) **activity, occupation** (of a person) Pl.
2 that which happens to or involves (someone), **occurrence, matter, business** Pi. Hdt. Trag. Th. Ar. +; (specif., ref. to a battle) **action, affair** Hdt. X. ‖ PL. matters, affairs, business A. Hdt. E. Th. +; (specif., ref. to war or fighting) Hdt.
3 (concr.) **thing** Ar. Pl. Arist.; (opp. its name) Pl. And.
4 (honorific, ref. to a person) μέγα πρᾶγμα, μέγιστον πρῆγμα (*very*) *important figure* Hdt. D. Men.
5 (derog., usu. w.pejor.adj.) **thing, creature** (ref. to a sophist) Pl.; (ref. to the populace) Pl. D.; (ref. to a woman) X.
6 (gener.) **situation, circumstance, fortune** (of a person or city) Pi. S. Pl.; (pl., of a person or persons) A. Hdt. E. Th. Ar. +; (opp. ἔργα *actions*) E.
7 ‖ PL. fortunes, position, power (of a state or nation) A. Hdt. Th. Ar.
8 ‖ PL. business of public life, affairs of state, government Hdt. E. Th. Pl. +; ἐν (or ἐπὶ) τοῖς πράγμασι (*be*) *in power or office* Th. D. Arist.; (also) ἐπὶ τῶν πραγμάτων D. Plb. Plu.; (w. νεώτερα) *innovations, revolution* Hdt. Lys. Isoc.
9 thing of consequence, **important** or **serious matter** Hdt. X.; οὐδὲν πρᾶγμα (πρῆγμα) *matter of no importance* Hdt. E. Ar. Pl.
10 (impers.phr.) πρῆγμά ἐστι *it is a serious matter* (*i.e. advantageous, desirable or necessary*) —W.DAT. or ACC. + INF. *for someone to do sthg.* Hdt.; (w.neg.) οὐδὲν πρᾶγμα (πρῆγμα) (*there is*) *nothing doing* —W.DAT. + (τε) καί + DAT. *betw. one person and another (i.e. they have nothing to do w. each other)* Hdt. D.; οὐδὲν πρᾶγμα τοῦ πολέμου (*someone has*) *nothing to do with the war* Plu.
11 matter at issue or under discussion, **question, issue** Pl. Arist.
12 (leg.) business at law, **case** Att.orats. Arist. Thphr. ‖ COLLECTV.PL. legal business Antipho Lys. Ar.

πρᾱγματείᾱ

13 ‖ PL. trouble, annoyance (freq. w. ἔχειν, παρέχειν *have, cause*) A.*satyr.fr.* Hdt. E. Ar. Pl. +; (sg.) Hdt.

πρᾱγματείᾱ ᾱς *f.* [πρᾱγματεύομαι] **1** effort devoted to a task, **effort, activity, application** Isoc. Pl. X. D. Plu.
2 occupation, business, concern (of persons or things) Isoc. Pl. D. Arist.; (ref. to a task imposed on a citizen by special decree, opp. an elective or allotted office) Aeschin.; (specif.) **legal business** Isoc. D.
3 way of doing things, **behaviour, procedure** Aeschin. Arist.
4 activity of investigating; **treatment, study** (W.GEN. of a subject) Pl.; comprehensive treatment of a subject (by a philosopher), **system** Arist.
5 product of philosophical investigation, **treatise, study, work** Arist. Plu.
6 product of (historical) research, **work** (of history) Plb.

πρᾱγματειώδης ες *adj.* (of an argument, envisaged as a pastime) **full of trouble or effort, laborious** Pl.

πρᾱγματεύομαι, Ion. **πρηγματεύομαι** *mid.vb.* [πρᾶγμα] | aor. ἐπρᾱγματευσάμην (X.), also ἐπρᾱγματεύθην (Isoc. Arist. Men.), Ion. ἐπρηγματεύθην (Hdt.) ‖ *neut.impers.vbl.adj.* πρᾱγματευτέον |
1 expend effort, **take pains** (in doing sthg.) Pl. X.; **take** (W.NEUT.ACC. some, much, this, or sim.) **trouble** Hdt. Ar. Isoc. Pl. X. D. +; **exert oneself** —W.INF. *to do sthg.* Plu.
2 (esp. of philosophers) **concern or occupy oneself** —W.PREP.PHR. *w. sthg.* Isoc. Pl. X. D. Arist. —W.NEUT.ACC. Isoc. Pl.
3 work hard, be busy X. Arist.; (specif.) **be engaged in business** Arist. NT. Plu.
4 (tr.) **occupy oneself with** —*a subject, an undertaking* Pl.; **work to achieve** —*sthg.* X. D.; **take in hand** —*funeral arrangements* Men. ‖ PASS. (of a subject) **be dealt with** Pl.; (of poems) **be worked on or elaborated** Pl.; (of a spear) **be adapted or modified** —W.ADV. *in a certain way* X.; (of crafts) **be practised** Arist.; (of turns of phrase) **be contrived** Aeschin.
5 (of a historian) **deal with** —*a subject, events, or sim.* Plb.; (intr.) **deal** —W.PREP.PHR. *w. a historical subject* Plb. ‖ MASC.PL.PTCPL.SB. **historians** Plb.

πρᾱγματικός ή όν *adj.* **1** (of persons) **practical, effective, capable** Plb.; **with practical experience** Plb.
2 (of persons, their speech) **statesmanlike** Plb.; (pejor., of a person's behaviour) **scheming, Machiavellian** Plb.
3 (of military forces) **capable, efficient** Plb.; (of an action, an attack, a fortified hill) **effective** Plb.; (of a consideration) **efficacious, practical** Plb.
4 (of pronouncements) **on political matters** Plb.
5 (of history) providing a narrative of events (esp. political and military, opp. a more specialised study), **systematic** Plb. Plu.

—**πρᾱγματικῶς** *adv.* **1 in a practical or effective manner** Pl.
2 in a statesmanlike manner Plb.

πρᾱγμάτιον ου *n.* [dimin. πρᾶγμα] **little problem** Ar.; (specif.) **petty lawsuit** Ar.

πρᾱγματο-δίφης ου *m.* [δῑφάω] **one who probes about for lawsuits, lawsuit-hunter** Ar.

πρᾱγματοκοπέω *contr.vb.* [κόπτω] **meddle in others' business or stir up trouble**; (in political ctxt.) **be meddlesome, be scheming** Plb.

πρᾱγματοποιίᾱ ᾱς *f.* [ποιέω] **scheming behaviour, intrigue** Plb.

πρᾱγματώδης ες *adj.* | compar. πραγματωδέστερος | **1** (of sophistic writings) **laborious, over-wrought** Isoc.
2 (of a task) **troublesome** D.

πρᾶγος ους *n.* **1 deed, action** Pi. S. Ar.(quot. E.)

2 matter, affair, business A. S. Ar.
3 fortune, fate (of a city) A.
4 distressing event, trouble A.

πρᾱεῖα *fem.adj.*: see πρᾶος

πράθον (ep.aor.2), **πραθέειν** (ep.aor.2 inf.): see πέρθω

πρακτέος ᾱ ον *vbl.adj.* [πράσσω] (of things) **to be done** Pl. Aeschin. D. Arist.

πρακτήριος ον *adj.* (of fortune) **bringing success in action, effective, successful** A.

πρᾱκτικός ή όν *adj.* | compar. πρᾱκτικώτερος | **1 fit for or concerned with action**; (of persons) **active, practical** Pl. X. Arist. Plu.; (of a type of life) Arist.
2 (of knowledge, thinking) **practical** (opp. intellectual or theoretical) Pl. Arist.; (of vigour, an impulse) **active** Pl. Plu.; (of first principles) **of action or conduct** Arist.; (of the iambic trimeter) **associated with or representative of action** (opp. dance) Arist.; (of songs, opp. those representative of character or emotion) Arist.
3 (of persons) **efficient** X. Men. Plb.; **capable** (W.GEN. of sthg.) Arist.; (of military forces) **effective** Plb.; (of wine, at stimulating ideas) Ar.; (of tact, as a course of action) Men.; (of a type of motion, compared w. others) Pl.

—**πρᾱκτικῶς** *adv.* **effectively** Plb. Plu.; **energetically** Plb.; **actively** Plu.

πρᾱκτός ή όν *adj.* (of things) **to be done** Arist.; (of good) **to be achieved by action, practicable** Arist. ‖ NEUT.SB. (sg. and pl.) **act or action** Arist.

πράκτωρ ορος *m.f.* **1** one who brings about (a certain result); (ref. to Zeus, Aphrodite) **accomplisher, agent** (W.GEN. of an event) S.; (ref. to a person) **cause** (W.GEN. of an accident) Antipho
2 one who collects payment of a penalty or exacts punishment (perh. influenced by legal usage, as 3); **avenger** A.; (W.GEN. of bloodshed) A. S. ‖ MASC. and FEM.ADJ. (of a spear and hand, periphr.ref. to the Trojan expedition) **avenging, vengeful** A.
3 ‖ PL. (at Athens, as title of officials who kept a register of state debtors) **registrars of debts** Att.orats.
4 bailiff, constable (assoc.w. a debtors' prison) NT.

Πράμνειος ου *masc.adj.* (of wine) **Pramneian** (a generic name for a type of wine, not assoc.w. any specific place) Hom. Pl.

—**Πράμνιος** ου *masc.adj.* (of a wine-god) **Pramnian** Ar.

πρᾶν *dial.adv.*: see πρώην

πρᾱνής, Ion. **πρηνής**, ές *adj.* **1 on the face or belly** (opp. on the back, supine); (quasi-advbl., of persons lying) **face down, prone** Il. AR.; (of persons falling) **head first, headlong** Hom. Hes. E. AR.
2 (quasi-advbl., of a palace that is thrown) **headlong to the ground** Il.; (of ships sinking) **bottom up** Tim.; (of a hand) **palm down** Plu.
3 (of a hill, a road) **steep** X.; (of an isthmus) **sloping steeply** (W.PREP.PHR. to the mainland) AR.; (prep.phr.) κατὰ πρανοῦς **downhill** X. Plu. ‖ NEUT.SB. **steep slope** X.

πρᾱξικοπέω *contr.vb.* [πρᾶξις, κόπτω] **1** (intr., of a commander) **employ trickery, behave treacherously** (in capturing a city) Plb.; (tr.) **capture** (W.ACC. a city) **through trickery or treachery** Plb.
2 (tr.) **trick, deceive, break faith with** —*a populace* Plb.

πράξιμος ον *adj.* [πράσσω] (of money owed) **able to be exacted, recoverable** Plb.(treaty)

πρᾶξις, Ion. **πρῆξις**, εως (dial. ιος) *f.* **1 doing, performance** (usu. W.GEN. of an action) Thgn. Antipho Pl.; (gener.) **acting, activity** Pl. Arist.

2 (specif., in drama) **action** (opp. speech) Arist.; (ref. to the action, single and complete in itself, which forms the plot in epic and dramatic poetry) Arist.
3 that which is performed or undertaken, **business, transaction, enterprise** Od. hHom. Thgn.
4 result or issue of an activity, **outcome** A. Pi. X.; beneficial outcome, **profit, benefit** (W.GEN. fr. lamentation) Il.; (W.DAT. for mourners) Od. B.; successful outcome, **success** X.; **fulfilment** (W.GEN. of oracles) A.
5 (specif.) **action, act** Pi. E. Att.orats. Pl. +; (pl.) Thgn. S. E. Att.orats. Pl. +; (W.GEN. of arms, legs, or sim.) Pl.; (opp. words) D.
6 (euphem.) **activity** (ref. to sexual intercourse) E.; (in a homosexual relationship) Aeschin.
7 **happening, event** Th.; (milit.) **action, engagement, fighting** Plb.
8 **fortune, condition** (W.GEN. of a person) A. Hdt. S.
9 capacity for action, **practical ability** Plb.
10 (pejor.) underhand dealings, **trickery, treachery** Plb.
11 (leg.) **enforcement, execution** (W.GEN. of a contractual agreement) And.; **exaction** (W.GEN. of a fee, a tax) Pl.; **action for recovery of a debt** D.(contract); **execution of judgement** (by a magistrate, W.GEN. against someone) Arist.
12 exaction of vengeance, **vengeance** (W.GEN. on someone) E. [or perh. *retribution because of someone, i.e. because of his crime*]

πράξω (fut.): see πράσσω
πρᾱόνως compar.adv.: see under πρᾶος
πρᾶος ον adj. —also **πρᾱΰς**, Ion. **πρηΰς**, εῖα ὺ adj. | compar. πρᾱότερος, also πρᾱΰτερος (Pl. Plb.), Ion. πρηΰτερος | superl. πρᾱότατος, Ion. πρηΰτατος (AR.) | Att.sg. only πρᾶος ον, fem. always πρᾱεῖα ‖ PL.: nom.masc. πρᾶοι, also πρᾱεῖς (NT.) | acc.masc. πρᾱους, also πρᾱεῖς (Plb.) | nom.acc.neut. πρᾱέα (X.) | gen.masc.neut. πρᾱέων (D.), πρᾱέων (X.) | dat.masc.neut. πρᾱέσι (Pl.) |
1 (of persons, their nature or character) **gentle, meek, mild** (sts. W.DAT. or PREP.PHR. towards someone) Pi. Hdt. Ar. Att.orats. Pl. +; (of goddesses) Call.; (of a person, likened to a wild animal) **tame** E.; (of a region, ref. to its inhabitants) **peaceable** Isoc.
2 (of dogs, horses, animals in general) **mild, gentle** (sts. W.PREP.PHR. towards humans) Isoc. Pl. X.; (of a certain kind of fish) **tame** X. ‖ NEUT.PL.SB. **calm behaviour** (by a horse) X.
3 (of a river) **gentle, calm** AR.; (of a season) **mild** X.
4 (of speech, words, a voice, commands given to a horse) **soft, gentle, soothing** Pi. Pl. X.
5 (of punishments, pleasures, or sim.) **mild, gentle** Pl.; (of a delight, ref. to wine) Philox.Leuc.; (fig., of a remedy for an untamed horse, ref. to a bridle) Pi.; (of forgiveness) Ar.; (of the art of agriculture) X.; (of government, laws) Isoc. D. Arist.; (of conditions in a state) **easy-going** D.

—**πρᾴως** adv. | compar. πρᾱότερον, also πρᾱΰτερον |
1 **mildly, meekly, gently** Isoc. Pl. X. +; (w. διακεῖσθαι) **be calm** (opp. angry) D.; (of lions) *behave gently* (towards their trainers) Isoc.
2 **leniently** —*ref. to judging* Pl.; (w. ἔχειν) *be lenient* (towards someone or sthg.) D.
3 **lightly, calmly** —*ref. to enduring sthg.* Pl. X. D. —*ref. to speaking of one's suffering* X.; (w. ἔχειν) *be indifferent* (towards sthg.) Pl.

—**πρᾱόνως** irreg.compar.adv. **more mildly** or **gently** (opp. angrily, terrifyingly) Lys. Ar.

πρᾱότης ητος f. **mild temper, mildness, meekness, gentleness** (of a person, a populace) Th. Att.orats. Pl. X. +; (opp. fierceness) Pl.; (opp. anger) Arist.

πραπίδες ων f.pl. | dat.pl. πραπίσι, ep. πραπίδεσσι ‖ also sg. πραπίς ίδος in 3 | **1** part of the body which surrounds the heart, **chest** (equiv. to φρήν, ref. to the thorax, perh. orig. more specif. to the lungs) Il.
2 emotional centre of the body, **breast, heart** (as the seat of sorrow) Il. AR.; (as the seat of desire) Melanipp.
3 **mind** (as the seat of thoughts, knowledge, plans) Hes.fr. A. Pi. Emp. E. Critias; (sg.) Pi. E. Ar.(cj.)
4 **good sense, common sense, intelligence** (possessed by a person) Od. Hes. A. Emp.; **cleverness, ingenuity, skill** Hom. Hes.fr. hHom.

πρασιά ᾶς, Ion. **πρασιή** ῆς f. [πράσον] **1** bed of leeks; (gener.) **vegetable-bed** Od.
2 (fig.) **group** (of people seated on grass) NT.

πράσιμος η ον adj. [πρᾶσις] (of things) **for sale** Pl. X.
πράσιος ᾱ ον adj. [app. πράσον] (of a colour) perh. **leek-green** Pl.
πρᾶσις εως, Ion. **πρῆσις** ιος f. [πέρνημι] **selling, sale** (of sthg., oft. opp. buying, purchase) Hdt. Att.orats. Pl. X. Arist. Plu.
πράσον ου n. a kind of vegetable, **leek** Ar.
πράσσω, Att. **πράττω**, Ion. **πρήσσω** vb. | iteratv.impf. πρήσσεσκον | fut. πράξω, Ion. πρήξω | aor. ἔπραξα, Ion. ἔπρηξα | pf.1 (tr.) πέπρᾱχα, Ion. πέπρηχα | pf.2 πέπρᾱγα, Ion. πέπρηγα | 3sg.plpf.1 (tr.) ἐπεπράχει | 3pl.plpf.2 (intr.) ἐπεπράγεσαν ‖ PASS.: fut. πράξομαι (Pl.), also πραχθήσομαι | fut.pf. πεπράξομαι | aor. ἐπράχθην, Ion. ἐπρήχθην | pf. πέπραγμαι, Ion. πέπρηγμαι ‖ neut.impers. vbl.adj. πρακτέον |
1 (of persons, gods, horses) undertake or accomplish a course of travel; **pass over, cross** —*the sea* Od.; **make** —*one's way* Hom. hHom.; (intr.) **make one's way** —W.GEN. *on a journey* Hom.
2 perform (an action); **perform, do, carry out** —*a task, activity, or sim.* Hom. +; **do** —W.DBL.ACC. *sthg., to someone* E. Ar.
3 bring about (a result); **bring about, cause, create** —*slaughter, revolt, peace, or sim.* Pi. Hdt. Att.orats. Pl.; **achieve, win** —*glory* Pi.; **achieve, effect, accomplish** —W.INDEF.NEUT.PRON. *sthg., nothing, or sim.* (ref. to an actual or expected result) Hom. +; (of Zeus) **make** —*a sea nymph* (W.PREDIC.ACC. *someone's wife*) Pi.; (intr.) **effect one's purpose, succeed** Il. Thgn. ‖ IMPERS.PF.PASS. *it is all over* E.
4 (intr.) perform an act or be active, **act** (sts. opp. speak) A. Pi. Hdt. +
5 (intr.) experience a certain fortune, **do, fare** —W.ADV. or PREP.PHR. *well, badly, or sim.* Simon. A. Pi. Hdt. + —W.NEUT.ACC.PRON. or ADJ. (*e.g.* χρηστόν τι *well*, εὐδαίμονα *happily*, πολλὰ καὶ ἀγαθά *very successfully*) A. E. Ar. X.
6 (specif.) **engage in** —*political activities* Att.orats. Pl. Arist.; (intr., of a politician) **be active, take action** (sts. opp. speaking) Pl. X. D.
7 **be busy with, mind** —*one's own affairs or business* S. Pl. X. —*many things* (i.e. meddle w. other people's business) Hdt. E. Ar. | cf. πολυπραγμονέω
8 (in military or political ctxts.) **transact** —*a matter* (W.PREP.PHR. *w. someone*) Th.; (intr.) **negotiate** (sts. W.PREP.PHR. *over some matter*) Hdt. Th. X. D. —W.DAT. or PREP.PHR. *w. someone* Th.; **arrange** —W. ὅπως + FUT.INDIC. or W.SUBJ. *that sthg. happens* Th. —W.ACC. + INF. D. ‖ IMPERS.IMPF.PASS. *negotiations were conducted* —W.PREP.PHR. *w. someone* Aeschin.
9 (in ctxts. of secrecy or intrigue) **negotiate** —*matters* (W.DAT. *w. someone, i.e. be in league w. him*) D.; **deal**

treacherously with, **betray** —*a city* (W.DAT. *to someone*) Plb.
‖ MASC.PL.PRES.PTCPL.SB. **conspirators** Th. ‖ PASS. (of matters) **be organised** or **fixed up** S. Th.; (of a revolt) **be engineered** Lys.
10 (in financial ctxts., act. and mid.) **exact, demand payment of** —*a debt, money, tribute, or sim.* (sts. W.ACC. *fr. someone*) Pi. Hdt. Th. Ar. Att.orats. Pl. +; (act.) **exact payment from** —*a debtor* Plb. ‖ PASS. **have exacted from oneself, be called upon to pay** —*tribute, a price* Th. Pl.
11 (in non-financial ctxts.) **exact** —*retribution* (W.GEN. *for men killed in war*) A.; (of Justice) —*a debt* A.; (of a person) **exact vengeance for, avenge** —*a murder* A. ‖ MID. **exact** —*a heavy penalty* Call. —W.DBL.ACC. *a deserved punishment, fr. someone* A.; **exact retribution for** —*a crime* (sts. W. 2ND ACC. *fr. someone*) A.

πρᾱτέος ᾱ ον *vbl.adj.* [πέρνημι] (of goods) **to be sold, for sale** Pl.

πρᾱτήρ ῆρος *m.* **seller, vendor** Pl. Is. D.

πρᾱτός ή όν *adj.* (of a person) **for sale** (as a slave) S.

πρᾶτος *dial.adj.,* **πράτιστος** *dial.superl.adj.*: see πρῶτος, πρώτιστος

πρᾱτοτόκος *dial.adj.*: see πρωτοτόκος

πράττω *Att.vb.*: see πράσσω

πρᾰΰ-γελως ωτος *masc.fem.adj.* [πρᾱΰς, γέλως] (epith. of Health) **gently laughing** Licymn.

πρᾰΰ-μητις ιος *dial.fem.adj.* [μῆτις] (epith. of Eileithuia, goddess of childbirth) **gently skilful** Pi.

πράυνσις εως *f.* [πρᾱΰνω] **making mild, calming** (of an angry person) Arist.

πρᾱΰνω, Ion. **πρηΰνω** *vb.* [πρᾱΰς] | fut. πρᾱϋνῶ | aor. ἐπρᾱϋνα, Ion. ἐπρηΰνα ‖ aor.pass. ἐπρᾱΰνθην |
1 make (someone) **mild** or **gentle; calm, soothe, mollify, pacify** —*an angry or distressed person* hHom. A. Pl. X. Arist. +; (of philosophy) **make** (W.ACC. *people*) **behave in a mild** or **civilised way** —W.PREP.PHR. *towards each other* Isoc. ‖ PASS. (of persons) **be calmed down** Hdt. Pl. X. Arist.
2 calm —*a horse* A. X.; **tame** —*animals, birds* Hes. Pl. X. Plu. ‖ PASS. (of horses) **be calmed** X.
3 calm, pacify —*one's own or another's anger* Pl. Plb.; **soothe** —*a painful wound* S.; (of Nereids) —*waves and winds* Hes.; (of Lawfulness) **tame** —*acts of violence* Sol. ‖ PASS. (of winter storms) **die down** Hdt.
4 (intr., fig., of speech, opp. force) **calm things down** AR.

πρᾱΰς *adj.,* **πρᾱΰως** *adv.*: see πρᾶος

πρᾱχθήσομαι (fut.pass.): see πράσσω

πρέμνον ου *n.* **1 bottom** or **stump of a tree trunk;** (gener.) **tree trunk** Lys. X. Hellenist.poet. Plb. Plu.; (appos.w. φηγός *oak*) Call.; **log** (for burning) hHom. Ar.
2 trunk (of a miraculous pillar which shoots up fr. the earth) Pi.*fr.*; (fig.) **basis** (W.GEN. of a great scheme) Ar.

πρεπόντως *ptcpl.adv.*: see under πρέπω

πρεπτός ή όν *adj.* [πρέπω] **1** (of conflicts in war) **glorious** A.
2 (of fantasies of sound, compared to flowers) **conspicuous** S.*Ichn.* | see also πρόοπτος 2

—πρεπτόν *neut.adv.* **in a manner appropriate** (W.DAT. *to someone*) Ar.

πρέπω *vb.* | dial.3sg.impf. πρέπε | fut. πρέψω | aor. ἔπρεψα |
1 stand out (against one's background or surroundings); (of a person likened to a figure in a painting) **stand out, be conspicuous** A.; (of a full moon depicted on a shield) A.; (of Zeus as a flying swan) —W.DAT. *by his snow-white wing* E.; (of persons) —*by their clothing, armour, or sim.* A. E. —*by their grief, their hair shorn in mourning* A. E.; (of a mourner's cheek) —*w. gashes* A.; (of bows and arrows) **be prominent** (in soldiers' hands) A.; (of gold on the touchstone) **shine forth** Pi.; (fig., of harm which is not hidden, compared to a light) A.; (of persons, a beacon) **be conspicuous** —W.PREDIC.PTCPL. *as doing sthg.* (i.e. *be clearly doing sthg.*) A.
2 (of individuals) **stand out, be pre-eminent** (among others) Il. E.*fr.*; (of a people) A.
3 (of a cry) **be loud and clear** A. S.*Ichn.*; (of a smell) **be distinct** or **strong** A.
4 be conspicuously like, resemble —W.DAT. *someone or sthg.* A. Pi. E. —W.NOM.PREDIC.ADJ. *such and such* (+ INF. *to observe*) A. E. —W. ὡς or ὥστε + NOM.PREDIC.SB. (sts. + INF. *to look at*) S. E.
5 (of things) **be fitting, appropriate** or **suitable** —W.DAT. *for someone or sthg.* Sapph. Pratin. Pi. Trag. Ar. Isoc. + —W.PREP.PHR. *among or for certain people* E. X. —W.PREDIC.PASS.PTCPL. *in being said* (i.e. *be appropriately said*) Pl. ‖ PRES.PTCPL.ADJ. **appropriate** or **suitable** (sts. W.DAT. for someone or sthg.) S. E. Th. Ar. Att.orats. Pl. +; (of an eventuality) **worthy** (W.GEN. of someone's fortune) S.
‖ NEUT.ACC.PTCPL. **it being** (i.e. since it is) **appropriate** E.
6 ‖ MASC.PTCPL. (of a person) **conspicuously suited** (W.INF. to do or be sthg.) S. Plu.; **matching** (W.DAT. a description) Plu.
7 ‖ IMPERS. **it is fitting, suitable** or **appropriate** A. E. Isoc. —W.ACC. or DAT. *for someone* (*to do sthg.*) A. Hdt. E. Pl. + —W.ACC. or DAT. (sts. understd.) + INF. (*for someone*) *to do sthg.,* (*for sthg.*) *to happen* Lyr. Hdt. Trag. Th. Ar. +
8 (tr.) **liken** —*someone* (W.DAT. *to sthg.*) A.

—πρεπόντως *ptcpl.adv.* **1 fittingly, suitably, appropriately** A. Pi. E. Th. Ar. Isoc. +
2 in a manner appropriate (W.DAT. to someone or sthg.) Pl. Arist. Plb. Plu.
3 in a manner worthy (W.GEN. of someone) Pl.

πρεπώδης ες *adj.* | compar. πρεπωδέστερος, superl. πρεπωδέστατος | (of things) **fitting, suitable, appropriate** (sts. W.DAT. for someone or sthg.) Isoc. Pl. X. Arist.
‖ NEUT.IMPERS. (w. ἐστί) **it is appropriate** —W.INF. or DAT. + INF. (*for someone*) *to do sthg.* Ar.

πρέσβα *ep.nom.voc.fem.adj.* [πρέσβυς] **1** (of a daughter) **eldest** Hom.
2 (of a goddess, ref. to Hera) **august, revered** Il.

πρεσβεία ᾱς *f.* [πρεσβεύω] **1 seniority** (as a criterion for office) A. Arist.
2 dignity, high rank Pl.
3 despatch of ambassadors, mission, embassy Ar. Att.orats. Pl. +
4 (collectv.) **body of ambassadors, embassy** Th. Ar. Att.orats. Pl. +

πρεσβεῖον, Ion. **πρεσβήιον,** ου *n.* **1 what is given as a mark of respect** (to a warrior), **prize of honour** Il.
2 mark of seniority (among brothers, ref. to the right to their father's name) D.; **mark of rank** (ref. to the Roman *fasces*) Plu.
3 ‖ PL. (gener.) **prerogative** or **privilege** (W.INF. to do sthg.) Pl.; (specif.) **privileges of seniority, precedence** (among brothers) E.*fr.* Arist.; (concr., appos.w. **house, empire**) **inheritance by right of seniority** D. Plu.

πρέσβειρα *nom.voc.f.* [πρέσβυς] **1 senior, chief** (W.GEN. of goddesses, ref. to Hestia) hHom.; (of Erinyes) E.; (of a collection of eels, envisaged as maidens) Ar.
2 (ref. to a nymph) **mistress, honoured lady** S.*Ichn.* ‖ ADJ. (of Themis) **august** AR.
3 prob. **high-ranking woman** (w. further connot. *ambassadress*) Ar.

πρέσβευμα ατος *n*. [πρεσβεύω] **1** (pl.) **embassy, mission** E. **2** (pl., ref. to a person) **ambassador, envoy** E. Plu.

πρεσβεύς έως *m*. | ep.Ion.nom.pl. πρεσβῆες | **elderly man** Hes.

πρέσβευσις εως *f*. **despatch of an embassy** Th.

πρεσβευτής οῦ *m*. **1 ambassador, envoy** (of a state, sent on a specific mission) Th. Att.orats. Pl. X. +
2 agent, representative (travelling abroad on another's behalf) D.
3 (ref. to a Roman *legatus* attached to a general) **legate** Plb. Plu.

πρεσβευτικός ή όν *adj*. **of or relating to ambassadors**; (of speeches) **by ambassadors** Plb.; (of contests) **diplomatic** Plb.

πρεσβεύω *vb*. [πρέσβυς] **1 have precedence in age**; (of a brother) **be the elder** (of two) S.; **be the eldest** —W.GEN. *of his siblings* Hdt.; (of a son) **be first in line of succession** —w. ἀπό + GEN. *to a father* Th.; (of birth) **have precedence** —W.DAT. *for particular brothers* (*so giving them the status of eldest brothers*) E.; (of persons) **be the most senior** (in a group) Pl.
2 have precedence in rank; (of inhabitants of a city) **have precedence** —W.GEN. *over other cities* Pl.; (of Zeus) **be supreme** —W.GEN. *in heaven* S. || IMPERS. **it is best** —W.ACC. + INF. *that sthg. shd. be the case* S.
3 (tr.) **give precedence to, honour** —*a deity* (*in a prayer*) A.; (of a wife) —*her husband* E.; (of persons) **pay special honour to** —*a tomb, a mother's name* A. S. —*a god, a craft, arguments* Pl.; (of Aphrodite) **give preference to, exalt** —*those who respect her power* E.; (of the Muses) **honour** —*a city* (*by their presence*) E.; (of a person) **attach greater importance to** —*one consideration* (w. πρό + GEN. *over another*) Plu.; (intr., of a god) **be honoured** Ion || PASS. (of a deity) **have pride of place** (in a speech) A.; (of old age) **be more honoured** —W.GEN. *than youth* Pl.; (of the last remnant of one's life) **be most highly prized** A.; (of a crime) **rank as most notable** —W.GEN. *of crimes* A.
4 be an ambassador or **envoy** (sts. W.PREP.PHR. **to** or **fr. a person** or **place**) Hdt. Ar. Att.orats. Pl. +; **serve** —W.COGN.ACC. *on embassies* Din.; (of a woman) **be spokesperson for, represent** —W.GEN. *her family* E.
5 || MID. **send envoys** (sts. W.PREP.PHR. **to a person** or **place**) Th. Ar. Pl. X. Hyp. D.; **send an intermediary** (to someone) Men.
6 (tr., of ambassadors) **negotiate** —*peace* Att.orats.; **do** (W.NEUT.ACC.PL.ADJ. *shocking things, exemplary service*) **as ambassador** D. || PASS. (of actions) **be performed by an ambassador** D.
7 (at Rome) **be a *legatus*** (attached to a general) Plu.

πρέσβη ης *f*. **company of envoys** A.(dub.)

πρεσβῆες (ep.Ion.nom.pl.): see πρεσβεύς

πρεσβήιον Ion.*n*.: see πρεσβεῖον

πρεσβηίς ίδος *fem.adj*. (of a privilege given to Hestia) **of seniority** (among the gods) hHom.

πρέσβις εως *f*. **seniority** (among gods, magistrates) hHom. Pl.

πρέσβιστος *superl.adj*.: see under πρέσβυς

πρέσβος ους *n*. **object of veneration** (W.DAT. to a people, ref. to a queen) A.; **venerable company** (W.GEN. of citizens) A.

πρεσβυγενείη ης Ion.*f*. [πρεσβυγενής] **seniority of birth** (betw. two related families) Hdt.

πρεσβυ-γενής ές *adj*. [γένος, γίγνομαι] **1** (of a son) **eldest-born** Il. E.
2 (at Sparta, of elders) **aged, old** Tyrt. || MASC.PL.SB. **elders** Plu.

πρέσβυς, Lacon. **πρέσγυς** (Alcm.), εως *m*. | voc. πρέσβυ | **1 old man** (oft. as a term of respect) Alcm. Pi. Trag. Ar. Hellenist.poet. || PL. (in voc. address) **old men, elders** Trag.
2 || ADJ. (of Agamemnon) **elder** (of two brothers) A.
3 (usu.pl.) **ambassador** Th. Ar. Att.orats. +

—**πρεσβύτερος** ᾱ ον *compar.adj*. **1** (of a person) **elder** (of two) Il. Hdt. Pl. +; **older** or **elderly** Hdt. Th. Ar. +; (of a deed) **too old** (W.COMPAR.GEN. for one's years) Pi.*fr*. || NEUT.SB. **time between youth and old age** Pl. || MASC.PL.SB. **older men, older generation** hHom. Pi. Hdt. Th. Ar. Att.orats. +
2 (of a person) **living earlier in time** (than someone else), **older** Hdt.; (of a people) **more ancient** Hdt.; (of an event) **earlier** (than someone's lifetime) Hdt.
3 (of a person's counsels) **mature beyond one's years** Pi.
4 (of a duty, a consideration) **more important** Hdt. Pl.; (of an evil) **graver** (W.GEN. than another) S.
5 || MASC.SB. perh., **senator** (at Rome) Plb.; **elder** (of the Jewish Sanhedrin NT.; in a Christian church) NT.

—**πρεσβυτέρως** *compar.adv*. **more highly** —*ref. to valuing sthg.* Pl.

—**πρεσβύτατος** (also **πρέσβιστος** hHom. A. Lyr.adesp.) η ον *superl.adj*. **1** (of a person, a deity) **eldest** Il. Hes. Pi. Hdt. Th. Ar. +; (of the leader of a flock of birds) E.; (of a motherland) Sol.
2 (of the moon) **most revered** (of stars) A.; (of Health) Lyr.adesp.; (of obligations to parents) **most sacred** Pl.; (of a prize) **foremost** B.; (of a consideration) **most important** Th.

πρεσβυτέριον ου *n*. **council of elders** NT.

πρεσβύτης ου *m*. **old man** (oft. as a term of respect, sts. appos.w. ἀνήρ, πατήρ, or sim.) Hdt. Trag. Th. Ar. Att.orats. Pl. +

πρεσβυτικός ή όν *adj*. **1 of or relating to an old man**; (of a crowd) **of old men** Ar.; (of a curse) **uttered by an old man** Plu.; (of troubles) **experienced in old age** Ar.; (of a song, a mode of expression, a way of playing a game) **typical of old men** Ar. Isoc. Pl.; (of gods) **of the elderly** Ar. || MASC.PL.SB. **elderly people** Arist.
2 (of a strategy) **belonging to a former age, antiquated** Plu.

—**πρεσβυτικῶς** *adv*. **in the manner of an elderly person** Plu.

πρεσβῦτις ιδος *f*. | acc. πρεσβῦτιν | **old woman** A. E. Lys. Pl. +

πρεσβῦτο-δόκος ον *adj*. [δέχομαι] (of hearths or altars) **welcoming the elders** (of a land) A.(dub.)

πρέσγυς Lacon.*m*.: see πρέσβυς

πρευμένεια ᾱς *f*. [πρευμενής] **goodwill, benevolence** E.

πρευμενής ές *adj*. [πρᾶος, μένος] **1** (of a person, a god; of a dead person, his feelings) **well-disposed, favourable** (sts. W.DAT. to someone) A. E.; (of Zeus' eye) A.; (of a person's friendship) **kindly** E.
2 (of fortune, an outcome) **favourable, propitious** A.; (of a journey home) E.(dub.)
3 (of offerings) **propitiatory** A.

—**πρευμενῶς** *adv*. **1 graciously, kindly** —*ref. to welcoming someone* A.; **benevolently** —*ref. to prophesying, giving advice* A.
2 in propitiatory fashion —*ref. to making an appeal to the underworld* A.

πρῆγμα Ion.*n*., **πρηγματεύομαι** Ion.mid.*vb*.: see πρᾶγμα, πρᾱγματεύομαι

πρηγορεών ῶνος *m*. [πρό, ἀγείρω] **pouch in the gullet of a bird** (for temporary storage of swallowed food), **crop, craw** Ar.

πρηθῆναι (Ion.aor.pass.inf.): see πέρνημι

πρήθω *vb*.: see πίμπρημι

πρηκτήρ ἦρος *Ion.m.* [πράσσω] **1 doer** (W.GEN. of deeds, opp. speaker of words) Il.
2 person engaged in commerce, **trader** Od.
πρημαίνω *vb.* [πρῆσαι, see πίμπρημι] (of squalls) **blow, swell, bluster** Ar.(mock-dithyramb)
πρηνής *Ion.adj.*: see πρᾱνής
πρῆξις *Ion.f.*, **πρήξω** (Ion.fut.): see πρᾶξις, πράσσω
πρῆσαι (aor.inf.): see πίμπρημι
πρῆσις *Ion.f.*: see πρᾶσις
πρήσσω[1] *Ion.vb.*: see πράσσω
πρήσσω[2] (v.l. **πρήσω**, cj. **πρήθω**) *vb.* [reltd. πίμπρημι] (of Hephaistos) **stir up, fan** —*the flames of a fire* AR.; (intr., of a wind) **blow** AR.
πρηστήρ ἦρος *m.* [πρῆσαι, see πίμπρημι] **1** that which burns, **burner, burning element** (app.ref. to a lightning storm) Heraclit.
2 storm accompanied by lightning; **hurricane** or **thunderstorm** Hdt.; (causing a fire) X.; (appos.w. ἄνεμος *wind*, as a weapon of Zeus, alongside his lightning) Hes.; (assoc.w. τυφώς *whirlwind*) Ar.
3 hot blast (of air fr. bellows) AR.
πρήσω[1] (fut.): see πίμπρημι
πρήσω[2] *vb.*: see πρήσσω[2]
πρητήριον ου *Ion.n.* [πέρνημι] **selling-place, market** Hdt.
πρηΰνω *Ion.vb.*, **πρηΰς** *Ion.adj.*: see πραΰνω, πρᾶος
πρηών *ep.m.*: see πρών
Πρίαμος ου (ep. οιο), Aeol. **Πέραμος** (also **Πέρραμος**) ω *m.* **Priam** (king of Troy) Hom. +
—**Πρῐαμίδης** ᾱο (also εω) *ep.m.* —also **Πρῐαμίδᾱς** ᾱ *dial.m.* **son of Priam** Il. E. ‖ PL. descendants of Priam (usu. ref. to the Trojan people) A. E. Theoc.
—**Πριαμικός** ή όν *adj.* (of misfortunes) **like those of Priam** Arist.
—**Πριαμίς** ίδος *fem.adj.* (of the land, gates) **of Priam** E.
πρίασθαι *aor.mid.inf.* | aor. ἐπριάμην, ep.3sg. πρίατο | imperatv. πρίω, dial. πρίασο | **1** conclude a purchase (of material things); **buy** —*goods, slaves, or sim.* Od. Pi. Hdt. S. E. Th. +
2 secure (sthg. immaterial) by payment; **buy** —*peace* (*by means of bribery*) Aeschin. —w. τό + INF. *an opportunity to do sthg.* X.; **pay for** —w. μή + INF. *sthg. not to happen* And.; **ensure by payment** (W.GEN. of a certain price) —w. ὥστε + INF. *that sthg. happens* X.
3 buy, bribe —*jurors* D.
πρίζω *vb.* [πρίω] **saw** (timber) Pl.(dub.)
Πρίηπος ου *Ion.m.* **Priapos** (son of Dionysus, ithyphallic god esp. assoc.w. sexuality and gardens) Theoc. Mosch.(pl.)
πρίν temporal *adv.* and *conj.* [reltd. πρό] | sts. πρίν Hom. |
—A *adv.* **1** at some time or times in the past, **earlier, formerly, previously** Hom. +; (also) τὸ πρίν Hom. + • (quasi-adj.) ἐν τοῖς πρὶν λόγοις *in the previous speeches* Th.
2 before a specified time (either past or future), **before then, beforehand, sooner, first** Hom. + • πρὶν κνέφας ἦλθε *darkness arrived first* (*before sthg. could happen*) Il. • πρίν μιν καὶ γῆρας ἔπεισι *old age will overtake him first* Il.
3 (in the first of two co-ordinated cls., as antecedent to conj. πρίν, freq. w.neg., chiefly ep.) • οὐδέ τις ἔτλη πρὶν πιέειν, πρὶν λεῖψαι *and no one presumed to drink first, before pouring a libation* Il.
4 (as prep.) **before** —W.GEN. *the due time* (*i.e. prematurely*) Pi.
—B *conj.* **1** (usu. after a positive main cl., sts. after neg.cl.) at a time preceding (an activity), **before** —W.INF. or ACC. + INF. *doing sthg., someone does sthg., sthg. happens* Hom. +; (also) πρὶν ἤ Il. Hdt.
2 up to a specified time, **until** —W.INDIC. (usu. AOR.) *someone did sthg., sthg. happened* hHom. +; (also) πρίν γ' ὅτε Hom.
3 (after neg.cl., ref. to pres. or fut. time) **until** or **unless** —W.SUBJ. (or ἄν + SUBJ.) or (after historic tenses) OPT. *someone does sthg., sthg. happens* Hom. +; (also) πρίν γ' ὅτε Hom.; πρὶν ἤ Hdt.
πρῑνίδιον ου *n.* [dimin. πρῖνος] **little holm-oak** Ar.
πρῑνινος η ον *adj.* [πρῖνος] **1** (of a plough-tree) **made of holm-oak** Hes.; (of charcoal) **from holm-oak** Ar.
2 (fig., of persons, their characters) **tough as holm-oak** Ar.
πρῖνος ου *f.* a kind of oak (usu. ref. to its timber, esp. as hard), **holm-oak** Hes. Simon. Ar. X. +
πρῑνώδης ες *adj.* (of a person's spirit) **tough as holm-oak** Ar.
πρίστις εως *f.* [prob. πρίω] perh. **sawfish** (ref. to a type of warship, app. w. a heavy ram) Plb.
πρῑστός ή όν *adj.* [πρίω] (of ivory) **sawn** Od.
πρίω (aor.mid.imperatv.): see πρίασθαι
πρίω *vb.* | du.ptcpl. πρίοντε | aor. ἔπρῑσα ‖ aor.pass.ptcpl. πρισθείς | **1 saw** (timber) Ar. —*a beam* (W.ADV. *in two*) Th.
2 grind, gnash —*one's teeth* (*in rage*) Ar.; (fig.) —*oneself* (*i.e. one's teeth*) Men.; **grind out** —*rage* (W.PREP.PHR. *against someone, i.e. gnash one's teeth in rage at him*) AR.
3 ‖ PASS. (of Hector, dragged behind a chariot) **be gripped tightly** (prob. w. further connot. of being cut) —W.DAT. *by a belt* (*attached to the rails*) S.
πρίων ονος *m.* tool for cutting wood, **saw** S. Arist. Plu.
πρό *prep.* | W.GEN. | sts. following loc.adv. |
—A | location |
at or near the front of, **in front of, before** —*persons, places, things* Hom. +; οὐρανόθι πρό *before the vault of the sky* (*ref. to birds flying*) Il.; (as adv.) **in front** Hom.; (phr.) πρὸ χειρῶν *in one's hands* S. E. | for πρὸ ποδός (ποδῶν) *at one's feet* see πούς 7, 8; see also καιρός 2
—B | movt. |
1 in front of, ahead of —*someone or sthg.* Hom. +; (as adv.) **forth** —*ref. to bringing a child into the light of day* Hom. hHom. | for πρὸ ὁδοῦ *ahead* (*in a journey, task, or sim.*) see ὁδός 12
2 at the head of —*people, warriors* Hom. Hes.; (as adv.) **at the front** Il.
—C | protection or support |
1 (ref. to holding shields) **in the way of** —*arrows* X.
2 (ref. to fighting or dying) **in defence of, for** —*people, places* Il. A. Pi. Hdt. +
3 (ref. to speaking, taking care, sacrificing, running risks, or sim.) **on behalf of** or **for the sake of** —*persons, places* Il. Hdt. Trag. +
—D | time |
1 earlier than, before —*an event, activity, period or point in time* Hom. +; (phrs.) πρὸ τοῦ *before that, previously* A. Hdt. E. Th. +; ἠῶθι πρό *before dawn* Hom.; (as adv.) **previously** Hom. Hes. A. | see also μοῖρα 2, φύσις 8
2 (phrs.) πρὸ πολλοῦ *before by much* (*time*), **long before** Hdt. +; πρὸ μιᾶς ἡμέρας *one day before* Plu.; πρὸ μιᾶς καλανδῶν Μαρτίων *pridie Kal. Mart.* Plu.; (W.DBL.GEN.) πρὸ ἓξ ἡμερῶν τοῦ πάσχα *before the Passover by six days* (*i.e. six days before the Passover*) NT.
3 before the time of, before —*a certain person, a generation* Th. Isoc. Plu.
4 (ref. to recognising sthg.) **earlier than, before** —*someone else* Il.

—**E** | comparison or preference |
1 rather than —*someone or sthg.* Hdt. E. Th. Pl. +; **better than** —*many shields* (*as a defence*) S.; (phr.) πρὸ πάντων *above all others* (*i.e. especially*) A. | see also πᾶς 9
2 (pleon., w.compar.adj.) **than** Hdt. Pl. • ἡ τυραννὶς πρὸ ἐλευθερίης ἦν ἀσπαστότερον *tyranny was more welcome than freedom* Hdt.
3 (ref. to esteeming sthg.) **above** —*sthg. else* Pi. Th. Pl.; πρὸ πολλοῦ ποιεῖσθαι *esteem above much* (*i.e. very highly*) Isoc.
—**F** | substitution |
in place of, instead of —*someone or sthg.* Simon. Hdt. E.; (phrs.) γῆν πρὸ γῆς *one land in place of another* (*i.e. land to land, in ctxt. of pursuit*) A. Ar.; πρὸ θυέλλα θυέλλης *gust after gust* Hes.
—**G** | cause |
1 out of, through —*fear* Il.
2 on account of, because of —*certain circumstances* S. E.
προ-αγγέλλω *vb.* **give advance notice** or **warning** (of sthg.) D. —W.ACC. *of sthg.* X. Plb. —*of someone* (*i.e. his arrival*) Thphr. —W.ACC. + FUT.INF. *that sthg. will happen* X. ‖ PASS. (of a circumstance) **be warned about in advance** Th.
προάγγελσις εως *f.* **advance notice, forewarning** (W.GEN. of sthg.) Th.
προ-άγνυμι *vb.* (of a deity, by sending a wind) **beat down** (W.ACC. *waves*) **in front** (of a swimmer) Od.(tm.)
προαγόρευσις εως *f.* [προαγορεύω] **1 foretelling** (of an event) Arist.
2 prediction (by a seer) Plu.
προ-αγορεύω *vb.* | aor. προηγόρευσα (Hdt. Plu.) | pf. προηγόρευκα (D.) ‖ In Att., mainly pres. and impf. (fut. and pf. being supplied by προείρω, aor. by προεῖπον). |
1 declare in advance (fr. foreknowledge or conjecture), **foretell, predict** —*good fortune, sufferings, the future* Hdt. Th. X. Plu. —W.ACC. + FUT.INF. *that sthg. will happen* Hdt.
2 (intr.) **give advance notice** (of one's intention) Isoc.
3 advise with foreknowledge (fr. a god), **give advice** or **warning** —W.DAT. + INF. *to someone to do sthg.* X.
4 (of persons in authority) **declare publicly, announce, proclaim** —*a message, a decision, equality under the law, contests* Hdt. X. —*war* Th. D. —W.COMPL.CL. or ACC. + INF. *that sthg. is the case* Th. Pl. X. D.
5 order publicly, issue an order Hdt. X. —W.INF. or W.DAT. or ACC. + INF. (*to someone*) *to do sthg.* Hdt. Th. Ar. Pl. X. Plb. ‖ IMPERS.PASS. **an order is given** —W.INF. *to do sthg.* X.
6 (leg., of a magistrate or prosecutor) **give public notice** —W.DAT. + INF. *to a person* (*awaiting trial for homicide*) *that he is excluded fr. certain places and rights* Att.orats. Pl. Arist.; **give** —W.COGN.ACC. *public notice* (*of such exclusion*) Pl.; **serve notice** —W.DAT. + INF. *on someone to appear for trial* Plu.; (of a law) **give instruction** —W.DAT. + INF. *to certain persons to do sthg.* Pl.
προ-άγω *vb.* | fut. προάξω | aor.2 προήγαγον | pf. προῆχα (D.) | **1 lead or take forward; move forward** —*one's troops* Th. X. Plb. Plu.; **conduct** —*someone* (*to a place*) Hdt. Pl.; **lead** (W.ACC. *someone*) **along** (in a particular direction) Hdt.; **move** (W.ACC. *a wall*) **further forward** (towards a road) D.
2 bring into the open; bring out —*a corpse* (*into the open streets*) Pl.; **lay out** —*a matter for discussion* Pl. ‖ PASS. (of a person) **be brought outside** Men.
3 (intr.) **lead the way** (in walking) Pl. X.; (fig., in disputation) Pl.; (of a commander) **lead an advance, push forward** Plb. Plu.; (of troops) **move forward** Men. Plb. Plu.; (gener., of persons) **walk on, move on** Men.
4 (intr., of a discourse) **be prior, precede** (another) Pl.

5 lead (someone) **on by persuasion or temptation; lead** (W.ACC. *someone*) **on** —W.DAT. *by subterfuge* Hdt. —W.ADV. *to a certain point* E.; **draw on, lure** —*an enemy fleet* (*into a bay*) Th.; (of hope) **lead on, encourage** —*someone* E.; (of need) **compel, prompt** (someone) Th. ‖ PASS. **be lured on** —W.DAT. *by good fortune* Men.
6 (act. and mid.) **induce, encourage, tempt** —W.ACC. + INF. *someone to do sthg.* Th. X. Aeschin. D. Arist. ‖ PASS. **be induced** —W.INF. *to do sthg.* D.
7 lead (someone) **towards some new emotion, state or activity**; (act. and mid.) **move, rouse** —*someone* (W.PREP.PHR. *to hatred, hostility, anger, jealousy, pity, laughter, or sim.*) Hdt. Att.orats. X. Arist.; (act.) **guide** (by example, opp. exhort) —*someone* (W.PREP.PHR. *to virtue*) X.; **draw** —*someone* (*into discussion*) Pl.; **throw** —*oneself* (*into unsuitable behaviour*) Hdt. ‖ PASS. (of a city) **be led** —W.PREP.PHR. *into disasters* And.
8 (of old age, time) **bring on, advance** —*someone, his life* (W.PREP.PHR. *to a certain point*) Isoc. X.
9 (intr., of a day) **be well advanced** Plb.
10 bring (sthg.) **to a more advanced state**; (of a populace) **advance, enhance** —*a city, its power* Th.; **extend** —*one's empire* Th.; (of mathematicians) **develop** —*mathematics* Arist.; (of poets) —*harmony and rhythm* Arist.; (of a writer) —*an outline account* (*into a detailed work*) Arist. ‖ MID. (of a nation) **advance** —*its power* (*to a certain height*) Hdt. ‖ PASS. (of malpractices) **develop, become rife** D.
11 advance (someone) **in status; promote, elevate** —*someone* Plb. —(W.PREP.PHR. *to a position of command*) Plu. —*money* (*to a position of honour*) Pl.; **lead** —*a city, a nation* (*to a reputation, a position of power, or sim.*) Isoc. Plu.
12 (of experience) **advance the growth of, mature** —*a person* Men. ‖ MID. (of a person) **develop, bring up** —*one's sons* (*in a certain way*) D. ‖ PASS. (of persons) **be developed** —W.DAT. *in character* Arist.
προαγωγεύω *vb.* [προαγωγός] **1** (pejor.) **procure** —*a woman, a boy* (*as a sexual partner for someone*) Aeschin. Plu.
2 (of a boy) **advertise** —*oneself* (*sexually,* W.DAT. w. *one's eyes*) Ar.
3 procure —*someone* (W.DAT. *for a sophist, i.e. as a besotted pupil*) X.
προαγωγή ῆς *f.* [προάγω] **prominent position, eminence** (of a person within a society) Plb.
προαγωγίᾱ (or **προαγωγείᾱ**) ᾱς *f.* [προαγωγεύω] (pejor.) **procuring** (for sexual purposes), **pimping** Pl. X. Aeschin. Arist.
προ-αγωγός οῦ *m.f.* **1 one who procures a sexual partner for another** (usu. in exchange for money), **procurer, pimp** Aeschin.; (*f.*) **procuress** Ar. Aeschin.
2 one who introduces someone to another for their mutual benefit, go-between X.
προ-άγων ωνος *m.* [ἀγών] **1 ceremony preceding a dramatic contest** (at which the competing dramatists, accompanied by actors and choruses, spoke about their plays), **preliminary ceremony** Aeschin.
2 (in ctxt. of gymnastic education) **preparatory contest** Pl.
3 preliminary defence (W.GEN. against an indictment) D.; **preliminary bout** (W.GEN. in a legal contest) Plu.
4 preliminary encounter (in a battle) Plu.; (fig., ref. to a battle, an enterprise, or sim.) **prelude, preliminary** (usu. W.GEN. to sthg. more significant) Plu.
προ-αγωνίζομαι *mid.vb.* **1 engage in an earlier contest** —W.DAT. w. *a nation* Th.; **engage beforehand** —W.COGN.ACC. *in contests* Pl. ‖ PASS. (of contests) **be fought earlier** Plu.

προαδικέω

2 fight on behalf of, champion (someone) Plu.

προ-αδικέω contr.vb. commit the earlier offence (opp. a retaliatory one) Plu. ‖ PASS. be victim of the earlier offence Aeschin.

προ-ᾴδω vb. be the leading singer (in a chorus) Aeschin.

προ-αιδεῦμαι Ion.mid.contr.vb. [αἰδέομαι] be under an obligation —W.DAT. to someone Hdt.

προαίρεσις εως f. [προαιρέω] 1 choosing one thing before another, act of choice Pl. Arist.
2 free or deliberate choice (opp. compulsion) Att.orats. Arist.; choice, purpose (as characteristic of moral action) Arist.
3 that which is chosen; choice (ref. to a decision taken) Hyp.; (ref. to a type of constitution adopted) D.; (W.GEN. of a profession, ref. to its nature) Aeschin.; predilection (ref. to a mode of behaviour) Aeschin.; chosen manner (W.GEN. of life) D.; chosen policy (W.GEN. of self-advancement) D.; chosen line (W.GEN. of argument) D.; chosen area (W.GEN. of political activity) D. ‖ PL. principles (of conduct) Isoc.
4 chosen basis for action, political attitude or principles (of a state or leader) Plb.; (specif.) character or reputation (of a military leader or army) Plb.
5 chosen course of political or military action, policy (of a state or leader) Aeschin. D. Plb.; (specif.) programme of action or conduct (of a leader) Plb.

προαιρετικός ή όν adj. 1 (of persons) inclined to a preference (W.GEN. for sthg.) Arist.
2 (of a disposition of mind, a part of the mind) concerned with choice or purpose, purposive Arist. Plu.

προαιρετός ή όν adj. (of an action or sim.) chosen, purposed Arist.

προ-αιρέω contr.vb. | aor.2 προεῖλον ‖ neut.impers.vbl.adj. προαιρετέον | 1 bring forth (supplies, fr. a storeroom or sim.); bring out, produce —grain, items of food or drink Th. Ar. Thphr. Men. ‖ MID. select for use, take —knucklebones (W.PREP.PHR. fr. baskets) Pl.
2 ‖ MID. have a preference (for one thing rather than another); choose, select —someone or sthg. Att.orats. Pl. X. + —(w. πρό or ἀντί + GEN. in preference to someone or sthg. else) Pl. X.; (intr.) exercise choice Arist.
3 ‖ MID. choose, decide —W.INF. to do sthg. Att.orats. Pl. X. + —W.NEUT.ACC. (to do) sthg. D. Arist.

προ-αισθάνομαι mid.vb. 1 perceive in advance; receive advance news, become aware earlier (of sthg.) Th. Att.orats. Arist. Plb. Plu. —W.ACC. of someone or sthg. Th. Isoc. X. D. Plb. Plu. —W.GEN. Th. X. —W.ACC. + PTCPL. that someone is doing sthg. Th.
2 (of a hearer) anticipate —sthg. being said Th.

προαίσθησις εως f. advance warning (W.GEN. of someone or sthg.) Plu.

προ-ακούω vb. 1 hear (W.ACC. sthg.) beforehand D.; listen (W.GEN. to someone) beforehand Pl.; (of a horse) hear (W.ACC. many things) before (its rider) X.
2 hear beforehand (about sthg.) Hdt. —W.PREP.PHR. about sthg. D. —W.GEN. Plb. —W.COMPL.CL. that sthg. is the case Hdt. Aeschin. D. Plb. —how things stand Hdt. —W.ACC. + FUT.PTCPL. that sthg. will be the case D.
3 (of ears) hear on behalf of, hear for (a person) X.

προ-αλής ές adj. [app. ἅλλομαι] leaping forward; (of terrain, over which water flows quickly down) sloping Il.; (of water) streaming (down a mountain) AR.

προ-αλίσκομαι pass.vb. 1 (of a person) be convicted beforehand D. Plu.
2 (of a fish) be caught earlier Plu.

προ-αμαρτάνω vb. sin previously NT.
‖ NEUT.PL.PF.PASS.PTCPL.SB. earlier offences Plu.

προ-αμείβομαι mid.vb. receive (W.ACC. a product or service) in advance (of payment) Pl.

προ-αμύνομαι mid.vb. take precautionary or pre-emptive action Th. —W.ACC. against someone Th.

πρόαν dial.adv.: see πρώην

προ-αναβαίνω vb. climb (W.ACC. a hill) beforehand Th.

προ-αναβάλλομαι mid.vb. (of a singer) strike up in advance, rehearse —a song Ar.; (of a speaker, comparing himself to a chorus rehearsing before a contest) say (W.ACC. sthg.) by way of prelude Isoc.

προ-ανάγομαι pass.vb. (of ships) put to sea beforehand Th.

προ-αναιρέω contr.vb. 1 destroy (W.ACC. an enemy) first (before he destroys you) Plu.; (of old age) carry off (W.ACC. someone) too soon (before he can do sthg.) Isoc. ‖ PASS. be killed too soon (to be able to do sthg.) Plu.
2 refute in advance —W.RELATV.CL. what someone will say Arist.
3 (of an ambassador) waste (W.ACC. a city's time) beforehand (i.e. before his return home) D.

προ-αναισιμόομαι pass.contr.vb. (of a period of time) elapse earlier Hdt.

προ-αναισχυντέω contr.vb. take the lead in shamelessness Hyp.

προ-ανακīνέω contr.vb. 1 ‖ PASS. (of a war against someone) be stirred up in advance, be prefigured —W.DAT. by a war against someone else Plu.
2 (fig., of an orator, envisaged as a fighter) limber up in advance Arist.

προ-ανακρίνω vb. (of magistrates) make preliminary decisions or judgements Arist.

προ-αναλίσκω vb. | fut. προαναλώσω | aor.ptcpl. προαναλώσᾱς ‖ aor.pass.inf. προαναλωθῆναι | 1 pay (W.ACC. a sum of money) in advance Aeschin. D.; spend money in advance Lys.
2 exhaust prematurely —one's resources Th. ‖ PASS. (of soldiers) give one's life prematurely (i.e. unnecessarily) Th.

προ-αναρπάζω vb. spirit away (W.ACC. an accuser) in advance (of a trial) D.; catch (W.ACC. someone) in advance (W.GEN. of his readiness) Plu.

προ-ανασείω vb. stir up (W.ACC. the populace) beforehand Plu. ‖ PASS. (of lawsuits) be already threatened —W.DAT. against someone Plu.

προ-αναφωνέω contr.vb. declare (W.ACC. sthg.) by way of preface Plu.

προ-αναχώρησις εως f. (milit.) premature retreat Th.

προ-ανέχω vb. (of headlands) project Th.

προ-ανύτω vb. [ἀνύω] succeed in accomplishing —sthg. X.

προ-απαγορεύω vb. give up (an activity) prematurely Isoc.

προ-απαντάω contr.vb. 1 advance to meet (an enemy) Th.
2 meet (W.DAT. ships) in advance (of reaching a place) Th.

προ-απεῖπον aor.2 vb. give up (an activity) prematurely Isoc.

προ-απείρω vb. | only pf. προαπείρηκα | ‖ PF. have retired from active life Isoc.

προ-απέρχομαι mid.vb. | aor.2 προαπῆλθον | depart beforehand Th. D.; depart before —W.GEN. the appropriate time Pl.

προ-απεχθάνομαι pass.vb. incur hostility beforehand D.

προ-απηγέομαι Ion.mid.contr.vb. [ἀφηγέομαι] explain beforehand —one's situation Hdt.

προ-αποδείκνῡμι vb. ‖ PASS. (of things) be demonstrated in advance Isoc.

προ-αποθνήσκω vb. **1 die before** —W.GEN. *someone or sthg.* Antipho Plu.; **die first** (before another) Hdt. Plu.; (before doing sthg.) Plb. Plu.; **take one's life first** (before being put to death) X.
2 sacrifice one's life —W.PREP.PHR. *on someone's behalf* Pl. —W.GEN. *for someone or sthg.* Arist. Plu.

προ-αποθρηνέω contr.vb. **bewail in advance** —*someone's imminent death* Plu.

προ-αποκάμνω vb. **grow tired before the end, give up too soon** Pl.; **give up before** —W.GEN. *the last hope* (*has been exhausted*) Plu.

προ-απολαύω vb. **enjoy a foretaste** —W.GEN. *of an event* Plu.

προ-απολείπω vb. **1 abandon** (W.ACC. *someone*) **prematurely** Plb.
2 (of winds) **fail first** (before reaching somewhere) Plu.; (of a person's spirit, while his body is still unwearied) Antipho

προ-απόλλῡμι vb. | pf. προαπόλωλα | (of an activity, a situation) **destroy** (W.ACC. *someone*) **first** (before sthg. happens) Men. Plu. || PASS. and PF.ACT. **be destroyed or die first** Antipho Th. Pl. X. D. +; **die before** —W.GEN. *someone* Lys.

προ-αποπέμπομαι mid.vb. **send** (W.ACC. *someone*) **on ahead** X. || PASS. **be sent on ahead** Th.

προ-αποπνέω contr.vb. (of a breeze) **blow early** (in the day) Plu.

προ-απορέω contr.vb. [ἀπορέω¹] **have preliminary doubts or uncertainties** Arist. || AOR.PASS. (w.mid.sens.) **raise a preliminary problem** Pl.

προ-αποστέλλω vb. **despatch in advance** —*troops, ships, messengers, or sim.* Th. D. Thphr. Plb. Plu. || PASS. **be despatched in advance** Th. Plb. Plu. —W.GEN. *of an event* Th.

προ-αποτρέπομαι mid.vb. **turn aside first** X.

προ-αποφαίνομαι mid.vb. **1 declare** (W.ACC. *one's opinion*) **at the start** Pl.; (intr.) **make one's position clear at the start** Pl.
2 pronounce an opinion —W.PREP.PHR. *on sthg.* Plu.

προ-αποχωρέω contr.vb. (of an army) **withdraw first** Th.

προ-αρπάζω vb. **snatch** (someone or sthg.) **in advance**; (fig.) **catch, ensnare** (W.ACC. *someone*) **earlier** Men.; **anticipate** —*someone's statements* Pl.

προ-ασκέω contr.vb. (of rulers, thinkers) **train in advance** —*persons, their mental dispositions* Isoc. Arist.

προ-άστιον (also **προάστειον**) ου *n.* [ἄστυ] **area outside a town, outskirts, suburb** Archil. Pi.fr. Hdt. S. E. Th. +

προ-αυδάω contr.vb. | inf. πρωυδᾶν | **declare** —*war* (W.DAT. *on someone*) Ar.

προ-αυλέω contr.vb. **play** (W.ACC. *a piece of music*) **as a prelude on the aulos** Arist.

προαύλιον ου *n.* [αὐλός] **prelude on the aulos** Pl. Arist.

προ-αφικνέομαι mid.contr.vb. (of a commander) **arrive first** (before others) Th.

προ-αφίσταμαι mid.vb. | act.athem.aor. προαπέστην |
1 depart first (before achieving sthg.) Pl.; **depart before** —W.GEN. *someone* Plu.
2 leave off first (fr. an activity, before achieving sthg.) Pl.
3 (of a populace) **take the initiative in seceding** (fr. an alliance) Th.

προβάδην adv. [προβαίνω] **1 while walking** —*ref. to urinating* Hes.
2 forwards, onwards Ar.

προ-βαθής ές adj. [βάθος] (of a river) **very deep** AR.

προ-βαίνω vb. | fut. προβήσομαι | also dial.act.fut. (causatv.) προβάσω (Pi.) || athem.aor. προύβην, imperatv. πρόβᾱ, pl. πρόβᾱτε || see also προβιβάω |
1 (of persons) **go forward, proceed** (on foot) Hdt. Trag. Ar. X. + —W.INTERN.ACC. *on a journey* E.; **advance** —W.INTERN.ACC. *a step* Thgn. Ar. —*a leg, a boot* E.
2 (of a ship) **proceed, move forward** Hdt.; (of stars, as a marker of time) Il.; (of speech) **come forth** (fr. the mouth) AR.
3 (of time, day, night) **move on, advance, pass** Hdt. S. X. D. Plb.
4 (of a person's age) **advance** X. Plb. || PF. (of persons) **be advanced** —W.DAT. *in age* Lys. —W.PREP.PHR. NT.
5 (of persons) **go forward in an activity or course of action; proceed** —W.PTCPL. *by acting in a given way* Hdt. —W.PREP.PHR. *fr. one part of the body to another* (*in cutting one's flesh*) Hdt. —*further in one's narrative* Hdt.; **make progress** (in an inquiry) Pl.
6 go forward (in a course of action or speech) **to a given point; advance** —W.ADVBL. or PREP.PHR. *further, to the extreme of boldness, or sim.* Trag. Pl. X. Aeschin. D.
7 (of work, a person's fortune) **proceed** Hdt. E.; (of a speech, a scheme, troubles, events) **progress, lead** —W.ADV. or PREP.PHR. *to some point* E. Ar. Plb. || IMPERS.PF. **things have gone** —W.PREP.PHR. *to a certain point* Pl.
8 progress in scope, intensity or extent; (of a person's power) **increase, grow** X.; (of a trouble) E. AR.; (of a custom) **gain ground** Aeschin.; (of the length of a war) **be extended** —W.PREDIC.ADJ. *greatly* Th.; (of a war) **be prolonged** Plb.
9 (of persons) **be ahead** (of others) **in some quality; be superior** —W.DAT. *in sthg.* Il. Call.epigr. —W.GEN. *to someone* (+ DAT. *in sthg.*) Il.; **be pre-eminent** —W.GEN. *in a place* (+ DAT. *for sthg.*) Hes.
10 (causatv., in fut.act., of a kind of behaviour) **advance, help** —*someone* (*towards an achievement*) Pi.
11 (of events) **go before, precede** (in time) Thgn.
12 (of a javelin-thrower) **go beyond, overstep** —*a starting-line* Pi. [or perh. **step up to**]

πρό-βακχος ου *masc.adj.* [Βάκχος] (of Bromios) **Bacchant-leading** E.

προ-βάλλω vb. | fut. προβαλῶ | aor.2 προύβαλον, ep. πρόβαλον, iteratv. προβάλεσκον || The sections are grouped as: (1–3) **throw forward or cast forth**, (4–10) **bring forward** (for some purpose), (11–16) **place in front.** |
1 throw forward, toss, cast —*items of food* (W.DAT. *to persons, dogs, birds*) Hdt. Ar.; (of a wind) **fling** —*a boat* (W.DAT. *to another wind*) Od. || MID. **sprinkle** —*barley grains* (*on a sacrificial victim*) Hom.; (fig.) **toss out, offer** —*a clever idea* (*envisaged as dogfood*) Ar.
2 (of a person) **cast forth, shed** —*a tear* (W.GEN. *fr. one's eyes*) Corinn.
3 throw (someone) **forth** (in abandonment or rejection); **cast out, expose** —*bodies* (*without burial*) Plu.; (fig.) **surrender** (W.ACC. *oneself*) **to despair** Hdt. || MID. **cast away, abandon** —*someone* (*on a desert island*) S.
4 put forward or offer (a person or thing, to someone); **present, offer** —*one's body* (W.DAT. *to someone, for sex*) E.fr. —(app.) *a right to do sthg.* S. —*a choice* Pl. —*a challenge* (*to someone*) AR.; **introduce** —*subjects of study* (W.DAT. *to children*) Pl.; **expose** —*someone* (W.DAT. *to the Nymphs, i.e. their influence*) Pl. —*oneself* (W.PREP.PHR. *to a curse*) S.; (of troops) perh. **bring to the fray** —*bitter contention* Il.; (fig.) **offer as a stake** (at dice), **risk** —*one's life* E.
5 bring forward (for the attention of others); **hold out, dangle** —*the name of peace* (W.DAT. *before someone*) D. || PASS. (of a saying) **be put about** Th.; (of a person) **have one's name brought up** —W.DAT. *before people* (*to remind them of sthg.*) Th.

πρόβασις

6 put forward, propound, pose (sts. W.DAT. for someone) —*a question, problem, riddle* Ar. Pl. Arist.
7 ‖ MID. put (someone) forward (for election or appointment); **propose** —*someone* Hdt. Pl. X. D. Din. Thphr. —(W.PREDIC.SB. *as an arbitrator*) D. —(W.INF. *to perform a public service*) And. ‖ PASS. (of persons) be proposed Hdt. Pl. Aeschin. D.
8 ‖ MID. **bring forward in one's support** —*witnesses* Isoc. Is.; **cite in one's support, appeal to, adduce** —*Homer* Pl.; **bring forward** (W.ACC. a nation, as an example) **to illustrate a point** Hdt.
9 put forward as an argument or excuse; **bring forward, appeal to, adduce** —*a sexual relationship* (*as creating an obligation*) E. ‖ MID. put (W.ACC. sthg.) **forward as an excuse** or **pretext** (for one's own behaviour) Th.; **put forward** —*an excuse, a pretext* Plb.
10 ‖ MID. (leg.) **present a preliminary accusation** —W.ACC. *against someone* D. —(W. 2ND ACC. *for some offence*) D. —(W.INF. *for committing some offence*) D.; (gener., in Roman ctxt.) **accuse, attack, censure** —*someone* Plu. ‖ PASS. (of a person) be the object of a preliminary accusation X. | see προβολή 8
11 cause (one thing) to go in front (of another); (of a charioteer) **get** (W.ACC. his horses' heads) **in front** (of rival horses) S.; (of a depicted horse, as an example of misunderstood movement) **move** (W.ACC. its right legs) **ahead** (of its left legs) Arist. ‖ MID. **lay** (W.ACC. a base of stones) **in front** (of a grave mound) Il.; (of a weaver) **set up** (W.ACC. one's work) **before oneself** Hes.; (of a rower) **stretch out** (W.DU. one's hands) **in front of oneself** Ar.; (fig.) get oneself in front of, **surpass, excel** —W.GEN. *someone* (+ DAT. *in sthg.*) Il.
12 ‖ MID. (milit.) **hold at the ready, level** —*one's weapons* X.; (intr.) **level one's spear** Plb.
13 ‖ MID. (milit.) place (someone or sthg.) in front of oneself (for protection); **put** (W.ACC. troops) **in front of oneself for cover** X.; **station** (W.ACC. troops, elephants) **in front** —W.GEN. or πρό + GEN. *of an army, its wings* Plb.; **protect oneself behind** —W.ACC. *a trench, wall, river* Plb.
14 ‖ MID. place (a shield) in front of oneself (for protection); **hold** (W.ACC. a shield) **in front of oneself** Carm.Pop. E.; (intr.) **provide protection** (w. one's shield) —w. πρό + GEN. *for vulnerable parts of one's body* X. ‖ PASS. (of a shield) be used for cover X. ‖ ACT. (gener.) **put up** —W.COGN.ACC. *a protective barrier* Pl.
15 ‖ MID. (fig.) use (sthg., as if a shield) for protection; **have** (W.ACC. cities, an island) **as a protective shield** —w. πρό + GEN. *for one's country* Isoc. D.; (intr.) **make protective arrangements** —w. ὑπέρ or πρό + GEN. *for a populace, a country* Aeschin. D.; (tr.) **shield oneself with, have for one's protection** —*hope, an alliance* D.; (intr., of a boxer) shield oneself with one's hands, **be on guard** D. ‖ PF. (of a soldier) have placed oneself (as a shield), stand as cover —w. πρό + GEN. *in front of someone* X.; (gener., of a person) be protector —W.GEN. *of someone* D. ‖ PF.PTCPL.ADJ. (of a person) on guard, wary Plu.; (fig., of a policy) guarded, cautious D.
16 ‖ MID. place (sthg.) in front of oneself for concealment; **hold out** (W.ACC. one's cloak) **in front of oneself** (to conceal an erect penis) Ar.; (of a naked youth) **use** (W.ACC. one's thighs) **for concealment** (of one's genitals) Ar.; (fig., of a person) **use** (W.ACC. sthg.) **as a cover** —w. πρό + GEN. *for one's shame* Aeschin.

πρόβασις ιος *Ion.f.* [προβαίνω] (collectv.) movable chattels, **cattle, livestock** (opp. κειμήλια *immovable property*) Od.

πρόβατα των *n.pl.* **1** walking animals (ref. to four-footed grazing animals), **cattle, livestock** Il. Hes. hHom. Hdt. Lyr.adesp.
2 (collectv.) **sheep** Th. Ar. Att.orats. Pl. X. +; (provbl., as a kind of animal preyed on by others) D. Plb. Plu. ‖ SG. **sheep** Ar. X. Men. Plb. Plu.
3 (fig.) **sheep** (derog., ref. to a group of stupid or lazy people) Ar.; (ref. to people viewed as under the guidance and protection of God or other leader) NT.

προβατείᾱ ᾱς *f.* **sheep-farming** Plu.(pl.)
προβατευτικός ή όν *adj.* (of the art) **of sheep-farming** X.
προβατική ῆς *fem.adj.* (w. πύλη understd.) **of the sheep** (ref. to a gate so-called at Jerusalem) NT.
προβάτιον ου *n.* [dimin. πρόβατον] **sheep** Ar. Pl. Men. Plu.; (provbl., as an example of a lazy animal) Ar.
προβατο-γνώμων ονος *m.* (fig., ref. to a king) **judge of the flock** (i.e. people) A.
προβατο-κάπηλος ου *m.* **sheep-dealer** Plu.
πρόβατον *n.sg.*: see πρόβατα
προβατο-πώλης ου *m.* [πωλέω] **sheep-seller** Ar.
προ-βέβουλα *pf.vb.* [βούλομαι] **prefer** —*someone* (W.GEN. *to another*) Il. —*death* (*to slavery*) Ion
πρόβημα ατος *n.* [προβαίνω] **step forward, step** Ar.(mock-trag.); (fig., ref. to an undertaking) E.(cj.)
προ-βιβάζω *vb.* | Att.fut. προβιβῶ | **1** cause (someone) to step forward; (of a blind man's guide) **lead** (him) **forward** S.; (of a commander) **lead forth** —*an army* Pi.*fr.*
2 cause (someone or sthg.) to advance towards a goal; **help** (W.ACC. someone) **forward** (in an investigation) Pl.; **lead** (W.ACC. someone) **on** —W.ADV. or PREP.PHR. *to some point, to virtue, or sim.* Ar. Pl. X.
3 advance, **make progress with** —*an undertaking* Plb.; **make** (W.NEUT.ACC. a little) **progress** (in solving a problem) Plb.
4 advance, **enhance** —*one's country* (*i.e. its prestige*) Plb. —*knowledge of sthg.* Plb.
5 lead on, egg on —*someone* (W.PREP.PHR. *to the divulging of secrets*) Plb. ‖ PASS. (of a person) be egged on (to do sthg.) NT.
προ-βιβάω *contr.vb.* | only masc.ptcpl. προβιβῶν | **go forward, advance** Hom. hHom.
—προβιβάς άντος *masc.athem.pres.ptcpl.* **go forward, advance** Hom.
προ-βιόω *contr.vb.* | pf.pass.ptcpl. προβεβιωμένος | ‖ NEUT.PL.PF.PASS.PTCPL.SB. one's earlier life Plb.
πρόβλημα ατος *n.* [προβάλλω] **1** that which is thrown forward or projects, **promontory** S.
2 (in military ctxts.) that which is placed in front (for protection); **protective device** (ref. to a shield made of animal-skins) Hdt.; **defence, protection** (W.GEN. for the body, ref. to a shield) A. Scol.; (W.GEN. for beached ships, ref. to palisades) E.; (W.GEN. against weapons, ref. to greaves) A.; **protective armour** (for a horse) X.; **protective barrier** (ref. to a river) Plb.
3 (gener.) means of protection, **protection, defence** Pl.; (W.GEN. against cold) E. Pl.; (W.GEN. against trouble, ref. to money) Ar.; (W.GEN. afforded by fear, i.e. by respect for military authority) S.; (fig.) **bulwark** (ref. to friends) Plu.
4 (fig., ref. to a person) **screen, cover** (W.GEN. for another person, i.e. to disguise his actions) S.; (ref. to a person's demeanour) **cloak** (W.GEN. for his real character) D.
5 question put forward for discussion and solution; **problem** (in geometry or sim.) Pl. Plu.; (in ethics, literary interpretation) Arist.
6 practical or theoretical difficulty, **problem, dilemma** Plb.

προβληματουργικός ή όν *adj.* [ἔργον] (of the capacity) for constructing defences Pl.

προβληματώδης ες *adj.* (of a circumstance) **problematical, hard to explain** Plu.

προβλής ῆτος *masc.fem.adj.* **1** (of a rock, a headland) **projecting, jutting** Hom. hHom. Archil. AR.; (of posts in a defensive wall) Il.
2 ‖ MASC.FEM.SB. **headland** S.

πρόβλητος ον *adj.* (of a corpse) **cast out, exposed** S.

προ-βλώσκω *vb.* | ep.aor.2 πρόμολον, ptcpl. προμολών | **come** or **go forward** or **forth** (fr. a place) Hom. AR. Theoc.

προ-βοάω *contr.vb.* **1 cheer on, shout encouragement** (to warriors) Il.
2 cry aloud —W.NEUT.ACC. *in a terrifying way* S.

προ-βοηθέω *contr.vb.* **bring help in advance** (before sthg. happens) Hdt.

προβόλαιος ον *adj.* [προβολή] **1** (of a spear) **held pointing forwards** (in readiness), **couched, levelled** Theoc.
2 ‖ MASC.SB. **levelled spear** Hdt.(oracle)

προβολή ῆς, dial. **προβολᾱ́** ᾶς *f.* [προβάλλω] **1 placing** (W.GEN. of a shield) **in front** (of oneself, for defence) Plb.
2 holding (of a spear) **forwards** (in readiness for defence or attack); **forward** or **levelled position** (opp. upright) X.; **stance with spear at the ready** (adopted by a body of soldiers) Plb. Plu.; **levelled spear** or **line of levelled spears** Plb. Plu.
3 (in boxing) **on-guard position** Theoc.
4 edging forwards (W.GEN. of one's body, by a boar-hunter) X.
5 (gener.) **what is placed in front** (of someone or sthg.) for protection or covering; **protection, defence** Pl. X. D.; (W.GEN. against terror and weapons, ref. to a person) S.; (against heat, ref. to flesh) Pl.; (against death, ref. to a plea for one's life) E.; (W.DAT. for one's eyes, afforded by eyelids) X.
6 projecting area or object; promontory, headland S.(cj.) Plb.; **spur** (W.GEN. of a mountain) Plu.; **pier** Plb.; **tip** (of a missile) Plb.
7 putting forward, proposal (of a person, for election to an office) Pl.
8 (leg.) **preliminary presentation of a case** (sts. W.GEN. against someone) Att.orats. X. Arist. [The term describes the procedure whereby an intending plaintiff might present an accusation against an individual before the Assembly, and thereby test public opinion before deciding whether to bring the case to a court of law. The vote of the Assembly had no binding legal force.]
9 (gener.) **prosecution** Plu.

προβόλιον ου *n.* **thrusting-spear** (for boar-hunting) X.

πρόβολος ου *m.* **1 projecting rock, headland** Od.
2 barrier, obstacle (fouling a harbour) D.; (W.GEN. of timber, breaking the force of a current) Plu.; (ref. to a nation lying betw. enemy nations) Plu.; (fig.) **stumbling-block** (ref. to a person) D.
3 fortress, bulwark (W.GEN. in war, ref. to a fort) X.; (fig., ref. to a person) Ar.
4 spear (for hunting) Hdt.

προ-βοσκίς ίδος *f.* [βόσκω] **trunk** (of an elephant) Plb. Plu.

προ-βοσκός οῦ *m.* **assistant herdsman** Hdt.

προβούλευμα ατος *n.* [προβουλεύω] **1 provisional resolution, preliminary decree, proposal** (of the Council, to be laid before the Assembly) Aeschin. D. Arist.
2 (gener.) **public decree** Plu.
3 (Lat.) *senatusconsultum* (recommendation of the Senate to a magistrate) Plu.

προ-βουλεύω *vb.* **1 plan in advance** —W.COMPL.CL. *how to do sthg.* Th.; **premeditate** (an action) Arist.(also mid.) ‖ MID. **decide** (W.ACC. sthg.) **provisionally** Hdt.; **think ahead** X. ‖ IMPERS.PF.PASS. **it has been planned** —W.COMPL.CL. *that sthg. shd. happen* Ar. ‖ PF.PASS.NEUT.PTCPL.SB. **premeditation** Arist.
2 (of official probouloi, at Athens) **hold preliminary discussion** Th.; (elsewhere) Arist.; (W.GEN. ahead of the popular assembly) Arist.; (of Spartan elders) Plu.
3 (specif., of the Council) **pass a preliminary decree, make a proposal** (to be laid before the Assembly) X. D. Arist.; **propose** —sthg. Aeschin. D. —W.ACC. + INF. *that someone shd. do sthg.* D.; **hold discussion ahead of** —W.GEN. *the Assembly* Plu. ‖ PASS. (of rewards) **be proposed** (by the Council) D. ‖ IMPERS.PF.PASS. **it has been proposed** —W.DAT. *by the Council* (W.ACC. + INF. *that sthg. shd. happen*) X. ‖ PF.PASS.NEUT.PTCPL.SB. (Lat.) *senatusconsultum* (recommendation of the Senate to a magistrate) Plb.
4 (of a person) **take precedence in policy-making** X.; **be chief counsellor** Plu.
5 think for or **about the interests of** —W.GEN. *someone* Ar. X.

προβουλή ῆς *f.* **premeditation** (of a crime) Antipho

πρό-βουλοι ων *m.pl.* [βουλή] **1 persons who discuss matters before others; preliminary counsellors** (officials who consider proposals before they are submitted to the people, playing the same role in an oligarchy as that of a council in a democracy) Ar. Arist. Plu.; (gener., in Roman ctxt.) **councillors** (of a city or nation) Plu.
2 (specif., committee of ten senior persons appointed at Athens in 413 BC after the Sicilian disaster) **counsellors** Lys. Ar. Arist.; (sg.) Ar.
3 persons who discuss matters on behalf of others, counsellors (W.GEN. of the people) A.
4 persons sent to a conference on behalf of others; delegates, representatives (W.GEN. of oneself, of Greece) Hdt.; (W.PREP.PHR. fr. Greece) Plu.
5 ‖ SG. (at Rome) **consul** Plu.

—**πρόβουλος** ον *adj.* (of Ruin) **who plans ahead, scheming** A.

προ-βράχεα (or **προβραχέα**) έων *n.pl.* [βράχεα or βραχύς] **shoals, shallows** Plb.

προ-βύω *vb.* | fut. προβύσω | **push forward** (a lamp-wick); **trim** —*a lamp* Ar.

προ-βώμιος ον *adj.* (of animal-sacrifices) **before altars** E. ‖ NEUT.PL.SB. **area before an altar** E. [or perh. *altar steps*]

προ-γαμέω *contr.vb.* (of a man) **marry earlier** (than a given time) Plu.

προ-γαργαλίζω *vb.* **tickle** (someone) **first** (before being tickled) Arist.(dub.)

προ-γένειος ον *adj.* [γένειον] (of a person) **with a prominent beard, full-bearded** Theoc.

προ-γενής ές *adj.* [γένος, γίγνομαι] (of gods) **ancestral** (w.connot. of being progenitors of a race, and perh. also protectors of it) S.

—**προγενέστερος** ᾱ ον *compar.adj.* **1** (of persons) **earlier in birth, older** (sts. W.GEN. than someone) Hom. Sapph. AR. Theoc.
2 living in an earlier time, earlier Plu.

—**προγενέστατος** η ον *superl.adj.* (of persons) **oldest** hHom. Plb.

προ-γεννήτωρ ορος *m.* **forefather, ancestor** E.

προ-γίγνομαι, Ion. **προγίνομαι** *mid.vb.* | pf. προγέγνημαι

|| pf.act. προγέγονα | 1 (of persons, animals) **come forth, come into view** Il. Hes. hHom. Call. Theoc.
2 (of persons) **be born earlier** (than a specified time) Hdt. || AOR. or PF.PTCPL.ADJ. (of persons, gods) **earlier** Hdt. Isoc. X. || MASC.PL.PF.PTCPL.SB. **predecessors** Isoc. X.
3 || MASC.PL.AOR.PTCPL.SB. **predecessors** (in a particular activity) Plb.
4 (of events, circumstances) **happen** or **arise earlier** Th. Pl. Aeschin. Arist. —w. πρό + GEN. *before sthg.* Pl. —W.GEN. Arist. || PRES.PTCPL.ADJ. (of examples) **previous** Th. || PF.PTCPL.ADJ. (of events, circumstances) **earlier** Th. + || NEUT.PL.PF.PTCPL.SB. **past events** Th. +

προ-γιγνώσκω, later **προγῑνώσκω** vb. | aor.2 προέγνων, ep.inf. προγνώμεναι | 1 **show forethought** E.; **think ahead** —w. ἐς + ACC. *to future glory* Th.
2 (tr.) **recognise in advance, foresee** —*a circumstance or eventuality* hHom. Th. Isoc. Pl. X. Plu. —W.ACC. + FUT.INF. *that someone will do sthg.* Th. —W.COMPL.CL. *that sthg. is the case* Pl. X.
3 **have prior knowledge of** —*sthg.* Pl. Arist. —*someone* NT. || PASS. (of things) **be already known** Arist.
4 || PASS. **be judged beforehand** —W.INF. *to be in the wrong* D.

πρόγνωσις εως *f.* **foreknowledge** (possessed by God) NT.
προγονικός ή όν *adj.* [πρόγονος] (of achievements, fame, friendships, a tomb) **of** or **relating to one's ancestors, ancestral** Plb. Plu.
πρό-γονος ου *m.f.* [γόνος] 1 (ref. to a lamb) **first-born, firstling** Od.
2 **child by a former marriage, stepchild** E. Is. Plu.
3 (oft.pl., of gods or humans) **forefather, ancestor** (of an individual or a nation) Callin. Pi. B. Hdt. Trag. Th. +; (appos.w. *cow, woman,* ref. to Io) **ancestress** A.
4 || PL. (fig., ref. to troubles) **parents** (W.GEN. of troubles) S.
πρόγραμμα ατος *n.* [προγράφω] 1 **written notice of business to be transacted, programme of business, agenda** (for an official body) D. Arist.
2 **edict** (of a Roman emperor) Plu.
προγραφή ῆς *f.* 1 **preface** or **list of contents** (of a historical work) Plb.
2 **public notice** X. Plb.
3 (at Rome) **proscription** (publication of the names of persons declared outlaws) Plu.
προ-γράφω vb. 1 (of a historian) **write about** (W.ACC. sthg.) **at the outset** Th.
2 (of officials) **announce publicly in writing, publish notice of** —*a trial, an Assembly, its agenda, or sim.* Ar. Aeschin. D. Arist. Plu. || PASS. (of business) **be put on the agenda** D.; (of garrison duty) **be posted up** D.; (of an indictment) **be published** Plu.
3 (in Roman ctxt.) **publish** (in a list of outlaws) **the name of, proscribe** —*someone* Plb. Plu. || PASS. (of persons) **be proscribed** Plb. Plu.
4 **write** (a name) **at the beginning of a document; prefix** —*someone's name* (*to authorise a decree*) Plu.
5 (of a Roman censor) **designate** (W.ACC. someone) **as leader** —W.GEN. *of the Senate* (*i.e. as princeps senatus*) Plu.
προ-γυμνάζομαι *mid.vb.* **take exercise earlier** Plu.
προ-δαῆναι aor.2 pass.inf. | ptcpl. προδαείς | **have foreknowledge** (of sthg.) Od. AR.; (tr.) **foresee** —*sthg.* AR.
προ-δανείζω vb. **lend in advance, lend, advance** —*money* (W.DAT. *to someone*) Arist.; (mid.) Hyp. || PASS. (fig., of an artist's time) **be given as an advance loan** —W.DAT. *for creative labour* Plu.

προ-δαπανάω contr.vb. **spend** (W.ACC. nothing) **in advance** X.
προ-δείδω vb. | aor.ptcpl. προδείσας | **be fearful in advance, be apprehensive** (of what is about to be heard) S.
προ-δείελος ον *adj.* (quasi-advbl., of a lion going to its den) **towards evening** Theoc.
προ-δείκνῡμι vb. —also (pres.) **προδεικνύω** (Hdt.) | Ion.aor. προέδεξα | 1 (of gods) **indicate in advance, foretell** —*coming events* Hdt. —W.COMPL.CL. or ACC. + FUT.INF. *that sthg. will happen* Plu.; **send in advance** —*a vision, warning signs* Hdt.; (of persons) **give advance notice** —W.ACC. + INF. *that sthg. is the case* Th. || PASS. (of an event) **be foretold** Plu.
2 **reveal** or **reveal first** —*the nature or identity of sthg.* A. S.
3 **show** (to someone) —*an object, an appropriate demeanour* (*for her to adopt*) Hdt.
4 (of a blind man) **reveal in front** (of himself), **point to** or **probe** —*the ground* (W.DAT. *w. a staff*) S.
5 **make a display** (to deceive); (of a boxer) **gesture** —W.NEUT.ADV. + DAT. *ineffectively, w. his hands* (*i.e. feint*) Theoc.; (of a cavalry commander) **feint** (by making deliberately misleading movements) X.; (tr., of a general) **feign** —*an intended attack* Plb.
προ-δειμαίνω vb. **fear in advance, be apprehensive of** —*everything* Hdt.
προδέκτωρ ορος *Ion.m.* [προδείκνῡμι] **forecaster** or **prophet** (ref. to the sun, its eclipse being regarded as an omen) Hdt.
προ-δέρκομαι *mid.vb.* **foresee** —*one's fate* A.
πρό-δηλος ον *adj.* [δῆλος] 1 (of future events or circumstances) **clearly foreseen** or **foreseeable**; (of danger, calamity, a person's fate, or sim.) **clear, plain, evident** Alc. E. Att.orats. X. Arist. +; (of actions) **deliberate** Is.; (of death in battle) **expected, certain** Plb.
2 (of present facts or circumstances) **plain to see, clear, evident** Att.orats. Pl. X.
3 (of enemies) **visible, open, declared** D.
4 (quasi-advbl., of persons) w. εἶναι + FUT.PTCPL. *be clearly about to do sthg.*, (of things) *be clearly about to happen* Att.orats.; (of a person) W.PTCPL. ὤν + ὅτι + PRES.INDIC. *it being clear that he is* (such and such) D.
5 || NEUT.SG.IMPERS. (usu. w. ἐστί) **it is clear** —w. ὅτι + FUT. *that sthg. will happen* X. D. —W.ACC. + FUT.INF. Pl. —w. ὅτι + AOR. *that sthg. was the case* Hyp.; (without COMPL.CL.) *the situation is clear* Men. || NEUT.PL.IMPERS. **it is clear** —w. ὅτι + PRES. *that someone intends* (*to do sthg.*) Hdt.
6 (prep.phr., ref. to seeing someone) ἐκ προδήλου **clearly** S.; (ref. to fighting) **openly** Plb. Plu.
—**προδήλως** adv. 1 **in full view, conspicuously** S.; **with conspicuous bravery** Plu.
2 **clearly, obviously, certainly** Isoc. Aeschin. Plb. Plu.
προ-δηλόω contr.vb. 1 (of persons) **make clear in advance** —W.COMPL.CL. *that they will do sthg., what they intend to do* Th.; (of omens, oracles, a dream) **foretell** —*future events* Plu. —W.ACC. + INF. *that someone is fated to do sthg.* Plu.
2 || PASS. (of news) **be clearly passed on** (by signallers) Plb.
3 || PF.PASS.PTCPL.ADJ. (of things) **previously described** Plb.
προδήλωσις εως *f.* **advance notice** (of one's prowess) Plu.
προ-διαβαίνω vb. (of a rider) **go across** (W.ACC. a ditch) **in advance** (of his horse) X.; (intr., of troops) **go across** (a sea, a river) **in advance** (of others) X. Plb. Plu.
προ-διαβάλλω vb. **take the initiative in slandering, create a prejudice against** —*someone* Th. Hyp. Plu. || PASS. **have prejudice created against one** Arist.

προ-διαγιγνώσκω vb. **1 fully understand** (W.ACC. the unpredictability of war) **first** (before engaging in it) Th. **2 decide** (sthg.) **in advance** Th.

προ-διαδίδωμι vb. **previously spread** —a report Plb.

προ-διαλαμβάνω vb. **1** (of a commander) **capture in advance** —narrow passes Th.(cj.) **2 decide in advance** (on sthg.) Plb. —W. περί + GEN. about sthg. Plb. —W. ὑπέρ + GEN. on a course of action Plb. —W.INF. to do sthg. Plb. —W.COMPL.CL. that sthg. is the case Plb. || IMPERS.AOR.PASS. a decision was reached earlier Plb. **3 recognise earlier** —W.COMPL.CL. that sthg. is the case Plb.

προ-διαλέγομαι mid.vb. | aor.pass.inf. (w.mid.sens.) προδιαλεχθῆναι | **1 speak by way of preface** Isoc. —W.NEUT.ACC. a few words Isoc. **2 have discussion beforehand** —W.DAT. w. someone Plu.

προ-διαλύω vb. (of soldiers) **break** (W.ACC. their ranks) **earlier** Plb.

προ-διαπέμπομαι mid.vb. **send on** (W.ACC. someone) **in advance** Plb.; (intr.) **send a message in advance** Plb.

προ-διασπείρω vb. **spread in advance** —a rumour Arist.

προ-διασύρω vb. **pull** (an opponent's arguments) **to pieces beforehand** (i.e. before they have been stated) Arist.

προ-διαφθείρω vb. **1 destroy beforehand** —ships Plb. || PASS. (of a city) be destroyed beforehand Th.; (of a person) be ruined beforehand Th.; (of troops, commanders) be killed previously Isoc. **2 corrupt beforehand** —judges, officers D. || PASS. (of a populace) be corrupted beforehand —W.DAT. by promises Plu.

προ-διαχωρέω contr.vb. **have a previous disagreement** —W.DAT. w. someone Arist.

προ-διδάσκω vb. | aor. προυδίδαξα | **give prior instruction** (for later application); **instruct, teach** —someone Ar.(also mid.) Pl. —W.DBL.ACC. someone, sthg. S.(also mid.) Ar. Aeschin. Plu. —W.ACC. + INF. someone to do sthg. S. D. || PASS. receive tuition D.; receive tuition first —w. πρότερον ἤ + INF. before doing sthg. Th.

προ-δίδωμι vb. | aor. προέδωκα, also προύδωκα || neut.impers.vbl.adj. προδοτέον | **1 give** or **pay in advance** —money, wages X. Plb. || PASS. (of money) be advanced Plb. **2 deliver up, hand over** —persons, places, possessions (sts. W.DAT. to someone) Hdt. Trag. Ar. Att.orats. Pl. +; **betray** —a cause Ar.; **surrender** —an opportunity (to an enemy) D.; (of a bribed charioteer) —victory (to a rival) Pl. || PASS. (of persons, places) be betrayed Hdt. +; (of secrets) E. **3** (intr.) **turn traitor** Hdt.; **be guilty of** —W.COGN.ACC. betrayal Din.; (fig., of an oracle, a hope) **prove false** A.; (of gratitude, meton. for those expected to show it) S. **4** (wkr.sens.) **desert** or **let down** —someone Thgn. Trag. Ar. Att.orats. Pl. + —oneself (i.e. give up) E. Ar. Pl.; **abandon** —W.ACC. + INF. someone to death E.; **give up** —a legal case Aeschin. **5 fail in loyalty or obligation; betray** —someone's kindness E. —truth, justice Pl. —an oath X. —an oracle Ar. —a vote (by disregarding it) D. **6 fall short of what is required or expected**; (of a barricade) **fail** (someone) Hdt.; (tr., of an eye, i.e. sight) —someone D.; (of lower bricks) —those above (by not supporting them) X.; (of a mattock) **disappoint** —its user's hopes (by failing to do its job) Ar.; (intr., of wine) **run out** Xenoph.; (of streams) **run dry** Hdt.; (of pleasures) **give out** S.

προ-διεξέρχομαι mid.vb. **1** (of foxes) **go across** (a hare's track) **before** (the hounds reach it) X. **2 go through an account beforehand**; **explain first** —W.INDIR.Q. how sthg. stands Aeschin.

προ-διεργάζομαι pass.vb. (of a pupil's mind, envisaged as land to be cultivated) **be worked on thoroughly in advance** Arist.

προ-διερευνάομαι mid.contr.vb. **reconnoitre thoroughly** X.

προ-διερευνητής οῦ m. **one who reconnoitres, scout** Plu.

προ-διέρχομαι mid.vb. | aor.2 προδιῆλθον | pf. προδιελήλυθα | **1 go through in advance** || PF. (of a person's prowess) **have already permeated** —the hearing of a nation X. **2 explain first** —W.INDIR.Q. how sthg. has been done Aeschin.

προ-διευκρινέομαι pass.contr.vb. (of political institutions) **be already well arranged** Plb.

προ-διηγέομαι mid.contr.vb. **recount** or **explain** (W.ACC. sthg.) **first** Hdt. D.

προ-διήγησις εως f. **preliminary exposition** (ref. to part of a speech) Aeschin. Arist.

προδικασία ᾶς f. [δικάζω] **preliminary hearing** (in a lawsuit) Antipho

πρό-δικος ου m. [δίκη] **1 principal in a lawsuit, prosecutor** A. **2** (at Sparta) **guardian** (of a young king) X. Plu.

προ-διοικέομαι mid.contr.vb. **arrange in advance** —W. ὅπως + FUT. that sthg. shd. happen Aeschin. || PASS. (of a decree) be planned in advance D.

προ-διομολογέομαι mid.contr.vb. **agree on** (W.ACC. sthg.) **beforehand** Pl. || PASS. (of a proposition) be already agreed on Pl. Arist.

προ-διώκω vb. (of troops) **pursue in advance** (of others), **break out in pursuit** Th.

προ-δοκαί ῶν f.pl. [δέχομαι] **place where one lies in wait** (for an animal), **place of ambush, hide** Il.

προ-δοκέομαι pass.contr.vb. (of things) **be already decided** Th.; **be already believed** Pl.

πρόδομα ατος n. [προδίδωμι] **advance payment** Plb.

πρό-δομος ου m. —or perh. **πρόδομον** ου n. [δόμος] | only dat. προδόμῳ | **1 porch, vestibule** (before the entrance to a hall or dwelling, sts. used as a sleeping-place for visitors) Hom. AR.; (before the entrance to a temple) AR. **2 ante-chamber** (of a bedroom) AR.

—**πρόδομος** ον adj. **1** (of songs of praise) **sung before a house** B. **2** (quasi-advbl., of a person coming) **in front of a house** E.

προ-δοξάζω vb. **form an opinion beforehand** Pl. Arist. || IMPERS.PF.PASS. an opinion has already been formed Arist.

προδοσία ᾶς, Ion. **προδοσίη** ης f. [προδίδωμι] **betrayal** (of persons or places) Hdt. E. Th. Att.orats. Pl. +; (of a nation's liberty) D.; (gener.) **treason, treachery** A.fr. Hdt. Th. Att.orats. Pl. +

πρόδοσις εως f. **1 that which is given in advance, advance payment** D. **2 act of betrayal, treason** Pl.

προδοτέον (neut.impers.vbl.adj.): see προδίδωμι

προδότης ου, dial. **προδότᾱς** ᾶ m. **traitor, betrayer** (usu. of persons, places or causes, sts. w.gener.ref. to one who is faithless or unreliable) Timocr. Hdt. Trag. Th. +

—**προδότις** ιδος f. **female traitor, traitress** E. Ar.

πρόδοτος ον adj. (of persons, their life) **betrayed, let down** S. E.

πρό-δουλος ον adj. [δοῦλος] (of footwear) **serving** (the feet) **like slaves** A.

προ-δραμεῖν aor.2 inf. | The pres. and impf. are supplied by προτρέχω. | **1** (of persons or animals) **run forward** Antipho X. Thphr. NT. Plu.; **run ahead** —W.GEN. of someone X.

2 (fig., of a report) **run ahead** (of more reliable information) Plu.

προδρομεύω *vb.* [πρόδρομος] (of cavalry) **serve as the advance contingent** Arist.

προδρομή ῆς *f.* **running forward, sally** (by an individual) X. ‖ PL. (fig.) **sallies** (W.GEN. of argument) Pl.

πρό-δρομος ον *adj.* [δραμεῖν] **1** (of a person, a group of horsemen) **running forward, rushing headlong** A. S.
2 (of an army, a herald, a messenger) **going on in advance** Hdt. E.
3 ‖ MASC.SB. (usu. W.GEN.) **forerunner** (of others, ref. to a person arriving earlier) Pl.; (of dawn, the sun, ref. to the morning star) Ion E.
4 ‖ MASC.PL.SB. **advance contingent** (of soldiers or horsemen) Hdt. Th. Plu.; (specif., ref. to a body of light-armed Athenian cavalry) X. Arist.; (ref. to scouts) Plb. Plu. ‖ SG. **advance skirmisher** Plu.

προ-δυστυχέω *contr.vb.* **suffer earlier misfortune** Isoc.

προδωσ-έταιρος ον *adj.* [προδίδωμι, ἑταῖρος] (of a fort) **that has betrayed one's comrades** Scol.

προ-εγείρω *vb.* **rouse** (W.ACC. oneself, one's reasoning faculty) **in advance** (of experiencing an emotion) Arist.

προ-εγκάθημαι *mid.vb.* (of passionate feelings) **be already settled** —W.DAT. *in people* Plb.

προ-εγχειρέω *contr.vb.* **attempt** (sthg.) **earlier** Plb.

προέδεξα (Ion.aor.): see προδείκνῡμι

προεδρεύω *vb.* [πρόεδροι] **1 act as a presiding officer** (of the Council or Assembly) Att.orats. Arist.
2 (of a tribe) **preside** (over the Assembly) Aeschin. D. [A law of 346/5 BC prescribed that members of a designated tribe should sit together near the speakers' platform and be responsible for the orderly conduct of the meeting.]

προεδρίᾱ ᾱς, Ion. **προεδρίη** ης *f.* ‖ ῐ *metri grat.* (Xenoph.) ‖ **1 right to a front seat** (at games, festivals, theatres, public assemblies, granted to distinguished foreigners; at Athens, also to certain officials and persons regarded as public benefactors) Xenoph. Hdt. Ar. Att.orats. Pl. +; (concr.) **front seat** or **seats** Ar. Pl. Aeschin. Din.
2 (concr.) **front seat** (of Darius, watching his troops cross the bridge over the Hellespont) Hdt.
3 presidency (of a tribe, in the Assembly) Aeschin.
4 position of importance (of a citizen, in the state) Arist.; (of the aulos, in education) Plu.; **pre-eminence** (of an individual, among others) Plu.; **first place** (for a month, in the calendar) Plu.
5 (in Roman ctxt.) **special privileges** (of a senator or official) Plb. Plu.; **seniority** (of the *princeps senatus*) Plu.

προεδρικός ή όν *adj.* (of a prosecution) **relating to presidency** (of the Council or Assembly) Arist.

πρό-εδροι ων *m.pl.* [ἕδρᾱ] **1 presiding officers** (of the Council or Assembly, ref. to a board of nine, who assumed this function, previously exercised by the πρυτάνεις, at the beginning of the 4th C. BC) Att.orats. Arist.; (sg.) Aeschin. D. Plu.
2 (ref. to five persons appointed at Athens in 411 BC to set up the oligarchy of the Four Hundred) Th.
3 (ref. to officials at Mytilene) Th.; (ref. to officials in a lawcourt) Pl.

προ-εέργω *ep.vb.* [εἴργω²] (of a warrior) **block by standing in front, bar** —W.ACC. + INF. *an enemy fr. making his way* Il.

προέηκα (ep.aor.1), **προεθείς** (aor.pass.ptcpl.): see προίημι

προ-εθίζω *vb.* ‖ neut.impers.vbl.adj. προεθιστέον ‖ **make** (someone) **accustomed** (to sthg.) **by prior training; accustom** —W.ACC. + INF. *oneself to do sthg.* Plu. ‖ PASS. **become accustomed** (to sthg.) X. Arist.

προεῖδον (aor.2): see προοράω

προ-εικάζω *vb.* **guess in advance** —*future events* Arist.

προεῖμαι (pf.pass.), **προείμην** (athem.aor.mid.): see προίημι

πρό-ειμι¹ *vb.* [εἰμί] ‖ only Ion.neut.pl.pres.ptcpl. (tm.) πρὸ ... ἐόντα ‖ (of events) **be earlier** (in time) Il. Hes. Sol.

πρό-ειμι² *vb.* [εἶμι] ‖ Only pres. and impf. (other tenses are supplied by προέρχομαι). The pres.indic. has fut. sense. ‖
1 (of persons, troops, animals) **go forward, advance, proceed** Hdt. Th. Ar. Pl. +
2 (of land, fr. the silting of the Nile Delta) **grow in extent, increase** Hdt.
3 (of time, days, night) **go on, pass** Hdt. Th. Att.orats. Pl. +; (of a person's age) **advance** Pl.
4 go forward in an activity or course of action; (of persons) **proceed, continue** Isoc. Pl. —W.PREP.PHR. *indefinitely* Arist.; (of a horse) **progress** —W.PREP.PHR. *to a further stage of training* X.
5 (of an activity, a speech, an acquaintance, or sim.) **go on, proceed, progress** Hdt. Att.orats. Pl. X.
6 (of persons) **move on ahead** (of others), **go in advance** or **in front** Hdt. X.; **go ahead** —W.GEN. *of someone* Hdt. Ar.; **go further ahead** —W.GEN. *than is appropriate* X.
7 come forth —W.ADV. *out of doors* Ar.; **come out** (fr. inside) Men.

προεῖναι (athem.aor.inf.): see προίημι

προ-εῖπον *aor.2 vb.* —also **προεῖπα** *aor.1 vb.* **1 foretell, predict** —*sthg.* Pl. D. —W.COMPL.CL. *that someone is close to death* Aeschin.
2 say (W.ACC. sthg.) **first** or **by way of preface** Att.orats. Arist.; **mention** (W.ACC. sthg.) **previously** Th. Att.orats. +; **say** (sthg.) **earlier** Att.orats. +
3 (of gods) **warn** (W.DAT. someone) **earlier** —W. μή + INF. *not to do sthg.* Od.(tm.)
4 give advance notice (of one's intention) Th.
5 (of persons in authority) **declare publicly, announce, proclaim** (oft. W.DAT. to someone) —*war, friendly relations* Hdt. X. —*a sentence of death* Ar. Pl. —*someone's commands, a decree* Hdt. S. —*contests, prizes* X. —W.COMPL.CL. *that sthg. is or will be the case* Hdt. Th. Isoc. Pl. —W.FUT.INF. *that one will do sthg.* Hdt. And.; **make** (W.NEUT.ACC. this) **proclamation** Hdt.
6 order publicly, issue an order —W.INF. or DAT. + INF. (*to someone*) *to do sthg.* Hdt. Th. Pl. + —W.ACC. + INF. *that someone shd. do sthg., that sthg. shd. happen* Hdt. Th. —W.ACC. + DAT. *for sthg., to someone* Th.; **issue** (W.ACC. sthg.) **as an order** Hdt.
7 (leg., of a prosecutor) **give public notice** —W.DAT. *to someone* (W.GEN. *of a charge of murder*) D. ‖ cf. προαγορεύω 6

προ-είρω *vb.* [εἴρω²] ‖ pres. not found ‖ fut. προερῶ ‖ pf. προείρηκα ‖ PASS.: aor. προερρήθην, also προυρρήθην, inf. προρρηθῆναι ‖ pf. προείρημαι ‖ neut.impers.vbl.adj. προρρητέον ‖
1 say (sthg.) **beforehand** Pl. X.; **mention** (W.ACC. sthg.) **beforehand** Pl. Aeschin.; **say** (W.ACC. sthg.) **at the outset** or **by way of preface** Att.orats. Pl. ‖ PASS. (of things) **be said or mentioned beforehand** Hdt. Att.orats. Pl. X.; **be said by way of preface** Isoc. Aeschin.
2 say (sthg.) **publicly; hold forth** —W.DAT. *to people* Ar.; **announce, proclaim** —W.DIR.SP. *sthg.* Ar. —W.DAT. + COMPL.CL. *to someone, that sthg. must be done* Hdt.; **declare** —*war* (W.DAT. *on someone*) Th. ‖ PASS. (of war) **be declared** X.

3 order publicly, **issue an order** —w.INF. or w.DAT. + INF. (*to someone*) *to do sthg.* Hdt. X. D. ǁ PASS. (of an item, a day, a place, or sim.) **be prescribed or pre-arranged** Hdt. Th. Att.orats. X. ǁ IMPERS.PASS. (AOR., PF. or PLPF.) **orders were, have or had been given** —w.INF. or w.DAT. + INF. (*to someone*) *to do sthg.* Hdt. Antipho Th. X. —w. ὅπως + FUT. *that someone shd. do sthg.* Pl.

προείς (athem.aor.ptcpl.): see προίημι

προ-εισάγω *vb.* **1** (of a writer) **bring in, introduce** (w.ACC. a subject) **first** (before other subjects) Plu.

2 ǁ PF.PASS. (of a child) **have been introduced already** (to members of a phratry, for enrolment in it) D.

3 (intr., of an actor) **come on stage earlier** —w.GEN. *than another actor* Arist.

προ-εισδέομαι *pass.contr.vb.* [δέω¹] (of a people) **be bound by previous ties** (of alliance) Plb.

προ-εισέρχομαι *mid.vb.* | aor.2 προεισῆλθον | pf. προεισελήλυθα | **go inside first** (before others) D. Plu.; **go on ahead and enter** (a city) Plu.

προ-εισπέμπω *vb.* **send** (w.ACC. someone) **inside first** (before oneself) X.

προ-εισφέρω *vb.* **1** (of a person) **make advance payment of emergency tax** (i.e. the total amount due fr. several individuals, whose contributions will be collected later) D.

2 (gener.) **make an advance contribution** (of money) Plu. —w.ACC. *of one's wealth* Plu.

προεισφορά ᾶς *f.* **advance payment of emergency tax** D.

προ-εκδαπανάομαι *pass.contr.vb.* (of a river, ref. to its water) **be exhausted in advance** (by canals, before reaching the sea) Plb.

προ-εκδίδωμι *vb.* **publish** (w.ACC. a treatise) **beforehand** Plb.

προ-εκδραμεῖν *aor.2 inf.* (of a soldier) **run out ahead** (of others) Plu.

προέκθεσις εως *f.* [προεκτίθημι] **preliminary summary** (of a historical narrative) Plb.

προ-εκθέω *contr.vb.* (of soldiers) **run out in front, sally forth** Th.

προ-εκκομίζω *vb.* **1 carry out** (w.ACC. a statue) **beforehand** (fr. a temple) Hdt.

2 ǁ PASS. (of a person) **be removed** —w.GEN. *fr. trouble* (w.PREP.PHR. *by good fortune*) Plu.

προ-εκλέγομαι *pass.vb.* | pf.ptcpl. προεξειλεγμένος | (of money) **be collected in advance** D.

προ-εκλύω *vb.* (of a commander) **weaken in advance** —*enemy soldiers' bodies* (by tiring them w. a preliminary attack) Plb.

προ-εκπέμπω *vb.* **send out ahead** —*troops, goods* Plu.

προ-εκπίπτω *vb.* (of gossip and rumour) **issue forth, spread** Plu.

προ-εκπλέω *contr.vb.* (of a person, a ship) **sail out ahead** (of others) Plu.

προ-εκπλήσσω *vb.* (of a politician seeking power) **startle** (w.ACC. people) **beforehand** (w. oracles) Plu.

προ-εκτίθημι *vb.* ǁ MID. (of a historian) **give a preliminary summary of** —*the contents of a work* Plb. Plu.

προ-εκφοβέω *contr.vb.* **terrify** (w.ACC. enemy troops) **beforehand** (w. sights or sounds) Plu.

προεκφόβησις εως *f.* **creation of early panic** (in enemy troops) Th.

προέλασις εως *f.* [προελαύνω] **riding forward, advance** (of cavalry) X.

προ-ελαύνω *vb.* **1 ride ahead** X. —w.GEN. *of someone* X.

2 ǁ IMPERS.PLPF.PASS. **the time was advanced** —w.PREP.PHR. *far into the night* Hdt.

προ-έλκω *vb.* | aor. προείλκυσα | **drag forth** —*someone* (*out of doors*) Men.

προ-εμβαίνω *vb.* **go on board** (a ship) **first** (before someone) Plu.

προ-εμβάλλω *vb.* **1 instil** (w.ACC. confidence) **beforehand** —w.DAT. *in someone* Plb. ǁ PASS. (of extra conjunctions, together w. their clauses) **be inserted before** —w.GEN. *a resumptive conjunction* (*and its clause*) Arist.

2 (intr., of the horns of certain grazing cows) **bump** (w.PREP.PHR. into the ground) **in front** (of them) Hdt.

3 ram (an opposing ship) **first** Th.; **inflict** (w.ACC. + DAT. a fatal blow on a ship) **by ramming** Plb.

4 (of a soldier) **get in the first blow** —w.DAT. *against an opponent* Plu.

προ-εμβιβάζω *vb.* **involve** (w.ACC. someone) **beforehand** —w. εἰς + ACC. *in hostility, war* Plb.

προέμεν (ep.athem.aor.inf.), **προέμενος** (athem.aor.mid.ptcpl.): see προίημι

προ-ενδείκνυμαι *mid.vb.* **put on a show in advance, ingratiate oneself beforehand** —w.DAT. *w. someone* Aeschin.

προ-ενεργέω *contr.vb.* **practise first** (certain abilities, as a necessary preliminary to possessing them) Arist.

προ-ενοίκησις εως *f.* **previous occupation** (w.DBL.GEN. of an island, by a people) Th.

προ-ενσείω *vb.* (fig., of a commander) **hurl** (w.ACC. one's troops) **first** —w.DAT. *at one's opponent* Plu.

προ-εντυγχάνω *vb.* **1** (of ambassadors) **have a meeting** (w.DAT. w. the Council) **first** (before the Assembly) Plu.

2 (of a person's appearance) **catch one's attention in advance** —w.GEN. *of his speaking* Plu.

προ-εξαγγέλλω *vb.* **report** (w.ACC. sthg.) **in advance** D.

προ-εξαγκωνίζω *vb.* (fig., of an orator, envisaged as a wrestler) **engage in a preliminary grapple** Arist.

προ-εξάγω *vb.* **1 bring out** (w.ACC. booty) **first** (fr. a city, before burning it) Hdt.

2 lead out (w.ACC. troops, fr. a city) **first** (before another manoeuvre) Th.

3 (euphem.) **remove** (w.ACC. oneself) **prematurely** —w.PREP.PHR. *fr. life* (*i.e. commit suicide*) Plb.

4 ǁ MID. (of sailors) **put out** (to sea) **in advance** Th.(dub., cj. προεξανάγομαι).

προεξαΐσσω *Ion.vb.*: see προεξάσσω

προ-εξαλείφομαι *pass.vb.* (of registers of payments due) **be wiped clean in advance, be cancelled prematurely** Arist.

προ-εξαμαρτάνω *vb.* **make a mistake at the outset** Isoc.

προεξανάγομαι *mid.vb.*: see προεξάγω

προ-εξανίσταμαι *mid.vb.* | athem.aor.act. προεξανέστην |

1 (of a combatant) **get up from the ground first** (before his opponent) Plu.

2 (of a soldier) **start forward from one's position first** (before others) Hdt.

3 (of a ruler, a populace) **make the first move, take the initiative** (in war) Plu.; (of persons) **spring into action first** (before sthg. happens) D. —w.GEN. *before others* Arist.

4 start prematurely; (of runners) **be too quick off the mark** Hdt. Plu.; (of ambushers) **spring out too soon** Plu.

προ-εξαποστέλλω *vb.* **send off** (w.ACC. someone) **in advance** Plb.

προ-εξάσσω, Ion. **προεξαΐσσω** *vb.* | aor.ptcpl. προεξάξας | (of soldiers) **dart out ahead** (of the main body) Hdt. Th.

προ-εξέδρη ης *Ion.f.* [ἐξέδρα] **prominent seat** (of white stone, fr. which Darius watched his troops cross the bridge over the Hellespont) Hdt.

προεξειλεγμένος (pf.pass.ptcpl.): see προεκλέγομαι

προ-έξειμι vb. [ἔξειμι²] (of troops) **advance out** —W.GEN. *of camp* Th.
προ-εξελαύνω vb. **1** (of soldiers) **ride out in front** Plu. **2 move out ahead** (of a fleet) —W.DAT. *w. one's ship* Plu.
προ-εξέρχομαι mid.vb. | aor.2 προεξῆλθον | pf. προεξελήλυθα | (of troops) **go out** (fr. a city) **beforehand** Th.; (of a person) **leave** (a country) **beforehand** Plb.
προ-εξορμάω contr.vb. **start out early** (on a journey) X.
προ-επαινέω contr.vb. (derog., of persons purporting to be connoisseurs of oratory) **praise** (a speaker's remark) **in advance** (of its being made) Th.
προ-επανασείω vb. [ἐπί, ἀνασείω] **wave** (sthg.) **threateningly at someone in advance** ‖ PASS. (of military preparations) **be set in motion as a warning** (to someone) Th.
προ-επιβάλλω vb. (fig.) **lay** (W.ACC. + DAT. hands, on someone) **in advance** (i.e. attack them first) Plb.
προ-επιβουλεύω vb. **form plans against** (W.DAT. someone) **in advance** Th. ‖ PASS. **be the victim of forward planning** Th.
προ-επιδείκνῡμι vb. **demonstrate beforehand** —W.COMPL.CL. *that sthg. is the case* Isoc.
προ-επιπλήττω (v.l. **προσ-**) Att.vb. [ἐπιπλήσσω] **rebuke** (W.DAT. oneself) **in advance** (as a rhetorical technique) Arist.
προ-επίσταμαι mid.vb. **know** (sts. W.ACC. sthg.) **already** Isoc. Pl. X. Arist.
προ-επιχειρέω contr.vb. **be first to attack** Th. Plu.
προ-εργάζομαι mid.vb. **1 do work in advance** —W.DAT. *for someone* (i.e. save him the trouble of doing it himself) Hdt.; (tr.) **work for** —*the common good* Hdt. **2 work on in advance, prepare** —*fallow land* (W.DAT. *for sowing*) X. **3** ‖ PF. or PLPF.PASS. (of work) **have already been done** Th.; (of a person's reputation) **have been already won** X.; (of an argument) **have been elaborated beforehand** Th.; (of actions) **have been performed in the past** Isoc. ‖ NEUT.PL.PF.PASS.PTCPL.SB. *past actions or achievements* Antipho Th.
προ-ερέσσω vb. **row** (sts. W.ACC. a ship) **ahead** Hom.
προ-ερευνάομαι mid.contr.vb. (of cavalry) **scout ahead** X.
προερρήθην (aor.pass.): see προείρω
προ-ερύω vb. | pf.aor. προέρυσσα | **haul forward** —*a ship* (to the sea, for launching) Il.
προ-έρχομαι mid.vb. | impf. προηρχόμην (NT.) | aor.2 προῆλθον | pf. προελήλυθα ‖ Fut. (and usu. impf.) are supplied by πρόειμι². | **1** (of persons, troops, animals) **go forward, proceed, advance** (sts. W.ADV. or PREP.PHR. to or fr. a place) Hdt. Th. Isoc. Pl. X. + —W.INTERN.ACC. *on a journey* Pl. —W.DAT. *in imagination* Aeschin.; (of a dangerous situation) **reach** —W.PREP.PHR. *as far as a certain region* Th. **2** (of a herald) **come forward** (to speak) Hdt. Aeschin.; (of a speaker) Th. Aeschin. Plb. **3** (of a person) **come forth** (fr. indoors) Men. **4 go in front** X. —W.GEN. *of someone* X.; **arrive ahead of** —W.ACC. *someone* NT. **5 arrive first** (before sthg. can happen) Th.; **travel first** (before others) —W.ACC. *on a road* Pl. **6** (of time) **go on, advance, pass** Th. Pl. D. Arist.; (of things) —W.PREP.PHR. *along w. time* Pl. ‖ PF. (of persons) **be advanced** —W.DAT. *in age* X. **7** (of persons) **proceed, progress** (in a course of action or in speech) Pl.; (of an activity, a discussion) Th. Pl. **8 go forward** (in a course of action or speech) **to a given point; proceed, advance** —W.ADVBL. or PREP.PHR. *further, to this point, to the extreme of audacity, or sim.* Isoc. Pl. X. D. Arist. **9** (of a person's conduct, a situation) **proceed, develop** —W.ADVBL. or PREP.PHR. *further, shamefully, to some point* Pl. D. **10** (of a country's power, a city) **increase, grow** —W.PREP.PHR. *to some point* Hdt. Arist.
προερῶ (fut.): see προείρω
πρόες (ep.athem.aor.imperatv.), **πρόεσαν** (ep.3pl.athem. aor.), **προέσθαι** (athem.aor.mid.inf.): see προίημι
πρόεσις εως f. [προίημι] **giving away** (opp. getting) Arist.
προετέον (neut.impers.vbl.adj.): see προίημι
προετικός ή όν adj. (of a person) **of the kind that gives away, inclined to be prodigal** or **generous** X. Arist.; (W.DAT. to people) Arist.
—**προετικῶς** adv. **generously, lavishly** —*ref. to spending* Arist.
προ-ετοιμάζομαι mid.vb. **arrange** (W.NEUT.ACC. sthg.) **in advance** Hdt. ‖ IMPERS.PASS. **advance arrangements are made** Hdt.
προέτω (ep.3sg.athem.aor.imperatv.): see προίημι
προ-ευλαβέομαι mid.contr.vb. | aor.pass.ptcpl. (w.mid.sens.) προευλαβηθείς | **take precautions in advance** D.
προ-εφίστημι vb. **direct the attention of** (W.ACC. + PREP.PHR. someone, to sthg.) **in advance** Plb.
προ-έχω, also contr. **προύχω** vb. | iteratv.impf. προύχεσκον | fut. προέξω | aor.2 πρόεσχον ‖ aor.2 mid. προυσχόμην, ep. προεσχεθόμην (Theoc.) | **1 have** or **hold** (sthg.) **in front** (of oneself); **hold** (W.ACC. a shield) **in front** —W.GEN. *of one's thigh* Ar.; **put out** —*one's hands* (as if a boxer, to fend off a blow) X. ‖ MID. **hold before oneself** —*one's spear* Il.(tm.) —*one's shield* AR. —*one's arrows and cloak* Theoc. —*a bearskin* (for protection) AR. —*a ram's head, a robe* (for concealment) Hdt. AR.; **stretch forth** —*one's head* (to hear) AR.; **hold at arm's length** —*a baby* (while it defecates) Ar.; app. **have before oneself** —*a sacrificial animal* Od. **2** ‖ MID. **put forward, propose, offer** —*terms* (W.DAT. *to someone*) Th. **3** ‖ MID. **put forward as an argument or excuse; allege** (W.NEUT.ACC. sthg.) **as an excuse** S.; **claim** or **pretend** —W.ACC. + INF. (w. ἄν) *that* (if some condition were fulfilled) *sthg. would happen* Th. **4** (intr., of a headland, hill, building, object) **project forward** (relative to its surroundings), **jut out, project** Hom. hHom. Hdt. E. Th. +; (of a broad hat) —W.GEN. *fr. someone's head* Call. **5 be ahead** (of others) **in distance** or **time**; (of a charioteer, a horse) **be in front** (in a race) Il.; (of a commander's horse) **be out in front** —W.GEN. *of other horses* Hdt.; (of troops) **keep ahead** (sts. W.GEN. of others) —W.DAT. *by a day's march* Hdt.; (of a ship) **be ahead** (of others) X. —W.DAT. *by a day and a night* Th. ‖ AOR. (of a runner) **be the winner** —W.DAT. *by a head* X. **6 have an advantage** (sts. W.GEN. over someone) Att.orats. ‖ IMPERS. **it is advantageous** —W.INF. *to do sthg.* Hdt. **7** (of a person) **be senior** (sts. W.GEN. to someone) —W.DAT. *in age* Pl. Men. —*by a number of years* Pl. **8 be ahead** (of others) **in rank** or **quality**; (of persons) **stand out** —W.GEN. *fr. the people* (i.e. be leaders) hHom.; (of a populace) **be the foremost member** —W.GEN. *of a race* Hdt.; (of persons or things) **be pre-eminent** or **superior** (usu. W.DAT. or PREP.PHR. in sthg.) Th. Isoc. Pl. X. Arist.; **be superior to, surpass** —W.GEN. *someone or sthg.* (sts. W.DAT.

or PREP.PHR. *in sthg.*) Hdt. S. Th. Isoc. X. Call. —(W.ACC. *in sthg.*) Hes.*fr.*; (of a system of government) **be best** Hdt.
‖ PRES.PTCPL.ADJ. (of kinds of life) **principal** Arist.
‖ NEUT.PTCPL.SB. **superiority** Th.
9 possess (sthg.) **beforehand**; **be the first recipient** (in an exchange) Arist.; **know already** —*someone's feelings* Hdt.

προήγαγον (aor.2): see προάγω

προ-ηγεμών όνος *m.* **leader, guide** (of persons celebrating mystery rites) D.

προ-ηγέομαι *mid.contr.vb.* **1** (in military ctxts.) **go first and lead the way**; (of a detachment) **lead the way** (in an army on the march) Hdt. X. —W.GEN. *ahead of others* X.; (of a bird of omen) **fly ahead as a guide** X.; (of a cavalry commander) **ride at the head** —W.GEN. *of his men* Plb.; (gener., of soldiers) **be in front** (sts. W.GEN. of others) Plb.
‖ PRES.PTCPL.ADJ. (of part of an army) **forming the vanguard** X.
2 go at the head of a procession; (of persons, objects carried by persons, or sim.) **lead the way** Hdt. X. Plb. Plu. —W.GEN. *in a procession* Plb. Plu. —W.DAT. *for a god* (i.e. *lead him in procession*) Ar.; (gener., of a swineherd) **go in front** (of his animals) Plb.
3 ‖ NEUT.PL.PTCPL.SB. **things providing guidance** (ref. to indications or data) Plb.

—**προηγουμένως** *mid.ptcpl.adv.* **first and foremost** Plu.

προηγητήρ ῆρος *m.* (ref. to a god) **leader** (W.GEN. into disaster) E.

—**προηγήτειρα** ης *Ion.f.* (ref. to a cow) **guide** (W.GEN. on a journey) AR.

προηγητής οῦ *m.* **1 guide** (for a blind man) S.
2 usher (preceding a bridal carriage) Hyp.

προ-ηγορέω *contr.vb.* [ἀγορεύω] **1 speak on behalf of others**; **be a spokesman** X. Plu. —W.GEN. *for someone* X.
2 (leg.) **speak in defence of others**; **be an advocate** —W.DAT. *for someone* Plu.

προ-ήδομαι *pass.vb.* **be pleased in advance** —W.DAT. w. sthg. Arist.

προῆκα (aor.1), **προηκάμην** (aor.1 mid.): see προΐημι

προ-ήκης ες *adj.* [reltd. ἀκίς, ἀκωκή] (of oars) **sharp-tipped, with sharp blades** Od.

προ-ήκω *vb.* **1** (of a person) **be advanced** —W.DAT. or PREP.PHR. *in age* Ar. Plu.
2 (of a day) **be far advanced** Plu.
3 (of a person) **have progressed** —W.ADV. or PREP.PHR. *this far in hope, so far in insensitivity* E. D.; (of a situation) **have developed** —W.PREP.PHR. *to a certain point* D.
4 (of a person) **be pre-eminent** —W.DAT. *in reputation* Th. Plu. —*in wealth* X.; (of a place) **be superior** —W.PREP.PHR. *in prestige* Plu.
5 (of the mouth of a purse-net) **extend forward, project** X.

προῆμαι (athem.aor.mid.subj.): see προΐημι

προ-ῆμαρ *adv.* **throughout the day, all day** Semon.

προήσθησις εως *f.* [προήδομαι] **anticipatory pleasure** Pl.

προ-ηττάω *Att.contr.vb.* [ἡσσάομαι] (of an event) **overpower beforehand**, **break in advance** —*the spirits of troops* Plb. ‖ PF. or PLPF.PASS. (of commanders, troops) **have been defeated earlier** Plb. Plu.; **have already been broken** —W.DAT. *in spirits* Plb. Plu.; (of spirits) Plb.

προ-θαλής ές *adj.* [θάλλω] (of a child) **maturing early, precocious** hHom.

προ-θέλυμνος ον *adj.* [app. θέλυμνον *foundation*] **1** (quasi-advbl., of hair or trees which are torn out) **roots-first, by the roots** Il. Ar.; (of mountain peaks, lifted by a god) **from the foundations** Call.; (fig., of a person who is destroyed) **root and branch** Ar.
2 (of shields, in a battle-line) **one upon another, overlapping** Il.

προθέμεν (dial.athem.aor.mid.): see προτίθημι

προ-θεραπεύω *vb.* **1 give preparatory treatment** (to wool before dyeing) Pl.
2 try to win over (W.ACC. someone) **in advance** Plu.

πρόθεσις εως *f.* [προτίθημι] **1 laying out** (of a body, before burial) Pl. D.
2 presentation, offering (of sacred bread) NT.
3 posting up in public (of the names of debtors) Arist.
4 that which is put forward, **preliminary notice, statement** (of a case to be proved, opp. its proof) Arist.; (gener., of a topic to be written about) Arist.
5 purpose, intention Plb. NT.; (W.GEN. of heart) NT.; (prep.phr.) κατὰ πρόθεσιν *purposely, deliberately* Pl.
6 good intentions (towards someone), **goodwill** Plb.
7 supposition, assumption Plb.

προ-θεσμία ᾶς *f.* [θεσμός] (leg.) **limit appointed in advance** (after which no further proceedings are allowed), **statute of limitations** Pl. Aeschin. D.; (W.GEN. *for a claim, a crime*) Lys. Pl.; (W.DAT. *to a person's liability*) Lys.

προ-θεσπίζω *vb.* | 3sg.plpf. προυτεθεσπίκει | **foretell** —*sthg.* Hippon. —W.INDIR.Q. *how the future will come to pass* A.

προ-θέω *contr.vb.* [θέω¹] | iteratv.impf. προθέεσκον | **1** (of a warrior) **run out in front** (of a body of soldiers) Hom.; (of a hunter, hounds, soldiers, a crowd) **run forward** X. AR.; (of a hunted animal) **run ahead** (of its pursuers) Il.
2 (fig., of the soul) **run ahead** (of happenings, opp. be left behind, ref. to its capacity for apprehending them) Pl.; (of arrows) **be precursors** —W.GEN. *of the appearance of the enemy* Plu.
3 (of abusive words) **spring forwards** —W.DAT. + INF. *for someone to utter* Il.(dub.)

προ-θνήσκω *vb.* | aor.2 προύθανον | **1 die earlier** (in a previous age) Pi.*fr.*; (in the present age) Th.
2 die on behalf of —W.GEN. *someone* E.

προ-θρῴσκω *vb.* | only aor.2 ptcpl. προθορών | (of a goddess, a warrior, an ox) **spring** or **leap forward** Il. AR.

πρόθυμα ατος *n.* [προθύω] **1 preliminary offering** Ar.; **preparatory sacrifice** (W.PREP.PHR. for the voyage to Troy, ref. to the killing of Iphigeneia) E.
2 sacrifice on behalf (W.GEN. of an army) E.*fr.*

προθυμέομαι *mid.contr.vb.* [πρόθυμος] | impf. προυθυμούμην, also προεθυμούμην ‖ aor.pass. (w.mid.sens.) προυθυμήθην ‖ neut.impers.vbl.adj. προθυμητέον, also pl. προθυμητέα |
1 be eager or **desire keenly** —W.INF. (sts. understd.) *to do sthg.* Hdt. S. E. Th. Ar. Att.orats. +; (wkr.sens.) **be ready** or **willing** —W.INF. *to do sthg.* Pl.
2 show eagerness, be keen, try one's best A. Hdt. Ar. Pl. X. D.
3 be enthusiastic or **in good spirits** (opp. ἀθυμέω) X.
4 be eager (for sthg. to happen) A. Th. Pl. Arist. —W.ACC. + INF. *for sthg. to happen* Pl. —w. ὥστε and ACC. + INF. Th. —w. ὅπῃ (ὅκως) ἄν + OPT. Hdt. Pl. —w. ὡς + OPT. X. —w. ὅπως + FUT.INDIC. Th.
5 (tr.) **be eager for, desire keenly** —*a peace agreement* Th. —W.NEUT.ACC. *sthg.* Antipho Th. Pl. X.

προθυμία ᾶς, Ion. **προθυμίη** ης *f.* **1 impatient haste** (to do or obtain sthg.), **eagerness, keenness** Il. Hdt. Trag. Th. Att.orats. Pl. +
2 (specif.) **eager desire** (W.GEN. of someone) Hdt. E.; (W.GEN. for sthg.) Hdt. S. E. Pl.

πρόθυμος

3 eagerness on another's behalf, **keen support, goodwill** (oft. w. εἰς + ACC. for someone) Hdt. E. Th. X. Plb.

πρό-θυμος ον *adj.* [θυμός] **1** (of persons) **eager, keen** (oft. W.INF. to do sthg.) Hdt. E. Th. Att.orats. Pl. +; (w. τό + INF.) Th.; (of a person's eye, conduct) E. ‖ NEUT.SB. eagerness E. Th.
2 eagerly desirous, eager (W.GEN. for sthg.) S.; **full of enthusiasm** (W.PREP.PHR. for sthg.) Hdt. Ar. Pl. +
3 eager on another's behalf, keen in support, full of goodwill (W.DAT. for someone or sthg.) S. E.*fr.* X.; (w. εἰς or περί + ACC.) Th. Att.orats. X.

—**πρόθυμα** *neut.pl.adv.* **eagerly** E.

—**προθύμως** *adv.* | compar. προθυμότερον, superl. προθυμότατα | **1 eagerly, keenly** A. Hdt. Th. Ar. Att.orats. Pl. +
2 heartily, enthusiastically —*ref. to welcoming someone* Hdt.

προθύραια ων *n.pl.* [πρόθυρον] **porches** or **porticoes** (of the gods) hHom.

πρό-θυρον ου *n.* [θύρᾱ] | oft. pl. for sg. | **1 gateway** (of a courtyard) Hom.
2 entrance door, doorway (of a house or hall) Hom. hHom. A.
3 space in front of a door, doorway or **porch** Pi. Hdt. E. Th. Ar. Pl. +
4 (fig.) **portal** (to the Isthmos, ref. to Corinth) Pi.

προ-θύω *vb.* [θύω¹] **1** make a sacrifice before an event (to promote its success); **make a preliminary sacrifice** —W.PREP.PHR. *for ploughing of the land* E.; (before a wedding) Plu. ‖ MID. sacrifice before a battle; **sacrifice** Plu. —*a horse* Plb.
2 make a sacrifice on behalf of (someone or sthg., to promote their success); **offer a sacrifice for** —W.GEN. *an army* E.*fr.*; **offer a sacrifice** —W.COGN.ACC. *of burnt offerings* (W.DAT. *for a city*) E.*fr.* ‖ MID. **offer a sacrifice for** —W.GEN. *someone's poetry* Ar.; (tr.) **sacrifice** —*one's daughter* (W.GEN. *for one's country*) E.*fr.*; (fig.) —*oneself* (W.PREP.PHR. *for one's country*) Plu.
3 make a sacrifice in honour of (someone); **celebrate with sacrifices** —W.COGN.ACC. *rites of welcome and birth* (W.GEN. *for a newly discovered son*) E.
4 sacrifice first —W.DAT. *to Hestia* (W.PREP.PHR. *before other gods*) Pl.

προ-ιάλλω *ep.vb.* | impf. προίαλλον | aor. προίηλα | **1 send forth, despatch** —*someone* (on an errand) Hom. Hes.*fr.* AR. —*a pig, gifts, phantoms* (*to someone*) Od. AR. Mosch.
2 discharge, shoot —*an arrow* Theoc.

προ-ιάπτω *vb.* | fut. προϊάψω | ep.aor. προίαψα | **hurl forth, despatch** (W.DAT. to Hades) —*warriors, their souls* Il. —*a city* A.

προϊδεῖν (aor.2 inf.), **προϊδην** (Aeol.aor.2 inf.), **πρόιδον** (dial.aor.2): see προοράω

προ-ίζομαι *mid.vb.* (of a king) **take the seat of honour** Hdt.

προ-ίημι *vb.* | pres.: ῑ usu. in Att. | ep.3sg. προίει, ep.3pl. προϊεῖσι | inf. προϊέναι | ep.impf. προΐειν | fut. προήσω | aor.1 προῆκα, ep. προέηκα | ATHEM.AOR.: ep.3pl. πρόεσαν, ep.2sg.imperatv. πρόες, ep.3sg.imperatv. προέτω, inf. προεῖναι, ep.inf. προέμεν, ptcpl. προείς ‖ MID.: impf. προϊέμην | aor.1 προηκάμην | athem.aor. προείμην, ptcpl. προέμενος, subj. προῆμαι, opt. προοίμην, inf. προέσθαι ‖ PASS.: aor.ptcpl. προεθείς | pf. προεῖμαι | neut.impers. vbl.adj. προετέον ‖ The sections are grouped as: (1–4) send forth, (5–7) let slip, (8–11) give up, abandon, (12–13) give away. |

1 send forth, let fly, discharge —*a spear, an arrow* Hom. hHom. B.; **fling** —*one's sandals* (*into a river*) hHom.; (of a fisherman) **cast** or **let down** —*one's tackle* (*into the sea*) Od.

2 send forth, despatch —*someone* (to a destination, or on an errand, sts. W.INF. to do sthg.) Hom. Pi. AR. —*ships* Il.; **send forward** —*troops* X.; (wkr.sens.) **let go, release** —*someone* Il.
3 (of a god) **send forth** —*a wind, a bird of omen* Hom. —*glory* (to someone) Il.; (of a baby) —*an omen* (fig.ref. to a fart) hHom.; (of a person) —*a message* Od.
4 (of a river) **pour forth** —*its waters* Il. Hes.*fr.*; (of a rock, a mountain) —*streams of water* E. Theoc.; (of a person) —*tears* E.
5 let slip (fr. one's grasp) —*a tiller, someone's foot* Od. ‖ MID. **let** (W.ACC. one's cloak) **slip off** D.
6 let slip, blurt out —*an injudicious or ominous remark* Od.; (of an animal) **utter** —*human speech* AR. ‖ MID. (of persons) **utter** —*a word, sounds* D. Plb.; **let slip** —*a secret* Plb.
7 ‖ MID. **allow** (W.ACC. someone) **to escape** Plb.; **allow** (W.ACC. time) **to slip by** Plb.
8 give up, hand over, surrender (sts. W.DAT. to someone) —*persons, possessions* Hdt. Th. Ar. —W.INF. (the right) to rule Pi. ‖ MID. **give up, let go of** —*persons, possessions* Hdt. Att.orats. X. + —*one's life* Plu.; (intr.) **put oneself into someone's hands** X.
9 ‖ MID. **desert, abandon, sacrifice** —*persons, places, possessions* Th. Att.orats. X. +; **betray** —*a cause, the public interest, or sim.* Att.orats.
10 ‖ MID. **abandon** —*someone* (W.PREP.PHR. to slavery) D.; **leave** —*someone* (W.PREDIC.PTCPL. to be treated wrongly, or sim.) Th. Plb. —(W.INF. to die) X.; (wkr.sens.) **allow** (sts. W.DAT. someone) —W.INF. to do sthg. Lys. D.; **leave** —*sthg.* (W.PREDIC.ADJ. in a certain state) Pl.
11 ‖ MID. **abandon, surrender** —*oneself* (to a disease, i.e. cease to fight it) Th. —(to a temptation) D. —(W.DAT. to the enemy, i.e. lose the will to fight) X.; (intr.) **succumb** (to illness) Arist. ‖ ACT. **give up, devote** —*oneself* (W.PREP.PHR. to immediate gratification) X.
12 ‖ MID. **give away freely, give away** (sts. W.DAT. to someone) —*money, property, or sim.* Att.orats. Pl.; **offer** —*a service* Pl. X. —*a contribution* (of one's valour, W.DAT. to a city) Th.; **lend** —*money* D.; (intr.) **lend money** Isoc.; **spend freely** Arist. ‖ PASS. (of money) be lent Isoc.
13 ‖ MID. **give away recklessly, throw away, squander** —*money or sim.* Att.orats.; **let slip, sacrifice** —*an opportunity, an advantage* Lycurg. D.; (intr.) **throw away an opportunity** Arist. ‖ PASS. (of opportunities or sim.) be thrown away D.

προΐκτης ου *m.* [προίξ] one who reaches out his hand (for a gift), **beggar** Od.

προίξ ικός *f.* **1** app., reaching out (of the hand, in making a gift) ‖ ADVBL.GEN. **as a gift**; (ref. to doing a favour) *without reward* Od.; (ref. to testing someone) *without cost or return* (i.e. w. impunity) Od.
2 ‖ ADVBL.ACC. **as a gift**; (ref. to giving, receiving, or doing sthg.) *without charge or reward, for free* Ar. Att.orats. Pl. X. Thphr. Plu.; (ref. to making political judgements) *with no eye to gain, disinterestedly* D.
3 dowry Att.orats. Pl. Arist. Thphr. Men. Plu.

προ-ιππάζομαι *mid.vb.* (of horsemen) **ride on ahead** Plu.

προ-ιππεύω *vb.* (of a horseman) **ride ahead** (sts. W.GEN. of other troops) Plu.; **ride out in front** —W.GEN. *of an army* Plu.; **ride in front** (of troops) Plu.

προΐσσομαι *mid.vb.* [reltd. προίξ] app., reach out (one's hand), **beg** Archil.(dub.)

προ-ίστημι *vb.* | aor.1 προέστησα ‖ also MID.: fut. προστήσομαι | aor.1 προεστησάμην, also προυστησάμην ‖ The act. and aor.1 mid. (sts. also pres. and fut.mid.) are tr.

For the intr.mid. see προΐσταμαι below. The act. athem.aor., pf. and plpf. are also intr. |
1 place (someone or sthg.) in front (of sthg.); **set forth, place** —*a warrior* (W.PREP.PHR. *in front of an army,* W.INF. + DAT. *to fight an enemy*) Il.; **place** (W.ACC. one's body) **in the way** (of a missile) Antipho; **station** (W.ACC. soldiers) **in front** —W.GEN. *of a wing* Plb. || MID. **station** (W.ACC. chariots) **in front** (of one's troops) X.; **set up** (W.ACC. a staff) **in front** (of one's house) Hdt.
2 || MID. **make** (W.ACC. someone) **patron** or **protector** —W.GEN. *of oneself* And. Pl. D.
3 || MID. **set** (W.ACC. an activity) **in the forefront** —W.GEN. *of one's life* Pl.; **make** (W.ACC. someone's enmity) **the foremost issue** —W.GEN. *of a lawsuit* D.; **make** (W.NEUT.ACC. sthg.) **the principal argument** E.*Cyc.*
4 || MID. **put** (W.ACC. sthg.) **forward as an excuse** or **pretext** D. —W.GEN. *for sthg.* Antipho.
5 || MID. **put forward as an authority, adduce** —*a writer* Pl.
6 || MID. **put** (one thing) **ahead** (of another); **regard** (W.ACC. one's ears) **as more reliable** —W.GEN. *than one's mind* Pl.
7 || MID. place (someone) at the head; **make** (W.ACC. someone) **one's leader** Hdt.

—**προΐσταμαι** *mid.vb.*| also ACT.: athem.aor. προέστην, also προΰστην | pf. προέστηκα, inf. προεστάναι | plpf.: 3sg. προειστήκει, 3pl. προεστήκεσαν || PASS.: aor.ptcpl. (w.mid.sens.) προσταθείς |
1 (of a warrior) come to stand before, **come to face** —W.DAT. *an opponent* S.; (of a suppliant) —W.ACC. *a god* S.
2 come to stand in front (of someone or sthg., so as to provide protection or concealment); (of bodyguards) **place oneself before** —W.GEN. *someone* Hdt.; (of a person) **stand in the way of** —W.GEN. *calamity (i.e. protect someone fr. it)* S.; **cover, conceal** (a character defect) E. || AOR.PASS. (of a god's arrows) form a protective guard S.
3 (gener.) **act as protector** or **champion** —W.GEN. *of someone* E. X. D. —*of freedom* Isoc. —*of peace* Aeschin. —*of an opinion* Plb.; **act as avenger** —W.GEN. *of someone's murder* S.
4 stand at the head, **be leader** —W.GEN. *of a country, populace, party, or sim.* Hdt. Th. Ar. Att.orats. + —*of an army, a chorus* X. —*of a revolution* Th. || MASC.PTCPL.SB. (usu.pl.) leader Hdt. Th. +
5 have charge —W.GEN. *of a shrine* X. —*of a war, education, affairs* Isoc. D.; have management of, **govern, direct** —W.GEN. *oneself, one's life* (W.ADV. *in some way*) Hdt. Isoc. X. —*a business* Plu.

προ-ιστορέω *contr.vb.* || PASS. (of events) be narrated previously Plb.

προ-ίσχω *vb.* **1** (of a boy playing a guessing-game) hold out —*items* (*concealed in his hand*) X. || MID. hold in front of oneself, **hold out** —*one's hands* (*in supplication*) Th. Plu. —*one's sword* Plu.; **hold** (W.ACC. one's hands, one's cloak) **in front** —W.GEN. *of one's face* (*for protection*), *of one's book* (*for concealment*) Plu.; **hold in front of oneself** —*draperies or sim.* (*for protection or concealment*) Plu.; **present, offer** —*a clod of earth* (*as a gift of friendship*) AR.
2 || MID. **put forward** —*a pretext* (or sthg. *as a pretext*) Hdt. Plu. —W.NEUT.ACC. sthg. (*as an argument, demand, proposal, or offer*) Hdt. Th. —*kinship* (*in support of a claim*) Th.

Προιτίδες ων *fem.pl.adj.* (of one of the seven gates of Thebes) of Proitos (a legendary Theban), **Proitid** A. E.

προ-ίωξις εως *f.* [reltd. ἰωκή, ἰωγμός] **pursuit** (opp. παλίωξις *counter-attack*) Hes.

πρόκα, also **πρόκατε** *Ion.adv.* [πρό] **at once, immediately** Hdt. Call. AR.

προ-καθεύδω *vb.* **have a sleep in front** (of a courthouse, while waiting for admittance) Ar.

προ-καθηγέομαι *mid.contr.vb.* **1** (of allied sailors) **take a leading role** Plb.
2 (of goodwill towards someone) **act as an incentive** (to do sthg.) Plb.; (of events) **influence in advance** —W.GEN. *purposes and decisions* Plb.

προ-κάθημαι, Ion. **προκάτημαι** *mid.vb.* **1** have a front seat (at a spectacle) Plu.; **sit in state** Plu.
2 (of officials) **preside** Plb. Plu.; (of a political body) —W.GEN. *over the state, the popular assembly* Pl. Arist.
3 (of the Thessalians) **lie in an advanced position** —W. πρό + GEN. *ahead of the rest of Greece* (*w. respect to an invader fr. the North*) Hdt.
4 be stationed in front (of someone) so as to offer protection; (of night-watchmen) **be stationed in front** —W.GEN. *of an army* E.; (of troops, a commander) **be stationed as a forward guard** Th. Plb. —W.GEN. *of people, a place* X. Plb. Plu.; (gener., of a nation) **stand guard over, protect** —W.GEN. *another nation* Hdt.; (of a god) —*his own property* Hdt.

προ-καθίζω, Ion. **προκατίζω** *vb.* **1** (of a flock of birds coming to ground) **settle ever further forwards** (in a meadow) Il.
2 (of a king, a judge) **sit in state** Hdt.(also mid.)
3 (tr., of a commander) **station** (W.ACC. troops) **as a forward guard** Plb.; (intr.) **take up a forward position** —W.PREP.PHR. *at a place* Plb.; **take up a position in defence** —W.GEN. *of a place* Plb. || MID. (of troops) **station oneself in a forward position** Plb.

προ-καθίημι *vb.* **1** cast down beforehand (before sthg. happens), **first plunge** —*a city* (W.PREP.PHR. *into confusion*) D.
2 put down (a bait) beforehand (or before someone); (fig.) **dangle** (W.ACC. someone) **as a bait** —W.INF. *to deceive other persons* D.
3 (wkr.sens.) **bring** (W.ACC. persons) **forward** —W.ACC.PTCPL. *begging someone to do sthg.* Plu.; **send** (W.ACC. a commander) **forward** —W.ACC.FUT.PTCPL. *to harass the enemy* Plu.

προ-καθίστημι *vb.* **1** place (persons) in front (for protection) || MID. **post** (W.ACC. sentries) **to guard oneself** X. || PF.ACT. (of a guard) be posted Th.
2 (fig.) **use** (W.ACC. a law) **as a protection** (for someone) or **as a screen** (for sthg.) Antipho (dub.)

προ-καθοράω *contr.vb.* | fut. προκατόψομαι | (of ships) take a look in advance, **reconnoitre** Hdt.

πρό-κακος ον *adj.* [κακός] (of evils) **beyond evils** A.

προ-καλέομαι *mid.contr.vb.* **1** call forth, summon —*someone* (W.PREP.PHR. *fr. a place*) X.; **call for** —*someone's inherited nobility* (i.e. *for a display of it*) E.
2 challenge —*someone* (sts. W.PREP.PHR. *to a contest*) Hom. Pl. X. Plb. —(W.INF. *to fight*) Il. Hdt.; **issue a challenge** Th. Pl. X.; (provbl.) **call forth** —*cavalry* (W.PREP.PHR. *into an open plain, i.e. challenge someone to a contest in which he is an expert*) Pl.
3 call, invite —*someone* (W.PREP.PHR. *to a discussion, a meal, an alliance, or sim.*) Hdt. Th. Pl. + —(W.INF. *to do sthg.*) Anacr. Th. Isoc. +; **call upon** —*someone* (W.ADV. *by name, in proposing a toast*) Critias; (intr.) **issue an invitation** (to do sthg.) Th. Ar. Isoc.; (of circumstances) **call for** —W.INF. (someone) *to do sthg.* Arist.; (of a person) **invite** (W.ACC. someone) **to come over** —W.PREP.PHR. *to oneself (i.e. to*

προκαλίζομαι

one's cause) Plb. ‖ PASS. (of a state) be invited —W.PREP.PHR. to arbitration Th.
4 (fig., of a baby) **invite, welcome** —sleep hHom.
5 call for help or advice, **appeal** —W.PREP.PHR. to someone Plb.
6 (of a state, negotiators, or sim.) make a call for, **offer, propose** —arbitration, a truce, or sim. Th. Ar. X. —W.NOM. or ACC. + INF. that one (or someone else) shd. do sthg. Th. X. Aeschin.; **invite** (W.ACC. someone) **to accept an offer** —W.ACC. of peace Ar.; (intr.) **make an offer** (of alliance) Th.
7 (leg.) issue a formal challenge to an opponent (to do or accept sthg., e.g. to give or accept an oath, to give up or accept slaves for interrogation); **challenge** (usu. W.ACC. someone) Att.orats. —W.PREP.PHR. to sthg. Att.orats. —W.INF. to do sthg. D.; **issue** (W.COGN. or INTERN.ACC. this or sim.) **challenge** (sts. W. 2ND ACC. to someone) Antipho Pl. D.; **challenge** (W.ACC. someone) **to accept an offer** —W.ACC. of sthg. D. —W.INF. to do sthg. D. —W.ACC. + INF. that someone shd. do sthg. D.

προκαλίζομαι mid.vb. [reltd. προκαλέομαι] **challenge** —someone (sts. W.INF. to fight or sim.) Hom.

προ-καλινδέομαι (v.l. **προκυλινδέομαι**) mid.contr.vb. (of Persians) roll on the ground in front (of someone), **grovel** Isoc.

προ-κάλυμμα ατος n. **1 curtain** (of a bed or bedchamber) A.
2 screen (of skins and hides, for protection fr. arrows) Th.; (to conceal light) Plu.; **covering** (of clothing and hides, to conceal armour) Plu.
3 (fig.) **screen, cloak** (for wrongdoing, ref. to elaborate speech) Th.

προ-καλύπτω vb. **1** conceal by placing (sthg.) in front; (of a cloud) **conceal, veil** —the sun X. ‖ MID. (of a woman) **veil** —one's eyes, cheeks E. ‖ PASS. (of a baggage-train) be concealed (fr. enemy view) —W.DAT. by soldiers (placed in front) X. ‖ PF.PASS. (fig.) have (W.ACC. one's eyes, ears, body) as a veil —W.PREP.PHR. before one's soul Pl.
2 place (sthg.) in front as a covering; **use** (W.ACC. one's cloak) **as a protective cover** (for someone) E. ‖ MID. (fig., of sophists) **use** (W.ACC. poetry) **as a veil** (to disguise their art) Pl.

προ-κάμνω vb. | aor.2 προύκαμον | **1 toil previously** Thgn.
2 have a previous illness Th.
3 grow weary first (before one has reached one's goal) A. E.
4 suffer in advance —W.DAT. for anticipated troubles Th.
5 toil on behalf of —W.GEN. someone S.

προκάς άδος f. [πρόξ] a kind of deer, **deer** hHom.

προ-καταγγέλλω vb. (of God, prophets) **make an announcement in advance** —W.ACC. or PREP.PHR. about a future event NT.

προ-καταγιγνώσκω vb. **1** make a presumption of guilt (against someone) in advance (before a trial or hearing); **presume** (usu. W.GEN. someone) **guilty** Ar. D. Plb. —W.ACC. of some crime Att.orats. —W.INF. of being or doing sthg. Th. And. Lys.
2 prejudge —nothing (i.e. be unprejudiced) Aeschin. D.

προ-κατακαίω vb. (intr., of troops) **burn all before one** X.

προ-καταλαμβάνω vb. **1** (of military forces) **capture** (W.ACC. a place) **in advance** (of others or of sthg. happening) Th. X. Plb.(also mid.) Plu.; **overpower** (W.ACC. a nation) **first** (before attacking another) Th. ‖ PASS. (of places, persons) be captured in advance Th. X. Plb. Plu.
2 (of a person) **occupy** (W.ACC. the speaker's rostrum) **first** (before anyone else) Aeschin.

3 (fig.) take under one's control in advance, **catch** (W.ACC. someone's ear, i.e. attention) **first** (before others do) Aeschin.; **pre-empt, appropriate** —an assembly (W.DAT. for ambassadors, i.e. for them to address when they arrive) Aeschin. —an honorific title Aeschin.; **prejudice** (in one's favour) —an audit Aeschin.; **anticipate, make provision for** —a contingency Aeschin. ‖ PASS. (of a topic) be already covered Isoc.; (of charges) be already detailed Din.
4 take measures in advance to prevent, **anticipate, forestall** —a revolt, a likely event Th. —someone Plb.(mid.) —w. ὅπως μή + SUBJ. or FUT.INDIC. sthg. happening Th.; (of winter) **overtake** —a commander Plb.; (intr.) **take pre-emptive action** Th. Pl. ‖ PASS. (of a person) be forestalled (in an action) Plb.; (of troops) be taken by surprise (by a sudden attack) Plb.
5 comprehend in advance; **foresee, anticipate** —someone's future power Pl. —someone's point of view Men.

προ-καταλέγομαι pass.vb. (of a country) **be described previously** Hdt.

προ-καταλήγω vb. (of a mountain range) **stop short** (of a place) Plb.

προ-καταλύω vb. **1** put an end to earlier, **annul** (W.ACC. laws) beforehand Th. ‖ MID. **settle** (W.ACC. one's enmity against someone) **beforehand** Hdt.
2 end prematurely, **cut short** —a voyage D.
3 end (W.ACC. one's life) **in advance** —W.GEN. of one's work Plu.

προ-καταπίπτω vb. (of rumours about someone) **arrive pell-mell** (W.PREP.PHR. at a city) **in advance** (of his arrival) Plu.

προ-καταπλέω contr.vb. **sail down the coast in advance** (of others) Plb.

προ-καταπλήττομαι Att.mid.vb. [καταπλήσσω] **throw** (W.ACC. enemy troops) **into panic first** (before attacking them) Plb.

προ-κατάρχομαι mid.vb. **1** (of colonists) **give priority** —W.GEN. + DAT. at sacrifices, to someone (fr. the mother city) Th.
2 (of a leader) **begin hostilities** Plb.

προ-κατασκευάζω vb. **1 make** (W.ACC. + PREDIC.ACC. one thing into another) **in advance** (of sthg. happening) X.
2 arrange in advance, ensure —someone's safety Plb. ‖ MID. **arrange** (W.ACC. sthg.) **in advance** Plb.; **devise in advance** —a pretext Plb.; **secure in advance** —friends, a reputation Plb. ‖ PASS. (of things) be arranged or secured in advance Plb. Plu.

προκατασκευή ῆς f. **1 preparatory training** Plb.
2 preparatory treatment (by a historian), **introduction** (sts. W.GEN. to a topic or work) Plb.

προ-κατασύρω vb. (of a commander) **ravage** (W.ACC. a region) **first** Plb.

προ-καταφεύγω vb. (of a person, ships) **escape first** (before they can be caught) Th.; (before others) Th.

προ-καταφθείρω vb. **destroy** (W.ACC. corn) **in advance** (of someone's arrival) Plb.

προ-καταχράομαι mid.contr.vb. **use up in advance** —W.DAT. a maintenance allowance Plu. ‖ PF.PASS. (of Assemblies, ref. to the permitted number of their meetings) have already been used up D.

πρόκατε Ion.adv.: see πρόκα

προ-κατελπίζω vb. **entertain a prior hope** or **expectation** (about sthg.) Plb.

προ-κατεργάζομαι pass.vb. (of a person's power and fame) **be achieved earlier** (by his father) Plu.

προ-κατέχω vb. **1** (of a commander, troops, sailors) **take prior control of** —*a city, high ground, a route, or sim.* Th. X. Plb. Plu.
2 ‖ PASS. (fig., of persons) **be prejudiced** or **biased** —W.DAT. *by friendly feelings* (*towards someone*) Plb.; **be already committed** (*to a cause*) Plb.
3 be superior (*to someone*) —W.DAT. *in age and reputation* Plb.
4 ‖ MID. **hold before oneself** —*a veil* hHom.

προ-κατηγορέω contr.vb. **1 accuse** (*someone*) **in advance** (*before he commits an offence*) D.
2 ‖ NEUT.PL.AOR.PASS.PTCPL.SB. **accusations made earlier** Hyp.

προκατηγορίᾱ ᾱς f. **earlier accusation** (W.GEN. *against someone*) Th.

προκάτημαι, προκατίζω Ion.vbs.: see προκάθημαι, προκαθίζω

προκατόψομαι (fut.mid.): see προκαθοράω

πρό-κειμαι mid.pass.vb. [κεῖμαι] | only pres. and impf.
 | impf. προυκείμην, also προεκείμην | **1 lie exposed to view**; (of a person) **lie** (on a bed or on the ground) Hdt. S.; (of a tuft of wool, on the ground) S.
2 (of a person) **lie dead** Trag.; (of a corpse) **lie exposed** (i.e. unburied) S. Ar.; **be laid out** (for burial) E. Antipho Ar.; (of the hands of a dead person) **lie** —W.PREDIC.ADJ. + PREP.PHR. *limp, in their joints* E.
3 lie or **be placed in front** (of someone); (of food) **be set before one** Hom. Hdt.; (of a cup) Thgn.; (of a tripod) **be set forth** (as a prize) Hes.; (of a person) **be exposed** or **offered** —W.DAT. *to a sea-monster* (*as food*) Ar.(mock-trag.); (fig., of a boy, compared to a suppliant's olive-branch) **be placed before** —W.DAT. *a jury* D.
4 lie in front (of sthg.); (of weapons) **lie in front** —W. πρό + GEN. *of a temple* Hdt.; (of a brooch or pin) —W.GEN. *of a woman's breasts* S.; (of screens) **stand in front** —W. πρό + GEN. *of people* Pl.; (of siege-towers) —W.GEN. *of besiegers' shelters* Plb.; (fig., of preludes) **stand at the head** (of poetical and musical works) Pl.
5 (of a place) **lie forward** (relative to another); (of a country, a coastal area) **project, jut out** (sts. W.PREP.PHR. *into the sea*) Hdt. X. —W.GEN. *beyond an adjacent landmass* Hdt.; (of an island) **lie in front** (of a coast), **lie offshore** X.; (fig., of a virtue) **stand out** —W.PREP.PHR. *fr. all others* B.
6 (of places or things) **lie in front** (of sthg.) so as to offer protection; (of mountains) **form a defensive shield** —W.GEN. *for a country* X.; (fig., of a goddess's bow and arrows) —*for her patron city* Call.
7 (of regulations or sim.) **be set forth**; (of laws) **be laid down** S. E. Th.; (of a punishment) S. Th. X. Aeschin.; (of a span of life) Hdt. ‖ PTCPL.ADJ. (of a task, a period of time, an end, a sign, or sim.) **prescribed** or **predetermined** Hdt. Trag. Pl.; (neut.ptcpl., w. ἦν) *it was laid down* —W.DAT. + INF. *that one shd. be liable to a certain punishment* A.
8 be put forward (for acceptance or competition); (of gifts, rewards, prizes) **be offered** Hdt. Lys. Pl. X.; (of an opinion) Hdt.; (of an alliance) Th.
9 (of matters) **lie before one** (for immediate or future attention); (of a task, a contest, or sim.) **lie ahead** (sts. W.DAT. for *someone*) Hdt. E. Lys. Pl.; (of a subject for discussion, a goal) **lie before** —W.DAT. *someone* Pl. Arist. ‖ PTCPL.ADJ. (of a matter) **under discussion** Hdt.
 ‖ NEUT.SG.PTCPL.SB. **question under discussion** Pl.
 ‖ NEUT.SG.GEN.PTCPL. (as impers. temporal phr.) **when the issue is** —W.PREP.PHR. *to do w. safety* Ar.

‖ NEUT.PL.PTCPL.SB. **present tasks** or **issues** S. E. Th. Isoc. Pl. +

προ-κέλευθος ον adj. (of a god) **guiding the journey** (W.GEN. *of someone*) Mosch.

προ-κήδομαι mid.vb. **be concerned for** or **take care of** —W.GEN. *someone* A. S. Plu.

προ-κηραίνω vb. **be anxious** —W.GEN. *about someone* S.

προ-κηρῡκεύομαι mid.vb. (of a negotiator) **make overtures** —W.PREP.PHR. *to someone* Aeschin. —*about sthg.* And.

προ-κηρύσσω, Att. **προκηρύττω** vb. **1** (of persons in authority) **make a public proclamation** S. Is. —W.ACC. *of an order, a race, rewards, or sim.* S. X. Aeschin. Plb. Plu. —W.DAT. + INF. *to people, to do sthg.* Plu.
2 (of smoke rising fr. a house) **give clear notice** (of what is happening inside) E.
3 (of a prophet) **proclaim** (W.ACC. sthg.) **beforehand** NT.

προ-κινδῡνεύω vb. **1** (of soldiers or sim.) **bear the brunt of danger** Th. Isoc. X. D. Plb. Plu. —W.DAT. *against the enemy* Th. —W.PREP.PHR. *on behalf of someone or sthg.* Att.orats. Plb. Plu.
2 face danger on behalf of, risk one's life for —W.GEN. *someone* And. Isoc. X. Plu.
3 (specif.) **fight in the front line** Plb.
4 begin the fighting (sts. W.DAT. *against someone*) Plb.

προ-κῑνέω contr.vb. **move forward** —*a body of troops* X.; (of a rider) **make** (W.ACC. *one's horse*) **advance** X. ‖ PASS. (of troops) **be moved forward** X.

προ-κλαίω vb. **1 weep in advance** (of someone's arrival) S.; **mourn** (W.ACC. *a wife*) **in advance** (of her death) E.; **mourn first** (before feasting) Hdt.
2 mourn (W.ACC. *someone*) **publicly** E.

πρόκλησις εως (Ion. ιος) f. [προκαλέομαι] **1 calling forth, challenge** (to a duel) Hdt. Plu.
2 (leg.) **challenge** (to an opponent, to do or accept sthg.) Att.orats. Arist. | cf. προκαλέομαι 7
3 (gener.) **invitation, offer, proposal** Th. Isoc. Arist. Plu.

προκλητικόν neut.adv. **as a means of laying down a challenge** —*ref. to shouting* (*by a commander*) Plu.

προ-κλίνω vb. (of an old man) **lean forward, lean** —*one's body* (W.PREP.PHR. *upon someone's arm*) S.

πρό-κλυτος ον adj. [κλυτός] (of stories) **heard in former times** Il.

Πρόκνη ης f. **Prokne** (mythol. princess of Athens, who killed her son Itys in order to punish her husband Tereus for raping her sister Philomela, and was turned into a swallow or nightingale by the gods) S.fr. E. Th. Ar. D.

προ-κνημίς ῖδος f. (collectv.sg.) **greaves** Plb.

προκοιτίᾱ ᾱς f. [πρόκοιτος] **sentry duty** Plb.

πρό-κοιτος ου m. [κοίτη] **one who keeps watch before a military camp, sentry** Plb.

προ-κολάζω vb. **inflict initial punishment** Arist.

προ-κολακεύω vb. **flatter in advance** —*someone's future power* Pl.

προ-κόλπιον ου n. [κόλπος] **bag-like fold made by drawing up the tunic through the belt, front pocket** Thphr. Men.

προ-κομίζω vb. ‖ PASS. (of persons and belongings) **be sent in an advance convoy** Hdt.

προ-κόμιον ου n. [κόμη] **1 forelock** (of a horse) X.
2 false hair, wig (worn as a disguise) Men.

προκοπή ῆς f. [προκόπτω] **progress** (in action, fortune, or sim.), **progress, advance, development** Plb.

προ-κόπτω vb. | aor.ptcpl. προκόψᾱς | **1 strike** or **cut one's way forward** (i.e. forge one's way ahead); (fig., of persons) **make** (usu. W.NEUT.ACC. no, much, or sim.) **progress** Alc. E.

X. Plb. —W.GEN. *in naval strength* Th. || PASS. (of an enterprise) *be successful* Hdt.
2 *make progress* (to another's benefit); **pave the way** —W.DAT. + GEN. *for someone, in domination* (i.e. *further his domination*) Th.
3 (gener.) **progress, advance** —W.DAT. (or perh. ἐν + DAT.) *in wisdom and age* NT.; (of fame, acquaintance) —w. ἐπί + ACC. *to some point* Plb.

πρόκοψις ιος Aeol.f. **progress** or **success** Sapph.

προ-κρίνω vb. | aor. προέκρινα, also προύκρινα | **1** choose in preference, **select, choose** —*someone or sthg.* Hdt. E. Th. Isoc. Pl.(also mid.) Arist. + —W.ACC. + INF. *someone to do sthg.* Is. D. || PASS. (usu. of persons) *be chosen* or *selected* Hdt. Isoc. Pl. X. Plb. Plu.
2 prefer —*someone or sthg.* (W.GEN. *to someone or sthg. else*) Xenoph. Isoc. Pl. Plu.
3 *judge to have pride of place*; **adjudge** —W.ACC. + INF. *someone or sthg. to be pre-eminent* (*in some quality*) Isoc. Pl. X. || PASS. (of a person, a virtue) *be adjudged* —W.INF. + PREDIC.ADJ. *to be best, finest* X. || PF.PASS. (of a nation) *be the most eminent* (sts. W.GEN. of nations) Hdt.; (of individuals) *be the pick* —W.GEN. *of a population* Hdt. X.
4 select (W.ACC. a candidate for office) **by a preliminary vote** (the final choice being determined by lot) D. Arist. || PASS. (of a person) *be selected beforehand* Isoc. D. Arist. —W.INF. *to draw lots for an office* D.

πρόκρισις εως f. **preliminary selection** (of candidates) Pl.

πρόκριτος ον adj. **1** (of persons) **chosen beforehand, preselected** Pl. D.
2 (of persons) **selected by preliminary vote** (to go into the lottery which determines the final choice) Arist.

πρό-κροσσοι αι α (also οι α) pl.adj. [κρόσσαι] (of beached ships) **in rows** or **ranks** Il.; (of moored ships) Hdt.; (of griffins' heads, as decoration around a bronze bowl) perh. **in a stepped pattern** Hdt.

προ-κρούω vb. | Lacon.impf. πρώκροον (or perh. πρωκρόγον) | **1** (intr., of a naval force) **strike first** —W.PREP.PHR. *against enemy ships* Ar.
2 (fig.) **shag first, screw first** —*an old woman* (*before a young one*) Ar.

προ-κυκλέω contr.vb. (fig.) **roll out** —*items of food and drink* (W.PREP.PHR. *fr. one's house*) Carm.Pop.

προ-κυλινδέομαι mid.contr.vb. **roll on the ground in front of, grovel before** —W.DAT. *someone* Ar. —W.GEN. D. | see also προκαλινδέομαι

προ-κυλίνδομαι mid.vb. (of sea-swell) **roll forward** Il.

προκύλισις εως f. **prostration** (as an act of worship) Pl.

προ-κύπτω vb. | aor. προύκυψα | **1** bend or stoop forward; (colloq.) **pop one's head** —W.PREP.PHR. *outside the city walls* Ar.; (of a woman's breast) **pop out** —W.GEN. *fr. her torn dress* Ar.
2 (of earth-born warriors) **emerge** —W.PREP.PHR. *into the upper air* AR.(cj.)

προ-κώμιον ου n. [κῶμος] **prelude** (W.GEN. consisting of a hymn) **to victory celebrations** Pi.

πρό-κωπος ον adj. [κώπη] (quasi-advbl., of a sword that is held) **with hilt forward** (the scabbard having been swivelled fr. perpendicular to horizontal), **with hilt to hand, ready to draw** A.; (of a person) A.(dub.)

προ-λαγχάνω vb. | pf. προείληχα | (of a dramatist) **draw the first lot** (for the order of performance of plays in a competition) Ar.

προ-λάζυμαι mid.vb. **seize earlier** (than otherwise), **grasp sooner** —W.GEN. *a pleasure* E.

προ-λαμβάνω vb. | aor.2 προύλαβον | **1** receive or take (sthg.) before (an event); **receive in advance** or **beforehand** —*money, pay, expenses* Aeschin. D. Arist. —*a favour* E. Plb.; **seize** or **capture in advance** —*places, possessions* D.
2 gain in advance —*a desired aim* Aeschin. —*someone's trust* D.; **ensure in advance** —w. ὅπως + FUT.INDIC. *that sthg. will be the case* D.
3 find in advance —W.ACC. + PF.PTCPL. *that someone has done sthg.* D.
4 receive first, listen to first —*someone's words* (w. πρό + GEN. *in preference to speaking w. someone else*) S.; (of the mind) **take in beforehand** —*items of knowledge* Plb.
5 act first in taking —*one's foot* (W.PREP.PHR. *out of a house*, i.e. *leave it before sthg. happens*) E.
6 act in advance (of the right or usual time); **take up prematurely** —*lamentation* E.; **anticipate, pre-empt** —*someone's prophecy* (by making one's own) E.; **arrive ahead of** —*the right time* Plb.; **anticipate, forestall** —W.GEN. *someone announcing a name* (by calling it out first) Arist.; (intr.) **prejudge** (an issue) D.; **act prematurely** —W.INF. *to do sthg.* (i.e. *do sthg. prematurely*) NT.
7 (w. positive connot.) **secure early** (in the day) —*a god's support* X.; **seize early** —*an opportunity* Plu.; **anticipate** (W.DAT. in imagination) —*future contingencies* Plb.; (intr., of a law) **anticipate** (a contingency) X.
8 be in advance (of others) in location or time; (of a person, an animal) **be** or **get ahead** Th. X. D. Plb. Plu.; (of a hare) —W.ACC. *of hounds* X.; (of a speaker) —W.GEN. *of someone else* (in the order of speakers) D.; (of persons) **get a head start** —W.GEN. *on a journey* Hdt. —*in flight* Th. Plu.
9 (usu. pejor.) **secure** (sthg.) in advance (so as to use it to one's advantage); **take advantage of, presume on, exploit** —*someone's goodwill* D.; (of an older man) —*someone's youth* Aeschin.; **steal a march on, gain an advantage over** —W.GEN. *someone* Aeschin. D.; (intr.) **gain an advantage** Isoc. D.
10 (intr., of a speaker) *take up a narrative at an earlier point in time*, **start earlier** Isoc.
11 (of one state of existence) **be earlier** —W.GEN. *in time* (than another) Arist.

προ-λέγω vb. | impf. προέλεγον, also προύλεγον | Aeol.aor.ptcpl. προλέξαις || pf.pass.ptcpl. προλελεγμένος | **1** pick out (someone) in preference to another || PF.PASS.PTCPL.ADJ. (of warriors, nobles) **chosen, select** Il. Theoc.
2 make special mention (of someone) || PASS. (of persons) *be renowned* —W.PREDIC.ADJ. *as most outstanding* Pi.
3 (of a person, an oracle) **foretell, predict** —*sthg.* Alc. A. Hdt. S. Pl. + —W.ACC. + FUT.INF. or COMPL.CL. *that sthg. will be the case* Hdt. Antipho Pl. Aeschin.
4 say beforehand —*sthg.* Aeschin. Hyp. —W.COMPL.CL. *that sthg. is the case* Hyp.
5 (of a leader) **give advance notice** (of one's intention) D.; (tr., of a state) **give** (to one's enemies) **advance warning of** —*war, battles, their location* Plb.
6 (usu. of persons in authority) **state publicly, proclaim, declare** —W.ACC. + INF. *that sthg. is the case* A. Th. —W.COMPL.CL. *that sthg. is* or *will be the case* Hdt. D. Plb.; (of a law) **prescribe, specify** —*a course of action, a punishment* Lycurg. D.; **order** —W.DAT. + INF. *someone to do sthg.* Din. || NEUT.PL.PF.PASS.PTCPL.SB. *pronouncements* Ar.
7 order publicly, issue an order —W.DAT. + INF. *to someone to do sthg.* X.
8 issue a warning or **advice** —W.INF. or W.DAT. + INF. (*to someone*) *to do sthg.* E.fr. Aeschin. D.

προ-λείπω *vb.* **1 abandon, forsake, desert** —*persons, a corpse, a city, one's possessions* Hom. Hes. Hdt.(quot.epigr.) Trag. Th. Ar. + —*one's post* Th. —*a friendship* Thgn. —*a marriage* E. —*a fight* Plu.
2 (wkr.sens., of persons departing) **leave behind, leave** —*persons, places* Od. Hes. hHom. Eleg. Parm. Trag. +; (of a rising star, Dawn) —*the stream of Okeanos* Hes. Mimn.; (of persons emerging) —*a cave* Pi. —*a temple, a tent* E. —*a chariot* A.; (of a dying person) —*one's youth, one's life* B. E.
3 leave off, give up —W.NEUT.ACC. + μή W.INF. *this, namely lamenting* S.
4 (tr., of a person's soul or spirit, w. further connot. of courage) **desert, fail** —*someone* Ar.; (of the bloom of youth, good fortune) Pl. Plu.; (of intelligence, stratagems) Od. Ar.; (wkr.sens., of a desire) **leave** —*someone* Plu.
5 (intr., of a person) **be faint** or **collapse** E.; (of a person's bodily strength) **give out** Th.; (of trouble) **cease** E.

προ-λεπτύνομαι *pass.vb.* (of particles of moisture) **be already made thin** (by decomposition) Pl.

προ-λεσχηνεύομαι *mid.vb.* **talk previously** —W.DAT. w. *someone* Hdt.

πρό-λεσχος ον *adj.* [λέσχη] **forward in speech, talkative** A.

προ-λεύσσω *vb.* **foresee** —*sufferings* S.

πρόλημμα ατος *n.* [προλαμβάνω] (in political ctxt.) **advantage** Plb.

πρόληψις εως *f.* **earlier apprehension** (of some future event), **anticipation, presentiment** Plb.

πρό-λογος ου *m.* [λόγος] **prologue** (of a tragedy, ref. to the opening speech) Ar.; (of a tragedy or comedy, ref. to the part preceding the entry of the chorus) Arist.

προ-λοχίζω *vb.* | *fut.* προλοχιῶ | **1 set an ambush beforehand** (in a place); **ambush** —*a road, a region* Th. Plu.
2 || PASS. (of ambushes) **be set beforehand** Th.

προ-λυμαίνομαι *mid.vb.* **ruin beforehand** —*an enemy's formation* Plb.

προ-λῡπέομαι *pass.contr.vb.* **feel antecedent pain** (before pleasure) Pl. Arist.; **feel anticipatory pain** (about the future) Pl.

προλύπησις εως *f.* **previous feeling of pain** Pl.

προμάθεια *dial.f.*: see προμηθίᾱ

προμᾱθεύς *dial.m.*, **προμᾱθίς** *dial.fem.adj.*: see under Προμηθεύς

προ-μαλάττομαι *Att.pass.vb.* [μαλάσσω] (fig., of a populace) **be softened up beforehand** (by an ambitious politician) Plu.

πρόμαλος ου *f.* **a kind of tree; perh. elm** AR.

προ-μανθάνω *vb.* **1 learn beforehand** (of sthg. in the future); **learn in advance** —*the struggles that lie ahead* E.*fr.*
2 learn (a lesson) **beforehand** (for later application); **gain learning in advance** Pi.; (of children) **learn** (their lessons) Thphr.; (tr.) **learn in advance** —*a song* Ar. —*nothing* Th. —W.INF. *to bear sufferings* S.; **gain in advance** —W.COGN.ACC. *knowledge* Pl.

προμαντείᾱ ᾱς, Ion. **προμαντηίη** ης *f.* [προμαντεύομαι] **right to consult an oracle first** (before others) Hdt. D. Plu.

προ-μαντεύομαι *mid.vb.* —also **προμαντεύω** *act.vb.* (of a person) **predict** (sthg.) Hdt. —W.COMPL.CL. *that sthg. will be the case* Plu.(act.)

πρό-μαντις εως (Ion. ιος) *m.f.* [μάντις] **1 one who makes prophecies on behalf of an oracular god; prophetess** (most freq. ref. to the Pythia at Delphi) Hdt. Th. Plu.; **prophet** (in Egypt) Hdt.
2 || MASC.FEM.ADJ. **predicting** or **having knowledge of a future event**; (of Apollo) **prophetic** E.; (fig., of Justice, a person's heart) S. E.; (of persons) **prescient** or **cognisant** (W.GEN. of future events) A. E.

προ-μάτωρ ορος *dial.f.* [μήτηρ] **female ancestor, foremother** A. E.

προμαχέω *contr.vb.* [πρόμαχος] **1** (of a detachment of troops) **fight in front** (of their army) X.
2 (of the Athenians) **fight as champions** —W.GEN. *of the Greeks* Lycurg.(quot.epigr.)

προμαχεών ῶνος *m.* **battlement** (of a wall) Hdt. X.

προμαχίζω *vb.* **1 stand forth as a champion** —W.DAT. *for one's side* Il.
2 fight as a champion —W.DAT. *against someone* Il.

προ-μάχομαι *mid.vb.* **1** (of a warrior) **fight in front** —W.GEN. *of others* Il.; (of troops) **fight in the front line** Plb.
2 (of specified troops) **fight before others, open the fighting** Th.
3 (of a guard dog) **fight for** or **in defence of** —W.GEN. *someone* Ar. || MASC.PL.PTCPL.SB. **defenders** (of a place) Plu.

πρόμαχος ου *m.* **1 one who fights at the front** (of an army) || PL. **leading ranks of warriors** Hom. Eleg. Pi.; **front ranks** (of an army) Plu. || ADJ. (transf.epith., of Herakles' spear) **in the forefront of battle** S.
2 one who fights in defence (of others); **champion, defender** (W.GEN. of Zeus, ref. to Herakles) Ibyc.; (of a city, homes, a country, ref. to a military commander) A. Plu.; (of aristocracy, ref. to a politician) Plu.; (pl., ref. to the loyal subjects of a king) X.

προ-μεθίημι *vb.* **let loose** —*a dove* (fr. a ship) AR.(dub.)

προ-μείγνῡμι *vb.* | *aor.2 pass.inf.* προμιγῆναι | || PASS. **have sexual intercourse** (W.DAT. w. someone) **first** (before another does) Il.

προ-μελετάω *contr.vb.* **practise beforehand** —W.COMPL.CL. *what one shd. say* Ar. —*a technique* Pl. —W.INF. *doing sthg.* X. NT.; (intr.) **practise** (doing sthg.) Pl.; (of a dancer) **rehearse** Ar.

προ-μεριμνάω *contr.vb.* **be anxious beforehand about** —W.INDIR.Q. *what one will say* NT.

προ-μετωπίδιον ου *n.* [*dimin.* μέτωπον] **1 scalp, skull** (of a horse) Hdt.; (of an ox) Thphr.
2 head-piece, frontlet (as protective armour for a horse) X.

προμήθεια *f.*: see προμηθίᾱ

Προμήθεια ων *n.pl.* [Προμηθεύς] **festival of Prometheus, Prometheia** Lys. X. Is.

προμηθέομαι *mid.contr.vb.* [προμηθής] | *Ion.aor.imperatv.* προμηθέσαι (Archil.) | **1 show forethought** or **foresight**; perh. **be cautious** Archil.; **be concerned** —w. μή + SUBJ. or GEN. and μή + SUBJ. (*for someone*) *in case sthg. shd. happen* Hdt. Pl. —W.PREP.PHR. *on someone's account* Pl. —W.ACC. or PREP.PHR. *about sthg.* Pl.
2 show regard or **respect for** —*someone* Hdt.

Προμηθεύς έως (Ion. έος) *m.* [*pop.etym.* προμηθής] **Prometheus** (brother of Epimetheus, son of the Titan Iapetos, punished by Zeus for giving fire to mortals) Hes. Trag. Ar. Pl. +
—**προμηθεύς** έως, dial. **προμᾱθεύς** έος *m.* **one who has foresight** or **forethought, forethinker** A.(dub.) Pi.
—**προμᾱθίς** ίδος *dial.fem.adj.* (of a kind of government) **forethinking, provident** A.(cj.)

προ-μηθής ές *adj.* [*perh.reltd.* μανθάνω] | *compar.* προμηθέστερος | (of a person) **showing foresight** or **forethought, far-sighted, prudent** Pl.; (of political caution) Th.; (of a person, in neg.phr.) **anxious** (W.GEN. about dying) S. || NEUT.SB. **forethought, prudence** Th.

προμηθίᾱ (also **προμήθεια**), dial. **προμάθεια** ᾱς, Ion. **προμηθίη** (also **προμηθείη**) ης f. **forethought, foresight** Pi. Hdt. Trag. Th. +; **concern, consideration** (W.GEN. for someone or sthg.) Xenoph. S. E. Pl.

προμηθικῶς adv. **with natural forethought** —ref. to the making of a suggestion (by Prometheus, w. play on his name) Ar.

προ-μήκης ες adj. [μῆκος] **1 extended in length**; (of an animal) **long** (opp. short) S.Ichn.; (of an animal's head) **elongated** Pl.; (of a person, W.ACC. in the head) Plu.
2 (geom. and math., of a shape, an area of land) **oblong, rectangular** Pl.; (of numbers, compared to the sides of a rectangle) **made up of unequal factors, oblong** Pl.; (of a right-angled triangle) **with sides of unequal length** (opp. isosceles), **scalene** Pl.

προ-μηνύω vb. (of a person, an oracle, or sim.) **indicate or disclose** (W.ACC. an action or event) **beforehand** S. Plu.

προμιγῆναι (aor.2 pass.inf.): see προμείγνῡμι

προ-μισθόομαι pass.contr.vb. (of a house) **be rented previously** Plu.

προ-μνάομαι mid.contr.vb. **1 court or woo (someone) on another's behalf**; (of a woman) **act as a matchmaker** X.; (fig., of a man) —W.DAT. **for people** (ref. to introducing them to teachers) Pl.
2 (gener.) **introduce, commend** —subjects for composition (W.DAT. to poets) Pl.; (of a person's mind) **encourage a belief** —W.DAT. and ACC. + FUT.INF. in oneself, that sthg. will happen S.
3 try to obtain, solicit —W.ACC. + DAT. a province, for someone (as governor) Plu.; **make solicitations** (for gifts) X.

προμνηστικός ή όν adj. || FEM.SB. **art of matchmaking** Pl.

προμνηστῖνοι αι masc.fem.adj. [perh.reltd. προμνάομαι] perh., relating to wooing (w.connot. of women filing past a suitor); (quasi-advbl., of men or women approaching or entering a place) **one after another** Od.

προμνήστρια ᾱς f. —also perh. **προμνηστρίς** ίδος (X.) f. [προμνάομαι] **woman who woos or courts someone on another's behalf, matchmaker** Ar. Pl. X.; (w.GEN. of evils, i.e. one who does evil while matchmaking) E.

προ-μοιχεύω vb. **seduce** (W.ACC. a woman) **first** —W.DAT. for another man (i.e. pave the way for his seducing her) Plu.

προμολή ῆς f. [πρόμολον, see προβλώσκω] | usu. pl. for sg. |
1 going forth, departure (of persons) AR.
2 (concr.) **entrance** (of a palace, a room) Call. AR.; (of a house) AR.(sg.)
3 foot (of a mountain) Call.

πρόμολον (ep.aor.2): see προβλώσκω

πρόμολος ον adj. (of a dream) **that comes forth** (W.GEN. fr. Hades) Ar.(dub.)

πρόμος ου m. [πρό; cf. πρόμαχος] **1 one who fights in front** (of an army), **leading fighter, champion** Hom.; (W.DAT. against an adversary) Il.; (appos.w. ἀνήρ) Il.
2 one who fights on another's behalf, champion (W.GEN. of one's comrades) AR.
3 (gener., oft.pl.) **chief, leader** A.; (W.GEN. of military forces) A. E. AR.; **ruler** (W.GEN. of a land) S. E. AR.; **captain** (W.GEN. of a ship) AR.; (as a servant's designation of his master) Ar.(mock-ep.) || ADJ. (of leaders) **foremost** A.; (of Helios, W.GEN. of all the gods) S.

προ-μοχθέω contr.vb. **toil on behalf of** —W.DAT. someone (W.INTERN.ACC. on some task) E.

πρό-νᾱος ον, also **Προνάος** ᾱ (Ion. η Call.) ον, Ion. **Προνήϊος** η ον adj. [νᾱός¹] **1** (of an altar) **before a temple** A.
2 (as a cult-title of Athena at Delphi) **Before the Temple** (i.e. that of Apollo, because her own temple, about a mile away, would seem to an approaching traveller to stand in front of it) A. Hdt. Aeschin. Call. | cf. Πρόνοια, under πρόνοια

—**προνήϊον** ου Ion.n. **temple porch** Hdt.

προ-ναυμαχέω contr.vb. **fight at sea in defence of** —W.GEN. a place Hdt.

προ-νέμω vb. **1 put forward, offer, present** —pure hands (as a mark of innocence) A.; (of a poet) —a choice song (W.DAT. to a place) Pi.
2 || MID. **move forward** (perh. w. allusion to animals grazing); (fig., of Ares, as an agent of bloodshed) **gain ground, advance** S.

προ-νεύω vb. (of a seated person) **lean or bend forward** Pl.; (of a rider) X.; (of rowers) X. Plb.

προνήϊον Ion.n., **Προνήϊος** Ion.adj.: see πρόνᾱος

προ-νηστεύω vb. (of persons about to sacrifice) **fast beforehand** Hdt.

προ-νῑκάω contr.vb. (of military forces) **win an earlier victory** Th. Plu.; (of a litigant) —W.ACC. over someone Is. || PASS. **be defeated earlier** Th. Plu.

προ-νοέω contr.vb. | aor.mid. προυνοησάμην || aor.pass. (w.mid.sens.) προυνοήθην || neut.impers.vbl.adj. προνοητέον | **1 perceive beforehand, foresee, anticipate** —a trick Il. —future events or contingencies Pi. Th. Pl.(mid.) X. Arist. —an order X. —W.COMPL.CL. that sthg. will be the case X.; (intr.) **think ahead, show forethought** Eleg. E. Th. X.(also mid.) Arist.
2 know or realise beforehand —W.COMPL.CL. that sthg. is the case Th. Pl. Plb.(mid.)
3 devise beforehand, think of —a better idea Od.; **plan** —a journey Emp.(tm.) —W.COMPL.CL. that sthg. shd. happen X.; **provide for** —someone's best interests Th.
4 || MID. **premeditate, plan, make provision for** —W.NEUT.ACC. this, nothing, everything, or sim. Th. Att.orats. X. Men.; **plan** —W.COMPL.CL. that sthg. shd. or shd. not happen Lys. Ar. D. —W.INF. to do sthg. E. Antipho; **take care** —w. μή + INF. not to do sthg. Ar. D.; (intr.) **plan ahead** Th. Ar.; **act with premeditation** Lys.
5 || MID. **think of in advance, anticipate** —W.GEN. someone's intention E.
6 || MID. **take thought, have concern** —W.GEN. for persons, property, a country S. Th. Lys. X.(also act.) Men. —for the future, a danger, a contingency Att.orats. —W.PREP.PHR. on someone's behalf Lys. D.

προνοητικός ή όν adj. **1** (of a person) **possessing forethought, foresighted, prudent, cautious** X.; **capable of planning** (W.NEUT.ACC. certain things) Men.
2 (of a capacity) **for forethought** Arist.
3 (of the provision of water) **indicative of forethought** or **concern** (on the part of the gods) X.

—**προνοητικῶς** adv. **with foresight** X.

πρόνοια ᾱς, Ion. **προνοίη** ης f. [πρόνοος] **1 perceiving beforehand, foreknowledge, prescience** (W.GEN. of what is fated, of nothing) A. S.; (on the part of an oracle) S.
2 thinking ahead, forethought, foresight (of humans) S. E. Th. Ar. Att.orats. +; (W.ADJ. θεία **god-like** or **god-given**) E.; (of gods) Pi.fr. Hdt. E. Pl.
3 (specif.) **deliberate intention, plan** or **planning** A. E. Th. Pl.; (W.GEN. of a person) Hdt. Th. Lys.; (opp. τύχη chance) Hdt. Antipho; (prep.phr.) ἐκ προνοίας (προνοίης) **purposely, deliberately** Hdt. E. Ar. Pl. +
4 premeditation (of a crime) Antipho Lys.; (prep.phr.) ἐκ προνοίας with premeditation Att.orats. Pl. Arist.

5 careful thought, **concern** (W.GEN. or PREP.PHR. for someone or sthg.) Hdt. S. E. Th. Att.orats. +; (W.INF. to act appropriately) E.; (gener.) **prudence, caution, care** Att.orats.
—**Πρόνοια** ᾱς *f.* (appos.w. Ἀθηνᾶ, as cult-title of Athena at Delphi, a later modification of her title Προναία) **Forethought** D.

προνομαίᾱ ᾱς *f.* [προνομή] **proboscis, trunk** (of an elephant) Plu.

προνομείᾱ ᾱς *f.* [προνομεύω] **foraging** or **plundering** Plb.

προνομεύω *vb.* [προνομή] **go foraging** or **plundering** Plb.; (tr.) **forage on** or **plunder** —*a coast* Plb.

προνομή ῆς *f.* **1 foraging expedition, foray, raid** X. Men. Plu.
2 foraging party X. Plb.
3 pasturage Plu.
4 proboscis, trunk (of an elephant) Plb. | cf. προβοσκίς

πρόνομος ον *adj.* [προνέμω] (of herds) app., **moving forward while feeding, grazing** A.

πρό-νοος ον *adj.* [νόος] | compar. προνούστερος | (of persons) **foresighted, prudent** A. Hdt. S.

προ-νύμφιος ον *adj.* [νύμφη] (of the sleep of a bride-to-be) **prenuptial** Call.

προ-νύξ *adv.* **all night long** Semon.

προ-νύττω Att.*vb.* [νύσσω] **goad on** —*someone* (*to do sthg.*) Plb.

προ-νωπής ές *adj.* [νωπέομαι *be downcast*] **1** (of Iphigeneia, held above the sacrificial altar) **bent forward** or **face down** A.; (of a dying woman) **slumping forwards, drooping** E.
2 (fig., of a person) **prone, inclined** (W.PREP.PHR. to abusive talk) E.

προνώπιον ου *n.* [perh. πρό, ἐνώπια] **1 open space in front of a house**; (pl. for sg.) **front** (of a house) E.
2 (fig.) **porch** or **forecourt** (W.GEN. of a land, ref. to the nearest part of it visible fr. across the sea) E.
—**προνώπιος** ον *adj.* (quasi-advbl., of a person appearing) **in front** (of a house), **outside** E.

πρόξ προκός *f.* **a kind of deer, deer** Od. Call. AR.; (fig.ref. to a coward) Archil.

πρόξεινος Ion.m.: see πρόξενος

προξενέω contr.*vb.* [πρόξενος] | impf. προυξένουν | aor. προυξένησα | **1 be a proxenos, be official representative** (of a people) X. —W.GEN. *of a person, a people* X. D. Plu.; **be official host** —W.GEN. *of ambassadors* D.
2 (of an official at Delphi) **be host** or **guide** —W.NEUT.ACC. *regarding certain matters* E.; (elsewhere, of a local resident) **arrange a visit, furnish an introduction** (to a prophetess, for a foreigner) E.
3 (gener., of a ruler) **be protector of, look after** —W.GEN. *someone* (*fr. abroad*) E.; (of a man) **represent the interests of** —W.GEN. *women* (*envisaged as outsiders in the community*) Ar.; (of a local citizen) **give help and advice** —W.DAT. *to someone* (*fr. abroad*) S.
4 (of human or divine agents) **bring about** (a benefit or consequence, W.DAT. for someone); **procure** —*an honour* Plu.; **supply** —*sources of entertainment* Plu. —*the opportunity to do sthg.* X.; **cause** —*danger* X.
5 (of the hands of a person who has blinded himself) **cause** —W.ACC. + INF. *his eyes to be sightless* S.
6 (of hope) **produce, lend** —*courage* S.; (of trade) **procure** —*friendship w. foreign kings* Plu.; (of a woman's beauty) —*an undesirable husband* Plu.
7 introduce, recommend (usu. W.DAT. to someone) —*a person* D. —(W.PREDIC.SB. *as a teacher or pupil*) Pl.
8 propose (to someone) —*the establishment of a tyranny, a disgraceful course of action* Plu.

προξενίᾱ ᾱς *f.* **1 office** or **status of proxenos** Th. Att.orats. X.; (pl., ref. to the records of appointments to this office) Arist. Plb.
2 (gener.) **tie of guest-friendship** Pi.

πρό-ξενος, Ion. **πρόξεινος**, ου *m.* (*also f.* S.) [ξένος²]
1 (local citizen appointed by another state to look after its interests and those of its citizens) **proxenos, official representative, honorary consul** (oft. W.GEN. of a people, a city) Hdt. Th. Ar. Att.orats. Pl. +; (W.DAT. to a people, a person) X. Aeschin.
2 || PL. (gener., ref. to members of a family) **hosts** (W.GEN. of neighbouring peoples) Pi.
3 (at Delphi, ref. to a local official who escorted visitors to the oracle) **official host** E.
4 (gener.) **sponsor, protector** (of foreigners) A.; (of women, envisaged as outsiders in the community) Ar.
5 (ref. to the mistress of a house) **hostess** S.

προξυγγίγνομαι mid.*vb.*: see προσυγγίγνομαι

προ-οδοποιέω contr.*vb.* | pf. προωδοπεποίηκα | **1** prepare a way in advance (for some activity); (of a person) **pave the way** —W.DAT. *for someone else* (W.ACC. or GEN. *in achieving sthg.*) Plu.; (of old age) —W.DAT. *for cowardice* Arist.; (of children's games) —W.PREP.PHR. *for later pursuits* Arist.
2 || PASS. (fig., of a person) **be prepared in advance** —W.PREP.PHR. *by sthg.* (sts. W. 2ND PREP.PHR. *for sthg.*) Arist.

πρό-οδος¹ ου *m.* [ὁδός] || COLLECTV.PL. **advance party** (of soldiers) X.

πρό-οδος² ου *f.* **1 journey forward, progress, advance** (of troops) X.
2 (app. collectv.) **advance guard** (of soldiers) Plb.

πρό-οιδα pf.*vb.* [οἶδα] **know beforehand** —*sthg.* Hdt. Th. Att.orats. Pl. + —W.INDIR.Q. or COMPL.CL. *what* (*or that sthg.*) *is the case* Lys. X. D. Arist. —W.ACC. + FUT. (or PRES.) PTCPL. *that sthg. will be* (*or is*) *the case* Th. Att.orats. Men.; (intr.) Hdt. Th. Att.orats. X.

προοίμην (athem.aor.mid.opt.): see προίημι

προοιμιάζομαι, also contr. **φροιμιάζομαι** (A. E. Arist.) mid.*vb.* [προοίμιον] | aor. ἐπροοιμιασάμην, also ἐφροιμιασάμην | pf. πεπροοιμίασμαι, also πεφροιμίασμαι |
1 deliver a preamble or **write a preface** Pl. X. Arist. Plu.; **say** (W.ACC. sthg.) **by way of preamble** E. Pl. X. Arist.; **mention** (W.ACC. certain gods) **in a preamble** (to a prayer) A. || PASS. (of things) **be said by way of preamble** Arist.
|| NEUT.PL.PF.PASS.PTCPL.SB. **prefatory remarks** Arist.
2 (fig.) **make a start, take the first step** (in an action) A.

προ-οίμιον, also contr. **φροίμιον** (A. E.), ου *n.* [οἴμη] **1** that which precedes an epic singer's narrative (ref. to an address or hymn to a god); **prelude** (W.GEN. to Zeus) Pi.; (specif.) **hymn** (W.GEN. to Apollo, ref. to one of the Homeric hymns, also to a composition by Socrates) Th. Pl.
2 prelude (on the lyre, before singing begins) Pi.
3 preamble, opening, introduction (of a poem, speech, or sim., sts. W.GEN.) A. Pi. E. Ar. Isoc. Pl. +
4 (fig.) **prelude** (W.GEN. to spear-fighting, ref. to a battle-cry) Pi.*fr.*; (W.GEN. to murder, ref. to a scream) E.; (without GEN., to some future activity, ref. to lamentation, dancing, a dream) A.; (ref. to the onset of madness) A.; **start, opening** (W.GEN. of hostilities, someone's reign) Plb.

προ-οίχομαι mid.*vb.* **depart previously** X.

προ-ομαλύνω *vb.* **first make** (W.ACC. a material to be moulded) **level** or **smooth** Pl.

προ-όμνῡμι *vb.* | aor.ptcpl. προομόσᾱς, also προυμόσᾱς | **swear an oath beforehand** A. D. —W.ACC. *by the gods* (w. ἦ μήν + INF. *that one expects sthg.*) Pl. —W.COMPL.CL. *that sthg. is the case* D.

προ-ομολογέω *contr.vb.* **agree beforehand** —W.ACC. + INF. *that sthg. is the case* Pl. ‖ PF. or PLPF.PASS. (of a proposition) **have already been agreed** Pl. Aeschin.; (of a person) —W.INF. *to be such and such* D. ‖ IMPERS. **it has already been agreed** —W.ACC. + INF. *that sthg. is the case* Pl.

προοπτέον (neut.impers.vbl.adj.): see προοράω

προόπτης ου *m.* [προόψομαι, see προοράω] **scout** Plb.

πρόοπτος, Att. **προῦπτος**, ον *adj.* **1** (of future events or circumstances) **foreseen** or **foreseeable**; (of death) **expected, certain** Hdt. S. E. Isoc. D. Plu.; (of danger, trouble) Th. D.
2 (of present facts or circumstances) **plain to see**; (of a messenger's report) **clear** (in significance) A.(v.l. πρεπτός); (of a portent) Plu.

προορᾱτός ή όν *adj.* [προοράω] (of circumstances) **foreseeable** X.

προ-οράω *contr.vb.* | fut. προόψομαι | aor.2 προεῖδον, dial. πρόιδον (Pi.), inf. προϊδεῖν, Aeol. προΐδην ‖ neut.impers. vbl.adj. προοπτέον |
1 **see ahead** (of oneself), **see before one** —*a person, the outline of a person, persons approaching, ships* Hdt. Antipho Th. —*the ground ahead* X. —*sthg. happening* Il.; (of birds) —*a hawk* Il.; (mid., of persons) —*a ship, a boar* Od. Hes.; (act., intr.) **look forward** or **before one** Od.; **see ahead** Th.
2 **see in advance** (of a stated or implied time); **see** (sts. W.ACC. someone or sthg.) **first** (before sthg. happens) Hom. Th.; (of a horse) **see** (W.ACC. many things) **before** (its rider) X.; **see** (W.ACC. someone) **previously** NT.
3 **see beforehand** (future events); **foresee** —*the future, one's fate, contingencies* Pi. Hdt. Th. Pl. + —W.COMPL.CL. *that sthg. will be the case* Th.; **look ahead to, anticipate** —*sailing weather* Alc. —*safety* Th.; (intr.) **see ahead** Isoc. Pl. Arist. ‖ MID. **foresee, anticipate** —*future events, contingencies* Th. D. Plb. —W.INDIR.Q. *what situation one is being led into* Th. —W.ACC. + PTCPL. *that one's death is close* Men.
4 **make provision, take thought, be concerned** —W.GEN. *for persons, food* (i.e. *its supply*) Hdt. —W.PREP.PHR. *on someone's behalf, against future dangers* Th. Lys.; (intr.) **show concern** (for others) Hdt. ‖ MID. **provide for, look after, attend to** —W.ACC. *one's interests* Th. —*contingencies or sim.* Pl. D.; **be attentive** —W.GEN. *to circumstances* Th.; **take care** —W. μή + INF. *not to do sthg.* D.; (of laws) **provide** —W. ὅπως + SUBJ. *that sthg. shd. happen* D. ‖ PASS. (of an offence) **be provided for, be covered** (by a law) D.

προ-ορίζω *vb.* (of God) **predetermine** —W.ACC. + INF. *that sthg. shd. happen* NT.

προ-ορμάω *contr.vb.* (of persons) **hasten ahead, push on** X. ‖ PASS. (of wagons) **be hurried on ahead** X.

προ-οφείλω, Att. **προυφείλω** *vb.* | 3sg.impf.pass. προωφείλετο | **1** **have a pre-existing debt or obligation; owe** —*a penalty* (W.DAT. *to someone; to one's ribs, in reparation for a past injury*) E. Ar. ‖ PASS. (of tribute, pay) **be owing** Hdt. X.; (of a penalty for a past injury) —W.DAT. *to someone* Antipho D.; (of a service, an alliance, for services previously rendered) Th.; (fig., of hatred) —W.PREP.PHR. *fr. one state towards another* Hdt.
2 **have a duty, owe it** (to someone) —W.ACC. + INF. *that they shd. be treated well* E. —W.DAT. + INF. *to a city, to give it good advice* Ar.

προοχή ῆς *f.* [προέχω] **promontory, headland** Plb.

πρό-οψις εως *f.* [ὄψις] **advance sight** (of enemy troops) Th.

προπαιδείᾱ ᾱς *f.* [προπαιδεύω] **preparatory teaching** or **study** Pl.

προ-παιδεύω *vb.* ‖ PASS. **be given** (W.COGN.ACC. *preparatory teaching*) **in advance** —W.GEN. *of dialectic* Pl.; **be given preliminary training** Arist.

προ-παλαιπαλαίπαλαι *adv.* [πάλαι] **for a very very very long time** —*ref. to being ready* Ar.

πρό-παππος ου *m.* [πάππος] **great-grandfather** Att.orats. Pl. Plu. ‖ PL. **forefathers** Call.

πρόπαρ *prep. and adv.* [reltd. προπάροιθε] **1** (prep., ref. to position) **before, in front of** —W.GEN. *a person, a group of people* Hes. A. E.
2 (ref. to the position of persons and things) **in front of, along** —W.GEN. *a shore* (since what is seen fr. inland appears in front of it) AR.; (ref. to the position of a river) **alongside** —W.GEN. *another river* (when the former is nearer) E.
3 (adv., ref. to time) **before then, sooner, first** A.; **formerly, once** E.(v.l. πρόπαν)

προ-παραβάλλομαι *mid.vb.* (of persons building a wall) **lay out** (W.ACC. *stones*) **earlier** —W.DAT. *for themselves* Th.

προ-παρασκευάζω *vb.* (of workers) **prepare beforehand** —*wool* (for dyeing, weaving) Pl.; (of a politician) **condition, accustom** —*people's minds* (W.COMPL.CL. *to accepting that sthg. will be the case*) Th.; (of a husband) **provide in advance** —*all that will be beneficial* (W.DAT. *for future children*) X. ‖ MID. **arrange beforehand** —*a funeral* Is.; **make** (W.NEUT.ACC. *these*) **prior arrangements** Th.; (of a commander) **make advance preparations** Plu. ‖ PF.PASS. (of people) **be already prepared** —W.COMPL.CL. *in case sthg. shd. happen* Th.

προ-παρέχω *vb.* **offer in advance** —W.DBL.ACC. *oneself as an ally* (W.DAT. *to someone*) X. ‖ MID. **provide for oneself in advance** —*a day's food* X.

προ-παρίστημι *vb.* | dial.athem.aor. προπαρέσταν | **stand by** (W.DAT. *someone*) **as champion** E.

προ-πάροιθε(ν) *adv. and prep.* **1** (adv., ref. to position) **before, in front** Hom. Hes. hHom. AR.; (prep.) **in front** —W.GEN. *of someone, sthg., somewhere* Hom. Hes. hHom. Pi.*fr.* B. Hellenist.poet.; **in front of, along** —W.GEN. *a shore* (since what is seen fr. inland appears in front of it) Il.
2 (prep.) perh. **on behalf** —W.GEN. *of someone* AR.
3 (ref. to time) **before then, beforehand, first** Hom. AR.; (prep.) **before** —W.GEN. *marriage* A.
4 **in time past, before, formerly** Od. Call. AR.; (quasi-adjl., of a noble family) **of a former age** E.

πρό-πᾱς πᾶσα πᾶν *adj.* [πᾶς] **1** (of a day) **all, whole, entire** Hom. Hes. hHom. AR. Theoc.; (of a land, house, populace, race) Trag.; (of time) A.; (of a family's destiny) S.
2 ‖ PL. (of ships) **all** Il.; (of sufferings) S.
3 ‖ MASC.PL.COLLECTV.PRON. **everyone, all** E.*fr.*

—**πρόπαν** *neut.adv.* **completely** E.(dub.) | see πρόπαρ 3

προ-πάσχω *vb.* **1** **suffer the first injury** (opp. *strike the first blow*) Hdt. Th.
2 **suffer an earlier injury** —W.PREP.PHR. *fr. someone* Th.; (tr.) **suffer earlier** —*a wrong or injury* S. Antipho Pl.; **experience earlier** —*some good* X.

προ-πάτωρ ορος *m.* [πατήρ] **1** (sg. and pl., ref. to humans) **forefather, ancestor** Pi. Hdt. E. Pl. Plu.; (ref. to Zeus) S.
2 **grandfather** (opp. πατήρ *father*) Pl.

πρό-πειρα ᾱς *f.* [πεῖρα] **1** **first test** (of troops in battle) Hdt.
2 **preliminary experiment** (to see whether sthg. is possible) Th.

πρό-πεμπτα *neut.pl.adv.* [πέμπτος] **five days before** D.(law)

προ-πέμπω *vb.* | aor. προέπεμψα, also προύπεμψα | **1** **cause** (someone) **to go forth** (on a mission or journey); **send forth** or **ahead, despatch** (sts. W.FUT.PTCPL. or INF. *to do sthg.*)

—heralds, messengers, scouts, ambassadors, soldiers Hom.(sts.tm.) Parm. Hdt. S. E. Th. +—*wagons, ships* Hdt. Th. X. || PASS. (of a messenger, a scout) be sent ahead Th. X.
2 see (someone) off on a journey; **send on one's way, send off** —*someone* (W.DAT. *w. horses and chariot*) Od.; **see off** —*someone* Hdt. Th. X. —(W.PREP.PHR. *out of a city*) Hdt. —(W.GEN. *fr. a land*) E. || MID. (of a commander) **send off** —*troops* (*who are filing past him*) X. || PASS. (of the Minotaur's victims, w. allusion to 4) **be seen off** —W.PREP.PHR. + ADV. *to certain death, by the whole populace* Isoc.
3 accompany (someone) on a journey; **conduct, escort, accompany** —*someone* (sts. W.PREP.PHR. *to a place*) A. Hdt. S. Ar. Att.orats. Pl. +; **follow** —*a retreating enemy* X.; (fig., of a diner) **help on the way, help down** —*a piece of bread* (W.DAT. *w. a relish*) X. || PASS. (of persons) be escorted Isoc.
4 (specif., of mourners, their lamentation) **escort** —*a dead person* (sts. W.PREP.PHR. *to the tomb*) A.; **accompany** —*the dead* (W.DAT. *w. dirges*) Pl. || PASS. (of dead persons) be escorted to the grave Pl.
5 convey or cause to be conveyed; **send off** —*drink-offerings* (W.DAT. *to the gods below*) A. —*a person's ashes* (*to someone*) S.; (of a messenger) **convey, bring** —*grievous news* S.; (of arrows) —*death* S.; send on (to a further destination), **pass on** —*sacred objects* Hdt.; (wkr.sens.) **hand over** —*a weapon* S.
6 cause (a message) to be conveyed; **send** —*messages* (W.DAT. *to someone*) S. —*peace proposals* (W.PREP.PHR. *to a city*) Th.; (intr.) **send a message** —W.PREP.PHR. *to a city* Th. X. || IMPERS.PF.PASS. a message has been sent Th.
7 propel (sthg.) forwards; **hurl** —*a spear* (W.PREP.PHR. *towards heaven*) B.; (of Zeus) —*lightning* (*fr. heaven*) B.; (of the embers of a burning city) **send forth** —*rich puffs of wealth* A.

προ-περιλαμβάνω *vb.* **envisage** (W.DAT. in one's mind) **beforehand** —*the completion of a project* Plb.

προ-πέρυσι(ν) *adv.* **the year before last, two years ago** Lys. Pl. D.

προ-πετάννῡμι *vb.* (of a contingent of troops) **spread** (W.ACC. themselves) **out at the front** —W.GEN. *of the army* X.

προπέτεια ᾱς *f.* [προπετής] **impetuosity, recklessness, rashness** Isoc. D. Arist. Call.*epigr.* Plb. Plu.

προπετής ές *adj.* [προπίπτω] | compar. προπετέστερος, superl. προπετέστατος | **1** (of a person slain as a sacrifice) **falling forwards, collapsed** (W.PREP.PHR. over someone's tomb) E.; (of a dying person) **prostrate** S.
2 (of a tuft of wool) fallen to the ground, **thrown down, discarded** S.
3 (of a horse's neck) inclined forwards, **drooping** X.
4 (fig., of a person) **verging** (W.PREP.PHR. on grey hairs) E.
5 (fig., quasi-advbl., of a listener who is swept) **headlong** (by a style of speech) Arist.; (of persons) rushing headlong, **ready, eager** (W.PREP.PHR. for sthg.) Pl. X. Men.; (W.INF. to do sthg.) X.
6 (fig., of persons) **impetuous, reckless, rash** D. Arist. Men. Plb.; (of behaviour) X. Hyp. Men. Plb. NT.; (of lack of restraint) Arist.; (of pleasures) Aeschin.; (of laughter) **uncontrolled** Isoc.
7 (of drawing of lots) perh. **random** Pi.

—**προπετῶς** *adv.* **1 headlong** —*ref. to a horse careering downhill* X.
2 impetuously, recklessly, over-hastily X. Isoc. Pl. D. Arist. Men. +

προ-πηλακίζω *vb.* [πηλός] | fut. προπηλακιῶ | aor. προυπηλάκισα | (fig.) **drag through the mud** or **throw mud at**, **scoff at, insult, abuse** —*persons, their words, their poverty, or sim.* S. Th. Att.orats. Pl. + || PASS. (usu. of persons) be abused Ar. Att.orats. Pl. +

προπηλάκισις εως *f.* **disrespectful attitude** (W.GEN. to old age) Pl.(pl.)

προπηλακισμός οῦ *m.* (sts.pl.) **contemptuous, abusive** or **insulting behaviour** Hdt. Pl. D. Arist.; **abusive treatment** (W.GEN. of someone) Plu.; **mockery, travesty** (W.GEN. of justice) Aeschin.

προπηλακιστικῶς *adv.* **in an insulting manner** D.

προ-πίνω *vb.* | impf. προύπινον | fut. προπίομαι | aor.2 προύπιον | **1 drink up** —W.INTERN.ACC. one long draught Anacr. || PASS. (of a cup) be drained Call.*epigr.*
2 drink first (in honour of or to the health of someone, usu. before handing over the cup to that person to drink from); **drink a toast** Hippon. Ar. X. —W.DAT. *to someone* Pi. Critias X. Plu.; (tr.) **drink as a toast** (to someone) —*a cup or horn of wine* X. Plu. —*loving-cups* D.
3 (fig., fr. the custom of sts. giving a precious cup, or some other gift, to the recipient of the toast) **make a present of** —*one's thighs* (*to a lover*) Anacr.; (pejor., w.connot. of irresponsibility) **give away** (W.DAT. to someone) —*war-spoils* D. —*one's freedom* D. —*money or sim.* Plu.; **betray, sacrifice** —*one's allies, one's country* (W.DAT. *to someone*) E. Plu. || PASS. (of a poem) be offered as a present Dionys.Eleg.; (of interests of state) be sacrificed —W.ADVBL.PHR. *for momentary popularity* D.

προ-πίπτω *vb.* | aor.2 προύπεσον | **1** fall forwards; (of rowers) **bend forwards, fall to the oars** Od.; (of a helpless person, a suppliant) **fall prostrate** E.; (of a fighting cock) **fall dead** Plb.; (of a pancratiast) **fling oneself** —W.PREP.PHR. *to the ground* Theoc.
2 intrude rashly, burst in —W.DAT. *on a sacred place* S.
3 (fig., of a politician) **thrust oneself forward** (opp. hang back) Plb.; (of an angry person) **act impetuously** Plu.
4 (of troops, ships) **advance rashly** or **too far** Plb. —W.GEN. *ahead of others* Plb.
5 (of a crag, a structure) **project** (sts. W.GEN. beyond a point) Plb.; (of a pike, held by a soldier) —W.ADVBL.ACC. *a certain distance* (w. πρό + GEN. *in front of his body*) Plb.; (of a wounded person's bowels) **protrude** Plu.
6 (of a horse's shadow) **fall in front** (of it) Plu.
7 (of a word) **be let fall, be uttered** (by someone) Plu.

προ-πιστεύω *vb.* **previously trust** or **believe** (someone) D. || PASS. be already trusted —W.INF. + PREDIC.ADJ. *to be worthy* X.

προ-πίτνω *vb.* (of subjects of an oriental king) **fall prostrate** A.; (of a suppliant) S. E.

προ-πλέω contr.*vb.* [πλέω¹] —also **προπλώω** Ion.*vb.* (of persons, ships) **sail in advance** or **ahead** (of others) Hdt. Th. Plb.

πρό-πλους ουν Att.*adj.* [πλόος] | masc.fem.nom.pl. πρόπλοι | (of ships) **sailing in advance** (of the main fleet) Th. Isoc.; sailing in front (of a fleet), **leading** X.

προ-ποδέω contr.*vb.* [πούς] (of Apollo) **set the foot forward, lead the way** (in dancing) Call.

προ-ποδίζω *vb.* (of a warrior) **set the foot forward, advance** Il.

προ-ποιέω contr.*vb.* **1 do** (W.ACC. a service) **previously** —W.PREP.PHR. *for someone* Hdt.
2 (intr.) **act first, make the first move** (in a war) Th.
3 || PASS. (of ships, a seat) **be constructed previously** Hdt.

προ-πολεμέω contr.vb. **make war in defence** —W.GEN. *of a country, of people* Isoc. Plb. Plu.; (of a class of persons) **be a state's defenders in war** Pl. Arist.
προπόλευμα ατος *n.* [πρόπολος] (ref. to a broom) **instrument of service, servant** E.
προπολέω contr.vb. (of Hekate) **be minister or attendant** (of a deity) S.*fr.*
προ-πολιτεύομαι mid.vb. || NEUT.PL.PF.PASS.PTCPL.SB. **former political services** Plb.
πρό-πολος ου *m.f.* [πέλω, πολέω] **1** app., **one who goes before** (someone); **minister, attendant, servant** (of a deity) hHom. A. Hdt. E. Ar.; (of a person) Xenoph. E. AR.; (W.GEN. of the Muses, ref. to a poet) B.; (fig., W.GEN. of lovers' brawls, ref. to wine) Ion
2 (appos.w. πάτρα *family*, ref. to a clan which habitually provided victors, composers or performers) **minister** (W.DAT. to victory songs) Pi.
3 || PL. **crewmen** (of a ship) Pi.
προπομπή ῆς *f.* [προπέμπω] **1 arrangement for departure** (made by a host for a guest) Plu.; **despatching** (W.GEN. of couriers) **on the next stage of a journey** Plu.
2 (concr.) **escort** (for a traveller) X. Plb.
3 procession Plu.
προπομπός οῦ *m.f.* **1** (appos.w. λόχον *detachment*) **escort** (for a commander) X. || PL. **escorts** (of a person or persons, on a journey, in a procession or as a guard) A. X. Plu.; (of a corpse, to the grave) A.; (appos.w. ἱππεῖς *cavalry*) Plu.
2 || ADJ. (of a person) **escorting** (W.ACC. drink-offerings) A.(dub.)
προ-πονέω contr.vb. **1 labour beforehand** (for sthg. subsequently obtained) X. || NEUT.PL.PF.PASS.PTCPL.SB. **earlier labours** X.
2 labour on behalf of —W.GEN. *someone* X.; (of mercenaries) **bear the brunt of fighting** X.
3 labour for (i.e. w. a view to obtaining) —W.GEN. *sthg.* X.
4 (act.) **tire** (W.ACC. oneself) **in advance** (of a battle) Plu.
Προ-ποντίς ίδος *f.* [Πόντος] **sea lying before the Pontos** (Black Sea), **Propontis** (now Sea of Marmara) A. Hdt. AR. Theoc. Plb. Plu.
προπορεία ᾶς *f.* [προπορεύομαι] **advance journey, reconnaissance expedition** Plb.
προ-πορεύομαι mid.pass.vb. | aor.ptcpl. προπορευθείς |
1 (of persons, esp. soldiers) **go forward, advance** Plb.; **go in front** (sts. W.GEN. of someone) Plb. NT.
2 (of an individual) **step forward** Plb.
3 proceed or **be advanced** —W.PREP.PHR. *to an office* Plb.; **come forward** (as a candidate for office) Plb.
πρό-ποσις εως *f.* [πόσις²] **drinking of a toast, toast** Simon. Critias
προ-πότης ου *m.* **one who drinks a toast** || PL. (appos.w. θίασοι *bands of revellers*) **toast-drinkers** E.
πρό-πους ποδος *m.* [πούς] **foot** (of a hill or mountain) Plb. Plu.
προ-πράκτωρ ορος *m.* **one who acts on behalf of another, protector, champion** A.*satyr.fr.*
προ-πράσσω vb. **do** (W.ACC. a favour) **in advance** A.(dub.) || NEUT.PL.PF.PASS.PTCPL.SB. **earlier events** (in a tragic plot) Arist.
προ-πρᾴων ον *adj.* [πρᾷος] (of a person) **very kindly** Pi.
προ-πρηνής ές *Ion.adj.* [πρανής] **1** (quasi-advbl., of a person lying) **face down, prone** Il.
2 (of a person) **stooping forwards** Od.
—**προπρηνές** *Ion.neut.adv.* **forwards** (opp. backwards) —*ref. to moving one's staff* Il.

προ-πρό adv. and prep. **1** (adv.) **on and on, deeply, far** —*ref. to going into a region* AR.
2 eagerly AR.
3 (prep.) **right before** —W.GEN. *someone's eyes* AR.
προπρο-βιάζομαι mid.vb. **laboriously heave** (a beached ship) **forwards** (to the sea) AR.
προπρο-καταΐγδην ep.prep. (ref. to a ship in a storm) **plunging ever further through** —W.GEN. *the hollow sea* AR.
προπρο-κυλίνδομαι mid.pass.vb. **1** (pejor., of a suppliant) **roll about before, grovel at the feet of** —W.GEN. *someone* Il.
2 (fig., of a wanderer) **roll ever onwards** Od.
πρό-πρυμνα adv. [πρύμνα] **from the stern** —*ref. to jettisoning cargo* A.
προ-πύλαιος ον *adj.* [πύλαι] **1** (of Apollo of the Street, i.e. his statue) **before the door** (of a house) Ar.
2 || NEUT.SB. (usu.pl.) **gateway** or **gatehouse** (of a temple or precinct) Hdt. Arist.(sg.) Men.; (of the precinct and theatre of Dionysus at Athens) And.(sg.); (of the pre-Periklean Acropolis) Hdt.; (specif.) **Propylaia** (ref. to the elaborate gateway on the Acropolis, commissioned by Perikles, built 437–432 BC) Th. Ar. Aeschin. D. Plu.
πρό-πυλον ου *n.* **gateway** (of the pre-Periklean Acropolis) Arist. || PL. **gateway** or **porch** (of a temple) Hdt.; **portals** (of a palace) S. E.
προ-πυνθάνομαι mid.vb. **learn beforehand** —*news, information* Hdt. X. —W.ACC. + PTCPL. *that sthg. is the case* Hdt. —W.COMPL.CL. *that sthg. will happen* Th.; (intr.) **gain advance information** (about sthg.) Th.
πρό-πυργος ον *adj.* [πύργος] (of sacrifices) **before the towers** (of a city) A.
προ-πωλέω contr.vb. **negotiate a sale, act as broker** (on someone's behalf) Pl.
προ-ρέω ep.contr.vb. | iteratv.impf. προρέεσκον | (of streams and rivers) **flow forth** Hom. Hes. AR.; (tr.) **pour forth** —*water* hHom. AR.
προρρηθῆναι (aor.pass.inf.): see προείρω
πρό-ρρησις εως *f.* [ῥῆσις] **1 statement made beforehand; earlier order** or **instruction** Th.; **prediction** (of a seer) Plu.
2 statement made publicly; declaration (of war) D.; **proclamation** (of the rules of a contest) Pl.; **homily** (giving advice and instruction) Pl.
3 (leg.) **public notice** (of a charge of murder) Antipho Pl. | see προαγορεύω 6, προεῖπον 7
4 app. **prompting** (W.GEN. of logic, ref. to an idea) Plu.
προρρητέον (neut.impers.vbl.adj.): see προείρω
πρό-ρρητος ον *adj.* [ῥητός] (of instructions) **previously told** (W.DAT. to someone) S.
πρό-ρριζος ον *adj.* [ῥίζα] **1** (of trees) **roots-first, uprooted** Il. Plu.; (fig., of shrines) Pl.
2 (quasi-advbl., of thickets falling in a forest fire) **in utter devastation** Il.
3 (fig., quasi-advbl., of persons or families destroyed, ruined or eliminated) **root and branch, utterly** Hdt. S. E. And.; (of a person flung fr. a chariot) **to utter destruction** S.
πρός, ep. and dial. **προτί** and **ποτί**, also dial. **πότ** prep. | πότ sts. written in combination w. following wd., e.g. ποττάν (for πρὸς τάν) | W.ACC., GEN. and DAT. |
—**A** | **space or location** |
1 up against and in contact; (ref. to clasping or clinging) **to** —W.DAT. *someone or sthg.* Hom. +
2 bordering on, by —W.DAT. *a country, the sea* Th. X. —W.ACC. *the sea* NT.
3 at —W.DAT. *a location* Hom. + | for πρὸς ποσί (*fig.*) *at one's feet* see πούς 8

4 close to, near —w.DAT. *someone, land, sea* S. Th. Men.
5 on the point of —w.DAT. *an activity (i.e. doing it)* S.
6 in —w.DAT. *a state of affairs* S.
7 in the presence of, before —w.DAT. *a judge or magistrate* D.
—**B** | direction |
1 on the side of or in the direction of, facing —w.ACC. or GEN. *a location, peoples, west, or sim.* Hom. +
2 (ref. to looking) **in the direction of, towards** —w.ACC. *someone or sthg.* Od. +
3 (ref. to speaking, replying, or sim.) **to** —w.ACC. *someone* Hom. +; (ref. to lamenting) **towards** —w.ACC. *heaven* Il.
4 (ref. to fighting or sim.) **against** —w.ACC. *someone (esp. an enemy)* Il. + | for πρὸς κέντρα *against the pricks* see κέντρον 1
5 (ref. to struggling) **in the face of, against** —w.DAT. *high seas* A.
—**C** | movt. |
1 in the direction of, towards —w.ACC. *someone or sthg.* Hom. + | see also αἶπος 2, ἀνάντης 3, λέπας, ὄπισθε(ν) 4, ὄρθιος 2, σιμός 5
2 all the way to (so as to reach), to —w.ACC. *someone or sthg.* Hom. +; (ref. to coming to sit down) **at** —w.ACC. *an altar, someone's knees* Od.
3 all the way to (so as to be in contact with), against —w.ACC. *sthg.* Hom. + —w.ACC. or DAT. *rocks* Od.; (ref. to misery alighting) **upon** —w.ACC. *someone* A.
4 (ref. to wounding or sim.) **in, at** —w.ACC. *a part of the body* Hom.
5 all the way down to (so as to be in contact with), down to or **upon, against** —w.DAT. *the ground* Hom.
6 (ref. to tearing the skin) **against** —w.DAT. *rocks* Od.; (ref. to forging sthg.) **on** —w.DAT. *an anvil* Pi.
7 (ref. to inviting someone) **to** —w.ACC. *dinner* Plu.
8 (ref. to things leading) **to** —w.ACC. *good repute* Arist.
—**D** | time |
1 towards, near to —w.ACC. *evening, dawn, daytime* Od. + | see ἑσπέρα 1, ἡμέρα 1
2 at the approach of —w.ACC. *the bloom of youth, old age* Pi. E. Pl.
3 in —w.DAT. *old age* Ibyc.
—**E** | origin |
1 (ref. to arriving) **from** —w.GEN. *a location* Od.
2 (specif., ref. to a guest arriving) **from** —w.GEN. *Zeus (i.e. under his protection)* Od.
3 (ref. to obtaining or inheriting) **from** —w.GEN. *a person or god* Hom. +
4 (ref. to learning or hearing) **from** —w.GEN. *someone* Il. +
5 (ref. to being descended fr. someone) **on the side of** —w.GEN. *one's father or mother* Hdt. Isoc. D.; **in the line of** —w.GEN. *men or women (i.e. in the male or female line)* Isoc. Pl. D.
6 characteristically deriving from or belonging to, **in the nature** or **way of, characteristic of, like** —w.GEN. *someone or sthg.* Hdt. Trag. Ar. +
—**F** | agency or cause |
1 by the agency of, by, at the hands of, from, through —w.GEN. *someone or sthg.* Il. +
2 at the instigation of —w.GEN. *someone* Il.
3 by reason of, because of —w.GEN. *sthg.* S.
—**G** | relationship |
1 in respect of, in relation to —w.ACC. *someone or sthg.* Pi. Hdt. Trag. Th. + | for πρὸς ταῦτα *in view of this, therefore* see οὗτος 11

2 (ref. to measuring the time allowed for a speech) **with reference to, by** —w.ACC. *a number of water jars or an amount of water* Aeschin. Arist.
3 (ref. to living) **in dependence upon** —w.ACC. *someone* Arist.
4 (ref. to having affection, enmity, or sim.) **towards** —w.ACC. *someone* Pi. Trag. +
5 (ref. to being occupied) **with** —w.DAT. *sthg.* Pl. Aeschin. Plb.
6 (ref. to being engaged) **in** —w.DAT. *an activity* X. D. —w.ACC. Plb. Plu.
—**H** | purpose or result |
with a view to, for —w.ACC. *some end* S. E. Pl. X. + | (phrs.) πρὸς ἔπος and πρὸς λόγον *to the point*, πρὸς καιρόν and πρὸς τὸ καίριον *(i.e. appropriately, effectively)*, πρὸς χάριν *with the aim or effect of pleasing* (see ἔπος 6, λόγος 23, καιρός 3, καίριος 4, χάρις 11)
—**I** | advantage or benefit |
1 to the advantage of —w.GEN. *someone* Hdt. Trag. + —*one's glory, argument* Th. Pl.
2 on the side of, in support of —w.GEN. *someone* A. Hdt. E. Pl.
—**J** | swearing, witnessing, judging |
1 (ref. to swearing or supplicating) **in the name of, by** —w.GEN. *a divinity, person, part of the body, or sim.* Od. +
2 (ref. to bearing witness) **in the presence of, before** —w.GEN. *a person or god* Il.
3 in the judgement of, in the eyes of —w.GEN. *a person or god* Hom. +
—**K** | attendant circumstances |
1 to the accompaniment of —w.ACC. *a musical instrument* Archil. Pi. E. X. +
2 by the light of —w.ACC. *the sun, moon, day, a lamp, torch* Th. And. Ar. X. +
3 in accordance with —w.GEN. *justice, impiety* Trag.; **consistent with** —w.GEN. *someone's reputation* Th. | see also τρόπος 6
4 in a state of —w.DAT. *fear* Plu.
5 (phrs.) πρὸς βίαν *through force, violence or defiance*, πρὸς καιρόν *on the spur of the moment*, πρὸς τὸ λιπαρές *insistently*, πρὸς μέρος *proportionately* (see βία 14, καιρός 7, λιπαρής 5, μέρος 15)
—**L** | addition |
1 in addition to, as well as —w.DAT. *sthg.* Od. +; (phr.) πρὸς τούτοις *on top of that, in addition* (see οὗτος 11); (w.vb. of adding) **to** —w.ACC. *sthg.* Hdt. Ar. Pl. +
2 (as adv.) **in addition, furthermore, besides** Hom. +
—**M** | exchange or reciprocal relations |
1 (ref. to making an exchange or agreement) **with** —w.ACC. *someone* Il. Hdt. Th. +
2 (ref. to exchanging sthg.) **for** —w.ACC. *sthg. else* Pl.
—**N** | comparison or relation |
1 (ref. to comparing sthg.) **with** —w.ACC. *sthg. else* Hdt.; (without a vb. expressing comparison) **compared with** —w.ACC. *someone* Hdt. Th. Pl. | (phr.) ἓν πρὸς ἕν *in a one-to-one comparison* (see εἷς 9)
2 (ref. to judging or sim.) **in relation to** —w.ACC. *a criterion* Emp. E. Isoc. +
—**O** | approximation |
close to, about —w.ACC. *a certain number* X. Plb.

προ-σάββατον ου *n.* **day before the sabbath** (i.e. Friday) NT.

προσ-αγγελία ᾱς *f.* **report, message** Plb. Plu.

προσ-αγγέλλω *vb.* **1 bring an announcement** or **report** Plb. —w.ACC. *of sthg.* Plb. Plu. —w.COMPL.CL. or ACC. + INF. *that*

προσαγόρευσις

sthg. is the case Plb. Plu. —W.ACC. + PTCPL. *that someone is doing sthg.* Plu. || PASS. (of facts, events) be reported D. Plb. Plu.; (of persons) —w. ὡς + NOM.PTCPL. *as doing sthg.* Plb.; (W.PTCPL. alone) Plu. || IMPERS.PASS. it is reported —W.COMPL.CL. or ACC. + INF. *that someone is doing sthg.* Plb.
2 publicly offer for sale —*someone's property* Plu.
3 denounce —*someone* (W.DAT. *to the Senate*) Plu.

προσαγόρευσις εως *f.* [προσαγορεύω] **address, greeting** (of a person by another, in a speech or letter) Plu.

προσαγορευτέος ᾱ ον *vbl.adj.* (of a thing) **to be called** (W.DAT. by a particular name) Pl.

προσ-αγορεύω *vb.* | fut. προσαγορεύσω (Pl. Arist.) | aor. προσηγόρευσα (X. +) || aor.pass. προσηγορεύθην (A.) || neut.impers.vbl.adj. προσαγορευτέον || mainly pres. (fut. and aor.pass. being usu. supplied by προσείρω, aor. by προσεῖπον) |
1 speak to; **address, greet** —*someone* Hdt. Ar. Pl. Men. —*a country* (*after absence*) Lycurg.; (intr.) **deliver a greeting** Th. Thphr. || PASS. be addressed or greeted Th. Thphr.
2 address by name; **address, greet** —*someone* (W.DAT. or ADV. *by name*) Antipho X. || PASS. be addressed (in greeting) —W.PREDIC.SB. *as such and such* (i.e. *by a particular title*) Plb. Plu.
3 bid —W.ACC. + INF. χαίρειν *someone 'good day'* Ar. —*sthg. 'goodbye'* (i.e. *dismiss it fr. consideration*) Pl.
4 designate, call —*someone or sthg.* (W.PREDIC.ACC. *such and such*, i.e. *give them a particular name, title or description*) A. Att.orats. Pl. + —(W.DAT. *by a particular name*) Pl. Lycurg. —(W.ACC.) Is. Plb.; **name** —*someone* (W.ADV. or ADVBL.PHR. *in a particular way*) Pl. || PASS. be called —W.PREDIC.SB. *such and such* A. Att.orats. Pl. + —W.DAT. *by a particular name* Isoc. Pl. Lycurg.
5 describe —*sthg.* (W.INF. + PREDIC.ADJ. or SB. *as being such and such*) Pl. —(w. ὡς + PREDIC.ADJ.) Pl. || PASS. be described —w. ὡς + ADJ. *as such and such* Pl. —W.ADV. *in some way* Pl.

προσ-άγω, dial. **ποτάγω** (Theoc.) *vb.* | fut.mid.inf. (sts. w.pass.sens.) προσάξεσθαι || neut.impers.vbl.adj. προσακτέον |
1 bring (material and non-material things, usu. welcome or beneficial) to (persons or gods); **bring** —*gifts, sacrifices, animals, food, or sim.* (*usu.* W.DAT. *to a person or god*) hHom. Hdt. S. Ar. X. —*hymns and dances* (*to a god*) Pl. —*honour* (*to a city*) Pi. —*death* (*to a person*) E.
2 bring (part of the body) into contact with or proximity to (W.DAT. another part of the body, a person or object); (of a crocodile) **bring** (W.ACC. its upper jaw) **to** (its lower) Hdt.; (of a person) **move** (W.ACC. his eye) **close** (to a shield's rim) E.; **put** (W.ACC. one's hand) **in** (fire) Thgn.; **lay** (W.ACC. one's hands) **on** (a person) Ar.
3 bring (someone) to (a place); **bring** or **take** (somewhere) —*persons, corpses* E. Ar. Is.
4 bring —*a people* (W.PREP.PHR. *into an alliance*) Th.; **lead** —*people* (W.PREP.PHR. *into danger*) Th. —*children* (*to learning*) Arist.
5 (gener.) **present** —*one's mouth* (*for kissing*) Ar.; **bring on, start up** —*a dance* Ar.; (of a day) **bring** —*an event* Hdt.; (of a god) —*a nuisance* (*fig.ref. to a person*) Od.; (of a need) —*a person* (i.e. *prompt him to come*) S.
6 bring forward —*someone* (W.PREP.PHR. *to the Assembly, the Council*) Th. Att.orats.; **introduce** —*a person* (W.DAT. *to someone*) X.
7 (in political or legal ctxt.) **bring forward** —*an item of business, a charge, evidence, or sim.* Ar. Att.orats.
8 (milit.) **bring up** —*troops* (*oft.* W.DAT. or PREP.PHR. *against a place*) E. Th. X. —*siege-engines* (W.DAT. *against a city, a wall*) Th. X. —*a ship* (*against harbour fortifications*) Th.; (intr., of a commander, troops) **move up** (sts. W.PREP.PHR. *near to a place, against the enemy*) Th. X. || PASS. (of a siege-engine) be brought up Th.
9 bring (sthg.) to bear (against a person or situation); **bring to bear, apply** —*one's sword* (*where it is needed*) E. —*a touchstone* (*to gold*) Pl. —*remedies* Hdt. —*boldness, coercion, spitefulness* E. Th. D.; (fig.) —*games* (*as a form of medicine*) Arist.; **offer** —*pleasures* (*as a temptation*) Pl.; **administer** —*an oath* (*to someone*) Hdt.; **put into effect** —*an action* Hdt.(dub.) || PASS. (of threats) be brought to bear X.
10 (intr.) move towards (somewhere); (of a naval commander) **approach** —W.DAT. *a coast* Plb.; (fig., of a person) —*a certain age* Plu. —W.PREP.PHR. *closer to one's goal* Plu. || IMPERATV. come —W.ADV. *here* Theoc.; (as a summons to action) come on Theoc.
11 || MID. bring to oneself; **draw** (W.ACC. someone) **close** —W.PREP.PHR. *to oneself* Pl.; **embrace** —*someone* Ar. X.; **draw** (W.ACC. a bow, i.e. bowstring) **towards oneself** Pl.; **draw** —*someone's cheek* (W.DAT. *to one's lips*) E.; cause to come (to oneself), **attract, entice** —*someone* Ar.
12 || MID. **bring over to one's side, win over** —*a person, a populace* (sts. W.DAT. *by shrewdness, virtue, kindness, deceit, favours*) Hdt. E. Th. Isoc. Pl. —*someone's mind* Ar.; **secure for oneself** —*allies, helpers* Th. X. —*an alliance* Th. —*goodwill* Isoc.
13 bring into line, bring to heel (sts. W.DAT. *by force*) —*cities, peoples, defectors* Hdt. Th. X.; **bring under control** —*a horse* (*by applying the bit gently*) X. || PASS. (of an enemy) be brought to heel Th.
14 induce —W.ACC. + INF. *someone to do sthg.* S. E. || PASS. be won over —W.DAT. *by pity or fairness* Th.
15 || MID. **secure for oneself, recover** —*wrecked ships* Th.; **gather for oneself** —*cremated bones* E.
16 || MID. **draw to oneself** —*the eyes of all* X.; **bring upon oneself** —*a misfortune* Antipho
17 || MID. (of a country) **attract, bring in, import** —*all that it needs* X. || NEUT.PL.AOR.PASS.PTCPL.SB. imports X.

προσαγωγεύς έως *m.* one who brings in or attracts; (pejor.) procurer (W.GEN. *of profits, for another person*) D.

προσαγωγή ῆς *f.* **1** bringing along, **ceremonial presentation** (of offerings to a god) Hdt.
2 bringing home (of cattle fr. pasture) Plb.
3 bringing over, **acquisition** (W.GEN. of allies) Th.; **inducement** (to become an ally) D.
4 presentation (of someone to another by an intermediary), **introduction** X.
5 bringing up (against enemy fortifications, W.GEN. of siege-engines) Plb.; (concr.) **apparatus for bringing up** (siege-engines, ref. to protective sheds) Plb.
6 assault (on a city) Plb.
7 opportunity for putting in (for ships) Plb.; **means of access** (to a place) Plu.
8 addition (of one thing to another); (prep.phr.) ἐκ προσαγωγῆς *cumulatively, gradually, in stages* (*opp. all at once*) Arist.

προσαγωγίδες, dial. **ποταγωγίδες**, ίδων *f.pl.* women who induce suspected persons to commit an incriminating act, **agentes provocatrices** (used by a Syracusan tyrant) Arist.; (ref. to men so-called) Plu.

προσαγώγιον ου *n.* a kind of woodworking tool (described as ingenious); perh. **callipers** (or other measuring device) Pl.

προσαγωγός όν *adj.* | compar. προσαγωγότερος | || NEUT.SG.COMPAR.SB. greater attractiveness, more alluring quality (of fictional narratives) Th.

προσ-ᾴδω, dial. **ποταείδω** vb. | dial.fut. ποταείσομαι | **1 sing** —W.DAT. *to someone* Theoc.
2 sing (perh. W.INTERN.ACC. cries) **in response** (to someone) Ar.
3 sing in accompaniment —W.DAT. *to a tragedy* (i.e. sing the odes in it) Ar.
4 sing in harmony (w. sthg.) Pl.; (fig.) **be in harmony, be of one accord** —W.DAT. *w. someone* S.; (of arguments) **strike the right note** Pl.

προσ-αιρέομαι mid.contr.vb. **1 choose** (someone) **to serve alongside** (oneself); (of a commander or official) **choose, co-opt** —*a person or persons* (as colleagues) Th. Pl. X. D. Arist. Plu. —(W.DAT. *for oneself*) Hdt. D. Arist. Plu. —W.DBL.ACC. *someone as one's secretary* Isoc.; (intr.) **make a choice** (of someone as colleague) Hdt.
2 choose (someone) **to serve alongside** (another); (of the people) **choose** —*a person or persons* (as colleagues, W.DAT. *for someone*) Th. X. Thphr. Plu. —W.DBL.ACC. *persons as advisers* (for someone) Th.
3 (of the people) **invite the cooperation of** —*the Council* D.
4 (of troops) **take with oneself as reinforcements** —*archers* Hdt.
5 make an additional choice; (of the people) **choose also** —*three commanders* (w. πρός + DAT. *in addition to the existing ones*) X. —*guardians of the laws* (in addition to making laws) X.

προσαΐσσω ep.vb.: see προσᾴσσω

προσ-αιτέω contr.vb. **1** (of a petitioner or needy person) **ask** or **beg for** —*sthg.* E. Ar. X. D. Plu.; **make a request to** or **beg from** —*someone* Hdt. Isoc. X.; **beg** —W.DBL.ACC. *for sthg. fr. someone* E. X.
2 (intr., of a suppliant or petitioner) **plead** (for sthg.) E. Pl. X.; (of a needy person) **beg** Ar. Pl. X. D. +
3 (fig., of bloodshed) **demand** —*other blood* (in requital) A.; (of building works) **require** —*a certain number of workmen* X.

προσαίτης ου m. **beggar** NT.

προσ-αιτιάομαι mid.contr.vb. **find fault with** (W.ACC. someone) **in addition** (to doing sthg. else) Plu.

προσ-ακούω vb. **hear** (W.COMPL.CL. that sthg. is the case) **in addition** (to seeing sthg.) X.; **hear** (W.ACC. sthg.) **in addition** (to sthg. else) X.

προσ-ακροβολίζομαι mid.vb. **mount an attack with missiles** Plb.

προσακτέον (neut.impers.vbl.adj.): see προσάγω

προσ-αλείφω vb. **smear** (W.ACC. an ointment) **on** —W.DAT. *someone* Od.

προσ-άλληλος ον adj. [ἀλλήλους] (of paving-stones) **placed one against another** X.

προσ-άλλομαι mid.vb. (of a small person, compared to a puppy) **jump up** (to kiss a tall wife) X.

προσαμβάσεις εων dial.f.pl. [προσαναβαίνω] **1** (milit.) **attacks by climbing, scaling** (W.GEN. of walls) E.
2 means of ascent; (periphr. W.GEN. κλίμακος or κλιμάκων) **scaling ladder** or **ladders** A. E.

προσ-αμύνω vb. **1 bring help** (sts. W.DAT. to someone) Il. Plu.
2 carry on a fight (against an attacker) Il.

προσ-αμφιέννῡμι vb. | fut. προσαμφιῶ | **put** (W.ACC. a cloak) **around** —*someone* Ar.; **provide clothes for** —*captives* Plb.

προσ-αναβαίνω vb. **1** (of persons) **climb up** —W.PREP.PHR. *to a place* Arist. Plb.
2 (of a river, lake water) **rise** Plb.
3 (of cavalrymen) **become mounted in addition, be recruited additionally** X.
4 (of a historian) **go back** (in time) —W.DAT. *to Romulus* Plu.

προσ-αναγκάζω vb. **1 compel** (W.ACC. someone else) **in addition** (to do the same as oneself) Th.
2 put (W.ACC. someone) **under an additional obligation** —W.DAT. *to undergo training* Th.
3 (gener.) **compel, force** —*someone* (to do sthg.) Th. Pl. —(W.INF. *to do sthg.*) hHom. Pl. X. Aeschin. D. Plu.; **constrain** —W.ACC. + NEUT.ACC. *someone, in a certain way* Pl. || PASS. **be forced** (to do sthg.) Th.
4 force a conclusion (by argument); **insist** —W.ACC. + INF. *that sthg. is the case* Pl.
5 urge (someone) —W.DIR.SP. '*do sthg.*' Ar.

προσ-αναγορεύω vb. **make an additional proclamation** Pl.

προσ-αναγράφω vb. || PASS. **have one's name inscribed additionally** (on a monument) Lycurg.

προσ-αναδέχομαι mid.vb. **wait for** —*reinforcements, a person* Plb.

προσ-αναδίδωμι vb. **distribute additionally** —*extra scaling ladders* Plb.

προσ-αναδραμεῖν aor.2 inf. (of a historian) **go back** (to an earlier time) Plb.

προσ-αναζητέω contr.vb. **search in addition for** —*earlier laws* Arist. [or perh. *also consult*]

προσ-αναιρέω contr.vb. **1** || MID. (of a people) **take on in addition** —*another war* Th.
2 (of theories which are at variance w. experience) **undermine** (W.ACC. the truth) **in addition** (to being held in contempt) Arist.
3 (of oracles) **command in addition** —W.DAT. + INF. *someone to do sthg.* D.; (of the Pythia) **give confirmation** (to a law) Pl.

προσ-αναισιμόω contr.vb. || PASS. (of money) **be spent in addition** Hdt.

προσ-ανακάμπτω vb. (of a mediator) **go back and forth** Plb.

προσ-αναλαμβάνω vb. **1** (of a ship's captain) **take on board additionally** —*items of cargo, a passenger* D. Plu.
2 (of a commander) **pick up in addition** —*troops, stragglers* Plb.; **also procure** —*grain* Plb. || PASS. (of Roman senators) **be recruited additionally** Plu.
3 (of officials) **also wear** —*certain clothes* Plb.
4 (fig., of a commander, a traveller) **restore, refresh** —*one's troops, oneself* Plb.; (intr., of troops) **be refreshed, recover** Plb.

προσ-αναλίσκω vb. **spend** (W.ACC. other people's money) **in addition** (to one's own) Pl.; **spend** (W.ACC. money) **as well** (as doing sthg. else) D.; (wkr.sens.) **spend** —*money* (on sthg.) X. Plu.

προσ-αναμιμνήσκω vb. **remind** —*someone* (sts. W.GEN. of sthg.) Plb.; (intr., sts. W.ADVBL.ACC. briefly) Plb.

προσ-ανανεόομαι mid.contr.vb. **recall to mind** —*a fact* Plb.(dub.)

προσ-αναπαύω vb. **1** (of a commander) **also rest** —*his forces* Plb.
2 || MID. (of a soldier) **rest on** —W.DAT. *his shield* (laid on the ground) Plu.; (of a historian) **create a break** (by introducing a digression) Plb.

προσ-αναπληρόω contr.vb. **fill up additionally, supplement** —*the defective parts of one's life* (w. extra activities) Arist. || MID. **add** (W.ACC. a square) **to fill in** (a shape) Pl.

προσ-αναρρήγνῡμι vb. **cause** (W.ACC. one's body) **to haemorrhage** (by shouting) Plu.; (of wounded men) **lacerate** (W.ACC. themselves) **further** Plu.

προσ-ανασείω vb. || PASS. **be stirred** —W.DAT. *by arguments* Plb.

προσ-αναστέλλω vb. hold in or back —one's horse Plu.
προσ-ανατείνω vb. | aor.pass.ptcpl. (w.mid.sens.) προσανατaθείς | 1 ‖ MID. hold out, proffer —a threat Plb.; threaten —W.DAT. someone Plb. ‖ AOR.PASS. engage in threatening behaviour —W.ADVBL.ACC. for a short time Plb. 2 (intr.) stretch out time, delay Plb.
προσ-ανατίθημι vb. 1 ‖ MID. take on oneself in addition —a task X. 2 ‖ MID. refer for advice —W.DAT. to someone Men.
προσ-ανατρέχω vb. (of a historian, in his narrative) go back (to an earlier time) Plb.
προσ-ανατρίβομαι mid.vb. (of a wrestler) rub up against (an opponent), grapple Thpr.; (fig., of a disputant) Pl.
προσ-αναφέρω vb. refer (a matter) for advice —W.DAT. to someone Plb.
προσ-άνειμι vb. (of troops) go uphill too (to join others) Th.
προσ-ανειπεῖν aor.2 inf. declare in addition —W.COMPL.CL. that sthg. will be the case X.
προσ-ανέρπω vb. (of a snake) creep up (someone's body) —W.DAT. to the neck Plu.
προσ-ανερωτάω contr.vb. ask (W.ACC. someone) additionally —W.INDIR.Q. what is the case Pl.
προσ-ανέχω vb. 1 hold on, wait Plb.; (tr.) wait for —an appointed time Plb. 2 hold on, cling —W.DAT. to hope, to brilliance of intellect Plb.; hold out for, cling to the hope of —W.DAT. survival, help, someone's arrival Plb.
προσανής dial.adj.: see προσηνής
προσ-ανοιμώζω vb. groan disapprovingly Plb.
προσ-αντέλλω dial.vb. [ἀνατέλλω] (of dust) rise up (fr. a battle) E.
προσ-αντέχω vb. (of troops) hold out Plb. —W.DAT. against siege-operations Plb.
προσ-άντης ες adj. [ἄντα] 1 (of a road, an ascent, ground) sloping upwards or steep Pi. Th. X. Arist. Plb. Plu. ‖ NEUT.SB. sloping ground Pl. 2 (fig., of a person) irksome, obstructive, unsociable E.; opposed, unreceptive (W.PREP.PHR. to good things) X.; inimical, unsympathetic (W.DAT. to someone) Plu. 3 (fig., of speech) antagonistic Hdt.; (of a circumstance, proposal, course of action) troublesome, awkward or unwelcome (sts. W.DAT. to someone) E. Isoc. Pl. Plu.; (of an investigation) Arist.
προσ-αντίσχω vb. (of troops) hold out, resist Plb.
προσ-αξιόω contr.vb. plead strongly (for a certain course of action) Plb.
προσ-απαγγέλλω vb. additionally announce —W.COMPL.CL. that sthg. is the case X.
προσ-απαιτέω contr.vb. demand (W.ACC. sthg.) in addition Thpr.
προσ-απειλέω contr.vb. threaten in addition —W.COMPL.CL. that one will do sthg. Is. ‖ MID. (intr.) make further threats NT.
προσ-απειπεῖν aor.2 inf. forbid in addition —w. μή + IMPERS.PASS.INF. that sthg. shd. be done Aeschin.
προσ-απερείδομαι mid.vb. also depend —W.PREP.PHR. on an existing agreement (to support one's case) Plb.
προσ-αποβάλλω vb. 1 throw away or lose in addition —a sum of money (w. πρός + DAT. on top of another sum) Ar. —one's friends (W.DAT. on top of one's money) Plu. 2 lose into the bargain, actually lose (i.e. not in addition to losing sthg. else, but in addition to failing to gain it) —existing resources X. —one's money and life Plb. —a country, a city Plu.

προσ-απογράφω vb. (leg., of an accuser) register in addition the names of —other persons Lys.
προσ-αποδείκνυμι vb. demonstrate in addition —W.COMPL.CL. that sthg. is the case Pl.
προσ-αποδίδωμι vb. 1 go so far as to pay, actually pay —money (W.DAT. to someone) Hyp. 2 ‖ PASS. (of money) be paid in addition D. 3 ‖ MID. actually sell —sthg. (to finance a repayment, opp. being able to afford it) Plb.
προσ-αποκρίνομαι mid.vb. | neut.impers.vbl.adj. προσαποκριτέον | make an addition to one's answer —W.DAT. to a question or questioner (i.e. give an answer that goes beyond the question asked) Pl. Arist.
προσ-αποκτείνω vb. kill (W.ACC. someone) in addition (to someone else) X. Plu.
προσ-απόλλυμι vb. —also (pres.) **προσαπολλύω** (Hdt.) 1 kill (W.ACC. someone) in addition (to someone else) Hdt. Plb. Plu. ‖ MID. and PF.ACT. perish too (as well as someone else) Hdt. Lys. Isoc. Plu. 2 also lose —cavalry (as well as other troops) Hdt. —one's empire (as well as being defeated) Hdt. —old possessions (w. πρός + DAT. in addition to recent acquisitions) Pl. ‖ MID. (of soldiers, isolated because of the destruction of their ships) be lost too Th.; (of allies, when one suffers a reverse) Th. 3 app., kill in addition (to wounding), finish off —someone E. 4 lose or destroy in the end or consequentially, go on to lose or destroy —possessions or sim. Att.orats. Pl. ‖ MID. perish into the bargain (as well as being reduced to slavery) D.
προσ-αποπέμπω vb. send (W.ACC. sthg.) in addition (to other things) Ar.
προσ-απορέω contr.vb. [ἀπορέω¹] pose a further question Arist.
προσ-αποστέλλω vb. despatch (W.ACC. troops) as reinforcements Th.
προσ-αποστερέω contr.vb. ‖ PASS. be robbed (W.GEN. of victory) in addition (to being abused) D.
προσ-αποτίνω vb. pay in addition —a fine, a sum of money Pl. Hyp. D.
προσ-αποφαίνω vb. demonstrate in addition —W.COMPL.CL. that sthg. is the case Pl.; (mid.) —W.INDIR.Q. what is the case Arist.
προσ-αποφέρω vb. ‖ PASS. (of a person's name) be reported back as well (as the names of others, to a central authority) D.
προσ-άπτω, ep. **προτιάπτω** vb. 1 fasten or attach (one thing to another); place —an offering (W.DAT. on a tomb) S.; fit, put —articles of clothing or adornment (W.DAT. on someone) E.; press —one's breast (W.PREP.PHR. to another's, in embracing her) E.; clasp —someone's hand (in one's own) E. 2 ‖ MID. lay hands on, touch —W.GEN. persons or things Plu.; (of a venomous spider) touch (someone's flesh) —W.DAT. w. its mouth X.; (gener., of persons) come into contact —W.GEN. w. persons or things Aeschin.; (fig.) light upon —W.GEN. a track (towards a goal), the truth Pl. 3 (gener., w. non-material objects) attach, add —a word (to others) Ar. Pl.; apply —one's mind (W.PREP.PHR. to sthg.) E.fr. —an allegory (W.DAT. to a line of argument) Pl.; associate —a word (W.DAT. w. a language) Pl.; (intr., of a new trouble) come as an addition —W.DAT. to older ones S. 4 bestow (a material or non-material object); assign, give —an ancestral home, a fleet (W.DAT. to someone) E. X. —a

festival and rituals (*to a land*) E.; **devote** —*an expansive narrative* (*to a subject*) Plb.
5 bestow (an abstr. entity); **grant** —*glory, fame, honour, praise* (W.DAT. *to someone or sthg.*) Il. Pi. S. Pl. —*happiness, pleasures* Pl. Arist. —*attributes or qualities* (*e.g. speed, length, fecundity*) Pl. Arist.
6 impose (sthg. undesirable); **impose** —*an obligation* (W.DAT. *on a city*) S. —*expense and suffering* (*on a populace*) Plb.; **inflict** —*pain* Pl.; **attach** —*blood-guilt* (W.DAT. *to someone*) E.
7 ascribe, attribute —*an observation, an opinion* (W.DAT. *to someone*) Arist. Plb. —*a quality* (*to sthg.*) Pl. —*someone's success* (*to luck*) Plb.; **impute** (usu. W.DAT. to someone) —*wrongful behaviour* S.*Ichn.* Isoc. Pl. Arist. —*blame, credit* Plu.

προσ-αραρίσκω *vb.* | PF.: inf. προσαραρέναι, Ion.ptcpl. προσαρηρώς ‖ MID.: Ion.3sg.pf.subj. (or perh. redupl.aor.subj.) προσαρήρεται | **1** ‖ STATV.PF. (of persons, compared to bats) **cling** —W.DAT. *to walls* X. ‖ PTCPL.ADJ. (of metal tyres) **fitted** (to wheels) Il.
2 ‖ MID. **attach** —*the plough-tree* (W.DAT. *to the yoke-pole*) Hes.

προσ-αράσσω *vb.* (of grappling-engines) **dash** —*ships* (W.DAT. *against cliffs*) Plu.

προσ-αρκέω *contr.vb.* **1 give help** (sts. W.DAT. to someone) S. E. Plu. —W.NEUT.ADVBL.ACC. *in every way, in small ways* S.
2 render —*a favour* (W.DAT. *to someone*) S.*fr.*

προσ-αρμόζω, Att. **προσαρμόττω** *vb.* **1 attach** —*a severed hand* (*to an arm*) X. —*an object* (usu. W.DAT. or PREP.PHR. *to another object*) Plb. Plu. ‖ PASS. (of an object) **be attached** —W.DAT. or PREP.PHR. *to another object* X. Plb.
2 (gener.) **press** —*a child* (W.DAT. *to one's breast, in suckling it*) E. —*one's lips* (*to someone, in kissing him*) E.; **apply** —*one's arms* (W.DAT. *to the oar*) E.; **put** —*one's arms* (*around someone, in an embrace*) E.; (of a commander) **bring** (W.ACC. *one's ships*) **into contact** —W.DAT. *w. an enemy fleet* E.
3 add or **bestow** —*gifts* S.
4 fit —*sthg.* (W.PREP.PHR. *into a matching place, envisaged as its footprint*) Pl.
5 match, accommodate —*sthg.* (W.DAT. *to sthg. else*) Pl. Plu.; (intr., of things) **fit, match** —W.DAT. or πρός + ACC. *other things* Pl. X.

προσ-αρτάω *contr.vb.* **1 attach** —*an object* (usu. W.DAT. *to another*) Arist. Plu. ‖ MID. (fig.) **attach oneself to, rely on** —W.DAT. *someone* Plu.; (of a commander) **hang on, cling** —W.DAT. *to an island* Plu. ‖ PASS. (of an object) **be attached** (usu. W.PREP.PHR. *to another*) Plb. Plu.
2 ‖ PASS. (of troops) **be positioned close** —W. πρός + DAT. *to the foot of a hill* Plb.
3 append —*further requirements* (W.DAT. *to the study of generalship*) Plb.
4 ‖ PASS. (fig., of intellect) **be attached, belong** —W.DAT. *to someone* Pl.; (of goodness) **be connected** —W.DAT. *w. beauty* X.; (of private gain) —*w. one's public actions and speeches* D.

προσ-άρχομαι *mid.vb.* app., **make offerings of first fruits**; perh. **offer honours** or **assistance** —W.DAT. *to someone* Th.(dub.) Pl.(dub.) | see also προσέρχομαι

προσ-ασκέω *contr.vb.* also **train** —*troops* Plb.

προ-σάσσομαι *mid.vb.* | aor. προεσαξάμην | **store up in advance, stock up on** —*provisions* Hdt.

προσ-άσσω, ep. **προσαΐσσω** *vb.* | aor. προσῆξα, ep.aor.ptcpl. προσαΐξας | (of a person) **rush up** (to someone) Od.; (fig., of a tearful mist) **rush upon** —W.DAT. *someone's eyes* A.

προσ-αυαίνομαι *pass.vb.* (of Prometheus' body) **wither away upon** —W.DAT. *a rock* A.

προσ-αυγάζω *vb.* (of the moon) **shine** —W.DAT. *on someone* AR.(tm.)

προσ-αυδάω *contr.vb.* | impf. προσηύδων, ep.3du. προσηυδήτην | **1 speak to, address** —*someone* Hom. Hes. hHom. Pi. Parm. Trag. —W.DAT. S.; (intr.) **deliver an address** or **speech** Hom. hHom. Call.
2 speak, utter —*words or sim.* Hom. Hes. hHom. E.; **address** —W.DBL.ACC. *words to someone* Hom. Hes. hHom.
3 call, name —*someone* (W.PREDIC.SB. *father, mother*) A. S. ‖ PASS. **be called** —W.PREDIC.SB. *nurse and sister* S.
4 speak of, describe —*someone's misfortune* (W.ADVBL.PHR. *in a particular manner*) E.

προσ-αύλειος ον *adj.* (derog., of fortunate events) **of the farmyard, merely rustic** E.

προσ-αυλέω, dial. **ποταυλέω** *contr.vb.* **pipe** (W.ACC. a tune) **in accompaniment** (to a song) Ar. Plu.; **pipe for** —W.DAT. *persons* (i.e. accompany their singing) Men. Theoc.

προσ-αυξάνω *vb.* | aor.ptcpl. προσαυξήσας | **1 show additional esteem for** —*someone* (W.DAT. *by privileges*) Plb.
2 give additional support to —*a proposal* Plb.

προσ-αύω *vb.* [αὔω¹] **burn** (W.ACC. one's foot) **in** —W.DAT. *a fire* S.

προσ-αφαιρέομαι *mid.contr.vb.* **1** (of a law) **take away** (W.ACC. some of one's existing resources) **too** —W. πρός + DAT. *in addition to doing other harm* D.
2 go on to steal —W.DBL.ACC. *sthg. fr. someone* Is.; **go on to annex** —*a city* D.

προσ-αφικνέομαι *mid.contr.vb.* (of ships) **arrive as reinforcements** —W.DAT. *for someone* Th.

προσ-αφίστημι *vb.* **cause** (W.NEUT.INTERN.ACC. no) **further defection** —W.GEN. *fr. an alliance* Th.

προσ-βαίνω *vb.* | athem.aor. προσέβην, dial. προσέβαν ‖ ep.3sg.aor.mid. προσεβήσετο, also προσεβήσατο |
1 set one's foot upon, step on (a corpse, while despoiling it) Il.; **step on to** —*a path* (*leading uphill, to climb it*) Od.; **step** —W. πρός + ACC. *against the lower part of a bow* (*to steady it while shooting*) X. ‖ MID. **set foot on** —*a threshold* (or perh. **approach it**) Od. —*a staircase* (or perh. **climb it**) Od.
2 ‖ MID. (of a deity) **go up to** —*Olympos, a mountain peak* Il. Hes.; (of Selene, the personif. moon) **ascend to** —*her vantage-point* hHom.
3 (of persons) **go up, climb** —*a mountain, its spurs, a hill* Hom. hHom. —W. πρός + ACC. *towards a mountain ridge* hHom.
4 (intr.) **ascend, climb** (a wall, ladder, hill) Hdt. S. E. Th. Plb. Plu. —W.DAT. *a tree* Plu. —W.DAT. *to someone* (*on a hill*) Th. —*to the Capitol* Plu.; (of a bull, being taken on board a ship) **go up** —W.PREP.PHR. *along a gangplank* E.
5 come to, approach —*a city, house, tent, plain* E. —*a crag* (*by air*) A.; perh. **go right up to** —W.DAT. *a city wall* Pl.
6 (intr., of a bird) **come, arrive** E.; (of persons) —W.INF. *in order to sing* E.*fr.*; **enter** —W.PREP.PHR. *into a grove, a country* S. X.
7 (of madness) **come upon** —*someone* S.; (of anguish) **come to** —W.DAT. *someone* E.

προσ-βάλλω, ep. **προτιβάλλω**, also (tm.) **ποτὶ ... βάλλω** *vb.* **1 throw, cast** —*one's staff* (W.DAT. *to the ground*) Il.(tm.)
2 strike, dash —*a chariot wheel* (W.DAT. *against a rock*) E.; (fig.) **wreck** —*one's prosperity* (W.DAT. *on the reef of Justice*) A.
3 (w. aggressive connot.) **lay** —*one's hand* (W.DAT. *on someone*) E.; **set** —*scaling ladders* (W.DAT. *against gates*) E.

—troops (against gates, the enemy) A. E. —people (compared to wild beasts, against someone) D.
4 place (a part of the body) against or on (someone or sthg.); **place, set** —one's breast (W.ADVBL.PHR. against an enemy's, in resistance) Archil. —one's belly and thighs (w. ἐπί + DAT. on someone's belly and thighs, in sexual intercourse) Archil. —one's cheek, breast (W.DAT. or πρός + ACC. against someone's cheek or breast, in an embrace) E. —(periphr.) one's foot (W.DAT. in a country, i.e. enter it) E.
5 cast —one's eyes (W.DAT. on someone) E.
6 impose or inflict (sthg. burdensome or undesirable, W.DAT. on someone); **impose** —a second journey (i.e. the need for one) A. —an oath S.; **inflict** —a slur, a stain, blood-guilt, disgrace E. Pl.; **cast** —blame Antipho; **bring** —an accusation Antipho; **cause** —distress, pain, alarm, or sim. Hdt. Trag. Antipho —anger and quarrelling E.
7 (w. reverse constr.) **place, lay** (W.ACC. someone) **under** —W.DAT. a compulsion (W.INF. to do sthg.) S.
8 bring to bear (sthg. welcome or useful); (of a doctor) **apply** —a gentle hand Pi.; (of a person) **apply** or **effect** —a love-charm, remedial measures, instructions S.; (gener.) **put** —a person (W.PREP.PHR. to some use) Ar.
9 bring —a benefit, fame (W.DAT. to someone) Hdt. S.; (of a charioteer) —an Olympic victory (to one's countrymen) Hdt.; (of heroes) **provide** —a theme (W.DAT. for poets) Pi.; (of a god) **add** —further land (W.DAT. to land, i.e. extend it) E.
10 (of the sun) **strike** —the earth (w. its rays) Hom.; (of an unexpected voice) **come to, reach** —someone Ar.
11 (intr., of a ship) **collide** —w. πρός + ACC. w. another ship Pl.; (of objects of perception, colours) **impinge** (sts. w. πρός + ACC. on one's sight or hearing) Pl.
12 (of soldiers) **make an attack** or **assault** Hdt. Th. X. Plb. Plu. —W.DAT. or πρός + ACC. on persons or places A. Hdt. E. Th. Att.orats. X. +; (of a ram or battering-ram, fig.ref. to a lover) **assault** —W.DAT. a woman's door Thphr.; (intr., of a whirlwind) **attack** Men.
13 (wkr.sens., of a person) **accost, tackle** —W.DAT. or πρός + ACC. someone Men.; **approach** —W.DAT. someone Aeschin. Plu.; (intr.) **have sex** (w. someone) Ar.
14 (of sailors) **put in** —w. ἐς + ACC. to harbour Th. —W.DAT. or πρός + ACC. at a place Th. Plu.
15 || MID. direct oneself against or towards (someone); **confront, oppose** —someone (W.DAT. in word or deed) Il.; **throw oneself upon the protection of** —someone AR.

πρόσβασις εως f. [προσβαίνω] **1** means of approach (usu. uphill); **approach, access** (to a cliff, hill, hill-town) Hdt. Th. Plb.; (W.GEN. to a house) E.; (to a peninsula, fr. the sea) Plb.; (to an enemy camp) Plb.
2 scaling (W.GEN. of ramparts) E.

προσβατός όν adj. **1** (of a mountain) **accessible, scalable** X.
2 || NEUT.IMPERS. (w. ἐστί) there is access (to a river, W.DAT. for someone) X.; (to a place, W.DAT. for death) X.

προσ-βιάζομαι mid.vb. **1 compel** (W.ACC. someone) **in addition** (to do the same as oneself) Ar. || PASS. (of retreating troops) be hard pressed into the bargain (as well as suffering defeat) Th.
2 apply additional force (in argument); **push** (W.NEUT.ACC. sthg.) **too far** Pl.; **force through** (a proposal) Aeschin.
3 use force or compulsion (sts. W.ACC. on someone) Plu.; **compel** —W.ACC. + INF. someone to do sthg. Plu.

προσ-βιβάζω vb. | fut. προσβιβῶ | **1** bring over (to one's side), **win over, persuade, convince** —someone S.Ichn. Ar. X. Plu. —(W.COMPL.CL. that it is necessary to do sthg.) Aeschin.

2 relate, connect —someone (W.DAT. to someone else, for purpose of comparison) Plu.; (of a creator of words) **assign** —appropriate letters (W.DAT. to words, w. sounds and shapes reflecting the meanings) Pl.; (of a sceptic) **bring** (W.ACC. mythical creatures) **into line** —W.PREP.PHR. w. probability Pl.
3 add, advance —an argument Pl.(dub.)

προσ-βιόω contr.vb. **live on** —W.ACC. for a short time Plu. —(W.DAT. after eighty) Plu.

προσ-βλέπω, dial. **ποτιβλέπω**, Lacon. **ποτιγλέπω** vb. | dial.inf. ποτιβλέπεν | fut. προσβλέψομαι | aor. προσέβλεψα | **1 look at** —someone or sthg. S. E. Ar. Pl. X. Theoc. Plu. —W.DAT. X. Plu. —w. πρός + ACC. Men.; (intr.) **look** (at someone) Alcm. Pl. X. Plu.; **see** —W.INDIR.Q. how someone fares S.
2 look upon —the light, sun and earth (periphr. for being alive) S. E.
3 take notice of —someone's words A.

προσ-βλώσκω vb. | aor.2 inf. προσμολεῖν | **come to, arrive at** —a place S.; (intr.) **come here, approach** S.

προσ-βοάω contr.vb. | Ion.3sg.aor.mid. προσεβώσατο | || MID. **call** (W.ACC. someone) **over to oneself** Hdt.

προσ-βοηθέω contr.vb. (of a commander, troops) **bring help** Th. X. D. Plb. Plu. —W.DAT. to someone Th. Plb. Plu. —W.PREP.PHR. to ships, a city Plb.

προσβολή ῆς f. [προσβάλλω] **1** forceful contact (of one thing w. another); **striking, knocking** (of objects against adulterated bronze, so revealing its impurity) A.; **collision** (of ships, opp. deliberate ramming) Th.
2 contact (without force); **physical contact** (w. an object, as a proof of its existence) Pl.; **point of contact** (of two items) Pl.; **touch** (of a child, by a mother) E.; (W.GEN. of someone's face, in a kiss) E.; **contact** (W.GEN. + PREP.PHR. of the eyes, w. sthg.) Pl.
3 bringing to bear (of one thing on another or on a person); **application** (W.GEN. of fire or cold, to someone) Pl.; (of a cupping-glass, to a body) Arist.; (of the tongue, to a part of the mouth, in articulating a sound) Arist.
4 (in military ctxt.) **attack, assault** A. Hdt. Th. +; (in wrestling) Ar.
5 attack (by a supernatural agent); **attack, visitation** (W.GEN. of Erinyes) A.; (of a god or gods, as a source of harm) E.fr. Ar.; (of pollution fr. bloodshed) A.; (W.ADJ. divine, ref. to pollution) Antipho; (W.ADJ. evil, ref. to a disastrous outcome, as foretold by sacrificial entrails) E.
6 means of approaching, **approach, access** (to a place) Plb. Plu.; (specif.) **point of access** (W.GEN. to an island, ref. to a city, an area of coast or sea) Th.
7 landing-place, port of call (W.GEN. for ships, ref. to an island) Th.
8 || PL. accessible or exposed parts (of stakes in a palisade) Plb.

πρόσ-βορρος ον adj. [Βορέας] (of the rock-face of the Acropolis, a cave within it) **north-facing** E. || NEUT.PL.SB. northern parts (of a country) Pl.

προσ-γελάω contr.vb. | fut. προσγελάσομαι | **1 smile at** —someone Hdt. Pl. Aeschin. —one's image in a mirror E.; **smile** (at someone) —W.COGN.ACC. a final smile E.
2 (fig., of a goddess's words) **greet** —someone S.Ichn.; (of the smell of bread) A.; (of plants and trees) **welcome** —the goddess Peace Ar.

προσ-γίγνομαι, Ion. **προσγίνομαι** mid.vb. **1 come as an addition;** (of a city, nation, person) **join, attach oneself** (in an alliance or sim., sts. W.DAT. to someone) Hdt. Th. X. D.

Plu.; (of troops, ships, or sim.) **come as reinforcements** (sts. W.DAT. to someone) Th. X. Plb. Plu.

2 (in judicial ctxt., of a populace) **support** —W.DAT. *someone* Hdt.; (of a magistrate's decision) **be in favour** (of a course of action) Hdt.

3 (of things) **come in addition, be added, accrue** (sts. W.DAT. to sthg. or for someone) Hdt. E. Th. Att.orats. Pl. X. +; (opp. ἀπογίγνομαι *be subtracted*) Pl.

4 (gener.) **come about** (for someone); (of toil, an evil end) **be in store** (sts. W.DAT. for someone) S.; (of hatred for one's child, in neg.phr.) **be associated** —W.DAT. *w. a parent* S.

5 (of a person) **become** (W.PREDIC.SB. a philosopher) **in addition** (to having some other quality) Pl.

προσ-γλίχομαι mid.vb. app. **be eager to connect** —sthg. (W.DAT. *w. sthg.*) Arist.; (intr.) **be eager to make a connection** Arist.

προσ-γράφω vb. **1** write in addition; **add** —*a phrase or sim.* (sts. W.DAT. or πρός + ACC. *to a document, law, or sim.*) Att.orats.; (intr.) **make additions** (to the text of a speech) Isoc. ‖ MID. **additionally mention** —W.ACC. + INF. *that sthg. is the case* Is. ‖ PASS. (of phrases or sim.) be added Att.orats. X.; (of things) be mentioned additionally D.

2 add a stipulation (to a law, decree, or sim.) —W.ACC. + INF. *that sthg. shd. be done* Aeschin. D. —W.COMPL.CL. Plu. ‖ MID. **additionally stipulate** —*a safeguard* D. ‖ IMPERS.PASS. it is further stipulated —W.ACC. + INF. *that sthg. shd. be done* Aeschin. D. Plu.

3 ‖ PASS. (of names) be added (on a monument) Lys. Plu.

4 ‖ PASS. (of a *cognomen*) be added —W.DAT. *to a Roman name* Plu.

5 add to a list; **enrol** —*someone* (W.DAT. *in the Senate*) Plu. —(W.DAT. *in the state, i.e. as a Roman citizen*) Plu.

6 add —*a month* (to the Roman calendar) Plu.

7 ascribe —*someone's popularity* (W.DAT. *to his exploits*) Plu.

προσ-γυμνάζω vb. also **train** —*someone* Pl.

προσγυμναστής οῦ m. **wrestling opponent** Hyp.

προσ-δανείζομαι mid.vb. **borrow a supplementary sum of money** Lys. X.; (tr.) **borrow** —*more money* Plu.

προσ-δαπανάω contr.vb. **spend** (W.NEUT.ACC. some) **additional amount** NT.

πρόσδεγμα ατος n. [προσδέχομαι] (pl. for sg.) act of welcoming, **reception** (W.GEN. of a stranger) S.

προσδεής ές adj. [προσδέω²] **in further need** (W.GEN. of sthg.) Pl.

προσδέκομαι Ion.mid.vb.: see προσδέχομαι

προσδεκτέος ᾱ ον vbl.adj. [προσδέχομαι] to be accepted; (of an activity) **acceptable** —W.DAT. to someone) Pl.

προσ-δέρκομαι, dial. **ποτιδέρκομαι** mid.vb. | act.aor.2 inf. προσδρακεῖν ‖ aor.pass. (w.mid.sens.) προσεδέρχθην | **1** look at or **see** —*someone or sthg.* Hom. A. E. Theoc.

2 (of a god, the sun and moon) **look upon** —*someone* A.

3 (intr.) **give a look** —W.ADVBL.ACC.PHR. *more melting than sleep and death* Alcm. ‖ IMPERATV. **look!** S.

πρόσδετος ον adj. [προσδέω¹] (of an object) **fastened** (W.DAT. to sthg.) E.

προσ-δέχομαι, Ion. **προσδέκομαι** mid.vb. | ep.athem. pres.ptcpl. ποτιδέγμενος ‖ neut.impers.vbl.adj. προσδεκτέον | **1** receive (someone) favourably; (of a person) **welcome home** —*someone* S.; (of a king) admit into one's presence, **receive** —*someone* X.; (of a populace) **welcome, admit** —*a herald, an ambassador* (sts. W.PREP.PHR. *into a city*) Th. Din.; (of a city, country, phratry) **accept** —*someone* A. E. Isoc.; (of earth, rain, light, in neg.phr.) —*someone's pollution* S.; (of persons) —*someone* (as a friend, pupil, teacher, or sim.) Ar. Pl. Aeschin.; (of a woman) —*a man* (as a sexual partner) Hdt.

2 (specif.) accept (someone) into membership of a group; **accept, admit** —*someone* (as a citizen) D. —(as an ally) Th. D. —(W.PREP.PHR. *into an alliance*) Aeschin.

3 receive (sthg.) favourably; **accept, welcome** —*an oracular response* Hdt. —*an alliance* X. Aeschin. —*a proposal, plea, settlement, or sim.* Th. Aeschin. Plb. —*someone's rule* Th. —*someone's company, his sophistries, or sim.* Att.orats.; **accept, allow** —*falsehood, truth* Pl.; (of things) **admit of, be susceptible to** —*creation, destruction* Pl.; (intr.) **accept** (a proposal) Th.

4 await (a coming or expected event or person); **await** —*someone or sthg.* Hom. Hippon. Hdt. S. E. Th. +; **expect** —W.FUT.INF. *to do sthg.* Hdt. —W.PRES.INF. X. —W.ACC. + FUT.INF. *someone to do sthg., sthg. to happen* Hdt. Th. X. —W.ACC. + FUT.PTCPL. or W. ὡς + FUT.INDIC. *that someone will do sthg.* Hdt.; (intr.) **expect** (sthg. to happen) Hdt. Th.

5 wait (in expectation) Hom. —w. ὁππότε + OPT. *for the time when someone would come* Il. —w. εἰ + OPT. or FUT.INDIC. *in case sthg. might happen* Od. Call.

προσ-δέω¹ contr.vb. **fasten on, attach** —*brailing rings and ropes* (W.ADV. *inside or outside of a sail*) Hdt. —*a myrtle-branch* (W.PREP.PHR. *to the top of a pole*) Hdt. ‖ PASS. (of a wineskin) be attached —W.DAT. *to a windlass* Hdt.

προσ-δέω² contr.vb. | 3sg.impf. προσέδει | 3sg.aor. προσεδέησε | The vb. is freq. qualified, in both act. and mid., by τι or οὐδέν *somewhat, not at all.* | **1 have further need** —W.GEN. *of sthg.* E.

2 ‖ IMPERS. there is (sts. W.DAT. for someone or sthg.) still need —W.GEN. *of someone or sthg.* Th. Att.orats. Pl. X. —W.INF. *to do sthg.* Pl.

—**προσδέομαι** mid.contr.vb. —also dial. **ποτιδεύομαι** mid.vb. | fut. προσδεήσομαι ‖ aor.pass. (w.mid.sens.) προσεδεήθην | **1** have further need; **still need** —W.GEN. *someone or sthg.* Th. Att.orats. Pl. X. Theoc. —W.INF. *to do sthg.* Th. X.; (intr.) X.

2 ‖ IMPERS. there is still need —W.GEN. *of sthg.* X.

3 (of a person) **want, desire** —W.GEN. *high office, pleasures, peace* X.

4 beg for, ask for —W.ACC. + GEN. *sthg. fr. someone* Hdt. —W.DBL.GEN. Hdt.; beg, ask —W.INF. or GEN. + INF. *(someone) to do sthg.* Hdt.

προσ-δηλέομαι mid.contr.vb. (of a naval force, through its defeat) also **harm** —*the land forces* Hdt.

προσ-διαβάλλω vb. **1 bring** (W.ACC. someone or sthg.) **into further discredit** (sts. W.DAT. w. someone) Plu. ‖ PASS. (of a person) be further discredited Plu.

2 also **discredit** —*sthg.* (W.INF. + PREDIC.ADJ. *as being such and such*) Antipho

προσ-διαιρέομαι mid.contr.vb. **divide** or **distinguish** (W.ACC. sthg.) **further** Arist.

προσ-διαλέγομαι mid.vb. | aor.pass. (w.mid.sens.) προσδιελέχθην | **1 respond** (sts. W.DAT. to someone) **in conversation** or **discussion** Hdt. Pl. ‖ MASC.PTCPL.SB. respondent, interlocutor Pl. Plb.

2 (gener.) **converse** —W.DAT. *w. someone* Pl. Plu.

προσ-διαμαρτυρέω contr.vb. (leg.) **testify further** —W.ACC. + INF. or COMPL.CL. *that sthg. is the case* Is. Aeschin.

προσ-διαμαρτύρομαι mid.vb. also **appeal urgently to** —*someone* Plb.

προσ-διανέμω vb. **1** (of a person) **additionally distribute** —*sthg.* (among a group) Plu.

προσδιανοέομαι

2 || MID. (of a group of persons) **distribute** (W.ACC. sthg.) **in addition among each other** Plu.; (intr.) **make another distribution** (of sthg.) **to one other** D.

προσ-διανοέομαι mid.contr.vb. **consider additionally** —W.ACC. + INF. or COMPL.CL. *that sthg. is the case* Pl.

προσ-διαπράσσομαι mid.vb. **exact** or **procure in addition** (for someone) —*other things* X.

προσ-διαρπάζω vb. **also plunder** —*houses* Plb.

προσ-διασαφέω contr.vb. **also explain** —*sthg.* Plb. —W.COMPL.CL. *that sthg. is the case* Plb.

προσ-διατρίβω vb. **1 spend time with, associate with** —W.DAT. *someone* Pl.
2 **spend more time alive, live longer** Men.

προσ-διαφθείρω vb. **1 cause the death of** (W.ACC. someone) **too** (as well as dying oneself, as well as the deaths of others) S. Plu.; **kill** (W.ACC. someone) **in addition** (to doing sthg. else) Plu. || PASS. **also be killed** (as well as others) Isoc.
2 (wkr.sens.) **further corrupt** —*someone* Plu.; (of news) **further demoralise** —*someone* Plu.
3 (of love) **finally destroy** —*someone's good qualities* Plu.

προσ-διδάσκω vb. **instruct** (W.ACC. someone) **further** —W.NEUT.ACC. *on a small matter* Pl.

προσ-δίδωμι vb. **1** (of a king) **additionally give** —*more land* (to someone) X.; (of a lawgiver) **add** —*a word of advice and encouragement* (W.DAT. *to the governed*) Pl.
2 **give** (W.PARTITV.GEN. *some of one's territory*) **as well** (as withdrawing fr. someone else's) Isoc.
3 **give a share** (of sthg., to someone); **share** —W.GEN. *a drink, one's pleasure* (W.DAT. w. someone) E. —*a sacrificial animal, its offal* (w. someone) Ar. —W.ACC. *a small amount of one's gains* (w. someone) Ar.; **give** —W.COGN.ACC. *a share* (W.GEN. *of food*) S.; (intr.) **give a share** (of food) —W.DAT. *to someone* E.Cyc. Ar.
4 (of a democratic ruler) **share** —W.GEN. *discussion* (w. the populace) E.; (of a person envisaged as responding to a beggar) **make a donation** —W.GEN. *of sthg. dishonourable* (ref. to sexual favours) X.
5 (gener.) **give, hand** —*a document* (W.DAT. *to someone*) Plu. —*sacrificial entrails* (to someone) Plu. || PASS. (of a document) **be handed** —W.DAT. *to someone* Plu.

προσ-διέρχομαι mid.vb. (fig.) **go through in addition, also describe** —*sthg.* Plu.

προσ-διηγέομαι mid.contr.vb. **add an account of** —*sthg.* Thphr.

προσ-δικάζομαι mid.vb. **make an additional claim** —W.GEN. *for a sum of money* D.

προσ-διορθόομαι mid.contr.vb. **add** (W.NEUT.ACC. sthg.) **by way of correction** (of one's own mistake) Aeschin.

προσ-διορίζω vb. **1** (of a lawmaker) **specify** (W.ACC. *a regulation*) **additionally** (to what is specified in an inscription) D.
2 **add** (W.NEUT.ACC. sthg.) **to a definition** Arist.
3 || MID. **add** (W.NEUT.ACC. sthg.) **by way of qualification** Arist. || PASS. (of things) **be added by way of qualification** —W.DAT. *to a premise* Arist.
4 || MID. **assert in addition** —W.FUT.INF. or ACC. + FUT.INF. *that one will do sthg., that sthg. will be the case* Plb. Plu.

προσ-δοκάω contr.vb. [reltd. δοκέω] | aor. προσεδόκησα |
1 **look forward** (in hope or fear); **expect** —W.FUT.INF. or ACC. + FUT.INF. (or AOR.INF. w. ἄν) *that one* (or someone) *will* (would) *do sthg., that sthg. will happen* A. Hdt. E. Ar. Att.orats. Pl. + —W.ACC. PREDIC.SB. *someone to be such and such* Pl.; (intr.) Lys. Isoc. Pl.

2 (wkr.sens.) **expect** —W.AOR.INF. *to do sthg.* And. —W.ACC. + PRES.INF. *someone to do sthg.* And. —W.ACC. + AOR.INF. *someone to arrive* A.(dub.)
3 **expect, anticipate** —*a future event* Trag. Ar. Att.orats. Pl. + || PASS. (of events) **be expected** Pl. X.
4 **wait for** (someone or sthg.); **look out for, expect** —*someone* E. Ar. X.; **wait in expectation** —W.COMPL.CL. *for the moment when sthg. will happen* Ar.; (intr.) Ar. Men.
5 (without ref. to the future) **expect, think, suppose** —W.PRES.INF. or ACC. + PRES.INF. *that one* (or someone) *is doing sthg.* E. Pl. X. —W.ACC. + PF.PASS.INF. *that sthg. has been done* Pl. || PASS. (of a person) **be supposed** —W.PRES.INF. *to have sthg.* Lys.; (of a house) —*to be worth such and such* Lys.

προσ-δοκέω contr.vb. (of further proposals) **also seem best** —W.DAT. *to someone* X. [perh. πρὸς δοκέω]

προσδόκημα ατος n. [προσδοκάω] **expectation** (W.GEN. of sufferings) Pl.

προσδοκητέος ᾱ ον vbl.adj. (of things) **to be expected** Din.

προσδοκητός όν adj. (of things) **expected** (W.DAT. by someone) A.

προσδοκίᾱ ᾱς f. **1 expectation** (freq. W.GEN. of sthg. either hoped for or feared) E.fr. Th. Att.orats. Pl. +; (w. ὡς + FUT.INDIC. *that someone will do sthg.*) Th. Isoc.; (W.ACC. + FUT.INF.) Plu.; **apprehension, anxiety** (W. μή + SUBJ. or OPT. *that someone may do sthg.*) Th.
2 (prep.phrs.) πρὸς (παρὰ) τὴν προσδοκίαν **in accordance with** (contrary to) **expectation** Th. Plb.

προσδόκιμος ον adj. (of a person, a military force, ref. to their arrival) **expected** (sts. W.DAT. by someone) Hdt. Th. D. Plu.; (of troubles, danger) Hdt. Plb.

προσ-δοξάζω vb. **make a further judgement** (about sthg.) Pl.

προσδρακεῖν (aor.2 inf.): see προσδέρκομαι

προσ-δραμεῖν, dial. **ποτιδραμεῖν** aor.2 inf. | fut. προσδραμοῦμαι | The pres. and impf. are supplied by προστρέχω. | **1 run up** (to a person or place) Hdt. X. D. Thphr. Men. Plb. + —W.DAT. or πρός + ACC. *to someone or sthg.* Ar. Pl. X. Plu. —W.ACC. Call.; (wkr.sens., of poison) **approach** —W.DAT. *someone's lips* Mosch.
2 (fig.) **align oneself, side** —w. πρός + ACC. w. *the opinion of the majority* Plb.
3 (fig.) **fawn (on), flatter** (someone) Plb.

προσ-εάω contr.vb. (of a wind) **allow** (W.ACC. sailors) **onwards** (i.e. to continue on their course) NT.

προσ-εγγίζω vb. **come near** (someone) Plb.

προσ-εγγράφω vb. **1 inscribe** (W.ACC. *a picture*) **as well** (as *a message*) —W.PREP.PHR. *on pillars* Hdt.
2 **add** —*someone's name* (in a document, W.PREP.PHR. *alongside someone else's*) Hyp. —*a qualifying expression* (sts. W.PREP.PHR. *to a decree*) Aeschin.

προσ-εγγυάομαι mid.contr.vb. **also act as surety for** —*someone* (W.GEN. *for a sum owed*) D.

προσ-εγκελεύομαι mid.vb. **give additional encouragement** —W.DAT. *to someone* Plu.; (tr., of trumpeters) **sound by way of encouragement** —*a rousing tune* Plu.

προσ-εδαφίζομαι pass.vb. | 3sg.pf. προσηδάφισται | (of a shield) **have the base decorated** —W.DAT. w. *coiling snakes* A.

προσεδρεύω vb. [πρόσεδρος] **1 sit beside** —W.DAT. *a pyre* E.
2 **besiege** —W.DAT. *a city* Plb.
3 **be in attendance** (as a servant) —w. πρός + DAT. *at a schoolroom* D.; **stick close** —W.DAT. *to someone* D.

4 (fig.) **dwell on** (people) —W.DAT. *in one's thoughts, one's memory* Democr.
5 keep a close watch —W.DAT. *on events, a dispute* D. Plb.; **be on the lookout** (for an opportunity) Plb.
6 apply oneself diligently (to study) Arist. —W.DAT. *to laborious exercises* Arist. —*to someone's writings* Plb. —w. πρός + ACC. *to one's private business* Arist.

προσεδρίᾱ ᾱς *f.* **1 attendance at the sick-bed** (sts. W.GEN. of someone) E.
2 blockade, siege Th.

πρόσ-εδρος ον *adj.* [ἕδρᾱ] (of smoke) **settled about** (someone), **enshrouding** S.

προσέειπον *ep.aor.2 vb.*: see προσεῖπον

προσ-εθίζω *vb.* **1 make** (W.ACC. persons) **accustomed** —W.INF. *to doing sthg.* X. || PASS. **become accustomed** —W.DAT. *to sthg.* X.
2 make (W.ACC. endurance and frugality) **second nature** (to Spartan youths) X.

προσ-είδομαι *mid.vb.* (of a lock) **be like, resemble** —W.DAT. *someone's hair* A.

προσεῖδον (aor.2): see προσοράω

προσ-εικάζω *vb.* | aor. προσήκασα | **1 make** (W.ACC. sthg.) **like** —W.DAT. *sthg. else* Pl. X. || PASS. **be associated** (through similarity of behaviour) —W.DAT. *w. one's ancestors, someone's cowardice* Aeschin.
2 liken, compare, identify —*someone or sthg.* (W.DAT. *w. someone or sthg. else*) A. E. Pl. Plu.; (intr.) **make a comparison** A.

προσ-είκελος η ον *adj.* (of objects, creatures, countries, or sim.) **like, comparable to** —W.DAT. *others* Hdt.

προσεικέναι (Att.pf.inf.), **προσεικώς** (ptcpl.): see προσέοικα

πρόσ-ειλος ον *adj.* [εἵλη] (of houses, opp. caves) **exposed to the sun's heat, sunny, warm** A.

προσείμην (athem.aor.mid.): see προσίεμαι

πρόσ-ειμι[1] *vb.* [εἰμί] **1 be additional**; (of bronze decorations) **be added** or **attached** —w. πρός + DAT. *to a helmet* Hdt.; (of a liver-lobe) —W.DAT. *to sacrificial entrails* E.; (of a harbour) **be an additional feature** (of a place) Th.; (gener., of material and non-material things) **be added** (sts. W.DAT. to other things) Hdt. E. Pl.
2 (of troops) **be reinforcements** (sts. W.DAT. for someone) Hdt. X.; (of money) **be surplus** (to requirements) X. D.
3 (of a person) app. **make oneself available** —W.DAT. *to one who visits* Hes.
4 (wkr.sens., of qualities, attributes, feelings, circumstances) **be attached, be applicable, belong** —W.DAT. *to someone or sthg.* Semon. S. E. Th. Critias Ar. +; **also be present** Trag. Th. Ar. + || IMPERS. **it is a quality inherent** —W.DAT. *in someone* (+ INF. *to do sthg.*) Pl.

πρόσ-ειμι[2] *vb.* [εἶμι] | impf. προσῄειν || Only pres. and impf. (other tenses are supplied by προσέρχομαι). The pres.indic. has fut. sense. | **1** (of persons, sts. troops) **come or go to or towards, approach** —W.DAT. *a person or persons* Hdt. Th. Ar. Att.orats. Pl. + —*the gods* (W.ACC. *w. processional hymns*) Ar. —*a wall* Th. —w. πρός + ACC. *a person or place* Hdt. Ar. Att.orats. Pl. + —W.ACC. *a person* And. —*a place* A. E.; (intr.) Hom. Hes. Hdt. E. Th. Ar. +
2 (intr., of war) **approach** Pi.*fr.*; (of danger) Lys. X.; (of a time) Hdt. X.; (of happy times) E.*fr.*; (of things conveyed by persons) S. Ar. Pl.; (of natural phenomena) Pl. X.; (fig., of Hope) —W.DAT. *a voting urn* A.
3 (specif., of people, troops) **come in support, join** —W.DAT. *someone* Th.; **come seeking support, apply** —W.DAT. *to someone* Th.

4 approach for the purpose of addressing, approach —W.DAT. or πρός + ACC. *the people, the Council, officials* Th. X. D. Plb.; **come forward** (to speak) And.
5 enter or **engage in** —w. πρός + ACC. *public life, politics* Isoc. Aeschin. Thphr. —W.DAT. D.
6 (of revenue, tribute, money) **come in, accrue** (freq. W.DAT. to someone) Hdt. Th. Ar. Att.orats. X.; (of goods) Ar.

προσ-εῖπον, ep. **προσέειπον** *aor.2 vb.* —also **προσεῖπα** *Att.aor.1 vb.* | ep. freq.tm. πρὸς ... ἔειπον | ep.3sg.opt. προτιείποι | **1 speak to, address** —*someone* Hom. + —*a place, a thing* S. Ar.; **say** —W.DBL.ACC. *sthg. to someone* Hom. hHom. Ar. Call. AR.
2 address, greet, hail —*someone* (W.PREDIC.ACC. *as emperor*) Plu. —(w. ὡς + PREDIC.ACC. *as a stranger*) Pl. —(W.ADV. *by name*) Aeschin.
3 bid —W.ACC. + INF. χαίρειν *someone 'good day'* E.*Cyc.* X.
4 (of a poet) **invoke, mention** —*a person, a place* Pi.; (of a person) **call** —*someone's name* E.
5 designate, call —*someone or sthg.* (W.PREDIC.ACC. *such and such, i.e. by a particular name, title, or description*) A. S. Pl. Aeschin. D. —(W.DAT. *by a particular name*) Isoc. Pl.; **name** —*someone or sthg.* (W.ADV. *in a particular way*) Isoc. Pl. D.
6 describe —W.ACC. + INF. *sthg. as being* (W.PREDIC.ACC. or ADV. *such and such, in a particular state*) Pl. Aeschin.

προσ-είρω *vb.* [εἴρω²] | pres. not found | fut. προσερῶ | pf. προσείρηκα || PASS.: fut. προσρηθήσομαι | aor. προσερρήθην || neut.impers.vbl.adj. προσρητέον |
1 speak to, address —*someone* Hdt. E. Isoc. Pl. || PASS. **be addressed** E.
2 designate, call —*someone or sthg.* (W.PREDIC.ACC. *such and such, i.e. by a particular name, title, or description*) Pl. —(W.ACC. *by a name*) Pl. || PASS. **be called** —W.PREDIC.NOM. *such and such* Pl. —W.ACC. or DAT. *by a particular name or word* Pl.

προσ-εῖσκομαι *pass.vb.* | 2sg.pf. προσήϊξαι | **be like, resemble** (someone) E.

προσ-εισπράσσω *vb.* **exact in addition** —*a further sum of money* Plu.

προ-σείω *vb.* **1 shake** or **wave** (W.ACC. a branch or fruit) **in front** (of hungry animals, to lead them to food) Pl.
2 shake forward —*one's hair* (*in practising the head-movements of a Bacchant*) E.; **shake, wave** (sts. W.DAT. at someone) —*one's hand* (*to discourage a closer approach*) E.
3 (fig.) **hold out** —*a threat* Th.

προσ-εκβάλλω *vb.* **1 expel** or **banish** (W.ACC. someone) **as well** (as someone else) D.
2 cast aside (someone's corpse) **as well** (as killing him) Plu.

προσ-εκκαίω *vb.* **further inflame** —*someone's ambition* Plu.

προσ-εκλέγομαι *mid.vb.* (of newly appointed officers) **go on to select** —*other officers* Plb.

προσ-εκπέμπω *vb.* **also send out** —*troops* X.

προσ-εκπονέω *contr.vb.* || PASS. (of a remaining section of wall) **be completed as well** Plu.

προσεκτικός ή όν *adj.* [προσέχω] (of persons) **attentive** (sts. W.DAT. to sthg.) X. Arist.

προσ-εκτίνω *vb.* **pay in addition** —*a penalty* Pl. —*a sum of money, a fine* Plu.

προσ-εκφέρω *vb.* **pay in addition** —*a sum of money* Plb.(treaty)

προσ-εκχλευάζω *vb.* [ἐκ, χλευάζω] **also jeer at** or **mock** —*someone* D.

προσ-ελαύνω *vb.* **1 drive ahead** —*wagons* X. —*oxen* (w. πρός + ACC. *to a place*) Plb.
2 (intr.) **ride up** Hdt. Th. X. Plu. —w. πρός + ACC. *to someone, to somewhere* Hdt. Th. X. Plu. —W.DAT. X. Plu.

3 ‖ PASS. (of feet) be nailed —w. πρός + ACC. *to the ground (by arrows)* Plu.

προ-σεληναῖος ον *adj.* [σελήνη] (of Pelasgos, mythol. ancestor of the Arcadians) existing before the moon, **older than the moon** Lyr.adesp.

—**Προυσέληνος** ου *Ion.m.* **Pre-lunar man** (ref. to an Arcadian) Call.

προσ-έλκομαι *mid.vb.* ǀ aor. προσειλκυσάμην ǀ **1 draw** (someone or sthg.) **to oneself; draw to one's bosom, embrace** —*someone* E. Ar.; (of an archer's hands) **pull towards oneself** —*a bow* Pl.

2 (fig.) **draw** —*someone* (w. εἰς + ACC. *into friendship*) Thgn.; (of a word) **attract, acquire** —*an extra letter* Pl.

προσ-εμβαίνω *vb.* **trample on** (W.DAT. a dead man) **as well** (as hating him when he was alive) S.

προσ-εμβάλλω *vb.* **1 also plunge** —*someone* (W.PREP.PHR. *into a vortex, after falling into it oneself*) Pl.

2 **also introduce** —*a garrison* (W.PREP.PHR. *into a place*) Plu. —*members of a certain class* (*into the courts, as jurors*) Plu.

προσ-εμπικραίνομαι *mid.pass.vb.* **feel further bitterness against** —W.DAT. *someone* Hdt.

προσ-εμφερής ές *adj.* ǀ superl. προσεμφερέστατος ǀ (of an object) **similar** (W.DAT. to another) Hdt.

προσ-ενθυμέομαι *mid.contr.vb.* **also bear in mind** —W.COMPL.CL. *that sthg. is the case* Lys. [perh. πρός ἐνθυμέομαι]

προσ-εννέπω (also **προσενέπω**), dial. **ποτενέπω** *vb.* ǀ 3sg.impf. προσέννεπε (AR.), προσήνεπε (Pi. B.), ποτήνεπε (Stesich.) ǀ **1 speak to, address** —*someone* Lyr. Trag. AR.; **greet** —*doors, a tomb* E.; (fig., of a house) —*someone* E.

2 **address** —W.DBL.ACC. *someone by a certain name* A.; **call** —*someone or sthg.* (W.PREDIC.ACC. *such and such*) A.; **address** —*palace gates* (W.PREDIC.ACC. *as if they were the doors of Hades*) A.

3 **call upon** —W.ACC. + INF. *a deity, to do sthg.* Pi.

4 **bid** —W.ACC. + INF. χαίρειν *someone 'good day'* E.

προσ-εννοέω *contr.vb.* **also have in mind** —*sthg. else* X.

προσ-εντείνω *vb.* **inflict** (W.ACC. + DAT. blows on someone) **in addition** (to other maltreatment) D.

προσ-εντέλλομαι *mid.vb.* ǀ aor. προσενετειλάμην ǀ **add an instruction** —W.DAT. + INF. *to someone, to do sthg.* X. Plb.

προσ-εννυβρίζομαι *pass.vb.* **be the victim of further outrage** Plb.

προσ-εννυφαίνομαι *pass.vb.* (of figures) **be woven into** (W.DAT. a robe) **in addition** (to others) Plu.

προσ-εξαιρέομαι *mid.contr.vb.* **select** (W.ACC. someone) **in addition** Hdt.

προσ-εξαμαρτάνω *vb.* **1 add crimes** —W.NEUT.ACC. *of a far greater kind* (w. πρός + DAT. *to one's original misdeeds*) D.

2 **make a further mistake** Plu.

προσ-εξανδραποδίζομαι *mid.vb.* **enslave** (W.ACC. certain cities) **into the bargain** (as well as failing to honour a promise to fortify others) D.

προσ-εξανίστημι *vb.* ǀ athem.aor.ptcpl. προσεξαναστάς ǀ ‖ ATHEM.AOR. (of a baby) **raise oneself up** —w. πρός + ACC. *to someone's knees* Plu.

προσ-εξαπατάω *contr.vb.* (of witty sayings) **have an additional element of trickery** Arist.

προσ-εξασκέω *contr.vb.* **also practise** —W.INF. *doing sthg.* Plu.

προσ-εξελίσσω *vb.* **wheel** (W.ACC. troops) **round further** Plb.

προσ-εξεργάζομαι *mid.vb.* **1 commit** (W.ACC. other crimes) **in addition** D. ‖ PASS. (of crimes) **also be committed** D.

2 (intr., of a writer) **take extra trouble** Plb.

προσ-εξερείδομαι *mid.vb.* (of a person who has fallen on ice) **support oneself** —W.DAT. *w. one's hands and knees* Plb.

προσ-εξετάζω *vb.* **inquire further** —W.INDIR.Q. *what is the case* D. ‖ PASS. (of actions) **be examined as well** (as others) D.

προσ-εξευρίσκω *vb.* **devise** (W.ACC. a new plan, way of behaving, or sim.) **in addition** Ar. Isoc. Plb.

πρόσεξις εως *f.* [προσέχω] **application** (W.GEN. + DAT. of the mind, to an activity) Pl.

προσ-έοικα, dial. **ποτέοικα** *pf.vb.* (w.pres.sens.) ǀ Att.inf. προσεικέναι, ptcpl. προσεικώς ǀ **1** (of persons or things) **be like, resemble** —W.DAT. *someone or sthg.* A. E. Ar. Isoc. Pl. Theoc. + ‖ PTCPL.ADJ. (of things) **fitting, appropriate** (sts. W.DAT. for someone) S.

2 (of a person) **seem** —W.INF. *to do sthg.* D.

προσ-επάγομαι *pass.vb.* (of misconduct) **be given further encouragement** Plb.

προσ-επαινέω *contr.vb.* **also praise** —*someone* Aeschin.

προσ-επαιτιάομαι *mid.contr.vb.* **also censure** —*someone* Plu.

προσ-επεῖπον aor.2 *vb.* **say in addition** —*sthg.* Plb. —W.COMPL.CL. *that sthg. is the case* Plu.

προσ-επεξευρίσκω *vb.* **devise** (W.ACC. sthg.) **in addition** Th.

προσ-επιβάλλω *vb.* **1 throw** (W.PARTITV.GEN. earth) **on top** (of someone) **in addition** (to throwing him into a well) Plb.

2 **impose** (W.ACC. + DAT. further conditions on someone) **in addition** —W.DAT. *to those originally envisaged* Isoc.

προσ-επιγίγνομαι *mid.vb.* **also** (as well as others) **attack** —W.DAT. *someone* Plb.

προσ-επιγράφω *vb.* **add to an inscription** —W.COMPL.CL. *that sthg. is the case* Thphr.

προσ-επιδείκνυω *vb.* [ἐπιδείκνυμι] **also point out** —W.DAT. + COMPL.CL. *to someone, that sthg. is the case* Plb.

προσ-επιδίδωμι *vb.* **also give** —*sthg.* (W.DAT. *to someone*) Pl.

προσ-επιδράττομαι *Att.mid.vb.* **also grasp for oneself, also appropriate** —*territory* Plb.; (fig.) **also attract** —*envy* Plb.

προσ-επιζητέω *contr.vb.* **also seek after** —*sthg.* Plb.

προσ-επίκειμαι *mid.vb.* (fig., of the state) **also press hard** (on someone, w. tax demands) D.

προσ-επικοσμέομαι *pass.contr.vb.* (of a soldier) **also be furnished** —W.DAT. *w. a type of helmet* Plb.

προσ-επικτάομαι *mid.contr.vb.* **1 acquire** (W.ACC. honour) **in addition** Arist.

2 (of a king) **add** (W.ACC. nations) **by acquisition** —W.DAT. *to one's own nation* Hdt.

προσ-επιλαμβάνω *vb.* **1 receive in addition** —*a rank* Plu. —W.GEN. *land belonging to the populace* Plu.

2 (of a lake) **also extend** —W.GEN. *into an area* Plb.

3 (of a form of government) **acquire in addition, increase** —W.ACC. *power* (W.DAT. *for the people*) Arist.(dub.)

4 ‖ MID. (of particles in the body) **also lay hold** (on sthg.) Pl.; (of a person) **continue to hold on** (to an office) Plu.

5 ‖ MID. (fig.) **take a hand** (W.GEN. in a war) **in addition** —W.DAT. *to someone* Hdt.

προσ-επιλέγω *vb.* **say in addition** —W.COMPL.CL. *that sthg. is the case* Plb.

προσ-επιμελέομαι *mid.contr.vb.* **take care** (W.GEN. of sthg.) **as well** —w. πρός + DAT. *on top of other things* Pl.

προσ-επιμετρέω *contr.vb.* **1 also confer** —*honours* (W.DAT. *on someone*) Plb.

2 **promulgate in addition** —*a further decree* Plb.

προσ-επινοέω *contr.vb.* **devise** (W.NEUT.ACC. sthg.) **in addition** Plb.

προσ-επιπλήττω Att.vb. [ἐπιπλήσσω] also **rebuke** —W.DAT. *oneself* Arist.(dub.) | see προεπιπλήττω
προσ-επιπονέω contr.vb. **take further trouble** Aeschin.
προσ-επιρρώννυμαι pass.vb. **be further strengthened** —W.DAT. *in one's inclinations* Plb.
προσ-επισῑτίζομαι mid.vb. (of a fleet) **take on further provisions** Plb.
προσ-επισκώπτω vb. **go so far as to jest** Plu.
προσ-επισπάομαι mid.contr.vb. (pejor., of a historian) **drag in** —W.DBL.ACC. *someone, as witness* Plb.
προσ-επίσταμαι mid.vb. **know in addition** —*sthg.* Pl. —W.INDIR.Q. *what is the case* Pl.
προσ-επιστέλλω vb. **also instruct** —W.DAT. + INF. *someone to do sthg.* Th. X. ‖ PASS. (of an instruction) **be given additionally** Th.
προσ-επιτάττω Att.vb. [ἐπιτάσσω] **1 impose an additional stipulation** —W.ACC. + INF. *that someone shd. do sthg.* Plb. ‖ PASS. (of a stipulation) **be imposed additionally** Plb.
2 ‖ MID. (of a naval commander) **also take one's place in a formation** Plb.
προσ-επιτείνω vb. (of negotiators) **impose stricter terms on** —*someone* Plb.; (intr.) **insist more stringently** (on sthg.) Plb.
προσ-επιτέρπομαι mid.pass.vb. (of a particular god, in addition to others) **also take delight in** (people) Ar.
προσ-επιτίθημι vb. **1 add** (W.ACC. sthg.) **further** (to an assertion, by way of qualification) Arist.
2 inflict —*punishment* (W.DAT. on someone) Plb.
προσ-επιτῑμάω contr.vb. **also criticise** —W.DAT. *someone* Plb.
προσ-επιφέρω vb. (of the earth, when farmed) **provide** (W.ACC. luxuries) **as well** (as necessities) X.
προσ-επιφθέγγομαι mid.vb. **also cry out** —W.DIR.SP. *sthg.* Plb.
προσ-επιφωνέω contr.vb. **add** (a remark) **at the end of a speech** Plu.
προσ-επιχαρίζομαι mid.vb. (of choral performers) **also** (in addition to others) **pay homage** —W.DAT. *to the gods* X.
προσ-εργάζομαι mid.vb. **1 do** (W.ACC. nothing) **in addition** —W.DAT. *to things done earlier* E.
2 procure or **earn** (W.ACC. sthg.) **additionally** X.; (of a sum of money) **make, earn** —*ten times the amount* NT.
3 (of a sculptor) **apply** (W.ACC. gold) **to** —W.DAT. *a statue* Plu.
4 treat —W.DBL.ACC. *someone in a very savage way* Plu.
προσ-ερείδω vb. | pf. προσήρεικα (Plb.), προσηρήρεικα (Plu.) | **1 prop up, support** —*one's body* (W.DAT. *against a wall*) Plu. ‖ PASS. (of ships) **be propped up** —W.DAT. *on land* Plu.; (of a trophy) **be supported** (on someone's shoulder) Plu.
2 set up, plant —*scaling ladders* (sts. W.DAT. *against walls*) Plb. Plu.
3 thrust, press home —*a javelin* Plb. —*the tip of a javelin* (W.DAT. or πρός + ACC. *into a shield or sim.*) Plb. Plu.; (intr.) **press** —W.DAT. + PREP.PHR. *w. one's hands against someone's back* Plb.
4 (intr.) **press home an attack** Plb. —w. πρός + ACC. *on a city* Plb.
προσ-ερεύγομαι mid.vb. (fig., of waves) **belch at, roar against** —W.DAT. *a shore* Il. [or perh. W.ACC. *a rock*]
προσ-έρομαι mid.vb. | 3sg.aor.opt. προσέροιτο | **ask in addition** —W.DBL.ACC. *someone sthg.* Pl.
προσ-έρπω, dial. **ποθέρπω** (also tm. **ποτὶ ... ἕρπω**) vb. | aor. προσείρπυσα | **1 creep up** —W.PREP.PHR. *nearer to a tomb* S.; (of a baby) **crawl up** (to someone) Plu.; (of an animal, a person envisaged as a crab) **creep up, sidle up** Ar.; (of a cow) **amble up** Theoc.
2 (fig., of pain) **creep on** S.; (of an action) —W.DAT. *by stealth* S.; (of a remedy, fig.ref. to punishment) **be on the way, be in store** —W.DAT. *for someone* S.; (tr., of poetic inspiration) **steal upon** —*someone* Pi. ‖ PTCPL.ADJ. (of fortunes, time) **coming**, future A. Pi. ‖ NEUT.PTCPL.SB. **what is coming** (ref. to sthg. arriving) A.; (ref. to a future event) S.
προσερρήθην (aor.pass.): see προσείρω
προσ-ερυγγάνω vb. **belch** (at someone) Thphr.
προσ-έρχομαι, dial. **ποτέρχομαι** mid.vb. | impf. προσηρχόμην (Th., dub.; see προσάρχομαι) | fut. προσελεύσομαι (Plb.) | aor.2 προσῆλθον, dial.2sg.subj. ποτένθῃς | pf. προσελήλυθα ‖ impf. and fut. are usu. supplied by πρόσειμι² |
1 come or **go to** or **towards, approach** —W.DAT. *someone* A. Hdt. S. Th. Ar. Att.orats. + —*a place* A. Th. Theoc.*epigr.* —W.ACC. *a place* E. —W. πρός + ACC. *someone* Ar. —*an object or place* Hdt. Ar. Thphr. —w. ἐπί + ACC. *a place* E.; (intr.) **come close, approach** (sts. W.ADV. or PREP.PHR, *hither, near to someone,* or sim.) Hdt. S. E. Th. Ar. Att.orats. +
2 (of a time) **approach** Hdt.; (of pain) S.; (of sthg. expected) E.; (of sleep) **come** —W.DAT. *to someone* E.
3 go to fight (an opponent) Th.; (of cavalry) —w. πρός + ACC. *against cavalry* X.
4 come in support, come over to, join —W.DAT. *someone* (as an ally) Th.
5 (of a speaker) **approach for the purpose of addressing, approach** —W.DAT. or πρός + ACC. *the people, the Council* Aeschin. D.; (intr.) **come forward to speak** D. Arist.
6 enter or **engage in** —w. πρός + ACC. *public life, politics* Att.orats. Arist. —W.DAT. Plu.
7 (of revenue) **come in, accrue** (sts. W.DAT. *to someone*) Hdt. Lys. X. D.
προσερῶ (fut.): see προσείρω
προσ-ερωτάω contr.vb. **ask** (W.ACC. someone) **an additional question** —W.INDIR.Q. *whether sthg. is the case* Pl.; **ask as an additional question** —W.ACC. *what is obvious* Arist. ‖ PASS. (of a person) **be asked an additional question** X.; (of a question) **be asked additionally** Arist.
προσ-εσπέριος ον adj. (of nations) **to the west, western** Plb.
προσ-εταιρίζομαι mid.vb. **gain** (someone) **as an additional friend** or **colleague**; (of conspirators) **recruit in addition** —*someone* Hdt.; (of a politician) **ally oneself with** —*the people* Hdt.; (of a person) **befriend** —*someone* Plu.
προσεταιριστός όν adj. (of soldiers) **joined in partisanship, of the same political persuasion** Th.
προσ-έτι adv. **furthermore, moreover, besides** Hdt. Th. Ar. Att.orats. Pl. X. +; (also tm.) πρὸς δ' ἔτι *and furthermore* Hdt. Pl. X. Mosch.
προσευθῦναι ῶν f.pl. [προσευθύνω] **further auditing** (W.GEN. of magistrates) Arist.(dub.)
προσευθύνω vb. **audit** (W.ACC. a magistrate) **in addition** (to receiving accounts) Arist.
προσ-ευπορέω contr.vb. **provide** (W.ACC. money) **additionally** —W.DAT. *for someone* D. ‖ PASS. (of money) **be additionally provided** D.
προσ-ευρίσκω vb. **find** —W.ACC. + PREDIC.ADJ. *someone trustworthy* S. ‖ PASS. (of funds) **be found** —w. πρός + ACC. *for a project* Plb.
προσευχή ῆς f. [προσεύχομαι] **1 offering of prayer** (to God), **prayer** NT.
2 place for communal prayer (unless perh. ref. to a meeting held there); **place of prayer** or **prayer-meeting** NT. | cf. συναγωγή 6

προσ-εύχομαι *mid.vb.* **1** offer prayers or vows, **pray** Hdt. S. E. Antipho + —W.DAT. *to a god or gods, a statue* A. E. Ar. Pl. + —W.DAT. + INF. *to a god, to do sthg.* E. Pl. X. Plu.; (tr.) **address in prayer** —*a god, an altar* A. Hdt. E. Lys. Ar.
2 pray for —*sthg.* X.

προσ-εφέλκω *vb.* (of a law) **draw in additionally**, also **invite** —*foreigners* (*to citizenship*) Arist.

προσεχής ές *adj.* [προσέχω] **1** closely connected; (of troops) **adjacent, next** (sts. W.DAT. to others) Hdt.
2 (of a populace, a place) **neighbouring, bordering** (sts. W.DAT. on a place) Hdt. D.

προσ-έχω, dial. **ποτέχω** *vb.* | aor.2 προσέσχον | **1** (of a woman) **apply, offer** —*her breast* (*to a suckling serpent*) A.
2 direct (a ship) to land; **bring in** —*one's ships* Hdt.; (fig., of a need) **bring** (W.ACC. someone) **to land** S.; (intr., of persons) **land, put in** (sts. W.DAT. w. one's ship or ships) Hdt. Th. —W. εἰς or πρός + ACC. *at a place* Hdt. D. Plb. —W.DAT. Th. Plb. Plu. —W.ACC. S. Plb.
3 direct (one's attention); **turn** —*one's eyes* (*towards someone*) E.; (phr.) προσέχειν τὸν νοῦν (or sts. τὴν γνώμην) *apply one's mind, pay attention* Th. Ar. Att.orats. Pl. + —(W.DAT. *to someone or sthg.*) Th. Ar. Att.orats. Pl. + —(w. πρός + ACC.) Antipho —(w. πρός + DAT.) Ar.(dub.) —(W.INDIR.Q. *to how sthg. happens or what happens*) Ar. X.; (of hungry persons, w. play on previous phr.) **focus** —*their stomachs* (W.DAT. *on a speaker, i.e. his argument*) Ar.
4 (intr.) **pay attention** Att.orats. X. + —W.DAT. *to someone or sthg.* Th. Ar. Att.orats. Pl. +; **apply oneself** (to a war) Hdt. —W.DAT. *to an activity* Hdt. Th. Ar. Pl. +
5 be on one's guard —w. ἀπό + GEN. *against someone or sthg.* NT.
6 ‖ MID. (of a person, compared to a limpet) **attach oneself, cling, stick** —W.DAT. *to a person, a pillar* Ar.; (of mud) —*to a pole* Hdt.; (fig., of a person) **adhere, devote oneself** —W.DAT. *to a god* Pi. ‖ PASS. (of a person) be stuck fast —W.DAT. *to a poisoned robe* E.; (of objects) be held in place (on someone's shoulder) E.; (fig., of a person) be implicated —W.DAT. *in a curse* Th.
7 (of a person, a science) **have** (W.ACC. sthg.) **besides** or **in addition** Pl. D.

προσ-ζημιόω *contr.vb.* **1 punish** (W.ACC. someone) **additionally** —W.DAT. w. *exile* Pl.
2 (of a vice) **actually punish** —*those who are guilty of it* Isoc.

πρόσ-ηβος ον *adj.* [ἥβη] (of a person) **approaching manhood** X.

προσηγορέω *contr.vb.* [προσήγορος] **address, greet** —*someone* S. E.

προσηγόρημα ατος *n.* **greeting** (to dead children) E.

προσηγορίᾱ ᾱς *f.* form of address, **designation, name, title** Isoc. D. Arist. Plb. Plu.

προσηγορικός ή όν *adj.* (of a name) **given as a surname** (ref. to Lat. *cognomen*) Plu.

προσ-ήγορος ον *adj.* [ἀγορεύω] **1** (of a person) **addressing** (W.DBL.GEN. prayers to a god) S.; (of the oaks at Dodona) **speaking** A.; (of an utterance) **by way of greeting** S.
2 (of a person) **addressed, greeted** (W.GEN. or DAT. by someone) S.
3 (of persons) **ready to talk, on familiar terms** (W.DAT. w. each other) Pl.; (fig., of things) **commensurate** (w. πρός + ACC. w. each other) Pl.
4 (fig., of Greek technical terms) **meaningful, intelligible** (when rendered in Latin) Plu.

προσήιξαι (2sg.pf.pass.): see προσείσκομαι

προσηκάμην (aor.mid.): see προσίεμαι

προσ-ήκω *vb.* | freq. w.neg. in senses 4–8 | **1** (of persons) **have come, have arrived** S. Ar.(cj.); (of a need) A.
2 (of high ground) **reach, extend** —W.PREP.PHR. *to a river* X.; (of a theatre) —*to other buildings* X.
3 (of persons, ref. to their parentage) **be related** (usu. W.DAT. to someone) Hdt. E. Th. Ar. +; (W.GEN.) Lys. ‖ NEUT.PTCPL.SB. **kinship** E. ‖ MASC.FEM.PL.PTCPL.SB. **relatives** A. Hdt. E. Att.orats. +; (W.GEN. of someone) Th. Pl.
4 (of persons) **be connected, have to do** —W.DAT. w. *someone, a city* E. Th. Ar. X.; **belong** —W.DAT. *to a nation* (W.INF. *to impose punishment, i.e. be subject to its authority*) E.
5 (of things) **belong** (by natural connection or by right, usu. W.DAT. to someone); (of an honour) **belong** —*to someone* Hdt.; (of a family tie) S.; (of a share in someone's folly) E.; (of a circumstance) **pertain, be relevant** —*to someone* Th.; (of a calamity) **have to do** —w. πρός + ACC. w. *someone* Hdt. ‖ PTCPL.ADJ. (of a circumstance, situation, or sim.) **relevant, pertinent** (usu. W.DAT. to someone) Att.orats. Pl. +; (of land, possessions, allies, safety) **belonging or relevant to oneself** (i.e. one's own) Th.; (of grievances) **genuine** Th.; (of virtues) **hereditary** Th.
6 ‖ IMPERS. **there is a connection** —W.DAT.PERS. + GEN. *betw. someone and sthg.* (*i.e. it is of concern to him*) Ar. Att.orats. +
7 be **suited to circumstances**; (of a certain kind of behaviour) **be appropriate** —W.DAT. *for someone* S. Pl. X.; (of equipment) —*for triremes* Pl.; (of a skill) —*for an occupation* Pl. ‖ PTCPL.ADJ. (of a person) **suitable, appropriate** (for sthg.) Pl.; (of a god) —W.INF. *for doing sthg.* A.; (of things, sts. W.DAT. for someone or sthg.) Th. Att.orats. Pl. + —W.INF. *to hear* Pl.; (prep.phr.) ἐκ προσηκόντων *appropriately or in character* Th. ‖ NEUT.PTCPL.SB. (sg. and pl.) **what is appropriate or right** Th. Att.orats. Pl. +
8 ‖ IMPERS. **it is appropriate or right** —W.DAT. + INF. *for someone to do sthg.* A. Hdt. S. Th. Ar. Att.orats. + —W.ACC. + INF. A. E. Th. Att.orats. Pl. + —W.ACC. or DAT. (alone) Th. Att.orats. + ‖ NEUT.ACC.PTCPL. in circumstances where it is **appropriate** Th. Pl. —W.INF. *to do sthg.* Th. Isoc. Pl.

—**προσηκόντως** *ptcpl.adv.* **1 suitably, appropriately, rightfully** Att.orats. Pl. X. Arist. Men. Plu.; **in a manner appropriate** (W.DAT. to a topic) Isoc.
2 in a manner worthy of or **doing credit to** (W.DAT. one's city) Th.

προσ-ήλιος ον *adj.* (of ground) **exposed to the sun, sunny** X.

προσ-ηλόω *contr.vb.* [ἧλος] **1 nail on** —*timbers* (*to a broken rudder*) Plu.; (fig., of pleasure and pain) —*the soul* (w. πρός + ACC. *to the body*) Pl.
2 ‖ PASS. (of a criminal) be **nailed up** (to a board, as a form of execution) D.
3 nail up —*passageways* (*in a theatre, to block them*) D.

προσήλυτος ου *m.* [προσελεύσομαι, see προσέρχομαι] one who has come over (to Judaism), **proselyte, convert** NT.

πρόσ-ημαι *mid.vb.* [ἧμαι] **1** (of suppliants) **sit** or **lie before** —W.DAT. *persons, altars* A. S.; (of Erinyes) **sit close to, beset** —W.DAT. *a house* A.; (fig., of the poison of ill-will) —W.ACC. *someone's heart* A.
2 (of troops) **be encamped by** —W.DAT. *enemy fortifications* E.
3 sit at —W.DAT. *an oar* A.
4 (of islands) **lie near** —W.DAT. *a land* A.

προ-σημαίνω *vb.* **1** (of a god, a seer) **indicate in advance, foretell** (sts. W.DAT. to someone) —*future events* Hdt. E. Plu. —W.COMPL.CL. or ACC. + INF. *that sthg. will happen* Plu.; (of

an eclipse) **portend** —*a calamity* Plb.; (intr., of a deity) **give an advance sign** or **warning** X. Plu. ‖ IMPERS. there is advance warning (of an impending disaster) Hdt.
2 (of an oracle, a god) give authoritative advice, **advise** —W.INF. or DAT. + INF. (*someone*) *to do sthg.* Hdt. Aeschin. —W.DAT. + INDIR.Q. *someone, what he shd. do* X.
3 (of a herald) indicate publicly, **proclaim** —*sthg.* (W.DAT. *to someone*) Hdt.

προσ-ήνεμος ον *adj.* [ἄνεμος] (of one side of a threshing-floor) facing the wind, **windward** X.

προσήνεπε (3sg.impf.): see προσεννέπω

προσηνής, dial. **προσᾱνής**, ές *adj.* [reltd. ἀπηνής]
1 friendly or favourable; (of a person) **easy-going, pleasant** (usu. W.DAT. *to people*) Anacr. Plu.; (of animals) **gentle** (W.DAT. *to people*) Emp.
2 (of hospitality) **comforting** Pi.; (of speech) **bland** Th.; (of words) **kind** Plu. ‖ NEUT.PL.SB. soothing drinks Pi.
3 (of an oil) **suitable** (W.DAT. *for a lamp*) Hdt.
—**προσηνεστέρως** *compar.adv.* **more gladly** or **readily** —*ref. to the sensation of taste accepting certain foods* Plb.

προσήρεικα and **προσηρήρεικα** (pf.): see προσερείδω

προσ-ηχέω *contr.vb.* (of a loud noise) **resound** Plu.

προσ-ηῷος, also **ποτᾱῷος**, ᾱ ον *dial.adj.* [ἑῷος] (of a temple) **facing dawn, east-facing** Theoc.; (epith. of Artemis in Euboea, fr. the position of her temple) Plu.

προσ-θᾱκέω *contr.vb.* **sit begging** —W.COGN.ACC. *in a suppliant posture* S.

πρόσθε(ν), dial. **πρόσθα** *adv. and prep.* [πρό] **1** (ref. to position) **before, in front** Hom. +; (also) τὸ πρόσθεν Thgn.; (prep.) **in front** —W.GEN. *of someone or sthg.* Hom. +
2 (prep.phrs., ref. to movt. or position) εἰς τὸ πρόσθε(ν) *forward, ahead* Hdt. E. Th. +; *to the front* S.; *in front* (W.GEN. *of someone or sthg.*) Hdt. E. +; (fig.) ἐς πρόσθεν *further on* (W.GEN. *in one's troubles*) E.; ἐν τῷ πρόσθε(ν) *in front* Th. Ar. —(W.GEN. *of someone or sthg.*) Lys. X.
3 (ref. to choice) **sooner, rather** —W. ἤ + CL. *than doing sthg.* X.; (prep.) **in preference** —W.GEN. *to someone or sthg.* E.
4 (ref. to time) in the past, **before, formerly, previously** Hom. +; (also) τὸ (sts. τὰ) πρόσθε(ν) Hom. Trag. +; (quasi-adj., of persons, events, statements, time, or sim.) **earlier, former** Il. +
5 before a specified time (either past or future), **before then, beforehand, first** Hom. +; (quasi-adj., of a person) **elder** E.; (prep.) **sooner than, before** —W.GEN. *someone* Il. A. S. —*a time* S. X.
6 (in the first of two co-ordinated cls., as antecedent to conj. πρίν or πρὶν ἤ, usu. w.neg.) Od. Pl. X. • οὐ γάρ μιν πρόσθεν παύσεσθαι ὀΐω ... πρίν γ᾽ αὐτὸν με ἴδηται *for I do not think he will stop until he sees me* Od.
7 πρόσθεν ἤ *earlier than, before* —W.INF. or ACC. + INF. *one (or someone) does sthg.* S. E. —W.INDIC. *sthg. has happened* S.; (co-ordinating two phrs.) • μηδὲν πρόσθεν ἢ τὰ Λοξίου (*do*) *nothing before Loxias' business* S.

πρόσθεσις εως *f.* [προστίθημι] **1** action of placing against; **application** (of one object to another) Arist.; **placing** (of a ladder against a wall) Th. Plb.; **bringing up** (of a siege-engine) Plb.
2 process of adding, **addition** (sts. W.GEN. + DAT. *of one thing to another*) Pl.; (of numbers) Arist. ‖ PL. (gener.) **additions** (to) or augmentation (of honours, contracts, or sim.) Plu.
3 addition of a limiting expression to a general term, **qualification** Arist.

πρόσθετος ον *adj.* **1** (of hair) added, **artificial, false** X.
2 (of a person) assigned to a creditor, **enslaved for debt** Plu.

προσ-θέω *contr.vb.* [θέω¹] **run up** X. —W.DAT. *to someone* X. Plu.

προσθήκη ης *f.* [προστίθημι] **1** addition (w. πρός + DAT. *to apparently favourable news, ref. to a messenger's confirmation of it*) A.; (of a name, to a person's title) Plu.
2 additional material (in an argument) Pl.; **digression** (in a narrative) Hdt.
3 (pejor.) that which is added as a merely subsidiary element, **appendage** Pl. Hyp. D. Arist. Plu.; (W.GEN. *of a woman, ref. to a man*) Plu.
4 additional help (W.GEN. fr. *a god, the laws*) S. D.; **additional source** (W.GEN. *of power, ref. to a person*) Plu.
5 addition of a limiting expression to a general term, **qualification** D.

πρόσθημα ατος *n.* **appendage, accessory** (ref. to a cuirass) X.; (ref. to a subsidiary virtue) Pl. ‖ PL. accessories (W.DAT. *to one's dress, ref. to jewellery*) E.

προσ-θιγγάνω *vb.* | fut. προσθίξομαι | dial.aor.2 (tm.) ποτὶ ... θίγον | **1** (of a person) **touch** (usu. W.GEN. *someone or sthg.*) Trag.
2 (of food) **touch** —W.ACC. *someone's lips* Theoc.(tm.)

πρόσθιος ᾱ ον *adj.* [πρόσθεν] **1** at the front; (of a quadruped's feet or legs) **front** E. X. Plu.; (of part of a military procession, i.e. its head, likened to that of terrifying mythical creatures) Plu.
2 (of members of a chorus, envisaged as teeth) **front** Ar.

προσθό-δομος ον *adj.* [δόμος] (of a dead king, ref. to the location of his tomb) **in front of the palace** A.

προσ-θροέω *contr.vb.* **address** —W.DBL.ACC. *the right words to someone* A.

προσ-ίεμαι *mid.vb.* [ἵημι] | pres. usu. ῑ | aor.1 προσηκάμην (E.), athem.aor. προσείμην | **1** let (someone) come to oneself; **admit, accept** —*someone* (*as a friend, lover, ally, or sim.*) Hdt. E. Ar.(cj.) Isoc. Pl. + —(W.PREP.PHR. *to one's society*) Pl. X.; **allow** (W.ACC. *the enemy*) **to come** —W.ADV. *close* X.; (of a woman) **accept** —*another's baby* (W.DAT. *at the breast*) Plu.
2 let in; **admit, allow** —*tender words* (W.DAT. *into one's heart*) E. —*a war* (W.PREP.PHR. *into one's country*) D. —*someone's entry* (*into a house*) Lys.(cj.); (of a wall) **admit of, permit** —*an assault by scaling ladders* Plb.
3 readily adopt or accept; **adopt** —*foreign customs* Hdt.; **accept** —*a proposal, an argument, a method of inquiry, or sim.* Th. Pl. X. Hyp. +; **believe** —*an account, a slander* Hdt.; **welcome** —*a statement* E. —*an outcome* Th.; **be willing to take** —*medicine, food, a joke* X. Arist. Plb.; **countenance, condone** —*treachery, wrongdoing, or sim.* Hdt. X. D. +; (of gods) —*a war* X.
4 take upon oneself, **venture** —W.INF. *to do sthg.* Pl. X.
5 (of an oracular response, a person's behaviour or speech) **appeal to, please** —*someone* Hdt. Ar.
6 (of a desire) **attract, induce** —*someone* (W.INF. *to do sthg.*) S.fr.

—**προσίημι** *act.vb.* allow (someone) to come (to a person or place); **admit** —*someone* (*to a person's presence*) X. —(w. πρός + ACC. *to a place*) X.

προσ-ιζάνω *vb.* **1** (fig., of a curse) **sit close by** —W.DAT. *someone* A.
2 (of blame) **alight, settle** —W.DAT. *on someone* Semon.; (of misery) —w. πρός + ACC. *on someone* A.

προσ-ίζω *vb.* **1** (of suppliants) **go and sit** or **lie before** —*an altar, a goddess* (i.e. *her statue or altar*) A. E.

προσικνέομαι

2 (of a crowd, envisaged as a swarm of bees) **settle** —w. περί + ACC. *around the speaker's rostrum* Pl.

3 (of a drop of rain) **alight, fall** —W.DAT. *on someone* E.; (fig., of a concern for sthg.) E.*fr*.

προσ-ικνέομαι *mid.contr.vb*. **1** approach in supplication, **approach** —*a temple* A.

2 (of a pang of grief) **reach** —w. ἐπί + ACC. *to someone's heart* A.

προσίκτωρ ορος *m*. one who approaches (a god or temple) in supplication, **suppliant** A.

προσ-ιππεύω *vb*. (of cavalry) ride against (the enemy), **charge** Th. Plu.; (of individuals) **ride up** —W.DAT. *to a person, a place* Plu.

προσ-ίστημι *vb*. | imperatv. προσίστη | (fig.) **set** (W.ACC. the prow of one's life) **against** —w. πρός + ACC. *the swell* (i.e. oppose the flow of fortune) E.

—**προσίσταμαι** *mid.vb*. | also ACT.: athem.aor. προσέστην | pf. προσέστηκα | Ion.3sg.plpf. προσεστήκεε | **1 come and stand near, station oneself close by** A. Hdt. Pl. X. Men. —W.DAT. *someone or sthg*. A. Hdt. Pl. Plu. —W.ACC. *an altar* A. —w. πρός + ACC. *a statue, a loom* Ar. X. —*a shop* Thphr.; **come and attend** (a meeting or sim.) X. D. Arist. —w. πρός + ACC. *a court* Aeschin. ‖ PF. and PLPF.ACT. (of persons or things) **stand close by** Ar. Pl. Plu. —W.DAT. *someone or sthg*. Hdt. Ar.; attend —W.DAT. *a court* Aeschin.

2 (fig., of a wave of bitterness) **reach** —W.DAT. *to someone's heart* A.; (of honour) **come** (to someone) E.; (of subjects for a speech) **occur** —W.DAT. *to someone* D.; (of a thought) —W.DAT. *to someone* Pl. —W.ACC. Hdt. ‖ IMPERS. it occurs —W.DAT. + INF. *to someone, to do sthg*. Pl.

3 (fig., of impeachments, eloquence) act adversely on, **offend, upset** —W.DAT. *someone* Hyp. D.

4 ‖ PF.ACT. (of a person's breathing) app., **be stopped short** (so that he cannot speak) Men.

προσ-ιστορέω *contr.vb*. (of a writer) **record in addition** —W.ACC. + INF. *that sthg. is the case* Plu.

προσ-ίσχω, ep. **ποτίσχω** *vb*. | impf. προσῖσχον (Hdt.) | **1** hold (sthg.) against (sthg. else); **hold** —*a shield* (w. πρός + ACC. *against the ground*) Hdt.

2 direct (a ship) to land; **bring in** —*one's ship* (W.DAT. *to a place*) E.; (intr.) **come to land, put in** Hdt. —W.DAT. *at a place* Hdt. Th. Plu. —w. ἐς or πρός + ACC. Hdt.

3 ‖ MID. attach oneself, **cling** (to someone) AR. ‖ PASS. (of impurities in water) be stuck fast —W.DAT. *to the inner lip of a cup* Plu.

προσιτός ή όν *adj*. [πρόσειμι²] (of a person's character) **approachable** Plu.

προσ-καθέζομαι *mid.vb*. | fut. προσκαθεδοῦμαι | **1** (of a commander, troops) take up a position nearby (for the purpose of besieging a place), **lay siege** Th. X. Arist. Plb. —W.DAT. *to a city, a person* Plb. Plu.; (tr.) **besiege** —*a city, an island* Th. X.

2 (fig.) **give close attention** —W.DAT. *to events* D.

προσ-καθέλκω *vb*. also **launch** —*ships* Plu.

προσ-κάθημαι, Ion. **προσκάτημαι** *mid.vb*. **1** (of a commander, troops) occupy a position nearby (for the purpose of besieging a place), **lay siege** Hdt. Th. X. Arist. Plu. —W.DAT. *to a city* Th. Plb. Plu.; (wkr.sens.) **be encamped nearby** Th. D. Plu.

2 (fig.) **beset, pester** (someone, w. warnings) Hdt.

3 (of flies) **settle** (on someone) Plu.; (of an evil, in sthg.) Pl.

προσ-καθίζω *vb*. | fut. προσκαθιζήσομαι | **1** (of a suppliant) **sit** or **lie before** (someone) —W.COGN.ACC. *in a posture of misery* E.

2 (of a commander, troops) **take a position before, besiege** —*a city* Plb. ‖ MID. (in fig.ctxt.) **lay siege** (to any place where money is on offer) Aeschin.

3 (fig., of Socrates) **beset, pester** (people) Pl.

προσ-καθίστημι *vb*. **appoint** (W.ACC. a priest) **additionally** —W.DAT. *to existing priests* Plu.

προσ-καθοπλίζω *vb*. (of a king) also **arm** —*a class of people* Plu.

προσ-καθοράω *contr.vb*. **perceive also** —*the underlying science* (w. πρός + DAT. *in addition to each separate thing*) Pl.

πρόσ-καιρος ον *adj*. [καιρός] **1** (of sallies by troops) **well-timed** Plu.

2 (fig., of a person, envisaged as a rootless plant) **lasting for a short time only, transitory** NT.

προσ-καίω *vb*. **burn additionally; burn, scorch** —*a pot* Ar. ‖ PASS. (fig., of a person) be inflamed (w. love for someone) X. ‖ PF.PASS.PTCPL.ADJ. (of utensils) burnt (app. w. pun on προσκεκλημένος *summoned to court*, cf. προσκαλέω 2-3) Ar.

προσ-καλέω *contr.vb*. **1** (of persons in authority) **call to, summon** —*someone* S. Th. Pl. X. D. +; (mid.) —*one's servant, one's dog* Thphr. —*someone* Plb. NT. Plu. ‖ PASS. be summoned X.

2 ‖ MID. (leg., of an accuser) call (someone) to court; **serve a summons** (usu. W.ACC. on someone) Ar. Att.orats. + —W.ACC. δίκην *to face a charge* (sts. W.GEN. *of sthg.*) Lys. D. —W.GEN. *on a charge of sthg*. Ar. —w. εἰς or πρός + ACC. *before a magistrate or court* Ar. Att.orats. —w. εἰς + ACC. *for a particular suit* X. Is. D. ‖ PASS. be served a summons Antipho Ar. D. —W.ACC. δίκην *on a charge* (sts. W.GEN. *of sthg.*) Arist. —W.GEN. *on a charge of sthg*. D. —w. εἰς + ACC. *to appear before a court* Arist.

3 ‖ MID. **summon** —*a witness* D. —*someone* (w. εἰς + ACC. *to give evidence*) D. ‖ PASS. be summoned (as a witness) —W.PREP.PHR. *fr. one's house* D.

προσ-καρτερέω *contr.vb*. **1 make additional effort** X.

2 **act resolutely, persevere, persist** (in doing sthg.) Plb. NT. —W.DAT. *in a siege, in mining operations* Plb. —*in prayer* NT.; **continue an attack** —W.DAT. *on the enemy* Plb.

3 **give careful attention** —W.DAT. *to someone's diet* Plb.; **be intent** —W.DAT. *on gain* Plb.

4 (of a friend, servant, or sim.) **remain loyal to, stick by, stay with** —W.DAT. *someone* D. Plb. NT. —*someone's teaching* NT.

5 (of a boat) **wait ready** —W.DAT. *for someone* NT.

προσ-κατάβλημα ατος *n*. [καταβάλλω] **supplementary payment** (to make up a shortfall) D.

προσ-καταγιγνώσκω *vb*. | fut. προσκαταγνώσομαι | **1** (leg.) **adjudge, award** —*property* (W.DAT. *to someone*) D.

2 ‖ PASS. (of a person who has lost his life) be convicted into the bargain Antipho

προσ-καταισχύνω *vb*. (of a badly made funeral monument for one's mistress) **bring further shame to** —*a tribute which was itself ignoble* Plu.

προσ-κατακλαίομαι *mid.vb*. also **lament** (someone) Plb.

προσ-κατακτάομαι *mid.contr.vb*. **gain** (W.ACC. someone's land) **in addition** (to recovering one's own) Plb.

προσ-καταλέγω *vb*. **enlist** (W.ACC. persons) **in addition** —W.DAT. *to others* Plu.; **enlist** (W.ACC. persons) **to serve beside** —W.DAT. *oneself* Plu. ‖ PASS. (of persons) be selected additionally Plu.

προσ-καταλείπω *vb*. **1** leave (W.ACC. + DAT. an empire to one's descendants) **as well** (as other possessions) Th.

2 **lose** (W.ACC. one's own possessions) **into the bargain** (as well as failing to win those of others) Th.

προσ-καταλλάττομαι Att.mid.vb. [καταλλάσσω] (leg., of disputants) **agree to a settlement** Arist.

προσ-καταμένω vb. **stay on for a longer time** (in a place) Hyp.

προσ-κατανέμω vb. **1 allocate** (to the populace) **in addition** —*a second Council* Plu.
2 also allocate —*land* (W.DAT. *to people*) Plu.

προσ-καταριθμέω contr.vb. **count** (W.ACC. sthg.) **in addition** —W.DAT. *to sthg. else* (i.e. add it to the total) Plu.

προσ-κατασκευάζω vb. **1 set up in addition** —*a trading depot* D.; **build in addition** —*another bridge* Plu.; **establish in addition** —*local rulers* Plb.; (intr., of besiegers) **add further structures to, build on** —W.DAT. *existing structures* Plb.
2 ‖ MID. **establish** (W.ACC. *bases for attack*) **in addition** (to existing ones) D.; **equip** (W.ACC. *three hundred cavalrymen*) **in addition** (to the existing number) Aeschin.
3 ‖ PASS. (of a plan) **be contrived additionally** D.; (of disgrace) **be cast** (W.DAT. *on a city*) **in addition** (to the wrongs which it has suffered) D.

προσ-κατασπάω contr.vb. **also draw down** (to the shore), **launch** (W.ACC. *ships*) **in addition** (to those already at sea) Plb.

προσ-κατατάττω Att.vb. [κατατάσσω] (of historians) **append, insert** —*speeches* (into a narrative) Plb.

προσ-κατατίθημι vb. **also put down, pay in addition** —*a sum of money* Ar.

προσ-καταψεύδομαι mid.vb. **make further false accusations against** —W.GEN. *someone* Plb.

προσ-κατηγορέω contr.vb. **1 bring a further accusation** (sts. W.GEN. against someone) —W.ACC. *of sthg.* Th. —W.COMPL.CL. *of doing sthg.* X. Plu.
2 ‖ PASS. (of an expression) **be given an additional predicate** (by having an extra word) Arist.

προσκάτημαι Ion.mid.vb.: see προσκάθημαι

πρόσ-κειμαι mid.pass.vb. [κεῖμαι] **1 be situated on or against**; (of handles) **be placed on** (tripods) Il.; (of timbers) **be placed against** —W.DAT. *a wall* Th.; (of documents) **be attached** —W.DAT. *to arrows* Plu.; (fig., of Socrates, perh. envisaged as a spur) **be applied** —W.DAT. *to a city* (W.PREP.PHR. *by a god*) Pl.; (of cities, envisaged as sick persons) **have** (W.ACC. *cupping-glasses*) **applied to oneself** Ar.; (of a person) **place oneself against, cling** (to a hanging corpse) S.
2 be located nearby; (of a person) **keep close** —W.DAT. *to a door* Ar.; (of a chariot-horse) **press close** (to the turning-post) S.; (of a place, a part of the body) **lie close** —w. πρός + DAT. *to a place, to another part* Hdt. Ar.
3 (in military ctxt., of assailants) **press hard, make an attack** Hdt. E. Th. Ar. X. + —W.DAT. *on opposing troops* Hdt. Th. Ar. Plb. Plu. —*on a city* Th. Plb. Plu. —*on a city's gates* E.; (fig., of compulsion) **press** (upon someone) Pl.; (of a misfortune) E. —W.DAT. *upon a house* E. ‖ NEUT.PTCPL.SB. **enemy pressure** Hdt.
4 (of persons, in seeking support or making a request) **press one's case** E. Th. D. Plu.; **make overtures** —W.DAT. *to someone* Hdt. X. Plu.
5 be keenly involved (W.DAT. in an activity or interest); (of a commander) **apply oneself** —*to a siege* Plb.; (of a political leader) **pay particular attention** —*to the navy* Th.; (of persons) **be given** —*to wine-drinking, divination, a certain kind of behaviour* Hdt. Th.; **be intent** —*on a futile hunt, a philosophical concept* S. Pl.; **place one's trust** —*in a story* Hdt.; (wkr.sens.) **be involved** —*in good fortune, trouble* S.

6 be closely associated (W.DAT. w. someone); (of a person) **be attached** or **devoted** —*to someone* Hdt.; (of a politician) **associate oneself** —*w. the people* Th.; (of a woman) **be assigned** —*to someone* (as a wife, by auction) Hdt. —(*as a slave, by lot*) Il.
7 (of things) **be associated** (w. someone or sthg.); (of a duty) **be attached** —W.DAT. *to high office* Arist.; (of gratitude, to a reward) S.; (of a reward) —w. πρός + DAT. *to an exploit* E.; (of a duty) **be assigned** —W.DAT. *to someone* Hdt.; (of an honour) **be due** —W.DAT. *to a god* Hdt.; (of a skill, of qualities or attributes) **belong** —W.DAT. *to someone* Hdt. S. E.
8 ‖ IMPERS. **a responsibility has been assigned** —W.DAT. *to someone* Hdt. —(W.INF. *to do sthg.*) Hdt. —(W.ACC. + INF. *to ensure that someone does sthg.*) E.
9 (of things) **be added** (to other things); (of a festival) **be added** (to existing ones) Arist.; (of suffering) —W.DAT. or ἐπί + DAT. *to suffering* E.; (of remarks) —W.DAT. *to earlier remarks* Isoc.; (of letters, words, phrases, to other words or sim.) Ar. Pl. X. Arist. Plb.; (of one term in a definition) **be combined** —W.DAT. *w. another* Arist.
10 (of a person) perh. **also be regarded** or **treated** —W.PREDIC.SB. *as an enemy* (W.DAT. *by someone, as well as by the speaker*) S.

προ-σκέπτομαι mid.vb. | fut. προσκέψομαι | aor. προυσκεψάμην | 3sg.plpf.pass. προύσκεπτο ‖ For pres. and impf. προσκοπέω is used. | **1 watch, keep an eye on** —*someone* Ar.
2 look (at sthg.) **beforehand** (w. the mind); **think things over first** Hdt.; (tr.) **first consider** —*all circumstances* Hdt. —W.COMPL.CL. *that sthg. is the case* Th. ‖ PASS. (of speeches) **be vetted in advance** Th. ‖ NEUT.PL.PF.PASS.PTCPL.SB. **earlier inquiries** Pl.
3 look out for, take thought for —*someone's interests* E.

προσ-κερδαίνω vb. **1** (of a money-lender) **make additional profit** D.
2 gain (W.ACC. *bodily health*) **as well** (as a good reputation) Plb.

προσ-κεφάλαιον ου n. **1 cushion to rest the head on, pillow** Lys. Ar.
2 cushion (for sitting or lying on) Ar. Pl. Aeschin. D. Thphr. +

προσ-κηδής ές adj. [κῆδος] **1 involving a close tie**; (of friendship) **warm** Od. [or perh. **full of sadness**, as 3]
2 (of a person) perh. **welcoming** AR.
3 perh. **careworn, anguished** AR.
4 related by marriage (W.DAT. to someone) Hdt.

προ-σκήνιον ου n. [σκηνή] **raised platform in front of stage buildings, proscenium, stage** Plb. Plu.

προσ-κηρυκεύομαι mid.vb. (of a people) **send heralds** (to another people), **make diplomatic overtures** Th.(treaty)

προσ-κινέομαι mid.contr.vb. (of a woman) **make responsive movements** (in sexual intercourse), **thrust back** Ar.; (of chariots, fig.ref. to bodies, w. sexual connot.) Ar.

προσ-κλάομαι pass.contr.vb. (of a rider) **suffer a fracture** (by striking one's leg against sthg.) X.

προσ-κληρόομαι pass.contr.vb. **become attached to, join** —W.DAT. *someone* (as a follower) NT.

πρόσκλησις εως f. [προσκαλέω] (leg.) **summons** (ref. to a document) Ar.; (ref. to the process) Pl. D. Arist.

προσ-κλίνω, dial. ποτικλίνω vb. | ep.3sg.pf.pass. ποτικέκλιται | **1 prop** or **lean** (W.ACC. *an arrow*) **against** —W.DAT. *part of a bow* (or perh. *a door-handle*) Od. ‖ PF.PASS. (of a king's seat) **be positioned beside** —W.DAT. *his wife* (i.e. her seat) Od.; (of a serpent's back) **be stretched over** (a bed of rocks) Pi.

πρόσκλισις

2 (intr., of persons) **incline towards, be sympathetic to** —w.DAT. *someone* Plb. ‖ PASS. **attach oneself to, join** —w.DAT. *a leader* NT.

πρόσκλισις εως *f*. **inclination** (towards a person or cause); **sympathy, support, favour** (sts. w.DAT. for someone) Plb.

προσ-κλύζω *vb*. (of the sea) **wash** (against a country) X. —w.DAT. or πρός + ACC. *against a place* Plb. Plu.

προσ-κνάομαι *mid.contr.vb*. scratch or rub oneself against; (fig., of a lover, compared to a pig rubbing itself against a stone to relieve an itch) **scratch oneself** —w.DAT. *against someone* (i.e. be unable to keep away fr. him) X.

προσ-κοινωνέω *contr.vb*. **1 share** —w.GEN. *in sthg*. Pl.; (of a city) **create involvement** (w.DAT. for itself) —w.GEN. *in civil strife* Pl.

2 be a partner (in an enterprise) —w.DAT. *w. someone* D.

προσ-κολλάομαι *pass.contr.vb*. **1** (of a soul) **be glued or welded** —w.DAT. *to a body* Pl.

2 (fig., of a person) **be closely attached, adhere** —w.DAT. *to someone* Pl.; (of a husband) —w.DAT. or πρός + ACC. *to one's wife* NT.

προσ-κομίζω *vb*. **1 convey to a destination** (by land); **transport** —*someone* (w.PREP.PHR. *to a place*) X.; **bring up** —*a siege-engine, stones* Th. D. Plu.; **bring in** —*crops* X. ‖ PASS. (of persons) be transported —w.DAT. or PREP.PHR. *to a place* Plu.; (of gifts) be brought along (to someone) Plu.

2 convey to a destination (by sea); **transport** —*corpses* (w.PREP.PHR. *to a place*) Th.; **bring up** —*ships* (w. πρός + DAT. *to join others*) Th. ‖ MID. **bring to land, bring home** —*corpses and wrecks* Th. ‖ PASS. (of ships, a naval commander) sail towards land Th. X. Plu.

3 ‖ MID. bring in for oneself, **import** —*necessary supplies* X.

4 bring over, attach —*a city* (w.DAT. *to a confederacy*) Plu.

προ-σκοπέω *contr.vb*. | impf. προυσκόπουν ‖ Only pres. and impf.; for other tenses see προσκέπτομαι. | **1** ‖ MID. **watch for, look out for** —*someone* (who is absent) E.; **look to see** —w.INDIR.Q. *where someone is* Thphr.

2 look out (for sthg.) beforehand (w. the mind); **look out for, take thought for** —*common interests* Th. —*another's interests* E.(mid.); **guard against** —*contingencies* E. Th. X. —w. μή + INF. *suffering harm* Th.; **consider** —w.INDIR.Q. *what will happen* X. Men.(mid.)

3 keep watch on (w.ACC. people's words, actions and criticisms) **on behalf of** —w.GEN. *someone* S.

προσκοπή[1] ῆς *f*. [προσκοπέω] **action of looking out, lookout, watch** (w.GEN. for ships) Th.

προσκοπή[2] ῆς *f*. [προσκόπτω] **taking of offence, offence, resentment** Plb.

πρό-σκοπος ου *m*. [σκοπός] **1** (perh. collectv.sg.) **guard posted in front of a camp, outpost** X. ‖ PL. scouts X.

2 ‖ ADJ. (of intelligence) **foreseeing** Pi.*fr*.

προσ-κόπτω *vb*. **1 strike** (a part of the body) **against** (an object); **strike** —*one's leg* (w.DAT. *against sthg*.) X. —*one's foot* (w. πρός + ACC. *against a stone*) NT.; **stub** —*one's toe* Ar.; (intr.) **stumble** NT.

2 (of winds) **strike against** —w.DAT. *a house* NT.; (of impurities in water) —*the inner lip of a cup* (and so be trapped by it) Plu.

3 (fig.) **give offence** Plb. —w.DAT. *to someone* Plb.

4 take offence Plb. —w.DAT. *at someone or sthg*. Plb.

προσ-κοσμέω *contr.vb*. **1 build** (w.ACC. a basilica) **as an additional ornament** —w.DAT. *for the forum* Plu.

‖ NEUT.PL.PF.PASS.PTCPL.SB. additional ornaments (w.DAT. for a theatre) Plu.

2 ‖ MID. or PASS. (of political supporters) **be drawn up additionally, be attached** —w.DAT. *to other supporters* Arist.

προσ-κρέμαμαι *pass.vb*. [κρεμάννῡμι] (of a ship) **hang on, be attached** —w.DAT. *to another ship* (after a collision) Plb.

πρόσκρουμα (also **πρόσκρουσμα** Plu.) ατος *n*. [προσκρούω] **1 striking against or collision with** (someone); (fig.) **antagonism, quarrel** D. Plu.

2 mishap, reverse (suffered by a city or army) Plu.

3 cause of offence (against gods or humans), **offence** Plu.

πρόσκρουσις εως *f*. **collision** (betw. people); (fig.) **antagonism** Plu.

προσ-κρούω *vb*. **1** (of a body) **strike against, collide with** —w.DAT. *fire* Pl.

2 (of a nation, a commander) **stumble, meet with a reverse** D. Plu.

3 come into collision, clash, quarrel, fall out (freq. w.DAT. w. someone) Att.orats. Pl. Arist. Plu.; **be averse** —w.DAT. *to philosophy* Plu.

προσ-κτάομαι *mid.contr.vb*. **1 acquire in addition** —*territory, power, slaves, wealth, or sim.* (sts. w.DAT. or πρός + DAT. *on top of what one currently possesses*) Hdt. Th. Att.orats. X. Arist. Plu.; **add** —*perjury* (w. πρός + DAT. *to other disgraces*) D.

2 win over to one's side —*a person, nation, country* (sts. w.PREDIC.SB. *as friend, ally*) Hdt.

προσ-κυλίνδω *vb*. —also **προσκυλινδέω** (Plu.) *contr.vb*. | aor. προσεκύλισα | **1 roll up** —*a millstone* (against a door) Ar. —*a boulder* (w.DAT. or ἐπί + ACC. *against a cave door*) NT.

2 ‖ MID. **roll on the ground** or **prostrate oneself before** —w.DAT. *temples* Plu.

προσ-κυνέω *contr.vb*. | fut. προσκυνήσω | aor. προσεκύνησα, also προσέκυσα, ptcpl. προσκύσᾱς, imperatv. πρόσκυσον, inf. προσκύσαι ‖ The vb. connotes *worship*, usu. w. no indication of the form which it takes, but oft. assoc.w. kneeling or prostration (esp. by orientals before their rulers). It sts. also connotes a reverential kiss. |

1 worship, make obeisance to, pay reverence to —*a god or gods, their statues or shrines, earth, heaven, sacred objects* Hippon.(tm.) A. Hdt. S. Ar. Pl. + —*a bow* (as if a god) S. —w.DAT. *God, Jesus* NT.; (intr.) **worship** (God) NT.

2 salute in farewell —*one's home* S.; (pejor.) **pay exaggerated respect to, revere** —*a person* Ar. Pl.; (of a politician) —*the Council building* D.; (wkr.sens., without pejor. connot.) **respect** —*a person* Aeschin.

3 (provbl., of a person seeking to avert retribution) **pay due respect to, humble oneself before** —*Adrasteia* A. Pl. D. Men. —*divine jealousy* S.

4 adopt a submissive posture (before a superior); (usu. of orientals) **bow down before, pay obeisance to** —*a ruler or sim*. Hdt. E. Isoc. X. Plu.; (of defeated persons) —*a Roman general* Plb.; (intr.) **make obeisance** (to someone) Hdt. X. Plu.; (tr., of persons likened to orientals) **kowtow to** —*assailants* D.; (of a suppliant) **prostrate oneself before** —*a person* S. ‖ PASS. **receive obeisance** E. X.

προσκύνησις εως *f*. **obeisance** (as an act of worship) Pl.; (before a ruler) Arist. Plu.

προσκυνητής οῦ *m*. **worshipper** NT.

προσ-κύπτω *vb*. **bend or stoop towards** (someone); **lean forward** (to give a kiss) Ar.; (to whisper in someone's ear) Pl. Thphr.

προσ-κυρέω *contr.vb*. —also (in aor., more freq.) **προσκύρω** *vb*. | aor. προσέκυρσα | **1 arrive at, reach** —w.DAT. *a place* Hes.; (of a ship) **run upon, strike** —w.DAT. *a rock* Thgn.

2 chance to meet with —W.DAT. *some experience* Emp.; **encounter** —W.ACC. *sufferings* S.; (of a disaster) **come upon, befall** —W.DAT. *a house* A.
3 (of islands) **be adjacent** —W.DAT. *to a region* Plu.

προσκύσαι (aor.inf.), **προσκύσᾱς** (ptcpl.), **πρόσκυσον** (imperatv.): see προσκυνέω

πρόσ-κωποι ὤν *m.pl.* [κώπη] **men at the oar, oarsmen** Th.

προσ-λαγχάνω *vb.* (leg.) **also** or **actually bring** —*a suit (against someone)* D. Plu.

προσ-λάζυμαι *mid.vb.* **take hold** —W.GEN. *of someone's hand* E.

προσ-λαλέω *contr.vb.* **talk, chat** (usu. W.DAT. to someone) Thphr. Men.

προσ-λαμβάνω *vb.* | fut. προσλήψομαι | aor.2 προσέλαβον | **1 take, receive** or **acquire** (sthg.) **in addition** (to sthg. else, specified or implied); **take** (W.ACC. *bread*) **as well** (as *meat*) X.; **receive** (W.ACC. *pay*) **as well** (as *other benefits*) X.; **gain** (W.ACC. *what one wants*) **in addition** (to *what one has*) And.; **gain** —*other glory* (w. πρός + DAT. *on top of an earlier achievement*) X.; **get** —*other troubles* (w. πρός + DAT. *on top of present ones*) A.
2 acquire (sthg.) **as an addition** (to *what one already has*); **acquire, gain** —*troops, power, money, help, experience*, or sim. Th. +; (intr.) **make gains** D.
3 add (a new factor) to an existing situation; **add** —*shamelessness* (W.DAT. *to one's predicament*) E. —*rational explanation* (*to true opinion*) Pl. —*what one has not yet learned* (*to one's knowledge*) Isoc.
4 make an addition to one's family; acquire, gain —*a wife, a marriage-alliance* S. E. —*brothers* (W.DAT. *for one's sons, by a second marriage*) X.
5 take or **gain** (someone) **as helper** or **assistant; enlist in support, get on one's side** —*a person or persons, a city, populace, fleet*, or sim. A. Th. Isoc. D. Arist.; **gain** —*someone* (W.PREDIC.SB. *as an ally*) X.; **enlist** —*someone* (as a *scrutineer*) Lys. || MID. **enlist** —*mercenaries* Plu.; **bring over** (to one's side) —*a city* Plb.; **get the benefit of** —*someone else's opinion* Plb.
6 || MID. **take physical hold of, grasp** —W.GEN. *an object, a part of the body* Ar.; (of a body) **come into contact** —W.GEN. *w. sthg. that will affect its health* Pl.
7 (intr.) **give help, lend a hand** S. Ar.(mid.) X. —W.DAT. *to someone* (W.GEN. *in some matter*) Pl.

προσ-λάμπω *vb.* (of a heavenly body) **shine upon, illuminate** (another) Pl.

προσ-λέγομαι *mid.vb.* | 3sg.aor. προσελέξατο, dial. ποτελέξατο | **1 speak to, address** —*someone* AR. Theoc. —W.DBL.ACC. *someone, w. certain words, w. no word* Call. Theoc.
2 speak, address —*reproaches* (W.DAT. *to one's heart*) Hes.

προσ-λείπω *vb.* || NEUT.PTCPL.SB. **deficiency** (of human nature) Arist.

προσ-λεύσσω *vb.* **look at** or **upon** —*someone or sthg.* S.

προσ-λέχομαι *mid.vb.* | 3sg.athem.aor. προσέλεκτο | **lie down beside** (someone) Od.

πρόσληψις εως *f.* [προσλαμβάνω] **additional acquisition** (of sthg.) Pl.

προσ-λιπαρέω *contr.vb.* **1 plead persistently** Plu.
2 (fig., of soldiers) **be keenly attentive to** —W.DAT. *their leader's money* (*as bees to the honeycomb*) Plu.

προσ-λογίζομαι *mid.vb.* | neut.pl.impers.vbl.adj. προσλογιστέα | **1 count** (W.ACC. sthg.) **in addition** —W.DAT. *to sthg. else* (*in reaching a total*) Hdt.; **include** (W.ACC. sthg.) **in one's calculations** (of a total) Hdt. Lys.
2 also reckon —W.COMPL.CL. *that sthg. is the case* Plu.
3 reckon up, estimate —*the shamefulness of an action* (W.DAT. *by some criterion*) Plu.

προσ-μανθάνω *vb.* **1 learn in addition** (to sthg. learned earlier) —*the rest of a story, another duty* A. X.
2 (wkr.sens.) **learn** —*sthg.* Ar. —W.INF. *how to do sthg.* Ar.

προσ-μαρτυρέω *contr.vb.* **1** (of a witness) **add in evidence** —W.DIR.SP. *sthg.* D. —W.ACC. + INF. *that sthg. is the case* Is.
2 testify to (W.ACC. *a will*) **as well** —W.DAT. *as to sthg. else* D.
3 corroborate by one's evidence —W.ACC. *another's testimony* D.
4 give (W.NEUT.INTERN.ACC. this) **evidence** —W.DAT. *in support of someone* Plu.; (of facts) **give evidence in support of, confirm, validate** —W.DAT. *someone's reasoning* Plb.

προσ-μάσσω *vb.* | dial.3sg.aor.mid. ποτεμάξατο | **1 create additionally by kneading**; (fig., of Themistokles, envisaged as a cook) **serve up as an extra dish** —*Peiraieus* (W.DAT. *for Athens, described as having lunch*) Ar.
2 impress (sthg.) upon (sthg. else); **press** —*one's lips* (W.DAT. *on another's lips*) Theoc. || MID. perh. **make** (W.ACC. *a leaf*) **adhere** (to sthg.) Theoc. || PASS. (of a poisoned robe) **be stuck fast** —W.DAT. *to someone's sides* S.

προσ-μάχομαι *mid.vb.* **1** (of troops) **fight in battle, fight against, attack** —W.DAT. *opponents* Plb. Plu. —*a place* Plb. Plu.; (intr.) **attack** X. Plb. Plu.
2 fight in single combat; (of boxers and wrestlers) **fight against** —W.DAT. *an opponent* Pl.; (fig., of a person) —*one's cowardice* Pl.

προσμείγνῡμι (sts. written **προσμίγνῡμι**) *vb.* —also (pres. and impf.) **προσμίσγω 1** (causatv.) **bring** (W.ACC. *someone or sthg.*) **close to** or **into contact** (W.DAT. w. *someone or sthg. else*); **link** —*city walls* (*to the sea*) Plu.; **extend** —*an army's wing* (*to a river*) Plu.; **attach** —*a city* (*to a league*) Plu.; **associate** —*oneself* (w. *someone*) Plu.
2 (fig.) **inflict** —*danger* (W.DAT. *on a city*) Aeschin.; (of a racehorse) **bring** —*its owner* (W.DAT. *to victory*) Pi.
3 (intr.) **come close** or **into contact; approach** —W.DAT. *someone or sthg.* S. Pl. —W.PREP.PHR. *close to a person or place* Th. Pl. X. Plb. Plu. —W.ACC. *a house* E.; (of troops) **come up close to, reach** —W.DAT. *a place* E. Th. Plb. Plu.
4 (of troops in the rear) **close up** (w. those ahead) X.; (of ships) **link up** —w. πρός + ACC. *w. other ships* Th.
5 (of a boundary) **come into contact** —W.DAT. *w. another boundary* Pl.; (of a soul) —*w. divine virtue* Pl.
6 (of a prophecy) **come home** —W.DAT. *to someone* S.
7 (of troops, sailors) **meet in battle, come to grips, engage** Hdt. Th. X. Plb. Plu. —W.DAT. *w. opponents* Hdt. Th. Plb. Plu. —w. πρός + ACC. *w. the enemy's disarray* Th.
8 (of sailors, ships) **arrive, land** Plu. —W.DAT. *at a place* Hdt. Th. Plb. Plu. —w. εἰς + ACC. Plu.

πρόσμειξις εως *f.* **approach, attack** (of enemy troops) Th.

προσ-μένω *vb.* **1** (of persons) **go on waiting, remain longer** Hdt. S. X. Men. +
2 wait for, await —*a person, ships* S. E. Th. X. + —*an event, a time, a request, evidence,* or sim. E. Isoc. Plu. —W.ACC. + FUT.INF. *someone to do sthg.* S.; **look to** or **count on** —*Hope* Thgn.
3 (of sufferings) **await, be in store** —W.DAT. *for someone* A.
4 (of a warrior) **stand firm against** —*the enemy's battle-cry* Pi.
5 (of hounds) **stick** —W.DAT. *to a quarry's tracks* X.; (of persons) **remain** —W.DAT. *alongside someone* NT.; **remain faithful** —W.DAT. *to God* NT.

προσ-μερίζω vb. apportion, **bestow** —*one's favour* (W.DAT. *on someone*) Plb. ‖ PASS. (of regions) be assigned or allocated —W.DAT. *to a kingdom* Plb.

προσ-μεταπέμπομαι mid.vb. send for (W.ACC. troops, cavalry) **as reinforcements** Th. Aeschin.

προσ-μηχανάομαι mid.contr.vb. 1 (of lawgivers) **also devise** —*a safe means* (W.DAT. *for someone, to do sthg.*) Pl.
2 ‖ PASS. (of an emblem) be artfully worked onto (a shield) A.; be artfully fastened on —W.DAT. *w. rivets* A.

προσμίγνῡμι, also **προσμίσγω** vbs.: see προσμείγνῡμι

προσ-μισθόω contr.vb. 1 lease (W.ACC. private capital) **in addition** (to leasing a business) D.
2 ‖ MID. hire (W.ACC. mercenaries, slaves) **besides** (to supplement other resources) Th. X. D.

προσμολεῖν (aor.2 inf.): see προσβλώσκω

προσ-ναυπηγέομαι mid.contr.vb. build (W.ACC. other ships) **too** Hdt.

προσνάχω dial.vb.: see προσνήχω

προσ-νέμω vb. 1 **assign additionally, add** —*a number of people* (W.DAT. *to others, in a register of citizens*) D. ‖ MID. grant (W.ACC. a small favour) **in addition** —w. πρός + DAT. *to other services* S.
2 assign —*territory or sim.* (W.DAT. *to someone*) Plb. Plu. —*persons and things* (*to specific places*) D. —*appropriate forms of celebration* (*to gods and seasons*) Pl. —*birds* (*to appropriate gods, i.e. match them to each other on the basis of shared attributes*) Ar.(mid.)
3 attach —*oneself* (W.DAT. *or ADV. to a leader or cause*) D. Plu. —*one's city* (w. πρός + ACC. *to a league*) Plb.; **devote** —*oneself* (W.DAT. *to justice*) Plb.; **offer** —*one's goodwill* (W.DAT. *to someone*) Plb. ‖ PASS. (of people) be attached —W.PREP.PHR. *to politicians* D.; (pejor., of friends) be made an appendage —W.DAT. *to things* (i.e. *be secondary to material things*) Arist.
4 drive on —*flocks* (*towards a place*) E.Cyc.

προσ-νεύω vb. incline one's head (towards someone) Plu.

προσ-νέω contr.vb. [νέω¹] | aor. προσένευσα | **swim up** (to a ship) Plu.

προσ-νήχω, dial. **προσνάχω** vb. 1 ‖ MID. **swim up** —W.DAT. *to a ship* Plu.; (of a floating island) —W.PREP.PHR. *to a place* Call.
2 (of the sea) flow up to, **lap** —W.ACC. *a place* Theoc.

προσνίσομαι mid.vb.: see ποτινίσομαι

προσ-νωμάω contr.vb. app. **make one's way** (to a place) S.

προσξυλλαμβάνω vb., **προσξυνοικέω** contr.vb.: see προσσυλλαμβάνω, προσσυνοικέω

προσόδιος ον adj. [πρόσοδος] (of trumpet-music) **processional, march-like** Plu. ‖ NEUT.SB. processional hymn Ar.

πρόσ-οδος ου f. [ὁδός] 1 action of approaching, **approach** (of a person, to a place) E. Th.
2 **means of approach** (offered by a place to persons) X. Plb. Plu.; (fig., for a poet, to his subject) Pi.
3 **approach, overtures** (of a wooer, a lover) Hdt. Theoc.
4 (milit.) **assault** (on an enemy) Hdt. X.
5 **procession** (to a place of religious celebration) Ar. Att.orats. Pl. X.
6 approach (to an official body, by persons presenting evidence, pleading a case, or sim.); **approach, address** (usu. w. εἰς or πρός + ACC. to the Assembly or Council) Att.orats.
7 (sg. and pl.) **income, revenue** (accruing to a private individual) Att.orats. Pl. +; (accruing to a ruler or the state) Hdt. Th. Att.orats. +

προσ-όζω, dial. **ποτόσδω**, Lacon. **ποτόδδω** vb. (of things) **smell** —W.NEUT.ADV. *sweetly* Ar. —W.GEN. *of sthg.* Theoc.

πρόσ-οιδα pf.vb. [οἶδα] owe (W.ACC. gratitude) **as well** (as payment) Ar. Pl.

προσ-οικειόω contr.vb. 1 associate —*oneself* (W.DAT. *w. a god*) Plu.
2 ‖ PASS. (of a people) become friendly —W.DAT. *w. a foreign ruler* Plb.

προσ-οικέω contr.vb. (of persons or peoples) **live nearby** Th. Isoc. X. Plu.; **live near** —W.DAT. *persons, places* Isoc. Pl. Plu. —W.ACC. Th. Arist.

προσ-οικοδομέω contr.vb. 1 **build on, add** —*an extension* (W.DAT. *to an altar*) Th.
2 build (W.ACC. a monument) **next to** —W.DAT. *a shrine* Plu.; build (W.ACC. a second temple) **close by** (a first) Plu.
3 construct (W.ACC. a mortal kind of soul) **as well** (as an immortal one) Pl.

πρόσ-οικος ον adj. [οἶκος] 1 (of peoples) **living close by, neighbouring** Hdt. Th. D. Plu.; **neighbouring on** (W.DAT. a place, a people) Hdt. Th. ‖ MASC.PL.SB. neighbours Th. Plu.
2 (of a region) **lying adjacent** Plu.; (of a sea, W.DAT. to a place) Pl. ‖ FEM.SB. neighbouring territory Plu.
3 (of a war) **with neighbouring people** Plu.

προσοιστέος ᾱ ον vbl.adj. [προσφέρω] 1 (of a further death) **to be added** (W.DAT. to an earlier one) E.
2 (of things) **to be brought into contact** (sts. W.DAT. w. sthg. else) Pl.

προσ-οίχομαι mid.vb. go on one's way —W.PREP.PHR. *to a place* Pi.

προσ-ολοφύρομαι mid.vb. express one's grief —W.DAT. *to someone* Th. Plu.

προσ-ομαρτέω contr.vb. (of a lie) **accompany** —W.DAT. *the one who tells it* Thgn.

προσ-ομῑλέω contr.vb. 1 (of persons) have dealings (w. others) Th. Pl.; (of a person, a god) **associate, have dealings** —W.DAT. *w. someone* Thgn. E.fr. Pl. —w. πρός + ACC. X.; (fig., of a Muse, as embodying wisdom) —W.DAT. *w. women* E.
2 (of an octopus) **cling** —W.DAT. *to a rock* Thgn.
3 **encounter, face** —W.DAT. *war, athletic training* Th. Pl. —*a practical test* (*of sthg.*) S.; **engage in** —W.DAT. *abusive behaviour* Pl.

προσομῑλητικός ή όν adj. (of the art) **of social relations** Pl.

προσ-όμνῡμι vb. —also (pres.) **προσομνύω** (D.) **swear in addition** —W.FUT.INF. *to do sthg.* X. —W.COGN.ACC. *an oath* D.

προσ-όμοιος ον adj. (of persons or things) **resembling, like** (W.DAT. someone or sthg.) E. Ar. Pl. D. Plu.

—προσομοίως adv. in a manner resembling (W.DAT. sthg.) Pl.

προσ-ομοιόω contr.vb. (of a person's attributes) **resemble** —W.DAT. *a man, a serpent* (in their attributes) D.

προσ-ομολογέω contr.vb. 1 make an additional agreement or admission; **agree to** or **admit** (W.NEUT.ACC. these things) **as well** D.; make a further confession —W.INF. *that one did sthg.* D. ‖ PASS. (of facts) also be admitted or acknowledged —W.DAT. *to someone* And.
2 agree or admit in response (to a statement, claim, or sim.); **concede, acknowledge** (sts. W.DAT. to someone) —W.INF. or ACC. + INF. *that sthg. is the case* Isoc. Pl. D.; **agree** Pl. D. —W.NEUT.ACC. *about sthg.* D. Men. —W.ACC. *a sum of money* (W.DAT. *to someone, i.e. agree that one owes it*) Isoc.
3 agree in response (to a request or sim.); **agree** Hyp. —W.FUT.INF. *to do sthg.* D.
4 (of defeated persons) agree to terms, **surrender** X.

προσομολογίᾱ ᾱς f. agreement or admission (by a litigant) D.

προσ-ομόργνυμαι mid.vb. (fig.) **wipe off** —*one's pollution* (W.DAT. *on people, i.e. implicate them in one's crime*) Plu.

προσ-όμουρος ον Ion.adj. [ὅμορος] (of a people) **bordering on** (W.DAT. *another people*) Hdt.

προσ-ονομάζω vb. **give a designation or name; call** —*objects of worship* (W.PREDIC.ACC. *gods*) Hdt.; **name** —*someone or sthg.* (*such and such*) Plu. ǁ PASS. (of a place) be named —W.PREDIC.SB. *such and such* Plb.; (of a person) be surnamed —W.PREDIC.SB. *such and such* Plu.

προσ-οράω, dial. **ποθοράω**, also **ποθορέω** (Theoc.) contr.vb. —**ποθόρημι** (Theoc.) Aeol.vb. | dial.pres.fem.ptcpl. ποθορεῦσα | dial.opt. ποθορῷμι | fut. προσόψομαι | aor.2 προσεῖδον, dial. ποτεῖδον |
1 look upon, see —*someone or sthg.* Hes.fr. Mimn. Sapph. Xenoph. B. Hdt. +; (mid.) A. Pi. S.; (of a girl) **have** (W.ACC. *beauty*) **in one's glance** Theoc.
2 (intr.) **have sight, see** Theoc.

προσ-οργίζομαι pass.vb. **be angry** —W.DAT. *at sthg.* Arist.

προσ-ορέγομαι mid.vb. **hold out, offer** (W.NEUT.ACC. *more*) **as an inducement** —W.DAT. *to someone* Hdt.

προσορέω contr.vb. [πρόσορος] (of peoples, places) **border on** —W.DAT. *places* Plb.

προσ-ορίζω vb. **1 include** (territory) **within boundaries; add** —*a region* (W.DAT. *to an empire*) Plu.; **give** (W.ACC. *land*) **additionally** (*to a city*) Plu. ǁ PASS. (of countries) be added (to an empire) Plu.
2 ǁ MID. (leg., of a mortgagee) **have** (W.ACC. *a house*) **marked with boundary-stones as well** (*as the land surrounding it*) D.
3 determine, prescribe —*a short period of mourning* Plu. ǁ MID. **define** (W.ACC. *a term*) **more precisely** Arist.

προσ-ορμέω contr.vb. (of sailors) **come to anchor** —W.DAT. *at a place* Plb.

προσ-ορμίζομαι mid.vb. | aor.pass. (w.mid.sens.) προσωρμίσθην | (of sailors, ships) **come to anchor** Arist. NT. —W. πρός + ACC. *at a place* Hdt. D. —W.DAT. Plb. Plu. —W.ADV. *somewhere* D.

προσόρμισις εως f. **coming to anchor** Th.

πρόσ-ορος, Ion. **πρόσουρος**, ον adj. [ὅρος] **1** (of a people, a region) **bordering** (usu. W.DAT. *on another people or region*) Hdt. X.
2 (of footsteps, as indicating the presence of others) **nearby** or **of neighbours** S.

προσ-ουδίζω vb. [οὖδας] **dash to the ground** —*a baby* Hdt. —*a statue* Plu.

προσ-ουρέω contr.vb. **piss** (*on someone*) D.; (fig., of bad dramatists) —W.DAT. *on Tragedy* Ar.

πρόσουρος Ion.adj.: see πρόσορος

προσ-οφείλω vb. **1 owe besides** —*a sum of money, gratitude* Th. X. D.; (intr.) **owe a further amount** (as a fine or penalty) Ar. ǁ PASS. (of wages) be still owing Th.
2 (fig., of a person) be in arrears, **fall short** (in some quality, by comparison w. someone else) Plb.

προσ-οφλισκάνω vb. **1** (leg.) **lose** (W.ACC. *one's case*) **as well** (as doing sthg. else) D.
2 (specif.) lose one's case and incur a penalty besides; **be sentenced to pay** —*a sum of money, a fine* Aeschin. D.; (intr.) **be sentenced to pay a fine** D.
3 (of the recipient of a favour) **become indebted** —W.DAT. *to someone* Arist.
4 (gener.) **incur** (W.ACC. *disgrace*) **besides** D.; **incur** (W.ACC. *a reputation for sthg.*) **in addition** —W.DAT. *to a reputation for sthg. else* Plu.; **incur a charge of** —W.ACC. *ostentation*

Plu.; **deserve to have applied to oneself** —W.ACC. *a proverbial saying* Plb.

προσόψιος ον adj. [πρόσοψις] (of a hill) **within sight, in full view** S.

πρόσ-οψις εως f. [ὄψις] **1** that which is looked upon, **sight, spectacle** Plb.
2 aspect, appearance (W.GEN. *of a person, assumed by a god*) Pi.; (*of siege-works*) Plb.
3 sight (ref. to a person, as seen by another) S. E.
4 personal appearance, aspect, looks S. E.
5 capacity or opportunity for looking, sight, view Th.; (W.GEN. *of a person, the enemy*) E. Th.
6 (concr.) **sight, eyes** (of a person) Plu.

προσ-παίζω vb. | aor. προσέπαισα, also προσέπαιξα (Plu.) |
1 behave or speak playfully to, joke with, tease —W.DAT. *someone* Pl. X. Men. Plb. Plu.; **play with, toy with** —W.DAT. *the state* (*i.e. treat politics lightly*) Plu.; (intr.) **be playful, have fun, joke** Pl. Plb. Plu.; (phr.) προσπαίζειν ὕμνον *sing a playful hymn to* —W.DAT. *a god* Pl.
2 make the object of a joke, make fun of —*someone* Pl.

πρόσ-παιος ον adj. [παίω] delivering a blow; (of troubles, an accident) app. **sudden, unexpected** A. Plb.; (prep.phr.) ἐκ προσπαίου *suddenly, unexpectedly* Arist.

—**πρόσπαιον** neut.adv. **suddenly, unexpectedly** S.Ichn.

—**προσπαίως** adv. **suddenly, unexpectedly** Arist.

προσ-παλαίω vb. **wrestle with** —W.DAT. *someone* Pl.; (fig., of Atlas) —*the sky* Pi.; (intr.) **compete in wrestling** Pi.; (fig., ref. to verbal argument) Pl.

προσ-παραβάλλομαι pass.vb. (of couches) **be placed beside** (a table) **additionally** (for extra guests) Plu.

προσ-παραγράφω vb. **1 make a further addition in writing; add** (W.ACC. *someone's name*) **as well** (as one already added) D.
2 (wkr.sens.) **add, insert** —*the names of sponsors* (*to a speech*) Pl.; **append** —*a further designation* (*to a name*) D.

προσ-παρακαλέω contr.vb. **1 call on additionally, summon** (W.ACC. *people, allies*) **as reinforcements** Th.
2 also call upon or **exhort** —W.ACC. + INF. *someone to do sthg.* Plb.

προσ-παρασκευάζω vb. **provide in addition** —*another military force* D.

προσ-παρατίθημι vb. **1 also set out** (w.connot. of inviting comparison); **also draw attention to** —*one's change of allegiance* Plb.
2 ǁ PASS. (of letters) be assigned (W.DAT. *to courts*) as well (as to jurors) Arist.

προσ-παρέχω vb. **provide** (W.ACC. *ships, provisions*) **in addition** —W.DAT. *for someone* Th. Plu. ǁ MID. (of heat, when combined w. a desire for a drink) **produce additionally** —*a desire for a cold drink* Pl.; (of a night's sleep) **produce** (W.ACC. + DAT. *courage in people's minds*) **as well** —W.PREP.PHR. *in addition to other benefits* Pl.

προσ-παροξύνω vb. (of a remark) **further irritate** —*someone* Plu.

προσ-πασσαλεύω, Att. **προσπατταλεύω** vb. **nail** —*Prometheus* (W.DAT. *to a rock*) A. —*a prisoner* (*to a board*) Hdt. —*shoes* (*to someone, like a dedicatory object to a tree*) Ar.; **nail up** —*a tripod* (*in one's house*) Hdt. —*an ox's skull* (*over a doorway*) Thphr. ǁ PASS. (of Prometheus) be nailed —W. πρός + DAT. *to rocks* Men.

προσ-πάσχω vb. **1 experience** (W.NEUT.ACC. *some feeling or thought*) **in addition** Isoc. Pl.
2 (of a lover) **feel affection** —W.DAT. *for someone* Plu.

πρόσ-πεινος ον adj. [πεῖνα] **hungry** NT.
προσ-πελάζω vb. **1** (of Poseidon) **drive** (W.ACC. a ship) **up against** —W.DAT. *a headland* Od.
2 come near, approach Plu. —W.DAT. *a person or place* Pl. X. Plb. Plu. —w. πρός + ACC. *a place* Plu.
προσ-πέμπω vb. **1 send** (esp. a herald or messenger) on an errand; **send along** —*a person or persons* (oft. W.DAT. *to someone*) S. Th. Ar. Isoc. +
2 send —*a message* (W.DAT. or PREP.PHR. *to someone*) Th. Plu.; (intr.) **send a message** (oft. W.DAT. or PREP.PHR. *to someone*) Th. Att.orats. X. Plb. Plu. —(w. ἐς + ACC. *to a place*) Th.; (of a suitor) **make overtures** Hdt.
3 send —*money, gifts* (usu. W.DAT. *to someone*) Plu.
προσ-πέρδομαι mid.vb. | act.aor.2 προσέπαρδον | (of an oarsman) **fart on** —W.DAT. *an oarsman below* Ar.
προσ-περιβάλλω vb. **1 build additionally** (W.ACC. a defensive wall) **around** —W.DAT. *a city* Th. ‖ PASS. (of a fortification) be built for additional protection around —W.DAT. *a camp and fleet* Th.
2 ‖ MID. put (sthg.) around oneself additionally (for protection); **also surround oneself** (i.e. one's city) —W.ACC. *w. walls* Isoc.; **have** (W.ACC. one's land troops) **for protection in addition** —W.DAT. *to one's fleet* Plu. ‖ PASS. (of persons, ref. to their homes) be surrounded additionally —W.DAT. *by an enclosing wall* Pl.
3 ‖ MID. **acquire** (W.ACC. possessions) **in addition** D.
προσ-περιγίγνομαι mid.vb. **1** (of a sum of money) **be an additional surplus** D.
2 (of expenses) **be paid in addition** (by someone) Plu.
προσ-περικόπτω vb. (colloq.) **take as an extra cut** (W.DAT. for oneself) —*a sum of money* Hyp.
προσ-περιλαμβάνω vb. **also include** or **incorporate** —*items* (in a proposal) D. —*places* (in a treaty) Plb.
προσ-περιποιέω contr.vb. **save** (W.ACC. a sum of money) **as surplus** D.
προσ-περονάω contr.vb. (of pleasure and pain) **pin** —*a soul* (w. πρός + ACC. *on a body*) Pl. ‖ PASS. (of hands) be pinned —W.DAT. *to shields* (by arrows) Plu.; (of bread) be fastened with skewers —w. πρός + DAT. *to pieces of meat* X.
προσ-πέτομαι mid.vb. | athem.aor. προσεπτάμην, also dial.athem.aor.act. προσέπταν | **1** (of birds) **fly up** (to someone, a place) Ar. Plu.; (of wasps) —W.PREP.PHR. *to a door* Ar.; (fig., of a person, compared to a fly) **wing one's way** —W.DAT. *to someone* X.; (of soldiers, compared to birds) **flock** —W.DAT. *to a commander* Plu.
2 (fig., of a sound, a scent) **be wafted** —W.ACC. *to someone* A.; (of a song, a story) —W.DAT. *to someone* A. —W.ACC. *to a country* Telest.; (of troubles) **swoop** (sts. W.DAT. on someone) Trag.
προσ-πεύθομαι mid.vb. [πυνθάνομαι] **press on with one's inquiries** S.
προσ-πήγνυμι vb. fasten to (a cross), **crucify** —*someone* NT.
προσ-πηδάω contr.vb. **leap** —w. πρός + ACC. *on an altar* And.
προσ-πηχύνομαι mid.vb. **take** (W.ACC. a baby) **in one's arms** Call.
προσ-πίλναμαι athem.pass.vb. [πιλνάω] (of a ship) be brought near, **reach** —W.DAT. *an island* Od.
προσ-πίπτω vb. | dial.aor.2 subj. ποτιπέσω (A.) | **1 fall to the ground** (before someone or sthg.); **fall to the ground, prostrate oneself** (in deference) Hdt.; (before a tomb) E.; (in supplication) S. X. —W.DAT. *before an altar, a person, knees* S. E. D. —W.ACC. *before someone's knees* E. —W.ACC. or πρός + ACC. *before a statue* A. Ar.
2 cast oneself eagerly (at someone); (of children) **rush up** Hdt. —W.DAT. *to someone* X. —w. πρός + ACC. *to their father's knees* E.; (of a father) **fall upon, embrace** —W.DAT. *his children* E.; (of a husband) —*a statue of his dead wife* E.
3 cast oneself aggressively (against someone or sthg.); (of persons, usu. troops) **fall upon, attack, assault** —W.DAT. *persons, troops* Th. X. D. + —*a city* Th.; (of a ship) —*another ship* Th.; (of persons) —w. πρός + ACC. *someone* D.; (intr., of soldiers, sailors, ships, animals) **attack** E. Th. X. D. +; (hyperbol., of a person) **storm** —w. εἰς + ACC. *into a country* Hyp.
4 come up against (an obstacle); **collide, stumble** —w. ἐς + ACC. *against the pedestal of Justice* (i.e. *offend against Justice*) S.; (of sailors) **run** —w. εἰς + ACC. *into shallows* Plb.; (of an object) **strike against** —W.DAT. *someone's leg* X.; (of a ramp) **rest against** (a wall) Th.; (of things) **come into contact** —W.DAT. *w. other things* Pl.; (of shadows) **be cast** —W.PREP.PHR. *against the side of a cave* Pl.
5 meet (oft. suddenly or unexpectedly); **fall in with, encounter** (usu. W.DAT. *someone*) S. Pl. Aeschin.; **accost, waylay** (usu. W.DAT. *someone*) Ar. X.; **find, gain** —W.ACC. *a particular kind of companionship* E.
6 meet with (a circumstance); **succumb** —W.DAT. *to pleasures, desires, abusive behaviour, or sim.* Isoc. Pl. X.; (of a captive) **fall victim** —W.DAT. *to an unwelcome allocation by lot* E.; (of a person's good fortune) **encounter** —W.DAT. *disaster* Hdt.
7 (of circumstances) suddenly come on; (of disaster, accidents, sickness, or sim.) **befall, strike** (oft. W.DAT. *someone*) Hdt. E. Th. Ar. +; (of pollution) **fall on** (someone) E. Antipho; (of expenses) Th.; (of old age) **come upon** (someone) E.*satyr.fr.*; (of emotions, sensations) **come over** (someone) Th. Pl. Men.; (of troubles) **impinge** —w. εἰς + ACC. *on human life* Hyp. ‖ NEUT.PL.PTCPL.SB. *circumstances that arise* Isoc. Arist.
8 (of information) **come to one's ears**; (of a statement) **be sprung upon** —W.DAT. *someone* Aeschin.; (of news or sim.) **reach** —W.DAT. *someone* Plb. Plu. —w. εἰς + ACC. *a place* Plb. ‖ IMPERS. *news comes* (sts. W.ACC. + INF. *that sthg. is happening*) Plb.
προσ-πίτνω vb. **1 fall to the ground** (before someone or sthg.); **prostrate oneself** (in supplication) Trag. —W.DAT. *before someone* S. —W.ACC. *before someone, knees* S. E. —*before a tomb* E.; **beseech** —W.ACC. + INF. *a god, that one may not be killed* E.
2 fall upon (a bed) E.; **embrace** —W.DAT. or ACC. *someone* E.
3 fall upon, attack —W.ACC. *someone* E.
4 (fig., of anger) **come over, assail** —W.DAT. *someone* E.
5 (of arrows) **rain down** A.; (of arrows in a quiver) **brush against** —W.ACC. *an archer's side* E.
προσ-πλάζω vb. (of waves) **beat against** (a shore) Il.; (of lake water) —W.DAT. *someone's chin* (as he stands in it) Od.
προσ-πλάσσομαι, dial. **ποτιπλάσσομαι** pass.vb. | dial.aor. ποτεπλάσθην | **1** (of nests made of mud) **be moulded** or **stuck** —w. πρός + DAT. *onto cliffs* Hdt.
2 (of a statue of a Grace) **be moulded besides** —w. ποτί + DAT. *in addition to three others* Call.*epigr.*
πρόσ-πλατος ον adj. [πλατός] (of a people, in neg.phr.) **approachable** (W.DAT. by strangers) A.
προσ-πλέκομαι pass.vb. (of soldiers scaling a wall) **cling on** Plb.
προσ-πλέω contr.vb. [πλέω¹] (of sailors, ships) **sail up** (to places or people, or against enemy ships) Hdt. Th. Att.orats. X. Plb. Plu.; **sail against, bear down on** —W.DAT. *the enemy* Th.
προσ-πληρόω contr.vb. **man** (W.ACC. other ships) **in addition** Th. X. Plb.; (mid.) X.

πρόσ-πλωτος ον *adj.* [πλωτός] able to be sailed up or to; (of a river) **navigable** (W.PREP.PHR. up to a certain point) Hdt.; **accessible** (W.PREP.PHR. fr. the sea) Hdt.

προσ-πνέω *contr.vb.* —also **προσπνείω** *ep.vb.* **1** (of a deity) breathe (into people), **inspire** —*soft passions* Theoc.
2 ‖ IMPERS. there is an aroma (W.GEN. of pork) wafting its way —W.DAT. *to someone* Ar.

προσ-ποθέω *contr.vb.* **desire in addition** —*an item of knowledge* Pl.

προσ-ποιέω *contr.vb.* | aor.pass. (w.mid.sens.) προσεποιήθην (Plb.) | **1** make (sthg.) belong (to someone); **bring over, annex** —*a city or sim.* (usu. W.DAT. *to someone*) Th. X.; **attach** —*credit for doing sthg.* (W.DAT. *to someone*) Th.
2 ‖ MID. **procure for oneself** —*a wooden foot* Hdt.
3 ‖ MID. **win over, get on one's side** —*persons or countries* Hdt. E.(dub.) Th. —*the people* Ar. —*gods* X.; **acquire, gain** —*a band of supporters* Hdt. —W.DBL.ACC. *someone as a friend* Hdt. —*cities as subjects* Th.; **bring** —*a region* (W.PREP.PHR. *into a confederacy*) Th.
4 ‖ MID. **lay claim to** —*a city, victory, reputation, or sim.* Th. Aeschin. Arist. —W.PARTITV.GEN. *a share of sthg.* Ar. Is.; **claim credit for** —*an action* Th.; (intr.) **claim credit** (for sthg.) D.
5 ‖ MID. **pretend, affect** —*anger* Hdt. —*need* Isoc. —*enmity* Th.
6 ‖ MID. **pretend, claim, profess** —W.INF. or ACC. + INF. *to do or be sthg., or that sthg. is the case* Hdt. Ar. Att.orats. Pl. + —W.FUT.INF. *that one will do sthg.* X. —w. ὡς + PTCPL. *to being such and such* Plb. —W.COMPL.CL. *that sthg. is the case* Pl.; (phr.) οὐ (or μή) προσποιεῖσθαι *pretend not, pretend otherwise* Th. Ar. Aeschin. D. Thphr. +

προσποίημα ατος *n.* **1** that which one claims for oneself, **assumption, claim** (by a person, to having certain qualities) Arist.
2 pretence Plu.; (W.GEN. of madness) Plu.

προσποίησις εως *f.* **1** advantageous action, **gain, advantage** (for a city, fr. making an alliance) Th.
2 verbal claim, **claim, pretension** (to superiority over others) Th.; (W.GEN. to kinship w. someone) Th.; (to knowledge) Pl.; (to noble actions) Plu.
3 pretence (of an emotion or intention) Arist. Plu.; (W.GEN. of anger) Plu.

προσποιητικός ή όν *adj.* (of a person) **of the kind who pretends** (W.GEN. to courage, good qualities) Arist.

προσποίητος ον *adj.* (of a lover) **pretended** (opp. genuine) Pl.; (of enmity, honesty) **affected** D. Din.
—**προσποιήτως** *adv.* **pretendedly, supposedly** (opp. really) Pl.

προσ-πολεμέω *contr.vb.* **1** go to war Th. Isoc. Pl. D. —W.ACC. *against someone* X. —W.DAT. Plb. Plu.
2 (fig., of a politician) **be engaged in a war** —W.DAT. w. *another politician* Aeschin.; (of people) **be hostile** —W.DAT. *to someone* Plu.; **be inimical** —W.DAT. *to a city's tranquillity, a country's peace* Aeschin. Plu.

προσ-πολεμόομαι *mid.contr.vb.* **go to war with** (W.ACC. a people) **in addition** (to one's other opponents) Th.

προσπολέω *contr.vb.* [πρόσπολος] **be an attendant at, serve** —W.DAT. *a house, a tomb* E. ‖ PASS. **be escorted by attendants** S.

πρόσ-πολος ου *m.f.* [πέλω, πολέω] **1 attendant, servant** S. E. Men.; **minister** (of a deity, assoc.w. a shrine) B. Trag.
2 (fig., ref. to a warrior) **servant, minister** (W.GEN. of slaughter) A.

προσ-πορεύομαι *mid.vb.* | aor.pass. (w.mid.sens.) προσεπορεύθην | **1 go up to, approach** (a person or place) Plb. —W.DAT. or πρός + ACC. *a person* Plb. NT.; (fig.) —w. πρός + ACC. *a paradoxical statement* (W.ADV. cautiously) Plb.
2 put oneself forward —w. πρός + ACC. *for enlistment in the army* Plb.
3 put oneself forward (as a candidate) Plb. —w. πρός + ACC. *for an office* Plb.

προσ-πορίζω *vb.* **supply in addition** —*sources of revenue* X. D. —*other sufferings* (*for oneself*) Men.

προσ-πορπατός όν *adj.* [πορπάω] (of Prometheus) **pinned, fastened** (to a rock) A.

προσ-πράττομαι *Att.mid.vb.* **exact in addition** —*a sum of money* And.

πρόσπταισις εως *f.* [προσπταίω] (fig.) **stumble** (by a listener, when a speaker pauses too soon) Arist.

πρόσπταισμα ατος *n.* **1 stubbing of one's toe** (as exemplifying a minor injury) Arist.
2 injury which results from stubbing one's toe, **bruise** or **lesion** Thphr.

προσ-πταίω *vb.* | pf. προσέπταικα | **1 strike** —*one's knee* (against the ground) Hdt.
2 stub —*one's toes* Men. —*one's foot* Plu.; (intr.) **stub one's toe** or **stumble** Ar. Pl. X. Arist. Thphr. Plu.
3 (fig.) **trip over** —W.DAT. *opponents* (described as stumbling-blocks) D.; (of a listener, when a speaker pauses too soon) **stumble** Arist.
4 (esp. in military ctxts.) **suffer a setback** Hdt. Isoc. Arist. Plu.
5 come into conflict, clash —W.DAT. or πρός + ACC. *w. someone* Plu.

πρόσπτυγμα ατος *n.* [προσπτύσσομαι] action of enfolding in one's arms, **embrace** (of one's mother, i.e. by her) E.; **embracing** (of one's sister) E.(dub.) [or perh. concr. *person being embraced*]

προσ-πτύσσομαι, ep. **ποτιπτύσσομαι** *mid.vb.* | fut. προσπτύξομαι | aor. προσεπτυξάμην, ep. προσπτυξάμην | 3sg.plpf. προσέπτυκτο | **1** enfold in a close embrace, **clasp to oneself, embrace** —*someone* Od. E. AR. Theoc. —W.DAT. S.; (of a poisoned tunic) **cling** —W.DAT. *to someone's sides* S.
2 hold close to oneself, **kiss** (someone's lips) E.
3 (wkr.sens.) **greet** —*someone* Od. hHom. AR.; **say** (W.DBL.ACC. sthg. to someone) **as a greeting** Od.; (intr.) **offer a greeting** Od.; (fig.) **welcome, gladly celebrate** —*feasts* (W.GEN. *in honour of the gods*) Pi.

—**προσπτύσσω** *act.vb.* **embrace** —*someone's body, a statue* E.

προσ-πτύω *vb.* **spit on** —W.DAT. *someone* (through aiming carelessly) Thphr.; **spit** (on someone or sthg., as a mark of contempt) Plu.

προσ-πυνθάνομαι *mid.vb.* **1 inquire in addition** —W.INDIR.Q. *whether sthg. is the case* Plu.
2 proceed to inquire —W.INDIR.Q. *what is the case* Plb.

προσ-ραίνω *vb.* **sprinkle** —*dye* (on people) Ar.

προσ-ράπτω *vb.* **sew** or **stitch** (W.ACC. a fox-skin) **on** (a lionskin, to patch it) Plu. ‖ PF.PASS.PTCPL.ADJ. (of cloaks) **patched** Plu.

προσ-ρέω *contr.vb.* | aor.2 pass. (w.act.sens.) προσερρύην | (fig., of people) **flood in** (to join someone's cause) Hdt. ‖ AOR.2 PASS. (of a person) **slip along** (to a place) Men.; **rush up** —W.DAT. *to someone* Plu.

προσ-ρήγνυμι *vb.* (of a river) **beat against** —W.DAT. *a house* NT.

προσρηθήσομαι (fut.pass.): see προσείρω

πρόσρημα ατος *n.* [προσείρω] **1 address, greeting** (to someone) Pl.
2 designation, name, title (of someone or sthg.) Pl. D. Plu.

πρόσρησις εως *f.* **1 address, greeting** E. X. Pl.; (W.GEN. to someone) Pl.; **right of address, audience** (granted to someone) E.
2 object of address or **greeting** (W.DAT. by someone, ref. to a tomb) Plu.(quot.com.)
3 way of describing, **designation, name, title** Pl.

προσρητέος ᾱ ον *vbl.adj.* **1** (of a person) **to be addressed** Pl.
2 (of a city) **to be described** (W.PREDIC.ADJ. as such and such) Pl.

προσ-ρίπτω *vb.* —also **προσρίπτέω** *contr.vb.* | impf. προσερρίπτουν (Plu.), dial. ποτερρίπτουν (Stesich.) | **1 throw** —*a purse* (to someone) Plu. —*a letter* (W.DAT. to someone) Plu. —*apples* (w. ποτί + ACC. *onto a chariot*) Stesich.; (fig.) **cast** —*reproaches* (W.DAT. *at someone*) Plb.
2 (hyperbol., of a people) **fling** —*treacherous generals* (W.DAT. *to the enemy*) Plu.; (of a commander) **fling back** —*unwanted soldiers* (W.DAT. *to their countries and parents*) Plu.
3 ‖ PASS. (of a message) **be passed on** —W.DAT. *to someone* Plu.
4 ‖ PASS. (fig., of the commander of a formerly large fleet) **be consigned or reduced** —W.DAT. *to a single vessel* Plu.

προσ-σαίνω, dial. **ποτισαίνω** *vb.* **1** (of a person) **fawn on** —*someone* A.; (of Ruin) **fawn** (*on her intended victim*) A.
2 (gener., of news) **gladden** —*someone* A.; (of the impression of a dead wife's signet-ring) **stir the feelings of** —*her husband* E.

προσ-σέβω *vb.* **revere, honour** —*a dead person* (w. *lamentations*) A.

προσ-σημαίνω *vb.* (of words) **signify additionally, connote** —*sthg.* Arist.

πρόσσοθεν *ep.adv.*: see πρόσωθεν

προσ-σπαίρω *vb.* (of a person's lustful nature) **pant after** —W.DAT. *prostitutes* Plu.

προσ-σταυρόω *contr.vb.* **surround** (W.ACC. *beached ships*) **with a stockade** Th.

προσ-στείχω *vb.* | ep.aor.2 προσέστιχον | (of a goddess) **go to** —*Olympos* Od.; (of persons) **approach** S.(v.l. προστείχω)

προσ-στέλλω *vb.* **1** (of a hoplite) **bring** (W.ACC. *his unprotected right side*) **up against** —W.DAT. *the shield of his comrade* Th. ‖ MID. (of a commander) **keep close** —W.DAT. *to hill-country* Plu.
2 ‖ PF.PASS.PTCPL.ADJ. (of a hound's loins) **drawn tight, taut** X.; (fig., of a skill) **unassuming, modest** Pl.

προσ-στρατοπεδεύω *vb.* **encamp near** —W.DAT. or PREP.PHR. *a place, the enemy* Plb.

προσ-συλλαμβάνω (-ξυλλαμβάνω) *vb.* ‖ MID. (of ships) **make an additional contribution** —W.GEN. *to an enterprise* Th.

προσ-συνοικέω (-ξυνοικέω) *contr.vb.* (of colonists) **join in a settlement** —W.DAT. *w. others* Th.

προσ-συρίζω *vb.* **whistle** (to someone) Plb. —W.ACC. *a signal* Plb.

προσ-σφάζω *vb.* **slaughter** (W.ACC. someone) **as a sacrificial offering** —W.DAT. *on someone's tomb* Plu.

πρόσσω *ep.adv.*: see πρόσω

πρόσταγμα ατος *n.* [προστάσσω] **order, command, instruction** Att.orats. Pl. +

προστακείς (aor.2 ptcpl.): see προστήκομαι

προστακτικός ή όν *adj.* [προστάσσω] (of a person's brevity of speech) **imperious** Plu.

προσ-ταλαιπωρέω *contr.vb.* **1 continue to endure hardship, hold out** Ar. Plu.
2 persevere —W.DAT. *in a course of action* Th. Plu.

πρόσταξις εως *f.* [προστάσσω] **1 order, command** Lys. Pl. Arist.; **demand, requisition** (W.GEN. for the building of ships) Th.
2 specific provision (made in a law, relating to individuals and their rights) And.

προστασίᾱ ᾶς, Ion. **προστασίη** ης *f.* [προίστημι] **1 position at the head, leadership** (W.GEN. of the people) Th.; (gener.) **leadership, authority** D.; **control, charge** (W.GEN. of state affairs) Plb.; **pre-eminence** (of a historian) Plb.
2 (at Rome) **status** or **position of a** *patronus* Plu.
3 (pejor., in political ctxt.) patronage offered from self-interest, **protection-racket** D.; (leg.) **crooked collusion** (to avoid paying a debt) D.
4 (w.pers.ref.) **protection** (i.e. protector, W.GEN. of young wives, ref. to an old priestess) Call.*epigr.*
5 that which stands in front, **area in front** (W.GEN. of the Theban acropolis) Aeschin.; **frontal area** (W.PREP.PHR. around a theatre) Plb.; **line** (W.GEN. of elephants) **standing in front** (of troops) Plb.
6 that which is placed in the forefront; **outward show, pomp, dignity** (of person, places, institutions) Plb.

πρόστασις εως *f.* **outward show, pompous appearance** (of a tyrant's life, opp. the reality) Pl.

προσ-τάσσω, Att. **προστάττω** *vb.* **1** assign (someone) to a post, rank or duty; **appoint** —*someone* (W.PREDIC.SB. *as commander, sts.* W.DAT. or PREP.PHR. *over others*) Hdt. Th.; **prescribe** —*someone* (W.RELATV.CL. *who will perform a task*) E. ‖ PASS. (of a commander) **be posted or assigned** —W.DAT. *to a gate* (i.e. to attack it) A.; (of persons, esp. troops) —W.ADV. or DAT. or PREP.PHR. *somewhere, to some task or department* Hdt. S. E. Th.
2 allocate (soldiers, peoples) to a certain grouping, leader or opponent; **assign, attach** —*neighbouring people* (w. πρός + DAT. *to tribes*) Hdt. —*soldiers* (W.DAT. *to a commander*) Th. —*enemy troops* (*to specified troops of one's own, for them to fight*) X. ‖ PASS. (of troops, ships, an individual) **be assigned** —W.DAT. *to a commander* Hdt. Th.
3 assign, apportion —*a task, duty, or sim.* (usu. W.DAT. *to someone*) Hdt. E. Att.orats. Pl. +; **prescribe** —*a ration* (*for an athlete*) Arist. —*a course of action* (sts. W.DAT. *for someone*) Att.orats. + ‖ PASS. (of a task or duty) **be assigned** —W.DAT. *to someone* A. Ar. Att.orats. +; (of expenditure) **be prescribed** —W.PREP.PHR. *by a city* Lys. ‖ NEUT.SG.PL.PASS.PTCPL.SB. (pres., aor., pf.) **order or orders** Hdt. S. E.*Cyc.* Att.orats. +; (fut.) **future orders** X.
4 give an order (usu. W.DAT. *to someone*) E. Th. + —W.INF. *to do sthg.* Hdt. S. E. Th. Ar. +; **order** —W.ACC. + INF. *someone to do sthg.* E. D.; **make demands for, requisition** —*sthg.* (W.DAT. *fr. someone*) And. ‖ PASS. (of persons) **be given orders** (sts. W.INF. to do sthg.) Hdt. E. Th. +; (of cavalry) **be requisitioned** —W.DAT. *fr. someone* Hdt. ‖ IMPERS.PASS. (impf., aor., pf., plpf.) **an order was** (has or had been) **given** (usu. W.DAT. + INF. to someone to do sthg.) Hdt. Ar. Att.orats. + ‖ NEUT.ACC.AOR.PASS.PTCPL. **an order having been given** —W.DAT. + INF. *to someone to do sthg.* Lys. D.

προστατείᾱ ᾶς *f.* [προστάτης] **position at the head, presidency** (of a local group) Th.; (in a civic or military ctxt.) **leadership** X.

προστατεύω *vb.* **1 stand at the head, be in charge, have control** —W.GEN. *of a city, an army, or sim.* X.; (of a city) **exercise authority** X.
2 take care to ensure —w. ὅπως + SUBJ. *that sthg. happens* X.

προστατέω contr.vb. **1** stand in front as protector; (of a warrior) **stand as defender** —W.GEN. *of a city's gate* A.; (of a goddess) **be protector** or **champion** —W.GEN. *of her city's soldiers* E.; (fig., of Shamelessness) **be the guardian deity** —W.GEN. *of politicians* Ar.
2 (of a time) stand in front (of the present moment), **be imminent** or **coming** (perh. w. further connot. of having control) S.
3 stand at the head, **be in charge, have control** —W.GEN. *of people, a city, house, or sim.* E. Pl. X. Thphr. Plb.; (intr.) Pl. Plu. ‖ PASS. (of the people) be governed —W.PREP.PHR. *by someone* X.
4 be responsible for ensuring —w. ὅπως + SUBJ. *that sthg. happens* X.

προστατήριος ᾱ ον adj. **1** (of Artemis) standing guard (over a city), **protective** A.; (of Apollo) **standing guard in front** (of a house) S. D.(oracle)
2 (fig., of fear) **standing guard before** or **having control of** (W.GEN. someone's heart) A.

προστάτης ου, dial. **προστάτᾱς** ᾱ m. [προΐσταμαι] **1** one who stands before and protects; **guardian, defender** A.; (W.GEN. of a city's gate) A.; (gener., ref. to a person or god) **protector** A. S.; (W.GEN. against sickness) S.; **champion** (W.GEN. of poetry) Pl.; (of someone's proposals, a peace treaty) Isoc. X.; (of a nation's happiness or freedom) Lycurg. D.
2 (specif., at Athens) **patron** (of a metic) Ar. Att.orats.; (elsewhere) Arist.; (at Rome) **patronus** Plu.
3 one who stands at the head (of others); **leader, ruler** (freq. W.GEN. of a people, city, land, or sim.) A. E. Att.orats. Pl. +; **champion** (of a nation) Hdt.
4 (in a democracy) **leader** (freq. W.GEN. of the people) E. Th. Ar. Att.orats. +
5 (gener.) one who has charge, **director** (W.GEN. of a trading-post) Hdt.; (of military operations) X.; (of religious observances) D.; (fig., ref. to the obligation of noble birth) **controller** (of one's life) E.; (ref. to a great passion) **manager** (W.GEN. of a person's conflicting appetites) Pl.
6 one who stands before (a god), **suppliant** S.; (W.GEN. of a god) S.

προστατικός ή όν adj. **1** (of a root, fig.ref. to the background fr. which a tyrant emerges) **as champion of the people** Pl.
2 (of a dead hero) **protective** Plu.
3 (of marks) **of honour** Plb. ‖ NEUT.SB. **dignity** (W.GEN. of an office) Plb. | cf. προστασία 6, πρόστασις
—**προστατικῶς** adv. **in a dignified manner** Plb.

προστάττω Att.vb.: see προστάσσω

προ-σταυρόω contr.vb. **fence off** (W.ACC. the sea, i.e. the shore) **with stakes** Th.

προ-στέγιον ου n. [dimin. στέγη] **porch** (of a cottage) Plu.

προσ-τειχίζομαι pass.vb. (of the outer part of a city) **be included within the walls** Th.

προστείχω vb.: see προσστείχω

προσ-τεκταίνομαι mid.vb. **contrive in addition** —*the remainder of a scheme* Plu.

προσ-τελέω contr.vb. **also make** —*a payment* X.

προ-στέλλω vb. ‖ MID. (of Justice) **send forth** —*someone* (W.INF. *to do sthg.*) A. ‖ PASS. (of a person) **venture forth** —W.INTERN.ACC. *on a long journey* S.

προ-στένω vb. **lament prematurely** A.

προ-στερνίδιον ου n. [dimin. στέρνον] **breast-piece** (as protective armour for a horse) X.

πρό-στερνος ον adj. [στέρνον] (of folds of a dress) **over the breast** A.

προστετᾱκώς (dial.pf.ptcpl.): see προστήκομαι

προσ-τεχνάομαι mid.contr.vb. **devise** (W.ACC. sthg.) **in addition** Plu.

προ-στηθίδια ων n.pl. [dimin. στῆθος] **breast-ornaments, pectorals** (worn by priests of Cybele) Plb.

προσ-τήκομαι pass.vb. | aor.2 ptcpl. προστακείς | dial.pf.act.ptcpl. (w.pass.sens.) προστετᾱκώς | (of corrosive poison fr. the robe of Nessos) **be liquefied against, soak** or **eat into** (Herakles' sides) S.; (of Herakles, i.e. his flesh) perh. **be dissolved** (by contact w. the poisoned robe) S.

προσ-τίθημι vb. | dial.aor. ποτέθηκα, athem.imperatv. ποτίθες (Theoc.) ‖ The sections are grouped as: (1–3) place (things) against or on (other things), (4–6) bring (persons or things) into close relationship with others, (7–9) give, confer or bestow, (10–12) impose, inflict or attribute, (13–16) add. |
1 place (sthg.) against or on (sthg. else); **place** (W.ACC. a boulder, plank, scaling ladder) **against** (a door, a wall) Od. Th. Ar.; **place** or **hold** —*a lock of hair* (W.DAT. *against another's hair*) A. E. —*one's arms* (*around someone's knees, in supplication*) E. —*one's shield* (*against one's chin*) E. —*a blind person's hand* (W.PREP.PHR. *on a dead person's face*) E.; **put, lay** —*clothes, decoration, fetters* (W.DAT. *on someone*) E. —*offerings* (*on a tomb*) S.; **apply** —*one's hands* (W.DAT. *to a tree, in order to uproot it*) S. —*spurs* (*to a horse*) Pl. —*pigments* (*to a statue*) Pl. —*a ruler* (*to a diagram, in making measurements*) Ar.; **take, put** —*horses* (W.DAT. *to mangers*) E.; **bring near** —*one's face* (*to get a better view*) E.fr.
2 ‖ MID. place (sthg.) against oneself; **draw to oneself, embrace** —*someone's breast* E.; **apply to oneself** —*a sponge* Ar.; **put** —*fine clothes* (W.DAT. *on one's body*) E.
3 put (a door) to (a closed position); **close** —*a door, a gate* Hdt. Th. Lys.
4 bring (someone or sthg.) into close relationship (W.DAT. w. someone or sthg. else); **attach, add** —*someone* (*to a group*) A.; (in military or political ctxt.) **ally** —*oneself* (*to someone*) Th.; (fig.) **link** —*an island* (*to praise*) Pi.
5 ‖ MID. bring over (someone) to one's side; **win over** —*the people* Hdt.; **take on** —*someone* (*as an ally*) Th.; **gain** —*someone* (W.PREDIC.SB. *as a friend, ally, enemy*) Hdt. E. X. —(W.PREP.PHR. *near one's land, i.e. as a neighbour*) S. —*military help* (*for one's city*) E.; **take** —*someone* (W.PREDIC.SB. *as a wife*) S.
6 ‖ MID. **attach oneself to, side with** —W.DAT. *someone* S. Th. D.; (gener.) **align oneself with, favour, support** —W.DAT. *persons, their opinion* Hdt. Th. X. D. —*a law* Pl.; **go along with, believe in** —W.DAT. *a story* Hdt.
7 confer or bestow (someone or sthg., usu. W.DAT. on someone or sthg. else); **hand over, assign** —*prerogatives of gods* (*to mortals*) A. —*one's daughter* (*to a suitor,* W.PREDIC.SB. *as wife*) Hdt. —*a marriage* (i.e. *wife, to someone*) E. —*one's son* (*to another father*) E. —*one's son* (*to a city, for sacrifice*) E. —*a city* (*to someone*) Th.; **bestow** —*credit, honour, one's due* (*on someone*) E.fr. Th. —*a specific rank* (*on ritual objects*) hHom.; **bequeath** —*a life of good repute* (*to one's children*) E.; **contribute** —*one's weight* (i.e. *help, to someone*) E. —*one's benevolence* (w. εἰς + ACC. *to public affairs*) D.; (wkr.sens.) **bring** —*an urgent message* E. ‖ MID. **grant** —*a favour* (W.DAT. *to someone*) S.; **contribute** —*sthg. further* S.
8 consign —*someone, one's body* (W.DAT. *to Hades, a funeral pyre*) E. —*someone* (*to punishment, demeaning work*) E.
9 ‖ MID. (specif.) **give, cast** —*a vote* (W.DAT. *for someone*) A. D. —(W.PREDIC.ADJ. + DAT. *in opposition to someone*) Th.; (intr.) app. **register one's view** —W.DAT. *by vote* Th.

προστῑλάω

10 impose (sthg. unasked for or unwelcome); **impose** —*a task* (W.DAT. *on someone*) Hdt. E. —W.DAT. + INF. *on someone the task of doing sthg.* Hdt.; **inflict** —*humiliation, punishment, grief, or sim.* (W.DAT. *on someone*) Hdt. E. Th.; **lay** —*a curse* (W. ἐπί + DAT. *on someone*) S.; **bring to bear, apply** —*force, compulsion* A. E. X.; (wkr.sens.) **cause** —*amazement, speechlessness, disquiet* (W.DAT. *for someone*) E. Antipho; (of dangerous situations) **prompt** —*hesitation* S.
11 ‖ MID. impose (sthg.) on oneself; **bring upon oneself** —*trouble, pain, or sim.* A. E. Th. —*dangers* Th. —*enmities* Pl.; **take upon oneself** —*concern for someone* S.; **undertake** —*war* (W.DAT. *against someone*) Hdt.; entertain in one's heart, **harbour** —*anger* (*against someone*) Hdt. —*pained feelings* Th.
12 attribute (a quality or fault, usu. W.DAT. to someone); **attribute** —*noble birth* E.*fr.*; **impute** —*boldness, stupidity, lust* E.; **attach** —*blame* E. Th. Ar.
13 make an addition; **add** —*sthg.* (countable or quantifiable, usu. W.DAT. to sthg. else) Thgn. Hdt. + —*good reputation* (*to the achievement of prosperity*) Pi. —*money* (fr. further sources) Th. —*a favour* (W.DAT. *to an earlier favour*) E. —*a funeral speech* (*to a ceremony*) Th. —*letters* (*to words*) Pl. —*a character* (*to a play*) Ar. —*a word* (W. πρός + ACC. *to a name*) Ar. —*a sum of money* (*to a payment*) X.; (intr.) **make an addition** or **additions** (sts. W.DAT. or πρός + ACC. to sthg.) Th. Arist.
14 add in speech or writing; **add** —*sthg., nothing, or sim.* Hdt. Th. + —w. ὅτι + INDIC. *that sthg. is the case* Antipho D.; **add a qualification** (sts. W.DAT. to sthg.) Pl.; **add a stipulation** —W.DAT. *to a law* (W.ACC. + INF. *that sthg. is to be the case*) Hdt. ‖ PASS. (of a stipulation or detail) be added —W.DAT. *to a law* Hdt. —w. πρός + ACC. *to a treaty* Plb.
15 add to what is given or offered; **also give, add** —*further gold* Hdt. —*an oath, pledge, assurance, favour* S. D.; **give** (W.ACC. *a dowry*) **as well** (as one's daughter) E. D.; **give** (W.ACC. a sum of money) **along with** —W.DAT. *one's daughter* Hyp.; **pay** (W.ACC. money) **as well** (as doing sthg. else) D.; (intr.) **pay money as well** Pl. Arist.
16 perform an additional act; **proceed, continue** (in speech) NT. ‖ MID. **proceed** —W.INF. *to do sthg.* NT.

προσ-τῑλάω contr.vb. (fig., of an exploding haggis) **shit** —w. πρός + ACC. *in someone's eyes* Ar.

προσ-τῑμάω contr.vb. **1** (of a jury) **impose an additional penalty** Lys.(law) D.; **impose in addition** —*an appropriate penalty* (usu. W.DAT. *on someone*) Pl. Arist. —W.ACC. or GEN. *a sentence of imprisonment* D.; **impose a fine** (sts. W.ACC. of a certain sum) **in addition** —W.DAT. *payable to the treasury* D.; **impose** (W.ACC. damages) **in addition** D. ‖ IMPERS.PASS. an additional penalty (W.GEN. of imprisonment, a fine) is imposed —W.DAT. *on someone* D.
2 (at Rome, of a judge) **impose** (W.ACC. a sum of money) **as a fine** Plu.; (of a censor) **impose** (W.ACC. a sum of money) **as a tax** —W.DAT. *on property worth a certain sum* Plu.

προστίμημα ατος *n.* (leg.) **additional penalty** D.

πρόστιμον ου *n.* **legal penalty** Plb. Plu.

προ-στόμια ων *n.pl.* **outer mouths** (of the Nile, ref. to the silt which extended the original outlet) A.

προσ-τρέπω vb. | aor.2 ptcpl. προστραπών | aor.2 mid.inf. προστραπέσθαι | **1** turn towards (a god) in supplication; **beseech, entreat** —*a god* (W.ACC. *for this much*) S. —(W.INF. *to do sthg.*) S.; **beg, pray** —W.ACC. + INF. *for sthg. to happen* E. ‖ MID. **entreat** (a god) Plu. —*a person* (*as if a god*) Plu.
2 ‖ MID. **approach as a suppliant** —*a temple* A.; (fig., of a murdered man) **appeal to** —*his suffering* (*i.e. claim atonement because of it*) Pl.
3 ‖ MID. (of a person wrongly sentenced to death) **turn, direct** —*the wrath of avenging spirits* (W.DAT. *against those who sentenced him*) Antipho (cj.) | see προστρίβω 4
4 approach as an enemy, **attack** —*a land* Pi.(dub.) | see προτρέπω 2

προσ-τρέφομαι pass.vb. | aor. προσεθρέφθην | (of a priest of Ruin, fig.ref. to a lion) **be reared as an additional inmate** —W.DAT. *for a house* A.

προσ-τρέχω vb. | The fut. and aor. are supplied by προσδραμεῖν. | **1 run up** (to a person or place) Men. NT. Plu. —W.DAT. or πρός + ACC. *to someone or sthg.* Ar. X. Plb.
2 (of sailors) sail quickly towards, **make for** —W.DAT. or πρός + ACC. *a place* Plb.
3 (fig.) **come close** —w. πρός + ACC. *to the truth* Plb.
4 align oneself, side —W.DAT. *w. the Senate* Plb.
5 fawn on, flatter (someone) Plb.

προσ-τρίβω vb. **1** wear away ‖ PF.PASS.PTCPL. (of a murderer who has been purified) worn away (by his travels in search of purification, perh.w. additional connot. that the blood-guilt is worn off) A.
2 rub off or inflict (sthg. on someone) ‖ MID. **have** (W.ACC. beatings) **inflicted** —W.DAT. *on people* Ar. ‖ PASS. (of punishment) be inflicted —W.DAT. *on a rash tongue* A.
3 ‖ MID. (fig.) cause (sthg.) to be imposed (on someone); (of an excess of property) **stamp** —*a reputation for wealth* (W.DAT. *on its owner*) D.; (of a teacher) **inculcate** —*a love of medicine* (W.DAT. *in someone*) Plu.
4 ‖ MID. (pejor.) **bring down, inflict, fasten** —*disaster and slander* (W.DAT. *on someone*) D. —*blame, scandal, a charge of murder, an avenging spirit, or sim.* (on someone) Plu. —*the wrath of avenging spirits* (on someone) Antipho (dub.) | see προστρέπω 3

πρόστριμμα ατος *n.* that which is rubbed off or inflicted on (persons), **affliction, harm** A.

προστρόπαιος, dial. **ποτιτρόπαιος**, ου *m.* [προστρέπω]
1 one who turns to another (in supplication), **suppliant** A. S. Plu.
2 (specif.) suppliant seeking purification (for murder), **polluted suppliant** A.
3 (w. no connot. of supplication) **polluted killer** E. ‖ NEUT.SB. polluting presence (of a person) Aeschin.
4 murdered person (who supplicates his next of kin for vengeance), **suppliant for vengeance** A. E. Antipho; **avenging spirit** (of the victim) Antipho Plb.

—προστρόπαιος ον *adj.* **1** (of prayers) **of supplication** S.
2 (of the seated posture) **of a suppliant for purification** A.
3 (of the blood of a murdered suppliant or other person) **calling for vengeance, polluting** E.

προστροπή ῆς, dial. **προστροπά** ᾶς *f.* **1** turning towards (someone, in supplication); **supplication, appeal, prayer** (for purification or help, made to a god, city or person) Trag. Aeschin.
2 service, duty (of a priestess, W.GEN. *to a goddess*) E.(dub.)

πρόστροπος ου *m.* **suppliant** (sts. W.GEN. of someone) S.

προσ-τυγχάνω vb. **1** (of trouble) **happen to, befall** —W.DAT. *someone* Pi.*fr.* ‖ NEUT.AOR.PTCPL.SB. chance or randomness (in events) Pl.; (prep.phr.) ἐκ τοῦ προστυχόντος *casually, randomly* Plu.
2 (of a person) **happen upon, meet with, encounter** —W.DAT. *someone or sthg.* Pl. Plu. ‖ NEUT.AOR.PTCPL.SB. that which gets in the way, obstacle Pl. Plu.
3 gain, obtain, get —W.GEN. *a fair reward* S.
4 meet with, get, find —W.GEN. + PREDIC.SB. *someone who will inflict punishment on one* S.

—προστυγχάνων οντος *masc.pres.ptcpl.sb.* **passer-by or chance acquaintance** Th. Pl. X. Plu.
—προστυχών οὖσα όν *aor.2 ptcpl.adj.* (of fare for a guest) **offered, provided** E.; (of a lawgiver, of bread) **ordinary** Plu. ‖ MASC.SB. passer-by or chance acquaintance Pl. Is. D. Plu.; ordinary person Plu.
προστυχής ές *adj.* **1** (of a person) having an encounter, **being in contact** (w. someone) Pl.
2 acquainted, familiar (W.DAT. w. places) Pl.; (W.GEN. w. crimes) Pl.
προ-στῷον ου *n.* [στοά] **colonnade, cloister** (of a house) Pl.
προσ-υβρίζω *vb.* **outrage** (W.ACC. the laws or sim.) **as well** (through treating office-holders outrageously) D. ‖ PASS. (of a person) suffer further outrage D.
προ-συγγίγνομαι (-ξυγγίγνομαι) *mid.vb.* **have a preliminary meeting** —W.DAT. w. someone Th.
προ-συγχέω *contr.vb.* (of elephants) **throw** (W.ACC. troops) **into confusion beforehand** Plb.
προ-συμμίσγω *vb.* [συμμείγνῡμι] (of rivers) **first unite** —their waters (before issuing into the sea) Hdt.
προ-συνοικέω *contr.vb.* previously cohabit (w. someone); (of a woman) **be previously married** —W.DAT. to someone Hdt. Plu.
προσ-υπακούω *vb.* (of a disputant) **also answer** —W.NEUT.ACC. a further point Pl.
προσ-υπάρχω *vb.* ‖ IMPERS. there is also an opportunity —W.DAT. + INF. for someone to do sthg. D.
προσ-υπισχνέομαι *mid.contr.vb.* **promise besides** —W.ACC. + FUT.INF. that sthg. will happen Plu.
προσ-υποδείκνῡμι *vb.* **also indicate** —another cause of complaint (W.DAT. to someone) Plb.
προσ-υπομιμνήσκω *vb.* **suggest additionally** —W.DBL.ACC. sthg. to someone Plb.; (of circumstances) **give a further reminder** (to someone of sthg.) Plb.
προσ-υφαίνω *vb.* **weave** (W.ACC. what is mortal) **into** —W.DAT. what is immortal Pl.
προσ-φάγιον ου *n.* [φαγεῖν] **food eaten in addition to bread), fish** NT.
πρόσφαγμα ατος *n.* [προσφάζω] **1** app. **preliminary sacrifice** (ref. to a murder which precedes either another's murder or another's funeral) A.
2 app., **victim sacrificed to a dead person** (at his tomb); **sacrificial offering, victim** (ref. to a person) E. Plu.; (ref. to an animal) E.
3 victim sacrificed at an altar, sacrificial offering, victim (ref. to a person) E.
4 (pl. for sg.) **sacrifice** (of a person) E.; (ref. to the murder of a person) E.(cj.)
προ-σφάζω *vb.* ‖ PASS. (of an animal's blood) **be shed in sacrifice** —W.DAT. to the dead E.
προσφάσθαι (*mid.inf.*): see πρόσφημι
πρόσ-φατος ον *adj.* [θείνω] **1** app., recently killed; (of a corpse) **not decomposed, fresh** Il. Hdt. Plu.; (of fish) Men.; (of the colour of old purple dye, a work of art) **as fresh as ever** Plu.
2 (fig., of a criminal described as recently caught) **fresh** (opp. one described as thoroughly pickled, i.e. long in prison) D.; (of a defendant on trial for a recent offence, opp. persons whose offences are stale and cold) D.; (of persons) **vigorous, enthusiastic** (opp. dulled by familiarity) Plu.
3 recent in date; (of an act of justice) **recent, fresh, new** A.; (of snow) Plb.; (of anger, jealousy) Lys. Plu.; (of inquiries and studies) Arist.; (of events) Plb. Plu.; (of a witness to an event) Arist. ‖ NEUT.SB. recentness (of an event) Plb.

—πρόσφατον *neut.adv.* **recently** Pi.
—προσφάτως *adv.* **recently** Plb. NT.
προσφερής ές *adj.* [προσφέρω] **1** (of persons or things) **like, similar to** (W.DAT. someone or sthg.) Hdt. Trag. Th. Ar. Pl. Plu.; (w. ὡς + DAT.) S.*Ichn*.; (W.GEN.) E.
2 (of an action) **serviceable, useful** (W.DAT. for someone) Hdt.
προσ-φέρω *vb.* | fut.mid. (w.pass.sens.) προσοίσομαι |
1 bring (sthg.) to a place; **bring** —objects (w. πρός + ACC. to a temple) Hdt.; **bring up** —stones (to build a wall) Th.; (of a hunter) **bring home** —food S.; (of an eagle) —prey (W.DAT. to a nest) A.
2 (w. aggressive connot.) **bring up** —siege-engines, scaling ladders (W.DAT. against a city, its walls) E. Th. Plb.; **bring** —weapons, missiles, fire, a torch (sts. W.DAT. against someone) E. Ar.
3 bring (part of the body) into contact or proximity (w. persons or parts of the body); **place** —one's lips (w. πρός + ACC. against another's lips) X. —one's hand (against a horse's nostrils) Hdt.; (w. aggressive connot.) **lay** —a hand, even a fingertip (usu. W.DAT. on someone) Pi. E. Ar.; (fig.) **get** —one's hands (W.DAT. on persons, i.e. attack them) X. Plb.
4 bring or apply (sthg. non-material, oft. W.DAT. to or against someone or sthg.); (of persons) **bring to bear, apply** —boldness Pi. —compulsion, force, a device, test, or sim. A. Hdt. E. Ar. Pl.(sts.mid.) Plb.(mid.) —medicine, a remedy Th. Pl. —sneezing (as a cure for hiccups) Pl. —a law or decree (w. πρός + ACC. against sthg.) D.
5 bring additionally; **add** —wine (to a libation) S. —a new trouble (W.DAT. to an old one) E.
6 present (sthg., oft. W.DAT. to someone); **offer, present** —a prize (fig.ref. to a victory ode) Pi. —libations, funeral offerings (to the dead) S. E. —gifts (to the infant Jesus) NT.; **hand over** —a bow, an urn, part of a sacrificed animal S. Ar.; **introduce** —clever new ideas (to fools) E.; (gener.) **bring** —a new message E.
7 offer —food Ar. Pl. X. —a cup (W.DAT. + INF. to someone, for a drink) E.*Cyc.* —W.DAT. + INF. to someone, (sthg.) to eat and drink X. —W.INF. (sthg.) to eat Men. ‖ MID. **take** —food, drink, poison X. Aeschin. Plu. ‖ PASS. (of food) be offered Pl. X.
8 bring, address, put —a proposal, argument, or sim. (usu. W.DAT.) Hdt. S. E. Th. +; **make a proposal** —W.COMPL.CL. that sthg. shd. be done Plb. ‖ PASS. (of business) be brought or put (to someone) Hdt.
9 contribute, pay —money, tribute, tax Hdt. Th. X.; (of slaves put out for hire, a business) **bring in** —an income X. D. ‖ PASS. (of gifts) be contributed Th.
10 ‖ PASS. be carried to or towards (someone or somewhere); (of a wounded man) be brought back (to camp) Thphr. —w. πρός + ACC. to the ranks X.; (of sailors, a ship) sail up (sts. W.DAT. to other sailors, a harbour) Hdt. X. Plb. Plu.
11 ‖ PASS. move with hostile intention (against someone); (of troops, ships) bear down, attack Hdt. Th.; (of a war) approach —W.PREP.PHR. fr. a particular region Plu.; (of troops, a commander) face, engage with, attack —W.DAT. or πρός + ACC. opponents, a city Hdt. Th.; (of a rider, a horse) come up against —w. πρός + ACC. an enemy Hdt.; (of a boxer) move to the attack Pl.; (fig., of a person) take the offensive (in attempting to persuade someone) Hdt.
12 ‖ PASS. conduct oneself towards, treat, deal with —W.DAT. or πρός + ACC. persons, situations, arguments, or sim. (W.ADV. or PREP.PHR. in a certain way) Th. Att.orats. Pl. + —(W.PTCPL.PHR. by acting in a certain way) X. —(W.NOM.

PREDIC.SB. *as a friend*) E.*Cyc.* —(w. ὡς + DAT.PREDIC.SB. *as an ally*) Isoc.
13 ‖ PASS. (of a person's features) come close in appearance, bear a resemblance —w. ἐς + ACC. *to someone* Hdt.; (act., of a person) **bear a resemblance** —W.DAT. *to someone* (W.ACC. *in some characteristic*) Pi.

προσ-φεύγω *vb.* **flee for refuge** —W.DAT. or πρός + ACC. *to a person or place* Plb. Plu.

πρόσ-φημι *vb.* [φημί | 3sg.aor. προσέφη, dial. προσέφᾱ (B.), also ποτέφᾱ (Stesich.), προσέφᾱσε (Call.) ‖ mid.inf. προσφάσθαι | **speak to, address** —*someone* Hom. Hes. hHom. Lyr. Call. Theoc.; **say** —W.DBL.ACC. *sthg. to someone* Hom.; (intr.) **speak** Hom. hHom. ‖ MID. (in neg.phr.) **say** —*a single word* Od.

προσ-φθέγγομαι *mid.vb.* **1 speak to, address** —*someone* E.; **greet** —*a land* E.; (intr.) **speak out** S.
2 call, name —*a hill* (W.GEN. *that of Kronos*) Pi.; **designate** —*a class of things* (W.PREDIC.SB. *such and such*) Pl.

προσφθεγκτός όν *adj.* **addressed, greeted** (W.GEN. by the voice of a particular person) S.

πρόσφθεγμα (or **πρόσφθεγγμα**) ατος *n.* (usu.pl.) **address or greeting** (to a person or god) Trag.; **shout, cry** A.

προσ-φθείρομαι *pass.vb.* | aor.2 ptcpl. προσφθαρείς | (of a person, as imprecation) **come into damned contact** —W.DAT. *w. someone* Ar.

πρόσφθογγος ον *adj.* [προσφθέγγομαι] (of words) **of greeting** A.; (of a cry) **in greeting** (W.GEN. of someone's return) A.

προσ-φθονέω *contr.vb.* **1 oppose** (W.DAT. someone) **from jealousy** Plu.
2 be jealous —W.GEN. *of someone's power* Plu.

προσφίλεια ᾱς *f.* [προσφιλής] **friendship, goodwill** (of the gods) A.

προσ-φιλής ές *adj.* [φιλέω] **1** (of persons) **held in great affection, beloved, dear** (W.DAT. to one's family, a god) S. E.; (gener.) **well-liked, likeable** Hdt.
2 (wkr.sens., of persons) **pleasing, congenial, welcome** (W.DAT. to someone) S. Th. Isoc. Pl. +; (of actions or things) Trag. Pl. +
3 on terms of friendship, friendly (W.DAT. w. someone) Hdt.
4 showing friendly feelings, friendly, kindly, well-meaning (W.DAT. to someone) S. E. Th.; (of words) S.

—**προσφιλῶς** *adv.* | compar. προσφιλέστερον, superl. προσφιλέστατα | **1 in a friendly manner, kindly** S. Pl. X.
2 in a manner that is pleasing (W.DAT. to someone) Pl. X. Plu.

προσ-φιλονικέω *contr.vb.* (of troops) **be eager for victory** —w. πρός + ACC. *in response to a previous defeat* Plb.

προσ-φοιτάω *contr.vb.* **1 go regularly** —W.ADV. or PREP.PHR. *to a shop, a barber's, a bank* Att.orats. Thphr.; **make visits** (to people) Plu.
2 come up to, accost (a person) Plu.; **come to join** (a military leader) Plu.

προσφορά ᾶς *f.* [προσφέρω] **1 bringing up** (W.GEN. of scaling ladders, in a siege) Plb.
2 manner of application, particular use (of a foodstuff) Pl.; **application** (of a cause, as an explanation for sthg.) Arist.
3 addition, increase (to or of crimes) S.
4 offering (of food or sim., by nurses to children) Pl.
5 what is offered, service, benefit (provided by a person) S.; (concr.) **wedding present** Thphr.; (in religious ctxt.) **offering** NT.

προσ-φορέω *contr.vb.* **bring in** —*captured weapons* (w. πρός + ACC. *to a camp*) Hdt.; **bring up** —*sheaves of corn* (*to fuel a fire*) X.

προσφορήματα των *n.pl.* **things offered** (to guests, W.DAT. for a meal) E.

πρόσφορος, dial. **ποτίφορος**, ον *adj.* [προσφέρω]
1 contributing to a given end; (of things) **useful, helpful, needful** (sts. W.DAT. for someone or sthg.) S. E. Th.
2 (of things) **suitable, appropriate** (sts. W.DAT. for someone or sthg.) Pi. S. E. Th. Ar. Pl. +
3 ‖ NEUT.SB. (sg. and pl.) **what is appropriate or needed** (sts. W.DAT. for someone or sthg.) A. Hdt. E. Th. Ar. Pl. +; (W.GEN. in present circumstances) E.(dub.)
4 (of persons) **suited, fit** (for a task) E.; (W.INF. to do sthg.) A. Pi.; **suited to dealing** (W.DAT. w. someone) E.
5 (of a person, in neg.phr.) **resembling, similar to** (W.DAT. persons of mortal birth) E.

—**πρόσφορα** *neut.pl.adv.* **suitably, properly** E.

προσφυής ές *adj.* [προσφύω] **1 naturally grown or grafted** (on sthg.); (of leaden weights, fig.ref. to physical pleasures) **attached** (to the soul) Pl.; (of a footstool) **fixed** (W.PREP.PHR. to a chair) Od.
2 (of things) **naturally akin** (W.DAT. to other things) Pl.

—**προσφυέως** *Ion.adv.* **appropriately, shrewdly** —*ref. to speaking* Hdt.

προσ-φῡσάομαι *pass.contr.vb.* (fig., of war, envisaged as fire) **be blown upon, be fanned** (by those who come near it, as if by winds) Plb.

πρόσφυσις εως *f.* [προσφύω] **grip** (of a rider, W.DAT. on a horse's shoulders) X.

προσ-φύω *vb.* | aor.1 προσέφῡσα | **make** (sthg.) **grow** (on sthg.); (fig.) **attach** or **graft on** —*an argument* (W.DAT. *to another argument*) Ar.; **add** —*sthg.* (W.DAT. *to a speech*) A.(dub.)

—**προσφύομαι** *pass.vb.* | also (most freq.) ACT.: athem.aor. προσέφῡν | pf. προσπέφῡκα | **1** (of horns) **grow** —W.DAT. on someone's head E.; (of hands and legs) —*on people* Pl.; (of barnacles or sim.) **adhere** (to someone) Pl.; (of an embryo, to the womb) Arist.; (of maggots, to entrails) Plu.; (of a wall) **be attached** —W.DAT. *to rocky ground* Plu.; (of a fish) **be fixed** —W.DAT. *to a hook* Theoc.
2 (of a person) **attach oneself, hold fast, cling** —W.DAT. *to a tree* Od.; (to a tree trunk) AR.; (to someone's body, w. one's teeth) Il.; (fig.) **associate closely** —W.DAT. *w. someone* Pl.; (fig., of a person's soul) **become attached** —W.DAT. *to other people* Plu.
3 (fig.) **severely criticise** —W.DAT. *someone* Plb.

προσ-φωνέω *contr.vb.* | ep.3sg.impf. προσεφώνεε | **1 speak to, address, greet** —*someone or sthg.* Hom. B. Trag. Isoc. AR. Mosch. NT. —W.DAT. NT.; **speak** (to someone) Od. ‖ PASS. be addressed or greeted S.
2 say —W.DBL.ACC. *sthg. to someone* Il. E. —W.ACC. *particular words* S.; **give voice to** —*song* S.*Ichn.*
3 designate, call —*someone* (W.PREDIC.ACC. *such and such, i.e. give him a particular name or title*) E. Plb.
4 address (someone) **in a dedication; dedicate a book** —W.DAT. *to someone* Plu.

προσφώνημα ατος *n.* **1** (sg. and pl.) **speech, talk, utterance** (of a person) S. E.
2 designation, name (W.GEN. of a person) S.; **title** (given to someone) Plu.

προσφώνησις εως *f.* **dedication** (W.GEN. of a book) Plu.

προσ-χαίρω *vb.* **take delight** —W.DAT. *in sthg.* Plu.

προσ-χαρίζομαι *mid.vb.* **gratify, satisfy** —W.DAT. *a horse's belly* X.

προσ-χάσκω *vb.* | aor.2 προσέχανον | pf. (w.pres.sens.) προσκέχηνα | **1 gape, gawp** —W.ACC. *w. grovelling acclaim* (W.DAT. *at someone*) A.

2 **gawp at, listen uncritically to** —W.DAT. *everything one is told* Plb.

πρόσχημα ατος *n.* [προέχω] 1 that which is put forward (for concealment or dissimulation); **pretext, pretence, excuse** Hdt. Th. Lys.; (as predic., ref. to a person or thing) **pretext** (sts. W.GEN. for sthg.) Hdt. S. Plb. Plu.; (ref. to prudence) **cover, screen, cloak** (W.GEN. for cowardice) Th.; (acc., quasi-advbl.) *as a pretext* —*ref. to doing sthg.* Hdt.; (dat.) *on the pretext, under the cover* (W.GEN.) *of sthg.*) D.
2 (gener.) **screen, disguise** Pl.; **pretence, mere show** Ar. Pl.
3 (without pejor. connot.) **motive** D.
4 perh. **introductory material** (W.GEN. of a speech) Pl.
5 that which is displayed (to be admired by others); (as predic., ref. to a town) **glory, ornament, showpiece** (W.GEN. of a country, a people) Hdt. Plb. Plu.; πρόσχημ' ἀγώνος *showpiece of games* (i.e. games which are the showpiece, W. 2ND GEN. *of Greece*) S.
6 (gener.) **respectability** (of a person) D.; **dignity, prestige** (of sthg.) Plb.; **pomp, show, majesty** Plu.

πρό-σχισμα ατος *n.* split in front; **forepart** (of a shoe, where there is an opening for the toes) Arist.

προσ-χλευάζω *vb.* **also react with ridicule** Plb.

πρόσ-χορδος ον *adj.* [χορδή] (of voices) concordant, **in unison** (W.DAT. w. other voices) Pl.

προσ-χόω *contr.vb.* —also (pres.) **προσχώννῡμι** (Plb.) *vb.* | nom.pl.ptcpl. προσχωννύντες | 1 **create** (sthg.) **by piling up earth; form by means of a dam** —*a bend in a river* Hdt.; **level** —*uneven ground* Plb. ‖ IMPERS.PASS. **a mound is raised** against (a wall) Th.
2 **create** (sthg.) **by piling up silt;** (of rivers) **form** (W.ACC. land) **by alluvial deposits** Hdt.; **form deposits against** (islands) Th.

προσ-χράομαι *mid.contr.vb.* | neut.impers.vbl.adj. προσχρηστέον | 1 **make additional use** (sts. W.DAT. of sthg.) Pl. Arist.
2 (wkr.sens.) **make use** —W.DAT. *of sthg.* Pl. Arist.

προσ-χρῄζω, Ion. **προσχρηΐζω** *vb.* 1 **desire, ask for, want** (W.GEN. someone or sthg.) **in addition** Hdt. S.
2 **beg** —W.GEN. + INF. *someone to do sthg.* Hdt.
3 **desire, want** —W.NEUT.ACC. *sthg.* A. S. —W.INF. *to do sthg.* S.

πρόσχωμα ατος *n.* [προσχόω] **alluvial deposit, silt** (of the Nile) A.

προσχώννῡμι *vb.*: see προσχόω

προσ-χωρέω *contr.vb.* | fut. προσχωρήσω, also mid. προσχωρήσομαι | 1 **come near, approach** (sts. W.DAT. someone or sthg.) Hdt. Th. Plu.; (of the sun in summer, opp. recede) X.
2 **come over** (to join someone); (of a nation) **join, combine** —W.DAT. w. *another nation* Hdt.; (of troops) **link up** —w. πρός + ACC. w. *other troops* Hdt.; (of people, cities, or sim.) **come over** (to someone, usu. a former enemy) Hdt. Th. X. Plb. Plu. —W.DAT. or πρός + ACC. *to someone* Hdt. Th. +; (of a politician) **ally oneself** —w. πρός + ACC. w. *certain people* D.
3 **give oneself over, turn** —w. πρός + ACC. *to a certain lifestyle* Pl.
4 **come in support or agreement;** (of a god) **side** —w. πρός + ACC. w. *human plans* Hdt.; (of a person) **agree** —W.DAT. w. *someone* Hdt.; **accede** —W.DAT. *to a plea* S.; (of a foreigner) **comply** —W.DAT. w. *a host city* E.
5 ‖ PF. (of people) **have come close to, be like, resemble** —W.DAT. or πρός + ACC. *a nation* (W.ACC. *in customs, speech*) Hdt.

πρόσ-χωρος ον *adj.* [χώρᾱ] (of a place) **nearby** A. S.; (W.DAT. another place) Plb.; (of persons) **living nearby** S. X.

‖ MASC.PL.SB. **neighbours** Hdt. S. Th. +; (W.DAT. to someone) Plb.

πρόσχωσις εως *f.* [προσχόω] 1 **piling up** (of sediment, in a river), **silting** Th.; (concr.) **silt** Th.
2 **earth piled up** (against a city wall, by besiegers) Th.

προσ-ψαύω, dial. **ποτιψαύω** *vb.* 1 **touch** (someone or sthg.) S. —W.DAT. *sthg.* NT.; **lay hands on** (someone, violently) S.
2 (fig., of songs of praise) **touch upon, bring about** —W.DAT. *everlasting honours* Pi.*fr.*

προσ-ψηφίζομαι *mid.vb.* **vote** or **decree in addition** —W.ACC. + INF. *that sthg. shd. happen* Lys. Plu.

πρόσω, ep. **πρόσσω**, Att. **πόρρω**, dial. **πόρσω** *adv.* and *prep.* [πρό] 1 (ref. to movt.) **forwards, onwards, ahead** Hom. Pi. Hdt. Trag. Ar. +; τὸ (and ἐς τὸ) πρόσω *forwards* Hdt.; (also) τοῦ πρόσω X.
2 (as prep.) **far** —W.GEN. *into a river* X.; (fig.) **far ahead** —W.GEN. *in virtue, wisdom, wickedness, skill, or sim.* Hdt. Ar. Pl. +; ἐς τὸ πρόσω *further ahead* —W.GEN. *in one's speech, one's affairs* Hdt.
3 (ref. to position or direction) **forwards, ahead** (opp. backwards) —*ref. to facing* Il.; **in front** (opp. behind) E.
4 (ref. to time) **forwards, ahead** —*ref. to thinking* Hom.; **in the time ahead, hereafter** A. Pi.; **for a longer time, further** —*ref. to speaking or doing sthg.* Trag.
5 (ref. to distance) **far away, far off** Pi. Hdt. Trag. Ar. +; πόρρω ἀπό *far away* —W.GEN. *fr. sthg.* Hdt. Antipho +
6 (as prep., oft. fig.) **far** —W.GEN. *fr. persons, places, dangers, or sim.* Hdt. E. Isoc. + —*fr. what is right* A. —w. τοῦ + INF. *fr. doing sthg.* Isoc. +
7 **for a long way, far** —*ref. to sthg. extending* A. Ar. Pl.
8 (quasi-adjl., of a person's life) **far advanced** E.; (of a day) Aeschin.(dub.); (as prep.) **far, late** —W.GEN. *into the night, the day* Hdt. Pl. X.; **far on** —W.GEN. *in life* E. Isoc. Pl. Plu.

—**προσωτέρω**, Att. **πορρωτέρω**, dial. **πόρσιον** (Pi.) *compar.adv. and prep.* **further** Pi. Hdt. Pl. + —W.COMPAR.GEN. *than sthg.* Hdt. Pl. X.; (also) τὸ προσωτέρω (sts. W.COMPAR.GEN.) Hdt.; (as prep.) **further** —W.GEN. *fr. sthg.* Plu.

—**προσωτάτω** (also **προσώτατα** Hdt. S. E.), Att. **πορρωτάτω**, dial. **πόρσιστα** (Pi.) *superl.adv. and prep.*
1 **furthest** or **very far** Hdt. S. E. X. Plu.; (also) τοῦ προσωτάτω S.; πορρωτάτω ἀπὸ *furthest away* —W.GEN. *fr. sthg.* Isoc. X. Men.; (as prep.) **furthest** or **very far** —W.GEN. *fr. sthg.* Isoc. Pl. D. +
2 **for a very long time ahead** Pi.

προσῳδίᾱ ᾱς *f.* [προσῳδός] 1 app. **address** or **manner of speaking** (to someone) A.*fr.*
2 **variation in pitch** (of the voice) Pl.; **intonation** (perh. ref. to the pitch accent) Arist.

προσ-ῳδός όν *adj.* [ἀοιδή] (fig., of a person's misfortune) **in harmony, comparable** (W.DAT. w. another's) E.

πρόσωθεν, ep. **πρόσσοθεν**, Att. **πόρρωθεν** *adv.* [πρόσω]
1 **from afar, at a distance** Pi. Trag. Pl. +
2 **from far back in time, from long ago** E. Att.orats. Pl. +
3 **from a remote source** or **in a far-fetched way** —*ref. to creating metaphors* Arist.; **from a distant starting-point** —*ref. to constructing an argument* Arist.
4 **ahead** or **before one** —*ref. to driving one's chariot-horses* Il.

—**πορρωτέρωθεν** Att.*compar.adv.* **from further back in time** Isoc.

προσ-ωνέομαι *mid.contr.vb.* **buy** (W.ACC. furniture) **additionally** (to that which one already has) X.

προσωνυμίᾱ ᾱς *f.* [ὄνομα] additional name, **nickname, sobriquet, epithet** Plu.

προσωπεῖον ου *n.* [πρόσωπον] **mask** (of an actor) Thphr.

προσωπο-λήμπτης ου *m.* [λαμβάνω] one who takes another's part, **one who shows partiality** or **favouritism** NT.

πρόσ-ωπον ου *n.* [ὤψ] | also irreg.ep.pl. προσώπατα, dat. προσώπασι | **1 face** (of a person) Il. +; (also pl., ref. to a single person) Hom. Hes. hHom. Semon. S. E.; (sg., of a bird, an animal) Hdt. X.; (of a Herm) Th.; (of a personif. song, Truth) Pi.; (of Modesty, Virtue) E.; (of dawn) E.; (pl., of the moon) S.*fr.*
2 (prep.phrs.) ἐς πρόσωπον *face to face* (W.GEN. *w. someone*) E.; κατὰ πρόσωπον *face to face, in person* Plu.; *facing, in front (of oneself)* Th. X. Plb.; (W.GEN. *of sthg.*) X. Plb.; *frontally (ref. to attacking)* Plb.; (also) πρὸς τὸ πρόσωπον X.
3 countenance (of a person, as reflecting one's feelings), **look, expression** Trag. Th. Ar. X. D. Thphr.
4 face, front, façade (of a temple) Pi. E.; (of a poetical composition, envisaged as a grand building) Pi.; **outward appearance** (of tyranny) E.
5 mask (of an actor) D. Arist.; (ref. to the death-mask of an ancestor, equiv. to Lat. *imago*) Plb.
6 character, figure, person (in historical or literary ctxt.) Plb.; **role** (played by a country, in a historical narrative envisaged as a drama) Plb.; (in political or military ctxt.) **leading figure, figure-head** Plb.
7 (phr.) λαμβάνειν πρόσωπον *take the part (of someone),* **show partiality** or **favouritism** NT.
8 (wkr.sens., in prep.phrs.) κατὰ πρόσωπον, ἀπὸ προσώπου *in* or *from the presence* (W.GEN. *of someone*) NT.; πρὸ προσώπου *before* (W.GEN. *someone*) NT.

προσωτέρω, προσώτατα, προσωτάτω *compar. and superl.advs.*: see πρόσω

προσ-ωφελέω *contr.vb.* **give help** E. X. —W.DAT. *to someone* Hdt. E.; (tr.) **help** —*someone* Hdt.

προσωφέλημα ατος *n.* (concr.) **help** (in the form of money) E.

προσωφέλησις εως *f.* provision of help (to someone), **help** S.

πρόταγμα ατος *n.* [προτάσσω] **vanguard** (of an army) Plu.

προταινί *prep.* [reltd. Boeot.adv. προτηνί *before this day, earlier*; cf. ποταίνιος] **in front** —W.GEN. *of the ranks* E.

πρότακτοι ων *m.pl.* [προτάσσω] soldiers stationed in the front ranks, **vanguard** Plu.

προ-ταμιεῖον ου *n.* **anteroom of a storehouse** or **treasury** X.

προ-ταρβέω *contr.vb.* **1 anticipate with fear, fear** —*one's fate* A. —*someone's death* E.*fr.*; (intr.) **fear** (imminent death) E.
2 fear on behalf of, fear for —W.GEN. *someone* S.

προ-ταρῑχεύω *vb.* **salt** or **pickle** (certain birds) **first** (before eating them) Hdt.

πρότασις εως *f.* [προτείνω] **term in a proposition, premise** Arist.

προ-τάσσω, Att. **προτάττω** *vb.* **1** (of a commander) **station** (W.ACC. troops) **in front** (sts. W.GEN. or πρό + GEN. of others) Th. X. Plb. Plu. || MID. **station** (W.ACC. cavalry) **in front** —W.GEN. *of one's battle-line* X. || PF.PASS. (of troops) be in the vanguard Plb. Plu. || NEUT.SG.AOR.PASS.PTCPL.SB. front rank, vanguard X. || MASC.PL.PF.PASS.PTCPL.SB. those in the front rank (of an army) X. Plb. Plu.; (of a procession) Ar.
2 place (someone) in front (of others, to protect or lead them); (of Athenians) **station** (W.ACC. themselves) **in the forefront** —w. πρό + GEN. *in defence of all Greeks* And.
|| MID. or PASS. (of a king, or perh. a god) **station oneself as defender** A. || PASS. (of Athenians) be appointed leaders —w. ὑπέρ + GEN. *on behalf of all Greeks* Isoc.
3 appoint (W.ACC. persons) **as spokesmen** —W.GEN. *on one's behalf* Th.
4 rank (W.ACC. one person or thing) **above** —W.GEN. *another* Aeschin. Plu.
5 || MID. set before oneself; **take** (W.ACC. sthg.) **as an example** Pl.; **propose to adopt** —*a way of life* Pl.
6 appoint or **order in advance** —W.ACC. + INF. *someone to do sthg.* Th.; **fix beforehand, prescribe** —*a time-limit* S.

προ-τείνω *vb.* **1 stretch forward** (a part of one's body); **stretch** or **hold out** —*one's hand (to receive sthg.)* Archil. S. Ar. D. —(*to touch sthg. or someone*) A.(dub.) E. —(*to greet someone*) E. X. D. —(*in making a pledge*) S. —*one's hands (in submission)* Hdt.(sts.mid.) —*one's feet (to have one's shoes removed)* Ar.; **stretch** or **lean** (W.ACC. oneself) **forward** Pl.
2 (fig., of a warrior) expose to danger, **risk** —*one's life* S.
3 stretch out —*someone* (W.DAT. *for the lash, i.e. for flogging*) NT.
4 hold forth (an object); **hold out** —*a corpse's severed hand* (W.DAT. *to someone*) Hdt. —*a shield* E. —*an olive branch* Call.; **thrust forward** —*a spear* X.; **offer** —W.PARTITV.GEN. *some barley meal (to someone)* Ar.; (of hands) —W.ACC. *money* Ar.; (intr., of land) **stretch out** (into the sea) Pl. Plb. || PASS. (of a bridle) be held out or offered (to a horse) X.
5 hold out (an offer or inducement, oft. W.DAT. to someone); **offer, propose, promise** —*an advantage* A. —*ecstatic rites (to young women)* E. —*someone's beauty (to a prospective husband)* E. —W.DBL.ACC. *someone as a husband (to a prospective bride)* E. —*reading-matter* Pl. —*terms or conditions* Hdt.(sts.mid.) —*freedom, independence, an assurance* Att.orats. —*friendship, rightful behaviour, or sim.* D.(mid.) —*hope* Plb.(sts.mid.); **offer** —W.DAT. + INF. *to someone an opportunity to do sthg.* X. || PASS. (of benefits, alternative courses of action) be offered Isoc.
|| NEUT.PL.PASS.PTCPL.SB. terms offered Plb.
6 hold out (as a reason); **offer** —*a pretext, an excuse* Hdt. E.; **put forward** (W.ACC. the gods) **as an excuse** S.; **claim, allege** —W.ACC. + INF. *that sthg. is the case* E.; (gener.) **offer, present** —*an illusion* Pl.
7 hold out (as a threat), **threaten** —*someone's death* E.
8 || MID. put forward, **propose, suggest** —*sthg.* (*in a discussion*) Pl. —*someone (as an instance of sthg.)* Pl. —W.DBL.ACC. *sthg. as a payment* Hdt.; (intr.) **make a proposal, offer a suggestion** Pl.
9 || MID. (of a speech) **present, portray** —*sthg.* Pl.

προ-τείχισμα ατος *n.* (sg. and pl.) **advanced fortification, outwork** Th. Plb.

προ-τέλεια ων *n.pl.* [τέλος] **1** sacrificial rites preceding marriage, **preliminary rites** Men.; (W.GEN. before marriage) Pl.; (W.GEN. for a daughter) E.; (W.GEN. on behalf of a fleet, ref. to the sacrifice of Iphigeneia) A.
2 (fig.) **first rites** (iron.ref. to warfare at Troy, perh. as if it were a celebration of the marriage of Helen and Paris) A.; (gener.) **prelude** (W.GEN. of a lion's life, before it turns to slaughter) A.

προ-τελέω *contr.vb.* **pay** or **spend** (W.ACC. a sum of money) **in advance** Th. X.

προτελίζω *vb.* [προτέλεια] **consecrate** (W.ACC. a girl) **before marriage** —W.DAT. *to Artemis* E.

προ-τεμένισμα ατος *n.* [τεμενίζω] **entrance to a sacred precinct** Th.

προ-τέμνω *vb.* | dial.aor.2 ptcpl. προταμών | **1 cut** (W.ACC. meat) **first** (for someone, before others) Il.
2 trim (W.ACC. a tree trunk) **straight up** —W.PREP.PHR. *fr. the roots* Od.
3 ‖ MID. **cut** (W.ACC. a furrow) **straight ahead** Od.
4 ‖ MID. (of enemy troops) **cut down, ravage** (W.ACC. fields) **in advance** (of the harvest) AR.

προτενής ές *adj.* [προτείνω] (of a spear, held in the hand) **pointing forward** AR.

προ-τένθαι ῶν *m.pl.* [τένθης] app. **pre-tasters** (officials having responsibilities of an unknown nature on the day before the festival of the Apatouria) Ar.

προτενθεύω *vb.* (fig., of corrupt magistrates) **get an advance taste of** —sureties (*deposited early, and fr. which they could make a profit*) Ar.

προτεραία ᾱς, Ion. **προτεραίη** ης *f.* [πρότερος] **1 previous day**; (dat.) τῇ προτεραίᾳ (προτεραίῃ) **on the day before** Hdt. Th. Att.orats. Pl. + —(W.GEN. *sthg.*) Hdt. And. Pl. Plu. —(w. ᾗ or ὅτε + INDIC. *the day or time when sthg. happened*) Lys. D.; (prep.phr., ref. to having a hangover) ἐκ τῆς προτεραίας *from the day before* Pl.
2 ‖ ADJ. (of a night) **previous** Plb.(dub.)

προτεραίτερος ᾱ ον *redupl.compar.adj.* (hyperbol., of a person) **even more first** (at doing sthg.), **firster** Ar.

προτερέω *contr.vb.* **1** (of troops) **be ahead** (of their expected position) Hdt.; (of a commander) **be further ahead** —W.GEN. *on his journey* Hdt.; (fig.) **have the advantage, come out on top** Plb.
2 act in advance of, forestall —W.GEN. *someone* Th.
3 act too quickly (opp. too slowly) Arist.; (of persons or actions) **be too early** (opp. too late) Plb.

προτερη-γενής ές *adj.* [γένος, γίγνομαι] (of persons) **of an earlier generation** Call. AR.

προτέρημα ατος *n.* [προτερέω] **success** (in war) Plb. ‖ PL. (gener.) **advantages** Plb. Plu.

πρότερος ᾱ (Ion. η) ον *compar.adj.* [πρό] **1 further ahead** (in position); (of a dog's paws, of wheels) **front** Od. Hdt.; (of racehorses) **ahead** (of others) B.
2 belonging to past time; (of persons, years, activities) **earlier, of old** Hom. Hes. A. Pi. ‖ MASC.PL.SB. (w.art.) **men of old** Il. Xenoph. Ar.; (without art.) S.*satyr.fr.*
3 belonging to time preceding or opposed to the present; (of a generation, people or gods) **preceding, former** Il. Hes. Ar.; (of a husband or wife, of children by a first husband) **earlier, previous** Hom. Hdt.; (of things, events, circumstances) Od. + ‖ MASC.PL.SB. (w.art.) **predecessors** (in an activity) Isoc.; (without art.) **ancestors** A.; **earlier poets** Pi.
4 (specif., of a day, a night) **previous, preceding** Il. Thgn. Hdt. Ar. +; (phrs.) τῇ προτέρᾳ ἡμέρᾳ *on the day before* (W.GEN. *sthg.*) Th. Arist.; τῷ προτέρῳ ἔτει *in the year before* (W.GEN. *sthg.*) Plb.; (w. ἤ + INDIC. *sthg. happened*) Hdt.; (w. ἡμέρῃ understd.) τῇ προτέρῃ *on the day before* Od.
5 (of persons) **earlier in birth, older** Hom. Hdt.; (W.GEN. than someone) Mimn.
6 (quasi-advbl., usu. of persons doing or suffering sthg., sts. of things happening) **before another or others, first** Hom. Hes. A. Hdt. Th. Ar. +; **before** (W.GEN. someone or sthg. else) Il. Alc. Hdt. Ar. +; (also) πρότερος ἤ Pl.
7 having priority (in rank, importance or choice); (of persons) **superior** (W.GEN. to others, w. πρός + ACC. in military expertise) Pl.; (W.GEN. to the law, i.e. above it) E.; **closer** or **with better claim** (sts. W.GEN. than someone else, in ctxts. of family relationship and inheritance) Is.; (of action) **superior** (to speech, W.DAT. in effectiveness) D.; (predic., of a route that is chosen) **for preference** Thgn.

—**πρότερον** *neut.adv.* **1 at an earlier time, previously, formerly, before** Eleg. Pi. Hdt. Trag. Th. +; (also) τὸ πρότερον Hdt. Pl. X.; (pl.) τὰ πρότερα *in earlier times* Th.; (sg., quasi-adjl., of persons or things) **earlier, previous, former** Hdt.
2 earlier (than sthg. else), **first** S.; **before** —W.GEN. *someone or sthg.* A.(dub.) Hdt. D. —w. πρό + GEN. Pl.; τὸ πρότερον —W.GEN. *someone or sthg.* Hdt.
3 (in the first of two co-ordinated cls., as antecedent to conj. πρίν or πρὶν ἤ *before*) **first** Hdt. S.; (w.neg., as antecedent to ἕως *until*) Lys.
4 (conj., co-ordinating two cls.) πρότερον ἤ *earlier than, before* —W.INDIC. or SUBJ. *sthg. happens* Hdt. Antipho Th. —W.INF. or ACC. + INF. *doing sthg., someone does sthg., sthg. happens* Hdt. Th.; (co-ordinating two phrs. or non-finite cls.) Hdt. Pl.; (also) τὸ πρότερον ἤ Hdt.

—**προτέρως** *adv.* (log.) **in a prior** (opp. posterior) **sense** Arist.

προτέρω *adv.* **1** (ref. to direction) **forwards, onwards, ahead** Hom. hHom. AR.; **further ahead** Hom. AR.; **further back** AR.
2 (ref. to duration of time) **further, longer** Hom. AR.
3 (ref. to past time) **earlier, once** Call.

—**προτέρωσε** *adv.* **1** (ref. to movt.) **forwards, onwards, ahead** hHom. AR. Theoc. —W.GEN. *on a path* AR.
2 (as prep., ref. to location) **beyond** —W.GEN. *a place* AR.

προ-τεύχομαι *pass.vb.* | pf.inf. προτετύχθαι | ‖ PF. (of circumstances) **exist in the past** (and so be now of less concern) Il.

προτί *dial.prep.*: see πρός

προτιάπτω, προτιβάλλω *ep.vbs.*: see προσάπτω, προσβάλλω

προτι-ειλέω *ep.contr.vb.* [εἰλέω¹] **press** or **force** —*an adversary* (W.PREP.PHR. *towards a place*) Il.

προτιείποι (ep.3sg.aor.2 opt.): see προσεῖπον

προ-τίθημι *vb.* | impf. προυτίθην, ep.3pl. πρότιθεν | aor. προὔθηκα | dial.athem.aor.mid. προθέμᾱν (E.) | ‖ The sections are grouped as: (1–4) set forth (persons or material things), (5–13) set forth (non-material things), (14–18) place ahead or in front. |
1 set (someone) **forth**; **put out** —*a corpse* (W.DAT. *for animals*) Il. S. E. —*an invalid* (*on a desert island*) S.; **expose** —*a baby* Hdt. ‖ PASS. (of a baby) **be exposed** —W.DAT. *for death* E.
2 ‖ MID. **lay out** —*a corpse* Hdt.(act.) E. Ar. Att.orats. —*bones* (*after cremation*) Th.
3 set forth —*tables* Od. —*an ox* (*to eat*) Hes.; **serve** —*a meal, food* (sts. W.DAT. *to someone*) Archil. Hdt. S. E.; (wkr.sens.) **present** —*a person's ashes* (W.DAT. *to someone*) S. ‖ MID. **have set before oneself** (or others), **serve** or **have served** —*food* Hdt. Ar.; **set out, make a display of** —*one's precious cups* Hdt. —*captured weapons* Th.
4 ‖ PASS. (of persons subject to judicial proceedings) **be publicly listed** Arist.
5 set forth (a non-material quality); **display, exhibit** —*integrity* Th. —*hostility* (W.DAT. *to someone*) Th.
6 offer —*a crown* (W.DAT. *to someone, as a reward*) Th. —*hope* Th. —*a choice* Pl. —*prizes* X. ‖ MID. **propose** —*a choice* Pl. ‖ PASS. (of a person) **be put forward** or **offered** —W.PREDIC.SB. *as a prize* E.
7 introduce, set up —*a competition* X. —*a debating contest* E. Th. ‖ PASS. (of a contest) **be introduced** Pl.
8 prescribe, set —*punishments, penalties* Th. D. —*a law* (W.DAT. *for oneself*) E. —*a task, mourning, a trial* (*for*

προτιμάω

someone) Hdt. S. Lys. —*a target* (*to be achieved during one's life*) Plb.
9 set —*the limit of human life* (W.PREP.PHR. *at seventy years*) Hdt. —W.DBL.ACC. *a year as a limit* Hdt.(mid.)
10 ‖ MID. set for oneself as a duty, **take upon oneself** —*the care of sthg.* S.; **set oneself, propose** —W.INF. *to do sthg.* Isoc. Pl.
11 bring forward (for discussion); **put** —*an issue* (W.DAT. *to people*) Hdt.; (esp. of presiding officials) **propose, give the opportunity for** —*a debate, a decision, expressions of opinion, or sim.* (sts. W.DAT. *to persons in the Assembly*) Th. Ar. X. Aeschin. D. —W.INF. *debating a topic, considering an issue* Th. Lys. D.; (of the Council) **put** (to the Assembly) —*matters for debate* Isoc.; (intr., of a city) **make a proposal** (to another city) —W.PREP.PHR. *about sthg.* D.(cj.) ‖ PASS. (of the opportunity to speak) be offered —W.DAT. *to someone* (*in the Assembly*) X. ‖ IMPERS.PASS. it is proposed —W.INF. *to hold a debate* (*about sthg.*) D.
12 (gener.) **propose** —W.INF. *that people shd. speak on a topic* Hdt. —W.ACC. or DAT. + INF. *that someone shd.* (or *to someone that they shd.*) *do sthg.* Hdt. ‖ MID. **propose** —*a conference* S. —*a time for sthg.* Th. D. —*a topic for discussion* Isoc.; **specify** —*a total, items required* E.
13 put forward —*an explanation, a reason, arguments* Hdt. S. E. ‖ MID. put forward as a reason, **plead** —*kinship* Plb. ‖ PASS. (of a charge) be preferred (against someone) Th.
14 (of an old woman) move forward, **advance** —*her steps* E.
15 place (sthg.) in front (of someone or sthg.); (act. and mid.) **place** (W.ACC. *one's cloak*) **in front** —W.GEN. *of one's eyes* E.; (act.) **place** (W.ACC. *a mirror*) **before** —W.DAT. *someone* E. ‖ MID. **place** (W.ACC. *troops*) **in the vanguard** Plb.
16 (of a speaker or writer) **put** (W.ACC. *sthg.*) **first** (opp. last) Arist. ‖ MID. **place** (W.ACC. *a preamble*) **in front** —W.GEN. *of a discourse* Pl.; **place first** —*reasons, an account of sthg.* Plb. ‖ PASS. (of a word) be placed in front —W.GEN. *of another word* Pl.; (of topics) be put first (in a speech) Arist.
17 place ahead (in preference), **prefer** —*sthg.* (W.GEN. *to sthg. else*) Hdt. S.(mid.) E. Th. —(w. ἀντί + GEN.) E. ‖ PASS. (of a person's courage) be given precedence (over his faults) Th.
18 ‖ MID. perh., place preferentially, **rank, count** —*mortals* (w. ἐν + DAT. *as deserving pity*) A. | cf. τίθημι 18

προ-τῑμάω *contr.vb.* | fut.mid. (w.pass.sens.) προτιμήσομαι (X.) | **1 honour** or **value more highly** —*someone* (W.GEN. *than someone else*) X. —(*than a certain sum of money*) X.(mid.) —*a son* (w. ἀντί + GEN. *than all other possessions*) Pl. —*a country* (w. πρό + GEN. *ahead of another*) X. ‖ PASS. (of persons) be honoured more highly —W.GEN. *than others* X.; be preferred (over others) —W.PREP.PHR. *for public office* Th.
2 honour (W.ACC. *someone*) **above all others** or **pre-eminently** E. Isoc. X. ‖ PASS. (of persons or things) be specially honoured Th. Lys. Isoc. X.; (iron.) be rewarded —W.INF. *w. dying* Th.
3 give precedence to, prefer —*safety, justice, or sim.* (W.GEN. *rather than the contrary*) Antipho Pl. Plu. —*brevity of speech* (w. μᾶλλον ἤ + ACC. *rather than length*) Pl. —*beauty* (w. πρό + GEN. *before virtue*) Pl.; (w. comparison not expressed but implied) —*truth, injustice, monarchy, the enjoyment of wealth, or sim.* (*rather than the contrary*) Th. Isoc. Pl. +; **regard as more important** —*someone's death* (*than another's, than her death*) A. E.

4 consider it more valuable or **important** —W.INF. + PREDIC.ADJ. *to be such and such* (w. ἤ + PREDIC.ADJ. *than to be sthg. else*) Hdt. —W.INF. + PREDIC.SB. or W.ACC. + INF. *to become such and such, or for someone to do sthg.* (W.GEN. *than a large sum of money, i.e. set greater store by that activity*) Hdt.; (w. no comparison expressed) **give priority** —W.INF. *to doing sthg.* Pl.
5 (freq. in neg.phrs.) **be concerned over, care about** —W.GEN. *someone or sthg.* A. E. Th. Ar. Pl. D. —W.ACC. + PASS.PTCPL. *someone being beaten* Ar. —W.INF. *doing or being sthg.* S. E. —w. ὅπως + FUT. *ensuring that sthg. happens* Ar.; **be concerned** (about sthg.) Ar.

προτίμησις εως *f.* **preference** (W.GEN. *for a particular kind of government*) Th.

πρότῑμος ον *adj.* (of an ability) **especially honoured** Xenoph. ‖ NEUT.SB. high honour or rank E.

προτι-μῡθέομαι *ep.mid.contr.vb.* **speak to, address** —*someone* Od.; **speak** —*a word* (sts. W.DAT. *to someone*) AR. Theoc.; (intr.) **speak** (to someone) AR.

προ-τῑμωρέω *contr.vb.* **1 lend help** or **support** (W.DAT. *to someone*) **earlier** (than the present time) Th.
2 ‖ MID. **take revenge** (W.ACC. *on someone*) **first** (before sthg. else happens) Th.

προτι-όσσομαι *ep.mid.vb.* **1** turn one's eyes towards, **look at** —*someone* Od.
2 (of a person, a heart) **foresee, anticipate** (sthg.) Il. AR. —W.ACC. *death, disaster* Od.; **expect** —W.ACC. + FUT.INF. *that sthg. will happen* AR.; **infer** —W.ACC. + PRES.INF. *that sthg. is the case* AR.

προ-τίω *vb.* **1 honour** (W.ACC. *semblance*) **more highly** (than reality) A.; **honour pre-eminently** —*the sanctity of parents* A.
2 deem (W.ACC. *someone*) **more deserving** —W.GEN. *of burial* (*than another person*) S.

πρότμησις εως *f.* [προτέμνω] cutting in front; (concr., ref. to the place where the umbilical cord is cut) **navel** Il.

προ-τολμάομαι *pass.contr.vb.* (of certain kinds of criminal activity) **be committed for the first time** Th.

πρότομα ων *n.pl.* [προτέμνω] **sacrifices performed in advance** (W.GEN. *of battle*) E.*fr.*

προτομή ῆς *f.* **1** front part which has been cut off, **scalp, skull** (of a wild animal) Plu.
2 cup, goblet (app. fr. its resemblance to a skull) Philox.Leuc.

πρότονος ου *m.* [προτείνω] **forestay** (rope extending fr. the masthead to the forepart of a ship, by which, along w. the ἐπίτονος backstay, the mast was held in position; the Homeric ship had two) A. E.*fr.*; (pl.) Hom. hHom. E. AR.; (pl., fig.ref. to the arms of a nautilus) Call.*epigr.*

προτρεπτικός ή όν *adj.* [προτρέπω] **1** (of a speech or argument) of the encouraging kind, **hortatory** Isoc.; (of skill) in making hortatory speeches or arguments, **in exhortation** Pl.
2 (of a proclamation) **inciting** (a populace, W.PREP.PHR. *to valour*) Aeschin.

προ-τρέπω *vb.* | aor.1 προύτρεψα | aor.2 ptcpl. προτραπών (Pi., cj.) ‖ mid.aor.2 προυτραπόμην, inf. προτραπέσθαι |
1 cause (someone) to turn (in a given direction) ‖ MID. or PASS. (of troops) **turn in flight** —W.PREP.PHR. *towards a place* Il. ‖ MID. (of the sun) **turn** —W.PREP.PHRS. *fr. heaven towards earth* Od.
2 ‖ MID. turn oneself, **give oneself up, yield** —W.DAT. *to grief* Il. ‖ ACT. perh., cause (someone) to yield (to sthg.); **subject** —*someone* (W.DAT. *to a constraint*) S. —*a land* (W.DAT. *to enemy force*) Pi.(cj.) | see προστρέπω 4

3 (act. and mid.) **urge on, incite, encourage** —*someone* Hdt. S. Isoc. Arist. —(W.PREP.PHR. *to sthg.*) Att.orats. Pl. X. + —W.ACC. + INF. *someone to do sthg.* A. Hdt. S. Th. Att.orats. Pl. + —W.ACC. + ὥστε W.INF. Th. ‖ MID. **prevail on oneself** —W.PREP.PHR. *to engage in debate* Pl. ‖ PASS. **be urged on or encouraged** X. —W.PREP.PHR. *to sthg.* D.

προ-τρέχω vb. | impf. προὔτρεχον | The aor. is supplied by προδραμεῖν. | **1** (of a person) **run forward** or **ahead** X. **2** (fig., of a person's tongue) **run ahead** —W.GEN. *of his thoughts* Isoc.

πρό-τριτα adv. [τρίτος] on the third day beforehand, **two days before** Th.

προτροπάδην, dial. **προτροπάδᾱν** adv. [προτρέπω] **headlong** —*ref. to fleeing, hurrying, or sim.* Il. Pi. Pl. Plb. Plu.

προτροπή ῆς *f.* **incitement, encouragement, exhortation** Pl. Arist. Plb. Plu.

προ-τυγχάνω vb. | aor.2 ptcpl. προτυχών | **happen to be encountered first** ‖ AOR.2 PTCPL.ADJ. (of a gift) **makeshift** Pi.

προ-τύπτω vb. | aor. προὔτυψα ‖ aor.2 pass.ptcpl. προτυπείς | **1** (of troops) **press forwards, rush onwards** Il.; (of a ship) AR. **2** (of a strong emotion) **burst forth** Od. **3** ‖ PASS. (of a city's bridle-bit or curb, fig.ref. to an attacking army) **be stricken (by divine resentment) beforehand** (i.e. before it can subdue the city) A.

προὔβαλον (aor.2), **προὔβην** (athem.aor.): see προβάλλω, προβαίνω

προυδίδαξα (aor.), **προὐδώκα** (aor.): see προδιδάσκω, προδίδωμι

προὔθανον (aor.2), **προὔθηκα** (aor.), **προυθῡμούμην** (impf.mid.), **προυθῡμήθην** (aor.pass.): see προθνῄσκω, προτίθημι, προθῡμέομαι

προὔκαμον (aor.2), **προὐκείμην** (impf.mid.pass.), **προὔκρῑνα** (aor.), **προὔκυψα** (aor.): see προκάμνω, πρόκειμαι, προκρίνω, προκύπτω

προὔλαβον (aor.2), **προὔλεγον** (impf.): see προλαμβάνω, προλέγω

προυμόσᾱς (aor.ptcpl.): see προόμνῡμι

προυννέπω vb. [πρό, ἐννέπω] **1 say in advance, foretell, predict** —*sthg.* A. **2 forewarn, proclaim** (that sthg. will be done) E. **3 say publicly, proclaim** —W.COMPL.CL. *that sthg. is the case* A. **4 order publicly, proclaim** —W.ACC. + PASS.INF. *that someone is to be exiled* E. **5 bid** —W.ACC. + INF. χαίρειν *a messenger 'good day'* S.

προυνοησάμην (aor.mid.), **προυνοήθην** (aor.pass.): see προνοέω

προυξένουν (impf.), **προυξένησα** (aor.): see προξενέω

προυξεπίσταμαι mid.vb. [πρό, ἐξεπίσταμαι] **know of** (W.ACC. sthg.) **in advance** A.

προυξερευνάω contr.vb. [πρό, ἐξερευνάω] **investigate** (W.ACC. a path) **in advance** (to see if it is unoccupied) E.

προυξερευνητής οῦ m. **advance scout** (W.GEN. of a route) E.

προυξεφίεμαι mid.vb. [πρό, ἐξεφίημι] | 2sg.impf. προυξεφίεσο | **command beforehand** (that sthg. shd. be done) S.

προϋπαρχή ῆς *f.* [προϋπάρχω] **previous service** (offered to someone) Arist.

προ-ϋπάρχω vb. **1 take the first step** (in an enterprise); **take the initiative** —W.GEN. *in sthg.* Th. Isoc. —W.DAT. D. —W.NEUT.ACC. Isoc. ‖ NEUT.PL.PF.PASS.PTCPL.SB. **previous services** (sts. W.PREP.PHR. *to someone*) D. Arist.

2 (of persons or things) **already exist** or **be already available** Pl. Aeschin. Arist. + ‖ PRES.PTCPL.ADJ. (of things) **existing** Th. D. Arist. +; (of officials) Arist. Plb. ‖ NEUT.PL.AOR.PTCPL.SB. **earlier events** D.

προὔπεμψα (aor.), **προὔπεσον** (aor.2), **προυπηλάκισα** (aor.): see προπέμπω, προπίπτω, προπηλακίζω

προὔπῑνον (impf.), **προὔπιον** (aor.2): see προπίνω

προ-υπισχνέομαι mid.contr.vb. **promise earlier** —W.INF. *to do sthg.* Plb.

προ-υπογράφομαι mid.vb. **sketch out** —*a plan for a city* Plu.

προ-υπολαμβάνω vb. **assume** or **suppose** (W.ACC. sthg.) **beforehand** Arist.

προ-υποτίθεμαι mid.vb. **posit** (W.ACC. many things) **in advance** Arist.

προὔπτος Att.adj.: see πρόοπτος

προὔργου adv. [πρὸ ἔργου] **1 tending to promote some enterprise; conveniently** or **purposely** (W.PREP.PHR. *for battle*) —*ref. to equipping oneself* E.; **opportunely** (for someone else) —*ref. to falling* E. **2** (quasi-adjl., as predic. to statements such as *one has sthg.* or *sthg. is*) **useful, worthwhile** Isoc. Pl. Arist. **3** (neut.sb.) τὰ προὔργου **useful, important** or **worthwhile things** Th. Ar. Men. Plb.; τι (or οὐδὲν) προὔργου *sthg.* (*nothing*) **useful** or **worthwhile** Isoc. Pl. X. Is. Arist. Plu. **4** ‖ IMPERS. (w. ἐστί) **it is worthwhile** —W. CONDITIONAL CL. *if one does sthg.* Pl.; (+ οὐδέν) **it is not helpful** or **worthwhile** —W.INF. or DAT. + INF. (*for someone*) *to do sthg.* And. D.

—προυργιαίτερος ᾱ ον compar.adj. (of activities or considerations) **more important** Th. Ar. Att.orats. Pl. Men. Plb.

προυρρήθην (aor.pass.): see προείρω

προυσελέω contr.vb. **treat contemptuously** or **outrageously** —*certain types of people* Ar. ‖ PASS. (of Prometheus) **be maltreated** A.

Προυσέληνος Ion.m.: see under προσεληναῖος

προὔσκεπτο (3sg.plpf.pass.), **προυσκεψάμην** (aor.mid.): see προσκέπτομαι

προυσκόπουν (impf.): see προσκοπέω

προὔστην (athem.aor.), **προυστησάμην** (aor.1 mid.): see προΐσταμαι

προὔσχον (aor.2): see προέχω

προυτεθεσπίκει (3sg.plpf.), **προυτίθην** (impf.), **προὔτρεχον** (impf.): see προθεσπίζω, προτίθημι, προτρέχω

προὔτρεψα (aor.), **προυτραπόμην** (aor.2 mid.): see προτρέπω

προὔτυψα (aor.): see προτύπτω

προὔφαινον (impf.), **προυφάνην** (aor.2 pass.), **προὔφηνα** (aor.): see προφαίνω

προ-υφαιρέω contr.vb. (of a politician) **get** (W.ACC. Assemblies) **out of the way in advance** (by holding them before some other event) Aeschin.

προυφασιζόμην (impf.mid.), **προυφασισάμην** (aor.mid.): see προφασίζομαι

προυφείλω vb., **προὔφερον** (impf.), **προὔφθην** (athem.aor.), **προὔφῦν** (athem.aor.), **προὔχω** vb.: see προοφείλω, προφέρω, προφθάνω, προφύομαι, προέχω

προυχειροτόνησα (aor.): see προχειροτονέω

προὔχρῑον (impf.): see προχρίω

προυχώρησα (aor.), **προυχώρουν** (impf.): see προχωρέω

προὔχω contr.vb.: see προέχω

προ-φαίνω vb. | impf. προὔφαινον, Ion. προέφαινον, dial. πρόφαινον | aor. προὔφηνα ‖ PASS.: aor.2 προυφάνην, dial. προφάνην | **1 make visible;** (of gods) **show forth, display**

προφανής

—*portents* (W.DAT. *to someone*) Od.; (of an upturned charioteer) —*his legs* (*to the sky*) S.; (fig., of a hero) **bring into the limelight, bring lustre to** —*one's ancestors and their homeland* Pi.
2 (intr., of the moon) **give forth light, shine** Od.; (of a person, a torch) **light the way** (for someone) Plu.
|| MASC.PTCPL.SB. torch-bearer Plu. || IMPERS.PASS. there is enough light —W.INF. *to see* Od.
3 || PASS. (of gods, persons, things) **come into view, be visible or appear** Hom. Alc. B. S. E. X. +; (of a person) **be revealed or exposed** —W.NOM.PTCPL. *as doing sthg.* S.; (of terrain) **be open to view** Il.; (of a person) **be seen to be, be sprung** —W.PREP.PHR. *fr. someone's blood* S.; (of a sound) **ring forth** S.
4 **reveal in advance**; (of a god) **give forewarning** (W.DAT. to someone) —W.ACC. *of sufferings* S.(cj.) —W.ACC. + INF. *that someone will do sthg.* Hdt. —W.COMPL.CL. *that sthg. will happen* Hdt.; **promise** —*benefits* X.; (of approaching Fate) **threaten** —*disaster* S.; (of a vision) **foreshadow, portend** —*sthg.* Hdt.
5 **make public**; (of a person) **reveal** —*one's state of mind* S.(dub.) —W.INDIR.Q. *what is the case* (W.DAT. *to someone*) Pi.*fr.* S.*Ichn.*; **give notice of** —*rewards, prizes* S.*Ichn.* X.; **offer** —*a song* Ar.; **declare, say** —*sthg.* S.; **indicate** —w. ὅπως + FUT. *that one will do sthg.* Hdt. || PASS. (of gods) **be indicated or specified** —W.PREP.PHR. *in an oracle* D.; (of an argument) **be formulated** Pl.; (of thoughts or considerations) **occur** —W.DAT. *to someone* Pl.

προφανής ἐς *adj.* **1** (of death) **visible in advance, foreseen** B. || NEUT.PL.SB. foreseen circumstances Arist.
2 (of a light) **clearly visible, conspicuous** X.; (of warfare) **open** (i.e. undisguised) D.; (prep.phrs.) ἀπὸ τοῦ προφανοῦς *visibly, openly* (opp. *secretly*) Th.; (also) ἐκ (τοῦ) προφανοῦς Th. D. Plb. Plu.
3 (of facts or circumstances) **plain to see, clear, evident** Pl. Plb. Plu.

—**προφανῶς** *adv.* **clearly, obviously, certainly** Plb. Plu.

—**πρόφαντος** ον *adj.* **1** (of a person) **conspicuous, famed** (W.DAT. *for wisdom*) Pi.
2 (of divine will) **revealed in advance, foretold** S.
|| NEUT.IMPERS. (w. ἦν) it was foretold or predicted (by a god) —W.DAT. + INF. *to someone that he would do sthg.* S.
|| NEUT.SB. oracular response Hdt.

προφασίζομαι *mid.vb.* [πρόφασις] | impf. προυφασιζόμην | fut. προφασιοῦμαι | aor. προυφασισάμην | **1 make excuses** Th. Ar. Isoc. —W.COGN.ACC. *excuses* Lys. Pl. Aeschin.; **allege, plead, use** (W.ACC. someone or sthg.) **as an excuse** Thgn. Th. Lys. Pl. X. +; **claim** (by way of excuse) —W.INF. *that one is unwell* D. —W.COMPL.CL. *that sthg. is the case* X. D.
2 **give a false explanation, allege, pretend** —W.ACC. + INF. *that sthg. is the case, that someone did sthg.* Pl. Is.; **devise** (W.COGN.ACC. a lie) **as a pretext** Is. || PASS. (of a story) **be devised as a pretext** Th.

πρόφασις εως (Ion. ιος) *f.* [προφαίνω] **1** explanation (true or false) offered in self-justification, **plea, ground, excuse** Thgn. Pi. Hdt. Th. Ar. Att.orats. +; (personif., as daughter of Epimetheus *Afterthought*) **Excuse** Pi.
2 (pejor.) explanation designed to conceal one's true purpose or intention, **pretext** Hdt. S. E. Th. +
3 **cause, reason** or **justification** (for doing sthg.) Hdt. Th. +; **circumstantial cause, occasion** (of an event) Pl. X. D.
4 || ADVBL.ACC. **as a reason or occasion** (for lamenting one's own sorrows) —*ref. to lamenting someone else* Il.; **for the sake or purpose** (W.GEN. of her bed) —*ref. to desiring a woman* Il.; **as a pretext** (W.INF. to do sthg.) Hes.*fr.*; **on the pretext or pretence** (of doing or being sthg.) Hdt. E. Th. Ar.; **in explanation or justification** (for doing sthg.) Ar.

προφᾱτεύω *dial.vb.*, **προφᾱ́τᾱς** *dial.m.*: see προφητεύω, προφήτης

πρό-φατος ον *adj.* [φατός] (of a person) **famed, renowned** Pi.

προφερής ἐς *adj.* [προφέρω] **1** brought into a more advanced position or state; (of one of the Fates) **superior** (W.GEN. to the others) Hes.
2 (of a person) **advanced, mature** (in appearance or growth) Pl. Aeschin.

—**προφερέστερος** ᾱ ον *compar.adj.* (of a person) **superior** (W.GEN. to someone, sts. also W.DAT. in a quality) Od.; (of mules, W.GEN. + INF. to oxen, at doing sthg.) Il.; (of a consideration) **more important** (W.GEN. than someone's life) AR.

—**προφερέστατος** (also **προφέρτατος** S.) η ον *superl.adj.* (of persons, deities, things) **most outstanding, foremost, best** (W.GEN. of all or sim., sts. W.DAT. in sthg.) Od. Hes. Ibyc. Lyr.adesp. AR. Theoc.; (of a son or successor) **foremost** or **eldest** S.

προ-φέρω *vb.* | impf. προύφερον, iteratv. προφέρεσκον | aor.2 προήνεγκον || The sections are grouped as: (1–3) carry or bring forward (persons or material things), (4–10) bring forward or make public (non-material things, esp. in speech), (11–15) bring (or be) ahead or in front. |
1 (of seers) **bring forward** —*sacrificial victims* Th.; (of a person) **bring forth** —*sthg.* (*fr. a storeroom*) Isoc.
2 (of a storm-wind) **carry off** —*someone* Hom.; (of love resulting in suicide, of death) —*a person, a corpse* (*to Hades*) Thgn. E.
3 **bring, present** —*a corpse* (W.DAT. *to someone*) Il.; (of a bird) —*a morsel* (*to its chicks*) Il.
4 **bring forward** (so as to make public); **display** —*one's head* (W.ADV. *without shaking, i.e. not have a head that shakes fr. old age*) Thgn.; **publish, issue** —*poetical compositions or sim.* Pl.; (of a god) perh. **flaunt** —*an honour* (*ref. to a musical tribute by worshippers*) Ar.
5 **exhibit or exercise** (qualities or behaviour); **display, bring to bear** —*one's strength* Il.; **engage in** —*rivalry* Od. —(W.DAT. w. *someone*) Od.(mid.); (of birds) **launch** —*an attack* Il.(mid.); (of a person) **threaten** —*war* Hdt.
6 **bring forward** (in speech); **utter** —*a word* (*of address*) E. —*reproaches* (sts. W.DAT. *against someone*) Il. AR.; **mention, speak** —*a name* (w. ὡς + SB. *as an insult*) D.; (of mouths) **proclaim** —W.DBL.ACC. *a country as someone's homeland* Pi.; (gener.) **describe** —*the length of a voyage* AR. || PASS. (of words) **be directed or applied** —W.PREP.PHR. *to a particular theme* Th. || IMPERS.PASS. it is claimed —W.COMPL.CL. *that sthg. will be the case* Th.
7 **bring forward by way of reproach, bring up** —*gifts received fr. Aphrodite, poverty, an activity or circumstance* (W.DAT. *against someone, i.e. cast such things in one's teeth*) Il. Thgn. Hdt. Att.orats.; **say reproachfully** —W.DIR.SP. *sthg.* Hdt.
8 **bring forward for consideration, put forward** —*a claim* (W.DAT. *against someone*) Th. —*a proposal* Hdt. —*concepts, topics* (*in a discourse*) Pl.(also mid.)
9 (act. and mid.) **bring forward in evidence, support or illustration**; (of a seer) **name** (as one's authority) —*a goddess* A.; (of persons) **cite, adduce, appeal to** —*oaths, an agreement, or sim.* Th. —*laws* X.(dub.) —*examples of behaviour or sim.* Arist. Plb. Plu.

10 (of an oracle) **propose, prescribe, indicate** —*a course of action* (W.DAT. *to someone*) Hdt. —W.DAT. + INF. *to persons that they shd. do sthg.* Hdt. ‖ NEUT.GEN.AOR.PASS.PTCPL. *when it was prescribed* (by an oracle) A.
11 bring to a more advanced position or state; (of a person) **move forward, advance** —*one's foot* (i.e. *walk ahead*) E.; (of dawn, as indicating an early beginning) **help** (someone) **progress, give** (someone) **a head start** —W.GEN. *on one's journey, in one's work* Hes.
12 (intr.) **get ahead, have a head start, be well on the way** —w. ἐς + SB. *towards acquiring sthg.* Th.
13 stand out, excel Pi. —W.DAT. *in some quality* Th.
14 surpass, be superior to —W.GEN. *someone or sthg.* (sts. W.DAT. or PREP.PHR. *in some quality*) B. Hdt. E. Th. Theoc.
15 be ahead in age, be older Theoc.

προ-φεύγω vb. **flee, escape** Il.; (tr.) **escape from** —*someone or sthg.* Hom. Thgn. AR. Theoc.; **elude, avoid** —*death, destiny, distress, or sim.* Od. Thgn. Lyr. AR. —*debts and hunger* Hes. —*wrongdoing* (i.e. *committing it*) Thgn.

προφητεύω, dial. **προφᾱτεύω** vb. [προφήτης] **1** (of a priest or official) **be spokesman** or **interpreter** —W.GEN. *of a god, an oracular shrine* Hdt. E.; (of a poet) —*of a Muse* (envisaged as delivering an oracle) Pi.*fr.*; (fig., of madness) **act as interpreter** (of divine will) Pl.; (tr., of priestesses) **interpret** —*the will of an oracular god* E.*fr.*
2 (of an official at Delphi) **be spokesman** —W.DAT. + ACC. *for someone, on some matter* (by putting one's question to the oracle) E.
3 proclaim through divine revelation, prophesy (about sthg.) NT.; **foretell** (future events) NT.
4 (derog.) **speak as if having prophetic powers, prophesy** NT. —W.INDIR.Q. *who has done sthg.* NT.

προ-φήτης ου (Ion. εω), dial. **προφᾱ́τᾱς** ᾱ *m.* [φημί] **1 one who speaks on behalf of a god** (in order to communicate his will to mortals); **interpreter, spokesman** (W.GEN. of Zeus, ref. to Apollo at Delphi, to the seer Teiresias) A. Pi.; (of Bacchus, ref. to a subterranean man-god, i.e. Rhesos) E.; (of Nereus, ref. to the sea god Glaukos) E.; (of Dionysus, ref. to the leader of his worshippers) E.; (of oracles, ref. to a seer; of an oracular shrine, ref. to a local demigod) Pi.*fr.* Corinn.; (ref. to the priest of an oracular god) Hdt.
2 one who interprets or predicts divine will; seer, prophet (sts. W.GEN. of the gods) A. Pl.; (W.GEN. of future events) Pl.
3 one who proclaims the will of God, prophet (ref. to Old Testament figures such as Moses or Isaiah; also to John the Baptist, Jesus, and others) NT.
4 one who interprets the words of a seer, interpreter Pl.; (W.GEN. of a seer's words) Ar.
5 spokesman (W.GEN. of the Muses, ref. to a poet) Pi.*fr.* B. Pl.; (pl., ref. to cicadas) Pl.; (W.GEN. of judges in athletic contests, ref. to a herald who proclaims the victor) B.
6 (gener., ref. to a person) **interpreter** (of events, for a blind man) E.; **spokesman** (for others) Pl.
7 (fig.) perh. **prompter** (W.GEN. of a revel, ref. to a wine-bowl, as helping the revellers to give voice) Pi.; **signifier** (W.GEN. of goodwill, ref. to applause) Men.

προφῆτις ιδος *f.* | acc. προφῆτιν | **1 interpreter** or **spokeswoman, priestess** (sts. W.GEN. of Apollo, ref. to the Pythia) E. Pl.; (of Apollo at Argos) Plu.
2 prophetess NT.

προ-φθάνω vb. | aor.ptcpl. προφθάσᾱς, subj. προφθάσω | athem.aor. προύφθην, inf. προφθῆναι, ptcpl. προφθάς ‖ athem.aor.mid. προφθάμενος |
1 (of a person's heart) **get ahead of, outpace** —*one's tongue* (i.e. *allow speech to be controlled by emotion*) A.
2 act in advance (of others), **act first** Th. AR.(mid.); **forestall** (an opponent) Th. Theoc. —W.NOM.PTCPL. *by doing sthg.* Th.; (of a warrior) **strike first** —W.DAT. *w. his spear* E.
3 (tr.) **anticipate** —*someone* (in doing or saying sthg.) Ar. Pl. NT.

προ-φοβέομαι pass.contr.vb. **fear in advance, be apprehensive of** —*punishments, sufferings, wars* A.

προφοβητικός ή όν *adj.* (of older people) **inclined to fear in advance** (W.ACC. *everything*) Arist.

προφορά ᾶς *f.* [προφέρω] **1 utterance, pronunciation, delivery** (of the words in an oration) Plu.
2 reproach, rebuke Plb.
3 perh. **proposition, claim** (in a rhetorical exercise) Plb.

προ-φορέομαι mid.pass.contr.vb. **be constantly carried forward;** (of persons) **travel back and forth** Ar.; (of hounds) **run to and fro** X.

προ-φράζω vb. | ep.pf.pass.ptcpl. προπεφραδμένος | (of priests) **foretell, give warning of** —*sthg.* (W.DAT. *to someone*) Hdt. ‖ PF.PASS.PTCPL.ADJ. (of prizes) **announced beforehand** Hes. ‖ IMPERS.PLPF.PASS. *an instruction had been given in advance* —W.DAT. *to someone* AR.

πρό-φρων ονος *masc.fem.adj.* —also **πρόφρασσα** ep.fem.nom.adj. [φρήν] (of gods, humans, their hearts, freq. in ctxts. of giving help or granting favours) **eager, earnest, willing, ready** Hom. Hes. Thgn. Pi. Trag. Ar. + • (freq. in quasi-advbl. sense) πρόφρων Δαναοῖσιν ἄμυνεν *he readily supported the Danaans* Il.

—**προφρόνως**, ep. **προφρονέως** adv. **earnestly, readily, willingly, gladly** Il. Hes. hHom. Semon. Thgn. A. +

προ-φύλακες ων *m.pl.* **advance guard, outpost** Th. X. Plu.

προφυλακή ῆς *f.* [προφυλάσσω] **1** (freq.pl.) **advance guard, outpost** Th. X. Plb. Plu.
2 means or function of protecting, protection (W.GEN. of cities) Plb.; (W.PREP.PHR. *against a danger*) Plb.

προφυλακίς ίδος *fem.adj.* (of ships) **acting as a lookout** Th.

προ-φυλάσσω, Att. **προφυλάττω** vb. | ep.2pl.imperatv. προφύλαχθε | **1 be on guard before, guard, watch over** —*a temple* hHom.; (of a dog) **protect** —*sheep* X.
2 (of soldiers) **act as advance guard, keep a lookout** Ar. X. Plu.; (of ships) Hdt. Th.; (fig., of laws) —W.GEN. *over people* X. ‖ IMPERS.PASS. *an advance watch is provided* —W.PREP.PHR. *by certain troops* X.
3 ‖ MID. **protect oneself** or **take precautions against** —*potential enemies* Hdt. —*missiles* X. —*hunger, thirst, cold, heat* X.; (intr.) **take precautions** Hdt. Th. Plu.

προ-φύομαι pass.vb. | act.athem.aor. προύφυν | **be born before;** (of a person) **be** —W.PREDIC.SB. *the father* (W.GEN. *of someone's father,* i.e. *be his grandfather*) S.

προ-φῡράω contr.vb. | pf.pass. προπεφύραμαι | **mix** (ingredients) **together in advance** (of kneading dough) ‖ PASS. (fig., of a speech) **be moulded into preliminary shape** Ar.; (of trouble) **be concocted beforehand** Ar.

προ-φυτεύω vb. (fig., of lust and cunning) **engender, bring forth** —*a monstrous form* (ref. to a scene of murder) S.

προ-φωνέω contr.vb. **1 foretell, predict, give warning of** —*sufferings* A.
2 announce publicly, proclaim —*someone's sufferings* A.; **call out, utter loudly** —*a cry* (W.DAT. *to everyone present*) S.
3 (of persons in authority) **announce, proclaim** —*an order* (W.DAT. *to someone*) A. S.
4 order publicly, issue an order or **warning** —W.DAT. + INF. *to someone to do sthg.* S. E.

προ-χαίρω vb. **feel anticipatory pleasure** (about the future) Pl.

προ-χαλκεύω vb. (of Fate, envisaged as a swordsmith) **forge in advance** (a weapon for an avenger) A.

προχάνᾱ ᾱς dial.f. [perh. προέχω] **excuse, pretext** Call.

προχειρίζομαι mid.vb. [πρόχειρος] | fut. προχειριοῦμαι | aor. προεχειρισάμην (Plb.) | **1 make** (sthg.) **ready or available** (for oneself or others); **get ready** —one's belongings Ar.; **mobilise** —troops D. Plb.; (of a clerk) **produce** —a document Plu.; (of a biographer) **make** (W.ACC. someone's life) **available** —W.DAT. for readers Plu. || PASS. (of a discourse) be embarked upon Pl.; (of benefits) be available D.
2 select, appoint —political leaders, officials, or sim. Isoc. Plb. Plu. —someone (W.PREP.PHR. for a specific task) D. Plb. Plu. —(W.PREDIC.SB. as commander, assistant) Plb. NT. —(W.INF. to do sthg.) NT. || ACT. **select** —someone (W.PREP.PHR. for punishment) Din. || PASS. (of persons) be selected or appointed Plb.; (of Jesus) be appointed or destined —W.DAT. for people (W.PREDIC.SB. as the Messiah) NT.; (of troops) be allotted or assigned —W.DAT. to someone Plb.
3 determine, decide —W.INF. to do sthg. Plb.

πρό-χειρος ον adj. [χείρ] **1** (of material things, esp. weapons) **ready to hand** Trag. Th. X. Men.; (of knowledge, stories, arguments, or sim.) Pl. D. Plb.
2 (of a person) **ready** (W.INF. to do sthg.) S.; (W.DAT. for flight) E.
3 (of a person) **forthcoming** (W.PREP.PHR. in conversation) Plb.; (pejor.) **headstrong, reckless** Plu.
4 (of things) **commonplace, everyday** Pl.; (of a course of action) **undemanding, straightforward** Xenoph. Isoc.; (of properties of things) **readily perceptible, obvious** Arist.; (of problems) **easy** Arist. || NEUT.IMPERS. (W. ἐστί) it is easy (freq. W.DAT. for someone) —W.INF. to do sthg. Isoc. Pl. +

—**προχείρως** adv. | compar. προχειρότερον, superl. προχειρότατα | **1 readily** Att.orats. +
2 casually, hurriedly, recklessly Att.orats. +; **offhand** —ref. to answering a question Pl.

προ-χειροτονέω contr.vb. | aor. προυχειροτόνησα | **1** (of presiding magistrates) **hold a preliminary vote** (by a show of hands) Aeschin.; (of the populace, in the Assembly) D. || PASS. (of a candidate for office) be selected by preliminary vote Pl.
2 || PASS. (gener., of persons) be chosen beforehand —W.PREP.PHR. by God NT.

προχειροτονίᾱ ᾱς f. **preliminary vote** (in the Assembly, by a show of hands) Arist.

προ-χέω contr.vb. **1** (of persons) **pour first** (W.PARTITV. GEN. + ADV. some water three times, i.e. three parts of water, before adding a fourth part of wine) Hes.; **pour** —libations (W.DAT. to a god) Hdt.
2 (of a river) **pour forth** —its waters (W.PREP.PHR. into the sea) Il. —(W.ADV. fr. a place) hHom.; (of rivers of volcanic lava) —a stream of smoke Pi.; (fig., of singers) —a poet's voice (i.e. his words) Pi.; (intr., of rivers) **flow forth** —W.PREP.PHR. into the sea AR. || MID.PASS. (of groups of people) pour or stream forth (sts. W.PREP.PHR. to a place) Il. AR.
3 (of persons) **shed** —tears AR.

πρό-χνυ adv. [γόνυ] **1 with the knees forward, on one's knees** —ref. to crouching Il.
2 utterly —ref. to one's enemies perishing Hom.
3 (intensv.) **thoroughly** (W.ADJ. old) AR.; (confirming a supposition) **really, in fact** AR.

προχοαί ῶν f.pl. [προχέω] | ep.dat. προχοῇς, προχοῇσι | **1 place where a river or lake flows forth into the sea, mouth** Hom. Sol. Pi. AR.
2 flowing waters, waters (of a river) Od. Hes. A. B. Ar. AR. +

προχοΐς ίδος f. [dimin. πρόχοος] **chamber-pot** X.

πρόχοος όου, contr. **πρόχους** ου f. [προχέω] **pitcher, jug** (for pouring water) Hom. Hes. E. Ar. Philox.Leuc. X.; (for pouring libations) S.; (for pouring wine) Od. AR.

προ-χορεύω vb. (iron., of Ares) **lead in the dance** —a band of revellers E.

προ-χόω contr.vb. (of soil being eroded fr. mountains) **pile up** (W.ACC. a mound) **in front** (of a place) Pl.

προ-χρίω vb. | impf. προύχρῑον | **smear ointment** (on a robe) **in advance** (of its being packed away) S.

πρόχυσις εως f. [προχέω] **1 pouring forth, sprinkling** (of barley grains at a sacrifice) Hdt.
2 alluvial deposit (of soil), **silt** Hdt.; **alluvial coast** AR.

προχύται ῶν f.pl. **1 barley grains for sprinkling** (over a sacrificial victim), **sacrificial barley grains** E. AR.
2 floral tributes (cast before a person) Plu.

προχυταῖος ᾱ ον (or ος ον) adj. (of an offering to a god of fruits and liquids) **poured and scattered forth** E.fr.

προχύτης ου m. **pitcher** Ion

προχυτός ή όν adj. (of rocks) **dislodged in a shower** (fr. a mountainside) hHom.

προ-χωρέω contr.vb. | impf. προυχώρουν | aor. προυχώρησα | **1** (of persons, esp. commanders or troops) **move forward, advance** S. Th. X. Plu.
2 advance in time; (of a treaty) **go on, last** Th.; (of a person's life) **proceed** —W.ADV. in a certain way X.; (of drinking) **be well under way** X.
3 (of that which is hotter or colder) **move between states, progress** (opp. remaining stationary) Pl.
4 progress (to a given state); (of persons) **come** —W.PREP.PHR. to such a depth of misfortune Th.; (of a country's fortunes) **advance** —W.PREP.PHR. to such a position of power Hdt.
5 move forward (usu. towards a favourable outcome, freq. W.DAT. for someone); (of a person's course, fig.ref. to one's fortunes; of situations, undertakings) **proceed, develop** —W.ADV. or W.ADVBL. or PREP.PHR. well, strongly, as wished or as hoped for, according or contrary to expectation E. Th. X. Plb. Plu.; (of civil unrest) —W.PREDIC.ADJ. w. such savagery Th.; (of situations) **develop successfully, go well** Hdt. Th. X. Thphr. Plu.; (of a hope) **be realised** Plb.
6 (of sacrifices) **be propitious** —W.DAT. for someone Th. X.; **turn out** —W.PREDIC.ADJ. propitious (for someone) Hdt.
7 || IMPERS. (esp. w.neg.) things go (do not go) well (sts. W.DAT. for someone) Hdt. Th. Pl. Plu.; things go (do not go) —W.ADVBL. in a certain way, as expected Th.; it proves (does not prove) possible Th. —W.DAT. + INF. for someone to do sthg. Th.
8 (of things) **be convenient** —W.DAT. for someone X. || IMPERS. it is convenient —W.DAT. for someone (to do sthg.) X.

προχώρησις εως f. **forward movement, direct motion** (opp. retrograde, in a planet's orbit) Pl.

προ-ψαλάσσω vb. [ψαλάσσω touch or pluck, reltd. ψάλλω] **threaten, bully** —someone S.Ichn.

προωδοπεποίηκα (pf.): see προοδοποιέω

προ-ωθέω contr.vb. **1** (of an animal) **push** or **thrust** (W.ACC. itself) **forward** X.; (fig., of a person) **egg on** —someone Pl. || PASS. (of weapons) be thrust forward (at the enemy) Plb.
2 (of rivers) **push forward** —silt (out to sea) Plb. || PASS. (fig., of persons) be swept forward (by circumstances, as if by a torrent) Plb.
3 (of persons) **push, jostle** —someone Plb.

προ-ώλης ες *adj.* [ὄλλυμαι] (of a person) **perishing prematurely** (or perh. *utterly*) D.

πρυλέες έων *ep.m.pl.* [reltd. πρύλις] **foot-soldiers, warriors** Il. Hes.

πρύλις εως *f.* **a kind of dance performed by armed warriors, war-dance** Call.

πρύμνα, Ion. **πρύμνη**, ης, dial. **πρύμνᾱ** ᾱς *f.* [πρυμνός] | acc. πρύμναν, Ion. πρύμνην (also cj. in S. Ar.) |
1 hindmost part of a ship, stern or **stern-deck** Hom. + | see also πρυμνός 3
2 (fig.) **stern** (W.GEN. of the city, i.e. of the ship of state, as battered by stormy seas) A.; (as the position of the helmsman, i.e. ruler) A.; (ref. to a garlanded altar or shrine, as if a sacred ship bedecked w. wreaths) A.
3 ‖ ADVBL.ACC. **stern foremost, sternwards** —*ref. to ships backing water* Hdt. Th. Plu. —(*fig.*) *ref. to a person retreating* E. Ar.
4 (prep.phr.) κατὰ πρύμναν **at the stern, astern, from astern** (*ref. to a wind blowing, a wave rising*) S. Th. Theoc.; (*ref. to attacking or following a ship*) Plb.; **stern-first** (*ref. to running into shallows*) Plb.; **at the stern** (*ref. to the position of rudders*) E.; **beside the stern** (W.GEN. *of a ship, ref. to where persons are standing*) Hdt.

—**πρύμνηθεν** *adv.* **1 from the stern** —*ref. to fleeing* A. —*ref. to shouting* E.
2 from astern, at the stern —*ref. to a wind blowing, a wave rising* E. AR.
3 by the stern —*ref. to taking hold of a ship* Il.
4 at the stern —*ref. to standing* E.

πρυμναῖος ᾱ ον *adj.* (of mooring-cables) **at the stern, stern** AR.

πρυμνήσιος ᾱ ον *adj.* (of mooring-cables) **at the stern, stern** E. ‖ NEUT.PL.SB. **stern cables** Hom. hHom. A. E. AR. Plu.

πρυμνήτης ου *m.* **1 man at the stern, helmsman** (W.GEN. of a land, fig.ref. to a ruler) A. | see πρωράτης
2 ‖ ADJ. (of a cable) **stern** E.; (of a wind) **from astern** AR.(dub.)

πρυμνόθεν *adv.* [πρυμνός] **1 at the base** —*ref. to a tree being broken off* (*by the wind*) AR.; **from the foundations** —*ref. to islands being rooted to the sea-bed* Call.; (fig.) **root and branch** —*ref. to destroying a city, a race* A.
2 [equiv. to πρύμνηθεν] **from astern** —*ref. to a wave rising* AR.

πρυμνός ή όν *adj.* | superl. πρυμνότατος | **1** (of parts of the body) **at the base** (i.e. furthest fr. their tip and closest to the torso); (of an arm) **upper** (by the shoulder) Il.; (of a leg) **at the top** (by the thigh) Il.; (of a tongue) **at the root** Il.; (of a shoulder) at its lower part (at the shoulder-blade), **lower** Od.; (of an ox's horns) **at the base** Il. ‖ NEUT.SB. **lower part** or **base** (W.GEN. of the palm, i.e. wrist) Il.; (W.GEN. of the head, appos.w. *neck*) Pi.*fr.*
2 (of things) **at the undermost part**; (of a boulder, W.PREDIC.ADJ. *broad*) **at the base** Il.; (of trees being cut off) **at the base** or **roots** Il.; (of a spear-shaft, or perh. a spear-head) at its lower part, **lower** (where the one joins the other) Il.; (prep.phr.) ἐκ πρυμνῆς φρενός *from the bottom of one's heart* A.(cj.)
3 (of a ship) at its hindmost part, **at the stern** Hom. [unless sb. πρύμνη *stern*, appos.w. νηῦς; cf. πρῷρα 3]
4 ‖ NEUT.PL.SB. **far end** (W.GEN. of a market-place) Pi.

πρυμνοῦχος ον *adj.* [πρύμνα, ἔχω] (of Aulis) **where the sterns of ships are held fast** (in their moorings, perh. also w. allusion to being delayed by adverse winds) E.

πρυμνώρεια ης *ep.Ion.f.* [πρυμνός, ὄρος] **base of a mountain; foot** (W.GEN. of Ida) Il.

πρυτανεία ᾱς, Ion. **πρυτανηίη** ης *f.* [πρυτανεύω] **1** (at Athens) **period of office of prytaneis, prytany, presidency** Att.orats. Arist.
2 (in other states) **office or government of an executive committee, presidency** Arist.
3 rotating headship of a board of commanders, presidency (W.GEN. of an individual) Hdt.; (W.GEN. for the day) Hdt.

πρυτανεῖον, Ion. **πρυτανήιον**, ου *n.* [πρύτανις] **prytaneion, town hall** (ceremonial headquarters of a city, housing its sacred hearth and public dining-rooms) Pi. Hdt. Th. Theoc. Plb.; (pl. for sg.) Hdt.(oracle) Call.; (specif., at Athens, a building on the Acropolis, rebuilt in the 5th C. BC, prob. on the north slope, where meals were offered to ambassadors, and to other individuals in gratitude for particular services, and where certain homicide trials were held) Hdt. Ar. Att.orats. Pl. +; (W.GEN. of wisdom, fig.ref. to Athens) Pl.; (ref. to a hospitable person's house) Plu.

—**πρυτανεῖα** ων *n.pl.* **court dues** (sum paid to the state by litigants before a trial, in cases involving monetary claims, w. the losing party reimbursing his opponent) Ar. Att.orats. X.

πρυτανεύω *vb.* | ep.fut.inf. πρυτανευσέμεν | **1** (of a god) **be chief, hold sway** —W.DAT. over gods and humans hHom.
‖ PASS. (of a person) **be under instructions** (fr. someone) D.
2 be chairman (of a board of arbitrators) D.
3 (at Athens, of an individual) **serve as a prytanis** Antipho And. Arist.; (of a tribe) **hold the presidency, preside** (in the Council and Assembly) Th.(decree) And.(law) Pl. Arist.; (elsewhere) **be a member of an executive committee** Plb.
4 (of a person serving as prytanis) **propose a debate** —W.PREP.PHR. *about peace* Ar.
5 (tr., of a person) **be the prime mover** or **instigator of** —*peace, a course of action* Isoc. D.

πρυτανηίη *Ion.f.*, **πρυτανήιον** *Ion.n.*: see πρυτανεία, πρυτανεῖον

πρύτανις εως *m.* (also *f.*) **1 leader of a people, ruler, lord** A. Pi.; (W.GEN. of people) B.; (ref. to Zeus) E.; (W.GEN. of the gods, of thunder and lightning, ref. to Zeus) A. Pi.; (of horses, ref. to Poseidon) Stesich.; (of drinking-parties, ref. to Dionysus) Ion; (of mankind, ref. to wine) Ion
2 (*f.*) **mistress** or **queen** (W.GEN. of evil days, ref. to the Sphinx) Ar.(quot. A.*satyr.fr.*)
3 (at Athens, usu.pl.) **prytanis** (one of the fifty members of the Council who formed its executive committee during the tenth part of the year that their tribe was in charge) Th. Ar. Att.orats. Pl. +; (in other states) **executive officer** Arist.
4 chairman or **president** (W.GEN. of a body of tax-commissioners) Hdt.

πρῴ *Att.adv.*: see πρωί

πρῳαίτερον, πρῳαίτατα *compar. and superl.advs.*: see under πρωί

πρώειραν (ep.acc.): see πρῷρα

πρώην (or **πρῴην**), dial. **πρωᾱν, πρόᾱν, πρᾶν** (Theoc. Mosch.) *adv.* [reltd. πρό] **1 lately, recently** Il. Ar. Att.orats. Pl. +; **before, previously** —*ref. to sthg. mentioned in a discussion* Arist.
2 (contrasted w. χθές *yesterday*) **the day before yesterday** Th. Plu.; (in phrs., combined w. *yesterday*) χθὲς καὶ πρώην, πρώην καὶ χθές (or sim.) *yesterday or the day before, a day or two ago, quite recently* Hdt. Ar. Isoc. Pl. D.

πρῳηρότης *m.*: see πρωιηρότης

πρωθ-ήβης ου *masc.adj.* —also **πρώθηβος** ον (B.) *adj.* [πρῶτος, ἥβη] | also fem.acc. πρωθήβην (Od.) | (of men) **in the first bloom of youth** Hom. hHom. B. AR.; (of a woman) Od.

πρωί (sts. written **πρῶι**), Att. **πρῴ** adv. [reltd. πρώην]
1 early (in the day) Il. Hes. Ar. Pl. X. +; (w.GEN. in the day) Hdt. X.
2 early in the year Th.
3 too early, too soon Od. A. S. Pl.
—**πρωαίτερον** (or **πρωιαίτερον**), also **πρωίτερον** (Th.) compar.adv. **earlier** (in the day) Th. Pl. X.; (gener.) **at an earlier time, earlier** (w.GEN. than midnight) Th.; (w.GEN. than necessary) Pl.; **too early** (in life) Plu.
—**πρῳαίτατα**, also **πρωίτατα** (Th.) superl.adv. **earliest or very early** (in the day) Pl. X.; (gener.) **at the earliest time or at a very early time** Th. Pl. X.

πρωΐᾱ ᾶς f. [πρῷος] **early morning** NT.
πρωϊζά neut.pl.adv. **1 on the day before yesterday**; χθιζά τε καὶ πρωιζά yesterday or the day before (i.e. not so long ago) Il. | cf. πρώην 2
2 before the due time, early Theoc.
πρωϊ-ηρότης (or **πρωηρότης**) ου ep.m. [ἀρότης] **one who ploughs early in the season, early ploughman** Hes.
πρώιμος η ον adj. | superl. πρωιμώτατος | (of a time for sowing) **early** (in the season) X.
πρώιος Ion.adj.: see πρῷος
πρωίτερον, πρωίτατα compar. and superl.advs.: see under πρωί
πρώκιος ον adj. [πρώξ] (of sustenance for a cicada) **from dewdrops** Call.
πρώκροον (Lacon.impf.): see προκρούω
πρωκτίζω vb. [πρωκτός] **bugger** —someone Ar.
πρωκτο-πεντετηρίς ίδος f. **four-year-festival arsehole; grand arse** (belonging to a character called Θεωρία Festival-goer) Ar.
πρωκτός οῦ m. **anus, arsehole** (of a human or animal) Hippon. Ar.
πρωκτο-τηρέω contr.vb. **be an arsehole-sleuth** (i.e. keep a watch out for buggers, ref. to corrupt politicians) Ar.
πρών ῶνος, ep. **πρηών** ῶνος (Hes.) and ὁνος (Call.) m. | ep.nom.acc.pl. πρώονες, πρώονας, ep.dat.pl. πρηόσι (Call.) |
1 protruding rock, ridge (of a mountain) Il. Hes. hHom. Alcm. B. Call.
2 rocky land projecting towards or into the sea, foreland, headland, promontory Pi. Trag. Ar.(quot. S.) Call.
πρώξ ωκός f. | PL. **dewdrops** (as food for a cicada) Theoc.; **drops** (of healing oil fr. Apollo's hair) Call.
πρῷος ᾱ ον, Ion. **πρώιος** η ον adj. [πρωί] **1 early in the day**; (of an afternoon) **early** Hdt.
2 early (in a given season); (of crops, vegetables, fruits) **early** Ar.; (of a rose) Call.; (quasi-advbl., of an army assembling) Hdt.
—**πρώιον** Ion.adv. **early** (in the day) Il.
πρῷρα ᾱς, Ion. **πρώρη** ης f. —also **πρῶρρα** ᾱς (Plb.) f. | also ep.acc. πρώειραν (AR., dub.) | **1 forepart of a ship, prow, bows** Hdt. Trag. Th. +
2 (fig.) **prow** (w.GEN. of life, envisaged as a ship meeting the waves of fortune) E.; (prep.phr.) ἐκ πρῴρας from the prow —ref. to a wind of anger blowing A.(dub.)
3 || ADJ. (of a ship) **at the prow** Od. [unless sb. prow, appos.w. νηῦς; cf. πρυμνός 3]
—**πρῴραθε(ν)**, Ion. **πρώρηθεν** adv. **1 from the prow, from the bows** —ref. to disembarking, dropping anchor, or sim. Pi. Plu.; ἐκ πρῴρηθεν from ahead, in front —ref. to waves rising Theoc.
2 at the prow or **bows** —ref. to strengthening ships Th.; (neut.sb.) τὰ πρῴραθεν bows Th.
πρῳρατεύω vb. [πρῳρατής] **act as bow-officer** Ar.

πρῳρατής ου m. **bow-officer** (of a trireme, second in command to the helmsman, whose duties included acting as a forward lookout and supervising the forward crew) X.; (fig.) **leader** (w.GEN. of an army) S.fr.(dub., cj. πρυμνήτης)
πρῳρεύς έως m. **bow-officer** X. D. Arist. Plu.
πρώρηθεν Ion.adv.: see πρῴραθεν
Πρωταγόρᾱς ου m. **Protagoras** (sophist fr. Abdera, c.490–420 BC) Isoc. Pl. +
—**Πρωταγόρειος** ᾱ ον adj. (of the teaching) **of Protagoras** Pl.
πρωτ-άγριον ου n. [πρῶτος, ἄγρᾱ] (concr.) **first capture** (in a hunt, ref. to deer) Call.
πρωταγωνιστέω contr.vb. [ἀγωνιστής] **1 take the leading role in a play**; (of an actor in a minor role) **be the star performer** Plu.; (of speech) **play the leading part** (in tragedy) Arist.
2 (fig., of a person, an honourable ideal) **play the leading part** (in an enterprise) Arist. Plu.
πρῶτ-αρχος ον adj. [ἀρχή] (of ruinous folly) **initial, original** (as starting a series of catastrophes) A.
πρωτεῖον ου n. [πρωτεύω] **1 first place, primacy, pre-eminence** (of a city) D.; (of persons or their qualities) Plb. Plu.
2 || PL. (usu.fig.) **first place or prize** Pl. D. Plb. Plu.
Πρωτεσίλᾱος ου, dial. **Πρωτεσίλᾱς** ᾱ, Ion. **Πρωτεσίλεως** εω m. **Protesilaos** (Greek warrior, first to leap ashore at Troy) Il. Hes.fr. Pi. Hdt. E. Th.
πρωτεύς έος masc.adj. (of a people) **first, foremost** (w. ἐκ + GEN. of the Achaeans) Tim.(dub.)
πρωτεύω vb. [πρῶτος] **1** (usu. of persons, also of cities or sim.) **hold first place, be pre-eminent, be foremost** (freq. w.DAT. or PREP.PHR. in a specific quality or activity, also freq. w.GEN. or PREP.PHR. among specific people) Att.orats. Pl. X. Arist. Plu.
2 (of avarice) **be foremost** (among a person's vices) Plu.; (of justice) —w.GEN. **among virtues** Plu.
πρώτιστος η ον (also ος ον hHom.), dial. **πράτιστος** ᾱ ον superl.adj. [πρῶτος] (of persons or things) **first in a series, first of all, very first** hHom. Parm. Ar. Men. Hellenist.poet.; (quasi-advbl., of persons doing or suffering sthg.) Hom. hHom. Pi. Ar. Theoc.
—**πρώτιστον, πρώτιστα** neut.sg. and pl.advs. | also τὸ πρώτιστον, τὰ πρώτιστα | **1 first** (in a series of actions), **first of all** Hom. Hes. Pi. Trag. Ar. +; (in a series of arguments) E.
2 at the start, in the first place, at the outset Hom. hHom. Ar. Call.
3 for the first time Hes. hHom. Simon. B. Ar. Hellenist.poet.
4 before another event, first, earlier S. Ar. D. Call.
πρωτο-βόλος ον adj. [βάλλω] (of a region) **first struck** (by the rays of dawn) E.(dub.)
πρωτο-γενής ές adj. [γένος, γίγνομαι] **first-born**; (of a class of things) **primary** Pl.
πρωτό-γονος ον adj. [γόνος] **1** (of a child) **first-born** (in a family) E.; (of a person, in a land) Lyr.adesp.; (of lambs, kids) **born first** (in a year), **firstling** Il. Hes.
2 (of a palm tree, created on Delos by Zeus) **first ever born** E.
3 (of a ceremony) **for the original creation** (of the Olympic games), **founding** Pi.
4 (of families) **of foremost lineage, high-born** S.
πρωτό-θρονος ον adj. [θρόνος] (of Artemis) **throned in majesty** Call.
πρωτο-καθεδρίᾱ ᾱς f. [καθέδρᾱ] **best seat, place of honour** (in a synagogue) NT.

πρωτο-κλισίᾱ ᾱς *f.* **place of honour** (at a meal) NT.
πρωτο-κτόνος ον *adj.* [κτείνω] (of Ixion's supplication for purification) **for the first killing** A.
πρωτό-λεια ων *n.pl.* [λεία] (collectv.) **first offering** or **first act** (by a suppliant) E.
πρωτό-μαντις εως *f.* [μάντις] (appos.w. *Earth*) **first prophetess** (at Delphi) A.
πρωτό-μορος ον *adj.* [μόρος] (of the inevitability) **of dying first** (before some other event) A.
πρωτο-παγής ές *adj.* [πήγνυμι] (of a chariot, a wagon) **newly made** Il.; (of poetic skill) **new-fashioned** (i.e. in a new style) Scol.
πρωτό-πειρος ον *adj.* [πεῖρα] (of troops) **having a first experience** (w.GEN. of hardship) Plb.
πρωτο-πήμων ον, gen. ονος *adj.* [πῆμα] (of mental derangement) **bringing the start of sufferings** A.
πρωτό-πλοος ον, Att. **πρωτόπλους** ουν *adj.* [πλόος] **1** (of a ship) **making a first voyage** Od. E.; **first that ever sailed** (i.e. the Argo) E.
2 ‖ MASC.PL.SB. **those commanding the leading ships** X.
πρωτο-πορεία ᾱς *f.* **vanguard** (of an army) Plb.
πρῶτος η (dial. ᾱ) ον, dial. **πρᾶτος** ᾱ ον *adj.* **1 foremost** (in position); (of warriors) **in the front ranks** Od.; (of a door) **outer** Il.; (of a bench at the Assembly) **front** Ar.; (of battle) **at the front** (of it) Il.; (of a chariot-pole) **at the end** (of it) Il. ‖ MASC.PL.SB. **men in the front rank** Il.
2 first (in a list or sequence of two or more); (of persons or things) **first** Hom. +; **earlier** (W.GEN. than another) NT.; (of a rank of soldiers) **front** Isoc. ‖ FEM.SB. **front rank** Lys. ‖ NEUT.SB. (sg. and pl.) **beginning** (of a poem or speech) Pl. Aeschin. ‖ NEUT.PL.SB. **first prize** Il.
3 (quasi-advbl., of persons doing or suffering sthg.) **first** Hom. +
4 occurring first (before other things); (of dawn) **early** S.
5 (advbl. and prep.phrs.) τὴν πρώτην *for a start, first of all* Hdt. Ar. D. Arist.; ἀπὸ πρώτης *from the start* Antipho Th.; κατὰ πρώτας *at the start* Pl.; ἐν πρώτοις *above all, especially* Hdt. Pl.
6 first in order of existence; (of households, cities, kinds of government) **original, primitive** Arist.; (philos., of matter, substance, a type of argument) **primary, fundamental** Arist.
7 first in rank or importance; (of persons) **foremost, leading** (sts. W.GEN. of a body of people, sts. W.DAT. in a quality) S. E. Th. +; (of cities) Th. ‖ MASC.SB. (sg. and pl.) **foremost person or leader** (sts. W.GEN. of a body of people, of a place) Hom. S. + ‖ NEUT.PL.SB. (ref. to persons) **leading citizens** (sts. W.GEN. of a place) E.; (ref. to a single person) **one of the leaders** (W.GEN. of a people) Hdt.; (fig.) **number one** (W.GEN. for villainy) Ar.
8 first in degree or quality; (of a person's fortune) **best, highest** S. ‖ NEUT.PL.SB. **peak** (W.GEN. of mental powers) Hdt.; (advbl. and prep.phrs.) τὰ πρῶτα, ἐς τὰ πρῶτα *to the highest degree, particularly* (*ref. to showing military prowess, to being honoured*) S. Th.
—**πρῶτον**, **πρῶτα** *neut.sg. and pl.advs.* ‖ also freq. τὸ πρῶτον, τὰ πρῶτα ‖ **1** (ref. to position) **at the front, in front** (opp. behind) Il.
2 first (in a series of actions), **first of all** Hom. +; (in a series of arguments) +
3 at the start, **in the first place, at the outset** Hom. +
4 for the first time Hom. +
5 before another event, **first, earlier** Hom. +
6 (gener., after relatv.prons.) **at an earlier time, once** Hom. + • ἀπειλάων τὰς ἀντιθέῳ Ὀδυσῆι πρῶτον ἐπηπείλησε *the threats which he once made against godlike Odysseus* Od.; (after temporal conjs.) **at the earliest time** Hom. • ἐπὴν τὰ πρῶτα γένηται *when once he is born* Hom. • εὖτ' ἂν πρῶτα (ὅτε πρῶτον or sim.) *as soon as* Od. +
—**πρώτως** *adv.* **primarily** (opp. secondarily) Arist.
πρωτο-στάτης ου *m.* [ἵσταμαι] **1** (milit.) **man who stands first in line** (W.GEN. on the right wing) Th.
2 ‖ PL. **men in the front rank** X. Plb.
3 ringleader (W.GEN. of a faction) NT.
πρωτο-τόκος, dial. **πρᾱτοτόκος**, ον *adj.* [τίκτω] (of a woman, cow, goat) **that has given birth for the first time** Il. Pl. Theoc.; (of a thinker, fig.ref. to having produced a doctrine) Pl.
—**πρωτότοκος** ον *adj.* (of a child) **first-born** NT.
πρωτουργός όν *adj.* [ἔργον] (of certain motions) **primary** Pl.
πρωτο-φυής ές *adj.* [φύω] (of a drug) **created for the first time** (fr. a supernatural source, rather than obtained fr. a plant) AR.
πρώτως *adv.*: see under πρῶτος
πρωυδᾶν (contr.inf.): see προαυδάω
πταῖσμα ατος *n.* [πταίω] **1 stumble** or **trip**; **slip, error** (of judgement) Thgn.
2 upset, mishap, setback Aeschin. D.; **disaster, catastrophe** Hdt. Plu.
πταίω *vb.* ‖ aor. ἔπταισα ‖ pf. ἔπταικα ‖ **1 stumble, trip** S.; (provb.) δὶς πρὸς τὸν αὐτὸν λίθον πταίειν *stumble twice against the same stone* (i.e. make the same mistake twice) Plb.; (fig., of a stone) **collide** —w. ποτί + DAT. w. *the boots of someone in a hurry* Theoc.
2 (fig.) **stumble** —w. πρός + DAT. *against an evil* (i.e. meet w. trouble) A.; (of a politician) **founder** —W.DAT. *against the state* (compared to a reef, i.e. wreck one's ambitions) Pl.; (of a country) **collapse** —w. περί + DAT. *on account of an enemy commander* (i.e. be defeated by him) Hdt.; (of persons) **fail** (in an enterprise) —w. περί + DAT. *by reason of themselves* (i.e. be the cause of their own failure) Th.
3 (of persons) **meet with failure** or **setback** E.fr. Th. D. X. Men.; **meet with disaster** Plb. Plu.; (of a person's body) **suffer ill health** Pl.
4 make a mistake (in answering a question) Pl. —W.DAT. *in one's thinking* Pl.; **commit an offence** Arist.
5 (tr.) **make** (W.ACC. someone's understanding) **stumble** —w. ποτί + DAT. *against rough falsehood* Pi.fr. ‖ PASS. be made to fail —w. διά + ACC. *through the agency of others* Plu.
πτάμενος (athem.aor.mid.ptcpl.): see πέτομαι
πτανός *dial.adj.*: see πτηνός
πτάξ ακός *f.* [perh. πτήσσω; cf. πτώξ] **hare** A.
πταρεῖν (aor.2 inf.): see πτάρνυμαι
πταρμός οῦ *m.* [πτάρνυμαι] **action of sneezing, sneezing, sneeze** Th. Pl.; (taken as an omen) Ar.; (as a good omen) Plu.
πτάρνυμαι *mid.vb.* ‖ mid. used only in pres. (X.) ‖ act.aor.2 ἔπταρον, inf. πταρεῖν ‖ **sneeze** Hdt. Ar. Pl.; (taken as a good omen) Od. X.; (as a bad omen) Men.
πτάτο (ep.3sg.athem.aor.mid.): see πέτομαι
πτελέα ᾱς, Ion. **πτελέη** ης *f.* **elm tree** Il. Ar. Hellenist.poet.; (ref. to the timber) Hes.
πτερινός ή όν *adj.* [πτερόν] **1** (of bird-gods) **equipped with feathers or wings, feathered** or **winged** Ar.
2 (of a fan) **made of feathers** E.; (of a head-dress) Plb.
πτέρις εως *f.* **plant with feather-like leaves, fern** Theoc. Plb.
πτέρνη (also **πτέρνα** Plb. NT.) ης *f.* **1 back part of the human foot, heel** (esp. in ctxt. of treading upon the ground) Il. A. D. Call. Theoc. NT.

2 prob. hoof (of a horse) Call.
3 foot, base (of a catapult) Plb.

πτερο-δόνητος ον *adj.* [πτερόν, δονέω] (of a dithyrambic poet and his poetry) **wing-propelled, high-flown** Ar.

πτερόεις εσσα εν, contr. **πτερούς** οὖσσα οὖν (A. E.) *adj.* **1** (of birds) **winged** A. Pi. E.; (of the Sphinx, Pegasos, the Sun's horses) Pi. S. E.; (of Khaos, Eros) Ar. Mosch.; (of a cowherd, fig.ref. to a gadfly) A.; (of the cicada) Call.; (of Perseus' sandals) Hes.; (of a thunderbolt) Ar.; (fig., of the foot of a person wishing to fly to safety, of an escape) E.
2 (of arrows) **feathered** Il. AR.; (of an arrow, fig.ref. to a song) Pi.; (fig., of a song, envisaged as flying fr. the composer to its recipient) Pi.
3 (fig., of words, as if flying to the listener) **winged** Hom. Hes. hHom.
4 (of Ixion's wheel) app. **speedy** Pi.
5 (of a person's heart) **fluttering** AR.; (of hope) **flighty, fleeting** B.
6 (of a kind of shield, w. sense uncert.) Il.

πτερόν οὗ *n.* [πέτομαι] **1** (usu. collectv.pl.) **feather** Hom. +
2 (usu.pl.) **wing** (of a bird or other flying creature) Hom. +; (of minor deities, supernatural horses, a dream-vision) A. Pi. E. Call.*epigr.* AR.; (fig., of a person or god, envisaged as providing protection for human nestlings) A. E.; (provbl., as exemplifying great speed) Od. E.
3 winged creature (ref. to the Sphinx, to Pegasos) E. Ar.(quot. E.)
4 (fig.) **wing** or **feather** (W.GEN. of trouble, prob. ref. to its hue, envisaged as changing when seen fr. different angles) A.; **wing** (W.GEN. of the Muses, ref. to a song, envisaged as flying fr. the composer to its recipient) B.
5 ‖ PL. **wings** (fig. or hyperbol., as a means of transporting a person beyond normal limits); (wished for by a person, as providing a means of quick escape) E.; (ref. to divinely made armour, as lifting the spirits of its recipient) Il.; (ref. to the fame conferred by poetry, as transporting the person commemorated in it over land and sea) Thgn.; (W.GEN. of the games, of victories, ref. to the victor's garland) Pi.
6 (fig.) **wing** (of a ship, by which it flies over the sea, ref. to an oar) Od.; (ref. to a sail) Hes.; (ref. to an oar or sail) E.; (pl., ref. to handles or straps of a wicker wine-flask) Ar.
7 feathered arrow, arrow E.
8 (meton.) **omen** S.

πτερο-ποίκιλος ον *adj.* [ποίκιλος] (of birds) **with dappled wings** (w. secondary ref. to persons wearing patterned cloaks) Ar.

πτερο-ρρυέω *contr.vb.* [ῥέω] (of a bird) **shed one's feathers, moult** Ar.; (w. secondary ref. to a person being stripped of his money) Ar.; (of the soul, envisaged as winged) Pl.

πτεροφίτωρ *masc.fem.adj.*: see πτεροφύτωρ

πτερο-φόρᾱς ου *masc.adj.* [φέρω] (of a military officer) wearing a feather, **with a plume in one's helmet** (as a mark of rank) Men.

πτερο-φόρος ον *adj.* **1** (of birds, their bodies) **feathered** or **winged** A. Ar.; (of deities) **winged** E.; (of the Sun's chariot team) E.*fr.*; (of Zeus' thunderbolt) Ar.
2 (of a reed, fig.ref. to an arrow) **feathered** Lyr.adesp.
3 ‖ MASC.SB. (in Roman ctxt.) **express messenger** Plu.

πτεροφυέω *contr.vb.* [πτεροφυής] (of a soul) **grow feathers** or **wings** Pl.

πτερο-φυής ές *adj.* [φύω] (of a class of creatures, ref. to birds or sim.) **that grows feathers** or **wings** Pl.

πτερο-φύτωρ (better **πτεροφίτωρ**) ορος *masc.fem.adj.* (of the need for Eros) **to grow wings** Pl.(quot.poet.)

πτερόω *contr.vb.* ‖ pf.pass.ptcpl. ἐπτερωμένος ‖ **1 equip with feathers** or **wings** —*a person, a soul* Ar. Pl. ‖ PASS. (of a person, a soul) **be given feathers** or **wings** Ar. Pl.
‖ PF.PASS.PTCPL.ADJ. (of a verse, which mentions flight) **winged** Ar.
2 put feathers on —*a letter* (wrapped round the butt-end of an arrow) Hdt.
3 (of a naval commander) **make** (W.ACC. a ship) **spread the oars like wings** (so as to be poised for a quick start) Plb.; **poise** (W.ACC. the oars) **at the ready** Plu. ‖ PF.PTCPL.ADJ. (of a ship) with oars poised at the ready Plb.
‖ PF.PASS.PTCPL.ADJ. (of a ship) **winged** (W.DAT. w. oars) E.(dub.)
4 ‖ MID.PASS. (fig., of a person) **wing one's way** —W.PREP.PHR. *to dinner* (w. further connot. of being aflutter for it) Ar. ‖ PASS. (of a person's mind) **be set aflutter** —W.DAT. *by words* Ar.; (of soldiers) be given wings (i.e. have one's spirits lifted, by a commander's example) Plu.

πτερυγίζω *vb.* [πτέρυξ] ‖ fut. πτερυγιῶ ‖ aor.ptcpl. πτερυγίσᾱς ‖ **1 use one's wings**; (fig., of persons) **take wing, fly away** Ar.
2 (prob. of an actor playing a bird) **flap one's wings** Ar.; (fig., of a person) **flap** or **flail about** Ar.

πτερύγιον ου *n.* [dimin. πτέρυξ] **1 wing** or **fin** (of wood, serving to stabilise the flight of a projectile) Plb.
2 pinnacle, summit (of a temple) NT.

πτερυγ-ωκής ές *adj.* [ὠκύς] (of a bird) **swift-winged** A.

πτερυγωτός ή όν *adj.* (fig., of an oracle concerning birds) **winged** Ar.

πτέρυξ υγος *f.* [reltd. πτερόν] **1** (usu.pl.) **wing** (of a bird or other flying creature) Hom. +; (of a bird, as observed in augury) Call.; (of minor deities) Hes. E. Ar.; (fig., of rising smoke) E.; (fig. or hyperbol., of a person, for transporting one out of danger or to somewhere desirable) Anacr. Thgn. A.
2 ‖ PL. (fig.) **wings** (W.GEN. of the Muses, ref. to a song for a victor, carrying his fame far afield) Pi.; (W.GEN. of lamentation, carrying it to listeners) S.
3 (fig.) **wing-like covering, wing** (W.GEN. of fabrics, for the roof of a tent) E.; (W.GEN. of the sun, perh. ref. to its light spreading across the sky) E.; (pl., of a mother, offered as protection to her child, envisaged as a chick) E.
4 (fig.) perh. **wing** (W.GEN. of Euboea, app. ref. to some geographical feature of Aulis) E.
5 flap (of a two-part tunic, ref. to its front or back part) Men. Plu. ‖ PL. **flaps** (of a cuirass) X.
6 broad edge (of a scimitar) Plu.

πτέρωμα ατος *n.* [πτερόω] **1 feathered object, arrow** A.*fr.*
2 plumage (W.GEN. of the soul) Pl.

Πτέρως ωτος *m.* [πτερόν, Ἔρως] **Pteros** (i.e. Winged Eros) Pl.(quot.poet.)

—πτερώνυμος ον *adj.* [ὄνομα] (of Pteros) **named after his wings** Pl.

πτέρωσις εως *f.* [πτερόω] (collectv.) **feathering, plumage** (perh. w. secondary ref. to a helmet plume) Ar.

πτερωτός ή όν (also ός όν S.) *adj.* **1 equipped with feathers**; (of wings) **feathered** Hdt.; (of a soul) Pl.; (of arrows) E.; (of a helmet crest) Plu.
2 equipped with wings; (of bat-like creatures, serpents, a class of creatures) **winged** Hdt. Arist.; (of Hades) E.; (of a carriage for deities, a team of chariot-horses) A. E.; (of Zeus' thunder) S.; (fig., of a person escaping troubles or abandoning others) E. ‖ NEUT.PL.SB. **winged creatures** (ref. to birds) A. E.
3 (of the sound) **made by wings** Ar.

πτέσθαι (aor.2 mid.inf.): see πέτομαι

πτηνός ή όν (also ός όν Pl.), dial. **πτᾱνός** ᾱ́ όν adj. [πέτομαι] **1** having the capacity to fly with wings; (of birds, other creatures, a class of creatures) **flying** or **winged** Trag. Ar. Pl. Arist.; (of Eros, of Zeus in the form of a swan) E.; (of the Muses' chariot team, of that of Zeus, of supernatural horses) Pi.fr. E. Pl. ‖ NEUT.PL.SB. winged creatures (ref. to birds) Trag. Ar. Pl. X.; (also masc.pl.sb.) E.; (neut.sg.sb.) Call. **2** (hyperbol., of persons or animals, in imagined situations) **winged** E. Pl. X.; (of poets) Pl.
3 (of arrows) **winged, flying** S. E.
4 (of the means of escape for birds) **by flying** Pl.
5 (pejor., of words) **fleeting, impermanent** E. Pl.; (of dreams) **flighty, capricious** E.

πτῆσις εως f. **flight** (of birds or sim.) A. Arist.

πτήσσω vb. [reltd. πτώσσω] | dial.impf. πτάσσον (B.) | aor. ἔπτηξα, ep. πτῆξα, dial. ἔπταξα | pf. ἔπτηχα | ep.pf.ptcpl. πεπτηώς | **1** **crouch down**; (of birds or animals) **cower** (in fear) A. B. S.fr. Ar. AR.; (of persons, sts. compared to birds) Pi. B. Trag. Ar. Pl. X.; (tr.) **cower before** —one's enemies Thgn. —a master's knee Scol.; **flinch at** —the threat fr. aggressors Lycurg. —battle AR.; (wkr.sens.) **be dismayed** —W.ACC. in one's heart S. ‖ PF. (of a person, a country) **be cowed** Isoc. Hyp.
2 (of a person) **crouch before** —an altar (fr. fear and for protection) E.; (of birds) **go cowering for protection** —W.PREP.PHR. to a place Ar.; (fig., of a city, envisaged as a storm-tossed ship) —to another city E.
3 (of persons) **crouch** (for concealment) Od. E. Ar.
4 ‖ PF.PTCPL. (fig., of headlands) **crouching** —W.PREP.PHR. away fr. a harbour (i.e. towards the sea) Od.(dub.) | see ποτιπεπτηυῖαι
5 (causatv., of a person) **strike with dismay, alarm** —someone's heart Il.(dub.)

πτῆται (ep.3sg.athem.aor.mid.subj.): see πέτομαι

πτίλον, dial. **ψίλον**, ου n. **1 soft** or **downy feather** Alcm. Ar. Plb.
2 **wing-like membrane, wing** (of an unknown kind of snake) Hdt.

πτισάνη ης f. [πτίσσω] **barley-gruel, porridge** Men.

πτίσσω vb. | aor. ἔπτισα ‖ pf.pass.ptcpl. ἐπτισμένος | **1 crush** —lotus seeds (to make loaves) Hdt.
2 **remove** (grain) **from its husk** ‖ PF.PASS.PTCPL.ADJ. (of barley) **shelled** Pl.

πτοέω, dial. **πτοάω**, ep. **πτοιέω**, **πτοιάω** contr.vb. | aor. ἐπτόησα, ep. ἐπτοίησα, Aeol.3sg. ἐπτόαισε ‖ PASS.: ep.pres. πτοιῶμαι (Mimn.) | aor. ἐπτοήθην, ep.3pl. ἐπτοίηθεν, ep.ptcpl. πτοηθείς | pf.: 3sg. ἐπτόηται, ep. ἐπτοίηται, Ion.3pl. ἐπτοέαται (Anacr.), ptcpl. ἐπτοημένος |
1 (of a circumstance, a dress, Aphrodite) **set aflutter, excite** —someone, the heart Sapph. AR. ‖ PASS. (of persons) **be excited** or **agitated** Hes. Mimn. E. Pl. Arist. Plu. —W.ACC. in one's mind Anacr. —W.DAT. by love E. Call. —by dreams AR. ‖ PF.PASS.PTCPL.ADJ. **excited** Men.; (W.ACC. in one's mind) A.; (of a person's step, hands) **agitated** E.; (of Erinyes) **aflutter** (W.DAT. w. serpents) E. ‖ AOR.PASS.PTCPL.SB. **state of agitation** or **giddiness** (in the mind) E.
2 (of a person, a dream) **alarm, frighten** —someone Plb. Mosch. ‖ PASS. (of persons, their minds) **be alarmed** or **frightened** Od. Plb. Plu.; (of a fawn, a horse) Anacr. Plu. ‖ PF.PASS.PTCPL.ADJ. (of persons) **alarmed** or **frightened** A. E. Plb. Plu.

πτοία ᾱς f. **alarm, panic** Plb. Plu.

πτοιάω, **πτοιέω** ep.contr.vbs.: see πτοέω

πτοίησις εως f. **strong agitation** or **excitation** (of a person's mind or body) Pl.

Πτολεμαῖος ου m. **Ptolemy** (name of successive Macedonian kings of Egypt) Call. Theoc. Plb. Plu.

πτολεμίζω ep.vb., **πτολεμιστής** ep.m., **πτολεμόνδε** ep.adv., **πτόλεμος** ep.m.: see πολ-

πτολίαρχος ep.m.: see πολίαρχος

πτολίεθρον ου ep.n. [πόλις] **city** or **town** Hom. Hes. Hellenist.poet. Plu.(oracle)

πτολι-πόρθης ου ep.m. [πέρθω, πορθέω] **destroyer** or **sacker of cities** A.

πτολί-πορθος (also **πτολιπόρθιος** Od.) ον ep.adj. **1** (epith. of Achilles and Odysseus) **city-sacking** Hom.; (of Ares, Enyo, Herakles, minor warriors) Il. Hes.; (of battles) Pi.
2 (of Agamemnon) **who sacked the city** (W.GEN. of Troy) A.

πτόλις ep.f.: see πόλις

πτόρθος ου m. **1 shoot** or **branch of a tree** or **shrub, shoot, sapling, twig** or **bough** Od. Ion E. Ar. Pl. +; (fig.) **offshoot, branch** (of a family) E.fr.
2 **putting forth of shoots, sprouting** Hes.

πτύγμα ατος n. [πτύσσω] **folded part, fold** (W.GEN. of a dress) Il.

πτύελος ου m. [πτύω] **saliva** Arist.

πτυκτός ή όν adj. (of a writing-tablet) **folding** Il.

πτύξ πτυχός f. | SG.: only acc. πτύχα, dat. πτυχί | PL.: only nom. πτύχες, acc. πτύχας | see also πτυχαί | **1** (sg. and pl.) **fold** (of a garment) hHom. E. Mosch.
2 (sg. and pl.) **fold, cleft, hollow, glen** (of a mountain) Hom. hHom. AR.
3 (pl.) **layer** (of hide or metal, in a shield) Il. Hes.

πτύον ου n. | ep.gen.dat.sg.pl. πτυόφιν | **winnowing-shovel** Il. Theoc. NT.

πτύρομαι pass.vb. | aor.2 ἐπτύρην | (of a horse) **be frightened** Plu.

πτύσμα ατος n. [πτύω] **spit, spittle** Plb. NT.

πτύσσω vb. | aor. ἔπτυξα | **1 fold up** —garments Od.
2 roll up —a scroll (after reading it) NT.
3 fold —one's arms (w. ἐπί + DAT. around someone) S.
4 ‖ MID. **fold round oneself, wrap oneself up in** —a cloak Ar.; (of a tunic) **enfold** —its wearer's thigh Plu.(quot. S.)
5 ‖ PASS. (of spears) app., **be layered** (i.e. be held by rank followed by rank, in a phalanx) Il.

πτυχαί ῶν f.pl. | in Trag., acc. πτυχᾱ́ς is sts. wrongly given as πτύχᾱς, as if fr. πτύξ | **1 folds, sheets** (W.GEN. of papyrus, as a place in which information is concealed) A.; **leaves** (of a writing-tablet) E.
2 folds (W.GEN. of sacrificial entrails, whose configuration was taken as having prophetic meaning) E.; (fig., of songs, ref. to intricacies of choral singing and dancing) Pi.
3 folds, clefts, hollows, glens (of a mountain or hillside) Simon. Pi. S. E. Tim.
4 folds, recesses (W.GEN. of heaven or the sky, w.connot. of remoteness) E.

πτύω vb. | aor. ἔπτυσα | **1 spit out** or **up** —blood Il.
2 discharge saliva, spit Hdt. X. Men. Call. NT. —W.DAT. in someone's face S.; (fig.) **repudiate** —someone S.(dub.)
3 (as a ritual act, to protect oneself against pollution, danger, Nemesis) **spit** —W.PREP.PHR. into one's bosom Thphr. Theoc.
4 (of waves) **splash** —W.PREP.PHR. against the shore Theoc.

πτωκάδες ων f.pl. [πτώξ] **timorous creatures** (ref. to birds) S.

πτῶμα ατος n. [πίπτω] **1 fall from a height, fall, plunge** (of a person) A.; (of a thunderbolt) Pl.

2 fall to the ground, **fall** (of a person or horse, caused by stumbling or sim.) E. Pl. Plu.; (of a person knocked down or killed) Trag. Plu.; (fig.) **downfall** (of a person) Plu.; (of a city) Pl.
3 (specif., in wrestling) **fall** Pl. Call.; (of a murdered person, envisaged as a wrestler) E.
4 **fallen body** (W.GEN. of a slain person) E.; **corpse** NT. ‖ PL. bodies of those who have fallen (in battle) Plb. Plu.
5 (collectv.sg.) **ruins** (of a wall) Plb.; (of a city) Plu.
6 that which falls out (for a person); **eventuality, chance, accident** (W.PREP.PHR. proceeding fr. the gods) E.(dub.)

πτώξ πτωκός *m.* [πτώσσω] cowering creature, **hare** Il. Theoc.; (appos.w. λαγωός *hare*) Il.; (fig., ref. to a person being hunted down) A.

πτώσιμος ον *adj.* [πίπτω] (of an army) **fallen** A.; (of soldiers, W.DAT. by the spear) A.

πτῶσις εως *f.* 1 fall from a height, **fall, plunge** (of Phaethon) Plb.
2 **fall** (W.GEN. of dice) Pl.
3 **fall, collapse** (of a house) NT.; **downfall** (of a person) NT.
4 (gramm.) **inflection** (ref. to the modification of a word's form, esp. its termination) Arist.
5 (philos.) specific instance (of a general category), **case, instance** Arist.

πτωσκάζω *vb.* [πτώσσω] (pejor., of a warrior) **cower** Il.

πτώσσω *vb.* [reltd. πτήσσω] ǀ only in pres. ǀ 1 (of persons) **cower** (in fear) Il. Hdt.; (of a bird) Archil.; (tr., of persons) **cower before, shrink from** —*someone* Il. E.; (of birds) **be terrified of** —*clouds* (*fr. which they fear that predators may emerge*) Od.
2 (of locusts threatened by fire) **fly terrified** —W.PREP.PHR. *to water* Il.
3 (pejor., of a beggar) **slink** —W.PREP.PHR. *around the town* Od.; (of a needy person) —W.ACC. *to people's houses* Hes.; (of women) **slink off** —W.PREP.PHR. *to deserted places* (*to meet their lovers*) E.; (of unsuccessful athletes) **skulk** —W.PREP.PHR. *down alleyways* Pi.
4 (of soldiers) **crouch** (for protection) —W.DAT. *beneath shields* Tyrt.

πτωχεία ᾶς, Ion. **πτωχηίη** ης *f.* [πτωχεύω] 1 state of being a beggar, **beggary** Hdt. Lys. Pl.; (personif., as sister of Poverty) Ar.
2 **Beggary** (as description or title of an unknown play by Sophocles, about Odysseus disguised as a beggar at Troy) Arist.

πτωχεύω *vb.* [πτωχός] ǀ iteratv.impf. πτωχεύεσκον ǀ 1 **be a beggar, beg, go begging** Od. +; (tr.) **beg for** —*a meal* Od.; **beg from** —*one's friends* Thgn.
2 (fig., of historians) **be badly off** —W.GEN. *for facts* Plb.

πτωχηίη Ion.*f*.: see πτωχεία

πτωχικός ή όν *adj.* (of clothing) suited to a beggar, **beggarly, beggar's** E. Lycurg.; (of a staff) Ar.; (of desires) Pl.

πτωχίστερος *compar.adj.*: see under πτωχός

πτωχο-μουσο-κόλακες ων *m.pl.* [μοῦσα, κόλαξ] **begging-song-flatterers** (as an example of a bathetic compound) Arist.(quot.)

πτωχο-ποιός οῦ *m.* [ποιέω] **beggar-maker** (ref. to Euripides, criticised for introducing too many such characters) Ar.

—**πτωχοποιός** όν *adj.* (of probity, as a lifestyle) **reducing a person to beggary** Plu.

πτωχός οῦ *m.f.* 1 **beggar** Od. +; (appos.w. ἀνήρ) Od.; (ref. to a woman) A. S.
2 ‖ PL. (as a class) **the poor** NT.; those who are wanting (W.DAT. in spirit) NT.

—**πτωχός** ή όν (also ός όν) *adj.* 1 (of a woman) reduced to beggary, **poor, destitute** S. NT.
2 (of a way of life) **beggarly, beggar's** S.

—**πτωχίστερος** ᾶ ον *compar.adj.* (of a person) **more beggarly** (W.GEN. than another person) Ar.

πυάνιος ον *adj.* [πύανος *bean*, reltd. κύαμος] (of a porridge) **made with beans** Alcm.

Πυανοψιών (later **Πυανεψιών**) ῶνος *m.* [πύανος *bean*; 2nd el. later reltd. ἕψω by pop.etym.] **Pyanopsion** or **Pyanepsion** (fourth month of the Athenian year, named after the festival Pyanopsia, in honour of Apollo, at which boiled beans were served) Thphr. Plu.

πῡγαῖον ου *n.* [πυγή] **rump** (of a bird) Hdt.

πῡγ-αργος ου *m.* [ἀργός] **white-rump** (name of a kind of antelope) Hdt.

πῡγεών ῶνος Ion.*m.* **arse** Hippon.

πῡγή ῆς, Lacon. **πῡγά** ᾶς *f.* **buttocks, rump, arse** (of a person) Hippon. Ar.; (of an ape, a dog) Archil. Ar.

—**πῡγίδιον** ου *n.* [dimin.] **arse** Ar.

πῡγίζω *vb.* **bugger** —*someone, his arsehole* Ar. Theoc.

πύγισμα ατος *n.* **act of buggery** Theoc.

πῡγιστί *adv.* **in the language of buggery** Hippon.

πυγμαῖος η ον Ion.*adj.* [πυγμή *cubit*; cf. πυγών] (of a person) cubit-tall, **pygmy, dwarfish** Hdt.

—**Πυγμαῖοι** ων *m.pl.* **Pygmies** (legendary race, notable for an attack on them by cranes) Il. Hes.*fr.* Call.

πυγμαχέω *contr.vb.* [πυγμάχος] **fight with one's fists, box** Hdt.(quot.epigr.) AR.

πυγμαχίᾱ ᾱς, Ion. **πυγμαχίη** ης *f.* **boxing** (as a sport) Il. hHom. Pi. AR.; **fist-fight** (of drunken youths) Pratin.

πυγ-μάχος ου *m.* [πύξ, μάχομαι] one who fights with his fists, **boxer** Od. Pi. Theoc.

πυγμή ῆς, dial. **πυγμά** ᾶς *f.* 1 (usu.pl.) **fist** E. Ar. Theoc. NT. Plu.
2 use of the fist; (sg.) **boxing** (as a sport) Il. Pi. S.*satyr.fr.* E. Th. Pl. +; (pl.) **fist-fighting** (by drunken revellers) E.*Cyc.*

πῡγο-στόλος ον *adj.* [πυγή, στολή] (of a woman) clothed in a way that draws attention to her arse, **fancy-arsed** Hes.

πυγούσιος ᾱ ον *adj.* [πυγών] (of a pit) **measuring a cubit in breadth** Od.

πυγών όνος *f.* (as a measure of length, distance fr. elbow to first joint of the fingers, twenty finger-widths) **cubit** Hdt. X. ǀ cf. πῆχυς

πύελος ου *f.* 1 **feeding trough** (for poultry) Od.
2 **bath-tub** Scol. Ar. Plb. Plu.

Πῡθαγόρᾱς ου, Ion. **Πῡθαγόρης** εω *m.* **Pythagoras** (religious and scientific thinker, born on Samos in the mid-6th C. BC, later migrated to Croton, where he founded the community that bore his name) Ion Hdt. Isoc. Pl. +

—**Πῡθαγόρειος** ον *adj.* (of ritual practices, a lifestyle, a precept) **Pythagorean** Hdt. Pl. Plu. ‖ MASC.PL.SB. **Pythagoreans** (ref. to his followers) Pl. Arist.

—**Πῡθαγορικός** ή όν *adj.* (of a precept or practice) **Pythagorean** Plu. ‖ MASC.PL.SB. **Pythagoreans** Plu.

—**Πῡθαγορικτᾱς** ᾶ *dial.m.* **follower of Pythagoras, Pythagorean** Theoc.

Πῡθαιεύς (also **Πῡθαεύς**) έως *m.* [Πυθώ] **Pythaieus** (cult name of Apollo) B.*fr.* Th.

Πῡθαΐς ΐδος *f.* **Pythian embassy** (ref. to a sacred embassy to Delphi) Is.

—**Πῡθαϊστής** οῦ *masc.adj.* (of feasting and dancing) **by members of the Pythian embassy** Call.

Πῡθίᾱ ᾱς, Ion. **Πῡθίη** ης *f.* **Pythia** (oracular priestess at Delphi) Hdt. Isoc. Pl. X. +

Πύθια ων *n.pl.* **Pythian games** (held quadrennially at Delphi) Pi. Th. X. +

Πυθιάς άδος *fem.adj.* **1** (of a cry) **Pythian** (ref. to a hymn in honour of Apollo at Delphi) Ar.(quot. S.); (of a victory in the games at Delphi) Pl.
2 ‖ SB. Pythian festival (at Delphi) Pi.

Πυθικός ή όν *adj.* of or relating to Pytho (i.e. Delphi); (of the land, the oracular shrine, a prophecy, officials, or sim.) **of Pytho, Pythian** Trag. Th. Ar. Pl. Plu.; (of the games, victories in them) S. Plu.

Πύθιοι ων *m.pl.* **Pythians** (four persons appointed by the Spartan kings to consult the Delphic oracle on affairs of state) Hdt. X.

Πύθιον ου *n.* **Pythium** (temple of Pythian Apollo at Athens) Th.

Πυθιο-νίκης ου, dial. **Πυθιονίκας** ᾱ *m.* [νίκη] **victor in the Pythian games** Pi. Hdt. Plb. Plu.

—**Πυθιόνῑκος** ον *adj.* (of a hymn or sim.) **for a Pythian victor** or **victory** Pi.; (of a person) **victorious in the Pythian games** B.

Πύθιος ᾱ ον *adj.* | also **Πύθῐος** hHom.(dub.) | **1** of or at Pytho (i.e. Delphi); (of the rock, ref. to Mt. Parnassos) **Pythian** E.; (of gods and goddesses, ref. to those assoc.w. Delphi, i.e. Apollo, Dionysus, Athena Pronaia) Ar.; (of the games, victory garlands) Pi.
2 (epith. of Apollo, as god of Delphi) **Pythian** hHom. A. Pi. B. E. Th. +; (of his temple, oracles, tripod, or sim.) Pi. E.; (of the swan, as sacred to him) Ar.; (of a shore) **of the Pythian god** (ref. to a region in Attica where he had a temple) S.; (of lightning over Mt. Parnes, watched out for as a signal fr. him) E. ‖ MASC.SB. Pythian god (i.e. Apollo) Pi. E.; (prep.phr.) ἐν Πυθίου *in the temple of the Pythian god* (ref. to the Pythium at Athens) Th. Pl. Is.

πυθμήν ένος, Aeol. **πύθμην** ενος *m.* **1 lowest part, bottom** (of a jar or chest) Hes. Alc. Theoc. Plb.; (gener., as an image of completeness) ἐκ νεάτου πυθμένος ἐς κορυφήν *from the very bottom to the top* Sol.
2 lowest region, depths (W.GEN. of Tartaros) Pi.*fr.*; **bottom, bed** (of the sea) Hes. Sol. Thgn. Pl. AR.; (of a river) Pl. ‖ PL. depths or foundations (of the earth) A.
3 that which acts as a base or support; **foot, leg** (of a tripod) Il.; (fig.) **base, foundations** (of Justice, envisaged as an edifice) A.; (gener.) **base, bottom** (of a metal spear-head) Plb. ‖ PL. supports (two in number, either for the base or for the handles of a large cup) Il.; (for doors, ref. to doorposts or sockets) S.; basic constituents (of flesh in the human body) Pl.
4 base, foot (of a tree, i.e. the part next to the ground) Od. Hes.*fr.*; (in fig.ctxt.) **stock** (ref. to a fully grown tree, opp. the small seed fr. which it grew) A.; (fig., of a family) A.; (of insolence) A.(dub.); (of blessings) B.
5 cluster of twigs, clump (of thornwood, used as a broom) Hippon.
6 (math.) **base** (of a series, i.e. the lowest term possessing a given property) Pl.

Πυθοῖ, Πυθοῖδε *advs.*: see under Πυθώ

Πυθό-κραντος ον *adj.* [Πυθώ, κραίνω] ‖ NEUT.PL.SB. things ordained at Pytho, Pythian ordinances A.

Πυθό-μαντις εως *m.* [μάντις] **1** (appos.w. Λοξίας, ref. to Apollo) **prophet at Pytho** A.
2 ‖ MASC.FEM.ADJ. (of the hearth) of the prophet at Pytho S.

πυθόμην (ep.aor.2 mid.): see πυνθάνομαι

Πυθό-χρηστος ον *adj.* [χράομαι] **1** (of oracular pronouncements) **delivered at Pytho, Pythian** A. Arist. Plu.; (of laws, games, a sacrifice) **prescribed at Pytho** X. Plu. ‖ NEUT.SB. oracle delivered at Pytho Plu.
2 (of a person) **instructed by the Pythian oracle** A.; **named by the Pythian oracle** E.

πύθω *vb.* | iterativ.impf. πύθεσκον | fut. πύσω | ep.3sg.aor. πῦσε (hHom.), πύσε (Call.) | **1** (causativ., of earth, sun) **cause to decay, rot** —*a dead person's bones, a slain monster* Il. hHom.; (of rain) —*a boat* Hes.; (of moisture) —*sandals* Call.; (of poison) —*flesh* AR.
2 ‖ PASS. (of the dead, their bones) **rot** or **putrefy** Hom. Hes. hHom.; (of wounds) **fester** AR.

Πυθώ *f.* | gen. Πυθοῦς only in late authors | acc. Πυθώ | dat. Πυθοῖ | —also **Πυθών** ῶνος *f.* | acc. Πυθῶνα | dat. Πυθῶνι | **Pytho, Python** (old names for Delphi) Hom. Hes. Thgn. Lyr. Hdt. Trag. +

—**Πυθοῖ** (also **Πυθόϊ** Pi.) *adv.* **1 at Pytho** Pi. Th.(treaty) Ar. Pl. +
2 to Pytho Plu.

—**Πυθοῖδε** *adv.* **to Pytho** Hes.
—**Πυθώδε** *adv.* **to Pytho** Od. S. Ar. Pl. AR.
—**Πυθόθεν** *adv.* **from Pytho** Pi.
—**Πυθωνάδε** *adv.* **to Python** Pi.
—**Πυθωνόθεν** *adv.* **from Python** Tyrt. Pi.

πύθων ωνος *m.* app., prophet or diviner; (quasi-adjl., appos.w. πνεῦμα *spirit, possessed by a person*) **of prophecy** or **divination** NT.

πύκα *adv.* [reltd. πυκνός] **1 in a close and compact manner; solidly** —*ref. to being armed w. a cuirass* Il. Aeschin.(quot. epigr.) —*ref. to buildings or shields being constructed* Hom. hHom.
2 closely —*ref. to doors fitting together* Il.
3 thickly —*ref. to covering sthg. w. fat* AR.
4 thick and fast —*ref. to a building being struck by missiles* Il.; with frequent rapid steps, **nimbly** —*ref. to dancing* hHom.
5 with close attention, carefully —*ref. to rearing a child* Il.
6 soundly, shrewdly, sensibly —*ref. to thinking* Il.

πυκάζω, dial. **πυκάσδω** *vb.* | dial.fut.inf. πυκαξεῖν | ep.aor. πύκασα, ep.aor.ptcpl. πυκάσσας (Hes.) ‖ PASS.: aor.ptcpl. πυκασθείς | pf.ptcpl. πεπυκασμένος, Aeol. πεπυκάδμενος |
1 cover closely (for protection or concealment); **cover up, wrap** —*a corpse* (*in garments*) Il.; (of a goddess) **envelop** —*herself* (W.DAT. *in a cloud*) Il.; (of whiskers) **cover** —*cheeks* (W.DAT. *w. thick down*) Od.; (fig., of grief) **envelop, overwhelm** —*someone's heart* Il.
2 ‖ AOR.PASS.PTCPL.ADJ. (of a person) wrapped (W.DAT. in a ragged cloak) E. ‖ PF.PASS.PTCPL.ADJ. covered (W.DAT. w. rags, W.ACC. on one's shoulders) Od.; (of a mountain) thickly clad (W.DAT. w. trees) Hes.; (of a bird) concealed (W.DAT. by branches) Il.; (of chariots) covered up (in storage) Il.; (of chariots, a miraculous fish) overlaid (W.DAT. w. gold) Il. Theoc.; (fig., of a person in the grave) wrapped (W.DAT. in silence) Mosch.
3 wreathe —*one's own or another's head, a house* (sts. W.DAT. w. *garlands*) E. D.(oracle) Men. Theoc.
‖ AOR.PASS.PTCPL.ADJ. (of persons) wreathed (W.DAT. w. garlands) Hdt. E. ‖ STATV.PF.PASS. (of an altar) be decked —W.DAT. w. *flowers* Xenoph. ‖ PF.PASS.PTCPL.ADJ. (of Dionysus) wreathed (W.DAT. w. ivy and laurel) hHom.
4 cover with protective armour; cover, shield —*one's body* (W.DAT. w. *armour*) E.; (of a helmet) —*someone's head* Il.
‖ MID. **shield oneself** —W.DAT. w. *armour* E.

5 (of persons) **huddle** or **pack** (W.ACC. themselves) **together** (for concealment) Od.; **pack closely** —*a beached ship* (W.DAT. + ADV. *w. stones all round*) Hes.; **pack, pad** —*boots* (W.DAT. *w. felt*) Hes.
6 make tight, close up (doors) S.
7 ‖ PF.PASS.PTCPL.ADJ. (of a person) **sound** (W.ACC. in mind) Hes. ‖ STATV.PF.PASS. (of the mind of a person who is described as naked in body) **be clothed** —W.ADV. *well* (i.e. w. *good sense*) Mosch.

πυκι-μήδης ες (or **πυκιμηδής** ές) *adj*. [πύκα, μήδομαι] (of a person) **shrewd in counsel, wise** Od. hHom.

πυκινός *adj*.: see πυκνός

πυκινό-φρων ονος *masc.fem.adj*. [φρήν] (of a person) **shrewd-minded** Hes.*fr*.; (of a plan) **carefully devised** hHom.

Πυκνίτης ου *masc.adj*. [Πνύξ] (of personif. Δῆμος *Populace*) **of the Pnyx** (as if that is his domicile) Ar.

πυκνό-πτερος ον *adj*. [πυκνός, πτερόν] (of nightingales) perh. **with fluttering wings** S.

πυκνός, also **πυκινός**, ή (dial. ά) όν, Aeol. **πύκνος** ᾱ ον *adj*. [reltd. πύκα] | compar. πυκνότερος, also πυκινώτερος | superl. πυκνότατος, also πυκινώτατος |
1 dense in texture; (of a corslet, woven fabric or cords) **close-textured** Il. X. Theoc.; (of a cake-mix) Ar.; (of a cloak) **thick** Od.; (of flesh, bone, minerals, a covering of hair) **dense** Pl. X.; (of a wood, bushes, thickets, or sim.) Hom. Hes.*fr*. hHom. Hdt. Theoc.; (of a region, W.DAT. w. glades) Call.; (of clouds) Il. Hes.; (fig., of darkness, a squall, a hailstorm) E. AR.; (of a cloud of shields, a snowstorm of missiles) E.
2 compact or solid in construction; (of a house, door, container, bed, or sim.) **solid, sturdy, secure** Hom. Hes. hHom.; (of a place of ambush) app. **secure** Od.; (of a shield) **closely fitted** (W.DAT. w. hides) Il.
3 (of persons, ranks of warriors, or sim.) **close-packed, massed** Il. Hes. Mimn. E. Ar. X.; (of an ambush) Il.
4 (of things) placed close together, **clustered together** Hom. A. Ion Hdt. Th. Pl. +; (of stones) **close-laid** Hom.; (of teeth, stakes, pegs, bonds) **close-set** Hom. Hdt. Ar. Pl. Theoc.; (of leaves, branches) **dense** Hom.; (of epithets) **abundant** Arist.
5 (of things, circumstances or actions) in close or rapid succession; (of stones, spears, arrows) **flying thick and fast** Hom. Hdt. E.; (of wings) **fast-beating** Hom. Sapph.; (of the wheel of fortune) **fast-turning** S.*fr*.; (of the steps of a blind old man) **short and frequent** E.; (of tears, dews, breezes, journeys, gatherings, requests) **frequent, repeated, constant** Od. Trag. Th. Ar. Isoc. Pl. +
6 (quasi-advbl., of warriors falling, envoys despatched) **in quick succession** Il. A. E.
7 (of grief, delusion) **intense, overwhelming, unrelenting** Il.
8 (of minds, plans, or sim.) soundly based, **shrewd, clever, wise, subtle** Hom. Hes.*fr*. Archil. Thgn. Lyr. Hdt.(oracle) E. +; (of words) Hom. AR.; (of an ambush) **cunning** AR. ‖ NEUT.PL.SB. **clever thoughts** Od.
9 (of persons) **shrewd, clever** Pi. Ar. AR.; (of a dog) **smart** (W.INF. at pursuing game) Pi.*fr*.; ‖ MASC.PL.SB. **clever people** S.

—**πυκνόν**, also **πυκινόν** *neut.sg.adv*. **1 repeatedly, constantly** Hes. hHom. Ar. Men.
2 deeply, intensely —*ref. to grieving* Od.
3 tightly —*ref. to being crammed together* Ar.

—**πυκνά**, also **πυκινά** *neut.pl.adv*. **1 repeatedly, constantly** Il. Pl. X. Aeschin. Thphr. +
2 with frequent rapid steps, nimbly —*ref. to dancing* hHom. Ar.

3 (intensv., W.ADJ. *torn*) **all over** Od.

—**πυκνῶς**, also **πυκινῶς** *adv*. **1 closely** —*ref. to doors fitting together* Hom.
2 deeply, intensely —*ref. to being distressed* Hom.
3 carefully —*ref. to rearing someone* Anacr.
4 in a tight group —*ref. to dogs running* X.
5 soundly, shrewdly, sensibly —*ref. to giving advice* Hom.

—**πυκνότερον** *compar.adv*. **more frequently, more regularly** Ar. Pl. D.

Πυκνός (gen.sg.): see Πνύξ

πυκνό-στικτος ον *adj*. [πυκνός, στικτός] (of deer) **thickly spotted, dappled** S.

πυκνότης ητος *f*. **1 thickness, density** (of clouds, minerals, flesh, bones, or sim.) Ar. Pl. Arist. Plu.; (of thickets) Plu.; (of a horse's hair) Plu.
2 closeness, compactness (of interlocking hoplite shields, or shields in a tortoise formation) Th. Plb.; **close formation, density** (of soldiers, wagons) Plu.
3 close spacing (of musical notes, adding variation to a melody) Pl. | cf. μανότης 2
4 frequency (of things occurring) Isoc. Pl.; **frequent repetition** (of a dance rhythm) Plu.
5 shrewdness, cleverness (of a person) Ar. Plu.

πυκνόω *contr.vb*. **1** (of soldiers) **compact, contract** —*themselves, their ranks* Hdt. Plb. Plu.; (intr.) **crowd together, close ranks** Plb.; (of a commander) **close up** —*the front line* Plu.; (fig., of a person) **concentrate** —*oneself* (*i.e. one's thoughts*) Ar.
2 ‖ PASS. (of air) **be condensed** (to form cloud and mist) Pl.; (of water, to form ice) Arist.; (of clay) **be contracted** (in fire) Plu.; (of iron) **be hardened** (by cold) Plu.
3 ‖ PASS. (of a breath taken by an orator) **be deep** Plu.
4 ‖ PASS. (of ground) **be thickly covered** —W.GEN. w. *tracks* X.

πύκνωμα ατος *n*. **1 concentrated formation** (of troops) Plu.; **dense line** (of pikes) Plu.
2 (mus.) **close spacing** (of the three lower notes in a tetrachord, when separated by a larger interval fr. the top note) Pl.

πύκνωσις εως *f*. **1 close order** (of troops, pikes) Plb.
2 thickening (of the skin, rendering it less permeable to heat) Plu.

πυκταλίζω *vb*. [πύκτης] **box** (as a sport) Anacr. Hippon.

πυκτεύω, Boeot. **πουκτεύω** *vb*. **fight with one's fists, box** Isoc. Pl. X. D. Corinn.; **land a blow** —w. ἐς + ACC. *on someone's head* E.*Cyc*.

πύκτης ου, dial. **πύκτᾱς** ᾱ *m*. [πυγμή, πύξ] **one who fights with his fists** (as a sport), **boxer** Xenoph. Pi. S. Pl. +

πυκτικός ή όν *adj*. (of a person) **skilled in boxing** Pl. Arist.; (of a fight) **for boxers** Pl. ‖ FEM.SB. **art of boxing** Pl.

πυκτοσύνη ης *f*. **art of boxing** Xenoph.

πύλᾱ *dial.f*.: see πύλαι

Πυλᾱγορέω *contr.vb*. [Πυλάγορος] **be a delegate at Pylai** Aeschin. D.

Πυλ-άγορος (or **Πυλᾱγόρος**) ου *m*. [Πύλαι, ἀγείρω] **delegate at Pylai** (ref. to a person attending the Amphictyonic Council held there) Hdt. Aeschin. D. Plu.

πύλαι ῶν (dial. ᾶν, ep. ἄων, Ion. έων) *f.pl*. —also sg. **πύλη** ης, dial. **πύλᾱ** ᾱς *f*. | ep.dat.pl. πύλῃς, πύλῃσι | **1 pair of double gates, gates** (of a city, military camp, or sim.) Hom. Hes. A. Pi. E. Th. + ‖ SG. **single gate** (of a pair) Hdt. ‖ COLLECTV.SG. **gate** (of a city) Plb. NT. Plu.
2 pair of double doors, doors (of a house) Pi. Trag.; (of a palace) Hdt. X. AR.; (of a temple) E. Call. ‖ COLLECTV.SG. **door** (of a house) S.; (of a treasury) E.*fr*.

3 gates (W.GEN. of Hades) Hom. Hes. Thgn. A. E. NT.; (of the dead, of darkness) E. ‖ COLLECTV.SG. gate (of Hades) Theoc.
4 sluice-gates Hdt.
5 (specif., fig.ref. to the Isthmos) **gates** (W.GEN. of Corinth) Pi.; (of the Peloponnese) B. X.; **gateway** (to the sea) Pi.
6 entrance into a country through mountains, pass Hdt.; (ref. to a named pass) **Gates** (W.GEN. or ADJ., as *of Syria and Cilicia, Caspian*) X. Plb. [such passes were sts. blocked by a gated wall] | see also Πύλαι
7 (fig.) **gates** (W.GEN. of spring, opened at its beginning) Alc.; (of song, thrown open by its composer) Pi.; (of new themes for poetry, sought by a poet) B.*fr.*; **doors** (to close one's ears, ref. to hands) Pl.
8 narrow passage (envisaged as a gateway), **neck, aperture** (W.GEN. of a water-container) Emp.; **gateway, entrance** (of a vagina) Archil.; (W.GEN. of a mouth, as a barrier for speech to pass beyond) E.; (W.GEN. to a lake, ref. to the head of a strait) A.
9 (medic.) **portal vein** (conveying blood to the liver) E. Pl.

Πύλαι ὧν *f.pl.* **Pylai, The Gates** (local name for the pass more widely called Θερμοπύλαι *Thermopylai*) Hdt. Ar. Att.orats. Plb. Plu.

—**Πυλαΐα** ᾱς, dial. **Πυλαίη** ης *f.* **Pylaia** (twice-yearly meeting of the Amphictyonic Council at Pylai) Hdt. Aeschin. D.; (fig. and pejor.) **gathering, medley, mishmash** (W.GEN. of stories) Plu.

—**Πυλαίη** ης *dial.fem.adj.* (epith. of Demeter) **of Pylai** Call.*epigr.*

—**Πυλαϊκός** ή όν *adj.* of or relating to Pylai or the Pylaia; (fig. and pejor., of rabble-rousing) **vulgar** or **indiscriminate** Plu.

—**Πυλᾶτις** ιδος *fem.adj.* (of an assembly, ref. to the Amphictyonic Council) **at Pylai** S.

πυλαι-μάχος, dial. **πυλᾱμάχος** (Stesich., dub.), ον *adj.* [μάχομαι] (epith. perh. of Ares) **fighting at city-gates** Stesich.; (of Athena) Call.

—**Πυλαιμάχος** ου *fem.adj.* [Πύλος] (epith. of Athena) **fighting at Pylos** Ar.

πυλ-άρτης ου *m.* [ἀραρίσκω] (ref. to Hades) **one who fastens gates, gatekeeper** (of the underworld) Hom.

Πυλᾶτις *fem.adj.*: see under Πύλαι

πυλαωρός *ep.m.*: see πυλωρός

πυλεών ῶνος *m.* **garland** Alcm. Call.

πύλη *f.*: see πύλαι

πυλη-δόκος ου *m.* [πύλη, see πύλαι; δοκεύω] (epith. of Hermes) **watcher at the door** hHom. [or perh. *one who waits in doorways*]

πυλίς ίδος *f.* [dimin. πύλη, see πύλαι] **little gate, postern** Hdt. Th. Att.orats. Pl. X. Plb.

Πυλοι-γενής ές, gen. έος *ep.adj.* [Πύλος; γένος, γίγνομαι] (of Nestor) **born at Pylos** Il.; (of people, horses) Il. hHom.

Πύλος ου *f.* (*perh. also m.* Hom.) **Pylos** (city and district in SW. Peloponnese, home of Nestor) Hom. +; (peninsula in Messenia) Hdt. Th. Ar. +

—**Πύλιος** ᾱ ον *adj.* (of Nestor) **from Pylos, Pylian** S. Call. ‖ MASC.PL.SB. **men of Pylos, Pylians** Hom. Hdt. X.

—**Πυλόθεν** *adv.* (ref. to movt.) **from Pylos** Od.

—**Πύλονδε** *adv.* **to** or **towards Pylos** Hom.

πυλουρός Ion.*m.*: see πυλωρός

πυλόω *contr.vb.* [Πύλαι] (of the Athenians) **furnish with gates** —*the Peiraieus* X. ‖ PASS. (of a city wall) **be furnished** —W.DAT. *w. gates* Ar.

πυλώματα των *n.pl.* [πυλόω] **1 gate, gateway** (of a city) A. E.
2 door, portal (of a house, palace, temple) E.

πυλών ῶνος *m.* [πύλαι] **1 gate-house** or **gate-tower** Plb. NT.
2 door or **doorway** (of a palace or house) Plb. NT.; (of a courtyard) NT. ‖ PL. **doors** or **portals** (of a temple) NT.

πυλωρός, ep. **πυλαωρός**, Ion. **πυλουρός**, οῦ *m.* (*also f.* E.) [οὖρος², ὁράω] **1 one who keeps watch over a gate** or **doorway, gatekeeper, doorkeeper** (of a city wall, palace, temple) Il. Hdt. E. AR. Plu.; (of Hades, ref. to Cerberus) E.; (of the Isthmos, ref. to Poseidon) Call.; **guardian of a gate** (ref. to a warrior) A.
2 (gener.) **warden, guardian** (of a person) S.

πύματος η (dial. ᾱ) ον *superl.adj.* **1 in last** or **most distant position**; (of ranks) **last, hindmost, rear** Il.; (of a limit) **furthest** Parm.; (of Aithiopians) **remotest** Theoc.; (of a rim) **at the outermost edge** (of a shield) Il.; (of a chariot-rail) **at the end** (or perh. *at the chariot's rear*) Il.; (of a nose) at the very top, **at the bridge** Il. ‖ MASC.PL.SB. **troops in the rear** Il.
2 last in time; (of a lap in a race, a meal, night-watch, song) **last** (of a series) Hom. AR. Theoc.; (quasi-advbl., of a person or thing to whom sth. is done) **last of all** Hom. Hes. hHom. Thgn. Theoc.; (of a sleep, a journey) **last** (before death) hHom. S.; (of old age) **coming at the last** S.; (prep.phr.) ἐν πυμάτῳ *at the last, finally* S.

—**πύματον**, **πύματα** *neut.sg. and pl.superl.adv.* **1 for the last time** Hom. B.; (also) τὸ πύματον Theoc. Bion
2 (fig.) ὅ τι πύματον *by the most extreme possible fate* —*ref. to perishing* S.

πύνδαξ ακος *m.* **bottom** (of a metal container) Thphr.

πυνθάνομαι, also (pres. and impf.) **πεύθομαι** *mid.vb.* | impf. ἐπυνθανόμην, also ἐπευθόμην, ep. πυνθανόμην, πευθόμην | fut. πεύσομαι, dial. πευσοῦμαι | AOR.2: ἐπυθόμην, ep. πυθόμην | imperatv. πυθοῦ, Ion. πυθεῦ | ep.3sg.redupl. opt. πεπύθοιτο, Ion.3pl.opt. πυθοίατο | pf. πέπυσμαι | plpf. ἐπεπύσμην, ep.3sg. πέπυστο, 3du. πεπύσθην ‖ neut.impers.vbl.adj. πευστέον |
1 hear or **overhear** (sounds); **hear** Hom. A. —*speech, sounds* Hom. —W.GEN. *shouting, fighting* Hom.
2 hear, learn (about sthg.) Hom. + —W.GEN. *of someone or sthg.* Hom. S. E. —W.GEN. + PTCPL. *of someone doing sthg., sthg. happening* Il. A. Th.
3 hear, learn —*sthg.* Hom. +. —(W.GEN. *about someone*) Hom. —(W.GEN. *fr. someone*) Il. Hdt. Trag. Ar. —(W.PREP.PHR.) Hdt. Trag. Th. + —W.ACC. + PTCPL. *that someone is doing sthg., that sthg. has happened* Hom. Hdt. Trag. Th. + —W.ACC. + PREDIC.ADJ. *that someone is such and such* Il. E. —W.COMPL.CL. or ACC. + INF. *that sthg. is the case* Il. Hdt. S. E. Antipho + —W.INDIR.Q. *what is the case* hHom. Hdt.
4 (pres. and impf.) **know** (as a result of having heard or learned) —W.GEN. *about someone or sthg.* Hom. Pl. —W.ACC. + INF. *that sthg. is the case* A. Pi. AR. —W.GEN. + COMPL.CL. *fr. someone that sthg. is the case* Hes.
5 seek information, make inquiries (sts. W.GEN. or PREP.PHR. fr. someone) Hom. Hdt. Trag. Pl. + —W.ACC. *about someone or sthg.* Hom. Trag. Ar. X. AR. Theoc. —W.GEN. *about someone* Od. S. —W. περί + GEN. *about someone or sthg.* Hdt. Antipho + —W.INDIR.Q. *whether sthg. is the case, what is the case* Hom. Hdt. Trag. Pl. +

πύξ *adv.* [πυγμή] **1 with the fist** —*ref. to striking someone or being struck* Lys. Ar. X. D. Theoc. Plu.
2 with the fist as used in boxing, **in** or **at boxing** —*ref. to excelling, contending, winning,* or *sim.* Hom. Hes. Pi. B. Theoc.

πύξινος η (dial. ᾱ) ον *adj.* [πύξος] (of a yoke for mules) **of boxwood** Il.; (of a lyre) Theoc.; (of a juror's ticket) Arist.

πύξος ου f. **box tree** Bion
πυός οῦ m. **rich milk produced by a she-goat or ewe immediately after giving birth (considered a delicacy), beestings, cream** Ar.
πυππάξ interj. (expressing admiration) **bravo!** Pl.
πῦρ πυρός n. | only sg.; for pl. see πυρά below | **1 visible state or condition of combustion, fire** or **flames** Hom. +; (as an element) Heraclit. A. Emp. +; (identified w. *aither*) Parm. E. [or perh. ref. to the sun E.]
2 fuel in a state of combustion (intentionally lit to provide heat or light), **fire** Hom. +; (assoc.w. the domestic hearth) A. E.; (on an altar) Hom. +; (used for testing the purity of precious metals) Thgn. Pi. Isoc. Plb.
3 fire (used as a destructive agent, esp. in war) Hom. +; (sent fr. heaven by God to punish sinners) NT.; (ref. to the conditions of Hell, as a place of eternal punishment) NT.
4 fire, flames (of a funeral pyre) Hom. S. E.; (of a torch) Trag.; (of a beacon) A. Th.; **watch-fire** (lit at night) Il.
5 fire or **lava** (of a volcano) A. Pi. S. Th.
6 heat or light of celestial phenomena; fire (of the sun) Pi. E.; (of stars) S. E.; (of lightning or thunderbolts) Pi. Trag. Ar.
7 fire, burning heat (of summer) Pi.
8 burning sensation (felt by a lover), **fire** Sapph.; (fig.ref. to love) Call.*epigr.* Theoc.; (ref. to hopeful anxiety) S.
9 high temperature (of a person), **fever** Call.; (specif.) **inflammation** (in the body) Pl.
10 (fig.) fiery behaviour or feelings; διὰ πυρὸς ἰέναι (or sim.) *go through fire* (i.e. burn w. hatred) —W.DAT. *against someone* E.
11 fire (as the exemplar of that which is hot) Ar.; (as the exemplar of that which is dangerous, destructive or irresistible) Il. +; διὰ πυρὸς ἰέναι *go through fire* (i.e. face any danger) Ar. X.; (ref. to a person, w.connots. of violence and ruthlessness) S.; (in a comparison w. a person, ref. to his inflammable nature) Plu.; (ref. to discord amongst mortals, brought by Jesus) NT.
12 fire (as a sign of divine inspiration, assoc.w. the Holy Spirit) NT.
—πυρά ῶν n.pl. | irreg.dat. πυροῖς (X.) | **watch-fires** (lit at night, usu. in a camp) Il. Hdt. E. Th. X. +
πυρά ᾶς, Ion. πυρή ῆς f. **1 funeral pyre** Hom. Pi. B. Hdt. S. E. +; **pyre** (for burning sacrificial oxen) Hdt.
2 tomb, grave (where the pyre stood) S. E.
3 altar (for burnt sacrifices) Od. E.
4 fire lit for warmth, bonfire NT.
πυρ-άγρη ης Ion.f. [ἀγρέω] **fire-tongs** (of a smith) Hom. Call.
πυρακτέω contr.vb. **harden with fire, scorch** —*the tip of a stake* Od.
πῦραμίς ίδος f. **pyramid** Hdt. X. Arist.; (as a geometrical figure) Pl.
πυραμοῦς οῦντος m. [πυρός] **a kind of cake** (app. made of roasted wheat and honey, given as a prize on social or festal occasions), **cake** Ar. Call.; (fig.) **prize** Ar.
πυργηδόν adv. [πύργος] **like a wall, in close-packed lines** —ref. to soldiers or hunters arranging themselves Il.
πυργηρέομαι pass.contr.vb. [ἀραρίσκω] **1** (of occupants of a city) **be enclosed within towers or walls, be besieged** A. E.; (of persons on a rooftop) **be under siege** (fr. persons below) E.
2 (fig., of persons, compared to a city) **have** (W.ACC. one's body) **under siege** —W.PREP.PHR. *fr. one's enemies* E.
πυργίδιον ου n. [dimin. πύργος] **little tower, garret** Ar.

πύργινος η ον adj. (perh. of cities) **towered** A.
πυργο-δάϊκτος ον adj. [δαΐζω] (of wars) **by which ramparts are torn apart** A.
πυργομαχέω contr.vb. [μάχομαι] **1 assault a tower** X.
2 fight from a tower (on an elephant's back) Plb.
πύργος ου m. **1 fortified wall or part of a wall** (securing a city or defensive position), **wall, fortification, rampart** Hom. Archil. Pi. Trag. AR. ‖ PL. **walls** or **ramparts** Hom. Hes. Hippon. B. Hdt. Trag. +
2 tower (as part of a city wall, or as a separate defensive fortification) Il. Hdt. Th. Ar. X. +; (of a palace or house) Hdt. Ar.
3 (gener.) **place of security, stronghold** E.
4 (fig., ref. to persons or their prosperity) **stronghold, tower of strength** Od. Eleg. E.; (W.GEN. for a city) Alc. Pi.; (W.GEN. in battle) Theoc.; **bastion, defence** (W.GEN. against death) S.; (ref. to a renowned island-state) **tower, bastion** (which its citizens may climb by their lofty achievements) Pi.
5 movable tower for storming a city, siege-tower X.
6 ‖ PL. **towers** (on boats transporting troops, perh.ref. to defensive structures) Hdt.
7 tower (ref. to a separate structure on a country estate, occupied by female slaves) D.; (in a vineyard, hired out to farmers) NT.
8 body of troops drawn up in close order, line Il.
πυργοῦχος ου m. [ἔχω] **tower, turret** (on a warship) Plb.
πυργο-φύλαξ ακος m. (ref. to a god) **guardian of the walls** (W.GEN. of a land) A.
πυργόω contr.vb. **1 fortify with walls** —*a city, a citadel, the Isthmos* Od. Thgn. Hdt.(oracle) E. ‖ MID. **create** (W.ACC. **strong positions**) **by building walls** X.
2 (fig., of a poet) **raise tower-high** —*majestic words, the art of comedy* Ar.; (of a city) —*a bride's and bridegroom's happiness* (w. wedding songs) E.; (of gods) **exalt** —*a city, things of no worth* E.; (of a father) **establish, set up strongly** —*his sons* (W.DAT. *in kingdoms*) E.
3 (pejor., of heralds) **build up** —*twice as much as happened* (i.e. magnify it in their narrative) E.; (of a person) —*a claim on someone's gratitude* (W.ADV. *excessively, i.e. exaggerate it*) E.
4 ‖ MID.PASS. (fig., of a woman envisaged as a horse in harness) **stand tall and proud** —W.DAT. *in her apparel* A.
‖ PF.MID.PASS. **be towering** —W.DAT. *in courage, brazenness* E.; **have an exaggerated pride** —W.DAT. *in one's words* E.
‖ PASS. (of wealth) **be raised tower-high** B.
πυργώδης ες adj. (of the top or platform) **of a tower** S.
πύργωμα ατος n. [πυργόω] **walled city, fortress** Hdt.(oracle) E. ‖ PL. **walls** or **battlements** A. E.
πυργωτίς ιδος fem.adj. (of a barricade, fig.ref. to an encircling army) **around the walls** A. [or perh. *forming a wall*]
πυρ-δαής ές adj. [πῦρ, δαίω] (of a person) **who kindles a fire** A.
πύρδανον ου n. prob. **firewood** Call.
πυρεῖα, Ion. πυρήϊα, ων n.pl. **firesticks** (generating fire fr. the friction of a drill of harder wood rotated against a softer wood) hHom. S. Pl. AR. Theoc.
πυρέσσω, Att. πυρέττω vb. **be feverish** or **fall ill with a fever** E.Cyc. Ar. Pl. +
πυρετός οῦ m. **1 burning heat** (brought by Sirius in the autumn) Il. [or perh. *fever*]
2 fever Ar. Pl. X. D. Arist. +

πυρευτικός ή όν adj. [πυρεύω] (of hunting) **of the firelit kind** (i.e. by torchlight, ref. to night-time fishing) Pl.
πυρεύω vb. **set fire to** —*timber* Pl.
πυρή Ion.f.: see πυρά
πυρήια Ion.n.pl.: see πυρεῖα
πυρήν ῆνος m. **stone** (of the olive, the wild cherry) Hdt.; (of the lotus) Plb.
πυρη-φόρος ον adj. [πυρός, φέρω] (of a plain) **wheat-bearing** Od. hHom.
πυρία ᾶς, Ion. **πυρίη** ης f. [πῦρ] **vapour-bath** (made by throwing aromatic substances on hot embers confined under a cloth) Hdt. Pl.
πυριάτη ης f. **beestings curdled by heating** (ref. to rich milk, eaten as a delicacy) Ar.
πυριατήριον ου n. **vapour-bath room** Plu.
πυρι-βόλος ον adj. [βάλλω] (of lightning-strokes) **hurling fire** E.fr.
πυρι-γενέτᾱς ᾱ dial.masc.adj. [γένος, γίγνομαι] (of a horse's bit) born in fire, **fire-forged** A.
πυρι-γενής ές adj. (of a horse's bit) born in fire, **fire-forged** E.; (of violence, meton. for a sword) E.
πυρι-γόνος ον adj. (of an oily kind of soil) **productive of fire** Plu.
πυρι-δαής ές adj. [δαίω] (of an eye) **blazing with fire** B.fr.
πυρί-δαπτος ον adj. [δάπτω] (of a torch, ref. to its wood) **devoured by fire** A.
πυρίδια ων n.pl. [dimin. πυρός] **little grains of wheat** Ar.
πυρι-έθειρα ᾱς fem.adj. [πῦρ] (of a lightning flash) **with tresses of fire** B.
πυρι-ήκης ες adj. [reltd. ἀκίς, ἀκωκή] (of a stake) **with fiery point** Od.
πυρι-θαλπής ές adj. [θάλπω] (of a rock) **heated by fire** (fr. the forge of Hephaistos) AR.
πυρί-καυτος (also **πυρίκαυστος**) ον adj. [καυτός] **1** (of a stake) **charred by fire** (at its end, to harden it) Il.; (of an ashen powder, ref. to its appearance) Plu.
2 (of diseases) **burning, inflammatory** Pl.
πυρί-κμητος ον adj. [κάμνω] (of basins and tripods) **fire-wrought** Call.
πυριμανέω contr.vb. [μαίνομαι] (of rays of heat, on meeting inflammable material) **break into a fierce fire** Plu.
πύρινος η ον adj. **1** (of elements within a substance) **made or consisting of fire** (opp. air, earth, or sim.) Arist.
2 (of a heavenly body, ref. to a meteorite) with the appearance of fire, **fiery** Plu.
3 (fig., as a nickname given to a particular war) **fiery** (because it spread like fire and could not be extinguished) Plb.
πύρινος η ον adj. [πυρός] (of a crop, loaves) **of wheat, wheaten** E.satyr.fr. X.
πυρί-στακτος ον adj. [πῦρ, στακτός] (of a rock, ref. to Aetna) **that drips with fire** E.Cyc.
πυρί-φατος ον adj. [θείνω] (of a land) **destroyed by fire** A.
Πυρι-φλεγέθων οντος m. [φλεγέθω] **Pyriphlegethon, Fireblazer** (one of the rivers of the underworld) Od. Pl.
πυρι-φλέγων οντος masc.ptcpl.adj. [φλέγω] (fig., of a fierce lion) **blazing with fire** E.
πυρί-φλεκτος ον adj. (of a torch) **blazing with fire** E.
πυρί-χρως ωτος masc.fem.adj. [χρώς] (of an angry face) **fire-coloured** Arist.(quot.)
πυρ-καϊά (also **πυρκαϊά** E.) ᾶς, Ion. **πυρκαϊή** ῆς f. [καίω] **1 funeral pyre** Il. E. Plu.; (fig.ref. to a pillaged city) Plu.; **pyre** (for an animal sacrifice) AR.
2 conflagration, fire Heraclit. Hdt. Plu.; (fig.ref. to a destructive war) Plu.

3 (leg.) **arson** D.(law) Arist.
4 burnt stump (of a sacred olive) Lys.(dub.)
πύρνον ου n. [πῦρός] (sg.pl.) wheaten bread, **bread** Od. Lyr.adesp.(cj.)
πυρο-βόλα ων n.pl. —also app. **πυροβόλοι** ων m.pl. [πῦρ, βάλλω] **incendiary arrows** Plu.
πυρο-ειδής ές adj. [εἶδος¹] **1** (of a substance) with the form or appearance of fire, **fiery** Pl.; (of a meteorite, fragments of it) Plu.
2 (of the sight of flashing armour and colourful military costumes) **fiery, flaming** Plu.
πυρόεις εσσα εν adj. **1** (of a star, ref. to a comet or meteor) **fiery** AR.
2 (of the snuff on a lamp-wick) **red-hot** Call.
πυρ-οπίπης ου m. [πυρός, ὀπῑπεύω] **wheat-snooper** (ref. to an Athenian σιτοφύλαξ *corn-inspector*) Ar.
πῡροπωλέω contr.vb. **sell wheat** D.
πυρο-ρραγής ές adj. [πῦρ, ῥήγνῡμι] (of a sound) **fire-cracked** (i.e. as of a pot cracked in firing) Ar.
πῡρός οῦ m. **wheat** (ref. to the grain) Hom. Hippon. Hdt.; (collectv.pl., ref. to the plant or the grain) Hom. Hippon. Hdt. Th. Ar. Pl. +
πῡρο-φόρος ον adj. [φέρω] **1** (of land, a country, or sim.) **wheat-bearing** Il. Hes. Eleg. Lyr. E. +
2 (of ships) **wheat-carrying** B.fr.
πυρόω contr.vb. [πῦρ] **1 set fire to, burn** —*a city, house, temples, ships, individuals* Hdt. S. E. —*parts of sacrificial animals* A.; **burn out** —*the Cyclops' eye* E.Cyc. ‖ PASS. (of a person, a city, its houses, sacrificial offerings, or sim.) be set on fire or burned Lyr.adesp. Pi. E. Plu.
2 cremate —*a person's bones* E.fr. ‖ PASS. (of a dead person) be cremated E.; (of a person's ashes, envisaged as gold-dust) be put to the fire (perh. w. secondary connot. *be tested in the fire*; see 6) A.
3 ‖ PASS. (of matter in the early universe) be made fiery Pl.
4 ‖ PASS. (fig., of a person) be inflamed (w. excitement) —W.ACC. *in one's heart* (W.DAT. *by a beacon-signal*) A.
5 subject (sthg.) to fire ‖ PASS. (of bronze) be made red-hot Plu.
6 test or prove (a precious metal) by applying fire; **prove the quality of** —*cups* Thphr. | see also 2
7 fumigate —*a house* (W.DAT. *w. sulphur*) Theoc.
πυρ-πάλαμος ον adj. [παλάμη] (of Zeus' lightning) perh. **flung with fiery hand** Pi.
πύρ-πνοος ον, also contr. **πύρπνους** ουν adj. [πνέω] (of mythical monsters, their mouths, or sim.) **fire-breathing** A. E.; (of Zeus' lightning) A.
πυρπολέω contr.vb. [πυρπόλος] **1 light a fire** or **keep a fire burning** Od. X.; (tr.) **light** or **burn** —*coals* Ar.
2 set fire to —*a house, city, country, an individual* Ar. Plb. Plu. ‖ PASS. (of a city, country, or sim.) be set on fire Hdt. Plb. Plu.
πυρπόλημα ατος n. **beacon-fire** E.
πυρ-πόλος ον adj. [πέλω, πολέω] (of a thunderbolt) **fiery** E.
πυρράζω vb. [πυρρός] (of the morning or evening sky) **be fiery red** (as a sign of coming weather) NT.
πυρρίας ου m. **redhead** (ref. to a slave w. red or auburn hair, characteristic of Thracians) Ar.
πυρρίχη ης f. **pyrrhic dance, war-dance** (energetic dance in hoplite armour, imitating movements of defence and attack, assoc. esp. w. the Panathenaic festival) Ar. Pl. X.; (pl., ref. to the defensive movements of an armed man under attack) E.; (ref. to the dance of Roman priests of Mars called Salii) Plu.; (fig.phr.) πυρρίχην βλέπειν **have a war-dance look** (i.e. *a fierce martial expression*) Ar.
πυρριχίζω vb. **perform a war-dance** Plu.

πυρριχιστής οῦ *m.* **pyrrhic dancer** Lys.; (pejor., opp. a true soldier) Plu. ‖ COLLECTV.PL. performance by pyrrhic dancers (at the Panathenaia) Is.

πυρρίχος η ον *adj.* [dimin. πυρρός] (of a bull) **ruddy** or **tawny** Theoc.

πυρρόθριξ *adj.*: see πυρσόθριξ

πυρρός ά (Ion. ή) όν *adj.* —also **πυρσός** ή (dial. ά) όν *adj.* [reltd. πῦρ] | superl. πυρσότατος (Plu.) | **1** yellow-brown in colour; (of a first beard, cheeks covered by it) **auburn, sandy** A. E.; (of a person w. such a beard) Theoc. ‖ FEM.SB. (w. θρίξ understd.) auburn hair (around the lips) Theoc.
2 (of a person) **auburn-haired** Plu.(quot.epigr.); (of a barbarian tribe, unless *with ruddy complexion*) Hdt.
3 (of a lion's jaws, its mane) **tawny** E. Theoc.; (of a bull's coat or head of hair) E.; (of a hound, its colour, its hair) X.; (of a horse's mane) Plu. ‖ MASC.SB. (ref. to a horse) chestnut, bay Theoc.
4 (of a colour, described as golden yellow blended w. grey) **auburn, sandy, chestnut, tawny** Pl.
5 (of shit, the colour of clothing stained by it) **brown** or **yellow** Ar.; (of a person, fr. shitting oneself or being shat on) Ar.
6 (of gold) **ruddy, reddish** Arist.; (of a cloak) perh. **red** Hdt.; (of a rose) Mosch.
7 (of a shooting star) **fiery, flaming** Theoc.; (of a person's eyes) **fiery** or **blood-shot** E.

πυρρό-τριχος ον *adj.* [θρίξ] (of a person) **red-haired** or **sandy-haired** Theoc.

πυρσαίνω *vb.* (of a river famed as rich in pigment) **colour** (W.ACC. hair) **auburn** —W.PREDIC.ADJ. *w. a golden hue* E.

πυρσεία ᾶς *f.* [πυρσεύω] **fire-signalling** Plb.

πυρσεύω *vb.* [πυρσός¹] **1 light beacon-fires, signal by beacons** X.
2 use a beacon to mark —*an island* (W.ACC. w. *its flaming light*) E.
3 (fig.) **raise like a beacon** —*a shout conveying news* (W.GEN. *of sthg.*) E.

πυρσό-θριξ (also **πυρρόθριξ** Arist.) τριχος *masc.fem.adj.* [πυρρός, θρίξ] (of a horse) **with coat of bay** or **chestnut hair** E.; (of a person) **red-haired** or **sandy-haired** Sol.(dub., v.l. ξανθόθριξ)

πυρσό-νωτος ον *adj.* [νῶτον] (of a dragon) **tawny-backed** E.

πυρσός¹ οῦ *m.* [πῦρ] | also neut.pl. πυρσά (E.) | **1 firebrand, torch** E. AR. ‖ PL. (fig.) fires (of love) Theoc.
2 beacon-fire Il. B. Hdt. E. Plb.; (fig., W.GEN. of hymns of praise) Pi.
3 ‖ NEUT.PL. watch-fires E.

πυρσός² *adj.*: see πυρρός

πυρσό-χαιτος ον *adj.* [πυρρός, χαίτη] (of a head) **with auburn hair** B.

πυρσώδης ες *adj.* [πυρσός¹] (of the flame) **of a torch** E.

πυρφορέω *contr.vb.* [πυρφόρος] **1 carry a torch** E.
2 bring fire (to burn a city) A.(dub.)

πυρ-φόρος ον *adj.* [πῦρ, φέρω] **1** carrying fire (fr. heaven); (of thunder or lightning) **fire-bearing** A. Pi. S.; (of Zeus, as sender of lightning; of his thunderbolt, envisaged as a spear) S. Ar.; (of lightning, described as a star) Ar.
2 carrying fire (against an enemy); (of arrows) **incendiary** Th.; (of eagles, acting as a substitute for arrows or thunderbolts) Ar.
3 carrying the fire of a torch; (of an assailant) **carrying a firebrand** A. S.; (epith. of Prometheus, of Demeter or Persephone) **torch-bearing** S. E.; (of the light of Artemis' torches) **fire-carrying** S.

4 ‖ MASC.SB. fire-bearer (military official in charge of the sacrificial flame, in Sparta and elsewhere) Hdt. X.
5 (epith. of deified Plague) **fire-bringing** (i.e. causing fever) S.

πυρώδης ες *adj.* (of flashes of lightning, beams of light) **fire-like, fiery** Ar. Pl. Plu.; (of the temperature of a person's body or of soil) Plu.; (fig., of a blush) Plu.

πυρ-ωπός όν *adj.* [ὤψ] (of a thunderbolt) **with fiery appearance, fiery** A.

πύστις εως *f.* [πυνθάνομαι] **1 inquiry, question** (sts. W.GEN. to someone) Th. Pl.
2 that which is learnt by inquiring, **information, news** (sts. W.GEN. of sthg.) Trag. Th.

πυτῑναῖος ᾱ ον *adj.* [πῠτίνη *wicker wine-flask*] (of wings, fig.ref. to straps or handles) **on wicker flasks** Ar.

πω, Ion. **κω** *enclit.adv.* **1** up to this time, so far; (only w.neg.) οὔ πω, οὔπω, μή πω, μήπω, οὐ ... πω, μή ... πω (or sim.) *not yet* Hom. + | see also πώποτε
2 (intensv., w.neg.) at all; οὔ πω, μή πω (or sim.) *not at all* Hom. Trag.; (in qs. implying neg. answer) S. Th.

πῶ *dial.interrog.adv.*: see πόθεν

πώγων ωνος *m.* **beard** (app. the projecting part, opp. γένειον, γενειάς, which include the facial area covered by it) Alc. Anacr. Hdt. Ar. Pl. Thphr. +; (of a he-goat) Hdt. S.*Ichn.*; (fig., W.GEN. of flame, ref. to its tapering shape) A.

πώεα (nom.acc.pl.): see πῶυ

πωλείᾱ ᾶς *f.* [πωλεύω] act of breaking in a horse, **horse-breaking** X.

πωλέομαι, Ion. **πωλεῦμαι** *mid.contr.vb.* [πέλω] | ep.2sg. πωλέαι, Aeol.3pl πώλενται | Ion.ptcpl. πωλεύμενος (Od. A.) | Ion.impf. πωλεύμην, ep.3sg. πωλεῖτο, 3sg.iteratv.impf. πωλέσκετο | fut. πωλήσομαι | (of persons) come or go regularly, **go about, keep coming** or **going** (oft. W.PREP.PHR. or ADV. to a place) Hom. Hes. Archil. Alc. Emp. Call.; (of nocturnal visions) —W.PREP.PHR. *into a girl's bedchamber* A.

πώλευσις εως *f.* [πωλεύω] **horse-breaking** X.

πωλεύω *vb.* [πῶλος] **break in a young horse** X.

πωλέω *contr.vb.* | iteratv.impf. πωλέεσκον (Hdt.) | fut.mid. (w.pass.sens.) πωλήσομαι (Arist.) | **1** be a seller (opp. ἀποδίδοσθαι *make a sale*), **offer for sale** or **sell** —*sthg.* or *someone* (sts. W.DAT. or PREP.PHR. *to someone*, sts. W.GEN. *at a certain price* or *for a certain return*) Hdt. E.*Cyc.* Th. Ar. Att.orats. Pl. +; (intr.) offer goods for sale, **sell, trade** Ar. X. ‖ PASS. (of persons or things) be offered for sale Hdt. Th. +
2 (of the Council, of a state official) sell the right to collect, **farm out** —*a tax* Aeschin. Arist.; sell the right to use, **let out** —*mines* Arist.; (of demes) **sell** or **farm out** —*offices* Arist.
3 (fig., of a politician) **sell out, betray** —*a city's interests* D. ‖ PASS. (of a populace) be sold out (by politicians) Ar.

πώλης ου *m.* **seller, 'monger'** (com. coinage, properly only as 2nd element of cpd. nouns such as βυρσοπώλης *leather-monger*) Ar.

πώλησις εως *f.* activity of selling, **selling, sale** X. Arist.

πωλητήριον ου *n.* **1** place where things are offered for sale, **shop** X.
2 sales office (W.GEN. for the metic tax, i.e. where it is farmed out) D.

πωλητής οῦ *m.* **1 seller** (of a house) Plu.
2 ‖ PL. (at Athens) sales officers (ten state officials responsible for farming out public contracts and taxes and selling confiscated property) Antipho D. Arist.

πωλητικός ή όν *adj.* (of sophistry as a technique) **which has to do with marketing** (W.GEN. of particular types of excellence) Pl.

πωλικός ή όν adj. [πῶλος] **1** related to young horses; (of a team, a yoked pair, the eyes, the hide) **of horses** E.; (of pursuit) **with horses** E.; (of a carriage or chariot) **horse-drawn** S. E.; (gener., of the rails) **of a chariot** E.
2 (of chambers) occupied by young women, **maiden** A.

πωλίον ου n. [dimin. πῶλος] **young colt, pony** And. Ar.

πωλοδαμνέω contr.vb. [πωλοδάμνης] **break in young horses** X.; (tr.) **break in** —horses E.; (fig.) —a child S.

πωλο-δάμνης ου m. [δάμνημι] **horse-breaker** X.

πῶλος ου m.f. **1** (sg. or pl.) young horse, **foal, colt** or **filly** Hom. + ‖ MASC.PL. (gener.) horses S. E. ‖ FEM.PL. (ref. to a team) horses (of either sex) Alc. Pi. S. E.
2 ass, donkey NT.; **foal** (of an ass) NT.
3 (fig., ref. to a young woman, w.connots. of immaturity and wildness) **foal, filly** Anacr. E.; (ref. to a young man) **colt** A. E.; (gener., ref. to a daughter) **girl, maiden** E.; (ref. to a son) **youth, boy** E.

Πωλυδεύκης dial.m.: see Πολυδεύκης

πώλυπος (Simon.), also **πούλυπος** (Thgn.), ου m. —also **πουλύπους** (Od. hHom. S.fr.), **πολύπους** (E.(cj.) Arist. +), ποδος m. [πολύς, πούς, by pop.etym.] **polyp, octopus** (oft. characterised by its ability to change colour) Od. + | cf. also adj. πολύπους[1]

πῶμα[1] ατος n. **cover, lid** (of a quiver) Hom. B.; (of a chest) Hom. Plu.; (of a jar or sim.) Od. Hes. Archil. Call. Plb.; (of a cauldron) Plu.

πῶμα[2], also **πόμα** (Pi. Hdt. +), ατος n. [πίνω] **drink, draught** Hdt. Trag. Philox.Leuc. Pl. X. Arist. +; **stream** (as providing drinking-water or fertilising the soil) A.; (fig.) **draught** (of song, as a refreshing mixture of ingredients) Pi.

πώ-μαλα adv. [πώ, see πόθεν; μάλα] (as colloq. expression of refusal or denial) **no way, not a chance** Ar. D.

πώνω Aeol.vb.: see πίνω

πώ-ποτε (also **πώ ποτε**) temporal adv. **1** at any time up to now (usu.w. past tense vb.); (in neg.cl.) **ever yet, ever before** Il. Hes. Trag. Th. Ar. Att.orats. +; (in qs. implying neg.) Ar. Att.orats. +; (in conditional cl.) Ar. Att.orats. +; (in relatv.cl.) Antipho Pl. D.; (in neg.cl., ref. to fut.) **ever** NT.
2 (w.art. and aor.ptcpl.) οἱ πώποτε γενόμενοι those who have ever existed (or sim.) Isoc. Pl.; (quasi-adjl.) οἱ πώποτε those who have ever existed X.; οἱ πώποτε προδόται those who have ever been traitors Lycurg.

πώρινος η ον adj. [πῶρος tufa] (phr.) πώρινος λίθος tufa-stone, tufa (as a building material) Hdt.

πωρόω contr.vb. petrify or harden; (fig.) **make dull** or **obtuse** —people's minds (so that they do not realise sthg.) NT. ‖ PASS. (of persons, their minds) be dulled NT.

πώρωσις εως f. **dullness, insensibility** (of people's minds) NT.

πῶς, Ion. **κῶς** interrog.adv. | used occas. in indir.qs. |
1 in what manner or by what means, **how?** Hom. +
2 (expressing surprise or incredulity, indignation, or a request for clarification) **how can it be that, for what reason, in what sense, why?** Hom. +; πῶς φῄς; πῶς εἶπας; (or sim.) what do you mean? Trag. +
3 (w.vb. be or sim.) in what state or condition, **how?** Hom. +; (W.GEN. w. regard to a contest, goodwill, magnitude) E. Pl.
4 (w. wd. repeated by a 2nd speaker, in asking for an explanation) • δίκαια ... πῶς δίκαια; (These actions are) just. —How can they be just? S.
5 (w. other interrogs.) • πῶς ἐκ τίνος νεώς ... ; How and by what ship ... ? E. • πῶς τί τοῦτο λέγεις; What is this you are saying and why? Pl. • τί τἀμά —πῶς ἔχει; —θεσπίσματα; What of my prophecies? How do they stand? E.
6 (w.adj. ὤνιος for sale) **for how much?** Ar. Men.
7 (expressing a wish, esp. a hopeless one) πῶς ἄν (w.opt.) if only I (or someone) could Trag. Ar. Men.; (expressing a courteous exhortation) I should be glad if you could Od.
8 (w. ellipse of vb.) **how so, how can that be?** S. E. Ar. Pl. +; (also) πῶς δή; Trag. Ar.; πῶς δαί; E. Ar.; πῶς δῆτα; Pl.; καὶ πῶς; A. E. Ar. Pl. +
9 (confirming a neg. statement) πῶς γάρ; how could that be so? S. E. Antipho +; (confirming a positive statement) πῶς γὰρ οὔ; how could that not be so? Trag. Pl. +; (also) πῶς γάρ; S.; πῶς δ' οὔ; Trag. Ar. Pl.
10 (transitional, oft. preceding a further q.) πῶς οὖν; what then (is to be done), what follows? E. Pl. +
11 (parenth., in intensv.phrs.) πῶς δοκεῖς, πῶς οἴει; (or sim.) you can't imagine how, remarkably, ever so E. Ar. Thphr. • ἐκ γαληνῶν πῶς δοκεῖς προσφθεγμάτων after such unimaginably calm talk E.; (non-parenthetically, W.ACC. + INF.) Ar. X. D. • πῶς οἴεσθέ μου τὴν καρδίαν ὀρεχθεῖν; you can't imagine how my heart palpitated Ar.
12 (exclam.) **how ... !** NT.

—**πως**, Ion. **κως** indef.enclit.adv. **1** in some or any way, by some or any means, at all Hom. + | see also οὔπως
2 (conveying indefiniteness, uncertainty or diffidence) **somehow, as it happens, so it seems** Il. +; (modifying another adv.) **somewhat** Hdt. +; (w. εἰ, ἐάν or sim.) if somehow, if perhaps Hom. +
3 (sts. written πῶς) in a particular way Arist.

πωτάομαι mid.contr.vb.: see ποτάομαι

πῶυ εος n. [reltd. ποιμήν] | nom.acc.pl. πώεα | **flock** (usu. W.GEN. of sheep) Hom. Hes. Philox.Leuc. AR. Theoc.

Ρ ρ

ῥα enclit.ep.pcl.: see ἄρα, also ἦ¹
ῥαββί, also **ῥαββουνί** indecl.m. [Semit.loanwds.] (term of respectful address) **master** NT.
ῥαβδίζω vb. [ῥάβδος] **beat** (w.ACC. someone) **with a stick** Ar. NT.
ῥαβδομαχίᾱ ᾱς f. [μάχομαι] **fighting with staves** (as a sport) Plu.
ῥαβδονομέω contr.vb. [ῥαβδονόμος] **act as umpire** (in an athletic contest) S.
ῥαβδο-νόμος ου m. [νέμω] attendant who carries the *fasces* (symbols of authority of a Roman magistrate), **lictor** Plu.
ῥάβδος ου f. **1 stick, branch** (perh. limed, used for trapping birds) Ar.; **rod** (for fishing) Od. Pl.; (pl., used for divination by Scythian seers) Hdt.
2 shaft (of a hunting spear) X.
3 stick, rod (used for control of people, horses, oxen) hHom. Pl. X. Mosch.; **wand** (for control or transformation of mortals by divinities) Hom. Pi.
4 stick, rod (used for inflicting pain or punishment) Plu.
5 stick (as a symbol or necessary accompaniment of office or rule); **rod, staff** (carried by the mythical judges Rhadamanthys and Aiakos) Pl.; (by Hermes, ref. to the caduceum) hHom.; (by a rhapsode) Pi. Call.; (by a gymnasiarch) Plu.; (by a traveller) NT. ‖ PL. *fasces* (carried by Roman lictors) Plb. Plu.
6 perh. **strip** (of gold) or **thread** (of gold wire, on a shield) Il.
ῥαβδουχέομαι pass.contr.vb. [ῥαβδοῦχος] **be accompanied by lictors** Plu.
ῥαβδουχίᾱ ᾱς f. insignia of a lictor, *fasces* Plu. ‖ PL. lictors with *fasces* Plu.
ῥαβδοῦχος ου m. [ἔχω] **1** one who holds a stick, rod or staff (as a symbol of office or the right to maintain discipline); **official** (esp. at athletic contests or festivals) Th. Ar. Plb.; (gener.) **judge, arbitrator** Pl.
2 (m.f., in Greek or Macedonian ctxt.) **attendant, official, bodyguard** Plu.
3 (at Rome) holder of *fasces*, **lictor** Plb. Plu.
ῥαβδο-φόρος ου m. [φέρω] **1** bearer of a stick, rod or staff, **attendant, bodyguard** Plu.
2 lictor Plb. Plu.
ῥάβδωσις εως f. (archit.) **fluting** (W.GEN. of a column) Arist.
ῥαβδωτός ή όν adj. (of coverings for horses) **striped** X.
ῥαγδαῖος ᾱ ον adj. [ῥάσσω] striking or beating; (of rain) **violent, furious** Plu.; (of a hurricane, fig.ref. to a person) Men.; (of a person) Plu.
ῥαγῆναι (aor.2 pass.inf.): see ῥήγνῡμι
ῥᾱγίζω vb. [ῥάξ] (of foxes) **steal grapes from, plunder** —*a vineyard* Theoc.
ῥαδαλός όν adj. [perh.reltd. ῥαδινός] (of a reed-thicket) perh. **waving, swaying** Il.(dub., v.l. ῥοδανός)

Ῥαδάμανθυς υος m. **Rhadamanthys** (son of Zeus and Europa, king of Crete and judge in the underworld) Hom. +
ῥαδιέστερος (compar.adj.): see ῥάδιος
ῥαδινάκη ης f. [Iran.loanwd.] a kind of natural mineral oil, **petroleum** Hdt.
ῥαδινός ή όν, Aeol. **βράδινος** ᾱ ον adj. **1** (of a whip, javelin, flower, sapling, cypress) app. **slender, slim** (perh. w.connot. of flexibility or suppleness) Il. Lyr. Theoc.
2 (of the feet, hands, arms or thighs of a girl or goddess) **slender, slim, shapely** Hes. hHom. Anacr. Thgn. AR. Theoc.; (of a cheek) A.(dub.); (of the body, through healthy diet) X.; (of a boy) Sapph.(cj.); (of a girl) Theoc.; (of colts) Anacr.
ῥᾴδιος ᾱ ον (also ος ον E. Pl. D.), Ion. **ῥηίδιος** η ον (**ῥῄδιος** Thgn.) adj. [reltd. ῥέα, ῥεῖα] ‖ compar. ῥᾴων, Ion. ῥηίων, also ῥηίτερος (ῥήτερος Thgn.), dial. ῥάτερος (Pi.), also ῥαδιέστερος (Plb.) ‖ superl. ῥᾷστος, Ion. ῥήιστος ‖ The compar. and superl. forms are very freq., as are advbl. forms. The simple adj. is relatively rare. ‖
1 (of the performance of an action) **not requiring great effort, easy** Hom. +
2 ‖ NEUT.IMPERS. (w. ἐστί, sts.understd.) **it is easy** —W.INF. *to do sthg.* Od. +; (pejor.) **it is all too easy** E.
3 (of a path) free of obstacles, **easy** Hes.; (of a message, departure, arrival) with an easy journey, **easy, fast** Thgn. +
4 (of an instruction, account, or sim.) free of complication, **easy, straightforward, simple** Hom. +; (of a judgement, decision) Att.orats. Pl.
5 (of a way of life, manner of death) free from difficulties or pain, **easy** Od. E.
6 (of an enemy or potentially difficult person or obstacle) easy to deal with, **easy** D.; (W.INF. to fight against, to kill) Il.; (to fend off) Th.; (to guard against) E.; (of a ditch, to cross) Il.
7 ‖ COMPAR. **easier in mind** (through relief fr. anxiety or distress) E. D.
8 (of manners or character) **easy-going, adaptable** E.
—**ῥᾳδίως**, Ion. **ῥηιδίως**, Aeol. **βραϊδίως** adv. ‖ compar. ῥᾷον, Ion. ῥήιον, ῥηιτέρως ‖ superl. ῥᾷστα, Ion. ῥήιτατα (Od.), dial. ῥάιστα (Theoc.) ‖ **1** without great effort, difficulty or obstacle, **easily, simply, quickly** —*ref. to performing an action* Hom. +
2 (in expressions indicating monetary value) **easily as much as** (W.SB. a specified sum) Is. D.
3 without feeling undue pain, **easily, lightly, patiently** —*ref. to bearing misfortunes* Lyr. Trag.; **comfortably** —*ref. to living one's life* X.; in a manner which brings relief, **well** —*ref. to coping, while recovering fr. the illness of love* Theoc.
4 without much resistance, **readily** —*ref. to yielding to pressure* Th.
5 willingly, recklessly —*ref. to doing sthg. criminal or not sensible* S. Ar. Pl.
6 without attempting to prevent or raise objections, **easily, lightly, uncaringly** E. Att.orats. Pl.

ῥᾳδιουργέω

7 without scruple or thought, **easily, carelessly** —*ref. to saying sthg.* E. Lys. Pl. —*ref. to swearing* D.
8 (neg.phr.) οὐ ῥᾳδίως *scarcely, rarely* Plu.

ῥᾳδιουργέω *contr.vb.* [ῥᾳδιουργός] **1** do (sthg.) the easy way ‖ PASS. (of things) be done lazily or negligently X.
2 (intr.) take things easily, **be lazy, self-indulgent** or **indifferent** X.
3 commit a crime Plu.

ῥᾳδιούργημα ατος *n.* unscrupulous act, **fraud, deception, double-dealing** NT. Plu.

ῥᾳδιουργίᾱ ᾱς *f.* **1 laziness, lack of discipline, self-indulgence** X. Plb.
2 double-dealing Plb. NT.; (ref. to a specific crime) perh. **fraud** Plu.
3 careless or cavalier behaviour, **unscrupulousness** (by historians, about facts) Plb.

ῥᾳδιουργός όν *adj.* [ἔργον] **1** (of sacrifices) **easy to perform, simple** X.
2 ‖ MASC.SB. unscrupulous person Plb.

ῥαθάμιγξ ιγγος *f.* [prob.reltd. ῥαίνω] **1** ‖ PL. sprinklings, drops or specks (of blood) Il. Hes.; (of dust) Il. Call.
2 drop (of water) Pi.*fr.* Bion

ῥαθα-πῡγίζω *vb.* [1st el.uncert. (v.l. ῥοθο-); πῡγή] **kick** (W.ACC. someone) **in the arse** Ar.

ῥᾳθῡμέω (or **ῥᾱθῡμέω**) *contr.vb.* [ῥᾴθυμος] **1 take things easily** X. +
2 be idle, slack off or **be remiss** Isoc. Pl. X. D. Arist. +

ῥᾳθῡμίᾱ (or **ῥᾱθῡμίᾱ**) ᾱς *f.* **1** ease of mind, **equanimity, composure** Th. Isoc.
2 (pejor.) **indifference, remissness, laziness** E. Att.orats. Pl. X. +; **carelessness** (W.GEN. in speech) Pl.
3 (oft.pl.) **freedom from cares, leisure** E. Isoc. Arist. Plb.

ῥᾴθῡμος (or **ῥᾱθῡμος**) ον *adj.* [ῥᾴδιος, θῡμός] **1** (of persons) easy in one's mind; (usu.pejor.) **indifferent, remiss, idle, lazy** S. Att.orats. Pl. Arist. +
2 (of life) **easy, carefree** Isoc.; (pejor., of a way of thinking, an excuse) **lazy** Isoc. ‖ NEUT.PL.SB. the easy life Arist.; (superl.) the easiest option Pl.

—**ῥᾳθῡμως** (or **ῥᾱθῡμως**) *adv.* | compar. ῥᾳθῡμότερον, also ῥᾳθῡμοτέρως (Arist.) | **1 in a relaxed manner** Isoc. Arist. Plb. Plu.
2 with equanimity, lightly —*ref. to bearing misfortunes* Pl. +
3 (pejor.) **casually, carelessly** Pl. +

ῥαΐζω, also **ῥᾴζω** *vb.* [ῥᾴδιος] (of a person, part of the body) **recover, get better** (after illness) Pl. D. Plu.

ῥαίνω *vb.* | dial.inf. ῥαινέμεν (Pi.) | fut. ῥανῶ | aor. ἔρρᾱνα, ep.pl.imperatv. ῥάσσατε ‖ PASS.: aor. ἐρράνθην | ep.3pl.pf. ἐρράδαται | ep.3pl.plpf. ἐρράδατο |
1 sprinkle, besprinkle or **spatter** —*sthg.* (W.DAT. *w. blood*) Pi. E. —(*w. perfumes*) Plb. Bion; (fig.) —(*w. song, praises*) Pi. Lyr.adesp. ‖ PASS. be sprinkled or spattered —W.DAT. *w. blood, dust* Hom. —*w. dew* Pi.
2 sprinkle with water, **wash down** —*a room, shrine* Od. Plb. Plu. ‖ PASS. (of ground) be sprinkled or washed down Plb. Plu.
3 sprinkle, spray —*vinegar, drugs* (W.PREP.PHR. *into or over the eyes*) Ar. AR.

ῥαιστήρ ῆρος *m.* [ῥαίω] implement which smashes, **hammer** Il. A. Call. AR.

ῥαιστήριος ᾱ ον *adj.* causing to smash or break up; (of drugs) **destructive** AR.; (W.GEN. to life) AR.; (of perils at sea, W.GEN. to ships) AR.

ῥαίω *vb.* | ep.3sg.subj. ῥαίησι | ep.fut.inf. ῥαισέμεναι | aor. ἔρραισα ‖ PASS.: aor. ἐρραίσθην | 3pl.pf. ἔρραινται (cj., for ἔρρανται) |
1 smash or break ‖ PASS. (of a sword) be shattered Il.; (of a brain, bone, spinal marrow) Od. Pi.*fr.* AR.
2 (of a god) **shatter, wreck** —*a ship* Od.; **shipwreck** —*a sailor* Od. ‖ PASS. (of a ship) be wrecked AR.; (of sailors) be shipwrecked Od. A.(cj.)
3 destroy, slay —*someone* AR. ‖ PASS. (of Zeus) be crushed A.; (fig., of a person, by an insult) S.(dub.)

ῥάκιον ου *n.* [dimin. ῥάκος] **1** (usu.pl.) **rag** Ar.
2 small piece of cloth Plu.

ῥακιο-συρραπτάδης ου *m.* [συρράπτω] **rag-stitcher** (ref. to Euripides, criticised for clothing his characters in rags) Ar.

ῥακό-δυτος ον *adj.* [ῥάκος, δύω¹] (of clothing) **ragged** E.

ῥάκος, Aeol. **βράκος**, εος (ους) *n.* **1** ragged or tattered garment, **rag** Od. Ar. Men. Call. Theoc. ‖ PL. rags Od. Hdt. S. E. Ar. Isoc.; (derog., ref. to a countrywoman's dress) Sapph.
2 ‖ PL. (ref. to women's dresses of good quality) garments Theoc.
3 strip or **piece of cloth** Hdt. NT.
4 (fig.) **tatters** (W.GEN. of a body, ref. to the flesh of Prometheus, torn by an eagle) A.; (of a house, ref. to a ruin) Arist.; (pl., of an old woman's face, stripped of cosmetics) Ar.

ῥακώματα των *n.pl.* tattered clothing, **ragments** Ar.(mock-trag.)

ῥάμνος ου *f.* a kind of prickly shrub; esp. **buckthorn** Theoc. Plb.

Ῥαμνοῦς οῦντος *m.* **Rhamnous** (a deme in Attica) Lys. D. Plu.
—**Ῥαμνούσιος** ᾱ ον *adj.* belonging to the deme Rhamnous, **Rhamnousian** Pl. Aeschin. D. Plu.
—**Ῥαμνουσίς** ίδος *fem.adj.* (of Helen) **Rhamnousian** (as daughter of Nemesis, whose temple was in the deme) Call.

ῥαμφή ῆς *f.* hooked knife, **billhook** Plb.

ῥάμφος ους *n.* curved beak of a bird, **beak, bill** Ar.

ῥανίς ίδος *f.* [ῥαίνω] **drop** (of water, dew, rain, blood) E. Ar.

ῥαντήριος ᾱ ον *adj.* (of the ground) **sprinkled** (w. blood) A.(dub.)

ῥάξ ῥᾱγός *f.* **grape** Pl.

ῥάξας (aor.ptcpl.): see ῥάσσω

ῥᾷον (compar.adv.): see ῥᾳδίως, under ῥᾴδιος

ῥαπίζω *vb.* | Ion.pf.pass.ptcpl. ρεραπισμένος (Anacr.) | **1 beat** (w. a stick or sim.) —*a person* Hippon. Hdt. D. Plu. —*a dog* Xenoph. —*an athlete* (*who starts too soon*) Plu. ‖ PASS. be beaten Anacr. Hippon. Arist. Plb.
2 strike (w. a whip), **lash** —*a person* Hdt. ‖ PASS. be lashed Hdt.
3 (fig.) **give a good bashing to** —*a siege-engine* (*w. play on sense 'harpist'*) Plu. ‖ PASS. (of a siege-engine) be given a good bashing Plb. | see σαμβύκη
4 strike with the hand (on the face or jaw), **strike, slap** —*a person* NT.

ῥάπισμα ατος *n.* **slap, blow** (to the face or jaw) NT.

ῥαπτός ή όν *adj.* [ῥάπτω] **1** (of a tunic) **stitched** Od.; (of leather leggings, perh. by mending) Od. ‖ NEUT.PL.SB. rugs (used by Persians for sitting on) X.
2 (fig., of verses as performed by rhapsodes) **stitched together** Pi.

ῥάπτω *vb.* | aor. ἔρραψα, ep. ῥάψα ‖ PASS.: aor. ἐρράφην | pf. ἔρραμμαι | **1 sew together, stitch** —*oxhides* Il.; (intr.) sew Ar. ‖ PASS. (of a saddle-cloth) be stitched X.; (of a torn lip) D.
2 make by sewing or stitching, **stitch together** —*a shoe* Hdt. ‖ MID. **stitch for oneself** or **have stitched** —*a water-pipe* (W.GEN. *fr. leather hides*) Hdt. —*a cushion, leather phallus* Ar. ‖ PASS. (of false beards) be stitched together Ar.
3 ‖ MID. **sew up** —*cups* (W.PREP.PHR. *in a bag*) Plu. ‖ PASS. (of baby Dionysus) be sewn up (in the thigh of Zeus) E.

4 (fig.) stitch together, **contrive, plot** —*evil, murder* Hom. Hdt. E.

Ῥάριον ου *n.* **Rarion** (name of an arable plain nr. Eleusis, where the first crops were sown by Triptolemos) hHom.

—**Ῥαριάς** άδος *fem.adj.* **Rarian** (cult title of Demeter) Call.

ῥάσσατε (ep.pl.aor.imperatv.): see ῥαίνω

ῥάσσω, Ion. **ῥήσσω** *vb.* | aor.ptcpl. ῥάξας | **1 strike, dash** —*a person* (w. εἰς + ACC. *into the mud*) D.; (of an evil spirit) **strike down** —*a person* NT.
2 (intr., of dancers) **beat the ground** Il. hHom. Call.; (tr.) **beat** —*the ground* (W.DAT. *w. their feet*) AR. ‖ PASS. (of an altar) app., **be shaken** (by the feet of dancers) Call.

ῥᾷστος (superl.adj.): see ῥᾴδιος

ῥᾳστωνεύω *vb.* [ῥᾳστώνη] **be easy-going** or **relaxed** (in one's frame of mind) X.

ῥᾳστώνη, Ion. **ῥηιστώνη**, ης *f.* [ῥᾴδιος] **1 lack of difficulty** (in performing or achieving sthg.); **ease, easiness** Pl. Plu.; (W.GEN. of an undertaking) Pl. Plu.; **opportunity** (W.GEN. for sthg., i.e. to do it) Plu.
2 facilitating condition, **ease, convenience** Hdt.(cj.) Lys. Isoc. Pl. X. Arist.; condition free from difficulty, **easy time** Lys. D. Plb.
3 ease, relaxation, rest (opp. hard work) Th. Pl. X. D. Arist. +; (pejor.) **idleness, nonchalance** X. D. Plu.
4 easing up (fr. heavy drinking) Pl.; **relief, respite, rest** (fr. troubles, pain, or sim.) Pl. D. Plb. Plu.

ῥάτερος (dial.compar.adj.): see ῥᾴδιος

ῥαφανιδόομαι *pass.contr.vb.* [ῥαφανίς] **be stuffed with a radish** (up the rectum, as a degradation inflicted on adulterers) Ar.

ῥαφανίς ῖδος *f.* **radish** Ar. Thphr. Plu.

ῥαφεύς έως *m.* [ῥάπτω] (fig.) **stitcher, contriver** (W.GEN. of murder) A.

ῥαφή ῆς *f.* **1 stitching, sewing** (as a handicraft) Pl.
2 (concr., usu.pl.) **stitching, stitches** Od. AR. Plu.
3 seamlike juncture (of bones in the skull), **suture** Hdt. E. Pl.

ῥαφίς ίδος *f.* **needle** NT.

ῥαχία ᾶς, Ion. **ῥηχίη** ης *f.* [ῥάσσω] **1** place beaten by the sea (or where the waves break), **shore** A. Th. Plb. Plu.
2 waves breaking on the shore, **flood-tide** (opp. ebb-tide) Hdt.

ῥαχίζω *vb.* [ῥάχις] **1** cut through the spine; **hack in two** —*persons* A. —*animals* S.
2 inflict (W.ACC. slaughter) **by hacking** (animals) S.

ῥάχις εως (Ion. ιος) *f.* **1 backbone, spine** (of humans and animals) Archil. A. E. Ar. Pl. +
2 backbone and adjoining flesh, **chine** (W.GEN. of a pig) Il.
3 ridge (of a hill or mountain) Hdt. Plb.

ῥαχός (or perh. **ῥάχος**), Ion. **ῥηχός**, οῦ *f.* growth of bushes, **thicket, brushwood** X.; (ref. to a fence) Hdt.

ῥάψα (ep.aor.): see ῥάπτω

ῥαψῳδέω *contr.vb.* [ῥαψῳδός] **1** be a composer or performer of epic poetry; (of Homer, Hesiod) **compose** or **recite epic poetry** Pl.; (of rhapsodes) **recite** Pl. Arist. —*epic poetry* Isoc. Pl. ‖ PASS. (of the poems of Homer) be recited (at the Panathenaia) Lycurg.; (of speeches about the rhapsodic art) be delivered by rhapsodes Pl.
2 (pejor.) speak in the manner of a rhapsode (w.connot. of repetition or excessive demonstrativeness); (of a forensic orator, ambassadors) **declaim** D.
3 (tr.) recite poetry in honour of, **celebrate** —*brave men* Ar.

ῥαψῳδία ᾶς *f.* **1** recitation of epic poetry by a rhapsode, **rhapsodic recitation** Pl.; (gener.) **poetic recitation** Pl.
2 rhapsodic art Arist.
3 composition in epic metre, **epic poetry** Pl.; (ref. to a polymetric poem) **composition** Arist.

ῥαψῳδικός ή όν *adj.* (of the art or profession) **rhapsodic** Pl.

ῥαψ-ῳδός οῦ *m.* (sts.*f.*) [ῥάπτω, ἀοιδή] **1 song-stitcher** (app.ref. to the formulaic nature of epic composition); composer of epic poetry, **bard** (ref. to the Homeric Phemios) Pl.; performer of epic poetry, **rhapsode** Hdt. Pl. X. Plu.
2 (*f.*) **songstress** (ref. to the Sphinx, who composed riddles in hexameter verse) S.

ῥᾴων (compar.adj.): see ῥᾴδιος

ῥέα *ep.adv.* [reltd. ῥεῖα, ῥᾳδίως] | sts. monosyllab. | **easily** Il. Hes. Call. AR.

Ῥέα ᾶς, Ion. **Ῥέη**, ep.Ion. **Ῥείη**, ης *f.* | also monosyllab.nom. Ῥέα (Il.), also gen. Ῥείας (Il.) | Ion.acc. Ῥέην, ep. Ῥείην (also Ῥείαν Hes.) | **Rhea** (daughter of Ouranos and Gaia; mother, by her brother Kronos, of the Olympian gods) Il. +

ῥέγκω (also **ῥέγχω** Plu.) *vb.* **1 snore** A. Ar.(sts.mid.) Plu.
2 (of horses) **snort** E.

ῥέγμα ατος *n.* [reltd. ῥέγος] **garment** Ibyc.

ῥέγος εος *n.* [reltd. ῥῆγος] app. **rug, coverlet** Anacr.

ῥέεθρον Ion.*n.*: see ῥεῖθρον

ῥέζω *vb.* [reltd. ἔρδω] | ep.impf. ἔρεζον, also ῥέζον | iteratv.impf. ῥέζεσκον | fut. ῥέξω | aor. ἔρρεξα, ep. ἔρεξα, also perh. ῥέξα (E., cj.) ‖ PASS.: aor.ptcpl. ῥεχθείς |
1 act —W.ADV. or PREP.PHR. *in a certain way* Hom.
2 (tr.) **do, accomplish, perform** —*sthg.* Hom. Hes. Sol. Pi. Trag. Hellenist.poet.
3 do —*harm* (W.DAT. *to someone*) E. —*harm or good* (W.ACC. *to someone*) Hom.; **treat** —*someone* (W.ADV. *badly*) Od.
4 offer —*a sacrifice, sacrificial animal* Hom. hHom. Pi. S. Hellenist.poet.; (intr.) **sacrifice** Il. Stesich. Call. AR.

Ῥέη Ion.*f.*: see Ῥέα

ῥέθος εος *n.* **1 face** S. E. Hellenist.poet.
2 ‖ PL. **limbs** Il. Theoc.

ῥεῖα, Aeol. **ῥήα** *adv.* [reltd. ῥέα] **1 without effort, difficulty** or **obstacle, easily, quickly** Hom. Hes. hHom. Alc. Emp. Hellenist.poet.
2 without physical or mental burden, **at ease, comfortably** —*ref. to how the gods live* Hom.
3 without resistance, **readily, willingly** hHom. AR.
4 without thought or trouble, **lightly, uncaringly** Od.

Ῥείη ep.Ion.*f.*: see Ῥέα

ῥεῖθρον, Ion. **ῥέεθρον**, ου *n.* [ῥέω] **1** (freq.pl. for sg.) flowing water or current, **river, stream** Hom. + [freq. w. name in GEN., e.g. *stream of Okeanos*]
2 ‖ PL. **streams** (of blood) A.
3 course, channel (of a river) Il. Hdt.

ῥεκτήρ ῆρος *m.* [ῥέζω] **doer** (W.GEN. of evil deeds) Hes.

ῥέκτης ου *m.* **active person** Plu.

ῥέμβομαι *mid.vb.* [reltd. ῥόμβος] **1 wander about, roam** Men. Plu.
2 (fig.) **be unsteady, waver** (in one's actions) Plu.

ῥεμβώδης ες *adj.* (fig., of a siege) **erratic** Plb.; (of amusements) **desultory** Plu.

ῥέξω (fut.): see ῥέζω

ῥέος ους *n.* [ῥέω] **1 flowing water, stream** A.
2 flood (of tears) A.

ῥέπω *vb.* | fut. ῥέψω | aor. ἔρρεψα | **1** (of one arm of the scales) **incline, tilt** Ar.; (of the scales of Justice) B.
2 (of what is weighed) turn the scales; (of a person's fate, when weighed by Zeus) **sink** Il.; (of wealth and virtue) **preponderate** (in alternation) Pl. ‖ PASS. (of good and bad) be balanced or weighed (in the scales of Zeus) A.

ῥεραπισμένος

3 (of things) have greater weight or influence; (of a cause) come out ahead, **prevail** Hdt.; (of the characters of citizens) **tip the balance** Pl.; (of one of two opposites) **preponderate** Pl.
4 (of a god or human) incline in support, **turn the scales** (in favour of someone or sthg.) A. X.
5 (of persons, ref. to conduct or feelings) **incline** —W.PREP.PHR. *towards someone or sthg.* Isoc. Pl. D. Arist. Plb.; (of love, that should have been shown to a certain person) —*towards another* A.; (of an action, the probability that one is responsible for it) **tilt** —W.ADV. or PREP.PHR. *this way, towards someone* S.
6 (of an oracle) **point** —W.PREP.PHR. *towards sthg.* Ar.; (of evil) **turn** —W.PREP.PHR. *into good* Men.
7 (of an issue or event) **be decided, fall out** (in a certain way) A. Pi. S. Pl.
8 (of a winged horse) **be weighed down, sink** Pl.; (fig., of sleep, onto the eyelids) Pi.

ῥεραπισμένος (Ion.pf.pass.ptcpl.): see ῥαπίζω

ῥερυπωμένος *ep.pf.pass.ptcpl.adj.*: see under ῥυπάω

ῥεῦμα ατος *n.* [ῥέω] **1 flow, stream** (W.GEN. of honey) S.; (of olive oil) Pl.; (of fire) Plu.; (fig., of beauty, other immaterial things) Pl.
2 flow of lava, **eruption** Th.
3 **flow, current** (of a stream or river) A. Hdt. X. Plb. Plu.; (fig., ref. to movement of an army) **flood** S.; **tide** (W.GEN. of Fortune) Men.
4 **stream, river** A. E. Pl. X. Plu.; (fig., of soldiers) A. E.
5 **flood** (caused by rainfall) Hdt. Th.
6 (medic.) flux or rheum || PL. rheumatic pains Plu.

—**ῥευμάτιον** ου *n.* [dimin.] **rivulet** Plu.

ῥεύσομαι (fut.mid.): see ῥέω

ῥευστικός ή όν *adj.* [ῥέω] **flowing, liquid** Plu.

ῥεχθείς (aor.pass.ptcpl.): see ῥέζω

ῥέω *contr.vb.* | The vb. does not contract εη, εο, εου, εω. | ep.3sg.impf. ἔρρεε, also ῥέε | iteratv.impf. ῥέεσκον | fut. ῥεύσομαι (Thgn.) | aor. ἔρρευσα | pf. ἐρρύηκα | PASS.: ῥέομαι (Hdt.(oracle) Plu.) | 3sg.impf. ἐρρεῖτο (E.) | fut. ῥυήσομαι (only in cpd. εἰσ-) | aor.2 (w.act.sens.) ἐρρύην, ep. ῥύην |
1 (act. and aor.2 pass., of rivers, streams, springs) **flow** Hom. + —W.DAT. *w. water or sim.* Hom. + —W.GEN. Pl. —W.ACC. *w. milk and honey* Theoc.
2 (act. and aor.2 pass., of blood, sweat, tears, wine) **flow, run, stream** Hom. +; (of lava, fire) Th. Plu.; (of Zeus, as liquid gold) Isoc. Men.; (fig., of missiles) **stream forth** Il. Archil.
3 (act. and aor.2 pass., of a river, W.ADJ. μέγας) *be in flood* Hdt. Th. D.; (fig., of an army, Aphrodite, an orator, W.ADJ. πολύς, πολλή) *come in full flood, be in full spate* A. E. D.
4 (act. and aor.2 pass., of persons, desires) **have an inclination** (towards), **rush, resort** —W.PREP.PHR. *to someone or sthg.* Isoc. Pl. Plu.
5 (of the earth) **run, stream** —W.DAT. *w. blood, water, milk, wine, honey* Il. E.; (of ravines) —*w. water* E.; (of a pot, roof) **leak** Pl. Men. || PRES. and IMPF.PASS. (of a ship) be drenched —W.DAT. *w. bloodshed* E.; (of persons, horses, a temple) —*w. sweat* Hdt.(oracle) Plu.
6 (fig., of a city) **overflow** —W.DAT. *w. gold* E.; (of a poet) —*w. praise* Ar.
7 (of speech) **flow** Il. Hes. hHom. Theoc.; (of braggart speech) **flood** A.
8 (of a poisoned swab of wool) flow away, **melt, dissolve** S.; (fig., of anxieties) **fly away** (on the wind) S.; (of a reputation) **fade** S.
9 (of hair) become loose, **fall, drop off** Od. Hes.*fr.* Theoc.; (of fruit, fr. the branch) Hes.*fr.* Plb.

10 (of things) **be in a state of flux** Pl. || MASC.PL.PTCPL.SB. Fluxionists (ref. to Heracliteans) Pl.
11 (fig., of expectations, activities) εὖ ῥεῖν *proceed well, prosper* Sol.(cj.) Thgn.
12 (provb., of rivers) ἄνω ῥεῖν *flow upwards or backwards* (*in inversion of the natural order*) E.; (fig., of circumstances) *be topsy-turvy* E.; (aor.2 pass., of speeches) D.

ῥήα *Aeol.adv.*: see ῥεῖα

ῥῆγμα ατος *n.* [ῥήγνυμι] **1 breach, fissure** (in a wall) Plb.; **collapse, ruin** (of a house) NT.
2 || PL. (fig.) split chunks (W.GEN. of words) Ar.
3 (medic.) **rupture** D.

ῥηγμίν (or perh. **ῥηγμίς**) ῖνος *f.* | nom. not found | in Hom. always W.GEN. ἁλός or θαλάσσης *of the sea* | **1** waves breaking on the shore (or place where the waves break), **breakers** or **shore** Hom. hHom. Hippon. Pi. E. AR.
2 (gener.) broken surface of the sea, **surf** Hom.

ῥήγνυμι *vb.* | ep.3sg.impf. ῥήγνυσκε | fut. ῥήξω | aor. ἔρρηξα, ep. ῥῆξα | pf. ἔρρωγα || MID.: fut. ῥήξομαι | aor. ἐρρηξάμην || PASS.: fut. (only in cpds.) ῥαγήσομαι | aor.2 ἐρράγην, inf. ῥαγῆναι |
1 **break, shatter, smash** —*a bone* Il. E. AR. —*a building, masonry* E. || PASS. (of bones) be broken E.; (of a toenail) Plu.; (of iron) be shattered S.; (of trees) —W.PREP.PHR. *by falling rocks* Hes.; (of a ship) be wrecked D. Plu.; (of a wave) break Il.; (fig., of hopes) be dashed A.
2 (of a warrior, weapon) **rend, perforate, pierce** —*armour, a shield* Il. Hes. E. Plu.
3 **rend, tear** —*skin, flesh* Il. E.; make by rending, **inflict** —*wounds* Pi.
4 **break** —*opposed ranks* Il. Hdt.; (mid.) Il. E.; (intr.) **break through** Il.
5 break down (a barrier); **break through, breach** —*a wall, door, gate* Il.(also mid.) || PASS. (of a wall) be breached (by a river) X.
6 **break up** —*the surface of the earth* (W.DAT. *w. a plough*) Ar.(mock-dithyramb)
7 **burst open, burst** —*a cloud* (envisaged as a balloon) Ar.; (of wine) —*wineskins* NT.; **rupture** —*an abscess* Plu. || PASS. (of a cloud) burst open Ar.; (of the heavens) Plu.; (of ground, a rock or mountain) Pl. Plu.; (of wineskins) NT.; (of a corpse, on a funeral pyre) Plu.; (of chilblains) Hippon.; (of a vein) be ruptured X.; (of air) be split open (by things passing through it) Plu.
8 **break in two, snap** —*a strap, tendon, bowstring* Il. —*a ship's ropes* Od. || PASS. (of a strap, thread) be snapped X. Plu.
9 **break into pieces, tear, rend** —*clothes* A. E. —*garlands* E. || PASS. (of clothes) be torn or rent X. Plu.
10 (of an animal) **maul** —*a person* NT.
11 **break off** —*a piece of aither* E.; (mid.) —*rocks* AR. || MID. **tear off** —*a lock of hair* AR.
12 damage the health or strength (of an animal) || PASS. (of an immature hound) damage or rupture oneself (through over-excitement) X.; (of a horse) be broken (by over-exertion) Plu.
13 cause (sthg.) to break out; **break into** —*speech* Hdt. E. Ar. D.; **burst into** —*streams of tears, weeping* S. Plu. || MID. **cause an outbreak of** —*strife* Il.
14 (of the earth) **emit** —*warm springs* Plu. || PASS. (of springs) burst forth (fr. the earth) Plu.; (of a fire) burst —W.PREP.PHR. *into flames* Plu.; (of thunder, a rainstorm) break out Ar.(quot. S.) AR. Plb.
15 (intr., of a river) **burst one's banks** Hdt.; (fig., of evils)

break forth S. ‖ PF. (of a stream of tears) have burst out S.; (fig., of evils, a sea of troubles) Trag.

ῥῆγος εος *n.* [reltd. ῥέγος] (usu.pl.) **rug, coverlet** (usu. as a blanket to sleep on) Hom.

ῥηθείς (aor.pass.ptcpl.), **ῥηθήσομαι** (fut.pass.): see εἴρω²

ῥηΐδιος (also **ῥῄδιος**) *Ion.adjs.*: see ῥᾴδιος

ῥηϊδίως *Ion.adv.*, **ῥήϊον** *Ion.compar.adv.*: see ῥᾳδίως, under ῥᾴδιος

ῥήϊστος (Ion.superl.adj.): see ῥᾴδιος

ῥηϊστώνη *Ion.f.*: see ῥᾳστώνη

ῥήϊτατα (ep.Ion.superl.adv.), **ῥηϊτέρως** (Ion.compar.adv.): see ῥᾳδίως, under ῥᾴδιος

ῥηΐτερος, ῥηΐων (Ion.compar.adjs.): see ῥᾴδιος

ῥηκτός ή όν *adj.* [ῥήγνυμι] **able to be broken**; (of a person) **vulnerable** (W.DAT. to weapons or stones) Il. AR.

ῥῆμα ατος *n.* [εἴρω²] **1** something said or spoken, **statement** Hdt. +; saying (by a wise person), **maxim** Pi. Pl. Men.
2 spoken word, **word** (usu.pl., sts. w.connot. of advice) Archil. +
3 spoken word, **mere word** (opp. actions, reality) Pi. +
4 (ref. to a word or phrase) **expression** Ar. +
5 (gramm.) **verb** (opp. ὄνομα noun) Pl. Arist.; **phrase** (opp. ὄνομα word) Pl.

—**ῥημάτιον** ου *n.* [dimin.] **little phrase** Ar.

—**ῥηματίσκιον** ου *n.* [dimin.] **little phraselet** Pl.

ῥήν ῥηνός *m.* [reltd. ἀρήν] | only ep.dat.pl. ῥήνεσσι | **sheep** or **lamb** AR.

ῥῆξα (ep.aor.): see ῥήγνυμι

ῥηξηνορίη ης *ep.Ion.f.* [ῥηξήνωρ] **strength to break the enemy** Od.

ῥηξ-ήνωρ ορος *ep.masc.adj.* [ῥήγνυμι, ἀνήρ] (epith. of Achilles) **breaker of men** (i.e. of enemy warriors or ranks) Hom. Hes.

ῥῆξις εως *f.* **1** process or action of breaking or bursting; **fracture** (in a statue) Plu.; **rupture** (of air, by a loud sound passing through it) Plu.
2 bursting (of a gall-bladder) E. [or perh. *fissure* (at the tip of a sacrificial flame)]
3 bursting out (of water fr. beneath the earth) Plu.
4 rending, tearing apart (of oxen, by Herakles) Call.

ῥήξω (fut.): see ῥήγνυμι

ῥησικοπέω contr.vb. [ῥῆσις, κόπτω] **coin phrases** Plb.

ῥῆσις εως (Ion. ιος) *f.* [εἴρω²] **1** act of speaking, **speech, talk** Od.
2 formal utterance or address, **speech** A. Hdt. +; (in a play) Ar. Pl. +
3 spoken account, **narration, tale** Pi.
4 declaration, **proclamation** Hdt.

Ῥῆσος ου *m.* **Rhesos** (king of Thrace, ally of the Trojans) Il. Hippon. E.

ῥήσσω *Ion.vb.*: see ῥάσσω

ῥητέος ᾱ ον *vbl.adj.* [εἴρω²] **to be spoken of** D.

ῥήτερος (Ion.compar.adj.): see ῥᾴδιος

ῥητήρ ῆρος *m.* **speaker** (W.GEN. of words) Il.; **orator** Call.

ῥητίνη ης *f.* **pine-resin** Plb.

ῥητορεία ᾱς *f.* [ῥητορεύω] **1** rhetoric, **oratory** Isoc. Pl. Arist. Plu.
2 public speech, **oration** Isoc. Arist. Plu.

ῥητορεύω *vb.* [ῥήτωρ] **1** be an orator, use rhetoric Isoc. Pl. Plu.
2 ‖ PASS. (of a speech) be delivered Isoc.

ῥητορικός ή όν *adj.* **1** (of the art, language or speech) of an orator, **oratorical, rhetorical** Pl. Arist. Plu. ‖ FEM.SB. art of rhetoric Pl. Arist. Plu. ‖ NEUT.SB. rhetoric Pl. Plu.
2 (of cowardice) **of a politician** (ref. to Demosthenes) Aeschin.
3 (of a person) **practising rhetoric, good at oratory** Isoc. Pl. Arist.

—**ῥητορικῶς** *adv.* in the manner of an orator, **rhetorically** Pl. Aeschin. Arist. Plu.

ῥητός ή όν *adj.* [εἴρω²] **1** (of persons) spoken of, **famed** Hes.
2 (of a payment, reward, sum of money) **stated, specified** Il. Th.; (of a time or day) Hdt. +; (prep.phr.) ἐπὶ ῥητοῖς (ῥητοῖσι) **on fixed terms** Hdt. E. Th. Att.orats. Pl. +
3 (of things) that may be spoken of or said, **speakable** (opp. what must be kept secret or unspoken) Trag. Isoc. D. Men.; (in terms of decency or propriety) S. D.; that may be expressed in language, **expressible** Pl.
4 (in neg.phr., of pain, grief) **describable** S. E.
5 (of an answer or order) **express, definite** Plb.
6 (math., of magnitudes and quantities) **rational** Pl.

—**ῥητῶς** *adv.* **expressly, distinctly** Plb. Plu.

ῥήτρᾱ ᾱς, Ion. **ῥήτρη** ης *f.* **1 verbal agreement** Od. Call.
2 prescribed code of conduct, **ordinance** X.
3 (at Sparta) **Rhetra, lawcode** (of Lykourgos) Plu.; (gener.) **decree, ordinance** Tyrt. Plu.

ῥήτωρ ορος *m.* **1 public speaker, orator** Pl. Arist. Men. +; **proposer** (W.GEN. of a motion) E.
2 speaker or proposer of a motion (in the Assembly); **politician** Th. Ar. Att.orats. Thphr. +

ῥηχίη *Ion.f.*: see ῥαχία

ῥηχός *Ion.f.*: see ῥαχός

ῥιγαλέος ᾱ ον *adj.* [ῥῖγος] (of rain) **cold, chilling** Emp.

ῥιγεδανός ή όν *adj.* causing a state of shivering or shuddering; (of Helen) **chilling** Il.; (of a voice) AR.

ῥιγέω contr.vb. | fut. ῥιγήσω | aor. ἐρρίγησα, ep. ῥίγησα | ep.pf.: 3pl. ἐρρίγᾱσι (Theocr.), dat.sg.ptcpl. ἐρρίγοντι (Hes.), 3sg.subj. ἐρρίγῃσι | ep.3sg.plpf. ἐρρίγει |
1 shiver, shudder (w. fear or apprehension) Hom. Hes. S. Theoc. —W.ACC. *at sthg.* Il.; **shrink** —W.INF. *fr. doing sthg.* Il. AR.
2 lack ardour (for a task) Pi.

ῥιγηλός ή όν *adj.* (of arrows) causing one to shiver or shudder, **chilling** Hes.

ῥίγιον neut.compar.adj. [ῥῖγος] **1** ‖ NEUT.IMPERS. (w. ἔσται) it will be colder (in the evening) Od.
2 (fig., of a situation or course of action) more chilling, **more dreadful** Hom. AR.; (W.GEN. than another) AR.; (of no other being, W.GEN. than a bad woman) Hes. Semon.; (of old age, than death) Mimn.

—**ῥίγιστος** η ον *superl.adj.* (of sufferings) most chilling, **most dreadful** Il.; (of a deity, W.DAT. to persons, gods) AR.

ῥῖγος εος (ους) *n.* **1 cold** (as affecting the body), **cold, chill** Od. Hippon. Hdt. Pl. X. Plu.
2 shivering Pl.

ῥιγόω contr.vb. | fem.ptcpl. ῥιγοῦσα, also ῥιγῶσα (Semon.), masc.dat. ῥιγοῦντι, also ῥιγῶντι (Pl.) | 3sg.subj. ῥιγοῖ, also ῥιγῷ (Pl.) | inf. ῥιγοῦν, also ῥιγῶν (Ar.) | fut. ῥιγώσω, ep.inf. ῥιγωσέμεν | (of persons, animals) **be cold, be frozen** Od. Semon. Hippon. Hdt. Ar. Pl. +

ῥίζα ης *f.* **1 root** of a tree or plant, esp. as the part which gives fixity or stability, **root** Hom. +; (prep.phr.) ἐκ ῥιζῶν *from the roots, roots and all* (ref. to a tree being pulled out of the ground) Il.; (fig.) root and branch, entirely Plu.
2 root (used for medicinal or magical purposes) Il. S.*fr.* AR.
3 lower part of a tree, **lower trunk, base** Od.
4 (fig.) **root** (ref. to the continent of Africa, app.fr. a conception of the earth as a plant w. three roots) Pi. ‖ PL.

ῥίζιον

roots (of the earth, i.e. depths) Hes. A.; (of Mt. Aetna) A.; (of the eyeball) Od.; (of feathers) Pl.; (ref. to feet planted in the sea by the floating island of Delos) Call.
5 perh. **base** (W.GEN. of a triangle, ref. to one of its sides) Pl.
6 root (fr. which sthg. originates); **root, source, origin** (of a shrine) B.fr.; (W.GEN. of cities, ref. to a land) Pi.; (W.GEN. of evils) E.fr.
7 (ref. to a person or persons) root (fr. which a family springs or through which it currently survives), **root, stock** Pi. Trag. D. +
8 ‖ PL. **veins** (in the eye) E.

—**ῥίζηθεν** adv. **from the roots** —ref. to plant-shoots being broken off AR.

ῥίζιον ου n. [dimin.] **little root** Ar.

ῥιζόω contr.vb. | aor. ἐρρίζωσα ‖ pf.pass. ἐρρίζωμαι | **1** ‖ PASS. (of a plant or tree) **take root** or **become rooted** X. AR.; (of human reproductive seed) Pl.; (gener., of a vineyard) be established Od.
2 fix immovably, **root** (to the sea-bed) —a petrified ship Od. —an island Call. ‖ PASS. (of rocks) be rooted (in the sea) AR.; (of a rock formation leading underground) —W.ADV. in the earth S.
3 (fig.) cause to take root, **firmly establish** —tyranny Hdt. ‖ PASS. (of rule) be firmly established Arist.

ῥίζωμα ατος n. **1 root** (fr. which a family springs) A. Arist.(quot.trag.)
2 ‖ PL. **roots, sources** (W.GEN. of all things in the world) Emp.

ῥίζωσις εως f. process of taking root; **firm rooting** (of an embryo in the womb) Plu.; (of logs thrown into a river, causing a blockage) Plu.

ῥικνός ή όν adj. [reltd. ῥοικός] (of Hephaistos, ref. to his deformed feet) **shrivelled, withered** hHom.; (of skin, feet, fr. old age) Call. AR.

ῥίμμα ατος n. [ῥίπτω] (pl.) **flinging** (of dolphins' feet, i.e. their fins) Lyr.adesp.

ῥίμφα adv. with a light and easy movement, **swiftly, lightly** Hom. Hes. hHom. A. Pi. AR.

ῥιμφ-άρματος ον adj. [ἅρμα] (of driving, careering) **with a chariot at full speed** Pi. S.

ῥινάω contr.vb. [ῥίς] lead (someone) by the nose, **deceive** Men.

ῥίνη ης f. a kind of tool, **file, rasp** X.

ῥινηλατέω contr.vb. [ῥίς, ἐλαύνω] trace with the nose (i.e. by smell), **scent out** —sthg. A. S.Ichn.

ῥινο-κόλλητος ον adj. [ῥινός, κολλητός] (of a lyre) **with glued hides** S.Ichn.

ῥινόν οῦ n. app. **shield** Od.

ῥινο-πύλη ης f. [ῥίς, πύλαι] app. **drainage-exit** (ref. to a small closable opening in a city wall, also used as an unofficial entrance) Plb.

ῥινός οῦ f. **1 skin** (of a person) Hom. Call.; (pl.) Od. AR.
2 skin (of a wolf, lion, horse) Il. Pi. E.; **hide** (of an ox) Hom. Hes. hHom. E.fr.
3 oxhide, leather (one of several layers covering a shield) Il. ‖ PL. **shield** (of oxhides) Il.

ῥινο-τόρος ον adj. [τορεῖν] (of Ares) **shield-piercing** Il. Hes.

ῥίον ου n. **1 peak, crag** (of a mountain) Hom. hHom. AR. Theoc.
2 headland Od. Hdt.(cj.)

—**Ῥίον** ου n. **Rhion** (name of both the N. and the S. headland at the W. entrance to the Corinthian gulf) E. Th. X. Plb.

Ῥῖπαι ῶν (dial. ἂν) f.pl. **Rhipai** (fabled mts. in the far north, beyond which the Hyperboreans live) Alcm. S.

—**Ῥίπαιος** ᾱ ον adj. (of the mountains) **Rhipaian** Call. AR. Plu.

ῥιπή ῆς f. [ῥίπτω] **1 forceful forward motion** (carrying a person or thing along); **throw, flight** (of a missile) Hom. Pi. E. AR.; **onrush** (of a warrior or god) Il. Hes. hHom.; (of feet) E.
2 impetus (of natural forces); **onrush** (of fire) Il. AR.; **surge** (of waves) Pi.; **gust, blast** (of winds, a storm) Il. Lyr. A. S. Call. AR.; (fig.) **blast** (of wine, ref. to its strong bouquet) Pi.fr.
3 (usu.pl.) rapid repeated movement, **whirring** (of wings, a gnat) A. AR.
4 ‖ PL. **flashes** (of light fr. stars) S.
5 ‖ PL. **notes** (of a lyre) Pi.

ῥιπίζω vb. [ῥιπίς] **1 fan** —a fire Plu. —food (on a fire) Ar. —a person Plu.
2 (fig.) **fan** (into flames) —civil strife Ar. —a city Plu.

ῥιπίς ίδος f. [ῥίψ] **fan** (to stir up a cooking-fire) Ar.

ῥιπτάζω vb. [ῥίπτω] | iteratv.impf. ῥιπτάζεσκον | **1** (of Zeus) **throw about** —gods Il.; (intr.) perh. **cast** (glances) hHom.
2 ‖ PASS. (of garments) be thrown —W.GEN. upon a corpse S.fr.
3 ‖ PASS. **toss and turn** (in bed, through anxiety) Plu.; (fig.) be tossed this way and that (by conflicting considerations) Plu.; (of a problem) be tossed around —W.DAT. in sleepless nights Ar.

ῥιπτέω contr.vb.: see ῥίπτω

ῥιπτός ή όν adj. (of a death) **by throwing** (fr. a height) S.

ῥίπτω vb. —also (pres. and impf.) **ῥιπτέω** contr.vb. | impf. ἔρριπτον, also ἔριπτον (Tim.), iteratv. ῥίπτασκον | fut. ῥίψω | aor. ἔρριψα, also ἔριψα (Mosch.), ep. ῥῖψα | pf. ἔρριφα ‖ PASS.: fut. ῥιφήσομαι (Plu.) | aor. ἐρρίφην, also ἐρρίφθην | pf. ἔρριμμαι |
1 throw (an object); **hurl, fling** —a weapon, missile, thunderbolt, discus, or sim. Hom. A. Pi. B. E. X. +; (wkr.sens.) **throw** —a ball Od. —an object (W.PREP.PHR. or DAT. in some direction or to someone) Hes. Hdt. S. E. Ar. +; **cast** (fr. a container) —water, lots E. Pl. ‖ PASS. (of objects) be hurled or thrown A. Pi.fr. E. Pl. X. + ‖ PF.PASS. (of the cast of a net) have been made Hdt.(oracle)
2 throw out, hurl —words (angry, abusive, demented) A. E. Plb. —curses E. ‖ PASS. (of words) be uttered —W.ADV. in vain E.
3 throw (a person); **fling down** —someone (usu. W.PREP.PHR. fr. or to a place) Il. Hes. hHom. Trag. Pl. +; **fling** —someone (W.PREP.PHR. into the sea) E. Lyr.adesp. —(W.PREDIC.ADJ. into the air) Hdt. ‖ PASS. be flung (down) E. Pl. +; be thrown —W.PREP.PHR. into the sea Pi.fr.
4 throw (oneself); **fling down** —oneself, one's body (sts. W.PREP.PHR. fr. or to a place) A. Hdt. E. Th. +; **fling** —oneself (W.PREP.PHR. into the sea, a river, or sim.) Hdt. Th. X. D. Plb.; (of a fugitive) —oneself (into a room) Hdt.; (intr.) **fling oneself down** (fr. or to a place) Thgn. E. Men.
5 throw (oneself) down (in pain or anguish); **fling** —oneself (W.DAT. to the ground) S. —(W.PREP.PHR. onto a bed) E.; (intr.) **throw oneself to the ground** E.
6 throw (a part of one's body) forward or backward; **fling out** —one's arms (W.PREP.PHR. to heaven) E.; (of Bacchants, Cassandra) —one's hair or neck (to the sky) E.; (of a dancer or runner) —one's leg Ar. Arist.; (wkr.sens.) **cast** —one's eye (W.ADV. everywhere) Ar.; **direct** —one's attention (W.PREP.PHR. to someone) Theoc.
7 throw dismissively, **throw down, throw away** —ears of corn (which one has plucked) Hdt. —parts of slaughtered animals S. —a musical instrument Melanipp.; **get rid of** —lice Hdt.; **waste** —money D.; (of trees) **shed** —their fruit Mosch.
8 throw (someone) out of a house or community; **cast out**

—*an unwelcome person, an unwanted child* Trag. D. —*a corpse* (W.PREDIC.SB. *as prey for animals*) E. ‖ PASS. (of a corpse, infants) be cast out (as prey for animals) S. Plu.
9 throw off (an encumbrance); **throw off** —*one's cloak* (*usu. to be ready for strenuous action or to run away*) E. Lys. Ar. Pl. +—*a garland, chaplets* E.; **throw away** —*one's shield, weapons* Anacr. Lys. Pl. +; (of a horse) **throw** —*its rider* Pi. Ar. ‖ PASS. (of weapons) be thrown away Pl. Plb.; (of a parasol, envisaged as a shield) Ar.
10 (fig., ref. to throwing dice) **run** —*a risk* E.; **risk** —*warfare* E. | cf. ἀναρρίπτω 3
—**ἐρριμμένος** η ον *pf.pass.ptcpl.adj.* **1** (of persons, corpses) **lying around, prostrate** Men. Plb. NT. Plu.
2 (of a shoe, cloak) **discarded** Ar.; (of old triremes, gold and silver) Plu.; (of building materials) **dumped** (on the ground) X.; (fig., of services deserving gratitude) **cast aside, wasted** S.

ῥίς ῥινός *f.* **nose** Hom. + ‖ PL. **nostrils or nose** (of humans and animals) Hom. +

ῥίσκος ου *m.* **storage box, chest** Men.

ῥίψ ῥιπός *f.* | dat.pl. ῥιψί, ep. ῥίπεσσι | (sg. and pl.) **wickerwork** (for making sandals) hHom.; (as bulwarks for a boat) Od.; (ref. to rush matting, used as a covering or to lash together the frame of a raft) Hdt.; (provb.) ἐπὶ ῥιπὸς πλεῖν *sail on wicker* (*ref. to a risky venture*) Ar.

ῥίψ-ασπις ιδος *m.* [ῥίπτω, ἀσπίς¹] (pejor.) **shield-dropper** Lys. Ar. Pl. Plu.

ῥίψ-αύχην ενος *masc.fem.adj.* [αὐχήν] (of ecstatic dancing) accompanied by throwing back of the neck, **neck-tossing** Pi.*fr.*

ῥῖψις εως *f.* **1 throwing** (of a weapon) Pl.; **flinging, throwing out** (W.GEN. of Hephaistos, fr. Olympos) Pl.
2 plunging (W.GEN. of heavenly bodies, to earth) Plu.
3 throwing away (W.GEN. of a shield) Plu.
4 casting about, **glance** (W.GEN. of the eye) Plu.

ῥιψο-κίνδυνος ον *adj.* (of a person, an action) dicing with danger, **reckless** X.

ῥιψολογέω contr.vb. [λόγος] **say** (W.ACC. sthg.) **rashly** Plb.

ῥίψ-οπλος ον *adj.* [ὅπλα] (of cowardly flight) **with weapons abandoned** A.

ῥοά dial.f., **ῥόα** Aeol.f.: see ῥοή

ῥόα ᾶς, Ion. **ῥοιή** ῆς, also **ῥοιά** ᾶς (Ar.) *f.* **1 pomegranate tree** Od.
2 pomegranate hHom. Hdt. Ar. Pl. Plu.; (ref. to an ornament of gold or silver in this form) Hdt.

ῥοδανός ή όν *adj.* [perh.reltd. ῥαδινός] (of a reed-thicket) **waving, swaying** Il.(dub., v.l. ῥαδαλός)

Ῥοδανός οῦ *m.* **Rhône** (river in S. France) AR. Plb. Plu.

ῥόδεος ᾱ (Ion. η) ον *adj.* [ῥόδον] (of a bud, flower, petal) of a rose, **rose** hHom. Ibyc. E. Mosch.

ῥοδή ῆς, perh. also **ῥοδέη** ης (AR.) *f.* **rose-bush** Archil. AR.(cj.)

Ῥοδιακός, **Ῥόδιος** *adjs.*: see under Ῥόδος

ῥόδινος η ον *adj.* [ῥόδον] **made or derived from roses**; (of a garland) **of roses** Anacr. Stesich.; (of an unguent) **rose-scented** Hippon. Plu.

ῥοδο-δάκτυλος, Aeol. **βροδοδάκτυλος**, ον *adj.* (of Dawn) **rose-fingered** Hom. Hes. Mimn.; (app. of the moon) Sapph.; (of Io) B.

ῥοδόεις εσσα εν *adj.* **1** (of a river bank) full of roses, **rosy** B.
2 (of a garland) rich with roses, **of roses** Theoc.
3 (of a flower) rich in rose-colour, **rosy** E.; (of Dawn) Theoc.
4 (of oil) **rose-scented** Il.

ῥοδό-κολπος ον *adj.* [κόλπος] (of Eunomia) **rosy-bosomed** Lyr.adesp.

ῥόδον, Aeol. **βρόδον**, ου *n.* **1 rose** (the flower or the bush; esp. assoc.w. surpassing beauty, fragrance and luxury) hHom. Thgn. Lyr. Hdt. Ar. + ‖ PL. (fig.) **roses** (fr. Pieria, ref. to poetry) Sapph.; (iron., ref. to unkind words, in allusion to the sprinkling of rose-petals) Ar.
2 rose-colour, rosiness (of the cheek or lip) Theoc. Bion

Ῥοδόπη ης, dial. **Ῥοδόπᾱ** ᾱς *f.* **Rhodope** (mt. range in Thrace) Hdt. Th. Theoc.

ῥοδό-πηχυς, dial. **ῥοδόπᾱχυς**, Aeol. **βροδόπᾱχυς**, υ *adj.* [ῥόδον, πῆχυς] (of Dawn, women and goddesses) **with rosy arms** Hes. hHom. Lyr.; (of Adonis) Theoc.

Ῥόδος ου *f.* **1 Rhodes** (island off the coast of Lycia, or its capital city) Il. Pi. Hdt. Th. +
2 Rhodos (daughter of Aphrodite, after whom the island was named) Pi.

—**Ῥόδιοι** ων *m.pl.* **Rhodians** (as a population or military force) Il. Th. Att.orats. +

—**Ῥόδιος** ᾱ ον *adj.* **1** (of a man or woman) **Rhodian** Th. X. Din. Call.*epigr.* + ‖ FEM.SB. **Rhodian territory** Th.
2 (of a perfume) made in or characteristic of Rhodes, **Rhodian** Ar.

—**Ῥοδιακός** ή όν *adj.* (of ships) of the Rhodian type, **Rhodian** Plu.

ῥοδό-χρως ωτος *masc.fem.adj.* [ῥόδον, χρώς] (of Helen) with rosy complexion, **rosy** Theoc.

ῥοδωνιά ᾶς *f.* **rose-garden** D.

ῥοή ῆς, dial. **ῥοά** ᾶς, Aeol. **ῥόα** ᾶς *f.* [ῥέω] | ep.dat.pl. ῥοῇς, ῥοῇσι |
1 (usu.pl.) **flow of liquid, stream** (of liquid) Il. Alc. Pi.; (of honey, wine) E.; (of blood) S. E.
2 ‖ COLLECTV.PL. **flowing waters, river or stream** (oft. w. name in GEN., e.g. *of Okeanos*) Hom. +
3 (fig.) **stream** (of words issuing fr. the mouth) Pl. ‖ PL. **streams** (of poetry, foreknowledge) Pi.; **currents** (of events) Pi.
4 (philos.) **flow** (of a river, as illustrating the changeable nature of things) Pl.; **flow, flux** (envisaged as engendering all things) Pl.

ῥοθέω contr.vb. [ῥόθος] make a confused or tumultuous noise; (of persons) **clamour, be in uproar** S.; (of words) **roar forth** S.

ῥοθιάζω vb. [ῥόθιον] make a confused noise, **create a hubbub** A.

ῥοθιάς άδος *fem.adj.* (of an oar) **dashing, splashing** A.

ῥόθιον ου *n.* [ῥόθος] **1 tumultuous and noisy movement, roar, surge** (of waves) A.; (sg. and pl.) **surging waves** S. E. AR.; (fig., ref. to waves of devastation) A.
2 dash, splash (ref. to the noise or propulsive effect of oars in water) E. Th. Plu.; (fig., ref. to applause or cheers) **roar** Ar.
3 noisy bluster (of winds) E.*fr.*
4 tumultuous noise, hubbub (W.GEN. of songs) Pi.*fr.*; **uproar** (ref. to civic commotion) E.

ῥόθιος ον *adj.* (of a wave) making tumultuous or noisy movement, **surging** Od.

ῥοθοπῡγίζω vb.: see ῥαθαπῡγίζω

ῥόθος ου *m.* **tumultuous noise, clamour, hubbub** Hes. A. Pi.*fr.* Plu.

ῥοιά *f.*: see ῥόα

ῥοιβδέω contr.vb. [ῥοῖβδος] make a noise while moving swiftly through the air; (of Athena) **whirr** (w. her aigis) A. | see also ῥυβδέω

ῥοίβδημα ατος *n.* **whistle** (of herdsmen) S.*Ichn.*

ῥοίβδησις εως *f.* **whistling** (W.GEN. of herdsmen) E.

ῥοῖβδος ου *m.* [reltd. ῥοῖζος] **noise associated with vigorous**

ῥοιζέω motion through the air; **whirr** (W.GEN. of wings) S.; **whistling rush** (of wind) Ar.

ῥοιζέω contr.vb. [ῥοῖζος] | iteratv.impf. ῥοίζεσκον | ep.aor. ῥοίζησα | (of a person) **whistle** (as a signal) Il.; (of a serpent or monster) **hiss** Hes. AR.; (of dung-beetles) **buzz** Hippon.

ῥοίζημα ατος n. **whirring** (of wings) Ar.

ῥοῖζος ου m. (f. Od.) [reltd. ῥοῖβδος] **noise associated with vigorous motion through the air**; **whizz** (of arrows, missiles) Il. Plu.; **whirr** (of wings) AR.; **whistle** (of a shepherd) Od.; **hiss** (of a serpent) AR.; perh. **screech** (of siege-engines) Plu.

ῥοιή Ion.f.: see ῥόα

ῥοικός ή (dial. ᾱ) όν adj. [reltd. ῥικνός] (of a hunter's throwing-stick) **bent** Theoc.; (of a person) **bandy** (W.PREP.PHR. around the shins, i.e. bow-legged) Archil.

ῥόμβος ου m. [ῥέμβομαι] **1 whirling or circular motion**; **whirl** (of javelins, tambourines) Pi.; **swoop** (W.GEN. of an eagle) Pi.
2 bull-roarer (a rhombus-shaped piece of wood whirled round on a string to make a whirring noise, used in mystery cults, esp. of Dionysus and Cybele/Rhea) E. AR.; (used in magic) Theoc.

ῥομφαία ᾱς f. **sword** NT.; (specif., ref. to a large sword used by non-Greeks) Plu.

ῥόος ου, Att. **ῥοῦς** οῦ m. [ῥέω] **1 flow of water**; **river, stream** (oft. w. name in GEN., e.g. of Okeanos) Hom. +; (fig., W.GEN. of smoke, fr. a volcano) Pi.
2 flow, current (of a river, the sea) Hom. Hdt. Th. Pl. +; (of air) Emp.
3 (abstr.) **flow** (as a universal principle) Pl.

ῥοπαλισμός οῦ m. [ῥόπαλον] **clubism, stiffitis** (com. pseudo-medical term for priapism) Ar.

ῥόπαλον ου n. [ῥέπω] **1 stick** (for support in walking) Od.
2 club, cudgel (for inflicting hurt or punishment) Hom. Pi.fr. X. Plu.; (as an offensive weapon, used by non-Greeks) Hdt.; (used for hunting) X.; (of Orion) Od.; (of Herakles) S. Ar. AR. Theoc. Plu.
3 (fig.) **bludgeon** (W.GEN. of the people, ref. to the sacred trireme Paralos, used for the transport of state offenders) Arist.(quot.)

ῥοπή ῆς f. **1 inclination of an arm of the scales**, **turn of the scales** Trag. Isoc. Pl. +; (W.GEN. of Justice) A.
2 decisive turn, influence, weight Isoc. Pl. X. D. +; **decisive influence** (W.GEN. on sthg.) Isoc. Arist. Plb.
3 uncertain turn, critical balance, knife-edge Alc. S. Th. Plu.; **critical point** (W.GEN. of life) S.
4 resting balance (of the scales), **equilibrium** Plu.

ῥόπτρον ου n. **1 object** (perh. hinged) which falls on an animal in a deadfall trap, **falling weight** Archil.; (fig., W.GEN. of Justice) E.
2 door-knocker E. Lys. X.
3 || PL. **resonant instrument** (used by Parthian troops); perh., **cymbal-clappers** Plu.

ῥοῦς Att.m.: see ῥόος

ῥοφέω, Ion. **ῥυφέω** contr.vb. [reltd. ῥυβδέω] | fut. ῥοφήσομαι | **1 gulp down eagerly or greedily, guzzle** —a gruel of blood S. —meat broth, lentil soup Ar. —(fig.) a bowlful of wages, peace) Ar.; (intr.) Ar. X.
2 (fig., of a poisoned robe) **drain** —bronchial tubes (i.e. empty them of breath) S.

ῥοχθέω contr.vb. | ep.3sg.impf. ῥόχθει | (of waves dashing against rocks) **roar** Od.; (of rocks dashed by waves) AR.

ῥοώδης ες adj. [ῥόος] (of a sea or river) **with a strong current** Th. Plu.

ῥύαξ ᾱκος m. [ῥέω] **1 watercourse, gully** Th.
2 lava-stream Pl.; (W.GEN. of fire) Th. Lycurg.

ῥύατο (ep.3pl.athem.impf.mid.): see ῥύομαι

ῥυάχετος ου Lacon.m. [ῥύαξ] (pejor., ref. to Athenians) perh., **lava-like stream, rabble** Ar.

ῥυβδέω Ion.contr.vb. [reltd. ῥοφέω] (w. play on the sound of the name *Charybdis*) **suck down** (water) Od.(v.l. ῥοιβδέω) | cf. ἀναρρυβδέω

ῥύβδην Ion.adv. with a gulp, **voraciously** Hippon.(cj.) | see ῥύδην

ῥύγχος εος (ους) n. [reltd. ῥέγκω] **1 snout** (of swine) Stesich. Philox.Leuc.; (of a dog) Thphr. Theoc.
2 beak (of a bird) Ar.

—ῥυγχίον ου n. [dimin.] **little snout** (of a young pig) Ar.

ῥύδην adv. [ῥέω] **1 in a flowing or continuous manner; steadily** —ref. to eating Hippon.(dub.) | see ῥύβδην
2 at full speed —ref. to riding Plu.
3 abundantly —ref. to being rich Plu.

ῥυδόν adv. **abundantly** —ref. to being rich Od. Call.

ῥύετο (ep.3sg.impf.mid.): see ῥύομαι

ῥύην (ep.aor.2 pass.): see ῥέω

ῥυηφενίη ης Ion.f. [ῥέω, ἄφενος] **flow of wealth, affluence** Call.

ῥυθμίζω vb. [ῥυθμός] | pf.pass. ἐρρύθμισμαι | **1 give shape or order** (to someone or sthg.); **put in order, bring into line** —a person (by punishment, training, instruction) Pl. X. Plu.; (of beauticians) **smarten up** —a person's appearance X. || MID. **arrange** —one's hair E. || PASS. **be brought into line** (by punishment) A.
2 give a clear shape (to sthg.); **define** —the location of pain S.
3 shape, compose —oneself (by adopting a deceptive facial expression and tone of voice) Plu.
4 (intr.) **make arrangements** —W.DAT. by legislation Arist.; **systematise, organise** (philosophical theories) Arist.

ῥυθμικός ή όν adj. (of motion) **rhythmical** Pl.

ῥυθμός, Ion. **ῥυσμός**, οῦ m. [perh. ῥέω] **1 orderly form or configuration, shape, pattern** (W.GEN. of a temple) Pi.fr.; (of written letters) Hdt.; (of matter) Arist.
2 characteristic appearance, style, mode (W.GEN. of clothing) E.
3 characteristic manner (of persons); **disposition** Anacr. Thgn.
4 characteristic method or manner (of behaviour, an activity); **manner** (of suffering) E.; (of killing) E. Theoc.; **pattern, tenor** (of human affairs) Archil.
5 orderly movement, motion, sweep (of an arm) E.Cyc.
6 rhythm (of verse, prose, music, or sim.) Lyr.adesp. Carm.Pop. Ar. Tim. Isoc. Pl. +; (of dance) Ar. Men. Plu.; (of a galloping horse) A.
7 (prep.phrs.) ἐν ῥυθμῷ, μετὰ ῥυθμοῦ **in time, in step** (ref. to marching, dancing, or sim.) Th. Pl. X. Plu.; (also) ῥυθμῷ Plu.; ἀπὸ ῥυσμοῦ app. **out of step, off the rails** (ref. to faulty judgement) Call.epigr.

ῥῦμα¹ ατος n. [ἐρύω] **1 that which is drawn**; (periphr.) τόξου ῥῦμα **drawn bow** (meton. for a body of archers) A.; (ref. to the distance of a bow-shot) X.
2 that which draws along, tow-line Plb.

ῥῦμα² ατος n. [ῥύομαι] **defence, protection** (ref. to an altar, shrine, tower) Trag. || PL. perh., **bodyguards** Sol.

ῥυμβέω contr.vb. [ῥόμβος] **whirl** Pl.

ῥυμβών όνος f. **coil** (of a serpent) AR.(pl.)

ῥύμη ης f. [ἐρύω] **1 force associated with onward movement; impetus, momentum, force** (of a falling beam) Th.; (imparted by a potter to his wheel) Ar.; (of a blow, weapon,

missile) X. Plu.; (of warships, due to their weight) Plu.; (of the wings of large birds) Ar.
2 forceful onward motion; **rush** (of horses, chariots, air escaping fr. a balloon) Th. Ar. X. Plu.; **acceleration, spurt, charge** (of soldiers) Th.; **sudden attack, onset** (of ships, soldiers) Th. Plu.; (fig., of war) Plu.
3 momentum (provided by a god, fortune, events, or sim.) E. Plu.; **vehemence** (of persons, their ambition or emotions) D. Plu.; **impulse** (opp. thought) Pl.
4 (concr.) place of onward motion (of people); **street, alley** NT.; (in a military camp) Plb.

ῥύμμα ατος *n*. [ῥύπτω] cleansing material, **soap, detergent** Ar. Pl.

ῥυμός οῦ *m*. [ἐρύω] **pole, shaft** (by which a chariot or wagon is attached to the yoke) Il. Hdt. Call. Plu.

ῥυμοτομία ᾱς *f*. [ῥύμη 4, τέμνω] **division by streets** (of a camp or town) Plb.

ῥυμουλκέω *contr.vb*. [ῥῦμα¹, ἕλκω] **draw by a tow-line, tow** —*a boat* Plb.

ῥύομαι *mid.vb*.: see ἔρυμαι

ῥύπα (ep.neut.pl.): see ῥύπος

ῥυπαίνω *vb*. [ῥύπος] **1** make dirty ‖ PASS. (of a shield) be tarnished X.
2 sully, spoil —*happiness* Arist.
3 (intr.) be abusive Arist.

ῥυπαρός ά όν *adj*. **dirty, filthy** Plu.

ῥυπάω, ep. **ῥυπόω** *contr.vb*. [ῥύπος] | ep.ptcpl. ῥυπόων | impf. ἐρρύπων | (of a person, clothes) **be dirty, be filthy** Od. Ar. Men. Plb.

—**ῥερυπωμένος** η ον *ep.pf.pass.ptcpl.adj*. (of clothes) **dirtied, dirty** Od.

ῥύπος ου *m*. | ep.n.pl. ῥύπα | **1 dirt, filth** (esp. on clothes or the body) Od.(pl.) Semon. Pl. Theoc. Plb.
2 ‖ PL. app., sealings (on containers for valuables) Ar.

ῥυπόω *ep.contr.vb*.: see ῥυπάω

ῥυππαπαῖ *interj*. (cry of Athenian rowers) **yo-ho-ho!** Ar. ‖ COLLECTV.NEUT.SB. yo-ho-hos (ref. to rowers) Ar.

ῥυπτικός ή όν *adj*. [ῥύπτω] (of particles in the body) having cleansing properties, **cleansing** Pl.

ῥύπτω *vb*. [ῥύπος] cleanse of dirt ‖ MID. wash oneself, **wash, bathe** Ar.

ῥῦσαι (aor.mid.imperatv.), **ῥυσάμενος** (aor.mid.ptcpl.), **ῥυσάμην** (ep.aor.mid.), **ῥύσασθαι** (aor.mid.inf.), **ῥυσεῦνται** (dial.3pl.fut.mid.), **ῥῦσθαι** (ep.athem.mid.inf.): see ῥύομαι

ῥυσιάζω *vb*. [ῥύσιον] **1** seize protected persons or property (in violation of religious law); **commit an unlawful seizure** or violation, **rob, steal** E. ‖ PASS. (of a person) be robbed E.
2 ‖ PASS. (of a protected person) be seized unlawfully A.
3 ‖ PASS. (of the persons of debtors) be seized (as security for debt) Plu.

ῥῡσί-βωμος ον *adj*. [ῥύομαι, βωμός] (of Athens) **guarding altars** A.

ῥῡσί-διφρος ον *adj*. [δίφρος] (of a charioteer's hand) **preserving the chariot** Pi.

ῥύσιον ου *n*. [prob. ἐρύω] **1** that which is seized by way of rightful or equivalent reprisal (for violent theft or murder, as sanctioned by religious law); **rightful compensation** or **forfeit** (ref. to cattle, for horses stolen) Il.; (ref. to a life, for a life) S.
2 that which is put up for lawful retaliatory seizure (in case of non-compliance or default); **pledge, security** (ref. to a hostage or hostages) S. AR.
3 ‖ PL. reprisals or property seizure (ref. to the rights or the acts themselves) Plb.

4 protected person or property seized (in violation of religious law); **unlawful seizure** (ref. to persons) A.

ῥύσιος ον *adj*. [ῥύομαι] (of a goddess) **protective** A.

ῥῡσί-πολις *masc.fem.adj*. [πόλις] | only nom. | (of Athena) **protecting the city** A.

ῥύσις εως *f*. [ῥέω] **1** action of flowing, **flow, stream** (of water, blood, fire) Pl. NT. Plu.; (fig.) **flood** (of sensual appetite) Plu.
2 flow, course (of a river) Plb.

ῥύσκεο (2sg.athem.iteratv.impf.mid.): see ῥύομαι

ῥυσμός *Ion.m*.: see ῥυθμός

ῥύσομαι (fut.mid.): see ῥύομαι

ῥυσός (also perh. dial. **ῥυσσός** Theoc.) ή όν *adj*. [reltd. ῥυτίς] (of persons, flesh, parts of the body) **wrinkled, shrivelled** Il. Hippon. E. Ar. Pl. Theoc.

ῥυσότης ητος *f*. **wrinkled appearance** (of a person) Plu.

ῥυστάζω *vb*. [ἐρύω; reltd. ῥυτήρ¹] | iteratv.impf. ῥυστάζεσκον | **1 haul, drag** —*a corpse, murderers* (W.PREP.PHR. *around a tomb*) Il. Call.
2 pull about, manhandle —*maidservants* Od.

ῥυστακτύς ύος *f*. **pulling about, manhandling** (of a person) Od.

ῥῡτ-αγωγεύς έως *m*. [ῥυτήρ¹, ἀγωγός] **leading-rope** (for a horse) X.

ῥῡτήρ¹ ῆρος *m*. —also **ῥύτειρα** ᾱς (Alcm.) *f*. [ἐρύω] **1** one who draws or pulls; **drawer** (W.GEN. of a bow) Od. Alcm.; **shooter** (W.GEN. of arrows) Od.
2 rein (for horses) Il. S. AR. Plu.
3 strap (for flogging) Aeschin. D.; (for attaching) Plu.

ῥῡτήρ² ῆρος *m*. [ῥύομαι] one who looks after or guards, **guardian** Od.

ῥυτίς ίδος *f*. [reltd. ῥυσός] **wrinkle** (in the skin) Ar. Pl.; (in leather) Pl.

ῥυτός ή όν *adj*. [ῥέω] (of water fr. a spring or river, seawater) **flowing, running** Trag. ‖ NEUT.SB. drinking-horn (ref. to a cup w. a small hole through which the liquid was drunk) D. Plb. Plu.

ῥῡτός ή όν *adj*. [perh. ἐρύω] **1** (of stones, too large to carry) dragged, **hauled up** Od.
2 ‖ NEUT.PL.SB. reins Hes.

ῥύτωρ¹ ορος *m*. [ἐρύω] one who draws or pulls; **drawer** (W.GEN. of a bow) Ar.

ῥύτωρ² ορος *m*. [ῥύομαι] **protector** (W.GEN. of a city, ref. to a god) A.

ῥυφέω *Ion.contr.vb*.: see ῥοφέω

ῥύψις εως *f*. [ῥύπτω] cleansing, **cleansing-power** (ref. to the action of alkalis on the tongue) Pl.

ῥυώδης ες *adj*. [ῥέω] (of semen) flowing fully, **copious** Pl.

ῥῶ *indecl.n*. [Semit.loanwd.] **rho** (letter of the Greek alphabet) Ar. Pl. Plb.

ῥωγαλέος η ον *Ion.adj*. [ῥώξ] (of a warrior's tunic) **split, rent** (by a weapon) Il.; (of clothing, a knapsack) **torn, tattered** Od.

ῥωγάς άδος *fem.adj*. (of a rock) **broken, cleft** AR.; **jagged** Theoc.

ῥωγμός *m*.: see ῥωχμός

ῥωμαλέος ᾱ ον *adj*. [ῥώμη] **1** (of persons, their bodies) having physical strength, **strong, robust** Plu.; (of a horse) Plu.
2 (of a public speaker) **powerful** Plu.
3 (of fetters) **strong** Hdt.

ῥώμη ης, dial. **ῥώμᾱ** ᾱς *f*. [ῥώννυμι] **1** physical strength (of persons), **strength** Xenoph. +
2 strength, power, might (of a nation, city, army, commander) Hdt. +; **influence, power** (of persons) E. Pl. Aeschin.

3 show of strength (by an attacker) S. Th. +
4 strength of heart, **confidence** Th. X. Plu.; **sturdiness, robustness** (of soul) Isoc. Pl. X. Plu.
5 strength, force, power (of speech, argument, a skill) Pl.; (of disbelief, a wish) Isoc. Pl.
6 strength or power (of objects, external forces); **strength** (of a spear, wall) E. Plu.; (of winds) E.; (of heat, pleasures) Pl.

Ῥώμη ης *f.* **Rome** (ref. to the city or state) Plb. NT. Plu.; (meton., ref. to its government, people or military power) Plb. Plu.

—**Ῥωμαῖοι** ων *m.pl.* **Romans** Plb. NT. Plu.; (sg., ref. to a citizen) Plb. NT. Plu.

—**Ῥωμαϊκός** ή όν *adj.* **1** of or belonging to Rome or the Romans; (of the race and history) **Roman** Plb. Plu.; (of a legion or military force, a camp, esp. opp. those of allies or the enemy) Plb. Plu.; (of spoils taken fr. Romans) Plu. ‖ NEUT.PL.SB. Roman history Plu.
2 characteristic or current among the Romans; (of a way of fighting, military equipment, formations, handling of weapons) **Roman** Plb. Plu.; (of customs, measures, the calendar, alphabet, language or literature) Plb. Plu.; (of manly principles and deeds) Plb.; (of a warship) Plb. Plu.
3 (of persons) on or from the Roman side (opp. another race); (of an officer) **Roman** Plb.; (of an informer, money-lender) Plu.; (of men in Plutarch's *Lives*, opp. Greek) Plu.
4 (of a historian) concerned with Roman affairs, **Roman** Plb.

—**Ῥωμαϊκῶς** *adv.* **in the Roman manner** —*ref. to using a sword* Plu.

—**Ῥωμαϊστί** *adv.* in the speech of the Romans, **in Latin** NT. Plu.

ῥώννῡμι *vb.* | aor. ἔρρωσα ‖ PASS.: ῥώννυμαι | aor. ἐρρώσθην | pf. ἔρρωμαι, imperatv. ἔρρωσο, pl. ἔρρωσθε | plpf. ἐρρώμην | **1 make strong** or **powerful** —*people, places* Plu.; **encourage, embolden** —*a person* Plu.
2 ‖ PRES. and AOR.PASS. (of a person or place) **be strengthened** (physically, or w. troops, manpower, money) Plu.; (spiritually or intellectually) Pl.; **be encouraged** or **emboldened** Th. Plu.; (of a desire) **be reinforced** Pl.
3 ‖ PF. and PLPF.PASS. (of a person, nation, troops) **be strong** Hdt. E. Th. X. D.; **have the strength** —W.INF. *to do sthg.* Pl.; **have a strong desire** —W.PREP.PHR. *for war* Th. —W.INF. *to do sthg.* Th. Lys. Pl.; **be confident** Th. X.; (of things) **be powerful** or **effective** X. Plu.
4 ‖ PF. and PLPF.PASS. **be in good health** Th. X.; (imperatv., as a parting salutation or at the end of a letter) **good health to you, keep well, goodbye** Isoc. X. Men. NT. Plu.; ἐρρῶσθαι φράζω (sts. λέγω) **bid** (W.DAT. *someone*) **keep well** Pl.; (w. sarcasm) *say good-day* —W.DAT. *to persons or things* (i.e. have no more time for them) D. Men. Plu.

—**ἐρρωμένος** η ον *pf.pass.ptcpl.adj.* | compar. ἐρρωμενέστερος, superl. ἐρρωμενέστατος | **1** (of persons) **in good health, robust** Lys. +; (of soldiers) **eager, fired up** E.; (of persons, ref. to their influence) **powerful** Pl. D. Plu.; **with a powerful capacity** (W.INF. to do sthg.) And.
2 (of things, activities) **powerful, vigorous** Hdt. +

—**ἐρρωμένως** *pf.pass.ptcpl.adv.* | compar. ἐρρωμενέστερον, also ἐρρωμενεστέρως (Isoc.), superl. ἐρρωμενέστατα | **forcefully, powerfully, vigorously** A. +

ῥώξ ῥωγός *f.* [ῥήγνῡμι] **break, cleft** ‖ PL. perh., **narrow passages** (in a palace) Od.

ῥώομαι *ep.mid.vb.* [perh.reltd. ῥώννῡμι] | 3pl.impf. ἐρρώοντο, ῥώοντο | 3pl.aor. ἐρρώσαντο, 3pl.aor.subj. ῥώσωνται | **1 move quickly** or **vigorously**; (of persons or gods) **charge, stream forward** Hom. Hes. hHom. Call.
2 (of nymphs) **move** or **dance nimbly** Il. hHom. AR.
3 (of limbs) **move vigorously** Hom.
4 (of a horse's mane) **stream out** Il.

ῥωπήια ων *ep.Ion.n.pl.* [ῥώψ] **place where there is brushwood, thicket** Hom. hHom.

ῥωπικός ή όν *adj.* [ῥῶπος] (of things) **cheap and tawdry, trashy** Plu.; (of an apparently competent man) **superficial, useless** Plb.

ῥῶπος ου *m.* [perh. ῥώψ] **merchandise of poor quality, trash, junk** D.

ῥωχμός (also perh. **ῥωγμός** Il.) οῦ *m.* [ῥήγνῡμι] **break, cleft** (in the ground) Il. AR.; (in a stone, in rock) Bion Plu.

ῥώψ ῥωπός *f.* **bush** or **shrub** ‖ PL. **brushwood** Od.

Σ σ

σά *dial.neut.pl.interrog.pron.*: see τά, under τίς
σᾶ (neut.nom.acc.pl.adj.): see σῶς
σά μάν (dial. form of τί μήν): see τά, under τίς
Σαβάζιος ου *m.* **Sabazios** (deity of Phrygian origin, sts. identified w. Dionysus) Ar. Thphr. ‖ PL. cries of 'Sabazios' Ar.
σάββατον ου *n.* [Semit.loanwd.] **1** (sts.pl.) **Sabbath day** (i.e. Saturday) NT.
2 (sts.pl.) **period of seven days ending with the Sabbath, week** NT.
σαβοῖ *interj.* **saboi!** (cry of the devotees of Sabazios) D.
σάγαρις εως (Ion. ιος) *f.* | Ion.acc.pl. σαγάρις | **light battle-axe** (used esp. by Scythians and Persians, app. sharpened along one edge), **sagaris** Hdt. X.
σαγή ῆς *f.* [σάσσω] **baggage** (carried on one's person, esp. for a journey); **equipment, kit** A. E. ‖ PL. **weaponry** A.
σαγηνεύς έως *m.* [σαγήνη] **drag-net fisherman** Plu.
σαγηνεύω *vb.* **1** (of a line of men w. joined hands) spread a drag-net over, **round up** —*a population* Hdt.
2 sweep clear, depopulate —*an enemy territory* Hdt. Pl.
σαγήνη ης *f.* **drag-net** (for fishing) NT. Plu.
σάγμα ατος *n.* [σάσσω] **1 case, cover** (for storing and transporting shields and weapons) E. Ar.
2 pack, knapsack (of a soldier) Ar.
3 saddle-bag, pack-saddle A.(cj.) Plu.
4 tightly packed heap, **heap** (W.GEN. of weapons) Plu.
σάγος ου *m.* [Lat. *sagus*] a kind of cloak (worn by Gauls and Roman soldiers), **coarse cloak** Plb. Plu.
σάγω *Lacon.vb.*: see θήγω
σάθη ης *f.* (colloq. term for penis) **dick, cock** Archil. Ar.
σαθρός ά όν *adj.* **1** (of pots, vessels) **flawed, defective** Pl.
2 (w.medic.connot., of a soul) **unsound, infirm** Pl.
‖ NEUT.PL.SB. **unsound or infirm parts** (of the body) D.
‖ NEUT.SG.SB. **infirmity** (W.GEN. of the soul) Plu.
3 (of the basis of a constitution) **defective, flawed** Pl.
‖ NEUT.PL.SB. **flaws, shortcomings** (W.GEN. of a tyranny) Plu.; **weak points** (W.GEN. in policy) D.
4 (of words and arguments) **flawed, hollow** E. D.; (of fame or reputation) Pi.; (of a person) **unsound** (in argument) Pl.
5 (of conduct or thinking) **corrupt, tainted** Hdt. D.; (of religious rites) **depraved** E.
6 (of soldiers) unsound (in loyalty), **disaffected** Plu.
—**σαθρόν** *neut.adv.* **with an untrue note** —*ref. to a theory* (envisaged as a pot) *ringing* Pl.
—**σαθρῶς** *adv.* (fig.) **unsoundly** —*ref. to a person being established in life* Arist.(quot.)
σαίνω *vb.* | aor. ἔσηνα, dial. ἔσᾱνα | **1** (of animals, esp. dogs) give a display of affection and delight (in greeting, expectation of food), **fawn** Od. hHom. A. AR.; (tr.) **fawn upon** —*a person* Hes. Ar. AR.
2 (of persons) adopt an attitude of deference or affection (in order to obtain sthg.); **fawn upon, flatter** —*a person* Pi. Call. Plb.; (intr.) **fawn** A. Pi.

3 adopt an attitude of submissiveness; (of animals) **cringe** (fr. fear) AR.; (tr., of persons) **cringe before** —*a deadly fate, battle* A.
4 show a warm welcome —w. ποτί + ACC. *to an announcement* (of an athletic victory) Pi.
5 (of persons or things) arouse excitement or delight; **thrill** —*a person, heart or soul* B. S. E. Arist.; (intr., of hope) Plu.
6 ‖ PASS. **be beguiled** —W.PREP.PHR. *by hope* A.
σαίρω *vb.* | aor. ἔσηρα | **1 brush, sweep** —*a house, temple, floor* E. Plu. ‖ PASS. (of ground) **be swept** Plu.
2 sweep off, brush away —*dust* S.
σάκ-ανδρος ου *m.* [perh. σάκος¹, see σάκκος; ἀνήρ] (colloq., ref. to a hairy vagina) **man-sack** Ar.
σακέσ-παλος ον *adj.* [σάκος², πάλλω] (of warriors) **shield-wielding** Il. Call. Mosch.
σακεσ-φόρος ον *adj.* [φέρω] **1** (of warriors) **shield-bearing, armed with a shield** B. S. E.
2 (as the comic title of a politician, fig.ref. to his large beard) **shield-bearing** Plu. | cf. σάκκος 3
σακεύω *vb.*: see σακκέω
σακίον ου *n.* [dimin. σάκος¹, see σάκκος] **1 piece of sackcloth** X.
2 sackcloth (worn as a punishment by Syrians who have offended a goddess) Men.
σᾱκίτᾱς ᾱ *dial.masc.adj.* [σηκός] (of a lamb) weaned in the pen, **stall-fed** Theoc.
σακκέω (v.l. **σακεύω**) *contr.vb.* [σάκος¹, see σάκκος] **pass through coarse cloth; strain** —*fruit* (for its juice) Hdt.
σάκκος, Att. **σάκος¹**, ου *m.* [Semit.loanwd.] **1 coarse animal-hair cloth, sackcloth** (esp. assoc.w. mourning) NT.
2 item made of sackcloth; sack Hdt. Ar.; **strainer** (for wine) Hippon.
3 (fig.) **long and coarse beard** Ar.
σᾱκός *dial.m.*: see σηκός
σάκος² εος (ευς Hes.) *n.* **1 body-shield of oblong or figure-of-eight shape** (usu. made of leather and oft. faced w. metal), **shield** Hom. Hes. Sol. Hdt. Trag. Hellenist.poet.
2 that which affords protection like a shield; shield (against enemies, ref. to an altar) A.
σάκτᾱς ου *m.* [σάσσω] **sack, bag** Ar.
σάκτωρ ορος *m.* (ref. to Xerxes) **packer** (W.DBL.GEN. of Hades, w. dead Persians) A.
σακχ-υφάντης (v.l. **σαχυφάντης**) ου *m.* [σάκκος] one who weaves sackcloth, **cloth-weaver** D.
σαλάκων ωνος *m.* [σάλος] **swaggerer, show-off** Arist.
σαλακωνίζομαι *mid.vb.* (of a woman, described as a whore) **swagger, strut** Hermipp.
Σαλαμῑν-αφέται έων *Ion.m.pl.* [Σαλαμίς¹, ἀφίημι] **abandoners of Salamis, Salamis-ceders** (ref. to the Athenians) Sol.
Σαλαμίς¹ ῑνος *f.* **Salamis** (island and its principal town in

Σαλαμίς

the Saronic Gulf, betw. Athens and Megara, site of a battle betw. Persian and Athenian fleets in 480 BC) Il. +
—**Σαλαμίνιος**[1] ᾱ (Ion. η) ον *adj*. **1** (of the territory) **of Salamis, Salaminian** Hdt. || FEM.SB. Saladminian territory Hdt.
2 (of a man or woman) **from Salamis, Salaminian** Pl. X. Plu.; (of a rower at the battle of 480 BC) Ar. || MASC.PL.SB. Salaminians (ref. to the inhabitants) Aeschin. D. Plu. || FEM.PL.SB. Women of Salamis A.(title)
—**Σαλαμινίᾱ** ᾱς *f*. **Salaminia** (name of one of two Athenian triremes, fast ships w. elite crews, used for state business as well as fighting) Th. Ar. X. Plu. | cf. Πάραλος[3]
—**Σαλαμινιάδες** ων *fem.pl.adj*. (of shores) **Salaminian** A.
Σαλαμίς[2] ῖνος *f*. **Salamis** (town on Cyprus, founded by Teucer of Grecian Salamis) hHom. Hdt. Th. Isoc.
—**Σαλαμίνιος**[2] ᾱ (Ion. η) ον *adj*. (of a man) **from Salamis, Salaminian** Hdt. Plb. Plu. || MASC.PL.SB. Salaminians (as a population or military force) Hdt. Isoc.
σάλεσσι (Lacon.dat.pl.): see θάλος
σαλεύω *vb*. [σάλος] **1** (intr., of sailors) **be tossed about** (at sea) X. Plu.
2 (fig., of persons, cities, an army, a system of government) **be storm-tossed, be in trouble** S. E. Isoc. Pl. Plu.; (of a household, relying on one son as its anchor) Plu. | see also ἁλύω 4
3 (tr., of a torrent) **shake** —*a house* NT. || PASS. (of ground, foundations) be shaken (by an earthquake) A. NT.; (of a reed) —W.PREP.PHR. *by the wind* NT.; (of a liquid measure) be shaken up NT.; (of an object) be agitated, oscillate Pl.
4 shake about, **brandish** —*weapons* Plu.
5 || PASS. (of troops) surge to and fro Plu.; (of a shadow) flicker Plu.
6 (fig.) **shake, destabilise** —*an empire* Plu. || PASS. (of the powers of heaven) be shaken NT.
7 stir up, agitate —*mobs* NT.; (of the soul) —*the body* Pl. || PASS. (of a person) be inwardly disturbed NT.
σάλλω *Lacon.vb*.: see θάλλω
σάλος ου *m*. **1 swell, surge** (of the sea) E. Ar. AR. NT. Plu.
2 tossing (of a voyager, by the sea) S.; (fig., of a city, envisaged as a ship, in terms of its politics) S.
3 turbulence (in politics) S. Lys. Plu.
4 tremor (in the earth) E.; **commotion** (in a celestial body) Plu.; **turbulence** (in the air) Plu.
5 loss of balance (by soldiers, on uneven ground) Plu.
6 (gener.) **disturbance, commotion** (in the state, a military formation, a soul) Plu.
7 area of open water (where a ship rides at anchor), **roadstead** (opp. harbour) Plb.
σαλπιγγο-λογχ-υπηνάδαι ῶν *m.pl*. [σάλπιγξ, λόγχη, ὑπήνη] **trumpet-lance-and-beard types** (as typifying the followers of Aeschylus) Ar.
σαλπιγκτής, Att. **σαλπικτής**, also perh. **σαλπιστής** (Plb.), οῦ *m*. **trumpeter** Th. X. D. Thphr. Plb. Plu.
σάλπιγξ ιγγος *f*. **trumpet** (usu. of bronze, used for giving signals, esp. in war and contests) Il. Ibyc. B. Trag. +
σαλπίζω *vb*. aor. ἐσάλπιγξα, ep. σάλπιγξα, also ἐσάλπισα (Plb. NT.) | **1 sound the trumpet** Plb. NT.; **play** (W.ACC. notes) **on the trumpet** X. || IMPERS.AOR. the trumpet sounded X.
2 (fig., of the heavens) **resound like a trumpet** Il.
σαλπικτής *Att.m*., **σαλπιστής** *m*.: see σαλπιγκτής
σᾶμα *dial.n*.: see σῆμα
σάμαινα ης *f*. [Σάμος 1] **ship of Samian style** Plu.
σαμαίνω *dial.vb*.: see σημαίνω
Σαμαῖοι *m.pl*.: see under Σάμη

σαμάντρια *dial.f*.: see under σημαντήρ
Σαμάρεια ᾱς *f*. **Samaria** (city and region of Palestine) Plb. NT.
—**Σαμαρίτης** ου *m*. inhabitant of Samaria, **Samaritan** NT.
—**Σαμαρῖτις** ιδος *f*. **Samaritan woman** NT.
σαμβαλίσκον *dial.n*., **σάμβαλον** *dial.n*.: see σάνδαλον
σαμβύκη ης *f*. [loanwd.] **1** a kind of arched harp, **sambuca** Arist.
2 female player of the sambuca, **harpist** Plb.
3 a kind of siege-engine (used to scale walls fr. ships, named because of its shape), **sambuca** Plb. Plu.
σαμβυκίστρια ᾱς *f*. female player of the sambuca, **harpist** Plb. Plu.
σάμερον *dial.adv*.: see σήμερον
Σάμη ης *f*. **Same** (old name for the island Kephallenia, also called Samos) Od. hHom.
—**Σαμαῖοι** ων *m.pl*. inhabitants of Same (a town on the island), **Samians** Th.
Σαμοθράκη, Ion. **Σαμοθρηίκη**, ης *f*. **Samothrace** (island off the coast of Thrace) Hdt. +
—**Σαμοθράκιος** ᾱ ον, Ion. **Σαμοθρηίκιος** η ον *adj*. of or relating to Samothrace; (of a city, shrine, ship, walls) **Samothracian** Hdt. Plu.
—**Σαμόθραξ** ακος, Ion. **Σαμόθρηξ** ηκος *masc.adj*. (of a person or deity) of or from Samothrace, **Samothracian** Call.*epigr*. Plu.
—**Σαμοθρήικες** ων *Ion.m.pl*. **Samothracians** Hdt.
Σάμος ου *f*. **1 Samos** (large island off the coast of Asia Minor) hHom. +
2 Samos (old name for Kephallenia, also called Same) Hom.
3 Thracian Samos, **Samos** (name for Samothrace) Il.; Σάμος Θρηικίη *Samothrace* Il. hHom.
—**Σάμιος** ᾱ (Ion. η) ον *adj*. (of persons or things) of or relating to (Ionian) Samos, **Samian** Stesich. Hdt. +; (as epith. of Dionysus) Call.*epigr*. || FEM.SB. Samian territory Hdt. Theoc. || MASC.PL.SB. Samians (as a population or military force) Hdt. +
σαμφόρᾱς ου *m*. [σάν, φέρω] one who bears the letter *san* (ref. to a horse, branded as a mark of its pedigree), **san-bearer** Ar.
σάν *indecl.n*. **san** (archaic letter of the Greek alphabet, used as the regular character for the sound *s* in several Doric scripts, later used as a Doric name for sigma) Pi.*fr*. Hdt.
σάνατος *Lacon.m*.: see θάνατος
σάνδαλον, dial. **σάμβαλον**, ου *n*. **sandal** hHom. Eumel. Sapph. Call. Theoc.
—**σανδάλιον** ου *n*. [dimin.] **sandal** Hdt. NT.
—**σανδαλίσκον**, dial. **σαμβαλίσκον**, ου *n*. [dimin.] **sandal** Hippon. Ar.
σανδαράκινος η ον *adj*. [σανδαράκη *arsenic sulphide, realgar*] (of painted ramparts) of the colour of realgar, **orange-red** Hdt.
σανίδιον ου *n*. [dimin. σανίς] **1** small flat piece of wood, **plank** (app. used as a work-surface) Ar.
2 gypsum-covered board (on which laws and lists were written), **tablet** Lys. Aeschin.
σανίδωμα ατος *n*. [σανιδόω *board over*] structure made with planks, **planking** Plb.
σανίς ίδος *f*. **1** piece of wood, **plank** Od. Call. Plb. Plu.; **timber** (fr. a shipwreck) NT.
2 boarding plank (for a ship), **gangplank** E.
3 board (to which offenders were bound or nailed) Hdt. Ar.
4 (usu.pl.) wooden door-panel, **door** Hom. E. AR.
5 writing-board, **writing-tablet** E.

6 gypsum-covered board (on which laws and lists were written), **tablet, notice-board** Ar. Att.orats. Arist. Plu.
7 app. **platform** or **shelf** Od.

σάος Aeol.adj.: see σῶς

σαοφροσύνη ep.f., **σαόφρων** dial.adj.: see σωφροσύνη, σώφρων

σαόω contr.vb. [σάος, reltd. σῴζω] | ep.2sg.opt. (or subj.) σαῷς, 3sg. σαῷ, imperatv. σάου, ep. σάω | ep.3sg.impf. σάω | fut. σαώσω | aor. ἐσάωσα, ep. σάωσα, ep.1pl.subj. σαώσομεν, 2pl. σαώσετε, inf. σαῶσαι, ep. σαωσέμεν, σαωσέμεναι ‖ PASS.: ep.2sg.fut. σαώσεαι | aor. ἐσαώθην | —also **σάωμι** Aeol.vb. | 2sg. σάως (or σάῳς) | —also **σώω** ep.vb. | pl.imperatv. σώετε | masc.nom.pl.pres.ptcpl. σώοντες | iteratv.impf. σώεσκον ‖ mid.pass.inf. σώεσθαι (AR.) |
1 (of persons, gods, other agents) save from imminent danger or death, **save, rescue** —persons Hom. Hes.fr. Pi.fr. —one's life D.(quot.epigr.) —ships, a city Il. Alc. Call. AR. ‖ PASS. be saved or survive Hom. Pi. AR.
2 bring (W.ACC. someone) **safely** or **in safety** —W.ADV. or PREP.PHR. to a place Hom.
3 save from enemy hands, rescue, recover —a corpse Il.
4 (of a person) preserve from harm, **keep safe, protect, look after** —a person, people Hom. Tyrt. AR. —possessions, a land and city Od. Thgn.; (of a god) —persons, places hHom. Call. Plb.(quot.epigr.); (of the head) —the body Hdt.(oracle)

σαπρός ά όν adj. [σήπω] **1** (of organic matter, material objects, buildings) **rotten, decayed** Thgn. Ar. D. Men. +
2 (of olive oil) **rancid** Thphr.
3 (gener., of fish) of poor quality, **poor, bad** NT.
4 (of fish platters) **worn-out** Ar.
5 (of a spoken phrase) **old-fashioned, dated** Ar.
6 (of old people) **decrepit** Ar.
7 (fig., of peace, envisaged as wine) **well-matured, mellow** Ar.

σαπρότης ητος f. **rottenness** (of food) Pl.

Σαπφώ οῦς, Aeol. **Ψάπφω** ους f. **Sappho** (lyric poet fr. Lesbos, late 7th–early 6th C. BC) Sapph. Alc. Hdt. Pl. Arist. +

σάπω dial.vb.: see σήπω

Σάραπις ιδος m. | acc. Σάραπιν | **Sarapis** (Greek name for the Egyptian deity Osiris–Apis) Call.epigr. Plu.
—**Σαραπιεῖον**, also **Σεραπεῖον**, ου n. **temple of Sarapis** Plb. Plu.

σαρδάνιον neut.adv. **scornfully, bitterly** —ref. to smiling, laughing Od. Pl. Plb.

Σάρδεις εων, dial. **Σάρδιες** ιων f.pl. | Ion.acc. Σάρδῑς (Hdt.), dial. Σάρδιας (Call.) | **Sardis** (capital city of Lydia) Alcm. +
—**Σαρδιᾱνός**, Ion. **Σαρδιηνός**, ή όν adj. **1** (of the city, region) of Sardis, **Sardian** Hdt. X.
2 (of a person) from Sardis, **Sardian** Hdt. Plu. ‖ MASC.PL.SB. Sardians X. Plu.; (sg.) Call.
—**Σαρδιᾱνικός** ή όν adj. (of a dye) of the Sardian type (i.e. reddish-purple), **Sardian** Ar.

σάρδιον ου n. Sardian stone, **cornelian** Pl.

Σαρδώ οῦς f. | acc. Σαρδώ | —also **Σαρδών** όνος (Plb. Plu.) f. **Sardinia** (island in the Mediterranean, S. of Corsica) Hdt. Ar. Call. Plb. Plu.
—**Σαρδόνιος** ᾱ ον adj. **1** of or relating to Sardinia; (of the sea) **Sardinian** Hdt. AR. Theoc. Plb. ‖ MASC.PL.SB. men of Sardinia, Sardinians (as a population or military force) Hdt. Plb.
2 (of laughter, by conflation w. σαρδάνιον) **sardonic** Plu.
—**Σαρδονικός** ή όν adj. (of linen) of the Sardinian kind, **Sardinian** Hdt.
—**Σαρδῷος** ᾱ ον adj. (of the sea) **Sardinian** Plb. ‖ MASC.PL.SB. Sardinians Plb.

σαρδών όνος f. **upper-cord** (of a hunting net) X.

σάρῑσα ης f. long battle-spear, **sarisa, pike** (used esp. by the Macedonian phalanx) Men. Plb. Plu.

σαρῑσο-φόρος ον adj. [φέρω] (of a phalanx) **sarisa-bearing** Plb.

σαρκάζω vb. [σάρξ] (of persons compared to dogs) app., pull back one's flesh (to reveal the teeth), **grimace** (fr. physical effort) Ar.

σαρκασμο-πιτυοκάμπται ῶν m.pl. [πιτυοκάμπτης] **snarling pine-benders** (as typifying the followers of Aeschylus) Ar.

σαρκίδιον ου n. [dimin. σάρξ] **piece of flesh** (W.GEN. of a bird or animal) Plu.

σαρκίζω vb. (of a warrior) **scrape out flesh** (fr. a dead enemy's skull) Hdt.

σάρκινος η ον adj. **1** (of persons, their bodies, a fish) **formed of flesh and blood, fleshy** Pl. Arist. Theoc.
2 (of persons) **flabby, corpulent** Plb.

σαρκίον ου n. [dimin. σάρξ] **poor flesh** (ref. to the human body as sthg. subject to decay) Plu.

σαρκο-ειδής ές adj. [εἶδος¹] (of body tissue) having the form of flesh, **fleshy** Pl.

σαρκο-φάγος ον adj. [φαγεῖν] (of birds and animals) **flesh-eating, carnivorous** Plu.

σαρκώδης ες adj. (of gods or humans) **made of flesh, corporeal** Hdt. Pl.; (of the rump or loins of a dog) **fleshy** or **sinewy** X.

Σαρμάτης m.: see under Σαυρομάται

σάρξ σαρκός f. **1** (oft.pl.) fleshy part (of the human or animal body), **flesh** Hom. +
2 (usu.sg., ref. to the physical human frame as a whole, oft. as the object of suffering) **flesh, body** Trag. Pl. NT.; (opp. mind) A. E.; (envisaged as a garment) E.
3 flesh (as a source of sin) NT.; (of sexual desire, without connot. of sinfulness) NT.
4 flesh (W.GEN. of Jesus, ref. to the Eucharist) NT.
5 (phrs.) πᾶσα σάρξ all mankind NT.; σάρξ καὶ αἷμα flesh and blood (ref. to a human being, opp. God) NT.; κατὰ τὴν σάρκα by human (opp. spiritual) standards NT.

σάρον ου n. [σαίρω] **sweepings, refuse** (W.GEN. of the sea, pejor.ref. to Asterie, i.e. Delos) Call.

σαρόω contr.vb. **sweep clean** —a house NT. ‖ PASS. (of a house) be swept clean NT.

Σαρπηδών όνος m. | also gen. Σαρπήδοντος, dat. Σαρπήδοντι | **Sarpedon** (ruler of Lycia and a Trojan ally) Il. +
—**Σαρπηδόνιος** ᾱ (Ion. η) ον adj. (of a headland in Thrace) **Sarpedonian** Hdt. AR.; (of a headland in Cilicia) A. Plb.

Σαρωνικός ή όν adj. (of the gulf betw. Athens and the Argolid) **Saronic** A. E. Call.

σαρωνίς ίδος f. a kind of tree; app. **oak** Call.

σᾱσαμίς dial.f., **σάσαμον** dial.n.: see σησαμή, σήσαμον

σᾱσαμό-παστος ον dial.adj. [σήσαμον, πάσσω] (of cakes) **sesame-sprinkled** Philox.Leuc.

σᾱσαμο-τῡρο-παγής ές dial.adj. [τῡρός, πήγνῡμι] (of cakes) **compounded of sesame and cheese** Philox.Leuc.

σᾱσαμό-φωκτος ον dial.adj. [φώγω roast, toast] (of cakes) **sesame-toasted** Philox.Leuc.

σάσσω, Att. **σάττω** vb. | aor. ἔσαξα ‖ PASS.: pf. σέσαγμαι | Ion.3pl.plpf. ἐσεσάχατο | **1 pack tightly, cram** —soil (W.PREP.PHR. around a plant) X. —fruit (into jars) Plb. ‖ MID. make compact, **strengthen** —a wall Hdt.

Σατανᾶς

2 fill up, **stock, provision** —*a route into a country* (W.DAT. *w. water*) Hdt.
3 ‖ PASS. (of a ship) be loaded —W.GEN. *w. men* X.; (of couches) —*w. cloaks and rugs* Ar.(cj.); (of baskets) —*w. straw* Plb.; (of a person) be weighed down —*w.* σύν + DAT. *w. wet clothing* Semon.(dub.); (fig.) be laden (in one's soul) —W.GEN. *w. riches* X.; be burdened —W.GEN. *w. sufferings* A.
4 ‖ PASS. (of soldiers) be equipped Hdt. —W.DAT. or ADVBL.PHR. *in a certain way, w. gear, weapons* Hdt. Theoc.

Σατανᾶς ᾶ *m.* [Semit.loanwd.] **Satan, the Devil** NT.

σατίνη ης, dial. **σατίνᾱ** ᾱς *f.* ‖ Ion.gen.pl. σατινέων ‖ only pl., sts. for sg. ‖ **carriage** or **chariot** (used esp. by women) hHom. Sapph. Anacr. E.

σάτον ου *n.* [Semit.loanwd.] unit of dry measure (approx. 13 litres); **measure** (W.GEN. of grain) NT.

σατραπείᾱ ᾱς, Ion. **σατραπηίη** ης *f.* [σατράπης] **office** or **province of a satrap, satrapy** Hdt. Th. X. Plb. Plu.

σατραπεύω *vb.* **rule as a satrap** X. —W.GEN. *over a region* X. Plu.

σατράπης ου *m.* [Iran.loanwd.] **satrap** (provincial governor in the Persian empire) Att.orats. X. Men. Plb. Plu.

σατραπικός ή όν *adj.* 1 (of a court) **of a satrap, provincial** Plu.
2 (of cuisine) fit for a satrap, **luxurious** Plu.
3 (pejor., of orders) of the kind issued by satraps, **from eastern lands** Plu.
4 (of sexual unions) **with orientals** Plu.

σάττω Att.*vb.*: see σάσσω

σατυρικός ή όν *adj.* [Σάτυροι] 1 (of persons) **satyr-like** (in appearance or behaviour) Pl. Plu.; (of leaps by revellers) Plu.
2 (of poetry) of the satyric kind, **satyric** Arist.; (of a piece of play-acting, fig.ref. to a comparison of Socrates w. a satyr) Pl. ‖ NEUT.SB. satyric drama X. Arist.

Σάτυροι ων *m.pl.* **satyrs** (group of mythol. rustic males, sts.w. animal features, oft. identified w. Silenoi) Hes.*fr.* E. Pl. +; (sons of Silenos in satyric drama, where they form the chorus) E.*Cyc.* Ar. ‖ SG. satyr Pl. X. Plu.; (ref. to Socrates, fr. his bullying style of argument) Pl. ‖ see also Σιληνός
—**Σατυρίσκοι** ων *m.pl.* [dimin.] **satyrs** Theoc. ‖ SG. satyr Mosch.; (ref. to a lecherous youth) Theoc.

σαυλόομαι mid.contr.*vb.* [σαῦλος] (of a band of satyrs) **swagger along** E.*Cyc.*

σαυλο-πρωκτιάω contr.*vb.* [πρωκτός] **wiggle one's arse** Ar.

σαῦλος η ον *adj.* moving in an affected manner; (of Bassarids) **hip-swaying, mincing** Anacr.
—**σαῦλα** neut.pl.*adv.* **mincingly** —*ref. to a person walking* Anacr.; **in a waddling manner** —*ref. to a tortoise walking* hHom.; **struttingly** —*ref. to a man walking like a horse* Semon.

σαυμαστός Lacon.*adj.*: see θαυμαστός

σαυνιαστάς ᾶ dial.*m.* [σαύνιον] **spear-fisher** Call.

σαύνιον ου *n.* **spear, javelin** Plu.

σαύρᾱ ᾱς, Ion. **σαύρη** ης *f.* **lizard** Hdt. Theoc.

Σαυρομάται ῶν (Ion. έων) *m.pl.* **Sauromatai, Sarmatians** (nomadic tribe, living originally NE. of the Black Sea) Hdt. AR.; (sg.) Hdt.
—**Σαρμάτης** ου *m.* Sarmatian man, **Sarmatian** Plb.
—**Σαυρομάτις** ιδος fem.*adj.* (of the land) **Sarmatian** Hdt. ‖ SB. Sarmatian woman Pl.

σαῦρος ου *m.* **lizard** Theoc.

σαυρωτήρ ῆρος *m.* **spike** (at the butt of a spear) Il. Hdt. Plb.

σαυτόν 2sg.acc.masc.reflexv.pron., **σαυτήν** fem.: see σεαυτόν

σάφα *adv.* [σαφής] 1 (w.vb. of knowing) **with certainty, reliably** Hom. hHom. Pi. Hdt.(oracle) Trag. Antipho +

2 (w.vb. of speaking or demonstrating) **reliably, unambiguously** Hom. Pi. Theoc.

σαφέως Ion.*adv.*: see σαφῶς, under σαφής

σαφήνεια ᾱς *f.* [σαφηνής] **sureness, reliability, clarity** (in perception or expression) A. Antipho Isoc. Pl. Arist. +

σαφηνής, dial. **σαφᾱνής**, ές *adj.* 1 (of a report or sim.) **sure, reliable** A. Pi. S.
2 (of shouts) **clear** (to hear and understand) A.
—**σαφηνῶς**, Ion. **σαφηνέως** *adv.* (w.vb. of knowing) **with certainty, reliably** Thgn.; (w.vb. of speaking) **distinctly, unambiguously** A. Hdt.

σαφηνίζω *vb.* ‖ fut. σαφηνιῶ ‖ 1 make (sthg.) sure or clear; **clarify, explain** —*sthg.* A. X. Plu. —W.COMPL.CL. *that sthg. is the case* X.; (intr., of a speaker) **be clear** (in meaning) Arist. ‖ IMPERS.PASS. it is made clear —W.INDIR.Q. *what is the case* X.
2 **indicate, specify** —*certain people* X.
3 (of the sun or moon) **illuminate** —*objects, places* X. Plu.

σαφής ές *adj.* ‖ compar. σαφέστερος, superl. σαφέστατος ‖ 1 (of persons, things, reports) **sure, reliable, trustworthy** Pi. Hdt. Trag. Th. +
2 **evident, clear** (to see, hear, understand) Pi. B. Trag. Th. +
—**σαφές** neut.*adv.* 1 **with certainty, reliably** hHom. Pi.
2 **clearly** Pi.
—**σαφῶς**, Ion. **σαφέως** *adv.* ‖ compar. σαφέστερον, also σαφεστέρως (Antipho Plb.) ‖ 1 (w.vb. of knowing or sim.) **with certainty, reliably** hHom. +
2 (usu. w.vb. of speaking) **clearly, unambiguously** A. +
3 (supporting a truth) **clearly, evidently** A. +

σαχυφάντης *m.*: see σακχυφάντης

σάω[1] contr.*vb.* ‖ only 3pl. σῶσι ‖ **strain** —*a powder* (*through linen*) Hdt.

σάω[2] (ep.2sg.imperatv. and 3sg.impf.), **σαῷ** and **σαῶς** (ep.3sg. and 2sg.opt. or subj.), **σάως** or **σῶς** (Aeol.2sg.pres.), **σάωσα** (ep.aor.), **σαώσω** (fut.): see σαόω

σαώτερος (compar.*adj.*): see σῶς

σαωτήρ *m.*: see σωτήρ

σβέννῡμι, also (pres. and impf.) **σβεννύω** (Pi. B.) *vb.* ‖ ep.impf. σβέννυον (B.) ‖ fut. σβέσω, ep. σβέσσω ‖ aor.1 ἔσβεσα, ep. σβέσα, ep.inf. σβέσσαι ‖ athem.aor. ἔσβην (Hom.) ‖ PASS.: aor. ἐσβέσθην ‖
1 **quench, extinguish, put out** —*fire, flames, burning objects* Heraclit. Pi. B. Hdt. Th. + ‖ PASS. and ATHEM.AOR.ACT. (of fire) be extinguished Il. NT.; (of lamps) NT.; (of heat) —W.DAT. *by cold* Plu.
2 (of windless weather) **quell, make calm** —*waves* Ar. ‖ ATHEM.AOR.ACT. (of wind) be stilled, subside Od.
3 **quench** —*thirst* (W.DAT. *w. water*) AR. ‖ PASS. (of goats) be drained dry (of milk) Hes.
4 **quell, stifle, put a stop to** —*anger, passion, grief, fear, strife, or sim.* Il. Heraclit. Hdt.(oracle) S. E. Pl. + ‖ PASS. (of a warlike spirit, political unrest) be quelled Plu.

σβέσις εως *f.* **extinguishing** (of fire) Plu.

σβεστήριος ᾱ ον *adj.* (of preventive measures) **serving to extinguish** (fire) Th. ‖ NEUT.SB. means of extinguishing (fire) Plu.

σέ, σε (acc.2sg.pers.pron.): see σύ

σεαυτόν (also **σαυτόν**), Ion. **σεωυτόν**, ἥν 2sg.acc. masc.fem.reflexv.pron. [σύ, αὐτός] ‖ gen. σεαυτοῦ (also σαυτοῦ), dial. σαυτῶ (Theoc.), Ion. σεωυτοῦ ῆς ‖ dat. σεαυτῷ (also σαυτῷ), Aeol. σαύτῳ, Ion. σεωυτῷ ῇ ‖ **yourself** (ref. to the subject of the main vb.) Alc. +; (phr.) γνῶθι σαυτόν *know yourself* (*inscription on the temple at Delphi*) Pl. X. +

σεβάζομαι *mid.vb.* [σέβας] | ep.3sg.aor. σεβάσσατο | feel inhibiting shame (in the face of), **shy from** —*sthg.* Il.

σέβας *n.* [σέβω] | SG.: only nom., voc., acc. σέβας | PL.: only acc. σέβη (A.) | **1** feeling of reverence or reverent awe (inhibiting a shameful action), **shame, respect** Il.
2 feeling of awe, **awe, wonder** (at the sight of a god) hHom.; (at the sight of a mortal, a palace worthy of Zeus) Od.
3 reverence, respect (due to gods, parents) hHom. A. S.; (due to a sister, ruler, strangers) A.
4 quality of arousing reverence or awe; **awesomeness, majesty, sanctity** (of gods) Trag. Arist.*lyr.*; (of a suppliant's hand, Justice) E.; (of religious rites) Ar.; (of a mother) A.
5 object of reverence or awe (ref. to a god, person or place) Trag. Theoc.; (ref. to a tomb) E.; **awesome sight** (ref. to a flower) hHom.; (ref. to armour, a person) S.

σεβάσματα των *n.pl.* [σεβάζομαι] **objects of veneration** or **worship** (such as statues) NT.

Σεβαστός οῦ *m.* **Augustus** (title of the Roman emperor, sts. appos.w. Καῖσαρ *Caesar*) NT. Plu.
—**Σεβαστή** ῆς *f.* (appos.w. σπεῖρα *cohort*) **Augusta** NT.

σεβίζω *vb.* [σέβας] | AOR.: subj. σεβίξω (A.), ptcpl. σεβίσας (S.), inf. σεβίσαι (Ar.) || PASS.: aor.ptcpl. (w.mid.sens.) σεβισθείς (S.) | **1** (act. and mid.) **revere, venerate, honour** —*gods, suppliants, persons* Pi. Trag. Ar. Call. || PASS. (of a person) be revered Emp.
2 (act., mid. and aor.pass.) regard (sthg.) as having a sacred or exalted character; **revere, respect, honour** —*a city* Pi. —*royal authority, a marriage* E. —*a parent's curse, a suppliant's claims* A. S.
3 reverently practise —*piety* S.; **reverently perform** —*sacrifices* E.

σέβω *vb.* | impf.mid. ἐσεβόμην || aor.pass.ptcpl. σεφθείς (Pl.) | **1** || MID. **feel awe or respect** (inhibiting a shameful action), **feel shame** Il.; feel too much shame (to do sthg.), **shrink in awe from** —W.INF. *doing sthg.* A. Pl. || AOR.PASS.PTCPL. awestricken (at a sight) Pl.
2 (act. and mid.) **revere, venerate, honour, respect** —*a god* Trag. + —*a person* (sts. as a god) Trag. —*a suppliant, parents, kin, a wife* Trag.; (act., intr.) show reverence to the gods, **act piously** Th.
3 revere, respect —*the authority or ordinances of gods or rulers* Pi. Trag. —*a holy place, city, country* S. E. —*a curse* E.; (mid.) —*objects, living things* (which have a religious or other claim to reverence) Hdt. +
4 (gener., without religious connot., act. and mid.) treat respectfully, **honour, respect** —*material and non-material things* (such as places, wealth, kinship, self-control, a person's love) Hdt. Trag. +
5 celebrate reverently —*a festival* Archil. —*a dirge, day of sacrifice* E. —*religious rites* Ar.(mid.)
6 (act. and mid.) **practise** —*honesty, justice* A. E. Pl. —*modest behaviour* E.
7 exercise —*royal authority* S.; **uphold, maintain** —*a political system* A. —*a custom* E.

σέθεν (ep.gen.2sg.pers.pron.): see σύ

Σειληνός *m.*: see Σιληνός

σεῖο (ep.gen.2sg.pers.pron.): see σύ

σεῖος Lacon.*adj.*: see θεῖος[1]

σειρά ᾶς, Ion. **σειρή** ῆς *f.* **cord, rope** Hom. Hdt. AR. Plu.

σειραῖος ᾱ ον *adj.* **1** (of a horse) **attached by trace-ropes** S.
2 (of a halter) **made of rope** E.

σειρα-φόρος, dial. **σηραφόρος**, Ion. **σειρηφόρος**, also **σειροφόρος** (E.), ον *adj.* [σειρά, φέρω] (of horses) **trace-bearing** (i.e. attached to a racing-chariot, one on either side of the two yoked horses) Alcm. A. E.; (of two camels on the outside of a third) Hdt. || MASC.SB. (fig., ref. to a person) **trace-horse** (implying the capacity for extra effort) A.; (pejor., perh. implying the need to be goaded into action) Ar.

Σειρῆνες ων *f.pl.* —also **Σηρηνίδες** ων *dial.f.pl.* | ep.du.gen. Σειρήνοιιν | **Sirens** (mythol. beings who lured sailors to their island and thus to death w. their enchanting song, becoming provbl. for their voices and deceptiveness) Od. Hes.*fr.* Alcm. Pl. X. +
—**Σειρήν**, dial. **Σηρήν**, ῆνος *f.* **1** (gener., ref. to a beautiful singer) **Siren** (appos.w. Μῶσα *Muse*) Alcm.; (sg. and pl., responsible for the music of the spheres) Pl.; (pl., summoned to accompany a dirge) E.; (sg., as a mourner) Mosch.
2 Siren (ref. to a deceitful temptress) E.(pl.)
3 enchanting music (W.GEN. of panpipes) Lyr.adesp.; **enchanting quality** (W.GEN. of a man's words) Plu. || ADJ. (of the sound of singing) **siren-voiced, enchanting** Pi.*fr.*
4 engrossing subject (for study) Plu.

Σείριος ου *m.* **Sirius** (name of the dogstar; oft. assoc.w. burning heat because its rising marks the hottest time of year) Hes. Archil. Alc. E. AR.; (appos.w. ἀστήρ *star*) Hes.; (w. κύων *dog*) A.
—**σείριος**, dial. **σήριος** (Alcm.), ᾱ ον *adj.* **1** (of a star, ref. to Sirius) **blazing** or **sparkling** Alcm.; (of a planet) E.
|| NEUT.PL.SB. sparkling stars Ibyc.
2 (of ships discharging burning arrows) perh. **scorching** Tim.
3 || NEUT.PL.SB. lightweight summer garments X.(cj.) | see σπειρία, under σπεῖρον

σειρίς ίδος *f.* [dimin. σειρά] **rope, cord** (in an animal-trap) X.

σειροφόρος *adj.*: see σειραφόρος

σεισ-άχθεια ας *f.* [σείω, ἄχθος] **shaking off of burdens, disburdenment** (name given to Solon's cancellation of debts) Arist. Plu.; (gener., ref. to relief fr. hardships) Plu.

σεισί-χθων ονος *masc.adj.* [χθών] (epith. of Poseidon) **earth-shaking** A.*satyr.fr.* Pi. B.

σεισμός οῦ *m.* **1 shaking, tremor** (W.GEN. of the earth) E. Th. Plu.; **earthquake** Hdt. S. Th. +
2 turbulence (W.PREP.PHR. in the sea) NT.
3 (gener.) **shaking, commotion, agitation** Pl.

σειστός ή όν *adj.* (of a cloak) **shaken, shaken out** Ar.

σείω, dial. **σίω** (Anacr.) *vb.* | impf. ἔσειον, ep. σεῖον | aor. ἔσεισα, ep. σεῖσα || PASS.: aor. ἐσείσθην | pf. σέσεισμαι | **1 move vigorously to and fro, shake** —*doors, the aigis* Il.; (of horses) —*the yoke* Od.; (of a charioteer) —*reins* S.; (of a warrior) —*helmet plumes* Alc. A.; **shake out** —*a cloak* Ar.
|| MID. (of a laurel branch) **shake** Call. || PASS. (of a helmet) shake Il.; (of teeth) be shaky or loose Hdt.
2 brandish —*a spear or sim.* Il. +
3 shake (part or the whole of one's body); **shake, toss** —*hair* Anacr. E. Ar. Theoc. —*the head* (in restiveness, agitation, dancing) S. E.; (of a poisoned bird) —*its body* E.; (of a bird) **flap** —*its wings* AR. Theoc.(mid.) || MID. (of Hera) **shake** (w. anger) Il.
4 shake (the ground or sim.) with some natural or supernatural force; (of Poseidon) **shake** —*the earth* (w. an earthquake) Hdt.; (of a person, envisaged as Zeus) —*the earth* (w. thunder) Ar.; (intr., of Poseidon) **cause an earthquake** Ar. X. || AOR.IMPERS. there was an earthquake Th. || PASS. (of ground, fixed objects) be shaken Il. +
5 shake (so as to weaken or cause to totter), **shake, rock** —*a city, household* Pi. S. || PASS. (of delight) be shaken (fr. its place), **be dislodged** Pi.

σελαγέομαι

6 shake (so as to confuse or distress); **shake, shock** —*the heart, brain* Ar.; (colloq., of persons using intimidation) **shake up, harass, rattle** —*rich people, magistrates* Antipho Ar.

σελαγέομαι *pass.contr.vb.* [σέλας] | ep.3sg.impf. σελαγεῖτο | (of fire, the sun) **shine** or **blaze brightly** E. Ar.; (of ships) **be lit up, blaze** (w. fire) Ar.; (of Dionysus, w. torches) Ar.

σελαγίζω *vb.* | ep.impf. σελάγιζον | (of lightning) **flash** Call.

σελάνά *dial.f.*, **σελάννά** *Aeol.f.*: see σελήνη

σελάναία *dial.f.*: see σεληναίη

σέλας αος *n.* | ep.dat. σέλαϊ, σέλᾳ | nom.acc.pl. σέλα (Plu.) |
1 **brightness, gleam, glow** (of fire, torches) Hom. Hes. Pi. Emp. Trag. +; (of the sun, moon, stars, day) Pi.*fr.* Trag. Ar. AR.; (emanating fr. a goddess) hHom.
2 **gleam, flash** (of light, lightning) Il. A. Hdt. S. Plu.
3 **brightness, light** (emanating fr. the eyes) A. Pi.*fr.* E.*fr.* Theoc.; (meton.) **sight** (W.GEN. of the eyes) E.*Cyc.*
4 **radiance** (of limbs) B.

σελασ-φόρος ον *adj.* [φέρω] (of torches) **light-bearing, gleaming, glowing** A.

σεληναίη ης *ep.Ion.f.* —also **σελάναία** ᾶς *dial.f.* [σελήνη] **moon** Praxill. Pl. AR. Bion; (personif.) **Selenaie** (moon-goddess) E. Ar. Call. Theoc.

σεληναῖος η ον *Ion.adj.* of or belonging to the moon; (of night) **moonlit** Hdt.(oracle)

σελήνη ης, dial. **σελάνά**, Aeol. **σελάννά**, ᾶς *f.* [σέλας]
1 **moon** Hom. +
2 **moon** (as source of light); (prep.phrs.) πρὸς τὴν σελήνην *by moonlight* And. X. Men. Plu.; (also) ἐν σελήνῃ Th.
3 period from one moon to the next, **lunar month, month** E.; (prep.phr.) κατὰ σελήνην *reckoning by the moon* Th. Ar. Arist.
4 moonlit night, **night** (ref. to the time of a ritual or festival) E.
5 (personif.) **Selene** (moon-goddess) Hes. hHom. Hdt. Ar. +

σεληνιάζομαι *pass.vb.* be moonstruck, **suffer from fits** NT.

σεληνιακός ή όν *adj.* (of the year) reckoned by the lunar month, **lunar** Plu.

σέλινον ου *n.* **wild celery** Hom. Hdt. Ar. Arist.(quot.com.) Theoc. Plu.; (pl., ref. to a garland of celery, esp. as awarded at the Nemean and Isthmian games) Anacr. Pi. Call. Theoc. Plu.

σελινο-φόρος ον *adj.* [φέρω] (of a victorious chariot) celery-bearing, **crowned with wild celery** Call.

σελίς ίδος *f.* [reltd. σέλμα] column of writing (in a papyrus roll), **column** Plb.

Σελλοί ῶν *m.pl.* —also **Ἑλλοί** (Pi.*fr.*) or **Ἑλλοί** ῶν (Call., v.l. in Il. S.) *m.pl.* **Selloi, Elloi** or **Helloi** (expounders of the oracle of Zeus at Dodona) Il. Pi.*fr.* S. Call. || SG. Sellian priest Call.

σέλμα ατος *n.* [reltd. σελίς] 1 plank or planking of a ship; perh. **deck** hHom.; (fig., of the belly of a person envisaged as a cargo ship) E.*Cyc.*
2 || PL. rowers' benches Archil. Dionys.Eleg. Trag. AR.
3 (in fig.ctxt.) **steersman's bench** (as a position of power) A.
4 || PL. planks, planking (to stand on, in a tower) A.

σέλω *Lacon.vb.*: see ἐθέλω

Σεμέλη ης, dial. **Σεμέλα** ᾶς *f.* **Semele** (daughter of Kadmos, mother of Dionysus by Zeus) Il. +

σεμνο-δότειρα ᾶς *fem.adj.* [σεμνός, δοτήρ] (of Fame) bestower of prestige, **glory-giving** B.

σεμνολογέομαι *mid.contr.vb.* [σεμνολόγος] **talk pompously, pontificate** Aeschin. D. —W.ACC. *about sthg.* Plu.

σεμνο-λόγος ου *m.* **pompous talker** D.

σεμνό-μαντις εως *m.* [μάντις] **pompous prophet** S.

σεμνομῦθέω *contr.vb.* [μῦθος] speak solemnly; (pejor.) **adopt a high and mighty tone** E.

σεμνοπροσωπέω *contr.vb.* [πρόσωπον] put on a solemn face, **look high and mighty** Ar.

σεμνός ή (dial. ά) όν *adj.* [σέβω] 1 (of gods) **worthy of reverence, venerable, august** hHom. Lyr. Trag. Ar.
2 (specif.) Σεμναὶ θεαί *Awesome Goddesses* (at Athens, usu. identified w. Erinyes) A. S. Th. Ar. Att.orats. Arist.
3 (of rites, hymns, places, or sim.) **solemn, holy** Sol. Pi. Trag. Licymn. +
4 (of human rulers, leaders) **august, grand, impressive** A. +; (of women) **grand, high-class** Ar. Isoc. X.; (of persons) **solemn, dignified** (in behaviour or speech) X. Arist.
5 (of things assoc.w. humans, esp. language) **stately, impressive** Pi. Hdt. +
6 (pejor., of persons) **proud, pretentious, standoffish** E. Ar. Isoc. X. D.; (of speech) **pompous** S. || NEUT.SB. pride or arrogance E.

—**σεμνῶς** *adv.* 1 **reverently, solemnly** A. Hdt. E. Isoc.
2 (sts.pejor.) **grandly, impressively, proudly** E. Ar. Pl. X. Aeschin. D. +

σεμνό-στομος ον *adj.* [στόμα] (of speech) solemn or proud of utterance, **high and mighty** A.

σεμνότης ητος *f.* 1 quality of inspiring awe, **awesomeness, solemnity** (of night) E.
2 awesomeness of appearance, **majesty, impressiveness** Pl. X. Plb. Plu.
3 **dignity** (of persons, behaviour, language) Isoc. Arist. Plb. Plu.; (pejor.) **standoffishness** E.

σεμνό-τιμος ον *adj.* [τιμή] (of Erinyes, Agamemnon in the underworld) **honoured with reverent awe** A.

σεμνόω *contr.vb.* make impressive, **embellish, elaborate** —*a story* Hdt.

σεμνύνω *vb.* 1 make impressive or exaggerate, **magnify, exalt** —*someone or sthg.* Pl. D.; **give an aura of solemnity** or **importance to** —*sthg.* Hdt. Pl. D.
2 || MID. be solemn, dignified or impressive, **give oneself airs, be proud** E. Ar. Isoc. Pl. +; (of a treatise) be pretentious Pl.

σέο, σεο (Ion.gen.2sg.pers.pron.): see σύ

σεπτός ή όν *adj.* [σέβω] (of the waters of the Nile) **revered, sacred** A.

Σεράπεῖον *n.*: see Σαράπειον, under Σάραπις

Σεράπνα *Lacon.f.*: see Θεράπνη, under θεράπνη

σέρφος ου *m.* small insect (perh. winged, esp. eaten by birds); perh. **gnat** Ar.

σέσαγμαι (pf.pass.): see σάσσω

σεσήμασμαι (pf.pass.): see σημαίνω

σέσηπα (pf.): see σήπω

σεσηρώς, dial. **σεσάρώς** *statv.pf.ptcpl.* | ep.fem. σεσαρυῖα | having the lips parted so that the teeth are bared; **grinning** (in malice, contempt or mockery) Hes. Ar. Theoc.

σεσοφισμένος *pf.mid.pass.ptcpl.adj.*: see under σοφίζομαι

σεσωπᾶμένος (dial.pf.pass.ptcpl.): see σιωπάω

σεσωφρονισμένως *pf.pass.ptcpl.adv.*: see under σωφρονίζω

σέτω (Lacon.3sg.athem.aor.imperatv.): see τίθημι

σεῦ, σευ (Ion.gen.2sg.pers.pron.): see σύ

σεῦτλον *dial.n.*: see τεῦτλον

σεύω *vb.* | dial.3pl. σεύοντι (B.) | ep.aor. ἔσσευα, also σεῦα || MID.: ep.3pl.impf. ἐσσεύοντο | ep.aor.: 3sg. σεύατο, ptcpl. σευάμενος | athem.aor.: ep.3sg. ἔσσυτο, σύτο, also ἔσυτο (E.), ptcpl. σύμενος (Pratin. A.) | ep.pf. (w.pres.sens.) ἔσσυμαι, ptcpl. ἐσσύμενος || PASS.: aor. (w.mid.sens.) ἐσύθην (E.), ep. ἐσσύθην (S.), σύθην (A.), ptcpl. συθείς | —also **σοέω** *contr.vb.*

| only ep.3sg.impf. σόει (B.) | —also **σόομαι** or **σέομαι** (A. S. Ar.) *mid.contr.vb.* | 3sg. σοῦται, 3pl. σοῦνται | imperatv. σοῦ, 3sg. σούσθω, 2pl. σοῦσθε, dial. σῶσθε (Call.) | —also **σώομαι** (AR.) *mid.vb.* | ptcpl. σωόμενος | inf. σώεσθαι | ep.3pl.impf. σώοντο |
1 set in rapid motion, **drive forward, urge on** —*troops, animals, a ship* Hom. B. AR.
2 (act. and mid.) **drive, chase** —*a person* Il.; **drive away** —*an animal* Hom.; (act., of rustlers) **drive off** —*cattle* B.
3 set in motion (by violent physical contact), **send spinning, flying** or **rolling** —*a person or corpse* Il.
4 make (W.ACC. blood) **spurt forth** Il.
5 ‖ MID. and AOR.PASS. move rapidly, **hasten, rush** Hom. hHom. Mimn. Pratin. Pi. Trag. +; **make haste** —W.INF. *to do sthg.* Il. Pi. Ar. ‖ AOR.PASS.PTCPL. gone (w. focus on departure rather than speed) Trag. ‖ MID.IMPERATV. be off! Ar.
6 ‖ STATV.PF.MID. be in a state of eagerness or excitement, be eager Hom.

—**ἐσσύμενος** η ον *ep.pf.mid.ptcpl.* **1** eager, in haste Hom. Pi. Lyr.adesp. AR.
2 eager (W.GEN. for sthg.) Hom. hHom.; (W.INF. to do sthg.) Hom.

—**ἐσσυμένως** *ep.pf.mid.ptcpl.adv.* eagerly, hastily Hom. Hes. hHom. Pi.*fr.* AR. Theoc.

σεφθείς (aor.pass.ptcpl.): see **σέβω**

σεωυτόν *Ion.2sg.acc.masc.reflexv.pron.*, **σεωυτήν** *fem.*: see σεαυτόν

σηκάζομαι *pass.vb.* [σηκός] | ep.3pl.aor. σήκασθεν | aor.ptcpl. σηκασθείς | (fig., of soldiers, compared to livestock) **be penned up** (by attackers) Il. X.

σηκίς ίδος *f.* female slave born in the household, **slave-girl** Ar.

σηκο-κόρος ου *m.* [κορέω¹] **sweeper of pens** Od.

σηκός, dial. **σᾱκός**, οῦ *m.* **1** enclosure (for sheep, goats or cattle), **pen, fold** Hom. Hes. Pl. Theocr.; **lair** (of a dragon) E.
2 nursery (for children) Pl.
3 sacred enclosure, **precinct** Trag. Theoc.*epigr.* Plu.; **shrine** E. AR.; **burial place, sepulchre** Simon.
4 stump of a sacred olive tree (in a temple-precinct or other enclosure), **olive stump** Lys.

σήκωμα¹ ατος *n.* **sacred enclosure, precinct** E.

σήκωμα² ατος *n.* [σηκόω *weigh*] **1** weight (used in scales); (gener.) **weight** (ref. to a lump of lead) Plb.
2 weight (of the rear part of a spear, counterbalancing the front part) Plb.
3 (fig.) weight or strength (contributed to sthg.); **weight** (of heavy infantry, contributed to an attack) Plb.; (of an individual, contributed to a cause) E.

σῆμα, dial. **σᾶμα**, ατος *n.* **1** sign enabling recognition; **distinguishing mark** (on a horse's forehead) Il.; (W.GEN. on a lot) Il.; **marker** (of place or distance) Hom.
2 device (on a shield) A. E.
3 emblem (on a ship's stern, ref. to a painted or carved figure) E.
4 sign from which a meaning or inference may be drawn; **sign** Hom. +; **indication** (W.GEN. of sthg.) hHom. + ‖ PL. signs, symbols (on a writing-tablet) Il.
5 sign as evidence or proof (esp. of identity); **evidence, proof, token** Od. S.; **password, watchword** E.
6 sign for action, **signal** Od.; (W.GEN. for ploughing, battle) Hes. E.
7 ‖ PL. signals (fr. a lyre to singers), **notes** Pi.
8 sign from heaven, **omen, portent** Hom. hHom. Pi. B. AR. Theoc.
9 ‖ PL. heavenly signs or bodies (i.e. constellations) Parm.
10 mound signalling a grave, **grave mound** Hom.; (gener.) **grave, grave monument, tomb** Hippon. Pi. Hdt. +

σημαίᾱ *f.*: see σημεῖᾱ

σημαιᾱφόρος *m.*: see σημειοφόρος

σημαίνω, dial. **σᾱμαίνω** *vb.* | fut. σημανῶ, Ion. σημανέω | aor. ἐσήμηνα, ep. σήμηνα ‖ PASS.: aor. ἐσημάνθην | pf. σεσήμασμαι | **1** indicate by visible signs, **indicate, point out** —*sthg.* Il. Trag. —W.COMPL.CL. *that sthg. is the case* Hdt. Trag. X. ‖ PASS. (of facts) be indicated —W.PREP.PHR. *in writing* Hdt.
2 indicate by language, **indicate, point out** —*persons, landmarks, or sim.* Od. Hdt. S. E. +; **explain** —*facts, reasons, or sim.* Hdt. Trag. +; (of a priestess) **communicate** —*an oracle* Thgn.; (intr.) **explain, say** Hdt. Trag. Th. +
3 (of things) **betoken, signify** —*sthg.* Hdt. +; (of words) **mean** —*sthg.* Pl. Arist. Plu.
4 (intr.) **make a signal** (for the purpose of communication) A. +; (of gods) **give a sign** —W.DAT. *to someone* X.; (of an earthquake, wind) **give a signal, be a sign** (of future events) Th. X. ‖ PASS. (of ships) be signalled —W.PTCPL. *as arriving* X. ‖ IMPERS.PASS. a signal is given X.
5 give signals or orders, **be in command, be in charge** Hom. AR. —W.GEN. or DAT. *of men, an army* Il.; **give orders** —W.DAT. *to someone* Il. —W.DAT. or ACC. + INF. *to someone to do sthg., that someone shd. do sthg.* Hdt. Trag. Th. X. ‖ NEUT.PL.PASS.PTCPL.SB. orders X.
6 (of a commander, trumpeter) **give a signal** (for action) Th. X. + —W.ACC. *for retreat* Th. ‖ IMPERS.AOR. a signal was given Hdt. E. X.
7 ‖ MID. use as a sign, **identify** —*footprints* (as someone's) S.
8 ‖ MID. **mark out, identify** —*the strongest men* (in an army) Plb.
9 ‖ MID. mark with a sign, **mark** —*an ox* Hdt. ‖ PASS. (of an ox) be marked Hdt.; (of slaves) —W.DAT. w. *a brand mark* X.
10 ‖ MID. mark with a seal (for identification or security), **seal** —*a document, container* Ar. Att.orats. + ‖ PASS. (of a document or container) be sealed Ar. Att.orats.

σημαιοφόρος *m.*: see σημειοφόρος

σημαντήρ ῆρος *m.* **master** (of sheep, ref. to a shepherd) AR.; (W.GEN. of a plot of land, ref. to a farmer) AR.

—**σημαντρίς** ίδος *f.* sealer; (appos.w. γῆ *earth*) **sealing clay** Hdt.

—**σᾱμάντρια** ᾱς *dial.f.* (ref. to smoke) **signaller, indicator** (W.GEN. of a funeral pyre) Call.

σημαντήριον ου *n.* [σήμαντρον] **seal** (as a mark of security) A.

σημαντικός ή όν *adj.* **1** (of sounds) conveying meaning, **significant** Arist.
2 (of a circumstance) **indicative** (W.GEN. of health) Arist.

σήμαντρον ου *n.* **1 seal** (on a document, container) Hdt. E. X.
2 brand mark (on a slave) X.; (fig.) **mark** (ref. to a bruise or wound) E.

σημάντωρ ορος *m.* **1** giver of signals or orders; **commander** (in war) Il.; **officer** (of a military unit) Hdt.
2 (gener.) **master, ruler** Od. hHom. AR.; (W.GEN. of the gods, ref. to Zeus) Hes. hHom.
3 (specif.) **master** (of animals, ref. to a shepherd, herdsman, charioteer) Il. AR.
4 informant S.

σημασίᾱ ᾱς *f.* verbal expression establishing identity, **designation** Plb.

σηματουργός οῦ *m.* [ἔργον] maker of devices (for shields), **emblazoner** A.

σημείᾱ (also **σημαίᾱ**) ᾱς f. **1 military standard** Plb. Plu. **2** (in the Roman army) company of soldiers belonging to the same standard, **maniple** Plb.

σημειο-γράφος ου m. [σημεῖον, γράφω] one who writes with symbols, **shorthand writer** Plu.

σημεῖον, Ion. **σημήιον**, ου n. [σῆμα] **1** physical sign (enabling recognition); **marking** (on an animal) Hdt.; **marker** (of place or distance) Hdt. X. D. Plu. **2 device** (on a shield) Hdt. E. **3 emblem** (on a ship, ref. to a painted or carved figure) E. Th. Ar.; **ensign** (on the commander's ship) Hdt.; **standard** (military or royal) X. Plu. **4** visible sign from which a meaning or inference may be drawn; **sign** E. Th. +; **indication** (W.GEN. of sthg.) A. + **5** sign as evidence or proof (in reasoning); **evidence, proof, token** Trag. Th. + **6** visible sign for the purpose of communication or command; **signal** (raised and lowered at the beginning and end of an attack) Hdt. Th.; (at sea, perh. given by flag) Hdt. Th. X.; (raised and lowered at the beginning and end of a meeting of the Assembly) And. Ar.; (given by fire, a beacon) Th. Ar. **7** (gener.) **signal** (for action) Th. +; (to a horse, fr. its rider) X.; **sign, guidance** (fr. a god) Pl. || PL. gestures (of a rhapsode) Arist. **8** sign from heaven, **omen, portent** Hdt. S. + **9 guiding sign** (ref. to a constellation) E. **10 seal** (ref. to wax bearing an impressed device) Ar. Pl. +; (ref. to the device itself) Ar.

σημειόομαι mid.contr.vb. **1** || PASS. (of a route) be marked (by milestones) Plb. **2** interpret from signs, **identify** —a place, route Plb.; **infer, interpret** —the future Plb. **3** interpret as a sign, **treat as an omen** —an event Plb.

σημειο-φόρος (also **σημαιοφόρος** or **σημαιᾱφόρος**) ου m. [φέρω] **standard-bearer** Plb. Plu.

σημερινός ή όν adj. [σήμερον] (of words) belonging to today, **today's** (i.e. spoken today) Call.

σήμερον, dial. **σάμερον**, Att. **τήμερον** adv. [ἡμέρᾱ] **today** Hom. hHom. Pi. Hdt. E. Ar. +

σημήιον Ion.n.: see σημεῖον

σηπεδών όνος f. [σήπω] **decay, rotting, putrefaction** Pl. Plb. Plu.

σηπίᾱ ᾱς, Ion. **σηπίη** ης f. **cuttlefish** Hippon. Ar.

σηπιο-πουλυπόδεια ων n.pl. [πουλύπους¹, πώλυπος] **many-armed cuttlefish** Philox.Leuc.

σήπω, dial. **σάπω** vb. | pf. σέσηπα || aor.pass. ἐσάπην | **1** make rotten or putrid; (of a woman, envisaged as an eel or viper) **rot, putrefy** —a person (by her touch) A.; (of faulty respiration) **cause decay** or **putrefaction in** —parts of the body Pl.; (intr., of stillness) **cause decay** or **decomposition** (in nature) Pl. **2** || STATV.PF. (of timber, blood) **lie rotted** Il. E. **3** || PASS. (of dead flesh) be made rotten, become putrid, rot Il. Hes. Hdt. Pl. Plu.; (of parts of the living body, timber, plants, substances) Hdt. Ar. Pl. X. Men.; (of stones and tiles, in neg.phr.) X.; (of seawater, in neg.phr.) **decay** B.

σῆραγξ αγγος f. [reltd. σεσηρώς] **1 hollowed rock, cave** E. Pl. Theoc. **2** || PL. **cavities, pores** (in the lungs) Pl.

σηραφόρος dial.adj.: see σειραφόρος

Σηρήν dial.f., **Σηρηνίδες** dial.f.pl.: see Σειρῆνες

σήριος dial.adj.: see σείριος, under Σείριος

σηροκτόνος Lacon.adj.: see θηροκτόνος

σῆς σεός m. | PL.: nom. σῆτες (Men.), gen. σέων (Ar.) | **moth** (esp.ref. to the larva of the clothes-moth) Pi.fr. Ar. Men. NT.

σησαμῆ ῆς f. —also **σᾱσαμίς** ίδος (Stesich.) dial.f. —also **σησαμοῦς** οῦντος m. [σήσαμον] **sesame cake** (unbaked cake made of roasted sesame-seeds, oil and honey; a symbol of fertility, served at Athenian weddings) Stesich. Ar. Men.

σησάμινος η ον adj. (of oil) **made from sesame, sesame** X.

σήσαμον ου, dial. **σᾱ́σαμον** ω (Alcm.) n. [Semit.loanwd.] **1 sesame** (as a plant) Ar. X. **2** || PL. or COLLECTV.SG. **sesame-seeds** or **sesame** Alcm. Sol. Hippon. Hdt. Ar. Men.

σηστέρτιον ου n. [Lat.loanwd.] **sestertium** Plu.

Σηστός οῦ f. **Sestos** (city and naval station of the Thracian Chersonese, facing Abydos) Il. Hdt. Th. +

—**Σήστιοι** ων m.pl. men of Sestos, **Sestians** D. Plu.

σθεναρός ά (Ion. ή) όν adj. [σθένος] **physically strong, strong, mighty** Il. S. E. AR.

σθένος εος (ους) n. **1** physical strength, **strength, might** (of gods, persons, animals) Hom. Hes. Lyr. Trag. + **2** (periphr.) **strength** (W.GEN. of a person or god) Il. Hes. Pi.fr. S.Ichn. Pl. AR. • σθένος Ἰδομενῆος **mighty Idomeneus** Il. Hes.fr. **3 strength, power, might** (of a river) Il. S.; (of the sun, snowfall, winter, flood-water, fertile land) Pi. **4 power, might, authority** (of gods and humans) hHom. Trag.; (of a country) S.; (of Necessity, Truth, Justice) Trag.; (of wealth) Pi. E. **5 military strength, strength** S. E. **6** use of strength (physical or military), **force** Trag.; (phr.) παντὶ σθένει **in full strength, with full force** (usu. ref. to allies or attackers) A. Th. Pl. X. D. AR.

σθένω vb. | only pres. and impf. | impf. ἔσθενον, ep. σθένον | **1** (of persons, their bodies) have physical strength, **be strong** S. E. **2** (of gods, persons, a city) **be strong, have power, be powerful** Trag.; (of a beacon) A.; (of proclamations) S.; (of self-will, the voice of the people, a plea for justice, arrogance) A. E. **3 have strength, be able** S. E. Ar.; (in neg.phr.) —W.INF. **to do** sthg. S. E. AR.

σιᾱ́ Lacon.f.: see θεᾱ́

σιαγών όνος f. **jaw-bone, jaw** Pl. X. NT. Plu.

σίαλον ου n. **spit, saliva** X. Arist.(quot.) Thphr.(cj.) Plb.

σίαλος ου m. (sts. appos.w. σῦς) **fatted pig, fat hog** Hom.

σιάλωμα ατος n. **edging, rim** (of a shield) Plb.

σίβδᾱ ᾱς dial.f. [reltd. σίδιον] **pomegranate** Call.

Σίβυλλα ης f. **Sibylla, Sibyl** Ar. Pl. Call. Plu. [One of a class of prophetesses, orig. fr. Asia Minor. The most famous was located at Cumae.]

Σιβύλλειος ον adj. (of books of oracles at Rome) **Sibylline** Plu. || NEUT.PL.SB. **Sibylline books** Plu.

σιβυλλιάω contr.vb. (of an oracle-monger) **be mad on the Sibyl, be Sibyllitic** Ar.

Σιβυλλισταί ῶν m.pl. **interpreters of the Sibylline oracles** Plu.

σιβύνιον ου n. [dimin. σιβύνης **hunting spear**] **small hunting spear** Plb.

σῑγᾱ́ dial.f.: see σῑγή

σῖγα adv. [reltd. σῑγή] **1 silently, in silence** Trag. Ar. AR. **2 quietly, secretly** A. S. **3** (as exclam.) **silence!** A. E. Ar.

σῑγάζω vb. (of the song of the Sirens) **make silent, silence** —the winds Pi.fr.; (of a person) —someone (in mid-speech) X.

σῑγᾰλόεις εν *ep.adj.* [reltd. νεοσίγαλος] | only masc. and neut.dat.sg. σῑγᾰλόεντι, and neut.nom.acc.pl. σῑγᾰλόεντα | (of textiles, leather items) with a gloss or shine, **glossy, shining** Hom. hHom. AR.; (of a seat) Od.; (of an upper room for women) Od.

σῑγάω *contr.vb.* [σιγή] | dial.2sg. σῑγῇς, 3sg. σῑγῇ, 3pl. σῑγῶντι | fut. σῑγήσομαι || PASS.: aor. ἐσῑγήθην, dial. ἐσῑγάθην, perh. dial.3pl. ἐσίγᾱθεν (E.) | pf. σεσίγημαι, dial.ptcpl. σεσῑγαμένος || neut.impers.vbl.adj. σῑγητέον |
1 (of persons) **make no sound, be** or **keep silent** Hom. hHom. Thgn. Pi. Hdt. Trag. +; (of Justice, in her operations) Sol.; (of a house, meton. for its occupants) E.; (of a personif. writing-tablet) E.
2 (of chariot hubs, in neg.phr.) **be silent** A.; (of the κερκίς *pin-beater*) Lyr.adesp.; (of air, winds, sea) **be silent** or **still** E. Theoc.; (fig., of pain, in neg.phr., contrasted w. winds and sea) Theoc. || PASS. (of a house) be hushed E.
3 (fig., of destruction) **work silently** A.; (of names whose significance is not apparent) **hold a secret** E.*fr.*
4 (tr.) **keep quiet about** —*sthg.* A. Pi. || PASS. (of a death, plans, actions) be kept secret or hushed up Hdt. E. Aeschin.; (of a customary proclamation) be suppressed Aeschin.; (of a happening, a person) go uncelebrated Pi. E. Theoc.; (of a silence) be kept E.

σῑγή ῆς, dial. **σῑγᾱ́** ᾱς *f.* [σῖγα] **silence** (of persons) Pi.*fr.* Hdt. + || PL. **silence, stillness** (W.GEN. of winds) E.

—σῑγῇ, dial. **σῑγᾷ** *dat.adv.* **1 in silence** (sts. w.connot. of secrecy) Hom. +; **quietly, in a whisper** Hdt.
2 without the knowledge (W.GEN. of someone) Hdt. E.
3 (as exclam.) **silence!** Od.

σῑγηλός, dial. **σῑγᾱλός**, όν *adj.* **1** (of persons) **silent** S. E.; (of a state of helplessness in a poet) **dumb** Pi.
2 (of a messenger, in neg.phr.) disposed to silence, **taciturn** S. E.

σιγῆν (Lacon.aor.2 inf.): see θιγγάνω

σῑγητέον (neut.impers.vbl.adj.): see σῑγάω

σίγλος ου *m.* [Semit.loanwd.] **siglos** (Persian coin said to be worth 7½ Attic obols) X.

σῖγμα (or **σίγμα**) *indecl.n.* [Semit.loanwd.] **sigma** (letter of the Greek alphabet) Hdt. Pl. X. Arist. Plu.

σιγῡ́νης (v.l. **σιγύννης**) ου *m.* —also **σίγυννος** ου (AR.) *m.* —also **σίγυνον** ου (Arist.) *n.* [loanwd., reltd. Σίγυνναι or Σίγυννοι, a tribe N. of the Istros] **spear** Hdt. Arist. AR.

σιδᾱ́ρεος, σιδᾱ́ρειος *dial.adjs.*, **σιδᾱ́ριος** *Aeol.adj.*: see σιδήρεος

σιδᾱρῑ́τᾱς ᾱ *dial.masc.adj.* [σίδηρος] (of war) **fought with iron, iron** Pi.

σιδᾱρόδετος *dial.adj.*: see σιδηρόδετος

σιδᾱρό-κωπος ον *dial.adj.* [κώπη] (of a soldier) **armed with an iron sword** Tim.

σιδᾱρο-νόμος ον *dial.adj.* [νέμω] (of a hand) **apportioning by the sword** A.

σιδᾱρό-πληκτος (v.l. **σιδηρό-**) ον *dial.adj.* [πλήσσω] (of the digging of a grave, w. further allusion to death by sword-stroke) **with blows of iron** A.

σίδᾱρος *dial.m.*: see σίδηρος

σιδᾱρόφρων *dial.adj.*: see σιδηρόφρων

σιδᾱρο-χάρμᾱς ᾱ *dial.masc.adj.* [χάρμη] (of men and horses) perh. **fighting in iron-mail** Pi.

σιδηρείᾱ ᾱς *f.* **iron-working** (of the Chalybes) X.

σιδηρεῖα ων *n.pl.* **iron-mines** Arist.

σιδήρεος ᾱ (Ion. η) ον, Att. **σιδηροῦς** ᾶ οῦν, ep. **σιδήρειος** η ον, dial. **σιδᾱ́ρεος** (also **σιδᾱ́ρειος**), Aeol. **σιδᾱ́ριος** ᾱ ον *adj.* **1** (of manufactured objects) of iron, **iron** Hom. +; (of heaven, as a solid firmament or vault) Od.
2 (of coinage) **iron** Plb. || MASC.PL.SB. iron coins (the currency of Byzantium) Ar.
3 (of mining or production work) relating to iron, **of iron** AR.
4 (of a mythol. race of men) **iron** Hes. Pl.; (of one of the four castes or breeds of men in the ideal state, or of persons belonging to it) Pl.
5 having the qualities of iron; (fig., of Herakles) **tough as iron, iron-hard** Simon.; (of a boxer's flesh) Theoc.; (of a heart, ref. to its capacity for endurance) Od.
6 (fig., of persons, their hearts, or sim.) **iron-hard, inflexible, unfeeling** Hom. Hes. Lys. Ar. Aeschin. Theoc. Plu.
7 (fig., of the din of war, the strength of a funeral pyre) **relentless** Il.
8 (fig., of an argument) **cast-iron, unshakeable** Pl.

σιδηρεύς έως *m.* **iron-worker** X.

σιδήριον ου *n.* [dimin. σίδηρος] **1** || PL. **pieces of iron** Pl.
2 || PL. **irons** (used for branding) Hdt.; (gener.) **tools** Th. Pl.
3 iron weapon, knife, dagger Hdt. Lys.

σιδηρῖτις ιδος *fem.adj.* (perh. of a craft) **iron-working** A.*satyr.fr.*

σιδηρο-βρῑθής ές *adj.* [βρῖθος] (of a wooden axe-haft) **iron-weighted** Ar.(quot. E.)

σιδηρο-βρώς ῶτος *masc.fem.adj.* [βιβρώσκω] (of a whetstone) **iron-eating** S.

σιδηρό-δετος, dial. **σιδᾱρόδετος**, ον *adj.* [δέω¹] (of wooden stocks) **bound with iron bands** Hdt.; (of a shield-handle) B.

σιδηρο-κμής ῆτος *masc.fem.adj.* [κάμνω] (of cattle) **slain by the sword** S.

σιδηρο-μήτωρ ορος *f.* [μήτηρ] **mother of iron** (ref. to Scythia) A.

σιδηρό-νωτος ον *adj.* [νῶτον] (of a shield) **iron-backed** E.

σιδηρόομαι *pass.contr.vb.* | 3sg.plpf. ἐσεσιδήρωτο | (of a wooden pipe) **be overlaid with iron** Th.

σιδηρόπληκτος *adj.*: see σιδαρόπληκτος

σίδηρος, dial. **σίδᾱρος**, ου *m.* **1 iron, steel** Hom. +; (exemplifying hardness or stubbornness in persons) Hom. Pi.*fr.* E.
2 iron implement or weapon; iron (ref. to an arrow-head) Il. Hdt.; (ref. to an axe or sickle) Il. Hes. hHom. E.; (ref. to a cuirass) Hes.; (ref. to a sword or knife) Il. Anacr. Hdt. S. E. Antipho +; (ref. to a hook) Hdt.; (pl., ref. to fishing-hooks) Theoc.
3 (collectv.sg.) **iron** (ref. to axe-heads) Od.; (ref. to tools) Pi. E.; (ref. to weapons) Alcm. Pi. Trag. Th. +; (ref. to fetters) X.

σιδηρο-τέκτονες ων *m.pl.* **iron-workers** (ref. to the Chalybes) A.

σιδηροῦς *Att.adj.*: see σιδήρεος

σιδηροφορέω *contr.vb.* [σιδηροφόρος] (of Greece, i.e. Greek men) **carry arms** Th.; (mid.) Th. Arist. || PASS. go with an armed escort Plu.

σιδηρο-φόρος ον *adj.* [φέρω] (of the land of the Chalybes) **yielding iron** AR.

σιδηρό-φρων, dial. **σιδᾱρόφρων**, ον, gen. ονος *adj.* [φρήν] (of a person, courageous spirit) **with a mind or will of iron, iron-hearted** A.; (of bloodshed) **pitiless** E.

σίδιον ου *n.* [reltd. σίβδα] **pomegranate peel** Ar.(pl.)

Σῑδών ῶνος *f.* **Sidon** (coastal city of Phoenicia) Od. Hdt. X. Plb. NT. Plu.

—**Σῑδόνες** ων *m.pl.* **men of Sidon, Sidonians** Il.

—**Σῑδονίηθεν** *adv.* **from Sidon** Il.

—**Σιδόνιος**, also **Σιδώνιος**, ᾱ (Ion. η) ον *adj.* **1** of or belonging to Sidon; (of the city) **of Sidon** E.; (of persons or things) **Sidonian** Il. A. Hdt. E. Isoc. Call.
2 ‖ FEM.SB. **land or city of Sidon** Od. NT.
3 ‖ MASC.PL.SB. **inhabitants of Sidon, Sidonians** Od. Hdt. NT.; (sg.) Pl.
—**Σιδωνιάς** άδος *fem.adj.* (of an oar) **Sidonian** E.
σιειδής Lacon.*adj.*: see **θεοειδής**
σιείκελος Lacon.*adj.*: see **θεοείκελος**
σίζω *vb.* | ep.3sg.impf. σίζε | dial.aor. σίξα (Theoc.) | **1** (of the Cyclops' burning eye) **sizzle** (the sound compared w. hot metal plunged into cold water) Od.; (of a cooking-pan, fish fresh fr. the pan) Ar.
2 whistle —W.DAT. **to a dog** (W.INF. *for it to bark at someone*) Theoc.
Σικανοί ῶν *m.pl.* **Sicanians** (name of early inhabitants of Sicily) Th. Call.
—**Σικανίᾱ** ᾱς, Ion. **Σικανίη** ης *f.* **Sicania** (old name of Sicily) Od. Hdt. Th.
—**Σικανικός** ή όν *adj.* **of or belonging to the Sicanians**; (of a settlement) **Sicanian** Th.
Σικελοί ῶν *m.pl.* **Sicels** (name of early settlers in Sicily, distinct fr. Sicanians; gener., name for native Sicilians) Od. Hdt. Th. Plb. Plu.
—**Σικελός** ή (dial. ᾱ́) όν *adj.* (of persons, the land, activities, or sim.) **Sicel, Sicilian** Od. Thgn. Lyr. E. Th. +
—**Σικελίᾱ** ᾱς, Ion. **Σικελίη** ης *f.* **country of the Sicels**; (gener., ref. to the whole island) **Sicily** A. Pi. Hdt. E. Th. +
—**Σικελικός**, also **Σῑκελικός** (Theoc. Mosch.), ή (dial. ᾱ́) όν *adj.* **of or belonging to Sicily or the Sicels**; (of a city, sea, ship, food, or sim.) **Sicel, Sicilian** Th. Ar. Pl. X. D. Thphr. +; (of Muses) Mosch.; (of a disaster, war, exploits) Th. Plb. Plu.
‖ NEUT.SB. **control of Sicily** Th.
—**Σικελιώτης** ου *m.* (usu.pl.) **Siceliot** (general name for Greek colonists, opp. native Sicilians) Th. Pl. X. Plb. Plu.
—**Σικελιῶτις** ιδος *fem.adj.* (of a city) **Siceliot** Plu.
σίκερα *indecl.n.* [Semit.loanwd.] **a kind of alcoholic drink, liquor** NT.
σίκινις (or **σίκιννις**) ιδος *f.* **sikinis** (dance performed by satyrs) E.*Cyc.*
σικύᾱ ᾱς *f.* **bottle-gourd**; (medic.) **cupping-glass** Pl. Arist.
σίκυος ου *m.* **cucumber** Praxill. Ar. Thphr. Plu.
Σικυών ῶνος *f.* (sts.m.) **Sicyon** (city NW. of Corinth) Il. Pi. B. Hdt. +
—**Σικυωνόθε** *adv.* **from Sicyon** Pi.
—**Σικυώνιος** ᾱ (Ion. η) ον *adj.* **1** (of persons or things) **of or belonging to Sicyon, Sicyonian** Hdt. Th. +
2 ‖ FEM.SB. **Sicyonian territory** Th. Plb. Plu.
3 ‖ MASC.PL.SB. **Sicyonians** (as a population or military force) Hdt. Th. +
σικχαίνω *vb.* [σικχός] **develop a dislike** (of expensive food) Plb.; (tr.) **have no taste for** —*common things* Call.*epigr.*
σικχός οῦ *m.* **one who is fastidious** (over food) Arist.
Σιληνός (also **Σειληνός**) οῦ *m.* **Silenos** (companion of Dionysus and father of the satyrs) Pi.*fr.* Hdt. E.*Cyc.* Pl. X. Call.; (ref. to Marsyas) Hdt.; **Silenos-figure** (ref. to a hollow statuette) Pl. ‖ PL. **Silenoi** (ref. to the satyrs, or Silenos and satyrs) hHom.
—**Σιληνικός** ή όν *adj.* **of or relating to Silenos or Silenoi**; (of a piece of play-acting, fig.ref. to a comparison of Socrates to a Silenos-figure) **Silenic** Pl.
—**Σιληνώδης** ες *adj.* (of the appearance or behaviour of Socrates) **Silenos-like** Pl.
σιλλικύπριον ου *n.* **castor-oil plant** (growing in Egypt) Hdt.

σίλλοι ων *m.pl.* **silloi** (satirical poems, of a kind assoc.w. Timon of Phleious) Plu.
σίλφιον ου *n.* [loanwd.] **silphium** (plant growing in Cyrenaica, related to asafoetida, used in cooking and medicine) Sol. Hdt. Ar.
σιλφιόομαι *pass.contr.vb.* (of a food dish) **be prepared with silphium** Philox.Leuc.
σιμαίνω *vb.* [σιμός] **wrinkle one's nose** (in impatience) Call.
σιμβλήιος η ον *Ion.adj.* [σίμβλος] **relating to a beehive**; (of honey) **from a hive** AR.
σιμβληίς ίδος *fem.adj.* (of a rock) **serving as a hive** AR.
σίμβλος ου *m.* **beehive** Hes. Hellenist.poet.; (fig.) **hive** (W.GEN. of money) Ar.
Σιμόεις εντος, contr. **Σιμοῦς** οῦντος (Hes. Call.) *m.* **Simois** (river nr. Troy) Il. Hes. Stesich. A. B. E. +
—**Σιμοεντιάς** άδος, also **Σιμοεντίς**, contr. **Σιμουντίς**, ίδος *fem.adj.* (of the banks, land) **of Simois** E. Ar.
—**Σιμούντιος** ου *adj.* (of the waters) **of Simois** E.
σιμο-πρόσωπος ον *adj.* [σιμός, πρόσωπον] (of a low-quality horse) **flat-faced** Pl.
σιμός ή όν *adj.* **1** (of peoples) **short-nosed** or **snub-nosed** Hdt.
2 (of a person) **snub-nosed** Ar. Pl. X. Men. Theoc.; (of a nose) **snub** Arist. ‖ NEUT.SB. **snubbiness or shortness** (of a nose) X. Arist.
3 (of several kinds of animals) **flat-nosed** or **blunt-nosed** Hdt. Lyr.adesp. Theoc.; (of the heads of hounds) X.
4 (of a place) **sloping** Ar. X. ‖ NEUT.PL.SB. **sloping ground, slopes** X.
5 (prep.phr.) πρὸς τὸ σιμόν (τὰ σιμά) **uphill** X. Plu.
6 (of an empty stomach) **concave, hollow** (opp. bulging) X.
σιμότης ητος *f.* **1 snubbiness** (of a nose) Pl. X. Arist. Plu.
2 upward curvature (W.GEN. of a boar's tusks) X.
Σιμοῦς *m.*: see **Σιμόεις**
σίμωμα ατος *n.* **snub end** (of a ship, ref. to its prow) Plu.
Σιμωνίδης ου (Ion. εω) *m.* **Simonides** (poet fr. Keos, 6th–5th C. BC) Hdt. Ar. Pl. X. Arist. +
σιναμωρέω *contr.vb.* [σινάμωρος] **1 ravage, plunder** —*a city, land* Hdt.
2 ‖ PASS. (of a woman) **be raped** Ar.
σιναμωρίᾱ ᾱς *f.* **destructiveness** (of animals) Arist.
σινά-μωρος ον *adj.* [σίνος; for 2nd el. cf. ἐγχεσίμωρος] (of a person) app., threatening harm; **trouble-making** Anacr.; **destructive** (W.GEN. of possessions) Hdt.
σίναπι εως *n.* [reltd. νᾶπυ] **mustard plant** NT.
σινδονίτης ου *m.* [σινδών] **linen garment** Men.
σινδον-υφής ές *adj.* [ὑφαίνω] (of towels) **of woven linen** Philox.Leuc.
σινδών όνος *f.* [Semit.loanwd.] **cloth of light texture; cloth, sheet** (oft. of linen) Hdt. S.*fr.* NT.; (covering a bed) Hdt. Th.; (for wrapping a mummy, used as a bandage) Hdt.; (as a garment, shroud) NT.; (for straining food) Hdt.; (used as a noose) S.; (as a sail) E.*fr.*; (as a signal flag) Plb.
σινιάζω *vb.* **sift** —*corn* NT.
σίνις ιδος *m.* [σίνομαι] | acc. σίνιν | **1 agent of destruction or plunder; scourge** (W.GEN. of cattle, ref. to a lion) Call.; (appos.w. ἀνήρ) Arist.(quot.poet.)
2 (mythol. pers. name) **Sinis** (robber and killer at the Isthmos) B. E. X. Plu. | cf. **πιτυοκάμπτης**
σίνομαι *mid.vb.* | 3pl.iteratv.impf. σινέσκοντο | aor. ἐσινάμην | **1** (of troops, animals) **ravage, plunder, destroy** —*people, cattle, property, land, crops* Od. Hdt. Pl. X. AR. +
2 (gener.) **harm, injure, damage** —*someone or sthg.* Il. Hes. Hdt. X. Call.

σίνος ους *n.* **harm, damage** A. Hdt. ‖ PL. physical impairments, defects Isoc.

σίντης εω *ep.m.* one who destroys or plunders; **marauder** (appos.w. λέων *lion*, λίς *lioness*, λύκος *wolf*) Il. ‖ PL. plunderers (ref. to mice) Call.

Σινώπη ης *f.* **Sinope** (city on the S. shore of the Black Sea) Hdt. Isoc. X. D. Plb. Plu.

—**Σινωπεῖς** έων *m.pl.* inhabitants of Sinope, **Sinopians** X. Plb. Plu.; (sg.) Plu.

σιόδματος *Lacon.adj.*: see θεόδμητος

σίον ου *n.* a kind of marsh plant, **reed** Theoc.

σιός *Lacon.m.*: see θεός

σιπύη ης *f.* storage container (for dry foodstuffs), **grain-tub** Ar.

—**σιπύηθεν** *adv.* (prep.phr.) ἐκ σιπύηθεν *from a grain-tub* Call.

σίραιον ου *n.* new wine boiled down (used in medicine and as a condiment in cooking), **condensed wine** Ar.

σιρός οῦ *m.* underground pit for storage, **store pit** (for grain) D.(pl.)

σισύμβριον ου *n.* a kind of mint, **calamint** Ar.

σισύρα ᾱς, Ion. **σισύρη** ης *f.* **goatskin** or **sheepskin** (used as a blanket or cloak) Ar. Call.

σίσυρνα, Ion. **σισύρνη**, ης, Aeol. **σισύρνᾱ** ᾱς *f.* **animal-skin cloak** Alc.; (as a characteristic garment of certain tribes) Hdt.

σισυρνο-φόρος ον *adj.* [φέρω] (of a foreign tribe) **wearing animal-skins** Hdt.

Σίσυφος ου *m.* **Sisyphos** (king of Corinth, a byword for trickery, condemned perpetually to push a rock uphill in Hades; sts. regarded as the true father of Odysseus) Hom. +

—**Σισυφίδης** ου *m.* | ep.gen.sg. Σισυφίδᾱο, dial.gen.pl. Σισυφιδᾶν | **son of Sisyphos** Hes.*fr.* ‖ PL. descendants of Sisyphos (of whom Odysseus was one) S.; (ref. to the Corinthians) Call.

—**Σισύφειος** ᾱ ον *adj.* 1 (of the son) **of Sisyphos** (ref. to Odysseus) E.; (of the rock) E.

2 (of a marriage characterised by deceit) **Sisyphean** E.

—**Σισυφίς** ίδος *fem.adj.* (of the coast of Corinth) **Sisyphean** Theoc.

σῖτα (nom.acc.neut.pl.): see σῖτος

σῑτ-αγωγός όν *adj.* [σῖτος] conveying grain or food; (of ships) **with a cargo of grain, carrying provisions** Hdt. Th. And. X. ‖ NEUT.PL.SB. supply-ships Plu.

σιτάρια ων *n.pl.* [dimin. σῖτος] **scraps of bread** Plb.

σιταρχίᾱ ᾱς *f.* [ἄρχω] 1 allowance to troops for buying food, **ration-money** Plb.

2 (gener.) **wages, pay** (for troops) Plb.

σῑτέομαι *mid.contr.vb.* | 3pl.iteratv.impf. σῑτέσκοντο | fut. σῑτήσομαι ‖ dial.aor.pass. (w.mid.sens.) σῑτήθην (Theoc.) |
1 **feed on, eat** —*sthg.* Hdt. Ar. X. Theoc. Plb. Plu. —W.DAT. X.
2 (fig.) **feed on** —*hopes* A.; **gobble up** —*wisdom* (W.ADV. *like a dog*) Ar.; (of war, in neg.phr.) **consume** —*fixed amounts* (*i.e. its consumption is not subject to regulation*) Plu.(quot.)
3 (intr.) **take one's meals, eat** Od. Hdt. Pl. X. Is. Plu.
4 (specif.) dine at public expense (in the prytaneion), **have free meals, receive official maintenance** Isoc. Pl.

σῑτευτός ή όν *adj.* [σῑτεύω] (of cattle) **fattened up** Plb. NT.; (of children) X.

σῑτεύω *vb.* | iteratv.impf. σῑτεύεσκον | **fatten up** —*beasts* Hdt. ‖ PASS. (of a bird) be fattened up Plu.

σῑτηγέω *contr.vb.* [σῑτηγός] **transport grain** Lycurg. D.

σῑτηγίᾱ ᾱς *f.* **transportation of grain** D.

σῑτ-ηγός όν *adj.* [σῖτος, ἄγω] (of ships) **transporting grain** D. ‖ NEUT.PL.SB. supply-ships Plu.

σῑτηρέσιον ου *n.* [σῑτηρός] 1 allowance (to troops and sailors) for buying food, **ration-money** X. D.
2 (at Rome) allowance of grain, **grain-dole** Plu.

σῑτηρός ᾱ όν *adj.* (of standard measures) **of grain** Arist.

σίτησις εως *f.* [σῑτέομαι] 1 action or habit of taking food, **eating, feeding** Hdt. X. Plu.
2 customary way of feeding, **diet** Hdt. Pl. Plb.
3 (specif.) privilege of being fed at public expense (in the prytaneion), **free meals, official maintenance** Ar. Pl. Att.orats. Plu.; **feeding, maintenance** (of public officials) Arist.

σῑτία ων *n.pl.* [dimin. σῖτος] 1 food made from grain, **bread** Hdt.
2 (gener.) **food** Hdt. Ar. +; (sg.) Pl. X. Arist. Plu.
3 **provisions, rations** (of soldiers) Hdt. Th. Ar. +

σῑτίζω *vb.* | aor. ἐσίτισα | 1 **feed** —*an infant* Hdt. Ar. Thphr. —*dogs* Isoc. —W.DBL.ACC. *gamecocks, w. garlic* X.
2 ‖ MID. **feed on** —*sthg.* Theoc.

σῑτικός ή όν *adj.* (of a market) **for grain** Arist.; (of export) **of grain** Plb.; (of a law) **relating to grain** Plu. ‖ NEUT.SB. grain trade Plu.

σῑτίον *n.sg.*: see σῑτία

σῑτο-βόλιον ου *n.* [βάλλω] place for storing grain, **granary** Plb. Plu.

σῑτοδείᾱ ᾱς, Ion. **σῑτοδείη** ης *f.* [δέω²] **food-shortage, famine** Hdt. Th. Isoc. D. Thphr. +

σῑτοδοτέομαι *pass.contr.vb.* [δοτήρ, δίδωμι] (of troops) **be provisioned** Th.

σῑτολογέω *contr.vb.* [λέγω] 1 (of troops) **collect grain or provisions, forage** Plb.
2 (tr.) collect forage from, **forage** —*land* Plb.

σῑτολογίᾱ ᾱς *f.* **foraging** Plb. Plu.

σῑτομετρέω *contr.vb.* [σῑτομέτρης] measure out food in fixed quantities; (tr.) **ration, provision** —*troops* Plb. ‖ PASS. (of troops) be rationed or provisioned —W.ACC. *w. a certain quantity of grain* Plb.

σῑτο-μέτρης ου *m.* [μετρέω] official in charge of grain-distribution, **grain-rationer** Arist.

σῑτομετρίᾱ ᾱς *f.* **rationing, provisioning** (of troops) Plb.; **distribution of grain** (to citizens) Plu.

σῑτομέτριον ου *n.* food-allowance, **rations** (for servants) NT.

σῑτο-νόμος ον *adj.* [νέμω] dealing out food; (of a hope) **affording the prospect of food** S.

σῑτοποιέω *contr.vb.* [σῑτοποιός] 1 **make bread** E. ‖ MID. make bread for oneself X.
2 **provide food** —W.DAT. *for someone* X. ‖ MID. **have a meal** X.

σῑτοποιίᾱ ᾱς *f.* **bread-making** X.

σῑτοποιικός ή όν *adj.* (of equipment) **for bread-making** X. Plb.

σῑτο-ποιός όν *adj.* [ποιέω] 1 (of an enforced labour) **of bread-making** E.
2 ‖ MASC.SB. bread-maker, baker Th. Pl. X. Plu. ‖ FEM.SB. Hdt. Thphr.; (appos.w. γυνή) Hdt. Th.

σῑτοπομπίᾱ ᾱς *f.* [πέμπω] conveyance of grain, **grain-supply** D.

σῑτο-πώλης ου *m.* [πωλέω] **grain-seller** Lys.

σῖτος ου *m.* | neut.nom.acc.pl. σῖτα | 1 **grain** (ref. to wheat or barley) Od. Hdt. +
2 food made from grain; **bread** (oft.pl., sts.opp. meat) Hom. +
3 (gener.) **food** (oft.pl., sts.opp. drink) Hom. +
4 **maintenance allowance** (for troops) Th. ‖ PL. provisions (for troops) Hdt.

σῑτουργός

5 (leg.) maintenance (for widows, divorced women, orphans, wards) Is. D. Arist.
σῑτουργός οῦ *m.* [ἔργον] bread-maker, baker Pl.
σῖτο-φάγος ον *adj.* [φαγεῖν] (of persons) bread-eating Od. Hdt.
σῖτο-φόρος ον *adj.* [φέρω] 1 (of camels, mules) carrying food or provisions Hdt.
2 (of a country) grain-producing Plb.
σῖτο-φύλακες ων *m.pl.* [φύλαξ] officials who supervise the sale and pricing of grain, grain-controllers Lys. D. Arist.
σίττα *interj.* sibilant signal (fr. shepherd to sheep or goats), sitta! Theoc.
σίττη ης *f.* a kind of bird; perh. nuthatch Iamb.adesp. Call.
σῑτ-ώνης ου *m.* [σῖτος, ὠνέομαι] official appointed to buy grain, grain-commissioner D.
σῑτωνίᾱ ᾱς *f.* purchase of grain D.
σιφλός ή όν *adj.* 1 app., injured or impaired; (of a son of Hephaistos) lame (W.DU.ACC. in both feet) AR.
2 (of Homeric Glaukos, who exchanged gold armour for bronze) mentally impaired, mad Call.
σιφλόω *contr.vb.* (of a god) app. injure, harm —*someone* Il.
σίφων ωνος *m.* tube or pipe; siphon (for drawing wine) Hippon.; (fig.ref. to a penis) spigot E.*Cyc.*
σιφωνίζω *vb.* siphon off —*wine* (*or perh.* corn) Ar.
σίω *dial.vb.:* see σείω
σιωπάω *contr.vb.* | *fut.* σιωπήσομαι ǁ PASS.: *dial.pf.ptcpl.* σεσωπᾱμένος (Pi.) | 1 make no vocal sound, be or keep silent Hom. Hdt. S. E. Ar. Att.orats. +
2 (tr.) be silent about, not speak of —*sthg.* Ar. X. D. Plu. ǁ PASS. (of facts, actions, or sim.) be kept quiet or hushed up Pi. E. Att.orats. X. Plu.
σιωπή ῆς, *dial.* **σιωπά** ᾶς, *also* **σωπή** ῆς (Call.) *f.* absence of speech, silence Pi. B. S. E. Th. Ar. +
—**σιωπῇ**, *dial.* **σιωπᾷ** *dat.adv.* in silence Hom. Pi. Lys. Ar. X. +
σιωπηλός ή όν (*also* ός όν E.) *adj.* (of a person) disposed to silence, taciturn E. Plu.; (of a lyre, an island) silent Call. ǁ NEUT.SB. taciturn character (of a person) Plu.
σιωπηρός ά όν *adj.* (of a person) silent, quiet X.
σκάζω *vb.* (of wounded soldiers) limp Il.
σκαιός ά (Ion. ή) όν *adj.* 1 (of a hand or other part of the body) left Hes. Hellenist.poet.; (of half of the body) Pl. ǁ FEM.SB. left hand Il. AR. Theoc.
2 (of a headland) on the left Od.
3 Σκαιαὶ πύλαι Skaian gates (*the main gate of Troy, perh.* Left gate) Il. Hes.*fr.*
4 (fig.) left-handed; (of persons) awkward, clumsy Alcm. Hdt. E. Lys. Ar. Pl. D. +; (of speech) S. E. Ar.; (of circumstances, attributes, conduct) Pi. Hdt. E. Pl. Plu.
—**σκαιῶς** *adv.* stupidly Ar. Plb.
σκαιοσύνᾱ ᾱς *dial.f.* stupidity S.
σκαιότης ητος *f.* stupidity Hdt. S. Th. Pl. D. +
σκαιουργέω *contr.vb.* [ἔργον] act rudely Ar.
σκαίρω *vb.* [*reltd.* σκιρτάω] | *iteratv.impf.* σκαίρεσκον | 1 (of dancers) skip Il. hHom. AR. | *see also* σπαίρω
2 (of calves, deer) frisk, gambol Od. Call. Theoc.
σκαλαθυρμάτια ων *n.pl.* [σκαλαθύρω] raked-up bits (of knowledge) Ar.
σκαλ-αθύρω *vb.* [σκάλλω] (fig.) have fun poking —*a woman* Ar.
σκαλεύς έως *m.* one who hoes, hoer X.
σκαλεύω *vb.* poke —*coals* (*fig.ref. to a vagina*) Ar. —*fire* (W.DAT. *w. a sword, ref. to a Pythagorean precept, i.e. do not provoke an angry man*) Plu.

σκαληνός ή όν *adj.* uneven; (math., of numbers) odd Pl. ǁ NEUT.PL.SB. (geom.) polygons (opp. triangles) Call.
σκάλλω *vb.* stir up (ground), hoe Hdt.
σκαλμός οῦ *m.* thole, thole-pin (to which the oar was fastened) hHom. A. E. AR.; (appos.w. θρᾱνίτης) top bench of oars Plb.
σκάλοψ οπος *m.* a kind of rodent; app. mole-rat Ar.
Σκάμανδρος ου *m.* Scamander (river nr. Troy) Il. Hes. A. Pi. B. Hdt. +
—**Σκαμάνδριος** ον *adj.* (of a meadow, plain, streams, banks) of Scamander, Scamandrian Il. Stesich. S. E.
σκάμμα ατος *n.* [σκάπτω] 1 product of digging, pit Pl.
2 sanded pit used by wrestlers, arena Plb.
σκᾱνᾱ́ *dial.f.:* see σκηνή
σκανδάληθρον ου *n.* [σκάνδαλον] trigger on which the bait is placed in a dead-fall trap; (fig.) trap (W.GEN. in words, ref. to a verbal ploy) Ar.
σκανδαλίζω *vb.* 1 cause (W.ACC. someone) to offend or sin NT. ǁ PASS. be led into sin NT.
2 give offence to, offend —*someone* NT. ǁ PASS. take offence NT.
σκάνδαλον ου *n.* 1 app., trap or snare (for an animal); (fig.) enticement to sin, temptation NT.
2 that which causes offence, offence, scandal NT.
σκάνδιξ ικος *f.* a kind of wild herb; perh. chervil Ar.
σκαπανεύς ῆος *ep.m.* [σκαπάνη] man who digs, digger Call.
σκαπάνη ης, *dial.* **σκαπάνᾱ** ᾱς *f.* [σκάπτω] 1 act of digging, digging Men.
2 implement for digging, pick Theoc.
σκαπτήρ ῆρος *m.* man who digs, digger Arist.(quot.poet.)
σκᾶπτον, **σκᾶπτρον** *dial.n.:* see σκῆπτρον
σκάπτω *vb.* | *aor.* ἔσκαψα ǁ PASS.: *pf.ptcpl.* ἐσκαμμένος |
1 hollow out (ground); (intr.) dig (w. an implement such as a spade or pick) hHom. E.*fr.* Ar. Pl. X. +
2 (tr.) create by digging, excavate, dig —*a trench* Th. ǁ NEUT.PL.PF.PASS.PTCPL.SB. pit (for the long-jump) Pl.
3 (tr.) dig (for cultivation), hoe —*a piece of land* Plu.
4 (tr.) dig the ground for, hoe —*plants* hHom. ǁ PASS. (of plants) be hoed X.
5 use a pick against, pick, break —*rocks* Hippon. Arist. —*a door* E.
σκαρδαμύσσω, *Att.* **σκαρδαμύττω** *vb.* | *aor.* ἐσκαρδάμυξα | blink E.*Cyc.* X.
σκαρθμός οῦ *m.* [σκαίρω] prancing (of a horse) AR.
σκαρῑφησμοί ῶν *m.pl.* [σκαρῑφάομαι *make a scratch*] (fig.) scratchings, chippings (W.GEN. of nonsense) Ar.
σκαταιβάτης ου *m.* [σκῶρ, βαίνω, w. play on καταιβάτης] (epith. of Zeus) lord of the thunder-crap Ar.
σκατοφαγέω *contr.vb.* [σκατοφάγος] (fig., of a person) eat shit (i.e. behave offensively) Men.
σκατο-φάγος ον *adj.* [σκατός, see σκῶρ; φαγεῖν] (of a person, as a term of abuse) shit-eating Ar. Men.
σκαφεῖον ου *n.* [σκάπτω] implement for digging, spade or pick Hyp. Plu.
σκαφεύομαι *pass.vb.* [σκάφη] be put to death in a trough (as a Persian method of execution) Plu.
σκαφεύς έως *m.* [σκάπτω] (pejor.) digger, labourer E.
σκάφη ης *f.* 1 concave domestic utensil; dish, bowl Hdt. Ar. Men.
2 tray or tub (holding items for sale, w. play on senses 3 and 4) Ar.
3 large tub or trough (capable of floating, in which the children of Tyro and Romulus and Remus were exposed); tub Ar. Arist. Plu.

4 small boat, **tub, skiff** Plb. NT. Plu.
5 trough (in which a live person was encased, as a Persian method of execution) Plu. | see σκαφεύομαι

σκαφίδιον ου n. [dimin.] small boat, **skiff** Plb.

σκάφιον ου n. **1** small bowl or basin; **basin** (ref. to a chamber-pot) Ar.
2 bowl (ref. to a convex mirror used as a burning-glass) Plu.
3 (fig.) a style of haircut which left the hair evenly short, **basin-cut** Ar.

σκαφίς ίδος f. **bowl** Od. Theoc.

σκάφος[1] ου m. [σκάπτω] digging (of the ground around plants); **hoeing** (W.GEN. of vines) Hes.

σκάφος[2] εος (ους) n. **1 hull** (of a ship) Trag. Th.
2 (gener.) **ship, vessel** Hdt. Trag. Ar. D. Plb. Plu.

σκεδάννῡμι vb. [reltd. κεδάννῡμι, σκίδναμαι] | fut. σκεδάσω, dial. σκεδασῶ (Alcm.), Att. σκεδῶ | aor. ἐσκέδασα, ep. σκέδασα ‖ PASS.: aor. ἐσκεδάσθην | pf.ptcpl. ἐσκεδασμένος |
1 cause to scatter in different directions; (of a commander) **cause to disperse, dismiss** —troops Il. ‖ PASS. (of persons, ships; of troops, sts. w.connot. of being routed) be scattered or dispersed Hdt. Th. Pl. X. Men. +
2 (of Ares) **disperse, scatter** —blood of slain warriors (W.PREP.PHR. all over a river) Il.; (of Pandora) —the contents of her jar Hes. ‖ PASS. (of the sun's rays) be spread wide A.; (of a report) be disseminated Hdt. Plu.; (of vision) be diffused (opp. concentrated) X.
3 separate into pieces, **shatter, shiver** —a trident A.
4 disperse (so as to remove); (of a god) **disperse** —mist (sts. W.GEN. fr. the eyes) Hom.; (of dawn) —things visible at night Sapph.; (of the sun) **melt, thaw** —frost A.
5 dispel —sleep (W.PREP.PHR. fr. the eyes) Alcm. S. —cares Thgn. —sedition Plu.

σκέδασις εως f. **scattering, rout** (of a crowd of persons) Od.

σκεδαστός ή όν adj. (of matter) that may be dispersed, **divisible** Pl.

σκέθοντες (Aeol.masc.nom.pl.aor.2 ptcpl.): see ἔχω

σκεθρῶς adv. **exactly, precisely** —ref. to knowing, discriminating A.

Σκείρων m.: see Σκίρων

σκελετός οῦ m. [σκέλλω] dried-up corpse, **mummy** Plu.

σκελίσκος ου m. [dimin. σκέλος] **slim leg** (of a female dancer) Ar.

σκέλλω ep.vb. [reltd. σκληρός] | 3sg.aor.opt. σκήλειε | pf.ptcpl. ἐσκληώς | plpf. ἐσκλήκειν | dry up (so as to harden); (of the sun) **dry up, shrivel** —flesh Il. ‖ STATV.PF. and PLPF. (of flesh, leather straps) be dried up or parched AR.

σκέλος ους n. | DU.: nom.acc. σκέλει, gen.dat. σκελοῖν | **1 leg** (of persons or animals) Il. +
2 (prep.phr.) ἐπὶ σκέλος **step by step, gradually** (ref. to retreating while still facing the enemy, by drawing one leg back to the other) E. Ar. Plu. | cf. πούς 14
3 ‖ PL. Legs (ref. to a pair of long walls linking a city to its port, such as Megara to Nisaia, Athens to Peiraieus) Ar. Plu.

σκέμμα ατος n. [σκέπτομαι] **1** subject for inquiry, **question** Pl.
2 inquiry, investigation Pl. Arist.

σκεπάζω vb. [σκέπας] | aor. ἐσκέπασα ‖ pf.pass. ἐσκέπασμαι | (of persons, defensive armour) give protective shelter or covering, **shield, cover** —persons, parts of the body, or sim. N. Plb. ‖ PASS. (of persons, horses) be covered or protected —W.DAT. by body armour Plb.; (of parts of the body, by clothing) X.

σκέπαρνος ου m. (or perh. **σκέπαρνον** ου n.) carpenter's **axe** Od. A.satyr.fr. Call. Plu.

σκέπας αος n. | acc.pl. σκέπᾰ (Hes.) | place offering shelter, **shelter, cover** Od. Hes.; (W.GEN. fr. wind) Od.

σκέπασμα ατος n. [σκεπάζω] that which affords shelter, cover or protection; **shelter** (ref. to a building) Arist.; **covering** (ref. to clothing or rugs) Pl. Arist.; (W.ADJ. of leather, W.GEN. for armour) Plu.; **protection** (W.ADJS. of bronze and steel, ref. to armour) Plu.

σκεπαστικός ή όν adj. (of a receptacle, ref. to a house) of the kind that offers protection, **protective** (W.GEN. to goods and bodies) Arist.

σκεπάω ep.contr.vb. [σκέπας] | 3pl. (w.diect.) σκεπόωσι | (of headlands) **give shelter from** —heavy waves Od.

σκέπη ης f. protective cover, **shelter, protection** Pl. X. Plb.; (W.GEN. fr. war, alarm) Hdt.; (W.GEN. offered by someone) Plb.

σκεπτέος ᾱ ον vbl.adj. [σκέπτομαι] **to be considered** or examined Antipho Pl.

σκέπτομαι mid.vb. [reltd. σκοπέω] | fut. σκέψομαι | aor. ἐσκεψάμην | pf.mid.pass. ἔσκεμμαι ‖ PASS.: 3sg.fut.pf. ἐσκέψεται ‖ neut.impers.vbl.adj. σκεπτέον ‖ For pres. and impf. Att. uses σκοπέω and σκοπέομαι. |
1 (intr.) look attentively; **look, look out** Hom. hHom. E. Ar. Call. Theoc.; (tr.) **look out for, watch for** —a person Thgn. —the whizz of arrows Il. —the light of dawn AR.
2 (gener.) **see, catch sight of** —a person hHom.
3 look at inquiringly; **look at, inspect** —objects, persons hHom. A. Hdt. E. Ar. +; **examine, see** —W.INDIR.Q. what (or whether sthg.) is the case Ar. X.
4 look at (w. the mind); **observe, consider** —sthg. S. E. Th. + —W.INDIR.Q. or COMPL.CL. what (whether, or that sthg.) is the case Trag. Th. +; (intr.) **take a look, observe, inquire** E. Th. + ‖ PF.PASS. (of things) have been considered D. Arist. ‖ IMPERS.PF. and FUT.PF.PASS. consideration has been (will be) given Pl. D.
5 decide after consideration, determine —W.INF. to do sthg. Th.
6 ‖ PF. have seen, have detected —foolishness (in a person) E.; have looked at, thought out or planned —a course of action, speech, arguments Pl. X. D. Plu.

—**ἐσκεμμένος** η ον pf.pass.ptcpl.adj. (of actions, speeches) **thought out, planned, designed** Th. X. D.; (of buildings) X.

—**ἐσκεμμένως** pf.pass.ptcpl.adv. in a way which has been thought out, **deliberately** D.

σκέπω vb. [σκέπας] | only pres. | **1** (of a harbour) **shelter** —those at anchor (W.PREP.PHR. fr. the wind) Plb.
2 (of soldiers) **give cover** or **protection to** —one's body (W.DAT. w. a shield) Plb.; (intr., of armour) **give protection** Plu.

σκερβόλλω vb. [σκέρβολος] app. **utter abuse** Ar.

σκέρβολος ον adj. [reltd. βάλλω] (of speech) app. **abusive** Call.

σκευᾱ́ dial.f.: see σκευή

σκευαγωγέω contr.vb. [σκευαγωγός] transport goods or property, **move one's belongings** Aeschin. D.

σκευ-αγωγός όν adj. [σκεῦος] transporting baggage (for an army) ‖ MASC.SB. baggage-master X. ‖ NEUT.PL.SB. baggage-trains or baggage-animals Plu.

σκευάζω vb. [σκεῦος, σκευή] | fut. σκευάσω | aor. ἐσκεύασα | pf. ἐσκεύακα ‖ PASS.: pf. ἐσκεύασμαι, Ion.3pl. ἐσκευάδαται | Ion.3pl.plpf. ἐσκευάδατο ‖ neut.impers.vbl.adj. σκευαστέον ‖
1 make ready, prepare —items of food, a meal Hdt. Ar. Pl. Thphr. Plu.; (also mid.) E. Pl. ‖ PASS. (of items of food, a meal) be prepared Ar. Pl. X.

σκευάριον

2 (app.fig.) make a dish of, **cheat** —*a person* Men.
3 (of an embalmer) **prepare** —*a corpse* Hdt. ‖ PASS. (of a corpse) be prepared Hdt.
4 ‖ MID. **plan** —*war, treason* Hdt. —*a pretence of madness* Plu.
5 ‖ MID. **make, get** —*one's weapons* (W.PREDIC.ADJ. *ready*) E.
6 fashion, create —*a statue, fountain, pigment, poison, bit (for a bridle)* Hdt. Th. Pl. Plu. —*pleasures* Pl.; **make** —*damage* (W.PREDIC.ADJ. *irreparable*) Plb. ‖ PASS. (of coffins) be fashioned —W.PREP.PHR. *fr. rock crystal* Hdt.
7 (iron., of Hermes in his role as a thief) **collect household property** hHom.
8 equip, clothe, dress —*persons, troops* (freq. W.ADV. or DAT. *in a certain style of dress or uniform*) Hdt. Ar. X. Plu. ‖ MID. **clothe oneself** Plu. —W.DAT. *in certain garments, a particular style of dress* Plu. ‖ PASS. (of persons, troops) be dressed or equipped (in a certain way) Hdt. E. Th. Ar. Plu.
9 ‖ MID. (of a commander) **equip oneself with supplies** Plu. ‖ PASS. be furnished —W.DAT. *w. provisions* Hdt.
10 ‖ PASS. (of a nation) be provided —W.DAT. *w. rivers* Hdt.; (of a temple) be equipped or decorated —W.ADV. *finely* Hdt.; (of a gateway) —W.DAT. *w. carved figures* Hdt.

σκευάριον ου *n*. [dimin. σκεῦος] **1 little** or **insignificant item of property** Ar. ‖ COLLECTV.PL. **pots and pans, bits and pieces** Ar. Aeschin.
2 [dimin. σκευή] ‖ PL. **bits of clothing** Pl.

σκευασία ᾶς *f*. [σκευάζω] **preparation** (W.GEN. of food) Pl. Plu.; (without GEN.) Men. Plu.

σκευαστός ή όν *adj*. (of a class of things) **man-made, manufactured** (opp. natural) Pl. ‖ NEUT.PL.SB. **manufactured objects** Pl. Arist.

σκευή ῆς, dial. **σκευά** ᾶς *f*. [reltd. σκεῦος] **1 personal equipment, dress, costume, outfit** (esp. of a particular role or profession) Hdt. S. E. Th. And. Lys. +
2 equipment (of soldiers) Hdt. Th. Pl. D.
3 style of dress or **equipment** Hdt. Th. Plu.
4 tackle (of a fisherman) Pi.; (W.GEN. of a ship) NT.
5 (gener.) **gear, goods and chattels** Plb.

σκευο-θήκη ης *f*. [σκεῦος, τίθημι] **place for storing equipment**; (specif.) **naval arsenal** Aeschin.

σκευοποιέω contr.vb. [σκευοποιός] ‖ PASS. (of military engines) **be constructed** Plu.

σκευοποιήματα των *n.pl*. **accoutrements, costume** (ref. to the clothing and mask of a tragic actor) Plu.

σκευο-ποιός οῦ *m*. [σκευή, ποιέω] **maker of theatrical costumes** (incl. masks), **costume-maker** Ar. Arist.

σκεῦος ους *n*. **1 manufactured object serving a specific purpose**; **household utensil** Ar.; **piece of furniture** Pl.; **item of military equipment** Th.; **vessel, container** NT. Plu.; (gener.) **piece of personal property, object, thing** NT. Plu.
2 (fig., derog.ref. to a person) **tool** Plb.; (in positive sense) **instrument, vessel** (of God) NT.
3 ‖ COLLECTV.PL. **utensils** Ar. X. Thphr. Men. Plu.; **furniture** Pl. D.; (gener.) **contents** (of a house), **belongings, goods and chattels** Lys. Ar. D. Plb. NT.
4 ‖ PL. **implements, tools** (for specific kinds of work) Th. Ar. Plu.; **equipment** (of soldiers, an army) Th. X.; (for a ship) Pl. X. D. Arist. Plb. +; (for a horse) X.
5 ‖ PL. **luggage, baggage, gear** Ar. Pl. X. Plb. Plu.
6 (gener.) **object** (opp. living thing) Pl. Arist. ‖ PL. **inanimate things** (as a class, opp. male and female) Arist.(quot.)

σκευουργία ᾶς *f*. [ἔργον] **utensil-making** Pl.

σκευοφορέω contr.vb. [σκευοφόρος] (of persons or animals) **carry baggage** X. ‖ MID.PASS. **have one's baggage carried** —W.DAT. *by camels* Plu.

σκευοφορικός ή όν *adj*. **1 of or related to baggage-carrying**; (of a train) **of baggage-carriers** X.
2 (of the weight) **of carried baggage** X.

σκευο-φόρος ον *adj*. [φέρω] **1** (of animals) **baggage-carrying** Hdt. X.
2 ‖ MASC.SG.SB. **baggage-carrier, porter** Ar. X. ‖ PL. **baggage-train** Hdt. Th. X.
3 ‖ NEUT.SG.SB. **baggage-train** Plb. ‖ PL. **baggage-animals, baggage-train** X. Men. Plb. Plu.

σκευοφυλακέω contr.vb. [φύλαξ] **guard baggage** Plu.

σκευωρέομαι mid.contr.vb. [οὖρος², ὁράω] **1 look after baggage or belongings**; (fig., w.connot. of intrigue or self-interest) **have an eye on, attend to, manage, plan** —*disreputable actions* D.
2 concoct, fabricate —*a lease* D. ‖ PASS. (of a lease) be fabricated D.
3 busy oneself, meddle —w. περί + ACC. *w. sthg*. D. Arist.; (in neutral sense) **negotiate** —*sthg*. Plu.
4 attend to, clean up —*devastated ground* Plu.
5 (pejor.) **clean out, ransack** —*a house* Plu.

σκευώρημα ατος *n*. **product of planning or scheming**; (ref. to a line of argument) **fabrication, concoction** D.

σκευωρία ᾱς *f*. **1 care, attention** (to an activity) Arist.
2 (pejor.) **scheming, intrigue** D. Plu.

σκέψις εως *f*. [σκέπτομαι] **1 process of perceiving or viewing** (w. the senses), **perception** Pl.
2 taking notice (W.GEN. of someone) X.
3 inspecting or examining (a subject) with the mind; **examination, inquiry** E. Ar. Pl. Arist. +
4 (ref. to a specific process) **forensic inquiry, investigation** Pl. Arist. Plu.

σκήλειε (ep.3sg.aor.opt.): see σκέλλω

σκηνάομαι mid.contr.vb. [σκηνή] **1 pitch one's tent, encamp** Pl.; (gener.) **take up quarters, settle oneself** (in a place) Th. Pl.
2 (tr.) **provide for oneself** (as shelter), **build oneself** —*a hut* Th.

—**ἐσκηνημένος** η ον pf.mid.pass.ptcpl.adj. (of persons in a carriage) **tented over, under awnings** Ar.

σκηνέω contr.vb. —also **σκηνόω** contr.vb. **1 encamp** (in a place) Th. X. D. Plb. Plu.
2 be quartered in a tent X.
3 (specif.) **dine in a tent** X.; **take one's meals** —W.ADV. *at home, outdoors* X.
4 (gener.) **take up quarters, be billeted, settle** X. Plu.

σκηνή ῆς, dial. **σκᾱνά** ᾶς *f*. **1 roofed structure providing temporary shelter; tent** (esp. for soldiers) Hdt. S. + ‖ PL. **place for tents, camping-ground** A.
2 dining-tent X. Plu.; (meton.) **banquet, entertainment** X.
3 shopkeeper's booth or **stall covered by an awning, stall** Ar. D. Thphr. Theoc.
4 tent-like covering for a carriage, awning, canopy X. Plu.; **covered carriage** A.
5 (specif.) **tent pitched in the agora for actors, tent** Pl.; (in the 5th-C. theatre) **stage building** (esp. as scenic background) X. Arist.; (phrs., ref. to the acting area) ἐπὶ τῆς σκηνῆς *on the stage* D. Arist.; οἱ ἀπὸ τῆς σκηνῆς *the characters in a play* D.
6 (gener., ref. to the acting profession) **stage, theatre** Plu.
7 tabernacle (W.GEN. of testimony, ref. to a portable sanctuary containing the Ark of the Covenant) NT.

σκηνήματα των *n.pl*. [σκηνέω] **quarters, shelter** (ref. to an eagle's nest) A.; (ref. to buildings assoc.w. a sanctuary) X.(v.l. σκηνώματα)

σκηνίδιον ου *n.* [dimin. σκηνή] **mere tent** Th.
σκηνικός ή όν *adj.* [σκηνή 5–6] **of or relating to the stage** ‖ MASC.SB. **actor** Plu.
σκηνίς ίδος *f.* [σκηνή 4] **awning, canopy** (on a boat) Plu.
σκηνίτης ου *m.* [σκηνή 3] **stall-holder, shopkeeper** Isoc.
σκηνογραφίᾱ ᾱς *f.* [σκηνή 5, γράφω] **scene-painting** (in the theatre) Arist. Plb.; (fig., ref. to mere show) Plu.
σκηνοπηγίᾱ ᾱς *f.* [σκηνή 7, πήγνῡμι] (as the name of a Jewish festival) **Building of Tabernacles** NT.
σκηνοποιέομαι *mid.contr.vb.* [σκηνή 1] **make oneself a tent or shelter** Plb.
σκηνοποιίᾱ ᾱς *f.* 1 **hut-building** (w. reeds) Plb.
2 arrangement of tents (in a camp), **tent-formation** Plb.
σκηνοποιός οῦ *m.* **tent-maker** NT.
σκηνο-φύλαξ ακος *m.* **guardian of tents, camp-guard** X. Plu.
σκηνόω *contr.vb.*: see σκηνέω
σκηνύδριον ου *n.* [dimin. σκηνή] **simple hut** Plu.
σκήνωμα ατος *n.* [σκηνόω] **tent, hut** X. Plu.; (poet.pl.) E.; **dwelling-place** (W.DAT. for the descendants of Jacob, ref. to a temple) NT. ‖ PL. **housing, lodgings** (ref. to a cave) E.*Cyc.* ‖ see also σκηνήματα
σκηπάνιον ου *n.* [σκῆπτρον] 1 **staff of office, staff, sceptre** Il.
2 **staff for support, staff, stick** Call.
σκήπτομαι *mid.vb.* | aor. ἐσκηψάμην | 1 (intr.) **support oneself with, lean on** —W.DAT. *a javelin, staff* Il. AR.; **lean on a staff** Od.; (fig.) **lean or depend on** —W.DAT. *a person* (W.PREDIC.SB. *as witness*) D.
2 **allege as excuse, claim, plead** —*ignorance, illness, lack of resources, or sim.* Hdt. Th. Pl. Plb. Plu. —W.INF., ACC. + INF. or COMPL.CL. *that sthg. is the case* Pl. Aeschin. D. Plb. Plu. —W.COGN.ACC. *an excuse* Plu.
3 **pretend** —*madness* Plu. —W.INF. or ACC. + INF. *that one is such and such, that sthg. is the case* Ar. Att.orats. Arist. Plu.
4 (intr.) **make a claim** or **plea** —W.PREP.PHR. *on another's behalf* Pl.
—**σκήπτω** *act.vb.* 1 **allege as excuse** —*the threat of violence* E.
2 (intr.) **move in the manner of a lightning-bolt**; (of Zeus' arrow, his strife w. a mortal in the form of lightning, a flash of light, plague) **shoot** or **swoop down** A. S.; (of a person) **plunge down** (fr. a rock) A.
3 (tr., of a god) **send down, launch** —*rancour, an avenging spirit* (W.DAT. or PREP.PHR. *against someone or sthg.*) A. E.
σκηπτός οῦ *m.* [σκήπτω 2] 1 **that which shoots down; lightning-bolt** X.
2 **violent storm** (of dust) S.
3 (fig.) **bolt, stroke** (W.GEN. of plague) A.; **thunderstorm, hurricane** (ref. to catastrophic events) D.; (ref. to a violent person) Men.; **storm, onslaught** (W.GEN. of enemies) E.; (of war) Plu.; (ref. to sickness or suffering) E.
σκηπτουχίᾱ ᾱς *f.* [σκηπτοῦχος] **bearing of a staff of office, military command** A.
σκηπτοῦχος ον *adj.* [σκῆπτρον, ἔχω] 1 **bearing a staff of office**; (of a king) **staff-bearing, sceptred** Hom. E.; (of Hera) Lyr.adesp. ‖ MASC.SB. **man holding a sceptre, king** Hom. Semon. Mosch. Plu.(quot.epigr.)
2 ‖ MASC.SB. (at the Persian court) **attendant bearing a staff, mace-bearer** X.
σκῆπτρον, dial. **σκᾶπτρον** (B.), also **σκᾶπτον** (Pi.), ου *n.* [σκήπτομαι 1] 1 **staff** (for support) Hom. Pi. Hdt. Trag.; (fig., ref. to a person) **prop, support** S.
2 (as a symbol of authority) **staff, sceptre** (of a king or ruler) Hom. Pi. Trag. +; (of Zeus) A. Pi. B.; (of Rhea) Call.; (of a priest or prophet) Hom. Hes.*fr.* A.; (of a herald) Il. AR.; (of a bard) Hes.; (held by a speaker in an assembly as a token of his right to speak) Hom.
3 **authority symbolised by a staff, royal power** Pi. Hdt. Trag. Ar.; (pl.) Hdt. Trag. Ar. AR.
σκήπτω *vb.*: see under σκήπτομαι
σκηρίπτω *vb.* [reltd. σκήπτομαι, στηρίζω] | only pres. | 1 (of cattle ploughing) **press** —*their hooves* (W.PREP.PHR. *in the ground*) AR.
2 ‖ MID. **support oneself** (w. a staff) Od. —W.DAT. *w. one's hands and feet* Od.
σκῆψις εως *f.* [σκήπτομαι 2] 1 **plea made in support of a claim or by way of excuse, plea, excuse, pretext** Hdt. Trag. Ar. Att.orats. Plb. Plu.
2 (leg.) **claim** (to exemption fr. a leitourgia) Arist.
σκιᾱ́ ᾶς, Ion. **σκιή** ῆς *f.* 1 **cover provided by objects intercepting light and heat, shade** Hes. hHom. A. Hdt. E. Ar. +
2 **image cast by a person or object intercepting light, shadow** Od. S. E. Pl. +
3 (fig.) **shadow** (opp. reality), **reflection** (of sthg.) Pl.; **mere shadow, faint trace** (of sthg.) P.
4 **shadow of a dead person, shade, ghost, phantom** Od. Trag.; (ref. to an emaciated person) **shadow** A.
5 (as a symbol of what is impermanent, insubstantial or unreal) **shadow** Pi. Trag.; (phrs.) καπνοῦ σκιά *shadow of smoke* S.; ὄνου σκιά *donkey's shadow* (provbl. *for sthg. not worth fighting for*) Ar. Pl.; ἡ ἐν Δελφοῖς σκιά *the phantom at Delphi* (ref. to the Amphictyonic council) D.
σκιᾱγραφέω *contr.vb.* [γράφω] | only pf.pass.ptcpl. ἐσκιᾱγραφημένος | **paint with shadows** (a technique in which alternating spots of contrasting colours appear to blend when viewed fr. a distance)
‖ NEUT.PL.PF.PASS.PTCPL.SB. **illusionistic paintings** Pl.
‖ PF.PASS.PTCPL.ADJ. (fig., of pleasure, justice and injustice) **created by illusionistic technique, illusory** Pl.
σκιᾱ́γραφημα ατος *n.* **piece of illusionistic painting** Pl.
σκιᾱγραφίᾱ ᾱς *f.* 1 **illusionistic painting, illusionism** Pl. Arist.
2 (fig.) illusory representation, **illusion** (of virtue) Pl.; (derog., ref. to a person) **cardboard figure** Plu.
σκιάδειον ου *n.* **sunshade, parasol** Ar.
σκιαδίσκη ης *f.* [dimin.] **parasol** Anacr.
σκιάεις *dial.adj.*: see σκιόεις
σκιάζω *vb.* | aor. ἐσκίασα ‖ PASS.: aor.ptcpl. σκιασθείς | pf. ἐσκίασμαι | 1 **provide with shade** (so as to protect fr. the sun), **shade** —*exposed parts of vines* X. ‖ PASS. (of persons) **be provided with shade** —W.DAT. *by branches* Plu.
2 (of the setting sun) **cast into shadows** —*the earth* Il.
‖ PASS. (of the moon) **be in shadow** (fr. clouds) Plu.
3 **cast a shade or covering over, shade, shadow, cover** —*the neck* (W.DAT. *w. locks of hair*) E.; (of a veil) —*the head* E.; (of a beard) —*a shield* Hdt.; (fig.) —*a people* (W.DAT. *w. garlands of blooming health*) Pi.*fr.* —*the mind* (w. *cheerfulness*) Pi.*fr.*
‖ PASS. (of persons) **be shaded** —W.DAT. *by laurels* E.; (of a place) —*by roses* Sapph.; (of hair) —*by flowers* Semon.; (of the cheek, by a beard) E.
σκιᾱμαχέω *contr.vb.* [μάχη] **fight with shadows** (ref. to imaginary opponents) Pl. Plu.; **fight about shadows** (ref. to empty causes) Pl.
Σκιά-ποδες ων *m.pl.* [πούς] **Shadefeet** (a fabled race in Africa or India w. large feet which could be used as sunshades) Ar.
σκιαρό-κομος ον *dial.adj.* [σκιερός, κόμη] **shady-haired**; (fig., of a forest) **with shady leaves** E.
σκιαρός *dial.adj.*: see σκιερός

σκιάς άδος *f.* [σκιά] **1** covering which gives shade; **arbour, bower** Theoc.
2 canopy (over a royal seat or couch) Plu.
σκίασμα ατος *n.* [σκιάζω] **shadow** (cast by the earth on the moon) Plu.
σκιᾱτροφέω (also **σκιᾱτραφέω** X.), Ion. **σκιητροφέω** *contr.vb.* [σκιᾰ́, τρέφω] | pf.ptcpl. ἐσκιᾱτροφηκώς | **live in the shade** (resulting in physical weakness) Hdt.; **live a sheltered** or **pampered life** Pl. ‖ MID.PASS. **stay in shade** (in a tent) Hdt.; **live indoors** X.
σκιᾱτροφίᾱ, also **σκιᾱτραφίᾱ**, ᾱς *f.* **sheltered** or **pampered lifestyle** Plu.
σκιάω *ep.contr.vb.* | 3sg. σκιάει, 3pl. σκιάουσι ‖ PASS.: 3pl.impf. (w.diect.) σκιόωντο | (of a horsehair crest) **shade** —*a helmet* Theoc.; (of the peak of Athos) **cast a shadow over** —*Lemnos* AR. ‖ PASS. (of streets) be plunged into shadows Od.
σκίδναμαι *pass.vb.* [reltd. σκεδάννῡμι] | impf.: ep.3sg. σκίδνατο, 3pl. ἐσκίδναντο | **1** be made to separate in different directions; (of groups of persons) **disperse** Hom. Hdt.; (of troops) **be scattered** (in disorder or flight) Plu.
2 (of a spring) **be dispersed** or **channelled** (through an orchard) Od.
3 (of sea-spray, corn-seed, grains of earth) **be scattered** Il. Hdt.(oracle) Plu.
4 (of a dust-storm, fragrance, the sound of a voice) **spread** Il. Hes. hHom.; (of the sun) **spread light** Hdt.
5 (of anger) **spread** (in the breast) Sapph.; (of sleep, over the eyes) E.
—**σκίδνημι** *act.vb.* (perh.intr.) **disperse** (opp. come together) Heraclit.
σκιερός, dial. **σκιαρός**, ᾱ́ (Ion. ή) όν *adj.* [σκιᾰ́] **1** (of wooded places, trees, or sim.) giving shade, **shady** Hom. Thgn. Ibyc. Pi. E. +
2 (of places) receiving shade, **shaded** Hes. Pi. Ar. Pl. Plu.
3 (of part of the sky) **in shadow** (fr. the earth) Plu.
4 (of the underworld) full of shadows, **shadowy** Thgn.
5 (of a colour) **shadowy, dark** Plu.
6 (of the limbs of primeval creatures) app., of a dubious nature, **shadowy** Emp.
σκιή Ion.*f.*: see σκιᾱ́
σκιητροφέω Ion.contr.vb.: see σκιᾱτροφέω
σκίλλα ης *f.* sea onion, **squill** (used in medicine and purificatory rituals) Hippon. Thgn. Thphr. Theoc. Plu.
σκιμαλίζω *vb.* [σκίμαλος *middle finger*] raise the middle finger (as an obscene gesture of defiance or contempt), **give** (W.ACC. someone) **the finger** Ar.; (fig.) —W.DAT. w. *one's turns of phrase* Ar.
σκίμπους ποδος *m.* [reltd. σκίμπτομαι] a simple kind of bed; **couch, pallet** Ar. Pl.; (for reclining on at dinner, in a military ctxt.) X.
σκίμπτομαι *mid.vb.* [reltd. σκίπων, perh. σκήπτομαι] | dial.3sg.aor. σκίμψατο | **1** (of Aietes) **plant, fix, place** —*a plough and oxen* (W.PREP.PHR. *in the midst of the Argonauts*) Pi.
2 lean on; (fig., of a city) **gain strength and confidence, take pride** —W.DAT. *in descent fr. its mother-city* Call.
σκινδάλαμοι (or perh. **σχινδάλαμοι**) ων *m.pl.* (fig.) **slivers, splinters** (fr. chariot linchpins, ref. to words as weapons) Ar.; (of the quibbling arguments of sophists) Ar.
σκιο-ειδής ές *adj.* [σκιᾰ́, εἶδος¹] (of races of humans, apparitions of souls) **shadow-like, shadowy** Ar. Pl.
σκιόεις (also dial. **σκιάεις** Pi.*fr.*) εσσα εν (ειν AR.) *adj.* **1** full of shade or shadows; (of mountains) **shaded, shady, shadowy** Hom. hHom. Pi.; (of groves) hHom. AR.; (of halls) Od. hHom.; (of animal dens) hHom.; (of Delphi) Pi.*fr.*; (of a city) Hes.*fr.*
2 (of clouds) casting shade, **shadowy, shadowing** Hom.
σκιό-θηρον ου *n.* [θηράω] **sundial** Plu.
σκιόωντο (ep.3pl.impf.pass.): see σκιάω
σκίπων ωνος *m.* [reltd. σκίμπτομαι] **1 stick, staff** (for support) Hdt. Ar. Call. Plu.; (as a symbol of rank) Plb.
2 (fig.) **prop, support** (ref. to a servant's arm) E.
Σκίρα ων *n.pl.* **Skira** (Athenian festival celebrated by women in the month Skirophorion, featuring a procession fr. the Acropolis to the suburb of Skiron) Ar. Men.
σκιραφεῖον ου *n.* [σκίραφος] **gambling-house** Isoc.
σκίραφος ου *m.* dice-box; (fig.) **trickery** Hippon. [or perh. *dice player, trickster*]
σκῖρον ου *n.* **cheese-rind** Ar.
Σκιροφοριών ῶνος *m.* **Skirophorion** (twelfth and last month of the Athenian year, June/July, named after the festival Skira) Att.orats. Arist. Plu.
σκιρτάω *contr.vb.* [reltd. σκαίρω] | dial.2pl.fut. σκιρτᾱσεῖτε (Theoc., cj. for dial.aor.subj. σκιρτᾱσῆτε) | **1** (of horses) **spring, bound** Il. E. Pl.; (of a filly, she-goats) **be frisky** Anacr. Theoc.; (of an ox) **thrash about** Plu.
2 (of Bacchants) **bound, gambol** E.; (of persons) **leap** (w. joy) NT.; (of a child in the womb) **kick** NT.
3 (of persons) **prance, skip about, kick up one's heels** Ar. Pl.; (fig., of persons, the bestial part of the soul) **be unruly** E.*fr.* Pl.
4 (of winds) **frolic** A.
σκίρτημα ατος *n.* **spring, bound, leap** (of a person or animal) A. E. Plu.
σκίρτησις εως *f.* **bounding, leaping** (of a bull) Plu.
Σκίρων (sts. written **Σκείρων**) ωνος *m.* **Skiron** (mythol. robber who threw travellers over cliffs nr. Megara) B. E. Isoc. Pl. X. +
—**Σκιρωνίς** (sts. written **Σκειρωνίς**) ίδος *fem.adj.* (of the cliffs assoc.w. Skiron) **Skironian** E. Plb.; (of the road by those cliffs) Hdt.
σκιώδης ες *adj.* [σκιᾰ́] (of a rocky place) **shady** E.
σκληροκαρδίᾱ ᾱς *f.* [σκληρός] **hardness of heart, stubbornness** NT.
σκληρός ᾱ́ όν *adj.* [reltd. σκέλλω] **1** (of material substances, opp. μαλθακός *soft*) hard to the touch, **hard, firm, solid** Thgn. Pi. Pl. +; (of a bed, w.connot. of disagreeable hardness) Pl.; (of earth in which a foreign soldier lies) A.; (of a boxer's fist) Theoc.
2 (of the body, in whole or part, opp. ὑγρός *supple, lithe*) inflexible, **stiff, firm** Ar. Pl. X.
3 (of a way of life) **hard, austere, severe** S. X. Plb. Plu.; (of a person, W.DAT. in his way of life) Men.
4 (of persons, their nature, behaviour, thoughts) **hard, stubborn, unyielding** S. E. Ar. Pl. Arist. +; (of compulsion) Antipho
5 (of a daimon responsible for a person's destiny) **hard, unfeeling, cruel** E. Ar. Theoc.; (of the Sphinx) S.; (of words) S. Arist.
6 (of thunder) **violent** Hdt.; (of climate) **harsh** Plb.
7 (of a voice) **harsh, rough** (in tone) Plu.
8 (of happenings) **harsh, unwelcome** Call.*epigr.*; (of the teaching of Jesus) NT.; (of an action) NT. ‖ NEUT.SB. harshness (of circumstances) Simon.
—**σκληρόν** *neut.adv.* **hard, violently** —*ref. to thundering* Hes.
—**σκληρῶς** *adv.* **1** in hard circumstances, **uncomfortably** —*ref. to sitting or sleeping on hard ground* Ar. X.

2 austerely —*ref. to living* X.
3 hardly, with difficulty E.*satyr.fr.*
4 harshly, unfeelingly Pl. Arist. Plu.

σκληρότης ητος *f.* **1 hardness** (as an abstr. quality) Pl. Arist. Plu.
2 stiffness, rigidity (of body-armour) Plu.
3 harshness, stubbornness (of persons) Pl. Arist.
4 unfeelingness, cruelty (of destiny) Antipho

σκληρο-τράχηλος ον *adj.* (fig., of persons) **stiff-necked, stubborn** NT.

σκληφρός ά όν *adj.* [reltd. σκληρός] (of a person) **slender, puny** Pl.

σκνιπός ή όν *adj.* (of a person) **dim-sighted** Semon.

σκνῑφαῖος (v.l. **σκνῑπαῖος**) ᾱ ον *adj.* (of a traveller) **in the twilight** Theoc.

σκόλιον ου *n.* [σκολιός] **1** lyric composition sung at a symposium (by a poet), **skolion** Pi.*fr.* Ar.; (appos.w. μέλος *song*) Arist.
2 short stanza in fixed metre sung at a symposium (by each guest in turn while holding a myrtle-branch), **drinking-song** Ar. Pl. Arist.

σκολιός ά (Ion. ή) όν *adj.* **1 not straight;** (of a person) **bent, crooked** Hes.; (of an iron hook) Hdt.; (of a supporting arm) E.; (of a staff) Thphr.; (of the needles of a fish's spine or fin) AR. ‖ NEUT.PL.SB. **crooked things** NT.
2 (of a slave's head) **crooked, askew** Thgn.; (of an ill-formed horse) Pl.
3 (of a river, canal) **curved, winding** Hdt.; (of a path, labyrinth) Call. AR.; (of twists of rope in a knot) Plu.; (fig., of paths, ref. to deviousness) Pi.
4 (of ground) **irregular, uneven** Plu.
5 (of judgements, words, actions, thoughts, or sim.) not straightforward, **crooked, devious** Il. Hes. Eleg. Pi.*fr.* E. Pl. +
—**σκολιῶς** *adv.* **crookedly, deviously** Hes.

σκολιότης ητος *f.* **crookedness** (W.GEN. of the curvature of a bow) Plu.

σκόλοψ οπος *m.* [reltd. σκάλλω] **1** pointed wooden stick or pole ‖ PL. **stakes, palisade** (for reinforcing a ditch or wall) Hom. Hdt. E. X. Plu.
2 stake (for impaling a head or body) Il. E.

σκολύθριον ου *n.* **little stool** Pl.

σκόλυμος ου *m.* a kind of edible plant, **golden thistle** Hes. Alc.

σκόμβρος ου *m.* **mackerel** Ar.

σκόπ-αρχος ου *m.* [σκοπός, ἄρχω] (milit.) **leader of scouts** X.

σκόπελος ου *m.* [reltd. σκοπός] rocky prominence; **rock, crag** (ref. to a cliff or headland) Hom. Ar. AR.; (ref. to a small island) Alcm. Pi.*fr.*; (ref. to a mountain) E. Ar. AR.; (ref. to an acropolis) Pi.*fr.* E. ‖ PL. **rocks** (in a river, on the coast) Hdt. Plu.; (on a mountainside) A. E. AR. Mosch.; (ref. to an acropolis) E.

σκοπεύω *vb.* **spy out, watch for** —*the enemy* X.; (intr.) **be on watch** E.(cj.)

σκοπέω *contr.vb.* ‖ Only pres. and impf.; for other tenses see σκέπτομαι. ‖ **1 look out for** —*someone or sthg.* Pi. S. Th. +; (mid.) Isoc.; (intr.) **look, be on the lookout** S. Ar. X.; (mid.) E.
2 (act. and mid.) **look at inquiringly, look at, inspect, examine** —*sthg.* Trag. Ar. Pl. ‖ MID. (intr.) **look inquiringly, look** E. Ar.
3 (act. and mid.) **look at** (w. the mind); **look at, consider, examine** —*sthg.* Hdt. S. E. Th. + —W.INDIR.Q. *what* (*or whether sthg.*) *is the case* Hdt. S. E. Th. +; (intr.) **consider,**

observe, inquire Trag. Th. + ‖ PASS. (of a person) be examined or considered —W.PREP.PHR. *by others* Pl.
4 (act. and mid.) direct one's consideration, **look** —W.PREP.PHR. *at or towards someone or sthg.* E.*fr.* Antipho Th. Pl. X. +

σκοπή ῆς *f.* **1 lookout-post** A. X.
2 ‖ PL. **acts of looking out, watches** A.

σκοπιά ᾶς, Ion. **σκοπιή** ῆς *f.* **1 lookout-place** Hom. hHom. Thgn. Hdt. Pl.
2 place providing a lookout, **hilltop** Il. hHom. Pi.*fr.* E. Ar.; **mountain peak** Hellenist.poet.; **pinnacle** (of Troy, ref. to its acropolis) E.; (fig.) **peak, pinnacle** (of fortune and success) Pi.
3 lookout, watch Od. Hdt. X. Call.
4 scouting expedition Plu.

σκοπιάζω *vb.* **be on the lookout** Hom.; (tr.) **spy out** —*the enemy* Il.; (act. and mid.) **watch for** —*fish, a lion* Theoc. ‖ MID. **watch** (fr. a vantage point) —*a ship* AR.

σκοπιωρέομαι *mid.contr.vb.* [οὖρος², ὁράω] **keep watch, be on the lookout** Ar. X.

σκοπός οῦ *m.* (sts.*f.*) [σκοπέω] **1** one who watches, **watcher, lookout** Hom. Hes.*fr.* S. E. X. +; **observer** (W.GEN. of someone or sthg.) Il. hHom. X.
2 watcher (ref. to Zeus, Apollo) A. Pi.
3 spy, scout Il. Scol. Trag. X. Men. Plu.
4 (*m.f.*) one who watches over; (ref. to a god or mortal ruler) **guardian, warden** (W.GEN. of a place, a people) A. Pi. Call.; **overseer** (of maidservants, slaves) Od. S.; (of a blind man) S.; (fig., W.GEN. of an edict, by ensuring it is carried out) S.
5 goal of looking (and aiming), **mark, target** Od. A. Pi. S. Antipho +; (prep.phr.) ἀπὸ σκοποῦ *wide of the mark* (*in speech*) Od. Pl. X.
6 (gener.) **aim, goal, purpose** Pl. Arist. Plb. Plu.

σκορακίζω *vb.* [ἐς κόρακας, see κόραξ 1] tell (someone) to go to the crows ‖ PASS. be told to go to hell D. Plu.

σκορδινάομαι *mid.contr.vb.* (of a bored or agitated person) prob. **twitch, fidget** Ar.

σκοροδ-άλμη ης *f.* [σκόροδον, ἅλμη] garlic-brine, **pickled garlic** Ar.

σκοροδίζω *vb.* ‖ pf.pass.ptcpl. ἐσκοροδισμένος ‖ feed or smear (a fighting-cock) with garlic (to stimulate aggression); (fig.) **make** (W.ACC. someone) **fighting mad** Ar. ‖ PF.PASS.PTCPL.ADJ. (of persons) fighting mad Ar.

σκόροδον, also **σκόρδον** (Plb.), ου *n.* (usu.pl.) **garlic, clove of garlic** Hdt. Ar. X. Thphr. Plb.; (fed to fighting-cocks, to stimulate aggression) X.

—**σκορόδιον** ου *n.* [dimin.] ‖ PL. **bits of garlic** Ar.

σκοροδο-πανδοκευτρι-αρτόπωλις ιδος *f.* garlic-innkeeper-breadseller, **garlicky bread-selling barmaid** Ar.

σκορπίδιον ου *n.* [dimin. σκορπίος 2] **small catapult** (for shooting arrows) Plb.

σκορπίζω *vb.* **1** (of a wolf) **scatter, chase in all directions** —*sheep* NT. ‖ PASS. (of troops) be scattered (in flight) Plu.; (of persons) be dispersed (to their homes) NT.
2 (intr., of a person) **scatter, divide** (people, opp. uniting them) NT.

σκορπίος ου *m.* **1 scorpion** (usu. w. allusion to its sting) Scol. Pl. D. NT. Plu.; **Scorpio** (the constellation) Plu.
2 catapult (for shooting arrows) Plu.

σκοταῖος ον *adj.* [σκότος] (quasi-advbl., of persons acting) **in darkness** (i.e. during the night) X. Plu.; (of activities being performed) Plu.

σκοτεινός ή όν *adj.* **1** (of night) **dark** Th. X.; (of night's chariot, a weapon of the underworld powers) A.; (of a dungeon, the inside of a scabbard) E.; (of places) Pl. X. Plu.; (of features in a painting, opp. light) X. || NEUT.SB. **darkness** (of night, a place) Th. Pl. X.
2 (of a person) **blind** S.; (fig., of a person's body, w. moral connot.) NT.; (of the vision of a dying person, the light seen by an ageing person) **darkened, dimmed** E.
3 (fig., of behaviour) **dark, secret** E.; (of a report, speech, procedure, or sim.) **obscure, unclear** Pl. Aeschin. Plu.
4 (of blame) **dismal, casting a shadow** Pi.
5 (of a person) **obscure** (opp. illustrious) Pl.
—**σκοτεινόν** *neut.adv.* **in privacy** Pl.
—**σκοτεινῶς** *adv.* **in the dark, blindly** —*ref. to conducting a discussion* Pl.
σκοτεινότης ητος *f.* **darkness, obscurity** Pl.
σκοτίᾱ ᾱς, Ion. **σκοτίη** ης *f.* **darkness** AR. NT.
σκοτίζομαι *pass.vb.* (of the sun) **be darkened** NT.
σκότιος ᾱ (Ion. η) ον (also ος ον E.) *adj.* **1** (of night, the night sky) **lacking light, dark** E. AR.; (of the underworld, a prison) E.
2 (of ragged clothes, worn in grief) **dark** E.
3 (of the afterlife) **dark** E.; (quasi-advbl., of persons fading away) **into darkness** (i.e. death) E.
4 (fig., of bastard children) **secret** Il. Call. AR.; (of sexual unions) **clandestine** E.
5 (fig., of perception through the senses) **bastard** (opp. γνήσιος *legitimate*, through the intellect) Democr.
6 (of a dithyramb) **obscure** Ar.
7 (of a person) **obscure** (opp. illustrious, in respect of ancestry) Plu.
—**σκότια** *neut.pl.adv.* **in the darkness** (of an inner room, a grave) E.
σκοτοβῑνιάω *contr.vb.* [βινέω; coined fr. σκοτοδινιάω] **be eager to fuck in the dark** Ar.
σκοτο-δασυ-πυκνό-θριξ τριχος *masc.fem.adj.* [δασύς, πυκνός, θρίξ] (of the cap of Hades) **dark-shaggy-thick-haired** Ar.
σκοτο-δῑνίᾱ ᾱς *f.* [δίνη] (fig.) **whirling in the dark, dizziness** (ref. to intellectual perplexity) Pl.
σκοτοδῑνιάω *contr.vb.* **suffer from a sensation of whirling in darkness, feel dizzy** or **have a black-out** Ar. Pl.
σκοτόεις εσσα εν *adj.* (of a cloud, gloomy sky) **full of darkness, dark** Hes. AR.
σκοτο-μήνιος ον *adj.* [μήν²] (of night) **in the dark part of the month** (i.e. when there is no moon), **moonless** Od. Hes.*fr.*
σκότος ου *m.* —also **σκότος** εος (ους) *n.* **1 lack of light, dark, darkness** Od. Lyr. Hdt. Trag. Th. +; (of death, which takes away sight) Il. hHom. E.; (of the underworld) Pi.*fr.* Trag. Call.*epigr.*; (of the domain of evil spirits) NT.; (of the womb) A.
2 lack of sight, blindness S. E.; **black-out** (ref. to dizziness or unconsciousness) Theoc.
3 (fig.) **dark, darkness** (in ctxts. of concealment or secrecy) Pi. B. Trag. Pl. X. Aeschin.
4 lack of renown, obscurity Pi.
5 (in ctxts. of perception) **obscurity, uncertainty, cloudiness** Pl. X. D.; **blindness** (in the mind) D.; (w. moral connot.) NT.
6 gloom, joylessness Theoc.
7 (ref. to a person) perh. **shady one** (i.e. of dubious repute) Hippon. [or perh. *bastard*; cf. σκότιος 4]

σκοτόω *contr.vb.* **1 make dark, blind** —*eyes* S. || PASS. (of a person) **be in the dark** (mentally) Pl.; (of the mind) **be blinded** Pl.
2 || PASS. (of a person knocked unconscious, or suffering fr. vertigo) **black out** Pl. Plb.
σκοτώδης ες *adj.* **1** (of a room) **dark** Plu.; (of things) **dimly visible** (W.DAT. to the eyes) Pl.
2 (fig., of things) **dark** (to the mind), **obscure** Pl.
σκότωμα ατος *n.* (medic.) **black-out** Plb.
σκυβαλισμός οῦ *m.* [σκύβαλον *dung*] **contemptuous treatment** (of a person) Plb.
σκυδμαίνω *vb.* [reltd. σκύζομαι] | ep.inf. σκυδμαινέμεν | **be angry** —W.DAT. *w. someone* Il.
σκύζομαι *mid.vb.* **growl** or **show resentment**; (of gods and humans) **be angry** Il. Theoc. —W.DAT. *w. someone* Hom.; (of a lion) **be enraged** Theoc.
Σκύθαι ῶν *m.pl.* **Scythians** (inhabitants of a region N. of the Black Sea, freq. characterised as savage and uncivilised) Hes.*fr.* +
—**Σκύθης** ου *m.* | voc. Σκύθα | **1 Scythian man** (sts. appos.w. ἀνήρ), **Scythian** Thgn. Hdt. Pl. X. +; (sg. and pl., ref. to archers used as police at Athens) Ar. And. Aeschin. | see τοξότης
2 || MASC.FEM.ADJ. (of a people, place, iron, bloodshed) **relating to Scythia** or **the Scythians, Scythian** A. E.
—**Σκυθίς** ίδος *fem.adj.* | acc. Σκύθιν | (of a woman) **Scythian** Aeschin. Plu.
—**Σκύθαινα** ης *f.* **Scythian woman** Ar.
—**Σκυθίᾱ** ᾱς, Ion. **Σκυθίη** ης *f.* **Scythia** Hdt. Call. Plu.
—**Σκυθίηνδε** *Ion.adv.* **to Scythia** Call.
—**Σκυθικός** ή όν, Aeol. **Σκύθικος** ᾱ ον *adj.* **1** (of people, places, things) **of or relating to Scythia** or **the Scythians, Scythian** Hdt. Theoc. Plu. || FEM.SB. **Scythian territory, Scythia** Alc. Hdt. Pl. Plu.
2 (of weapons, clothes, behaviour) **in the Scythian style, Scythian** Alc. Anacr. A.(cj.) Plu.
—**Σκυθικῶς** *adv.* **in Scythian fashion** Plu.
—**Σκυθιστί** *adv.* **in Scythian language** Hdt.
σκυθίζομαι *pass.vb.* | pf.ptcpl. ἐσκυθισμένος | (of hair) **be treated in Scythian fashion, be cropped** or **shorn** (ref. to the practice of scalping enemies) E.
σκυθράζω *vb.* [reltd. σκυδμαίνω] **scowl angrily** (on seeing an ill omen) E.
σκυθρωπάζω *vb.* [σκυθρωπός] **look surly** or **sullen, scowl** Ar. X. Aeschin. D. Thphr. Men. +
σκυθρ-ωπός όν *adj.* [σκυθράζω, ὤψ] **1** (of persons) **with a surly** or **sullen look, grim-faced, scowling** E. Ar. Isoc. Pl. X. D. + || NEUT.SB. **sullenness** E.
2 (of the council of the Areopagus) **stern-faced** Aeschin. || NEUT.SB. **sternness** (in the exercise of authority) Plu.
3 (of eyes, old age) **sullen** A. E.; (of mental anxiety) Arist.(quot.)
4 (of omens, a day of fasting) **grim, gloomy** Plu.
5 (of actions) **harsh, unpleasant** Plu.
—**σκυθρωπῶς** *adv.* **sullenly** X.
σκυλακείᾱ ᾱς *f.* [σκυλακεύω] **puppyhood** Plu.
σκυλακεύω *vb.* [σκύλαξ] **cause to produce puppies, mate** —*bitches* X.
σκυλάκιον ου *n.* [dimin. σκύλαξ] **young puppy** Pl. X.
σκυλακο-κτόνος ον *adj.* [κτείνω] (of a boar's tusk) **dog-killing** Lyr.adesp.
σκυλακώδης ες *adj.* **like a puppy** || NEUT.SB. **puppy-like behaviour** X.

σκύλαξ ακος *m.f.* **1** young dog, **puppy** Od. Hes. Xenoph. Hdt. +; (w. no connot. of youth) **dog** E. Pl. +; (ref. to Cerberus) S.; (fig.) **pup** (ref. to a young dolphin) Lyr.adesp. **2 collar** (W.ADJ. *of iron*, for a prisoner's neck) Plb.

σκυλεύματα των *n.pl.* [σκυλεύω] things stripped from an enemy; **spoils** (ref. to arms) Th.; (ref. to valuable captured items used for ornament or dedicated to gods) E.

σκυλεύω *vb.* [σκῦλον] **1 despoil, strip** (usu. of weapons) —*a dead or fallen person* Hdt. E. Th. Ar. Pl. Arist. +; **strip** —*arms or sim.* (W.GEN. or PREP.PHR. *fr. someone*) Hdt. Lys. X. —W.DBL.ACC. *someone of arms* Hes.
2 despoil —*a city* Plb.; (fig.) —*a cunt* Hippon.

Σκύλλα, Ion. **Σκύλλη**, ης *f.* **Scylla** (mythol. monster, barking like a puppy, w. six heads and twelve feet, a threat to sailors) Od. A. E. Pl. X. +

σκύλλω *vb.* | pf.pass.ptcpl. ἐσκυλμένος | **1** || PASS. (of corpses) **be torn or skinned** —W.PREP.PHR. *by fish* A.
2 trouble, harass —*someone* NT. || PF.PASS.PTCPL.ADJ. (of persons) **harassed** NT.

σκυλοδεψέω *contr.vb.* [σκυλοδέψης] **tan hides** Ar.

σκυλο-δέψης ου, also **σκυλοδεψός** οῦ (Pl. D.) *m.* [σκύλος, δέψω] one who kneads (untanned) hide, **tanner** Ar. Pl. D. Thphr. Plu. [sts. wrongly written as σκῠτο-]

σκῦλον ου *n.* [perh.reltd. σκύλλω] **1** || PL. arms stripped from a slain enemy or valuable items captured in war (oft. in ctxts. of dedication to gods), **spoils** S. E. Th. +; (ref. to dedicated skulls) E.
2 (sg.) **spoil, booty** (ref. to captured horses) E.; (ref. to a lost sword, a consulship) Plu.; (ref. to a corpse) **prey** (W.DAT. for birds) E.

σκύλος εος *n.* [σκύλλω] animal skin, **hide** (of a lion, worn as a cloak) Call. Theoc.

σκύμνος ου *m.* (*also f.* E.) **1** young of a wild animal, **cub, whelp** E.; (of a lion) Il. Hdt. S. E. Ar.(quot. A.); (of a wolf, bear, fox) E. Call. Theoc. Plu.; **creature** (belonging to the sea) E.(cj.)
2 (ref. to a human child) **whelp** E.

σκύπφος *m.*: see σκύφος

Σκῦρος ου *f.* **Skyros** (island in the Aegean, E. of Euboea) Hom. hHom. Pi. S. E. Th. +
—**Σκύριος** ᾱ ον *adj.* of or relating to Skyros; (of a person) **Skyrian** Hdt.; (of goats) Pi.*fr.*; (of a love-affair) **on Skyros** Bion ||. MASC.PL.SB. men of Skyros Plu.
—**Σκυρόθεν** *adv.* (ref. to movt.) **from Skyros** Il. Pi.*fr.*

σκῠρωτός ή (dial. ᾱ́) όν *adj.* [σκῦρος *stone-chip*] (of a road) made with stone-chips, **gravelled** Pi.

σκυτάλη ης, dial. **σκυτάλᾱ** ᾱς *f.* **1** (at Sparta) stick around which a strip of writing material with a message was wrapped (in Plu., misinterpreted as a means of transmitting a secret message), **despatch-staff** Th. Ar. X. Plu.; material on which the message was written, **despatch-scroll** Plu.
2 (gener.) **despatch, message** Archil.
3 (personif., ref. to the bearer of an ode) **courier** (of the Muses) Pi.
4 prob. **stick** or **baton** Pl.
5 (at Rome) **stick, stave** (for use as a club) Plu.
6 a kind of snake (w. body of uniform thickness), **stick-snake** Plu.

σκυτάλιον *n.*: see under σκύταλον

σκυταλιοφορέω *contr.vb.* [σκυτάλιον, φέρω] (of Athenians imitating Spartan manners) **carry a little stick** or **baton** Ar.(cj.)

σκυταλίς ίδος *f.* [dimin. σκυτάλη] **stick** (used to tighten a noose round the neck of an animal) Hdt.

σκύταλον ου *n.* **club, cudgel** Hdt. Ar. X.; (of Herakles) Pi. Theoc.

—**σκυτάλιον** ου *n.* [dimin.] **little stick** or **baton** Ar.(dub., see σκυταλιοφορέω)

σκυτεύς έως *m.* [σκῦτος] **leather-worker** (sts. ref. to a shoemaker) Ar. Pl. X. Arist.

σκύτευσις εως *f.* [σκῠτεύω] **leather-working** (specif.ref. to shoemaking) Arist.

σκυτεύω *vb.* be a leather-worker X.

σκυτικός ή όν *adj.* related to leather-working || FEM.SB. craft of shoemaking Pl. Arist.

σκυτινος ή όν *adj.* [σκῦτος] (of shoes, clothing, equipment, or sim.) made of leather, **leather** Anacr. Hdt. Ar. X. Plb. Plu.

σκυτίον ου *n.* [dimin. σκῦτος] **bit of leather** (ref. to the phallus worn by comic actors) Ar.(dub.)

σκυτοδέψης, σκυτοδεψός *m.*: see σκυλοδέψης

σκυτόομαι *pass.contr.vb.* (of wooden practice swords) **be covered with leather** Plb.

σκῦτος εος (ους) *n.* **1** tanned hide, **leather** (usu. ref. to shoe-leather) Od. Ar. Pl. X. Arist.
2 leather lash, **whip** Ar. D. Plu.

σκυτοτομεῖον ου *n.* [σκυτοτόμος] **shoemaker's shop** Lys.

σκυτοτομέω *contr.vb.* cut shoe-leather, **be a shoemaker** Ar. Pl. Arist.; (tr.) **make** —*shoes* (*fr. leather*) Pl.

σκυτοτομία ᾱς *f.* **shoemaking** Pl.

σκυτοτομικός ή όν *adj.* of or relating to a shoemaker; (of a group, a person) **engaged in shoemaking** Ar. Pl.; (of the craft) **of shoemaking** Pl. Aeschin. || FEM.SB. craft of shoemaking Pl. Arist.

σκυτο-τόμος ου *m.* [τέμνω] **1** one who cuts leather, **leather-worker** Il. Pl. X.
2 (specif.) **shoemaker** Ar. Pl. Arist. Plu.

σκύφος ου *m.* | also neut.acc.sg. σκύφος | —also **σκύπφος** ου (Hes.*fr.* Anacr.) *m.* **1** deep cup or bowl (usu. assoc.w. rustics), **bowl, tankard** Od. Hes.*fr.* Lyr. E.; (used as a milking-pail) E.*Cyc.* Theoc.
2 (gener.) **cup** Arist. Plu.

—**σκύφιον** ου *n.* [dimin.] **cup** Stesich.

σκωληκό-βρωτος ον *adj.* [σκώληξ, βιβρώσκω] (of a person) **worm-eaten** NT.

σκώληξ ηκος *m.* **worm** Il.; (ref. to a creature that torments the damned) NT. || PL. larvae (of insects), **grubs** or **maggots** Ar. Plu.

σκῶλος ου *m.* [reltd. σκόλοψ] **1 stake** (w. a sharpened end) Il. Call.
2 thorn Ar. Call.

σκῶμμα ατος *n.* [σκώπτω] **jest, joke, gibe** Ar. Pl. X. Aeschin. D. Arist. +

—**σκωμμάτιον** ου *n.* [dimin.] **little joke** Ar.

σκωπτικός ή όν *adj.* (of persons) **witty, facetious** Plu. || NEUT.SB. propensity to make jokes Plu.

σκωπτόλης ου *m.* **joker, jeerer** X.

σκώπτω *vb.* | fut. σκώψομαι | aor. ἔσκωψα || PASS.: aor. ἐσκώφθην | **1 mock, jeer at** —*someone or sthg.* Ar. Pl. X. D. + —(w. εἰς + ACC. *for sthg.*) D. Plu.; (intr.) **jest, joke, jeer** Eleg.adesp. E.*Cyc.* Ar. Isoc. Pl. + —w. εἰς + ACC. *at someone or sthg.* Ar. Aeschin. Arist. Plu. || PASS. be mocked or jeered at Ar. Pl. X. +
2 address playfully, joke or **banter with** —*someone* Hdt.

σκῶρ σκατός *n.* **dung, shit** Ar.

σκωρ-αμίς ίδος *f.* [ἀμίς] **shit-pot** (ref. to a person) Ar.

σκώψ ωπός *m.* a kind of small owl, **little owl** Od. Theoc.

σμᾶμα *dial.n.*: see σμῆμα

σμᾶνος *dial.n.*: see σμῆνος

σμάομαι *mid.contr.vb.* [reltd. σμήχω] | Ion.3sg. σμᾶται | aor.ptcpl. σμησάμενος, dial. σμᾱσάμενος | **smear oneself**

σμάραγδος

(w. soap or unguents); **cleanse, soap** —*one's head, hair* Hdt. Call.

σμάραγδος ου *f.* [loanwd.] green jewel, **emerald** Pl. Plu.; (appos.w. λίθος) *emerald stone* Hdt.

σμαραγδο-χαίτᾱς ᾱ *dial.masc.adj.* [χαίτη] (of the sea) **emerald-tressed** Tim.

σμαραγέω *contr.vb.* **1** give out a loud noise; (of thunder, sea breaking on the shore, the earth during the Titanomachia) **crash** Il. Hes.
2 (of a meadow) **ring, resound** (w. cries of birds) Il.
3 (of Ares) perh. **raise a thunderous battle-cry** Call.
4 (of clods being broken apart) **rasp** AR.

σμαραγίζω *vb.* (of the earth, burning fr. a lightning-bolt) **crash, roar** Hes.

σμερδαλέος ᾱ (Ion. η) ον *adj.* (of beasts, monsters, parts of their bodies) **awe-inspiring, terrible, dread** Hom. AR.; (of weapons, armour) Hom.; (of the domain of Hades) Il.; (of Odysseus, emerging fr. the sea) Od.; (of battle-strife, physical strength) Hes. AR.; (of a cry, words) B. AR.; (of lightning) AR.; (of a city) Ar.(mock-ep.)
—**σμερδαλέον**, **σμερδαλέα** *neut.sg.pl.adv.* **terrifyingly, mightily, loudly** —*ref. to shouting, weapons clashing, or sim.* Hom. Hes. hHom. AR.

σμερδνός ή όν *adj.* (of the Gorgon's head, the jaws of Typhon) **fearsome, terrifying** Il. A.
—**σμερδνόν** *neut.adv.* **fearsomely** —*ref. to shouting, gazing* Il. hHom.

σμῆμα (also **σμῆγμα** Plu.), dial. **σμᾶμα**, ατος *n.* [σμάομαι, σμήχω] that which is smeared on the body (as a cleansing agent), **unguent** or **soap** Philox.Leuc. Theoc. Plu.

σμῆνος, dial. **σμᾶνος**, εος (ους) *n.* **1 beehive** Hes. Pl. X. Theoc. Plu.
2 swarm (of bees) A. Pl. X. AR. Plb.; (of wasps) Ar.; (of gods, ref. to clouds) Ar.; (fig., W.GEN. of pleasures, virtues, wisdom) Pl.

σμήρινθος *f.*: see μήρινθος

σμήχω *vb.* [reltd. σμάομαι] **wipe off** —*scurf left by sea-water* (W.PREP.PHR. *fr. one's head*) Od.

σμῑκρολογίᾱ *f.*, **σμῑκρολόγος** *m.*, **σμῑκρομέρης** *adj.*: see μῑκρο-

σμῑκρός *adj.*, **σμῑκρότης** *f.*: see μῑκρός, μῑκρότης

σμῖλαξ *f.*: see μῖλαξ

σμῑλεύματα των *n.pl.* [σμίλη] (fig.) **chisellings, chisel-shavings** (ref. to verbal quibbles of sophists) Ar.

σμίλη ης *f.* a kind of cutting tool, **knife** or **chisel** Pl. Call.; (used for incising letters on wood) Ar.; (used by leather-workers) Pl.

Σμινθεύς έως *m.* **Smintheus** (epith. of Apollo, assoc. by pop.etym. w. a town named Sminthe in the Troad, or w. Mysian σμίνθος *mouse*) Il.

σμινύη ης *f.* heavy tool used for digging, **mattock** Ar. Pl. X. Call.

σμῡγερός ά (Ion. ή) όν *adj.* [reltd. μογερός] **1** afflicted with pain and toil; (of Philoktetes, Pineus) **careworn, miserable** S.(cj.) AR.
2 (of the Chalybes) **painstaking, tireless** AR.
3 entailing pain and toil; (of a widow's fate) **painful, laborious** AR.
—**σμυγερῶς** *adv.* **painfully, with difficulty** S.(cj.) AR.

σμυρίζω *dial.vb.*: see μυρίζω

σμύρνα (also **ζμύρνα** Hyp.), Ion. **σμύρνη**, ης (dial. ᾱς) *f.* [loanwd., reltd. μύρρᾱ] gum of an Arabian tree, **myrrh** (used for embalming, as a salve for wounds, a perfumed unguent, and burnt as incense) Emp. Hdt. E. Ar. Hyp. +

Σμύρνα, Ion. **Σμύρνη**, ης *f.* **Smyrna** (city on W. coast of Asia Minor, mod. Izmir) hHom. Mimn. Hippon. Thgn. Hdt. +
—**Σμυρναῖος** ου *masc.adj.* (of a man) from Smyrna, **Smyrnaean** Plu. ‖ PL.SB. inhabitants of Smyrna, Smyrnaeans Callin. Pi.*fr.* Hdt. +

σμυρνίζομαι *pass.vb.* (of wine) **be flavoured with myrrh** NT.

σμύχω *vb.* (intr.) burn in an intense smouldering fire; (fig., of a person) **smoulder** —W.ACC. *in one's heart* (W.DAT. *w. the pain of love*) AR.; (of the pain of love) AR. ‖ PASS. (of a city) be set burning —W.DAT. *w. fire* Il.; (of Eros) smoulder Mosch.

σμῶδιξ ιγγος *f.* swollen bruise (caused by a blow), **weal** Il.

σμώχω *vb.* [reltd. σμήχω] (intr.) perh. **grind away** —W.DAT. *w. both jaws* (*ref. to eating vigorously*) Ar.

σοβαρός ά όν *adj.* [σοβέω] **1** perh., having an impressive or powerful effect (so as to inspire fear or awe); (of a wind) **powerful, blustering** Ar.; (of persons, their manner) **tempestuous** Ar. D. Men.; (of a song) **rumbustious** Ar.
2 (of persons, their behaviour) **haughty, proud** Plu.; (of a horse) **spirited** X.
3 (of speech, dress, or sim.) **impressive, pompous, showy** Men. Plu.
—**σοβαρόν** *neut.adv.* **insolently** —*ref. to laughing at someone* Theoc.
—**σοβαρῶς** *adv.* **impressively, awe-inspiringly** Ar. Plb. Plu.

σοβέω *contr.vb.* [reltd. σέβω] **1** perh., cause to shrink away in fear or reverence; (gener.) **scare away, shoo** —*birds* Ar. Men.; **keep off** —*flies* (W.PREP.PHR. *fr. a wound*) Thphr.; **clear off** —*dust* (*fr. a horse*) X.
2 strut, swagger D. Thphr. Plu.
3 ‖ PASS. (fig.) be agitated or excited (in pursuit of glory) Plu.

σόει (ep.3sg.impf.): see σεύω

σοί, σοι (dat.2sg.pers.pron.): see σύ

σοῖο (ep.masc.gen.sg.possessv.pron.adj.): see σός

σολοικίζω *vb.* [σόλοικος] **1 make mistakes** —W.DAT. *in the Scythian language* Hdt. —*in speech* (*so as to appear a barbarian*) D.
2 use language incorrectly, commit a solecism (in style or syntax) Arist.

σόλοικος ον *adj.* [assoc. by pop.etym. w. Σόλοι *Soli* (a town in Cilicia, whose inhabitants were alleged to speak bad Greek)] **1** incorrect in language; (of speech) **non-Greek, barbarian** Anacr. ‖ MASC.PL.SB. non-Greek speakers, barbarians Hippon.
2 (of persons, their actions) incorrect in behaviour, **ill-mannered** X. Arist. Plu. ‖ NEUT.SB. inappropriate behaviour Plu.

σόλος ου *m.* lump of iron (used for throwing, as a test of strength), **weight** Il.; (specif.) **discus** AR.

Σόλων ωνος *m.* **Solon** (Athenian politician and poet, 7th–6th C. BC) Sol. Hdt. +

σόος *Ion.adj.*: see σῶς

σορο-πηγός οῦ *m.* [σορός, πήγνῡμι] **coffin-maker** Ar.

σορός οῦ *f.* **1 cinerary urn** Il.
2 coffin Hdt. Ar. Aeschin. NT. Plu.

σός σή (dial. σά) σόν *possessv.pron.adj.* [σύ; cf. τεός] | ep.masc.gen.sg. σοῖο (Od.) | **1** of or belonging to you (sg.), **your** (oft. w.art. ὁ σός) Hom. +; (ref. to particular classes of persons, interests or concerns) ὁ σός *your husband* E.; (pl.) οἱ σοί *your people* (i.e. friends, followers, kin) Hdt. S. E.; (neut.sg.) τὸ σόν *your meaning, interest, decision* S.; (pl.) τὰ σά *your interests, affairs* Hdt. S. X.; (without art.) σά *your property* Od.
2 (w. force of an objective gen.) directed towards you (sg.) Hom. + • σὴ ποθή, σὸς πόθος *longing for you* Hom. • σὴ

προμηθία, ἡ σὴ πρόνοια concern, forethought for you S. E. • ἡ σὴ εὔνοια goodwill towards you Pl.
σοῦ[1], **σου** (gen.2sg.pers.pron.): see σύ
σοῦ[2] (mid.imperatv.): see σεύω
σουδάριον ου n. [Lat. sudarium] **towel, cloth** NT.
Σούνιον ου n. **Sounion** (southernmost headland of Attica, w. a temple of Poseidon) Od. Hdt. S. E. Th. +
—**Σουνιακός** ή όν adj. of or relating to Sounion; (of the headland) **Sounian** Hdt.
—**Σουνιεύς** έως m. man from Sounion, **Sounian** Pl. Aeschin.
—**Σουνιάρᾱτος** ον adj. [ἀράομαι] (epith. of Poseidon) **prayed to at Sounion** Ar.
—**Σουνιέρᾱκος** ον adj. [ἱέραξ] (com.epith. of a bird-god) **Hawk of Sounion** Ar.
σοῦνται (3pl.mid.): see σεύω
Σοῦσα ων n.pl. **Sousa** (city N. of the Persian Gulf, residence of Persian kings fr. Cyrus onwards) A. Hdt. Tim. X. +
—**Σούσιος** ου masc.adj. (of a man) **from Sousa** X.
—**Σουσίς** ίδος fem.adj. (of a woman) **from Sousa** X. ‖ SB. region of Sousa A.
—**Σουσιγενής** ές adj. [γένος, γίγνομαι] (of Darius I) **born in Sousa** A.
σούσθε, σούσθω (2pl. and 3sg.mid.imperatv.), **σοῦται** (3sg.mid.): see σεύω
σοφίᾱ ᾱς, Ion. **σοφίη** ης f. [σοφός] **1** practical cleverness or technical skill; **expertise, skill** (in handicrafts) Il. Stesich. Pi. Pl. +; (in music, poetry) hHom. Sapph. Sol. +; (in medicine, divination, other arts and activities) Pi. S. Pl. +
2 sound sense, **cleverness, intelligence** Sol. Thgn. + ‖ PL. (personif.) intellects, wits (ref. to members of an audience) Ar.
3 quality of intelligent thought or understanding, **wisdom** S. E. Pl. +; (ref. to speculative thought) Arist.; (personif., as a deity) **Wisdom** Lyr.adesp. E. Ar.
σοφίζομαι mid.vb. | aor. ἐσοφισάμην ‖ PASS.: aor.inf. σοφισθῆναι ‖ neut.impers.vbl.adj. σοφιστέον | **1** (of a poet) **practise one's skill** Thgn.; (of thinkers, sophists) Pl. X. Arist.
2 (usu.pejor.) act or speak subtly, **be smart, be tricky** E. Ar. Pl. D. Arist. +
3 (tr.) devise (w.ACC. sthg.) **cleverly** or **skilfully** Hdt. Ar. Pl. X. Arist. Plu. ‖ PASS. (of a stratagem) be devised cleverly Hdt. S.
—**σεσοφισμένος** η ον pf.mid.pass.ptcpl.adj. (of Muses) **skilled** Ibyc.; (of a person, W.GEN. in seamanship) Hes.
—**σεσοφισμένως** pf.mid.pass.ptcpl.adv. **with subtlety** or **sophistication** —ref. to using language X.
σόφισμα ατος n. **1 invention, device** A. Pi. Ar. Pl.
2 (usu.pejor.) **artifice, stratagem, trick** Hdt. Trag. Th. Lys. Ar. +
3 (ref. to a person) **model of cleverness** Ar.
4 captious argument, quibble, sophism Pl. D. Plu.
σοφιστεύω vb. [σοφιστής] (of rhetoricians) **give lectures, teach rhetoric** Plu.
σοφιστής οῦ m. **1** master of a craft, **expert** (ref. to a musician or poet) Pi. E.; (ref. to a diviner) Hdt.; (ref. to the creator of the universe) Pl.
2 inventor, deviser (W.GEN. of troubles) E.
3 wise man, teacher (ref. to Solon, Pythagoras, the Seven Sages) Hdt. Isoc.
4 (gener.) clever person, **expert** (w. hint of sense 5) A. E.
5 (fr. late 5th C. BC) **sophist** (freq. w.pejor.connot., ref. to an expert who teaches undesirable or superfluous skills for a fee) Th. Att.orats. Pl. X. +; (gener.) **quack, charlatan** Ar. D. Plu.
6 teacher of rhetoric or **declaimer** Plu.
—**σοφίστρια** ᾱς f. (iron., ref. to the Hydra) **professoress** Pl.

σοφιστικός ή όν adj. **1** of or relating to a sophist; (of a life, the class or category of persons) **sophistic** Pl.; (of the art or profession) Pl. Arist. ‖ FEM.SB. art of sophistry Pl. Arist.
2 (pejor.) with the characteristics of a sophist; (of a person, opp. σοφός) **sophistical** Pl. X.; (of an argument, mode of arguing) Arist.
3 (of literary rivalry) **quibbling, niggling** Plu.
4 (of stratagems) **contrived, deceptive** Plu.
5 (of a route) **over-complicated** Plu.
—**σοφιστικῶς** adv. **1** in the manner of a sophist, **sophistically** —ref. to arguing Pl. Arist. —ref. to declaiming Plu.
2 cunningly —ref. to deceiving Plu.
Σοφοκλῆς, also **Σοφοκλέης** (Ar.), έους m. | voc. Σοφόκλεις, acc. Σοφοκλέα, dat. Σοφοκλεῖ | **Sophocles** (tragic poet, 490s–406 BC) Ar. Pl. D. Arist. Plu.
—**Σοφόκλειος** ᾱ ον adj. of or relating to Sophocles; (of a verse, a city described by him) **Sophoclean** Plu.
σοφός ή (dial. ᾱ́) όν adj. **1** skilled in an art or craft; (of a horseman, his technique) **clever, skilful, expert** Alcm. Anacr.; (of a charioteer) Pi.; (of a helmsman) Archil. A. B.; (of an assayer) Thgn.; (of musicians, poets) Pi. E. Ar.; (of an actor) Ar.; (of a prophet, an augur) Trag.; (of hunting dogs) X.
2 (gener., of persons) **skilled, expert** Pi. E. Pl. Arist.; (W.GEN. in sthg.) A. Pl.; (W.INF. at doing sthg.) E. Pl.
3 (of persons, their minds, judgements, words, actions, inventions) showing sound sense, **sensible, wise** Thgn. Simon. Pi. Trag. +
4 (of persons) endowed with intelligent thought or understanding, **clever, learned, wise** Pl. X. +; (of Athena) Telest.
5 (of a musical instrument, ref. to the aulos) **clever** Telest.
6 (pejor., of persons, their judgements, actions, or sim.) **too clever, cunning** S. E. Ar. Pl. D. ‖ NEUT.SB. cleverness (opp. σοφία wisdom) E.
—**σοφῶς** adv. | compar. σοφώτερον, superl. σοφώτατα | **cleverly, sensibly, wisely, subtly** Hdt. E. Ar. +
σπαδίζω vb. [σπάω; reltd. σπάδιξ torn-off branch] | aor.ptcpl. σπαδίξας | **strip off, flay** —someone's skin Hdt.
σπάδων ωνος m. | acc. σπάδοντα (Plu.) | **eunuch** Plb. Plu.
σπαθάω contr.vb. [σπάθη] **1** (intr.) use a batten to pack the threads of the weft together, **weave close** Ar.; (w.connot. of extravagance, as using more wool) Ar.; (tr., fig.) **squander** —money Plu.
2 ‖ PASS. (fig., of a report) be packed with lies D.
σπάθη ης f. **1** broad wooden slat or blade (used to pack together the threads of the weft on the loom), **batten** A. Pl.
2 broad blade (of a sword), **sword-blade** Alc.; **sword** Thphr. Men.
3 stem (of a palm-frond) Hdt.
σπαίρω vb. | reltd. ἀσπαίρω | (of persons dying or threatened w. death) **gasp, writhe** AR. Plb.; (of a wounded snake's tail) **thrash** AR.(cj., for σκαίρω)
σπάκα acc.f. [said to be Median for κύνα] **bitch** Hdt.
σπανίζω vb. [σπάνις] | fut. σπανιῶ | aor. ἐσπάνισα ‖ pf.pass. ἐσπάνισμαι | **1** (of things) **be rare, be scarce** Pi. Ar. Plu.
2 (of persons) **be in want** or **need** —W.GEN. of someone or sthg. A. Hdt. E. Th. Ar. + ‖ PASS. be in want or destitute E. —W.GEN. of everything X. ‖ PF.PASS. have been deprived, be short —W.GEN. of helpers, friends A. E.
σπάνιος ᾱ ον (also ος ον) adj. **1** scarce in number; (of persons, animals or things) **scarce, scanty, rare** Hdt. E. Th. Isoc. Pl. +; (w.sg. nouns, of a desirable possession or sim.) E. Th. Isoc. +

σπανιότης

2 scanty in amount; (of precious metal, water, fodder, provisions) **in short supply, scarce** Lyr.adesp. Hdt. Th. Pl. X.; (of a Muse, ref. to the music of the seven-stringed lyre) **scanty, meagre** (compared w. that of the eleven-stringed lyre) Ion
3 (of a person) **keeping oneself scarce** (through limited accessibility or cooperation) E. Pl. X. Plu.
4 scarce in occurrence; (quasi-advbl., of persons or things) **infrequent, at rare intervals** Hdt. Pl. ‖ NEUT.IMPERS. (w. ἐστί, sts. understd.) it is rare —W.INF. *to do sthg.* Th. Isoc. X. +
—**σπάνιον** neut.adv. **rarely** Plu.
—**σπανίως** adv. | compar. σπανιώτερον | **rarely** Th. X. Plb. Plu.
σπανιότης ητος f. **scarcity** (W.GEN. of land) Isoc.
σπάνις εως f. **1 scarcity, shortage** (W.GEN. of provisions, persons, other resources) Hdt. S. E. Th. Att.orats. +
2 (specif.) **shortage of food** Plb. Plu.
3 (in neg.phr.) infrequent occurrence, **rarity** (W.INF. *to have a bad wife*) E.
σπανιστός ή όν adj. [σπανίζω] (of gifts) **scanty** (i.e. given scantily) S.
σπανοσῑτίᾱ ᾱς f. [σπάνις, σῖτος] **shortage of grain** X.
σπάραγμα ατος n. [σπαράσσω] **1 tearing** (W.GEN. of hair, in grief) E.
2 tearing apart, mangling (of animals, by Bacchants) E.
3 product of tearing; **piece torn away** (W.GEN. fr. a cliff) Plu.
4 app. **mangled body** S.
σπαραγμός οῦ m. **1 rending, tearing** (of cheeks or hair, in grief) E.
2 tearing apart, mangling (of animals, a person, by Bacchants) E.
3 tearing off (of garlands, armour) E. Plu.; **tearing away** (of a bridge's supports) Plu.
4 (medic.) **convulsion** S. Plu.
σπαράσσω, Att. **σπαράττω** vb. | fut. σπαράξω | aor. ἐσπάραξα | **1 tear, rend** —*one's hair, cheeks, breasts* (in grief) E.(mid.) Ar. Plu. —*one's flesh* (W.PREP.PHR. *fr. the bones*) E. —*one's intestines* (during disembowelling) Plu.
2 (fig., of a commander, compared to a carrion-bird) **tear to pieces, maul** —*the remnants of wars* Plu. ‖ PASS. (of a person or corpse) **be mauled** —W.PREP.PHR. *by a carnivorous animal or bird* Plu.
3 (of Zeus) **tear apart, shatter** —*a rocky ravine* (W.DAT. *w. thunder and lightning*) A.
4 ‖ PASS. (of a person) app., **be clawed** —W.GEN. *by the hair* E.(dub.)
5 (fig., of persons) **tear apart, maul** (w. verbal aggression) —*persons, their behaviour* Ar. Pl. D. Plu. ‖ PASS. **be mauled** —W.PREP.PHR. *by false accusers* Plu.
6 (of an evil spirit) **convulse** —*someone* NT.
σπαργανάω contr.vb.: see σπαργανόω
σπαργανίζω vb. [σπάργανον] | only aor.ptcpl. σπαργανίσας | **wrap** (W.ACC. a stone) **in swaddling-clothes** Hes.
σπαργανιώτης ου m. **baby in swaddling-clothes** hHom.
σπάργανον ου n. [σπάργω] **1 swaddling-cloth** (for wrapping a baby in) hHom. Pi. ‖ PL. **swaddling-clothes, baby clothes** hHom. A. Pi. E. Men. Plu.; (meton.) **baby in swaddling-clothes** S.*Ichn.*; **babyhood** S.
2 ‖ PL. **tattered rags** (of a beggar) Ar.
σπαργανόω, also **σπαργανάω** (Pl.) contr.vb. **wrap** (W.ACC. a baby) **in swaddling-clothes** E. Pl. NT. Plu. ‖ PASS. (of a baby) **be wrapped in swaddling-clothes** NT.
σπαργάω contr.vb. **1** (of a breast, an udder) **swell, be full to bursting** (w. milk) E.; (of a nursing mother) Pl.; (of one who is pregnant) **swell with child** Pl.

2 (fig.) **swell** (w. sexual passion) Pl.; (w. arrogance) Pl. Plu.; (w. eagerness) Plu.
σπάργω vb. | only ep.3pl.aor. σπάρξαν | **wrap** (W.ACC. a baby) **in swaddling-clothes** hHom.
σπαρείς (aor.pass.ptcpl.): see σπείρω
σπαρνός ή όν adj. [σπείρω] **1** (of cloaks) app. **sparse, scarce** Hes.*fr.*
2 (of ships' walkways) perh. **narrow** A.
3 (of an event) **rare** Call.
Σπάρτη ης, dial. **Σπάρτᾱ** ᾱς f. **Sparta** (chief city of the Peloponnese and capital of Laconia) Hom. + | see also Λακεδαίμων
—**Σπάρτηθεν** adv. **from Sparta** Od. AR.
—**Σπάρτηνδε** adv. **to Sparta** Od.
Σπαρτιᾱ́της ου, Ion. **Σπαρτιήτης** εω m. **citizen of Sparta, Spartiate, Spartan** Tyrt. Hdt. E. +
—**Σπαρτιᾶτις** ιδος f. **Spartan woman** E. ‖ ADJ. (of a woman, the land) Spartan E.
—**Σπαρτιητικός** ή όν Ion.adj. **of or belonging to Spartiates**; (of troops, behaviour) **Spartan** Hdt.
σπάρτον ου n. [σπάρτος] **rope, cord, cable** (of esparto grass) Il. Hdt. Th. Pl. X. Call.
—**σπαρτίον** ου n. [dimin.] **little cord** Ar.
σπαρτός ή όν (also ός όν E.) adj. [σπείρω] **1 created by sowing** (of seeds) ‖ MASC. or NEUT.PL.SB. **living beings** A.
2 (of Ekhion, the men of the Theban race in general) **sown** (i.e. created by the sowing of a dragon's teeth by Kadmos at Thebes, fr. which the race sprang) Trag. Pl. ‖ MASC.PL.SB. **Sown Men** (ref. to the original race or their descendants, the Thebans) A. Pi. E.
3 belonging to the race of Sown Men; (of a spear) **Theban** E.
σπάρτος ου m.f. **esparto grass** Pl. X.
σπάσμα ατος n. [σπάω] **1** (medic.) **wrench** (of muscles in a joint), **sprain** Pl. D. Plu.
2 that which is torn off, **shred, fragment** (of sthg.) Plu.
3 sword-blade drawn from a scabbard, **unsheathed blade** Plu.
σπασμός οῦ m. **1** (medic.) **spasm, convulsion** Hdt. S. Th. Plu.; (W.GEN. of physical torment) S.
2 erection of the penis, **hard-on** Ar.
3 convulsion (W.GEN. of the sea, accompanying an earthquake) Plu.
σπαταλάω contr.vb. **live luxuriously** or **indulgently** Plb.
σπατίλη ης f. **excrement** (caused by diarrhoea) Ar.
σπάω contr.vb. | aor. ἔσπασα, ep. σπάσα ‖ MID.: aor. ἐσπασάμην, ep. σπασάμην, also σπασσάμην ‖ PASS.: aor. ἐσπάσθην | **1 pull** (out of a scabbard), **draw** —*a sword* E.; (mid.) Hom. Hdt. Ar. X. + ‖ PASS. (of a sword) **be drawn** X. Plu.
2 ‖ MID. **draw, pull** —*a spear* (w. ἐκ + GEN. *out of a body, hand, spear-case*) Il. —*one's hand* (*out of another's*) Od. ‖ PASS. (of a spear) **be pulled out** (of a body) Il.
3 draw —*a lot* (fr. a helmet) A.
4 ‖ MID. **pull to oneself, grasp** —*brushwood and twigs* Od. —*a plough* Pi.
5 pull on, tug —*a rope* Hdt. —*a horse's bit* Pl. —*a horse, its mouth* (W.DAT. *w. a bit*) X. —*someone's elbow* AR.; (intr.) **pull** (on a rope) Ar.
6 (w. stronger connot. of force or violence) **pull, drag** —*someone or sthg.* (W.PREP.PHR. *fr. someone or sthg.*) E. Pl.; **pull up, uproot** —*an olive tree* Theoc.; (of persuasion, passions) **pull, tug** —*a person* S. Pl. ‖ PASS. (of a person) **be dragged away** E.
7 (of an angler, his line) **pull up, catch** —*sthg.* Ar.

8 pull at, pluck —*foliage* hHom. —*one's hair, a tuft of wool (fr. a sheep or cloak)* S. Plu.; (of animals) **pluck at, tear** —*a corpse* S.; (of birds) —*each other (w. talons)* S.
9 (medic.) **wrench, sprain, put out of joint** —*one's leg* Plu. ‖ PASS. suffer a sprain in, have put out of joint —W.INTERN.ACC. *one's thigh, feet* Hdt. E.*Cyc.*
10 ‖ PASS. (medic.) be pulled about, be convulsed S.
11 draw in through the mouth, **suck in** —*a clot of blood* A. —*air* Men.; **suck on** —*a breast* Call.; **quaff, drain** —*a draught of wine, a cup* E.*Cyc.* Men.

σπεῖο (ep.aor.2 mid.imperatv.): see ἕπομαι
σπεῖος *ep.n.*: see σπέος
σπεῖρα ᾱς (Ion. ης) *f.* **1 rope, cable** (of a ship) Od.(v.l. σπεῖρον)
2 (usu.pl.) **coil** (of a serpent) S.*fr.* E. AR. Theoc.
3 ‖ PL. **coils, mesh** (of a fishing-net) S.
4 ‖ PL. **straps** (coiled about a boxer's fist) Theoc.
5 (in the Macedonian army) **battalion** (of prob. 256 men) Plb.; (in the Roman army) **maniple** Plb.; **cohort** NT. Plu.
σπειράματα των *n.pl.* **coils** (W.GEN. of a viper) A.
σπειρηδόν *adv.* [σπεῖρα 5] **in battalions** Plb.
σπεῖρον ου *n.* [reltd. σπεῖρα] **1 piece of cloth that envelops; shroud** (for a corpse) Od. ‖ PL. **cloth wraps** (as a rudimentary kind of clothing) Od.
2 sail (of a ship) Od. | see also σπεῖρα 1
—**σπειρία** ων *n.pl.* [dimin.] **light clothes** (worn by soldiers in summer) X.(dub.) | see σείριος 3
σπειρόω *contr.vb.* | only ep.3sg.aor. σπείρωσε | **envelop in cloths, swaddle** —*a baby* Call.
σπείρω *vb.* | iteratv.impf. σπείρεσκον | fut. σπερῶ | aor. ἔσπειρα | pf. ἔσπαρκα ‖ PASS.: aor. ἐσπάρην, ptcpl. σπαρείς | pf. ἔσπαρμαι | **1 scatter on or deposit in the ground, sow** —*seeds or sim.* Hes. Hdt. +; (mid.) AR.; (act., intr.) Hes. Ar. X.; (fig.) —*words (in a soul)* Pl. ‖ PASS. (of seeds or sim.) be sown Ar. Pl. +
2 produce by sowing, sow —*grain, other edible products* Hdt. E. X.; (of Kadmos) —*a crop (of men, fr. a dragon's teeth)* E. ‖ PASS. (of plants) be sown Hdt.
3 strew with seeds, sow —*ground, fields, or sim.* Hes. Hdt. S. E. + —*the sea (provbl. for futile labour)* Thgn. ‖ PASS. (of ground) be sown Hdt. Ar. X. +
4 (of a father) **sow** —*a mother's field or furrow (i.e. womb)* A. E. —*a marriage bed (i.e. wife)* E.
5 produce by sowing seed, beget, sire, father —*a child* S. E. —*a race* E.; (intr.) Pl. ‖ PASS. (of a child) be begotten, be fathered S. E. Pl.; (fig., of a soul) Pl.
6 (fig.) **create or spread by sowing**; (of Aphrodite) **sow** —*desire* E.; (of a poet) —*splendour* (W.DAT. *in an island*) Pi. —*brand-new ideas* Ar.
7 scatter like seed, scatter —*gold and silver* (W.PREP.PHR. *fr. a city wall*) Hdt.; **sprinkle** —*water* (W.PREP.PHR. *fr. a vessel*) E.; **spread** —*a flame* Lyr.adesp. —*a tale* A.*satyr.fr.* S. ‖ PASS. (of arrows) be scattered —W.DAT. *on the ground* E.; (of a report) be disseminated or spread far and wide Ar.(quot. E.) X.
8 (of war) **disperse, separate** —*people (fr. each other)* Men. ‖ PASS. (of people, troops) be scattered or dispersed Th. Pl. X. Plu.
9 (intr.) **sow** (assoc.w. θερίζειν *reap*, in fig.ctxts., usu. of benefiting fr. one's own work) Hes.*fr.* Ar. Pl. NT.

σπένδω *vb.* | iteratv.impf. σπένδεσκον | aor. ἔσπεισα, ep. σπεῖσα, ep.3sg.iteratv. σπείσασκε ‖ MID.: aor. ἐσπεισάμην | pf. ἔσπεισμαι ‖ PASS.: aor. ἐσπείσθην |
1 pour out a drink-offering, make a libation (oft. W.DAT. to a god or gods) Hom. + —W.DAT. *w. water* Od.; (fig., of a poet) —W.PREP.PHR. *over Aigina* (W.DAT. *w. songs*) Pi.
2 (tr.) **pour out, make a libation of** —*wine, a cup of wine* Hom. hHom. Thgn. —*a drink-offering* S. E. Ar. —*an offering to the dead or the underworld gods* E. ‖ PASS. (of Dionysus, meton. for wine) be poured out as an offering E.
3 pour, sprinkle —*goat's urine (as a medical cure)* Hdt.
4 ‖ MID. **pour libations one with another**; (intr., of combatants) **agree to a truce, make peace** (oft. W.DAT. or πρός + ACC. w. someone) Hdt. E. Th.(also act.) Ar. +; **agree to** —W.COGN.ACC. *a truce* Th.; **pledge** —W.FUT.INF. *to abide by a truce* Th.; (fig.) **cease fighting against, be reconciled to** —W.DAT. *events, oracles* E.
5 ‖ MID. **give or gain permission under truce** —W.INF. *to do sthg.* Th.
6 ‖ MID. **give safe conduct under truce** X. —W.DAT. *to an embassy, a herald* X. Aeschin.
7 ‖ MID. (tr.) **achieve by truce** —*peace* Hdt. —*a retreat, recovery of the dead, a day to recover the dead* Th.; (of a husband and wife) **agree to end** —*a dispute* E. ‖ PASS. (of a truce) be agreed Th. Plu.

σπέος, also **σπεῖος**, ους *ep.n.* [app.reltd. σπήλαιον] | dat.sg. σπῆι, pl. σπέεσσι, σπήεσσι | **cave, cavern, grotto** Hom. Hes. hHom. Call. AR.
σπέρμα ατος *n.* [σπείρω] **1 that which is sown, seed** (of plants) Hes. +; **sowing** Hes.
2 generative seed (of gods and humans), **semen, sperm** A. Pi. Hdt. E. +
3 parentage, lineage Pi. Trag. X.
4 offspring, race Trag. NT.; **child** Pi. Trag. Th.(oracle); **breed** (of seers, demagogues, jurors) E. Ar.
5 (fig.) **origin, germ, seed** (of fire, flame) Od. Pi.; (of salvation, prosperity) A. Pi.; (of troubles, an evil person) D.; (of a feud, ill conduct) Plu.
σπερμ-αγοραιο-ληκιθο-λαχανοπώλιδες ων *f.pl.* [ἀγοραῖος, λέκιθος, λαχανόπωλις] **market-breed of porridge-and-vegetable-saleswomen** Ar.
σπερμαίνω *vb.* (of a man) **produce by sowing seed, beget, father** —*offspring* Hes. Call.
σπερμολογίᾱ ᾱς *f.* [σπερμολόγος 2] **gathering of germs of ideas at random** (w.connot. of recycling them for gain or to make trouble); **gossip, tittle-tattle** (of sailors) Plu.
σπερμο-λόγος ον *adj.* [λέγω] **1** (of birds) **seed-gathering** Plu. ‖ MASC.SB. **seed-picker** (ref. to a type of bird, such as a jackdaw or starling) Ar.
2 ‖ MASC.SB. (fig.) **one who picks up seeds or scraps of food, scrounger** D.; **scrapmonger or idle gossiper** NT.
σπερχνός ή όν *adj.* [σπέρχω] (of a messenger's report) **hasty, hurried** A.
—**σπερχνόν** *neut.adv.* **furiously** —*ref. to being angry* Hes.
σπέρχω *vb.* | only pres. and impf., and aor.pass.ptcpl. σπερχθείς | **1** (intr., of gusts of wind) **rush furiously** Hom. hHom.
2 ‖ MID.PASS. (of a person) **make eager haste, hurry** Hom. E. AR. Theoc. —W.INF. *to do sthg.* Il. Parm. AR.; (of a ship) **speed on** Od. AR.
3 ‖ MID.PASS. **be of hasty temper, be angry** Il. Hdt. E. Call. —W.DAT. *w. someone* Hdt. Call. ‖ AOR.PASS.PTCPL. **stung to anger** Pi. Hdt.
σπερῶ (fut.): see σπείρω
σπέσθαι (aor.2 mid.inf.), **σπέσθω** (ep.3sg.aor.2 mid.imperatv.): see ἕπομαι
σπεύδω *vb.* | ep.inf. σπευδέμεν | fut. σπεύσω, also mid. σπεύσομαι (Il.) | aor. ἔσπευσα, ep. σπεῦσα |
1 perform with haste or eagerness, press on with —*an activity* Hom. Hdt. —*war* E.; **hasten on** —*a marriage* Od. Hdt. —*death* E.

σπευσίδωρος

2 strive to achieve (for oneself), **be eager for, pursue** —*wealth, nothing to excess* Sol. Thgn. —*immortality, excellence* Pi. —*a marriage* Hdt. —*bravery, pleasures* E. —*political leadership* Th.; (of Artemis) —*a sacrifice* A.(mid.) ‖ PASS. (of a goal) be pursued Hdt.
3 strive to accomplish, **pursue, urge on, promote** —*an interest, ambition, course of action* Hdt. Trag. +
4 (intr.) **press on, hasten** Hom. + —W.INF. *to do sthg.* Hes. Pi. Trag. X.; **hasten to ensure** —W.ACC. + INF. *that someone does sthg.* S.
5 (intr.) exert oneself (physically or mentally), **strive hard** Il. +; **be eager** —W.PREP.PHR. *for some activity or acquisition* Il. + —W.INF. *to do sthg.* Hes. A.(mid., dub.) Hdt. S. E. + —W.ACC. + INF. or FINAL CL. *that sthg. shd. happen* A. Hdt. Ar. Pl. +; (of bees) **be busy** Hes.

σπευσί-δωρος ον adj. [δῶρον] (of Prometheus) **eager to provide gifts** (W.DAT. to mortals) A.*satyr.fr.*

σπευστικός ή όν adj. (of a person) of the hurrying kind, **prone to hurry** Arist.

σπῆι, σπήεσσι (dat.sg.pl.): see σπέος

σπήλαιον ου n. [app.reltd. σπέος] **cave, cavern** Pl. NT. Plu.; (fig.) **den** (W.GEN. of robbers) NT.

σπηλαιώδης ες adj. (of an underground dwelling) **cave-like, cavernous** Pl.

σπῆλυγξ υγγος f. **cave** AR. Theoc.

σπιδέος gen.neut.adj. [app. fr. unattested nom. σπιδής or σπιδύς] (of a plain) perh. **wide** or **vast** Il.

σπιθαμή ῆς f. distance between the tips of thumb and little finger when the hand is fully extended (as a unit of measurement, about 20cm), **span** Hdt. Pl. Arist. Plu.

σπιθαμιαῖος ᾱ ον adj. (of an object) **measuring a span** Arist. Plb.

σπιλάδες ων f.pl. ‖ dat. σπιλάσι, ep. σπιλάδεσσι ‖ **rocks** (in or projecting into the sea) Od. Call. AR. Plb.; (ref. to the Πλαγκταί *Wandering Rocks*) AR.; (in a garden, w. a stream issuing fr. them) Theoc.*epigr.* ‖ SG. σπιλάς (appos.w. πέτρῃ) *rugged rock* (*in the sea*) AR.; **stone** S.(dub.)

σπιλώδης ες adj. (of a hill) **rocky** Plb.(dub., cj. σπιλαδώδης)

σπινθαρίς ίδος f. [σπινθήρ] **spark** (fr. a comet or meteor) hHom.

σπινθάρυξ υγος f. **spark** (W.GEN. of fire) AR.

σπινθήρ ῆρος m. **1 spark** (fr. a comet or meteor) Il.; (of fire) Ar.
2 (fig.) **spark, flashpoint** (ref. to a circumstance which ignites a war) Ar. Plb.

σπίνος ου m. perh. **chaffinch** Ar.

σπλαγχνεύω vb. [σπλάγχνον] (of a participant at a sacrifice) **eat the entrails** Ar.

σπλαγχνίζομαι pass.vb. ‖ aor. ἐσπλαγχνίσθην ‖ **have sympathy, feel pity** NT.

σπλάγχνον ου n. [reltd. σπλήν] **1** ‖ PL. internal organs of a sacrificial animal; **innards, offal** (eaten by participants at a sacrifice) Hom. Hdt. Ar.; (inspected in divination) A. E. Aeschin. Plb. Plu.; (gener.) **sacrificial feast** Ar.
2 (collectv.sg., ref. to human organs) **lungs** or **guts** A.; **spleen** Pl. Plu. ‖ PL. **innards** Hdt. E.*Cyc.* Ar. NT. Plu.
3 womb A. ‖ PL. **womb** Pi. AR.; **loins** (of a father) S.
4 (fig., sg. and pl.) inner organs as the seat of emotions; **heart, guts** (as the seat of anxiety) A.; (of impetuousness or violence) A. E.; (of anger) E. Ar. AR.; (of pity) S. NT.; (of love) Theoc. Mosch.; (of eager enthusiasm) Philox.Leuc.; (ref. to one's innermost nature or character) **heart** E.

σπλεκόω contr.vb. [perh. fr. phr. ἐς πλέκος] perh., get into a sexual embrace; **have a fuck** Ar.

σπλήν ηνός m. [reltd. σπλάγχνον] **1 spleen** (of animals or humans) Hdt. Pl. Men. Plu.
2 perh. (fig.) **anger, annoyance** Ar.

σπληνιάω contr.vb. suffer from a disorder of the spleen or an associated ill-humour, **be splenetic** Plu.

σπογγιά ᾶς f. [σπόγγος] **sponge** (for wiping and cleaning) Ar. Aeschin. Plu.

σπογγίζω vb. ‖ fut. σπογγιῶ ‖ **sponge down** —*sthg.* Ar. D.

σπογγίον ου n. [dimin. σπόγγος] **little sponge** (used as a medicine-bottle stopper) Ar.

σπογγιστικός ή όν adj. [σπογγίζω] of or related to sponging ‖ FEM.SB. **art of using a sponge** Pl.

σπόγγος ου m. **sponge** (for wiping and cleaning) Hom. A. Ar. Pl. NT.

σποδέω contr.vb. [σποδός] **1 crush to ashes** or **powder; crush, crunch** (w. the teeth) —*food* Ar.
2 pound, batter —*a person, his flanks* Ar.; (of a floating corpse) —*an island* A.(cj.) ‖ MID. **smash** —*one's head* (W.PREP.PHR. *against rocks*) E. ‖ PASS. (of a fleet) be pounded (by stormy weather) A.; (of a person) —W.DAT. *by a hail of missiles* E.
3 (fig.) **fuck hard, bang** —*a woman* Ar. ‖ PASS. (of a man or woman) be banged Ar.

σποδιά ᾶς, Ion. **σποδιή** ῆς f. **1** smouldering ashes, **ashes, embers** Od. E.*Cyc.*
2 ash (used to blacken the skin) Call.
3 human ashes, **ashes, dust** Call.*epigr.*

σποδίζω vb. ‖ fut. σποδιῶ ‖ aor.imperatv. σπόδισον ‖ **roast on ashes, roast, toast** —*berries and nuts* Pl.; (fig., of Zeus) —*a person* (W.DAT. *w. his lightning-bolt*) Ar.

σποδός οῦ f. **1 ashes, embers** (of burnt wood) Od. hHom. Hdt. Theoc.; (of a burnt city) A.; (of an altar-fire) Hdt. S.
2 ashes (sprinkled over the head or body by mourners) E. NT.
3 human ashes, **ashes, dust** Trag.
4 dust (of the earth) Hdt.

σποίμην (ep.aor.2 mid.opt.): see ἕπομαι

σπόλα Aeol.f.: see στολή

σπολάς άδος f. sleeveless leather jacket, **jerkin** (worn by a slave) Ar.; (worn by soldiers) X.

σπόμενος (ep.aor.2 mid.ptcpl.): see ἕπομαι

σπονδ-αρχίη ης Ion.f. [σπονδή, ἄρχω] **right to pour the first libation** (claimed by Spartan kings) Hdt.

σπονδεῖος ᾱ ον adj. associated with libations ‖ NEUT.SB. **libation-cup, chalice** Plu.

σπονδή ῆς f. [σπένδω] **1 drink-offering, libation** (usu. of wine) Hes. + [The offering was made before wine was drunk, and to accompany prayers and sacrifices.]
2 ‖ PL. libations made by two or more parties (to solemnise an agreement); **agreements, contracts** (made by allies) Il.; (collectv.) **treaty, truce** (betw. combatants) Il. Hdt. +; (W.GEN. or πρός + ACC. w. someone) Th. X.; (ref. to a sacred truce during the Panhellenic games or Eleusinian Mysteries) Th. Aeschin.

σπονδο-φόρος ου m. [φέρω] one who brings a truce, **truce-bearer** (ref. to an official who proclaimed a temporary peace during the games or Mysteries) Pi. Aeschin.; (ref. to the bearer of a private peace treaty) Ar.

σπορά ᾶς f. [σπείρω] **1 product of sowing, crop** E.
2 place of sowing, sowing-place (of a dragon's teeth at Thebes) S.
3 time of sowing, seed-time (meton., ref. to one year in a chronological sequence) E.
4 sowing of human seed, **procreation** (of offspring) Pl. Men.

5 origin, **lineage** A.(dub.) S. | see σπόρος 5
6 (concr.) offspring, **child** S. E.
7 (collectv., W.ADJ. *female*) **sex** E.

σποράδην *adv.* [σποράδες] 1 in a scattered condition or manner, **here and there** —*ref. to living* (*i.e. not in communities*) Isoc. Pl. —*ref. to persons or things being distributed* Arist. Plu.
2 **in loose order, in scattered groups** —*ref. to troops moving* Plb. Plu.

σποράδες ων *masc.fem.pl.adj.* [σπείρω] 1 (of persons, soldiers, animals, ships) **scattered, dispersed, here and there** Hdt. Th. Plb. Plu.; (of islands, streams of fire) Pi.*fr.* Plu.
2 (of people) **scattered about, isolated** (opp. living in communities) Arist. Plu.
3 (of events) **separate, unconnected** Plb.
4 (of rain-showers) **intermittent, occasional** Plu.

—**σπορά**ς άδος *masc.fem.adj.* (of the life of an islander, opp. city-dweller) not communal, **isolated** or **lonely** E.

—**Σποράδες** ων *f.pl.* **Sporades** (a chain of islands NW. of Rhodes) AR.

σποραδικός ή όν *adj.* (of animals) of the scattered kind (opp. belonging to a herd or flock), **ungregarious** Arist.

σπορεύς έως *m.* **sower** (of seeds) X.

σπορητός οῦ *m.* 1 **sown crop, corn** A.
2 **sowing** (of corn) X.

σπόριμος ον (also η ον Call.) *adj.* (of land, a furrow) such as may be sown, **fit for sowing, sown** X. Call.; app. **sown, cultivated** Theoc. ‖ NEUT.PL.SB. **cornfields** NT.

σπόρος ου *m.* 1 process of sowing, **sowing** (of seeds) Hdt. Pl. X. Theoc. Plu.
2 time of sowing, **seed-time** X. Theoc.
3 that which is sown, **seed, seeds** Hellenist.poet. NT.
4 product of sowing, **crop** Hdt. S.
5 (perh.fig., ref. to a person) **offspring** A.(cj.) | see σπορά 5

σπουδά *dial.f.*: see σπουδή

σπουδάζω *vb.* [σπουδή] | fut. σπουδάσομαι, also σπουδάσω (Plb.) | aor. ἐσπούδασα | pf. ἐσπούδακα ‖ neut.impers. vbl.adj. σπουδαστέον | 1 **be in earnest, be serious** (freq. W.PREP.PHR. about someone or sthg.) E. Ar. Att.orats. Pl. X. + ‖ STATV.PF. **be in a state of eagerness** Ar. Pl. +
2 **be serious** (opp. playful) Ar. Pl. X. + ‖ STATV.PF. be in a serious mood Pl. + ‖ PF.PTCPL.ADJ. (of a face) serious X.
3 **be eager** —W.INF. *to do sthg.* S. E. Lys. Ar. X. + —W.ACC. + INF. or FINAL CL. *that sthg. shd. be done* Pl. X. +
4 (tr.) **do earnestly, pursue seriously, busy oneself with** —*an activity or interest* E. Isoc. Pl. X. +
5 ‖ PASS. (of an activity) **be pursued earnestly** E. Pl. X.; (of comedy, a game) **be taken seriously** Arist.; (of things) **be designed seriously, be produced elaborately** Isoc. Pl. X.
6 ‖ PASS. (of persons) **be treated seriously** Arist. Plu.; (of a woman) **be the object of serious attention, be fancied** Plu.

σπουδαιολογέω *contr.vb.* [σπουδαῖος, λόγος] (act. and mid.) **talk seriously** X. ‖ PASS. (of talk) **be serious** X.

σπουδαῖος ᾱ (Ion. η) ον *adj.* [σπουδή] | compar. σπουδαιότερος, Ion. -έστερος | superl. σπουδαιότατος, Ion. -έστατος | 1 (of persons, their attributes) earnest in disposition or appearance, **serious** X. Plu.
2 (of a person or god, their behaviour) earnest in purpose, **energetic, zealous** S.*fr.* D. Plu.
3 associated with earnest thought or purpose; (of speech, advice, or sim.) **earnest, serious** Thgn. Pi. Ar. Isoc. Pl. +
4 (of undertakings, decisions, or sim.) serious (opp. trivial), **important, weighty** hHom. Thgn. Hdt. +
5 (of persons, their attributes and activities) deserving of serious regard (for moral character or other excellence), **admirable** Hdt. Att.orats. Pl. X. +
6 (of pastures, a country, technique, acquisition) **excellent, admirable** Hdt.; (of a gift) S.; (of seeds) X.; (of abstr. concepts, such as justice) Pl. Arist.; (of customs, laws, government) Plb.

—**σπουδαίως** *adv.* **earnestly, in a serious manner** Pl. X. NT. (w. ἔχειν) **be earnest or serious** Arist.

σπουδαρχίᾱ ᾱς *f.* [ἄρχω] app. **canvassing** (of political support) Plu.

σπουδαρχίας ου *m.* **would-be politician** X.

σπουδαρχιάω *contr.vb.* **be ambitious for public office** Arist.

σπουδαρχίδης ου *m.* the kind of man who seeks public office, **office-hunter** Ar.

σπούδασμα ατος *n.* [σπουδάζω] that which is pursued earnestly, **pursuit, concern** Pl.

σπουδαστέος ᾱ ον *vbl.adj.* (of wealth) **to be pursued seriously** X.

σπουδαστής οῦ *m.* one who is earnest in some cause; **keen supporter** (of someone's interests) Plu.; **enthusiast** (W.GEN. for sthg.) Plu.

σπουδαστικός ή όν *adj.* [σπουδαστός] (of a person) **earnest, energetic** Arist.; **serious** (opp. playful) Pl.

σπουδαστός ή όν *adj.* [σπουδάζω] (of a goal) **to be pursued seriously** Pl.; (of a duty) **to be undertaken eagerly** Arist.

σπουδή ῆς, dial. **σπουδά** ᾶς *f.* [σπεύδω] 1 eager haste, **haste** A. Hdt. +; (prep.phrs.) διὰ σπουδῆς *with eager haste* E. Th. X. Plu.; (also) κατὰ σπουδήν Th. X. Plb. Plu.; μετὰ σπουδῆς D. Plb. NT. Plu.; σὺν σπουδῇ S.; ὑπὸ σπουδῆς Th. Plu.
2 eager effort, **effort, exertion** (sts. W.GEN. or PREP.PHR. over someone or sthg.) Od. +; eager attempt or strenuous undertaking, **enterprise** E.; (phr.) σπουδὴν ποιεῖσθαι *take trouble* Hdt. + —W.PREP.PHR. *about sthg.* Isoc. + —W.INF. *to do sthg.* Hdt. —W. FINAL CL. *that sthg. shd. be done* D.
3 eager concern, **interest, enthusiasm, keenness** (sts. W.GEN. or PREP.PHR. for someone or sthg.) Trag. Th. +; (phr.) σπουδὴν ἔχειν *be eager* —W.INF. or ACC. + INF. *to do sthg., for sthg. to happen* Hdt. E. Isoc. +; (prep.phrs.) κατὰ σπουδήν *eagerly* Thphr.; (also) μετὰ σπουδῆς Aeschin. Arist.
4 **seriousness, earnestness** (opp. playfulness, nonchalance) E. Ar. Pl. +; (prep.phrs.) ἀπὸ σπουδῆς *seriously, earnestly* Il.; (also) μετὰ σπουδῆς Pl. X. Arist.; σὺν σπουδῇ Pl.
5 (in political, forensic or competitive ctxts.) eagerness for a cause, **zeal, partisanship** Antipho Pl. D. Plu. ‖ PL. **contentions, rivalries** Hdt.; **contentious issues** Plu.; **shows of support** E.; (prep.phr.) κατὰ σπουδάς *through personal influence* Ar.

—**σπουδῇ**, dial. **σπουδᾷ** *dat.adv.* 1 in eager haste, **hastily** Od. hHom. Archil. Trag. +
2 with strenuous effort, **strenuously** Tyrt.; **hardly, scarcely** Hom.
3 **earnestly, seriously** Pi. E. Pl. +

σπυρίς (also **σφυρίς** Men.) ίδος *f.* **basket** (for catching fish) Hdt.; (for transporting eels) Ar.; (for carrying food) Men. NT.

—**σπυρίδιον** ου *n.* [dimin.] (pejor.) **tattered basket** Ar.

σπώμην (ep.aor.2 mid.subj.): see ἕπομαι

στάγες (fem.nom.pl.): see σταγών

στάγμα ατος *n.* [στάζω] **distillation** (of a bee, ref. to honey) A.

σταγών όνος *f.* | irreg.nom.pl. στάγες (AR.) | (freq.pl.) **drop** (of blood) Trag. AR. Plu.; (of tears) A.; (of water, rain) E.; (of wine) E.*Cyc.* Tim.; (of oil) AR.

σταδαῖος ᾱ ον *adj.* [reltd. στάδιος] 1 (of Zeus, represented in the act of throwing his thunderbolt) **standing upright** A.

σταδιεύς

2 associated with a standing posture; (of spears) used in hand-to-hand fighting (opp. missile-throwing), **for close fighting** A.; (of a battle) **fought at close quarters** Th.

σταδιεύς έως *m.* [στάδιον] **sprinter** Plb.

σταδιοδρομέω *contr.vb.* [σταδιοδρόμος] **be a sprinter** D.

σταδιο-δρόμος ου *m.* **runner in a single-lap race, sprinter** Pl. Aeschin.

στάδιον ου *n.* —also **στάδιοι** ων *m.pl.* [perh. στάδιος]
1 stade as a measure of distance (100 ὀργυιαί or 6 πλέθρα, i.e. 600 Greek feet, approx. 185 metres), **stade** Hdt. Th. + ‖ DAT. σταδίῳ (as an exaggerated measure of comparison) **by a great distance, by a mile** Ar.
2 stade as the length of the running-track at Olympia; (meton.) single-leg race (opp. δίαυλος two-leg race), **sprint** Thgn. Lyr. Hdt. E. +; **racecourse** Ar. Arist.
3 ‖ PL. (gener.) **spaces (for dancing)** E.

στάδιος ᾱ (Ion. η) ον *adj.* [reltd. ἵστημι] **1** standing or stand-up; (of fighting) **close-range** (opp. w. missiles at a distance) Il. ‖ FEM.SB. **close-range fighting** Il. AR.
2 (of buildings) **steadfast, secure** Pi.
3 (of a cuirass) **stiff, rigid** AR.
4 (of a garment) perh., falling straight, **full-length** Call.

στάζω *vb.* | *fut.* στάξω, dial.1pl. σταξεῦμες (Theoc.), Aeol.3pl. στάξοισι (Pi.) | *aor.* ἔσταξα, ep. στάξα | **1** (of persons or things) let fall in drops, **drip** —*nectar and ambrosia* Il. Hes.fr. Pi. —*sperm* Pi. —*blood* A. AR. —*water, tears, sweat* E. —*oil* Theoc.; (fig., of Eros) —*longing* E.
2 (intr., of persons, parts of the body) **drip** —W.DAT. *w. blood* Trag. —*w. sweat* S. —*w. tears, foam* E.; (of a person) **drip tears** E.; (of a vine) perh. **drip wine** E.
3 (of liquids, blood and tears) fall in drops, **drip, trickle** Hdt. S. E. Pl. X.; (fig., of pain) A.
4 (of sound) **trickle** —W.PREP.PHR. *through the ears* E.

στάθεν (dial.3pl.aor.pass.): see ἵσταμαι, under ἵστημι

σταθερός ά όν *adj.* [σταθμός] **1** standing fast, stationary; (of noon) **high** (perh. because the sun at its highest appears to stand still) Pl.; (phr.) σταθερὸν ἦμαρ **midday** (*ref. to the sun reaching its highest point*) AR.
2 (of good weather) **settled** Plu.

σταθευτός ή όν *adj.* [σταθεύω] (of Prometheus) **scorched** (W.DAT. by the sun's flame) A.

σταθεύω *vb.* **1** grill or roast —*cuttlefish* Ar.
2 scorch —*a person* (W.DAT. *w. a torch*) Ar.

σταθήσομαι (fut.pass.): see ἵστημι

στάθητι, στάθητε (2sg. and pl.aor.pass.imperatv.), **στάθι** (dial.athem.aor.imperatv.): see ἵσταμαι, under ἵστημι

σταθμάω *contr.vb.* —also **σταθμέομαι, σταθμόομαι** *Ion.mid.contr.vbs.* [στάθμη] **1** (act.) **mark out** —*the length of a plethron* E. ‖ PASS. (of poetry) **be measured** (*on the scales*), **be weighed** Ar.(dub., cj. σταθήσεται)
2 ‖ MID. **mark out, map out** —*a sacred precinct* Pi. —*the stars in the Little Bear* (*for navigation*) Call.; (intr., of a carpenter) **use a chalk-line** Pl.
3 ‖ MID. (intr.) calculate using observation as a guide-line; **make an estimate** or **calculation** Hdt. S. —W.COMPL.CL. *how to do sthg.* Hdt.; **make an inference, judge** —W.DAT. *fr. facts or observations* Hdt. Pl. —W.COMPL.CL. *that sthg. is the case* Hdt. —*fr. the fact that sthg. is the case* Hdt.
4 ‖ MID. (tr.) use (sthg.) to make an inference; **judge by** —*a person's words* Pl.

στάθμη ης, dial. **στάθμᾱ** ᾱς *f.* [ἵστημι] **1** that which provides a guide-line, **chalk-line** or **plumb-line** (used by a carpenter or stone-mason) Hom. Thgn. Pi. Pl. X. [The line was used both horizontally, as a string smeared w. chalk or ochre and drawn tight along a surface so as to leave a straight line marked on it, and vertically, as a plumb-line for testing straightness.]
2 (provbl.) λευκὴ στάθμη **white line** (*leaving no visible mark on white stone, ref. to a person unable to discriminate*) Pl.
3 (ref. to a guide-line for behaviour) **standard** (for a son) Pi.; **ordinance, guidance** (for a ruler's descendants) Pi.
4 (fig., in ctxt. of running the course of life) **guide-line** or **goal** Pi.
5 (prep.phrs.) παρὰ στάθμην **in a straight line** (*ref. to movt.*) Thgn.; **strictly, exactly** (*ref. to judging or sim.*) Thgn. A.; παρὰ στάθμην βίου **following a straight line in life** (*ref. to conduct which leads straight towards sthg.*) E.; κατὰ στάθμην **accurately** (*ref. to guessing*) Theoc.

σταθμητός ή όν *adj.* [σταθμάω] **able to be finely judged, capable of being discriminated** Pl.

σταθμο-δότης ου *m.* [σταθμός 2, δίδωμι] one who assigns a soldier's billet or quarters, **quartermaster** Plu.

σταθμός οῦ *m.* [ἵστημι] | nom.pl. σταθμοί, also neut.nom.acc. σταθμά | **1** establishment of a shepherd or herdsman, **steading, farmstead** Hom. Hes. hHom. ‖ PL. farm buildings, cattlesheds, pens Hom. Hes. A. Hellenist.poet.; stables (for horses) Thgn. A. E. X.(also sg.)
2 dwelling (W.GEN. of Hades) Pi. ‖ PL. **dwelling-place, halls** Pi. S. E. Ar.; **stations** (W.GEN. for ships) E.; **quarters, billets** (for soldiers) Plb.
3 place for standing or resting, **stopping-place, staging-post, lodging** (sited at intervals on roads in the Persian empire) Hdt. X. Plu.
4 distance between stops, **stage** (of a journey) X.
5 that which stands, **column, pillar** Od. hHom. E.
6 (usu.pl.) upright post, **doorpost** Hom. Hdt. S. E. AR. Theoc.
7 that which is placed in the balance, **weight** (as a property of objects) Hdt. Th. +; (as a measure of quantity) **heavy amount, weight** (W.GEN. of sthg.) Hdt. E.
8 object of known weight used as a standard of measurement (such as on a balance), **weight** Il. E. +
9 weighing device, **balance, scales** Hdt. Ar. Thphr.
10 use of scales or process of weighing, **weighing** D. Arist.

—σταθμόνδε *adv.* **to the sheepfold** Od.

σταίην (athem.aor.opt.): see ἵσταμαι, ἵστημι

σταῖς αἰτός *n.* **kneaded flour, dough** Hdt.

σταιτινο-κογχο-μαγής ές *adj.* [σταίτινος, κόγχος, μάσσω] (of a cake) **of dough moulded into a boss** Philox.Leuc.

σταίτινος η ον *adj.* (of figurines substituted for sacrificial animals) **made of dough** Hdt. Plu.

στακτός ή όν *adj.* [στάζω] **1** (of perfumed unguents, juices) **oozing in drops, dripping** Ar. Pl.
2 ‖ FEM.SB. (w. σμύρνα understd.) the kind of myrrh which drips, **oil of myrrh** Plb.; (fig., ref. to its being a superior and expensive oil) **superlative quality, quintessence** (W.GEN. of intelligence) Men.

στάλᾱ *dial.f.*: see στήλη

στάλαγμα ατος *n.* [σταλάσσω] that which has been dripped, **drip, drop** (of poisonous saliva, blood) A. S. Tim.

σταλαγμός οῦ *m.* **1** process of dripping, **drip** (of poisonous saliva) A.; (of saliva fr. a horse) A. Plu.
2 drip, droplet (of blood) A. E.; (of water) Plb.; (fig., of peace) Ar.

σταλάσσω *vb.* [reltd. στάζω] **1** let fall in drops, **drip** —*tears* E.; (fig., of a storm of suffering) —*bloodshed* E.
2 (intr., of a napkin) **drip** Sapph.
3 (of sweat) fall in drops, **drip** E.(dub.)

σταλάω *ep.contr.vb.* | 3sg. σταλάει | (of a tear) **drip** AR.

στάλιξ ικος *f.* [perh. ἵστημι] **stake** (for supporting a hunting net) Theoc.epigr. Plu.

στάμεν (dial.athem.aor.inf.): see ἵσταμαι, under ἵστημι
σταμίνες ων *m.pl.* [ἵστημι] | ep.dat. σταμίνεσσι | supports; perh. **ribs** (of a ship's hull) Od.
στάμνος ου *m.* large jar for storing and transporting wine, **wine-jar** Ar. D.
—**σταμνίον** ου *n.* [dimin.] **wine-jar** Ar. Men.
στάμων *dial.m.*: see στήμων
στάν (dial.athem.aor.), **στάν** (ep.3pl.athem.aor.), **στάς** (athem.aor.ptcpl.): see ἵσταμαι, under ἵστημι
στάσα (dial.aor.1): see ἵστημι
στασιάζω *vb.* [στάσις] | aor. ἐστασίασα | **1** (in political ctxts., of individuals or groups) **be at variance, engage in factional strife** (freq. w.DAT. or PREP.PHR. w. someone) Hdt. Th. Ar. Att.orats. +
2 (of a city or populace) **be divided into factions, engage in civil conflict** Th. Lys. Ar. Isoc. +; (of a country) **be divided** Lys.
3 (gener.) **be at variance, be in dispute** (freq. w.DAT. or PREP.PHR. w. someone, or w.PREP.PHR. about sthg.) Hdt. Ar. Pl. X. +
4 (of persons or things) **be in a state of discord** or **conflict** (within themselves) Pl. Arist.
5 (tr.) **cause a disturbance in, revolutionise** —*someone's affairs* D.
στασί-αρχος ου *m.* [ἄρχω] **leader of a factional group, rebel-leader** A.
στασιασμός οῦ *m.* [στασιάζω] **1 state of factional conflict** Th.
2 political rivalry, feuding (w.PREP.PHR. betw. individuals) Plu.
στασιαστής οῦ *m.* **one who stirs up sedition, rebel, revolutionary** NT.
στασιαστικός ή όν *adj.* **1** associated with factional strife; (of persons, speeches) **factious, partisan** Pl. Aeschin. Plu.
2 (of speeches, behaviour) **seditious, mutinous** Plu.
—**στασιαστικῶς** *adv.* **in a factious manner** or **spirit** D. Arist.
στάσιμος ον *adj.* [στάσις] **1** (of water) **standing, stagnant** X.
2 (of a state of certainty; of motion, as an absurdity) **stationary, at rest** Pl.
3 (of persons, their natures) **steady, steadfast** Pl. Arist. Plb. Plu.
4 (of water of a particular consistency) **stable** Pl.
5 (of a spear) **sturdy, firm** Plb.
6 (of a harmony, metre, rhythm, way of speaking) **sedate, stately** Arist.
7 || NEUT.SB. **stationary song, choral song, stasimon** (sung by the chorus when it has reached its station in the orchestra, opp. parodos, sung as it enters) Arist.
8 (in military ctxts.) of the kind that holds its position; (of a section of cavalry in the centre, opp. lighter horse on the flanks) **standing, immobile** Plb.; (of a fighting force, ref. to heavily armed troops, opp. lighter skirmishers) Plu.
9 (of a loan) app., put out (at a regular rate of interest), **standing** Lys.(law of Solon)
10 || NEUT.SB. (fig.) **weight, gravity** (of a situation) Plb.
—**στασιμωτέρως** *compar.adv.* **more stably** Pl.
στάσις εως *f.* [ἵστημι] **1 setting up, placing** (of nets, traps, ladders) X. Plb.
2 placing on the scales, weighing Ar.
3 process of standing up, standing A.; (in the sun, as a punishment) Plu.
4 way of standing, posture E.
5 place where someone or something stands, position, post, station Hdt. Ar. D.
6 relative position or direction, **lie** (w.GEN. of winds, seasonal weather) Alc.(unless fig., sense 15) Hdt.

7 taking of a settled position, **setting in** (w.GEN. of a wind) Plb.
8 position of advantage, **position** (for which boxers vie) Aeschin.
9 state (of an argument, over whose nature opponents wrangle) Aeschin.
10 position reached, **stage** (w.GEN. in a conversation) S.
11 state, condition (of a horse) Pl.
12 position, standpoint (w.GEN. of a philosopher) Plu.
13 fixed intonation (of voice) Plb.
14 standing still, **state of rest** (opp. κίνησις *motion*) Pl. Arist.
15 action of rising up (i.e. uprising, within a community); **discord, factional strife** Alc. Eleg. Scol. Pi. Hdt. Trag. +; (betw. persons, without political connot.) **dissension, division, conflict** A. S. Th. Ar. Pl. Plu.; (fig.) **strife** (of winds) Alc.(unless sense 6) A.; **disorder** (in the human body) Pl.
16 group of persons engaged in a political uprising or dispute, **faction** Hdt. Th. Plu.
17 (without political connot., ref. to persons w. common purpose) **band, company** A. S.(cj.); (perh. derog.) **group, set** (w.GEN. of Euripidean lyrics) Ar.
Στασίχορος *dial.m.*: see Στησίχορος
στασιώδης ες *adj.* **1** (of persons, troops) **seditious, mutinous** Plb. Plu.
2 (of persons, speeches) **divisive, trouble-making** X. D.
στασιωρός οῦ *m.* [οὖρος², ὁράω] **guardian of the fold** (ref. to Silenos or perh. a ram) E.*Cyc.*
στασιῶται ῶν (Ion. έων) *m.pl.* **1 partisans, supporters** (freq. w.GEN. of someone) Hdt.
2 (fig., ref. to laws enacted in the interest of a part of a citizen-body) **partisans, factionists** Pl.
3 (ref. to adherents to the doctrine of Parmenides, opp. οἱ ῥέοντες *the Fluxionists*, w. play on στάσις 14) those who stand in support, **partisans** (w.GEN. of The Whole) Pl.
4 dissidents, rebels Plb.
στασιωτεία ᾱς *f.* **1 faction-state** (opp. πολιτεία *city-state*) Pl.
2 factionalism And.
στασιωτικός ή όν *adj.* (of speeches, situations) predisposed towards faction, **factious, factional** Th. Arist.
—**στασιωτικῶς** *adv.* (w. ἔχειν) **be at odds, disagree** Pl.
στάσκον (iterat.athem.aor.), **στάσομαι** (dial.fut.mid.), **στάσω** (dial.fut.): see ἵσταμαι, under ἵστημι
στατέον (neut.impers.vbl.adj.): see ἵστημι
στατήρ ῆρος, Aeol. **στάτηρ** ηρος *m.* [ἵστημι] a kind of heavy coin, **stater** Alc. Hippon. Hdt. Th. Ar. Att.orats. + [The name was given to a variety of non-Athenian coins, mostly of high value, accepted at Athens and elsewhere: esp. gold coins, incl. the Persian Δαρεικός *Daric*; also coins of electrum, fr. Cyzicus and Phocaea, and of silver, fr. Aigina and elsewhere.]
στατίζω *vb.* [στατός] **1** (tr.) **place** —*a foot* (w.ADV. somewhere) S.*satyr.fr.*
2 (intr.) **be stationary, stand** E.; (also mid.pass.) E.
στατικός ή όν *adj.* [ἵστημι] **1** related to standing still; (of a condition, first principle) **static, of rest** Arist.
2 related to weighing; (of a skill) **of weighing** Pl.
στατός ή όν *adj.* **1** (of water) standing still, **still, stagnant** S. E.*fr.*
2 (of a horse) kept in a stall, **stalled** Il.
3 || MASC.SB. full-length robe (of a musician or actor) Plu. | cf. στάδιος 4
σταυρός οῦ *m.* [reltd. στῦλος] **1** || PL. **upright poles, stakes, palisade** (for reinforcing a wall or ditch) Hom. Th. X. Plu.(also sg.)

σταυρόω

2 ‖ PL. piles (supporting a platform) Hdt.; (in a harbour, for protecting ships) Th.
3 stake (for impaling a body) Plu.
4 cross (as the instrument of crucifixion) Plb. NT. Plu.; (fig., ref. to voluntary suffering) NT.

σταυρόω contr.vb. 1 ‖ PASS. (of a wall) be fenced with stakes Th.
2 (intr.) drive in piles (in a harbour) Th.
3 crucify —a person Plb. NT. ‖ PASS. be crucified NT.

σταύρωμα ατος n. that which is built with stakes, **palisade, stockade** Th. X. Plu.; (in a harbour, as protection for ships) Th.

σταύρωσις εως f. process of building a stockade; (concr.) **stockading** (in a harbour) Th.

σταφίς ίδος f. [reltd. ἀσταφίς; cf. σταφυλίς] dried grape, **raisin** Theoc.

σταφυλή ῆς, Aeol. **σταφύλᾱ** ᾶς f. (usu.pl.) **ripe grape** Hom. Hes. Alc. Pl. X. +

σταφύλη ης f. [perh.reltd. σταφυλή] stone-mason's instrument for determining the horizontal, **plumb-level** Il. Call. [The instrument consisted of a level w. a plumb-line attached, and perh. took its name fr. the likeness of the bob to a grape.]

σταφυλίς ίδος f. [σταφυλή] **ripe grape** (opp. σταφίς raisin) Theoc.

στάχυς υος m. | also στάχῡς (E.) ‖ PL.: acc. στάχῡς (Ar.) | ep.dat. σταχύεσσι | 1 (usu.pl.) **ear of corn** Il. Hes. Lyr.adesp. A. Ar. Arist. +; (pl., fig.ref. to prisoners, envisaged as the harvest of war) Ar.
2 (collectv.sg.) **ears of corn, crop** Trag. Hellenist.poet.
3 **crop** (W.GEN. of men, fr. a dragon's teeth sown by Kadmos or Jason) E. AR.; (fig., of children) E.fr.; (W.GEN. of ruin, produced by hubris) A.

στέαρ ᾱτος n. 1 hard fat, **lard** (used in cooking) Scol.
2 tallow (for greasing a bow) Od.
3 blubber (of dolphins) X.

στέγᾱ dial.f.: see στέγη

στεγάζω vb. [στέγη] | aor. ἐστέγασα ‖ neut.impers.vbl.adj. στεγαστέον | 1 (of shields, body-armour and persons using it) **cover, protect** —parts of the body X. ‖ PASS. (of a boat) be covered over (w. an awning, as protection against rain) Antipho; (of exposed olive shoots, w. protective clay) X.
2 (of sleep) **cover, veil in darkness** —a person S.

στεγανός ή όν adj. [στέγω] 1 (of a hare's coat) **affording protective cover** (against moisture) X.; (of a shield-formation, against arrows) Plu. ‖ NEUT.SB. impermeability or watertightness Pl.
2 (of a net, ref. to darkness, cast by Night over a city) affording cover, **covering** A.; (of an eagle, W.DAT. w. its wings, imagined as covering the earth below) S.
3 (of buildings) with a roof-covering, **roofed over** E.fr. Th. Call.; (of cakes) **coated** Philox.Leuc.

—στεγανῶς adv. in an enclosed manner, **without escaping** —ref. to air being pumped through tightly fitting tubes Th.

στέγ-αρχος ου m. [στέγη, ἄρχω] master of a house, **householder** Hdt.

στέγασμα ατος n. [στεγάζω] 1 that which affords cover, **covering** Pl. X.; **protective covering** (ref. to body-armour) Plu.
2 roof Plu.

στεγαστρίς ίδος fem.adj. (of hides stretched over the wooden frame of a boat's hull) **affording watertight cover** Hdt.

στέγαστρον ου n. **covering** (ref. to the robe or net in which Agamemnon was trapped) A.; (ref. to a garment lent to a traveller) Plu.

στέγη ης, dial. **στέγᾱ** ᾱς f. [στέγω] 1 that which affords cover, **roof** Alc. A. Hdt. E. X. +
2 roof over one's head, **shelter** Anacr. E. X. Plu.
3 **chamber, room** Hdt. S. X.; (ref. to a cave) S.
4 **floor, storey** (in a siege-engine) Plu.
5 (gener.) **building, dwelling, house** Hippon. Hdt. Trag.(freq.pl.) X. NT.
6 (fig.) **cover** (for the Hellespont, ref. to a bridge of boats) Tim.; **shelter** (for items being cooked, ref. to a pot) Tim.

στεγνός ή όν adj. affording cover (against rain); (of felt cloth) **watertight** Hdt.; (of a cave-dwelling) E.Cyc.
‖ NEUT.SB. (sg. and pl.) structure affording cover, shelter X.

στέγος ους n. [στέγω, reltd. τέγος, στέγη] 1 structure affording cover; **building, dwelling, house** Trag. Call. Theoc.; (fig., ref. to a funeral urn) S.
2 perh. roof E.

στέγω vb. | aor. ἔστεξα (Plb. Plu.) | 1 cover closely (so as to keep sthg. out); (of a ship) **keep out** —water A.; (of certain elements in the natural universe) **be impermeable to** —other elements Pl.; (intr., of a ship) **be watertight** Th. Plu.; (of a rampart) **hold** (against assaults, imagined as waves) A.
2 (of fortifications, armour, soldiers) **fend off, withstand** —weapons, missiles, enemies, an attack A. Th. X. Plb. Plu.; (of a tortoise's shell) —blows Ar.; (intr., of sleeping quarters) **provide shelter** (against heat and rain) Pl. ‖ MID. (of a person) keep off from oneself, **shelter oneself against** —rain Pi.; (of a city) **fend off** —a foreign incursion E.
3 keep (sthg.) in; (of containers) **keep in, hold in, prevent from leaking out** —water, poison Pl. Plu.; (of the stomach) —food and drink Pl.; (of a person) **hold in, hold back** —tears E.; (intr., of soil) **be retentive, hold moisture** Pl.
4 (fig., of a soul, compared to a sieve, in neg.phr.) **be without leakage** (in respect of memory) Pl.; (without explicit comparison, of a soul attempting to satisfy its appetites) **keep in** —nothing (i.e. be insatiable) Pl.; (of a person, in respect of memory) Plu.
5 (of a house) **hold, contain** or **shelter** —a crowd of slaves E.; (of a storehouse, ref. to a cave) —an infant S.Ichn.; (of an urn) —a person's remains S.; (of a cradle) —sthg. (opp. be empty) E.; (of rivers, as geographical limits) **enclose** —land E.fr.; (of soil) **welcome, be receptive to** —sthg. planted Plu.
6 veil in silence, **conceal** —news, events, words S. E. Plb. ‖ PASS. (of things) be kept secret Th.; (of a person) have one's secrets kept S.

στείβω vb. | ep.impf. στεῖβον | 1 (of horses) **tread under foot, trample on** —corpses and shields Il.; (of women) —clothes (in washing) Od.
2 (of persons) **tread** —places, ground Call. AR. —grassy spaces (W.INTERN.ACC. in dancing) E. ‖ PASS. (of roads) be trodden or frequented X.; (of dust) be trodden into or trampled upon Theoc.
3 (intr., of persons, dogs) **tread, go about** hHom. E.

στεῖλα (ep.aor.): see στέλλω

στειλειή ῆς ep.Ion.f. —also **στελεή** ῆς (AR.) Ion.f. [reltd. στέλεχος] **haft** (of an axe, or perh. ref. to the socket in the axe-head into which the handle was fitted) Od.; **handle** (of a hammer) AR.

στειλειόν οῦ ep.Ion.n. **haft, handle** (of an axe) Od.

στείνομαι Ion.pass.vb. [στενός] 1 (of doors) be made narrow, **become too narrow** (for a crowd fleeing through them) Od.

2 (of persons, sheep) be confined within a narrow space, **be penned in** Il. AR.

3 (of Gaia) **be cramped, be crowded** (by her children within her) Hes.; (of a river) —W.DAT. *w. corpses* Il.; (of islands) —*w. people* AR.; (of fields) —*w. bellowing* (*i.e. bellowing cattle*) Theoc.; (of pens) —W.GEN. *w. lambs and kids* Od.; (of a ram) **be encumbered** —W.DAT. *by its fleece and by Odysseus hanging underneath* Od.

στεινόπορος, στεινός *Ion.adjs*.: see στενόπορος, στενός

στεῖνος εος *Ion.n*. —also **στένος** ους (A.) *n*. **1 narrow** or **confined space** Hom.; **narrow place** (in a road) Il.; **narrow street, alleyway** Call.; **narrow strip of land** (ref. to the Isthmos of Corinth) Call.

2 (fig.) difficult or painful circumstances, **straits, distress, anguish** Il. A. ‖ PL. **hardships** hHom.

στεινότης *Ion.f*.: see στενότης

στεινωπός *Ion.adj*.: see στενωπός

στείομεν (ep.1pl.athem.aor.subj.): see ἵσταμαι, under ἵστημι

στεῖρα[1] ᾱς *fem.adj*. [reltd. στερρός] (of a cow) which has not given birth, **barren** Od. Theoc.; (of a woman) NT. Plu.

στεῖρα[2] ᾱς, Ion. **στείρη** ης *f*. [reltd. στερεός] **keel** (of a ship, app. incl. the timbers extending above the waterline) Hom. AR.

στείχω *vb*. —also **στίχω** (Hdt.) *vb*. | ep.impf. στεῖχον | ep.aor.2 ἔστιχον | **1** (of animate and quasi-animate subjects) make one's way, **proceed, come, go** (freq. W.ADV. or PREP.PHR. to or fr. a place) Hom. Hes. Lyr. Hdt. Trag. + —W.ACC. *to a place* B. Trag. Call. AR. —W.COGN.ACC. *on a path or sim.* B. Trag.

2 go away, depart Trag.

3 (of a wave, storm, sunlight) **come, approach** Alc. A. E.

4 (of a song, report) **go out, travel** Pi. B.

5 (of troubles, ruin) **advance** —W.DAT. or PREP.PHR. *against someone* S.

6 (of a first beard) **spread** —W.PREP.PHR. *over cheeks* A.

7 (of time) **move on, advance** AR.

στεκτικός ή όν *adj*. [στέγω] (of techniques) **providing shelter** (W.GEN. fr. inundations) Pl.

στελγίς *f*.: see στλεγγίς

στελεή *Ion.f*.: see στειλειή

στέλεχος εος (ους) *n*. [reltd. στειλειή] **1 trunk** (of a growing tree) Pi. D. Arist. Plu.

2 stump (of a burned olive tree) Hdt.

3 trunk of a felled tree, **log** Ar. Men. Plu.

στέλλω *vb*. | fut. στελῶ, ep. στελέω | aor. ἔστειλα, ep. στεῖλα | pf. ἔσταλκα ‖ PASS.: aor. ἐστάλην ‖ MID.PASS.: pf. ἔσταλμαι | Ion.3pl.plpf. ἐστάλατο |

1 arrange or put in order; **make ready, marshal** —*soldiers* Il.

2 fit out, equip —*a ship* Od. Hdt. S. —*an army* A. Hdt.

3 prepare for —*a journey home* E.

4 ‖ MID. **get oneself ready, prepare** Il. —W.INF. *to do sthg*. Hdt. E.

5 fit out, equip, dress —*a person* (W.DAT. or COGN.ACC. or ADVBL.PHR. *in clothes, in a certain way*) Hdt. S. E. X. ‖ MID. **dress oneself** —W.COGN.ACC. *in clothes* E. ‖ PASS. be dressed or equipped —W.ADVBL.PHR. or DAT. *in a certain way, in clothes* A. Hdt. Pl. Plu. —W.PREP.PHR. *for war* X.

6 arrange in the earth, **bury** —*the dead* AR.

7 ‖ MID. **gather up, hitch up** —*one's clothes* Hes. AR.

8 gather up, **draw in, furl** —*a sail* A. E.; (mid.) Call. AR.

9 ‖ MID. **take in, shorten** —*a ship's reefing ropes* (so as to shorten the sail by running it up to the yard-arm) Plb.; (fig.) **curtail** —*one's speech* E. —*one's customary respect* Plb.; **reduce, play down** —*the impact of a military defeat* Plb.

10 despatch, send (freq. W.PREP.PHR. to a place) —*persons* Il. Hdt. S. E. Plu. —*ships, a fleet, troops* Hdt. E. Th. Lys. —*a gift* S. —*an embassy* Plb.; **direct** —*a ship* E.; **lead on** —*a horse* (*into an arena*) AR.

11 urge or cause to set forth, **urge on** —*someone* (W.PREP.PHR. *into battle, homewards*) Il. A.

12 cause to come, **summon, fetch** —*someone* S. ‖ MID. cause to come to oneself, **have** (W.ACC. someone) **fetched** S.

13 (intr., usu.mid.pass.) **set out, go** or **travel** Pi. Hdt. Trag. + —W.COGN.ACC. *on a journey, voyage, march* Trag. AR. Plb.

14 ‖ MID.PASS. **direct oneself, aim** —W.PREP.PHR. *towards a goal or activity* Hdt. Ar. Pl.

στελμονίαι ῶν *f.pl*. broad belts for hunting dogs, **girths** X.

στέμμα ατος *n*. [στέφω] **1** (usu.pl.) band of wool, **fillet** (as a symbol of holiness, assoc.w. priests, prophets, or sim.) E. Ar. Call. Plu.; (used in supplication to wreathe an olive branch, also a priest's staff) Il. E. Plb.; (to wreathe a sacrificial victim) Hdt. Ar. Thphr. Plu.; (hung in the oracular chamber and on sacred objects at Delphi) E. Ar.; (assoc.w. the temple of Hera at Argos) Th.; (worn on the head by the Fates) Pl.

2 ‖ PL. tufts of wool, wool (for spinning of threads by Ἔρις Discord) E.; (as the fringe of a cloak) Ar.

3 garland (of wild celery, won by a victor at the Isthmian games) Plu.

4 ‖ PL. (in Roman ctxt.) **family tree** Plu. [Displayed in entrances to houses; so called because the names were illuminated w. painted garlands.]

στεμματόω *contr.vb*. **wreathe with a fillet** —*a sacrificial victim* E.

στέμφυλον ου *n*. [reltd. ἀστεμφής] (sg. and pl.) edible mass of olives from which the oil has been pressed, **pressed olives** Ar. Arist.

στενάγματα των *n.pl*. [στενάζω] **groans, moans** S. E. Ar.

στεναγμός οῦ *m*. **1 groaning, moaning** Pi.*fr*. S. E. Plb. NT. Plu. ‖ PL. **groans, moans** Trag. Pl. Plu.

2 bellowing (of rowers) E.

στενάζω *vb*. [στένω] | fut. στενάξω | aor. ἐστέναξα ‖ neut.impers.vbl.adj. στενακτέον | **1** utter a deep or loud sound of grief; **groan, moan** Trag. Ar. Aeschin. D. NT. Plu.; utter with groans, **groan forth** —W.COGN.ACC. *a dirge, death-cry, curses* E.

2 (tr.) **bemoan, bewail** —*persons, their fate* S. E.

στενακτός ή (dial. ά) όν *adj*. **1** associated with or fit for moaning; (of a cry) **mournful** E.; (of actions) **lamentable** E.

2 (of a person on the way to death) provoking moans, **lamented** S.

στεναχίζω *vb*.: see στοναχίζω

στενάχω *vb*. [στένω] | only pres. (usu.ptcpl.) and impf. | iteratv.impf. στενάχεσκον | ep.3pl.impf.mid. στενάχοντο | **1** (intr.) utter a loud sound of grief; **groan, wail, roar** Hom.(sts.mid.) S. AR.; (of a hungry wild animal) AR.; (of horses running scared) Il.(mid.)

2 (tr.) **bemoan, bewail** —*dead men* Od.(mid.) Callin. —*a person, fate, suffering* Trag.; (of Zeus) **groan at the thought of** —*the goddess Ate* Il.

3 (of mountain torrents) **roar, resound** Il.; (of a portico, through overcrowding) Ar.; (of rollers, beneath the weight of a ship) **screech** AR.(mid.)

στενο-κώκῡτος ον *adj*. [app. στένω, κωκυτός] (quasi-advbl., of hair that is to be pulled out) **with groaning and lamentation** Ar.

στενολεσχέω *contr.vb*. [στενός, λέσχη] discourse in a finicky manner or about narrow subjects, **chatter narrowly** Ar.

στενό-πορθμος ον *adj.* [πορθμός] (of the currents of the Euripos) **narrow-channelled** E.

στενοπορίᾱ ᾱς *f.* [στενόπορος] narrowness of the way through or past (a place), **narrow terrain** X.

στενό-πορος, Ion. **στεινόπορος**, ον *adj.* [πόρος] **1** (of an entrance, exit, defile, the Clashing Rocks) **affording a narrow passageway** A. E. Arist.(quot.) Plu.
2 (of a country) **full of narrow defiles** Plu.
3 (of Aulis, its moorings) **on a narrow strait** E.
4 ‖ NEUT.SG. and PL.SB. narrow pass (on land) Hdt. Th. X.; (sg.) narrow strait (at sea) X.

στενός, Ion. **στεινός**, ή όν *adj.* | compar. στενότερος, Ion. στεινότερος, superl. στενότατος, Ion. στεινότατος | also στενώτερος, στενώτατος (Plb. Plu.) | **1** (of areas of land or sea, passageways, or sim.) **narrow** Hdt. E. Th. + ‖ FEM.SB. narrow strip of land Th. ‖ NEUT.SG.SB. narrow part (W.GEN. of a country, a road) Hdt. X. ‖ NEUT.SG. and PL.SB. narrow pass (on land), narrows or strait (at sea) A. Hdt. Th. +
2 ‖ NEUT.SG.SB. confined or difficult situation (military or financial), tight position Hdt. D.
3 limited in scope or amount; (of topics for discussion or writing) **narrow, constricted** Pl. Plb.; (of speeches) **thin, poor** Arist.; (of resources) **meagre** Plu.

στένος *n.*: see στεῖνος

στενότης, Ion. **στεινότης**, ητος *f.* **narrowness** (usu. W.GEN. of a harbour, strait, pass, passage) Hdt. Th. Lys. X. Plb. Plu.

στενοχωρίᾱ ᾱς *f.* [χῶρος] **1 narrowness of space, lack of room** Th. Pl. X. Plb.; **cramped quarters** Plu.
2 (fig.) financial straits, **lack of resources** Plb.

Στέντωρ ορος *m.* **Stentor** (a Greek at Troy, famous for his loud voice) Il.

—Στεντόρειος ᾱ ον *adj.* (of a herald) **Stentorian** (i.e. loud-voiced) Arist.

στενυγρός ή όν *Ion.adj.* [στενός] (of a path) **narrow** Semon.

στένω *vb.* | only pres. and impf. | **1** make a deep sound of grief; (of persons, peoples) **moan, groan** Trag. Ar. D. Men. Call. + —W.GEN. *for sthg.* E.; (mid.) A.
2 (of a turtle-dove) **moan** Theoc.; (of the sea, a headland) Il. Trag. AR.
3 express sorrow inwardly; (of a person, a lion's spirit) **moan, groan, sigh** —W.ACC. or PREP.PHR. *in the heart* Hom.
4 (tr.) **moan for, grieve for, lament** —*someone or sthg.* Trag. Call.*epigr.* Plu.; (mid.) E.

στεν-ωπός, Ion. **στεινωπός**, όν *adj.* [στενός, ὀπή] **1** with a narrow opening; (of a road) **narrow** Il.
2 ‖ MASC.SB. narrow path or passage (on land) S. Plu.; lane Plu.
3 ‖ MASC.SB. narrow channel, strait Od. A. AR.
4 ‖ MASC.PL.SB. narrow channels (ref. to blood-vessels) Pl.

στέργηθρον ου *n.* [στέργω] (sg. and pl.) **love, affection, fondness** A. E.; (W.GEN. for someone or sthg.) A.

στέργημα ατος *n.* app., thing which produces love, **love-charm** S.

στέργω *vb.* | fut. στέρξω | aor. ἔστερξα | pf. ἔστοργα (Hdt.) ‖ PASS.: aor.ptcpl. στερχθείς (Plu.) ‖ neut.impers.vbl.adj. στερκτέον | **1 be fond of, feel affection for, love** —*a child, parent, brother* S. E. Pl. + —*a wife, husband* Hdt. S. E. Men. +; (of subjects, citizens) —*a ruler, city* Hdt. S. Isoc.; (of a dog) —*the person who feeds it* X. ‖ PASS. (of persons) be held in affection, be loved (sts. W.PREP.PHR. by someone) Th. Pl. X. Plu.; (of a dog) Plu.
2 (of patron deities) **cherish** —*a nation, a person* A. Ar.; (fig., of Self-Control) —*a person* E.
3 (of a man) **love** (w. sexual passion) —*a male lover* X.; (of a horse) —*a mare* Hdt.
4 (wkr.sens.) **be fond of, have a liking for** —*a person, quality, way of behaving* Thgn. A. Hdt. S. +
5 welcome warmly, appreciate —*someone's goodwill* Hdt.
6 accept, put up with, acquiesce in —*sthg.* Semon. Hdt. Trag. + —*a rival wife* S.; (intr.) **be satisfied, be content** S. E. Pl. D. —W.DAT. *w. sthg.* E. Ar. Att.orats. Pl. + —W.INF. *to do sthg.* E. —W.PTCPL. *w. doing (or suffering) sthg.* E. Plu.; **be resigned** —W.PTCPL. *to doing (or suffering) sthg.* S. E.
7 desire —W.ACC. + INF. *someone to do sthg.* S.

στερεο-ειδής ές *adj.* [στερεός, εἶδος¹] (of the body of the cosmos) **solid in shape** Pl.

στερεο-παγής ές *adj.* [πήγνυμι] (of missiles) **solid-hard** Tim.

στερεός ᾱ (Ion. ή) όν *adj.* [reltd. στερρός] **1 hard to the touch**; (of oxhide shields, thongs on a boxer's hands) **firm, hard** Il. Theoc.; (of ground, soil) E. Pl. X. Plb. Plu.; (of bones, a horn) Pl. Plu.; (of a shield, ship's beak) Plu.
2 (of the warp-thread of twisted wool, a military cloak) **tough, robust** Pl. Plu.
3 (of a type of Roman javelin) **solid, stout** (opp. light or slender) Plb.
4 (of stone, the class of non-fusible minerals, adamant) **hard, solid** Od. Pl. Theoc.; (of gold objects, a stone tower) Hdt.
5 (of a formation of ships) **solid, compact** Plb.
6 (of persons, animals, parts of their bodies) **hard, tough** Pl. X. Theoc. Plu.; (of a person's temperament) Pl.
7 (of a heart) **hard, unyielding** Od.
8 (of words of reproach, threats) **hard, harsh** Il. A.; (of fire, pain) **cruel, relentless** Pi.; (of faults) **stubborn, obstinate** S.; (of a proposition) **tough** Pl.
9 (geom., of a body or figure) having three dimensions, **solid** Pl. Arist. ‖ NEUT.PL.SB. cubes Pl.
10 (math., of a number) **cubic** Arist.

—στερεῶς *adv.* **1 firmly, tightly, hard** —*ref. to stretching, pulling, binding, pressing* Hom. Theoc.
2 stoutly —*ref. to armour resisting a blow* Plu.
3 stubbornly, hard-heartedly —*ref. to saying no* Il. hHom.

στερεότης ητος *f.* **hardness, solidity** Pl. Plu.

στερεό-φρων ονος *masc.adj.* [φρήν] (of Ajax) **stubborn-minded** S.

στερεόω *contr.vb.* **1** (of stones) **harden** —*a horse's feet* X.
‖ MID. (of a person) **toughen up** —*one's body* X.
2 (of the name of Christ) **make firm, strengthen** —*an infirm person* NT. ‖ PASS. (of feet) be made firm or strengthened NT.; (fig., of churches) be strengthened —W.DAT. *by faith* NT.

στερέω *contr.vb.* | pres. perh. only 3sg.imperatv. στερείτω (Pl.); for other pres. forms see στερίσκω | fut. στερήσω, also στερῶ (A., unless prophetic pres.) | aor. ἐστέρησα, ep.inf. στερέσαι | —also **στέρομαι** *pass.vb.* | fut. στερήσομαι | aor. ἐστερήθην, ptcpl. στερηθείς, aor.2 ptcpl. στερείς | pf. ἐστέρημαι | fut.pf. ἐστερήσομαι |
1 deprive, rob —*someone* (W.GEN. *of someone or sthg.*) Od. Trag. Th. + ‖ PASS. be deprived or robbed —W.GEN. *of someone or sthg.* Hes. Pi. Hdt. Trag. + —W.ACC. *of sthg.* A.(dub.) S.
2 ‖ PASS. be bereaved, suffer loss A. S.; be left wanting (in knowledge) S.; be defrauded X.

στέρησις εως *f.* **1 deprivation, loss** (W.GEN. of sthg.) Th. Pl. D. Arist. Plu.
2 (log.) **privation** Arist.
3 (gramm.) **negation** Arist.

στερητικός ή όν *adj.* (of a proposition, principle) **privative** Arist.

—στερητικῶς *adv.* **privatively** Arist.

στερίσκω vb. [reltd. στερέω, στέρομαι] | only pres. | deprive, rob —a city (W.GEN. of sthg.) Th. ‖ PASS. be deprived or robbed —W.GEN. of someone or sthg. Hdt. E.(dub.) Th. Pl. X. Arist.(quot.trag.)

στέριφος η ον adj. **1** [reltd. στερεός, στερρός] (of ground, a ship's prow, its beak) **firm, hard** Th.; (of a woman's breast) Ar.
2 [reltd. στεῖρα¹, στερρός 4] (of a woman) **barren** Ar. Pl.

στερκτέον (neut.impers.vbl.adj.): see στέργω

στερκτικός ή όν adj. [στέργω] relating to love or affection ‖ NEUT.SB. affectionate feeling Plu.

στερκτός ή όν adj. **to be cherished** S.

στερνο-κτύπος ον adj. [στέρνον] (of lamentation) **with the thud of breast-beating** Tim.

στέρνον ου n. **1** (sts. pl. for sg.) front of the thorax or chest, **breast, chest** (of men) Hom. Archil. Tyrt. Lyr. Trag. +; (of animals) Hom. Hdt. X. Plu.
2 breast (of a woman) E. ‖ PL. breasts, bosom S. E. Plu.
3 (fig., ref. to mountains in a dark northern land) **breast** (W.GEN. of Night) Alcm.
4 (sg. and pl.) breast as the seat of emotions, **heart** hHom. Trag. AR. Theoc.

στερνο-τυπής ές adj. [τύπτω] (of the sound of mourning) **from the beating of breasts** E.

στερνοῦχος ον adj. [ἔχω] having a bosom; (of the land of Attica, ref. to its hills) **bosomy** S.

στέρομαι pass.vb.: see στερέω

στεροπή ῆς, dial. **στεροπά** ᾶς f. [reltd. ἀστεροπή]
1 lightning flash Il. Hes. Ibyc. Pi. Trag. AR.
2 flashing light, gleam (of bronze) Hom.; (of sunlight) S.

στεροπηγερέτα ep.m. [ἀγείρω] | only nom. | (epith. of Zeus) **lightning-gatherer** Il.

στέροψ οπος masc.fem.adj. [ὤψ] (of a smoky flame) **gleaming, flashing** S.

στερροποιέομαι mid.contr.vb. [στερρός] (of a commander) make firm or solid, **strengthen** —his rearguard Plb.

στερρός ά όν (also ός όν E.) adj. **1** [reltd. στερεός] (of a bed, fig.ref. to the ground) **hard** E.; (of a body of spearmen) **hard, solid** E.; (of a shin) **rigid, stiff** (through old age) Ar.
2 (of a person's nature or spirit) **hard, tough, unyielding** E. Ar. Plu.
3 (of an upbringing) **hard, harsh** E.; (of compulsion, destiny, pains) **cruel, relentless** A. E.
4 [reltd. στεῖρα¹] (of a heifer, fig.ref. to a woman) **barren** E.

—στερρῶς adv. **firmly, obstinately** —ref. to resisting temptation X.

στέρφος εος n. **skin, hide** (W.ADJ. of a goat, as a garment) AR.

στεῦμαι ep.vb. | only 3sg. στεῦται, 3pl. στεῦνται (A.), 3sg.impf. στεῦτο | **1** perh., be eager or make as if (to do sthg.); **be set** or **threaten** —W.FUT.INF. to do sthg. Il. A.
2 claim —W.AOR.INF. to have done sthg. Od. —W.PRES.INF. to be someone AR.
3 perh. **be eager** (to do sthg.) Od.

στεφάνη ης, dial. **στεφάνα** ᾶς f. [στέφω] **1** that which encircles a warrior's head; **helmet** Il.
2 metal band encircling a woman's head (to keep her hair or veil in place); **diadem, tiara** Il. Hes. hHom. Ar.
3 diadem (ornamenting a commander's helmet) Plu.
4 (fig.) **crown** (W.GEN. of towers, ref. to battlements encircling a city) E.
5 rim (of a snare) X.; (W.GEN. of a basket) Mosch.
6 prob. **brim, edge** (of a plateau) Il.
7 brow (W.GEN. of a hill) Plb.; **crest** (W.GEN. of a burial mound) AR.
8 upper tier (W.GEN. of a theatre) Plb.

στεφανηπλοκέω contr.vb. [στέφανος, πλέκω] **plait garlands** Sapph. Ar.

στεφανηφορέω, dial. **στεφαναφορέω** contr.vb. [στεφανηφόρος] **wear a garland** E. D. Plu.

στεφανηφορία, dial. **στεφαναφορία** ᾶς f. **garland-wearing** (by victorious athletes) Pi. E.(dub.); (in a civic ctxt.) D.

στεφανη-φόρος, dial. **στεφαναφόρος**, ον adj. [φέρω] **1** (of singers and dancers, times of celebration, Peace) **wearing a garland, garlanded** Scol. B. E.; (of victorious horses) Theoc.
2 (of a contest) **with a garland for the victor** Hdt. And. ‖ NEUT.PL.SB. contest with a garland for the victor E.(cj.)
3 (of the office of archon) **marked by the wearing of a garland** Aeschin.

στεφανίζω vb. | dial.aor. ἐστεφάνιξα | **crown** —someone Ar.(perh.quot.com.)

στεφανίσκος ου m. [dimin. στέφανος] **garland** Anacr.

στεφανίτης ου masc.adj. (of a contest) **which has a garland as the prize** Att.orats. X. Arist. Plu.

στέφανος ου m. [στέφω] **1** that which surrounds or encircles (the head); **garland** (usu. of flowers or leaves, worn esp. on festive and religious occasions) Hes. +; (worn by an archon when performing official duties) D. Arist.
2 garland (awarded to victorious athletes) Pi. B. Hdt. +; (to an individual as a mark of honour) Hdt. +
3 garland of gold (awarded by a city or ruler for exceptional service), **crown** Hdt. E. Att.orats. +
4 diadem (of gold, worn by a woman) E.; **crown** (of stars, ref. to the bridal crown of Ariadne, transformed into the constellation Corona Borealis) AR.
5 (fig.) **crown** (of a city, ref. to battlements which encircle it) Anacr. Pi.
6 (fig.) **circle, ring** (W.GEN. of war) Il.
7 (fig., ref. to the olive, Ajax, lives given in war) **crown, crowning glory** (of a country) E. Lycurg.; (ref. to a person's children) E.
8 (gener.) **prize, reward** Pi. S. E. Th.; (W.GEN. of glory) S. E.

στεφανόω contr.vb. **1 garland, crown** —a person, head, hair (oft. W.DAT. w. a garland, flowers, or sim.) Pi. Hdt. + ‖ MID. garland oneself, **put on a garland** Anacr. S.fr. E. + ‖ MID.PF.PTCPL.ADJ. wearing a garland Hdt. +
2 garland, crown —a victor (esp. an athlete) Pi. B. + ‖ MID. have oneself garlanded, **win a victor's garland** Pi. B.
3 honour with a garland for exceptional service, **crown** —someone E. Ar. Att.orats. +; (gener.) **reward** —someone (W.DAT. w. money) Plb. Plu.
4 (fig.) **adorn, honour** —persons, places (by one's conduct) E. Ar. Att.orats. —a tomb (W.DAT. w. sacrificial blood) E. —a victor or sim. (w. song) Pi. Critias
5 ‖ STATV.PF. and PLPF.PASS. (of decorative figures) be set in a circle or as an edge (around a shield, an aigis) Il.; (of a cloud, crowd of spectators, the sea) form a circle (around a person, an island) Hom. hHom.; (of snakes) be entwined as a garland (around the head of Hekate) AR.
6 ‖ PF.MID. (of heaven) have circles or garlands —W.ACC. of stars Il. Hes.

στεφανώδης ες adj. **like a garland**; (of foliage) **fashioned as a garland** E.

στεφάνωμα ατος n. **1** that which encircles (the head), **garland** Thgn. S. Ar. Plu.
2 garland awarded to a victorious athlete, **garland, crown** Pi.; (fig., ref. to a song in honour of the victor) Pi. E.
3 (fig.) **crown** (W.GEN. of towers, ref. to battlements encircling a city) S.

4 (fig.) **ring, circle** (W.GEN. of altars) Pi.
5 (fig.) **crowning glory** (W.GEN. for wealth, ref. to honour) Pi.

στεφανωτρίς ίδος *fem.adj.* (of papyrus) **used to make garlands** Plu.

στέφος εος (ους) *n.* [στέφω] | PL.: nom.acc. στέφη (also στέφεα E.) | gen. στεφέων | **1** wreath made of flowers or leaves (worn on the person or hung about an object); **garland** (assoc.w. a festal or religious occasion) Emp. E. Call. Bion; (worn by a victor, or to celebrate a victory) E.
2 band of wool, fillet (carried by suppliants) Trag.; (worn by a priestess) A. E.; (worn by a sacrificial victim) E. | see στέμμα 1
3 || PL. **honours paid to gods, offerings** A.

στέφω *vb.* | fut. στέψω | aor. ἔστεψα || PASS.: aor.ptcpl. στεφθείς | pf.ptcpl. ἐστεμμένος | **1 set in a circle** or **place as a garland** —*decorations* (W.PREP.PHR. *around a chariot*) A. —*a golden cloud* (*around a hero's head*) Il. —(*fig.*) *beauty* (W.DAT. *around someone's speech*) Od. || PASS. (of ivy leaves) **be set as a crown** —W.PREP.PHR. *on a fennel rod* (*to create a thyrsos*) E.
2 encircle with foliage, garland (oft. W.DAT. w. leaves or sim.) —*a person, head, object* Hes. Hdt. E. Pl. + —*a victor, his head* E. Call.; (fig., of battlements) **encircle** or **crown** —*a city* S.(cj.) || MID. **garland** —*one's head* E. Plu.; **garland oneself** AR. || PASS. (of a victor) **be garlanded** —W.DAT. w. *olive* E.*lyr.* || PF.PASS.PTCPL.ADJ. (of a person) **wreathed** or **garlanded** (W.DAT. w. foliage) A.*satyr.fr.* AR.; (w. garlic, for apotropaic purposes) Thphr.; (of a chariot) X.; (of a ship's stern) Pl.; (of the stern of a city, fig.ref. to a shrine, w. suppliants' branches) A.
3 encircle with woollen fillets (as a symbol of holiness); **garland** (sts. W.DAT. w. wool) —*a sacrificial victim, a maenad's fawnskin* E. —*a venerable person* Pl. —*an object used in magical rites* Theoc. || PF.PASS.PTCPL.ADJ. (of a suppliant's branch) **garlanded** (W.DAT. w. wool) A.; (of a sprig, used in a purificatory ritual) **wool-bound** Theoc.
4 garland or **crown with offerings, crown, deck, honour** —*a god, temple* (W.DAT. w. spoils) S. E. —*a corpse, tomb* (w. *libations or other offerings*) S. E.

στέωμεν (ep.1pl.athem.aor.subj.), **στῇ** (3sg.), **στήῃ** (ep.3sg.), **στήῃς** (ep.2sg.), **στῆθι** (athem.aor.imperatv.): see ἵσταμαι, under ἵστημι

στῆθος εος (ους) *n.* | ep.gen. στήθεσφι | **1** (sts.pl. for sg.) **front of the thorax, breast, chest** (of men, women, animals) Hom. Hes. Archil. Tyrt. Lyr. A. +; (as the seat of the heart) Hom. hHom. Sapph. Alc.; (as the seat of the voice) Il. hHom. A. B.
2 (as the seat of emotions and thoughts) **breast, heart** Hom. Hes. Archil. Thgn. Lyr. Parm. +

στήλη ης, dial. **στάλα** ᾱς *f.* [reltd. στέλλω] **1 wooden post** or **stone block supporting a rampart, buttress** Il.; **temple pillar** (of precious mineral) Hdt.
2 block (of hollowed crystal for displaying mummies) Hdt.; (of stone, marking a reef) Hdt.; (marking a boundary) X.; (marking the turning-point in a horse-race) S. X.
3 pedestal (for a statue) And.
4 upstanding monolith set on a funeral mound or tomb, grave-pillar, stele Hom. Hippon. Simon. Th. +
5 inscribed or **commemorative pillar** Hdt. X. Plb.; (esp. at Athens) pillar of stone or bronze inscribed with public records (incl. laws, decrees, treaties and the names of individuals being honoured or disgraced), **official pillar, stele** Hdt. Th. Ar. Att.orats. +; (meton., w. primary ref. to the text inscribed) **official notice** or **decision** Att.orats. Plb.;

(fig., ref. to commemorative poetry) **memorial, monument** Pi.
6 || PL. στῆλαι Ἡράκλειαι, Ἡρακλέος (or sim.) **Pillars of Hercules** (ref. to the promontories flanking the Strait of Gibraltar) Pi. Hdt. Isoc. Pl. Arist. +

—**στηλίδιον** ου *n.* [dimin.] **little gravestone** (for a dog) Thphr.

στηλίτης ου *m.* **one whose name is inscribed on a pillar** (for public dishonour), **posted delinquent** Isoc. D. Arist.

στήμεναι (ep.athem.aor.inf.): see ἵσταμαι, under ἵστημι

στημόνιος ᾱ ον *adj.* [στήμων] **of** or **relating to the warp**; (of wool) **used for the warp-thread** Arist.

στημονο-νητικός ή όν *adj.* [νέω²] (of the art) **of spinning the warp-thread** Pl.

στημονο-φυής ές *adj.* [φυή] (of a sturdy temperament) **with a warp-like nature** (since the warp-threads are tauter than those of the weft) Pl.

στημορραγέω *contr.vb.* [ῥήγνῡμι] (of the rending of clothes) **tear apart the threads** A.

στήμων, dial. **στάμων**, ονος *m.* **1** (in weaving) **threads which extend lengthwise in the loom** (opp. the crosswise threads of the weft or woof), **warp** Hes. Pl. Bion; (gener.) **thread** Ar.
2 (fig.) **thread** (by which a country's fortune hangs) Plu.

στῆν (ep.athem.aor.), **στῆναι** (athem.aor.inf.): see ἵσταμαι, under ἵστημι

στήριγγες ων *f.pl.* [στηρίζω] **supports, props** (W.GEN. of a horse's body, ref. to its shanks) X.

στήριγμα ατος *n.* **1 support** (W.GEN. fr. a hand) E.(pl.)
2 prop (ref. to a forked support, Lat. *furca*) Plu.

στηρίζω *vb.* | aor. ἐστήριξα, ep. στήριξα, also ἐστήρισα (NT. Plu.) || PASS.: aor.ptcpl. στηριχθείς | pf. ἐστήριγμαι |
1 (of Zeus) **set firm, fix** —*a stone* (W.PREP.PHR. *in the ground*) Hes. —*rainbows* (*in a cloud*) Il.; (of Eris) —*her head* (W.DAT. *in heaven*) Il.
2 || STATV.PF.PLPF.PASS. (of a rock, the cosmic sphere) **be set firm, stand fixed** Emp. Call.; (of an abyss) NT.; (of the moon) —W.DAT. *in heaven* hHom.; (of anger) —*in a person* AR.; (of evil) —*on evil* Il.
3 set firm —*one's face* (*i.e. fix one's purpose*, W.GEN. *on sthg.*) NT.; **give firmness of purpose to** —*someone* NT.
4 (intr.) **get a firm footing** Od.; (mid.pass.) Il. Hes. Tyrt. Plu.
5 || MID. (of a person) **sit fixed, be rooted** (in a place) S.
6 (of a column of supernatural light) **stand fixed** —W.PREP.PHR. *betw. earth and heaven* E.; (of a wave; fig., of glory) **be set fast in** or **tower to** —W.DAT. *heaven* E.; (of flames) **tower** —W.PREP.PHR. *towards heaven* Plu.
|| MID.PASS. (of the abode of Styx) **tower, reach up** —W.PREP.PHR. *towards heaven* Hes.; (of a pine tree) E.
7 (of a disease) **become fixed, settle** —W.PREP.PHR. *in a part of the body* Th.

στῇς (2sg.athem.aor.subj.): see ἵσταμαι, under ἵστημι

στῆσα (ep.aor.), **στῆσαι** (aor.inf.), **στησάμην** (ep.aor.mid.), **στῆσαν** (ep.3pl.aor.), **στήσᾱς** (aor.ptcpl.), **στησάτω** (3sg.aor.imperatv.): see ἵστημι

Στησίχορος, dial. **Στᾱσίχορος**, ου *m.* **Stesichorus** (early 6th-C. BC lyric poet, assoc.w. S. Italy and Sicily) Simon. Isoc. Pl. Arist.

στήσομαι (fut.mid.), **στῆσον** (aor.imperatv.), **στήσω** (fut., also aor.subj.): see ἵστημι

στῆτε, στήτω (2pl. and 3sg. athem.aor.imperatv.): see ἵσταμαι, under ἵστημι

στία ᾱς *f.* [perh.reltd. στέαρ] | only ep.gen.pl. στιάων | **small stone, pebble** AR.

στιβάδιον ου *n.* [dimin. στιβάς] **pallet** or **bed of leaves** Plu.
στιβαδοκοιτέω *contr.vb.* [στιβάς, κοίτη] **lie on a pallet** or **bed of leaves** Plb.
στιβαρός ά (Ion. ή) όν *adj.* [στείβω] **1** compressed to form a solid mass; (of parts of the body) **sturdy, stout, strong** Hom. Hes. hHom. Pi.*fr.* Emp. Hellenist.poet.; (of a person) Ar.; (of weapons, hammers) Hom. Hes. AR.; (of a door-bolt) Theoc.; (of a bulwark, ref. to Apollo) Call.
2 (of a discus) massive, **mighty** Od.; (of trees, rocks, or sim.) AR.
—**στιβαρῶς** *adv.* **strongly, firmly** —*ref. to fitting double gates together* Il.
στιβάς άδος *f.* **bed of straw, rushes or leaves** (sts. covered w. a garment or rug), **pallet** or **bed of leaves** Hdt. E. Ar. Pl. X. Men. +
στιβέομαι (or **στιβάομαι**) *pass.contr.vb.* [στίβος] | only 3sg.pf. ἐστίβηται | (of an area) **be paced** or **trodden** S. [or perh. *be scoured for tracks*]
στίβη ης *f.* [app.reltd. στείβω, στιβαρός] **frozen dew, hoarfrost, rime** Od. Call.*epigr.*
στιβήεις εντος *masc.adj.* (of the time before dawn) **frosty** Call.
στίβος ου *m.* [στείβω] **1** trodden way, **track, path** hHom. S. E. AR.
2 mark of treading, **footprint, track** (of humans and animals) hHom. Hdt. Trag. X. Plb. Plu.; (prep.phr.) κατὰ στίβον *on the track, in the footsteps* (sts. w.GEN. *of someone*) Hdt. AR.
στιγεύς έως (Ion. έος) *m.* [στίζω] **tattooer** Hdt.
στίγματα των *n.pl.* **1 tattoo-marks, tattoos** Hdt. Plu.
2 marks, spots (on serpents) Hes.
στιγματίας ου, Ion. **στιγματίης** εω *m.* **tattooed slave** or **criminal** Asius Ar. X. Thphr.(cj.)
στιγμή ῆς *f.* **1** minimal mark; (geom.) **point** Arist.
2 moment (w.GEN. of time) NT.
3 (fig.) **jot, tiniest scrap** (w.GEN. of sthg.) D.
στιγμός οῦ *m.* **tattooing** (as a punishment) A.(pl.)
στίζω *vb.* | fut. στίξω | aor. ἔστιξα || PASS.: pf. ἔστιγμαι |
1 prick, **tattoo** —*a person* Hdt. || PF.PASS. be tattooed Hdt. —w.ACC. on the head Hdt. —w.INTERN.ACC. *w. flower patterns* X.
2 tattoo (as a punishment or mark of disgrace) —*a person or slave, an arm* Ar. Call. —w.COGN.ACC. *w. a tattoo* Hdt. —w.INTERN.ACC. *w. an animal figure* (w.PREP.PHR. *on the forehead*) Plu. —*the Hellespont* (as a punishment inflicted by Xerxes) Hdt. || PF.PASS.PTCPL.ADJ. (of a runaway slave) tattooed Ar. Aeschin.
3 (fig.) beat severely (so as to leave bruises resembling a tattoo), **beat black and blue** —*a slave* Men. || PASS. be beaten black and blue —w.DAT. *by a staff* Ar.
4 (fig., of wind) **stipple** —*the sea* Simon.
στικτός ή όν *adj.* **1** (of a deer, bird's wing, fawnskin) marked with spots, **dappled** S. E.
2 (of the hundred eyes of Argus) marking (his body) with spots, **dappling** E.
στίλβω *vb.* | only pres. and impf. | **1** (of clothes anointed w. oil, polished metal, colours, or sim.) **glitter, glisten, gleam** Il. E. Philox.Leuc. Pl. Plb. +; (of light, fire) hHom. B.
2 (of persons, horses, or sim.) **be resplendent** Hom. E. Ar. Theoc. Plu.
3 (of a person) **glint** —w.INTERN.ACC. *w. a flashing look* E.
στίλη ης *f.* app. **moment, instant** (of time) Ar.
στιλπνός ή όν *adj.* (of dewdrops) **glittering, glistening** Il.

στιλπνότης ητος *f.* **lustre, gloss** (of oil) Plu.
στίξ στιχός *f.* [στιχάομαι] | only gen.sg., and nom.acc.pl. στίχες, στίχας | **1** (usu.pl.) **row, line, rank** (of combatants, oft. as collectv.pl. *ranks, forces*) Il. Hes. A. Pi. E.; (of ships) Il.; (of hunters, dancers) Il.; (of spectators in a theatre) Ar.; (of winds, oracle-like words) Pi.
2 || PL. **classes, species** (of primordial creatures) AR.
στιπτός ή όν *adj.* [στείβω] **1** (of a bed of leaves) **pressed down, compressed** S.
2 (fig., of a person) **tough** Ar.
στίφος εος (ους) *n.* [perh. στείβω] **1** compacted body, **massed ranks, solid column, close array** (of soldiers, ships) A. Hdt. Th. X. Plb.; (of people) Ar.
2 band (of soldiers united by close ties) Plu.
στιφρός ά όν *adj.* **1** compressed; (of an animal's leg, thigh) **firm, tough** X.
2 (of a noose, javelin shaft) **strong** X.
στιχάομαι *mid.contr.vb.* —also **στιχάω** *act.contr.vb.* [reltd. στείχω; cf. στίξ] | only (w.diect.) ep.3pl.impf. ἐστιχόωντο, ep.act.3pl. στιχόωσι | **1** (of soldiers, herdsmen, ships) **go, make one's way, proceed** (sts. perh. w.connot. *in line, in column*) Il. AR.; (of cattle, dolphins, nymphs) Hellenist.poet.
2 (of trees) **stand in line** AR.
στιχάς άδος *f.* [reltd. στίχος] || PL. **rows, lines** (of birds) E.(cj.) | see στολάς
στίχες, στίχας (nom.acc.fem.pl.): see στίξ
στίχος ου *m.* [στείχω; cf. στίξ] **1 row, line** or **file** (of soldiers) X.; (of trees) X.
2 series (of numbers) Pl.
3 line (of verse) Ar. Pl. Call.*epigr.* Plb. Plu. || COLLECTV.PL. verse Plu.
—**στιχίδια** ων *n.pl.* [dimin.] **verselets** (fr. a play of Aristophanes) Plu.
στίχω *vb.*: see στείχω
στλεγγίς (also **στελγίς** Plb.) ίδος *f.* [prob.loanwd.]
1 scraper, strigil (usu. of metal, used to remove sweat, sand and oil when bathing after exercise) Pl.; (of reed, also used to siphon liquid) Ar.
2 a kind of tiara overlaid with metal; **tiara** (of gold) X. Plb.
στοά, dial. **στοιά** (Ar.), ᾶς, Ion. **στοιή** ῆς *f.* [reltd. ἵστημι]
1 roofed colonnade, **portico, stoa** Hdt. Th. Ar. Att.orats. +; (serving as a place where corn was stored and sold) Ar.
2 (milit.) **shed** (to protect siege-workers) Plb.
στοιβή ῆς *f.* [reltd. στείβω] **1** a kind of thorny bush, **burnet** Plu.; (used as a broom) Hippon.
2 (fig., ref. to superfluous language, fr. the use of the bush for stuffing and packing) **padding** Ar.
στοιχεῖον ου *n.* [στοῖχος] **1** length of a shadow as a means of measuring time, **shadow** (app. cast by the gnomon of a sundial) Ar.
2 one component in a complete series; (in speech) indivisible sound which may be represented by a single letter, **element** (of a syllable or word) Pl. Arist.
3 letter Pl. Arist. Plb.
4 (philos.) component into which matter is divisible, **element** Pl. Arist. Plu.
5 (in reasoning, geometry) element on which others depend, **basic proposition** Arist.
6 (gener.) **elementary** or **fundamental principle** Isoc. X. Arist.; **element, component** Plu.
στοιχειώδης ες *adj.* (of a body of matter) **elementary** Arist.
στοιχέω *contr.vb.* **1** (of cavalry) **form a line** X.
2 (fig.) **be in line, comply** —w.DAT. *w. sthg.* Plb.
3 go straight ahead, not deviate —w.PTCPL. *in doing sthg.* NT.

στοιχηγορέω *contr.vb.* [ἀγορεύω] speak in an unbroken series, **recite without a break** A.

στοιχηδόν *adv.* [στοιχέω] **in a row** or **rows** AR.

στοιχίζω *vb.* [στοῖχος] | *aor.* ἐστοίχισα | **1 set in a row** —*hunting nets* X.
2 line up, classify, distinguish —*methods of divination* A.

στοῖχος ου *m.* [στείχω] **1 line, file, column** (of ships, soldiers) A. Th. X.; **row, line** (of hunting nets) X.; (prep.phrs.) κατὰ στοῖχον *in a line* Th.; (also) ἐπὶ στοίχου Ar.
2 row, tier (W.GEN. of the steps of a pyramid) Hdt.
3 series (of numbers) Arist.

στολάς άδος *fem.adj.* [reltd. στόλος] (of birds) **in close array** E.(dub.) | see στιχάς

στολή ῆς, *dial.* **στολά̄** ᾶς, *Aeol.* **στόλᾱ** (or **σπόλᾱ**) ᾱς *f.* [στέλλω] **1 equipment** or **outfit, garb, attire, dress** (of a man or woman, oft. w.adj. specifying its type) Sapph. B. Hdt. Trag. Ar. Pl. + || PL. **robes, clothes** (of a single person) S.
2 perh., equipping to go forth, **despatch** (W.GEN. of a fleet) A.

στολιδόομαι *mid.contr.vb.* [reltd. στολίζω] **dress oneself in** —*a fawnskin* E.

στολιδωτός ή όν *adj.* (of a tunic) **hanging in folds, pleated** X.

στολίζω *vb.* [στολίς] | *aor.ptcpl.* στολίσᾱς || *pf.pass.ptcpl.* ἐστολισμένος | **1** prob. **fold up, stow away** —*sails* Hes.
2 || PF.PASS.PTCPL. (of a warrior) **equipped** —W.DAT. *w. a spear* E.; (of ships) —*w. emblems* E.

στολίς ίδος *f.* [στέλλω] **1** (sg. and pl.) **garment, dress, robe** E.
2 || PL. **folds, pleats** (W.GEN. of a garment) E.

στόλισμα ατος *n.* [στολίζω] **equipment, weaponry** (ref. to spears) E.

στολμός οῦ *m.* [στέλλω] **1** (sg. and pl.) **attire, apparel** E.; (W.GEN. of robes or sim.) A. E.; (for corpses) E.
2 perh., arrangement, **rig** (of a sail) A.

στολοκρός όν *adj.* (of a person) app., shorn of hair, **close-cropped** Anacr.

στόλος ου *m.* [στέλλω] **1 travel by sea or land** (usu. for a stated purpose), **journey, expedition** Pi. Hdt. Trag. +
2 purpose or cause of a journey, **mission, errand** S. E.
3 sending, despatch (of someone by another) S.
4 military expedition, campaign (by sea or land) Hdt. Trag. Th. X.
5 (fig.) **contest** (ref. to the pankration) Pi.
6 expeditionary force (of soldiers or ships), **force, armament** Hdt. Trag. Th. Pl. X. +
7 troop, band, host, company (usu. ref. to people travelling or gathered for a specific purpose) Hdt. Trag. Ar.
8 prow or **beak** (of a ship) A. Pi. E.

στόμα, *Aeol.* **στύμα**, ατος *n.* | oft.pl. for sg. | **1 mouth** (of a person or animal) Hom. +; (fig.) **jaws** (of battle, war) Il.
2 mouth as the organ of speech; mouth, lips, voice Hom. +; **voice, mouthpiece** (of the Muses, ref. to a poet) Theoc. Mosch.; (personif., in voc.) ἀνόσιον στόμα *you impious mouth* S.
3 (phrs.) ἔχειν ἀνὰ στόμα, διὰ στόμα, διὰ στόματος, ἐν στόματι *have on one's lips, i.e. often speak of* (someone or sthg.) Il. Hdt. E. Ar. X. Plb.; ἀπὸ στόματος εἰπεῖν *speak off the cuff, extemporise* Pl. X. Plu.; ἐξ ἑνὸς στόματος *with one voice, in unison* Ar. Pl.
4 aperture or opening of objects or natural features; mouth (of a river or canal) Hom. +; (of a harbour or bay) Hom. Th. Ar. D. Plb.; (of a lake or sim.); oft. of Pontos, the Black Sea, ref. to the Bosporos) Pi. Hdt. E. Th. +; (of a passageway or street) Od. Pl. X.; (of a city, ref. to a gate) S.; (of the underworld) Pi. E.; (of a well) X.
5 aperture (of a trench, ref. to the span betw. its sides) Hdt.
6 foremost part of an object; point, tip (of a spear) Il.; **edge** (of a sword) NT.; **front line, fighting edge** (of an army) X. Plb. Plu.
7 (fig.) **keen edge** (ref. to a steely temper) S.; **cutting edge** (of a fighting force, ref. to its best men) Plb.
8 edge (of battlements, ref. to their top) E.; (fig.) **edge, end** (of life) X.(dub.)
9 (prep.phrs.) ἐπὶ στόμα *on one's face, face down* Il. Hippon. X. Men. Plu.; κατὰ στόμα *face to face, head-on* Hdt. E. Pl. +

στομά-λιμνον ου *n.* [λίμνη] **salt-water lake, lagoon** (perh. as a place name) Theoc.

στόμ-αργος ον *adj.* [perh. ἀργός] perh., with a swift tongue; (of a person) **voluble** or **loud-mouthed** A. S.; (of tiresome talk) E.

στοματουργός όν *adj.* [ἔργον] (of a tongue) **working in the mouth** Ar.

στομαυλέω *contr.vb.* **pipe** (W.ACC. an aulos-prelude) **with the lips** (opp. the aulos) Pl.

στόμαχος ου *m.* [reltd. στόμα] **1 throat** (of a person or animal, as the vulnerable part) Il.
2 stomach (as the organ of digestion) Plu.

στόμιον ου *n.* [*dimin.* στόμα] **1 mouth, opening** (of a subterranean chamber, chasm, or sim.) A. S. Pl. Plb.; (of a harbour) E.
2 mouthpiece of a horse's bridle, bit Hdt. Trag. X.; (fig.) **curb** (ref. to control imposed on a city or persons) Trag. Philox.Leuc.

στομόω *contr.vb.* | *pf.pass.* ἐστόμωμαι | **1 stop the mouth of, gag** —*a person* Hdt.
2 give a sharp edge; (fig.) **whet, sharpen** —*a person, his jaws* (*i.e. tongue*) Ar. || PF.PASS. have been given a sharp edge, have had one's tongue sharpened E.*fr.*
3 || PASS. (of babies) be given a hard edge or be tempered —W.ACC. *in their physique* Plu.
4 provide a fighting edge; **line** —*the rear and sides of an army* (W.DAT. *w. spearmen and slingers*) Plu. || PF.PASS. (of an Erinys) be aggressively fringed —W.DAT. *w. vipers* E.

στομφάζω *vb.* [στόμφος *pompous language*] **rant bombastically** Ar.

στόμφαξ ᾱκος *m.* **bombastic ranter** (ref. to Aeschylus) Ar.

στόμωμα ατος *n.* [στομόω] **1 mouth** (of Pontos, the Black Sea, ref. to the Bosporos) A.
2 hard edge or **hardness, temper** (W.GEN. of steel) Plu.
3 (fig.) **cutting edge** (ref. to a military force) Plu.

στόμωσις εως *f.* **hardening of iron** (so as to provide an edge); (fig.) **sharpness of edge, sharpness** (of speech) S.

στοναχέω *contr.vb.* [στοναχή] | *aor.inf.* στοναχῆσαι || MID.: *ep.3pl.impf.* στοναχεῦντο | **1** (of mourners) **groan, wail, moan** Il. Mosch.
2 || MID. (tr.) **lament, sigh for** —*a dead poet's singing* Mosch.

στοναχή ῆς *f.* [reltd. στενάχω] **groaning, moaning** Hom. E. || PL. **groans, moans** Hom. Sol. Stesich. Pi. S. E. AR.

στοναχίζω (v.l. **στεναχίζω**), *dial.* **στοναχίσδω** (cj.) *vb.* | only pres. and impf. | **1** (act. and mid., of a person) **groan, wail, moan** Hom. Sapph.
2 (of earth) **groan** (under the tread of feet, the weight of a falling Titan) Il. Hes.; (of Gaia, under the pressure of her children within her) Hes.

στονόεις εσσα εν *adj.* [στόνος] **1 full of the sound of moaning;** (of song, speech) **mournful, sorrowful** Il. S. AR.;

(of the nightingale) S.; (of a sea-channel) **moaning, groaning** S.
2 causing moaning; (of arrows, missiles) **grievous, painfraught** Hom. Hes. hHom.; (of fighting, war, the turmoil of battle) Il. Hes. Pi. AR.; (of a sword) S.; (of tests of endurance) Hes. AR.
3 associated with moaning; (of sorrows, sufferings, a wakeful night) **painful** Od. Archil. Tim. AR.; (of a bed) **grief-filled, sorrowful** Od.; (of breast-beating) A.
—**στονόεν** neut.adv. **with moans** —ref. to crying out A.
στόνος ου m. [στένω] **moaning, groaning** (of persons, fr. pain or grief) Hom. A. S. Th.; (fr. painful exertion) Call.; (of the sea) S.
στόννξ υχος m. **sharp point** (of a rock) E.Cyc. AR.
στοργή ῆς f. [στέργω] **love, affection** (opp. strife) Emp.
στόρνη ης f. [στόρνυμι] **waist-band, girdle** (of a woman) Call.
στόρνῡμι vb. | inf. στορνύναι, imperatv. στόρνῡ, ptcpl. στορνύς | dial.fut.: 3pl. στορεσεῦντι, inf. στορεσεῖν (Theoc.) | aor. ἐστόρεσα, ep. στόρεσα ‖ mid.pass.impf. ἐστορνύμην | —also **στρώννῡμι**, and (impf.) **στρωννύω** | 3sg. στρώννῡσι (X., perh. false reading for στόρνυσι) | ptcpl. στρωννύς (Plu.) | impf. ἐστρώννυον (NT.) | aor. ἔστρωσα ‖ MID.: aor.ptcpl. στρωσάμενος ‖ PASS.: 3sg.impf. ἐστρώννυτο (Men., cj.) | 3sg.pf. ἔστρωται, ptcpl. ἐστρωμένος | 3sg.plpf. ἔστρωτο |
1 spread with coverings, **make up** —a bed, couch Hom. hHom. Hdt. S. E. Ar. +; (mid.) Theoc.; **spread out** (on a bed) —rugs or sim. Hom.; (intr.) **spread out a bed** (on the ground) Od. AR.(mid.) NT. ‖ PASS. (of a bed or couch) be made up Hdt. E. Th. Men. Call. Theoc. +; be spread —W.DAT. w. blankets, foliage hHom. Pl.
2 cover by spreading, **strew** —the ground (W.DAT. w. fabrics) A. —a road (w. myrtle branches) Hdt. ‖ PASS. (of a road) be paved (w. stone) Hdt. Plu.
3 spread out —hot embers (in cooking) Il. —branches (on an altar) AR. —branches, cloaks (W.PREP.PHR. in the road) NT.; **lay out in a line** —rollers (for launching a ship) AR.(mid.)
4 (of gods, halcyons, winds, lack of winds) **make smooth, calm** —the sea, waves Od. hHom. B. AR. Theoc. ‖ PASS. (of waves) subside Hdt. AR.
5 (of Zeus) **calm, soothe** —his anger A.
6 (of Herakles) cause to stretch out, **lay low** —Centaurs (W.DAT. w. arrows) E.; (of the Athenians) **overthrow** —the might of the Persians Lycurg.(quot.epigr.); (of persons, time) **humble** —a proud spirit E. Th.
στοχάζομαι mid.vb. [στόχος] | aor. ἐστοχασάμην ‖ neut.impers.vbl.adj. στοχαστέον | **1 aim** (w. a missile or blow) —W.GEN. at a target or person Antipho Pl. X. Plb.
2 (fig.) **aim** —W.GEN. or PREP.PHR. at sthg. (as a desirable goal or acquisition) Isoc. Pl. D. Arist. Plb. Plu.
3 (fig.) **aim at, target** —W.GEN. someone (w. a view to securing favour) X. Arist. Plb. Plu.
4 aim with the mind, **conjecture, make an inference, guess** S. Pl. X. Aeschin. Plb. —W.GEN. about sthg. Isoc. Pl. —W.INDIR.Q. or ACC. + INF. what (or that sthg.) is the case Arist. Plb.
5 get the measure of, **judge** —W.GEN. someone (W.ADV. correctly) Plu.
6 have in one's sights, **take notice of** —W.GEN. sthg. Plb.
στόχασις εως f. **guessing, guesswork** Pl.
στόχασμα ατος n. weapon for aiming, **javelin** E.
στοχασμός οῦ m. use or power of guessing, **guesswork** Pl.
στοχαστικός ή όν adj. **1** (of persons, virtue) **aiming at, trying to hit** (W.GEN. a desirable goal) Arist.

2 (of a mind) good at guessing, **intuitive** Pl. ‖ FEM.SB. art of guesswork, conjecture Pl.
—**στοχαστικῶς** adv. (w. ἔχειν) *be good at guessing, be intuitive* Arist.
στόχος ου m. **1 target** (for archers and javelin-throwers) X.
2 act of aiming, **targeting** E.
3 act of guessing, **guess** A.
στραγγάλη ης f. [reltd. στράγξ *squeezed-out drop*] **noose for strangling** Plu.
στραγγεύομαι mid.vb. prob., trickle drop by drop; (fig.) **hesitate, loiter, dawdle** Ar. Pl.
στραγγουρίᾱ ᾱς f. [οὐρέω] condition of slow and painful urination, **strangury, difficulty in pissing** Ar.
στραγγουριάω contr.vb. **suffer from strangury** Ar. Pl.
στράπτω vb. [reltd. ἀστράπτω] | ep.3sg.impf. στράπτε | aor.ptcpl. στράψᾱς | (of lightning, torch-light, armour) **flash** S. AR.
στρατ-ᾱγέτᾱς ᾱ dial.m. [στρατός, ἡγέομαι] leader of an army, **military chief** B.
στρατᾱγός dial.m.: see στρατηγός
στρατ-άρχης εω Ion.m. [ἄρχω] **commander of an army** Hdt.
στρατ-αρχος ου m. **commander of an army** (W.GEN. of Aithiopians) Pi.
στρατείᾱ ᾱς, Ion. **στρατηίη** ης f. **1 military expedition, campaign** (ref. to a specific undertaking) A. Hdt. E. Th. Att.orats. +
2 going on a campaign, **period of military service** Hdt. Th. Att.orats. + | see also στρατιά 4
3 (concr.) **expeditionary force, military force** E. | see also στρατιά 3
στράτευμα ατος n. [στρατεύω] **1 military expedition, campaign** A. Hdt. E.Cyc.
2 armament, army (ref. to land forces) Hdt. Trag. Th. +; (ref. to ships or sailors) Trag. Th.
3 ‖ PL. **troops, soldiers** NT.
στρατεύσιμος ον adj. (of a person's age) **suitable for military service** X. ‖ MASC.PL.SB. men liable to military service Plb.
στράτευσις ιος Ion.f. **expedition** Hdt.
στρατεύω vb. [στρατός] | MID.: pf. ἐστράτευμαι ‖ PASS.: aor. (w.mid.sens.) ἐστρατεύθην (Pi.) | **1** (act. and mid., of commanders) **take the field** or **go on campaign** (oft. W.PREP.PHR. to or against a place, person or people) Pi. Hdt. Trag. +; **march out** —W.COGN.ACC. on a campaign E. Att.orats. Arist.; **embark on** —a war Th.
2 ‖ MID. **serve in an army, do military service** Th. Ar. Pl. +
στρατηγέω contr.vb. [στρατηγός] **1** (gener.) **be a military commander** or **general** A. Hdt. E. + —W.ACC. in a war, seabattle D. —W.DAT. for someone (i.e. be in charge of his forces) D.; **conduct one's generalship** —W.NEUT.ACC. or ADV. in a particular way Hdt. X. D.; (fig., of Fortune) **take command** —W.ADV. more effectively X. ‖ NEUT.PL.PASS.PTCPL.SB. (pres. and pf.) achievements or conduct of a commander Isoc. D.
2 be in command —W.GEN. of persons, troops, ships Hdt. S. Th. Ar. + —of a place Hdt. Plu. —W.DAT. of persons, troops A. E.; **lead** —W.DAT. troops (W.PREP.PHR. to a place) Hdt.
3 (specif., at Athens) hold the office of strategos, **be a general** Th. Ar. Att.orats. Pl. X. Arist.
4 (at Rome) **be a consul** Plb.; **be a praetor** Plu.
5 (of a commander) use a stratagem or pursue a strategy against, **outmanoeuvre** —an enemy, fellow commander Plb.; (intr.) **pursue a strategy, manoeuvre** —W.INF. so as to achieve sthg. Plu.

στρατήγημα

6 ‖ PASS. serve under a general Arist.; (of an expedition, a city) be commanded —w. ὑπό + GEN. *by specified leaders* Isoc. Pl.; (fig., of the Athenians) —*by Philip* D.; (of the journeying of fugitives) —W.DAT. *by an old man and woman* E.
7 (fig., of a money-lender) **be in command** —W.GEN. *of market-traders* Thphr.

στρατήγημα ατος *n.* **1** act or **display of generalship** Isoc.
2 stratagem, tactic X. Aeschin. Plb. Plu.

στρατηγίᾱ ᾱς, Ion. **στρατηγίη** ης *f.* **1 office of general, generalship, military command** Hdt. E. Th. +; (at sea) X.
2 (specif., at Athens) office of strategos, **generalship** Th. Att.orats. Pl. Plu.
3 (at Rome) **praetorship** Plu.
4 tenure and performance of the office of general, **period of generalship, command, campaign** Th. Isoc. X. +
5 practice, skill or theory of being a general, **generalship, leadership** Pl. X. D. Arist.

στρατηγιάω contr.vb. **itch to be a general** X. D. Plu.

στρατηγικός ή όν *adj.* **1** (of things, actions, abstr. concepts) of or relating to a general, **of a general** Pl. X. Arist. +
‖ FEM.SB. **art of generalship** Pl. Arist. ‖ NEUT.PL.SB. **functions and duties of a general, generalship, strategy, tactics** Isoc. Pl. X. Plb.
2 (of persons) like or suitable to be a general, **general-like** Isoc. Pl. X. Arist. +
3 (at Rome) of or belonging to a praetor; (of insignia, cohorts, or sim.) **praetorian** Plu.; (of persons) **of praetorian rank** Plu. ‖ MASC.PL.SB. **praetorian guards** Plu.

—**στρατηγικῶς** *adv.* | compar. στρατηγικώτερον | in the manner of a general, **like a general** Ar. Plb.

στρατήγιον ου *n.* **1 general's quarters** or **command post** S.
2 (at Athens) headquarters of the generals, **war office** Aeschin. D. Plu.
3 headquarters of a Roman general, **praetorium** Plb.

στρατηγίς ίδος *fem.adj.* **1** (of a ship) **of a general** Th. And. D. Plu. ‖ SB. **flagship** Hdt.
2 (of doors) **of generals** (i.e. of their headquarters) S.
3 (of a cohort) **praetorian** Plu.
4 ‖ SB. **female general** (of a gynaecocracy) Ar.

στρατ-ηγός, dial. **στρατᾱγός**, οῦ *m.* [στρατός, ἄγω]
1 leader of an army, **general, commander** Archil. Ibyc. Carm.Pop. Hdt. Trag. +
2 (at Athens) **general** (one of ten officers elected annually to command the army and navy and war department at home) Hdt. Th. Ar. Att.orats. +; (*f.*) **female general** Ar. | see στρατηγίς 4
3 (at Rome) **consul** Plb.
4 one who holds military command within a prescribed territory, **military governor** Hdt. Plb.; **chief magistrate** NT.
5 officer, commander (W.GEN. of the temple in Jerusalem, responsible for maintaining order) NT.

στρατηίη Ion.*f.*: see στρατεία

στρατηλασίη ης Ion.*f.* [στρατηλάτης] **1 military expedition, campaign** Hdt.
2 expeditionary force Hdt.

στρατηλατέω contr.vb. **1 lead an army** (freq. W.ADV. to a place, or W.PREP.PHR. to or against a place or people) A. Hdt. E.
2 be leader E. —W.GEN. *of troops* E.; **lead** —W.DAT. *troops* E.

στρατ-ηλάτης ου, dial. **στρατηλάτας** ᾱ *m.* [στρατός, ἐλαύνω] **1** leader of an army, **commander, general** S. E. Plu.; (W.GEN. of troops, Greece) E.; (of ships) A. E.
2 (fig., ref. to the aulos) **commander** (W.DAT. of revels and brawling) Pratin.

στρατιᾱ́ ᾱς, Ion. **στρατιή** ῆς *f.* **1 military force** (on land or sea), **armament, army** A. Pi. B. Hdt. E. Th. +
2 host, multitude (of competitors in a foot-race) Pi.
3 military expedition, campaign Ar. [also Hdt., unless the correct form is στρατηίη]
4 period of going on campaign, **military service** Ar. [also Hdt. Th. Pl. And., unless the correct forms are στρατηίη, στρατεία]

στρατι-άρχης εω Ion.*m.* [ἄρχω] **commander of an army** Hdt.

στρατί-αρχος ου *m.* **commander of an army** (of mercenaries) X.

στράτιος ᾱ ον *adj.* [στρατός] | Aeol.compar. στροτιώτερος |
1 (epith. of Zeus in Asia Minor) **of armies, of battle** Hdt. Plu.
2 (prob. of persons) **martial** Alc.

—**στράτιον** *neut.adv.* **belligerently** —*ref. to farting* Ar.

στρατιώτης ου *m.* [στρατιᾱ́] member of an armed force, **soldier** Hdt. Th. +; **professional soldier, mercenary** Arist.

στρατιωτικός ή όν *adj.* **1** (of things, activities, abstr. concepts) of or relating to a soldier, **military** Ar. Att.orats. Pl. X. + ‖ NEUT.SG.SB. **soldiers as a group, soldiery** Th. Plu. ‖ NEUT.PL.SB. **military affairs** Pl. X.; **military funds** Arist.
2 (of a person's age) **suitable for military service** X.
3 (of persons, their behaviour) of a soldierly nature, **soldier-like, military** Arist. Plb. Plu.

—**στρατιωτικῶς** *adv.* **1 in a soldierly way** Isoc. Plb.
2 like a common soldier —*ref. to behaving brutishly* Plb.

—**στρατιωτικώτερον** *compar.adv.* **more for soldiers** (than for a sea-fight) —*ref. to equipping ships as troop-carriers* Th.

στρατιῶτις ιδος *fem.adj.* [στρατιώτης] | acc. στρατιῶτιν |
1 of or relating to soldiers; (of aid) **military** A.; (of a skill) Plu.
2 (of a ship) **for troops** (i.e. troop-ship) Th. X. Plu.

στρατολογέω contr.vb. [στρατός, λέγω] **enlist, levy** —*soldiers* Plu.; (intr.) **levy soldiers** Plu. ‖ PASS. (of soldiers) **be levied** Plu.

στρατό-μαντις εως *m.* [μάντις] **seer of the army** (ref. to Calchas) A.

στρατόομαι *mid.contr.vb.* | ep.3pl.impf. (w.diect.) ἐστρατόωντο, also στρατόωντο ‖ PASS.: aor.ptcpl. στρατωθείς | **1** (of troops, commanders) **be on campaign, be in the field** Il. AR.
2 ‖ PASS. (of a military force) be formed as an army, **be mustered** A.

στρατοπεδείᾱ ᾱς *f.* [στρατοπεδεύω] **encampment, camp** X. Plb. Plu.

στρατοπέδευσις εως *f.* **1** process of making a camp, **encamping** Pl. X.
2 place of encamping or fact of having encamped, **encampment** X.

στρατοπεδευτικός ή όν *adj.* (of the layout) **of an encampment** Plb.

στρατοπεδεύω *vb.* [στρατόπεδον] **1** (usu.aor., of troops, commanders) set up camp, **encamp** X. Plb. Plu.; (mid.) Hdt. Th. Isoc. Pl. X. +
2 (pres. and impf.) **lie encamped** Plb. Plu.; (mid.) Hdt. Th. X. Plu. ‖ PF.MID. **have set up camp, be encamped** Th. Pl. X.

στρατό-πεδον ου *n.* [στρατός, πέδον] **1** place of encampment (or the persons encamped there), **military encampment, camp** Hdt. Trag. Th. +
2 (gener.) **army** Hdt. E. Att.orats. +; (ref. to naval forces) Hdt. Th. Lys. X.
3 (at Rome) **legion** Plb.

στρατός οῦ, Aeol. **στρότος** ου *m.* **1 host of troops, army** Hom. +; (ref. to a naval force or fleet) A. Hdt. E. Th.; (fig., ref. to an advancing body of rain) Pi.

2 multitude, host (w.GEN. of cavalry, infantry, ships) Sapph.; (of Amazons, Centaurs, or sim.) A. Pi. E.
3 host of people (belonging to a city or nation), **people** A. Pi.; **host, crowd** (at a public gathering) Alcm. Pi. S.

στρατωνίδης ου *m.* type of man who serves as a soldier, **soldier-man** Ar.

στρέβλη ης *f.* [στρεβλός] **1** app., tensioning device, **twister** (used to maintain the tension on a trireme's undergirding cables) A.
2 instrument of torture, **wheel** or **rack** Plb.

στρεβλός ή όν *adj.* **1** (of a penis) **twisted, warped, bent** Ar.; (of a straight-rule) Arist.
2 (fig., of wrestling tricks) **crooked, cunning** Ar.

στρεβλότης ητος *f.* **twist, curve** (of a bent spear-point) Plu.

στρεβλόω contr.vb. | fut.mid. (w.pass.sens.) στρεβλώσομαι |
1 twist (so as to make taut), **twist tight** —*cables* (W.DAT. w. windlasses) Hdt. —*strings of a musical instrument* (W.PREP.PHR. *on pegs, w. allusion to sense 2*) Pl.; (of a doctor) **twist, wrench** —*a dislocated foot* Hdt.
2 twist or stretch in torture (usu. on the wheel), **stretch, torture** —*a person* Ar. Att.orats. Pl. Plb. Plu. || PASS. be stretched Ar. Att.orats. Pl. Plb. Plu.

στρέμμα ατος *n.* [στρέφω] (medic.) **wrench, sprain** D.

στρεπτ-αίγλᾱ ᾱς *dial.fem.adj.* [στρεπτός, αἴγλη] (of the onset of clouds) app. **with twists of radiance** Ar.(mock-dithyramb)

στρεπτικός ή όν *adj.* of or related to twisting; (of one part of the art of weaving) **of twisting** (threads) Pl.

στρεπτός ή όν *adj.* [στρέφω] **1** capable of being turned (by entreaty); (of a god, a mind) **turnable** Il.
2 capable of turning; (of a tongue) **voluble, glib** Il.
3 (of a χιτών, uncert. whether corslet or tunic) **flexible, pliant** Il. [or perh. *woven*]
4 (of a bow-string) **twisted** Hes.*fr.*; (of osiers, used as ropes) E.*Cyc.*
5 (of iron, ref. to a pick-axe or similar tool) **bent, curved** E.; (of the tip of a bow) Theoc.
6 || MASC.SB. rolled or twisted pastry D.
7 || MASC.SB. collar or necklace of twisted metal, torque Hdt. Pl. X. Plu. || NEUT.SB. Men. Plu.

στρεπτο-φόρος ον *adj.* [στρεπτός 7, φέρω] (of Persian soldiers) **wearing a torque** Hdt.

στρεύγομαι *pass.vb.* **1** **be exhausted** or **worn out** —W.PREP.PHR. *in combat* Il. —W.DAT. *through toils* AR.
2 **be in pain** or **distress** Od. AR. —W.DAT. *through shortage of breath, a disease* Tim. Call.

στρεφεδῑνέομαι *pass.contr.vb.* [στρέφω, δῑνέω; cf. στροφοδῑνέομαι] | only ep.3pl.aor. στρεφεδίνηθεν | (of the eyes of one stunned by a blow) be made to whirl round, **go spinning** Il.

στρέφω *vb.* | fut. στρέψω | aor. ἔστρεψα, ep. στρέψα | ep.iteratv.aor.2 στρέψασκον || PASS.: aor.1 ἐστρέφθην, dial. ἐστράφθην (Theocr.) | aor.2 ἐστράφην | pf. ἔστραμμαι |
1 (usu. of persons) turn in some direction (freq. specified by ADV. or PREP.PHR.), **turn, direct** —*objects, persons, animals, parts of the body, eyes* Hom. + || PASS. (of a person) turn oneself, have recourse —W.PREP.PHR. *to arguments* Ar.
2 || PF.PASS.PTCPL.ADJ. (of a place) turned or facing (W.PREP.PHR. in some direction) Plb.
3 direct (someone's) attention; **turn** —*someone, oneself* (W.PREP.PHR. *towards some activity*) E. || PASS. (of a person) turn oneself, have recourse —W.PREP.PHR. *to arguments* Ar.
4 turn with a circular motion; **revolve, rotate** —*a spindle* Hdt.; (of the universe) —*itself* Pl.; (of the Great Bear) —*its tail* (*around the pole*) E.; (of the Euripos channel) **whirl round** —*eddies* E.; (of a boy) **spin** —*a top* Call.*epigr.*; (fig., of whirls of madness) **throw into turmoil** —*a person* S.*Ichn.* || PASS. (of a spindle, the universe, heavenly bodies) revolve, rotate Hom. Pl. Theoc.
5 || MID.PASS. (of persons or animals) **go this way and that, range about, roam** Il. hHom. Sol. S. Call.*epigr.*; (of a person lying asleep or restless) **toss about** Il. E. Ar. Men.; (of a joint in the body) **move freely** Ar.
6 (fig., of evils) **roam at large, be rife** Sol.
7 (of persons, their concerns) **be involved** or **engaged** —W.PREP.PHR. *in sthg.* Ar. Pl.
8 turn in the opposite direction; **turn round, turn back** —*an army, troops, a horse* S. X. —*one's steps* E.*fr.*; (of an earthquake) **reverse** —*a statue* E.; (of the sun) —*its position* E.; (intr., of a commander, soldiers, horsemen) **turn round** X. Plu.; (of a charioteer or ploughman) turn round one's team, **turn** Il. || PASS. (of persons, soldiers) turn or wheel round Hom. S. X. Theoc. Plb. Plu.; (of a horse) X.
9 turn round (a situation); (of a god) **turn** —*a person* (W.ADV. + PREP.PHR. *back to happiness*) Thgn.; **reverse** —*a state of affairs* Pl.; (of reports) —*a person's life* (W.INF. *so that it has repute*) E. || PASS. (of Justice and the natural order) be turned —W.ADV. *back* E.; (of an angry person's temper) be turned about or change S.; (of a person) change one's mind or attitude S.
10 **change, distort** —*words* (*by altering letters*) Pl.
11 **turn over** —*ground* (*by digging*) X.
12 **turn** —*a boat, bag* (w. κάτω *upside down*) S. Ar.; (fig.) —*a person, the established order, arguments, laws, or sim.* (w. κάτω or ἄνω (τε καὶ) κάτω *upside down*) A. E. Pl. D.; (of a god) **overturn** —*a situation* S. E.
13 twist (a part of the body) so as to cause pain; (of a person, pain) **torment, rack** —*someone* Ar.; (fig., of stories) —*the soul* Pl.; (of moving words) **wring** —*the heart* Plu. || PASS. (of limbs) be strained or sprained Pl.; (of a person) suffer a sprain or wrench —W.INTERN.ACC. *in one's foot* (*i.e. twist one's ankle*) Hdt.
14 || PASS. (of osiers) be twisted or entwined —W.DAT. w. *each other* hHom.; (of cords of esparto grass) be plaited X.
15 (of a wrestler preparing for a throw) **twist** —*his backside* (*i.e. turn his hip*) Thphr.; (phr.) ἔριδα στρέφειν *twist* (*one's body*) *in a contest* Pi.
16 (fig., pejor.) **twist** —*one's arguments* (w. ἄνω κάτω *this way and that*) Pl. —*an accusation* (W.ADV. *in all directions*) D.; (of a questioner, compared to a dancer) —*his questions* (W.PREDIC.ADJ. *double*) Pl. || MID.PASS. **twist and turn, wriggle** (i.e. be evasive or scheming) S.*Ichn.* Ar. Pl. —w. ἄνω (καὶ) κάτω *this way and that* Pl.
17 (w. no pejor.connot.) turn over in the mind, **ponder** —*some matter* E. Plu.; **try out** —*every device* Plu.
18 **return, give back** —*money* (W.DAT. *to someone*) NT.

στρεψοδικέω contr.vb. [δίκη] twist justice, **pervert the course of justice** Ar.

στρεψοδικο-πανουργίᾱ ᾱς *f.* **justice-perverting villainy** Ar.

στρηνές *neut.adv.* app. **with a harsh sound** AR.

στρῐβῐ-λῐκίγξ *adv.* [app. στρίβος *thin shrill cry*, λίκιγξ *faint bird sound*] (in neg.phr., expressing emphatic refusal) **with a peep** or **tweet** (i.e. not even in the faintest possible way or to the slightest degree) Ar.

στρίγξ ιγγός *f.* [reltd. τρίζω] | acc. στρίγγα | a kind of owl; app. **screech-owl** Carm.Pop.

στριφνός ή όν *adj.* [perh.reltd. στῖφρός] (of a toy cockerel) **tough, firm, solid** Men. [or perh. *lean, scrawny*]

στροβέω *contr.vb.* [στρόβος] **1 whirl round, spin** —*someone, oneself* Ar.; (intr., of a dancer) **whirl, spin** Ar. ‖ MID. (of eyes) **whirl about** (in frenzy) Ar.
2 (fig., of fancies, prophetic frenzy) put into a whirl, **throw into turmoil** —*a person* A.; (of a plague) —*a city* Plu. ‖ PASS. (of persons in distress, compared to sailors in a storm) be tossed this way and that A.; (of a person continuously disturbed by anxious thoughts) be in a turmoil Plb.

στρόβῑλος ου *m.* **1 spinning-top** Pl. Plu.; (fig., ref. to a dancer who performs pirouettes) Ar.
2 whirlwind Men.; (fig., ref. to a tempestuous person) Men.

στροβῑλώδης ες *adj.* (of a mountain) shaped like a spinning-top, **conical** Plu.

στρόβος ου *m.* [reltd. στρεβλός] **whirling round** (of ships, by a storm) A.

στρογγύλος η ον *adj.* [reltd. στράγξ; cf. γογγύλος] **1 with curved or spherical shape**; (of pots) **round, rounded** Pl. Thphr.; (of the earth, opp. flat; of a shape) Pl.; (of hailstones, a mortar, other natural or manufactured objects) Hdt. Ar. X. Arist. Plb. Plu. ‖ NEUT.SB. curvature (opp. straightness) Pl.; roundness Arist.
2 (of a boat, i.e. merchant ship) **round-hulled** Hdt. Th. X. D. Plb. Plu.
3 (of a dog's legs, haunches, a horse's feet) well-rounded, **well-formed** X.
4 (fig., of verbal expressions) **compact, terse** Ar. Pl.

—**στρογγυλώτατα** *superl.adv.* **most tersely** Arist.

στρογγυλότης ητος *f.* **roundness** Pl. Arist.

στρόμβος ου *m.* [reltd. στρεβλός] **1 spinning-top** Il.
2 whirlwind A.
3 large spiral shell of a mollusc, **trumpet-shell** Theoc.

στροτιώτερος (Aeol.compar.adj.), **στρότος** Aeol.*m.*: see στράτιος, στρατός

στρουθός οῦ *m.f.* **1 house sparrow, sparrow** Il. Sapph. Hdt. Ar. Plu.
2 (W.ADJ. κατάγαιος *terrestrial*) **ostrich** Hdt.; (w. μεγάλη) Ar. X.; (w. no ADJ.) Ar. Plb.

—**στρουθίον** ου *n.* [dimin.] **sparrow** NT.

στροφαῖος ᾱ ον *adj.* [στροφεύς, στροφή] (epith. of Hermes) **of the pivoting door** (w. further fig.connot. *twister and turner*) Ar.

στροφάλιγξ ιγγος *f.* [στρέφω] **1 whirl, whirlpool** Emp.
2 whirling cloud (W.GEN. of dust) Hom.; (of smoke) AR.
3 swirl (of water in a bucket) AR.

στροφαλίζω *vb.* **twist, spin** —*wool* Od.

στροφάς άδος *masc.fem.adj.* (of the paths of the Great Bear) **revolving, circling** S.

στροφεῖον ου *n.* **twisted cord** X.

στροφεύς έως *m.* **door-socket** (hole set in a threshold and lintel into which fitted the στρόφιγξ, the pivot on which the door turns) Ar. ‖ PL. sockets and pivots Plb.

στροφή ῆς *f.* **1 turning, turn** (of a horse) X.
2 twirl, pirouette (of a dancer) Ar.
3 whirl (W.GEN. of madness) S.*Ichn.*
4 rolling (W.GEN. of the eye) E.
5 change (W.GEN. of season) Pl.
6 (gener.) **twisting, turning** Pl.
7 (ref. to evasive or underhand behaviour) **twist, dodge, trick** Ar. Pl. Plu.
8 (ref. to a mode of argument) **twist, turn** A. Ar. Pl.
9 (ref. to a form of elaboration or modulation in new-style music) **twist, turn** Ar.

στρόφιγξ ιγγος *f.* **1 pivot** (fitting into the στροφεύς *door-socket*) Plu.; (for a moving figure on a shield) E.; (ref. to a vertebra) Pl.
2 (fig.) **pivot, hinge** (W.GEN. of a tongue, in a versatile speaker) Ar.

στρόφιον ου *n.* [dimin. στρόφος] **1** broad band of cloth (worn by women to support the breasts), **breast-band, bra** Ar.
2 headband (of a priest) Plu.

στροφίς ίδος *f.* [στρέφω] **twisted cord** E.

στρόφις *m.* | only nom. | **twister** (ref. to an evasive or deceitful person) Ar.

στροφοδῑνέομαι *mid.pass.contr.vb.* [στρόφος, δῑνέω; cf. στρεφεδῑνέομαι] (of vultures) **wheel round and round** A.

στρόφος ου *m.* [στρέφω] **1** twisted rope or band, **cord** Od. hHom. Hdt.
2 prob. **breast-band** (of a woman) A. | cf. στρόφιον
3 twisting of the bowels, **colic** Ar.

Στρῡμών όνος *m.* **Strymon** (a river in Thrace) Hes. A. Hdt. Th. +; (name of the river god) E.

—**Στρῡμονίης** εω Ion.masc.*adj.* (of a wind blowing fr. the north) **from the Strymon, Strymonian** Hdt.

—**Στρῡμόνιος** ᾱ ον *adj.* (of a sea or lake, a wind, swans) **Strymonian** A. Call. Mosch.; (of Rhesos, son of the river god) E. ‖ MASC.PL.SB. people living near the Strymon, **Strymonians** Hdt.

στρυφνός ή όν *adj.* | compar. στρυφνότερος | **1** (of foodstuffs, their constituent particles) harsh to the taste, **astringent** Pl. X.
2 (fig., of persons, their characters) **austere, acerbic** Ar. X. Arist.

στρυφνότης ητος *f.* **acerbity, harshness** (of character) Plu.

στρῶμα ατος *n.* [στόρνῡμι] **1** that which is spread with coverings, **bed, mattress** Thgn. Thphr.
2 ‖ PL. fabrics spread as coverings, **bedding, bedclothes** Lys. Ar. Pl. X. D. Thphr. +; coverlets, rugs Ar. Men. Plu.; (ref. to coverings for horses) X.
3 ‖ COLLECTV.PL. **luggage, baggage** (as travellers regularly transported belongings in their bedding) Ar.

στρωματό-δεσμον ου *n.* —also **στρωματόδεσμος** ου (Plu.) *m.* [δέω¹] bag for packing bedclothes, **bedding-bag, bed-pack** Pl. X. Aeschin. Plu.

στρωματο-φύλαξ ακος *m.* servant in charge of royal coverlets and bed furnishings (in Alexander's army), **furnishing-superintendent** Plu.

στρωμνή ῆς, dial. **στρωμνᾱ́** ᾶς, Aeol. **στρώμνᾱ** ᾱς *f.* **1** that which is spread with coverings; **bed** Sapph. A. Pi. Th.; **couch** (for reclining or dining) Plu.; (gener., ref. to a sleeping-place) E.; (ref. to the ground on which Typhon lies) Pi.
2 that which is spread as a covering; (usu.pl.) **bedding** Pl. X. Plu.; **coverlet** (for a couch) Plu.; (ref. to the Golden Fleece) Pi.

στρώννῡμι, στρωννύω *vbs.*: see στόρνῡμι

στρωτήρ ῆρος *m.* timber cross-beam, **floor-beam, joist** Plb.

στρώτης ου *m.* (appos.w. θεράπων *servant*) **person responsible for spreading coverlets** Plu.

στρωτός ή όν *adj.* **1** (of a bed) spread with coverings, **laid, made up** Hes. E. Mosch.
2 (of garments) **spread as coverings** (on a bed) S.

στρωφάω *contr.vb.* [reltd. στρέφω] **1** keep turning, **spin** —*wool* Od.
2 ‖ MID.PASS. turn this way and that, **go about, range, roam** Il. Hes. hHom. Thgn. B. Hdt. +; (of a lion, fig.ref. to an adulterer) **roam freely** —W.PREP.PHR. *in another's bed* A.

στυγ-ἄνωρ ορος *masc.fem.adj.* [στυγέω, ἀνήρ] (of the Amazonian army) **man-hating** A.

στυγερός ά (Ion. ή) όν *adj.* [στύγος] **1** (of persons, deities, things, circumstances) **loathsome, hateful** (sts. W.DAT. to someone) Hom. Hes. Eleg. Lyr. Parm. Trag. +
2 (of words, lamentation, grief, or sim.) **dread, harsh, bitter** Hom. hHom. B. S. Ar. AR.

—**στυγερῶς** *adv.* in a manner causing distaste or dread or bitterness (for oneself or others), **with grim consequences** Hom. AR.

στυγερ-ώπης ες *adj.* [ὤψ] (of Envy) showing hatred in the face, **scowling with hate** Hes.

στυγέω *contr.vb.* | aor.1 ἐστύγησα, ep. στύξα, opt. στύξαιμι | aor.2 ἔστυγον ‖ PASS.: fut. στυγήσομαι (S.) | aor. ἐστυγήθην | **1** shudder at or regard with loathing or aversion, **hate, detest, abhor** —*someone or sthg.* Il. + ‖ PASS. be hated or abhorred (freq. W.DAT. by someone) Trag. AR.
2 shrink from, fear, dread —*someone or sthg.* Hom. Hes. Thgn. Simon. AR.
3 shrink from —W.INF. *doing sthg.* Il. S. AR.
4 (causatv., in ep.aor.1) cause to be hateful; **make** (W.ACC. one's physical strength) **an object of dread** —W.DAT. *to someone* Od.

στύγημα ατος *n.* (ref. to a person) **object of hatred, abomination** (to someone) E.

στυγητός όν *adj.* [στυγέω] (of a person) **hated, abominated** (W.DAT. by someone) A.

Στύγιος *adj.*: see under Στύξ

στύγιος ον *adj.* [στύγος] (of grief, the anger of a goddess) **hateful, bitter, dread** E.

στυγνάζω *vb.* [στυγνός] **1** (of a person) **look grim** (at an unwelcome command) NT.
2 (of the sky) **be gloomy** or **overcast** NT.

στυγνός ή (dial. ά) όν *adj.* [στύγος] **1** (of gods, persons, places, things) **hateful, dreadful, horrendous** Archil. Trag. Theoc. Plb. Bion
2 (of a person) showing hatred, **resentful, bitter** S.
3 (wkr.sens., of a face or brow) **sullen, gloomy** A. E.; (of a person) X. Plu.; (of mourners) Mosch.
4 (of a day) producing gloom (in people), **grim** Plu.

—**στυγνόν** *neut.adv.* **grimly, dreadfully** —*ref. to uttering a cry of grief* S.

στυγνότης ητος *f.* **1 sullenness** (of people, their looks) Plb. Plu.
2 gloominess (of a place) Plb.

στύγος ους *n.* **1** feeling of hatred, **hate, loathing** A.
2 feeling of despondency, **gloom** A.
3 cause of hatred or revulsion, **abomination, horror** (ref. to a serpent, murder, squalor and discomfort, sthg. in the imagination) A.
4 (ref. to a person, a race) object of hatred, **abomination** A.; (W.GEN. to the gods) A.; (ref. to a god, W.DAT. to men) AR.

στυλίς ίδος *f.* [dimin. στῦλος] app. **flag-pole** (at a ship's stern) Plu.

στῦλος ου *m.* [reltd. στύω] **1 pillar** (esp. as support for a building) A. Hdt. E.; (W.GEN. of a house, fig.ref. to a son) E.
2 pole (part of a device used to board enemy ships) Plb.; see κόραξ.

στύμα *Aeol.n.*: see στόμα

Στύμφαλος, Ion. **Στύμφηλος**, ου *m.* **Stymphalos** (town in Arcadia) Il. Plb.

—**Στυμφάλιος** ᾱ ον *adj.* of or belonging to Stymphalos; (of a person) **Stymphalian** X.; (of the city walls) Pi. ‖ FEM.SB. territory of Stymphalos, **Stymphalia** Plb. ‖ MASC.PL.SB. people of Stymphalos, **Stymphalians** Plb.

—**Στυμφαλίς**, Ion. **Στυμφηλίς**, ίδος *fem.adj.* (of a nearby lake) **Stymphalian** Hdt. AR.; (of the nymph Metope, who gave her name to the lake) Pi.

Στύξ Στυγός *f.* [pop.etym. στυγέω] **Styx** (eldest daughter of Okeanos, a goddess resident in the underworld, in whose name the gods swore oaths; also the name of the underworld river) Hom. Hes. Pi.*fr.* B. Hdt. Ar. +

—**Στύγιος** ᾱ ον *adj.* **1** of or relating to Styx; (of the river, its waters) **Stygian** A.*fr.* Pl.; (of the abode of Hades) S.
2 (of darkness) **deathly** A.

στύξα (ep.aor.): see στυγέω

στύπος εος (ους) *n.* **1 trunk** (of a tree) AR. Plb.
2 beam (W.GEN. of a battering-ram) Plb.

στυππεῖον (also **στυππίον** Plb.) ου *n.* **coarse fibre of hemp or flax, tow** Hdt. X. D. Plb. Plu.

στυππειο-πώλης ου *m.* [πωλέω] **seller of tow** Ar.

στυπτηρίη ης *Ion.f.* [στύφω *contract, draw together*] a kind of astringent mineral, **alum** Hdt.

στύραξ[1] ακος *m.* lower end (usu. spiked) of a spear or similar weapon; **butt** (of a javelin or spear) Pl. X. Plu.; (of a Roman standard) Plu.

—**στυράκιον** ου *n.* [dimin.] **butt** (W.GEN. of a javelin) Th.

στύραξ[2] ακος *m.f.*—also **στυρόν** οῦ (Call.) *n.* **1** (*f.n.*) a kind of aromatic gum, **storax** Hdt. Call.
2 (*m.*) tree producing this gum, **storax tree** Plu.

στυφελιγμός οῦ *m.* [στυφελίζω] **buffeting, maltreatment** (of a comic poet by an audience) Ar.

στυφελίζω *vb.* | aor. ἐστυφέλιξα, ep. στυφέλιξα | **1** (of a god or human, a weapon) **strike hard, thump, batter** —*a person, shield* Il. AR.; (of Poseidon, perh. w. his trident) —*the sea* Alc.; (of wind) —*clouds* Il.; (fig., of a god) —*a person's heart* (w. adversity) Pi.*fr.*; (intr., of Ares) **batter away** S. ‖ PASS. (of a dog) be beaten Xenoph.
2 (of a god or human) **shove, dislodge** —*someone or sthg.* (W.PREP.PHR. *fr. a place*) Hom. AR.
3 (gener.) treat roughly; (of a god) **assault, maltreat** —*a fellow god* Il.; (of humans) —*strangers, servants* Od. —*a stepdaughter* (W.DAT. *w. rebukes*) AR. ‖ PASS. (of strangers) be maltreated Od.

στυφελός ή όν (also ός όν A.) *adj.* **1** (of earth, rocks) **hard** AR.; (of a shore) **rough, rugged** A. AR.
2 (fig., of military commanders) **tough, stalwart** A.

στύφλος ον *adj.* (of earth) **hard** S.; (of a shore) **rough, rugged** A.; (of a rock or cliff) A. E.

στυφο-κόπος ου *m.* [κόπτω] **hard-hitter** (ref. to an ὀρτυγοκόπος *quail-tapper*) Ar.

στύω *vb.* [reltd. στῦλος] | aor.inf. στῦσαι | pf. ἔστυκα, ptcpl. ἐστυκώς | **1** ‖ AOR.ACT. and PRES.MID.PASS. **get an erection, get a hard-on** Ar.
2 ‖ PF.ACT. **have an erection** Ar.

στῶ (athem.aor.subj.): see ἵσταμαι, under ἵστημι

Στωικός ή όν *adj.* [στοά] belonging to the Stoa (ref. to the Stoa Poikile, in which Zeno of Kition taught); (of a philosopher) **Stoic** NT. Plu.; (of a doctrine) Plu. ‖ MASC.PL.SB. **Stoics** Plu.

στωμυλίᾱ ᾱς *f.* [στώμυλος] **wordiness, prattle, babble** Ar. Plb. Plu.

στωμυλιο-συλλεκτάδης ου *m.* [συλλέγω] **prattle-collector** (ref. to Euripides) Ar.

στωμύλλω *vb.* | aor.mid. ἐστωμυλάμην | (act. and mid., of persons) **chatter, prattle, babble** Ar.; (of halcyons) Ar.

στωμύλματα των *n.pl.* (ref. to Euripidean poetry) **chit-chat** Ar.; (ref. to poets) **chatterboxes** Ar.

στωμύλος ον *adj.* [στόμα] **1** (of a Euripidean character) **mouthy, prattling on, having the gift of the gab** Ar.; (of a rustic) Theoc.
2 (of a person, as an individual and a historian) **wordy** Plb.

σύ, dial. **τύ**, Boeot. **τού** *2sg.pers.pron.* | acc. σέ (enclit. σε), dial. τέ (enclit. τε, also τυ), also τεί (Alcm.), τίν (Corinn. Theoc.) | gen. σοῦ (enclit. σου), ep. σεῖο (also τεοῖο Il.), Ion. σέο, σεῦ (enclit. σεο, σευ), ep. σέθεν, dial. τέο (Alcm.), τεοῦ (Call.), τεῦ, τεῦς (enclit. τευ, τευς) (Theoc.), Boeot. τεοῦς | dat. σοί (enclit. σοι), dial. τοί (enclit. τοι), also τίν (enclit. τιν Stesich.), τεΐν ‖ See also nom.sg. τύγα, τύνη, du. σφώ, pl. ὑμεῖς | The nom. is used to draw attention to a particular person, esp. in contrast w. another pron. Non-enclitic forms of other cases are used to draw attention, or w. preps. | **you** (sg.) Hom. +

συβαριάζω *vb.* [Σύβαρις] **play the Sybarite, live in the lap of luxury** Ar.

Σύβαρις εως (Ion. ιος) *f.* **1 Sybaris** (Greek city in S. Italy, a byword for wealth and luxury) Hdt. Ar. Arist. Plb. Plu.; (name of the river on which it stood) Th.
2 (fig., ref. to a wagon-train of concubines) **a very Sybaris** Plu.

—**Συβαρίτης** ου (Ion. εω), dial. **Συβαρίτᾱς** ᾱ *m.* **man of Sybaris, Sybarite** Hdt. Ar. Arist. Theoc. Plu. ‖ PL. **people of Sybaris, Sybarites** Hdt. Arist. Plb. Plu.

—**Συβαρῖτις** ιδος *f.* **woman of Sybaris** Ar. ‖ ADJ. (of a spring, a lake, taking their names fr. the town) **of Sybaris, Sybaritic** Theoc.

—**Συβαριτικός** ή όν *adj.* **of or relating to Sybaris**; (of a kind of story) **in the Sybaritic style** Ar.; (of a war) **against Sybaris** Hdt.

συβήνη ης *f.* **a kind of carrying-case; bow-and-arrow case** Ar.

συ-βόσιον ου *n.* [σῦς, βόσκω] | ῐ *metri grat.* (Hom.) | **herd of pigs** Hom. Plb.

συ-βώτης (also **συβότης** Arist.) ου *m.* **swineherd** Od. Hdt. Pl. Arist.

σύγ-γαμος (**ξύγ-**) ον *adj.* [σύν, γάμος] **1** (of a woman) **in married union** (W.DAT. w. someone) E.
2 (of Zeus) **sharing a wife** (W.DAT. w. a mortal) E. ‖ FEM.SB. **woman who shares a husband with another woman, rival wife** E.

συγ-γείτων ον, gen. ονος *adj.* (of a land) **neighbouring** E.

συγ-γελάω *contr.vb.* **laugh together, share a laugh** E.*fr.* —W.DAT. **over wine** Call.*epigr.*

συγγένεια (**ξυγ-**) ᾱς *f.* [συγγενής] **1 common ancestry, kinship** (betw. persons or races) E. Th. Att.orats. Pl. +
2 natural relationship, kinship (betw. things) Pl. Arist.
3 (collectv.sg.) **kin, kinsfolk** E. Pl. Men. NT.; kin occupying the same house, **family** D.; (ref. to a single person) **kin** (W.GEN. of someone) E.

συγ-γενέτειρα ᾱς *f.* [γενετήρ] (ref. to Clytemnestra) **kinswoman** (W.GEN. of the Dioscuri) E.

συγ-γενής (**ξυγ-**) ές *adj.* [γένος, γίγνομαι] **1 associated by birth**; (of character, nobility, a capacity to do sthg., one's destiny) **innate, inherited, natural** Pi.; (of a mode of behaviour) A.; (of fear, in a community) A.; (of an ability, a desire) Arist. ‖ NEUT.SB. **inherited ability, natural genius** Pi.
2 (of persons) **of the same ancestry, related** (oft. W.DAT. to someone) Hdt. Trag. ‖ MASC.FEM.SB. (oft.pl.) **kinsman or kinswoman, relation** (oft. W.GEN. of someone) Pi. Hdt. E. Th. Ar. Att.orats. +; (fig., of months that are connate w. Oedipus) S. ‖ NEUT.SB. **kinship** Trag. Th.
3 (of things) **belonging to or involving someone related by birth**; (of a marriage) **kindred** A.; (of a lock of hair, a hand) A. S.; (of murder) E.; (of communications) **between kinsfolk** E.
4 (of the union of Zeus and Amphitryon w. the same woman) **related, shared** E.
5 (gener., of persons or things) **akin, related, similar** (oft. W.DAT. to someone or sthg.) Ar. Pl. Arist. ‖ MASC.FEM.SB. **associate, affiliate** (W.GEN. of someone's lifestyle, truth) Ar. Pl.
6 (honorific title for the associates of the Persian king) **brother** or **cousin** X.

—**συγγενῶς** *adv.* **1 innately, as one's birthright** —*ref. to being plagued by misfortune* E.
2 in a naturally related way —*ref. to heavenly bodies moving* Pl.

συγγένησις εως *f.* [συγγίγνομαι] **association, meeting** (of people w. each other) Pl.

συγγενικός ή όν *adj.* [συγγενής] **1** (of ailments) **congenital, inherited** Thphr. Plu.
2 of or relating to kin; (of friendship, affection, disputes, warfare) **between kin** Arist. Plb. Plu.

—**συγγενικῶς** *adv.* **on terms of family relationship** —*ref. to managing civic life at Athens* D.

συγγενίς ίδος *f.* **female relative** NT.

συγ-γεννάω *contr.vb.* **1** (of an aspect of seeing) **cooperate** (w. the eye) **in producing** —*colour* Pl.
2 ‖ PASS. (of a person) **be born contemporaneously** —W.DAT. w. *an event* Plu.
3 ‖ PASS. (of a vice) **be engendered** —W.DAT. *in a constitution* Plb.

συγγεννήτωρ ορος *f.* **joint parent** (W.GEN. of children, ref. to a wife) Pl.

συγγεωργέω *contr.vb.* [συγγέωργος] **be a fellow farmer** Is.

συγ-γέωργος (**ξυγ-**) ου *m.* [γεωργός] **fellow farmer** Ar.

συγ-γηθέω (**ξυγ-**) *contr.vb.* | only pf. (w.pres.sens.) ξυγγέγηθα | (of a slave) **join in rejoicing** (at his master's good fortune) L.

συγ-γηράσκω *vb.* | aor.inf. (tm.) σὺν ... γηράναι (or perh. γηρᾶναι) (A.) | **1** (of the mental faculties) **grow old together** —W.DAT. w. *the ageing body* Hdt.; (of a mother) **grow old alongside** (a son) A.
2 (fig., of virtue) **live on** (w. someone) **in old age** Isoc.

συγ-γίγνομαι (**ξυγ-**), Ion. and dial. **συγγίνομαι** *mid.vb.*
1 (of people) **come together, associate, meet** Hdt.
2 associate, keep company, consort —W.DAT. w. *a person* E. Ar. Att.orats. Pl. +; (of a pupil or follower) —w. *a teacher* Isoc. Pl. X.
3 come into contact with, meet —W.DAT. *someone* Hdt. E. Th. Ar. +
4 (of a man or woman) **have sexual intercourse** —W.DAT. w. *someone* Hdt. Lys. Ar. Isoc. +
5 (in an appeal to a god or supernatural agent) **be an ally, come to help** S. Ar. —W.DAT. *someone* A.
6 become familiar —W.DAT. w. *want, water-drinking* Pl.; **be wrapped** —W.DAT. *in thoughts* Ar.

συγ-γιγνώσκω (**ξυγ-**), Ion. and dial. **συγγινώσκω** *vb.*
| fut. συγγνώσομαι | athem.aor. συνέγνων | pf. συνέγνωκα |
1 think together (w. others), **share in a judgement or decision; agree, concur** Hdt.(also mid.) Th. —W.DAT. w. *someone* X. (W.ACC. *about sthg.*) Is. —w. μετά + GEN. w. *many* (W.ACC. *in a mistake of judgement*) Th.
2 share thoughts (w. oneself, usu. W.DAT.REFLEXV.PRON. ἑαυτῷ or sim.), **be conscious of, recognise, admit** —W.NOM.PTCPL. *having done sthg.* S. —w. ὡς + NOM.PTCPL.

Lys. —W.DAT.PTCPL. Hdt. —W.NOM. + INF. Hdt.(mid.) —W.ACC. + INF. *that sthg. is the case* Plu.
3 be conscious of, be aware of —*sthg. shameful* (W.DAT. *in someone*) Plu.; (intr.) be privy (to sthg.), **have guilty knowledge** Plu.
4 recognise, acknowledge, admit —*sthg.* Hdt. Th. —W.ACC. + INF. *that sthg. is the case* Hdt.(also mid.) —W.ACC. + INF. *that someone is doing sthg.* Hdt. Plu. —W.DAT. + INF. Hdt. —W.NOM. + INF. *having done sthg.* Hdt.(mid.) —W.COMPL.CL. *that sthg. is the case* Pl. Plu.
5 (of a person, one's judgement) admit to an error, **give way** Hdt.(also mid.)
6 have fellow feelings, **show compassion, be sympathetic** —W.DAT. *to someone* A.(also mid.) —*to an object* (*as if a person*) Ar.
7 be indulgent, be forgiving S. E. Ar. Pl. +; **pardon, forgive, excuse** —W.DAT. *someone* Simon. Hdt. + —(W.ACC. *for sthg.*) E. X. —(W.GEN.) Pl. —W.DAT. *sthg.* E. Pl. Arist. —W.DBL.DAT. *someone, for sthg.* E.
8 form a reasoned conclusion Ar.
σύγγνοια (**ξύγ-**) ᾱς *f.* **sympathy** or **forgiveness** S.
συγγνώμη (**ξυγ-**) ης *f.* **1 recognition, acknowledgement** (of an error) Hdt.
2 fellow feeling, **compassion, sympathy** Ar. +; (phr.) συγγνώμης τυγχάνειν *win sympathy* Th. And. Lys. X.
3 forgiveness, pardon Hdt. +; (phrs.) συγγνώμην ἔχειν *show forgiveness, offer pardon* (oft. W.DAT. *to someone, sts.* W.GEN. *for sthg.*) Hdt. S. E. Th. Ar. Att.orats. +; (also) συγγνώμην διδόναι Lys. Aeschin. Men. Plb. Plu.; συγγνώμης τυγχάνειν *receive forgiveness, be pardoned* E. Att.orats. X. Plb. Plu.; (also) συγγνώμην λαμβάνειν Th. Pl.
4 (phr.) συγγνώμην ἔχειν *have a claim on forbearance or forgiveness* S. E. Antipho D.
5 (phr.) συγγνώμη (w. ἐστί, freq. understd.) *it is pardonable or excusable* —W.INF. *to do sthg.* D. Arist. —W.DAT. + INF. *for someone to do sthg.* Hdt. E. Lys. Isoc. X. + —W.ACC. + INF. Th. —W. CONDITIONAL CL. *if sthg. is the case* Th. Pl.
συγγνωμονικός ή όν *adj.* [συγγνώμων] **1** (of persons) **of the indulgent** or **forgiving kind** Arist.
2 (of things) **pardonable** Arist.
συγγνωμοσύνη ης *f.* sympathetic understanding, **forgiveness** S.
συγγνώμων (**ξυγ-**) ον, gen. ονος *adj.* [συγγιγνώσκω] **1** (of persons) **in agreement** (W.DAT. w. *someone*) Pl.; (W.GEN. *about sthg.*) Plu.; (phr.) ξυγγνώμονες ἔστε (in a solemn appeal to the gods) *concur* —W.DAT. + INF. *that someone shd. be punished* Th.
2 (of a person or god) **indulgent, forgiving** Pl. Arist.; (W.DAT. *to someone*) X.; (W.GEN. *for sthg.*) E. X. ‖ NEUT.SB. **indulgence, spirit of forgiveness** Pl.
3 (of actions) entailing forgiveness, **pardonable** Th.
συγ-γνωρίζω *vb.* **share in knowledge** Arist.
συγγνωστέος ᾱ ον *vbl.adj.* [συγγιγνώσκω] (of remarks) **to be pardoned, pardonable** Pl.
συγγνωστός όν *adj.* (of an action or emotion) **pardonable, forgivable** E. Ar. Plu.; (of a person) Plu.
συγ-γογγύλλω (**ξυγ-**) *vb.* | aor.ptcpl. συγγογγύλας | **twist** (someone) **around** Ar.
συγ-γομφόομαι *pass.contr.vb.* (of a bridge) **be bolted together** Plu.; (fig., of a mass of soldiers) Plu.
σύγ-γονος (**ξύγ-**) ον *adj.* [γόνος] **1** associated by birth; (of a mode of behaviour, fearlessness, a skill) **innate, inherited, natural** A. Pi.
2 associated with a race or family; (of Erinyes, either as closely assoc.w. the house of Atreus, or gener. as avengers of crimes against kin) **of the race, familial** A.; (of the taint of bloodguilt) E.
3 (of a hearth) **native** (to someone) Pi.
4 related by birth; (of a tortoise shell) **akin, related** (W.GEN. to an oyster shell) S.*Ichn.* ‖ MASC.SB. **kinsman** (W.GEN. of someone) Pi. ‖ MASC. or FEM.SB. **brother or sister** E. ‖ MASC.PL.SB. **kinsmen, relations** Pi. E. Ar.
5 belonging to or involving someone related by birth; (of feelings) **kindred** A.; (of bloodshed) E.
σύγγραμμα ατος *n.* [συγγράφω] **1** something written down, **written information, writing** Hdt. X.
2 written work on a particular subject, **essay, treatise** Isoc. Pl. X. Arist. Plb. Plu.
3 prose composition (opp. poetry) Isoc. Pl.; (prep.phr.) κατὰ τὰ συγγράμματα *according to the handbooks* (i.e. prescribed forms or written rules), *by the book* Pl.
συγγραφεύς (**ξυγ-**) έως *m.* **1 writer, composer, author** Ar. Isoc. Pl.
2 (specif.) **writer of prose** (opp. poetry) Pl.; (ref. to a historian) X. Plb. Plu.
3 draftsman, commissioner (ref. to a member of a board appointed to draft specialised legislation) Th. Isoc.
συγγραφή (**ξυγ-**) ῆς *f.* **1 writing down, recording** (of notable things) Hdt.
2 written record, **history, chronicle** (ref. to a work by an earlier historian) Th.
3 written agreement, contract Th. Att.orats. Pl. Arist.
συγγραφικῶς *adv.* **with studious accuracy** —*ref. to speaking* Pl.
συγ-γράφω (**ξυγ-**) *vb.* **1** (act. and mid.) **write down, record** —*an oracle, message, evidence, or sim.* Hdt. Antipho X. D. ‖ PASS. (of sayings) be written down X.
2 (act. and mid., of a prose-writer) **compose an account of, write about** —*a war, cookery, a person's life, or sim.* Th. Pl. Plb. Plu.; (of a poet) —*a person* Theoc.*epigr.* ‖ PASS. (of an event) be written about Plu.
3 (act. and mid.) **compose** —*a speech, letter, treatise, or sim.* Isoc. Pl. D. Plu. ‖ PASS. (of speeches) be composed Isoc. Pl.
4 (intr.) **be a writer** Pl.; **write in prose** (opp. verse) Isoc. Pl.; **write a work** —W. περί + GEN. *about sthg.* X. Plb.
5 compose by drawing or painting ‖ PASS. (of a bird) be drawn or painted Ar.(dub.)
6 (of a member of a legislative commission) **draft** —*laws, proposals* And. Ar.(mid.) X. Arist.; (intr.) **make draft proposals** Th.; **act as a draftsman** Pl.(mid.) ‖ PASS. (of a law) be drafted Plu.
7 ‖ MID. **make a written agreement**; (of combatants) **agree on terms, sign a treaty** Th. Isoc. —W.ACC. *for peace* Isoc.; (of merchants or sim.) **make a contract** (sts. W.COGN.ACC.) D.; (tr.) **stipulate** (W.ACC. *sthg.*) **in a contract** X. D. ‖ NEUT.PL.PF.PASS.PTCPL.SB. terms of an agreement or contract Isoc. D.
8 ‖ PF.PASS.PTCPL.ADJ. **enrolled**; (phr.) πατέρες συγγεγραμμένοι *patres conscripti* (i.e. Senators, at Rome) Plu.
συγ-γυμνάζω *vb.* **1 train together** —*regular troops and mercenaries* Plb.
2 ‖ MID. **take exercise together** Pl. Arist. Plu. —W.DAT. w. *someone* Pl.
συγγυμναστής οῦ *m.* **exercise-partner** Pl. X. Aeschin.
συγ-καθαγίζω *vb.* (of lightning) **burn up** (W.ACC. *a sacrifice*) **as well** (as the altar) Plu.

συγ-καθαιρέω (ξυγ-), Ion. **συγκαταιρέω** contr.vb. **1 help** (sts. W.DAT. or μετά + GEN. someone) **to bring down** or **destroy** —opponents, their power, walls Th.
2 (of a seer) **help** (W.DAT. an army) **to win** —a fight Hdt.
3 help (W.DAT. someone) **to take down** —a hanged person Plu.

συγ-καθάπτω vb. **fasten together, link** —one's hand (W.DAT. to someone, in a dance) Men.

συγ-καθαρμόζω vb. **join** (w. someone) **in arranging for burial** —a corpse S.

συγ-καθέζομαι mid.vb. **1** (of persons) **sit down together** Isoc. Pl.
2 (of the Roman Senate) **be in session** Plu.

συγκαθείργω Att.vb.: see συγκατείργω

συγ-καθέλκομαι (ξυγ-) pass.vb. | fut. -καθελκυσθήσομαι | (of a good man) **be dragged down together** (w. evil associates) A.

συγ-καθεύδω (ξυγ-) vb. **sleep together** (w. sexual connot., oft. W.DAT. w. someone) A. Ar. Pl. X. Plu.

συγ-κάθημαι (ξυγ-), Ion. **συγκάτημαι** mid.vb. **1** (of persons in a group) **sit together** E. X.; (of members of a deliberative assembly) Th. Ar. X. Aeschin. D. Thphr.; (of members of an audience) Thphr.
2 (of women) **reside together** Hdt.
3 (of a person or persons) **sit with** —W.DAT. or μετά + GEN. someone NT. Plu.

συγ-καθιερόω contr.vb. **assist in dedicating** —an offering Plu.

συγ-καθίζω vb. **1** (of persons) **sit down together** NT. Plu.
2 (of Roman senators) **sit together** (w. someone) Plu.
3 || MID. (of a court) **be in session** X.

συγ-καθίημι vb. **1 help to let down** —funeral offerings (into the sea) E.
2 (of a mind) **lower** —itself (W.PREP.PHR. to a less elevated level of contemplation) Pl.; (intr., of a person) lower oneself (to the level of an inferior), **be accommodating** Pl. —W.DAT. to someone Pl.
3 (intr., of ambushers) **crouch down** Plb.

συγ-καθίστημι (ξυγ-) vb. **1 help to establish** or **set up** —forms of government, persons of authority A. Th. Att.orats. Pl. X. Arist.
2 help to arrange —transport, military matters, training E. Th. Plu.
3 help to treat —a sickness E.

—**συγκαθίσταμαι** mid.vb. | also ACT.: athem.aor. συγκατέστην | pf.ptcpl. συγκαθεστώς | **position oneself for confrontation**; (of troops, athletes, boxers, ambassadors) **confront, face** —W.DAT. or πρός + ACC. an enemy, opponent, audience Plb.; (of a commander, boxer, fleet) **get in position** —w. εἰς + ACC. for fighting Plb. || PF.PTCPL.SB. opponent Plb.

συγ-καθορμίζομαι pass.vb. **come to anchor alongside** Plb.

συγ-καίω vb. (of the sun) **burn up** —the earth's surface Pl. || PASS. (of air) be burnt up Pl.

συγ-καλέω (ξυγ-) contr.vb. **1 call together, convoke, convene** —persons Il. A. Hdt. Th. Ar. Att.orats. +; (mid.) Hdt. NT.
2 convene —an assembly, a meeting Plb. NT. Plu.
3 invite jointly (to a feast) —someone (W.DAT. w. others) X.

συγκαλυμμός οῦ m. [συγκαλύπτω] **shrouding** (of the head by a cloak) Ar.

συγκαλυπτέος ᾱ ον vbl.adj. (of a story) **to be covered up, to be concealed** A.

συγκαλυπτός όν adj. (of thigh-bones of sacrificial animals) **wrapped up** (W.DAT. in fat) A.

συγ-καλύπτω vb. **1** (of Poseidon) **veil, shroud** —earth and sea (W.DAT. in clouds) Od.(tm.)
2 (of persons) **cover up, conceal** —nakedness Pl.; (of a personif. dessert) —its face (W.DAT. under a veil) Philox.Leuc.
3 || MID. **shroud one's head** (in a cloak) X. Plu.
|| PF.PASS.PTCPL. with one's head shrouded Plu.
4 conceal from the knowledge of others, conceal, hide —secret rites Plu. —events, facts E. Plu. || PASS. (of a truth) be concealed NT.

συγ-κάμνω vb. **1 share in physical labour, toil together** S. E. Plu. —W.DAT. w. a person, country S. E.
2 share in suffering, sympathise with, feel anguish over —W.DAT. a person's troubles A. E.

συγκαμπή ῆς f. [συγκάμπτω] **bend, joint** (where a horse's neck meets its body) X.

συγ-κάμπτω vb. **bend** —one's leg (at the knee) Pl. X. || PASS. (of a person, i.e. his limbs; of a leg) bend Pl. X.; (of an armoured gauntlet) X.

συγ-κασιγνήτη ης f. **one's own sister** E.

σύγ-κασις εως f. [κάσις] (appos.w. κούρα girl) **one's own sister** E.

συγ-καταβαίνω (ξυγ-) vb. **1 go down together** (w. others, to or fr. a place) Th. NT. Plu. —W.DAT. w. someone (to Hades) E.
2 (of a deity or supernatural power) **come down in support, join forces** (w. someone) A.
3 (of persons) **arrive together** —W.PREP.PHR. at a particular time of life Arist.
4 descend (to lower ground) **for battle**; (of a commander, troops) **take the field** Plb.; **venture** —w. εἰς + ACC. upon a fight, risk Plb.
5 (of a person) **stoop, sink, resort** —w. εἰς + ACC. to sthg. Plb.
6 submit, consent (to sthg.) Plb.
7 come down (in one's demands) Plb.
8 degrade oneself (through associating w. lower classes) Plb.

συγ-καταβάλλω vb. (fig., of a ruler) **throw** (W.ACC. himself) **down together** —W.DAT. w. people unable to stand (i.e. associate w. a weaker ally) Plu.

συγ-καταβιβάζω vb. **make** (W.ACC. enemy troops) **come down too** (i.e. entice them down after one) Plb.

συγκαταγήρᾱσις εως f. [συγκαταγηράσκω] **companionship in old age** Pl.

συγ-καταγηράσκω vb. **1** (of a person) **grow old together** —W.DAT. w. someone Is.
2 (of dyed figures in a woollen garment) **age with, last as long as** —W.DAT. the wool Hdt.; (of suffering) —a life of poverty Men.

συγ-κατάγω vb. **1 help to bring to shore** —a ship Plu.
2 help to bring back or **restore** —a tyrant Ar. —exiles Isoc. Plu. —democracy Aeschin.

συγ-καταδαρθάνω (ξυγ-) vb. (w. sexual connot.) **sleep with** —W.DAT. someone Ar.

συγ-καταδιώκομαι (ξυγ-) pass.vb. (of ships) **be chased into port together** —w. μετά + GEN. w. their commander Th.

συγ-καταδουλόω (ξυγ-) contr.vb. **help to enslave** —a region, people Th.(also mid.)

συγ-καταζεύγνῡμι vb. **yoke together, force into marriage** —bachelors (W.DAT. w. widows) Plu. || PASS. (of a person) be yoked, be fastened inescapably —W.DAT. to delusion S.

συγ-καταθάπτω vb. **1 join in burying, take part in the funeral of** —someone Isoc.
2 bury (W.ACC. clothes) **together** —W.DAT. w. someone Hdt. || PASS. (of clothes) be buried together —W.DAT. w. someone Hdt.; (fig., of freedom) —w. valour Lys.

συγκατάθεσις εως *f.* [συγκατατίθημι] **1 assent, approval** Plb. Plu.
2 (in Stoic philosophy) assent given by the mind to a natural impulse, **assent** Plu.
συγ-καταθέω *contr.vb.* (of troops) **join in a foray** X.
συγ-καταθνήσκω *vb.* (fig., of music and poetry) **die together** —W.DAT. *w. a poet* Mosch.
συγ-καταίθω *vb.* **burn together** or **completely** —*the collected remains of a corpse* S.
συγ-καταινέω *contr.vb.* (of gods, men) **give approval** or **assent** Plb. Plu. —W.DAT. *to someone* X. Plb. —W.ACC. *to sthg.* Plb.
συγκαταιρέω Ion.contr.vb.: see συγκαθαιρέω
συγ-καταίρω *vb.* (of ships) **put in to land together** Plu.
συγ-κατακαίω *vb.* **1** also **burn** —*tents* X. ‖ PASS. (of persons or things) also **be burned** Plu.
2 burn (W.ACC. *a cloak*) **together** —W.DAT. *w. a corpse* Plu. ‖ PASS. (of things) **be burned together** —W.DAT. *w. people* Hdt. Plu.
συγ-κατάκειμαι *mid.pass.vb.* **1** (of a person) **lie together** (w. someone, for sexual intercourse) Pl. —W.DAT. *w. someone* Ar. Pl.
2 recline alongside (someone, at a symposium) Plu.
συγ-κατακληίομαι Ion.pass.vb. [κατακλείω] (of a priestess) **be shut up** (w. a god, in his temple) Hdt.
συγ-κατακλίνομαι (**ξυγ-**) *pass.vb.* | aor.2 ptcpl. ξυγκατακλινείς | **1** (of a husband) **share a bed** (w. his wife) Ar.
2 (of a person at a symposium) **share a couch** Ar.
συγ-κατακόπτομαι *pass.vb.* (of persons) **be cut down together** (w. others, in battle or sim.) Plu.
συγ-κατακτάομαι *mid.contr.vb.* **share in acquiring** —*sthg.* (W.DAT. *w. someone*) D.
συγ-κατακτείνω *vb.* **1 kill together** —*cattle and men* S.
2 kill (W.ACC. *two sons*) **as well** (as their father) E.*fr.*
3 join in a killing E.
συγ-καταλαμβάνω (**ξυγ-**) *vb.* **help to capture** —*a place, plunder* Th. Isoc. X.
συγ-καταλείπω (**ξυγ-**) *vb.* (of allies) **jointly leave behind** —*a garrison* (W.DAT. *for a place*) Th.
συγ-καταλύω (**ξυγ-**) *vb.* **1 help to bring to an end** —*democracy* Th. Att.orats. Plu.
2 bring down also —*a further opponent* Plu.
3 ‖ PASS. (of a city's fortunes) **be brought down simultaneously** —W.DAT. *w. someone's death* Plb.
συγ-καταμείγνυμι *vb.* (of a poet) **mingle together, blend** —*the Graces* (W.DAT. *w. the Muses*) E.; (of a carefree person) —*one's soul* (w. singing, revelry, dancing) X.; (mid., of foodstuffs) —*particles of the body* (w. particles of themselves) Pl.
συγ-καταναυμαχέω *contr.vb.* (of a naval commander) **join** (W. μετά + GEN. w. an allied commander) **in defeating at sea** —*an opponent* Aeschin.
συγ-κατανέμομαι (**ξυγ-**) *mid.vb.* (of settlers) **share in the distribution of** —*land* Th.
συγ-κατανεύω *vb.* **agree, assent** —W.DAT. *to someone or sthg.* Plb.
συγ-καταπίμπλημι *vb.* (of a polluted person) **infect also** —*innocent people* Antipho
συγ-καταπλέκω *vb.* **interweave** —*political themes* (W.DAT. *in poems*) Plu.; (of Chance) —*an event* (w. another) Plu.
συγ-καταπράσσω *vb.* **help to accomplish** —*sthg.* D.
συγ-κατασκάπτω *vb.* **1 help to demolish** —*walls* E. And.
2 destroy also —*someone* (along w. oneself) E. ‖ PASS. (of a city) also **be destroyed** (along w. its soldiers) E. [or perh. *be utterly destroyed*]
συγ-κατασκεδάννυμαι *mid.vb.* **sprinkle over the ground together** (w. μετά + GEN. w. someone) —*a drinking-horn (i.e. its contents)* X.
συγ-κατασκευάζω (**ξυγ-**) *vb.* **1 help** (sts. W.DAT. someone) **to found** or **establish** —*an empire, institution* Th. Isoc. X. Plb.
2 help (sts. W.DAT. someone) **to achieve** —*sthg.* D. Plb.
3 help to promote —*human life* Pl. —*a war* D.; (of income) **help to provide** —*what is needed* X.
συγ-κατασκηνόω *contr.vb.* (of a commander) **accommodate in one's tent** —*soldiers* X.
συγ-κατασκήπτω *vb.* (of a pair of eagles) **swoop down together** Plu.
συγ-καταστασιάζω *vb.* **help** (W.DAT. someone) **to raise a faction against** —*a city* Plu.
συγκατάστασις εως *f.* [συγκαθίσταμαι] **confrontation** (w. military opponents, wild animals) Plb.
συγ-καταστρέφω (**ξυγ-**) *vb.* **1 bring** (W.ACC. one's life) **to an end simultaneously** —W.DAT. *w. loss of liberty* Plu.
2 ‖ MID. **help** (sts. W.DAT. someone) **to conquer** —*a place, kingdom, people* Th. Isoc. X.
συγ-κατατάττω Att.vb. **draw up together** —*two detachments of cavalry* X.
συγ-κατατίθεμαι *mid.vb.* **1 be a party to a deposition** (of a will) Is.
2 lay down jointly —*the same opinion* (W.DAT. as someone, i.e. agree completely) Pl.
3 give one's agreement or **assent** Plb. Plu. —W.DAT. *to someone or sthg.* Plb.
συγ-κατατρίβω *vb.* (of soldiers) **completely crush** —*crops* Plu.
συγ-καταφαγεῖν aor.2 inf. **eat up** (W.ACC. a communal dish) **together** —W.DAT. *w. one another* Plu.
συγ-καταφέρομαι *pass.vb.* **1** (of sailors in a storm) **be carried into harbour together** —W.PREP.PHR. *w. their enemies* Plb.
2 be carried away —W.DAT. *by a person's trickery, a mistaken belief* Plb.
συγ-καταφθείρω *vb.* **lose** (W.ACC. one's soldiers) **as well** (as sthg. else) Plb.
συγ-κατά-φυρτος ον *adj.* [φύρω] (of a cheesecake) **well mixed together** (W.DAT. w. milk and honey) Philox.Leuc.
συγ-καταψεύδομαι *mid.vb.* **join in telling lies against** —W.GEN. *someone* Aeschin.
συγ-καταψηφίζομαι *mid.vb.* **1 join in a vote of condemnation** Plu.
2 ‖ PASS. (of the twelfth apostle) **be voted in also** —w. μετά + GEN. *alongside the eleven* NT.
συγ-κατείργω, Att. **συγκαθείργω** *vb.* | aor. συγκατείρξα (Philox.Cyth., cj.), Att. συγκαθεῖρξα | (of a god) **shut up** (W.ACC. Odysseus) **together** —W.DAT. *w. a monster (i.e. Polyphemos)* Philox.Cyth.; (fig., of a man who makes someone else the close custodian of an irresistible woman) **coop up** —*someone* (W.DAT. *in an impossible situation*) X. ‖ PASS. **be shut in together** (sts. W.DAT. w. someone) Aeschin. Plu.
συγ-κατεξανίσταμαι *mid.vb.* | athem.aor.act.ptcpl. συγκατεξαναστάς | **join in opposition** (to a proposal) Plu.
συγ-κατεργάζομαι (**ξυγ-**) *mid.vb.* **1 collaborate with, help** —W.DAT. *someone* Hdt.
2 help (W.DAT. someone) **to gain** —*kingship* Hdt.
3 help (sts. W.DAT. someone) **to achieve** or **perform** —*an aim or undertaking* Th. Plb. Plu.

4 help to conquer —*a country* Plu.
5 kill together (i.e. at the same time) —*one's children* E.
συγ-κατέρχομαι *mid.vb.* **return together from exile** (sts. w.dat. or μετά + gen. w. someone) Lys. Aeschin. Arist. Plu.
συγ-κατεύχομαι *mid.vb.* **sum up in a prayer** —*one's wishes* S.
συγ-κατέχω *vb.* **keep** (w.acc. someone) **under control alongside** —w.dat. *oneself* Pl.
συγ-κατηγορέω *contr.vb.* **join** (sts. w.dat. or μετά + gen. w. someone) **in making an accusation** Hyp. D. —w.gen. or κατά + gen. *against someone* Hyp. D.
συγ-κατήγορος ου *m.* **joint accuser, fellow prosecutor** Hyp.
συγκάτημαι Ion.*mid.vb.*: see συγκάθημαι
συγ-κατοικέω *contr.vb.* (of colonists) **settle down with, take up residence with** —w.dat. *the local population* Plu.; (fig., of old dirt) —*an old man* S.
συγ-κατοικίζω (ξυγ-) *vb.* **1 join in colonising, help to settle** —*a land* Hdt.
2 help to found —*a city* Th.
3 help to resettle, help to restore —*a displaced population* Th.
4 settle together —*wild beasts* (w.dat. w. people) E.
5 set up, establish (abroad) —(fig.) *memorials to one's conduct* Th.
συγ-κατοικτίζομαι *mid.vb.* **lament jointly** (w. others) —*one's sufferings* S.
συγ-κατορθόω *contr.vb.* (of a god) **help to bring to a successful issue** —*someone's activities* Isoc.
συγ-κατορύττω *Att.vb.* **bury together** —*one's wealth* (w.dat. w. oneself) Men. —*a speech* (w. a corpse) Plu.
σύγκαυσις εως *f.* [συγκαίω] **burning, combustion** Pl.
σύγ-κειμαι (ξύγ-) *mid.pass.vb.* **1** (of corpses) **lie together** S.; (of an object) **be placed together** (w. other objects) X.
2 (of an item taken as a whole) **be composed or compounded** —w. ἐκ + gen. *of constituent parts* Isoc. Pl. X. Arist. +; (fig. and pejor., of an orator) —*of mere words* Aeschin.; (of a soul) —*of vice and cruelty* Plu.
3 (of constituent parts) **be placed together** (to form a unity) Pl.
4 (of writings, poems, speeches) **be composed** Th. Isoc. Pl. Arist. Plu.
5 (of an artifice, report, argument) **be contrived, be concocted** E. Th. Att.orats.
6 (of a treaty, signal, time, place) **be agreed on, be arranged** (sts. w.dat. by someone) Hdt. Th. Ar. Pl. + ‖ neut.pl.ptcpl.sb. **terms agreed** Hdt. Th. Att.orats. + ‖ impers. **it is** (was, had been) **agreed** Hdt. Th. Ar. Pl. X. Plu. —w.dat. *by someone* (w.inf. or acc. + inf. *to do sthg., or that someone shd. do sthg.*) Hdt. Th. Plb.
συγ-κελεύω (ξυγ-) *vb.* **1 join in giving an order** Th.
2 give the same order (as an earlier one) E.
συγ-κεντέω *contr.vb.* (of attackers) **stab to death** —*a person or persons* Hdt. Plb. ‖ pass. (of one person) **be stabbed to death** (by a single attacker) Hdt.
συγ-κεράννῡμι (ξυγ-) *vb.* | neut.impers.vbl.adj. συγκρᾱτέον | **1 mix together, blend, combine** —*colours, abstr. entities* Pl. —*several things* (sts. w.prep.phr. *into one*) Isoc. Pl.(also mid.) —*sthg.* (w.dat. w. sthg. else) Pl.
2 form by blending —*sthg.* (w.prep.phr. *fr. two ingredients*) Pl.(also mid.); **temper** —*the characters of youths* Plu.
3 ‖ pass. (of milk and honey) **be mixed together, blended or combined** Plu.; (of the generative seed of husband and wife) E.; (of the nature of a dog and a fox) X.; (of personal qualities, abstr. entities) Th. Pl.; (of sufferings) A.; (of an aspect of character) —w.dat. w. *another aspect* Men. Plu.; (of a husband) **be united in loving harmony** (w. a wife) S.(dub.)
4 ‖ mid. **form by close union, form, forge together, cement** —*friendship* Hdt. ‖ pass. (of friendship) **be formed** Hdt.; (of enmity) Hdt.
5 ‖ pass. (of a person) **be closely associated** —w.dat. w. *someone* X.; **be deeply involved or be steeped** —w.dat. *in anguish, lamentation* S. —*in ill-fortune* Ar.; (of a person's love) **be interfused** —w.dat. *through cities* Call.
συγ-κεραυνόομαι *pass.contr.vb.* **be struck with a thunderbolt**; (fig., of a person) **be blitzed** —w.acc. *out of one's mind* (w.dat. *by wine*) Archil.
συγ-κερκίζω *vb.* (fig.) **weave together** —*different temperaments* Pl.
συγ-κεφαλαιόομαι *mid.contr.vb.* **1 bring together under one head, sum up, summarise** —*arguments, events, or sim.* Pl. Plb.; (intr.) Arist. ‖ pass. (of ways of doing sthg.) **be summarised** Arist.
2 total up —*what is owed* Plb. ‖ pass. (of an account) **be totalled up** Aeschin.
3 amalgamate, centralise —*administrative activities* X. ‖ pass. (of administrative activities) **be centralised** —w. εἰς + acc. *in a few officials* X.
συγκεφαλαίωσις εως *f.* **summary, résumé** (w.gen. of sthg.) Plb.
συγκεχυμένως *pf.pass.ptcpl.adv.*: see under συγχέω
συγ-κηδεστής οῦ *m.* **relation by marriage; brother-in-law** (ref. to a wife's sister's husband) D.
συγ-κινδῡνεύω (ξυγ-) *vb.* **share a risk, incur danger together** (oft. w.dat. or μετά + gen. w. someone) Th. Isoc. Pl. X. D. +
συγ-κῑνέω *contr.vb.* **1** (of extravagant behaviour) **move strongly** —*those who witness it* Plb.; (of accusers) **stir up** —*people* NT.
2 ‖ pass. (of rebels, troops) **be stirred up in support** Plb. —w.dat. *for someone* Plu.
συγ-κλάω *contr.vb.* **break into pieces** —*vine-twigs* Ar. —*spears* Plu. ‖ pass. (fig., of slaves, persons engaged in menial occupations) **become stunted** Pl.
σύγκλεισις, Att. **ξύγκλησις**, εως *f.* [συγκλείω] **1 closing up** (of neighbouring shields), **closing of ranks** Th.
2 locking together (w.gen. of components, w. πρός + acc. w. each other) Pl.
3 app., **place where mountains close in, narrow pass, defile** Plb.(dub.) | see σύγκλισις
συγ-κλείω, Att. **συγκλῄω** (ξυγ-), Ion. **συγκληίω** *vb.* [κλείω¹] **1 shut in, hem in, coop up** —*people, esp. troops* (sts. w.prep.phr. *in a place*) Plb. Plu. ‖ pass. **be cooped up or hemmed in** Arist. Plb.
2 confine, hem —*an Assembly* (w.prep.phr. *into an area*) Th.
3 (fig., of fortune) **hem** —*someone* (w.prep.phr. *into a perilous position or sim.*) Plb. ‖ pass. (of a person) **be cramped** —w.prep.phr. *by circumstances* Plb.
4 (of troops) **enclose** —*an inner body of their own troops* Hdt. Plu.
5 (of groves, mountains) **enclose, surround** —*a place* Hdt. Plb. ‖ pass. (of a region) **be enclosed** —w.dat. *by mountains* Hdt.; (of a river current) **be constricted** (by topography) Plb.
6 enclose (in a net), **catch** —*fish* NT.
7 ‖ pf.pass.ptcpl. (of a woman lying on the ground) **wrapped up** —w.dat. *in her garments* E.
8 shut, close —*doors, gates* X. Aeschin.; (of a physical cause) —*portals in an organ of the body* Pl.; (intr.) **close the doors**

Ar. ‖ PASS. (of gates) be closed Th.; (of a prison, i.e. its doors) And.
9 (of a political leader) **close tight, shut up** —*a city* (*by keeping the occupants inside and securing its defences*) Plb.
10 close down —*courts* Ar.
11 shut, close —*one's mouth* E. Ar. —*one's eyes* E. —*a dead person's eyes* E.; (of an assailant) —*someone's eyes* (*w. a blow*) D. ‖ PASS. (of eyelids) be closed X.
12 (of an hour) **bring a day to a close, get late** Plb.
13 bring together so as to close up a gap; (of soldiers) **lock together** —*shields* X.; **close up** —*a battle-line* Plb.; (intr.) **lock shields, close ranks** Th. Plb. ‖ PASS. (of a section of an army) be formed into close ranks Th.
14 (intr., of the ends of a wall forming a circle) **close up a gap, converge** Pl.
15 (of enemy territory lying betw. allies) **block the line of communication** Th.
16 connect together —*part of a discourse* (W.DAT. *w. another part*) Isoc.; (of a physical cause) —*skin* Pl.; (of troubles) **lock together** —*rival wives* (W.DAT. *in conflict*) E. ‖ PASS. (of cities) be linked —W.DAT. *through intermarriage or sim.* X. ‖ PF.PASS.PTCPL. (of a dismembered body) fitted together E.; (of part of a discourse) connected —W.DAT. *to another part* Isoc.

συγ-κλέπτω *vb.* **join in theft** —w. μετά + GEN. *w. someone* Antipho

σύγ-κληρος ον *adj.* [κλῆρος] **1** (of land) **having adjoining portions** (w. another), **bordering** E.
2 ‖ NEUT.PL.SB. **fortune shared jointly** (W.DAT. *w. someone*) S.(cj.) | see ἔγκληρος 3

συγκληρόω *contr.vb.* **1 apportion together** —*both halves of an allotment of land* Pl.
2 allot —*ships* (W.DAT. *to groups of people*) D.
3 (of fortune) **throw together** —*someone* (W.DAT. *w. another*) Aeschin.

συγκλητικός ή όν *adj.* [σύγκλητος 3] **belonging to the Roman Senate**; (of a person) **of senatorial rank** Plu. ‖ MASC.PL.SB. **senators** Plu.

σύγκλητος ον *adj.* [συγκαλέω] **1** (of a meeting of the Assembly) **specially summoned, extraordinary** (opp. statutory) Aeschin. D.; (of a conference) S.
2 (of an army) **assembled** E.
3 ‖ FEM.SB. **specially convened meeting** (of the Assembly or Council) Arist. Plb.; (at Rome) **Senate** (ref. to the institution itself) Plb. Plu.

συγκλινής ές *adj.* [συγκλίνω] **inclining together**; (app. of a group of people) perh. **converging** Ar.(quot. A.)

συγκλινίᾱ ᾱς *f.* **convergence of slopes** ‖ PL. **depressions, hollows** (sts. W.GEN. in the landscape) Plu.

συγ-κλίνω *vb.* | fut.pass. συγκλιθήσομαι | **1** (fig., of nations) **lean together, show a joint inclination** —W.DAT. *towards a ruler* Plb.
2 ‖ PASS. (of a man or woman) **lie together** (for sexual intercourse, usu. W.DAT. w. someone) Hdt. E. Men.

σύγκλισις εως *f.* **convergence of slopes** ‖ PL. **depressions, hollows** Plb.(cj.) Plu. | see σύγκλεισις 3

συγ-κλονέω *contr.vb.* (of arrows) **throw completely into disarray** —*enemy troops* Il.

σύγ-κλυς (ξύγ-) υδος *masc.fem.adj.* [κλύζω] **washed together**; (fig., of troops, people, a crowd) **scraped together, nondescript** Th. Pl. Plu.

συγκλυσμός οῦ *m.* **process of being washed over by waves, swamping** Men.

συγ-κοιμάομαι *mid.contr.vb.* **1** (of a man or woman) **sleep together** (w. sexual connot.) —W.DAT. *w. someone* Hdt. Trag. Plu.
2 (fig., of inattentive historians) **doze over, sleep through** —W.DAT. *the events described* Plb.

συγκοίμημα ατος *n.* (poet.pl., ref. to a woman) **bedfellow** E.

συγκοίμησις εως *f.* (w. sexual connot.) **sleeping together** (sts. W.GEN. w. someone) Pl.

συγ-κοιμίζω (ξυγ-) *vb.* (of the Fates) **make to sleep together, unite in the marriage bed** —*Zeus* (W.DAT. *w. Hera*) Ar.

συγ-κοινόομαι (ξυγ-) *mid.contr.vb.* **share** —*activities and risks* (W.DAT. *w. someone*) Th.; **discuss** —*sthg.* (W.DAT. *w. one another*) Men.(dub.)

συγ-κοινωνέω *contr.vb.* **have a share** —W.GEN. *in someone's reputation* D.

σύγ-κοιτος ου *m.* [κοίτη] (appos.w. ὕπνος *sleep*) **bedfellow** Pi.

συγ-κολάζω *vb.* **help** (W.DAT. someone) **to exact punishment** Pl.

συγ-κολλάω *contr.vb.* **1 glue together**; (of a divine creator) **stick together** —*natural elements* Pl.; (of a writer) —*literary leftovers* Pl.
2 (of litigious persons) **cobble together, fabricate** —*lawsuits* Ar.

συγκολλητής οῦ *m.* **one who glues together**; **fabricator** (W.GEN. of lies) Ar.

συγκόλλως *adv.* **1 in a way that creates coherence**; **in harmony, in agreement** (W.DAT. *w. someone*) —*ref. to speaking* A.
2 (of a dream portent, w. ἔχειν) **be in harmony** (w. known facts) A.

συγ-κομιδή (ξυγ-) ῆς *f.* **1 collecting together, gathering in, harvesting** (W.GEN. of crops) Th. Isoc. Pl. X. Arist. Plb.; **harvest, harvest-time** Plb.
2 collecting together (of people); **crowding** (W.PREP.PHRS. into the city, fr. the countryside) Th.

συγ-κομίζω (ξυγ-) *vb.* **1 bring together** —*all the grain in a city, items of furniture* (w. εἰς + ACC. *to a place*) Hdt. Plu. ‖ PASS. (of persons) be conveyed together —W.ADV. *to a place* X.
2 collect up —*spilled wine, items of plunder, firewood* Hdt. Plb. Plu.
3 collect together —*prisoners, corpses* Th. ‖ PASS. (of corpses) be collected together Hdt. Plu.
4 gather in, harvest —*crops* X. Plu.(mid.) ‖ PASS. (of crops) be gathered in Hdt. X. Plu.
5 ‖ MID. **collect for oneself, acquire** —*oil fr. a plant, grain* Hdt. X. —*persons, advantages, personal attributes* X. ‖ PASS. (of promised benefits) be gathered in, be reaped S.
6 help in burying —*a corpse* S. NT.
7 ‖ PASS. (of a corpse) be completely cremated Plu.

συγκοπή ῆς *f.* [συγκόπτω] (gramm.) **cutting short** (of a word, by omission of letters), **syncope** Plu.

συγ-κόπτω *vb.* **1** (of a storm) **break up** —*a bridge* Hdt.; (of a woman) —*her jewellery* X.
2 strike, thrash, beat up —*a person* Att.orats. Pl. X. Plu. ‖ PASS. **be thrashed** E.Cyc. Lys. Ar. Pl. X. +
3 ‖ PASS. (fig., of a commander) **be depleted** —W.PREP.PHR. *by earlier battles* Plu.

συγ-κορυβαντιάω *contr.vb.* **share in a mania** (for sthg.) Pl.

συγ-κοσμέω *contr.vb.* (of soldiers) **help to confer honours on** —*their commanders* X.

σύγ-κρᾱσις (ξύγ-) εως *f.* [συγκεράννῡμι] **1 mixing together, blending, combining** (sts. W.GEN. of things) Th. Pl. Men. Plu.

συγκρατέον

2 (ref. to a person) **harmonising influence** (W.GEN. on events) Plu.
συγκρατέον (neut.impers.vbl.adj.): see συγκεράννῡμι
σύγκρᾱτος ον *adj.* (of a pair of people) **closely joined** E.
συγ-κρημνίζομαι *pass.vb.* (of troops) **be flung down together** (into a trench) Plb.
συγ-κρίνω *vb.* **1** (philos., opp. διακρίνω *separate, segregate*) **combine, aggregate** —*particles, matter* Pl. Arist. ‖ PASS. (of things) **be combined** Pl. Arist.
2 judge (sthg.) **in relation to** (sthg. else); **compare** —*one thing or person* (W.DAT. or πρός + ACC. w. another) Arist. Plb. Plu. —*needs, statements, achievements* Arist. Plb. Plu. ‖ PASS. (of persons or things) **be compared** Plb.
3 ‖ PASS. (of persons) **be brought for examination** —w. πρός + ACC. *before someone* Plb.
4 combine (by comparing like w. like); (of Time) **arrange** (into classes) —*primordial creatures* AR.
σύγκρισις εως *f.* **1** (philos., opp. διάκρισις *separation*) **combination, aggregation** Pl. Arist.
2 comparison (sts. W.GEN. and DAT. or πρός + ACC. of one thing or person w. another) Arist. Plb. Plu.
συγκριτικός ή όν *adj.* **1** (of an art or technique) **of the combining kind** (opp. διακριτικός *of the separative kind*) Pl. Arist.
2 (of a dark colour) **causing compression** (of the stream of sight) Arist.
σύγκριτος ον *adj.* (of a person) **comparable** (W.DAT. to someone) Plb.
συγ-κροτέω (ξυγ-) *contr.vb.* **1 strike together with a clashing sound, clap** —*one's hands* X. ‖ PASS. (of a person) **be clapped, be applauded** X.
2 (fig.) **knock together, hammer into shape** —*a plan* Ar. —*the etymological components of a word* (into its final form) Pl. ‖ PASS. (of a shield) **be hammered into shape** Plu.; (of a word) Pl.
3 (fig.) **knock into shape, co-ordinate, organise** —*a chorus* D. —*a body of soldiers* Plu. ‖ PASS. (of political clubs) **be organised** Plu. ‖ PF.PASS.PTCPL.ADJ. (of soldiers) **knocked into shape, well-trained, disciplined** D.; (of a ship, its crew) X. Plb.; (of a chorus) Plu.
σύγκρουσις εως *f.* [συγκρούω] **collision, conflict** (W.GEN. betw. opposing factions) Plu.
συγκρουσμός οῦ *m.* **collision** (W.GEN. betw. ships) Plu.
συγ-κρούω (ξυγ-) *vb.* **1 strike together, clap** —*one's hands* Ar.
2 (of persons) **bring into collision** —*ships* (W.DAT. w. each other) Plu.; **bring about a collision** (betw. ships) Th.; (intr., of ships) **collide** —W.DAT. w. each other Plb. ‖ PASS. (of sailors' teeth) app., **be brought into collision** (w. oars), be knocked Tim.
3 keep together —*a herd of oxen* (on the move) Plb.
4 (fig.) **bring into conflict, set at loggerheads** —*persons, cities, or sim.* (sts. W.DAT. or πρός + ACC. w. someone) Th. Isoc. D. Arist. Thphr. Plu.; (intr., of people) **come into collision, be at loggerheads** Plu.
συγ-κρύπτω *vb.* (of persons or things) **help** (sts. W.DAT. someone) **to conceal** —*facts, feelings, defects, crimes* E. Att.orats. X. Men. Plu.; (intr.) Antipho
συγ-κτάομαι (ξυγ-) *mid.contr.vb.* **1 help** (W.DAT. someone) **to gain** —*an objective, territory* Th.
2 (of a group of people) **acquire** —*all the land* Arist.
συγ-κτερεΐζω *vb.* **perform burial rites jointly** —W.PREP.PHR. w. someone AR.
συγ-κτίζω (ξυγ-) *vb.* **help** (W.DAT. someone) **to found** or **colonise** —*a place* Hdt. Th.

συγκτίστης εω *Ion.m.* **joint founder** (of a colony) Hdt.
συγκυβευτής οῦ *m.* [συγκυβεύω] **dicing-companion, fellow gambler** Aeschin.
συγ-κυβεύω *vb.* (of persons) **play dice together** Arist.; (of a person) —W.DAT. w. someone Hdt. Plu.
συγ-κυκάω (ξυγ-) *contr.vb.* **1** (of a god) **mix together, mash up** —*people* (W.PREP.PHR. in a bowl) Ar.; **mix up together** —*different sounds* Pl.
2 stir up, throw into a ferment —*Greece* Ar.
συγ-κυκλέω *contr.vb.* (of a god) **help to revolve** —*the universe* Pl.
σύγ-κύνᾱγος (ξυγ-) ου *dial.m.f.* —also **συγκύνηγος** ου (Men.) *m.f.* **fellow hunter, hunting companion** E. Men.
συγκυνηγετέω *contr.vb.* [συγκυνηγέτης] **be a hunting companion** Plu.
συγ-κυνηγέτης ου *m.* **fellow huntsman** X. Aeschin. Men.
συγκυνηγέω *contr.vb.* [συγκύνᾱγος] (of people) **hunt together** Arist.
συγ-κύπτω *vb.* **1** (of persons) **bend or stoop together, cower together** Ar.
2 (fig.) **act in a common cause, conspire** Hdt. Ar.
3 (of the wings at the front of a square formation of troops) **draw together** X.
4 (of an infirm person) **be bent double** NT.
συγ-κυρέω (ξυγ-) *contr.vb.* —also (aor.) **συγκύρω** *vb.* ‖ aor. συνεκύρησα, ep. συνέκυρσα ‖ **1 come together by chance or accident**; (of horses) **collide** Il.; (of ships) **meet** Hdt.; (of primordial elements) Emp.
2 (of persons) **meet with** —W.DAT. *a fate* S. —W.PREP.PHR. *one and the same fate* (W.DAT. as someone) E.
3 happen to be in the way (of a missile) Plb.
4 happen to arrive at the same time (as others) Plb.
5 (of a ship) **happen, chance** —W.NOM.PTCPL. *to get in the way* Hdt.; (of aither) —*to be moving* Emp.
6 (of events, accidents) **happen** Thgn. Hdt. Plb. —W.DAT. *to someone* Hdt. E. Plb.; (of a military disaster) **chance** —W.INF. *to happen* Hdt. ‖ IMPERS.AOR. **it chanced** —W.ACC. + INF. *that someone did sthg.* Plb.
7 (of a place, a people) **be contiguous, be adjacent** —W.DAT. or PREP.PHR. *to a place* Plb. Plu.
συγκύρημα ατος *n.* **coincidence, accident** Plb.
συγκύρησις εως *f.* **coincidence, accident** Plb.
συγκυρίᾱ ᾱς *f.* **coincidence** NT.
σύγ-κωλος ον *adj.* [κῶλον] **with limbs together**; (of a dog's legs) **close together** X.
συγκωμάζω *vb.* [σύγκωμος] ‖ dial.2pl.aor.imperatv. συγκωμάξατε ‖ **join in the revels** Pi.
σύγ-κωμος (ξύγ-) ου *m.f.* [κῶμος] **partner in revels, fellow reveller** E. Ar.
συγ-χαίρω (ξυγ-) *vb.* **1 rejoice together** (sts. W.DAT. w. someone) A. Ar. X. D. Arist. —W.DAT. *over sthg.* Isoc.
2 feel or express delight (for another); **offer congratulations** (oft. W.DAT. to someone, sts. w. ἐπί + DAT. over sthg., or ὅτι because he has done sthg.) Att.orats. X. Plb. NT.
συγ-χειμάζομαι *mid.vb.* (of shoes) **go through the winter together** (w. their wearer) Ar.
συγ-χειρίζω *vb.* **assist** (W.DAT. someone) **in managing** —*a kingdom* Plb.
συγ-χειρουργέω *contr.vb.* **lend a hand in performing** —*sacrifices* Is.
συγ-χέω (ξυγ-) *contr.vb.* —also (pres. and impf.) **συγχύννω** (NT.) *vb.* ‖ ep.3sg.athem.aor. (w.pass.sens., tm.) σὺν ... χύτο ‖
1 pour together, mix together, combine (opp. separate)

—*sensations* Pl. ‖ PASS. (of warp and weft, objects of perception) **be combined** Pl.; (of eyebrows, i.e. have nothing separating them) Plu.; (of causes and pretexts) **be confused** (by historians) Plb.
2 mix up together at random, jumble together —*votes* Is. —*remnants of a shattered object* E. ‖ PASS. (of reins) **be tangled together** Il.; (of minerals) **be jumbled together** Pl.; (of impressions made in soft wax) **run together** Pl.
3 throw into turmoil, create havoc in —*a house, city, constitution, affairs* E. D. Plu. —*a military formation* Plb. Plu. ‖ PASS. (of a city, fleet, troops) **be thrown into confusion** NT. Plu.; (of affairs) Isoc. D. Plu.
4 demolish —*a sandcastle* Il. —*tombs, a road* Hdt.; **erase** —*writing* E. ‖ PASS. (of a city) **be demolished** (by an earthquake) Plu.
5 ‖ PASS. (of gold) **be melted down** —W.PREP.PHR. *by a fire* Plu.
6 destroy, overthrow —*a political system, a country's supremacy* Plu.
7 make ineffectual —*weapons* Il.; **nullify** —*a court* D. —*someone's efforts* Il. E.; (of behaviour) **efface, destroy** —*a feeling of gratitude* S.; (of time) —*all things* S.
8 set at naught, annul, violate —*a treaty, law, oath, or sim.* Il.(tm.) Hdt. E. Antipho Th. +; **be responsible for a violation** —W.COGN.ACC. Pl. ‖ PASS. (of oaths, rights, or sim.) **be annulled or violated** Att.orats. Plu.
9 (of the sea) **shake, shatter, weaken** (mentally and physically) —*a person* Od.
10 confound, disturb —*persons, their feelings, beliefs* Il. Hdt. Men. NT. Plu. ‖ PASS. (of persons) **be thrown into confusion** NT.; **be troubled or distraught** Il.(tm.) E. Plu.; (of a mind, opinions) **be confounded** Il.(tm.) Hdt.; (of a person) —W.DAT. *in his hopes* Plu.; (of spirits) **be dashed** AR.(tm.)
11 ‖ PASS. (of vision) **become confused or blurred** Arist. Plu.; (of writing, sounds, or sim.) **be confused or unclear** Plu.
12 ‖ PASS. (of a war) **be stirred up** Plb.
—**συγκεχυμένως** *pf.pass.ptcpl.adv.* **confusedly, indiscriminately** —*ref. to using words* Arist.
συγ-χλιδάω *contr.vb.* (of banquet tables) **luxuriate with** —W.DAT. *an array of foods* Philox.Leuc.(tm.)
συγχορευτής οῦ *m.* [συγχορεύω] **fellow dancer, dancing partner** Pl. X.
συγ-χορεύω *vb.* **1 join in a dance** Ar.
2 (specif.) **be a member of a chorus** Arist.
συγχορηγέω *contr.vb.* [συγχορηγός] **1 provide help** (esp. w. money or supplies); **help out** Plu. —W.DAT. *someone* Plb. Plu.; **contribute towards** —W.DAT. *a wedding* Plu.
2 (tr.) **help out with, supply** —*nourishment* Plu.
συγ-χορηγός οῦ *m.* one who shares in defraying expenses, **contributor to one's costs** D.
σύγ-χορτος ον *adj.* [χόρτος] (of land, settlements) having pastures adjoining, **bordering, adjacent** E.; (W.DAT. to a country) A.
συγ-χόω *contr.vb.* **1 cover by heaping up earth; cover with earth** —*a coffin, tomb* Hdt. Plu.
2 fill with earth; block up, choke —*wells, springs* Hdt. X. Plu.; **block** —*a road* Hdt.; (fig., of storm-waves) **engulf** —*the paths of the stars* A.
3 reduce to a heap, demolish —*statues, buildings* Hdt.
συγ-χράομαι *mid.contr.vb.* **1 make use of, employ** —W.DAT. *someone or sthg.* Plb.
2 have dealings with, associate with —W.DAT. *people* NT.
3 borrow at the same time (fr. several sources) —W.DAT. *ships* Plb.

σύγ-χρους ουν *Att.adj.* [χρώς] (of earth) **having the same colour or appearance** (W.DAT. as sthg.) Plb.
συγχύννω *vb.*: see συγχέω
σύγχυσις (ξύγ-) εως *f.* [συγχέω] **1 confusion, turmoil** (among people or things) Plb. NT. Plu.
2 consternation (in a person) E.
3 ruin (W.GEN. of a life, house) E.
4 breach, violation (W.GEN. of oaths, laws, treaties, a constitution) Th. Isoc. Pl. Plu.
συγ-χωνεύω *vb.* [χοανεύω] **melt down** —*objects of gold or bronze* Lycurg. D. ‖ PASS. (of gold) **be melted down** Plu.
συγ-χωρέω (ξυγ-) *contr.vb.* | fut. συγχωρήσω, also συγχωρήσομαι | neut.impers.vbl.adj. συγχωρητέον, also pl. συγχωρητέα (S. Pl.) | **1** (of the Clashing Rocks) **come together** E.; (of chorus members) **close ranks** Ar.; (of ambassadors) **meet** Ar.
2 fall in with, agree with —W.DAT. *someone* Hdt. E. Th. Att.orats. Pl. +; **go along with, agree to** —W.DAT. *a proposal, request, argument, or sim.* Hdt. E. Th. Att.orats.
3 (of combatants) **come to terms** (sts. W. πρός + ACC. w. someone) E. Th.
4 agree, consent Hdt. S. Th. + —W.INF. or ACC. + INF. *to do sthg., that sthg. shd. be done* E. Th. + —W.DAT. + INF. *that someone shd. do sthg.* Att.orats. X. ‖ IMPERS. **it is agreed** Th. ‖ IMPERS.PASS. **it is agreed** Th. —W.ACC. or DAT. + INF. *that someone shd. do sthg.* Plb. Plu.
5 agree to, concede, allow (sts. W.DAT. to someone) —*requests, money, peace, or sim.* Hdt. E. Ar. Att.orats. + ‖ PASS. (of things) **be agreed** X. D. Arist. Plb. Plu.; **be conceded** —W.DAT. *to someone* D. Plb.
6 concede in argument, concede, grant —*a point, argument, or sim.* (sts. W.DAT. *to someone*) Att.orats. Pl. —W.ACC. + INF. *that sthg. is the case* Hdt. Pl. Is. ‖ PASS. (of a point) **be conceded** —W.DAT. *to someone* Pl.
συγχώρημα ατος *n.* formal allowance or permission, **concession** Plb. Plu.
συγχώρησις εως *f.* **agreement, assent** (to an argument or proposition) Pl. Plu.
σύδην *adv.* [σεύω] **in a rush, in eager haste** —*ref. to fleeing* A.
σύειος ᾱ ον *adj.* [σῦς, see ὗς] **of swine**; (of an oil) **made of pork fat** X.
συ-ζεύγνῡμι *vb.* [σύν] **1 yoke together** —*horses* Hdt. X. ‖ MID. **have** (W.ACC. a chariot) **yoked** X. ‖ PASS. (of horses) **be yoked together** X.
2 lash together —*rafts* Plb. ‖ PASS. (of ships) **be lashed together** Plb.
3 yoke in marriage, pair —*a wife* (W.DAT. *w. a husband*) E. —*Ares* (w. πρός + ACC. *w. Aphrodite*) Arist. —*men and women* X. Arist. NT. ‖ PASS. (of a woman) **be coupled** —W.DAT. *w. a god* E.; (of a man and boy) **be paired** (in sexual partnership) X.; (of slaves) **mate** X.; (fig., of a number) **be coupled** —W.DAT. *w. another* (i.e. be multiplied by it) Pl.
4 ‖ PASS. (of persons) **be yoked, be fastened inescapably, be bound** —W.DAT. *to a fate, calamity* E.; (of Herakles) —*to wanderings* E.
5 (intr.) **make a connection** (betw. two considerations) Arist. ‖ PASS. (of two aspects of character or behaviour) **be inseparably united** Arist.; (of one aspect) —W.DAT. *to another* Arist.
6 ‖ PASS. (of a legion) **be drawn up alongside** (another) Plu.
σύζευξις εως *f.* **1 yoking together, union, pairing** (of men and women) Pl. Arist.
2 pairing, combination (of things) Pl. Arist.

συ-ζητέω contr.vb. **1 search** or **inquire together** —W.DAT. or μετά + GEN. w. someone Pl.
2 inquire, debate NT. —W.INDIR.Q. *what is the case* NT.; **dispute, debate, argue** —W.DAT. or πρός + ACC. w. someone NT.

συ-ζυγέω contr.vb. [ζυγόν] (of cavalry) **stay together in rank** Plb.

συζυγία ᾱς f. [συζεύγνῡμι] **1 yoke-team** (W.GEN. of chariot-horses) E.; **team** (W.GEN. of mares going to pasture) E.fr.
2 pairing, union (of Muses and Graces) E.
3 pair (of related or opposed entities) Pl.; (of people, for comparison in biography) Plu.

συζύγιος ᾱ ον adj. **yoked together**; (of the Graces) **joined hand in hand** E.

σύζυγος (ξύ-) ον adj. **1 yoked together**; (of unions) **wedded** A.
2 || MASC.FEM.SB. **yoke-mate** (ref. to a wife, brother) E.; (ref. to a comrade, partner) E. Ar.

σύζυξ ζυγος masc.fem.adj. **1** (of husband and wife) **united in marriage** E.
2 (of two kinds of exercise) **paired, linked** Isoc.
3 || MASC.SB. (ref. to a chariot-horse) yoke-fellow, partner Pl.

σύζωμα (or **ξύ-**) ατος n. [συζώννῡμι] **girdle, sash** (of a woman) A.

συ-ζώννῡμι (ξύ-) vb. **1 fasten a girdle on** (a man, being dressed as a woman) Ar.
2 || MID. (of a woman, a man dressed as a woman) **hitch up one's dress** Ar.

συ-ζώω vb. | Att.3sg. συζῇ, 3pl. συζῶσι, inf. συζῆν, ptcpl. συζῶν | **1** (of a person) **live together** —W.DAT. or μετά + GEN. w. someone D. Arist. Plu.
2 live in, pass one's life in —W.DAT. *restless activity* D.; (of a constitution) χαλεπὴ συζῆν *difficult to live with* (i.e. live in) Pl.
3 (of people) **live together** (in society) Arist.

συθείς (aor.pass.ptcpl.), **σύθην** (ep.aor.pass.): see σεύω

σῡκάζω vb. [σῡκῆ] **pluck ripe figs** (w. pun on συκοφάντης) Ar. —W.COGN.ACC. X.

σῡκάμῑνον ου n. [prob.loanwd.] **fruit of the mulberry tree, mulberry** Hippon. Arist. Plu.

σῡκάμῑνος ου f. **mulberry tree** NT.

σῡκῆ ῆς, Ion. **σῡκέη** ης f. **fig tree** Od. Hippon. Hdt. Ar.

σῡκίδιον ου n. [dimin. σῡκῆ or σῡκίς] **little fig tree** or **fig slip** Ar.

σῡκινος η ον adj. [σῡκῆ] **1** (of wood) **of the fig tree** Ar. Pl.; (of a dog's collar, w. pun on συκοφάντης) **of fig-wood** Ar.; (of a ladle) Pl.; (of a statue) Theoc.*epigr.*
2 (fig., of a person, ref. to the low quality of fig-wood) **frail, feeble, useless** Hippon. Ar. Theoc.

σῡκίς ίδος f. **cutting from a fig tree, fig slip** Ar.

σῡκολογέω contr.vb. [σῡκον, λέγω] **pick figs** (w.connot. of σῡκον 3) Ar.

σῡκο-μορέᾱ ᾱς f. [σῡκῆ; μορέα *mulberry tree*] **fig-mulberry tree, sycamore-fig tree** NT.

σῡκον ου n. **1 fruit of the fig tree, fig** Od. Iamb. Hdt. Ar. Pl. +
2 (app. fr. its appearance) **inflammatory swelling on the eyelid, sty** Ar.
3 (fig.) **cunt** Ar.

σῡκο-πέδῑλος ον adj. [πέδιλον] (of the goddess Bribery, w. pun on συκοφάντης) **figwood-sandalled** Ar.(quot.com.)

σῡκοτραγέω contr.vb. [τρώγω] **eat figs** Thphr.

σῡκοφαντέω contr.vb. [σῡκοφάντης] **1 act as a sycophant; inform on, denounce, slander** or **blackmail** —someone Ar. Att.orats. X. Arist. Thphr. Plu.; **denounce** —sthg. (*as contraband*) Ar.; (intr.) **be a slander-monger, informer** or **blackmailer** Ar. Att.orats. Pl. X. Men. || PASS. **be denounced** or **slandered** Att.orats. Thphr.
2 extort —money Lys. NT.
3 (wkr.sens.) **attack** (W.ACC. someone) **with fraudulent** or **quibbling arguments** Pl. D.; **quibble about** —sthg. D.; **quibble with, carp at** —poets Arist.; **find fault with, criticise** —someone Plu. || PASS. **be criticised** X.; **be accused** —W.INF. *of doing sthg.* Plu.

σῡκοφάντημα ατος n. **malicious accusation, slander** Aeschin. D. Plu.

σῡκο-φάντης ου m. —also **σῡκοφάντρια** ᾱς (Ar.) f. [σῡκον, φαίνω] **1 one who brings a malicious charge or allegation** (against another, at Athens); **false accuser, informer, slanderer** Ar. Att.orats. Pl. X. Arist. +
2 one who behaves in a discreditable or petty fashion; trickster, quibbler, petty critic Pl. D. Men.

σῡκοφαντίᾱ ᾱς f. **1 behaviour or action of a false accuser; making of a malicious accusation, slander** Att.orats. X. Arist. Plu.
2 (log.) **trickery, fallaciousness** Arist.

σῡκοφαντίᾱς ου m. (com. name for a wind, fig.ref. to a person) **slanderer** Ar.

σῡκοφαντικός ή όν adj. (of a lawsuit) **trumped up, malicious** D.

—σῡκοφαντικῶς adv. **in the manner of a sycophant** —ref. *to a way of living* Isoc.

σῡκοφάντρια f.: see σῡκοφάντης

σῡλάω contr.vb. [σῡλη] | iteratv.impf. σῡλασκον | aor. ἐσῡλησα, dial.ptcpl. σῡλάσαις (Pi.) | PASS.: aor. ἐσῡλήθην, dial.ptcpl. σῡλᾱθείς | **1** (of soldiers) **despoil** —*a slain enemy* Il. —*a corpse* Pl.; **strip away** —*armour* Il. E.; **strip** —W.DBL.ACC. *a slain enemy, of his armour* Il. || PASS. (of a slain enemy) **be stripped of armour** X.
2 (of Perseus) **strip away** —*the head of Medusa* (fr. her body) Pi.
3 strip off —*a lid* (W.GEN. fr. a quiver) Il.; **strip off the cover from** —*a bow* Il.
4 (gener., of a person or god) **strip, rob** —W.DBL.ACC. *someone, of sthg. or someone* E. D. || PASS. **be stripped** or **robbed** —W.ACC. *of sthg.* Hdt. Trag. Isoc. D.
5 (of persons, armies) **strip bare, pillage, plunder** —*temples* or *sim.* A. Hdt. + —*ships* D. —*people* Arist. Plb. Plu.; (fig., of detractors) —*the achievements of ancestors* D. || PASS. (of persons, places, ships) **be plundered** or **robbed** Hdt. E. Isoc. D.; (of an altar, by the abduction of suppliants fr. it) E.
6 seize as spoil, carry off —*property (of gods or humans)* Hes. Thgn. Hdt. S.; (of a god) **steal** —*a person* (W.GEN. fr. a country) E.; (of a person) **appropriate** —*another's rights* A. S. || PASS. (of a statue) **be carried off** or **stolen** Hdt.; (of an exposed baby) —W.DAT. *by birds of prey* E.; (fig., of a person's life) E.; (of sleep) —W.PREP.PHR. *fr. the eyelids* B.; (of a boy) —W.GEN. *fr. among the boys* (*to compete w. grown men*) Pi.

σῡλέομαι dial.mid.contr.vb. **steal** —*honey* (W.PREP.PHR. fr. a hive) Theoc.

σῡλεύω vb. **1 strip** —*a slain enemy (of his armour)* Il.
2 rob, cheat —*someone (of gifts due to him)* Il.

σῡλη ης f. **1 seizure of goods in reprisal** || PL. **reprisals** Lys. D.
2 || PL. **rights of reprisal** D.

σῡλησις εως f. **plundering** (of cattle, temples) S.*Ichn.* Pl.

σῡλήτωρ ορος m. **plunderer, robber** (W.GEN. of the gods, ref. to an abduction of suppliants fr. an altar) A.

—**συλήτειρα** ᾱς *f.* **plunderer** (W.GEN. of countrymen, ref. to a hind) E.

συλλαβή ῆς *f.* [συλλαμβάνω] **1** that which holds together; **fastening** (W.GEN. of robes, ref. to a woman's girdle) A.
2 that which is held together; set of sounds or letters comprising a unified element in speech, **syllable** A. Pl. D. Arist. Plu.; (as the minimal portion of speech) Aeschin. D. Thphr.

συλ-λαγχάνω *vb.* [σύν] **1 share a common lot** or **fortune** —W.DAT. *w. people, animals* Pl.
2 happen to be associated —W.DAT. *w. a particular time or circumstance* Plu.

συλ-λαλέω *contr.vb.* **talk together, converse** —W.DAT. or PREP.PHR. *w. someone* Plb. NT.

συλ-λαμβάνω (ξυλ-) *vb.* **1 gather up** (and take w. one) —*troops, followers, one's children, or sim.* Hdt. S. E. Ar. X. Arist.
2 pack up, carry off with one —*a bridle* Pi. —*wings* Ar.; (dismissively) —*oracles, curses* S. —*books* Ar.
3 get together (in preparation for an undertaking), **rally** —*oneself* S.; **muster** —*an implacable heart* E.
4 put together, close —*the mouth and eyes* (*of a corpse*) Pl.; **shut** (forcibly) —*a speaker's mouth* Ar.
5 put together —*syllables* (*so as to pronounce them as a single word*) Ar.
6 put together (in speech), **embrace, include** —*all or many topics* (sts. W.DAT. or PREP.PHR. *in a brief statement, into one thing, or sim.*) Hdt. E. Pl. Aeschin.; (intr.) **sum up** Arist. ‖ PASS. (of terms or definitions) be combined or included (sts. W.DAT. or PREP.PHR. *w. others*) Arist.
7 (of rhetoric) **embrace, incorporate** —*all spheres of activity* Pl.; (of a civic honour) —*all other honours* D.
8 (of a fortunate man, throughout his life) **gather** or **acquire together** —*all advantages* Hdt.
9 lay hands on, seize, capture —*persons* Hdt. S. E. Th. Ar. Att.orats. + —*ships* Hdt. Th. D. —*birds* Ar. ‖ PASS. (of persons, ships) be seized or captured Th. Ar. Att.orats. +
10 get one's hands on —*objects* Ar.; **grasp** —*one's hair* S. —*things which fly* (in neg.phr., fig.ref. to thwarted aspirations) Theoc. ‖ PASS. (of a memorandum) be laid hands on Isoc.
11 grasp with the mind, grasp, comprehend —*an oracular response, meaning, language, or sim.* Hdt. Pl.
12 (of a person, god, fortune, circumstances) **lend a hand, give help** (oft. W.DAT. to someone or sthg.) Hdt. S. E. Ar. Isoc. Pl. +—W.PREP.PHR. *towards sthg.* Hdt. X. —W.ACC. *in sthg.* Ar. X. Is. D. —W.GEN. *in trouble or an undertaking* E. —*w. a stake* E.*Cyc.* —*w. ropes* Ar.
13 ‖ MID. **lend a hand, give help** (sts. W.DAT. *to someone*) A. Th. Pl. —W.GEN. *w. logs* (i.e. w. carrying them) Ar. —*w. a sickness* S. —*w. a story* Pl.(tm.); (of circumstances) **contribute** —W.GEN. *towards an outcome* Th.
14 ‖ MID. **take part, join** —W.GEN. *in an expedition, hunt* Hdt. E.*fr.*

Συλλάνιος *Lacon.adj.*: see Ἑλλήνιος

συλ-λέγω (ξυλ-) *vb.* | aor. συνέλεξα | pf. συνείλοχα ‖ PASS.: fut. συλλεγήσομαι | aor. συνελέχθην | aor.2 συνελέγην ‖ mid.pass.pf. συνείλεγμαι, ptcpl. συνειλεγμένος, also συλλελεγμένος |
1 (act. and mid.) **bring** or **gather together, collect** —*material things* Il. Hdt. Th. Ar. X. + ‖ PASS. (of things) be collected Hdt. X.
2 (act. and mid.) **collect, acquire** —*money, financial contributions* Hdt. Th. Ar. Att.orats. Pl. X. +—*dowries* Hdt.

—*property* Hyp. —*a livelihood* Sol. E. Pl. D.; (intr.) **accumulate wealth** Men. ‖ PASS. (of money) be collected Hdt.; (of property) be acquired Din.
3 collect —*words and phrases, lines of verse, instances of behaviour* D.; (pejor., of a poet) —*songs, versicles* Ar.; (intr.) **collect information** D.
4 (of an accuser) **build up** —*anger and hatred* (W.DAT. *against someone*, W.PREP.PHR. *fr. jurors*) Hyp. ‖ MID. **acquire** —*benefits, skills* Ar. Isoc.; **gather, rally** —*one's strength* E. ‖ PASS. (of mistakes) be accumulated D.; (of fame) be acquired Lycurg.; (of a habit of talkativeness) —W.DAT. *by someone* X.
5 collect, gather together, assemble —*groups of people, companions, supporters, or sim.* Hdt. E. Th. Ar. Pl. +; (mid.) Od. Call. ‖ PASS. (of people) gather together, assemble Hdt. Th. Ar. Att.orats. Pl. +; (of birds) Ar.
6 convene —*an assembly, council, meeting* Th. Pl. X. ‖ PASS. (of an assembly or council) be convened Hdt. Th. Isoc. D.
7 assemble, levy, muster —*an army, troops, ships* Hdt. Th. Isoc. X. +; (mid.) —*a company of soldiers* X. ‖ PASS. assemble or be assembled Hdt. Th. Att.orats. X. +
8 recruit —*a chorus* Antipho
9 ‖ PASS. (of a soul) gather together —W.PREP.PHR. *into itself* Pl.
10 ‖ PASS. (of rivers) meet Hdt.

σύλ-λεκτρος ου *m.f.* [λέκτρον] **1** (ref. to Hera) sharer of a bed, **bedfellow, wife** (W.GEN. of Zeus) E.
2 (ref. to Amphitryon) sharer of a wife (i.e. Alkmene), **wife-sharer** (W.GEN. w. Zeus) E.

συλλήβδην *adv.* [συλλαμβάνω] **1** in a comprehensive manner; **collectively, altogether, in one swoop** Thgn. A. Ar. Att.orats. +
2 in sum, in short Lys. Isoc. Pl. +
3 in general, simply Plb.

σύλληξις εως *f.* [συλλαγχάνω] **pairing by lot** (of husbands and wives, boxers) Pl.

συλλήπτωρ ορος *m.* [συλλαμβάνω] **helper, accomplice** A. Antipho; (W.GEN. in sthg.) Pl.; (W.DAT. + GEN. for someone, in sthg.) E. Pl. X.

—**συλλήπτρια** ᾱς *f.* (ref. to Virtue) **helper** (W.GEN. in sthg.) X.

σύλληψις (ξύλ-) εως *f.* **1 forcible seizure, apprehension, arrest** (of a person) Th. Att.orats. Arist. Plb. Plu.; (of a ship) Plb.
2 receiving (of seed, in the womb); **conception** (W.GEN. of a child) Plu.

συλλογή (ξυλ-) ῆς *f.* [συλλέγω] **1 gathering, collection** (of firewood) Th.; (of scattered bones) Plu.; (of instances of outrageous behaviour) D.
2 accumulation, growth (W.GEN. of a beard) A.
3 selecting (W.GEN. of citizens) Pl.
4 levying, mustering (W.GEN. of confederates) Hdt.; (of an army, soldiers) X. Plu.
5 convening of a meeting Pl.

συλ-λογίζομαι *mid.vb.* | aor. συνελογισάμην ‖ PASS.: aor. συνελογίσθην | **1 estimate** or **determine** (fr. evidence), **calculate, take stock of** —*achievements, circumstances, consequences* Hdt. Att.orats. Pl. Plb. Plu.
2 calculate, conclude, deduce —*sthg.* Isoc. Pl. Arist. Plb. —W.COMPL.CL. *that sthg. is the case* Pl. Arist. Plb. —W.INDIR.Q. *what is the case* Pl. Hyp. D. Arist.; (intr.) **make an inference, draw a conclusion** Pl. Arist. Plb. ‖ PASS. (of things) be deduced Pl. ‖ IMPERS.PLPF.PASS. it had been

συλλογισμός

concluded (i.e. decided) —W.DAT. + INF. *by someone, to do sthg.* Plb.
3 infer (W.ACC. sthg.) **syllogistically** (fr. two logical premises) Arist.; (intr.) **argue by deduction** Arist.

συλλογισμός οῦ *m*. **1 forming of a conclusion, process of reasoning** Pl. Plb.
2 conclusion, inference Arist. Plb. Plu.
3 (log.) a kind of deductive argument (in which a conclusion is drawn fr. two premises), **syllogism** Arist.

συλλογιστέος ᾱ ον *vbl.adj.* (of a concept) **to be inferred** (as being the cause of sthg.) Pl.

συλλογιστικός ή όν *adj.* (of principles) **of syllogistic reasoning** Arist.

—συλλογιστικῶς *adv.* **syllogistically** Arist.

σύλλογος (ξύλ-) ου *m*. [συλλέγω] **1 gathering, assembly, meeting** (of people, gods, troops, oft. for the purpose of deliberation) Hdt. E. Th. Att.orats. Pl. +
2 mustering (of troops) Th. X.; (of ships) And.
3 (fig.) **pulling together, rallying** (W.GEN. of one's spirits) E.

συλ-λούομαι *mid.vb.* **bathe together** —W.DAT. w. *someone* Plu.

συλ-λοχίζω *vb.* **incorporate** —*troops* (w. εἰς + ACC. *into a legion*) Plu. || PASS. (of troops) **be incorporated** —w. εἰς + ACC. *into companies of a hundred* Plu.; **be formed into companies** —w. κατά + ACC. *by clans and tribes* Plu.

συλ-λοχίτης εω *Ion.m.* **soldier of the same company** Hdt.

συλ-λῡπέω *contr.vb.* | *fut.pass.* συλλυπηθήσομαι, also συλλυπήσομαι | **1 make** (W.ACC. one's friends) **share in pain or grief** —W.DAT. w. *oneself* Arist.
2 || PASS. **share in pain or grief** Hdt. Antipho Pl. —W.DAT. w. *someone* Arist.
3 || PASS. **condole, commiserate** —W.DAT. w. *people, their sufferings* Hdt. Thphr. Plu.
4 || PASS. **be deeply grieved** —W.PREP.PHR. *over sthg.* NT.

συλ-λύω (ξυλ-) *vb.* **1 help to release** —*someone's bonds* E.; (intr., fig.) **help to loose** (a knot, i.e. a problem or quarrel), **help with the resolution** S.
2 share a lodging (w. someone) A. | cf. καταλύω 15

σῡμα *Lacon.n.:* see θῦμα

συμ-βαίνω (ξυμ-) *vb.* [σύν] | PASS.: 3sg.aor.subj. ξυμβαθῇ | *pf.inf.* ξυμβεβάσθαι (Th.) | **1** (of natural elements) **come together, meet** Emp.; (of two sets of people) —W.DAT. w. *each other* X.; (of arrangements) —W.PREDIC.ADJ. *in a close fit* A. || STATV.PF. (of a person) **stand with feet together** X.
2 (of persons, usu. adversaries) **come together in agreement, come to terms, make an agreement** (oft. W.DAT. w. someone, also w. πρός + ACC.) E. Th. Ar. Pl. —W.NEUT.ACC. *on sthg.* Th. Ar. —W.INF. *to do sthg.* Th. —W.ACC. + INF. (also w. ὥστε) *that someone shd. do sthg.* Hdt. Th. || PASS. (of peace terms) **be agreed** Th.
3 (of a god or human) **be on close terms** —W.DAT. w. *someone* E. Ar.
4 (of time, reports, oracles) **correspond, match, tally** —W.DAT. w. *sthg.* Hdt. S. Lys.; (of periods of time, oracles) **come out right, tally** Hdt. S. Ar.; (of a god's plans) **coincide, chime in** —W.DAT. w. *someone's troubles* E.
5 (of events, circumstances) **happen, occur** Th. Att.orats. Pl. +; **happen** —W.INF. *to occur* Hdt. Th.; (of things) —W.NOM.PTCPL. *to be* (i.e. *exist*) Pl. D. || IMPERS. **it happens, it turns out** —W.ACC. + INF. (sts. w. ὥστε) *that someone does sthg., that sthg. is the case* Hdt. S. Th. Att.orats. +
|| NEUT.PTCPL.SB. **chance event, contingency** Pl. X. Is. Arist. Plb.
6 (of sufferings, pleasures, responsibilities) **fall to the lot of, befall, come the way of** —W.DAT. *someone* E. Th. Att.orats. + || IMPERS. **it falls** —W.DAT. + INF. *to someone, to do sthg.* Hdt. Th. Att.orats. X. Arist. Theoc.
7 (of persons, events, predictions, or sim.) **turn out** —W.PREDIC.SB. *as such and such* S. E. Pl. —W.ADV. **well, badly, contrary to expectation,** or sim. Hdt. E. Th. X.; (of oracles) **be fulfilled** A.
8 (of things, in measurement or calculation) **add up** —w. εἰς + ACC. *to some result* A. X. D.
9 (of consequences) **result, follow** Th. D.; (of logical conclusions) Pl. D. Arist.; (of a process) **turn out** —W.INF. *to consist of sthg.* Pl. || IMPERS. **it follows** —W.ACC. + INF. *that sthg. is the case* Pl. Arist. || NEUT.PTCPL.SB. **contingent attribute, property** (of sthg.) Arist.

συμ-βακχεύω *vb.* (of a mountain) **join in the Bacchic revelry** E. —W.DAT. w. *Dionysus* E.; (of a person) **share in the ecstasy** —w. μετά + GEN. w. *someone inspired by a god* Pl.

σύμ-βακχος ου *masc.fem.adj.* [βάκχος, βάκχη] (of Cassandra) **sharing inspiration** (W.DAT. w. gods) E.

συμ-βάλλω (ξυμ-) *vb.* | only ep. forms fr. stem βλη- are given here (for others see βάλλω) | *inf.* ξυμβλήμεναι | 3du.aor. ξυμβλήτην || MID.: *aor.*3sg. ξύμβλητο, 3pl. ξύμβληντο, 2sg.subj. ξυμβλήεαι, 3sg.subj. ξύμβληται, *ptcpl.* ξυμβλήμενος |
1 throw or bring together; (of combatants) **strike together, clash** —*shields* Il.(tm.) E. X.; (of mountain torrents, confluent rivers) **dash together** —*their waters* Il.; (perh.fig., of a god) **join** —*tears* (W.DAT. w. *tears, envisaged as streams*) E.; (intr., of roads) **come together, meet** S.
2 bring together, join —*hands* (*in a pledge*) E.; **shut tight** —*one's eyes* (*in death*), *one's eyelids* (W.DAT. *in sleep*) A.; **twist together** —*ropes* (i.e. *cords, so as to produce ropes*) Ar. || PASS. (of barley) **be brought together** (for storage) X.
3 (of gods or humans) **bring together in conflict, match** —*persons, animals* Il. X. Aeschin.; **set** (W.ACC. a person, an animal) **to fight** —W.DAT. *against another* Hdt.; (fig.) **bring** (W.ACC. a person) **face to face** —W.DAT. w. *shamelessness* (*envisaged as a combatant*) Pl.
4 (intr., of combatants) **come together, join battle, clash** (sts. W.DAT. or πρός + ACC. w. someone) Il. Hdt. E. Th. +; (of ships) Plb.; (of Violence, Justice) —W.DAT. w. *Violence, Justice* A.; (of the universe, i.e. its individual parts) **collide** Pl.
5 (tr.) **engage in** —*war* Il. —*battle, a contest, enmity, strife* (W.DAT. w. *someone*) E. —*insults* S. —*counsel, talk* (W.DAT. or πρός + ACC. w. *someone*) E.; (perh.) —*eye-contact* E.
6 (without adversative connot.) **have contact with, fall in with, meet** (sts. W.DAT. someone) Il. A. E.*fr.* X. Plu.; (mid.) Hom. AR.; **converse** —w. πρός + ACC. w. *someone* NT.
7 || MID. **add** (sthg.) **to a collective stock or situation; contribute** —*goods, money, help,* or sim. (sts. W.DAT. *to someone*) Hdt. Att.orats. Pl. X. —*an opinion* Hdt. S. Pl. —*arguments, remarks* (*to a discussion*) Isoc. Pl. X. —*a song* Philox.Cyth.; (of tributaries) —*water* Hdt.; (of fortune, circumstances) —*sthg.* (sts. w. εἰς or πρός + ACC. *towards sthg.*) Th. Isoc. Pl. X. D. +; (of a poet) **throw in, include, add** —*sthg.* (*in an account*) Pi.; (intr., of persons or things) **contribute, help** (sts. W.DAT. someone or sthg., or w. εἰς + ACC. *towards sthg.*) A. Hdt. E. Att.orats. Pl. +
8 make a contract (usu. ref. to lending money on security) Pl. Hyp. —W.COGN.ACC. Pl. D.
9 loan on contract, lend —*goods, money* Ar. Att.orats. Pl.; (intr.) **make a loan** Isoc.

10 ‖ MID. **come to terms** (sts. W. πρός + ACC. w. someone) Th.(decree); (tr.) **agree upon, arrange** —*a rendezvous* X.
11 **put together** (for the purpose of comparison); **compare** —*sthg.* (W.DAT. or πρός + ACC. *w. sthg. else*) Hdt. Pl. Lycurg.; (intr.) **be an object of comparison** Hdt. ‖ PASS. (of one thing) **be compared** (sts. W.DAT. or πρός + ACC. w. another) Hdt.
12 **class together** —*different things* Pl.
13 **put together in the mind, conjecture, infer** —*sthg.* Hdt.(mid.) S. Ar. —*someone's ancestry* Pi. —W.COMPL.CL. *that sthg. is the case* Hdt. —W.INDIR.Q. *what is the case* Hdt. Pl.(mid.); (intr.) **make an inference** Hdt.; **interpret, understand** —*a situation, oracle, dream, sickness* Hdt. E. Ar. Pl. Call.
14 ‖ MID. **reckon, calculate** Hdt. —*months* Hdt. ‖ PASS. (of a distance) **be calculated** Hdt.

συμ-βασιλεύω *vb.* **share kingship** (usu. W.DAT. w. someone) Plb. Plu.

σύμβασις (ξύμ-) εως (Ion. ιος) *f.* [συμβαίνω] 1 **agreement** (to do sthg.) Th.
2 **terms of agreement, treaty** Hdt. E. Th. X. Plu.
3 **friendly terms, reconciliation** E.

συμβατήριος (ξυμ-) ον *adj.* relating to agreement; (of a proposal) **offering peace terms** Th.

συμβατικός (ξυμ-) ή όν *adj.* 1 (of the efforts of ambassadors, a reply given to them) **conducive to an agreement** Th.; (of a state of affairs) Plb.
2 (of a proposal) **offering peace terms** Th. Plu.; (of speech, a proposal) **conciliatory** Plu.

—**συμβατικῶς** *adv.* (w. ἔχειν) *be disposed to come to terms* Plu.

συμβατός όν *adj.* ‖ NEUT.IMPERS. (w. ἐστί) **it can fall to the lot** —W.DAT. + INF. *of someone, to do sthg.* Plb.

συμ-βελής ές *adj.* [βέλος] (of attackers) **under fire from a variety of missiles** Plb.

συμβησείω (ξυμ-) *vb.* [desideratv. συμβαίνω] (of a military leader) **wish to agree on terms** Th.

συμ-βιάζομαι *pass.vb.* (of elements in a city) **be forced into conformity** D.

συμ-βιβάζω (ξυμ-) *vb.* 1 **bring together, bring to terms, reconcile** —*enemies, disputants* Hdt. Pl. Arist. —*someone* (W.DAT. w. others) Th.
2 **put together, compare, examine** —*statements* Pl.
3 **put together in the mind, conclude, infer** —W.COMPL.CL. or INDIR.Q. *that* (or *whether*) *sthg. is the case* Pl. Arist. NT.

συμβιβαστικός ή όν *adj.* conducive to reconciliation ‖ NEUT.SB. reconciliation Plu.

σύμβιος ου *m.* [συμβιόω] one who lives together (w. someone), **close companion** Arist.

συμ-βιόω *contr.vb.* 1 (usu. of comrades, male friends) **live together** Pl. Arist. —W.DAT. or μετά + GEN. *w. someone* Isoc. Plb. Plu.
2 **be associated with in life; spend one's life in** —W.DAT. *good fortune* D. —*doctrines and arguments* Plu.

συμβίωσις εως *f.* **life together** Plb. Plu.

συμβιωτής οῦ *m.* one who lives together (w. someone), **close companion** Plb. Plu.

συμβλητός ή όν *adj.* [συμβάλλω] (of things) capable of being compared, **comparable** (sts. W.DAT. w. sthg.) Arist.; (w. πρός + ACC.) Theoc.

συμ-βοάω *contr.vb.* 1 **shout in unison** —W.DAT. *w. someone* X.
2 (of people separated by darkness or distance) **call** (W.ACC. one another) **together** X.

συμ-βοήθεια (ξυμ-) ᾱς *f.* **joint military help, reinforcements** Th.

συμ-βοηθέω (ξυμ-) *contr.vb.* 1 (usu. of troops) unite in giving help, **rally in support** or **defence** Th. Ar. X. Plu. —W.DAT. *of someone* Th.
2 **join** (W.DAT. someone) **in giving help** —W.DAT. *to others* X.

συμβόλαιον ου *n.* [reltd. σύμβολον] 1 that which tallies, **token** (ref. to a choice of words, taken as proof that sthg. is true) Hdt. ‖ PL. indications, symptoms (of an apparently dead person) S.; proofs (fr. comparable situations) Plu.
2 (oft.pl.) **contract** (for an interest-bearing loan) E.*fr.* Att.orats. Pl. X. +
3 ‖ PL. (gener.) transactions, dealings Att.orats. Pl. Arist.; (euphem., for sexual intercourse) E.
4 **relationship** (betw. people) Plu.

συμβολαῖος (ξυμ-) ᾱ ον *adj.* [συμβολή] (of legal cases) **arising from inter-state agreements** Th.(v.l. ξυμβολιμαῖος) | see σύμβολον 5

συμβολεύω *vb.* (of Spartan youths) **contribute** —*food* (*to a common meal*) X.

συμβολέω (ξυμ-) *contr.vb.* [reltd. συμβάλλω] (of persons) **fall in with, meet** —W.DAT. *someone* A.; (intr.) A.

συμβολή (ξυμ-) ῆς *f.* 1 coming together, **meeting** (of roads) X.
2 **juncture, clasp** (of a belt) Hdt.; **link** (in a horse's bit) X.; **socket** (in a joint of the human body) Pl.
3 **encounter between soldiers, engagement, clash** Hdt. Th. Ar. X. Plb.; (betw. ships) A.
4 **inter-state agreement** or **treaty** Arist.(cj. σύμβολα) | see σύμβολον 5
5 ‖ PL. contributions (towards a shared meal) Ar. Men.; (towards communal enjoyment) X.; (by gamblers, ref. to a jackpot) Men.; (to the state, a war) Plu.

συμβολιμαῖος *adj.*: see συμβολαῖος

σύμβολον ου *n.* 1 **tally** (each of two corresponding halves of a small object, such as a knucklebone, kept separately by the parties to a transaction, which might later be put together to guarantee the credentials of the holder) Hdt. E. Arist.; (fig.) **tally, counterpart** (W.GEN. of a person, oneself, ref. to a human being imagined as half of an original whole) Pl.
2 something which tallies; **counterpart** (W.GEN. of a happening, ref. to what must happen in requital for it) A.; **matching evidence** (W.GEN. of suffering, recognised by one whose own suffering comes fr. the same source) S.; perh., shared connection, **binding link** (betw. Oedipus and the Thebans) S.
3 object or circumstance serving as proof of identity, **token** E. Lys. X. Plu.
4 object or document indicating authorisation; **token, ticket** (given to a juror entering court, perh. for random assignment of seats) Ar. D. Arist.; (given to a person attending the Assembly, also to a juror when he votes, exchanged later for daily pay) Ar. Arist.; **entry-pass** (to Cloudcuckoo City) Ar.; **admission ticket** (to an entertainment) Thphr.
5 (usu.pl.) **reciprocal agreement** or **treaty between states** (providing for the settlement by individuals of commercial and other disputes in the courts of either state) Att.orats. Arist. Men. Plb.
6 (gener.) **contract, compact** hHom.
7 **criminal design** Thgn.
8 **prearranged sign** (indicating a fact or initiating action, esp. in military ctxt.); **signal** (fr. a beacon) A.; (for sthg. to be done) Plu.; **password** E.

σύμβολος

9 indication of a future event; **sign, evidence** (W.GEN. of divine intent) Pi.; **omen** hHom. Archil.
10 indication of truth or meaning; **token, evidence, proof** (usu. W.GEN. of sthg.) E. Isoc. Pl. D. +

σύμβολος (**ξύμ-**) ον *m.* [reltd. συμβολέω, σύμβολον] chance encounter (usu. w. a particular kind of person or animal, regarded as a portent), **coincidental** or **significant meeting** A. Ar. X.

συμβούλευμα ατος *n.* [συμβουλεύω] **piece of advice** X. Arist. Plb.

συμβουλευτέος (**ξυμ-**) ᾱ ον *vbl.adj.* (of policies) **to be advised** or **counselled** Th.

συμβουλευτής οῦ *m.* **1** (ref. to a law) **adviser, counsellor** Pl.
2 colleague in the Council, **fellow councillor** Aeschin.

συμβουλευτικός ή όν *adj.* **1** (of a law) **of the advisory kind** Pl.
2 (of a kind of rhetoric) **deliberative** Plb.; (contrasted w. forensic and epideictic) Arist.

συμ-βουλεύω (**ξυμ-**) *vb.* **1 give advice** (oft. W.DAT. to someone) Thgn. Hdt. S. Att.orats. Pl. + —W.INF. *to do sthg.* Hdt. Th. + —W.ACC. + INF. *that someone shd. do sthg.* Hdt. Lys. Isoc. Pl.
2 advise, recommend —*sthg.* (oft. W.DAT. *to someone*) Hippon.(tm.) Hdt. Ar. Att.orats. Pl. +
3 (of an orator) **make a deliberative speech** Arist. | see συμβουλευτικός 2
4 (of a written composition) **have a didactic purpose** Isoc.
5 || MID. **ask advice** (oft. W.DAT. fr. someone) Hdt. Lys. Pl. X. —W.ACC. *on some matter* Hdt. Th.; **deliberate together** X. —w. μετά + GEN. *w. someone* Ar.

συμβουλή (**ξυμ-**) ῆς *f.* **1** giving of advice; **advice** Hdt.(v.l. συμβουλίη) Pl. X. D. +
2 deliberative rhetoric Arist.
3 seeking of advice, **deliberation together, consultation** Pl.

συμβουλίᾱ ᾱς, Ion. **συμβουλίη** ης *f.* **1** (sg. and pl.) **advice** Hdt. Att.orats. X. Arist. +
2 deliberation together, consultation Hdt.

συμβούλιον ου *n.* **1** (usu. derog.) result of consultation, **plan, plot** NT.
2 council NT. Plu.

συμ-βούλομαι *mid.vb.* **1 be united in wishing** —W.ACC. + INF. *that sthg. shd. happen* Pl. D.
2 share a wish (sts. W.DAT. w. someone) Pl. Plu. —W.INF. *for someone to die* E. —W.ACC. *for sthg.* X.

σύμ-βουλος (**ξύμ-**) ου *m.f.* [βουλή] **1 adviser, counsellor** (in private or public affairs, usu. without ref. to a specific office, oft. W.DAT. to someone or sthg., sts. W.GEN. of someone) Anacr. Hdt. Trag. Th. Ar. Att.orats. +; (W.GEN. about sthg.) A. Isoc. X. Men.
2 member of an advisory board; **adviser** (accompanying a Spartan general) Th.; (accompanying a consul) Plb.
3 deliberative orator Arist. | see συμβουλευτικός 2

συμ-βύω (**ξυμ-**) *vb.* || PASS. (of jurors) **be crammed together** Ar.

σύμ-βωμος ον *adj.* [βωμός] (of the Muses) **sharing an altar** (w. Phoibos) Lyr.adesp.

σύμενος (athem.aor.mid.ptcpl.): see σεύω

συμ-μαθητής οῦ *m.* **fellow student** Pl.

συμ-μανθάνω *vb.* **1 share lessons** —W.DAT. *w. someone* X.
2 understand fully; **be accustomed** (to a strong drink) X.
3 learn fully or **share in knowledge** S.(dub.)

συμ-μάρπτω *vb.* **1 grasp together, gather handfuls of** —*reeds and branches* Il.
2 (of Polyphemos) **snatch up together** —*two men* Od.(tm.) E.*Cyc.*; (of a punitive deity) —*a whole family* Hdt.(oracle)
3 (of Zeus) **snatch up** —*Metis* (*to swallow her*) Hes.*fr.*

συμ-μαρτυρέω (**ξυμ-**) *contr.vb.* **1** bear witness alongside or in confirmation; **attest, confirm** —*sthg.* Sol. —W.ACC. (or COMPL.CL.) + DAT. *sthg.* (*or that sthg. is the case*) *for someone* E. Pl. X.
2 attest to, agree with, confirm —W.DAT. *sthg.* Isoc. Plu.; **provide confirmation** (of sthg.) Th.
3 agree (about sthg.) S. —W.DAT. *w. someone* S.

σύμ-μαρτυς (**ξύμ-**) υρος *m.f.* one who gives evidence in addition or confirmation, **joint witness** (W.GEN. of or to sthg.) Pl.; (also W.DAT. for someone) E.; (W.INDIR.Q. to what is the case) S.

συμμαχέω (**ξυμ-**) *contr.vb.* [σύμμαχος] **1** (of a country, military leader, or sim.) **be an ally, be in alliance, form an alliance** (oft. W.DAT. w. someone) A. Hdt. S. Th. Pl. X. +
2 (gener., of people, gods) **support, help** (usu. W.DAT. someone or sthg.) S. E.*fr.* Pl. X.
3 (of a circumstance) **help, contribute** —w. ὥστε + INF. *towards sthg. being the case* Hdt.

συμμαχίᾱ (**ξυμ-**) ᾱς, Ion. **συμμαχίη** ης *f.* **1** union between people or states for defensive or offensive purposes; **alliance, confederacy** Simon. Hdt. E. Th. Att.orats. X. +; (ref. to allied territory) Th.; perh. **one's duty as ally** A.
2 whole body of allies, **allied forces** Hdt. E. Th. Aeschin.; group of allies, **allied** or **auxiliary force** Th. Pl. X.; (collectv.) **fellow soldiers** Pi.
3 (without military connot.) **support, help** Pl.

συμμαχικός (**ξυμ-**) ή όν *adj.* **1** of or relating to allies; (of gods) **who witness an alliance** Th.
2 (of affairs, a dispute, law) **relating to allies** Isoc. Plb. Plu.; (alternative title of a speech of Isocrates, usu. known as *On the Peace*) **On the Alliance** Arist.
3 (of troops) **allied** Plb. Plu.
4 (of a war betw. allies) **social** Plb. Plu.
5 || NEUT.SB. **alliance, confederacy** Th. Ar. X. D. Arist.; allied forces, **allies** Hdt. Th.; (pl.) X. Plb. Plu.

—**συμμαχικῶς** *adv.* **in the spirit of allies** (opp. masters) Isoc. Plb.

συμμαχίς (**ξυμ-**) ίδος *fem.adj.* [σύμμαχος] **1** (of a city, territory) **allied** Th. Att.orats. X. Plb. Plu.; (of a ship) Th. X.
2 || SB. allied city or territory Th. X. D. Plb.; body of allies, **alliance, confederacy** Th.

συμ-μάχομαι (**ξυμ-**) *mid.vb.* **1 fight alongside, be an ally, provide support** (oft. W.DAT. for someone) Hdt. Th. Pl. X. Arist. Plu.; (fig., of probability) **be on the side of** —W.DAT. *someone* Hdt.
2 join in fighting —W.COGN.ACC. *a battle* Aeschin. D. Arist. Plu.; **fight together** (as allies) Arist.

σύμ-μαχος (**ξύμ-**) ον *adj.* [μάχη] **1** fighting alongside, allied || MASC.FEM.SB. (in military or gener. ctxts.) ally, supporter (oft. W.DAT. to someone) Archil. Sapph. Pi. Hdt. Trag. Ar. + || PL. (of persons united in a defensive or offensive alliance) allies Hdt. Trag. Th. Ar. Att.orats. +
2 (of places, weapons) **allied** (sts. W.DAT. to someone or sthg.) Hdt. Trag.; (of a law, circumstance) **supportive, helpful, favourable** (usu. W.DAT. to someone) Hdt. S. Th. Ar. Att.orats. X.

συμμέθεξις εως *f.* [συμμετέχω] **sharing together** (W.GEN. of hardships) Arist.

συμ-μεθίστημι *vb.* || MID. **change one's position to match** (another's change) Plu.

συμ-μείγνῡμι (**ξυμ-**) *vb.*, sts. written **συμμίγνῡμι** *vb.* —also (pres. and impf.) **συμμειγνύω** (X.), also **συμμίσγω** (Il. +)
1 mix together, commingle —*two or more things* hHom. Anacr. Pi. Hdt. Pl. —*sthg.* (W.DAT. *w. sthg. else*) A. Hdt. Pl.

‖ PASS. (of things) be mixed together or commingled Thgn. Hdt. Lys. —W.DAT. *w. other things* Il. Thgn.(tm.) Hdt. E. Pl.
2 mix in —*sthg.* (*as a constituent in sthg. else*) Hdt. Pl. ‖ PASS. (of cakes) be mixed —W.DAT. *w. lentils* Sol.; (of misfortune) be blended in —W.DAT. *w. someone* (*at birth*) Hdt.
3 form by combination, blend —*a temper of mind* Thgn.; **put together** —*contracts* Pl. ‖ PASS. (of things) be formed by combination Pl.
4 ‖ PASS. (of troops) **unite, join forces** Hdt. Th.
5 ‖ PASS. (of events) **happen concurrently** Hdt.
6 join in marriage or sexual union; (of Eros) **unite** —*all things* Ar.; (of Aphrodite) —*gods* (W.DAT. *w. women*) hHom.; (of a woman) —*her body* (*w. her husband, in death*) E.; **contract** —*a sexual union* (W.DAT. *w. someone*) Ar.; **link in marriage** —*a person, house* (W.DAT. *w. another*) E. ‖ PASS. (of heaven and earth) be joined in sexual union E.*fr.*; (of a person) have sexual relations —W.DAT. *w. someone* Hdt. Ar. Pl.
7 associate, introduce —*someone* (W.DAT. *to good fortune*) Pi.; **communicate** —*some business* (W.DAT. *to someone*) Thgn. Hdt.
8 (intr.) **mix, associate, have contact** —W.DAT. or πρός + ACC. *w. someone or sthg.* Thgn. Hdt. E. Ar. Pl. +; **have sexual relations** —W.DAT. *w. someone* Pl.; (of a sea) **meet** —W.DAT. *another sea* Hdt. ‖ MID.PASS. **associate, consort** —W.DAT. *w. someone* A. Hdt.
9 (of combatants) **come together, engage, clash** Hdt. Th. X. D. —W.DAT. *w. someone* Hdt. Th. X. Plb. ‖ PASS. (of bronze) **clash** —W.DAT. *w. bronze* Hdt.(oracle)

σύμ-μεικτος, also written **σύμμικτος** (**ξύμ-**), ον *adj.* [μεικτός] **1 mixed together indiscriminately**; (of the produce of the earth) **mixed, of various kinds** Hes.; (of cattle) S.; (of bronze vessels) **miscellaneous** Lys.; (of a rabble, shouting) **confused** Plb.
2 consisting of a mixture or blend; (of an army, race, population) **of mixed origin** Hdt. Th. Plb. Plu.; (of the form of the Minotaur) **mixed** E.*fr.*; (of things) **compounded** (fr. specific elements) Pl.; (of an evil) **mixed** (i.e. containing some good) Pl.; (of sacrifices) **combined** (W.DAT. *w. rites*) Pl. ‖ NEUT.SB. **mixed dialect** (of Ionic and Doric) Call.

σύμμειξις *f.*: see σύμμιξις

συμ-μελετάω *contr.vb.* (of javelin-throwers) **practise together** Antipho

συμ-μένω (**ξύμ-**) *vb.* **1** (of an army, troops) **stay together** (in good order) Th. Isoc. Plb. Plu.; (opp. be disbanded) D.
2 (of a person) **stay together** —W.DAT. *w. someone* Plb. Plu.
3 (of a pontoon) **hold together, hold firm** Plb.
4 (of an empire, change of government) **hold together, last** Th. Arist.
5 (of an alliance, agreement, friendship) **hold up, hold fast, endure** Hdt. Th. Pl. X.
6 (of persons) **hold firm** (in friendship) X.
7 (of persons, a city) **stand united** (through reciprocal obligations) Arist.

συμ-μεταβάλλω *vb.* **1 change** (W.ACC. *sthg.*) **simultaneously** or **for conformity** (usu. W.DAT. *w. someone or sthg.*) Plu.
2 (intr.) **change at the same time** Arist. —W.DAT. *as sthg.* Plu.(mid.)
3 ‖ MID. (of combatants) **change sides to join** —W.DAT. *w. someone* Aeschin.

συμ-μεταδίδωμι *vb.* **give (someone) a share** (in sthg.); **communicate with, confide in** —W.DAT. *someone* (W.GEN. or περί + GEN. *about sthg.*) Plb.

συμ-μεταίτιος ον *adj.* (of circumstances) **contributing jointly** (w. πρός + ACC. *towards sthg.*) Pl.

συμ-μετακοσμέομαι *mid.pass.contr.vb.* **change one's style of life for conformity** —W.DAT. *w. someone* Plu.

συμ-μεταπίπτω *vb.* (of the public record) **change together with** —W.DAT. *political turncoats* Aeschin.; (of the characters of cities, the dispositions of subjects) —*changes of ruler* Plb.

συμ-μετασχηματίζομαι *mid.vb.* **adapt oneself correspondingly** —w. πρός + ACC. *to a particular way of life* Plu.

συμ-μετατίθεμαι *mid.vb.* **1** (of a ruler) **change together with** —W.DAT. *changes in circumstances* Plb.
2 (of a soldier) **change one's position correspondingly** —w. πρός + ACC. *to match an expected blow* Plb.

συμ-μεταφέρομαι *pass.vb.* **be carried along together** (w. *someone*) Plu.

συμ-μεταχειρίζομαι *mid.vb.* **share in the handling of** —*a corpse* Is.

συμ-μετέχω *vb.* **share** —W.GEN. *in sthg.* E. Pl. Arist. Plu. —(W.DAT. *w. someone*) E. Plu.; (intr.) **join in** (w. someone, in holding an opinion) Pl.

συμ-μετίσχω (**ξύμ-**) *vb.* **share** —W.GEN. *in responsibility* S.

συμ-μετοικέω *contr.vb.* **change residence along with** —W.DAT. *someone* Plu.

συμ-μετρέω (**ξύμ-**) *contr.vb.* **1** ‖ MID. **measure against something** (or by comparison w. sthg.); **reckon up** —*the time of day* (against the time needed for a journey) Hdt.; **calculate** —*the height of a wall* (W.DAT. *by layers of bricks*) Th. —*the circuits of stars* (w. πρός + ACC. *relative to each other*) Pl. —*distances travelled* (*by reference to celestial phenomena*) Plb.
2 ‖ PASS. (of a day) be calculated —W.DAT. *against time elapsed* (*since someone's departure*) S.; (of a person, ref. to his age) be commensurate —W.DAT. *w. a long passage of time* (i.e. be ripe for death) S.; (of life) be measured out Th.

συμμέτρησις (**ξύμ-**) εως *f.* **measuring by comparison**; **measurement** (of the required length for ladders, based on the thickness of bricks) Th.

συμμετρίᾱ ᾱς, Ion. **συμμετρίη** ης *f.* [σύμμετρος]
1 sameness in measurement, commensurability Arist.
2 proper measure, proportion or **symmetry** Democr. Isoc. Pl. X. +
3 appropriateness, suitability Pl.
4 appropriate length or **height** Plb.

σύμ-μετρος (**ξύμ-**) ον *adj.* [μέτρον] **1 having the same measure**; (math., and in gener. ctxts., of things) **of equal extent** or **magnitude, commensurate** (sts. W.DAT. or πρός + ACC. *w. sthg.*) Pl. Arist. Plu.; (of a footprint, W.DAT. *w. another's foot*) E.; (of a person, ref. to moral stature, W.DAT. *w. other persons*) Isoc.
2 (math.) **reducible to a common measure, commensurable** Pl. Arist.
3 of equal duration; (of a firebrand) **coterminous** (w. someone's life) A.; (of a person) **equal in age** (W.DAT. *to someone*) S.
4 of corresponding extent, magnitude or degree; (of height) **proportionate** (to length and breadth) Pl.; (of things, w. πρός + ACC. *w. sthg.*) Arist.; (gener., of a lock of hair) **matching, comparable** (W.DAT. *to another's hair*) A.(dub.)
5 of suitable or sufficient measure; (of advice) **suitable, appropriate** A.; (of food and drink, exercise, terrain, resources) Critias Isoc. Pl. Arist. Plb. Plu.; (of words of praise) **adequate** (W.DAT. *for someone*) Isoc.; (of a speech) **consistent** (W.DAT. *w. sthg.*) Isoc.

6 in due proportion; (of things, a shape, person) **suitably proportioned** Pl. Arist.; (of a dining-room) X.; (of hares, their rib-cages) X.; (of things, places) **suitably sized** (w.connot. of moderate in size) Plb. Plu. || NEUT.SB. **due proportion** Pl.
7 (of a person, ref. to his arrival) **suitably timed** (W.DAT. for sthg.) S.; **at a suitable distance, within range** (for hearing) S.
8 in accord with metre; (of the spelling of a name) **suited to the metre** S.*eleg.*; (of dancers) **keeping in time** Tim.

—**συμμέτρως** *adv*. **1** to a degree that suits the circumstances, **suitably, appropriately** Plb. Plu.
2 in the right proportion Isoc. Pl. X.
3 at the right time E.

συμ-μήστωρ ορος *m*. **fellow counsellor** AR.

συμ-μητιάομαι *mid.contr.vb*. **join in giving counsel, share in deliberations** Il.

συμ-μηχανάομαι *mid.contr.vb*. **1 help to procure** —*supplies* X.
2 devise (W.ACC. sthg.) **together** —W.DAT. *w. someone* Plu.

σύμμιγα *adv*. [συμμείγνῡμι] **mixed up together** (W.DAT. w. women) —*ref. to men congregating* Hdt.

συμμιγής ές *adj*. **1 mixed together indiscriminately**; (of cattle) **mixed, of various kinds** S.; (of cheese-baskets) **mixed up, in disarray** E.*Cyc*.; (of unnatural creatures) **blended, jumbled together** (fr. assorted limbs) AR.; (of a noise) **confused** Plu.; (of a theatre) **with mixed seating** (W.DAT. for men and women) Plu.
2 (of a population) with a variety of trades, **heterogeneous** Plu.
3 mixed (w. other things); (of shed blood) **mingled, mixed** (w. other blood) E.; (of new sufferings, W.DAT. w. old troubles) A.; (of shouting, w. screaming) Tim.(cj.)
4 (of evils) **shared** (W.DAT. by a man and a woman) S.(dub.)
5 (of the sound of swans, ref. to cries accompanied by wing-beats) **harmonious** Ar.
6 consisting of a mixture; (of a substance) **compound** (opp. simple) Pl.; (of shade, opp. pure sunlight) app. **murky, gloomy** Pl.; (of woods) **thick, dense** Plu.

συμμίγνῡμι *vb*.: see συμμείγνῡμι

σύμμικτος *adj*.: see σύμμεικτος

συμ-μῑμέομαι *mid.contr.vb*. **imitate** —W.DAT. sthg. Pl.

συμ-μιμνήσκομαι *mid.pass.vb*. | 2pl.pf.imperatv. (w. pres.sens.) συμμέμνησθε | **call to mind, bear in mind** (W.ACC. sthg.) **together** —W.DAT. *w. someone* D.

σύμμιξις (also written **σύμμειξις**) εως *f*. [συμμείγνῡμι]
1 mixing together, commingling, combining (of things) Pl.
2 sexual intercourse Pl. Plu.
3 union (of marriage partners, without sexual connot.) Pl. Arist.

συμμίσγω *vb*.: see συμμείγνῡμι

συμ-μῑσέω *contr.vb*. **join** (W.DAT. w. someone) **in hating** —*someone* Plb.

σύμ-μολπος ον *adj*. [μολπή] (of Apollo's lyre) **singing in harmony** (w. the song of swans) E.

συμ-μορίᾱ ᾱς *f*. [μόρᾱ] **1 allotment, division** (of ships in the charge of individual commanders) X.
2 (at Athens, in the 4th C. BC) **symmory, taxation-group** (of those liable to pay a property-tax or contribute to a trierarchy) Att.orats. Arist.

σύμ-μορος (**ξύμ-**) ον *adj*. (of certain Boeotian troops) **in the same division** (W.DAT. as Thebans) Th.

συμ-μοχθέω *contr.vb*. **share in toils** or **troubles** —W.DAT. *w. someone* E.

συμ-μυέομαι *pass.contr.vb*. **be initiated together** —W.DAT. *w. someone* Plu.

συμ-μύω *vb*. | pf. συμμέμῡκα | **1** (intr., of wounds) **close up** Il.(tm.); (of pores) Pl.; (of eyelids) **close** Pl.
2 (of a person) **close one's lips** (opp. be open-mouthed) Pl.; **keep one's mouth shut** (in obedience) Plb.

συμ-παγής ές *adj*. [πήγνῡμι] (of natural elements) **compacted, compounded** Pl.

συμπάθεια ᾱς *f*. [συμπαθής] **fellow feeling**; (fig.) **reverberation** (of bronze plates, in response to noise) Plb.

συμπαθέω *contr.vb*. **have fellow feeling, sympathise** (sts. W.DAT. w. someone or sthg.) Plb. Plu.

συμ-παθής ές *adj*. [πάθος] **1** (of persons listening to music) **affected by corresponding feelings** Arist.
2 (of persons) with fellow feeling, **sympathetic** Plb. Plu.

συμπαιᾱνίζω *vb*.: see συμπαιωνίζω

συμ-παιδεύω *vb*. **1** (of farming) **help to train** —*people* (W.PREP.PHR. *for supporting one another*) X.
2 || PASS. (of children) **be educated together** (sts. W.DAT. or μετά + GEN. w. someone) Isoc. Is.
3 || PASS. (of a populace) **be brought up** —W.DAT. *in violence and passion* Plb.

συμ-παίζω (**ξυμ-**) *vb*. | dial.inf. συμπαίσδεν (Theoc.) | (of gods, humans, children) **play together** (ref. to revelry, carefree behaviour, child's play, or w. sexual connot.; sts. W.DAT. or μετά + GEN. w. someone) Anacr. Hdt. S. Ar. Thphr. Men. +

συμπαιστής οῦ *m*. **playmate** (ref. to a drinking-companion) Pl.

—**συμπαίστρια** ᾱς *f*. **playmate** (ref. to a Bacchic dancer) Ar.

—**συμπαίστωρ** ορος *m*. **playmate** (ref. to a child) X.

συμ-παίω *vb*. **1** (of horses) **clash, dash** —*foreheads* (W.DAT. *against chariots*) S.
2 (intr., of waves of strife) **clash together** E.

συμ-παιωνίζω (also **συμπαιᾱνίζω**) *vb*. **1 sing the paean together** —W.DAT. *w. someone* D.
2 (of Celtic soldiers) **cry out together** Plb.

σύμπᾱκτος *dial.adj*.: see σύμπηκτος

συμ-παλαίω *vb*. **wrestle with** —W.DAT. *someone* Plu.; (fig.) —*foreign domination* Plb.

συμ-πανηγυρίζω *vb*. **attend a festival together** —W.DAT. *w. someone* Plu.

συμ-παραγγέλλω *vb*. **help** (W.DAT. someone) **in canvassing for office** Plu.

συμ-παραγίνομαι (**ξυμ-**), Ion. and dial. **-παραγίνομαι** *mid.vb*. **1 stand by in support**; **stand by, support** —W.DAT. *someone* D.
2 || AOR. (of troops) **arrive in support** Th.
3 (of a new crop) **be ready at the same time** (as the old crop has been consumed) Hdt.
4 (of crowds) **congregate** NT.

συμ-παραθέω *contr.vb*. **run along together** (sts. W.DAT. w. someone) D. Plu.

συμ-παραινέω (**ξυμ-**) *contr.vb*. **join in recommending** —*sthg*. (W.DAT. *to someone*) Ar. —W.ACC. + INF. *that sthg. be done* Ar.

συμ-παρακαθέζομαι *mid.vb*. **also sit down beside** (someone) —w. μετά + GEN. *along w. someone else* Pl.

συμ-παρακαθίζομαι *mid.vb*. **make** (W.ACC. someone) **sit down too** D.

συμ-παρακαλέω *contr.vb*. **1 call upon** (W.ACC. someone or sthg.) **for support** Pl. X. Din. Plu.; **invite** (someone) **in addition** X.
2 make an appeal together —W.DAT. *w. someone* Plb.

συμ-παράκειμαι *mid.pass.vb.* (of magisterial insignia) be positioned alongside in accompaniment, **be in attendance** Plb.

συμ-παρακελεύομαι *mid.vb.* **help to encourage** —*sthg.* Isoc.

συμ-παρακολουθέω *contr.vb.* **1 follow closely or attend upon** (someone); (of a supervisor) **keep in close attendance** Pl.; (of fear, an oath) **haunt** (someone) X. Aeschin.; (of an ill fate) **stick** —W.DAT. *to someone* Aeschin.
2 (of memory) **keep pace** —W.DAT. *w. the passage of time* Isoc.; (of a listener) —*w. an argument* Pl.

συμ-παρακομίζω (ξυμ-) *vb.* **convey along with one, provide a convoy for** —*ships* Th. || PASS. (of ships) be provided with a convoy Th.

συμ-παραλαμβάνω *vb.* **take along with one** —*someone or sthg.* (*as an adjunct or assistant*) Pl. Arist. NT. —*ships, troops* (*as reinforcements*) X. Plb.

συμ-παραμειγνύω *vb.* [παραμείγνῡμι] **mix in as well** —*liquid items* (*in a concoction*) Ar.

συμ-παραμένω (ξυμ-) *vb.* **1** (of leadership) **remain securely** —W.DAT. *w. someone* Th.
2 (of a wife) **stand by and support** —W.DAT. *her husband in trouble* Men.
3 (of cities) **remain loyal** Isoc.

συμ-παρα-νεύω *vb.* (of seers uttering riddles) **express assent at the same time** Arist.

συμ-παραπέμπω *vb.* **1 help to escort** —*a convoy* Aeschin. —*a procession of revellers, funeral-urn* Plu.
2 send along as an escort; (fig.) **keep fixed** —*one's sight* (*on a person, i.e. follow him w. one's eyes*) Plu.

συμ-παραπλέω *contr.vb.* **sail alongside in support** (of an army on shore) Plb. Plu.

συμ-παραπόλλυμαι *mid.vb.* (of a person) **be ruined too** D.

συμ-παρασκευάζω (ξυμ-) *vb.* **1 help** (oft. W.DAT. someone) **to arrange** or **procure** —*sthg.* And. X. D. Plb. Plu.
2 (of a group of people) **devise together** —*sthg.* D.
3 || MID. **equip oneself with** —*a military force* Isoc.

συμ-παραστατέω *contr.vb.* **stand by so as to assist** Ar. —W.DAT. *someone* A. Ar.

συμπαραστάτης (ξυμ-) ου *m.* **one who stands by in support, assistant, supporter** S. Ar.

συμ-παρατάττομαι *Att.mid.vb.* [παρατάσσω] (of troops) **station oneself alongside** X. D. —W.DAT. *someone* Isoc. Lycurg.

συμ-παρατηρέω *contr.vb.* **watch out at the same time, also take care** —W.COMPL.CL. *that sthg. shd. happen* D.

συμ-παρατίθημι *vb.* **place** (W.ACC. infantry) **alongside in support** Plb.

συμ-παρατρέφω *vb.* (of the produce of the earth) **feed** (W.ACC. wild animals) **at the same time** (as hunting dogs) X.

συμ-παρατρέχω *vb.* **run alongside in company with** (i.e. keep up with) —W.DAT. *persons, animals* Plu.

συμ-παραφέρομαι *pass.vb.* **be swept along together** —W.DAT. *w. the flow* (*of events and people fleeing*) Plu.

συμ-παραχωρέω *contr.vb.* **go along with, assent to** —W.NEUT.PL. *this* (*request*) Plu.

συμ-πάρειμι[1] (ξυμ-) *vb.* **1** (of persons) **be present as well** (as others) Th. And. X. +
2 (of a group of persons) **be present together** X.
3 (of modesty and obedience) **be present at the same time** (in someone) X.
4 (of troops, a legal helper) **be present in support** —W.DAT. *for someone* X. D.

συμ-πάρειμι[2] *vb.* **go along together** (w. someone) X. Aeschin.

συμ-παρέπομαι *mid.vb.* **1** (of persons) **follow along together** (w. someone) X.
2 (of rewards, abstr. qualities) **go along with, accompany** —W.DAT. *someone* Pl. X.

συμ-παρέχω *vb.* **1 help to cause** —*fear* X.; **help to provide** —*security* X.
2 || MID. **help to procure** —*glory* X.

συμ-παρίσταμαι (ξυμ-) *mid.vb.* **stand beside in support; assist, support** —W.DAT. *someone's wishes* S.; (of a god) —*a person* Men.

συμ-παρομαρτέω *contr.vb.* **1** (of fear, beauty, scents) **keep company** —W.DAT. *w. someone or sthg.* X.
2 (of kinds of behaviour) **go hand in hand** (w. a person) X. —W.DAT. *w. kingship* X.

συμ-παροξύνω *vb.* (of farming) **help to stimulate** —*someone* (W.PREP.PHR. *to sthg.*) X.

συμ-παρορμάω *contr.vb.* (of people) **join in urging** (someone to do sthg.) Plu.

σύμ-πᾱς (ξύμ-) πᾱσα πᾱν *adj.* [πᾶς] | For the use of the art. w. this wd. see πᾶς. || see also συνάπᾱς | **1** || PL. (of persons or things) **all together, all** Hom. +; (w. numbers) **altogether, in total** Hdt. S. +
2 (sg., w. collectv.sb., of a city, nation, army) **whole, total, all** Hes. +; (of places or things) Hdt. +; (of time) Pi. E. Isoc.; (of a city, the purport of a speech) **taken as a whole, in general** Th.; (of virtue, vice, a subject of study) Isoc. Pl.; (of sthg. quantifiable) **total, in total, in all** Hdt. +
3 || NEUT.SB. (w.art.) **the sum of the matter** Hdt. Th.; **the universe** Isoc.; (as adv.) **altogether, on the whole, in general** Th. Isoc. +; **in total** D.

συμ-πάσχω *vb.* **1 suffer jointly** (w. others); **also experience** —*sthg.* Pl.; (of a whole army) **be affected together** (by dangers) Plb.
2 have fellow feeling, sympathise Pl.; **feel for** —W.DAT. *one's country, someone's misfortunes* Plb.

συμ-πατάσσω *vb.* (of commanders) **cause** (W.ACC. a whole army) **to clash** (in the field of battle) E.

συμ-πατέω *contr.vb.* (of persons, animals) **trample** (W.ACC. someone) **under foot** Plb. Plu. || PASS. (hyperbol., of a commander) be trampled under foot —W.PREP.PHR. *by enemy cavalry* Aeschin.

συμ-πείθω *vb.* **1 help** (someone) **to persuade** (another) Isoc. —W.ACC. *about sthg.* X.
2 help to persuade —*someone* (W.INF. *to do sthg.*) X.
3 persuade (W.ACC. someone) **as well** (as others) Pl.
4 persuade —*someone* Isoc. Pl. Lycurg. Arist. Men. + —(W.INF. *to do sthg.*) Att.orats. Arist. Men. + —(W.ACC. *about sthg.*) Men. || PASS. **be persuaded** Arist. Men. —W.INF. *to do sthg.* Arist. Men. —W.ACC. *about sthg.* D. Men. —W.ACC. + DAT. *about sthg., by someone* Men.

συμ-πείρομαι *pass.vb.* (of soldiers, shields) **be pierced** (by weapons) Plu.

σύμ-πειρος ον *adj.* [πεῖρα] (of an athlete's spirit) **experienced** (W.DAT. in competition) Pi.

σύμπεισις εως *f.* [συμπείθω] **persuasion** Men.

συμ-πέμπω (ξυμ-) *vb.* **1 send together** or **at the same time** —*someone or sthg.* (oft. W.DAT. *w. someone or sthg. else*) A. Pi. Hdt. E. Th. + || PASS. (of a person) be sent together —W.DAT. or PREP.PHR. *w. someone* Th. X. Aeschin.
2 help in conducting, join in —*a procession* Lys. Is.

συμ-πενθέω *contr.vb.* **1 join in mourning** E. D. —W.DAT. *someone* A. —W.ACC. *for the dead, a country's misfortunes* Isoc. Lycurg.
2 sympathise —W.DAT. *w. someone's misfortunes* Isoc.

συμ-πένομαι *mid.vb.* share (W.DAT. w. someone) in being poor —W.GEN. *in knowledge* Pl.
συμ-περαίνω (ξυμ-) *vb.* **1** help to accomplish —*sthg.* E. Isoc. ‖ MID. help (W.DAT. someone) to create —*enmity* D. ‖ PASS. (of the speeds of different planetary orbits) be achieved simultaneously Pl.
2 accomplish completely, complete —*a plan, the barring of doors* E. ‖ PASS. (of activities) be brought to completion X. Plu.
3 ‖ MID. (log.) conclude (syllogistically) —*sthg.* Arist.
συμπέρασμα ατος *n.* conclusion (in a syllogism) Arist.
συμπερασματικῶς *adv.* in the form of a syllogistic conclusion Arist.
συμ-πέρθω (ξυμ-) *vb.* help to sack —*a city* E.(tm.)
συμ-περιάγω *vb.* (of a ship) carry around with itself —*weapons* X. ‖ PASS. (of bodyguards, concubines, crowds) be taken around with one X. Plu.
συμπεριαγωγός όν *adj.* (of arts) assisting in a process of conversion Pl.
συμ-περίειμι *vb.* [περίειμι²] go around together —W.DAT. w. *a dog* X.
συμ-περιλαμβάνω *vb.* **1** (of a creator god) enclose, envelop —*bones and marrow* (W.DAT. w. *sinews*) Pl. ‖ PASS. (of a kind of bile) be enveloped (by fluid) Pl.
2 (of a person) embrace (someone) NT.
3 (of a whole) embrace, encompass —*separate types* Pl.; (of an actor) —*characterisation* Arist.; (of a writer) include —*someone or sthg.* Plb.
συμ-περιπατέω *contr.vb.* walk around together (sts. W.DAT. w. someone) Pl. Arist. Men. Plu.
συμ-περιποιέω *contr.vb.* help (W.DAT. someone) to secure —*sovereignty* Plb.
συμ-περιστέλλω *vb.* help to screen or cover up —*faults* Plb.
συμ-περιτειχίζω *vb.* help to wall in —*a person* (under siege) Plu.
συμ-περιτίθημι *vb.* help to bestow —*pompous dignity* (W.DAT. on someone) Plu.
συμ-περιφέρω *vb.* **1** carry around with one —*pots* Pl. ‖ PASS. (of things sharing the motion of sthg. which revolves) be carried round together Pl.; (of dogs) scamper around together X.; (fig., of a person, city) adapt oneself —W.DAT. *to changing circumstances* Aeschin.
2 ‖ PASS. (of a person) go around together, associate (sts. W.DAT. w. someone) Plb.; go along (w. an activity), join in Plb.
3 ‖ PASS. go along with (in obedience or comprehension), follow —W.DAT. *orders, words* Plb.
συμπεριφορά ᾶς *f.* **1** association (betw. people), companionship, intimacy Plb.
2 willingness to go along (w. another's circumstances), adaptability Plb.
συμ-πήγνῡμι *vb.* | dial.aor. συνέπᾱξα | **1** fix together, put together, construct —*a tomb, shelter, shepherd's pipe* E. Pl. Theoc. —(fig.) *a false story* Pi. ‖ STATV.PF. (of substances) be compounded or compacted Pl. ‖ MID. cause (W.ACC. a chariot) to be constructed Critias ‖ PASS. (of light) coalesce —W.DAT. w. *an object* Pl.
2 cause to stick together; (of juice) curdle —*milk* Il.; (of fibrous matter) congeal —*blood* Pl. ‖ PASS. (of substances) be condensed or solidified Pl.
σύμπηκτος, dial. **σύμπᾱκτος**, ον *adj.* **1** (of houses) put together, constructed (W.PREP.PHR. fr. stalks and reeds) Hdt.
2 (of milk) curdled Philox.Leuc.

σύμπηξις εως *f.* compacted mass (of debris) Plu.
συμ-πιέζω *vb.* press together (w. one's hands), squeeze —*things, a person's hair* Pl. ‖ PASS. (of parts of the body represented in sculpture) be compressed or contracted (opp. extended) X.
συμπίεσις εως *f.* compression (of the tongue, in pronunciation) Pl.
συμ-πιλέω *contr.vb.* **1** force together into felt; (of things, actions) compress, constrict —*a substance* Pl. ‖ PASS. (of substances) be compressed Pl.
2 ‖ PASS. (of a cloak) be made of felt Plu.
συμ-πίνω (ξυμ-) *vb.* drink together (freq. W.DAT. or PREP.PHR. w. someone) Alc. Scol.(tm.) Hdt. Ar. Pl. +
συμ-πίπτω (ξυμ-) *vb.* **1** (of winds) dash together Od.(tm.)
2 (of boxers, warriors) fall upon one another Il.(tm.); (of a pancratiast) get to grips (w. an opponent) Pi.
3 (of combatants) clash, engage (freq. W.DAT. w. opponents) Hdt. S. Th. X. +; (fig., of quarrelling persons) Hdt.
4 (of a ship) collide (sts. W.DAT. or PREP.PHR. w. another) Th. Plb. —W.DAT. w. *a wave* E.
5 (of a person) fall in with, meet (a wild animal) Semon.; (fig.) meet with —W.DAT. *misfortunes, accidents* Hdt. S.
6 (of misfortunes, events) befall, happen (usu. W.DAT. or PREP.PHR. to or for someone) A. Hdt. Th. Isoc. +; happen —W.NOM.PTCPL. *to occur* Hdt. ‖ IMPERS. (or W.NEUT.PRON.) it happens —W.ACC. + INF. (sts. w. ὥστε) *that sthg. is the case* Hdt. Th. Arist. +
7 (of the practices of different nations) coincide, be consistent (w. each other) Hdt.; (of a circumstance, account) —W.DAT. w. *sthg.* Hdt.; (of persons or things) coincide (in agreement) E. Pl.
8 (of a building, city) fall in, collapse E. Th. X. D. NT.
9 ‖ PASS. (of a dead body) shrink Pl.; (of a horse's nostrils) be shrunken or narrow X.
10 (of the sides of a triangle) converge Plb.; (of a river) —W.DAT. w. *another* Plu.; (of things) impinge —W.PREP.PHR. *on one another* Pl.
συμ-πίτνω (ξυμ-) *vb.* **1** (of waves) fall together, break upon one another A.
2 (of a person) fall in with, meet —W.DAT. *someone* E.
3 (of desires, obligations, circumstances) converge, coincide A. E.
συμ-πλανάομαι *mid.contr.vb.* **1** (of a person) wander around together —W.DAT. w. *someone* Plu.
2 (fig.) go astray (in understanding) Plu.
συμ-πλάσσω, Att. **συμπλάττω (ξυμ-)** *vb.* **1** (of Hephaistos) mould or put together, fashion —*an object* (W.GEN. *fr. earth*) Hes.; (of river currents) mould into a mass —*debris* Plu. ‖ PASS. (of sesame-balls) be moulded Ar.
2 (of a person) make up, invent —*a dream, accusations* Aeschin. D.
3 (intr., of persons) conspire in a fiction or pretence Pl.
συμ-πλαταγέω *contr.vb.* make a noise by striking together; clap —W.DAT. w. *one's hands* Il.
συμ-πλείονες ονα *pl.compar.adj.* (of persons) several together Arist.
συμπλεκτικός ή όν *adj.* [συμπλέκω] (of a skill) of interweaving (threads, opp. twisting) Pl.
συμ-πλέκω (ξυμ-) *vb.* **1** twine or plait together, weave —*a web* (W.PREP.PHR. *on a loom*) Theoc. —(fig.) *stories, aspects of personality, or sim.* Pl.; (of a historian) —*separate events* Plb.; interweave, entangle —*laws* (W.DAT. w. *complicated language*) D. ‖ PASS. (of animals' tracks, their scents) be tangled or mixed together S.*Ichn.* X.

2 create by interweaving, plait —*a suppliant's branch and herald's wand* Din. —*a garland* Plu.
3 link or connect, interlock —*one's hands* (W.PREP.PHR. *behind one's back*) Th.; (fig.) **link** —*hands* (W.DAT. *w. someone, i.e. form friendship*) Plb. ‖ PF.PASS. (of lambs) have (W.ACC. their bodies) bound together —W.DAT. *w. twisted osiers* E.*Cyc.*
4 link, combine —*elements of language, terms for things* Pl. Arist.; (of circumstances) **connect** —*events in different countries* Plb. ‖ PASS. (of physical processes) be linked or interrelated Pl.
5 ‖ PASS. (of a person) be in a clinch, wrestle —W.DAT. *w. someone* Hdt.; (of a lover) be locked in an embrace —W.DAT. *w. one's beloved* Pl.
6 ‖ PASS. (of combatants) come to close quarters, come to grips (oft. W.DAT. w. an enemy) D. Plb. Plu.; (of a war in neighbouring territory) come threateningly close D.
7 ‖ PASS. (of a ship) become entangled, run foul (of another) Hdt. Plb.
8 ‖ PASS. (fig., of a person) be entangled —W.DAT. *w. a troublesome person* E. Ar. Aeschin. Men. +; be embroiled —W.DAT. *in verbal abuse* Pl. —*in a war* Plu.

συμ-πλέω (**ξυμ-**) *contr.vb.* [πλέω¹] **1** (of persons, ships) **sail together** (w. others, usu. W.DAT. or μετά + GEN.) Hdt. E. Antipho Th. +
2 (of a group of persons) **sail together** (w. each other), **be shipmates** Hdt. X.
3 (fig., of a person) **sail together** —W.DAT. *w. friends in trouble (i.e. support and sympathise w. them)* E.

σύμ-πλεως ων *Att.adj.* [πλέως] (of a plain) **very full** (W.GEN. of trees and vines) X.

Συμ-πληγάδες (**Ξυμ-**) ων *f.pl.* [πλήσσω] **Symplegades, Clashing Rocks** (at the entrance to the Black Sea) E.

συμ-πληθύνω *vb.* (of stubble) **help to increase in amount, augment** —*manure* X.

συμ-πληθύω *vb.* (of tributaries, snow and rain) **help to swell** —*a river* Hdt.

συμ-πληρόω (**ξυμ-**) *contr.vb.* **1 help to fill; help** (W.DAT. others) **to man** —*ships* Hdt.
2 fill completely, fully man —*ships* Th. X. Plb. ‖ PASS. (of ships) be fully manned Th. X.
3 ‖ PASS. (of the universe) be filled out or completed Pl.; (of bones) —W.DAT. *w. flesh* Pl.
4 fill in, fill up (a space) Pl. —*a space, an interval, outline* Pl.(sts.mid.) Plu. —*the Senate* Plu.
5 ‖ PASS. (of sailors) be swamped (by waves) NT.
6 ‖ PASS. (of a day) be fulfilled, arrive NT.

συμπλήρωσις εως *f.* **fulfilment, completion, achievement** (W.GEN. of prosperity) Plb.

συμπλοϊκός ή όν *adj.* [σύμπλοος] (of friendship) **of the kind that exists between shipmates** Arist.

συμπλοκή ῆς *f.* [συμπλέκω] **1 intertwining** (as a generic term for weaving and associated arts) Pl.
2 combination (of letters to form a word, or of words to form a proposition) Pl.; (of concepts, in thought) Arist.
3 connection, interrelationship (of things w. each other) Plb.
4 close engagement (of soldiers, ships) Pl. Plb. Plu.; (gener.) **military engagement** Plb.
5 sexual embrace Pl.

σύμ-πλοος, Att. **σύμπλους** (**ξύμ-**), ου *m.f.* [πλόος] **one who shares in a voyage, fellow sailor, shipmate** (sts. W.DAT. *w. someone*) Hdt. E. Att.orats. Pl. +; (fig.) **fellow voyager** (W.GEN. *in suffering*) S.

συμ-πνέω *contr.vb.* **1** (fig.) **breathe together, conspire, go along together** —W.DAT. *w. the blasts of fortune (i.e. accept what they bring)* A.
2 (fig., of different races, a city) **breathe as one, achieve unity** Pl. Arist. Plu.; (of states) **act in unison, cooperate** D. Plb.

συμ-πνίγω *vb.* **1** (of thorns) **choke** —*seed* NT.; (fig., of cares and temptations) —*the word of God* NT. ‖ PASS. (of those who hear the word) be choked —W.PREP.PHR. *by cares or sim.* NT.
2 (of crowds) **press closely on** —*someone* NT.

συμ-ποδηγετέω *contr.vb.* [reltd. ποδηγέω] **go along with** (someone) **as guide** S.*Ichn.*

συμ-ποδηγέω *contr.vb.* (of a god) **accompany as a guide** —*the whole universe* Pl. ‖ PASS. (of the universe) be guided —W.PREP.PHR. *by a divine cause* Pl.

συμ-ποδίζω (**ξυμ-**) *vb.* **1 fetter by tying the feet together**; (gener.) **bind hand and foot, tie up** —*someone* Ar. Pl. ‖ PASS. (of horses) get entangled (in nets) X.; (fig., of a person) be tied in knots —W.PREP.PHR. *by a disputant* Pl.
2 (fig.) **incapacitate** —*someone* (W.DAT. *w. drugs or drink*) Pl.; (of deep snow) **handicap, hobble** —*baggage-animals* X.

συμ-ποιέω *contr.vb.* **1 help to do** —*sthg.* And. Is. Men.
2 collaborate —W.DAT. *w. someone* Ar.

συμ-ποιμαίνομαι *pass.vb.* (of lynxes) **be shepherded together** (w. the flocks) E.(tm.)

συμ-πολεμέω (**ξυμ-**) *contr.vb.* **join together** (freq. W.DAT. or μετά + GEN. w. someone) **in war** Th. Att.orats. Pl. X. Arist. +

συμ-πολιορκέω (**ξυμ-**) *contr.vb.* **help** (sts. W.DAT. someone) **to besiege** —*a person, place* Hdt. Th. D. Plu.; **help to blockade** —*ships* Th. ‖ PASS. be besieged together (w. others) Th. Plb.

συμ-πολιτείᾱ ᾱς *f.* **1 union of states, confederation** Plb.
2 reciprocity of civic rights (among states) Plb.

συμ-πολῑτεύω (**ξυμ-**) *vb.* **1 live as a fellow citizen, live as a member of the same state** (sts. W.DAT. w. others) Th. X.; (mid.) Att.orats. Arist. Plu.
2 ‖ MID. (of a state) **belong to a confederacy** Plb.; **share reciprocal civic rights** (w. another state) Plb.
3 ‖ MID. (fig., of crimes) **be associated with political life** Plu.

συμ-πολίτης (**ξυμ-**) ου *m.* **fellow citizen** E.

σύμ-πολλοι αι α *pl.adj.* [πολύς] (of persons or things) **many together** Pl.

συμ-πομπεύω *vb.* **join in a procession** Aeschin. Plu.

συμ-πονέω (**ξυμ-**) *contr.vb.* **share in toil** or **suffering** (sts. W.DAT. w. someone) Trag. Ar. Pl. +

συμ-πονηρεύομαι (**ξυμ-**) *mid.vb.* **join** (w. others) **in depravity** Ar. Isoc.

συμ-πορεύομαι (**ξυμ-**) *mid.vb.* **1 travel together** E. Th. Pl. X. +
2 come together, meet (oft. W.DAT. or πρός + ACC. w. someone) Plb. Plu.
3 (of a deliberative body) **convene** Plb.

συμ-πορθέω *contr.vb.* **help** (W.DAT. someone) **to devastate** —*a people* E.

συμ-πορίζω (**ξυμ-**) *vb.* **procure** (fr. someone) —*troops* Th. ‖ MID. **procure for oneself** —*timber* Th. —*a style of life* Isoc. ‖ PASS. (of things) be provided or procured Plu.

συμ-πορσύνω *vb.* (of a person) **help to arrange** —*someone's journey* AR.(tm.)

συμποσίᾱ ᾱς *f.* [συμπότης] **drinking together** Alc. Pi. B.*fr.*(cj.)

συμποσιαρχέω *contr.vb.* [συμποσίαρχος] **be toast-master** Arist.

συμποσί-αρχος ου *m*. [συμπόσιον, ἄρχω] ruler of a drinking-party (who prescribed toasts and determined the strength of wine), **toast-master** X.

συμπόσιον (ξυμ-) ου *n*. [συμπίνω] **1 drinking-party, symposium** (of male guests after a banquet, garlanded and reclining on couches; accompanied by ritual prayers and libations, also games and entertainments) Eleg. Lyr. Hdt. Ar. Pl. +
2 group of diners NT.

συμπότης (ξυμ-) ου *m*. **drinking companion** (habitual or on a specific occasion, such as a symposium) Eleg.adesp. Lyr. Hdt. E. Ar. Pl. +

συμποτικός (ξυμ-) ή όν *adj*. **1** of or relating to drinking-companions; (of the toast-master's rules, musical modes) **for drinking-parties** Pl.; (of circumstances) **ripe for a party** Ar.
2 (of a person) **convivial, party-going** Ar. Plb.

συμ-πρᾱγματεύομαι *mid.vb*. do business together, **cooperate** (sts. W.DAT. w. someone) Plu.

συμπράκτωρ, Ion. **συμπρήκτωρ**, ορος *m*. [συμπράσσω] one who acts together (w. someone); **assistant, helper** Hdt. X.; **companion** (W.GEN. on a journey) S.; **accomplice** (W.GEN. in a blameworthy act) Antipho

συμ-πράσσω (ξυμ-), Att. **συμπράττω**, Ion. **συμπρήσσω** *vb*. **1 act together, cooperate, be in league** (freq. W.DAT. w. someone) S. Th. Att.orats. +
2 fare (W.ADV. badly) **in company** —W.PREP.PHR. *w. others faring badly* (i.e. share their ill-fortune) E.
3 help (freq. W.DAT. someone) **to do** or **achieve** —sthg. Trag. Th. X. Arist.
4 ‖ MID. **help** (W.DAT. someone) **to exact a penalty for, help to avenge** —a crime Hdt.

συμπρεπής ές *adj*. [συμπρέπω] (of clothes, a state of affairs) **appropriate, fitting** A.

συμ-πρέπω *vb*. **1** (of acclaim) **befit, be suited to** —W.DAT. *someone* Pi.(tm.); (of a lisp) —*someone's speech* Plu.
2 (of high poetic language) **accord with** —W.DAT. *the splendour of the performer's voice* Plu.

συμ-πρεσβευτής οῦ *m*. **fellow ambassador** Aeschin. Arist. Plb.

συμ-πρεσβεύω (ξυμ-) *vb*. (of a person) **be on an embassy together, be a fellow ambassador** (sts. W.DAT. w. someone) Aeschin. D. Thphr. ‖ MID. (of a state) **join in an embassy** (w. another state) Th.

σύμ-πρεσβυς (ξύμ-) εως *m*. [πρέσβυς] (only pl.) **fellow ambassador** Th. X. Aeschin. D.

συμπρήκτωρ Ion.*m*., **συμπρήσσω** Ion.*vb*.: see συμπράκτωρ, συμπράσσω

συμ-πρίασθαι *aor.mid.inf*. | aor. συνεπριάμην | **buy up** —grain Lys. —iron, land Arist.

συμ-προάγω *vb*. **join in escorting** (someone) Plu.

συμ-πρόεδρος ου *m*. **fellow president, joint chairman** (of the Assembly) Aeschin.

συμ-προθῡμέομαι (ξυμ-) *mid.contr.vb*. **1 share in enthusiasm, show the same eagerness** X. —W.ACC. *for sthg*. Th. X. —W.INF. or COMPL.CL. *to do sthg., that sthg. shd. happen* Th. Pl. X.
2 show keen support (oft. W.DAT. for someone) Th. Arist. Plu.

συμ-προπέμπω (ξυμ-) *vb*. **help to send on one's way** or **help to escort** —persons, troops Hdt. Th. Ar. X. Men. +

συμ-προσμείγνῡμι *vb*. **have contact with, meet** —W.DAT. *someone* Pl.

σύμ-πτυκτος (ξύμ-) ον *adj*. [συμπτύσσω] (of a wooden frame used in brick-making) **folding** Ar.

συμ-πτύσσω *vb*. **fold up** —a garment S.

σύμπτωμα (ξύμ-) ατος *n*. [συμπίπτω] **1 chance occurrence, accident, incident** Arist. Plb. Plu.
2 critical circumstance Th.
3 mischance, mishap D. Arist. Men.
4 calamity, disaster Plb. Plu.

σύμπτωσις εως *f*. **1 convergence** (of rivers, mountains) Plb.
2 clash (betw. troops, ships) Plb.

σύμ-πυκνος ον *adj*. [πυκνός] (of fittings around an aperture on a bridle) **crowded together, tight** X.

συμ-πυνθάνομαι *mid.vb*. **hear together** (w. someone) —*a prophecy* E.

συμ-πυρόω (ξυμ-) *contr.vb*. **burn together** (w. a corpse) —*precious garments* E.; (of Polyphemos) **burn up all together** —*a band of men* E.*Cyc*. ‖ PASS. (of a husband) share a funeral pyre (w. his wife) E.

συμ-φαγεῖν *aor.2 inf*. | *aor.2* συνέφαγον | The pres. is supplied by συνεσθίω. | **eat together** Pl. —W.DAT. *w. someone* NT.

συμ-φανής ές *adj*. [φαίνομαι] **1** (of an action or person) **visible** Pl. Plb.
2 (of a subject of inquiry) **clarified, illuminated** Arist.; (of a fact or conclusion) **clear** Plb.

συμφερόντως *ptcpl.adv*.: see under συμφέρω

συμφερτός ή όν *adj*. [συμφέρω] (of valour) brought together or combined (w. that of others), **united, joint, communal** Il.

συμ-φέρω (ξυμ-) *vb*. | fut.mid. (w.pass.sens.) συνοίσομαι |
1 bring together (to a single place) —*financial contributions* Hdt. —*corpses* X. —(fig.) *troubles, lamentations, hopes* Hdt. E. Plu.; **lump together** —*crimes* D. ‖ MID. **assemble** —*attendants* Plu.; **concentrate** —*all power* (w. εἰς + ACC. *in oneself*) Plu.
2 (gener.) **get together, contribute** —*money* Hdt. Th. —*counsel* A.
3 ‖ PASS. (of an entity) **come together** (opp. be separated) Heraclit. Pl.; (of sailors, i.e. their ships) be clustered together (in a narrow space) Th.; (of debris in a river) be accumulated Plu.
4 (of warriors) **join** —*battle* Tyrt.; **bring together in conflict** —*gods* (emblazoned on their shields) A. ‖ PASS. (of warriors) meet in conflict (sts. W.DAT. w. someone) Il. Hes. A. AR. Plu.
5 ‖ PASS. (of a person) meet with, encounter —W.DAT. *someone* Theoc.*epigr*. —(fig.) *misfortune* Hdt.
6 ‖ MID. (of a river) **unite** —*its waters* (W.DAT. *w. another river*) AR. ‖ PASS. (of a river) be united —W.DAT. *w. the sea* Call.
7 help (sts. W.DAT. someone) **to carry** —sthg. Ar. X.
8 help (sts. W.DAT. someone) **to bear** —*grief* S. E.; **share responsibility for** —*someone's mistakes* Antipho; (intr., of gods) **help** —W.DAT. *someone* S.
9 app. **bear** (W.DAT. along w. persons) —*their anger* (i.e. be sympathetic or indulgent towards it) A.
10 comply —W.DAT. *w. someone* S. E.
11 (of things) confer a benefit, **be useful, profitable** or **advantageous** (oft. W.DAT. to someone or sthg.) A. Hdt. S. Th. Ar. Att.orats. + ‖ IMPERS. it is beneficial or advantageous (oft. W.INF. or ACC. + INF. to do sthg., that sthg. shd. be the case) A. S. Th. Ar. Att.orats. + ‖ PRES.PTCPL.ADJ. (of things, situations) beneficial, advantageous S. Th. Ar. Att.orats. + ‖ NEUT.PTCPL.SB. (sg.pl.) benefit, advantage S. Th. Att.orats. +
12 be in accord; (of a name) **correspond with, match, suit** —W.DAT. *a circumstance* S.; (of a person) —*an oracle* (i.e. be the person to whom it alludes) Ar.; (of a husband or wife) **be**

suited —w.DAT. *to one's partner* Ar. X.; (of clothes) —*to a city* Ar.
13 ‖ PASS. (of a person) **agree, concur** (w. a decision) S. —w.ACC. *about sthg.* E. —w.DAT. *w. someone, a statement, or sim.* Hdt. Antipho Pl. Plu.; (of persons) **be in agreement** Th. Pl. Plu.
14 ‖ PASS. (of persons) **correspond** —w.ACC. *in customs* (sts. w.DAT. *w. each other*) Hdt. Plu.; (of locks of hair, circumstances) E. —w.DAT. *w. others* Plu.; (of a name) —*w. a guess, an activity* A. Call.*epigr.*
15 ‖ PASS. (of persons) **get along, live harmoniously** (w. each other) Hdt. —w.DAT. *w. others* Hdt. Pl.; (of a person) **adapt oneself** —w.DAT. *to circumstances* Plu.; (of a soul) **be in harmony** —w.DAT. *w. the universe* Pl.
16 ‖ PASS. (of events, circumstances) **happen, turn out** (sts. w.DAT. *for someone*) Hdt.(sts.act.) Th. Plu. —(w.PREP.PHR. *for the better*) Ar.; (of changes) **happen concurrently** Pl.
‖ IMPERS. **it happens** —w.ACC. + INF. (sts. w. ὥστε) *that someone does sthg., that sthg. is the case* Hdt. Th.; **it turns out** —w.ADVBL. or PREP.PHR. *better, for the better* Hdt.
—**συμφερόντως** *ptcpl.adv.* **usefully, profitably, advantageously** (sts. w.DAT. for someone or sthg.) Att.orats. Pl. +

συμ-φεύγω *vb.* (of individuals) **share flight** or **exile** (usu. w.DAT. or PREP.PHR. w. someone) Hdt. E. Pl. Lycurg. Plb. Plu.; (of groups) **flee together** Plb. Plu.

σύμ-φημι (ξύμ-) *vb.* [φημί] **1 agree, concur** (in a statement of fact) A. S. Pl. X. D. + —w.DAT. *w. someone* S. E. Pl. —w.ACC. *about sthg.* Pl. X. —w.ACC. + INF. *that sthg. is the case* S. Pl. Arist.
2 agree, promise —w.FUT.INF. *to do sthg.* X.

συμ-φθέγγομαι *mid.vb.* (of the lyre) **speak in harmony** —w.DAT. *w. the lyre-player* Plu.

συμ-φθείρω *vb.* **1** (of a woman) **destroy utterly** or **help to destroy** —*another's marriage* E.
2 ‖ PASS. (of arts and crafts) **perish together** (w. the human race, in a natural disaster) Plb.

σύμ-φθογγος (ξύμ-) *ον adj.* [φθόγγος] (of a choir of Erinyes) **chanting together** A.

συμ-φιλέω *contr.vb.* **share in loving** (opp. hating) S.

συμ-φιλοκαλέω *contr.vb.* **share in a love of beauty** Plu.

συμ-φιλονικέω *contr.vb.* **1 support in a desire for victory, side with, cheer on** —w.DAT. *a competitor* And. Pl.
2 join in a disputation (betw. rhetoricians) Plu.

συμ-φιλοσοφέω *contr.vb.* **study philosophy together** Arist. Plu. —w.DAT. *w. someone* (i.e. a teacher) Plu.

συμ-φιλοτῑμέομαι *mid.contr.vb.* **show enthusiastic support** (freq. w.DAT. for someone or sthg.) Plu.

συμ-φλέγω *vb.* (of a god) **burn up, consume in flames** —*a building, person* E. Theoc. ‖ PASS. (of a person) **be burned to death** —w.PREP.PHR. *by lightning* Plu.

συμ-φοβέομαι (ξύμ-) *pass.contr.vb.* (of troops) **be thrown into panic as well** (as others) Th.

συμ-φοιτάω (ξύμ-) *contr.vb.* **1** (of persons) **go together regularly** (to a place), **assemble periodically** Hdt.
2 go together —w.DAT. *w. someone*, w.PREP.PHR. *to the same school* X.; **go to school together, be a schoolmate** Ar. Pl. D.
3 (of a person) **regularly associate** —w.DAT. *w. someone* Plu.

συμφοίτησις εως *f.* **attendance at school together; companionship formed at school** Aeschin.

συμφοιτητής οῦ *m.* **fellow pupil, schoolmate** Pl. X. Arist.

συμ-φονεύω *vb.* **1 help to kill** —*someone* E.
2 kill (w.ACC. someone) **together** —w.DAT. *w. another victim* E.

συμφορά (ξυμ-) ᾶς, Ion. **συμφορή** ῆς *f.* [συμφέρω] **1 set of circumstances, event, incident** Hdt. Trag. Th.
2 unfortunate event, mishap, misfortune, calamity Hippon. Lyr. Hdt. Trag. Antipho Th. +; (fig., ref. to a person) **disaster** Aeschin.
3 fortunate event, happy chance, good fortune Simon. Trag. Ar.

συμφορεύς έως *m.* ‖ PL. **aides-de-camp** (ref. to officers accompanying or assisting a Spartan military commander) X.

συμ-φορέω (ξυμ-) *contr.vb.* **1 bring together** (in one place), **collect, gather up** —*bones, goods, or sim.* Hdt. Th. Pl. Plu.; (of wind) **heap up** —*snow* X.
2 (of soldiers) **bring close together** —*shields* (as a barricade) Hdt.
3 lump together —*accusations, gibes and abuse* D.
4 ‖ PASS. (of nations) **be mixed together** Pl.; (of an ugly horse, a disordered mixture) **be thrown together** (fr. random parts) Pl.; (of rivers) **come together** AR.
5 (of embassies) **be united in bringing** —*garlands* (w.DAT. *for someone*) Plb.

συμφόρησις εως *f.* **1 collecting together** (of corpses) Plu.
2 crowding together (w.GEN. of countryfolk into a city) Plu.

συμφορητός όν *adj.* (of dining, meals) **based on contributions** Arist.

σύμφορος (ξύμ-) *ον adj.* **1 corresponding** or **matching**; (of wives) **suitable, appropriate** (w.GEN. to circumstances of wealth, not poverty) Hes.; (of hunger, w.DAT. for an idle man) Hes.; (of an activity, for someone) Ar.; (in neg.phr., of a young wife, for an old man) Thgn.; (of a pair of items) **well-matched** Ar. ‖ NEUT.IMPERS. (w. ἐστί understd.) **it is suitable** —w.DAT. + INF. *for someone to do sthg.* Thgn.
2 making a contribution; (of actions, words, things) **beneficial, profitable, advantageous** (oft. w.DAT. for someone or sthg.) Hes. Hdt. S. E. Th. +; (of a nation) **convenient** —w.DAT. + INF. *for another nation to make war on* Th. ‖ NEUT.SB. **expediency** or **advantage** Th.
‖ NEUT.IMPERS. (w. ἐστί, sts. understd.) **it is beneficial** —w.INF. or ACC. + INF. *to do sthg., that someone shd. do sthg.* E. Th.
—**συμφόρως** *adv.* | compar. συμφορώτερον, superl. συμφορώτατα | **profitably, advantageously** Th. Isoc. X. D. Men. Plb.

συμ-φράδμων ονος *m.* **one who joins (others) in taking counsel, counsellor** Il. Call.

συμ-φράζομαι (ξυμ-) *mid.vb.* **1 take counsel together; devise together** (sts. w.DAT. w. someone) —*plans, actions, or sim.* Hom. Hes. AR.
2 take counsel with oneself, consider, ponder —w.COMPL.CL. *how to do sthg.* Od.; **devise** —*cures for sickness* S.
3 (intr.) **devise a plan** hHom.(tm.)
4 offer counsel —w.DAT. *to someone* AR.(sts.tm.)

συμ-φράσσω, Att. **συμφράττω** *vb.* **1 press** or **pack close together** —*cloths* (forming an awning, to make them airtight) Hdt. —*pikestaffs* (in a line) Plb. —*ships* (as a barrier) X.
2 (intr., of troops) **close ranks, close up** Plb. Plu.
3 fence in, enclose —*an object* (w.DAT. w. a wall) Pl. —*bones* (w. flesh) Pl. —*a person* or *place* (w. armed men or sim.) Plu.
4 block up —*gaps* (in netting) X. ‖ PASS. (of pores in the body, unworked ground) **be blocked up** Pl. Plu.; (of gaps in a military formation) **be closed up** Plu.

συμ-φρονέω contr.vb. **1** (of people) be of one mind, **agree or come to an agreement** (sts. W.DAT. or πρός + ACC. w. someone) Plb.
2 become aware of, reflect on, understand —sthg. Plb. Plu.
3 collect one's wits, come to one's senses Plu.

συμφρόνησις εως f. sense of agreement, **spirit of unity** (among cities) Plb.

σύμ-φρουρος (**ξύμ-**) ον adj. [φρουρός] (of a personif. cave) sharing watches, **companion in watching and waiting** (W.DAT. w. someone) S.

σύμ-φρων (**ξύμ-**) ον, gen. ονος adj. [φρήν] **1** (of a shared military command) **of one mind** A.
2 (of gods) of one mind (w. those addressing them), **favouring, sympathetic** A.

συμ-φυγάς (**ξύμ-**) άδος m.f. **companion in exile** E. Th. Isoc. X.

συμ-φυής ές adj. [φύω] **1** (of a vice) born with one, **innate, natural** Arist. Plb.
2 (of persons or things) **naturally related** or **united** (sts. W.DAT. or GEN. to someone or sthg.) Pl. Plb. Plu.

συμ-φύλαξ (**ξύμ-**) ακος m. **1 fellow guard**; **member of the same garrison** Th.; (fig., ref. to fear) X.
2 fellow guardian (ref. to an official in the state) Pl.; **fellow protector** (W.GEN. of sthg.) X.

συμ-φυλάσσω vb. **1** (of persons, dogs) **help to guard** —a place, property Hdt. Pl. X.
2 (of a woman) **act as a fellow guardian** (along w. a man) Pl.

σύμ-φυλος ον adj. [φῦλον] (of phantoms of the same stock as humans), **kindred** Plu.

συμφυρτος ον adj. [συμφύρω] (of parts of a crashed chariot and its driver) **tangled together** E.

συμ-φύρω vb. **1 mix together** (usu. so as to spoil or defile); (fig., ref. to a process of reasoning) **knead** —many things (W.PREP.PHR. **into one**) Pl. ‖ PASS. (of blood) be mixed or mingled —W.DAT. w. *fire* E.; (of air) —w. *dust* Plu.; (fig., of pleasures) be tainted or contaminated —W.DAT. w. *pains* Pl.; (of the soul) —w. μετά + GEN. *in the company of evil* Pl.
2 (of a boxer) **mess up, disfigure** —a face (W.DAT. w. *blows*) Theoc. ‖ PASS. (of a wounded man) be fouled —W.DAT. w. *blood* Plu.; (of a city) be turned into an ugly mess —W.DAT. *by randomly located buildings* Plu.

συμ-φῡσάω contr.vb. **1 blow together**; (of persons, envisaged as a team of horses) pant as one, **work together** Pl. ‖ PASS. (of a strong wind) be created by converging winds Plu.
2 (of a blacksmith) **fuse** or **weld together** —human bodies Pl. ‖ PASS. (fig., of a plan) be welded together Ar.

σύμφυσις εως f. [συμφύω] growing together (of two substances); **organic union, coalescence** Pl. Arist.

συμ-φυτεύω (**ξύμ-**) vb. **1 plant** or **engender together**; (of a god) **help to produce** —glory (W.DAT. *for someone*) Pi.(tm.); (fig., of a person) **help to plot** —a deed S.
2 ‖ PASS. (of pleasures) be planted together —W.DAT. w. the *soul* (W.PREP.PHR. *in the same body*) X.

σύμφυτος ον adj. [συμφύω] **1 born with one**; (of virtues, vices, behaviour) **congenital, innate, natural** (sts. W.DAT. in someone) Pi. Lys. Pl. Aeschin. Arist. Plu.; (of a cause of strife in a family) A.; (of a lifetime, ref. to old age) **growing with one** A.
2 (of attributes, qualities) **naturally associated** (W.DAT. or GEN. w. sthg.) Pl.
3 (of parts of the body, emotions, sensations) born or grown together (w. sthg. else), **naturally united, kindred** Pl. Arist. ‖ NEUT.SB. one's own sex (ref. to women) E.
4 (of a hill) **overgrown, thickly covered** Plb.

συμ-φύω vb. | athem.aor. συνέφῡν | pf. συμπέφῡκα ‖ PASS.: aor.2 συνεφύην | **1** (tr.) engender or cause to grow together; (of water) **help** (W.DAT. the earth and the seasons) **to bring forth** —produce X.
2 ‖ PASS. and ATHEM.AOR.ACT. (intr., of biological forms, a political community, a citizen-body) grow together, **become united, coalesce** Pl. Arist. Plb. Plu. ‖ PF.ACT. (of biological forms) have grown together, **be united** Pl. X. Plu. ‖ AOR.PASS. (of understanding) become ingrained Arist.; (of thorns) grow together (w. seeds) NT.

συμ-φωνέω contr.vb. **1** sound together; (of the notes or intervals in a musical mode, the mode itself) **sound in concord** Ion Pl.
2 (fig., of things) **be in accord** or **harmony** (usu. W.DAT. or πρός + ACC. w. sthg.) Isoc. Pl. Aeschin. Arist. +
3 (of persons) **be in accord, agree** —W.DAT. w. *persons, statements* Pl. Arist.; **be of one voice, agree** (w. one another) Pl. Arist. Thphr. Plb. Plu. ‖ PASS. (of a fact) be agreed —W.PREP.PHR. *by all* Plb. ‖ IMPERS.PASS. it is agreed —W.DAT. *by people* (W.INF. *to do sthg.*) NT.
4 (of persons) **come to an agreement** (on a price, wage, course of action) Plb. NT.

—συμφωνούντως ptcpl.adv. **in accord, in agreement** (W.DAT. w. someone) —ref. to speaking Pl.

συμφωνίᾱ ᾱς f. **1** sounding together; **concord** (of certain notes or intervals) Pl. Arist.
2 (fig.) **concord, harmony** (among persons or things) Pl. Arist. Plb.
3 group of musicians, band Plb.
4 (gener.) **music** NT. [or perh. concr., as 3]

σύμ-φωνος (**ξύμ-**) ον adj. [φωνή] **1** sounding together; (of lyre-strings) **sounding in harmony** hHom.; (of sounds) **concordant** Pl.
2 (of a lyre) **in harmony** (w. a singer) S.*Ichn.*; (of a singer, W.DAT. w. another) Ar.; (of choral singing) **harmonious** Ar.; (of a place) **echoing in harmony** S.
3 (fig., of peace, pledges) **harmonious** Pi. S.
4 (fig., of statements, behaviour, or sim.) **in harmony, in accord** (sts. W.DAT. or GEN. w. sthg.) Pl. Plb.; (of numbers) **harmonious, concordant** Pl.; (of a person, in lifestyle) **consistent** Plb.
5 (of persons) **of one voice, in agreement** Plb.; (of a person) **in accord** (W.DAT. w. a message) Plb.; (of a decision, an action) **agreed** Plb.

συμ-ψαύω vb. **1** (of the sides of adjacent ships) **touch, be in contact** Plb.
2 (of sections of a camp) **be contiguous** —W.DAT. w. each *other* Plb.

συμ-ψάω contr.vb. | only aor.inf. συμψῆσαι, ptcpl. συμψήσᾱς | **1 rub** or **scrape together**; **rake over** (sand, so as to remove imprints of one's body) Ar.
2 (of a torrent) **sweep away** —a horse Hdt.

συμ-ψεύδομαι mid.vb. **conspire in falsehood** Plb.

συμ-ψηφίζω vb. **1 count up, calculate** —prices NT.
2 ‖ MID. **vote together, take sides** —W.DAT. w. *someone* Ar.

σύμ-ψηφος ον adj. [ψῆφος] **1 voting together**; (of persons) **taking the same side, in agreement** (usu. W.DAT. w. someone, sts. also W.GEN. over sthg.) Pl. D. Plb. Plu.
2 being in favour (W.DAT. of sthg.) Pl.

συμ-ψοφέω contr.vb. make a noise by clashing together; **clash noisily, rattle** —a shield (W.DAT. w. *one's sword*) Plb.; **make a loud crash** —W.DAT. w. *weapons* (on *weapons*) Plb.

σύν, also **ξύν** prep. | W.DAT. |
—**A** | accompaniment (in movt., position, activity or experience) |

1 together with, with —*someone or sthg.* Hom. +; (w.art.) οἱ σὺν (ξὺν) αὐτῷ *those with him, his companions, soldiers, allies* X. +
2 with the help of —*a deity, divine support* Hom. +; **by the will of** —*a god* Pi. S. E.; **with the consent of** —*the government* Hdt.
3 in support of, on the side of —*someone* X. NT.
4 side by side with —*someone, others* Od. + —*sthg.* A. Call.
5 (as adv., ref. to joint or simultaneous action) **together** Hom. S. Th. AR.
—**B** | accompaniment (in wearing, carrying or possessing) |
1 with (on one's person) —*equipment, armour, clothing* Hom. +
2 with (in one's possession) —*an object, offering, message, or sim.* Hom. +
—**C** | means or instrument |
1 by, on —*an animal or vehicle* Hom. +
2 by means of —*the excellence of a horse, praise, force, kindness* Hdt. X.
3 by, with —*a weapon* A.
—**D** | manner or attendant circumstances |
1 with —*virtue, freedom* Od. Pi. S.; (phr.) σὺν (ξὺν) νόῳ (νῷ) *with good sense* Heraclit. Hdt. E. Ar. Pl. + | see also σπουδή 1, 4, τάχος 5
2 in accordance with —*just conduct, the laws, orderliness, propriety* Pi. Hdt. X.; **on** —*oath* Od. Plu. | see also δίκη 2, καιρός 4, χρόνος 6
—**E** | coincidence or consequence |
1 with (as a concurrent circumstance) —*a storm, noise* Hom. —*a circumstance, condition, state, activity, or sim.* Od. Hdt. Trag. +
2 with (as a necessary consequence) —*pollution, harm, benefit, or sim.* Il. Thgn. Hdt. S. X. +
—**F** | time |
1 at the same time as —*nightfall, a night, day, the break of a wave* Pi. E. Theoc. —*someone's arrival* Pi.
2 during —*a period of time, one's youth* Lyr. X.
—**G** | inclusion or addition |
1 including (as a part of a total) —*members of a group, a period of time, sum of money, asset, cost of sthg.* Hdt. Th. Att.orats. + —*a district* Th.
2 together with or alongside, in addition to —*someone or sthg.* A. +
3 (as adv.) **besides, in addition** Trag. AR.

συν-αγανακτέω contr.vb. **share** (sts. W.DAT. w. someone) **a feeling of annoyance or indignation** Plb. Plu.
συν-αγαπάω contr.vb. **join** (W.DAT. w. someone) **in feeling affection for** —*someone* Plb.
συν-άγγελος ου m. **fellow messenger** Hdt.
συν-αγείρω (ξυν-) vb. | MID.: ep.aor.2 ptcpl. συναγρόμενος || PASS.: ep.3pl.aor. συνάγερθεν | Aeol.3sg.pf. συναγάγρεται |
1 gather together, assemble —*persons, a meeting, or sim.* Il. Hdt. Lys. Ar. AR. —*soldiers, an army, fleet, or sim.* Il. Hdt. Th. Isoc. Aeschin. Plb. || MID.PASS. (of persons or things) **gather or be gathered together** Il. Pl. X. Theoc. | see also συναίρω 2
2 gather, get together, collect —*a livelihood* Od. —*goods* Od.(mid.) || PASS. (of fruit) be gathered in Alc.
3 (fig.) **gather together, collect** —*oneself* Pl. —*one's wits* AR.(mid.) || MID.PASS. (of a person) **collect oneself, recover** Theoc. || PASS. (of boldness) be mustered Pl.
συν-αγελάζομαι pass.vb. [ἀγέλη] (of animals) **herd together** —W.DAT. w. *animals of the same kind* Democr.; (fig., of persons) —W.PREP.PHR. w. *one's own kind, w. one another* Plb. Plu.

συναγελασμός οῦ m. **herding together** (of children, into groups) Plu.
συν-άγκεια ας f. [ἄγκος, cf. μισγάγκεια] place where mountain gullies meet, **gorge** Plb. Plu.
συν-άγνῡμι (ξυν-) vb. | only ep.aor. συνέαξα, inf. (tm.) σὺν ... ἆξαι |
1 break in pieces, shatter —*one's spear* Il. —*a chariot* Il.(tm.); (of a storm) —*ships* Od.
2 (of a lion) **crunch up** —*the young of a hind* Il.
συν-αγορεύω (ξυν-) vb. | aor. συνηγόρευσα (Plu.) || The aor. is usu. supplied by συνεῖπον, fut. and pf. by συνείρω². |
1 speak in support (oft. W.DAT. of someone) Th. Att.orats. X. Plu. —W.ACC. *on some matter* Th. X.
2 advocate —*a course of action* Plu. —W.INF. or COMPL.CL. *doing sthg., that sthg. shd. be done* X.
3 speak in support of, favour —W.DAT. *someone's interests, wishes, arguments* Isoc. D. Plu.
συναγυρμός οῦ m. [συναγείρω] **gathering together, consolidation** (W.GEN. of wisdom) Pl.
συναγυρτός όν adj. (of water) **collected** (in a pond or reservoir, opp. flowing in a stream) Pl.
συν-άγχη ης f. [ἄγχω] constriction of the throat; **quinsy** Plu.
συν-άγω (ξυν-) vb. | dial.inf. συνάγεν (Pi.) | impf. συνῆγον, dial. συνᾶγον, ep. σύνᾱγον | aor.2 συνήγαγον, dial. συνάγαγον | pf. συνῆχα (X.) |
1 bring or **gather together** —*persons, animals, ships, or sim.* Il. Hdt. E. Th. + || PASS. be brought or gathered together X. Men. +
2 gather, assemble —*an army, troops, or sim.* Alc. E. Isoc. X. Aeschin. + || PASS. (of military forces) be gathered Hdt. Isoc. D. +
3 bring together, convene —*persons in authority, a court, an assembly, or sim.* Sol. Hdt. Th. + || PASS. (of an assembly, council, or sim.) be convened Plb. NT. Plu.
4 (of a host) **assemble** —*guests* (for a dinner or drinking-party) Thphr. Men.; (intr., of guests) Thphr. Men.
5 gather together (things); **collect, assemble** —*property, books* X. —*subjects* (for study, historical writing) Isoc. Pl. —*financial contributions, money* Arist. Men.; (of Zeus) —*clouds* Od. || PASS. (of money or sim.) be collected Men. Plb. Plu.; (of subject matter) Arist.
6 gather up —*the remains of a meal* NT.; **gather in** —*fruits, crops* Plb. NT.; (of a net) **take in** (a catch of fish) NT.
7 cause (persons) **to come together** (in a union or bond); (of persons, gods, circumstances) **bring together, unite** (in friendship, marriage, or sim.) —*persons* hHom. A. E. Ar. X. +; (of a matchmaker) **arrange** —*marriages* X.
8 bring together (separated items); **unite, combine** —*things, places* Th. Isoc. Pl. +; (of a poet) **link** —*voices* (W.DAT. by means of *the aulos and his craft*) Pi.fr. || PASS. (of things) be combined Pl. D. Arist. Plu.
9 (of a person in a state of grief and weakness) **pull** (W.ACC. *oneself*) **together** Plu.
10 bring together in conflict, match —*combatants* A. E.; (of a god) **bring about** —*fighting, a war* Archil. Isoc.; (of combatants) **join, engage in** —*battle or sim.* Il. hHom.; (intr.) **engage in combat** Theoc. Plu. —W.DAT. w. *someone* Plb.
11 cause (things) **to come together; draw close** —*wings* (of an army or fleet) Hdt. E. —*sterns of ships* Hdt.; (of rivers) —*their courses* Hdt.
12 contract, knit —*one's brow* Ar.; **close** —*one's anus* (after defecating) Ar.; (of dogs) **prick up** —*their ears* X. || PASS. (of ears, compared to a parasol) close up Ar.
13 draw together (so as to lessen in extent); **contract, narrow** —*a prow, the edges of a canal* Hdt.; **reduce** (in size) —*a city* Plb. || PASS. (of a sea, an area of ground) be narrowed

συναγωγεύς

Hdt. Plb.; (of eyes, compared to a sputtering flame) Arist.; (of expenditure) be reduced or restricted Plu.; (of proof) —W.PREP.PHR. *to a brief statement* Plu.; (of a style of writing or speech) be condensed Plu.
14 ∥ PASS. (fig., of persons) be cramped or hard pressed —W.DAT. or PREP.PHR. *by shortage of food or sim.* Plb. Plu.
15 carry (sthg.) together (w. someone); **help** (W.DAT. someone) **to carry** —*a cargo* Od.(tm.)
16 take together (w. oneself, into one's house); **entertain** —*someone* NT.
17 put together (a conclusion); **deduce, infer, conclude** —W.ACC. or COMPL.CL. *sthg., that sthg. is the case* Arist.; (intr.) Arist.

συναγωγεύς έως *m.* **1** one who brings together; (ref. to an official) **assembler, organiser** (W.GEN. of citizens) Lys.
2 (ref. to mutual love) **uniter, restorer** (W.GEN. of the original state of being) Pl.

συν-αγωγή (**ξυν-**) ῆς *f.* **1** bringing together, **assembling** (of persons, troops, animals) Plb.
2 uniting (of a man and woman, in marriage) Pl.
3 process of bringing together, **collection** (opp. division) Pl.; **combining** (of things) Arist.
4 collecting, **gathering** (of supplies, taxes) Plb.; **accumulation** (of money) Plu.; **gathering in** (of the harvest) Plb.
5 (concr.) **collection** (of documents) Arist.
6 place of assembly (among Jews), **synagogue** NT.
7 bringing about, **setting on foot** (of a war) Th.
8 drawing together, **concentration** (of troops, in a tight formation, opp. extension, i.e. deployment, of them) Pl.
9 pursing up, **knitting** (of the face, i.e. brow, in a frown) Isoc.
10 bringing together (of opposing statements, in a refutative argument) Arist.

συν-αγωγός όν *adj.* bringing together; (of ties of friendship) **uniting** (people) Pl.; (of a bond) **providing a connection** (W.GEN. betw. two things) Pl.

συν-αγωνιάω *contr.vb.* **share in anxiety** Plb. —W.DAT. *w. someone* Plu.

συν-αγωνίζομαι (**ξυν-**) *mid.vb.* **1** (lit. and fig., of persons) join in a contest (freq. W.DAT. together w. someone); (in military ctxt.) **fight alongside** or **offer support** Th. Isoc. X. Plb. Plu.; (in legal ctxt.) Att.orats.; (in political ctxt.) Th. Arist.; (in dramatic ctxt., of a goddess in a play) **support** —W.DAT. *the dramatist* Ar.; (of tragic choruses) **back up the plot** Arist.
2 (gener., of persons, their conduct, circumstances) **collaborate, be in league** or **agreement** (oft. W.DAT. w. someone or sthg.) Att.orats. Men. Plu.

συναγώνισμα ατος *n.* **supporting circumstance** Plb.

συν-αγωνιστής οῦ *m.* (lit. and fig.) one who shares in a contest; (in military ctxt.) **fellow combatant** Isoc. Pl. Hyp. Plb.; (in legal ctxt. or gener.) **collaborator, accomplice, supporter** Att.orats. Plb. Plu.; **supporter in a struggle** (W.GEN. for sthg.) Aeschin. D.

συν-άδελφος ον *adj.* [ἀδελφός] (of a person) **with a brother** or **brothers** (opp. having none) X.

συν-αδικέω (**ξυν-**) *contr.vb.* **1** share in wrongdoing, **be a partner in crime** (sts. W.DAT. w. someone) Th. Isoc. Pl. X. D. Plu.; (tr.) **join in wronging** —*someone* Men.
2 ∥ PASS. be a fellow victim Isoc. D. Men. Plu.

συν-ᾁδω (**ξυν-**), also **συναείδω** *vb.* **1** (of a person) **sing together** (w. someone) —*a paean* Aeschin.; (tr., of the Muses) sing (w. someone) about, **celebrate together** —*a person* Lyr.adesp. Theoc.
2 (of a lyre) **respond in harmony** —W.DAT. *w. a lyre-player* Plu.
3 (fig., of circumstances, arguments, or sim.) **be in accord, be in harmony, agree** —W.DAT. *w. sthg.* Pl. Arist. Plu.; (of things, persons, statements) **be in accord** (w. each other) Heraclit. Pl. Plb.; (of a person, malady) **match, tally, be identical** —W.DAT. *w. another person or malady* S. Ar.

συναείρω *ep.vb.*, **συναέρρω** *Aeol.vb.*: see συναίρω

συν-αθροίζω (**ξυν-**) *vb.* **1 gather together, assemble** —*persons, troops, ships, or sim.* Lys. Pl. X. Aeschin. Plb. + ∥ PASS. (of persons, troops) gather or be gathered together Th. Isoc. Pl. X. +; (of a commander) be stationed together —W.DAT. *w. his troops* E.
2 gather together (things); **unite, combine** —*separate items* (W.PREP.PHR. *into one*) Ar. —*revenues* Arist.; **collect** —*corpses, spoils, equipment, or sim.* Plb.; (of the gods) **put together, assemble** —*the human body* Pl. ∥ PASS. (of things, facts) be collected together or combined Pl. Arist.; (of a soul) be unified Pl.; (of glory) be accumulated Lycurg.

συν-αθύρω *vb.* (of a girl) **play together** —W.DAT. *w. other girls* Mosch.

συναίγδην *ep.adv.* [συναΐσσω] **with a rush together** —*ref. to combatants engaging* Hes.

σύν-αιμος (**ξύν-**) ον *adj.* [αἷμα] **1** (of a person) sharing the same blood, **related by blood, kindred** (W.DAT. to someone) S.
2 of or relating to kin; (of a face) **of a kinsman** S.; (of strife) **between kin** S.; (of Zeus) **protector of kin** S.
3 ∥ MASC.FEM.SB. blood-relative, kinsman or kinswoman (ref. to a brother or sister) S. E. ∥ PL. kinsfolk, kin S.

συν-αίμων ον, gen. ονος *adj.* **related by blood** E.(dub.) [or perh. masc.sb. *kinsman*]

συν-αινέω (**ξυν-**) *contr.vb.* **1 give one's assent** or **approval** A. S. Pl. X. Call. Plu. —W.DAT. *to someone* Hdt. Plb.
2 join (W.DAT. w. someone) **in giving approval** S.
3 (tr.) **consent to, approve** —*a thanksgiving* A.; **approve of, agree with** —*someone's words* X.
4 agree (sts. W.DAT. w. someone) **over** —*a request, offer, arrangement* S. E. X. AR.
5 consent, agree —W.INF. *to do sthg.* X. Plb.

συν-αίνυμαι *mid.vb.* **gather up** (fr. the ground) —*a bow and arrows* Il.

συν-αιρέω (**ξυν-**) *contr.vb.* | aor.2 συνεῖλον, ep. σύνελον |
1 take (several things) together; (of a person) **gather up** —*a cloak and sheepskins* Od.; (of plague) **seize without discrimination** —*weak and strong bodies* Th. ∥ PASS. (of a notion) be brought together (into a unity, through reasoning) Pl.
2 (of a stone) app., smash together, **smash, crush** —*a person's brows* (*i.e. forehead*) Il.
3 (of a suicidal impulse) **seize** or **carry off, destroy** —*a person* S.
4 help to capture —*a city* Hdt.
5 defeat, destroy —*enemies* Plu.; **capture** —*a city* Plu.
6 (fig.) seize in the mind, **grasp** —*a situation* Plu.
7 draw together (so as to contract or shorten) Th.; (aor.ptcpl.) συνελών (intr., w.vb. of speech) *in short, in a word, concisely* Th.; (also) ὡς συνελόντι εἰπεῖν *to put it concisely* X.; συνελόντι (συνελόντα Hyp.) εἰπεῖν (or sim.) Hyp. D. Plu.; συνελόντι Is. D.
8 ∥ PASS. (of the circumference of a city) be contracted or shrink Plb.
9 bring to an end —*a war, siege, business* Plu.; **complete** —*a journey, an enterprise* Plu. ∥ PASS. (of a war, an activity) be brought to an end Plu.; (of a distance) be covered Plu.

συν-αίρω (ξυν-), ep. **συναείρω**, Aeol. **συναέρρω** vb. | aor. συνῆρα, ep. (tm.) σὺν ... ἤειρα, Aeol.fem.nom.ptcpl. συναέρραισα | **1** jointly lift up —*a corpse* Il.(tm.) —*a stake* (W.DAT. *w. someone*) Od.(tm.) ‖ MID. app. **lift up** or **take hold of** —*a person* (W.GEN. *by the legs*) Plu.
2 harness together —*horses* (W.DAT. *w. straps*) Il.(tm.); (also mid.) Il.(dub., v.l. συναγείρομαι); **bind together, twine** —*shoots of anise* Sapph. | cf. συνάορος
3 ‖ MID. **engage together in, undertake together** (sts. W.DAT. *w. someone*) —*a love affair* A. —*murder, warfare* E. —*danger* Th. —*action* D.
4 ‖ MID. (intr., of cities) **undertake things together, cooperate** X. D.; (of persons) **conspire** (sts. W.DAT. *w. someone*) Plu.; **take part** or **share in** —W.GEN. *war, danger* Th.
5 take up together; settle —*financial accounts* (W. μετά + GEN. *w. someone*) NT.

συν-αισθάνομαι mid.vb. **1 share in perceptions** or **feelings** (sts. W.DAT. *w. others*) Arist. Plu.; **share in consciousness** —W.GEN. + COMPL.CL. *of one's friend, that he exists* (i.e. *of his existence*) Arist.
2 (gener.) **become aware** —W.ACC. or GEN. or W.GEN. + PTCPL. *of sthg., of sthg. happening* Plb. Plu.

συναίσθησις εως *f.* sharing of perception (w. other persons), **joint perception** Arist.

συν-αΐσσω ep.vb. [ᾄσσω] **rush in company** (w. someone) AR.

συν-αιτιάομαι mid.contr.vb. **accuse in addition** (to someone) —*others* Plu.

συν-αίτιος (ξυν-) ᾱ ον (also ος ον) adj. **1** being jointly a cause (of sthg.); (of persons or things) **jointly responsible, sharing responsibility** (usu. W.GEN. for some result or outcome, sts. also W.DAT. *w. someone*) Isoc. Pl. X. D. Arist. Plu.
2 sharing culpable responsibility, **equally to blame** (W.GEN. for a murder, plot) A. Plu.

συν-αιωρέομαι mid.contr.vb. **1** (of wind) **oscillate together** —W.DAT. *w. water* (*of rivers*) Pl.
2 (of persons) **be united in suspense** —W.DAT. *over an outcome* Plu.

συναιώρησις εως *f.* **oscillation together** (of one process w. another) Pl.

συν-ακμάζω vb. **1** flourish together; (of persons) **achieve eminence at the same time** (as each other) Plu.
2 (of a city's fortunes, a person) **reach a peak** or **prime** —W.DAT. *during someone's lifetime* Plb. Plu.; (of a person's popularity) —W.DAT.PTCPL. *while he is successful* Plu.
3 (of a person) **keep pace** —W.PREP.PHR. *w. increasing demands* Plb.

συν-ακολασταίνω vb. **share a life of debauchery** —W.DAT. or μετά + GEN. *w. other persons* Plu.

συν-ακολουθέω (ξυν-) contr.vb. **1 follow along together, keep company** (oft. W.DAT. or μετά + GEN. w. someone or sthg.) Th. Ar. Att.orats. +
2 follow (in the mind), **keep up with** —W.DAT. *a person, an argument* Pl.
3 go along with, be guided or **directed by** —W.DAT. *a person, god, fortune* Pl. Arist.
4 (of effects) **follow along** —W.DAT. or μετά + GEN. *in the wake of their cause* Pl.; (of principles) **follow together logically, be mutually implied** Arist.

συν-ακοντίζω vb. **1** (of youths) **throw javelins together** Antipho
2 (of soldiers) **throw a hail of javelins** Plb. ‖ PASS. (of persons, elephants) be struck by a hail of javelins Plb.

συν-ακούω (ξυν-) vb. **1** (of a person) share in hearing (sthg. heard by others), **also hear** —*some news* X.; (intr.) **overhear, listen in** Plu.
2 (of persons) hear simultaneously, **hear** —W.GEN. *each other shouting* X.

συν-ακροάομαι mid.contr.vb. **be a fellow listener** (to orations) Pl.

συν-αλαλάζω vb. **1** (of singers of a wedding song) **blend one's cries** —W.DAT. *w. the aulos* E.
2 (of troops) **raise a combined battle-cry** Plb. Plu.

συν-αλγέω (ξυν-) contr.vb. **1 share in suffering** or **sorrow** S. E. Antipho Pl. D. + —W.DAT. *w. someone* Arist. Plu.; **sympathise** —W.DAT. *w. someone's misfortunes* A. E. Arist. Plu.
2 (of limbs) **be all in pain** (fr. fighting) E.

συναλγηδών (ξυν-) όνος *f.* shared suffering ‖ PL. (personif., ref. to women) fellow mourners E.

συν-αλείφω vb. **1 help to put oil on** —*someone* Plu.
2 anoint thoroughly; (fig.) **gloss over, whitewash** —*bad qualities* Arist.

συν-ᾱλιάζω vb. [ἁλία] | dial.aor. συνᾱλίαξα (spoken by a Spartan, prob. com. coinage) | **assemblify** —*a troop of women* Ar.

συν-ᾱλίζω vb. [ἁλίζω] | aor. συνήλισα | **bring together, collect, assemble** —*people, soldiers, animals* Hdt. X. ‖ PASS. (of persons) assemble or be assembled Hdt. X.; (of an individual, together w. others) NT.

συναλλαγή (ξυν-) ῆς *f.* [συναλλάσσω] **1** association involving exchange; **interchange, exchange** (W.GEN. of words, ref. to peace negotiations) E.(pl.)
2 conversion from a state of hostility; (periphr.) **conciliation** (W.GEN. of speech, i.e. conciliatory speech) S.; (sts.pl.) **reconciliation** (betw. enemies) Th. X.
3 ‖ PL. exchanges, dealings (betw. persons, men and gods) S.
4 ‖ PL. trafficking (in), procuring (W.GEN. of sexual partners) E.
5 association between persons and circumstances; **visitation** (W.GEN. of a disease) S.; **conjunction of events, juncture** S.

συνάλλαγμα ατος *n.* **1** (in commercial or legal ctxts.) **dealing, transaction** (usu. betw. individuals) D. Arist. Plb.
2 (specif.) **contract** Arist.

συνάλλαξις εως *f.* (in commercial ctxt.) **exchange, transaction** Pl.

συν-αλλάσσω (ξυν-), Att. **συναλλάττω** vb. **1** associate (persons) by way of an exchange; (of fate) **cause** (W.ACC. a just man) **to associate** or **have dealings** —W.DAT. *w. impious men* A. ‖ PASS. (of a woman) be united (in sexual partnership) —W.DAT. *w. a man* S. E.
2 reconcile —*opposed or alienated persons* Lys. Pl. X. NT. —W.DAT. *w. others* Th. ‖ PASS. be reconciled or make peace (sts. w. πρός + ACC. w. someone) Th. X.
3 settle —*points of contention* Th.
4 (intr.) engage in an exchange, **have dealings** (w. someone) S. E. —W.DAT. *w. someone* Plu.; (specif.) **have business dealings** or **enter into a contract** D. Arist. —W.DAT. *w. someone* Men.

συν-άλλομαι mid.vb. (of soldiers) **leap up and down together** (in a kind of war-dance) Plu.

συν-αλοάω, dial. **συναλοιάω** contr.vb. **thrash** —*someone* (W.DAT. *w. a branch*) Hippon.; (of a boxer) **crush, smash** —*an opponent's cheeks* Theoc.; (of stones) —*a siege-engine* Plu.

συν-αλύω vb. **loaf about together** —W.DAT. *w. someone* Plu.

σύν-άμα prep. [ἅμα] (ref. to cattle coming fr. pasture) **together at the same time** —W.DAT. *w. others* Theoc.

συν-αμαθύνω vb. (of fire) **destroy together, consume** —*a heap of twigs* AR.(tm.)

συν-αμάομαι *mid.contr.vb.* (of the child Eros) **gather up** —*knucklebones* AR.

συν-αμιλλάομαι *mid.contr.vb.* (fig., of a suppliant's embrace, envisaged as a wrestler's hold) **fight in addition** —W.DAT. *to his tears* (*in pressing his plea*) E.

σύν-αμμα ατος *n.* [ἅμμα] that which is tied together, **fastening** (ref. to the Gordian knot) Plu.

συν-αμπέχω (**ξυν-**) *vb.* wrap up closely; (fig.) **enshroud in secrecy** —*a fact* A.

συν-αμπίσχομαι *mid.vb.* **veil** —*one's eyes* (*in grief and horror*) E.

συν-αμύνω *vb.* (of persons) **join in giving support** —W.DAT. *to someone* E.

συν-αμφότεροι (**ξυν-**) αι α *pl.adj.* **1** (of persons or things) **both together** Thgn. Hdt. Th. Pl. X. Is. +
2 ‖ SG. (of an entity) containing two in one, combined, dual Pl. D. Plb. ‖ NEUT.SG.SB. **the two combined** Arist.

συν-άμφω *indecl.du.demonstr.pron.* **1** (ref. to persons or things) **both together** Pl. Arist. AR. Plb.
2 ‖ NEUT.SG.SB. **the two combined** Arist.

συν-αναβαίνω (**ξυν-**) *vb.* **1** (of persons, soldiers) go up-country together, **travel inland together** (fr. the coast, into central Asia; sts. W.DAT. w. someone) Hdt. Isoc. X. Plu.; (to Jerusalem, w. Jesus) NT.
2 go up together (to the Capitol) Plu.; (of troops using scaling-ladders) **climb up together** Plb.

συν-αναβοάω *contr.vb.* **join in the shouting** X.

συν-αναγιγνώσκω *vb.* **read** (W.ACC. a letter) **together** (w. someone) Plu.

συν-αναγκάζω *vb.* **1 join in compelling** —W.ACC. + INF. *someone to do sthg.* D.
2 (of persons, circumstances) **compel** —W.ACC. + INF. *someone to do sthg.* Arist. Plb. Plu.; (intr., of need) **exercise compulsion** Arist. ‖ PASS. (of persons) **be constrained or compelled** D. Arist. —W.INF. *to do sthg.* X. Arist.
3 (of a person) **achieve** (W.ACC. sthg.) **by force as well** (as planning it) Isoc.

συν-ανάγομαι *pass.vb.* **1** (of troops) **be taken back together, be withdrawn together** —W.PREP.PHR. *to a place* Plb.
2 (of a person) embark together (w. others), **join in a voyage** D.

συν-αναγράφομαι *pass.vb.* (of a person) **also be enrolled** (as an ally, together w. someone else) Aeschin.

συν-αναγυμνόω *contr.vb.* (of open flaps on a tunic) **expose** —*the whole thigh* Plu.

συν-αναδέχομαι *mid.vb.* undertake together, **share** —*a danger* Plb.; **accept** —*war* Plb.

συν-αναδραμεῖν *aor.2 inf.* **run a race together** (w. someone) Plu.

συν-αναζεύγνυμι *vb.* (of a commander) decamp together (w. someone), **set out together** Plu.

συν-αναιρέω *contr.vb.* **1 help** (W.DAT. someone) **to pick up** —*a dead body* Antipho
2 destroy or **ruin in addition** (to sthg. else) —*success, property* Isoc.; **destroy** (W.ACC. someone or sthg.) **together** —W.DAT. *w. someone or sthg. else* Plb. ‖ PASS. (of a person, potential success) be destroyed together —W.DAT. *w. someone* Lycurg. Plu.; (log., of a species) —*w. its genus* Arist.
3 ‖ PASS. (of the power of a state) **be destroyed completely** Th.
4 (of the Pythian priestess) give an oracle in support (of an action), **respond with approval** Pl.

συν-ανακάμπτω *vb.* (of persons) **turn back together** (w. someone) Plb.

συν-ανάκειμαι *mid.pass.vb.* **recline together** (at a meal), **dine together** (sts. W.DAT. w. someone) NT.

συν-ανακομίζομαι *mid.vb.* **help** (W.DAT. someone) **to recover** —*sthg.* Plb.

συν-ανακυκλέομαι *mid.contr.vb.* (of a process) **come round again together** —W.DAT. *w. sthg.* Plb.

συν-αναλίσκω *vb.* **1** expend or use up jointly; **share in defraying** —*expenses* X. D.; (provbl.) **consume together** —*salt* (i.e. spend time in someone's company) Arist.
2 (fig.) use up in addition (to one's wealth), **also exhaust** —*one's sense of gratitude for it* D.

συν-αναμείγνυμι *vb.* ‖ PASS. (of persons) join up together —W.DAT. *w. others* Plu.

συν-αναμιμνήσκομαι *mid.vb.* | aor.pass. (w.mid.sens.) συναναμνησθείς | **recall** or **remember** (W.ACC. sthg.) **together** —W.DAT. *w. someone* Pl.

συν-ανανεόομαι *mid.contr.vb.* **join in renewing** or **reproducing** —*relationships* Plb.

συν-αναπαύομαι *mid.contr.vb.* (of a woman) rest alongside, **sleep together** (sts. W.DAT. w. a man) Plu.; (of a Spartan) —W.DAT. *w. his male comrades* Plu.

συν-αναπείθω (**ξυν-**) *vb.* **1 help to persuade** —W.ACC. + INF. *someone to do sthg.* Th.; (of an experience) **help to make** (W.ACC. an opinion) **convincing** Plu.
2 persuade in addition —W.ACC. + INF. *others to do sthg.* Isoc. Plu.

συν-αναπέμπω *vb.* **send up** (to heaven) **together** —*bodies* (*along w. souls*) Plu.

συν-αναπληρόω *contr.vb.* **make up the full amount of, equalise** —*someone's achievement* (W.DAT. *w. some quality of one's own*) Plb.

συν-αναπράσσω *vb.* **help to exact** —*pay* (fr. someone) X.

συν-αναστρέφω *vb.* **1 go along together** (w. someone) Plu.
2 ‖ MID. **keep company, associate** —W.DAT. *w. someone* Plu.

συν-ανασῴζω *vb.* **help** (W.DAT. someone) **to recover** or **save** —*a city or territory* Isoc. Plb.

συν-ανατήκω *vb.* (of molten bronze) **also melt down** (as well as softening) —*sthg.* Plu.

συν-αναφέρω *vb.* **refer to** (W.ACC. sthg.) **at the same time** Plb.

συν-αναφθέγγομαι *mid.vb.* (of persons) **cry out together** Plu.

συν-αναχρώννυμι *vb.* [ἀνά, reltd. χρῴζω] apply a colour or stain ‖ PASS. (of behaviour) **be allowed to infect** —W.DAT. *someone* Plu.

συν-αναχωρέω *contr.vb.* (of a soldier) **retreat together** (w. someone) Pl.

συν-ανδάνω *vb.* | only ep.aor.2 συνεύαδον | (of a plan) **be pleasing also** —W.DAT. *to someone* AR.

συν-ανέρχομαι *mid.vb.* | ep.aor.2 συνανήλυθον | **return together** —W.DAT. *w. someone* AR.

συν-ανθέω *contr.vb.* (of a city) **flourish concurrently** —W.DAT. *w. someone's good governance* Plb.

συν-ανίστημι *vb.* **1 raise up together; make** (W.ACC. someone) **stand up too** (along w. oneself) X.
2 help (W.DAT. someone) **to rebuild** —*walls* X.
3 ‖ ATHEM.AOR. **stand up too** X. —W.DAT. *w. someone* X.

συν-αντάω (**ξυν-**) *contr.vb.* | ep.3pl.impf. (tm.) σὺν ... ἤντεον (AR.), 3du. συναντήτην | **1** (of two persons) **meet, come face to face** Od.
2 meet, encounter (usu. W.DAT. someone or sthg.) Il.(mid.) E. Ar. X. Men. +; **come into contact** —W.DAT. *w. bloodshed* E.
3 ‖ PASS. (of an envoy's statement of position) **be received** Plb.

4 (of things) **happen** —W.DAT. *to someone* NT. Plu.
συνάντησις εως *f.* **meeting, encounter** (w. someone) E.
συν-αντιάζω (**ξυν-**) *vb.* **meet, encounter** —W.DAT. *someone* S.
συν-αντιλαμβάνομαι *mid.vb.* **take a hand** (in sthg.) **together; assist, help** —W.DAT. *someone* NT.
συν-αντλέω *contr.vb.* **bail out** (bilgewater) **together;** (fig.) **help** (W.DAT. Herakles) **to bear** —*his labours* E.
συν-άντομαι *mid.vb.* | only pres. and impf. | **1 meet, encounter** (usu. W.DAT. someone or sthg.) Hom. Hes. Archil. Pi. E.(dub.) Call. Theoc.
2 come into contact; (of singers) **lay hands on** —W.DAT. *a lyre* Pi.; (of Excess, in neg.phr.) **have dealings** —W.DAT. *w. Justice* Pi.
συν-ανύω, also **ξυνανύτω** (A.) *vb.* **1 work together, cooperate** —W.DAT. *w. someone* Plu.
2 coincide in one's arrival —W.DAT. *w. a critical time* Plu.; (of the blood of a dying man, flowing to the heart) **arrive together** —W.DAT. *w. the end of life* A.
συν-αξιόω *contr.vb.* **join in thinking** (W.ACC. someone) **worthy** or **entitled** —W.INF. *to do sthg.* X.
συναοιδός *adj.*: see συνῳδός
συναορέω *contr.vb.* [συνάορος] (of hope) **accompany** —W.DAT. *someone* Pi.*fr.*
συνάορος (**ξυν-**), Ion. **συνήορος**, ον *adj.* [συναίρω 2] **1 harnessed** or **linked together;** (of a lyre) **accompanying** (W.DAT. a feast) Od.; (of praise, W.DAT. a lyre) Pi.; (of the philosopher-poet in his chariot) **accompanied** (W.DAT. by divine charioteers) Parm. | cf. παράορος
2 || MASC.FEM.SB. **partner, spouse** (usu. wife) E.
συν-απάγω *vb.* **help to take away, escort away** —*a horse* X.; (of triremes) —*merchant ships* X.
συν-απαίρω *vb.* **depart together** (w. someone) Plb.
συν-απαιτέω *contr.vb.* **join in a claim** (for sthg.) Men.
συν-άπας ἅπασα ἅπαν *adj.* | cf. σύμπας | **1** || PL. (of persons or things) **all together, all** Thgn. Hdt. Pl.; (w. numbers) **altogether, in total** Hdt.
2 (sg., w. collectv.sb., of an army, country, place) **whole, total, all** Hdt.; (of music) **taken as a whole** Pl.
συν-απατάομαι *pass.contr.vb.* **be deceived together** —W.DAT. *w. others' hopes* (i.e. have one's own hopes frustrated too) Plu.
συν-άπειμι *vb.* [ἄπειμι²] **depart together** (w. someone) Lys. X.
συν-απεργάζομαι *mid.vb.* **1** (of actions, causes) **help to produce** or **create** —*sthg.* Pl.
2 (of a playwright, orator) **contribute to** or **complete the effect** (of sthg.) —W.DAT. *by language, gestures, or sim.* Arist.
συναπίστημι Ion.*vb.*: see συναφίστημι
συν-αποβαίνω *vb.* **disembark together** —W.DAT. *w. someone* Hdt.
συν-αποβάλλω *vb.* **lose also** (as well as one's leader) —*supremacy* Plu.
συν-απογράφομαι *mid.vb.* **register oneself together** (w. others), **be a fellow candidate** Plu.
συν-αποδημέω *contr.vb.* **go abroad together** (sts. W.DAT. or μετά + GEN. w. someone) Arist. Thphr. Plu.
συν-απόδημος ον *adj.* **going abroad together** || MASC.PL.SB. **fellow travellers** Arist.
συν-αποδιδράσκω (**ξυν-**) *vb.* | aor.inf. ξυναποδρᾶναι | **run away** or **escape together** —W.DAT. *w. someone* Ar.
συν-αποδοκιμάζω *vb.* **agree** (W.DAT. w. governments) **in rejecting** or **belittling** —*mechanical crafts* X.
συν-αποδύομαι *mid.vb.* **join** (w. another) **in stripping off** (for a contest); (fig.) **join in preparing** —W.PREP.PHR. *for an undertaking* Plu.
συν-αποθνῄσκω *vb.* (of a person, soul) **die together** (sts. W.DAT. w. someone) Hdt. Pl. X. Arist. NT. Plu.; (fig., of fire, physical faculties, memory) Hdt. Isoc. Aeschin.
συν-αποκάμνω *vb.* (of limbs) **be all exhausted** (by fighting) E.
συν-αποκηρύττω Att.*vb.* [ἀποκηρύσσω] **disown** (W.ACC. a son) **at the same time** (as selling off his mistress) Men.
συν-αποκτείνω *vb.* **be an accomplice in killing** —*someone* Antipho Aeschin.
συν-αποκτίννῡμι *vb.* (of persons committing suicide) **kill at the same time** —*their lovers* Arist.
συν-απολαμβάνω *vb.* **receive** (W.ACC. sthg.) **at the same time** (as someone else) X.
συν-απολαύω *vb.* **1 share in enjoyment** —W.GEN. *of sthg.* Arist.
2 (of a state) **share in the consequences** (of faction betw. individuals) Arist.
συν-απόλλῡμι (**ξυν-**) *vb.* **1 destroy together, involve in one's own destruction** —*someone* Antipho Th. Plu. || PASS. (of persons or things) **be destroyed** or **perish together** (sts. W.DAT. w. others) Hdt. Th. Lys. D. Plb. Plu.; (of abstr. qualities) Pl.
2 help to destroy —*someone* Hyp.
3 lose (W.ACC. sthg.) **together** (sts. W.DAT. w. sthg. else) D. Plu.
συν-απολογέομαι *mid.contr.vb.* (leg.) **join in a defence** (sts. W.DAT. of someone) Att.orats.
συν-απομαραίνομαι *mid.vb.* (of affection) **wither away together** (w. the bloom of youth) X.; (of diseases) **decline in virulence** —W.DAT. *w. fading bodily strength* Plu.
συν-απονεύω (**ξυν-**) *vb.* **sway together;** (of spectators at a naval battle) **sway** (W.DAT. w. their bodies) **in sympathy** —W.ADVBL.PHR. *w. their hopes and fears* Th.
συν-αποπέμπω *vb.* **despatch together** (w. someone) —*equipment* X.
συν-απορρήγνῡμι *vb.* **tear off together** (w. an earring) —*an ear-lobe* Plu.
συν-αποσβέννῡμι *vb.* | athem.aor.inf. συναποσβῆναι | || ATHEM.AOR. (of war) **be extinguished simultaneously** —W.DAT. *w. the exhaustion of a country* Plu.
συν-αποστέλλω (**ξυν-**) *vb.* **1 despatch together** (sts. W.DAT. or PREP.PHR. w. someone) —*envoys, troops, or sim.* Th. X. Plb. Plu. || PASS. (of a body of citizens) **be despatched as a unit** D.
2 despatch jointly (w. others) —*an army* X.; **join in sending off** —*someone* (on a journey) Is.
συν-αποστερέω *contr.vb.* **1 join** (W.DAT. or μετά + GEN. w. someone) **in depriving** or **robbing** —*someone* (W.GEN. *of sthg.*) D.
2 help (someone) **to steal** —*money* Pl.
συν-αποτελέω *contr.vb.* (of a skill) **help to complete** —*sthg.* Pl.
συν-αποτίκτω *vb.* **1** (of the processes of vision) **help to produce** —*a colour* Pl.
2 (of a person's nature) **produce** (W.ACC. bad things) **together** —W.DAT. *w. good* Plu.
συν-αποφαίνομαι *mid.vb.* **1 declare together; express the same opinion** (as someone) Isoc.; **declare** (W.ACC. sthg.) **in support** Aeschin.
2 register one's support (sts. W.DAT. for someone) —W.INF. *for a course of action* Plb.
συν-απόφασις εως *f.* (log.) **joint negation** Arist.
συν-αποχωρέω *contr.vb.* **go away together** —W.DAT. *w. someone* Plb.

συναπτός όν *adj.* [συνάπτω] (of sandal-thongs) fastened together, **tied, knotted** Ar.

συν-άπτω (**ξυν-**) *vb.* **1** fasten together (one thing to another); **tie together** —*tables* Ar.; (provbl.) **tie** —*thread* (W.DAT. *to thread, i.e. compare like w. like*) Pl.
2 (of persons) **link** —*their hands* Pl.; (of a single person) —*one's hand* (W.DAT. *to another's*) E. Ar.
3 fasten, tie up —*a person, hands* (w. ἐν + DAT. *in ropes*) E.
4 fasten —*one's lips* (W.DAT. *to someone, in a kiss*) E.
5 bring tightly together, close tight —*one's eyelids* E.
6 (of troops) **close up** —*the edges of a formation* X.
7 connect —*a place* (W.DAT. or PREP.PHR. *to another*, W.DAT. *by walls*) Plu.; (of a stretch of land) —*a place* (*to another*) Plb.
8 (of friendship) **unite** —*people* X.; (of a god) —*everyone* (W.PREP.PHR. *in a single catastrophe*) E. —*a lost son* (W.DAT. *w. his father*) E.; (of bloodshed) —*dead persons* (w. *earth*) E.
9 connect (esp. immaterial things, to persons or things); (of fate) **fasten** —*calamity* (W.DAT. *on someone*) E.; (of a person) **link** —*calamity* (W.DAT. *to calamity*) E.; **associate** —*oneself and one's country's interests* (W.DAT. *w. senseless behaviour*) D. —*hatred and malice* (w. *ambition*) Plu. —*manly valour* (w. *music*) Plu.; (intr., of anxiety and toil) **be associated** —W.DAT. *w. the care of sickness* E.; (of abstr. things) **be linked** (sts. W.DAT. to other things) Arist. ‖ PASS. (of a person) be linked —W.DAT. *to another* (*by family connections*) Plu.; (of livestock-breeding) —*to farming* X.; (of abstr. things, to each other) Pl.; (of terms in a syllogism) Call.*epigr.*; (of desire for wealth, to people) Plu.
10 attach (as an addition); **add** —*a remark* E.; (of thought) —*an aspect of meaning* (*to a given subject*) Arist. —*exploits, spoils* (W.DAT. *to other exploits, spoils*) Plu. —*interest* (*to a capital sum*) Plu.
11 bring close —*one's foot or step* (W.DAT. *to someone, i.e. meet him*) E. —*one's leg* (*to a tomb, i.e. reach it*) E.; (of two persons) —*their feet* (*i.e. meet*) E.
12 (intr.) **come up close; meet up** (usu. W.DAT. w. someone) Plb. Plu.; **arrive** (sts. W.DAT. or PREP.PHR. at a place) E. Plb. Plu.
13 (intr., of a place) **be adjacent, lie next** —W.DAT. or PREP.PHR. *to somewhere* A. Hdt. Plb. Plu.
14 (intr., of time) **be close, press** Pi.; (of a specific time) **approach** Plb.
15 join, unite —*three things* (W.PREP.PHR. *into one*) Pl.
16 compound —*one thing* (W.PREP.PHR. *fr. two*) E.; **create** —*two things* (W.PREP.PHR. *fr. one*) E. ‖ PASS. (of a single entity) be compounded (fr. other things) Pl.
17 (fig.) **put together, devise** —*a plan* A. E.
18 join together (in conflict); (of combatants) **engage** —*their armies* Hdt.; **clash** —*swords* E.; (of Hope) **embroil** —*cities* E.; (intr., fig.) **create a tangle** (i.e. conflict) S.
19 engage in —*fighting, war, or sim.* (sts. W.DAT. *w. someone*) A. Hdt. E. Th. X. Plu.; (intr.) **join battle** (sts. W.DAT. *w. someone or sthg.*) Hdt. E. Ar. Plb. Plu. ‖ MID. perh. **bring on oneself** —*blows* D. ‖ PASS. (of a war, battle, dispute) be joined or set on foot Hdt. Plu.
20 engage, involve —*oneself* (W.PREP.PHR. *in conversation*, W.DAT. *w. someone*) Ar.; (intr.) **engage, join** —W.PREP.PHR. *in conversation* (W.DAT. *w. someone*) E.; (of persons) —W.DAT. *in conversation* (w. *each other*) S. —W.PREP.PHR. *in dancing* E.
21 effect (a joint arrangement); **contract** —*a marriage, marriage-alliance* (sts. W.DAT. or PREP.PHR. *w. someone*) E. Th.(mid.) Plu.(mid.); **cement** —*friendship* (*by marriage*) Plu.; **exchange** —*oaths* E.; **arrange** —*common ownership* (of hounds) X. —*a feast* (W.PREDIC.ADJ. *shared*, W.DAT. *w. someone*) E.
22 ‖ MID. take hold together; **lend a hand, assist** A. —W.DAT. *someone* E.; (of a god) **have a hand in** —W.GEN. *a decision, an action* A. Plu.(quot. S.)
23 ‖ MID. **involve oneself in, join in** —W.GEN. *the beginning of a war* Plb. —*a supplication* Plu.
24 ‖ MID. **grasp** —W.GEN. *an opportunity* Plb.

συν-αραρίσκω *vb.* ‖ pf. συνάρηρα ‖ fit (objects) together ‖ STAT.V.PF. (of a song) be constructed hHom.; (of a ship's timbers) be held together —W.DAT. *by bolts* AR.; (of earth, heaven and sea) be united —W.DAT. *in a single form* AR.

συν-αράσσω *vb.* **1** dash together, **crush, smash** —*bones, skulls, timbers* Hom.(tm.); **wreck** —*a house* E. ‖ PASS. (of bones) be smashed Od.(tm.); (of ships) be wrecked (by a storm) Hdt.; (of persons) have (W.ACC. their heads) smashed Hdt.
2 [as if reltd. συναραρίσκω] **fasten together** —*a ship* (W.DAT. *w. bolts*) AR.; **attach, fit** —*a pole* (W.ADV. *to a yoke*) AR.

συν-αρέσκω (**ξυν-**) *vb.* ‖ ep.fut. συναρέσσω ‖ ep.aor. συνάρεσσα ‖ **1** (of things) **be equally pleasing** —W.DAT. *to someone* (*as to someone else*) X. D. Men.
2 ‖ PASS. be satisfied or content —W.DAT. *w. sthg.* Arist.
3 approve jointly (sts. W.DAT. *w. someone*) —*a sacred duty* AR. —*a plan* AR. ‖ MID. **make an agreement** —W.DAT. *w. someone* AR.

συνάρηρα (pf.): see συναραρίσκω

συν-αρθμέω *contr.vb.* fit together; **bring** (W.ACC. a person) **into contact** —W.DAT. *w. someone's words* AR.

συν-αριθμέω *contr.vb.* **1** count together, **count up** —*votes* Is. ‖ MID. **reckon up** —*instructions, a tally* Aeschin.; (intr.) **do a count** Pl. ‖ PASS. (of items) be counted or added in (sts. W.DAT. *w. other items*) Arist.; (of an activity, an abstr. quality) be included in the reckoning Arist.; (of a person) be counted together (as an adherent) —W.DAT. *w. someone* Plu.
2 count (W.ACC. someone) **in** Call.

συν-ἀριστάω (**ξυν-**) *contr.vb.* **take lunch together** —W.DAT. or μετά + GEN. *w. someone* Ar. Aeschin.

συν-αριστεύω *vb.* **join in a valiant exploit** E.

συν-αρμογή ῆς *f.* **arrangement together, collocation** (of objects) Plu.

συν-αρμόζω (**ξυν-**), Att. **συναρμόττω** *vb.* ‖ aor. συνήρμοσα, dial. συνάρμοξα (Pi.) ‖ **1** (of builders, engineers) **fit together** —*stones, timbers* Hdt. Th. X.; (intr., of parts, sts. W.DAT. *w. one another*) Pl. ‖ PASS. (of components of a military formation) be fitted together Plb.
2 close tight —*one's eyes, another's eyes* E.
3 couple, combine —*force and justice* Sol. —*good sense* (W.DAT. *w. justice*) Pi.; **compound** —*a word* (W.PREP.PHR. *fr. two words*) Pl. ‖ PASS. (of a body, an object) be compounded or composed (of certain materials or physical qualities) X. Plu.
4 put together, construct —*a ship, the Trojan Horse* E.; (of god) —*the universe* Pl.
5 bring into harmony ‖ PASS. (of a lyre) be tuned —w. πρός + ACC. *to the aulos* X.
6 (fig.) **harmonise, unite** —*different things, a plurality of things* Isoc. Pl.(also mid.) —*citizens* Pl. —*a city* Plu.(mid.) ‖ PF.PASS. (of parts of a kingdom) be harmonious or united D.
7 (fig.) bring (someone or sthg.) into harmony (w. someone or sthg. else); **harmonise** —*abstract principles* (W.DAT. or πρός + ACC. *w. each other*) Pl. Plb.; (of an event) **attune**

—*mortals* (W.DAT. *to unscrupulousness*) A.; (intr., of statements) **be in accord, harmonise** —W.DAT. *w. each other* Pl.; (of a person) **fit in, get along** (sts. W.DAT. *w. someone*) X. Arist. ‖ PASS. (of a person) **be attuned** —w. πρός + ACC. *to circumstances* X.
—**συναρμοττόντως** Att.ptcpl.adv. **fittingly, appropriately** Pl.
συν-αρπάζω (ξυν-) vb. **1** forcefully **take hold of** or **carry off** (persons or things); **seize, snatch, grab** —*someone* S. E. Lys. Ar. X. D. + —*a cockerel* Ar.; (of an eagle) —*a hare* X.; (of an evil spirit) **take hold of, possess** —*a person* NT.; (of a person, compared to a whirlwind) **carry clean away** (by his death) —*everything* S.; (of a woman in a dream-vision, seen as a horse) perh. **drag off** —*a chariot's gear* A. ‖ PASS. (of a person or animal) **be seized** or **carried off** S. Plb. Plu.; (of a ship) **be caught** (in a storm) NT.
2 (of a victor) **carry off** —*all the spoils* X.; **plunder** —*a city* E.
3 (fig.) **carry away, win over** (by persuasion or beguilement) —*an army, a lover* E. Call.*epigr.*
4 (of multiple assailants) **seize simultaneously** —*hands and legs* E.
5 snap up, appropriate —*intelligence* X.; **grab hold of** —*a problem* Ar.
6 grasp (w. the mind), **recognise** —*a voice* S.
συν-αρτάω (ξυν-) contr.vb. **1 fasten together, unite** —*a family* E.
2 ‖ PASS. (of ships) **be entangled** or **locked together** Th.; (of a hill) **be linked** (by a ridge) —W.DAT. *to a place* Plu.
3 ‖ PASS. (of a commander) **be locked in conflict, be occupied** —W.DAT. *w. an enemy* Plu.; (of persons) **be involved** —W.DAT. *in war or sim.* Plu.
4 ‖ PASS. (of virtues) **be linked** —W.DAT. *to feelings* Arist.; (of a type of behaviour) **be connected** —w. πρός + ACC. *w. someone* Arist.
συν-αρτύνω vb. **1** (of sailors) **fit together** (shields, to provide cover for a boat) AR.
2 ‖ MID. **devise together** —*a plan* AR.
συναρχίᾱ ᾱς f. [συνάρχω] ‖ PL. **board of magistrates** Arist. Plb.
σύναρχος ου m. **fellow ruler, partner in office** Arist.
συν-άρχω (ξυν-) vb. **1 share command** (at sea) —W.DAT. *w. someone* Hdt.
2 be a colleague in office (usu. W.DAT. *w. someone*) Th.
—**συνάρχων** (ξυν-) οντος m. **colleague in office, fellow official** Th. Att.orats. Pl. X. Arist. +
συν-ασεβέω contr.vb. **be linked in impiety** —W.DAT. *to someone* Antipho
συν-ασκέω contr.vb. **1 help** (someone) **in the practice of** —*virtues, skills* Isoc. D.
2 ‖ PASS. (of a phalanx) **be well trained** or **highly disciplined** Plu.
συν-ασοφέω contr.vb. [ἄσοφος] **share in folly** —W.DAT. *w. the foolish* E.
συνασπιδόω contr.vb. [reltd. συνασπίζω] **1** (of soldiers) **bring shields close together, form in close order, close up** X.
2 (of allies) **fight side by side** X.
συν-ασπίζω vb. [ἀσπίς¹] **1** carry a shield alongside (someone); (fig., of a crowd of revellers) **be comrades in arms** —W.DAT. *to their leader* E.Cyc.
2 (of soldiers) **bring shields close together, form in close order** or **with interlocked shields** Plb. Plu.
συνασπισμός οῦ m. **close-order formation** or **formation of interlocked shields** Plu.

συν-ασπιστής (ξυν-) οῦ m. **comrade in arms** S.
συν-ασχαλάω (ξυν-) contr.vb. —also **συνασχάλλω** vb. | fut.ptcpl. συνασχαλῶν | **be distressed** or **feel grief together, sympathise** —W.DAT. *w. someone's troubles* A.
συν-ασχολέομαι mid.contr.vb. **busy oneself together, engage in business** —W.DAT. *w. someone* Plu.
συν-ατῑμάζω vb. —also **συνατῑμόω** contr.vb. ‖ PASS. **share in dishonour** —W.DAT. *w. someone* Plu.
συν-ατῠχέω contr.vb. **share in misfortune** —w. μετά + GEN. *w. someone* Lycurg.
συν-αυαίνω vb. **dry up completely; burn out** —*the Cyclops' eyeball* E.Cyc. ‖ PASS. (of pores) **be dried up** Pl.
συν-αυδάω (ξυν-) contr.vb. **speak in accord, agree, concur** S.
συν-αυλέω contr.vb. **play the aulos in accompaniment** —W.DAT. *to a song* Ar.
συναυλίᾱ¹ (ξυν-) ᾱς f. [σύναυλος¹] **1 concord of aulos-players; aulos-duet** (ref. to aulos-music wailed by two persons) Ar.; (fig.) **duet** (W.GEN. of spears, ref. to a duel) A.
2 (gener.) **concord of instruments** (opp. performance on one) Pl.
συναυλίᾱ² ᾱς f. [σύναυλος²] **cohabitation** (of husband and wife) Arist.
σύν-αυλος¹ (ξύν-) ον adj. [αὐλός] **in harmony with the aulos**; (gener., of song) **concordant, harmonious** Ar.; (of the cry of singers) **in concert** (W.DAT. *w. their joy*) E.
σύν-αυλος² (ξύν-) ον adj. [αὐλή] **having an abode together**; (of a shepherd) **sharing a haunt** (w. his flocks) S.; (fig., of a person) **living together** (W.DAT. *w. madness*) S.
συναύξησις εως f. [συναύξω] **increase, expansion** (of power and territory) Plb.
συναύξω, also **συναυξάνω** vb. | aor. συνηύξησα | **1** (of persons or things) **help to increase, enlarge** or **enhance** —*property, strength, repute, or sim.* X. Arist. Plb. Plu.; (of water) **help** —W.DAT. *the earth and the seasons* **to increase** —*produce* X.
2 ‖ PASS. (of things) **increase** or **grow together** (usu. W.DAT. *w. sthg.*) Hdt. E. Att.orats. +
συν-αφαιρέω (ξυν-) contr.vb. **1 remove** (W.ACC. *someone's head*) **at the same time** (as his armour) Plb.
2 ‖ MID. **help to rescue** —*someone* Th.
συνάφεια ᾱς f. [συνάπτω] **connection, contiguity** (of activities and territories) Plu.
συναφή ῆς f. **point of contact** (betw. blade and haft of a pike, two sets of troops) Plb.
συν-αφίημι vb. **launch at the same time** (as the enemy) —*one's cavalry* Plb.
συν-αφίστημι (ξυν-), Ion. **συναπίστημι** vb. **1 cause** (W.ACC. *others*) **to join in a revolt** Th.
2 ‖ ATHEM.AOR. and MID. **join in a revolt** (sts. W.DAT. *w. someone*) Hdt. Th. ‖ PF.ACT. **be jointly in revolt** Th.
συν-άχθομαι mid.pass.vb. | fut. συναχθεσθήσομαι or perh. συναχθέσομαι | aor. συνηχθέσθην | **be troubled** or **grieved together; condole, sympathise** (oft. W.DAT. *w. someone*) Hdt. Att.orats. X. Arist. Thphr. Plu. —W.DAT. *over sthg.* D. —W.DBL.DAT. *w. someone, over sthg.* X.
σύναψις εως f. [συνάπτω] **1 contact** or **combination** (W.GEN. + PREP.PHR. *of one thing w. another*) Pl.
2 conjunction (of stars) Pl.
3 contiguity Arist.
συν-δαΐζω vb. **join together in slaying** —*someone* S.
συν-δαίνῡμι vb. | aor.ptcpl. συνδαίσᾱς | **join** (W.DAT. *w. someone*) **in celebrating with a feast** —*a marriage* E.
συνδαίτωρ ορος m.f. **fellow diner, table companion** A.

συν-δάκνω vb. bite together (on sthg.); (of a horse) take (W.ACC. the bit) **between the teeth** X.

συνδακρύω vb. (of a person) **weep together** (w. someone) E. X. —W.ACC. **over** sthg. Plu.

συν-δανείζομαι mid.vb. **collect** (W.ACC. money) **by borrowing** Plu.

συν-δειπνέω contr.vb. **dine together** (oft. W.DAT. or μετά + GEN. w. someone) Att.orats. Pl. X. Arist. Thphr. Plu.

σύν-δειπνον, also **ξυνδείπνιον** (Call.), ου n. [δεῖπνον] **common meal, banquet** Pl. Call. Plu.

σύνδειπνος ου m. one who shares a meal, **fellow banqueter** E. X.

συν-δεκαδίζω vb. [δεκαδιστής] meet together (as a member of a dining-club) on the tenth day of the month, **dine together on the tenth** —W.DAT. w. someone D.

συν-δεκάζω vb. (leg.) bribe all together; **bribe** —jurors, the Assembly, a court X. Aeschin. D.(law) —the populace (W.DAT. w. handouts or sim.) Plu.

σύν-δενδρος ον adj. [δένδρεον] (of an island) **densely wooded** Plb.

συν-δέομαι mid.contr.vb. [δέω²] **join** (sts. W.DAT. w. someone) **in pleading** or **begging** Pl. Aeschin. Plu. —W.ACC. **for** sthg. (W.GEN. fr. someone) D.

σύνδεσις εως f. [συνδέω] **connecting link** Pl.

συν-δεσμεύω vb. **tie together** —logs Plb.

σύν-δεσμος (ξύν-) ου m. [δεσμός] | neut.nom.acc.pl. σύνδεσμα (E.) | **1** that which binds together; **frame, framework** (ref. to timbers supporting a wall) Th.; **binding** (W.GEN. of heaven, ref. to a light) Pl.; (W.GEN. for silt deposits, fig.ref. to closely adjacent islands, serving to prevent their dispersal) Th.
2 ‖ NEUT.PL. **fastenings** (ref. to knots, bodily sinews) E.; **bands** (of a crown) E.
3 process of binding; **binding together** (W.GEN. of a city, parts of virtue) Pl.; (of one thing w. another) Arist.; (opp. fastening by glue or nails) Arist.
4 bond (betw. parents, ref. to children) Arist.; (betw. nations) Plu.
5 bondage, fetter (W.GEN. of unrighteousness) NT.
6 (gramm.) connecting word, **connective** (ref. to a particle or conjunction) Arist.; (gener.) **connection, combination** (of words or phrases) Arist.

συν-δεσμώτης (ξύν-) ου m. **fellow prisoner** Th. Pl.

συνδετέος ᾱ ον vbl.adj. [συνδέω] (of things) **to be tied together** Ar.

συνδετικός ή όν adj. ‖ NEUT.SB. that which is capable of binding, **bond** (ref. to education) Plu.

σύνδετος ον (also **συνδετός** όν) adj. **1** (of animals) **bound, tied up** S.; (of materials) **fastened** (sts. W.DAT. to each other) Pl.
2 ‖ NEUT.PL.SB. **fastenings** or **bands** (of a cradle) E.

συν-δέω (ξύν-) contr.vb. [δέω¹] **1 tie together** —feet, hands Od.(sts.tm.) Pl.
2 lash together —ships Hdt. —logs Plu. ‖ PASS. (of ships) be lashed together Plu.
3 tie up, bundle together —twigs hHom. —luggage Men. ‖ PASS. (of weapons) be tied up in a bundle X.
4 (of sailors, grapnels) **grapple together** —ships, sailors (i.e. their ships) Plb. ‖ PASS. (of sailors, i.e. their ships) be grappled Plb.
5 tie up —persons, animals Il. Hdt. S. E.Cyc. Ar. Pl. +; (fig., of wine) **bind, fetter** —the feet, hands, tongue and mind Hes.fr.(tm.) ‖ PASS. (of persons) be tied up Pl. Plu.
6 (of a hare) **entangle** —itself (in a net) X.
7 bind up —a wounded hand Il. —a wound AR.
8 fasten up —a robe E. —a bed-pack (W.DAT. w. a strap) Plu.; **seal up** —a writing-tablet E.
9 (of a god, physical substance, or sim.) **bind together, combine** —sthg. (W.DAT. w. sthg. else) Pl.; (intr.) Pl. ‖ PASS. (of a piece of defensive armour) be combined —W.DAT. w. another X.; (of things) be bound together (sts. W.DAT. w. others) Pl.
10 (of good, the public interest, or sim.) **bind together, unite** —natures, cities, or sim. Pl.; (of Equality) —friends, allies, cities (W.DAT. to each other) E. ‖ PASS. (of persons) be bound together (in marriage) Pl.; (of a city) —W.DAT. by customs or sim. Pl.
11 ‖ PF.PASS.PTCPL.ADJ. (of a hound's haunches) **close-knit, compact** X.

σύν-δηλος ον adj. [δῆλος] (of the plot of a tragedy) **wholly clear, perspicuous** Arist.; (of a circumstance) **fully apparent** Plu.

συν-δηλόω contr.vb. **make wholly clear** —a purpose Arist.

συν-δημαγωγέω contr.vb. **join in winning over the people**; (of a speech) **conspire** (W.DAT. w. an event) **in winning over** —the public at large Plu.; (of one's looks) **contribute to one's popularity** Plu.

συν-δημιουργός οῦ m. **one who works hand in hand** or **cooperates** (W.DAT. w. laws) Pl.

συν-διαβαίνω (ξυν-) vb. **go across** (a ditch, water) **together** (sts. W.DAT. w. someone) Th. X. Plu.

συν-διαβάλλω (ξυν-) vb. **1** (of ships) **cross** (W.ACC. a sea) **together** Th.
2 bring into disrepute —one's righteousness Plu.
3 ‖ PASS. be criticised or slandered together (w. another); be jointly accused Th.; share in opprobrium Att.orats.

συν-διαβιβάζω vb. **help to convey** (W.ACC. persons, an army) **across** (a river, sea) Pl. X. Plu.

συν-διαγιγνώσκω (ξυν-) vb. **share** (W.DAT. w. someone) **in a decision** —W.INF. to do sthg. Th.

συν-διάγω vb. **spend time together, live together** (sts. W.DAT. or PREP.PHR. w. someone) Arist. Plu.

συν-διαθέω contr.vb. **run together in a race** (W.PREP.PHR. w. others) Pl.

συν-διαιτάομαι (ξυν-) mid.pass.contr.vb. **live together** (sts. W.DAT. or PREP.PHR. w. someone) Isoc. Pl. Plu.; (of dogs, w. humans) Th.

συνδιαίτησις εως f. spending time together, **intimacy** Plu.

συν-διαιτητής οῦ m. **co-arbitrator** D.

συν-διακινδῡνεύω vb. **share in danger** Hdt. Pl.

συν-διακομίζομαι pass.vb. **be conveyed across** (a river, sea) **together** Plb. Plu.

συν-διακοσμέω contr.vb. **help to arrange** or **set in order** —a city and its laws, a political system, festival Pl. Plu.

συν-διακυβερνάω contr.vb. (of oratory) **help to steer** —matters of state Pl.

συν-διαλαμβάνω vb. **engage in joint discussion** Plb.

συν-διαλλάττω Att.vb. [διαλλάσσω] **help to reconcile** —a person (sts. W.DAT. to someone) D. Plu.

συν-διαλύω vb. **help to put an end to** —disturbances Isoc.

συν-διαμάχομαι mid.vb. **fight to the end in support** —W.DAT. of sthg. Pl.

συν-διαμένω vb. **1** (of an envoy) **stay on together** (w. someone, as a guest) X.
2 continue to stand by (someone, in misfortune) Arist.

συν-διαμνημονεύω vb. **join** (sts. W.DAT. w. someone) **in recollecting** —W.COMPL.CL. or INDIR.Q. that (or whether) sthg. is the case Aeschin. D.

συν-διανεύω *vb.* **1** nod together; (of grapnels) app. **drop down together** Plb.
2 (of a person) **incline** —w.DAT. + PREP.PHR. *in the mind, towards certain regions (i.e. direct one's attention to them)* Plb.

συν-διανοέομαι *mid.pass.contr.vb.* think (about sthg.) together; **deliberate together** (sts. w.DAT. w. someone) Plb.

συν-διαπεραίνω *vb.* **help to bring to an end** —*an argument* Pl.

συν-διαπέτομαι *mid.vb.* (fig., of kinds of ignorance, envisaged as birds) **fly about together** Pl.

συν-διαπολεμέω (ξυν-) *contr.vb.* (of ships) **serve through a war together** —w. μετά + GEN. *w. a commander* Th.

συν-διαπονέω *contr.vb.* **work together** —w.PREP.PHR. *w. someone* Pl.

συν-διαπορέω *contr.vb.* **discuss a problem together** Plu.

συν-διαπράττω *Att.vb.* [διαπράσσω] **1** (of a city) **contribute to bringing about** —*the greatest results* Isoc.
2 ∥ MID. **take part in transactions** or **negotiations** X.

συν-διαρθρόω *contr.vb.* **piece together, articulate precisely** —w.INDIR.Q. *what someone means* Arist.

συν-διασκέπτομαι *mid.vb.* ∣ only aor.inf. συνδιασκέψασθαι ∣ **join in examining** or **investigating** —*sthg.* Pl.

συν-διασκοπέω *contr.vb.* (act. and mid.) **join** (w.DAT. or μετά + GEN. w. someone) **in investigating** or **examining** —*sthg.* Pl.

συν-διαστρέφομαι *pass.vb.* (of parts) **be distorted together** —w.DAT. *w. the whole* Plu.

συν-διασώζω (ξυν-) *vb.* **1 help to preserve** —*what is good, a form of government, property* Th. Isoc. D.
2 rescue jointly —*a person and his weapons* Pl.

συν-διαταλαιπωρέω *contr.vb.* **persevere to the end** (in bringing up children) Pl.

συν-διαταράσσω *vb.* **scatter at one throw** —*a collection of adversaries (compared to a flock of birds)* Plu.

συν-διατελέω *contr.vb.* (of a foolish belief) **persist** (w.DAT. w. someone) **until the end** (of his life) Pl.

συν-διατηρέω *contr.vb.* **help in maintaining** —*the established government* Plb.

συν-διατίθημι *vb.* **help** (w.DAT. someone) **to arrange** —*a truce, points of law* Plu.

συν-διατρίβω *vb.* **1 spend time together, consort together** (usu. w.DAT. or μετά + GEN. w. someone) Att.orats. Pl. X. Plb. Plu.
2 spend time on, occupy oneself with —w.DAT. *stories, follies, or sim.* Isoc.

συν-διαφέρω (ξυν-) *vb.* **1 help** (w.DAT. someone) **to continue** —*a war* Hdt.
2 endure together —*invasions, suffering* (w.DAT. or μετά + GEN. *w. someone*) Ar. Plu.
3 (of conspirators) **carry through together** —*an undertaking* Plu.

συν-διαφθείρομαι *pass.vb.* **be corrupted together, share the taint of depravity** —w.DAT. *w. someone* Isoc. Din.

συν-διαφυλάττω *Att.vb.* [διαφυλάσσω] **1 help to defend** —*a city's walls* Lycurg.
2 help (sts. w.DAT. someone) **to preserve** —*his authority, control of affairs* Plb. Plu.

συν-διαχειμάζω *vb.* **spend the winter together** —w.DAT. or PREP.PHR. *w. someone* Plu.

συν-διαχειρίζω *vb.* **help to deal with** —*remaining business* Hdt.

συν-διεκπίπτω *vb.* **break out through** (a crowd of assailants) **together** (w. someone) Plu.

συν-διέξειμι *vb.* **go through** (W.ACC. a topic of conversation) **together** —w.DAT. *w. someone* X.

συν-διηθέομαι *pass.contr.vb.* (of a smell) **be strained through** (a respiratory blockage) **together** (w. the breath) Pl.

συνδιημέρευσις εως *f.* [συνδιημερεύω] spending of days together ∥ PL. **days spent together** or **social recreations** Plu.

συν-διημερεύω *vb.* **spend one's days together** (sts. w.DAT. or PREP.PHR. w. someone) X. Arist.

συν-δικάζω *vb.* **1** (of a person) **share in judicial decisions** Pl.; (of the Council) **share** (w. a court) **in a decision** Lys.
2 be a member of a jury, serve as juror Thphr.

συν-δικαστής (ξυν-) οῦ *m.* **fellow juror** Ar.

συνδικέω (ξυν-) *contr.vb.* [σύνδικος] **1** (leg.) **support a case, act as advocate** (oft. w.DAT. for someone) A. E. Att.orats. Pl. X. Plu.
2 (of an official appointed by the state) **be a public advocate** or **commissioner** D.; **act as advocate** —w.DAT. *for the public* Aeschin. —*for a law* D.

συνδικίᾱ ᾱς *f.* **advocacy** Pl.

σύν-δικος (ξύν-) ου *m.f.* [δίκη] **1 one who gives assistance in a legal case, advocate, supporter** A. Pl. D.; (fig., ref. to a law) Isoc.; (ref. to a place) **witness** (w.DAT. to a person's achievements) Pi.
2 (specif.) **official appointed by the state** (in an international dispute), **state advocate** D.; **advocate, commissioner** (in cases of confiscated property) Lys.; (for a law to which preliminary approval has been given) D.; (w.DAT. for a law, other undefined business) D.
3 ∥ ADJ. (of the lyre, as a possession of Apollo and the Muses) **shared by right** Pi. [or perh. *acting as spokesman*]
—**συνδίκως** (ξύν-) *adv.* **entailing equal right** or **delivering a joint sentence** (w.DAT. w. a curse) —*ref. to performing a retaliatory action* A.

συν-διοικέω *contr.vb.* **1 help** (w.DAT. someone) **to manage** —*business, responsibilities* Is. D. Arist. Plb. Plu.
2 ∥ MID. **arrange jointly** (w. μετά + GEN. w. someone) —w.COMPL.CL. *that one shd. do sthg.* Thphr.

συν-διοράω *contr.vb.* **join in an attempt to discern** —w.INDIR.Q. *what might be the case* Isoc.

συν-διορθόω *contr.vb.* **help to straighten out** —*a situation* Men.

συν-διψάω *contr.vb.* **share thirst** —w.DAT. *w. a thirsty friend (i.e. in sympathy w. him)* Arist.

συν-διώκω (ξυν-) *vb.* **1 join in pursuit** (of an enemy) Th.
2 pursue all the way (to a place) —*fleeing troops* Plb. ∥ PASS. (of troops, a person) **be pursued all the way** Plb. Plu.

συν-δοκέω (ξυν-) *contr.vb.* **1** (of proposals or decisions, expressed as indef.neut.pron. *this* or sim.) **seem equally good, be agreed** —w.DAT. (oft. w. καί) *by someone (too)* Th. Ar. Att.orats. Pl. +; (of a period of time, an idea) Pl. Arist.
2 ∥ IMPERS. **it is agreed** Pl. Men. —w.DAT. (oft. w. καί) *by someone (too)* E. Th. Ar. Att.orats. Pl. + —w.INF. *to do sthg.* X. Plu. —w.ACC. + INF. or COMPL.CL. *that sthg. is the case* Pl. X. Arist.
3 ∥ PF.PASS.PTCPL.ADJ. (of an argument or sim.) **agreed upon** Pl.

συν-δοκιμάζω *vb.* **1 help to test** or **examine** —*an opinion or sim.* Isoc. Pl.
2 approve, sanction —*a proposal* Plu.

συν-δοξάζομαι *pass.vb.* (of laws) **be ratified** Arist.

συν-δουλεύω *vb.* **share slavery** —w.DAT. *w. someone* E.

σύν-δουλος (ξύν-) ου *m.f.* —also **συνδούλη** ης (Hdt.) *f.* [δοῦλος] **fellow slave** Hdt. E. Ar. Arist. Men. NT.

συν-δραμεῖν (ξυν-) aor.2 inf. | The pres. and impf. are supplied by συντρέχω. | **1** run or come together (in conflict); (of opposing warriors) **rush together** Il.; (of troops, a commander) **engage** —w. εἰς (τὰς) χεῖρας *in close combat* Plb. Plu.
2 come together in one place; (of people, a crowd) **come together, gather** (sts. W.PREP.PHR. at a place) Hdt. Th. Att.orats. X. +; **flock** —w. πρός + ACC. *to a person* Plb.; **unite** —w. ἐπί + ACC. *against someone* Plb.; (gener.) **rush up** (in a group or to a place) Plb. Plu.
3 (of clouds) **gather** Hdt. Plu.; (fig., of collective sorrow or troubles) —W.ADV. or PREP.PHR. *at a place* Archil. Isoc.
4 (fig., of humans) run in company, **associate** —W.DAT. w. *a class of animals* Pl.
5 (of opinions, circumstances) **come together** —w. εἰς ταὐτόν (ἐς τωὐτό) *to the same point* (i.e. *coincide*) Hdt. D.
6 (of spoils) **arrive together** (fr. different locations) Plb.
7 (of virtues) **come together, be combined** Plb.
8 (of prophecies) **correspond, tally** —w. πρός + ACC. w. *events* Plu.; (of a circumstance) **conspire** —w. πρός + ACC. w. *another* Plb.
9 (gener., of enthusiasm, reputation) **accrue** Plb. Plu.
συν-δράω (ξυν-) contr.vb. **1 help** (sts. W.DAT. someone) **to do** or **perform** —sthg. E. Th. Ar.
2 (intr.) **act in partnership, lend a hand** S. E.
3 (of a circumstance) **entail joint action** E.
συν-δρήστειρα ης *Ion.f.* | only tm. σὺν ... δρήστειρα | active helper, **helpmate** AR.
συν-δρομάδες ων *fem.pl.adj.* [δρομάς] (of rocks, ref. to the Clashing Rocks) running together, **colliding, clashing** E. Theoc.
συνδρομή ῆς *f.* [συνδραμεῖν] running together; (gener.) **gathering** (of people, birds) Plb. NT. Plu.; (pejor.) **concourse** (ref. to an assembly of citizens) Arist.(quot.)
σύνδρομος ον *adj.* **1** (of rocks, ref. to the Clashing Rocks) **colliding, clashing** Pi. || NEUT.PL.SB. **collisions** or **clashes** (of rocks) AR.
2 (of the time of gathering in grapes) **coinciding** (W.DAT. w. the rising of Arcturus) Pl.
3 || MASC.SB. one who runs in accompaniment, **hunting companion** (of Artemis, ref. to Aktaion) Call.
4 || NEUT.PL.SB. **running-track that is shared** (W.DAT. w. another athlete) Pl.
—συνδρόμως adv. **in close pursuit** —ref. *to following a scent* A.
συνδυάζω vb. [σύνδυο] **1 combine, couple, pair** —things Arist. —one thing (w. πρός + ACC. w. another) Arist. || PASS. (of persons or animals, usu. w. sexual connot.) **be paired, couple** X. Arist. —W.DAT. w. *another person or animal* Pl. Arist.
2 (intr., of a nation) **pair up, collude** (sts. W.DAT. w. another nation) Plb.
συνδυάς άδος *f.* pairing, **partnership** (W.GEN. w. a wife) E.
συνδυασμός οῦ *m.* **pairing, combination, coupling** (of persons or things) Arist.
συνδυαστικός ή όν *adj.* (of human beings) disposed to live in pairs, **pairing** Arist.
σύν-δυο indecl.num.adj. [δύο] (of animals) **two together, two at once, in pairs** hHom.; (of persons, companies, tribes) Pl. X. Hyp. D.; (of things) Hdt. Pl. Plb.; (of sufferings) Pi.
συν-δυστυχέω contr.vb. **share in misfortune** E. Is.
συν-δώδεκα indecl.num.adj. (of monthly festivals) **twelve in all** E.

συν-εγγίζω vb. (of persons) **draw near, come close** (sts. W.DAT. to a place or person) Plb.; (of a future contingency) Plb.
συν-εγγυάω contr.vb. **join in giving away** (in marriage) —*a woman* Plu.
σύν-εγγυς (ξύν-) *adv. and prep.* [ἐγγύς] | sts. quasi-adjl., w.art. | **1** (ref. to place) **nearby, close** Th. X. Plb.; (as prep.) —W.GEN. or DAT. *to somewhere, someone* Plb.
2 (ref. to time) **near at hand** Arist. Plb.
3 (ref. to relationships betw. persons) **close** Arist.; (as prep.) —W.GEN. or DAT. *to someone or sthg.* Arist. Plu.
4 in close approximation, closely, narrowly Plu.
συνεδρείᾱ *f.*: see συνεδρίᾱ
συνεδρεύω vb. [σύνεδρος] | impf. συνήδρευον | **1** (of persons) **sit together in council, take part in a conference** Aeschin. D.
2 (of a juryman) **sit together** (w. other jurors) —w. ἐπί + DAT. *for underhand purposes* Thphr.
3 deliberate, confer (oft. w. μετά + GEN., sts. W.DAT. w. someone) Plb. Plu.
4 (of philosophers) **debate** —W.DAT. *an argument* Arist.
συνεδρίᾱ (also **συνεδρείᾱ**) ᾱς *f.* **1 sitting together, perching together** (of birds, regarded as a favourable omen) A. Arist.
2 company, gathering (of friends) X.
3 sitting together in a council, **membership of a council** Aeschin.
4 conferring, consultation (of a person, w. others) Plb.
συνεδριακός ή όν *adj.* [συνέδριον] (of a system of government) managed by a council, **representative** Plb.
συνεδριάομαι mid.contr.vb. [συνεδρίᾱ] | only ep.inf. (w.diect.) συνεδριάασθαι | **sit together in council** AR.
συνέδριον ου *n.* [σύνεδρος] **1 council** (gener., or ref. to minor administrative bodies) Att.orats. X. NT.; (ref. to the Areopagus) Att.orats.; (ref. to the Roman Senate, assemblies in various regions, the Jewish Sanhedrin) Plb. NT. Plu.
2 (iron.) **conclave** (of philosophical debaters) Pl.
3 congress (of allies) Hdt. Att.orats. X. Plu.
4 (concr.) **council-chamber** or **meeting-place** Hdt. Att.orats. Pl. X. Men.; **meeting-house** (of Pythagoreans) Plb.
σύν-εδρος (ξύν-) ον *adj.* [ἕδρᾱ] **1** (of the two Ajaxes) **sitting together** E.
2 (of persons) **sitting together** (W.DAT. w. a king, perh. as his counsellors) Hdt.; (of Justice) **sitting as partner** (W.GEN. of Zeus) S.
3 (of a circle of chiefs) **sitting in council** S.
4 || MASC.SB. one who sits in negotiation (w. others), **fellow commissioner** (sts. W.DAT. w. someone) Th. Isoc.
5 || MASC.SB. one who sits in discussion (w. others), **delegate** (to a congress) Att.orats. Plb.
6 || MASC.SB. (in political and military ctxts.) **adviser** Plb. Plu.
συνέεργον (ep.impf.), **συνέεργαθον** (ep.aor.2): see συνείργω
συν-εθέλω, also **συνθέλω** (ξυν-) vb. **share in a wish, approve, concur, consent** S. E. Antipho Ar.(quot. S.) X. Arist.
συν-εθίζω (ξυν-) vb. **accustom** —someone or sthg. (W.DAT. or πρός + ACC. *to someone or sthg.*) Pl. Arist. Plb. Plu. —(W.INF. *to do sthg.*) Aeschin. D. Plb. Plu. || PASS. **become accustomed** or **habituated** (usu. W.INF. to doing sthg.) Th. Att.orats. Pl. +
συνείδησις εως *f.* [σύνοιδα] **moral consciousness, conscience** NT.
συνειδήσω (fut.): see σύνοιδα
συνείκω vb. **yield, give way** Plb. —W.DAT. *to circumstances* Plb.

συν-ειλέω contr.vb. [εἰλέω¹] **1 crowd together** or **shut up** —*people* (*in a place*) Hdt. ‖ PASS. (of people) **be crowded** or **pressed together** X. Plu.
2 gather together, collect —*rods* Hdt.

σύν-ειμι¹ (**ξύν-**) vb. [εἰμί] | neut.impers.vbl.adj. συνεστέον |
1 (of a person) **be together, consort, associate, keep company** (usu. W.DAT., sts. w. μετά + GEN. w. someone) Thgn. Eleg.adesp. S. E. Th. +
2 be together (w. others), **be present** Hdt. S. Ar. +
3 (of colleagues, lovers) **be together** Ar. Pl.; (of a commander) **get together** (for negotiation) —W.DAT. *w. someone* Th.
4 be an associate or **adherent** (i.e. pupil or follower, oft. W.DAT. of someone) Ar. Att.orats. Pl. X.
5 (of gods, Justice, a city, physical force) **be with, side with, support** —W.DAT. *someone* Trag.
6 live together —W.DAT. *w. a husband, wife, lover* Hdt. S. E. Ar. D.
7 copulate, have sex (usu. W.DAT. w. someone) Ar. Pl. D. Arist. Plu.
8 be afflicted or **beset** —W.DAT. *by sorrow, dreams, sickness* Od. Trag.; **be occupied** —W.DAT. *w. work, pleasures, or sim.* Ar. Pl. X. —*w. horses* Pl.; **be consumed** —W.DAT. *by ambition* Plu.
9 be familiar —W.DAT. *w. ideas, arguments, activities* Ar.; **be used** —W.DAT. *to certain food* Plu.
10 (of time, disasters, sickness, hope) **keep company, be associated** (usu. W.DAT. w. someone) S. E. Plu.; (of grief) —W.DAT. *w. a life of luxury* Men.

σύν-ειμι² (**ξύν-**) vb. [εἶμι] | ep.3pl.impf. σύνισαν, ξύνισαν ‖ Only pres. and impf. (other tenses are supplied by συνέρχομαι). The pres.indic. has fut. sense. |
1 (of persons) **go** or **come together, meet, assemble** Hdt. Th. Pl. +; (of ships) Plu.; (of a crowd) NT.
2 (of things) **come together, unite** Pl. Arist.
3 (of opposing troops) **meet in battle, engage** Il. Hes. Hdt. Th. +; (of cities) **come into conflict** Th.; (of rocks, ref. to the Clashing Rocks) **collide** AR. Theoc.
4 (of persons, a council) **meet** (for consultation or discussion) Th. Pl. X. Lycurg. +
5 (of a person or persons) **meet** (secretly or for a subversive purpose), **conspire** (sts. W.DAT. w. someone) Att.orats.
6 (of revenues) **come in, be gathered in** Hdt.; (of the harvest) Hdt.(oracle)

συν-εῖπον aor.2 vb. **1 say** (W.ACC. sthg.) **in support** Hyp. —W.DAT. *of someone* Isoc.
2 speak in support Att.orats. X. Plu. —W.DAT. *of someone or sthg.* Att.orats. X. Plb. Plu. —W.ACC. *of sthg.* D.
3 second an account, confirm —W.COMPL.CL. *how sthg. happens* E.

συν-είργω (**ξυν-**), ep. **συνεέργω** vb. | ep.impf. συνέεργον | fut. συνείρξω | aor. συνεῖρξα | ep.aor.2 συνεέργαθον ‖ PASS.: fut. συνείρξομαι | aor. συνείρχθην ‖ The Att. form is sts. wrongly given as συνέργω. |
1 (of headlands) **shut in, enclose, bound** —*a bay* Il.; (of skin) —*bones* AR.(tm.)
2 shut in, confine —*someone* (*in a building*), *everyone* (w. εἰς + ACC. *inside a single city*) Plu. ‖ PASS. (of people) **be kept in close confinement** Plu.
3 ‖ PASS. (of bride and groom) **be shut up** —w. εἰς + ACC. *inside the bridal chamber* Plu.; (of a man) —W.DAT. *w. wild beasts* (*fig.ref. to women*) Ar.
4 (intr., of a legislator, a god) **arrange a union** (betw. a man and a woman, body and soul, w. allusion to 3) Pl.
5 close up (a hut, by shutting the door) S.

6 secure or **fasten together** —*a keel and mast, rams* Od. —*a tunic* (W.DAT. *w. a belt*) Od.

σύνειρξις (less correctly **σύνερξις**) εως f. **legally arranged union** Pl.; (W.GEN. of marriage) Pl.

συν-είρω¹ (**ξυν-**) vb. **1 fasten together in a row**; (of a seller) **string together** —*finches* Ar.; (of gods) **link together** —*human beings* (w. each other, in singing and dancing) Pl.; (of an etymologist) —*components of words* Pl.
2 (of a hunter) **keep** (hounds) **in a line** (fr. a fixed point) X.
3 (of pupils) **synthesise** —*what they have learned* Isoc.; (of mathematicians) **put together** —*a numerical system* Arist.
4 (pejor., of an orator) **string together** —*words and phrases* D.; (of an uncomprehending student) **reel off** —*expressions* Arist.; (of a reader) —*several lines of text* Plb.
5 (intr.) **link together the components of an argument, follow the connection of thought** Arist.; **draw out a string of conclusions** Arist.
6 continue without interruption —W.NOM.PTCPL. *doing sthg.* X.

συν-είρω² vb. | only fut. συνερῶ, pf. συνείρηκα | **speak in support** (oft. W.DAT. of someone or sthg.) Att.orats. X.; **support** (W.DAT. someone) **in pleading** —*a case* D.

συνείς (athem.aor.ptcpl.): see συνίημι

συν-εισάγω vb. (of two sets of people) **bring in together** —*provisions* (*into a fort*) X.; (of a person) —*someone* (*into a city*, w. μετά + GEN. w. oneself) Arist.

συν-εισβαίνω (**ξυν-**) vb. **embark together** —W.ACC. or εἰς + ACC. *on a ship* (sts. W.DAT. *w. someone*) A. E. Antipho

συν-εισβάλλω (**ξυν-**) vb. **1 join in an invasion** (sts. W.DAT. or PREP.PHR. w. someone, oft. w. εἰς + ACC. into a region) Hdt. Th. Isoc. X. D. +
2 (of charioteers) **join in a charge** X.

συν-εισελαύνω vb. (of troops) **march together** (w. someone) —w. εἰς + ACC. *to a place* Plu.

συν-εισέρχομαι (**ξυν-**) mid.vb. | aor.2 συνεισῆλθον | **enter together** (sts. W.DAT. w. someone, usu. W.ACC. or εἰς + ACC. a house, fortification, or sim.) E. Th. And. X. NT. Plu.

συνείσομαι (fut.): see σύνοιδα

συν-εισπίπτω (**ξυν-**) vb. **1** (of pursuers or attackers) **burst in** (to a city or sim.) **together** (oft. W.DAT. w. persons in flight) Hdt. Th. Lys. X. Plb. Plu.
2 (of a person) **plunge inside** (a house, city) **together** —W.PREP.PHR. *w. someone, a crowd* Ar. X.
3 plunge in (the sea) **together** (w. others) X.

συν-εισπλέω contr.vb. (of a commander) **sail in** (w. εἰς + ACC. to a harbour) **at the same time** (as others) X.

συν-εισπράττω Att.vb. [εἰσπράσσω] **help** (W.DAT. someone) **to exact** —W.DBL.ACC. *money, fr. debtors* D.

συν-εισφέρω vb. **1** (of the citizen-body) **join in making a financial contribution** D.; (of persons) **contribute** —*money, food* Plu.; (mid., of a person) —*one's own lineage* (*to a common stock*) Hyp.
2 (of a wounded fugitive) **get** (W.ACC. himself) **inside** —w. εἰς + ACC. *into a building* Plu.

συν-εκβαίνω vb. (of troops) **also push out** (fr. a place, in pursuit of enemy troops) X.

συν-εκβάλλω (**ξυν-**) vb. **1** (of a lioness giving birth) **expel** (W.ACC. the uterus) **together** —W.DAT. *w. the cub* Hdt.
2 also banish —*lending and borrowing* (W.PREP.PHR. *at the same time as money*) Plu.
3 help (sts. W.DAT. someone) **to drive out** or **expel** —*enemies, rulers, or sim.* Ar. X. Arist. Plb. Plu.

συν-εκβιβάζω vb. **help to extricate** —*wagons* (*fr. mud*) X.

συνεκδημέω contr.vb. [συνέκδημος] **be a travelling companion** Plu.

συν-έκδημος ου *m.* one who goes abroad together, **travelling companion** NT. Plu.

συν-εκδίδωμι *vb.* **1** help to give away in marriage; **share** (sts. W.DAT. w. someone) **the expense of a dowry for** —*a daughter or sister* Lys. D. Plu.
2 give away —*one's wife* (W.DAT. *to another husband*) Plu.
3 surrender up (W.ACC. oneself) **as well** (as others) Plu.

συν-εκδραμεῖν *aor.2 inf.* | The pres. is supplied by συνεκτρέχω. | **1** run out together; (of troops) **take part in a sortie** X.
2 (of a statesman) **proceed together** —W.DAT. *w. someone* (W.PREP.PHR. *to the highest offices*) Plu.
3 (of good fortune, honours, or sim.) fall to the lot of, **accrue to** —W.DAT. *someone* Plb.

συν-εκδύομαι *mid.vb.* (of a woman) **divest oneself** (W.ACC. of modesty) **at the same time** (as divesting oneself of clothes) Hdt.

συν-εκθερμαίνω *vb.* **help to foment** —*military ardour* (*in someone*) Plu.

συν-εκθνῄσκω *vb.* **die together**; (fig., of a drinker) **give out together** —W.DAT. *w. the drink* E.*Cyc.*

συν-εκκαίδεκα *indecl.num.adj.* (of persons) **sixteen at a time, in groups of sixteen** D.(dub.)

συν-εκκαίω *vb.* **1 set on fire also** —*sthg. else* Plu.
2 (fig.) **help to inflame** —*persons, their spirits* Plb. Plu.

συν-εκκαλέομαι *mid.contr.vb.* **1 call forth** (someone) as participant; (of troops) **call on the assistance of** —*other troops* Plb.
2 (of a list of contents) **invite the attention of** —*readers* Plb.

συν-έκκειμαι *mid.pass.vb.* (of a child) **be exposed together** —W.PREP.PHR. *w. a trinket* Men.; (of trinkets, w. a child) Men.

συν-εκκλέπτω *vb.* **1** join in stealing away; **help to smuggle away** —*someone* E.
2 join in concealing —*someone's presence* E.
3 share in the pretence of —*a marriage* E.

συν-εκκλησιάζω *vb.* **share in membership of the Assembly** Plu.

συν-εκκομίζω *vb.* **1 help** (W.DAT. someone) **to transport away** —*persons and property* Isoc.
2 help to carry out for burial, **attend the funeral of** —*someone* Plu. || PASS. **have one's funeral attended** Plu.
3 help (sts. W.DAT. someone) **to bear** —*labours, troubles, sexual passion* E.

συν-εκκόπτω *vb.* **help to cut down** —*trees* X.

συν-εκκρίνομαι *pass.vb.* (of a disease) **be secreted or discharged together** (w. a poison) Plu.

συν-εκκρούομαι *pass.vb.* (of a person) **be knocked off course** —W.DAT. *by circumstances* Plu.

συν-εκλείπω *vb.* (of a goal set by a ruler for his country) **fade at the same time** (as his death) Plu.

συν-εκμοχλεύω *vb.* **help to lever open** (doors) Ar.

συν-εκπέμπω *vb.* | also *tm.* συνεκ ... πέμπω (Call.) | **1 help to escort away** —*non-combatants* X.; (of the olive, ref. to its use in funerals) **help to escort to the grave** —*dead soldiers* Call.
2 help (W.ACC. persons in danger) **to escape** X. Plu.
3 (of a bodily canal) **help to discharge** —*drink* Pl.
4 send out together —*warriors* (*to battle*), *slaves* (*fr. a house*) Isoc. X.
5 despatch also —*a commander, soldiers* X. Plu.

συν-εκπεράω *contr.vb.* go forth together; (of hounds) **run close** —w. μετά + GEN. *w. the hare* X.

συν-εκπίνω *vb.* | neut.pl.impers.vbl.adj. συνεκποτέα (Ar.) | **1 drain** (W.ACC. a drinking-horn) **together** —w. μετά + GEN. *w. someone* X.
2 drink up (W.ACC. the dregs) **as well** (as the wine) Ar.

συν-εκπίπτω *vb.* **1 fall out together**; (of opinions, envisaged as votes being emptied fr. an urn) **come out in agreement** Hdt.; (of persons) **concur** Hdt.
2 (of a runner) **come out equal, tie** —W.DAT. *w. another* Hdt.
3 (of one of a pair of nascent qualities) **emerge together** —w. μετά + GEN. *w. the other* Pl.
4 (of flashes of lightning) **break out as well** (as thunder) Plu.
5 (of diseased flesh) **fall away together** (w. what holds it to the bones) Pl.
6 (of a soldier) **sally forth together** (sts. W.DAT. w. others) Plu.; (of troops) **sally forth in close pursuit** —W.DAT. *of an enemy in flight* Plu.
7 get out (of a place) **together** —W.DAT. *w. others* Plu.; **go into exile together** —W.DAT. *w. someone* Plu.; (fig., of arts) —*w. coinage* Plu.
8 (fig.) **be carried away, go overboard** (in enthusiasm) Plb. Plu.

συν-εκπλέω *contr.vb.* —also **συνεκπλώω** *Ion.vb.* **sail out together, share a voyage** (sts. W.DAT. or μετά + GEN. w. someone) Hdt. Th. Att.orats. Plu.

συν-εκπληρόω *contr.vb.* **1** fill out completely; **satisfy to the full** —*someone's desire* Plb.
2 fulfil —*a promise* Plb.
3 supplement, compensate for —*sthg. deficient* Plb.

συν-εκπνέω *contr.vb.* **breathe one's last together, expire together** —W.DAT. *w. someone* E.

συν-εκποιέομαι *pass.contr.vb.* be made complete; **be fully furnished** —W.DAT. *w. supplies* Plb.

συν-εκπονέω *contr.vb.* **1 work together, cooperate** —W.DAT. *w. someone* E.
2 (tr.) **join in performing** —*a service* E.; **help** (W.DAT. persons) **to achieve** —*their escape* E.; **help** (W.DAT. an old man) **to work** —*his limbs* (i.e. help him to walk) E.

συν-εκπορεύομαι *mid.vb.* (of troops) **march forth together, join in a campaign** Plb.

συν-εκπορίζω *vb.* **help to provide** —*sthg.* (W.DAT. *for someone*) X.

συνεκποτέα (neut.pl.impers.vbl.adj.): see συνεκπίνω

συν-εκπρήσσομαι *Ion.mid.vb.* [ἐκπάσσω] **help** (W.DAT. someone) **to avenge** —*a death, abduction* Hdt.

συν-εκπυρόομαι *pass.contr.vb.* (of bodily substances) **be fully inflamed together** (w. body heat) Pl.

συν-εκσῴζω *vb.* **1 help to rescue** —*someone* S. Men.
2 (of a person's spirit) **come to the aid of** —*his wearied body* Antipho

συν-εκτάττω *Att.vb.* [ἐκτάσσω] **help to draw up** (an army) **in line** X.

συν-εκτίθημι *vb.* || PASS. (of trinkets) **be put out together** —W.DAT. *w. an exposed baby* Men.

συν-εκτίκτω *vb.* (of oviparous animals) **bring forth together** (w. their offspring) —*sustenance for them* Arist.

συν-εκτίνω *vb.* **help** (sts. W.DAT. someone) **to pay** —*a fine, debt* Pl. D. Plu.

συν-εκτραχύνομαι *pass.vb.* (of a river) **become rough on converging** (w. another river) Plu.

συν-εκτρέφω *vb.* **1** || PASS. (of a person) **be brought up together** (sts. W.DAT. w. someone) E. And.
2 help to bring up or **nurture** —*a child* Plu.; (of a city) —*orphaned children* Pl.; (of a man) **share** (W.PREP.PHR. w. another) **in nurturing** —*the* (*abstract*) *product of their union* Pl.
3 (of persons) **help to feed** —*a fire* Plu.

συν-εκτρέχω vb. | Only pres. (the aor. is supplied by συνεκδραμεῖν). | (of benefits) fall to the lot of, **accrue to** —w.dat. *careful readers* Plb.

συν-εκφέρω (ξυν-) vb. **1** carry out (a corpse) together, **join in a funeral procession** Th. Lycurg.
2 (of soldiers) **join in carrying** (a wounded man) **out** (of the fighting) Plu.
3 ‖ pass. (fig., of a person) be carried away —w.dat. *by victory, ambition* Plu.
4 (of inventions) **bring out at the same time** —*loftiness of conception* (w.dat. *alongside technical skill*) Plu.

συν-εκχέομαι pass.contr.vb. (of troops) **pour** or **rush out together** Plb.; (of a commander) **rush forward together** —w.dat. *w. his troops* Plb.

συν-ελαύνω (ξυν-) vb. | ep.inf. ξυνελαυνέμεν | ep.aor. συνέλασσα, also tm. σὺν ... ἤλασα, ep. σὺν ... ἔλασα | **1 drive** (w.acc. animals) **together** —*into a pen or area of land* hHom. X.
2 round up —*cattle* Hes.fr. —(*as booty*) Il.
3 (of river currents) **push together** —*debris* Plu.
4 (of a person) **grind together** —*one's teeth* Od.(tm.)
5 bring together, **match** —*gods, men* (*usu.* w.dat. *in conflict*) Hom.; (of combatants) dash together, **clash** —*their spears and shields* (w.dat. *against each other*) AR.(tm.); (intr., of warriors) **clash** Il.
6 squeeze together, **compress** —*one's limbs* (w.prep.phr. *in a small space*) hHom. ‖ pass. (of an island's width) be compressed —w. εἰς + acc. *into a narrow isthmus* Plu.
7 drive or **force** —*a person, fleeing opponents, or sim.* (w.prep.phr. *to a place*) Plu. ‖ pass. (of a person) be driven or forced (by a storm) —w.prep.phr. *into a house* Plu.; (of troops) —*to a place* Plb.
8 ‖ pass. (of a person) be forced —w.prep.phr. *into war or battle* Plu.; be brought —w.prep.phr. *close to death* Plu.
9 ‖ pass. (of a person) be confined —w. εἰς + acc. *to a country* (i.e. be forced to stay within its limits) Plb.

συν-ελευθερόω (ξυν-) contr.vb. **help to free** —*persons, places* Hdt. Th. D. Plu.

συν-ελίσσομαι pass.vb. (of a driver thrown fr. a chariot) be wound round with, **be entangled in** —w.dat. *the reins* S.(tm.)

συν-έλκω (ξυν-) vb. | aor. συνείλκυσα ‖ neut.impers.vbl.adj. συνελκυστέον | **1 draw** or **pull together** —*skin* Pl.; (of the sun, envisaged as a lamp) **draw in, retract** —*its wick* Ar.
2 help to haul —*someone* (fr. a pit) Ar.; (fig., of a person envisaging a verbal tug-of-war) **join** (w. μετά + gen. *w. persons on one side*) **in bringing over** —*oneself* (*to their point of view*) Pl.
3 (of soldiers, sailors) **drag** (w.acc. corpses, ships) **all together** —w.prep.phr. *to a place* X. Plu.
4 (of an oriental ruler) **draw together** —*his enjoyments* (w.prep.phr. *fr. the ends of the earth*) X.

συν-εμβαίνω vb. **join** (sts. w.dat. someone) **in embarking** —w.prep.phr. *on the sea* (i.e. developing naval power), *on war, hostile relations* Plb.

συν-εμβάλλω (ξυν-) vb. **1 help** (w.dat. someone) **to put in place** —*door-bars* Ar.
2 throw (w.acc. snakes) **in** (to a receptacle) **as well** (as a person) Plu.
3 (intr., of troops) **join in an assault** or **incursion** X. D. Plb. Plu.

συν-εμβολή (ξυν-) ῆς f. act of bending jointly (to the oar); **dash** (w.gen. of oars) **in unison** A.

συνέμεν (dial.athem.aor.inf.): see συνίημι

συν-εμπίμπρημι vb. | aor.inf. συνεμπρῆσαι | **help to burn** —*ships* E.

συν-έμπορος (ξυν-) ου m. **1 fellow traveller, companion** Trag. Pl. Call. Plu.; (fig., ref. to grief) A.
2 (ref. to Dionysus) **partner** (w.gen. in a dance) Ar.

συν-ενδίδωμι vb. **give in, give way** (sts. w.dat. to sthg.) Plu.

συν-ενείκομαι pass.vb. [reltd. συμφέρω] (of a falling rock) be brought into contact with, **meet** —w.dat. *a crag* Hes.(dub.)

συν-ενθουσιάω contr.vb. **be filled with the same fervour** (sts. w.dat. as someone) Plb. Plu.

συν-εννέπω vb. speak in agreement, **agree** —w.dat. *w. someone* AR.(tm.)

συν-εξάγω vb. **1 lead out together, be in joint command of** —*an army* Hdt.
2 (of a person, envisaged as a midwife) **help to bring out** —*someone's opinion* (w. εἰς + acc. *into the light*) Pl.

συν-εξαιρέω (ξυν-) contr.vb. **1 help** (sts. w.dat. someone) **to remove** —*a wild beast* (w.prep.phr. *fr. a country*), *an enemy* (w.gen. *fr. a house*) Hdt. E. ‖ mid. (of various impediments) **combine to take away** (fr. a hare) —*the capacity for foresight* X.
2 ‖ mid. remove from harm, **rescue** (w.acc. the guilty) **together** —w.dat. *w. the innocent* Plb.
3 help (oft. w.dat. someone) **to capture** or **destroy** —*people, animals, places* E. Th. Att.orats. X. Plb. Plu.
4 help to put an end to, help to win —*a war* E.

συν-εξαίρω vb. **1** ‖ pass. be lifted up —w.prep.phr. *by one's companions* Plu.
2 help to raise —*someone's reputation* Plu.
3 (intr.) move away together, **leave together** —w. μετά + gen. *w. colonists* Plb.

συν-εξακολουθέω contr.vb. **1** be fully in attendance (on someone or sthg.); (of effects, consequences) **follow** —w.dat. *for someone* Plb. —*on sthg.* Plb.
2 (of results) **turn out in accordance** —w.dat. *w. plans, predictions* Plb.
3 (of behaviour) **be associated** —w.dat. *w. someone* Plb.

συν-εξακούω vb. (of people) **listen together to** —*someone's words* S.

συν-εξαλείφομαι pass.vb. (of a tyranny) **be wiped out at the same time** (as its functionaries) Plu.

συν-εξαμαρτάνω (ξυν-) vb. **1 be associated in wrongdoing** (usu. w.dat. or μετά + gen. w. someone) Att.orats. Arist. Plu.; **abet** —w.dat. *someone's crimes* Plb.
2 (of judgements) **be equally mistaken** Th.

συν-εξανίσταμαι mid.vb. | also athem.aor.act. συνεξανέστην | **1** (of a seated person) **rise together** (w. someone) Plu.
2 (of a commander) **stir into action at the same time** (as others) Plu.
3 (of people, a country) **be roused in support** Plb. Plu. —w.dat. *for someone* Plb. —*in response to circumstances* Plb.

συν-εξαπατάω contr.vb. **be party to a deception** D. ‖ pass. be deceived as well (as others) D. Plu.

συν-εξαποστέλλω vb. **send out** (w.acc. persons) **together** (sts. w.dat. w. someone) Plb.

συν-εξεγείρομαι pass.vb. (of a people) **be roused into action together** Plb.

συν-έξειμι (ξυν-) vb. [ἔξειμι²] **go out together** (fr. a camp, house, on a hunt) —w.dat. or μετά + gen. *w. someone* Th. X.

συν-εξελαύνω vb. **drive** (w.acc. a person) **out together** (w. someone) A.

συν-εξερευνάω *contr.vb.* ‖ MID. help (W.DAT. someone) to search after —*the truth of sthg.* Pl.
συν-εξέρχομαι (ξυν-) *mid.vb.* | aor.2 συνεξῆλθον | (of persons, troops) go or come out together (oft. W.DAT. w. someone or sthg.) Hdt. E. Th. X. D. + —W.ACC. *on an expedition* Th.
συν-εξετάζω *vb.* **1** examine together —*a question* Pl.
2 ‖ PASS. be reckoned together with, be an adherent of —W.DAT. or μετά + GEN. *someone* D. Plu.
3 ‖ PASS. be measured alongside, be a rival (of someone) Plu.
συν-εξευρίσκω (ξυν-) *vb.* help to find —*someone or sthg.* Ar. Isoc. —W.COMPL.CL. *how sthg. may be achieved* E.
συν-εξημερόομαι *pass.contr.vb.* (of a people) be tamed together —W.PREP.PHR. w. *the land (which is being tamed by agriculture)* Plu.
συν-εξίσταμαι *mid.vb.* | also pf.act. συνεξέστηκα | be moved to enthusiastic support, side keenly —W.DAT. w. *people, their aims* Plb.
συν-εξιχνεύω *vb.* help (W.DAT. someone) to keep track of —*events* Plu.
συν-εξομοιόομαι *pass.contr.vb.* **1** be made equal with (someone or sthg.); behave in the same way —W.DAT. *as someone* Plb.
2 be assimilated, become adapted —W.DAT. *to the environment* Plb.
συν-εξορμάω *contr.vb.* **1** (of gods) join in urging on —*warriors (to battle)* Isoc.; (of a person) help to spur on —*someone (to an undertaking)* Plu.; (of a commander) urge on —*troops, cavalry* Plu.
2 help to stir up —*dissension* Plu.
3 (intr., of charioteers) sally forth together (w. someone) X.; (of a person) go out together (w. someone, on a sortie or expedition) Plb.; (of troops) march out in support (sts. W.DAT. of someone) Plb.
4 (of a ship) put out to sea at the same time —W.DAT. *as oneself* Plb.
5 (of weeds) spring up among —W.DAT. *corn* X.
συν-εορταστής οῦ *m.* [ἑορτάζω] (ref. to a god) participant in a festival Pl.
συνεοχμός οῦ *m.* [reltd. συνέχω] juncture, joint (W.GEN. of head and neck) Il.
συν-επάγω (ξυν-) *vb.* **1** bring in —*stronger states* (w. ἐπί + ACC. *against weaker*) Th.
2 join in bringing in (a foreign commander or foreign troops), join in inviting outside help Th.
3 ‖ MID. take (W.ACC. someone) with one (on a campaign) Plu.
συν-επαγωνίζομαι *mid.vb.* (fig., of Fortune) conspire (W.DAT. w. events) in putting up a struggle Plb.
συν-επαείδω *vb.* [ἐπᾴδω] join in hymning —*a goddess* E.
συν-επαινέω (ξυν-) *contr.vb.* **1** consent, approve, assent (sts. jointly w. others) A. X. D. Plb. Plu.
2 approve of —*sthg.* Pl. X. —W.INF. *doing sthg.* Th. X.
3 join in praising —*someone or sthg.* Pl. Arist. ‖ PASS. be praised jointly (w. someone) Arist.
συν-έπαινος ον *adj.* disposed to give approval or consent, approving, consenting (sts. W.DAT. to sthg.) Hdt.; (of a dream, W.ACC. + INF. to someone doing sthg.) Hdt.
συν-επαίρω *vb.* **1** lift up (W.ACC. oneself) at the same time (as doing sthg. else) X.
2 (fig., of things) help to arouse or incite (someone) —W.INF. *to do sthg.* X. ‖ PASS. (of a mob) be stirred up —W.DAT. *by popular leaders* Plu.

συν-επαιτιάομαι (ξυν-) *mid.contr.vb.* **1** accuse (W.ACC. someone) as well (as another) —W.GEN. *of a crime* Th. Plu.
2 join (someone) in making an accusation Plu.
συν-επαιωρέομαι *pass.contr.vb.* (of an eagle, as a favourable omen) soar in support Plu.
συν-επακολουθέω *contr.vb.* (of persons or things) be in close attendance (on someone, the soul) Pl. Plu.
συν-επαμύνω (ξυν-) *vb.* (of assailants) join in with help (against someone) Th.
συν-επανίστημι (ξυν-) *vb.* | only athem.aor. συνεπανέστην | join in revolt (sts. W.DAT. w. someone) Hdt. Th.; join together in revolt Hdt.
συν-επανορθόω *contr.vb.* | aor. συνεπηνώρθωσα | **1** help to restore —*a city's fortunes, a fallen city* D. Plb.
2 help (the laws) to put things right D.
συνέπαξα (dial.aor.): see συμπήγνυμι
συνεπάπτομαι *Ion.mid.vb.*: see συνεφάπτομαι
συν-έπειμι (ξυν-) *vb.* [ἔπειμι²] join (w. μετά + GEN. w. others) in attacking —W.DAT. *someone* Th.
συν-επείσειμι *vb.* (of dancers) go together onto —*a stage* Plb.
συν-επεισπίπτω *vb.* burst in (w. εἰς + ACC. to a city) together —W.PREP.PHR. w. *troops in flight* Plu.
συν-επελαφρύνω *vb.* [ἐλαφρός] help to lighten (a burden); give help (W.DAT. to someone) in bearing —*a war* Hdt.
συν-επεμβαίνω *vb.* **1** (fig., of people) pounce together upon —W.DAT. *opportunities to harm others* Plb.
2 (of a person) trample upon, exult over —W.DAT. *people's misfortunes* Plb.
συν-επερείδω *vb.* **1** help (someone) to drive home —*a sword* Plu.; drive home —*one's spear* Plu.; (intr.) contribute to the force (of a spear-thrust) —W.DAT. w. *the impetus of one's horse* Plu.
2 (fig.) help to fix —*suspicion* (W.DAT. or ἐπί + ACC. *on someone*) Plu.
συν-επευθύνω *vb.* (of a god) help to direct —*events* Plu.
συν-επεύχομαι (ξυν-) *mid.vb.* **1** join in praying (w. others) Th. —W.ACC. + INF. *that sthg. may happen* Ar.
2 vow at the same time (as making another vow) —W.FUT.INF. *to do sthg.* X.
συν-επηχέω *contr.vb.* join in the chanting (of a paean) X.
συν-επιβαίνω *vb.* **1** mount (a ladder, wall) together (sts. W.DAT. w. someone) Plb. Plu.
2 (fig., in legal ctxt.) come on in support —W.DAT. *of someone's attack* Antipho
3 get on one's feet with help (fr. someone) Men.
συν-επιβάλλω *vb.* **1** (of a person) direct one's attention together, connect mentally (w. sthg.) Plb.
2 (of events) fall out together with, occur within —W.DAT. *periods of time* Plb.
συν-επιβλάπτομαι *pass.vb.* (of a constitution) share in further damage Arist.
συν-επιβοηθέω *contr.vb.* come to offer help against (someone) Plb.
συν-επιβουλεύω *vb.* join in a plot X. —W.DBL.DAT. w. *someone, against sthg.* Is.
συν-επιγίγνομαι *mid.vb.* (of troops) come up together (in reinforcement) Plb.
συν-επιγραφεύς έως *m.* fellow registrar (of property) Isoc.
συν-επιδείκνυμι *vb.* also indicate —*sthg.* Plb. ‖ PASS. (of things) also be indicated Plb.
συν-επιδίδωμι *vb.* devote (W.ACC. oneself) to helping Plb. —W.DAT. *someone* Plb. —w. εἰς + ACC. *to achieve some goal* Plb.

συν-επιθειάζω vb. also give credit to the gods —W.ACC. *for one's achievements* Plu.

συν-επιθῡμέω contr.vb. share (W.DAT. w. someone) in a desire —W.GEN. *for sthg.* X.

συνεπιθῡμητής οῦ m. fellow aspirant (after knowledge) Pl.

συν-επίκειμαι (ξυν-) mid.pass.vb. join in an attack (on someone) Ar.

συν-επικλάω contr.vb. help to break down; (fig., of physical sensations) help to weaken or frustrate —*serious thought* Plu.

συν-επικοσμέω contr.vb. (of honour, success) help to adorn or embellish (a man, his life) X. Arist.

συν-επικουρέω contr.vb. 1 (of persons) come to the rescue (of someone) X.
2 help to relieve —W.DAT. *someone's difficulties* X.

συν-επικουφίζω vb. 1 help to lighten —*a body* (w. corks, to make it float) Plu. ‖ PASS. (fig., of persons) become unburdened too Plu.
2 (fig., of success) help to lift up, help to puff up —*persons petty by nature* Plu.

συν-επικραδαίνω vb. (of hounds) make (W.ACC. their whole bodies) quiver together —w. σύν + DAT. w. *their tails* X.

συν-επικρίνω vb. help to adjudicate between —*persons (i.e. their views)* Pl.

συν-επικρύπτω vb. (of persons, weather) help to conceal —*someone or sthg.* Plu.

συν-επικῡρόω contr.vb. 1 confirm, ratify —*a decree, treaty, or sim.* Plb. Plu.
2 help (W.DAT. the people) to enact —*laws* Plu.

συν-επιλαμβάνω (ξυν-) vb. 1 take hold together; join in (an enterprise) —W.DAT. *alongside someone* Th. ‖ MID. (usu. in military ctxt.) join in, lend a hand, offer support (sts. W.DAT. to someone) Th. Thphr. Plb. Plu.
2 ‖ MID. take part in, help with —W.GEN. *a war, campaign, bringing down a state, or sim.* Hdt. Th. Plb. Plu.; (of nurture) lend help towards —W.GEN. *education* Pl.
3 ‖ MID. contribute towards (sthg.); (of a god) help (W.DAT. someone) to gain —W.GEN. *safety* Plb.; (of thunder) contribute to —W.GEN. *fear* (W.DAT. *for persons, i.e. help to alarm them*) Th.
4 ‖ MID. help to lay hold of (by persuasion), help to win over —W.GEN. *someone* Plu.

συν-επιμαρτυρέω contr.vb. (of ambassadors) join (W.DAT. w. others) in giving evidence Pl.

συν-επιμελέομαι (ξυν-) mid.contr.vb. —also (pres.) **συνεπιμέλομαι** (Th.) mid.vb. | aor.pass. (w.mid.sens.) συνεπεμελήθην | 1 help to look after, share responsibility for, have joint charge of —W.GEN. *activities, troops, or sim.* Th. X. D. Arist. Thphr.
2 help to arrange —W.COMPL.CL. *that sthg. shd. be done* Pl. X.
3 attend to or look after (W.GEN. someone or sthg.) at the same time (as sthg. else) X.

συνεπιμελητής οῦ m. one who shares responsibility (for supervising sthg.), fellow supervisor X.

συν-επινοέω contr.vb. help to devise —W.COMPL.CL. *how sthg. might be done* Plb.

συν-επιπλέω contr.vb. sail on board too (w. others) D.

συν-επιρρέπω vb. (fig., of persons) incline towards (sthg.) together; be indulgent to —W.DAT. *people's faults* Plu.

συν-επιρρώνῡμι vb. 1 lend one's strength to —*another's sword-thrust* Plu.; (intr., of cavalry) lend strength (to an attack) Plu.
2 (of a god) give strength to —*troops* Plu.

συν-επισημαίνομαι mid.vb. join in signifying disapproval Plb.

συν-επισκέπτομαι mid.vb. join in investigating or examining Pl. —W.ACC. or INDIR.Q. *sthg., what is the case* Pl.

συν-επισπάω contr.vb. 1 (of a horse) drag along (after it) —*a person (holding its reins)* Plu.
2 ‖ MID. (of persons or things) draw (W.ACC. someone or sthg.) along after oneself Pl. X.
3 ‖ MID. (of a commander) carry along with one —*troops* Plu.; (of fleeing troops) —*pursuers* Plu.
4 ‖ MID. draw along (in agreement), carry (W.ACC. someone) along with one Pl. Plb. Plu.
5 ‖ MID. draw along (into error or harm), drag (W.ACC. someone) down with one Pl. D.
6 ‖ MID. (of a defecting city) bring (W.ACC. other cities) over with one Plb.
7 ‖ MID. also drag in —*an issue (into a discussion)* Plb.

συνεπίσπεο (dial.aor.2 mid.imperatv.): see συνεφέπομαι

συν-επισπεύδω vb. help to get moving —*wagons (stuck in mud)* X.

συνεπισπόμενος (aor.2 mid.ptcpl.): see συνεφέπομαι

συν-επίσταμαι mid.vb. 1 share (w. others) in knowing, also be aware of —*sthg.* X.
2 (of everyone) know —*sthg.* Pl.

συν-επιστατέω contr.vb. (of the state) help to supervise (a course of study) Pl.

συν-επιστένω vb. join in lamenting —W.DAT. w. *someone (over his sufferings)* Plu.

συν-επιστρατεύω (ξυν-) vb. join in making war (usu. W.DAT. on someone) Th. Aeschin. D.

συν-επιστρέφω vb. 1 (of one of the Fates) help to turn round —*a spindle* Pl.
2 (of people) turn —*their faces* (W.PREP.PHR. *towards sthg.*) Plb.
3 cause (someone) to turn; (of a shout) help to gain the attention of —*people* Plu.
4 ‖ PASS. (of people) be directed together —W.PREP.PHR. *towards a single goal* Plu.
5 (intr., of military formations) turn about together Plb.
6 (of rims of a shield) curve together —W.PREP.PHR. *towards each other* Plu.
7 (of the breath in a diseased lung) distort —*veins* Pl.

συν-επισχῡ́ω vb. (of persons) lend strong support (to someone) X. Plb. —W.DAT. *to someone or sthg.* Plb.

συν-επιταχῡ́νω vb. join in spurring on —*someone (to achieve a goal)* Plu.

συν-επιτείνω vb. (of an event) help to intensify —*people's anger* Plb.

συν-επιτελέω contr.vb. 1 (of a person) join in performing —*a paean* X.
2 (of a goddess) help in the completion (of a work) Plu.

συν-επιτίθημι (ξυν-) vb. 1 place on (an altar) together (w. others), join in offering —*sacrifices* Is.
2 ‖ MID. lend a hand —W.DAT. *in an enterprise* Th.; reinforce, aid and abet —W.DAT. *someone's accusations* Plu.
3 ‖ MID. (of people, cities, in military ctxts.) join (sts. w. μετά + GEN. w. someone) in an attack (sts. W.DAT. on people, places) Th. X. Hyp. Arist. Plb. Plu.; (in non-military ctxts., ref. to criticising, abusing, intriguing) Pl. Is. NT.
4 ‖ MID. attack with help (fr. sthg.); use to one's advantage in an attack —W.DAT. *someone's mistakes, difficulties, or sim.* Plb.
5 ‖ MID. (of natural disasters) attack jointly —w. μετά + GEN. w. *a war* Th.; (of sickness) —W.DAT. w. *famine* Plu.

συν-επιτῑμάω *contr.vb.* join in censuring (someone) Plu.
συν-επιτρίβω *vb.* (of mistakes) completely ruin —everything X.
συν-επίτροπος ου *m.* co-trustee (of property) D.
συν-επιφέρω *vb.* join in giving —*a name* (*to someone*) Plu.
συν-επιφθέγγομαι *mid.vb.* (of a god) give voice at the same time (as a human) Plu.
συν-επιχειρέω *contr.vb.* make a concerted attack —W.DAT. *on enemies* (W.ADVS. *simultaneously, fr. all sides*) Plb.
συν-επιψεύδομαι *mid.vb.* (of material evidence) support (W.DAT. someone) in a lie Call.
συν-επιψηφίζω *vb.* vote in support Plb. —W.ACC. *of a resolution* Arist.
συν-έπομαι (**ξυν-**) *mid.vb.* **1** (of persons, troops, or sim.) follow along with, accompany (oft. W.DAT. someone or sthg.) Od.(tm.) Hdt. Trag. Th. Ar. + **2** (of an object, an art) go along with, be a natural accompaniment for —W.DAT. *sthg.* Pl.; (of circumstances, consequences) accompany —W.DAT. *someone or sthg.* S. Pl. **3** (of a person) follow compliantly, go along —w. μετά + GEN. *w. received opinions* Th. —W.DAT. *w. a law, events* Pl. Arist. **4** (of a listener) follow (sts. W.DAT. an argument) Pl.
συν-επόμνῡμι *vb.* **1** (of persons) join in swearing an oath Ar. **2** (of a person) swear at the same time (as swearing another oath) —W.INF. *that one has not done sthg.* X.
συν-ερανίζομαι *mid.vb.* collect contributions for oneself (fr. friends) Plu.
συν-εραστής οῦ *m.* fellow lover, one who shares (W.DAT. w. a city) a love (W.GEN. of virtuous men) X.
συν-εράω (**ξυν-**) *contr.vb.* **1** help (sts. W.DAT. someone) in a love affair E. Plu. **2** share (W.DAT. w. someone) a mutual love Theoc. **3** go a-loving together —W.DAT. *w. someone* Scol.
συν-εργάζομαι (**ξυν-**) *mid.vb.* **1** (of a person) work together, collaborate, cooperate (sts. W.DAT. w. someone) S. Plb. Plu.; (of an object) contribute —W.PREP.PHR. *towards an effect* X. **2** ‖ PF.PASS.PTCPL.ADJ. (of building-stones) made to fit together Th.
συν-εργάτης (**ξυν-**) ου *m.* fellow worker, assistant (W.DAT. to someone) S.; (W.GEN. in a hunt) E.; (fig., ref. to darkness) accomplice E.
—**συνεργάτις** ιδος *f.* accomplice (W.GEN. in murder) E.
συνεργέω (**ξυν-**) *contr.vb.* [συνεργός] **1** (of persons, gods) work together, collaborate, cooperate (oft. W.DAT. w. persons, their actions) E. X. Aeschin. D. Arist. +; (of feet) —W.DAT. *w. each other* X.; (of a man's spirit) —*w. himself* Arist. **2** (of circumstances) assist (usu. W.DAT. someone) Plb.(also mid.) Plu.; contribute —W.PREP.PHR. *towards sthg.* Plb.(also mid.) Plu.
συνέργημα ατος *n.* cooperative action, assistance, contribution Plb.
συνεργίᾱ ᾱς *f.* **1** working together, cooperation or assistance Plb. **2** collusion, conspiracy D. Din.
συν-εργός (**ξυν-**) όν *adj.* [ἔργον] **1** working together or helping with work; (of crafts, circumstances, or sim.) cooperative, contributory (sts. W.GEN. or PREP.PHR. towards sthg.) Pl. X. Arist. Plb. **2** ‖ MASC.FEM.SB. (ref. to a person or god, sts. w. sinister connot.) collaborator, assistant, accomplice (sts. w. W.DAT. someone) E. Th. And. Ar. +; (W.GEN. in crime, in sthg. undertaken or sought for) E. Pl. X. D. Plu. **3** ‖ MASC.FEM.SB. joint maker (W.GEN. of a wall) Pi.; joint creator (W.GEN. of excellence, ref. to the Erotes) E.; (of trust) D. **4** ‖ MASC.FEM.SB. (ref. to a hound) partner (of another) X.; (ref. to a nightingale, W.DAT. + GEN. for a person, in lamentation) E.
συνέργω *vb.*: see συνείργω
συν-έρδω (**ξυν-**) *vb.* | fut. συνέρξω | work together, cooperate (sts. W.DAT. w. someone) S.
συν-ερείδω *vb.* **1** press together —*one's hands* Theoc.(tm.); press closed —*a dead person's mouth* Od.(tm.) ‖ PASS. have (W.ACC. one's hands) pressed together (i.e. bound) —W.DAT. *by bonds* E. **2** (of Zeus) close up —*Dionysus* (*in his thigh*, W.DAT. w. *pins*) E. **3** (of a boxer) press (W.ACC. his fists) close —W.DAT. *to an opponent* Theoc. **4** (intr., of troops in a line) press close together —W.PREP.PHR. *against each other* Plb. **5** (of elephants, in battle) press close to, jostle —W.DAT. *opposing elephants* Plb. **6** (of troops) give a concerted push Plu. **7** (of ships) collide Plu.
συν-έρῑθος ου *f.* (ref. to Athena, a Muse) fellow worker, assistant (to someone engaged in a task or art) Od. Ar.; (ref. to Kypris, W.GEN. in a contest) AR.; (ref. to a girl) fellow worker or companion Call.*epigr.*
—**συνέριθος** ου *fem.adj.* | dial.superl. συνεριθοτάτᾱ | (of an art) assisting, helping Pl. ‖ SUPERL. (of the music of the aulos) being of most helpful service (W.DAT. to Bromios) Telest.
σύνερξις *f.*: see σύνειρξις
συνέρρηξα (aor.): see συρρήγνῡμι
συνερτικός ή όν *adj.* [συνείρω[1]] (of a person) good at stringing words together, cohesive Ar.
συν-έρχομαι (**ξυν-**) *mid.vb.* | impf. συνηρχόμην (NT Plu.) | aor.2 συνῆλθον | Fut. (and usu. impf.) are supplied by σύνειμι[2]. | **1** (of two persons) go along together Il.(tm.) **2** (of persons) come together, meet, assemble Eleg.adesp. Hdt. E. Th. Ar. +; (of an army) muster Hdt. Th. Isoc. **3** (of persons, official bodies) meet (for consultation, discussion, formal business) Hdt. Th. Ar. Att.orats. + **4** (of a person) come close (to another) E. **5** meet —W.DAT. or PREP.PHR. *w. someone* (for negotiation or discussion) D. **6** (of a person or persons) meet (secretly or for a subversive purpose), conspire Isoc. Aeschin. —W.DAT. *w. someone* S. **7** join in —W.DAT. *dances* E. **8** (of armies) meet in battle, engage Hdt.; (fig., of disputants) Pl. **9** (of a battle) be brought about —W.PREP.PHR. *by states* Th. **10** come together so as to combine; (of troops) join forces Hdt.; (of families, populations) unite Pl. X.; (of people) form a community Isoc. Arist.; (of cities) form a coalition D. **11** (of natural elements, objects) combine, form a unity Emp. Ar. Pl.; (of the gratitude or efforts of two persons) be combined S. E.; (of items, so as to make up a total) Hdt. **12** (fig., of people) rally together (after a setback) D. **13** come together in a marital or sexual union; (of a woman) come to share —W.ACC. *someone's bed* S.; (of a man) form a union —W.DAT. *w. a male lover, a wife* Pl. X.; (of man and wife) X. NT.

14 (of events or circumstances) come together, **coincide** Hdt.; (of fortune) **turn out** —W.ADV. *in a particular way* Plu.

συνερῶ (fut.): see συνείρω²

σύνες (athem.aor.imperatv.): see συνίημι

συν-εσθίω *vb.* | Only pres. (the aor. is supplied by συμφαγεῖν). | **eat together** Arist. —W.DAT. *w. someone* NT.

σύνεσις (**ξύν-**) εως (Ion. ιος) *f.* [συνίημι] **1** rushing together, **confluence** (of rivers) Od.
2 faculty of understanding, **understanding, intelligence** Pi. Dionys.Eleg. Hdt. E. Th. +
3 consciousness of guilt, **conscience** E. Men. Plb.
4 branch of knowledge, **subject** (ref. to music) Arist.

συνεστάθην (aor.pass.): see συνίστημι

συνεστέον (neut.impers.vbl.adj.): see σύνειμι¹

συνεστηκότως *pf.ptcpl.adv.*: see under συνίστημι

συνέστην (athem.aor.), **συνέστηκα** (pf.): see συνίσταμαι, under συνίστημι

συν-εστιάομαι *pass.contr.vb.* **1** (of the Council) **dine together** D.; (of persons) —W.DAT. *w. one another* Plu.
2 share in a feast (w. others) Is.

συν-έστιος (**ξύν-**) ον *adj.* [ἑστίᾱ] **1** (of a guest or resident in a house) **sharing a hearth** (sts. W.DAT. w. someone) S. E. Pl. AR.; (epith. of Zeus) **of the common hearth** A.
2 (of gods) **sharing an altar** A.(dub.)
3 (of a person) **sharing as a guest** (W.GEN. in a feast) E.

συνεστραμμένως *pf.pass.ptcpl.adv.*: see under συστρέφω

συνεστώ όος *Ion.f.* [σύνειμι¹] being together (regularly); **company**, **gathering** (of guests) Hdt.

συν-έταιρος ου *m.* **comrade, companion** Sapph. Hdt.

συνετός (**ξυν-**) ή όν, Aeol. **σύνετος** ᾱ ον *adj.* [συνίημι] **1** (of persons) with the capacity to understand, **intelligent, astute** Thgn. Pi. Hdt. E. Ar. +; (W.GEN. in sthg.) E.; (W.ACC. in sthg.) E. Th.; (of gods) S. E.(cj.); (of minds) Ar. || NEUT.SB. intelligence or astuteness E. Th. Plu.
2 (of speech or sim.) **intelligible, comprehensible** Sapph. Thgn. B. Hdt. E. +

—**συνετῶς** *adv.* **1** intelligently E. Ar. Plb.
2 intelligibly Plu.

συνέτρησα (aor.): see συντετραίνω

συνεύαδον (ep.aor.2): see συνανδάνω

συν-ευδαιμονέω *contr.vb.* **share in good fortune** X.

συν-ευδοκέω *contr.vb.* **give consent** or **approval** (sts. W.DAT. to someone or sthg.) Plb. NT.

συν-εύδω (**ξύν-**) *vb.* **1** **sleep together, share a bed** —W.DAT. *w. a wife or husband* Hdt. S. E.
2 (fig., of time) **share in** (someone's) **sleep** (i.e. be spent in sleep) A.

συν-ευημερέω *contr.vb.* **share in** (someone's) **success** Plu.

συν-ευνάζομαι (**ξύν-**) *mid.vb.* | 3pl.aor.pass. (w.mid.sens.) συνηυνάσθησαν, ep. συνεύνασθεν | (of a man) **share a bed, sleep together** (w. a woman) Pi. —W.DAT. *w. a woman* S.

συν-ευνάομαι *pass.contr.vb.* (of a man) **share a bed** (sts. W.DAT. w. a woman) Hdt.

συν-ευνέτης (**ξύν-**) ου *m.* **bedfellow** (ref. to a husband) E.

—**συνευνέτις** (**ξύν-**) ιδος *f.* | acc. ξυνευνέτιν | **bedfellow** (ref. to a wife) E.

σύν-ευνος (**ξύν-**) ου *m.f.* [εὐνή] **bedfellow** (ref. to a wife or concubine) Pi. Trag.; (ref. to a husband or male lover) A. Ar.

συν-ευπορέω *contr.vb.* **1** help by supplying, **contribute** —*money* D.; **make a financial contribution** Lycurg.
2 help out —W.DAT. *someone* (*in need*) Din. —(W.GEN. *w. a dowry, money, expenses*) Is. D.
3 help to arrange —W.COMPL.CL. *how sthg. may be done* Plu.

συν-ευρίσκω *vb.* **find together** (w. an exposed child) —*trinkets* Men.

συν-ευτυχέω *contr.vb.* **share in the good fortune** (of the present day) —W.ACC. *throughout one's life* E.

συν-ευφραίνομαι *pass.vb.* **share in festive spirit** —W.DAT. *w. someone* D.

συν-εύχομαι (**ξυν-**) *mid.vb.* **join** (sts. W.DAT. w. someone) **in a prayer** E. Pl. —W.ACC. *for sthg.* E. Ar. Pl. X. D. —W.ACC. + INF. *for sthg. to happen, for someone to do sthg.* Ar. Pl. Plu.

συν-ευωχέομαι *pass.contr.vb.* **feast together** Arist.

συν-εφάπτομαι, Ion. **συνεπάπτομαι** *mid.vb.* **1** grasp (W.GEN. a sword) **jointly** —W.DAT. *w. someone* Plu.
2 (fig., of dilatory allies) **join in** —W.GEN. *the rites* (W.DAT. *w. those offering peace libations, i.e. arrive in time to enjoy the fruits of victory*) Aeschin.
3 (of a poet) **lend a helping hand, join in** (w. praise) Pi.; (of persons, gods) **lend a hand** (usu. W.GEN. in an activity or undertaking) Plu.; **help** (W.DAT. a country) **to gain** —W.GEN. *freedom* Plu.
4 join in laying hands on, **help to attack** —W.GEN. *an army* Hdt.

συν-εφεδρεύω *vb.* **1** (of soldiers) **be in reserve to offer support** (sts. W.DAT. to someone) Plb.
2 (of a person) **keep close watch** —W.DAT. *over allied tribes, a situation* Plb.

συν-εφέλκω *vb.* **1** (of the soul departing fr. the body) **drag with one, have in tow** —*nothing of the body* Pl.; (mid., fig., of political agitations) —*the common people* Plu.; (of the common people) —*the whole state* Plu.
2 || PASS. be indulgent —W.DAT. *to people's faults* Plu.

συν-εφέπομαι *mid.vb.* | aor.2 ptcpl. συνεπισπόμενος, dial.imperatv. συνεπίσπεο | **1** (of troops) **join in pursuit** Hdt.
2 (of troops, persons) **follow along** (sts. W.DAT. after someone) X.; (of Memory) **keep company** —W.DAT. *w. the Muses* Scol.
3 (of disputants) **follow up** —W.DAT. *an argument* Pl.
4 (of freedom) **follow in consequence** Pl.

συν-έφηβος ου *m.* **fellow ephebe** Aeschin.

συν-εφιστάνω *vb.* apply oneself, **be fully attentive** (sts. W.DAT. to a topic) Plb.

συν-εφίστημι (**ξύν-**) *vb.* **1** (of a person) **apply, direct** —*oneself, someone* (i.e. one's own or his attention, W.PREP.PHR. *to sthg.*) Plb.; (intr.) **direct one's attention, pay attention** (usu. W.DAT. or PREP.PHR. to sthg.) Plb.
2 (of a person, events) make attentive, **catch the attention of** —*someone* Plb.
3 || PF. (of officers) share in the role of superintendent —W.GEN. *over each contingent* (*of a coalition*) Th.
4 || ATHEM.AOR. (of a crowd) **rise up together** or **join in an attack** —W.PREP.PHR. *against someone* NT.

συνέχεια ᾱς *f.* [συνεχής] **1 continuity** (of motion, substance) Arist.
2 continuity of effort, **persistence, perseverance** D. Plb.
3 continuance, persistence (of dangers, wars, or sim.) Plb.
4 close sequence (of buildings, troops in formation) Plb. Plu.
5 mere sequence (of words without grammatical structure) Pl.

συνεχής (**ξυν-**) ές *adj.* [συνέχω] **1 continuous in space**; (of Being, a surface, entities) **continuous** Parm. Pl. Arist. || NEUT.SB. continuity or continuum (of elements which form a unity, by having common boundaries and moving simultaneously) Arist.
2 (of buildings) in unbroken series, **continuous, contiguous** Hdt. Th.; (of people, places, things) **adjacent** (usu. W.DAT. to someone or sthg.) Hdt. E. Pl. Plb.

3 (of troops) **next in line** (sts. W.DAT. to other troops) Plb.
4 (of speech) continuous, **uninterrupted** Th.
5 (of a narrative, events) following on immediately, **successive** (sts. W.DAT. to sthg.) Plb.; (prep.phr.) κατὰ τὸ συνεχές **sequentially, as a natural sequel** Plb. ‖ NEUT.SB. continuity (of a series of letters) Plu.
6 continuous in time; (of efforts, activities) **continuous** Th. X. Men.; (of war) Th. Pl. D.; (of sicknesses) Pl. D.; (prep.phr.) κατὰ τὸ συνεχές **continuously, without break** Plb. ‖ NEUT.SB. continuing state, continuance (of sthg.) Th.; continual association (w. someone) Plu.
7 (of a person) **constant, persevering** X.

—**συνεχές** (**ξυν-**) neut.adv. | ep. σῦν- metri grat. | **1** in unbroken sequence (of space), **continuously** Theoc.
2 in unbroken sequence (of time), **continuously, continually** Hom. Pi. Ar. Call. AR.

—**συνεχῶς**, Ion. **συνεχέως** adv. | ep. σῦν- metri grat. | **1** in unbroken sequence (of space), **continuously** Plb.
2 in unbroken sequence (of time), **continuously, continually** Hes. Hdt. E. Th. +
3 (w. numerals) **in succession, without break** B. Antipho Th. Ar. +

συν-έχθω vb. **share in hating** (opp. loving) S.

συν-έχω (**ξυν-**) vb. | ep.du.pf.ptcpl. συνοκωχότε (v.l. συνοχωκότε) ‖ aor.2 mid. (w.pass.sens.) συνεσχόμην | **1** hold together (parts of the body); **hold** or **keep tightly together** —one's thighs, fingers Ar.; close up by holding together, **shut** —one's ears NT.
2 (intr., of tendons, belt-buckles) come together, **join, meet** Il. ‖ PF.PTCPL.ADJ. (of shoulders) hunched together (over the chest) Il.
3 keep together (groups of persons or things); **keep together** —people, troops, ships (in a place, under arms) Plb. Plu. —an army (instead of dispersing or disbanding it) X. D.
4 keep together (in a condition of stability or unity); (of a god) **hold together** —the universe X.; (of a person, institution, lawful behaviour, friendship, or sim.) —a state, household, persons or things E. Att.orats. Pl. Arist. Plu.; (of oarsmen) **keep together** —their rowing (i.e. keep time w. each other) Th.; (of a goddess) **keep united** —former enemies Ar.; (of persons) **maintain** —a partnership Arist. ‖ PASS. (of the human body) be held together —W.PREP.PHR. by certain physical conditions Pl.; (of a situation) —by goodwill D.; (of Being) cohere Parm. [or perh. be continuous]
5 hold together (several things at the same time); (of a single expression) **contain, comprise, embrace** —a plurality of things Pl. ‖ NEUT.PTCPL.SB. that which comprises (everything), the chief matter, the essential point or reason (sts. W.GEN. of or for sthg.) Plb.
6 keep enclosed or within boundaries; (of skin) **encompass, confine** —bones Pl.; (of Aetna) —Typhon Pi.; (of a representation of Okeanos) —a shield Hes.; (of a crowd) **surround, press upon** —a person NT.; (of authorities) **hold in custody** —a person NT. ‖ PASS. be trapped —W.PREP.PHR. in a well Pl.
7 occupy, engage —oneself (W.DAT. w. someone or sthg.) Plu.
8 ‖ PASS. be brought into close contact; (of combatants) get to grips, engage closely Hdt.; (of women, compared to dogs) couple (w. men) Thphr.
9 ‖ PASS. be entangled or embroiled —W.DAT. w. a violent-tempered father Hdt. —w. a trouble (ref. to a troublesome person, perh. w. sexual connot.) Ar.
10 ‖ PASS. be gripped or afflicted —W.DAT. by anxiety, dreams, disease, drought, war, or sim. A. Hdt. E. Th. Att.orats. Pl. +

συν-ηβάω contr.vb. **enjoy the fun of youth together** —W.DAT. w. someone Anacr. Scol.
συν-ηβολίη ης Ion.f. [ἀβολέω] **meeting, encounter** AR.
σύν-ηβος ου m. [ἥβη] **youthful companion** E.
συνηγορέω (**ξυν-**) contr.vb. [συνήγορος] (leg., sts. in non-legal ctxts.) **plead** or **speak in support, be an advocate** (usu. W.DAT. or PREP.PHR. of someone or sthg.) S. Ar. Att.orats. Pl. Arist. +
συνηγορίᾱ ᾱς f. process of speaking in support, **advocacy** Aeschin. D. Plu.
συνηγορικός ή όν adj. of or relating to an advocate ‖ NEUT.SB. advocate's fee Ar.
συν-ήγορος (**ξυν-**) ου m. [ἀγορεύω] **1** (leg., at Athens) **advocate, supporter** (ref. to a friend or relative who speaks for an accused person) Att.orats.
2 state advocate (appointed to prosecute crimes against the state) Ar. Hyp. Din. Plu.; (appointed to defend a law whose repeal has been proposed) D.; (chosen by lot to oversee the examination of a magistrate's accounts) Arist.
3 (at Rome) **advocate, counsel** Plu.
4 (gener.) **advocate, supporter** (of someone or sthg.) A. Isoc. Aeschin. Plu.

—**συνήγορος** ον adj. speaking in support; (of new oracles) **providing corroboration** (W.DAT. for old ones) S.
συνηδέατε (Ion.2pl.pf.), **συνήδη** (1sg.plpf.): see σύνοιδα
συν-ήδομαι (**ξυν-**) pass.vb. **1** share (sts. W.DAT. w. someone) a feeling of pleasure; **share** (someone's) **pleasure** E. Pl. X. D. + —W.DAT. or ἐπί + DAT. in sthg. S. X. Arist.
2 express one's delight (in someone's good fortune); **offer congratulations** (sts. W.DAT. to someone) Hdt. X. Thphr. Plu.
3 be pleased (at sthg. which has happened) Antipho D.; **take pleasure** —W.DAT. in a resolution, someone's actions Isoc. —in someone's misfortunes E. Isoc.
συν-ηδύνω vb. help to sweeten or season; (fig.) **contribute pleasure** (opp. pain) Arist.
συνήθεια ᾱς, Ion. **συνηθείη** ης f. [συνήθης] **1 intimacy, acquaintance, familiarity** (betw. people) Isoc. Aeschin. Arist. Men. Plb. Plu.; (betw. a lyre and its player) hHom.
2 group of associates, **club, guild** Plb.
3 habituation, acquaintance, familiarity (sts. W.GEN. w. sthg.) Att.orats. Pl. X. +
4 customary usage, ordinary meaning (of language) Pl.
5 customary practice, **custom** Plb. NT. Plu.
συν-ήθης (**ξυν-**) ες adj. [ἦθος] **1** (of Lawlessness and Madness) having common haunts, **neighbouring** (W.DAT. on each other) Hes.
2 (of nations) having common habits or characters, **alike, akin** (to each other) Th.
3 (of persons) **well acquainted, familiar** (sts. W.DAT. w. or to someone) Isoc. Pl. X. Arist. +; (of a voice, the mental image of a person) **familiar** S. E. ‖ MASC.SB. (sg.pl.) acquaintance or friend X. Men. Plu.
4 (of persons) **habituated, accustomed** (usu. W.DAT. to sthg.) Pl. Arist. Plb.; (W.INF. to doing sthg.) Pl. Plb.
5 (of behaviour, circumstances) **habitual, customary, familiar** (sts. W.DAT. for someone) S. Th. Att.orats. Pl. + ‖ NEUT.IMPERS. (w. ἐστί understd.) it is customary —W.DAT. + INF. for someone to do sthg. E. Arist.

—**συνήθως** adv. **customarily, habitually** Aeschin. Plu.; (w. ἔχειν) be on familiar terms —W.DAT. w. someone D.
συνῆκα (aor.): see συνίημι
συνήκοος ον adj. [συνακούω] **1** (of persons) **listening together** (W.GEN. to sthg.) Pl. Plu.
2 (of a person) **overhearing** (W.GEN. sthg.) Plu.

συν-ήκω (ξυν-) *vb.* [ἥκω] **1** (of delegates) **have come together, be assembled** Th.
2 (of separate building-works) **meet, join up** X.
συν-ήλικες (ξυν-) ων *m.f.pl.* [ἧλιξ] **1** persons of the same age (as oneself), **coevals, peers** A. Plu.(quot.com.)
2 (ref. to lambs) **equals in age** (W.DAT. to a boy) Call.
συνήλισα (aor.): see συναλίζω
συνημέρευσις εως *f.* [συνημερεύω] spending the day together, **daily association** (betw. people) Arist.
συνημερευτής οῦ *m.* daily associate, **constant companion** Arist.
συν-ημερεύω *vb.* **1 spend a day together** (w. someone) Pl.
2 spend one's days together, associate daily (sts. W.DAT. w. someone) Isoc. Pl. X. Arist.
συνημοσύνη ης *f.* [συνήμων] ‖ PL. pacts, agreements (betw. people) Il. AR.; pledges of support (fr. a goddess) AR.
συνήμων ον *adj.* [συνίημι] forming a pact ‖ MASC.PL.SB. **friends, allies** AR.
συνήορος Ion.*adj.*: see συνάορος
συν-ηπεροπεύω *vb.* **help** (perh. W.DAT. someone) **to beguile** or **cajole** (another) Ar.
συν-ηρετέω (ξυν-) *contr.vb.* [ἐρέτης] row together; (fig., of a person, wealth) **be a partner** —W.DAT. *to someone* S. E.*fr.*
συν-ηρεφής (ξυν-) ές *adj.* [ἐρέφω] **1** (of mountains) **thickly covered** (W.DAT. w. trees, snow) Hdt.; (of ground) **thickly shaded** Plu.; (of a wood) **dense** Plu.
2 (fig., of a person's face) **shadowed, clouded** E.
συνῆστε (2pl.plpf.): see σύνοιδα
συν-ηττάομαι Att.*pass.contr.vb.* [ἡσσάομαι] (of enemies) **be defeated together** X.
συν-ηχέω *contr.vb.* (of voices, trumpets, or sim.) **ring out together** Plb. Plu.
συνθᾱκέω *contr.vb.* [σύνθᾱκος] (fig., of a person) **sit in council** —W.DAT. *w. night (i.e. deliberate at night)* E.
σύν-θᾱκος ον *adj.* [θᾶκος] **1** (of Helen) **seated together** (W.DAT. w. the Dioscuri, in heaven) E.; (of Shame, W.DAT. + GEN. w. Zeus, on a throne) S.
2 (gener., of a goddess) **companion** (of a mortal devotee) E.
συν-θάλπω (ξυν-) *vb.* warm thoroughly; (fig.) **cheer up** or **soothe** —someone (W.DAT. *w. lies*) A.
συν-θαμβέω *contr.vb.* **follow in amazement** —W.DAT. *a rhapsodic narrative* Pl.
συν-θάπτω (ξυν-) *vb.* **1** join (w. others) in burying, **help to bury** —someone Trag. Pl.; (intr.) **attend a funeral** Is. Plu.
2 bury together; bury (W.ACC. someone or sthg.) **together** (sts. W.DAT. w. someone) E. Plu. ‖ PASS. (of a person, armour, or sim.) be buried together (usu. W.DAT. w. someone) Hdt. Th. Hyp. NT. Plu.; (fig., of freedom) Lycurg.
3 bury (W.ACC. someone) **in** —W.DAT. *funeral attire* E.
συν-θεάομαι *mid.contr.vb.* **1 view together, be a fellow spectator** (at a performance) Antipho Pl. X.
2 join in examining —*sthg.* Pl. X.
3 (gener.) **view, examine** —*sthg.* Plb.; **notice, see** —*someone or sthg.* Plb.
συν-θεατής οῦ *m.* **1 fellow spectator** (at a performance) Pl.
2 fellow examiner (of sthg.) Pl.
συνθέλω *vb.*: see συνεθέλω
συν-θερίζω *vb.* (fig.) **reap** (a benefit) Ar.
συνθεσίη ης Ion.*f.* [συντίθημι] **formal agreement, compact** (betw. people) Il. AR.
σύνθεσις εως *f.* **1** process of putting together, **combination, composition** (of stones in a building) Arist.; (of harmonies, abstr. entities) Pl.

2 structuring, organisation (of syllables or words, into sentences) A. Pl. Arist.; (derog., of words, by a deceptive speaker) Aeschin.; (gener.) **composition** (of speeches) Isoc.
3 organisation of parts (into a structure), **composition** Arist.; **structure** (W.GEN. of wicker screens) Plb.
4 social or political agreement (betw. persons), **compact** Pi. Plu.
συνθέτης ου *m.* **composer** (of a literary work) Pl.
συνθετικός ή όν *adj.* (of an art) **constructive, manufacturing** Pl.
σύνθετος ον (also η ον), or perh. **συνθετός** ή όν *adj.* **1 put together**; (of material things, a centaur) **compounded, composite** Pl. X. Arist.; (of syllables, words, harmonies) **compound** Pl. Arist.; (of the soul, abstr. entities, non-prime numbers) Pl. Arist.
2 (of stories) **made up, false** A.; (of an event) **contrived, pre-arranged** Hdt.
συν-θέω *contr.vb.* [θέω¹] | fut. συνθεύσομαι | **1** (of persons) **run with others** (in a race, or to help someone) Plu.
2 (fig., of a plan) **run in harmony** —W.DAT. *w. people (i.e. run their way, run smoothly for them)* Od.
3 (of the jointed components of a horse's bit) **run smoothly** X.
συν-θεωρέω (ξυν-) *contr.vb.* **1 be a member of a sacred delegation** (sts. W.DAT. w. someone) Lys. Ar.
2 be a fellow spectator (at a performance) Thphr.
3 (of friends) contemplate together, **study together** Arist.
4 get a comprehensive view —W.COMPL.CL. *of how sthg. is the case* D.
5 (gener.) **see** —*someone or sthg.* Plb. ‖ PASS. (of places, events) be viewed or examined together Plb.; (gener., of things) be studied or investigated Plb. ‖ IMPERS.PASS. it is seen or realised —W.COMPL.CL. *that sthg. is the case* Plb.
συν-θήγω *vb.* fully whet or sharpen ‖ PASS. (fig., of a person, ref. to his mind) be whetted to a fine edge —W.DAT. *w. anger* E.
συνθήκη (ξυν-) ης *f.* [συντίθημι] **1** (oft. collectv.pl.) article of agreement; **agreement, compact, treaty** (betw. states or sim.) Hdt. Th. Ar. Att.orats. +; **arrangement, contract** (betw. individuals) A. Att.orats. Pl. +
2 (gener.) agreement (among people), **convention** Pl. Arist.
σύνθημα (ξύν-) ατος *n.* **1** that which is agreed on or pre-arranged; (in military ctxt.) **signal** (ref. to a visual sign) Hdt. Th. Din. Plb.; (gener., for battle) Plu.
2 (specif.) **password, watchword** Hdt. E. Th. X. Plb.; **tablet with password** (Lat. *tessera*) Plb.
3 despatch in cipher, coded message Plb.
4 (ref. to writing) **sign, symbol** S.
5 symbol, token (W.GEN. of a person's destiny) S.
6 (in military or political ctxt.) **agreed plan, arrangement** Hdt. Th. X. Plb.; (gener.) **agreement, covenant** (betw. people) S. Isoc.
7 that which exists by convention, **conventional sign** (ref. to a word) Pl.; **convention** (ref. to behaviour) Pl.
συνθηματιαῖος ον *adj.* (of garlands) agreed on (betw. manufacturer and buyer), **contracted for** Ar.
συνθηματικός ή όν *adj.* (of writings) **in cipher, coded** Plb.
—**συνθηματικῶς** *adv.* **in cipher** Plb.
συνθηρᾱτής οῦ *m.* [συνθηράω] (fig.) **partner in a hunt** (for friends) X.
συν-θηράω (ξυν-) *contr.vb.* **1 go hunting together** (sts. W.DAT. w. someone) X.; **join in a search** (for an escaped bird) Plu.

συνθηρευτής

2 ‖ MID. hunt down, catch —*someone* S.(tm.) ‖ PASS. (fig., of a person's hands) become a prey (to a captor) S.

συνθηρευτής οῦ *m*. [συνθηρεύω] hunting companion X.

συν-θηρεύω *vb*. **1** go hunting together Pl. Plu.

2 ‖ MID. (fig., of imitation) help to hunt down —*an attribute that one does not naturally possess* Ar.

σύν-θηρος ον *adj*. [θήρᾱ] (of a person) hunting together (W.DAT. w. someone) X.; (fig., W.GEN. for friends) X.

συν-θιασώτης (ξυν-) ου *m*. member of the same religious association; (gener.) associate, brother (sts. W.GEN. in sthg.) Ar.

συν-θλάω contr.vb. smash, break —*a seal* Men.; pound to pieces —*someone's face and head* Plu. ‖ PASS. (of a person) be crushed NT.

συν-θλίβω *vb*. press together; (of a person) compress, crush (sthg.) Arist.; (of a crowd) press upon —*someone* NT. ‖ PASS. (ref. to the brains of lower animals) be crushed or damaged Pl.

συν-θνῄσκω (ξυν-) *vb*. (of a person) die together (sts. W.DAT. w. someone) Trag.; (fig., of piety) —W.DAT. w. *people* S.; (of poetry) —w. *its composer* Ar.

συν-θοινάτωρ ορος *m*. fellow diner E.

συν-θρᾱνόομαι pass.contr.vb. [θρᾶνος] ‖ 3sg.pf. συντεθράνωται ‖ (of a building) app., have the supporting timbers cave in, be shattered to pieces E.

συν-θραύω *vb*. break in pieces, shatter —*a skull* E. —*spears* Plu. ‖ PASS. (of a spear, siege-engine) be shattered X. Plb.

σύν-θρηνος ον *adj*. [θρῆνος] (of friends) sharing in one's grief Arist.

συν-θριαμβεύω *vb*. share in a military triumph Plu.

συν-θρύπτω *vb*. (fig.) break —*someone's heart* NT.

συν-θύω *vb*. [θῠ́ω¹] join in a sacrifice (sts. W.DAT. w. someone) E. Att.orats. X. Men. Plb. Plu.

συν-ιερεύς έως *m*. fellow priest Plu.

συν-ιεροποιέω contr.vb. join (W.DAT. w. someone) in the performance of religious rites Is.

συν-ιζάνω *vb*. (of flesh, clay) settle together, contract, shrink (through loss of moisture) Theoc. Plu.

συνίζησις εως *f*. [συνίζω] collapse (of buildings) Plu.

συν-ίζω *vb*. **1** (of an electoral assembly) sit together, hold a sitting Hdt.

2 (of a spleen) shrink Pl.

συν-ίημι (ξυν-) *vb*. [ἵημι] ‖ PRES.: ῐ usu. in Att. (also Hes. Archil.) ‖ inf. συνιέναι, ep. συνιέμεν (Hes.), also συνιεῖν (Thgn.) ‖ imperatv. ξυνίει (Od. Thgn.) ‖ IMPF.: ep.3pl. ξύνιεν ‖ AOR.1: συνῆκα, also ξυνῆκα, ep. ξυνέηκα ‖ ATHEM.AOR.: imperatv. σύνες ‖ ptcpl. συνείς ‖ dial.inf. συνέμεν (Pi.) ‖ AOR.MID.: ep.3sg. ξύνετο, 1pl.subj. συνώμεθα ‖

1 bring (persons) together; (of a god) set together, match —*combatants* Il.

2 ‖ MID. come together in agreement, come to terms Il.

3 put together mentally; hear, recognise —*a voice* Il. S.; hear —W.GEN. *someone (speaking)* Od.(also mid.)

4 be aware or take notice of Hom. —W.ACC. *someone's words* Od. Archil. Ar. —W.GEN. *someone, advice* Il. Thgn. —W.ACC. + COMPL.CL. *someone, how she behaves* S.

5 comprehend, understand Hes. Thgn. Hdt. Trag. + —W.ACC. *things, actions, words (esp. their implication or meaning)* Thgn. Pi. Hdt. Trag. + —W.GEN. *persons (i.e. their language or meaning)* Hdt. Th. Pl. —*speech* Pl. —W.INDIR.Q. *what is the case, how or that sthg. is the case* Heraclit. Hdt. Democr. Ar. + —W.ACC. + PTCPL. *that someone is doing sthg.* Hdt.

συν-ικετεύω *vb*. join (W.DAT. w. someone) in making a plea Plu.

συν-ικνέομαι mid.contr.vb. (of events) be pertinent or relevant (sts. W.DAT. to someone) Arist.

συν-ίππαρχος ου *m*. joint commander of cavalry Hdt.

συν-ιππεύς έως *m*. fellow cavalryman D.

σύνισαν (ep.3pl.impf.): see σύνειμι²

συνίσᾱσι (3pl.pf.), **σύνισθι** (pf.imperatv.): see σύνοιδα

συν-ισθμιάζω (ξυν-) *vb*. join in the celebration of the Isthmian games A.*satyr.fr.*

συν-ίστημι (ξυν-) *vb*. —also (pres. and impf.) **συνιστάνω** (Plb.) *vb*. —**συνιστάω** (Plb.) contr.vb. ‖ impf. συνίστην, also 3sg. συνίστανε, συνίστᾱ ‖ fut. συστήσω ‖ aor.1 συνέστησα ‖ also MID.: aor.1 συνεστησάμην ‖ PASS.: fut. συσταθήσομαι ‖ aor. συνεστάθην ‖ The act. and aor.1 mid. are tr. For the intr.mid. see συνίσταμαι below. The act. athem.aor., pf. and plpf. are also intr. ‖

1 set (persons or things) together (to form a unity); combine, unite (for a common purpose, such as war, conspiracy) —*people, cities, or sim.* Hdt. Th. Isoc. + ‖ AOR.PASS. (of a coalition or alliance) be put together D.

2 bring into harmony —*lyre-strings* (W.DAT. w. *each other*) Pl.

3 marshal —*troops* Plb.

4 combine or associate (one person or thing w. another); introduce (usu. W.DAT. to someone) —*a person (for friendship or business)* Att.orats. Pl. X. ‖ FUT. and AOR.PASS. be introduced —W.DAT. *to someone* Att.orats. X. Plb.

5 associate (W.DAT. w. oneself), appropriate, acquire —*a country, the art of prophecy* Hdt.

6 associate (sts. W.DAT. or μετά + GEN. w. people), assign (to them) —*a commander, guide, or sim.* Plb. ‖ AOR.PASS. (of a person) be assigned Plb.

7 (sts.mid.) put (things) together (constructively); construct, create —*material things, arts* Isoc. Pl.; compose —*a plot or literary work* Arist.; establish, set up —*an oligarchy* Th. —*a political club* D.(law) —*a constitution* Arist. ‖ AOR.PASS. (of things) be composed or compounded (of certain elements) Pl. X. Arist.

8 get together, muster —*military forces* Isoc. D. Plb.

9 (gener., sts.mid.) get together, organise —*a war, attack, financial contributions, or sim.* Att.orats. X. Arist. +; arrange —*someone's death* Hdt. —(perh.) *a sexual liaison* E.*fr.*; fix, settle —*the price of sthg.* D. ‖ AOR.PASS. (of a war) be set on foot Plb.

10 (of a speaker) establish, demonstrate —*sthg.* Plb. —W.COMPL.CL. *that sthg. is the case* Plb.

11 (of a wind) concentrate —*an animal's scent* X.

—συνίσταμαι mid.vb.| fut. συστήσομαι ‖ also ACT.: athem.aor. συνέστην ‖ pf. συνέστηκα ‖ 3sg.plpf. συνειστήκει, Ion. συνεστήκεε ‖

1 (of people, cities, a country) unite (for a common purpose) Th. X. D. Arist.; collude, conspire (for an underhand purpose) Th. Ar. Att.orats. X. +

2 (of a wife) unite (in marriage) —W.DAT. w. *a husband* S.

3 (of people, troops, animals) gather together Th. Isoc. X. ‖ PF.ACT. (of statues) stand together Hdt.; (of an army) stand assembled E.; (of cavalry) stand united X.; (of an assembly) be in session Plu. ‖ PF.ACT.PTCPL.ADJ. (of a military force) organised or regular, standing X. D.

4 (of combatants) meet in conflict, engage (usu. W.DAT. w. someone) A. E. Ar. ‖ PF. and PLPF.ACT. (of combatants) be engaged in conflict Hdt.; (of persons) be in conflict, be at odds (sts. W.DAT. w. someone) Hdt.; (of opinions, sts. W.DAT. w. *other opinions*) Hdt.

5 (of persons) **meet, struggle** —W.DAT. *w. hunger and weariness* Hdt. —*w. pain* S. ‖ PF. and PLPF.ACT. (of persons) **be engaged** or **involved** —W.DAT. *in hard work, fighting* Hdt. Th.; **be afflicted** —W.DAT. *w. hunger* Hdt.
6 (of war, fighting) **be joined, break out, begin** Hdt. Th. Isoc. + ‖ PF. and PLPF.ACT. **be under way** Il. Hdt. Pl. +
7 (of parts) **be put** or **come together** (to form a whole) Emp. Arist.; (of whole things) **be composed** or **formed** E.*fr.* Isoc. Pl. X. +; (of threats, dangers, or sim.) **take shape, arise** E. D. Plb.
8 (of Being) **be made compact** Parm.; (of moisture) **be condensed** X.; (of blood, liquids) **be clotted** or **coagulated** Arist. ‖ PF.ACT. (of a body) **be solid** or **firm** X.; (of snow) **be frozen solid** Plb.
9 ‖ PF.ACT.PTCPL.ADJ. **clotted, stodgy**; (fig., of a state of mind) **glum, gloomy** E.; (of a person) Men.; (of a face) Plu. —**συνεστηκότως** *pf.ptcpl.adv.* **in a grave** or **gloomy state of mind** —*ref. to listening to a type of music (which induces that state)* Arist.

συν-ίστωρ (ξυν-) ορος *m.f.* [ἵστωρ] **one who knows along with another**; (ref. to a god, dead person) **witness** S.; (W.COMPL.CL. to what is the case) S. E. Th.; (ref. to a person, W.GEN. of sthg.) Plb.; (ref. to a house, W.ACC. of crimes) A.

συν-ισχναίνω *vb.* | fut. συνισχνανῶ | (fig., of custom or habituation) **join** (W.DAT. *w. time*) **in reducing** —*sad feelings* E.

συν-ισχυρίζω *vb.* [ἰσχυρός] | fut. συνισχῡριῶ | (of soldiers) **help to give strength to** —*their commanders* X.

συν-ίσχω *vb.* ‖ PASS. **be gripped** or **afflicted** —W.DAT. *by diseases* Pl.

συν-ναίω (ξυν-) *vb.* **live together** —W.DAT. *w. someone* A. S. AR.; (fig.) —*w. good fortune, old age* S.

συν-νάσσω *vb.* | aor.ptcpl. συννάξᾱς | **pack close together** —*ten thousand men* Hdt.

συν-ναυβάτης (ξυν-) ου *m.* **shipmate** S.

συν-ναυμαχέω (ξυν-) *contr.vb.* **fight together at sea** (sts. W.DAT. *w. an ally*) Hdt. Th. Ar. D. Arist.

συν-ναυστολέω *contr.vb.* (of persons) **sail together** —W.DAT. *w. someone* S.

συν-ναύτης ου, dial. **συννᾱύτᾱς** ᾱ *m.* **shipmate** S. E.*Cyc.* Pl.

συν-νέμω *vb.* **1 divide, distribute** —*citizens* (w. εἰς + ACC. *into tribes*) Arist. ‖ PASS. **be distributed** (into tribes) Arist.
2 (fig., of Rome) **make a partner, incorporate** (W.DAT. *w. oneself*) —*conquered people* Plu.

σύννευσις εως *f.* [συννεύω] **convergence; union** (W.GEN. + PREP.PHR. of cities, w. each other) Plb.

συν-νεύω (ξυν-) *vb.* **1 nod in agreement, signify consent** S.
2 (of the sides of an object) **converge** —W.PREP.PHR. *towards a single point* Plu.; (fig., of two factions) —*on a person* (i.e. unite behind him) Plu.
3 (of separate events) **incline, tend** —W.PREP.PHR. *towards a single purpose* Plb.

συν-νέφελος (ξυν-) ον adj. [νεφέλη] (of the state of the sky) **cloudy, misty** Th.

συν-νεφής ές adj. [νέφος] **1** (of night, day) **cloudy** Plb. Plu.; (of the atmosphere) **misty** Plb.
2 (fig., of a person) **clouded with gloom, scowling darkly** E.

συν-νέφω (ξυν-) *vb.* **1** (of Zeus) **gather clouds together** Ar. ‖ IMPERS. **it is cloudy** Arist.
2 (fig., of a person) **be gloomy** (W.ACC. *in one's expression*), **scowl darkly** E.

συν-νέω (ξυν-) *contr.vb.* [νέω³] | Ion.3pl.pf.pass. συννενέαται | **pile together** —*weapons* Hdt.; **heap up** —*a pyre* Hdt. ‖ PF.PASS. (of objects, corpses) **lie heaped up** Hdt. Th.

συν-νικάω *contr.vb.* **share in a victory** (sts. W.DAT. or μετά + GEN. *w. someone*) E. And. X.

συν-νοέω *contr.vb.* **1 think about, reflect on** —*sthg.* S. Pl.; (mid.) E. Ar.
2 understand Pl. —*sthg.* Pl. —W.INDIR.Q. *what is the case* Pl. —W.COMPL.CL. *that sthg. is the case* Pl. Arist. —W.ACC. + PTCPL. Pl. Plu.

σύννοια (ξύν-) ᾱς, Ion. **συννοίη** ης *f.* [σύννους] **1 thinking, thought** Hdt. S. Pl.
2 (specif.) **anxious thought, anxiety** A. E.

συννομή ῆς *f.* [σύννομος] **1 shared management, partnership** Pl.
2 (ref. to a person and his property) **pairing, partnership** Pl.

συν-νομοθετέω *contr.vb.* **help in making rules** Pl.

σύν-νομος (ξύν-) ον adj. [νέμω, νομός; sts. perh. νόμος *melody*] **1** (of animals, flocks) **grazing** or **herding together** Pl. Theoc.; (of lions) **roaming together** S.; (fig., of children) **reared together** Pl. Plu. ‖ MASC.FEM.PL.SB. (ref. to birds) **creatures who flock together, fellows, mates** Ar.
2 (gener.) **consorting together** (w. someone or sthg.); (of cliffs) **bordering** (W.DAT. on the sea) E.; (of birds) **keeping pace** (W.DAT. *w. racing clouds*) E.; (of passions) **in partnership** (W.DAT. *w. ruinous madness*) A.; (of persons) **partnered** (by birth), **related** (W.DAT. *to someone*) Pi.
3 (of a bird) perh. **sharing in melodies** (W.GEN. *of songs*) Ar.
4 ‖ MASC.FEM.SB. (ref. to a person) **partner** (in plunder) A.; **partner, mate** (ref. to a wife or husband) S. Pl.; (W.GEN. of a husband's bed) A.; (ref. to a lioness) AR.; (ref. to a bird) perh., **singing partner** (W.DAT. *to another bird*) Ar.
5 (of things) **corresponding, matching** or **in common** Pl.; (of stones in a wall) **evenly fitted** Plb.

συν-νοσέω *contr.vb.* (of persons) **share in sickness** (fig.ref. to folly, vice, misfortune) —W.DAT. *w. persons, places* E. Plu.

σύν-νους ουν Att.adj. [νόος] **1 deep in thought, thoughtful** Isoc. Men. Plu.
2 taking thought, considering carefully Arist.

συν-νυκτερεύω *vb.* **keep** (someone) **company at night** Plu.

συν-νυμφοκόμος ου *m.* (ref. to a servant) **attendant to a bride** E.

συν-οδεύω *vb.* **travel together** (sts. W.DAT. *w. someone*) NT. Plu.

συνοδίᾱ ᾱς *f.* **1 shared travel** Plu.
2 (concr.) **party of travellers** NT.

συν-οδοιπόρος ου *m.* **travelling companion** X. Thphr.

σύν-οδος (ξύν-) ου *f.* [ὁδός] **1 coming together** (of people, esp. for deliberation), **meeting, assembly, congress** Alc. Hdt. E. Th. Ar. Att.orats. +
2 meeting (betw. individuals) Th. Isoc. D. Plu.
3 gathering (for social purposes) Pl. D. Arist. Men.
4 private meeting, association, cabal (for secret or conspiratorial purposes) Sol. Th. Ar. Att.orats. +
5 meeting (betw. opposing armies), **encounter, clash** Th. Ar. X. Plu.
6 coming together, meeting (of things, ref. to their juxtaposition, unification, or sim.) Pl. Arist.; (concr.) **confluence** (W.GEN. *of the sea, ref. to the Bosporos*) E.
7 condensation (of water) Pl.
8 (astron.) **conjunction** (of sun and moon, causing an eclipse) Plu.
9 coming in, receipt (W.GEN. *of revenue*) Hdt.

συν-οδύρομαι *mid.vb.* **join in lamentation** Pl.

σύν-οιδα (ξύν-) *pf.vb.* [οἶδα] | 1pl. σύνισμεν, Ion. συνοίδαμεν, 3pl. συνίσᾱσι, also συνοίδᾱσι (Lys. Plb.)

συνοικειόω 1338

| imperatv. σύνισθι, inf. συνειδέναι, ptcpl. συνειδώς ‖ PLPF.: 1sg. συνῄδη, 2pl. συνῇστε, Ion. συνῃδέατε ‖ FUT.: συνείσομαι, also συνειδήσω (Isoc.) |
1 be aware (of generally known facts, situations, esp. as being true); **share in knowledge, be a witness, be in the know** S. E. Th. Ar. Att.orats. + —W.ACC. or COMPL.CL. *about sthg., that sthg. is the case* Sol. Hdt. S. E. Th. Ar. + ‖ NEUT.PTCPL.SB. knowledge or awareness (of sthg.) D. Plu.
2 share knowledge (w. others); **be complicit** —W.DAT. *w. someone* (sts. + ACC. or COMPL.CL. *about sthg.*) E. Th. Att.orats. X. Men.
3 (gener.) be aware (of facts about other persons); **know** —W.ACC. + DAT. *sthg. (oft. discreditable) about someone* Hdt. Ar. Att.orats. Pl. X. —W.DAT. or ACC.PTCPL. *that someone is doing sthg., or is such and such, or that sthg. is the case* A. Hdt. S. Att.orats. +
4 have personal knowledge (of external facts, situations); **know, be conscious** (W.DAT.REFLEXV.PRON. in one's own mind) —W.ACC. or COMPL.CL. *of sthg., that sthg. is the case* Sapph. Att.orats. Pl. X. Arist.; (w. moral connot.) **have** (W.ACC. sthg.) **on one's conscience** Ar. Att.orats. Pl. X.
5 have personal knowledge (of facts about oneself); **be conscious** (W.DAT.REFLEXV.PRON. in one's own mind) —W.NOM. or DAT.PTCPL. *of doing sthg., of being such and such* Att.orats. Pl. X.; (W.NOM.PTCPL. only) E.

συν-οικειόω contr.vb. **1** ‖ PASS. (of relatives) be associated or connected Arist.; (of pleasure, virtue) —W.DAT. *w. sthg.* Arist.; (of people) be united in friendship Plb. Plu.
2 (fig.) associate (by way of likeness), **relate** —*a person or thing* (W.DAT. *to another*) Plb. Plu.

συν-οικέω (ξυν-) contr.vb. | Aeol.inf. συνοίκην | **1** (of a person) **live together** (oft. W.DAT. w. someone) A. S. Ar. Pl. +
2 (of a husband or wife) **make one's home together, cohabit** (usu. W.DAT. w. one's partner) Sapph. Hippon. Hdt. E. +; (of both partners) Hdt. Pl. Arist.
3 (of outsiders) **live together, settle** (in a place) Th. Arist. —W.DAT. *w. the local inhabitants* Hdt. Th. —W.ACC. *in a place* (W.DAT. *w. the locals*) Hdt. X. —*in a place* (w. *other settlers*) Arist. ‖ PASS. (of a region) be populated Pl. X. Plu.
4 (fig.) be associated (in one's life), **live together** —W.DAT. *w. a burden* S. —*w. fear, old age, the ways of horses* E. —*w. pleasures, ignorance, monarchy* Th.
5 (of miseries) **consort** (w. old age) S.; (of helplessness, poverty, physical attributes) **attend** —W.DAT. *on someone* E. Pl.; (fig. of a poisoned robe) make a home (in one's flesh), **cling close** S.

συνοίκημα ατος n. (ref. to the common people, for a tyrant) **thing to live with** Hdt.

συνοίκησις εως (Ion. ιος) f. **1** living together, **cohabitation** (of marital partners) Hdt. Pl.
2 group living together, **settlement, community** Pl.

συνοικητήρ ῆρος m. (fig., ref. to hunger) **housemate** Semon.

συνοικήτωρ (ξυν-) ορος m. (ref. to a tutelary deity) **sharer of a home** (in a city), **fellow resident** (W.DAT. w. another deity) A.

συνοικίᾱ (ξυν-) ᾱς f. **1** sharing of a home (in a city), **co-residency** (of a tutelary deity, W.GEN. w. another) A.
2 house of multiple occupation (esp. for renting), **tenement-house** or **boarding-house** Th. Ar. Att.orats. X. Men. Plu.
3 group living together, **settlement, community** A. Pl.; (ref. to a place) **settlement, hamlet** Plb. Plu.

συνοίκια (ξυν-) ων n.pl. **Settlement** (name of an Athenian festival commemorating the political unification of Attica by Theseus) Th. | see μετοίκιον 2

συν-οικίζω (ξυν-) vb. **1** cause (someone) to live together (w. someone); **settle together, unite in marriage** —*a woman* (W.DAT. *w. a man*) Hdt. E. Isoc. Pl. + —*slaves* (w. *free women*) Plb.; (fig., of a god) **wed** —*a type of behaviour* (W.DAT. *to a person*) Men.; **wed together** —*opposing elements in nature* Pl.
2 furnish with inhabitants or settlers, **settle, colonise, found** —*a city* E. Th. Aeschin. +
3 settle together (in political union), **unite** —*people, a place* (*into a single city-state*) Th. D.; (gener.) **settle** —*people* (*in a place*) Plb. Plu. ‖ PASS. (of people) form a political unity Th. D.; settle together (in cities) Isoc.; (of the inhabitants of individual cities) form a coalition (in war) X.; (of a city, ref. to Sparta) be concentrated (in a single place) Th.
4 join (sts. W.DAT. w. someone) **in colonising** or **founding** (a place) Th.

συνοίκισις (ξυν-) εως f. **political unification** (of a place) Th.

συνοικισμός οῦ m. **1 cohabitation** (of husband and wife) Plu.
2 foundation (of a city) Plb. Plu.

συνοικιστήρ ῆρος m. **joint founder** (of a city) Pi.

συν-οικοδομέω (ξυν-) contr.vb. **1** (of Theseus, fig.ref. to his unification of Attica) **build together** —*a single house* (out of many) Plu.
2 ‖ PASS. (of stones in a wall) be built up close together Th.

σύν-οικος (ξύν-) ον adj. [οἶκος] **1** living together in the same house; (of Justice) **living together** (W.GEN. w. the gods below) S. ‖ MASC.FEM.SB. (ref. to a person or god) **housemate** (oft. W.DAT. w. someone) A. S. Ar. Isoc.
2 (of the temple of Erekhtheus) providing a shared home, **shared** (W.DAT. w. Athena) E.
3 living together in the same city or country; (fig., of a war) in one's own country, **domestic** Plu. ‖ MASC.FEM.SB. (ref. to people, a god, Justice) **fellow inhabitant** (oft. W.DAT. w. someone) A. B. Hdt. E. Th. +; (W.GEN.) Lycurg.; (W.GEN. of a country) Th. ‖ MASC.SB. **joint settler** or **coloniser** Arist.
4 (fig., of a person or god) dwelling together, **associated, familiar** (W.DAT. w. harm, want, truth, or sim.) S. Pl. Din.; (of sufferings, pleasures, or sim., w. someone) S. Pl. X. Plu.; (of hunger, w. darkness) A.

συν-οίκουρος (ξυν-) ου m. [οἰκουρός] **fellow guardian of a house**; (pejor., ref. to a man) **household partner** (W.GEN. in evil) E.

συν-οικτίζω vb. **show compassion for** —*someone* X.

συν-οίμιος ον adj. [οἶμος] (of a hymn) **with the same strain, accompanied** (W.DAT. by a lyre) AR.

συν-οίομαι mid.vb. agree in thinking, **concur, assent** (sts. W.NEUT.ACC. to sthg.) Pl.

συνοίσομαι (fut.mid.): see συμφέρω

συνοκωχότε (ep.du.pf.ptcpl.): see συνέχω

συν-ολισθάνω vb. **1** slip together; (of an animal's brain) **contract** (into an egg-shape) Plu.
2 (of ground) **be shifting** or **slippery** Plu.

συν-όλλῡμι (ξυν-) vb. **lose** (W.ACC. one's beauty) **as well** (as sthg. else) Bion ‖ MID. **die together** —W.DAT. *w. someone* E.

συν-ολολύζω vb. (of women) **raise a cry at the same time** (as men) X.

σύν-ολος η ον (also ος ον Arist.) adj. [ὅλος] (of a craft, substance, or sim.) **taken as a whole, all together** Pl. Arist. ‖ NEUT.ADV. (w.art.) as a whole, in general, altogether Pl. D. Arist. Men.

—**συνόλως** adv. **in general, in sum** Isoc.

συν-ομαίμων (ξυν-) ον, gen. ονος adj. of the same blood ‖ MASC.SB. **brother** A. E. ‖ FEM.SB. **sister** Mosch.

συν-ομᾶλιξ ικος *dial.m.f.* [ὁμῆλιξ] person of the same age (as someone) || FEM.PL. (ref. to girls) coevals, peers Theoc. Bion

συν-ομαλύνω *vb.* **1** level completely —*ground* Plu.
2 raze (to the ground) —*a wall* Plu.

συν-ομαρτέω *contr.vb.* (of friends) keep company (w. someone) E.(tm.); (of gods) —W.DAT. w. *someone* Sol.

συν-ομηρεύω *vb.* be a fellow hostage Plb.

συν-ομῑλέω *contr.vb.* converse —W.DAT. w. *someone* NT.

συν-όμνῡμι (**ξυν-**) *vb.* —also (pres. and impf.) **συνομνύω** (D. Plb.) **1** (of persons) swear together —*an oath* Hdt. Aeschin. Plu. —W.ACC. + INF. *that sthg. is the case* X.
2 promise on oath, swear, pledge —*sthg.* A. Ar. —W.FUT.INF. *to do sthg.* A. Lycurg. Plb. Plu.(mid.); (of a single person) —*sthg.* S.
3 (of states) swear alliance, enter into confederacy (sts. W.DAT. w. others) Hdt. Th. Plu.(mid.); (fig., of fire and sea) A.; (of a woman) pledge oneself —w. πρός + ACC. *to a lover* Hyp.
4 (in sinister sense, of a person or persons) conspire (sts. W.DAT. w. someone) Ar. D. Arist.; (mid.) Men. Plu. || PASS. (of an action) be the product of conspiracy Ar.

συνομοιοπαθέω *contr.vb.*: see συνομοπαθέω

συν-ομολογέω (**ξυν-**) *contr.vb.* **1** (of persons) speak in agreement, tell the same story —W.DAT. *as others* Hdt.
2 (esp. of disputants) concur, agree (oft. W.DAT. w. someone) Pl. X. Arist. —W.ACC. or ACC. + INF. *about sthg., that sthg. is the case* Th. Pl.(sts.mid.) X. || PASS. (of things) be agreed Isoc. Pl. X. +
3 assent, agree —W.ACC. or FUT.INF. *to sthg., to do sthg.* X.

συνομολογίᾱ ᾱς *f.* agreement (among disputants) Pl.

συν-ομοπαθέω *contr.vb.* sympathise —W.DAT. w. *someone or sthg.* Arist.(v.l. συνομοιο-) Plu.

συν-ομορέω *contr.vb.* (of a house) be adjacent —W.DAT. *to a building* NT.

συν-οξύνομαι *pass.vb.* (of the head of a javelin) be sharpened to a fine point Plb.

συν-οπηδός, dial. **συνοπᾱδός**, όν *adj.* **1** (of a soul, god, person) following along with, accompanying (W.DAT. a god or person) Pl. AR.
2 || MASC.SB. companion or follower (W.GEN. of someone) Hes.*fr.* Telest.

σύν-οπλος (**ξύν-**) ον *adj.* [ὅπλα] (of spears) being joint weaponry, allied, united E.

συνοπτικός ή όν *adj.* [συνοράω] (of a person skilled in dialectic) capable of taking a comprehensive view Pl.

συνοπτός όν *adj.* (of persons, places, things) in full view, clearly visible (sts. W.DAT. to someone) Arist. Plb. Plu.

συν-οράω (**ξυν-**) *contr.vb.* | aor.2 συνεῖδον, inf. συνιδεῖν |
1 (of persons) see clearly, have in view —*each other* X. —*a place* Plb.; (gener., of a person) see, observe —*an event, a situation* Plb. Plu. || PASS. (of a person) be observed Plu.
2 see in the mind, take a comprehensive view (of a matter) D. Arist.; take in, comprehend —*many things, a whole picture, or sim.* Pl. D. Arist. Plb. || PASS. (of a beginning and an ending) be viewed at the same time Arist.
3 observe with understanding, understand, comprehend —*persons or things* Att.orats. Arist. Men.; (gener.) observe —*sthg.* X.(mid.) Arist. Plb. Plu. —W.INDIR.Q. or COMPL.CL. *what, whether or that sthg. is the case* Isoc. X. Arist. Plu. —W.ACC. + PTCPL. *that sthg. is the case* Plb. || PASS. (of a situation) be observed Plb.

συν-οργίζομαι *pass.vb.* share in anger or indignation (sts. W.DAT. w. someone) Isoc. D. Call. Plb.

συνορέω *contr.vb.* [σύνορος] (of a region, its ruler) share a boundary, be adjacent (sts. W.DAT. to a region) Plb. Plu.

σύν-ορθρος ον *adj.* [ὄρθρος] (of a future event) coinciding in the morning twilight, arriving together at dawn (W.DAT. w. the rays of the sun) A.

συν-ορίνω *vb.* **1** rouse or stir up —*someone's feelings* Il.(tm.) || PASS. (of hearts) be stirred or troubled AR.
2 || PASS. (of opposing ranks of soldiers) be stirred at the same time (into movement) Il.

σύν-ορκος ον *adj.* [ὅρκος] (of people) bound together by oath X.

συν-ορμέω *contr.vb.* (of ships, sailors) be moored together (sts. W.DAT. w. others) Plb.

συν-ορμίζω *vb.* moor together —*ships* X. Plb.

συν-όρνυμαι *mid.vb.* | aor.2 ptcpl. συνόρμενος | (of persons) start out together (for war) A.

σύν-ορος, dial. **ξύνουρος** (A.), ον *adj.* [ὅρος] **1** (of a region) sharing a boundary, bordering, neighbouring (W.GEN. or DAT. on a region) Plu.
2 (fig., of dust, as sister of mud) neighbouring A.; (of species of things) adjacent (sts. W.DAT. to each other) Arist.

συν-ορούω *vb.* (of two combatants) rush together (at one another) AR.

συνουσίᾱ (**ξυν-**) ᾱς, Ion. **συνουσίη** ης *f.* [σύνειμι¹] **1** being together; (oft.pl.) social intercourse, association, company (of people, w. each other) Hdt. Trag. Ar. Isoc. +
2 association, communion (W.GEN. w. someone or sthg.) S. E. Lys. Pl. X.
3 (oft.pl.) social gathering, party Hdt. Isoc. Pl. D. +
4 association for the purpose of talk or learning; association (w. Socrates, by his pupils) Pl. X.; conversation, discussion Isoc. Pl.
5 sexual relationship or sexual intercourse Pl. X. D.(oath) +

συνουσιάζω *vb.* have sexual intercourse Plu.

συνουσιαστής οῦ *m.* **1** adherent (W.GEN. of Socrates) X.
2 fellow member (of an association) Lys.(title)

συνουσιαστικός (**ξυν-**) ή όν *adj.* (of a person) of the sociable kind Ar.

συν-οφρυόομαι *pass.contr.vb.* [ὀφρῦς] | pf.ptcpl. συνωφρυωμένος | draw one's brows together
|| PF.PTCPL.ADJ. (of a person, face) with knitted brow, frowning S. E.

σύν-οφρυς υ, gen. υος *adj.* (of a girl) with meeting eyebrows Theoc.

συν-οχέομαι *pass.contr.vb.* travel together in the same carriage Plu.

συνοχή (**ξυν-**) ῆς *f.* [συνέχω] **1** holding together or joining || PL. narrowing (W.GEN. of a track) Il. [or perh. *meeting (of one track w. another)*]
2 narrow mouth (W.GEN. of a harbour) AR. || PL. narrows (W.GEN. of the sea) AR.
3 meeting, confluence (of rivers) AR.
4 fastening (W.GEN. of a tunic) AR.
5 engagement, grip (W.GEN. of war) AR.
6 affliction, distress (W.GEN. of nations) NT.

σύνοχος ον *adj.* joined together; (of sacred music, tears) in concert (W.DAT. w. worshippers, sufferings) E.

συνοχωκότε (ep.du.pf.ptcpl.): see συνέχω

σύν-οψις εως *f.* [ὄψις] **1** comprehensive view (offered by a location) Plb.; (prep.phr.) ἐν συνόψει in full view (sts. W.GEN. or DAT. *of someone*) Plb.
2 general survey (of things, w. the mind) Pl. Plb.

σύνστομος *adj.*: see σύστομος

σύνταγμα ατος *n.* [συντάσσω] **1** body of troops arranged in order, contingent, company X. Plb. Plu.
2 arrangement, organisation (of the mode of government) Isoc.; constitution (of a state) Plb.

συντακείς

3 overall arrangement (of a written work) Plb.
4 (mus.) arrangement of notes, **modal arrangement** or **scale** Arist.
5 written composition, **treatise, work** Plu.
6 that which has been pre-arranged, **arranged payment** or **contribution** Aeschin. | cf. σύνταξις 5
7 ‖ PL. things prescribed, precepts (of the Pythagoreans) Plu.

συντακείς (aor.2 pass.ptcpl.): see συντήκω

συν-ταλαιπωρέω (**ξυν-**) *contr.vb*. **share in distress** or **hardship** S. Ar.

συνταλαιπωρίᾱ ᾱς *f*. **distress** Plb.

συντάμνω *dial.vb*.: see συντέμνω

συν-τανύω *vb*. stretch together; (fig., of a poet) twist together, **combine** —*strands of many topics (for the sake of brevity)* Pi.

σύνταξις (**ξύν-**) εως *f*. [συντάσσω] **1** putting together in order (of people or things); **arrangement, organisation, system** Isoc. Pl. X. D. Arist.
2 (milit.) **formation, disposition** (of troops, ships) Th. X. Arist. Plb.
3 body of troops arranged in order, **contingent** X.
4 combined forces (of a nation) Plu.
5 (in financial ctxts.) **arranged payment, agreed contribution** Att.orats. Plu.
6 (gener.) arrangement (to do sthg.), **agreement, plan** Plb.
7 written composition, **treatise, work** Plb.

συν-ταράσσω (**ξυν-**), Att. **συνταράττω** *vb*. **1** create physical confusion or disorder; **throw into confusion, disturb, upset** —*horses, a feast, a fight* Il.(tm.) Theoc.(tm.) —*a water-source* Hdt.; (of sickness or sim.) —*persons, their mental functions* Hdt. Pl. ‖ PASS. be upset —W.PREP.PHR. *by sickness* Pl.
2 throw into confusion or disorder —*enemy troops or sim.* Plb. Plu. ‖ PASS. (of troops) be thrown into disorder Plb. Plu.
3 ‖ PASS. (of the sky) be mixed confusedly, be confounded —W.DAT. *w. the sea* A.; (of separate pools) be muddled together (by trampling soldiers) E.*fr*.
4 (in political and social ctxts.) **throw into confusion, disturb, upset** —*a city, established institutions* Hdt. And. D. Plu. ‖ PASS. (of customs, civic life, government) be thrown into confusion Th. X.; (of good order) be disturbed D.; (of a house, city) be thrown into turmoil E. Plu.
5 (gener.) **confound, overturn** —*plans or arguments* Ar. ‖ PASS. (of plans) be overturned Hdt.
6 (of a speaker) **muddle together** —*topics* D.; **muddle** —*his language or manner of speech* Plu.; (of poets) **confuse** —*people* Plu.
7 have a disturbing effect on the emotions; **disturb, alarm** —*a country, city, army* Hdt. Isoc. Plu. ‖ PASS. (of troops) be thrown into panic Th. Plu.; (of persons) become distraught or disturbed (w. grief, anxiety, or sim.) Hdt. Ar. Isoc. Plu.
8 stir up (to hostility) —*people, a city* E. Aeschin. Plb. ‖ PASS. (of persons) be stirred up Aeschin.; (of cities) —W.DAT. *in hostility* S.
9 stir up —*war* Plb. Plu.

σύντασις (**ξύν-**) εως *f*. [συντείνω] **tension, intensity** (of feelings or purpose) E. Pl.

συν-τάσσω (**ξυν-**), Att. **συντάττω** *vb*. **1** (sts.mid., of a commander) put together in order, **arrange in formation, marshal, draw up** —*troops* Hdt. Th. Isoc. X. Plb. Plu. ‖ MID. (intr.) **arrange one's troops in formation** Th. X. Plb. Plu.; (of troops) **get in formation, fall in line** Th. Ar. X. ‖ PASS. (of troops) be put in formation, be drawn up X. Plb. Plu.
‖ PF.PASS.PTCPL.ADJ. (of troops) in formation Th. X. Plb. Plu.; (of an advance) orderly Plb.; (gener., of citizens) mobilised, in the army X. D.
2 station together —*troops* (W.DAT. *w. others*) X. ‖ PASS. (of troops) be stationed together E. ‖ PF.PASS. (of charioteers, at the start of a race) be stationed in line Pl.
‖ PF.PASS.PTCPL.ADJ. (fig., of things) stationed together, in combination (W.DAT. w. other things) Isoc. Pl.
3 (in political and social ctxts., sts.mid.) **arrange, organise, regulate** —*activities, institutions, or sim.* Isoc. Pl. X. Lycurg. Plu. ‖ MID. **arrange** —*a course of action (for oneself)* Isoc. ‖ PASS. (of people, institutions) be organised or put in order D. Arist. Plb. Plu. ‖ PF.PASS.PTCPL.ADJ. (of a constitution) well organised Arist.
4 include, incorporate —*the poor* (w. εἰς + ACC. *in political activity*) Plu. ‖ PASS. (of people) be included or incorporated —w. εἰς + ACC. *among others* (i.e. become members of a confederacy) Plu.
5 (gener.) **arrange, prescribe, order** —W.ACC. + INF. *that someone shd. do sthg.* X. Aeschin. Plb.; **give an order** —W.DAT. (usu. + INF.) *to someone (to do sthg.)* Thphr. Plb. NT. Plu.
6 ‖ MID. **make an arrangement** or **agreement** (w. someone) Plb. —W.ACC. *on a course of action* D. —W.INF. *to do sthg.* D. Men. Plb. ‖ PASS. (of things) be pre-arranged or agreed upon Isoc. Pl. D. Arist. Plb.
7 (in financial ctxts.) **arrange** —W.COGN.ACC. *an agreed payment* Aeschin. ‖ MID. **make an arrangement** or **agreement** (sts. W.DAT. w. someone) —W.ACC. *for a payment* Aeschin. D. —W.INF. *to pay sthg.* D.
8 (sts.mid.) **put together, compose** —*a speech or written work* Pl. Aeschin. Plb. Plu.; **concoct** —*a false charge* Aeschin. ‖ MID. compose a work Plb. ‖ PASS. (of a speech) be composed Plu.

σύν-ταφος ον *adj*. [τάφος¹] (of a person) **sharing a grave** Pl.

συν-ταχύνω *vb*. **1 hasten on, be impatient for** —*an undertaking* Hdt.; (intr.) **hurry** (to do sthg.) Hdt.
2 (of destiny) **shorten** —*someone's life* Hdt.

συν-τείνω (**ξυν-**) *vb*. **1 draw tight, tighten** —*a noose* Plu.; (fig.) **bind fast** —*affectionate feelings* E.; (intr., of muscles) **tighten, contract** Pl.
2 apply pressure or stress; **intensify** or **increase** —*one's walking pace, the running of one's hounds* E. —*someone's emotions* Pl. —*one's tone of voice* Plu.; (fig., of the Fates) —*a hard upbringing* (i.e. make it even harder) E.; (intr., of trouble) Plu. ‖ PASS. (of character traits) be intensified Pl.
3 draw together or focus (one's efforts); **strain, exert** —*physical or mental efforts* (W.PREP.PHR. *to some end*) Pl. Arist. —*oneself* Pl. Plu.; **earnestly direct** —*cities (to war)* Pl. ‖ PASS. (of persons, their mental faculties) be or become intent Th. Pl. X. —W.INF. *on doing sthg.* Pl.
4 (intr.) **make an intense effort** Pl.; **hurry** Men. Plu.; **speed** (in a chariot) —W.ACC. *to a place* Pi.*fr*. [or perh. tr. *speedily drive (a chariot)*]
5 (intr., of thoughts, words, facts) **tend, point** or **converge** (usu. W.PREP.PHR. *in a certain direction*) E. Isoc. Pl. X. D. Arist. +

—**συντεταμένως** *pf.pass.ptcpl.adv*. **intently, urgently** Ar. Pl. X.

συν-τειχίζω (**ξυν-**) *vb*. **join** (sts. W.DAT. w. someone) **in building a wall** or **fortification** Th. X.

συν-τεκμαίρομαι (**ξυν-**) *mid.vb*. **make a calculation** (about distance or time) Th. X.

συν-τεκνοποιέω *contr.vb*. (of a woman) **have children together** —W.DAT. *w. a man* X.

συν-τεκνόω (**ξυν-**) *contr.vb.* (of Air) **join** (w. Earth) **in producing** —*living creatures* Ar.

συν-τεκταίνομαι *mid.vb.* **1** (of gods) **construct, assemble** —*sthg., everything* Pl.
2 help (sts. W.DAT. someone) **to devise** —*a plan, trick* Il.(tm.) AR.

συν-τελέθω *vb.* (of a piece of land) **belong** (to someone) Pi. | cf. συντελέω 7

συντέλεια (**ξυν-**) ᾱς *f.* [συντελέω] **1** shared payment, **contribution** (of money, by states) D.; (by individuals, towards a leitourgia) D.; (fig.) **cooperative effort** Pl.
2 group sharing a common function, **partnership, company** (ref. to a city's gods) A.; **league** (of states) Plb. Plu.
3 overall accomplishment, **completion, close** (of events or sim.) Plb. NT. Plu.

συν-τελέω (**ξυν-**) *contr.vb.* **1** (of gods) **help to bring fulfilment** (to the plans of humans) Pi.*fr.*
2 (of persons) bring to completion, **accomplish, finish** —*a plan, activity, or sim.* Plb.(sts.mid.) NT. Plu. ‖ PASS. (of buildings, ships, activities) be completed Hyp. Plb. NT. Plu.
3 perform —*a sacrifice* Plu.; **celebrate** —*a festival* Plu.
4 (of a sum of money) pay off completely, **cover** —*an expense* D.
5 (of persons, cities) **contribute** —*money* Aeschin. D. —*chariots* X.; (intr.) **contribute** (financially) D. Arist.; (gener., of things) **make a contribution** —W.PREP.PHR. *to sthg.* Arist.
6 make a contribution (according to rateable property); (gener.) **be assessed as belonging, be ranked** —w. εἰς + ACC.PERS. *in the listing of grown men, bastards* Isoc. D.
7 (of a city, its people) be tributary, **belong** —W.DAT. or εἰς + ACC. *to a city, league, or sim.* Th. Isoc. X. Plu.

συντελής ές *adj.* **1** sharing payment; (fig., of Troy) **jointly liable** (w. Paris, for the settlement of a due payment) A. ‖ MASC.SB. contributor (to a joint leitourgia) D.
2 (of a city) **tributary** (w. ὡς + ACC. to another city) D.

συν-τέμνω (**ξυν-**), dial. **συντάμνω** *vb.* **1** make short by cutting down; **cut down** —*a ship's prow* (W.PREP.PHR. *to a shorter length*) Th.
2 cut out —*uppers* (*of shoes*) X.
3 cut short (in size or distance); (of a boundary) **cut short, curtail** —*a realm* A.; (intr., of a fleet) **take a short-cut** Hdt.
4 cut short (in quantity or extent); **cut down, curtail** —*privileges* A. —*lyrics* Ar. —*pay, expenses* Th. X.; **shorten** —*someone's labours* E.
5 cut short (in speech); **curtail, abridge** —*one's words or sim.* E. Ar. Pl. Aeschin. D.; (intr.) cut things short, **be brief** E. Aeschin. D.
6 (of Kypris) **stop short** —*the plans of men and gods* S.*fr.*(mid.); (of avenging spirits) —*the criminally foolish* S.
7 (intr., of a period of time before an event) **be short** Hdt.
8 join in cutting; (intr., of a disputant) **help to make a distinction** (betw. categories) Pl.

συν-τερετίζω *vb.* **hum along** (in accompaniment to an aulos-girl) Thphr.

συν-τερμονέω *contr.vb.* [τέρμων] (of a people, a place) be coterminous with, **border on** —W.DAT. *another* Plb.

συντεταμένως *pf.pass.ptcpl.adv.*: see under συντείνω

συν-τετραίνω *vb.* | aor. συνέτρησα ‖ pf.pass. συντέτρημαι |
1 join (two things) by boring or drilling (a passage betw. them); **bore** (W.ACC. a passageway, mine) **through** —W.PREP.PHR. *into a place* Pl. D.; (fig., of two gulfs) **unite** (W.ACC. their heads) **by boring through** —*the intervening land* (i.e. *by penetrating inland*) Hdt. ‖ PASS. (of places underground) be connected by tunnels Pl.; (of a house) be provided with tunnels Plu.
2 (fig.) **drill, channel** (W.ACC. a story) **through** —W.DAT. + PREP.PHR. *to the mind, by way of the ears* A.

συν-τεχνάζω *vb.* **collude in a trick** (sts. W.DAT. w. someone) Plu.

συν-τεχνάομαι *mid.contr.vb.* **give technical help** Plu.

σύν-τεχνος ου *m.f.* [τέχνη] **fellow craftsperson** Ar. Pl.

συν-τήκω *vb.* | aor.2 pass.ptcpl. συντακείς, perh. also aor.1 ptcpl. συντηχθείς (E.) | **1 fuse** or **weld together** —*material objects* Pl. ‖ PASS. (fig., of a spouse, lover, friend) be fused together or joined as one —W.DAT. w. *another, another's feelings, or sim.* E. Pl.
2 ‖ PASS. (of flesh) be decomposed —W.PREP.PHR. *by fire* Pl.; (of tracks in snow) melt away X.
3 make (someone or sthg.) dissolve; (fig., of days and nights) **dissolve** or **waste away** —*a person* (W.DAT. *through tears*) E.; (of a person) **wear away** —*the whole time* (W.DAT. *in tears*) E. ‖ PF. (intr., of a person, body, looks) be wasted, be worn (sts. W.DAT. or PREP.PHR. through grief or anxiety) E. Plu. ‖ PASS. waste away —W.DAT. *through sickness, starvation* E.; melt away (through sorrow) E.

σύντηξις εως *f.* **liquefaction** (of flesh) Plu.

συν-τηρέω *contr.vb.* **1** watch over closely, **maintain, preserve** —*relationships, one's power, or sim.* Plb.
2 protect —*a person* NT.
3 keep to oneself —*an opinion, a message* Plb. NT.
4 ‖ PASS. (of two items) be preserved together NT.

συν-τίθημι (**ξυν-**) *vb.* **1 place together** —*material objects* Hdt. X. —*ships* (to form a bridge) Hdt. —*timbers, stones, bricks* (for the purpose of construction) Hdt. Th. X. —*syllables* (in constructing words) Pl.; (of a seated hare) —*its front legs* X. ‖ PASS. (of things) be placed together Pl. Arist.
2 seal —*one's lips* E.Cyc.
3 add together —*sums of money* D.; **make up** —*a sum total* D. ‖ PASS. (of numbers, quantities) be added together Hdt.; (of a sum total) be made up Hdt.; (of a sum of money) be added —w. πρός + ACC. *to another* D.
4 gather together —*all that was dear to one* (W.PREP.PHR. *in a small compass, ref. to a funeral urn*) E.
5 join (things) together; **combine** —*items, words, propositions, or sim.* Pl. X. Arist. + —*a notion* (W.DAT. w. *another*) Pl. ‖ PASS. (of things) be combined Pl. Arist.
6 join (things) together (mentally or in speech); **join together** —*all considerations* (W.PREP.PHR. *into one*) E.; **take together** —*the whole race of gods, the whole female sex* E.; (intr.) put (everything) together, **summarise** S. ‖ PASS. (of a speech) be taken as a whole E.
7 treat as a unity, **combine** —*the pursuit of two aims* E.
8 create by joining together; **compose, compound** —*things, words* (sts. W.PREP.PHR. *fr. constituent parts*) Pl. X. Arist. ‖ PASS. (of things) be composed or compounded Pl. Arist.
9 create (one thing, out of another); **make** —*cakes* (W.PREP.PHR. *fr. a juice*) Hdt. —*a phantom* (fr. *the upper air*) E.
10 (gener.) **construct** —*a wall* Th.; **create** —*the human race* Pl. —*laughter* S.
11 ‖ MID. app., put together for oneself, **accumulate, acquire** —*power* X.
12 compose —*a speech, letter, literary or dramatic work* Isoc. Pl. Arist. Call. Plu. ‖ PASS. (of dramas) be composed Arist.
13 compose an account of, **narrate** —*events* A. Th.
14 (pejor.) **make up, concoct** —*stories, charges, or sim.* E. Ar. Att.orats. Pl. + ‖ PASS. (of a report) be concocted Plu.

συντῑμάω

15 (freq.pejor.) **contrive, plan** —*an activity* S. E. Antipho Th. Ar. D. ‖ PASS. (of an undertaking) **be coordinated** D.
16 app. **arrange neatly** or **fold** (opp. shake out) —*clothes and bedding* X.
17 ‖ MID. **put in order, settle** —*one's own and one's city's interests* X.
18 ‖ MID. put together in one's mind, **take in, understand** —*sthg. which one has heard* Il.; **take to heart, heed** —*someone's words* Od. Pi. Call.*epigr*.; (wkr.sens.) **hear** —*singing, a voice, bird-cry* Od. Alcm.; (intr.) **pay heed, take note** Hom. ‖ ACT. **conclude, infer** —W.ACC. + INF. *that sthg. is the case* Plb.
19 ‖ MID. **agree on, arrange** —*an alliance, friendship, or sim.* (oft. W.DAT. w. someone) Thgn. Hdt. Th. And. X. + —*peace* Att.orats. Plb. Plu. —*an action, place, fee, or sim.* Hdt. Th. Pl. X. + —W.NEUT.PRON. *sthg.* Hdt. E. Th. Ar. + —W.PRES. or FUT.INF. *to do sthg.* Pi. Hdt. Th. Att.orats. + —W.ACC. + INF. *that sthg. shd. happen* And. X. —W.COMPL.CL. *that or how sthg. shd. be done* Hdt. X.; (intr.) **make a contract, agreement** or **arrangement** Pi. Hdt. Th. Pl. + ‖ PASS. (of a time) **be agreed upon** Pl.
20 make over, commit, entrust (usu. W.DAT. to someone) —*money, letters, or sim.* Plb.

συν-τῑμάω contr.vb. ‖ MID. (of persons) **agree jointly to an assessment** —W.ACC. *for a certain level of tax* D. ‖ PASS. (of the price of corn) **be set by joint assessment** D.

συν-τιτρώσκω vb. **1** (of persons) **inflict wounds on** —*persons, parts of the body* X. Plu. ‖ PASS. (of persons) **be wounded** Plu.
2 (of a naval commander) **cripple, disable** —*ships* Plu.

συν-τλῆναι athem.aor.inf. ǀ dial.2sg.athem.aor. συνέτλᾱς ǀ **endure together** —*sufferings* (W.DAT. w. someone) E.

συντομίᾱ ᾱς f. [σύντομος] **1 shortness** (W.GEN. of a route) Plu.
2 conciseness (of language) Pl. Lycurg. Arist.

σύντομος (ξύν-) ον adj. [συντέμνω] **1** cut short; (of a route, path, or sim.) **short, direct** Hdt. Ar. X. Plb. Plu. ‖ FEM.SB. (w. ὁδός understd.) **short-cut** or **direct route** Hdt. X. Plu. ‖ SUPERL.FEM.SB. **shortest route** X. ‖ NEUT.PL.SB. **direct route** X.; (w. τῆς ὁδοῦ) Hdt.; (superl.) **shortest route** Th.
2 (of speech, language) **concise, brief** Trag. Isoc. Arist. Plu.; (of a speaker, writer) Aeschin. Call.*epigr*.
3 (of activities or results) **quickly performed** or **achieved, quick, rapid** E. Th. Plb.

—**συντόμως** adv. ǀ compar. συντομώτερον, also συντομωτέρως (Is.) ǀ superl. συντομώτατα, also συντομωτάτως (S.) ǀ **1 concisely, briefly** A. S. Att.orats. Pl. + **2 rapidly, with despatch** S. X. Plb. Plu.

συντονίᾱ ᾱς f. [σύντονος] **1 strain** (suffered by bodily organs) Pl.
2 tension (in the mind) Arist.
3 intensity (of effort) Arist.; **strenuous activity** (of a person) Plu.

συντονο-λῡδιστί adv. (quasi-adjl., of a musical mode) **in tense Lydian manner** (assoc.w. lamentation) Pl.

σύντονος ον adj. [συντείνω] **1 strained tight**; (of the material of sinews) **taut, firm** Pl. ‖ NEUT.SB. **tautness** or **tension** (of a stake supporting a hunting net) X.
2 (of the use of a hand, Bacchic dancing) **vigorous** S. E.; (of activities, processes) **strenuous, rigorous** Men. Plb. Plu.; (of a march) **forced** Plb.
3 (of feelings) **intense, ardent** Pl.
4 (of poverty, physical afflictions) **extreme** Plu.
5 (of Eros, a person) **intense, energetic** Pl. Arist.
6 (of Muses, ref. to proponents of Heraclitean doctrines) **earnest, severe** Pl.; (of a person) **strict, rigid** Plu.; (of a form of government, assoc.w. a tense musical mode) Arist.
7 (of music, a musical mode, involving a greater number of high notes) **tense** (i.e. straining the voice and stimulating the emotions, opp. ἀνειμένος *relaxed*) Pratin. Arist.
8 (of lamentation) **high-pitched** Tim.
9 (fig.) sharing the same pitch; (of a verbal message) **consonant, in tune** (W.DAT. w. a written message) E.

—**σύντονα** neut.pl.adv. **with muscles tensed** —*ref. to carrying someone* E.

—**συντόνως** adv. ǀ compar. συντονώτερον ǀ **1 using intense effort, strenuously, vigorously** Pl. Arist. Plu.
2 intently —*ref. to looking* Pl.
3 rapidly Plb. Plu.

συν-τραγῳδέω contr.vb. **collude in solemnly acting out** —*a pretence, a supplication* Plu.

συν-τράπεζος (ξυν-) ον adj. **sharing a table**; (of domestic life) **with shared meals** E. ‖ MASC.SB. **table companion, messmate** X.

σύν-τρεις τρια pl.num.adj. (of sheep) **three together** Od.; (of geometric angles) Pl.

συν-τρέφω vb. **1** (of water) **help to nourish** —*people* X.; (of farming) **help to feed** —*a horse* X.
2 ‖ PASS. (of a person) **be brought up** or **grow up together** (sts. W.DAT. w. someone) Isoc. X. Men. Plb. Plu.; (of animals) **be fed** or **reared together** E. X.; (of a person) **live and eat together, grow familiar** (sts. W.DAT. w. someone) E. X. Plu.
3 ‖ PASS. (of living beings) app., **be nourished through a combination** (of elements) Pl.
4 ‖ PASS. (of natural qualities, feelings) **grow up together, be inbred** (sts. W.DAT. in someone) Pl. Arist. Plu.; (of a character trait) **become familiar** (to one's associates) Plu.; (of a person) **become habituated** —W.DAT. *to sthg.* Plb. Plu.

συν-τρέχω (ξυν-) vb. ǀ Only pres. and impf. (other tenses are supplied by συνδραμεῖν). ǀ **1 run together in partnership**; (of hounds) **run together** X.; (of persons) **run alongside** (someone) X.
2 come together in one place; (of people, a crowd) **come together, gather** (sts. W.PREP.PHR. at a place) Hdt. Isoc. Arist. Plb. Plu.; **flock** —w. πρός + ACC. *to a person* Plu.; **rush up** (in a group or to a place) Plb. Plu.
3 (of water) **mingle, blend** —W.DAT. *w. a stream of honey* S.
4 (of a person) **meet** —W.DAT. *w. death* S.
5 (of people) **concur** —W.DAT. *in sthg.* X.
6 (of behaviour, time) **correspond, tally** (w. expectation or sim.) S. E.; (of an event) —W.DAT. *w. a specified time* E.; (of two circumstances) **coincide** Plu.
7 (of events) **turn out** —W.PREP.PHR. *according to plan* Plb.
8 (of hairs, under heat) contract, **shrivel up** X.

συν-τριαινόω contr.vb. **lever up** —*foundations, roots* E.

συν-τρίβω (ξυν-) vb. **1 smash to pieces, shatter** —*pottery, equipment, weapons, or sim.* Hippon. Ar. Pl. X. Aeschin. D. + —*persons* (w. a boulder) E.*Cyc*.; (specif.) **break open** —*a jar of perfume* NT. ‖ PASS. (of objects) **be smashed** or **shattered** D. Arist. Men. Plb. NT. Plu.; (fig., of an established practice) **be broken down** D.
2 (specif.) **smash** —*someone's forehead, nose, mouth* Lys. Men. Plu.; **break** —*someone's leg* Plb.; **crack** —*someone's head* Plu. —*someone* (W.PARTITV.GEN. *on the head*) Isoc.; (gener.) **beat to death** —*a person* Plu. ‖ PASS. (of parts of the body) **be smashed** or **crushed** Pl.; (of a bone, vertebrae) **be broken** NT. Plu.; (of a person) **suffer a fracture** —W.ACC. *of the collar-bone* And. —*of the legs and ribs* X.; **receive a crack**

συνῳδός

—W.ACC. or PARTITV.GEN. *on the head* Lys. Ar.; (fig., of a person) **be maimed or deformed** —W.ACC. *in character* Plb.
3 wreck —*ships* Th. Plb.; (fig., of a poet envisaged as a charioteer) **crash** —*an idea* Ar. ‖ PASS. (of chariots, ships) **be wrecked or crashed** X. Plu.
4 crush (by military force) —*enemies* Plb. Plu. ‖ PASS. (of a city, commander, troops, or sim.) **be crushed** Plu.
5 crush (in spirit), **demoralise** —*someone* Plb. ‖ PASS. (of persons) **be demoralised** Plb.
6 (of circumstances) **wear out, grind down** —*an estate, a person* X. Men.; (of an evil spirit) —*a person* NT.; (of a person, fallen on ill luck) **shatter** —*many blessings* Men.; (of sufferings) —*mental powers* Plu.

συντριηραρχέω contr.vb. [συντριήραρχος] **be a fellow trierarch** (sts. W.DAT. w. someone) Lys. Isoc.

συν-τριήραρχος ου *m*. **fellow trierarch** D.

συντροφίᾱ ᾱς *f*. [σύντροφος] **1 feeding together; common nurture** (of infants, at the same breast) Plu.
2 living together; familiarity, association (betw. people) Plb.; **habituation** (W.DAT. to sthg.) Plb.

σύντροφος (**ξύν-**) ον *adj*. [συντρέφω] **1** (of a person) **sharing** (W.DAT. w. someone) **in the rearing** (W.GEN. of a herd) Pl.; (of earth, sun, winds) **jointly** (W.DAT. w. water) **providing nourishment** (W.GEN. for plants) Pl.
2 (of a person, a people) **brought up together** (oft. W.DAT. w. someone) Hdt. S. Ar. Arist. Men. ‖ NEUT.SB. **common upbringing** Arist.
3 (of an animal or bird, a person envisaged as a bird) **reared together** (w. another), **fellow** Ar. Pl. X.
4 (of animals) **living together** (w. people, sts. W.DAT.), **domestic** Hdt. Plu.
5 (of a person) **living together** (W.DAT. w. someone) S.; (fig., w. old age) S.(cj.); (of the sight, i.e. presence) **of one living together** (w. oneself) S.
6 (of a person) **habituated** (sts. W.GEN. or DAT. to sthg.) E. Plb. Plu.
7 (of a temperament) **innate** S.; (of poverty) **endemic** (W.DAT. in a country) Hdt.; (of an element) **inherent** (W.GEN. in nature) Pl.
8 (of illnesses, activities, haunts, or sim.) **habitual, regular** Th. Plu.; (of a sound, W.GEN. for one in pain) S.

—**σύντροφος** ου *m.f*. **1 person brought up with one; associate, companion** (sts. W.GEN. of someone) NT. Plu.
2 (at a Hellenistic court) **foster-brother** or **foster-sister** (W.GEN. or DAT. of the heir to the throne) Plb.

συν-τροχάζω vb. (of persons) **run together** Plu.

συν-τυγχάνω (**ξυν-**) vb. **1** (of people, natural elements) **come together, meet, encounter** (usu. W.DAT. someone or sthg.) Hdt. S. E. Antipho Ar. +; **meet with** —W.DAT. *a destiny* S.
2 (of events, misfortunes) **occur, turn out, happen** (sts. W.DAT. to or for someone) A. Hdt. S. Th. + ‖ IMPERS. **it happens** —W.ACC. + INF. *that sthg. is the case* Th. Plb. Plu.
3 (of food) **happen to be available, come to hand** X.
4 ‖ AOR.PTCPL.ADJ. (of a piece of workmanship, in neg.phr.) **casual, ordinary** Hdt.

συν-τῡρόω contr.vb. **make into cheese, curdle** ‖ PASS. (fig., of a plan) **be concocted** Ar.

συντυχίᾱ (**ξυν-**) ᾱς, Ion. **συντυχίη** ης *f*. [συντυγχάνω] **1** (w. neutral connot.) **happening, turn of events, occurrence, circumstance** Pi. Hdt. S. E. Th. +
2 luck, fortune Hdt. E.; (prep.phr.) κατὰ συντυχίην *by chance* Hdt.; (also) κατά τινα συντυχίαν Plb.
3 happy or **unhappy event** (as defined by qualifying epith.), **outcome, fortune** Sol. Thgn. Pi. Hdt. Th. Ar.

4 misfortune Lyr.adesp. Hdt. E. Pl.
5 fortunate circumstance, success Pi.

συν-υπακούω vb. **join in complying** (sts. W.DAT. w. someone or sthg.) Plb.; **join in agreeing** —w. πρός + ACC. *to sthg.* Plb.

συν-υπάρχω vb. **1** (of things) **coexist** Arist.
2 (of things) **exist in addition** (to other things) Plb.

συν-υπατεύω vb. **be fellow consul** Plu.

συν-υπερβάλλω vb. **cross** (W.ACC. a mountain range) **together** —W.PREP.PHR. *w. someone* Plb.

συν-υπηρετέω contr.vb. **join in helping** —W.DAT. *someone* Pl.

συν-υποδείκνῡμι vb. —also (pres.) **συνυποδεικνύω** **1 be in agreement in pointing out**; (of speakers) **jointly emphasise** —W.COMPL.CL. *that sthg. is the case* Plb.
2 (of a man's ill-repute) **help** (W.DAT. his enemies) **by laying evidence** (against him) Plb.
3 give full or definitive information; (of a writer) **describe fully** —*some particular* (about a battle), *the nature and location of places* Plb.; **demonstrate** —W.INDIR.Q. *how sthg. may be done* Plb.; (of a guide) **identify** —*roads* (W.DAT. *for an invading army*) Plb.

συν-υποδύομαι mid.vb. **join in undergoing** —*a danger* Plu.

συν-υποκρίνομαι mid.vb. ‖ aor.pass. (w.mid.sens.) συνυπεκρίθην ‖ **1 play a role jointly** (w. someone); **play along** —W.DAT. + ACC. *w. a person, in a pretence* Plu.; **join in a pretence** Plu.
2 put on an accommodating pretence (before other people or in the face of circumstances); **dissemble, put on an outward show** Plb.; **pretend to go along** —W.DAT. *w. persons* Plb.; **pretend** —W.INF. *to be doing sthg.* Plb. —w. ὡς + FUT.PTCPL. *that one is about to do sthg.* Plb.

συν-υπονοέω contr.vb. **come to a conclusion, infer** —W.COMPL.CL. *that sthg. is the case* Plb.

συν-υποπτεύω vb. **suspect, guess** —*what is happening* Plb.

συν-υποτίθεμαι mid.vb. **help in devising** —*a speech* Plu.

συν-υφαίνω vb. **1** ‖ MID. (of the creator god) **put together for one's purposes by weaving, weave** —*a mesh* (*of physical elements*) Pl.
2 (fig.) **weave or fit** (things) **together in order to make a whole**; (of statecraft) **unite harmoniously** —*all the elements in a state* Pl. ‖ PASS. (of a philosophical argument) **be constructed** Pl.
3 (pejor.) **weave** (things) **together in a deceptive or secret way**; (of a person) **weave** or **fit together** —*elements* (*to make a good story*) Plu. ‖ PASS. (of an enterprise) **be devised** Hdt.
4 devise (W.ACC. a plan) **jointly** —W.DAT. *w. someone* Od.(tm.)

συνύφανσις εως *f*. (fig.) **weaving together, uniting** (of things) Pl.

συνυφή ῆς *f*. **woven fabric, web** Pl.

συν-υφίσταμαι mid.vb. **join** (W.DAT. w. someone) **in undertaking** —*sthg.* Plb.

συνῳδίᾱ ᾱς *f*. [συνῳδός] **concord, agreement** Pl.

συν-ωδίνω vb. **1** (of birds) **share grief, feel pain together** Arist.
2 (of a person) **grieve in sympathy** —W.DAT. *w. someone's troubles* E.

συν-ῳδός (**ξυν-**), also **συναοιδός** (E.), όν *adj*. [ἀοιδή] **1** (of a person, a bird) **singing in unison, responsive** (W.DAT. to someone's laments, woes) E.; (w. force of tr.vb., of persons) **jointly singing** (W.ACC. of sthg.) E.
2 (of speech, argument, thoughts) **being in harmony** or **accord** (W.DAT. w. someone or sthg.) Hdt. E. Ar. Arist.; (of woes) **consonant** (w. crimes) E.

συνωθέω

3 (of an argument) in harmony (w. itself), **harmonious, in tune, concordant** Pl.

συν-ωθέω (ξυν-) *contr.vb.* **1** push or force together, compress —*natural elements, objects* (*oft.* W.PREP.PHR. *into a constricted space*) Pl.; **sweep together** —*grain* (*into a heap*) X. ‖ PASS. (of things) be compressed Pl.; (of an object) be crammed together (w. others) Plu.
2 forcefully drive (a group of people) all at once; (of soldiers) **push** or **drive back together** —*opposing troops* (*into difficult country or a limited area*) Plu.; **push** —*one another* Plu.; (of storms) **drive** —*sailors* AR. ‖ PASS. (of troops, elephants) be pushed or driven back together Plb.

συνώμεθα (1pl.aor.mid.subj.): see συνίημι

συνωμίαι ὧν *f.pl.* [ὦμος] area between the shoulder blades, **upper back** (of a bull) Plb.

συνωμοσία (ξυν-) ᾱς *f.* [συνόμνῡμι] **1 swearing of oaths together** Plb.
2 confederacy (betw. states) Th.
3 conspiracy Th. Ar. D. Plb. Plu.
4 group of conspirators, **political club, cabal** Th. Pl.

συνωμότης (ξυν-) ου *m.* **1** one who is linked by oath, **sworn ally, confederate** (in war) Hdt. S.
2 (in political ctxts.) **confederate, associate** And. Lys. Ar.; (pejor., ref. to a political opponent) **revolutionary** Ar.
3 conspirator, fellow conspirator Th. Plb. Plu.; (W.GEN. w. someone) Plu.; (pl., fig.ref. to toil and sleep) A.

συνώμοτος (ξυν-) ον *adj.* linked by oath ‖ NEUT.SB. sworn agreement (betw. states) Th.

συν-ωνέομαι *mid.contr.vb.* **1** buy in a large or excessive amount; **buy up** —*cavalry forces, wild animals* Hdt. Plu. —*grain* Lys. X. —*land* D. Plu. —*knowledge* (*i.e. education*) Pl.
2 buy together; **be a companion in shopping** —W.ACC. *for shoes* Thphr.

συνωνυμία ᾱς *f.* [συνώνυμος] (rhet.) use of a different word with the same sense, **synonymy** Arist.

συν-ώνυμος (ξυν-) ον *adj.* [ὄνομα] **1** (of a land) **having the same name** (W.GEN. as another) E.; (of a river, W.DAT. as a city) Plb.; (of persons) Plu.
2 (of a word, concept, or sim.) having the same sense (as another), **synonymous** Arist.

—**συνωνύμως** *adv.* by application of the same name Plb.

συνωρίζομαι (ξυν-) *mid.vb.* [συνωρίς] make into a pair, **pair, join** —*one's hand* (w. *another's*) E.

συνωρικεύομαι (ξυν-) *mid.vb.* **go in for driving pairs** (of horses) Ar.

συνωρίς (ξυν-) ίδος *f.* [συνάορος] **1 pair of horses** or **chariot and pair** E. Ar. Pl. Plb. Plu.
2 chariot drawn by a pair (of elephants) Plb.
3 (gener., sts. W.GEN.) **pair** (of persons) S. E.; (of weapons, hands and feet) A.; (of military divisions) E.

σύνωσις εως *f.* [συνωθέω] forcing together (of physical particles), **compression** Pl.

συν-ωφελέω (ξυν-) *contr.vb.* **1** (of persons) **join together in helping** —*one another* X. ‖ PASS. share in receiving help or benefits Lys.
2 (of persons or things) **give help, be of use** X. —W.DAT. *to someone* S.; (tr.) **help, assist, benefit** —*someone or sthg.* X.

συνωχαδόν *adv.* [συνέχω] **continually** or **continuously** Hes.

συο-κτόνος ον *adj.* [σῦς, see ὗς; κτείνω] (of Atalanta, Herakles) **boar-slaying** Call.

συο-φόνος ον *adj.* [θείνω] (of a spear) **boar-killing** E.*fr.*

συοφορβός *m.*: see ὑφορβός

Συράκουσαι, Ion. **Συρήκουσαι**, ῶν, dial. **Συράκοσαι** (Pi.), **Συράκοσσαι** (Pi. B.), **Συράκουσσαι** (Theoc.*epigr.*), ᾱν *f.pl.* Syracuse (chief city of Sicily) Pi. B. Hdt. Th. +

—**Συρᾱκόσιοι** (also **Συρᾱκούσιοι** Arist. Plu.), Ion. **Συρηκόσιοι**, ων *m.pl.* Syracusans (as a population or military force) Pi. B. Hdt. Th. +; (sg., as ethnic adj.) Pi. Hdt. Th. +

—**Συρᾱκόσιος** ᾱ ον *adj.* of or relating to Syracuse or the Syracusans; (of the city) **of Syracuse** B.; (of warships) **Syracusan** Th. X.; (provbl., of a table laden w. food) Pl. ‖ FEM.SB. Syracusan territory Th. Plu.

σύρδην *adv.* [σύρω] **1 in a long trailing line** —*ref. to an army moving* A.
2 in one fell swoop —*ref. to a warrior destroying an army* E.

Συρία *f.*, **Συριακός** *adj.*: see under Σύροι

σύριγμα ατος *n.* [σῡρίζω] **1 piping** (ref. to the sound or activity) E. Ar.
2 whistle (of a hunter to his dogs) S.*Ichn.*

συριγμός οῦ *m.* **whistling, hissing** (in derision) X. Plb. Plu.

σῦριγξ ιγγος *f.* **1** (oft. collectv.pl.) **shepherd's pipes, panpipe** (a set of tubes, usu. of reed) Il. +
2 (meton.) sound resembling that of a panpipe; **whistle, hiss** (in derision) Pl.
3 (ref. to other tubular objects) **spear-case** Il.; **socket** (for a doorpost) Parm.
4 duct, channel (in the body) Emp. S.; **vein** AR.
5 nave, hub (of a chariot wheel) Trag. Call. Theoc.
6 underground passage, tunnel Plb.
7 covered gallery or **passageway** Plb.

σῡρίζω, Att. **σῡρίττω**, dial. **σῡρίσδω** *vb.* ‖ dial.inf. σῡρίσδεν ‖ aor. ἐσύριξα ‖ **1** play the panpipe, **pipe** E. Hellenist.poet. —W.INTERN.ACC. *wedding music* E.; (of a panpipe) **make a shrill sound** E.
2 (of horses' mouth-bands, constricting their breath) **scream, whistle** A.
3 (of a dog, a person, both compared to a snake) **hiss** Hippon. Ar.; (of a monster) —W.INTERN.ACC. *terror* A.; (of steering-oars, as they move through the sea) E.
4 (of spectators) **hiss at** —*a person* D. Thphr. Plu. ‖ PASS. be hissed at Aeschin.
5 (of the tongue) **make a sibilant sound** Pl.

Συρη-γενής ές *adj.* [Συρία; γένος, γίγνομαι] (of a team of chariot-horses) **of Syrian breed** Hdt.(oracle)

σῡρικτάς ᾶ *dial.m.* [σῡρίζω] panpipe player, **piper** Theoc.

Σύριος *adj.*: see under Σύροι

Συριστί *adv.* [reltd. Σύροι] **in the Syrian language** X. Plu.

σῡρίττω Att.*vb.*: see σῡρίζω

συρμαία ᾱς, Ion. **συρμαίη** ης *f.* [σύρω] that which scours one's insides; **purgative** (either laxative or emetic, assoc.w. Egypt) Hdt. Ar.; (ref. to a radish fr. which purgatives were made) Hdt.

συρμαΐζω *vb.* **use a purgative** Hdt.

συρμός οῦ *m.* [σύρω] **trail** (left by a snake) Plu.

Σύροι ων *m.pl.* Syrians (tribes living betw. the Tigris and the Mediterranean, incl. mod. Syria, Assyria and Cappadocia) Hdt. +; (sg., as ethnic adj.) NT. Plu.

—**Σύρος** ου *m.* Syros (pers. name of a male slave) D. Men.

—**Σύρᾱ** ᾱς *f.* Syra (pers. name of a female slave) Ar.

—**Σύριος** ᾱ (Ion. η) ον *adj.* of or relating to the Syrians; (of incense, perfume) **Syrian** A. E. Melanipp. Theoc. Bion; (of a chariot) A. ‖ MASC.PL.SB. Syrian peoples Hdt.

—**Συρίᾱ** ᾱς, Ion. **Συρίη** ης *f.* land of the Syrians, **Syria** A. Hdt. +

—**Συριακός** ή όν *adj.* of or relating to the Syrian peoples or Syria; (of a war, political affairs, a region) **Syrian** Plb. Plu.

σύρραξις εως *f.* [συρράσσω] **clash** (of opposing armies) Plu.

συρ-ράπτω *vb.* [σύν] **1 stitch together** —*goatskins, scalps*

Hes. Hdt. Plu. ‖ PASS. (of parts of a tunic) be stitched together Plu.
2 stitch up —*a stomach, sack* Hdt. Plu.; (fig.) —*someone's mouth* (*i.e. restrain him fr. speaking*) Pl.

συρ-ράσσω (ξυρ-) vb. **1** (of a commander, troops) **clash together, engage** (sts. W.DAT. w. someone) X. Plu.
2 (of people) **come to blows** —W.DAT. w. *each other* Th.

συρ-ρέπω vb. **incline** (w. the mind) —W.PREP.PHR. *towards certain regions* (i.e. *direct one's attention to them*) Plb.

συρ-ρέω contr.vb. | pf. συνερρύηκα ‖ aor.2 pass. (w.act.sens.) συνερρύην | **1** (of rivers, liquids, vapours) **flow** or **stream together** (to a place) Pl. Plb.
2 (of metals) **become molten** Plb.
3 (of people) **stream together** (to a place or person) Hdt. Isoc. Pl. X. Plu.; (of a fleet) **assemble** Hdt.
4 (fig., of troubles) **stream together** —w. εἰς + ACC. *into old age* (*envisaged as a receptacle*) X.; (of interest payments) **accumulate** Is.; (of vices or sim.) **be concentrated** —w. εἰς + ACC. *in a person* Plu.; (of wealth) —*in the hands of a few* Plu.

συρ-ρήγνῡμι (ξυρ-) vb. | aor. συνέρρηξα | 3sg.plpf. ξυνερρώγει (Th.) ‖ PASS.: aor.2 συνερράγην | **1 crack** —*a skull* (*one's own or another's*) Plu. ‖ PASS. (of a ship's turrets) be smashed Plb.; (fig., of a person) be broken down —W.DAT. *by sufferings* Od.
2 break up and merge —*everything* (W.PREP.PHR. *into a single whole*) Ar.
3 (intr., of rivers) **burst together** —W.PREP.PHR. *into another river* Hdt.
4 ‖ PASS. (of troops, commanders) clash, engage (sts. W.DAT. w. someone) Plu.
5 (intr., of war) **break out** Th. ‖ PASS. (of war, shouting, a drinking bout) break out Plu.

συρροή ῆς f. [συρρέω] **confluence** (W.GEN. of fluids in the body) Plu.

σύρροια ᾱς f. **confluence** (W.GEN. of rivers) Plb.

σύρρους ουν Att.adj. (of a lake) flowing together, **merging** (W.DAT. w. the sea) Plb.

σύρρυσις εως f. confluence, **collection** (W.GEN. of winter rains, in a river) Plb.

σύρτις εως f. [σύρω] trailing line, **line** (of ships) Tim.

Σύρτις εως (Ion. ιος) f. **Syrtis** (name of two dangerous sandbanks off N. Africa) Hdt. AR. Plb. NT. Plu.

σύρφαξ ᾱκος m. [συρφετός] **rubbish, litter, scum** (ref. to the populace) Ar.

συρφετός οῦ m. [σύρω] **1** that which is dragged or swept together; **sweepings, litter** (for farm animals) Hes.; **refuse** (carried down a river) Call.
2 rabble, mob Pl.; (ref. to a single person) **riff-raff, pleb** Pl.

συρφετώδης ες adj. (of a crowd) **rag-tag** Plb.

σύρω vb. | aor. ἔσυρα | **1** draw (sthg.) along behind one; (of a woman) **trail along** —*her dress* Theoc.; (of a bull) **draw along** —*a plough* Mosch.
2 (of fishermen) **drag in** —*a net* NT.
3 drag along by force; (of a god or human) **drag, drag away** —*a person, corpse* S.fr. NT. Plu. ‖ PASS. (of a corpse) be dragged along Plu.; (of objects) be swept along (by the current of a river) Plu.

σῦς m.f.: see ὗς

συ-σκεδάννῡμι vb. [σύν] | fut.inf. συσκεδᾶν | scatter completely; (fig., of a poet) **scatter to the winds** —*dust-grounds of words* Ar.

συ-σκεπτέον neut.impers.vbl.adj. [σκέπτομαι] **it is necessary to investigate together** Pl.

συ-σκευάζω (ξυ-) vb. **1** make ready by putting (things) together; **pack up** —*food* (for someone to take to a party), *presents* (for a departing guest) Ar. X.; (fig.) **package together, bundle up** —*all topics* (W.PREP.PHR. *into a single decree*) D. ‖ PASS. (of various arrangements) be packaged together X.
2 ‖ MID. pack up one's baggage (in preparation for departure); **pack, get ready** —*belongings, bedding, or sim.* Att.orats. Pl. X. Plu.; (intr.) Th. X. Plu. —W.ACC. *for a journey* X.
3 ‖ MID. get together (before departure), **equip oneself with** —*provisions, money, or sim.* X. Din.; (fig., of an orator) —*effrontery, an accusation* D.
4 (pejor., sts.mid.) **put together, fabricate** —*intrigues, slanders, or sim.* Hyp. D. Plu. ‖ PASS. (of things) be devised or contrived D.
5 ‖ MID. (fig. or gener.) package up, **take control of, manage, organise** —*persons, affairs, a state* X. Hyp. D. Plu.

συσκευασίᾱ ᾱς f. **packing up** (of baggage) X.

συ-σκευοφορέω contr.vb. **help to carry baggage** X.

συ-σκευωρέομαι mid.contr.vb. (pejor.) **help to put together** —*an initiation ceremony* D.

συσκηνέω, also **συσκηνόω** contr.vb. [σύσκηνος] **1** share a tent, **be quartered together** (sts. W.DAT. w. someone) X. Plu.
2 dine together regularly X.

συσκηνήτρια ᾱς f. **tentmate** (ref. to a woman attending the Thesmophoria) Ar.

συσκηνίᾱ ᾱς f. sharing of a tent; **shared quarters** X.

συσκήνια ων n.pl. (at Sparta) places for communal dining, **messes** X.

σύ-σκηνος (ξύ-) ου m. [σκηνή] one who shares a tent, **tentmate** or **messmate** Th. Lys. X. Plu.

συσκηνόω contr.vb.: see συσκηνέω

συ-σκιάζω vb. **1 put in full shade** —*grapes* (after harvesting) Hes.; (intr., of a valley) **be fully shaded** —W.DAT. *by trees* E.; (of the moon, by clouds) Plu.
2 (of a young man) **darken** —*his cheek* (w. a beard) E. ‖ PASS. (of the head) be completely shrouded (by flesh) Pl.
3 (fig., of success) **shroud, disguise** —*mistakes* D.

σύ-σκιος ον adj. [σκιά] **1** (of places) **thickly shaded, very shady** X. Plu.
2 (of trees) providing shade, **shady** Plu. ‖ NEUT.SB. thick shade (W.GEN. of a tree) Pl.

συ-σκοπέω contr.vb. **1 share in an inquiry** Pl.
2 examine together (sts. W.DAT. w. someone) —*an argument or sim.* Pl.

συ-σκοτάζω (ξυ-) vb. [σκότος] | aor. συνεσκότασα | (of the day) **grow dark** Plb. ‖ IMPERS. it grows dark Th. X. D. Plu.

συ-σκυθρωπάζω vb. **share gloomy looks** X.

συ-σπαράσσω vb. (of an evil spirit) **convulse** —*someone* NT.

σύσπαστος ον adj. [συσπάω] pulled together; (of a purse) **shut by a draw-string** Pl.

συ-σπάω contr.vb. **1 pull together** —*hides stuffed w. hay* (i.e. their edges, for sewing up) X.
2 contract, tighten —*parts of the body* Pl.

συ-σπειράομαι pass.contr.vb. [σπεῖρα] **1** (of soldiers) **form into a compact body, close up** X. Plu.
2 (fig., of a person) draw in on oneself, **become withdrawn** Pl.

συ-σπένδω vb. **pour libations together** (sts. W.DAT. w. someone) Aeschin. D.

συ-σπεύδω vb. **cooperate eagerly** —W.DAT. w. *someone* (W.ACC. + INF. *in the achievement of some result*) Hdt.

συ-σπλαγχνεύω vb. (of a participant at a sacrifice) **join in eating the entrails** Ar.

συ-σπουδάζω (ξυ-) vb. **share the same eagerness** (sts. W.ACC. for sthg.) Ar. X. Arist. Plu.(cj.)

συσ-σαίνομαι pass.vb. (of listeners) feel comfortable —W.DAT. w. a dialect (through long habituation to it) Plb.
συσ-σημαίνομαι mid.vb. join in sealing —a document D.
σύσ-σημος ον adj. [σῆμα] corroboratively significant || NEUT.SB. (ref. to a statement) corroboration, endorsement Men.; (ref. to a kiss) signal, sign NT.
συσσῑτέω (ξυν-) contr.vb. [σύσσῑτος] 1 (of ambassadors, magistrates, ephebes, prisoners, members of a dining club) dine together (sts. W.DAT. w. someone) Att.orats. Arist. Thphr. 2 (of soldiers, Spartans) take meals together or share quarters (sts. W.DAT. w. someone) Lys. Ar. Pl. Plu.
συσσίτησις εως f. communal dining (at Sparta) Plu.
συσσῑτίᾱ ᾱς f. (in official or military ctxt.) communal dining Pl. X.
συσσίτιον (ξυσ-) ου n. 1 place of communal dining, dining-area (ref. to a tent) E. || PL. mess-rooms Pl. Plu.(also sg.) 2 || PL. (in official or military ctxt., or at Sparta) communal meals or messes Hdt. Ar. Isoc. Pl. +; (also sg.) Plu.
σύσ-σῑτος (ξύσ-) ου m. [σῖτος] 1 one who dines together (w. another, usu. on a regular or formal basis); dinner companion Thgn. Hdt. Ar. Arist. 2 (in official or military ctxt., or at Sparta) messmate Ar. Att.orats. X. Plu.
συσ-σῡκοφαντέω contr.vb. collude in blackmail D.
συσ-σῴζω (ξυσ-) vb. 1 help to save or protect —a person, city, or sim. E. Ar. Pl. Plb. 2 save at the same time; save jointly —people, things Th. Plb. —one's reputation (w. one's life) E.Cyc. —someone (w. oneself) E. —(W.DAT. w. someone else) Plb. 3 preserve, adhere to —a plan, rules Plb.
συσ-σωφρονέω contr.vb. share in good sense —W.DAT. w. someone E.
συστάδες ων f.pl. [συνίστημι] close arrangements, clumps (W.GEN. of vines, ref. to quincunx formations) Arist.
συσταδόν (ξυσ-), also συστάδην (Plb.) adv. at close quarters, hand to hand —ref. to fighting Th. Plb.
συ-σταθεύω (ξυ-) vb. (fig., of a person) help to grill or roast —someone (by causing sexual frustration) Ar.
συσταθήσομαι (fut.pass.): see συνίστημι
συ-στασιάζω (ξυ-) vb. 1 join (sts. W.DAT. w. someone) in factional strife Th. Lys. D. 2 support (W.DAT. someone) in sedition Plu.
σύστασις (ξύ-) εως f. [συνίστημι] 1 group of people standing together; gathering, group E. Th. X. 2 (in political ctxt.) grouping, association Isoc. D.; (of nations) Plb.; (fig.) coalition (W.GEN. of arguments) Pl. 3 faction, conspiracy D. Plu. 4 coming together (of combatants); engagement, close combat Hdt. Pl. Plu.; (fig.) conflict (W.GEN. of emotions, ref. to the involvement of onlookers in a battle) Th. 5 bringing together (of one person w. another); introduction Plb. Plu.; connection, tie of friendship Plb. 6 result of bringing (things) together; formation, arrangement, structure Pl. Arist. Plb. Plu.; (of events in a dramatic plot) Pl. Arist. 7 process of bringing together, emergence, formation (of cities, a constitution, or sim.) Pl. Plb.
συ-στασιώτης ου (Ion. εω) m. member of the same faction, fellow partisan Hdt.
συστατικός ή όν adj. [συνίστημι] (of good looks) capable of bringing people together, conducive to familiarity Plb.
συ-σταυρόομαι pass.contr.vb. be crucified together —W.DAT. or σύν + DAT. w. someone NT.

συ-στεγάζω vb. (of creator gods) completely cover or protect —the human head (W.DAT. w. a thin layer of bone) Pl. || PASS. (of a charioteer) be completely protected —W.DAT. by cuirass and helmet X.
συ-στέλλω (ξυν-) vb. 1 || PASS. (of a phalanx) be contracted or narrowed Plu. 2 || PASS. (of an area, a kingdom) be reduced, contract, shrink X. Plb. 3 draw together (sails, i.e. shorten them, in a high wind); (fig., of a sausage-seller) reef in, shorten —his sausages (envisaged as sails) Ar.; (intr.) shorten sail (so as not to be carried away by passion) Ar. 4 restrict, limit, curtail —persons, activities, behaviour Isoc. Pl. D. Plu. || PASS. cut back (on expenses) Th.; put a check on one's behaviour Plb. Plu.; be restricted —W.PREP.PHR. to sthg. Plu.; (of activities) be curtailed Plu. 5 humble —persons, pride, or sim. Isoc. Pl. Plu. || PASS. be humbled or brought low E. Isoc. Plu. 6 restrict (persons) to a limited area; confine —people (usu. W.PREP.PHR. to or within a place) Plu. || PASS. be confined or limited (usu. W.PREP.PHR. to or within a place) Plu. 7 || PASS. (of persons) huddle together or close ranks E. Ar. 8 pull (clothing) together || MID. draw (W.ACC. one's cloak) tightly around oneself Ar.; wrap (W.ACC. oneself) up tightly Ar. || PASS. (of corpses) be wrapped —W.DAT. in funeral robes E.
συ-στενάζω vb. lament together, share in sorrow —W.DAT. w. someone E.
συ-στένω vb. share in lamentation Arist.
συ-στεφανηφορέω contr.vb. wear a garland together —W.DAT. w. someone Scol.
συ-στεφανόομαι pass.contr.vb. wear a garland together —W.DAT. w. someone D.
σύστημα ατος n. [συνίστημι] 1 whole composed of several parts, organisation, structure (of an entity, a literary plot) Arist.; (of numbers) Pl.; (of government) Plb. 2 system (of notes and intervals, ref. to a musical scale) Pl. 3 association of homogeneous parts; organisation (ref. to a specific government) Pl.; confederacy (of cities) Plb.; college (of priests) Plb.; collection (of animals) sorted by type, herd (of swine) Plb. 4 (milit.) body, regiment (usu. W.GEN. of mercenaries, cavalry, or sim.) Plb. 5 (gener.) body (of people, troops) Plu.; (ref. to the Roman Senate) Plu.; (W.GEN. of houses, ref. to a city) Plu.
συστήσω (fut.): see συνίστημι
συστοιχέω contr.vb. [σύστοιχος] (of soldiers) remain in column Plb.
συστοιχίᾱ ᾱς f. listing or series (of cognate things or ideas) Arist.
σύ-στοιχος ον adj. [στοῖχος] 1 (of things or ideas) belonging to the same column or series, coordinate Arist. 2 (of behaviour) in line, consistent (W.DAT. w. other behaviour) Plb.
συστολή ῆς f. [συστέλλω] 1 reduction, curtailment (of honours) Plu. 2 thriftiness Plb.
συ-στολίζω vb. make up (by weaving), fabricate —fine robes E.
σύ-στομος (unless σύνστομος) ον adj. [στόμα] (of a person) with closed mouth, tight-lipped Men.
συστρατείᾱ ᾱς f. [συστρατεύω] partnership (w. someone) in an expedition X.

συ-στρατεύω (**ξυ-**) *vb.* (act. and mid., of soldiers, commanders) **go on campaign together, serve together** (sts. W.DAT. w. someone) Hdt. Th. Att.orats. Pl. X. +

συστρατηγέω *contr.vb.* [συστράτηγος] (milit.) **be in joint command** (sts. W.DAT. w. someone) D. Plu.; (fig., of Fortune) Plu.

συ-στράτηγος (**ξυ-**) ου *m.* [στρατηγός] **joint commander** E. Th. X. Plu.

συ-στρατιώτης ου *m.* **fellow soldier** Pl. X. Is. Arist. Plu.

συ-στρατοπεδεύω (**ξυ-**) *vb.* (of armies) **camp together** X.(mid.) Plb.

σύστρεμμα ατος *n.* [συστρέφω] **1 tight group, close body** (of soldiers) Plb.
2 mêlée or **pressure** (of combatants) Plb.

συ-στρέφω (**ξυ-**) *vb.* **1** turn (sthg.) together (in on itself); (of soldiers) **form** (W.ACC. themselves) **into a tight unit** Hdt.; (of a commander) **close up** —*his forces* Plu. ‖ PASS. (of soldiers) band together or close ranks Hdt. Th. X. Plb. Plu.; (of people) Hdt. Th. Plu.; (of persons) perh., gather together NT.
2 (of a ruler) **unite** —*a nation* Hdt.; (of demagogues) **cause** (W.ACC. people) **to unite** (in a common cause) Arist. ‖ PASS. (of people, commanders) unite or make common cause Hdt. Th. Aeschin. D. Plb.
3 gather together —*a bundle of sticks* NT.
4 (of a disputant, compared to an animal) **gather** (W.ACC. oneself) **together** (before pouncing) Pl.; (of a rider) app. **make ready** —*a horse* (*for a charge*) Plu. ‖ PASS. (of a whirlwind) gather Men.
5 (of a hurricane) **sweep up, catch up** —*someone* A.*fr.* Ar.
6 screw up —*one's face* (*in pain*) Plu.
7 condense, make concise —*syllogisms* Arist.; (intr., of a person) **be concise** Aeschin. ‖ PF.PASS.PTCPL.ADJ. (of a saying) concise, pithy Pl.

—**συνεστραμμένως** *pf.pass.ptcpl.adv.* **concisely** —*ref. to forming a syllogism* Arist.

συστροφή ῆς *f.* **1 twisting** (of threads) Pl.
2 uniting (of people); **massing** (W.GEN. of a population) Hdt.; **gathering, mob** Plb. NT.
3 build-up (of rain), **squall** Plb.; (fig., ref. to trouble) **storm, imbroglio** Plb.

συ-σφάζομαι *pass.vb.* (of a person) **be slaughtered together** —W.DAT. w. someone E.

συ-σχολάζω *vb.* **1 share one's leisure pursuits** (esp. philosophical studies, sts. W.DAT. w. someone) Plu.
2 be a pupil —W.DAT. of a philosopher or orator Plu.

σύτο (ep.3sg.athem.aor.mid.): see σεύω

σῦφαρ *n.* | only nom.acc. | **skin** (of an old crow) Call.

συφεός, also **συφειός**, οῦ *m.* [reltd. συφορβός] **pig-sty** Od. Thphr.(cj.)

—**συφεόνδε** *adv.* **to the pig-sty** Od.

συφορβός *m.*: see ὑφορβός

συχνός ή όν *adj.* **1** ‖ PL. (most freq.) **great in number;** (of persons or things) **many, numerous** Hdt. Th. Ar. Pl. X. D. +
2 (sg.) **great in duration;** (of time) **long** Hdt. Pl. X. D. Plu.; (of speech, argument) Pl.; (of a piece of business) **prolonged** D.
3 great in size or extent; (of a crowd, city, army, or sim.) **large, great** Hdt. Pl. Plu.
4 great in amount; (of money, property, other collectv.sg. nouns) **much** Hdt. Ar. Plb. Plu.
5 great in degree; (of caution, falsehood, persuasion) **great, much** Pl.; (of madness) Men.; (of a task, an activity) **demanding** Pl. D.
6 ‖ SG.SB. (in same gender as GEN.) **large amount** (W.GEN. of charcoal dust) Ar.; **large part** (of a herd) Plu.

—**συχνόν** *neut.sg.adv.* **by quite a distance** —*ref. to being separate, missing someone's meaning* Pl. X.

—**συχνά** *neut.pl.adv.* **1 heartily** —*ref. to bidding farewell* Pl.
2 at length —*ref. to speaking* Men.

—**συχνῷ** *dat.neut.sg.adv.* (modifying COMPAR.ADJ. **better, younger**) **by far** Pl. D.

—**συχνῶς** *adv.* **1 completely** Antipho(dub.)
2 frequently Plu.

σφαγεῖον ου *n.* [σφαγεύς] **bowl for the blood of a sacrifice; blood bowl** (for animal offerings) E. Ar.; (for humans) E.

σφαγεύς έως *m.* [σφάζω] **1 one who cuts the throat** (in a ritual sacrifice); **butcher, slaughterer** (of a person, in a real or fig. sacrifice) E.; (personif., ref. to the sword of one who commits suicide) S.
2 murderer And.(decree) D.
3 (gener.) **cut-throat, killer** E. X. Plu.

σφαγή ῆς, dial. **σφαγά** ᾶς *f.* | freq.pl. for sg. | **1 throat-cutting** (in a ritual sacrifice); **slaughter, sacrifice** (of an animal) Trag. Ar. NT.; (of a person) E.
2 (gener.) **slaughter, murder** Trag. Isoc. Pl. X. +
3 fatal or **bloody wound** S. E.
4 place of wounding (in sacrifice or murder), **throat, neck** E. Antipho Th. X. Plu.

σφαγιάζω *vb.* [σφάγιον] **ritually slaughter** (a victim) by cutting the throat; **sacrifice, slaughter** —*an animal* Ar. —*a person* Plu.; (mid.) —*an animal* Hdt. Plu. ‖ MID. (intr.) **offer a sacrifice** (of an animal) Hdt. X. Plb. Plu. ‖ PASS. (of an animal) be sacrificed Ar. X.; (of a person) Hdt. Plu.

σφαγιασμός οῦ *m.* **1 ritual slaughter, sacrifice** (of a person) Plu.
2 (pl. for sg.) **slaying, murder** (of a person) E.

σφάγιον ου *n.* [σφάζω] **1 object of ritual slaughter;** (ref. to an animal) **victim, offering** Trag. Ar. Plu.; (ref. to a person) E. Plu.; (ref. to a group of persons) D.
2 ‖ PL. **sacrifice or sacrificial victims** A. E. Antipho Ar. Plb. Plu.
3 ‖ PL. (before a battle) **sacrifices, offerings** A. Hdt. E. X.; (concr.) victims Th. X.
4 victim of murder, victim E.; (ref. to a person who commits suicide) S.
5 ‖ PL. **slaughter** (of a person or persons) E.

σφαγίς ίδος *f.* **sacrificial knife** E.

σφαδάζω *vb.* | only pres. and impf. | **1 toss one's body about;** (of a horse or a person likened to a horse which is new to the bridle or yoke) **plunge about** A. E.*fr.*; (of a wounded horse) X.
2 (of a dying man) **writhe** Plu.
3 (of cavalry, a soldier, person) **be desperate** or **impatient** —W.PREP.PHR. *for battle, acquisitions* Plu.

σφαδασμός οῦ *m.* **bodily spasm, convulsion** Pl.

σφάζω, Att. **σφάττω** *vb.* | fut. σφάξω | aor. ἔσφαξα ‖ PASS.: fut. σφαγήσομαι | aor. ἐσφάχθην, aor.2 ἐσφάγην | pf. ἔσφαγμαι |
1 slaughter by cutting the throat, slaughter, kill —*animals* (*for food*) Hom. hHom. Ar. Pl. ‖ PASS. (of animals) be slaughtered Hom.
2 ritually slaughter by cutting the throat, slaughter, sacrifice —*animals* Od. Hdt. E. Pl. X. + —*persons* Hes.*fr.* A. Emp. Hdt. E. Plu.; (intr.) **perform ritual slaughter** Hom. E. X. ‖ PASS. (of animals) be slaughtered D. Plu.; (of persons) A. Pi. Hdt. E.
3 (gener.) **slay, butcher** —*persons* A. Hdt. E. Th. +; (of a frenzied person) —*animals* (*mistaken for persons*) S.; (of a boar) —*sheep, persons* B. ‖ PASS. (of persons) be slain E. Antipho D. Plu.
4 cut —*someone's throat* E.

σφαῖρα ᾶς (Ion. ης) *f.* **1 ball** (as a plaything) Od. Anacr. Hdt. Pl. +
2 (gener.) **globular object, sphere** Parm. Pl. Arist. Plu.
3 (astron.) **sphere** (revolving around the earth, carrying the heavenly bodies) Arist.
4 boxing-glove (used in practice, instead of leather thongs) Pl.; (in fig.ctxt.) Dionys.Eleg.
σφαιρηδόν *adv.* **like a ball** —*ref. to throwing an object* Il.
σφαιρίζω *vb.* **play ball games** Pl. Plu.
σφαίρισις εως *f.* **ball playing** or **ball game** Arist.
σφαιριστήριον ου *n.* (in a gymnasium or palaestra) **area** or **room for boxing practice** Thphr.
σφαιρο-ειδής ές *adj.* [εἶδος[1]] (of a shape, the human head, heaven) **globular, spherical** Pl.; (of the butt-end of a spear) X.
σφαιρομαχέω *contr.vb.* [μάχομαι] fight with gloves, **practise boxing, spar** Pl. Men. Plb.
σφαῖρος ου *m.* **sphere** (ref. to the shape of the cosmos) Emp.
σφαιρόομαι *pass.contr.vb.* | pf. ἐσφαίρωμαι | 3sg.plpf. ἐσφαίρωτο | ‖ PF.PLPF. (of a javelin or spear used for practice) **be equipped with a spherical knob** (instead of a point), **be buttoned** X. Arist. Plb.; (of a boxer's chest and back, app. w. allusion to σφαῖρα 4) **be cushioned** —W.DAT. *w. iron-hard flesh* Theoc.
σφαιρωτός ή όν *adj.* (of a javelin or spear used for practice) **buttoned** X.
σφακελίζω *vb.* [σφάκελος] (of parts of the body) **become gangrenous** or **mortify** Hdt. Pl.
σφάκελος ου *m.* **1** (medic.) **gangrene** or **necrosis**; (gener.) **convulsion** (in the brain or whole body) A. E.
2 convulsive power (W.GEN. of gales) A.
σφάκος ου *m.* a kind of wild herb, **sage** Ar. Men.
σφακτός ή όν *adj.* [σφάζω] (of persons) **slaughtered** E.
σφαλερός ά όν *adj.* [σφάλλω] **1 liable to cause a slip**; (of a condition, situation, course of action) **precarious, full of pitfalls, fraught with danger** Hdt. E. Th. Att.orats. Pl. +
2 (of the feet of Erinyes) **liable to cause a trip** (W.DAT. for someone) A.
3 liable to make a slip; (of a person) **fallible, prone to error** E.; (of a protecting tower, allies) **unreliable, unsafe** S. D.; (of a criterion) **deceptive** E.
—σφαλερῶς *adv.* **precariously** Isoc. D.
σφάλλω *vb.* | fut. σφαλῶ | aor. ἔσφηλα, ep. σφῆλα, dial. ἔσφᾱλα, also σφᾶλα | pf. ἔσφαλκα ‖ PASS.: fut. σφαλοῦμαι, fut.2 σφαλήσομαι | aor.2 ἐσφάλην | pf. ἔσφαλμαι |
1 cause to totter or **fall**; **bring down** —*a warrior* Pi. —*a bull* AR. —*someone's knees* (i.e. bring him to his knees) E. ‖ PASS. (of a bull) **be brought down** E.
2 (of a wrestler) **catch off balance, throw** —*an opponent* Il. Theoc. ‖ PASS. **be tripped up** —W.DAT. *by someone's wrestling tricks* (fig.ref. to wiles) Ar.
3 (of a horse) **unseat, throw** —*its rider* X. ‖ PASS. (of a rider) **be thrown** X.
4 (of a missile) **knock over** —*a person* Od.
5 (of a bull) **upset, overturn** —*a chariot* E.
6 ‖ PASS. (of a drunkard, blind man, horse) **stagger** or **stumble** Heraclit. E. Ar. X. Plu.+; (fig., of an irresolute person) **lose one's footing** E.
7 (usu. of abstr. things, such as ill fortune, inexperience, bad company; also of persons or gods) **bring down, ruin** —*persons, houses, cities* Pi. Hdt. S. E. Th. + ‖ PASS. **be brought down, ruined** or **suffer a reverse** Pi.*fr.* Hdt. S. E. Th. Ar. +; **be blighted** —W.PREP.PHR. *by sickness, misfortune, or sim.* Pl.
8 (of excessive wine-drinking) **undermine** —*bodies and minds* X.
9 (of persons) **overthrow** —*justice* E.
10 (of soldiers as passengers) **hamper** —*ships* Th.
11 (gener.) **cause** (a person) **to fail** (in action or thought); (of a god, an oracle) **trip up, lead astray, frustrate** —*a person* Hdt. S. E. Pl. +; (of a person) —*the Fates* E. ‖ PASS. (of persons, thoughts, or sim.) **be proved wrong** or **go astray** Hdt. S. E. Th. Isoc. +; **fail** or **be frustrated** Antipho Th. Ar. —W.GEN. *in sthg.* A. E. Th. Pl. Plu.
12 ‖ PASS. **be cheated** or **deprived** —W.GEN. *of someone or sthg.* S. E.
σφάλμα ατος *n.* **1 slip, stumble** (by a person) Plu.
2 slip-up, mistake, blunder E. Pl. Plu.
3 failure, defeat, calamity Hdt. Th. Pl. X. Plu.
σφάξ *dial.m.*: see σφήξ
σφαραγέομαι *mid.contr.vb.* | only ep.3pl.impf. σφαραγεῦντο | (of the roots of an eye being burned, sheep's udders) **be swollen to bursting** Od.
σφαραγίζω *vb.* **cause to swell up, stir up** —*earth tremors, dust-clouds, thunder and lightning* Hes.
σφάττω *Att.vb.*: see σφάζω
σφεδανός ή όν *adj.* [reltd. σφοδρός] (of conflict) **vehement, violent** Xenoph.(cj.)
—σφεδανόν *neut.adv.* **furiously** —*ref. to pursuing someone* Il.
σφεῖς 3pl.pers.pron. | MASC.FEM.: acc. σφᾶς (enclit. σφᾶς, also σφάς), Ion. σφέας (enclit. σφεάς) | acc. also enclit. σφε (sts. as sg.), Aeol. ἄσφε, dial.enclit. ψε (Theoc.) | gen. σφῶν, Ion. σφέων (enclit. σφεων), ep. σφείων | dat. σφίσι(ν), enclit. σφισί(ν), also σφι(ν) (sts. as sg.), dial. φιν (Emp. Call.), Aeol. ἄσφι ‖ NEUT.: acc.enclit. σφεά (Hdt.), σφε (Theoc.) ‖ DU.: ep.nom.acc.enclit. σφωέ, gen.dat.enclit. σφωίν |
1 (pl. and du., ref. to persons; also ref. to things denoted by masc.fem. sbs., and in neut. forms) **they, them** Hom. +
2 (reflexv.pl., in ACC.GEN.DAT.) **themselves** (sts. w. αὐτούς, αὐτῶν, αὐτοῖς) Hom. +; (as 2nd pers.pron.) **yourselves** Il. And.; (as 1st pers.pron.) **ourselves** AR.
3 ‖ SG. (in ACC.DAT. forms σφε, σφι) **him, her** hHom. Pi. Trag.; (ref. to a masc.sb.) **it** S.
σφέλας *ep.n.* | only acc. σφέλας, dat. σφέλαϊ, acc.pl. σφέλᾱ | **stool, footstool** Od. AR.
σφενδάμνινος η ον *adj.* [σφένδαμνος *maple tree*] (fig., of persons) **tough as maple** Ar.
σφενδονάω *contr.vb.* [σφενδόνη] **1** (of soldiers) **use a sling, cast a sling-shot** Pi.*fr.* Th. X.; (of a person) **let fly** —W.DAT. *w. sods, stones, pears* Men.
2 cause to whirl round like a sling, swing to and fro —*a club* E. ‖ PASS. (of the limbs of a person struck by lightning) **be catapulted** (fr. a ladder) E.(dub.)
σφενδόνη ης, dial. **σφενδόνᾱ** ᾱς *f.* **1 leather strap** (held by a thong at each end), **sling** (for projecting stones) Archil. E. Th. Ar. X. +; (used as an improvised bandage) Il.
2 sling-stone X.; (pl., fig.ref. to hail) Ar.
3 tackle for loading a ship; (in fig.ctxt., ref. to ropes around an object to be jettisoned) **sling** A.
4 seal (on a signet-ring, perh. fr. resemblance of their combined shape to a military sling) E. Pl.
σφενδόνησις εως *f.* **use of a sling, slinging** Pl.
σφενδονήτης ου *m.* **soldier who uses a sling, slinger** Hdt. Th. Pl. X. D. +
σφενδονητικός ή όν *adj.* (of the skill) **of slinging** Pl.
σφεός ή (dial. ἅ) όν *possessv.adj.* [σφεῖς, σφώ; reltd. σφέτερος, σφός, σφωίτερος] **1** [σφεῖς] (3sg.) **her, her own** Alcm.; (3pl.) **their, their own** Alcm.
2 [σφώ] (2du.) **of you both** Alcm.
σφετερίζω *vb.* [σφέτερος] | aor. ἐσφετέρισα ‖ MID.: aor. ἐσφετερισάμην, dial.aor.ptcpl. σφετεριξάμενος (A.) | **1 make**

one's own, **appropriate** —*others' property, management of civic affairs* Pl.; (mid.) —*others' property* D. Plb. Plu. —*an uncle's children* (*in forced marriage*) A.

2 ‖ MID. **annex** —*territory* X. D. Arist. Plb. Plu.

σφετερισμός οῦ *m.* **personal gain** Arist.

σφετεριστής οῦ *m.* **appropriator** (of a state's property, opp. a guardian of it) Arist.

σφέτερος ᾱ (Ion. η) ον *possessv.adj.* [σφεῖς] **1** (3pl., sts. strengthened by αὐτῶν or ἑαυτῶν) **their own** Hom. + ‖ FEM.SG.SB. their own land Hdt. Th. Lys. Isoc. ‖ MASC.PL.SB. their own people Hdt. Th. X. ‖ NEUT.SG.PL.SB. their own property, interests, business Th. Att.orats. Pl. X. Arist.

2 (3sg.) **his** or **her own** Hes. A. Pi. B. Hellenist.poet. Plb.

3 (2pl.) **your own** Hes. AR.; (2sg.) Theoc.; (2du.) Alcm.

4 (1pl.) **our own** AR. Plb.; (1sg.) **my own** Theoc.

σφέων, σφεων (Ion.gen.3pl.pers.pron.): see σφεῖς

σφηκιά ᾶς *f.* [σφήξ] **wasps' nest** E.*Cyc.* Ar.

σφηκίσκος ου *m.* **1 pointed stake** Ar.

2 piece of squared-off timber (used for building); **lintel** (W.GEN. of a doorway) Arist.; **plank** or **beam** (prob. for shipbuilding) Plb.

σφηκόομαι *pass.contr.vb.* | 3pl.plpf. ἐσφήκωντο | (of a cloak) be pinched in like a wasp's waist, **be wasp-waisted** Anacr.; (of locks of hair) **be bound wasp-like** —W.DAT. *w. gold and silver bands* Il.

σφηκώδης ες *adj.* (of persons, their appearance) wasp-like, **slim-waisted** Ar.

σφήκωμα ατος *n.* **collar** (on a helmet, ref. to a metal band or sim. holding the plume and constricting it) Ar.

σφῆλα (ep.aor.): see σφάλλω

σφήν ηνός *m.* | ep.dat.pl. σφήνεσσι | **wedge** (securing a mast at its base) AR.; (as a geometrical instrument, perh. for drawing angles) Ar.; (used for impaling) A.

σφηνόομαι *pass.contr.vb.* (of wing-shaped pieces of wood) **be wedged in** —w. εἰς + ACC. *to the shaft of an arrow* Plb.

σφήξ ηκός, dial. **σφάξ** ᾱκός (Theoc.) *m.* **wasp** Il. Hdt. Ar. Pl. X. +

Σφήττιος ᾱ ον *adj.* (of a person) of or from Sphettos (an Attic deme), **Sphettian** Ar. Att.orats. Pl. (of vinegar) Ar.

—**Σφηττόθεν** *adv.* **from Sphettos** Plu.

—**Σφηττοῖ** *adv.* **in** or **at Sphettos** Lys. Aeschin.

σφι(ν) (enclit.dat.3sg.pl.pers.pron.): see σφεῖς

σφίγγω *vb.* **1 bind tight** —*a person* A. —*sheaves* Theoc. ‖ PASS. (of a cloak) be bound tight Theoc.; (of land) be constricted or reduced to a narrow width (by seas on either side) Plu.

2 (of enveloping aither, circular motion) **bind** or **hold together** —*everything* Emp. Pl. ‖ PASS. (of stars) be held in place —W.DAT. *by circular motion* Plu.

Σφίγξ ιγγός, Boeot. **Φίξ** ῑκός *f.* [prob.orig. Σφίξ, then reltd. by pop.etym. to σφίγγω] | acc. Σφίγγα, Boeot. Φῑκα |

1 sphinx (representation of a hybrid creature, usu. a lion w. a woman's head and wings, common fr. early times in Egyptian, Mesopotamian and Greek art) Hdt. E. Plu.

2 (in Theban legend) **Sphinx** (daughter of Chimaira or Echidna, sister of the Nemean lion; her riddle was solved by Oedipus) Hes. Trag. Ar.(quot. A.) Pl.

σφίσι(ν), σφισί(ν) (dat.3pl.pers.pron.): see σφεῖς

σφόδρα *adv.* [σφοδρός] **1** (w.vbs.) **to an intense degree, strongly, very much, certainly** Pi. Hdt. S. Th. Ar. +

2 (w.adj. or adv.) **extremely, very** Ar. Att.orats. Pl. + • (w.sb.) ἡ σφόδρα μανία *complete madness* Pl.

3 (w. emph. force, in answers, oft. σφόδρα γε, καὶ σφόδρα γε) **very much so, yes indeed** Pl. X.

σφοδρός ά όν (also ός όν Pl.) *adj.* [reltd. σφεδανός] | compar. σφοδρότερος, superl. σφοδρότατος | **1** (of feelings, behaviour) **vehement, intense, strong** Th. Pl. X. +; (of punishment, a blow) **heavy, powerful** Men. Plb. Plu.; (of poison, a guarantee) **strong, effective** Plu.; (of cold) **extreme** Plu.

2 (of persons, their bodies, natures, sts.pejor.) **intense, energetic, impetuous** Pl. X. D. Men. Plu.; (of an orator) D.; (of a horse) X.

—**σφοδρῶς** *adv.* | compar. σφοδρότερον | **1 vigorously, violently, impetuously** —*ref. to performing actions* Od. Pl. X. D. +

2 intensely, powerfully —*ref. to suffering or feeling emotions* Pl. Arist. Plu.; (w. ἔχειν) be intensely eager X.

σφοδρότης ητος *f.* **1 intensity, vehemence** (of feelings, behaviour) Pl. Arist. Plu.; (as shown by the use of hyperbole) Arist.

2 vehemence, impetus (of a military attack) X. Plu.

σφοδρύνομαι *pass.vb.* **gain excessive strength** or **confidence** —W.DAT. *fr. a weak stratagem* A.

σφονδύλη ης *f.* a kind of insect (emitting a foul smell); perh. **beetle** Ar.

σφονδύλια ων *n.pl.* [dimin. σφόνδυλος] **vertebrae** Il.

σφόνδυλος ου *m.* **1 bone of the spinal column, vertebra** Pl. Plu.; (collectv.sg.) vertebral column, **spine** Ar.; (collectv.pl.) E.

2 fly-wheel (fixed around a spindle), **whorl** (named fr. its resemblance to a vertebra) Pl.

σφός ή όν *possessv.adj.* [σφεῖς; reltd. σφεός, σφέτερος]

1 (3pl.) **their, their own** Hom. Sapph. Pi. AR.

2 (3sg.) **his, his own** or **her, her own** Hes. Alcm. Thgn.

σφρᾱγίδιον ου *n.* [dimin. σφρᾱγίς] **signet-ring** Ar.

σφρᾱγῑδ-ονυχ-αργο-κομήτης ου *m.* [σφρᾱγίς, ὄνυξ, ἀργός] **long-haired layabout with signet-ring of onyx** Ar.

σφρᾱγίζω *vb.* | aor. ἐσφράγισα ‖ MID.: fut. σφραγιοῦμαι (Plu.) ‖ PASS: pf.ptcpl. ἐσφραγισμένος | **1 mark with a seal** (for identification or security), **seal** —*a document* E. —*a boulder* (blocking an entrance) NT.; (mid.) —*a document* Plb. Plu. —*the doors of a storeroom* E.fr. ‖ PASS. (of Zeus' thunderbolt) be sealed away (in a storeroom) A.

2 (fig.) **mark with a seal** (for authentication or approval); (of God) **mark with His seal** —*Christ* NT.; (of a person) **certify** —W.COMPL.CL. *that sthg. is the case* NT.

3 ‖ PASS. (fig., of persons who have been in a fight) **be stamped** —W.DAT. *w. marks of injury* E.

σφρᾱγίς, Ion. **σφρηγίς**, ῖδος *f.* **1 signet-ring** Hdt. S. Ar. Pl. Plu.

2 seal, signet (ref. to the stone or gem in such a ring) Hdt. Plu.

3 impression of a signet-ring, **signet, seal** E. Th. Ar. Pl. +

4 seal (of state) Arist. Plb. Plu.; (of office) Plu.

5 (fig.) **seal** or **sign** (as a means of safeguarding poems against theft, perh. ref. to stylistic evidence) Thgn.; (as an instrument for conveying or stopping speech; ref. to the tongue or mouth) Critias Tim.

σφράγισμα ατος *n.* **impression** or **use of a seal; sealing** E. X.

σφρῑγάω *contr.vb.* | only pres. | ep.fem.nom.pl.ptcpl. (w.diect.) σφριγόωσαι (AR.) | **1 be swollen;** (of young persons, their bodies or arms) **be bursting with health, be full of vigour** E. Ar. Pl. AR.

2 (fig., of a heart) **be swollen** (w. rage) A.; (of a speech) **be puffed up** (w. overconfidence) E.

σφυγμός οῦ *m.* [σφύζω] (medic.) **throbbing** (fr. emotion, inflammation) Plu.

σφυδόομαι *pass.contr.vb.* | pf.ptcpl. ἐσφυδωμένος | ‖ PF. (of an ithyphallic god) be at bursting-point Carm.Pop.

σφυδρόν *n.*: see σφυρόν

σφύζω, dial. **σφύσδω** *vb.* (of veins or arteries) **pulse, throb** Pl.; (of the head and feet) Theoc.

σφῦρα ᾶς (Ion. ης) *f.* **1 hammer** Od. B. Hdt. AR.
2 heavy wooden mallet, **mallet** (to break up earth) Hes. Ar.

σφυράς άδος *f.* **dung-ball** (of sheep or goats) Ar.

σφυρ-ήλατος ον *adj.* [σφῦρα, ἐλαύνω] (of a sword, fetters, statues of gold or other metal) beaten out with a hammer, **hammer-wrought** A. Hdt. Pl. Theoc.; (fig., of compulsion) Pi.*fr.*

σφυρίς *f.*: see σπυρίς

σφυρόν (also **σφυδρόν** NT.) οῦ *n.* **1 ankle** (of a person) Il. Archil. E. Ar. X. +; (of a fawn, horse) E.
2 (fig.) **footing** (on which a country stands) Pi.
3 (fig.) **foothill** (of a mountain) Pi.; **edge** (of a country) Theoc.

σφύσδω *dial.vb.*: see σφύζω

σφώ, ep. **σφῶι** (also perh. **σφῶιν** Od.) **2du.pers.pron.** | acc. σφώ, ep. σφῶι | gen.dat. σφῶν, ep. σφῶιν | **the two of you, you both** Hom. Trag. Ar. Pl. Theoc.

σφωέ (ep.nom.acc.3du.enclit.pers.pron.), **σφωίν** (gen.dat.): see σφεῖς

σφωίτερος ᾱ (Ion. η) ον *possessv.adj.* **1** [σφώ] (2du.) **of you both** Il.
2 [as if reltd. σύ] (2sg.) **your own** AR.
3 [σφεῖς] (3pl.) **their own** AR.; (3sg.) **his** or **her own** Theoc.

σφῶν, σφῶιν (gen.dat.2du.pers.pron.): see σφώ

σφῶν (gen.3pl.pers.pron.): see σφεῖς

σχαδών όνος *f.* honey-cell; (collectv.pl.) **honeycomb** Theoc.

σχάζω *vb.* —also (impf.) **σχάω** *contr.vb.* | impf. ἔσχων (Ar.) | aor. ἔσχασα, Aeol.ptcpl. σχάσαις (Pi.), dial. σχάσσᾱς (Call.) |
1 release (pressure or tension, by cutting); **slit open** —*a vein* X. Plu. —*a haggis* Ar.
2 cause to relax, **relax, ease up on** —*fierce looks and angry breathing* E. —*anxious thinking* Ar.; **ease off** —*an oar* Pi. E. Call.; **rest** —*one's voice* (i.e. stop speaking) E.
3 (of Peleus wrestling w. Thetis) cause to become limp, **weaken the power of, foil** —*her fire, claws and teeth* Pi.; (of a person) —*an adversary* (W.PREP.PHR. *in his thinking, i.e. sap his confidence*) B.
4 (of hounds) **lower, let drop** —*their tails* X.
5 ‖ MID. **give up** —*horse-racing* Ar.
6 (of a commander) **let off, discharge** —*engines of war* Plu.

σχαλίς ίδος *f.* **stake** (supporting a hunting net) X.

σχαστηρίᾱ ᾱς *f.* [σχάζω 6] **release-mechanism** or **trigger** (in a military catapult) Plb.

σχάω *contr.vb.*: see σχάζω

σχέδην *adv.* [σχεῖν, see ἔχω] in a restrained manner, **slowly** —*ref. to persons, horses or ships moving* X. Plu.

σχεδίᾱ ᾱς, Ion. **σχεδίη** ης *f.* [perh. σχεδόν] **1** improvised vessel (built fr. timbers pinned and tied together), **boat** Od.; **raft** Th. Pl. Plb. Plu.; (made of hides) X.
2 craft, vessel (of Charon) Theoc.; (gener.) **ship** E.
3 pontoon-bridge (of boats, built by Darius across the Hellespont) A. Hdt.

σχεδιάζω *vb.* [σχεδόν] **1** act on the spur of the moment; (of officials) **behave perfunctorily** Plb.
2 (of a historian) **make a careless statement** Plb.

σχέδιος ᾱ ον *adj.* (of a sword) **used at close quarters** A.
—**σχεδίην** *adv.* **at close quarters** —*ref. to striking w. a spear* Il.

σχεδόθεν *adv. and prep.* **1** from close at hand; (in ctxt. of fighting) **at close quarters** Il.
2 (ref. to location) **close by** AR.
3 (as prep., ref. to location or motion towards) **close, near** —W.GEN. or DAT. *to someone* Hom.
4 (ref. to time) **at once, without delay** AR.

σχεδόν *adv. and prep.* [σχεῖν, see ἔχω] **1** (ref. to location) **close, near** Hom. hHom. Pi. AR. Theoc. —W.GEN. *to someone or sthg.* Od. hHom. AR. —W.DAT. Hom. Hes. Pi. Hdt. AR.; (in ctxt. of fighting) **at close quarters** Il.
2 (ref. to motion towards) **close, near** Hom. Hes. AR. —W.GEN. *to someone or sthg.* Hom. AR. —W.DAT. Il. Hes.
3 (ref. to an impending event) **close, near** (sts. W.DAT. *to someone*) Hom. Hdt. E.; (ref. to a person) **near** —W.GEN. *to an impending event* Theoc.
4 (ref. to family relationship) closely connected, **close** Od.
5 (modifying assertions) to a close degree or extent; (w.adj., adv., advbl. or prep.phr.) **nearly, about, roughly** Stesich. Hdt. S. E. +
6 (w.vbs., esp. of speaking, thinking, knowing, sts. softening an assertion) **nearly, more or less, one might almost say** Hdt. S. E. +
7 (as an answer, in dialogue) **more or less, perhaps so** Pl.

σχεθέειν, σχεθεῖν, σχεθέμεν (ep.aor.2 inf.), **σχεθέτω** (3sg.imperatv.), **σχέθοιμι** (opt.), **σχέθον** (1sg.), **σχέθω** (subj.), **σχεθών** (ptcpl.): see ἔχω

σχεῖν (aor.2 inf.): see ἔχω

σχελίδες ίδων *f.pl.* **sides of beef** (or other meat) Ar. Philox.Leuc.

σχέμεν (ep.aor.2 inf.), **σχέο** (ep.aor.2 mid.imperatv.): see ἔχω

Σχερίη ης *Ion.f.* **Scherie** (land of the Phaeacians, oft. identified w. Corcyra, mod. Corfu) Od.

σχερός οῦ *m.* [perh. falsely derived fr. ἐπισχερώ; cf. ἐνοσχερώ] (only in phr.) ἐν σχερῷ in unbroken line (ref. to creating a myriad of poetic themes) Pi.; **uninterruptedly, continuously** (ref. to a sequence or duration of events) Pi.

σχές (aor.2 imperatv.), **σχέσθαι, σχέσθε** (aor.2 mid.inf. and 2pl.imperatv.): see ἔχω

σχέσις εως *f.* [σχεῖν, see ἔχω] **1 possession** (W.GEN. of a style of military equipment) Pl.; **bearing** (W.GEN. of arms) A. Pl.
2 state, condition (W.GEN. of hair and clothing) X.
3 state, demeanour (of a person) D.
4 holding back, restraint (as a concept, opp. flow, motion) Pl.

σχετήριον ου *n.* means of stopping; (ref. to meat) **remedy** (W.GEN. for hunger) E.*Cyc.*

σχετλιάζω *vb.* [σχέτλιος] | aor. ἐσχετλίασα | consider (sthg.) cruel or shocking; **complain, protest** Ar. Att.orats. Pl. Thphr. Plb. Plu.

σχετλιασμός οῦ *m.* venting of indignation or complaint, **complaining, protesting** Th. Arist.

σχέτλιος ᾱ (Ion. η) ον (also ος ον E.) *adj.* | oft. in voc. address, w. strong emotional force | **1** (of a person or god) **enduring, obstinate, tireless** Hom. S.; (W.GEN. in daring) E.
2 hard-hearted, unfeeling, cruel Hom. +; (of the nature of a bird of prey, wild creatures) **savage** Thgn. Hdt.
3 (of actions) **cruel** Od. Hes. Thgn. Hdt. E. Ar.; (of sleep, as having unfortunate consequences) Od.
4 (of persons) **wicked, villainous** Ar. Att.orats. Pl.; (of actions, words) Ar. Att.orats. Pl. Plu.
5 (of persons) **unfortunate, miserable, wretched** A. E. Ar. Hellenist.poet.; (W.GEN. in sufferings) E.
6 (of pain, sufferings) **harsh, cruel, pitiable** B. S. E. Ar. +

—**σχέτλιον** neut.adv. **cruelly, shockingly** hHom.
—**σχετλίως** adv. (w. ἔχειν) *be heartless* Isoc.
σχέτο (ep.3sg.aor.2 mid.): see ἔχω
σχῆμα ατος *n.* [σχεῖν, see ἔχω] **1 form, shape** (of physical objects, sts. also ref. to their appearance) E. Ar. Pl. +; (of things, opp. their colour) Pl.; (as an element of art, opp. colour) Pl. Arist.
2 visual impression, **appearance, bearing** (of a person) Hdt. Trag. Ar. +; **build** (of a horse) X.; **outward manifestation** (of an empire) Pl.; (periphr., in voc. exclam.) **sight** (W.GEN. of a familiar place, seen anew in emotional circumstances) S. E.; (phr., ref. to Erinyes) μορφῆς σχήματα *form-shapes* E.
3 appearance (opp. reality); **show, pretence** Th. Pl. Plu.; **outward appearance, guise** (of sthg. else) Isoc. Pl. Arist.; (fig., ref. to a person) **mere figure** E.*fr.*
4 good impression (created by an action) E.
5 manner, style (of dress) S. E. Ar.; **item** (of clothing) E.; **dress, clothes** (of an individual) Theoc.
6 lifestyle Pl. X.; **role, function** (of a person in society) Pl.; (of a camel as a pack-animal) X.
7 specific form, type (of government) Th. Pl. Arist.; (oft.pl.) **style, form** (of rhetorical or poetic diction) Arist.; (sg.) **characteristic form** (of a legal speech or proclamation, a literary genre) Isoc. Pl. Arist.
8 posture (ref. to bodily movement or position) Ar. Isoc. X.; **gesture** (by an orator) D.
9 (usu.pl.) **dance-figure, dance-step** Hdt. E.*Cyc.* Ar. Pl. X.; (fig., ref. to exaggerated behaviour) Pl.
10 (phr.) οὐ κατὰ σχῆμα *not in due form, inappropriately* Plb.
σχηματίζω vb. | pf.mid.pass. ἐσχημάτισμαι | **1** adopt a certain shape; (of armies) **adopt a formation** —W.NEUT.ACC. *of a certain kind* Pl.; (of the body) **adopt** —W.COGN.ACC. *a shape or posture* Pl.; (of the soul) **shape** —*perception* Plu. ‖ MID. **shape, arrange** —*one's hair* E. ‖ PASS. (of a shield) be emblazoned (in a particular way) A.
2 pose or gesture (w. one's body), **dance** Ar.; **make a gesture** (of an abusive kind, w. one's arm or hand) Plu. ‖ MID. (of spectators) **react with body language** X. ‖ PASS. (of dance-rhythms) be expressed by steps and gestures Arist.
3 ‖ MID. **put on a show** —W.ACC. *of authority* Pl.; **put on a pretence** Pl. —W.INF. or ὡς + NOM.PTCPL. *of being or doing sthg.* Pl.
σχημάτιον ου *n.* [dimin. σχῆμα] **dance-figure, dance-step** Hdt.
σχηματισμός οῦ *m.* [σχηματίζω] **1** assumption of a certain form, **bearing, deportment** (of the body) Pl.; **demeanour** (of a person) Plu.
2 assumption of a false form, **affectation, airs** Pl. Plu.
σχηματοποιέομαι mid.contr.vb. [σχῆμα] (of a horse) adopt a certain bearing, **show off** X.
σχήσω (fut.2): see ἔχω
σχίζα ης *f.* [σχίζω] **split piece of wood** (esp. used for fire at sacrifices) Hom. Ar. AR. Theoc.
σχιζοποδίᾱ ᾶς *f.* [πούς] **cloven-footedness** (of animals) Arist.
σχίζω vb. | aor. ἔσχισα, ep. σχίσσα ‖ PASS.: aor. ἐσχίσθην | pf. ἔσχισμαι | **1** split by cutting; (of Zeus) **split, cleave** —*the earth* (W.DAT. *w. a thunderbolt*) Pi.; (of a person) —*a head* (w. *an axe*) S. —*tree-bark* Hdt.; **cut up** —*portions of sacrificial meat* hHom.; **cut** —*shoe-leather* X.; **chop** —*wood* X.
—W.PARTITV.GEN. Plu. ‖ PASS. (of the earth) be split open (by ploughing) AR.; (of rocks, by an earthquake) NT.; (of the heavens) NT. ‖ PF.PASS.PTCPL. (of a torch) split (i.e. app. consisting of pieces of split wood) Ar.

2 split by tearing; (of a lion) **rend** —*an animal's hide* (W.DAT. *w. its claws*) Hes.; (of a person) **tear** —*a garment* NT. ‖ PASS. (of a shawl, cloak, curtain, fishing-net) be torn Theoc. NT. Plu.
3 divide into parts; (of the creator god) **split, divide** —*veins* (*in the body*), *the fabric of the soul* Pl.; (of a river) —*a country* Hdt. —*its stream* AR. ‖ PASS. (of a river) be divided Hdt. Pl. AR. Plb.; (of a road) Hdt.; (of an army) Hdt.; (of troops) be separated Plu.
4 make a mental or logical division; **divide** —*a class or category* Pl. ‖ PASS. (of classes or categories) be divided Pl.
5 ‖ PASS. (of opinions) be divided Hdt.; (of people, in their opinions) X. NT.; (of good news and truth) be kept separate A.
σχινδάλαμοι *m.pl.*: see σκινδάλαμοι
σχῖνο-κέφαλος ον *adj.* [σχῖνος, κεφαλή] **onion-headed** or **squill-headed** (epith. of Perikles) Plu.(quot.com.)
σχῖνος ου *f.* **1** a kind of resinous shrub, **mastic** Hdt. Ar. Call. Theoc.
2 a kind of bulbous plant (sts. identified w. σκίλλα *squill, sea-onion*) Plu.
σχίσις εως *f.* [σχίζω] **1 division** (of a number or entity) Pl.
2 fork (in a road) Pl.
σχίσμα ατος *n.* **1 rent, tear** (in a garment) NT.
2 division of opinion, **dissension, schism** (W.PREP.PHR. among people) NT.
σχισμός οῦ *m.* **cleaving** (of a body, by a sword) A.
σχιστός ή (dial. ᾱ́) όν *adj.* **1** (of a road) **branching, forked** S. E.
2 (of a chariot rail) perh. **branching** (to the right and left side) E.
3 (of animals) **cloven-hoofed** Pl.
σχοίατο (ep.3pl.aor.2 mid.opt.), **σχοίην** (aor.2 opt.): see ἔχω
σχοίνινος η ον *adj.* [σχοῖνος] (of a basket) **made of rushes, rush** E.*Cyc.*
σχοινίον ου *n.* [dimin. σχοῖνος] **rope, cord** Hdt. Ar. D. Men. NT. Plu.; (fig.ref. to a phallus) Ar.
σχοινίς ῖδος *f.* **rope** Theoc.
σχοινισμός οῦ *m.* app., a form of torture using ropes, **rope-treatment** Plu.
σχοῖνος ου *m.f.* **1** a kind of marsh-plant, **rush** Hdt. Ar. Theoc.; (as being sharp) app. **reed** Ar.
2 place where rushes grow, **bed of rushes** Od. Pi.
3 rope, cord (oft. made fr. rushes) Hdt. Pl. Theoc.
4 measuring-rope (for land) Hdt.
5 (ref. to an Egyptian unit of measurement, 60 stades) **schoinos** Hdt.; (in fig.ctxt.) σχοῖνος Περσίς *Persian yardstick* (*as a criterion by which poetry shd. not be judged, i.e. by amount, opp. by quality*) Call.
σχοινο-τενής ές (also fem. -τένεια Pi.) *adj.* [reltd. τείνω] like a stretched measuring-rope; (of a canal, gangway) **in a straight line** Hdt.; (of the singing of dithyrambs, ref. to the original arrangement of the singers in a line rather than a circle) Pi.*fr.*; (phr., of engineers) σχοινοτενὲς ποιεῖσθαι *make a straight line* Hdt.
σχολᾱ́ dial.*f.*: see σχολή
σχολάζω vb. [σχολή] | aor. ἐσχόλασα | **1 be at leisure, be unoccupied** Th. Lys. Ar. Pl. X. D. +
2 have leisure or **time, be available** —W.INF. *to do sthg.* Pl. X. Arist. Plu. —W.DAT. *for one's friends* X. Men. Plu. —W.PREP.PHR. *for an activity* X. Aeschin. Arist.
3 devote one's time —W.DAT. or PREP.PHR. *to an activity* D. Plu.

σχολαῖος

4 take one's time, **delay, linger, hesitate** A. E. ‖ MID. (of the growth of the baby Hermes, in neg.phr.) **be slow** S.*Ichn.*
5 **have a respite, be free** —w. ἀπό + GEN. *fr. an activity* X. —W.GEN. Plu.
6 (of land) **be unoccupied** or **uninhabited** Plu.; (of a place) **be vacant, be free** —W.DAT. *for someone* Plu.

σχολαῖος ᾱ ον *adj.* [σχολή] | compar. σχολαίτερος | 1 (of persons) proceeding at a leisurely pace, **slow** Th.; (of a march) X.
2 (of actions) **delayed, tardy** Hdt.

—**σχολαίως** *adv.* | compar. σχολαίτερον, superl. σχολαίτατα |
1 **slowly** Th. Pl. X. D. Plu.
2 **tardily, reluctantly** X. Arist.

σχολαιότης ητος *f.* **leisurely progress** (on a march) Th.

σχολαστήριον ου *n.* [σχολάζω] **study-room** Plu.

σχολαστής οῦ *m.* 1 **scholar** Plu.
2 ‖ ADJ. (of a style of life) **leisured** or **scholarly** Plu.; (of the masses) **with time on one's hands** Plu.

σχολαστικός ή όν *adj.* 1 (of a person or city) of the kind which has leisure or free time, **leisured** Arist.
2 ‖ NEUT.SB. **leisureliness** (as one of the attributes of intellectual activity) Arist.
3 (of a gathering) for leisured discussion, **leisured, scholarly** Arist.
4 (pejor., of a person) **scholarly, intellectual** Plu.

σχολή ῆς, dial. **σχολᾱ́** ᾶς *f.* 1 **leisure, free time** A. Pi. Hdt. E. Th. +; (prep.phr.) ἐπὶ σχολῆς *at leisure or in a leisurely way* E. Pl. Aeschin. Plu.; (also) κατὰ σχολήν Ar. Pl. D. Men. Plu.
2 **rest, respite** S.; (W.GEN. fr. sthg.) S. E. Pl. Arist. Plu.; (w. ἀπό + GEN.) Pl. X.
3 **leisureliness, slowness, delay** Trag.
4 **leisure, enough time** (W.INF. to do sthg.) A. S. Ar. Pl. X.
5 use of free time, **leisure pursuit, pastime** Pl.
6 **leisured discussion, session** (required for expounding a topic) Arist.
7 **group of scholars** (studying philosophy or rhetoric) Arist.; **School** (under a particular teacher) NT. Plu.

—**σχολῇ** *dat.adv.* 1 in a leisurely way, **slowly** S. Th. +; **with reluctance** X.
2 (ref. to the improbability of sthg. happening) not in a hurry, **scarcely, hardly** S. And. Pl. X. Arist.; (introducing an *a fortiori* argument in an apodosis, usu. after a neg. protasis 'if not ...') **then hardly** Pl. X. Arist.

σχόμενος (aor.2 mid.ptcpl.), **σχῶ** (aor.2 subj.), **σχών** (aor.2 ptcpl.): see ἔχω

σώεσθαι[1] (mid.pass.inf.): see σαόω

σώεσθαι[2] (mid.inf.): see σεύω

σώεσκον (iteratv.impf.), **σώετε** (2pl.imperatv.): see σαόω

σῴζω *vb.* [σῶς] | fut. σώσω | aor. ἔσωσα | pf. σέσωκα ‖ MID.: fut. σώσομαι | aor. ἐσωσάμην ‖ PASS.: fut. σωθήσομαι | aor. ἐσώθην | pf. σέσωμαι, later σέσωσμαι ‖ neut.impers.vbl.adj. σωστέον ‖ This vb. is found only once in Hom. For the ep. forms see σαόω. |
1 (of persons, gods, other agents) save (someone or sthg.) from imminent danger or death; **save, rescue** —*persons, someone's life* Hdt. S. E. + —*a country, city, or sim.* Hdt. S. E. + —(W.GEN. *fr. enemies*) S.; (of a person, truce) —W.ACC. + INF. (sts. w. μή) *someone fr. being killed* E. ‖ MID. **save** —*one's life* E. —*one's eyelids* (*i.e. skin*) Ar. ‖ PASS. (of persons, cities, or sim.) be saved, be safe, survive Thgn. Hdt. Trag. +
2 save from an unwelcome situation; **save, rescue** —*someone* Trag. —(W.GEN. or PREP.PHR. *fr. troubles*) S. ‖ PASS. be saved —W.GEN. *fr. troubles* E.

3 get (sthg.) back safely; **rescue, recover** —*corpses* E. —*a lost opportunity* D.
4 **bring** (W.ACC. someone) **safely** —W.ADV. or PREP.PHR. *fr. or to a place* S. E. Pl. ‖ PASS. get safely —W.ADV. or PREP.PHR. *fr. or to a place* Hdt. Trag. + —W.DAT. *to someone* Theoc.
5 preserve from harm; (of persons or gods) **keep safe, protect, look after** —*possessions or sim.* Hdt. S. E. + —*persons, cities, or sim.* Lyr.adesp. Hdt. Trag. Ar. +; (of a city) —*its inhabitants* S. Th.; (of a class of people) —*a city* E.; (of a countryman) —*a source of fire* Od.; (of a dragon) —*the Golden Fleece* E.; (of a pregnant woman) —*an embryo* A.; (mid.) —*one's treasures* E.*fr.* —*one's guard dog* (*fig.ref. to a person*) Ar.; (of a country) —*its spoils of war* E. ‖ PASS. (of a person) be kept safe E.; (of inactivity, ref. to inactive persons) be safe Th.
6 (of things) keep (someone or sthg.) safe; (of corks) **keep secure** —*a fishing-line or net* A.; (of an anchor) —*a ship* E.*fr.*; (of weapons) **protect** —*parts of the body* E.; (of a quiver) —*an arrow* E. ‖ PASS. (of objects) be kept safe S. E. —W.DAT. *for someone* Ar.
7 (of abstr. things, such as obedience, caution, good order) **keep safe, protect** —*people* S. Th. Ar. X.; (of laws and customs) —*a constitution, democracy* Arist.; (of the ability to light a fire) **keep alive** —*a person* S.; (of time) —*hopes* E.
8 keep safe (non-material things); **preserve, maintain** —*one's marriage bed* (*i.e. remain faithful*) E. —*one's father's reputation* E. —*one's present way of thinking* A. —*silence* E.; (mid.) —*caution* S. —*a memory* (*of sthg.*) E. Pl.; (act.) **fulfil** —*what is ordained* E.
9 keep to oneself, **keep safe, guard** —*information, secrets* A. S.
10 preserve by obedience, **observe** —*instructions* Trag. —*laws* S. E.; (mid.) —*proverbial advice* A.*satyr.fr.*
11 (act. and mid.) preserve in one's mind, **remember** —*sthg.* E. Pl.
12 (of God or Christ) keep safe from eternal death, **save** —*a person* NT. ‖ PASS. be in a state of salvation NT.

σωκέω *contr.vb.* [σῶκος] (of a person) **have strength** A. —W.INF. *to do sthg.* A.

σῶκος ου *masc.adj.* (epith. of Hermes) app. **strong** Il.

σωκρατάω (or **σωκρατέω**) *contr.vb.* [Σωκράτης] | 3pl.impf. ἐσωκράτων (v.l. ἐσωκράτουν) | (pseudo-medic., of Athenians imitating Spartan manners) **have Socratitis** (i.e. either *long to be like Socrates* or, as v.l., *behave like Socrates*) Ar.

Σωκράτης ους *m.* | voc. Σώκρατες | acc. Σωκράτη, also Σωκράτην | **Socrates** (Athenian philosopher, 469–399 BC) Ar. Isoc. Pl. X. +

—**Σωκρατίδιον** ου *n.* [dimin.] | only voc. Σωκρατίδιον | **dear Socrates** Ar.

Σωκρατικός ή όν *adj.* (of dialogues, precepts) of or relating to Socrates, **Socratic** Arist.; (epith. of Aeschines and Antisthenes, followers of Socrates, to distinguish them fr. namesakes) Plu.

σωλήν ῆνος *m.* **pipe** (for water, other liquids) Hdt. Plu.; (app. colloq.ref. to a penis) Archil.

σῶμα ατος *n.* | dial.dat.pl. σωμάτεσσι (Pi.) | 1 **dead body, corpse** Hom. +; **carcass** (of an animal) Il. Hes. Pi. Hdt.
2 **living body, body** (of a person) Hes. +; (opp. soul) Pi.*fr.* Isoc. Pl. X.; (pl., ref. to creatures, opp. plants) Pl.
3 (periphr.) **body, form** (W.GEN. of Cerberus, the Sphinx, implying strength or bulk) S. E.; (phr., fig.) σῶμα πόλεως **body politic** Hyp. Din.

4 body (of Christ, ref. to bread in the Christian sacrament) NT.
5 (as a tangible manifestation of the individual self, which one saves, risks, fights for) **life, skin** E. Th. X.; (in legal ctxts.) Att.orats.
6 personal rights, civil status Att.orats.
7 person, individual, human being S. E. Aeschin.; (w. epith. *free, slave, captive*) Att.orats. X. Plb.; (without epith.) **slave** Plb.; (periphr.) ἀνθρώπου σῶμα *a person* Hdt.
8 body of matter, substance, mass, body Pl. Arist.; (geom.) **solid** Arist.
9 whole body, frame (of the universe) Pl.
10 (fig.) **essence** (of a proof, ref. to syllogisms) Arist.

σωμ-ασκέω *contr.vb.* **1** train the body (for athletic or military purposes), **take exercise** X. Plb. Plu.
2 (fig., of a commander) **put in good shape** —*a war* (*in terms of training and equipment*) Plu.

σωμασκίᾱ ᾱς *f.* **bodily exercise, physical training** Pl. X.

σωματικός ή όν *adj.* **1** of or relating to the body; (of activities, pains, pleasures, strength) **bodily** Arist. Plb. Plu.; (of a person's name) **relating to a bodily feature** Plu.
‖ NEUT.PL.SB. bodily features Plu.
2 having body or substance; (of an entity) **corporeal, physical** Arist.; (of the form of the Holy Spirit) NT.
‖ NEUT.PL.SB. material things (opp. abstr. notions) Plu.

σωμάτιον ου *n.* [dimin. σῶμα] **poor body** (of an infirm person) Isoc.

σωματο-ειδής ές *adj.* [εἶδος¹] **1** having bodily form; (of the soul, entities) **corporeal** Pl. ‖ NEUT.SB. (w.art.) the corporeal Pl.
2 (of historical inquiry, a character sketch) having an organic form, **unified, systematic** Plb.

σωματοποιέω *contr.vb.* **1** give body or substance (to someone or sthg.); (fig.) **build up the strength of, consolidate** —*a commander, troops, a kingdom* Plb. ‖ PASS. (of a person) be strengthened —w. διά + ACC. *by someone* (*i.e. by his help*)
2 (fig.) **strengthen, bolster** —*downcast spirits* Plb.; **give credibility to** —*every hope* Plb.

σωματο-φύλαξ ακος *m.* **bodyguard** Plb. Plu.

σωόμενος (mid.ptcpl.): see σεύω
σώοντες (ep.masc.nom.pl.ptcpl.): see σαόω
σώοντο (ep.3pl.impf.mid.): see σεύω
σῶος Att.*adj.*: see σῶς
σωπή *dial.f.*: see σιωπή
σωρείᾱ ᾱς *f.* [σωρεύω] **heaping up** (of dead bodies) Plu.
σώρευμα ατος *n.* **heap** (of dead bodies and armour) X.
σώρευσις εως *f.* **accumulation** (of concepts) Arist.
σωρεύω *vb.* [σωρός] **1** form into a heap; **heap** or **pile up** —*spoils of war, corpses* Plb. Plu. ‖ PASS. (of soil) be piled up Plb.
2 ‖ PASS. (of beaches) be covered with heaps —W.GEN. *of corpses, weapons, wreckage* Plb.
3 heap (sthg. on sthg. else); (fig., intr.) **build, capitalise** —W.PREP.PHR. *on a natural advantage* Arist.

σωρηδόν *adv.* **in heaps** Plb.
σωρός οῦ *m.* **1 heap, pile** (of grain, wood, earth, or sim.) Hes. Hdt. Ar. X. Plb. Plu.; (of troubles, blessings) Ar.
2 entity accumulated from separate parts, **aggregate** (opp. unity) Arist.

σῶς σῶν *adj.* | masc.acc. σῶν ‖ PL.: masc.nom. σῷ (dub.), acc. σῶς | neut.nom.acc. σᾶ | —also Ion. **σόος** η ον —also Att. **σῶος** ᾱ ον —also Aeol. **σάος** ᾱ ον | compar. σωότερος (AR., v.l. X.), σαώτερος (Il. Theoc., perh. X.) |

1 (of a person, animal, army, ship) **safe, unharmed** Hom. Hdt. S. E. Th. +
2 (of a region, building, or sim.) **safe, secure** E. Pl. X. D.; (of possessions, money) Hom. Pi. Hdt. E. Lys. +; (of a seal) **secure, unbroken** Hdt.; (of relics) still existing, **intact** Hdt.; (of an old cloak) Pl.; (of a water-source) S.; (of snow) Pl.; (of a sacred trust) **inviolate** D.
3 (of death) certain to come, **sure, certain** Hom.

σῶσθε (dial.2pl.mid.imperatv.): see σεύω
σῶσι (3pl.): see σάω¹
σωσί-πολις *masc.adj.* [πόλις] | only nom. | (of the upper bank of rowers in a trireme) **city-saving** Ar.

σῶστρα ων *n.pl.* **1** (collectv.) payment for saving (someone or sthg.); **reward for safekeeping** (of lost horses) Hdt.; **reward for recovery** (W.GEN. of a runaway slave) X.
2 thank-offerings (to the gods) **for saving a life** (W.GEN. of a child) Hdt.

σώτειρα ᾱς *f.* [reltd. σωτήρ] **1** (ref. to a goddess) **saviour** or **protectress** (sts. W.GEN. or DAT. of someone or sthg.) Hdt. E. Pl.; (ref. to a woman, acting in specific circumstances) Pi. E.
2 (epith. of Fortune, Eunomia, Themis) **Saviour, Protectress** Pi.; (title of Athena) Lycurg.; (without name, app.ref. to Athena) Ar.; (ref. to a goddess of the Mysteries) Arist.; (as the name of a road, in Tarentum) Plb.

σωτήρ (also **σαωτήρ** Call.) ῆρος *m.* [σῴζω] | voc. σῶτερ |
1 (ref. to a god, acting or appealed to in specific circumstances) **saviour, protector** (sts. W.GEN. or DAT. of someone or sthg.) hHom. Ion Hdt. Trag. Pl. +; (gener.) **tutelary god** Hdt. X.
2 (ref. to a person, a people) **saviour, protector** (sts. W.GEN. or DAT. of persons, a city, or sim.) Trag. Th. Ar. Att.orats. +; (ref. to a person or place, W.GEN. against harm) E.; (fig., ref. to earth and sea) Antipho; (ref. to reason, W.GEN. of virtue) Pl.
3 (title of Zeus) **Saviour, Protector** Pi. E. Ar. Att.orats. +; (specif., as recipient of the third libation) A. Pi. Pl.; (title of the Ptolemies) Call.; (title of God, Christ) NT.
4 (epith. of Fortune, of εὐπραξία *success*) **Saviour, Protector** A. S.; (appos.w. πρότονος *forestay*) **protector** (W.GEN. of a ship) A. ‖ PL. (w. τιμαί *functions of gods*) protectors (W.GEN. of mortals) E.

σωτηρίᾱ ᾱς, Ion. **σωτηρίη** ης *f.* **1** state or achievement of safety; **safety, preservation** or **rescue** (of a person, country, or sim.) Hdt. Trag. Th. Ar. Att.orats. +
2 means of safety (for someone) A. Hdt. E. Th. +
3 safe return (W.ADV. or PREP.PHR. homeward, to a place) Th. D.; (phr.) νόστιμος σωτηρία *safe return home* A.
4 activity of preserving; **preservation, safeguarding, security** (of buildings or sim.) Hdt. Arist.; (of the community) Th.; (of laws, life, an opinion) Pl.
5 means of safeguarding; safeguard (for a city, constitution) Pl. Arist.; **safekeeping** (of prisoners) Pl.
6 preservation from eternal death, salvation NT.

σωτήριος ον *adj.* **1** (of a person or god) **bringing safety, protective** (sts. W.GEN. or DAT. of someone) S. E. Th.
2 (of actions, circumstances, places, or sim.) **ensuring safety** (oft. W.DAT. for someone) Heraclit. Trag. Th. Att.orats. + ‖ NEUT.SG.SB. salvation NT. ‖ NEUT.PL.SB. means of safety S. Din.
3 (of tyrannical behaviour) **preservative** (W.GEN. of power) Arist.
4 (of a person's character) **conservative** Pl.
5 ‖ NEUT.PL.SB. thank-offerings for safety X. Plu.

—**σωτηρίως** adv. in a salutary way —ref. to handling a political affliction Plu.

σωφρονέω contr.vb. [σώφρων] | aor. ἐσωφρόνησα | pf. σεσωφρόνηκα ‖ PASS.: pf.ptcpl. σεσωφρονημένος | **1** (of sound mind, **be sane** Hdt. E. Antipho Pl. NT.
2 show good sense, **be sensible** Hdt. Trag. Th. +
3 (aor. and pf.) **come to one's senses** Hdt. Pl.
4 show self-control, **behave sensibly, modestly** or **discreetly** Scol. S. Antipho Ar. Pl. X. +
‖ NEUT.PL.PF.PASS.PTCPL.SB. sensible or modest behaviour Aeschin.
5 (specif., of women) show sexual restraint, **be chaste** Semon. A. E. D.; (of men) E.

σωφρόνημα ατος n. **act of self-control** X.

σωφρονίζω vb. | fut. σωφρονιῶ | aor. ἐσωφρόνισα | **1** (of a person, misfortune, or sim.) **bring to one's senses, teach a lesson to, chasten** —someone Att.orats. Pl. X. Plu. ‖ PASS. be brought to one's senses, be taught a lesson Th. Pl. X. Plu.
2 teach (W.ACC. someone) **self-control** Aeschin. Plu. ‖ PASS. be taught self-control Pl.
3 (of Spartan ephors) **keep** (W.ACC. people) **under control** X.
4 (of citizens) **moderate, temper** —public expenditure Th.; (of potential danger and disgrace) —a person's anger Antipho
5 (of a madman) **control** —his panting breath E.; (of masters) —the sexual desires of their slaves (W.DAT. by short rations) X.
—**σεσωφρονισμένως** pf.pass.ptcpl.adv. **in a controlled** or **sensible manner** —ref. to examining a situation A.

σωφρονικός ή όν adj. **1** (of persons) **self-controlled** X. Arist. Plu.
2 (of behaviour) **restrained** Pl. X.; (of a woman's demeanour) **modest** Plb.
—**σωφρονικῶς** adv. **in the manner of one who is self-controlled, with restraint** Ar.

σωφρόνισμα ατος n. [σωφρονίζω] **lesson, piece of advice** (W.GEN. fr. a father) A.

σωφρονισμός οῦ m. **moral improvement** (sts. W.GEN. of someone) Plu.

σωφρονιστήρ ῆρος m. **moderator** (for overconfidence, ref. to fear, envisaged as a bridle) Plu.

σωφρονιστήριον ου n. **reformatory** (ref. to a prison) Pl.

σωφρονιστής οῦ m. **1** one who inculcates good sense or moderation; (in political ctxt.) **monitor, moderator** (of people, conduct, policies) Th. Pl.
2 moral guide (for the young) D.
3 (specif.) **disciplinary officer** (for ephebes) Arist.; (ref. to the Roman censor, Spartan governors elsewhere in Greece) Plu.

σωφρονιστύς ύος f. **moral improvement** Pl.

σωφροσύνη ης, dial. **σωφροσύνᾱ** ᾱς, ep. **σαοφροσύνη** ης f. [σώφρων] **1 soundness of mind, rationality** (opp. madness) Pl. X. NT.
2 sound thinking, **good sense, prudence** Od. Thgn. +
3 good sense (leading to good conduct, esp. through mastery of one's natural desires or emotions); **self-control, moderation, temperance** E. Th. Ar. Att.orats. Pl. +; (gener.) good behaviour, decency Ar. Att.orats.
4 (specif.) **chastity** E.
5 (in political ctxt.) **sensible government** (ref. to oligarchy) Th.

σώφρων, dial. **σαόφρων**, ον, gen. ονος adj. [σῶς, φρήν] **1** (of persons, their minds) sound in thinking, **sensible, prudent** Hom. +; (of thought, behaviour, speech, advice) Thgn. Pi.fr. Hdt. Trag. Th. + ‖ NEUT.SB. good sense E.
2 (of personal qualities and attributes, such as courage, scepticism) **judicious** Pi.fr. E. Th.
3 (of persons, their behaviour) sensible or restrained (esp. through mastery of natural desires and emotions), **temperate, sober** Scol. Trag. Ar. Att.orats. Pl. +; (gener.) **virtuous, decent, respectable** E. Ar. Att.orats. ‖ NEUT.SB. virtue E.; moderation Th.
4 (esp. of women) sexually restrained, **chaste** Trag. Ar. Att.orats. +
5 (in social or political ctxt.; of Eunomia, as principle of civic order) **prudent** Pi.fr. B.; (of aristocratic government) **moderate** Th.; (of a decree) **judicious** Aeschin.
—**σωφρόνως** adv. | compar. σωφρονέστερον, also σωφρονεστέρως (E.), superl. σωφρονέστατα | **1 sensibly** Hdt. S. E. Th. Isoc.
2 prudently, cautiously X.
3 soberly, modestly, temperately A. E. Ar. Att.orats. Pl. +
4 decorously —ref. to wreathing a suppliant's olive branch A.
5 (in political ctxt.) **moderately** Th.

σώω ep.vb.: see σαόω

Τ τ

τά[1] (neut.nom.acc.pl.): see ὁ
τά[2] *dial.neut.pl.interrog.pron.*: see under τίς
τᾱ́ (fem.nom.acc.du.), **τᾷ** (dial.fem.dat.art., also adv.): see ὁ
τᾱγᾱ́ (**τᾰγᾱ́** Ar.) ᾶς *dial.f.* [app. τάσσω; cf. τᾱγός] **1 military command** (w.GEN. of soldiers) A.
  2 (as Lacon.wd.) **military posting** Ar.
τᾱγείᾱ ᾱς *f.* [τᾱγεύω] **office of *tagos*** X.
τᾱγεύω *vb.* [τᾱγός] | aor.mid.imperatv. τᾱ́γευσαι (unless aor.act.inf. τᾱγεῦσαι) A. | **1** (of Jason of Pherai) **hold the office of *tagos*** X. ‖ PASS. (of Thessaly) **be subject to a *tagos* or *tagoi*;** (gener.) **be in a state of war or mobilisation** X.
  2 ‖ MID. **station** —*defenders* (w. ἐπί + DAT. *at gate entrances*) A. | cf. τάσσω 1–2
τᾱγέω *contr.vb.* (of the Persian king) **have command** —w.GEN. *of Asia* A.
τάγηνον ου *n.* **frying-pan** Ar.
τάγμα ατος *n.* [τάσσω] **1 positioning, configuration** (of footprints) S.*Ichn.*
  2 arrangement by which something is done, **system** Arist.
  3 (milit.) **formation, division, detachment** (in an army) X. Plb. Plu.; **legion** (in the Roman army) Plu.
τᾱγός οῦ *m.* [perh.reltd. τάσσω] **1 *tagos*** (in Thessaly, civic magistrate w. military responsibilities; title adopted by Jason of Pherai, on assuming military leadership in early 4th C. BC) X.
  2 commander (of the gods, ref. to Zeus) A.; (of troops or ships, ref. to a Persian) A.; (ref. to Menelaos) E.
  3 head of state (of Thebes) S.; (of Athens, as comic title) Ar.
τᾱγοῦχος ου *m.* [τᾱγά, ἔχω] (appos.w. ἀνήρ) **military commander** A.
τᾷδε *dial.fem.dat.adv.*: see τῇδε, under ὅδε
ταθείς (aor.pass.ptcpl.), **τάθην** (ep.aor.pass.), **ταθήσομαι** (fut.pass.): see τείνω
ταί (dial.fem.nom.pl.), **ταῖν** (fem.gen.dat.du.): see ὁ
Ταίναρος ου *m.f.* —perh. also **Ταίναρον** ου *n.* | gender usu. indeterminate | **Tainaros, Tainaron** (southernmost point of the Peloponnese, site of a temple of Poseidon, also an entrance to the underworld) hHom. Pi. Hdt. E. +
  —**Ταινάριος** ᾱ (Ion. η) ον *adj.* (of the headland, region) **of Tainaros** Lyr.adesp. AR.
ταινίᾱ ᾱς *f.* [reltd. τείνω] | ταινίᾱ *metri grat.* (Emp.) |
  1 ribbon, band (tied around the head of a victor in a contest) Emp. Pl. X. Plu.; (worn by Nereids) B.; (decking a funeral urn, votive or ritual object) Plu.; (as a typical item sold by the poor) D.
  2 strip of cloth (as a bandage for the neck) Plu.; (used for concealing sthg.) Men.
  3 strip of wood (for an inscription) Thphr.
  4 strip of land (separating two stretches of water) Plu.; (ref. to a long sandbank) Plb.
ταινιό-πωλις ιδος *f.* [πωλέω] **ribbon-seller** D.

ταινιόω *contr.vb.* **deck or wreathe with ribbons** —*a victorious athlete or commander* Th. X. —*a victorious chorus* Ar. ‖ MID. (of a woman) **put on ribbons** Ar.
ταῖς (Aeol.fem.acc. and dat.pl.), **ταῖς**, **ταῖσι** (fem.dat.pl.): see ὁ
ταισίδε (poet.fem.dat.pl.): see ὅδε
τακερός ά όν *adj.* [τήκω] (of Eros) **melting, languid** Anacr.
  —**τακερά** *neut.pl.adv.* | compar. τακερώτερα | **meltingly** —*ref. to gazing* Alcm. Ibyc.
τακτέον (neut.impers.vbl.adj.): see τάσσω
τακτικός ή όν *adj.* [τακτός] **1** of or relating to the drawing up of troops; (of a commander) **good at tactics** X. Plu.; (of an action) **demonstrating good tactics** X.; (of the skill, theoretical study) **of tactics** Plu.; (of manoeuvres) **tactical** Pl. ‖ NEUT.PL.SB. **tactics** X.; (as the title of a treatise) Plu.
  2 (of military units) of the kind that are drawn up in order, **regular** X.; (of the movements of a phalanx) **well-drilled** Plu.
τακτός ή όν *adj.* [τάσσω] **1** (of a sum of money, quantity of grain or food, penalty) **prescribed, fixed** Th. Pl. X. Plb.; (of a day or time) **appointed** Aeschin. D. Plb. NT.; (of a route, place) D. Plb.
  2 (of a person) **under orders** (to do sthg.) X.(dub.)
τάκω *dial.vb.*: see τήκω
ταλα-εργός όν *adj.* [τλῆναι, ἔργον] **enduring labour**; (of a mule) **hard-working, hardy** Hom. Hes. hHom.; (of a spinning-woman) AR.; (of Herakles) Theoc.; (of the necks of oxen) Mosch.
τάλαινα *fem.adj.*: see τάλᾱς
ταλαιπωρέω *contr.vb.* [ταλαίπωρος] **1** (of persons) **suffer hardship** E. Democr. Th. Att.orats. X. +; (of troops) **be in difficulties** or **suffer a reverse** Th.
  2 (tr., of war) **cause hardship to** —*persons* Isoc. ‖ PASS. (of persons) **suffer hardship** or **be distressed** Th. Ar. Isoc. Pl. D. Plu.
ταλαιπωρίᾱ ᾱς, Ion. **ταλαιπωρίη** ης *f.* (sg. and pl.) **hardship, distress** Hdt. Th. Att.orats. Plb. Plu.
ταλαί-πωρος ον *adj.* [τλῆναι, 2nd el.uncert.] **1** (of a person, country, city) **long-suffering, distressed, miserable** Trag. Ar. Att.orats. Pl. +; (in mock sympathy or as a serious reproach, esp. in voc.) **wretched, foolhardy, reckless** S. E. Aeschin. D. Plu.
  2 (of activities) **toilsome, wearisome** Ar. Plu.; (of life) S. Men.
  3 (of blinded eyes) **wretched, pitiable** E.; (of news) **sad** Men.
  4 ‖ NEUT.SB. **capacity for endurance** Ar.
  —**ταλαιπώρως** *adv.* **with discomfort and difficulty, wearisomely** Th. Ar. Plb. Plu.; **miserably** Arist. Plb.
τάλαις (Aeol.masc.nom.): see τάλᾱς
ταλαί-φρων ον, gen. ονος *adj.* [φρήν] **with enduring mind;** (of a person) **long-suffering, wretched** S. E. ‖ VOC.SB. (perh. w. a hint of reproach) **poor woman** S.

τᾰλα-κάρδιος ον *adj.* [καρδίᾱ] **1** with enduring heart; (of Herakles) **stout-hearted, valiant** Hes.; (of soldiers) Aeschin.(quot.epigr.) Plu.(quot.epigr.)
2 (of Oedipus) **long-suffering, wretched** S.
τάλαν *neut.adj.*, **τάλανι** (masc.dat.adj.): see τάλᾱς
τᾰλαντεία *f.*: see ταντᾰλεία
τᾰλαντιαῖος ᾱ ον *adj.* [τάλαντον] **1** (of property, a crown) **worth a talent** D. Plb. Plu.
2 (of a stone, armour) **weighing a talent** Plb. Plu.
τάλαντον ου *n.* [τλῆναι] **1** (sg. and pl.; in Hom. always pl.) pair of scales, **scales** Il. Ar.; (of Justice) hHom. B.; (of Zeus, for weighing the fortunes of mortals) Il. Archil. Thgn. A.
2 definite (but unspecified) weight, **talent** (W.GEN. of gold) Hom.
3 commercial weight (varying according to the system used; in Attica, weight about 26kg, value 16 minae), **talent** Hdt. Th. X. Arist.; sum of money represented by the corresponding weight of gold or silver, **talent** Hdt. +
τᾰλαντόομαι *pass.contr.vb.* (of Space) **sway as if in a balance, oscillate** Pl.
τᾰλαντοῦχος ου *m.* [ἔχω] **holder of scales** (ref. to Ares, envisaged as trading lives for ashes) A.
τᾰλαός ά όν *adj.* [reltd. τάλᾱς] (of mortals) **suffering, wretched** Ar.
τᾰλα-πείριος ον *adj.* [τλῆναι, πεῖρα] (of persons) **enduring trials, long-suffering** Od. hHom.; (of Troy) Ibyc.
τᾰλα-πενθής ές *adj.* [πένθος] **1 enduring grief**; (of a heart) **patient in sorrow** Od.; (of a person) **cruelly suffering** B.
2 (of news) **grievous** B.
τᾰλᾰρίσκος ου *m.* [dimin. τάλαρος] **basket** or **pot** (for plants) Theoc.
τάλαρος ου *m.* [reltd. τλῆναι] **receptacle for holding or carrying things** (usu. made of wicker); **basket** (for cheese, grapes) Hom. Hes. Ar. Theoc.; (as a woman's possession, made of silver or gold) **work-basket** (for spinning-thread) Od. Theoc.; **flower-basket** Mosch.
τάλᾱς τάλαινα τάλᾰν *adj.* [τλῆναι] | Aeol.masc.nom. τάλαις (Alc.), dial. τάλᾱς (Theoc.) | masc.voc. τάλᾰν | fem.gen. ταλαίνης (dial. ταλαίνᾱς) | masc.dat. τάλᾰνι, also τάλαντι (Hippon.) || superl. ταλάντατος |
1 (of persons) **enduring misfortune, unhappy, miserable, wretched** Semon. Alc. Thgn. Simon. Trag. Ar. +; (of a heart, stomach, hand) S. E. Ar.; (of a city) E.; (of a life, destiny) E.
2 || voc. (τάλαν, ὦ τάλαν or fem. equiv., in mock sympathy or as a serious reproach) **poor fool** (spoken by a woman) Od. Trag. Ar. Call.; (spoken by a man) Call. Theoc.; (masc., in very mild remonstrance, spoken by a woman) **my good man** Ar.; (masc. or fem., by a woman to a woman) **poor dear** Ar.; (masc., as exclam. by a woman) **oh dear!** Men.
3 (of states or situations, such as madness, sickness, strife, a curse) **wretched, remorseless, cruel** Trag.; (of calamities) S. E. Ar.
4 (pejor., of a person, hand) **provoked by suffering to reckless action, hard-hearted, relentless, cruel** Trag. Theoc.; (gener.) **wretched** Hippon.
τᾰλᾰσήιος η ον *ep.Ion.adj.* [ταλασίᾱ] (of the task) **of wool-working** AR.
τᾰλᾰσίᾱ ᾱς *f.* [app.reltd. τάλαντον] perh., **weighed amount of wool; wool-working, wool-spinning** (by women) Pl. X. Plu.
τᾰλάσιος ᾱ ον *adj.* (of the task) **of wool-working** X.
τᾰλᾰσιουργέω *contr.vb.* [ταλασιουργός] (of a woman) **be a wool-worker** X.
τᾰλᾰσιουργίᾱ ᾱς *f.* **wool-working** (incl. spinning and weaving) Pl.

τᾰλᾰσιουργικός ή όν *adj.* (of the craft) **of wool-working** Pl.; (of implements) **for wool-working** X.
τᾰλᾰσιουργός οῦ *f.* [ταλασίᾱ, ἔργον] **wool-worker** Pl.
τᾰλᾰσί-φρων ον, gen. ονος *adj.* [τλῆναι, φρήν] **with enduring mind**; (of Odysseus) **stout-hearted** Hom. Hes. Alcm.; (of Herakles, Neleus) Hes.*fr.*; (of servants) Theoc.; (of a soldier, his heart) **steadfast** Il. Tyrt.
τᾰλάσσω (ep.aor.subj.): see τλῆναι
τᾰλαύρῑνος ον *adj.* [τλῆναι, ῥῑνός] (of a warrior, ref. to Ares) **shield-bearing** Il.; (of War, a commander) **belligerent, redoubtable** Ar.
—τᾰλαύρῑνον *neut.adv.* **like a true warrior** *—ref. to fighting* Il.
τᾰλά-φρων ον, gen. ονος *adj.* [φρήν] (of a warrior) **stout-hearted** Il.
τᾱλῐκος *dial.demonstr.adj.*: see τηλίκος
τᾱλις ιδος *f.* [perh. Aeol.wd.] | acc. τᾱλιν (Call.) | **fiancée** or **bride** S. Call.
τᾰμέειν (ep.aor.2 inf.), **τᾰμεῖν** (dial.aor.2 inf.): see τέμνω
τᾰμεῖον *n.*: see ταμιεῖον
τᾰμεσί-χρως χροος *masc.fem.adj.* [τέμνω, χρώς] (of weapons) **flesh-cutting, piercing** Il.
τᾰμίᾱ ᾱς, Ion. **τᾰμίη** ης *f.* [ταμίᾱς] **female servant in charge of household stores, housekeeper** Hom. hHom. Ar. X.; (appos.w. γυνή or ἀμφίπολος) Hom. Alcm.; **steward** (W.GEN. + DAT. of wealth, for men, ref. to Peace) Pi.; (W.GEN. of activities in heaven, ref. to the Graces) Pi.
τᾰμίᾱς ου, Ion. **τᾰμίης** εω *m.* [prob.reltd. τέμνω] **1** one who has management of supplies; **steward** (ref. to a person apportioning food to troops) Il.; (ref. to a servant in charge of household stores) Ar.
2 one who has management of some activity; (ref. to a god) **steward, custodian, controller** (W.GEN. of men and war, oaths, good and evil, rains and droughts) Il. E. Isoc. Pl.(quot.poet.); (of the winds, the trident, ref. to Aiolos, Poseidon) Od. Ar.; **guardian** (of a place, ref. to the Dioscuri, Battos, Pan) Pi. E.; **master, lord** (ref. to Iacchus) S.
3 steward, controller (W.GEN. of many things, ref. to a king) Pi.; (of revels, the Muses and athletic contests, ref. to a poet, a populace) Pi.; (of one's mind and tongue, of love, ref. to oneself) Thgn.; (of one's desires, of circumstances) Th.; **dispenser** (W.GEN. of news, ref. to a messenger) E.; **minister** (of Zeus, ref. to a sacred official) Pi. [or perh. *dispenser* of Zeus' oracle]
4 steward, controller (W.GEN. + DAT. of breath to the body, ref. to the lungs) Pl.; (W.GEN. of prizes, ref. to a contest) Carm.Pop.; **custodian** (of victory-garlands, ref. to a house) Pi.
5 person entrusted with financial management (of private or public funds), **treasurer** Hdt. Att.orats. X. Arist.; (ref. to an official in charge of the treasury of a temple, esp. at Athens) Hdt. Att.orats. Pl. Arist.; **steward, keeper** (of temple property) E.
6 (at Rome) **quaestor** Plb. Plu.
τᾰμιείᾱ ᾱς *f.* [ταμιεύω] **1** exercise of the office of steward, **household management** Pl. X.; **stewardship** Arist.
2 (at Rome) **quaestorship** Plu.
τᾰμιείδιον ου *n.* [dimin. ταμιεῖον] **storeroom** (in a house) Men.
τᾰμιεῖον (also **τᾰμεῖον** NT.) ου *n.* [ταμιεύω] **1** building or room where goods are stored, **storehouse** Th. Isoc. Pl. X.; **storeroom** Pl. X. Thphr. Men. NT.; (gener.) **inner room** NT.
2 treasure-house, treasury Th. Pl.; (fig., ref. to a source of good things) Lyr.adesp. Plu.

3 (at Rome) public treasury, *aerarium* Plb. Plu.; (in a military camp) quaestor's quarters, *quaestorium* Plb.

ταμιεύματα των *n.pl.* **housekeeping responsibilities** (of a wife) X.

ταμιευτικός ή όν *adj.* **1** (of a law) **relating to the public treasury** Plu.
2 (of laws) **relating to the office of quaestor** Plu.; (of the office) **of quaestor** Plu.

ταμιεύω *vb.* [ταμίας] | iteratv.impf. ταμιεύεσκον (S.) | **1** exercise the duties of a housekeeper or storeroom-keeper; (of a wife) **run a household, look after stores** Ar.; (tr.) **look after, manage** —*domestic affairs and finances* (sts. W.DAT. *for a husband*). Ar. Pl.; (of a male servant) **be a steward** (w.connot. of financial responsibility) —W.DAT. *for someone* Ar.
2 (gener., sts. w.connot. of financial responsibility) **manage, have charge of, look after** (sts. W.DAT. for someone) —*property or sim.* Lys. Ar. Is.; (of politicians or officials) —*public affairs or finances* Lys.; (of Danae) **have custody of, treasure** —*the golden seed of Zeus* S. || MID. (of a politician) **exercise stewardship** (in the state) Hyp. || PASS. (of a land) be ruled —W.DAT. *by a people* Pi. [or perh. *be held in trust (for a people)*]
3 || MID. (fig.) **draw as if from a storehouse** —*laws* (W.PREP.PHR. *fr. someone's hand*) Lys. —*things of value* (fr. one's *soul*) X. || PASS. (of the power of sight) **be drawn or dispensed** (fr. the sun) Pl.
4 || MID. **manage one's affairs** (as if a household budget); **regulate** or **carefully calculate** —W.INDIR.Q. *to what extent one wishes to do sthg.* Th. X.; **regulate a situation** —w. ὥστε + INF. *so as to be able to do as one wishes* X. || ACT. (of a river, as a barrier) **give the opportunity** —W.DAT. + INF. *for someone to do sthg.* Plu.
5 be a treasurer or **paymaster** (sts. W.DAT. for someone) Ar. D. —W.GEN. *of an official ship* D.; **have charge of the state treasury** D. Arist.
6 (at Rome) **serve as quaestor** Plu.

ταμίη Ion.*f.*, **ταμίης** Ion.*m.*: see ταμία, ταμίας

τάμισος ου *f.* **rennet** (substance taken fr. the stomach of a young animal, used to set cheese) Theoc.

τάμνω *dial.vb.*, **τάμον** (ep.aor.2): see τέμνω

τᾶμος *dial.adv.*: see τῆμος

τἄν, **τἄν**: crasis for τὰ ἐν, τοι ἄν

τἄν[1] (dial.fem.acc., also Aeol.fem.gen.pl.), **τᾶν**[1] (dial.fem.gen.pl.): see ὁ

τᾶν[2] *Att.interj.* | only in phr. ὦ τᾶν | ostensibly a polite form of address, but oft. condescending or impatient | **my good man, my dear fellow** S. E. Ar. Pl. D. Men. Plu.

τανα-ήκης ες *adj.* [ταναός; ἀκίς, ἀκωκή] (of bronze, ref. to spears, perh. also swords) **sharp-pointed** Hom. Hes.*fr.*; (ref. to an axe) **sharp-edged** Il. | see also τανυήκης

τᾱναό-δειρος ον *adj.* [ταναός, δέρη] | ᾱ metri grat. | (of birds) app. **long-necked** Ar.

ταναός όν (also ἡ όν AR.) *adj.* **1** (of a javelin) **long and slender** Il.; (of ears of corn) hHom.; (of a Triton's conch) Mosch.; (of a poplar) **tall and slender** AR.; (of locks of hair) **long** E. AR.; (of feet, w.connot. of gracefulness) **slim** Alcm.
2 (of a ray of light, flame of fire) **thin, fine** Emp.
3 [perh. assoc.w. τανύω] (of the upper air) app. **outspread, extensive** E. Men.

τανaύ-πους ποδος *masc.fem.adj.* [πούς] (of sheep) perh. **thin-legged** or **nimble-footed** Od. hHom.

τανα-υφής ές *adj.* [ὑφή] (of a robe) perh. **finely woven** S.

τανα-ῶπις ιδος *fem.adj.* [ὤψ] (of a female deity) **far-sighted** Emp.

τανηλεγής ές *adj.* [perh. fr. false division of τ' ἀνηλεγής] (of death) app. **uncaring, pitiless** Hom. Tyrt.

τᾱνίκα *dial.adv.*: see τηνίκα

τανί-σφυρος (also **τανύσφυρος**) ον *adj.* [ταναός, σφυρόν] (of young women, nymphs) **slim-ankled** Hes. Ibyc. B.; (of Persephone) hHom. B.

τανί-φυλλος (also **τανύφυλλος**) ον *adj.* [φύλλον] (of an olive tree) **slender-leaved** or **long-leaved** Od.; (gener., of a mountain) **leafy** B. Theoc.

τανταλεία ᾱς *f.* [Τάνταλος; perh. also assoc.w. τάλαντον] app. **swaying** (of the rock above Tantalos) Pl. [perh. better ταλαντεία *balancing*]

τανταλόομαι *pass.contr.vb.* | aor.ptcpl. τανταλωθείς | perh., **suffer the fate which threatened Tantalos** (ref. to the suspended rock above his head); (of Kapaneus, knocked by a thunderbolt fr. the walls of Thebes) **be struck down** S.

Τάνταλος ου *m.* **Tantalos** (mythol. king of Phrygia, son of Zeus, father of Pelops, noted for wealth; punished in Hades by food and drink eluding his grasp or by a rock suspended above his head) Od. +

—**Ταντάλειος** ον *adj.* derived from or relating to Tantalos; (of his son Pelops, his descendants, their palace) **of Tantalos, Tantalean** E.; (of the punishment) Plb.

—**Ταντᾰλίδης** ου (Ion. εω), dial. **Ταντᾰλίδᾱς** ᾱ (E.) *m.* **son of Tantalos** (ref. to Pelops) Tyrt. Simon. || PL. descendants of Tantalos A. E.

ταννάκης *dial.adj.*: see τανυήκης

τανύ-γλωσσος ον *adj.* [ταναός or τανύω; γλῶσσα] (of seabirds) **with long or outstretched tongue**; app. **screeching** Od.

τανυ-γλώχῑν (or perh. **τανυγλώχῑς**) ινος *masc.fem.adj.* [γλωχίν] (of an arrow) **with slender point, sharp-pointed** or **long-barbed** Il.

τανύ-δρομος ον *adj.* [τανύω, δρόμος] (of a person) **running at full stretch** A.

τανυ-έθειρα ᾱς *fem.adj.* [ταναός, τανύω] (of Semele) **long-haired** Pi.

τανυ-ήκης, dial. **ταννάκης**, ες *adj.* [ἀκίς, ἀκωκή] (of a sword, arrows) **sharp-pointed** Hom. B.; (of branches, jostling in the wind as if in combat) Il. | see also ταναήκης

τανύ-θριξ τριχος *masc.fem.adj.* [θρίξ] (of a goat) **long-haired, shaggy** Hes.; (of a pig) **long-bristled** Semon.

τάνυμαι (athem.pres.pass.): see τανύω

τανύ-πεπλος ον *adj.* [πέπλος] (of women, goddesses) **with fine** or **long-flowing robes** Hom. Hes. Stesich. B.

τανύ-πους ποδος *masc.fem.adj.* [πούς] (of Erinyes) **far-striding** S.

τανύ-πτερος ον *adj.* [πτερόν] (of birds) **long-winged** or **spread-winged** Hes. hHom. Ibyc. Pi.; (of arrows) perh. **swift-flying** Tim.

τανυ-πτέρυξ υγος *masc.fem.adj.* —also **τανυπτέρυγος** ον *adj.* (of birds) **long-winged** or **spread-winged** Il. Alcm.; (of a fly) Simon.

τανύ-ρριζος ον *adj.* [ῥίζα] (of poplars) **long-rooted** Hes.

τανυσί-πτερος ον *adj.* [πτερόν] (of birds) **spread-winged** Od. Hes. hHom. Lyr. Ar.; (of the moon, as the goddess Selene) hHom.

τανυστύς ύος *f.* **tautening, bending** (of a bow, in order to string it) Od.

τανύσφυρος *adj.*: see τανίσφυρος

τανύ-φλοιος ον *adj.* [ταναός, τανύω; φλοιός] (of trees) app., **with fine bark, smooth-barked** Il. Theoc.

τανύφυλλος *adj.*: see τανίφυλλος

τανύω *vb.* [reltd. τείνω] | fut. τανύω | aor. ἐτάνυσα, ep.

ταξιαρχέω

ἐτάνυσσα, also τάνυσα, τάνυσσα ‖ PASS.: athem.pres. τάνυμαι | aor. ἐτανύσθην, ep.3pl. τάνυσθεν | 3sg.pf. τετάνυσται, 3sg.plpf. τετάνυστο |

1 (sts.mid.) pull so as to make tight, **stretch tight** —*a lyre-string, strap* Od. hHom. —*a veil (around one's body)* Od. —*a sail (w. ropes)* AR.; (of a charioteer) **make taut, tighten** (opp. slacken) —*a rein* S.(cj.); (of a weaver) **pull** (to oneself) —*the loom-rod* Il. ‖ PASS. (of cheeks) app., be pulled tight (opp. being flaccid or shrunken) Od.; (of sails) be stretched tight (by the wind) AR.; (of a muscle) Theoc.
2 bend —*a bow (in order to string it)* Od. AR.; (mid.) Il.; (by drawing back the bow-string, in order to shoot) AR.; (intr., fig., of a poet) bend the bow, **take aim** Pi.
3 (fig., of gods, ref. to conflict envisaged as a tug-of-war) **pull tight** —*the rope of strife* Il.; pull tight (as if a rope), **intensify** —*strife, fighting, toil* Il. ‖ PASS. (fig., of indecisive fighting) be stretched tight Il.
4 (of a charioteer) maintain tautness (w. the reins); perh., impart intense effort to, **drive at full stretch** —*horses* Il. —*a chariot* Pi. ‖ PASS. (of horses) be kept taut (under the reins) Il. ‖ IMPF.MID. or PASS. (of horses and mules) stretch out into a gallop, **go at full stretch** Hom.
5 (tr.) stretch out flat, **spread out, lay out** —*spits, a spear, corpse, sacrificial animal* Hom. AR.(mid.); (of a boxer) —*an opponent* Od. ‖ MID. (of a person) **stretch oneself out** Od. ‖ PASS. (of a rug, distaff, spear) be laid out Hom. AR.; (of fallen warriors, roasting hogs) be stretched out Il.
6 pull so as to expand, **stretch** —*oxhide (for curing)* Il. ‖ ATHEM.PRES.PASS. (of oxhide) be stretched Il.
7 (sts.mid.) extend (sthg.) to full length; (of Zeus) **stretch out, spread out** —*a rainbow* Il.; (of sailors) —*a sail* AR.; (of Iris, a bird) —*one's wings* AR.; (of a child) —*one's hand (to touch sthg.)* Call.; (wkr.sens., of a musician) **hold up** (in one's hands) —*a lyre* AR.; (fig., of a host) **offer** —*good cheer* Pi. ‖ MID. (of a person) **stretch upwards** (on tiptoe) AR. ‖ PASS. (of Ouranos) be stretched out (around Gaia) Hes.
8 ‖ PASS. (of a vine, island, path, quiver, dragon's coils) stretch or extend (in some direction) Od. AR. Theoc.

ταξιαρχέω contr.vb. [ταξίαρχος] **serve as a taxiarch** Th. Lys. Ar. X. D. Arist.

ταξιαρχίᾱ ᾱς f. **office of taxiarch** Arist.

ταξί-αρχος ου m. [τάξις, ἄρχω] **1 commander of a detachment of troops**; (gener.) **company commander** (of infantry, cavalry, sailors) Hdt. X.
2 (at Athens) commander of a contingent (usu. of infantry) supplied by one of the ten tribes, **company commander, taxiarch** Th. Ar. Att.orats. Pl. Arist.; (ref. to a naval commander) X.
3 (at Rome) **centurion** Plb. Plu.; mid-ranking commander (sts. app. ref. to a military tribune) Plu.

ταξιόομαι mid.contr.vb. (of a warrior) **station oneself** (in battle) Pi.

τάξις εως (Ion. ιος) f. [τάσσω] **1** (milit.) process of arranging in order, **organising, disposition** (of troops, by a commander) Th. Ar. Pl. X.
2 arranged order, **formation, battle order** Th. Ar. X. +; (of ships) Hdt. Th.; (gener.) **good order** (in a military formation) Th. X.
3 (oft.pl.) **rank, line** (of troops) Hdt. E. Th. Ar. +; **bank** (of rowers) A.
4 contingent (of troops) Hdt. S. Th. Lys. X. +; (ref. to members of a tragic chorus) **company** A.
5 station, post (of troops) Hdt. S. E. Th. Pl.; (of ships) Hdt.; (of a soldier, oft. ref. to his maintaining or abandoning it) A. Hdt. E. Att.orats. Pl.; (ref. to the subterranean location of Erinyes) A.; (fig., ref. to a moral stance or principle, either maintained or abandoned) Att.orats. Pl.
6 (in non-military ctxts.) **order, arrangement** (of one's personal life, things in the physical world) Ion Isoc. Pl. X.; (of a speech) Aeschin. D. Arist.; **organisation, system** (of government) Arist.; (as a more gener. organising principle, sts. assoc.w. law) **good order, regularity** Pl. Arist.
7 (leg.) imposed arrangement, **ordinance, regulation** Pl. Arist.; **assessment** (of tribute) X.
8 designated location or **spatial position** (of sthg.) Pl. Arist.
9 (in political ctxt.) **chosen position, stance** (of a person) D.
10 class, category (of persons, ref. to their character or social position) Att.orats. X.; (prep.phr.) ἐν τάξει **in the class, in the guise** (W.GEN. *of an enemy*) D. —*by way* (W.GEN. *of malice and spite*) D.

ταπεινός ή όν *adj.* **1** (of ground) **low-lying** Pi. Hdt.
2 (of a river in summer) **low** Plb. ‖ NEUT.SB. (geom.) shallowness (opp. depth) Arist.
3 (of a horse's hoof, the bone in its lower leg) **low** (relative to the ground) X.; (of disks on the bit of a bridle, app. relative to their axis) X.; (of spears) **carried in lowered position** (opp. upright) X.
4 (of persons, their fortunes, cities) brought low, **humbled, abased, humiliated** A. Hdt. E. Att.orats. Pl. X.; (of persons) **downcast, dejected** Isoc. X.; (of the will to persevere) **weakened** (by adversity) Th.
5 (of persons, their character, behaviour or speech, w. moral connot.) **mean, degraded, base** Att.orats. Pl. X. +; (in neutral or good sense) **submissive, self-effacing, humble** Att.orats. Pl. X. +
6 (of a person, style of life, or sim.) **humble, mean, poor** Att.orats. Pl. X. +; (of a city, a country, military power) **weak, insignificant** Isoc. D.; (of a subject of study, material for a speech) **trifling, modest** Isoc.; (of a style of writing or speaking) **low, plain, ordinary** Isoc. Arist.

—**ταπεινά** *neut.pl.adv.* **humbly, abjectly** —*ref. to crouching in supplication* E.

—**ταπεινῶς** *adv.* **1 at a low ebb** —*ref. to how one is faring* Isoc.; **meanly, poorly** —*ref. to living* Isoc. X.
2 self-effacingly, humbly Isoc. Plb.; **abjectly** Arist. Men.
3 in a low style —*ref. to giving a speech* Arist.

ταπεινότης ητος f. **1 low position, lowness** (of the stance of a horse, to avoid being seen) Hdt.
2 loss of power and reputation (through military or other reversal); **abasement, humiliation** (of persons, cities) Th. Isoc. D. Men. Plu.
3 lowness of spirits, dejection X.
4 lowly or **humble condition** (of persons, cities) Isoc. Arist.
5 moral abasement (of the human spirit), **baseness** Pl. Arist.

ταπεινο-φροσύνη ης f. [φρονέω] humble state of mind (as a good quality), **humility** NT.

ταπεινόω contr.vb. **1 make lower** ‖ PASS. (of a body) be reduced (in size) Pl.; (hyperbol., of a mountain) be made low or levelled NT.
2 lessen —*someone's jealousy* Plu.; reduce in effect or importance, **play down, minimise** —*a factor, an event, someone's success* Arist. Plb.
3 bring low, humble, abase, humiliate —*persons, their power* Att.orats. Pl. X. +; (intr.) **belittle** (persons or things, as a rhetorical strategy) Arist.; (in good sense) **make** (W.ACC. oneself) **humble** NT. ‖ PASS. (of persons) be humbled or humiliated Pl. X. +; abase oneself Men.

ταπείνωσις εως f. **1 lowering** (of the body, in dancing), **crouching** Pl.

2 process of abasing (someone or sthg.), **humbling, abasement, humiliation** (of a person, city, power) Plb. NT. Plu.
3 humble status (of a person) NT.

τάπης ητος *m.* [loanwd., reltd. δάπις] rug or blanket (for a bed or seat), **coverlet** Hom. Thgn. B.*fr.* Ar. Theoc.

τάπις ιδος *f.* **rug, carpet** (as used in Asia) X.

ταρ (sts. wrongly divided as **τ' ἄρ**) *enclit.pcl.* (following interrog.wds., perh. giving a lively or surprised tone) **then** Hom. hHom.

τἄρα: crasis for τοι ἄρα

τάραγμα ατος *n.* [ταράσσω] **disturbance, confusion, turmoil** (in a collapsing house) E.; (W.GEN. of the mind) E.

ταραγμός οῦ *m.* state of disorder, **disturbance, confusion, turmoil** E.; (in the mind) A. E.

ταρακτικός ή όν *adj.* (of the sense of hearing) **able to cause a disturbance** (W.GEN. in the mind) Plu.; (of a malaise in the state) Plu.

—**ταρακτικῶς** *adv.* (w. ἔχειν) *be intent on causing a disturbance* Men.

τάρακτρον ου *n.* tool for causing disturbance; (fig., ref. to a troublemaker) **agitator** Ar.

τaράκτωρ ορος *m.* **agitator, disturber** (W.GEN. of a city) A.

ταραντῖνον *n.*, **Ταραντῖνος** *adj.*: see under Τάρας

ταραξι-κάρδιος ον *adj.* [καρδίᾱ] (of words) **heart-shaking** Ar.

ταραξ-ιππό-στρατος ον *adj.* [ἵππος, στρατός] (of Kleon) **confounder of the cavalry corps** (i.e. enemy of the Ἱππεῖς *Knights*) Ar.

τάραξις εως *f.* **confusion** (W.GEN. of lifestyles) Ar.

Τάρας αντος *m.* **Taras, Tarentum** (mod. Taranto, town on southern coast of Italy) Hes.*fr.* Hdt. Th. Pl. +

—**Ταραντῖνοι** ων *m.pl.* inhabitants or citizens of Tarentum, **Tarentines** Hdt. Arist. Plb. Plu.

—**Ταραντῖνος** η ον *adj.* (of a man or woman from Tarentum, **Tarentine** Hdt. Pl. Plb. Plu.

—**ταραντῖνον** ου *n.* **tarentine, silk gown** (worn by women, made of costly diaphanous fabric resembling silk, fr. the fibres secreted by a large shellfish assoc.w. Tarentum) Men.

ταράσσω, Att. **ταράττω** *vb.* | dial.inf. ταρασσέμεν (Pi.) | fut. ταράξω | aor. ἐτάραξα | ep.pf. τέτρηχα, ptcpl. τετρηχώς | ep.3sg.plpf. τετρήχει ‖ PASS.: fut. ταράξομαι | aor. ἐταράχθην | pf. τετάραγμαι |
1 agitate (sthg.) so as to create disorder; (of Poseidon, Zeus) **disturb, stir up** —*the sea* Od. E.; (of Zeus) **wreak havoc on** —*the whole world* A.; (of persons) —*a country, populace* Hdt.; (of a person, likened to a hurricane) —*land and sea* Ar.; (of persons) **disturb, trouble** —*land and sea* (*by farming and navigation*) Pi. ‖ PASS. (of the sea) be disturbed (by wind) Archil. Sol. E.; (of a person) be churned up (in one's stomach, w. flatulence) Ar.; (of the stomach itself) Ar.
2 create disorder or confusion (among persons or things); (of troops) **throw into disorder** —*an enemy* Hdt.; (of wreckage and corpses) —*banks of oars* Hdt.; (of donkeys) **confuse, upset** —*cavalry* (*by braying*) Hdt.; (of a boxer) **confuse** —*an opponent* Theoc.; (of an orator) **jumble up** —*topics* D. ‖ PASS. (of troops, ships) be thrown into disorder Hdt. Th. X. Plb. Plu.; (of a skein of wool) be tangled Ar.; (of horses) be panicked Theoc.
3 (in political ctxts.) create unrest; **throw into confusion, disturb** —*a city, civic affairs, people* E. Ar. Att.orats.; (intr.) **create unrest, cause trouble** Ar. Pl. ‖ PASS. (of a city, populace, situation) be thrown into turmoil Thgn. Th. D. Arist. Din.
4 (of persons, events, fears) **disturb, agitate, confuse** —*a person, heart or mind* Trag. Ar. Pl. +; (in philosophical debate) **perplex** —*a person* Pl.; (intr.) **create perplexity** Pl. ‖ PASS. (of persons, their thinking) be confused or disturbed Thgn. S. E. Att.orats. +; be perplexed Pl.; (of a person's sight) be disturbed (by madness) E.
5 (of gods or humans) **stir up, incite** —*a quarrel, bloodshed* S. E. —*war* Pl. —*trouble* X. D. —*accusations* Plu.; (of the Muse) **rouse** —*her voice* Pi. ‖ PASS. (of lamentation) be stirred up A.; (of war) D.
6 ‖ STATV.EP.PF. or PLPF. (of an assembly) be in confusion or disorder Il.; (of the sea) be turbulent AR.; (of soil) be disturbed or broken AR.; (of Eros, compared to a gadfly) be in a frenzy AR.; (of sorrows) have been aroused AR.

—**τεταραγμένως** *pf.pass.ptcpl.adv.* **confusedly** Isoc. Pl. Plu.

ταραχή ῆς *f.* **1** confused and disturbing state of affairs, **confusion, complication, trouble** Hdt. E. Th. +
2 (in military ctxt.) **disorder, confusion** Th. X. Plb.
3 (in political or civic ctxt.) **disorder, upheaval, unrest** Hdt. Th. Att.orats. +
4 disturbance, confusion (W.GEN. of the mind) Pi.; (gener.) **confusion, perplexity** Isoc. Pl.

τάραχος ου *m.* **1** disordered behaviour (among a group of people), **disturbance, confusion, commotion** X. NT. Plu.
2 disorder, confusion (in the state) Plu.
3 confusion, perplexity (in the mind) X. NT.

ταραχώδης ες *adj.* **1** causing disturbance and confusion; (of god) **confusing, baffling** Hdt.; (of human fortunes, activities) Isoc.; (of a hare's scent-trail) X.; (of a verdict, an inquiry) Arist.; (of an emotion) **disturbing** Arist.; (of sights and sounds, dreams) Plu.
2 full of disturbance and confusion; (of a battle) **full of confusion** Th. Plu.; (of troops) **prone to confusion** X.; (of troops, a manoeuvre) **disorderly** Plb.; (of plans) **confused** Plu.; (of a person) prone to be upset, **full of disquiet** Plu.
3 (in political ctxt., of a speech) **troublemaking, inflammatory** D.; (of public affairs, an assembly, a person) **turbulent** Arist. Plu.

—**ταραχωδῶς** *adv.* | superl. ταραχωδέστατα | **in a confused, disorderly** or **disturbed manner** Isoc. Plu.

ταρβαλέος ᾱ ον *adj.* [ταρβέω] (of persons) **frightened, fearful** hHom. S.

ταρβέω *contr.vb.* —**τάρβημ(μ)ι** Aeol.vb. **1 be fearful, be afraid** Hom. hHom. Alc. Trag. Plu. —W.DAT. *for someone* AR. —W.INF. *to do sthg.* E.
2 be afraid of, fear —*someone or sthg.* Il. hHom. Pi.*fr.* Trag. AR. Theoc.

τάρβος εος (ους) *n.* **1 fear, alarm, fright** Il. A. S. AR.; **fear** (W.GEN. of someone or sthg.) A. Mosch.; (W.INF. of doing or suffering sthg.) E. AR.
2 (ref. to a person) cause of fear, **terror** (W.DAT. to a city) E.

ταρβοσύνη ης *f.* state of alarm, **fear** Od.

ταρβόσυνος η ον *adj.* (of fear) **terrifying** A.

Ταργήλια *Ion.n.pl.*, **Ταργήλιος** *Ion.m.*: see Θαργήλια

ταρίχευσις εως (Ion. ιος) *f.* [ταριχεύω] **1 preserving** (of fish, by salting or other means) Hdt.
2 embalming (of corpses) Hdt.

ταρῑχευτής έω *Ion.m.* **embalmer** Hdt.

ταρῑχεύω *vb.* [τάριχος] **1** preserve (food) by drying, smoking, pickling or salting; **preserve** —*fish* (*by pickling in brine*) Hdt. —*sorb-apples* (*by drying*) Pl. —*slices of dolphin* X.
2 preserve (a body) by embalming (usu. for the purpose of mummification); **embalm** —*a dead person or animal* Hdt. Pl. —*a head* Hdt.

ταρίχιον

3 ‖ PASS. (of a person against whom death and total extinction are invoked) be preserved —W.ADV. κακῶς *in ill manner* (*i.e. be shrivelled or dried up, like a mummy or preserved fish*) A. ‖ PF.PASS.PTCPL. (fig., of a person long in prison) thoroughly pickled D.

ταρίχιον ου *n.* [dimin. τάριχος] **piece of salt fish, piece of kipper** Ar.

ταριχοπωλέω *contr.vb.* (pejor.) be a seller of preserved fish, **sell kippers** Pl.

ταριχοπώλιον ου *n.* place where preserved fish is sold, **kipper-shop** Thphr.

τάριχος ους *n.* —also **τάρῑχος** ου *m.* [perh.loanwd.]
1 (collectv.neut.sg.) fish (usu. tunny or mackerel) preserved by drying, smoking, pickling or salting; **dried fish, salt fish, kippers** Ar. D. Thphr. Men. Plb. Plu.
2 ‖ MASC.PL. preserved fishes Hdt.; (sg., fig.ref. to a dead person) Hdt.

τάρπην (ep.aor.2 pass.), **ταρπῆναι, ταρπήμεναι** (ep.aor.2 pass.inf.), **ταρπώμεθα** (ep.1pl.aor.2 mid.subj.): see τέρπω

ταρσός, Att. **ταρρός**, οῦ *m.* [perh.reltd. τέρσομαι] 1 slatted or interwoven framework; **rack** or **tray** (for stacking and perh. drying cheeses) Od. Theoc.
2 matted arrangement of reeds ‖ COLLECTV.PL. matting (laid betw. courses of bricks in a wall) Hdt.; (as casing for improvised mud-bricks) Th.
3 **crate, basket** or **mat** (in or on which Socrates sits suspended) Ar.
4 **array, row** or **bank** (of oars) Hdt. E. Th. Plb. Plu.
5 part of the human foot, app. **sole** (perh. fr. its bone structure) Il. Hdt. AR.
6 **spread, array** (of feathers, on a bird's wing, a peacock's tail) AR. Mosch.

ταρτάρειος ᾱ ον *adj.* [Τάρταρος] (of confusion, caused by a collapsing house) **hellish** E.

Τάρταρος ου *m.* (*also f.* Pi.) —also **Τάρταρα** *n.pl.* [loanwd., unless reltd. ταράσσω] **Tartaros** (one of the primeval beings, orig. ref. to the lowest depths of the earth, beneath Hades; later, gener., the mythical underworld) Il. +; (father of Typhon, by Gaia) Hes.; (father of Death) S.
—**τάρταρα** *n.pl.* **lowest depths** (W.GEN. of the earth) Hes. E.

τάρφεα *n.pl.* [reltd. ταρφέες] ‖ only nom. and dat. τάρφεσι ‖ thick growths, **thickets** (W.GEN. of a wood) Il. AR.; **clumps** (of seaweed) AR.

ταρφέες ειαί έα *ep.pl.adj.* —also **ταρφύς** (A.) *nom.fem.sg.adj.* [τρέφω] 1 (pl.) thick, densely packed or abundant; (of arrows) **coming thick and fast** Hom.; (of thunderbolts) Hes.; (of snowflakes falling; of helmets of densely massed warriors, compared to snowflakes) **in profusion** Il.
2 (sg., of hair) **thick, abundant** A.; (of a multitude of soldiers) **dense** A.
—**ταρφέα** *neut.pl.adv.* 1 **constantly** Hom. AR.
2 **thick and fast** —*ref. to handfuls of corn falling* Il.
—**ταρφέως** *adv.* **frequently, often** B.

τάρφθην (ep.aor.pass.): see τέρπω

ταρφύς *fem.sg.adj.*: see ταρφέες

ταρχύω *vb.* ‖ fut. ταρχύσω ‖ aor.inf. ταρχῦσαι ‖ ep.aor.mid. ταρχῡσάμην ‖ **bury** (w. due solemnity) —*a person* Il. AR.(also mid.)

τάς (fem.acc.pl. and Aeol.fem.gen.sg.), **τᾶς** (dial.fem.gen.): see ὁ

τᾶσδε (dial.fem.gen.): see ὅδε

τάσις εως *f.* [τείνω] tension or intensity; **propulsive force** (needed to despatch missiles) Plu.

τάσσω, Att. **τάττω** *vb.* ‖ fut. τάξω ‖ aor. ἔταξα ‖ pf. τέταχα ‖ PASS.: fut. ταχθήσομαι ‖ aor. ἐτάχθην ‖ pf. τέταγμαι ‖ fut.pf. τετάξομαι ‖ neut.impers.vbl.adj. τακτέον ‖
1 (of a commander) put in order, **arrange in formation, draw up, marshal** —*an army, soldiers, ships* (sts. W.PREP.PHR. *for battle, or in a particular way*) A. Hdt. E. Th. +; (mid.) E.; (intr.) **marshal troops** Th. X. ‖ MID. (of a commander) **get one's troops in formation** Th.; (of troops) **get in formation, fall in** (sts. W.ADVBL. or PREP.PHR. in a particular way) Hdt. Th.; (tr., of sailors) **draw up** —*their ships* (*in a particular formation*) Th.; **form** —*a circle* (*of ships*) Th. ‖ PASS. (of troops, ships) be drawn up or be in position Hdt. Th. X.; (gener., of people, birds) get in position or be ready (to do sthg.) A. Ar. ‖ PF.PASS.PTCPL.ADJ. (of troops, an army) in formation or in good order E. Th. X.
2 (of a commander) assign to a particular position, **post, station** —*troops, ships* (usu. W.ADVBL. or PREP.PHR. *somewhere, against someone*) A. Hdt. E. Th. +; (fig., of circumstances) A.; (of officials) —*a watch* (*in a temple*) E.(mid.) ‖ PASS. (of troops, ships) be posted or stationed (somewhere, or for a particular objective) Hdt. Trag. Th. +; (of soldiers, sailors) be posted or drafted —W.PREP.PHR. *into the infantry, the fleet* Hdt.
3 (of a commander) put in the ranks, **enlist, enrol** —*a person* Att.orats.
4 (of a politician) **position** —*oneself* (*in a political stance or alliance*) D. Din. ‖ PASS. (of a person) be assigned a position (in the performance of a task) E.
5 (gener.) assign to a particular position (in space or time); **place** —*people, things* (W.ADV. or PREDIC.ADJ. *in different positions or order*) Hdt. E. X. +
6 place in a class or category; **assign** —*someone* (W.PREP.PHR. *to the ruling class, a menial role, or sim.*) Pl. X.; **rank** —*someone* (W.INF. + PREP.PHR. *as being among the wisest*) Aeschin.; **class** —*sthg.* (W.INF. + PREDIC.ADJ. *as being such and such*) Pl. ‖ PASS. (of cities) be included —W.PREP.PHR. *in an alliance* Th.
7 place (someone) in an official or specific role; **appoint** —*someone* (W.PREDIC.SB. *as a commander*) X. Aeschin. D. —(W.PREP.PHR. *to a post or for a task*) Isoc. Pl. X. D. ‖ PASS. be appointed (usu. W.PREDIC.SB. or PREP.PHR. as holder of a post, or for a task) Hdt. Trag. X. + —W.INTERN.ACC. *for a task* E.
8 **appoint, instruct, order** —W.ACC. + INF. *someone to do or be sthg.* Hdt. S. E. X. Corinn. —W.DAT. + INF. Hdt. X. ‖ PASS. be appointed or be under orders —W.INF. *to do sthg.* Hdt. Trag. X. ‖ IMPERS.PF. and PLPF.PASS. an order has (had) been given —W.DAT. + INF. *to someone to do sthg.* Th. X.
9 (of a person, law, argument) **order, ordain, prescribe** —*rules, arrangements, or sim.* Hdt. S. E. Att.orats. Pl. +; (of parties to an agreement) **stipulate** —W.ACC. + INF. *that each shd. do sthg.* E.; (intr., of a person) **give orders** S. ‖ PASS. (of immortal life) be ordained —W.DAT. *for someone* Pi.
‖ PF.PASS.PTCPL.ADJ. (of a time, place) prescribed or fixed A. Hdt. E. Pl. +; (of a diet, sacrifices) established or regular Pl. X.; (of a craft) with fixed rules Isoc.; (of a system of government) well-ordered Isoc. Pl.; (of words) accepted or conventional Isoc. ‖ NEUT.PASS.PTCPL.SB. (sg. and pl.) what is (was, has been) prescribed S. Ar. X.
10 (of persons) arrange for or specify a fee or payment; **fix** —*tribute, a sum of money, material items* (usu. W.DAT., sts. also W.INF. *for someone, to contribute*) Hdt. Th. Att.orats. —*a payment* (W.DAT. *to someone*) X.; (intr.) **fix a payment** —W.GEN. *at a certain sum* Th. ‖ MID. **fix, stipulate** —*a fee* E. Pl.; **arrange** —W.INF. *to pay* Th. —W.ACC. + INF. *for tribute to*

be paid Hdt.; **arrange to pay** —*tribute or sim.* Hdt.; (intr.) **arrange to make** or **receive payment** Th. Pl.; (gener.) **contract, arrange** —W.FUT.INF. *to do sthg.* Plb. ‖ PASS. (of tribute, a price, or sim.) be fixed Hdt. Th. Pl.; (of persons) be assessed or required —W.INF. *to pay tribute* Hdt.
11 fix, prescribe —*a penalty, punishment* Ar. Att.orats. Pl.; (mid.) Hdt.
—**τεταγμένως** *pf.pass.ptcpl.adv.* **in an orderly** or **regular manner** Isoc. Pl. X. Arist. Plb. Plu.
τᾱτάομαι *dial.pass.contr.vb.*: see τητάομαι
ταῦ *indecl.n.* [Semit.loanwd.] **tau** (letter of the Greek alphabet) Pl.
Τάϋγετον, Ion. **Τηΰγετον**, ου *n.* **Taygeton** (mt. range betw. Laconia and Messenia) Od. +
ταύρειος ᾱ (Ion. η) ον (also ος ον E.) *adj.* [ταῦρος] **1** (of the body, foot, horns, blood) **of a bull** Trag. Ar. Plu.; (of the slaughter) E.; (of herds) **of bulls** Theoc.; (of the dragging of Dirke) **by a bull** E.*fr.*
2 (of a shield, helmet) **of bull's hide** Il.
—**ταύρεος** ον *masc.adj.* (epith. of Poseidon) associated with bulls (prob. as sacrificial offerings), **of the bulls** Hes.
ταυρηδόν *adv.* **like a bull** —*ref. to glowering fiercely* Ar. —*ref. to a way of looking, habitual to Socrates* (perh. w. head thrust forward) Pl.
Ταυρικός *adj.*: see under Ταῦροι
ταυρό-δετος ον *adj.* [δέω¹] (of glue) made from bull-hide and providing a bond, **bull-hide bonding** E.*fr.*
Ταῦροι ων *m.pl.* **Tauri, Taurians** (inhabitants of the mountainous headland of Crimea) Hdt. E. Call.
—**Ταυρικός** ή όν *adj.* (of the race) **Taurian** Hdt.; (of the mountains) Hdt.; (of the land) Hdt. E.
ταυρό-κερως ων *adj.* [κέρας] (epith. of Dionysus) **bull-horned** E.
ταυρό-κολλα ης *f.* [κόλλα] **bull-hide glue** Plb.
ταυρό-κρᾱνος ον *adj.* [κρᾱνίον¹] (epith. of Okeanos) **bull-headed** E.
ταυροκτονέω *contr.vb.* [ταυροκτόνος] **slay bulls** (as sacrifices) A.(dub.) —W.COGN.ACC. S.
ταυρο-κτόνος ον *adj.* [κτείνω] (of lions) **bull-slaying** S.
ταυρό-μορφος ον *adj.* [μορφή] (of the face of a river god) **bull-shaped** E.
ταυρόομαι *mid.pass.contr.vb.* **1 become a bull** ‖ PF. (of Dionysus) be changed into a bull E.
2 (of a person) **be savage as a bull** A. —W.ACC. *in one's gaze* (i.e. look savagely) E.
Ταυρο-πόλος ου, dial. **Ταυροπόλᾱ** ᾱς (S.) *f.* [πέλω] **Tauropolos** (i.e. Bull-herd, cult-title of Artemis, under which she was worshipped at Halai Araphenides in Attica) S. E. Ar. [also explained by E. as *Taurian-roaming* (Ταῦροι, πολέω)]
—**Ταυροπόλια** ων *n.pl.* **Tauropolia** (festival in honour of Artemis Tauropolos, held at Halai) Men.
ταυρό-πους πουν, gen. ποδος *adj.* [πούς] (of an image of a river god) **bull-footed** E.
ταῦρος ου *m.* **bull** Hom. +; (appos.w. βοῦς) Il.; (as the form taken by a river god, by Dionysus) Carm.Pop. S. E.; (ref. to the bronze bull of Phalaris) Pi.; (ref. to the Minotaur, to a sea-monster) E.
ταυροσφαγέω *contr.vb.* [ταυροσφάγος] **cut a bull's throat** (in sacrifice) Ar.
ταυρο-σφάγος ον *adj.* [σφάζω] (of a day) **when bulls are slaughtered** (as sacrifices) S.
ταυρο-φάγος ον *adj.* [φαγεῖν] (com.epith. of the poet Cratinus) **bull-devouring** Ar.

ταυρό-φθογγος ον *adj.* [φθόγγος] (perh. of bull-roarers) **bellowing like bulls** A.*fr.*
ταυρο-φόνος ον *adj.* [θείνω] (of a festival) **where bulls are slain** Pi.
ταυρ-ωπός όν *adj.* [ὤψ] (of Dionysus) **bull-faced** Ion
τᾱΰσιος *dial.adj.*: see τηΰσιος
ταῦτα (nom.acc.neut.pl.): see οὗτος
ταὐτά: crasis for τὰ αὐτά
ταυταγί (neut.pl., w.pcl. γε): see οὑτοσί, under οὗτος
ταύτην, ταύτης, ταύτῃ (acc., gen., dat. fem.sg.), dial. **ταύτᾱν, ταύτᾱς, ταύτᾳ**: see οὗτος
ταυτηνδί (fem.acc., w.pcl. δέ): see οὑτοσί, under οὗτος
ταὐτό, Att. **ταὐτόν**: crasis for τὸ αὐτό(ν)
ταυτολογέω *contr.vb.* [ταὐτόν, λόγος] **say the same thing**; (of a historian) **repeat what has been said before** Plb.; **repeat oneself** Plb.
ταυτότης ητος *f.* **sameness, identity** Arist.
ταφεῖν *aor.2 inf.* [reltd. θάμβος] | *aor.2* ἔταφον, dial. τάφον, *ptcpl.* ταφών | *pf.* τέθηπα, *ptcpl.* τεθηπώς | *plpf.* ἐτεθήπεα |
1 (aor., of a person, heart) be struck with amazement, **be amazed, be astonished** Hom. Pi. B. Call. AR. —W.ACC. *at sthg.* B. —W.ACC.PTCPL. *at someone doing sthg.* A.
2 ‖ PF. (of a person, heart) be in a state of wonder or amazement Hom. Emp. Hdt. AR. —W.ACC. *at sthg.* AR.; be bewildered or dazed Il. Parm.; (fig., of a person's style of speech) Plu.
ταφεύς έως *m.* [τάφος¹] one who gives burial, **burier** S. Plu.; (iron. ref. to dogs and birds, to which an exposed corpse is prey) S.
ταφή ῆς *f.* [θάπτω] **1** act of burial, **burial, funeral** Hdt. Trag. Th. Att.orats. +; (pl. for sg.) E.; (ref. to the right or opportunity to bury someone) S. ‖ COLLECTV.PL. public burial-rites (for the war-dead) Th. Pl. D.
2 mode of burial, **funeral practice** Hdt.(pl.)
3 (pl.) burial-place, **grave** Hdt. Ar.; (pl. for sg.) Hdt. S.
4 payment for burial, **burial-fee** D.
ταφήιος η ον *ep.adj.* [τάφος¹] relating to burial; (of a shroud) **for a funeral** Od.; (of sacrificed sheep) AR.
ταφῆναι (aor.pass.inf.), **ταφήσομαι** (fut.pass.): see θάπτω
τάφιος ον *adj.* [τάφος¹] (of festivals) **funerary** Call.
τάφον (dial.aor.2): see ταφεῖν
τάφος¹ ου *m.* [θάπτω] **1** funeral rites or ceremony, **funeral** Hom. Trag. Th. Lys.; (ref. to a feast) Hom.; (pl. for sg.) S. Pl.
2 (concr.) **grave, tomb** Hes. +; (pl. for sg.) S.
τάφος² εος *n.* [ταφεῖν] **astonishment, amazement** Od. hHom. Ibyc.
ταφρείᾱ ᾱς *f.* [ταφρεύω] **provision of trenches** (for a city's defence) D.; **digging of trenches** (by soldiers) Plb. Plu.
τάφρευμα ατος *n.* **trench, ditch** Pl.
ταφρεύω *vb.* [τάφρος] (milit.) **dig a trench** Pl. X. —W.COGN.ACC. Aeschin.
τάφρος ου *f.* (also *m.* Call.) —also **τάφρη** ης *Ion.f.* [θάπτω]
1 ground excavated by digging; **trench** (for defence of a city, camp or land) Il. Hdt. S. E. Th. +; (as a moat) Hdt.
2 (gener.) **trench** (in which axes are set up for an archery contest) Od.; **ditch** or **trench** (on a farm) Pl.; (ref. to a grave) E.
ταφών (aor.2 ptcpl.): see ταφεῖν
τάχα *adv.* [ταχύς] **1 with speed, quickly** —*ref. to the bloom of youth passing* Theoc.
2 (ref. to a fut. event) following quickly (upon a preceding event), **soon** Hom. +; (w. past tenses, in narrative) Hom. +
3 (ref. to a fut. event) with great likelihood, **probably** S. E. Th. Lys. Ar. Pl. +; (more commonly) τάχ' ἄν Hdt. Trag. Th.

Att.orats. Pl. +; (τάχα or τάχ' ἄν modified by ἴσως) *quite possibly* S. Th. Ar. Pl. +

ταχέως *adv*.: see under ταχύς

ταχινός ή (dial. ά) όν *adj.* [ταχύς] **1** (of an arrow, a bird) **swift** AR. Theoc.
2 (of a person) quick in action, **quick** Call.
3 (of whiskers) early to grow, **early** Call.
4 (of a lover's mind) quick to change, **fickle** Theoc.

τάχιστος (superl.adj.): see ταχύς

τάχος εος (ους) *n*. **1** quickness of movement (by persons, animals, objects), **quickness, swiftness, speed** Il. A. Pi. Hdt. S. Th. +; **rapidity** (of a river) Hdt.
2 quickness, speed (in the performance of an action) Th. X. Men. Plb. Plu.; (of apprehension) Pl.
3 (pejor.) **hastiness, haste** (of thought, behaviour) E. Th.
4 ‖ ACC.SG.ADV. quickly or without delay Scol. A. E. Telest.; (advbl.phrs.) ὡς τάχος *with all speed, at once* Pi. Hdt. Trag. +; ὅ τι τάχος Hdt. Th.; ὅσον τάχος S. E. Ar.; ᾗ (ᾇ) τάχος Pi. Theoc. Plu.
5 (prep.phrs.) ἐν τάχει *with speed, quickly* A. Pi. S. Th. +; διὰ τάχους S. Th. Pl. +; κατὰ τάχος Hdt. Th. Plb. Plu.; σὺν τάχει S. Plu.; εἰς τάχος Ar. X.; μετὰ τάχους Pl. Plb. Plu.

ταχύ *neut.adv.*: see under ταχύς

ταχυ-άλωτος ον *adj.* [ἁλωτός] (of a country) **quickly conquerable** Hdt.

ταχυ-βάτᾱς ᾱ *dial.masc.adj.* [βαίνω] (of a spy) stepping quickly, **swift-footed** E.

ταχύ-βουλος ον *adj.* [βουλή] (pejor.) **hasty in reaching a decision** Ar.

ταχυεργίᾱ ᾱς *f.* [ἔργον] **speed of action** (by a person) X.

ταχυ-ήρης ῆρες *adj.* [ἐρέσσω] (of a ship) **swift-rowed** A.

ταχύ-μορος ον *adj.* [μόρος] (of a rumour) swift-doomed, **short-lived** A.

ταχυναυτέω *contr.vb.* [ναύτης] have the capacity to sail quickly ‖ PTCPL.ADJ. (of ships) fast Th. Aeschin. Plb. ‖ INF.SB. speed at sea Th. Plb. Plu.

ταχύνω *vb.* | aor. ἐτάχῡνα | **1** (intr.) **go** or **act quickly, make haste** Trag. Ar. X. Plb. Plu.
2 (tr.) **hurry on** —*a person* E.; **quickly make** —*a trench* S.

ταχυ-πειθής ές *adj.* [πείθω] quickly persuaded, **credulous, gullible** Theoc.

ταχυπλοέω *contr.vb.* [ταχύπλους] (of a ship) have the capacity to sail quickly, **be fast** Plb.

ταχύ-πλους ουν *Att.adj.* [πλόος] sailing swiftly; (of a command to rowers) **to make a ship speed along** E.*fr.*

ταχύ-πομπος ον *adj.* [πέμπω] (of pursuit) prob., offering swift escort (to those pursued), **swiftly accompanying** A.

ταχύ-πορος ον *adj.* [πόρος] (of Achilles; of an oar, i.e. ship) travelling swiftly, **swift-moving** E.; (of flight) Tim.; (app. of a woman's mind) A.

ταχύ-ποτμος ον *adj.* [πότμος] (of the human race) **swift-doomed, short-lived** Pi.

ταχύ-πους πουν, gen. ποδος *adj.* [πούς] (of a god, horses) **swift-footed** E.; (of a dog-fox, fig.ref. to a person) Ar.; (of a hind) Lyr.adesp.; (of a footstep, leg) **swift, nimble** E.

ταχύ-πτερνος ον *adj.* [πτέρνη] (of horses) with swift heels, **swift-footed** Thgn.

ταχύ-πτερος ον *adj.* [πτερόν] (of breezes) **swift-winged** A.

ταχύ-πωλος ον *adj.* [πῶλος] (epith. of the Greeks, the Myrmidons) **swift-horsed** Il.; (of Kastor) Theoc.

ταχύ-ρροθος ον *adj.* [ῥόθος] (of a messenger's report) quickly creating a hubbub, **panic-making** A.

ταχύ-ρρωστος ον *adj.* [ῥώννυμι] (of a dove) strengthened in speed, **gaining swift strength** (fr. the wind) S.

ταχύς εἶα ύ *adj.* | compar. θάσσων (Att. θάττων), also ταχύτερος (Hdt.) | superl. τάχιστος, also ταχύτατος (Pi.) ‖ sts. quasi-advbl., as e.g. ἀφίξεται ταχύς *he will come quick, i.e. quickly* |
1 (of gods, humans, animals) quick in movement, **swift, fast** Hom. +; (W.ACC. on foot, i.e. swift-footed) Il. Hdt. E. AR.; (W.INF. at running) Hom. ‖ NEUT.SB. speed (of a horse) X.
2 (of feet) **swift** Hom.; (of wings) B. Ar.; (of rowers' hands) Pi.; (of a mind) **quick, nimble** E.
3 (of arrows) **swift** Hom.; (of a chariot) Pi.; (of ships) A. Hdt. S. Th. Ar. D.; (of an oar) E.; (of a wind) AR.; (of a river) **rapid** Hdt. ‖ NEUT.SB. quickness (in music) Pl.
4 (of persons) quick in action, **quick** S. X.; (W.INF. to do sthg.) E. Th. Ar.; (pejor.) **quick, in haste** (W.INF. to make a decision) S. Th.; **quick, prone** (W.PREP.PHR. to anger) Plu. ‖ NEUT.SB. speed or haste E.
5 (of running, a leap, flight) quickly moving, **quick, rapid** B. S. Th.; (of the flow of tears) E.; (of rumour) E.
6 (of ruin, punishment, instructions) quick to arrive, **quick, prompt** A. Th. D.; (of perception) Th.; (of death) **quick, sudden** E. X. Mosch.; (of change) And. Pl.; (of war, danger) **sudden, immediate** Th.
7 (of a disease) quick to depart, **short-lived** S.; (of gratitude) S.; (of hopes) Pi.
8 (of an outcome, decision, undertaking) quickly achieved, **quick, rapid** A. Hdt. Th.; (of pleasures) **quickly realised** or **enjoyed** Th.; (pejor., of actions) **quick, hasty** Hdt.
9 (of a message) quickly told or completed, **quick, short** S.; (of a narrative) Arist.; (of a period of time) S.
10 (of a route) **quick, short** Ar. X.; (advbl.acc.) τὴν ταχίστην *in the quickest way, with all speed* Hdt. Ar. Att.orats. X. Thphr. +
11 (prep.phrs.) διὰ ταχέων *quickly* Th. Isoc. Pl. X. D.; ἐκ ταχείας S.

—**ταχύ** *neut.adv.* **1** with speed, **swiftly** Ar. X.
2 quickly, without delay, soon Pi. Hdt. S. E. Th. Ar. +

—**ταχέως** *adv.* **1** with speed, **swiftly** Il. +
2 quickly, without delay, soon Hes. +
3 (pejor.) **hastily** Th.
4 probably Plb.; cf. τάχα 3

—**θᾶσσον** (Att. **θᾶττον**), also **ταχύτερον** (Hdt.) *compar.adv.* **1** with greater speed, **more quickly, faster** Pi. +
2 within a shorter time, **sooner** Hdt. +; **more readily** S.
3 (with little or no compar. connot.) **speedily, quickly** Hom. +
4 within a short time (fr. a given moment), **quickly, soon** Hom. +; ὅτι θᾶσσον *quickly, at once* Theoc.; (w. temporal or conditional conj.) ἐπειδή (ἐπειδάν) θᾶττον *as soon as* Pl. D.; ὡς θᾶττον Plb.; ἐάν (ἄν, ἤν) θᾶττον Pl. X. Men.

—**τάχιστα** *superl.adv.* **1** very quickly, **at full speed** Hom. hHom.
2 with least delay, **straightaway, at once** Hom. +
3 (w.relatv.adv.) ὅτι (ὅττι) τάχιστα *as quickly as possible, with all speed* Hom. +; ὡς τάχιστα Alc. +; ὅπως τάχιστα Trag. Ar.; ὅσον τάχιστα Trag.; ᾇ τάχιστα Pi.
4 (in vbl.phrs.) ὡς δυνατόν ἐστι τάχιστα (or sim.) *as quickly as is possible* Hdt. Th. Pl. X.; (w. temporal conj.) ἐπεί, ἐπεάν (ἐπειδή, ἐπειδάν or sim.) τάχιστα *as soon as* A. Hdt. Att.orats. Pl. X.; ὡς τάχιστα Hdt. X. Aeschin. D.; ὅπως τάχιστα A.; (w.ptcpl.) ἀπαλλαγεὶς τάχιστα *immediately after departing* Plu.

ταχυτής ῆτος, dial. **ταχυτᾱς** ᾶτος *f.* **1 quickness, swiftness, speed** (of runners, their feet) Il. Xenoph. Pi. B.; (of a dog, camels, ants) Od. Hdt.; (as a concept) Pl.

2 speed (in working) Plu.; **hastiness** (in behaviour) Arist.

τᾰ́ων (ep.fem.gen.pl.): see ὁ

ταῶς ταῶ, also **ταῶν** ταῶνος m. [loanwd.] **peafowl, peacock** (esp. as an ornamental pet) Ar. Plu.

τε¹ *enclit.pcl.* | The wd. is used (1–3) as a conjunction, connecting parallel items, and (4) w. a universalising function but no specific sense of its own. There are numerous applications of the wd. in both uses: only the most common are illustrated. |
1 (single τε, connecting wds., phrs., cls., sts. sentences; typically placed following 1st wd. of the 2nd item) **and** Hom. + • Ζεῦ ἄλλοι τε θεοί *Zeus and other gods* Il. • ἀνοικίσασθαι ἐς Ὄλυνθον μίαν τε πόλιν ταύτην ἰσχυρὰν ποιήσασθαι *to settle inland at Olynthos and make that one city strong* Th.
2 (similarly) τε ... τε **both ... and** Hom. + • ἀνδρῶν τε θεῶν τε *of both men and gods* Hom. Hes. • Πριηνέας τε εἷλε ἐς Μίλητόν τε ἐσέβαλε *he both captured the inhabitants of Priene and attacked Miletos* Hdt.
3 τε (...) καί **both ... and** Hom. + • Ἀτρείδης τε ἄναξ ἀνδρῶν καὶ δῖος Ἀχιλλεύς *both the son of Atreus, lord of men, and noble Achilles* Il. • βούλεταί τε καὶ ἐπίσταται *he both wishes and knows* Th.
4 (mainly ep., usu. marking a statement as general or gnomic, or an action as habitual or characteristic, usu. following relatv.pron. or conj., esp. ὅς τε, δέ τε, γάρ τε, καί τε, ἀλλά τε) • θεοὶ δέ τε πάντα ἴσασι *but the gods do know everything* Od. • πάντων ὅσσα τε γαῖαν ἔπι πνείει τε καὶ ἕρπει *of all things that both breathe and walk on earth* Il. • καὶ Λιβύην, ἵνα τ᾽ ἄρνες ἄφαρ κεραοὶ τελέθουσι *and Libya, where lambs become horned straightaway* Od. • ἑστήκει ὥς τίς τε λέων *he stood like a lion* Il. [This use of τε is seen in later ἅτε, ὥστε, ἐφ᾽ ᾧτε, οἷός τε, and in occas. use of ὅς τε (or ὅστε) for ὅς in Lyr. Trag.]

τέ, τε² (dial.acc. 2sg.pers.pron.): see σύ

τεαύτᾱ *Aeol.fem.adj.*: see τοιοῦτος

τέγγω *vb.* | fut. τέγξω | aor. ἔτεγξα ‖ PASS.: aor. ἐτέγχθην |
1 make wet by immersion in water; wet —*one's feet* (usu. W.PREP.PHR. *in the sea*) E. Pl. AR.; (of halcyons) —*their wings* (W.DAT. *w. seawater*) Ar.(quot. E.); **soak, steep** —*clothes* (W.DAT. *in river water*) E.; (fig., of a poet) —*an account* (*in falsehood*) Pi.
2 (gener.) **make wet**; (of a wine-drinker) **soak** —*one's lungs, belly* (sts. W.DAT. *w. wine*) Alc. E.Cyc.; (of a stream) **water** —*a land, foliage* E. ‖ PASS. (of a head) be made wet or be drenched —W.DAT. *w. rain or sea spray* S.; get (W.ACC. one's hair, feet) wet —W.DAT. *w. dew, seawater* S. AR.
3 (specif.) **make wet with tears**; **moisten, water** —*one's eyes, cheek, dress, or sim.* (freq. W.DAT. *w. tears*) B. Trag.; (fig., of a raincloud of sorrow) —*a cheek* S. ‖ PASS. (of a person, eyes) be drenched (w. tears) A. E.
4 shed —W.INTERN.ACC. *tears* Pi. S.
5 make wet with blood; (of a person, gouged eyes) **drench, stain** —*one's* (or *another's*) *hand, beard, cheek* (sts. W.DAT. *w. blood*) Trag. AR.; (of blood) —*an altar* E.
6 ‖ PASS. (fig., of an obdurate person) **be softened** (into compliance) A. E. Ar. Pl. Plu.

Τεγέα ᾱς, Ion. **Τεγέη** ης f. **Tegea** (city in SE. Arcadia) Il. +
—**Τεγεᾶται** ῶν, Ion. **Τεγεῆται** έων *m.pl.* **men of Tegea, Tegeans** Hdt. Th. + ‖ SG. (sts. appos.w. ἀνήρ) **Tegean** Hdt. Th.
—**Τεγεᾶτις** ιδος f. **woman of Tegea** E.*fr*.; **region of Tegea** Th. ‖ ADJ. (of the region) **of Tegea** X. Plb.
—**Τεγεητικός** ή όν *Ion.adj.* (of the borders) **of Tegea** Hdt.

τέγεος ον *adj.* [τέγος] (of chambers, halls) **roofed** Il. Emp.

τέγος εος (ους) n. [reltd. στέγος] **1 roof** (of a house, esp. as a place for standing or sleeping on) Od. hHom. Th. Lys. Ar. +
2 roofed building; **chamber** (in the temple at Delphi) Pi.; (ref. to a cave) Pi.
3 brothel Plb.

τέθᾱλα (dial.pf.), **τεθᾱλώς** (dial.pf.ptcpl.), **τεθᾰλυῖα** (ep.fem.pf.ptcpl.): see θάλλω

τέθαμμαι (pf.pass.), **τεθάφθαι** (pf.pass.inf.), **τεθάψομαι** (fut.pf.mid.): see θάπτω

τεθαρρηκότως *Att.pf.ptcpl.adv.*: see under θαρσέω

τέθεικα and **τέθηκα** (pf.), **τέθειμαι** (pf.pass.): see τίθημι

τεθηγμένος (pf.pass.ptcpl.): see θήγω

τέθηλα (pf.): see θάλλω

τέθηπα (pf.): see ταφεῖν

τεθήσομαι (fut.pass.): see τίθημι

τέθλασμαι (pf.pass.): see θλάω

τέθμιος *dial.adj.*, **τεθμός** *dial.m.*: see θέσμιος, θεσμός

τέθναθι (pf.imperatv.), **τεθνάτω** (3sg.pf.imperatv.), **τεθναίην** (pf.opt.), **τέθνηκα** (pf.), **τεθνᾶσι** (3pl.pf.), **τεθνήξω** (fut.pf.): see θνήσκω

τεθνάναι (pf.inf.), **τεθνάμεναι, τεθνάμεν** (ep.pf.inf.), **τεθνάκην** (Aeol.pf.inf.): see θνήσκω

τεθνεώς (pf.ptcpl.), **τεθνειώς, τεθνηώς** (ep.pf.ptcpl.): see θνήσκω

τεθορυβημένως *pf.pass.ptcpl.adv.*: see under θορυβέω

τέθραμμαι (pf.pass.), **τεθράφθαι** (pf.pass.inf.): see τρέφω

τεθριππο-βάμων ον, gen. ονος *dial.adj.* [τέθριππος; βῆμα, βαίνω] **going in a four-horse chariot**; (of travel) **in a chariot and four** E.

τεθριππο-βάτης εω *Ion.m.* **driver of a four-horse chariot** Hdt.

τέθρ-ιππος ον *adj.* [τέσσαρες, ἵππος] **1 having four horses yoked abreast**; (of a chariot, the light of the sun) **drawn by four horses** Pi. E.; (of a race) **for four-horse chariots** E.
2 ‖ NEUT.SB. **four-horse chariot** Pi. Hdt. E. Ar. Pl. +; (pl. for sg.) Pi. E.

τεθριπποτροφέω *contr.vb.* [τεθριπποτρόφος] **maintain a four-horse team** Hdt.

τεθριππο-τρόφος ον *adj.* [τρέφω] (of a household) **maintaining a four-horse team** (for chariot-racing, a mark of great wealth) Hdt.

τεθυμένος (pf.pass.ptcpl.): see θύω

τεί (dial.acc.2sg.pers.pron.), **τεΐν** (dial.dat.sg.): see σύ

τεῖδε *dial.adv.* **1 in this place, here** Theoc.
2 to here, hither Hes.(dub.) Theoc.

τείνυμαι *Ion.mid.vb.*: see τίνω

τείνω *vb.* [reltd. τανύω] | fut. τενῶ | aor. ἔτεινα, ep. τεῖνα | pf. τέτακα ‖ MID.: fut. τενοῦμαι | aor. ἐτεινάμην, ep. τεινάμην ‖ PASS.: fut. ταθήσομαι | aor. ἐτάθην, ep. τάθην, ptcpl. ταθείς | pf. τέταμαι | ep.3sg.plpf. τέτατο, 3pl. τέταντο, 3du. τετάσθην |
1 pull so as to make tight, stretch tight, draw tight —*reins* (to fasten them to a chariot-rail) Il. —*a cable* (around a ship) AR.(mid.); **make taut** —*a ship's rigging* S.; (intr.) **pull** (on a rope, a fishing-line) Ar. Theoc. ‖ PASS. (of straps) be stretched tight Il.; (of sails, by the wind) Od. AR.
‖ AOR.PASS.PTCPL. (of a person) **strung up** —W.PREP.PHR. *in bonds* Od. ‖ PF.PASS.PTCPL. (of a rock, in mid-air) **suspended** (w.connot. of tension) —W.DAT. *by chains* E.
2 (specif.) **pull back** (a bow-string); **bend** —*a bow* (in order to shoot) Il. A. AR.(mid.); **aim, direct** —*arrows* S.
3 (fig., of gods, in a conflict envisaged as a tug-of-war) **pull tight** —*the issue of war* (W.PREDIC.ADJ. *so that it is equal on both sides*) Il. ‖ PASS. (of war and fighting) be pulled tight

(and so equal) Il. Hes.; (of fighting) be intensified Il.; (of the din of battle) S.
4 intensify, raise high, heighten —*one's voice, shouts* A. E. Tim.
5 (intr.) **exert oneself, strive hard** S. Ar. Pl.; **press on, hasten** (to a place or goal) E. Ar. X. || PASS. (of the pace of horses and sprinters) be strained to the utmost Hom.; (of persons) be intensely concentrated —W.PTCPL. *on doing sthg.* Pi.; (of persons, their efforts) —W.PREP.PHR. *on a goal* Pi. Pl. Plu.
6 extend or **spread out** (objects) in space; (of persons) **spread out** —*hunting nets* X. —*a sail* Call.; **lay out** —*planks (in a specific configuration)* Hdt.; **place** or **fit** —*a bridle (around a horse's jaws)* Pi.; (of Zeus) **send forth** —*a tempest* Il.; (usu.mid.) **stretch out** —*one's hands, limbs, items held in the hand* Hellenist.poet.; (mid., of a dragon) —*its neck* AR.
7 (intr., of mountains, regions, buildings, roads) **stretch, extend** (in a certain direction) A. Hdt. X. AR. Plu.; (of pleats in a dress) E.; (of a geometrical line) Pl.; (fig., of the paths of Zeus' mind) A.; (of a god, ref. to his sphere of influence) Pl. || PASS. (of darkness, mist, light) be spread out Od. Hes. Thgn. S.; (of fallen warriors, sleepers, or sim.) be stretched out Il. Simon. E. AR.; (of a sword) lie extended (by one's side) Il.; (of a mountain, an island) stretch (in a certain direction) Hdt. E.; (of paths, a column of light) Pl.; (of an eyebrow, across the face) Theoc.
8 extend (sthg.) in time; **draw out, prolong** —*one's speech* A. E. Pl. —*bloodshed* E.; **draw out, pass** —*one's life* A. E.; (intr., of time) **stretch on** A.; (of a speaker) **run on** (at length) A. S. || PASS. (of life) be drawn out A.
9 direct (speech, actions) to a particular goal; **aim, direct** —*an argument (against someone)* Pl.; **plan, intend** —*bloodshed (for someone)* E.; (intr., of thoughts, words, facts) **tend, point** —W.PREP. or ADVBL.PHR. *in a certain direction, to a certain goal* Pl. D. Arist. Plb.; **relate, pertain** —W.PREP.PHR. *to someone (i.e. concern one)* Hdt. E. Pl. X.; (of a person) **approach** —W.PREP.PHR. *close to someone (in respect of likeness)* Pl. || PASS. (of speech) be directed (at someone) E.

τεῖος *ep.adv.*: see τέως

τείρεα (ep.nom.acc.pl.), **τείρεσι** (ep.dat.pl.): see τέρας

Τειρεσίας ου (ep. ᾱο) *m.* **Teiresias** (mythol. blind Theban prophet) Od. +

τείρω *vb.* | aor.ptcpl. τείρᾱς (Lyr.adesp.) | otherwise only pres. and impf. | **1** (of warriors, their weapons, oppressors) **wear down, exhaust, harass** —*a person* Il. A.
2 (of wounds, discomforts, old age) **distress, pain** —*a person* Il. E. AR.; (of hunger, need) —*a person, belly* Od. E.; (of a song, cares, another's fate) —*a person, mind* Od. Mimn. A.; (of love, a beloved) —*a person* Hes.*fr.* Alcm. Telest. || PASS. (of a person, heart, animal) be in pain or distress Hom. Anacr. Eleg. Pi. Trag. Ar. +
3 bruise, crush, trample —*flowers* (W.DAT. *underfoot*) Lyr.adesp.

τείσω (fut.): see τίνω

τειχεσι-πλήτης ου *m.* [τεῖχος, πελάζω] | only voc. τειχεσιπλῆτα | (epith. of Ares) **approacher of walls, attacker of cities** Il.

τειχέω *contr.vb.* | Ion.impf. ἐτείχεον | **1 equip with a wall** or **walls, wall, fortify** —*a city, region* Hdt.
2 build —W.COGN.ACC. *a wall* or *walls (for fortification)* Hdt.

τειχ-ήρης ες *adj.* [ἀραρίσκω] (of a populace) **confined within one's walls** (by the enemy) Hdt. Th. And. X. Plb.

τειχίζω *vb.* | fut. τειχιῶ | aor. ἐτείχισα | **1 equip with a wall** or **walls, wall, fortify** —*a city, camp, region* Hdt. Th.(also mid.) Att.orats. + || PASS. (of a populace, city, place) **be fortified** Hdt. Th. Att.orats. +; (fig., of Egypt) —W.DAT. *by the Nile* Hdt.; (of a city's safety) —*by military strength* D.
2 (act. and mid.) **build a wall** or **walls** (for fortification) Th. Ar. Pl. X. D.; **build** —W.COGN.ACC. *a wall* Il. Th. And. X. —*a fortification* Th. X. Plu. || PASS. (of a wall) be built Th. And. X. Aeschin.; (fig., of a treasury of songs; of a tower, ref. to Aigina) Pi.

τειχιόεις εσσα εν *adj.* (of a city) **with good walls** Il.

τειχίον ου *n.* [dimin. τεῖχος] **wall** (of a building, or on open land, opp. city wall or fortification) Od. Th. Ar. Pl. +

τείχισις εως *f.* [τειχίζω] **wall-building** Th. X.

τείχισμα ατος *n.* **walled place, fortification** Th. Call. Plu.

τειχισμός οῦ *m.* activity of building walls, **wall-building** (for fortification) Th. D. Plu.; **fortification** (W.GEN. of a city) Th. Plb.

τειχοδομία ᾱς *f.* [τεῖχος, δέμω] **wall-building** (for fortification) Plu.

τειχ-ολέτις ιδος *f.* [ὄλλυμι] **destroyer of the walls** (W.GEN. of Rome, ref. to a traitoress) Plu.(quot.poet.)

τειχο-μάχᾱς ᾱ *dial.m.* [μάχομαι] (appos.w. ἀνήρ) **stormer of walls, siege-engineer** Ar.

τειχομαχέω *contr.vb.* **attack a wall, assault a fortification, conduct siege operations** Hdt. Th. X. Plu.; (fig., of an aggressor) **lay siege** —W.DAT. *to someone* Ar.

τειχομαχίᾱ ᾱς, Ion. **τειχομαχίη** ης *f.* **1 assault on a wall** (as a specific event) Hdt. Plu.; (as general title for the narrative of the Trojan attack on the Greek defensive wall in *Iliad* 12) Pl.
2 (as a military technique) **storming of walls** Plu.

τειχο-ποιός οῦ *m.* [ποιέω] **Superintendent of Walls** (official appointed to oversee the repair of city walls) Aeschin. D. Arist.

τεῖχος εος (ους) *n.* **1 defensive** or **protective wall, wall** Hom. +
2 (specif., oft.pl.) **city wall** Hom. +
3 improvised or **temporary wall** (for defensive or offensive purposes), **wall, fortification** Il. +
4 (meton.) **place protected by a wall, fortress** Hdt. X.
5 μακρὰ τείχη **Long Walls** (connecting Athens to Peiraieus and Phaleron) Th. Lys. X.; (also) μακρὸν τεῖχος **Long Wall** (ref. to the wall to Peiraieus) Th. And. Plu.
6 (fig.) ξύλινον τεῖχος **wooden wall** (ref. to a fleet) Hdt.(oracle) Arist.; (ref. to a pyre) Pi.
7 (fig.) defensive wall, **protection** (against sthg. undesirable) D.

τειχοφυλακέω *contr.vb.* [τειχοφύλαξ] **guard a wall, do sentry duty** Plu.

τειχο-φύλαξ ακος *m.* **1 wall-guard, sentry** Plu.
2 military governor (of Babylon) Hdt.

τειχύδριον ου *n.* [dimin. τεῖχος] **small wall** or **fortified place**; app. **small fort** X.

τείως *ep.adv.*: see τέως

τεκεῖν (aor.2 inf.), **τεκέμεν** (dial.aor.2 inf.): see τίκτω

τεκμαίρομαι *mid.vb.* [τέκμαρ] | fut. τεκμαροῦμαι | aor. ἐτεκμηράμην, ep. τεκμηράμην | **1 mark out an end or goal**; (intr., of Zeus) **mark a limit, ordain a time** (by which sthg. must be done) Il.; (tr., of a king) **decide the time of, prescribe, fix** —*the escorting of a guest on his way* (W.PREP.PHR. *for a particular day*) Od.
2 (gener., of gods) **mark out, decree, ordain** (usu. W.DAT. for someone) —*evils* Il. —*war, justice* Hes. —W.ACC. + FUT.INF. *that someone will do sthg.* AR.; (of a goddess) **ordain, prescribe** —*a journey* Od.; (of officials) **designate** —*places (for things)* Pl.

3 (of Apollo) prescribe for oneself, **determine** —w.inf. *to do sthg.* hHom.
4 (of a goddess, prophet) **predict** —*destruction* (*for someone*) Od.
5 judge (sthg.) from visible signs; **calculate** —*assaults on battlements* (*by measuring their height*) E. —*a land* (*i.e. its location,* w.dat. *by the stars*) S. —*a voyage* (*i.e. its direction,* w.dat. *by the sun and stars*) AR.; **estimate** —*leaves* (*i.e. their number*) AR.
6 make a mental judgement or inference; **infer, conjecture, deduce** (usu. w.dat. or prep.phr. fr. or by reference to sthg., or w. ὡς or ὅτι fr. the fact that sthg. is the case) —*facts, happenings* Hdt. S. Ar. Isoc. Pl. + —w.acc. + pres. or fut.inf. *that sthg. is or will be the case* Pl. X. Plu.; (intr.) **make an inference** or **deduction** Pi. Hdt. Trag. Th. Att.orats. Pl. +
7 recognise —*a voice* AR.

—**τεκμαίρω** *act.vb.* **1** give visible proof of —*hereditary qualities* (*by one's actions*) Pi.; (intr., of an action) **give proof** (of sthg.) Pi.
2 indicate (to someone) —w.compl.cl. *what suffering awaits* A.

τέκμαρ, ep. **τέκμωρ** (Hom. Alcm. AR.) *indecl.n.* **1** fixed mark determining an end or goal; **limit set by destiny, fated end** (w.gen. of Ilion) Il.; (of life) Pi.*fr.*
2 end to a situation, **conclusion, solution** Hom.; **goal** (ref. to a place reached) Il.; (ref. to a god's purpose) Pi.; **useful end** or **purpose** (in doing sthg.) AR.
3 (personif., in a cosmogony) **Tekmor, End** (assoc.w. Πόρος *Means*) Alcm.
4 visible sign or confirmation that an end or goal has been determined; **sign, token** (of Zeus' word or decree, ref. to his nod) Il.; (gener., of Zeus' purpose for mortals) Pi.
5 distinguishing mark, **sign, marker** (w.gen. of individual seasons, ref. to the weather) A.; (of good and bad things) Hes.*fr.*
6 guiding or helpful sign; (ref. to the moon, a constellation, bird, torch) **sign** hHom. AR.; (ref. to a grave) **landmark** (for sailors) E.; (gener.) **indication** (of how sthg. can be done) AR.
7 corroborating sign; **mark, track** (of a hunted man) A.; **proof** (of a statement) A.
8 app. **position** (of the sun, moon, stars) AR.

τέκμαρσις εως *f.* making of an inference, **inference, deduction** Th.

τεκμήριον ου *n.* **1** sure sign or principle, **criterion** (for adopting a particular course of action) A.
2 piece of evidence seen or heard, **sign, evidence, proof** (of sthg.) Hdt. Trag. Men.
3 evidence from facts or logic, **evidence, proof** (of sthg.) Hdt. Trag. Th. Ar. Att.orats. +
4 evidence which constitutes proof in a logical argument, **necessary sign** Arist.

τεκμηριόω *contr.vb.* **offer evidence** (of sthg.) Th. —w. ὅτι *to prove that* (*sthg. is the case*) Th.

τεκμηριώδης ες *adj.* (of arguments) **derived from evidence** Arist.

τέκμωρ *ep.indecl.n.*: see τέκμαρ

τεκνία ων *n.pl.* [dimin. τέκνον] (as an affectionate address by Christ to his disciples) **children** NT.

τεκνίδιον ου *n.* [dimin. τέκνον] (as an affectionate address by a mother) little child, **baby** Ar.

τεκνο-γόνος ον *adj.* [τέκνον, γίγνομαι] (of women who have given birth) **child-bearing** A.

τεκνο-κτόνος ον *adj.* [κτείνω] (of pollution) **incurred by killing one's children** E.

τεκν-ολέτειρα ᾱς *f.* [ὀλετήρ] **slayer of one's child** (ref. to Prokne) S.

τέκνον ου *n.* [τίκτω] **1** that which is born, **offspring, child** (of divine or human parents) Hom. +
2 ‖ voc. (as a familiar address by an older person) **my child** Hom. Trag. Ar. Men. +
3 ‖ pl. children or young people (w. no parental relationship implied) Pi.
4 (usu.pl.) **young** (of an animal) Hom. Semon. Stesich. A. Hdt. +
5 (fig.) **child** (of rock and sea, ref. to a limpet) Alc.; (of earth, ref. to flowers) A.; (of air, ref. to birds) E.; (of springs, ref. to frogs) Ar.

τεκνοποιέομαι *mid.contr.vb.* [τεκνοποιός] (of a man) **father children** X.; (of an older man) **get children** (by employing a proxy) X.; (of both parents) **produce children** X.

τεκνοποιητικός ή όν *adj.* (of a science or skill, regarded as part of household management) **progenitive** Arist.

τεκνοποιΐα ᾱς *f.* production of children, **parenting, childbearing** X. Arist. Plb.

τεκνό-ποινος ον *adj.* [ποινή] (of Wrath) **child-avenging** A.

τεκνο-ποιός όν *adj.* [ποιέω] **1** (of a wife) **child-bearing** Hdt.; (of a husband) **child-begetting** E.
2 (of sexual relationships) **procreative** X.

τεκνοῦσσα ης *contr.fem.adj.* (of a woman) having a child or children, **of parental status** S.

τεκνόω *contr.vb.* | aor. ἐτέκνωσα, ep. τέκνωσα | **1** produce a child; (sts.mid., of a god or man) **beget, father** —*a child* Hes.*fr.* S. E. Plu.; (of a woman) **give birth to** —*a child* E.*fr.*; (intr., of a marriage) **produce children** S. ‖ pass. (of persons) be born Pi. Plu.; (fig., of a marriage) app., be created by a child (i.e. consist of the union of a son and his mother) S.
2 (fig., of Orpheus) **create** —*a lyre* Tim. ‖ mid. (of time) **give birth to** —*nights and days* S.; (of Gaia) —*dreams* E.; (intr., of prosperity) **produce offspring** (ref. to misery) A. ‖ pass. (of lamentation, divine laws) be generated A. S.
3 provide with children; (of the Sown Men, as founders of the Theban race) **stock, populate** —*a city* (w.dat. *w. their descendants*) E. ‖ pass. (of a man) become a father E.

τέκνωσις εως *f.* procreation, **fathering** (of a child or children) Th. Plu.

τεκόμην (ep.aor.2 mid.), **τέκον** (ep.aor.2): see τίκτω

τέκος εος (ους) *n.* [τίκτω] | ep.dat.pl. τέκεσσι, τεκέεσσι |
1 offspring (of divine or human parents), **child** Hom. Hes. Thgn. Lyr. Trag. Hellenist.poet.
2 ‖ voc. (as a familiar address by an older person) **my child** Hom. Call. AR.
3 (usu.pl.) **offspring, young** (of an animal) Il. E. Ar.(quot. Philox.Cyth.) AR. Theoc.*epigr.*
4 (of hubris) **child** (w.gen. of impiety) A.

τέκταινα ης *f.* [τέκτων] (ref. to a goddess, or perh. a mortal woman) **producer, provider** (w.gen. of a livelihood) Call.

τεκταίνομαι *mid.vb.* | fut. τεκτανοῦμαι | aor. ἐτεκτηνάμην, ep. τεκτηνάμην | **1** make (sthg.) in wood; (of a carpenter) **build, construct** —*ships* Il. Ar. —*items of furniture* Plu.; (intr.) **practise carpentry, be a carpenter** Ar. Pl. X. Plb. ‖ pass. (fig., of a plan) be carpentered E.
2 (gener., of gods or humans) **craft, fashion, create** —*a singing tortoise* (i.e. tortoise-shell lyre) hHom. —*the universe, subjects of study, desire for sthg.* Pl. —*a tomb* Call.; (fig.) —*a beloved person* (envisaged as a statue) Pl.
3 (fig., of a person) **devise, contrive** —*all manner of harm* (against someone) Ar.(quot. E.) —*sedition* Plu.; (of fate)

—*change* Plu.; (of persons) —W.ACC. + PREDIC.ADJ. *that a guest shd. be excluded fr. conversation* E. ‖ PASS. (pejor., of evidence) **be fabricated** D.

—**τεκταίνω** *act.vb.* **build** —*wooden houses* AR.; (fig.) **contrive** —*deceptions* AR.

τεκτονεῖον ου *n.* **carpenter's workshop** Aeschin.

τεκτονικός ή όν *adj.* (of a person) **skilled in carpentry** Pl. X.; (of the skill) **of carpentry** Pl. ‖ MASC.SB. **carpenter** Pl. ‖ FEM.SG.SB. **craft of carpentry** Pl. X. Aeschin. Arist. ‖ NEUT.SG.SB. **carpentry** (as an occupation) Pl.; (pl., ref. to the tasks involved) Pl.

τεκτοσύνη ης, dial. **τεκτοσύνᾱ** ᾱς *f.* **1** ‖ PL. **carpentry** (ref. to shipbuilding) Od. **2 craftsmanship** (ref. to the building of Troy) E.(dub.)

τέκτων ονος *m.* (*also f.* A. E.) [reltd. τέχνη] **1 builder in wood, carpenter, joiner** Hom. +; (W.GEN. of ships, i.e. **shipwright**) Il.; (of timbers) Od. **2 skilled worker in other materials; artificer, craftsman** (ref. to a worker in horn) Il.; (ref. to a sculptor, stonemason) E.; (without ref. to specific material) Pi. Trag. ‖ PL. **makers** (W.GEN. of Zeus' thunderbolts, ref. to the Cyclopes) E. **3** (gener.) **craftsman** (ref. to a poet, trainer of athletes) Pi.; (W.GEN. of songs, ref. to a singer) Pi. Ar.(quot.com.); (of relief fr. pain, ref. to a doctor) Pi.; (appos.w. χείρ *hand*) **perpetrator** (of murder) A. **4** (pejor., fig.ref. to persons, actions) **creator, author, architect** (W.GEN. of quarrels) A.; (of harm) E. **5** (ref. to Zeus) **ancestor** (of the Danaids) A.

τεκών (aor.2 ptcpl.): see τίκτω

τελαμών ῶνος *m.* [reltd. τλῆναι] **1** (milit.) **supporting strap** (passing over the shoulder and across the chest); **strap, belt** (for a sword) Hom. Hes. AR. Theoc.; (for a shield) Il. Hdt. **2 linen band, bandage** (for wounds) Hdt. E.; (for wrapping mummies) Hdt.

Τελαμών ῶνος *m.* **Telamon** (ruler of Salamis, father of Ajax and Teucer) Hom. +

—**Τελαμωνιάδης** ᾱο *ep.m.* —also **Τελαμωνιάδᾱς** ᾱ *dial.m.* **son of Telamon** (ref. to Ajax) Hom. Pi.; (ref. to Teucer) Pi.

—**Τελαμώνιος** ᾱ ον *adj.* (of Ajax) **son of Telamon** Il. Ibyc. S. E. Pl.; (of Teucer) Il.

τελέεις εσσα εν *adj.* [τελέω, τελήεις] (of oracular words) **bringing fulfilment or carrying authority, authoritative, sure** Tyrt.

τελέθω *vb.* [reltd. πέλω] ‖ iteratv.impf. τελέθεσκον ‖ **1 come into being**; (of night) **draw on** Il. **2 come to be** (sthg.); (of persons or things) **become, turn out to be, be** —W.PREDIC.ADJ. or SB. *such and such* Hom. Hes. Thgn. A. Pi. E. +; (of a person) —W.PREP.PHR. *among the dead* A.; (of sacrifices) **turn out to be favourable** —W.INF. *for sthg. to be done* X.

τέλειος (also **τέλεος**) ᾱ (Ion. η) ον (also ος ον) *adj.* [τέλος] ‖ only τέλειος in Hom., thereafter both forms regularly used ‖ compar. τελειότερος, τελεώτερος, superl. τελειότατος, τελεώτατος ‖ **1 having reached one's appointed end**; (of persons, animals) **complete in growth, full-grown, adult, mature** A. Pl. X.; (of sacrificial animals) Hdt. **2** (of persons) **complete in quality, accomplished, perfect** (sts. W.PREP.PHR. in respect of sthg.) Isoc. Pl. Arist. Plb. Plu.; **perfect in goodness** NT. **3** (of sacrificial goats) **perfect, unblemished** Il.; (formulaic, in oathtaking) κατὰ ἱερῶν τελείων *over unblemished sacrifices* Th.(treaty) And.(law) D. Arist. **4** (gener., of objects, activities) **complete in extent or quality**; (of a piece of weaving) **complete, finished** E.; (of education, an inquiry) **comprehensive** Pl.; (of a misfortune) D.; (of a banquet) **full-scale** Hdt.; (of a month) **whole** B. Ar. **5** (of values, relationships, abstract qualities) **complete in every respect**; (of fame) **consummate** Pi.; (of justice, injustice) **absolute** Pl.; (of virtue, friendship, or sim.) **perfect** Pl. Arist. **6 having reached fulfilment**; (of sexual passion) **fulfilled, satisfied** Thgn.; (of justice, sufferings, the act of a god) **accomplished, fulfilled** A.; (of a prayer, wish, curse) A. Pi. E. Ar.; (of what is forecast in a dream) Hdt. Pl. **7 relating to fulfilment of marriage**; (of a song) **marking fulfilment** (W.GEN. of marriage) E.*fr.*; (of time) **ripe** (for a marriage) A.*satyr.fr.* **8** (of gods) **bringing fulfilment** (of their own purposes or the prayers of others); (of gods in general, also of the Eumenides) **with power to fulfil, wielding authority** A.; (of Apollo) Theoc.; (as cult-title of Zeus, esp. in voc. address) **fulfiller, accomplisher** A. Pi.; (as cult-title of Hera, who brings marriage to fulfilment) A. Pi. Ar.; (of the power of Zeus) **carrying authority** A.; (of the thoughts of the infant Zeus, w. play on sense 1) **fully grown** Call. **9** (of an eagle, as a bird of augury) **bringing fulfilment** (fr. Zeus), **carrying authority** Il.; (of a divine ordinance) A.; (of a person) **in authority** A.; (of a human vote, i.e. decision) **final, authoritative** A. S.

—**τέλειον** ου *n.* (transl. of a Persian wd. transliterated as τυκτά) perh. **feast of completion** or **perfection** (given on the king's birthday) Hdt.

—**τελείως, τελέως** *adv.* **1 completely, absolutely, thoroughly** Isoc. Pl. + **2 with full authority, decisively** A. **3 perfectly, faultlessly** Ar. X. **4 in the end, by way of fulfilment** —*ref. to dreams coming to nothing* Hdt.

τελειότης ητος *f.* **completeness** (of someone's life, in terms of its achievements) Plu.

τελειόω (also **τελεόω**) *contr.vb.* ‖ aor. ἐτελείωσα, also ἐτελέωσα ‖ pf. τετελείωκα ‖ PASS.: aor. ἐτελε(ι)ώθην ‖ pf.ptcpl. τετελειωμένος ‖ **1 complete successfully, accomplish** —*appointed or appropriate tasks* Hdt. NT. —*libations* Th. —*an ambush* S.; **complete** —*unfinished columns* Plb.; (gener.) **carry out** —*plans, intentions* Plb. ‖ PASS. (of an arrangement, activity) **be completed** Hdt. S. Plb.; (of a prophecy) **be fulfilled** NT.; (of a person) **be finished, reach one's goal** NT. **2 come to the end of, complete** —*a period of time* NT. ‖ PASS. (of a time for sthg.) **be completed** Pl. **3** (of activities, emotions, seen as complete in themselves) **make perfect** —*their own form or quality* Arist. ‖ PASS. (of a person, soul) **attain perfection or maturity** S.(dub.) Pl.; **be perfected** NT.; (of a fruit) **be fully grown** Plb. ‖ PF.PASS.PTCPL.ADJ. (of a substance) **complete** Arist. **4** (of portents) **put the final seal on, validate** —*someone aspiring to become king* Hdt.

τελείω *ep.vb.*: see τελέω

τελείωσις (or **τελέωσις**) εως *f.* [τελειόω] **1 state of completion or perfection, perfection** (sts. W.GEN. of sthg.) Arist. **2 fulfilment** (of sthg. foretold) NT.

τελεό-μηνος ον *adj.* [μήν²] (of a year) **with its full complement of months, fully completed** S.

τελεό-πορος ον *adj.* [πόρος] (of a bridge) **providing a passage** (over the Hellespont) Tim.

τέλεος *adj.*, **τελεόω** *contr.vb.*: see τέλειος, τελειόω

τέλεσα and **τέλεσσα** (ep.aor.), **τελέσθην** (ep.aor.pass., also Aeol.aor.pass.inf.): see τελέω

τελεσιουργέω contr.vb. [τελεσιουργός] **effect, achieve** —the capture of a city Plb. ‖ PASS. (of peace) **be arranged** Plb.

τελεσιούργημα ατος n. **final achievement, end product** (of historical inquiry) Plb.

τελεσιουργός όν adj. [τελέω, ἔργον] **1** accomplishing an action; (of persons, their capacities or efforts) **effective** (sts. W.GEN. or PREP.PHR. in accomplishing sthg.) Plu. ‖ NEUT.SB. **capacity to achieve one's purpose** Pl. Plu.
2 ‖ MASC.SB. **practitioner or executor** (of an undertaking) Plb.

τέλεσκον (iteratv.impf.): see τελέω

τελεσσι-δώτειρα ᾱς fem.adj. [δωτήρ] (of Fate) **who gives completion** E.

τελεσσι-επής ές adj. [ἔπος] (of a shrine of Apollo) **word-fulfilling** Pi.fr.

τελεσσί-φρων ονος masc.fem.adj. [φρήν] (of Wrath) bringing thoughts to fulfilment, **purposeful** A.

τελεστήριον ου n. **1 place for initiation or mystery rites, initiation chamber** Plu.
2 ‖ PL. **offerings made on completion** (of enterprises) X.

Τελέστης ου m. **Telestes** (of Selinus, dithyrambic poet, active c.400 BC) Plu.

τελεστικός ή όν adj. of or relating to initiation or mystery rites; (of inspiration, wisdom) **mystical** Pl. Plu.; (of a person's life) **involved with mystery rites** Pl.

τελεσφορέω contr.vb. [τελεσφόρος] **1 bring to maturity**; (of persons, compared to plants) **bear fruit** NT.
2 (of a sum of money) **be paid as tax** or **duty** X.

τελεσφορής ές adj. (of a worshipper) **initiated** Call.(cj.)

τελεσφορίη ης Ion.f. **1 rite that brings accomplishment or fulfilment, initiation** (in the mysteries) AR.
2 perh. **outcome** (ref. to punishment) Call.(cj.)

τελεσ-φόρος ον adj. [τέλος, φέρω] **1** (of a year) **bringing completion** (to the cycle of seasons and the growth of crops), **complete** Hom. Hes. hHom.; (of a prescribed period of days) **completed** E.
2 bringing or entailing fulfilment; (of a prayer, curse, dream, desire, oracle) **fulfilled, accomplished** Trag.; (of eddies of thought) **moving to fulfilment** A.; (of a life) **of fulfilment** or **contentment** AR.; (of thanks or repayment) **in fulfilment** of a promise) S. ‖ NEUT.SB. **fulfilment** A.
3 with power to fulfil; (of Zeus, Fate, Justice) **wielding authority** hHom. A. S.; (of a king) **in authority** Simon.; (of a person, W.GEN. over a house) A.
4 (of zeal, persuasive language) **end-accomplishing** Arist.(quot.)

τελετή ῆς f. [τελέω] **1** (freq.pl.) rite associated with an exclusive cult (oft. entailing initiation); **mystic rite** or **ritual** (of Demeter) Hdt. Isoc.; (ref. to her mysteries at Eleusis) And. Ar. Isoc. Plu.; (of Dionysus, the Corybants, Orpheus) Hdt. E. Ar. Pl. D.; (assoc.w. the Tauropolia) E.; (fig., ref. to an improvised legal action dedicated to Apollo) Ar.; (w. no ref. to a specific god) Pi. Pl. Arist. Plu.; (ref. to a rite belonging to a particular family) D.(decree)
2 ‖ PL. (gener., w. no connot. of exclusiveness) **rites, rituals, festivals** Alcm. Pi. Ar. Pl. D.

τελευτά dial.f.: see τελευτή

τελευταῖος ᾱ ον adj. [τελευτή] **1** last in order or position; (of persons or things) **last, in final place** Hdt. Lys. Pl.; (of soldiers) **in the rear** Th. X. ‖ NEUT.PL.SB. **final letters** (of words), **terminations** Hdt.
2 last in time; (of a day) **last, final** Hdt. Lys. X. D.; (of the light of the setting sun) E.; (of a harvest, libation) Hdt. S.; (of a night-watch, council) X.; (of a speech, argument) Hdt. And. Pl.
3 last before death; (of a day) **last, final** E.; (of life, ref. to its final period) S.; (of the light of day) S.; (of a message) S.; (of an illness) Antipho; (of advice) X.; (of a military campaign) Is.
4 (quasi-advbl., of persons or things) **last** (to do sthg. or happen, as τελευταῖος ἦλθε he was last to come) A. Hdt. Th. Ar. Att.orats. +
5 (of events, circumstances, arguments) last in time (relative to the present), **last, latest, most recent** S. Th. Att.orats.
6 last and greatest; (of an outrage) **final, culminating** S.; (of an act of folly) Aeschin.; (of democracy, oligarchy) **in extreme form** Arist.
7 ‖ NEUT.SG.ADV. τὸ τελευταῖον **finally** Hdt. Th. Ar. Att.orats. Pl. +; (also) τελευταῖον Att.orats. Pl. + ‖ NEUT.PL.ADV. τὰ τελευταῖα Th. Pl. D.

τελευτάω contr.vb. | fut. τελευτήσω | aor. ἐτελεύτησα, ep. τελεύτησα, dial. τελεύτᾱσα ‖ PASS.: fut. τελευτήσομαι, dial. τελευτάσομαι | aor. ἐτελευτήθην, dial.3pl. τελεύτᾱθεν (Pi.) |
1 bring to a desired end or goal; (of humans, gods) **accomplish, carry through** —tasks, promises Hom. E.; (of Zeus) **fulfil, bring to fruition** —someone's wish or intention Hom.; (of a person) —someone's oath Call.; (of Philoktetes) **bring to a successful conclusion** —the toils of war (W.DAT. for the Greeks) Pi. ‖ PASS. (of a wish, promise) **be fulfilled** Il. Pi.
2 bring to completion or a conclusion; complete —the swearing of an oath Hom. hHom.; **finish off** —a boat (w. gunwales) Od.; **bring to an end** (w. ποῖ to what place, i.e. to what particular conclusion) —an activity, speech, one's life S. E. ‖ PASS. (of a killing) **be completed** E.
3 (of Zeus) **bring about** —someone's doom Od. ‖ PASS. (of events) **happen** Hom. E.; (of excellence) **be achieved** B.
4 come to the end of (an allotted period of time); **end, reach the end of** —one's life (usu. fr. natural causes) A. Hdt. E. Th. +; (of rays of sunlight) E.; (of a person) —a day (in peace and prosperity) Pi.
5 (intr.) **end one's life, die** (fr. natural or other causes) A. Hdt. S. Th. +; **come to the end** —W.GEN. of one's life X.
6 (intr., of an event, narrative, period of time) **come to an end, end** A. Hdt. Th.
7 (of events, circumstances, hopes) **end, turn out** —W.ADV. or PREP.PHR. in a certain way A. Hdt. E. Th. Pl.; (of persons or things) **come in the end** —W.PREP.PHR. to some goal or state Xenoph. Pl.; **end as, become finally** —W.PREDIC.ADJ. such and such Sol. Pl.; (of names) **end** —W.PREP.PHR. in the same letter Hdt.
8 (of a person) **end a speech, end** —W.ADV. well (i.e. finally say sthg. which meets w. approval) S.; **come to the end** —W.GEN. of one's speech, praise Th.
9 ‖ PRES.PTCPL. (quasi-advbl., of persons or things) **in the end, finally** (as τελευτῶν ἔλεγε finally he said) Hdt. S. Th. Ar. +
10 (w. spatial ref., of a building, country, river) **come to an end** (sts. W.PREP.PHR. at a certain place) Hdt. Th.; (of a promontory) **be the limit** —W.GEN. of a country Hdt.

τελευτή ῆς, dial. **τελευτά** ᾱς f. [τελέω] **1** process or result of bringing (sthg.) to an end; **accomplishment, fulfilment** (W.GEN. of a mission, oracle) Il. A.; (W.GEN. entailed by marriage) A. Pi.

τελέω

2 outcome, result (W.GEN. of a situation, marriage, speech, emotion) Thgn. Pi. Hdt. Trag.; (gener.) **outcome** A. B. E. Th. Isoc.
3 ending in time; ending, end (of a situation) Od. Lys.; (of strife) Hes. A.; (of toils, sufferings) E.; (of a war, an empire) Th.; (of a voyage, journey) Pi. Ar.
4 ending of life, end, death Pi. Hdt. S. E. Th. +; **end** (W.GEN. of life) Il. Hdt. S. Att.orats. Pl. +; (periphr.) **final end, finality** (W.GEN. of death) Hes. E.
5 (prep.phrs.) εἰς τελευτήν **in the end, finally** Hes. hHom. Thgn. S.; (also) ἐν τελευτᾷ Pi.; ἐπὶ τελευτῆς **at the end** Isoc. Pl. Aeschin. Arist.
6 last part, end (of a speech, song, literary work) E. Isoc. Pl. Aeschin. Arist. Call.
7 outermost part, extremity (of a wall) Th.; (of shapes, a solid object) Pl.

τελέω contr.vb. —also **τελείω** ep.vb. [τέλος] | ep.impf. ἐτέλειον, also τέλεον, iteratv. τελέσκον (Call.) | fut. τελῶ, also τελέσω (Pi.), ep. τελέω | aor. ἐτέλεσα, ep. ἐτέλεσσα, also τέλεσα, τέλεσσα | pf. τετέλεκα ‖ PASS.: fut. τελοῦμαι, also τελεσθήσομαι (Thphr.), inf. τελεῖσθαι, ep. τελέεσθαι | aor. ἐτελέσθην, ep. τελέσθην, Aeol.inf. τελέσθην | pf. τετέλεσμαι |

1 bring to an end or goal; complete, accomplish, perform —an action or undertaking Hom. +; **complete** —a piece of craftsmanship, a building Od. hHom. Theoc. —a journey, course Hom. Mimn. Thgn. S. Plb.; (intr.) **complete a journey** Od. Th. ‖ PASS. (of actions) be completed or performed Hom. +; (of building operations) be completed Th.; (of a wall's intended height) be achieved or reached Th.; (of corpses) app., be finished off (i.e. be consumed, on a funeral pyre) Pi.
2 bring (someone's words, feelings) **to completion or fruition**; (esp. of gods) **fulfil** —a promise, prediction, wish, prayer, curse Hom. +; **give effect to, vent** —one's anger Il.; (intr., of a curse) **be effective** S.; (of a predictive sign) **be fulfilled, turn out** (in a particular way) A. ‖ IMPERS.FUT. **things will turn out** (in some way) A. ‖ PASS. (of things) be fulfilled Hom. +
3 (usu. of gods) **bring about, produce** —harm, good fortune, fame (for someone) Hom. + ‖ PASS. (of a family, attacks by Erinyes) be produced (fr. a particular source) A.; (of imitations of things, by painting and music) Pl.
4 ‖ PASS. app., be given authority (by a god) ‖ PF.PTCPL.ADJ. (of a messenger) authorised hHom.; (of a day) appropriate or marked with authority Hes.
5 (of a mother, Zeus, the Fates) **bring to full term** —an unborn child Pi. E.; (fig., of Dawn) **bring on** or **bring to birth** —day Od.; (of time) **bring to maturity** or **perfection** —excellence Pi. ‖ PASS. (of a thing) be completed or made perfect Arist.; (fig., of prosperity) reach full growth A.
6 reach the end of —one's life or a part of it, a period of time Sol. Simon. B. S. —an illness Hes.; **reach** —the end of one's life S. ‖ PASS. (of a year) be completed Hes.
7 ‖ MID. **bring to fruition**; (leg.) **get** (W.ACC. a lawsuit) **heard** D. ‖ PASS. (of a lawsuit) be heard D.
8 pay (what is owed); **make good, discharge** —a promised payment, promised gifts (to a person) Hom. —gifts (i.e. offerings, to a god) hHom.
9 (specif.) **pay** —money, a fee Hdt. Ar. Isoc. Pl. X. —a reward S.; (fig.) **render up** (as if in discharge of a debt) —one's soul (to Hades) Pi.; (of a hired poet) —a song Pi. ‖ PASS. (of money) be paid or spent Hdt. X.; (fig., of hostile words) be given in payment (in return for hostile words) A.

10 pay —taxes (of various kinds) Att.orats. Arist. —tribute, levies, or sim. X. Aeschin. Plb. Plu. —interest D.; (intr.) **pay a tax** Hdt.
11 be classed for purpose of taxation; (of ethnic groups) **be classed, be reckoned as belonging** —w. εἰς + ACC. among Greeks, Boeotians Hdt.; (of an outsider) —among citizens S.; (of a man) —among women E.; (of a child) —among adults Pl.
12 (of a civic assembly) app. **pay out, dole out** —a corn allowance X.
13 introduce (someone) **to a rite; initiate** —someone (sts. W.DAT. to a god, i.e. into his cult) Pl. D.; (intr.) **perform initiation rites** D. ‖ PASS. be initiated (sts. W.ACC. into rites) Ar. Pl. D. Plu. —W.DAT. to a god (i.e. into his cult) Hdt. X. Thphr.; (fig.) —W.DAT. into self-control X.; **be consecrated** —W.PREDIC.SB. as a general D.
14 perform —sacred or mystery rites E. Call. Plu. —a sacrifice Plu.; **celebrate** —a feast (for a god), a marriage Call. Theoc. ‖ PASS. (of mystery rites; of sacrifices, esp. those assoc.w. marriage) be performed E.fr. Pl. X. Plu.; (of a festival) be celebrated —W.DAT. in someone's honour Plu.

τελέως adv.: see under τέλειος
τελέωσις f.: see τελείωσις
τελήεις εσσα εν adj. [τελέω, reltd. τελέεις] **1** (of hecatombs of sacrificial animals) **bringing fulfilment, effective** Hom. hHom. [or perh. perfect, unblemished]
2 (of birds of omen) **bringing fulfilment, carrying authority** hHom.
3 (of the river Okeanos) perh. **unending** Hes.
τέλθος εος dial.n. [τέλος] **payment, debt** Call.
τέλλομαι pass.vb. [reltd. τέλος] | dial.3sg.impf. τέλλετο (Pi.) | **1** app., **be accomplished or brought about**; (of good news) **result** (fr. oracles) A.(cj.); (of gifts) **turn out, count** —W.PREP.PHR. in one's favour Pi.; (of a song) **become** —W.PREDIC.SB. a starting-point (for sthg.) Pi.
2 (of men sown fr. a dragon's teeth) **rise up** AR.; (of dawn) **arise, appear** AR.
3 (of a family) **live on** Pi.; (of a year) **pass** AR.
—τέλλω act.vb. | aor. ἔτειλα (Pi.) | **1 travel** or **follow** (to its end) —a path Pi.
2 (intr., of the sun) **rise** S.
τέλμα ατος n. **1 stagnant water, pond, marsh, lagoon** Hdt. Ar. Pl. X. Men. +
2 mortar Hdt.
τελματώδης ες adj. (of water) **marshy, muddy** Plu.
τέλος εος (ους) n. | The sections are grouped as: (1–6) fulfilment, completion, end, (7–12) office, service, (13–14) tax, payment. |
1 achievement or fulfilment of an end or goal (oft. through the agency of a god); **fulfilment, accomplishment, execution** (of a prayer, promise, hope) Hom. +; **achievement, attainment** (of a return home, marriage, other desired goals) Hom. +; **resolution** (of a war) Il. Hes.; (gener.) **issue, outcome, result** (sts. W.GEN. of an activity) Sol. +
2 power of decision, authority (belonging to a god) Alcm. +; (belonging to a human) Sol. S. E.; (belonging to appointed officials) Th.(treaty) Arist.; **validity** (of terms of a treaty or contract; of an accusation) Antipho Th. D.
3 process or result of bringing to completion; completion (of speech or action) Il. +; (of an artefact or building) Il. Hdt.; **maturity** (of persons, plants, animals) Pl.; (W.GEN. of youthful manhood, old age) Mimn. E.
4 ending in time; end (W.GEN. of life, i.e. death) Thgn. +; **end, death** Hdt. Pl. X.; (periphr.) **final end, finality** (W.GEN.

of death) Hom. Hes. Mimn. Thgn. A.; (gener.) **end, cessation** (of lamentation, sufferings, speech, or sim.) S. E.
5 end which is reached or sought for; finish, goal (in a race) Pi. B. Pl.; (fig., W.GEN. of life, envisaged as a racecourse) E.; **end, limit** (of a journey) Pi.; **goal** (of ambitions) Pi.; (philos.) **end, purpose** (of an activity) Pl. Arist.
6 ‖ NEUT.SG.ADV. τέλος *finally* or *at last* Thgn. +; (prep.phrs.) εἰς τέλος *in the end* Hes. +; *for ever* hHom. +; *completely* Plb.; διὰ τέλους *for ever* or *completely* Trag. Att.orats. Pl. +
7 office carrying authority; post, position (of a local councillor) Pi.; **magistracy** Th.(treaty); (collectv.sg.) **authorities** A.; (phr.) οἱ ἐν τέλει *those in authority or office* Hdt. S. Th. X. Plu. ‖ PL. magistrates (at Sparta) Th. X.
8 (gener.) **duty, service, task** A.
9 (milit.) place where a service is performed, **post** (of sentinels, troops) Il.
10 (milit., perh. w.connot. of performing a specific service, or of comprising a complete unit) **company, detachment, division** (of soldiers, cavalry, chariots, ships) A. Hdt. E. Th. Plb.; **legion** (in the Roman army) Plu.
11 ‖ PL. services or tributes due to the gods, offerings A. S.; rites (sts. of mystery cults) S. E. Pl.; (ref. to marriage rites) S.
12 (in the Solonian constitution) rating according to service rendered to the state, **rating, class** Arist.
13 dues exacted by the state; **tax** (of various kinds) Ar. Att.orats. Pl. +
14 ‖ PL. payments or expenditure Th. D. Plu. ‖ IMPERS. τέλη λύει *it pays expenses or dues* (i.e. it pays, it is profitable) S. | cf. λυσιτελέω 2

–τέλοσδε adv. **to the finality** (W.GEN. of death) Il.
τέλσον ου n. land at each end of a field where the plough turns, **turning-point** Il. AR.
Τελχῖνες ων m.pl. **Telkhines** (mythol. inventors of metalwork, reputed as malignant sorcerers) Call.; (as a name applied to literary enemies) Call.
τελωνέω contr.vb. [τελώνης] **be a tax-collector** D. Thphr.
τελ-ώνης ου m. [τέλος, ὠνέομαι] one who buys the right to collect taxes, **tax-farmer, tax-collector** Ar. Aeschin. D. Arist. Men. +
τελωνία ᾱς f. **tax-farming** D.
τελωνικός ή όν adj. (of laws) **relating to tax-collection** D. ‖ NEUT.PL.SB. business of tax-collection Pl.
τελώνιον ου n. place where taxes are collected, **tax-office** NT.
τέμαχος ους n. [τέμνω] **slice** (of fish, other seafood) Ar. X.
–τεμάχιον ου n. [dimin.] **little slice, offcut** (of sthg.) Pl.
τέμει (3sg.pres.): see τεμεῖν
τεμενίζω vb. [τέμενος] **create or mark off** –W.COGN.ACC. *a sacred precinct* Pl.
τεμένιος ᾱ ον adj. (of a grove) **serving as a sacred precinct** S.
τέμενος εος (ους) n. [app.reltd. τέμνω] **1** piece of land marked off for use by a king or chieftain, **private estate, domain** Hom. Hdt. E. Arist.
2 piece of land dedicated to a god or hero (oft. containing a shrine or temple), **sacred precinct** Hom. +
3 (gener., ref. to a city, region) **precinct, domain** (of a particular god) Pi.; (ref. to the racecourse at Delphi) Pi.; (ref. to the Acropolis) Ar.; (ref. to a place of dedicated trophies) Tim.(dub.); (W.GEN. of the sky) A.
τέμνω, dial. **τάμνω** vb. | iteratv.impf. τέμνεσκον | fut. τεμῶ ‖ AOR.2: ἔτεμον, dial. ἔταμον, ep. τάμον, dial.inf. ταμεῖν, ep. ταμέειν, Aeol.masc.nom.pl.ptcpl. τάμοντες | pf. τέτμηκα | ep.pf.ptcpl. (w.pass.sens.) τετμηώς (AR.) ‖ MID.: fut.

τεμοῦμαι | aor.2 ἐτεμόμην, dial. ἐταμόμην ‖ PASS.: aor. ἐτμήθην, ptcpl. τμηθείς | pf. τέτμημαι, dial.3pl. τέτμανται (Pi.) ‖ neut.impers.vbl.adj. τμητέον ‖ The sections are grouped as: (1–7) cut (someone or sthg.) in various ways, (8–10) cut to clear, harvest or destroy, (11–13) make (sthg.) by cutting, (14–15) cut a path (through sthg.), (16–17) separate or divide. |
1 make an incision; cut open –*flesh, a throat* Il. E. Ar. AR.; (of a person committing suicide) **pierce** (w. a sword) –*one's valour* (i.e. valiant body) Pi.; (intr., of teeth, a knife) perform the function of cutting, **cut** X. D. ‖ PASS. (of a person) be cut (w. a razor) Ar.
2 (medic.) **perform surgery** Pl. X.; (fig., on the body of a diseased state) A. ‖ PASS. (of a person) undergo surgery Pl.
3 castrate, geld –*an animal* Hes.
4 cut into (a sacrificial animal, i.e. at its throat); **slaughter, sacrifice** –*a victim* Il. E.
5 solemnise (by sacrifice) –*an oath, treaty, truce* Hom. Alc. Hdt.(also mid.) Plb.; (gener.) **conclude** –*a pact of friendship* E. Call.; (of soldiers) app. **decide, determine** –*the outcome of battles* Pi.
6 (act. and mid.) **cut up, cut in pieces** –*meat, fish, animals* (for food) Hom. + –*oxhide* Od. AR.; cut into portions, **divide** (usu. w. δίχα *in two*, or sim.) –*a person, an egg, other objects* Pl. ‖ PASS. (of a fish) be cut up Philox.Leuc.
7 cut so as to remove, **cut off** –*hair* Il. Trag. –*a head* Il. Trag. –*body-parts* AR.; **decapitate** –*the hydra* Pl.; **cut out** –*an arrow-head* (fr. flesh) Il. –*a tongue* Od. Ar.; **cut** –*the threads of a web* (fr. a loom) Theoc.; (fig., of soldiers) **remove, put an end to** –*a danger* (w. swords) E. ‖ PASS. (of a person) have (W.ACC. one's hair) cut E.; (of a purse) be cut (i.e. stolen) Pl.
8 (of woodcutters) **cut down, fell** –*trees* Il. Simon. E. Th. +
9 (act. and mid.) cut for one's own use, **cut** –*timber, logs, stakes* Od. Hes. Hdt. E. Th. + –*branches, foliage, plants* Il. Hellenist.poet.; **cut, harvest** –*corn* X.; **quarry** –*stones* Hdt. Pl. ‖ PASS. (of a vine) be cut or harvested S.fr.
10 (esp. of soldiers) **cut down, destroy** –*crops, vines* E. Ar. X.; **ravage, lay waste** –*land* Hdt. Th. Att.orats. +
11 make by cutting, **cut** –*a staff, mortar and pestle, spear* Od. Hes. Pi. –*straps* Hdt. –*ribs of willow* (for a ship) Hdt. –*a pine-torch* Call.
12 make (a medicine) by cutting up a plant; **produce** –*a drug* Pl.; (fig.) **find** –*a remedy* (for troubles) E.
13 make or open up by cutting, **cut** –*roads* Pi. Hdt. Th. Call. –*channels* Pl. –*a well* X. –*a mine* Hyp. –*a furrow* Call.
14 cut through (the earth); (of a ploughman, his oxen) **cleave** –*the soil* Sol. Call. AR.(also mid.); (of a hoe) A.fr.
15 cut through (to create a path); **cut through, cleave** –*sea, waves* Od. Pi. B. AR. –*air* hHom. Ibyc. B.; **cut** –*a furrow* (through air, sea) Lyr.adesp. Ar.; (sts.fig.) construct by cutting, **carve out** –*a route, road, voyage* Hdt. E. Ar.(quot. E.) AR. –*a path of escape* A. –*a path of speech* E. –*a middle course, middling lifestyle* Pl.; (fig., of hopes) **follow the road of** –*falsehoods* Pi.; (intr.) **cleave one's way** AR.
16 make separate; **set aside** (for someone) –*a private estate* Il.; (mid., for oneself) Il. ‖ MID. **separate off** –*parts of a kingdom* (for distribution) Pl.
17 separate into parts; (of a river) **divide** –*a country* (down the middle) Hdt. –*the borders of two regions* E.; (of persons) –*a number, an abstract entity or concept* Pl. ‖ PASS. (of a line) be divided Pl.; (of the world, into two parts) Isoc.

Τέμπη ῶν, Ion. **Τέμπεα** έων n.pl. **1 Tempe** (valley of the R. Peneios in Thessaly, famed for its beauty) Hdt. Call. Plb. Plu.
2 valley (W.GEN. of the Peneios) Theoc.

—**Τεμπόθεν** *adv.* from Tempe Call.
τεναγίζω *vb.* [τέναγος] (of a stream) **be shallow** Plu.
τέναγος εος (ους) *n.* (oft.pl.) **shoal, shallow water, shallows** (in a sea or river) Pi. Hdt. Th. X. AR. +
τεναγώδης ες *adj.* (of a sea, river or lake) **shallow** AR. Plb.
τένδω *vb.* [perh.reltd. τένθης] (of an octopus) app. **gnaw** —*its foot* Hes.
τενθεία ᾶς *f.* [τένθης] gluttonous behaviour, **gorging session** Ar.
τένθης ου *m.* **glutton** Ar.
τενοῦμαι (fut.mid.): see τείνω
τένων οντος *m.* [τείνω] **tendon, sinew** (in various parts of the body) Hom. Hes. Archil. A. AR.; (ref. to the Achilles tendon) Il. E. Call. AR.
τέξω (fut.): see τίκτω
τέο[1], enclit. **τεό** (Ion.gen.pron.adj.): see τίς, τις
τέο[2], **τεοῖο**, **τεοῦ**, **τεοῦς** (dial.gen.2sg.pers.pron.): see σύ
τέοισι, enclit. **τεοισί** (Ion.dat.pl.pron.adj.): see τίς, τις
τεός ά (Ion. ή) όν, Aeol. **τέος** ᾱ ον, Boeot. **τιός** ά όν *possessv.pron.adj.* [reltd. σός] | Boeot.masc.acc.pl. τιώς (Corinn.) | of or belonging to you (sg.), **your** Hom. Hes. Lyr. A. S. Ar. Hellenist.poet.
τέουτος *Aeol.demonstr.adj.*: see τοιοῦτος
τεράζω (or **τεράζω**) *vb.* [τέρας] **interpret a portent** A.
τέραμνα ων *n.pl.* **1 halls, chambers** Lyr.adesp.; (W.GEN. of Hades, Apollo at Delphi, Troy) E.
2 timbers (of a house) E.; (ref. to roof-beams) E.
τεράμων ωνος *m.* app. **reed** (used as a fishing-rod) Pl.
τέρας εος (also ατος Hdt. +) *n.* | PL.: nom.acc. τέραα, τέρεα (ep. τείρεα), contr. τέρᾱ (AR., perh. Ar.), also τέρατα (Hdt. +) | gen. τεράων, τερέων, also τεράτων (Plb. +) | dat. τέρασι (Men. NT.), ep. τεράεσσι, τείρεσι |
1 significant sign from a god, sign, portent Hom. Lyr. Hdt. S. E. +
2 ‖ PL. signs in heaven (ref. to stars or constellations) Il. Call. AR.
3 (gener., ref. to an object, sight, occurrence, oft. w. supernatural connection) **marvel** A. Pi. B. S. Ar. Call.*epigr.*; (ref. to a human artefact) Theoc.
4 (w.neg.connot.) **monstrous sight** (ref. to the Gorgon's head on the aegis) Il.; (ref. to the underworld) Hes.; **monster, prodigy** (ref. to various mythical creatures) hHom. Trag. Philox.Cyth. Isoc.; product of unnatural birth (ref. to deformed offspring), **monstrosity** A. E. Pl. Aeschin. Men.
5 extraordinary situation or statement Pl.
τερα-σκόπος ου *m.f.* [σκοπέω] **1** one who observes signs or portents, **seer, diviner** Pi. Trag.; (ref. to Apollo) A.
2 ‖ ADJ. (of a heart) **divining or prophetic** A.
τερατεία ᾶς *f.* [τερατεύομαι] **1 creation or narration of marvels, fantasy** (ref. to fictional narrative) Isoc. Plb.
2 capacity for fantasy or **fiction** (as a useful human attribute) Ar.; (pejor., in a political opponent) Aeschin.
τεράτευμα ατος *n.* **fairy-tale, tall story** Ar.
τερατεύομαι *mid.vb.* [τέρας] **1** (of an orator, dramatist) **tell tall stories** or **fairy-tales** Ar.; (of a historian) Plb. Plu.; (of a political opponent) Aeschin. Hyp.
2 have a portentous manner, **put on airs, posture** Aeschin.
τερατολογία ᾶς *f.* [τερατολόγος] **outlandish fiction** (of philosopher-poets) Isoc.
τερατο-λόγος ον *adj.* [λέγω] (of species of mythical creatures) marvellous to speak of, **of outlandish description** Pl.
τερατο-σκόπος ου *m.* [reltd. τερασκόπος] **seer, diviner** Pl. Plu.

τερατώδης ες *adj.* **1** (of a heavenly sign, apparition) **portentous** Plu.; (of prehistoric times) **full of marvels and monsters** Plu.
2 (of the sound of a voice) **portentous, wondrous** Ar.; (of exploits, feats of trickery) **miraculous, superhuman, spectacular** Isoc. Plu.; (of circumstances) **extraordinary** Arist. ‖ NEUT.SB. (pejor.) portentousness, **cheap thrills** (as a product of dramatic spectacle) Arist.
3 (of persons) **prodigious** (W.PREP.PHR. in cleverness) Pl.
τερατ-ωπός όν *adj.* [ὤψ] (of Pan) **wondrous-looking** hHom.
τερετίζω *vb.* **hum** —W.DAT. *to oneself* Thphr.; (perh. tr.) —*a song* Men.
τέρετρον ου *n.* [τετραίνω] **tool for boring timber, auger** Od.
τερέων (gen.pl.): see τέρας
τερηδών όνος *f.* [τετραίνω] **1 woodworm** Ar. Plb.
2 Woodworm (com. name for a player of wooden pipes) Ar.
τέρην εινα εν *adj.* [app.reltd. τείρω] | gen. τέρενος τερείνης (dial. τερείνᾱς, Aeol. τερένᾱς) τέρενος ‖ compar. τερενώτερος (Lyr.adesp.) ‖ **1** (of tears) **soft, gentle** Hom. AR.; (of flesh) Il. Hes.; (of a mouth, body) AR.; (of eyes) E.
2 (of foliage, plants, flowers, grass) **soft, tender** Hom. hHom. Lyr. E. AR.; (of fruit) Alc. A.; (of grains of cinnamon) Melanipp.; (of vine-blossom) Pi.; (of the bloom of youth) Hes. hHom.
3 (of a girl) **tender** Archil. Hippon. Thgn. E.*Cyc.* [or perh. *slender*]
4 (of blood; of a body, i.e. mass, of water) **smooth** Emp. [or perh. *thin*]
5 (of half-size auloi) **slender** Anacr. [or perh. *thin*, ref. to their sound]
—**τέρεν** *neut.adv.* **tenderly, delicately** —*ref. to a girl speaking* Thgn.
τερθρεία ᾱς *f.* [τερθρεύομαι *quibble*] **quibbling, hair-splitting** Isoc.
τέρθριος ου *m.* [τέρθρον] **brailing-line** (at the end of a sailyard, used for reefing) Ar.
τέρθρον ου *n.* [reltd. τέρμα] **edge** (W.GEN. of a doorway) Apollod.Lyr.; (of Olympos) hHom. [or perh. *summit*]
τέρμα ατος *n.* | oft. pl. for sg. | **1** end of a lap in a racecourse (where horses or runners turn), **turning-point, end** Il. Anacr. Pi. S. Arist.
2 end of a race or racecourse, **finish, finishing-line** X. Plb.
3 end which is reached or sought for; **end, goal** Semon. Thgn. S. E.; (of a journey) Thgn. A.; (periphr., W.GEN. of salvation, i.e. final salvation) S. E.; (W.GEN. of death) Tyrt. E.; **achievement** (of heroism) Tyrt.; **successful conclusion** (to one's efforts) E.
4 extreme part (of a place or object) ‖ PL. **limits, edges or borders** (of a continent, mountain range) Hdt.; (app., of an area betw. two rivers) Hdt.; (of a land) E.; **boundaries** (of a city) Plu. ‖ SG. **edge or border** (of a cloak) AR.
5 end as a limit; **limit** (to wealth) Sol.; (to boldness) E.; (concr.) **line, mark** (beyond which a javelin-thrower must not step) Pi.; **marker** (of the distance reached by a discus) Od.
6 end as cessation; **end** (of sufferings or sim.) Thgn. A. E.; (of life) Simon. Trag. X. Call. Plu.; (periphr.) **finality** (W.GEN. of hanging, i.e. death by hanging) A.
7 final part (in time); **end, extremity** (of old age, youthfulness) E. Ar.; **conclusion** (of a speech, literary work) A. Plb.
8 final and greatest part, **culmination, climax** (of athletic events) Pi.; (of troubles) E.
9 end, outcome, issue (of events) A.; power (of the gods) to determine an outcome, **final authority** (W.GEN. over all things) E.; (appos.w. Τύχη *Fortune*) Lyr.adesp.

τερμίνθινος η ον *adj.* [τέρμινθος] (of resin) **turpentine** X.
τέρμινθος ου *f.* **terebinth, turpentine tree** Theoc.*epigr.* Plu.
τερμιόεις εσσα εν *adj.* [τέρμις *edge*, reltd. τέρμα] **1** (of a shield) **edged** (w. an elaborate border) Il. [or perh. *fringed*, w. a leather apron to protect the legs]
2 (of a tunic) app. **edged, bordered** Od. Hes.
τέρμιος ᾱ ον *adj.* [τέρμα] having an end; (of a day) **last** (of one's life) S.; (of a place) providing both a goal (for one's travels) and an end (for one's life), **of final rest** S.
τερμόνιος ᾱ ον *adj.* [τέρμων] (of a crag) **at the end** or **edge** (of the earth) A.
τέρμων ονος *m.* [reltd. τέρμα] **1** (oft.pl.) **limit, boundary** (of a region) E. Plu.
2 (pl. for sg.) **goal, finishing-line** (of a racecourse) E.
3 end, outcome (of events) A. E.
Τέρπανδρος ου *m.* **Terpander** (musician and poet fr. Lesbos, 7th C. BC) Pi.*fr.* Tim. Plu.
τερπι-κέραυνος ον *adj.* (app. τέρπω; κεραυνός] (epith. of Zeus) **who delights in the thunderbolt** Hom. Hes. hHom.
τερπνός ή (dial. ἅ) όν *adj.* [τέρπω] | superl. τερπνότατος, also τέρπνιστος, τερπνίστατος (Call.) | **1** (of things, activities, experiences) giving pleasure, **pleasant, delightful** Eleg. Pi. Trag. Ar. Philox.Leuc. Pl. +; (of Hebe, meton. for youth) Pi. ‖ NEUT.SB. pleasure or enjoyment Pi. Th.
2 (of a person, referring to the way he died) **pleasing** (W.DAT. to himself) S.; (of sons, W.DAT. to parents) Call.
3 (of Artemis) perh. **delighting** (W.DAT. in young animals) A.
—**τερπνῶς** *adv.* **pleasantly** Thgn. S.*fr.* Lyr.adesp. AR.
τέρπω *vb.* | fut. τέρψω | aor. ἔτερψα ‖ MID.: fut. τέρψομαι | ep.aor.subj. τέρψομαι, 3sg.opt. τέρψαιτο, ptcpl. τερψάμενος | ep.aor.2: 1pl.subj. ταρπώμεθα | ep.redupl.aor.2: 3sg. τετάρπετο, 1pl.subj. τεταρπώμεσθα, ptcpl. τεταρπόμενος ‖ PASS.: aor. ἐτέρφθην, ep. τάρφθην | ep.aor.2 ἐτάρπην, also τάρπην, inf. ταρπῆναι, ταρπήμεναι, 1pl.subj. τραπείομεν |
1 (of persons, things, circumstances) **delight, gladden, give pleasure to** —*someone, a heart* Hom. Hes. Hdt. S. E. Ar. Isoc. +; (sts.mid., of a person) —*one's heart* Hom. Eleg. Lyr. S.*Ichn.* E. Hellenist.poet.; (intr., of a singer, poet, speaker) **give pleasure** Od. Th.; (of words, things, circumstances) S. E. Th. X. +
2 comfort, solace —*someone grieving* Il. ‖ MID. **comfort** —*one's heart* (W.DAT. w. *lamentation*) Od. ‖ MID.PASS. **take comfort** Hom.; **take comfort from** or **have one's fill of** —W.GEN. *lamentation* Hom.
3 ‖ MID.PASS. **have pleasure** or **enjoyment, be delighted, enjoy oneself** Hom. Hes. Thgn. Hdt. S. E. +; **enjoy** —W.INTERN.ACC. *a benefit* E.; **enjoy, take pleasure in, delight in** —W.DAT. or PREP.PHR. *activities, experiences, persons, things* Hom. Hes. Eleg. B. Hdt. Trag. + —W.GEN. *song, one's youth* Od. —*life* E. —W.PTCPL. *doing or experiencing sthg.* Hom. Eleg. E. X.
4 ‖ MID. **satisfy, content** —*one's heart* (W.GEN. w. *food and drink*) Il. ‖ PASS. **enjoy to the full, have one's fill of** —W.GEN. *food, drink, sleep, lovemaking* Hom. —W.PTCPL. *doing sthg.* Hom.
τερπωλή ῆς *f.* **joy, delight** Od. Archil. Thgn. AR.
τερσαίνω *vb.* [τέρσομαι] | ep.aor. τέρσηνα | **dry up, staunch** —*blood (fr. a wound)* Il. ‖ PASS. (of flies, on a poisoned wound) be dried up, wither AR.
τέρσομαι *pass.vb.* | aor.inf. τερσῆναι, ep. τερσήμεναι | (of blood, a wound) **be dried up, be staunched** Il.; (of clothes, a warm spot in a vineyard, a crop) **be dried** (by the sun) Od.

AR.; (of teardrops of amber) AR.; (of eyes) **be dry** (W.GEN. of tears) Od.
—**τέρσω** *act.vb.* | 3sg. (app.fut.) τέρσει | (of thirst) **parch** —*lips* Theoc.
τέρτατος, τέρτος *Aeol.adjs.*: see τρίτατος, τρίτος
τέρχνος εος *n.* **young shoot** (of a tree) Call.(pl.)
τερψι-επής ές *adj.* [τέρπω, ἔπος] (of songs) **delightfully worded** B.
τερψί-μβροτος ον *adj.* [βροτός] (epith. of Helios) **bringer of gladness to mortals** Od. hHom.; (perh. of songs) B.
τέρψις εως (Ion. ιος) *f.* **1 pleasure, joy, delight** Hes. Archil. Lyr. Hdt. Trag. Isoc. +; (W.GEN. fr. or in sthg.) Hes. Thgn. Pi. Trag. Th. Ar.; (W.INF. in doing sthg.) S. E.
2 satisfaction, gratification (W.GEN. of a longing) E.
Τερψι-χόρᾱ ᾱς, Ion. **Τερψιχόρη** ης *f.* [χορός] **Terpsichore** (Muse of the dance) Hes. Pi. Pl. Corinn. AR.
τεσσαρά-βοιος ον *adj.* [τέσσαρες, βοῦς] (of a prize) **worth four oxen** Il.
τεσσαράκοντα (Att. **τετταρά-**), Ion. **τεσσεράκοντα** *indecl.num.* **forty** Hom. + ‖ ATT.MASC.PL.SB. (w.art.) **the Forty** (a body of Athenian magistrates, four fr. each tribe, who adjudicated private cases) Isoc. D. Arist.
τεσσαρακοντα-ετής, Ion. **τεσσερακονταετής**, ές *adj.* [ἔτος] (of a man) **forty years old** Hes.; (of a period of time) **of forty years** NT.
—**τετταρακοντοῦτις** ιδος *Att.fem.adj.* (of a woman) **forty years old** Pl.
τεσσαρακοντ-ήρης ες *adj.* [ἐρέσσω] (of a ship, app. a catamaran) **forty-rowed** (w. three banks of oars, and rowers seated in groups of twenty, on each side of both hulls) Plu.
τεσσαρακοστός, Att. **τετταρακοστός**, ή όν *num.adj.* **1** (of a year, day, Olympiad) **fortieth** Th. Aeschin. Plb. Plu.
2 ‖ FEM.SB. (w. μοῖρα understd.) **fortieth part**; (specif.) **tax of one fortieth** (i.e. of two and a half percent) Ar.; **fortieth** (name of a coin fr. Chios) Th.
τεσσαράκυκλος *adj.*: see τετράκυκλος
τέσσαρες, Att. **τέτταρες**, Ion. **τέσσερες**, ep. **πίσυρες**, dial. **τέτορες**, α *pl.num.adj. and sb.* | dat. τέσσαρσι, τέτταρσι, also τέτρασι, Ion. τέσσερσι | **four** Hom. +
τεσσαρεσ-καί-δεκα (Att. **τέτταρες-**, Ion. **τέσσερες-**) *indecl.num.adj.* **fourteen** Hdt. Plb.
—**τεσσαρεσκαιδέκατος** (Att. **τέτταρες-**, Ion. **τέσσερες-**) η ον *num.adj.* **fourteenth** Hdt. Plb. NT. Plu.
—**τεσσαρεσκαιδεκ-ετής** ές *adj.* [ἔτος] (of a boy) **fourteen years old** Plu.
τεσσεράκοντα *Ion.indecl.num.adj.*, **τέσσερες** *Ion.num.adj.*: see τεσσαράκοντα, τέσσαρες
τεσσεράκοντ-όργυιος ον *Ion.adj.* [ὄργυια] (of a pyramid) **forty fathoms high** Hdt.
τεταγμένως *pf.pass.ptcpl.adv.*: see under τάσσω
τεταγών *masc.sg.redupl.aor.2 ptcpl.* [reltd. Lat. *tetigi*] **seizing** (someone) Il.
τέτακα (pf.), **τέταμαι** (pf.pass.): see τείνω
τέτᾱκα (dial.pf.): see τήκω
τετανό-θριξ τριχος *masc.fem.adj.* [reltd. τείνω; θρίξ] (of a person) **straight-haired** or **stiff-haired** Pl.
τέτανος ου *m.* [τείνω] **1** (medic.) **convulsive muscular tension, tetanus** Pl.
2 tautness, stiffness (of the penis) Ar.
τεταραγμένως *pf.pass.ptcpl.adv.*: see under ταράσσω
τετάρπετο (ep.3sg.redupl.aor.2 mid.), **τεταρπόμενος** (ptcpl.), **τεταρπώμεσθα** (1pl.subj.): see τέρπω

τεταρταῖος, dial. **τετόρταιος** (Theoc.), ᾱ (Ion. η) ον *adj.* [τετάρτη, see under τέταρτος] **1** (quasi-advbl., of persons) **on the fourth day** (since departure or sim.) Pl. X. Plb. Plu. **2** (of corpses) **four days old** Hdt. NT. **3** (of a fever) returning on the fourth day, **quartan** Pl. Call.; (fig., of erotic passion) Theoc.

τεταρτη-μόριον ου *n.* **fourth part, quarter** (of a sum of money) Hdt.; (of an obol, ref. to a trifling sum) Arist.; *quadrans* (quarter of a Roman *as*) Plu.

τέταρτος, dial. **τέτρατος**, η ον *num.adj.* [τέσσαρες] **fourth** Hom. +
—**τετάρτη** ης *f.* **1 fourth day** Hes. Th. X. Plb.
2 fourth part, quart (ref. to a Laconian liquid measure) Hdt.
—**τέταρτον**, dial. **τέτρατον** *neut.sg.adv.* **1 for the fourth time** Hdt. Call.; (w.art.) Hom.
2 (w.art.) **on the fourth occasion** Il. Hes. Call. AR.
3 fourthly (in the structure of a speech) Pl.
—**τέταρτα** *neut.pl.adv.* **fourthly** (in order of importance) Hdt.
—**τετάρτως** *adv.* app. **fourthly** Pl.

τετάσθην (ep.3du.plpf.pass.), **τέτατο** (ep.3sg.plpf.pass.): see τείνω

τετάφαται (Ion.3pl.pf.pass.): see θάπτω

τέταχα (pf.): see τάσσω

τετεύξεται (ep.3sg.fut.pf.pass.): see τεύχω

τέτευχα[1] (pf.): see τυγχάνω

τέτευχα[2] (pf.), **τετεύχαται** (ep.3pl.pf.pass.), **τετεύχατο** (ep.3pl.plpf.pass.): see τεύχω

τετευχῆσθαι *ep.pf.pass.inf.* [τεύχεα] **wear armour** Od.

τετίημαι *ep.pf.pass.vb.* | only ptcpl. τετιημένος, 2du. τετίησθον | **be sorrowful** Hom. Hes. hHom. AR.

—**τετιηώς** ότος *ep.pf.act.masc.ptcpl.adj.* (of a person, heart) **sorrowful** Il. hHom.

τέτλαθι (ep.pf.imperatv.), **τετλαίην** (ep.pf.opt.), **τέτλαμεν** (ep.1pl.pf.), **τετλάμεν** and **τετλάμεναι** (ep.pf.inf.), **τέτληκα** (pf.), **τετληώς** (ep.pf.ptcpl.): see τλῆναι

τέτμανται (dial.3pl.pf.pass.): see τέμνω

τετμεῖν *ep.aor.2 inf.* | aor.2 ἔτετμον, also τέτμον | perh. also 3sg.pres. τέμει (Il.) | (of a person) **reach, find** —*someone* (*usu. somewhere or doing sthg.*) Hom. hHom. Hellenist.poet.; (of old age) **come upon** —*someone* Od.; (of a man) come to have, **end up** —W.GEN. *w. an unsuitable type of wife* Hes.
|| PRES. (of a plough) perh., reach —*the turning point* (*of a field*) Il.

τέτμηκα (pf.), **τέτμημαι** (pf.pass.), **τετμηώς** (ep.pf.ptcpl.): see τέμνω

τέτοκα (pf.): see τίκτω

τετολμηκότως *pf.ptcpl.adv.*: see under τολμάω

τέτορες *dial.num.adj. and sb.*: see τέσσαρες

τετορήσω (redupl.fut.): see τορεῖν

τετόρταιος *dial.adj.*: see τεταρταῖος

τετρα-βάμων ον, gen. ονος *dial.adj.* [τέσσαρες; βῆμα, βαίνω] (of horses, the Trojan Horse) **four-footed** E.; (of a bear's paws, the Sphinx's talons) **four** E.

τετρα-βόειος ον *adj.* [βοείη] (of a shield) **made from four oxhides** Call.

τετρά-γυος ον *adj.* [γύης] (of an orchard, ploughland) of **four measures, four-acre** Od. Call. AR. || NEUT.SB. **four-acre field** Od.

τετραγωνίζω *vb.* [τετράγωνος] (of lines) **form four sides of** —*a specific shape or square number* Pl.; (intr., of a mathematician or geometrician) **perform the activity of squaring** (shapes or numbers) Pl. Arist.

τετραγωνο-πρόσωπος ον *adj.* [πρόσωπον] (of a species of furred animal) **square-faced** Hdt.

τετρά-γωνος ον *adj.* [τέσσαρες, γωνία] **1** with four corners; (of a city, building, piece of land, or sim.) **four-sided** or **square-shaped** Hdt. Pl. Plb. Plu.
2 (of timber) **square-cut** (as planks) Hdt. Th. Plb. Plu.; (of the stonework of Herms) Th.
3 (milit., of a formation of troops) **square-shaped** Th. Plu.
|| NEUT.SB. **square** (ref. to the layout of a camp) X. Plb.
4 (geom., of a shape) **quadrangular** or **square** Ar. Pl.
|| NEUT.SB. **quadrilateral** Arist.; **quadrangle** or **square** Pl. Arist.
5 (math., of a number which is formed by multiplying equal factors) **square** Pl.
6 (fig., of a person) **perfect as a square, four-square** Simon. Arist.

τετράδιον ου *n.* [dimin. τετράς] (milit.) **four-man detachment** NT.

τετρά-δραχμος ον *adj.* [τέσσαρες, δραχμή] **1** (of a soldier) **earning four drachmas a day** Men.
2 || NEUT.SB. **coin of four drachmas, tetradrachm** Plu.

τετρα-έλικτος ον *adj.* [ἑλικτός] (of a race) **turning four times, of four laps** B.

τετρά-ενος ον *adj.* —perh. also **τετραένης** ες (Theoc.) *adj.* [ἐνιαυτός] (of a child) **four years old** Call.; (of a seal on a wine-jar) Theoc.

τετρα-ετής ές, Att. **τετραέτης** ες *adj.* [ἔτος] (of a period of time) **of four years** Hdt. Plb.; (of children) **four years old** Hdt. Pl. Men. Call.

τετραετίᾱ ᾶς *f.* **period of four years** Plu.

τετρά-ζυγος ον *adj.* [ζυγόν] (of a chariot team) **of four yoked horses** E.

τετρα-θέλυμνος ον *adj.* [app. θέλυμνον *foundation*] (of a shield) **with four layers of hide** Hom.

τετραίνω *vb.* [reltd. τορεῖν | aor. ἔτρησα | ep.redupl.aor. τέτρηνα || pf.pass. τέτρημαι | **1 bore through, perforate** —*a tendon* Il. —*timber* Od. Ar. —*a jar, its cover* Hippon. Plb.
2 || PF.PASS. (of things) **be perforated with a hole or holes** Hdt. Ar. Plu.; (of a wounded man, compared to a net) A.; (of heaven) be full of holes or be leaky Hdt.; (of jars, a sieve, a soul compared to a sieve) Pl.; (provbl.) πίθος τετρημένος *leaking jar* (*in ctxt. of insatiable behaviour*) Pl. Arist. Thphr.; (*in ctxt. of wasted labour*) X.
3 || PF.PASS. (of the chasm of Tartaros) **be bored** —W.PREP.PHR. *right through the earth* Pl.

τετρα-και-δεκέτις, Att. **τετταρακαιδεκέτις** (Arist.), ιδος *fem.adj.* [τέσσαρες, καί, δεκέτης] (of a girl) **fourteen years old** Isoc. Arist.

τετράκις (also **τετράκι, τετράκιν**) *num.adv.* **1 four times** Od. Pi. Hdt. Th. Ar. Att.orats. +
2 (in multiplication) τετράκις τρία *four times three* Pl.; τετράκις ... χίλιοι *four thousand* Th.

τετρακισ-μύριοι αι α *pl.num.adj.* [μῡρίος] **four times ten thousand, forty thousand** X.

τετρακισ-χίλιοι αι α *pl.num.adj.* **four thousand** Hdt. +

τετρά-κναμος ον *dial.adj.* [κνήμη] (of the wryneck woodpecker) **of the four spokes** (of a wheel, to which it is bound as a love-charm) Pi.; (of the binding of Ixion) **four-spoked** Pi.

τετρακόσιοι αι α *pl.num.adj.* **1 four hundred** Hdt. +; (sg., of ἀσπίς *a body of soldiers*) X.
2 || MASC.PL.SB. (w.art.) **the Four Hundred** (ref. to an oligarchy established at Athens in 411 BC) Th. Att.orats. X. Arist.

τετρακοσιοστός ή όν *adj.* (of a year) **four hundredth** Din.
τετρά-κυκλος ον *adj.* [κύκλος] | τετράκυκλος *metri grat.* Od.(cj. τεσσαρά-) | (of a wagon, carriage) **four-wheeled** Hom. Hdt.
τετραμαίνω *vb.* [reltd. τρέμω | aor.subj. τετραμήνω | **tremble** Ar. —w.ACC. *at a rumour, before divinities* Archil. Ar.(v.l. τετρεμαίνω)
τετρά-μετρον ου *n.* [τέσσαρες, μέτρον] verse consisting of four metrical units, **tetrameter** (usu. ref. to trochaic tetrameter) Ar. X. Arist. Plu.
τετρά-μηνος ον *adj.* [μήν²] (of a truce) **lasting four months** Th. Plb.; (of a year, in some calendars) **with four months** Plu. || FEM.SB. period of four months NT.
τέτραμμαι (pf.pass.): see τρέπω
τετραμοιρία ᾶς *f.* [τετράμοιρος] fourfold portion, **four times as much** (of sthg.) X.
τετρά-μοιρος ον *adj.* [μοῖρα] relating to the fourth part; (of a night-watch) **fourth** (of five) E.
τέτραξ ακος *m.* **grouse** Ar.
τετραξός ή όν *adj.* [τέτραχα] (of lines) **fourfold, in four sets** Arist.
τετραορία ᾶς *dial.f.* [τετράορος] | sts. quadrisyllab. w. synizesis of αο | **four-horse chariot** Pi.
τετρ-άορος, also contr. **τέτρωρος**, ον *adj.* [αἴρω; cf. συνάορος] | also τετράορος (or trisyllab. w. synizesis of αο) Pi. | **1** (of horses) **yoked four together** Od. E.; (of a chariot) **four-horse** Pi. E. Tim.
2 (of a river god in the form of a bull) **four-legged** S.
τετρά-παλαι *adv.* [πάλαι] (w.pres.vb., ref. to an action lasting to the present) for four ages, **for a very long time** Call.*epigr.*
τετρα-πάλαστος (or **-πάλαιστος**) ον *adj.* [παλαστή] (of a foot, as a unit of measurement) **equal to four palm-breadths** Hdt.
τετρά-πεδος ον *adj.* [πούς] (of an object, a dimension) **measuring four feet** Plb. Plu.(quot.epigr.)
τετρά-πηχυς υ, gen. ους (Ion. εος) *adj.* [πῆχυς] (of things) **measuring four cubits** Hdt. Arist.; (of a person) four cubits tall, **six feet tall** Pl.; (of men, as commendatory epith.) Ar.
τετραπλάσιος ᾱ ον *adj.* (of time and effort, periods of time, a legal penalty, or sim.) **fourfold, four times as great, quadruple** Pl.; (of water in a klepsydra) **four times more** (W.GEN. than for someone else) D.
τετρά-πλεθρος ον *adj.* [πλέθρον] (of an area) **measuring four plethra** Plb.
τετραπλοῦς ῆ οῦν *Att.adj.* (of a sum of money) **fourfold, four times as much, quadruple** X. NT. Plu.; (of a noun) **quadruply compounded** Arist.
—**τετραπλῆ** *adv.* in a fourfold manner or amount, **fourfold, four times over** —*ref. to making recompense* Il.
τετρα-ποδηδόν *adv.* [πούς] **on all fours, doggy-style** (ref. to a position in sexual intercourse) Ar.
τετρα-ποδητί *adv.* **on all fours** —*ref. to scrambling up a cliff* Plb.
τετρά-πολις (also **τετράπτολις** E.) εως *masc.fem.adj.* [πόλις] **1** (of Kephallenia) **comprising four cities** Th.
2 || FEM.SB. Tetrapolis, Four Towns (a confederacy of neighbouring towns in NE. Attica: Marathon, Oinoe, Probalinthos, Trikorythos) Ar. Plu. || MASC.ADJ. (of the people) of the Four Towns E.
τετρά-πολος ον *adj.* [πολέω] (of land) **ploughed four times** Theoc.
τετρά-πους πουν, gen. ποδός *adj.* [πούς] | nom.acc.neut.pl. τετράποδα | **1** (of animals, a species) **four-footed** Hdt. E. Pl. Arist.; (of a wolf's gait) E.

2 (of booty) **consisting of cattle** Plb.
3 || NEUT.SB. quadruped or beast Hdt. Th. Ar. Pl. X. Call. +
4 (geom., of a space, line) **four-foot** Pl.
τετρα-πτερυλλίδες ίδων *f.pl.* [πτερόν] **four-winged creatures** Ar.
τετρά-πτιλος ον *adj.* [πτίλον] with four wings or feathers; (of an imaginary four-bodied opponent of Geryon) prob. **four-plumed** (i.e. w. four helmets, a match for three-winged Geryon) Ar.
τέτραπτο (ep.3sg.plpf.pass.): see τρέπω
τετράπτολις *adj.*: see τετράπολις
τετραπυργία ᾶς *f.* [πύργος] **square building with a tower at each corner, castle** (in Asia Minor) Plu.
τετρά-ρρυμος ον *adj.* [ῥυμός] (of a chariot) **with four poles** (and eight horses) X.
τετραρχία ᾶς *f.* [ἀρχή] **1** rule over the fourth part of a region; (in Thessaly) prob., fourth part of a kingdom, **tetrarchy** (anachronistic ref. to the fourfold division of the country in the 6th C. BC; less likely, four-part kingdom) E.; (ref. to one of the four regions into which the country was divided in the 4th C.) D.
2 (in Roman ctxt.) region in a province (not always a fourth part of it) in the charge of a dependent ruler, **tetrarchy, principality** Plu.
—**τετραρχέω** *contr.vb.* **be tetrarch, have charge** —W.GEN. *of a region* NT.
—**τετράρχης** ου *m.* **tetrarch, local ruler** NT. Plu.
τετράς άδος *f.* **1 fourth day** (of the month, or of its mid or last ten days) Hes. hHom. Th. Ar. +
2 fourth numeral, **four** Arist. Plu.
τετρα-σκελής ές *adj.* [σκέλος] (of an animal, a species) **four-legged** Trag.; (of war) **against four-legged beasts** E.; (of a calf's collapse) **on all four four legs** E.
τετρα-στάδιον ου *n.* **distance of four stades** Plb.
τετρα-στάτηρος ον *adj.* [στατήρ] (of a cloak) **four-stater** (perh. ref. to the stater as a unit of weight rather than value, i.e. *heavy, warm*) Ar.
τέτρατος *num.adj.*: see τέταρτος
τετρά-τρυφος ον *adj.* [θρύπτω] (of a loaf of bread) **broken or breakable into four pieces** Hes.
τετραφαλαγγία ᾶς *f.* [φάλαγξ] **quadruple phalanx formation** Plb.
τετρα-φάληρος ον *adj.* [φάλαρα] (of a helmet) perh. **four-plated** Il. AR.
τετρά-φαλος ον *adj.* [φάλος] (of a helmet) perh. **four-ridged** Il. AR.
τετράφαται (ep.3pl.pf.pass.), **τετράφατο** (ep.3pl.plpf.pass.), **τετράφθω** (ep.3sg.pf.pass.imperatv.): see τρέπω
τετρά-φυλος ον *adj.* [φυλή] (of the Athenians) **divided into four tribes** Hdt.
τέτραχα, also **τετραχῇ** *adv.* **in four ways, into four parts** —*ref. to dividing sthg.* Pl. X. Plu.
τετραχθά *ep.adv.* **in four ways, into four pieces** —*ref. to breaking or tearing sthg.* Hom.
τετραχῶς *adv.* **in four ways, in a fourfold manner** —*ref. to making distinctions or sim.* Arist.
τετρεμαίνω *vb.*: see τετραμαίνω
τέτρημαι (pf.pass.), **τέτρηνα** (ep.redupl.aor.): see τετραίνω
τετρ-ήμερος ον *adj.* [ἡμέρᾱ] || FEM.SB. fourth day Arist.
τετρ-ήρης ους *f.* [ἐρέσσω] **four-rowed ship** (w. three banks of oars, and rowers seated in groups of four along each side of the hull, so that the oars at one level were operated by two men) Arist. Plb.
τετρηρικός ή όν *adj.* (of a ship) **four-rowed** Plb.

τέτρηχα (ep.pf.): see ταράσσω
τέτρῖγα (pf.): see τρίζω
τέτριμμαι (pf.pass.), **τετρίφαται** (Ion.3pl.pf.pass.): see τρίβω
τετρ-όροφος ον *adj.* [ὀροφή] (of a house) **four-storeyed** Hdt.(v.l. τετρώροφος)
τέτροφα[1] (pf.): see τρέπω
τέτροφα[2] (pf.): see τρέφω
τετρ-ώβολος ον *adj.* [ὀβολός] **1** (of honey) **costing four obols** Ar.; (derog., of soldiers) **earning four obols a day** (a low rate of pay) Men.
2 ‖ NEUT.SB. **four obols** (as a sum of money) Plu.
τέτρωμαι (pf.pass.): see τιτρώσκω
τέτρωρος *adj.*: see τετράορος
τετρώροφος *adj.*: see τετρόροφος
τετρ-ώρυγος ον *adj.* [ὄργυια] (of hunting nets) **four fathoms** (in length) X.
τέττα *voc.* (in an address by one warrior to another) **my friend** Il.
τεττάρα-, τέτταρεσ- (Att.): see τεσσαρα-, τεσσαρεσ-
τετταρακαιδεκέτις *Att.fem.adj.*: see τετρακαιδεκέτις
τετταράκοντα *Att.num.adj.*, **τέτταρες** *Att.pl.num.adj.*: see τεσσαράκοντα, τέσσαρες
τετταρακοντα-και-πεντακισ-χῑλιοστός όν *Att.adj.* **forty-five thousandth** Pl.
τεττῑγο-φόρᾱς ου *m.* [τέττιξ, φέρω] **wearer of the cicada** (ref. to an old-fashioned Athenian) Ar.
τέττῑξ ῑγος *m.* **1 cicada** Il. + [Ref. is most freq. to its sound, a shrill chirruping by the male, sts. described as singing.] **2 cicada badge** (golden badge or brooch in the form of a cicada, worn by Athenians, perh. in the hair, a custom which became obsolete in the early 5th C. BC) Th.; (w.connot. of old-fashioned behaviour) Ar.
τέτυγμαι (pf.pass.), **τετύγμην** (ep.plpf.pass.), **τετυκεῖν**, **τετυκέσθαι** (ep.redupl.aor.2 act. and mid.inf.), **τετύκοντο** (ep.3pl.redupl.aor.2 mid.): see τεύχω
τετυγμένος *pf.pass.ptcpl.adj.*: see under τεύχω
τέτυμμαι (pf.pass.), **τετύποντες** (nom.masc.pl.redupl.pf.ptcpl.): see τύπτω
τετυφωμένως *pf.pass.ptcpl.adv.*: see under τῡφόω
τετύχηκα (pf.), **τετυχηώς** (ep.pf.ptcpl.): see τυγχάνω
τετύχθαι (pf.pass.inf.), **τετύχθω** (3sg.pf.pass.imperatv.), **τετύχμενος** (Aeol.pf.pass.ptcpl.): see τεύχω
τεῦ[1], enclit. **τευ**[1] (dial.gen.2sg.pers.pron.): see σύ
τεῦ[2], enclit. **τευ**[2] (dial.gen.pron.adj.): see τίς, τις
τευθίς ίδος *f.* —also **τευθιάς** άδος (Philox.Leuc.) *f.* **squid** Semon. Ar. Philox.Leuc. Plu.
Τεῦκρος ου *m.* **1 Teucer** (son of Telamon, half-brother of Ajax, founder of Salamis on Cyprus) Il. Pi. S. E. Ar. +
2 Teukros (eponymous ancestor of the Trojans) Hes.*fr.*
—**Τεῦκροι** ων *m.pl.* **Teucrians, Trojans** Hdt. Call. ‖ SG.ADJ. (of a man) **Trojan** Hdt.
—**Τευκρίς** ίδος *fem.adj.* (of the land of Troy) **Teucrian** A. Hdt.
τευκτικός ή όν *adj.* [τυγχάνω] (of excellence in deliberation) **capable of attaining** (W.GEN. a good result) Arist.
τεύξασθαι (aor.mid.inf.), **τεύξεσθαι**[1] (fut.mid.inf.): see τεύχω
τεύξεσθαι[2] (fut.mid.inf.), **τεύξομαι** (fut.mid.): see τυγχάνω
τεῦς, enclit. **τευς** (dial.gen.2sg.pers.pron.): see σύ
τευτάζω *vb.* ‖ pf. τετεύτακα ‖ **be occupied** —w. περί + ACC. or GEN. *w. a subject of study or form of behaviour* Pl.; (of gymnastics) **be connected** or **concerned** —w. περί + ACC. *w. bodily change* Pl.
τεῦτλον, dial. **σεῦτλον**, ου *n.* **beet** Ar. Plu.
—**τευτλίον** ου *n.* [dimin.] **small beet** Ar.
τεύχεα *n.pl.*: see under τεῦχος
τευχεσ-φόρος ον *adj.* [τεύχεα, φέρω] (of soldiers) **bearing arms** or **wearing armour, armed, armoured** A. E.
τευχηστήρ ῆρος *m.* (appos.w. ἀνήρ) **armed warrior** A.
τευχηστής οῦ *m.* (appos.w. ἀνήρ) **armed warrior** A. AR.; (without ἀνήρ) Call.
τεῦχος εος (ους) *n.* [τεύχω] **receptacle** or **container**; **urn** (for ashes) A. S. Plu.; (for votes) A.; **pitcher** (for liquids) A. E. Call.; **tub** (for bathing) A.; **goblet, cup** (for wine) E.; **pot, jar** (for foodstuffs or sim.) X. Plb.; **bucket** (made of rushes, for cheese) E.*Cyc.*; **chest** (made of wood) X.; **chest** or **basket** (used for hiding a baby) E.; **container** (for chicks, ref. to an egg) E.
—**τεύχεα** (also **τεύχη**) έων *n.pl.* **1 collection of equipment** (for fighting); **armour, weaponry** (for individuals or an army, freq. in ctxts. of putting it on or stripping it fr. a corpse) Hom. Hes. B. Hellenist.poet.
2 equipment, gear (for sailing or travelling) Od. E.
τευχο-φόροι ων *m.pl.* [φέρω] **men bearing arms** or **wearing armour, soldiers in arms** E.
τεύχω *vb.* ‖ fut. τεύξω ‖ aor. ἔτευξα, ep. τεῦξα ‖ ep.redupl.aor.2 inf. τετυκεῖν ‖ pf. τέτευχα, ptcpl. (w.pass.sens.) τετευχώς ‖ MID.: fut.inf. (also w.pass.sens.) τεύξεσθαι ‖ aor.inf. τεύξασθαι ‖ ep.redupl.aor.2 inf. τετυκέσθαι, 3pl. τετύκοντο ‖ PASS.: ep.3sg.fut.pf. τετεύξεται ‖ aor. ἐτύχθην ‖ pf. τέτυγμαι, ep.3pl. τετύχαται, 3sg.imperatv. τετύχθω, inf. τετύχθαι, Aeol.ptcpl. τετύχμενος ‖ plpf. ἐτετύγμην, ep. τετύγμην, ep.3pl. ἐτετεύχατο, also τετύχατο ‖
1 construct (material things); **build, construct** —*a house, temple, or sim.* Hom. Pi. B. E. Theoc.; **create, fashion** —*objects in metal, wood, or sim.* Hom. Hes. Call. AR. —*a song, music* A. Pi.; **make** —*clothes* Od.; (of a miller) —*barley-meal* Od. ‖ MID. **make** —*an altar, horse-trough* Call. AR.; **build oneself** —*a house* Call.
2 ‖ PF.PASS. (of structures) **be built** Hom. Theoc.; (of clothes) **be made** Od.; (of objects, decorations) **be created** or **fashioned** Il. A. E. AR. Theoc. —W.GEN. *fr. some material* Hom. Hes.; (also) —w. ἐκ + GEN. Theoc. —W.DAT. Od.; (of Nymphs) —w. ἐκ + GEN. *by Zeus* Alc. ‖ PF.ACT.PTCPL. (of a rope) **made** —W.GEN. *fr. oxhide* Od.
3 make ready, prepare (for someone) —*a meal* Od. —*a potion* Hom. —*a drug* A.; (of a lion) —*a feast* (*of slaughtered sheep*) A. ‖ MID. **make for oneself, prepare** —*a meal* Hom. ‖ PF.PASS.PTCPL. (of cakes) **prepared, made** Philox.Leuc.
4 cause (sthg.) **to happen**; (of gods) **cause, bring about** —*rain, wind, or sim.* Il. A.; (of gods, humans, circumstances) **cause, create** —*suffering, evils, dissension, fear, war, laughter* (*usu.* W.DAT. *for someone*) Hom. Hes. Archil. Lyr. A. E. + —*a deceitful character* (*in someone*) Hes.; **contrive** —*murder, a trap* (*for someone*) Od. Call.; **arrange, effect** —*a marriage, transport, hospitality, burial, sacrifices, offerings* Od. Pi. S. E. Theoc.; **secure** —*honour* (*for someone*) Pi. AR. ‖ PASS. (of actions, events) **occur** or **happen** Hom. Hes. AR. Theoc.
5 cause (a person or thing) **to be** (such and such); **make** —*someone or sthg.* (W.PREDIC.ADJ. or SB. *such and such*) Hom. Pi. B. Trag. Critias AR. Theoc. ‖ PF.PASS. (of a person) **be made** —W.PREDIC.ADJ. *flawless* Simon.
6 ‖ PF. and PLPF.PASS. (of gods, persons, things) **have been created; be** —W.PREDIC.ADJ. or SB. *mortal, a suppliant, or*

sim. Hom. hHom. Eleg.adesp. AR. Theoc.; (also aor.pass.) Hes. A. ‖ PF.PASS. (of a saying) **exist** A.

—**τετυγμένος** η ον *pf.pass.ptcpl.adj.* **1** (of a structure, object) **well-made** Hom.
2 (of a mind) **well-balanced, steady** Od.

τέφρᾱ ᾱς, Ion. **τέφρη** ης *f.* **ash, ashes** Il. E.*Cyc.* Ar. Pl. Call. Plu.; (ref. to the remains of a cremated person) Theoc.*epigr.* Plu.

τεφρώδης ες *adj.* (of soil, silt) **like ash, ashy** Plu.

τέχνᾱ *dial.f.*: see τέχνη

τεχνάζω *vb.* [τέχνη] | aor. ἐτέχνασα | **1 practise an art** or **craft** Arist.
2 be cunning, use subterfuge Hdt.(also mid.) Ar. Pl. X. D. Plu.
—W.NEUT.ACC. *in some way* Ar. X. Is. D.
3 contrive, plan —*deception* Plu. —W.INF. *to do sthg.* Plu. —W.ACC. + INF. *that sthg. shd. happen* Arist. Plu. —W.COMPL.CL. *how sthg. may happen* Arist. Plu.(mid.)

τεχνάομαι *mid.contr.vb.* **1** make with skill, **craft, fashion** —*an artefact* Od. S.*Ichn.* S. Call. AR.
2 undertake with skill or cunning, **contrive, devise** —*a plan, course of action* Il. S. Th. AR. Plu.; **devise a way** —W.INF. *to do sthg.* Th. —W.COMPL.CL. *how sthg. may be done* hHom. X.; (intr.) **plan** or **plot** E. Th. Ar.

τεχνάσματα των *n.pl.* [τεχνάζω] **1** (concr.) **skilled work** (W.GEN. in cedar wood, ref. to a coffin) E.
2 contrivances, tricks E. Ar. X.

τέχνη ης, dial. **τέχνᾱ** ᾱς *f.* [reltd. τέκτων] **1 technical skill, craftsmanship, art, skill** (in any profession or occupation, whether manual, business, artistic, intellectual, sporting) Hom. +; (gener.) **expert knowledge** or its application, **expertise** Th. Pl. Arist.
2 sphere of expertise or branch of craftsmanship, **art, craft** (esp. as a profession or occupation) Hdt. Ar. Att.orats. +; **technique, system** (of rhetoric or sim.) Arist.
3 art, design (opp. nature or chance) Pl.
4 (concr.) product of craftsmanship, **handiwork** (of a skilled man) S.
5 (pejor.) **craft, artifice, trickery** Od. +
6 (wkr.sens.) **manner** or **means**; (phrs., oft. in commands) μηδεμιᾷ (μηδεμιῇ) τέχνῃ **by no means, on no account** Hdt. Th.(treaty) Lys.; πάσῃ (παντοίᾳ) τέχνῃ **by every possible means** (i.e. urgently) S. Lys. Ar. X.; ἰθέῃ τέχνῃ **in a direct** or **true way** (i.e. in actual fact) Hdt.

τεχνήεις εσσα εν *adj.* | fem.nom.pl. τεχνήσσαι | **1** (of chains) **skilfully made** Od.; (of toys) Call.
2 (of Hephaistos) **skilled** AR.; (of women, W.GEN. at the loom) Od.

—**τεχνηέντως** *adv.* **skilfully** —*ref. to steering a boat* Od. AR.

τέχνημα ατος *n.* [τεχνάομαι] **1** product of craftsmanship, **handiwork** (W.GEN. of someone) S.; (ref. to the organisation of the human body) X.; (fig.) **masterpiece** (W.GEN. of villainy, ref. to a person) S.
2 product of craft or artifice, **trick, stratagem** E. Plu.
3 piece of skill, **technique, device** Pl.

τεχνητός ή όν *adj.* (of things) **artificial** (opp. created by a god) Plu.

τεχνικός ή όν *adj.* [τέχνη] **1** (of persons) **having technical skill** or **knowledge, skilled, expert, professional** Isoc. Pl. Arist.
2 (of actions, occupations) entailing technical skill or knowledge, **professional, scientific** Isoc. Pl. Arist.; (of a work of art) **technically accomplished** Plb. Plu.; (of a naval stratagem, Fortune) **crafty** Plb.
3 (of things) **artificial** (opp. natural) Pl.

—**τεχνικῶς** *adv.* | compar. τεχνικώτερον | **1 in an expert, professional** or **scientific manner** Isoc. Pl. X. Plu.

2 artfully, craftily D.

τεχνίον ου *n.* [dimin. τέχνη] **insignificant skill, minor art** Pl.

τεχνίτης ου *m.* **1** one who practises an art or craft; **craftsman, artisan** X. Arist. Thphr. Plb. NT. Plu.; (milit.) **engineer** Plu.
2 skilled practitioner (of an art or craft), **expert, professional** Pl. X. Arist.; (W.GEN. in military affairs) X.
3 (pejor.) **clever manipulator** (W.GEN. of language) Aeschin. D.
4 ‖ PL. **artists** (ref. to practitioners of the fine arts, esp. painters, sculptors) Plu.; (specif., ref. to a group of professional actors or musicians) D. Arist. Plb. Plu.

τεχνολογέω *contr.vb.* [λόγος] **be a prescriber of techniques, lay down artistic rules, systematise** Arist.

τεχνο-πωλικός ή όν *adj.* [πωλέω] (of the name of an activity) **of expertise-selling** Pl.

τεχνύδριον ου *n.* [dimin. τέχνη] **insignificant skill, minor art** Pl.

τέω, τέων, enclit. **τεω, τεων** (Ion.dat.sg. and gen.pl.pron.adj.): see τίς, τις

τέως, ep. **τείως** (AR.) *temporal adv.* | In Hom., τέως is of variable scansion (iambus, monosyllable, trochee) and is sts. written τῆος or τεῖος when trochaic. | see also ἕως¹ |
1 (ref. to a time already specified) **during that time, in the meantime** Hom. hHom. S. E. Th. Ar. +; (correlatv. w. preceding ἕως *as long as, while*) **for just so long, meanwhile** Hom.; (ref. to a time about to be specified) **for such time** (followed by ὄφρα, ἕως *until*) Il. Ar.
2 (w. gener. ref. to earlier time) **up to this time, hitherto** Hdt. Th. Ar. Pl. +; ἐν τῷ τέως χρόνῳ *in the time leading up to this* Lys.
3 for a time, for a while (usu. w. a corresponding phr. *but now, but later, but when,* or sim.) Od. A. Hdt. Th. Lys. Ar. +
4 ‖ CONJ. (used like ἕως, W.INDIC. or ἄν + SUBJ.) **while** or **until** Hdt. Pl. D. AR. Plb.

—**τέωσπερ** *conj.* [περ¹] **right up to the time when** —w. ἄν + SUBJ. *someone shd. do sthg.* D.

Τέως ω *f.* **Teos** (city on the coast of Asia Minor) Hdt. Th. Theoc.*epigr.*

—**Τήιος** ᾱ (Ion. η) ον *adj.* (of Anacreon) **of Teos, Teian** Lyr.adesp. Hdt. Ar. Pl.; (of other persons) Arist. Plu.; (of cups) Alc.; (of the city) Mosch. ‖ MASC.PL.SB. **men of Teos, Teians** Iamb.adesp. Hdt. Th. Plb.

τῆ *adv.* [reltd. τῆ, see under ὁ] (exclam.) **there!** (when handing sthg. to someone, w.imperatv. *drink, pour, take,* or sim.) Hom.; (drawing attention to sthg., without imperatv.) Call.*epigr.*

τῇ (fem.dat.art., also adv.): see ὁ

τήβεννα ης *f.* —also **τήβεννος** ου (Plu.) *f.* **Roman cloak, toga** Plb. Plu.

τηγανίτης ου *m.* [reltd. τάγηνον] **a kind of bread cooked in a frying-pan, flatbread** Hippon.

τῇδε *fem.dat.adv.*: see under ὅδε

τήθεα έων *n.pl.* **marine animals of the mollusc family, ascidians, sea-squirts** Il.

τήθη ης, also **τηθή** ῆς *f.* **grandmother** Ar. Att.orats. Pl. Men.

τηθίᾱ ᾱς *f.* perh. **old woman** or **nurse** Men.

τηθίς ίδος *f.* **father's** or **mother's sister, aunt** Is. D. Men.

Τηθύς ύος *f.* **Tethys** (daughter of Gaia and Ouranos, sister and wife of Okeanos, mother of river gods and sea nymphs) Il. Hes. A. +

Τήιος *adj.*: see under Τέως

τηκεδών όνος *f.* [τήκω] **1 wasting sickness** Od.

τηκτός

2 wasting away (through desire for the Sirens' song) AR.
3 putrefaction (of flesh) Pl.

τηκτός ή όν *adj.* **1** (of lead) **melted, molten** E.
2 (of substances) **soluble** Pl. Arist.; (of minerals) **capable of being melted, fusible** Pl.

τήκω, dial. **τάκω** *vb.* | aor. ἔτηξα | pf. τέτηκα, dial. τέτᾱκα ‖ PASS.: dial.impf. τᾱκόμᾱν (E.) | aor. ἐτήχθην (Pl.), aor.2 ἐτάκην |
1 cause (sthg.) **to melt or dissolve; melt, melt down** —*metals* Hdt. —*wax* Theoc.; **dissolve** —*material substances* Pl.; (of winds) **dissolve into rain** —*water in the atmosphere* Hdt. ‖ PASS. (of snow) melt Od. Hdt. E. Theoc.; (of metal, earth, through heat) Hes.; (of fat) liquefy or ooze S.; (of dew) evaporate AR.; (of flesh, a corpse, material substances) be decomposed or dissolved S. Pl. X.; (of barley-groats) be consumed (in a fire) Theoc.
2 ‖ STATV.PF. (of snow) be melted X.; (of flesh) be tender (fr. boiling) E.*Cyc.*; (of bodies) be consumed (by fire) E.; (of bile) be dissolved (fr. flesh into blood) Pl.; (of metal) be molten Plb.
3 cause (someone) **to waste away** (fr. a physical cause); (of sickness) **waste away** —*a body, a person* Pl. Call. ‖ PASS. (of persons, their looks) be wasted (by sickness, hunger, desire) Od. Hdt. Call. Theoc. ‖ STATV.PF. (of women) be wasted away (w. weeping) Il. S.
4 cause (someone or sthg.) **to pine away or weaken** (fr. a strong emotion); (of a person) **waste away, wear out** —*one's heart, life* (*in grief, jealousy*) Od. E. Call. ‖ PASS. waste or pine away (through grief, desire, jealousy) S. E. Ar. Theoc.; melt (w. compassion, love) Pi.*fr.* E. AR.; melt in tears Od.; (of skin, cheeks) run with tears Od.; (of a lover's look) be languid Plu.; (fig., of self-conceit) be brought to nothing A.
5 make (W.ACC. a lamentation) **while wasting away** (i.e. waste away lamenting) S.

τηλ-αυγής ές *adj.* [τῆλε, αὐγή] **1 with beams visible far off;** (of the Sun's face, the Moon's raiment) **beaming afar, far-shining** hHom. Lyr.adesp.; (of the sun's rays) Ar.; (of a lookout post, ref. to a beacon) Thgn.; (fig., of a family's radiance, i.e. glory; of garlands, the face of a work of art) Pi.
2 visible far off; (of a peak, sail) **far-visible** Pi.*fr.* B.; (of a hill) S.
—**τηλαυγῶς** *adv.* **clearly, distinctly** —*ref. to seeing* NT.

τῆλε *adv.* **1 far off, far away, at a distance** Hom. Hes. A. Tim. AR. —W.GEN. *fr.* **someone or somewhere** Hom. Pi.
2 to a place far away, far Il. Hes. hHom. Parm. AR. —W.GEN. *fr. someone or somewhere* Od. hHom. Pi.
3 from afar Il. AR.

τηλε-βόλος ον *adj.* [βάλλω] (of a stone) **striking from afar, far-flung** Pi.

τηλεδαπός ή όν *adj.* (of persons) **from afar, foreign** Od. Dionys.Eleg.; (of islands) **far off, distant** Il.

τηλεθάης ες *adj.* [τηλεθάω] (of flowers) **blooming** Archil.

τηλεθάω *ep.contr.vb.* [reltd. θάλλω] | 3sg. τηλεθάει | (of a stream) **be richly furnished** —W.DAT. *w. various trees* (*on its banks*) Theoc.*epigr.*

—**τηλεθάων** ουσα ον *ep.pres.ptcpl.adj.* | also (w.diect.) τηλεθόων, fem. τηλεθόωσα, neut.pl. τηλεθόωντα | **1** (of trees, vegetation) **flourishing, growing profusely** Hom. hHom. AR. Mosch.; (of a lock of hair) **luxuriant** Il.
2 (fig., of persons) **in the bloom of youth** Il.; (of cities) **flourishing** Emp.

τηλε-κλειτός ή όν *adj.* (of persons) **far-famed** Hom. Hes. AR.

τηλε-κλυτός ή όν *adj.* (of a person, horses) **far-famed** Hom.

Τηλέμαχος ου *m.* **Telemachus** (son of Odysseus) Hom. +

τηλέ-πλαγκτος ον *adj.* [πλαγκτός] (pleon., of wanderings) **with wandering far and wide, far-flung** A.

τηλέ-πομπος ον *adj.* [πέμπω] (of a beacon's light) **sent from afar** A.

τηλέ-πορος ον *adj.* [πόρος] **1** (of a sound) **far-travelling** Ar.(quot.lyr.)
2 entailing a far journey; (of a cave) **far distant, remote** S.

τηλέ-σκοπος ον *adj.* [σκοπέω] (of light fr. fire) **seen from afar, far-visible** Hes.

—**τηλεσκόπος** ον *adj.* (of the eye of heaven) **far-seeing** Ar.

τηλε-φανής ές, Aeol. **πηλεφάνης** ες *adj.* [φαίνομαι] **1** (of a tomb, hilltop, rock, or sim.) **seen from afar, far-visible** Od. Alc. Ar. Men.
2 (of fire) **far-shining** Pi.*fr.*
3 (of Echo) **appearing far off** (perh. ref. to sound as well as sight) S.

τηλέ-φαντος ον *adj.* (of a star) **far-shining** Pi.*fr.*; (fig., of an honour) Pi.*fr.*

τηλέ-φιλον ου *n.* [φιλέω] plant, flower or leaf (perh. poppy-petal) used by lovers to divine whether their love is returned, **love-in-absence** Theoc.

τηλία ᾱς *f.* **1 board or tray with raised edges; tray** (used by a market-trader for displaying wares) Ar.; (fig.) **bread-tray** (W.GEN. of the Peiraieus, ref. to Sestos, which, by its strategic position, controlled grain imports to the Athenian market) Arist.(quot.)
2 dicing-table Aeschin.
3 chimney-board (used as a cover when the fire is not alight) Ar.

τηλίκος η ον, dial **τᾱλίκος** ᾱ ον *demonstr.adj.* [reltd. ἡλίκος] **1** (of persons) **of such an age** (whether young or old, as indicated by the ctxt.); **of the right age** (sts. W.INF. to do sthg.) Od. Thgn.; **of the same age** (w. ὡς + PERS.PRON. as someone) Il. hHom.
2 (of wild animals) **so great** (as one previously mentioned) Theoc.

τηλικόσδε ἥδε ὅνδε *demonstr.adj.* (of persons) **of such an age, at this age** (whether young or old, as indicated by the ctxt.) S. E. Pl.; (of an object) **of such-and-such a size** Arist.

τηλικοῦτος αὕτη (also οὗτος S.) οὗτον (also οὗτο) *demonstr.adj.* [οὗτος] | also masc. and neut. acc. τηλικουτονί (Ar. Isoc.) | **1** (of persons) **of such an age** (whether young or old, as indicated by the ctxt.) A. S. Ar. Att.orats. Pl. +; (of a mind) **of one of such an age** S.
2 of such a magnitude; (of a wall) **so large** Ar.; (of cities, places) **so great** Att.orats. Pl. +; (of power, punishment, crimes, lies, sufferings) Ar. Att.orats. Pl. +; (of persons, a god) **so grand** Pl. Men.
3 (of islets) **so small** or **insignificant** Isoc.

τήλινος η ον *adj.* [τῆλις *fenugreek*] (of unguents) **made from fenugreek** Plb.

τηλόθε(ν), Aeol. **πήλοθεν** *adv.* [τῆλε] **1 from afar** Hom. Hes. Sol. Lyr. S. E. +
2 far off, far away Il. AR. —W.GEN. *fr. someone or somewhere* Pi. E. AR.

τηλόθι *adv.* **1 far off, far away, afar** Hom. hHom. AR. Mosch. —W.GEN. *fr. somewhere* Hom.
2 to a place far away, far AR.

τηλορός *adj.*: see τηλουρός

τηλόσε *adv.* **to a place far away, far** Hom. hHom. E. AR.

τηλοῦ, Aeol. **πήλοι** *adv.* **1 far off, far away, afar** Hom. Hes. Thgn. E.*fr.* Arist.(quot.) AR. —W.GEN. *fr. someone or somewhere* Od. hHom. E.*Cyc.* —W.GEN. *in the countryside, in a land* Ar. AR.

2 to a place far away, **far** Od. AR. Theoc.
3 from afar —*ref. to hearing a voice* Sapph.
—**τηλοτάτω** *superl.adv.* **furthest away** Od.
τηλουρός (also **τηλορός** E.) όν *adj.* [ὅρος] **1** with distant boundaries; (of a region, land) **far off, distant** A. E. AR.
2 (of a person) **far off, distant** E.; (W.GEN. fr. somewhere) E.
τηλύγετος η ον *adj.* **1** (of a special or favourite child, whether an only child, last-born, born to aged parents or spoilt) perh. **beloved, darling** Hom. hHom. AR. Mosch.
2 [as if reltd. τῆλε] (of a person) app. **far away** (W.PREP.PHR. fr. one's native country) E.
τηλ-ωπός όν *adj.* [ὤψ] **1** (of a person) visible far off, **far away, distant** S.; (perh. of a place) Lyr.adesp.
2 (of a shout) ringing out over a distance, **far-sounding** S.
τημελέω *contr.vb.* **look after, take care of, attend to** —W.ACC. *one's daughters* E. —*one's head (i.e. hair, w. a comb)* Plu. —W.GEN. *arrangements for visitors* Pl.; **protect** —W.GEN. *the body of a fallen comrade* E.
τήμερον *Att.adv.*: see σήμερον
τῆμος, dial. **τᾶμος** *adv.* **1 at that time, then** (ref. to the past, sts.w. correlative. ἦμος) Hom. Hes. Thgn. S. Even. Hellenist.poet.
2 at the present time, **now** AR.
—**τημόσδε** *adv.* **at that time, then** Hellenist.poet.
—**τημοῦτος** *adv.* **at that time, then** Hes. Call.
τηνεί *dial.demonstr.adv.*: see ἐκεῖ
τήνελλα *interj.* **hurrah!** (ritual cry heralding a victor) Lyr.adesp. Ar.
τήνελλος ου *m.* **hurrah man, Mr Victor** Ar.
τηνίκα, dial. **τανίκα** *temporal adv.* [reltd. ἡνίκα] **at that time, then** (sts. answering *when*) Corinn. AR. Theoc.; (also) τὸ τηνίκα S.
τηνικάδε *temporal adv.* **1** (usu. τὸ τηνικάδε) **at that time, then** (sts. answering *when*) Men.(dub.) Plb.
2 at this time (of day, ref. to an early hour) Pl.; **by this time** (tomorrow) Pl.
τηνικαῦτα *temporal adv.* **1 at that time, then** (sts. answering *when*) Hdt. S. E. Ar. Att.orats. Pl. +; (also) τὸ τηνικαῦτα Plb.
2 at this or that time (of day) Lys. Men.; **at that time** (W.GEN. of summer) Ar.
τηνόθι *dial.demonstr.adv.*: see ἐκεῖθι
τῆνος *dial.demonstr.pron. and adj.*: see ἐκεῖνος
τηνῶ, **τηνῶθε**, **τηνῶθεν** *dial.demonstr.advs.*: see ἐκεῖθεν
τῆος *ep.adv.*: see τέως
τῆπερ *fem.adv.*: see under ὁ
τηρέω *contr.vb.* | fut.pass. τηρήσομαι (Th.) | **1 watch over with protective care; watch over, look after, take care of** —*a house, city* hHom. Pi. —*persons* Ar. Men. Theoc. Plu. —*hounds* X. —*someone's seat* Ar. —*a will* D. —*keys, records, money, possessions* Arist. Plu. ‖ PASS. (of persons, money, places) be looked after Men. Plb.
2 look after, preserve or maintain (abstr. things); **safeguard** —*laws, life, peace, security, tranquillity, a mode of behaviour, or sim.* Att.orats. Arist. Men. Plb.; **observe, keep** —*oaths, secrets, promises, or sim.* Lys. Isoc. Men. Plb. NT. Plu.; **preserve** —*a feeling of grievance, way of thinking* D.; **maintain** —*a military formation* Plu. ‖ PASS. (of a person's interests, prosperity) be safeguarded D. Arist.
3 watch vigilantly; watch closely, keep an eye on —*someone or sthg.* Thgn. Ar. Pl. D. Arist. Men. +; (of soldiers) **watch, guard** —*passes, entrances, military positions* Hdt. Ar. Plb.; (intr.) **keep watch, be on the alert** Th. Arist. Plb.; (mid.) Lys. ‖ PASS. (of persons) be closely watched Ar.; (of prisoners) be held in custody Th. Plb. NT. Plu.; (of a wall) be under guard Th.; (of a potential base of operations) be kept in view D.
4 (gener.) **be watchful, take care** —W.COMPL.CL. *that sthg. shd. not happen* Ar.(also mid.) Isoc. Pl. D. Arist. —*that sthg. shd. happen* D. Arist.; **guard against** —*some eventuality* Arist.
5 look out for, watch for —*someone* (whom one wishes to meet) Lys. Ar. Men. Theoc. —*someone's arrival* Th. —*someone's mistakes* Th. —*contradictions in speech* Isoc.; **watch for, wait for** —*a particular kind of weather* Th. D. Plb. Plu. —*a particular occasion* Th. D. Plu. —*an opportunity* Arist. —W.ACC. + PTCPL. *someone doing sthg.* S. Th. D. Arist.; **watch for an opportunity** —W.INF. *to do sthg.* Th. ‖ PASS. (of an opportunity) be watched for Lys.
τήρησις εως *f.* **1** careful watching; **custody, confinement** (of prisoners) Th. NT.; (in protective sense) **safeguarding** (of a constitution) Arist.; (of a bridge, as a task entrusted to priests) Plu.; **safekeeping** (of poison) Plu.
2 preserving (of fruit) Plu.
3 alertness, vigilance (in keeping watch) Th.
τηρός οῦ *m.* **warden** (ref. to a priestly superintendent) A.
τῆς (fem.gen.), **τῆς** (ep.fem.dat.pl.), **τῇσι** (Ion.fem.dat.pl.): see ὁ
τῆσδε (fem.gen.), **τησίδε** (Ion.fem.dat.pl.): see ὅδε
τητάομαι, dial. **τᾱτάομαι** *pass.contr.vb.* | only pres. | **1 be in want, suffer deprivation** Hes. S. X.
2 be deprived —W.GEN. *of persons or things* Pi. S. E. Pl. Arist.
τητέρη (Ion.fem.dat.): see ἕτερος
τῆτες *adv.* [ἔτος] in this year, **this year** —*ref. to a past or future happening* Ar. Plu.
Τηΰγετον *Ion.n.*: see Ταΰγετον
τηΰσιος η ον *Ion.adj.* —also **ταΰσιος** ᾱ ον *dial.adj.* serving no purpose; (of a journey) **idle, vain, fruitless** Od.; (quasi-advbl., of an arrow being shot) B.; (of feet moving) AR.; (of speech and action) **idle, rash** hHom.
—**τηϋσίως** *adv.* **to no purpose, in vain** —*ref. to shooting an arrow* Theoc.
τί *neut.interrog.pron.adj. and adv.*, **τι** *neut.indef.pron.adj. and adv.*: see τίς, τις
τιάρα, dial. **τιήρᾱ** (A.), ᾱς *f.* —also **τιάρης** (v.l. **τιάρᾱς**, **τιήρης**) εω *Ion.m.* [loanwd.] peaked cap worn by Persian soldiers (and by the king, w. more ornamentation), **tiara** A. Hdt. Pl. X. Plu.
τιαρο-ειδής ές *adj.* [εἶδος¹] (of helmets worn by a people of Asia Minor) **tiara-shaped** X.
τίη, Att. **τιή** *interrog.adv.* [τί] for what reason, **why?** Hom. Hes. Ar. AR.
τιήρᾱ *dial.f.*, **τιήρης** *Ion.m.*: see τιάρα
τιθαιβώσσω *vb.* (of bees) perh. **store up honey** Od.
τιθασείᾱ ᾱς *f.* [τιθασεύω] taming or domestication ‖ PL. rearing or farming (W.GEN. of fish) Pl.
τιθασευτής οῦ *m.* one who tames (animals); (fig.) **tamer or trainer** (of the populace, ref. to a politician) Ar.
τιθασεύω *vb.* [τιθασός] **1 tame, domesticate** —*animals* Pl. X.
2 (fig., of politicians, rulers, or sim.) **tame, make docile** —*people, their tempers, or sim.* D. Plu. ‖ PASS. (of a wife) be domesticated X.; (of a people) be made docile (by a ruler) Plu.
3 (of a farmer) **domesticate, train** —*cultivated* (opp. *wild*) *trees or plants* Pl.; **reclaim, cultivate** —*wild trees* Plu.
τιθασός ή όν *adj.* [perh.reltd. τιθήνη, θήμαι] **1** (of animals) **tamed, domesticated** (opp. wild) Pl. Plu.
2 (fig., of a person, populace) **tame, docile** Plu.; (of Violence) reared tamely at home, **domestic** A.
3 (of trees) **domesticated, cultivated** Plu.

—**τιθασῶς** adv. (of trees, plants, seeds, w. ἔχειν) *be domesticated* Pl.

τίθημι vb. | 2sg. τίθης, ep. and Aeol. τίθησθα, 3sg. τίθησι, dial. τίθητι (Theoc.), 1pl. τίθεμεν, 2pl. τίθετε, 3pl. τιθέᾱσι | also dial. (esp. Ion.) contr.pres. (as if fr. τιθέω) 2sg. τιθεῖς, 3sg. τιθεῖ, 3pl. τιθεῖσι | imperatv. τίθει, dial. τίθη (Alcm.) | opt. τιθείην, 1pl. τιθεῖμεν | inf. τιθέναι, ep. τιθήμεναι, τιθέμεν | ptcpl. τιθείς | impf. ἐτίθην, 2sg. ἐτίθεις, 3sg. ἐτίθει, ep. τίθει, 3pl. ἐτίθεσαν, ep. τίθεσαν, dial. τίθεν (Pi.) | fut. θήσω, dial. θησῶ (Call. Theoc.), ep.inf. θησέμεναι, dial. θησέμεν | aor.1 ἔθηκα, Lacon. ἔσηκα (Alcm.), 3pl. ἔθηκαν, ep. θῆκαν ‖ ATHEM.AOR. (as if fr. ἔθην): 3du. ἐθέτην, 1pl. ἔθεμεν, 2pl. ἔθετε, 3pl. ἔθεσαν, ep. θέσαν | imperatv. θές, 3sg. θέτω, Lacon. σέτω | subj. θῶ, ep. θείω, dial. θέω, ep. 2 and 3sg. θήῃς, θήῃ, ep.1pl. θέωμεν (disyllab.), also θείομεν | opt. θείην | inf. θεῖναι, ep. θέμεναι, θέμεν, ptcpl. θείς ‖ pf. τέθηκα, also τέθεικα (NT. Plu.) ‖ MID.: τίθεμαι, imperatv. τίθεσο, also τίθου, ptcpl. τιθέμενος, ep. τιθήμενος | fut. θήσομαι, dial.1pl. θησεύμεσθα (Theoc.) | aor.1: dial.2sg. ἐθήκαο (Theoc.), ep.3sg. θήκατο, ptcpl. θηκάμενος (Thgn. Pi.) ‖ ATHEM.AOR.: ἐθέμην, ep.3sg. θέτο | imperatv. θοῦ, ep. θέο, 3sg. θέσθω, 2pl. θέσθε | ptcpl. θέμενος | subj. θῶμαι, ep.2sg. θῆαι | opt. θείμην | inf. θέσθαι ‖ pf. τέθειμαι ‖ PASS.: fut. τεθήσομαι | aor. ἐτέθην ‖ neut.impers.vbl.adj. θετέον ‖ The sections are grouped as: (1–3) put (both material and abstr. things) in a place, (4–6) put down (money), reckon up (an account), or sim., (7) ground arms or sim., (8–12) set up or establish (dedications, prizes, laws and practices), (13–16) arrange (persons, things, situations) in a certain way, (17–19) reckon (persons or things) to be in a certain state, (20–21) bring about (events or actions). |

1 put in a place, **put in place, set, place** —*a stone, marker, foundations* Hom. —*a chair (for someone)* Od. —*(for oneself)* Od.(mid.) Hdt.(mid.) —*sthg.* (W.ADV. or PREP.PHR. *elsewhere, on the ground, in someone's hands, into a box, or sim.*) Hom. +—*garlands* (W.PREP.PHR. *on one's brows, around one's breast*) Anacr.(mid.); **bury** —*a body, bones* (W.ADV. or PREP.PHR. *somewhere, in the ground, or sim.*) Il. A. Th. Pl.; (gener.) **put** —*sthg.* (w. εἰς μέσον *into the public domain, i.e. make it common property*) Hdt. Pl.

2 put in the mind; **put** —*understanding, courage, anger, or sim.* (W.PREP.PHR. *in someone's mind or heart*) Hom. ‖ MID. **harbour** (W.PREP.PHR. *in one's mind or heart*) —*anger, shame* Il. —W.INF. *the idea of doing sthg.* Od.; (without PREP.PHR.) —*anger, a pure or unbending mind* Il. Thgn. A. Scol.

3 ‖ MID. **place** —*one's voting-pebble* (W.PREP.PHR. *in an urn*) A.; **cast** —*a vote* A. Hdt. E. Att.orats. Pl. +; **give** —*an opinion* Hdt. S. And. Ar.; (intr.) **give one's decision** Pl. ‖ PASS. (of votes) be cast E. Pl.

4 (in financial ctxts.) put down or deposit; **deposit** —*a sum of money* (W.PREP.PHR. *in a bank*) D.; **put down** —*sthg.* (W.PREDIC.SB. *as a security, i.e. place it in pawn*) Ar. D.; (intr.) give security (for a loan), **borrow on security, take out a mortgage** Pl. ‖ MID. get security given to one, **lend money on security** Pl. D.; **deposit, lodge** —*goods, money, contracts* (*somewhere, w. someone*) Od. Hdt. Lycurg.; (fig.) χάριν τίθεσθαι *lodge a favour, create a debt of gratitude* (*usu.* W.DAT. *w. someone*) A. Hdt. E.

5 put down money in payment; **pay** —*interest, a tax, a sum owed* D.

6 (in drawing up accounts) **set down, reckon** —*an amount* (*as covering an item of expenditure*) Lys. D. ‖ MID. (fig.) reckon up, put a figure against —*an obligation* (W.ADV. *too precisely*) E.

7 ‖ MID. (milit.) τὰ ὅπλα τίθεσθαι *ground arms* (i.e. halt and take up a position) Hdt. Th. X.; (gener.) *stand ready to fight* —W.PREP.PHR. *alongside someone, on behalf of one's city, or sim.* Th. Att.orats. Arist.; (in naval ctxt.) Plu.; (fig., of passion, in aid of reason) Pl.; (also) ὅπλα ἱππικὰ τίθεσθαι *serve in the cavalry*, τὴν ἀσπίδα τίθεσθαι *serve in the ranks* Pl.

8 place or set up in a temple, **dedicate** —*offerings* Od. Hdt.(quot.epigr.) E.

9 set up for competition, **offer** —*a prize, sthg. as a prize* Hom. Pi. Hdt. S. Th. +

10 institute, establish —*an athletic festival* Pi.; **set up, hold** —*assemblies* A. —*a contest* Hdt. E. X.

11 (act. and mid., of a legislator, person in authority, state) **lay down, make** —*a law or sim.* Hdt. Trag. Ar. Att.orats. Pl. +; (act.) **prescribe** —W.ACC. + INF. *that someone shd. do sthg.* X. —W.DAT. + INF. E.

12 (usu.mid.) **assign, give** —*a name* (W.DAT. *to sthg., one's child*) Od. Hdt. E. Pl.

13 arrange (in a certain way); (of gods) **arrange matters** —W.ADV. *in some way* Hom.; **arrange** —*an outcome, events* (W.ADV. or PHR. *in some way*) Semon. Hdt. Trag.; (usu. of gods) **bring it about** —W.ACC. + INF. *that someone shd. do sthg., that sthg. shd. be the case* A. E.; (oft.mid., of humans) **arrange, manage** —*affairs, situations* (W.ADV. *well, badly, or sim.*) Eleg. Hdt. Trag. Th. Ar. Pl. +; εὖ τίθεσθαι *keep in good order* —*one's shield, house, arms* Il. Hes. X.

14 ‖ MID. (fig.ref. to moving counters in a board-game, determined by the throw of dice) **place** —*a lucky throw* (prob. w. ellipse of √ψῆφον + πρός, *i.e. place one's counter according to a lucky throw, capitalise on good luck*) A.; (gener.) **take advantage of** —*a situation* Th. Pl. Plu.

15 (sts.mid.) **make** —*someone or sthg.* (W.PREDIC.SB. or ADJ. *such and such, e.g. make someone a priestess, turn a ship into stone, make someone immortal, make a curse come true*) Hom. Stesich. Pi. Hdt. Trag. Ar. +

16 ‖ MID. **make** —*someone* (W.PREDIC.SB. *one's wife or husband*) Od. A. B. —*(one's son, by adoption)* Pl.; **adopt** —*someone* Plu.

17 (act. and mid.) make out (mentally) a thing or person to be such and such; **regard, reckon, count** —*someone or sthg.* (W.PREDIC.SB. *as such and such, e.g. regard sthg. as an insult, count someone as a friend*) Od. Hdt. S. E. Pl. D.

18 (act. and mid.) place (mentally) a thing or person in a class; **place, rank, count** —*someone or sthg.* (W.ADV. or PREP.PHR. *nowhere, i.e. as of no account, ahead of sthg., or sim.*) Trag. Pl. D. —(W.PREP.PHR. *among one's friends*) Pl. X. —(w. ἐν + DAT. *as deserving of account, honour, blame, laughter*) Tyrt. Hdt. Plu. —(*as a minor concern, a light matter*) S. —(*as shameful, a crime, an omen*) E. Th. D. Plu. —(W.PARTITV.GEN. *as belonging to a class of person, as characteristic of a type of behaviour*) Pl. D.

19 (act. and mid.) **count, regard** —*someone or sthg.* (W.INF. *as doing sthg., being such and such*) S. Pl. D.; (also W.PTCPL.) Pl. D.; assume (hypothetically), **assume, posit** —*sthg.* Pl. D. Arist.

20 (of gods or humans) **make, create, cause** (for someone) —*events, situations, sufferings* Hom. Alcm. Pi. Trag. ‖ MID. **make, create, get** (for oneself) —*a house, meal, or sim.* Hom.; (of a goddess) **get, conceive** —*a child* (W.PREP.PHR. *beneath her girdle*) hHom.; (of a god) **assume** —*someone's appearance* Pi.

21 (act. and mid., periphr.) **create** —*fighting* (i.e. *fight*), *effort* (i.e. *exert oneself*), *slowness*, *haste* (i.e. *be slow, hasty*), *forgiveness, thoughtfulness* (i.e. *show these qualities*) Hom. Pi. Trag. Tim.

τιθηνέομαι mid.contr.vb. [τιθήνη] **1** (of a wet-nurse) **suckle, nurse** —*a baby* hHom. Thgn. Men. Plu.
2 (of a boy) perh. **cuddle** or **pet** —*a baby girl* X.
3 (fig., of Demeter and Persephone) **act as nurses** —W.DAT. + ACC. *for initiates, in Eleusinian rites* S.

τιθήνη ης, dial. **τιθήνᾱ** ᾱς *f.* [θῆμαι] **1** woman who suckles a child, **wet-nurse, nurse** Il. hHom. S. E. Call. AR.; (ref. to nymphs of Mt. Nysa who nursed Dionysus) Il. S. Plu.
2 (fig.) **nurse** (of Apollo, ref. to Delos) Call.; **nurse, nurturer** (of snow, ref. to Aetna) Pi.; (of Becoming, ref. to Space) Pl.

τιθήνημα ατος *n.* object of nursing, **nursling** (ref. to a baby) E.*fr.*

τιθήνησις εως *f.* activity of nursing, **nursing** Pl. Plu.

τιθηνός όν *adj.* (of a father's nurture of his daughter) **nurse-like** E. ‖ MASC.SB. tutor (in the Egyptian royal court) Plu.

τιθύμαλλος ου *m.* a kind of plant (w. a pungent sap, used for medicinal purposes), **spurge** Ar.

Τῑθωνός οῦ *m.* **Tithonos** (brother of Priam, father of Memnon by Eos, who gained eternal life for him fr. Zeus, but not eternal youth) Hom. Hes. hHom. Tyrt. Mimn.; (provbl. for senility) Ar. Call.

τίκτω vb. | fut. τέξω, also mid. τέξομαι, inf. τεκεῖσθαι (hHom.) | aor.2 ἔτεκον, ep. τέκον, ptcpl. τεκών, inf. τεκεῖν, dial. τεκέμεν (Pi.) | pf. τέτοκα ‖ MID.: aor.2 ἐτεκόμην, ep. τεκόμην |
1 (of a woman or goddess) **bear** —*a child* Hom. +; (intr.) **give birth** Hdt. + ‖ AOR.FEM.PTCPL.SB. mother Hdt. Trag. Lys. Ar.; (also pres.ptcpl.) S.
2 (of a man or god) **beget, father** —*a child* Hom. + ‖ AOR.MASC.PTCPL.SB. father Trag. Theoc.
3 (of both parents together) **produce** —*a child* Hom. E. ‖ MASC.PL.AOR.PTCPL.SB. parents Trag.
4 (pres. and impf.) bear or beget a child and so be its parent (ref. to both the original act and the continuing relationship); **be mother** or **father of** —*a child* Hom. Hes. Lyr. Trag.
5 (of animals) **give birth to** —*young* Hom. +; (intr.) **give birth** Od. +; (of reptiles, primordial Night) **lay** —*an egg* Hdt. Ar.
6 (of earth, heaven, or sim.) **give birth to, produce** —*living and growing things* A. E.; (of vines) —*fruit* Ar.; (of a city, country) —*a person* Thgn. Pi. E. Pl.; (of night) —*day, the sun* A. S.; (of a torch) —*fire* X.
7 (fig., of persons) **give birth to, create** —*songs, words, speeches, laws, calamities* S. E. Ar. Pl. Call.; (of a country) —*famine* Hdt.; (of a torrent) —*destruction* Ar.; (of death) —*poison* S.; (of circumstances, behaviour) —*consequences* (material or abstract, welcome or unwelcome) Eleg. B. Hdt. Trag. Pl.

τῑλάω contr.vb. [τῖλος *diarrhoea*] empty the bowels of, **shit** —*bile* Hippon.

τίλλω vb. | aor. ἔτιλα ‖ aor.pass. ἐτίλθην ‖ **1** (of a person, in mourning or distress) **pluck, pluck out, tear** —*one's hair* Il. Men.; (mid.) Od. AR. ‖ MID. tear one's hair (in mourning) —W.ACC. *for someone* Il.
2 pluck (a person, so as to remove hair); (of a person in distress) **pluck, tear** —*oneself* (i.e. *one's hair*) Ar.; (fig., of a pathic's arse) —*its cheeks* (i.e. *buttocks*, prob. ref. both to depilation, assoc.w. women, and to unmanly lamentation) Ar. ‖ PASS. (of a man) be plucked or depilated (ref. to removal of his bodily hair, so that he may pass for a woman) Ar.; (ref. to forceful removal of his pubic hair as a punishment) Ar.
3 pluck (a bird, so as to deprive it of feathers); (of a hawk) **pluck, pluck at** —*a bird, its head* Od. A. Hdt.
4 (of a chorus of birds) **pluck at** (i.e. *assault*) —*a person* Ar.; (of persons) **defoliate** or **prune** —*a plane tree* (fig.ref. *to a person, i.e. treat him w. disrespect*) Plu.; (fig.) app., harass verbally, **mock** —*people* Anacr. ‖ PASS. (fig., of a person, compared to a bird) be plucked or fleeced —W.PREP.PHR. *by false accusers* Ar.
5 pluck (sthg.) from where it is growing; **pluck** —*squills* Theoc. —*ears of corn* NT.
6 pluck to pieces, **shred** —*a piece of cloth* Theoc. —*a garland* Theoc.(or perh.tm. κατατίλλω)

τιλμός οῦ *m.* **plucking out of hair** (of women, as a punishment by men) A.; **tearing of one's hair** (by a man in distress) Men.

τίλσις εως *f.* **plucking out** (of one's hair, as an example of pathological behaviour) Arist.

τίλων ωνος *m.* a kind of fish (found in a Thracian lake) Hdt.

τῑμά dial.*f.*, **τῑμάεις** dial.adj.: see τῑμή, τῑμήεις

τῑμαλφέω contr.vb. [τῑμαλφής] **richly honour** —*gods* (W.DAT. w. *tapestries*) A. —*Apollo* (on his arrival at Delphi) A. —*a victory* (W.DAT. *in words*) Pi.; (of persons, in particular rites) **offer worship to** —*gods* Arist. ‖ PASS. (of the Eumenides) be richly honoured A.; (of a king) —W.DAT. w. *the sceptre of authority given by Zeus* A.

τῑμ-αλφής ές adj. [τῑμή, ἀλφάνω] (of a possession) fetching a high price, **costly, valuable, precious** Pl.

τῑμάορα (dial.masc.acc.sg.), **τῑμάορος** dial.adj.: see τῑμωρός

τῑμάοχος ον dial.adj. [ἔχω] (of goddesses) having honour, **honoured** hHom.

τῑμαρχίᾱ ᾱς *f.* [ἀρχή] constitution based on rivalry for distinction and honours, **timarchy** Pl.

τίμᾱτος Aeol.adj.: see τῑμητός

τῑμάω contr.vb. [τῑμή] | fut. τῑμήσω, dial.3pl. τῑμᾱσεῦντι (Theoc.) | aor. ἐτίμησα, ep. τίμησα, dial. τίμᾱσα | pf. τετίμηκα, dial. τετίμᾱκα ‖ MID.: fut. (usu. w.pass.sens.) τῑμήσομαι ‖ PASS.: fut. τῑμηθήσομαι | aor. ἐτῑμήθην, dial. ἐτῑμάθην, dial.3pl. τίμᾱθεν (Pi.) | pf. τετίμημαι, dial.3sg. τετίμᾱται ‖ neut.impers.vbl.adj. τῑμητέον |
1 (of humans and gods) **pay honour** or **respect to, honour** —*a god, ruler, parent, guest, place* Hom.(sts.mid.) +; (of the Muses) —*a song* hHom.; (of Paian) —*the skill of a doctor* (fig.ref. *to a ruler*) Pi.; (of a poet, through his song) —*a hero* Pi.
2 honour in a specified manner (freq. W.DAT. w. an act or reward); **honour** —*the dead* (w. *rites of burial, lamentation, or sim.*) Trag. Th. —*a city* (w. *a military alliance*) A.; **reward** —*someone* (w. *gifts, an office*) Isoc. X.; (intr.) **confer honour** or **give rewards** Pl. X. D.
3 hold (material or abstr. things) in honour; (of persons) **honour, value, prize** —*money* Thgn. —*modesty, excellence, piety, heedlessness, tyranny* A. Pi. E. —*one's birthday* Hdt.; **respect** —*a plea, wish, obligation* Trag.; (wkr.sens.) **esteem** or **observe** —*customs, a sacrificial art* E.
4 put a value or price on; **value, assess** —*goods, property* Is. D. —(W.GEN. *at a certain sum*) Pl. ‖ MID. **value, assess** —*sthg.* Plb. —(W.GEN. *at a certain sum*) Lys. X. D.; (gener.) **rate, rank** —W.INF. or ACC. + INF. *doing sthg. or that sthg. shd. happen* (W.PREP.PHR. *above a large sum, one's life, or sim.*) Th. Isoc. D. ‖ PASS. (of things) be valued, rated or

assessed Pl. D. —W.GEN. *in monetary terms* Th.; (of persons) —W.PREP.PHR. *above a certain sum* Plb.
5 (leg.) assess the amount of punishment due to a criminal; (of jurors) **assess, fix, award** —*a penalty, sentence* Ar. Pl. D.(law); (intr., w. δίκην understd.) **fix a penalty** Ar.; **award a sentence** or **penalty** (sts. W.DAT. to someone) —W.GEN. *of death, a sum of money* Att.orats. Pl. ‖ PASS. (of persons) be sentenced —W.DBL.GEN. *to a fine, for sthg.* D.(law) ‖ IMPERS.PASS. a sentence (W.GEN. of death or sim.) is fixed —W.DAT. *for someone* Antipho Pl.
6 ‖ MID. (of a prosecutor or defendant) estimate (as the appropriate penalty), **ask for a sentence** (sts. W.DAT. for someone, oneself) —W.GEN. *of death, imprisonment, a fine* Att.orats. Pl. Arist.(act.); **ask for** —w. δίκην + GEN. *a penalty of a certain sum* Plu.; **rate** (W.ACC. one's actions) as deserving a sentence —W.GEN. *of death* Plu.

τῑμή ῆς, dial. **τῑμά** ᾶς *f.* [reltd. τίω] **1 honour, esteem** (paid by men to gods or superiors, or by gods to men as a reward for services) Hom. + ‖ PL. honours or marks of honour Hes. Thgn. Pi. Hdt. Trag. +
2 (oft.pl.) **honour, prerogative, privilege** (attaching to a specific position or office, esp. that of a god or king) Hom. Hes. Thgn. A. Pi. Emp. + ‖ PL. honoured powers (of underworld gods) A.; honours or privileges (meton. for those who hold them, i.e. rulers and gods) S.
3 office (civic or other) Hdt. Th. +
4 price, value, worth (of things) hHom. Hdt. Ar. Att.orats. Pl. +; **return, profit** (fr. an activity) Ar.
5 assessment of value (of material or abstr. things) Pl.; (ref. to wealth) **criterion** or **standard of valuation** (W.GEN. for things) Arist.
6 recompense, compensation (esp. for damage to one's personal honour) Hom.

τῑμήεις, dial. **τῑμάεις**, εσσα εν *adj.* | also contr.nom. τιμῆς, acc. τιμῆντα | compar. τῑμηέστερος, superl. τῑμηέστατος |
1 (of persons and gods) **honoured, esteemed** Hom. Pi. Call. AR.; (of a marriage) AR. ‖ NEUT.IMPERS. (w. ἐστί) it is an honour —W.INF. *to fight for one's country* Callin.
2 (of gold, gifts) **costly, precious** Hom. Hes.*fr.* hHom. Eleg. Call.
3 (of youth) **precious** Eleg.

τίμημα ατος *n.* [τῑμάω] **1 assessed value, valuation** (of a specific property) Att.orats. Plb. Plu.
2 valuation of a citizen's whole estate (by which his tax obligations and political rights are determined), **property rating** Att.orats. Pl. X. Arist. Plu.
3 financial means (of a person, based on his property rating) E. [or perh. *valuation* (of an item for purchase)]
4 (leg.) sum assessed as damages or penalty (as determined by law or by a jury, or proposed by a prosecutor or defendant); **damages, penalty** Ar. Att.orats. Pl. Plb. Plu.
5 compensation (to a tomb for earlier neglect, fig.ref. to a lament) A.

τῑμήορος Ion.*adj.*: see τῑμωρός

τῑμῆς (fem.gen.sg. and contr.*adj.*): see τῑμή, τῑμήεις

τίμησις εως *f.* **1 honouring** (of persons) Pl.
2 assessment of value, **valuation** (of property) Pl. Plb. Plu.
3 valuation of a citizen's property (for political purposes), **property rating** Arist. ‖ COLLECTV.PL. (at Rome) census Plu.
4 (leg.) **fixing of a penalty** or **claim for damages** Att.orats. Pl.

τῑμητείᾱ ᾱς *f.* [τῑμητεύω] (at Rome) office of censor, **censorship** Plu.

τῑμητέος ᾱ ον *vbl.adj.* [τῑμάω] (of persons or things) **deserving to be honoured** or **esteemed** E. Pl.

τῑμητεύω *vb.* **be censor** Plu.

τῑμητής οῦ *m.* **1 valuer of land** Arist.
2 assessor of penalties or **damages** Pl.
3 (at Rome) **censor** Plb. Plu.

τῑμητικός ή όν *adj.* **1** (of a writing-tablet, on which a juror marked his vote) **for a penalty** Ar.
2 (of a Roman) **of censorial rank** Plu.; (of the office) **of censor** Plu.; (of the dedication of a building) **by a censor** Plu.

τῑμητός ή όν, Aeol. **τίμᾱτος** ᾱ ον *adj.* **1** (of a person) **worthy of honour, honourable** Arist.
2 (of a penalty) **to be assessed** (by the jury) D.
3 (of gifts fr. friends) **highly valued** Theoc.

τίμιος ᾱ (Ion. η) ον (also ος ον) *adj.* [τῑμή] **1** held in honour; (of persons) **honoured, esteemed** Od. +; (of gods, their temples, or sim.) Hes.*fr.* hHom. A. Pi. E. Pl. +; (of a city, country) S. D.; (of actions) Pi. S.; (of a contract) **honoured** hHom.
2 (of commodities, possessions, personal qualities, or sim.) **valuable, prized, precious** Archil. Hdt. S. E. Att.orats. Pl. +; **of high price, costly, expensive** Sapph. Lys. Ar. Pl. X. D.
3 bringing honour; (of a place of burial, an abode for deities) **honourable** A.; (of a prize, royal gifts, a seat) Xenoph. Hdt. X.; (of a privilege accorded to someone) **full of honour** A.; (of the future) **bringing honour** (to a people) A.; (of thanks) **giving honour, respectful** A.; (of a marriage feast) **impressive, splendid** hHom. ‖ NEUT.PL.SB. honours Plb.

τῑμιότης ητος *f.* **preciousness, value** (of sthg.) Arist.

Τῑμόθεος ου *m.* **Timotheus** (of Miletus, dithyrambic poet, c.450–360 BC) Arist. Plb. Plu.

τῑμοκρατίᾱ ᾱς *f.* [κράτος] constitution based on rivalry for distinction and honours, **timocracy** Pl.; (ref. to a state in which rulers are chosen on the basis of a property qualification) Arist.

τῑμοκρατικός ή όν *adj.* (of a person whose ideals conform w. those of timocracy) **timocratic** Pl.; (of a form of constitution, in which rulers meet a property qualification) Arist.

Τῑμοκρέων οντος *m.* **Timocreon** (of Rhodes, lyric poet, early-5th C. BC) Timocr. Plu.

τῖμος ου *m.* **price, payment** (in a commercial exchange) Archil. A.

τῑμωρέω contr.*vb.* [τῑμωρός] | neut.impers.vbl.*adj.* τῑμωρητέον, pl. τῑμωρητέα (Th.) | **1** (of persons, sts. in legal ctxt.) **seek** or **take vengeance** Hdt. Antipho Pl. —W.DAT. *on someone* Hdt. S.(also mid.) E.(also mid.) Att.orats. Pl. —w. ὑπέρ + GEN. *on behalf of someone* Lys. Pl. Arist. —W.DAT. *for someone* (+ ACC. *for his murder, i.e. avenge it*) E. Pl.
2 (tr., esp.mid.) **exact vengeance from, take revenge on, punish** —*someone* Hdt. S. E. Th. Ar. Att.orats. + —(W.GEN. *for sthg.*) Hdt. E. Lys. Pl. X. —(w. 2ND ACC.) E. —(W.PREP.PHR.) Hdt. Lys. ‖ MID. **exact vengeance, take revenge, be punitive** Hdt. E. Th. Att.orats. Pl. X. ‖ PASS. be punished And. Lys. Pl. X.
3 (esp. in military ctxt.) **give help** (to those who have been attacked or wronged); **lend help** or **support** (usu. W.DAT. to someone) Hdt. E. Th. Arist. Plb. Plu.

τῑμώρημα ατος *n.* **1** (sts. in legal ctxt.) **punishment, penalty** Pl.
2 help in taking revenge (given to someone) Hdt.

τῑμώρησις εως *f.* **1 vengeance, revenge** (W.GEN. for someone, i.e. for his murder) X.
2 (leg.) **punishment** Pl.

τῑμωρητέος ᾱ ον *vbl.adj.* (of a person) **deserving punishment** D.

τῑμωρητήρ ῆρος *m.* **helper in taking revenge** Hdt.
τῑμωρητικός ή όν *adj.* (of a person) **vengeful** Arist. Plu. ‖ NEUT.PL.SB. **acts of revenge** Arist.
τῑμωρίᾱ ᾱς, Ion. **τῑμωρίη** ης *f.* **1** (freq.pl.) **revenge, retribution, punishment** A. Hdt. E. Th. Att.orats. Pl. +; (W.GEN. for sthg.) Hdt. E. Att.orats. Men. Plu.; (for a murdered person) E. Antipho
2 revenge (W.GEN. taken on someone) E. Att.orats. Men. Plu.
3 help (given to those who have been attacked or wronged) Hdt. Th.
τῑμωρός, dial. **τῑμάορος**, Ion. **τῑμήορος** (AR.), ου *m.f.* [τῑμή; οὖρος², ὁράω] | also (as if fr. τῑμάωρ) dial.masc.acc.sg. τῑμάορα (A.) | **1** app., one who watches over honour; (specif.) **avenger** (oft. W.GEN. of a wrong, someone who has been wronged) Hdt. Trag. Antipho X. Plu.; (W.DAT. of someone) Antipho X. Plu.; (W.DAT.PERS. + GEN. for someone, of his murder) S.; **punisher** (W.GEN. of someone) E. Lys. Plb.
2 ‖ MASC.FEM.ADJ. (of justice) **avenging, bringing vengeance** (sts. W.GEN. for someone or sthg.) E. Pl. Call.; (of a hand) helping to bring vengeance E.; (of a plea) for vengeance Hdt.; (of talk) vengeful Plb.
3 helper, supporter, champion (of persons who have been attacked or wronged, usu. in DAT.) Hdt. Th.; (in GEN.) And.
4 (gener., ref. to a god or demigod) **protector, defender** A.; (W.GEN. of a place) AR.; (W.DAT. of supplications) AR.; (ref. to a person, W.GEN. of the truth) Antipho
5 (fig., ref. to a poet) **supporter** (W.DAT. of or at the crowning of a victor, i.e. eulogist of his victory) Pi.
τίν, enclit. **τιν** (dial.acc. and dat.2sg.pers.pron.): see σύ
τινάκτωρ ορος *m.* [τινάσσω] (ref. to Poseidon) **shaker** (W.GEN. of the earth) S.
—τινάκτειρα ᾱς *f.* (prob. ref. to Poseidon's trident) **shaker** (W.GEN. of the earth) A.
τινάσσω *vb.* | fut. τινάξω | aor. ἐτίναξα, ep. τίναξα ‖ MID.: ep.3du.aor. τιναξάσθην ‖ PASS.: aor. ἐτινάχθην, ep.3pl. ἐτίναχθεν | **1 cause** (sthg. fixed or stable) **to tremble or shake**; (of Poseidon, Zeus) **shake** —*the earth* Il. Hes.*fr.* Lyr.adesp.; (of a dolphin, rower) —*a ship's timbers* hHom. AR.; (of debris in a river) —*a bridge* Plu.; (of a person) —*a chair* (w. a kick) Od. —*a tree* (w. a club) AR. —*a woman* (by tugging her robe) Il.; (of wind) —*a heap of chaff* Od. —*heifers* (W.PREP.PHR. *fr. a rock, i.e. dislodge them*) Theoc.; (fig., of love) —*the mind* Sapph.
2 ‖ PASS. (of a mountain) **be shaken** (by Titans, an earthquake) Hes. Plu.; (of a mountain, leaves) be buffeted (by winds) Od. AR.; (of a person) shake (w. emotion) Plu.; (fig.) quake (w. fear) AR.
3 move (sthg.) vigorously to and fro; (of Zeus) **shake** —*the aigis* Il.; (of Dionysus) —*the thyrsos* E.; (of a person) —*reins, a rattle* AR.; (of wind) —*leaves* AR.; (of an eagle, w. its flapping wings) —*a sail* AR.; (of a dancer) **shake, toss** —*hair, a garland* Alcm. Ar.; (of a madman, distraught cattle) —*their heads* E. Plu.; (of a bird) **set in motion** —*the flap of its wings* (i.e. flap them) AR. ‖ MID. (of a bird) **flap** —*its wings* Od. AR. ‖ PASS. (of a warrior's helmet) shake Il.; (of sea, a ship's tackle) be agitated (by wind) AR.; (of a sunbeam reflected by water) tremble AR.
4 (of a warrior) **brandish, flourish threateningly** —*a spear, sword, shield* Hom. Tyrt. Pi. AR.; (of Herakles) —*a club, bow, spears* Pi. S.; (of Zeus) —*a lightning-bolt* Il. A. ‖ MID. **flourish** —*the point of a spear* Theoc.; **make a flourish** —W.DAT. w. one's weapons (i.e. brandish them) Plu.
τινθαλέος ᾱ ον *adj.* [τινθός app. *boiling water, steam*] (of bathwater) **steaming hot** Call.

τινθυρίζω *vb.* (of birds, in a fable) **chirrup** —*a message* Call.
τίνω, Ion. **τίνω**, also **τιννύω** (Plu.) *vb.* —also **τίννυμαι** or **τείνυμαι** Ion.mid.vb. | iteratv.impf. τίνεσκον (AR.) | fut. τείσω | aor. ἔτεισα ‖ MID.: fut. τείσομαι | aor. ἐτεισάμην | fut. and aor. sts. wrongly written as τίσω, τίσομαι, ἔτισα, ἐτισάμην; cf. τίω |
1 make recompense for what is owed; pay —*a reward, debt, fine, fee, compensation, or sim.* Hom. Pi. Trag. X. Call. AR. —*a penalty* (sts. W.GEN. *for sthg., in requital for someone*) Pi. Hdt. Trag. Pl. AR. + —*a blow* (W.PREP.PHR. *for a blow*) A.
2 pay the penalty or **atone for** —*a crime or other transgression* (which one has committed) Hom. Thgn. A. E. AR. —*someone* (whom one has killed) Il. —*a crime committed by an ancestor* Sol.; (intr.) **pay the penalty, pay** Sol. —W.DAT. w. one's head (i.e. life) Od.
3 get recompense or **retribution; exact vengeance** (for a wrong one has suffered) S. ‖ MID. **exact vengeance** Od.; (tr.) **avenge** —*a wrong* (to oneself or another) Hom. Hes. Thgn. Trag. AR.; **exact** —*punishment* (W.GEN. *for a wrong*) E.; (intr., gener.) **get oneself repaid, recoup one's expenses** Od.
4 ‖ MID. **take vengeance on, punish** —*someone* Hom. Thgn. Hdt. Trag. Ar. X. + —(W.GEN. *for a wrong*) Hom. Thgn. Hdt. —(w. 2ND ACC. *for a wrong*) Od.; **pay back** (an offender) —W.NEUT.ACC. *double* (the amount of the offence) Hes.
5 (in positive sense) **make a return** (for kindness) S. ‖ MID. **repay, requite** —*a benefactor* (W.DAT. w. returns of kindness) Pi.
τίοισι (Aeol.dat.pl.interrog.pron.adj.): see τίς
τίπτε (also **τίφθ'** before an aspirate) *interrog.* **1** (adv.) **why ever, why?** Hom. hHom. A. Hellenist.poet.
2 (pron. and adj.) **whatever, what?** Od. S. AR.
τίς τί *interrog.pron.adj.* | SG.: masc.fem.acc. τίνα, neut. τί | gen. τίνος, τοῦ, Ion. τέο, τεῦ | dat. τίνι, τῷ, Ion. τέῳ, Aeol. τίῳ ‖ DU.: nom.acc. τίνε ‖ PL.: masc.fem.nom. τίνες, acc. τίνας | neut.nom.acc. τίνα, Boeot. τά (Pi.), Megar. σά (Ar.) | gen. τίνων, Ion. τέων | dat. τίσι, τοῖσι, Ion. τέοισι, Aeol. τίοισι ‖ Used in both dir. and indir.qs. An acute accent on the final syllab. always remains acute. |
1 (as pron.) **who, what?** Hom. +; (w.partitv.gen.) τίς θεῶν; *which of the gods?*
2 (as adj.) **which, what?** Hom. + • τίς θεός; *which god?*
3 (w. other interrogs.) • τίς πόθεν εἰς ἀνδρῶν; *who and from where are you?* Hom.
4 (for relatv.pron., rarely before Hellenist.poet.) • οὐδὲ κελεύθῳ χαίρω τίς πολλοὺς ... φέρει *I do not delight in the road which carries many people* Call.*epigr.*
—τί neut.sg.interrog.pron. (standing alone or introducing a cl.) **for what reason, why?** Hom. + • (freq. w.pcl.) e.g. τί γάρ; or τί μήν; *how else?* (see γάρ D, μήν¹ 3); (introducing a conditional cl.) τί δ' εἰ ... ; *but what if ... ?* E. +; (w. wd. repeated in an indignant or incredulous q.) • ζῶσι ... τί ζῶσι; *They are alive.* — *What do you mean, 'they are alive'?* E.
—τά, also **σά** (Ar.) dial.neut.pl.interrog.pron. **why?** Pi.; (w.emph.pcl., equiv. to τί μήν;) σά μάν; *how else?* (i.e. certainly) Ar. | see μήν¹ 3

τις τι *enclit.indef.pron.adj.* | SG.: masc.fem.acc. τινά, neut. τι | gen. τινός, του, Ion. τεό, τευ | dat. τινί, τῳ, Ion. τεῳ ‖ DU.: nom.acc. τινέ, gen.dat. τινοῖν ‖ PL.: masc.fem.nom. τινές, acc. τινάς | neut.nom.acc. τινά, Att. non-enclit. ἄττα, Ion. ἄσσα | gen. τινῶν, Ion. τεων | dat. τισί, Ion. τεοισί ‖ The most general uses are illustrated in 1–2, and specific uses in 3–11. |
1 (as pron.) **someone** or **something, anyone** or **anything** Hom. +

τίσις

2 (as adj.) **a, any, some** • θεός τις *a god* Hom. +
3 (collectv.) **a person** (i.e. people in general, or everyone) Hom. + • ὧδε δέ τις εἴπεσκε *so people said* Hom. • εὖ μέν τις δόρυ θηξάσθω *let each man sharpen his spear well* Il.; (w.demonstr.) πᾶς τις, ἕκαστός τις (or sim.) *every one, each one* Sol. +
4 (ref. to a specific person whom one does not wish to name) **someone, one** Il. + • ποῖ τις τρέψεται; *where is one (i.e. where am I) to turn?* Ar. • δώσει τις δίκην *someone (i.e. you) will be punished* Ar. || NEUT. (euphem.) **something** (w.neg.connot.) Th. + • ἄν οὗτός τι πάθῃ *if he comes to any harm (i.e. dies)* D.
5 (opp. οὐδείς, οὐδέν) **someone** (or **something**) **important** or **of substance** E. + • ηὔχεις τις εἶναι *you prided yourself on being someone* E. • λέγουσί τι *there is something in what they say* Pl. Arist.
6 (w. proper names) **a certain, someone called** Hom. + • ἦν δέ τις ... Δόλων *there was one Dolon* Il.; **a, someone like, a type of** A. + • Ὀδυσσεύς τις *another Odysseus* Ar.
7 (w.predic.adj., adding a note of indefiniteness) **a type of, a somewhat** Hom. + • ἐγώ τις ... δυσμαθής *I am the sort of person who learns slowly* Pl.
8 || PL. (w. numerals, to indicate inexactness) **some, about** • ἡμέραι ἑβδομήκοντά τινες *seventy or so days* Th.; (without numeral) • ἡμέραι τινές *several days* Th. +
9 (w.demonstr. or interrog.adj., adding indefiniteness) Hom. + • τοιήδε τις αἰτίη *some such reason* Hdt. • ποῖόν τι κινδύνευμα; *what sort of risk?* S.
10 (philos., w.art., to show that the art. denotes a particular representative of a general class) • τὸ τὶ μέγεθος *some particular height* Arist.
11 (in opposed cls.) ὁ μέν τις ... ὁ δέ *one person ... another* (or sim.) Hdt. +
—**τι** neut.adv. (with vbs., advs., adjs.) **to some extent, somewhat, at all** Hom. +

τίσις εως *f.* [τίνω] **1 repayment, recompense** (for financial or material loss) Od.
2 **retribution, vengeance, revenge** Hom. Hdt. S. Pl. AR. Plu.; (W.GEN. fr. a god or gods) Alcm. Sol.; (for a crime) Hes. Hdt. E. Pl.; (for a murdered man) Od. Hdt.(pl.)
3 **revenge** (W.GEN. taken on someone) hHom. Thgn. S.
4 (in positive sense) **repayment** (for benefits received, W.GEN. to friends) Thgn.

τίσω (fut.): see τίω

τιταίνω *vb.* [reltd. τείνω, τανύω] | aor.ptcpl. τιτήνᾱς |
1 **stretch so as to make tight**; (sts.mid.) **bend** —*a bow* (*in order to string it*) Hom. —(*in order to shoot, by drawing back the bow-string*) Il. hHom. B.
2 (of Zeus) **stretch out, hold out** —*scales* Il.; (of a servant) **set up** —*tables* Od.
3 **stretch** —*one's hands* (w. περί + DAT. *around someone's waist*) Il.
4 (of a horse) **strain at, pull** —*a chariot* Il. Parm.; (of oxen) —*a plough* Il. || MID. (of a person) **exert oneself, strain** Od.; (of horses, birds, hounds, a person in flight) **go at full stretch, speed on** Hom. Hes. AR.; (also act.) Il.
—**τῑταίνω** *vb.* (of Titans, in a pop.etym. of their name) app. **strain** (to do sthg.) Hes.

Τῑτᾶνες, Ion. **Τῑτῆνες**, ων *m.pl.* **Titans** (children of Heaven and Earth, who preceded the Olympian gods, and after an unsuccessful assault on Olympos were imprisoned by Zeus in Tartaros) Il. +
—**Τῑτᾱ́ν** ᾶνος *m.* **Titan** (ref. to Atlas, son of the Titan Iapetos) A.; (ref. to Prometheus, son of Iapetos) S. E.; (ref. to the aither) Emp.

—**Τῑτᾱνίς**, Ion. **Τῑτηνίς**, ίδος *f.* —also **Τῑτηνιάς** άδος (Call.) Ion.*f.* **female Titan, Titan** A. E. Call. AR. || ADJ. (of a city, the root of a plant, assoc.w. one of the Titans) **Titanian** AR.
—**Τῑτᾱνικός** ή όν *adj.* **of the Titan kind**; (of a person's nature) **Titan-like** (i.e. lawless) Pl.; (of civic calamities caused by internal strife) Plu.

τίτανος ου *f.* **a kind of white earth**; prob. **gypsum** (app. used as coating on a shield) Hes.

τίτᾱς ᾱ *dial.masc.adj.* [τίνω] (of bloodshed) **avenging** (earlier bloodshed, perh. also w.connot. of itself requiring further vengeance), **vengeful** A.

Τῑτῆνες ων *Ion.m.pl.*, **Τῑτηνίς**, also **Τῑτηνιάς** *Ion.f.*: see Τιτᾶνες

τιτθεῖᾱ ᾱς *f.* [τιτθεύω] **activity of a wet-nurse, nursing** D.
τιτθεύω *vb.* [τίτθη] **be a wet-nurse** D.; (tr.) **nurse** —*a baby* D. Plu.
τίτθη ης *f.* [τιθήνη] **wet-nurse** (usu. ref. to a slave) Ar. Pl. Aeschin. D. Arist. Thphr. +
τιτθός οῦ *m.* **woman's breast**; **breast** (as evidence of female gender) Ar.; (of a mother, given to a baby) Lys.
—**τιτθίον** ου *n.* [dimin.] **1** (colloq.) **tit, titty** Ar.
2 breast (of a wet-nurse) Men.

τίτλος ου *m.* [Lat. *titulus*] **inscription, notice** NT.

τιτρώσκω *vb.* —also **τρώω** *ep.vb.* | fut. τρώσω | aor. ἔτρωσα || PASS.: fut. τρώσομαι, τρωθήσομαι | aor. ἐτρώθην | pf. τέτρωμαι | **1 cause** (someone or sthg.) **physical injury**; (of a person, weapon) **wound, injure** —*a person, part of the body, an animal* Hom. +; (fig., of love, the arrows of love, a handsome person likened to an archer) —*someone* E. X. Mosch.; (of money-makers, likened to bees) **sting** —*someone* Pl. || PASS. (of persons, animals) **be wounded** Il. +
2 cause by wounding —*fatal bloodshed (i.e. inflict a fatal wound)* E.
3 damage, cripple, disable —*ships* (*in battle*) Th. Plb. || PASS. (of ships) **be damaged or disabled** Hdt. Plb.
4 (gener., of persons, ref. to their behaviour; of an argument or sim.) **damage, harm** —*someone* E. Pl.; (of faction) —*a race* Call.; (of wine) **overpower, undo** —*someone* Od. E.*Cyc.*
5 (fig., w. sexual connot., of heaven) app. **penetrate** (for procreation) —*the earth* A.*fr.*

Τιτυο-κτόνος ον *adj.* [Τίτυος, κτείνω] (epith. of Artemis) **Tityos-slaying** Call.

Τίτυος ου *m.* **Tityos** (son of Earth, punished in Hades for attempting to rape Leto) Od. Pi. Pl. AR. Theoc. Plu.

τίτυρος ου *m.* app. **pheasant** Thphr.

τιτύσκομαι *mid.vb.* [reltd. τεύχω, τυγχάνω] **1 make ready, prepare** —*horses* (*for a chariot-yoke*) Il. —*fire* Il. —*things needed for a sacrifice* AR.
2 (of a warrior) **take aim, aim** (w. a weapon, sts. W.GEN. at someone or sthg.) Hom. Theoc.; (of a boxer, w. his fists) Theoc.; (of an archer shooting an arrow, a person inserting a key into a lock) —W.ADV. **straight** (*at a target, the aperture*) Od.
3 (of ships, credited w. thought) **aim for a destination** Od.
4 (fig.) **take aim** (in one's mind), **consider** —W.INF. *doing sthg.* Il.
—**τιτύσκω** *act.vb.* (of a racehorse) **provide** or **win** —*a victory* (*for someone*) B.

Τιτώ οῦς *f.* **Tito** (a name for Ἠώς *Dawn*) Call.

τίφη ης *f.* **a kind of beetle, also a kind of small boat**; (w. play on both senses) **beetle-boat** Ar.

τίφθ᾽ interrog.: see τίπτε

τῖφος εος *n.* **marsh** AR. Theoc.

τίω, ep. **τἴω** vb. [reltd. τῑμή] | ep.inf. τἴεμεν | impf. ἔτιον, ep. τίον, also ἔτῑον, τῖον | iteratv.impf. τίεσκον, also τἴεσκον | fut. τίσω | aor. ἔτῑσα ‖ PASS.: pf. τέτῑμαι |
1 (of humans and gods) **pay honour** or **respect to, honour** —*a god, ruler, guest, place, or sim.* Hom. Hes.(also mid.) Thgn. A. Pi.*fr.* Hdt.(oracle) + ‖ PASS. (of persons, gods, places) be honoured Hom. Hes. hHom. A. Emp.
2 hold in honour or **esteem, honour** —*justice, laws* Od. AR. —*the interests of mortals* A.; consider valuable, **value** —*victory* A.; (wkr.sens.) **celebrate** —*a wedding song* A.
3 put a value or price on; **rate** —*sthg.* (W.PREDIC.ADJ. or PREP.PHR. **at a certain value**) Il.

τίῳ (Aeol.dat.interrog.pron.adj.): see τίς

τιώς (Boeot.masc.acc.pl.possessv.pron.adj.): see τεός

τλᾱ-θῡμος ον *dial.adj.* [τλῆναι, θῡμός] (of a fighter's valour) **stout-hearted** Pi.

τλᾱτός *dial.adj.*: see τλητός

τλημοσύνη ης *f.* [τλήμων] **endurance, patience** hHom.(pl.) Archil. Plu.

τλήμων, dial. **τλᾱμων**, ον, gen. ονος *adj.* [τλῆναι] | compar. τλημονέστερος, superl. τλημονέστατος | **1** (of a person, heart) capable of endurance, **patient, steadfast, stalwart** Il. Tyrt. Thgn. A. Pi. Plu.
2 (of a person, city) enduring misfortune, **unhappy, miserable, wretched** B. Trag. Ar. X. Theoc. Plu.; (of life, circumstances, words) associated with misfortune, **unhappy, pitiful** S. E.
3 ‖ VOC. (w. a mixture of reproach and sympathy) **poor fool** S. E. X.; (also nom. in self-address) S.
4 (of a person, heart) hard and unfeeling, **over-bold, reckless, relentless** Trag.; (of a murderer's hand, war) A. E.
5 (derog., of a fart) **insolent** hHom.; (of wine) **pernicious** Call.*epigr.*

—**τλημόνως** *adv.* **1 patiently** A. E.
2 piteously, ruthlessly E.

τλῆναι athem.aor.inf. [reltd. τάλᾱς, τάλαντον, τόλμα] | ep.inf. τλήμεναι | 1sg. ἔτλην, dial. ἔτλᾱν, ep. τλῆν | 3pl. ἔτλησαν, dial. ἔτλᾱσαν, ep. ἔτλαν | imperatv. τλῆθι, dial. τλᾶθι, 3sg. τλήτω, 2pl. τλῆτε | 2sg.subj. τλῇς | opt. τλαίην | ptcpl. τλάς, fem. τλᾶσα | fut. τλήσομαι, dial. τλᾱσομαι | ep.aor.1 ἐτάλασσα, subj. ταλάσσω ‖ PF.: τέτληκα, ep.1pl. τέτλαμεν | ep.inf. τετλάμεν, τετλάμεναι | ep.imperatv. τέτλαθι, 3sg. τετλάτω | ep.opt. τετλαίην | ep.ptcpl. τετληώς, fem. τετληυῖα | ep.1pl.plpf. ἐτέτλαμεν ‖ The ep.pf. forms are used w. pres. sense, the plpf. w. impf. sense. |
1 (oft. imperatv.) **hold out, endure, be patient** Hom. Archil. Thgn. S. E. AR.; **bear, put up with** —W.PTCPL. *seeing sthg.* Od. Tyrt.
2 (tr.) **submit to, endure, suffer** —*evils, labours, battles, sickness, marriage* Hom. hHom. Pi. Trag. Arist.*lyr.* AR.; (intr.) **suffer** Il.
3 submit to acting in a manner contrary to one's own feelings; (oft. in neg.phr.) **endure, bear** —W.INF. *to do sthg.* Hom. Sapph. Thgn. Pi. Trag. Ar. Isoc. —W.PTCPL. Simon. A. S.
4 bring oneself to act in a manner contrary to the feelings of others; **have the heart** or **nerve, bring oneself** —W.INF. *to do sthg.* Hom. Hes. hHom. Thgn. Trag.; **dare** —*a reckless or wrongful action* A. E. Men.
5 have courage or hardihood, **dare** —W.INF. *to do sthg.* Hom. Hes. Pi. Trag. Ar. X. AR. —W.ACC. *a deed* Theoc.

τλησι-κάρδιος ον *adj.* [καρδίᾱ] **1** (of a god) **hard-hearted** A.
2 (app. of a mourner) **with an enduring heart** A.

τλητός ή όν, dial. **τλᾱτός** ά όν *adj.* **1** (of a heart) capable of endurance, **patient, enduring** Il.

2 capable of being endured; (in neg.phrs., of an action, assertion, slavery, grief, stench) **endurable, tolerable** Trag. Ar. AR.

τμήγω *ep.vb.* [τμητός, τέμνω] | aor.1 ἔτμηξα ‖ PASS.: aor.2 ἐτμάγην, 3pl. τμάγεν | also aor.2 ἐτμήγην | **1 cut down, fell** —*a tree* AR.
2 ‖ PASS. (of fleeing soldiers) be scattered (into groups) Il.; (of clouds) be rent asunder or dispersed Call.

τμήδην *adv.* [τέμνω] in a cutting manner, **so as to cut** (the skin) —*ref. to a spear striking the neck* Il.

τμηθείς (aor.pass.ptcpl.): see τέμνω

τμῆμα ατος *n.* **1 cut, incision** (in flesh) Pl.
2 part cut off, section, piece (of a material object) Pl. Plu.
3 (geom.) **section, segment** (of a line, circle) Pl. Arist. Plu.
4 division (into parts, of an abstr. entity or a concept) Pl. Arist.

τμῆσις εως *f.* **1 cutting down, ravaging, laying waste** (of land) Pl.
2 cutting into parts, **division** (of a material object) Pl.; (of an abstr. entity) Pl.

τμητέον (neut.impers.vbl.adj.): see τέμνω

τμητικός ή όν *adj.* **1** (of things) **able to cut** Arist.
2 (of geometrical solids) **sharp, pointed** Pl.

τμητός ή όν *adj.* **1** (of leather reins) made by cutting, **cut** S. E.
2 (of things) **able to be cut** Arist. Theoc.

Τμῶλος ου *m.* **Tmolos** (mt. in Lydia, assoc.w. Dionysus) Il. Thgn. A. Hdt. E. Call.

τό (neut.nom.acc., also neut.adv.): see ὁ

τόδε (neut.nom.acc.): see ὅδε

τοδί (neut.nom.acc.): see ὁδί, under ὅδε

τόθεν *demonstr.adv.* [reltd. ὅθεν] **1 from there, thence** Hes.; (also) ἐκ τόθεν AR. Theoc.
2 (as relatv.) **from where, whence** A. Call. AR.
3 (ref. to cause or agency) **from that source** B.; (ref. to derivation of a name) AR.
4 (ref. to time) **from then on, thereupon, thereafter** A.; (also) ἐκ τόθεν AR.

τόθι *demonstr.adv.* [reltd. ὅθι] **1 in that place, there** Od. hHom. Pi. B. E. +; **to that point** (in an argument) Parm.
2 (as relatv.) **where** hHom. Mimn. Lyr. Hellenist.poet.

τοι[1] *enclit.pcl.* [dat. σύ] | The pcl. is used to bring home a truth to an addressee, whether real or imaginary ('I tell you'). It may add slight emphasis to an assertion, or indicate the applicability of a general reflection to the matter in hand. It is uncommon in prose, except w. a conj. or other pcl. |
1 I tell you, for sure, in truth, indeed Hom. + • βαρείας τοι τύχας προταρβῶ *heavy indeed is the fate that I dread* A. • σέ τοι κικλήσκω *it is to you that I am calling* S. • τίκτει τοι κόρος ὕβριν *excess, you may be sure, begets insolence* Thgn.
2 (in subordinate cls., esp. w. causal conj. ἐπεί or conditional εἰ) Hom. + • ἐπεί τοι δεινὸν ἂν εἴη *since it would indeed be dreadful* Lys. • εἴ τοι νομίζεις *if you really think* (*sthg. to be the case*) S.
3 (w. another pcl., which has its normal force, τοι directing focus on the addressee) ἀλλά τοι, ἀλλά ... τοι, γάρ τοι, γέ τοι, δέ τοι, δή τοι, τἄρα (τοι ἄρα) Hom. + | see also ἤτοι, καίτοι, μέντοι, οὔτοι

τοι[2] (dial.enclit.dat.2sg.pers.pron.): see σύ

τοί[1] *adv.*: see τοιγάρ

τοί[2] (dial.dat.2sg.pers.pron.): see σύ

τοί[3] (dial.masc.nom.pl.): see ὁ

τοίαδε, τοιαδί (nom.acc.neut.pl.): see τοιόσδε

τοιαῦτα, τοιαυτί (nom.acc.neut.pl.): see τοιοῦτος

τοιγάρ (**τοὶ γάρ** Hom.) *conj.* [τοί¹, γάρ] | The conj. is always 1st wd. in sentence, giving a strong logical connection to the previous one. | **for that reason, therefore** Hom. hHom. Hdt. Trag. Ar. Arist.*lyr.* +

—**τοιγαροῦν**, Ion. **τοιγαρῶν** *conj.* [οὖν] **for that very reason, therefore** Hdt. S. Ar. Att.orats. Pl. +

—**τοιγάρτοι** (or **τοιγάρ τοι**) *conj.* [τοι¹] **for that very reason, therefore** A. Hdt. Th. Ar. Att.orats. +

τοῖν (gen.dat.du.), **τοῖιν** (ep.gen.dat.du.): see ὁ

τοίνυν (also **τοίνῦν**) *conj.* [τοι¹, νυν] | The conj. has a colloq. tone, giving a weak logical connection to the previous sentence, and is never 1st wd. in its sentence until late authors. | **1** (in narrative) **so, then, therefore** Pi. Hdt. Antipho Pl. +
2 (in dialogue, introducing an answer, responding to an invitation, or sim.) **so, well then** Hdt. Trag. Th. Ar. Pl. +
3 (passing to a new point) **well then** Hdt. Trag. Ar. Att.orats. Pl. +

τοῖο (ep.masc.neut.gen.): see ὁ

τοῖος ᾱ (Ion. η) ον *demonstr.adj.* **1** (of persons or things) **of such a kind, such** (correlatv. w. οἷος, ὅς, or sim.) Hom. Hes. Eleg. AR. Theoc.; (without correlatv., ref. to someone or sthg. mentioned earlier or implied) Hom. hHom. Semon. Mimn. A. Pi. +; (ref. to sthg. following) A. Hellenist.poet.; τοῖος ἤ (or καὶ) τοῖος *of this or* (*and*) *that kind* Pl.
2 (at start of sentence, giving reason for a preceding statement) **because this kind of** Hom. Hes. Archil. Sol. Trag. Ar. +
3 (in agreement w. another adj., denoting that it is to be taken in its full or exact sense) **so very, ever so** Hom. Hes. hHom.

—**τοῖον** *neut.adv.* **1** in **such a way** Od. hHom. AR.; **to such an extent, so much** Il. AR.
2 (w. another adv.) **so very, ever so** Od.

—**τοίως** *adv.* **in such a way** AR.

τοιόσδε ᾅδε (Ion. ἥδε) όνδε *demonstr.adj.* | 1st syllab. sts. scanned short in Trag. | **1** (of persons or things) **such as this, of such a kind, such** (correlatv. w. οἷος, ὅς, or sim.) Hom. +; (without correlatv., ref. to someone or sthg. mentioned earlier or implied) Hom. +; (ref. to sthg. following) Hdt. +
2 ‖ NEUT.ACC.PL. (introducing dir.sp., w.vb. of speaking) like this, as follows Hdt. S. E. Th. +

—**τοιοσδί** ᾱδί ονδί *demonstr.adj.* (w. stronger force) **just such as this** Ar. D. Arist.

τοιοῦτος αὕτη οὗτο (also οὗτον), Aeol. **τέουτος** αὐτᾱ ουτο *demonstr.adj.* [τοῖος, οὗτος] | 1st syllab. sts. scanned short | **1** (of persons or things) **such as this, of such a kind, such** (correlatv. w. οἷος, ὅς, or sim.) Od. +; (without correlatv., ref. to someone or sthg. mentioned earlier or implied) Hom. +; (ref. to sthg. following) Pi. Hdt. +
2 ‖ NEUT.ACC.PL. (after dir.sp., w.vb. of speaking) **such words as these, like this** Hom. A. Pi. Hdt. +

—**τοιουτοσί** αυτηί ουτί (also ουτονί) *demonstr.adj.* (w. stronger force) **just such as this** Ar. Att.orats. Pl. Men.

—**τοιαῦτα** *neut.pl.adv.* **in such a way** S.

τοιουτό-τροπος ον *adj.* [τρόπος] (of things, words, events) **of such a kind** Hdt. Th. Pl. Men.

τοῖς (Aeol.masc.acc.pl., also masc.neut.dat.pl.), **τοῖς, τοῖσι¹** (masc.neut.dat.pl.): see ὁ

τοῖσι² (dat.pl.): see τίς

τοίσδεσι and **τοίσδεσσι** (ep.masc.neut.dat.pl.), **τοισίδε** (Ion. and poet.masc.neut.dat.pl.): see ὅδε

τοῖχος ου *m.* [reltd. τεῖχος] **1** (oft.pl.) **wall** (of a house, building, room) Hom. +; (of a courtyard) Od. Hes. Hdt. Ar. AR.; (of a tent) E.; (ref. to a retaining wall for earthworks) Th.
2 side (of an altar) Call.
3 side (of a ship, ref. to the framework) Hippon. AR.; (fig., w. εὖ πράττων *successful*, as a desirable place to move to) Ar. ‖ PL. **sides** (of a ship) Hom. Thgn. E. Th. Theoc. Plb.; (fig., of the human body) E.

τοιχωρυχέω *contr.vb.* [τοιχωρύχος] **be a housebreaker, commit burglary** Ar. Pl. X.; (tr.) **break through** —*a house-wall* Arist.; (fig., of a swindler) **make a smash-and-grab raid** D.

τοιχωρυχίᾱ ᾱς *f.* **housebreaking, burglary** X.

τοιχωρύχος ου *m.* (*also f.* Men.) [τοῖχος, ὀρύσσω] **1** one who digs through a wall, **housebreaker, burglar** Ar. Pl. D. Plb. Plu.
2 (gener., as a term of abuse) **crook** Ar. Men.

τοίως *adv.*: see under τοῖος

τόκα *dial.adv.*: see τότε

τοκάς άδος *fem.adj.* [τίκτω] having given birth or capable of giving birth; (of a sow) **kept for breeding** Od. Plb.; (of a lioness, bitch, goat) **with newborn young** E. Call. Theoc. ‖ SB. **mother** (sts. W.GEN. of a child) E.; (ref. to a sheep) **dam** E.*Cyc.*

τοκεύς έως (ep. ῆος), Aeol. **τόκευς** ηος *m.* | DU.: ep.nom.acc. τοκῆε ‖ PL.: nom. τοκέες (A. Hdt.), ep. τοκῆες | gen. τοκέων, ep. τοκήων | dat. τοκεῦσι, ep. τοκέεσσι (Theoc.) | man who begets, **father** Hes. Hdt. AR.; (in neg.phr., ref. to a woman) **true parent** (W.GEN. of a child) A. ‖ PL. **parents** Hom. +

τοκεών ῶνος *Ion.m.* **father** Call.

τοκίζω *vb.* [τόκος] **lend money at interest** D. ‖ PASS. (of money) **be lent at interest** Plu.

τοκισμός οῦ *m.* **money-lending** X. Arist.

τοκιστής οῦ *m.* **money-lender** Arist.

τόκος ου *m.* [τίκτω] **1** giving birth, **childbirth, childbearing** Il. hHom. Parm. Hdt. Trag. Ar. +; (by an animal) Il. Pl.; (fig.) **begetting** or **bringing to birth** (of an abstr. concept) Pl.
2 (hendiadys) γενεή τε τόκος τε *lineage and parenthood* or *race and kin* (*denoting a family line or its members*) Hom.
3 (concr.) **offspring** (of human or divine parents, i.e. son or daughter) Semon. Trag.; (of sheep, i.e. a lamb) E.*Cyc.*; (collectv.) **children** AR.; **litter** (of a sow) X.; **young** (of bees) X. ‖ PL. **descendants** A.
4 (sg. and pl.) product of money lent, **interest** Pi. Ar. Att.orats. Pl. +; (w. play on sense 3) Ar. Pl.; (fig., ref. to a return or profit fr. circumstances envisaged as a financial transaction) X. Men.; (phr.) τόκος τόκου or τόκοι τόκων *interest on interest* (i.e. compound interest) Ar. Thphr.

τοκοφορέω *contr.vb.* [φέρω] **pay interest** (on money owed) D.

τόλμα ης, dial. **τόλμᾱ** ᾱς *f.* [reltd. τλῆναι] **1 boldness, courage** A. Pi. Hdt. E. Th. +; (W.GEN. for an undertaking) A. Pi.
2 bold or **daring act** Trag. Isoc. Pl.
3 over-boldness, audacity, brazenness, recklessness Hdt. Trag. Th. Ar. Att.orats. Pl. +

τολμάεις, τολμᾱρός *dial.adjs.*, **τόλμᾱτος** *Aeol.adj.*: see τολμήεις, τολμηρός, τολμητός

τολμάω, Ion. **τολμέω** *contr.vb.* | dial.2sg. τολμῇς (Theoc.) | fut. τολμήσω, dial. τολμᾱσῶ (Theoc.) | aor. ἐτόλμησα, dial. ἐτόλμᾱσα (Pi.) | pf. τετόλμηκα, dial. τετόλμᾱκα (Pi.) ‖ neut.impers.vbl.adj. τολμητέον |

1 have the hardihood to bear (sthg. difficult or unpleasant); **put up with, bear** —*one's lot, sufferings, or sim.* Thgn. E. Pl.
—W.PTCPL. **doing** or **suffering sthg.** Od. Thgn. E.; (intr.) **endure, bear up, hold out** (against sufferings, hardships) Od. Thgn. E.
2 bear, bring oneself, be patient enough —W.INF. *to do sthg.* Od. Thgn. Trag. Att.orats.

3 **dare to undertake, boldly venture on** —*an action or activity* Od. Archil. Pi. E. Th. Isoc.; (intr.) **have courage, be bold, be daring** Il. Trag. Th. Ar. Att.orats.; **be bold enough** —W.INF. *to do sthg.* Hom. Tyrt. Scol. Hdt. Trag. Th. +
4 (pejor.) **have the effrontery to perform** —*an action* Trag. Antipho Ar.; **dare, have the effrontery** —W.INF. *to do sthg.* Il. Thgn. Hdt. S. E. Ar. Att.orats. +

—**τετολμηκότως** *pf.ptcpl.adv.* **boldly, courageously** Plb.

τολμήεις, dial. **τολμάεις**, εσσα εν *adj.* [τόλμα] | also perh.contr. τολμῆς (A.), superl. τολμήστατος (S.) | 1 (of a heart) **enduring, steadfast, staunch** Od.
2 (of a person, heart) **bold, daring, courageous** Il. A.(dub.) Pi.; (pejor.) **brazen** S.(dub.)

τόλμημα ατος *n.* [τολμάω] 1 **brave deed, courageous exploit** E. Th. Ar. Plb. Plu.
2 (pejor.) **brazen act, audacious exploit** E. Ar. Pl. D.; **reckless statement** E.

τολμηρός, dial. **τολμᾱρός** (Bion), ά όν *adj.* [τόλμα] 1 (of a person) **bold, courageous** E. Th. Pl. Plb. Plu.; (of military enthusiasm) Th. ‖ NEUT.SB. **daring, courage** Th.
2 (pejor., of a person) **audacious, brazen, reckless** Ar. Att.orats. Plb. Bion; (of an action, accusation, statement) Att.orats. Pl. Arist. Men.

—**τολμηρῶς** *adv.* | compar. τολμηρότερον | 1 **boldly, courageously** Th. X. Plb. Plu.
2 **audaciously, brazenly** Lys. Din.

τολμητής οῦ *m.* [τολμάω] person of bold character, **daredevil** Th. Plu.

τολμητός ά όν (also ός όν), Aeol. **τόλματος** ᾱ ον *adj.* 1 (of a situation) perh. **endurable** or **to be endured** Sapph.
2 (of actions) **capable of being dared** (W.DAT. by someone) S.; (of a hope of safety) **achieved by daring** E.

τολυπεύω *vb.* [τολύπη] 1 wind spun thread into a ball (for weaving), **wind balls of wool** Ar.
2 (fig., of Penelope) **spin out** —*ruses* (*as if on her loom*) Od.; (of warriors) spin out or wind up, **carry through to the end** —*wars, hardships* (*perh. as if the threads of fate*) Il.; **wind up, bring to a close** —*a war* Od.; **spin** —*sorrow* (*as if a thread or skein,* W.DAT. *for someone*) E.

τολύπη ης *f.* ball of spun thread, **ball of wool** Ar.

τομαῖος ον *adj.* [τομή] 1 (of a lock of hair) **cut off, shorn** A. E.
2 effected by cutting; (of a cure for infestation by snakes) **by the knife** (prob. ref. to cutting of medicinal plants) A.; (fig., of a cure for troubles) prob. **by surgery, surgical** A.

τομάω *contr.vb.* (of a disease) be in need of cutting, **require surgery** S.

τομεύς έως *m.* cutting-instrument, **knife** or **blade** Pl. X.

τομή ῆς, dial. **τομά** ᾶς *f.* [τέμνω] 1 position at which a cut has been made; **cut** (in a tree, plant) Il. S.*fr.*; (in hair, ref. to a place fr. which a lock has been cut) A.(cj.); **cut end** (of a beam) Th.; (of a sheaf of corn) Theoc.; **cut section** (of a bisected body) Pl.
2 act or process of cutting; **cutting, cut** (usu. W.GEN. by an axe, sword, or sim.) Anacr. S. E.; (concr.) **cut, gash, wound** (in a body) Plu.; (fig., in a state) Plu.
3 cutting of a specific object; **cutting** (W.GEN. of wood, leather) S. Pl.; **cutting down, ravaging** (of crops) Archil.; (periphr.) ῥιζῶν τομαί *cuttings of roots* (*i.e. cut roots*) S.*fr.*
4 (oft. collectv.pl.) cutting by the knife (in surgery), **cutting, surgery** Pi. Isoc. Pl. Arist. Plu.
5 separation into parts, **division** (of a number, abstr. entity or concept) Pl. Arist.; (of a state into two parts) Plu.
6 **section** (of a populace) Plu.
7 (geom.) **dividing line** (betw. two things) Arist. Plb.

τόμια ων *n.pl.* 1 **severed pieces** (usu. testicles, of a sacrificial animal, over which oaths were sworn) Ar. Att.orats. Pl. Arist.
2 ‖ SG. (ref. to the animal) **oath-sacrifice** Ar.

τόμοντες (Aeol.masc.pl.aor.2 ptcpl.): see τέμνω

τομός ή όν *adj.* | compar. τομώτερος, superl. τομώτατος |
1 (of a slayer, personif.ref. to a sword) with the capacity to cut, **cutting, sharp** S.; (of fire, ref. to its effect on the body) **piercing** Pl.
2 (fig., of a person) app. **sharp, smart** Call.
3 (of an utterance) app. **clear** Call.

τόμος ου *m.* cut piece, **cut, slice** (of meat, cake) Ar.

τονθορύζω *vb.* | aor.ptcpl. τονθορύσᾱς | (of persons) make an inarticulate sound, **mumble** or **grumble** Ar.

τόνος ου *m.* [τείνω] 1 that which is stretched tight or made taut; **strand** (of rope) X.; **rope** (used in a military catapult) Plu.; **cord, strap** (for a bed, attached to the frame and supporting the bedding) Hdt.; (collectv.sg.) cordage, **bedcords** Ar.
2 state of being taut, **tension** (of cables, lyre-strings) Hdt. Ar.; (of a bow) Plu.
3 state of being intensified, **volume, power** (of a voice) Ar. Aeschin. D. Plu.
4 **pitch** (in speech or music) Pl. X. Arist. Plu.; **music** (fr. a lyre) S.*Ichn.*; (fig.) **note, tenor** (ref. to a mode of behaviour) Plu.
5 **metre** (of prophetic or inscriptional verses) Hdt.
6 going full stretch, **straining of every nerve** (ref. to running) Pi.; concentrated effort, **eager striving** (W.PREP.PHR. for excellence) Xenoph.(dub.)
7 (gener.) **impetus** (ref. to movt.) Plu.; **intensity** (of emotions) Plu.

τοξάζομαι *mid.vb.* [τόξον] | ep.fut. τοξάσσομαι | ep.aor. ἐτοξασσάμην | shoot with a bow, **shoot an arrow** or **arrows** Od. —W.GEN. *at someone* Od.

τόξ-αρχος ου *m.* [ἄρχω] 1 (ref. to the Persian king) **archer lord** A.
2 (in the Athenian army) **captain of archers** Th.

τοξεία ᾱς *f.* [τοξεύω] **shooting of arrows** Plu.

τόξευμα ατος *n.* 1 that which is shot by a bow, **arrow** Hdt. E. Th. Ar. Pl. X. Plu.
2 distance which an arrow can be shot, **bowshot** E. Th. X. Plu.
3 ‖ COLLECTV.PL. **company of archers** Hdt. Plu.
4 (fig.) **arrow** (shot fr. the tongue, ref. to praise and blame) Pi. S. E.*fr.*; (shot fr. the eye, ref. to an alluring look) A.

τοξευτής οῦ *m.* **bowman, archer** (in a contest) Il.; (fig., ref. to a person who wounds others w. arrows of love) Call.

τοξευτός ή όν *adj.* (of a person) **struck by an arrow** S.

τοξεύω *vb.* 1 shoot with a bow, **shoot an arrow** or **arrows** Hdt. Ar. X. + —W.GEN. or PREP.PHR. *at someone or sthg.* Il. Hdt. S. X. Plu.
2 (tr.) **shoot an arrow at, shoot at** —*a person or animal* X. ‖ PASS. (of a person or animal) be shot at by an archer Th.; be struck by an arrow X. D. Plu.
3 (fig.) **shoot** —W.ADV. *surpassingly well* (*in exercising one's judgement*) S.; (tr., of a poet) —*songs* (*of love, at someone*) Pi.; (of a tongue, mind) —*words, thoughts* A. E.; (of love) **shoot at** —*a person* E. ‖ PF.PASS. (of an arrow, fig.ref. to a resource) have been shot (i.e. used) A.
4 (fig.) **shoot at, aim for, aspire after** —W.GEN. *a good reputation, welcoming embrace* E. ‖ PASS. (of friendship) be aimed for Plu.

τοξ-ήρης ες *adj.* [τόξον, ἀραρίσκω] 1 (of Apollo, his hand) **equipped with a bow** E.

τοξικός 1386

2 (gener., of the twang) **of a bow** E.; (of the equipment) **of an archer** E.

τοξικός ή όν *adj*. **1** of or relating to a bow; (of the string) **of a bow** A.; (of an arrow) **from a bow** A.*fr*.; (of the equipment) **of an archer** Pl. ‖ FEM.SB. **archery** Pl. X.
2 (of a person) **skilled with the bow** X.
3 ‖ NEUT.COLLECTV.SG.SB. **archer corps** Ar.

τοξο-δάμᾱς αντος *masc.adj*. [δάμνημι] **conquering with the bow, invincible in archery** A. B.

τοξό-δαμνος ον *adj*. (epith. of Artemis) **who conquers with the bow** E.; (of the Persian army) **of invincible archers** A.

τοξό-κλυτος ον *adj*. [κλυτός] (epith. of Artemis) **famed with the bow** B.

τόξον ου *n*. **1 bow** Hom. + [Used as a military weapon, in hunting, and in archery contests. It is assoc.w. particular heroes (esp. Herakles, Philoktetes), gods (esp. Apollo, Artemis), and peoples (esp. Amazons, Cretans, Persians, Scythians).]
2 ‖ PL. **bow** Hom. +; (w. wider ref. to an archer's equipment) **bow and arrows** Il. Hdt.; (specif.) **arrows** Il. S. E. Mosch.
3 ‖ PL. (fig.) **arrows** (ref. to words) E.; (of the sun, ref. to its rays) E.; (W.ADJ. *of the vine*, ref. to the capacity of wine to overpower) Pi.*fr*.; (of wine-dregs aimed in the game of kottabos) Critias
4 (fig.) **shot** (at sthg., ref. to an attempt at description) A.

τοξοποιέω *contr.vb*. **make into the shape of a bow, arch, knit** —*one's brows* (*in sadness or anger*) Ar.

τοξοσύνη ης, dial. **τοξοσύνᾱ** ᾱς *f*. **bowmanship, archery** Il. E.

τοξο-τευχής ές *adj*. [τεύχω] (of women, ref. to Amazons) **armed with a bow** A.

τοξότης ου, dial. **τοξότᾱς** ᾱ *m*. **1 bowman, archer** (in military ctxt.) Hdt. E. Th. +; (pejor., in contrast w. a fully armed warrior) Il. S. E.; (ref. to Herakles) Alcm.; (ref. to Philoktetes) Pi.; (in fig. ctxts., ref. to one who hits the mark in judgement, or who assails w. words) A. S. Pl. Arist.; (as a device on Persian coins) Plu. ‖ MASC.ADJ. (of a host) of archers (ref. to Amazons) Pi.
2 bowman, policeman (ref. to Scythian bowmen employed at Athens to maintain public order) And. Ar. Aeschin.
‖ COLLECTV.PL. **police-force** Ar. Pl. | cf. Σκύθης

—**τοξότις** ιδος *f*. **1 female archer, archeress** (ref. to Atalanta) Call.
2 opening in a fortification through which arrows may be shot, loophole Plb.

τοξουλκός όν *adj*. [ἕλκω] **1** (of the prowess of Persians) **in drawing the bow, in archery** A.
2 (of arrows) **shot from the drawn bow** A.

τοξο-φόρος ον *adj*. [φέρω] (of gods, persons, peoples) **bow-bearing** Il. hHom. Pi. Hdt.(oracle) E. Ar. ‖ MASC.PL.SB. **archers** Hdt. E.

τοπάζω *vb*. [τόπος] | aor. ἐτόπασα | **try to place** (sthg.) **mentally; make a guess, guess, conjecture** A. Ar. Pl.
—W.PREP.PHR. *about sthg*. Pl. —W.INDIR.Q. *whether sthg. is the case* Pl. —W.ACC. + INF. *that sthg. is the case* Pl.

τόπ-αρχος ον *adj*. [ἄρχω] (of a woman, ref. to the mistress of a household) **in charge of a place** A.(dub.)

τοπαστικός ή όν *adj*. [τοπάζω] (of a person) **good at making guesses, intuitive, ingenious** Men.

τοπήια ων *Ion.n.pl*. [app. τόπος] **rigging** (of a ship) Call.

τοπικός ή όν *adj*. [τόπος] **1** of or relating to a place; (of the matter of which a physical body is made) **that allows change of place** Arist.
2 (of a method of selecting material for deductive arguments) **with reference to specific topics** Arist.
‖ NEUT.PL.SB. **Topics** (title of treatise) Arist. | see τόπος 5

τοπογραφίᾱ ᾱς *f*. [γράφω] **description of a locality, topography** Plb.

τοπομαχέω *contr.vb*. [μάχη] (of a commander) **conduct one's fighting with an eye to location, manoeuvre for position** Plu.

τόπος ου *m*. **1** (sg. and pl.) **geographical locality, place, region, area** Hdt. Trag. Th. Ar. Att.orats. Pl. +; (periphr. W.GEN., as Κιθαιρῶνος τόπος, Ἑλλάδος τόποι *region of Kithairon, land of Greece*) Trag.
2 place occupied by someone or something; place, position, location Parm. S. Isoc. Pl. X. Aeschin. +; (ref. to a place of burial) NT.; (prep.phr.) ἐπὶ τόπου *in that place, on the spot* Plb.
3 allotted place (in a dwelling or at table), **place, space** NT.
4 place, passage (in a book) X.(dub.) Plb. NT.
5 point under discussion, subject, topic Isoc. Aeschin.; (specif.) **topic** (as the basis of a kind of deductive argument) Arist.
6 occasion or opportunity (for behaviour); **place, scope, room** (W.GEN. for pity, forgiveness, defending oneself) Plb. NT.
7 position, role (W.GEN. in a ministry) NT.

τορείᾱ ᾱς *f*. [τορεύω] **embossed metalwork** Plu.

τορεῖν *aor.2 inf*. [reltd. τετραίνω] | 3sg.aor.2 ἔτορε (Il.), ep. τόρε (AR., cj.) | redupl.fut. τετορήσω (Ar.) | **1** (of a warrior) **pierce** (w. a spear) —*an opponent's belt* Il.; (intr., of a spear) **pierce** —W.PREP.PHR. *beneath a belt* AR.
2 cry out piercingly, shrill out —*a message* Ar.(mock-trag.)

τορευτής οῦ *m*. [τορεύω] **craftsman in embossed metalwork** Plu.

τορεύω *vb*. [τορεῖν] **1 emboss a metal object** (i.e. carve or mould ornamentation in relief, by chasing or in repoussé); **emboss metalwork** Plu.
2 (fig., of a theatrical chorus) prob. **beat out** —*a dance-song* Ar.

τόρμος ου *m*. **hole, socket, mortise** (into which the end of a stake is fitted) Hdt.

τόρνευμα ατος *n*. [τορνεύω] **turning motion of a lathe**; (fig.) **rapid circling** (of persons running round a pillar) E.

τορνευτο-λυρ-ασπιδο-πηγός οῦ *m*. [λύρᾱ, ἀσπίς¹, πήγνῡμι] **lyre-turner-and-shield-maker** Ar.

τορνεύω *vb*. [τόρνος] **1 rotate a lathe** (fig.ref. to rotating a stake in the Cyclops' eye) E.*Cyc*.
2 create (sthg.) **on a lathe**; (fig., of a poet) **round out, turn out** —*verbal timbers* Ar.; (of a god) —*concentric circles of sea and land* Pl.; (mid.) —*a spherical figure* Pl.

τορνόομαι *mid.contr.vb*. **use a peg-and-string device** (to trace a circumference); (of grave-diggers, a shipwright) **mark out, round off** —*a burial mound, the curved bottom of a ship* Hom.

τόρνος ου *m*. [app. τορεῖν] **1 peg-and-string** (a device for tracing circles, w. a string extending fr. a central fixed peg or pin, and a chalk or sim. attached to the free end of the string) Thgn. Hdt. E.; (fig.) **central point** (W.GEN. of a circle, ref. to the geographical position of Athens, envisaged as the peg in a surrounding world) X.
2 lathe (on which wood was turned for chiselling) A.*fr*. Pl.

τορός ά όν *adj*. [τορεῖν] **1 with a piercing sound**; (fig., of a terrifying prophetic dream) **shrill** A.
2 communicating sharply and directly; (of an interpreter) **clear, plain** A.; (of speech, a message) A.; (of a poem) Call.
3 (of a Spartan youth) **sharp, keen** X.

—τορῶς adv. **1 clearly, plainly, distinctly** —ref. to speaking, communicating, hearing, knowing A. Emp. E.
2 decisively —ref. to a decree being nailed up A.
3 keenly, smartly, briskly —ref. to making an attack, performing a service Ar. Pl.
τορύνη ης f. **stirring spoon, ladle** (for soup) Ar. Pl. Plu.
τορύνω vb. **stir** —soup Ar.
τοσαυτάκις demonstr.adv. [τοσοῦτος] **so many times, so often** And. Pl. X. Plu.
τοσαυταχῶς demonstr.adv. (sts. correlatv.w. ὁσαχῶς) **in so many ways, so often** Arist.
τόσος, ep. **τόσσος**, η (dial. ᾱ) ον demonstr.adj. [reltd. ὅσος] **1 of such a magnitude or number; (of persons or things) so much, so large, so great** (in size or importance) or (pl.) **so many** (i.e. as someone or sthg. mentioned earlier or implied) Hom. Hes. Archil. Lyr. A. Hellenist.poet.; (at start of sentence, oft. w. γάρ, giving reason for a preceding statement) Hom. hHom. A. Theoc.
2 as much, as large, as great, as many (correlatv.w. ὅσος) Hom. Sol. Thgn. Emp. Hellenist.poet.; (correlatv.w. ὡς) A.; **great enough** (w. ὥστε + INF. to do sthg.) Alcm.
3 (w.num.adv., e.g. δὶς τόσος **twice as much**) Hom. Hes. Thgn. Pi. S. E. AR.
4 (in pl., as relatv., for ὅσοι) **as many as** B. Call.; (w.correlatv. τόσοι **as many**) **as** Call.
5 τόσος καὶ τόσος **such and such** (in amount or number, which one does not wish to specify) Pl. D.
6 (prep.phrs.) ἐκ τόσου **ever since that time** Hdt. Pl.; ἐπὶ τόσσον **to such an extent** AR.
—τόσον, ep. **τόσσον** neut.adv. **1 to such an extent, so much** Hom. Hes. Archil. A. Emp. Call.; **to such a distance, so far** Hom. hHom. S.; **so loudly** Hom.
2 as much, as greatly (correlatv.w. ὅσον or ὡς) Hom. Emp. Hellenist.poet.; **as far** Hom. Hes. Emp. AR.
3 δὶς τόσον **twice as much** E. Call.
4 (as relatv., for ὅσον) **as much as** Pi. Call.
—τόσῳ neut.dat.sg.adv. (correlatv. after ὅσῳ + compar. adv. or adj.) **by that much, to that extent** (w. further compar.) Pl. X.; (without further compar.) **all the more** Th.
—τόσως adv. (w. δίς **twice**) **as much** E.
τοσόσδε, ep. **τοσσόσδε**, ἥδε ὁνδε demonstr.adj. **1 of such a magnitude or number; (of persons or things) so much, so great** (in size or importance) or (pl.) **so many** (i.e. as someone or sthg. mentioned earlier or implied) Hom. Hdt. Trag. Th. Ar. Pl. +; (as sthg. following) Hdt. Th.
2 as much, as large, as great, as many (correlatv.w. ὅσος or sim.) Il. E. Call.; **great enough** (W.INF. to do sthg.) Od. —(w. ὥστε + INF.) A. S.
3 || NEUT.ACC.SG.SB. (introducing a statement in dir. or indir.sp., w.vb. of speaking or knowing) **just this, this much, as follows** Hdt. S. E. Th. Pl.
4 (prep.phr.) ἐς τοσόνδε **to such an extent, so much** Hdt. S.; **to such a state** E.Cyc.; **so far** (W.GEN. in speech, circumstances) Hdt. S. E.; **for so long** S.
—τοσοσδί ηδί ονδί demonstr.adj. (w. stronger force) **so much** Pl. Arist.
—τοσόνδε, ep. **τοσσόνδε** neut.sg.adv. **1 to such an extent, so much, so greatly** Hom. Trag. Pl. Call.
2 so long (in time) A.
3 so loudly Ar.
—τοσάδε, **τοσσάδε** neut.pl.adv. **so many times, so often** Simon. Pi.
—τοσῷδε neut.dat.sg.adv. (w.compar.adv. or adj., sts. after ὅσῳ + compar.) **by that much, to that extent, so much** Hdt. E. Plb.

τοσουτ-άριθμος ον adj. [τοσοῦτος, ἀριθμός] (of a multitude of men) **of such large number, so numerous** A.
τοσοῦτος, ep. **τοσσοῦτος**, αύτη οῦτον (also οῦτο) demonstr.adj. [τόσος, οὗτος] **1 of such a magnitude or number; (of persons or things) so much, so great** (in size or importance) or (pl.) **so many** (i.e. as someone or sthg. mentioned earlier or implied) Hom. B. Hdt. Trag. Th. Ar. +; (correlatv.w. ὅσος, ὡς, ὥστε, or sim.) Od. Hdt. S. E. Th. +
2 || NEUT.ACC.SG. or PL.SB. (ref. to what precedes, w.vb. of speaking or knowing) **this much** Archil. Hdt. Trag. Th. Ar.; (ref. to what follows) Hdt. S. E. Antipho Th. Ar. +
3 (w.num.adv., e.g. δὶς τοσοῦτος **twice as much**) Th. Isoc. Pl.
4 (prep.phrs.) εἰς τοσοῦτον **so far** (oft. W.GEN. in folly, hope, or sim.) Hdt. S. E. Ar. +; ἐπὶ τοσοῦτον, κατὰ τοσοῦτον **to such an extent, so far** Hdt. Th. And. +; διὰ τοσούτου **at so small a distance** Th.; ἐκ τοσούτου **from so far off** X. Plu.; ἐν τοσούτῳ **in the meantime** Th. Ar.; μέχρι τοσούτου **for so long** Th. X.; παρὰ τοσοῦτον **so close** Th. Plu. —W.GEN. **to danger** Th. | for τοσούτου δεῖν **fall so short** see δέω² 2
—τοσουτοσί αυτηί ουτονί demonstr.adj. (w. stronger force) **so much** Pl. D.
—τοσοῦτον (also τοσοῦτο Pi.), ep. **τοσσοῦτον** neut.adv. **1 to such an extent, so much, so greatly** Hom. Hdt. S. E. Th. Att.orats. +
2 to such a distance, so far Od. Pi. Antipho Th.
3 so long (in time) Ar.
—τοσούτῳ neut.dat.sg.adv. (usu. w.compar.adv. or adj.) **by that much, to that extent, so much** Hdt. Th. Isoc. +
τόσσαι Aeol.aor.inf. | app. equiv. to aor. τυχεῖν (see τυγχάνω) | ptcpl. τόσσαις | (of a person) **happen to be** (in a place) Pi.
τοσσάκι ep.demonstr.adv. [τόσος] (sts. correlatv.w. ὁσσάκι) **so many times, so often** Hom. Call.
τοσσάτιος η ον ep.adj. (of time) **so much, so long** (correlatv.w. ὅσος) AR.
τοσσῆνον dial.demonstr.adv. [reltd. τοσοῦτος, τῆνος] **so much** (correlatv.w. ὅσον) Theoc.
τόσσος, **τοσσόσδε**, **τοσσοῦτος** ep.adjs.: see τόσος, τοσόσδε, τοσοῦτος
τότε, Aeol. **τότα**, dial. **τόκα** temporal adv. **1** (ref. to an event or circumstance in the past) **at that time, then** Hom. +
2 (gener.) **formerly** (opp. now) Hdt. Trag. Th. Ar. Pl. +; (w.art.) οἱ τότε (or sim.) **the men of that time** Hom. +; τότε ἢ τότε **at one time or another** A. E.
3 (ref. to an event succeeding another in the past) **then, after that, thereupon** Hom. +
4 (ref. to fut. time or imagined circumstances) **then, in that event, in that case** Hom. +
5 (strengthened w.pcl. or temporal adv.) δὴ τότε Hom. Hes. A. Pi. Ar.(mock-epic) Hellenist.poet.; ἤδη τότε or τότε ἤδη Il. Hes. A. E. Th. Ar. +; τότ' ἔπειτα Hom. Hes. AR.
6 (prep.phrs.) εἰς (ἐς) τότε **until then** Hdt. E. Pl.; (w.fut.vb.) **at that time** Pl. D.; ἀπὸ τότε **from that time on** NT.; (also) ἔκτοτε Plu.
—τοτέ indef. temporal adv. **1** (in corresponding cls.) τοτὲ μὲν ... τοτὲ δέ **at one time ... at another, now ... then** Od. Pi. Emp. Trag. Ar. Att.orats. +
2 (w. variation on the basic pattern) τοτὲ μὲν ... τότ' αὖτε Pi.; ... ἄλλοτε δέ (or sim.) Pl. X.(quot.) D.; ... ὅταν δέ A. Pl.; τοτὲ (μὲν) ... ἄλλοτε S.; ἄλλοτε ... τοτὲ δέ Il.; νῦν μὲν ... τοτὲ δέ Thgn.; (without first element) τοτὲ δέ Il. hHom. Pl.
τοτοῖ, also **τοτοτοῖ** interj. (expressing grief or pain) **ah, ah!** A. S.
του (gen.enclit.indef.pron.adj.): see τις
τού Boeot.2sg.pers.pron.: see σύ

τοῦ[1] (gen.interrog.pron.adj.): see τίς
τοῦ[2] (masc.neut.gen.art.): see ὁ
τοῦδε (masc.neut.gen.): see ὅδε
τοὔνεκα (or τοὕνεκα), Boeot. τώνεκα *demonstr.conj.* [corresponding to relatv. οὕνεκα, as if fr. τοῦ ἕνεκα] **for that reason, therefore** Hom. Hes. Thgn. Pi. Corinn. Call. AR.
—τοὔνεκεν *conj.* [ἕνεκεν] **1 therefore** Xenoph. Simon. Call. AR.
2 (as relatv.conj., for οὕνεκεν) **that** Call.
τουτάκις, also τουτάκι *demonstr.adv.* [οὗτος] **1 at that time, then** Thgn. Pi. Call.
2 (app. for οὕτως, correlatv.w. ὡς *just as*) **so** Ar.(oracle)
τουτεί *dial.demonstr.adv.* [οὗτος] **here** Theoc.
τουτέστι *adv.* [τοῦτ' ἔστι] **that is, that means, i.e.** Plu.
τοὔτερον (Ion.neut.nom.acc.): see ἕτερος
τουτί *neut.nom.acc.*: see οὑτοσί, under οὗτος
τοῦτο (neut.nom.acc.): see οὗτος
τουτογί, τουτοδί (neut.sg., w.pcl. γε or δέ): see οὑτοσί, under οὗτος
τουτόθε, also τουτῶθεν *dial.demonstr.adv.* [οὗτος] **from this place, from here** Theoc.
τοῦτον, τούτου, τούτῳ (masc.acc.sg., masc.neut.gen. and dat.sg.): see οὗτος
τουτονγί (masc.acc., w.pcl. γε): see οὑτοσί, under οὗτος
τουτουμενί (masc.gen., w.pcl. μέν): see οὑτοσί, under οὗτος
τούτους, τούτων, τούτοις (masc.acc.pl., gen.pl., masc.neut.dat.pl.): see οὗτος
τόφρα *ep.demonstr.adv.* [reltd. ὄφρα] **1 up to or during that time**; (correlatv.w. ὄφρα *as long as, until*) **all that time** or **meanwhile** Hom. hHom. Emp. Call.; (correlatv.w. ἕως, ἧος, πρίν *while, until*) Hom. AR.; (correlatv.w. ὅτε *when*) **then** AR.
2 (without correlatv.) **all that time** or **meanwhile** Hom. Semon. Call. AR.
3 (app. as relatv.adv., W.OPT.) **while** AR.
4 (w. contrastv. pcls.) τόφρα μέν *while* (answered by τόφρα δέ *for so long*) Call.
5 (as final conj., W.OPT.) **so that** AR.
τραγαλίζω *vb.* [τρώγω] **nibble, munch** —*scraps of food* Ar.
Τραγασαῖος ᾶ ον *adj.* [Τραγασαί] **from Tragasai** (a town in the Troad); (of swine, ref. to their appetite, w. play on τρώγω) **Tragasaian** Ar.; (of a person, ref. to the smell of his armpits, w. play on τράγος *goat*) Ar.
τραγεία ᾶς *f.* [τράγος] **goatskin** (as a garment or rug) Theoc.
τραγ-έλαφος ου *m.* [ἔλαφος] **goat-stag** (imaginary animal, represented in art, esp. oriental) Ar. Pl. Plu.
τραγήματα των *n.pl.* [τρώγω] **items of food which can be nibbled** (such as fruits, various raw or cooked delicacies, usu. as a dessert), **dainties, sweetmeats, nibbles** Ar. Pl. X. Men. Plu.
τραγηματίζω *vb.* nibble delicacies; (of bored spectators in the theatre) **eat sweets** Arist. ‖ MID. (of a diner, a pilferer fr. a fruit stall) **treat oneself to dessert** Thphr. Men.
τραγικός ή όν *adj.* [τράγος] **1 relating to the composition or performance of tragic drama**; (of a poet, poetry, play, language, or sim.) **tragic** Ar. Pl. +; (of a chorus) Hdt. D. Arist. Plu.; (of a stage, mask, costume, or sim.) Pl. X. Plu.; (of an actor, character in a play) Call.*epigr.* Plu.; (of a speech, curse) **from tragedy** Men. Plu.; (of the act of being a spectator) **at tragedies** Pl. ‖ FEM.SB. **tragedy** Pl. Arist. ‖ MASC.PL.SB. **tragic poets** Pl. Arist. Plu.
2 productive of the true essence of tragedy (i.e. of pity and fear); (of a play, an action in a play) **tragic** Arist.; (superl., of Euripides) Arist.
3 conveying the same effects or having the same associations as tragic drama; (of a person, ref. to his appearance) **like a tragic hero** Ar.; (of a tyrant) **straight out of tragedy** (because he suffered a sudden reversal of fortune) Plu.; (of a ranting accuser) **histrionic** D.; (of a style of speech) **high-flown** Pl. Arist.; (of behaviour, circumstances) **theatrical, spectacular** Plb. Plu.; (of a person's temperament) **imperious** Plu.; (of a spectacle, events, sufferings) **distressing, pathetic** Plb. Plu.; (of circumstances) **as if belonging to drama** (rather than real life) Plu.
4 (of falsehood) **tragical** (w. allusion both to the fictional nature of tragic drama and to the double nature of the goatlike Pan) Pl.
5 belonging to a goat; (of horns on a helmet) **of a goat** Plu.
—τραγικῶς *adv.* | compar. τραγικώτερον | **theatrically, in the high style, with poetic exaggeration** —*ref. to speaking* Pl. Men. Plu.; **spectacularly** —*ref. to living in a house at a commanding height* Plu.
τραγίσκος ου *m.* [dimin.] **young he-goat** Carm.Pop. Theoc.
τραγο-ειδής ές *adj.* [εἶδος[1]] (of Pan) **goat-like** Pl.
τραγο-κτόνος ον *adj.* [κτείνω] (of bloodshed) **from the killing of goats** (by Bacchants) E.
τραγο-μάσχαλος ον *adj.* [μασχάλη] (of persons, likened to mythical monsters) **with armpits that smell like goats** Ar.
τράγον (dial.imperatv.): see τρώγω
τράγος ου *m.* [τρώγω] app., animal which nibbles; (specif.) **he-goat** (in pl. sts. gener. *goats*) Od. Alc. Pi.*fr.* Hdt. S.*Ichn.* E.*Cyc.* +
τραγο-σκελής ές *adj.* [σκέλος] (of Pan) **goat-legged** Hdt.
τραγῳδέω *contr.vb.* [τραγῳδός] **1** prob. **be a tragic actor** Ar. Plu.; **be a tragic poet** Call.
2 make (W.ACC. women) **the subject of tragedies** Ar. ‖ PASS. (of persons or things) **be celebrated in tragedy** Isoc. Plu.
3 (fig.) **wax histrionic** Plu. —W.ACC. *about alleged crimes* D. Plb.; **declaim melodramatically** —*speeches (of indignation)* D. Thphr.; **enact** (a pretended event) in a tragic manner, **stage** —*a calamity* Men.; **dress up, vamp up** —*a word (by changing its original form)* Pl. ‖ PASS. (of a word) **be vamped up** Pl.
τραγῳδία ᾶς *f.* **1 tragic drama, tragedy** (ref. either to a single play or to the genre) Ar. Att.orats. Pl. X. Arist. +; (also as including the poetry of Homer) Pl.
2 speech or action that outdoes reality and stirs emotion; **melodramatic language** or **behaviour** (by an individual) Hyp. Men.; **high drama** (ref. to circumstances which encourage fear of the gods) Plb.; **theatrical display, play-acting** (ref. to a person's behaviour, a country's public image) Plu.
τραγῳδικός ή όν *adj.* of or relating to tragic drama; (of the art) **of tragedy** Ar.; (of a throne in the underworld, awarded to the best dramatist) Ar.; (of a look, pain) **straight out of tragedy** Ar.
τραγῳδιο-γράφος ου *m.* [γράφω] **writer of tragedies** Plb.
τραγῳδο-διδάσκαλος ου *m.* [τραγῳδός] **teacher or trainer of the tragic chorus** (usu. the poet himself), **tragic dramatist** Ar. Isoc. Arist.
τραγῳδο-ποιός οῦ *m.* [ποιέω] **tragic poet** Ar. Pl.; (incl. Homer) Pl.
τραγ-ῳδός οῦ *m.* [τράγος, ἀοιδή] **1 goat-singer** (orig., prob. singer at a goat-sacrifice or for a goat-prize, or for a goat awarded as prize and then sacrificed); **tragic performer** (ref. to a member of the chorus) Ar.; **actor** Plu. ‖ PL. **tragic performers** (actors, chorus-members, or both) Ar. X. D. Men. Call. Plu.

2 app. **tragic poet** Arist.
3 ‖ COLLECTV.PL. (meton., ref. to the plays themselves) tragedies Ar. Pl. Arist. Men. Plu.; (ref. to the occasion) tragic performances Att.orats. Thphr. Plu.
—**τραγῳδός** όν *adj.* (of a Muse, or perh. of poetry) **tragic** Call.
τράμις *f.* | only acc. τράμιν | anus or perineum, **arse** or **crotch** Ar.
τρᾱνής ές *adj.* (of information) **clear, exact, precise** S.
—**τρᾱνῶς** *adv.* **clearly** —*ref. to knowing or explaining* A. E. Plb. Plu.
τρᾱνώματα των *n.pl.* [τετραίνω] piercings, **pores** (of the tongue) Emp.
τρά-πεζα ης, dial. **τράπεσδα** ᾱς (Alcm.) *f.* [app. τέσσαρες, πούς] **1** object which has four legs, **table** (esp. for serving food) Hom. +
2 provision of food (for guests), **table, board, hospitality** Od. Archil. A. Pi. E. X. +; (specif.) **board** (opp. bed) Hdt. Plu.
3 food set on the table, **meal, food** Pi. Hdt. S. E. Thphr. Theoc.; δεύτεραι τράπεζαι *second course* Plb.
4 style of meal (assoc.w. a specific country or city), **cuisine** Th. Pl.
5 table in a sanctuary (on which offerings are placed), **offertory table** Ar. Din. Plb.
6 table of a banker, **bank** Att.orats. Pl. Thphr. Plu.; **table** (w.GEN. of a money-changer) NT.
7 shop **counter** or **stall** (of a butcher) Thphr.
8 perh. **table** or **plinth** (of bronze, for a statue in a temple) D.(oracle)
τραπεζεύς ῆος *ep.masc.adj.* (of dogs) **fed at table** Hom.
τραπέζιον ου *n.* [dimin. τράπεζα] **small table** Plu.
τραπεζῑτεύω *vb.* [τραπεζίτης] **be a banker** D.
τραπεζίτης ου *m.* [τράπεζα] **money-changer, banker** Att.orats. Plb. NT. Plu.
τραπεζῑτικός ή όν *adj.* (of a speech, lawsuit) **concerning a banker** Isoc.(title) Arist.; (of accounts) **of a banker** Hyp. D.
τραπεζο-κόμος ου *m.* [κομίζω] **table-attendant, waiter** Plu.
τραπεζο-ποιός οῦ *m.* [ποιέω] one who prepares a table (but not the food) and serves a meal, **waiter** Men.
τραπείομεν (ep.1pl.aor.2 pass.subj.): see τέρπω
τράπεσδα *dial.f.*: see τράπεζα
τραπέσθαι (aor.2 mid.inf.): see τρέπω
τραπέω *ep.contr.vb.* | 3pl. τραπέουσι, subj. τραπέωσι | 3pl.impf. ἐτράπεον | **tread, trample** —*grapes* Od.; (intr.) **tread grapes** Hes.
τραπῆναι (aor.2 pass.inf.), **τραπήσομαι** (fut.pass.): see τρέπω
τράπομαι *Ion.pass.vb.*: see τρέπω
τράπον (ep.aor.2), **τραπόμην** (ep.aor.2 mid.), **τραποῦ** (ep.aor.2 mid.imperatv.): see τρέπω
τράπω *Ion.vb.*: see τρέπω
τρασιά ᾶς *f.* [reltd. ταρσός] fig-drying rack; (meton., collectv.sg.) **drying figs** Ar.
τραυλίζω *vb.* [τραυλός] | aor. ἐτραύλισα | (of children) **lisp** or **stammer** Ar.; (of Alkibiades) lisp (by mispronouncing ρ as λ) Ar.; (act. and mid.) Plu.(quot.com.)
τραυλός ή όν *adj.* (of a child) **lisping** or **stammering** Hdt.
τραυλότης ητος *f.* **lisp** Plu.
τραῦμα, dial. **τρῶμα**, ατος *n.* [τιτρώσκω] —also **τρώμᾱ** ᾱς (Pi.) *dial.f.* **1 wound** (usu. sustained in battle) A. Pi. Hdt. E. Th. +; (fr. a lightning-bolt) AR.; (fr. a bee-sting, Eros) Call.*epigr.* Theoc.
2 (leg.) **wounding, bodily harm** Att.orats. Pl. Arist.
3 blow, damage (to ships) Hdt. Plb.
4 (fig.) **disaster** (suffered by an army) Hdt.
τραυματίας ου, Ion. **τρωματίης** εω *m.* **wounded man** (usu.pl., ref. to soldiers) Hdt. Th. Arist. Thphr. Plb. Plu.
τραυματίζω, Ion. **τρωματίζω** *vb.* | aor. ἐτραυμάτισα | **wound** —*someone* Hdt. E. Th. Plb. NT. Plu. ‖ PASS. (of persons, animals) be wounded A. Hdt. Th. X. Plb. +
τράφε (dial.3sg.impf.), **τραφέμεν** (ep.aor.2 inf.): see τρέφω
τραφερός ά (Ion. ή) όν *adj.* [τρέφω] **1** (of a path) solid, **over dry land** AR. ‖ FEM.SB. **dry land** (opp. ὑγρή *sea*) Hom. hHom. AR. Theoc.
2 (of fish) app. **well fed, fat** Theoc.
τράφην (ep.aor.2 pass.), **τράφον** (ep.aor.2): see τρέφω
τράφω *dial.vb.*: see τρέφω
τραχέως *adv.*: see under τραχύς
τραχήλια ων *n.pl.* [dimin. τράχηλος] scraps of animal meat (app. fr. the neck); (gener.) **scrag-ends** (thrown to a dog) Ar.
τραχηλίζω *vb.* take (someone) by the neck; (ref. to a move in wrestling) **put a neck-lock on** —*a person* Plu. —*an ox* Thphr.
τράχηλος ου *m.* | also neut.nom.acc.pl. τράχηλα (Call.) |
1 neck (of a person, animal, bird) Hippon. Hdt. Ar. Pl. X. +; (put in a noose) D. Theoc. Plu.; (fig., as trampled on by a victor) Iamb.adesp.; (of a nation, persons, as bearing the yoke of servitude) NT. Plu.
2 (gener., ref. to the upper part of the body when being embraced) **neck** NT.
3 throat (cut by a weapon) E. Plu.
4 (gener.) **head** (of a person or animal, as cut off) Hdt. E. Aeschin. Plu.; (as fallen on fr. a height, w.connot. of breaking the neck) E.
5 neck (of an animal, as a joint of meat) Plu.
Τρᾱχίς, Ion. **Τρηχίς**, ῖνος *f.* **Trakhis** (city and region in S. Thessaly) Il. Hes. Hdt. S. E. +
—**Τρᾱχίνιος** ᾱ ον (also ος ον Theoc.), Ion. **Τρηχίνιος** η ον *adj.* from or belonging to Trakhis; (of a person) **Trakhinian** Hdt. Th.; (of the region, a mountain range, colony, Herakles' funeral pyre) Hdt. S. X. Theoc. ‖ FEM.SG.SB. region of Trakhis Hdt. Th. ‖ MASC.PL.SB. inhabitants of Trakhis Hdt. S. Th. ‖ FEM.PL.SB. Women of Trakhis S.(title)
τραχύνω, Ion. **τρηχύνω** *vb.* [τραχύς] | PASS.: aor. ἐτραχύνθην | pf.inf. τετραχύνθαι | **1** make rough or harsh; (of physical phenomena) **have an astringent effect on, roughen** —*parts of the body* Pl.; (of wind) **make rough** —*the sea* AR.; (intr., of a river) **be rough** Plu.(dub.) ‖ PASS. (of parts of the tongue) be roughened Pl.; (of a river) be turbulent Pl. Plu.
2 ‖ PASS. (of a speaker) use harsh tones or rasp —W.DAT. in his speech Plu.
3 (of a person) **be harsh** A.(dub.) [or perh. (of a populace) *call (someone) harsh*] ‖ PASS. (fig., of persons) become exasperated Pl. Is. Plb. Plu.
τραχύς εῖα ύ (also ύς ύ Theoc.), Ion. **τρηχύς** έα ύ *adj.* [perh. reltd. θράσσω] **1** rough in texture or to the touch; (of substances or surfaces) **rough** (opp. smooth) Sol. Pl. X. Arist.
2 (of terrain) **rough, rugged** Hom. +; (fig., of the path to a goal) Hes. Pl. NT.; (of falsehood, envisaged as a stone to trip over) Pi.*fr.*
3 (of a stone, rock, cliff, or sim.) **rough, jagged** Il. Archil. Pi. Hdt. AR. +; (of a horse's bit) X.; (of a staff) **knotted** Theoc.; (of a cloak) **coarse** Plu.
4 (of dust-filled air) **rough, harsh** (to the breather) Plu.
5 (of Pan) bristling with hair, **shaggy** Pl.; (of a hedgehog) **spiky** Ar.

τραχύτης

6 (of natural phenomena) exerting rough strength; (of a wave, its surge, a sea) **rough** A. AR. Plb. Plu.; (of storm-winds, a river) **powerful, raging** AR. Plu.; (fig., of war, envisaged as a blizzard) Pi.

7 (of persons, warriors, their weapons) **grim, violent, savage** Tyrt. A. Pi. B. Ar. D. +; (of a wolf) Theoc.*epigr.*; (of fighting) Hes.; (of a disease, passion) Pl. AR.; (wkr.sens., of a colt) **wild** Plu.

8 (of a judge, mind, words) **harsh, stern, severe** Sol. A. Plu.; (of laws, government, tyranny) Pl. Arist.; (of anger) B. E.; (of a labour of Herakles) Call. ‖ NEUT.SB. harshness (of a law) Pl.

9 harsh to the ear; (of a sound, voice) **harsh, rasping** Pl. Plu.; (of a person, W.DAT. in his voice) X.; (fig., of a poet, in neg.phr.) perh. **out of tune** (i.e. unfit, W.INF. to praise someone appropriately) Pi.

10 (of circumstances) **harsh, unfavourable** Pi. Isoc.; (of a red blotch on the face) **violent, unsightly** Plu.

—**τρηχύ** Ion.neut.adv. **roughly** —*ref. to making a threat* Theoc.

—**τραχέως**, Ion. **τρηχέως** adv. | compar. τρᾱχύτερον, also τρᾱχυτέρως (Pl.) | **1 roughly, harshly** —*ref. to handling or dealing w. someone, speaking, ruling* Hdt. Isoc. Plu.; **fiercely, savagely** —*ref. to barking* Plu.

2 (w. ἔχειν) **be exasperated** (w. someone or at sthg.) Pl. D. Plu.; (w. ἔχειν, διακεῖσθαι) **be harshly disposed** (towards someone or sthg.) Isoc.; (w. φέρειν) **take** (sthg.) **badly** Plu.

τρᾱχύτης ητος, Att. **τρᾱχυτής** ῆτος f. **1 roughness** (opp. smoothness) Pl. Arist.

2 **ruggedness** (of terrain) X. Plb. Plu. ‖ PL. rugged regions Plu.

3 **roughness, sharpness** (of a horse's bit) X.; (of ice) Plu.

4 **physical power, violence** (of a military attack) Plu.; (of a river) Plu.

5 **roughness, harshness** (of a person's manner, speech, anger, or sim.) A. Isoc. Plu.

6 **sharp peal** (W.GEN. of thunder) Plu.

τράχω dial.vb.: see τρέχω

τρεῖς τρία pl.num.adj. and sb. | masc.fem.acc.pl. τρεῖς, Boeot. τρίς | gen. τριῶν | dat. τρισί, dial.masc. τριοῖσι (Hippon.) | **three** Hom. +

—**τρεισ-καί-δεκα** (or **τρῐσκαίδεκα**) τριακαίδεκα num.adj. —or **τρεῖς καὶ δέκα** τρία καὶ δέκα num.adj. | gen. τριῶν καὶ δέκα | **thirteen** Hom. +

—**τρῐσκαιδεκάπᾱχυς** υ dial.adj. [πῆχυς] (hyperbol., of a big man) **thirteen cubits tall** Theoc.

—**τρῐσκαιδεκαστάσιος** ον adj. [ἵστημι] (of gold, weighed against silver) **worth thirteen times as much** Hdt.

—**τρεισκαιδέκατος** (or **τρῐσ-**) η ον num.adj. **thirteenth** Hom. Plu. ‖ FEM.SB. thirteenth day Od. Hes.

—**τρῐσκαιδεκέτης** (or **τρῐσκαιδεκαέτης**) ες adj. [ἔτος] (of a child) **thirteen years old** Lys. Is.

—**τρῐσκαιδεκήρης** ου f. [ἐρέσσω] **thirteen-rowed ship** (app. w. three banks of oars, and rowers seated in groups of thirteen, so that one level of oars had five men per oar and two levels had four) Plu.

τρέμω vb. | only pres. and impf. | **1** (of mountains or sim.) **tremble, shake, quiver** (fr. the footsteps of gods, or in fear at their actions) Il. Call. AR.; (of the robe of a person weeping) Il.; (of a person suffering a fit) —W.ACC. *in one's hands, legs* E.; (of persons, their limbs, fr. age and infirmity) E. Arist. AR.; (of hounds, fr. excitement) X.; **shiver** (fr. a soaking in cold water) Ar. Men.

2 (of persons, their limbs) **tremble with fear** Hom. E. Ar. D. Men. Theoc. +; **be afraid of, fear** —*someone* Plu.; (of mice) —*a cat* Call.

3 (gener.) **tremble in anticipation of some event**; **be afraid of, fear, dread** —*the future, divine punishment, censure, an undertaking* S. E. Ar. Pl. —W.ACC.PERS. and μή + SUBJ. or OPT. *someone, in case he shd. do sthg. or one shd. do sthg. to him* S. E.; **be afraid** —W.INF. *to do sthg.* A. S. —W.PREP.PHR. *for sthg.* (i.e. for its possible loss) Antipho Pl.

τρέπω, Ion. **τράπω** vb. | iteratv.impf. τρέπεσκον | fut. τρέψω | aor.1 ἔτρεψα, ep. τρέψα | aor.2 ἔτραπον, ep. τράπον | pf. τέτροφα ‖ MID.: aor.1 (tr. and intr.) ἐτρεψάμην | aor.2 (intr.) ἐτραπόμην, ep. τραπόμην, inf. τραπέσθαι, imperatv. τραποῦ ‖ PASS.: Ion.pres. τράπομαι | fut. τραπήσομαι | aor.1 ἐτρέφθην, Ion.inf. τραφθῆναι | aor.2 ἐτράπην, inf. τραπῆναι | pf. τέτραμμαι, ep.3pl. τετράφαται, ep.3sg.imperatv. τετράφθω | ep.plpf.3sg. τέτραπτο, 3pl. τετράφατο ‖ neut.impers.vbl.adj. τρεπτέον |

1 cause to turn (in some direction); **turn, direct** —*someone or sthg.* (W.PREP.PHR. or ADV. *towards sthg. or somewhere*, e.g. one's eyes towards a city, sheep to a mountain, a weapon against enemies) Hom. +

2 ‖ PF.PASS. (of a person, place) **be turned, face** —W.PREP.PHR. *in some direction* Hom. Hes. Hdt. Th. AR. Theoc. +

3 turn (someone or sthg.) away (fr. their course); **turn, turn away, divert** —*persons, their attention, a weapon, horses, rivers* (W.PREP.PHR. or ADV. *in some direction*) Hom. —*a person* (fr. a course of action) Il. ‖ PASS. (of a weapon) be turned aside Il.

4 ‖ MID.PASS. (of a person) **turn round, turn back** Il.; (of the sun, on reaching the solstice) Pl. X.; (of troops) **retreat** Plb.

5 ‖ MID.PASS. (of persons) **turn one's steps, turn, move** —W.PREP.PHR. or ADV. *to some place, in some direction* Hom. +

6 ‖ MID.PASS. (esp. in deliberative qs.) **turn for help, turn** A. E. Ar. Att.orats. Pl. +

7 ‖ MID.PASS. turn upon, **follow** —W.INTERN.ACC. *a path* (fig.ref. to a course of action) Hdt. E. Ar. Pl.

8 turn (someone or sthg.) towards a course of action, state or feeling; **turn, direct** —*persons, their heart, one's heart, speech* (W.PREP.PHR. or ADV. *to work, insolence, disaster, joy, or sim.*) Hom. +; (of gold, an impulse) **prompt** —W.ACC. + INF. *someone to do sthg.* Pi. ‖ MID.PASS. (of persons, their minds) **be turned** or **turn** —W.PREP.PHR. *to dancing, thought, plunder, drink, or sim.* Hom. + —W.INF. *to doing sthg.* Th.

9 direct (an emotion or action) upon someone; **turn, direct** —*blame, anger, or sim.* (W.PREP.PHR. *onto or against someone*) Att.orats.; (of gods, in an imprecation) **direct, visit** —*retribution* (W.PREP.PHR. *on someone's head*) D. ‖ MID.PASS. (usu. in imprecations; of harm, trouble, debts) be visited, **fall** (on someone's head) Hdt. Ar.

10 direct (a product or resource) to some purpose; **use** —*an item* (W.ADV. or PREP.PHR. *for sthg.*) Hdt. Ar.

11 transform (a state of affairs); **turn** —*a situation* (W.PREP.PHR. *into a joke*) Hdt. Ar. —*someone's mistakes* (*to the good*) Ar. ‖ MID.PASS. (of flesh) **change colour** Hom. Ar.; (of weather) **change** Plu.; (of clouds) —W.PREP.PHR. *into mist* Plu. ‖ PF.MID.PASS. (of spring) have turned (to summer) Theoc.

12 alter, change —*someone's mind or opinion* Il. Archil. X. ‖ MID.PASS. (of a mind) **change** or **be changed** Hom.; (of a person) **change one's mind** or **attitude** Hdt. Th.; **change** —W.ACC. *in one's opinions* Th.; **change in behaviour** —W.PREP.PHR. *for the better* Ar.

13 (milit., act. and mid.) **turn** —*enemy soldiers* (W.PREP.PHR. *to flight*) E. X. Plb.; **put to flight, rout** —*troops or sim.* Il. Tyrt.

Pi. Hdt. Th. Ar. +; (fig.) **vanquish** —*perils on the sea* AR. ‖ MID.PASS. **turn** —W.PREP.PHR. *to flight* Hdt. Th. X. Plb. Plu.; **turn** or **be put to flight** A. Hdt. Th. X. Plb. Plu.

τρέφω, dial. **τράφω** *vb.* | ep.inf. τρεφέμεν, dial. τράφειν, also τράφεν | dial.3sg.impf. ἔτραφε, also τράφε | fut. θρέψω | aor.1 ἔθρεψα, ep. θρέψα | ep.aor.2 (w.pass.sens.) ἔτραφον, τράφον, inf. τραφέμεν | pf. τέτροφα ‖ PASS.: fut. θρέψομαι, also τραφήσομαι | aor.1 ἐθρέφθην, ep. θρέφθην | aor.2 ἐτράφην, ep. τράφην, ep.3pl. ἔτραφεν, τράφεν (dub., v.l. ἔτραφον, τράφον) | pf. τέθραμμαι, inf. τεθράφθαι ‖ neut.impers.vbl.adj. θρεπτέον |

1 thicken or solidify (a liquid); **curdle** —*milk* Od.; make by curdling milk, **set** —*cheese* Theoc. ‖ PF.ACT. (of brine) be congealed or caked (on someone's body) Od.

2 (sts.mid.) help (someone) to grow; (of a parent or sim.) **bring up, rear, raise** —*a child* Hom. +; (fig., of a country, city, region) Pi. Trag. Th. +; (fig., of a person) —*virtue* (*which one has fathered*) Pl.; (of a mother) **nurture** —*a child in the womb* A. ‖ PASS. (of a child in the womb) be nurtured A.

3 ‖ PASS. (of children, persons in general) be brought up or grow up (oft. W.ADV. or PREP.PHR. in some way, under particular circumstances) Hom. +; (w. focus on the parent, whose qualities a child inherits) be the child —W.GEN. or PREP.PHR. *of a specific parent* S.; (of a slave) be bred or brought up (in a house) S. Pl.

4 bring up animals; **bring up, rear, keep** —*cattle, horses, dogs, birds, fish* Hom. A. Hdt. E. Ar. Pl. + —*a lion cub* (*as an example of a dangerous activity*) A. Ar. ‖ PASS. (of a horse) be reared Plu.

5 (of earth, sea, parts of the natural world) **breed, nourish, produce** (esp. in great abundance) —*persons, wild creatures, medicines, dyes, spices* Hom. Hes. Alcm. A. Hdt. E. +

6 foster growth (in sthg.); **grow** —*one's hair* (*to be an offering to a god*) Il. E.; **grow long** —*one's beard, hair* Hdt. Ar. Plu.; **tend** —*a plant* Il. —*a person* (*compared to a plant*) Hom. Theoc.; (of the sun) **foster, nurture** —*life on earth* A.; (of food and drink) **engender** —*fat* (W.DAT. *in swine*) Od.

7 (fig., of a prophet) **nourish, foster** —*truth* S.; (of a person, esp. poet) —*an emotion* (*in others*) Pl.; (of the Muses) —*a poet's weaponry* (*i.e. his poetry*), *someone's fame, his excellence* Pi. B.; (of a person's tongue, ref. to mere words) **feed, fuel** —*his passionate spirit* S.; (of education, opp. nature) **develop** —*a person* Pi.

8 provide (someone, esp. a dependent) with food and shelter; (of a son) **maintain, support** —*a parent* Hdt. Att.orats. Pl. Thphr. Plu.; (of a husband, his labour) —*a wife* A. E.; (of a relative or friend) —*a person, household* Att.orats.; (of a populace, persons in general) —*an individual* Ar. Att.orats. Pl. —*a populace* Plu.; (of persons) **maintain, keep** (in one's household) —*slaves, a tutor for one's son* X. Aeschin. —*bodyguards* Plu.; (fig., of a juror) **hoard, maintain** (as if part of the household) —*a beach of voting-pebbles* (*i.e. a great supply, for future use*) Ar.

9 (gener., of a demigoddess) **care for, tend** —*a mortal* Od.; (fig., of hope) **sustain** —*someone* Semon.; (of troubles) **attend** —*mortals* E. ‖ PASS. (fig., of a blind man) be cared for or sustained —W.PREP.PHR. *by darkness* S.

10 (of foodstuffs) **provide nourishment** Hdt.; (of land, an estate) **feed, maintain** —*a populace, an individual* Thgn. Hdt. Th. Isoc. Pl. Men. Plu.; (of the sea) —*a fisherman* Pi. ‖ PASS. (of persons, animals, souls) be nourished or fed (oft. W.DAT. on sthg.) E. Pl. X. Plu.; (fig., of a craving) be fed or fostered A.

11 (of a state, person) **maintain, provision, supply** —*an army, fleet, persons serving in them* Th. Ar. Isoc. X. D. Plb. Plu.

12 (gener., of a person) **maintain** —*a dignified name* S.; **keep** —*one's tongue* (W.PREDIC.ADJ. *quiet*) S.; **have, endure** —*sickness, fear, ruin, menial tasks* S.; (phr.) ἐν ἐλπίσιν τρέφειν **have hopes** —W.FUT.INF. *of doing sthg.* S. ‖ PF. (of a city) hold —*sthg.* (W.PREDIC.ADJ. *disliked, i.e. in dislike*) S.

τρέχω, dial. **τράχω** *vb.* | fut. (only in cpds.) θρέξομαι | aor. (usu. in cpds.) ἔθρεξα | iterat.v.aor. θρέξασκον ‖ The fut., aor. and pf. are supplied by δραμεῖν. |

1 (of a drill) **rotate, spin** Od.; (of a line of dancers, whose movement is compared to a potter's wheel) **wheel** or **circle round** Il.; (gener., of dancers) move quickly, **skip** Il.

2 (of persons) proceed quickly on foot, **run** A. E. Ar. Pl. +; (of animals, birds) Il. Pi.*fr.* E.*Cyc.* Ar. X. Theoc.; (of charioteers, meton. for their horses) Call.; (of persons envisaged as hounds or horses) A. Ar.; (of personif. Oath) —W.PREP.PHR. *along w. crooked judgements* (*i.e. keep pace w. them, so that they are redressed*) Hes.

3 (specif., of athletes) run in a race, **run** Pi. Ar. X. Thphr.; (fig., of persons) —W.PREP.PHR. *for one's life* (*i.e. be in a life-or-death situation*) Hdt. —W.INTERN.ACC. *the last available route* (*i.e. try the last possible course of action*) Plb.

4 (gener.) **rush, be quick, hurry** (oft. to do someone's bidding) Ar. X. Men.

5 (of sailors) sail quickly, **run** (over the sea, or w. the wind) Scol. Plb.

6 (fig., of a poetic narrative) **run on, proceed** Pi.; (of speech) E.

τρέω contr.*vb.* [perh.reltd. τρέμω] | ep.impf. τρέον, 3du. τρεέτην | aor. ἔτρεσα, ep. τρέσσα | **1** (of persons, animals) **shrink back** (in fear) Hom. Hes. Tyrt.; (of a lion) —W.ACC. *before burning torches* Il.

2 be struck with fear, **be afraid** Trag. Pl. AR. Theoc. —W.ACC. *of someone or sthg.* Pi.*fr.* B. Trag. X. Plu. —W.GEN. *because of sthg.* Hes. —W. μή + SUBJ. or ὅπως + FUT.INDIC. *that sthg. may happen* A. E. —W.INF. *to do sthg.* E.

3 ‖ MASC.AOR.PTCPL.SB. (at Sparta) runaway or coward Hdt. Plu.

τρῆμα ατος *n.* [τετραίνω] **1** that which is created by drilling or piercing, **aperture, hole** (for letting out water) Emp. Ar. Pl.; (in a wooden or metal object) Plb.

2 arrow-slit, **loophole** (in a wall) Plb. Plu.

3 eye (W.GEN. of a needle) NT.

4 orifice, **hole** (ref. to a vagina) Ar.

τρήρων ωνος *m.f.* [perh. τρέω] **1** app. **pigeon** (always appos.w. πέλεια or πελειάς, perh. *dove, a species of pigeon*) Hom. hHom. Ar. AR. [or perh.adj., as epith. of doves or pigeons, *timorous, tremulous, shy*]

2 (appos.w. κέπφος, *a kind of sea-bird*, a byword for imbecility) **birdbrain, stupid coot** (ref. to a person) Ar.

τρῆσις εως *f.* [τετραίνω] process of perforating, **perforation, piercing** Pl.

τρητός ή όν *adj.* perforated with a hole or holes; (of a stone) **perforated, pierced** Od.; (of ear-lobes) hHom.; (of a bedframe, prob. w. holes for cords to support the bedding) Hom.; (of garments, w. holes for stitching) Pl.; (of the labour of bees, ref. to a honeycomb) Pi.; (of furnaces) AR.; (of panpipe reeds) Theoc.*epigr.*

Τρηχίνιος *Ion.adj.*, **Τρηχίς** *Ion.f.*: see Τραχίς

τρηχύνω *Ion.vb.*, **τρηχύς** *Ion.adj.*: see τραχύνω, τραχύς

τρία *neut.pl.num.adj. and sb.*: see τρεῖς

τρίαινα ης (dial. ας) *f.* [τρεῖς] three-pronged fish-spear, **trident** (of Poseidon) Hom. A. E. Ar. Lyr.adesp. Plu.; (of a fisherman) Archil.; (of a politician, as symbolising Athenian naval power) Ar.

τριαινόω *contr.vb.* use a trident (on sthg.); (gener.) **prise up** —*a stone seat* (W.DAT. *w. crowbars*) E.; **turn up** —*earth* (W.DAT. *w. a mattock*) Ar.

τριακαιδεκ-έτης ες *adj.* [τρεισκαίδεκα, ἔτος] (of a girl) **thirteen years old** Pl.

τριᾰκάς, Ion. **τριηκάς,** άδος *f.* [τρεῖς] **1** group of thirty; thirty-strong squadron (W.GEN. of ships) A.; (at Sparta) perh. **company of thirty men** Hdt. **2 thirtieth day of the month** Hes. Plu.

τριᾱκονθ-άμματος ον *adj.* [τρίᾱκοντα, ἅμμα] (of hunting nets) **with thirty knots** (app. as an indication of height) X.

τριᾱκονθ-ήμερος, Ion. **τριηκοντήμερος,** ον *adj.* [ἡμέρα] (of a month) **lasting thirty days** Hdt.; (of a truce) Plb. Plu.

—**τριακονθήμερον** *neut.adv.* **for thirty days** Plb.

τριάκοντα, Ion. **τριήκοντα** *indecl.num.adj.* | also Ion.gen. τριηκόντων (Hes. Call.) | **1 thirty** Hom. + **2** ‖ MASC.PL.SB. **the Thirty** (commonly called the Thirty Tyrants, a group of oligarchs imposed on Athens by the Spartans in 404 BC after the Peloponnesian war) Att.orats. Pl. X. Arist. Plu.

τριᾱκονταέτης *adj.,* **τριᾱκονταέτις** *fem.adj.*: see τριᾱκοντούτης

τριᾱκοντά-ζυγος ον *adj.* [ζυγόν] (of the Argo) **with thirty benches of rowers** Theoc.

τριᾱκοντάκις *num.adv.* **thirty times** Plu.

τριᾱκοντα-μναῖος ον *adj.* [μνᾶ] (of stones) **weighing thirty minae** Plb.

τριᾱκονταρχίᾱ ᾱς *f.* [ἀρχή] **rule exercised by thirty people, government of thirty** X.

τριᾱκόντ-ερος (later **-ορος**), Ion. **τριηκόντερος,** ου *f.* [ἐρέσσω] **thirty-oared ship, triaconter** (w. fifteen rowers' seats on each side of the hull) Hdt. Th. X. D. Plu.

—**τριᾱκοντόριον** ου *n.* [dimin.] **triaconter** (ref. to a sacred ship sent to Delos) Arist.

τριᾱκοντούτης (or **τριᾱκονταέτης**) ες *adj.* —also **τριᾱκοντοῦτις** (or **τριᾱκονταέτις**), Ion. **τριηκοντοέτις,** ιδος *fem.adj.* [ἔτος] **1** (of a person) **thirty years old** Pl. Is. **2** (of a truce) **lasting thirty years** Hdt. Th. Ar. X.; (of sexual abstinence) Plu.

τριᾱκοντ-ώρυγος ον *adj.* [ὄργυια] (of hunting nets) **measuring thirty fathoms** (in length) X.

τριᾱκόσιοι, Ion. **τριηκόσιοι,** αι α *pl.num.adj.* **1 three hundred** Hom. + **2** ‖ MASC.PL.SB. (w.art.) **the Three Hundred** (ref. to the wealthiest Athenian citizens, who were liable to finance certain state duties, such as the equipping of triremes) Att.orats.; (ref. to a judicial body in Megara) D.

τριᾱκοστός, Ion. **τριηκοστός,** ή (dial. ᾱ́) όν *num.adj.* **1 thirtieth** Pi. Hdt. Th. X. D. + **2** ‖ FEM.SB. (w. μοῖρα understd.) **duty of one thirtieth** (i.e. of three and a third percent) D.

τριακτήρ ῆρος *m.* [τριάζω *perform a triple throw*] **wrestler who gains victory by throwing an opponent three times, champion wrestler, overthrower** (ref. to Zeus as supplanter of Kronos) A.

τρι-άρμενος ον *adj.* [ἄρμενα, under ἀραρίσκω] (of a ship) **with three sails, masts** or **decks** Plu.

τριάς άδος *f.* **1** the number three, **three** Pl. Arist. Plu. **2 set of three, trio** Theoc.

Τριβαλλοί ῶν *m.pl.* **Triballians** (a Thracian tribe w. a reputation for savagery) Th. Ar. Isoc. D. Plu.; (name adopted by a gang of aristocratic Athenian hooligans) D. ‖ SG. **Triballian man** Ar.

—**Τριβαλλικός** ή όν *adj.* (of a region) **belonging to the Triballians** Hdt.

τριβή ῆς, dial. **τριβά** ᾶς *f.* [τρίβω] **1 process of rubbing** or **wearing out;** (fig.) **wearing away, attrition, erosion** (W.GEN. of a person's life, his property) A. **2** (ref. to a baby) **cause of wearing away, waster** (W.GEN. of the life and soul of its nurse) A. **3 time spent in acquiring a skill, practice, experience** X. Plb. Plu.; **exercise** (of an acquired skill) Plu.; (pejor.) **result of mere practice, knack, routine** (opp. true skill) Pl. Plb. **4 spending of time; lapse** (W.GEN. of time) S.; **expenditure** (W.GEN. of time, on sthg.) Pl.; **use of one's time, occupation, activity** A.; **way of spending time, mode** (of life) Ar. **5** (sg. and pl.) **drawing out of time, delay** S. Ar. D. Plb. Plu.; **protraction** or **long duration** (of a war) Plb. Plu.

τριβολ-εκτράπελος ον *adj.* [τρίβολος] (pejor., of topics of disputation) **thorny-outlandish** Ar.

τρίβολος ου *m.* **1 thistle** Alc. NT. **2 thorn** or **burr** Ar.

τρίβος ου *m.f.* [τρίβω] | gender oft. indeterminate | **1 rubbing, wear** (of metal) A.; (fig.) **wearing out, attrition** (of persons) A. **2 trail created by the repeated passage of persons or animals, track, path** E. X. Theoc. NT. Plu.; (fig., ref. to the passage of armies) Hdt. **3 path, course** (followed by an inventor) hHom.; (W.GEN. of love) A.(dub.)

τρίβω *vb.* | ep.inf. τρῑβέμεναι | iteratv.impf. τρίβεσκον | fut. τρίψω | aor. ἔτρῑψα ‖ MID.: fut. τρίψομαι ‖ PASS.: fut. τρῑβήσομαι | aor.1 ἐτρίφθην | aor.2 ἐτρίβην | pf. τέτρῑμμαι, Ion.3pl. τετρίφαται | **1 subject** (sthg.) **to pressure and friction;** (of a person) **rub** —*one's leg, head, an itch* Pl. Aeschin. —*someone's penis, feet* Ar. Plu. —*a horse's coat* X.; **chafe** —*one's arse* (by sitting) Ar.; (of a strap) —*a dog's flanks* X.; **rub together, wring** —*one's hands* Men. ‖ PASS. (of a penis) **be rubbed** Ar.; (of stone) —W.DAT. *by a hand* Plu.; (of gold) —*on a touchstone* Thgn.; (of rollers) **be scraped** (by a hull sliding over them) AR. **2 cause** (one thing) **to press hard against** (another); **grind** —*a stake* (w. ἐν + DAT. *into the Cyclops' eye*) Od.; **rub** —*sthg.* (*against sthg. else, to create a spark*) Pl. ‖ PASS. (of timber in a forest) **be rubbed together** (by winds, so as to catch fire) Th. **3 smear** (a substance) **over** (sthg.) ‖ MID. **rub on oneself** —*unguents* Call.(dub., cj. ἐντρίβω); (fig.) **rub off** —*one's pollution* (W.DAT. *on someone*) A. **4 reduce** (a substance) **to small pieces by grinding; grind, pound** (in a mortar) —*herbs, medicine, poison* Hdt. Ar. Pl. Theoc. Plu. —*ink* (i.e. the substances fr. which it is made) D.; (fig.) —*cities* Ar.; (of oxen) **thresh** —*barley* (by trampling on it) Il. ‖ PASS. (of poison) **be pounded** Pl. Plu.; (of a fruit) **be crushed** Plb.; (of fishes) **be bruised** (fr. contact w. a river bank) Hdt. ‖ PF.PASS.PTCPL.ADJ. (of spices) **crushed** Hdt. **5 cause to decay** or **weaken by constant use; wear out** —*personal possessions* Hdt. —*one's feet* Theoc.; (of cattle) —*ploughshares* Theoc.; **wear down** —*someone's sceptre* (i.e. power) Ar. ‖ PF.PASS.PTCPL. (of the path to Hades) **well worn, well pounded** (w. play on sense 4 *pound poison*) Ar. **6 wear down** (persons, their strength) **by constant harrassment;** (of litigants) **grind down, wear down, wear away** —*one another* (W.DAT. *w. crooked judgements*) Hes.; (of a god) —*a family* (w. *murders*) A.; (of a commander) —*troops, their strength* Th. Plu. ‖ MID. (of a city, troops, a commander) **allow oneself to be worn down** Il. Th. Plu. ‖ PASS. (of persons, troops) **be worn down** Hdt. Arist. Plu. ‖ PF.PASS. (of a person, ref. to his appearance) **be ravaged** (by a life of warfare) Plu.

7 (of troops) **ravage** —*a region* E.

8 **use up time** (usu. w.connot. of waste or delay); **drag out, pass** —*one's life* (*in misery or toil*) S. E. Ar.; (without neg.connot.) AR.; **draw out, prolong** —*a war* Plb. Plu.; (app. intr.) **waste time** A.

9 **keep** (W.ACC. persons) **occupied** (so as to leave them no free time) Plu. ‖ MID. **engage** or **exercise oneself** —W.PREP.PHR. *in an activity* Thgn. ‖ PASS. (of a populace) be occupied —W.DAT. *w. war* Hdt.

τρίβων[1] ωνος *m.* [τρίβω] **short cloak** (worn esp. by the poor), **cloak, tunic** E.*satyr.fr.* Ar. Is. Thphr. Men. +; (worn by ascetics, such as Socrates) Pl.; (worn by Spartans) D. Plu.; (fig., ref. to a locust's wings) Ar.

—**τριβώνιον** ου *n.* [dimin.] **cloak** Lys. Ar. Men. Plu.

τρίβων[2] ωνος *masc.fem.adj.* (of a person) **familiar** (W.GEN. w. someone or sthg.) Hdt. E.*Cyc.* Ar.; **practised, skilled, experienced** (usu. W.GEN. or NEUT.ACC. in an activity) E. Ar.

—**τριβωνικῶς** *adv.* in a practised manner; (w. pun on τρίβων[1]) **cloakwisely** —*ref. to putting on a χλαῖνα* (*a superior cloak, in place of the τρίβων*) Ar.

τρί-γαμος ον *adj.* [τρεῖς, γάμος] (pejor., of a woman) **thrice-wed** Stesich. Theoc.

τρι-γέρων οντος *masc.fem.adj.* (of a saying) triply old, **of immemorial age** A.

τρί-γληνος ον *adj.* [γλήνη; cf. γλήνεα] (of earrings) **with three drops** Hom.

τρί-γλυφοι ων *f.pl.* [γλύφω] **triglyphs** (in Doric architecture, triple-grooved beam-ends, visible on the facade of a building) E.

τρίγλυφον ου *n.* (collectv.) **band of triglyphs** Arist.

τρι-γλώχῑν (or **τριγλώχῑς**) ῑνος *masc.fem.adj.* [γλωχίν]
1 (of an arrow) **three-barbed** Il. Simon.
2 (of a sword, fig.ref. to Poseidon's trident) **three-pronged** Call.
3 (of an island) **three-cornered** Call. AR.

τριγονίᾱ ᾱς *f.* [τρίγονος] **third generation** Plu.; (quasi-adjl., of a villain, perfume-seller) ἐκ τριγονίας **third-generation** Hyp. D.

τρί-γονος ον *adj.* [γονή] entailing three births; (of a person's children) **three** E.

τριγωνο-ειδής ές *adj.* [τρίγωνος, εἶδος[1]] (of a country or region) **triangular in shape** Plb.

τρί-γωνος ον *adj.* [γωνία] **1** (of the Nile Delta) **three-cornered, triangular** A.; (of a shape, space) Hdt. Pl. Plb. ‖ NEUT.SB. **triangle** Pl. Arist. Call. Plb. Plu.
2 ‖ NEUT.SB. triangular oriental harp, **spindle harp** Pl. Arist.

τρι-δάκτυλος ον *adj.* (of a measured length) **of three finger-breadths** Plb.

τρί-δουλος ον *adj.* [δοῦλος] (of a person) triply a slave, **a slave through and through** A.*satyr.fr.* S.

τρί-δραχμος ον *adj.* [δραχμή] (of an item for sale) **priced at three drachmas** Ar.

τρι-έλικτος ον *adj.* [ἑλικτός] (of a serpent) **thrice-coiled** Hdt.(oracle)

τρι-έμβολον *neut.adv.* [ἐμβολή] (fig.) **hard enough for three rammings** —*ref. to having an erection* Ar. [or perh. *like a triple-size ram*]

τριετηρίς ίδος *f.* [τριετής] **1** festival held every three years (counting inclusively, i.e. in alternate years), **biennial festival** Pl.; (ref. to the Isthmian games) Pi.; (ref. to festivals in honour of Dionysus) hHom. Hdt. E.

2 period of three years Arist.

τριέτηρος ον *adj.* (of a girl) **three years old** Call.

τρι-ετής ές, Att. **τριέτης** ες *adj.* [ἔτος] **1** (of a period of time) **lasting three years** Hdt. Pl.; (of a friend) **of three years' standing** Theoc.
2 (of a child) **three years old** Pl. Plu. ‖ NEUT.SB. **age of three** Pl.
3 (of a garland) awarded (at the Nemean games) every three years (counting inclusively, i.e. in alternate years), **biennial** B.

—**τρίετες** *neut.adv.* **for three years** Od.

τριετίᾱ ᾱς *f.* **period of three years** NT. Plu.

τρί-ζυγος ον *adj.* [ζεύγνῡμι] yoked or joined together as three; (of Aphrodite, Athena and Hera, at the judgement of Paris) **triply teamed, three** E.

τρίζυξ ζυγος *masc.fem.adj.* (of a path) **where three roads join** S.*Ichn.*

τρίζω *vb.* ‖ pf. (w.pres.sens.) τέτρῑγα, ep.masc.acc.pl.ptcpl. τετρῑγῶτας ‖ ep.3sg.plpf. (w.impf.sens.) τετρῑγει ‖ **1** emit a shrill or thin sound; (of the shades of the dead) **squeak, gibber** Hom.; (of bats, a race of troglodytes who sound like bats) Od. Hdt.; (of fledgling birds, threatened by a snake) **squawk** Il.; (of barbarian women) **squeal** Plu.
2 (of wrestlers' backs) **creak, groan** (through strain) Il.; (of an axle) Call.
3 (of a person) **gnash, grind** —*one's teeth* NT.

τριηκ- (Ion. forms): see τριᾱκ-

τρι-ημιολίᾱ ᾱς *f.* [τρεῖς, ἡμιόλιος 3] a kind of swift trireme (used by the Rhodians for policing the seas) Plb.

τρι-ημιπόδιος ον *adj.* [ἡμιπόδιον] (of a trench) of three half-feet, **measuring a foot and a half** (in depth) X.

τριηραρχέω *contr.vb.* [τριήραρχος] ‖ aor. ἐτριηράρχησα ‖
1 command a trireme Hdt. Th. Plu.; **be commander** —W.GEN. *of a ship* (ref. *to a trireme*) Hdt. Plb.
2 (of an Athenian citizen) **serve as a trierarch** Ar. Att.orats. X. Arist. Thphr. —W.GEN. *of a ship* Is.; (of a family estate) **be capable of funding the duties of trierarchy** Is.
3 ‖ PASS. (of a populace) **be provided with trierarchs** X.

τριηράρχημα ατος *n.* (collectv.) app., skilled crew, **officers** (on a trireme) D.

τριηραρχίᾱ ᾱς *f.* **1 command of a trireme** Arist.
2 (at Athens) duty of a trierarch, **trierarchy** Att.orats. X. Thphr. Plu.

τριηραρχικός ή όν *adj.* (of an Athenian law) **relating to the trierarchy** D.; (of legal cases) **concerning trierarchs** Arist.

τριήρ-αρχος ου *m.* [τριήρης, ἄρχω] **1 commander of a trireme, trierarch** Hdt. Th. X. Plb. Plu.
2 (specif.) **trierarch** (wealthy Athenian citizen who, as a leitourgia, i.e. public duty, took command of a trireme for a year and paid for its maintenance and repair) Th. Ar. Att.orats. X. Arist.

τριηρ-αύλης ου *m.* [αὐλέω] **trireme-piper** (who set time for the rowers) D.

τρι-ήρης εος (ους) *f.* [ἐρέσσω] **three-rowed ship, trireme** (w. oars arranged in three tiers, ref. to the principal Greek warship of the 5th C. BC) Hippon. Hdt. Th. Ar. Att.orats. +

τριηρικός ή όν *adj.* (of gear) **belonging to a trireme** D. Plu.; (of a class of person) **such as serves on a trireme** (opp. fishing or merchant vessel) Arist.

τριηρῖται ῶν *m.pl.* (collectv.) **crew of a trireme** Hdt. Th. X. Plu.

τριηρο-ποιοί ῶν *m.pl.* [ποιέω] (appos.w. ἄνδρες) **officials responsible for the building of triremes** Arist.

—**τριηροποιικά** ῶν *n.pl.* **funds for the building of triremes** D.(cj.)

τρι-κάρηνος, dial. **τρικάρᾱνος**, ον adj. [κάρηνον] (of a serpent) **three-headed** Hdt.; (transf.epith., of a cavern in the mountains) **three-peaked** Pi.fr.

τρι-κέφαλος ον adj. [κεφαλή] | ᾱ metri grat. | (of Geryon) **three-headed** Hes.

τρί-κλῑνον ου n. [κλίνη] **1** arrangement of couches on three sides of a table (for the purpose of dining); **dining-area** Plu. || PL. dining tables Plb. Plu. **2** dinner-party Men.

τρι-κόρυθος ον adj. —also **τρίκορυς** υθος masc.adj. [κόρυς] (of Ajax, Corybants) **with triple helmet** (i.e. wearing a helmet w. three crests) E. [or perh. more loosely *impressively helmeted*]

τρι-κότυλος ον adj. [κοτύλη] **1** (of a large cup) **holding three-quarters of a litre** Men. **2** (of wine) app. **sold at three-quarters of a litre per obol** (i.e. cheap) Ar.

τρί-κρᾱνος ον adj. [κρᾱνίον¹] (of Cerberus) **three-headed** S. E.

τρι-κύαθος ον adj. (of a cup) **holding three ladlefuls** (of wine) Anacr.

τρι-κῡμίᾱ ᾱς f. [κῦμα] series of three waves; **huge wave, mighty swell** E. Men.; (fig., W.GEN. of evils) A.; (of an argument) Pl.; (fig.ref. to a swell of opposition to a series of three arguments) Pl.

τρι-λάγῡνος ον adj. (of a cup) **holding three flagonfuls** Stesich.

τρί-λλιστος ον ep.adj. [λίσσομαι] (of a goddess) **thrice invoked** Call.; (of night) thrice prayed for, **earnestly wished for** (as bringing an end to battle) Il.

τριλοφίᾱ ᾱς f. [λόφος] **1 three-crested helmet** Plu. **2 triple crest** (of a bird, as similar to that on a military helmet) Ar.

τρι-μερής ές adj. [μέρος] (of a branch of learning) **tripartite** Plb.

τρί-μετρος ον adj. [μέτρον] consisting of three metrical units; (of iambic verse, a metre) **in trimeters** Hdt. Pl. || NEUT.SB. (in iambic verse) trimeter Ar. Arist. Plu.

τρί-μηνος ον adj. [μήν²] (of a journey) **lasting three months** Hdt.; (quasi-advbl., of a person being absent) **for three months** S. || FEM.SB. period of three months Hdt. Aeschin. Men.(cj.) Plb. Plu.

τρῖμμα ατος n. [τρίβω; cf. τρίβων²] that which is well rubbed; (fig., ref. to a person) **old hand** Ar.; (W.INF. at making speeches) Ar.

τρῖμμός οῦ m. beaten path, **track** (in hunting) X.

τριμοιρίᾱ ᾱς f. [τρίμοιρος] threefold portion, **triple pay** X.

τρί-μοιρος ον adj. [τρεῖς, μοῖρα] (of a cloak, fig.ref. to earth covering each of the three bodies of the dead Geryon) with triple share, **threefold** A.

τρί-μορφος ον adj. [μορφή] (of the Fates) **who take three different forms** A.

Τρῑνακρίᾱ ᾱς, Ion. **Τρῑνακρίη** ης f. [app. τρεῖς, ἄκρᾱ] Trinakria (old name of Sicily) Th.; (equiv. to Θρινακίη *Sicily*) Call. Theoc.

—Τρῑνάκριος η ον Ion.adj. (of the sea) of or around Trinakria, **Trinakrian** AR.

τριξός Ion.num.adj.: see τρισσός

τρί-οδος ου f. [τρεῖς, ὁδός] **1** (oft.pl.) place where three roads meet or one road branches into two (esp. in ctxts. of persons meeting); **fork in the road** Pl. Call.epigr.; (as a place of burial) E.; (assoc.w. Hekate, superstitions) S.fr. Thphr. Theoc.; (frequented by beggars and loungers) Call. Mosch. **2** (fig., ref. to a place of choice, perplexity, error) **fork** Thgn. Pi. Pl.

3 || PL. app., three junctures or concordances (W.GEN. of musical modes, on an eleven-stringed lyre) Ion

τριοδοντίᾱ ᾱς f. [τριόδους] use of a trident (in fishing), spearing, **tridentry** Pl.

τρι-όδους οντος m. [ὀδούς] three-pronged implement, **trident** (of Poseidon) Pi. B.; (of a fisherman) Pl.

τριοῖσι (dial.masc.dat.pl.): see τρεῖς

τρι-όροφος ον adj. [ὀροφή] (of a house) **three-storeyed** Hdt.

τριόρχης (also **τρίορχος**) ου m. a kind of hawk; prob. **buzzard** Semon. Ar.; (ref. to a lecherous person, w. play on τρεῖς ὄρχεις *three testicles*) Ar. Plb.(quot.); (pl., ref. to three persons dancing, w. play on ὀρχεῖσθαι *dance*) Ar.

τρί-παις παιδος masc.fem.adj. [παῖς¹] (of a mother) **with three children** Plu.

τρί-παλαι adv. [πάλαι] **for three ages, for a very long time** Ar.

τρι-πάλαστος ον adj. [παλαστή] (of a measurement) **of three palm-breadths** Hdt.

τρί-παλτος ον adj. [παλτός] **thrice brandished**; (fig., of sufferings) **striking thrice, repeated** A.(dub.)

τρι-πάχυντος ον adj. [παχύνω] (of an evil daimon) **thrice-gorged** (on blood) A.(cj.)

τρί-πεδος ον adj. [πούς] (of a measurement) **of three feet** Plb.

τρι-πέτηλον ου n. [πέταλον] plant with triple leaves, **clover** Call.

τρι-πέτηλος ον adj. (of Hermes' wand) app. **with three branches** (one forming the handle, the other two springing fr. it and meeting at the top) hHom.

τρί-πηχυς υ adj. [πῆχυς] (of an object) **three cubits long** or **tall** (about four and a half feet) Hes. Hdt. E.Cyc. X. +; (of a crocodile) Hdt.

τρί-πλαξ ακος masc.fem.adj. [πλάξ] (of the rim of a shield) perh. **with three layers** (of metal) Il.

τριπλασιάζομαι pass.vb. [τριπλάσιος] (of an amount) **be trebled** Plu.

τριπλάσιος ᾱ ον adj. (of distance, quantity, strength) **three times as great, threefold, triple** Pl. X. D. Arist. Plb.; (of things, amounts) **three times greater** (W.GEN. than sthg.) Ar. Pl.; (w. ἤ + ADV. than formerly) D.; (of persons) **three times more numerous** (W.GEN. than another group) Pl.

—τριπλάσιον neut.adv. **three times as loud** (W.GEN. as someone) —ref. to shouting Ar.

τρί-πλεθρος ον adj. [πλέθρον] (of the width of a temple or river) **measuring three plethra** Pl. X.

τριπλοῦς ῆ οῦν Att.adj. —also **τριπλόος** ᾱ ον (Pi.) dial.adj. **1** (of things) having three parts, **threefold, triple** Pl. X.; (of a compound word) Arist.; (of a group) **of three persons** E.fr.; (of a battle order) **in three divisions** Plu.; (of a highway) **where three roads meet** S.

2 (of a refrain) **sung three times** Pi.

3 (of sufferings, repayments) **treble in amount, threefold** A.; (of a quantity, measurement) **three times as great** (sts. W.GEN. as sthg.) Pl.

—τριπλῇ fem.dat.sg.adv. **in a threefold manner or amount, threefold, three times over** —ref. to making recompense Il.

τριποδήιος ον Ion.adj. [τρίπους] (of the oracular seat of Apollo at Delphi) **consisting of a tripod, tripodal** Call.

τρι-πόδης ου masc.adj. [πούς] (of a mortar) **of three feet** (prob. in height) Hes.; (of a trench, in depth and width) X.

τρι-πόθητος, dial. **τριπόθᾱτος**, ον adj. [ποθέω] (of persons) **thrice-desired, deeply yearned for** Mosch. Bion; (of spring) Bion

τρί-πολις εως *masc.fem.adj.* [πόλις] (of the island of Rhodes) **with three cities** Pi.

τριπόλιστος ον *adj.* [reltd. τρίπολος] (fig., of a person's fate, or perh. of lamentation) thrice renewed, **constantly revisited** S.

τρί-πολος ον *adj.* [πέλω, πολέω] (of fallow land) thrice turned over, **thrice ploughed** Hom. Hes. Call. Theoc.

τρί-πους, ep. **τρίπος,** ποδος *m.* [πούς] **1** cauldron on three legs (for heating water), **tripod-cauldron, tripod** Hom. Hes.*fr.* hHom. Alcm. S. Call.; (as a gift) Hom.; (as a votive offering in a temple) hHom. Pi. B. Hdt. E. Th. +; (as a prize for an athlete or poet) Il. Hes. Pi. Hdt.; (for a khoregos, and usu. then dedicated to a god or erected as a monument in a public place) Att.orats. Pl. Theoc.*epigr.* Plu.
2 seat on three legs (fr. which the Delphic priestess delivered oracles), **tripod** E. Ar. X. Corinn. Call.; (fig., ref. to a place fr. which authoritative pronouncements are made) Pl. Plu.
3 three-legged table Ar. X. Men. Plu.

—**τρίπους** πουν, gen. ποδος *adj.* | acc. τρίπουν | **1** (of an old man w. a walking-stick) **three-footed, three-legged** Hes.; (of the way such a person walks) A.
2 (of a tunnel) **of three feet** (in width) Hdt.; (of a line, in length) Pl.; (of the square root of a number, measured in foot-lengths) Pl.

τρῑπτήρ ῆρος *m.* [τρίβω] **mortar** (W.GEN. for lawsuits, i.e. in which they are ground out, fig.ref. to an informer) Ar.

τρίπτης ου *m.* slave who rubs down (a person's body after bathing), **masseur** Plu.

Τριπτόλεμος ου *m.* **Triptolemos** (mythol. Eleusinian noble, to whom Demeter taught the mysteries and the art of agriculture) hHom. S.(title) Ar. Pl. X. Call.; (as a judge in the underworld) Pl.

τριπτός όν *adj.* [τρίβω] (of a highway) **trodden** Pi.*fr.*(cj.)

τρί-πτυχος ον *adj.* [τρεῖς, πτύξ] **1 with three folds;** (of an elaborate helmet) **three-layers thick** Il.
2 (of dirges) **threefold** (i.e. for three persons) E.; (gener., of persons or things) **triple, three** E.

τρί-πωλος ον *adj.* [πῶλος] consisting of three horses; (fig., of a group of goddesses, envisaged as a team) **of three** E.

τρί-ρρῡμος ον *adj.* [ῥῡμός] (of squadrons) **of chariots with three poles** (app. pulled by six horses) A.

τρίς *num.adv.* [τρεῖς] **1** on three occasions, **three times, thrice** (sts. ref. to ritually repeated acts) Hom. +; (prep.phrs.) εἰς τρίς, ἐς τρίς (usu. written ἐστρίς in Pi.) *thrice* Pi. Hdt. S.*fr.* E. X. Theoc.; ἐπὶ τρίς NT.
2 (w.demonstr.adj., ref. to quantity) τρὶς τόσσος *three times as much or as many* Hom. X. AR.; (w.relatv.adj.) τρὶς ὅσα *three times as many as* (one currently possesses) X.
3 (in multiplication) **three times** (a certain number) Hes. Emp. S. + • τρὶς ἐννέα *three times nine, twenty-seven* S. Th.
• τρὶς ἕξ *triple six* (as a throw of the dice) A.
4 (w.adjs., multiplying or intensifying) **three times, three times over** or **utterly, thoroughly** Hom. + | see also τρισάθλιος, τρισκακοδαίμων, τρίσμακαρ

τρῖς (Boeot.masc.fem.acc.pl.): see τρεῖς

τρισ-άθλιος (also written **τρὶς ἄθλιος**) ᾱ ον *adj.* | superl. τρισᾱθλιώτατος | (of persons, a town) thrice-unhappy, **thoroughly wretched** S. Ar. Men.

τρισ-άσμενος η ον *adj.* thrice-glad, **most willing** (to do sthg.) X.

τρισ-εινάς άδος *Ion.f.* [ἐννεάς] **thrice-ninth day** (i.e. 27th of the month) Hes.

τρισ-ευδαίμων ον, gen. ονος *adj.* thrice-fortunate, **as fortunate as can be** B.

τρισί (dat.pl.): see τρεῖς

τρῐσκαίδεκα (and cpds.): see τρεισκαίδεκα

τρισ-κακοδαίμων (also written **τρὶς κακοδαίμων**) ον, gen. ονος *adj.* thrice-unfortunate, **as unfortunate as can be** Ar. Aeschin. Men.

τρί-σκαλμος ον *adj.* [σκαλμός] **1** (of a boat) with three thole-pins (prob. on each side), **with three pairs of oars** Plu.
2 (of ships, ref. to triremes) with three rows of thole-pins, **three-banked** A.

τρισ-κατάρατος ον *adj.* thrice-cursed, **utterly damnable** D. Men.

τρίσ-μακαρ (also written **τρὶς μάκαρ**) αρος *masc.fem.adj.* thrice-blest, **blest beyond measure** Od. Hes.*fr.* Ar. Call.

τρισ-μακάριος ᾱ ον *adj.* **blest beyond measure** Archil. Ar.

τρισμός οῦ *m.* [τρίζω] **squeak** (of a mouse) Plu.

τρισ-μύριοι αι α *pl.num.adj.* [μῡρίος] three times ten thousand, **thirty thousand** Hdt. Lys. Ar. Pl. X. +; (sg., w.collectv. ἵππος *cavalry*) X.

τρισμῡριό-παλαι *adv.* [πάλαι] **for thirty thousand ages, for a long long time** Ar.

τρισ-οιζυρός ή όν *Ion.adj.* (of an island) thrice-miserable, **deeply wretched** Archil.

τρισ-όλβιος ᾱ ον *adj.* (of persons) thrice-happy, **deeply fortunate** Ar.

τρισ-ολυμπιονίκᾱς ᾱ *dial.m.* [Ὀλυμπιονίκης] (of a family) **thrice victorious in the Olympic games** Pi.

τρι-σπίθαμος ον *adj.* [σπιθαμή] (of a wheel) **measuring three spans** (in diameter, i.e. a little more than two feet) Hes.; (of a piece of wood, in length) X.

τρί-σπονδος ον *adj.* [σπονδή] consisting of three libations; (of a drink-offering to the dead) **thrice-poured, triple** S.

τρισσός, Att. **τριττός,** Ion. **τριξός,** ή όν *num.adj.* [τρίχα¹] **1** (of land which is divided) **in three parts** Hes.*fr.*; (of a desire) consisting of three parts, **threefold** Pl.; (of a group of three goddesses) E.
2 (of persons, deities, things, places) **three** hHom. Pi. Hdt. S. E. Pl. +

τρι-στάδιος ον *adj.* [στάδιον] (of a circle) **measuring three stades** (in diameter) Pl.

τρί-στεγον ον *n.* [στέγη] **third storey** (of a house) NT.

τρί-στοιχος ον *adj.* [στοῖχος] (of Scylla's teeth) **in three rows** Od.

—**τριστοιχεί** (also **τριστοιχί**) *adv.* **in three rows** —*ref. to armour laid on the ground* Il.; **in three layers** —*ref. to night encircling the entrance to Tartaros* Hes.

τρισ-χίλιοι αι α *pl.num.adj.* **1 three thousand** Il. Hdt. Th. +
2 ‖ MASC.SB. (w.art.) the Three Thousand (ref. to persons granted Athenian citizenship by the Thirty Tyrants in 404 BC) Lys. X. Arist.

τρισχῑλιοστός ή όν *adj.* (of a year) **three-thousandth** Pl.

τρι-σώματος ον *adj.* [σῶμα] (of Geryon) **three-bodied** A. E.; (of Cerberus, Typhon, the Chimaira) E.

τριταγωνιστέω *contr.vb.* [τριταγωνιστής] **be a bit-part actor** D.

τριτ-αγωνιστής οῦ *m.* [τρίτος] third actor (taking the least important roles); (pejor.) **bit-part actor** D.

τριταῖος, Aeol. **τρίταιος** (Theoc.), ᾱ ον *adj.* [τρίτη, under τρίτος] **1** on the third day; (quasi-advbl., of persons arriving or sim.) **in three days' time, on the day after next** Hdt. Th. X. Plb. Plu.; (of a prospective wind, a festival) Pi. E.; (of a funeral) **on the third day** (after death) Pl.
2 (of a fever) returning on the third day, **tertian** Pl.
3 (reckoning backwards in time; quasi-advbl., of persons having arrived) **on the day before last, three days ago** Hdt.

τριταλαντιαῖος

Plb.; (of corpses) **three days old** Hdt.; (of a wound) Men.; (of a report) Plb.; (of a friend) **of three days' standing** Theoc. **4** (of a day) **third** A.*fr.*(cj.) E.

τριταλαντιαῖος ον *adj.* [τριτάλαντος] (of a container) **holding three talents** (of gold) Plu.

τρι-τάλαντος ον *adj.* [τάλαντον] **1** (of a weight) **of three talents** Ar.
2 (of a container) **holding three talents** (of silver) Plu.
3 (of a property) **worth three talents** Is.

τρίτατος, Aeol. **τέρτατος** (Pi., dub.cj.), η (dial. ᾱ) ον *num.adj.* [τρίτος] (of persons or things) **third** (in a list or sequence) Hom. hHom. Sol. Pi. B. E. +
—**τρίτατα** *neut.pl.adv.* (w. δραμεῖν) **come third** (*in a race*) E.*lyr.fr.*

τριτεῖα ων *n.pl.* **third prize** or **place** Pl.

τριτη-μόριον ου *n.* **third part, third** (of sthg.) Hdt. Th. Pl. Arist. Plu.

τριτημόριος ον (Ion. η ον) *adj.* having a third part; (of a country, ref. to its resources) **providing a third** (W.GEN. of a continent, i.e. of its total resources) Hdt.

τριτη-μορίς ίδος *f.* [reltd. μέρος] **third part, third** (of an army) Hdt.

τριτο-βάμων ον, gen. ονος *dial.adj.* [βῆμα, βαίνω] (of a walking-stick) **acting as a third foot** (for an old woman) E.

Τρῖτο-γενής έος *f.* —also **Τρῑτογένης** ευς (Lyr.adesp.) *dial.f.* [pop.etym. Τρίτων, Τρῑτωνίς; γένος, γίγνομαι] **Tritogenes** (name of Athena) hHom. Hdt.(oracle) Lyr.adesp. Ar.
—**Τρῑτογένεια** ᾱς *f.* **Tritogeneia** (name of Athena) Hom. Hes. Scol. Ar.

τρίτος, Aeol. **τέρτος**, η (dial. ᾱ) ον *num.adj.* [τρεῖς] **1** (of persons or things) **third** (in a list or sequence, oft. as last item) Hom. +
2 (of Zeus, as recipient of the last libation) **third** A. Pl.; (of the bowl fr. which it was poured) Pi.; (of the libation) X. ‖ NEUT.SB. **third libation** Pl. | see σωτήρ 3
3 ‖ NEUT.PL.SB. **third-day offerings** (made two days after death) Ar. Is.
4 third in importance or merit; (of a person) **in third place, third** (in a competition) Isoc. Plu.; (of an actor) τὰ τρίτα λέγειν *speak* (i.e. act) *the third part, i.e. take the most minor role* (in a play) D.; (fig., of a person) **come third in pecking order** Men.
5 (phrs.) τρίτον μέρος *third part, one third* (of an object, country, group of persons, or sim.) Pi. Hdt. +; (also) τρίτη αἶσα Hes.
6 (math.) ἥμισυ τρίτον *a half coming third* (after two full units, i.e. two and a half) Archil.; τρίτον ἡμιτάλαντον *half-talent coming third* (i.e. two and a half talents) Hdt.
7 (prep.phrs.) ἐκ τρίτου, ἐκ τρίτων *in third place, thirdly* (in a sequence) E. Pl.; ἐκ τρίτου *a third time* NT.
—**τρίτη** ης *f.* **third day** (of a month) Aeschin. D.; **day after tomorrow** Ar. X.; **day before yesterday** X.
—**τρίτον** *neut.sg.adv.* **1 thirdly, third** (in a sequence) Pi. Hdt. Trag. Att.orats. Pl. AR.; (also) τὸ τρίτον Hom. Hes. Hdt. Th. Ar. Call.
2 for a third time B. E. Antipho X. Men. Theoc.; τὸ τρίτον *for the third time* Il. Hdt. Ar. X. Call. Theoc.
—**τρίτα** *neut.pl.adv.* **thirdly** (in order of importance) Hdt.
—**τρίτως** *adv.* (ref. to classification) **in third place** Pl.

τριτό-σπονδος ον *adj.* [σπονδή] (of a paean) **accompanying the third libation** A.

τριτό-σπορος ον *adj.* [σπόρος] (of a generation) **produced by the third sowing, third** A.

τριτο-στάτης ου *m.* [ἵσταμαι] person standing third; (ref. to a member of a chorus) **next but one neighbour** (to the koryphaios) Arist.

τριττός *Att.num.adj.*: see τρισσός

τριττυαρχέω *contr.vb.* [τριττύς, ἀρχή] **be leader of a trittys** (as a minor military command) Pl.

τριττύς ύος *Att.f.* [τρισσός] | acc.pl. τριττῦς | (at Athens) **third part of a tribe, trittys** Aeschin. D. Arist.

Τρίτων ωνος *m.* **1 Triton** (sea god, son of Poseidon and Amphitrite) Hes. E.*Cyc.* AR. Plb. ‖ PL. Tritons (minor sea gods) Mosch.
2 Triton (river in N. Africa) Hdt. Call.; (assoc.w. Athena) A.; (identified w. the Nile) AR.
—**Τρῑτωνίς** ίδος, also **Τρῑτωνιάς** άδος (E.) *fem.adj.* **1** (of a lake, adjoining the river Triton) **of Triton, Tritonian** Pi. Hdt. E. AR.; (of a nymph assoc.w. this lake) AR.
2 (epith. of Athena, perh. fr. a river Triton in Boeotia) **Tritonian** Call. AR.
3 ‖ FEM.SB. daughter of Triton (ref. to Thebe, eponymous heroine of Egyptian Thebes) AR.

τρι-φαλαγγίᾱ ᾱς *f.* [τρεῖς, φάλαγξ] **three-column formation** (of troops) Plb.

τρι-φάσιος η ον *Ion.adj.* [perh.reltd. φημί or φαίνω] **1** (of a duel, fought by pairs of men, horses and dogs) **threefold, triple** Hdt.
2 (of names, substances, opinions, versions of a story) **of three different kinds** Hdt.; (wkr.sens., of things, places) **three** Hdt.

τρι-φίλητος ον *adj.* [φιλητός] (of Adonis) **thrice-loved, deeply beloved** Theoc.

τρί-φυλλον ου *n.* [φύλλον] **three-leaved plant, trefoil, clover** Hdt.

τρί-φῡλος ον *adj.* [φυλή] (of a people) **composed of three tribes** Hdt.

τρίχα[1] *adv.* **1 into three parts** —*ref. to dividing or separating things or people* Hom. Pi. Hdt. Isoc. X. D.; **in three ways** —*ref. to formulating a plan* Od.
2 in the third (i.e. last) **part** (W.GEN. of night) Od.

τρίχα[2] (acc.sg.): see θρίξ

τριχᾱΐκες ων *m.pl.* [θρίξ, ἄσσω] (epith. of Dorians) perh. **with streaming hair** Od. [or perh. *with waving horsehair plumes*; unless τρίχα[1], 2nd el.reltd. οἶκος, *living as three tribes*]

τρί-χαλκον ου *n.* [τρεῖς, χαλκός] **three-khalkous coin** Thphr. | see χαλκοῦς, under χάλκεος

τρί-χᾱλος ον *dial.adj.* [χηλή] (fig., of the swell of the sea) app. **three-taloned, triple** A. | cf. τρικυμία

τριχῇ *dat.adv.* [τρίχα[1]] **1 into three parts** —*ref. to dividing or apportioning* Hdt. Isoc. Pl. Arist. Plu.
2 in three divisions —*ref. to stationing troops* X.
3 in three places —*ref. to laying an ambush* Th.
4 in a threefold manner, **in three ways** Pl.

τριχθά *adv.* [reltd. τρίχα[1]] **1 into three parts** —*ref. to dividing, breaking or tearing* Hom.
2 in three divisions —*ref. to a population being settled according to tribes* Il.

τριχινός ή όν *adj.* [θρίξ] (of clothing) **made of hair** Pl. X.

τριχίς ίδος *f.* [app. θρίξ] **small fish of the herring family with hair-like bones, sardine, sprat** or **anchovy** Ar.

τριχό-βρως ωτος (v.l. **τριχοβρώς** ῶτος) *m.f.* [βιβρώσκω] hair-eater, **clothes-moth** Ar.

τρι-χοίνικος ον *adj.* [χοῖνιξ] consisting of three khoinix-measures (in volume); (of a loaf) **three-litre size** X.; (fig., of a periphrastic phrase, app. envisaged as a large quantity of vegetables) Ar.

τριχορρυέω contr.vb. [θρίξ, ῥέω] shed hair; (of feathered helmet-crests) **moult** Ar.

τριχός (gen.sg.): see θρίξ

τρί-χους ουν Att.adj. [τρεῖς, χοῦς¹] (of a water-clock) **holding three khoes** (approx. ten litres) Arist.

τρίχωμα ατος n. **1** (collectv.sg.) **hair** (of the human head) Hdt. Thphr.; (of the beard) A.
2 coat (of a hare or hound) X.
3 ‖ PL. (fig.) **streaks of blood** E.(dub., cj. θριγκώματα)

τριψημερέω contr.vb. [τρίβω, ἡμέρᾱ] waste the day, **fritter time away** Ar.

τρῖψις εως f. **1 rubbing, friction** (of one thing against another) Pl.
2 capacity to sustain being rubbed, **durability, toughness** (of animal-hides) Hdt.
3 rubbing (of an itch) Pl.; **rubbing down, massaging** (of the body) Arist. Plu.

τρίψω (fut.): see τρίβω

τρι-ώβολον ου n. [τρεῖς, ὀβολός] **three-obol coin** (equal to half a drachma) X. Aeschin. Plu.; (as daily pay for jury-service) Ar.; (for attendance at the Assembly) Ar. Arist.; (for soldiers, sailors) Th. X. Plu.; (as an example of a paltry sum) Ar. Men.

τριῶν (gen.pl.): see τρεῖς

τρι-ώρυγος ον adj. [ὄργυια] (of structures) **measuring three fathoms** (in length, height) X.

Τροζήν (also later **Τροιζήν**) ῆνος f. **Troizen** (town in Argolis) Il. Hes.fr. Hdt. Th. Att.orats. +

—**Τροζήνιοι** (also **Τροιζήνιοι**) ων m.pl. **Troizenians** (as a population or military force) Hdt. +

—**Τροζήνιος** (also **Τροιζήνιος**) ᾱ (Ion. η) ον adj. of or from Troizen; (of a person, ship, the city, land) **Troizenian** B. Hdt. E. Th. Plu.

—**Τροζηνίς** (or **Τροιζηνίς**) ίδος fem.adj. (of the land) **Troizenian** Th.

Τροίᾱ, dial. **Τροΐᾱ**, also **Τρωΐᾱ**, ᾱς, Ion. **Τροίη** ης f. **Troy** (city in Asia Minor, reputedly captured after a ten-year siege by the Greeks in the Mycenaean age; sts.ref. also to its territory, the Troad) Hom. +

—**Τροίᾱθεν**, dial. **Τροΐᾱθεν**, Ion. **Τροίηθεν** adv. **from Troy** Od. Hes.fr. Pi. E.; (also) ἀπὸ Τροίηθεν Hom.

—**Τροίᾱνδε**, Ion. **Τροίηνδε** adv. **to Troy** Hom. Pi.

Τρόιος dial.adj.: see Τρώιος, under Τρώς

τρομερός ᾱ́ όν adj. [τρόμος] **1** (of limbs, footsteps) **trembling, shaking, tottering** (through age and infirmity) E.; (of the feet of a dying lion) Theoc.
2 (of persons, their bodies or minds) **trembling** (w. fear) E.
3 (of fear) that makes one tremble, **quaking** AR.; (of the lash of Pan) causing fear, **terrifying** E.
4 (of a city) **shivering** (w. cold) Ar.

—**τρομερά** neut.pl.adv. **with faltering steps** E.

τρομέω contr.vb. | only pres. and impf. | Ion.fem.nom.pl. ptcpl. τρομεῦσαι (Call.) | 3sg.iteratv.impf. τρόμεσκε (Hes.) | Usu. the vb. does not contract. |
1 (of the natural world, mountain peaks) **tremble, shake, quiver** (at the advent of violent wind, of the huntress Artemis) Hes.fr. hHom.
2 (act. and mid., of persons, their heart or limbs, animals) **tremble with fear, be frightened** Il. hHom.; (tr.) **tremble before, be afraid of, fear** —a person, god, behaviour, circumstances Hom. hHom. Sol. Ibyc. A. Pi. +
3 (act. and mid.) tremble in anticipation of some event; **be afraid of, fear, dread** —death, the future Od. A. AR.; **be afraid** —W.INF. to do sthg. Theoc. —W.COMPL.CL. that sthg. may happen Call.

τρόμος ου m. [τρέμω] **trembling** (fr. fear) Hom. A. E. AR. NT. Plu.; (fr. love) Sapph.; (fr. cold) Pl.

τροπαίᾱ ᾱς f. [τρέπω] **1 wind which changes direction, changing wind** (fig.ref. to a sudden change of fortune) Plu.
2 change (W.GEN. of wind) Plu.; (fig.) **veering, shift, change** (W.GEN. of one's mind or resolution) A.; (fr. troubles) A.

τρόπαιον, Att. **τροπαῖον**, ου n. **1** memorial marking the rout of an enemy (set up on the battlefield, orig. consisting of captured armour, later sts. a more permanent monument); **trophy, memorial** (oft. w. ἱστάναι set up) A. E. Th. Critias Ar. Tim. +; (W.GEN. of a battle) Th.; (W.GEN.PERS. over defeated enemies) E. Att.orats. Pl. X.; (w. κατὰ or ἀπὸ + GEN.PERS.) Att.orats. Plu.; (at Rome) **emblem of victory** (carried by a triumphant general) Plu. ‖ PL. **spoils** (W.GEN. of victory) S.
2 victory E. Ar.; (phr.) τρόπαιον ἱστάναι **win a victory** Pl. —W.GEN. over someone or sthg. S. E. Ar. Isoc.
3 (gener.) record of prowess or excellence, **memorial** Lys. Isoc. Arist.

τροπαῖος ᾱ ον adj. **1** (of Zeus) turning enemies to flight, **causing the rout** S. E. Men.; (W.GEN. of enemies) E.; (of a monument to Zeus, i.e. the trophy dedicated to him) **in thanks for victory** E.
2 (of a sacrifice before battle) **ensuring the rout** (W.GEN. of the enemy) E.
3 (of sun and stars as devices on a shield) **turning to flight** (an adversary) E.

τροπαιοφορίᾱ ᾱς f. [τροπαιοφόρος] **carrying of trophies** Plu.

τροπαιο-φόρος ον adj. [φέρω] (of a Roman commander) **carrying a trophy** (i.e. emblems of victory, in a procession) Plu.

τροπαλίς ίδος dial.f. [reltd. τρέπω] app. **bunch** (W.GEN. of garlic) Ar.

τροπέω contr.vb. [τρέπω] | Aeol.inf. τρόπην | ep.3pl.impf. τρόπεον | (of horses) **turn** —a chariot (W.ADV. back) Il.; (of Ares) —persons (W.PREP.PHR. to arms) Alc.

τροπή ῆς f. | dial.acc.pl. τροπάς (Hes. Alcm.) | **1** ‖ PL. **turnings** (freq. W.GEN. of the sun); **time of the solstice** (i.e. midsummer or midwinter day) Hes. Alcm. Th. Arist.; (distinguished as θεριναί summer or χειμεριναί winter) Hdt. Th. Pl. Plb. Plu.; **solstice-point** (app. place on the horizon where the sun was seen to rise or set at this time) Od.
2 reversal, alteration, change (of heavenly bodies, in their courses) Pl.; (in a process of nature) Pl. Arist. Plu.; (W.GEN. of opinion) Plu.; (fig., ref. to a person's behaviour, compared w. the movements of the Euripos, the transformations of a chameleon) Aeschin. Plu.
3 (milit.) putting to flight, **rout** (oft. W.GEN. of an enemy) Hdt. Trag. Th. +
4 (philos., as a term used by Atomists) **turn, relative inclination** (of elements, equiv. to θέσις position) Arist.

τρόπις εως (Ion. ιος) f. [reltd. τρέπω] | dat. τρόπιδι (AR.) |
1 keel (of a ship, sts. gener.ref. to its underside) Od. Hippon. Hdt. E. Arist. +
2 (fig.) **bottom line** (W.GEN. of a situation) Ar.

—**τροπιδεῖα** ων n.pl. **keel** Pl.

τροπόομαι mid.contr.vb. [τροπός] (of a sailor) **strap** —an oar (W.PREP.PHR. to a thole-pin) A. ‖ PASS. (of oars) be strapped to thole-pins Ar.(dub.)

τροπός οῦ m. [reltd. τρέπω] **oar-strap** (securing the oar to the thole-pin) Od.

τρόπος ου *m.* [τρέπω] **1 turn, direction** (taken by a canal, passageway, mountain range) Hdt.
2 way (of doing sthg.); **way, fashion, manner** Pi. Hdt. Trag. Lyr.adesp. Th. Critias +; (ref. to a musical mode) Pi.; (gener., ref. to musical style) Pl.; (ref. to a manner or style of speech) Isoc. Pl.
3 way (in which sthg. is constituted); **manner, nature, style** (of things, activities, circumstances) Trag. Th. Ar. Pl. +
4 (sg. and pl.) **way** (one is or behaves); **ways, habits, character** (of a person) Semon. Thgn. Pi. Hdt. Trag. Th. +
5 (advbl.phrs.) τίνι (τέῳ) τρόπῳ; *in what way, how?* Hdt. Trag. +; (also) τίνα τρόπον; E. Ar. +; οὐδενὶ τρόπῳ *by no means, on no account* Hdt. +; παντὶ τρόπῳ *in every possible way* (or in urgent appeals, *at all costs*) A. Th. Ar. Att.orats. +
6 (prep.phrs.) ἐκ παντὸς τρόπου *in every way* Th. Att.orats. Pl. +; κατὰ τρόπον *in the right way, appropriately* Isoc. Pl. Hyp. Men.; πρὸς τρόπου *in character, appropriately, suitably* Pl. Thphr.; ἀπὸ τρόπου *inappropriately* Pl. Plu.
7 (advbl.acc.) *in the manner of or like* (W.GEN. *someone or sthg.*) A. Pi. Hdt. E.
τροποφορέω *contr.vb.* [φέρω] bear the ways of, **tolerate** —*someone* NT.
τροπωτήρ ῆρος *m.* [τροπόομαι] **oar-strap** Th. Ar.
τροφά *dial.f.*: see τροφή
τροφαλίς ίδος *f.* [perh. τρέφω] app. **wedge, slice** (W.GEN. of cheese) Ar.
τροφεῖα ων *n.pl.* [τρέφω] **1** recompense (by an action or offering) for care and upbringing; **repayment for nurture** (to a parent, fr. a child) Men.; (to a master, fr. a slave) E.; (to one's fatherland or city) A. Att.orats. Pl. Plu.; (ref. to a rite in memory of the she-wolf who nurtured Romulus) Plu.
2 repayment for nurture (of one's own children, ref. to an offering to the Nymphs fr. a parent) E.
3 (gener.) **nourishment, nurture, sustenance** S. E.
τροφεύς έως *m.* **1** one who brings up a male child; **foster-father** E. Plb. Plu.; **tutor** S. E.; (ref. to a woman) **nurse** A.; (gener.) **educator** (of citizens) Pl. ∥ PL. foster-parents or parents Pl.; nurses, nurturers (of Ajax, ref. to the rivers and plains of Troy) S.; (of mankind, ref. to land and sea) Antipho Pl.
2 rearer, keeper (of a lion cub, horses, dogs) A. Pl. Plu.; (pejor., of prostitutes) Plu.; (fig.) **breeder** (of wickedness) Pl.
τροφή ῆς, dial. **τροφά** ᾶς *f.* **1 nourishment, food** (as sustenance) Hdt. S. E. Th. Att.orats. Pl. +
2 means of sustenance (ref. to a bow) S.; **source of sustenance** (ref. to a city, an altar) E.
3 condition in which one lives, **way** or **state of life** S. Pl.
4 (oft.pl.) **upbringing, nurture, nurturing care** (of children, by parents or sim.) Hdt. Trag. Lys. Pl. X. Arist. +; **maintenance** (of a parent, by a child) A. S. Att.orats.; (of birds, by their young) S.; (of citizens, at public expense) Arist.
5 rearing, keeping (of animals) Pi. Hdt. Plu.
6 (concr.) **nursling** (of a sheep, ref. to a lamb) E.*Cyc.*; (collectv.sg.) **nurslings, brood** (of an animal) S.*Ichn.*; (of the founder of a race, ref. to a populace) S.
τροφίας ου *masc.adj.* (of oxen) **stall-fed** (opp. grazing) Plu.
τρόφιμος η ον (also ος ον E.) *adj.* **1** providing nourishment or nurture; (of water) **nourishing** Pl.; (of a house) **providing nurture** (for slaves) E.; (of a land, W.GEN. for children) E.
2 (of a vessel, ref. to the stomach) **alimentary** Tim.
3 (of a child) receiving nurture, **brought up** (in a temple) E. ∥ MASC.M.SB. nurslings (ref. to persons reincarnated as babies) Pl.; pupils (of philosophers in an ideal state) Pl.; foster-children (ref. to poor children brought up at others' expense at Sparta) X.
4 ∥ MASC.SB. young master (term used by a slave to refer to his owner's son) Men. ∥ FEM.SB. young mistress Men.
τρόφις ι, gen. ιος *adj.* (of children) **adult** Hdt.; (of a wave) full-grown, **huge** Il.
τροφόεις εσσα εν *adj.* (of waves) **huge** Hom.
τροφός οῦ *f.* **1** servant-woman who feeds or rears a child (oft. described as acting as confidante and adviser to the family and her former charges), **nurse** Od. hHom. Pi. Hdt. Trag. Pl. +; (ref. to a mother) S. Theoc.; (iron., ref. by a man to himself) E.; (W.GEN. of cattle, horses, fig.ref. to a herdsman or sim.) Pl.
2 (ref. to the earth, foodstuffs) **giver of nourishment** or **nurture** A. Pl.; (ref. to a city, region) **nurturer, nurse** (of persons, animals) Pi. Trag. Isoc. Pl. Call. +; (fig., of the other arts, ref. to agriculture) X.
3 (fig., ref. to a place, as custodian or protector of sthg.); **nurse** (of a spring, ref. to a city) E.; (of stars, ref. to night) E.; (of festivities, ref. to a sacred grove) Pi.*fr.*
Τροφώνιος ου *m.* **Trophonios** (assistant builder of Apollo's temple at Delphi, who became an underground oracular god at Lebadeia in Boeotia) hHom. Pi.*fr.* Hdt. E. Ar. Plu.
τροχάζω *vb.* [τρέχω, τροχός] **1** proceed quickly on foot, **run** E.
2 (of children) **run races** Thphr.
3 (of a commander, troops) **go at the double** Hdt. X. Plb.
4 (tr., of a god or fate) **hurry, drive** —*someone* (W.PREP.PHR. *along a path*) E.*fr.* [or perh. *bowl like a hoop*]
τροχαῖος ου *m.* **1** metrical foot consisting of a long and short syllable, **trochee** Pl.
2 trochaic rhythm Arist.
τροχαλός ή όν *adj.* **1** (of an old man, buffeted by the wind) **wheeling** or **bowling along** (like a wheel or hoop) Hes. [or perh. *curved, bent*]
2 (app. of an old man, animated by rejoicing) perh. **running** E.*fr.*
3 (of a carriage) with running wheels, **swiftly running** E.
τροχάω *contr.vb.* ∣ ep.masc.acc.sg.ptcpl. (w.diect.) τροχόωντα ∣ (of a person) **run** Od.
τροχερός ά όν *adj.* (of trochaic tetrameter rhythm) **running, tripping** Arist.
τροχηλατέω *contr.vb.* [τροχηλάτης] (fig., of Erinyes, the guilt of bloodshed) **drive on** —*someone* (*in fits of madness*) E. [or perh. *bowl along*]
τροχ-ηλάτης ου *m.* [τροχός, ἐλαύνω] driver of a wheeled vehicle; (specif.) **charioteer** S. E.
τροχ-ήλατος ον *adj.* **1** (of tented carriages) driven on wheels, **wheeled** A.
2 (of a chariot) wheeling along, **speeding** S.; (fig., of madness) **wheeling, whirling** E.
3 (of a person's death) caused by being dragged behind a chariot, **chariot-drawn** E.
4 (of a lamp, envisaged as the Sun-god) **driven on the wheel** (i.e. the potter's wheel, w. further allusion to the Sun's chariot) Ar.
τροχίζομαι *pass.vb.* ∣ aor. ἐτροχίσθην ∣ (of a person) **be put on the wheel** (for torture) Antipho Arist.
τροχιλεῖα (also **τροχιλιά** Plb. Plu.) ᾶς *f.* **pulley-hoist** (used in building-work) Ar.; **pulley** Plb. Plu.
τροχιλεῖον ου *n.* **pulley** Pl.
τροχίλος ου *m.* a kind of small bird; perh. **sandpiper** Ar.; (ref. to the Egyptian plover, also called *Crocodile bird*) Hdt. Arist.
τρόχις *m.* [τρέχω] ∣ only acc. τρόχιν ∣ **courier, errand-runner** (of Zeus, ref. to Hermes) A. S.*satyr.fr.*

τροχοδῑνέομαι pass.contr.vb. (of a mad person's eyes) **roll around** A.

τροχο-ειδής ές adj. [εἶδος¹] **1** (of the lake on Delos) in the shape of a wheel, **circular, round** Thgn. Hdt.; (of a discus) B. **2** (of the city of Athens) **encircling** (the Acropolis) Hdt.(oracle)

τροχόεις εσσα εν adj. (of the lake on Delos) **circular** Call.

τροχοποιέω contr.vb. be a maker of wheels, **be a wheelwright** Ar.

τροχός οῦ m. [τρέχω] **1 wheel** (of a carriage or chariot) Il. Simon. S. E. Ar. Pl. +; (on which Ixion was perpetually spun) Pi.; (fig., of fortune) S.fr.
2 wheel (of a potter) Il. Critias Ar. Pl. X. Plb.
3 wheel (as an instrument of torture, on whose rim the victim was stretched) Anacr. Ar. Att.orats. Plu.
4 circular band, **hoop** X.
5 circular zone or belt, **circle** (of land, sea) Pl. Plu.
6 circular object; **round piece, circle, cake** (of wax, tallow) Od.; app. **orb, disc** (of the sun) Ar.; **disc** (fitted on a horse's bit) X.

τρόχος ου m. **1** activity of running, **running** (as a sport) E.
2 circular journey, **course, circuit** (W.GEN. of the sun, ref. to a day's length) S.
3 place for running, **racecourse** (for horses) E.

τρύβλιον ου n. small shallow vessel, **dish, bowl** Ar. NT. Plu.; (W.GEN. of a woman, w. allusion to cunnilingus) Ar.

τρυγάω contr.vb. [reltd. τρύξ] | ep.3pl. (w.diect.) τρυγόωσι, ep.3pl.opt. (w.diect.) τρυγόωεν | **1** gather in (fruit) at the vintage; **gather** —grapes Od. NT.; (fig., w. sexual connot.) **harvest** —Fruity Autumn Ar.; (intr.) **gather in the vintage** Ar. Pl.; (fig., ref. to making a profit) Ar. ‖ PASS. (of fruits) be gathered Hdt.; (of honey) be collected (fr. the hive) Mosch.
2 gather fruit from, **harvest** —a vineyard Il. —vines Hes. X.; (provbl., of persons who achieve success unopposed) —unwatched vines Ar.

τρύγη ης f. grape crop, **harvest** hHom.

τρυγητήρ ῆρος m. | ῠ metri grat. | **grape-gatherer** Hes.

—τρυγήτρια ᾱς f. **female grape-gatherer** D.

τρύγητος ου m. time of year when grapes are gathered, **vintage** Th.

τρυγη-φόρος ον adj. [φέρω] (of a region) prob. **grape-producing** hHom.

τρυγικός ή όν adj. [τρύξ] (of a chorus) **comic** Ar. | cf. τρυγῳδός

τρυγο-δαίμων ονος m. [conflation of τρυγῳδός and κακοδαίμων] **goddamned comic poet** Ar.

τρύγοιπος ου m. filter for straining must from grape-skins, **wine-strainer** Ar.

τρυγῳδίᾱ ᾱς f. [τρυγῳδός] **comedy** (ref. either to a single play or to the genre) Ar.

τρυγῳδικός ή όν adj. (of a chorus) **comic** Ar.

τρυγ-ῳδός οῦ m. [ἀοιδή] must-singer or lees-singer (w. play on τραγῳδός), **comic poet** Ar.

τρυγών όνος f. [τρύζω] **turtle-dove** Ar. Theoc. NT.; (pl., pejor.ref. to women chattering in dialect) Theoc.

τρυμαλιά ᾶς f. [τρύμη] hole, **eye** (W.GEN. of a needle) NT.

τρύμη ης f. [τρύω] drill (or perh. hole); (pejor.ref. to a person) **gimlet, sharper** Ar. [or perh. needle's eye, w.connot. of elusiveness]

τρύξ τρυγός f. [reltd. τρυγάω] **1** unfermented grape-juice, **must** Anacr. Ar. Call.
2 lees, dregs (of wine) Archil. Semon. Theoc.; (of the juice fr. a Scythian fruit) Hdt.; (fig.ref. to a decrepit old woman) Ar.

τρύξω (fut.): see τρύχω

τρύπανον ου n. [τρυπάω] tool for boring timber, **drill** (usu. rotated by a strap) Od. Pratin. E.Cyc. Pl. Arist.; (fig.ref. to Pan) **tool** (w. allusion to his sexual exploits) Call.

τρυπάω contr.vb. [τρύω] **1 drill a hole through, bore** —timber or sim. Od. Pl. Plb. ‖ PASS. (of a cup) be holed or pierced Arist.
2 (of a he-goat) **penetrate** —she-goats Theoc.

—τετρῡπωμένος η ον pf.pass.ptcpl.adj. (of a person) **pierced** (W.ACC. in one's ears, for earrings) X.; (of a voting-token, cast for the plaintiff) **perforated, with a hole** (opp. πλήρης **solid**, cast for the defendant) Aeschin. Arist.

τρύπημα ατος n. **1** hole (W.GEN. in a ship, ref. to an oar-hole) Ar.; (in a counting-board, to receive a voting-token) Arist.
2 hole (ref. to the vagina) Ar.
3 eye (W.GEN. of a needle) NT.

τρύπησις εως f. **boring** (of holes) Arist.

τρυπητά ῶν n.pl. **perforated voting-tokens** (ref. to metal discs w. a central hole) Arist. | see ψῆφος 4

τρυπητής οῦ m. one who drills holes, **hole-maker** Pl.

τρῡσ-άνωρ ορος dial.masc.fem.adj. [τρύω, ἀνήρ] (of a cry) wearing down men, **distressing** S. [or perh. of a man in distress]

τρῡσί-βιος ον adj. [βίος] (of a poor man's stomach) wearing down life, **debilitating** Ar.

τρῠτάνη ης f. app., tongue or pointer of a balance; **balance, scales** Ar. D. Plu.

τρυφάλεια ᾱς (Ion. ης) f. [app.reltd. τετράφαλος] app., helmet with four plates or ridges, **helmet** (w.connot. of impressive or elaborate design) Hom. Hes. Stesich. Ar. AR. Theoc.

τρυφάω contr.vb. [τρυφή] | aor. ἐτρύφησα | **1** experience soft or luxurious living; (of a child; iron., of a person as if a child) **be coddled** or **pampered** E.; (of persons) **be spoilt** or **indulged** Ar. Isoc. Pl. D. Arist. Plu.; (of a populace, by flattery) D.; (of the upbringing of a Persian king) Pl.
‖ NEUT.PTCPL.SB. **luxurious living** Ar.
2 delight in luxury; (of a ruler, landowners) **be sumptuous** or **extravagant** (in dress, expenditure) Isoc. Arist.; (of a goddess) **preen oneself** —W.PREP.PHR. on one's power E.; (of a city) **enjoy luxury** Pl.
3 behave in a self-indulgent way; (of women) **take liberties, get out of hand** Ar.; (of persons who are not satisfied w. the life which a god has given) **act like spoilt children** E.
4 (wkr.sens.) **be self-indulgent, be indolent, have an easy life** E. Att.orats. Pl. Men. Plu.
5 (of disputants) **lack rigour** Pl.

τρυφεραίνομαι pass.vb. [τρυφερός] | aor.ptcpl. τρυφερανθείς | (of a person) be made soft or delicate in manner, **be pansified** Ar.

τρυφερός ά όν adj. [τρυφή] **1** (of persons, their lifestyle, or sim.) **pampered, luxurious** Ar. Arist. Men. Plu.; (of a person who cannot endure pain) **soft** Arist. ‖ COMPAR.NEUT.SB. more luxurious way of life Th.
2 (of a seat) **comfortable** (for the limbs) Critias
3 (of Dionysus' hair) **luxuriant** E.
4 ‖ NEUT.SB. voluptuousness (of female thighs) Ar.

—τρυφερόν neut.adv. **1 in a delicate manner** —ref. to walking Ar.
2 in soft tones —ref. to speaking Theoc.(dub.)

—τρυφερῶς adv. **luxuriously** —ref. to living Arist.

τρυφερότης ητος f. indulgence in luxury, **luxuriousness** Arist.

τρυφή ῆς *f.* [θρύπτω] **1 luxuriance** (of a person's clothing) E. || PL. **luxuries or comforts** (esp. as exotic, opp. Greek) E. Isoc. Pl.
2 (freq.pejor.) **enjoyment of** (or **indulgence in**) **luxury, luxurious living** (esp. as an exotic or female trait) E. Ar. Att.orats. Pl. +
3 (personif., without pejor. connot.) **Luxury, Delight** Ar.
4 self-indulgent behaviour, irresponsibility (of women) Ar.

τρύφημα ατος *n.* [τρυφάω] **object of luxury; plaything** (W.GEN. of Zeus' bed, ref. to Ganymede) E.

τρύφος εος *n.* [θρύπτω] **that which is broken off; chunk** (of a rock, mountain) Od. Call.; **lump** (of rock-salt) Hdt.; **piece** (of an oar) AR.

τρῡχηρός ά όν *adj.* [τρῦχος] (of clothes) **worn out** E.; (of flesh, by age and suffering) E.

τρύχνος ου *f.* app., **plant of the nightshade family** Theoc.

τρῡχόομαι *pass.contr.vb.* [τρύχω] (of a person's property or livelihood) **be worn away, become exhausted** Mimn.
—**τετρῡχωμένος** η ον *pf.pass.ptcpl.adj.* (of persons, cities) **worn out** (by war or sim.) Th. Pl. Plu.

τρύχος εος (ους) *n.* (pl. and collectv.sg.) **rags, tatters** E. Ar.

τρύχω *vb.* [reltd. τρύω] | fut. τρύξω (Od.) | iteratv.impf. τρύχεσκον | only pres., fut. and impf. | **1 wear away** (resources) by attrition; (of unwanted guests) **wear out, exhaust** —*a person's property or livelihood* Od. —*a person* (i.e. *his resources*) Od.; (of drones) **consume** —*the work of bees* (i.e. *honey*) Hes. || PASS. (of a person, i.e. his resources) **be worn down** Od.
2 wear down (someone) with hardships; (of a rough wind) **wear down, wear out** —*people's strength* Hes.*fr.*; (of a commander) —*his troops* (w. *long campaigns*) X.; (of poverty) —*a person* AR.; (of a person) **distress** —*oneself* (w. *grief*) E.; (of blighted crops) —*people's hearts* S.; (of a person) **grind out** —*one's life* (*in misery*) Thgn.
3 || PASS. (of persons) **be worn down** or **worn out** (by hunger, sickness, travel, or sim.) Od. Thgn. S. E. Th. Ar. Plu.; (of a city, by faction) Sol.; (of a lover) **pine away** with desire —W.GEN. *for someone* Ar.

τρύω *vb.* [reltd. τρύχω] | fut. τρύσω (A.) | aor. ἔτρῡσα (Lyr.adesp.) || pf.pass. τέτρῡμαι | **weary, tire** —*someone's feet* (*or perh. horses*) Lyr.adesp.; (of a burden of suffering) **wear out, wear down** —*a person* A. || PF.PASS. **be worn out** (by famine, war, exertions, or sim.) Hdt. Pl. Plb. Plu.; (of military strength) Plb.; (of a farmer's knees) **be wearied** (by toil) AR.

Τρῳάς *fem.adj.*: see Τρωιάς, under Τρώς

τρωγάλιον ου *n.* [τρώγω] **item of food which can be nibbled** (such as fruits, various raw or cooked delicacies, esp. as a dessert); **sweetmeat, nibble** Pi.*fr.* Ar.(pl.)

τρώγματα των *n.pl.* **items of food for munching, munchables** (ref. to a dessert) Philox.Leuc.; (ref. to sausages or sim.) Ar.(cj.)

Τρωγοδύται (v.l. **Τρωγλοδύται**) έων *Ion.m.pl.* [app.loanwd.] **Trogodutai** (name of a people in Aithiopia, i.e. Egypt and to the south of it) Hdt. [The v.l., reltd. τρωγλοδύτης *animal which goes down a hole* (Arist.), usu.interpr. as *cave-dwellers*, is not appropriate to inhabitants of these regions.]

τρώγω *vb.* | fut. τρώξομαι | aor.2 ἔτραγον (in cpds.), dial.imperatv. τράγον (Carm.Pop.) | **1 take repeated small bites; nibble, chew** —*beans, fruits, delicacies* Sol. Hippon. Carm.Pop. Hdt. Ar. X. +; (fig.) **nibble on** —*someone's inferior ideas* (*as if scraps of food*) Ar.; (intr.) **have a snack** D.
2 (of herbivorous animals) **gnaw, munch** —*grass, plants, fruits* Od. Ar. Theoc.
3 (gener., tr. and intr.) **eat** Plb. NT.

τρωθήσομαι (fut.pass.): see τιτρώσκω

Τρωϊά *dial.f.*: see Τροία

τρώκτης ου *m.* [τρώγω] **one who nibbles** or **gnaws**; (pejor., fig.ref. to a foreign trader) **rodent** Od.

τρωκτός ή όν *adj.* **1 such as may be nibbled**; (of walnuts) **for nibbling** Philox.Leuc.
2 || NEUT.PL.SB. **edible seeds** (of lotus plants) Hdt.; **sweetmeats** (of sesame and honey) Hdt.; **dessert fruits** X.

τρῶμα *dial.n.*, **τρῶμα** *dial.f.*: see τραῦμα

τρωματίζω *Ion.vb.*, **τρωματίης** *Ion.m.*: see τραυματίζω, τραυματίας

τρώξιμος ον *adj.* [τρώγω] **such as may be nibbled** || COLLECTV.FEM.SG.SB. (perh. w. σταφυλή understd.) **grapes grown** (or **ripe**) **for eating** Theoc.

τρῶξις εως *f.* **gnawing** (W.GEN. of one's nails) Arist.

Τρώος (or **Τρωός**) *m.*, **Τρωός** *Ion.adj.*: see Τρώς

τρωπάω *contr.vb.* [τρέπω] | ep.3sg.mid.iteratv.impf. τρωπάσκετο | (of a nightingale) **twist and turn, modulate** —*its voice* Od. || MID. (of a person) **turn one's steps, turn** —W.ADV. or PREP.PHR. *back, in flight, to a place* Hom.
—W.INF. *to flee* Il.

Τρώς ωός *m.* —also **Τρώως** ου (or **Τρωός** οῦ) (Hes.*fr.*) *m.* [reltd. Τροία] **Tros** (mythol. ancestor of the Trojans) Il. Hes.*fr.* hHom.
—**Τρῶες** ων *m.pl.* **descendants of Tros, Trojans** Hom. +
—**Τρωιάς**, contr. **Τρῳάς**, άδος *fem.adj.* **1** (of women) **descended from Tros, Trojan** Il. hHom. E. || PL.SB. **Trojan women** Il. E.
2 (of the land, city, acropolis) of Tros, **Trojan** Hdt. S. E.; (of spoils) from the land of Tros, **Trojan** Od.; (of a town) in the land of Tros, **in the Troad** Th. || SB. **Troad** (ref. to NW. corner of Asia Minor) Hdt. X. Plb. NT. Plu.
—**Τρωικός** ή όν *adj.* (of the people, city, land, things assoc.w. them) **Trojan** Il. Hdt. Trag. Aeschin.(quot.epigr.) Plu.; (of the war, things assoc.w. it) Hdt. E. Isoc. || NEUT.PL.SB. **events at Troy** (ref. to the Trojan war) Hdt. Th. Isoc. Pl. Arist.
—**Τρώιος** η ον, also **Τρωός** ή όν *Ion.adj.* —also **Τρόιος** ᾱ ον (Alc.) *dial.adj.* (of horses, dogs, spears) **Trojan** Il.; (of the plain) Pi.*fr.*; (of a man, ref. to Paris) Alc. || FEM.PL.SB. **Trojan women** Hom.

τρῶσις εως *f.* [τιτρώσκω] (pl.) **wounding** Arist.

τρώσομαι (fut.pass.), **τρώσω** (fut.): see τιτρώσκω

τρωτός ή όν *adj.* (of persons, their flesh or body) **able to be wounded, vulnerable** Il. E. X.

τρωχάω *ep.contr.vb.* [τρέχω] (of maidservants, horses, mules) **run** Hom. AR.

τρώω *ep.vb.*: see τιτρώσκω

τύ *dial.2sg.nom.pers.pron.*, **τυ** (dial.enclit.acc.): see σύ

τύγα, also **τύγε** *dial.2sg.nom.pers.pron.* [σύ, γε] (emph.) **you** Theoc.

τυγχάνω *vb.* [reltd. τεύχω] | fut. τεύξομαι | ep.aor. ἐτύχησα, τύχησα | aor.2 ἔτυχον, ep. τύχον | pf. τετύχηκα, also τέτευχα (Arist. Plb.), ep.ptcpl. τετυχηώς | Ion.3sg.plpf. ἐτετεύχεε
|| The vb. reflects a passive sense of τεύχω. The sections are grouped as: (1–5) occur, happen, (6–9) hit the mark, be successful, (10–14) encounter. |
1 (of good or bad things) **happen** Trag. —W.DAT. *to someone* Hom. Hdt. Trag.
2 (usu. of persons) **happen** (by coincidence), **chance** —W.PTCPL. *to be doing* or *have done sthg.* Od. +; **be in the course of, happen in fact to be** —W.PTCPL. *doing sthg.* Hdt. +

3 (of persons or things, oft. w. no notion of coincidence) **happen** (w. ὤν *to be* understd.) —W.ADVBL.PHR. *somewhere* Hom. + —W.PREDIC.SB. or ADJ. *such and such* S. +
4 ‖ PF. (of a headland, cliff) **be set** or **lie** (in a specific position) Hom.
5 (freq. in ellipt.phrs., ref. to casual or unpredictable action) • ὅτι ἂν τύχωσι τοῦτο λέγουσι *they say what they happen to* (*say, i.e. they speak at random*) Pl. • ὅταν τύχω (τύχῃ), ὁπότε τύχοιεν *when I happen to, when one happens to, whenever they happen to* (*do sthg., i.e. on occasion, or in the end*) E. Th. Isoc. Pl.
6 **be successful in one's aim** (w. a spear or arrow), **hit one's target** Hom.; **hit** —W.GEN. *someone or sthg.* Il. Hdt. Pl. X. ‖ AOR.PTCPL. (w.aor.vb. *strike* or sim.) **hitting the mark, on target** Hom.
7 (fig., of a speaker) **hit the mark** (in looking for the right word) Trag.; **hit** —W.GEN. *the mark* (*i.e. speak to the point*) S.; **hit upon, meet** —W.GEN. *a listener's wishes and expectations* Th.; **hit upon, succeed in giving** —W.GEN. *good advice* Th.; (of a listener) **apprehend** —W.GEN. *someone's meaning* Pl.; (of a biographer) **capture** —W.GEN. *a person's qualities* X.
8 (gener.) **achieve one's aim, be successful, succeed** Anacr. Pi. E. Th. Pl. Arist. —W.PTCPL. *in doing sthg.* Il. A. Pi.
9 **make a successful plea, have one's request granted** Hdt.; **gain permission** —W.INF. *to do sthg.* Plu.
10 **happen to meet** (someone or sthg.); **fall in with, meet, encounter** (usu. W.GEN. someone) Od. A. Lys.; (of a person falling fr. a chariot) **meet, hit** —W.GEN. *deep sand* Il.
11 **meet with, experience, suffer** —W.GEN. *violence, wounds, misfortunes, death, punishment, or sim.* A. Hdt. E. Pl. X.
12 (gener.) **meet with** (sthg. welcome or desired); **gain, obtain, get** —W.GEN. *sthg.* Od. + —W.NEUT.ACC.ADJ. or PRON. *sthg.* Trag. —W.GEN. or ACC. *sthg.* (W.GEN. *fr. someone*) S.; **prevail** —W.GEN. *on someone* (W.INF. *to do sthg.*) Pl.
13 **get, win** —W.GEN. *a god or person* (*i.e. their support or compliance*) A. E.
14 **find** —W.GEN. *someone* (W.PREDIC.ADJ. *such and such, e.g. the Muses favourable*) Pi. S. E. And. Ar. +
—**τυχών** οὖσα όν *aor.2 ptcpl.adj.* (of things) **ordinary** Pl. Lycurg. Arist. ‖ MASC.SB. **person who happens to come by** Hes.; **casual** or **ordinary person** Isoc. Pl. X. D.
—**τυχόν** *aor.2 neut.ptcpl.adv.* **maybe, perhaps** Isoc. Pl. X. D. +
—**τυχόντως** *aor.2 ptcpl.adv.* **haphazardly, randomly, casually** Arist. Plb.
Τυδεύς έως (ep. έος) *m.* | acc. Τυδέα, ep. Τυδῆ | ep.dat. Τυδέϊ, also Τυδῆϊ (Theoc.) | **Tydeus** (one of the Seven against Thebes) Hom. Hes.*fr.* Ibyc. Hdt. Trag. Theoc.
—**Τυδεΐδης** εω *ep.m.* **son of Tydeus** (ref. to Diomedes) Hom. Scol.
τυΐδε (or **τυῒδε**), perh. also **τυΐδε** Aeol.*adv.* 1 **to this place, hither** Hes.(cj.) Sapph.
2 **to that place, thither** Theoc.
τυκίζω (or perh. **τυχίζω**) *vb.* [τύκος] **work** (stone) **with a mason's hammer**; (of birds) **work, chisel** —*stones* (W.DAT. *w. their beaks*) Ar.
τύκισμα (or perh. **τύχισμα**) ατος *n.* **that which has been chiselled**; (sg. and pl.) **stoneworkings, chiselled work** E.
τύκος (or perh. **τύχος**) ου *m.* [perh.reltd. τεύχω] 1 **tool for working stone, mason's hammer** or **chisel** E.
2 **battle-axe** Hdt.
τυκτά: see τέλειον, under τέλειος
τυκτός ή όν *adj.* [τεύχω] 1 (of a ground for sports) **constructed** or **prepared** Od.; (of a tombstone) **hewn,**

carved Theoc.; (of a plough-handle) **fashioned** (fr. adamant) AR.; (of an oxhide shield, a fountain) **crafted, well-made** Hom.
2 (of an evil, ref. to Ares) **complete, consummate** Il.
τύλη ης, dial. **τύλᾱ** ᾱς *f.* 1 **pillow, cushion** Sapph.
2 **hardened skin, callus, hump** (on a baggage-carrier's shoulder) Ar.
τύλος ου *m.* 1 **wooden bolt** (used in fastening ships' timbers), **trenail, dowel-pin** Ar.
2 **lump of hardened skin, callus** X.
τυλόω *contr.vb.* (of a bit) **make callous, harden** —*a horse's mouth* X.
—**τετυλωμένος** η ον *pf.pass.ptcpl.adj.* (of a workman) **with calluses** (W.ACC. + DAT. *on his hands, fr. the mattock*) Theoc.; (of wooden clubs) **studded** (W.DAT. *w. iron*) Hdt.
τυλωτός ή όν *adj.* (of clubs) **knurled** or **studded** Hdt.
τύμβευμα ατος *n.* [τυμβεύω] 1 **tomb, burial-chamber** S.
2 **that which is placed in a tomb, corpse** E.
τυμβεύω *vb.* [τύμβος] 1 **place in a tomb, entomb, bury** —*a dead person, a body* S. E. ‖ PASS. **be entombed** Ar.(mock-trag.)
2 **pour as an offering at a tomb** —*libations* S.
3 (intr., of a living person) **dwell entombed** S.
τυμβ-ήρης ες *adj.* [ἀραρίσκω] 1 (of a corpse) **entombed, buried** S.
2 (of an underground chamber) **entombing, tomb-like** S.
3 (of a suppliant's seat) **at a tomb, sepulchral** Ar.(mock-trag.)
τύμβος ου *m.* 1 **mound of earth or stones marking a grave, burial mound, barrow** Hom. S. AR.
2 (gener.) **grave, tomb** Hippon. Eleg. Pi. Hdt. Trag. +; (specif.) **tombstone** E.
3 (fig., in voc., as derog. address to an old man) **tombstone, sepulchre** Ar.; (appos.w. γέρων *old man*) **with one foot in the grave, at death's door** E.
τυμβοχοέω *contr.vb.* [τυμβοχόος] **heap up a burial mound** Hdt.
τυμβοχοή ῆς *f.* **heaping up of a burial mound** Il.
τυμβο-χόος ον *adj.* [χόω] (of a group of servants) **for heaping up a burial mound** A.
τυμβό-χωστος ον *adj.* [χωστός] (of a cave, in which a living person is to be immured) **as a burial mound** S.
τυμβ-ωρύχος ου *m.* [ὀρύσσω] **one who digs up graves, tomb-robber** Ar.
τύμμα ατος *n.* [τύπτω] 1 **blow, stroke** (of a weapon) A.
2 **prick, wound** (fr. a thorn) Theoc.
τυμπανισμός οῦ *m.* [τύμπανον] **drum-beating** (in orgiastic rites) Ar.
τυμπανίστρια ᾱς *f.* **drummer** (ref. to a woman who participates in orgiastic rites) D.
τύμπανον (also **τύπανον**) ου *n.* [τύπτω] 1 **hand-drum, drum** hHom. A.*fr.* Pi.*fr.* Hdt. E. Ar. + [The drum, of eastern origin, was held in the left hand and struck w. the right. It was used mainly by women, almost exclusively in orgiastic rites, such as those of Cybele, Dionysus, Sabazios.]
2 **war-drum** (of a Parthian army) Plu.
3 **stretching-frame, garrotte** Ar. Arist. [Instrument of execution, comprising a vertical plank to which the victim was clamped, w. feet off the ground, and perh. strangled by a collar round the neck.]
Τυνδάρεος ου, Att. **Τυνδάρεως** ω *m.* **Tyndareos** (husband of Leda) Od. +
—**Τυνδάρειος** ᾱ ον (also ος ον) *adj.* (of a child, the name) **of Tyndareos** E. Ar.; (of an oath of allegiance) **to Tyndareos** E.

—**Τυνδαρίδης** ου, dial. **Τυνδαρίδας** ᾶ m. son of Tyndareos (ref. to one of the Dioscuri) Pi. AR. Theoc.; (pl., ref. to the Dioscuri) Hes.fr. +

—**Τυνδαρίς** ίδος f. daughter of Tyndareos (ref. to Helen or Clytemnestra) E. Theoc.

τύνη ep.2sg.nom.pers.pron. [σύ] **you** (oft. w. peremptory or contemptuous tone) Il. Hes. Call. AR.

τυννός ή (dial. ᾱ́) όν adj. (of a child, meal) **small, little** Call. Theoc.

τυννοῦτος ον (also ο) adj. [οὗτος] (of persons or things) **as small as this, so small** Ar.

—**τυννουτοσί** ονί adj. (w. stronger force) **as small as this** Ar.

τυντλάζω vb. [τύντλος mud] (of a farm-worker) perh., **walk in mud, get mucky** Ar. [or perh. *break up the soil*]

τύπανον n.: see τύμπανον

τυπή ῆς f. [τύπτω] | only ep.dat.pl. τυπῇσι | **blow, stroke** (of a weapon or sim.) Il. AR.

τυπίς ίδος f. **hammer** (of a smith) Call. AR.

τύπος ου m. **1 blow** (of a smith's hammer) Hdt.(oracle)
2 visible trace of a blow or of pressure; **impression, imprint, mark** (of the bezel of a ring) E.; (of a footprint) S.(v.l. κτύπος); (on the handle of a shield, left by its bearer) E.; (of nails) NT.; (of a javelin) Plu.; (fig., made on the soul by things learned) Pl.
3 shape created by moulding, modelling or sculpture; **figure, model** (of a man, in wood; in stone, perh. as bas-relief) Hdt. || PL. carved figures (in stone) Hdt.; bas-reliefs E.fr. Plb.; mouldings (in metal, on a shield) E.; figurines (worn by priests of Cybele) Plb.; idols NT.; (periphr.) forms (w.GEN. of statues) E.; (gener.) images (ref. to statues) Isoc.
4 shape, outline (of an incomplete primeval being) Emp.; **shape, appearance** (of a person, Gorgons) A.; (of an unripe grape) S.fr.; (of an arm, a serpent) E.; (of letters of the alphabet, shorthand symbols) Plu.
5 (ref. to the contents of a document) **form** (of wording) NT. [or perh. *import, tenor*]
6 archetype or example (which may be reproduced or imitated); **pattern, model, type** (of persons, speech, or sim.) Pl. Plb. NT. Plu.; type (as recognisable fr. examples), **general character, type** Pl. || PL. general principles (of conduct) Plb.
7 outline, sketch, general idea (of a topic) Isoc. Pl. Arist. Men. Plb. Plu.; τύπῳ (sts. ἐν τύπῳ) *in outline, speaking generally* Pl. Arist. Plb. Plu.

τυπόω contr.vb. (of gods) **form, mould, model** —*humans* Pl. || NEUT.PTCPL.SB. that which gives shape (to a foetus) Plu. || PASS. (of objects) be sculpted (opp. painted) Pl.; (of physical things) be formed (as copies of eternal things) Pl.; (fig., of children) be moulded (by training) Plu.

τυπτητέος ᾱ ον vbl.adj. [τύπτω] (of a person) **who must be beaten** D.

τύπτω vb. | Att.fut. τυπτήσω | aor.1 ἔτυψα, ep. τύψα | aor.2 ἔτυπον (E.) | nom.pl.redupl.pf.ptcpl. τετυπόντες (Call.) || PASS.: fut. τυπτήσομαι (Ar.) | aor.2 ἐτύπην | also aor.1 ἐτύφθην (Plu.) | pf. τέτυμμαι, inf. τετύφθαι |
1 strike (someone or sthg.) with an implement; **strike, smite** (w. a sword, spear) —*a person, part of the body, shield* Hom. A. Hdt. X. Call. Plu.; (w. a cudgel, rod) Il. Arist. NT.; (w. stones) Plb.; (fig., w. a goad) —*a populace* (envisaged as a horse) Thgn. || PASS. be struck (by a weapon) Hom. Hes. Pi. Hdt. Trag. +; (by stones) S.; (by a boar's tusk) Bion; receive (by being struck) —w.ACC. *lashes* Pl. Aeschin.(law) —*wounds* Il.
2 strike (someone) with the hand or fist; **strike, beat** —*a person, part of the body* Hdt. Th. Ar. Att.orats. Pl. + —(W.INTERN.ACC. w. *a blow*) Antipho || PASS. be struck or beaten Hdt. E.Cyc. Att.orats. Ar. + —W.INTERN.ACC. w. *blows* Ar.
3 strike (sthg.) with deliberate purpose; **strike, beat** —*the sea* (W.DAT. w. *oars*) Od. —*the ground, a rock* (w. *the foot*) Il. AR. Plu.; (of a smith) —*metal* Call. || PASS. (of a cock, in a cock-fight) be struck Ion; (of timbers) —W.DAT. *by axes* AR.
4 strike (someone or sthg.) through accidental collision; (of a person falling) **strike, hit** —*the ground* (w. *one's forehead*) Od.; (of a discus) —*a person* Call.; (of a wind) **buffet** —*clouds* (w. *a storm-blast*) Il.; (of the rim of a shield slung over the back) **tap** —W.DBL.ACC. *someone, on his ankles and neck* Il. || PASS. (of a ship) be battered (by a reef) Alc.; (of a place) be buffeted (by a storm) Pi.
5 (usu. of a mourner) **beat** —*one's breast* Men. NT.; (mid.) —*one's breast, forehead* Plu. || MID. **beat one's breast** (in mourning) Hdt. —W.ACC. *for a god* Hdt.
6 pierce (someone or sthg.) with a sharp point; (of a thorn) **prick** —*a foot* Call. Theoc. || PASS. (of a person) be pricked (by a thorn) Theoc.; be stung (by a wasp, gadfly) X. AR.
7 have a powerful effect on the mind or emotions; (of grief, pain) **strike, smite** —*someone* Il. E. AR.; (of a reproach, envisaged as a goad) A.; (of realisation of the truth) Hdt. || PASS. (of persons) be struck —W.DAT. *by disaster* A. —*w. anguish* Pi.

τύπωμα ατος n. [τυπόω] **1** object which is shaped; **moulded urn** S.
2 shape, outline (of a person's body) E.

τύπωσις εως f. **impression** (made by a sight or feeling on the mind, compared to one made on wax) Plu.

τῠρακίνας ᾱ dial.m. [τῡρός] **cheesecake** Philox.Leuc.

τυραννεῖον ου n. [τύραννος] (sg. and pl.) **tyrant's palace** or **quarters** Plu.

τυραννεύω vb. —also **τυραννέω** contr.vb. [τύραννος] **1** (of an oriental monarch or satrap) **be ruler, rule** —W.GEN. *over a people or place* Hdt. Ar. || AOR. become ruler Hdt. Isoc.
2 (in Greek states) **be tyrant** (oft. W.GEN. over a people or place) Alc. Hdt. Th. Ar. Att.orats. Pl. + || AOR. become tyrant Sol. Hdt. Th. + || PASS. (of people, places) be subject to a tyrant Hdt. Th. +
3 (of kings or sim.) **be ruler, rule** (oft. W.GEN. over a people or place) S. E.; (of Kypris) —W.GEN. *over the heart of Zeus* S.fr.; (of a princess) **enjoy royal power** E.
4 (pejor.) **exercise despotic control** —W.GEN. *over someone* Isoc. Pl. X.; (fig., of a person, desire) **be imperious** Pl. || PASS. (of a person) be tyrannised —W.PREP.PHR. *by someone* D. —*by a passion* Pl.

τυραννίη ης Ion.f. **1** rule of a tyrant, **tyranny** Xenoph.
2 (gener.) **sovereignty, dominion** Archil.

τυραννίζω vb. **be an apologist for tyrants** D.

τυραννικός ή όν adj. | superl. τυραννικώτατος |
1 (freq.pejor.) of or relating to a tyrant; (of a person) **of the tyrannical kind** Pl.; (of a person's temperament or behaviour, laws, power, happenings) of the kind associated with tyrants, **tyrannical** Anacr. Att.orats. Pl. X. Arist. +; (of a person, sentiments or behaviour, a conspiracy) **supportive of tyranny** Th. Ar. Pl. X. || NEUT.PL.SB. time of the tyrants (in Athens, Syracuse) Isoc. Arist.
2 of or relating to a ruler; (of a dwelling, throne, blood, power, or sim.) **ruling, royal** Trag. Isoc.; (of a possession, ref. to a counsellor) **princely** Isoc.

3 (of a ruler, ref. to his temperament) **princely, noble** Isoc.; (pejor., of persons, their temperaments) **imperious, despotic** E. Pl.

—**τυραννικῶς** *adv.* | compar. τυραννικώτερον | **in the manner of a tyrant** (opp. a king) Isoc. Arist.; (opp. constitutionally) Arist.; **high-handedly, despotically** Isoc. Pl. Plu.

τυραννίς ίδος *f.* **1** (in oriental ctxt.) **kingship, absolute rule** Hdt.
2 (in Greek states) **rule by a tyrant, tyranny** Archil. Sol. Simon. Pi. Hdt. Th. +
3 (gener., usu. without pejor.connot.) **sovereignty, dominion, monarchy** (of men or gods) Trag. Ar.; (concr., ref. to the office itself) Trag.
4 (pejor.) **despotism** Th. Ar. +; (as the worst type of government) Pl.; (fig., as exercised by a desire) Pl.

τυραννοκτονία ᾱς *f.* [κτείνω] **killing of a tyrant** Plu.
τυραννο-ποιός οῦ *m.* [ποιέω] **tyrant-maker** Pl.
τύραννος ου *m.* (sts.*f.*) [loanwd.] **1** (ref. to an oriental ruler) **king, monarch** (sts. W.GEN. of a people or place) Hdt.; (ref. to a satrap) **ruler** Hdt.
2 (ref. to a Greek autocrat) **tyrant** Semon. Alc. Thgn. Scol. Pi. Hdt. +; **despot** Att.orats. Pl. Arist. + [The name was first applied to usurpers who established autocratic rule in Greek states in the 7th and 6th C. BC. At first neutral in tone, it later acquired a pejor. sense.]
3 (gener.) **monarch, sovereign, ruler** Trag. Isoc.; (ref. to a god) hHom. Trag. Ar.; (ref. to Persuasion) E.; (*f.*) **queen** S. E.; **princess** E. || COLLECTV.MASC.PL. **royal family** S. E.
4 || ADJ. (pejor., of a city) **despotic, tyrannical** Th.
5 || ADJ. (of a dwelling, sceptre, conduct, or sim.) **royal, kingly** Trag.

τυρβάζω *vb.* [τύρβη] **create disorder or mess**; (of a person, compared to a marsh-bird) **stir up** —*mud* Ar. || PASS. (of persons in a crowd) **be made to jostle, be thrown together** —W.DAT. *w. others* Ar.

τύρβη ης *f.* **confusion, disorder, turmoil** (created by a mob or mass of people) Isoc. X. Plb.

τυρεύματα των *n.pl.* [τυρεύω] **cheeses** E.

τυρεύω *vb.* [τυρός] **make (or make into) cheese**; (fig.) **curdle up a plot, concoct mischief** D.

τῡρέω contr.vb. **make cheese** —W.COGN.ACC. Alcm.

Τύριος *adj.*: see under Τύρος

τυρόεις εντος (or perh. dial. **τῡρῶς** ῶντος) *masc.adj.* [τυρός] (app.w. ἄρτος *cake* understd.) **of cheese** Theoc.

τυρό-κνηστις ιδος *f.* [κνῆστις] | acc. τυρόκνηστιν | **cheese-grater** Ar. Plu.

τυρό-νωτος ον *adj.* [νῶτον] (of a cake) **cheese-topped** Ar.

τυροπωλέω contr.vb. [τυροπώλης] **1 sell cheese, be a cheesemonger** Men.
2 (tr., fig.) **peddle like cheese** —*the art of poets* (i.e. sell it by weight) Ar.

τῡρο-πώλης ου *m.* [πωλέω] **cheese-seller, cheesemonger** Ar.

τῡρός οῦ *m.* (oft.pl.) **cheese** Hom. +

Τύρος ου *f.* **Tyre** (city in Phoenicia) Hdt. Isoc. Plb. NT. Plu.

—**Τύριος** ᾱ (Ion. η) ον *adj.* (of a person, ship, sea) **from or relating to Tyre, Tyrian** A. Hdt. E. Plb. Plu. || MASC.PL.SB. **Tyrians** Hdt. Plb. NT. Plu.

Τυρσηνοί, dial. **Τυρσᾱνοί** (Pi.), Att. **Τυρρηνοί**, ῶν *m.pl.* **Tyrsenians, Tyrrhenians** (Greek name for pre-Roman inhabitants of W. and NW. Italy, i.e. Etruscans) Hes. hHom. Pi. Hdt. +

—**Τυρσηνός** ή όν *adj.* (of a man) **Tyrsenian, Etruscan** Plu.; (of a bowl) Critias

—**Τυρσηνίᾱ**, Att. **Τυρρηνίᾱ**, ᾱς, Ion. **Τυρρηνίη** ης *f.* **Tyrrhenia** (i.e. Etruria) Hdt. Th. Pl. Arist. +

—**Τυρσηνικός**, Att. **Τυρρηνικός**, ή όν *adj.* (of a trumpet) **Tyrrhenian** Trag.; (of pirates) E.*Cyc.*; (of the sea N. of Sicily and W. of Italy) Th. Plb. Plu.; (of types of sacrifice) Pl.; (of a city, spear, war, property) Plu.

—**Τυρσηνίς**, Att. **Τυρρηνίς**, ίδος *fem.adj.* (of Scylla, located in the Strait of Messene) **Tyrrhenian** E.; (of the land, cities, or sim.) AR. Plb. Plu.; (of clothing) Plu.

τύρσις ιος *f.* **1 tower** (W.GEN. of Kronos, on the Isle of the Blessed) Pi.
2 tower, turret (usu. on a wall or house) X.

Τυρταῖος ου *m.* **Tyrtaeus** (Spartan elegiac poet, mid-7th C. BC) Pl. Lycurg. Arist. Plu.

τῡρῶς *dial.masc.adj.*: see τυρόεις

τυτθός όν (also ή όν Call. AR.) *adj.* **1** (of children) **little, young** Hom. Hes.*fr.* A. Call. Theoc.; (of a creature, ref. to a bee) **tiny** Theoc.; (of the arrow of Eros, contrasted w. its long reach) Mosch. || NEUT.SB. **bit** (W.GEN. of food) AR.
2 (of fear, shame) **slight** AR.; (of time) **short** Simon. AR.; (of a means of escape fr. death, ref. to a safe course betw. Scylla and Charybdis) **narrow** AR.; (of meat) **sparse** Theoc.
3 (prep.phr.) ἐπὶ τυτθόν *for a short time* AR.; *on a small scale* Call.

—**τυτθόν** *neut.sg.adv.* **1** (ref. to quantity, distance, time) **a little, slightly** Hom. Hes. S.*fr.* Hellenist.poet.
2 by a little, only just, barely —*ref. to missing or avoiding sthg., being alive* Il. AR.
3 softly —*ref. to speaking* Il.

—**τυτθά** *neut.pl.adv.* **1 into small pieces** —*ref. to cutting or breaking* Od.
2 only just, barely —*ref. to escaping* A.

Τυφάων *ep.m.*, **Τυφᾱόνιος** *ep.adj.*: see Τυφῶν

τῡφεδανός ή όν *adj.* [τῦφος] (of a person) **stupid or demented** Ar.

τῡφεδών ῶνος *f.* **stupidity, nonsense** (in speech) Call.

τυφλό-πους ποδος *masc.fem.adj.* [τυφλός, πούς] (of the foot of Oedipus) **stepping blindly** E.

τυφλός ή όν *adj.* **1** (of persons, animals, eyes) **unable to see, blind** Il. +; (fig., of a person able to see only a lover) **blind** (W.GEN. to all else) X.
2 (of a blinded person's hand, foot, staff) **not guided by sight, blind** E. || NEUT.PL.SB. **blind side** (W.GEN. of a soldier's body, i.e. his back) X.
3 (of persons, their heart or mind) **lacking comprehension or foresight, blind, undiscerning, uncomprehending** Pi. Parm. Hdt. E.*fr.* NT.; (of a person, W.ACC. in ears and mind, prophetic skill) S.; (W.GEN. in relation to the future) Plu.; (of hopes, opinions, or sim.) **blind, misdirected, deluded** A. Pl.
4 (of deities or personif. abstractions) **blind or acting as if blind**; (of Wealth) **blind, random, undiscriminating** Hippon. Timocr. E.*fr.* Ar. +; (of Eros) Theoc.; (of Fortune) Men.; (of human nature, when controlled by passion) Plu.
5 (of missiles) **aimed blindly** B.
6 unable to be seen; (of arrows) **unseen, unforeseen** (by their target) E.; (of ruin, by its victim) S.; (of rope-ends) **not visible, concealed** Plu.; (of internal injuries) Plu.; (of political unrest) **covert, secret** Plu.
7 (of marshes, shorelines) **full of hidden dangers, unpredictable, treacherous** Plu.; (of a stormy sea) Plu.

—**τυφλόν** *neut.adv.* **indistinctly, with a muffled sound** —*ref. to a dog growling* Plu.

—**τυφλῶς** *adv.* (fig., w. ἔχειν) **be blind** (to sthg.) Pl.

τυφλότης ητος *f.* **blindness** (sts. compared w. ignorance) Pl. Arist. Plu.

τυφλόω contr.vb. **1** make blind, **blind** —persons, their eyes or sight Hdt. E. Arist. NT. ‖ PASS. (of a person) be blinded or become blind Hdt. E. Isoc. Pl. Plu.; (fig., in one's perceptions) Pl.; (of a wound) be inflicted by blinding S.
2 make (sthg.) invisible ‖ PF.PASS. (of the gods' intentions) be hidden from view Pi.; (of the results of human toil) be consigned to obscurity Pi.
τύφλωσις εως f. blinding (of a person) Isoc.
τυφλώττω Att.vb. (fig.) be blind, lack discrimination Plb.
τῦφο-γέρων οντος m. [τῦφος] stupid old man, dotard Ar.
τῦφος ου m. **1** (medic.) delirium; (wkr.sens.) **delusion, humbug, baloney** Men. Plu.
2 false pride, conceit, vanity Plb. Plu.
τυφόω contr.vb. | pf.pass. τετύφωμαι | **1 delude** —a person or mind Alc.(dub.) ‖ PF.PASS. (of persons) be crazed or crazy Pl. D.; suffer from self-delusion or conceit Plb. Plu.
2 ‖ PASS. (of a bird) be stunned senseless (by a noise) Plu.
—**τετυφωμένως** pf.pass.ptcpl.adv. stupidly, crazily D.
τύφω vb. | only pres. and impf. | **1** create smoke; (of persons) **cause smoke** (maliciously or dangerously, in a mine) D.; **raise** —W.INTERN.ACC. smoke (as a signal) Hdt.; (of sacrificial fat) give off smoke S.
2 (tr.) expose (sthg.) to smoke; **smoke out** (W.DAT. w. smoke) —wasps Ar.; (fig., of an enemy) —a city Ar. ‖ PASS. (of bees) be overcome —W.DAT. by smoke AR.
3 cause to give off smoke, **send up in smoke, incinerate** —the Cyclops (by burning out his eye) E.Cyc. ‖ PASS. (of the Cyclops) be burned up E.Cyc.; (of a city or ruin) smoulder E.; (of Aetna) Call.; (of a person blasted by a thunderbolt, of a forest) AR.; (of a lamp-wick) NT.; (fig., of a war, opp. blaze up) Plu.
Τῡφῶν ῶνος, ep. **Τῡφάων** ονος m. —also **Τῡφώς** ῶ, ep. **Τῡφωεύς** έος m. | acc. Τῡφῶνα, also Τῡφῶ | **Typhon, Typhaon**, also **Typhos, Typhoeus** (giant w. a hundred serpent-heads, son of Gaia and Tartaros, blasted beneath the earth by Zeus; assoc.w. elemental forces such as volcanoes and hurricanes) Il. Hes. hHom. A. Pi. Hdt. +
—**Τῡφᾱόνιος** η ον ep.adj. (of a rock in the Caucasus) **of Typhon** AR. ‖ NEUT.SB. Typhonian hill (in Boeotia) Hes.
τῡφωνικός ή όν adj. [τῡφώς] (of a wind) **with the force of a hurricane** NT.
τῡφώς ῶ m. hurricane, whirlwind Trag. Ar.
τυχαῖος ᾱ ον adj. [τύχη] (of an encounter, event) **fortuitous, accidental** Plu.
τύχη ης, dial. **τύχᾱ** ᾱς f. [τυγχάνω] | The wd. refers to an agency or force, unseen and beyond human control, acting deliberately or at random; also to events befalling persons which are attributed to that agency, and gener. to unpredictable happenings. |
1 (personif., as a deity determining human fortune) **Fortune, Providence** Hes. hHom. Alcm. Archil. S. E. +; (w.epith. σωτήρ, σώτειρα Saviour) A. Pi. S.; (as a semi-personif. agent) fortune, providence, luck B. Hdt. Trag. Th. Att.orats. Pl. +; (periphr.) ἀναγκαία τύχη inescapable fortune, fate S.
2 fortune as dispensed or controlled by the gods; **fortune, fate** (sts. W.GEN. fr. a god or gods) Pi. Trag. +; (W.ADJ. θεία god-sent) Hdt. S. Pl. X.
3 fortune ascribed to some unforeseen or unpredictable cause, **fortune, chance, accident** Hdt. Trag. Th. Ar. +
4 (semi-personif.) random chance, **chance, luck** (opp. divine providence) E.; (as a capricious or malignant agent) E. Men. Plb.; (personif., as a deity) **Chance, Luck** Men.
5 (specif., oft.pl.) that which befalls an individual, **fortune, lot, circumstance** Simon. Pi. Hdt. Trag. Att.orats. +
6 favourable outcome of fortune; **good luck, success** hHom. Thgn. Pi. Hdt. Trag. Th. +; (W.ADJ. ἀγαθή good or sim.) Sol. Carm.Pop. A. Hdt. Ar. +; ἀγαθῇ τύχῃ (usu. in prayers and wishes) with fortune's blessing Th.(treaty) Ar. Att.orats. Pl. +
7 unfavourable outcome of fortune; **mischance, misfortune** Hdt. Trag. Att.orats. Pl. +; (W.ADJ. κακή bad or sim.) Trag.; (personif.) **Misfortune** E.
τυχηρός ά όν adj. **1** (of a person) enjoying good fortune, **fortunate, successful** A.; (of resources) **favourable** Arist.
2 ‖ NEUT.PL.SB. accidents of fortune, coincidences Plu.
—**τυχηρῶς** adv. with good fortune, successfully Ar.
τύχησα (ep.aor.): see τυγχάνω
τυχίζω vb., **τύχισμα** n.: see τυκίζω, τύκισμα
τυχικός ή όν adj. [τύχη] (of an incident) **fortuitous** or **fortunate** Plb.
—**τυχικῶς** adv. fortuitously, by chance Plb.
τυχόν aor.2 neut.ptcpl.adv., **τυχόντως** aor.2 ptcpl.adv.: see under τυγχάνω
τύχον (ep.aor.2): see τυγχάνω
τύχος m.: see τύκος
τω (dat.enclit.indef.pron.adj.): see τις
τώ[1] (Aeol.masc.neut.gen.art.), **τῶ**[1] (dial.): see ὁ
τώ[2] (nom.acc.du.): see ὁ
τώ[3], **τῶ**[2] neut.adv.: see under ὁ
τῷ[1] (masc.neut.dat.art., also neut.adv.): see ὁ
τῷ[2] (dat.interrog.pron.): see τίς
τωθάζω vb. | fut. τωθάσομαι | aor. ἐτώθασα | engage in mockery or scurrility; **jeer, scoff, sneer** Arist. —W.ACC. at someone Hdt. Pl. Theoc.; **play a dirty trick** Ar. —W.ACC. on someone Ar. ‖ PASS. be jeered at Pl.
τωθασμός οῦ m. mockery, scurrility Arist.
τωνδέων (Aeol.masc.gen.pl.): see ὅδε
τώνεκα Boeot.demonstr.conj.: see τούνεκα
τώς[1] dial.adv. **1** (as demonstr.adv., equiv. to οὕτως, w.vb.) **in this way, thus, so** Hom. Hes. A. B. S.Ichn. Call. AR.; (correlatv.w. ὡς or sim.) Il. Alcm. Archil. A. Parm. Call. AR.
2 (intensv., w.adj.) **so** Od.
3 (summing up an argument) **thus, therefore** Parm. S.(cj.)
4 (in comparisons, equiv. to ὡς, w. noun) **as, like** A.(dub.) S.Ichn. Ar.; (w.adv.) Men.
τώς[2] (dial.masc.acc.pl.): see ὁ

Υ υ

ὔ (also **ὗ**) *interj.* **1 ow!** (repeated as an expression of alarm) S.*Ichn.*
2 hu (repeated to represent the sound of sniffing a scent) Ar.
Ὑάδες ων *f.pl.* [prob. ὗς; pop.etym. ὔω] | also Ὗάδες (E.) | **Hyades** (stars in a constellation betw. the Pleiades and Orion, assoc.w. rainfall) Il. Hes. E.
ὕαινα ης *f.* **hyena** Hdt.
Ὑακίνθια ων *n.pl.* [Ὑάκινθος] **Hyacinthia** (Lacedaemonian festival in honour of Hyacinthos) Hdt. Th. X. Plu.
Ὑακινθίδες ων *f.pl.* daughters of Hyacinthos, **Hyacinthids** (title given to the daughters of Erekhtheus) E.*fr.* D.
ὑακινθινο-βαφής ές *adj.* [ὑακίνθινος, βάπτω] (of a helmet plume) **dyed hyacinthine** (i.e. blue-black or perh. dark red) X.
ὑακίνθινος, Aeol. **ϝακίνθινος**, η (dial. ᾱ) ον *adj.* [ὑάκινθος] **1** (of blossom, flower-petals) **of hyacinths** Od. E. Theoc.; (of fields) Anacr.
2 (of an egg) **of hyacinth colour** Sapph.(dub.)
ὑάκινθος, Aeol. **ϝάκινθος**, ου *m.f.* a kind of flower, **hyacinth** (prob. ref. to an iris or orchid) Il. hHom. Sapph. Thgn. Theoc. Mosch.
—**Ὑάκινθος** ου *m.* **Hyacinthos** (Laconian youth, loved by Apollo but accidentally killed by him w. a discus) Hes.*fr.*(cj.) E. AR. Plu.; (as a cult title of Apollo) Plb.
ὑάλινος η ον *adj.* [ὕαλος] (of drinking-vessels) **made of glass** Ar.
ὕαλος ου *f.* **1** a kind of transparent fusible mineral, **glass** Ar. Pl. Call.
2 a kind of crystalline stone, **rock crystal** Hdt.
ὑββάλλω *ep.vb.*: see ὑποβάλλω
ὑβός οῦ *m.* **hump-back** (derog., ref. to a person, perh. w.connot. of being a passive homosexual) Theoc.
ὑβρίζω, dial. **ὑβρίσδω** *vb.* [ὕβρις] | fut. ὑβριῶ | aor. ὕβρισα | pf. ὕβρικα ‖ MID.: fut. ὑβριοῦμαι ‖ PASS.: fut. ὑβρισθήσομαι | aor. ὑβρίσθην | freq. w.COGN.ACC. or w. εἰς + ACC. *towards* or *against someone* |
1 behave arrogantly or **insolently** Od. +
2 be self-indulgent or **excessive** (in one's appetites) Antipho X.
3 be rebellious (against one's superiors) Hdt. X.; (of women) **be unruly** S. E. Ar.; (of an animal) Hdt. X.
4 inflict insult or **dishonour** S. E. Lys. Pl. X. +; **insult, dishonour** —*someone* Od. +; (of a man) **degrade** —*himself* (*by working as a prostitute*) Aeschin. ‖ PASS. **be insulted** or **dishonoured** S. E. Th. +
5 (in legal ctxt.) **be slanderous** Lys. Pl. Aeschin.; **slander, defame** —*someone* Is.
6 behave violently or **outrageously** E. Th. Ar.(also mid.) +; (of a river w. a strong current) **be violent** Hdt.
7 treat with violence (physically or sexually), **assault, abuse, maltreat, outrage** —*persons* Il. + ‖ PASS. **be treated violently, be abused** E. Th. +; (of a man who has shaved off his facial hair) **have** (w.ACC. his cheeks) **violated** Ar.
8 (in legal ctxt., as a punishable offence) **commit an assault** Att.orats. X.; **assault** —*someone* Lys. Pl. D.
9 (of soldiers) **ravage, pillage** —*cities, islands* Isoc. ‖ PASS. (of a city, populace) **be oppressed** (by a tyrant, foreign power) Isoc. X.
—**ὑβρισμένος** η ον *pf.mid.pass.ptcpl.adj.* **1** (of a design on a shield) **aggressive, offensive** E.
2 (of a style of clothing) **ostentatious, excessive** X.
3 ‖ NEUT.PL.SB. **outrageous acts** Lys.
ὕβρις, Aeol. **ὔβρις**, εως (dial. ιος, also εος Ar.) *f.* **1 arrogance, insolence** Od. +; (appos.w. ἀνήρ) **man who is an exemplar of insolence** Hes.
2 unruliness (of animals) Archil. Hdt. X.
3 instance of arrogant behaviour (in speech or action), **abuse, insult** Hom. +
4 violence, assault, outrage Hes. +
5 violence (of animals) Pi.; (of a storm) NT.
6 (in legal ctxt.) **physical violence, assault** (sts. punishable by death) Ar. Att.orats.
7 (specif.) **violation** (ref. to adultery or rape) Att.orats. +
8 crime involving disrespect (of the state and public religion), **sacrilege** Pl.
9 self-inflicted dishonour, degradation (of the body of a man working as a prostitute) Aeschin.
10 (personif.) **Hybris** B.; (mother of Κόρος *Excess*) Pi. Hdt.(oracle)
ὕβρισμα ατος *n.* [ὑβρίζω] **1 outrageous action** or **behaviour** Hdt. E. X. D. Plu.
2 insult (in speech) Hdt.
3 (ref. to a person) **object of abuse, victim of dishonour** (at the hands of an enemy) E.
4 affront (to humans, ref. to Centaurs) E.; (to the gods, ref. to an over-populated earth) E.
ὑβριστέος ᾱ ον *vbl.adj.* (of persons) **to be maltreated** D.
ὑβριστής οῦ *masc.adj.* | ep.gen.pl. ὑβριστάων ‖ irreg. compar. ὑβριστότερος (Hdt. Pl. X.), irreg.superl. ὑβριστότατος (Ar. Pl. X.) | **1** (of persons) **arrogant, insolent, abusive** or **violent** Hom. Hes. Anacr. Eleg. Hdt. Trag. +; (of Typhon) Hes.
2 (of an army) **rampaging** Thgn.
3 (of bulls, horses, satyrs) **restive, unruly** E. Pl. X. Plu.; (of a crowd) Hdt.
4 (of a Bacchant's thyrsos) **violent** E.
5 (of persons) **liable to** or **guilty of violent conduct** (such as is punishable by law) Att.orats.
6 lacking in sexual restraint, wanton, outrageous And. Ar. X.
7 (wkr.sens.) **mocking, sarcastic** Ar. Pl.

ὑβριστικός ή όν adj. **1** (of words, actions, a frame of mind, or sim.) **insolent, insulting** or **outrageous** Att.orats. Pl. X. Arist. Plu. || NEUT.SB. insolence X. || NEUT.PL.SB. outrageous treatment (at someone's hands) D.
2 (of ideas, lines of verse) **outrageous, monstrous** Pl. Plu.
—**ὑβριστικῶς** adv. | compar. ὑβριστικώτερον | **insolently, insultingly** or **outrageously** Pl. X. D. Plb. Plu.
ὑβριστότατος superl.adj., **ὑβριστότερος** compar.adj.: see ὑβριστής
ὑγιάζω vb. [ὑγιής] make healthy, **cure, heal** —*the sick, a physical condition* Arist. Plb.; (intr.) heal Arist. || PASS. be made healthy, be cured Arist. Plb.
ὑγιαίνω vb. | fut. ὑγιανῶ | aor. ὕγίᾱνα | **1** (of persons, their bodies, or sim.) **be healthy** Thgn. Scol. Hdt. Th. Ar. Pl. +
2 be able-bodied (opp. disabled) Lys.
3 (of a mind) **be sound** Hdt.; (of a person) **be of sound mind** Ar. Pl. D. Men. Plu. || NEUT.PTCPL.SB. reasonable part (of the populace, an army) Plu.
4 (fig., of a city, its condition, a form of government, or sim.) **be stable** X. D. Plu.; (of a policy) **be sound** Plu.; (of ambition, in neg.phr.) **be sane** Plu.
5 be healthy (in one's allegiance), **be sound** or **loyal** Plb. Plu. || NEUT.PTCPL.SB. sound part (of Greece, i.e. that which remains loyal against a foreign enemy) Hdt.; (of the Senate, a populace) Plu.
6 || IMPERATV. (in taking leave) fare well! Ar. || INF. (as a greeting, w. double meaning) health and sanity! Plu.
ὑγίανσις εως f. **process of becoming healthy** Arist.
ὑγίεια, also **ὑγιείᾱ** (Ar.), **ὑγεία** (Plu.), ᾱς, Ion. **ὑγιείη** ης f.
1 state of being healthy, **good health** Lyr. A. Hdt. E. Ar. Isoc. + || PL. instances of good health Pl.
2 soundness (W.GEN. of mind) A.
3 (as a deity) **Hygieia, Health** Lyr. Critias Hyp. Plu.; (Lat. *Salus*) Plu.
ὑγιεινός ή όν adj. **1** good for the health; (of foods, places, activities, or sim.) **healthy, wholesome, salubrious** Isoc. Pl. X. Arist. Men. Plu. || NEUT.SB. that which promotes good health Pl. Arist.
2 (of matters) **relating to health** Pl. Arist. || NEUT.SB. health (as a condition or subject of study) Pl.
3 having good health; (of persons, their bodies, or sim.) **healthy** Isoc. Pl. X. Arist. Plb. Plu.; (fig., of a city) Pl. || NEUT.SB. condition of being healthy, state of good health Pl. Arist.
—**ὑγιεινῶς** adv. | compar. ὑγιεινότερον, also ὑγιεινοτέρως (X.) | **1 with a concern for health** —*ref. to a doctor applying treatment* Pl.
2 healthily —*ref. to living* X.; (w. ἔχειν) be in good health Pl.
3 soundly —*ref. to walking* Arist.; (fig.) —*ref. to understanding* Arist.
ὑγίεις εσσα εν adj. (of prosperity) **healthful, sound** Pi.
ὑγιηρός ά (Ion. ή) όν adj. | superl. ὑγιηρότατος, also ὑγιηρέστατος | **1** (of a remedy) good for the health, **wholesome, healing** Pi.
2 (of a people) **healthy** Hdt.
ὑγιής ές adj. | masc.fem.acc.sg. ὑγιῆ, Att. ὑγιᾶ, Ion. ὑγιέα |
1 (of persons, animals, their bodies) **healthy** Sol. Simon. Hdt. Th. Att.orats. + || NEUT.SB. condition of being healthy Pl. Arist.
2 (of persons) **cured** (of lovesickness) X. Theoc.
3 (of persons, their mind, soul, character) **sane** Simon. E. Pl.; (of thoughts, plans, or sim.) Hdt. Th. Pl.; (of a city, its character) Pl.
4 in good or undamaged condition; (of ships, a wall) **in good repair, sound** Th.; (of objects, a corpse) **undamaged, intact** Lys. Pl. X.; (of a substance) **unaltered** Pl.; (of sthg.

previously damaged) **restored** Pl.; (of virtue as a concept) **whole** (i.e. not analysed into its constituents) Pl.
5 (of advice, criticism) **sound, beneficial** Il. Pl.; (of a message, an account) **true** D. Plb.
6 (neg.phr.) οὐδὲν ὑγιές **no health** (*in a person's body or soul, an animal's womb*) Hdt. E. Ar. Pl. D.; *nothing true* (*in words, thoughts or appearances*) S. E. Th. Ar. Att.orats. +; *nothing beneficial* (*in certain merchandise, pleasure*) Ar. Pl.; *nothing honest* (*in or fr. a person's actions*) E. Ar. Pl. +
—**ὑγιές** neut.adv. with a true tone, **soundly** —*ref. to an object ringing (when tested by tapping)* Pl.
—**ὑγιῶς** adv. **1 healthily, soundly** Pl.
2 sensibly —*ref. to thinking, deciding* Pl.
3 with integrity —*ref. to managing public finances* D.
4 accurately —*ref. to making a calculation* D. —*ref. to narrating history* Plb.
ὑγραίνω vb. [ὑγρός] | aor. ὕγρᾱνα | **1 make wet; moisten** —*one's eyes, cheeks* (W.DAT. w. *tears*) E.; (of a river) **water, irrigate** —*areas of land* E.; (intr., of south winds) **bring moisture** X.; (of things) **cause moistness** Pl. || PASS. be moistened Pl.
2 pour —*libations* E.
ὑγρο-βόλος ον adj. [βάλλω] (of drops of water) **moisture-spreading** E.*fr.*
ὑγρο-μελής ές adj. [μέλος] (of a newborn hare) **soft-limbed** X.
ὑγρός ά (Ion. ή) όν adj. **1** consisting of flowing liquid; (of a sea, waterfall, wave, stream) **flowing, running** Hom. hHom. Iamb.adesp. Pi. Trag. Ar. +; (of boundaries formed by bodies of water) **watery** E. || FEM.SB. sea Hom. hHom. E. Ar. Call.*epigr.* AR.
2 (of the air, its consistency) **fluid** Pi. Emp. E. Call.; (of an admixture, in the air) **of moisture** E.*fr.*
3 consisting of a liquid; (of drops of water, tears, sweat) **wet** E. Arist.(quot.); (of a drink, agricultural produce) **liquid** E. X.; (of a substance, its nature) X. Arist. || NEUT.SB. moisture (in the body of a person or animal, in the ground) Pl. X. Plu.
4 in liquid or soft form; (of oil, wax, or sim.) **liquid** (opp. solid or viscous) Hom. hHom. Pl. Theoc.; (of water, opp. frozen) Pl.; (of organic matter, as an ingredient for a dye) Simon.; (of mud, blood, bile) Pl. Plu.; (of nourishment) Arist. || NEUT.SB. liquid (esp. water) Hdt. Pl. X. +
5 covered in or permeated by moisture; (of a surface, piece of ground, or sim.) **damp, moist** S. Pl. X. Plu.; (of eyes) **wet** (w. tears) AR.; (of a corpse) AR.; (of dust) E. || NEUT.SB. damp place Pl.; dampness (of a region) Hdt.; moistness (of the tongue, w.connot. of fluency) Thphr.
6 full of moisture; (of a night, clouds) **wet, rainy** Ar. Pl.; (of a mist) **thick** Plu.; (of a storm) **torrential** Plu.; (of fruits) **succulent** Plu.; (fig., of poems) **saturated** (as if w. water, so as to be heavier) Ar. || NEUT.SB. wetness (as a property, opp. dryness) Pl. Arist.
7 of or relating to liquids; (of measures) **liquid** Pl. Arist.
8 (of a kind of motion) **flowing** Pl. Plu.
9 (of plants, trees) well-watered (so as to be pliant), **supple, green** (opp. dry and brittle) Theoc. NT.
10 flexible and soft (as if a liquid); (of a person's body) **relaxed** Ar.; (of a dying person's body, a limb) **languid** S. E.; (of Eros) **gentle, tender** Pl.; (of desire) hHom.
11 flexible and easily moved; (of persons, their limbs, muscles, joints) **supple** B. Pl. X.; (of a bow) **pliant** Theoc.; (of a horse's bit) **flexible** (in its joints) X.; (fig., of the back of a sleeping eagle) **rippling** Pi.
12 (fig., of a person, soul) **easy-going** Heraclit. Plu. || NEUT.SB. easy-going nature Plu.; lavishness (in lifestyle) Plu.

13 (fig., of perception) **flexible, fluid** (i.e. unstable) Plu.

–ὑγρόν neut.adv. **with mist and rain** —*ref. to a wind blowing* Od. Hes. hHom.

–ὑγρῶς adv. | compar. ὑγροτέρως | **in a supple manner** —*ref. to a horse bending its knees* X.

ὑγρότης ητος f. **1 moistness** (as a condition) Arist.
2 moisture (in soil, clay, mould) X. Plu.
3 fluid (inside the body or eyes) Pl. Arist. Plu.
4 sweat (on the skin) Plu.
5 glaze, sheen (in the eyes, on the face) Plu.
6 flowing or **flickering motion** (of a flame) E.
7 quality of being pliant, **suppleness** (in the body's joints) X.; (fig.) **softness, sympathetic nature** (of a jury) Lycurg.; **relaxed character** (shown in generosity) Plu.

ὑγρο-τροφικός ή όν adj. [τρέφω] (of a category of animal husbandry) **concerned with the rearing of aquatic animals** Pl.

ὑγρώσσω vb. (of a sponge) **be wet** A.

ὑδαρής ές adj. [ὕδωρ] **1** (of a honey drink) **diluted with water** Arist.; (of wine) **watery** X.
2 (fig., of friendship) **watery** A. Arist.; (of a narrative plot) **diluted** (by being told at length) Arist.

ὑδατ-ηγός οῦ m. [ἄγω] (appos.w. ἀνήρ) **one who draws water** (fr. a well) Call.

ὑδάτινος η ον, Aeol. **ὑδάτινος** ᾱ ον adj. | ῡ- metri grat. | (of garments) **as if made of water, flowing, rippling** Call. Theoc.

ὑδάτιον ου n. [dimin. ὕδωρ] **small river, rivulet** Pl.

ὑδατόεις εσσα εν adj. | ῡ- metri grat. | (of clouds) **rain-charged** Theoc.

ὑδατο-θρέμμων ον, gen. ονος adj. [τρέφω] | ῡ- metri grat. | (of fish) **water-bred** Emp.

ὕδατος (gen.sg.): see ὕδωρ

ὑδατο-τρεφής ές adj. [τρέφω] (of trees) **nourished by water** Od.

ὑδατώδης ες adj. (of ice) **watery, slushy** Th.

ὕδει (ep.dat.sg.): see ὕδωρ

ὑδερικός ή όν adj. [ὕδερος] (of an ailment) **dropsical** Plu.

ὕδερος ου m. [ὕδωρ] ailment involving a build-up of water (in parts of the body), **dropsy** Arist. Plu.

ὑδέω contr.vb. —also **ὑδείω** ep.vb. [perh.reltd. ᾄδω, αὐδή] **sing of, celebrate** —*a person* Call. || PASS. (of a people) **be reported** —W.INF. *to have existed* (*since the distant past*) AR.; (of events) **be recounted** AR.

ὕδιον (unless **ὐίδιον**) ου n. [dimin. ὗς] **piglet** X.

ὕδρα ᾱς, Ion. **ὕδρη** ης f. [ὕδωρ] **monstrous water-serpent, hydra** (assoc.w. Lerna nr. Argos) Hes. S. E. AR.; (as the exemplar of an invincible opponent) Pl. Plu.

ὑδραγωγία ᾱς f. [ἀγωγή] **conveyance of water; system of irrigation** (in the veins) Pl.

ὑδραίνω vb. | aor.mid. ὑδρᾱνάμην, Ion. ὑδρηνάμην |
1 sprinkle with water —*a person* (*as a sacrificial victim*) E.
2 || MID. **wash oneself** Od. —W.INTERN.ACC. *in bathing-water* E.

ὑδρεία ᾱς, Ion. **ὑδρείη** ης f. [ὑδρεύω] **1 supplying of water; provision of water** Pl.; **fetching water** (using a water-jar or sim.) Th. AR. Plb. Plu.; **water-supply** Plb.
2 place with a supply of water, **watering-place** Plb. Plu.
3 conveyance of water (fr. one part of the body to another), **irrigation** Pl.
4 means of supplying water (for agriculture), **channel, conduit** Pl.

ὑδρεύω vb. [ὕδωρ] **1 draw** or **fetch water** (esp. fr. a spring or well) Od. Thgn.; (mid.) Od. hHom. Hdt. E. Th. Pl. +
2 || MID. (fig., of organs of the body) **draw nutrients** (fr. the blood stream) Pl.

ὑδρήιον ου Ion.n. **container for water, water-jar** Hdt.

ὑδρηλός ή όν adj. **1** (of meadows, an island) **well-watered** Od. hHom.
2 (of clouds, drops) **watery** A. E.
3 (of jars) **for water** E.Cyc.

ὑδρηνάμην (Ion.aor.mid.): see ὑδραίνω

ὑδρίᾱ ᾱς, Ion. **ὑδρίη** ης f. **1 pot for carrying or storing water, water-jar, pitcher** Ar. D. Arist.(provb.) Men.(cj.) Plb. +; (for storing treasure) Ar. | for the provb. see θύρα 8
2 pot shaped like a water-jar; **voting-urn** Isoc. X. Arist. Plu.; **funeral-urn** (for ashes) Plb. Plu.

ὑδριᾱ-φόρος ου m. [φέρω] **one who carries a water-jar** (in a religious procession), **jar-carrier** Ar.

ὑδρίον ου n. [dimin. ὑδρίᾱ] **small container for water, water-jar** (for an individual) Plu.

ὑδρο-ειδής ές adj. [εἶδος¹] (of a river god) **in watery form** E.

ὑδρόεις εσσα εν adj. (of reeds) **well-watered** E.

ὑδρο-μέλαθρος ον adj. [μέλαθρον] (of fish) having a home under water, **water-dwelling** Emp.

ὑδροποσίᾱ ᾱς f. [ὑδροπότης] **1 practice of drinking only water** (i.e. abstaining fr. wine), **water-drinking** X. Plu. || PL. periods of drinking water only (during campaigns) Pl.
2 drink of water Plu.

ὑδροποτέω contr.vb. **drink only water** (i.e. abstain fr. wine) Hdt. Pl. X.

ὑδρο-πότης ου m. **one who drinks only water** (i.e. not wine), **water-drinker** X.

ὑδρο-ρρόᾱ ᾱς f. [ῥοή] **course for water; drain** (at the base of a wall) Ar. Men.; **irrigation channel** Ar.

ὑδρόρροια ᾱς f. [ῥόος] **structure for the conveyance of water, aqueduct** Plb.

ὕδρος ου m. [ὕδρᾱ] **1 water-snake** Il. Hdt. Call.
2 monstrous water-serpent, **hydra** (at Lerna) Hippon.

ὑδροφορέω contr.vb. [ὑδροφόρος] (of women) **fetch water** X.

ὑδρο-φόρος ου f. [φέρω] **water-carrier** (ref. to a woman) Hdt. X. Call.; (as the name for a type of female statue) Plu.

ὑδρό-χυτος ον adj. [χυτός] (of springs) **pouring forth water** E.Cyc.

ὑδρωπικός ή όν adj. [ὕδρωψ *dropsy*] **suffering from dropsy** Plb. NT.

ὕδωρ ὕδατος, Aeol. **ὕδωρ** ὕδατος n. | ep.dat.pl. ὑδάτεσσι | —also ep. **ὕδος** εος (Call.) | dat. ὕδει (Hes. Thgn.) | sts. ῡ- metri grat. | **1 water** (esp. for washing, drinking, diluting wine) Hom. +; (given w. earth as a token of submission to a Persian conqueror) Hdt. Att.orats. +
2 water (in or fr. a spring, stream, river, lake or well) Hom. +; (in or fr. the sea) Od. +
3 water (in the form of rain) Il. Xenoph. Hdt. Ar. Pl. X.; **rain, rainfall** Pi.fr. Hdt. Th. Ar. + || PL. showers of rain X. D.
4 water (in the form of flooding) Pi. D.; **flooding** Th. X. D. || PL. floods X. D.
5 water (as an element, opp. fire) Archil. Thgn.; (as one of four elements) Pl. Arist.; (as a deity) Men.
6 source of water, **water-supply** Hdt. Th. Pl. X.
7 water (opp. dry land); **body** or **stretch of water** (ref. to a spring, stream, river or waterfall) Hom. Hdt. Trag. X. +; (ref. to a pond, lake) Od. S. E. X.; (ref. to the sea, its current) Od. Hes. Mimn. A. E.
8 water (used as a measure of time, esp. in a lawcourt); **water** (in a clock) Att.orats.; (ref. to a period of time allotted for hearing a case or speech) Att.orats. Pl.; (ref. to an opportunity to speak) Att.orats.

ὑεῖ (Att.du.nom.acc.): see υἱός

ὕειος ᾱ ον *adj*. [ὗς] **1** of or from a pig; (of tripe) **pig's** Ar.; (of meat, i.e. pork) Plu.
2 (of a beast, to which a soul wallowing in ignorance is compared) **pig-like** Pl.
ὕεσιν (Att.du.gen.dat.), **ὕεος** (Att.gen.): see υἱός
ὕεσσι (ep.dat.pl.): see ὗς
ὑέτιος ᾱ (Ion. η) ον *adj*. [ὑετός] (of a wind) bringing rain, **rainy** Hdt.
ὑετός οῦ *m*. [ὕω] heavy rain, **downpour** Il. Hes. Antipho Th. Ar. X. +
ὑηνέω *contr.vb*. [ὑηνός] **act like a pig** Pl.
ὑηνίᾱ ᾶς *f*. [ὑηνός] **piggishness, boorishness** (W.GEN. of a person) Ar.
ὑηνός ή όν *adj*. [ὗς] (of animals) of the pig kind, **swinish** Pl.
Ὕης *interj*. **Hyes!** (w. Ἄττης, as a ritual cry in the cult of Sabazios) D.
ὑθλέω *contr.vb*. [ὕθλος] **talk nonsense** or **twaddle** Ar.
ὕθλος ου *m*. **idle talk, twaddle, drivel** Pl. D.; (provbl.) γραῶν ὕθλος **old wives' tale** Pl.
υἷα (ep.acc.sg.), **υἷας** (ep.acc.pl.), **υἱάσι** (ep.dat.pl.): see υἱός
υἴδιον (unless ὑΐδιον) ου *n*. [dimin. υἱός] young male child; (derog., ref. to an adult) **little son** Ar.
ὑΐδιον *n*.: see ὕδιον
ὑϊδοῦς οῦ *Att.m*. son of a son, **grandson** Pl. X. D. Men.
υἱῆες *ep.m.pl*.: see υἱός
υἱιδεύς έως *m*. **grandson** Isoc.
ὑϊκός ή όν *adj*. [ὗς] **1** (of sacrificial victims) **consisting of pigs** Plb.
2 (of a person's excitement over food and drink) **pig-like, swinish** X.
—**ὑϊκόν** *neut.adv*. **like a pig** —*ref. to behaving* X.
υἱοποιέομαι *mid.contr.vb*. [υἱός] **make (someone) one's son; adopt** —*a boy* Plb.
υἱός, Att. **ὑός**, οῦ *m*. —also **υἱύς** υἱέος (Att. ὑέος) *m*. | dat. υἱεῖ || Att.du.nom.acc. ὑεῖ, gen.dat. ὑέοιν || PL.: nom. υἱεῖς, ep. υἱέες | dat. υἱέσι, ep. υἱάσι | —also **υἷς** υἷος *ep.m*. | acc. υἷα, acc.pl. υἷας, du. υἷε | —also **υἱῆες** υἱήων (AR.) *ep.m.pl*. | ep. υι-sts. scanned short *metri grat*. |
1 male offspring (by birth or adoption, regardless of age), **son** Hom. +; (appos.w. ἀνήρ) D.; (fig., ref. to Koros, in relation to Hubris) Hdt.(oracle)
2 offspring (of an animal) NT.
3 || PL. **sons** (W.GEN. of the Achaeans, ref. to their warriors) Hom. Ibyc.; (of the Colchians, Hyperboreans, ref. to peoples) Call. AR.
4 (gener.) **descendant** (of a well-known ancestor) NT.
5 one associated or affiliated (w. someone); **son** (ref. to a disciple or follower) NT. || PL. **members** (W.GEN. of a group) NT.
6 (ref. to Jesus) **son** (W.GEN. of mankind) NT.
7 one who is characterised (by a phenomenon or quality); **son** (W.GEN. of pain) Men.; (of thunder, peace, light, encouragement) NT.
8 one who belongs (to an era or sim.); **son** (W.GEN. of the current age, the resurrection, God's kingdom or covenant) NT.
υἱωνός οῦ *m*. **1** son of a son, **grandson** Hom. Hes.*fr.* AR. Plu.; (by adoption) Plb. Plu.
2 (gener.) **descendant** Hellenist.poet.
ὐκτρῶς *Boeot.adv*.: see οἰκτρῶς, under οἰκτρῶς
ὕλᾱ *dial.f*.: see ὕλη
ὑλάγματα των *n.pl*. [ὑλάω] **barks** (of dogs) E.; (fig., derog.ref. to hostile speech) A.
ὑλαγμός οῦ *m*. **barking** (of dogs) Il.(dub.) X. Theoc. Plu. | see κυνυλαγμός

ὑλαγωγέω *contr.vb*. [ὕλη, ἀγωγός] **haul timber** D.
ὑλαῖος ᾱ ον *adj*. [ὕλη] (of a wild animal) inhabiting woodland, **of the woods** Theoc.
ὑλακή ῆς *f*. [ὑλάω] **barking** (of dogs) Pl. AR. Plu.
ὑλακό-μωρος ον *adj*. [for 2nd el. cf. ἐγχεσίμωρος] | ῡ *metri grat*. | (of dogs) app. **known for barking** Od.
ὑλακτέω *contr.vb*. [ὑλάω, ὑλακή] **1** (of dogs) **bark** Il. Ar. X. Arist. Theoc. Plu. —w. πρός + ACC. *at someone* Plu.; (tr.) **bark at** —*someone* Ar. Isoc. Theoc.
2 (of a heart) **growl** (w. anger) Od.; (of a woman) **bark out** —W.INTERN.ACC. *threats* S.; (of a king) **bark at** —*his subjects* Plb.
3 (of a drunken man) **howl** —W.ADV. *tunelessly* E.
ὑλᾱτόμος *dial.m*.: see ὑλοτόμος
ὑλάω *contr.vb*. | ep.impf. ὕλαον | (of dogs) **bark** (as a hostile reaction to a stranger) Od.(also mid.) Theoc.; (tr.) **bark at** —*someone* Od.
ὕλη ης, dial. **ὕλᾱ** ᾱς *f*. **1 thick vegetation** (esp. assoc.w. mountains), **scrub, brush, woodland, forest** Hom. + || PL. areas of scrub or woodland Plb. Mosch. Plu.
2 wood, brushwood (cut or collected for fuel or sim.) Hom. hHom. A. Hdt. S. Pl. +; (for use in construction) Od. Hes. hHom. Hdt. Th. Call.
3 wood (as a commodity, for use in the construction of ships, buildings, defences), **timber** E. Th. Pl. D. Plu.
4 (gener.) raw material, **material** (for construction or decoration) Pl. Plu.; (collectv.sg.) **material things** (ref. to wealth or sim.) Plu.
5 subject matter (of a narrative) Arist. Plb.
6 (philos.) **matter** (as a component of objects in the natural world) Arist.
ὑλήεις εσσα εν (also εις εν Od.) *adj*. | Ion.neut.nom.sg. ὑλέειν (Archil., cj.) | dial.neut.nom.sg. ὑλᾶεν (S.), dial.neut.acc.pl. ὑλᾶντα (E.) | (of locations) **thickly covered with vegetation, scrub-covered** or **wooded** Hom. Hes. Archil.(cj.) S. E. AR. Theoc.
ὑλη-κοίτης ου *m*. [κοίτη] one who has a sleeping-place in the woods, **woodland-dweller** (app.ref. to a deer) Hes.
ὑληουργός *ep.m*.: see ὑλουργός
ὑλη-φόρος ου *f*. [φέρω] woman who carries timber, **timber-carrier** Ar.
ὑληωρός *ep.m*.: see ὑλωρός
ὑλικός ή όν *adj*. (of substance) **consisting of matter, material** Arist. || NEUT.SB. **matter** Arist.
—**ὑλικῶς** *adv*. **as matter, materially** —*ref. to an entity existing* Arist.
ὕλιμος ον *adj*. (of a valley) **scrub-covered** or **wooded** E.; (of foliage) **shrubby** E.*fr.*
ὑλο-δρόμος ον *adj*. [δραμεῖν] (of beasts) **woodland-ranging** Ar.
ὑλό-κομος ον *adj*. [κόμη] (of a valley) with leafy woodland, **leafy, wooded** E.
ὑλοτομέω *contr.vb*. [ὑλοτόμος] **cut wood** Hes.
ὑλοτομίᾱ ᾶς *f*. **wood-cutting** Arist.
ὑλο-τόμος, dial. **ὑλᾱτόμος**, ου *m*. [τέμνω] **1 woodcutter** Il. Hes. Simon. S. AR. Theoc.; (as an ancillary in the Roman army) Plu.
2 || ADJ. (of an axe) **for wood-cutting** Il.
3 (app., ref. to a person) **herb-cutter** hHom.
ὑλουργός, ep. **ὑληουργός**, οῦ *m*. [ἔργον] **1** one who works in woodland, **woodsman** E.
2 one who works with timber, **carpenter** (appos.w. ἀνήρ) AR.
ὑλο-φάγος ον *adj*. [φαγεῖν] (of a cow) **scrub-feeding** (opp. stall-fed) Hes.

ὑλο-φορβός όν *adj.* [φέρβω] (of cattle) **scrub-grazing** E.

ὑλο-φόρος ον *adj.* [φέρω] (of regions) scrub-bearing, **covered with scrub** Plb.

ὑλώδης ες *adj.* (of regions) **scrub-covered** or **wooded** S.*Ichn.* Th. X. Plb. Plu.; (of a river) **shaded by trees** Plu. ‖ NEUT.PL.SB. areas of scrub or woodland X.

ὑλ-ωρός, ep. **ὑληωρός**, οῦ *m.* [οὖρος², ὁράω] one who guards woodland areas; **woodland-guardian** (title of a magistrate) Arist.; (ref. to a nymph) AR.

ὑμᾶλιξ *Aeol.m.f.*: see ὁμῆλιξ

ὑμάρτη (Aeol.imperatv.): see ὁμαρτέω

ὑμεῖς, Aeol. **ὔμμες**, dial. **ὑμές**, Boeot. **οὐμές** 2pl.pers.pron. | acc. ὑμᾶς (enclit. ὕμας), Ion. ὑμέας, Aeol. ὔμμε, dial. ὑμέ | gen. ὑμῶν (enclit. ὕμων), Ion. and dial. ὑμέων, ep. ὑμείων, Aeol. ὑμμέων, Boeot. οὑμίων | dat. ὑμῖν (enclit. ὕμιν), Aeol. ὔμμῑν and ὔμμῐ, dial. ὑμίν (enclit. ὕμιν) ‖ See also sg. ἐγώ, du. σφώ | The nom. is used to draw attention to particular persons, esp. in contrast w. another pron. Non-enclitic forms of other cases are used to draw attention, or w. preps. | **you** (pl.) Hom. +; (in an address to an individual) **you and your crew** or **people** Od. +

ὑμέναιος, dial. **ὑμήναιος** (Call.), Aeol. **ὑμήναος**, ου *m.* [Ὑμήν] **1** song in honour of Hymen, **hymeneal song, bridal song** (sung by the bride's attendants) Il. Hes. Sapph. A. Pi. E. + **2 wedding** S. E. Call.*epigr.*; (iron., ref. to rape, adultery) E. ‖ PL. wedding-rites S. E.

—**Ὑμέναιος** ου *m.* **Hymenaios** (name for Hymen) Pi.*fr.* E. Ar. Theoc. Bion Plu.

ὑμεναιόω *contr.vb.* **1** (of young women) **sing the bridal song** A.

2 (of a young man) take as one's bride, **marry** —*a woman* Theoc.; (of a wolf, as an example of impossibility) —*a sheep* Ar.

ὑμές *dial.2pl.pers.pron.*: see ὑμεῖς

ὑμέτερος ᾱ (Ion. η) ον *possessv.adj.* [ὑμεῖς, ὑμός] **1** of or belonging to you (pl.), **your** Hom. +; (sts. followed by a pron. in gen.) ὑμέτερος ... ἑκάστου θυμῷ *the courage of each one of you* Il. ‖ MASC.PL.SB. your people (i.e. allies) X. ‖ NEUT.SG.SB. your business or interest Antipho Pl.; your opinion Ar. ‖ NEUT.PL.SB. your interests or affairs Hdt. Th. +; your possessions Att.orats.

2 (used for sg., when the subject is a figure of authority or when other persons beside the subject are implied) hHom. Sol. Pi. Call.; (for sg., w. respectful ref. to one deity) Call.

3 ‖ NEUT.SB. your home Hdt.

4 ‖ FEM.SB. your land or territory Hdt. Th.

5 (w. objective force) relating to you (pl.); ἐπὶ τῇ ὑμετέρᾳ παρακελεύσει *for the purpose of exhorting you* Pl.; τὸ δέος τὸ ὑμέτερον *fear of you* Lys.

—**ὑμέτερόνδε** *adv.* **towards your house** Il.

ὑμήν ένος *m.* fine layer of skin or tissue, **membrane** Call. AR.

Ὑμήν ένος *m.* | sts. ῡ metri grat. | voc. Ὑμήν | **Hymen** (deity assoc.w. marriages, invoked in wedding-hymns) E. Ar. Hellenist.poet.

ὑμήναιος *dial.m.*, **ὑμήναος** *Aeol.m.*: see ὑμέναιος

ὔμμες, ὔμμε, ὔμμι (Aeol.nom.acc.dat.2pl.pers.pron.): see ὑμεῖς

ὑμνέω *contr.vb.* [ὕμνος] | PRES. Ion.3pl. ὑμνεῦσι | Ion.fem.ptcpl. ὑμνεῦσα, Lacon. ὑμνίοισα (Alcm.) | Lacon.imperatv. ὕμνη (Ar.) | dial.inf. ὑμνῆν (Ibyc.), Aeol. ὔμνην | dial.1pl.subj. ὑμνέωμες (Lyr.adesp.), Lacon. ὑμνίωμες (Ar.) | IMPF.: Aeol.3pl. ὔμνην | AOR.: ὕμνησα ‖ PASS.: Ion.3pl. ὑμνέαται | fut. ὑμνηθήσομαι, also ὑμνήσομαι (E.*fr.*) | —also **ὑμνείω** (Hes.) *ep.vb.*

1 commemorate in song; (of gods or humans, esp. poets) **sing of** —*persons, gods, deeds, events, or sim.* Hes. hHom. Xenoph. Lyr. Hdt. S. +; (of a nightingale) —*her cares* E.; (intr.) **sing** Hes. Th. Pl. ‖ PASS. (of persons or things) be commemorated in song E.*fr.* Isoc. X.

2 sing —W.COGN. or INTERN.ACC. *a song or sim.* Alcm. Stesich. Heraclit. A. E. X. + —(w. 2ND ACC. about sthg., in honour of a god) A. E.

3 celebrate in song —*a wedding* Pi.*fr.* X.; (of a wedding-song) —*a bride* S.

4 (of Apollo) **chant** (an oracle) A.*fr.*

5 celebrate in speech; (esp. of orators and historians) **sing the praises of, hymn** —*a city, persons, their virtues, achievements, or sim.* Th. Att.orats. Pl. + ‖ PASS. (of persons or things) be celebrated Hdt. E. Lys. Pl. X. +

6 (gener.) **repeat aloud, recite** —*a story, statement, maxim* E.*fr.* Pl. X. —*the law* Pl.; (intr., of legends) **resound, ring** (in people's ears) Pl. ‖ PASS. (of a name, saying, or sim.) be repeated aloud Trag. Pl.; (of a tale) be recited Pl. ‖ IMPERS.PASS. there is chatter (about sthg.) Pl.

ὕμνησις ιος *dial.f.* singing (of hymns) Pi.*fr.*

ὑμνητής οῦ *m.* one who sings the praises, **eulogist** (W.GEN. of tyranny, ref. to a tragic poet) Pl.

ὑμνητός ή όν *adj.* (of persons) **celebrated in song** Pi.

ὑμνο-άνασσα ᾱς *dial.f.* [ὕμνος] **queen of song** (ref. to the Muse Clio) B.

ὑμνο-θέτης ου *m.* [τίθημι] composer of songs of praise, **poet** or **eulogist** (ref. to the author of a laudatory epigram) Theoc.*epigr.*

ὑμνο-ποιός οῦ *m.f.* [ποιέω] **song-maker** (ref. to a Muse or poet) E.

ὑμνο-πόλος ου *m.* [πέλω] one who is engaged in composing songs, **bard** Emp.

ὕμνος ου *m.* **1 song** (usu. of praise or commemoration, sts. in narrative form); **poem, hymn** (about deities, heroes, warriors, athletes, nobles) Od. Hes. hHom. Lyr. A.*fr.* Hdt. +; (in praise of women, a river, a location) A. E. Ar.; (by Orpheus) Pl.; (fig., envisaged as a draught of wine) Dionys.Eleg.

2 song for a group or chorus; **choral song** (usu. accompanied by dancing) Alcm. Lyr.adesp. E. Ar. Pl.; (for a bride, ref. to a wedding-song) S. Pl.; (sung by birds or frogs) Ar.

3 song of lamentation, **dirge** A. Pi. E.

4 song (inspired by or in honour of Eros), **love-song** Lyr.adesp. Pl.; **praise song** (for honouring desirable young men) Pi. B.*fr.*; (in a poetic competition) Thgn.

5 song (related to magic); **chant** (sung to invoke Erinyes and other infernal deities) A.; **spell** (cast by Erinyes) A.; (for charming someone, esp. the infernal deities) Pi. E.

6 song of triumph, **victory-song** A. Pi. Isoc.

7 sound (fr. a musical instrument), **tune** Pi. Ar. Theoc.*epigr.*

ὑμνῳδέω *contr.vb.* [ὑμνῳδός] **1** (of Apollo) **chant** (prophecies, through an oracle) E.; (of inspired poets) sing Pl.

2 sing —*a dirge* A.

ὑμνῳδίᾱ ᾱς *f.* **1** singing (at a wedding) E.

2 sung prophecy, **oracle** E.

ὑμν-ῳδός όν *adj.* [ὕμνος, ἀοιδή] (of the Hesperides) song-singing, **songful** E.

ὕμοι *Aeol.adv.*: see ὁμοῦ, under ὁμός

ὕμοιος *Aeol.adj.*: see ὁμοῖος

ὑμός ή (dial. ᾱ) όν *ep. and dial.possessv.adj.* [ὑμεῖς, ὑμέτερος] **1** of or belonging to you (pl.), **your** Hom. Hes. Pi. AR.

2 (for sg.) **your** (w. respectful ref. to an honoured athlete and his ancestors) Pi.

ὅμως Aeol.conj.: see ὅμως
ὅν (acc.sg.): see ὕς
ὗνις εως f. [perh.reltd. ὗς] **ploughshare** Plu.
ὑομουσίᾱ ᾱς f. [μοῦσα; cf. εὐμουσίᾱ] **swinish education** Ar.
ὑό-πρῳρος ον adj. [πρῷρα] (of a ship) having a prow shaped like a pig's snout, **pig-snouted** Plu.
ὑός (gen.sg.): see ὗς
ὗός Att.m.: see υἱός
ὑοσ-κύαμος ου m. [ὗς] plant that induces delirium, **hog's bean, henbane** X. Plu.
ὑπά Aeol.prep.: see ὑπό
ὑπ-άγγελος ον adj. [ὑπό] acting in response to a messenger, **summoned** A.
ὑπ-αγκαλίζω vb. (of a man) **place one's arm around** —a friend (perh. to steady himself in his drunkenness) E.Cyc. ‖ MID. (of a woman) **shield in one's arms** —children E.
ὑπαγκάλισμα ατος n. (ref. to a child or female sexual partner) object of one's embrace, **darling, beloved** S. E.
ὑπ-αγορεύω vb. **1** speak (w. the effect of laying a foundation for future action); (of an instructor) **suggest** —W.DAT. + INDIR.Q. *to someone what he shd. do* D.; (of seers) **prescribe** —*religious rites* Plu.
2 dictate —*letters* Plu. ‖ PASS. (of information) **be dictated** X.
ὑπ-άγω, Aeol. **ὐπάγω** vb. | aor.2 ὑπήγαγον | **1 lead or bring under** (a yoke); **bring** (W.ACC. *horses*) **under** —*a yoke* Il.; **bring** (W.ACC. *mules*) **under the yoke** Od.; **yoke** —*horses* (w. ὑπά + ACC. *to chariots*) Sapph.
2 bring under (someone's power); **bring** —*someone* (w. εἰς + ACC. *into another's hands*) Hdt. —(w. ὑπό + ACC. *under the sway of one's argument*) Plu. ‖ MID. **bring under one's control** —*a city* Th. —*regions, peoples* Plu.; (of a woman) **captivate** —*a man* Plu.; (wkr.sens.) **win over** —*a person* (W.DAT. *by embassies and honours*) Plu.
3 bring under (judicial authority); **bring** —*someone* (w. ὑπό or εἰς + ACC. *before a court, magistrates, to trial*) Hdt. Th. Plu.; **subject** —*someone* (W.DAT. *to prosecution*) Plu.; **bring** (W.ACC. *someone*) **to trial** X. ‖ MID. (of Justice) **bring** (W.ACC. *someone*) **to account** E. ‖ PASS. **be brought** —W.PREP.PHR. *before a court, jury* Hdt. X.; **be brought to trial** X. D.
4 lead gradually onwards; lead on —*a person, hounds* X. Plu.; (fig., of wine) —*a person* (W.PREP.PHR. *to a revel*) E.Cyc.; (intr.) **lead the way** Pl.
5 (of a river current, the splash of oars) **carry along** —*debris, a ship* Plu.
6 lead gradually (to an action or state); **lead** —*someone* (W.PREP.PHR. *to a hope*) E. —*a city* (*towards a particular policy*) Plu. ‖ MID. **induce, prompt** —*someone* (*to admit sthg.*) —(W.PREP.PHR. *to an action*) Plu. ‖ PASS. **be prompted** (to do sthg.) Isoc.; **be led on** —W.PREP.PHRS. *fr. one state to another* D. —W.DAT. *by desire for victory* D.; **be guided** —W.DAT. *by certain principles of conduct* Plu.; (of affairs) **be brought** —W.PREP.PHR. *to a certain state* D.
7 lead off, start off —*a hunt* X.; **start up** —*the rhythm of a dance* Ar.
8 (intr.) **go forward, move on** X. NT. Plu.; (of soldiers) app. **march on slowly** X. ‖ IMPERATV. (addressed to a person or animal) **get a move on!** E.Cyc. Ar.
9 lead on furtively or by underhand means; (of a god, an evil spirit) **draw on, lure, entice** —*a person* E. Lys.; (of a commander or troops) —*enemy soldiers, ships* (sts. W.PREP.PHR. *into an ambush or vulnerable position*) Th. X. Plu. ‖ PASS. **be lured on** —W.DAT. *by a sight* Plu.

10 lead by underhand means (to an action or state); **mislead** —*someone* Hdt. D.; **induce** —*someone* (W.INF. *to do sthg.*) E. ‖ MID. **offer inducements** X.; **entice** —*someone* (W.DAT. *w. hopes*) Isoc. —(W.PREP.PHR. *into servitude*) D.; **tempt** —*someone* (W.INF. *to do sthg.*) X. Plu. ‖ PASS. **be led astray** D. —W.DAT. or PREP.PHR. *by false hopes, cajoleries, promises, or sim.* Aeschin. D.; **be enticed** —W.PREP.PHR. *into servitude, enmity, or sim.* D.; **be tempted or induced** —W.INF. *to do sthg.* D.
11 lead away; (of a god) **draw away** —*a warrior* (w. ἐκ + GEN. *out of missiles and dust*) Il.; (of a person) **draw** (W.ACC. *someone*) **aside** —w. ἀπό + GEN. *fr. others* Plu. ‖ PASS. **be taken away** —W.PREP.PHR. *to prison* Plb.
12 (of a commander) **withdraw** —*an army* Th.; (intr., of a commander, troops) **withdraw, retreat** Hdt. Th. Plu.
13 (intr.) **depart, go away, be off** Thgn. Ar. Men. NT.; (euphem., of Jesus, ref. to his death) NT. ‖ IMPERATV. **be off!** NT.; **go** —w. 2ND IMPERATV. (without copula) *and do sthg.* NT.
14 ‖ PASS. (of earth) **be surreptitiously removed** —W.ADV. *fr. beneath* (*a mound*) Th.
ὑπαγωγεύς έως m. perh. **trowel** (for applying plaster) Ar.
ὑπαγωγή ῆς f. **1 starting-point** (W.GEN. *of a hunt*) X.
2 withdrawal, retreat (by troops) Th. Plu.
3 journey down (W.PREP.PHRS. *to the sea, by means of rivers*) Plu.
ὑπαδεδρόμηκα (Aeol.pf.): see ὑποδραμεῖν
ὑπαδέω Aeol.contr.vb.: see ὑποδέω
ὑπ-ᾴδω, ep. **ὑπαείδω** vb. | ep.3pl. ὑπᾱείδουσι metri grat. (Call.) | ep.aor. ὑπάεισα | **1 sing** (sts. W.INTERN.ACC. *a song*) **as an accompaniment** (for a musical instrument, religious ceremony, dancing) Il.(tm.) hHom.(tm.) Ar. Call. —W.DAT. *for dancing* E.(cj.) Ar.
2 (of panpipes) **play an accompaniment** (for dancers) Call.
3 (of a bowstring, when twanged) **resound in response** Od.(tm.)
ὑπάθῡμις Aeol.f.: see ὑποθῡμίς
ὑπαί ep.prep.: see ὑπό
ὑπαιδείδοικα (ep.pf.): see ὑποδείδω
ὑπ-αιδέομαι mid.contr.vb. **treat** (W.ACC. *a person*) **with a measure of respect** X.
ὕπαιθα adv. [ὑπαί, see ὑπό] **1 away from under** (an attack or threat); **out of the way, out of reach** —*ref. to escaping* Il.; (as prep.) —W.GEN. *of someone or sthg.* Il.
2 underneath, below Il. AR. —W.GEN. *a person* (i.e. acting as support) Il.
ὑπ-αίθριος ον (also ᾱ ον E.) adj. [ὕπαιθρος] **1 under a clear sky**; (of persons or things) **out in the open air** (sts. w.connot. of being exposed to the elements) A. Pi. Hdt. Th. Pl. X. +; (of reservoirs, opp. roofed over) Pl.; (of objects, tasks) **outdoors** Hdt. Pl. X. Plb.
2 (of dew, frost) **of the open air** A. E.
—**ὑπαίθρεια** ων n.pl. **exposed conditions** (W.GEN. *of hills*) S.(cj.) [or perh. *of frosts, i.e. exposure to frosts*]
ὕπ-αιθρος ον adj. [αἴθρᾱ] **1 under a clear sky**; (of wintering) **in the open** Plb.; (of standing, as a form of torture) Plu.; (quasi-advbl., of troops bivouacking) Plu.
2 (of military forces) **in the field** (i.e. out on campaign) Plb.
3 ‖ NEUT.PL.SB. (in military ctxt.) **open country** (opp. cities, fortifications, or sim.) Plb.
4 (fig., of conduct) **public** Plu.; (of folly) **manifest** Plu. ‖ NEUT.PL.SB. **public conduct** Plu.
5 (prep.phrs.) ἐν (τῷ) ὑπαίθρῳ *in the open air* Antipho X. Plu.; (in military ctxt.) *in the field* (opp. *in camp*) Plu.; εἰς

ὕπαιθρον into public view (w. further military connot., into the field) Plb.
ὑπ-αίθω vb. **light a fire beneath** —a body (on a pyre) S.
ὑπ-αινίττομαι Att.mid.vb. [αἰνίσσομαι] **speak enigmatically** D. Plu.
ὑπαιρέω Ion.contr.vb.: see ὑφαιρέω
ὑπ-αΐσσω ep.vb. [ἄσσω] | fut. ὑπαΐξω | aor.ptcpl. ὑπαΐξας |
1 (of a fish) **dart along beneath** —the rippling surface of a river Il.
2 (of a serpent) **dart from beneath** —w.GEN. an altar Il.
ὑπ-αισχύνομαι mid.vb. **feel a little ashamed** —w.DBL.ACC. before someone, about sthg. Pl.
ὑπ-αίτιος ον adj. 1 (in legal ctxt.) having culpable responsibility, **blameworthy, to blame** (sts. w.GEN. for sthg.) Antipho
2 (of a person, behaviour) **subject to censure** (w.DAT. or πρός + GEN. by someone) X.; (of a person, w.GEN. + DAT. for sthg. by someone) Plu.
ὑπακουός όν adj. [ὑπακούω] (of a poet) **obedient** (w.GEN. to the Muses) AR.
ὑπ-ακούω, Aeol. **ὑπακούω** vb. | dial.inf. ὑπακουέμεν (Pi.) | fut. ὑπακούσομαι, also ὑπακούσω (Plu.) | 1 **give heed by listening; listen, pay attention** Hom.(sts.tm.) E. Ar. X. + —w.GEN. or DAT. to someone Sapph. Ar. Pl. X. +; **pay heed** —w.GEN. or DAT. to sthg. Pl. X. +
2 **hear** —w.ACC. footsteps Od.(tm.); (of distant locations) —w.GEN. a person shouting Lyr.adesp.
3 **make a response** (in words or action, to a call, invitation, question, or sim.); **respond** (sts. w.DAT. to someone) Od. hHom. Th. Att.orats. + —w.DAT. to an interlocutor (in dialogue) Pl.; (of Echo) —to cries S.(cj.)
4 **respond** (to a knock at the door); **answer** Ar. Pl. X. D. NT. —w.DAT. someone (at the door) Ar. Pl. Plu. —the door Thphr. Men.
5 **respond compliantly; consent, accede** (sts. w.NEUT.ACC. to sthg., nothing) Hdt. Th. Isoc. X. D. +; **comply** —w.DAT. w. someone or sthg. Th. Pl. X. +
6 **respond** (to an official summons); (of commanders, magistrates, citizens) **report** (for duty) X. Arist. Plu.; **answer a summons** (to appear in court) Att.orats. X. Plu. —w. εἰς + ACC. for a trial, to a court X. Hyp.
7 **be obedient, obey** Th. Ar. X. D. + —w.GEN. or DAT. someone Th. X. D. + —w.DAT. a request, an order X. Plb.
8 **submit** Th. Lys. D. Plu. —w.GEN. or DAT. to someone Th. Plb. Plu.
9 **be subject** —w.GEN. or DAT. to someone Hdt. Th. D. Plb.; (of a garden) —w.DAT. to the sun's rays Pi.
10 **understand** —w.ACC. sthg. (w.PREDIC.ADJ. as meaning such and such) Pl. —(w.PREP.PHR. in relation to certain words) Pl.
ὑπ-αλαζών όνος masc.fem.adj. (of a doctor) **somewhat of an impostor** Men.
ὑπ-αλείφω vb. | pf.pass.ptcpl. ὑπαληλιμμένος | 1 **apply a little ointment;** (fig.) **anoint** —a person (w.ACC. on the eyes, w.DAT. w. peace, as a cure for eye-problems caused by war) Ar.
2 ‖ MID. **anoint oneself** (i.e. one's eyes) —w.INTERN.ACC. w. a salve Pl.
3 ‖ MID. (of a wrestler) **rub oneself with oil** Ar. Plu.(quot.com.)
4 ‖ MID. **make up** —one's eyes (w.DAT. w. a cosmetic) X. ‖ PF.PASS.PTCPL. (of eyes) made-up X.
ὑπ-αλέομαι ep.mid.contr.vb. | imperatv. ὑπαλέυεο | aor.inf. ὑπαλεύασθαι | **evade, avoid** —death (w.GEN. at someone's hands) Od. —evil talk (fr. others) Hes.; (intr.) **take evasive action** Hes.
ὑπαλλαγή ῆς f. [ὑπαλλάττω] **that which is taken in exchange, replacement** (w.GEN. for one's troubles, ref. to a marriage) E.
ὑπάλλαγμα ατος n. **that which is exchanged, medium of exchange** (w.GEN. for a need, ref. to coinage) Arist.
ὑπ-αλλάττω Att.vb. [ἀλλάσσω] 1 **take** (w.ACC. looted armour) **as replacement** (for one's own) Plb.
2 ‖ PASS. **be rid** —w.GEN. of a person Plu.
ὑπ-άλληλος ον adj. [ἀλλήλους] (of things) **subordinate to one another** Arist.
ὑπ-άλπειος ᾱ ον adj. [Ἄλπεις] **under the Alps** ‖ FEM.SB. **sub-Alpine region** (w.GEN. of Italy) Plu.
ὑπάλυξις ιος Ion.f. [ὑπαλύσκω] **escape** (fr. death) Il.; (w.GEN. fr. troubles, ruin) Od. AR.
ὑπ-αλύσκω vb. 1 **avoid, evade, escape** —death, one's fate, someone's hands or wrath Hom.(sts.tm.) Thgn. AR.
2 **get free from, escape** —storms, a wave Od. —a debt Od.
3 (intr.) **escape, get away safely** Od. Hes. AR.(sts.tm.)
ὑπ-αμάω contr.vb. **slice** (w.ACC. an animal's throat) **from below** A.fr.(tm.)
ὑπ-αναγιγνώσκω vb. 1 (of a court-clerk) **read out** —a legal document Hyp.
2 (of a plaintiff) **read out** (through a clerk), **have read out** —a law or decree Is. Aeschin.
ὑπ-αναδύομαι mid.vb. (of a person) **draw back a little** Men.
ὑπ-ανακινέω contr.vb. **start to limber up** —w.PREP.PHR. for dinner Ar.
ὑπ-αναλίσκω vb. 1 (of soldiers) **gradually use up** —provisions Plu.
2 (of a commander) **gradually drain** —an opponent's resources Plu. —w.PARTITV.GEN. his strength Plu.
3 (of campaigns) **put a drain on** —one's finances Th. ‖ PASS. (of finances) be drained away Th.
ὑπανάστασις εως f. [ὑπανίσταμαι] **rising from one's seat out of respect** (before one's elders) Pl. Arist.
ὑπ-αναχωρέω contr.vb. (of troops, ships) **withdraw a little** Th. X.
ὑπ-ανδρος ον adj. [ἀνήρ] (of a woman) **subject to a man, married** Plb. Plu.
ὑπᾱνέμιος dial.adj.: see ὑπηνέμιος
ὑπ-ανιάομαι mid.contr.vb. **feel a certain discomfort** Ar.
ὑπ-ανίημι vb. 1 (of a tyranny) **gradually ease** —its excessive inhumanity Plu.
2 (intr., of fear) **abate, subside** Plu.
ὑπ-ανίσταμαι mid.vb. | athem.aor.act. ὑπανέστην | pf.act. ὑπανέστηκα |
1 **rise** (freq. w.GEN. or PREP.PHR. fr. one's seat) **out of respect** (freq. w.DAT. for someone) Hdt. Ar. X.
2 **stand up to leave** (a symposium) Thgn.
3 (of a hare) **start up** —w.DAT. before someone X.
ὑπ-ανοίγνῡμι, also **ὑπανοίγω** vb. **secretly open** —a sealed urn or document Isoc. D.
ὑπ-αντα adv. [ἄντα] **in a way which meets** or **fits** (w.DAT. w. one's plans) —ref. to someone arriving E.(cj.)
ὑπ-αντάω contr.vb. | aor. ὑπήντησα, dial. ὑπάντᾱσα |
1 **come face to face** (intentionally or accidentally); **meet, come** or **go to meet** (usu. w.DAT. w. someone) Pi. X. Hyp. NT. —w.DAT. w. a city (meton. for its occupants) Plu. —w.GEN. w. a person S.(dub.) —w.ACC. Theoc.
2 (of troops, a commander) **meet** or **advance to meet** (sts. w.DAT. w. the enemy) X. Plb. NT. Plu.
3 (of a hunter) **intercept** (a hare) X.

ὑπάντησις εως *f.* meeting (W.DAT. or GEN. w. someone) NT.
ὑπ-αντιάζω *vb.* | aor. ὑπηντίασα, dial. ὑπᾱντίασα | dial.aor.fem.ptcpl. ὑπαντιάξαισα | **1 meet, come** or **go to meet** (usu. W.DAT. someone) A. Pi. X. —W.ACC. A.(cj.) Pi.
2 meet, advance to meet, confront (an enemy) Il. X. Plu. —W.DAT. *enemies, their might* Pi. Plu. —W.ACC. *enemies* Hdt. Plu.; (fig., of battle cries) A.
ὑπ-αξόνιος ον *adj.* [ἄξων] (of the noise of a hub) **beneath the axle** Call.
ὑπ-απειλέω *contr.vb.* **give a threatening hint** —W.DAT. *to someone* (W.FUT.INF. *that one will do sthg.*) X.
ὑπ-άπειμι *vb.* [ἄπειμι²] (of soldiers) **withdraw stealthily** Th.
ὑπ-αποκῑνέω *contr.vb.* **sneak off** Ar.
ὑπ-αποτρέχω *vb.* **run furtively away** Ar.
ὑπάπτω *Ion.vb.*: see ὑφάπτω
ὕπαρ *indecl.n.* [reltd. ὕπνος] **1 vision seen while awake, waking** or **true vision** (opp. ὄναρ *illusory dream-vision*) Od. Pi. Pl. Mosch.
2 || ADVBL.ACC. in a waking state, awake Pl. Theoc. Plb.
3 || ADVBL.ACC. in reality A. Pl. Plu.
ὑπ-άργυρος ον *adj.* **1** (of a rock, land, hills) **having silver beneath the surface, silver-veined** E. X.
2 (fig., of the child of a man belonging to the bronze or iron caste in the ideal state) **alloyed with silver** Pl.
3 (of a Muse's voice) subject to silver, **hired for money** (perh. w. further connot. *silvery, i.e. attractive to the ear*) Pi.
ὑπ-άρκτιος ον *adj.* [Ἄρκτος] (of latitudes, frosts) **of the far north, subarctic** Plu.
ὑπ-αρνος ον *adj.* [ἀρήν] (of a ewe) **with a lamb at the teat** E. Call.
ὕπαρξις εως *f.* [ὑπάρχω] means of subsistence, **means, resources** Plb.; (concr.) **property, possessions** Plb.
ὑπαρπάζω *Ion.vb.*: see ὑφαρπάζω
ὑπαρχή ῆς *f.* point in time which is a beginning; (prep.phr.) ἐξ ὑπαρχῆς *from* or *at the beginning* Arist.; (ref. to a starting-point in an undertaking, line of argument, or sim., usu.w. αὖθις or πάλιν *again*) *from the beginning afresh* S. D. Arist. Plu.
ὕπ-αρχος ου *m.* [ἄρχω] **1 subordinate commander** (in an army) X. Plb.; **second-in-command** (W.GEN. to the Persian king) X.; (to other commanders) S.(dub.)
2 (in the Persian empire) **subordinate ruler, governor** (sts. W.GEN. of a region, ref. to a satrap) Hdt. X. D. Plu.
3 deputy (to a Persian satrap) Hdt. Th. X.
4 (gener.) **ruler** (in a region of Greece) X.
5 || PL. (gener.) officers (of a king) E.
6 || PL. (ref. to a people) subjects (W.GEN. of another) Plb.
ὑπ-άρχω *vb.* | impf. ὑπῆρχον, dial. ὑπᾶρχον || pf.mid.pass. ptcpl. ὑπηργμένος, Ion. ὑπαργμένος | **1 begin (an activity), take the initiative** Od. E.(dub.) Th. D.
2 take the initiative in, begin —W.GEN. *sthg.* Hdt. Th. D. +; **lay the foundation** —W.GEN. *of troubles, freedom, noble lineage* E. And. Pl.; (of an event, for subsequent events) A.
|| IMPERS.PLPF.PASS. a start had already been made —W.GEN. *on sthg.* Th.
3 act first —W.PTCPL. *in doing sthg.* Hdt. X.; **be the first** —W.PTCPL. *to die* E.
4 (specif.) **initiate a conflict, be the aggressor** (in a war or personal dispute) Th. Att.orats. Pl. || PASS. (of an action) be performed as provocation Antipho
|| NEUT.PL.PASS.PTCPL.SB. initial acts of aggression Hdt.
5 || MID. (of the creator god) **bring about the beginning** (of a certain element in human life) Pl.
6 (tr.) take the initiative in performing, **initiate** —*favours or services* E. Aeschin. D. || PF.PASS. (of services) have already been performed (for someone) Aeschin.
|| NEUT.PL.PF.PASS.PTCPL.SB. services already performed or benefits already received Ar. Lys. D. Arist.
7 (of material and non-material things) **be in existence, exist, be available** or **at hand** (sts. W.DAT. for someone) Pi. Hdt. Trag. Th. Ar. Att.orats. + || PTCPL.ADJ. (of persons or things) existing Hdt. Th. Isoc. + || NEUT.PL.PTCPL.SB. existing circumstances or resources Democr. Th. Att.orats. +
8 (gener., of persons or things) **be** (usu. W.PREDIC.ADJ. or SB. *such and such*) S. E. Th. Ar. +
9 (of things) **happen** (in fact) —W.PRES.PTCPL. *to exist* (W.DAT. *for someone, i.e. be available for him*) Hdt.; (of persons) —W.PRES.PTCPL. + PREDIC.ADJ. *to be such and such* D. —W.PF.PTCPL. *to be in such and such a state* D.
|| PASS. (of things) have already been —W.AOR. or PF.PASS.PTCPL. *made* or *done* Hdt.
10 (of persons) be available in support, **support, side with** —W.DAT. *someone* X. D.
11 (of a proposition) **be assumed** or **granted** (as a hypothesis) Pl.
12 (philos., of things) **exist** (in actual fact) Arist.
13 (of an attribute) **belong** —W.DAT. *to sthg.* Arist.
—ὑπάρχει *impers.vb.* **1** the situation exists, **the fact is** —W.ACC. or DAT. + INF. *that sthg. is the case, that someone is such and such* S. Att.orats.
2 the possibility exists, **it is possible, there is an opportunity** Th. —W.INF. or DAT. + INF. (*for someone*) *to do sthg., to be such and such* Th. Att.orats. Pl.
ὑπασδεύξαισα (Aeol.aor.fem.ptcpl.): see ὑποζεύγνῡμι
ὑπ-ασπίδιος ον *adj.* [ἀσπίς¹] (of body-armour) **worn under a shield** S.; (of sleeping) **under a shield** E.
—ὑπασπίδια *neut.pl.adv.* **under the cover of a shield** —*ref. to advancing* Il.
ὑπασπίζω *vb.* [ὑπασπιστής] **serve as a shield-bearer** —W.DAT. *for a warrior* Pi. E.
ὑπ-ασπιστήρ ῆρος *masc.adj.* (of a throng) **protected by shields** A.
ὑπ-ασπιστής οῦ (Ion. έω) *m.* **1** one who carries a shield (for a soldier), **shield-bearer** Hdt. E. X. Plu.
2 || PL. body of soldiers armed with shields, shield-men (opp. cavalry and heavy infantry) Men.; (ref. to elite soldiers, esp. a Macedonian king's bodyguard) Plb. Plu.
3 || PL. (without military connot.) attendants (to a king, in Ptolemaic Egypt) Plb.
ὑπ-αστρος ον *adj.* [ἄστρον] (app. of flight fr. pursuers) **under the stars** (i.e. anywhere under the heavens) A. [or perh. *as far as the stars*]
ὑπατείᾱ ᾱς *f.* [ὑπατεύω] office or rank of consul, **consulship** Plu.
ὑπατεύω *vb.* [ὕπατος²] **hold the office of consul** Plu. —W.COGN.ACC. Plu.
ὑπατικός ή όν *adj.* **1** (of a province, election, rank, robes) of or for a consul, **consular** Plu.
2 (of a man) of consular rank, **consular** Plu.
ὕπατος¹ η (dial. ᾱ) ον *superl.adj.* [reltd. ὑπέρ, ὑπό]
1 uppermost (in power or authority); (of Zeus) **highest, supreme** Il. hHom. Pi. B.*fr.* E. +; (W.GEN. of or among the gods) Hom.; (W.GEN. over a land) A.; (of his power, plans) Thgn. Pi.*fr.*; (of Athena) D.(oracle); (of divine fathers) Pi.*fr.*; (of a god, Sleep, W.GEN. of gods) E. AR.
2 uppermost (in quality or distinction); (of a person, offspring, death) **best, finest** Pi. S. Call.; (of an athletic festival, a blessing) **greatest** Pi.

3 (of a mountain) **highest** hHom.
4 in a very high position; (of gods) **high up, on high** A.; (opp. infernal) A.; (of the house of Zeus) Pi.; (of vultures) **high above** (W.GEN. their nests) A.
5 (of a pyre) at its highest point, **at the top** Il.; (of a mountain or sim.) Call. AR.; (of a part of the body) AR. Theoc.
6 (of an island, river) **furthest, remotest** AR. [or perh. *most northerly*]
7 (of the infernal regions) **lowest** AR.
8 [ὕπατος²] (of a magistracy) **consular** Plu.(quot.epigr.)
—**ὑπάτη** ης *f.* (mus.) **top string** (of a lyre, closest to the player's body in position and lowest in musical pitch) Arist.; **lowest note** (in a scale) Pl.
—**ὕπατος²** ου *m.* highest-ranking magistrate (at Rome), **consul** Plb. Plu.; (appos.w. ἀρχή *magistracy*) Plb.

ὑπ-αυγάζω *vb.* **1 inspect** (W.ACC. a cloak) **under the light** Ar.(cj.)
2 (of a shooting star) light up behind, **illuminate** —*a furrow* (*in the sky*) AR.

ὑπ-αυλέω *contr.vb.* | dial.inf. ὑπαυλῆν | dial.3sg.fut. ὑπαυλήσει | **play** (sts. W.ACC. a tune) **on an aulos in accompaniment** Alcm.

ὕπ-αυλος ον *adj.* [αὐλή] **under the shelter** (W.GEN. of a tent) S.

ὑπ-αφίσταμαι *mid.vb.* | athem.aor.act. ὑπαπέστην | **1** (of an accused man) **quietly withdraw** (into exile) Antipho
2 step back, get out of the way Men.

ὑπ-αφρονέστερος ᾱ ον *compar.adj.* [ἄφρων] (of a people) **rather unintelligent** Hdt.

ὕπ-αφρος ον *adj.* [ἀφρός] (of eyes) perh., with a foam-like appearance, **rheumy** E. [unless (of a reef) *concealed beneath foam*, hence (fig.ref. to a face) *under cover* or *disguised*]

ὕπεας *Ion.n.*: see ὄπεας
ὑπέασι (ep.3pl.): see ὕπειμι¹

ὑπ-έγγυος ον *adj.* [ἐγγύη] **1** (of a person persuaded to leave sanctuary) **under an assurance** or **guarantee** (about the nature of the punishment to be faced) Hdt.
2 (of dream interpreters) **accountable** (to the gods, for an honest interpretation) A. || NEUT.SB. accountability (W.DAT. to Justice and the gods) E.

ὑπέδδεισα (ep.aor.), **ὑπεδείδισαν** (ep.3pl.plpf.), **ὑπέδεισα** (aor.): see ὑποδείδω
ὑπέδεκτο (ep.3sg.athem.aor.mid.): see ὑποδέχομαι
ὑπέδῡν (athem.aor.): see ὑποδύομαι, under ὑποδύω
ὑπέθηκα (aor.), **ὑπεθέμην** (athem.aor.mid.): see ὑποτίθημι
ὑπειδόμην (aor.2 mid.): see ὑφοράω

ὑπ-είκω, ep. **ὑποείκω** *vb.* | fut. ὑπείξω, ep. ὑποείξω, also ὑπείξομαι, ep. ὑποείξομαι | aor. ὑπεῖξα, ep. ὑπόειξα | aor.2 ὑπείκαθον (S. Pl. AR.), ep. ὑποείκαθον (AR.) || neut.impers. vbl.adj. ὑπεικτέον |
1 give way (before an enemy) Pl. X.; **withdraw, retreat** —W.GEN. *fr. a place* Il. || NEUT.PTCPL.SB. group in retreat E.
2 hold back —W.GEN. *fr. battle* Il.
3 (tr.) give way before, **shrink from, avoid** —*an enemy's hands* Il.
4 give way (to another, over sthg.); **give up, surrender** —W.GEN. one's seat (W.DAT. *to someone*) Od. Plu.; **give precedence** —W.DAT. *to one's elders* (W.GEN. *on the road, in seating or speaking*) X.; **back down** —W.GEN. *over one's original proposal* Hdt.
5 concede, grant —W.DAT. *to someone* (W.ACC. + INF. *that someone may do sthg.*) S.
6 give way (under physical pressure); (of armour, carpets, flesh, substances, or sim.) **yield, give way** Il. Pl. X. Arist. AR.; (of wood covering a trap) —W.DAT. *beneath an animal's foot* X.; (of soil) —*to a plough* Od.(tm.); (of river water, to a ship) AR.; (of trees) **be pliant** (before a flood) S. || PTCPL.ADJ. (fig., of persuasion) pliant, accommodating Plu.
7 (of a sailor) **slacken off** (i.e. loosen the rigging, in a storm) S.; (fig., of a person, envisaged as a sailor) —W.DAT. *before a populace* (*envisaged as a storm-wind*) E.
8 slacken off, relent —W.PTCPL. *in one's anger* Il.
9 give way (by acknowledging another's superior power or authority); **give in, yield, submit** (freq. W.DAT. to someone or sthg.) Hom. A. Hdt. S. Th. Ar. + || NEUT.SB. submissiveness Th.
10 give way (to external circumstances); (of a horse) **give in, yield** —W.DAT. *to a whip* Pl.; (of a ship) —*to rowers* (*i.e. move forwards*) AR.; (of a person) —*to old age, persuasion, pleasures, protests, or sim.* E. Pl. D. Plu. —*to sorcery* (W.PASS.INF. *so as to be overpowered by it*) AR.; (of an enemy's numbers and resources) —*to an opponent's valour* Pl.; (of Fortune) —*to a person's ambitions* Plu.; (of passion, in neg.phr.) —*to reason* Arist.; (of arms and the military laurel) —*to the toga and the tongue* Plu.(quot.)
11 (of a person's speech, in neg.phr.) **be humbled** —W.DAT. *by his misfortunes* S.
12 (of a region) **yield to pressure** —w. πρός + ACC. *for revolt* Plu.

ὕπ-ειμι¹ *vb.* [εἰμί] | ep.3pl. ὑπέᾱσι | ep.3sg.impf. (tm.) ὑπό ... ἦεν | dial.3sg.fut. ὑπεσσεῖται (Theocr.) | **1 be under** —W.DAT. *a roof* (i.e. in a house) Il.; (of young animals) —*their mothers* Il.; (of a stool) —*feet* Hom.(tm.); (of claws) —*a monster's hands* Hes.; (of chambers) —w. ὑπό + ACC. *the ground* Hdt.; (of goatskins) **be underneath** (a person, to lie on) Theoc.; (of the Cyclops' eye) **be below** (his brow) Theoc.
2 (of horses) **be under** (the yoke) Ar. —w. ὑπό + DAT. *chariots* (i.e. yoked to them) Hdt.
3 be under (as a support); (of supports) **be underneath** (a cup or its handles) Il.(tm.); (of a foundation of stone, for a brick wall) X.; (fig., of a foundation of troubles) A.(dub.)
4 (of young men) **be available in support** (for a city) E.; (of an extra leader) E.*fr.*; (of material resources, physical strength) —W.DAT. *for someone* Hdt. Th.; (of the achievements of others) —*for a speaker* (*i.e. as subject matter*) Isoc.
5 (of a character trait, enmity, envy, or sim.) **subsist, be underlying** E. Is. D. Plu.; (philos., of matter) Arist. —W.DAT. *in sthg.* Arist.
6 (gener., of hope, confidence, the prospect of punishment) **exist, be available** (usu. W.DAT. for someone) S. Th. Isoc. D. Arist.; (of arguments) **come to hand** Plb.
7 (of accusations) **be consequential** (on an action) D.
8 (of an ambush) **be concealed** X.

ὕπ-ειμι² *vb.* [εἶμι] | Only pres. and impf. (other tenses are supplied by ὑπέρχομαι). The pres.indic. has fut. sense. | **1** (of soldiers) **proceed gradually** or **stealthily** Hdt.
2 (of love) **steal up on** —*someone* AR.; (fig., of tyrannical behaviour) **creep up** Ar.
3 (of considerations) **occur to** —*someone* Plu.
4 insinuate oneself into the favour of —*someone* Plu.

ὕπειξις εως *f.* [ὑπείκω] **1 giving ground** (in a war-dance) Pl.
2 concession, compliance Pl.

ὑπείξομαι (fut.mid.), **ὑπείξω** (fut.): see ὑπείκω

ὑπ-εῖπον aor.2 *vb.* —also **ὑπεῖπα** (Men.) aor.1 *vb.* **1 speak** (w. the effect of laying a foundation for future speech or action); **say** or **speak** (usu. W.ACC. sthg.) **at the outset** Th. Ar. Pl. Aeschin. D. Men. Plu.

ὑπείρ

2 begin by saying —W.INDIR.Q. or COMPL.CL. *what (or that sthg.) is the case* Plu.
3 begin by calling for —*a hearing* E.
4 speak (w. the effect of offering a suggestion, explanation or addition); **suggest, indicate, intimate** —*sthg.* D. Plu. —W.COMPL.CL. or ACC. + INF. *that sthg. is or will be the case* Th. Ar. Plu. —W.INDIR.Q. *what is the case* D.; (intr.) **make a suggestion** S.
5 prescribe —*instructions* (W.DAT. *to someone*) E.

ὑπείρ *ep.prep.*: see ὑπέρ
ὑπειρέβαλον (ep.aor.2): see ὑπερβάλλω
ὑπειρέχω *ep.vb.*: see ὑπερέχω
ὑπείροχος *ep.adj.*: see ὑπέροχος
ὑπείρω¹ *vb.*: see ὑφείρω

ὑπ-είρω² *vb.* [εἴρω²] | only pf.pass.ptcpl. ὑπειρημένος | ‖ PF.PASS.PTCPL. (of an argument or proposition) **suggested at the outset** Isoc. Is. | cf. ὑπεῖπον

ὑπείς (Ion.athem.aor.ptcpl.): see ὑφίημι

ὑπ-εισέρχομαι *mid.vb.* | aor.2 ptcpl. ὑπεισελθών | **stealthily enter** —*a house* E.

ὑπ-έκ (unless **ὕπεκ**), also (before a vowel) **ὑπέξ**, Aeol. **ὑπέξ** *prep.* [ὑπό, ἐκ] | W.GEN. | **1 out** or **away from beneath** —*clouds, a vehicle, helmet, foot* Il. hHom. Theoc.
2 out of the protection of, away from —*an animal* Il. Thgn. Hdt.
3 up out of —*Erebos, the sea* Od. AR. Mosch.
4 out of reach of, away from —*the enemy, projectiles, fire, danger, suffering, death* Hom. Alc. AR.
5 out from —*a hand* Theoc. —*a serpent's jaws* AR. —*a mother's womb* Mosch.
6 free or **away from** —*a rock, forestays* AR.
7 app. **away from** —*a chariot* Il.
8 at a distance from —*a wall* Il. —*a place* AR.

ὑπεκ-βαίνω *vb.* **steal away from** —W.GEN. *home* E.(cj.)
ὑπεκ-βάλλω *vb.* (of sailors) **pass by** —*a river (i.e. its mouth)* AR.(tm.)
ὑπεκ-διδράσκω *vb.* | athem.aor.ptcpl. ὑπεκδράς | **flee to safety** —w. ἐκ + GEN. *fr. a city* Plu.
ὑπεκ-δραμεῖν *aor.2 inf.* **1** (fig., of a person, envisaged as helmsman) **run out from under, outrun, escape** —*a verbal tirade (envisaged as a storm at sea)* E.
2 (gener.) **escape, elude** —*the gods (as avengers)* E. —*shafts of verbal abuse* S. —*the appointed end (of a period of time, i.e. survive it)* S. —*current danger, death* Hdt. E. —w. μή + INF. *being put to death* E.
3 (of a horse) **run from under (its rider), bolt** Plu.
ὑπεκ-δύομαι *mid.vb.* [δύω¹] | athem.aor.act. ὑπεξέδῡν | pf.act. ὑπεκδέδῡκα | **1 slip furtively out** or **away** Lycurg. Men. Plu. —W.GEN. *fr. a gathering* Plu.
2 creep out from hiding Hdt.
3 (tr.) **escape** —*hardships* E.Cyc.
ὑπεκεχύμην (plpf.pass.): see ὑποχέω
ὑπεκ-θέω *contr.vb.* [θέω¹] **1** (of water) **run out** (fr. a klepsydra, under the pressure of air) Emp.
2 (of sailors, i.e. their ships) **run out** (to sea, under a strong wind) Plu.
ὑπεκ-καίω *vb.* (fig.) **inflame** —*persons (for combat)* Plu.
ὑπέκκαυμα ατος *n.* **1 combustible matter** (ref. to wood or sim.) Plu.; (ref. to bitumen) X.
2 cause of combustion, fuel (W.GEN. *for a flame*, ref. to *naphtha*) Plu.
3 (fig.) **incentive, incitement, provocation** (freq. W.GEN. *to sthg.*) X. Plu.
ὑπέκ-κειμαι *mid.pass.vb.* [κεῖμαι] **1** (of women and children) **be placed out of reach (of danger), be removed for safety** —W.ADV. or PREP.PHR. *to a place* Hdt.
2 (of property, money) **be removed for safekeeping** Hdt. Th. —w. παρά + DAT. *w. someone* Isoc.
ὑπεκ-κλέπτομαι *pass.vb.* | aor.2 ptcpl. ὑπεκκλαπείς | (of money) **be smuggled out for safety** Plu.
ὑπεκ-κλίνω *vb.* **1** perh. **sneak away to safety** Ar. [or perh. *duck away (fr. a blow)*]
2 (tr., of troops) **wheel away to avoid** —*an attack* Plu.
ὑπεκ-κομίζω *vb.* **transport to safety** —*women and children* Th. Plu. ‖ MID. **have** (W.ACC. *one's property*) **transported to safety** Hdt. X. ‖ PASS. (of a person) **be carried to safety** Plu.
ὑπεκ-λαμβάνω *vb.* **take** (W.ACC. *someone*) **away into safety** E.
ὑπεκ-λύω *vb.* **undermine** or **gradually weaken** —*an army's resolve* Plu.
ὑπεκ-πέμπω *vb.* **1 send away covertly** or **for safety** —*a child, wife* (W.ADV. or PREP.PHR. *to a place*) E. Plu. —(W.GEN. *fr. a country*) E. ‖ PASS. (of a child) **be sent away covertly** or **for safety** —W.ACC. *to a place* S.
2 covertly dispatch —*ships* (W.INF. *to take a message*) Th.
ὑπεκ-πλέω *contr.vb.* [πλέω¹] **sail away covertly** or **to safety** Plu.
ὑπεκ-προθέω *contr.vb.* **1 run out in front** (in a race or to escape pursuit) Hom. Emp.; (tr., of Ate) **outrun** —*Prayers* Il.
2 (of Nereids) **dart up from below in front** (of a ship) AR.
ὑπεκ-προλύω *vb.* **release** (W.ACC. *mules*) **from under** —W.GEN. *a wagon* Od.
ὑπεκ-προρέω *ep.contr.vb.* (of water) **flow out from below** Od.
ὑπεκ-προτάμνω *dial.vb.* [προτέμνω] (of a ship) **cleave through** (W.ACC. *the sea*) **ahead** AR.(tm.)
ὑπεκ-προφεύγω *vb.* **flee onwards out of reach** (of a person or threat); **escape** Hom.; (tr.) **escape from** —*a sea-monster, whirlpool, misery* Hom. Hes.
ὑπεκ-ρέω *contr.vb.* | aor.2 pass.ptcpl. (w.act.sens.) ὑπεκρυείς | **1** (of acquisitions) **trickle away** Pl.; (tr., of happenings) **slip away from** —*forgetful or thoughtless persons* Plu.
2 ‖ AOR.2 PASS. (of persons) **slip out of** —W.GEN. *a tent* Plu.
ὑπεκ-ρήγνυμαι *pass.vb.* (of a dam) **be broken away from below, burst** Plu.
ὑπεκ-ρίπτω *vb.* **cast out** (fr. office), **oust** —*a person* Plu.
ὑπεκ-σαόω *ep.contr.vb.* **remove safely out of reach** (of danger), **rescue** —*someone* Il.
ὑπεκ-σῴζω *vb.* **remove safely out of reach** (of danger); **rescue** —*sailors* (W.GEN. *fr. the sea*) A.
ὑπεκ-τίθεμαι *mid.vb.* **1 remove to safety** —*persons, property* (sts. W.PREP.PHR. *to or fr. a place*) Hdt. Th. Att.orats. X. Plu. ‖ PASS. **be removed to safety** Hdt. Lys.
2 remove covertly, smuggle away —*a child* (sts. W.PREP.PHR. *to or fr. a place*) S. E.
ὑπεκ-τρέπω *vb.* | aor.2 mid.opt. ὑπεκτραποίμην | **1 turn** (W.ACC. *one's step*) **away** —W.GEN. *fr. someone* S.
2 ‖ MID. **turn away from** —*someone* Pl. —(w. μή + INF. *so as not to help in rescuing him*) S.
ὑπεκ-φέρω *vb.* **1 take out of reach** (of danger); (of a horse) **carry away** —*a person* (fr. his pursuers) Plu.; (of a god) —*a warrior* (W.GEN. *fr. battle*) Il.
2 (of feet) **carry along** —*a runner* AR.; (fig., of a person's spirited nature) —*his ambition* (W.PREDIC.ADJ. *so as to render it invincible*) Plu.
3 (intr., of horses) **speed onwards** Od. [or perh. tr. *carry (someone) onwards*]

4 move (W.ACC. a shield) **aside a little** Il.
5 (of superstition) **gradually draw away** —someone (W.GEN. fr. a philosophical doctrine) Plu.(cj.)
6 (intr.) **keep ahead** (of pursuers) Hdt.

ὑπεκ-φεύγω vb. **1 flee out of reach** (of a person or threat); **escape** Hom. S. Pl. Plu.; (tr.) **escape from** —persons, war, a place Hom. Plu.; (of ships) —the enemy's wing, a manoeuvre Th. | see also ὑπερφεύγω
2 avoid, evade, escape —death, destruction, misery Hom.(sts.tm.) E. —pollution, reproach S. E.
3 (of the Muses) **flee from** —a loveless poet Bion

ὑπεκ-χέομαι mid.contr.vb. | 3sg.athem.aor. ὑπεξέχυτο | (of tears) **well up and pour forth** AR.

ὑπεκ-χωρέω contr.vb. **1** (of a commander, his army) **withdraw** (from before the enemy) Hdt. Plu.
2 (of an abstr. entity, such as largeness or heat) **withdraw** (in the face of its opposite) Pl.; **withdraw before** —W.DAT. its opposite Pl.; (of the immortal part of the soul) —death (i.e. escape it) Pl.
3 (euphem.) **retire** —W.GEN. fr. life (i.e. die) Pl.

ὑπέλυντο (3pl.athem.aor.mid.): see ὑπολύω
ὑπεμνάασθε (ep.2pl.impf.mid.): see ὑπομνάομαι
ὑπέμνασα (dial.aor.): see ὑπομιμνήσκω

ὑπ-εμνήμῡκα pf.vb. [ὑπό, app.reltd. ἠμύω] (of an orphan) prob., **have bowed one's head** (w. sorrow), **be downcast** Il.

ὑπέμνησα (aor.): see ὑπομιμνήσκω

ὑπ-εναντιόομαι mid.pass.contr.vb. | aor. ὑπηναντιώθην |
1 act in opposition (sts. furtively or underhandedly); **be opposed** or **resistant** (to someone or sthg.) Plu.; **oppose** —W.DAT. persons, plans, decision, or sim. Plu.
2 (of things) **be opposite in nature**, **be opposed** (to one another) Arist.

ὑπ-εναντίος ᾱ ον adj. **1 opposite** (in position); (of horses) **facing** (W.DAT. each other) Hes.
2 (of persons, their behaviour, things, circumstances) **opposed, hostile, unfavourable** (sts. W.DAT. to someone or sthg.) Th. X. Hyp. D. Arist. + ‖ MASC.PL.SB. **opponents** (in politics) D. Plu.; **opposing** or **enemy forces** X. Plb. Plu. ‖ NEUT.SB. **contrasting trait** (in someone's character) Hdt.
3 (of things) of the opposite or contrasting kind, **opposite, reverse** (usu. W.DAT. of specified things) Hdt. Pl. Aeschin. D. Arist.; (W.GEN.) Men.; **self-contradictory, inconsistent** Arist. ‖ NEUT.SB. **opposite side** (of a person's character) Hdt.
4 (advbl.neut.pl.acc.) τὰ ὑπεναντία τούτων **on the contrary** Hdt.

—**ὑπεναντίως** adv. **1 in the opposite way, contrarily** (usu. W.DAT. to someone or sthg.) Aeschin. D. Plu.; (W.GEN.) Arist.
2 contradictorily, inconsistently Arist.

ὑπεναντίωμα ατος n. [ὑπεναντιόομαι] **self-contradiction, inconsistency** Arist.

ὑπεναντίωσις εως f. **opposition** (betw. two feelings) Arist.

ὑπ-ενδίδωμι vb. **give ground, make some concession** Th.

ὑπένδυμα ατος n. [ὑπενδύομαι] **undergarment** Plu.

ὑπ-ενδύομαι mid.vb. | pf.ptcpl. ὑπενδεδυμένος | ‖ PF.PTCPL. **wearing** (W.ACC. a tunic) **underneath** (one's armour) Plu.

ὑπ-ένερθε(ν) adv. and prep. **1 beneath, below** Hom. hHom. Thgn. Ar. Hellenist.poet. —W.GEN. the chin, navel Hes. Ar.
2 under —W.GEN. the earth Stesich. Pi.; **in the underworld** Il. AR.
3 under the shelter, in the lee —W.GEN. of an island Od.
4 from below Simon. AR. —W.GEN. feet Il.

ὑπέξ prep.: see ὑπέκ

ὑπεξ-άγω vb. **1 lead out of range** (of danger); **take** (W.ACC. persons) **to safety** Od. Hdt.(mid.) Plu.
2 draw (W.ACC. one's step) **back from** —someone E.
3 (intr., of soldiers) **withdraw, retreat** Hdt. X. Plu.

ὑπεξαίρεσις εως f. [ὑπεξαιρέω] app. **removal** (W.GEN. of impossible tasks, fr. possible ones) Plu.

ὑπεξ-αιρέω contr.vb. **1 remove from beneath** (one's feet, i.e. fr. one's path); **remove, get rid of** —opponents Pl. X.(mid.) —dangers (W.DAT. facing someone) Th. —an accusation (against oneself) S. —a source of fear Arist.(mid.) ‖ PASS. (of opponents) **be removed** Hdt. Th.
2 ‖ MID. (fig., of a person, envisaged as a midwife) **quietly** or **surreptitiously take away** —a mistaken belief (envisaged as an unwanted baby) Pl.
3 (of a man) **gradually remove, drain** —wealth (W.GEN. fr. his house, through marriage) E.; (of the dead) —their killers' blood S. [perh. w. futher connot. fr. below]
4 ‖ MID. **remove from danger, rescue, secure** —a possession (ref. to a region) D.
5 ‖ MID. **make an exception of, exempt** —someone (fr. a regulation, punishment) Plu. ‖ PASS. **be exempted** Plu.
6 ‖ MID. **set apart for oneself** —some special provision (in an agreement) Plu.

ὑπ-εξακρίζω vb. [ἄκρος] (of cattle) **gradually move off uphill** E.

ὑπεξ-αλέομαι ep.mid.contr.vb. | only aor.inf. ὑπεξαλέασθαι | **keep clear of, avoid** —the hands of Zeus Il.

ὑπεξ-αλύσκω vb. **escape, avoid** —the wrath of Zeus, death Hes. AR.

ὑπεξ-αναβαίνω vb. **step back from danger** Theoc.

ὑπεξ-ανάγομαι mid.vb. (of a ship) **steal away** Th.

ὑπεξ-αναδύομαι mid.vb. | athem.aor.act. ὑπεξανέδῡν |
1 come up from under —W.GEN. the sea Il.
2 duck away (fr. a blow) Theoc.

ὑπεξ-ανίσταμαι mid.vb. | athem.aor.act. ὑπεξανέστην | **stand up from one's seat in respect** (for a person arriving); **stand up** (sts. W.DAT. for someone) Plu.

ὑπεξ-αντλέω contr.vb. **bail out from below**; (fig.) **drain away** —a wave of troubles (W.DAT. fr. one's mind) E.

ὑπεξ-αφύομαι mid.pass.vb. [ἀφύσσω] (of streams) **drain away** AR.

ὑπεξέδῡν (athem.aor.): see ὑπεκδύομαι

ὑπέξ-ειμι vb. [εἶμι] | Only pres. and impf. (other tenses are supplied by ὑπεξέρχομαι). The pres.indic. has fut. sense. |
1 (of troops) **withdraw** (before the enemy), **retire, retreat** Hdt. Plu.
2 (of a person) **gradually withdraw** (fr. a crowd) Plu.
3 (of beauty) **leave gradually, pass away** Pl.
4 (of magistrates) **make way** —W.DAT. for their successors D.; (of fire, snow, water, before cold, heat, new water) Pl. Arist.
5 (of a person) **get away surreptitiously, slip away** Arist. Plu.
6 go out from under cover (to fight), **sally forth** Hdt.(dub.)

ὑπεξ-είρυμαι ep.mid.vb. [ἔρυμαι] | 3sg.athem.aor. ὑπεξείρῡτο | **bring out from danger**; (of Zeus) **save** —someone (W.GEN. fr. murder) AR.

ὑπεξ-ειρύω Ion.vb. [ἐρύω] **drag to safety** —a corpse Hdt.

ὑπεξ-ελαύνω vb. **ride off in retreat** Hdt.

ὑπεξ-έρχομαι mid.vb. | The impf. is supplied by ὑπέξειμι. |
1 (of combatants, opponents, or sim.) **withdraw, retire, retreat** Th. Pl. —W.PREP.PHR. to a region Hdt. —W.ACC. before others Th.
2 (gener.) **withdraw** (fr. a room or building) Th. Plu.
3 withdraw covertly, slip away Th. And. Arist. Plu. —W.GEN. fr. a place Plu. —W.PREP.PHR. to or fr. a place Plu.
4 withdraw for safety —W.PREP.PHR. to a place Hdt. Th. D.

ὑπεξέχυτο

5 (of beauty) leave gradually, **pass away** Pl.
6 (of a concept) slip away from, **elude** —W.GEN. *a speaker* Pl.
7 withdraw in deference to, **keep out of the way of** —W.DAT. *someone* Pl.
8 give way in favour of, **back down before** —W.DAT. *someone* D.
ὑπεξέχυτο (3sg.athem.aor.mid.): see ὑπεκχέομαι
ὑπεξ-έχω vb. go out covertly, **slip out** (of a city) Hdt.; **slip away** —W.PREP.PHR. *to or fr. a place* Hdt.
ὑπεξ-ίσταμαι mid.vb. | athem.aor.act. ὑπεξέστην |
1 withdraw (sts. W.GEN. fr. a place) Plu. —W.GEN. *fr. public life* Plu.
2 renounce one's claim —W.GEN. *to kingship* Hdt.
3 stand aside, make way —W.DAT. *for someone* X. Plu.
4 give way —W.DAT. *to the demands of a situation* Plu.
5 get out of the way of, be rid of —W.DAT. *problems* Plu.
6 (tr.) **evade** —*an argument it is bearing down* Pl.
ὑπέρ, ep. **ὑπείρ**, Aeol. **περί** (also **πέρ** and **πέρρ**) *prep.* | W.ACC. and GEN., also DAT. (Pi.) | ὑπέρ sts. follows its noun (w. anastrophe of the accent), e.g. γουνὸς ὕπερ *above the knee* Od. |
—A | location |
1 at a position or height above, above, over —W.GEN. *a place, object, person, part of the body* Hom. + —W.ACC. *water-level* Plb. —app. W.DAT. *mountain look-outs* Pi.fr.; (ref. to placing an arrow) **on** —W.GEN. *a bow* Mosch.; (app.adv.) **above, overhead** Pi.
2 at a position further than, beyond —W.GEN. *a sea, an island* Od. Pi. —W.ACC. *a place* Hdt. Pl. AR. Plb.
3 inland of —W.GEN. *coastal places or people* Hdt. Th. —W.ACC. Plb.
4 off —W.GEN. *a coastal location* Hdt. Th.
5 immediately above (on the body), **above, over** —W.GEN. *a part of the body* Hom. X.
6 at a height above, above —W.GEN. *sthg.* Hom. —*someone's head* Hdt. E. —W.DAT. *someone* Pi.(dub.); **overlooking** —W.GEN. *a location, a sea, an enemy* Od. Pi. X. —W.ACC. *a location* Plb.
7 at the end or top of, at —W.GEN. *the head (of someone lying asleep)* Hom.
—B | movt. |
1 over, across —W.ACC. *a space, object, location, part of the body* Hom. + —W.GEN. Hom. Hes.fr. Anacr. A. Pi. S. +
2 further than, beyond, past —W.GEN. *a place* Pi. —W.ACC. AR. Plb.
—C | excess |
1 exceeding in degree, beyond —W.ACC. *a limit or criterion (such as the appropriate measure, what is best, truth, expectation, financial resources)* Thgn. Pi. Trag. Th. Ar. Pl. + —*a human being* (i.e. to a superhuman degree) Hdt. X. —*one's age* (i.e. precociously) Aeschin. D. Men. Plb.; (phr.) πέρ (cj. for πρὸς) βίαν (app.) *with excessive might* Alc. | see also καιρός 1, μόρος 1
2 beyond (so as to transgress), **beyond, in violation of** —W.ACC. *oaths, destiny, or sim.* Hom. Hdt.(oracle) | see αἶσα 7, μοῖρα 2, μόρος 1
3 in defiance of —W.ACC. *a god* Il.
4 beyond the capacity of, beyond —W.ACC. *persons, a human being* Il.
5 exceeding in number, more than, beyond —W.ACC. *a certain number* Hdt. Th. Pl. X. +
6 exceeding in age, beyond —W.ACC. *a certain time of life* X. Aeschin.

—D | superiority |
1 to a superior extent, above, beyond —W.GEN. *other people* Pi.
2 beyond or **superior to** —W.ACC. *someone or sthg. else* (sts. W.DAT. *in a particular quality*) Pl. Plb. NT.
3 (after compar.adj.) **than** —W.ACC. *someone* NT.
—E | time |
beyond (retrospectively), **earlier than** —W.ACC. *a certain event* Th. Pl.
—F | protection or support |
1 (ref. to fighting, dying, running risks, or sim.) **in defence of, for** —W.GEN. *persons, places, things* Il. Hes. Pi.fr. Hdt. Trag. Th. +
2 (ref. to speaking or acting) **on behalf of, for the sake of, in support of, in the interest of** —W.GEN. *persons, places* Il. Anacr. Pi. Hdt. Trag. Th. +
3 (ref. to entreating) **in the name of, by** —W.GEN. *someone or sthg.* Hom. AR. Theoc.
—G | specification |
1 (ref. to fearing, grieving, quarrelling, supplicating, or sim.) **in respect of, with regard to, over** —W.GEN. *someone or sthg.* Pi. Hdt. Trag. +
2 (ref. to hearing, speaking, knowing, or sim.) **about** —W.GEN. *someone or sthg.* Il. Hdt. Lys. Pl. +
—H | cause |
(ref. to killing, dying, fighting, punishing, or sim.) **on account of, because of** —W.GEN. *someone or sthg.* Pi. S. E. Lys. +
—I | purpose or motive |
for the purpose of achieving, **for the sake of** —W.GEN. *some goal* Th. Isoc. Pl. X. +
ὕπερ (prep. w. anastrophe): see ὑπέρ
ὑπέρᾱ f.: see ὑπέραι
ὑπερ-αβέλτερος ον adj. (of excuses and accusations) **exceedingly silly** D.
ὑπερ-άγαμαι mid.vb. | aor.pass. (w.mid.sens.) ὑπερηγάσθην | **be exceedingly impressed** Pl.
ὑπερ-αγανακτέω contr.vb. **be exceedingly annoyed** —W.GEN. *w. someone* Pl. —W.DAT. *at sthg.* Aeschin.
ὑπερ-αγαπάω contr.vb. **1** (of a populace) **have an excessive affection for** —*a military leader* D.; (of poets) —*their own poems* Arist.
2 (wkr.sens.) **have an extremely high regard** or **affection for** —*someone or sthg.* Plu.; **be extremely delighted by** —*sthg.* Plu.
ὑπερ-άγω vb. go beyond, **surpass** —W.GEN. *others* Plb.
ὑπερ-αγωνιάω contr.vb. **be extremely anxious** Pl. Men.
ὑπερ-ᾱής ές, gen. έος adj. [ἄημι] (of a storm-wind) **exceedingly blustery** Il.
ὑπέραι ῶν f.pl. upper ropes (attached to the yard arm of a ship's mast, i.e. at the top of the sail), **braces** Od.
ὑπερ-αιδέομαι mid.contr.vb. **be too much in awe of** —*someone* (W.INF. *to address him*) AR.
ὑπερ-αιμέω contr.vb. [αἷμα] (of a horse's body) **have an excess of blood** X.
ὑπερ-αίρω vb. **1 raise** (W.ACC. *sthg.*) **higher** (than its current position) Pl.
2 (intr.) **rise above** (a normal level); (of a stream) **overflow** —W.PREP.PHR. *into fields* D.
3 (of a person) **be taller** —W.GEN. *than a certain height* Plu.
4 (of a horse) **jump over** —*walls* X.; (of persons) **go over** —*mountains* Plb.; **advance beyond** —*a location* Plb.
5 go over or **across** —*a sea* Plb.; (intr.) **cross the sea** Plb.
6 go beyond; (of soldiers) **advance beyond** —*others, a*

ὑπερβαίνω

location Plb.; **outflank** —*the enemy* Plb.; (of a line of soldiers) **be stationed further back than** —*another line* Plb.
7 go past, round —*a headland* Plb.
8 go past, exceed —*an appointed time* Plb.
9 go further (in quality); **excel** —W.DAT. *in sthg.* D. Plu.; **surpass** —*persons, their qualities* D. Plb. Plu.; (of a city) —W.GEN. *others* D.
10 go further (than a standard or limit); (of a family's size) **go beyond, exceed** —*its resources* Arist.; (of persons) —*proper or customary behaviour* A. Plb. —W.GEN. Pl.; (of demands) —W.GEN. *another's offer* Plb.; (intr., of emotions, pride) **be excessive** Plb. Plu. ‖ NEUT.PTCPL.SB. **exaggeration** (in a historical account) Plb.

ὑπέρ-αισχρος ον *adj.* [αἰσχρός] **exceedingly ugly** X.

ὑπερ-αισχύνομαι *mid.vb.* | aor.pass.ptcpl. (w.mid.sens.) ὑπεραισχυνθείς | **1 be exceedingly ashamed** (sts. w. ἐπί + DAT. *over sthg.*) Aeschin.
2 (of a young man) **be extremely shy** (before women) —W.PREP.PHR. *in the presence of women* Men.

ὑπερ-αιωρέομαι *pass.contr.vb.* **1** (of a severed head) **be suspended over** —W.GEN. *a house* Hdt.; (of crane beams) —*walls* Plu.
2 (of sailors) **lie at anchor off** —W.GEN. *a harbour* Hdt.

ὑπερ-ακοντίζω *vb.* (fig.) **shoot beyond, surpass** —*someone* (W.DAT. *in or w. sthg.*) Ar. —(W.PTCPL. *in doing sthg.*) Ar.

ὑπερ-άκρια ων *n.pl.* [ἄκρος] **uplands** (above the plain of Attica), **hill-country** Hdt.
—**ὑπεράκριοι** ων *m.pl.* **inhabitants of the hill-country** (ref. to an Athenian political faction in the 6th C. BC, also called διάκριοι) Hdt.

ὑπερ-ακρίζω *vb.* **1** (of a horse-rider) **jump over** —*walls* X.
2 (of a cliff) **tower above** —W.GEN. *a temple* E.

ὑπεραλγέω *contr.vb.* [ὑπεραλγής] **1 feel excessive grief, grieve too much** E. Arist.
2 feel extreme grief, be distraught E. —W.DAT. *over sthg.* Hdt. Arist. Plu. —W.GEN. S.
3 feel pain or **grief for** —W.GEN. *someone* E. Ar.

ὑπερ-αλγής ές *adj.* [ἄλγος] **1** (of a person) **in extreme pain** Plb.
2 (of anger) **extremely painful** S.

ὑπερ-αλκής ές *adj.* [ἀλκή] (of military positions) **extremely strong** Plu.

ὑπερ-άλλομαι *mid.vb.* | ep.athem.aor.: 3sg. ὑπέραλτο, ptcpl. ὑπεράλμενος | **1 leap over** —*men and horses, a fence* Il. X. —W.GEN. *a wall* Il.
2 leap beyond —*a certain distance* X.

ὑπέρ-αλλος ον *adj.* [ἄλλος] (of a spear) **superior to others, matchless** Pi.

ὑπερ-αμπέχω *vb.* ‖ PTCPL.ADJ. (of the sky) **providing a cover above, over-arching** Tim.

ὑπερ-αναιδεύομαι *pass.vb.* [ἀναιδής] **be surpassed in shamelessness** Ar.

ὑπερ-αναίσχυντος ον *adj.* (of an action) **exceedingly impudent** D.

ὑπερ-ανατείνω *vb.* **stretch out, expose** —*one's neck* X.

ὑπερᾱνόρεος Aeol.*adj.*: see ὑπερήνωρ

ὑπέρ-αντλος ον *adj.* [ἄντλος] **1** (of a ship) with bilge-water coming over (the deck or sides), **waterlogged** Plu.
2 (fig., of a person) **foundering** (W.DAT. *under misfortune, anxieties*) E. Plu.

ὑπερ-άνω *adv. and prep.* **1 over and above, on top of** —W.GEN. *a trap-door* Plu.
2 over and above (what is necessary); (quasi-adjl., of repetitiousness by a writer) **to excess** Plb.

ὑπερ-ᾱ́νωρ dial.masc.*adj.*: see ὑπερήνωρ

ὑπερ-αποθνήσκω *vb.* **die on behalf** (of someone or sthg.); **give one's life** Pl. Arist. —W.GEN. *for someone, one's country* Pl. X. Arist. —w. ὑπέρ + GEN. *for the sake of fame* Pl.

ὑπερ-αποκρῑ́νομαι *mid.vb.* **answer** (charges) **on behalf of, defend** —W.GEN. *someone* Ar.

ὑπερ-απολογέομαι *mid.contr.vb.* **make a defence speech on behalf of** —W.GEN. *someone or sthg.* Hdt. Antipho X.

ὑπεραρρωδέω Ion.contr.*vb.*: see ὑπερορρωδέω

ὑπερ-ασθενής ές *adj.* (of a person) **exceedingly weak** Arist.

ὑπέρ-ασθμος ον *adj.* [ἄσθμα] (of a wild animal) **panting excessively, short of breath** X.

ὑπερ-ασπάζομαι *mid.vb.* **give an extremely warm welcome to** —*someone* X.

ὑπερ-ασπίζω *vb.* [ἀσπίς¹] (of a soldier) **place a shield over, shield, protect** —*someone* Plb. Plu.

ὑπερ-άστειος ον *adj.* [ἀστεῖος] (of a person) **exceedingly refined** (W.ACC. *in appearance*) Men.

ὑπερ-άτοπος ον *adj.* (of a state of affairs) **exceedingly odd** D.

ὑπερ-αυξάνομαι *mid.pass.vb.* (of persons) **grow excessively powerful** And.

ὑπεραυχέω *contr.vb.* [ὑπέραυχος] **be overconfident** or **overproud** Th.

ὑπέρ-αυχος ον *adj.* [αὐχή] (of persons, speech) **excessively self-confident, overconfident** or **overproud** A. S. X.

ὑπεράφανος dial.*adj.*: see ὑπερήφανος

ὑπερ-αχθής ές *adj.* [ἄχθος] (of racks) **excessively heavy, overloaded** (w. *cheeses*) Theoc.

ὑπερ-άχθομαι *pass.vb.* **be extremely upset** —W.DAT. *by an event* Hdt.; **be excessively angry** —W.DAT. *w. someone* S.

ὑπερ-βαίνω, Aeol. **περβαίνω** *vb.* | 3sg.aor.1 imperatv. (causatv.) ὑπερβησάτω | athem.aor. ὑπερέβην, ep. ὑπέρβην, ep.3pl. ὑπέρβασαν, ep.3sg.subj. ὑπερβήῃ ‖ Aeol.3sg.pf.pass. περβέβαται |

1 go up and over; get over, scale —*a wall, fortification, roof* Il. E. Th. X. D. Plu.; (intr.) Th. X. Plu.; **step over** (seated people, corpses) Ar. Plb. —*a corpse* Plu.; (of a river) **overflow** Hdt. —w. εἰς + ACC. *onto land* Hdt.
2 (aor.1, causatv.) **put** (W.ACC. *one's leg*) **over** (a horse's back) X.
3 go over, cross —*a ditch, road, river, mountain* Hdt. E. X. Theoc. Plu. —*a boundary or border* E.*fr.* Th.(treaty) Pl. Lycurg. Plb. Plu. —*a threshold* Od. hHom. E.(cj.) Plu. —*a house or shrine* (i.e. its threshold, on entering or leaving) E.; (intr.) **go across** (fr. one place to another) Hdt. —w. εἰς + ACC. *to another region or sea* Hdt. X.
4 (of a people) **be situated beyond** —*a mountain* Th.
5 travel beyond —*people living in a certain place* Hdt.; (fig., of a king, ref. to his sphere of influence) **go beyond** —*neighbouring peoples* Hdt.; **go past, pass by** —*sthg.* Plu.
6 pass over, ignore, omit —*someone or sthg.* Att.orats. Pl. Plu.
7 go beyond (proper limits); **overstep** —*the boundaries* (W.GEN. *of a wife, i.e. of what she is permitted*) Men.; (of the sun, in a hypothetical situation) —*its limits* Heraclit.
8 exceed —*an age limit, period of time, price* Pl. Arist. Plb. ‖ PASS. (of time) **have been exceeded, be past** —W.DAT. *for someone* Alc.
9 outdo, surpass —*someone or sthg.* Pl. Plb.; (of one state of affairs) —*another* Pl.
10 go beyond (what is right or legal), **transgress** Il. Thgn. Pl. —*a law, agreement, oath, justice* Pi. Hdt. S. E. Pl. +; (gener.) **go too far** or **to an extreme** (in behaviour) Pl.

ὑπερ-βάλλω vb. | aor.2 ὑπερέβαλον, ep. ὑπέρβαλον, also ὑπειρέβαλον | **1** (of a competitor) **throw further** —w.gen. *than others* Il.; **out-throw** —*others* (i.e. *outdistance them*) Il. **2 throw beyond, overshoot** —*the markers of others* Il. **3** (of Sisyphos) **push** (w.acc. a boulder) **over** —*the crest of a hill* Od. **4** (esp. in military ctxts.) **go across** —*mountains, boundaries, rivers* A. E. X. + —*a stretch of land or water* AR.(tm.); **cross** (into another country) Hdt. +; (of a beacon-signal) **cross over** —*a headland* A. **5 get beyond, sail round** —*a headland* Hdt. Th. **6** (of a charioteer) **get ahead of, outstrip** —*other chariots* S. **7** (of hounds, tracking a quarry) **get too far ahead, overrun** X. **8** (of rainfall) **rise above** —*a certain level* Hes.; (of a river) **flood over** —*fields* Hdt.; (of a stormy sea) **rise higher** —w.gen. *than a ship's sides* Thgn.; **rise too high** E.; (of cooking pots) **boil over** Hdt. **9** (of persons) **outdo, surpass** —*others, their achievements, or sim.* Isoc. X. +; **be superior** E. Isoc. Pl. +; (of Time) —w.gen. *to all the gods* Pi.*fr*.; (of things) **be outstanding** —w.dat. *in some quality* Isoc. Pl. X. **10** ‖ mid. **come out ahead or on top, prevail** Hdt. Ar.; **prevail over** —*others* Hdt. S. E. +; **outdo, surpass** —*persons, their achievements* (sts. w.dat. *by some achievement*) Hdt. Isoc. Pl. X.; (of a king) —*others* (w.dat. *in the height and size of his buildings*) Hdt. ‖ act. (of old age) **overwhelm** —*a person* (w.dat. *w. hardships*) E.*fr*. **11** ‖ mid. (of a leader, an army) **be greatly superior** (in resources) Hdt. Pl. **12** (of emotions) **outdo** or **outnumber** —*others* Pl.; **be greater** —w.gen. *than others* Pl.; (of a crash) **be louder** —w.gen. *than thunder* A.; (of an action) **have a greater effect** —w.gen. *than another* Pl. ‖ pass. (of feelings) **be outnumbered** (by others) Pl. **13 go higher** (w. a sum of money), **offer a larger amount** Hdt. And.; **outbid** —*others* Hdt. Att.orats. **14 go beyond** (a limit); (of persons) **exceed** —*an appropriate level* (*in drinking, emotions*) Thgn. D.; (of wealth, enjoyment, or sim.) —*what is sufficient, appropriate or customary* X.; (of a state or condition) —*a mean* Pl.; **be excessive** (relative to another state) Arist.; (of a detail in a painting) **be larger** —w.gen. *than the demands of symmetry* Arist. ‖ pass. **be exceeded** (by a mean, i.e. *fall short of it*) Pl. **15 go too far** (in speech), **exaggerate** Pi. Th. Isoc.; (of an expression) **be an exaggeration** Pl. **16 go too far** (in behaviour); **be excessive** (in one's demands, zeal, bad behaviour) Th. Ar. X. Arist.; (in one's grief) E.; (act. and mid.) **outdo** —*others* (*in extravagance, wickedness, or sim.*) Ar. X. D. **17 be excessive** (in intensity); (of the sun) **be exceedingly hot** Hdt.; (of an affliction or sim.) **be extreme** A. E. Th.; (of a law) **be too severe** And. **18 go beyond, exceed** —*a period of time* X. —*one's normal life expectancy* Hdt. **19** ‖ mid. **put off, postpone** —*sthg.* Hdt. X. Arist.; (intr.) **delay** Hdt. Pl. +

—**ὑπερβάλλων** ουσα ον pres.ptcpl.adj. **1** (of persons, an army) **outstanding, exceptional** Th. Isoc.; (of a wild boar, w.dat. in its strength) X.; (of a face, in its ugliness) X.; (of abilities, pleasures, happiness, cowardice) E. Pl. Aeschin. **2** (of praise, pleasures, expenditure, or sim.) **excessive, extravagant** Th. Isoc. Pl. X. + ‖ neut.sb. **excess** (in wealth, behaviour) E. Pl.; (in speeches of praise) Th.

3 (of a person's death) **overwhelming** (in its effect on others) And. **4** (of fire, shouting) **of extraordinary intensity** Plb.
—**ὑπερβαλλόντως** pres.ptcpl.adv. **1 outstandingly** Isoc. **2 exceedingly, extremely** Pl. X. D. Plb. **3 excessively** Isoc. Pl.
—**ὑπερβεβλημένος** η ον pf.mid.ptcpl.adj. **1** (of a woman) **outstanding, exceptional** E.(dub.); (of natural ability) Pl. **2** (of a funeral) **extravagant** Pl.
—**ὑπερβεβλημένως** pf.mid.ptcpl.adv. **excessively** Arist.
ὑπερ-βαρής ές adj. [βάρος] (quasi-advbl., of a deity falling on a victim) **with overwhelming weight** A.
ὑπερβασίᾱ ᾱς, Ion. **ὑπερβασίη** ης f. [ὑπερβαίνω] **attitude or behaviour that goes beyond** (what is proper or lawful), **transgression, offence** Hom. Hes. Thgn. S. Call. AR.
ὑπέρβασις εως f. **1 transporting** (w.gen. of boats) **across** (the Isthmos) Plb.(dub., cj. ὑπερβίβασις) **2 transgression, offence** Thgn. [or perh. *excessive temper* or *superiority*]
ὑπερβατός ή όν adj. | compar. ὑπερβατώτερος | **1** (of a wall) **able to be got over, scaleable** Th. **2** (of a word) **transposed** (fr. its normal place in a sentence) Pl. **3** ‖ compar. (of sorrows) **surpassing** (w.gen. other sorrows) A.
ὑπερβεβλημένως pf.mid.ptcpl.adv.: see under ὑπερβάλλω
ὑπερβῆ (ep.3sg.athem.aor.subj.), **ὑπέρβην** (ep.athem.aor.): see ὑπερβαίνω
ὑπερ-βιάζομαι mid.vb. (of a calamity) **be overwhelming** Th.
ὑπερ-βιβάζω vb. **1 transport** (w.acc. ships) **across** (to the other side of a breakwater) Plb. **2 send** (w.acc. soldiers) **over** (a wall) Plu.
ὑπερβίβασις f.: see ὑπέρβασις
ὑπέρ-βιος ον adj. [βίᾱ] **1 of extraordinary power**; (of gods, persons, their strength, deeds, or sim.) **overpowering, overwhelming, mighty** Pi. B. AR.; (of a burden) Hes.; (of a wave, pain, quarrel, oath) AR. **2** (pejor.) **of excessive power or violence**; (of persons, their spirit, behaviour, or sim.) **violent, arrogant** or **insolent** Hom. Hes. AR.
—**ὑπέρβιον** neut.adv. (pejor.) **violently, high-handedly** or **insolently** Hom.
ὑπερ-βιόω contr.vb. **outlive** —w.gen. *someone* Plb.
ὑπερβολάδην adv. [ὑπερβολή] **to excess** —*ref. to drinking wine* Thgn.
ὑπερβολή ῆς, dial. **ὑπερβολά** ᾶς f. [ὑπερβάλλω] **1 going over, crossing** (w.gen. of a mountain) X. Plb.; **place for crossing, pass** X. Plb. Plu. **2 going beyond** (others); **superiority** (of persons or things) Th. Isoc. Pl. Arist. **3 potential to go beyond** (others), **opportunity to surpass** (sts. w.gen. in sthg.) Att.orats. **4 exceeding** (of what has gone before); **further degree** (of sthg.) Isoc. D. Men. **5 going beyond** (what is needed), **surplus, surfeit, excess** (opp. deficiency) Isoc. Pl. Arist. **6 going too far, excess, extreme** or **extravagance** (of material and non-material things, esp. aspects of behaviour) E. Th. Att.orats. Pl. Arist. Men. + **7 extravagant language, exaggeration** Isoc. D.; (as a figure of speech) **hyperbole** Arist. **8 going higher, increase** (w.gen. in price) Arist. **9** (gener.) **extremely great amount or degree**; **surpassing degree** (w.gen. of honour) Plu.; **surpassing volume** (w.gen. of a voice) Plu.

10 putting off, **delay, postponement** (sts. W.GEN. of sthg.) Hdt. Plb.

11 (advbl. and prep.phrs.) ὑπερβολῇ *to a surpassing or excessive degree,* **extremely** or **excessively** Arist. Men. Plb.; (also) εἰς ὑπερβολήν E. Isoc. Aeschin. Arist.; *in excess* (W.GEN. *of someone*) E.; (also) ἐξ ὑπερβολῆς Plb.; καθ' ὑπερβολήν S. Att.orats. Arist. Plb.; *in an excess* (W.GEN. *of sthg.*) Aeschin.; (also) πρὸς ὑπερβολήν Isoc.; *in an excess* (W.GEN. *of sthg.*) Is.

ὑπερβολικός ή όν *adj.* (of an expression of gratitude) **excessive, extravagant** Plb.

–**ὑπερβολικῶς** *adv.* | compar. ὑπερβολικώτερον | **with exaggeration** Plb. ‖ COMPAR. **more extravagantly** Plb.

Ὑπερβόρεοι ων *m.pl.* [Βορέας] **Hyperboreans** (a people thought to live in the extreme north and to be particularly blessed) Hes.*fr.* hHom. Pi. B. Hdt. Call. +; (sg., as ethnic adj.) Pl.

–**ὑπερβόρεος** ον *adj.* (of prosperity) like that of the Hyperboreans, **hyperborean, out of this world** A.

ὑπερ-βριθής ές *adj.* [βρίθος] (of a burden of grief) **very heavy** S.

ὑπ-εργάζομαι *mid.vb.* [ὑπό] **1 plough up** (W.ACC. fallow land) **in preparation** —W.DAT. *for sowing* X.

2 (fig., tr.) **prepare the ground for** —*a future action* Plu.; (intr.) **do the groundwork** Plu. ‖ PF.PASS. (of a woman) have been made ready (for a love affair) —W.ACC. *in her soul* (W.DAT. *by desire*) E.; (of acts of kindness) have been done in the past (W.DAT. *by two people*) as a basis (for mutual tolerance now) E.

ὑπερ-γέλοιος ον *Att.adj.* [ὑπέρ, γελοῖος] (of a situation) **exceedingly ridiculous** D.

ὑπερ-γεμίζομαι *pass.vb.* (of silver-mines) **be over-manned** (w. slave labour) X.

ὑπερ-γέμω *vb.* (of an army) **be overloaded** —W.GEN. *w. plunder* Plb.

ὑπερ-γήρως ων, gen. ω *adj.* [γῆρας] **extremely old** ‖ NEUT.SB. **extreme old age** A.

ὑπέρ-δασυς υ, gen. εος *adj.* [δασύς] (of a man) **very hairy** X.

ὑπερ-δεής ές *adj.* [δέος] | only ep.masc.acc. ὑπερδέα | (of a people) **exceedingly fearful** Il. [or perh. fr. δέω² *very wanting in numbers*]

ὑπερ-δείδω *vb.* | aor. ὑπερέδεισα | statv.pf. ὑπερδέδοικα |
1 be afraid for —W.GEN. *someone* S.; (of a dove) **fear** (W.ACC. snakes) **on account of** —W.GEN. *her offspring* A.
2 be extremely afraid Hdt.

ὑπερ-δειμαίνω *vb.* **be extremely afraid of** —*someone* Hdt. —*the law* Hdt.(cj., for ὑπο-)

ὑπέρ-δεινος ον *adj.* [δεινός] (of a situation, an action) **exceedingly dreadful, appalling** D.

ὑπερ-δειπνέω *contr.vb.* **dine too well** Men.

ὑπερ-δέξιος ον *adj.* [δεξιός] **1** (in military ctxts.) being in a favourable position above (the enemy); (of ground) **higher** X. Plb. ‖ NEUT.PL.SB. **higher ground** X.

2 (of a hill) **in a commanding position** Plb.; (W.GEN. above the enemy) Plb.

3 (of troops) **on higher ground** Plb.; (W.GEN. than the enemy) Plb.; (of men on a siege-engine) **at a higher level** (W.GEN. than a wall) Plb.

4 (of ground) **favourable** (W.DAT. to the enemy, because of its height) Plb.

5 (of a gate) **higher up** (a hill) Plb.

6 (prep.phrs.) ἐξ ὑπερδεξίου *from a higher position, from the high ground* X. Plb.; (also) ἐξ ὑπερδεξίων Plb.; (also, sg.) *higher upstream* Plb.

7 (fig.) **having the upper hand** (W.DAT. in a war) Plb.; (in terms of right) (W.GEN. of virtue) **triumphant** (W.GEN. over vice) Plu.; (of the effectiveness of troops) **superior** Plb.

8 (epith. of Apollo) **supreme** Plu.

ὑπερ-διατείνομαι *mid.vb.* **over-exert oneself** D.

ὑπερδικέω *contr.vb.* [δίκη] **make a case in defence of, plead for** —W.GEN. *someone* or *sthg.* A. Pl.

ὑπέρ-δικος ον *adj.* **1** (of Nemesis) **more than just, severely just** Pi.

2 (of painful words) **more than fair** S.

–**ὑπερδίκως** *adv.* **more than fairly** A.

ὑπερ-δραμεῖν *aor.2 inf.* | aor.2 ὑπερέδραμον | **1 run beyond the reach of, escape** —*poverty* Thgn.

2 overcome, prevail over —*stronger powers, adversaries* E. —*the gods' decrees* S.; (intr., of military forces) **prevail** E.

3 surpass —*goddesses* (W.DAT. *in beauty*) E.

Ὑπερείδης ου *m.* **Hypereides** (Athenian orator and politician, 389–322 BC) Plu.

ὑπερεῖδον (aor.2): see ὑπεροράω

ὑπ-ερείδω *vb.* [ὑπό] **1 act as a support from underneath;** (of a pillar) **support** —*a roof* Plu.; (fig., of a military leader) —*the state* Plu.

2 cause to be supported from underneath; support, prop up —*the pole of a wagon* (W.DAT. *w. a piece of wood*) Plu.; (fig., of mathematicians) —*problems in geometry* (W.PREP.PHR. *by means of mechanical illustrations*) Plu.

3 put under as a support; (of a philosopher, in his doctrine) **place** (W.ACC. air) **as a support** (for the earth, compared to a base beneath a dough-trough) Pl.; (of a poet) **place** (W.ACC. a stone of the Muses) **as a foundation** (W.DAT. for a person and his homeland, as if for a statue, i.e. exalt them in poetry) Pi.

ὑπ-ερείπω *vb.* | impf. ὑπήρειπον | aor.2 ὑπήριπον | **1** (of a person, sickness, news) **cause to give way, undermine** —*courage, strength of mind* Plu.

2 (aor.2, of limbs) **give way beneath one** Il.

3 ‖ PASS. (of a person) **totter, collapse** Plu.; (of limbs) **give way beneath one** Lyr.adesp.

4 ‖ PASS. **be undermined** —W.DAT. *by old age* Plu.; (fig.) —*by fears and threats* Plu.; (of a commander, by an opponent's tactics) Plu.

ὑπερ-εκθεραπεύω *vb.* **go to extravagant lengths to court the favour of** —*someone* Aeschin.

ὑπερ-εκπλήττομαι *Att.pass.vb.* [ἐκπλήσσω] **1 be overwhelmed with astonishment** —w. ἐπί + DAT. *at someone* X.

2 be unduly alarmed by —W.ACC. *someone* (w. ὡς + PREDIC.ADJ. *in the belief that he is invincible*) D.

ὑπερ-εκχύννομαι *pass.vb.* [ἐκχέω] (of the contents of a container) be poured out over (the rim), **run over, overflow** NT.

ὑπερ-έλαφρος ον *adj.* [ἐλαφρός] (of a hare) **exceedingly nimble** X.

ὑπερ-εξακισχίλιοι αι α *pl.num.adj.* **more than six thousand** D.

ὑπερ-εξηκοντέτης ες *adj.* [ἐξηκοντούτης] **over sixty years old** Ar.

ὑπέρ-εξις εως *f.* [ἕξις] **excessiveness** (in size) Pl.

ὑπερ-επαινέω *contr.vb.* **praise extravagantly** or **over-praise** —*someone* or *sthg.* Hdt. Ar. Isoc. Pl. +

ὑπερ-επιθῡμέω *contr.vb.* **desire above all else** —W.INF. *to do sthg.* X.

ὑπερέπτᾱ (dial.3sg.athem.aor.), **ὑπερέπτατο** (3sg.athem.aor.mid.): see ὑπερπέτομαι

ὑπ-ερέπτω *vb.* [ὑπό] (of a river) **eat away** (W.ACC. ground) **from under** —W.GEN. *feet* Il.

ὑπερ-εράω *contr.vb.* **be exceedingly passionate** (W.GEN. about sthg.) Plu.(cj.)

ὑπερ-έρχομαι *mid.vb.* **1 go beyond** —*a place* X.
2 excel —W.DAT. *in achievements* Pi.
3 (of desires) **come in excess** E.(tm.)
ὑπερ-εσθίω *vb.* **overeat** X.
ὑπερέσχεθον (ep.aor.2): see ὑπερέχω
ὑπέρ-ευ *adv.* [εὖ] **surpassingly well** Pl. X. D. Men.
—ὑπέρευγε *interj.* [εὖγε] **very well said!, bravo!** Men.
ὑπερ-ευγενής ές *adj.* (of persons) **exceedingly well-born** Arist.
ὑπερ-ευδαιμονέω *contr.vb.* **be exceptionally prosperous** Arist.
ὑπερ-ευδοκιμέω *contr.vb.* **have an exceptionally good reputation** Lys.
ὑπερ-εχθαίρω *vb.* **detest beyond measure** —*boastful language* S.
ὑπερ-έχω, ep. **ὑπειρέχω**, Aeol. **περρέχω** *vb.* | Aeol.3sg. (tm.) πὲρ ... ἔχει | aor.2 ὑπερέσχον, ep. ὑπερέσχεθον, Aeol.fem.ptcpl. περσκέθοισα | **1 hold** (W.ACC. sthg.) **above** or **over** —W.GEN. *someone* Ar. Plb. Plu. —*a fire* Il. Plu.
2 (of a god) **bring** (W.ACC. a cloud) **over** (a land) A.*fr.*; **hold** (W.ACC. a shield, hand, strength, or sim.) **over** —W.GEN. or DAT. *a person or place* (*for protection*) Hom. Thgn. A. Ar.
3 (of a star) **rise** Od.; **rise above** —W.ACC. *mountains* AR.; (of the sun) —W.GEN. *the earth* Il.; (of a person) **be above** —W.GEN. *the ground* (*by a certain height*) Theoc.(dub.); (of things) —*a certain level* Pl.; (of bilge-water) —W.ACC. *the mast-support* Alc.(tm.); (of a suspended object) **be high up** —W. ὑπέρ + GEN. *above a house* Hdt.; (of areas in a city) **have an elevated position** X.; (of a cliff) **tower** (*above a road*) X.; (of sea-swell, above rocks) AR.
4 (of things) **project, stick out** (fr. the ground, a body) Hdt.; **protrude above** (a barrier) X. —W.GEN. *a shield, wall* E. Pl.; (of parts of a soldier's body) **extend beyond** —W.GEN. *his protective armour* X.; (of ears of corn) **stand out** (above others) Hdt.
5 (specif.) **be or rise above** (the surface of water); (of objects) **stick out** (of water) X. —W.GEN. *of water* Hdt. Th.; (of land) **be above** —W.GEN. *water* Hdt.; (of towns, an island) **be above water** Hdt.; (of a person) **keep oneself** (i.e. one's body) —w. ὑπέρ + ACC. *above water* Plb.; **keep one's head above** —W.GEN. *water* Ar. X.; **keep one's head above water** Th.
6 (milit.) **extend beyond, outflank** (the enemy) Th. X. —W.GEN. *the enemy* X.
7 stand out in physique; stand out beyond —W.GEN. *others* (W.ACC. w. *one's broad shoulders, i.e. be broader in the shoulders*) Il. —(W.ACC. w. *one's head and forehead, i.e. be a head taller*) Od.(tm.)
8 (of persons, places, things) **excel, be superior or pre-eminent** (freq. W.DAT. or PREP.PHR. in some quality or asset) A. Hdt. Isoc. Pl. X. D. +; **be superior to, surpass** —W.GEN. *all or others* (freq. W.DAT. or PREP.PHR. *in sthg.*) Att.orats. Pl. X. Arist. + —(W.ACC. *in sthg.*) Sapph. A. —W.ACC. *all* (W.DAT. *in sthg.*) E.; (of the moon) —*all the stars* Sapph.; (of expensive clothing) **exceed** —W.ACC. *one's means* Plb.
|| PASS. (of persons or things) **be surpassed or exceeded** Pl. Arist.
9 (of the gods' will) **prevail** Thgn.; (of a stormy sea) **get the better** (of a ship) D.
ὑπερ-ζέω *contr.vb.* (fig., of a person) **boil over** (w. rage) Ar.
ὑπερ-ηδέως *adv.* **with especial pleasure** X.
ὑπερ-ήδομαι *pass.vb.* **be overjoyed** Hdt. X. Plu. —W.DAT. *at sthg.* Hdt.
ὑπερημερίᾱ ᾱς *f.* [ὑπερήμερος] **1** (leg.) **going beyond the due day** (for a payment), **defaulting, default** D. Thphr.

2 right to execute proceedings for defaulting D.; (concr.) **penalty for defaulting** Thphr.
ὑπερ-ήμερος ον *adj.* [ἡμέρα] **1** (leg., of persons) **beyond the day** (for a payment), **defaulting, in arrears** Lys. D. Plu.; (W.GEN. for a specified sum) Antipho
2 (fig., of unmarried girls) **overdue** (W.GEN. for marriage) Arist.(quot.com.)
ὑπερ-ημίσεις, Ion. **ὑπερημίσεες**, εων *m.pl.* [ἥμισυς] **more than half of the men** (usu. W.GEN. of a specified group or number) Hdt. Plu.
ὑπ-έρημος ον *adj.* [ὑπό, ἐρῆμος] (of cities, a room) **rather desolate** Plu.
ὑπερηνορέη ης *ep.Ion.f.* [ὑπερήνωρ] **insolence** AR.
ὑπερ-ηνορέων οντος *ep.masc.ptcpl.adj.* (of persons, Cyclopes) **overbearing, insolent, arrogant** Hom. || PL.SB. (iron.) **supermen** (ref. to dignitaries in a theatre audience) Ar.
ὑπερ-ήνωρ ορος *ep.masc.adj.* —also **ὑπερᾱ́νωρ** ορος *dial.masc.adj.* —also perh. **ὑπερᾱνόρεος** ον *Aeol.adj.* [ἀνήρ] app., exceeding (the limits of) a man; (of persons) **overbearing, insolent, arrogant** Hes. AR. Theoc.(dub.); (of boasting) E.
ὑπερηφανέω *contr.vb.* [ὑπερήφανος] **1** (of warriors) **be arrogant** Il.; (of kingship) Plb.
2 (of writers) **be excessively proud of** —*themselves and their works* Plb.
ὑπερηφανίᾱ ᾱς *f.* **1 arrogance** Att.orats. Pl. X. Arist. Plb. +; (W.GEN. towards gods and men) Pl. D.
2 ostentation, extravagance Pl.
ὑπερήφανος, dial. **ὑπερᾱ́φανος**, ον *adj.* **1** (of the Giants, the power of Zeus) **overbearing, insolent, arrogant** Hes. A.; (of persons, their actions, words, or sim.) Sol. Pi. Att.orats. Pl. X. Arist. +
2 (of houses, expenditure) **ostentatious** D. Plu.
3 (w. positive connot., of valour, courage) **proud** Ibyc. B.
4 (of buildings, achievements, empire, a piece of handiwork) **magnificent, glorious** Plb. Plu.; (iron., of wisdom, an achievement) Pl.
—ὑπερηφάνως *adv.* **1 arrogantly** Isoc. Pl. D. Plb. Plu.
2 magnificently Plu.
ὕπερθε(ν) *adv. and prep.* [ὑπέρ] **1 from above** Hom. hHom. Thgn. AR.
2 up above, above Hom. Hes. Sol. Pi. E. + —W.GEN. *someone or sthg.* Simon. A. Pi. AR. Theoc.
3 higher up (on the body) Hom. Pi.; **above** —W.GEN. *the nose* Theoc.
4 over (a surface) Hom. hHom. AR. —W.GEN. *someone's eyes* A.
5 on top Il. —W.GEN. *of sthg.* Hes. AR.
6 over, across —W.GEN. *the sea* AR.
7 further on Il. AR.; **beyond** —W.GEN. *a place* Pi. Hdt.
8 to a greater degree, further S. E.
9 beyond the reach —W.GEN. *of hardships* E.
ὑπερ-θερμαίνομαι *pass.vb.* (of a person) **get too hot** Arist.
ὑπέρθεσις εως *f.* [ὑπερτίθημι] **1 putting further ahead** (in time); **postponement, delay** Plb.; **adjournment** (of a debate) Plb. Plu.; **temporary relief** (W.GEN. fr. present troubles) Plb.
2 putting further ahead (in urgency); **intensity** (W.GEN. of the pursuit of an aim) Plb.
ὑπερ-θέω *contr.vb.* [θέω¹] **1** (fig.) **run over, surmount** —*the crest of a wave* (*of misfortune*) A.
2 (fig.) **run beyond, outrun** (i.e. not be overtaken by) —*the strength of wine* Pl.
ὑπερθέωμαι (dial.athem.aor.mid.subj.): see ὑπερτίθημι

ὑπερ-θνῄσκω vb. | aor.2 ὑπερέθανον | **1 die on behalf of, die for** —W.GEN. *someone, a land* E.
2 die because of —W.GEN. *sthg.* E.
ὑπερ-θρῴσκω vb. | fut. ὑπερθοροῦμαι, ep. ὑπερθορέομαι | aor.2 ὑπερέθορον, ep. ὑπέρθορον | **1** (of persons, animals) **jump over** —*a fence, wall, trench, line of people* Il. A. Hdt.; (of evil) —W. ὑπέρ + ACC. *a barrier* Sol.
2 jump over the side of, **jump out of** —*a ship* A.
3 (of a beacon-light) **leap across** —*a plain* A.
4 (of smoke) **leap up above** —W.GEN. *a city* E.
ὑπερ-θυίω vb. (of seawater) **bubble over** (W.GEN. fr. the mouth of a drowning man) Tim.
ὑπέρ-θυμος ον adj. [θυμός] | superl. ὑπερθυμέστατος (Stesich.) | **1 great-hearted, bold** Hom. Hes. Lyr.; (of strength) B.(cj.)
2 (pejor.) **proud-hearted, overbold** Hom. Hes.
3 (of horses) **excessively high-spirited** X.
—**ὑπερθύμως** adv. **with excessive anger** A.
ὑπερ-θύρον (also **ὑπερθύριον** Od. Hes.) ου n. **lintel** (above a door or gate) Od. Hes. Carm.Pop. Parm. Hdt. Arist.
ὑπερ-θωμάζω Ion.vb. [θαυμάζω] **feel** or **express extreme admiration** Hdt.
ὑπερ-ίημι vb. **throw** (a discus) **beyond** —*a marker* Od.
ὑπερ-ικταίνομαι mid.vb. [perh. ἴκταρ] (of feet) perh. **move with extraordinary speed** Od.
Ὑπερϊονίδης m.: see under Ὑπερίων
ὑπερ-ίπταμαι mid.vb.: see ὑπερπέτομαι
ὑπερ-ισθμίζω vb. [ἰσθμός] (of a commander) **transport** (W.ACC. his ships) **across the Isthmos** Plb.; (intr.) **transport one's ships across the Isthmos** Plb.
ὑπερ-ίσταμαι mid.vb. | athem.aor.act. ὑπερέστην | **1** (of a dream figure) **come and stand over** —W.GEN. *someone* Hdt.
2 stand in front (so as to protect); **provide protection** AR. —W.GEN. *for someone* S.
ὑπερ-ίστωρ ορος masc.fem.adj. **knowing too well** (W.GEN. about sthg.) S.
ὑπερ-ίσχυρος ον adj. [ἰσχυρός] (of persons) **exceedingly strong** Arist.; (of a fortress) X.
ὑπερ-ίσχω vb. **1** (of Zeus) **hold** (W.ACC. a hand) **above** (as protection) —W.DAT. *for guests and suppliants* AR.
2 keep (W.ACC. one's head) **up** —W. ὑπέρ + ACC. *above water* Plb.
3 (of justice) **prevail over** —W.GEN. *violence* Hes.(tm.)
Ὑπερίων ονος m. **1 Hyperion** (a Titan, father of Helios) Hes. hHom. Mimn.
2 Hyperion (the sun-god, freq. appos.w. Ἥλιος) Hom. hHom.
—**Ὑπεριονίδης** ου (ep. ᾱο), dial. **Ὑπεριονίδᾱς** ᾱ m. **son of Hyperion** (ref. to Helios) Od. Hes. hHom. Stesich. Pi.
ὑπερ-κάθημαι mid.vb. (of soldiers) **occupy a higher position** —W.GEN. *than the enemy* X. —W. ἐπί + GEN. *on hilltops* X.
ὑπέρ-καλος ον adj. [καλός] **exceedingly beautiful** Arist.
ὑπερ-κάμνω vb. **toil on behalf of** —W.GEN. *one's children, city* E.
ὑπερ-καταβαίνω vb. **come down over** —*a wall* Il.
ὑπερ-καταγέλαστος ον adj. (of legal proceedings) **utterly ridiculous** Aeschin.
ὑπερ-κατάκειμαι mid.pass.vb. **recline in a higher position** (at a dinner) Plu.
ὑπέρ-κειμαι mid.pass.vb. [κεῖμαι] **1 be situated above**; (of a hill or sim.) **overlook** (a place) Plb. —W.GEN. *a city, the enemy* Plb. || PTCPL.ADJ. (of places) **high up** Plb.; (of cliffs) **overhanging** Plb.

2 (of a people or region) **lie beyond** Isoc. Plb. —W.GEN. or DAT. *a location* Plb.
ὑπερκέρασις εως f. [ὑπερκεράω] **outflanking** (of an enemy) Plb.
ὑπερ-κεράω contr.vb. [κεράω²] **outflank** Plu. —*the enemy* Plb.
ὑπερ-κολακεύω vb. **flatter extravagantly** —*someone* D.
ὑπέρ-κομπος ον adj. [κόμπος] (of armour, a shield-device, thoughts, rashness) **over-boastful, vainglorious** A.
ὑπέρ-κοπος ον adj. [κόπτω] **1 striking with excessive force**; (of a weapon) **brutal** A.; (of an abduction) A.
2 (of speech) **arrogant** S.
3 (of ships) **outstanding** (W.DAT. in speed) A.
—**ὑπερκόπως** adv. **excessively** A.
ὑπερ-κορέννυμι vb. **completely satisfy** —*one's appetite* (W.GEN. w. wealth) Thgn.
ὑπερκότως adv. [κότος] **with excessive anger** E.
ὑπερ-κρεμάννυμαι mid.vb. (of old age) **hang over** —W. ὑπέρ + GEN. *one's head* Hom. Thgn.
ὑπερ-κτάομαι mid.contr.vb. **bring upon oneself** (W.ACC. much suffering) **beyond one's need** S.
ὑπερ-κυβιστάω contr.vb. **plunge head over heels**; (fig., of politicians) **take the plunge** Plb.
ὑπερ-κύδᾱς αντος masc.adj. [κῦδος] **far-famed, renowned** Il. Hes.
ὑπερ-κύπτω vb. **1 bend one's head over** (an obstacle); **crane one's neck** (to see sthg.) Pl.
2 (tr., of an impossibly large bull) **crane one's neck over** —*a mountain* Plu.
ὑπέρ-λαμπρος ον adj. [λαμπρός] **1** (of the sun's rays) **exceptionally bright, brilliant** Ar.
2 (of an achievement) **exceptionally glorious** Plu.
—**ὑπέρλαμπρον** adv. **with exceptional clarity** —*ref. to howling* D.
ὑπερ-λαμπρύνομαι mid.vb. (of hounds) **make too much of a show** —W.PREP.PHR. *over sthg. they find* X.
ὑπερ-λῡπέομαι mid.contr.vb. **be extremely upset** Hdt.
ὑπερ-μαίνομαι mid.vb. | aor.2 pass. ὑπερεμάνην | || PASS. **be driven utterly mad** (w. enthusiasm) Ar.
ὑπερμάκης dial.adj.: see ὑπερμήκης
ὑπερμαχέω contr.vb. [μάχομαι] **1 fight on behalf of, fight for** —W.GEN. *one's city, freedom, a political leader, the enemy* S. E. Plu.
2 fight for (in argument), **champion** —W.GEN. *someone* (W.DAT. against someone else) S.
ὑπερμαχητικός ή όν adj. (of courage) **that prompts one to fight in defence** (W.GEN. of what is one's own) Plu.
ὑπερ-μάχομαι mid.vb. **fight on behalf of, fight for** —W.GEN. *someone* S. —*freedom* Plu.
ὑπερμεγάθης Ion.adj.: see ὑπερμεγέθης
ὑπέρ-μεγας μεγάλη μέγα adj. [μέγας] (of a person) **exceedingly important** Ar.
ὑπερ-μεγέθης, Ion. **ὑπερμεγάθης**, ες adj. [μέγεθος] **1** (of things) **extremely large** Hdt. Philox.Leuc. X. Plu.
|| NEUT.PL.SB. **huge masses** (of matter in the universe) X.
2 (of preparations, services to one's city) **extremely great** Isoc. D.
3 (of a task) **extremely demanding** X.
4 (of a crime, lie, damage) **extremely serious** Aeschin. D.
ὑπερ-μεθύσκομαι pass.vb. **become extremely drunk** Hdt.
ὑπερμενέων οντος masc.ptcpl.adj. [ὑπερμενής] (of men) **extremely aggressive** or **boisterous** Od.
ὑπερ-μενής ές adj. [μένος] (epith. of Zeus) **all-powerful, mighty** Il. Hes.; (of kings, warriors) Hom. Pi.fr.

ὑπέρ-μετρος ον adj. [μέτρον] (of senility) beyond due measure, **extreme** Pl.
ὑπερ-μήκης, dial. **ὑπερμάκης**, ες adj. [μῆκος] **1** (of a course) **exceedingly long** A.; (fig., of the Persian king's reach) Hdt.
2 (of mountains) **exceedingly high** Hdt.
3 (of a shout) **exceedingly loud** Pi.
ὑπερ-μῑσέω contr.vb. **show especial loathing for** —someone Lys.
ὑπέρ-μορα neut.pl.adv. [μόρος] **1 beyond what is fated** Il.
2 beyond the normal limit, excessively B.(cj.)
ὑπερ-νεωλκέω contr.vb. **haul** (W.ACC. ships) **over land** Plb. Plu.
ὑπερ-νότιος ον adj. (of a people) **in the far south** Hdt.
ὑπέρ-ογκος ον adj. [ὄγκος²] **1** of excessive bulk; (of an army) **oversized** (for its resources) D.; (of masses of stones) **immense, huge** Plu. ‖ NEUT.SB. **excessive mass** (W.GEN. of possessions) Pl.
2 (of a shin) **extremely swollen** X.
3 (of good fortune) **exceedingly great** Plu.; (of a person) **overloaded** (w. material benefits) Plu.
4 (of an office) **over-powerful** Plu.; (of a state of mind) **overbearing** or **excessively self-important** Plu.
—**ὑπερόγκως** adv. **with excessive self-importance** Plu.
ὑπερ-οικέω contr.vb. (of a people) **live beyond** —W.GEN. others Hdt. —W.ACC. a mountain range Hdt.
ὑπέρ-οικος ον adj. [οἶκος] (of a people) **living beyond** (W.GEN. a certain region) Hdt.
ὕπερον ου n. —perh. also **ὕπερος** ου (Hes.) m.
1 pestle Hes. Hdt. Pl. Plb.
2 weapon resembling a pestle, club Plu.
ὑπεροπλήεις εσσα εν adj. [ὑπέροπλος] | only superl. ὑπεροπληέστατος | **arrogant, aggressive** AR.
ὑπεροπλίη ης ep.Ion.f. —also perh. **ὑπεροπλίᾱ** ᾱς dial.f. | -ῑ- metri grat. | **1 arrogance, insolence, presumption** Il. S.(cj.) | see ὑπεροπτεία
2 aggressiveness or **mettle** (of a bull) Theoc.
ὑπεροπλίζομαι mid.vb. | ep.3sg.aor.opt. ὑπεροπλίσσαιτο | **show disdain for** —a palace Od. [or perh. as if reltd. ὁπλίζω *overpower by force of arms*]
ὑπέρ-οπλος ον adj. [ὅπλα] **1 superior in weapons**; (gener., of persons, strength, valour) **overbearing, mighty** Hes. Mimn. Pi. AR. Theoc.; (of a serpent) B.
2 (of ruin) **overwhelming** Pi.
3 (of youthfulness) **arrogant, presumptuous** Pi.
—**ὑπέροπλον** neut.adv. **arrogantly, presumptuously** Il.
ὑπέροπτα neut.pl.adv. [ὑπερόπτης] **haughtily, disdainfully** S.
ὑπεροπτείᾱ ᾱς f. **arrogant defiance** S.(dub.) | see ὑπεροπλίη
ὑπερόπτης ου m. [ὑπερόψομαι, see ὑποράω] **1 disdainful person** Arist. Theoc. Plu.
2 disparager, despiser (W.GEN. of persons or things) Th. Plu.
ὑπεροπτικός ή όν adj. **1** (of persons) **disdainful, scornful** Isoc.
2 (of an action) **overbearing** D.
—**ὑπεροπτικῶς** adv. | compar. ὑπεροπτικώτερον | **with disdain** or **scorn** Plb. Plu. —W.GEN. *for someone* X.
ὑπερ-οράω contr.vb. | fut. ὑπερόψομαι | aor.2 ὑπερεῖδον |
1 (of animals crossing a bridge) **look over** (the sides) **at** —the sea Hdt.
2 (of a soul) **look beyond** —present existence Pl.
3 look beyond (so as to ignore, usu. out of wilfulness or a sense of superiority), **disregard, disdain, scorn** —someone or sthg. Hdt. Th. Att.orats. Pl. X. + —W.GEN. Antipho Pl. X. D. Plu.; (intr.) **take no notice** (of someone) Plu.; **be scornful** Th. ‖ PASS. **be scorned** Th. Pl. Plu.
ὑπεροριᾱ f.: see under ὑπερόριος
ὑπερ-ορίζω vb. **cast beyond the borders** (of a country) —*objects considered impure* Aeschin.; (of fallacious arguments) **banish, expel** —*virtues* (fr. the soul) Pl. ‖ PASS. (of persons) **be banished** (fr. a city) Aeschin. —W.PREP.PHR. *fr. the inhabited world* Isoc.
ὑπερ-όριος, Ion. **ὑπερούριος**, ον adj. **1 beyond the borders** (of a city or region); (of persons, activities) **abroad** Th. D.; (of a public office) **exercised abroad** Aeschin.(law) Arist. ‖ NEUT.PL.SB. **foreign regions, abroad** X.; **property** or **assets abroad** X.
2 (quasi-advbl., of ashes thrown out) **beyond the borders** Theoc.
3 (of gossip) **about foreign affairs** Aeschin. ‖ NEUT.PL.SB. **foreign affairs** Arist.
—**ὑπεροριᾱ** ᾱς f. **foreign land, abroad**; (prep.phrs.) εἰς τὴν ὑπεροριαν *to a foreign land, abroad* Lys. Pl. X. D.; ἐκ τῆς ὑπεροριας *from abroad* And. Lys.; (also ἀπό) X.; ἐν τῇ ὑπεροριᾳ *abroad* X. Is.; (advbl.acc.) ὑπεροριαν *to a foreign land* Pl.(dub.)
ὑπερ-όρνυμαι mid.vb. (of ruin) **rise overhead, loom up** —W.DAT. *against a city* S.(dub.cj.)
ὑπερ-ορρωδέω, Ion. **ὑπεραρρωδέω** contr.vb. **be afraid on behalf** or **account of, fear for** —W.GEN. *someone* E. —W.DAT. *one's country* Hdt.
ὕπερος m.: see ὕπερον
ὑπερ-ουράνιος ον adj. (of a region) **above** or **beyond heaven** Pl.
ὑπερούριος Ion.adj.: see ὑπερόριος
ὑπεροχή ῆς f. [ὑπέροχος] **1** (concr.) **piece of high ground, height** Plb.; (periphr., W.GEN. of a hill, i.e. **high hill**) Plb.
2 (abstr.) **superiority** (sts. W.GEN. of or in sthg.) Isoc. Pl. Arist. Plb. Plu.
3 (specif., in political or military ctxt.) **pre-eminence, supremacy** Arist. Plb. Plu.
4 excess (opp. ἔλλειψις *deficiency*, sts. W.GEN. of sthg.) Pl. Arist.
ὑπέροχος, ep. **ὑπείροχος**, Boeot. **πέροχος**, Aeol. **πέρροχος**, ον adj. [ὑπερέχω] **1** (of a person) **superior** (W.GEN. to others) Il.
2 (of persons, deities, their attributes, or sim.) **outstanding, pre-eminent** hHom. Lyr. A. Hdt. Theoc.; (of Zeus' eagle, W.GEN. among birds) Call.; (of Centaurs, W.ACC. in might) S.
3 (of sea-beasts) **monstrous** Pi.
4 (of a building) **tallest** AR.
5 (of a headland) **jutting out** AR.
ὑπεροψίᾱ ᾱς f. [ὑπερόψομαι, see ὑπεροράω] **disdain, scorn** Att.orats. Plb. Plu.; (W.GEN. for someone or sthg.) Th. Isoc. Plu.
ὑπερ-παγής ές adj. [πάγος] **exceedingly frosty** ‖ NEUT.SB. **bitter frost** X.
ὑπερπᾱδάω dial.contr.vb.: see ὑπερπηδάω
ὑπερπαθέω contr.vb. [πάθος] **be overcome with grief** E.
ὑπερ-παίω vb. | only pf. ὑπερπέπαικα | **strike with superior force**; (fig.) **beat** —*everyone else* (W.DAT. *in wealth, wickedness*) D. Men.; (of a disaster) —*all other events* (*in horror*) Plb.; (of a particular wine) —W.GEN. *all others* Ar.
ὑπέρ-παχυς υ, gen. εος adj. [παχύς] (of a person) **excessively fat** Plu.
ὑπερ-πέλομαι mid.vb. | ep.aor.2 ὑπερεπλόμην | (of Crete) **be greater** (in height and size) —W.GEN. *than other islands* AR. [or perh. *lie beyond*]
ὑπερ-περισσῶς adv. **exceedingly** NT.

ὑπερπετής ές adj. [ὑπερπέτομαι] **1** (of projectiles) **flying overhead** Plb. Plu.
2 (of defensive walls) **rising high** Plb.
ὑπερ-πέτομαι mid.vb. | 3sg.athem.aor. ὑπερέπτατο, ep. ὑπέρπτατο | dial.3sg.athem.aor.act. ὑπερέπτᾱ | —also (pres.) **ὑπερίπταμαι** (Plu.)
1 (of a bird) **fly overhead** Alcm. Plu.; **fly above** or **over** —W.GEN. *a ship, the forum* AR. Plu.; (of Perseus) —W.ACC. *a land* AR.; (fig., of a warrior, compared to an eagle) **fly across** —W.PREP.PHR. *into a land* S.
2 (of a spear) **fly overhead** Hom.
3 (of a discus) **fly beyond** —*a marker* Od.
ὑπερ-πηδάω, dial. **ὑπερπᾱδάω** contr.vb. **1** (of persons, animals) **leap over** —sthg. Ar. X. Theoc.
2 (of hounds) **bound about overexcitedly** X.
3 transgress —*laws* Att.orats.; **bypass** —*the defence's case* Aeschin.; **jump** (in an argument) —W.PREP.PHR. *to another topic* Arist.
4 (of an inventor) **surpass** —*all others* Pl.
ὑπέρ-πικρος ον adj. [πικρός] **exceedingly bitter-tempered** A. Men.
ὑπερ-πίμπλαμαι pass.vb. **1 become over-full** (fr. eating and drinking) X. Arist. —W.GEN. *of wine* S.
2 (of hubris) **be glutted** —W.GEN. w. *plenty* S.
ὑπερ-πίνω vb. **drink** (wine) **to excess** X.
ὑπερ-πίπτω vb. **1** (of water) **overflow** Plb.
2 (of a day) **slip past** (before a task is done) Hdt.
ὑπερ-πληθής ές adj. [πλῆθος] (of crimes) **exceedingly numerous, beyond number** D.
ὑπερ-πληρόω contr.vb. (of security and good repute, in neg.phr.) **fill to excess** (their possessor, i.e. one cannot have enough of them) X. || PASS. be filled to excess (w. food) X.
ὑπερ-πλούσιος ον adj. **extremely wealthy** Arist.
ὑπερπλουτέω contr.vb. [ὑπέρπλουτος] **be extremely wealthy** Ar.
ὑπέρ-πλουτος ον adj. [πλοῦτος] **1 extremely wealthy** Pl.
2 (of luxuriousness) **over-opulent, extravagant** A.
ὑπέρ-πολυς πόλλη πολυ adj. [πολύς] **1** (of persons, cattle) **exceedingly numerous, beyond number** A. X.
2 (of money) **prodigious in amount** D.
ὑπερ-πονέω contr.vb. **1 labour on behalf** (of someone) Pl. —W.GEN. *of someone* S.(mid.)
2 bear on behalf (of someone) —*that person's afflictions* S.
3 exercise too hard X.
4 be tired from over-exertion X.; **be worn out** —W.DAT. *by a war* Plu.
ὑπέρ-πονος ον adj. [πόνος] (of a horse) **worn out** (W.PREP.PHR. through old age) Plu.
ὑπερ-πόντιος ᾱ ον adj. **1** (of a person) **overseas** A.
2 (of a person) **from overseas** A.; (of speech, w.connot. of outlandishness) Pi.
3 (quasi-advbl., of Eros roaming) **across the seas** S.
ὑπέρπτατο (ep.3sg.athem.aor.mid.): see ὑπερπέτομαι
ὑπέρ-πτωχος ον adj. [πτωχός] **extremely poor** Arist.
ὑπερ-πυππάζω vb. [πυππάξ] **cheer on** (W.ACC. someone) **rapturously** Ar.
ὑπερ-πυρριάω contr.vb. [πυρρός] (of a cloak) **turn ruddy brown on behalf of** —W.GEN. *its wearer* (*who has soiled himself in fear*) Ar.
ὑπερ-πωτάομαι mid.contr.vb. (of Erotes) **flit around overhead** Theoc.
ὑπερράγην (aor.2 pass.): see ὑπορρήγνυμαι
ὑπερ-σεμνύνομαι mid.vb. (of an actor) **give oneself extraordinary airs** X.

ὑπερ-σκελής ές adj. [σκέλος] **with excessively long legs** Pl.
ὑπέρ-σοφος ον adj. [σοφός] **exceptionally wise** or **clever** Ar. Pl.
ὑπερ-σπουδάζω vb. **be extremely eager** —W.INF. *to do sthg.* Men.
ὑπερ-στατέω contr.vb. [ἵσταμαι] (of Justice) **stand in defence** —W.GEN. *of her allies* A.
ὑπέρτατος, also **ὑπερώτατος** (Pi.), η (dial. ᾱ) ον superl.adj. [ὑπέρ] | for compar. see ὑπέρτερος | **1** (of a man, as a lookout) **highest up** Il.; (of a stone, in a wall) Il.; (of a mountain) E.Cyc.
2 (of Zeus, his home, other deities) **highest, most exalted** (in position, w. further connots. of power and status) Hes. Pi. Ar.; (of Rhea's throne) Pi.
3 highest (in power, status or distinction); (of persons) **greatest, mightiest** A. Pi. E. Ar.; (of a god's mind) Diagor.; (of a star, ref. to the sun) Pi.fr.; (of a city) S.; (of monarchy) S.fr.; (of the hand of Law, the keys of Hesychia, the light of victory) Pi.
4 highest (in quality or extent); (of prosperity, fame, deeds of prowess, or sim.) **greatest** Pi. B. S.; (of an honour, gift, possession, or sim.) **most valuable, most highly esteemed** B. S. AR. Plu.(quot.epigr.)
5 (of Earth) **oldest** (W.GEN. of the gods) S.
6 (of afflictions) **most extreme, worst** S.
—**ὑπερτάτως** superl.adv. **above all** —*ref. to revering Zeus* A.
ὑπερ-τείνω vb. **1 stretch** (sthg.) **over**; **stretch out** (W.ACC. one's foot) **over** —W.GEN. *the shore-line* (*into the sea*) E.; **hold** (W.ACC. a person) **outstretched over** —W.GEN. *an altar* E.; **extend** (W.ACC. planks) **over** —W.GEN. *a corpse* (*in a grave*) Hdt.; **cause** (W.ACC. balconies) **to project** —w. ὑπέρ + GEN. *over roads* Arist.
2 (specif.) **stretch over** (as protection); **stretch** (W.ACC. a shield, hand) **over** —W.GEN. or DAT. *a person, head* E.; (of a tree) **extend** (W.ACC. shade) **over** (a house) **as protection** —W.GEN. *against Sirius* A.
3 (of troops) **extend beyond, outflank** —*an enemy's wing* X.; (of sailors, in a line of ships) —*opposing sailors* Plb.
4 (intr., of objects) **extend over** (a pit) X.; **extend** —w. ὑπέρ + GEN. *over a wall* Th.
5 (of land) **stretch further** (into the distance) AR.
6 (of a king's reign) **stretch beyond** (in time), **antedate** —*another's* Arist.
7 make more severe, extend, increase —*a penalty* Plu.
8 (of circumstances) **overstrain** —*human nature* Arist.; (of danger) **impose an excessive strain** (on soldiers) Arist.
9 (intr.) **be superior** or **greater** (sts. W.DAT. in sthg.) Arist.; **be in excess** —W.GEN. *of sthg.* Arist.
ὑπερτελέω contr.vb. [ὑπερτελής] **rise above** —*a net of slavery* (*i.e. escape fr. it*) A.
ὑπερ-τελής ές adj. [τέλος, also reltd. ὑπερτέλλω] **1** (of Herakles) **beyond the completion of, past, over** (W.GEN. his labours) S. [or perh.fig. *above, having surmounted*]
2 (of a beacon-flame) **rising high** A.; (of a deity) **high above** (W.GEN. a temple) E.
ὑπερ-τέλλω vb. **1** (of the sun) **rise high** Hdt.; **rise above** —W.GEN. *the earth* E.fr.
2 (of the Sown Men) **rise up, emerge** —w. ἐκ + GEN. *out of the ground* E.; (of a woman's breast) —*out of her robes* E.
3 (of a rock formation) **rise high above** —W.GEN. *the ground* E.; (of a boulder) **loom over** —W.GEN. *someone's head* E.
ὑπερτερίᾱ ᾱς, Ion. **ὑπερτερίη** ης f. [ὑπέρτερος] **1 upper part, body** (of a chariot) Od. Pl.
2 superior quality, superiority Thgn.

ὑπέρτερος ᾱ (Ion. η) ον *compar.adj.* [ὑπέρ] | for superl. see ὑπέρτατος | **1** higher (opp. lower) || NEUT.PL.SB. what is above (opp. below) Ar.(mock-oracle)
2 upper (opp. inner); (of an animal's flesh, opp. entrails) **outer** Od.
3 (prep.phr.) καθ' ὑπέρτερον *above, over* (W.GEN. *sthg.*) Theoc.
4 higher (in status, quality or power); (of persons or things) **higher, greater** or **stronger** Il. Archil. Ibyc. Pi. Trag. Plu.; **superior** (W.GEN. to others) A. S. AR. Plu.
5 coming out on top, **victorious, triumphant** (W.GEN. over someone or sthg.) Pi. E. AR. Plu.
6 (of the gods) **having control** (W.GEN. of human affairs) Theoc.
7 (of the performance of a task for a deity) **more important** (W.GEN. than one's own engagements) Pi.
8 (of information) **additional, further** S.
9 (of troubles) **worse** (W.GEN. than war) AR.
—ὑπέρτερον *neut.adv.* to a further degree, **more** or **better** (W.GEN. than someone or sthg.) A. S.

ὑπερ-τίθημι *vb.* | *dial.inf.* ὑπερτιθέμεν | Ion.impf. ὑπερετίθεα || *dial.athem.aor.mid.subj.* ὑπερθέωμαι |
1 place above or over; (fig.) **place** (W.ACC. a god) **over** —W.DAT. *everything* (W.PREDIC.ACC.ADJ. *as its cause, i.e. ascribe responsibility for everything to a god*) Pi. || MID. **place** —*the rim of a shield* (W. ὑπέρ + ACC. *over a railing*) Plb.
2 (act. and mid.) place (information) in the charge of someone), **communicate** —*one's intention, concerns, experiences, or sim.* (usu. W.DAT. *to someone*) Hdt.
3 place beyond; **place** (W.ACC. an object) **on the other side** (of a space) Plu. || MID. **transport** —*persons and property* (W.PREP.PHR. *to the other side of a river*) Plb.
4 || MID. go beyond, **surpass** —*someone or sthg.* (usu. W.DAT. or PREP.PHR. *in some quality*) Plb.
5 || MID. put further ahead (in time), **put off, postpone, defer** —*a narrative, payment, discussion, election, attack, or sim.* (sts. W.PREP.PHR. *to a specified time*) D. Plb. Plu. —W.INF. *doing sthg.* Plb.; (intr.) **defer matters, delay** Plb. Plu.

ὑπερ-τῑμάω *contr.vb.* **pay especial honour to** —*someone* S.
ὑπέρ-τολμος ον *adj.* [τόλμα] (of a man's spirit) **over-bold** A.
ὑπέρ-τονος ον *adj.* [τόνος] **1** (of a trumpet blast, a shout) **exceedingly loud** A. Ar.(quot. S.)
2 (of an athlete's strength) **overstrained** Plu.
ὑπερτοξεύσιμος ον *adj.* [ὑπερτοξεύω] possible for an archer to surpass; (fig., of a pollution, in neg.phr.) **surpassable** A.
ὑπερ-τοξεύω *vb.* surpass in archery, **outshoot** —*someone* Ar.(cj., for περι-)
ὑπ-ερυθριάω *contr.vb.* [ὑπό] **blush a little** Ar.
ὑπ-έρυθρος ον *adj.* [ἐρυθρός] (of the body of a plague victim) **reddish** Th.; (of a cosmic sphere) Pl.
ὑπερ-ύψηλος ον *adj.* [ὑπέρ, ὑψηλός] (of mountains) **extremely high** X.
ὑπερ-φαίνομαι *mid.pass.vb.* | *fut.*2 ὑπερφανήσομαι | *aor.*2 ὑπερεφάνην | **1** be or become visible over or above (a place); (of troops) **appear over** —W.GEN. *a hill, mountain range* Th. Plu.; (of a commander) **appear above** —W.GEN. *the enemy* Plu.; (of shields) —*a river* (i.e. *on the bank*) Plu.; (of persons inside a city) —W.ACC. *defensive walls* Plu.; (of cavalry) **appear on higher ground** Th.
2 (of the site of a battle) **overlook** —W.GEN. *a place* Plu.
ὑπερφαλαγγέω *contr.vb.* [φάλαγξ] form a phalanx reaching beyond (the enemy's battle-line); **outflank** (the enemy) X. —W.GEN. *an army* X.

ὑπερφανής ές *adj.* [ὑπερφαίνομαι] (of a cavalryman's spear) visible above (the rank in front), **protruding into view** X.
ὑπέρ-φατος ον *adj.* [φατός] beyond what can be expressed in words; (of a man) **indescribable** (W.DAT. for his beauty and achievements) Pi.; (of the strength of a snowstorm) Pi.*fr.*
ὑπερ-φέρω *vb.* **1 carry over or across**; **haul** (W.ACC. ships) **over** —*an isthmus* Th. || PASS. (of ships) be hauled over —*an isthmus* Th.; (of chaff) be carried across (by the wind) —w. εἰς + ACC. *to a place* X. —(w. ὑπέρ + ACC. *over the grain*) X.; (of a torch-like fire, in the sky) be carried along over —W.ACC. *a camp* Plu.
2 be superior (freq. W.DAT. in some quality or attribute); (of persons or things) **surpass** —*others* E. Isoc. Call. Plu. —W.GEN. Hdt. S. X.; (of persons, places) **be pre-eminent, excel** Hdt. Trag. Th. Ar. X. Aeschin.; (of a plant, in height) Hdt.
ὑπέρ-φευ *adv.* [app. φεῦ] beyond the appropriate limit (for mortals), **excessively** A. E.
ὑπερ-φεύγω *vb.* **escape over the top** (of the nets of Ruin) A.(tm., v.l. ὑπεκ-)
ὑπερ-φθίνομαι *mid.vb.* **die in defence** —W.GEN. *of someone* Pi.
ὑπερ-φίαλος ον *adj.* [ὑπερφυής, unless ὑπὲρ φιάλην] **1** (of persons, hearts, words) **overbearing, presumptuous, insolent** or **violent** Hom. hHom. Stesich. Pi. AR.; (of the Cyclopes, Giants) Od. Hes.*fr.* B.
2 (without pejor.connot., of persons) **superior** Od.; (of a person, the Cyclopes as builders of city-walls) **mighty** B. Theoc.
3 (of the bond fettering Typhon, fig.ref. to Aetna) **overwhelming** Pi.*fr.*; (of a task) AR.
—ὑπερφιάλως *adv.* **1 arrogantly, presumptuously** Od.
2 excessively Hom.
ὑπερ-φιλέω *contr.vb.* **1 be passionately in love** Arist. —W.ACC. *w. a woman* Ar. X.
2 adore beyond measure —*a leader* X.
ὑπερ-φοβέομαι *mid.contr.vb.* **be extremely fearful** A. X.
ὑπέρ-φοβος ον *adj.* [φόβος] (of a horse) **over-timid** X.
ὑπερ-φορέω *contr.vb.* (of wind) **carry** —*snow* (w. ὑπέρ + GEN. *over terrain*) X.
ὑπερ-φρονέω *contr.vb.* **1** think oneself superior (to others); **be proud, haughty** or **overconfident** A. Pl. Plb. —W.DAT. *because of one's wealth* Hdt.
2 look down on, **disdain, scorn** —*persons, behaviour* Th. Plu. —*one's present fortune* A. —*the common people* (W.DAT. *because of one's learning*) Aeschin. —W.GEN. *persons, gods, laws, an activity* E. Ar. Pl. X. || PASS. be looked down on —W.PREP.PHR. *by someone* Th.
3 (of Socrates, represented at an elevated position above the stage) perh. **think loftily about** —W.ACC. *the gods* Ar.
ὑπερφροσύνη ης *f.* **disdain** (for one's enemy) Plu.
ὑπέρ-φρων ον, gen. ονος *adj.* [φρήν] **1** thinking oneself superior || NEUT.SB. consciousness of superiority Th.
2 (of words, thoughts) **proud, arrogant, haughty** Trag.
3 (of a design on a shield) reflecting arrogance, **arrogant, grandiose** A.
ὑπερ-φυής ές *adj.* [φυή] | *masc.fem.acc.sg.* ὑπερφυῆ, Att.*masc.fem.acc.sg.* and *neut.pl.* ὑπερφυᾶ | **1** beyond what is natural (in scale); (of serpents, objects, things) **enormous** (W.ACC. or DAT. in size) Hdt. Ar. Plu.; (of a crowd) Ar.; (of the strength of elephants) Plb.; (of thunder, a shout, in volume) Plu. | see also ὅσος 4
2 (of persons or things) **exceptional, extraordinary** Hdt. Ar. Pl. Plu.; (W.ACC. or DAT. in some attribute) Plu.

3 (pejor., of things) **monstrous, preposterous, scandalous** Hdt. Ar. Att.orats. Pl. Plu.
4 (of a flatterer) **extravagant** Plu.

–ὑπερφυῶς *adv.* **1** to an extraordinary degree, **extraordinarily, exceedingly** Ar. Pl. Plu.; (also) ὑπερφυῶς ὡς Ar. Pl.
2 extravagantly —*ref. to welcoming or praising* Plu.
3 in an extraordinary way, **extraordinarily, remarkably** Pl.
4 (in dialogue, as an affirmative answer, sts. followed by μὲν οὖν) **decidedly so** Pl.

ὑπερ-φύομαι *mid.vb.* | athem.aor.act. ὑπερέφῡν | (of a person) be superior by nature, **surpass** —*all others* (W.DAT. *in strength*) Hdt.

ὑπερ-χαίρω *vb.* be extremely delighted, **be overjoyed** X. Plu. —W.DAT. *w. sthg.* E. —W.PTCPL. *doing sthg.* X.

ὑπερχαρής ές *adj.* **overjoyed** Plb.

ὑπερ-χέομαι *pass.contr.vb.* **1** (of a river) **overflow** Plu.
2 (fig., of persons) **stream forth in abundance** Plu.

ὑπερ-χλίω *vb.* luxuriate to excess, **run riot** —W.PREP.PHR. *w. wicked speech* S.

ὑπερ-χολάω *contr.vb.* **be extremely angry** Ar.

ὑπ-έρχομαι *mid.vb.* [ὑπό] | aor.2 ὑπῆλθον, ep. ὑπήλυθον || Impf. and fut. are supplied by ὕπειμι². | **1 go beneath** —*bushes* Od. —*a roof* (*i.e. into a house*) Od.
2 go down to —*the abode of Hades* Od.; (of a dead person) **go below** —*the earth* A.; (of an army) **go down** —W.DAT. *into a defile* (*betw. mountains*) Plu.
3 come unnoticed —w. εἰς + ACC. *into a javelin's path* Antipho —w. ὑπό + ACC. *under* (or *under the threat of*) *a javelin, its trajectory, impact* Antipho
4 (of soldiers) **arrive unnoticed** or **advance stealthily** X.; (of a person) **go over secretly** —w. πρός + ACC. *to the enemy* Plb.; **sneak up** —w. ὑπό + ACC. *to a litter* Plu.; **sneak one's way into** —W.ACC. *the position of tyrant* Plu.
5 (of feelings) **steal up on, come over** —*persons, their limbs* Hom.(sts.tm.) Hdt. S. E. Pl. AR.(cj.); (of an idle thought; of an event, i.e. the memory of it) —*a person* E. Plu.; (of a sickness) —W.DAT. *a person* Men.; (of a tickling sensation) **steal up** —w. ὑπό + ACC. *under the buttocks* Ar.
6 (intr., of silence) **come over** (a company) E.; (of fear) **spread** —w. ἐς + ACC. *to the tips of one's hair* S.; (of covert talk) **steal on** S.(cj.)
7 approach submissively, **be deferential towards** —*magistrates* X.
8 (pejor.) **worm oneself into the favour of, pander to** —*someone* And. Ar. Pl. X. D. Plu.; (without pejor.connot.) **win over** —*the populace* (W.DAT. *by friendly familiarity*) Plu.; (intr.) **ingratiate oneself** D.
9 (of a person, god, riddling oracle) **catch unawares** or **at a disadvantage, trap, trick** —*a person* S. E. Plu.

ὑπέρ-χρεως ων, gen. ω Att.adj. [χρέος] **deep in debt** D. | see also ὑπόχρεως

ὑπερ-ψύχομαι *pass.vb.* [ψύχω¹] (of a person) **get too cold** Arist.

ὑπέρ-ψυχος ον *adj.* [ψυχή] (of the body) **surpassing the soul** (in strength of appetite) Pl.

ὑπερῴᾱ ᾶς, Ion. **ὑπερῴη** ης *f.* [ὑπερῷον] **upper part of the mouth, palate** Il. Plu.

ὑπ-ερωέω *contr.vb.* [ὑπό, ἐρωέω²] (of horses) **draw back** (under a threat), **shy** Il.

ὑπερ-ωμόκρεως ων, gen. ω *adj.* [ὑπέρ, ὦμος, κρέας] (of a sausage) **of the flesh above the shoulder, shoulder-meat** Philox.Leuc.

ὑπερῷον, ep. **ὑπερώιον**, ου *n.* upper part of a house, **upper room** (esp. as the place where women work and sleep) Hom. Lys. Ar. Men. NT.; (as a storage space, perh. ref. to an attic) Ar.; (rented out to a man) Antipho; (as a meeting place) NT. || COLLECTV.NEUT.PL. upstairs Hom.

–ὑπερωιόθεν *ep.adv.* **from upstairs** Od.

ὑπερῷος ᾱ ον *adj.* (of a room) **upstairs** Plu.

ὑπερώτατος *superl.adj.*: see ὑπέρτατος

ὑπ-ερωτάω *contr.vb.* [ὑπό] **slyly ask a question** Pl.

ὑπ-εσθίω *vb.* **eat** or **lick up** —*everything* (w.connot. of *cunnilingus*) Ar.

ὑπ-εσπάνισμαι *pf.pass.vb.* [σπανίζω] **1 be short, be deprived** —W.GEN. *of food* A.; (of an Erinys, in neg.phr.) —*of blood* A.
2 (of part of a duty) be left short, **be stinted** S.

ὑπεσσεῖται (dial.3sg.fut.): see ὕπειμι¹

ὑπέσταν (ep.3pl.athem.aor.), **ὑπέστᾱν** (dial.1sg.athem.aor.): see ὑφίσταμαι

ὑπεστόρεσα, also **ὑπέστρωσα** (aor.): see ὑποστόρνῡμι

ὑπέσχεθον (ep.aor.2): see ὑπέχω

ὑπεσχόμην (aor.2 mid.), **ὑπέσχημαι** (pf.mid.): see ὑπισχνέομαι

ὑπ-εύδιος ον *adj.* (of a shoreline, meadow, breeze) **under a clear sky, calm** AR. || NEUT.SB. **calmness** (W.GEN. *of a sea*) Plu.

–ὑπεύδια *neut.pl.adv.* **in calm weather** AR.

ὑπ-εύθῡνος ον *adj.* [εὔθυνα] **1** subject to an investigation (sts. W.DAT. to someone, sts.W.GEN. for one's conduct or character); (of persons, esp. magistrates and politicians, their proposals) **accountable, answerable** A. Th. D. Plu.; (of authority in a democracy) **subject to scrutiny** Hdt.; (of the lifestyle of youths at Sparta) Plu.
2 (specif., of magistrates at Athens) **accountable, subject to an audit** (for their administration) Ar. Att.orats. Arist.
3 (of a witness) answerable (to a court or prosecutor, esp. for false evidence), **under oath** Aeschin. D.; (of a defendant) **answerable, responsible** (for a summons, false deposition, an action) D.
4 (of the body of a slave or retired commander) **subject to punishment** (for actions) D. Plu.; (of a traitor's supporter) **liable** (W.DAT. *to divine vengeance*) Lycurg.; (of survival in war, to disgrace and death) Lycurg.

ὑπέφθην (athem.aor.): see ὑποφθάνω

ὑπέχευε (ep.3sg.aor.): see ὑποχέω

ὑπ-έχω *vb.* | fut. ὑφέξω | aor.2 ὑπέσχον, ep. ὑπέσχεθον, also ὑποέσχεθον (AR.), ptcpl. ὑποσχών, imperatv. ὑπόσχες || neut.impers.vbl.adj. ὑφεκτέον || Only act.; for mid. forms see ὑπισχνέομαι. | The sections are arranged as: (1-7) hold (sthg.) under (sthg. else), hold out, offer, submit, (8-14) hold from underneath, support, undergo, submit to |
1 put (a mare) under (a stallion); **mate** —*mares* Il.
2 put (W.ACC. wax) **underneath** —W.DAT. *one's perceptions and thoughts* (*for them to be impressed on it*) Pl.
3 hold (a container) under (another vessel, to receive its contents); **hold out** —*a cup, bowl, bag* Hdt. Ar. Plb. —*one's cloak* (*for someone to vomit into*) Plu.
4 hold out —*one's hand* (*for a token, bribe, clod of earth, dole*) Il. D. AR. Plu. —*a truce* (w. play on 'hand') Ar.
5 (of a she-wolf) **offer** —*her breast* (W.DAT. *to babies*) Plu.; (of a woman) —*sexual favours* Ar.; (of an island) —*its ground* (*as birthplace for a god, w. further connot. 'place beneath'*) Call.; (of a baby) **lend** —*its ear* (W.GEN. *to a mother's words*) Simon.; (of an army) **present** —*a show of boldness* (W.DAT. *to the enemy*) Th.(dub.)

ὑπήεισα

6 submit —*oneself* (W.DAT. *to others, i.e.* put oneself at their service, for consultation, help, or sim.) Pl. X.; (intr.) submit —W.DAT. *to another* (W.INF. *for questioning, i.e.* give him permission to question one) Pl.
7 (app., for purpose of contrast w. ὑπερέχω *be superior*) **make** (W.ACC. one's smallness of stature) **submissive** —W.DAT. *to another's largeness* (W.INF. *for that to be superior to it*) Pl.
8 hold from underneath; (of a structure) **support** —*sthg.* Hdt.; (fig., of wealth) —*ambition* Pi.
9 sustain, maintain —*a line of argument* Arist.
10 bear, endure —*disaster, affliction* S. Ar.
11 incur —*blame, reproach* Antipho Pl. X.
12 submit to, undergo, face —*prosecution or sim.* E. Th. And. Pl. X. D. +; (of an official) —*an audit or scrutiny* Lys. D. Plb. Plu.
13 be liable to render —*an account* (i.e. be accountable, sts. W.DAT. *to someone, sts.* W.GEN. *for sthg.*) And. Pl. X. D. Plb. Plu.
14 pay —*a penalty* Hdt. S. E. Th. Att.orats. Pl. +; **pay for** —*a crime* E.; **be liable** —W.INF. *for payment of a fine* Pl.
ὑπήεισα (ep.aor.): see ὑπᾴδω
ὑπ-ηέριος ον *Ion.adj.* [ἀέριος] (of a sea) **somewhat misty** AR.
ὑπήκοος ον *adj.* [ὑπακούω] **1** (of tribes, regions, cities, kings) in a subordinate relationship (to a foreign power, through defeat or an alliance), **subject** Hdt. Th. +; (W.GEN. to a ruler, people) A. Hdt. E. Th. +; (W.DAT. to a city, king) Th. X. D. ‖ MASC.PL.SB. subjects Hdt. Th. X.; subject allies (opp. self-governing ones) Th. ‖ NEUT.SB. subject part (of members of an alliance) Th.
2 (of soldiers) **subordinate** (to their commander) X.; (of a satrap, to a Persian noble) X.; (of employees, to a businessman) X.; (of the passionate part of the soul, W.DAT. to the rational part) Pl.; (of everything, W.DAT. to being wealthy) Ar.
3 (of children, persons under instruction) **subject** (W.GEN. to parents, instructors) Pl.
4 (of ideal citizens, a kind of man) having an obedient attitude, **obedient** (W.GEN. to magistrates, laws) Pl. Arist.; (of an island) **compliant** (W.GEN. w. those who rule the sea) X.
5 (of a people) **in subjection** (W.GEN. to illegitimate rulers) A.
ὑπῆλθον (aor.2), **ὑπήλυθον** (ep.aor.2): see ὑπέρχομαι
ὑπηνέμιος, dial. **ὑπᾱνέμιος**, ον *adj.* [ὑπήνεμος] **1** (of beetles) subject to the wind, **on the wind** Theoc.
2 (fig., of soldiers skirmishing) **nimble** or **agile** (as though on the wind) Plu.
3 (of an egg, laid by Night) having wind underneath (i.e. inside its shell, to fertilise it), **fertilised by the wind** Ar.
ὑπ-ήνεμος ον *adj.* [ἄνεμος] **1** sheltered from the wind; (of persons) **to leeward** (w. ἐκ + GEN. of hills, i.e. sheltered by them) S.; (of the side of a threshing-floor, a shore) **leeward, sheltered** X. Theoc. | see προσήνεμος
2 (of a breeze) **gentle** E.*Cyc.*
ὑπήνη ης, dial. **ὑπήνᾱ** ᾱς *f.* **1 beard** Ar. Call. Plu.
2 area of the face covered by a beard, **chin** Theoc.
ὑπηνήτης ου *m.* one who is growing a beard, **youth** Hom. Pl.(quot. Hom.)
ὑπ-ηοῖος, also **ὑπηῷος** (AR.), η ον *Ion.adj.* [ἠῷος] near dawn; (of frost) **in the early morning** Od.; (quasi-advbl., of a person doing sthg.) Hom. AR.
ὑπηργμένος (pf.mid.pass.ptcpl.): see ὑπάρχω
ὑπηρεσίᾱ ᾱς *f.* [ὑπηρέτης] **1** performance of service (for another or in some cause); **service** Ar. Pl. Aeschin. D. Arist. Plb. Plu.

2 (collectv.) **body of assistants** (to a magistrate) Pl.; **body of servants** (in a royal household) Plb.
3 (specif.) body of assistants (to a trierarch), **specialist crew** or **petty officers** (opp. oarsmen) Th. Att.orats.
4 perh. **naval arm** or **capability** (of a ruler) Plb. ‖ PL. perh., defensive equipment (on a ship) Plb.
ὑπηρέσιον ου *n.* **rower's cushion** (on a trireme) Th. Isoc. Plu.
ὑπηρετέω *contr.vb.* **1** perform a service; **serve, assist** (sts. W.INTERN.ACC. or PREP.PHR. in sthg.) Hdt. S. Lys. Ar. Pl. X. + —W.DAT. *a person, city, god, or sim.* Hdt. S. E. Th. Att.orats. Pl. + ‖ PASS. (of things) be done as a service Hdt. Isoc. X. Arist. Plu.
2 (of hands) **serve** —W.DAT. *persons, their minds, needs* X. NT.; (of the body) —*the mind* X.
3 (of women) **serve, pander to** —W.DAT. *the lusts of males* E.
4 serve the cause of, **serve, support** —W.DAT. *a proposal, justice* E.; **aid, abet** —W.DAT. *unholy deeds* S.
5 minister to —W.DAT. *a disease* (i.e. treat it) S.
6 comply with, obey —W.DAT. *a teacher* X. —*an oracle, prophecies, laws, reason* Hdt. Lys. Pl. D. —*the will of God* NT.; (of the body) —*the decisions made by the mind* Isoc.; **humour** —W.DAT. *someone's ways* Ar.
7 (of a branch of knowledge) **be subsidiary** (to another) Arist.
ὑπηρέτημα ατος *n.* **act of service** (by a person) Antipho Pl. Plu.; (W.GEN. by a messenger's feet) S.
ὑπ-ηρέτης ου (Ion. εω), dial. **ὑπηρέτᾱς** ᾱ *m.* [ἐρέτης]
1 perh., rower under orders; (gener.) one who provides service in response to another's bidding, **servant, assistant, attendant** (sts. specif. of a ruler, commander, soldier, magistrate, god, or sim.) Hdt. Trag. Th. Ar. Att.orats. Pl. +; (W.GEN. in crime, an enterprise) E. X.
2 (ref. to an aulos) **servant** (of a performer) Pratin.; (ref. to wealth) **minister, agent** (W.GEN. of vice) Isoc.
ὑπηρέτησις εως *f.* [ὑπηρετέω] **putting** (W.GEN. of one's body or disgraceful actions) **at the service of another** Arist.
ὑπηρετικός ή όν *adj.* [ὑπηρέτης] **1** (of responsibilities, a category of persons or activities) **providing service** Pl. Arist.; (of feet, W.DAT. for the body) Pl.; (of a skill, w. εἰς + ACC. towards a particular end-product) Pl.; (of a tool, fig.ref. to a person) **serviceable** Plb. ‖ FEM.SB. skill entailing service (sts. W.DAT. to persons or gods) Pl.
2 (of a small boat) **attendant, ancillary** (ref. to a dispatch-boat, conveying messages fr. the flagship) X. ‖ NEUT.SB. attendant or ancillary vessel (usu. ref. to a dispatch-boat) Aeschin. D. Plb. Plu.
3 (of weapons) **suitable for subordinates** X.
4 (of a skill) **subsidiary, subordinate** (to another) Pl. Arist.
5 (of a virtue) **entailing subordination** (opp. command) Arist.
6 (of persons) **obedient** (W.DAT. to the law) Arist.
ὑπηρέτις ιδος *f.* | acc. ὑπηρέτιν | **servant** (W.GEN. of a disastrous message, ref. to a writing-tablet) E.; (of royal power, ref. to that of jurors) Pl.
ὑπήριπον (aor.2): see ὑπερείπω
ὑπήσω (Ion.fut.): see ὑφίημι
ὑπ-ηχέω *contr.vb.* **1** (of places) **reverberate in response, echo** (to a loud noise) Hes.(tm.) E. —W.DAT. *to the chirping of cicadas* Pl.
2 (of weapons, striking against each other) **resound** Plu.
ὑπηῷος *Ion.adj.*: see ὑπηοῖος
ὑπ-ιάχω *vb.* (of a house) make a loud sound in response, **resound** —W.DAT. *w. a bridal song* Theoc.(tm.)
ὑπίημι *Ion.vb.*: see ὑφίημι

ὑπ-ίλλω vb. app. **curb** (w.ACC. one's speech) **in deference** —w.DAT. *to someone* S.

ὑπίσᾱς (Ion.aor.ptcpl.): see ὑφίζω

ὑπίσσω Aeol.adv.: see ὀπίσω

ὑπίστημι Ion.vb.: see ὑφίστημι

ὑπ-ισχνέομαι mid.contr.vb. [ἴσχω; cf. ὑπέχω] | impf. ὑπισχνούμην, Ion. ὑπισχνεόμην | fut. ὑποσχήσομαι | aor.2 ὑπεσχόμην, ep.2sg. ὑπέσχεο, ep.imperatv. ὑπόσχεο, ptcpl. ὑποσχόμενος, inf. ὑποσχέσθαι | pf. ὑπέσχημαι | plpf. ὑπεσχήμην | —also (pres. and impf.) Ion. **ὑπίσχομαι** (also A.), ep. **ὑποΐσχομαι** (AR.) mid.vb. | impf.: Ion.2sg. ὑπίσχεο, 3sg. ὑπίσχετο, ep. ὑποΐσχετο, Ion.3pl. ὑπίσχοντο |
1 take upon oneself, **undertake** —*an action* Il. Hes. —w.INF. *to do sthg.* AR.; **undertake to fulfil** —*a plan, threat* Il.
2 make a promise (sts. w.DAT. to someone); **promise** Hom. Sol. Hdt. Th. Att.orats. + —w.FUT.INF. *to do sthg.* Hom.(sts.tm.) hHom. Hdt. S. E. Th. + —w.ACC. + FUT.INF. *that sthg. will be the case* Hom. A. E. Lys. X. D. —w.COMPL.CL. *that one will do sthg.* D.
3 promise (an action or gift); **promise** —*sthg.* (freq. w.DAT. *to someone*) Hom.(sts.tm.) hHom. Hdt. S. E. Th. +
4 profess or claim —w.INF. *to do sthg. or be such and such* hHom. Hdt. Isoc. Pl. X. —w.COMPL.CL. *that one knows sthg.* Pl.
5 take hold of from below; **catch** —*blood* (fr. a wound, w.DAT. *in one's hands*) AR. —*moonlight* (w.DAT. *on one's dress*) AR.

ὑπνο-δότᾱς ᾱ dial.m. [ὕπνος, δίδωμι] **giver of sleep** (appos.w. νόμος *melody*) A.

—**ὑπνοδότειρα** ᾱς f. (epith. of Night) **giver of sleep** E.

ὑπνομαχέω contr.vb. [μάχομαι] **resist falling asleep** X.

ὕπνος ου, Aeol. **ὕπνος** ω m. **1 sleep** Hom. +; (fig. or euphem., ref. to death) Hom. A. Call. Theoc.; (w.GEN. of death) Hes.fr.; (as an exemplar of softness) Theoc.
2 (personif.) **Sleep** (son of Night, twin-brother of Death) Il. Hes. S. E.Cyc. +
3 sleepiness, drowsiness (caused by tiredness) Hom.
4 (prep.phrs.) ἐν ὕπνῳ *in a state of sleep, asleep* Hdt. X. Theoc.; ἐν (τῷ) ὕπνῳ *in (i.e. during) sleep* (assoc.w. *dreaming*) A.(cj.) Hdt. E. Pl. +; (also) ἐν (τοῖς) ὕπνοις Isoc. Pl. Theoc. Plu.; καθ' ὕπνον *in a state of sleep, asleep* S.; *during sleep* (usu. assoc.w. *dreaming*) E. Pl. Arist. Plb. Plu.; (also) κατὰ τὸν ὕπνον, κατὰ τοὺς ὕπνους (assoc.w. *dreaming*) Plb. Plu.; περὶ πρῶτον ὕπνον *around (the time of) first sleep (i.e. early in the night)* Th. Ar. Plu.; (also) ἀπὸ πρώτου ὕπνου *after people had gone to sleep* Th.
5 dream Theoc.(pl.)

ὑπνόω contr.vb. | Lacon.inf. ὑπνῶν (Ar.) | aor. ὕπνωσα ‖ pf.pass.ptcpl. ὑπνωμένος | **sleep** or **fall asleep** Ar. Call.epigr. Plb. Plu. ‖ PF.PASS.PTCPL. **fast asleep** Hdt.

ὑπνώδης ες adj. **1** (of a person) inclined to sleep, **somnolent** Plu.
2 (of a diet) inducing sleep, **soporific** Pl.
3 (of a stupor) sleep-like, **sleepy, drowsy** Plu.

—**ὑπνώδεα** dial.neut.pl.adv. **in a sleep-like state** E. [or perh. masc.acc.adj., of a person]

ὑπνώσσω, Att. **ὑπνώττω** vb. be in a state of sleep, **be sleepy** or drowsy, **slumber** A. E.; (fig., of a non-philosophical person) —w.ACC. *throughout his life* Pl.; (of a heart, in neg.phr.) —w.DAT. *through fear (i.e. not rest or be at ease)* A.

ὑπνωτικός ή όν adj. (of a drink or drug) **sleep-inducing** Plu.

ὑπνώω ep.vb. **be asleep** Hom. Mosch. Bion

ὑπό, Aeol. **ὑπά**, ep. **ὑπαί** prep. | w.ACC., GEN. and DAT. | ὑπό and ὑπά sts. follow their noun (w. anastrophe of the accent), e.g. γαῖαν ὕπο *beneath the earth* Od. |

—**A** | location or space |
1 at a position beneath, **below, under** —w.ACC., GEN. or DAT. *the sun, earth, a place, object, part of the body, or sim.* Hom. +; (as adv.) **underneath** Od. Hdt.
2 (ref. to an island lying) **close to** —w.ACC. *a country* Isoc.
3 (ref. to examining sthg.) **under, in** —w.ACC. *the light* E. Pl.

—**B** | movt. |
1 to a position beneath, **below, under** —w.ACC. *the earth, sea, an object, or sim.* Hom. +
2 close beneath, up close to —w.ACC. *a city, wall* Hom. Plb. —*a pillar* S. —*a coast* Hdt.
3 so as to be in a position beneath, **under** —w.DAT. *a tree, shield, wheel, yoke, or sim.* Hom. + —w.GEN. *ashes, the earth* Od. Hes. Semon.
4 from under —w.GEN. *the earth, an object, animal, or sim.* Hom. + —*a womb, tent (i.e. out of it)* Pi. E.
5 (adv.) **from below** (a lowered brow) —*ref. to looking* Il. | cf. ὑπόδρα

—**C** | protection or shelter |
1 under the shelter of, behind —w.DAT. *defences* Plb.
2 (w.vb. of movt.) **under the shelter of** —w.ACC. *one's mother* Il. —*a door (i.e. behind it, ref. to being put in hiding)* Hdt.; **under the protection of** —w.ACC. *land-based troops (ref. to ships seeking refuge)* Hdt.; (gener.) **to** —w.ACC. *a place of safety* Plb.
3 from under the shelter of —w.GEN. *a person* Il. —*a mother bird's wings* E.

—**D** | subjection, control, dependence |
1 under the control of, subject to —w.DAT. *someone or sthg.* Hom. Hdt. Th. Lys. Pl. X. NT. —w.ACC. Hdt. Th. Pl. X. —*someone's power* Call. | see also χείρ 9
2 from under the control of —w.GEN. *someone or sthg.* Il.
3 (ref. to bringing a person) **under the jurisdiction of, before** —w.ACC. *a court, magistrates* Hdt. | see ὑπάγω 3
4 (ref. to a position at a symposium) **below** —w.DAT. *another symposiast (in ctxt., reflecting the order of speakers)* Pl.
5 (ref. to things being) **subordinate** —w.DAT. *to other things* Pl.; **within** —w.ACC. *a single category* Arist.

—**E** | sexual relations |
(ref. to a woman having sex) beneath, **with** —w.DAT. *someone* Od.; (ref. to bearing a child) conceived under, **to** —w.DAT. *someone* Hom.

—**F** | time |
1 in the course of, **during** —w.ACC. *the night (or a particular night)* Il. Hdt. Th. Lys. +; **in** —w.ACC. *a single breath* Plb.
2 for the duration of, **throughout** —w.ACC. *a particular circumstance* Il. —*a war* Hdt.
3 at or about —w.ACC. *a certain time* Hdt. Th. Ar. +
4 at the time of —w.ACC. *a certain event* Th Ar. X. + —w.ACC. + PTCPL. *an event happening* Hdt.

—**G** | agency or cause |
1 through the agency or compulsion of, **by, through** or **because of** —w.GEN. *someone or sthg.* Hom. + —w.DAT. Hom. +
2 through (a subordinate agent); **through** —w.GEN. *a messenger, herald, auctioneer* Hdt. Trag. Th. Pl. D.
3 under the impulse of (an emotion or state); **out of, through** —w.GEN. *fear, joy, anger, insolence, laziness, ignorance, or sim.* Il. hHom. Sol. Pi. Hdt. Trag. + —w.DAT. *sleep, grief, fear, mental impairment* Hom. A. E.

—**H** | attendant circumstances |
1 to the accompaniment of —w.GEN. *an aulos, aulos-player, lyre, pipes, drums, or sim.* Hes. Archil. Anacr. Thgn. Pi. Hdt. + —w.DAT. *an aulos-player* Hes.

ὕπο

2 in response to, at the sound of —W.GEN. *a trumpet* S. Ar.
3 accompanied by, with —W.GEN. *torches* Hom. E. X. —*dances* E. —*lamentation* A. —*holy silence* S. —*the flutter of wings* Ar. —*a procession* Hdt. —W.DAT. *singing and dancing* Hes. —*flashing rays, torchlight* B. Plu. —*lictors' rods and axes* Plu. —W.ACC. *singing and dancing* Pl.
4 (ref. to dying) **in a condition of, with** —W.GEN. *honour* E.
5 (ref. to travelling or sim.) **under** —W.DAT. *a breeze* Od.; **under, with** —W.DAT. *an escort* Hom. A. E.fr.(cj.); **in** —W.DAT. *darkness, night* A. AR. —W.ACC. Plu.
6 under the cover of —W.DAT. *darkness* (i.e. *in secrecy*) E. Plu.
—I (advbl.phr.) ὑπό τι *just a bit, somewhat* (qualifying an ADJ. or ADV.) Ar. Pl.

ὕπο (prep. w. anastrophe): see ὑπό
ὑπο-αμουσότερος ᾱ ον compar.adj. [ἄμουσος] (of a person) **somewhat less cultured** Pl.
ὑπό-βαθρον ου n. [βάθρον] **base** (for a couch) X.
ὑπο-βαίνω vb. (of the builder of a pyramid) **go lower** —W.GEN. *than another pyramid* (W.ACC. *by a certain distance*) Hdt. ‖ STATV.PF. (of a person) **be inferior to** —W.ACC. *someone* Pl.; (of a valuation) **be lower** Pl.
ὑπο-βάλλω, ep. **ὑββάλλω** vb. **1 put** (sthg.) **beneath** (someone or sthg.); **place** (W.ACC. *a cloth*) **underneath** (other coverings) Od.; **set down** (on the ground) —W.PARTITV.GEN. *some mats* (for sitting on) X.; **lay down** (W.PARTITV.GEN. *some prepared soil*) **as a bed** (for plants) X. ‖ MID. **set down for oneself** —*a kind of plant* (to sleep on) Plu. ‖ PASS. (of soil) **be laid as a bed** X.; (of cushions and rugs) **be spread** —W.DAT. *for someone* Plu.
2 place (W.ACC. *one's side*) **under** —W.DAT. *another's* (to support it) E.
3 put —*crowbars* (w. ὑπό + ACC. *under gates, to force an entry*) Ar.; **put** (W.ACC. *one's arm or shoulder*) **under** —W.DAT. *a mountain peak* (to wrench it fr. the ground, as a fantasy) E.
4 put (W.ACC. *a spear*) **under** —W.DAT. *a sword* (to block a downward stroke) Plu.; **present, expose** —*one's throat* (W.DAT. *to a sword*) Plu.
5 put —*a finger* (w. ὑπό + ACC. *under an eyeball, to distort vision*) Arist.
6 throw —*grain* (w. ὑπό + ACC. *under animals' feet, to be trampled*) X. —*captives* (W.DAT. *under elephants*) Plb. —*a prisoner* (under a heavy object, to crush him) Plu.
7 expose —*troops* (W.DAT. *to an enemy*) Plb. Plu. —(w. ὑπό + ACC. *to an attack*) Plu.
8 put (someone) **under the control** (of someone or sthg.); **subject** —*oneself* (W.DAT. *to another*) E. Aeschin. Plu. —(*to another's mercy*) E. —(w. ὑπό + ACC. *to calamities*) Isoc. —*persons* (W.DAT. *to the mob, its malice*) Plb. Plu. —(*to the laws, ostracism*) Plb. Plu. —*one's country* (w. ὑπό + ACC. *to a superior power*) Plb.
9 (fig.) **allow** (W.ACC. *one's past achievements*) **to be trampled underfoot** —W.DAT. *by an enemy* (w. whom one has foolishly engaged) Plu.
10 put (a baby) **to the breast; put** —*a puppy* (w. ὑπό + ACC. *under a bitch, for suckling*) X. ‖ PASS. (of a child) **be put** —W.DAT. *to a woman's breast* E.
11 (of a mother) **clasp** —*the ashes of a dead son* (w. ἀμφί + ACC. *to her breast*) E.
12 ‖ MID. **put to one's breast** (another's baby); **pass off** (W.ACC. *a child*) **as one's own** Ar.; **palm off** —*a child* (w. εἰς + ACC. *on a family*) Thphr.; (intr.) **pass off a child as one's own** Hdt. Ar. Pl. D. Plu.

13 ‖ MID. **pass off** (W.ACC. *one's own child*) **as another's** Arist.
14 ‖ MID. (fig.) **claim as one's own, appropriate** —*credit for another's achievements* Plu.
15 ‖ MID. (gener.) **be deceitful** S.
16 fraudulently cast —*voting-tokens* (into urns) Arist. ‖ MID. **furtively spread** —*rumours* S.
17 ‖ MID. app. **cast at the outset** (of a trial) —*a share of the votes* (W.DAT. *in favour of a man on a capital charge*) Isoc.
18 ‖ MID. **lay down** —*a foundation* (W.GEN. or DAT. *for a future course of action or sim.*) Plb. Plu.; app. **build** —*walls* Call.
19 ‖ MID. **undertake** —*an activity* Plu.
20 cast (words or sim.) **in a person's way** (as an interruption, retort, suggestion or offer); **interrupt** (a speaker) Il.
21 retort —W.DAT. *to someone* (W.ACC. or DIR.SP. *in certain terms*) Aeschin. D. —(W.COMPL.CL. *that sthg. is the case*) Aeschin.
22 make a suggestion Pl. X. Aeschin. Arist.; **suggest** —*names, a line of argument, course of action, or sim.* Att.orats. Arist. Plu.
23 mention, supply —*a name* (W.DAT. *to someone*) Plu.; **recall** —*a line of verse* (W.DAT. *to oneself*) Plu.; **offer** —*pleasures* (to someone, by way of temptation) Plu.
24 dictate —*a speech* Isoc.
25 secretly induce, suborn —*someone* (to make accusations) NT.

ὑπο-βαρβαρίζω vb. **speak somewhat like a barbarian, speak broken Greek** Pl.
ὑπόβασις εως f. [ὑποβαίνω] **crouching motion** (made by a horse, w. its hind legs) X.
ὑπο-βεβρεγμένος η ον pf.pass.ptcpl.adj. [βρέχω] **somewhat drunk, tipsy** Men.
ὑπο-βιβάζομαι mid.vb. (of a groom) **cause** (W.ACC. *a horse*) **to crouch** (for a rider to mount) X.
ὑπο-βινητιάω contr.vb. (of foods) **arouse the desire to be fucked** (in effeminate men) Men.
ὑπο-βλέπω vb. | fut. ὑποβλέψομαι | **1 look with eyes half open** (or fr. the corner of the eye, askance); **look at** (W.ACC. *someone*) **with suspicion** or **hostility** Ar. Pl. Arist.(quot.) Call.; **watch** (W.ACC. *events*) **with a suspicious eye** Plu. ‖ PASS. **be viewed with suspicion** E.
2 (without hostile connot.) **look with narrowed eyes** —w. πρός + ACC. *towards someone* (W.ADV. *bullishly, i.e. app. w. head thrust forward*) Pl.
ὑποβλήδην adv. [ὑποβάλλω] **1 by way of interruption** Il.
2 in response AR.
3 perh. **furtively** —*ref. to looking* hHom.
ὑποβλητέος ᾱ ον vbl.adj. (of prepared soil) **to be placed as a bed** (W.DAT. *for a plant*) X.
ὑπόβλητος ον adj. **1** (of a child) **passed off as one's own, supposititious** Plu. | see ὑποβάλλω 12
2 (of the speech of one who is suborned) **fraudulent** S.; (of speech) **false** (to one's true self) S.; (of identities) **fictitious** Plu.
ὑποβολή ῆς f. **1 placing underneath** (opp. περιβολή *placing around*, W.GEN. *of coverings*) Pl.
2 secretive adoption (of a child) Pl. Arist.
3 substitution (W.GEN. *of keys*) Plu. [or perh. *counterfeiting*]
4 placing in concealment, posting (W.GEN. *of ambushers*) Plb.; **place of hiding** or **ambush** Plb.
5 prompting, influence (W.GEN. *of circumstances*) Plb.; (prep.phr.) ἐξ ὑποβολῆς *under prompting* X.

ὑποβολιμαῖος ον *adj*. **1** (of a son) **supposititious** Pl. D. Plb. **2** (of crimes against parents) **committed by supposititious sons** Hdt.

ὑπο-βρέμω *vb*. (of the caverns of Hades) **rumble below** A. [or perh. *rumble in response*]

ὑπο-βρομέω *contr.vb*. (of mountain valleys) **resound in response** —W.DAT. *to a lion's roar* AR.(dub.) | see βρομέω

ὑπο-βρόχιος η ον *Ion.adj*. [βρόχος] (quasi-advbl., of oxen being dragged) **by a noose** hHom.(cj., for ὑποβρύχιος)

ὑπό-βρυχα *masc.fem.acc.sg.adj*. [reltd. βρύχιος] (of a person, region) **underwater** Od. Hdt.

ὑπο-βρύχιος ᾱ (Ion. η) ον *adj*. **1** (quasi-advbl., of Typhon lying) **underwater** AR.; (of a ship swept by a storm, a horse by a river, a clod thrown) hHom. Hdt. AR. Plb. Plu. | see also ὑποβρόχιος
2 (of souls moving around) **under the surface** (of heaven) Pl.

ὑπό-γαιος (also **ὑπόγειος** Plu.) ον *adj*. [γῆ] (of an object or area) **underground** Hdt. Plu.; (of thunder, ref. to seismic rumbling) A.*fr*.

ὑπο-γάστριον ου *n*. [γαστήρ] **underbelly** (of a person, envisaged as that of a fish) Ar.

ὑπο-γαστρίς ίδος *f*. **underbelly** (of a tunny, as a delicacy) Philox.Leuc.

ὑπόγειος *adj*.: see ὑπόγαιος

ὑπο-γελάω *contr.vb*. **laugh a little** Pl.

ὑπο-γενειάζω *vb*. **touch** (W.ACC. a man) **under the chin** (as a gesture of affection or supplication) Aeschin.

ὑπο-γίγνομαι, Ion. **ὑπογίνομαι**, ep.Ion. (tm.) **ὑπαὶ ... γίνομαι** *mid.vb*. **1** (of a sound of gnashing tusks) **come in response** (to a threat) Il.(tm.)
2 (of a new generation) **be born in succession** —W.DAT. *for a people* Hdt.
3 (of thoughts, feelings, situations) **arise, develop** Plb. Plu.
4 (of resources) **be available** Plb.

ὑπό-γλαυκος ον *adj*. [γλαυκός] (of a hound's eyes) **greyish-green** X.

ὑπο-γλαύσσω *vb*. [reltd. γλαυκός] | iteratv.impf. ὑπογλαύσσεσκον | (of the eyes of Zeus, in the form of a bull) **shine out beneath** (his forehead) Mosch.; (of the eyes of the Cyclopes) —w. ὑπό + ACC. *their brows* Call.

ὑπο-γλυκαίνω *vb*. sweeten (food) a little; (fig., of a demagogue) **sweeten up** —*the populace* (W.DAT. *w. tasty words*) Ar.

ὑπό-γραμμα ατος *n*. [γράμμα] **inscription at the foot** (of a pillar) Lycurg.

ὑπο-γραμματεύς έως *m*. **assistant clerk** or **secretary** (to an administrative body) Att.orats.; (pejor.) **petty bureaucrat** Ar.

ὑπογραμματεύω *vb*. serve as assistant clerk —W.DAT. *to a magistrate or official body* Att.orats. Plu.

ὑπογραφεύς έως *m*. [ὑπογράφω] **1** one who writes under orders; **signer** (W.GEN. of indictments, ref. to one who puts his name to a prosecution on another's behalf) Ar.
2 amanuensis Plu.

ὑπογραφή ῆς *f*. **1** impression underneath, **imprint** (W.GEN. fr. a foot) A.
2 underlining (W.GEN. of the eyes, w. make-up) X.
3 perh. **outlining** (in paint, of facial features on a mask) Plb.
4 tracing out (of areas of the sky, for divination) Plu.; **area traced out** (for a city) Plu.
5 preliminary sketch (by a painter) Plb.
6 general description, sketch (by a historian, W.GEN. of the lie of the land) Plb.
7 brief verbal description, **outline** (of an accusation, argument, political system, or sim.) Pl. Arist.

ὑπο-γράφω *vb*. **1** write underneath (sthg. written above); **write out** (W.ACC. a decree) **underneath** (another text) Hyp.; **append** —W. ὅτι + CL. *that a treaty was not honoured* (W.DAT. *to a pillar inscribed w. it*) Th.; **add one's signature** —W.DAT. *to a letter* Plu. ‖ PASS. (of a statement) be appended Plb. —W.DAT. *to a treaty* Plb.
2 ‖ MID. have (W.ACC. an epigram) **written at the foot** (of one's funerary monument) Plu.
3 use a lining-pencil on —*a face* Plu.
4 ‖ PASS. (of an upper jawbone) be marked on the underside —W.DAT. *by fissures* Plu.
5 trace on the ground —*the shape or position of places* Plu.
6 (of a teacher) **trace** (W.ACC. lines, on a wax tablet) **as a guide** (for a pupil learning to write) Pl.; (fig., of a city, ruler) **trace out** —*laws, rules of conduct* Pl.
7 ‖ MID. **draw in outline** —*the shape of a ship* Pl.; (fig.) —*the shape of a political system* Pl.(also act.) —*a likeness of the soul* Plu.
8 briefly describe in words, **give a sketch** (of a topic) Isoc.; **sketch, outline** —*an argument, political system, treaty, topographical details, or sim*. Pl. Plb. Plu. —*a change in someone's life* E.(mid.) —*hopes* (for the future, W.DAT. *to someone*) Plb. ‖ PASS. (of topographical details, hopes) be sketched or outlined Plb. ‖ PF.PASS. (of a system of conduct) exist in outline (in certain cities) Arist.
9 create an impression of —*oneself* (W.PREDIC.ADJ. *as being such and such*) Plb.; (of an accuser) **create an impression, imply** (opp. γράφειν *state in writing*) —W.ACC. + INF. *that someone did sthg*. D.
10 write from dictation, act as amanuensis Plu.

ὑπόγυιος, also **ὑπόγυος**, ον *adj*. **1** (of death, an appointed time) **close at hand, imminent** Isoc. D.
2 (of a way of achieving sthg.) **ready to hand** Arist.
3 (of an event or achievement) **recent** Isoc. D.
‖ NEUT.IMPERS. (w. ἐστί) it is a short time (since an event) Isoc.; (neut.superl.advbl.phr.) τὸ ὑπογυιότατον *in the very recent past* Isoc.
4 (of persons) **recently inflamed** (W.DAT. w. anger, i.e. in the first flush of it) Arist.
5 (of occurrences) **sudden** Arist.; (prep.phr.) ἐξ ὑπογυίου (ὑπογύου) *all of a sudden, on the spur of the moment* Isoc. Pl. X. Arist.

ὑπο-δαίω *vb*. **set fire to** (W.ACC. wood) **underneath** (a cauldron) Hom.(tm.)

ὑπό-δακρυς υ, gen. υος *adj*. [δάκρυ] (of a look) **somewhat tearful** Men.

ὑπο-δάμναμαι *pass.vb*. [δάμνημι] | aor.ptcpl. ὑποδμηθείς |
1 (w. sexual connot., of a woman) **be overpowered by, surrender to** —W.DAT. *a god or man, desire* Hes. hHom.; (of Zeus) —*Aphrodite's arrows* Mosch.
2 (of a person) **be oppressed** Od.
3 (of a bull) **be brought under the yoke** Mosch.

—**ὑποδάμναμαι** *Aeol.mid.vb*. (of Eros) **overpower** —*minds* Theoc.

ὑπο-δαμνάω *contr.vb*. (of a river god, fatigue) **weaken** (W.ACC. a warrior's knees) **beneath** (him) Il.(tm.)

ὑποδέγμενος (ep.athem.pres.ptcpl.): see ὑποδέχομαι

ὑποδέδρομα (pf.2): see ὑποδραμεῖν

ὑπο-δεέστερος ᾱ (Ion. η) ον *compar.adj*. [δέω²] **rather or more lacking** (in some quality); (of persons or things) **inferior** (sts. W.GEN. to others, in status, quality, value, size, number, or sim.) Hdt. Antipho Th. Pl. X. Plu.; (of a war) **less impressive** (W.GEN. than its reputation) Th.; (of a report) **falling short** (W.GEN. of the truth) Plu.

—ὑποδεέστερον *neut.compar.adv.* **more needily** —*ref. to living* Isoc.
—ὑποδεεστέρως *compar.adv.* **1 less forcefully** —*ref. to defending oneself* Antipho
2 with less strength in numbers —*ref. to fighting* Th.
ὑπόδειγμα ατος *n.* [ὑποδείκνῡμι] **1** example (offering instruction or proof); **example, illustration, indication** (sts. W.GEN. of sthg.) Plb. Plu.
2 (ref. to a person, behaviour) **good example, model** (for imitation) Plb. NT.
3 (ref. to a written treatise) **outline** (of the writer's doctrine) Plu.
ὑπο-δείδω *vb.* | aor. ὑπέδεισα, ep. ὑπέδδεισα | ep.statv.pf. ὑποδείδια, also ὑπαιδείδοικα (hHom.) | ep.3pl.statv.plpf. ὑπεδείδισαν | **be fearful** (before or under a threat); **be afraid** Od. AR. Plu.; (tr.) **be afraid of, fear** —*someone or sthg.* Hom. Hes. hHom. AR. Plu.; (of birds) **take fright before** —*a vulture* S.
—ὑποδεδιώς *nom.masc.pf.ptcpl.sb.* (as comic name of a bird) **fearfowl** Ar.
ὑποδεικτέος ᾱ ον *vbl.adj.* [ὑποδείκνῡμι] (of a technique) **to be outlined** Plb.
ὑπο-δείκνῡμι *vb.* —also (pres. and impf.) **ὑποδεικνύω**
1 (of a lion) perh. **gradually show** —*his teeth* Theoc.
2 show to a limited degree; (of a god) **give a glimpse of** —*prosperity* (W.DAT. *to people*) Hdt.
3 give an indication or **hint of** —*virtue, one's attitude* Th.; (intr., of a situation) **give a first sign** (of turning out in a certain way) X.
4 offer the prospect of, **hold out, offer** —*hope* Men.(cj.) Plb. —*benefits, opportunities* Plb. || PASS. (of immunity) be offered as a prospect Plb.
5 indicate (by way of guidance or as a preliminary measure), **mark out** —*channels* Hdt.
6 outline, adumbrate —*a constitution, the form of comedy* Arist.; **initiate, introduce** —*a literary technique* Arist.
7 point out, indicate —*a route, underground passage* Plb.
8 (of gods) **indicate** —W.ADV. *in a certain way (i.e. that sthg. is the case)* X. —*a means of safety* Plu.
9 point out, suggest —*arguments (for others to use)* Isoc. —W.COMPL.CL. *that sthg. will be the case* Isoc. —W.INDIR.Q. *what (or how sthg.) shd. be done* Isoc.; (intr.) **give advice** or **make a suggestion** Plb.
10 (of a teacher) **demonstrate** —*sthg.* X.; (of a master, envisaged as the teacher of his slave) —W.INF. *how to do sthg.* X.
11 demonstrate by way of example; do (W.ACC. sthg.) **as an example** —W.DAT. *for others* Isoc.; (intr.) **set an example** —W.DAT. *for others* Isoc.
12 (gener.) **reveal, indicate** or **demonstrate** —*a truth, fact, future contingency, form of behaviour, or sim.* Plb. —W.INDIR.Q. or COMPL.CL. *what (or that sthg.) is the case* Plb. NT. —W.ACC. + PREDIC.ADJ. *that someone is such and such* Plu. || PASS. (of things) be demonstrated or indicated Plb.
13 instruct —W.DAT. *someone* (W.INF. *to do sthg.*) Plb. NT.
ὑποδειμαίνω *vb.*: see ὑπερδειμαίνω
ὑποδέκομαι *Ion.mid.vb.*: see ὑποδέχομαι
ὑπο-δέμω *vb.* **build at the base** (of a pyramid) —*a first course of stone (of a particular variety)* Hdt.
ὑποδεξίη ης *ep.Ion.f.* [ὑποδέχομαι] | -ῑ- *metri grat.* | **hospitality** Il.
ὑποδέξιος ον *adj.* (of harbours) **able to take in** (a large fleet), **sufficiently capacious** Hdt.

ὑπόδεσις εως *f.* [ὑποδέω] **1 wearing of shoes** Arist.
2 (concr.) **footwear** Pl. X. Plb.
ὑποδεσμός οῦ *m.* **footwear, shoe** (of a soldier, distinguished fr. κρηπίς *heavy shoe*) Plb.
ὑπο-δέχομαι, Ion. **ὑποδέκομαι** *mid.vb.* | ep.athem.pres.: ptcpl. ὑποδέγμενος, inf. ὑποδέχθαι | ep.athem.aor.: 2sg. ὑπέδεξο, 3sg. ὑπέδεκτο || aor.pass.ptcpl. (w.mid.sens.) ὑποδεχθείς (E.) |
1 receive in a friendly or hospitable manner (esp. under one's roof or into one's care and protection); (of persons, cities, or sim.) **receive, welcome** —*visitors, guests, exiles, suppliants, or sim.* Hom. Hes.*fr.* Pi. Parm. Hdt. E. +; (fig., of native soil, envisaged as a mother) —*the dead* Pl.
2 (specif.) **entertain** —*a guest (w. a meal)* Antipho Plu.; (of a city) **play host** (to an army, by provisioning it) Th.
3 (of communities) **have relations with** —*each other* Th.
4 (iron., of enemies) **welcome** —*a person returning home* Hdt.; (of a hateful resting-place, ref. to a trap) —*a bird* Od.
5 (of an island, harbour) **provide a haven** or **refuge for** —*a ship* AR.; (of a glen) —*fugitive troops* X.
6 (of a populace) **take in, admit** —*a foreign garrison* D.
7 receive (fr. another); **receive, accept** —*an object or gift* Hes. hHom. Lyr.adesp. Pl. D. AR.(sts.tm.) —*military command* X.; (of a woman) —*a baby (for nursing)* hHom.
8 receive sympathetically, give ear to, hearken to —*the song of suppliants* A.; (of a god) —*prayers* Hes.; (of a hound) —*its master's call* Call.
9 (intr.) **accept** (a challenge to a duel, a challenging task) Il. AR.; (tr.) —*a proposal* Hdt.
10 (intr.) **accept, admit** (that one is responsible, that a suggestion is true) Hdt.
11 (of a woman) **conceive** (a child, envisaged as a burden that is taken up and carried) X.
12 receive submissively, submit to, endure —*violence, someone's anger* Od. AR.
13 make an undertaking or promise (freq. W.DAT. *to someone*); **undertake, promise** (to do sthg.) Od. Hdt. Th. —W.FUT.INF. or ACC. + FUT.INF. *that one (or someone) will do sthg.* hHom. Hdt. Th. AR. Plu. —W.PRES. or AOR.INF. *to do sthg.* Plu.; (tr.) **promise** —*a sum of money, support for a cause, or sim.* Hdt. Th.
14 (gener.) **undertake** —*public office* Plu.; **undergo** —*dangers* Plb.
15 be ready to receive; await (an enemy's attack) Hes. —*an enemy* X.; (of hunters) —*game (that is started up)* X.; (fig., of trouble, posthumous fame) —*a person* Od. E.
16 (of a rush of water) **catch, overwhelm** —*people* Pl.
17 receive (sthg. fr. above); **catch** —*a falling object* (W.DAT. *in one's cloak*) Plu.; (of Thetis) —*a child (who has leapt into the sea,* W.DAT. *in her bosom)* Il.; (of the gaping earth) **swallow up** —*a person* Pi.
18 (of a trench) **receive, take in** —*mountain streams* Pl.; (of a river) —*sewage* Plb.; (intr., of a watercourse) **take in water** (fr. nearby land) D.
19 (intr., of topographical features, such as a marsh or desert) **come next** (for one travelling in a given direction) Hdt. Plu.
ὑπο-δέω, Aeol. **ὐπαδέω** *contr.vb.* [δέω¹] **1 fasten** (W.ACC. a little cart) **beneath** —W.DAT. *a sheep's (preternaturally long) tail (to keep it fr. trailing on the ground)* Hdt.
2 fit with footwear; shoe —*someone* (W.DAT. *in a particular kind of footwear*) Plu.; (of a creator god) —*creatures* (w. *hooves or pads*) Pl. || MID. **put one's shoes on** Ar. Pl. Men.; **put on** —*shoes, boots, sandals, or sim.* Alc. Hdt. Ar. X. NT. Plu.

|| PF.MID.PASS. (esp. PTCPL.) wear shoes, be shod Pl. X.; wear a shoe —W.ACC. *on a particular foot* Th.; wear, be shod in —W.ACC. *shoes or sim.* Pl. D. NT.

ὑπο-δηλόω contr.vb. **1 covertly show** —*a signal* Ar. **2 hint at, allude to** —*someone, a character trait, an approaching death* Plu. || IMPERS.PASS. it is hinted (by a god, through dreams) —W.ACC. + FUT.INF. *that sthg. will happen* Plu.
3 suggest, intimate —W.DAT. *by one's silence, facial expression* (W.PRES.PTCPL. or ὡς + FUT.PTCPL. *that one is in a certain state of mind, that one will do sthg.*) Plu.

ὑποδήλωσις εως f. **covert allusion** (as a rhetorical technique) Pl.

ὑπόδημα ατος n. [ὑποδέω] that which is bound beneath the foot; **sandal** or **shoe** (of various kinds, worn by a man or woman) Od. Hdt. Lys. Ar. Pl. X. +; (collectv.sg.) **footwear** NT.

ὑπο-διδάσκαλος ου m. **assistant master** (for a chorus) Pl.

ὑπό-δικος ον adj. [δίκη] **1 liable to prosecution** (freq. W.GEN. for a crime or sim., sts. W.DAT. by the injured party or sim.) A. Att.orats. Pl. Arist.; **liable, answerable** (W.DAT. to a law) Pl.
2 liable to payment (W.GEN. of a fine, sts. W.DAT. to the injured party) Pl.

ὑπο-δινέομαι pass.contr.vb. perh. **be spun off one's feet** (by a thunderbolt) Call.

ὑποδμηθείς (aor.pass.ptcpl.): see ὑποδάμναμαι

ὑπο-δμώς ωός m. (ref. to a sea god) **servant, vassal** (W.GEN. of Poseidon) Od.

ὑπό-δοσις εως f. [δόσις] app., giving way, **decrease** or **remission** (W.GEN. of troubles) A.(dub, v.l. ὑπόδυσις *escape*)

ὑποδοχή ῆς f. [ὑποδέχομαι] **1 reception, welcoming** (to one's house or city, of visitors, foreigners, or sim.) Pl. Arist. Plu.; (W.GEN. to one's house) E.
2 provision of hospitality, entertainment (for guests) Hdt. Ar. Men. Plb. Plu.
3 harbouring (of a runaway slave or exile) Th. Pl.
4 haven (for ships, ref. to a harbour) X.; **shelter** (W.DAT. for a garrison, ref. to a stronghold) Pl.
5 support (for a person's aims) Aeschin. Plb.
6 reservoir (W.DAT. for rainwater) Arist.; (fig., ref. to a valley into which all kinds of knowledge flow) Pl.
7 receptacle (for food and drink, ref. to the abdomen) Pl.; (W.GEN. of all that becomes visible and tangible, ref. to Space) Pl.
8 acceptance (W.GEN. of a proposition) D.
9 interception (W.GEN. of an advancing army) Th.

ὑπόδρα, also **ὑποδράξ** (Call.) adv. [ὑπό, app.reltd. δέρκομαι] perh., with a glance from below (lowered or contracted brows); **grimly, angrily** —*ref. to looking* (at someone) Hom. Hes. hHom. Call.

ὑπο-δραμεῖν aor.2 inf. | Aeol.pf. ὑπαδεδρόμηκα | statv.pf. ὑποδέδρομα || Pres. and impf. are supplied by ὑποτρέχω. |
1 run underneath (an enemy's weapon, to clasp his knees in supplication) Hom.
2 run under —w. ὑπό + ACC. *the path of a javelin* Antipho; (of a dog) —*a horse's feet* Hdt.
3 (of sailors) **run under the shelter of** —*an island* NT.
4 (statv.pf., of a glen) **extend below** (a mountain) hHom.
5 run surreptitiously Ar.
6 run ahead of, cut in before —*someone* E. Ar.(dub.)
7 run into the way of, intercept —*brigands* X.
8 (fig.) sneak under (a person's defences); **ingratiate oneself with, wheedle** —*someone* E. Pl.
9 (of a hot flush, assoc.w. desire) **steal beneath** —W.DAT. *the flesh* Sapph.; (of darkness) **suffuse** —W.DAT. *a person's sight* Plu.
10 (of an idea) **occur** —W.DAT. *to someone* Plb. || IMPERS. it occurs —W.DAT. *to someone* (W.ACC. + FUT.INF. *that sthg. will be the case*) Plb.
11 (of despair) **steal over** —*people* Plb.; (of resentment) **spring up** Plb.

ὑπο-δρήσσω Ion.vb. [δράω] do the bidding of, **serve** —W.DAT. *a king* AR.

ὑποδρηστήρ ῆρος Ion.m. **servant** Od.

ὑποδρομή ῆς f. [ὑποδραμεῖν] **running into the path** (of a javelin) Antipho

ὑπόδρομος ον adj. (of a stone) **slipping under** (W.GEN. a person's step, causing unstable footing) E.

ὑπό-δροσος ον adj. [δρόσος] **under the dew, dewy** Theoc.

ὑπο-δρώω ep.vb. [δράω] do the bidding of, **serve** —W.DAT. *a person* Od.

ὑποδύω vb.: see ὑποδύω

ὑπόδυσις f.: see ὑπόδοσις

ὑποδύτης ου m. [ὑποδύω] **inner garment** (worn by soldiers, opp. outer cloak), **tunic** Plu.

ὑπο-δύω, also **ὑποδύνω** (Hdt.) vb. [δύω¹] | only pres. and impf. | **1 put on** (W.ACC. a tunic) **underneath** —W.DAT. *a cloak* Hdt.
2 crawl in —w. ὑπό + ACC. *underneath mats* Hdt.
3 (fig.) **edge one's way into** —*leadership* Hdt.
4 take on, undertake —*a risky enterprise* Hdt.
5 (of a bolting horse) **slip from underneath** (its rider) X.
—**ὑποδύομαι** mid.vb.| ep.3sg.aor. (tm.) ὑπό ... ἐδύσετο || athem.aor.act. ὑπέδυν, 3pl. ὑπέδῡσαν, imperatv. ὑπόδῡθι | pf.act. ὑποδέδυκα |
1 go downwards into, plunge into —*the sea* Hom.(sts.tm.) —*the earth, a cave* AR.
2 (of pain) **go deeply into, sink into** —*a person's side* A.
3 put oneself under (persons or objects, for the purpose of lifting or carrying); **go beneath** —w. ὑπό + ACC. *a yoke* Hdt. —W.DAT. Plu.; **shoulder** —W.ACC. *a wounded man, corpse, bier* Il. Plu.; **put one's shoulder to** —*a rock* Plu.
4 go under (an object, freq. for the purpose of concealment); **slip underneath** (an animal, parasol) Ar. —w. ὑπό + ACC. *a cloth, bed* Ar. D. —W.DAT. *a horse* Plu.; (of a scorpion) —w. ὑπό + DAT. *a stone* Scol.; (fig., of degenerate descendants) **take cover under** —W.ACC. (or perh. DAT.) *the virtues of their ancestors* Plu.
5 undertake —*war, danger, toil, action* Hdt. X. Plb. Plu. —W.INF. *to do sthg.* Hdt. X.
6 make oneself liable to, incur —*a criminal charge* D.
7 come under —*someone's guardianship* Plu.; **submit** —W.DAT. *to a person, a foreign power* Plu.; **be dependent on** —W.DAT. *foreign troops* Plu.
8 get inside (an enemy's ranks) Plu.; **enter into** —*politics* Plu.; **enter upon, adopt** —*a policy* Plu.
9 get inside (clandestinely or subversively); (of an art) **infiltrate** —W.ACC. or ὑπό + ACC. *another art* (so as to usurp its appearance and function) Pl.; (of dialecticians and sophists) **assume** —W.ACC. *the appearance of philosophers* Arist.; (of rhetoric) —w. ὑπό + ACC. *the appearance of politics* Arist.
10 insinuate oneself into the favour of, **ingratiate oneself with** —W.ACC. or ὑπό + ACC. *persons, the populace* Plu.; **seek to win** —*popular favour* Plu.; **worm one's way** —w. εἰς + ACC. *into an alliance* Plu.
11 (of deceitful words) perh., sneak up on, **beguile** —W.DAT. *a person* S.

ὑποείκω

12 (of a person) **slip** —w. παρά + ACC. *past legal constraints* D.; (of a proposal) **slip through** D.
13 (of weeping) **come over** —W.DAT. *someone* Od.; (of an illness) **come on** X.; (of a sense of wonder) Pl.
14 **come out from under** —W.GEN. *bushes* Od.; **slip out** —w. ὑπό + GEN. *fr. under roof tiles* Ar.; **escape** —W.GEN. *fr. afflictions* Od.

ὑποείκω *ep.vb.*: see ὑπείκω
ὑποεργός *ep.m.*: see ὑπουργός
ὑποέσχεθον (ep.aor.2): see ὑπέχω
ὑπο-ζάκορος ου *f.* **assistant temple-keeper** or **priestess** Hdt.
ὑπο-ζεύγνῡμι *vb.* | Aeol.aor.fem.ptcpl. ὑπασδεύξαισα ‖ aor.2 pass. ὑπεζύγην | **1** (act. and mid.) **put under the yoke**, **yoke** —*horses, oxen* Od. Hdt. Plu. —*mules* (sts. W.DAT. *to a cart*) Od.(tm.) AR. ‖ PF.PASS. (of lions) **be yoked** —W.DAT. *to chariots* Plu.
2 attach (to animals), **yoke** —*a chariot* Sapph.
3 (fig., of the art of kingship) **harness** —*certain people* (w. εἰς + ACC. *to the servile class*) Pl. ‖ AOR.PASS. (w.mid.sens.) **harness** or **submit oneself** —W.DAT. *to a task* S.
ὑπο-ζύγιον ου *n.* **animal placed under a yoke**, **draught animal**, **beast of burden** Thgn. Hdt. Th. Pl. X. Arist. +
ὑποζώματα (also **ὑποζώσματα** Plu.) των *n.pl.* [ὑποζώννῡμι]
1 undergirding cables (fitted around a ship's hull, to strengthen it) Pl.
2 braces, **bands** (of bronze, on a wooden trough) Plu.
ὑπο-ζώννῡμι *vb.* —also (pres.) **ὑποζωννύω** (Plb.) | pf.mid. pass.ptcpl. ὑπεζωμένος (Hdt.), also ὑπεζωσμένος (Plu.) |
1 secure with undergirding cables, **undergird**, **brace** —*a ship* Plb. NT.
2 undergird —*a horse* (W.DAT. w. *straps, for lifting its foreparts*) Plu.
3 ‖ MID. **fasten** (W.ACC. *a dagger*) **to one's belt** Plu.
‖ PF.MID.PASS.PTCPL. **wearing a belt** or **waistband** Hdt.; **wearing** (W.ACC. *a cloak*) **belted at the waist** Hdt.; **carrying** (W.ACC. *a sword, thongs, gold coins*) **attached to one's belt** Plu.
ὑπο-θάλπω *vb.* (of bouts of madness) **heat inwardly**, **inflame** —*a person* A.(tm.)
ὑπόθεο (ep.athem.aor.mid.imperatv.), **ὑποθέοιτο** (Ion.3sg.athem.aor.mid.opt.): see ὑποτίθημι
ὑπο-θερμαίνομαι *pass.vb.* (of a sword) **be warmed** —W.DAT. *by the blood it draws* Il.
ὑπό-θερμότερος ον *compar.adj.* [θερμός] (of a person) **somewhat overheated**, **rather incensed** Hdt.
ὑπόθεσις εως *f.* [ὑποτίθημι] **1 act of setting** (sthg.) **underneath** (as a basis for sthg.); **basis** (for a claim to property) D.; **foundational principle** (behind laws, a constitution, political actions) Pl. D. Arist.
2 proposal (for settling a dispute) X.; **pretext** (for a war) Plu.
3 foundation (in an argument); **assumption** Pl.; **premise**, **initial statement** (in a syllogism, an account of events) Arist. Plb.; **presupposition** (in an argument, mathematics) Arist.
4 foundational subject or **question**; **subject** (for a discourse or philosophical discussion) Isoc. X. Plu.; (for deliberation by a court or assembly) Aeschin. D.
5 initial status (in life), **origin**, **background** Plb.
6 that which is set down (as a goal to reach); **purpose** (in doing sthg.) Plu.
7 proposition (in a debate) Arist.; **hypothesis** (in a philosophical argument) Pl. X. Arist.
8 role (adopted by an actor) Plu.
9 current condition (of an empire) Plu.
10 subject matter, **content** (appropriate for prose, opp. poetry) Arist.

ὑπο-θέω *contr.vb.* [θέω¹] **1 make a stealthy rush** —W.PREP.PHR. *against an enemy* Pi.
2 run ahead unfairly, **cut in** (before another runner) Ar.
3 (of hounds) app. **run too far ahead** X.
ὑποθήκη ης *f.* [ὑποτίθημι] **1** that which is put into (someone's mind), **advice**, **suggestion** Hdt. Antipho Isoc. Arist. Plb.
2 that which is set down as a guarantee (for a loan), **security** D.
ὑπόθημα ατος *n.* **security** (for a stake, in gambling) Men.
ὑποθημοσύνη ης *f.* **advice**, **suggestion** or **instruction** Hom. X. AR.
ὑπο-θορυβέω *contr.vb.* (of a populace) **behave somewhat rowdily** —w. ἐς + ACC. *towards a politician* Th.
ὑπο-θράττω *Att.vb.* [θράσσω] (of circumstances) **somewhat disturb** —*a person* Plu.
ὑπο-θρύπτομαι *mid.vb.* (of political leadership) **be somewhat indulgent** (opp. authoritarian) Plu.
ὑπο-θυμίς ίδος *f.* [θύμον] **unidentified bird** (app. nesting on the ground under herbs); perh. **wheatear** Ar.
ὑπο-θῡμίς ίδος, Aeol. **ὑπᾱθῡμις** ιδος *f.* [reltd. θυμιάω] **fragrant garland** (worn around the neck) Sapph. Alc. Anacr.
ὑποθύψᾱς (aor.ptcpl.): see ὑποτύφω
ὑπόθυψις εως *f.* [ὑποτύφω] **incentive** (W.GEN. *to sthg.*) Plb.
ὑπο-θωπεύω *vb.* **subtly flatter** Hdt. —*someone* Ar.
ὑπο-θωρήσσομαι *Ion.mid.vb.* **arm oneself in secret** Il.
ὑπ-οίγνυμι *vb.* **stealthily open** —*a door, storeroom* Ar.
ὑπ-οικουρέω *contr.vb.* **1** (of a wife) **practise deception in the household** Ar.; (of a daimon) **cause trouble in the home** Plu.
2 secretly work upon —*soldiers, magistrates* (sts.W.DAT. w. *bribes*) Plu.; (of soldiers) **scheme**, **plot** Plu.
3 (of a disease) **lurk among** —*soldiers* Plu.
4 ‖ PASS. (of anger, feelings of estrangement) **be secretly nurtured** Plb.
ὕπ-οινος ον *adj.* [οἶνος] (of satyrs) **under the influence of wine**, **drunken** S.*Ichn.*
ὑπο-ισχάνω *ep.vb.* **hold** (W.ACC. *the palm of one's hand*) **beneath** —w. ὑπό + DAT. *one's chest* AR.
ὑποΐσχομαι *ep.mid.vb.*: see ὑπισχνέομαι
ὑπο-κάθημαι, Ion. **ὑποκάτημαι** *mid.vb.* **1** (of a person) **be ready and waiting** —W.PREP.PHR. *in a city* Hdt.; (of an army) **lie in wait for** —*invaders* Hdt.
2 lie concealed (in ambush) X.; (of anger) **lurk within** —W.DAT. *someone* Plb.
ὑπο-καθίεμαι *mid.vb.* [καθίημι] ‖ athem.aor.inf. ὑποκαθέσθαι | (of a king) app. **leave at large** —*no element of disaffection* Plb.(dub., cj. ὑποκαθῆσθαι *lie hidden*)
ὑπο-καθίζω *vb.* **1** (of a robber) **lie in wait** Plb.
2 ‖ MID. (of troops) **take up a concealed position** —w. ὑπό + DAT. *beneath a wall* X.
ὑπο-καίω *vb.* **1 burn** (W.ACC. *bones, as fuel*) **underneath** (*meat, a cooking-pot*) Hdt.
2 light (W.ACC. *a fire*) **underneath** (an object) Plb.
3 (intr.) **light fire underneath** (offerings), **make burnt offerings** A.
ὑπο-κάμπτω *vb.* **1 fall below** or **short of**, **undershoot** —*the mark* A.
2 (of a hare) **double back** X.
ὑπο-κάρδιος ον *adj.* [καρδίᾱ] (of anger, a wound fr. Eros) **deep in the heart** Theoc.

ὑπο-καταβαίνω vb. 1 gradually descend (fr. higher ground) Th. X.
2 (of a population) gradually migrate downstream Hdt.
ὑπο-κατακλίνομαι mid.vb. lie down in submission; (gener.) give in, defer D. Plu. —w.DAT. to someone Pl. Plu. —w. πρός + ACC. to a prophecy Plu.
ὑποκάτημαι Ion.mid.vb.: see ὑποκάθημαι
ὑπο-κάτω adv. and prep. 1 at a lower level than, below —W.GEN. a location Pl.; (quasi-adjl., of persons or things) below, lower Pl. Arist. Plb. Plu.
2 directly below, underneath —W.GEN. an object, tree, feet NT.
3 at the bottom (of a document) Hyp.
4 (ref. to being seated at a symposium) down (by one place) from, below —W.GEN. someone Pl.
5 less far inland than, down from —W.GEN. a place Plb.
—**ὑποκάτωθεν** adv. (quasi-adjl., of fields) lower Pl.
ὑπό-κειμαι mid.pass.vb. [κεῖμαι] 1 lie or have been placed in a position underneath; (of firewood) be placed under (a cauldron) Il.(tm.)
2 (of foundations, for a wall or house) be laid Th. X.
3 lie at a lower level; (of a location) lie below Plb. Plu. —W.DAT. another Aeschin. Plu. ‖ NEUT.SG.PTCPL.SB. tissue lying beneath (the flesh) Plb.
4 lie nearby; (of an island) lie close —w. ὑπό + ACC. to a country Isoc.; (of a river) be close behind (an army) Plb.
5 (of a challenge) lie before —W.DAT. someone Pi.
6 (of a course of action) be set down (for consideration), be suggested Hdt.
7 (of things) be laid down or prescribed (as a basis, starting-point or principle) Pl. D. + ‖ IMPERS. it is a basic principle —W.DAT. for someone (W.COMPL.CL. that he does such and such) Hdt. —W.ACC. + INF. that sthg. must be done Pl.
8 be established at the outset ‖ PTCPL.ADJ. (of a plan or sim.) original Plb. ‖ NEUT.PL.PTCPL.SB. original position (of an army) Plb.; original plan or decision Plb.
9 be assumed as a hypothesis; (of things) be assumed (sts. W.INF. to be such and such) Pl. Arist. ‖ IMPERS. it is assumed —W.COMPL.CL. or ACC. + INF. that sthg. is the case Arist.
10 (philos., of things) form the basis of or be fundamental to, underlie —W.DAT. other things Pl. ‖ NEUT.SB. substrate (ref. to Matter in relation to Form) Arist.; substance (ref. to Matter and Form in relation to contingencies) Arist.
‖ NEUT.PL.SB. (philos.) particulars underlying (universals) Arist.
11 ‖ PTCPL.ADJ. (of material) forming the subject (of a branch of philosophy), underlying Arist. ‖ NEUT.PL.SB. subject matter (of a speech) Isoc.
12 (pejor., of an art) exist under the guise of —W.DAT. another art Pl.
13 (of persons) be submissive Pl. —W.DAT. to someone Pl.
14 (of assets) be pledged as security (for a loan) Is. D.
15 (of circumstances) be current Plb. Plu.; (of a period in history) be the subject of current discussion Plb.
‖ NEUT.PL.SB. current state of affairs Plb.; resources currently available Plu.
16 (of things) remain as a possibility, be in prospect Th. D.; be in store —W.DAT. for someone Lycurg. D. Plb.
ὑπο-κηρύττομαι Att.mid.vb. [κηρύσσω] 1 announce, advertise —oneself (as a sophist) Pl.
2 have a herald announce —one's slaves (to be free) Aeschin.
ὑπο-κίνδῡνος ον adj. 1 (of missiles used in training) carrying a limited risk Pl.
2 (of a witness) at risk, in danger (because of his testimony) D.
ὑπο-κῑνέω contr.vb. 1 gently prompt —a person (to speak) Pl.
2 stir up —people (to rebel or join one's cause) Plu.
3 play on —someone's vanity Plu.
4 (intr.) make a slight movement or begin to move; flinch (after being struck) Ar.; (of a hare) make a move, start up X.; (of a city) stir (in rebellion) Hdt.
5 ‖ PASS. be somewhat excited (at an announcement) Plu.
6 ‖ PF. be disturbed mentally Pl.
ὑπο-κλάζω vb. | aor.2 ὑπέκλαγον | (of a satyr) make little screeches S.Ichn.
ὑπο-κλέπτομαι pass.vb. 1 be furtively robbed —W.ACC. of one's marriage bed (by an adulterer) S.
2 (of a sense of honour) be furtively stolen —W.DAT. by greed for gain Pi.(tm.)
ὑπο-κλίνομαι mid.vb. | aor.pass. (w.mid.sens.) ὑπεκλίνθην | lie down in —W.DAT. a bed of rushes Od.
ὑπο-κλονέομαι pass.contr.vb. be driven in confusion —W.DAT. by a warrior Il.
ὑπο-κλοπέομαι mid.contr.vb. [ὑπόκλοπος] conceal oneself, lurk Od.
ὑπόκλοπος ον adj. [ὑποκλέπτομαι] (of speech) deceitful B.fr.
ὑπο-κλύζομαι pass.vb. (of a ship's keel) be made to sink deep in the water (by the weight of Herakles) AR.
ὑπο-κνίζομαι pass.vb. (of a man) be somewhat excited (fr. meeting a beautiful woman) X. Plu.
ὑπο-κολακεύομαι pass.vb. receive some flattery Plb.
ὑπο-κόλπιος ον adj. 1 (of a lover) held to one's bosom, in one's embrace Theoc.
2 (of a baby) within the womb Call.
ὑπο-κονίομαι mid.vb. (of a wrestler) rub (W.ACC. his hands) with dust Plu.(quot.com.)
ὑπό-κοπος ον adj. [κόπος] (of hounds) somewhat tired X.
ὑπο-κόπτω vb. strike under —the hollow of someone's thigh (w. a sword) Plu.
ὑπο-κορίζομαι, dial. **ὑποκουρίζομαι** mid.vb. 1 (of young women) express affectionate sentiments —W.DAT. in songs Pi.
2 (of a father) use a pet name (for a baby son) Thphr.; (of a lover) use the pet names —W.INTERN.ACC. duckie and dovey Ar.
3 give the name (W.INTERN.ACC. such and such) as a mark of affection Plu.; (app. iron., of persons using a disparaging name) X.; convey in an affectionate name —a person's character traits Plu.
4 use a polite term (for sthg. disagreeable), speak euphemistically Pl. Plu. —W.ACC. of friendly relations (instead of slavery) D. —of allies (instead of masters) Plu.
5 use diminutive word forms Arist.
ὑποκόρισμα ατος n. 1 pet name (for a child, given by a nurse) Aeschin.
2 (ref. to a proconsulship) euphemism (W.GEN. for exile) Plu.
ὑποκορισμός οῦ m. 1 pet name (for a young person) Plu.
2 use of diminutive word forms Arist.
ὑποκουρίζομαι dial.mid.vb.: see ὑποκορίζομαι
ὑπό-κουφος ον adj. [κοῦφος] (of a person) rather weak (W.ACC. in judgement) Plu.; weak-minded Plu.
ὑπο-κρέκω vb. (of inappropriate boasting) sound in response, chime in —W.DAT. w. madness Pi.
ὑπο-κρητηρίδιον ου Ion.n. [dimin. κρᾱτήρ] stand for a bowl Hdt.

ὑπο-κρίζω vb. | aor.2 ὑπέκριγον | (of a satyr) **make little shrieks** S.*Ichn.*

ὑπο-κρῑ́νομαι *mid.vb.* | aor.pass. (w.mid.sens.) ὑπεκρίθην (Plb.) | **1 speak in response** (freq. W.DAT. to someone); **reply** Hom. hHom. Hdt. Theoc.; **say in reply** —W.NEUT.PL.ACC. or DIR.SP. *sthg.* Hdt. —W.INDIR.Q., COMPL.CL., INF. or ACC. + INF. *what* (*or that sthg.*) *is the case* Hdt.
2 respond with an interpretation or explanation (of an omen or dream); **interpret, explain** (an omen) Hom. AR. —*an omen* Plu. —*a dream* Od. Ar. —W.INDIR.Q. *what will happen* Theoc.
3 give an interpretation (of a riddling remark) Ar.(dub., v.l. ἀπο-)
4 be an actor, act Arist. Plu.; **act in** —*a play* D. Arist. Plu.; **play** —*a character* Aeschin. Plu.
5 (pejor., of an orator) **use histrionic arts, put on a performance** D. Plu.; (without pejor. connot.) **speak expressively, declaim** Arist. Plu.
6 (fig., of persons) **engage in a show of pretence, put on an act** Arist. Plb. Plu.; **act like** —*a certain kind of person, a legendary character, royalty* Arist. Plb. Plu.; **play out** —*another's grandeur* Plu.
7 (gener.) **pretend** —W.INF. *to do or have done sthg.* D. Plb.

ὑπόκρισις εως (Ion. ιος) *f.* **1 response, reply** (by a person or oracle) Hdt.
2 interpretation (of a dream) AR.
3 performance (by an actor) Arist.
4 performance of a role (W.GEN. of or by a dolphin) Pi.*fr.*
5 delivery (by an actor or orator, ref. to expressiveness of manner in putting across a speech) Arist. Plb. Plu.
6 elocution, expression (of a person reading aloud) Plb.
7 (pejor.) **play-acting, pretence, hypocrisy** Plb. NT.

ὑποκριτής οῦ *m.* **1 interpreter** (W.GEN. of riddling voices and visions, ref. to a seer) Pl.
2 actor Ar. Att.orats. Pl. X. Arist. Plu.
3 one who makes an excessive or false display (esp. of piety), **hypocrite** NT.

ὑποκριτικός ή όν *adj.* **1 of or relating to being an actor;** (of a person) **with a gift for acting** Arist. ‖ FEM.SB. **art of acting or performing** Arist.
2 of or relating to delivery (of a speech); (of features of style, a style used in debating) **suited for delivery** Arist. ‖ FEM.SB. **art of delivery** Arist. ‖ NEUT.PL.SB. **matters relating to delivery** Arist.; **things designed for delivery** Arist.

ὑπο-κρούω *vb.* **1 knock up** (against a person); **interrupt** Ar. Aeschin. —*a speaker* Plb.; (of a man, w. further sexual connot., as 2) **butt in on** —*a woman* Ar.
2 (w. sexual connot.) **knock off, bang** —*a woman* Ar.
3 (of a person reciting a piece of metrical prose) **beat time** Plu.

ὑπο-κρύπτομαι *mid.vb.* **hide, conceal** —*someone* Isoc.
‖ PASS. (of a ship) **be hidden beneath** —W.DAT. *spray* Il.

ὑπό-κυκλος ον *adj.* [κύκλος] (of a basket) **with wheels underneath, running on wheels** Od.

ὑπο-κύομαι *mid.vb.* (in aor., of a woman, a mare) **become pregnant, conceive** Hom. Hes. hHom.

ὑπο-κύπτω *vb.* **1** (of suppliants) **bow the head** or **stoop low** Ar.
2 (tr.) **stoop** (W.ACC. one's shoulder) **under** (a carrying-stick) Ar.
3 (of a people) **bow down, submit** —W.DAT. *to someone* Hdt.; (of a city) **surrender** Hdt.

ὑπο-κώλια ων *n.pl.* [dimin. κῶλον] **lower thighs** (of a hound or hare) X.

ὑπό-κωφος ον *adj.* [κωφός] **rather deaf** Ar. Pl. Arist. Plu.

ὑπο-λαμβάνω *vb.* **1 take up from underneath;** (of a dolphin) **take up** —*a person* (*on its back*) Hdt. Pl.; (of a boar) **pick up** —*a body* (*w. its tusks*) X.
2 support —*a drunk or wounded man* Pl. Thphr. Plu.; (of a structure) —*an object placed on it* Hdt.
3 take up and carry away; pick up and remove —*weapons* Th.; (of a river) **carry away** —*soil dumped in it* Hdt.; (of a cloud) —*Christ* (*during the Ascension*) NT.
4 (of a wind) **catch hold of** —*wrecked ships* Hdt. —*moisture* Hdt.; (of a wind, storm) —*sailors* Hdt.; (of plague, madness) —*persons* Hdt.; (of trembling) —*persons, limbs* Il.(tm.); (intr., of a sea-battle, envisaged as an affliction) **come on** Hdt.
5 (of a fleet) **catch up with** —*enemy ships* Th.
6 (of difficult terrain) **confront** —*an advancing army* X.
7 catch by underhand means, entice, seduce —*foreign sailors* (*w. higher wages*) Th. —*a state* (*fr. its previous allegiance*) Th.
8 take into one's protection, take in —*exiles* X.
9 (of a rider) **hold back, check** —*his horse* X.
10 (of hounds) **pick up** —*traces* (*of a quarry*) X.; (intr.) **pick up traces** X.
11 pick up, seize on —*allegations* Th.; **take up, accept** —*a proposal* Hdt.
12 take up (a speaker's words, w. a verbal response); **reply, retort** Hdt. Th. Pl. X. + —W.COMPL.CL. *that sthg. is the case* Th. Pl. X. D. —W.ACC. + INF. Th.; **retort by asking** —W.INDIR.Q. *whether sthg. is the case* Lys.
13 react —W.ADV. *in a hostile way* D.
14 (of a singer) **take up** —*a song of response* Theoc.
15 make a mental response (to another's words); **take, understand** —*a statement or sim.* (W.ADV. *in a certain way*) E. Pl. —(w. εἰς + ACC. *as applying to someone*) Aeschin. —*sthg.* (W.INF. *to be such and such*) Pl.; (intr.) **understand** —W.ADV. *correctly or sim.* Pl.
16 take up a notion (freq. mistakenly); **make a supposition** (sts. W.ADV. unfairly or sim.) Isoc. Pl. Arist. Thphr. Men. +; **suppose, imagine** —*sthg.* Lys. D. Arist. —W.INF. + PREDIC.ADJ. *that one is or will be such and such* X. Thphr. —W.COMPL.CL. or ACC. + INF. *that sthg. is the case, or is such and such* Hdt. Th. Att.orats. Pl. X. + ‖ PASS. (of persons or things) **be imagined** D. —W.ADV. *in a certain way* Isoc. D. —W.PREDIC.ADJ. *as such and such* Isoc. —W.INF. + PREDIC.ADJ. *to be such and such* Isoc. Arist. —W.INF. *to do such and such* Isoc. Arist. ‖ NEUT.AOR.PASS.PTCPL.SB. **supposition** Men.

ὑπολαμπής ές *adj.* [ὑπολάμπω] (of a shield) **shining** (W.DAT. w. various materials) Hes.

ὑπο-λάμπω *vb.* **1** (of the sun in winter) **shine at a low elevation** X.
2 (of the moon) **give light below** (clouds) Plu.
3 (of day) **begin to brighten, break** Plu.; (of dawn) AR.(mid.)
4 (of spring) **begin to appear** Hdt.

ὑπόλειμμα ατος *n.* [ὑπολείπω] **remnant** (W.GEN. of a faction) NT. Plu.

ὑπό-λειος ον *adj.* [λεῖος] (of a youth) **rather smooth-faced** Men.

ὑπο-λείπω *vb.* | fut.pass. ὑπολειφθήσομαι, also ὑπολείψομαι (Od.) | **1** (act. and mid., of departing or departed persons) **leave behind** —*persons or things* Hdt. Th. Lys. D.; (of deserting sailors) —*arrears of pay* Th. ‖ PASS. (of persons, occas. of things) **be left or remain behind** Od. Hdt. Th. Isoc. Pl. X. +; **stay behind and be left out** —W.GEN. *of an expedition* A. Hdt.

2 ‖ PASS. be outdistanced (by others); (of a runner, troops, or sim.) fall behind Th. Ar. Pl. X. Plu.; (of children) —W.GEN. *their fathers* (W.DAT. *by a certain number of years*) Arist.; (fig., of persons) be inferior (to others, in beauty) Arist.; be behind or deficient —W.DAT. *in sthg.* D.
3 **leave behind** (after death) —*a war, disgrace* (W.DAT. *to one's children*) Antipho Th.; (of a murdered man) —*spirits of vengeance* Antipho —*a mark* (*on one's murderer, as evidence of self-defence*) Antipho
4 leave (sthg.) remaining (for others); **leave behind** —*portions of food, sums of money, a share of property, or sim.* Od. Att.orats. Plu.; (of a jury) leave —*a murderer* (W.DAT. + INF. *for the victim's next of kin to punish*) Antipho ‖ MID. **leave an opportunity** —W.DAT. + INF. *for someone to do sthg.* Plu.
5 ‖ MID. leave remaining for oneself, **retain** —*money, property* Isoc. Is. Plu. —*military forces* Plb.; (of the sun) —*moisture* (W. περί + ACC. *around itself, opp. dispersing it*) Hdt.
6 ‖ PASS. (of persons or things) be left, remain (out of a larger number or amount) Il. Hdt. Th. Att.orats. Pl. +
7 leave (non-material) things remaining (for others); **leave** —*an excuse, argument, means of defence, or sim.* Th. Att.orats. Plb.(mid.) ‖ MID. leave for oneself, **leave oneself with** —*an accusation* (*i.e. be liable to it*) Th. —*great labours* Isoc. —*a guilty conscience* Antipho —*a line of argument or sim.* Att.orats. ‖ PASS. (of an argument, excuse, course of action, danger, or sim.) be left (freq. W.DAT. for someone) Att.orats. Pl. Plu.; (of tears, i.e. sorrow) E.; (of a person) be left with —W.ACC. *a particular fate* E. ‖ IMPERS.PASS. it remains —W.DAT. *for someone* (W.INF. *to do sthg.*) Lys. Plu.
8 **leave out, omit** (for others to deal with) —*arguments, topics, or sim.* Lys. Pl. ‖ MID. **leave** (W.ACC. sthg.) **out of account** Plb. ‖ PASS. (of a number) be left out Pl.
9 (of a water supply) fail —*a population* Arist.; (of words) —*a person* Arist.(quot.); (of a lifetime) be **insufficient for** —*a person enumerating infinite possibilities* Arist.
10 (intr., of provisions) **run out** Plu.
11 ‖ PASS. (of night-time) come to an end S.

ὑπό·λειψις εως f. **failure** (W.GEN. *of vision*) Plu.

ὑπο·λευκαίνομαι pass.vb. (of heaps of chaff) gradually become white Il.

ὑπο·λήνιον ου n. [ληνός] receptacle below a wine-press, **wine-press trough** NT.

ὑπο·ληνίς ίδος f. **water-trough** (for animals) Call.

ὑπό·ληψις εως f. [ὑπολαμβάνω] **assumption, supposition, conception, notion** (concerning persons or things) Hyp. D. Arist. Plb.

ὑπολιπής ές adj. [ὑπολείπω] (of tasks) remaining Plu.

ὑπό·λισφος ον Att.adj. [λίσπος] (of a rower's rump) somewhat flattened Ar.

ὑπο·λογίζομαι mid.vb. 1 calculate (credit or debit); **credit** (to someone) —*a sum of money* Plu.; **deduct** —*expenses* (W. ἐκ + GEN. *fr. wages*) Plb.
2 employ rational calculation, **think, reflect, reason** —W.PREP.PHR. *on the basis of probabilities* Isoc.
3 **take into account, bear in mind, consider** —*sthg.* Att.orats. Pl. X. Plu. —W.COMPL.CL. or INDIR.Q. *that* (or *whether*) *sthg. is the case* Pl.

ὑπό·λογος[1] ον adj. [λόγος] (of circumstances) **held accountable** (W.DAT. to persons, either to their credit or discredit) Lys. Pl. D.; (gener.) **taken into account** Pl. D. Din.

ὑπό·λογος[2] ου m. taking into account, **reckoning, consideration** (of persons or things) D. Din. Arist.(cj.); (specif.) **credit** (W.DAT. to someone, W.GEN. for sthg.) Lys.

ὑπό·λοιπος ον adj. [λοιπός] 1 (of persons or things) **left, remaining** (out of a larger number or amount) Hdt. Th. Att.orats. Pl. X. + ‖ NEUT.SG.SB. what is left, **remnant** (of a people's self-esteem) Th. ‖ NEUT.PL.SB. **remnants** (of a people or empire) Th. D.; **residue** (of a mixture) Pl.
2 **left over** (for the future); (of a task, course of action, occasion, hope, or sim.) **remaining** Hdt. Th. Ar. Att.orats. Pl. + ‖ NEUT.IMPERS. (w. ἐστί, sts.understd.) it remains —W.INF. or DAT. + INF. (*for someone*) *to do sthg.* Att.orats.
3 **left to come** (within a specific period); (of time, life) **still left, remaining** Th. Hyp. Plu.
4 **left to come** (in the future); (of persons) **future, subsequent** Hdt.

ὑπο·λόχᾱγος ου dial.m. [λοχᾱγός] **assistant commander** (of a company of soldiers) X.

ὑπο·λύριος ον adj. [λύρᾱ] (of reed) **for the inside of a lyre** (supporting its arms) Ar.

ὑπο·λύω vb. | dial.3sg.opt. (tm.) ὑπαὶ ... λύοι (A.) | 3pl.athem.aor.mid. (w.pass.sens.) ὑπέλυντο | 1 cause (a body or its strength) to be weakened or collapse; (of a warrior, wrestler, war, or sim.) **undermine** —*limbs, knees, strength* Hom.(sts.tm.) Hdt.(oracle, tm.) ‖ PASS. and ATHEM.AOR.MID. (of limbs, knees) give way, collapse (through wounding, fatigue, fear) Hom.(sts.tm.) Ar.
2 release (an animal) from beneath (the yoke); **unyoke** —*horses, oxen* Il.(tm.) Th. —*mules* (W.GEN. *fr. wagons*) Call.
3 release (W.ACC. persons) **from underneath** (sheep) Od. ‖ MID. release —*someone* (W.GEN. *fr. bonds*) Il.; **rescue** —*someone* (W.GEN. *fr. a dire situation*) AR.
4 untie from the feet, **take off** —*someone's shoes* A.(tm.) Ar.; **unshoe** —*someone* Pl. Plu.; (intr.) Ar. ‖ MID. **take off** —*one's shoes* Ar. Plu.; (intr.) **take off one's shoes** Ar. X.

ὑπο·μαίνομαι mid.vb. **be a bit mad** Men.

ὑπό·μακρος ον adj. [μακρός] (of a rod) **fairly long, longish** Ar.

ὑπο·μαλακίζομαι mid.vb. **be rather faint-hearted** X.

ὑπο·μαργότερος ον compar.adj. [μάργος] a little short of rather mad, **more or less insane** Hdt.

ὑπο·μάσσω vb. **gently** or **surreptitiously knead** —*magic herbs* Theoc.

ὑπο·μείγνῡμι vb. 1 **mix in, infuse** —*a substance* (W.DAT. *into another*) Pl.
2 (of the mind) **suffuse** —*bitterness* (W.PREP.PHR. *throughout the liver*) Pl.
3 ‖ NEUT.PF.PASS.PTCPL.SB. small admixture (W.GEN. of pain) Pl.
4 (of a fleet) **stealthily come close** —W.DAT. *to a place* Th.

ὑπο·μειδιάω contr.vb. **give a little smile** Plb. Plu.

ὑπο·μείων ον, gen. ονος compar.adj. somewhat lesser (in status) ‖ MASC.PL.SB. **inferiors** (ref. to men debarred fr. full citizenship at Sparta) X.

ὑπο·μέμφομαι mid.vb. **be rather reproachful** Plu.

ὑπομενετικός ή όν adj. [ὑπομένω] (of a courageous man) **characterised by endurance** (W.GEN. *of dangers*) Arist.; (w. πρός + ACC. *in the face of discomforts*) Arist.

ὑπο·μένω vb. 1 remain where one is, **remain behind, stay** Od. Hdt. S. Th. Att.orats. Pl. +
2 remain in an unchanged condition; **continue** —W.PREP.PHR. *in a position of leadership* Th.
3 remain alive; (of children) **survive** (after infancy) Hdt.
4 **wait** (for someone to arrive); **wait for, await** —*a person* Thgn. X. Thphr. —*an enemy army, its commander* Hdt.
5 **wait for** —*a festival* (app. to end) Th. —*punishment* Isoc.
6 (specif.) **remain to stand trial** (opp. flee abroad) And. Lys.; **remain to face** —*a trial* Att.orats.

ὑπομιμνήσκω

7 (of evils, punishment) **await, be in store for** —*someone* Pl. Plb.
8 keep one's ground, **stand fast** or **firm** (in the face of an enemy) Il. Hdt. Th. Pl. +; (fig., of a disputant) Pl.; (of a fleet) **hold position** Th.
9 stand firm against, **face, stand up to, withstand** —*a warrior, his spear, enemy troops, an attack, or sim.* Il. Hdt. E. Th. + —*a wild animal* Isoc. Theoc. —(fig.) *a disputant* Pl.
10 be patient under, **endure** —*unwelcome circumstances (such as war, danger, hostility, slavery, surgery)* Hdt. Th. Att.orats. Pl. X. +; **bear, be prepared** —W.INF. *to do sthg.* Att.orats. Pl. X. +
11 (wkr.sens.) **put up with, tolerate** —*a person* Thphr. —*an argument, bribes, advice, free speech, or sim.* Isoc. Pl. + —W.ACC. + PTCPL. *someone doing sthg., sthg. happening* Isoc. Pl. + —W.PASS.INF. *being helped* Pl. —*being mocked* Thphr.
12 (iron.) **bear with, cope with** —*one's prosperity* Pi.
13 sit patiently through —*several performances of a show* Thphr.

ὑπο-μιμνήσκω, dial. **ὑπομιμνάσκω** (Theocr.) *vb.* | aor. ὑπέμνησα, dial. ὑπέμνᾱσα (S.) | **1** cause (someone) to remember; **remind** —*a person (of sthg.)* Pl. X. Is. Aeschin. Thphr. + —(W.ACC. *of sthg.*) Hdt. Th. Att.orats. Pl. + —(W.GEN. *of someone or sthg.*) Od. X. Aeschin. D. —(W. περί + GEN. *about sthg.*) Pl. Plb. —(W.COMPL.CL. or INDIR.Q. *what, or that sthg., is the case*) Att.orats. Pl. + —W.ACC. *oneself* (w. ὡς + NOM.PTCPL. *that one is such and such*) Isoc.
2 give a reminder or **make mention** (of sthg.) Th. And. Pl. X. +; **recall, mention** —W.ACC. *sthg.* A.(dub.) Hdt. S. Att.orats. Pl. + —W.GEN. Th. D. Theoc. Plu. —W.COMPL.CL. *that sthg. is the case* Pl. X. Is.
3 prompt —W.ACC. + INF. *someone to do sthg.* Aeschin.
4 ‖ MID.PASS. **remember** —W.ACC. *sthg.* Pl. X. Plb. —W.GEN. NT.
5 ‖ AOR.PASS. (w.mid.sens.) deliver a report —w. περί + GEN. *about sthg.* A.(dub.)

ὑπο-μνάομαι *mid.contr.vb.* | only ep.2pl.impf. (w.diect.) ὑπεμνάασθε | **court** (W.ACC. *a married woman*) **behind the back** (of her husband) Od.

ὑπόμνημα ατος *n.* [ὑπομιμνήσκω] **1** (concr. and abstr.) that which provides a reminder or record, **reminder, memorial** (freq. W.GEN. *of someone or sthg.*) Th. Att.orats. Pl. X. Arist. Plb. Plu.
2 (freq.pl.) written record, **memorandum, note** Pl. X. D. Plb. Plu.
3 (usu.pl. for sg.) written work on a technical subject, **treatise** Plb. Plu.

ὑπομνηματίζομαι *mid.vb.* **make a record of** —*events* Plb.

ὑπομνηματισμός οῦ *m.* **1 note, memorandum** Plb. Plu.
2 ‖ PL. memoirs (of a statesman's life) Plb.
3 written report, **report** (fr. a commission) Plb.

ὑπόμνησις εως *f.* [ὑπομιμνήσκω] **1** process or instance of recalling to mind, **reminding** or **reminder** (freq. W.GEN. *of sthg.*) E. Th. Pl. X. Plb. Plu.
2 recollection or **recording** (of past events, by a historian) Plb.
3 bringing (of sthg.) to notice; **prompting** or **warning** (W.GEN. *of readers, about sthg.*) Plb.

ὑπο-μνηστεύομαι *mid.vb.* (of a father) **betroth** (his daughter) Arist. ‖ PASS. (of a man) be betrothed Arist.

ὑπ-όμνυμαι *mid.vb.* **1** make an objection on oath (to delay or disrupt proceedings); **make a sworn objection** (in the Assembly) X.; **disrupt** (W.ACC. *the Assembly*) **with a sworn objection** Ar.
2 swear an oath justifying postponement (of a lawsuit); (of a litigant) **enter a sworn plea for postponement** D.; (of a proxy) **swear as ground for postponement** —W.ACC. + INF. *that a litigant is abroad* D. —W.ACC. and ὡς + PTCPL. *that a litigant is ill* D. ‖ PASS. (of a plea) be entered as ground for postponement D.

ὑπομονή ῆς *f.* [ὑπομένω] **1 staying behind** (opp. ἀκολούθησις *following*) Arist.
2 endurance or **capacity for endurance** (of hard work, sickness, war, or sim.) Plb. NT. Plu.
3 capacity for resistance (W.GEN. *to blows, as a property of a sword*) Plb.
4 (gener.) **steadfastness** NT.; (specif., in facing death) Plu.
5 (pejor.) **passivity, tolerance** (opp. fighting back) Arist.

ὑπο-μῡκάομαι *mid.contr.vb.* (of bull-roarers) **bellow in answer** A.fr.

ὑπο-νείφω *vb.* **1** ‖ IMPERS. it snows a little Th.
2 ‖ MID. (of a night) **be rather snowy** Th.

ὑπο-νήχομαι *mid.vb.* **1 swim underwater** Plu.
2 dive underwater Plu.

ὑπο-νοέω *contr.vb.* **1** have a partial or hesitant notion (of what is possible or likely); **imagine, surmise, infer, suspect** —*sthg.* Hdt. E. Th. And. Ar. Men. + —W.ACC. + INF. *that someone is doing sthg., that sthg. is the case* Hdt. Th. Att.orats. Men. Plb. + —W.COMPL.CL. *that sthg. is or will be the case* X. D. Plu. —W.INDIR.Q. *what is the case* Plb.
2 make an inference or **guess** Ar. Pl. Men. Plu.
3 ‖ PASS. (of things) be inferred or imagined Th. Plb. Plu.
4 (specif.) have an apprehension of guilt or fault, **be suspicious** Th. Lys. Plu. —w. περί + GEN. *in regard to sthg.* And. —W.GEN. + COMPL.CL. *in regard to persons, that they are doing sthg.* (i.e. suspect them of it) Th.
5 (tr.) view with suspicion, **be suspicious of** —*statements, a story* Antipho And. Plu.; **suspect** —*a person* Plu. —(w. ὡς + PTCPL. *of doing sthg.*) Plu. ‖ PASS. (of a person) be under suspicion Plu.
6 apprehend with suspicion, **suspect** —*a lie* Pl. —*treachery, poisoning, or sim.* Plu.
7 have in mind (a course of action); **think** —W.INF. *of doing sthg.* Plb.(dub., cj. ἐπινοέω)

ὑπόνοια ᾱς *f.* | The sections are grouped as: (1–4) notion suggested by one's own thinking, (5–10) notion suggested by an external source. | **1** uncertain notion, **impression, surmise, conjecture** Ar. Isoc. D. Plu.; (W.GEN. *about the future*) Th.
2 partial understanding, **general idea, impression** (of a topic or issue) Plb.
3 apprehensive notion, **suspicion** (W.GEN. *of what is to happen*) Plb.; (W.COMPL.CL. *that sthg. is the case*) Th.; (W.ACC. + INF.) Plu.; (prep.phr.) παρὰ τὴν ὑπόνοιαν *contrary to expectation* Plb.
4 state of being suspicious (about persons or things), **suspicion** Men. Plb. Plu.; (W.GEN. *about what is happening*) Plu.
5 suggested meaning, **impression, interpretation** (W.GEN. *of the facts, conveyed by a poet, opp. the truth*) Th.
6 deeper meaning (of a poem) X.; (specif.) **allegory** Pl. Plu.
7 suggestion (conveyed allegorically by a design on a shield), **hint** (W.INDIR.Q. *of what will happen*) E.
8 impression (of a person, conveyed to another); **impression, hint, suspicion** (W.GEN. *of drunkenness*) Men.;

(of naivety, stupidity) Plu.; (of a humble and timid person, i.e. of being such) Plu.

9 innuendo (opp. foul language, in comedy) Arist.

10 (prep.phr.) καθ' ὑπόνοιαν *by indirect suggestion, by implication* Plb.

ὑπονομηδόν *adv.* [ὑπόνομος] **by underground channelling** Th.

ὑπό-νομος ου *m.* [νέμω] **1** underground passage, **tunnel** Th. X. Plb. Plu.

2 vein, seam (of silver, in a mine) X.

ὑπο-νοστέω *contr.vb.* **1** (of a river, pile of wood, ground) subside Hdt. Th.

2 (of a cloud) sink down (to earth) Plu.

ὑπονόστησις εως *f.* reduction in level (W.GEN. of a sea) Plu.

ὑπο-νύσσω *vb.* prick on the underside, **prick** —*a bull's flanks* (W.DAT. *w. a spear*) AR.(tm.); (of a bee) **sting** —*fingertips* Theoc.

ὑπο-νυστάζω *vb.* **be rather drowsy** Pl. Plu.

ὑπό-ξυλος ον *adj.* [ξύλον] wooden underneath; (of necklaces) **of plated wood** (i.e. fake) X.; (fig., of a person) **phoney** Men.

ὑπο-ξυρέω, Ion. **ὑποξυράω** *contr.vb.* **1** shave (W.ACC. the temples) underneath (the hair on the crown) Hdt.

2 ‖ PF.PASS.PTCPL.ADJ. (of a man) shaven in part, with trimmed beard (as a sign of affectation) Archil.

ὑπο-παρωθέω *contr.vb.* (fig.) push aside in an underhand way, **sideline** —*a person* Is.

ὑπο-πάσσω *vb.* scatter (W.ACC. grass) **underneath** Hdt.

ὑπο-πεινάω *contr.vb.* **be half-starved** Ar.

ὑπόπεμπτος ον *adj.* [ὑποπέμπω] (of a messenger) **sent with intent to deceive** X.

ὑπο-πέμπω *vb.* **1** send (W.ACC. someone) **covertly** Th. X. Plu.; send a covert message X. Plu. ‖ PASS. (of a person) be sent covertly Lys.

2 send (W.ACC. someone) **with intent to deceive** X.

3 ‖ PASS. (of a dead person) be sent beneath —*the darkness of earth* E.

ὑποπεπτηῶτες (ep.masc.nom.pl.pf.ptcpl.): see ὑποπτήσσω

ὑποπεπτωκότως *pf.ptcpl.adv.*: see under ὑποπίπτω

ὑπο-πέρδομαι *mid.vb.* **fart in response** (to blows) Ar.

ὑπο-περκάζω *vb.* (of grapes) **gradually darken** Od.

ὑπο-πετάννυμι *vb.* spread (W.ACC. a cloth) **beneath** (a person, for him to sit on) Od.(tm.)

ὑποπετάσματα των *n.pl.* **things spread beneath** (persons, i.e. rugs or sim.) Pl.

ὑπο-πετρίδιος ον *adj.* [πέτρᾱ] (of dreams) perh. **in the shade of rocks** or **inside a cave** Alcm.

ὑπό-πετρος ον *adj.* [πέτρος] (of a region) **with a stony subsoil** Hdt.

ὑπο-πίμπλαμαι *pass.vb.* **1** gradually become full (of sthg.); begin to be filled —W.GEN. *w. an emotion or physical sensation* Pl. Plu. —*w. high-flown talk and speculation* Plu.; (of eyes) —*w. tears* Plu.

2 begin to have a full growth —W.GEN. *of beard* Pl.

3 (of a group of women) bear a large number (W.GEN. of children) **over the course of time** Hdt.

ὑπο-πίμπρημι *vb.* apply fire from below; **set fire to** —*persons* or *things* Hdt. Ar. Plu.

ὑπο-πίνω *vb.* **have a little drink** (of wine) Anacr. Ar. Pl. X. ‖ STATV.PF.PTCPL.ADJ. a little drunk Ar. Pl. X.

ὑπο-πίπτω *vb.* **1** (of props in a building) **collapse underneath** (a superstructure) Pl.

2 (of a person) **fall down in front** (of an animal) X.

3 (of an object) **fall under** —W.DAT. *the path of a wagon* Plu.

4 fall down (before someone, in a servile or obsequious manner); (fig.) **grovel** Ar. Pl. Plu. —W.DAT. *to someone* Is. D. Plu.

5 (of sailors, in small boats) **get in low and close** —W. ἐς + ACC. *to the oars of enemy ships* Th.

6 (of an individual, a people) **fall under the influence** or **control of** —W.ACC. *another* Aeschin. Hyp. —W.DAT. D.; (of Greece) fall —W. ὑπό + ACC. *under the control of Athens* Isoc.

7 (of a population) **succumb** (to an enemy) Plb. Plu.; (of individuals) **fall captive** Plb.; **fall victim** —W.DAT. *to ostracism, votes* Plu.

8 come in the way (of elephants, missiles) Plb. Plu. —W.DAT. *of the enemy, weapons, the impact of ships* Plu.; (of a ship) —*another ship* Plb.

9 ‖ STATV.PF. and PLPF. (of a region) lie close beneath —W.DAT. *mountains* Plb.; (of an area) lie close —W. ὑπό + ACC. *to another* Plb.

10 (of an idea) occur (to a person) Isoc.; (of need, opportunity, or sim.) **arise** Plb. ‖ NEUT.PL.PTCPL.SB. things arising or occurring, events or circumstances Plb.

—ὑποπεπτωκότως *pf.ptcpl.adv.* **submissively** —*ref. to addressing someone* Plb.

ὑπο-πιττόω *Att.contr.vb.* [πίσσα] seal (a ship) with pitch on the underside; (fig., w. sexual connot.) **caulk the underside of** —*a woman* Ar.

ὑπο-πλέω *contr.vb.* [πλέω¹] **sail in the lee of** —*an island* NT.

ὑπό-πλεως ων *Att.adj.* —**ὑπόπλεος** ον *Ion.adj.* [πλέως] **1** (of a person) **quite full** (W.GEN. of fear, hesitancy) Hdt. Plu.

2 quite loaded (W.GEN. *w. money*) Timocr.; (of an oracle-monger, w. prophecies) Plu.

ὑπό-πλους ου *Att.m.* [πλόος] **subterranean seaway** (ref. to a roofed channel) Pl.

ὑπο-πνέω *contr.vb.* (of wind) **blow gently** NT.

ὑπο-πόδιον ου *n.* [πούς] **footstool** NT.

ὑπο-ποιέω *contr.vb.* **1** (of behaviour) **gradually produce** —*a certain effect* Plu.

2 ‖ MID. bring under one's influence or control, **win over** —*persons* D. Arist. Plu.

3 ‖ MID. assume, take on —*the office and title of tutor* Plu.; affect, put on —*another's bold manner of speech* Plu.

ὑπο-πόλιος ον *adj.* [πολιός] (of a beard) **greying** Anacr.

ὑπο-πορεύομαι *mid.vb.* (of troops, boats) **proceed in secret** Plu.

ὑπό-πορτις ιος *fem.adj.* [πόρτις] **with a suckling calf**; (fig., of a servant-woman) **with a babe in arms** Hes.

ὑπό-πους πουν, gen. ποδος *adj.* [πούς] (of certain kinds of animals) having feet underneath, **footed** Arist.

ὑπο-πρίασθαι *aor.mid.inf.* perh. **purchase craftily** Thphr.

ὑπο-πρό *prep.* **immediately in front** —W.GEN. *of someone's feet* AR.

ὑπόπτᾱς *dial.masc.adj.*: see ὑπόπτης

ὑπό-πτερος ον *adj.* [πτερόν] **1** equipped with wings; (of doves, drone-bees) **winged** S. Pl.; (of Arabian serpents) Hdt.; (of supernatural horses) Pl.; (of the sun's bed) Mimn.; (of Perseus' feet) Ar.(quot. E.)

2 (of a person, body or back, in fantasy or sarcasm) **winged** (and thus able to fly) E. Ar. Pl.

3 (fig., of a ship) **winged** (ref. to its sails or oars) Pi.; (of love, likened to a bird) Pl.

4 (fig., of a victor's prowess, envisaged as raising him aloft) **taking wing** Pi.; (of a quarrel, envisaged as departing) E.

5 (fig., of a person) **flighty** (W.DAT. in thoughts) A.

ὑπ-οπτεύω *vb.* **1** view with suspicion, **suspect** —*a person* Hdt. S. Th. Plb. —(W.PTCPL. *of doing sthg.*) X. ‖ PASS. be

viewed with suspicion Th. X. D.; be suspected —W.INF. *of doing sthg.* Th.
2 view with apprehension, **be suspicious of** —*a situation, location, behaviour, or sim.* Th. X. D. Plb. Plu. ‖ PASS. (of a speech) be viewed with suspicion Th.
3 (intr.) **be suspicious** Lys. Plb. Plu.
4 (of a horse) **be nervous** or **wary of** —*sthg.* X. ‖ PASS. (of things) be regarded warily (by a horse) X.
5 (of a person) view with dislike, **look askance at** —*a situation* Hdt.; (of a wild animal) **look with suspicion** or **hostility at** —*hunters* Theoc.
6 be apprehensive about —*what is to happen* E.; **suspect** —*a trap* E.*fr.*
7 have a notion (based on conjecture), **assume, suppose, surmise, suspect** —W.ACC. + INF. *that someone is doing or will do sthg., that sthg. is or will be the case* Hdt. Th. Lys. Pl. X. Aeschin. + —W. μή + SUBJ. or OPT. Hdt. Th. Pl. X. Plb.
8 suspect —W.ACC. + COMPL.CL. *someone of being such and such* Hdt. —W.INDIR.Q. *who someone is, what is the case* Hdt. X. ‖ PASS. (of an effort) be suspected —W. μή + SUBJ. *of turning out to be great (i.e. it is suspected that it will turn out so)* Th. ‖ IMPERS.PASS. it is suspected (that sthg. is the case) X.
9 have a suspicion or inkling of —*sthg.* E. Pl. X. Arist. Plb. ‖ PASS. (of a conclusion) be imagined (before being proved) Pl.

ὑπόπτης ου, dial. **ὑπόπτας** ᾱ *masc.adj.* [ὑπόψομαι, see ὑφοράω] **1** (of a person, populace) full of suspicion, **suspicious** S. Th.
2 (of a horse) **nervous** X.

ὑπο-πτήσσω *vb.* | ep.masc.nom.pl.pf.ptcpl. ὑποπεπτηῶτες |
1 crouch or **cower beneath** —W.DAT. *a tomb* E. ‖ PF.PTCPL. (of young birds) cowering beneath —W.DAT. *leaves* Il.
2 cower E.; (tr.) **cower before** —*persons* X. —*the gods, their anger* A. —*a people's reputation* Aeschin.; **cower away from** —*battle* AR.(cj.)
3 bow down, show respect —W.DAT. *to someone* X.; **submit, surrender** —W.DAT. *to someone* Plu.
4 (intr.) **be cowed** Plu.; (of a boy) **be shy** X.

ὕποπτος ον *adj.* [ὑπόψομαι, see ὑφοράω] **1** (of persons) viewed with suspicion, **suspected** (sts. W.DAT. by someone) A. E. Antipho Th. X. +; (W.INF. of doing sthg.) Th. X.
2 (of speech, behaviour, circumstances) attracting suspicion, **suspicious** E. Th. X. Plu.
3 (of persons) having a suspicion; **suspecting** (W.GEN. an imminent catastrophe) E. ‖ NEUT.SG.PL.SB. suspicion (about someone or sthg.) E. Th. Plu.

—**ὑπόπτως** *adv.* **1** in a manner attracting suspicion, **suspiciously** Th. Plu.; (w. ἔχειν or διακεῖσθαι) *be suspected* —W.DAT. *by someone* Th.
2 in a manner showing suspicion, **with suspicion** Th.; (w. ἔχειν) *be suspicious* —w. πρός + ACC. *of someone or sthg.* Isoc. D. Plb. —W.DAT. X.

ὑπο-πτυχίς ίδος *f.* [πτύξ] **lower joint** (W.GEN. of a cuirass) Plu.

ὑπουργέω Ion.contr.vb., **ὑπόργημα** Ion.n.: see ὑπουργέω, ὑπούργημα

ὑπ-όρνυμι *ep.vb.* | 3sg.redupl.aor.2 ὑπώρορε | 3sg.pf. (tm.) ὑπὸ ... ὄρωρε | 3sg.plpf. (tm.) ὑπὸ ... ὀρώρει ‖ MID.: 3sg.aor.2 (tm.) ὑπὸ ... ὦρτο |
1 stir up, **arouse** —*a desire for weeping* (W.DAT. *in someone*) Hom.(tm.); (of a Muse) **arouse emotions** Od.
2 ‖ MID. (of a thud) **arise from beneath** —W.DAT. *the feet of men on the march* Il.(tm.); (of a desire for weeping) **arise** —W.DAT. *in someone* Od.(tm.)
3 ‖ PF. and PLPF. (of a noise, perh. of applause) arise in accompaniment (to dancing) Od.(tm.); (gener., of a din) arise Hes.(tm.); (of beauty) emerge (fr. the light of the moon) hHom.(tm.)

ὑπ-όροφος ον *adj.* [ὀροφή] (of a person, the sound of a voice) under a roof, **indoors** E.

ὑπο-ρράπτω *vb.* [ῥάπτω] underhandedly stitch together, **fabricate** —*a speech* E.

ὑπο-ρρέω contr.vb. [ῥέω] | aor.2 pass. (w.act.sens.) ὑπερρύην | **1** (of a spring) **flow at the base** (of a cliff) Plu.; (of a liquid) **flow from underground** —w. ἐκ + GEN. *out of the earth* Plu.
2 (fig., of a commander, envisaged as a river) **flow quietly on** (opp. be in full flood) Plu.
3 (fig., of error, corruption) **drift imperceptibly** (into a community) D. Plu.; (of lawlessness) —W.PREP.PHR. *into a person's character and habits* Pl.; (of poverty) —*into a city* Plu.
4 ‖ AOR.2 PASS. (fig.) drift over (in one's allegiance) —w. εἰς + ACC. *to a political leader* Plu.
5 (fig., of a legend) **be current** Pl.
6 (of props in a building) **slip out of position** Pl. [or perh. *give way underneath (a superstructure)*]
7 (fig., of the constituents of stable government) **gradually slip away** D.; (of time) **trickle away** Ar.
8 (fig., of a historian) **lapse, sink** —w. εἰς + ACC. *to another writer (i.e. to his level or into his manner)* Plu.

ὑπο-ρρήγνυμαι *pass.vb.* [ῥήγνυμι] | aor.2 ὑπερράγην | **1** (of the upper air, as clouds clear) **burst open below** (the heavens) Il.; (of the sky, as a prodigious event) Plu.
2 (of chasms) **break open** (in the ground) Plu.

ὑπό-ρρηνος ον *adj.* [ῥήν, ἀρήν] (of a ewe) **with a lamb beneath** Il.

ὑπο-ρρίπτω *vb.* —also **ὑπορριπτέω** (Plb.) contr.vb. [ῥίπτω]
1 throw down —*bait (fig.ref. to an inducement)* Plb.
2 throw (W.ACC. someone) **down before** —W.DAT. *elephants, the populace* Plu.
3 cast (W.ACC. oneself) **down before** —W.DAT. *a conqueror (in surrender)* Plu.
4 (fig.) **cast** (W.ACC. oneself and one's country) **down before** —W.DAT. *symbols of despotism* Plu.

ὑπ-ορρωδέω contr.vb. **be rather afraid of** —*sthg.* Plu.(quot.com.)

ὑπ-ορύσσω, Att. **ὑπορύττω** *vb.* **1 dig under** —*a wall* Hdt. Plb.
2 (fig.) **undermine** —*a peace-agreement* Plu.

ὑπ-ορχέομαι mid.contr.vb. **dance in accompaniment** (to music or singing) —W.COGN.ACC. *a particular dance* Plu.; (fig., of fear) **dance to the tune of** —W.DAT. *anger* A.

ὑπόρχημα ατος *n.* song accompanied by dancing, **dance-song** Pl.

ὑπο-σημαίνω *vb.* **1** indicate discreetly or subtly; (of persons or things) **hint at, suggest** —*sthg.* Th. Pl. Plu.; (of a word) **imply** (sthg.) Arist.
2 (of a trumpet) **sound** —*the signal for retreat* Plu. ‖ PASS. (of a call for silence) be sounded —W.DAT. *by a trumpet* Th.

ὑπο-σιγάω contr.vb. **keep silent in response** (opp. singing along w. others) Aeschin.

ὑπο-σίδηρος ον *adj.* (fig., of the child of a man belonging to the gold or silver caste in the ideal state) **alloyed with iron** Pl.

ὑπο-σιωπάω contr.vb. **keep suspiciously silent about** —*a sum of embezzled money* Aeschin.

ὑπο-σκαλεύω *vb.* stir up from beneath, **rake up** —*a fire* Ar.

ὑπο-σκάπτω vb. dig —a jumping-pit Pi.
ὑπο-σκελίζω vb. [σκέλος] cause legs to give way beneath, **trip up** —someone D.; (fig., w. words or sim.) Pl. D.
ὑπο-σκιάομαι pass.contr.vb. | ep.3pl. (w.diect.) ὑποσκιόωνται | (of fields) **begin to fill with shadows** —W.DAT. fr. rocks AR.
ὑπό-σκιος ον adj. [σκιά] **1** (of the lips of suppliants) **shaded** (prob. by veils) A.; (of a land) **put under shadow** (W.DAT. by a hail of stones) A.fr.
2 (of a place) **shady** Men. Plu.
ὕπ-οσμος ον Att.adj. [ὀδμή] **close upon the scent** (of an animal) S.Ichn.
ὑπο-σμύχομαι mid.vb. (of a blinded man's eyes) **slowly waste away** AR.
ὑπο-σπάω contr.vb. **1 drag** (W.ACC. bedclothes) **from under** (people sleeping on them) D.; **pull** (W.ACC. stools) **from under** —W.GEN. people about to sit down Pl.
2 snatch away, filch —a lamb (W.GEN. fr. a flock) E.
3 pull away —one's foot (W.DAT. in flight, i.e. take to one's heels) E.
4 ‖ MID. (of a horseman who has just mounted) **pull out from under oneself** —anything requiring it (i.e. bunched-up clothing) X.
ὑπο-σπείρω vb. **1** (of Eros) **sow** —a sweet harvest (W.DAT. in a heart's desire) Melanipp.
2 (fig., of a person) **subtly plant** —ideas, doctrines, or sim. (in people, communities) Plu.
ὑπό-σπονδος ον adj. [σπονδή] (of persons) **protected by a truce** Isoc. Plb.; (quasi-advbl., of troops withdrawing, persons travelling, or sim.) **under a truce** Hdt. E. Th. X. Aeschin. D. +; (of war-dead or wrecks being recovered) Th. X. Plb. Plu.
ὑπο-σσαίνω ep.vb. [σαίνω] **be soothing** or **reassuring** (in speech) AR.
ὑπο-σσείω ep.vb. [σείω] **spin** (W.ACC. a stake) **at its lower end** —W.DAT. by means of a strap Od.
ὑπο-στάθμη ης f. that which settles at a low level; **sediment** (W.GEN. of aither, ref. to water, mist and air) Pl.; (fig.) **dregs** (W.GEN. of Romulus, ref. to the Roman republican constitution, opp. the Republic of Plato) Plu.
ὑπόστασις εως f. [ὑφίσταμαι] **1** that which forms a foundation or basis, **groundwork** (of a historical narrative, ref. to introductory material) Plb.
2 capacity to put up resistance, **endurance, steadfastness** (of people) Plb.
3 thick soup Men.
ὑποστάτης ου m. **prop** (ref. to a forked support, Lat. furca) Plu.
ὑποστατικός ή όν adj. (of persons) capable of endurance, **hardy** Arist.
—**ὑποστατικῶς** adv. **firmly** —ref. to making a statement Plb.
ὑποστατός όν adj. able to be withstood or borne; (in neg.phr., of a city, ref. to its military strength) **resistible** E.; (of insolent behaviour) **bearable** Men.
ὑπο-σταχύομαι mid.pass.vb. [στάχυς] (fig., of cattle) app., grow like ears of corn, **gradually yield increase** Od.
—**ὑποσταχύω** act.vb. | iteratv.impf. ὑποσταχύεσκον | (of the down of a beard) **begin to sprout** AR.(dub., v.l. ἐπι-).
ὑπο-στεγάζω vb. (of Atlas) **support from below** —the earth and the vault of the sky (W.DAT. w. his back) A.(cj.)
ὑπό-στεγος ον adj. [στέγη] **1** (of possessions) beneath the roof, **inside** (a cave) S.
2 (quasi-advbl., of trouble, fig.ref. to a person, being taken in) **beneath one's roof** S.; (of Erinyes going) **inside** (W.GEN. a house) S.

3 (of a cave) covered with a roof, **roofed** Emp.; (of reservoirs) Pl.
ὑπο-στέγω vb. place under a covering, **cover up** —part of the body X.
ὑπο-στέλλω vb. **1** (of a wind) **draw in, furl** —a sail (i.e. cause a sailor to do so, fig.ref. to a host cutting back on entertainment) Pi.
2 ‖ MID. (fig.) shorten sail, **restrain** or **curtail oneself** —W.DAT. in speech E.; (gener., in neg.phrs.) **exercise restraint, hold back** (in speech) Att.orats. Pl. Plu.; (in behaviour) D. Plu.; **shrink** —w. τοῦ + INF. fr. declaring sthg. NT.
3 ‖ MID. **give way, give in** —w. πρός + ACC. to someone Din. —W.ACC. to someone's influence Din.
4 (of a commander) **station** (W.ACC. troops, oneself) **in concealment** or **for protection** —w. ὑπό + ACC. under a hill or sim. Plb. —behind others Plb. —W.DAT. in a place, behind others Plu.; (intr.) **take cover** —w. ὑπό + ACC. beneath a hill Plb.; **withdraw for safety** —W.DAT. to a place Plu. ‖ STATV.PF. (of a baggage train) have cover —w. ὑπό + ACC. behind troops Plb.
5 (of a ruler) **place** —himself (w. ὑπό + ACC. under the protection of others) Plb.; (of a populace) **shelter** (W.ACC. itself) **behind** —W.DAT. the military strength of others Plu.
ὑπο-στενάζω vb. **moan softly** S.; (of a person compared to a bull) **utter deep moans** S.
ὑποστεναχίζω vb.: see ὑποστοναχίζω
ὑπο-στένω vb. **1 moan softly** S.
2 moan in response (to news) Ar.
ὑπο-στολίζω vb. **furl** —a sail Lyr.adesp.
ὑπο-στοναχίζω (v.l. **ὑποστεναχίζω**) vb. (of the ground) **groan beneath** (men on the march) Il.
ὑπο-στόρνυμι vb. | aor. ὑπεστόρεσα | —also **ὑποστρώννυμι** | aor. ὑπέστρωσα | —also (impf.) **ὑποστρωννύω** (NT.)
1 spread (sthg.) beneath (someone); **spread out** —cushions (on seats) Thphr. —cloaks (W.PREP.PHR. on the ground) NT.; **strew** —laurel (w. ὑπό + ACC. beneath a corpse) Call. ‖ MID. **spread** —a mattress (W.DAT. for oneself) Thphr.
‖ PF.PLPF.PASS. (of an oxhide) lie spread beneath (a person) Il.(tm.); (of bronze, ref. to a cauldron) —W.DAT. food being cooked Hdt.(oracle); (of a priestess) have (W.ACC. laurel) spread as one's bed Call.
2 (of Zeus, in the form of a bull) **present** (W.ACC. his back) **as a seat** Mosch.
3 spread with coverings, **make up** —a bed or couch Od. Plu.; (euphem., of a woman) —a bed (W.DAT. for a man, by taking him as her lover) E.; (intr.) **make up a bed** Plu. ‖ MID. **have** (W.ACC. one's bed) **made up** —W.ADV. softly (i.e. w. soft coverings) X.; **strew one's bed** —W.GEN. w. herbs Ar.
‖ PF.PASS.PTCPL.ADJ. (of a couch) made up Plu.
ὑποστρατηγέω contr.vb. [ὑποστράτηγος] **be second-in-command** Plu. —W.DAT. to someone X.
ὑπο-στράτηγος ου m. [στρατηγός] **1** (in a Greek army) **second-in-command** X. Plb.
2 (in the Roman army) **legate** (as second-in-command to a praetor) Plu.
ὑπο-στρέφω vb. | PASS.: aor. ὑπεστρέφθην (Il.) | aor.2 ὑπεστράφην (S. X.) | **1 turn back, turn round** —one's horses Il. —one's step E.fr. —one's life (W.PREP.PHR. fr. Hades, i.e. return alive) E.
2 (fig., of ivy, worn by a dancer) **whirl** (W.ACC. a person) **around** —W.INTERN.ACC. in the rapid movement of a Bacchic dance S.
3 (intr.) **turn around, turn back** Hdt. Antipho Th. X. Aeschin. Plb. + ‖ MID.PASS. (of horses, hares) **turn around** Hdt. X.

ὑποστροβέω

4 (intr., also aor.pass., of troops, cavalry, charioteers) **wheel round** Il.(sts.tm.) Hdt. Th. X.
5 ‖ AOR.PASS. (of a person) **recoil, be startled** —W.GEN. *because of some concern* S.
6 (intr.) retrace one's steps, **go back, return** Od. E. NT. Plu. —W.ACC. *to a place* Il. —W.PREP.PHR. Od.(mid.) Hdt. AR. Plb. NT. Plu.
7 (intr.) **make an about-turn** (in attitude or behaviour) E. Ar.
8 (intr.) **shy away** (fr. a proposal, i.e. decline to accept it) X.

ὑπο-στροβέω *contr.vb.* (fig., of the agony of prophecy) **whirl around** —*a prophetess* A.(tm.)

ὑποστροφή ῆς *f.* [ὑποστρέφω] 1 **wheeling round** (of cavalry) Hdt.
2 (prep.phr.) ἐξ ὑποστροφῆς *with a turning-manoeuvre* (by a team of chariot-horses in a race) S.; *with an about-turn* (by a commander, troops, ships) Plb.; (by a current of water) Plb.; (of fortune) Plb.

ὑποστρώματα των *n.pl.* [ὑποστρώννῡμι] **bedding** (W.GEN. of a horse) X.

ὑποστρώννῡμι, also **ὑποστρωννύω** *vb.*: see ὑποστόρνῡμι

ὑπο-στύφω *vb.* [στύφω *contract, draw together*]
‖ PTCPL.ADJ. (of a seasoning) **somewhat astringent** Plu.

ὑπο-σῡρίζω *vb.* (of the air) **whistle softly** —W.DAT. *w. the beating of wings* A.

ὑπο-σύρω *vb.* **drag down** —*wagons* (W.PREP.PHR. *to a river*) Plu.

ὑπόσχεο (ep.aor.2 mid.imperatv.), **ὑποσχέσθαι** (aor.2 mid.inf.): see ὑπισχνέομαι

ὑπόσχες (aor.2 imperatv.): see ὑπέχω

ὑποσχεσίη ης *Ion.f.* [ὑπισχνέομαι] **promise** Il. Call. AR.

ὑπόσχεσις εως *f.* **promise** Hom. A. Th. Att.orats. Pl. X. +

ὑποσχήσομαι (fut.mid.), **ὑποσχόμενος** (aor.2 mid.ptcpl.): see ὑπισχνέομαι

ὑποσχών (aor.2 ptcpl.): see ὑπέχω

ὑποτάμνω *dial.vb.*: see ὑποτέμνω

ὑπο-τανύω *vb.* **lay out** (W.ACC. props) **beneath** (a beached ship) Il.(tm.)

ὑπο-ταράττω *Att.vb.* [ταράσσω] **harry** (W.ACC. someone) **into submission** (w. verbal abuse) Ar.

ὑπο-ταρβέω *contr.vb.* **be afraid before** —*one's enemies* Il.

ὑπο-ταρτάριος ον *adj.* [Τάρταρος] (of the Titans) **down in Tartaros** Il. Hes.

ὑποτάσεις εων *f.pl.* [ὑποτείνω] **low stretches** (W.GEN. of plain, ref. to an area beneath a mountain) E.

ὑπο-τάσσω, Att. **ὑποτάττω** *vb.* | aor.2 pass. ὑπετάγην (Plu., quot.com.) | 1 **make** (persons) **subordinate** (to others); **subjugate** —*a foreign ruler* Plb.; **make** (W.ACC. oneself or another) **subject** —W.DAT. *to someone* Plb. Plu. ‖ PASS. **be submissive, obedient or subject** (freq. W.DAT. to someone) Plb. NT.; **be subordinate** (to others, in rank) Plb.; **be cowed** Plu.(quot.com.) ‖ PRES. or PF.MASC.PL.PASS.PTCPL.SB. **persons** (esp. troops) **under one's command** Plb. Plu.; **subject peoples** Plb.
2 (of a philosopher) **subject** —*the compulsions of the physical world* (W.DAT. *to higher principles*) Plu.
3 **classify** —*certain people* (w. ὑπό + ACC. *under a certain title*) Plb.
4 **assign** —*regions of the earth* (W.DAT. *to the cardinal points*) Plb. —*causes* (to events) Plb.

ὑπο-τείνω *vb.* 1 **extend** (W.ACC. struts) **beneath** (cat-heads, on a warship) Th.
2 (of the creator god) **make** (W.ACC. vertebrae) **extend** (along the spine) Pl.
3 ‖ FEM.PTCPL.SB. **side extending beneath** (the right angle), **hypotenuse** (of a right-angled triangle) Pl.
4 **hold out, offer** —*a prospect, promise, hope, reward* (to someone) Ar. Isoc. D. Plu.; **hold out the prospect** or **promise** —W.PRES. or FUT.INF. *of doing sthg.* Hdt. Th.
5 **supply** —*arguments* (to someone) E.(tm.); (intr.) perh. **suggest an answer** (to a question or issue) Pl.(also mid.)
6 (of observation of self-inflicted sufferings) **lay** (W.ACC. pain) **deep inside** (the observer) S.
7 (intr.) perh. **strain, pull hard** (on a rope) Ar.

ὑπο-τειχίζω *vb.* **build a wall to subvert** (the purpose of an enemy wall), **build a counter-wall** Th.

ὑποτείχισις εως *f.* **counter-wall** Th.

ὑποτείχισμα ατος *n.* **counter-wall** Th.

ὑπο-τελέω *contr.vb.* 1 (of a city or country) **pay** —*tribute or sim.* (to a superior power) Hdt. Isoc. X. Plb. Plu.; (intr.) **pay tribute** Th.
2 **pay** —*a contribution* (W.DAT. *to one's parents, for their maintenance*) D.

ὑποτελής ές *adj.* 1 **subject to payment** (W.GEN. of tribute) Th. Plu.; **tribute-paying** Th. Plu.
2 (of persons) **subject to taxation** Plu.

ὑπο-τέλλομαι *pass.vb.* (of rattling of teeth) **result** (fr. boxers' punches) AR.

ὑπο-τέμνω, dial. **ὑποτάμνω** *vb.* 1 **cut low down or from below**; **cut** —*the base of a tree* Od.(tm.); **cut away** —*anchors, door-pivots* Plu.; (of a spear) —*a tongue* Il.(tm.) ‖ PASS. (of sinews) **be cut away** Aeschin.(quot. D.)
2 ‖ MASC.PTCPL.SB. **cutter of roots** (for use in magic) hHom.(cj.)
3 (of a cobbler) **cut** (W.ACC. leather) **in a deceptive way** Ar.
4 **cut off** or **intercept** —*another's sources of water* Pl. ‖ MID. **cut off** —*a route* Hdt. Ar. X. —*persons* X. Plu.
5 **cut short, curtail** —*another's hopes* X.; (mid.) —*sources of booty, plans, demands* Plb. —*time available* Aeschin.

ὑπο-τίθημι *vb.* | aor.1 ὑπέθηκα (E. +) | 3pl.athem.aor. ὑπέθεσαν (Pl. Aeschin.) ‖ MID.: aor.1 ὑπεθηκάμην (Hes. hHom. Hdt.) | athem.aor. ὑπεθέμην, imperatv. ὑπόθου, ep. ὑπόθεο (Od., cj. for ὑπόθεν) | Ion.3sg.opt. ὑποθέοιτο (Hdt.) |
1 **place underneath**; **place** (W.ACC. sthg.) **under** —W.DAT. or PREP.PHR. *someone or sthg.* Il.(tm.) Pl. X. Plb. Plu.; **place** —*a city* (w. ὑπό + ACC. *below mountain rivers*) Pl.; (of an animal) —*its hind legs* (under part of its body) X. ‖ MID. **place** (W.ACC. sthg.) **underneath** (oneself, one's shoes or clothing) Ar. X. Plb.
2 (fig.) **place** (W.ACC. a calm foot) **under** —W.DAT. *one's anger* (i.e. *go easy with it*) E.(dub.)
3 **lay** (W.ACC. oneself) **before** (someone, i.e. as a suppliant) Plu.; **place** (W.ACC. oneself) **under** —W.DAT. *a burden* (i.e. *take it upon oneself*) Plu.; **put** (W.ACC. one's country) **under** —W.DAT. *one's enemies* (W.PREDIC.ADJS. *as their slave and subject to their control*) Pl.
4 **classify** (W.ACC. sthg.) **under** —W.DAT. *a particular art* Pl.
5 **set** (sthg.) **before** (someone); **hold out, offer** —*hope* (sts. W.DAT. *to someone*) E. Th. X. D. Plu.; (of hope) **hold out the prospect of** —*success* Th.; (of success) **encourage** —*strength* (W.GEN. *of hope*) Th.
6 **set out, put forward** —*an argument* E. —W.COGN.ACC. *a proposal* X.
7 (pejor., of a god) **put forward surreptitiously or with subversive purpose**, **infiltrate** —*his arts* (W.DAT. *among people*) E.
8 ‖ MID. **put** (sthg.) **into** (someone's mind); **suggest, propose** —*sthg.* (freq. W.DAT. *to someone*) Hom. hHom. Thgn.

Hdt. Ar. Isoc. +; (intr.) **make a suggestion, give advice** (freq. W.DAT. to someone) Hom. Thgn. Hdt. Ar. Pl. Arist.
9 ‖ MID. (of a deity) give information or instruction about, **explain** —*a trick, one's rites* Hes. hHom.
10 set down as a foundation; **lay** (W.ACC. tree trunks) **as a foundation** (for towers) X.; **set down** (W.ACC. rhythms) **as a basis** (for tunes) Pl. ‖ MID. **lay down** —*a beginning* (*before moving on*) D.; (of a historian) **adopt** —*a historical event* (W.PREDIC.SB. *as the starting-point of a narrative*) Plb.
11 ‖ MID. (usu. of a speaker or disputant) set for oneself, **propose** —*a subject or goal* Att.orats. Pl. X. +; (intr.) have (sthg.) as one's subject or goal, **propose** Isoc. Pl. Aeschin. ‖ PASS. (of a subject or goal) be proposed Pl. Arist.
12 set down as a basis (for argument or conduct); **set down** (W.ACC. sthg.) **at the outset** (of a speech) And.(mid.) Aeschin.; **fix** (W.DAT. in one's mind) **at the outset** —*a particular question* D. ‖ MID. take as a basis (for one's conduct), **make it one's policy** —W.INF. *to do sthg.* Th.
13 ‖ MID. assume as a premise (to one's argument); **assume** —sthg. Pl. Hyp. D. —W.COMPL.CL. or ACC. + INF. *that sthg. is the case* Isoc. Pl. X. Arist.; (intr.) **make an assumption** Pl. Arist. ‖ PASS. (of things) be assumed (to be such and such) Pl.
14 put down (as a guarantee for a loan); **pledge** —*a security* Hdt.; **pledge as security** —*property, goods, oneself* (sts. W.DAT. *to someone*) Att.orats. Plu.(also mid.) ‖ MID. **take** (W.ACC. sthg.) **as security** D.; (intr.) lend money on security, **be a mortgagee** D. ‖ PASS. (of things) be pledged as security, be mortgaged D.
15 put down (as a stake); **stake, risk** —*one's life* Pl.; **face** —*personal risk* D.
16 perh. **put down surreptitiously** or **at the bottom of the bill** —*a sum* (W.GEN. *for hospitality*) Thphr.(dub.)

ὑπο-τῑμάομαι *mid.contr.vb.* (of a condemned man) **suggest a lesser penalty** (than a death sentence) X.

ὑποτίμησις εως *f.* **plea to be excused** (fr. accepting an appointment) Plu.

ὑπο-τίτθιος ον *adj.* [τιτθός] (of a child) **at the breast** Theoc.(v.l. ἐπι-).

ὑπο-τμήγομαι *mid.vb.* **cut off** —*routes* AR.

ὑπ-οτοβέω *contr.vb.* (of a reed-pipe) **sound** (W.ACC. a melody) **in accompaniment** A.(tm.)

ὑπο-τοπέω *contr.vb.* [reltd. τοπάζω] | *aor.pass.* (w.mid.sens.) ὑπετοπήθην (Hdt.) | **1** (act., mid., aor.pass.) **guess, imagine, suspect** —W.INF. *that one will be* (*or has been*) *treated in a certain way* Th. Lys. —W.ACC. + INF. *that someone is doing sthg., that sthg. is* (*or will be*) *the case* Hdt. Th. Ar. —W. μή + SUBJ. *that sthg. may be the case* Th.
2 (aor.pass.) **have a suspicion** or **inkling of** —*someone's intentions* Hdt.
3 (act.) be apprehensive of, **suspect** —*hostility* Th.; (mid.) —*evil intentions* Ar.
4 (act.) view with apprehension, **be suspicious of** —*a request* Plu.

ὑπο-τρέμω *vb.* **1** (of limbs) **tremble beneath** (a person) Hom.(tm.)
2 (of a person) **tremble a little** Pl.

ὑπο-τρέφω *vb.* **1** ‖ MID. **nourish within oneself** —*boldness* X.
2 ‖ PASS. (of desires) be nourished in secret Pl.
3 ‖ PASS. (of wonder) grow gradually Call.
4 ‖ PASS. (of a child) be brought up Plu.

ὑπο-τρέχω *vb.* | Aor. and pf. are supplied by ὑποδραμεῖν. |
1 run under —W.DAT. *falling rocks* Plu.; (fig.) **run for protection beneath** —W.DAT. *a statesman* (*envisaged as a tree giving shelter in a storm*) Plu.
2 (fig.) sneak under (a person's defences); **ingratiate oneself with, wheedle** —W.ACC. *someone* E. Pl. Aeschin. Plu.
3 (of emotions) **steal over** —*persons, their minds* Plb.
4 (of a notion) **occur** (to someone) Plb.

ὑπο-τρέω *contr.vb.* **1** (of persons, animals) **shrink back** (in fear) Il. Call. AR. —W.ACC. *before an enemy, a deity* Il. Call. —*at a display of an enemy's power* Plu.; (of doves) —*before hawks* AR.
2 shrink from —*burdensome tasks* Plu.

ὑπό-τρῑμμα ατος *n.* [τρῖμμα] **sauce made by grinding or grating** (app. w. pungent taste); (fig.phr.) βλέπειν ὑπότριμμα *give a look of piquant sauce* Ar.

ὑπο-τρομέω *contr.vb.* | *iteratv.impf.* ὑποτρομέεσκον | **1** (of limbs) **tremble beneath** (a person) Il.(tm.)
2 (of persons) **tremble** (in fear) Il.; (tr.) **tremble before** —*a warrior* Il.; (of animals) —*a goddess* AR.

ὑπότρομος ον *adj.* [ὑποτρέμω] (of a person) **trembling** Aeschin.; (W.DAT. in voice) Plu.; (of a voice) Plu.

ὑποτροπή ῆς *f.* [ὑπότροπος] **1** turning back, **repulse** (in a battle) Plu.
2 return (W.GEN. of past diseases, fig.ref. to political unrest) Plu.

ὑποτροπίη ης *Ion.f.* **retreat** (W.GEN. fr. a battle) AR.

ὑπό-τροπος ον *adj.* [τρέπω] **1** turning back, **returning** (esp. to one's home) Hom. hHom. AR.; (W.PREP.PHR. fr. battle) Il.
2 (of a homeward voyage) **returning** AR.
3 (of a lion) **rallying** (after a blow) Theoc.

ὑπο-τροχάω *contr.vb.* (of the R. Alpheios) **run beneath** —*the sea* Mosch.

ὑπό-τροχος ον *adj.* [τροχός] (of devices for conveying ships across land) with wheels underneath, **wheeled** Plb.

ὑπο-τρώγω *vb.* **1** eat in small bites, **nibble on** —*an onion* X.
2 (of a river) eat away from below, **undermine** —*a wall* Call.*epigr.*

ὑπο-τυγχάνω *vb.* meet (sthg.) with a response, **reply** Plu.

ὑπο-τυπόω *contr.vb.* **1** give a general impression of, **sketch out** —*the Good* Arist.; (mid.) —W.INDIR.Q. *what 'substance' is* Arist. ‖ PASS. (of peace terms) be sketched out Plb.
2 ‖ MID. (creator gods) **design in a rudimentary way** —*the growth of nails* (W.DAT. *in humans*) Pl.

ὑπο-τύπτω *vb.* **1** strike beneath (a surface); (intr.) **dip** (into a lake, well, chest of gold) —W.DAT. *w. a pole, wineskin, bowl* Hdt.
2 (of geese) **dig** (into clay) —W.DAT. *w. their feet* (*compared to shovels*) Ar.

ὑπό-τῡφος ον *adj.* [τῦφος] (of a manner of conversation) **rather pompous** Plu.(quot.)

ὑπο-τύφω *vb.* | aor.ptcpl. ὑποθύψας | (fig.) ignite into a smouldering fire, **incite** —*slander* Plb. ‖ PASS. (of a war) smoulder (before breaking out) Plu.

ὕπ-ουλος ον *adj.* [οὐλή] **1** beneath a scar (i.e. w. scar tissue covering a wound that is partially or superficially healed); (of a body, spleen) **festering inside** Pl. Plu.
2 (fig., of a soul) **festering** (w. the disease of wrongdoing) Pl.; (of cities, w. faction, envy, luxury, or sim.) Pl. Plu.; (of beauty, W.GEN. w. evil) S. ‖ NEUT.PL.SB. **festering sores** (W.GEN. caused by wealth) Plu.
3 (of places) **unhealthy** Plu.
4 (of persons) festering with resentment, **secretly hostile** Plu. ‖ NEUT.PL.SB. lurking hostility Plu.
5 (of law and order) **specious, phoney** Th.; (of a person's silence) **deceptive, insidious** D.

ὑπουράνιος

6 (of a flaw in a state, compared to one in metal) **beneath the surface** Plu.; (of mud) **soft under the surface, treacherous** Plu.
—**ὑπούλως** adv. **1 with lurking hostility** Plb. Plu.
2 in a hollow or **deceptive manner** Plu.
ὑπ-ουράνιος ον adj. [οὐρανός] **1** (of birds) **under the heavens, in the sky** Il.
2 (of fame) beneath the whole extent of heaven, **worldwide** Hom. Plu.
3 (of the vault of the sky, a journey) **under heaven** Pl.
ὑπουργέω, Ion. **ὑποργέω** contr.vb. [ὑπουργός] **1 render service** or **assistance** (sts. W.NEUT.PL.INTERN.ACC. in sthg.) Hdt. S. E. Th. Ar. X. + —W.DAT. *to a person, country, or sim.* Hdt. Trag. Th. Isoc. X. + —w. ἐς + ACC. S.; (phr.) ὑπουργεῖν χάριν *render a service in gratitude, do a favour* (W.DAT. *to someone*) A. E. Plu. ‖ NEUT.PL.PF.PASS.PTCPL.SB. *services* or *favours* Hdt.
2 (euphem.) **do a favour** (for a lover) Pl. X.
3 (of hands) **serve** —W.DAT. *a person* (W.INTERN.ACC. *in sthg.*) Antipho
ὑπούργημα, Ion. **ὑπόργημα**, ατος n. **service rendered, service** (to a person, city, or sim.) Hdt. And. X. Plu.
ὑπουργίᾱ ᾱς f. **1 rendering of service, service, assistance** S. X. Arist. Plu.
2 (euphem.) **favour** (granted to a lover) X.
ὑπουργός, ep. **ὑποεργός**, οῦ m. [ἔργον] **1 one who works under the direction or in the service (of another); assistant** (for a builder) Plb.; (W.GEN. of Athena, ref. to a craftsman) AR.
2 agent, henchman (of a person) Plb.
3 ‖ ADJ. (of inactivity) **conducive** (W.DAT. *to a certain physical state*) X.
ὑπο-φαίνω vb. **1 bring out into view** (W.ACC. *a stool*) **from under** —W.GEN. *a table* Od. ‖ MID.PASS. (of the feet of men and horses) **be visible under** —w. ὑπό + ACC. *gates* Th.
2 show a little of, give a glimmer of —*hope* (W.DAT. *to someone*) D.; **give a glimpse of** —*one's thigh, scars, cuirass, or sim.* Plu. —*personal qualities* Plb. Plu.; (of a helmet) **allow a view of** —*the eye* Plu. ‖ MID.PASS. (of a speck of cloud) be glimpsed Call.; (of personal qualities, the prospect of safety) Isoc. Plb.; (of ground for disagreement) begin to appear Arist.; (of streams) become visible Plu.; (of a particular facial expression) be shown Plu.
3 (intr., of dawn, daylight, spring) **begin to appear** Pl. X.(also mid.pass.) Plb.; (fig., of hopes) **dawn** Din.
‖ NEUT.PL.PTCPL.SB. *things becoming apparent* (in an argument, ref. to difficulties) Pl.
4 (of a calm sea) **reflect** —*the whiteness of teeth* Theoc.(dub.)
ὑποφατις dial.f.: see under ὑποφήτης
ὑπό-φαυσις ιος Ion.f. [φάω] **small amount of visibility, narrow gap** (W.GEN. betw. ships) Hdt.
ὑπο-φείδομαι mid.vb. **show some restraint** X.
—**ὑποφειδομένως** mid.ptcpl.adv. **somewhat sparingly** Plu.
ὑπο-φέρω vb. **1 carry from under** (a threat); (of feet) **carry** (W.ACC. *a person*) **to safety** Il.
2 place under; put (W.ACC. *a torch*) **under** (a bier) Plu.; **place** (W.ACC. *one's spear*) **under** —W.DAT. *a sword-stroke* Plu.
3 ‖ PASS. (of streams) **travel underground** Plu.
4 carry (by being under); (of soldiers) **bear** —*arms* X.; (of props) **support** —*a weight* Plb.; (of a pole) —*a legionary standard* Plu.
5 bear up against, endure, tolerate —*hard work, disasters, terrors, dangers, or sim.* Isoc. Pl. X. Arist. Plu. —*reproof* Plb.
6 bear the burden of —*public services, financial contributions, living costs* Isoc. X. D.
7 (of a city or people) **sustain, maintain** —*a war* Arist. Plb.
8 put up with —*persons, their behaviour* Isoc. X. Men. Plb.
9 cope with, be able to control —*one's anger* Pl.
10 hold out, offer —*a hope* S.; **propose** —*a truce* X.; **adduce** —*a festive period* (as the reason for a truce) X. ‖ PASS. (of a truce) be proposed X.
11 (of a river) **carry** (W.ACC. *a ship*) **down** —W.PREP.PHR. *to the sea* Plu. ‖ PASS. (of a person) be carried downstream Plu.; be carried down (a mountainside, on a sledge) Plu.
12 ‖ PASS. (of kings) be brought down or humbled Plu.; (of a city) —W.DAT. *by adversities* Plu.; (of a city, a form of government) decline, degenerate Arist.; (of a faction, a political or military cause) lose strength Plu.
13 ‖ PASS. be carried away or descend —W.PREP.PHR. *into a certain kind of behaviour or attitude* Plu.
14 ‖ PASS. (of a city, compared to a ship without a helmsman) drift along Plu.; (of the dates of festivals) gradually drift (later into the year) Plu.
15 perh. **gradually draw out** —*a tangled skein of spun yarn* (W.ADVS. *this way and that,* W.DAT. *w. spindles*) Ar.; (of an activity) **gradually lead** —W.PREP.PHR. *to a particular outcome* Plu.
16 ‖ PASS. (of fastenings in a knot) be turned over and under (one another) Plu.
ὑπο-φεύγω vb. **1 flee** (fr. a pursuer); **flee** or **escape from** —*enemies, Erinyes, an amorous god* Il. E. Plu.
2 escape, avoid —*death* Il.(tm.)
3 (of troops) **retreat** or **withdraw** Hdt.; **retire gradually** Plu.; (of a boxer) retreat a little, **give ground** Pl.
4 (gener., of persons, troops, ships) **take flight** Hdt. Th. X. Plu.
5 abscond (before one's trial) Pl.
6 evade —*a responsibility* Th.
ὑπο-φήτης ου m. [φημί] **1 one who speaks under inspiration** (fr. a god); **interpreter** (of Zeus' oracle at Dodona) Il.; (W.GEN. of a sea god) AR.; (of the Muses, ref. to a poet) Theoc.
2 interpreter (of the Muses, W.GEN. for others, ref. to a poet) Theoc.
—**ὑποφᾶτις** ιος dial.f. **purveyor** (W.GEN. of slanders) Pi.
ὑποφήτωρ ορος m.f. **inspirer** (W.GEN. of a song, ref. to a Muse) AR.
ὑπο-φθάνω vb. | aor. ὑπέφθασα | athem.aor. ὑπέφθην ‖ MID.: athem.aor.ptcpl. (w.act.sens.) ὑποφθάμενος ‖ For the constrs. of the vb. see φθάνω. |
1 get ahead of, outpace —*someone* AR. Plu.
2 do (sthg.) **before** (someone else); **get in first** (w. a spear, arrow, message) Il. AR. Plu.; (tr.) **anticipate** —*someone* (*in speaking*) Od.; **steal a march on** —*someone* (*in raising support*) Plu.
3 do (sthg.) **before** (sthg. else happens); **act in advance** Od. Plu.; (of the sun) **be earlier** (in its setting, than someone's departure) AR.
ὑπο-φθέγγομαι mid.vb. **1** (of a ventriloquist) **speak from deep within** Pl.
2 (of a statue) **speak in response** (to a prayer) Plu.; (of an apparition) —W.DAT. *to a questioner* Plu.; (of a dog) **growl in response** (to other dogs) Plu.
ὑπο-φθονέω contr.vb. **1 be somewhat jealous** or **resentful** X.
2 be secretly envious —W.DAT. *of someone* (W.GEN. *on account of sthg., i.e. begrudge his having it*) X.
ὑποφθόνως adv. [φθόνος] **somewhat jealously** X.
ὑπο-φοβέομαι mid.contr.vb. **be rather afraid** Men.

ὑπό-φονος ον adj. [φόνος] (of the pains caused by a poison) **secretly fraught with death** S.(cj.)

ὑποφορά ᾶς f. [ὑποφέρω] **putting forward, adducing** (w.GEN. of a festival, as a reason for a truce) X.

ὑπο-φράζομαι mid.vb. **observe** (w.ACC. someone) **with suspicion** AR.

ὑπο-φύω vb. (of the ground) **cause** (w.ACC. grass and flowers) **to spring up beneath** —w.DAT. *a pair of lovers* Il.(tm.) || PASS. (of a crop) **grow** Plu.

ὑπο-φωνέω contr.vb. **call out in response** Plu.; (of birds) **sing in response** (to others) Mosch.

ὑπο-χάζομαι mid.vb. | ep.3pl.redupl.aor.2 (tm.) ὑπὸ ... κεκάδοντο | **1** (of warriors) **shrink back, give ground** Il.(tm.)

2 (of Zeus) **step back in respect** —w.DAT. *for the Mother of the gods* AR.

ὑποχαλῑνιδίᾱ ᾱς f. [χαλῑνός] strap under a horse's bit, **chin-strap** X.

ὑπό-χαλκος ον adj. [χαλκός] (fig., of the child of a man belonging to the gold or silver caste in the ideal state) **alloyed with bronze** Pl.

ὑπο-χαράττω Att.vb. [χαράσσω] **carve** (w.ACC. an epitaph) **below** (another) Plu.

ὑπο-χάσκω vb. **open one's mouth a little** Ar.; (of a horse) X.

ὑπό-χειρ χειρος masc.fem.adj. [χείρ] **under the hand** (of one's enemies) S.(cj.)

ὑπο-χείριος ον (Ion. η ον) adj. **1 under the hand**; (quasi-advbl., of gold coming) **into one's hands** Od.

2 (quasi-advbl., of an enemy coming) **into one's hands, under one's control** Thgn.

3 under the control (of another); (of persons, peoples, animals, places) **under one's control** Hdt. E. Th. Att.orats. Pl. X. +

4 (of knowledge of arithmetic) **in one's grasp** Pl.

ὑπο-χέω contr.vb. | ep.3sg.aor. ὑπέχευε, also (tm.) χεῦεν ὕπο || PASS.: pf. ὑποκέχυμαι | plpf. ὑπεκεχύμην | **1 spread** (w.ACC. oxhides, brushwood) **beneath** (a person, to lie on) Hom.(sts.tm.) || PF.PASS. (of leaves) lie strewn —w. ὑπό + DAT. *under one's feet* Hdt.

2 || MID. (fig., of a statesman) **subtly infuse** —*scientific knowledge* (compared to a dye, w.DAT. *into his rhetoric*) Plu.

3 || PASS. (fig., of disbelief) **flood over, engulf** —w.DAT. *someone* Hdt.

ὑπο-χθόνιος ον adj. **1** (of persons) **beneath the earth** (i.e. in Hades) Hes. AR.; (of daimons) Pl.(quot. Hes., v.l. ἐπι-)

2 (quasi-advbl., of persons going) **beneath the earth** (i.e. to their deaths) E.

ὑπ-οχλέομαι pass.contr.vb. (of pebbles) **be disturbed** or **jostled below** (by flowing water) Il.(tm.)

ὑπό-χλοος ον adj. [χλόος] (of a cheek) greenish, **pale** Call.

ὕποχος ον adj. [ὑπέχω] **1** (of kings) **subject** (w.GEN. to the Great King of Persia) A.; (of human affairs, w.DAT. to the gods) X.

2 (of perjurers) **liable** (w.GEN. to utter destruction) D.

ὑπό-χρεως ων, gen. ω Att.adj. —also ὑπόχρεος ον (Plb.) adj. [χρέος] **1** subject to a debt; (of persons) **in debt** Ar. Plu.; (w.GEN. to others) Plu.; (of property) **mortgaged** Is.(v.l. ὑπέρ-) D. Plb.

2 (of persons) indebted, **under an obligation** (sts. w.DAT. to someone) Plb.; (w.DAT. for favours) Plb.; (w.GEN. for friendship and favours) Plu.; (of the populace, w.DAT. to the Senate) Plb.

ὑπο-χρίω vb. **1 smear the underside** (of bandages) —w.DAT. *w. gum* Hdt.

2 apply make-up to (w.ACC. a person) **underneath the eyes** X. || MID. **apply make-up under** —*one's eyes* X.

ὑπό-χρῡσος ον adj. [χρῡσός] **1** (fig., of the child of a man belonging to the bronze or iron caste in the ideal state) **alloyed with gold** Pl.

2 (of a ring) with a covering of gold, **gilt** Men.

ὑπο-χωρέω contr.vb. **1** (of persons, esp. combatants) **go back, withdraw, retire** Il.(sts.tm.) Hes.fr. Hdt.(oracle) Th. Ar. X. + —w.GEN. *fr. a place* Hdt. X.; (of a hunted animal) X.; (of water) Pl.

2 give way —w.DAT. *before an enemy* Pl. Plu.; **give way before** —w.ACC. *enemy ships* Th.; (of a river) **make way** —w.DAT. *for a commander* (i.e. allow his army to cross) X.

3 (of a person facing trial or sim.) **slip away, abscond** Th. Is. D.

4 back away from —w.GEN. *a throne* (w.DAT. *in deference to another, i.e. cede it to him*) Ar.

5 give in, yield (usu. w.DAT. to someone or sthg.) Th. Pl. D. Plu.

6 (of rowing) **give place** (to the use of sails, as soon as there is no wind) Pi.

7 (of a swollen river) go down, **subside** Plu.

ὑποχωρήματα των n.pl. bodily matter discharged from below, **faeces** Thphr.

ὑποχώρησις εως f. (in military ctxt.) **retreat** Plb.

ὑπο-ψαλάσσω vb. [ψαλάσσω **touch** or **pluck**, reltd. ψάλλω] **finger, paw** —*a person* (envisaged as a sacrificial animal being tested for plumpness) Ar.

ὑπό-ψαμμος ον adj. [ψάμμος] **with sand beneath**; (of earth) **with a sandy subsoil** Hdt.; (of a sea, lake) **with a sandy bottom** X. Plu.

ὑποψίᾱ ᾱς, Ion. ὑποψίη ης f. [ὑπόψομαι, see ὑφοράω] **1** apprehending of guilt or fault (in relation to persons or their behaviour), **suspicion** Hdt. E. Th. Att.orats. Pl. X. +; (w.GEN. of revolution, bribery, treachery, or sim.) Th. Plu.; (w.INF. of doing sthg.) D. Plu.

2 apprehensive notion (of a present or future possibility); **suspicion** (w.GEN. of a shortage) X.; (of the truth) Plb.; (w.COMPL.CL. or ACC. + INF. that sthg. is the case) Pl. X. D.

3 misgiving (about the correctness of an argument) Pl.

ὑπόψιος ον adj. (of a person) **looked at askance** or **with contempt** (w.GEN. by others) Il.

ὑπόψομαι (fut.mid.): see ὑφοράω

ὑπ-οψωνέω contr.vb. app. **buy tasty foodstuffs by underhand means** (perh. by outbidding others or jumping the queue) Ar.

ὑπτιάζω vb. [ὕπτιος] **1** (of a speaker) **lean back** (languidly and arrogantly), **have a laid-back manner** Aeschin.

2 || PASS. (of a person's head) **sink backwards** (w. tiredness) S.

ὑπτίασμα ατος n. **1 supine position** (w.GEN. of a corpse) A.

2 upturning (w.GEN. of hands, i.e. their palms, in prayer) A.

ὑπτιόομαι pass.contr.vb. (of a ship's hull) **be turned upside down, capsize** A.

ὕπτιος ᾱ (Ion. η) ον adj. [ὑπό] **1** (usu. predic., of a person or animal lying, falling, pushed or turned) **on one's back** Hom. Archil. Hdt. S. E. Ar. +; (of a statue) Hdt.; (prep.phr., ref. to swimming) ἐξ ὑπτίας *on one's back* Pl.

2 (of a horse-rider) **leaning backwards** (to keep his balance) X.; (of a stake) **sloping, at an incline** X.

3 (of the stomach of a person lying down) **upturned** E.Cyc.; (of a hand, i.e. w. palm uppermost) Ar. Plu.; (of a person's foot, when kicking, i.e. w. sole uppermost) Call.

ὑπωλένιος

4 (of persons) **upside down** (i.e. standing on their heads) Pl.; (of primordial creatures in motion) Pl.; (of an object reflected by a concave mirror) Pl.
5 (of a shield) **face-down** Th. Ar. X. Plb.; (of a cup, envisaged as a shield) **base-down** Ar.; (of a helmet) **upturned** A.; (of a wheel sawn in half) **inverted** (i.e. w. the curved side down) Hdt.; (of rowers' benches, in a capsized ship) **upside down** S.; (of a letter shape) X.
6 (of land) horizontal, **flat** Hdt.

ὑπ-ωλένιος ον *adj*. [ὠλένη] (of a lyre) **under one's arm** hHom.; (of a quiver) Theoc.

ὑπωμοσία ᾱς *f*. [ὑπόμνυμαι] 1 objection made on oath to an allegedly illegal or unconstitutional law or decree (w. an undertaking to prosecute the proposer), **sworn objection** D.
2 **sworn plea for postponement** (of a lawsuit) Hyp. D.

ὑπωπιάζω *vb*. [ὑπώπιον] 1 strike under the eyes || PASS. be given a black eye Ar. Arist.
2 (fig.) **wear out, browbeat** —*a person* (w. *persistent requests*) NT.

ὑπ-ώπιον ου *n*. [ὤψ] 1 area under the eyes || PL. (gener.) **face** Il.
2 bruising below the eye, **black eye** Lys. Ar. Arist.

ὑπ-ώρεια (also perh. **ὑπώρεα** Hdt.) ᾱς, Ion. **ὑπωρείη** ης *f*. [ὄρος] 1 (sg. and pl.) **foothills** or **lower slopes** (freq. W.GEN. of a mountain) Il. Hdt. Pl. AR. Plb. Plu.
2 **foot** (W.GEN. of a cliff) Plu.

ὑπώρορε (ep.3sg.redupl.aor.2): see ὑπόρνυμι

ὑπ-ωρόφιος ον (also ᾱ ον Pi.) *adj*. [ὀροφή] 1 (of persons) **beneath the roof** (W.DAT. of a person, as his guest) Il.; (of lyres, firelight) **indoors** Pi. AR.
2 (of a woman's bedchamber) directly under the roof, **upstairs** AR.(cj.) Mosch.
3 (of spiders, swallows) in the roofing, **under the eaves** Ar. Theoc.

ὑπ-ώροφος ον *adj*. 1 (of a house) surmounted by a roof, **roofed** E.
2 (of treasures) **beneath the roof** (of a shrine) Call.
3 (of a shout) beneath the roof (of a house), **indoors** E.

ὕρχη ης *f*. **transport-jar** (for pickled fish) Ar.

ὗς υός *m.f.* | acc. ὗν || PL.: nom. ὕες | acc. ὕας, also ὗς | gen. ὑῶν | dat. ὑσί, ep. ὕεσσι | —also **σῦς** συός *m.f.* | acc. σῦν || PL.: nom. σύες | acc. σύας, also σῦς | gen. συῶν | dat. συσί, ep. σύεσσι | swine (male or female, wild or domesticated), **boar, sow, pig, hog** Hom. +; (fig., ref. to an uncivilised person) Pi.; (to an aggressive person) Ar. Men.; (to a stupid person) Pl. Theoc. Plu.; (to an ugly person) Men.

ὑσγινο-βαφής ές *adj*. [ὕσγινον *crimson dye*; βάπτω] (of trousers) **dyed with crimson** X.

ὕσδος Aeol.m.: see ὄζος

ὕσθην (aor.pass.): see ὕω

ὑσμίνη ης, dial. **ὑσμίνᾱ** ᾱς *f*. | also dat. ὑσμῖνι (Il.) | **combat, battle, warfare** Hom. Hes. Mimn. B. AR. Theoc.; (concr.) **battle-line** Il.

—**ὑσμίνηνδε** *adv*. **into battle** Il.

ὕσπληγίς ίδος *dial.f*. [ὕσπληξ] **starting-line** or **gate** Ar.

ὕσπληξ ηγος, dial. **ὕσπλᾱγξ** ᾱγγος *f*. 1 perh. **starting-line** or **starting-gate** (for a chariot-race) Pl.
2 **snare** (for catching birds) Theoc.

ὕσσακος ου (unless **ὕσσαξ** ακος) *m*. [ὗς, perh. σάκος¹] | only gen.pl. ὑσσάκων | **piggy-bag** (ref. to a woman's genitals) Ar.

ὑσσός οῦ *m*. **spear, javelin** (equiv. to Roman *pilum*) Plb. Plu.

ὕσσωπος ου *f*. **hyssop** NT.

ὑστάτιος η ον *Ion.adj*. [ὕστατος] 1 (of cattle) furthest back (in a herd), **last** Il.

2 (quasi-advbl., of a person arriving) **last** AR.
3 (of old age) extreme, **uttermost** Bion

—**ὑστάτιον** *neut.adv*. 1 **at the last moment** Il.
2 **for the last time** Call.
3 **last of all, at the end** —*ref. to narrating sthg.* Od.

ὕστατος η ον *superl.adj*. [reltd. compar. ὕστερος] 1 **last** (in position); (of persons, cavalry, ships) **at the back** or **rear, hindmost** Il. Th. Pl. X.; (W.GEN. of a group) Il.; (of a rudder) **at the stern** (W.GEN. of a ship) A.
2 **last** (in a sequence of two or more); (of persons or things) **last** Hdt. Trag. Pl. D. +; (of a competitor) Is. D. || FEM.SB. **last day** (of a trial) Plu. || NEUT.PL.SB. **last part, end** (of a speech) Ar.
3 (quasi-advbl., of persons or animals arriving, doing or suffering sthg., of things happening) **last** Hom. A. Hdt. Ar. Isoc. Pl. +; (of ships putting out to sea) Hdt.; (prep.phr., litotes) οὐκ ἐν ὑστάτοις *not among the last* (i.e. *before anyone else*) E.
4 (quasi-advbl., of a person meeting w. his downfall) **at last, in the end** Pi.
5 **last** (in one's life); (of a sleep) **last, final** hHom.; (of a drink) Antipho; (of a day, journey, lament, words) Trag.; (of a person's end) S.
6 || SG.SB. (w.art., in same gender as GEN.) **last part** (W.GEN. of sthg.); ὁ ... ὕστατος ... τοῦ χρόνου *last part of life* A.; τῇ ὑστάτῃ τῆς ὁρτῆς *at the end of the festival* Hdt. [unless *last day*, as 2] | cf. λοιπός 2
7 (of an event) **latest, most recent** Hdt. Plu.
8 last in rank or importance; (of persons) **lowest, basest** S.

—**ὕστατον** *neut.sg.superl.adv*. 1 **for the last time** Hom. E. Pl. AR.
2 at the end of a series of actions, **last of all, finally** Hes. hHom. Thgn. AR.

—**ὕστατα** *neut.pl.superl.adv*. 1 **for the last time** Hom. Callin. Hdt. AR. Theoc.; (w.art.) Lys.
2 **most recently** Hdt.

ὑστέρᾱ ᾱς, Ion. **ὑστέρη** ης *f*. **womb** Hdt. Pl.

ὑστεραῖος ᾱ (Ion. η) ον *adj*. [ὕστερος] 1 (of a day) **later** (than the previous one), **following, next** Aeschin.
2 (of an event) **on the next day** Th. X.

—**ὑστεραίᾱ** ᾱς, Ion. **ὑστεραίη** ης *f*. **next day** Hdt. Th. Att.orats. Pl. X. +; **day after** (W.GEN. an event) And. Pl.; (w. ἥ or ᾗ or ᾗ ᾗ *the one on which sthg. happened*) Antipho Pl. D.

ὑστερέω *contr.vb*. 1 **be late** (in arriving) Hdt. Th. Pl. Aeschin. Plu. —W.DAT. *for someone* Th.
2 **arrive too late** —W.GEN. *for a battle* X. Plb. Plu. —*for a person* (i.e. *to meet him*) X. —*for a place* (i.e. *to save it*) Th. X.; **arrive later** —W.GEN. *than an agreed day* Hdt. —*than the appropriate time* (i.e. *miss it*) Plb. —*than ships* (i.e. *miss them*) Plb.; (gener.) **miss, avoid** —W.GEN. *sthg. dangerous* Plu.(quasi-oracular)
3 **fail to keep pace** (w. a fugitive) —W.DAT. *in one's pursuit* Th.; **lag behind** (on a journey) E.(cj.)
4 **be late** —W.GEN. *in taking action* D.; **act too late** E. D. Plb.
5 **be past** —W.GEN. *one's prime* Isoc.
6 **be inferior** (sts. W.GEN. to someone) —W.DAT. or PREP.PHR. *in some respect* Pl.
7 **be in need** NT.(also mid.pass.) —W.GEN. *of sthg.* NT.
8 (of wine) **run out** NT.
9 (of a personal quality) **be lacking** —W.ACC. *in someone* NT.

ὑστέρημα ατος *n*. **lack** (of money), **poverty** NT.

ὑστέρησις εως *f*. **lack** (of money), **poverty** NT.

ὑστερίζω *vb*. | fut. ὑστεριῶ | aor. ὑστέρισα | 1 **be late** (in arriving) Th. X. Men. Plu.; (of seasons) **come late** Plu.

2 (of a hunter's shout) **fail to keep pace** —w.GEN. *w. a hare* X.
3 be too late —w.GEN. *for action* (i.e. *fail to take it in time*) Isoc. D. —*for the appropriate time* (i.e. *miss it*) D. —*for everything, nothing* D. —w.DAT. *in giving help* D.; **act too late** or **too slowly** X. D. Arist.; (gener.) **be behind** —w.DAT. or ἐν + DAT. *in sthg.* X.
4 be past —w.GEN. *one's prime* Isoc.
5 be late in comprehension —w.GEN. *of sthg.* Arist.; (of comprehension) **come later** (opp. be instantaneous) Arist.
6 not be up to date —w.GEN. *w. affairs* Men.
7 (of an athlete) **be inferior** —w.GEN. *to a rival* X.
8 be unequal —w.GEN. *to an enemy* D. —*to a task* D.

ὑστερο-γενής ές *adj.* [γένος, γίγνομαι] (of a concept) **later in origin** (than another) Arist.

ὑστερό-ποινος ον *adj.* [ποινή] (of Ruin, an Erinys) **exacting belated vengeance** A.

ὑστερό-πους πουν, gen. ποδός *adj.* [πούς] (of a person) **stepping in too late** (to help) Ar.

ὕστερος ᾱ (Ion. η) ον *compar.adj.* [reltd. superl. ὕστατος]
1 later (in position); (of persons, troops, horses) **behind, at the back** or **in the rear** Od. Hdt. S. Th. Ar. X. +; **behind** (w.GEN. others) Th. Ar. Pl. X. +; (of feet) **following** or **lagging behind** E.
2 (of persons, in neg.phr.) **lagging behind** (a speaker's arguments, w.DAT. in understanding, i.e. keeping abreast of them) Th.; (of Erinyes, in neg.phr.) **slower** (w.GEN. than a ship, litotes for swifter than one) A.
3 immediately after (in a sequence); (of persons or things) **next** Thgn. Hdt. E. Th. Att.orats. +; (of an event) **subsequent** (w.GEN. to another) Th.; (of a day, to an event) X.
‖ NEUT.PL.SB. **subsequent events** E.
4 (specif.) **second, latter** (of two) Hdt. Antipho Ar. X. +
5 (quasi-advbl., of a person attacking) **next** Il.; (of a ship putting in) **after** (w.GEN. another) Th.
6 later (in time); (of persons) **later, future** E.; (of time, events, thoughts, words, or sim.) Pi. Hdt. Trag. Th. Ar. +; **later** (w.GEN. than others) Hdt. Th. ‖ MASC.PL.SB. **future generations** E.
7 (quasi-advbl., of persons or animals arriving, doing or suffering sthg., things happening) **later** Il. A. Hdt. S. Ar. +; (w.GEN. than others) Il. E.*Cyc.* Ar. Att.orats. Pl. +
8 (quasi-advbl., of a person arriving, bringing help) **too late** E. Th. Ar.; (w.GEN. for sthg.) Hdt. E. Ar. Pl.
9 (of a person) **late** (to learn sthg.) S.
10 later (in birth, i.e. younger) Il.
11 inferior (to another); **second** (w.GEN. to none, usu. w.DAT. in a particular quality) S. Th. Isoc. Pl. X.; (in neg.phr., w.GEN. to Zeus the Saviour) E.
12 lesser (in status); (of a politician) **taking second place** (w.GEN. to the laws) Aeschin.; (of a man's character, to a woman) S.; (of the body, in relation to the soul) Pl.; (of affairs, w. πρός + ACC. in relation to others) Th.; (phr.) ἐν ὑστέρῳ τίθεσθαι *regard* (sthg.) *of less importance* (usu. w.GEN. *than sthg. else*) Plu.
13 (prep.phrs.) ἐς (εἰς) ὕστερον **afterwards** Od. Hes. S. E. Pl. +; (also) ἐς τὸ ὕστερον Th.; εἰς τό γ' ὕστερον S.; ἐν ὑστέρῳ Th.; ἐξ ὑστέρης Hdt. | see also ἐσύστερον

—ὕστερον, Aeol. **ὕστερον** *neut.sg.compar.adv.* **1** later (in time) Hom. +; (w.art.) Th. Att.orats. Pl.; **after** (w.GEN. sthg. else) B. Hdt. Th. Ar. Att.orats. +; **later** (w. ἤ + CL. than sthg. happened) Th. Isoc. Pl. D.; (w.ACC. + INF.) Plu.; (quasi-adj.) Antipho + • οἱ ὕστερον *the successors* (of a person) Th. Pl. • τὰ ὕστερον γράμματα *the later inscriptions* Pl.

2 in second place (in importance) Pratin.
—ὕστερα *neut.pl.compar.adv.* **later** Od. S.*Ichn.* Call.

ὑστερο-φθόρος ον *adj.* [φθείρω] (of Erinyes) **bringing belated destruction** S.

ὕστριξ ιχος *m.f.* [perh.reltd. θρίξ] **porcupine** A.*satyr.fr.* Hdt. Call.

ὑστριχίς ίδος *f.* **bristle-whip** (used for punishing slaves) Ar.

ὑφ' *prep.*: see ὑπό

ὑφᾱγέο (dial.mid.imperatv.): see ὑφηγέομαι

ὕφ-αιμος ον *adj.* [ὑπό, αἷμα] **1** (of arms and wrists) **made bloody** D. [or perh. *bruised*]
2 (of a horse) **with bloodshot eyes** Pl.; (phr.) βλέπειν ὕφαιμον *give a bloodshot look* (as a sign of frenzy) Men.

ὑφαίνω *vb.* | ep.inf. ὑφαινέμεναι | iterativ.impf. ὑφαίνεσκον | fut. ὑφανῶ | aor. ὕφηνα, dial. ὕφᾱνα ‖ PASS.: aor. ὑφάνθην |
1 weave Od. Hdt. Ar. Pl. Plu. —*clothing or sim.* Hom. Hes. E. Ar. Pl. Call. Plu. —*a design* (in woven cloth) E. —*a headband* (fig.ref. *to a poem*) Pi.*fr.* ‖ MID. **weave** —*a cloak* Pl.; (of a spider) —*a web* X. ‖ PASS. (of clothing or sim.) **be woven** Ar. Arist. Plu.
2 (fig.) **weave, create** —*foundations* Call. —*buildings* (w.PREDIC.ADJ. *w. a pattern, fr. coloured stones*) Pl. —*a snare* X.(mid.) —*a song* B.; (of trees) —*a shady grove* (*w. their leaves*) Theoc. ‖ PASS. (of a honeycomb) **be woven** (by bees) X.; (of the spleen, so as to have a certain texture) Pl.; (of a story) Call.
3 (fig.) **weave, contrive** —*a trick, plan, or sim.* Hom. Hes. B. Ar. —*future happiness* Pi.

ὑφαίρεσις εως *f.* [ὑφαιρέω] **removal** (w.GEN. of conditions, fr. a treaty) Plb.

ὑφ-αιρέω Ion. **ὑπαιρέω** contr.vb. [ὑπό] **1 seize in response** (to some event); (of fear, trembling) **seize** —*someone* Hom.(tm.).
2 take from beneath; remove (w.ACC. props) **from under** —w.GEN. *ships* Il.(tm.); **take** (w.ACC. coral) **from under** —w.GEN. *the sea* Pi.; **remove** —*objects* (fr. *under a rock*) Plu.
3 take from under (the breast); **remove** —*a baby* (w.GEN. fr. *its mother*) Pl.
4 (gener.) **take away** (material or quasi-material things); **remove** —*a pillar, ladder, timbers* Plu. —*a club* (w.GEN. fr. *someone*) Plu. —*a source of income* Th.; (of war) —*the comforts of life* Th.; **cut off** —*supplies* Plu.; **detach** —*allies* (w.GEN. fr. *an enemy*) Th.
5 take away (non-material things); **take away** —*hope* Plu. —*time allowed for a procedure* Arist.; **curtail** —*idleness* (in others) Plu. —*aspects of one's behaviour* Plu.; **dispel** —w.PARTITV.GEN. *some suspicion* Th.
6 ‖ MID. **take away** for one's own advantage or by underhand means, **steal** —*a corpse, money, object, line of defence, or sim.* (sts. w.GEN. fr. *someone*) Hdt. Ar. Att.orats. Pl. X. +; (of hope) —(perh.) *thought* B.; (of a person) **stealthily remove** —*someone* (fr. *a gathering*) Ar.
7 ‖ MID. **rob** —*someone* (w.ACC. of sthg.) E. ‖ PASS. **be robbed** —w.ACC. of sthg. (w.PREP.PHR. *by someone*) Hdt.
8 ‖ MID. (intr.) **commit robbery, steal** Ar. D. Plu.
9 ‖ MID. **undermine** —*someone's judgement* E.
10 ‖ PASS. (of a person) **be removed** (by assassination) Hdt.
11 ‖ PASS. (of a word) **be shortened** (by removal of an element) Arist.

ὕφ-αλος ον *adj.* [ἅλς] **1** (of darkness) **in the depths of the sea** S.
2 (of a woman, on board a ship) **below the waterline** A.*satyr.fr.*; (of damage to a ship) Plb.

ὕφ-αμμος ον *adj.* [ἄμμος] (of a plain) **rather sandy** Plu.

ὕφανσις εως *f.* [ὑφαίνω] activity of weaving, **weaving** Arist.

ὑφάντης ου *m.* **weaver** Pl. Arist. Plu.

ὑφαντικός ή όν *adj.* **1** (of a person) **skilled at weaving** Pl. **2** of or relating to weaving; (of a κερκίς *pin-beater*) **for use in weaving** Pl. ‖ FEM.SB. craft of weaving Pl. Arist.
—**ὑφαντικῶς** *adv.* **in the manner of a weaver** Pl.

ὑφαντο-δόνητος ον *adj.* [ὑφάντης, δονέω] (of a garment) **weaver-agitated** (i.e. made by the weaver rapidly moving the shuttle to and fro) Ar.(mock-lyr.)

ὑφαντός ή όν *adj.* [ὑφαίνω] **1** (of clothing) made by weaving, **woven** Od. hHom. A. S. NT.; (fig., of warmth provided by clothing) Tim. **2** (of textiles) with an inwoven decoration, **brocaded** Th. Men.; (W.DAT. w. designs) E.

ὑφ-άπτω, Ion. **ὑπάπτω** *vb.* [ὑπό] **1** set on fire from below, **set alight, ignite** —*a building, city, pyre, or sim.* Hdt. E. Th. X. Plb. Plu. —*a person or corpse* E.*Cyc.* Th. Ar.; (intr.) **light a fire** Ar. ‖ PASS. (of a city) be set on fire E.; (fig., of insolent behaviour, compared to a fire) blaze up E. **2** (fig., of beautiful persons) **inflame** —*viewers* X. **3** ‖ PF.PASS.PTCPL. (of hounds) attached —W.DAT. *to leashes* X.

ὑφ-αρπάζω, Ion. **ὑπαρπάζω** *vb.* **1** seize furtively or by underhand means; **snatch up** —*an animal's young* Il.(tm.); **filch** —*objects, food* Ar. —*women's sexual rights* Ar.; (mid.) —*women's sexual partners* Ar. ‖ see also ἀφαρπάζω 3 **2** ‖ MID. **snap up** —*a piece of knowledge (envisaged as a morsel thrown to a dog)* Ar. **3 usurp** —*someone's place (at dinner)* X. **4 cut off** —*the remainder of someone's speech (by interruption)* Hdt. **5** (intr.) **interpose** (by giving an answer, before another can do so) Pl.

ὕφασμα ατος *n.* [ὑφαίνω] **woven cloth** Od. E. Pl. Plb.; (ref. to a robe) A. E. Pl.; (ref. to a tapestry) E.; (fig., ref. to a spider's web) A.

ὑφάω *ep.contr.vb.* ‖ ep.3pl. (w.diect.) ὑφόωσι ‖ (of women, on a loom) **weave** —*webs* Od.

ὑφειμένως *pf.mid.ptcpl.adv.*: see under ὑφίημι

ὑφ-είρω (unless **ὑπείρω**) *vb.* [ὑπό, εἴρω¹] **stick out** (W.ACC. one's hand) **furtively** or **from under cover** Ar.(cj.)

ὑφείς (athem.aor.ptcpl.): see ὑφίημι

ὑφεκτέον (neut.impers.vbl.adj.): see ὑπέχω

ὑφ-έλκω *vb.* **1 drag away** —*a corpse* (W.GEN. *by the feet*) Il.; **pull away** —*a yoke (fr. a wagon)* Plu. **2 drag out** (W.ACC. a person) **from underneath** (an animal) Ar.; **pull out** (W.PARTITV.GEN. some firewood) **from underneath** (a pot) Ar.; **draw away** (W.ACC. earth) **from underneath** (a mound) Th. **3** ‖ MID. **pull on** —*slippers* Ar.

ὑφέξω (fut.): see ὑπέχω

ὑφ-έρπω *vb.* (of resentful grief, an anxious feeling) **steal over** (a person) A.(tm.) S.; (of joy, trembling) —W.ACC. *a person* A.

ὕφεσις εως *f.* [ὑφίημι] **making concessions** Plu.

ὑφή ῆς *f.* [ὑφαίνω] **1 weaving** (as a craft) Pl.; **interweaving** (of gold and purple on a shield) Plu. **2 woven cloth** (ref. to a garment, tapestry) A. E. Pl.

ὑφ-ηγέομαι *mid.contr.vb.* [ὑπό] ‖ dial.imperatv. ὑφᾱγέο ‖ **1 lead the way** or **act as a guide** S. Pl. X. Theoc. Plu. —W.DAT. *for someone* E. Plu. **2** (of a horse) **go ahead** (of the man leading it) X.; (of hunted animals) **lead** (pursuers) —W.ADV. *in certain directions* X. **3 take the lead** or **initiative** (in an action) Th. Lys. **4** (gener., of gods, persons, abstract things) **point the way, lead on** A. Pl. Plu.; (tr.) point the way to or give some intimation of, **indicate, suggest** —*sthg.* Pl. X. Is. Arist. Plu. —W.INDIR.Q. *what is the case* Pl. **5** ‖ PF.PTCPL.ADJ. (of a principle) guiding Arist.

ὑφήγησις εως *f.* **1 guidance** (W.GEN. of lines, ruled by teachers for boys learning to write) Pl. **2 guidance, instruction** (W.GEN. given by someone) D. Plb.

ὑφηγητής οῦ *m.* **1 guide** (for a blind man) S. **2** (ref. to a past orator) **guide, model** (for an aspiring orator) Plu.

ὑφ-ηνίοχος ου *m.* **1 charioteer** (as subordinate to a warrior) Il. **2** perh. **under-coachman** X.

ὑφ-ήσσων ον, gen. ονος *compar.adj.* (of the Fate Atropos) **somewhat smaller** (in stature, than her two companions) Hes.

ὑφ-ιζάνω *vb.* **crouch under the cover of** —W.DAT. *a shield* E.

ὑφ-ίζω *vb.* ‖ Ion.aor.ptcpl. ὑπίσᾱς ‖ **1 set** (W.ACC. men) **in hiding** (for an ambush) Hdt. **2** (intr.) **crouch down** (in ambush) E.

ὑφ-ίημι, Ion. **ὑπίημι**, Aeol. **ὑπίημι** *vb.* ‖ Aeol.2sg. ὑπίης, dial.3sg. ὑφίητι (Theoc.) ‖ fut. ὑφήσω, Ion. ὑπήσω ‖ aor. ὑφῆκα (Plu.) ‖ athem.aor.: ptcpl. ὑφείς, Ion. ὑπείς, inf. ὑφεῖναι ‖ MID.: impf. ὑφιέμην ‖ aor. ὑφηκάμην (Plu.) ‖ athem.aor.: 3sg. ὑφεῖτο, ptcpl. ὑφέμενος, 1pl.subj. ὑφώμεθα, opt. ὑφείμην, pl.imperatv. ὕφεσθε, inf. ὑφέσθαι ‖ pf.mid.pass.ptcpl. ὑφειμένος ‖ PASS.: aor. ὑφείθην, 3pl.aor.imperatv. ὑφείσθωσαν (X.) ‖ pf.inf. ὑφεῖσθαι (Plu.) ‖ **1 let down, lower** —*a mast* Il. hHom.; (of an elephant) —*itself* (W.PREP.PHR. *to the ground*) Plu.; (of a Roman consul) —*his fasces* Plu. ‖ PASS. (of sails) be lowered Plu.; (fig., of the dignity of a magistracy) Plu. **2 put** (W.ACC. a stool) **under** —W.DAT. *someone's feet* Hom.(tm.); **throw** (W.ACC. a torch) **under** —W.DAT. *a pyre* Plu. ‖ PASS. (of cords) be put under —w. ὑπό + ACC. *the meshes of a net* X. **3 set** (W.ACC. a young animal) **under** (its mother, to be suckled) Theoc. —W.DAT. *its mother* Od.(tm.) Theoc. ‖ MID. **put** (W.ACC. a baby) **to suckle** —W.DAT. *at one's breast* E. ‖ PF.MID.PASS.PTCPL. (of children, envisaged as chicks) nestling beneath (their mother) E. **4 set in concealment, lay** —*an ambush* (sts. W.DAT. *for someone*) Plu. ‖ PF.MID.PASS.PTCPL. (of a snake) lurking in ambush (under a stone) S. **5 send secretly or with an underhand purpose; suborn** —*a person (to act as one's henchman)* S. Plu.; **send out** —*soldiers* (W.PREDIC.SB. *as bait,* W.DAT. *for an enemy*) Plu.; **send** (W.ACC. peacocks) **as a bait** or **bribe** —W.DAT. *to women* Plu. ‖ PASS. (of a woman) be set —W.PREDIC.SB. *as a bait* (W.DAT. *for someone*) Plu. **6 give up, surrender** —*one's body* (W.DAT. *to pain*) E. **7** ‖ MID. **give way, give in** (sts. W.DAT. to someone) X. Plu. —W.DAT. *to no one* (W.GEN. *in bravery*) Plu.; **yield** —W.GEN. *ground, victory, glory, or sim.* (sts. W.DAT. *to someone*) X. Plu.; **waive** —W.GEN. *one's rights* Plu. **8** make an admission or concession; **admit** —W.ACC. + INF. *that land belongs to someone* X. ‖ MID. **concede** —*a point (in argument)* X. —W.DAT. *to no one* (W.INF. *that he has had a happier life*) X. **9** ‖ MID. **leave, allow** —W.DAT. + INF. *someone to do sthg.* X.; **condone** —W.ACC. + INF. *someone doing sthg.* X. **10** ‖ MID. **submit, resign oneself** —W.INF. *to being deprived of territory* X. ‖ PF.MID.PASS.PTCPL.ADJ. resigned —W.INF. *to dying* E.

11 slacken —*a sheet* (*on a ship, so as to ease strain on a sail in high wind*) Scol. ‖ MID. **slacken off, ease off** —W.GEN. *on a sail* Archil.; (fig., of a person envisaged as a ship in a storm) **slacken sail** S. Ar. [or perh. **lower sail**]
12 let up, slacken off —W.GEN. *in one's course or running* Alc.; **relent** (in one's demands) Hdt. —W.GEN. *fr. one's anger, stubbornness* Hdt.; **flinch** —W.GEN. *fr. a task* E.(dub.) ‖ MID. **relent** —W.GEN. *fr. one's anger* Hdt. Plu.; **let up on, give up** —W.GEN. *a particular kind of behaviour or state of mind* X. Plu. —W.INF. *trying to do sthg.* X.
13 ‖ MID. **lower** —W.GEN. *one's tone of voice* Ar.
14 ‖ MID. (of spring water) **gradually lose** —W.GEN. *its coldness* Hdt.

—**ὑφειμένως** *pf.mid.ptcpl.adv.* **in a cowed** or **submissive manner** X.

ὑφ-ικάνω *vb.* (of trembling) **come over** —*a deer* Il.(tm.)

ὑφ-ίστημι, Ion. **ὑπίστημι** *vb.* | fut. ὑποστήσω | aor.1 ὑπέστησα, dial. ὑπέστᾱσα ‖ also MID.: aor.1 ὑπεστησάμην ‖ The act. and aor.1 mid. are tr. For the intr. mid. see ὑφίσταμαι below. |
1 place underneath (as a support); **set** (W.ACC. columns, bronze figures) **beneath** —W.DAT. *a porch, votive offering* Pi. Hdt.; **set** (W.ACC. posts, sticks) **as support** (for a structure) Hdt. X.; (fig., of a divine ordinance) **establish** —*an island* (W.PREDIC.SB. + DAT. *as a pillar for foreigners*) Pi.
2 lay down (sthg. non-material) as a foundation or support; (fig.) **lay down** —*wise precepts* S.; **give** (W.ACC. a pledge) **in support** —W.DAT. *to someone* A.(cj.) ‖ AOR.MID. (of a historian) set up as a basis (for one's narrative), **base oneself on** —*false and improbable premises, certain kinds of subject matter* Plb.; **introduce** —*events* Plb.
3 ‖ AOR.MID. **set** (W.ACC. a great man) **before oneself** (as a model or basis for one's conduct) Isoc.
4 post (W.ACC. persons) **in hiding** or **ambush** Hdt. X.; **lay** —*a trap* (W.DAT. *for someone*) E.
5 station (W.ACC. a ship) **opposite** —W.DAT. *the enemy* Plb. ‖ AOR.MID. **set** (W.ACC. one's way of life) **in opposition** —W.DAT. *to another's* X.

—**ὑφίσταμαι**, Ion. **ὑπίσταμαι** *mid.vb.*| also ACT.: athem.aor. ὑπέστην, dial. ὑπέστᾱν, Aeol.1pl. (tm.) ὑπὰ ... ἔσταμεν (cj.), ep.3pl. ὑπέστᾱν, 3sg.imperatv. ὑποστήτω, ep.3sg.subj. ὑποστήῃ (AR., cj.), opt. ὑποσταίην, ptcpl. ὑποστάς, inf. ὑποστῆναι | pf.: Ion.3pl. ὑπεστᾶσι, ptcpl. ὑφεστώς, Ion. ὑπεστεώς, ep.inf. ὑφεστάμεναι | plpf.: 3sg. ὑφειστήκει, 3pl. (tm.) ὑπὸ ... ἕστασαν (Pi.) ‖ AOR.PASS. (w.mid.sens.): ὑπεστάθην |
1 ‖ STATV.PF. (of columns) **stand as support** Pi.*fr.*; (of statues) —W.DAT. *for a building* Hdt.; (of posts) —*for platforms* Hdt.
2 (of a person) **take one's place below, submit** —W.DAT. *to someone* (*of higher rank*) Il. ‖ NEUT.PTCPL.SB. section (of milk) that settles below (the cream) Hdt.
3 act as a substitute (for another) Pl.
4 ‖ STATV.PLPF. (of armed men) **lie in ambush** —W.DAT. *for someone* E.
5 (in military ctxt.) **stand one's ground, offer opposition** or **resistance** Hdt. E. Th. Lys. X. Plb. +; (aor.pass.) E.; **oppose, resist** —W.DAT. *an enemy* A. Th. X.; **stand firm against, withstand** —W.ACC. *an enemy, weapons, attack* E. Th. D. AR. Plb. Plu.
6 (of a boxer) **stand one's ground** AR.
7 (gener.) **offer resistance** (to a proposal) X.; **stand up to, resist** —W.DAT. *calamities* E. Th.
8 give an undertaking, promise (sts. W.DAT. to someone) Hom. Hes. Th. AR. —W.COGN. or INTERN.ACC. *sthg.* Hom. AR. —*a gift or reward* Il. Theoc.*epigr.* —W.FUT.INF. *to do sthg.* Il. Hdt. E. Ar. Pl. X. +
9 promise to accept, agree to —*the smallest sum of money* Hdt. —*someone's demands* Hdt.
10 offer to undertake (a responsibility); **volunteer** Hdt. Lys. X. —W.PREDIC.SB. *to be a host, trierarch, khoregos, vendor* A. Lys. D.
11 give an undertaking to perform or endure (sthg. unwelcome or burdensome); **undertake, accept** —*a task, challenge, leitourgia, military command, or sim.* Hom. Alc.(tm.) Hdt. E. Th. Lys. +; **be ready to face** —*danger* Th. Isoc. D. Plu. —*a trial* Lys. —*the clamour of slanderers* Aeschin. —*ignominy and hostility* Plu.; (iron.) **take on** —*a passion* (*for someone*) E.; app. **endure** —*one's longing* (*for someone*) Theoc.
12 undertake, be prepared —W.PRES. or AOR.INF. *to do sthg.* Il. E. Isoc. X. D. Plb.; **consent** (to sthg.) Aeschin.
13 ‖ PF. (of resources) **be available** Plu.
‖ NEUT.PL.PF.PTCPL.SB. **business in hand** Plb.

ὑφόρᾱσις εως *f.* [ὑφοράω] **suspicious attitude** Plb.

ὑφ-οράω *contr.vb.* | dial.aor.2 (tm.) ὑπό ... ἴδον (S.*Ichn.*) | ep.iteratv.aor.2 (tm.) ὑπαὶ ... ἴδεσκον ‖ MID.: impf. ὑφεωρώμην | fut. ὑπόψομαι | aor.2 ὑπειδόμην |
1 look downwards Il.(tm.)
2 look askance at, glower at —*someone* S.*Ichn.*(tm.)
3 view with suspicion, be suspicious of —*persons* X.; (mid.) —*persons, behaviour, actions, situations* X. D. Plb. Plu. ‖ PASS. **be viewed with suspicion** Plu.
4 ‖ MID. (intr.) **be suspicious** Plb. Plu.
5 ‖ MID. **view with apprehension** —*one's circumstances* Is. —*a proposed course of action, future contingency, or sim.* Plb. Plu.
6 ‖ MID. **be apprehensive of, suspect** —*danger, unrest, or sim.* Th. Plu.
7 ‖ MID. **have a suspicion or inkling of, suspect, surmise** —W.INTERN.ACC. *sthg.* E. —W.ACC. *a person's plight* E.*fr.* —W.ACC. + PTCPL. *that sthg. is happening* E. —W.COMPL.CL. *that sthg. may be the case* Plb.

ὑ-φορβός, also **συφορβός** (and **συοφορβός** Plb.), οῦ *m.* [ὗς, φέρβω] one who provides fodder for pigs, **swineherd** Hom. Theoc. Plb. Plu.

ὑφ-ορμέω *contr.vb.* [ὑπό] (of boats) **lie at anchor undetected** Plb.

ὑφ-ορμίζομαι *mid.vb.* **come to anchor close to** —W.DAT. *an island* Plu.

ὕφος εος (ους) *n.* [ὑφαίνω] **woven cloth** S.*fr.*

ὑφόωσι (ep.3pl.): see ὑφάω

ὑφ-υδρος ον *adj.* [ὑπό, ὕδωρ] (quasi-advbl., of divers swimming) **underwater** Th.

ὑψ-αγόρης εω Ion.*m.* [ὕψι, ἀγορεύω] one who speaks loftily, **high and mighty speaker** Od.

ὑψαυχενία ᾱς *f.* [ὑψαύχην] **upright carriage of the neck** (of a horse) X.

ὑψ-αύχην ενος *masc.fem.adj.* [αὐχήν] (of a horse) with a long and upright neck, **high-necked** Pl.; (fig., of a tree, ref. to a long trunk) E.

ὑψ-αυχής ές *adj.* [αὐχέω] (of a girl, singing in praise of her homeland) **with deep pride** B.

ὑψ-ερεφής, ep. **ὑψηρεφής**, ές *adj.* [ἐρέφω] (of a building, room, cave) **high-roofed** Hom. Lyr.adesp. Ar.

ὑψ-ήγορος ον *adj.* [ἀγορεύω] (of speech, boasts) **lofty, haughty** A.

ὑψηλό-κρημνος ον *adj.* [ὑψηλός, κρημνός] (of cliffs) **lofty-cragged** A.

ὑψηλολογέομαι *mid.contr.vb.* [λόγος] **speak in a lofty style** Pl.

ὑψηλό-νους νουν *Att.adj.* [νόος] ‖ NEUT.SB. **high-mindedness** Pl.

ὑψηλός ή (dial. ά) όν *adj.* [ὕψι] **1** extending far upwards; (of mountains, trees, buildings, objects, or sim.) **high, tall** Hom. +
2 (of a person) **tall** Plu.; (pejor., of a hound) **long-limbed, lanky** X.; (of a nose) **high-bridged** (opp. snub) X.
3 (of a horse's hoof) **high** (relative to the ground) X.
4 having a high position (above the ground); (of mountain peaks, cities, regions, or sim.) **high up** Il. +; (of a roof, roof-beam) Od. A.; (of a platform or shelf) Od. ‖ NEUT.SB. **high position** Pl. X. Plu. ‖ NEUT.PL.SB. **highlands, high ground** Hdt. Pl. X. +
5 (of javelins) **pointing upwards** Plu.; (of God's arm) **uplifted** NT.
6 (of a harp) **high-pitched** Pi.*fr.*
7 elevated in status or prosperity; (of a person) **exalted** E.; (quasi-advbl., of a god, person or populace being raised, by good fortune or praise) **to a great height** E. And. Aeschin.; (of prosperity, by Fate) Pi. ‖ NEUT.SB. **exalted state** (of persons) NT.; (pl.) E.
8 elevated in quality or degree; (of fame, achievements) **lofty** Pi. Theoc.; (of athletic contests) Pi.; (of a mind) Pi.*fr.*; (of a skill) Pl.; (of a style of speaking) Plu.
9 (of a person) **high-minded** Plu.
10 (pejor., of a person) **high and mighty, haughty, arrogant** E. Pl. Men. Plu.; (fig., of words, compared to trees) **lofty** Plu. ‖ NEUT.SG.SB. **haughty demeanour** Plu.
—**ὑψηλά** *neut.pl.adv.* **1 high in the air** —*ref. to leaping* X.
2 (sts.pejor.) **loftily** —*ref. to thinking or speaking* Anacr. S.

ὑψηλό-φρων ον, *gen.* ονος *adj.* [φρήν] **1** (of a heart) **with lofty thoughts** E.
2 (of a person) **arrogant** Pl.

ὑψηρεφής *ep.adj.*: see ὑψερεφής

ὑψ-ηχής ές *adj.* [ὕψι, ἠχή] (of horses) **neighing proudly** Il.

ὕψι *adv.* **1 high up in the air, on high, aloft** Hom. Hes. hHom. AR.
2 to a high position, **high** —*ref. to raising, leaping, stepping in a dance* Il. hHom. AR.
3 out from shore —*ref. to anchoring ships* Il.

—**ὑψόθεν**, also **ὑψόθε** (Call. Theoc.), Boeot. **οὐψόθεν** *adv.*
1 from on high, from above Hom. Hes. Lyr. A. E. Pl. +
2 high up, **on high, aloft** Il. A. AR.
3 (as prep.) **above** —W.GEN. *one's brows* Pi.; **on top** —W.GEN. *of a headland* AR.

—**ὑψόθι** *adv.* **1** high up, **on high, aloft** Il. AR. Theoc.
2 at the top (of a bowl) Theoc.
3 to a high position, **high** —*ref. to raising, leaping, or sim.* Hellenist.poet.; (as prep.) **high above** —W.GEN. *a ship, cliff, the earth, or sim.* AR.
4 out from shore —*ref. to anchoring a ship* AR.

—**ὑψόσε** *adv.* to a high position, **high** —*ref. to raising, leaping, or sim.* Hom. AR. Mosch.

—**ὑψοῦ**, Aeol. **ἴψοι** *adv.* | *superl.* ὑψοτάτω (B.*fr.*) | **1** high up, **on high, aloft** Hom. B. Hdt. E. AR. Mosch.; (fig.) —*ref. to walking (i.e. enjoying greatness)* Pi.
2 to a high position, **high** —*ref. to raising, jumping, or sim.* Hes. Sapph. Hdt. AR. Plu.
3 (fig.) **to a height** —*ref. to exalting someone or sthg.* (by one's conduct or praise) Pi. Hdt.; **to a heightened state** —*ref. to rousing emotions* B.(superl.) S. AR.
4 out from shore —*ref. to anchoring a ship* Od.; **high up** (on dry land) —*ref. to beaching a ship* Il. hHom.
5 northwards —*ref. to sailing* AR.

ὑψι-άγυια ᾶς *fem.adj.* (of a city) **with stately streets** B.

ὑψί-βατος ον *adj.* [βαίνω] **1** (of cities) **set high** (i.e. in the hills) Pi.
2 (of a tripod-cauldron) **standing tall** S.

ὑψι-βρεμέτης ου (Ion. εω) *m.* [βρέμω] (epith. of Zeus) **high-thunderer** Hom. Hes. hHom. Ar.(mock-oracle)

ὑψι-γέννητος ον *adj.* [γεννητός] (of an olive branch) **tall-grown** A.

ὑψί-γυιος ον *adj.* [γυῖα] (of a sacred precinct, fig.ref. to a city) **with tall limbs, tall-timbered** or **towering** Pi.

ὑψι-δαίδαλτος ον *adj.* [δαιδάλλω] (of tripods) **tall and elaborate** B. [or perh. *decorated at the top*]

ὑψί-δειρος ον *adj.* [δειράς] (of a region) **high-ridged** B.

ὑψί-ζυγος ον *adj.* [ζυγόν] on the high bench (of the helmsman); (fig., epith. of Zeus) **seated in authority on high** Il. Hes. B.

ὑψί-θρονος ον *adj.* [θρόνος] (epith. of a Nereid, a Fate) **high-throned, august** Pi.

ὑψι-κάρηνος ον *adj.* [κάρηνα] (of oak trees) **high-topped, tall** Il. hHom.; (of a mountain glen) **high-peaked** Call.

ὑψί-κερως ων, *gen.* ω *adj.* —also **ὑψικέρᾱς** ᾱτος *masc.fem.adj.* [κέρας] | *acc.* ὑψικέρων, also ὑψικέρᾱτα, ὑψικέρᾱν | (of a deer) **with tall antlers** Od.; (of a bull) **high-horned** B. S.; (fig. of a mountain, i.e. w. high peaks) Ar.(quot. Pi.)

ὑψί-κομος ον *adj.* [κόμη] **1** (of a woman) **with hair tied high** Pi.*fr.*
2 (of trees) **tall and leafy** Hom. Hes. E.

ὑψικόμπως *adv.* [κόμπος] **in a proudly boastful manner** S.

ὑψί-κρημνος ον *adj.* [κρημνός] (of a city) **high on a cliff** A.

ὑψί-κροτος ον *adj.* [κρότος] (of dance-steps) **high-pounding** Tim.

ὑψί-λοφος ον *adj.* [λόφος] (of a mountain) **high-crested** Pi.; (fig., of speech) Ar.(v.l. ἱππόλοφος *horse-hair crested*)

ὑψί-λυχνος ον *adj.* [λύχνος] (of light) **from a lamp high above** Philox.Leuc.

ὑψι-μέδων οντος *masc.ptcpl.adj.* **1** (epith. of Zeus) **ruling on high** B. Ar. | see also μέδων, under μέδω
2 (of Mt. Parnassos) **of lordly height** Pi.

ὑψι-μέλαθρος ον *adj.* [μέλαθρον] (of a cow-shed) **high-roofed** hHom.

ὑψι-νεφής ές *adj.* [νέφος] (epith. of Zeus) **high in the clouds** Pi.

ὑψί-νοος ον *adj.* [νόος] (of violence) **arrogant** B.

ὑψί-πεδος ον *adj.* [πέδον] (of a dwelling-place) **on high ground, highland** Pi.

ὑψι-πετήεις εσσα εν *adj.* [πέτομαι] (of an eagle) **high-flying, soaring** Hom.

ὑψι-πέτηλος ον *ep.adj.* [πέταλον] (of a tree) **tall and leafy** Hom.

ὑψι-πετής ές *adj.* [πέτομαι] (of the vault of heaven) **high-flying, soaring** E.

ὑψι-πέτης ου, *dial.* **ὑψιπέτᾱς** ᾱ *masc.adj.* (of an eagle) **high-flying, soaring** Hom. Ar.(quot. S.); (of winds) Pi.

ὑψί-πολις εως *masc.fem.adj.* [πόλις] (of a citizen) **of a proud** or **prosperous city** S. [or perh. *exalted in his city*]

ὑψί-πους πουν, *gen.* ποδος *adj.* [πούς] (of laws, envisaged as begotten in heaven) **walking on high** S.

ὑψί-πυλος ον *adj.* [πύλαι] (of a city) **tall-gated** Il. Ibyc. B. Lyr.adesp.; (of a palace) E.

ὑψί-πυργος ον *adj.* [πύργος] (of a city, country) **tall-towered** Trag.; (fig., of hopes) **towering** A.

ὕψιστος *superl.adj.*, **ὑψίτερος** *compar.adj.*: see under ὑψίων

ὑψι-τέχνᾱς ᾱ *dial.masc.adj.* [τέχνη] (of Asklepios) **highly skilled** Lyr.adesp.

ὑψι-φανής ές *adj.* [φαίνομαι] (fig., of a person) **shining on high** (i.e. illustrious) B.

ὑψί-φρων ον, gen. ονος *adj.* [φρήν] (of mortals) with lofty thought, **arrogant** Pi.

ὑψι-χαίτᾱς ᾱ *dial.masc.adj.* [χαίτη] (of warriors) app. **with hair tied high** Pi.

ὑψίων ον, gen. ονος *compar.adj.* [ὕψι] (of a wall) **higher** Pi.fr.
—**ὑψίτερος** ᾱ ον *compar.adj.* (of oak trees) **higher, taller** Theoc.
—**ὕψιστος** η (dial. ᾱ) ον *superl.adj.* **1** rising to the greatest height; (of a mountain, wall, tower) **highest** A. Pi.fr. AR. **2** located at the greatest height ‖ NEUT.PL.SB. highest heavens NT. **3** most elevated (in status); (of Zeus) **highest** A. Pi. S. Theoc.; (of Poseidon) Lyr.adesp.; (of the goddess Health) Licymn.; (of God) NT.; (of a prize, reward) Pi. **4** most heightened in degree; (of fear of Zeus) **highest** (for mortals) A.; (of disasters) **greatest** (W.GEN. of disasters) A.

ὑψόθε(ν), **ὑψόθι** *advs.*: see under ὕψι

ὑψ-όροφος ον *adj.* [ὀροφή] (of a building or room) **high-roofed** Hom. E.(cj.) AR.; (of ships, W.DAT. w. decks, i.e. w. high decks) Plu.

ὕψος εος (ους) *n.* **1** quality of being high, **height** E. Pl. X. Plb. Plu. **2** distance from bottom to top (as a dimension), **height** A. Emp. Hdt. Th. Pl. +; (advbl.acc., sts. w.art.) *in height* Hdt. X.; (also) ἐς (εἰς) ὕψος Hdt. Plu. **3** high place, **height** Pl.; (ref. to heaven) NT. **4** (fig.) **height** (ref. to exalted status) E. **5** high degree, **height** (W.GEN. of a person's excellence) Plu.

ὑψόσε *adv.*: see under ὕψι

ὑψοτάτω *superl.adv.*: see ὑψοῦ, under ὕψι

ὑψοῦ *adv.*: see under ὕψι

ὑψόω *contr.vb.* **1 lift up** —a serpent NT. ‖ PASS. (of a person) be lifted up NT.; be elevated —W.PREP.PHR. *into heaven* NT. **2** (fig.) **exalt** —a person, oneself, a people Plb. NT. ‖ PASS. (of a person) be exalted NT.

ὕω, Aeol. **ὔω** *vb.* | fut. ὕσω | aor. ὗσα ‖ PASS.: fut. ὕσομαι | aor. ὕσθην | **1** (of Zeus, unspecified gods) **send rain** Hom. Hes. Alc. Thgn. Hdt. Ar. +; (of clouds) Ar.; (of Zeus) **rain** —W.INTERN.ACC. *gold* Pi. —*fresh water* (*every day*) Ar. **2** (of sea-spray) **rain down** Tim.(cj.) **3** ‖ IMPERS. it rains, rain falls Hes. Hdt. Ar. X. Arist. —W.ACC. *on a place* Hdt. **4** (of a rainstorm) **drench** —*a place* AR. **5** ‖ PASS. (of an animal, a place) be rained upon Od. Hdt.; (of a city) be drenched —W.DAT. *w. drops of blood* Plu.

ὑῶν (gen.pl.): see ὗς

φᾶ (dial.3sg.athem.aor.): see φημί
φαάνθην (ep.aor.pass.): see φαείνω
φαάντατος (ep.superl.adj.), **φαάντερος** (ep.compar.adj.): see φαεινός
φαγεῖν aor.2 inf. | aor.2 ἔφαγον, ep. φάγον | ep.inf. φαγέμεν, also φαγέειν | ep.3sg.subj. φάγῃσι, dial.3pl.subj. φάγωντι | also fut. φάγομαι (NT.), 2sg. φάγεσαι ‖ Other tenses are supplied by βιβρώσκω, ἔδω, ἐσθίω. |
 1 (of persons, animals) **eat** —sthg. Hom. hHom. Hippon. Pi. Ar. Pl. + —W.GEN. sthg., part of sthg. Od. A. E.fr. Pl. Arist.; (intr.) Hom. E.Cyc. Ar. Isoc. Pl. +
 2 (of guests) **feast on, enjoy** —hospitalities Od.
 3 eat up, consume, use up —a household's resources Od.
φᾱγός dial.f.: see φηγός
φάγος ου m. (appos.w. ἄνθρωπος) **glutton** NT.
φάε (ep.3sg.aor.2): see φάω
φάεα (ep.neut.nom.acc.pl.): see φάος
φαέθων ουσα ον ptcpl.adj. **1** (epith. of the sun, sts. personif. as Helios) **shining, radiant** Hom. Hes. Emp. S. E.; (of dawn) AR.
 2 (of utterances) **in the light of day** (opp. at night) S.
—**Φαέθων** οντος m. **1 Phaethon** (son of Eos and Kephalos) Hes.
 2 Phaethon (son of Helios and Klymene, who crashed his father's chariot) E. Pl. AR. Plb.
 3 Phaethon (a horse of Eos) Od.
—**Φαέθουσα** ης ep.f. **Phaethousa** (daughter of Helios) Od. AR.
φαεινός, dial. **φαεννός** (Sapph. Pi. Trag.), Att. **φᾱνός**, ή (dial. ά) όν adj. [φάος] | compar. φαεινότερος, Att. φᾱνότερος, ep. (w.diect.) φαάντερος | superl. φαεννότατος, Att. φᾱνότατος, ep. (w.diect.) φαάντατος |
 1 (of the sun, moon, stars, or sim.) **shining, radiant** Hom. Lyr. S. E. Pl. AR.; (of fire) **glowing** Il. Pl.; (of air, sky, aither) **bright, clear** Pi. E. Call.; (of a higher plane of existence) **full of light** Pi.; (of places) **well-lit** (opp. shadowy) X. ‖ NEUT.SB. light Pl. X.
 2 (of eyes) **shining, gleaming** Il. Pi. AR.; (of metal, esp. arms and armour) Hom. Hes. E. Ar. Call. AR.; (of amber, dew) **glistening** AR.; (of hair) **glossy** Il.
 3 (of dyed leather, helmet-plumes, furniture, or sim.) **bright, brightly coloured** Hom. hHom. Pl.; (of the appearance of sthg.) Parm.; (of garments, blankets) **dazzling** (fr. dye, or fr. being spotlessly clean) Hom. hHom. Ar. AR. ‖ NEUT.SB. bright colour (of an animal's fur) X.
 4 (of festivities, a happy life) **bright, sunny** (opp. gloomy) A. Pl.
 5 (of a person, an island, liberty, valour, or sim.) **splendid, illustrious** Pi. Pl.
 6 (fig., of statements, informed opinion) **enlightened** Pl.
 7 (of evil speech) **strident** Pi.

φαείνω ep.vb. | aor.pass. (w.diect.) ἐφαάνθην, also φαάνθην |
 1 (of the sun, dawn, sts. personif.; of lanterns) **give out light, shine forth** Od. Hes. Call. AR.; (fig., of Odysseus) **blaze** (w. fury or majesty) Od. ‖ PASS. (of eyes) shine, gleam Il.
 2 ‖ PASS. (of dawn, stars) shine forth, appear AR.; (of persons, gods, an island) be or become visible, appear (usu. W.DAT. to someone) Hellenist.poet.
 3 (tr., of a boy) **display** —spirit Call.
φάεσι (ep.dat.pl.): see φάος
φαεσί-μβροτος, dial. **φαυσίμβροτος**, ον adj. [φάω, βροτός] (of dawn, the sun, its beams) **shining on mortals, bringing light to men** Hom. Hes. Thgn. Pi. B. E.
φαεσφορίη ης ep.Ion.f. [φωσφόρος] **role of light-bearer** (awarded to Artemis, as lunar goddess) Call.
φαεσφόρος adj.: see φωσφόρος
φαθί or **φάθι** (imperatv.): see φημί
Φαίᾱκες, Ion. **Φαίηκες**, ων m.pl. | Ion.dat.pl. Φαίηξι, ep. Φαιήκεσσι | men of Phaeacia, **Phaeacians** (inhabitants of a mythical island named Scherie, later identified w. Corcyra) Od. Th. Call. AR. Plb.
—**Φαίηξ** ηκος Ion.masc.adj. (of a harbour) **Phaeacian** Call.
—**Φαιηκίς** ίδος Ion.fem.adj. (of women, the island) **Phaeacian** Call. AR.
φαιδιμόεις εσσα εν adj. [φαίδιμος] (of a people) **glorious, famous** Il.
φαίδιμος ον (also dial. ᾱ ον) adj. [reltd. φαιδρός] **1** (of Apollo's bow, Pelops' ivory shoulder) **gleaming, splendid** hHom. Pi.; (of horses, hair) **glossy** Pi.
 2 (of heroes, their limbs, or sim.) **splendid, mighty, glorious** Hom. Hes. Lyr. +
Φαίδρᾱ ᾱς, Ion. **Φαίδρη** ης f. **Phaidra** (wife of Theseus and stepmother of Hippolytos, w. whom she fell in love) Od. S.(title) E. Ar. Plu.
φαιδρό-νους ουν Att.adj. [φαιδρός, νόος] (of Clytemnestra) **gleeful** A.(dub.)
φαιδρόομαι pass.contr.vb. (of a person) **be amused, be gladdened** X.
φαιδρός ά όν adj. [reltd. φαίδιμος] **1** (of the sun's rays, the moon) **radiant, shining** A.; (fig., of the light of Peace) Pi.fr.
 2 (of gifts) **splendid** AR.; (of omens) **positive** Plu.
 3 (of persons, animals, their expressions) **beaming, cheerful** Trag. Ar. X. D. AR. Plu.; **jaunty** (in one's gait) X.; (of a horse's ears) **pricked up** Ar.; (quasi-advbl., of persons doing sthg.) **in a cheerful spirit** Plu.
—**φαιδρά** neut.pl.adv. **cheerfully** S.
—**φαιδρῶς** adv. **cheerfully** A. X.
φαιδρότης ητος f. **cheerfulness** Isoc.
φαιδρύντρια ᾱς f. [φαιδρύνω] **washerwoman, laundress** (W.GEN. of baby-clothes) A.
φαιδρύνω vb. [φαιδρός] | iteratv.impf. φαιδρύνεσκον |
 1 make radiant, wash clean, wash —a person, body A. Call.

φαιδρωπός

—*one's body, hair, clothes* E. AR. ‖ MID. **wash** —*one's body* Hes. Mosch.; (intr.) AR.
2 make (someone) beam; (of words) **gladden** —*someone* A. ‖ MID. (of a person) **brighten up** —*one's life* (*by fulfilling duties*) Pl. ‖ PASS. **be gladdened** (by sthg.) X.
3 touch up —*a painting* Pl.

φαιδρ-ωπός όν *adj.* [ὤψ] (of a lion-cub) **bright-eyed** A.; (of eyes) **glinting** E.

φαίην (pres. and athem.aor.opt.): see φημί

Φαίηξ *Ion.masc.adj.*: see under Φαίᾱκες

φαικάσια ων *n.pl.* shoes (app. white, worn by gymnasiarchs and Egyptian priests), **shoes** Plu.

φαῖμι *Aeol.vb.*: see φημί

φαινόλις ιδος *fem.adj.* [φαίνω] (of dawn) **shining, radiant, light-giving** hHom. Sapph. Mosch.

φαινο-μηρίς ίδος *fem.adj.* [μηρός] (of Spartan women) **thigh-flashing** Plu.(quot. Ibyc.)

φαίνω *vb.* | The vb. has two main usages: (i) tr. or causatv., in pres., impf., fut., aor.: *make appear, make shine*; (ii) intr., in mid.pass. and pf.act.: *shine forth, appear*. The intr. usages are given under φαίνομαι below. The pres., impf. and fut. act. can also sts. occur in the intr. sense, esp. in poetry.
‖ ACT.: dial.pres.inf. φαίνην (Alcm.) | fut. φανῶ, opt. φανοίην | aor. ἔφηνα, dial. ἔφᾱνα, inf. φῆναι ‖ MID.: aor. ἐφηνάμην ‖ PASS.: aor. ἐφάνθην |
1 (of gods, persons) **make visible, reveal** —*sthg.* (*to someone*) Pi. +; (of persons, animals) **expose** —*one's head, legs, or sim.* Od. +; (of water) **reflect the image of** —*sthg.* Th.; (of a youth) **show, display** —*maturity* (*on his cheeks*) Pi. ‖ MID. **display, show off** —*a weapon* (*to someone*) S.
2 (of persons, time, a household) **bring to light** —*sthg.* S. +; **reveal, expose** —*wrongdoers* S. Antipho; **denounce, report** (to the authorities) —*criminals, contraband, or sim.* Ar. Att.orats.; (intr.) **denounce people, be an informer** Isoc. X.
3 (of gods, persons) **make known, reveal, indicate** —*sthg.* (*to someone*) Od. +; reveal in words, **describe** —*events, one's thoughts, or sim.* Il. + ‖ PASS. (of statements) **be uttered** Il. S.
4 reveal by one's actions, **display** —*courage, anger, insolence, or sim.* Od. +; turn into visible results, **fulfil** —*fine words* S.
5 (of gods) **reveal, send** —*a portent* (*to someone*) Hom. Hdt. X.; **provide, supply** —*a wife, child* (*for someone*) Od.; (of a champion) —*material for a victory-song* Pi.; (of gods, persons, time, puberty) **bring about, produce** —*sthg.* Archil. +; (of a person) **perform** —*a song* Od.; (of a trumpet) **sound** —*its note* A.
6 (of leaders) **declare** —*a state of war* X. Plu. ‖ PASS. (of a state of war) **be declared** X.
7 cause to appear (to be); (of persons) **portray** —*someone or sthg.* (W.PREDIC.ADJ. *as such and such*) S.
8 cause to shine, kindle —*fire* S.; **brandish** —*torches* Ar.

—**φαίνομαι** *mid.pass.vb.*| fut. φανοῦμαι, Ion. φανέομαι, opt. φανοίμην | fut.2 φανήσομαι | aor. ἐφάνθην | aor.2 ἐφάνην, ep. φάνην, ep.3pl. ἔφανεν, also φάνεν, inf. φανῆναι, ep. φανήμεναι, dial. φανῆμεν, imperatv. φάνηθι, pl. φάνητε | aor.2 subj. φανῶ, ep.3sg. φανήῃ, Ion.3pl. φανέωσι | ep.3sg.iteratv.aor.2 φάνεσκε | pf. πέφασμαι, 3sg. πέφανται, also πέφαται (B. AR.), inf. πεφάνθαι, ptcpl. πεφασμένος | plpf. ἐπεφάσμην | fut.pf. πεφήσομαι ‖ also PF.ACT.: πέφηνα |
1 (of the sun, moon, stars, fire, torch-bearers, or sim.) **shed light, shine forth** Hom. Hes. S.; (act.pres., impf. and fut.) Od. Alcm. Ar. Pl. Theoc.
2 (of persons or things) **be or become visible, appear** Hom. +; **appear, turn up, show up** (in a place) Hom. Timocr. S. Pl. X.; (phr.) οὐδαμοῦ φαίνεσθαι *be nowhere to be seen* Pl. X.; (of persons, possible scenarios) *be nowhere in the running, get nowhere* Pl. D.
3 (of persons) **come into existence, be born** S.; (of winds) **rise up** Od.
4 (of an opportunity) **arise, appear** Hdt.; (of things) **be brought about, come about, happen** Il. S.; (of a task, fate, prize, or sim.) **be set, be ordained** (for someone) Hom. +
5 (of persons) **become** —W.PREDIC.SB. *a guide, commoner, trierarch* S. X. D.
6 (of persons or things) **be clearly seen to be, be shown to be** —W.PTCPL. *doing sthg.* A. +
7 be found to be, prove to be —W.PREDIC.ADJ. *tame, immortal, possible, or sim.* Thgn. A. S. Th. Pl. Plb.; **prove oneself to be** —W.PREDIC.ADJ. or SB. *good in battle, a skilful charioteer* Pi. Pl. —*a laughing-stock* Archil.
8 (of things) **be evident, be obvious** A.; (of deceit) **be revealed** Hippon.
9 (of persons or things) **seem** —W.INF. *to be sthg., to be doing sthg.* Od. +
10 seem to be —W.PREDIC.ADJ. *good, bad, or sim.* Hom. Archil. Thgn. E. X. —W.SB. *a good commander* X. —W.ADV. *in a certain condition* Pl.
11 (of a person) **appear to be, look like** —W.PREDIC.SB. *a beggar* Ar.; (of persons or things) **look** —W.ADJ. *unfamiliar* (*to someone*) Od.
12 (of examples of sthg.) **be apparent** (opp. genuine) Arist.; (of things) **seem to be the case** Pl. Arist. ‖ IMPERS. it seems so Pl.
13 (philos., of things) **seem to exist** Pl. Arist.; **be observable, have a detectable existence** Pl. Arist.
‖ NEUT.PL.PASS.PTCPL.SB. **phenomena** Arist.

—**πεφασμένως** *pf.pass.ptcpl.adv.* **manifestly, expressly** (in quot. fr. a law of Solon) Lys. Plu.

φαιός ά όν *adj.* **dark grey**; (of clothes, esp. those of mourning) **grey** Plb. Plu.; (of a person's complexion) **dark, swarthy** Plu. ‖ NEUT.SB. **grey** (ref. to the colour, as a mixture of white and black) Pl. Arist.

φαιο-χίτων ωνος *masc.fem.adj.* [χιτών] (of Erinyes) **wearing dark robes, grey-cloaked** A.

φαῖσθα (Aeol.2sg.), **φαῖσι** (Aeol.3sg. and pl.): see φημί

φάκελος ου *m.* **bundle** (of sticks, esp. for firewood) Hdt. E.*Cyc.* Th. Arist. Plu.

φακῆ ῆς *f.* [φακός] **lentil soup** Ar. Thphr. Men.

φακός οῦ *m.* (pl. and collectv.sg.) **lentils** (as food) Sol. Hdt. Thphr. Men. Theoc. Plu.

φαλαγγηδόν *adv.* [φάλαγξ] **in ranks, in close formation** —*ref. to troops charging or sim.* Il. Plb. Plu.

φαλάγγιον ου *n.* **venomous spider**; app. **black widow** Pl. X. D.

φαλαγγίτης ου *m.* **soldier in a phalanx, heavy infantryman** Plb.

φαλαγγιτικός ή όν *adj.* (of a cohort) **of infantrymen** Plb.

φαλαγγομαχέω *contr.vb.* [μάχομαι] (of troops) **fight against phalanxes** X.

φάλαγξ αγγος *f.* **1** (pl. and collectv.sg.) **rows, ranks** (of troops on the battlefield) Il. Hes. Tyrt. +
2 body of troops drawn up in ranks (opp. columns); **phalanx** (ref. to the heavy infantry, as the main body of an army) X. D. Din. Plb. Plu.; close-order formation, **phalanx formation** (assumed by troops, by a fleet) X.
3 (gener.) **area of ground occupied by a body of troops, encampment** or **lines** X.
4 log or **block** (of wood) Hdt.; **timber, spar** (fr. a ship) AR. ‖ PL. **rollers** (used to launch a ship) AR.
5 spider Ar. X. | see φαλάγγιον

φάλαινα f.: see φάλλαινα

φαλακρόομαι pass.contr.vb. [φαλακρός] (of men) **go bald** Hdt.

φαλακρός ά όν adj. [reltd. φάλαρος] (of a man, his head) **bald** Anacr. Hdt. E.Cyc. Pl. Plu. ‖ MASC.SB. **bald man** Hdt. Ar. Pl. Arist. ‖ NEUT.SB. (fig.) app., **phallus** A.satyr.fr. S.Ichn.

φαλακρότης ητος f. **baldness** (of a person) Plu.

φάλαρα ων n.pl. [reltd. φάλος] **1** parts of a helmet; perh. **metal plates** or **ridges** Il.
2 parts of a horse's headgear; app. **bosses** or **brasses** Hdt. E. X. Plb. Plu.
3 ‖ SG. **ridge** or **crest** (of a Persian tiara, indicating royalty) A.

φαλαρίς dial.f.: see φαληρίς

φαλαρῖτις ιδος fem.adj. (epith. of Athena) with a plate-metal helmet, **helmeted** Call.

φάλαρος ᾱ ον dial.adj. [reltd. φαλακρός] (of a dog) **white-headed** Theoc.; (as the name of a ram) Theoc.

φαληριάω Ion.contr.vb. | only ep.neut.nom.acc.pl.ptcpl. (w.diect.) φαληριόωντα | be **white-capped** Il.

φαληρίς, dial. **φαλᾱρίς**, ίδος f. white-headed bird; **coot** Ar.

Φάληρον ου n. **Phaleron** (harbour SW. of Athens, across the bay fr. Peiraieus) Hdt.

—**Φαληρόθεν** adv. **from Phaleron** Pl.
—**Φαληροῖ** adv. **at Phaleron** X. Plu.
—**Φαληρόνδε** adv. **to Phaleron** Th.
—**Φαληρεύς** έως m. man from Phaleron, **Phalerian** Lys. Pl. D. Plb. Plu. ‖ PL. **people of Phaleron** Hdt.
—**Φαληρικός** ή όν adj. **of** or **relating to Phaleron**; (of whitebait) **from Phaleron** Ar.; (of a marsh) **at Phaleron, Phalerian** X.; (of a wall, stretching fr. Athens to Phaleron) Th. Antipho ‖ NEUT.SB. **Phalerian harbour** Plu.

φάλης ητος (Ion. εω) m. [reltd. φαλλός] **phallus** Hippon. S.Ichn. Ar. Theoc.epigr.

—**Φαλῆς** ῆτος m. **Phales** (personif. of the phallic effigy carried in Dionysiac processions) Ar.

φαλιός ά όν adj. [reltd. φάλαρος] (of a bull) **white-headed** or **with a white blaze** (on its head) Call.

φάλλαινα (also **φάλαινα**) ης f. **whale** A.satyr.fr. Ar.

φαλλικόν οῦ n. [φαλλός] **phallic hymn** (sung to accompany the phallic effigy carried in processions) Ar. Arist.

φαλλός οῦ m. **phallic effigy** (carried in Dionysiac processions) Hdt. Ar.; (ref. to a phallic apparition which fathered Romulus and Remus) Plu.

φάλος ου m. part of a helmet; app. **metal plate** or **ridge** Il.

φᾱ́μᾱ dial.f.: see φήμη

φαμέν (1pl.), **φάμεν** (ep.1pl.impf. and athem.aor., also ep.pres. and athem.aor.inf.), **φάμενος** (pres. and athem.aor.mid.ptcpl.): see φημί

φᾱ́μις dial.f.: see φῆμις

φάν (ep.3pl.impf. and athem.aor.), **φάναι** (pres. and athem.aor.inf.): see φημί

φαναῖος ᾱ ον adj. [φανή] (epith. of Zeus) **light-giving** E.

φάνεν (ep.3pl.aor.2 pass.), **φανέομαι** (Ion.fut.mid.pass.): see φαίνομαι, under φαίνω

φανερο-μῑσής ές adj. [φανερός, μῖσος] (of persons) **open in showing hatred** (opp. concealing one's true feelings) Arist.

φανερός ά (Ion. ή) όν (also ός όν) adj. [φαίνω] **1** (of persons or things) **clearly visible** (sts. W.DAT. to people) Hdt. E. +; **for all to see, clearly present** (in a place) Hdt. S.; (of a route, view) **clear** Hdt. E.
2 (of justice, deeds, signs, opportunities, reasons, or sim.) **apparent, clearly evident, clear** Eleg.adesp. Hdt. S. E. +; (of conspirators, liars) **exposed, revealed** Hdt. Lys.; (of facts) **clearly established** Pl.; (prep.phr.) ἐπὶ φανεροῖς **on clear terms** (ref. to a meeting being convened) Th.
3 (of persons) φανεροί εἰσι + NOM.PTCPL. **they are clearly doing sthg., it is clear that they are doing sthg.** Hdt. Att.orats. X. ‖ NEUT.IMPERS. (w. ἐστί, oft. + COMPL.CL.) **it is clear (that sthg. is the case)** Isoc. Pl. X.
4 (of a spring) **uncovered** Th.; (of hatred, quarrels) **overt, unhidden** Th.; (of a vote) **open** (opp. secret) Th. Pl. D.; (of a person's death) **straightforward** (opp. murky) Antipho
5 (of a person) **open, transparent** (opp. crafty) Arist.
6 (prep.phrs.) ἐς τὸ φανερόν, ἐκ τοῦ φανεροῦ, ἐν τῷ φανερῷ **openly** Hdt. Th. +
7 (of assets, esp.ref. to property) **tangible, concrete, material** Att.orats.; φανερὰ οὐσία **real estate** Att.orats.; (of money, funds) **in ready cash** D.
8 (of a front-row seat at the games) **conspicuous, prominent** Xenoph.
9 (of a soldier) **conspicuous, distinguished** (for brave deeds) Th.; (of achievements, deeds, cities) **illustrious, famous** Pi. Th. X.

—**φανερῶς** adv. **1 plainly, openly, clearly** A. Hdt. S. +; **publicly, formally** Isoc.
2 seemingly, ostensibly Th.

φανερό-φιλος ον adj. [φίλος] (of a person) **open in showing friendship** Arist.

φανερόω contr.vb. **1** (of God, Jesus) **reveal** —sthg., oneself (sts. W.DAT. to people) NT.; **make known** —God's name NT. ‖ PASS. (of persons or things) **be revealed** NT.
2 ‖ PASS. (of a person) **become famous** —W.DAT. for sthg. Hdt.

φανή ῆς f. [φαίνω] **1 torch** Hes.fr.
2 ‖ PL. **torchlight rituals** E.

φάνεσκε (3sg.iteratv.aor.2 pass.), **φανέωσι** (Ion.3pl.aor.2 pass.subj.): see φαίνομαι, under φαίνω

φανήη (ep.3sg.aor.2 pass.subj.), **φάνηθι** (aor.2 pass.imperatv.), **φανήμεν** and **φανήμεναι** (dial. and ep.aor.2 pass.inf.), **φάνην** (ep.aor.2 pass.), **φανῆναι** (ep.aor.2 pass.inf.), **φανήσομαι** (fut.2 pass.), **φάνητε** (2pl.aor.2 pass.imperatv.), **φανοίμην** (fut.mid.pass.opt.): see φαίνομαι, under φαίνω

φανοίην (fut.opt.): see φαίνω

φᾱνός[1] Att.adj., **φᾱνότερος** (compar.), **φᾱνότατος** (superl.): see φαεινός

φᾱνός[2] οῦ m. [φαίνω] **torch** Ar. X. Men. NT. Plu.

φανοῦμαι (fut.mid.pass.): see φαίνομαι, under φαίνω

φαντάζομαι pass.vb. | Megar. φαντάδδομαι (Ar.) |
1 (of persons, objects) **be** or **become visible** (sts. W.DAT. to someone) Hdt. E. Pl.; (of visions, gods) **show oneself, appear** (sts. W.DAT. to someone) Hdt. Pl.; (of persons) **appear, turn up** (in a certain place) E. Men.; (in a certain category or area of investigation) Pl.
2 (of examples) **be apparent** Pl.; (of ghostly groans) **be heard** AR.
3 (of a seller of contraband) **be exposed** Ar.
4 (of proud beings) be conspicuous, **show off** Hdt.
5 (of persons or things) **appear** (to the eye), **seem** (to be) —W.PREDIC.ADJ. the same, different, in a particular condition E. Pl.; **appear** (to the mind), **seem** (to be) —W.PREDIC.ADJ. of a particular nature Pl.
6 (of an apparition) **take the form** —W.DAT. of someone A.

φαντασίᾱ ᾱς f. **1 forming of images** (in the mind), **imagining, visualising** Pl. Arist. Plu.
2 mental picture, image (as a product of the imagination, sts. in a poem) Arist. Plu.

φάντασις

3 form in which a person or thing appears, **physical appearance, look** (of a person, animal, river) Plb.
4 **image, likeness, semblance** (of sthg.) Pl. Arist.; **vision** (sent by god) Pl.
5 **impression, appearance** (of sthg., whether true or false) Pl. Arist. Plb. Plu.
6 **public image, reputation** Plb.; **good reputation, esteem** Plb.
7 **pomp, ceremoniousness** NT.; **ostentation** Plb.

φάντασις εως f. **supernatural manifestation** (ref. to apparitions or sim., seen by a soothsayer) Pl.

φάντασμα ατος n. 1 **likeness** (of a person), **apparition, phantom, spectre** A. E. Pl. NT. Plu.; **vision seen in a dream, dream** Arist. Theoc.
2 **image, likeness** (esp.ref. to a reflection, painting, or sim.) Pl.
3 **appearance, semblance** or **illusion** (of an object, opp. an image, ref. to the product of certain arts) Pl.
4 **mental image, impression** (of sthg.) Pl. Arist.

φανταστικός ή όν adj. 1 (of the art) of **being able to create semblances** (of things), **of illusions, of impressions** Pl.
2 || NEUT.SB. **imagination** (as the part of the mind which creates images of sensations or sim.) Plu.

φαντί (dial.3pl.), **φάντο** (ep.3pl.impf. and athem.aor.mid.), **φάο** (2sg.pres. and athem.aor.mid.imperatv.): see φημί
φανῶ (fut. and aor.2 pass.subj.): see φαίνω
φάος, dial. **φῶς**, ep. (w.diect.) **φόως**, φάεος (φάους) n. | dat. φάει | nom.acc.pl. φάη, ep. φάεα (ᾱ *metri grat.*) | ep.dat.pl. φαέεσσι, also φάεσι | —also **φῶς** φωτός Att.n. | dat. φωτί |
1 **light** (of day), **daylight** Hom. +; (in phr. *to see the light of day* or sim., ref. to being alive) Hom. +
2 **broad daylight** (w.connot. of full public view) S. E. X.
3 (prep.phr.) ἐς φάος *into existence,* (*back*) *to life* Hes. Archil. Pi. B. Trag. +; (also) *into sight* Hes.; *into the public sphere* Pi.
4 **period of daylight, day** Trag.
5 **light** (of the moon, stars, or sim.) Hes.*fr.* Pi. +; (concr., ref. to the moon) Parm.
6 **light** (fr. torches, fires, or sim.) Od. Alc. Hdt. Trag. X.
7 **light, torch, lamp** Od. +
8 (fig.) **brilliance, splendour** Alcm.; **shining light** (of victory, deliverance, hope, joy, valour, or sim.) Il. Lyr. Trag.; (ref. to persons) Hom. Anacr. Pi. Trag.; (ref. to God) NT.; (ref. to spiritual illumination, the light of truth) NT.
9 **light, gleam** (of a person's eyes, ref. to their gaze) Pi.
10 (usu.pl.) **eye** Od. E.*Cyc.* Call. Mosch.

—**φόωσδε** (sts. written **φόως δέ**) ep.adv. **into the light of day, into the world** (usu. fr. the womb, or fr. the underworld) Hom. Hes. hHom.

φαραγγώδης ες adj. [φάραγξ] (of a river) **passing through a ravine** Plb.

φάραγξ αγγος f. 1 **ravine, gully** Alcm. E. Th. X. D. +
2 **cave** (in a mountain) E.*Cyc.*
3 **crag, cliff-face** A. E.
4 (fig., ref. to an embezzler) **bottomless pit** Ar.

φαρέτρα ᾱς, Ion. **φαρέτρη** ης f. [φέρω] **carrying-case, quiver** (for arrows) Hom. +

φαρετρεών ῶνος m. **quiver** Hdt.

φαρέτριον ου n. [dimin. φαρέτρᾱ] **miniature quiver** (carried by Eros) Mosch.

φαρκίς ίδος f. **wrinkle** Simon.

φαρμακάω contr.vb. [φάρμακον] **be drugged** (opp. be in sound mind) D.

φαρμακείᾱ ᾱς f. [φαρμακεύω] 1 **administering of drugs, medication** Pl. X. Arist. Plu.; **medical treatment, therapy** (ref. to exercise) Arist.
2 **poisoning** Pl. D. Arist. Men. +; (concr.) **poison** Plu.
3 **state of bewitchment** or **distraction** (afflicting a nation in crisis) Plb.

φαρμακεύς έως m. [φάρμακον] **maker of potions** S.; **sorcerer** Pl.; **poisoner** Plu.

φαρμάκευσις εως f. [φαρμακεύω] **casting of spells, witchcraft** Pl.

φαρμακευτικός ή όν adj. (of a branch of medicine) **relating to the use of drugs** Plb.; (of purging) **by means of drugs** Pl.

φαρμακεύτρια ᾱς f. **woman who casts a love-spell** Theoc.(title)

φαρμακεύω vb. [φαρμακεύς] 1 **administer medicine** (to someone) Pl. Arist. || MID. **take medicine** Arist. Plu.
2 **poison, drug** —a person E. Pl.
3 **cast** (W.NEUT.PL.ACC. these) **spells** —w. ἐς + ACC. *on a river* Hdt. || PASS. **be bewitched** Men.

φαρμάκιον ου n. [dimin. φάρμακον] **medicine, drug** Pl.

φαρμακίς ίδος f. [φαρμακεύς] **sorceress** Ar. D. AR.

φαρμακόεις εσσα εν adj. [φάρμακον] (of an arrow) **poisoned** Mosch.

φάρμακον ου n. 1 **drug, potion** (ref. to herbs, medicines, poisons, or sim.) Hom. Hdt. E. Att.orats. +; (ref. to wine) Hdt.
2 **drug, poison** (administered to harm or kill) Hom. A. E. Th. Ar. Att.orats. +
3 **magic herb** or **potion** Od. S. E. Ar. AR.; **spell** Theoc.; **charm** (ref. to a magic bridle) Pi.
4 **medicine** (ref. to healing potions, ointments, or sim.) Hom. Sol. Pi. Trag. Ar. +
5 **treatment, cure, remedy** (for a disease or symptom) Thgn. Trag. Ar. Pl.; (ref. to surgery or sim.) A.
6 (fig.) **remedy** (for bad situations, troubles, cold, sadness, love, or sim.) Hes. Archil. Hippon. Lyr. Trag. Pl. +
7 **means of producing** (a desirable result); **prescription** (w.GEN. for safety, peace, wisdom, or sim.) Ion E. Pl. Arist.
8 **means of reviving, revival** (W.GEN. of life, for the dead) Ibyc.; (of valour, for an ageing hero) Pi.
9 **pigment, paint, dye** Emp. Hdt. Ar. Pl.

φαρμακοποσίᾱ ᾱς f. [πίνω] **taking of medicine as a draught** Pl. X.

φαρμακο-πώλης ου m. [πωλέω] **seller of medicines, apothecary** Ar. Aeschin.; (pejor.) **mountebank, quack** Plb.

φαρμακός, also **φαρμᾱκός**, οῦ m. **remedy** (for evils); **scapegoat** (ref. to a person who symbolically took on the sins of the people, and was driven out of the community after being ritually beaten or stoned) Hippon. Ar. Call.; (pejor., as the type of an accursed person, needing to be driven out) Lys. Ar. D.

φαρμακο-τρίβης ου m. [τρίβω] **grinder of drugs** or **pigments** D.

φαρμακόω contr.vb. (of Medea) **concoct** —antidotes Pi.

φαρμακώδης ες adj. (of plants, river water) **poisonous, noxious** Plu.

φάρμαξις εως f. [φαρμάσσω] **treatment** (for an itch) Pl.

φαρμάσσω, Att. **φαρμάττω** vb. [φάρμακον] 1 (of the god of medicine) **administer treatment** (to a person) AR.
2 **administer poison** Pl. || PASS. (of food) **be poisoned** Plu.
3 **practise witchcraft** AR.(also mid.); (fig.) **befuddle** —a person Pl. || PASS. **be bewitched** Ar.
4 **treat** —an axe-head (by plunging it in cold water) Od.; **season** —food (w. sesame) Hippon. || PASS. (fig., of an altar-flame) **be dosed** —W.DAT. w. sacred oil A.

φάρος[1] εος n. **plough** Alcm.(dub.) [perh. φᾶρος 3 *cloak*]
φάρος[2] Att.n.: see φᾶρος
Φάρος ου f. **Pharos** (small island nr. Alexandria, site of a famous lighthouse) Od. Th. Call. Plu.

φᾶρος, Att. **φάρος**, εος (ους) n. **1** large piece of cloth, **cloth** Od. Hdt.; sailcloth, **sail** B.
2 bedspread, **coverlet** S. Bion
3 cloak Hom. Hes. Xenoph. Lyr. Trag. Hellenist.poet.; (w. play on meaning *sailcloth*) E.; (pulled across the face in mourning) Od. E. Ar. | see also **φάρος**¹
4 shroud (for a corpse) Hom. S.

φαρόω contr.vb. [φάρος¹] | only ep.3pl. (w.diect.) φαρόωσι | **plough** —*land* Call.

φάρσος εος Ion.n. **sector** (of a city divided by a river) Hdt.

φάρυγξ υγγος, also **φάρυξ** υγος f. (sts.m.) **1 throat** (of a person or snake; ref. to the front of the neck, grabbed by someone) Od. Theoc.; (ref. to the internal throat, as affected by illness or strained by singing) Th. Ar.
2 gullet (of the Cyclops, gluttons) Od. E.*Cyc.* Arist.; (voc., meton. for a glutton) Ar.

φᾱ́ς (pres. and athem.aor.ptcpl.), **φάσαν** (ep.3pl.impf. and athem.aor.): see φημί

φάσγανον ου n. **sword** Hom. Pi. B. Trag. Hellenist.poet.

φασγανουργός όν adj. [ἔργον] (fig., of Fate) **forging swords** A.

φάσηλος ου m. a kind of **bean or nut** Ar.

φάσθαι (pres. and athem.aor.mid.inf.), **φάσθε** (ep.2pl.impf. and athem.aor.mid.), **φάσθω** (3sg.pres. and athem.aor.mid.imperatv.), **φᾶσί** (3pl.): see φημί

Φᾱσιᾱνικός ή όν adj. [Φᾶσις] (of a bird) from the Phasis region, **Phasian** (ref. to the pheasant) Ar.

φᾱσιᾱνός οῦ m. Phasian bird, **pheasant** Ar.; (fig.ref. to a man, w. play on φάσις¹ 1) **canary, stool-pigeon** Ar.

φάσις¹ εως f. [φαίνω] **1 denunciation** (by an informer) Att.orats.
2 appearance, visibility (of torch-signals) Plb.

φάσις² εως f. [φημί] **1 description** (of sthg.) Pl.
2 statement, proposition Arist.
3 pronouncement (that sthg. is the case), **affirmation** (opp. denial) Pl. Arist.; **mere pronouncement, unsupported statement** Plb.
4 (gener.) **report, message** NT.

Φᾶσις ιδος (Ion. ιος) m. | acc. Φᾶσιν | **Phasis** (river in Colchis) Hes. Pi. Hdt. Trag. +

φάσκω vb. [φημί] **1 say, assert, declare** —W.ACC. + INF. *that sthg. is the case* Hom. + —w. ὡς + INDIC. Mosch. —W.ACC. *sthg.* A. E.; (intr., esp. in phr. ὡς ἔφασκε or sim.) **say** S. E.; **affirm, confirm** (sthg.) Pl.; οὐ φάσκειν **deny** (sthg.) Pl.
2 say (that one will do sthg.), **promise** —W.FUT.INF. *to do sthg.* Hom. E.*Cyc.* Th. Pl.; (w.inf.understd.) Ar.
3 profess, claim —W.INF. *to have done sthg., to be doing sthg.* Od. A. E. Ar. Pl.; **pretend** —W.ACC. + INF. *that sthg. is the case* E.
4 (esp. in neg.phrs.) **deem, expect, believe** —W.ACC. + INF. *that sthg. is or will be the case* Hom.

φάσμα ατος n. [φαίνω] **1 vision** (in a dream) Trag. Plu.
2 apparition, phantom A. Hdt. E. Pl. +
3 portent A. Pi. Hdt. Pl. Plu.; **prodigy** (ref. to a marvellous lamb, a supernatural bull) E.
4 manifestation, supernatural form (W.GEN. of a bull, a hydra) S.; (taken by shape-shifting deities) Plu.
5 sight, spectacle S. E. Pl.
6 discovery, revelation E.
7 (fig.) **fantasy** (of sound, ref. to music) S.*Ichn.* || Pl. **mental pictures** (ref. to thoughts) Pl.

φάσομαι (dial.fut.mid.): see φημί

φάσσα, Att. **φάττα**, ης f. **wood-pigeon, ring-dove** Ar. Philox.Leuc. Theoc.; (opp. περιστερά *pigeon*) Pl.

φασσο-φόνος ον adj. [θείνω] (of the hawk) **pigeon-killing** Il.

φάσω (dial.fut.), **φατέ** (2pl.): see φημί

φατειός ή όν Ion.adj. [φημί] (of Terror, Cerberus, snakes, in neg.phr.) **able to be spoken of, describable** Hes.

φατέον (neut.impers.vbl.adj.), **φᾱτί** (dial.3sg.): see φημί

φατίζω vb. **1 speak of** (sthg.) **as** (sthg.); **declare** —*sthg.* (W.PREDIC.ACC. *to be such and such*) Parm. S. —(W.INF. κεκλῆσθαι + PREDIC.ACC. *to be called such and such*) Hdt. || PASS. (of a person) **be said** —W.INF. *to have done sthg.* AR.
2 || PASS. (of a philosophical proposition) **be stated** Parm.; (advbl.acc.) τὸ φατιζόμενον *as the saying goes* S.
3 || PASS. (of a city, rock, harbour) **be called** —W.PREDIC.SB. *such and such* Call. AR.
4 promise —*one's daughter* (W.PREDIC.ACC. *as a wife*, W.DAT. *to someone*) E. || PASS. (of a woman) **be promised** (as a wife, to someone) E.

φάτις f. | only nom., voc. φάτι, acc. φάτιν, acc.pl. φάτῑς |
1 common talk, talk (about someone, w.connot. of admiration) Od. B.; (w.neg.connot.) **gossip, rumour** Od. Archil. A. Pi. S.
2 repute, reputation (of a person) S.
3 rumour, report (about someone or sthg.) Sol. Hdt. Trag. Ar.; **tidings, news** Od. Hdt. Trag.
4 something to relate; occurrence S.; **subject matter** (of stories, ref. to heroes) Pi.
5 story, account Hdt. S. E.; (w. ἔχει understd.) *the story has it, people say* (W.ACC. + INF. *that sthg. is the case*) Pi. AR.
6 pronouncement (ref. to an oracle, a curse) Trag. AR.; **interpretation** (of a dream, an omen) A. S.; **description, appellation** (of a person) E.
7 speech, words (of a person) S.; (of the Muses, ref. to poetry) Ar.; **language** (W.ADJ. Ἕλλην *Greek*) A.

φάτνη ης f. **1 manger** (esp. for horses; oft. ref. to stalls) Hom. Pi. Hdt. E. Pl. +; (meton.ref. to fodder, as a crippling expense) Ar.; (fig., ref. to the shore) **dinner-table** (for a poor fisherman) E.*fr.*
2 Manger (name of the star cluster *Praesepe*) Theoc.

φάτνωμα ατος n. [reltd. φάτνη] (archit.) **compartment in a panelled ceiling, coffer** Plb.

φατνωματικός ή όν adj. (of a ceiling) **coffered, panelled** Plu.

φάτο (ep.3sg.impf. and athem.aor.mid.), **φατόν** (2 and 3du.): see φημί

φατός ή όν adj. [φημί] **1** (of persons) **spoken of, famed** Hes.
2 (of Gorgons, war, anger, sorrow, beauty, an impossible scenario, in neg.phr.) **describable** Hes. Pi. Parm. Ar.

φᾱτρίᾱ Att.f.: see φρᾱτρᾱ́

φάττα Att.f.: see φάσσα

φάττιον ου Att.n. [dimin. φάσσα] (as a term of endearment) **little dove, lovey-dovey** Ar.

φάτω (3sg.imperatv.): see φημί

φαυλίζω vb. [φαῦλος] **portray as being of poor quality, belittle, be disparaging about** —*persons, their diet* Pl. X.

φαῦλος η ον (also ος ον) adj. **1** (of persons) **inferior** (to others, in respect of social standing, intellectual ability, or sim.), **simple, common, ordinary** E. Th. Ar. Isoc. Pl. +; (W.ACC. in intelligence) Th.; (opp. σοφός *clever*) E.; (pejor.) **worthless, petty** E. Isoc. +
2 unskilled (in a particular activity) Pl.; **inadequate, poor** (W.INF. at doing sthg.) E. Pl.; (gener.) **weak, feeble, useless** Hdt. E.; (of a sheep-dog) D.
3 (w. moral connot.) **bad, disreputable** Isoc. +; (of horses) **badly behaved** X.

φαυλότης

4 (of things) poor in quality; (of a defensive wall, an army, shields, food, drink, clothing, or sim.) **poor** Th. X. +; (of vision) Pl.; (of equipment) **scanty, meagre** Th.
5 poor in terms of importance, significance or worth; (of activities, achievements, troubles, or sim.) **trivial, paltry** Hdt. E. Ar. Att.orats. +; (of a city) **obscure, insignificant** Isoc.; (of wounds) **slight** D.; (of the words of a barbarian woman) **worthless** E.; (of a style of behaviour) **mean, unimpressive** E. ǁ NEUT.SB. trivial or useless behaviour Hdt.; casualness or shallowness (of thinking, opp. rigorousness) Th.
6 (of tasks, undertakings, or sim.) not difficult, **simple, slight, easy** E. Ar. Pl. +
7 (w. moral connot., of behaviour) **disreputable** Isoc.; (of blame) **mean-spirited** E.; (of a reputation) **bad** D. ǁ NEUT.SB. perversity (of a people's behaviour) E.
8 (of an outcome) **bad, unfavourable** Arist. ǁ NEUT.PL.SB. ill fortune X.

—**φαύλως** adv. | compar. φαυλότερον, also φαυλοτέρως (Pl.) | superl. φαυλότατα | **1** in a simple manner, **simply** Pl. X. +
2 without difficulty, **easily** Ar.
3 in a casual manner, **casually, half-heartedly, lightly, indifferently** A. E. Ar. Pl. +
4 in an unimpressive or unsatisfactory manner, **unimpressively, poorly, badly** E. Isoc. Pl. +; (w. ἔχειν, of persons or situations) *be in a bad way, be in a sorry plight* Isoc. D. Men.

φαυλότης ητος *f.* **1 poor quality** (of soil) Pl.
2 meagreness (of resources) Isoc.
3 plainness, simplicity (of food, clothing) X. Plu.
4 inadequacy, ineffectiveness (of persons) Pl. X. D. Plb.
5 (w. moral connot.) **baseness, badness** (of persons, actions) Pl. D. Arist.
6 (ref. to tyranny) **bad form** (W.GEN. of monarchy) Arist.

φαυσίμβροτος *dial.adj.*: see φαεσίμβροτος
φάω *ep.contr.vb.* [reltd. φάος] | only 3sg.aor.2 φάε | (of Dawn) **shine forth, appear** Od.
φέβομαι *mid.pass.vb.* [reltd. φόβος] **be put to flight** —w. ὑπό + GEN. *by an enemy* Il.; **flee in terror** Hom. AR. —W.ACC. *fr. an enemy* Il.
φέγγος εος (ους) *n.* **1 radiance, glow** (given off by a god, young skin, the Forms, the Golden Fleece) hHom. Eleg.adesp. Pl. AR.; (fig.) **radiance, brilliance** (of the Graces, valour, or sim.) Pi. B.; **glory, blessedness** Pi.
2 light (of day) Trag. X. AR.; (in phr. *to see the light of day* or sim., ref. to being alive) Pi. B. S. E.; **gleam** (of dawn) AR.; (gener.) **day** (as a unit of time) A. E.
3 light (of the moon, stars, or sim.) E. Pl. X. NT.
4 light (of torches, fires, or sim.) A. Call.*epigr.*; (concr.) **torch** Ar. X. Plu.; (fig.) **shining light, beacon** (ref. to a city, god, person) Pi. Ar.
5 light, gleam (of a person's eyes, ref. to their sight) E. Theoc.
φέγγω *vb.* (of a meadow, the dawn) **gleam** (w. torches, sunlight) Ar. AR.
φεῖ *indecl.n.* [Semit.loanwd.] **phi** (letter of the Greek alphabet) Pl.
φείδομαι *mid.vb.* | fut. φείσομαι | ep.redupl.fut. πεφιδήσομαι | fut.pass. (w.mid.sens.) φεισθήσομαι | aor. ἐφεισάμην, ep.redupl.aor.2 πεφιδόμην ǁ neut.impers.vbl.adj. φειστέον |
1 leave unharmed, **spare** (fr. death) —W.GEN. *persons, animals, their lives* Hom. Anacr. Hdt. Trag. + —*persons (fr. punishment)* Att.orats. —*cities, buildings, possessions (fr. destruction or seizure)* Il. Sol. Th.
2 preserve from risk or loss, **spare, keep back** —W.GEN. *persons, horses, ships (fr. battle)* Il. Hdt. X.; (oft. in neg.phr.)

hold back, decline to give away —W.GEN. *precious items* Il. Hdt. —*one's life, resources, or sim.* (*for a particular cause*) Tyrt. Carm.Pop. E. Att.orats. Pl. +
3 (esp. in neg.phr.) **use sparingly, hold back with** —W.GEN. *the bow, the lash, stones* Pi. S. Ar.; use or give sparingly, **be sparing** (usu. W.GEN. w. food, drink, resources, or sim.) Hes. Th. Att.orats. —W.ACC. *w. one's time on Earth* Thgn.; (intr.) **live sparingly, be thrifty** Thgn. Ar. Att.orats.; **be stingy** Ar.
4 (oft. in neg.phr.) **hold back, refrain** —W.GEN. or INF. *fr. an activity, fr. doing sthg.* Pi. Hdt. S. E. Pl. +; (intr.) Scol. E. X.

—**φειδομένως** *ptcpl.adv.* **sparingly** Plu.
φειδώ οῦς *f.* **1** practice of being sparing, **thrift, economising, restraint** (w. household supplies or sim.) Od. Plu.; (w. an empire's finances) Plu.; (w.neg.connot.) **parsimony** Hes.
2 act of sparing, **sparing** (of corpses, fr. fire) Il.; (of citizens, fr. conflict) Plu.; sparing one's efforts, **holding back** (in battle) Th.
3 (gener.) **concern, consideration** (W.GEN. for sthg.) Plu.
φειδωλή ῆς *f.* **sparing, holding back** (W.GEN. of one's spears, in battle) Il.; **refusal to risk** (W.GEN. one's life, at sea) Sol.
φειδωλία ᾱς *f.* **thriftiness, frugality** Ar. Pl. Men.
φειδωλός ή όν (also ός όν) *adj.* **1** (of persons, their nature, or sim.) **thrifty** Lys. Pl.; (fig., of a poor man's stomach) Ar. ǁ NEUT.SB. thrift Plu.
2 (of a person's tongue) **restrained** (opp. loose) Hes.
3 (of persons, their actions, or sim.) **miserly, ungenerous** (sts. W.GEN. w. money) Pl. Men. ǁ MASC.SB. miser Ar. Pl. Arist. Men.

—**φειδωλῶς** *adv.* **in a miserly fashion, meanly** Pl.
Φείδων ωνος *m.* **Pheidon** (king of Argos, reputed inventor of a system of weights and measures) Hdt. Arist.
—**Φειδώνειος** ᾱ ον *adj.* (of weights and measures) **Pheidonian** Arist. Thphr.
φειστέον (neut.impers.vbl.adj.): see φείδομαι
φελλεύς έως *m.* area of stony ground, **rocky ground** Ar. Pl. Is.
φελλίον ου *n.* area of stony ground, **rocky ground** X.
φελλός οῦ *m.* **cork** (esp. used as a float, on a fishing-net) A. Pi. Pl. Plb. Plu.
φενακίζω *vb.* [φέναξ] **deceive, trick, fool** —*persons, the state* Ar. Att.orats. Men.; (intr., of persons, an indirect answer) Ar. Att.orats. Arist. ǁ PASS. (of persons, the state) be fooled Ar. Att.orats. Plu. —W.DAT. *by sthg.* D.
φενακισμός οῦ *m.* **deception** Ar. Att.orats.
φέναξ ᾱκος *m.* **deceiver** Ar.; (as the name of an exotic bird in a tall tale, w. play on φοῖνιξ 3) **cock-and-bull-finch** Ar.
φέρ-ασπις ιδος *masc.fem.adj.* [φέρω, ἀσπίς[1]] (of Ares, men) **shield-bearing** hHom. A.
φέρβω *vb.* | only pres. and impf., also 3sg.plpf. ἐπεφόρβει (hHom.) | **1** (of persons) **feed** —*animals* (sts. W.GEN. w. *fodder*) hHom. E. Call. AR.; (of Prometheus) —*an eagle* (W.DAT. w. *his liver*) AR.; (of Mother Earth, Demeter) **sustain** —*persons, animals, all living things* hHom. Call.; (of altars, w. their food-offerings) —*a person* E.; (of water) —*flowers* (*app. ref. to waterlilies*) Pi.
2 (of persons, a house) **nourish, nurture, rear** —*a child, a servant* E. AR.; (of a son) **sustain, preserve** —*a household* Hes.; (of Demeter) —*peace* Call.; (fig., of a person) **harbour** —*a wise mind and tongue* Pi.
3 ǁ MID. (of animals) **feed oneself, graze** AR. Theoc.; (tr., of a person) **sustain oneself on, feed on** —*sthg.* Theoc.; (fig., of an enlightened people) —*wisdom* E.
4 ǁ PASS. (of persons, all living things) be sustained —W.PREP.PHR. *by sthg.* hHom. S.; (wkr.sens.) exist, live (in a certain state or place) AR.

φερ-έγγυος ον *adj.* [φέρω, ἐγγύη] giving assurance; (of a warrior, an ally) **dependable** A. Th.; (of a god's ability to do sthg.) **assured, certain** A.; (of a person) **able** (W.INF. to do sthg.) A. Hdt.; (of a harbour, to protect ships) Hdt.; (of a person) **capable** (W.GEN. of sthg.) S.

φερέ-ζυγος ον *adj.* [ζυγόν] (of a horse) **bearing a yoke** Ibyc.

φερέ-κακος ον *adj.* [κακός] (of troops) able to endure hardships, **hardy** Plb.

φερε-κῡδής ές *adj.* [κῦδος] (of an island) bearing renown, **renowned, famous** B.; (of victory) **bringing renown** B.

φερέ-μηλος ον *adj.* [μῆλα] (of islands) bearing flocks, **with many flocks** Pi.*fr*.

φερε-μμελίης Ion.masc.*adj.* [μελίᾱ] | only acc. φερεμμελίην | (of a man) **spear-bearing** Mimn.

φερέ-οικος ον *adj.* [οἶκος] (of a people) carrying one's house with one, **nomadic** Hdt. ‖ MASC.SB. (ref. to the snail) house-carrier Hes.

φερέ-πονος ον *adj.* [πόνος] (of wrongdoing) **bringing trouble** (for the offender) Pi.

φερες-ανθής ές *adj.* [ἄνθος] (of choirs of girls) **bedecked with flowers** hHom.

φερέσ-βιος ον *adj.* [βίος] (of crops, fruit, Prometheus, Hera, Demeter) **life-giving** (sts. W.DAT. to men) hHom. A.*satyr.fr*. Emp.; (of ploughland, the earth) **fertile** Hes. hHom. AR.

φερε-σσακής ές *ep.adj.* [σάκος²] (of warriors) **shield-bearing** Hes.

φερε-στέφανος ον *adj.* bearing garlands; (of the Graces) app. **bringing awards** (for a poem) B.

φερετρεύομαι *pass.vb.* [φέρετρον] (of a trophy) **be carried on a stretcher** or **pallet** Plu.

φέρετρον *n*.: see φέρτρον

φέριστος *superl.adj.*: see under φέρτερος

φέρμα ατος *n.* [φέρω] **produce** (of the earth) A.; **progeny** (of a hare) A.

φερνή ῆς *f.* **1 dowry** (of a woman; sts.ref. to lands or persons) A. Hdt. E. Aeschin. +
2 gifts (of clothes or sim.) for a bride, **trousseau** E.

Φερρέφαττα, Φερσέφασσα, Φερσεφόνη (or sim.) *f.*: see Περσεφόνη

Φερρεφάττιον ου *n*. [Περσεφόνη] **shrine of Persephone** D.

φέρτατος *superl.adj.*: see under φέρτερος

φέρτερος ᾱ (Ion. η) ον *compar.adj.* [app. φέρω] **1** (of warriors, gods) **mightier** (sts. W.DAT. in strength) Hom. hHom.; (of persons, gods, a spell) **more powerful** Hom. hHom. A. Pi.; (of persons) **better** (W.DAT. w. the spear) Il.; (of horses, in a race, i.e. faster) Il.; (of the gods) **more able** (W.INF. to do sthg.) Od.
2 (of persons) **nobler** Il.; (in neg.phr., of a contest) **more important** (than the Olympics) Pi.
3 (gener., of options, outcomes, situations) **better** Hom. Pi. B. E.
—**φέρτερον** neut.*adv.* **better** —*ref.* to singing Theoc.

—**φέριστος**, also **φέρτατος**, η (dial. ᾱ) ον *superl.adj.* **1** (of warriors, gods) **mightiest** Hom. Hes. B. Call. AR.; (of men) **best** (W.DAT. w. the spear, the discus) Hom. ‖ VOC. mighty one Hom.
2 (of gods, men, glory, words) **noblest, most excellent** Il. Hes. Lyr. Emp. S. + ‖ VOC. (as a respectful term of address) good sir, noble sir Hom. hHom. Xenoph. A.; (to a horse) noble steed Il.; (informal, to a person) my dear friend Pl. Theoc.
3 (of water, a sheep) **finest** Pi. Lyr.adesp. AR.; (of options, outcomes) **best** Il. Pi. B.

φερτός ή (dial. ᾱ́) όν *adj.* [φέρω] (of slavery, in neg.phr.) **endurable** E.

φέρτρον (also **φέρετρον** Plb.) ου *n.* **bier** (for a fallen warrior) Il.; **stretcher** (to carry a dead boar)

φέρω *vb.* | PRES.: 2pl.imperatv. φέρετε, ep. φέρτε, ep.2sg.subj. φέρησθα, ep.3sg.subj. φέρῃσι, IMPF.: ἔφερον, iteratv. φέρεσκον ‖ FUT.: οἴσω, 2sg.imperatv. οἶσε, 3sg.imperatv. οἰσέτω, inf. οἴσειν, ep. οἰσέμεν, οἰσέμεναι | dial.fut. οἰσῶ, 1pl. οἰσεῦμες (Theoc.) | AOR.1 and AOR.2: ἤνεγκον, also ἤνεγκα, dial. ἤνεικα, ep. ἔνεικα | imperatv. ἔνεγκε, dial. ἔνεικε, also ἔνεικον (Anacr.) | inf. ἐνεγκεῖν, ep. ἐνεικέμεν, Aeol. ἐνείκην, also ἐνέγκαι, dial. ἐνεῖκαι | ptcpl. ἐνεγκών, also ἐνέγκᾱς, dial. ἐνείκᾱς | opt.3sg. ἐνέγκοι, also ἐνέγκαι, dial. ἐνείκαι, also ἐνείκειε ‖ PF.: ἐνήνοχα ‖ MID.: fut. (sts. w.pass.sens.) οἴσομαι | aor. ἠνεγκάμην, dial. ἠνεικάμην ‖ PASS.: φέρομαι | fut. οἰσθήσομαι | aor. ἠνέχθην, inf. ἐνεχθῆναι | pf. ἐνήνεγμαι ‖ neut.impers.vbl.adj. οἰστέον ‖ The sections are grouped as: (1–2) carry, hold, have, possess, (3–4) support, bear, (5) bear in a certain way, (6–7) endure, tolerate, (8–14) transport, propel, take away, (15) bring forth, produce, (16–26) bring, bring forward, bring about, bring to bear, or sim., (27–33) lead (tr. and intr.) |

1 carry, hold —*sthg.* (*in one's hands, on one's shoulders*) Hom. + —*a child* (*in one's womb*) Il. A. E. —*a quantity of food* (*in one's stomach*) X.

2 bear, have —*a name* E.; **possess** —*a discreet tongue, an impulsive heart, unseeing eyes* A. E.

3 support, bear —*a burden, a yoke* Pi. Trag. +

4 bear —*sufferings or sim.* (W.ADV. *easily, w. difficulty, fortitude, anger, bitterness, or sim.*) Hdt. Trag. +

5 bear (sthg.) in a certain way; **react to** —*sthg.* (*badly, well, w. anger, zeal, or sim.*) Hdt. +; (intr.) **react, feel** —W.ADV. *badly or sim.* (W.GEN., DAT. or PREP.PHR. *to sthg., about sthg.*) Th. Att.orats. X.; (W.NOM.PTCPL. *to seeing sthg., about doing sthg.*) Pi. Hdt. Ar. Pl. ‖ PASS. (of a person) be received —W.ADV. *well* (W. παρά + DAT. *by persons*) X.; (of the laws, a person's affairs; sts. of a person) be in a (certain) state, fare —W.ADV. *well, badly* S. Th. X.

6 endure —*misfortune, sufferings, or sim.* Od. +; (of good wine) **tolerate** —*dilution w. water* Ar.; (fig., of a speech) —*equal-parts dilution* (*ref. to sharing the floor*) Ar.

7 cope with, be able to control —*arrogance* (*in oneself*) Hes.; **bear the responsibility for, shoulder** —*mistakes* Antipho; (of a single factor) φέρειν τὸ πᾶν *have everything depending on it* Hdt.

8 (of a ship, feet, or sim.) **carry, transport** —*a person* (*to a place*) Hom. +; (of horses) **pull** —*a chariot, person* (*in a chariot*) Il.; (of winds, waves) **carry, propel** —*ships, sailors* Hom. E.; (of wind) **blow** (ships) —w. εἰς + ACC. *in a certain direction* X. ‖ PASS. (of a cloud) be blown or drift Hdt.; (fig., of persons distracted by grief or sim.) wander aimlessly (to a place) S. E.; (of a matter) be allowed to drift D.

9 (act. and mid.) **take away with one** —*a gift* Hom. E.; **gain, win** —*a prize, reward, advantage* Hom. +; (phr.) πλέον φέρεσθαι *have the advantage* Hdt. S. E.

10 earn, receive —*wages* E. Th. Ar. X. Men.; (of an Erinys) —*a drink of blood* (*fr. a murderer*) A.; **incur** —*respect, renown, hatred, reproach, or sim.* Il. +

11 seize and carry off; (act. and mid., of persons, monsters, lions, Death) **carry off** —*spoils, food, prey, victims* Hom. +; **plunder, rob** —*temples, persons* E. Th. | For φέρειν καὶ ἄγειν (or sim.) *plunder and pillage* see ἄγω 11.

12 carry away —*a wounded man* (*fr. a battle*) Il.; (of a raging river) **carry off, sweep away** —*a horse* Hdt.; (provbl., of the winds) —*harsh words* Od.; (fig., of fury, one's racing mind) —*a person* A. ‖ PASS. (of persons) be swept away (by storms,

waves, rivers, or sim.) Hom. A. Pl.; (of persons, their limbs, objects) be sent flying Hom.; (of a dust-storm, a squall) be driven —w. ὑπό + GEN. *by a gale* Pl.; (of a lion, boar, horse, soldiers) rush forwards, charge Il. Pl. X.; (of a spark) leap forth (fr. an anvil) Pi.; (of things) be in motion Pl.
13 (pres.ptcpl., adding emph. to a vb. of motion) rush off (and), **go right on ahead** (and) hHom. Hdt. + • (νηῦς) φέρουσα ἐνέβαλε νηὶ φιλίῃ (*the ship*) *went and rammed a friendly ship* Hdt.; (w.pass.ptcpl.) ἀπ' ἐλπίδος ᾠχόμην φερόμενος *I was utterly frustrated in my hopes* Pl.
14 ‖ IMPERATV. **come, come now** (introducing another imperatv., or a hortative subj.) Hdt. Trag. +; (introducing a q.) E. Ar. Att.orats. Pl. +
15 (of the earth, trees, vines, or sim.) **bring forth, bear** —*crops, flowers, fruit, wine* Od. +; (of a region) **produce** —*great men* Pl.; (intr., of vines, the earth) **bear fruit** hHom. Hdt. X.
16 (act. and mid.) **bring with one, bring** —*sthg.* (*to a place*) Hom. +; **go and get, fetch** —*sthg.* Od. S.; **bring for one's own use, bring along** —*supplies, equipment, or sim.* Od. Alc. Hdt. X.
17 deliver —*news, a message* (*to someone*) Hom. +; **announce, report** —*a disaster* A.; **spread** —*a person's fame* Od.
18 provide, offer, present —*gifts, songs, libations* (*to someone*) Od. +; **grant, do** —*a favour* (*for someone*) Il. +; **provide, supply** —*examples, parallels* Att.orats. Arist.
19 contribute, pay —*a sum of money* Th. +; (of a property) **bring in** —*rent* Is.
20 cast —*one's vote* A. Att.orats. ‖ PASS. (of a vote) be cast E.
21 bring, level —*charges, accusations* (*against someone*) D. Plb. ‖ PASS. (of a charge) be brought Arist.
22 bring forward, propose, nominate —*a person* Pl. Arist. —(W.PREDIC.SB. *as a chorus-master or sim.*) D.; (of a person) **bring up, mention** —*persons* (*in one's accusations*) Aeschin.
23 (of persons, monsters, arrows, events) **cause, spell** —*death, disaster, deliverance, or sim.* (W.DAT. *for someone*) Hom. B. Hdt. Trag.
24 wage —*war* (W.DAT. *on someone*) Il. Hes.
25 show —*gratitude, anger* (W.DAT. *towards someone*) A.fr. Pi.
26 apply, bring to bear —*one's opinion* (w. ἐπί + ACC. *on sthg.*) Pl.; **confer** —*a name* (*on sthg.*) Pl.; **attribute, relate, refer** —*one thing* (*to another*) Pl. Plb.; **entrust** —*matters* (*to someone*) Plb.
27 (of a god) **lead** —*a person* (*to a place*) Od.; (of a principle) **steer** (things, in a certain direction) Pl.; (of a leader) —*a city* Plu.
28 direct —*one's steps* S. E. —*one's full force, one's anger* (*at someone*) Il. Plb.
29 ‖ PASS. (of birds) be drawn (to a decoy) X.; (of one's memory) be drawn back —w. πρός + ACC. *to a subject* Pl.; (of a person) descend —w. ἐς + ACC. *to verbal abuse* E.
30 (intr., of roads, gateways, doors) **lead** —W.PREP.PHR. *to a place* Hdt. +; (fig., of an argument) —W.ADV. *in a certain direction* Pl.; (of regions) **extend** —W.PREP.PHR. *to a place* Hdt.
31 (intr., of a person, public opinion) **incline** —W.DAT. or ἐπί + ACC. *towards a conclusion or course of action* Hdt. Th.; **incline to the belief, hold** —W.INF. or COMPL.CL. *that sthg. shd. be done* Hdt.; (of justice) **dictate** (sthg.) Hdt.
32 (intr., of suspicion, facts) **point** —W.PREP.PHR. *to someone or sthg.* Hdt. Antipho; (of an oracle, a vision, an analogy) **refer, relate** —W.PREP.PHR. *to sthg.* Hdt. Pl.; (of a disembodied voice) **address oneself** —W.PREP.PHR. *to someone* Hdt.
33 (intr., of actions, things) **lead** —w. εἰς + ACC. *to harm, terror, disgrace, self-improvement* Hdt. S. E. Pl.; (of water, diet, behaviour, upbringing) **be conducive** —w. εἰς + ACC. *to health, valour, or sim.* Hdt. E. X.; (of good or bad management) **have consequences** —w. εἰς + ACC. *for the state* Pl. ‖ IMPERS. it is beneficial —W.DAT. + INF. *for someone to do sthg.* Hdt.

φεῦ *interj.* | expression of intense emotion, oft. doubled, sts. W.GEN. of the person or thing provoking the emotion |
1 (expressing dismay, grief or pain) **ah me!, alas!** Trag. Ar. X. +; (expressing anger or exasperation) **good grief!, by god!** Trag. Ar.
2 (expressing astonishment, wonder or admiration) **oh my!** B. S. E. Ar. +

φεύγω *vb.* | iteratv.impf. φεύγεσκον | fut. φεύξομαι, also φευξοῦμαι | aor.2 ἔφυγον | 3sg.iteratv.aor. φύγεσκε | pf. πέφευγα, masc.nom.pl.ptcpl. πεφευγότες, ep. πεφυζότες ‖ mid.pass.pf.ptcpl. πεφυγμένος ‖ neut.impers.vbl.adj. φευκτέον |
1 run away in order to escape (fr. a person, place or present danger); **flee** Hom. + —W.GEN. or PREP.PHR. *fr. a place* Od. +; (tr.) **flee from, flee** —*a person, place, or sim.* Hom. + —*an accusation,* (*the consequence of*) *a crime* Hdt. E.
2 be put to flight —w. ὑπό + GEN. *by someone* Il. Hdt.; (of a fish) —*by a dolphin* Il.
3 (without connot. of escape) **fly, speed** —W.ACC. *in a race* Pi.
4 (act. and mid., esp. aor. and pf.) **get away, escape** —W.GEN. or ἐκ + GEN. *fr. a battle, war, death, sufferings, or sim.* Hom. Hdt. S. +; (tr.) **escape from** —*war, the sea* Od. Callin.
5 escape or try to escape (some circumstance or future event); **avoid, evade** —*death, old age, enslavement, reproach* Hom. hHom. Eleg. Pi. Hdt. S. + —*the gods, their will, fate* Il. hHom. A. + —*an obligation* Att.orats.
6 shun —*wickedness* Pl. D.; **shrink from, avoid** —W.INF. *doing sthg.* Hdt. Att.orats. Pl.
7 (of things) **escape** (someone); (of reins) **slip from** —*someone* (i.e. *his grasp*) Il. —w. ἐκ + GEN. *someone's hands* Il.; (of unwise words) **escape from** —W.DBL.ACC. *a person, his mouth* (i.e. *fr. his mouth*) Il.; (intr., of a horse's bit) **slip** X.
8 (specif., esp. aor.) **be driven into exile** —W.PREP.PHR. *by persons* Hdt. + —*by a court* Din. —*fr. a place* Th.; (tr.) **go into exile from** —*one's native land* Th. X. —*persons* Hdt.
9 (esp. pres.) **live in exile** (sts. w. ἐκ + GEN. fr. one's native land) Thgn. A. +
10 (leg., opp. διώκειν *bring charges*) **face charges, be prosecuted, be a defendant** Ar. Att.orats. +; (tr.) **face** —*a charge* (sts. w. ὑπό + GEN. *fr. someone, also* sts. W.GEN. *of the alleged crime*) Ar. Att.orats. +; (fig., of a decree) **be challenged** D.
11 take refuge —w. ἐς + ACC. *in a certain defence* E.; **plead in defence** —W.COMPL.CL. *that sthg. is the case* A. S.

φεύζω *vb.* [φεῦ] | aor. ἔφευξα | **cry 'alas'** A. [or perh. ἔφῡξα (reltd. φῦ¹) **cry out in disgust**]
φευκτός ή (dial. ᾱ́) όν *adj.* [φεύγω] **1** (of disagreeable things) **needing to be avoided** or **shunned** Arist. Plb.
2 (of news, in neg.phr.) **escapable** S.
φευξείω *vb.* [desideratv. φεύγω] **wish to flee from** —*persons* E.
φεῦξις εως *f.* **escape** (fr. death) S.
φεύξομαι and **φευξοῦμαι** (fut.): see φεύγω
φεψαλόομαι *pass.contr.vb.* [φέψαλος] (of Typhon's strength) **be reduced to ashes** (by Zeus' bolt) A.

φέψαλος ου *m.* spark (fr. a fire) Ar.
φεψάλυξ υγος *m.* spark (fr. a fire) Archil. Plb.; (fig., in neg.phr.) **glimmer, trace** (of sthg.) Ar.
φή *adv.* (introducing a simile) **like, as** —*someone or sthg.* (*in same grammatical case as the person or thing compared*) Il. hHom. Call.
φη (Ion.enclit.3sg.), **φῆ** (ep.3sg.impf. and athem.aor.), **φῇ** (3sg.pres. and athem.aor.subj.): see φημί
φήγινος η ον *adj.* [φηγός] (of an axle, a branch) made of oak-wood, **of oak** Il. Call.*epigr.*
φηγός, dial. **φᾱγός**, οῦ *f.* **1 oak tree, oak** Il. Hellenist.poet.; (ref. to the sacred tree at Dodona) Hdt. S. E.*fr.* Call.
2 (pl. and collectv.sg.) **acorns** (roasted and eaten) Ar. Pl. Theoc.; (eaten raw by early man) AR.
φήῃ (ep.3sg.pres. and athem.aor.subj.): see φημί
φήληξ ηκος *m.* **wild fig** (ref. to the fruit) Ar.
φηλητεύω *vb.*, **φηλήτης** *m.*: see φιλητεύω, φιλήτης
φηλόω *contr.vb.* **deceive, mislead** —*someone* S.*satyr.fr.* —(W.DAT. *w. words*) AR.; (of fire-signals) —*someone's mind* A. || PASS. (of the public) **be deceived** —W.DAT. *by the tongues of political leaders* E.
φήμη ης, dial. **φᾱ́μᾱ**, also **φήμᾱ**, ᾱς *f.* [φημί] **1 prophetic pronouncement, prophecy, pronouncement** (by a person, oracle or god) Hdt. S. E. Isoc. +; **prophetic message** (of a dream) Hdt.; **oracular voice** S. E. Pl. X.; (personif., as an object of worship) Plu.
2 auspicious utterance (esp. ref. to chance remarks taken as good omens) Od. Ar.; **auspiciousness in speaking, propitiousness** Pl.
3 (gener.) **utterance** (sts.ref. to song) Pi. Trag. Ar. Pl. Plu.; **description, appellation, name** Pl.
4 saying, proverb A.; **story, legend** E. Isoc. Pl. Plb.; **testimony, content** (of sacred writings) Pl.
5 news, message Trag. Ar. Men. Call. Plb.; **report, rumour, claim** (oft. proved false) Sapph. Hdt. S. E. +
6 word of mouth, popular rumour, talk (about someone or sthg.) Hes. A. E.(pl.) Telest. Att.orats. +; (personif.) **Word of Mouth** Hes. Aeschin.
7 repute, reputation (of a person) Hes. Pi. E. Att.orats. +; (of a campaign) Th.; **good reputation, renown** Hdt. E. Att.orats. Plb.; (personif.) **Fame** B.
φημί, dial. **φᾱμί**, Aeol. **φαῖμι** *vb.* | In all dialects except Aeol. the pres.indic. is enclitic, apart fr. the 2sg. The past tense ἔφην was orig. an impf., but is oft. used as though an athem.aor., because of its resemblance to athem.aor. forms such as ἔβην. || PRES.: 2sg. φῄς, ep. φῆσθα, Aeol. φαῖσθα (perh. also φᾷ Alc.), 3sg. φησί, Ion. φη (Anacr.), dial. φᾱτί, Aeol. φαῖσι, 2 and 3du. φατόν, 1pl. φαμέν, 2pl. φατέ, 3pl. φᾱσί, dial. φαντί, Aeol. φαῖσι || IMPF. and ATHEM.AOR.: ἔφην, ep. φῆν, dial. ἔφᾱν, 2sg. ἔφης, ep. φῆς, also ἔφησθα, ep. φῆσθα, 3sg. ἔφη, ep. φῆ, dial. ἔφᾱ, also φᾶ, 1pl. ἔφαμεν, ep. φάμεν, 2pl. ἔφατε, 3pl. ἔφασαν, ep. φάσαν, also ἔφαν, φάν || PRES. and ATHEM.AOR.: subj. φῶ, 3sg. φῇ, ep. φήῃ, φῇσι, 1pl. φῶμεν, 3pl. φῶσι, opt. φαίην, 1pl. φαῖμεν, 3pl. φαῖεν, imperatv. φαθί (sts. written φάθι), 3sg.imperatv. φάτω, inf. φάναι, ep. φάμεν, ptcpl. φάς || FUT.: φήσω, dial. φᾱ́σω, also φᾱσῶ || AOR.: ἔφησα, dial. ἔφᾱσα, subj. φήσω, opt. φήσαιμι, 3sg. φῆσαι, also φήσειε, inf. φῆσαι, ptcpl. φήσᾱς || MID.: dial.fut. φᾱ́σομαι | IMPF. and ATHEM.AOR.: ἐφάμην, 3sg. ἔφατο, ep. φάτο, 2pl. ἔφασθε, ep. φάσθε, 3pl. ἔφαντο, ep. φάντο | PRES. and ATHEM.AOR.: imperatv. φάο, 3sg.imperatv. φάσθω, inf. φάσθαι, ptcpl. φάμενος || PASS.: 3sg.pf.imperatv. πεφάσθω || neut.impers.vbl.adj. φατέον

|| Mid. (in same senses as act.) is freq. in poetry and Hdt., rare in other prose writers. |
1 say, assert, declare —*sthg.* Hom. + —W.DIR.SP. *sthg.* Hom. + —W.ACC. + INF. *that sthg. is the case* Hom. + —W. ὅτι or ὡς + INDIC. Att.orats. Pl. +; (intr., oft.parenth.) Hom. + || IMPERS.PF.PASS.IMPERATV. **let it stand affirmed** (that sthg. is the case) Pl.
2 speak about, mention —*someone* Pl. +; **say** —W.DBL.ACC. *sthg. about someone* X.
3 say yes, agree or **assent** Hdt. S. +; **agree, confirm** —W.ACC. + INF. *that sthg. is the case* S.
4 (neg.phr.) οὔ φημι **deny** —W.ACC. + INF. (sts.understd.) *that sthg. is the case* A. Hdt. +; **refuse** —W.FUT.INF. *to do sthg.* Hdt. +
5 deem, think, suppose —W.INF. or ACC. + INF. *that one will do sthg., that sthg. is the case* Hom. +
φημίζω *vb.* [φήμη] | aor. ἐφήμισα, ep. ἐφήμιξα | **1 utter, spread** —W.COGN.ACC. *a rumour* Hes. || MID. **utter** —*words* A.; express in words, **describe, tell of** —*sufferings* A.
2 (of Apollo) **prophesy** A.
3 (of a person) **promise, pledge** —*a woman* (as a wife, W.DAT. *to someone*) E.
4 call, name —*sthg.* (W.PREDIC.ADJ. or SB. *such and such*) Call.
φῆμις, dial. **φᾶμις**, ιος *f.* | acc. φήμιν | **1 general talk, talk, discussion** Il. Ibyc.; (w.neg.connots.) **gossip** Od.
2 popular opinion Od.; (w.neg.connots.) **general censure, reproach** Od.
3 (concr.) **debating-place** Od.
φῆν (ep.1sg.impf. and athem.aor.): see φημί
φῆναι (aor.inf.): see φαίνω
φήνη ης *f.* **large bird of prey**; perh. **lammergeier** or **sea-eagle** Od. Ar.
φήρ Aeol.*m.*: see θήρ
φῄς (2sg.), **φῆσθα** (ep.2sg.), **φῇς**, **φῆσθα** (ep.2sg.impf. and athem.aor.): see φημί
φῆσαι (aor.inf.), **φήσαιμι** (aor.opt.), **φήσᾱς** (aor.ptcpl.): see φημί
φῇσι (ep.3sg.subj.), **φήσω** (fut., also aor.subj.): see φημί
φθάνω, ep. **φθᾱ́νω** *vb.* | fut. φθάσω | aor. ἔφθασα, dial. ἔφθασσα (Theoc.), ptcpl. φθάσᾱς, inf. φθάσαι || ATHEM.AOR.: ἔφθην, dial. ἔφθᾱν, 3sg. ἔφθη, ep. φθῆ, 1pl. ἔφθημεν, 3pl. ἔφθησαν, ep. φθάν | subj. φθῶ, 3sg. φθῇ, ep. φθήῃ, φθῇσι (sts. written φθήῃσι), ep.1pl. φθέωμεν, ep.3pl. φθέωσι | opt. φθαίην | inf. φθῆναι | ptcpl. φθᾱ́ς | plpf. ἐφθάκη (Plu.) || MID. (w.act.sens.): fut. φθήσομαι | athem.aor.ptcpl. φθάμενος (Hom. Hes.) || The sections are grouped as: (1–2) overtake or keep ahead, (3–8) act first, (9–10) be timely or premature. The vb. is common in constructions w. another vb., either as ptcpl. w. finite vb., or as finite vb. w.ptcpl.: as φθάσαντες ἀφίκοντο, ἔφθασαν ἀφικόμενοι *they arrived first.* |
1 (tr., of a rush of water) **outstrip, overtake** —*someone* Il.; (fig., of death) **overtake, catch up with** —*someone* Il.
2 (tr.) **keep physically or temporally ahead** (of someone or sthg.); (of Ate, in her travels over the earth) **outpace, stay one step ahead of** —*benign deities* (W.PTCPL. *and bring harm to mankind*) Il.; (of persons, ships) **keep ahead of** —*fellow travellers, enemy troops* (W.PTCPL. *and reach a place before them*) Hdt. + —*a storm* (W.PTCPL. *in finishing one's work, beaching one's ships*) Hes. Hdt. —*the swallow* (i.e. the arrival of summer, in pruning one's vines) Hes.; **be ahead of** —*a person* (in a train of thought) E.; **act before** —*thought* (i.e. thinking, W.PTCPL. *in committing an offence*) D.

φθαρτικός

3 do (sthg.) before (sthg. happens); **finish** —W.PTCPL. *doing sthg. (before being caught)* Antipho; (neg.phr.) οὐ φθάνειν (W.PTCPL.) καί (W.VB.) *no sooner finish (doing sthg.) than (do or suffer sthg. else)* E. Ar. Isoc. D.
4 do (sthg. before (someone else); **be first** (to do sthg.) A. E. + —W.PTCPL. *to do sthg.* Hom. + —W.INF. Th.; **act before** —*someone (in doing sthg.)* Hom. +; **catch** (someone) **unawares** (in doing sthg.) Hom. +
5 take preliminary action (before a second action); **take the prior step** —W.PTCPL. *of doing sthg.* (oft. w. πρίν and ACC. + INF. *before sthg. can happen*) Hdt. + —W.INF. *of doing sthg.* AR.; **take prior action** —w. πρίν + INF. *before dying* Antipho
6 have a prior experience; (of persons, cities) **already be in the position** —W.PASS.PTCPL. *of being destroyed, enslaved, or sim.* (oft. W.COMPL.CL. *before one can do sthg., before sthg. else can happen*) Il. +
7 (of the Kingdom of Heaven) **already arrive** —W.PREP.PHR. *for someone* NT.
8 (of persons or things) **be quicker** or **earlier** (W.GEN. or ἤ + NOM.PERS. *than someone or sthg.*) —W.PTCPL. *in doing sthg.* Hom. +
9 be timely, be in good time —W.PTCPL. *in doing sthg.* Ar. +
10 (in neg.phr.) be premature (in doing sthg.); οὐκ ἄν φθάνοις or φθάνοι *you (he) wouldn't be a moment too soon* —W.PTCPL. *in doing or suffering sthg.* (i.e. *may you or he lose no time in doing or suffering it*) Hdt. E. Ar. Pl. +; (wkr.sens.) οὐκ ἄν φθάνοιμι, φθάνοις, φθάνοι *I (you, he) won't lose time* —W.PTCPL. *in doing sthg.* (i.e. *will do it right away*) Pl. D.

φθαρτικός ἡ όν *adj.* [φθείρω] (of emotions, qualities, or sim.) **destructive** (oft. W.GEN. *to someone or sthg.*) Arist.

φθαρτός ἡ όν *adj.* (of things) **perishable** Arist. || NEUT.SB. *that which is perishable* (opp. *eternal Forms*) Arist.

φθᾶς (athem.aor.ptcpl.): see φθάνω

φθέγγομαι *mid.vb.* | fut. φθέγξομαι | aor. ἐφθεγξάμην | pf. ἔφθεγμαι | **1** utter one's characteristic call; (of animals or birds) **call, bark, low** (or sim.) Xenoph. Hdt. Ar. +
2 (of musical instruments) **sound, play** hHom. Thgn. X. Arist. —W.INTERN.ACC. *a melody* Thgn. E.
3 (of a melody) **ring out** E.; (of thunder, a door being hit) **resound** Ar. X.; (fig., of a theory) **ring** —W.ADV. *true, false* Pl.
4 utter an articulate sound; (of persons or gods, esp. in neg.phrs.) **make a sound, say** (sthg.) Od. Hes. Hdt. E. +; **call out, cry out** Hom. Pl. X.; **speak** Hom. hHom. Thgn. B. + —W.ADV. *well, loudly, quietly, or sim.* Il. Pi. E. Ar. +; (of Typhon's heads, a dove) Hes. —W.DAT. *in a human voice* Hdt.; (of a shout) **ring out** E. || NEUT.PTCPL.SB. *voice* Hdt.
5 (of a choir, Muse, frog chorus) **sing, chant** Alcm. Stesich. Ar. X. —*a song, a hymn* Ar.
6 (tr., of persons) **utter** —*laments, curses, oracles, war-cries, or sim.* A. Pi. E. Th. +; **say** —sthg. (sts. w. περί + GEN. *about sthg.*) Hdt. S. E. +
7 speak of, mention —sthg. E.; speak about, sing about, **celebrate** —*persons, deeds* Pi. —W.ACC. + INF. *how someone was victorious in the games* Pi.
8 call, name —sthg. (W.PREDIC.SB. or ADV. *such and such, in this way*) Pl.; **give the name, use the term** —W.ACC. *such and such* (W.DAT. or ἐπί + DAT. *to sthg., for sthg.*) Pl.; (of names) **convey** —*the same thing* (W.DAT. *in meaning*) Pl.

φθέγμα (or **φθέγγμα**) ατος *n.* **1** characteristic sound, **cry** (of a bird or animal) S. E. Ar.; **voice** (of a dead tortoise, ref. to the sound of a lyre) S.*Ichn.*; **sound** (of thunder, sthg. rattling, a grinding mortar) Pi. S.*Ichn.* Ar.; **note** (of a musical instrument) Ar. Pl.
2 voice (of a person or god) Trag. Ar.; (ref. to an oracle) S. Pl.; **human voice** (opp. the sound of a lyre) Pi.; **speech, language** S.

3 cry (of a troubled man) Pl.; (of a boatswain, keeping time for rowers) E.; **utterance** S. E.; (ref. to Bacchic hymns) S.

φθείρ ειρός *m.* **louse** Archil. Hdt. Ar. Men. Plu.

φθειρίασις εως *f.* [φθειριάω] **infestation by lice** (supposedly causing the flesh to rot) Plu.

φθειριάω *contr.vb.* [φθείρ] **suffer from louse infestation** Plu.

φθειριστικός ἡ όν *adj.* || FEM.SB. **art of catching lice** (as a trivial example of hunting) Pl.

φθειροτραγέω *contr.vb.* [τρώγω] (of an eastern tribe) **eat lice** (perh. orig. *eat pine-cones*, said to be another meaning of φθείρ) Hdt.

φθείρω *vb.* | fut. φθερῶ | aor. ἔφθειρα | pf. ἔφθαρκα || PASS.: fut. φθαρήσομαι, also mid. (w.pass.sens.) φθεροῦμαι | aor.2 ἐφθάρην, dial.3pl. ἔφθαρεν (Pi.) | pf. ἔφθαρμαι, 3pl. ἐφθάραται, inf. ἐφθάρθαι |
1 (of persons, gods, gales, diseases, poisons) **destroy, kill** —*persons, animals* Hes. Semon. Hdt. S. + || PASS. (of persons, armies, races, herds) be wiped out, destroyed or perish Pi. Hdt. Trag. Th. +
2 (of persons) **exhaust, consume, use up** —*flocks, money, possessions* Od. A.*satyr.fr.* Th.
3 (of gods, persons, misplaced hopes) **ruin** —*persons, households, one's body and soul, a city's prosperity* E. Th. X. Din.; (of troops, pests, a volcanic eruption) **lay waste to, ravage, destroy** —*places, property, orchards, crops* Th. Ar. X. + || PASS. (of goods, objects, virtues, unions, a common cause) be destroyed, lost or broken up Th. Pl. X. Arist.; (of factions, cities, plans, achievements) be ruined Th. Pl. X.; (of a person) be ruined, be done for Men.; (imperatv., as a curse) be damned Il. Ar.
4 (wkr.sens., of troops) **harry, inflict losses on** —*enemies, cities* Th. || PASS. (of an army, a state) be harried —w. ὑπό + GEN. *by enemies* Th.; be harmed, suffer losses Th. Arist. —W.DAT. *fr. plague and expenditure* Th.
5 (of persons, things, civil strife, bad influences) **damage, spoil, harm** —*persons, cities, laws, good habits, or sim.* Sol. Thgn. Trag. Th. +; (intr., of so-called benefits) **cause harm** Pl. || PASS. (of a person's body) be ravaged (by the effects of poison) E.; be reduced to a wretched state S.; (of a cursed land) be blighted S.
6 || PASS. (of childless women) waste away, languish S.; (of exiles, seafarers) wander wretchedly, be worn out E.; be a castaway, be shipwrecked A. E.
7 || PASS. (imperatv.) be gone E. Ar. —w. ἀπό + GEN. *fr. a house* E.; move away —W.GEN. *fr. a person* E.
8 || MID. or PASS. go (to someone) to be corrupted; (of an obsequious man) **sidle up** —w. πρός + ACC. *to the rich and powerful* D. Plu.; (of a woman) **yield up one's honour** —w. πρός + ACC. *to a debauched commander* Plu.

φθειρώδης ες *adj.* [φθείρ] (of armpits) **louse-infested** Arist. Thphr.(cj.)

φθεῖσα (ep.aor.): see φθίνω

φθεισ-ήνωρ (or **φθῑσήνωρ**) ορος *ep.masc.fem.adj.* [φθίνω, ἀνήρ] (of war) **destroying men, deadly** Il. Hes.

φθεισί-μβροτος (or **φθῑσίμβροτος**), also **φθῑσίβροτος** (Plu.), ον *ep.adj.* [βροτός] (of battle, Ares, Athena's aigis) **destroying mortals, deadly** Hom. AR. Plu.(oracle)

φθείσομαι (fut.mid.), **φθείσω** (fut.): see φθίνω

φθερσι-γενής ές *adj.* [φθείρω, γένος] (of Erinyes) **wiping out a race** A.

φθέωμεν, φθέωσι (ep.1pl. and 3pl.athem.aor.subj.), **φθῇ** (ep.3sg.athem.aor.), **φθῇ** (3sg.athem.aor.subj.), **φθήῃ, φθῇσι** (ep.3sg.athem.aor.subj.), **φθῆναι** (athem.aor.inf.), **φθήσομαι** (fut.mid.): see φθάνω

Φθίᾱ ᾱς, Ion. **Φθίη** ης *f.* Phthia (region in southern Thessaly, home of Achilles) Hom. Pi. E. Pl. +

–**Φθίηνδε** *adv.* to Phthia Il.

–**Φθίηφι** *adv.* at Phthia Il.

–**Φθῖος** ᾱ ον *adj.* (of a town) **Phthian, in Phthia** Plb. ‖ MASC.PL.SB. men of Phthia Il. Call.

–**Φθιάς** άδος *fem.adj.* (of women, horses, the land) **of Phthia, Phthian** E. AR.; (of a sacrificial axe) **of the Phthian type** E.

–**Φθιώτης** ου, dial. **Φθιώτᾱς** ᾱ *masc.adj.* (of persons) **of Phthia, Phthian** E. Ar.(quot. A.) Call.; (of Achaeans, ref. to a particular tribe or population) Hdt. Plb. Plu. ‖ PL.SB. men of Phthia E. Th.

–**Φθιῶτις** ιδος *fem.adj.* (of the land, the shores) **of Phthia, Phthian** Hdt. E. Plb.; (of women, a fleet, a town) E. Plb. ‖ SB. region of Phthia Th. ‖ PL.SB. Phthian women Arist.

φθίεται (ep.3sg.athem.aor.mid.subj.), **φθίης** (ep.2sg.aor.2 subj.), **φθίμενος** (athem.aor.mid.ptcpl.): see φθίνω

φθινάς άδος *fem.adj.* [φθίνω] **1** waning; (of a day) **marking the end** (W.GEN. of a month) E.

2 (of diseases) **wasting, consumptive** S. Plu.

φθίνασμα ατος *n.* **dying, sinking** (W.GEN. of the sun, ref. to its setting) A.

φθινό-καρπος ον *adj.* [καρπός¹] (fig., of a felled tree) **stripped of fruit, rendered barren** Pi.

φθινοπωρινός ή όν *adj.* [φθινόπωρον] (of an equinox, rain) **autumnal** Plb. Plu.

φθινοπωρίς ίδος *fem.adj.* (of a storm, olives, a season) **autumnal** Pi. Call.

φθιν-όπωρον ου *n.* [ὀπώρᾱ] **end of the harvest season, autumn** Hdt. Th. Call. Bion

φθινύθω *vb.* [φθίνω] **1** (of persons) **consume, exhaust** —*wine, a household* Od.; **fritter away, waste** —*one's life* (*in mourning*) Od.; **gnaw away at** —*one's heart* (*in anger and dissatisfaction*) Il.; (of suffering friends) **gnaw at, tug at** —*one's heart* Od.; (of the Sirens) **cause** (W.ACC. persons) **to waste away** or **perish** —W.DAT. *through pining* AR.

2 (intr., of a person's cheeks) **waste away, be hollowed** —W.DAT. *through grief* Od.; (of flesh) **shrivel** —w. ἀμφί + DAT. *on one's bones* (*through grief*) Od.; (of persons, animals) **perish, die** Hom.

φθίνυλλα ης *f.* **emaciated hag** Ar.

φθίνω, ep. **φθίνω** *vb.* | fut. φθείσω (v.l. φθίσω) | ep.aor.1 φθεῖσα (v.l. φθῖσα) | ep.2sg.aor.2 subj. φθίῃς ‖ MID.: fut. φθείσομαι (v.l. φθίσομαι) | athem.aor.: 3sg. ἔφθιτο, ep.3pl. ἐφθίατο, 3sg.imperatv. φθείσθω (AR.), inf. φθίσθαι, also φθεῖσθαι (AR.), ptcpl. φθίμενος, ep.subj.3sg. φθίεται, 1pl. φθιόμεσθα, ep.3sg.opt. φθῖτο ‖ mid.pass.pf. ἔφθιμαι |

1 (of natural phenomena) **come towards an end**; (act. and mid., of a lunar month) **wane, draw to a close** Od.; (specif.) **be in the final week** Th.; (of months, days, nights) **come to an end, pass** Od. Hes. S.; (of the stars) **set** A.; (of one's life) **pass by, drift by** Od.

2 (of persons, animals, plants, other physical things) **waste away, wither, decline, decay** Il. Emp. S. E. Pl.; (of youth, strength, excellence, insolence) Pi. S. ‖ MID.PASS. (of a person) **be wasted** or **withered** —W.ACC. *in arms and neck* Hippon.; (of life-force) **ebb away** —w. ἀπό + GEN. *fr. the limbs* Od.

3 (of oracles, prophecies) **fade, come to nothing** S.; (of an evil fate) **wane** S.; (of persons, their achievements and fortunes) **come to ruin, end in disaster** S. E.

4 (of persons) **perish, die** Od. Pi. Hdt. S. + ‖ MID.PASS. **perish, die, be killed** Hom. hHom. Eleg. Pi. Hdt. Trag. + ‖ MASC.PL.AOR.2 MID.PTCPL.SB. the dead Od. A. B. E. X.

5 ‖ FUT. and AOR.1 (causatv., of gods, persons, one's own might) **kill, destroy** —*persons* Hom. hHom. S.; **nullify, overturn** —*fate's edicts* A.

φθισήνωρ *ep.masc.fem.adj.*: see φθεισήνωρ

φθισικός, dial. **φθιτικός**, ή όν *adj.* [φθίσις] (of a sickness) **consumptive** Men.; (fig., of a person) **eaten away** (by envy) Men.

φθισίμβροτος, φθισίβροτος *ep.adj.*: see φθεισίμβροτος

φθίσις εως *f.* [φθίνω] **1 wasting sickness, consumption** (ref. to tuberculosis or sim.) Hdt. Arist. Plu.; **shrinking, wasting** (W.GEN. of the body) Pl.; **shrivelling, failure** (W.GEN. of crops) Pi.*fr.*

2 (gener.) **shrinking, shrinkage, diminution** (opp. increase or growth) Pl. Arist. Plb.; (fig.) **waning** (of a person's fortunes) Plu.

3 (concr.) **bodily waste** (of an animal) Pl.

φθιτικός *dial.adj.*: see φθισικός

φθῖτο (ep.3sg.athem.aor.mid.opt.): see φθίνω

φθιτός ή όν *adj.* [φθίνω] ‖ MASC.SB. **dead person** S. E. ‖ PL. **the dead** (esp. as the recipients of religious offerings) A. E. Plu.

Φθιώτης *masc.adj.*, **Φθιῶτις** *fem.adj.*: see under Φθίᾱ

φθογγάζομαι *mid.vb.* [φθογγή] (of a cockerel) **cry out, crow** Ion; (of Athena's snake-fringed aigis) **be noisy** —W.DAT. *w. hisses* Pi.*fr.*

φθογγή ῆς, dial. **φθογγά** ᾶς *f.* **1 voice** (of a person or god) Il. Trag. AR. Plu.; **voice, song** (of Orpheus) A.; **call, cry** (of an animal, a bird) Od. E.

2 something spoken, utterance A. E. AR.; **exclamation, cry, groan, shout** A. S.

φθόγγος ου *m.* **1 voice** (of a person, the Cyclops) Hom. Trag. Pl. Plu.; **song** (of the Sirens) Od.; **cry, call** (of animals, birds) Thgn. S. E. Pl. X.

2 utterance (of a person) A. S. NT.; **cry, exclamation** S. Pl.

3 speech (of a person) Od. Pl.; **language** (of a people) Anacr. A. Plu.

4 roar (of the sea, a tidal wave) E.; **sound** (of the wind, sthg. moving) Simon. Ar. Pl. Call.; (of music or sim.) Pl. X.

5 sonorous quality, sonorousness (possessed by certain letters of the alphabet) Pl.

6 musical sound, note (esp. played on an instrument) Lyr.adesp. E. Pl. Arist. Plu.; (fig., ref. to the emotions, as notes produced by the soul) Arist.; **individual sound** (in a word), **sound, letter** (ref. to a phoneme) Pl. Arist. Plu.

φθόη ης *f.* [φθίνω] **wasting disease, consumption** Isoc. Pl. Plu.

φθόϊς ιος *m.* | Att.contr.acc.pl. φθοῖς | **a kind of cake** (made w. cheese and honey), **cheesecake** Ar.

φθονερός ά (Ion. ή) όν *adj.* [φθόνος] **1** (of gods, persons, their feelings and actions) **jealous, envious** (of another's happiness or success) A. Pi. Hdt. S. Ar. +; (of reversals of fortune, sent by the gods) **spiteful** Pi.; (fig., of reins) **of spitefulness** (wielded by someone) Ar.(mock-trag.) ‖ MASC.SB. **envious man** Pi. Arist. Men. Theoc. Plu.

2 (of a person) **jealously holding back, selfish** (W.GEN. w. one's wisdom) Thgn.

–**φθονερά** *neut.pl.adv.* **enviously** Pi.

–**φθονερῶς** *adv.* **enviously, jealously, spitefully** Isoc. Pl. X. D.

φθονέω *contr.vb.* **1 feel envious desire** (of the success or possessions of others); **be envious** Il. + —W.DAT. *towards someone* Hes. + —W.GEN., DAT. or ἐπί + DAT. *of someone's achievements* Od. + —W.ACC. *of sthg.* E. ‖ PASS. **be envied** (oft. W.DAT. or ὑπό + GEN. by someone) Hdt. Th. X.

2 feel resentment (W.DAT. towards someone) —w. εἰ or ὅτι + VB. *that sthg. shd. be the case* Hdt. E. Lys. Ar. +; (esp. in neg.phr.) **resent, begrudge** —W.ACC. + INF. *that sthg. shd. be the case* Od. Hdt. S. E. —W.DAT. + INF. or PTCPL. *that someone shd. do sthg.* Lys. Pl. —W.DAT. or GEN. *someone's success* Th. Isoc. X.; **object to** —W.DAT. + GEN. *someone (having) sthg.* E. Isoc.; (intr.) **object** (to someone having sthg.) Od. Ar.; **resent** —W.ACC. *sthg.* E.; (in neg.phrs.) **think it amiss** —W.DAT. + INF. *for someone to do sthg.* Od. A.
3 (of a woman) **feel jealous hatred** —W.DAT. *towards one's stepchildren, one's husband* (W.GEN. *over a love affair*) E.; (of persons, gods) **feel indignation** or **hatred** —W.DAT. *towards someone* E. Att.orats. ‖ PASS. **be hated** —W.DAT. *for a crime* E.
4 (of the gods) **feel spite** Hdt. Arist. —W.DAT. *towards mortals* Ar.
5 (of persons, esp. in neg.phr.) **spitefully hold back, withhold** —W.GEN. *sthg.* (W.DAT. *fr. someone*) Od. A. E. Pl. X. Plb. —W.ACC. *sthg.* S.
6 spitefully refuse —W.INF. *to do sthg.* Od. Scol. Pi. E. Ar. +; **refuse** (to do sthg.), **say no** Pl.; **hold back, forbear** —W.PTCPL. *fr. doing sthg.* A.

φθόνησις εως *f.* (in neg.phr.) **begrudging, refusal** (W.GEN. of sthg. sought by a person) S.

φθόνος ου *m.* **1 envy, jealousy** (of the success or possessions of others) Pi. B. Hdt. Trag. +; (personif.) E. Call.
2 malicious desire to frustrate another's success, **spite** B. Trag. Th. Att.orats. Pl. X.; (as the gods' motivation for harming mortals; oft. w. θεῶν understd.) Pi. Trag.
3 spiteful refusal (of sthg.) A.; (wkr.sens., in neg.phr.) **begrudging** (of sthg.), **objection** (to granting sthg.) A. Ar. Pl.
4 resentment, offence (taken at sthg.) S. D.
5 cause of offence, **reproach** E.

φθορά ᾶς, Ion. **φθορή** ῆς *f.* [φθείρω] **1 destruction** (of a city, camp, crops) A. Plb. Plu.; **death and destruction** (esp. caused by wars, floods, fires, or sim.) Hdt. Pl. Plb. Plu.
2 (gener.) **destruction, obliteration** (of sthg.) Pl. Arist. Plu.; (philos., oft. as a description of death, opp. birth and creation) Pl. Arist. Plb. NT.
3 death (of a certain person) S. X.
4 loss of life (suffered by a population or army) Th. Pl. D. Plb. Plu.
5 ruin, doom (of a race, a house) S.
6 disaster (ref. to shipwreck) E. Arist.
7 pestilence, plague Arist. Plu.
8 wasting, squandering (of money) Arist. Plu.
9 decay (of a corpse, matter) Plu.; (fig., of a state) Plb.
10 degeneration, corruption (of a form of government) Arist. Plu.
11 seduction (of a woman, a boy) Aeschin.(law) Plu.

φθόρος ου *m.* **1 destruction** (of a fleet, a state's power) Plb. Plu.; (of persons and property) Plu.; (gener.) **destruction or obliteration** (of a person) Pl.
2 loss of life (in a plague, war) Th. Plb. Plu.
3 ruin, doom Thgn. A. B.
4 (fig., ref. to a person) destructive creature, **pestilence** Ar.; (ref. to a spendthrift) **ruin** (W.GEN. of money) Theoc.

φιάλη ης, dial. **φιάλα** ᾱς *f.* **1 saucer-like vessel, shallow goblet, phiale** (usu. of precious metal, esp. for pouring libations) Xenoph. Pi. Hdt. E. Th. Ar. +; (W.GEN. of Ares, fig.ref. to a shield, fr. the similarity of shape) Tim.
2 urn (of precious metal, esp. for cremated bones) Il.

φιαλη-φόρος ον *adj.* [φέρω] ‖ MASC.FEM.SB. phiale-bearer (as the title of a Laconian priest or priestess) Plb.

φιαρός ά (Ion. ἡ) όν *adj.* | compar. **φιαρώτερος** | (of dawn) **bright** Call.; (of a girl) app. **sleek** Theoc.

φιδάκνη Att.*f.*: see πιθάκνη

φιδίτιον (v.l. **φιλίτιον**) ου *Lacon.n.* **communal canteen, mess** (for Spartan men; ref. to the building, meal, or body of men) X. Arist. Plu.

φιλ-άγαθος ον *adj.* [φίλος, φιλέω; ἀγαθός] **loving goodness, prizing goodness** Plb. Plu.

φιλ-άγλαος ον *adj.* [ἀγλαός] (of cities) **delighting in splendour** Pi. B.; (of hospitality) **splendid, glorious** B.

φιλ-άδελφος ον *adj.* [ἀδελφός] **loving one's brothers and sisters, brotherly** X. Plu.; (of tears) **of love for one's brother** S. ‖ NEUT.SB. love for one's brother Plb.

φιλ-αθήναιος ον *adj.* [Ἀθηναῖος] (of peoples, individuals) **pro-Athenian** (politically or culturally) Ar. Pl. D. Plu.

φίλαι (ep.aor.mid.imperatv.): see φιλέω

φιλ-αίακτος ον *adj.* [αἰάζω] (of sufferings) **lamentable** A.

φιλ-αίματος ον *adj.* [αἷμα] (of Rout, as a son of Ares; of the earth, as recipient of sacrifices) **eager for blood** A. E.; (of deeds) **bloodthirsty, bloody** E.

φιλαίτερος (compar.adj.), **φιλαίτατος** (superl.adj.): see φίλος

φιλ-αίτιος ον *adj.* [αἰτία] **1** fond of making accusations, **fault-finding, quick to blame** A. Att.orats. X.; **quick to level a charge** (W.GEN. of neglect, against the gods) Pl. ‖ NEUT.SB. censoriousness Plu.
2 (of a politician) app., attracting blame, **liable to be criticised** D.

φιλ-ακόλαστος ον *adj.* **fond of self-indulgence** Plu. ‖ NEUT.SB. lasciviousness Plu.

φιλ-ακόλουθος ον *adj.* **fond of processions** Ar.

φιλ-ᾱλάκατος ον *dial.adj.* [ἠλακάτη] (of a woman) **fond of the distaff** (as exemplifying household tasks) B.

φιλ-αλέξανδρος ον *adj.* **fond of Alexander** Plu.

φιλ-αλήθης ες *adj.* [ἀληθής] **truth-loving, honest, sincere** Arist. Plu.

φίλᾱμα *dial.n.*: see φίλημα

φιλ-άμπελος ον *adj.* (of the goddess Peace) **fond of the vine** Ar.

φιλ-αναγνώστης ου *masc.adj.* **fond of reading** Plu.

φιλ-ανᾱλωτής οῦ *masc.adj.* **fond of spending; profligate** (W.GEN. w. other people's money) Pl.

φιλανδρίᾱ ᾱς *f.* [φίλανδρος] **love of one's husband or love for men, passionate love** (w. play on both senses) E.

φίλ-ανδρος ον *adj.* [ἀνήρ] **1** (of a land) **loving one's men, holding one's men dear** A.
2 (of the Amazons) **fond of men, not scared of men** Plu.; (pejor., of certain women) **promiscuous** Pl.
3 (of a woman) **fond of one's husband, doting** Plu.

φιλ-ανθρακεύς έως *m.* [ἄνθραξ] (ref. to a basket for carrying charcoal, or perh. to a person, w. play on φιλάνθρωπος) one who likes charcoal-sellers, **charcoal-sellers' friend** Ar.

φιλανθρώπευμα ατος *n.* [φιλανθρωπεύομαι] **act of kindness** or **charity** Plu.

φιλανθρωπεύομαι *mid.vb.* [φιλάνθρωπος] **be generous** Men. —w. πρός + ACC. *towards someone* D.

φιλανθρωπέω *contr.vb.* **show kindness** or **generosity** Plb. —W.ACC. *towards persons, cities* Plb.

φιλανθρωπίᾱ ᾱς *f.* **1** friendly attitude or behaviour, **kindness, benevolence, generosity** (shown by persons or gods) Att.orats. Pl. X. +
2 act of kindness or **generosity** D. Plb. Plu.; **generosity, altruism** (as a character trait) Plu.

φιλέω

3 **leniency** (towards prisoners or sim.) X. Plb. Plu.
4 **benevolent nature** (of the art of agriculture) X.; **benevolent associations** (of the term *law*) D.
5 (wkr.sens.) **friendliness, courtesy, politeness** D. Plb. Plu.

φιλ-άνθρωπος ον *adj*. 1 (of gods, their actions) **benevolent** (towards mankind) A. Ar. Pl. Plu.
2 (of persons, their actions) **benevolent** (towards other people), **humane, kind, generous** Att.orats. X. Arist. Men. Plb. Plu.
3 **lenient** (towards enemies, captives) D. Plb. Plu.
4 (of the art of agriculture, envisaged as a teacher) **benevolent, altruistic** X.; (of legislation) **humane, considerate** X.
5 (wkr.sens., of persons, letters, speeches, or sim.) **friendly, courteous, polite** D. Men. Plb. Plu.
6 (of dogs, horses) **fond of people, friendly** X.
7 (of wine, offered to guests) perh. **welcoming** Plu.
8 (of a situation in a drama) **appealing to** or **satisfying human feelings** Arist.

—**φιλανθρώπως** *adv*. 1 **humanely, benevolently** Att.orats. Plb. NT. Plu.
2 **in a friendly manner** Aeschin. Arist. Men. Plb.; **politely** D. Men. Plb.

φιλ-άνωρ ορος *dial.masc.fem.adj*. [ἀνήρ] 1 (of feelings) **of love for one's husband** A.; (of the footsteps) **of a devoted wife** A.
2 (of honour accorded to guests) **kindly, respectful** B.

φιλ-άοιδος ον, Att. **φιλῳδός** όν *adj*. [ἀοιδή] 1 (of a person) **fond of music, music-loving** Arist.; (of a lyre) **musical, tuneful** Sapph.
2 (of persons, frogs) **fond of singing** Ar.
3 (of a person) **poetry-loving, poetic** Theoc.

φιλαπεχθημοσύνη ης *f*. [φιλαπεχθήμων] **belligerence, aggression** Isoc. D.

φιλ-απεχθήμων ον, gen. ονος *adj*. [ἀπεχθάνομαι] (of persons, speeches) **belligerent, antagonistic** Att.orats.; (of statements) **contentious** Isoc.

—**φιλαπεχθημόνως** *adv*. **belligerently** Pl.

φιλ-απεχθής ές *adj*. (of persons, accusations, abuse) **antagonistic** Plb.

—**φιλαπεχθῶς** *adv*. **aggressively, antagonistically** Plb.

φιλ-απόδημος ον *adj*. **fond of travel** X.

φιλαργυρία ᾱς *f*. [φιλάργυρος] **love of money, covetousness, avarice** Att.orats. Arist. Plb. Plu.

φιλ-άργυρος ον *adj*. [ἀλέω] **greedy for money, avaricious** S. Pl. X. +

φιλ-άρετος ου *m*. [ἀρετή] **lover of virtue** Arist.

φιλ-άρματος ον *adj*. [ἅρμα] (of Thebes) **chariot-loving** Pi. E.

φιλαρχέω *contr.vb*. [φίλαρχος] **desire** or **be addicted to power** Plb. Plu.

φιλαρχίᾱ ᾱς *f*. **love of power, desire for power** Plb. Plu.; **desire for supremacy** (w. ἐν + DAT. over a people) Plb.; **pursuit of office** Plu.

φίλ-αρχος ον *adj*. [φιλέω, ἀρχή] (in political ctxt., of persons, peoples) **desiring power** Pl. Plb.

φίλατο (ep.3sg.aor.mid.): see φιλέω

φίλ-αυλος ον *adj*. [αὐλός] (of persons, the Muses, dolphins) **fond of the aulos** S. E. Ar. Arist.

φιλαυτίᾱ ᾱς *f*. [φίλαυτος] **self-regard, egotism** Plu.

φίλ-αυτος ον *adj*. [αὐτός] 1 (of persons) **self-regarding, selfish, egotistical** Arist. Plu.
2 (as a positive quality) **self-respecting** Arist. ‖ NEUT.SB. **self-respect** Arist.

φιλ-εγκλήμων ον, gen. ονος *adj*. [ἔγκλημα] **fond of making accusations** ‖ NEUT.SB. **fault-finding** (as a character trait) Plb.

φιλ-ελεύθερος ον *adj*. (of a people, a city) **fond of liberty** Plb. Plu.; (of a faction) **supportive of liberty, liberal, democratic** (opp. oppressive) Plu. ‖ NEUT.SB. **love of liberty** Plb. Plu.

φιλ-έλλην ηνος *masc.fem.adj*. [Ἕλλην] (of foreigners) **having an admiration for Greek culture, Hellenophile** Hdt. Isoc. X. Plu.; (of Greeks) **patriotic** Isoc. Pl. X.

φιλ-έορτος ον *adj*. [ἑορτή] (of Peace) **festival-loving** Ar.

φιλ-επιτιμητής οῦ *masc.adj*. **quick to find fault** Isoc.

φιλ-επίτιμος ον *adj*. **delighting in finding fault** ‖ NEUT.SB. **censoriousness** Plb.

φιλ-εραστής οῦ *masc.adj*. (of boys) **enjoying male lovers** Pl.; (of men) **glad to have male admirers** Arist.

φιλεραστίᾱ ᾱς *f*. **amorous behaviour** (of a male admirer) Pl.

φιλέραστος ον *adj*. **fond of having love-affairs, amorous** Plb.

φιλεργίᾱ ᾱς *f*. [φιλεργός] **industriousness** (as a character trait) X. D. Plb. Plu.

φιλ-εργός όν *adj*. [ἔργον] **loving hard work, industrious** D.

φιλ-έριθος ον *adj*. (fig., of a distaff) **loyal to wool-spinners** Theoc.

φιλεταιρίᾱ ᾱς *f*. [φιλέταιρος] **love for one's comrades, comradeship** X. Arist.

φιλ-έταιρος ον *adj*. [ἑταῖρος] 1 **fond of one's comrades** Pl. X. Arist.
2 (w.connot. of partisanship, esp. in political ctxts.) **loyal to one's comrades, loyal** Thphr. Plu.; (of courage) Th. ‖ NEUT.SB. **loyalty** Plu.

—**φιλεταίρως** *adv*. (iron.) **in loyal partnership** —*ref. to a pair of embezzlers stealing money* Aeschin.

φιλ-ευτράπελος ον *adj*. (of young men) **fond of being witty, facetious** Arist.

φιλ-εχθής ές *adj*. [ἔχθος] **fond of showing hostility, quarrelsome** Theoc.

φιλέω *contr.vb*. [φίλος] | dial.3pl. φιλέοντι, also φιλεῦντι, Ion. φιλεῦσι, Aeol. φιλέοισι | ep.inf. φιλήμεναι, Aeol. φιλέην (Theoc., cj.) | Ion.masc.nom.pl.ptcpl. φιλεῦντες, dial.fem.ptcpl. φιλεῦσα, Aeol.fem.ptcpl. φιλέοισα | iteratv.impf. φιλέεσκον, Ion.impf. ἐφίλευν | fut. φιλήσω, ep.inf. φιλησέμεν | aor. ἐφίλησα, dial. ἐφίλᾱσα (Theoc.) | pf. πεφίληκα ‖ MID.: ep.3sg.aor. ἐφίλατο, also φίλατο (also w.pass.sens. AR.), imperatv. φῖλαι, ptcpl. φιλάμενος | mid.pass.pf. πεφίλημαι | mid.pass.fut.pf. πεφιλήσομαι ‖ PASS.: fut. φιλήσομαι | aor. ἐφιλήθην ‖ neut.impers.vbl.adj. φιλητέον | —also **φίλημι** (or **φίλημμι**) Aeol.vb. | 2sg. φιλήσθα (or φίλησθα) | masc.acc.sg.ptcpl. φιλέντα |

1 (act. and mid.) **feel affection for, love, hold dear** —*one's child, father, master, a friend, servant* Hom. + —*a house, city, one's native land* E. Att.orats. Men.; (of gods) —*persons, peoples, good men, a city* Hom. +; (of a politician) —*the People* Ar. ‖ PASS. (of a person, land, animal) **be held dear, be loved** (oft. W.DAT. or PREP.PHR. by a parent, person, god) Il. +

2 **hold dear, look after** —*oneself* E.; **prize, value, guard zealously** —*one's life* S. E. NT.; **respect** —*oneself* (as a quality desirable in a public official) Arist.

3 **be a friend to** —*someone* Hes. +; (fig., of poverty) Thgn. ‖ MID. (of a god) **show one's care for, look after** —*a person* Od.

4 (of a host, city) **welcome, show hospitality to** —*a guest* Hom. Thgn.; (mid.) hHom. ‖ PASS. (of a guest) **be shown hospitality** —w. παρά + DAT. *by someone* Hom.

φιληδέω

5 love (romantically, sexually) —*one's wife, husband, lover* Hom. + ‖ PASS. be loved (by someone) Hdt. +
6 kiss —*a person, head, neck* Hippon. Thgn. Hdt. Trag. Ar. + ‖ MID. (of persons) **kiss one another** Hdt.
7 (of persons, gods, oft. in neg.phr.) **approve of, admire** —*persons, things, actions* Od. +; (of gods, Peace, Triumph) **love, prize** —*dance, song, celebration, food* (*as offerings*) Stesich. Pi. Philox.Leuc.; (of persons, gods, oft. in neg.phr.) —*peace, justice, treachery, conflict, or sim.* Hes. Sapph. Thgn. E. ‖ PASS. (of song) be enjoyed —W.DAT. *by certain places* Pi.
8 delight in (an activity); **enjoy** —*the spear* (*i.e. warfare*), *work, recreation, revelry* Anacr. Pi. E.*Cyc.* —W.INF. *doing sthg.* Hes. Pi. Hdt. S. +
9 take frequent delight in, make a habit of —W.PTCPL. *doing sthg.* Ar.; (of revels, an idle army) **be prone to** —*scuffles, rumour-mongering* E. ‖ IMPERS. **it is usual** —W.INF. or ACC. + INF. *for sthg. to be the case, for someone to do sthg.* A. Hdt. Th. Pl. +; (w.inf.understd.) Pl. Plu.
10 (of persons or things) **be accustomed, tend** —W.INF. *to do sthg., to happen* B. Hdt. Trag. Th. +; (w.inf.understd.) E.

φιληδέω *contr.vb.* [φιληδής] (of a person) **take delight** —W.DAT. *in battles* Ar.; (of a god) —*in new cities* Call.

φιλ-ηδής ές *adj.* [ἧδος] **fond of pleasure** Arist.

φιληδία ᾶς *f.* [φιληδέω] **pleasure, delight** (in sthg.) Ar.

φιληδονία ᾶς *f.* [φιλήδονος] **love of pleasure, sensual indulgence** Plu.

φιλ-ήδονος ον *adj.* [ἡδονή] **pleasure-seeking** (opp. self-disciplined) Plb. Plu.

φιληκοέω *contr.vb.* [φιλήκοος] **be an attentive listener** or **reader** Plb.

φιληκοΐα ᾶς *f.* **art of listening keenly** (W.GEN. to discussions) Isoc.

φιλ-ήκοος ον *adj.* [ἀκούω] **1 fond of listening** (to philosophical discussions and speeches, music, fine speaking, or sim.) Pl. ‖ MASC.SB. **keen listener** (to philosophical discussions) Pl. Plu.; **attentive reader** (of a book) Plb.
2 (of a philosopher) **attentive to detail** Plu.

φιλ-ηλιαστής οῦ *masc.adj.* **fond of jury duty in the Heliaia** Ar.

φίλημα, dial. **φίλαμα**, ατος *n.* **kiss** E. X. Men. Hellenist.poet. NT. Plu.

φιλημοσύνη ης *f.* **friendliness** (of a person) Thgn.

φιλ-ήνεμος ον *adj.* [ἄνεμος] (of cliffs) **wind-loving** Lyr.adesp.

φιλ-ήνιος ον *adj.* [ἡνία] (of horses) **loyal to the reins, accepting the reins** A.

φιλ-ήρετμος ον *adj.* [ἐρετμόν] (of peoples) **oar-loving, seafaring** Od.

φιλησί-μολπος ον *adj.* [μολπή] (of Euphrosyne) **delighting in the dance** Pi.

φίλησις εως *f.* **affection** (for someone) Arist.

φιληση-στέφανος ον *adj.* (fig., of a feast) **delighting in garlands, with abundant garlands** Pi.*fr.*

φιλητεύω (v.l. **φηλητεύω**) *vb.* **be a bandit** hHom.

φιλήτης (v.l. **φηλήτης**) ου *m.* **bandit, robber, thief** hHom. Archil. Hippon. Trag. Call.; **crook, conman** Hes.

φιλητικός ή όν *adj.* [φιλητός] **inclined to be fond** (W.GEN. of honours, learning) Arist.; **affectionate** (sts. W.GEN. towards someone) Arist. Plu.

φιλητός ή όν *adj.* [φιλέω] (of persons, qualities) **worthy of being loved, capable of inspiring affection** Arist. ‖ NEUT.SB. **that which is loved** Arist.

φιλήτωρ ορος *m.f.* **lover** A. Call.

φιλία ᾶς, Ion. **φιλίη** ης *f.* **1 existence of friendly feelings, friendship** (w. a person, betw. persons) Thgn. E. Th. Ar. +
2 friendly relationship (betw. gods and men, a person and a household) E.
3 love, loving relationship (betw. siblings, husband and wife) E. Arist.
4 entente, alliance, pact of friendship (betw. nations, rulers) Hdt. Th. And. Pl. +; (betw. plotters) Hdt.
5 friendliness, amiability E. Pl. Arist.
6 (philos., opp. νεῖκος *strife*) **friendliness, attraction** (as a force holding particles together) Emp. Isoc.
7 demonstration of friendly feelings, fondness, affection (for someone) Thgn. Th. Isoc. Pl. +; **love** (for one's husband, child, followers) E. X.; **devotion** (to one's husband, master or ruler) Pl. X.; **goodwill** (towards cities, peoples, foreign rulers) Th. Isoc. X.
8 love (of profit, goodness) Pl.

φιλικός ή όν *adj.* [φίλος] **1 relating to friends;** (of a group) **of friends** Arist.; (of help) **for friends** Plu.; (of matters) **involving friends** Plu.
2 relating to friendship; (of persons, actions, relationships, criticisms) **friendly** Pl. X. Arist. Plb. Plu.; (of qualities, feelings) **stemming from friendship** Arist. ‖ NEUT.SB. **friendliness** Arist.; **act of friendship, favour** X. ‖ NEUT.PL.SB. **feelings of friendship** X. Arist.
3 (of a song) **of love** Theoc.

—**φιλικῶς** *adv.* | compar. φιλικώτερον, superl. φιλικώτατα | **in a friendly manner** Isoc. Pl. X. Is. Arist. +

φίλιος ᾱ (Ion. η) ον (also ος ον) *adj.* **1 showing friendship;** (of persons, their eyes, words, or sim.) **friendly** A. Pi. Hdt. S. Pl. +
2 consisting of friends; (of a pair) **of friends** E.
3 (of Night, a person's destiny) **kindly** A. Pi.
4 (in military ctxt., of people, cities, ships, or sim.) **friendly** (opp. hostile) Hdt. E. Th. X. +; (of voyages, shipwrecks, flags, signals, property) **of friendly forces, of allies** Th. Lys. X. D. Plb. Plu.; (of delegations) **to allies** X. ‖ FEM.SB. **allied territory** X. D. ‖ MASC.PL.SB. **allies** Hdt. Pl. Plb. ‖ NEUT.PL.SB. **friendly ties, alliance** (betw. peoples) Hdt. E.
5 (wkr.sens., of things) **compatible** (w. other things, w. each other) Pl.
6 showing love or affection; (of the embrace or kiss of a wife or mother) **loving** E.
7 associated with love; (of the gifts of Kypris) **loving** or **lovely** Pi.
8 being the object of love or affection; (of a woman, wife, child) **beloved, dear** A. E.; (of a girl's companions) Mosch.; (of the mouth, head, cheek, hands of one's child) E.; (of a marriage bed) E.; (of the form of Virtue) Arist.*lyr.*
9 (wkr.sens., of a song, the light of dawn) **welcome** E.

—**Φίλιος** ου *m.* (epith. of Zeus) **guardian of friendships** E. Ar. Pl. Men. Plu.

—**φιλίως** *adv.* **1 gratifyingly, in an acceptable way** —*ref. to speaking* Pl.
2 in a friendly manner Plu.
3 (in military ctxt.) **in the manner of allies** Th. X.

φίλ-ιππος ον *adj.* [ἵππος] (of persons) **horse-loving, fond of horses** Pi. B. E. Pl. +; (of a god) **benign towards horses** (opp. towards humans) Plu.

Φίλιππος ου *m.* **Philip** (name of several rulers of Macedonia, after 350 BC usu. ref. to Philip II, 382–336 BC) Hdt. +

—**Φιλιππεῖος** ου *m.* **stater of Philip, Macedonian stater** (ref. to gold coins used to fund Philip's campaigns) Plu.

—**Φιλιππίζω** *vb.* (of persons, the Pythian oracle) **support Philip, be on Philip's side** Att.orats. Plu.

—**Φιλιππικός** ή όν *adj.* (of a war) **against Philip** Plb.
 || MASC.SB. (w. λόγος understd.) speech against Philip, Philippic D.(title)
—**Φιλιππισμός** οῦ *m.* **support for** or **alliance with Philip** D.
—**Φίλιπποι** ων *m.pl.* **Philippi** (city in Macedonia, site of a battle in which Julius Caesar's assassins were defeated) NT. Plu.
φιλίτιον *n.*: see φιδίτιον
φιλίων (compar.adj.): see φίλος
φιλο-βασιλεύς έως *masc.adj.* (of persons, a people) **loyal to one's king** Plu.
φιλο-γαθής ές *dial.adj.* [γηθέω] (of a cry) **of joyful delight** A.
φιλό-γαμος ον *adj.* [γάμος] (of suitors) **eager for marriage** E.
φιλο-γέλοιος ον *adj.* [γελοῖος] (of old people, in neg.phr.) **fond of joking** Arist.
φιλό-γελως ωτος *masc.fem.adj.* [γέλως] (of persons, Victory) **fond of laughter** Pl. Arist. Men. Plu.
φιλογεωργία ᾶς *f.* [φιλογέωργος] **love of growing crops** X.
φιλο-γέωργος ον *adj.* [γεωργός] **fond of growing crops** X.
φιλό-γλυκυς υ, gen. εος *adj.* [γλυκύς] (of a person) **fond of sweet things, sweet-toothed** Arist.
φιλογραμματέω *contr.vb.* [γράμμα] **be fond of reading, be studious** Plu.
φιλογυμναστέω *contr.vb.* [φιλογυμναστής] **devote oneself to gymnastic exercise** Pl. Plu.
φιλο-γυμναστής οῦ *masc.adj.* **devoted to gymnastic exercise, fond of exercise** Pl.
φιλογυμναστία ᾶς *f.* [φιλογυμναστέω] **devotion to gymnastic exercise** Pl.
φιλογυμναστικός ή όν *adj.* [φιλογυμναστής] **devoted to gymnastic exercise** Pl. Arist.
φιλο-γύναιξ αικος *masc.adj.* —also **φιλογύνης** ου *masc.adj.* [γυνή] (of men) **fond of women, womanising** Pl. Plb.
φιλο-δέσποτος ον *adj.* [δεσπότης] (of a slave) **loyal to one's master** Hdt.; (pejor., of the populace) **servile** Thgn.
φιλό-δημος ον *adj.* [δῆμος] (of a politician, an action) **loving the people, looking after the interests of the people** Ar.
φιλο-δίκαιος ον *adj.* (of persons, the Athenian people) **prizing justice, loving to see justice done** Arist. Plu.
φιλοδικέω *contr.vb.* [φιλόδικος] **be litigious** Th. Arist.
φιλό-δικος ον *adj.* [δίκη] **fond of lawsuits, litigious** Att.orats. Arist.
φιλοδοξέω *contr.vb.* [φιλόδοξος] **be desirous of glory, seek acclaim** Arist. Plb.
φιλοδοξία ᾶς *f.* **1** (usu. w.neg.connots.) **desire for glory** Plb. Plu.; **concern for one's reputation** Plu.
2 illustrious reputation (of a person) Plb.
φιλό-δοξος ον *adj.* [δόξα] **desirous of glory, ambitious** Pl. Arist. Plb. Plu.
φιλ-όδυρτος ον *adj.* [ὀδύρομαι] **devoted to lamenting, immersed in laments** A.
φιλό-δωρος ον *adj.* [δῶρον] **1 fond of giving gifts** Plu.
2 generous X.; (W.GEN. w. one's goodwill) Pl.; (of an action) **done out of generosity** D.
—**φιλοδώρως** *adv.* **generously** Pl.
φιλοζωέω *contr.vb.* [φιλόζωος] **be concerned with saving one's life** Plb.
φιλοζωία ᾶς *f.* **desire to save one's life** Plb.
φιλό-ζωος ον *adj.* [ζωή] **fond of one's life, scared of death** Arist.
φιλό-ζωος ον *adj.* [ζῷον] (of the creator god) **holding all living things dear, beneficent** X.

φιλο-θεάμων ον, gen. ονος *adj.* [θέαμα] **fond of spectacle, fond of watching performances** Pl.; (fig., of philosophers) **fond of the spectacle** (W.GEN. of the truth) Pl.
φιλό-θεος ον *adj.* [θεός] (of fortunate men) **loving the gods, grateful to the gods** Arist.
φιλο-θέωρος ον *adj.* [θεωρός] **fond of spectacle, fond of watching performances** (in the theatre) Arist.
φιλοθηρία ᾶς *f.* [φιλόθηρος] **love of hunting** X.
φιλό-θηρος ον *adj.* [θήρα] **fond of hunting** Pl. X.
φιλο-θρηνής ές *adj.* [θρῆνος] **fond of lamenting** Mosch.
φιλό-θυρσος ον *adj.* [θύρσος] (of the devotees of Cybele) **delighting in the thyrsos** Lyr.adesp.
φιλοθύτης ου *masc.adj.* [φιλόθυτος] **fond of offering sacrifices** (w.connot. of piety) Antipho Plu.; **fond of holding sacrificial banquets** Ar. Plu.
φιλό-θυτος ον *adj.* [θύω¹] (of rites) **of pious sacrifices** or **accompanied by sacrifices** A.
φιλ-οίκειος ον *adj.* [οἰκεῖος] **holding one's family dear, loyal to one's family** Plu. || NEUT.SB. **loyalty to one's family** Plb.
φιλ-οικοδόμος ον *adj.* **fond of erecting buildings** X. Plu.; **fond of engaging in architecture** Arist.
φιλ-οικτίρμων ον, gen. ονος *adj.* **quick to show pity, compassionate** E. Pl. Plu.
φιλ-οίκιστος ον *adj.* [οἰκτίζω] (of women) **quick to show pity, easily moved to tears** S.
φίλ-οικτος ον *adj.* [οἶκτος] (of a glance) **stirring pity, piteous** A.
φιλοινίη ης Ion.*f.* [φίλοινος] **fondness for wine** Hdt.
φίλ-οινος ον *adj.* [οἶνος] **fond of wine, bibulous** Pl. Arist. Plu.
φιλ-οίφᾱς ᾶ *dial.masc.adj.* [οἴφω] (of a man) **liking a fuck, lecherous** Theoc.
φιλό-καινος ον *adj.* [καινός] || NEUT.SB. **love of novelty** or **change** Plb.
φιλοκαλέω *contr.vb.* [φιλόκαλος] **be fond of beauty, be an aesthete** Th.; **make it one's aesthetic mission** —W.INF. **to decorate a palace w. gardens** Plu.
φιλό-καλος ον *adj.* [καλός] **1** (of persons, a city) **appreciative of fine things, refined** Isoc. Pl. X. Plu.; (of a soldier) **meticulous** (in dress and equipment) X.
2 (of persons, their nature) **fond of that which is noble** Arist. Plu.; **fond of noble actions, heroic** X.
φιλοκέρδεια ας (Ion. ης) *f.* [φιλοκερδής] **love of profit, greediness** Pl. X. Theoc. Plu.
φιλοκερδέω *contr.vb.* **pursue profit, be a profiteer** X.
φιλο-κερδής ές *adj.* [κέρδος] (of persons, their nature) **greedy for profit** Thgn. Ar. Pl. X. Plu.; (fig., of the Muse) Pi.
φιλο-κέρτομος ον *adj.* **fond of jeering** or **mocking** Od. Theoc.
φιλο-κηδέμων ον, gen. ονος *adj.* [κηδεμών] **holding one's relatives dear, loyal to one's family** X.
φιλο-κίνδυνος ον *adj.* **1 fond of danger, bold, intrepid** (in battle, hunting, or sim.) X. D. Plb. Plu.; (of a person's life) **adventurous** Isoc.
2 prone to take risks, foolhardy D. Arist.
—**φιλοκινδύνως** *adv.* **intrepidly, boldly** Isoc. X. Plb.
φιλο-κισσοφόρος ον *adj.* (of Dionysus) **fond of wearing ivy** E.Cyc.
φιλο-κόλαξ ακος *masc.fem.adj.* **fond of flatterers** or **flattery** Arist.
φιλοκοσμία ᾶς *f.* [κόσμος] **love of adornment** Plu.
φιλό-κροτος ον *adj.* [κρότος] (of Pan) **noisy, rowdy** hHom.
φιλο-κτέανος ον *adj.* [κτέανα] **eager for possessions, covetous** Il.

φιλο-κτήμων ον, gen. ονος *adj.* [κτῆμα] eager for possessions, **covetous** Sol.

Φιλοκτήτης ου (ep. ᾱο) *m.* **Philoktetes** (warrior and archer, abandoned on Lemnos after suffering a snakebite on the way to Troy) Hom. +

φιλό-κυβος ον *adj.* [κύβος] fond of playing dice, **addicted to gambling** Ar.

φιλο-κῡδής ές *adj.* [κῦδος] exulting in glory; (of revels, youth) **glorious, splendid** hHom.

φιλο-κυνηγέτης ου *masc.adj.* **fond of hunting** X.

φιλο-κύων ον, gen. κυνος *adj.* **fond of dogs** Pl.

φιλο-λάκων ωνος *masc.adj.* [Λάκων] (of politicians, writers) **pro-Spartan** Plu.

φιλο-λήιος ον *adj.* [λείᾱ] **obsessed with amassing spoils** hHom.

φιλολογέω *contr.vb.* [φιλόλογος] **engage in study** or **philosophical discussion** Plu.

φιλολογίᾱ ᾱς *f.* **1 love of discussions** (esp. philosophical) Isoc. Pl.
2 love of learning (ref. to scholarship in general, incl. literature) Plu.

φιλό-λογος ον *adj.* [λόγος] **1** (of the Athenians, opp. Spartans) **fond of talking, articulate** Pl.
2 (of persons) **fond of** (philosophical) **discussions** Pl.
3 fond of learning Arist. Plu.; **learned, erudite** Plu.

φιλο-λοίδορος ον *adj.* **fond of abusive language** D.

φιλομαθέω *contr.vb.* [φιλομαθής] **be fond of studying** Pl. Plb.; **engage in study** Plb. Plu.

φιλο-μαθής ές *adj.* [μανθάνω] **fond of learning** Isoc. Pl. X. Arist. Plu.; **eager to learn** (W.GEN. the arts of war) X.
|| NEUT.SB. **love of knowledge** Pl. Plu.

φιλομαθίᾱ (also **φιλομάθεια**) ᾱς *f.* **love of learning** Pl. Arist.; **pursuit of knowledge** Pl.

φιλο-μαντευτής οῦ *masc.adj.* [μαντεύομαι] **concerned about omens, superstitious** Pl.

φιλό-μαστος ον *adj.* [μαστός] (of young animals) **desiring the breast** A.; (gener.) **of suckling age, unweaned** A.

φιλομαχέω *contr.vb.* [φιλόμαχος] (of a commander) **be hungry for battle** Plu.; (specif.) **take the offensive** Plu.

φιλό-μαχος ον *adj.* [μάχη] (of a race, a goddess) **fond of battle, warlike** A. Pi.*fr.*; (of persons) **eager for battle** A.

φιλο-μεμφής ές *adj.* [μέμφομαι] | superl. φιλομεμφότατος | **quick to apportion blame, critical** Plu.

Φιλομήλᾱ ᾱς *f.* **Philomela** (mythol. princess of Athens, raped by her brother-in-law Tereus and turned into a swallow or nightingale by the gods) D. Arist.

φιλο-μήτωρ ορ, gen. ορος *adj.* [μήτηρ] **loving one's mother, dutiful to one's mother** Plu.; (as the title of a king) Plu.

φιλο-μμειδής ές *adj.* [μειδάω] (of Aphrodite, a Nereid) **fond of smiles, ever-smiling** Hom. Hes. hHom.

φιλό-μολπος ον *adj.* [μολπή] (of a goddess, a city) **music-loving** Lyr. Call.

φιλό-μουσος ον *adj.* [Μοῦσα] **1** (of persons, dolphins) **fond of music** Lyr.adesp. Pl. X. Arist. Men.
2 (of persons) **cultured, sophisticated** Pl. Arist. Theoc.; (of a speech) **sophisticated, artful** Ar.

φιλό-μῡθος ον *adj.* [μῦθος] **fond of myths, interested in stories** Arist.

φιλό-μωμος ον *adj.* [μῶμος] **fond of criticising** Pl.

φιλονῑκέω (v.l. **φιλονεικέω**) *contr.vb.* [φιλόνῑκος] **1** (of persons, oft. pejor.) **strive for victory, thirst for supremacy** (in battles, contests, games, or sim.) Th. X. D. Plb. Plu.; (of factions, in a political struggle) Plb.; (fig., of arguments in a discussion) Pl.
2 (of persons) **compete with one another, engage in rivalry** (esp. in games, political contests, or sim.) Th. Att.orats. X. Plu.; **contend with one another** (in battle) Isoc. D.
3 strive —W. πρός + ACC. *for sthg.* Pl. —W. ὅπως + SUBJ. or FUT.INDIC. *to ensure that one does sthg., that sthg. happens* Isoc. X. —W.INF. *to do sthg.* Plu.; **stubbornly argue** —W. πρός + ACC. *for sthg.* Plu.
4 (pejor.) **be stubbornly belligerent, be spitefully adversarial** (towards persons, their proposals, or sim.) Th. Att.orats. Pl. Plb. Plu. —W.ACC. *in* (*choosing*) *a certain course of action* Th.; **stir up hatred** —W.DAT. *against someone* Arist. || PASS. **be stubbornly opposed** Pl.

φιλονῑκίᾱ (v.l. **φιλονεικίᾱ**) ᾱς *f.* **1 desire for success, ambition** Simon. Pl. Plu.
2 rivalry, competition (betw. workers, chorus-directors, athletes, or sim.) Att.orats. Pl. X.; **contention** (betw. factions, empires) Th. Att.orats. Arist.
3 action of striving for supremacy, **struggle for victory** (in battle, or in a personal rivalry) Th. Pl. Men.
4 belligerence Th. Att.orats. Pl. Plb. Plu.

φιλό-νῑκος (v.l. **φιλόνεικος**) ον *adj.* [νίκη] **1** (of persons, their souls, horses) **eager for victory, ambitious** Lys. Pl. X. Arist. Plu.; **eager not to be outdone** (in generosity) X.
|| NEUT.SB. **eagerness for victory, fighting spirit** X.
2 competitive Isoc. Pl. Arist. Plu. || NEUT.SB. **competitiveness** Pl. Plu.
3 belligerent, argumentative Pi. Pl. Arist. Plu.

—**φιλονίκως** *adv.* | compar. φιλονῑκότερον | **with great eagerness for victory** Plu.; **competitively** Pl. X.

φιλοξενίᾱ ᾱς, Ion. **φιλοξενίη** ης *f.* [φιλόξενος] **1 kindness to visitors, hospitality** B. Call. AR. Plb. Plu.; (concr., ref. to amenities) Pl.
2 (gener.) **open-heartedness, generosity** Thgn.

φιλό-ξενος, Ion. **φιλόξεινος**, ον *adj.* [ξένος²] | superl. φιλοξενώτατος, also φιλοξεινώτατος (Call.) | (of persons, places, speeches, acts) **welcoming to strangers, hospitable** Od. A. Pi. B. E. Ar. +

—**φιλοξένως** *adv.* **with a policy of welcoming strangers** —*ref. to a state being organised* Isoc.

Φιλόξενος ου *m.* **1 Philoxenus** (of Cythera, dithyrambic poet, c.435–380 BC) Arist. Plb. Plu.
2 Philoxenus (of Leucas, lyric poet, contemporary of the above) Plu.

φιλο-παίγμων, Att. **φιλοπαίσμων**, ον, gen. ονος *adj.* [παῖγμα] **1** (of persons or gods) **fond of playful joking** Hes.*fr.* Pl.
2 (of a nuptial or Bacchic dance) **exuberant** Od. Ar.

φιλό-παις παιδος *masc.fem.adj.* [παῖς¹] (of a man) **fond of boys** Pl. Theoc.; (of the sickness) **of love for boys** Call.*epigr.*

φιλοπαίσμων Att.*adj.*: see φιλοπαίγμων

φιλο-παράβολος ου *adj.* (of soldiers' spirits) **ready to face dangers, emboldened, fired up** Plu.

φιλο-πατρίᾱ ᾱς *f.* [φιλόπατρις] **love for one's native land** Ar.

φιλό-πατρις ι, gen. ιδος *adj.* [πατρίς] | acc. φιλόπατριν | **loyal to one's native land, patriotic** Plb. Plu.

φιλο-πάτωρ ορος *masc.fem.adj.* [πατήρ] **loving one's father, loyal to one's father** E. X. Arist. Plu.; (as the title of a king) Plb. Plu.

φιλοπευστέω *contr.vb.* [reltd. πυνθάνομαι] (of a historian's audience) **be interested in research** Plb.

φιλό-πικρος ον *adj.* [πικρός] **fond of sour** or **savoury tastes** Arist.

φιλοπλουτίᾱ ᾱς *f.* [φιλόπλουτος] **love of riches, avariciousness** Plu.

φιλό-πλουτος ον *adj.* [πλοῦτος] (of persons, their efforts) devoted to amassing wealth, avaricious E. Plu.

φιλοποιέω *contr.vb.* [φιλοποιός] befriend, win over —*someone* Plb.

φιλο-ποιητής οῦ *masc.adj.* fond of poetry Pl.

φιλο-ποίμνιος ον *adj.* [ποίμνιον] (of a sheepdog) protective of the flock Theoc.

φιλο-ποιός όν *adj.* [ποιέω] (of a dinner-table) conducive to forming friendships Plu.

φιλο-πόλεμος, ep. **φιλοπτόλεμος**, ον *adj.* (of persons, peoples, gods) war-loving, warlike Il. Pl. X. AR. Theoc. Plu.
—**φιλοπολέμως** *adv.* in a warmongering manner Isoc.

φιλό-πολις, ep. **φιλόπτολις**, ι, gen. ιδος *adj.* [πόλις] | masc.fem.acc. φιλόπολιν | masc.nom.pl. φιλοπόλιδες, also φιλοπόλεις | **1** (of a god, guardian spirit) showing love for a (particular) city, **protecting a city** A. Ar.
2 (of persons) showing love for one's native city, **patriotic** E. Th. Att.orats. Pl. X.; (fig., of peaceableness) Pi.; (of a virtue) of love for one's city, **of patriotism** Ar. || NEUT.SB. patriotism Th.

φιλο-πολίτης ου, dial. **φιλοπολίτᾱς** ᾱ *masc.adj.* devoted to one's fellow citizens, **patriotic** Plu.

φιλοπονέω *contr.vb.* [φιλόπονος] **be industrious, be energetic** Pl. X. Plu.; **strive diligently** —W.PREP.PHR. *in pursuit of virtue* Isoc. || MID. **devote one's efforts** (to sthg.) Arist.

φιλο-πόνηρος ον *adj.* [πονηρός] **friendly with villains** Arist. Thphr. Plu.

φιλοπονίᾱ ᾱς *f.* [φιλοπονέω] **industriousness** Isoc. Pl. X. Plb. Plu.; **energetic behaviour** (of a person, hound) X. || PL. industrious efforts Isoc. Plb.; arduous exercises (of the Spartans) Arist.

φιλό-πονος ον *adj.* [πόνος] **1** (of persons, hounds) **hard-working, industrious, energetic** (as a character trait, or in a particular activity) S. Isoc. Pl. X. Arist. +
2 (of work) **painstaking** X.
3 (of war) **arduous, exhausting** X.
—**φιλοπόνως** *adv.* | compar. φιλοπονώτερον, superl. φιλοπονώτατα | **industriously, diligently, doggedly** Isoc. X. D. Men. Plb. Plu.

φιλοποσίᾱ ᾱς *f.* [φιλοπότης] **drunkenness** or **heavy drinking** Pl. X.

φιλο-πότης ου *masc.adj.* **fond of drink** Hdt. Ar. Plu.

φιλοπρᾱγμοσύνη ης *f.* [φιλοπράγμων] **meddlesomeness** (as the reason for filing a lawsuit) D.; **jostling** (for power or sim.) Pl.; **compulsion to pursue one's objectives** D.

φιλο-πρᾱ́γμων ον, gen. ονος *adj.* [πρᾶγμα] (of litigious men) **meddlesome** Is. Lycurg.

φιλοπροσηγορίᾱ ᾱς *f.* [φιλοπροσήγορος] **approachability, geniality** (opp. aloofness) Isoc.

φιλο-προσήγορος ον *adj.* **approachable, genial** (opp. aloof) Isoc.

φιλό-πρωτος ον *adj.* [πρῶτος] || NEUT.SB. **desire for pre-eminence** (as a character trait) Plu.

φιλοπτόλεμος *ep.adj.*: see φιλοπόλεμος

φιλόπτολις *ep.adj.*: see φιλόπολις

φιλορνῑθίᾱ ᾱς *f.* [φιλόρνις] **love of birds, bird-fever** (among impressionable Athenians) Ar.

φίλ-ορνις ῑθος *masc.fem.adj.* [ὄρνις] **1** (of a crag) **loved by birds** A.
2 (of a god) **benign towards birds** (opp. humans) Plu.

φιλ-όρτυξ υγος *masc.fem.adj.* **fond of quails** Pl.

φιλο-ρώμαιος ον *adj.* [Ῥωμαῖοι] **fond of the Romans, pro-Roman** Plu.

φίλος η (dial. ᾱ) ον *adj.* | voc. φίλε, also φῐ́λε *metri grat.* (Il.) || COMPAR.: φίλτερος, also φιλαίτερος (X. Call.), φιλώτερος (X.) | also masc.nom. φιλίων (Od.) | SUPERL.: φίλτατος, also φιλαίτατος (X. Theoc.) |

1 (of one's spouse, lover, friend or family member; oft. in addresses) held in great affection, **beloved** Hom. +; **dear** (W.DAT. to someone, the gods) Hom. + || MASC.FEM.SB. **dear one** (ref. to a lover, spouse, friend or family member) Hom. + || NEUT.SB. **beloved** (as a term of address) Ar. || NEUT.SUPERL.SB. **dearest** (as a term of address) Ar. || NEUT.PL.SB. (w.art.) **dear one** (ref. to a person) E. || NEUT.PL.SUPERL.SB. (w.art.) **nearest and dearest** (ref. to one's children, wife, or sim.) Trag.

2 || MASC.SB. (sts. also FEM.SB.) **friend** (sts. opp. relative; oft. as a formally codified relationship implying reciprocal loyalty and support) Hom. +; (fig.) **supporter, fosterer, patron** (W.GEN. of justice, truth, or sim.) Pl. +

3 (milit., of persons, forces, states) **friendly** (opp. hostile) Hdt. Th. +

4 (of persons, their mind or thoughts) **friendly, kindly, well-meaning** Hom. + || NEUT.PL.SB. (as quasi-advbl. intern.acc., w.vbs. of thinking, seeing, or sim.) **kindly thoughts, actions, glances** Hom. +

5 (of a person) **welcome** Od.; (of things, words, events) **welcome, gratifying, pleasant** Hom. + || NEUT.IMPERS. (w. ἐστί, sts.understd.) **it is pleasant** (oft. W.INF. to do sthg.) Hom. +; **it is beneficial** Hom. +

6 (of one's native land) **beloved** Hom. +; (of things, values, ideals) **held dear, treasured** Tyrt. +

7 (of one's heart, limbs, life) **dear** Hom. +; (wkr.sens., merely indicating possession; of clothes, toils, destiny) **personal, one's own** Il. Theoc.

—**φίλως** *adv.* **1 gladly** —*ref. to doing sthg.* Il. Hes.
2 welcomely, in a manner that is pleasing (W.DAT. to someone) A. E. Pl.
3 in a friendly manner Trag. Ar. X.; **lovingly** A.

φιλό-σῑτος ον *adj.* [σῖτος] **1** (of merchants) **devoted to grain** (i.e. to buying and selling it) X.
2 (of a person) **fond of food** Pl.

φιλο-σκώμμων ον, gen. ονος *adj.* [σκῶμμα] **fond of joking** Hdt. Plu.

φιλο-σκώπτης ου *masc.adj.* [σκώπτω] **fond of making jokes** Plu.

φιλοσοφέω *contr.vb.* [φιλόσοφος] | pf. πεφιλοσόφηκα | **1 be a lover of wisdom** Hdt. Isoc. Pl. X. Arist. Plu.; (of persons, their souls) **engage in the pursuit of knowledge** (oft. as a pure and lofty occupation) Th. Isoc. Pl. X. Plu.; (pejor.) **theorise** Lys.
2 (of a person) **be a philosopher** Pl. Arist. Plu.; (of a class of men) **be naturally inclined to philosophy** (w.connot. of superiority) Pl.; (gener., of a doctor, commander) **be learned** Men. Plu.
3 teach philosophy Isoc.; (of a parent) **give a lecture** (to one's son) Men.
4 study philosophy Isoc. Pl. Arist. Plb. Plu.
5 (gener.) **be a student, engage in study** Isoc. Pl. Arist. Plb.
—W.ACC. *of a particular subject or topic* Isoc. Plu.
—W.COGN.ACC. X. —W. περί + ACC. Isoc. Arist. || PASS. (of a subject) be investigated (by someone) Plu.
6 learn, work out —*sthg.* X. Arist. —W.COMPL.CL. *how to do sthg.* Isoc.; **reason, conclude** —W.COMPL.CL. *that sthg. is the case* Plu.
7 contrive (usu. W.ACC. τοῦτο *this*) —W.COMPL.CL. *that sthg. is the case* Att.orats. Men.; **devise** —*a strategy* (w. πρός + ACC. *to achieve sthg.*) Arist.

φιλοσοφίᾱ ᾱς *f.* **1 love of wisdom** Pl.; **pursuit of knowledge, scientific inquiry** (as an activity) Isoc. Pl. X. Arist. Plu.; (specif.) **scientific analysis** (of a particular subject) Isoc.
2 philosophy (as a discipline or field of science) Isoc. Pl. X. +; (ref. to a philosophical framework or outlook, esp. that of a particular person or school) X. Arist.

φιλό-σοφος ον *adj.* [φιλέω, σοφός] **1** (of persons, their mind, nature, way of life) **loving wisdom, seeking wisdom, eager for knowledge** Pl. Arist.; **learned** Ar. Isoc. Pl. Aeschin. Plu. ‖ NEUT.SB. **love of knowledge** Pl.
2 ‖ MASC.SB. **lover of wisdom, seeker for truth, learned man** Isoc. Pl. X. +; **philosopher** (as a profession; sts. opp. sophist, but oft. incl. all those who make a living fr. lectures, classes, or sim.) Isoc. Pl. X. +; (ref. to a specific historical figure or adherent of a specific school) Pl. Arist. Plb. NT. Plu.
3 (of discussions, studies) **on philosophical topics, philosophical** Pl. Plu.
4 (of speeches; of poetry, as a genre) **scientific** Isoc. Arist.

—**φιλοσόφως** *adv.* | compar. φιλοσοφώτερον |
1 scientifically (opp. casually) —*ref. to stating sthg.* Arist.; **in a spirit of scientific inquiry** Isoc.
2 in a balanced manner, open-mindedly (opp. contentiously) Pl. Plu.
3 on philosophical principles —*ref. to refusing to bow to someone* Plu.
4 wisely, profoundly Plu.
5 philosophically —*ref. to bearing a defeat* Plu.

φιλό-σπονδος ον *adj.* [σπονδή] (of a draught of liquid) **dedicated to libations, for libations** A.

φιλοστεφανέω *contr.vb.* [φιλοστέφανος] **1 be eager for garlands, be an avid competitor** —W.PREP.PHR. *in athletic contests* Plb.
2 (of a ruler) **behave** (w. εἰς + ACC. towards people) **in a way that solicits acclamation** Plb.

φιλο-στέφανος ον *adj.* (of goddesses, revellers) **delighting in garlands, garlanded** hHom. B. Ion E.*fr.*

φιλοστόνως *adv.* [στόνος] **with sighs and groans** —*ref. to praying* A.

φιλοστοργέω *contr.vb.* [φιλόστοργος] **show devoted affection to, love and cherish** —*the old, an adopted daughter* Pl. Plb.

φιλοστοργίᾱ ᾱς *f.* **1 affectionate nature** (of a boy) X.
2 devoted affection (for a family member, one's native land) Plb. Plu.

φιλό-στοργος ον *adj.* [στοργή] **affectionate, loving** (esp. towards family members) X. Theoc. Plu. ‖ NEUT.SB. **affectionate nature** (of a person) X. Plu.

—**φιλοστόργως** *adv.* **lovingly** Plu.

φιλο-στρατιώτης ου *masc.adj.* **1** (of a commander) **loyal to one's soldiers, soldiers' friend** X. Plu.
2 (of a person) **fond of the military** Plu.

φιλο-σώματος ον *adj.* [σῶμα] (of a person who fears death) **loving one's body** (opp. loving wisdom) Pl.

φιλότᾱς *dial.f.*, **φιλοτάσιος** *dial.adj.*: see φιλότης, φιλοτήσιος.

φιλό-τεκνος ον *adj.* [τέκνον] | compar. φιλοτεκνότερος, superl. φιλοτεκνότατος | (of persons, animals) **loving one's children** or **offspring** Hdt. E. Ar. +

φιλοτεχνέω *contr.vb.* [φιλότεχνος] (of persons) **engage in craftsmanship** Plb.; (of a god) **practise one's craft** Pl.

φιλοτεχνίᾱ ᾱς *f.* **love of practising one's craft** Pl.

φιλό-τεχνος ον *adj.* [τέχνη] (of persons) **devoted to crafts** (opp. pure wisdom) Pl. ‖ NEUT.SB. **craftsmanship, skill** (involved in painting or sim.) Plu.

φιλότης ητος, *dial.* **φιλότᾱς** ᾱτος *f.* [φίλος] **1 friendship** (betw. persons) Hom. +; (betw. states or sim.) Il. Hdt. And.; (personif.) **Friendship** Hes.
2 love (betw. two people) Od. Sapph. Thgn. Pi. AR. +; (ref. to a specific relationship) Thgn. Pi. AR.
3 spirit of friendliness, friendliness, friendship Hom. AR.; **affection, love** (for someone, sts. w.gen.pers.; esp. in dat., as the motivation for an action) Hom. Thgn. Pi. Trag. +; (philos.) **Love** (as the attraction betw. the elements) Emp.
4 physical affection, love (shown to someone, ref. to embraces) E.; (ref. to lovemaking) Hom. Hes. Archil. Mimn. +
5 (ref. to the object of one's affection) **dear friend** (as a term of address) Pl.; **nearest and dearest** (ref. to one's wife and children) Lys.

φιλοτήσιος, *dial.* **φιλοτάσιος**, ᾱ ον (also ος ον) *adj.* (of deeds) **of love** Od.; (of behaviour) **loving** S.; (of a cup) **of friendship** (ref. to a loving cup) Ar. ‖ FEM.SB. (w. κύλιξ understd.) **loving cup** (used to pledge friendship) Thgn. Ar. D.

φιλοτῑμέομαι *mid.contr.vb.* [φιλότιμος] | aor.pass. (w.mid.sens.) ἐφιλοτιμήθην, also mid. ἐφιλοτιμησάμην (Plb.) | **1** value honours, **pursue honours** Att.orats. Pl.; **court acclaim** —w. πρός or εἰς + ACC. *fr. someone* Lys. D. Plu.
2 engage in keen rivalry —w. πρός + ACC. w. *persons* Pl. Arist. Plb.
3 pride oneself —w. ἐπί + DAT. *on sthg.* Att.orats. Pl. X. Arist. —w. ὅτι + INDIC. *that one is able to do sthg.* Lys.; **take pride** —W.PTCPL. *in doing sthg.* Pl. X.
4 feel a threat to one's pride, feel jealous Ar.; **feel piqued** —w. ὅτι + INDIC. *that sthg. is the case* X.
5 be eager —W.INF. *to do sthg.* Pl. X. D. Arist. + —W.COMPL.CL. *that sthg. shd. be the case* Plb. Plu. —W.PREP.PHR. *for a task, war, victory* Plb. Plu.; (intr.) **be eager, be enthusiastic** (about sthg.) Plu.
6 strive assiduously (sts. W.INF. to do sthg.) Men. Plu.; **work zealously** —W.ACC. *at sthg.* X.; **devote oneself zealously** —W.PREP.PHR. *to sthg.* Plb. Plu. —w. πρός + ACC. *to the state* Lys. D. Plu.
7 be assiduously accommodating (towards someone) Plb. Plu.
8 perform a public service Is. D. —W.DAT. *by the staging of choruses or sim.* Plu.; **make a show of one's patriotism** —w. πρός + ACC. *to jurors* D.

φιλοτίμημα ατος *n.* **instance of lavish spending, lavish benefaction** (ref. to buildings, public spectacles) Plu.

φιλοτῑμίᾱ ᾱς, Ion. **φιλοτῑμίη** ης *f.* **1 love of honour** (freq. seen as selfish and discreditable), **desire for honour** or **acclaim, ambition** E. Th. Ar. Att.orats. +
2 result of striving for honour, honour, distinction, acclaim Att.orats. X. Plu.
3 self-centred attitude, stubborn pride Hdt.
4 ambitious rivalry, competition (betw. persons or cities) Isoc. X. Plb. Plu.; (esp. pl.) **rivalry, feud** Th. Isoc. Pl. Men. +; **contest** (W.GEN. of wealth, ref. to the costs of participating in the Olympic games) Lys.
5 determination, fighting spirit (of troops, boxers) Plb. Plu.; **determined effort, exertion** Plb. Plu.
6 ambition that is directed to the public good (and deserves to be honoured in return), **public-spirited ambition, patriotic zeal** D. Plb.
7 lavish generosity, generous spending, munificence (for the public good) Aeschin. D. Men. Plu.; (gener.) **generosity** Plu.

φιλό-τῑμος ον *adj.* [τῑμή] **1** (of Erinyes) **honour-loving** A.
2 (of persons, their nature, life, freq. pejor.) **eager for honour** or **acclaim, ambitious** E. Att.orats. Pl. +; (of a type of society, such as the Spartan) **based on the love of honour** Pl. ‖ NEUT.SB. **love of honour, ambition** E. Th. Pl. Plu.
3 (gener., of persons) **ambitious, keen, competitive** Att.orats. Pl. X. +; **eager** (W.INF. to do sthg.) X.
4 (of a request) app., self-centred, **presumptuous** Pl.; (of a remark, an inscription) **self-congratulatory, boastful** Plu.
5 (of intellects) app., deserving of honour, **honourable** Ar.
6 directing one's ambition to the public good (and deserving honour in return), **honourable, public-spirited** Att.orats.
7 generous (in expenditure on others) Plu.
8 (of a prayer) **eager to pay honour** (to those on whose behalf it is uttered) A.
—**φιλοτίμως** *adv.* | compar. φιλοτῑμότερον, also φιλοτῑμοτέρως (Isoc.) | superl. φιλοτῑμότατα | **1** with eager competition for distinction, **emulously** or **ambitiously** Isoc. Pl. X. Plb. Plu.
2 eagerly, enthusiastically Isoc. X. Plb. Plu.
3 honourably, with public-spiritedness, patriotically Att.orats.
4 with a sense of pride (in dead sons) Plu.
5 with due honours —*ref. to burying someone* Plu.
φιλο-τοιοῦτος ον *adj.* (of persons) **fond of such and such a thing, fond of some particular thing** Arist.
φιλοττάριον ου *n.* [dimin., reltd. φιλότης] (as a term of address) **dearest** Ar.
φιλο-τύραννος ον *adj.* **sympathetic towards tyrants** Plu.
φιλο-υγιής ές *adj.* (of a mental attitude) **conducive to health** Arist.
φιλό-φιλος ον *adj.* [φίλος] **loyal to one's friends** Arist. Plb.
φιλο-φόρμιγξ ιγγος *masc.fem.adj.* (of a chant) **in harmony with the lyre** A.
φιλοφρονέομαι *mid.contr.vb.* [φιλόφρων] | aor.pass. (w.mid.sens.) ἐφιλοφρονήθην | **1** (of persons, their souls) **feel friendliness, have kindly intentions** (sts. W.DAT. towards someone) X. Plu.; **show kindness, be friendly** —W.ACC. or DAT. *to someone* Hdt. X. Plu.; **fraternise** (w. one another) X. Plu. —W.ACC. *w. one another* Pl.; (fig., of laws) **treat kindly** —W.ACC. *persons* Pl.; (fig., of a person) **pander to, indulge** —W.DAT. *one's appetites* Pl.
2 express goodwill in greeting or parting (esp. w. an embrace); **greet, welcome** —*someone* X. Plu.; **bid a fond farewell to** —*someone* Plb. Plu.; (fig.) **embrace, welcome** —*bad habits* (in oneself) Pl.
φιλοφροσύνη ης *f.* **1 friendliness, good-naturedness** Il. X. Plu.; **friendliness** (towards a person) Pl. Plu.; **affection** (for a person) Hdt. Plu.; **friendship, friendly relations** (betw. persons) Plb. Plu.
2 ‖ PL. **demonstrations of friendship or affection** (ref. to friendly greetings or sim.) Pi. Plu.
3 festivity, revelry Ion Critias
φιλό-φρων ον, gen. ονος *adj.* [φρήν] **1** (of persons, their nature, personif. Calm) **having friendly intentions, well-meaning, kindly** Anacr. Pi. E. X. Men.
2 (of Delusion) **ingratiating, beguiling** A.
—**φιλοφρόνως** *adv.* | compar. φιλοφρονεστέρως (X.) | **in a kindly** or **friendly manner** (esp.ref. to greeting someone) Hdt. Lyr.adesp. S. X. +
φιλο-χορευτής οῦ *masc.adj.* (of Bacchus) **fond of dancers** Ar.
φιλό-χορος ον *adj.* [χορός] (of gods, revellers, a lyre) **fond of the dance** A. E. Ar.

φιλοχρηματέω *contr.vb.* [φιλοχρήματος] **be avaricious** Pl. Is.
φιλοχρηματία ᾱς *f.* **love of money, avarice** Pl. Arist. Plu.
φιλοχρηματιστής οῦ *masc.adj.* **fond of making money** Pl.
φιλο-χρήματος ον *adj.* [χρῆμα] **1 fond of money** Pl. Arist.
2 (of persons, their actions) **avaricious** Att.orats. Pl. X. Arist. Plu. ‖ NEUT.SB. **avarice** Pl. Arist.
—**φιλοχρημάτως** *adv.* **avariciously** Isoc.
φιλοχρημοσύνη ης *f.* **love of money** Pl. Plu.; **avariciousness** (as a state or activity) Plb.
φιλό-χρηστος ον *adj.* [χρηστός] **1 honest** (opp. unscrupulous) X.
2 (of fortune) **benevolent** Plu.
φιλοχωρέω *contr.vb.* [χώρᾱ] **feel affection for a place**; **feel at home** (sts. W.DAT. in a region) Plb. Plu.; (of persons; fig., of Poverty and Famine) **make one's home** (in a region) Hdt. Plu.; (fig., of a writer) **feel in one's element** (writing biographies) Plu.
φιλοχωρίᾱ ᾱς *f.* **affection for a place** Ar.
φιλο-ψευδής ές *adj.* (of gods, persons, their nature) **fond of lies** Il. Pl. Arist.
φιλό-ψογος ον *adj.* [ψόγος] (of persons, a city) **quick to criticise** E. Pl.
φιλοψῡχέω *contr.vb.* [φιλόψῡχος] **be overfond of one's life, show a cowardly concern with saving one's life** Tyrt. E. Att.orats. Pl. Plu.; **try to preserve one's life** (opp. fight) E.; (wkr.sens.) **be faint-hearted** Isoc.
φιλοψῡχίᾱ ᾱς, Ion. **φιλοψῡχίη** ης *f.* **overfondness for one's life, cowardly concern with saving one's life** Hdt. Pl. Plu.
φιλό-ψῡχος ον *adj.* [ψῡχή] **overfond of one's life, scared of death, cowardly** E. Plu.
φιλό-ψῡχρος ον *adj.* [ψῡχρός] (of ivy) **cold-loving, intolerant of heat** Plu.
φιλτάτιον ου *n.* [dimin. φίλτατος] (as a term of address) **dearest** Ar.
φίλτατος (superl.adj.), **φίλτερος** (compar.adj.): see φίλος
φίλτρον ου *n.* [reltd. φίλος, φιλέω] **1 potion, charm** or **spell to inspire love** (usu. romantic, but sts. affection for a friend or family member); **love-potion, love-charm** S. E. X. Arist. Theoc. Mosch.; (fig., ref. to sthg. that inspires love) E. Men. ‖ PL. **personal charms** (of a woman) Plu.
2 (gener.) **charm, spell** Pi. E.; (W.ADJ. *for a horse*, ref. to the magic bridle used to tame Pegasos) Pi.; (fig., ref. to sthg. that inspires courage or sim.) A. E. Plu.
3 ‖ PL. **feelings of love** (for a person, a city) E. Antipho; (sg.) Bion
φιλ-υπήκοος ον *adj.* (of a king) **kind to one's subjects, benign** Plu.
φίλ-υπνος ον *adj.* [ὕπνος] **fond of sleep, lazy** Theoc.
φιλύρᾱ ᾱς, Ion. **φιλύρη** ης *f.* **1 lime tree** or **linden tree** Hdt.
2 linden-bark, bast (ref. to the inner bark, cut into weavable strips) Hdt.
φιλύρινος η ον *adj.* (fig., of a person) **made of linden-bark, paper-thin, skinny** Ar.
φιλῳδός *Att.adj.*: see φιλάοιδος
φίλων ωνος *m.* perh. **braggart** Alc.
φῑμός οῦ *m.* **1 muzzle** (worn by a horse) A.
2 dice-box, shaker Aeschin.
φῑμόω *contr.vb.* | pf.pass.imperatv. πεφίμωσο | **1 muzzle, enclose** —*someone's neck* W.DAT. *in a pillory*) Ar.
2 (of Jesus) **silence** —*the Sadducees* (w. criticisms) NT. ‖ PASS. (of a person) **be silent** NT.; (in imperatv., as a command to a person, a gale) NT.
φιν (dial.enclit.dat.3pl.pers.pron.): see σφεῖς

φίντων ωνος *dial.m.* [reltd. φίλτατος] (as a term of address to a baby) **darling, dearest** A.*satyr.fr.*

Φίξ *Boeot.f.*: see Σφίγξ

φιτρός οῦ *m.* **log** (oft. as firewood, usu.pl.) Hom. B. Call. AR.

φῖτυ *n.* [perh.reltd. φύω] | only nom.sg. | **plant** Ar.

φίτυμα ατος *n.* [φῖτῡω] **scion** (ref. to a son) A.

φῖτυ-ποίμην ενος *m.* [φῖτυ, ποιμήν] (appos.w. ἀνήρ) **one who tends plants, gardener** A.

φῑτύω *vb.* | aor. ἐφίτυσα | (of a father) **beget** —*a child* Trag. Pl.; (of a god) **create** —*a race* Pl. ‖ MID. (of a woman) **bear** —*a child* (W.DAT. or ἐκ + GEN. *to someone, by someone*) Hes. AR. Mosch.

φλάζω *vb.* | aor.2 ἔφλαδον | (of the tearing of a mourner's clothes) **make a ripping sound** A.

φλᾶμιν ινος *m.* —also **φλᾱμίνιος** ου *m.* [Lat.loanwd.] *flamen* (Roman priest) Plu.

φλαυρίζω *vb.* [φλαῦρος] **disparage** —*someone or sthg.* Plu.

φλαῦρος ᾱ (Ion. η) ον *adj.* **1 poor in quality or status**; (of persons, troops) **poor, ineffective** Hdt.; (of a family) **lowly, undistinguished** Hdt.; (of a girl) **unattractive** (W.ACC. in appearance) Hdt.; (of land) **of poor quality** Hdt.
2 (of circumstances) **slight, trifling** Sol. Pi. Hdt.
3 (w. moral connot., of persons) **bad, worthless** E.; (of thoughts) **base** Men.
4 (of actions, conditions, consequences) **bad, harmful** E. Ar. Isoc. Pl. D.
5 (of a dream) **unfavourable, sinister** A.; (of news) **bad, unwelcome** S. D.; (of a state of affairs) **poor, wretched, pitiful** S.
6 (of words, speech) **disparaging, derogatory** S. Ar. Att.orats. X. Plu.

—φλαύρως *adv.* **1 with unhappy consequences, wretchedly** Hdt. Ar.; (w. ἔχειν, of persons) *be in a wretched condition* Hdt. Th. Pl.
2 to a slight extent, inadequately Hdt.
3 disparagingly, abusively Hdt.

φλαυρουργός όν *adj.* [ἔργον] (of the maker of a cup) **showing poor workmanship, unskilled** S.

φλάω *contr.vb.* | 3sg.impf. ἔφλᾱ | fut. φλάσω, dial. φλάσσω | aor. ἔφλασα, dial. φλάσα, also ἔφλασσα | **1 crush** —*a person* (w. a stone slab) Pi.; **crush up, pound** —*garlic or sim.* (in a mortar) Ar.; **pummel** —*a person* Ar.; **bruise** —*someone's shins* Ar.
2 (specif.) **crush or clamp the testicles; geld, castrate** —*a goat* Theoc.
3 munch, chomp down —W.ACC. or GEN. *food* Ar. Men.

φλέβιον ου *n.* [dimin. φλέψ] **small channel, small vein** (as a vessel for particles or sim., within the body) Pl.

φλεγέθω *vb.* [φλέγω] | ep.3pl.opt.pass. φλεγεθοίατο | **1** (of fire) **burn up** —*cities* Il. ‖ PASS. (of corpses) be burned up —W.DAT. *by fire* Il.
2 (intr., of fires, the sun, stars) **blaze** Il. Hes. Ibyc. S. AR.; (of a warrior) **gleam** (in his armour) E.; (fig., of Zeus' will) **blaze forth** A.

φλέγμα ατος *n.* **1 flame, fire** Il.
2 inflammation (in the body); **phlegm** (ref. to catarrh or sim.) Hdt.; (as one of the four humours) Pl. Arist.

φλεγμαίνω *vb.* | aor. ἐφλέγμηνα | **1** (of sore, sprained or infected parts of the body) **be inflamed** Ar. Plu.; (of diseases) **cause inflammation, be inflammatory** Pl. ‖ NEUT.PTCPL.SB. *inflammation* Pl.
2 (fig., of a city, regime, excessive wealth) **become inflamed, fester** (before being cured by a reformer) Pl. Plu.; (of a situation, a person's mind, the public reaction to a disaster) **be inflamed** (w. anger, grief, or sim.) Plb. Plu.; (of superstition) **be feverish** Plu.

φλεγματώδης ες *adj.* **1** (of certain foods) **causing an excess of phlegm** Pl.
2 (of persons) **suffering from an excess of phlegm** (as a humour), **phlegmatic** Arist.

φλεγμονή ῆς *f.* **inflammation** (of part of the body) Plu.; (fig., affecting scorched earth, a troubled city) Plu.

Φλέγρᾱ ᾱς, Ion. **Φλέγρη** ης *f.* **Phlegra** (westernmost of the three headlands of Chalcidice, site of a plain where a mythical battle was fought betw. the gods and the giants) Hes.*fr.* Pi. Hdt. E. Ar.; (pl.) Pi.

—Φλεγραῖος ᾱ (Ion. η) ον *adj.* (of the plain, battle) **Phlegraian** A. E. AR.; (of a person) **from Phlegra** AR.

φλεγύᾱς ᾱο *ep.masc.adj.* [φλέγω] (of an eagle) **fiery-coloured, tawny** Hes.

φλεγυρός ά όν *adj.* (of a Muse, invoked by charcoal-burners) **fiery, fired-up** Ar.

φλέγω *vb.* | fut. φλέξω | aor. ἔφλεξα ‖ 2du.pass.imperatv. φλέγεσθον | **1** (of a fire) **burn up, consume** —*locusts, persons* Il. Tim.; (of Sirius, ref. to summer heat) **scorch** —*islands* AR.; (of a person) **burn** —*persons or things* (sts. W.DAT. *w. fire*) Pratin. A. AR.; (of a commander) **set on fire, sack** —*a country* Plu. ‖ PASS. (of objects, cities, countries) be set on fire Il. Plu.
2 (fig., of Ajax, Ares) **kindle, stir up** —*ruin, bloody conflict* S. E.; (of Ares, messengers, news) **fire up** —*persons* (w. *fighting spirit, urgency*) A. S.; (of a satyr) **inflame with passion** —*a nymph* Mosch. ‖ PASS. (of persons) be fired up (w. anger, pride, fighting spirit) Ar. Pl. Plu.; be inflamed with emotion (fr. grief) S.
3 ‖ PASS. (of parts of the body) be inflamed (by infection) Pl.
4 ‖ PASS. (of a person) blush (fr. love or sim.) Pl. Theoc.
5 make (sthg.) **blaze or shine** (w. light); (of persons) **light** —*torches* E.; (of Zeus) **flash** —*a lightning-bolt* A.; (of day) **kindle** —*its light* S. ‖ PASS. (of altars) blaze —W.DAT. *w. offerings* A.; (fig., of hymns) blaze forth B.*fr.*
6 (intr., of fires, torches, or sim.) **blaze, gleam, flash, shine** (sts. W.DAT. w. *fire*) A. S. Tim.; (of the sun, lightning) A. S.; (of the night sky) —w. ὑπό + DAT. w. *stars* A.; (of Zeus) —W.DAT. w. *fire* Ar.; (of a gale) Plu. —w. ὑπό + GEN. w. *lightning* Ibyc.; (of armour, golden flowers) Pi. E. Plu.; (fig., of the gods) **blaze** —W.DAT. w. *fury* Ar.; (of fury, love, in someone's breast) A. AR.
7 (of the moon) **light up, illuminate** —*the evening* Pi.; (of the sun) —*the earth* (W.DAT. w. *its rays*) A.; (of a person) —*a temple* (w. *torches*) E.
8 (fig., of the Graces) **make** (W.ACC. *a victorious athlete*) **blaze with glory** Pi.; (intr., of a victor) **blaze with glory** —W.DAT. *in the songs of the Graces* Pi. ‖ PASS. (of a victor) be made to blaze with glory —W.DAT. *by the Muses* Pi.; (of a place) —*w. deeds of valour* Pi.

φλέδων ονος *m.f.* [app.reltd. φλέω] **prattler** (ref. to a false prophet) A.

Φλειοῦς (v.l. **Φλιοῦς**) οῦντος *m.* **Phleious** (a city near Argos) Pi. B. Hdt. Th. +

—Φλειάσιος (v.l. **Φλιάσιος**) ᾱ ον *adj.* (of persons) **from Phleious, Phleian** X. Plu. ‖ FEM.SB. *region of Phleious* Th. Plb. ‖ MASC.PL.SB. *men of Phleious* Hdt. Th. +

—Φλειούντιος ᾱ ον *adj.* (of the land) **of Phleious** E.*fr.*

—Φλειουντίς ίδος *fem.adj.* (of the land) **of Phleious** AR.

φλέξις ιδος *f.* a kind of bird Ar.

φλέψ φλεβός *f.* **1 vein** (also incl. arteries) Il. Hdt. S. Ar. Pl.; κοίλη φλέψ *hollow vein* (ref. to the vena cava, through which

blood flows to the heart) E.; (as a channel for air, nutrients, or sim., as well as blood) Pl.; (ref. to a milk duct) Hdt.
2 vein (of ore, in rock) X.
3 channel (of an underground spring) Plb.

φλέω *contr.vb.* **1** (of flocks) **be abundant** A.
2 (of houses) **be prosperous** A.

φλέως ω *Att.m.* [app.reltd. φλοῦς] a kind of reed; **reed, bulrush** Ar.

φληναφάω *contr.vb.* [φλήναφος] talk nonsensically, **babble** Ar.

φλήναφος ου *m.* **1** nonsensical talk, **nonsense, rubbish** Men.
2 (ref. to a person) **blatherer** Men.

φλιᾱ́ ᾱ̂ς, Ion. **φλιή** ῆς *f.* **1** part of a door-frame; (usu.pl.) **doorpost, jamb** Od. Hellenist.poet. Plb.
2 lintel AR.; **threshold** Theoc.

Φλῑάσιος *adj.*: see Φλειάσιος under Φλειοῦς

φλίβομαι *dial.mid.vb.* [reltd. θλίβω] | fut. φλίψομαι | (of a beggar) **press, rub** —*his shoulders* (W.DAT. *against doorposts*) Od.(v.l. θλίβ-) ‖ PASS. (of a woman) get squashed (in a jostling crowd) Theoc.

Φλιοῦς *m.*: see Φλειοῦς

φλόγεος ᾱ ον *adj.* [φλόξ] (of Athena's golden chariot) **blazing** or **gleaming** Il.; (of torches, lightning-bolts, starlight) E. Ar. Theoc.

φλογερός ά (Ion. ή) όν *adj.* (of a beacon-fire, beams of sunlight, the starry heavens) **blazing** E. AR.; (fig., of the fire of Eros) Theoc.

φλογίζω *vb.* (of Zeus) **burn** —*a person* (w. *a lightning-bolt*) S. ‖ MID.PASS. (of the sun) be on fire, **blaze** S.

φλόγιος ᾱ ον *dial.adj.* (of summer) **blazing, scorching** Alc.

φλογιστός ή όν *adj.* [φλογίζω] (of a body) **consumed by fire, burnt** S.

φλογμός οῦ *m.* [φλέγω] **blaze, flash** (sts. W.GEN. of fire, ref. to a lightning-bolt) E.; **flaming heat** (sts. W.GEN. of fire) E. AR.; **scorching heat** (as harmful to plants) A.

φλογο-ειδής ές *adj.* [φλόξ, εἶδος¹] (of supernatural or celestial phenomena) **fiery, glowing** Plu.; (of troops in armour) **gleaming** Plu.

φλογόεις εσσα εν *adj.* (of the eyes of Eros) **blazing, gleaming** Mosch.

φλογώδης ες *adj.* (of a fireball) **fiery, blazing** Plu.

φλογ-ωπός όν *adj.* [ὤψ] (of fire) of flaming appearance, **flaming** A.; (of omens) **seen in flames** A.

φλόγωσις εως *f.* **inflammation** (W.GEN. of the eyes) Th.

φλογ-ώψ ῶπος *masc.fem.adj.* (of the region of sunrise) of flaming appearance, **blazing** A.

φλόϊνος η ον *Ion.adj.* [φλέως] (of clothes) **made of reeds** Hdt.

φλοιός οῦ *m.* [app.reltd. φλέω] (sts.pl.) **bark** (of a tree) Il. hHom. Hdt. X. +

φλοῖσβος ου *m.* **1 din** or **turmoil of battle** Il.
2 roaring swell (of the sea) A.

φλοιστική ῆς *f.* **art of stripping bark** (W.GEN. fr. trees) Pl.

φλονίδες ων *f.pl.* [φολίς] **scales** (on an animal's limbs) Emp.(cj.) | see λεπίς 2

φλόξ φλογός *f.* [φλέγω] **1 flame** (sts. W.GEN. of fire, of Hephaistos) Hom. +; (ref. to a torch) E. Ar.(mock-trag.); (philos., as an element) Parm. Emp.
2 flame, flash (of a lightning-bolt) Hes. A. E. Plu.
3 (fig.) **flame** (flashing fr. the eyes of a fearsome person or snake) B. E. Plu.; (W.ADJ. of war) E.*fr.*; (W.GEN. of Aphrodite, i.e. love) Theoc.; (of wine, ref. to its warming power) E.; (of suffering) S.
4 blaze (of the sun) Simon. Trag. Arist. +; **gleam** (of gemstones) Pi.*fr.*; **beaming light** (emanating fr. an object, according to the Platonic theory of vision) Pl.; **radiance** (emanating fr. a person, by Eros' doing) AR.
5 (medic.) **inflammation** (in the body) Pl.

φλοῦς *m.* [app.reltd. φλέως] | only acc. φλοῦν | a kind of reed; **reed, bulrush** Hdt.

φλυᾱρέω, Ion. **φλυηρέω** *contr.vb.* [φλύαρος] **1 talk nonsense** Hdt. Ar. Isoc. +—W.COGN.ACC. Pl. —W.ACC. *about sthg.* Isoc. Pl.; (gener.) **talk** or **act foolishly** Ar. Pl. X. Men.
2 (w. affectionate connot., of friends) **talk foolish nonsense** —w. ἐς + ACC. *to one another* Eleg.adesp.

φλυᾱρίᾱ ᾱς *f.* (oft.pl.) **idle talk, empty nonsense** (esp. ref. to useless advice or meaningless sophistries) Ar. Isoc. Pl. +; (gener.) **rubbish, nonsense** Timocr. Pl. Plb. Plu.

φλύαρος ου *m.* **idle talk, twaddle** Ar. Men. Plu.

φλυᾱρώδης ες *adj.* (of minds) **foolish, distracted** Plu.

φλυηρέω *Ion.contr.vb.*: see φλυᾱρέω

φλύκταινα ης *f.* **blister** Ar.; (ref. to blood-blisters, liver-spots, or sim.) Ar.; **pustule** (on a plague victim) Th.

φλύω *vb.* | aor. ἔφλῡσα | **bubble up**; (fig., of a person) **babble, talk nonsense** A.; (of an inscription) **make an idle claim** A.

φόβᾱ *dial.f.*: see φόβη

φοβερός ά όν *adj.* [φόβος] **1** causing fear; (of persons, things, circumstances) **terrifying, frightening, alarming** (sts. W.DAT. to someone) A. Hdt. E. Th. Ar. Att.orats. +; (W.INF. to behold or sim.) A. E. X. D. Theoc. ‖ NEUT.SB. capacity to inspire fear (W.DAT. in people) Th.; frightening or dangerous situation Th. X.
2 causing fear (that sthg. may happen); (of persons, a horse) **creating a fear, threatening a possibility** (w. μή + SUBJ. or OPT. that they may or might do sthg.) X.; (of disasters) feared as likely, **threatening** (W.INF. to happen) X.
‖ NEUT.IMPERS. (w. ἐστί understd.) there is reason to fear —w. μή + SUBJ. *that sthg. may happen* X.
3 being fearful (by nature); (of persons, animals, their hearts, eyes) **afraid, timid** Alc. Anacr. E. Pl. X. +
4 experiencing fear; (of persons, their minds) **frightened, terrified, afraid** S. Th. Pl. X. +; **fearful** (W.GEN. of bloodshed) E.*fr.*; (w. εἰς τό + INF. of doing sthg.) Pl.; (prep.phr.) ἐπὶ τὸ φοβερώτερον *rather timorously* Th.
5 (of a tearful mist over the eyes) **caused by fear** A.; (of a retreat) caused or accompanied by fear, **panic-stricken** Th. X.

—**φοβερῶς** *adv.* | compar. φοβερώτερον, superl. φοβερώτατα | **1 in a terrifying manner, alarmingly** Lys. X. Plu.
2 in a terrified state X.

φοβερότης ητος *f.* **formidable appearance** (of a person) Arist.

φοβεσι-στράτη ης *f.* [φοβέω, στρατός] (epith. of Athena) **router of armies** Ar.

φοβέω *contr.vb.* [φόβος] | iteratv.impf. φοβέεσκον ‖ MID. and PASS.: Ion.imperatv. φοβεῦ, also φοβέο | fut. φοβήσομαι, also pass. (w.mid.sens.) φοβηθήσομαι (Plu.) | aor.pass. (freq. w.mid.sens.) ἐφοβήθην | 3pl.plpf. ἐπεφόβηντο, ep. πεφοβήατο ‖ neut.impers.vbl.adj. φοβητέον |
1 (of warriors, gods, their tricks) **put to flight** —*troops* (sts. W.DAT. w. *the spear*) Il. —*persons* B.; (of a lion, bird of prey) —*animals, birds* Il. ‖ MID.PASS. (of persons, animals) **run away in fear** or **be put to flight** (sts. W.PREP.PHR. by enemies, lions, or sim.) Il. hHom. Tyrt.; **flee from** —W.ACC. *someone* Il.

φόβη 1472

2 (of warriors, snakes on a shield) **terrify** —*troops* Hes. Hdt.; (of persons, animals, words, news, or sim.) —*persons, animals* (sts. W.DAT. w. *boasts, threats, or sim.*) Trag. Th. +; (intr., of persons, actions) **create fear** S. D. ‖ MID.PASS. (of troops, their hearts) **be terrified** (esp. before battle) Il. Hdt.; (of persons, animals) **be frightened, be alarmed** (oft. W.DAT. or PREP.PHR. by or at sthg.) Hdt. Trag. + —W.COGN.ACC. *by shameful fears, w. a great fear* Pl. NT.
3 ‖ MID.PASS. (of persons, animals) **be afraid of, fear** —*persons, animals, things* Hdt. Trag. Isoc. +; **be afraid** —W.INF. *to do sthg.* (sts. w. μή + VB. *in case sthg. shd. happen*) Trag. Th. Pl. X. —w. μή or ὅπως μή + VB. *that sthg. may happen or be the case* E. Th. Ar. X. —w. ὅτι or ὡς + VB. *that sthg. may be the case* Th. X. —W.ACC. *for this reason* (W.COMPL.CL. *namely that sthg. may be the case*) S. Th.
4 ‖ MID.PASS. **be afraid, be anxiously concerned** —W.PREP.PHR. *for oneself* (i.e. one's safety) Th.
5 ‖ MID.PASS. **be anxiously concerned** —W.ACC. *about someone* (w. μή + VB. *in case they may do sthg.*) Hdt. Th. Pl. —W.PREP.PHR. *about someone or sthg., for someone* (sts. w. μή + VB. *that sthg. may happen to them*) Hdt. S. Th. + —W.COMPL.CL. *how to achieve sthg.* X.
—**πεφοβημένως** *pf.mid.pass.ptcpl.adv.* **in fear, timorously** X.

φόβη ης, dial. **φόβα** ᾱς *f.* **1 lock of hair** Sapph. A. Pi. S. Call.; (gener.) **hair** (of a person) S.
2 mane (of a horse) S.*fr.* E.; **crest of hair** (of a bullock) E.
3 spray, sprig (of a plant) Pi.*fr.* E.; (gener.) **foliage** (of trees, plants) S. E.

φόβημα ατος *n.* [φοβέω] (ref. to the sacred olive) **object of awe** (W.GEN. for invading soldiers) S.

φοβητέος ᾱ ον *vbl.adj.* (of things) **to be feared** Pl.

φοβητικός ή όν *adj.* (of persons) **inclined to feel fear, timid** Arist.

φοβητός ή όν *adj.* (of a hunter) **to be feared, dangerous** (W.DAT. for game animals) S.

φόβητρα ων *n.pl.* **terrifying sights** (ref. to supernatural portents) NT.

φόβος ου *m.* [φέβομαι] **1 flight** (fr. the battlefield) Hom.; **putting to flight, rout** (of troops) Il. Hdt.
2 (personif., as son of Ares) **Rout, Panic** Il. Hes. A. Plu.
3 panic, fear (felt by troops in battle) Il. Tyrt. A. Pi. B. Hdt. +; (gener., felt by persons, animals, communities, places) Archil. Hdt. Pi. B. Trag. +; (W.GEN. or PREP.PHR. at sthg., about sthg.) S. Th.; (fig., as emanating fr. a warrior's eyes, a monster's jaws, jangling bells on a shield) A.
4 respectful fear, awe (of the gods, God) Th. Isoc. Pl. NT.
5 fear (W.GEN. or PREP.PHR. of someone or sthg.) Trag. Th. Att.orats. Pl. X. +; (W.INF. of doing sthg.) E. X.; (w. μή or ὅπως μή + VB. that sthg. may happen) Pl. X.
6 (wkr.sens.) **fear** (ref. to a particular anxiety) S. E. Att.orats. Pl. X. +; **anxiety, apprehension** (w. ὅπως + VB. about how sthg. can be achieved) Hdt.; **concern** (W.PREP.PHR. for sthg.) A. Th. Pl. X.; **apprehension, wariness** (about doing sthg. potentially risible) Pl.
7 something which inspires fear; terror, nightmare (esp. ref. to a sight or vision) Trag.; (ref. to an utterance) **something terrifying** (sts. W.INF. to hear) Hdt. S. E.; **terrifying threat** (made to someone) X.; **terrifying crime** E.
8 danger, threat (faced by a people) Hdt.
—**φόβονδε** *adv.* **to flight** —*ref. to turning, urging someone to turn* Il.

φοιβάς άδος *fem.adj.* [Φοῖβος] (of Cassandra, the prophetic art) **inspired by Phoibos** E.; (perh. of Artemis) **possessed** Tim.

φοιβαστικός ή όν *adj.* (of a woman) **inspired to utter prophecies** (W.GEN. in oracular verse) Plu.

φοιβάω *contr.vb.* [φοιβός] (of persons) **clean** —*domestic objects* E.*fr.* —*someone's skin* AR. —*one's hands* (W.DAT. w. *ointments*) Theoc.; **wipe** —*foam* (W.PREP.PHR. *fr. a horse's muzzle*) Call.

Φοίβειος ᾱ ον (also **Φοιβήιος** ον E.) *adj.* [Φοῖβος] (of a temple, a temple servant) **of Phoibos** Hdt. E.; (of the land and towers of Troy) **sacred to Phoibos** E.; (of duties) **serving Phoibos** (in his temple) E.

Φοίβη ης *f.* [reltd. Φοῖβος] **1 Phoibe** (goddess, daughter of Ouranos and Gaia) Hes. A.
2 Phoibe (one of the Leukippides, two sisters abducted by the Dioscuri) Alc.
3 Phoibe (mortal daughter of Leda) E.

φοιβό-ληπτος, Ion. **φοιβόλαμπτος**, ον *adj.* [ληπτός] (of persons) **inspired by Phoibos** (w. the gift of prophecy) Hdt. Plu.

φοιβός ή (dial. ᾱ́) όν *adj.* (of sunlight) **radiant** A. B.

Φοῖβος ου, Boeot. **Φῦβος** ω (Corinn.) *m.* **Phoibos** (epith. and alternative name of Apollo, sts. as a sun-god in his own right) Hom. +

φοῖδες *Ion.f.pl.*: see φῳδες

φοινήεις εσσα εν *adj.* [reltd. φοινός] (of a serpent, blood) **crimson** Il. Mosch.

φοινῑκ-άνθεμος ον *adj.* [φοῖνιξ, ἄνθεμον] (of spring) **with crimson flowers** Pi.

φοινῑκ-ασπις ιδος *masc.fem.adj.* [ἀσπίς¹] (of heroes) **with crimson shields** B.

φοινίκεος ᾱ ον, also contr. **φοινικοῦς** ῆ οῦν *adj.* (of flowers, lotus-fruit) **deep red, crimson** Pi. B. Plb.; (of painted walls) Hdt.; (of dyed fabrics and helmet crests) Simon. Hdt. X. AR. Plb. Plu.; (of dyed wool) Theoc. ‖ NEUT.SB. **crimson colour** Arist. Plu.

Φοινίκη *f.*, **Φοινίκηιος** *Ion.adj.*: see under Φοῖνιξ

φοινίκηιος η ον *Ion.adj.* [φοῖνιξ] (of clothing, barrels, wine) **made from palm** (i.e. fr. the leaves, wood, sap) Hdt.

Φοινῑκικός *adj.*: see under Φοῖνιξ

φοινῑκιοῦς οῦν *adj.* (of a bird, app. the flamingo) **crimson** Ar.

φοινῑκίς ίδος *f.* **crimson cloak** (esp. as battle-dress) Lys. Ar. X. Arist. +; (used as a rug, or worn by a horse in a ritual) X. Aeschin.

φοινῑκιστής οῦ *m.* [perh. φοῖνιξ 4] (ref. to a Persian) perh. **lyre-player** X. [unless *wearer of crimson robes*, indicating noble status]

Φοινῑκιστί *adv.*: see under Φοῖνιξ

φοινῑκο-βάλανος ου *f.* **palm-nut, palm-fruit, date** Plb.

φοινῑκό-βαπτος ον *adj.* [βαπτός] (of robes) **dyed with crimson** A.

Φοινῑκογενής *adj.*: see under Φοῖνιξ

φοινῑκο-δάκτυλος ον *adj.* (of dawn) **crimson-fingered** (cited as a less appropriate epith. than ῥοδοδάκτυλος *rosy-fingered*) Arist.

φοινῑκόεις εσσα εν *adj.* | ῐ *metri grat.* | (of clothes, reins) **crimson** (fr. dye) Hom. Hes. hHom.; (of wounds, Ares, W.DAT. w. blood) Il. Hes.

φοινῑκό-θριξ τριχος *masc.fem.adj.* [θρίξ] (of oxen) **red-haired** B.

φοινῑκο-κρήδεμνος ον *dial.adj.* [κρήδεμνον] (of Leto, the Muses) **with crimson head-scarf** B.

φοινῑκό-κροκος ον *adj.* [κρόκη] (of a woman's waistband) **woven with crimson** Pi.

φοινῑκό-λοφος ον *adj.* [λόφος] (of a dragon, birds) **crimson-crested** E. Theoc.

φοινῑκό-νωτος ον *adj.* [νῶτον] (of oxen) **red-backed** B.
φοινῑκο-πάρηος ον *Ion.adj.* [παρήιον] (of ships) **crimson-cheeked** (ref. to their painted prows) Od.
φοινῑκό-πεδος ον *adj.* [πέδον] (of the Red Sea) **having a crimson bed** A.*fr*.
φοινῑκό-πεζα ᾱς *dial.fem.adj.* [πέζα] (of Demeter, Hekate) **with crimson feet** Pi.
φοινῑκό-πτερος ον *adj.* [πτερόν] **with crimson plumage** ‖ MASC.SB. **red bird** (app. the flamingo) Ar.
φοινῑκο-πτέρυξ υγος *masc.fem.adj.* (of a nymph) **with crimson wings** Lyr.adesp.
φοινῑκό-ροδος ον *adj.* [ῥόδον] (of meadows) **with crimson roses** Pi.
φοινῑκο-σκελής ές *adj.* [σκέλος] (of a bird's claws) **on crimson legs** E.
φοινῑκο-στερόπᾱς ᾱ *dial.masc.adj.* [στεροπή] (of Zeus) **with crimson lightning-bolts** Pi. B.
φοινῑκό-στολος ον *adj.* [στόλος] (fig., of swords, or transf.epith. of the Carthaginians who wield them) **clothed in crimson** Pi.
φοινῑκοῦς *contr.adj.*: see φοινίκεος
φοινῑκο-φαής ές *adj.* [φάος] (of a swan's foot) **bright crimson** E.
Φοῖνιξ (v.l. **Φοίνῑξ**) ῑκος *m.* [app.reltd. φοῖνιξ] 1 (usu.pl., oft. appos.w. ἄνδρες) **man from Phoenicia, Phoenician** Hom. +; (ref. to Carthaginians) Pi. Plb. Plu.
2 **Phoinix** (ancestor of the Phoenicians, father of Europa) Il. Hes.*fr*. B. E.*fr*. Mosch.
3 **Phoinix** (tutor of Achilles) Il. S. Ar. Pl. X. Plu.; (title of a play by Euripides) Aeschin. D.
—**Φοίνισσα** ης *fem.adj.* (of women, ships, merchandise, a cry) **Phoenician** Od. A. Pi. B. Hdt. +; (of the land; of an island, ref. to Tyre) E.; (of Corsica, as a Carthaginian colony) Call. ‖ PL.SB. **Phoenician Women** (title of a play by Euripides) Arist.
—**Φοινίκη** ης, dial. **Φοινίκᾱ** ᾱς *f.* **Phoenicia** Od. Hdt. E.*fr*. +; (app.ref. to the Phoenician colony of Carthage) E.
—**Φοινίκήιος** η ον *Ion.adj.* (of ships, carvings) **Phoenician** Hdt.; (of letters, ref. to the Greek alphabet) Hdt.; (of a disaster) **affecting the Phoenicians** Hdt.
—**Φοινικικός** ή όν *adj.* 1 (of mines, cities, a ship) **belonging to the Phoenicians, Phoenician** Hdt. Th. X.
2 (of a tale) **of the Phoenician kind** (i.e. like the story of Phoenician Kadmos' Sown Men), **fantastical, outlandish** Pl.; (of a ruse) **outlandishly crafty** Plb.
—**Φοινικιστί** *adv.* **in the Phoenician language** (ref. to Punic, the form of Phoenician spoken in Carthage) Plb.
—**Φοινῑκογενής** ές *adj.* [γένος, γίγνομαι] (of Europa) **sired by Phoinix** E.*fr*.
φοῖνιξ (v.l. **φοίνῑξ**) ῑκος *m.* [app.reltd. φοινός] 1 **crimson dye** or **pigment** (used to dye crests, leather cords, or sim., also to stain ivory or rouge the cheeks) Hom. Call.; **crimson colour** (of blushing cheeks) E. ‖ MASC.ADJ. (of reins, robes, a helmet crest, plumb-line) **red** or **crimson** (fr. dye or pigment) Simon. E. AR. Theoc.; (of horses) **chestnut, bay** Il.; (of cows) **tawny** Theoc. ‖ FEM.ADJ. (of the blast of fire) **red** or **crimson** E.
2 **date-palm, palm tree** (esp. assoc.w. Apollo or Leto, who clung to the tree in her labour pains) Od. +; **palm-wood** Hdt. X.; **palm-frond** (given to victors in athletic games) Plu.; **palm-fruit, date** Melanipp. Thphr. Plu.
3 **phoenix** (a mythical bird) Hes.*fr*. Hdt.
4 **a kind of lyre** (perh. of Phoenician origin) Alc. Hdt.
φοίνιος ᾱ ον (also ος ον) *adj.* [reltd. φοινός] 1 (of blood) **crimson** or **gory** Od. Trag. Theoc. Bion; (of a drop of blood) S.; (of dew, fig.ref. to blood) A.
2 **stained with one's own blood**; (of eyeballs, flesh, severed veins, a wound) **bloody, bleeding** S. E. Ar.(mock-trag.) AR.; (of a feast for scavenging animals, ref. to corpses, an exposed child) E.; (of cheek-tearing) **bloody, bloodying** E.
3 **stained with another's blood**; (of a murderer's hand) **bloody, bloodstained** S. E.; (of a butcher's block) A.(cj.); (of the abode of a murderess) E.
4 **causing bloodshed**; (of Ares) **bloody, murderous, deadly** S. E.; (of a person) A. Pi.; (of hands, weapons, battle) Trag.; (of a bite) A.; (fig., of the shouting of attackers) E.
5 **causing death**; (of poison, a storm, a turbulent sea) **murderous, deadly** S.; (fig., of a vote) E.; (of a serpent's glare) E.
φοίνισσα ης *fem.adj.* [φοῖνιξ] (of cheeks) **red, crimson** (w. blood) A.; (of flames) Pi. B.; (of a herd of bulls) **tawny** Pi.
Φοίνισσα *fem.adj.*: see under Φοῖνιξ
φοινίσσω *vb.* ‖ fut. φοινίξω ‖ aor. ἐφοίνιξα ‖ aor.pass. ἐφοινίχθην ‖ 1 **make red** (w. blood or dye); (of Ares, a warrior) **dye red** (w. blood) —*a river, the sea* B. Hdt.(oracle); (of a person) —*a part of his body* (W.DAT. w. *mulberry juice*) Hippon.; **make bloody** —*sacrificial victims* E. ‖ PASS. (of persons, their bodies, the sea) **be dyed red** (w. blood) S. E. Tim. Theoc. Bion
2 (of a girl) **redden** —*her cheek* (w. *a blush*) E.; (of a weapon) —*a soldier's flesh* (W.DAT. w. *a bruise*) Plu. ‖ MID. (fig., of flowers) **put on red** —W.ACC. as *mourning garments* Mosch. ‖ PASS. (of a girl, a spurned lover) **turn red** (by blushing) AR. Theoc.
φοινός ή όν *adj.* (of wolves' jaws, a monster's last breath) **bloodied** Il. hHom.
φοιτᾰλέος (also **φοιτᾱλέος** AR. Mosch.) ᾱ (Ion. η) ον (also ος ον E.) *adj.* [φοιτάω] 1 (of a woman) **rushing** or **fleeing frantically** AR.; (of Io, as a heifer, W.PREP.PHR. **across the sea**) Mosch.
2 (of a gadfly's tormenting stings) **causing wild flight** (for Io) A.
3 (of madness) **that makes the mind wander** E.
φοιτάς άδος *fem.adj.* (*also neut.* E.) 1 (of a beggar) **vagabond** A.
2 (of Bacchants) **rushing wildly** (to the mountains) E.; (of the Sphinx's wings) **wildly roving** E.
3 (of a sickness) **coming and going, periodic, recurrent** S.
φοιτάω, Ion. **φοιτέω** *contr.vb.* ‖ dial.inf. φοιτῆν (Bion) ‖ dial.3sg.impf. ἐφοίτη (Theoc.) ‖ fut. φοιτήσω, dial.3sg. φοιτᾱσεῖ (Call.) ‖ neut.impers.vbl.adj. φοιτητέον —also **φοίτημι** *Aeol.vb.* ‖ 2sg. φοίταις ‖ 2sg.aor.subj. φοιτάσῃς ‖
1 **come and go repeatedly**; (of persons) **pace up and down, go back and forth** Hom. Archil.; (of Ares or warriors, in battle) Il.; (of persons searching for someone, hounds following a scent) **run back and forth** Od. X. AR. Plu.
2 **go about in various directions**; (of gods, persons, ghosts, animals) **roam about** Il. Hes. hHom. Sapph. S. E. +; (of birds) **fly about** Od. E.; (of distracted persons) **rush this way and that** S. Mosch.
3 (fig.) **wander in one's mind, be distracted, rave** S. E.
4 (wkr.sens., of persons) **make one's way, go along** Od. Thgn.; (of time) **go, move** —W.ADV. *forwards* Call.
5 (of a group of people or things) **come in a throng**; (of persons, ghosts, Cyclopes, birds) **come thronging** (usu. W.PREP.PHR. to a place or person) Od. Hdt. E. Th. Pl. +; (of arrows) B.; (of password tesserae) **be sent out in batches** Plu.

φοίτησις — 1474

6 go regularly or habitually; (of persons, gods, animals) **keep going** or **coming** (freq. W.PREP.PHR. to a place, an activity) Hdt. Th. Ar. Att.orats. Pl. +; (of reports) **arrive regularly** (fr. the battlefield) Th. Plu.
7 (of persons) **pay visits** (to a person or place) Hdt. S. X. Men. —W.PREP.PHR. *to a person* (*esp. a friend*) E. Th. Pl. Bion Plu.
8 (of dreams, apparitions, diseases) **visit, haunt** —W.DAT. or PREP.PHR. *persons* Hes. Hdt. E. Pl. Theoc.
9 (of persons, esp. boys) go (for lessons) —W.PREP.PHR. *to a teacher, to school* Ar. Att.orats. Pl. X. Plu.; (intr.) **go to school, be a pupil** Ar. Att.orats. Pl.
10 go (to someone) for sexual purposes; **have sexual relations** —W.DAT. or PREP.PHR. *w. someone* Hdt. Lys. Pl. Theoc. Plu.; (of female cats) —*w. tomcats* Hdt.; (of a couple) go —W.PREP.PHR. *to bed* (*on a particular occasion*) Il.
11 (of a petitioner or sim.) **go as a suppliant** or **pay court** —W.PREP.PHR. *to or at someone's door* Hdt. X. Plu.; (of ambassadors) **make visits** —W.PREP.PHR. *to a people* Th.
12 (of commodities) come as an import, **be imported** —W.PREP.PHR. *fr. somewhere, by sea* Hdt. Lys. X.; (of money) **come in** (as tribute) —W.DAT. *to a person, a people* Hdt. Th.
13 come again (in accordance w. a regular pattern of behaviour); (of the phoenix) **appear, arrive** or **return** Hdt.; (of Artemis) —W.DAT. *for a woman in labour* E.; (of a servant) Hdt.; (of an attack of pain) S.

φοίτησις εως *f.* ‖ PL. attendances (of a person, at weddings or sim.) Pl.; (at the gate of a king) X.

φοιτητής οῦ *m.* one who goes for regular lessons (to someone), **pupil** Pl.

φοιτίζω *vb.* | iteratv.impf. φοιτίζεσκον | (of gods and humans) **roam** hHom.; **pay visits** AR.; **habitually turn** —W.PREP.PHR. *to conversation* Call.

φοῖτος ου *m.* [φοιτάω] **derangement** (W.GEN. of the mind) A.

φολιδωτός ή όν *adj.* [φολίς] (of an iron corslet) **made of scales** Plu.

φολίς ίδος *f.* **scale** (on a dragon, the wings of the Boreads) AR.

φολκός οῦ *masc.adj.* (of a person) perh. **bandy-legged** Il.

φοναί ῶν *f.pl.* [θείνω] **1 massacre, general slaughter** (of battle, birds tearing one another apart) Il. A. Hdt. S.; (of garden pests) Ar.
2 slaughter (of a person, by a killer; of animals, by a hunter, sacrificer, lion) Il. E.; **bloody death** (of a person) S.
3 (concr.) **carnage, gore** Pi. S.

φονάω *contr.vb.* [φόνος] (of a mind; fig., of spears) **be thirsty for blood** S.

φόνευμα ατος *n.* [φονεύω] that which is slaughtered, **victim** E.

φονεύς έως (ep. ῆος) *m.* [φόνος] | acc. φονέα (also φονέᾱ E.), ep. φονῆα | nom.pl. φονῆς (also φονεῖς NT.), Ion. φονέες, ep. φονῆες | acc.pl. φονέας (also φονεῖς NT. Plu.), ep. φονῆας |
1 killer, murderer (freq. W.GEN. of a person) Hom. Archil. Hdt. Trag. +; (ref. to a woman) A. Antipho; (ref. to a sword, hand) S. E.
2 slayer (of enemies, a dragon) AR. Plu.; (of mice, ref. to a mousetrap) Call.
3 destroyer (of a living person, a land) S. E. Plu.; (W.GEN. of other people's integrity) Antipho

φονεύω *vb.* **1 kill, murder** —*a person* Hdt. S. E. Th. X. +; (intr.) **kill, commit murder** X. NT.; **be a murderer** S. ‖ PASS. (of a person) be killed Pi. E. Th. Theoc. +
2 (of persons, esp. troops) **slaughter** —*persons, animals* A. Hdt. E. Th. +; (intr.) **carry out a slaughter** Hdt. Plb. Plu.; (of an animal) **kill** —*a person, an animal* Pl. Plu.; (hyperbol., of a name, a person's cunning) **cause the death of** —*a person, the Sphinx* E.
3 make bloody, **slash** —*someone's throat* E.

φονικός ή όν *adj.* **1** (of persons, esp. tyrants; of barbarian peoples) **bloodthirsty, murderous** Th. Pl. Plu.; (of crimes) **of murder** Lycurg. ‖ NEUT.PL.SB. murderous acts Plu.
2 (of charges) **of homicide** Att.orats. Arist. ‖ NEUT.PL.SB. charges of homicide D. Arist. Plu.
3 (of laws) **relating to homicide** D. Arist. Plu.; (of a court) **for homicide trials** D. Arist.

φόνιος ᾱ ον (also ος ον) *adj.* **1** (of blood or drops of blood, fr. persons or animals) **shed in murder** or **slaughter** A. E. AR.; (of a libation) **of shed blood** E.(dub.)
2 stained with one's own blood; (of flesh, a wound) **bloody, bleeding** E.
3 (of nails) drawing blood, **bloody, bloodying** E.; (of cheek-tearing) E.(cj.)
4 stained with another's blood; (of a murderer's hand) **bloody, bloodstained** A.; (of the bed of a murderess) E.; (of the mangers of man-eating horses) E.
5 (of the lot, ref. to exile) **of a murderer** E.
6 causing bloodshed; (of Ares, Hades, an Erinys, a person, monster, serpent) **bloody, murderous, deadly** Trag.; (of a weapon, blow, activity) Trag. Ar. Tim.; (of Vengeance, curses, situations) Trag.; (of a wail) indicating bloodshed, **deathly** E.
7 causing death; (of old age) **deadly** E.
—**φόνια** *neut.pl.adv.* **murderously** —*ref. to a spectre glaring* Ar.

φονο-λιβής ές *adj.* [λείβω] (of a seat) **dripping with blood** A.; (fig., of a deed) A.

φονό-ρυτος ον *adj.* [ῥυτός] (of earth) **blood-soaked** A.

φόνος ου *m.* [θείνω] **1** act of killing, **killing, slaying** (of a person) Hom. +; **slaughter** (of an animal, esp. as a sacrifice) Emp. S.; (gener.) **slaughter, killing** (of persons) Hom. +
2 murder (as a crime) Hdt. Trag. +; **homicide** (as a legal charge) Att.orats. Pl. +; **manslaughter** (ref. to an unintentional killing) Pl.
3 (gener.) **death** (of a person or animal, as sthg. dealt, avoided, or sim.) Hom. +; (ref. to a death sentence, by public stoning) S.
4 bringer of death, **cause of death** (for someone, ref. to weapons, persons, things) Hom.
5 murdered body, **corpse** E.
6 general slaughter, **mass slaughter** (of captives, or in civil war) Hdt.
7 carnage (ref. to heaps of bodies or sim.) Hom. Tyrt. A.
8 spilt blood, **gore** Il. Trag. +; **blood** (as being shed) Alc.; (gener.) **blood** (in the body) Emp.

φοξός ή όν *Ion.adj.* pointed; (of a person) **dome-shaped** (W.ACC. in his head) Il.

φορᾱ́ ᾶς, Ion. **φορή** ῆς *f.* [φέρω] **1** act of carrying, **carrying** (of a person, on a stretcher) S.
2 that which is carried, **shipment, load** (ref. to a ship's cargo) Plu.
3 casting (W.GEN. of votes) E. Pl.
4 act of bringing; (specif.) **contribution, payment** (W.GEN. of money, tribute) Th. Pl. X.; (concr., ref. to that which is contributed) Th. Att.orats. X.; (fig.) **reimbursement** (ref. to one's just deserts) D.
5 act of producing, **fecundity, productivity** (of animals, plants) Pl.
6 (concr.) that which is produced, **crop** (of olives) Arist.; (fig., of traitors, wretches, fine men) Att.orats. Arist. Men.

7 act of moving, **move** (of a counter in a game, fig.ref. to a step taken by someone) Pl.; **step, action** (taken by someone) Plu.
8 motion (of stars, planets, the cosmos, or sim.) Pl. Arist. Plu.; (of objects, or gener. as a concept) Pl. Arist.; **trajectory** (of a javelin) Antipho
9 (fig.) **leaning** (of a people, ref. to their political loyalties) Plb.
10 issuing forth, projection (of one's voice, in speech) Pl.; **flow** (of blood, water) Plu.; **rushing movement** (of a fireball, a falling object) Plu.; **onrush** (of a crowd, an invading army) Plu.
11 driving motion, **impetus, momentum** (of charging soldiers) Plu.; **current** (of rivers or the sea) Plb.; **driving force** (of a wind) Plb.; (specif.) propelling wind, **favourable wind** Plu.
12 (fig.) **carrying tide** (of events) D.; **irresistible impulse** (affecting persons) Plu.; **impetuousness** (as a character trait) Plu.; **impetuous act** (esp. as causing civil strife or sim.) Plb. Plu.

φοράδην, dial. **φοράδᾱν** adv. **carried aloft** —ref. to a dead, sick, old or injured man being conveyed E. D. Plu. —ref. to a voice being borne by the air S.
φορβαῖος ᾱ ον adj. [φορβή] (of mountains) **rich in pastures** Call.
φορβάς άδος masc.fem.adj. **1** (of the earth) **nurturing** S.
2 (of horses, cows) **grazing** E. Pl. AR.; (of pigs) **foraging** AR. ‖ MASC. or FEM.SB. grazing animal AR.
3 (fig., of a herd of prostitutes dedicated to Aphrodite) **grazing** (in a sanctuary) Pi.fr.
φορβειά ᾶς f. **1 halter** (to tether a horse to a manger) X. Arist.
2 headstall, mouth-strap (worn by aulos-players, to hold the instrument in place and assist in production of the sound) Ar.
φορβή ῆς, dial. **φορβά** ᾶς f. [φέρβω] **1 pasture, food** (for horses, ref. to grass and crops in fields) Il. hHom.; (for birds, ref. to human bodies) S. Ar.
2 (gener.) **food** (for persons) Hdt. S. AR.
φορειᾱ-φόρος ου m. [φορεῖον, φέρω] **litter-bearer** Plu.
φορεῖον ου n. [φορεύς] **litter** (for conveying persons) Din. Plb. Plu.
φορεύς έως (ep. ῆος) m. [φέρω] **1** one who carries; (specif.) carrier of grapes to the press, **vintager** Il.
2 bearer (of a warrior's weapons, ref. to his squire) AR.
3 litter-bearer Plu.
4 pack-horse Plu.
φορέω contr.vb. ‖ ep.inf. φορήμεναι, also φορῆναι ‖ ep.3sg.subj. φορέῃσι ‖ Ion.3pl.impf. ἐφόρευν ‖ iterATV.impf. φορέεσκον ‖ fut. φορήσω ‖ aor. ἐφόρησα, also ἐφόρεσα (Plu.) ‖ MID.PASS.: Ion.1sg. φορεῦμαι ‖ —also **φόρημμι** Aeol.vb.
1 (of persons, esp. servants or labourers) bring repeatedly, or as one's accustomed role, or in quantities, **bring, carry** —water, fodder, spoils, messages, or sim. Hom. Hes. Stesich. Hdt. +; (of a woman) **regularly bring** —a child (to a place) Hdt. ‖ MID. **fetch for oneself** —water Hdt. E.; **lift** (food) —W.ADV. to one's mouth AR.
2 habitually carry; (of persons, gods) **carry** —provisions, a staff, shield, weapon, or sim. Hom. Anacr. Scol. Hdt. +; (of ships) —tackle Od.
3 (of a tree) **bear** —fruit Hdt.
4 (of persons) **wear** —clothes, jewellery, armour, or sim. Hom. Thgn. Hdt. S. +; **bear** —a device (on one's shield) B. Hdt.; (of persons, gods, animals) **have** —a thick skull, dark skin, wings, a tail, or sim. Hdt. E. Ar.; **have, show, display** —pompous airs, courage, a certain attitude Od. S. Ar.
5 (of persons) **carry** —an object, a sick person, a child Archil. Scol. Hdt. S.
6 (of horses) carry as one's accustomed role, **carry, bear** (usu. in a chariot) —persons, gods Il. hHom.; (fig.) —the panic of war Il.
7 (gener., of dolphins) **carry** —a person (across the sea) Lyr.adesp.; (of the wind) —a fire Il.; (of the Fates) **bring** (to Troy, in ships) —dogs (pejor.ref. to the Greeks) Il.; (of a rock) **dash** —a person (W.PREP.PHR. down into the sea) Od. ‖ PASS. (of a charioteer) be dashed —W.PREP.PHR. to the ground E.
8 (of waves, winds) **carry about** —sailors (in ships), corpses Od. ‖ PASS. (of seafarers, the sea) be swept about (usu. W.DAT. by waves, winds) Semon. Alc. Sol. Anacr. E.
9 (fig., of a poet, envisaged as a torrent) **sweep away** —trees, persons Ar. ‖ PASS. (of persons under a curse) be swept away (to destruction) A.
10 (of the wind) **carry about** (in the air) —chaff, sand, thistledown Hom. Hdt. ‖ PASS. (of dust) be carried about (by the wind) S.; (fig., of old age, in a wish) be carried —W.DAT. + PREP.PHR. on wings, in the air (instead of visiting people on earth) E.
11 ‖ PASS. (of grieving or lovesick persons) wander about Theoc. Bion; (fig., of ignorant persons) Parm.; (of entities, similar to the ideal Forms) be in motion Pl.
12 (of persons) **carry off** —spoils, valuables Hes. E.Cyc. Ar. ‖ PASS. (of produce) be carried off (in pillaging) A.; (of wool, by hens) Ar.; (of earth) be carried away (fr. a mound) Th.
φορή Ion.f.: see φορά
φόρημα ατος n. **1** that which is carried, **cargo** (ref. to a person) S.
2 burden, encumbrance X.; (fig., ref. to fear) X.; **imposition** (for subjects, ref. to the upkeep of a royal guard) X.
3 that which is worn, **piece of jewellery** Plu.
4 stretcher (to carry spoils, offerings or sim., in a procession) Plu.
5 team of stretcher-bearers Plb.
6 carrying (of weapons) X.
φορητός ή όν (also ός όν) adj. to be endured; (in neg.phrs., of a person; of Kypris, ref. to love) **bearable** A. E.
φορίνη ης f. **carapace, shell** (of a tortoise) S.Ichn.
Φόρκῡς υος (also ῠνος), also **Φόρκος** ου m. **Phorkys** (mythol. Old Man of the Sea, also known as Proteus) Hom. Hes. Pl. AR.
—Φορκίδες ων f.pl. **daughters of Phorkys** (ref. to the three Graiai) A.; (title of a lost tragedy by Aeschylus) Arist.
φορμηδόν adv. [φορμός] **criss-crossed** —ref. to timber or bodies being stacked Th.
φόρμιγξ ιγγος f. **phorminx, lyre** (esp.ref. to the archaic round-based lyre of the early poets, opp. the box-lyres of the classical period) Hom. Hes. Thgn. Pi. +
φορμίζω vb. (of Apollo, Orpheus, a bard) **play the lyre** Od. hHom. AR. Mosch.
φορμικτᾱ́ς ᾶ dial.m. **lyre-player** (ref. to Orpheus, Apollo) Pi. Ar.
φορμίς ίδος f. [dimin. φορμός] **small basket** Ar.
φορμίσκος ου m. **little basket** Pl.
φορμο-ρραφέομαι pass.contr.vb. [ῥάπτω] be woven into basket-work; (fig., of citizens) app. **be parcelled up** (by those in power) Aeschin.(quot. D.)
φορμός οῦ m. **1** woven basket, **basket** Hes. Hdt. Plb.
2 basketful, basket measure (of corn) Lys. Ar.
3 woven mat Hdt. Ar. Arist. Theoc.

φορολογέω contr.vb. [φορολόγος] (of a people, a leader) exact tribute from, levy taxes on —*a place* Plb. Plu.

φορο-λόγος ου *m.* [φόρος, λέγω] tribute-collector Plu.

φόρον (or **Φόρον**) ου *n.* [Lat.loanwd.] forum NT.

φορός όν *adj.* [φέρω] (of a wind) carrying forward, favourable Plb. Plu.

φόρος ου *m.* 1 payment (to a state or ruler, by a subject community), tribute Hdt. Th. Ar. Att.orats. Pl. +
2 financial contribution (to the state, by an individual, ref. to a leitourgia, envisaged as tribute) X.
3 instalment (of a payment) Plb.

φορτηγέω contr.vb. [φορτηγός] transport cargo (by boat) Hdt.

φορτηγία ᾱς *f.* transport of cargo (as an enterprise) Arist.

φορτηγικός ή όν *adj.* (of a ship) for transporting cargo Th. X.

φορτ-ηγός όν *adj.* [φόρτος, ἄγω] 1 (of ships) for transporting cargo Critias Plb. Plu. ‖ FEM.SB. cargo ship Plu.
2 ‖ MASC.PL.SB. porters; (gener., pejor.) rabble Thgn.

φορτίζω vb. 1 transport by sea —*goods* Hes.
2 load, weigh down —*a person* (W.INTERN.ACC. *w. burdens*) NT. ‖ PASS. (fig., of persons) be weighed down NT.

φορτικός ή όν *adj.* 1 burdensome (to persons of taste); (of comic poets) vulgar, lowbrow (in a rival poet's judgement) Ar.; (of their comedies) Ar.; (of a piece of comic business) Ar.; (of comedy in general) Pl.; (of other art forms) Arist.
2 (of people) vulgar, common (as lacking education or other accomplishments) Arist. Plu.
3 (of behaviour, speech, or sim.) vulgar, unsophisticated Pl. D. Arist.; (of a statement, question, way of arguing, or sim.) Pl. Arist. ‖ NEUT.PL.SB. mundane or everyday things Arist.
4 (of behaviour, esp. that which is self-promoting) vulgar, tasteless D. Arist. Men. Plb. Plu.; (of a form of praise) Arist.
5 (of a remark) coarse, crude Men. ‖ NEUT.SB. coarse gossip Aeschin.
6 (gener., of persons, their behaviour, speeches, or sim.) tiresome, annoying Plu.

—φορτικῶς *adv.* ‖ compar. φορτικώτερον ‖ in a vulgar, unsophisticated or tasteless manner Isoc. Pl. Arist. Plb. Plu.

φορτικότης ητος *f.* lack of sophistication (in an audience) Arist.

φορτίον ου *n.* 1 (sg. and pl.) cargo (of a ship) Hes. Archil. Sapph. Alc. Hdt. X. +; (gener.) wares Hes. Hdt. Ar. Hyp. +; (ref. to a large amount of anything) shipload Ar.
2 burden, load (carried by a person or pack-animal) Ar. X. Lycurg. Thphr. +; (ref. to an unborn child) X.; (fig., ref. to sthg. that one must endure) Ar. D. NT. Plu.

φορτίς ίδος *fem.adj.* (of a ship) for carrying cargo Od.

φόρτος ου *m.* [reltd. φέρω] 1 goods carried on a ship, freight, cargo Od. Hes. Hdt. S. Plu.; (fig., ref. to a bellyful of wine) E.*Cyc.*
2 (fig., ref. to a person) app. piece of merchandise (to be bought and sold, i.e. duped or sim.) Call.
3 (fig.) burden (W.GEN. of Love, i.e. borne by one in love) Anacr.; (of need, troubles) E.
4 vulgar or lowbrow material (in a comedy) Ar.

φορτοφορέω contr.vb. (of a ship) carry cargo Plu.(cj.)

φορύνομαι mid.pass.vb. (of food, knocked to the floor) be befouled, become dirty Od.

φορύσσω vb. [reltd. φορύνομαι] ‖ aor. ἐφόρυξα ‖ defile, befoul —*someone* (W.DAT. *w. blood, by beating him*) Od.

φορυτός οῦ *m.* [reltd. φορύσσω] scraps, rubbish Ar. Call.; (used as packing material for shipping pottery) Ar.

φοῦσα (Boeot.fem.athem.aor.ptcpl.): see φύομαι, under φύω

φόως *ep.n.*, **φόωσδε** *ep.adv.*: see φάος

φραγέλλιον ου *n.* [Lat. *flagellum*] multi-thonged whip, scourge NT.

φραγελλόω contr.vb. beat with a scourge, whip —*a person* NT.

φράγμα ατος *n.* [φράσσω] 1 protective screen; (milit.) barricade, fortification Hdt.
2 (gener.) defensive screen (ref. to any form of protection, incl. blankets) Pl.

φραγμός οῦ *m.* 1 blocking (of one's ears) S.
2 screen, fence (on either side of a walkway) Hdt.; fence or hedge (around a vineyard, orchard, or sim.) Hdt. X. Theoc. NT. Plu.

φράγνυμαι mid.vb.: see φράσσω

φραδάζω vb. [φράζω] ‖ dial.3sg.aor. φράδασσε ‖ (of an explorer) make known —*a remote land* Pi.

φραδή ῆς *f.* 1 (usu.pl.) advice (of a god, to a mortal) A. B. E. Theoc.
2 (fig.) indication (for trackers, provided by a scent) A.
3 ‖ PL. knowledge, information (about the future) Pi.

φραδής ές *adj.* (of a mind) shrewd Il.

φραδμοσύνη ης *f.* 1 (sg. and pl.) advice, counsel, urging (of a person or god) Hes. AR.
2 ‖ PL. designs, contrivances (of a god) Hes. hHom.
3 skill, expertise (of a helmsman) AR.

φράδμων ον, gen. ονος *adj.* (of persons) shrewd Il. Hdt.(oracle)

φράζω, Aeol. **φράσδω** (Theoc.) vb. ‖ fut. φράσω ‖ aor. ἔφρασα, ep. ἔφρασσα ‖ ep.redupl.aor.2 ἐπέφραδον, 3sg. πέφραδε, 2sg.imperatv. πέφραδε, inf. πεφραδέμεν, also πεφραδέειν ‖ pf. πέφρακα ‖ MID.: φράζομαι, Ion.imperatv. φράζευ ‖ 3sg.iteratv.impf. φραζέσκετο ‖ fut. φράσομαι, ep. φράσσομαι ‖ aor. ἐφρασάμην, dial. ἐφρασάμᾱν, ep. ἐφρασσάμην, ep.3sg.subj. φράσσεται, Ion.3pl.opt. φρασαίατο ‖ pf. πέφρασμαι ‖ PASS.: aor. (w.mid.sens.) ἐφράσθην ‖
1 indicate by pointing, point out —*an object, a person* Hom. Theoc.; signal —W.DAT. *w. one's hand* A. —W.INF. (*to someone*) *to do sthg.* Hdt.; show (a blind man) —W.INF. *how to do sthg.* Hdt.
2 (of persons or gods) indicate (in words) —*a place, a route,* (*where to find*) *a person* Od.; designate —*honours* (*for gods*) Hes.; (of a phrase) signify, mean —W.COMPL.CL. *that sthg. is the case* X.
3 announce, deliver —*a challenge, a verdict* Od. A. Pi.; (of persons, letters) reveal, announce, tell —*sthg.* (W.DAT. *to someone*) Il. Hes. A. Ar. Pl. —W.COMPL.CL. *that sthg. is the case* Od. A. Parm. E. Pl. +; (intr.) Od. Hes. hHom. A. S.
4 (of persons) mention —*sthg.* A. S. Antipho; speak —W.GEN. *about a person* S.; (of a poet) tell of —W.ACC. *sthg.* Pi.
5 describe, explain —*sthg.* (W.DAT. *to someone*) Od. Pi. Hdt. Trag. + —W.INDIR.Q. *what sthg. is like* Heraclit.; teach —*sthg.* (W.DAT. *to someone*) hHom. Pl.; (intr.) give an explanation hHom. A. Att.orats. Pl.
6 advise —W.DAT. *someone* (W.INF. *to do sthg.*) A.; (fig., of treachery) counsel (someone) or instigate (sthg.) S.; (of commanders, oracles, messengers) instruct, order —W.DAT. *someone* (W.INF. *to do sthg.*) Il. Th. Ar.; (intr.) give advice Hes. Pi.; prescribe, order (sthg.) Pl.
7 ‖ MID. and AOR.PASS. (w.mid.sens.) notice, observe (someone or sthg.) Od. Hes. Pi. Hdt. E. —*someone or sthg.* Hom. hHom. Pi.; discern —*tracks* Theoc.; take notice, be aware —W.GEN. *of sthg.* Theoc.
8 ‖ MID. watch or listen out (for sthg.) Hes.; keep watch on —*a door* Od.

9 ‖ MID. **take care** —W.INF. *to do sthg.* Hdt.(oracle) S. —W.DAT. + INF. *for someone not to suffer sthg.* Sol.; (intr.) **take care, watch out** Thgn. A.; **beware** —w. μή + SUBJ. *in case sthg. shd. happen* Il. hHom. Scol. Ar. Call.; **beware of, be wary of** —*a person, dog, thing* Il. Thgn. Hdt.(oracle) Ar.
10 ‖ MID. **take note of, consider** —W.ACC., COMPL.CL. or PREP.PHR. *sthg.* Od. Hes. hHom. Thgn. Parm. S.
11 ‖ MID. **deliberate** —W.INDIR.Q. *whether sthg. is the case, how to do sthg.* Hom. +; (intr.) Il.
12 ‖ MID. **deem, think** —W.COMPL.CL. *that sthg. is the case* Od. Hdt.
13 ‖ MID. (of persons or gods) **devise, think up** —*plans or sim.* Hom. Hes. hHom. Archil. Sol.; **plan** —*death or sim.* (W.DAT. *for one's enemies*) Od. —*a tomb* (W.DAT. *for oneself and one's comrade, in a particular place*) Il.; (intr.) **form a plan** Od.; **work out** —W.INF. or COMPL.CL. *how to do sthg.* Hom.; (of persons or gods) **think up and implement, contrive, come up with** —*a scenario, boon, strategy* Od. Hes.
14 ‖ AOR.PASS. (w.mid.sens.) **call to mind or mention** (sthg.) Od.

φρασί (dial.dat.pl.): see φρήν

φράσις εως *f.* **1 action of telling or presenting, exposition** (of events, in a play) Ar.
2 action of speaking, way of speaking, speech (of a person) Plu.
3 phraseology, style (of a writer) Plb.

φράσσεται (ep.3sg.aor.mid.subj.), **φράσσομαι**¹ (ep.fut.mid.): see φράζω

φράσσομαι² (mid.pass.): see φράσσω

φράσσω, Att. **φράττω** *vb.* | aor. ἔφραξα, also ἔφαρξα (A. Th. Ar.) ‖ MID.: aor. ἐφραξάμην, also ἐφαρξάμην (Alc. A. Th.) ‖ PASS.: aor. ἐφράχθην | pf. πέφραγμαι, also πέφαργμαι (E. Ar.) —also **φράγνυμαι** (Plu.) *mid.vb.* | impf. ἐφραγνύμην |
1 make a defensive barrier; (of troops, in combat) **make a barrier of** —*shields* Hdt. —*shield* (W.DAT. *upon shield*), *spear* (*upon spear*) Il. ‖ MID. and PASS. **fence oneself or be fenced** —W.DAT. *w.* (*i.e. behind*) *shields* Il. Tyrt. Mimn.
2 (fig.) **make a fence of** —*hunting nets* (W.GEN. *of harm, i.e. protect oneself w. traps to harm an enemy*) A.
3 (act. and mid.) **protect with a barrier; barricade, fence in, secure, protect** —*battlements* (W.DAT. *w. oxhide-shields, i.e. a rank of shield-bearers*) Il. —*beached ships* (*w. a barrier of bronze, i.e. armed defenders*) Il. —*an acropolis* (*w. doors and planks*) Hdt. —*the Capitol* (*w. weapons and ramparts*) Plu.; (fig., of a leader, compared to a helmsman) **make tight, batten down** —*a city* (*against the squalls of war*) A. ‖ PASS. (of the Acropolis) **be fenced in** —W.DAT. *by a wooden stockade* Hdt.
4 ‖ MID. **protect with a barrier** (of persons or troops); **secure, protect** —*a city's gates* (W.DAT. *w. defensive champions*) A. ‖ PF.PASS. (of an army) **be fenced round** —W.DAT. *by its chariot forces* E.; (of troops) **be protected or supported** —W.DAT. *by cavalry* Plu.
5 ‖ MID. (of occupants of a city, troops in action) **protect oneself** —W.ADV. *better* Th. Plu.; (of a person) —W.DAT. *w. soldiers* Plu. ‖ AOR. and (more freq.) PF.PASS. (of occupants of a city) **be securely protected** Hdt. —W.DAT. *by walls and gates* Pl.(aor.); (of persons in their houses) **be securely barricaded** Plu.; (of a nation) **be defended** —W.ADV. *better* (*i.e. be in a better state of defence*) Th.; (of a commander, *i.e. the city which he is defending*) —W.ADV. *well* Plu.
6 (gener.) **fortify** —*a city* Ar. ‖ MID. **secure, reinforce** —*walls, harbours, gates, a camp* Hdt. Th. Plu. —*river banks* (*to prevent a crossing*) Plu.
7 (act. and mid., in non-military ctxts.) **fence** —*a boat* (*i.e. its sides*, W.DAT. *w. twigs*) Od.; (prob.) **strengthen, make watertight** —*a ship* (*or its sides*) Alc.; **fence in** —*a pit* X.; **wall in** —*a piece of land* D.; (intr.) **build an enclosing wall** D. ‖ PASS. (of a river) **be fenced in** (by embankments) Hdt.
8 protect (one's person) **with defensive armour; clad** —*one's body* (W.DAT. *in armour*) A. ‖ PF.PASS. (of an army) **be protected** —W.DAT. *by armour* (*i.e. be armed for defence*) E.; (of soldiers) **be armoured** —W.DAT. *w. shields* E. —*w. helmets, breastplates, greaves* Plu.
9 ‖ PF.PASS. (fig., of a person) **be fortified, bolstered or supported** —W.DAT. *by wealth, friends, family, or sim.* Plu. —*by a particular circumstance* (w. πρός + ACC. *against a particular contingency*) Plu.; (of a city's supremacy) —*by alliances, subject nations, or sim.* Plu.
10 barricade, block —*a route, passageway, entrance* Hdt. Th. X. D. —*a mountain pass* (W.DAT. *w. a wall*) Hdt. —*a harbour mouth* (*w. rocks*) AR. —*a mountain range* (*i.e. its passes*) Plu.(mid.); **dam** —*a river* Plb. ‖ MID. (intr.) **bar the way** Plu. ‖ AOR. and (more freq.) PF.PASS. (of the lungs, i.e. their airways) **be blocked** Pl.(aor.); (of a house, i.e. its exits) Ar.; (of escape routes) X.; (of streets) —W.DAT. *by armed men* E.
11 (gener.) **hedge about** (a part of the body); **wreathe** —*one's hand* (W.DAT. *w. garlands*) Pi.; (of a hound) **tuck away** —*its tail* (*betw. its legs*) X.

φραστήρ ῆρος *m.* [φράζω] **1 one who provides information, guide** (W.GEN. *to local customs, roads, or sim., for persons in a foreign region*) X.
2 ‖ PL. app., **teeth showing one's age, adult teeth** X. | see φράτηρ 2

φράστωρ ορος *m.* **guide** (for persons in a foreign region) A.

φράτηρ ερος, also **φράτωρ** ορος *m.* **1** (usu.pl.) **member of a particular clan** or **phratry** Ar. Att.orats. Plu.; **member of the same phratry** (as oneself, a particular person), **fellow clansman** A. Ar. Att.orats. Pl. +; (fig.) **member of the brotherhood** (W.GEN. *of the stipend, ref. to a juror*) Ar.
2 ‖ PL. **initiation-teeth** (w. play on φραστῆρες *adult teeth*) Ar.

φρατορικός ή όν *adj.* [φράτωρ] (of an enrolment register) **of a clan** or **phratry** D.

φράτρα ᾱς, Ion. **φρήτρη** ης, Att. **φρατρίᾱ** (var. **φᾱτρίᾱ**) ᾱς *f.* [φράτηρ] **1 clan** (in Homeric society) Il. Plu.; (among the Persians) Hdt.
2 clan, phratry (esp. at Athens, as a subdivision of the tribe to which one was admitted on reaching adulthood) Att.orats. Pl. Arist.
3 (at Rome) **curia** (one of the thirty divisions of the people) Plu.

φρατρί-αρχος ου Att.*m.* [ἄρχω] **clan president** D.

φρατρίζω *vb.* [φράτηρ] **be a fellow clansman** D.

φράτριος ᾱ ον *adj.* (of gods, as protectors or patrons) **of the clan** Pl. D.

φράττω *Att.vb.*: see φράσσω

φράτωρ *m.*: see φράτηρ

φρέαρ ατος, also **φρέᾱρ** ᾱτος, ep. **φρεῖαρ** ατος *n.* | also contr.dat. φρητί (Call.) | **1 well** (for water) Il. +; (for rock-oil) Hdt.
2 water-tank, reservoir Th.; (app.ref. to a smaller indoor tank or cistern) Ar.

φρεατίᾱ ᾱς *f.* **reservoir** (for water) X. Plb.

Φρεαττώ οῦς *f.* —also **Φρέατος** ου *m.* | only in phr. ἐν Φρεαττοῖ (Φρεάτου) | **Phreatto** (name of an Athenian homicide court, which sat by the sea, the accused conducting his defence fr. the deck of a ship) D. Arist.

φρεῖαρ *ep.n.*: see φρέαρ

φρεν-ήρης ες *adj.* —also **φρενοάρᾱς** ᾱ *dial.masc.adj.* [φρήν, ἀραρίσκω] (of a person) **of sound mind** B. Hdt. E. Plu.

φρενῑτιάω *contr.vb.* [φρενῖτις *brain-fever*] (of a sick man) **be delirious** Plu.

φρενο-βλαβής ές *adj.* [φρήν, βλάβη] **mentally impaired, deranged** Hdt. Plu.(quot.com.)

φρενοβόρως *adv.* [βιβρώσκω] **with mind-gnawing madness** —*ref. to being sick* S.

φρενο-δᾱλής ές *dial.adj.* [δηλέομαι] (of derangement) **mind-destroying, robbing one of one's wits** A.

φρενόθεν *adv.*: see under φρήν

φρενο-μανής ές *adj.* [μαίνομαι] **deranged in one's mind, crazed** A.

φρενό-πληκτος ον *adj.* [πλήσσω] **smitten in one's wits, deranged** A.

φρενο-πλήξ ῆγος *masc.fem.adj.* —or perh. **φρενοπληγής** ές *adj.* (of bouts of frenzy) **smiting one's mind** A.

φρενο-τέκτων ονος *m.* (appos.w. ἀνήρ) **mind-crafter** (ref. to Aeschylus, as creator of characters w. psychological depth) Ar.

φρενόω *contr.vb.* **1 share one's wisdom with, give advice to, instruct** —*persons* Trag.; (intr.) **give advice** A. S. X.
2 give admonitory advice to, warn, admonish —*persons* A. X.

φρεν-ώλης ες *adj.* [ὄλλῡμι] (of madness) **mind-destroying** A.

φρέω *contr.vb.* [app.reltd. προΐημι]: only in cpds. διαφρέω, εἰσφρέω, ἐκφρέω, ἐπεισφρέω

φρεωρυχέω *contr.vb.* [φρέαρ, ὀρύσσω] (hyperbol., of a gnat) **bore wells in** —*a person* Ar.

φρήν φρενός *f.* | usu.pl. | dat.pl. φρεσί, dial. φρασί | **1 area of the body which surrounds the heart, chest** (ref. to the thorax, perh.orig. specif. the lungs) Hom. A. Pl.; **physical centre of the body, heart, core** A.
2 emotional centre of the body, breast, heart (as the seat of courage, anger, emotions and impulses) Hom. +; (as the seat of sincerity) ἐκ φρενός *from the heart* A.; (in litotes) οὐκ ἀπ' ἄκρας φρενός *from the bottom of one's heart* A.; (as the place where a secret is kept) Od.
3 mind (as the seat of one's thoughts, opinions, knowledge and plans) Hom. +; **senses** (ref. to the faculty of perception, as registering sounds, smells) Il. Hdt.(oracle)
4 wits, senses (ref. to one's right mind, esp. as being lost fr. fear, drunkenness, infatuation) Hom. +
5 good sense, common sense, intelligence (possessed by a person) Trag. +; (gener.) **prudence, reason** Pi.
6 mental faculty, rational intellect (of a person) A. Hdt.; **intellect, intelligence** Hom. Ar.; **compass of one's intellect, comprehension** A.
7 disposition (of a person, ref. to character or outlook) Il.
8 direction or focus of one's thoughts, intention, inclination, will (of a person or god) Hom. S.; (phr.) μιᾷ φρενί *with one accord* A.
—**φρενόθεν** *adv.* of one's own accord, **spontaneously** S.

φρήτρη *Ion.f.*: see φρᾱτρᾱ

φρίκη ης, dial. **φρίκᾱ** ᾱς *f.* **1 shivering fit** (as though fr. fever) Pl.
2 shuddering fear; fear Hdt. E. Pl. Plu.; (w.GEN. of someone) E.; **horror** (at sthg.) S. Plu.; **awestruck trepidation** (at sthg. supernatural) X. Plu.

φρικτός ή όν *adj.* [φρίσσω] | compar. φρικτότερος | **1** (of an act, an ominous sight) causing one to shudder, **horrifying** Plu.
2 (of a goddess) **awe-inspiring** Call.

φρικώδης ες *adj.* [φρίκη] **1** causing one to shudder; (of fevers) **shivering** Plu.
2 (of sights, sounds, punishments, tales) **horrifying** E. And. Ar. Plu.
3 (of an army, person, sight) **terrifying, awe-inspiring, formidable** Plu.; (of imprecations) **terrible** Plu.
4 (of oaths, matters within a court's remit) **solemn, grave** D. Plu.
5 (of a temple) **venerable, sacred** Plu.
—**φρικωδες** *neut.adv.* **horrifyingly** E.

φρῑμάσσομαι *mid.vb.* (of a frisky stallion or goat) **snort** Hdt. Theoc.

φρίξ φρῑκός *f.* **ruffling, rippling** (sts. W.GEN. of the wind, on the surface of a sea or river) Hom.

φρῑξ-αύχην ενος *masc.fem.adj.* [αὐχήν] (of dolphins) **with rippling neck** Lyr.adesp.

φρίσσω, Att. **φρίττω** *vb.* | aor. ἔφριξα | pf. πέφρικα, dial.masc.acc.pl.ptcpl. πεφρίκοντας | **1** (of lions, boars) **bristle up** —W.ACC. *their mane* (fr. fury or sim.) Hom. Hes.; (of a person) —*one's ridge of hair* Ar.(mock-trag.); (of an animal, its mane) **bristle** (fr. fury) Theoc. Plu.; (of a person's hair) **stand on end** (fr. cold) Hes.
2 (of corn, cornfields) **bristle** (w. ears of corn) Il. E.; (of battle-lines) —W.DAT. w. *spears* Il. AR.; (of the air) —w. *raised hands* A.; (of a lion's pelt) —w. *its mane* E.; (of the Boreads) —w. *wings* (W.ACC. *on their backs*) Pi.; (of snakes) —w. *scaly coils* Theoc.; (fig., of a goblet) **bristle, abound** (i.e. be decorated all over) —W.DAT. w. *gold* Pi.
3 (fig., of a dying warrior) **rasp out** —*his last breaths* Pi.
4 (of waves) **ripple** AR.
5 (of wild beasts) **shiver** (fr. cold) Hes.; (of rain) **be chilling** Pi.
6 (of a person) **shiver, thrill** —W.DAT. *fr. love* S.; (of persons, animals; fig., of the earth and sea) **shudder** (fr. fear, awe, dismay, or sim.) hHom. Trag. Pl. D. + —W.PREP.PHR. or COMPL.CL. *at sthg.* D. Plu.; **shudder at** —W.ACC. *sthg., an event* S. E. Ar. Call. Plu. —W.ACC. + INF. *the thought that someone shd. do sthg.* A.
7 tremble before, shrink from —*a person, a god* Il. Pi.; (iron., of the Fates) —*an old crone* AR.; (of a person) **shun** —*politics* Plu.; **balk at** —W.INF. *doing sthg.* D.

φροιμιάζομαι *mid.vb.*: see προοιμιάζομαι

φροίμιον *n.*: see προοίμιον

φρονέω *contr.vb.* [φρήν] | ep.3sg.subj. φρονέῃσι | iteratv.impf. φρονέεσκον | aor. ἐφρόνησα | pf. πεφρόνηκα || neut.impers.vbl.adj. φρονητέον |
1 (of persons) **have good sense, be sensible** or **wise** Il. Semon. Trag. Pl. +; (phr.) εὖ (ορ καλῶς, ὀρθῶς) φρονεῖν *have good sense* Trag. And.; **give good counsel** Il. X.; **have insight** (about sthg.) Isoc. Pl.
2 (esp. of adults, opp. babies) **have understanding, have intellect** A. Parm. Is.; **understand** (a situation) Od. —*sthg.* Od. E.; (of persons) **have feelings** Il.; **experience** —*sufferings or sim.* S.; (gener.) **be sentient** A. Critias Pl. Aeschin.
3 be in one's right mind S. E. Isoc. X.; (phr.) εὖ, ὀρθὰ φρονεῖν *be of sound mind* E. Lys. Ar.
4 be in a (W.ADV. or NEUT.ACC.ADJ. particular) **frame of mind** Il. Hes.
5 (phrs.) εὖ φρονεῖν *be glad* —W.DAT. *about sthg.* A.; (of warriors, lions, bulls) μέγα φρονεῖν (or sim.) **be high-spirited or fierce** Il. X.; (of persons) **be confident** —W.PREP.PHR. or COMPL.CL. *about sthg.* Pl. X. D.; (oft. pejor.) **be proud** Il. S. Ar. Att.orats. Pl.; *pride oneself* —W. ἐπί + DAT. *on*

sthg. Pl. X. Aeschin.; *think highly* —w. ἐπί + DAT. *of sthg., of oneself* Th. X. D.; (esp. in neg.phr.) μικρὸν φρονεῖν *be humble* S. E. Att.orats.
6 have a (W.NEUT.ACC. particular) **outlook, disposition** or **character** Hom. S. E. Th. +; **have an outlook** —w. κατά + ACC. *appropriate to one's status* A. S.; (phr.) φρονεῖν μεῖζω τῆς δίκης (μεῖζον τῆς δυνάμεως) *get ideas above one's station or capacity* E. Isoc.
7 have (W.ADV. or NEUT.ACC.PL.ADJ. particular) **feelings** or **intentions** (sts. W.DAT. towards someone) Hom. hHom. Eleg. Lyr. Ar. Isoc.; (phrs.) εὖ φρονεῖν *be well-disposed* —W.DAT., ACC. or εἰς + ACC. *towards someone* Od. Thgn. A. S. And.; ἴσον φρονεῖν *be on the same side* —W.DAT. *as someone* Il. S. Ar.; (esp. in political or military ctxts.) τὰ σά (or τὰ σοῦ, τὰ ἐκείνου) φρονεῖν *be on the same side as you* (*as that man*) Hdt. Th. Ar. D.; (of separate factions) ταὐτό (or κατὰ ταὐτό) φρονεῖν *make common cause* Hdt.
8 be minded, desire —W.INF. *to do sthg.* Il. —W.ACC. + INF. *that sthg. shd. happen* Il.; (phr.) ἰθὺς φρονεῖν *be resolved* Il.; **be deliberate, be intentional** (in doing sthg.) S.; **plot** —*evil* (W.DAT. *for someone*) Il.; (of an event) **signify, mean** —*sthg.* Th.
9 (of persons) **be aware** (of sthg.) S.; **recognise** —W.COMPL.CL. *that sthg. is the case* S.; (of oracles) **have knowledge of, know** —*sthg.* Hdt.
10 consider, deem (oneself) —W.INF. *to have been honoured* Il.; (phr.) εὖ φρονεῖν *be right* (*about sthg.*) Hdt.
11 think about, contemplate —*sthg.* Hom. —W.COMPL.CL. *how someone died* S.; **have** (W.NEUT.ACC.PL.ADJ. particular) **thoughts** Emp. Hdt. E. Att.orats. Pl.; (intr.) **make up one's mind, come to a conclusion** (about sthg.) S.
12 be concerned with —*transitory things* Od. —*human* (opp. *divine*) *matters* NT.
—**φρονούντως** *ptcpl.adv.* **wisely** —*ref. to speaking* A. S.
φρόνημα ατος *n.* **1 mind** (of a person or god) Trag.; **mentality, state of mind, outlook** (of a person) Hdt. Trag. Pl. Arist.; **attitude** (towards someone) A. S.
2 will (of a god, a person) Trag. ‖ PL. **intentions** Hdt. Pl.; **ambitions** (usu. w.pejor.connot.) A. Hdt. E. Th. +
3 spirit, confidence (of a person or nation) Th. Pl.; **pride** (as a positive trait) E. Th. Pl. Arist.
4 arrogance A. E. Ar. Isoc. Plu.
φρονηματίας ου *masc.adj.* (of persons) **self-assured, confident** Arist.; (w. ἐπί + DAT. in horsemanship) X.
φρονηματίζομαι *pass.vb.* (of persons, armies, races) **become proud-spirited** or **self-confident** (oft. W.PREP.PHR. due to military success or sim.) Arist. Plb.
φρόνησις εως *f.* [φρονέω] **1 thought, intention** (of a person) S.; **attitude** (W.DAT. towards someone) S.; (gener.) **state of mind, mentality** Arist.
2 way of thinking, mind (ref. to a person's individual mental faculty) Heraclit.; (gener., opp. body) Pl.; **mental faculty, intelligence** (as possessed by all animals) Emp.
3 wisdom, prudence Att.orats. Pl. X. Arist. +
4 perception (of sthg.) Isoc.; **understanding** (of sthg.) Isoc.
5 self-regard, arrogance, presumptuousness E.
φρόνιμος ον *adj.* **1** (of persons, actions, attitudes) **wise, sagacious** S. Ar. Att.orats. Pl. +; (of persons) **knowledgeable** (W.PREP.PHR. about sthg.) Isoc. Pl. X.; (of animals) **intelligent** Isoc. Pl. ‖ NEUT.SB. **reason** Pl.; **wisdom** X.; **prudence** Plu.; (specif.) **organ of intelligence** (in the body) Pl.
2 (of persons) **sensible, rational** (opp. mad) S. Ar.; **composed** (in the face of danger) X. ‖ NEUT.SB. **rationality** Pl.; **composure** X. ‖ NEUT.PL.SB. **rational thoughts** S.

3 (of birds) **thoughtful, enlightened** (in showing care for their aged parents) S.
—**φρονίμως** *adv.* | compar. φρονιμώτερον, superl. φρονιμώτατα | **wisely** Ar. Att.orats. Pl. X. +; **with intelligence** —*ref. to animals behaving* X.
φρόνις *f.* | only acc. φρόνιν | **wisdom, knowledge** Od.
φρονούντως *ptcpl.adv.*: see under φρονέω
φροντίζω, Aeol. **φροντίσδω** *vb.* [φροντίς] | Aeol.inf. φροντίσδην (cj.) | fut. φροντιῶ | aor. ἐφρόντισα | pf. πεφρόντικα ‖ MID.: fut. φροντιοῦμαι ‖ neut.impers.vbl.adj. φροντιστέον |
1 ponder in one's mind, deliberate —W.INDIR.Q. *what to do* Thgn. Hdt.; (intr.) **engage in deliberation** A. E. Isoc.; **wonder** —w. μή + SUBJ. *whether sthg. may not be* (*i.e. probably is*) *the case* Hdt. X. —W.INDIR.Q. *what might be the case* X.
2 contemplate, consider —W.ACC., GEN. or INDIR.Q. *sthg., how sthg. is the case* Trag. Pl.; (gener.) **think about** —W.ACC. or GEN. *sthg., a person, an event* Sapph. Hdt. Ar.; (intr.) **engage in contemplation** A. Hdt. Isoc.; **calculate, reason, reckon** (w. πρός + ACC. to oneself) —W.COMPL.CL. *that sthg. is the case* Hdt.
3 make plans, make decisions —W.PREP.PHR. *for oneself* Hdt.; **work out, think up, devise** —W.ACC. or INDIR.Q. *a strategy, how to do sthg.* Hdt. Ar. X.; (of two men) **have in mind** —W.ACC. *the same plan* E.
4 take care of, see to —*sthg.* E.(also mid.); **see to it, contrive** —W.COMPL.CL. *that sthg. is the case* Plb.; **take pains** —W.INF. *to do sthg.* Plu.
5 be or **become aware of, notice** —W.ACC. or COMPL.CL. *someone* or *sthg., that sthg. is the case* Thgn. E. Pl.; **direct one's attention** —W.PREP.PHR. *to sthg.* E.; **be concerned with, take an interest in** —W.ACC. or GEN. *sthg.* Ar. Att.orats. Pl. +
6 be concerned about —W.ACC. *sthg.* Ar. Men.; (esp. in neg.phr.) **show concern** —W.GEN., PREP.PHR. or COMPL.CL. *for someone, about sthg.* Hdt. E. Ar. Att.orats. Pl. +; (intr., esp. in neg.phr.) **pay attention, show concern** S. E. Ar. Att.orats.; (phr.) πεφροντικὸς βλέπειν *look careworn* E. ‖ PASS. (of a person) **be the object of concern** X.
—**πεφροντισμένως** *pf.pass.ptcpl.adv.* **with careful thought, earnestly** Plu.
φροντίς ίδος *f.* [reltd. φρονέω, φρήν] **1 faculty of thinking, thought** Pi. Lyr.adesp. Trag. Ar. +
2 application of thought, thought, contemplation, consideration (of sthg.) Pi. Hdt. Trag. X. D. +
3 thinking (of a philosophical or scientific kind) Ar.; perh. **thinking, wisdom** (of a particular person) Xenoph.
4 (freq.pl.) **thought** (ref. to a particular reflection or idea) Pi. Trag. Ar. Plu.
5 cogitation, deduction (ref. to a particular scientific argument or conclusion) Ar.
6 expressed thought, sentiment S. Men.
7 concerned or **anxious thought, concern** or **anxiety** (freq. W.GEN. about someone or sthg.) Thgn. Simon. Hdt. Trag. Antipho Pl. +
φρόντισμα ατος *n.* [φροντίζω] **deduction** (ref. to an example of Socratic wisdom) Ar.
φροντιστήριον ου *n.* **thinking-shop, thinkery** (com.ref. to a school for philosophy) Ar.
φροντιστής οῦ *m.* **thinker, intellectual** (esp.ref. to one who fancies himself a philosopher) Ar. X.; **contemplator** (W.GEN. or ACC. of celestial phenomena) Pl. X.
φροντιστικῶς *adv.* **attentively** —*ref. to visiting a sick friend* X.

φροῦδος η (dial. ᾱ) ον (also ος ον S. E.) *adj.* [πρὸ ὁδοῦ *on the road, on one's way*] **1** (of persons, gods, animals, a corpse; esp. w.vbs. of motion) **gone** (sts. W.PREP.PHR. fr. or to a place) S. E. Antipho Ar. Men. Plu. ‖ NEUT.PL.ADV. **away** A. E.
2 (specif., of dead persons) **departed** S. E. Call.; (W.PREP.PHR. to Hades) E.
3 (of things, evils, former blessings, hopes, fears) **no longer present, gone, past, lost** S. E. Ar.
4 (of a person's voice, limbs) **lost, not functioning** (fr. shock) E.; (of a person) **at a loss, unsuccessful** (w. ἐς + ACC. in sthg.) E.
5 (of bodies) **ravaged, ruined** (by sufferings) E.; (of a person) **done for** Ar. Men.

φρουρά ᾶς, Ion. **φρουρή** ῆς *f.* [φρουρός] **1 guard duty** (of watchmen, bodyguards, border guards) A. Hdt. E. Ar. X.; **act of standing guard** (over a fallen commander, in battle) Plu.; (specif.) **stint of garrison duty, garrison posting** Lys. X. D.
2 act or means of protection; **protection** (of a place, person, modesty, virtue, noble values, or sim.) E. Aeschin. D. Plu.; **housing** (for an eternal flame) Plu.
3 protective guard (of troops), **guard detail** E. Pl. Plu.; **garrison** Hdt. E. Th. Att.orats. X. +; (ref. to a naval guard) Hdt. Plu.
4 (in Laconia) mobilisation of troops, **military campaign** X.; (of the ephors) φρουρὰν φαίνειν *declare a general mobilisation of troops* X. Plu.; **body of mobilised troops** X.
5 act of keeping watch, **vigil** A. S.; (concr.) **lookout unit** (ref. to a body of men) A.
6 prison Pl. Plu.

φρουραρχέω *contr.vb.* [φρούραρχος] **serve as commander of a garrison** Plu.

φρουραρχίᾱ ᾶς *f.* **command of a garrison, post of garrison-commander** X. Plu.

φρούρ-αρχος ου *m.* [φρουρά, ἄρχω] **1 commander of a garrison** X. Din. Men. Plb. Plu.; (fig.ref. to a person's character) Men.
2 ‖ PL. **marshals or guardians** (title of officials in a proposed republic) Pl.

φρουρέω *contr.vb.* [φρουρός] | fut.pass. φρουρήσομαι | **1** (in military ctxt.) **provide or act as a guard**; (of troops, ships) **guard, defend** —*cities, passes, or sim.* Hdt. Th. X. D. Plu.; (intr.) **stand guard** Eleg.adesp. Hdt. E. Th. Pl. +
2 (of commanders or sim.) **defend with a garrison, furnish with a garrison** —*cities or sim.* Th. Isoc. X. Plu.; **station a garrison** —W.PREP.PHR. or ADV. *in a place* Th. X. ‖ PASS. (of cities, passes, or sim.) be guarded or garrisoned Hdt. S. Th. Att.orats. +
3 (specif., of persons) **serve in the civil guard** Pl.; **serve as a garrison-soldier** Ar. X. Arist. Plu.; **serve as a garrison-commander** X.
4 (in non-military ctxts.) act as a guard; (of a dragon) **guard** —*golden apples, the Golden Fleece* E.; (of a person) **keep under protective guard** —*one's wife, child* Plu.; (of gods, persons, cities) **protect** —*a person, city* S. E.Cyc. X. D. Plu.; (wkr.sens.; of Prometheus) **guard, man** —*the rock to which he is chained* A. ‖ PASS. (of women, objects) be guarded or kept safe E. Plu.
5 hold in safekeeping; (of priestesses) **look after** —*an image of a god, an eternal flame* A. Plu.; (of persons) **keep safe** —*a book* Plu.; (wkr.sens.) **maintain** —*an auspicious mouth (i.e. avoid unpropitious speech)* E. ‖ PASS. (of a corpse) be held in safekeeping (by a sea or river) Plu.; (of a marriage) be safeguarded —W.DAT. *by justice* A.
6 (w. hostile connot., of troops, commanders) **besiege,**

blockade —*a citadel, pass* Plu.; **occupy** —*a place* Plu.; (gener., of a crowd) **surround** —*a person* E. ‖ PASS. (of cities, harbours, persons) be blockaded, besieged or surrounded —w. ὑπό + GEN. *by enemies* Pl. Plu.; (of forts, cities, regions) be occupied by a hostile garrison Isoc. Plb. Plu.
7 (of persons, the crags of the underworld) **hold captive** —*a person* Ar. Plu.; (of a commander) **keep in check** —*enemies* (W.DAT. *w. fear*) Plb. ‖ PASS. (of persons) be held captive X. Plu.; (of soldiers) be press-ganged Plu.; (of a politician) be kept in check —W.DAT. *by votes* E.
8 keep watch (on someone) S. —w. ἐπί + DAT. *at someone's door* Theoc. ‖ PASS. be kept under surveillance E. Plu.
9 show vigilance, **be on one's guard, be poised for action** E. ‖ MID. **watch out for, dodge** —*weapons* E.
10 look out —W.PREP.PHR. or COMPL.CL. *for someone's best interests, a way of doing sthg.* S. E.
11 look out for, wait for —*a certain day* E.
12 see to, take care of —*a task* S.; **take care, ensure** —W.COMPL.CL. *that sthg. will not happen* S. E.

φρούρημα ατος *n.* **1 that which is looked after, ward, charge** (of a herdsman, ref. to cattle) S.
2 task of keeping watch E.
3 (ref. to a tribunal, warriors, bodyguards) **defender, protector** (of a person or land) A. E.

φρούριον ου *n.* [φρουρός] **1 place acting as a guard; fort, fortress** Th. Lys. Ar. D. +; **fortified outpost** (ref. to an island) Th.; **citadel** Pl. Men. Plu.; **fortified refuge** (for the gods, ref. to Athens) A.
2 guard provided by persons or deities; garrison A. Th. Arist. Plu.; (fig., ref. to the Gorgons, as occupying a particular place) A. ‖ PL. (ref. to persons) **guards** E.
3 garrison-duty X.

φρουρίς ίδος *f.* (usu. appos.w. ναῦς) **guard-ship** Th. X. Arist.

φρουρός οῦ *m.* [πρό, οὖρος²] **1 guard, watchman** (esp.ref. to troops stationed at city gates) Eleg.adesp. E. Arist. Plu. ‖ PL. **guardsmen** (ref. to members of a civil guard or sim.) Pl. X. Arist.; **garrison troops, garrisons** Th. Pl. X. Arist. Plu.
2 (ref. to a serpent) **guardian** (of a baby, golden apples, the Golden Fleece) E. AR.; (ref. to noble precepts, as protectors of the soul) Pl.
3 (ref. to a commander) **safekeeper, defender** (of a province) Plu.
4 watcher, lookout Call.

φρύαγμα ατος *n.* [φρυάσσομαι] **1 snorting, whinnying** (of excited horses) A. S. X.
2 vainglorious behaviour (of victorious young officers) Plu.; **insolent behaviour** Men.

φρυαγματίᾱς ου *masc.adj.* (of a way of life) **vaunting, vainglorious** Plu.

φρυαγμο-σέμνακος ον *adj.* [σεμνός] (of a person's attitude) **haughty-snorty** Ar.

φρυάσσομαι, Att. **φρυάττομαι** *mid.vb.* (of excited horses) **snort, whinny** Ar.(cj.) Call. Plu.
—**φρυάσσω** *act.vb.* **act insolently** NT.

φρυγανισμός οῦ *m.* [φρύγανον] **act of gathering firewood, firewood-gathering** Th.

φρύγανον ου *n.* **brushwood, firewood** Ar.; (collectv.pl.) Hdt. Th. Ar. X.

φρυγίλος ου *m.* **a kind of bird** (w. play on Φρύγιος *Phrygian*) Ar.

Φρύγιος *adj.*, **Φρυγίᾱ** *f.*, **Φρυγιστί** *adv.*: see under Φρύξ

φρύγω *vb.* | fut. φρύξω, dial. φρῡξῶ ‖ MID.PASS.: pf. πέφρυγμαι | **1** (of persons, esp. women) **cook** (food) Hdt.(oracle) Ar.

2 (specif.) **roast** —*beans, nuts, or sim.* Hdt. Ar. Theoc.; **dry** (in the sun) —*barley* Plu.(quot.com.) ‖ PASS. (of sweetmeats) be roasted Ar. ‖ PF.PASS.PTCPL.ADJ. (of barley, a food dish) roasted Th. Philox.Leuc.
3 (intr., of the sun, summer heat) scorch (the earth), **beat down** Theoc.

φρυκτός οῦ *m*. **1 beacon-fire** A. Th.
2 small fish for roasting, **roast sprat** Ar.

φρυκτωρέομαι *pass.contr.vb.* [φρυκτωρός] (of ships, i.e. their approach) **be signalled by beacon-fires** Th.

φρυκτωρίᾱ ᾱς *f*. **lighting of beacon-fires** Trag. Th. Ar.

φρυκτώριον ου *n*. **beacon-tower** (as the site of a prepared fire) Plu.

φρυκτωρός οῦ *m*. [φρυκτός, οὖρος²] **beacon-fire** A. Th.

φρῡνεός οῦ *m*. **toad** Pratin.

φρύνη ης *f*. **toad** (pejor.ref. to a repulsive old crone) Ar.

Φρύνιχος ου *m*. **1 Phrynichus** (tragic poet, 6th–5th C. BC) Ar. Plu.
2 Phrynichus (comic poet, late 5th C. BC) Ar. Plu.

—**Φρυνίχειος** ᾱ ον *adj*. ‖ NEUT.SB. (ref. to a high-kick in a dance) **the Phrynichus special** Ar.

Φρύξ Φρυγός *m*. **1 Phrygian man** Hdt. +; (as the name of a slave, ref. to his ethnic origin) Ar.
2 ‖ PL. **Phrygians** (as a population or military force) Il. +

—**Φρύγιος** ᾱ (Ion. η) ον *adj*. (of persons, places, things) from or belonging to Phrygia, **Phrygian** (in poetry oft. equiv. to *Trojan*) Hdt. S. E. Th. Ar. +; (of music, ref. to a mode, esp. assoc.w. the aulos) Alcm. Stesich. E. Arist. ‖ FEM.SB. **Phrygia** (as the name of a slave, ref. to her ethnic origin) Theoc.

—**Φρυγίᾱ** ᾱς, Ion. **Φρυγίη** ης *f*. **Phrygia** (region in Asia Minor) Il. +

—**Φρυγιστί** *adv*. (quasi-adjl., of music) **in the Phrygian mode** Pl. Arist.

φῦ¹ *interj*. (expressing discomfort or pain fr. smell, smoke, fire) **phew!** A.(cj.) Ar.

φῦ² (ep.3sg.athem.aor.): see φύομαι, under φύω

φυᾱ *dial.f.*: see φυή

φῡᾱτήρια ων *Lacon.n.pl*. [φῡσάω] **pipes** (ref. to a Spartan wind instrument, perh. similar to bagpipes) Ar. | see φυσαλλίδες

Φῦβος *Boeot.m*.: see Φοῖβος

φυγᾱ́ *dial.f.*: see φυγή

φύγαδε *adv*.: see under φυγή

φυγαδείᾱ ᾱς *f*. [φυγαδεύω] **banishment, exile** (of a person) Plb.

φυγαδεύω *vb*. [φυγάς] **1 banish, send into exile** —*a person* Att.orats. X. Arist. + ‖ PASS. (of persons) be sent into exile X. Plb. Plu.
2 live in exile Plb.

φυγαδικός ή όν *adj*. (of the wanderings, hopes, finances, or sim.) **of an exile** Th. Isoc. Plu. ‖ MASC.PL.SB. **persons in exile** Plb.

—**φυγαδικῶς** *adv*. **in exile** —*ref. to living* Plu.

φυγαδο-θήρᾱς ου *m*. [θηράω] **hunter of fugitives, bounty-hunter** Plb. Plu.

φυγ-αίχμᾱς ᾱ *dial.masc.adj*. [φεύγω, αἰχμή] **fleeing from the spear, scared of battle, cowardly** A. Call.

φυγαρχέω *contr.vb*. [ἀρχή] **shun political office** Arist.

φυγάς άδος *m.f*. [φεύγω] | *dial.dat.pl.* φυγάδεσσι (A., cj.) |
1 one who is forced to flee from his homeland (esp. by an official decree or death sentence), **exile** (esp. W.GEN., PREP.PHR. or ADV. fr. a place) Hdt. Trag. Th. Att.orats. +; (ref. to a voluntary exile, one shunning wickedness or sim.) S. E.; (W.GEN. fr. mankind) Plu.
2 one who flees (fr. war or persecution), **refugee** A. E.; one who flees (fr. battle), **fleer, runaway** S. E.; (fig., fr. bad influences, fr. one's former excesses and pledges) Th. Pl.
3 deserter (W.PREP.PHR. fr. an army) X.; (fig., fr. someone's service) Th.
4 ‖ MASC.FEM.ADJ. (quasi-advbl., of persons going or being driven) **in flight, fleeing** (fr. danger, fr. the scene of a crime) E.; (of a person's foot) E.(cj.)

φυγγάνω *vb*. **1 escape from** —*one's bonds* A.
2 (of a fact) **escape** (the notice of) —*someone* S.

φύγδα *adv*. **by fleeing** A.

φυγή ῆς, dial. **φυγᾱ́** ᾱς *f*. **1 action** or **instance of escape, flight** (of persons, animals, ships, or sim., esp. fr. battle, predators, dangers) Od. Tyrt. Hdt. Trag. +
2 avoidance (of pain or sim.) Arist.
3 means of escape (W.GEN. fr. a marriage, slavery, sufferings, or sim.) Trag. Arist.; (fr. divine justice or sim.) S.; (fr. predators or sim., ref. to a bird's wings) Pl.
4 enforced flight (fr. one's native land), **exile, banishment** (of a person, sts. W.GEN. or PREP.PHR. fr. one's homeland) Thgn. Hdt. Trag. +; (as cogn.acc.) φυγὰς φεύγειν *go into exile* Lys. Pl. Arist.
5 group or **body of exiles** Th. Att.orats. Pl. X. +

—**φύγαδε** *adv*. **to flight** (esp. fr. the battlefield) —*ref. to being driven* Il. AR.

φυγοδικέω *contr.vb*. [δίκη] **fail to appear at one's trial** D.

φυγομαχέω *contr.vb*. [φυγόμαχος] **1** (of troops, commanders) **avoid engaging in battle** (fr. fear or strategic considerations) Plb. Plu.; (gener.) **be reluctant to engage in battle** Plb. Plu.
2 (of wrestlers) **lack fighting spirit, be cowardly** Plu.

φυγό-μαχος ον *m*. [φεύγω, μάχη] **one who flees from battle, coward** Simon.

φυγό-ξεινος ον *Ion.adj*. [ξένος²] (of a people) **shunning foreign visitors, inhospitable** Pi.

φυγοπονίᾱ ᾱς *f*. [φυγόπονος] **work-shy attitude** (of Celts) Plb.

φυγό-πονος ον *adj*. [πόνος] (of a person) **work-shy** Plb.

φυγο-πτόλεμος ον *ep.adj*. [πόλεμος] (of a person) **avoiding war, cowardly** Od.

φύζα ης *f*. [φεύγω] **panicked flight** (of troops, fr. battle) Hom.; (of Medea, fr. Colchis and her pursuers) AR.

φυζακινός ή όν *adj*. (of deer) **flighty, timid** Il.

φυή ῆς, dial. **φυᾱ́** ᾱς *f*. [φύω] **1 physical appearance, physique** (of a person, a god, esp. as advbl.acc. *in appearance*) Hom. Hes. Tyrt. Lyr. A.*fr*. Hellenist.poet.; **physical form** (of a creature, a plant) hHom. S.*Ichn*. AR. Mosch.; **appearance** (of a herald) hHom.
2 frame, bulk (of an ox) Pi.
3 physical prime (of youth) Pi.
4 natural disposition, essential quality, nature (of a person, the sea) Archil. Semon. Pi.; φυᾷ *by nature* Pi.

φύη (dial.3sg.athem.aor.opt.): see φύομαι, under φύω

φῡκία ων *n.pl*. [φῦκος] **seaweed** Hippon. Pl. Theoc.

φῡκιόεις εσσα εν *adj*. (of beaches, a fisherman's bait) **covered in seaweed** Il. Theoc.

φῡκί-οικος ου *m*. [οἶκος] **dweller in seaweed** (ref. to Poseidon) Call.

φῦκος εος *n*. | *dial.dat.pl*. φύκεσσι | **1 seaweed** Il. Alcm.
2 orchil (a red dye extracted fr. coastal lichens); **red pigment, rouge** Theoc.

φυκτός ή όν *adj*. [φεύγω] **1 avoidable** ‖ NEUT.PL.SB. **possibility of escape** Hom.
2 (of a bold course of action, in neg.phr.) **to be shrunk from** AR.

φυλάζω *vb.* [φυλή] (of Lykourgos) **divide** (the Spartans) **into tribes** (W.COGN.ACC. φυλάς) Plu.(oracle)

φυλακεῖον ου *n.* [φύλαξ] **guard-post** (ref. to a fortified structure manned by troops) Plb.; **guard-detail** (ref. to a unit of soldiers) Plb.

φυλακή ῆς, dial. **φυλακά** ᾶς *f.* [φυλάσσω] **1** act of keeping safe, **guarding, protection** (of a city, person, cargo) Thgn. Hdt. E. X. Men.; **policing** (of the seas, against pirates) D.; protective overseeing, **stewarding** (of a political process) Pl.; role of guarding, **stewardship, trusteeship** Pl. Arist. **2** state of protecting or being protected, **protective guard** (over a person, object or place) Hdt. D.; state of being preserved, **preservation, survival** (of a language) Hdt.; **protection** (provided by sthg.) Isoc.; that which protects, **safeguard** (W.GEN. of sthg.) Att.orats. Arist. **3** act of keeping watch (esp.ref. to guard duty) Il. Archil. E. Th. +; **watch** (of the night, ref. to a military duty) E.; (as a unit of time, the night being divided into four or five watches) Hdt. E. NT. **4 guard-detail** (ref. to troops) Il. Hdt. E. +; **guard-post, checkpoint** Hdt. E. Th. +; **garrison** (ref. to troops, ships) Hdt. Th. +; **personal guard** (ref. to a body of troops) Hdt. Pl. D. **5 defensive vigilance** (against attack or sim.) Il. Thgn. Pi. Hdt. Pl.; (gener., as an attitude) Th. Pl.; **precautionary measure** Th.; (W.GEN. against suspicion) Antipho **6 vigilant surveillance** (of a flood-prone river, a person, nets in a hunt) Hdt. E. X. **7** hostile vigilance, **surveillance** (in a blockade) Th.; **guard, blockade** (ref. to people or ships keeping watch on a door, pass, harbour, or sim.) E. Th. Lys. X. **8 close guard** (over prisoners) E. Th.; **detention** (of a person) Hdt. Th.; **imprisonment, captivity** Plb.; (concr.) **prison** Plb. NT. **9** (fig.) **guard** (over one's own or another's tongue or mind) Thgn. A.

φυλακίζω *vb.* **imprison** —*someone* NT.

φυλακικός ή όν *adj.* [φύλαξ] **1 protective** (W.GEN. of the state, one's patriotic convictions) Pl. **2** (of persons, a class of people) **performing the role of guardian** (esp. of the state, ref. to philosopher-kings) Pl. ‖ FEM.SB. art of being a guardian Pl.

φυλακίς ίδος *f.* **female guardian** (of the state) Pl.

φυλακός οῦ *m.* (also *f.* Call.) **1 guard, sentry** Il. Hdt. **2 guardian, guard** (assigned to watch over a person, corpse, bridge) Hdt. **3 protector** (W.GEN. of a house, ref. to severed heads, as trophies) Hdt. **4 keeper, custodian** (of a chest, bow, sacred flock) Hdt. Call. AR. **5** (as the title of an official) **warden** (of the mouth of the Nile) Hdt. **6 warder** (of a captive) Hdt.; (of the dead, ref. to Cerberus) Theoc.

φυλακτέος ᾱ ον *vbl.adj.* [φυλάσσω] **1** (of plots) **needing to be guarded against** E. **2** (of privileges, a military formation) **needing to be preserved** X. D. **3** (of respect for a god) **needing to be observed** S.

φυλακτήρ ῆρος *m.* **sentry** Il. AR.

φυλακτήριον ου *n.* **1 guard-post, guard-tower, garrison-post** Hdt. Th. Pl. + **2 bulwark** (ref. to popular goodwill, as shoring up a ruler's position) Plu.; **safeguard** (against exploitation) Pl. D.; (ref. to a capsule of poison, as insurance against capture) Plu. **3** ‖ PL. **phylacteries** (ref. to leather boxes containing passages fr. the Torah, worn on the arm and forehead by Jews during worship) NT.

φυλακτήριος ᾱ ον *adj.* (of a person) **acting as protector** (of flocks or sim.) Pl.

φυλακτικός ή όν *adj.* **1** (of strength) **providing protection** Arist. **2** (of persons or things) **able to preserve** or **retain** (sthg., esp. advantages) X. Arist.; (of persons) **liable to hold on** (W.GEN. to grudges, anger) Arist. **3** (of persons) **cautious, wary** X. Arist.

—**φυλακτικῶς** *adv.* ‖ compar. φυλακτικώτερον ‖ **1 protectively** Plb. **2 cautiously, warily** Men. Plb.

φύλαξ ακος *m.* (*sts. f.*) **1 sentinel, sentry** Il. E. Th. Ar.; **lookout** (ref. to a guard in a watchtower) A. **2 guard, defender** (of a place or military position) Thgn. Hdt. S. E. Th. X.; (W.GEN. against enemies) E.; **guard, garrison** (ref. to a body of troops, a fleet) Hdt. Th. **3** (gener.) **watchman** (assigned to guard a tomb, an empty house) S. Lys. NT. **4 protector, bodyguard** (of a person) Hdt. E. Pl. X.; (ref. to a giant) **defender, supporter** (of Zeus, in a battle) Hes.; (milit., appos.w. λόχοι) **back-up** (ref. to reserve troops) X. **5** (ref. to a god, daimon, king) **patron, protector** (of persons, ships, places) Hes. Trag.; (ref. to a handmaid or sim.) **carer** (for a helpless old person) S. E. **6** (ref. to a god, person, dragon, or sim.) **guardian, keeper** (of shrines, sacred flocks, golden apples, or sim.) Pi.*fr.* Hdt. Trag.; (ref. to a person, a hero, Virtue) **protector** (of valuables, a house) Pi. E. X. **7** (ref. to a person) **defender, upholder** (of laws, noble precepts, or sim.) And. Pl. X.; (ref. to an edict carved in stone) **safeguard** (of a benefaction) Plu.; (ref. to an army) **preserver, enforcer** (of tyrants' rule, the subjugation of the populace) Lys. **8** (ref. to a privy councillor, queen, or sim.) **overseer, steward** (of a palace, household) A. E. **9** (ref. to a helmsman) **controller** (of the rudder) E. **10** (ref. to a market official) **overseer, monitor** (of commercial transactions) Lys. **11** (ref. to a daimon) **observer** (of mortals, their deeds) Hes. **12 warden** (of a prison, captives) Pl. X.; (ref. to Cerberus) S.

φύλαξις εως *f.* **defensive strategy, expedient** E.

φυλαρχέω *contr.vb.* [φύλαρχος] **serve as captain of a cavalry regiment** Ar. X. Is. Men.

φυλαρχία ᾱς *f.* **post of regiment-captain** Arist.

φύλ-αρχος ου *m.* [φυλή, ἄρχω] **1 leader of a tribe** (as one of the rulers of a city) Arist.; (ref. to an Arab chieftain) Plu. **2** (specif., at Athens) **president of a phyle** Hdt. Lys. X. Arist.; (as commander of the cavalry regiment provided by each phyle) **regimental commander** Ar. Att.orats. X. Arist. **3** (in Roman ctxt.) **commander of a tribal contingent, tribunus (militum)** Plu.

φυλάσσω, Att. **φυλάττω** *vb.* ‖ ep.inf. φυλασσέμεναι ‖ aor. ἐφύλαξα ‖ pf. (in cpds.) -πεφύλαχα ‖ MID.: fut. (sts. w.pass.sens.) φυλάξομαι ‖ aor. ἐφυλαξάμην ‖ pf. πεφύλαγμαι, imperatv. πεφύλαξο ‖ PASS.: aor. ἐφυλάχθην ‖ neut.impers.vbl.adj. φυλακτέον ‖ The sections are grouped as: (1–4) stand guard over, protect, defend (persons or things), (5–12) keep, hold, maintain (objects, emotions, customs, or sim.), (13–17) keep watch (for or on persons or things), (18–22) take precautions, be careful. ‖

1 keep a protective watch; (of sentries, shepherds, dogs, or sim.) **stand guard over, keep watch over** —*persons, animals, objects, places* Hom. Hes. A. Pi. +; (intr., sts. W.COGN.ACC.) **stand guard, keep watch** Hom. Hes. Th. X. —W.PREP.PHR. *over flocks, herds* Hom. NT. ‖ MID. (of sentries) **stand guard** Il. ‖ PASS. (of ships, a camp) be guarded Il. X.
2 keep safe from harm; (of gods, persons, things) **protect, defend** —*persons, places* Hom. Thgn. Pi. Hdt. Trag. +; (of a person's name) —*someone* (W. μή + INF. *against ill-treatment*) S.; (of persons) **act as bodyguard to** —*someone* Isoc. X. ‖ MID. **protect** —*one's head* Hdt.(oracle); (intr.) **defend oneself** or **get into a defended position** (against a military offensive) Hdt.(oracle) +.
3 keep safe in one's charge; (of gods, persons) **keep safe, look after, act as custodian of** —*objects, an estate, a contract* hHom. Lys. Isoc. X.; **take charge of, be responsible for, manage** —*a household, a city's affairs* Od. A.
4 (of gods and daimons) **keep a watch on, oversee** —*men's deeds and oaths* Il. Hes.
5 **preserve** or **keep stored** —*fine wine* Od. —*someone's words* (in the writing-tablets of one's mind) A. —*statements* (W.DAT. in one's memory) Pl.
6 (wkr.sens.) **keep, hold** —*apples* (W.PREP.PHR. *in one's lap*) Theoc.; **wear** —*a garland* Theoc.
7 **ensure the continued existence** (of sthg.); **hold on to, retain** —*another's love, one's fortune, one's ancestral language* Il. Hdt. D.
8 **maintain, preserve** —*rites* Pi. —*manners of behaviour* E.; (mid.) —*due measure* (in behaviour) Hes.
9 **keep, maintain** —*one's attitude* (W.PREDIC.ADJ. *reliable, i.e. remain true to one's word*) S. ‖ MID. **keep** —*someone's words* (W.PREDIC.ADJS. *unspoken and ineffective, i.e. keep them secret and not act upon them*) S. —*one's lips* (W.PREDIC.ADJ. *silent*) E.
10 **store up, harbour** —*anger* Il. Pl.; **preserve, maintain** —*silence* E.; **cling to** —*stupidity* S. ‖ PASS. (of hatred) be stored up —W.PREP.PHR. *by someone* S.
11 **uphold, respect, observe** —*an instruction, an oath, a law, justice* Il. Hdt. S. Pl.; (mid.) —*justice, an obligation* Sol. Pi.
12 **bear in mind, pay due attention to, take heed of** —*a saying, threats* Pi. Call.; (mid.) —*instructions, advice, or sim.* Hes. hHom. Thgn.
13 **keep watch** (without protective purpose); **keep vigil** (esp. at night) Od. A.; **watch for** —*a signal, persons (i.e. their arrival)* Od. A. E. X.; **keep a lookout** —W.DAT. *for the enemy* Th.; **be vigilant** (against corruption) And. ‖ MID. **look carefully to see** —W. μή + ἐστί (understd.) *if anyone is nearby* E. ‖ PASS. (of persons) be watched out for —W.DAT. *by sentinels* E.
14 **keep a careful watch on** —*someone* E. Lys. Pl. Thphr. —(W.INDIR.Q. *to see whether he will do sthg.*) Pl. ‖ MID. (wkr.sens., of a cicada) **watch** —*shepherds* Theoc.
15 **keep a custodial watch on, keep in custody** —*a person* E. Antipho ‖ PASS. be held in custody Hdt. Ar.
16 **keep** (W.ACC. someone) **safely away** —W. ἀπό + GEN. *fr. wine-jars* Men. ‖ MID. (of troops) **keep away** —W. ἀπό + GEN. *fr. crops* (W. μή + SUBJ. *to avoid trampling them*) X.
17 **watch and wait** (for a future event); **watch for the chance of** —*returning home* Il. —*vengeance* D.; **wait for** —*nightfall* E. Th. —*winds* D. —*an event* (to happen) Hdt. E. —*a specific day* Hdt. Antipho; **wait to see** —W.INDIR.Q. *what someone will do, when sthg. will happen* Hdt. Pl. D. —W.ACC. + PTCPL. *someone doing sthg., sthg. happening* Hdt. D. ‖ MID. **wait for the right moment, bide one's time** Ar.
18 **take precautions, be careful** —W.INF. *to do sthg.* S.; (mid.) Hes. A.
19 **take precautions** (against sthg.); **guard against** —W.INF. or ACC. + INF. *sthg. happening, someone doing sthg.* Th. Pl. D. —W. μή + SUBJ. *doing sthg., someone doing sthg.* E. Pl.; **protect, keep** —*someone, oneself* (W. μή or ὅπως μή + SUBJ. *fr. doing sthg.*) Pl.
20 ‖ MID. **be on one's guard, take precautions** Il. + —W.GEN. w. regard to one's ships (W. μή + SUBJ. *in case sthg. shd. happen to them*) Th.; **take care to ensure** —W. μή or ὅπως μή + SUBJ. *that sthg. does not happen* A. E. Ar. +; **protect oneself** —W. ἀπό + GEN. *fr. sthg.* X.
21 ‖ MID. (tr.) **be on one's guard** (against sthg.); **be wary of, avoid** —*persons, places, things* Hes. Hdt. Trag. Ar. +
22 ‖ MID. **be on one's guard** (against doing sthg.); **guard against, avoid** —*certain speech or behaviour* Sapph. Hdt. Ar. + —W.INF. or μή + INF. *doing sthg.* Hdt. Antipho D.; **guard** —W. πρός + ACC. *against sthg.* (i.e. avoid doing it) Th.

—**πεφυλαγμένος** η ον *pf.mid.ptcpl.adj.* (of a companion) **watchful, protective** Simon.

—**πεφυλαγμένως** *pf.mid.ptcpl.adv.* **guardedly, cautiously** Isoc. X. D. Plu.

φυλετεύω *vb.* [φυλέτης] (of a ruler) **accept as a phyle member** (i.e. grant Athenian citizenship to) —*foreigners, slaves* Arist.

φυλέτης ου *m.* [φυλή] **1** (usu.pl.) **member of the same phyle** (as another person), **fellow tribesman** Ar. Att.orats. X. Arist. Thphr. Plu.
2 **member of a** (particular) **phyle** Att.orats. Pl. Arist.

φυλετικός ή όν *adj.* (of courts) **serving a particular phyle** Pl.; (of ties of friendship) **between members of the same phyle** Arist.

φυλή ῆς *f.* [φύω] **1 tribe** (ref. to a distinct subgroup within a population) Hdt. Arist. Plu.; (ref. to the twelve tribes of Israel) NT.; (gener., ref. to all the peoples on earth) NT.
2 tribe, phyle (as an administrative division, at Athens) Hdt. Th. Ar. Att.orats. +; (in other cities or states) Pl. X. Arist. +
3 (milit.) **regiment** (of the Athenian land forces, esp. the cavalry; ref. to the detachment of troops fr. a single phyle) Hdt. Th. Lys. X.; (gener.) **regiment, battalion** Th. Pl. X.
4 (fig.) **type, category** (of furniture) X.

Φυλή ῆς *f.* **Phyle** (deme on the NW. border of Attica, w. a fort controlling the route to Thebes) Ar. Att.orats. X. Arist. Men. Plu.

φυλίη ης *Ion.f.* a kind of shrub; perh. **wild olive** or **buckthorn** Od.

φυλλάς άδος *f.* [φύλλον] **1 pile of leaves** (esp. used as a bed) Hdt. S. AR. Bion.
2 mass of leaves, foliage (esp. of a sacred grove or sim.) Trag.; (fig.) **vigour** (as withering in old age) A.
3 leafy branch (esp. as held by a suppliant) E. Ar.; (collectv.sg.) **brushwood** Plb.

φυλλεῖα ων *n.pl.* **greens, salad** Ar.

φύλλινος η ον *adj.* (of a shed-wall made fr. wattle) **leafy** Theoc.

φυλλοβολέω *contr.vb.* [βάλλω] (of roses) **shed petals** Call.*epigr.*; (gener., of a poplar in spring) **shake the leaves** Ar. [or perh. *shed catkins* or sim.]

φυλλό-κομος ον *adj.* [κόμη] (of plants) **covered in foliage, leafy** Ar.

φύλλον ου *n.* [φύω] **1 leaf** (of a tree or plant) S. Arist. Call. Theoc. Plb. ‖ PL. leaves (oft. as image for groups of people or mortals in general, ref. to their countless numbers, sts. also their ephemerality) Hom. +; (ref. to garlands, wreaths) E.;

(fig., ref. to songs, as victory-garlands) Pi.; foliage, sward (of a meadow) Theoc.
2 ‖ PL. **ears** (of corn, barley) Hdt.; **petals** (of flowers) Hdt.; **flowers** (of plants) Theoc.; **branches** (of fir) E.*Cyc.*
3 plant, herb (ref. to particular species, esp. used as medicine) S. Pl.

φυλλορροέω *contr.vb.* [ῥέω] (of vines) **shed leaves** X.; (fig., of a cowardly person, imagined as a tree) **shed** —*shields* Ar.

φυλλό-στρωτος ον *adj.* —also **φυλλοστρώς** ῶτος (Theoc.) *masc.fem.adj.* [στρωτός] (of a bed) **of spread** or **heaped leaves** E.; (of the ground) **heaped with leaves** (as a bed) Theoc.*epigr.*

φυλλο-φόρος ον *adj.* [φέρω] (fig., of contests) bearing leaves, **bringing wreaths** (of victory) Pi.

φυλλο-χόος ον *adj.* [χέω] (of the month) **of leaf-fall** (i.e. autumn) Call. AR.

φῡλο-βασιλεύς έως *m.* [φυλή] **chieftain of a tribe** (in Athens; ref. to the leaders of the original four tribes) Arist.

φῡλοκρινέω *contr.vb.* [κρίνω] **distinguish between tribes, be ethnically partial** Arist. —W.INDIR.Q. *about whom one shd. support* Th.

φῦλον ου *n.* [φύω] **1 tribe, clan** (within a population) Il.; (ref. to a person's kinsmen, ancestors or descendants) Od. Call.
2 tribe, race, nation (ref. to an ethnic group) Il. Hdt. Trag. X. Call. +
3 particular type, race, breed (of creatures, birds) Alcm. A. E.*fr.* Ar. X.
4 breed, class (of mankind, womankind) Il. Hes. Ar. X.; **class, category** (of persons, animals, things) Od. Semon. Pi. Pl. +
5 (sg. and pl.) **race** (of men, ref. to the human race) Hom. +; (of gods, giants, birds, or sim.) Hom. Hes. S. Ar. Pl. AR.; (of gods, as a community in a specific place) Il. hHom.
6 people, population Od. Hes. S. Plb.
7 group, crowd, throng (of followers) Pl. Plb.
8 contingent (of troops) E. X.

φύλοπις ιδος *f.* | acc. φυλόπιδα, also φύλοπιν | **uproar, tumult** (of battle) Hom. Hes.; (gener.) **combat, battle, conflict** Hom. Hes. Mimn. S. Ar.(mock-oracle) Theoc.

φῦμα ατος *n.* [φύω] **growth** (on the body), **tumour** Hdt. Pl. Plb.

φῦν (dial.athem.aor.inf.), **φῦναι** (athem.aor.inf.): see φύομαι, under φύω

φυξ-ᾱνορίᾱ ᾱς *dial.f.* [φεύγω, ἀνήρ] **act of fleeing from a husband, desire to avoid marriage** A.

φύξηλις *masc.fem.adj.* | only acc. φύξηλιν | (of a warrior) **cowardly** Il.

φύξιμος ον *adj.* **1** (of a place) **providing a safe refuge** Od. Plb. Plu.; (specif.) **providing sanctuary** (to fugitives) Plu.
2 (of a smell) needing to be avoided, **loathsome** Simon.
3 (of the gods) **able to escape** (W.ACC. love) S.

φύξιος ον *adj.* **1** (of a fate) **of being a fugitive** AR.
2 (as a title of Zeus) **protector of fugitives** AR.

φύξις εως *f.* **flight** (fr. battle, harm) Il. B.; (into exile) AR.

φῡράω *contr.vb.* [φύρω] | fut. φῡράσω | aor. ἐφύρᾱσα |
1 knead —*dough* Hdt.; (intr.) X.; **knead into a paste** —*earth* Pl. —*earth, a root* (W.DAT. *w. blood, milk*) A. Plu.; (fig.) **get the dough ready** (ref. to acquiring funds, as a necessary first step for assembling a fleet) Plu.(quot.) ‖ PASS. (of barley, earth) be kneaded —W.DAT. *w. water, wine, oil* Th. Pl.
2 ‖ MID. (fig., of a lascivious boy) **make syrupy, sweeten** —*his voice* Ar.

φύρδην, dial. **φύρδᾱν** *adv.* **1 in chaotic confusion, pell-mell** —ref. *to fighting or attacking, beaches being strewn w. bodies, events unfolding in a civil war* X. Plb. Plu.

2 headlong —*ref. to statues being toppled, a person being dragged* A. S.*fr.*

φύρω *vb.* | fut. φύρσω | aor. ἔφυρσα ‖ PASS.: aor. ἐφύρθην | pf.pass.ptcpl. πεφυρμένος | fut.pf.inf. πεφύρσεσθαι (Pi.*fr.*) |
1 mix up (w. liquid); **mix** —*earth* (W.DAT. *w. water*) Hes.
2 soak, sully —*one's clothes* (W.DAT. *w. tears*) Il.; **spatter, defile** —*persons, their faces, or sim.* (W.DAT. *w. blood*) Od. AR. —*one's head* (*w. dust*) E. ‖ PASS. (of persons, their faces, beds, objects) be soaked or stained (w. tears, blood, dye) Od. Simon. A. E. X. +; be defiled —W.DAT. *w. mud, dust* Semon. Pi.
3 (of early man) **jumble together** —*everything* (W.ADV. εἰκῇ *at random*) A.; (of a playwright) —*material in his plays* Ar.; (of a god) —*mortals' good and bad fortune* E.; (of a person attempting scientific inquiry) **muddle together** —*a methodology* (W. εἰκῇ *at random*) Pl.; (of a friendly god) **throw into confusion** —*an enemy* Pi. ‖ MID. or PASS. **get oneself in a muddle** Pl. ‖ PASS. (of a chariot's wheels) be entangled —W.DAT. *w. dead bodies* Plu.; (of the soul) —*w. the corporeal body* Plu.; (of the life of early man) be disordered or senselessly chaotic E.
4 ‖ PASS. (of sophists and orators) be **lumped together** Pl.; (of a population) be subject to **admixture** (opp. be isolated) Pl.; (of a person) **get mixed up** —*w.* πρός + ACC. *w. someone* Pl.

φύς (athem.aor.ptcpl.): see φύομαι, under φύω

φῦσα[1] ης *f.* | ep.gen.pl. φῡσάων (Call.) | **1** ‖ PL. **bellows** (as used by a blacksmith) Il. Hdt. Th. Call. AR.
2 gust (W.GEN. of fire) hHom. AR.
3 (sg. and pl.) **wind, flatus** (in the digestive tract) Pl. X.

φῦσα[2] (fem.athem.aor.ptcpl.): see φύομαι, under φύω

φῡσαλλίδες ων *f.pl.* [φῡσάω] **pipes** (ref. to a Spartan wind instrument, perh. similar to bagpipes) Ar. | see φυᾱτήρια

φῡσάω, Ion. **φῡσέω** (Call.) *contr.vb.* [φῦσα[1]] | dial.masc.nom.pl.ptcpl. φυσᾶντες | dial.inf. φυσῆν ‖ neut.impers.vbl.adj. φυσητέον | **1** (of winds, bellows) **blow** Il. Plb.; (of persons, w. their mouths, w. bellows) Hdt. Th. Plb.
2 (tr.) **blow on** —*a painful hand* Theoc. —*a sacred flame* Plb. —*a fire, torch* (to kindle it) Ar. Plb. Plu.(quot. A.)
3 blow (to produce a sound); **blow, play** —*a wind instrument* E. Plu. —*a tune* Ar.; (intr., of pipers) Plb.; (w.pejor.connot.) **puff away** Eleg.adesp. Ar. ‖ PASS. (of a conch shell) be blown Theoc.
4 (of the dying Ajax, his arteries) exhale, **spray out** —*blood* (fr. *his nostrils, his wound*) S.; (fig., of Ares) **breathe out** —*bloodshed* S.
5 (of horses) **pant** Ar.; (of persons, sts. w. μέγα, app.ref. to vociferous protest) **huff and puff** E. Call.
6 (of persons, wind) **inflate with air** —*objects* Ar.; **inflate, puff out** —*one's cheeks* (to be shaved, or fr. conceit) Ar. D. ‖ PASS. (of skins, a person's belly) be inflated with air Ar. X.; (of a lazy man) be bloated or puffy (opp. in good physical condition) X.; (of veins) be distended (opp. narrow) Hdt.
7 (of persons, w. μέγα) **swell up with conceit** Men.; (tr., of persons) **inflate the pride** or **confidence of** —*someone* D. ‖ PASS. (of persons) become puffed up with pride or overconfidence —*w.* ἐπί + DAT. *at sthg.* X. D. Plu.

φύσγων (v.l. **φύσκων**) *m.* [φύσκη] (ref. to a pot-bellied man) **stuffed sausage** Alc.

φύσημα ατος *n.* [φῡσάω] **1 gust, blast** (of wind) E.; (pejor., ref. to a tragedian's recital) Ar.
2 gasp (of a dying man) E.; **snort** (W.GEN. of a horse) X.; **spray** (W.GEN. of blood, fr. slaughtered cows) E.
3 swell (of the sea), **billow, wave** E.

φῡσητήρ ῆρος *m.* **blowing straw, tube** (used to inflate sthg.) Hdt.

φῡσίᾱμα ατος *n.* [φῡσιάω] **wheezing, snorting** (of sleeping Erinyes) A.

φῡσιάω *contr.vb.* [φῡσάω] | ep.ptcpl. (w.diect.) φῡσιόων |
1 (of horses, cows) **snort** (fr. exertion or fear) Il. hHom.; (of persons, Erinyes, their chests) **pant, heave** (fr. exhaustion) A. AR.; (of a dying man) **gasp** S.
2 (of fabled oxen) **snort, breathe out** —*fire* AR.

φῡσίγγομαι *pass.vb.* [φῦσιγξ *garlic shoot*, perh. also reltd. φῡσάω] (of the Megarians, famous as garlic producers) app. **be riled, be fired up** —W.DAT. *by an affront* (perh. alluding to the practice of stimulating fighting-cocks w. garlic) Ar.

φυσι-γνώμων ονος *m.* [φύσις] **physiognomist** (i.e. one who deduces character fr. physical appearance) Theoc.*epigr.*

φῡσί-ζοος ον *adj.* [φύω; app. ζειαί, by pop.etym. ζωή] (of earth) **life-giving** Hom. hHom. Hdt.(oracle); (of Zeus) A.

φυσικός ή όν *adj.* [φύσις] **1 naturally inherent;** (of personal qualities) **innate** X. Arist. Plb. Plu.; (of urges) **natural, universal, common to all** Arist. Plu.
2 occurring naturally; (of objects, fortifications) **natural** (opp. man-made) Arist. Plb.; (of phenomena, opp. due to human involvement) Arist.; (of the cause of a disaster, opp. supernatural) Plu.; (of practices, opp. arising fr. social conventions) Plu.; (of justice or sim., opp. being artificial concepts) Arist.
3 (of objects) belonging to the physical world, **physical** Arist.; (of phenomena) **relating to the physical plane** Plu.
4 (of science) **relating to the natural world** Arist.
|| MASC.SB. natural scientist or natural philosopher Arist. Plb. Plu. || FEM.SB. natural science, physics Arist.
|| NEUT.PL.SB. (as the subject and title of a work) Physics Arist. Plu.
5 (of investigation, teachings, jargon) relating to the natural sciences, **scientific** Arist. Plu.

—**φυσικῶς** *adv.* **1 innately, naturally, spontaneously** Plb.
2 universally Plb.
3 on the physical plane Plu.

φυσιογνωμονέω *contr.vb.* [γνώμων] (of onlookers) **recognise by appearance** or **look** —*a corrupted voter* D.

φυσιολογέω *contr.vb.* [φυσιολόγος] **conduct scientific investigation** Arist.

φυσιολογίᾱ ᾶς *f.* **natural science** Plu.

φυσιο-λόγος ου *m.* [λέγω] one who investigates the nature and workings of the universe, **natural scientist, natural philosopher** Arist.

φῡσιόων (ep.ptcpl.): see φῡσιάω

φύσις εως (dial. εος, Ion. ιος) *f.* [φύω] | dat.sg. φύσει, Ion. φύσῑ | nom.acc.du. φύσει |
1 natural configuration, **natural layout** (of sthg.) X.; physical nature, **physical characteristics** (of a place or object) Od. +
2 physical characteristics or appearance (of a person), **physique, appearance, look** A. +; (concr.) physical form, **body** (of a person) Pl.
3 material from which something is composed; **substance** (of an object) Arist.; (gener.) physical substance, **matter** (of sthg.) Pl.; (wkr.sens.) **essence** (W.GEN. of sthg.) A. Pl.; (periphr.) **entity, phenomenon, concept** (W.GEN. of sthg.) S. Pl.
4 inherent or essential character, **nature** (of sthg.) Heraclit. Isoc. Pl. X.; φύσει *by nature, intrinsically* S. Ar. Pl. Arist.; (also) ἐκ φύσεως Aeschin.; φύσιν A.
5 innate disposition, **character** (of a person) Pi. +; defining character, **temperament** (of a particular class, such as tyrants, philosophers) Pl.; ἀνθρωπεία φύσις *human nature* Th.
6 natural instinct (of a person); **instinct** (opp. artifice, as the instrument of the poet) Pl.; (pejor.phr.) χρῆσθαι τῇ φύσει *indulge one's base nature, show one's true colours* Ar. Isoc. Plu.
7 natural order of things, **nature** (esp. opp. human convention) E.*fr.* Ar. Pl.; (ref. to the laws of nature as a governing force) Heraclit. S. D.
8 (prep.phrs.) κατὰ φύσιν *in accordance with nature, naturally* Hdt. E.*fr.* Att.orats. Pl. +; παρὰ φύσιν *contrary to nature, unnaturally* E. Antipho Th. Pl. X. +; πρὸ τῆς φύσεως *before the natural term, prematurely* (ref. to dying) Plu.
9 (of a circumstance) φύσιν ἔχειν *be natural* D.; (impers.) *it is natural* —W.ACC. + INF. *that sthg. shd. be the case* Hdt. Pl.
10 nature, the natural world (ref. to the universe) E.*fr.* Pl.
11 creation (of the universe, its contents) Pl. Arist.
12 origin, birth (of persons, living things) Emp.; φύσει (also φύσιν, κατὰ φύσιν) *by birth* (ref. to being noble or sim.) Hdt. S.; **parentage** Isoc.; ὁ κατὰ φύσιν πατήρ *one's biological father* Plb.; **stock** (fr. which someone is descended) S.
13 tribe, race (of animals, envisaged as a group) S. Pl.; θνητὴ φύσις *human race* S.; **species, variety** (of animals, plants) Isoc.; **type, genus, category** (of sthg.) S. Pl.; (specif.) **class, sex, gender** (of males, females) S. Pl. X.
14 (w.pejor.connot., ref. to persons) **type, character** Isoc.; αἱ τοιαῦται φύσεις *people of such a type* S. Isoc. Aeschin.

φύσκη ης *f.* [φῦσα¹] **sausage of stuffed intestine, sausage** Ar.

φύσκων *m.*: see φύσγων

φυστή ῆς *fem.adj.* (of a barley-cake) **light, spongy** Ar. || SB. **sponge-cake** Philox.Leuc.

φῡσώδης ες *adj.* (of things) **full of air, puffed up** Pl.

φῡταλιή ῆς Ion.*f.* [φυτόν] | ῡ *metri grat.* | **1 plantation, orchard** or **vineyard** Il. AR.
2 planting, cultivation (of orchard fruits) AR.
3 that which is planted, **plant** (ref. to the olive tree) Call.

φυτάλμιος ον *adj.* **1** (of parents) producing offspring, **procreative** A.; (fig., of a bed) **fruitful, fecund** E.
2 app., naturally developing, **endowed from birth** (W.GEN. w. blind eyes) S.

φυτείᾱ ᾶς *f.* [φυτεύω] **1 planting** (of vines, fruit trees, or sim.) X. Plu.
2 that which is planted, **plant** NT. Plu.

φύτευμα ατος *n.* that which is planted, **plant** Pi. S. Pl.; (fig.) **offspring** (ref. to a child) A.*fr.*

φύτευσις εως *f.* (concr.) **plantation** (W.GEN. of trees) Pl.

φυτευτήριον ου *n.* **sapling** X.; **plantation, nursery** (of olive saplings) D.

φυτευτός ή όν *adj.* (of a category of things, ref. to plants) **grown** Pl.

φυτεύω *vb.* [φυτόν] **1 plant** —*trees, vines, plants,* or *sim.* Hom. Alc. Thgn. Carm.Pop. Pi. Ar. +; (fig., of God) NT.; (intr.) X. Arist. NT. || MID. (of personif. Libya) **plant in one's soil** —*the root of a great city* Pi. || PASS. (of trees) **be planted** D. Plb. NT.
2 (fig., of a teacher) **implant** —*teachings* (in a pupil's soul) Pl.; (of the laws of reincarnation) —*a soul* (w. εἰς + ACC. *into an animal*) Pl. || PASS. (fig., of a potential philosopher) **be planted** (in the wrong environment) Pl.
3 plant with crops (esp. w. fruit trees, vines, or sim., opp. cereals) —*a piece of land* Tyrt. Th. X.(mid.) Is. —*a vineyard* NT. || PASS. (of land) **be planted with crops** Hdt. X. D. Arist. Thphr.
4 (of persons or gods) **beget, father** —*a child* Hes. hHom. Pi. E. Ar. +; (intr.) Hes. S. E. Lys. Pl.; (of parents, a marriage) **produce** —*a child* S. —(of a woman) **bear** —*a child* (W.DAT. *to someone*) B.; (fig., of the Muses) **give birth to** —*Harmony* E.;

φυτικόν

(of Hubris) —*a tyrant* S. ‖ PASS. (of a person) be begotten Pl.; (fig.) be the child —W.GEN. *of an evil fate* S.
5 (gener., of men) **father** —*a race of people* Hdt. ‖ PASS. (of persons) **be descended** —W.GEN. or ἐκ + GEN. *fr. someone* Pl.
6 (of god, molecular processes) **create** —*plants, objects* Pl. ‖ PASS. (of things) **be created** —w. ὑπό + GEN. *by god* Pi.
7 (of persons or gods) **sow, prepare** —*sufferings, death, glory, respite, a marriage* (freq. W.DAT. *for someone*) Hom. Lyr. S. E. ‖ PASS. (of honours, prosperity) **be prepared** —W.DAT. *for persons* Pi.; **be attained** —w. σύν + DAT. *w. the help of a god* Pi.

φυτικόν οῦ *n.* **vegetative principle** (as part of the soul, ref. to the unconscious processes necessary for life and growth) Arist.

φύτλᾱ ᾱς *dial.f.* **stock** (ref. to a person's ancestry) Pi.

φυτόν οῦ *n.* [φύω] **1** that which grows, **plant, crop** (ref. to cultivated plants, vines, fruit trees, or sim., oft. to saplings requiring tender care) Hom. +; **tree** Theoc. Plu.; **timber** Pi.
2 (gener.) **plant** (sts.opp. animals) Pl. X. Arist. Theoc. Plu.
3 (fig.) **plant** (ref. to man, as a type of organism) Pl.; **vegetable** (ref. to a person in a state of permanent sleep) Arist.; **crop** (of the earth, ref. to iron) Call.; **phenomenon** (ref. to the cancellation of debts, seen as a blight) Plb.
4 (gener.) **being, living thing** Pl.
5 (pejor.) **creature** (ref. to a woman) E.
6 **breed, race** (ref. to womankind, a group of people) A. E.; (ref. to springs and rivers) Theoc.
7 **growth, tumour** (perh. fig.ref. to an erect penis) Archil.
8 (fig., ref. to a poet) **offspring, scion** (of the Graces) Theoc.

φυτο-σκάφος ου *m.* [σκάπτω] (sts. appos.w. ἀνήρ) one who tends plants, **gardener, nurseryman, orchardman** AR. Theoc.

φυτο-σπόρος ου *m.* [σπείρω] **sower** (fig.ref. to a father) S.

φυτο-τρόφος ον *adj.* [τρέφω] (of a landowner) **raising plants** AR.

φυτουργός οῦ *m.* [ἔργον] **planter** (of vines or sim.); (fig., sts. appos.w. πατήρ) **begetter** (of a son or daughter) Trag.; (gener., ref. to a carpenter) **creator** (of a piece of furniture) Pl.

φύτωρ ορος *m.* [φύω] **begetter, father** S.

φύω (also **φῡ́ω**), Aeol. **φυίω** (dub.) *vb.* ‖ The tr. usages are given first: act. (pres., impf., fut., aor.1). For the intr. usages (pass., fut.mid., also act.athem.aor. and pf.plpf., sts. pres.) see φύομαι below. ‖ dial.3pl. φύοντι | impf. ἔφυον | fut. φύσω | aor. ἔφυσα |
1 (of a father) **beget** —*a child* (sts. W.GEN. *by a mother*) Thgn. E.; **be the father** (of a child) Trag. +; (of parents) **produce** —*a child* S.; **be the parents** (of a child) E.; (fig., of a day) **establish the parentage of** —*a child* S.
2 (of the earth, a land) **produce** —*crops or sim.* Il. +; (of plants) **grow** —*leaves, branches* Il.; (of persons, animals) —*hair, teeth, horns, feathers, or sim.* Sol. +; **develop, acquire** —*intelligence* S.; (wkr.sens., of persons, animals) **have** —*a tongue, youthful body, mature mind* A. Hdt.
3 (of god, nature, or sim.) **create** —*the universe, its contents, mankind* Trag. +; (of a person, a city) **create, sow** —*troubles* S.; **win** —*glory* Hdt.
4 (of a magic drug, the bloom of youth) **cause to grow, produce** —*hair* (on someone's body) Od. A.; (of summer breezes, spring) —*fruits, leaves* Od. Mimn.

—**φύομαι** (also **φῡ́ομαι**) *pass.vb.*| aor.2 ἐφύην, ptcpl. φυείς ‖ fut.mid. (w.pass.sens.) φύσομαι ‖ also ACT.: athem.aor. ἔφῡν, 3sg. ἔφῡ, ep. φῦ, 3pl. ἔφῡσαν, also ἔφυν (Od.), ἔφυν (Pi.), inf. φῦναι, dial. φύμεναι (Theocr.), also φῦν (Parm.), ptcpl. φῡ́ς (fem. φῦσα, Boeot. φοῦσα), dial.3sg.opt. φῡ́η (Theocr.) | pf. πέφῡκα, ep.3pl. πεφύᾱσι, masc.acc.pl.ptcpl. πεφυῶτας, fem.ptcpl. πεφυυῖα | plpf. ἐπεφύκειν, ep. πεφύκειν, ep.3pl. ἐπέφῡκον ‖ The pres.act. is also sts. intr., esp. in poetry. |
1 (of persons, animals) **be born** Il. +—W.GEN. or w. ἐκ or ἀπό + GEN. *to a mother or father* Pi. +—W.PREP.PHR. *fr. noble stock or sim.* E. +
2 (of plants) **grow** (in a place) Hom. +; (of flowers, on a plant) Sol. +; (of hair, horns, a tumour, on someone's body) Il. +
3 (of the universe) **come into being** Parm.; (gener., of objects) Pl.; (of a cry) **rise, form** (in someone's breast) Alc.; (of phenomena, situations, events) **arise, develop, come about** Pl. D.; (of a person) **flourish** (at other people's expense) D.
4 **be naturally present**; (of limbs) **grow** (on the body) Hes.; (of the roots of the earth and sea) **be situated** (in a place) Hes.; (of death) **be a fact of life** S.
5 (wkr.sens., of persons or things) **be** or **become present, exist** Thgn. +
6 (of persons, places, things, personal qualities; esp. W.DAT. φύσει, oft. W.ADV. ἱκανῶς, εὖ, κάλλιστα, or sim.) **be naturally destined, suited** or **inclined** —W.DAT. or PREP.PHR. *to a particular activity* Pi. +—W.INF. *to do sthg.* S. +; (of persons or things) **naturally have a certain character** or **form** Att.orats. X. ‖ IMPERS. (esp. PF.) it is natural —W.ACC. + INF. *for sthg. to be the case* S. Arist.
7 (of persons, places, things, situations) **be naturally** —W.PREDIC.ADV. *of a particular nature, in a particular state* Hdt. +; (of persons or things) **be naturally** or **inherently** —W.PREDIC.ADJ., SB. or PTCPL. *good, bad, wise, or sim.* Sol. +
8 (wkr.sens., of persons, things, situations) **be** —W.PREDIC.ADV. *in a particular state, engaged in a particular activity* A. +—W.PREDIC.ADJ. *good, bad, astonishing, or sim.* Alc. +—W.PREDIC.SB. *a messenger, woman, delight, or sim.* Archil. +

—**πεφυκότως** *pf.ptcpl.adv.* **naturally** (opp. artificially) Arist.

φῶ (pres. and athem.aor.subj.): see φημί

φῷδες, Ion. **φοῖδες**, ων *f.pl.* **chilblains** Hippon.; **blisters** Ar.

Φώκαια ᾱς (Ion. ης), Aeol. **Φώκᾱα** ᾱς *f.* **Phocaea** (city on the coast of Asia Minor) hHom. Sapph. Hdt. Th. +

—**Φωκαιεύς**, Att. **Φωκᾱεύς**, έως *m.* | Att.nom.pl. Φωκᾱῆς (Th.), also Φωκᾱεῖς (Isoc.), Ion. Φωκαιέες | acc.pl. Φωκαιᾱ́ς (D.) | **1** man from Phocaea, **Phocaean** Hdt. ‖ PL. Phocaeans (as a population or military force) Hdt. Th. Isoc. Call. Plb.
2 ‖ ADJ. (of gold staters) **Phocaean** D.

—**Φωκᾱίς** ίδος *f.* **1 Phocaean woman** X. Plu.
2 region of Phocaea or **Phocaean coast** Th.

Φωκεύς *m.*: see under Φωκίς

φώκη ης *f.* **seal** (ref. to the marine mammal, esp. the Mediterranean monk seal) Od. hHom. Hdt. Ar. Call. Theoc.

Φωκίς ίδος *f.* **1 Phocis** (region of mainland Greece, on the north coast of the Corinthian gulf) Hdt. S. Th. +
2 ‖ ADJ. (of the land) of Phocis Hdt. E. Th.; (of a road) in or at Phocis E.; (of a dialect) Phocian A.

—**Φωκεύς** έως (Ion. έος) *m.* | Ion.nom.pl. Φωκέες, ep. Φωκῆες | man from Phocis, **Phocian** Trag. + ‖ PL. Phocians (as a population or military force) Il. +

—**Φωκικός** ή όν *adj.* **1** (of persons) **from Phocis, Phocian** Aeschin.; (of a desperate act) **of the Phocians** Plb.
2 (of a war) **Phocian** (ref. to the Third Sacred War of 356–346 BC) Aeschin. D. Plu.; (of losses) **in the Phocian War** Plu.

φωλάς άδος *fem.adj.* [φωλεός] (of bears) **lurking in a den** Theoc.

φωλεός οῦ *m.* **1 hole, burrow, den** (of a wild beast, snake) NT. Plu. **2 school** (for a boy) Call.

φωλεύω *vb.* (of snakes) **lurk in a burrow** Theoc.

φῶμεν (1pl.subj.): see φημί

φωνᾱ́εις *dial.adj.*: see φωνήεις

φωνασκέω *contr.vb.* [φωνή, ἀσκέω] | pf.ptcpl. πεφωνασκηκώς | (of a singer, an orator) **train one's voice** Pl. D.

φωνασκίᾱ ᾱς *f.* **vocal training** (of an orator) D.

φωνασκικός ή όν *adj.* (of an instrument) **for training the voice** (ref. to a pitch-pipe, to help a speaker pitch his voice) Plu.

φωνέω *contr.vb.* [φωνή] | aor. ἐφώνησα, ep. φώνησα, dial. φώνᾱσα (Pi.) | —also **φώνημμι** Aeol.vb. | fem.ptcpl. φώνεισα | aor.inf. φώναισαι (cj.) | **1** use one's voice, **speak** (sts. W.ADV. or PREP.PHR. *thus, quietly, loudly, or sim.*) Hom. +; **sound** —W.COGN.ACC. *one's voice* Od. **2** (in neg.phr.) **communicate by speech** (w. someone who does not understand one's language) Hdt. **3** (of persons or things) **have a voice, speak** (opp. be mute) Hdt. **4** (fig., of thunder) **have a voice** (i.e. communicate a message, as a portent) X. **5 speak** (opp. be silent) A. S. Ar. X. **6 say** —W.ACC. or DIR.SP. *sthg.* Hom. + —(W.ACC. *to someone*) AR. **7** (of a singer) **give voice to** —*varied sounds* Theoc.; (of the personif. voice of a lyre) **say** —*sthg.* S.*Ichn.* **8** ‖ AOR.PASS.PTCPL.SB. **words or sounds uttered** Pl. **9 speak about, mention, describe** —*sthg.* A. S. **10 call out** —*a named person* (*i.e. that person's name*) S. **11 tell, order** —*someone* (W.INF. *to do sthg.*) S. **12 call, address** —*someone* (W.PREDIC.ACC. *by a certain title*) Scol. —(W.PREDIC.NOM., *as if in* DIR.SP.) NT. **13 speak to, address** —*someone* NT.; **call, summon** —*someone* (*esp. a servant*) NT. —*one's sheep* NT.; **invite** —*persons* (*to a meal*) NT. ‖ PASS. (of servants) **be summoned** NT. **14** (ref. to non-human utterance; of swineherds) **call out** (w. a horn) Plb.; (of a cockerel) **give voice** (i.e. crow) NT.

φωνή ῆς, dial. **φωνᾱ́** ᾶς *f.* [φημί] **1 faculty of utterance** (as that which may be given, taken away, temporarily lost, or imagined as acquired by an inanimate object), **speech** Hom. Hes. Trag. Ar. + **2 voice** (as the instrument of speech or other utterances); **voice** (of gods or humans, oft. qualified as loud, quiet, shrill, or sim.) Hom. + **3 voice** (of an animal, ref. to its characteristic sound) Od. Iamb.adesp. Hdt. Ar. **4 sound produced by the voice, utterance** or **speech** (of gods or humans) Hom. + **5 speech, language** (as the medium of human communication) Hdt. Pl.; (specif., ref. to the dialect of a particular population) A. Hdt. Th. Ar. Isoc. Pl. + **6 shout, shouting, cry** (ref. to a battle-cry, cry of distress, shout of praise, hunting-call, or sim.) Hom. + **7 cry, call** (of an animal) Od. Hdt. Ar.; (of a bird) Od. Hes. hHom. Thgn. Ar. **8 sound, strain** (of a musical instrument) E. Pl. **9** (gener.) **sound, noise** Pl. Arist.; φωνῇ *by sound* (*ref. to how a blind person sees*) S. **10 vocalic quality** (possessed by vowels, opp. consonants) Pl.

φωνήεις, dial. **φωνᾱ́εις**, εσσα εν *adj.* | neut.nom.acc.pl. (trisyllab., w. synizesis) φωνάεντα (Pi.) | **1** (of living creatures) **possessing a voice** (characteristic of their kind), **able to speak** Hes.; (of animals) **possessing a human voice, articulate** X. **2** (of an audience) **vociferous, noisy** (opp. silent) Pl.; (of a rabble, compared to a cicada) Plu.; (fig., of grapes, envisaged as children) Ion **3** (of a victory-song) **resounding** Pi. **4** (of a lyre) **vocal, musical** Sapph. **5** (of a statement or utterance) **clear-voiced** Pi. B.; (of arrows, fig.ref. to a poet's words) **speaking loud and clear** (W.DAT. *to those who understand*) Pi. **6** (of speech-sounds) **vocalic** (opp. consonantal) Pl. ‖ NEUT.SB. **vowel** Pl. Arist.

φώνημα ατος *n.* [φωνέω] **sound** or **speech uttered, utterance** S.

φώρ φωρός *m.* [φέρω] **thief** Hippon. Hdt. Pl. D. Call.*epigr.* AR.

φωρᾱ́ ᾶς, Ion. **φωρή** ῆς *f.* **act of theft** hHom. Bion

φωράω *contr.vb.* | fut. φωρᾱ́σω | aor. ἐφώρᾱσα | **1 search for stolen goods** Ar. Pl. **2 detect, discover** —*a trespasser, plot, someone's true character* Plu. —W.ACC. + PTCPL. *money being embezzled, someone doing sthg. treacherous* X. Arist. Plu. ‖ PASS. **be caught** —W.PTCPL. *doing sthg.* E.*fr.* D. Arist. Plu.; **be found out** (sts. W.PTCPL. + PREDIC.ADJ. or SB. *as being such and such*) E. Th. D. Plb. Plu.; (of plots or sim.) **be detected** Plu. **3** (gener.) **discern, observe** —W.ACC. + PTCPL. *someone doing sthg.* Pl.; **find** —*someone's remains* Plu. ‖ PASS. (of facts) **be found out** Plu.

φωριαμός οῦ *m.* **chest, trunk** (for storing clothes) Hom.; **casket** (for storing medicines and poisons) AR.

φώριος ον *adj.* [φώρ] (of lovemaking) **secret, clandestine** Theoc.

φώς φωτός *m.* **1 man** Hom. Hes. Mimn. Lyr. Parm. Trag. +; (wkr.sens., appos.w. a term of kinship or occupation, e.g. υἱός, ἀρχηγός, ἰατρός) Hom. hHom. A. Pi. E. AR.; (as pers.pron.) **that man, he, him** Hom. Hes. A. S. **2 mortal man, man** (opp. god) Il. Hes. A. Pi. E. Theoc.; **human** (opp. animals) hHom. S.; (ref. to a man or woman) **person** E. **3 man** (of a particular woman), **husband** Trag.

φῶς Att.*n.*: see φάος

φῶσι (3pl.subj.): see φημί

φωσ-φόρος, also **φαεσφόρος**, ον *adj.* [φάος, φέρω] **1** (epith. of Hekate, Artemis) **torch-bearing** E. Ar. Call. **2 bringing light**; (of Dawn, daylight, the sun's course, torches, a star) **light-bearing, bright, blazing** A. E. Lyr.adesp. Ar. AR.; (of eyes) **shining, gleaming** E.*Cyc.*; (specif.) **emitting light** (in the Platonic theory of vision) Pl.

φωτεινός ή όν *adj.* [φάος] **1** (of the sun) **bright, shining** X.; (of a cloud) NT.; (of paintings) **brightly coloured** X. **2** (fig., of a pure person) **full of light** NT.

φωτίζω *vb.* | aor. ἐφώτισα | **1** (of a lamp, God's light) **illuminate, shine on** —*persons* NT. **2** (of a person) **bring to light, reveal, make public** —*secret instructions* Plb.; **set out** —*arguments* Plb. ‖ PASS. (of facts or sim.) **be made public** Plb.

φωτός[1] (gen.sg.), **φωτί** (dat.): see φάος

φωτός[2] (gen.sg.), **φωτί** (dat.): see φώς

X χ

χάδε (ep.3sg.aor.2), **χαδέειν** (ep.aor.2 inf.): see χανδάνω
χάζω vb. | ep.redupl.fut. κεκαδήσω | ep.redupl.aor.2 κέκαδον
|| MID.: χάζομαι, imperatv. χάζεο, Ion. χάζευ | impf.
ἐχαζόμην, ep.3sg. χάζετο, ep.3du. χαζέσθην | fut. χάσομαι,
ep. χάσσομαι | aor. ἐχασάμην, ep. ἐχασσάμην || For
ep.3pl.redupl.aor.2 κεκάδοντο see ὑποχάζομαι. |
1 (causatv.) make (someone) withdraw (fr. sthg.); (of a
person, weapon) **deprive** —someone (W.GEN. *of life*) Hom.
2 || MID. (of warriors) **be forced to retreat** —w. ὑπό or
ὑπέκ + GEN. *by an enemy's spear, a blast of fire* Il. AR.; **give
ground, shrink back** (fr. the front line) Il. —W.GEN. or
PREP.PHR. *fr. a place, battle* Il.; (gener., of persons, gods)
back away Call.
3 || MID. **pull out** —W.GEN. *of a test of strength* AR.; **hold
back, refrain** (sts. W.INF. fr. doing sthg.) AR.
χαῖον ου n. **staff, stick** (of a shepherd or traveller) Call. AR.
χάϊος ᾱ ον *Lacon.adj.* —also **χαός** όν *dial.adj.* | compar.
χαϊώτερος | **1** (of ancestors) **noble, well-born** Theoc.; (of a
woman, w. play on sense 2) Ar.
2 (of a woman) **stunning, well-endowed** (in physique) Ar.
χαιρετισμός οῦ m. [χαίρω] (in Roman ctxt.) **formal visit** (to
a superior, Lat. *salutatio*) Plb.
χαιρηδών όνος f. **enjoyment** (of sthg.) Ar.
χαίρω vb. | imperatv. χαῖρε, Boeot. χῆρε (Corinn.), dial.inf.
χαίρην | iteratv.impf. χαίρεσκον | fut. χαιρήσω | aor.
ἐχαίρησα | pf. κεχάρηκα, ep.ptcpl. κεχαρηώς | fut.pf.
κεχαρήσω, ep.inf. κεχαρησέμεν || MID.: fut. χαρήσομαι (NT.)
| ep.redupl.fut. κεχαρήσομαι | ep.3sg.aor. χήρατο
| ep.redupl.aor.2 κεχαρόμην, opt.3sg. κεχάροιτο, 3pl.
κεχαροίατο | pf. κεχάρημαι, ptcpl. κεχαρημένος, also
κεχαρμένος | plpf. ἐκεχαρήμην, ep.3pl. κεχάρηντο || PASS.:
aor.2 ἐχάρην, ep.3sg. χάρη, inf. χαρῆναι || Mid. and aor.2
pass. are used in the same senses as act. |
1 be glad, rejoice Hom. + —W.ACC., DAT. or ἐν + DAT. *in one's
heart* Hom. +; **take delight** (W.DAT. or PREP.PHR. *in sthg.*
Hom. + —W.DAT. (or ἐπί + DAT.) + PTCPL. *at someone doing
sthg.* Hom. + —W.ACC. + PTCPL. *that sthg. is the case* E.;
(imperatv., as the bard's invocation to gods, nymphs, or
sim.) —W.DAT. *in this song* Od. hHom. Ar.
2 enjoy the company of, be on good terms with —W.DAT.
people Hdt. S.
3 take pleasure —W.DAT. *in (doing) sthg.* Hes. Pi. E.; **enjoy**
—W.NOM.PTCPL. *doing sthg.* Il. +; **like** —W.PTCPL. *calling
sthg. by a certain name* Pl.; **favour** —W.DAT. *a certain name*
(*as a description of sthg.*) Pl.
4 take habitual delight —W.NOM.PTCPL. *in doing sthg.* Ar. +;
(wkr.sens.) **make a habit** —W.PTCPL. *of doing sthg.* Hdt. +
5 express one's delight —W.DAT. *in songs, laughter* E. X.
6 (usu. in neg.phrs., oft. w.fut. or in ptcpl., predicting
deserved retribution) **be gleeful** (i.e. unpunished) Hom. +
• οὐ χαιρήσεις (or sim., to a jeering opponent) *you won't be
so gleeful* (when sthg. happens), *you'll be laughing on the
other side of your face* Ar.; οὐ χαιρήσουσι (or sim., as a
prediction of an imminent reversal of fortune) *they won't
be celebrating* (when sthg. happens) Il. Hdt.; οὐ χαίρων
(esp.w. ἀπαλλάσσομαι *get off*) **not scot-free, not unpunished**
Hdt. +
7 be of good cheer (esp. in imperatv. χαῖρε, when
presenting someone w. food or gifts) Od. +; (as a greeting,
esp. in imperatv.) **hail** Hom. +; (in ritual greetings to the
sun, moon, one's native land, or sim.) Trag.; χαίρειν λέγω (or
sim., sts. w. λέγω understd.) *extend greetings* —W.ACC. or
DAT. *to someone* Sapph. Ar. +; **have a good day** (w.
implication *receive the greeting* χαῖρε), **be bid good day**
—W.DAT. or παρά + GEN. *by someone* S. Men.
8 (in farewells) **rejoice in good fortune**; (esp.imperatv.
χαῖρε, as a parting salutation) **farewell** Od. +; (in ptcpl. w.vb.
of motion, esp.imperatv.) χαίρων ἴθι (or sim.) *farewell, go in
peace, godspeed* Od. +; χαίρειν λέγω (or sim., dismissive) **bid
farewell to, dismiss, shun** —W.ACC. or DAT. *someone or sthg.*
A. +; ἐῶ χαίρειν *let go, put out of one's mind, forget about*
—W.ACC. *persons, things, difficulties, or sim.* Hdt. +; **ignore,
shun, avoid** (sthg.) Pl. +; (of questions, objections, plans,
reports, or sim., usu. in 3pl.imperatv.) **be bid farewell, be
dismissed, be discounted** Hdt. + || 3SG.IMPERATV. **let it be,
leave it alone** A. Hdt.
χαίτη ης, dial. **χαίτᾱ** ᾱς f. **1** (sg. and pl.) **flowing locks, hair**
(of a person, oft. torn out in grief or cut off as a vow; also
adorned, combed, shaken, or sim.) Hom. +; (sg., ref. to an
individual lock) Il. A. E. || PL. (fig.) **locks** (ref. to trembling
foliage, envisaged as tossed hair) Call.
2 mane (of a horse) Il. X. AR. Plu.; (of a lion) E. Theoc.; (fig., of
Aeschylus, as a fierce opponent) Ar.; **bushy hair** (on a
Cyclops' chest) Call.
3 crest (of a helmet) Plu.
4 thistledown Theoc.
χαιτήεις, dial. **χαιτάεις**, Ion. **χαιτέεις**, εσσα εν adj. (of
Apollo) **with flowing locks** Pi.; (of a horse) **with flowing
mane** Semon. AR.
χαίτωμα ατος n. **crest, plume** (W.GEN. of a helmet) A.
χᾱλᾱ́ dial.f.: see χηλή
χάλαζα ης f. **1** (sg. and pl.) **hail, hailstorm** Il. Sol. S. E. Pl. X. +;
(of blood, fig.ref. to slaughter on the battlefield) Pi.
2 hailstone Ar.
χαλαζάεις εσσα εν dial.adj. (fig., of slaughter on the
battlefield) **falling like hail** Pi.
χαλαζάω contr.vb. **have cysts** (as a sign of infestation by
parasites) Pi.
χαλαίνω vb. [χαλάω] (of charioteers) **slacken** —*reins* Hes.
χᾰλ-αργος ον dial.adj. [χηλή, ἀργός] (of a contest) **of swift
hooves** (i.e. a horse-race) S.

χαλαρός ᾱ́ όν *adj.* [χαλάω] **1** (of sandals, a cuirass, bridle) **loose-fitting** Ar. X.; (of a halter, chains) **loose, slack** Th. X.; (of a rider's legs) **slack, relaxed** (opp. held stiff) X.
2 (of a hip-joint) **supple, flexible** Ar.
3 (fig., of a musical mode) **lax, dissolute** Pl.

χαλαρότης ητος *f.* **looseness** (of a horse's bit, bridle, or sim.) X.

χάλασις εως *f.* **weakening** (of an instinct, as the result of luxurious living) Pl.

χάλασμα ατος *n.* **loose spacing** (W.GEN. of soldiers in a battle-line) Plb.; (of weapons, stacked on a wagon) Plu.

χαλάω *contr.vb.* | aor. ἐχάλασα, ep. χάλασσα, dial. ἐχάλαξα, ptcpl. χαλάξαις (Pi.) || MID.: aor. ἐχαλασάμην, ep.3pl. χαλάσαντο || MID.PASS.: ep.3sg.plpf. κεχάλαστο || PASS.: aor. ἐχαλάσθην | — also **χόλαιμι** *Aeol.vb.* | 3pl. χόλαισι |
1 make (sthg.) slack or loose; **unstring** —*a bow* hHom.
2 loosen —*a slipper, belt, sandal-strap, noose, bonds, or sim.* S. E. Ar. Pl. X.; (intr., of a ship's tackle, a girdle) **come loose** Alc. E. || PASS. (of bonds) be loosened A.
3 unstop —*a wineskin* E.*Cyc.*; **open** —*a pouch* Men.; **draw back** —*door-bolts, a shroud* S. E. Ar.; (intr., of gates, doors) **open up** X. Plu.
4 (of soothing tastes) **dilate, relax** —*constricted parts of the tongue* Pl.
5 release —*a person* (W.GEN. *fr. bonds*) Thgn. A.; (in neg.phr., of Justice) —*that which exists* (W.DAT. *fr. her bonds*) Parm.; (intr.) **loosen one's hold** (on a prisoner) A.
6 (specif.) **unfurl, let down** —*a ship's sails* Theoc. NT.; **lower** —*a lifeboat, person in a basket, stretcher, ship's mast* AR.(mid.) NT.; **let out, cast** —*fishing-nets* NT.
7 slacken, stop pulling on —*a rope* E.(dub.); (fig.) —*the reins* (W.DAT. *of one's argument, i.e. give it free rein*) Pl.; (intr.) **stop pulling** (on a hooked fish's line) Theoc.
8 (of an eagle) **relax, rest** —*its wings* Pi.; (of a horse) **open** (opp. clench shut) —*its mouth* X.; (of a person) **unfurrow** —*one's brow* Ar.; (of a ewe) **unburden** —*its udder* (*by letting its lamb suckle*) E.*Cyc.*; (intr., of tendons) **relax, slacken** Pl.; (of a person) **be at ease** S.; (of the structure of a particle) **loosen, weaken** Pl. || PASS. (of the soul, as having a natural resonance) become unstrung or detuned Pl.; (of the body) be weakened (by disease) Pl.
9 (of persons) **relax** —*a rigid law or principle* Pl. Plu.; **quell** —*feelings of anger or love* Ar. Pl.; (of a single night) **lessen** —*an aversion to one's husband* E.; (intr., of desires) **weaken, abate** Pl. || PASS. (of strict discipline) be relaxed Pl.
10 ease off, draw back —W.GEN. *fr. anger, sedition, or sim.* Alc. A. Ar. Plu.; **let up** —W.GEN. *on sufferings* (*inflicted on another*) A.; **be lenient** —W.DAT. *to persons* (w. τὸ μή + INF. *by letting them off doing sthg.*) A.; **show leniency** (sts. W.DAT. towards someone) —W.GEN. *in a certain respect* Pl. Plu.; **give way, yield** (sts. W.DAT. to someone) E.

Χαλδαῖοι ων *m.pl.* **1 Chaldaeans** (ref. to a Babylonian people famous for their priestly learning) Hdt. X.; (as a general term for Eastern priests and astrologers) Plb. Plu.(also sg.)
2 Chaldaeans (ref. to a people of eastern Anatolia) X. Plu.

—**Χαλδαϊκός** ή όν *adj.* (of a chart) of the kind used by Chaldaeans, **astrological** Plu.

χαλεπαίνω *vb.* [χαλεπός] | fut. χαλεπανῶ | aor. ἐχαλέπηνα || PASS.: aor. ἐχαλεπάνθην | **1 feel anger**; (of gods, persons, peoples; fig., of one's native land) **be angry** Hom. Th. Pl. X. D. + —W.DAT. or πρός + ACC. *w. someone* Hom. Thgn. Th. Att.orats. Pl. + —w. *a river* Hdt. —w. *the truth* Pl. —W.DAT. + PTCPL. *w. someone, for doing sthg.* Pl. Plu. —W.DAT., PREP.PHR. or COMPL.CL. *at or about sthg., that sthg. shd. be the case* Od. Th. Pl. X. + || PASS. be moved to anger —W.DAT. or πρός + ACC. *w. someone* X.
2 vent one's anger; (of persons, animals) **rage** Arist. —W.DAT. *at someone or sthg.* Pl. Plu.; (of the wind) Il.
3 be **harsh** or **hostile** (freq. W.DAT. towards persons) Th. Ar. Att.orats. X. Arist. Plu. || PASS. be treated harshly Pl.
4 (of winter weather) **be harsh** or **severe** Od.

χαλεπ-ήρης ες *adj.* [ἀραρίσκω] (of a task) **fraught with difficulty, arduous** Mimn.

χαλεπός ή (dial. ά) όν *adj.* **1** difficult (opp. easy); (of tasks, decisions, or sim.) **difficult, hard** Th. Ar. +; (of hares, to hunt) X.; (of gods, persons, W.INF. to oppose, subdue, expose, or sim.) Il. +; (of things, plans, W.INF. to find, achieve, or sim.) Od. + || NEUT.IMPERS. (w. ἐστί, sts. understd.) it is hard —W.INF. or W.DAT. or ACC. + INF. (*for someone*) *to do sthg.* Hom. + || NEUT.SB. difficulty Arist.
2 difficult to endure; (of grief, sufferings, old age, or sim.) **hard to bear** Hom. Hes. A. E.; (of boorish persons) **hard** (W.INF. to put up with) Pl.; (of neighbours, daughters) **troublesome** Th. Men.; (of ill-fitting kit) **irksome** X. || NEUT.PL.SB. sufferings, hardships Pi.*fr.* Hdt. +
3 physically difficult or harsh; (of terrain, roads, journeys, or sim.) **difficult, arduous** Th. Pl. +; (of life) **hard, harsh** Pl.; (of a person's touch) **rough** (opp. gentle) Ar.
4 (of storms) **severe, fierce** Hom. A. || NEUT.SB. severity (of a storm) X.
5 (of gods, beasts) **terrible** (W.INF. to behold) Il. +; (of the anger of Zeus, his bolt) **formidable** Il.
6 showing hostility or harshness (towards people); (of persons or peoples) **hostile** (sts. W.DAT. or πρός + ACC. towards others) Od. +; (wkr.sens.) **bad-tempered, irascible** Hdt. Isoc. Arist.; **angry** (sts. W.DAT. w. someone) Th.; (of dogs, wild animals) **fierce** Pl. X.; (of words, reproaches) **harsh, angry** Hom. +
7 (of gods, rulers, critics, or sim.) **harsh, strict** Od. Ar. Pl.; (of judges, laws, or sim.) Hdt. Th. Pl. D. +; (of a punishment, reproach) Od. Pl.; (of the voice of the people) **stern** Od.
8 (gener., of persons, things, places, situations) threatening danger or harm, **dangerous, pernicious** Pi. +

—**χαλεπῶς** *adv.* | compar. χαλεπώτερον, also χαλεπωτέρως (Th. D.) | superl. χαλεπώτατα | **1 with difficulty** (opp. easily) Il. +; (w. ἔχειν, of a task) be difficult Th. || IMPERS. (w. ἔχει) it is difficult —W.ACC. + INF. *for someone to do sthg.* X.
2 barely, scarcely, hardly Hdt. Lys. Pl. +
3 reluctantly (opp. readily) Th. X. +
4 with hardship, painfully Thgn. Th. X. +; (w. ἔχειν) *be in a bad way* Pl. Men.
5 roughly, severely, harshly Hdt. E. Th. Ar. Pl. X. +
6 (w. ἔχειν or διακεῖσθαι) *be angry or hostile* (freq. W.DAT. or PREP.PHR. *towards someone, over sthg.*) Att.orats. Pl. X. +
7 (w. φέρειν) *be indignant or resentful* Th. Att.orats. Pl. X. + —W.ACC. *at sthg.* Th. Pl. X. + —W.GEN. Th. —W.DAT. X. —W.PREP.PHR. X. + —W.PTCPL. *at doing or experiencing sthg.* Th. Pl. X. + —W.COMPL.CL. *that sthg. is the case* Lys. D. Plu.; (also w. λαμβάνειν) —w. περί + GEN. *over someone* Th.

χαλεπότης ητος *f.* **1 difficulty** (of doing or understanding sthg.) Pl. Arist. Plu.
2 roughness (of terrain) Th. Plu.
3 arduousness (of a journey) Plu.; **dreadfulness** (of a situation) Plu.
4 fierceness (of a people) Plu.; **bad-temperedness** (of persons, horses, dogs) Pl. X. Arist. Plu.; **anger, bitterness** Isoc. Plu.

5 harshness (of persons, regimes, punishments) Isoc. X. Arist. Plu.; **strictness, self-discipline** Th.

χαλέπτω vb. | aor. ἐχάλεψα ‖ MID.: aor. ἐχαλεψάμην ‖ PASS.: aor. ἐχαλέφθην | **1** (of gods, persons, things) **harass** —*someone* Od. AR.; (of things) **annoy** —*a god* Call.; (of a god) **cause trouble** —W.DAT. *for gods and men* Bion
2 (of a god) **strike down, ruin** —*someone* Hes.; (of a snake) **attack** —*someone* AR.
3 ‖ MID.PASS. **be angry** (sts. W.DAT. w. someone) Thgn. S.*Ichn.* Call. AR.

χαλεστραῖον ου n. [Χαλέστρᾱ Khalestra (town in Thrace)] Khalestrian soda, **detergent** Pl.

χαλί-κρητος ον Ion.adj. [χάλις, κεράννῡμι] (of wine) unmixed, **neat, pure** Archil. AR.

χαλῑνο-ποιικός ή όν adj. [χαλῑνός, ποιέω] ‖ FEM.SB. **art of making bridles** Arist.

χαλῑνός οῦ m. | nom.pl. χαλῑνοί, also nom.acc.neut.pl. χαλῑνά (Call. AR.) | **1 bit** (for a horse) Il. Anacr. Thgn. Trag. Pl. X. +; (pl. for sg.) AR.
2 (usu. pl. for sg.) **bridle** (incl. bit) Pi. Hdt. Trag. Ar. Call.
3 (fig., ref. to objects which constrain or control, sg. and pl.); **bridle** (ref. to a muzzle placed on a person, preventing speech) A.; (W.GEN. of a ship, ref. to an anchor) Pi.; (of virginity, ref. to a girdle) Pi.; (ref. to a ship's mooring-cables) E.; (du., ref. to two straps used to rotate a drill) E.*Cyc.*; (W.ADJ. *of rock*, ref. to the fetters of Prometheus) A.
4 (fig.) **bridle** (W.GEN. of Zeus, ref. to his compelling will) A.
5 (fig.) **curb** (on behaviour) Pl. Plu.(quot. S.); (W.GEN. on unruly behaviour) Plu.

χαλῑνο-φάγος ον adj. [φαγεῖν] (of horses' mouths) **champing at the bit** Call.

χαλῑνόω contr.vb. **1 fit a bridle** (and bit) on, **bridle** —*a horse* X. Plb. ‖ PASS. (of a horse) **be bridled** X. Plb.
2 (fig.) **bridle, curb** —*a river* (*by bridging it*) Plu. ‖ PASS. (of a people) **be bridled** or **constrained** (by the imposition of a garrison and taking of hostages) Plu.

χαλίνωσις εως f. **fitting a bit** or **bridle** (on a horse) X.

χαλῑνωτήρια ων n.pl. (fig.) **bridling-ropes** (W.GEN. of ships, i.e. mooring-cables) E.

χάλιξ ικος f. (collectv.sg. and pl.) **gravel, rubble** (as a building material) Th. Ar. Plu.

χάλις ιος Ion.f. | acc. χάλιν | **undiluted wine** Hippon.

χαλιφρονέω contr.vb. [χαλίφρων] (of a person) **be simple-minded** or **stupid** Od.

χαλιφροσύνη ης f. **weakness of will, lack of resolve** Od.

χαλί-φρων ον, gen. ονος adj. [χαλάω, φρήν] (of a person, child) loose-thinking, **simple-minded** Od.

χαλκ-άρματος ον adj. [χαλκός, ἅρμα] (of Ares) **with bronze chariot** Pi.

χάλκ-ασπις ιδος masc.fem.adj. [ἀσπίς¹] (of warriors, Ares, Herakles) **with bronze shield** Lyr. S. E.; (of an athlete in the full-armour race) Pi. ‖ MASC.PL.SB. **bronze-shields** (as the name of heavily armed Macedonian troops) Plb. Plu.

χαλκ-εγχής ές adj. [ἔγχος] (of soldiers) **with bronze spears** E.

χαλκεία ᾱς f. [χαλκεύω] **art of the smith, metalworking** Pl.

χαλκεῖον, Ion. **χαλκήιον**, ου n. [χαλκεύς] **smith's forge, smithy** Hdt. And. Pl. Aeschin. | see also χαλκίον

χάλκειος ᾱ (Ion. η) ον adj. [χαλκός] **1** made from or consisting of copper or bronze; (of arms, armour, tools, objects, figures on a shield, or sim.) **of bronze** Hom. Hes. hHom. Tyrt. X. Hellenist.poet.
2 (of a mythol. race of men) **of bronze** Hes.
3 (of a gleam fr. a helmet) **of bronze** Il.

χαλκέλατος adj.: see χαλκήλατος

χαλκ-έμβολος ον adj. —also **χαλκεμβολάς** άδος (E.) fem.adj. (of a ship, i.e. warship) **with bronze beak** Lyr.adesp. E. Plu. ‖ FEM.SB. **warship** Plu.

χαλκ-εντής ές adj. [ἔντεα] (of an army, war) **in bronze armour** Pi.

χαλκεό-γομφος ον adj. [χάλκεος, γόμφος] (of a chest) **with bronze bolts** or **rivets** Simon.

χαλκεο-θώρηξ ηκος Ion.masc.fem.adj. [θώραξ] (of warriors, demigods) **with bronze cuirass** Il. Theoc.

χαλκεο-κάρδιος ον adj. [καρδίᾱ] (of Herakles) **bronze-hearted, stout-hearted** Theoc.

χαλκεό-κρᾱνος ον adj. [κρᾱνίον¹] (of an arrow) **bronze-tipped** B.

χαλκεό-κτυπος ον adj. [κτύπος] (of battle) **with the clash of bronze** B.

χαλκεο-μήστωρ ορος m. (ref. to Hector) **skilled with bronze weapons, master warrior** E.

χαλκέ-οπλος ον adj. [ὅπλα] (of soldiers) **armed** or **armoured with bronze** E.

χάλκεος ᾱ (Ion. η) ον (also ος ον Il.), contr. **χαλκοῦς** ῆ οῦν, Aeol. **χάλκιος** ᾱ ον adj. [χαλκός] **1** made from or consisting of copper or bronze; (of arms, armour, tools, vessels, objects) **of bronze, brazen** Hom. +; (of lavish or mythol. buildings and structures) Hom. +; (of heaven, as a solid firmament or vault) Il. Thgn. Pi.; (of the aither) Call.; (of fig. walls protecting a state) Aeschin.
2 (of gods, persons, animals) **cast in bronze** (as statues) Hdt. Att.orats. Pl. X. Arist. Theoc.*epigr.* Plu.
3 (of one of the four castes or breeds of men in the ideal state, or of persons belonging to it) **of bronze** Pl.
4 (of a contest) concerning bronze (i.e. a shield), **over bronze** Pi.
5 (of a battle) fought with bronze (arms or armour), **bronze** Pi.
6 (of Ares, warriors) **bronze-clad** Il. Pi. Hdt.(oracle) Plu.(quot.epigr.) [or perh. fig. *indomitable*]
7 (fig., of singers' voices) like bronze, **ringing, pealing** Pi.*fr.*; (of a warrior's cry) **resounding** Il.
8 as strong or unyielding as bronze; (fig., of the shoulders of Atlas, the heart of a person or god, the sleep of death) **brazen, steely** Il. Hes. E.
9 (fig., of thieves or sim.) **brazen** Ar. Plu.

—**χαλκοῦς** οῦ m. **copper coin, khalkous** (worth 1/8 of an obol) Ar. D. Thphr. Plb. Plu.; (ref. to the Roman bronze *as*) Plu.

χαλκεό-στερνος ον adj. [στέρνον] (of Ares) **bronze-breasted** (i.e. w. bronze cuirass) B.

χαλκεο-τευχής ές adj. [τεύχεα] (of a warrior) **with bronze armour, armed in bronze** E.

χαλκεό-φωνος ον adj. [φωνή] (of Stentor, Cerberus) **brazen-voiced, loud-voiced** Il. Hes.

χάλκευμα ατος n. [χαλκεύω] **item of bronzework; brazen sword** A. ‖ PL. **brazen fetters** A.

χαλκεύς έως (Ion. έος, ep. ῆος) m. | nom.pl. χαλκεῖς, Att. χαλκῆς, ep. χαλκῆες | **1 bronze-smith** Hom.
2 (gener.) metalworker, **smith** or **blacksmith** Hom. Anacr. Hdt. Ar. Pl. X. +

χαλκευτικός ή όν adj. **1** (of the products) **of bronze-working** (ref. to bronze objects) X.
2 (of persons) **skilled at metalwork** X. ‖ FEM.SB. **art of metalwork** X.

χαλκεύω vb. [χαλκεύς] **1 engage in metalworking, be a smith** Th. Ar. Pl. X. Plb.
2 (tr.) **create in bronze or other metal, forge** —*swords, shields, objects* Il. S. Call.; (fig.) —*one's tongue* (W.PREP.PHR. *on the anvil of truth*) Pi.

χαλκεών

3 (as an intentional absurdity) **forge** —*a smith* Pl.
4 ‖ MID. **forge for oneself** —*a metal object* Ar.; (of a commander) **have** (w.ACC. helmets) **forged** (W.DAT. for his troops) Plu.; (fig.) **forge** —*fetters* (W.DAT. *for oneself*) Thgn.
5 ‖ PASS. (fig., of a plot) **be forged** Ar. ‖ PF.PASS. (of a person) **have** (W.ACC. a heart) **forged** —W.PREP.PHR. *fr. steel* Pi.*fr.*

χαλκεών ῶνος *m.* **forge, smithy** (of Hephaistos) Il. AR.
χαλκήιον *Ion.n.*: see χαλκεῖον, χαλκίον
χαλκήιος η ον *Ion.adj.* (of the tools, seat, dwelling) **of a smith** Od. Hes.
χαλκ-ήλατος, also **χαλκέλατος** (Pi.), ον *adj.* [χαλκός, ἐλαύνω] (of arms, armour, objects) **of beaten bronze** Pi. Trag. Ar.
χαλκ-ήρης ες *adj.* [ἀραρίσκω] **1 fitted with bronze**; (of arrows, spears) **bronze-tipped** Hom.; (of a warship, its prow) **fitted with a bronze beak** A. Plu.
2 (gener., of helmets, shields, armour) **bronze** Hom.
Χαλκιδεύς *m.*, **Χαλκιδικός** *adj.*: see under Χαλκίς
χαλκί-οικος ου *f.* [οἶκος] (epith. of Athena) **goddess with a bronze dwelling-place** (ref. to her shrine in Sparta) E. Th. Ar. Plb. Plu.
χαλκίον (sts. wrongly written **χαλκεῖον**, Ion. **χαλκήιον**) ου *n.* **1 bronze vessel** (ref. to a bowl, cauldron, or sim.) Hdt. Pl. X. NT.; (specif., for hot water, in the public baths) Thphr.
2 bronze object, bronze (ref. to a shield, helmet) Ar.; (specif., ref. to a resonant object at Dodona) Men.
3 (specif.) **bronze token** (to identify and allocate jurors) D.
4 bronze reflector (in a lamp) X.
5 ‖ PL. **bronze coins** Ar.
χάλκιος *Aeol.adj.*: see χάλκεος
χαλκίς ίδος *f.* **khalkis** (the gods' name for a bird which mortals call κύμινδις) Il.
Χαλκίς ίδος *f.* **1 Chalcis** (town in Euboea) Il. Hes. A. Hdt. E. +
2 Chalcis (town in Aetolia) Od. hHom. Th.
—**Χαλκιδεύς** έως *m.* **1 man from Chalcis** (in Euboea) Att.orats. Pl. Plu. ‖ PL. **inhabitants of Chalcis** Carm.Pop. Hdt. +
2 ‖ PL. **Chalcidian colonists** (in Sicily), **Chalcidians** Th. +; (on the peninsula of Chalcidice in Thrace) Hdt. +
—**Χαλκιδικός** ή όν *adj.* **1 of or relating to Chalcis** (in Euboea); (of swords, a cup) **made in Chalcis** Alc. Ar.; (of a woman) **from Chalcis** Plb.; (of a strait) **of Chalcis** (ref. to the Euripos) Call.; (of colonies, customs, language) **Chalcidian** Th. Arist. ‖ FEM.SB. **Chalcidice** (peninsula in Thrace, colonised by settlers fr. Chalcis) Th. +
2 relating to the Chalcidian colonies in Sicily; (of a mountain) **Chalcidian** Plb.
3 relating to Chalcidice (in Thrace); (of a town, war) **in Chalcidice** Th.; (of the people) **of Chalcidice** Hdt. +; (of cavalry) **Chalcidian** Th.
χαλκο-άρας ᾶ *dial.masc.adj.* [χαλκός, ἀραρίσκω] | gen.pl. **χαλκοαρᾶν** | (of warriors) **bronze-clad** Pi.
χαλκο-βαρής ές *adj.* —also **χαλκοβάρεια** ης *ep.fem.adj.* [βάρος] (of an arrow, spear, helmet, club) **heavy with bronze, bronze-tipped** or **bronze-covered** Hom. AR.
χαλκο-βατής ές *adj.* [βαίνω] (of a palace) **bronze-floored** Hom.
χαλκο-βόας ᾶ *dial.masc.adj.* [βοή] (of Ares, meton. for battle) **with the din of bronze** S.
χαλκό-γενυς υ *adj.* [γένυς] (of an anchor) **with bronze flukes** Pi.
χαλκο-γλώχιν (or perh. **-γλώχις**) ῖνος *masc.fem.adj.* [γλωχίν] (of a spear) **with bronze point** Il.
χαλκο-δαίδαλος ον *adj.* (of a spear) **of intricately worked bronze** B.

χαλκο-δάμας αντος *masc.fem.adj.* [δάμνημι] (of a whetstone) **able to tame bronze** Pi.
χαλκό-δετος ον *adj.* [δέω¹] **fastened with bronze**; (of a shield) **rimmed with bronze** A.; (of door-bolts) perh. **bound with bronze** E.; (of a room) perh. **secured with bronze** (i.e. w. bronze doors or bolts) S.; (gener., of castanets) **wrought from bronze** A.*fr.*
χαλκο-θώραξ ακος *masc.fem.adj.* (of Ares, a warrior) **with bronze cuirass** Pi.*fr.* B. S.
χαλκο-κνημίς ῖδος *masc.fem.adj.* [κνημίς] (of warriors) **with bronze greaves** Il.
χαλκο-κορυστής οῦ, dial. **χαλκοκορυστάς** ᾶ *masc.adj.* (of warriors) **armed** or **armoured with bronze** Il. Hes. Pi.*fr.*
χαλκό-κρας ατος *masc.fem.adj.* [κράς] (of arrows) **bronze-headed, bronze-tipped** Tim.
χαλκό-κροτος ον *adj.* [κρότος] **1** (of Demeter) **accompanied by clashing bronze** (ref. to the cymbals used in her worship) Pi.
2 (of horses) **with clattering hooves** Ar.
3 (of a sword) **of beaten bronze** E.
χαλκό-κτυπος ον *adj.* [κτύπος] (of the clang) **of clashing bronze** B.
χαλκο-κώδων ωνος *masc.fem.adj.* (of a trumpet) **with bronze bell** (i.e. bell end), **bronze-mouthed** B.
χαλκο-μίτρας ᾱ *dial.masc.adj.* [μίτρα] (of a warrior) **with bronze waist-guard** Pi. B.*fr.*
χαλκό-νωτος ον *adj.* [νῶτον] (of a shield) **bronze-backed** E.
χαλκόομαι *pass.contr.vb.* (of a warrior) **be decked out in bronze armour** Pi.
χαλκο-πάρηος, dial. **χαλκοπάραος**, ον *adj.* [παρήιον] **1** (of helmets) **with bronze cheek-plates** Hom.
2 (gener.) **with bronze sides or surfaces**; (of a javelin) **with bronze blade** Pi.; (of castanets) **with bronze plates** Lyr.adesp.
χαλκό-πεδος ον *adj.* [πέδον] (of the home of the gods) **bronze-floored** Pi.
χαλκό-πλευρος ον *adj.* [πλευρά] (of an urn) **bronze-sided** S.
χαλκο-πληθής ές *adj.* [πλῆθος] (of an army) **forming a bronze-armed mass, massed in bronze** E.
χαλκό-πληκτος ον *adj.* [πλήσσω] (of an axe) **of beaten bronze** S. [or perh. *striking with bronze blade*]
χαλκό-πους ποδος *masc.fem.adj.* [πούς] **1** (of the horses of a god, fire-breathing cattle) **bronze-hooved** Il. AR.; (of a tripod) **with bronze feet** E.; (of an Erinys, app.ref. to her unwearying pursuit of wrongdoers) S.
2 (of a threshold) **furnished with bronze steps** S.
χαλκό-πυλος ον *adj.* [πύλαι] **1** (of a temple) **with bronze gates** Hdt.; (epith. of Athena) **of the bronze gates** (ref. to her temple) E.
2 (of water) **bronze-gated** (ref. to the Kastalian spring, issuing fr. the mouths of bronze lions) Pi.*fr.*
χαλκο-πώγων ωνος *masc.adj.* **bronze-bearded** (as transl. of Lat. *Ahenobarbus*) Plu.
χαλκός οῦ *m.* | ep.gen.dat. χαλκόφι | **1 bronze** (perh. orig.ref. to copper, but later ref. to an alloy of copper and tin, as the material of armour, weapons and tools) Hom. +; (ref. to weapons and armour) Hom. +; (ref. to a fish-hook, a tool) Il.
2 bronze (as a precious metal, used to make vessels, tripods, decorations, or sim.) Hom. +; (as the material of musical instruments) Pi. E.; (ref. to bronze vessels, tripods, or sim., esp. as spoils, gifts, prizes) Hom. +; (ref. to a mirror) Call.
3 (collectv.sg., as a commodity) **bronzeware, bronze plate** Hom. +

4 (specif.) bronze vessel, **cauldron** Hom. E.*Cyc.*; **bronze urn** (for ashes) S.
5 (collectv.sg.) **copper money** Ar. Thphr. NT.

χαλκό-στομος ον *adj.* [στόμα] 1 (of a trumpet) **with bronze mouth** S.
2 (of a ship's beak) **tipped with bronze** A.

χαλκο-τειχής ές *adj.* [τεῖχος] (of a courtyard) **with bronze walls** B.

χαλκό-τευκτος ον *adj.* [τεύχω] (of doors) **made from bronze** E.

χαλκό-τοξος ον *adj.* [τόξον] (of the might of the Amazons) **in bronze bows** Pi.

χαλκό-τορος ον *adj.* [τορεῖν] (of swords) **of piercing bronze** Pi.

χαλκοτυπική ῆς *f.* [χαλκοτύπος] **art of bronzeworking** Pl.

χαλκο-τύπος ου *m.* [τύπτω] one who beats out bronze, **bronze-smith** Att.orats. X. Arist. Plu.

—**χαλκότυπος** ον *adj.* (of wounds) **inflicted by bronze weapons** Il.

χαλκουργεῖον ου *n.* [χαλκουργός *bronze-smith, copper-miner*] app. **copper-mine** Plb.

χαλκουργική ῆς *f.* **art of casting bronze** Arist.

χαλκοῦς *adj. and m.*: see χάλκεος

χαλκο-φάλαρος ον *adj.* [φάλαρα] (of a house) **adorned with bronze bosses** (perh. ref. to armour hung on walls) Ar.(mock-trag.)

χαλκόφι (ep.gen.dat.): see χαλκός

χαλκο-χάρμᾱς ᾱ *dial.masc.adj.* [χάρμη] (of warriors, war) **bronze-armed** Pi.

χαλκο-χίτων ωνος *masc.fem.adj.* [χιτών] (of warriors) **with coats of bronze-mail** Hom. Hes.*fr.* Aeschin.(quot.epigr.)

χάλκωμα ατος *n.* [χαλκόομαι] 1 **bronze object** ‖ PL. **bronzeware** (ref. to vessels, armour, or sim.) Lys. Ar. X.
2 **bronze vessel, cauldron** Plu.
3 **sheet of bronze** Plb.; (ref. to a writing-tablet, cuirass) Plb.; (ref. to armour-plating on a warship) Plu.
4 **bronze beak** (on a warship) Plu.

χαλυβδικός ή όν *adj.* [Χάλυβες] (of a contest, i.e. battle) **of iron, of steel** E.

Χάλυβες ων *m.pl.* **Chalybes, Chalybians** (a people of Asia Minor, supposedly the first to mine and smelt iron) A. Hdt. X. Call. AR.

—**Χάλυβος** ον *adj.* 1 from the land of the Chalybes; (of a stranger, fig.ref. to iron) **Chalybian** A. ‖ MASC.PL.SB. Chalybians E.
2 made from Chalybian metal; (of an axe) **iron, steel** E.*fr.*

χάλυψ υβος *masc.adj.* (of a clang) **of iron, of steel** A. ‖ SB. iron, steel S.

χαμάδις *adv.* [χαμαί] 1 **to** or **onto the ground** Hom. A. AR.
2 **on the ground** Call. AR.

χαμᾶζε *adv.* **to** or **onto the ground** Hom. E. Ar. AR. Plu.

χαμᾶθεν, also **χαμόθεν** (X. Plu.) *adv.* 1 (ref. to movt.) **from the ground** Hdt. Ar. Plu.
2 **from** or **at ground level** X. Arist.

χαμαί *adv.* [χθών] 1 **on the ground** Hom. +
2 **at ground level** (opp. in the air) Ar. Men.
3 **from ground level** (opp. fr. a rooftop) Call.
4 **on the earth** (as the location of mortals, opp. in heaven) Il. Hes. hHom.
5 **in the ground** —*ref. to burying sthg.* Pi.
6 **to** or **onto the ground** Hom. hHom. Pi. Hdt. E. Ar. +; (fig., ref. to thoughts or statements falling, i.e. going to waste) Pi. Pl.

χαμαι-γενής ές *adj.* [γένος, γίγνομαι] (of mortals, esp. opp. gods) **earth-born** Hes. hHom. Pi. | see also παλαιγενής 1

χαμαι-εύνης ου *masc.adj.* —also **χαμαιευνάς** άδος *fem.adj.* [εὐνή] (of lions, pigs, ascetic priests) making one's bed on the ground, **sleeping on the ground** Hom. Emp.

χαμαί-ζηλος ου *m.* [app.reltd. ζῆλος] **low stool** Pl.

χαμαι-κοίτης ου *masc.adj.* [κοίτη] (of ascetic priests) **sleeping on the ground** S.

χαμαι-λέων οντος *m.* **chameleon** (as the exemplar of changeability) Arist. Plu.

χαμαι-πετής ές *adj.* [πίπτω] 1 (of blood) **fallen on the ground, spilt** E.; (fig., of words) **wasted, ineffectual** Pi.
2 (fig., of a house) **prostrate** (opp. flourishing) A.; (of praise) **grovelling** A.
3 (of a bed) **on the bare earth** E.; (of a person) **sleeping on the earth** (opp. in a bed) Pl.

χαμαι-ριφής ές *adj.* [ῥίπτω] (of a person) **flung to the ground** E.

χαμαι-τύπη ης *f.* [τύπτω] ground-banger (i.e. woman who has sex on the ground), **cheap whore** Men. Plu.

—**χαμαιτύποι** ων *m.pl.* **rent boys** (pejor.ref. to Philip of Macedon's troops) Plb.

χάμ-εννα ης (dial. ᾱς) *f.* [εὐνή] 1 bed made on the ground, **simple bed, pallet** (of strewn foliage, used by soldiers, travellers, or sim.) E. AR. Theoc.
2 (gener.) **low bed, mattress** Ar.; (fig.) **lowly bed** (ref. to the bath in which Agamemnon was killed) A.

—**χαμεύνιον** ου *n.* [dimin.] **low bed, mattress** Hippon. Pl.

χαμευνίς ίδος *f.* **makeshift bed** (of strewn foliage) Theoc.

χαμηλός ή όν *adj.* 1 (of a horse's hooves) **close to the ground, low** (opp. tall) X.
2 (of a person's aspirations) **lowly** Pi.

χαμόθεν *adv.*: see χαμᾶθεν

χᾶν *dial.m.f.*: see χήν

χανδάνω *vb.* | fut. χείσομαι | aor.2 ἔχαδον, ep.3sg. χάδε, ep.inf. χαδέειν | ep.pf.ptcpl. κεχονδώς (cj., for κεχανδώς) | ep.3sg.plpf. κεχόνδει (v.l. κεχάνδει) | 1 (of a vessel, hands) **be able to hold** —*a certain amount of liquid or meat* Hom.; (of a beach) **hold, have room for** —*a fleet* Il.; (of a threshold) —*two people* Od.
2 (gener., of a house, storeroom) **contain** —*precious things* Hom.; (of a hand) **hold** —*a club* Theoc.
3 (fig., of the heart of a goddess, in neg.phr.) be able to hold in, **contain** —*her anger* Il.
4 (of the vocal organs) have the capacity, **be able** (to do sthg.) Il. Ar. —W.INF. hHom.

χανδόν *adv.* [χάσκω] **in great gulps** —*ref. to drinking wine* Od. Call.

χανεῖν (aor.2 inf.): see χάσκω

χάος *dial.adj.*: see χάϊος

χάος εος (ους) *n.* 1 **Khaos** (as the primordial state in the universe) Hes. Ar. Arist. Call.; (as a region in the cosmos) Hes.
2 **empty expanse of air, void, open sky** (as the domain of birds) B. Ar.; (personif., as an improbable deity) Ar.
3 **yawning blackness, impenetrable darkness** (of a starless night) AR.

χαρά ᾶς, Aeol. **χάρᾱ** ᾱς *f.* [χαίρω] 1 state of joy, **joy, delight** Trag. Lyr.adesp. Pl. X. D. +; (W.GEN. at sthg.) E. Plu.; (w. ἀπό + GEN. caused by sthg.) A.; (pejor.) **glee** (of an impudent attacker, a man taking revenge) A. S.
2 (ref. to a person) **cause of joy, joy** (for others) Sapph. E.*fr.*

χάραγμα ατος *n.* [χαράσσω] 1 **mark, imprint** (W.GEN. of a serpent, i.e. of its bite) S.
2 **stamped** or **engraved figure**; **stamp, design** (on a coin) Plu.; **brand-mark** (on cattle) Plu.
3 **engraved** or **sculpted product** (W.GEN. of craftsmanship, ref. to an image in metal or stone) NT.

χαράδρā ᾱς, Ion. **χαράδρη** ης *f.* **1 mountain torrent** Il. Anacr. Thgn. Ar. +
2 bed of a torrent, **gully, ravine** Il. Alcm. Hdt. Th. X. +
3 watercourse, channel (on private land) D.

χαραδριός οῦ *m.* perh. **stone curlew** Hippon. Ar. Pl.

χαραδρόομαι *pass.contr.vb.* (of a region) **be filled with ravines** Hdt.

χάραδρος ου *m.* **ravine** Plu.

χαρακοποιίᾱ ᾱς *f.* [χάραξ, ποιέω] **construction of a palisade** (around a military camp) Plb.

χαρακόω *contr.vb.* **1** surround with a palisade, **fortify** —*a city* Aeschin.
2 build fortifications in —*a mountainous region* Plb.

χαρακτήρ ῆρος *m.* [χαράσσω] **1** stamped or engraved design, **stamp, imprint** (as a distinguishing mark, on a coin, seal, or sim.) E. Pl. Arist. Plb.; (fig., w.GEN. of glory, impressed on deeds) Isoc.; (of excellence, as carried by the truly excellent) E.; (of noble birth, manifested by deeds) Plu.
2 (specif.) **coin type, issue** (ref. to a coin of specific value) Arist.; (fig.) **type** (of behaviour) Plb.
3 (fig.) **stamp** (of facial or bodily features, by which kinship, race or moral qualities are distinguished) A.(dub.) Hdt. E.
4 stamp (W.GEN. of speech, as marking a local dialect) Hdt.; (of words, i.e. style of expression, as typical of a people) Ar.
5 distinguishing mark (W.GEN. of each of two classes of things) Pl.; **characteristic feature** (distinguishing people, portents) Plu.

χαράκωμα ατος *n.* [χαρακόω] **1** protective barrier of stakes, **palisade** X. D. Plb. Plu.
2 palisaded camp, **stockade** X. Plu.

χαράκωσις εως *f.* **construction of a palisade** Lycurg. Plu.

χάραξ ακος *m.f.* **1** (*f.*) pointed wooden stake (for training vines), **vine-stake** Th. Ar. D. Men.
2 (*m.*, collectv.sg.) protective barrier of stakes, **palisade** D. Men. Plb. NT. Plu.; palisaded camp, **stockade** Men. Plb. Plu.

χαραξί-ποντος ον *adj.* [χαράσσω, πόντος] (of a ship's oars) **raking the sea** Lyr.adesp.

χαράσσω, Att. **χαράττω** *vb.* [χάραξ] | fut. χαράξω | aor. ἐχάραξα ‖ PASS.: aor. ἐχαράχθην | pf. κεχάραγμαι | **1 sharpen** —*sickles, the points of missiles* Hes. Plu. ‖ PASS. (of iron) be sharpened Hes.
2 (of snakes) perh., sharpen (by grinding together), **gnash** —*their teeth* Hes.
3 engrave or stamp (a mark or design); **scratch, carve** —*an inscription* (W.DAT. *on a wall*) Theoc.; (of a snake) **leave a mark on** —*flesh* (w. *its bite*) AR. ‖ PASS. (of metal) be stamped —w. εἰς + ACC. *to form money* Plb.
‖ PF.PASS.PTCPL.ADJ. (of a club) app., marked (W.DAT. w. protuberances) Theoc.
4 (of a bed of rock) **gash, lacerate** —*a back* Pi. ‖ PASS. (of the earth) be scratched or gashed (by the hands of mourners) A.; (of a person) be pierced (by a spear) —W.ACC. *in the back* E.; (fig.) be lacerated, be cut to the quick —w. ὑπό + GEN. *by one's misfortunes* Plu.
5 (fig., of an orator) sharpen the anger of, **incite** —*the people* (W.PREP.PHR. *against someone*) Plu. ‖ PASS. be exasperated —W.DAT. *w. someone* Hdt. E.

χάρη (ep.3sg.aor.2 pass.), **χαρῆναι** (aor.2 pass.inf.), **χαρήσομαι** (fut.mid.): see χαίρω

χαρι-δώτης, also **χαριδότης**, ου *m.* [χάρις] (epith. of Hermes) **bestower of favour** hHom.; (epith. of Dionysus) **bestower of joy** h.

χαρίεις εσσα εν *adj.* | compar. χαριέστερος, superl. χαριέστατος | **1** possessing visible grace or beauty; (of persons or gods, their face, physique, youth, or sim.) **graceful, charming, attractive, beautiful** Hom. Hes. Archil. Eleg. Lyr. E.*fr.* +; (of a bird) Anacr.
2 (of clothes) **fine, beautiful** Hom. hHom.; (of tapestries) Theoc.; (of fruit) hHom.
3 (of places, features of the natural world) **lovely, pleasant** Hes. Sapph. Pl.
4 (of dancing) **graceful** Alcm.; (of the bathing of a goddess) **beautiful** Call.
5 giving pleasure; (of wine, songs, stories, or sim.) **pleasing, delightful** Od. hHom. Thgn. Lyr. Ar. +
6 giving gratification; (of offerings, gifts, or sim.) **gratifying, pleasing, welcome** Hom. Ar. Pl.; (of a task) Pi.
7 possessing grace of manner or intellect; (of persons, their minds) **refined, sophisticated** Ar. Isoc. Pl. Arist. Plu.
8 (of poets, doctors, speakers, or sim.) **accomplished** Isoc. Pl. Arist. Plu.
9 (of ideas, remarks, or sim.) **neat, elegant, clever** Ar. Isoc. Pl. X. +; (of persons, jokes) **witty** Pl.
10 (gener., of abstr. things, such as activities, interests, reputation) **admirable, excellent** Ar. Isoc. Pl.
11 (iron., of situations, actions, consequences) **fine, nice, pretty** Ar. X.
—**χαριέντως** *adv.* | compar. χαριέστερον, also χαριεστέρως (Arist.) | **1** gracefully, elegantly, pleasingly or cleverly Isoc. Pl. Arist. Men. Plu.
2 (w. ἔχειν) *be in fine condition* (*physically*) Pl.

χαριεντίζομαι *mid.vb.* **make a joke, jest** Pl.

χαριεντισμός οῦ *m.* **light-heartedness, jesting** Pl.

χαρίζομαι *mid.vb.* [χάρις] | fut. χαριοῦμαι | aor. ἐχαρισάμην, ep.3sg. ἐχαρίσσατο (Call.), ep.inf. χαρίσσασθαι (hHom.), ep.imperatv. χάρισσαι (Sapph.), dial.2sg.subj. χαρίξῃ (Theoc.) | pf.mid.pass. κεχάρισμαι ‖ PASS.: fut. χαρισθήσομαι | aor. ἐχαρίσθην ‖ neut.impers.vbl.adj. χαριστέον |
1 (of a person, wine) **be pleasing** —W.DAT. *to someone* Od. Thgn. X.
2 make oneself agreeable, **gratify** or **seek to gratify** (oft. W.DAT. someone) Att.orats. Pl. + —W.PARTITV.GEN. *w. idle talk* Theoc. ‖ PLPF.PASS. (of a person) be dear —W.DAT. *to someone's heart* Od.
3 indulge, satisfy, **gratify** —W.DAT. *one's belly or body* X. —(W.PARTITV.GEN. *w. food*) Thgn. —*one's soul* (W.GEN. *w. good things*) Simon. —*one's anger, lust, or sim.* Thgn. S. Antipho Pl. X. +; **indulge in, yield to** —W.DAT. *pleasures* X.; **give free rein to** —W.DAT. *one's tongue* E.
4 (specif.) give sexual favours to, **gratify** —W.DAT. *a lover* Ar. Pl.; (fig., of Comedy) —*few* (*of those aspiring to be comic poets*) Ar.
5 perform a welcome act, **do a favour** (sts. W.COGN.ACC.) —W.DAT. *for someone* Hom. +; do (W.INTERN.ACC. sthg.) **as a favour** —W.DAT. *for someone* Th. Ar. Pl. X. + ‖ PASS. (of persons) be done a favour X. ‖ IMPERS.PASS. a favour is done —W.DAT. *to someone* Hdt.
6 do a favour by giving; **give** —*gifts, a ransom, or sim.* (W.DAT. *to someone*) Hom. Archil. Semon. Ar.; **be generous** (sts. W.PARTITV.GEN. w. sthg.) Od.; **grant** —W.INF. *the faculty of seeing* (W.DAT. *to the blind*) NT. ‖ PASS. (of a speech) be presented as a tribute —W.DAT. *to memory* Pl.
7 (specif.) **give up** (W.ACC. someone) **as a favour** —W.DAT. *to his enemies* NT. —*to his mother* (*to spare him fr. prosecution*) Plu. ‖ PASS. (of a criminal) be given up as a favour —W.DAT. *to the populace* (*to spare him fr. punishment*) NT.
—**κεχαρισμένος** η ον *pf.mid.pass.ptcpl.adj.* **1** (of a person) **dear** (W.DAT. to someone's heart) Hom.

2 (of a suitor) **pleasing, acceptable** (W.DAT. to a woman's father) Od.; (of gifts, offerings, actions, words, to persons or gods) Hom. Anacr. Thgn. Hdt. E. Lys. +
3 (of food or drink) **enjoyable** X.
—**κεχαρισμένως** *pf.mid.pass.ptcpl.adv.* **in a manner that is pleasing** (usu. W.DAT. to someone) Ar. Isoc. Pl. Plu.
χάρις ιτος *f.* [reltd. χαίρω] | acc. χάριν, rarely χάριτα (Hdt. E. X. NT.) ‖ PL.: dat. χάρισι, dial. (as name) Χάρισσι (Pi. B.), ep. χαρίτεσσι | **1 grace, gracefulness, beauty, charm** (of persons, objects, deeds, words) Hom. +; (w. stronger sense) **splendour, glory** Pi.
2 (personif., as a goddess) **Grace** Pi. Lyr.adesp.
3 ‖ PL. **Graces** (usu. three, daughters of Zeus and Eurynome, assoc.w. the Muses and Aphrodite) Hom. +
4 (as a name) **Kharis** (wife of Hephaistos) Il. Call.
5 gracious feelings (shown to or received fr. another), **goodwill, kindness, favour** A. +
6 (concr.) **favour, service** (offered to a person or god) Hom. +
7 (specif.) **sexual favour** Il. Pi. X.
8 feeling of gratitude (for a favour or service), **gratefulness, gratitude, thanks** (sts. W.GEN. for sthg.) Hom. +
9 feeling or source of gratification; satisfaction, pleasure, joy (sts. W.GEN. afforded by someone or sthg.) Il. +
10 ‖ ADVBL.ACC. **as a favour** (W.GEN. to someone) Il.; **in honour** (W.GEN. of a god) Pi.; (gener., as prep., usu. placed after its noun) **for the sake of, for the purpose of, because of** (W.GEN. someone or sthg.) A. + • γλώσσης χάριν *for the sake of talking* A.; ὀργῆς χάριν *out of anger* E.; (W.POSSESSV.ADJ.) Alc. + • ἔμαν χάριν *as a favour to me, for my sake* Alc.; χάριν σήν *for your sake* E.
11 (prep.phrs.) πρὸς χάριν **with the aim or effect of pleasing**, **to court popularity** S. E. Th. Isoc. Pl. +; (also) εἰς (ἐς) χάριν S. Th.
χαρίσιος ᾱ ον *adj.* (of a gift) given as a token of thanks, **of gratitude** Call.
χαριστήρια ων *n.pl.* **thank-offerings** (to the gods) X. Plb. Plu.; **placatory offerings** Plu. ‖ SG. (ref. to a temple) token of gratitude Plu.
χαριτίᾱ ᾱς *f.* **amusing story, anecdote** (W.GEN. about sthg.) X.
χαριτογλωσσέω *contr.vb.* [γλῶσσα] **speak to please** A.
χαριτόομαι *pass.contr.vb.* **be shown favour** (by God) NT.
χαριτό-φωνος ον *adj.* [φωνή] (of a nymph) **with charming voice** Philox.Cyth. [or perh. *with the voice of the Graces*]
χαριτ-ώνυμος ον *adj.* [ὄνομα] (of a message) with gratifying name (i.e. that of victory), **of pleasing import** B.
χάρμα ατος *n.* [χαίρω] **1** (ref. to persons, gods, things, situations) **source of joy, joy, delight** (freq. W.DAT. to someone) Hom. Hes. Archil. Semon. Thgn. Lyr. +; (ref. to corpses, W.GEN. for wild beasts, an Erinys) E.
2 (specif.) **reason for celebration, joyful news** A. E.
3 source of malignant glee (W.DAT. for one's enemies) Il. Hes. A.
4 (gener.) **feeling of joy, joy, delight** Od. hHom. Xenoph. A. Pi. E. +
χάρμη ης *f.* [app. χαίρω] **1 exultation in battle, battle-lust, battle-frenzy** Il.
2 fighting, combat Hom.
3 (specif.) **battle** Il.
4 (ref. to a wrestling match) **victorious bout** Pi. [or perh. abstr. *cause for celebration, success*]
χαρμονή ῆς, dial. **χαρμονά** ᾶς *f.* **1 feeling of joy, joy, delight** E. X.

2 source of joy S. E. Pl.
χαρμόσυνα ων *n.pl.* **thanksgiving celebrations** Hdt.
χαρμό-φρων ονος *masc.fem.adj.* [φρήν] **glad-hearted** hHom.
χαροπός ή (dial. ά) όν *adj.* [perh.reltd. χάρμη, ὄψις] **1** (of lions, wild animals, dogs, monkeys) perh. **fierce** Od. Hes. hHom. Lyr.adesp. S. Ar. Theoc. [or perh. *bright-eyed*]
2 (of hounds, horses) perh. **pale-eyed** X.
3 (of Ganymede) perh. **bright-eyed** Theoc.; (of a girl's eyes) **bright** Theoc.
4 (of dawn) **bright, radiant** AR.
χαροπότης ητος *f.* **paleness, blueness** (W.GEN. of the eyes of invaders fr. the north) Plu.
χαρτός ή όν *adj.* [χαίρω] **1** (of news, experiences, or sim.) **joyful, pleasing** S. Pl. ‖ NEUT.PL.SB. joyful experiences Archil. E.
2 (of persons) **causing malignant joy** (W.DAT. to their enemies) Call.
Χάρυβδις εως (Ion. ιος) *f.* **1 Charybdis** (whirlpool near Scylla's crag, sts. located in the Strait of Messina) Od. E. Th. AR.
2 (gener.) **yawning abyss** (ref. to a chasm which swallowed up a warrior) E.; (fig., ref. to a disastrous fate) Simon.; (ref. to an embezzler) Ar.
Χάρων ωνος *m.* [pop.etym. χαίρω, esp. in word-play] **Charon** (ferryman who took souls over the Styx) E. Ar. Call.
—**Χαρωνῖται** ῶν *m.pl.* **Infernals** (transl. of Lat. *Orcini*, sarcastic description of senators appointed posthumously by Caesar) Plu.
χασκάζω *vb.* [χάσκω] **open one's mouth wide; gape at** —*a pay-clerk* (*in the hope of pay*) Ar.
χάσκω *vb.* | aor.2 ἔχανον, inf. χανεῖν | statv.pf. κέχηνα, pl.imperatv. κεχήνετε | plpf. ἐκεχήνη | **1** (of the earth) **gape open** (usu. W.DAT. for persons, to swallow them) Il. hHom.; (of a boxer's temple, fr. a blow) Theoc.; (of a pathic's anus) Ar. ‖ PF. (of a pathic, ref. to his anus) be agape Ar.
2 open the mouth wide; (of a wounded person) **gape** Il.; (of a drowning man) **gape open-mouthed** —w. πρός + ACC. *at a wave* Od. ‖ PF.PTCPL. (of a wounded man) gaping Il.
3 (of a horse) **open the mouth** (to take the bit) X.; (of a lion or dog, to bare its teeth) Il. Ar. Theoc.; (of a crocodile, to yawn) Hdt.; (of a wolf, in anticipation of food) Men. ‖ PF. (of a bird) gape with open beak Ar. ‖ PF.PTCPL. (of a wolf) open-mouthed (i.e. ravening) Ar.; (of a seagull, fig.ref. to a haranguing orator) Ar.; (of a wine-jar of the type called ὄνος *donkey*) Ar.
4 gape, gawp (esp. in bewilderment, simple-minded admiration or eager anticipation) Sol. Hippon. —w. πρός + ACC. *after a girl* Anacr. ‖ PF. and PLPF. be open-mouthed, sit or stand gawping Semon. Ar. Men. —w. πρός + ACC. *at someone or sthg.* Ar. —(W.ADV. ἄνω *upwards, while looking at the heavens*) Ar. Pl. ‖ PF.PTCPL. open-mouthed Ar.; (of a tragic mask) Call.*epigr.*
5 gape (fr. inattention or boredom); **gape** —W.ADV. *in another direction* (*so as to overlook sthg.*) Ar. ‖ PF. sit yawning Ar.
6 open the mouth wide (to speak loudly); (pejor.) **bawl out** —*threatening words or sim.* S. Ar.
7 (of Niobe) **gasp out** —*a pitiful cry* Call. [or perh. *gape* (*pitifully*)]
χάσμα ατος *n.* **1 yawning chasm, abyss** (of Tartaros) Hes. E.
2 chasm (in the earth, sts. W.GEN.) Hdt. E. Pl. Plu.; (W.GEN. in a rock-face) E.; (W.GEN. in the heavens, to let souls through) Pl.; (betw. heaven and hell, in the afterlife) NT.

χασμάομαι

3 open expanse (W.GEN. of sea) Hdt.
4 gap (betw. open double doors) Parm.
5 open jaws, **gaping maw** (of a lion or wolf, worn as a head-dress) E. Plu.

χασμάομαι, also **χασμέομαι** (Theoc.) *mid.contr.vb.*
| dial.ptcpl. χασμεύμενος | 1 be open-mouthed, **gape, gawp** (absent-mindedly) Ar. —w. εἰς + ACC. *at sthg*. Theoc.; (in befuddlement) Pl.
2 **yawn** Pl.

χάσμη ης *f.* **yawning** Pl.

χάσμημα ατος *n.* **gape** (of a bird's beak) Ar.

χάσομαι (fut.mid.), **χάσσομαι** (ep.fut.mid.): see χάζω

χατέω *contr.vb.* 1 **be in need** (of help) Hom. AR. —w.GEN. *of someone or sthg.* Od. AR.
2 (in neg.phr.) be wanting in, **lack** —w.GEN. *sthg.* AR.
3 **need** (to do sthg.) AR. —w.INF. *to take food* Od
4 **long** —w.INF. or ACC. + INF. *to do sthg., for sthg. to happen* Od. AR.

χατίζω *vb.* 1 **be needy** (i.e. destitute) Hes.
2 **be in need** (of sthg.) Hom. —w.GEN. *of someone or sthg.* Il. Pi. E.
3 **long for, wish for** —w.GEN. *a return home, supper, marriage, work* Od. Hes. AR.
4 **long, want** —w.INF. *to do sthg.* Hes.*fr.*

χαυλι-όδων ον, gen. οντος *Ion.adj.* [1st el.uncert.; ὀδούς] (of a boar) **tusked** Hes. || MASC.PL.SB. **tusks** (of a crocodile or hippopotamus) Hdt.

χαυνο-πολίτης ου *m.* [χαῦνος] **empty-headed citizen** Ar.

χαυνό-πρωκτος ον *adj.* [πρωκτός] (of a man) **slack-arseholed** (i.e. accustomed to buggery) Ar.

χαῦνος η ον (also ος ον) *adj.* 1 (of the twisting of threads) **loose** Pl.
2 (of thoughts, purposes) **empty, foolish, futile** Sol. Pi. Plu.; (of the outcome of empty hopes) **vain** Pi.
3 (of a name, assoc.w. clouds) **airy, vacuous** Ar.
4 (of persons, their attitude) **puffed-up, conceited** Pl. Arist. Plu.

χαυνότης ητος *f.* 1 **loose texture, sponginess, porousness** (of soil) Plu.
2 **emptiness, foolishness** (w.GEN. of an ignorant mind) Pl.
3 **vanity, conceitedness** Arist. Plu.

χαυνόω *contr.vb.* **fill with vanity or conceit, puff up** (a person) E. Pl. || PASS. **become puffed up or conceited** Plb. Plu.

χαύνωμα ατος *n.* **loosened earth** Plu.

χαύνωσις εως *f.* **bamboozling** (of a jury, by a clever speaker) Ar.

χεζητιάω *contr.vb.* [desiderat.v. χέζω] (of a man, his anus) **need a shit** Ar.

χέζω *vb.* | fut. χεσοῦμαι | aor. ἔχεσα, inf. χέσαι | also aor.2 inf. χεσεῖν | pf. (in cpds.) -κέχοδα || MID.: 3sg.aor.opt. χέσαιτο || PASS.: pf. κέχεσμαι | **defecate, shit** Ar. Men.(cj.); (fr. fear) Ar.(also mid.) || PASS. (of a turd) **be shat** Ar.

χεῖ *indecl.n.* [Semit.loanwd.] **chi** (letter of the Greek alphabet) Pl.

χειά ᾶς, Ion. **χειή** ῆς *f.* **hole** (in the ground, as a snake's lair) Il.; (for burying or concealing sthg.) Pi.

χείλιοι *Ion.pl.num.adj.*: see χίλιοι

χεῖλος εος (ους, dial. ευς) *n.* | ep.dat.pl. χείλεσσι | 1 (usu.pl.) **lip** (of a person) Hom. +; (bitten in astonishment, steadfastness or exertion) Od. Tyrt. E.; (as the source of insincere laughter or speech, opp. that which comes fr. the heart) Il. NT. Plu.
2 **lip** (of a horse) X.; **beak** (of a bird) Call.; (pl. for sg.) E.
3 **lip, brim** (of a bowl, jar, basket, or sim.) Od. Hes. Semon. Hdt. Ar. Theoc. +; perh. **lip** (of a panpipe) Theoc.

4 **rim, outer edge** (of a spindle-whorl, circle of land) Pl.
5 **edge** (of a ditch) Il. Th.; (of Okeanos) Mimn.; **bank** (of a moat or river) Hdt. AR. Plb.
6 **tongue, spit** (of land, betw. two bodies of water) Plb.

χεῖμα ατος *n.* [reltd. χειμών] 1 **season of winter, winter** Od. Hes. Alcm. A. S. Hellenist.poet.
2 **cold weather, winter cold** Od. E.
3 (gener.) **storm, stormy weather** (esp. at sea) Lyr.adesp. A. E. AR.

χειμάδιον ου *n.* **winter quarters** (for troops) D. Plu.(pl.)

χειμάζω *vb.* | aor. ἐχείμασα | pf. κεχείμακα (Plu.) || PASS.: aor. ἐχειμάσθην | pf. κεχείμασμαι (Men.) | 1 (of persons, esp. troops) **pass the winter** (usu. W.ADV. or PREP.PHR. in a certain place or condition) Hdt. Th. Ar. Isoc. X. D. +
2 (of a god) **send a storm** S. X. || IMPERS. **it is stormy** Hdt.
3 || PASS. (of persons, ships) **be caught in a storm, suffer stormy weather** (at sea) Th. Pl. Arist. NT. Plu.; (on land) A. S. Plu.; (fig., of a city, as the ship of state) E. Ar.
4 (fig., of an act of bloodshed) **bring a storm of trouble upon** —*a city* S. || PASS. (fig., of persons, their health or prosperity) **be storm-tossed, be buffeted** (sts. W.DAT. or PREP.PHR. by fortune, sufferings, or sim.) Trag. Pl. Arist. Men. Plb.; (of the cosmos) Pl.

χειμαίνω *vb.* 1 || IMPERS. **it is winter** Theoc.
2 || PASS. **be caught in a storm** Hdt.; (fig., of a person's mind) **be storm-tossed or buffeted** —W.DAT. *by fear* Pi.
3 (fig., of a person in trouble) **express distress** —W.ADV. *most realistically* Arist.

χείμαρος ου *m.* **bilge-plug** (in a boat) Hes.

χειμά-ρροος, also **χείμαρρος**, ον, contr. **χειμάρρους** ουν *adj.* [ῥέω] 1 (of rivers, their waters) **in winter flood, torrential** Il. Thgn. Hdt. S. E. Theoc. + || MASC.SB. **torrent** Isoc. Pl. X. D. AR. +
2 (of a valley or ravine) **where torrents flow** E. Plb. || MASC.SB. **gully or valley** NT.
3 **storm-drain** (carrying heavy rain fr. a house) D.

χειμασίᾱ ᾶς, Ion. **χειμασίη** ης *f.* 1 **spending of the winter, wintering** (of birds, in warmer regions) Hdt.
2 **establishing of winter quarters** (for troops) Plb.; (concr.) **winter quarters** Plb.

χειμασκέω *contr.vb.* [ἀσκέω] (of an army) **perform winter exercises, spend the winter in training** Plb.

χειμερίζω *vb.* **spend the winter** —W.ADV. or PREP.PHR. *in a particular place* Hdt.

χειμερινός ή όν *adj.* 1 (of the season, months) **of winter** Hdt. Th.; (of the solstice) **winter** Th. Plb. Plu.; (of the sun, the position of sunrise and sunset, rainstorms, a battle) **in winter** Hdt. X. D. Plb. || FEM.SB. **season of winter** Hdt. || NEUT.PL.SB. **winter-time** Pl.
2 (of mess-halls, reservoirs) **for use in winter** Pl.
3 (of a region) **subject to harsh weather, wintry** Th.

χειμέριος ᾱ (Ion. η) ον (also ος ον) *adj.* 1 (of a month, day, the season, gloom) **of winter** Hom. Hes. Simon. Pi.; (of wind, snow, rain, a night, fire, or sim.) **in winter** Il. Hes. hHom. Archil. Pi. Emp. +
2 (of a headland) **in winter storms** S.; (of a river) **in winter flood** AR.
3 (of months) **wintry, chilly** Hdt.; (of a torrent) Anacr.; (fig., of a situation) **chill, grim** Ar.
4 (of a night, wind, sea-spray) **stormy** Pi. Th. AR. Plu.; (fig., of pain) **storm-like** S. [or perh. *chilling*]

χειμών ῶνος *m.* 1 **season of winter, winter** Il. +
2 **cold of winter, winter chill** Pi. Th.; (pl.) Pl.; (gener.) **bitter cold** (of a mountainous region) Hdt.

3 winter storm Hom. Anacr. Hdt. S.; (gener.) **storm** Hom. +; (fig., ref. to adversity, disaster, madness, or sim., esp. sent by the gods) Pi. Trag.; (W.GEN. of battle) S.

χειμωνο-τύπος ον *adj.* [τύπτω] (of a squall) **storm-battering** A.

χείρ χειρός (also poet. χερός), Lacon. **χήρ** χηρός, Aeol. **χήρ** χέρρος *f.* | acc. χεῖρα, poet. χέρα | dat. χειρί, χερί ‖ DU.: nom.acc. χεῖρε, χέρε | gen.dat. χεροῖν, also χειροῖν ‖ PL.: nom. χεῖρες, poet. χέρες | acc. χεῖρας, χέρας | gen. χειρῶν, χερῶν | dat. χερσί, ep. χείρεσσι, χείρεσι, χέρεσσι |
1 hand (of a person) Hom. +; (clasped in greeting or making a pledge, sts. meton. for such a pledge) Hom. +; (raised to heaven, held out to persons in supplication, flung around a person in an embrace or clasping the knees in supplication, used to signal or beckon) Hom. +; (raised to indicate assent, esp. in a group vote, sts. meton. for a vote) A. +; (prep.phr., ref. to counting) ἀπὸ χειρός *by means of one's hand (i.e. on one's fingers)* Ar.
2 hand and forearm, **arm** Hom. +
3 (phr.) ἄκρα (ἄκρη) χείρ *tip of the arm (i.e. hand or fingers, opp. forearm)* Il. Hdt. Th. Pl. X. AR.; (also) *fingertip* E. Ar. AR.
4 object resembling or functioning as a hand or arm; **gauntlet** (protecting a cavalryman's arm) X.; **grappling-claw, grapnel** (used by warships) Th. ‖ PL. arms (fig.ref. to oars) Tim.
5 hand as denoting one side of the body; **hand, side** Od. + | see ἀριστερός 2, δεξιός 7
6 hand as a measure of nearness; (prep.phrs.) ἀνὰ χεῖρας *close at hand, by one's side* Plb.; ἐς χεῖρα *within reach* E.; ἐκ χειρός *at close range or close quarters* X. Plb. Plu.; (also) ἐν χερσί (sts. W.GEN. or DAT. *to an enemy*) Th. X. Plb. Plu.; (ref. to nearness in time) ἐν χερσί *close at hand* Plu.; ἐκ χειρός *immediately* Plb.; ὑπὸ χεῖρα *on the spot, extempore* Plu.
7 hand as a symbol of engagement in an activity; (prep.phrs.) ἐν χερσί, εἰς χεῖρας, μετὰ χεῖρας (ref. to having or taking a matter) *in hand* Hdt. E. Th. Pl. +; (also) πὰρ χειρός B.
8 hand (as the instrument of giving and taking, sts. W.ADJ. *generous, full, empty*, or sim.) Od. +
9 hand (as the instrument of possession or control, freq. in ctxt. of falling into someone's hands) Il. +; (prep.phrs.) διὰ χειρός (χειρῶν) *in one's control* Th. Arist. Plu.; ὑπὸ χεῖρα *under one's control* X. D. Plu.
10 hand (as the instrument of violence or harm, esp. in phrs. *lay hands on, keep hands off*) Hom. +
11 hand as the instrument of combat; (phrs.) εἰς χεῖρας ἐλθεῖν (or sim.) *engage in combat* (oft. W.DAT. w. someone) A. Th. +; ἐκ χειρός *hand to hand* Th. X. Plb.; (also) ἐν χερσί Th. Plu. | see also νόμος 4
12 hand as a symbol of strength; (sg. and pl.) **physical force** or **might** Hom. + | see also νόμος 4
13 (concr.) body of men (esp. soldiers, usu. W.ADJ. *large*), **force, band** Hdt. E. Th. +
14 hand as a symbol of action (esp. opp. speech); **action** Il. +
15 hand (as a symbol of agency) Il. +; (phrs.) μιᾷ χειρί *single-handedly* D.; ἐκ (διά, πρός) χειρός *by the hand* (W.GEN. or POSSESSV.ADJ. *of oneself or another*) A. +
16 hand (as the instrument of manufacture or craftsmanship) Od. +; (concr.) product of craftsmanship, **handiwork** Theoc.*epigr.*
17 hand as the instrument of writing; (concr.) **handwriting** (of a particular person) Hyp.

χειραγωγέω *contr.vb.* [χειραγωγός] **1 lead** (W.ACC. a blind man, a woman) **by the hand** NT. Plu. ‖ PASS. (of a blind man) be led by the hand NT.

2 (of recollection of incidental events) **lead on** (i.e. astray) —*an informant (in his narrative of the main event)* Plb.

χειρ-αγωγός οῦ *m.* one who leads by the hand; **guide** (for a blind man) NT.

χειρ-απτάζω *vb.* [ἅπτω] touch with one's hand, **handle** —*a corpse* Hdt.

χειρί (dat.sg.): see χείρ

χειριδωτός όν *adj.* [χειρίς] (of tunics) furnished with sleeves, **sleeved** Hdt.

χειρίζω *vb.* [χείρ] | fut. χειριῶ | aor. ἐχείρισα | pf. κεχείρικα ‖ PASS.: aor. ἐχειρίσθην | **handle, manage, direct** —*military operations, the running of a city*, or sim. Plb. ‖ PASS. (of things) be managed Plb.

χείριος ᾱ ον *adj.* **1** (of a woman) in the hands (of a captor), **captive** S. E.
2 (of a woman) **obedient** (W.DAT. to someone's words) A.

χειρίς ῖδος *f.* **1 glove** (worn by a gardener) Od.
2 sleeve (worn by foreigners, esp. Persians) Hdt. X. Plu.

χειρισμός οῦ *m.* [χειρίζω] **1 handling, managing** (of a matter) Plb.; **treatment** (of persons, by fortune) Plb.; **presentation** (of events, in a historical work) Plb.
2 showing (of goodwill) Plb.
3 arrangement, disposition (of forces, in a battle) Plb.

χειριστής οῦ *m.* **director** (of military operations or sim.) Plb.

χείριστος *superl.adj.*: see under χείρων

χειρό-γραφον ου *n.* [χείρ, γράφω] **document written in one's own hand** Plb.

χειρό-δάικτος ον *adj.* [δαΐζω] (of sacrificial victims) **torn apart by hand** S.

χειρό-δεικτος ον *adj.* [δείκνῡμι] (of fulfilled oracles) **able to be pointed to** (as proof of the gods' infallibility) S.

χειρο-δίκης ου *m.* [δίκη] (of a mythol. race of men) deciding justice by strength of hand, **holding that might is right** Hes.

χειρο-δράκων οντος *masc.fem.adj.* (of Erinyes) **with serpent-coiled arms** E.

χειρο-ήθης ες *adj.* [ἦθος] **1** (of animals) accustomed to the hand, **tame** Hdt. X. Plu.; (derog., of the god Apis, incarnated as a calf) Hdt.
2 (of persons, a populace) **submissive, obedient** (sts. W.DAT. towards someone) X. D. Plu.; (of a river, quasi-personif.) **docile** Plu.
3 (of things) **manageable, tolerable** (W.DAT. to persons, their minds or bodies) Plu.

χειροῖν (gen.dat.du.): see χείρ

χειροκρατίᾱ ᾱς *f.* [κράτος] **rule of force** (as a type of government) Plb.

χειροκρατικός ή όν *adj.* (of a tendency) **towards rule by force** Plb.

χειρο-κτύπος ον *adj.* (of a satyr) **hand-clapping** Telest.(dub., cj. χοροιτύπος)

χειρό-μακτρον ου, Aeol. **χερρόμακτρον** ω *n.* [μάσσω] **1 hand-wiper, handkerchief, napkin** Hdt. X.
2 app. **head-scarf** Sapph. Hdt.

χειρο-μύλη ης *f.* **handmill** (for grinding grain) X.

χειρονομέω *contr.vb.* [νέμω] **1** make gestures with one's hands; (of a man standing on his head) **gesticulate** —W.DAT. *w. his legs* Hdt.
2 make movements with one's arms, **perform exercises** (such as shadow-boxing) Pl. X.

χειρόομαι *mid.contr.vb.* [χείρων, or perh. χείρ] **1** get the better of (or perh. overcome by strength of hand); **overpower, subdue, conquer** —*persons, peoples, animals,*

χειροπληθής

places Hdt. S. E. Th. Isoc. Pl. + ‖ PASS. be overpowered, subdued or conquered Hdt. Trag. Th. D. +
2 bring under one's control, **take captive, capture** —*persons, ships, animals* Hdt. S. E. Pl. X. + —*prey (ref. to persons)* S. ‖ PASS. be captured A. Hdt. Pl. +
3 (specif., of a hunter) **bring down** —*a boar* (W.DAT. w. *arrows*) E.; (fig., of a curse, envisaged as an archer) —*a person* A.
4 (gener., of certain arts) **exercise coercion over** —*situations* (W.DAT. or PREP.PHR. *by words or deeds*) Pl.

—**χειρόω** *act.contr.vb.* **manhandle** —*someone* Ar. ‖ PASS. be manhandled Ar.

χειρο-πληθής ές *adj.* [χείρ, πλῆθος] filling the hand; (of sling-stones) **palm-sized** X.; (gener., of a club) **large, broad** Theoc.

χειροποιέομαι *mid.contr.vb.* **use one's hand to perform** —*an act* S.

χειροποίητος ον *adj.* **1** (of a staff, lake, path, structure, or sim.) made by hand, **man-made** (opp. natural) Hdt. X. D. Plb. NT.; (of a conflagration) Th.
2 (of charges) **trumped-up** Plb.

—**χειροποιήτως** *adv.* by handiwork, **artificially** (opp. naturally) Plb.

χειρότερος *ep.compar.adj.*: see under χείρων

χειρο-τέχνης ου *m.* [τέχνη] **1 craftsman** Pl. X.; **skilled practitioner** (W.GEN. of medicine, warfare) S. Plu.
2 (gener.) **artisan, workman** Hdt. Th. Ar. Pl. +; (opp. master-craftsman) Arist.

χειροτεχνίᾱ ᾱς *f.* **handicraft, artisanship** (as a skill or activity) Pl.

χειροτεχνικός ή όν *adj.* **1** relating to artisanship ‖ FEM.SB. manual skill Pl. ‖ FEM.PL.SB. crafts, manual arts Pl.
2 (of contracts) relating to handicraft or artisans, **concerning handicraft** or **with workmen** Pl.
3 (gener., of persons) **skilled, proficient** Ar.

χειροτονέω *contr.vb.* [χειρότονος] **1** (of an assembly, the people, or sim.) hold a show of hands, **vote** Ar. D. Plb. Plu. —W.INF. or ACC. + INF. *to do sthg., that sthg. shd. be done* Aeschin. D. ‖ PASS. (of an act) be voted, be ruled —W.INF. *to be an outrage* D.
2 (tr., of the Assembly, the people, or sim.) **vote for** —*a proposal, war, form of government, or sim.* Ar. Att.orats. Arist. ‖ PASS. (of a proposal) be voted for Lys.
3 elect by a show of hands, **elect** —*a person* (sts. W.PREDIC.SB. *as commander or sim.*), *officials* Ar. Att.orats. Pl. X. Arist. Plu. —(W.INF. *to do sthg.*) D. ‖ PASS. be elected Ar. Att.orats. Pl. + —W.ACC. *to a particular office* Ar. Aeschin.
4 appoint —*church elders* NT.

χειροτονητός ή όν *adj.* (of an official or office) chosen by vote, **elected** Aeschin. Arist. Plu.

χειροτονίᾱ ᾱς *f.* **1** show of hands, **voting, vote** Th. X. Arist. Din. Plb. Plu.
2 result of voting, **election** (of a person) Att.orats.
3 vote (cast for someone, by an individual) Pl.; (collectv.sg.) **votes cast** Pl.

χειρό-τονος ον *adj.* [τείνω] (of prayers) **offered with outstretched hands** A.

χειρουργέω *contr.vb.* [ἔργον] **1** construct with one's hands ‖ PASS. (of buildings, gardens, gymnasia) be constructed Pl.
2 be the perpetrator (opp. planner, of an act of violence) Antipho Th. Aeschin.
3 be a performer (of music) Arist.

χειρούργημα ατος *n.* manual work, **handiwork** Pl.

χειρουργίᾱ ᾱς *f.* **1** practice of working with the hands, **handiwork** Pl.; (by women, w. sexual innuendo) Ar.
2 handicraft (ref. to a particular craft) Isoc. Pl.
3 (specif.) **surgery** Plu.

χειρουργικός ή όν *adj.* **1** (of skill in playing a musical instrument) **manual** Arist.
2 (of a branch of medicine) **surgical** Plb.

χειρόω *contr.vb.*: see under χειρόομαι

χείρωμα ατος *n.* [χειρόομαι] **1** (ref. to a murder) act of overpowering, **conquest** A. S.
2 (concr.) person in subjection, **slave** A.

χείρων, ep. **χερείων**, ον, gen. ονος *compar.adj.* ‖ used as compar. of κακός ‖ SG.: masc.fem.acc. χείρονα, ep. χερείονα, Att. χείρω, irreg. χέρεια (Hom.) ‖ dat. χείρονι, ep. χερείονι, irreg. χέρηι (Il.) ‖ PL.: masc.fem.nom. χείρονες, ep. χερείονες, Att. χείρους, ep. χερείους (AR.), irreg. χέρηες (Od. AR.) ‖ neut.nom.acc. χείρονα, ep. χερείονα, Att. χείρω, irreg. χέρεια (Hom.) ‖ dat. χείροσι, ep. χειρόνεσσι (Pi.) ‖
1 (of persons) of lower standing, **inferior, lesser** (in birth, rank, martial prowess, natural endowments) Hom. Hes.*fr.* Pi. AR. Theoc.
2 inferior in status, **lowlier, humbler** E.; **lower-class** Pl. +
3 (gener.) less good, **inferior** (sts. W.DAT. or PREP.PHR. in some quality or activity, sts. W.GEN. to someone else) Hom. Thgn. E. Th. +; **worse** (W.INF. at doing sthg.) Ar. X.
4 (w. moral connot.) less good, **worse, baser** Att.orats. +; (w. little compar. sense) **bad** (rather than good) S. Th. +
5 (of things) of inferior quality or worth, **inferior, worse** Il. Th. +
6 (of circumstances, courses of action) **less good, worse** Od. Hes. Hdt. Th. +; (of a sickness) **more severe** E.
7 (neg.neut.impers., phr.) οὐ χεῖρον or χέρειον (w. ἐστί, freq. understd.) *it is not worse* (i.e. it is better or no bad thing, sts. W.INF. *to do sthg.*) Od. Ar. Pl. X. Arist. Plu.
8 ‖ NEUT.SB. (sg. and pl.) the worse or the bad Hom. E. Th. +; (prep.phr., esp. ref. to things changing or being interpreted) ἐπὶ τὸ χεῖρον (also τὰ χείρω) *for the worse* Isoc. Pl. X. D. Arist. Thphr. +

—**χεῖρον** *neut.adv.* less well, **worse** Antipho Th. +

—**χειρότερος** (also **χερειότερος**) η ον *ep.compar.adj.* (of persons or things) **inferior** or **worse** Il. Hes. hHom. Eleg.adesp. Parm.

—**χερειότερον** *ep.compar.adv.* less well, **worse** Mosch.

—**χείριστος** η ον *superl.adj.* **1** (of persons or things) **worst** Att.orats. Pl. X. +
2 lowliest, humblest Lys. X.
3 (w. moral connot.) **worst, basest** Plb.

—**χείριστα** *superl.adv.* **in the worst possible manner** Arist.

Χείρων, dial. **Χίρων**, Aeol. **Χέρρων**, ωνος *m.* **Chiron** (centaur, teacher of Asklepios and Achilles) Il. Hes. Alc. Pi. S. E. +

χειρῶναξ ακτος *m.* [χείρ, ἄναξ] master of handiwork, **handcraftsman** Hdt.

χειρωναξίᾱ ᾱς, Ion. **χειρωναξίη** ης *f.* **1 handiwork, handicraft** A. Hdt.
2 (gener.) **occupation** (of a nurse or laundress) A.

χειρωτικός ή όν *adj.* [χειρόομαι] (of an art) of the kind that overpowers, **coercive** Pl. ‖ FEM.SB. art of coercion Pl.

χείσομαι (fut.): see χανδάνω

χείω *ep.vb.*: see χέω

χελῑδόνιον ου *n.* [χελιδών] a kind of plant, **celandine** Theoc.

χελῑδών όνος *f.* ‖ voc. χελιδοῖ ‖ **1 swallow** (esp. as the harbinger of spring) Od. +; (its twittering compared to the

unintelligible speech of foreigners) A.; (fig.ref. to a foreigner) Ar.; (pl., pejor.ref. to tragic poets) Ar.
2 tender area on the underside of a horse's hoof, **frog** X.

χέλιοι *Aeol.pl.num.adj.*: see χίλιοι

χελιχελώνη ης *f.* [redupl. χελώνη] **torty-tortoise** (refrain of a children's game) Carm.Pop.

χελῡ́νᾱ *dial.f.*, **χελύννᾱ** *Aeol.f.*: see χελώνη

χελύνη ης *f.* [reltd. χεῖλος] **lip** (of a person) Ar.

χέλῡς (also **χέλυς**) νος *f.* | acc. χέλῡν, also χέλυν | **1 tortoise** hHom.; (W.ADJ. *of the sea*, ref. to a turtle, or perh. fig.ref. to a limpet) Alc.
2 lyre (w. tortoise-shell bowl) hHom. Sapph. E. Tim. Call. Bion
3 breastbone (of an animal, fr. its resemblance to a tortoise shell) E.

χελώνη ης, dial. **χελῡ́νᾱ**, Aeol. **χελύννᾱ**, ᾱς *f.* **1 tortoise** hHom. Hdt. Ar. Call. Plu.
2 lyre (w. tortoise-shell bowl) Sapph.
3 movable armoured shed (to protect besieging troops fr. missiles), **mantlet** X. Plb.

χέρα (acc.sg.): see χείρ

χέραδος εος *n.* [app.reltd. χερμάς] **shingle, gravel** (esp. on a beach or river-bed) Il. Sapph. Alc. AR.; **debris** (washed into the sea by a storm) Pi.

χέρας (acc.pl.), **χέρε** (nom.acc.du.): see χείρ

χερείων and **χερειότερος** *ep.compar.adjs.*: see χείρων

χέρες (nom.pl.), **χέρεσσι** (ep.dat.pl.), **χερί** (dat.sg.): see χείρ

χέρηες (nom.pl.compar.adj.), **χέρηι** (dat.sg.compar.adj.): see χείρων

χερι-άρᾱς ᾱ *dial.masc.adj.* [χείρ, ἀραρίσκω] | gen.pl. χεριαρᾶν | (of craftsmen) **constructing by hand, dextrous, skilled** Pi.

χερμάς άδος *f.* [app.reltd. χέραδος] **rock, stone** (used as a missile) A. Pi. E.; (used to build an altar) AR.

—**χερμάδιον** ου *n.* [dimin.] **stone** (used as a missile) Hom. Tyrt.

χερνής ῆτος *masc.adj.* [perh.reltd. χείρ] **1** (of a household) **lowly, poor** E.
2 || SB. **craftsman, artisan** (as a category of slaves) Arist.

χέρνησος (also **Χέρν-**) *dial.f.*: see χερσόνησος (Χερσό-)

χερνήτᾱς ᾱ *dial.m.* **poor man, pauper** A. [or perh. *poor labourer*]

χερνητικός ή όν *adj.* || NEUT.COLLECTV.SB. **lower classes, working classes** Arist.

χερνῆτις ιδος *f.* (appos.w. γυνή) **labouring woman** (ref. to a wool-spinner) Il. AR.

χέρνιβον ου *n.* [χέρνιψ] **metal bowl for washing hands, hand-basin** Il.

—**χερνίβιον** ου *n.* [dimin.] **hand-basin** And.

χερνίπτομαι *mid.vb.* | aor. ἐχερνιψάμην | **1 wash one's hands** (in a basin of holy water, before a sacrifice) Il. Lys. Ar.
2 sprinkle holy water —W.PREP.PHR. *on the hair of a sacrificial victim* E.

χέρ-νιψ ιβος *f.* [χείρ, νίζω] | dial.dat.pl. χερνίβεσσι | **1 water for washing the hands** (before a meal) Od. Thgn.
2 (freq.pl.) **holy water, lustral water** (esp. for washing the hands before a sacrifice, or for sprinkling on participants or the victim) Od. Simon. Trag. Th. Ar. +
3 lustral libation (of holy water, to gods or the dead) A. E.*fr.*

χεροῖν (gen.dat.du.): see χείρ

χερο-μυσής ές *adj.* [μύσος] (of bloodshed) **polluting the hand** A.

χερό-πληκτος ον *adj.* [πλήσσω] (of thuds) **of hands beating** (against the chest, in mourning) S.

χερός (gen.sg.): see χείρ

χερο-τεκτοσύνᾱ ᾱς *dial.f.* [τεκτοσύνη] **craftsmanship** (ref. to the building of Troy) E.(cj.)

χερρόμακτρον *Aeol.n.*: see χειρόμακτρον

χέρρονδε *dial.adv.*: see χέρσονδε, under χέρσος

χερρόνησος (also **Χερρό-**) *Att.f.*: see χερσόνησος (Χερσό-)

χέρρος (Aeol.gen.): see χείρ

Χέρρων *Aeol.m.*: see Χείρων

χερσαῖος ᾱ ον *adj.* [χέρσος] **1** (of animals, birds) **living on dry land** (opp. in water, the air) Hdt. Pl.; (of hunting) **on land, of land animals** Pl.; (fig., of a wave of troops) **on dry land** A.
2 (of persons, esp. troops) used to land (opp. sea), **land-based** Th. Plu. || MASC.SB. **landsman, land-lubber** E.
3 (of forts, cities) **inland, landlocked** (opp. coastal) Pl. Plu.

χερσεύω *vb.* (of farmland) **lie barren** X.

χερσί (dat.pl.): see χείρ

χέρσοθεν *adv.*, **χέρσονδε** *adv.*: see under χέρσος

χερσονησίζω *vb.* [χερσόνησος] (of a city, mountain) **form a peninsula** Plb.

χερσονησο-ειδής ές *adj.* [εἶδος¹] (of a mountain) **forming a peninsula** Hdt.

χερσό-νησος, Att. **χερρόνησος**, dial. **χέρνησος** (AR.), ου *f.* [χέρσος, νῆσος] **peninsula** Hdt. Th. AR. Plb. Plu.

Χερσόνησος, Att. **Χερρόνησος**, dial. **Χέρνησος** (AR.), ου *f.* **Chersonese** (ref. to the Thracian Chersonese, mod. Gallipoli) Hdt. Th. Ar. Att.orats. X. +; (ref. to the Tauric Chersonese, in the Crimea) Hdt.; (ref. to the peninsula of Methana, near Troizen in the Peloponnese) Th.; (ref. to a promontory in Bithynia) X.

—**Χερσονήσιος** ᾱ ον *adj.* (of land, the plains) **of the Chersonese** (in Thrace) E.

—**Χερσονησίτης**, Att. **Χερρονησίτης**, ου (Ion. εω) *m.* (usu.pl.) **inhabitant of the (Thracian) Chersonese, Chersonesian** Hdt. X. D. Plb. Plu.; (appos.w. ὄλεθρος *pest*, ref. to a person) Plu.

χέρσος ου *f.* **1 dry land, land** (opp. sea) Hom. Lyr. Trag. Hellenist.poet. Plb. Plu.(quot.trag.); (ref. to Hades, opp. the river by which it is reached) A. || PL. **stretches of dry land** (ref. to coastal areas) E.
2 (appos.w. Εὐρώπα *Europe*) **mainland** Pi.
3 || ADJ. (of dust) **of dry land** (opp. sea) Pi.(dub.) [perh. *f.*, see κόνιος]
4 || ADJ. (of earth) **dry** Hdt. S.; **bare, barren** Hdt.
5 || ADJ. (of women) **barren, childless** S.
6 || ADJ. (of an altar) **bare, empty** (W.GEN. of offerings) E.

—**χέρσοθεν** *adv.* **1 from dry land** E. AR.
2 on dry land Pi.

—**χέρσονδε**, dial. **χέρρονδε** (Alcm.) *adv.* **onto dry land** Il. hHom. Alcm. AR. Theoc.

χερύδριον ου *n.* [dimin. χείρ] **tiny hand** (of a baby) Mosch.

χερῶν (gen.pl.): see χείρ

χέσαι (aor.inf.), **χέσαιτο** (3sg.aor.opt.), **χεσεῖν** (aor.2 inf.): see χέζω

χεσείω *vb.* [desiderativ. χέζω] **need a shit** Ar.

χεσοῦμαι (fut.mid.): see χέζω

χεῦμα ατος *n.* [χέω] **1 that which is poured** (into a mould); **cast vessel** (of silver) Hdt.; **cast design** (W.GEN. of tin, on a bronze shield) Il.
2 pouring (W.GEN. of a libation) E.; (fig.) **outpouring** (W.GEN. of victory songs) Pi.
3 draught (of water fr. a spring, to pour as a libation) S.
4 water pouring forth, **stream, flood** Call.
5 (gener., freq.pl.) **water** (esp. W.GEN. of a river, lake or sea) A. Pi. E. AR.

χέω contr.vb. —also **χείω** (Hes.) ep.vb. —also **χεύω** (Hes.fr., perh. AR.) ep.vb. | ep.impf. χέον | fut. (in cpds.) -χέω, ep. χεύω (Od., dub.) | aor. ἔχεα, dial. ἔχευα, ep. χεῦα, ep.1pl.subj. χεύομεν ‖ MID.: fut.ptcpl. χεόμενος (Is.) | aor. ἐχεάμην, dial. ἐχευάμην, ep.3sg. χεύατο, 3pl. χεύαντο | athem.aor. (as pass.): 3sg. ἔχυτο, ep. χύτο, 3pl. ἔχυντο, ep. χύντο, ptcpl. χύμενος ‖ PASS.: ep.3sg.impf. χεύετο (Hes.fr.) | fut. (in cpds.) -χυθήσομαι | aor. ἐχύθην, ep. χύθην | pf. κέχυμαι, ptcpl. κεχυμένος | plpf.: ep.3sg. κέχυτο, 3pl. ἐκέχυντο, ep. κέχυντο |

1 pour (liquids); pour —*water, wine, or sim.* (fr. vessels, onto hands, the ground, or sim.) Hom. Sapph. Alc. Call.(mid.); (of the Muses) —*dew, nectar* (W.PREP.PHR. on a poet's tongue or lips) Hes. Theoc.; (act. and mid., of persons) —*a libation* Od. Hdt. Trag. AR. ‖ MID. pour a libation Is. Plu. ‖ PASS. (of nectar, wine, water, libations) be poured A. Pi.fr. S. E.(cj.) Tim. AR.
2 (of a spring or river) pour forth —*water* Il. A. Theoc. ‖ PASS. (of springs) pour forth E.; (fig., of persons) —W.PREP.PHR. fr. a place Hom.; (of races, in the process of creation) Emp.
3 ‖ PASS. (of bodily substances) flow, be liquid Pl.; (of soil) become moist or loose X.; (fig., of a heart) melt AR. ‖ PF.PASS. (of organs in the body) be loose-textured or dilated Pl.
4 pour forth, shed —*tears* Hom. B. E. AR. Bion ‖ PASS. and ATHEM.AOR.MID. (of tears) pour forth, be shed Hom. Mosch. Bion
5 shed, spill —*blood* Bion ‖ PASS. and ATHEM.AOR.MID. (of blood) be spilled E. Call. —W.ADV. or PREP.PHR. on the ground A.
6 (of Zeus, the north wind) pour down —*rain, snow* Il. E.Cyc.
7 (of a runner) pour —*his breath* (W.PREP.PHR. over the head of the runner in front) Il.; (mid., of a person) —*dust* (W.PREP.PHR. over his head) Hom. ‖ PASS. (of a disease) be diffused (through the body) S.
8 (of persons, birds, cicadas) pour forth —*their voice, a lament, prayer, or sim.* Od. Hes. Lyr. A. S. AR.; (mid.) —*comic words* Ar.
9 (of a tide) cast up —*seaweed* (W.PREP.PHR. alongside the sea) Il. ‖ PASS. (of a clod of earth) be cast up —W.PREP.PHR. on an island Pi.
10 (of trees) cause (W.ACC. fruit) to hang down (fr. their branches) Od. AR.; (of sailors) let (W.ACC. sails) hang down —W.PREP.PHR. fr. a mast AR.; (of a sacrificial victim, held above the altar) app. let (W.ACC. her robe) fall —W.PREP.PHR. towards the ground A.; (of a girl) shed —*her robe* Ar.(cj.) ‖ PASS. (of branches) hang down (under the weight of fruit) Theoc.; (of hair) dangle down —W.PREP.PHR. over cheeks E.
11 (of gods) pour, shed, spread —*mist, darkness, sleep, beauty* (W.DAT. or PREP.PHR. over persons, eyes) Hom. —*a magic net* (over a bed) Od. ‖ MID. (of ripples) spread —W.PREP.PHR. over the sea Il. ‖ PASS. and ATHEM.AOR.MID. (of darkness, death, sleep) be spread —W.DAT. or PREP.PHR. over persons, eyes Hom. AR.; (of love) —*over a face* Sapph.; (of pallor) —*over cheeks* AR.; (of night) —*around the edges of Tartaros* Hes.; (of mist) be poured —W.ADV. back (i.e. be dispersed) Od.
12 (of trees, wind) shed, scatter, strew —*leaves* (W.ADV. or PREP.PHR. on the ground) Il. Hes. AR.(mid.); (of weapons) —*the straw of war* (fig.ref. to slain soldiers) Il. ‖ PASS. (of leaves) be shed (by trees) Hes.fr.; (of snow, frost, dew, dung, grain, stones) be spread or scattered (sts. W.PREP.PHR. in or over places) Hom. Sapph. S. X. AR.; (of corpses, fish, sheep) be strewn (on the ground) Hom. ‖ ATHEM.AOR.PTCPL. (of a person) sprawled —W.PREP.PHR. on the ground E.
13 ‖ PASS. (of a vine) spread Theoc.epigr.; (of hair) —W.PREP.PHR. over one's temples Theoc.
14 ‖ MID. cast —*one's arms* (W.PREP.PHR. around someone) Il. ‖ ATHEM.AOR.MID. cast one's arms —W.PREP.PHR. around someone Hom.
15 ‖ PF.PASS. (fig., of a poet) be engrossed —w. ἐν + DAT. in a subject Pi.; (of a mind) be intent —w. ἐπί + ACC. on someone Lycophronid.
16 heap up —*a burial mound* Hom. Pi.fr. Hdt. Call. —*meat* (W.PREP.PHR. on plates) Il. ‖ PASS. (of a burial mound) be heaped up AR.; (of feathers, a pile of food) Hdt.; (of gold) Theoc.

χἠ: crasis for καὶ ἡ

χηλευτός ή όν adj. [χηλεύω weave, plait] (of helmets) woven, plaited Hdt.

χηλή ῆς, dial. **χᾱλά** ᾶς f. **1** hoof (of an animal) Hes. A.satyr.fr. E. AR. Mosch. Plu.; (ref. to the trampling foot of fate) A.
2 claw (of a lion, wolf, crab, the Sphinx) Scol. E. Theoc.epigr.; talon (of a bird) Trag.
3 breakwater, mole (natural or man-made) Th. X. Plu.

χηλός οῦ f. chest, trunk (used for storage) Hom. Call. Theoc.

χήν χηνός, dial. **χᾱν** χᾱνός m.f. goose (ref. to both wild and domesticated birds) Hom. Semon. Hdt. Ar. Pl. +; (invoked in an oath) Ar.

χην-αλώπηξ εκος m. fox-goose, Egyptian goose Hdt. Ar.

χήνεος η ον Ion.adj. (of meat, eggs) of a goose Hdt.

χηνοβωτίᾱ ᾱς f. [βόσκω] goose-rearing Pl. [or perh. concr. goose-farm]

χήρ Lacon.f., **χήρ** Aeol.f.: see χείρ

χηραμός οῦ f. hollow, cleft (in a rock or sim.) Il. AR.

χήρατο (ep.3sg.aor.mid.): see χαίρω

χῆρε (Boeot.imperatv.): see χαίρω

χηρεία ᾱς f. [χηρεύω] widowhood Th.

χηρεύω vb. [χῆρος] **1** (of a woman) be a widow Is. D. Plu.
2 (of a man) be a widower Plu. ‖ MID. remain widowed —W.ACC. w. regard to the marriage bed (i.e. not remarry) E.
3 (fig., of a satyr) be widowed (i.e. lack a sexual partner) —W.ACC. w. regard to one's spigot (i.e. penis) E.Cyc.
4 (of an outlaw) live alone S.
5 (of a place) be without, lack —W.GEN. men Od. Plu.

χηρός (Lacon.gen.): see χείρ

χῆρος ᾱ (Ion. η) ον adj. **1** (of a woman) widowed Il. S. E. Lys. Hyp. Men. +; bereft (W.GEN. of her husband) Il.; (gener.) manless A.satyr.fr. ‖ FEM.SB. widow NT. Plu.
2 (of a man) widowed Call.epigr.
3 (fig., of a house, bed) widowed, bereft E. Call.epigr. AR.; (of cattle-pens) desolate Call.

χηροσύνη ης f. state of being widowed or bereaved; loss (W.GEN. of one's husband) AR.

χηρόω contr.vb. **1** make into a widow, widow —*a woman* Il.
2 (of Troy) leave (W.ACC. Greece) bereft E.Cyc.; (of a warrior) leave desolate —*the streets of Troy* Il.; (of a person, by his death) —*the rays of the sun* Arist.lyr.
3 ‖ PASS. (of a city) be bereft —W.GEN. of men Sol. Hdt.; (of a person) —*of possessions* Thgn.

χηρωσταί ῶν m.pl. heirs of a vacant inheritance, next of kin Il. Hes.

χῆτος εος n. [reltd. χατέω] only dat. χήτει, ep. χήτεϊ | lack, want (W.GEN. of someone or sthg.) Hom. Hes. Hdt. Pl. AR.

χθαμαλός ή (dial. ά) όν adj. [χθών] **1** (of a bed) on the ground Od.
2 (of a stool) close to the ground, low AR.

3 (of a cliff, wall, or sim., freq. compar. or superl.) **low** Hom. X. Plb. Plu.
4 (of an island, a region) **low-lying** Od. AR. Theoc.
—**χθαμαλώτερον** *compar.adv.* **to a lower depth, deeper** —*ref. to digging* AR.
χθές (also **ἐχθές**) *adv.* **yesterday** hHom. Hdt. S. Th. Ar. Isoc. +; (quasi-adjl., of events or sim.) relating to or happening yesterday, **yesterday's** Pl. • ἡ χθὲς ὁμολογία *yesterday's agreement* Pl.
χθιζινός ή όν *adj.* [χθιζός] (of food, a person) that was present yesterday, **yesterday's** Ar.(cj.)
χθιζός ή όν *adj.* [χθές] (of things) relating to or happening yesterday, **yesterday's** Il. Hdt. Call.; (quasi-advbl., of a person departing or sim.) **yesterday** Hom. hHom. Hellenist.poet.
—**χθιζόν, χθιζά** *neut.sg. and pl.advs.* **yesterday** Hom. Call.*epigr.* AR.
χθόνιος ᾱ (Ion. η) ον (also ος ον) *adj.* [χθών] **1** in or beneath the earth; (of a cave, foundations, the entrance to Hades) **in the earth, under the ground, subterranean** Pi. Call. AR.
2 (of a noise, thunder, ref. to the sound of an earthquake) **from beneath the earth** A. E. Ar.; (of the sound of cymbals, envisaged as thunder) **as if from the earth** E.
3 belonging to a particular land; (of goddesses, nymphs) **of the land, local** AR.; (of the Areopagus, as hill and tribunal) **native, indigenous** S.
4 sprung from the earth; (of the descendants of Erekhtheus, the sown-man Ekhion and the ancestry of his son) **earth-born** S. E.; (of a serpent) AR.
5 ‖ FEM.SB. (personif., as a goddess) **Earth** Emp.
6 of or relating to the goddess Earth; (of the anger) **of Earth** E.; (of the Gorgon) **Earth-born** E.
7 in or belonging to the underworld; (of the dead, their minds) **in the underworld** A. Pi. E.; (of a lake, path, dwelling, darkness) S. E. Pl.; (of a message) **for those in the underworld** S. ‖ MASC.PL.SB. **inhabitants of the underworld** A. E.*fr.*
8 (of the Titans, Typhon) **beneath the earth** (as a punishment) Hes. A.
9 (of deities, such as Hades, Hekate, Persephone, the Fates) **of the underworld, chthonic** Hes. B. Lyr.adesp. Hdt. Trag. Pl. +; (of dogs, accompanying Hekate) AR. ‖ MASC.PL.SB. **gods of the underworld, chthonic gods** A. Pi. Pl. Plu. ‖ FEM.SB. **chthonic goddess, Chthonia** (ref. to Demeter) E. Plu. ‖ FEM.DU.SB. **chthonic goddesses** (ref. to Demeter and Persephone) Ar.
10 (specif., of Zeus) **chthonic** (responsible for subterranean thunder, sts. identified w. Hades) Hes. A.*fr.* S.; (of Hermes, as conductor of the dead to Hades) Trag. Ar. Plu.; (of his function) Ar.
11 having characteristics associated with the underworld; (of a person's disposition) **gloomy, sullen** Anacr.
χθονο-στιβής ές *adj.* [στείβω] (of all things) **that walk on earth** (opp. those in the heavens) S.
χθονο-τρεφής ές *adj.* [τρέφω] (of a herb) **produced by the earth** A.
χθών ονός *f.* **1 surface of the earth, ground, earth** (on which persons and things fall, lie, walk, or sim.) Hom. +; (beneath which lies the underworld, in phr. ὑπὸ χθονός or sim.) Il. +; (beneath which one is buried) Od. Pi. Trag. +; (as broken up by a plough) Hes.
2 earth as the abode of man, **earth** (esp. in formulaic expressions for being alive, or for everyone on earth) Hom. +

3 entire earth, **world** A. +
4 earth as nourisher (of plants, livestock, or sim.), **earth** Il. +
5 Earth (as a goddess) A. E.
6 land (opp. sea) Hes. +
7 land, country, region (sts. ref. to a city) Od. +; **homeland** S.
χῖδρον ου *n.* (pl. and collectv.sg.) **porridge made from unripe grains of wheat, porridge, frumenty** (as a rustic food) Alcm. Ar.; (fig.ref. to peace, as the staple of country folk) Ar.
χῑλί-ανδρος ον *adj.* [χίλιοι, ἀνήρ] (of a city) **of a thousand men** Pl.
χῑλιαρχέω *contr.vb.* [χιλίαρχος] **serve as military tribune** (in the Roman army) Plu.
χῑλιάρχης εω *Ion.m.* **commander of a thousand men** Hdt.
χῑλιαρχίᾱ ᾱς *f.* **1 command of a thousand men** X.
2 post of military tribune (in the Roman army) Plu.
χῑλί-αρχος ου *m.* [ἄρχω] **1 commander of a thousand men** A. X. Men.
2 tribunus militum, military tribune (in the Roman army) Plb. NT. Plu.
3 captain, chief of staff (in the service of a foreign ruler) NT. Plu.
χῑλιάς άδος *f.* **thousand** (usu. W.GEN. of sthg.) A. Hdt. Ar. Pl. +; (gener., as a very large number) Call. Theoc.
χῑλι-έτης ες *adj.* [ἔτος] (of a journey, an interval of time) **of a thousand years** Pl.
χίλιοι, Ion. **χείλιοι**, Aeol. **χέλιοι**, αι α *pl.num.adj.* | Aeol.masc.acc.pl. χελίοις | —also **χίλιος** ᾱ (Ion. η) ον *sg.num.adj.* **1** (of persons or things) **thousand** Hom. +; (collectv.sg., of cavalry) Hdt. X. ‖ PL.SB. **a thousand** (W.GEN.PL. of persons or things) Hdt. Th. + • χίλιοι Μακεδόνων *a thousand Macedonians* Th.
2 ‖ FEM.PL.SB. (w. δραχμαί understd.) **a thousand drachmas** Pl. Is. D. Thphr.(cj.) Plu.
χῑλιό-ναυς εως *masc.fem.adj.* [ναῦς] (of a military expedition) **of a thousand ships** E.
χῑλιοναύτης ου, dial. **χῑλιοναύτᾱς** ᾱ *masc.fem.adj.* (of a fleet, perh. a commander) **of or with a thousand ships** A. E.
χῑλιό-παλαι *adv.* [πάλαι] (hyperbol.) **for a thousand aeons** —*ref. to being ready* Ar.
χίλιος *sg.num.adj.*: see χίλιοι
χῑλιοστός ή όν *adj.* (of a year) **thousandth** Pl.; (of a person, in ranking) X.
χῑλιοστύς ύος *f.* (milit.) **company of a thousand men** X.
χῑλιο-τάλαντος ον *adj.* [τάλαντον] (of temples) **costing a thousand talents** Plu.
χῑλός οῦ *m.* **green fodder** (for animals) Hdt. X. Plu.; (W.ADJ. ξηρός *dry*, ref. to hay) X.
χῑλόω *contr.vb.* **give fodder to** —*horses* X.
Χίλων (also **Χῖλων** Call.) ωνος *m.* **Khilon** (of Sparta, one of the Seven Sages, 6th C. BC, said to be the originator of the maxim μηδὲν ἄγαν *nothing to excess*) Hdt. Pl. Arist. Call.
—**Χιλώνειος** ᾱ ον *adj.* ‖ NEUT.SB. **maxim of Khilon** Arist.
χίμαιρα ᾱς (Ion. ης) *f.* [app.reltd. χεῖμα (w.connot. of an animal in its first winter)] **1 young she-goat** (esp. as a sacrifice to Artemis) Il. Hes. Trag. X. +
2 Chimaira (a fire-breathing monster, usu. described as part lion, part goat and part serpent) Il. Hes. hHom. Pi. Pl.
χίμαρος ου *m.f.* **he-goat** or **she-goat** Ar. Theoc.
χίμετλον, also **χίμεθλον**, ου *n.* [χεῖμα] **chilblain** Hippon. Ar. Arist.(quot.poet.)
χιόνεος η ον *ep.Ion.adj.* [χιών, w. ῐ *metri grat.*] (of skin) **white as snow** Bion
χιονίζει *impers.vb.* **it snows, snow falls** Hdt.

χιονό-βλητος ον *adj.* [βάλλω] (of mountain peaks) **snow-struck** Ar.

χιονό-βοσκος ον *adj.* [βόσκω] (of a meadow) **fed by snow** (i.e. streams of melted snow) A.

χιονο-θρέμμων ον, gen. ονος *adj.* [τρέφω] (of crags) **snow-nurturing** E.

χιονό-κτυπος ον *adj.* [κτύπος] (of a mountain) **snow-beaten** S.

χιονο-τρόφος ον *adj.* [τρέφω] (of a mountain) **snow-nurturing** E.

χιονό-χρως ωτος *masc.fem.adj.* [χρώς] | dat.sg. χιονόχρῳ | irreg.acc.pl. χιονόχροας | (of a swan's wing, barley-cakes) **snow-coloured** E. Philox.Leuc.

χιονώδης ες *adj.* (of places) snowy, **snow-covered** E. Call. AR.

Χίος ου *f.* Chios (island in the Aegean, famous for its wine and as the supposed birthplace of Homer) Od. hHom. A. Hdt. Th. +

—**Χῖος** ᾱ (Ion. η) ον *adj.* 1 (of persons, wine) **from Chios, Chian** Hippon. Hdt. Ar. +; (of a poet, ref. to Homer) Simon. Theoc.; (of ships) **of the Chians** Th.; (of the land) **of Chios** Hdt. ‖ MASC.PL.SB. **men of Chios, Chians** (as a population or military force) Hdt. Th. Ar. +

2 ‖ MASC.SB. (w. βόλος understd.) **Chian** (ref. to the worst possible throw in a dice-game, i.e. a one) Ar.

Χίρων *dial.m.*: see Χείρων

χιτών, Ion. **κιθών**, ῶνος, Aeol. **κίθων** ωνος *m.* [Semit. loanwd.] 1 **khiton** (a tunic-like garment worn by men) Hom. +; (worn by women) Sapph. +; (ref. to similar garments worn by foreign men, oft. described as decadently long or luxurious) A.*satyr.fr.* Hdt. X. Plb. Plu.; (ref. to the hunting garb of Artemis) Call.

2 (fig.) **garment** (ref. to the body, as the clothing of the spirit) Emp.; (ref. to the walls of a house, as keeping in warmth) X.

3 **corslet, coat of armour** Il. Hdt. X.; (fig.ref. to defensive walls) Hdt.

4 part of the shoe which covers the foot, **upper** X. Arist.

Χιτώνη ης *f.* **Wearer of the Khiton** (ref. to Artemis, as wearing the short tunic of a hunter) Call.

χιτώνιον ου *n.* [dimin. χιτών] 1 **dress** (worn by a woman) Ar. Theoc. Plu.

2 **humble tunic** (as a makeshift shroud) Plu.

χιτωνίσκος ου *m.* 1 **undershirt, vest, singlet** (worn under a cloak) Ar. Pl. D. Thphr.

2 (gener., equiv. to χιτών) **tunic, shirt** (worn by a man) Att.orats. Pl. X. Plb. Plu.; **dress** (worn by a woman) D. Men. Plu.

χιών όνος *f.* 1 (usu.sg.) **snow** (falling or lying on the ground) Hom. +; (in comparisons, metaphors, or sim., as the exemplar of purest white) Il. S. E. Pl. Arist. NT.

2 **icy water** (fr. melting snow) E. X.

χλαῖνα ης *f.* [χλανίς; perh. also reltd. χλαμύς] 1 **cloak** (worn over a khiton or sim.) Hom. +; (as a fine garment, opp. the heavy and coarse σισύρα) Ar.; (used as a blanket) Hom. +

2 (fig.) **blanket** (W.GEN. of earth, covering a dead man) A.

χλαμυδη-φόρος ον *adj.* [χλαμύς, φέρω] (of men) **wearing capes** Theoc.

χλαμύδιον ου *n.* [dimin. χλαμύς] **rough cape, gaberdine** Men. Plu.

χλαμυδουργία ᾱς *f.* [ἔργον] **cape-making** (as a profession) X.

χλαμύς ύδος *f.* | Aeol.acc. χλάμυν | **cape, cloak** (esp. of a soldier) B. Ar. X. Arist. Men. +; (of fine quality, as worn by a king) Sapph. NT. Plu.

χλανίδιον ου *n.* [dimin. χλανίς] **cloak** (worn by a man or woman, sts. used as a blanket) Hdt. E. Ar. Men.

χλανιδοποιΐᾱ ᾱς *f.* [ποιέω] **cloak-making** (as a profession) X.

χλανίς ίδος *f.* [reltd. χλαῖνα] **fine cloak** Simon. Hdt. Ar. D. Men. Plu.

—**χλανίσκιον** ου *n.* [dimin.] **fine little cloak** Ar.; (pejor., as if an unmanly garment) Aeschin.

—**χλανισκίδιον** ου *n.* [dimin.] **fine little cloak** Ar.

χλᾱρόν *dial.neut.adv.* [perh.reltd. χαλάω] perh. **softly, merrily** —ref. *to laughing* Pi.(dub., cj. χλοαρόν)

χλευάζω *vb.* [χλεύη] 1 (of persons, a frog chorus) **engage in jesting** Ar. Plb.

2 **mock, jeer** Arist. NT. Plu. —W.ACC. *at someone or sthg.* D. Plb. Plu. ‖ PASS. **be mocked** Din. Plu.

3 **make a fool of** —*oneself* Men.

χλευασίᾱ ᾱς *f.* **taunting, mockery** D.

χλευασμός οῦ *m.* 1 **act of poking fun, mockery** Plb. Plu.; **ridicule** (suffered by a city) D.

2 **instance of mockery, mocking joke** Plu.; (wkr.sens.) **jest** Plb. Plu.

χλευαστής οῦ *m.* **mocker, scoffer** Arist.

χλεύη ης *Ion.f.* 1 **ribaldry** hHom.

2 **act of poking fun, mockery** AR.

χλῆδος ου *m.* **rubble** D.

χλιαίνω *vb.* | fut. χλιᾰνῶ | **warm** —*oneself* (*by a fire*) Ar.

χλιαρός, Att. **χλῑαρός**, ά όν *adj.* (of soup, food, water) **warm** Alcm. Hdt. Ar.

χλιδᾱ *dial.f.*: see χλιδή

χλιδαίνομαι *mid.vb.* [χλιδανός] **lounge about** —W.DAT. *in luxury* X.

χλιδανός ή (dial. ᾱ́) όν, Aeol. **χλίδανος** ᾱ ον *adj.* [χλιδή] 1 (of persons) **soft-living, luxurious** (as an Ionian trait) Plu.

2 (of women, their youthfulness) **voluptuous** Sapph. A. E.*Cyc.*

χλιδάω *contr.vb.* 1 **live in luxury** Ar.; **luxuriate, revel** —w. ἐπί + DAT. *in the trappings of wealth* S. —W.DAT. *in one's sufferings* A.; (of Silenos, compared to a goat) —*in his beard* S.*Ichn.*

2 (fig., of singing) **swell** Pi.

χλιδή ῆς, dial. **χλιδᾱ́** ᾶς *f.* [reltd. χλιαίνω] 1 (freq.pejor.) **luxurious indulgence, luxury** (esp. as a lifestyle) A. Hdt. Pl. X.; **indulgent pleasure** (of a lover's bed, beauty contest) A. E.

2 (concr.) **luxury** (ref. to a ritual bath) E.; **luxurious ornament** (ref. to jewellery, fine clothes, a woman's flowing hair) Trag.

3 (ref. to Bacchants) **pride, glory** (W.GEN. of the place to which they belong) E.

4 **insolence, arrogance, pride** A. S.

χλίδημα ατος *n.* **luxurious adornment** (worn by a man) E.

χλιερο-θαλπής ές *dial.adj.* [χλιαρός, θάλπος] (of water for washing the hands) **warm** or **lukewarm** Philox.Leuc.

χλίω *vb.* [reltd. χλιαίνω] **luxuriate** —W.DAT. *in oriental robes* A. —w. ἐν + DAT. *in the fruits of another's labour* A.

χλόᾱ *dial.f.*: see χλόη

χλοαρόν *dial.neut.adv.*: see χλᾱρόν

χλοερός ά όν *adj.* [χλόη] 1 (of branches, leaves) **green, verdant** Hes. E. AR.; (of meadows, hills, valleys, or sim.) **green with vegetation** S.*Ichn.* E. AR. Plu.; (of streams) **verdant** or **fresh** E.

2 (of crumpets) **yellow** Philox.Leuc.

3 (of limbs) **fresh, youthful** Theoc.

χλοερο-τρόφος ον *adj.* [τρέφω] (of a plain) **grass-nourishing, grassy** E.

χλόη ης, dial. **χλόᾱ** ᾱς *f.* 1 **green shoot** (of a plant) Iamb.adesp. Hdt. X. Plu.

2 **green foliage** (esp. used in wreaths or rituals) E.

3 grass and plants of a meadow, **grass, sward** (esp. as forming a soft surface to lie on) E. Pl. Plu.; **greenery, plants** (eaten by herbivores) Pl.

—**Χλόη** ης *f.* (as a title of Demeter) **Verdant One** Ar.

χλο-ήρης ες *adj.* [ἀραρίσκω] (of a plant) covered in greenery, **verdant** E.

χλοη-φόρος ον *adj.* [φέρω] (of fields, ivy shoots) bearing greenery, **verdant** E.

χλόος ου *m.* pale green colour, **pallor** (on cheeks, fr. fear, sickness, or sim.) Call. AR.

χλούνης ου *m.* (appos.w. σῦς or κάπρος) **wild boar** Il. Hes. Call.

χλούνις ιος *f.* [app.reltd. χλόη] **virility** (of young men) A.

χλοώδης ες *adj.* [χλόη] (of bile) **greenish** Pl.

χλωρ-αύχην ενος *masc.fem.adj.* [χλωρός, αὐχήν] 1 (of nightingales) **green-throated** Simon.
2 (of a woman) **pale-necked** B.

χλωρηίς ίδος *fem.adj.* (of nightingales) **of the greenwood** Od. Lyr.adesp. [or perh. fig. *bursting with verdant song*]

χλωρό-κομος ον *adj.* [κόμη] (of laurel wreaths) **with green foliage** E.

χλωρός ά (Ion. ή) όν *adj.* [reltd. χλόη] | The adj. embraces both green and yellow. | 1 (of woods, plains, mountains, or sim.) **green** Od. hHom. Anacr. Pi.*fr.* S. +; (of leaves, plants, grass) Trag. Hellenist.poet. NT. Plu.; (of a river, W.DAT. w. reeds) E.; (of wheat, wheatfields, i.e. unripe) Th. Plu.; (of wood, i.e. living) Od. Hes. Ar.
2 (of flowers) **blooming** E.; (of cheese) **fresh** Lys. Ar.; (of limbs) **youthful** Theoc.; (of blood in a hero's veins) **full of life** S.; (of blood, as an offering) **freshly spilt** E.
3 (of honey, sand, beads of frankincense) **yellow** Hom. hHom. Stesich. Pi.*fr.* S.
4 (of steel) **pale, shining** Hes.; (of tears, dew, drops of wine) **glistening** Pi. S. E.
5 (of persons) **pale, pallid** (fr. fear, sickness, or sim.) Il. Sapph. Th.; (of fear, a personif. Death-mist) Hom. Hes. A. E. Theoc.
6 (fig., of affairs) **colourless, dull** Arist.(quot.)

χλωρότης ητος *f.* **fresh green colour** (of a wood) Plu.

γναυμάτιον ου *n.* [γναύω] piece of food to nibble, **titbit** Philox.Leuc.

γναύω *vb.* (of the Cyclops) **gnaw** —*human limbs* E.*Cyc.*

γνοάζω *vb.* [γνόος¹] **get the first hairs of old age** —W.ACC. *on one's greying head* S.

γνοάω *contr.vb.* | only ep.ptcpl. γνοάων | 1 (of a boy) **have the first down** —W.ACC. *on his cheeks* AR.; (of a first beard) **be downy** AR.
2 (of apples, fig.ref. to a girl's breasts) **be velvety** Theoc.

γνόη, Ion. **γνοίη**, ης *f.* 1 centre of a wheel (through which the axle passes), **nave, hub** Parm. Trag.
2 || PL. (fig.) sockets (W.GEN. of feet, i.e. feet in motion envisaged as chariot-wheels) A.

γνόος¹ ου, Att. **γνοῦς** οῦ *m.* 1 **scurf, dried foam** (of seawater, on a person's body) Od. Hippon.
2 **first down** (on a boy's cheeks) Call.; (on a boy's genitals) Ar.

γνόος² (perh. better **κνόος**) ου *m.* app. **creak** (W.GEN. of an axle) Call.

χοᾶ (acc.sg.): see χοῦς¹

χοανεύω (also contr. **χωνεύω**) *vb.* [χόανος] (of a person casting in bronze, fig.ref. to a poet composing verses) **pour molten metal into a mould**, **cast in a mould** Ar.; (fig., of a penis, in a threat of anal rape) **fill a channel** Ar. || PASS. (of silver, silver-ore) be smelted, be cast (into ingots) Plb. Plu.

χοάνη (also contr. **χώνη**) ης *f.* **funnel** Pl.; (W.GEN. for the hearing, ref. to the ear canal) Ar.

χόανος ου *m.* [χέω] **smelting-vat, crucible** Il. Hes. AR.; (fig., ref. to a place within the earth where substances are formed) Emp.

χόες (nom.pl.): see χοῦς¹

χοή ῆς *f.* [χέω] (usu.pl.) poured offering, **libation** (to the dead) Od. Hdt. Trag. X. Plu.; (to the gods of the underworld) A. S.; (to Earth or the earth) A. E.

χο-ήρης ες *adj.* [χοῦς¹, ἀραρίσκω] (of a vessel) **used in the Feast of Pitchers** (at Athens) E.

Χοη-φόροι ων *f.pl.* [φέρω] **Libation-bearers** A.(title)

χοΐ (dat.sg.): see χοῦς¹

χοινικίς ίδος *f.* [χοῖνιξ] app., cup-shaped stand, **stand** (for a crown on public display) D.

χοῖνιξ ικος *f.* 1 **khoinix** (a dry measure, sts. specified as Attic, approx. one litre, but varying in other Greek states) Hippon. Hdt. Ar. X. Plu.; (specif., ref. to a measure of grain as a person's daily ration) Hdt. Th. Ar. Men.; (gener.) **grain-ration** Od.
2 **khoinix cup** or **scoop** (used to measure out dry goods) Plu.
3 **leg-iron, shackle** (perh. named fr. its resemblance to a scoop) Ar. D.

χοιράς άδος *f.* [χοῖρος] 1 protruding ridge of rock (resembling a hog's back); **rock** or **reef** (either submerged or above sea-level, as a danger to ships) Archil. Thgn. A. Hdt. E.; (appos.w. πέτρα) Pi.; (pl., ref. to the Clashing Rocks) Theoc.
2 **rocky isle** (W.ADJ. *of Delos*) A. E.(pl.)
3 **swelling, growth** (on the neck, caused by scrofula) Plu.

χοίρειος α ον, ep. **χοίρεος** η ον *adj.* (of meat) of a pig, **pork** Ar. X. || NEUT.PL.SB. pork Od.

χοιρίδιον ου *n.* [dimin. χοῖρος] young pig, **piglet** Ar. Pl. Men. Plu.; (w. play on χοῖρος 2) **pussy** Ar.

χοιρίνᾶς ᾶ *dial.m.* (perh. w. πλακοῦς understd.) a kind of fried snack, **rissole** Philox.Leuc.

χοιρίνη ης *f.* **mussel shell** (used for voting in Athenian courts) Ar.

χοιρίον ου *n.* young pig; (w. play on χοῖρος 2) **pussy** Ar.; (as a term of endearment for an aulos-girl) **piggywig** Ar.

χοιρό-θλιψ θλιβος (or perh. -**θλῖψ** θλίβος) *f.* [θλίβω] (ref. to a lecherous old man) **pussy-pesterer** Ar.

χοιρο-κομεῖον ου *n.* [κομέω, κομίζω] **pig-pen** Ar.

χοιρό-κτονος ον *adj.* [κτείνω] (of a purificatory offering) **of slaughtered pigs** A.

χοιρο-πώλᾶς ᾶ *dial.m.* [πωλέω] **pig-seller** Ar.

χοῖρος ου *m.* (sts. *f.*) 1 **pig, porker** (esp. ref. to a young pig) Od. +; (W.ADJ. ἄγριος *wild*, ref. to a boar) Hippon.
2 **pussy** (ref. to female genitals) Ar.

χολᾶ *dial.f.*: see χολή

χολάδες ων *f.pl.* [χολή, χόλιξ] **intestines** (of a person or animal) Il. hHom.

χόλαισι (Aeol.3pl.): see χαλάω

Χολαργεύς έως *m.* man from Kholargos (an Attic deme), **Kholargian** Ar. Att.orats. Pl. Men. Plu.

χολάω *contr.vb.* [χολή] 1 have an excess of bile (believed to cause madness), **be demented** Ar. Men.
2 **be angry** —W.DAT. *w. someone* NT.

χολή ῆς, dial. **χολᾶ** ᾶς *f.* 1 **gall** (of a sacrificial animal, inspected in divination) Trag.; **gall-bladder** (of an animal) Men.
2 **bile, gall** (in the body, esp. as an indicator of health) Hippon. Th. Pl. Arist. Thphr. Men.; (fig.ref. to sthg. harsh,

χολίκιον

unpleasant or distasteful) Ar. Mosch. NT.; (ref. to a bitter substance, perh. myrrh) NT.
3 bile (as the source of anger, oft. described as rising within one) Ar. Men. Theoc.; **anger, bitterness** A. D. Men.; **raging anger, fury** (let loose on someone) Ar.
4 bile (as the source of fighting spirit) Archil.; **fighting spirit** Ar. Men.
5 (medic.) **excess of bile** (believed to cause madness) Men.; **madness, episode of madness** Ar.

χολίκιον ου *n*. [dimin. χόλιξ] **intestines** (of an animal, as offal) Thphr.

χόλιξ ικος *f*. [reltd. χολάδες] (pl. and collectv.sg.) **intestines** (of a person) Ar.; (of an animal, as offal) Ar.

Χολλῄδης ου *m*. **man from Kholleidai** (an Attic deme), **Kholleidian** Lys. Ar. D.

χόλος ου *m*. [reltd. χολή] **1 bile, gall** (of the hydra, used as arrow-poison) AR.; (as the source of bitter anger) Il.
2 bitter anger, rage Hom. Hes. Thgn. Lyr. Hdt. Trag. +; (W.GEN. because of someone or about sthg.) Il. S.; **fierceness** (of a dog) Call.
3 bitterness, bitter pain (W.GEN. of conflict) Sol.

χολόω contr.vb. | ep.fut.inf. χολωσέμεν ‖ MID.PASS.: ep.fut.pf. κεχολώσομαι | ep.3pl.plpf. κεχολώατο | **1 make angry, anger** —*someone* Hom. AR. —(W.ACC. *in his heart*) Hes. —*the heart* (W.DAT. *of someone*) B.
2 drive (W.ACC. *someone*) **into a rage** or **frenzy** —W.DAT. *w. agony* (*caused by a poisoned robe*) S.
3 ‖ MID.PASS. **be made angry, be** or **become angry** (oft. W.DAT. or GEN. by, with or at someone or sthg.) Hom. Hes. Iamb. Eleg. Lyr. Hdt. + —W.GEN. or PREP.PHR. *about or because of someone or sthg*. Hom. hHom. Pi. E. AR.

χολώδης ες *adj*. **1** (of humours in the body) **similar to bile, bilious** Pl.; (of colours) **bile-like** Pl.
2 (of persons) characterised by an excess of bile (as an indicator of health), **choleric** Arist.

χολωτός ή όν *adj*. (of words) **angry** Hom.

χονδρός ά όν *adj*. (of salt) **in crystals** or **blocks** Ar.

χόνδρος ου *m*. **1** (collectv.sg.) grains of salt, **rock salt, salt crystals** Plb.; **block** (of rock salt) Hdt.
2 grains of cereal (boiled in water or milk, as a dish), **barley-groats** Stesich. Ar. Men.

χοός (gen.sg.): see χοῦς²

χοραγός dial.m.f.: see χορηγός

χορ-αύλης ου *m*. [χορός, αὐλός] one who plays the aulos to accompany a chorus, **aulos-player** Plu.

χόρδευμα ατος *n*. [χορδεύω] **sausage** Ar.

χορδεύω vb. [χορδή] (fig., of a sausage-maker turned politician) stuff into sausage-casings, **make baloney out of** —*matters of state* Ar.

χορδή ῆς *f*. **1** intestine; (specif.) length of animal intestine twisted into a string, **catgut string** (of a lyre or harp) Od. hHom. Anacr. Pi. E. Telest. +; (meton.) **musical note** Pl. Arist.
2 stuffed length of intestine, **sausage** Ar. Philox.Leuc.

χορεία ᾶς, Ion. **χορείη** ης *f*. [χορεύω] **1 choral singing and dancing** (as an art form or activity) Pl. Theoc.
2 dance performed by a chorus, **choral dance** (usu. as part of a religious ceremony) E.(dub.) Ar. Tim. Pl. Plu.
3 (gener.) **dance, dancing** Plu.
4 song performed by a chorus, **choral song** Pratin. Ar.

χορεῖος ᾱ (Ion. η) ον *adj*. (of a song) performed by a dancing chorus, **choral** AR.

χόρευμα ατος *n*. dance performed by a chorus, **choral dance** Pratin. E. Ar. Pl.

χόρευσις ιος dial.f. **choral dancing** Pi.fr.

χορευτής οῦ, dial. **χορευτᾶς** ᾶ *m*. **1 chorus-member, choral dancer** Pi. Ar. Att.orats. Pl. X. +
2 (fig.) member of a train of followers, **acolyte** (W.GEN. of a god) Pl.

χορεύω vb. [χορός] **1** (of men or women) take part in a choral dance (esp. at a religious ceremony or public festival), **dance, join in the dance** Pi.fr. Hdt. Trag. Ar. Isoc. Pl. + —W.DAT. *in honour of a god* E. Pl.; (of Dionysus) E. Ar.; (of animals) Pi.fr. E.; (of dolphins) —w. περί + ACC. *around Poseidon* Lyr.adesp.; (fig., of the moon, earth) E.
2 dance —W.COGN.ACC. *a choral dance* Pl. Plu.
‖ AOR.PASS.PTCPL.SB. performances of choral dancing Pl.
‖ IMPERS.PF.PASS. there has been dancing Ar.
3 (tr.) **honour with dancing** —*a god* Pi. S. E.(mid.); **celebrate with dancing** —*a wedding* E. —*the rites of the Muses* Ar.; **accompany with dancing** —*a song* Ar.(mid.) ‖ PASS. (of Kithairon, the Delphic tripod) be honoured with dancing S. E.
4 (specif.) **be a member of a chorus** (performing in a competitive event at a religious festival) D. Plu.; (fig.) —w. ἐν + DAT. *in a particular band* (*of philosophers*) Pl.
5 (gener., of individuals) **dance** (for joy) E. Ar. Theoc. —W.INTERN.ACC. *a prelude* (*to a celebration*) A.(mid.); (of an avenging spirit) —W.PREP.PHR. *into a house* E.
6 (fig., of an aulos) **dance** (i.e. accompany the dancers) Pratin.
7 (causatv., of Dionysus, the Muses, Frenzy) cause to dance, **set dancing** —*persons, regions* E.; (perh. of wine) A.satyr.fr.
‖ PASS. be set dancing —W.DAT. *by aulos-accompanied madness* E.

χορηγέω contr.vb. [χορηγός] **1** (of gods) **lead** or **manage the dancing** —W.GEN. *of humans* Pl.; (fig., of adherents of a philosopher) **champion** —W.GEN. *a doctrine* Pl.
2 (at Athens) fund a choral performance, **act as khoregos** (freq. W.COGN.ACC.) Ar. Att.orats. X. Arist. + ‖ PASS. (of boys) be provided for by a khoregos Antipho; (of the populace) be served by khoregoi X.
3 (at Rome and elsewhere) **put on a theatrical performance** Plu. ‖ PASS. (of public spectacles) be put on Plu.
4 ‖ PASS. (of a public banquet) be financed (by an individual) Arist.
5 (fig.) **fund, finance** —W.DAT. *one's lusts* Aeschin.
6 (gener.) supply (someone, w. sthg.); **furnish, supply** —*troops, commanders* (W.DAT. *w. provisions*) Plb.; (of a region) —*all Asia* (w. horses) Plb. ‖ PASS. (of troops, commanders) be supplied (sts. W.DAT. w. provisions or sim.) Plb. Plu.; (of persons) —W.DAT. w. necessities Arist.; (of a building project) —*w. mules* Plu.; (of a person) be endowed —W.DAT. *w. natural abilities* Plb. ‖ PF.PASS.PTCPL.ADJ. (of a person) furnished, equipped, endowed (in terms of natural ability, W.ADV. to the highest degree) Arist.; (of virtue) well endowed (w. the capacity to do sthg.) Arist.
7 supply (sthg., to someone); **furnish, provide** —*supplies, money* (W.DAT. *to someone*) D. Plb. Plu.; (intr.) **provide supplies** or **money** (sts. W.DAT. to someone) Plb. Plu. ‖ PASS. (of provisions, clothing) be supplied —W.DAT. *to people* Plb. Plu.

χορήγημα ατος *n*. (ref. to an empire) means of funding, **funder** (W.GEN. of an emperor's lusts and vices) Plu.

χορηγία ᾱς *f*. **1** (at Athens) **duty of a khoregos** Th. Att.orats. X. + ‖ COLLECTV.PL. public services (ref. to leitourgiai in general, other than the trierarchy) Lys. D.

2 (gener.) **generous expenditure** (esp. on public works) Arist. Plu.; (wkr.sens.) **resources** or **extra resources** Arist. Plb. Plu.; **supply** (of things) Arist.

3 (concr.) **supplies** (esp. for an army) Plb. Plu.; **furnishings, equipment** (for a dining-room) Plu.

χορηγικός ή όν *adj.* (of competitions, thank-offerings for success) **in staging choruses** X. Plu.

χορήγιον ου *n.* **1 training-room for a chorus** D.

2 ‖ PL. **supplies** (for an army) Plb.

χορηγός, dial. **χοραγός**, οῦ *m.f.* [χορός, ἄγω] **1 leader of the dance, chorus-leader** Alcm. Lyr.adesp. Ar. Pl.; (fig., W.GEN. of the stars, ref. to Dionysus) S.; (of dolphins, ref. to a ship) E.

2 (at Athens) **khoregos** (wealthy citizen who, as a leitourgia, i.e. public duty, paid for the maintenance, training and costuming of a chorus for a competitive performance at a festival) Ar. Att.orats. X. Arist. Plu.; (elsewhere) **organiser of a chorus** Hdt. Theoc.*epigr.*

3 (ref. to the funder of any other leitourgia, apart fr. the trierarchy) **contributor, donor** D.

4 (gener., ref. to a person, his largesse, a war) **provider of funds, funder, financer** (of a person, lifestyle, celebrations, military defences) Aeschin. D. Plb. Plu.; (pejor.) **paymaster, bankroller** (of political agitators, petty tyrants, or sim.) D. Plb. Plu.

5 (fig., ref. to the subject matter of history) **generous provider, rich source** (W.GEN. of striking coincidences) Plu.

χορικός ή όν *adj.* relating to a chorus; (of a Muse, songs) **choral** Pl. Arist. ‖ NEUT.SB. **choral section** (of a play) Arist. ‖ NEUT.PL.SB. **staging of choruses, choral competitions** X.; **choral songs** Ar.(dub.)

χόριον ου *n.* perh., **intestine of an animal, guts** Theoc. ‖ PL. **pudding** (perh. similar to a haggis) Theoc.

χορῖτις ιδος *f.* [χορός] girl who dances in a chorus, **choral dancer** Call.

χορο-γήθης ες *adj.* [γηθέω] (of nymphs) **delighting in the dance** hHom.(cj.)

χοροδιδασκαλία ᾱς *f.* [χοροδιδάσκαλος] **art of training a chorus** Pl.

χοροδιδασκαλικός ή όν *adj.* (of the art) **of the chorus-trainer** Pl.

χορο-διδάσκαλος ου *m.* **chorus-trainer** Ar. Pl. Aeschin. Arist.

χοροιτυπίη ης *ep.Ion.f.* [χοροιτύπος] **beating the ground in choral dancing** ‖ PL. **choral dances** Il.

χοροι-τύπος ον *adj.* [τύπτω] (of Silenos) **beating the ground in the dance** Pi.*fr.*; (fig., of the tortoise, whose shell was used to make the lyre, envisaged as a girl) hHom. | see also χειροκτύπος

χορο-μανής ές *adj.* [μαίνομαι] (of a style) **of maddened dancing** Ar.

χορόνδε *adv.*: see under χορός

χορο-ποιός όν *adj.* [ποιέω] **1** (of Pan, the Graces) **directing the dance** S. E.

2 (of young persons) **performing the dance** Ar.

3 ‖ MASC.SB. **chorus-master** X.

4 (of sacrifices) **with choral dancing** E.

χορός οῦ *m.* **1 dance** (sts. incl. song) performed by a group of persons, **choral dance** Hom. +

2 dancing-ground, dance-floor Hom. Hes.

3 group of dancers or singers, **chorus, choir** Pi. B. Hdt. Trag. Th. +

4 (specif., in tragic and comic drama) **chorus** Hdt. Ar. Att.orats. +; (in a dithyrambic contest, freq. W.ADJ. κύκλιος *cyclical*) Ar. Att.orats. + ‖ PL. (meton.) **performances of drama** Ar. Men.

5 (fig.) **chorus-line, row** (of teeth) Ar.; (of utensils) X.

6 (gener. or fig.) **entourage** (of a sophist) Pl.; **group, circle** (of persons, gods) Hes. Pi. E. Pl.; (of stars) E.; **class** (of things) Pl.

–χορόνδε *adv.* **to a dance** Il.

χορο-στάς άδος *masc.fem.adj.* [ἵστημι] (of festivals) **celebrated with choral performances** Call.

χοροστασία ᾱς *dial.f.* **staging of a dance** ‖ PL. **dances** Call.

χορο-στάτις ιος *dial.f.* **leader of the dance** Alcm.

χορτάζω *vb.* [χόρτος] **1 feed up** —*animals* (sts. W.ACC. or DAT. *w. fodder*) Hes. Ar. Pl. ‖ PASS. (of unenlightened people) **be fed like cattle** Pl.

2 (gener.) **fill up with food, feed** —*a person* Men. —*a crowd* NT. —(W.GEN. *w. bread*) NT. ‖ PASS. **eat one's fill, be fed** NT. —W.PREP.PHR. *fr. pig-swill, table-scraps* NT.

χορτάσματα των *n.pl.* **fodder** (for cattle) Plb. Plu.; (gener.) **food** (for people) NT.

χορτολογία ᾱς *f.* [λέγω] **collecting of fodder, foraging** (by soldiers) Plb.

χόρτος ου *m.* **1 enclosed space, yard** Il.

2 ‖ PL. **places where animals are pastured, pastures** E.; (W.GEN. of a lion, ref. to Nemea) Pi.

3 fodder (for animals) Hes. Hdt. E. X. Plb. Plu.; (for a slave, ref. to poor fare) Hippon.

4 hay X. Theoc. Plu.

5 (gener.) **grass** NT.; (specif.) **blade of corn** NT.

χορῳδία ᾱς *f.* [χορός, ἀοιδή] **choral singing** Pl.

χορ-ωφελήτᾱς ᾱ *dial.masc.adj.* [ὠφελέω] (of the noise of clapping hands) **helping the dance along** Ar.

χοῦν[1] (acc.sg.): see χοῦς[2]

χοῦν[2] (inf.): see χόω

χοῦς[1] χοῶς *m.* [χέω] | acc. χοᾶ, dat. χοΐ ‖ PL.: nom. χόες, acc. χοᾶς, gen. χοῶν, dat. χουσί | **1 jar, jug, pitcher** (esp. ref. to a wine-jar) Ar.; **measuring-jug** Ar. D.

2 khous-measure (approx. 3.2 litres in volume), **jarful, pitcherful** (of liquid) Ar. Pl. D. Men. Plu.

3 ‖ PL. **Pitchers** (Athenian festival in honour of Dionysus and the new vintage) Ar. D. Call. Plu.

χοῦς[2] χοῦ (also χόος Plb.) *m.* | acc. χοῦν | **1 loose soil, earth** (esp. fr. digging a trench or tunnel) Hdt. Th. Plb. Plu.

2 silt (in an estuary) Plb.

3 dust NT.

χόω *contr.vb.* —also (pres.) **χώννυμι, χωννύω** (Plb.) *vbs.* | ptcpl. χῶν, inf. χοῦν | fut. χώσω | aor. ἔχωσα ‖ PASS.: fut. χωσθήσομαι | aor. ἐχώσθην | pf. κέχωσμαι |

1 heap up, build —*a burial mound* (oft. W.DAT. *for someone*) Hdt. S. E. Pl. X. + —*earthworks, mounds, or sim.* Hdt. Th. Plu. —*an artificial island* Hdt.; (intr., of troops) **heap up earth, build a mound** —W.PREP.PHR. *against a defensive wall* Th. ‖ PASS. (of a burial mound) **be heaped up, be built** (oft. W.DAT. *for someone*) E. X. Plu.(quot.); (of a city) **be raised up on embankments** Hdt.

2 bury, cover —*someone* (W.DAT. *w. a burial mound*) E. Pl. Call.*epigr.*

3 fill in, block up —*trenches, harbours, wells, or sim.* D. Plb. Plu. ‖ PASS. (of ditches, wells) **be filled up** (by troops) Plb.; (of a passageway for water) **be blocked** (by a hand) Emp.

4 ‖ PASS. (of bays, seas) **become silted up** Hdt. Plb.; (of an island) **be formed** (fr. deposited silt) Th.

χοῶν (gen.pl.), **χοῶς** (gen.sg.): see χοῦς[1]

χρᾷ (Ion.3sg.): see χράω, under χράομαι

χραεῖν aor.2 inf. | 3sg. ἔχραε, 2pl. ἐχράετε | **1** (of a daimon) **inflict torment** —W.DAT. *on someone* Od.

χραίνω

2 [perh. a separate wd., possibly reltd. χράομαι, χρήζω] (of persons) app. **desire** —w.inf. *to do sthg.* Il.; **covet** —w.acc. *a household* (w.inf. *so as to eat and drink up its resources*) Od.

χραίνω *vb.* | fut. χρανῶ | aor. ἔχρᾱνα | **1** (of a country-dweller, in neg.phr.) **come into contact with** —*a town, its places of business* E.
2 stain —*an altar, sword* (w.dat. *w. blood*) B. E.; (of foam fr. horses' mouths) —*the ground* (w.dat. *w. drops*) A. ‖ mid. **stain** —*one's hand* (w.dat. *w. blood*) S.
3 (intr.) **apply colour** (to a painting) Pl. ‖ mid. **darken oneself, get a tan** Ar. ‖ pass. (of a city) **be blackened** —w.dat. *by smoke* A.
4 defile —*a shrine, priestess, gods, their names, another man's bed* (sts. w.dat. *w. impious behaviour, the taint of pollution, or sim.*) Trag. Pl.; (of a goddess) —*her eyes* (w.dat. *w. a man's dying moments*) E. ‖ pass. (of a city) **be defiled** (by a polluted person) S.; (of the earth) —w.dat. *by the pollution of spilt blood* A.

χραισμέω *contr.vb.* | aor. ἐχραίσμησα, aor.2 ἔχραισμον | usu. in neg.phr. | **1** (of persons, gods, weapons) **ward off** —*death* (w.dat. *fr. someone*) Il. —*Zeus* (*fr. Hera*) Il.
2 (of persons, gods, a defensive wall, or sim.) **protect, save** —w.dat. *someone* (*esp. in battle*) Il. AR.; **be of help** (to someone, in a battle or contest) Il. AR.

χράομαι *mid.contr.vb.* [χρή] | 2sg. χρῇ, 3sg. χρῆται, Ion. χρᾶται, 2pl. χρῆσθε, Ion.3pl. χρέωνται | imperatv. χρῶ, Ion. χρέο, 3pl. χρήσθων | inf. χρῆσθαι, Ion. χρᾶσθαι | ptcpl. χρώμενος, Ion. χρεώμενος | impf. ἐχρώμην, 2sg. ἐχρῶ, 3sg. ἐχρῆτο, Ion. ἐχρᾶτο, 3pl. ἐχρῶντο, Ion. ἐχρέωντο | fut. χρήσομαι | aor. ἐχρησάμην, imperatv. χρῆσαι | pf. κέχρημαι, ptcpl. κεχρημένος, plpf. ἐκεχρήμην, 3sg. ἐκέχρητο, 3pl. ἐκέχρηντο | fut.pf. κεχρήσομαι ‖ pass.: aor. ἐχρήσθην ‖ neut.impers.vbl.adj. χρηστέον ‖ For the act.vb. see below. |
1 seek a prophecy from, consult —w.dat. *an oracle, god, seer, the movements of birds* Od. Hdt. Ar. Pl. X. Aeschin.; **consult an oracle** Od. hHom. Hdt. Th. Arist.; **consult a seer** E.
2 use, employ —w.dat. *someone or sthg.* (freq. w.adv. or prep.phr. *in a certain way, for a certain purpose*) Il. Hdt. S. E. Th. Ar. +—(w.predic.sb. *as someone or sthg.*) Th. Isoc. X. ‖ pass. (of things) **be made use of** Hdt. D.
3 (of a historian) **use as one's source** —w.dat. *epic poets* Hdt.
4 (of a people) **make habitual use of, use, have** —w.dat. *certain foods, clothing, customs, or sim.* Hdt. Ar.
5 (esp. statv.pf.) **have** —w.dat. *a good mind, bad mind, certain qualities, differences* Od. Thgn. Arist.
6 engage in, practise —w.dat. *trades, activities, or sim.* Hdt. E. Att.orats. Pl. +; **act** —w.adv. *in a certain way* X.
7 be familiar with —w.dat. *someone or sthg.* Th. And. Ar. X. ‖ pres.ptcpl.sb. **associate, companion** Hdt.
8 have sexual relations with —w.dat. *a man or woman* Hdt. Att.orats. X.
9 deal with, handle —w.dat. *someone or sthg.* Hdt. Att.orats. Pl. +
10 treat —w.dat. *someone* (w.adv. *in a particular way*) Hdt. Pl. —(w.predic.sb. *as a friend, enemy, teacher, or sim.*) A. Hdt. E. Th. Att.orats. +
11 indulge, give in to —w.dat. *desires, anger, pride* Hdt. S. Th.
12 be subject to, suffer —w.dat. *sthg.* A. Pi. Hdt. E. Th. Att.orats. +; **experience** —w.dat. *sthg.* Hdt. S. E. And. Pl. +
13 (esp. statv.pf.) **long for, be eager for** —w.gen. *oracular pronouncements, food, drink, a safe return home* Hom. Hes. Emp. E.; **need, want** —w.gen. *someone or sthg.* Od. Hes. Anacr. Asius S. E. Theoc. —*someone* (w.predic.sb. *as a poet, to commemorate one's deeds*) Theoc.; (intr.) **be in need, be destitute** Od. Hes. E. Pl.

—χράω *act.contr.vb.* | 3sg. χρῇ (S.), Ion. χρᾷ | Ion.ptcpl. χρέων (ep. χρείων), fem. χρέωσα | impf. ἔχρεον (also ἔχραον AR.), 3sg. ἔχρη | fut. χρήσω | aor. ἔχρησα | pf. κέχρηκα ‖ pass.: aor. ἐχρήσθην | pf.ptcpl. κεχρησμένος (Hdt.) | 3sg.plpf. ἐκέχρηστο | —also (pres., in sense 6) **χρηννύω**, **χρήννῡμι** *vb.* | only inf. χρηννύειν and χρηννύναι (Thphr.) | —also (pres., in sense 6) **κίχρημι** (D.)| ptcpl. κιχράς (Plu.), mid.inf. κίχρασθαι (Thphr.) |
1 (of gods, oracles, seers) **deliver a prophecy** Od. hHom. A. Hdt.; (tr.) **deliver** —*an oracle, a prophecy* Thgn. E.; **declare in an oracle** —*the will of Zeus* hHom. ‖ pass. (of oracles) **be delivered** Hdt.
2 prophesy (usu. w.dat. *to someone*) —*sthg.* Pi. Hdt. E. —w.acc. + inf. *that sthg. will happen* A. Ar. Lycurg. ‖ pass. (of things) **be prophesied or foretold** (in an oracle) Pi. Hdt. S. E. ‖ impers.pass. **it is foretold** (w.dat. *to someone*) —w.acc. + inf. *that sthg. will happen* Hdt. Th.
3 ordain, proclaim —*someone* (w.predic.sb. *as such and such*) Pi.
4 ordain, decree —*sthg.* Hdt. S. E.
5 instruct, command —w.dat. + inf. *someone to do sthg.* A. Th. ‖ pass. (of a person) **be instructed** (by an oracle) —w.inf. *to do sthg.* A. ‖ impers.pass. **an instruction is given** (in an oracle) —w.dat. + inf. *for someone to do sthg.* Hdt.
6 lend, make available, furnish —*money, commodities, a building, or sim.* (freq. w.dat. *to someone*) Hdt. Ar. X. D. Thphr. + —*one's name* (*to persons, their activities*) Plu.; (of Fortune) —*her gifts* Men. Plb. ‖ mid. **borrow** —*sthg.* (w.prep.phr. *fr. someone*) E. Thphr.

χραύω *vb.* [reltd. χραεῖν] | only 3sg.aor.subj. χραύσῃ | (of a shepherd) **graze with a blow, wound** —*a lion* Il.

χράω *contr.vb.*: see under χράομαι

χρέα (nom.acc.pl.), **χρέᾰ** (ep.): see χρέος

χρείᾱ ᾱς, Ion. **χρείη**¹ ης *f.* [χρή] **1 necessity, need** (w.gen. *for someone or sthg.*) Iamb.adesp. A. E. Pl. +; (w.inf. or compl.cl. *to do sthg., for someone to do sthg.*) NT.
2 (gener.) **necessity** (esp. as the reason for doing sthg.) S. E. Att.orats. +
3 (specif.) **need for action** A.; **stress** (of battle or sim.) A. S.
4 state of need, need, want (w.gen. of sthg.) S.; **lack, absence** (of sthg.) A. S.; (gener.) **indigence, destitution** S. E. Ar.
5 (concr.) **that which is needed, need, requirement** (of a person, a state; ref. to food, money, or sim.) Pl. X. Arist.; (specif.) **request** A. Th.
6 specific need or reason (for doing sthg.), **reason, purpose** S.; **task, errand** Plb. NT.; (wkr.sens.) **matter, business** Plb.
7 (gener.) **engagement in activity, activity** Arist. Plu.; (specif.) **military service** Arist. Plb.; **military engagement** Plb.
8 function or purpose (of a person or object); **function** (of sthg.) X.; **use, benefit, advantage** (of sthg.) S. Critias Pl. D.; (of a friend, child) Thgn. Pi. Antipho; **service** (provided by someone or sthg., esp. to the nation, a particular cause) Plb.
9 utilisation, profitable use (of sthg.) Pl.; (of friends, children, ref. to availing oneself of their talents) Pl. X.; (gener.) **use, employment** (of sthg.) Pl.
10 treatment (meted out to someone) Pl.
11 relationship (w. someone) Antipho; (betw. persons or things) Pl. Arist. Plu.

χρείη² (3sg.opt.): see χρή

χρειοῖ (ep.dat.sg.): see χρεώ
χρεῖος[1] *ep.n.*: see χρέος
χρεῖος[2] ον *adj.* [χρείᾱ] (of a person) **needy, destitute** A.; **in need** (W.GEN. of friends, supplies) E.
χρεισμολόγος *Boeot.adj.*: see under χρησμολόγος
χρειώ *ep.f.* (*or n.*): see χρεώ
χρειώδης ες *adj.* **1 necessary** ‖ NEUT.PL.SB. **necessities** Plu. **2 useful** ‖ NEUT.SB. **usefulness, helpfulness** (of someone or sthg.) Plu.; **expediency** Plu.
χρειῶν (ep.gen.pl.): see χρέος
χρείων (ep.ptcpl.): see χράω, under χράομαι
χρεμετίζω *vb.* (of horses) **neigh, whinny** Il. Hdt. Pl.
χρεμετισμός οῦ *m.* **neighing, whinnying** Ar. Plu.
χρέμπτομαι *mid.vb.* **clear one's throat** E.*Cyc.* Ar.
χρέο (Ion.mid.imperatv.): see χράομαι
χρεο-κοπίδαι (v.l. **χρεω-**) ῶν *m.pl.* [χρέος, κόπτω] **debt-cutters** (pejor. name for people who run up debts which they have no intention of repaying) Plu.
χρεόν *Ion.indecl.n.*: see χρεών
χρέος χρέους, ep. **χρεῖος** χρείους, Att. **χρέως** χρέως *n.* [χρή] | nom.acc.pl. χρέᾰ, ep. χρέᾱ (Hes.) | gen.pl. χρεῶν, ep. χρειῶν | ep.dat.pl. χρήεσσι (AR.) |
1 need (W.GEN. for a person, an object) Od. Ar.; **request, requirement** A.
2 (usu. w.neg.connot.) **debt, obligation to pay recompense** (esp. for stolen cattle) Hom.; (fig., ref. to payback, in the form of revenge for a massacre) Il.; **obligation to give requital** (for crimes or sim.), **burden of guilt** (incurred by someone) Thgn.; **curse** (incurred by a person or city) S.; **burden, penalty** (W.GEN. of a curse) A.; that which is to be exacted, **requital** (owed by someone) S. Plu.
3 (w. positive connot.) **sacred duty, sacred obligation** (to build a temple, sing a praise-song) Pi. B.; (ref. to a praise-song) Pi.
4 obligation, indebtedness (to someone) Thgn. A. Hdt.
5 (specif.) **debt** (of money) Hes. Hdt. Ar. Att.orats. Pl. +; **loan** Hdt. Is.
6 purpose, goal (of a person) Trag.; **reason** (for sthg.) Parm.
7 task, duty (entrusted to a person) Trag.; **function, role** (of a person) Pi. E.; **use, employment** (W.GEN. of a person, to do sthg.) Bion
8 concern, business (in which one is engaged) Od. A. E.
9 (gener.) **matter, thing** A.; (phr.) τί χρέος; *what's the matter?, what's happened?* A.
10 occurrence, event Theoc.; (specif.) **unfortunate occurrence, stroke of misfortune** E. Ar.
11 remarkable or formidable thing, **wonder, marvel** (ref. to a huge herd of deer) Call.
12 (prep.phrs.) κατὰ χρέος *as required* hHom.; παρὰ χρέος *right away* Call. | cf. παραχρῆμα
χρεώ, ep. **χρειώ**, οὓς *f.* (perh. also *n.*) [χρή] | ep.dat.sg. χρειοῖ | χρειώ is usu. monosyllab. | **1 need** (oft. W.GEN. of someone or sthg.) Hom. AR. Theoc.; (W.INF. to do sthg.) Od. AR.
2 lack, want (W.GEN. of sthg.) Il.; (gener.) **state of need** Hom.
3 necessity (as the reason for sthg.) Hom. Sol. Call. AR.; **compulsion, act of being compelled** (by the Muses, to do sthg.) AR.; compulsion of fate, **destiny** AR.
4 ‖ ELLIPT. (w. vb. understd.) **there is a need, it is necessary** —W.INF. or ACC. + INF. (*for someone*) *to do sthg.* Hom. Parm. Call. AR.
5 ‖ ELLIPT. (w. vb. understd.) **a need or necessity affects** —W.ACC. *someone* Hom. • τίπτε δέ σε χρεώ; *what do you want?* Hom. • χρεὼ βουλῆς ἐμὲ καὶ σέ *you and I need a plan* Il.
6 purpose, goal AR.; **reason** (W.GEN. for sthg.) AR.

7 (wkr.sens.) **concern, matter** AR.; (gener.) **thing** AR.
8 [χράομαι 1, χράω 1–2] **prophecy** AR.
χρεωκοπίδαι *m.pl.*: see χρεοκοπίδαι
χρεωλυτέω *contr.vb.* [χρέος, λύω] **pay off debt**; **pay for** —*a purchase made on credit* Plu.
χρεώμενος (Ion.mid.ptcpl.): see χράομαι
χρεών, Ion. **χρεόν** *indecl.n.* [χρή, reltd. χρεώ] | Usu. as nom. or acc.; sts. w. ἐστί, but more oft. w. quasi-vbl. force. The form χρεών is oft. monosyllab. |
1 ‖ IMPERS. (sts. w. ἐστί) **it is necessary** —W.INF. *to do sthg.* Pi. Hdt. Trag. Th. + —W.ACC. + INF. *for someone to do sthg., that sthg. shd. be the case* Parm. Hdt. Trag. +; (quasi-ptcpl.) **it being necessary, since it is or was necessary** (to do sthg.) Hdt. ‖ SB. **that which is necessary or inevitable** E.
2 ‖ IMPERS. **it is predestined** —W.ACC. + INF. *that someone shd. do sthg., that sthg. shd. be the case* Trag. +; **it is inevitable** —W.COMPL.CL. *that sthg. shd. be the case* Pl. ‖ SB. **that which is predestined** E.; (ref. to the content of an oracle) Plu.; **inescapable destiny** Pl.
3 ‖ IMPERS. **it is right or fitting** —W.INF. *to do sthg.* Hdt. Trag. + —W.ACC. + INF. *for someone to do sthg., that sthg. shd. be the case* Pi. Hdt. Trag. +; **it is right** (for someone to do sthg.) Sol.; (quasi-ptcpl. or quasi-advbl., ref. to someone being in power) **rightfully** Th. ‖ SB. **that which is fitting** A.
4 ‖ IMPERS. (wkr.sens., equiv. to *you should, one should*) **it is advisable** —W.INF. *to do sthg.* Thgn. A. +
χρεών (gen.pl.): see χρέος
χρεών (Ion.ptcpl.): see χράω, under χράομαι
χρέωνται (Ion.3pl.mid.): see χράομαι
χρέως *Att.n.*: see χρέος
χρέωσα (Ion.fem.nom.ptcpl.): see χράω, under χράομαι
χρεώστης ου *m.* [χρέος] **debtor** Plu.
χρεωφειλέτης ου *m.* [χρέος, ὀφειλέτης] **one who is in debt, debtor** (sts. W.GEN. by a certain amount or to someone) NT. Plu.; (fig.) **person who is in one's debt** (opp. benefactor) Plu.
χρή, Aeol. **χρῆ** *3sg.impers.vb.* | subj. χρῇ, opt. χρείη, inf. χρῆναι, also χρῆν | impf. χρῆν, also ἐχρῆν | fut. χρήσται (sts. written χρῇσται), also χρήσει | The wd., originally a noun in impers. constr. χρή (ἐστί), came to be treated as a vb., its forms originating in contractions: χρῆν for χρὴ ἦν, χρήσται for χρὴ ἔσται. From these developed alternative vbl. forms ἐχρῆν and χρήσει. ‖ The impf. is oft. used as a simple past tense, *it was necessary* or *fitting*, but can also have counterfactual force: see section 4. |
1 it is necessary (to do sthg.) Hom. + —W.INF. or ACC. + INF. (*for someone*) *to do sthg.* Hom. + ‖ NEUT.SB. **necessity** E.
2 it is predestined (for sthg. to happen) E. —W.ACC. + INF. *for someone to do sthg., for sthg. to happen* A. Hdt. + ‖ NEUT.SB. **destiny** E.
3 it is right, it is fitting (for someone to do sthg.) Trag. + —W.INF. or ACC. + INF. (*for someone*) *to do sthg.* Hom. +
4 ‖ IMPF. (w. counterfactual force, esp. in phr. ὡς χρῆν or sim., ref. to present or past) **it would be or would have been fitting** (for sthg. to happen), **it ought to be or ought to have been the case** A. Hdt. +
5 (gener., oft. equiv. to *you should, one should*) **it is best, it would be best** —W.INF. *to do sthg.* Hom. + —W.ACC. + INF. *that someone shd. do sthg.* Sol. +; (wkr.sens., equiv. to *you could, one might, or sim.*) Hdt. Th. +
6 there is a need —W.GEN. + ACC. *of sthg. for someone* (i.e. *someone needs sthg., or sthg. is fitting for someone*) Hom. • τί με χρὴ μητέρος αἴνου; *why need I praise my mother?* Od. • οὐδέ τί σε χρὴ ταύτης ἀφροσύνης *and you should not show such folly* Il.

χρή[1] (2sg.mid.): see χράομαι
χρή[2] (3sg.): see χράω, under χράομαι
χρή[3] (3sg.): see χρήω
χρή[4] (3sg.subj.): see χρή
χρήεσσι (ep.dat.pl.): see χρέος
χρῄζω[1], Ion. **χρηΐζω**, Megar. **χρῄδδω** (Ar.), dial. **χρῆσδω** (Theoc.) vb. [χρή] | Ion.fut. χρηΐσω | Ion.aor. ἐχρήϊσα |
1 have need of, need —W.GEN. *a doctor* Il. —*someone* (W.PREDIC.SB. *as a teacher*) A.
2 need, lack —W.GEN. *clothes, a means of making a living* Od. Hes.; (intr.) **be in need, be destitute** Od. Hes. Thgn.
3 desire, want —W.GEN. sthg. Od. Hes. Hdt. Trag. + —W.ACC. sthg. Trag. + —W.INF. *to do sthg.* Sol. Trag. Th. + —W.DBL.GEN. *sthg., fr. someone* Hdt.; (intr.) **feel desire** (for someone) Thgn.
4 ask for —W.GEN. or ACC. sthg. Hdt.; **ask** —W.GEN. or ACC. + INF. *someone, to do sthg.* Hdt. || NEUT.PTCPL.SB. **desire or request** E.
5 be willing (oft. in ptcpl. w. quasi-conditional force, *if willing*) A. E. X.
χρῄζω[2] vb. [χράομαι] **prophesy, deliver a prophecy** E.
χρηΐσκομαι Ion.mid.vb. [χρή] (of farmers) **be in need** —W.DAT. *of water* Hdt.
χρῆμα ατος n. [χράομαι] **1 material possession** || PL. **possessions, belongings, property** (of a person) Od. +; **resources** (of a person) Od. +; **valuables, treasure** Od. +; **stock** (ref. to cattle) hHom.; **goods, merchandise** hHom. +
2 || PL. **riches, wealth** Od. +; (gener.) **money** Hdt. + || SG. **sum of money** Hdt. +
3 matter, issue, event Hes. +
4 undertaking Hes. Thgn. +
5 act, action Alc. +
6 thing, happening Archil. +; τί χρῆμα ...; *what (thing)?* Trag. Ar.; τί χρῆμα; *what?* S. E.; (also) *why?* E.
7 striking thing, thing, creature (appos. W.ADJ. specifying the noteworthy quality) Hdt. + • σοφόν τι χρῆμ' ἄνθρωπος *man is a clever creature* Theoc.; (periphr., W.GEN. of the thing referred to) • ὑὸς χρῆμα μέγιστον *a monster of a boar* Hdt. • λιπαρὸν τὸ χρῆμα τῆς πόλεος *a splendid sort of city* Ar.
8 (esp. W.ADJ. πολλόν, μέγα *great* or ὅσον *how great*) **striking quantity, swarm, mass** (W.GEN. of animals, persons, objects) Hdt. +
9 oracle Emp.
χρηματίζω vb. | fut. χρηματιῶ | aor. ἐχρημάτισα || neut.impers.vbl.adj. χρηματιστέον | **1** (of rulers, envoys, councils, or sim.) **conduct one's business** Th. Att.orats. +; **conduct, deal with** —W.INTERN.ACC. *a particular piece of business* Th. Isoc. Plu.
2 deliberate —W. περί + GEN. *about sthg.* Ar. D. Arist.; **discuss, deliberate on** —W.ACC. sthg. D. Arist.
3 (of an individual) **raise a matter** —W.DAT. *w. the Council or Assembly* X.
4 (act. and mid., of envoys, leaders, assemblies, or sim.) **engage in negotiations** Th. D. —W.DAT. *w. someone, rival states* Hdt. Th. D.; (act., of an assembly) **give an audience** —W.DAT. *to someone* X. Plb. || MID. (of a person) **get an audience** —W.DAT. *w. someone, an assembly* Hdt. X.
5 || MID. **make money** Th. Pl. Is. —W.DAT. *for someone, oneself* Pl. —W.PREP.PHR. *fr. sthg.* Isoc. Pl. —*at the expense of someone or the state* Att.orats. Arist.; **make, generate** —W.COGN. or INTERN.ACC. *profit, returns, money* Pl. X. Arist.; **extort money from** —W.ACC. *someone* Plb.
6 assume the title of —W.PREDIC.SB. *king, the new Isis* Plb. Plu.; (of the followers of Jesus) **call oneself, be called** —W.PREDIC.SB. *Christians* NT.

7 || PASS. **be told in a divine message** (fr. an angel or sim.) —W.INF. *to do sthg.* NT. || IMPERS.PASS. **a divine message is given** (to someone, fr. the Holy Spirit) —W.INF. *that sthg. will happen* NT.
χρηματικός ή όν adj. **1** (of a penalty) **of money** (i.e. a fine) Plu.; (of contracts) **commercial** Plu.
2 (of persons) **wealthy through commerce** Plu.
χρημάτισις εως f. **money-making** X.
χρηματισμός οῦ m. **1** (freq.pejor.) **money-making** Isoc. Pl. X. D. Arist. +; **opportunity to make money** D. Plu.; **generation of revenue** Plu.
2 conducting of business, negotiation (w. envoys) Plb.
χρηματιστήριον ου n. **place of business** Plu.
χρηματιστής οῦ m. **1** (freq.pejor.) **money-maker** Pl. X. D. Arist. Plu.
2 (w. neutral connot.) **businessman** Pl.
3 | ADJ. (of a lifestyle) **devoted to making money** Arist.
χρηματιστικός ή όν adj. **1** (of persons) **devoted to making money** Pl.; (of the art, a strategy) **of** or **for making money** Pl. Arist. Plu.; (of activities) **money-making, profiteering** Plu.
2 (of a category of seafarers) **involved in commerce** (opp. warfare) Arist.
3 (of an omen) **predicting profit** X.
4 (of persons) **moneyed, rich** Pl.; (of dwellings) **of rich men** Pl.
5 (of activities, inclinations) **productive, beneficial, positive** Pl.
6 (of a tent, hall) **for conducting state business, for holding negotiations** Plb.
χρηματο-δαίτᾱς ᾱ dial.m. [δαίομαι²] **divider of possessions**; (fig., ref. to a sword, as settler of a dispute about inheritance) **divider** (W.GEN. of property) A.
χρηματο-ποιός όν adj. [ποιέω] **1** (of a trade) **profitable** X.
2 (of women) **industrious** Ar.
χρηματο-φθορικός ή όν adj. [φθείρω] (of a category of debating) **wasting money, financially harmful** Pl.
χρήμη ης Ion.f. [χρή, χράομαι] **need, lack** (W.GEN. of subsistence) Archil.
χρημοσύνη ης f. **state of need, need, indigence** Thgn.
χρῆν (pres.inf. and 3sg.impf.), **χρῆναι** (pres.inf.): see χρή
χρηννύειν, **χρηννύναι** (infs.): see χράω, under χράομαι
χρῇς (2sg.): see χρήω
χρῆσαι (aor.mid.imperatv.): see χράομαι
χρήσει (3sg.fut.): see χρή
χρῆσθα (Megar.2sg.): see χρήω
χρῆσθαι (mid.inf.), **χρῆσθε** (2pl.), **χρήσθων** (3pl.imperatv.): see χράομαι
χρήσιμος η ον (also ος ον) adj. [χράομαι] | compar. χρησιμώτερος, superl. χρησιμώτατος | **1** (of objects, tools, stratagems, circumstances, advice, or sim.) **useful, helpful, handy** (sts. W.DAT. for someone, sts. W.PREP.PHR. for or in response to sthg.) Thgn. Hdt. S. E. Th. +; (gener.) **advantageous, beneficial** Hdt. Th. || NEUT.IMPERS. (w. ἐστί, sts. understd.) **it is beneficial** —W.INF. *to do sthg.* E. Th. Ar. + —W.ACC. + INF. *that sthg. shd. be the case* Th. || NEUT.SB. **that which is in the interest** (of someone) Th.; **advantage, usefulness** (of sthg.) E. Th. Att.orats. +; **expediency** Th.
2 (of persons) **useful, helpful, obliging** (oft. W.DAT. to someone) Hdt. E. Pl. +; (W.DAT. to the state) E. D. || MASC.SB. **useful or productive citizen** Att.orats. +
3 (of a person's physique) **of service, serviceable** (W.DAT. to the state) E.; (of persons) **able-bodied** X. Aeschin.
4 (of persons) **excellent, praiseworthy** S. || NEUT.SB. **excellence, praiseworthiness** (of one's attitude) E.
5 able to be used; (of money) **legal tender** X.

6 made use of; (of medicinal substances) **used** (W.DAT. by people, w. ἐς + ACC. to treat certain diseases) Hdt.; (of resin, w. ἐς + ACC. for perfumes) Hdt.; (of a sacred site) **visited** (by people) Hdt.
—**χρησίμως** *adv.* **usefully, productively, with beneficial effects** (sts. W.DAT. for someone or sthg.) Th. X. Plu.
χρῆσις εως (Ion. ιος) *f.* **1** act of making use, **use, employment** (of an object, stratagem, or sim.) Isoc. Pl. X. Arist. +
2 productive use, **enjoyment** (esp. of wealth) Pi. Isoc. X. Arist. Plu.; (gener.) **possession** (of wealth, a lawcode) Isoc. Pl.
3 engagement (in an activity, civic life, military operations, sexual acts) Th. Isoc. Pl. Arist. Plb.; **behaviour** (ref. to sexual practices) Plb.
4 (sg. and pl.) **interaction, dealings** (w. someone, betw. people) X. Arist.; state of intimacy, **familiarity, intimacy** (w. a person, rival power) Isoc. Arist.; act of intimacy, **intimate contact** (w. someone) Arist.
5 need (for sthg.) Pi. X. Plu.
6 usefulness, advantage (of sthg.) Th. D.
7 oracular command (fr. a seer) Pi.
8 lending (of money without interest, opp. δανεισμός *lending at interest*) Arist.; (of books) Plb.
χρησμολογέω *contr.vb.* [χρησμολόγος] **prophesy** —*sthg.* Ar.; (intr.) **deliver a prophecy** Ar.
χρησμολογίᾱ ᾱς *f.* **interpretation of oracles** Plu.
χρησμο-λόγος ου *m.* [χρησμός, λέγω] **1** one who utters prophecies, **seer** Hdt. Arist.
2 one who collects and interprets oracles, **oracle-monger** Hdt. Th. Ar. X. Arist. Plu.
—**χρεισμολόγος** ον *Boeot.adj.* (of truth) **prophetic, oracular** Corinn.
χρησμός οῦ *m.* [χράομαι] **oracular message, oracle, prophecy, oracular command** Pi. Hdt. Trag. Th. Ar. +
χρησμοσύνη ης *f.* [χρή] **1 state of need, want** Tyrt. AR.
2 request (to someone, to do sthg.) Hdt.
3 help (given to someone) AR.
χρησμῳδέω *contr.vb.* [χρησμῳδός] **1 utter prophecies** Hdt. Ar. Pl. X. D.; **speak in an oracular fashion** Pl. X.
2 describe (W.ACC. sthg.) **in prophetic terms** Pl. ‖ PASS. (of a statement) be taken as an oracle (i.e. as a truth gnomically expressed) Pl.
χρησμῳδίᾱ ᾱς *f.* **prophecy** A. Pl.
χρησμ-ῳδός όν *adj.* [χρησμός, ἀοιδή] **1** (of the Sphinx) **singing prophetically** S.
2 (of songs) **prophetic, oracular** E.*fr.*
3 ‖ MASC.SB. **chanter of oracles** Pl.
χρήσομαι (fut.mid.): see χράομαι
χρῆσται, χρῆσται (3sg.fut.): see χρή
χρηστέον (neut.impers.vbl.adj.): see χράομαι
χρηστηριάζομαι *mid.vb.* [χρηστήριον] **consult an oracle** (sts. W.PREP.PHR. about sthg.) Hdt. X. Arist.; **seek an oracle** —W.DAT. *fr. a god* Hdt. —W.DAT. *fr. sacrificial offerings* Hdt.
χρηστήριον ου *n.* [χράομαι] **1 oracle** (ref. to the place, as a source of prophecies) Hes.*fr.* hHom. A. Pi. Hdt. E. +
2 oracular pronouncement, oracle, prophecy Hdt. Trag. Th. Lycurg.
3 divinatory sacrifice, sacrificial victim A. E.; (fig., ref. to sheep butchered by Ajax in his madness) S.
χρηστήριος ᾱ ον (also ος ον) *adj.* **1** giving an oracle; (of Apollo, the Delphic tripod, birds) **oracular, prophetic** A. Hdt. E.; (of a name) E.
2 given in an oracle; (of instructions) **oracular** A.
3 (of the robes) **of a prophet** A.

χρήστης ου *m.* [χράω] ‖ gen.pl. χρήστων (so accented) ‖
1 one who has lent money, **creditor** Ar. Att.orats. Plu.
2 one who owes money; **ower** (W.GEN. of money) D.; **debtor** D.
χρηστικός ή όν *adj.* [χρηστός] **1** (of a way of life) **making use** (of things, opp. manufacturing them) Arist.; (of a skill) **in making use** (W.GEN. of slaves) Arist.
2 (of a person's physique) **serviceable** Plu.
χρηστογραφίᾱ ᾱς *f.* [γράφω] **skill in painting** Plu.
χρηστο-ήθης ες *adj.* [ἦθος] (of a person) **of good character** Arist.
χρηστός ή όν *adj.* [χράομαι] ‖ The wd. is freq. contrasted w. πονηρός *bad.* ‖ **1** (freq. in neg.phr., of things) **useful, of use, serviceable** Xenoph. Hdt. +; (of things, circumstances) **helpful, beneficial** Hdt. +
2 (of situations, results, or sim.) **favourable, successful** Hdt. Trag. +
3 (of things) of good quality, **good, excellent** Hdt. Ar. +; (of food) **delicious** Hdt. Ar. Thphr.
4 (of gods, as patrons) **helpful, beneficial** Hdt. +; (of persons, God) **kind** (W.PREP.PHR. to someone) D. NT.
5 (of persons) fulfilling one's duty, **dutiful, upstanding** Hdt. +; (W.ACC. in a particular respect) Th.; (W.PREP.PHR. towards the state) Th. +; (iron., of feckless or villainous persons) **fine, admirable** Ar. Pl. D. + ‖ MASC.SB. **upstanding citizen** Ar. + ‖ NEUT.SB. **upstanding sector** (of the populace) Ar.
6 (w. moral connot., of persons) **good, honest** Hdt. +; (of a person's actions, lifestyle, or sim.) S. E. +
7 (iron., of persons) **kind-hearted, generous** (w.connot. of naivety) Pl.
8 (of persons) **noble, well-bred** X.
—**χρηστῶς** *adv.* **1** in a good or helpful manner, **well** Hdt. Ar. Arist.; (iron.) Hdt.
2 well and truly, thoroughly Ar. Men.
χρηστότης ητος *f.* **1 excellence of character, goodness, probity, honesty** E. Is. Plb. Plu.
2 goodness of heart, kindness Plu.
χρηστοφιλίᾱ ᾱς *f.* [χρηστόφιλος] **friendship with good men** Arist.
χρηστό-φιλος ον *adj.* [φίλος] (of a person) **having good men as friends** Arist.
χρήσω (fut.): see χράω, under χράομαι
χρῆται (3sg.mid.): see χράομαι
χρήω *vb.* [χρή, χρήζω] ‖ only 2sg. χρῇς, Megar. χρῆσθα, 3sg. χρῇ ‖ **want** (to do sthg.) S. Ar. —W.INF. *to do sthg.* S.
χρῖμα (sts. written **χρῖσμα**) ατος *n.* [χρίω] **unguent, ointment** (usu. ref. to perfumed oil or ointment intended for everyday use, such as after a bath or in religious rites) Xenoph. A. Philox.Leuc. X. Thphr. Call.
χρίμπτω *vb.* ‖ aor. ἔχριμψα ‖ PASS.: aor. ἐχρίμφθην ‖
1 (tr.) **bring** (sthg.) **near** (to sthg. else); **keep** (W.ACC. one's feet) **close** —W.DAT. *to a shore* A.; (of a charioteer) **bring close** —*the hub of his chariot wheel* (*to the turning-post*) S.; (of a hoplite) —*his flanks* (W.DAT. *to his neighbour's*) E.(cj.) ‖ MID. (of a bull) **dash, butt** —*its head* (W.PREP.PHR. *against a person's ribs*) Theoc.
2 (of ground struck by hooves) **send** (W.ACC. a noise) **right up** —W.DAT. *to the ear* A.
3 graze —*one's ankle* (W.DAT. *against a rock*) AR.
4 (intr.) **draw near, come close** AR. —W.DAT. or PREP.PHR. *to a person or place* E. AR.; **meet with, encounter** —W.DAT. *a storm* AR.

χρῖσμα

5 ‖ MID. and AOR.PASS. **draw near, come close** Od. —W.DAT. or PREP.PHR. *to a person or place* hHom. A. E.; (of a noise) Pi.; (fig., of a speaker) —W.PREP.PHR. *to a person's mind* (*i.e.* stir memory or feelings) E.(cj.)

χρῖσμα *n.*: see χρῖμα

Χριστιᾱνός οῦ *m.* [χριστός] follower of the teachings of Christ, **Christian** NT.

χριστός ή όν *adj.* [χρίω] (of medicine) to be used as ointment, **in the form of ointment** A. E.

—Χριστός οῦ *m.* he who has been anointed (by God, investing him w. divine authority on earth; ref. to the Jewish Messiah), **the anointed one** NT.; (as the title of Jesus) **Christ** NT.

χρίω *vb.* | impf. ἔχρῑον, iteratv. χρίεσκον | fut. χρίσω | aor. ἔχρῑσα ‖ PASS.: aor. ἐχρίσθην | pf. κέχρῑμαι, also κέχρῑσμαι | **1 anoint** *—someone* (W.DAT. *w. oil, usu. after a bath*) Hom. hHom. AR. *—a person, corpse or wound* (*w. ambrosia, as a protective or immortalising agent*) Il. hHom. AR. Bion *—gravestones* (*w. perfume*) Plu. ‖ MID. **anoint** *—one's body* (*w. oil*) Plu. *—one's breast* (W.DAT. *w. perfume*) Anacr.; **anoint oneself** (freq. W.DAT. w. oil or perfume) Od. Hes. Pi. X. Call. Theoc. Plu. ‖ PASS. be anointed —W.PREP.PHR. *by someone* Hdt.
2 (fig., of God) **anoint, consecrate** *—Jesus* NT. —(W.DAT. *w. the Holy Spirit*) NT. *—Isaiah* (W.INF. *to preach*) NT.
3 anoint *—garments* (W.DAT. *w. poison*) S. E. Plu.; (of Aphrodite) *—an arrow* (*w. desire*) E.; (mid.) *—arrows* (*w. poison*) Od.
4 ‖ MID. **smear** *—one's face* (W.DAT. *w. soot*) Plu. *—one's body* (*w. red ochre*) Hdt.; **smear oneself** —W.DAT. *w. soot* Plu. ‖ PASS. (of a person) be smeared —W.DAT. *w. ashes* Call.; (of a knife) *—w. poison* Plu.; (of objects) *—w. pitch, bitumen, madder, gold paint* Hdt. X.
5 (of a gadfly) **sting** *—someone* A.; (app., of a poisoned robe, also w. allusion to sense 3) *—a person's sides* S. ‖ PASS. be stung —W.DAT. *by a gadfly* A.

χρόᾱ Att.f.: see χροιά

χρόα (acc.sg.), **χροΐ** (dat.sg.): see χρώς

χροιά (also dial. **χροιά** Call.) ᾶς, Ion. **χροιή** ῆς, Att. **χρόᾱ** ᾱς *f.* [χρώς] **1 skin** (of a person) Mimn.(or Thgn.) Ar. AR.; (gener.) **body** Il.
2 surface (of an object) Thgn. Pl. Arist.
3 colour (of things) Sapph. A. Pi. Emp. E.*Cyc.* Pl. +
4 complexion (of a person) Sol. A. E. Ar. Pl. AR. +; **facial expression** E.

χροΐζω *vb.* [χρώζω] | dial.fut.mid.pass. χροΐζοῦμαι (Theoc.) | **caress** *—a sexual partner* E. ‖ MID.PASS. give or enjoy caresses Pi. Call. Theoc.

χρόμαδος ου *m.* [χρεμετίζω] grinding sound, **crunching** (W.GEN. of jaws, in a fistfight) Il.

χρονίζω *vb.* [χρόνος] | aor. ἐχρόνισα | pf. κεχρόνικα ‖ PASS.: aor.ptcpl. χρονισθείς | **1 spend time** —W.PREP.PHR. *in a place* Hdt. Plb.
2 spend a long time, **linger** E. —W.PREDIC.ADJ. *away fr. home* E. —W.PTCPL. *doing sthg.* E.
3 keep on —W.PTCPL. *doing sthg.* Pl.; **persist** —W.DAT. *in a state of anger* Arist.; (of a state of affairs) **last, continue** A. ‖ PASS. (of a war) be prolonged And.; (of friendship) Arist.
4 ‖ PASS. (of a lion cub, Justice) be matured by time A.
5 spend a long time (before doing sthg.), **delay** A. E.
6 take a long time (to arrive), **delay, be late** Th. NT. —W.INF. *in arriving* NT.; (of punishment) **be delayed** A.(dub.); (of peace) **be overdue** E.*fr.* ‖ PASS. (of information) be delayed A.

χρονικός ή όν *adj.* (of criteria) based on time, **chronological** Plu. ‖ NEUT.PL.SB. chronological data Plu.

χρόνιος ᾱ ον (also ος ον) *adj.* **1** happening after a long time; (of events or circumstances) **long-awaited, long-delayed, eventual** A. Pi. E. Th.
2 (quasi-advbl., of persons arriving, being seen, or sim.) **after a long time, at last** Od. Lyr.adesp. S. E. Ar.(quot. E.) Theoc.
3 taking a long time (before doing sthg.); (of persons) **slow** (to act) S. Th.
4 extending over a long time; (of events or circumstances) **long, lengthy, drawn-out** A. Th. Pl. Arist. Plb. Plu.; (of an old man's years) Ar.
5 (quasi-advbl., of a person being in a certain place or condition) **for a long time** E.
6 existing for a long time; (of a marriage) **of long duration** E.
7 belonging to a past time; (of an object) **from long ago** E.
8 (quasi-advbl., of a person suffering sthg.) **long ago** S.
9 continuing for a long time (into the future); (of circumstances) **enduring, lasting** Pi. E. Arist. Plu.
—χρόνια *neut.pl.adv.* after a long time, **at last** E.
—χρονιώτερον *compar.adv.* for a longer time, **longer** Pi.

χρονισμός οῦ *m.* [χρονίζω] **long-term stay** (of an army, in a place) Plb.

χρονογραφίᾱ ᾱς *f.* [χρόνος, γράφω] **chronological record** (of events) Plb.(dub.)

χρόνος ου *m.* **1** (abstr.) **time** (as that which passes) Eleg. Lyr. Hdt. Trag. +
2 (personif.) **Time** (as an agent of change or sim., sts. envisaged as a primordial deity) Sol. Lyr. Trag. +
3 period of time (of specified or unspecified duration), **time, length of time** Hom. +; (specif.) long time, **delay** D. Men.
4 specific point or period in time, **time, moment, occasion** Pi. Hdt. Trag. +; (advbl.phr.) ἕνα χρόνον *once and for all* Il.; (specif.) **date** (of a particular event) Hdt. Th. +
5 time during which or at which one is alive; **life, lifetime** (of a person) Pi. S.; **age** (esp. old age) A. S.
6 (advbl. and prep.phrs.) χρόνον *for a time* (usu. *a long time*) Od. Hdt. E.; (also) ἐπὶ χρόνον Hom. Hdt. AR.; (τῷ) χρόνῳ *in time, eventually, at last* Sol. Pi. Hdt. Trag. Th. +; (also) ἀνὰ χρόνον Hdt.; εἰς (ἐς) χρόνον Hdt. Arist. Men.; ἐν χρόνῳ Pi. Trag. Pl. +; μετὰ χρόνον Hdt. Call. AR.; σὺν (ξὺν) χρόνῳ A. S. Plb.; διὰ χρόνου *after an interval* (usu. *a long interval*) S. E. Th. Lys. Ar. Pl. +

χρονοτριβέω *contr.vb.* [τρίβω] **1 waste time** Arist. NT.
2 (tr.) **deliberately protract, spin out** *—a war* Plu.

χροός (ep. and dial.gen.sg.): see χρώς

χρουσοφαῖς (Boeot.masc.fem.acc.pl.): see χρῡσοφαής

χρῡσ-αιγις ιδος *fem.adj.* [χρῡσός, αἰγίς[1]] (of a goddess, perh. Athena) **with golden aigis** Ibyc.; (of Itonia, ref. to Athena) B.*fr.*

χρῡσᾰλάκατος *dial.adj.*: see χρῡσηλάκατος

χρῡσ-αμοιβός όν *adj.* (of Ares) **giving gold in exchange** (W.GEN. for bodies; fig.ref. to Ares as a money-changer, who gives gold dust, i.e. ashes, for the bodies of dead warriors) A.

χρῡσ-άμπυξ υκος *masc.fem.adj.* (of female deities) **with golden headband** Hes. hHom. Pi. B.; (of horses) Il.; (of a bridle) **forming a golden headband** Pi.

χρῡσάνιος *dial.adj.*: see χρῡσήνιος

χρῡσ-ανταυγής ές *adj.* (of flowers) **reflecting golden light** E.

χρῡσ-άορος ον *adj.* [ἄορ] (of a god or goddess) **with golden sword** Il. hHom. B. Hdt.(oracle) AR.

χρῡσ-άρματος ον *adj.* [ἅρμα] (of Athena, the Moon, Kastor, the descendants of Aiakos) **with golden chariot** Pi. B.

χρῡσ-ασπις ιδος *masc.fem.adj.* [ἀσπίς¹] (of Ares, Athena, Thebe) **with golden shield** Pi. B. E.

χρῡσ-αυγής ές *adj.* [αὐγή] (of flowers, the course of a star) **gold-gleaming** S. Ar.

χρῡσ-άωρ ορος *masc.fem.adj.* [ἄορ] **1** (of Apollo) **with golden sword** Hes. hHom. Pi.
2 (of Orpheus) app. **with golden lyre** Pi.*fr.*

χρῡσειος¹ (sts. written **χρῡσεῖος**) ᾱ ον *adj.* **of or for gold**; (of mines) **gold** Th. ‖ NEUT.PL.SB. **gold-mines** Pl. X. Plb. Plu.

χρῡσειος² *ep.Ion.adj.*: see χρῡσεος

χρῡσ-ελεφαντ-ήλεκτρος ον *adj.* [ἐλέφας, ἤλεκτρον] (of shields) **decorated with gold, ivory and amber** Plu.(quot.epigr.)

χρῡσ-ένδετος ον *adj.* [ἐνδέω¹] (of an emerald) **set in gold** Plu.

χρῡσεο-βόστρυχος ον *adj.* [χρῡσεος] (of Artemis) **with golden tresses** E.; (of Galateia) Philox.Cyth.

χρῡσεό-δμητος ον *adj.* [δέμω] (of a necklace) **fashioned in gold** A.(cj. χρῡσεόκμητος *worked in gold*)

χρῡσε-όδους οντος *masc.fem.adj.* [ὀδούς] (of a trident) **with golden teeth** Lyr.adesp.

χρῡσεο-κίθαρις ιδος *fem.adj.* [κιθάρᾱ] ‖ acc. -κίθαριν ‖ (of a Muse) **with golden kithara** Tim.

χρῡσεόκμητος *adj.*: see χρῡσεόδμητος

χρῡσεο-κόμᾱς ᾱ *dial.masc.adj.* [κόμη] (of Apollo) **golden-haired** Lyr.adesp.

χρῡσεό-κυκλος ον *adj.* [κύκλος] (of the light of the moon) **with golden disc** E.(v.l. χρῡσό-)

χρῡσεό-μαλλος, perh. also **χρῡσεόμαλλος** (cj. **χρῡσό-**), ον *adj.* [μαλλός] (of a sheep, sheepskin) **with golden fleece** E.

χρῡσεο-πήληξ ηκος *masc.fem.adj.* (of Athena) **with golden helmet** Call.

χρῡσεο-πήνητος ον *adj.* [πήνη] (of a robe) **woven with gold** E.

χρῡσεό-πλοκος ον *adj.* [πλέκω] (of ribbons) inwoven with gold, **gold-braided** B.

χρῡσεος ᾱ (Ion. η) ον, also contr. **χρῡσοῦς** ῆ οῦν, ep.Ion. **χρῡσειος** η ον, Aeol. and Lacon. **χρῡσιος** ᾱ ον *adj.* [χρῡσός] ‖ sts. ῠ *metri grat.* ‖ **1** made from or consisting of gold; (of objects) **of gold, golden** Hom. +; (of the possessions and attributes of the gods) Hom. +; (hyperbol., of the gods) Ar.
2 (of objects) ornamented with gold, **golden, gilded** Hom. +
3 (of a mythol. race of men) **of gold, golden** Hes. Pi. Plu.; (of one of the four castes or breeds of men in the ideal state, or of persons belonging to it) Pl.
4 ‖ MASC.SB. **gold coin** (ref. to a stater) Plb. Plu.
5 like gold (in colour); (of hair, flowers, objects) **golden** Hom. +; (of the sun, its might) Pi.
6 (of Aphrodite, the Muses) **golden** (i.e. radiant, perh. also w.connot. *golden-haired*) Hom. Hes. Mimn. Thgn. Pi.
7 (fig.) having the value or quality of gold; (of hope, honour, health, laws, or sim.) **golden** Pi. B.*fr.* S. Ar. Pl.; (of a person) Pl.

χρῡσεο-σάνδαλος, also **χρῡσεοσάμβαλος**, ον *adj.* [σάνδαλον] (of a person's steps) **in golden sandals** E.

χρῡσεό-σκᾱπτρος ον *dial.adj.* [σκῆπτρον] (of Zeus) **with golden sceptre** B.

χρῡσεό-στολμος ον *adj.* [στολμός] (of a house) **gold-decked** A.

χρῡσεό-στολος ον *adj.* [στόλος] (of a garment) **gold-decked** E.

χρῡσεόστροφος *adj.*: see χρῡσόστροφος

χρῡσεο-φάλαρος ον *adj.* [φάλαρα] (of the Trojan Horse) **with gold plates** or **bosses** E.(cj. χρῡσο-)

χρῡσ-ηλάκατος, dial. **χρῡσᾱλάκατος**, ον *adj.* [χρῡσός, ἠλακάτη] **1** (epith. of Artemis) **with golden distaff** Od.; (of goddesses and mythol. women) Pi. B.
2 (of Artemis) **with golden arrows** Il. Hes.*fr.* hHom. B. S.

χρῡσ-ήλατος ον *adj.* [ἐλαύνω] (of brooches, vessels, or sim.) **of beaten gold** Trag. Ar. Plu.; (of Apollo's bow-string) A.

χρῡσ-ήνιος, dial. **χρῡσᾱνιος**, ον *adj.* [ἡνία] (of a god or goddess) **with golden reins** Hom. Pi.*fr.* S.

χρῡσ-ήρης ες *adj.* [ἀραρίσκω] (of a temple, its friezes) fitted out with gold, **golden, gilded** E.; (fig., of the tail of the constellation Bear, depicted on a tapestry) E.

χρῡσῑδάριον ου *n.* [dimin. χρῡσίδιον] **little bit of gold** Arist.(quot. Ar.)

χρῡσίδιον ου *n.* [dimin. χρῡσίον] **1** ‖ COLLECTV.PL. **small items of gold, jewellery** Is. D.
2 small sum of money Plu.
3 (pejor.) **petty money** (dismissive ref. to wealth) Isoc.

χρῡσίον ου *n.* [dimin. χρῡσός] **1 gold** (ref. to the metal, as a commodity or a material for making coins and other objects) Hdt. Th. Ar. Att.orats. Pl. +
2 gold (ref. to a sum of money) Hdt. E.*Cyc.* Ar. Att.orats. Pl. +; (ref. to a particular issue or coinage) Ar.
3 object made of gold, **golden bowl** Scol. ‖ COLLECTV.PL. **gold ornaments, jewellery** Th. Ar. Is. D. Men. Plu.
4 (fig., ref. to a person, as a term of endearment) **jewel, treasure** Ar.

χρῡσιος Aeol. and Lacon.*adj.*: see χρῡσεος

χρῡσίς ίδος *f.* **golden bowl** or **goblet** Ar. D.

χρῡσῖτις ιδος *fem.adj.* (of sand) **containing gold** Hdt.

χρῡσο-βαφής ές *adj.* [βάπτω] (of slippers) **dyed golden** Plu.

χρῡσό-βωλος ον *adj.* [βῶλος] (of Mt. Pangaion) **with soil rich in gold** E.

χρῡσό-γονος ον *adj.* [γόνος] (of the Persian race) **descended from gold** (ref. to a shower of gold, in which form Zeus visited Danae and fathered Perseus) A.

χρῡσο-δαίδαλτος ον *adj.* [δαιδάλλω] (of horses' bits) ornamented with gold, **gold-chased** E.; (fig., of a beloved person) Ar.

χρῡσό-δετος ον (also ᾱ ον Alc.) *adj.* [δέω¹] **1** fastened with gold; (of a seal-stone) **set in gold** Hdt.
2 (of a necklace, brooch, sword-hilt) encased in gold, **gilded** Alc. S. E.
3 (of a warrior's body) **clad in gold** (i.e. golden armour) E.

χρῡσο-δῑνᾱς ᾱ *dial.masc.adj.* [δίνη] (of the river Paktolos) **with golden eddies** B.

χρῡσο-έθειρα ᾱς *fem.adj.* (of Kypris) **golden-haired** Ibyc.

χρῡσο-ειδής ές *adj.* [εἶδος¹] (of an object or colour) with the appearance of gold, **golden** Pl. X.

χρῡσό-ζυγος ον *adj.* [ζυγόν] (of a chariot) **with golden yoke** hHom. X.

χρῡσό-θρονος ον *adj.* [θρόνος] (of female deities) **golden-throned** Hom. hHom. Lyr. Ar.

χρῡσό-κᾱρᾱνος ον *dial.adj.* [κάρηνον] (of a supernatural deer) **golden-headed** (i.e. golden-horned) E.

χρῡσό-καρπος ον *adj.* [καρπός¹] (of trees) **with golden fruits** Pi.*fr.*

χρῡσό-κερως ων, gen. ω *adj.* [κέρας] ‖ nom.pl. χρυσόκερῳ ‖ —also **χρῡσοκέρᾱς** ᾱτος (E.) *masc.fem.adj.* (of a supernatural deer) **golden-horned** Pi. E.; (of an animal

χρῡσοκόλλα

prepared for sacrifice) **with gilded horns** Plu.; (fig., of a man in danger of his life) Aeschin.

χρῡσο-κόλλα ᾱς *dial.f.* **golden paste** (name of a dish made fr. linseed and honey) Alcm.

χρῡσο-κόλλητος ον *adj.* [κολλητός] (of decorations on a shield) **soldered** or **inlaid with gold** E.; (of the Sun's chariot) E.(dub.)

χρῡσο-κόμης ου, dial. **χρῡσοκόμᾱς** ᾱ *masc.adj.* [κόμη] (epith. of Apollo) **golden-haired** Scol. Lyr. E. Ar.; (of Dionysus, Eros, Zephyros) Hes. Alc. Anacr. E.

χρῡσό-κομος ον *adj.* (of a phoenix's feathers) **golden-haired, of golden plumage** Hdt.

χρῡσόκυκλος *adj.*: see χρῡσεόκυκλος

χρῡσό-λογχος ον *adj.* [λόγχη] (of Athena) **with golden spear** E. Ar.

χρῡσό-λοφος ον (also dial. ᾱ ον) *adj.* [λόφος] (of Ares, Athena) **with golden helmet-crest** Anacr. B.*fr.* Ar.

χρῡσο-λύρᾱς ᾱ *dial.masc.adj.* [λύρᾱ] (of Apollo) **with golden lyre** Ar.

χρῡσό-μαλλος ον *adj.* [μαλλός] (of a lamb) **with golden fleece** E. | see also χρῡσεόμαλλος

χρῡσο-μηλολόνθιον ου *n.* [dimin. μηλολόνθη] (as a term of endearment for a girl) **little golden cockchafer** Ar.

χρῡσο-μίτρᾱς ᾱ *dial.masc.adj.* [μίτρᾱ] (of Bacchus) **with golden headband** S.

χρῡσό-νωτος ον *adj.* [νῶτον] (of the Sun-god's reins) **with golden back, gold-covered** S.

χρῡσόομαι *pass.contr.vb.* (of statues, columns, objects) **be covered with gold, be gilded** Hdt. Ar. Pl. Plb. Plu.

χρῡσο-πάρυφος ον *adj.* [παρυφή *hem*] (of robes) **with golden borders** Plu.

χρῡσό-παστος ον (also dial. ᾱ ον) *adj.* [πάσσω] (of garments, rooms, objects) **sprinkled with gold, gold-spangled** Alc. A. Hdt. D. Plu.

χρῡσό-πᾱχυς υ *dial.adj.* [πῆχυς] (of Dawn) **golden-armed** B.

χρῡσο-πέδιλος, Aeol. **χρῡσοπέδιλλος**, ον *adj.* [πέδιλον] (of Hera, Dawn) **with golden sandals** Hes. Sapph.

χρῡσό-πεπλος ον *adj.* [πέπλος] (of goddesses) **golden-robed** Anacr. Pi. B.

χρῡσο-πήληξ ηκος *masc.fem.adj.* (of Ares, the Sown Men) **golden-helmeted** A. E.

χρῡσο-πλόκαμος ον *adj.* (of Apollo, a woman or goddess) **with golden tresses** hHom. B.(cj.) Tim.

χρῡσό-πλοκος ον *adj.* [πλόκος] (of Muses) **with golden tresses** Pi.*fr.*(cj.)

χρῡσό-πους πουν, gen. ποδος *adj.* [πούς] (of litters) **with golden feet** Plb.

χρῡσό-πρυμνος ον *adj.* [πρύμνα] (of a royal barge) **with golden stern** Plu.

χρῡσό-πτερος ον *adj.* [πτερόν] (of Iris, Eros, a Muse) **with golden wings** Il. hHom. Stesich. Ar.

χρῡσόραπις *adj.*: see χρῡσόρραπις

χρῡσό-ροος ον *adj.* [ῥόος] (of Mt. Tmolos) **with streams of gold** E.

χρῡσ-όροφος ον *adj.* [ὀροφή] (of chambers, awnings) **gold-roofed** Philox.Cyth. Plu.

χρῡσό-ρραπις, also **χρῡσόραπις** (Pi.), ιδος *masc.fem.adj.* [ῥαπίς *rod*] (of Hermes) **with golden wand** Od. hHom. Pi.

χρῡσό-ρρυτος, also **χρῡσόρυτος** (S.), ον *adj.* [ῥυτός] **1** (of a river) **flowing with gold** A.
2 (of Zeus's seed, its drops) **flowing as gold** S. E.*fr.*

χρῡσός οῦ, Aeol. **χρῡσος** ω *m.* | also χρῡσός (Pi.) | **1 gold** (ref. to the metal, esp. as the material fr. which an object is made) Hom. + | see also λευκός **4**

2 gold (meton. for a gold object, esp. armour) Il. hHom. Pi. S. E. +

3 gold (as a valuable commodity, sts. equiv. to *money, a fortune*) Hom. +; (as exemplifying sthg. precious, in comparisons describing people, objects, circumstances) Sapph. Thgn. A. +; (as exemplifying sthg. pure or purely good, oft. as being tested in the fire or sim.) Thgn. Pi. +; (exemplifying the colour of a girl's hair) Alcm.

χρῡσο-στέφανος ον *adj.* (of goddesses) **with a garland of gold** Hes. hHom. Sapph. Pi. E.; (of cavalry in a procession) Plb.; (of Olympic contests, w. allusion to the victor's crown) Pi.

χρῡσο-στεφής ές *adj.* [στέφος] (of a prize) **of a golden wreath** S.*Ichn.*

χρῡσό-στροφος ον *adj.* [στρόφος] **1** (of a mythol. woman) **with golden girdle** Ibyc.(v.l. χρῡσεό-)
2 (of Apollo's bow-string) **of twisted gold** S.

χρῡσότερος ᾱ ον *compar.adj.* (app. of a girl) **more golden** (w.GEN. than gold) Sapph.

χρῡσό-τευκτος ον *adj.* [τεύχω] (of objects) **made from gold** A. E.

χρῡσο-τευχής ές *adj.* [τεύχεα] (of a warrior) **with golden armour** E.

χρῡσό-τοξος ον *adj.* [τόξον] (of Apollo) **with golden bow** Pi.

χρῡσο-τρίαινα ᾱ *dial.masc.adj.* —also perh.

χρῡσοτρίαινος ου *masc.adj.* | voc. χρῡσοτρίαινα, also perh. -τρίαινε | (epith. of Poseidon) **with golden trident** Stesich. Ar. Lyr.adesp.

χρῡσό-τυπος ον *adj.* [τύπτω] (of a helmet, bowl) **of beaten gold** E. Critias

χρῡσοῦς *contr.adj.*: see χρῡσεος

χρῡσο-φάεννος ον *dial.adj.* [φαεινός] (of wings) **gold-gleaming** Anacr.; (of castanets) Lyr.adesp.(cj.)

χρῡσο-φαής ές *adj.* [φάος] | Boeot.masc.fem.acc.pl. χρουσοφαῖς | (of Hekate, Eros, Helen) **gold-gleaming** Sapph.(or Alc.) E.; (of urns) Corinn.; (of a garland) Plu.(quot.epigr.)

χρῡσο-φάλαρος ον *adj.* [φάλαρα] (of cavalry in a procession) **with gold trappings** Plb. | see also χρῡσεοφάλαρος

χρῡσό-φαντος ον *adj.* [φαίνω] (of riches) **of gleaming gold** S.*Ichn.*

χρῡσο-φεγγής ές *adj.* [φέγγος] (of the light of a beacon) **with golden radiance** A.

χρῡσοφορέω *contr.vb.* [χρῡσοφόρος] (of women) **wear gold jewellery** Hdt.

χρῡσο-φόρμιγξ ιγγος *masc.fem.adj.* (of Apollo) **with golden lyre** Simon.

χρῡσο-φόρος ον *adj.* [φέρω] (of foreign peoples, girls, a girl's neck) **wearing gold jewellery** Hdt. E. Lycophronid. Lycurg.(quot.epigr.)

χρῡσο-φύλαξ ακος *masc.fem.adj.* **1** (of griffins) **gold-guarding** Hdt. || MASC.SB. **guardian of the gold** (w.GEN. of Apollo, in his temple at Delphi) E.
2 (of a purse) **to hold money** Plu.

χρῡσο-χαίτα *dial.nom.masc.adj.* [χαίτη] (epith. of Apollo) **golden-haired** Pi.

χρῡσο-χάλῑνος ον *adj.* [χαλῑνός] (of a horse) **with golden bridle** Hdt. X. Plu.; (of the jingle) **of a golden bridle** Ar.

χρῡσο-χίτων ωνος *masc.fem.adj.* [χιτών] (of Thebe) **with golden robe** Pi.*fr.*

χρῡσοχοεῖον ου *n.* [χρῡσοχόος] **goldsmith's workshop** Plb.

χρῡσοχοέω *contr.vb.* **1 smelt gold** Ar. X.
2 (provbl.) **smelt ore for gold** (i.e. engage in a futile treasure-hunt, go on a fool's errand) Pl.

χρῡσο-χόος ου *m.* [χέω] one who smelts or casts gold, goldsmith Od. Ar. D. Plu.

χρῡ́σωμα ατος *n.* [χρῡσόομαι] object made of gold; gold ornament E.; gold phial E. ‖ COLLECTV.PL. gold plate Plb. Plu.

χρῡσ-ωνέω *contr.vb.* [ὠνέομαι] convert one's money into gold; buy —*gold staters* (*fr. a money-changer*) Isoc.

χρῡσ-ωπός όν *adj.* —also **χρῡσώψ** ῶπος *masc.adj.* [ὤψ] with golden face or appearance; (of the sun) gold-faced E.; (of the thyrsos of Dionysus) golden E. ‖ NEUT.SB. golden appearance (of hair) Plu.

—**χρῡσῶπις** ιδος *fem.adj.* | acc. χρῡσῶπιν | (of Justice) golden-eyed Simon.; (of a woman) Ar.

χρῡ́σωσις εως *f.* [χρῡσόομαι] covering of gold (on an object), gilding Plu.

χρῶ (mid.imperatv.): see χράομαι

χρῷ (dat.sg.): see χρώς

χρῴζω *vb.* [χρώς, reltd. χροΐζω] | PASS.: aor.inf. χρωσθῆναι | pf. κέχρωσμαι (perh. better κέχρωσμαι) | **1 touch, clasp** —*someone's knees* (*in supplication*) E. ‖ PASS. (of a person) be clasped (in supplication) E.

2 ‖ PASS. (of an object) be coloured —W.DAT. *w. a certain hue* Pl.

χρῶμα ατος *n.* [χρώς] **1 colour, hue** (of the skin of foreign peoples) Hdt. Plb.

2 colour, complexion (of a person, esp. as subject to change through emotion) E. Ar. Pl. X. Arist. Men. +

3 colour (of things, sts. opp. σχῆμα *shape*) E. Pl. X. Arist. Plb. Plu.

4 (fig.) **hue, shade** (W.GEN. of character) Plu.

5 (concr.) that which gives colour, **colouring, pigment** (ref. to a paint, cosmetic, or sim.) Pl. X.

6 ‖ PL. (fig.) colours, colourings (W.GEN. of poetry, ref. to ornamentation which distinguishes it fr. prose) Pl.

χρώς χρωτός (also ep. and dial. χροός) *m.* | acc. χρῶτα, also χρόα | dat. χρωτί, also χρῷ, χροΐ | **1 skin, flesh** (of a person, sts. meton. for the whole person or body) Hom. +; (of a bird's wings) Ar.(quot. E., or mock-trag.)

2 (prep.phr., w.vb. *shave*) ἐν χρῷ (χροΐ) **right down to the skin** Hdt. X. Plu.; (fig., ref. to a contingency coming close; see ξυρέω 4) S.; (w. other vbs.) **right up close** (*ref. to tracking, sailing, fighting*) S.Ichn. Th. Plu.

3 outward appearance of the skin, **complexion** (esp. as subject to change through emotion) Hom. E. Ar.(mock-trag.) X. Theoc.; (of an octopus, able to change it at will) Pi.*fr.*; (of a person, envisaged as an octopus) Thgn.

4 colour (of things) A. Parm.

χρωτίζομαι *mid.vb.* (fig.) **add colour to one's nature** —W.DAT. *w. new-fangled interests* Ar.

χυδαῖος ον *adj.* [χύδην] (of gossip) **random, indiscriminate** Plb.

χύδην, dial. **χύδᾱν** *adv.* **1 in profusion, abundantly** Philox.Leuc. Call.

2 in random heaps or **groups** X. Plb. Plu.

3 at random, indiscriminately —*ref. to speaking, selecting, learning, or sim.* Isoc. Pl. Arist.

4 (specif.) without the formality or constraints of verse, **in ordinary speech, in prose** Pl. Arist.

χύθην (ep.aor.pass.): see χέω

χῡλός οῦ *m.* [reltd. χῡμός] **sap, juice** (extracted fr. plants and fruits) Pl.; (fig., W.GEN. of friendship, for combatants after a war) Ar.; (of verbiage, as medicine for the art of tragedy, envisaged as sick) Ar.

χύμενος (athem.aor.mid.ptcpl.): see χέω

χῡμίζω *vb.* [χῡμός] (fig., of poets) **add flavour to, spice up** —*the art of musical composition* Ar.

χῡμός οῦ *m.* [reltd. χῡλός] **1 sap, juice** (extracted fr. plants and fruits, used to add flavour) Pl. Arist.

2 flavour (as apprehended by the sense of taste) Pl. Arist.

3 bodily fluid, **humour** Pl.

χύντο (ep.3pl.athem.aor.mid.): see χέω

χύσις εως *f.* [χέω] **1 outpouring** (ref. to a libation) A.; (W.GEN. of water, fr. a rock) AR.

2 heap, pile (W.GEN. of leaves) Od. Call.

χύτλα ων *n.pl.* **1** water that is poured, **water for washing** Call.

2 poured offerings, **libations** AR.

χυτλάζω *vb.* (fig.) pour out, **stretch out** —*oneself* (W.PREP.PHR. *on a couch*) Ar.

χυτλόομαι *mid.contr.vb.* **1 anoint oneself** (w. oil, while bathing) Od.

2 (tr.) **wash, bathe** —*a person* AR.; **wash off** —*defilement* (*fr. one's body*) Call.

χύτο (ep.3sg.athem.aor.mid.): see χέω

χυτός ή όν *adj.* **1** (of nectar) **poured** Pi.

2 (of blood) **shed** A.

3 molten or cast; (of ἀρτήματα *pendants*) λίθινα χυτά *of cast stone* (*ref. to glass*) Hdt.; χυτὴ γῆ *earthenware* Pl.

4 (of metals, glass, or sim., classed as solid forms of water) capable of being melted, **fusible** Pl.

5 (of earth) **heaped up** (as a burial mound) Hom. AR.

6 ‖ MASC.SB. mound of earth, mole or breakwater (at the mouth of a canal) Hdt.

χύτρᾱ ᾱς *f.* earthenware vessel (esp. for heating liquids or cooking), **pot** Ar. Pl. X. Thphr. Plu.

χύτρειος ᾱ ον *adj.* (of the clatter) **of pots** Ar.

χυτρεοῦς ῆ οῦν *Att.adj.* (of an object) **of earthenware, pot-like** Ar.

χυτρεύς έως *m.* **potter** Hippon. Pl.

χυτρίς ίδος *f.* earthenware vessel (for holding or heating liquids), **jug, pot** Hdt. Call.

—**χυτρίδιον** ου *n.* [dimin.] **little jug** Ar.

χυτρό-γαυλος ου *m.* [χύτρος, γαυλός] **cooking-pot** Men.

χυτρό-πους ποδος *m.* [πούς] earthenware vessel with legs, **pot** Hes.

χύτρος, Ion. **κύθρος**, ου *m.* earthenware vessel (for heating liquids or cooking), **pot** Hippon. ‖ PL. Pots (name of an Athenian festival) Ar.; Basins (name of a bathing-place at Thermopylai) Hdt.

χυτρώδης ες *adj.* (of a tortoise) **pot-shaped** S.Ichn.

χὠ: crasis for καὶ ὁ

χωλαίνω *vb.* [χωλός] (of persons, their feet) **limp** (on a specific occasion rather than through permanent lameness) Pl. Arist.

χωλείᾱ ᾱς *f.* [χωλεύω] **lameness** (W.GEN. of the feet) Pl.

χωλεύω *vb.* [χωλός] **1 limp** (through permanent lameness) Il.

2 become lame X. ‖ PASS. (of souls, as winged beings) be lamed Pl.

χωλο-ποιός οῦ *m.* [ποιέω] **creator of cripples** (ref. to Euripides, criticised for depicting too many such characters) Ar.

χωλός ή όν *adj.* **1** (of Hephaistos, persons, animals) **lame** Hom. Hippon. Asius Hdt. S. E.*Cyc.* +; (W.ACC. in the foot, legs) Il. Ar.; (of a leg) Plu.

2 (fig., of a lame king's rule) **lame** X.(oracle) Plu.(oracle); (of Greece) **crippled** (by the defeat of Athens) Plu.

χωλότης

3 (fig., of persons) **limping** (W.PREP.PHR. in respect of their hands, ref. to the asymmetry of being either right- or left-handed) Pl.; (gener., of persons or things) **handicapped** Pl.
4 (of verses) **limping** (ref. to the choliambic metre) Call.

χωλότης ητος *f.* **lameness** Plu.

χῶμα ατος *n.* [χόω] 1 (gener.) **artificially created heap of earth or sand, mound** Plb. Plu.
2 (specif.) **mound** (of earth, above a tomb, i.e. burial mound) Hdt. Trag. Pl. Arist. Theoc. Plu.
3 **mound, earthwork** (thrown up against the walls of a city, as an assault ramp) Hdt. Th. Plb. Plu.
4 **dyke** (to prevent a river fr. overflowing) Hdt.
5 **dam** (to divert a river) Hdt.
6 **mole** or **breakwater** (in a harbour) Hdt. X. D. Plu.
7 **causeway** (across a channel) Hdt. Plu.
8 **mass of earth or sand formed naturally** (on a coast or in a river), **mound, bank** or **sandbank** A. Pl. Plb.

χῶν (ptcpl.): see χόω

χωνεύω *vb.*: see χοανεύω

χώνη *f.*: see χοάνη

χώννυμι, χωννύω *vbs.*: see χόω

χώομαι *mid.vb.* | fut. χώσομαι | aor. ἐχωσάμην | **be angry** (sts. W.INTERN.ACC. or DAT. in one's heart) Hom. Hes. hHom. Hellenist.poet. —W.GEN. or PREP.PHR. *about sthg., because of someone* Il. Hes. hHom. AR. —W.DAT. *w. someone* (sts. W.INTERN.ACC. *about sthg.*) Hom. AR.

χώρᾱ ᾱς, Ion. **χώρη** ης *f.* [reltd. χῶρος¹, perh. also χωρίς]
1 **land under one's control, territory, land** (esp. of a particular people or ruler) Hom. Pi. Hdt. +; **estate** (of a particular person) X.
2 **territory controlled by a city; countryside** (opp. the city itself) Th. Att.orats. +
3 **land, country, region** (ref. to a particular place) Pi. Lyr.adesp. Trag. +
4 **area, space** (occupied by sthg., or in which sthg. takes place) Il. +
5 **empty space, space** (ref. to the distance or gap betw. two things) Il.
6 **position, place** (of someone or sthg., esp. as that which is yielded to another) Hom. Alcm. Tyrt. Thgn. Hdt. +; (ref. to the pre-existing position or status of sthg.; oft. w.connot. of stability, as in phr. μένειν κατὰ χώραν *remain in place*, sts. of laws, truces, or sim. *remain in force*) Hdt. Th. +
7 (ref. to a particular location) **place, spot** Hom. hHom.; (specif.) **military position** X.
8 **suitable location** (for a particular kind of plant) Pl.
9 **proper place, proper configuration** (of sthg., esp. in ctxts. of setting sthg. to rights) Pi. X.
10 (specif.) appointed **position, station, post** (of a soldier; also fig., of Ares) A. Hdt. +; **post** or **position** (within an army, as filled by a soldier) Aeschin.
11 **position, status, esteem** (accorded to a person) Thgn. X. Plb.; (W.GEN. of a slave, i.e. equiv. to that of a slave) X.

χωρέω *contr.vb.* [χώρᾱ, χῶρος¹] | fut. χωρήσω, also χωρήσομαι | aor. ἐχώρησα | pf. κεχώρηκα | 1 (of warriors) **give ground, withdraw, retire** (sts. W.GEN. or PREP.PHR. fr. a place) Il. A. E.; **give way** —W.DAT. *before someone* Il.
2 (of the earth) **give way** (i.e. open up) hHom.
3 (of persons) **go away** (freq. W.ADV. or PREP.PHR. fr. somewhere) Hdt. Trag. +
4 (gener., of persons or things) **go, proceed, move, travel** (freq. W.ADV. or PREP.PHR. somewhere) Pi. Hdt. Trag. Th. + | also freq.w. ὁμόσε 3

5 **go** —w. διά + GEN. *through murder, destruction* (i.e. be involved in it) E. —w. πρός + ACC. *to work* (i.e. get started on it) S.; (of a contest, i.e. get underway) Ar.
6 (of things) **be in motion** Pl.(quot. Heraclit.)
7 (of a night) **proceed, pass** A.
8 (of rumours, shouts, or sim.) **spread, grow** Hdt. E. X. Plu.; (of a fire) Call.; (of an evil) Ar.
9 (of opinions) **move, tend** —W.ADV. or PREP.PHR. *in a certain direction* E.
10 (of interest on a loan) **mount up** Ar.; (of expenses) **be paid out** —w. ἐκ + GEN. *fr. an estate* X.
11 (of a task) **go** —W.ADV. *forward* (i.e. *progress*) A.satyr.fr.; **proceed** Ar.
12 (of events) **go, turn out** —W.ADV. *happily, badly* Hdt. Pl.
13 (of an enterprise) **come off, succeed** Hdt.; (of wishes, intentions) **come to fruition** Hdt. || IMPERS. it turns out successfully —W.DAT. *for someone* Hdt.
14 (of Jesus' teaching, in neg.phr.) **make headway** —w. ἐν + DAT. *among people* NT. [or perh. *find a place*]
15 (tr., of containers) **have room for, hold** —*a commodity, a certain amount* Hdt. Ar. Pl. +
16 (usu. in neg.phr., of a city or land) **have enough room for, be able to contain** —*a large population* Th. —*all the wrongdoers that exist* E. —*a person, his ambition or ostentatious behaviour* Aeschin. D.; (of the universe) —*books to be written in the future* NT.; (intr., of a space) **be large enough, be sufficient** (for a crowd of people) NT.
17 (in neg.phr.) have the mental capacity for, **take in, grasp, apprehend** —*a person's teachings or thoughts* NT. Plu.

χώρι *dial.adv.*: see χωρίς

χωρίδιον ου *n.* [dimin. χωρίον] **small plot of land** (owned by a person) Lys. Men. Plu.

χωρίζω *vb.* [χωρίς] | pf.pass. κεχώρισμαι, Ion.3pl. κεχωρίδαται || neut.impers.vbl.adj. χωριστέον | 1 **keep separate, set apart** —*a tomb, drink* (W.DAT. *for a person*) E.
2 **separate** —*persons or things* (freq. W.GEN. or PREP.PHR. *fr. others, one another*) E. Isoc. Pl. X. + || PASS. (of persons or things) **be separated** or **kept separate** (freq. W.GEN. or PREP.PHR. fr. *others, one another*) Hdt. E. Isoc. Pl. X. +
3 || PASS. (specif., of a woman) **be divorced** Is. —w. ἀπό + GEN. *fr. her husband* Plb.
4 || PF.PASS. (of opinions) **be divided** Hdt.
5 **distinguish, differentiate** —*sthg.* (sts. W.GEN. or PREP.PHR. fr. *sthg. else*) Pl. Arist. || PF.PASS. (of persons or things) **be different** (freq. W.GEN. fr. *others, one another*) Hdt. Att.orats. Pl. X. + —(W.DAT.) Hdt.
6 || PASS. **go away, depart** Plb.

—**κεχωρισμένως** *pf.pass.ptcpl.adv.* **separately, individually** Arist.

χωρικός *adj.*: see χωρῑτικός

χωρίον ου *n.* [dimin. χώρᾱ or χῶρος¹] 1 (gener.) **physical location** (of persons, places, things, events), **place, spot, location** Hdt. Th. Ar. Att.orats. X. +; (specif.) **site** (of a banker's business) D.
2 **geographical area** (of any size), **area, place, region** Hdt. Th. Ar. Att.orats. Pl. X. +
3 **plot of land** (belonging to a person, usu. ref. to farmland), **land, estate** Th. Ar. Att.orats. Pl. +
4 (abstr.) **area, space, room** Th.
5 **extent of space** (betw. locations), **distance** Dionys.Eleg. Ar. X.
6 (geom.) **area, space** Pl.; (specif.) **figure** (delimiting a particular space) Pl.
7 **particular place** (in a literary work), **passage** Hdt.

8 subject, topic (for a historian or orator) Th. Lycurg.
9 routine (ref. to a piece of comic business) Ar.
χωρίς, Aeol. **χῶρις**, dial. **χῶρι** (Call.) *adv. and prep*. **1** in a separate place, **separately, apart** Od. Tyrt. Sapph. Hdt. E. Th. + —W. ἀπό + GEN. *fr. someone or sthg., one another* Hes.*fr*. Pl.; (as prep.) —W.GEN. Pi. Hdt. S. E. Ar. Isoc. +; (predic., w. εἶναι) Hdt. E. Ar. • χωρὶς ξενῶνές εἰσι *the guest-rooms are set apart* E.
2 as part of a separate process, **separately, independently** Hom. Hdt. S. E. Th. +
3 as a separate consideration, **separately, additionally, besides** Od. A. Hdt. Th.
4 separately (so as to be different), **separately, differently** Semon. —W. ἀπό + GEN. *fr. one another* Parm. —W.GEN. *fr. someone* S.; (predic., w. εἶναι or sim., sts. understd.) Trag. Ar. Pl. • χωρὶς τό τ' εἰπεῖν πολλὰ καὶ τὰ καίρια *there is a difference between saying much and speaking to the point* S.
5 otherwise (equiv. to *if this is not the case*) Pl.
6 (prep.) **apart from, except for** —W.GEN. *sthg*. Hdt.
7 (introducing the first of two considerations) **apart from, irrespective of, as well as** —W.GEN. *sthg*. A. Hdt. E. Att.orats. +
8 (phrs.) χωρὶς ἢ ὅτι *except for the fact that* Hdt.; χωρὶς ἢ ὁκόσοι *except for as many as* Hdt.
9 (prep.) in a state of separation from, **without** —W.GEN. *sthg*. S. Ar. —*a person or god* (*i.e. without their help*) S. E. Isoc.
χωρισμός οῦ *m*. [χωρίζω] **1** act of separating; **separation** (of sthg., fr. sthg. else) Pl. Arist.; (of sthg., into its component parts) Arist.
2 act of taking one's leave; **departure** (of a person) Plb.
χωριστός ή όν *adj*. **1** (of things) able to exist or be considered in isolation, **separable** (fr. other things) Arist.; (specif., of a class of possessions) separable (fr. their owners), **alienable** Arist. ‖ NEUT.SB. separability Arist.
2 (of things) existing independently, **separate** Arist.
χωρῖται ῶν *m.pl*. [χώρα, χῶρος¹] **1** inhabitants (of a particular region), **countrymen** A.
2 (pejor.) inhabitants of the countryside, **country folk, rustics** X. Plu.(dub.)

χωρῑτικός ή όν *adj*. (of a mass of people) **from the countryside** Plu.(v.l. χωρικός)
—**χωρῑτικῶς** *adv*. **in a rustic fashion** X.
χῶρος¹ ου *m*. [reltd. χώρα, perh. also χωρίς] **1 area of ground** Hom. A.*fr*. S.; (ref. to a plot of sacred land, such as a temple precinct) Simon. Pi. S.; **plot of land** (ref. to real estate) X.
2 (specif.) **country estate** X.
3 countryside (opp. city) X.
4 surface of the ground, **ground, earth** hHom.
5 area of open ground, **space, empty space** (betw. two things) Il.
6 particular piece of ground, **place, site, spot** Hom. Hes. Thgn. Hdt. S. E. +; (ref. to a mother's womb) A.
7 (ref. to a larger area) **place, area, locale** Hom. Hes. Archil. Sapph. A. +; (pl., in phr. *these parts* or sim.) Hdt. S. Th. +
8 region, land, country Hes. hHom. Mimn. Hdt. S. +; (of the dead, i.e. the underworld) Thgn. ‖ PL. lands (of a particular people), **territories** Hdt.
9 land (of a particular person), **homeland, native land** X.
10 proper place, **home** (of a young soul, ref. to the environment in which it can blossom) S.; (of a tree, i.e. its original location in the forest) Pi.
χῶρος² ου *m*. [Lat. *caurus, corus*] **north-west wind; north west** (as a direction) NT.
χωροφιλέω *contr.vb*. [χῶρος¹, χώρα] **feel affection for a place; feel at home** —w. ἐν + DAT. *in a particular place* Antipho
χωσθήσομαι (fut.pass.): see χόω
χῶσις εως *f*. [χόω] **1 building of a mound** (against a city wall, as an assault ramp) Th.
2 fortifying (W.GEN. of harbours) **with moles** Th.
χωστός ή όν *adj*. **1** (of burial mounds) **of heaped earth** E.
2 (of the road to a fortress in a marsh) **built up as a causeway** Plb.
χωστρίς ίδος *fem.adj*. (of armoured sheds) **used in making earthworks** Plb.
χώσω (fut.): see χόω
χὥτε: crasis for καὶ ὅτε

Ψ ψ

ψ *interj.* (repeated as an exclam. by a chorus of satyrs) **pst!** S.*Ichn.*

ψάγιος ᾱ ον *dial.adj.* (of a song) app. **skewed, unbalanced** (in content and harmony) Pi.

ψαίρω *vb.* [perh.reltd. ψάω] (of a mythic animal, app. a griffin) **fan** —*the air* (W.DAT. *w. its wings*) A.

ψαιστόν οῦ *n.* [ψαίω *grind*, reltd. ψάω] **barley-cake** (as a very cheap religious offering) Ar.

ψακάζω *vb.* [ψακάς] (of clouds) **drizzle** Ar. ‖ MID. (of a lamp, w. water dripping on it) **sputter** Arist.

ψακάς άδος *f.* **1 raindrop**; (collectv.) **drizzle, light shower** A. Hdt. X.(pl.); (gener.) **rain** E.
2 (fig.) **shower** (W.GEN. of bloody dew, ref. to bloodshed) A.
3 Spit-shower (comic name for a man who sprays saliva when speaking) Ar.
4 (fig.) **tiny drop, speck** (W.GEN. of money) Ar.

ψάλιον ου *n.* [app.reltd. ψαλίς, ψέλιον] **1** part of a bridle (app. U-shaped or circular); perh. **noseband** X.; (sg. and pl., gener.) **bridle** E. Ar.
2 (as the instrument of taming) **bridle, curb** E. Pl.; (fig.ref. to sthg. which subjugates or restrains persons) A.

ψαλίς ίδος *f.* vaulted underground space, **tunnel, sewer** Plu.; **vault, crypt** Pl.

ψάλλω *vb.* | aor.inf. ψῆλαι | **1 pluck** —*a lyre or harp* Anacr. Ion; (opp. κρούω *strum*, w. a plectrum) Pl.; (intr.) **play the lyre** or **harp** Hdt. Ar. Men. Plu. ‖ PASS. (fig., of the soul's constituents) be plucked (by passions) Pl.
2 twang —*a bowstring* E.; (fig., of men's censure) —*a baseless shot* (W.PREP.PHR. *at women*) E.*fr.*
3 pluck or **pull at** —*one's hair* (*in mourning*) A.

ψαλμός οῦ *m.* **1 twanging, plucking** (of a lyre or sim., ref. to the sound) A.*fr.* Pi.*fr.* Telest.; **harp-playing** Plu.
2 song with lyre or harp accompaniment, **melody** (about love) E.
3 psalm NT.
4 twanging shot (fr. a bow) E.

ψαλτήριον ου *n.* [ψάλτης] **harp** Plu.

ψάλτης ου *m.* **harpist** Plu.

ψάλτρια ᾱς *f.* female harpist (hired to perform at banquets or similar occasions), **harp-girl** Pl. Arist. Men. Plu.

ψάμαθος ου *f.* [reltd. ψάμμος] **1** (sg. and pl.) **sand** (of the shore, a river) Hom. hHom. S. E. +
2 (collectv.sg. and pl.) **grains of sand** (exemplifying that which is innumerable) Il. Pi. Call.

ψαμαθώδης ες *adj.* (of places by the sea) **sandy, full of dunes** hHom. AR.

ψαμμακοσιο-γάργαροι αι α *pl.adj.* [ψάμμη, w. 2nd el.reltd. to that of διᾱκόσιοι; γάργαρα *heaps*] (of sufferings) as innumerable as the sands, **umpteen zillion** Ar.

ψάμμη ης, dial. **ψάμμα** ᾱς *f.* [reltd. ψάμμος] **sand** (of the shore, a desert) A. Hdt.; (exemplifying that which is innumerable) Ar.

ψάμμινος η ον *adj.* (of a mountain range) **sandy** Hdt.

ψάμμος ου *f.* **1 sand** (of the shore, sea-floor, desert) Od. Hdt.; (exemplifying that which is innumerable) Pi. Lyr.adesp. Hdt.
2 desert Hdt. Plu.

ψαμμώδης ες *adj.* (of a region, ref. to a desert) **sandy** Hdt.

ψάρ ψᾱρός, also **ψήρ** ψηρός *m.* **starling** Il.

ψᾱρός ά όν *adj.* speckled like a starling; (of a horse) **dapple-grey** Ar.

ψαῦσις εως (Ion. ιος) *f.* [ψαύω] **1 touch** (as a sense) Democr.
2 touch (of man, as sthg. avoided by wild animals) Plu.; **caress** (of a lover) Plu.

ψαύω *vb.* | Aeol.inf. ψαύην | fut. ψαύσω | aor. ἔψαυσα |
1 make physical contact (by hand); **touch** —W.GEN. *someone, a part of the body* B. Hdt. S. E. Call. Plu. —*an animal* Mosch. —*an object* S. AR. —*the gods* (*i.e. their altars*) E. —W.DAT. *someone's robe* Pi.; (of a boxer) **merely touch** (opp. strike hard) —W.GEN. *an opponent's face* Plb.
2 (specif.) touch so as to make use or take charge (of sthg.); **set one's hand to** —W.GEN. *one's spear* E.; **lay one's hands on** —W.GEN. *food* (*to partake of it*) S. AR. —*a corpse* (*to take possession of it*) Plu.; **dip one's hands in** —W.GEN. *a spring* (*to wash them*) A.
3 touch (someone) aggressively; (of persons, Erinyes) **lay hands on** —W.GEN. *someone* Trag.; (fig., of a person) **assail** (a god) —W.PREP.PHR. *w. taunts* S.
4 touch (someone) lasciviously; (of a man) **paw at, grope** —W.GEN. *a woman, her body* Hdt. S. E.*Cyc.*
5 (of persons) come into physical contact (W.GEN. w. someone or sthg.); **touch, reach** —*an opponent's entrails* (w. a spear) Il.(dub.) —*a land* (W.DAT. *w. one's foot*) A.; (of a sailor) —*a land* E.; (of a person) touch accidentally, **brush against** —*a pig* Hdt.; (fig., of two rulers) **brush up against** —*one another* (*by controlling adjacent regions*) Plu.
6 (fig.) **touch, reach** —W.GEN. *heaven* (*i.e. achieve supreme felicity*) Sapph. Hdt.; **attain, experience** —W.GEN. *victory-songs, love* Pi.
7 put one's hand to, attempt —W.GEN. *great deeds* Plb.
8 (of things) come into physical contact (w. other things); (of the plumed helmets of warriors in close formation) **touch** (each other) Il.; (of a horse's tail) —W.GEN. *a chariot wheel* Il.; (of fish) —*a river bank* Hdt.; (of the tongue) —*one's mouth* (*in speaking*) X.; (of water) —*high ground* Plu.; (of a scimitar blade which has severed an opponent's helmet) —*the hair on his head* Plu.; (fig., of paintings) **touch, reach** —W.GEN. *heaven* (*i.e. be of highest quality*) Plu.
9 ‖ W.NEG. (usu. hyperbol.) have not even the slightest contact (W.GEN. w. sthg.); (of a person) not touch —*the earth* (W.DAT. *w. one's feet, because travelling so fast*) hHom.; not even touch (let alone throw) —*a javelin* Antipho; not even set foot in —*a place* Plb.; have no grasp on —*sanity* Call.; (of a woman) have nothing to do with —*a millstone* (*i.e. grinding of corn*) Semon.; (of a man) —*marriage* E.

ψαφαρόθριξ

10 affect emotionally; (of an event) **make an impression on, touch** —W.GEN. *someone's heart* E.
11 touch on (in speech), **bring up, allude to** —W.GEN. *sthg. painful* S. E.
12 touch on (in writing), **give a cursory treatment of** —W.GEN. *events, their motivation* Plb.
ψαφαρό-θριξ τριχος *masc.fem.adj.* [ψαφαρός, θρίξ] (of sheep) perh. **rough-fleeced** hHom.
ψαφαρός ά όν *adj.* (of a sacked city's ashes) **powdery, crumbling** A.
ψαφαρό-χρους ουν *masc.fem.adj.* [χρώς] (of a beggar's head) perh., rough-skinned, **leathery** E.
ψᾶφος *dial.f.*: see ψῆφος
ψάω *contr.vb.* | 3sg. ψῇ | aor. ἔψησα | **1** (of a midwife) **wipe** —*a baby* Hippon.
2 (intr., of a clump of wool dipped in corrosive poison) **crumble away, disintegrate** S.
ψε (dial.enclit.acc.pl.pers.pron.): see σφεῖς
ψέγω *vb.* **blame, criticise, find fault with** —*persons, gods, acts, things* Thgn. Trag. Ar. + —W.DBL.ACC. *someone (or sthg.), for sthg.* S. Pl. —W.ACC. + INF. *the fact that someone does sthg.* Pl.; (intr.) **find fault** Pl. ǁ PASS. (of persons or things) be criticised Isoc. Pl. Arist. +; be challenged Th.
ψεδνός ή όν *adj.* (of a person's hair) **sparse, scanty** Il.
ψεδυρός ά όν *adj.* [perh.reltd. ψιθυρός] (app. of the behaviour of lovers) **whispering** A.
ψεῖ *indecl.n.* [Semit.loanwd.] **psi** (letter of the Greek alphabet) Pl.
ψέκτης ου *m.* [ψέγω] **criticiser** (W.GEN. of sthg.) Pl.
ψεκτός ή όν *adj.* (of persons, actions, behaviour) deserving to be criticised, **blameworthy, deplorable** Pl. Arist. Plb. Plu.
ψέλιον, also **ψέλλιον**, ου *n.* [app.reltd. ψάλιον] **bangle, bracelet** or **anklet** (of precious metal, worn by women and Persian men) Hdt. X. Plb. Plu.
ψελιο-φόρος ον *adj.* [φέρω] (of Persians) **wearing bangles** or **bracelets** Hdt.
ψελλίζομαι *mid.vb.* [ψελλός] speak falteringly or unclearly, **stammer, stutter** Pl.; (fig., of early philosophy) Arist.; (of Empedocles) **say** (W.ACC. sthg.) unclearly Arist.
ψελλισμός οῦ *m.* (fig.) first murmuring (of gout, ref. to its symptoms) Plu.
ψελλός ή όν *adj.* (fig., of a narrative) **stuttering, unclear** A.
ψευδαγγελέω *contr.vb.* [ψευδάγγελος] **be a false messenger** Ar.
ψευδαγγελίᾱ ᾱς *f.* **false news, misinformation** (to trick an enemy) X.
ψευδ-άγγελος ου *m.f.* [ψευδής, ἄγγελος] **false messenger, bringer of false news** Il. Arist.
ψευδ-αμάμαξυς υος *m.* [ἀμάμαξυς *vine that grows up trees*] (pejor., ref. to a social climber) **lying climber-vine** Ar.
ψευδ-ατράφαξυς υος *f.* [ἀτράφαξυς *orache, a plant thought to make the eater turn pale*] **false orache** Ar.
ψευδ-αυτόμολος ου *m.* **bogus deserter** X.
ψευδ-εγγραφή ῆς *f.* **charge of false registration** (of a person's name on the list of public debtors) Arist.
ψευδ-ενέδρᾱ ᾱς *f.* **fake ambush** X.
ψευδ-επίγραφος ον *adj.* [ἐπιγραφή] falsely attributed or credited; (of an apparently competent man) **sham, counterfeit** Plb.
ψευδ-επίτροπος ου *m.* one pretending to be legal guardian (of a young king), **sham guardian** Plb.
ψευδηγορέω *contr.vb.* [ἀγορεύω] (of persons, the mouth of Zeus) **speak falsely, tell lies** A. Arist.(quot. E., dub.)
ψευδής ές *adj.* [ψεῦδος] **1** (of persons) **lying, false, deceptive** Hdt. S. E. Th. +

2 (of oracles, statements, accusations, reputations, or sim.) **false, untrue, mistaken** Trag. + ǁ NEUT.PL.SB. **lies** Hdt. Trag. +; (w. λέγειν *speak* or sim., esp. quasi-advbl.) Trag. + • εἰ δ' ἐγὼ ψευδῆ λέγω *if I am lying* E.*Cyc.*
3 (of a course of action) **of falsehood** or **dishonesty** Hdt.
4 (of a gift) **pretended** E.; (of a shore) **imaginary** Pi.*fr.*
—**ψευδῶς** *adv.* **1 falsely, lyingly** E. Th. Isoc. Plb. Plu.
2 mistakenly E. Pl. Arist. Plb. Plu.
3 groundlessly Plb. Plu.
ψεῦδις ιος *dial.masc.adj.* (of a witness) **lying, false** Pi.
ψευδο-βοήθεια ᾱς *f.* pretended help, **faked arrival of reinforcements** X.
ψευδογραφέω *contr.vb.* [γράφω] be a writer of falsehoods, **make false statements** Plb.
ψευδογραφίᾱ ᾱς *f.* **writing of falsehoods** Plb.
ψευδοδοξέω *contr.vb.* [δόξα] **hold a false opinion** Plb.
ψευδο-κῆρυξ ῡκος *m.* **false** or **lying herald** S.
ψευδοκλητείᾱ ᾱς *f.* [κλητεύω] (leg.) false claim to have witnessed the serving of a summons (for someone to appear in court) And. D. Arist.
ψευδο-κύων κυνός *m.* **imitation Cynic** Plu.
ψευδό-λιτρος ον *adj.* [λίτρον] (of detergent) **made from adulterated soda** Ar.
ψευδολογέω *contr.vb.* [ψευδολόγος] **make false statements** Isoc. Aeschin. Plb.
ψευδολογίᾱ ᾱς *f.* **telling of lies, mendacity, dishonesty** Isoc. D. Plb. Plu.; **telling of tall tales** (esp. in a literary work) Isoc. Plb.
ψευδο-λόγος ου *m.* **false talker, liar** Ar. Plb.
ψευδό-μαντις εως (Ion. ιος) *m.f.* [μάντις] **false prophet** (ref. to one whose predictions are not fulfilled) Hdt. Trag. Plu.
ψευδομαρτυρέω *contr.vb.* [ψευδομάρτυς] be a dishonest witness, **give false evidence** Pl. X. Arist. NT.
ψευδομαρτυρίᾱ ᾱς *f.* **giving of false evidence** Arist. NT. Plu. [apparent instances of pl. are prob. to be corrected to n.pl. ψευδομαρτύρια]
ψευδομαρτύρια ων *n.pl.* (leg.) **false evidence** Att.orats. Pl. Arist. Plu.
ψευδο-μάρτυς υρος *m.* witness who lies, **false witness** Pl. NT.
ψευδο-νύμφευτος ον *adj.* [νυμφεύω] (of a gift fr. Kypris) **of a false marriage** (ref. to the union of Paris and Helen) E.
ψευδο-πάρθενος ου *f.* [παρθένος] **pretended virgin** Hdt.
ψευδο-πάτωρ ορος *m.* [πατήρ] false father, **unfatherly father** Call.
ψευδοποιέω *contr.vb.* **1** prove (W.ACC. statements or opinions) **to be false** Plb.
2 discredit —*someone's services* Plb.
ψευδο-προφήτης ου *m.* **false prophet** NT.
ψευδό-πτωμα ατος *n.* [πτῶμα] **feigned fall** (as a wrestler's trick, fig.ref. to pretended losses as a military tactic) Plu.
ψευδορκέω *contr.vb.* [ψεύδορκος] **be a perjurer** Ar.
ψευδ-όρκιος ον *adj.* [ὅρκος] false to an oath by which one is bound, **guilty of breaking one's oath** Hdt.
ψεύδ-ορκος ου *m.* **oath-breaker, perjurer** E.
ψεῦδος εος (ους) *n.* **1** intentionally false or deceitful statement, **falsehood, lie** Hom. Hes. Thgn. +; (pl., personif.) **Falsehood** Hes.
2 factually untrue statement, **false statement** S. Att.orats. Pl. Plb.
3 falsehood, error (opp. truth) Pl. X. Arist. Din. Plb.
4 (concr.) **deception, deceit, illusion** (ref. to an imitation Hera, made fr. cloud) Pi.
5 sign or token of mendacity, **pimple** (on the nose of a liar) Theoc.

ψευδοστομέω contr.vb. [στόμα] **speak falsely, tell lies** S.
ψευδουργός οῦ m. [ἔργον] **practitioner of deceitful arts** Pl.
ψευδό-φημος ον adj. [φήμη] (of prophecies) **with a false message** S.
ψευδό-χριστος ου m. [Χριστός] **false Christ** NT.
ψεύδω vb. | fut. ψεύσω | aor. ἔψευσα ‖ PASS.: fut. ψευσθήσομαι | aor. ἐψεύσθην | pf. ἔψευσμαι, 3sg.imperatv. ἐψεύσθω | **1** (of gods, persons, signs) **deceive** —someone S. X. —(W.ACC. over sthg.) S. ‖ PASS. **be deceived** E. X.
2 prove false, belie —a report E.; (of second thoughts) **give the lie to** —first thoughts S.
3 (of persons or gods) **cheat** —someone (W.GEN. of wits, hopes, material things) A. Hdt. S. Ar. Plb. —(W.ACC. of hopes) X.; (of hope) —someone (W.GEN. of an aim) E. ‖ PASS. **be cheated** —W.GEN. of hopes, material things Hdt. S. Ar. Att.orats. X. + —of a person Ar.
4 ‖ PASS. **be mistaken or proved wrong** A. Hdt. S. Antipho Pl. + —W.GEN. in one's judgement, belief, or sim. Hdt. S. Th. Isoc. + —W.DAT. Hdt. —W.GEN. about someone or sthg. Antipho Th. Lys. Pl. + —W.ACC. Th. ‖ PF.PASS. (of a theory) **be wrong** Hdt.
5 ‖ PASS. **be let down or failed** —W.GEN. by lookouts Th.
6 ‖ PASS. (of a promise) **be broken** Th.
7 ‖ PASS. (of statements) **be fabricated** —W.PREP.PHR. by someone Antipho
—**ψεύδομαι** mid.vb.| fut. ψεύσομαι | aor. ἐψευσάμην, 2sg. ἐψεύσω (E.), ep.3sg.subj. ψεύσεται (Hes.) | pf. ἔψευσμαι | **1 tell falsehoods, lie** Hom. +
2 make false statements (unintentionally), **be mistaken** Hom. +
3 say (W.ACC. sthg.) **deceitfully** or **mistakenly** Ar. Att.orats. Pl. +; **lie about** —a marriage E.
4 lie to, deceive —someone A. E. Ar. X. —(W.ACC. about sthg.) S. Pl.; **cheat, disappoint** —someone (in an expectation) E. —(W.ACC. over sthg.) And.
5 break —an oath Il. X.; **renege on** —an alliance, agreement, payments Th. X.; **break with, violate** —a custom Plu.; **fail to deliver on** —one's threats Hdt.
—**ἐψευσμένως** pf.pass.ptcpl.adv. **mistakenly** —ref. to holding an opinion Pl.
ψευδ-ώνυμος ον adj. [ψευδής, ὄνομα] (of Justice, a river) falsely named, **untrue to one's name** A.
—**ψευδωνύμως** adv. **by the wrong name** A.
ψεῦσμα ατος n. [ψεύδω] **false statement** Pl. Plb.; **lie** Plu.
ψευστέω contr.vb. [ψεύστης] **be a liar** Il.
ψεύστης ου, dial. **ψεύστᾱς** ᾱ m. [ψεύδω] **liar** Il. Timocr. Hdt. S. D. Arist. + ‖ ADJ. (of a story) **false** Pi.
ψεφεννός ά όν dial.adj. (fig., of a person) **shadowy** (i.e. feeble or ineffective) Pi.
ψῆ (3sg.): see **ψάω**
ψῆγμα ατος n. [ψήχω] **1** (collectv.) **shavings, filings** (of gold) Hdt. Plu.; **gold dust** Hdt.
2 ashes (fr. a cremation, envisaged as a pile of gold dust and also as the fig. currency of war) A.
ψήκτρᾱ ᾱς f. **curry-comb, horse-comb** E.
ψῆλαι (aor.inf.): see **ψάλλω**
ψηλαφάω contr.vb. [perh.reltd. ψάλλω, ἁφάω] | ep.ptcpl. (w.diect.) ψηλαφόων | **1** (of a person in the dark) **grope around** Ar. Arist.; (of a blinded person) —W.DAT. w. his hands Od.
2 (fig., of persons envisaged as in the dark) **grope around** (for explanations) Pl.; (tr.) **grope at** —problems Ar.
3 feel with one's hands —the resurrected Christ NT.; (fig.) **seek to grasp, reach out for** —God NT.
4 ‖ PASS. (of a horse's body) **be stroked** X.
5 (fig.) **examine** —a dead boar Plb. —every option Plb.
ψηλάφημα ατος n. **caress** (of a lover) X.
ψηλάφησις εως f. **probing, disturbing** (of earth) Plu.
ψήν ψηνός m. **insect which lives in fruit, fig-wasp** Hdt. Ar.
ψηνίζω vb. (app. of the writer of a play Fig-wasps) **do one's fig-wasp act** Ar.
ψῆξις εως f. [ψήχω] **curry-combing, grooming** (of horses) X.
ψήρ m.: see **ψάρ**
ψῆττα ης Att.f. **flatfish** Ar. Pl.
ψηφῐδο-φόρος ον adj. [ψηφίς, φέρω] (of an official) **possessing a right to vote** Hdt.
ψηφίζω vb. [ψῆφος] | aor. ἐψήφισα ‖ MID.: fut. ψηφιοῦμαι | pf. ἐψήφισμαι | **1 do calculations** (on an abacus) Plb.
2 ‖ MID. **cast one's vote** (usu. by ballot), **vote** Hdt. Th. Ar. Att.orats. +
3 procure by vote —a judgement (W.PREP.PHR. against someone) S.
4 ‖ MID. **settle by vote** —an issue, a lawsuit Att.orats.
5 ‖ MID. **decide by vote, vote** —W.INF., ACC. + INF. or COMPL.CL. to do sthg., that sthg. shd. be done A. Hdt. Th. Ar. + —W.ACC. + INF. that sthg. is the case Th.
6 ‖ MID. **vote in favour of, vote for** —sthg. Th. Att.orats. X. +
7 ‖ PASS. (of a person) **be voted** —W.PREDIC.SB. a murderer Antipho; **be sentenced** —W.INF. to die E.
8 ‖ PASS. (of measures, motions, decrees) **be voted for** or **passed** Att.orats. Plu. ‖ NEUT.PL.AOR. and PF.PASS.PTCPL.SB. **resolutions** or **decrees** Th. Att.orats.
9 ‖ MID. **award by vote, vote for** —honours, property, an expedition (i.e. charge of it), a fine, immunity, or sim. (usu. W.DAT. for someone) Th. Ar. Att.orats. Plb. Plu. ‖ PASS. (of funds, immunity, or sim.) **be awarded by vote** —W.DAT. or PREP.PHR. to someone Th. Att.orats. X. Plu. ‖ IMPERS.PASS. **it is authorised by vote** —W.DAT. + INF. for someone to do sthg. Ar. Plu.
ψηφίς ῖδος f. [dimin. ψῆφος] **1 pebble** (in a stream or on a beach) Il. Democr. AR.
2 vote (taken by the populace) Hippon. Call.
ψήφισμα ατος n. [ψηφίζω] **1 proposal put to the vote** (usu. in the Assembly), **decree** A. Th. Ar. Att.orats. +
2 edict (W.GEN. of the gods) Emp. Ar.
ψηφισματο-πώλης ου m. [πωλέω] **decree-seller** Ar.
ψηφισματώδης ες adj. ‖ NEUT.PL.SB. **regulations in the form of decrees** Arist.
ψηφο-ποιός όν adj. [ψῆφος, ποιέω] (of a person) **rigging the vote** S.
ψῆφος, dial. **ψᾶφος**, ου f. **1 pebble** Pi. Hdt.
2 counter (in a game) Pl.
3 (collectv.sg. and pl.) **counters, set of counters** (for calculating sums) Hdt. Ar. +; result of using counters, **calculations, accounts, figures** D.; **reckoning** (of the value of sthg.) Pi.; means of calculating value, **criterion** Plb.
4 pebble cast as a ballot; ballot, voting-token A. Hdt. Att.orats. + [Orig. ref. to simple pebbles, but later to purpose-made metal discs w. a central axle, hollow to signify a vote for the plaintiff, solid to signify a vote for the defendant.]
5 individual vote (by a juror or member of a political assembly), **vote** A. +; (collectv.sg. and pl.) **votes cast** (in a ballot) E. Att.orats. +; **share of the vote** (received by a particular candidate or option) Pl.
6 holding of a ballot, vote (on an issue) A. +
7 place of voting, tribunal, court (ref. to the Areopagus) E.

ψηφοφορία

8 outcome of a vote, **verdict, decision** A. +; **sentence** S. E.; (phr.) μία ψῆφος *unanimous verdict* A. Ar.
9 motion voted into law; **ruling, decree** (of an assembly) A.; (ref. to the text, carved in stone) Pi.
10 verdict, opinion (of a person, on a question) Pl.; **decision, edict** (of a ruler) S. E.

ψηφοφορίᾱ ᾱς *f.* [φέρω] voting by ballot, **ballot** Arist.; (gener.) **voting** Plu.

ψήχω *vb.* [perh.reltd. ψάω] **1** (of time) **grind down, wear away** —*everything* Simon. ‖ MID.PASS. (of diseased bone) **crumble** Pl.
2 rub down, groom —*a horse* Pl. X.; (of Naiads) —*deer (pulling the carriage of Artemis)* Call. ‖ PASS. (of a horse) be rubbed down X.
3 stroke —*a horse's neck and forehead* E. —*a sausage (app. fig.ref. to a penis)* Hippon.; **rub** —*one's cheeks* AR.
4 smear —*a serpent's head* (W.DAT. w. *a magic potion*) AR.
5 (fig., pejor.) **scratch away at, scribble** —*impious books* Call.

ψιάδδω *Lacon.vb.* **play, sport** Ar.

ψίαθος ου *f.* | dial.acc.pl. ψιάθως | **reed-mat** (to sleep on) Ar.

ψιάς άδος *f.* **drop** (of rain) Il. Hes.

ψιθυρίζω *vb.* | dial.1pl.impf. ἐψιθυρίσδομες | **whisper** —*sthg.* Plb. Plu.; (intr.) **talk in whispers** Pl. Theoc.; (fig., of a tree, w. its rustling leaves) Ar.

ψιθύρισμα ατος *n.* (fig.) **whisper** (of a tree, fr. its rustling leaves) Theoc.

ψιθυρισμός οῦ *m.* **whispering** Men. NT.

ψιθυριστής οῦ *m.* **whisperer** (epith. of Hermes, perh. ref. to a specific statue) D.

ψίθυρος ον *adj.* (pejor., of words) **whispered** (because slanderous) S. ‖ MASC.SB. **whisperer** (i.e. slanderer) Pi.

ψῑλο-κόρσης εω *Ion.m.* [ψῑλός, κόρση] **bald-headed man** Call.

ψῑλομετρίᾱ ᾱς *f.* [μέτρον] poetry without instrumental accompaniment, **unaccompanied verse** Arist.

ψῑλόν *dial.n.*: see πτίλον

ψῑλός ή όν *adj.* **1** without vegetation; (of land, regions) **bare, treeless** Hdt. +; **devoid** (W.GEN. of trees, soil) Hdt. Pl.; (of ploughland) **open** Il. ‖ NEUT.PL.SB. **open ground** X.
2 (of land, agriculture) **devoted to grain-crops** (opp. fruit-farming) D. Arist.
3 without hair or feathers; (of birds, animals, parts of their bodies) **bald** Hdt. Pl. X.; (of dogs) **thin-coated** X.; (of a horse's tail) **stripped** (W.GEN. of all its hair) Plu.
4 (of persons, their faces) **hairless, shaven** Ar.; **smooth, soft** Ar.
5 (of animal-skin, worn as clothing) **hairless** (i.e. stripped of hair) Hdt.; (as worn by a beggar) **bare, bald, mangy** Od. Anacr.
6 without foliage ‖ NEUT.PL.SB. **bare stems** (of shrubs) X.
7 without the usual or appropriate covering; (of a sword) **bare, naked** (i.e. without scabbard) X.; (of a horse) **bare-backed** X.; (of a corpse, bone, soldier's head) **exposed, unprotected** S. Pl. X.; (of a spear, used as a pole) **bare** (opp. carrying flags) Plb.
8 (of the eye of a blind man, fig.ref. to his daughter acting as his guide) **defenceless** S.(dub.)
9 without the necessary equipment or accoutrements; (of persons) **unequipped, unprepared** S.; **lacking** (W.GEN. weapons, cavalry) Pl. X.; **without armour, unarmed** S. Th.
10 (of troops) without heavy armour, **light-armed** Hdt. +; (of armour) **light** Th.; (of military exercises) **for light-armed troops** Arist. ‖ MASC.PL.SB. **light-armed troops** Hdt. +; (sg.) X. D. ‖ NEUT.SB. **light infantry** Arist.
11 devoid or **bereft** (of sthg. integral or usu. present); (of a ship's keel) **stripped bare, alone** (i.e. w. the rest of the hull broken away) Od.; (of elephants) **bereft** (W.GEN. of their riders) Plb.; (of statements) **bare, mere, unsupported** Pl. D.; (of a soul) **devoid** (W.GEN. of a corporeal body) Pl.; (of pure sciences, W.GEN. of applications) Pl.
12 (of poetry, a singing voice) **unaccompanied** (by music or musical instruments) Pl.; (of music) unaccompanied (by singing), **instrumental** Pl. Arist.; (of language) **plain** (ref. to prose, opp. poetry) Pl. Arist.
13 (of certain sciences, incl. arithmetic) undertaken for the sake of knowledge alone, **pure** Pl.
14 (gramm.) without aspiration ‖ NEUT.SB. unaspirated consonant (ref. to π, opp. φ) Plu.

—ψῑλῶς *adv.* **1 baldly, simply** —*ref. to stating sthg. (without giving supporting evidence or sim.)* Pl. Plb.
2 (gener.) **merely, solely, purely** Pl. Plb. Plu.

ψῑλότης ητος *f.* **1 lack of vegetation** (on a plain) Plu.; **baldness** (of a head) Plu.
2 (gramm.) **lack of aspiration** (of consonants and vowels) Arist.; **smooth breathing** Plb.

ψῑλόω *contr.vb.* **1 strip** (sthg.) **bare** (of its usual covering or accompaniment); **strip** —*a head (of hair)* Hdt. —*a vine (of grapes)* X. ‖ PASS. (of heads) be stripped of hair, become bald Hes.*fr.*; (of a horse's fetlocks) X.; (of the side of a ship) be left bare (of oars) Plb.; (of a part of the body, a plant's roots) be left uncovered or exposed X. ‖ PF.PASS. (of a plant) have (W.ACC. its roots) exposed X.
2 (in military ctxt.) **leave** (a person or place) **devoid** (of persons); **strip** (W.ACC. a commander, an army) **of support** Th. X. ‖ PASS. (of an army's wing) be left bare Plb. —W.GEN. *of cavalry* Plu.; (of a rearguard) —*of camp-followers* X.; (of a hill) —*of cavalry* X.
3 strip (sthg.) **away** (fr. sthg. else); **strip away** —*most of a person's power* Hdt. ‖ PASS. (of meat) be stripped —W.GEN. *fr. bones* Hdt.; (of the wings) —W.DAT. *fr. a phalanx* Plb.

ψῑμύθιον ου *n.* **white lead** (in paste or powder form, applied to the face by women as a cosmetic) Ar. X. Arist.; (applied to blonde hair) Pl.

ψῑμυθιόω *contr.vb.* apply white lead to, **paint** or **powder with white lead** —*a face* Plu. ‖ MID. (of a woman) **paint** or **powder oneself** Lys.

ψίσδομαι *Aeol.mid.vb.* **weep** Sapph.

ψιττακός οῦ *m.* **parrot** Call.

ψιχίον ου *n.* [dimin. ψίξ *crumb*] **crumb** (of food) NT.

ψογερός ά όν *adj.* [ψόγος] finding fault (w. a person), **censorious** Pi. Plu.

ψόγος ου *m.* [ψέγω] **1** that which attracts blame, **cause for reproach, disgrace, fault** or **flaw** Xenoph. Simon. E. Th.
2 blame (directed at others), **blame, reproach, criticism** Pi. Trag. Th. Ar. Isoc. Pl. +
3 (specif.) **speech of condemnation** (of a person) Pl. Plb.; **satirical attack, lampoon** (in verse) Arist.

ψολόεις εσσα εν *adj.* [ψόλος *smoke, soot*] (of the lightning-bolt of Zeus) **smoking** Od. Hes. hHom. Pi.

ψολοκομπίᾱ ᾱς *f.* [κόμπος] smoky boasting, **empty bluster** Ar.

ψοφέω *contr.vb.* [ψόφος] | pf. ἐψόφηκα | **1** (of objects, natural phenomena) **make a noise, sound, resound** E. Lys. Ar. Pl. X. Men. Mosch.
2 (of a song) **sound forth** —W.ADV. *loudly* Call.
3 (of a person or mouse) **make a sound** E. Arist. Men.
4 (of a person, by opening a door) **make a noise** Men.; (tr.) **make a noise opening** —*a door* Men. Plu.

5 (of a person) **make a meaningless noise** (opp. say sthg. sensible) Pl.
6 (of satyrs) perh. **fart** (fr. fear) S.*Ichn.* [also interpr. as *die*]
ψοφήματα των *n.pl.* **noises** (made by a person) S.*satyr.fr.*
ψοφο-δεής ές *adj.* [ψόφος, δέος] (of persons, animals) **afraid of the slightest noise** Pl. Plu.; (gener., of a city) **nervous** Plu. ‖ NEUT.SB. **timidity** Plu.
ψόφος ου *m.* **1 sound, noise** (of objects, musical instruments, natural phenomena, activities) hHom. Sapph. Pi.*fr.* Hdt. S.*Ichn.* E. +
2 mere sound (W.GEN. of a voice, fig.ref. to an ineffective person) E.
3 empty bluster (of a person or his language) S. Ar.
ψοφώδης ες *adj.* (of dithyrambic poets) **full of noise, bombastic** Arist.
ψυδρός ά όν *adj.* [ψεῦδος] (of a mind) **false, deceitful** Thgn.
ψύθος εος (ους) *n.* [reltd. ψεῦδος] **falsehood, untruth** A. Call.
ψυκτήρ ῆρος *m.* [ψύχω¹] **wine-cooler** Pl. Men. Plu.
ψυκτικός ή όν *adj.* (of things) **having a cooling effect** Arist.
ψύλλα ης *f.* **flea** Ar. X.
ψύξις εως *f.* [ψύχω¹] **1 process of cooling down** Pl.
2 coldness (opp. heat) Pl.; (as a bodily sensation) Pl.
ψύττα *interj.* (as a shepherd's call) **hey!** E.*Cyc.*
ψυχά *dial.f.*: see ψυχή
ψῡχαγωγέω *contr.vb.* [ψῡχαγωγός] **1 summon spirits** Ar.; (tr.) **summon the spirits of** —*the dead* Pl.
2 draw to oneself souls (of living people, through artistic skill); (of poets, orators, forms of literature or art) **captivate, entrance** —*people* Isoc. X. Arist. Plb.; (intr.) Arist. Plb. ‖ PASS. (of the impressionable part of the human soul) **be spellbound** —W.PREP.PHR. *by illusions* Pl.
3 charm, win over —*someone* Plb.; (pejor.) **beguile, cajole** —*someone* Pl. Lycurg. Plb. ‖ PASS. **be won over** Plb.; **be beguiled or cajoled** —W.DAT. *by arguments, flattery, deceptive behaviour* Aeschin. D.
ψῡχαγωγία ᾱς *f.* **1 captivation of the soul, allurement** (ref. to rhetoric, its aim) Pl.
2 allure, fascination (of hunting, a narrative) Plb.
ψῡχαγωγικός ή όν *adj.* (of the visual element of drama) **captivating** Arist.
ψῡχ-αγωγός όν *adj.* [ψῡχή] (of cries) **summoning the spirits of the dead** A. ‖ MASC.SB. **necromancer** E.
ψῡχάριον ου *n.* [dimin. ψῡχή] (pejor.) **mean little soul** (of an unscrupulous or small-minded man) Pl.
ψύχεινός ή όν *adj.* [ψύχος] (of places) **cool** X.
ψῡχ-εμπορικός ή όν *adj.* [ψῡχή] ‖ FEM.SB. **trade in intellectual wares** (as practised by itinerant teachers, esp. sophists) Pl.
ψῡχή ῆς, dial. **ψῡχά** ᾶς *f.* [app.reltd. ψύχω²] **1 life-force or animating principle, soul, spirit** (of a person or animal) Hom. +; (as leaving the body in death, sts. breathed out or even escaping through a wound) Hom. +; (as leaving a fainting person) Il.; (as having wings) Pl.
2 (fig.) **soul, lifeblood** (W.GEN. of a state, ref. to a constitution) Isoc.; (of tragedy, ref. to plot) Arist.
3 soul which has left the body, spirit (esp. as going down to Hades or sim.) Hom. +; **ghost** (resembling an insubstantial image of a dead person) Hom. +
4 state or fact of being alive, life (as sthg. risked, spared, or sim.) Hom. +
5 (hyperbol., exemplifying what is most dear to a person; ref. to profit, children) **life itself, one's very life** Hes. E.
6 (ref. to a person, esp. in ctxt. of life or death) **living soul** Trag. +

7 (periphr.) **person** (W.GEN. of a specific named individual) S. E.
8 conscious self (as centre of emotions, desires, thoughts), **soul, heart, mind** hHom. +; **all one's heart** (put into doing sthg.) X. Theoc. Bion
9 (in self-address, sts. W.ADJ. φίλη *dear*) **heart** Pi. Trag. Ar.(mock-trag.)
10 spirit, strength of character, courage (of persons, animals) Pi. +
11 character, personality (of an individual) Thgn. +
12 (philos.) **primary source of life and consciousness** (assoc.w. fire), **soul** Heraclit.; (assoc.w. νοῦς *mind*, as animating the body, in the doctrine of Anaxagoras) Pl.; (as immortal, opp. body) Pl.; (as the underlying substance of living things) Arist.; (ref. to the all-pervading animating principle, which determines the structure of the cosmos) **world-soul** Pl.
ψῡχικός ή όν *adj.* **1 relating to the soul** (opp. the body); (of pleasures, achievements, or sim.) **of the soul** Arist.
2 (of inclinations, boldness) **of the mind** Plb.
ψῡχομαχέω *contr.vb.* [μάχομαι] **1** (of troops, roosters) **fight for one's life, fight to the death** Plb.
2 throw one's whole heart into a struggle Plb.
ψῡχομαχίᾱ ᾱς *f.* **fight for one's life** Plb.
ψῡχο-πομπός οῦ *m.* (ref. to Charon) **ferryman of souls** E.
ψῡχορραγέω *contr.vb.* [ψῡχορραγής] **breathe one's last, be at the point of death** E. AR. Plu.
ψῡχο-ρραγής ές *adj.* [ῥήγνῡμι] (of persons) **giving up the ghost, breathing one's last** E.
ψῦχος εος (ους) *n.* **1 cold** (opp. heat) Pl.
2 cold weather S. Ar. X. Arist. Plb. NT. Plu.; (pl.) Hdt. X. Arist.
3 cool, coolness (as a welcome relief fr. heat) Od. A. Pl. X.
ψύχόομαι *pass.contr.vb.* **become cold** Plu.
ψῡχρ-ήλατος ον *adj.* [ψῡχρός, ἐλαύνω] (of swords) **cold-forged** (i.e. dipped while hot in cold water, for hardening) Pl.
ψῡχρίᾱ ᾱς *f.* **frigidity, ineptitude** (of a remark) Plu.
ψῡχρολουτέω *contr.vb.* [λούω] **bathe in cold water** Plu.
ψῡχρός ά (Ion. ή) όν, Aeol. **ψῦχρος** ᾱ ον *adj.* [ψῦχος]
1 naturally cold; (of places, natural phenomena, such as snow, winds, water) **cold** Hom. Hes. Eleg. Lyr. Hdt. E. + ‖ NEUT.SB. **coldness** Hdt. Pl. X.(also pl.) Arist.; **cold water** Thgn. Hdt. Thphr. NT. Plu.
2 cold to the touch; (of an object) **cold** Plu.; (of a bronze spear-tip) Il.; (of a snake) Thgn. Theoc.; (of a drink) Pl.
3 causing a feeling of coldness; (of a path, fig.ref. to death by hemlock) **chilling** Ar. ‖ NEUT.PL.SB. (fig.) **chilling deeds** S.
4 lacking or having lost warmth; (of meat, an oven) **cold** Timocr. Hdt.; (of blood, a corpse) S. E.; (of knees) Theoc.; (of sweat) Sapph.; (of a flame, fig.ref. to passionate feelings) Pi.*fr.*; (fig., of crimes, envisaged as food) **gone cold** (i.e. of long standing) D.
5 (of persons) **lacking ardour or intensity of feeling, frigid, unresponsive** Isoc. Pl. X. Arist.
6 (as a term of aesthetic criticism) **lacking the power to excite an appropriate response**; (of a poet, play, music) **frigid, lifeless, boring** Ar. Pl.; (of remarks) X.; (of an expression) **trite, cliché** D. ‖ NEUT.SB. (sg. and pl.) **frigidity** (of style) Arist.
7 lacking the power to give pleasure or comfort; (of the object of one's embraces, ref. to an evil wife) **chill, joyless** S.; (of a life) Ar.; (of a path, fig.ref. to a way of life) Pi.*fr.*(dub.)
8 lacking effectiveness; (of help, victory) **ineffectual, empty, vain** Hdt.; (of pleasure, hope) E. Plu.

—ψῡχρῶς adv. **frigidly, feebly, boringly** —ref. to writing, speaking, joking Ar. Pl. Thphr.

ψῡχρότης ητος f. **1 quality of being cold, cold, coldness** Pl. Arist.
2 coldness (of natural phenomena) Plb. Plu.
3 cold state of the body, chill Plu.
4 want of feeling, **insensitivity** (in behaviour) D.
5 lack of ardour (in a commander) Plu.

ψῡχω[1] vb. [ψῦχος] | aor. ἔψῡξα ‖ PASS.: fut. ψυγήσομαι (NT.) | aor. ἐψύχθην | aor.2 ἐψύχην (Ar.) | pf.ptcpl. ἐψυγμένος |
1 make cold, **chill** —wine Isoc.; (of a doctor) **cool down** —a body Pl.; (intr., of the setting sun) **have a cooling effect** Hdt.; (of various agents and forces) Pl. ‖ MID. (of a boar) **cool down** —its flanks and belly (W.DAT. in mud) AR. ‖ PASS. (of substances, water) **be cooled down or become cold** Hdt. Ar. Pl. Arist.; (of overheated persons) Arist.; (of a fire) die down Pl.
2 ‖ MID. **feel cold** (as one of the body's senses) Pl.
3 ‖ PASS. (of a person) turn cold (fr. a snake-bite) AR.; (of a lover) shiver (w. emotion) Theoc.
4 ‖ PASS. (fig., of brotherly love) grow cold NT.
5 ‖ PASS. (of wet ground) dry out X.; (of wet curtains) be dried out Plu.

ψύχω[2] vb. [app.reltd. ψῡχή] (of Athena) **exhale, breathe out** Il.

ψωλή ῆς, dial. **ψωλά** ᾶς f. **penis with foreskin retracted** (fr. erection), **dick** Ar.

ψωλός οῦ masc.adj. [reltd. ψωλή] with the end of the penis exposed, **with exposed penis** (fr. circumcision) Ar.; (fr. an erection) Ar.

ψωμίζω vb. [ψωμός] **feed morsels to** —a baby Ar. ‖ PASS. (fig., of the populace) be fed —W.DAT. w. titbits (by demagogues) Ar.

ψωμίον ου n. [dimin.] **piece of bread** NT.

ψώμισμα ατος n. [ψωμίζω] **morsel of food** (fed to a baby) Arist. Plu.

ψωμός οῦ m. **1 morsel** (of human flesh, vomited up by Polyphemos) Od.
2 morsel of food (fed to a baby) Arist.
3 piece of bread (eaten w. the main course) X.

ψώρᾱ ᾶς, Ion. **ψώρη** ης f. itchy skin disease, **mange, scabies** (in persons or horses) Hdt. Plb.; **itch** (in persons) Pl.

ψωραλέος ᾱ ον adj. (of animals) **mangy** X.

ψωράω contr.vb. (of persons) **have an itch** Pl.

ψώχω vb. **rub** —ears of grain (W.DAT. in one's hands, to separate the husks) NT.

Ω ω

ὤ *dial.relatv.adv.*: see ὡς B
ὥ (nom.acc.du.relatv.pron.): see ὅς[1]
ὤ (sts. written ὦ) *interj.* **1** (on its own, expressing surprise, joy, pain) **oh!** E. +
2 (w. another exclam.) ὢ πόποι *ah me!, alas!* Hom. +; ὤ μοι (also written ὤμοι or ὢμοι) Hom. +; ὢ πρὸς τῶν θεῶν *ah by the gods!, in heaven's name!* S. E. Ar. Pl. +
3 (w.pron. or noun, usu. in NOM.) ὤ μοι ἐγώ, ὢ τάλας ἐγώ *ah me!, ah wretched me!* Hom. +; ὢ ἐμὲ δειλάν *ah unhappy me!* Call.
—ὤαι *dial.interj.* [ὤ, αἰαῖ] (expressing pain) **ah me!** Theoc.
ὧ[1] *dial.relatv.adv.*: see under ὅς[1]
ὧ[2] (dial.masc.neut.gen.relatv.pron.): see ὅς[1]
ὦ[1] *interj.* (as a form of address, w.VOC.) **O ...** Hom. + • ὦ θεοί *O gods* S. E. Ar. + • ὦ ἄνδρες Ἀθηναῖοι *O men of Athens* Th. Att.orats. + • ὦ Ζεῦ *O Zeus* Archil. +; (sts. also W.IMPERATV.) Trag. + • ὦ χαῖρ' Ἀθάνα *hail, Athena!* S.
ὦ[2] (1sg.subj.): see εἰμί
Ὠαρίων *dial.m.*, Ὠαριώνειος *dial.adj.*: see Ὠρίων
ὤατα (dial.nom.acc.pl.): see οὖς
ὠβά ᾶς *Lacon.f.* [perh.reltd. οἴη] subdivision of a Spartan clan (ref. to the people or their territory), **village, oba** Plu.(law)
ὠβάζω *vb.* (of Lykourgos) **divide** (the Spartans) **into obas** (W.COGN.ACC. ὠβάς) Plu.(oracle)
ὠγμός οῦ *m.* [ᾤζω] **sound of groaning** (of a chorus of Erinyes, as a stage-direction) A.
ὠγύγιος ον (also ᾱ ον A.) *adj.* (of the water of the Styx, of Earth, fire) **ancient, primordial** Hes. A.*fr.* Emp.; (of caverns, mountains, sacred lands) A. Pi. Call.; (of Thebes, Athens) A. S. AR.; (of one of the gates of Thebes, sts. also assoc.w. a fabled Boeotian king Ogygos) E.; (of god-given authority) S.
—Ὠγυγίη ης *Ion.f.* **Ogygia** (appos.w. νῆσος, Calypso's island, where Odysseus stayed for seven years) Od.
ᾠδά *dial.f.*: see ἀοιδή
ὧδε *demonstr.adv.* [reltd. ὅδε] **1** (in dir.sp., calling attention to the way in which sthg. is happening) **in this way, like this** Hom. + • πλάζομαι ὧδ' ἐπεὶ οὔ μοι ἐπ' ὄμμασι νήδυμος ὕπνος ἱζάνει *I am wandering like this because carefree sleep does not settle on my eyes* Il. • ὧδε περιυβρίσμεθα *we have been outraged in such a terrible way* Hdt.
2 (in narrative or dir.sp., introducing an explanation) **in the following manner, as follows, like this, thus** Hom. + • μετέβαλον δὲ ὧδε ἐς εὐνομίην *but they changed to good government in the following way* Hdt. • ἐν χρησμῷ ἦν γεγραμμένον περὶ αὐτῆς ὧδε *there was an oracle concerning it, written as follows* Hdt.
3 (in narrative or dir.sp., referring back to sthg. just said) in the way just indicated, **in that way, like that, thus** Hom. + • κατὰ μὲν τὸν … πόλεμον Ἀλυάττῃ ὧδε ἔσχε *that is the story of Alyattes' war* Hdt. • γένους μὲν ἥκεις ὧδε τοῖσδε *that is how things stand between you and them in family terms* E.
4 (correlatv., preceding cl. w. ὡς) **in such a way** (that or as) Hom. Hdt. + • ἀλλά μοι ὧδ' ἀνὰ θυμὸν οἴεται, ὡς ἔσεταί περ *but it seems to me in my mind exactly as it will be* Od.
5 (in dir.sp., calling attention to one's person or the immediate location) **before** or **in front of one, here** Hom. + • ἐν ἡμετέροισι δόμοισιν ἥμενος ὧδε *sitting here like this in our house* Od. • Δάφνις ἐγὼν ὅδε τῆνος ὁ τὰς βόας ὧδε νομεύων *I am that Daphnis who herded his cows here* Theoc.
6 (ref. to movt. towards the immediate location) **here** Hom. + • ἔρχεό μοι, τὸν ξεῖνον ἐναντίον ὧδε κάλεσσον *go, please, call the stranger here before me* Od. • προσάγαγε ὧδε τὸν υἱόν σου *bring your son here* NT.
7 (modifying an adj. or ptcpl.) **so, such** Hom. • ἀνὴρ πεπνυμένος ὧδε *such a wise man* Od.
—ὡδί *adv.* **1** in the way now being demonstrated (by the speaker, illustrating or imitating actions, pronunciation, or sim.), **like this, exactly like this** Ar. • ὡδὶ κελεύεις κατακλινῆναι; *are you telling me to recline like this?* Ar.
2 (introducing an illustrative statement or quotation) **exactly as follows, like this** Pl. Arist.
3 (introducing an explanation or expansion of what has been said) **more precisely as follows, like this** Ar. Pl. D. Arist. • ὡδὶ λέγεις *what you're saying amounts to this* Ar. • σκοπεῖτε γὰρ ὡδί *look at it this way* D. • (of persons) ὡδὶ ἔχειν **have this attitude, feel like this** (about sthg.) D. Arist.
Ὠδεῖον ου *n.* [ἀοιδή] **Odeion** (public building in Athens, constructed by Perikles c.440 BC to host musical performances; also used for other civic purposes, incl. grain distribution and legal hearings) And. Ar. X. D. Arist. Thphr.
ᾠδή *f.*: see ἀοιδή
ᾠδικός οῦ *m.* one skilled in singing; (gener.) **musician** Arist.
ὠδίνω *vb.* [ὠδίς] | only pres. and impf. | impf. ὤδινον (Thphr.) | **1** (of a woman) **suffer labour pains, be in labour** Il. Ar. Pl. +; (fig., of thinkers, w. ideas or sim.) Pl.; (provbl., of a mountain, w. a mouse) Plu. | see μῦς 2
2 (tr.) **be pregnant with, carry** —*an unborn child* hHom.; **give birth to, bear** —*a child* E.
3 feel intense physical or mental pain as though in labour; (of a woman) **labour painfully** —W.INTERN.ACC. w. *a burden of misfortune* S.; (of a person's mind) —w. *a fear* Plu.; (of the blinded Polyphemos) **be in agony** —W.DAT. *fr. pain* Od.
4 suffer anguish, be distressed E. Pl. —W.INDIR.Q. *over what someone is saying* S.
ὠδίς ῖνος *f.* | ep.dat.pl. ὠδίνεσσι | **1** pain or process of labour in childbirth, **labour, labour pains, delivery** Il. hHom. Pi. S. E. +
2 (concr.) child resulting from delivery or yet to be delivered, **child, offspring** A. Pi. E.
3 anguish Trag. Pl. NT. Plu.

ᾠδο-ποιός οῦ *m*. [ἀοιδή, ποιέω] song-maker, **singer** Theoc.*epigr*.

ᾠδός *Att.m.f*.: see ἀοιδός

ὠδύσατο (ep.3sg.aor.mid.): see ὀδύσασθαι

ὠδώδει (3sg.plpf.): see ὄζω

ὠείγοντο (ep.3pl.impf.pass.): see οἴγω

ὤεον *dial.n*.: see ᾠόν

ὤζω *vb*. [ὤ] (of Erinyes, in their sleep) **groan** A.; (of theatrical spectators, in surprised wonder) **cry oh!** Ar.

ὠή *interj*. (rousing or drawing the attention of persons or animals) **hey there!** A. E. X.; (as a nervous reaction to a sound) E.

ᾠήθην (aor.pass.): see οἴομαι

ὠθέω *contr.vb*. | impf. ἐώθουν, ep. ὤθουν, iteratv. ὤθεσκον | fut. ὠθήσω, also ὤσω | aor. ἔωσα, Ion. ὦσα, iteratv. ὤσασκον ‖ MID.: aor. ἐωσάμην, Ion. ὠσάμην ‖ PASS.: fut. ὠσθήσομαι | aor.ptcpl. ὠσθείς, inf. ὠσθῆναι | pf.ptcpl. ἐωσμένος |

1 propel (persons or things) with physical force; **push**, **thrust** —*someone or sthg*. (*freq.* W.ADV. or PREP.PHR. *specifying direction*) Hom. Hdt. E. Ar. + —*a weapon or sim*. (*at or into someone*) Hdt. E. Theoc. Plu.; (wkr.sens.) —*rocks (against a door, to keep it shut)* Ar. —*sthg*. (*into one's mouth, to smother laughter*) Thphr.; (of Polyphemos) **project, vomit** —*food* (*fr. his gullet*) E.*Cyc*. ‖ PASS. (of persons) be pushed (in some direction) Hdt. E. X. Plu.; be thrust or flung (to one's death) Plu.; (of corpses, fr. a cliff) Hdt.

2 push aside or away —*a person, weapon, object* (*freq.* W.ADV. or PREP.PHR. *specifying direction*) Hom. E. Ar. —*a door-bar* Parm.; (of a goddess) **dispel** —*a mist (fr. someone's eyes)* Il. ‖ MID. **push away** —*a person* Il. —*a veil (fr. one's head)* Parm.; (of a horse) **throw** —*a rider* Thgn. ‖ PASS. (of a person) be pushed away E.

3 thrust or force open —*a door* E. Lys. Ar.

4 cast out or drive away (fr. one's presence, house, community or country, sacred places and rituals) —*a person* Il. Trag. Ar. Pl. + —*an unburied corpse* S.; (fig.) —*a quality (fr. oneself, one's soul)* Pl. ‖ PASS. be cast out (of a house) S.*fr*.

5 (act. and mid., of soldiers or sim.) **fend off, push back, force away** —*adversaries* Il. Hdt. E. Th. Ar. X. +; (intr., act. and mid.) **push, shove** (against the enemy, in a skirmish) X. ‖ PASS. be pushed or driven back (by the enemy or a mob) Pl. X. Plu.

6 (wkr.sens., of persons) **push, jostle** (someone) X. Thphr.; (tr., of people in a crowd) **push against** —*others* Plu.; (fig., of a wine-cup) —*another (in eagerness to be filled)* Alc. ‖ MID. (of persons) **push, jostle** (each other) X. Theoc.

7 push or drive forward —*a warrior, one's comrades (to hasten a military advance)* Il. X. Plu.; (of a mother) —*an unwilling bride (to her wedding)* E. ‖ MID. (of soldiers) push oneself forward, **push forward, force a passage** Hdt. Th. X. Plu.; (tr., of persons) **force one's way through** —*a crowd* Plu. ‖ PASS. (of soldiers) be pushed forward (by those behind) X.; (of boars) be driven forward (by hunters) Pl.

8 (of water or wind) **sweep** or **drive along** —*someone or sthg*. Hom. E.(dub.) Theoc.; (of a person envisaged as a storm) —*a wave* Ar.

9 (fig., of a populace) **drive on, hurry** —*events* Hdt. ‖ MID. (of a writer) **press ahead** (in a narrative) Plu.

ὠθίζομαι *mid.vb*. (of persons) jostle (in words), **argue, dispute** (w. each other) Hdt.

ὠθισμός οῦ *m*. **1** hard pushing or clashing against another (in a hostile encounter or competition for space); **close engagement, mêlée** (of combatants, their shields) Hdt. Th. X. Plb. Plu.; (of ships in battle) Plu.; (of a crowd) Plu.

2 fierce verbal confrontation, **heated argument** Hdt.

ὠίγνυντο (ep.3pl.impf.pass.): see οἴγω

ὠίετο (ep.3sg.impf.mid.): see οἴομαι

ὤιξα (ep.aor.): see οἴγω

ὤιον *Aeol.n*.: see ᾠόν

ὠισάμην (ep.aor.mid.), **ὠίσθην** (ep.aor.pass.): see οἴομαι

ὦκα *adv*.: see under ὠκύς

ὠκεῖα (fem.adj.), **ὠκέα** (ep.fem.adj.), **ὠκειάων** (ep.fem.gen.pl.adj.): see ὠκύς

Ὠκεανός οῦ *m*. **1** Okeanos, **Ocean** (god of the primeval waters, also as a river encircling the world) Hom. +

2 (gener.) external sea, **ocean** (opp. the Mediterranean) Pi. AR. Theoc. Plb. Plu.

–Ὠκεανόνδε *adv*. **towards Ocean** hHom. Call.

–ὠκεανίς ίδος *fem.adj*. (of breezes) **of Ocean** Pi. ‖ SB. daughter of Ocean or Ocean nymph AR.

–Ὠκεανίνη ης *f*. **daughter of Ocean** or **Ocean nymph** Hes. Call.

ὤκειλα (aor.): see ὀκέλλω

ὠκέως *adv*., **ὤκιστα** (superl.adv.): see under ὠκύς

ὤκιστος (superl.adj.): see ὠκύς

ὤκτειρα, ὤκτῑρα (aor.): see οἰκτίρω

ὠκύ-αλος ον *adj*. [perh. ἅλς or ἅλλομαι] (of a ship) **speeding across the sea** Hom. S. Mosch.; (of a blast of wind) Pi.*fr*.(dub.)

ὠκυ-βόλος ον *adj*. [βάλλω] (of a bow) **quick-shooting** or **quick-striking** S.

ὠκυ-δίνᾱτος ον *dial.adj*. [δινάω] (of contests betw. ships or chariots) **swiftly speeding** or **turning** Pi.

ὠκύ-δρομος ον *adj*. [δρόμος] (of dolphin pups, the exertions of a hunted animal) **swift-running** Lyr.adesp. E.

ὠκύ-θοος ον *adj*. [θέω¹] (of clover) **fast-growing** Call.

ὠκύ-μορος ον *adj*. [μόρος] **1** with the fate of an early death; (of Achilles) **fated to die young** Il.; (of Penelope's suitors) **fated to die soon** or **quickly** Od.; (of mortals, a generation of heroes) soon to die, **short-lived** Simon. Emp.

2 (of arrows, poison) **carrying swift death** Hom. Plu.; (of a burning log, coterminous w. the life of Meleager) B.

ὠκυ-πέτης ου *masc.adj*. [πέτομαι] | nom.acc.du. ὠκυπέτα | (of a hawk) **swift-flying** Hes. AR.; (fig., of death) S.; (of a team of horses) **swiftly running** Il.

ὠκυπόδᾱς *dial.masc.adj*.: see under ὠκύπους

ὠκύ-ποινος ον *adj*. [ποινή] (of a transgression) app. **swiftly punished** A.

ὠκύ-πομπος ον *adj*. [πομπός] (of ships) providing swift conveyance, **swiftly moving** B. E.

ὠκύ-πορος ον *adj*. [πόρος] **1** (of a ship) **swift-travelling** Hom. hHom. Pi.; (of a person) E.*fr*.

2 (of currents of wave and wind) **swift-flowing** Pi.; (fig., of a stream of woe) A.

ὠκύ-πους πουν, gen. ποδος *adj*. [πούς] | acc. ὠκύπουν | ep.dat.pl. ὠκυπόδεσσι | (of animals, esp. horses) **swift-footed** Hom. Hes. Thgn. Lyr. S. E. AR.; (of Hermes, an athlete) E.

–ὠκυπόδᾱς ᾱ *dial.masc.adj*. (of a warrior) **swift-footed** E.*fr*.

ὠκύ-πτερος ον *adj*. [πτερόν] (of a hawk) **swift-winged** Il.; (of a ship, ref. to its sails) A. ‖ NEUT.PL.SB. flight feathers (of a bird's wing) Ar. AR. Plu.

ὠκύ-ροος ον *adj*. —also **ὠκυρόης** ου (AR.), dial. **ὠκυρόᾱς** ᾱ (E.) *adj*. [ῥόος] (of rivers) **swift-flowing** Il. E. AR.

ὠκύς εῖα (ep. ἑα) ύ *adj*. | ep.fem.gen.pl. ὠκειάων ‖ compar. ὠκύτερος, superl. ὠκύτατος, also ὤκιστος |

1 (of persons or things) characterised by the ability to move quickly; (of divinities, esp. Iris and Ares, of heroes, esp. Achilles, their limbs, feet or wings) **quick, speedy** Hom. Hes. Ibyc. Emp. E. AR.; (of persons, esp. messengers, their limbs or feet) Hom. Hes. Thgn. B.*fr.* E. Theoc.; (of chariots, horses or their feet, of ships or oars) Hom. Hes. Archil. Thgn. Lyr. E. +; (of arrows) Hom. Pi. Call.; (of movement or change) Simon.
2 (of birds, esp. the hawk or eagle, of wings) **quick** Hom. Lyr.; (of other animals, esp. deer, hounds, of their limbs, snakes' jaws) Od. Pi. Call. AR.
3 (of the sun's rays, blasts of wind, turbulent water) **quick** Eleg. Lyr.adesp. Pi.*fr.* AR.; (fig., of the word of the Muses) Ar.
4 (of persons, other agents) moving or acting quickly (in performing a task, going somewhere, or sim., freq. quasi-advbl.), **quick, speedy** Simon. S. E. Hellenist.poet.; (of persons in their actions, of minds or thought) hHom. Pi. AR.; (of Ares, meton.ref. to an army) E.
5 (of incantations) taking effect speedily, **swift-working** AR.
6 (of events, processes) occurring within a short space of time; (of a marriage, decided in a race) **quick, speedy** Pi.; (of the accomplishment of what is ordained) Pi.; (of death) Il.; (quasi-advbl., of life leaving a body) Il.; (of an opportunity) A.
7 passing quickly; (of the flower of youth) **fleeting** Thgn.
—ὦκα *adv.* | *superl.* ὤκιστα | **1** (ref. to movt.) **quickly, swiftly** Hom. hHom. Call. AR.
2 (ref. to time) **without delay, at once, straightaway** Hom. hHom. Thgn. Call. AR.
3 soon, before long Hom. hHom. AR. Theoc.
—ὠκέως *adv.* **quickly, swiftly** Archil. Pi.
ὠκύτης ητος, *dial.* **ὠκύτᾱς** ᾱτος *f.* **swiftness, speed** (in running) Pi. E.; (w.GEN. of hands, in playing the aulos) Telest.
ὠκυτόκιον ου *n.* [ὠκυτόκος] that which promotes a quick birth (ref. to a drug or amulet), **birth-charm** Ar.
ὠκυ-τόκος ον *adj.* (of the moon, app. identified w. Artemis) **giving a quick** or **easy birth** Tim.; (of a river) **swiftly bringing fertility** (to crops) S. ‖ NEUT.SB. quick birth or easy delivery Hdt.
ὠλένη ης *f.* **arm** (of a person, usu.pl., esp. in ctxt. of embracing someone) hHom. Trag. Ar.(mock-trag.)
ὤλεσα (aor.): see ὄλλῡμι
ὠλεσί-καρπος ον *adj.* [ὄλλῡμι, καρπός¹] (of a willow) **shedding fruit** (before it ripens) Od.
ὠλεσί-οικος ον *adj.* [οἶκος] (of an Erinys) **house-destroying** A.
ὤλισθον (aor.2): see ὀλισθάνω
ὦλξ ὠλκός *f.* [reltd. αὖλαξ] | *only acc.* ὦλκα, *pl.* ὦλκας | **furrow** (in the ground) Hom. Hellenist.poet.
ὠλόμενος Aeol.aor.2 mid.ptcpl.adj.: see ὀλόμενος, under ὄλλῡμι
ὠλόμην (aor.2 mid.): see ὄλλῡμι
ὦμεν (1pl.subj.), **ὦμες** (dial.): see εἰμί
ᾤμην (impf.mid.): see οἴομαι
ὠμ-ηστής οῦ, *dial.* **ὠμηστᾱ́ς** ᾶ, Aeol. **ὠμήστᾱς** ᾱ *masc.fem.adj.* [ὠμός, ἐσθίω] (of animals, birds, fishes) **eating raw flesh** Il. Hes. A. B. Hdt.(oracle) S. AR.; (hyperbol., of Achilles, ref. to his savagery) Il.; (as epith. of Dionysus) Alc. Plu.; (of Mark Antony) Plu.
ὠμο-βοέη ης *Ion.f.* [βόειος] **untanned oxhide** Hdt.
ὠμο-βόειος ᾱ ον *adj.* (of skins) **of untanned oxhide** X.; (of wicker shields, a trumpet) X.
ὠμο-βόινος η ον *Ion.adj.* (of shields) **made of untanned oxhide** Hdt.
ὠμο-βόλος ον *adj.* [βάλλω] (of a disease) **savagely attacking** Pi.*fr.*(dub.)

ὠμο-βόρος ον *adj.* [βιβρώσκω] (of Bacchants) **eating raw flesh** AR.
ὠμο-βρώς ῶτος *masc.fem.adj.* (of birds, Polyphemos) **eating raw flesh** E. Tim.; (of Erinyes) E.
ὠμό-βυρσος ον *adj.* [βύρσα] (of cuirasses) **of raw hide** Plu.
ὠμο-γέρων οντος *masc.adj.* (of men) not being a ripe old age, **on the verge of old age** Il. Call.
ὠμο-δακής ές *adj.* [δάκνω] (of a lust for killing) **savagely biting** A.
ὠμό-δροπος ον *adj.* [δρέπω] (of girls taken captive in war) **plucked unripe** (i.e. before marriage) A.
ὠμοθετέω *contr.vb.* [τίθημι] **1** (act. and mid.) **set in place the raw flesh** (on the fat-covered thigh-bones of a sacrificed animal) Hom.
2 sacrifice —*a ewe* AR.
ὠμόθην (aor.pass.): see ὄμνῡμι
ὠμό-θῡμος ον *adj.* [θῡμός] (of Ajax) **savage-hearted** S.
ὤμοι, ᾤμοι *interj.*: see ὤ
ὠμο-κρατής ές *adj.* [κράτος] (of Ajax) **fiercely mighty** S.
ὠμο-πλάτη ης, *dial.* **ὠμοπλάτᾱ** ᾱς *f.* [ὦμος] **shoulder-blade** (of a person or animal) X. Theoc.
ὠμός ή (*dial.* ά) όν *adj.* **1** (of animal flesh as food) not cooked over fire, **raw, uncooked** Od. Arist.; (of fish or birds) Hdt.; (perh. of human flesh) Hdt.
2 (hyperbol., of the flesh of one's enemies, as thrown to dogs or eaten by oneself) **raw** Hom. X. Call.
3 (of persons, divinities, their spirit, conduct, or sim.) not civilised, **savage, cruel** (sts. W.DAT. or εἰς + ACC. towards someone) Trag. Th. Pl. +; (of strife, civil war) A. Th.
4 not treated, processed or refined; (of earth) **unturned** X.; (of leather items) **raw** AR.; (of pitch) Plb.
5 (of fruit, crops) not fully grown or ripened, **unripe** Alc. X. AR. Theoc.; (fig., ref. to a person) Ar.
6 (of old age) not ripe, **early** or **premature** Od. Hes.
—ὠμῶς *adv.* | *superl.* ὠμότατα | **1 cruelly, savagely** Th. Ar. Att.orats. X. Plb. Plu.
2 rudely, coarsely —*ref. to speaking* D.
ὦμος ου *m.* **shoulder** (of a person or animal, freq.du. or pl.; sts.fig. or in fig.phrs., w.connot. of strength) Hom. +
ὤμοσα (aor.), **ὠμόσθην** (aor.pass.): see ὄμνῡμι
ὠμό-σιτος ον *adj.* [σῑτέομαι] **1** (of hounds, the Sphinx) **eating raw flesh** A. E.; (of the Sphinx's claws) **for eating raw flesh** E.
2 (of flesh) **eaten raw** E.*fr.*
ὠμο-σπάρακτος ον *adj.* [σπαράσσω] (fig., of a lawsuit about to be prepared, envisaged as meat before cooking) **torn into raw pieces** Ar.
ὠμότης ητος *f.* **wild behaviour, fierceness, savagery, cruelty** E. Att.orats. X. Arist. Men. +
ὠμο-τόκος ον *adj.* **1** (of a lioness) **having just given birth** Call. [or perh. *fierce after giving birth*]
2 (of lion cubs) perh. **raw, unformed** Call.
ὠμο-φάγος ον *adj.* [φαγεῖν] **1** (of wild animals, esp. lions) **eating raw flesh** Il. hHom. Theoc.; (of the Centaurs, an Anatolian tribe) Thgn. Th.; (of fishes) Ibyc.
2 (of pleasure) **in eating raw flesh** E.; (of initiatory feasts) **where raw flesh is eaten** E.*fr.*
ὠμό-φρων ονος *masc.fem.adj.* [φρήν] (of persons, Ares, a wolf, the Theban dragon) **savage-hearted** Trag.; (of iron, fig.ref. to war) A.
—ὠμοφρόνως *adv.* **savagely** A.
ὤν (masc.nom.sg.ptcpl.): see εἰμί
ὦν *dial.pcl.*: see οὖν
ὠνάθην (dial.aor.pass.), **ὠνάμην** (aor.2 mid.), **ὤνᾱσα** (dial.aor.act.): see ὀνίνημι

ὤνατο (3sg.aor.mid.): see ὀνομαι
ὧνδρες (voc.pl., w. crasis): see ἀνήρ
ὧνεκα *dial.conj.*: see οὕνεκα¹
ὠνέομαι *mid.contr.vb.* [ὦνος] | impf. ἐωνούμην, Ion. ὠνεόμην | aor. ὠνησάμην, also ἐωνησάμην (Plb. NT. Plu.) | pf.mid.pass. ἐώνημαι, ptcpl. ἐωνημένος | 3sg.plpf.mid. ἐώνητο ‖ PASS.: aor. ἐωνήθην ‖ The aor.mid. is usu. supplied by ἐπριάμην (see πρίασθαι). |
1 obtain for a price, **buy, purchase** —*goods, property, persons* (as slaves), *state contracts, favours, advancement*, or *sim.* Heraclit. Hdt. E. Ar. Att.orats. Pl. + ‖ PASS. (of persons or things) be bought Pl. X. Is. D.
2 (pres. and impf.) offer to buy, **bid** or **bargain for** (w. money or by barter) —*goods, property* (sts. W.DAT. or PREP. + GEN. *fr. someone*) Hes. Hdt.
3 avert, buy off —*a risk, legal claim* D.; **pay** —W.ACC. and μή + INF. *for sthg. not to happen* D.
ὦνερ (voc., w. crasis): see ἀνήρ
ὠνή ῆς *f.* [ὦνος] **1 buying, purchase** (of goods) E.*Cyc.* Att.orats. Pl. +
2 (phr.) ὠνὴ καὶ πρᾶσις (πρῆσις) *buying and selling, commerce* Hdt. Pl. X. Hyp. Arist.; (advbl.phr., ref. to buying or selling) ὠνῇ καὶ πράσει *outright* Hyp.
3 contract (awarded by the state, esp. for public works) Plb. Plu.; **contract for tax-collection** (sold annually by the state treasury) And. D.
ὠνήθην (aor.pass.), **ὠνήμην** (aor.2 mid.), **ὤνησα** (aor.act.): see ὀνίνημι
ὠνητέος ᾱ ον *vbl.adj.* [ὠνέομαι] (of merchandise) **which can be bought** Pl.
ὠνητής οῦ *m.* **buyer** or **bidder** (sts. W.GEN. for sthg.) X. Aeschin. Thphr. Plu.
ὠνητιάω *contr.vb.* **wish to be a buyer** (of sthg.) Thphr.
ὠνητός ή όν (also ός όν) *adj.* **1** (of persons) **bought** (as a slave, opp. free or hired) Od. S. E. Pl. Plu.; (of horses, grain) Plu.
2 (of hope, safety, political or military power, reputation) **able to be bought** (sts. W.GEN. or DAT. for or w. money) E. Th. Isoc. Pl. Arist. Plu.
ὠνινάμην (impf.mid.): see ὀνίνημι
ὤνιος ᾱ ον (also ος ον) *adj.* [ὦνος] **1** (of goods, slaves) available for purchase, **for sale** Ar. Pl. X. Is D. +; (fig., of valour, W.GEN. at the cost of blood) Aeschin.; (of elections, w.connot. of bribery) Plu. ‖ NEUT.PL.SB. merchandise Lys. Pl. X. D. Arist. Plu.
2 (of persons) capable of being bribed, **corrupt, venal** Arist. Din. Plu.
ὠνομασμένως *pf.pass.ptcpl.adv.*: see under ὀνομάζω
ὠνόμηνα (aor.): see ὀνομαίνω
ὦνος ου *m.* **1** purchase or barter price, **price** (sts. W.GEN. for sthg.) Hom. Hes.*fr.* AR. Theoc.; (W.GEN. for someone, as ransom) Il.
2 action of buying, **purchase** (of a cargo) Od.
ὠνοσάμην (aor.mid.): see ὀνομαι
ὠνούμηνα (Boeot.aor.): see ὀνομαίνω
ᾦξα (aor.): see οἴγω
ᾠόν οῦ, dial. **ὤεον** ου, Aeol. **ὤιον** ω *n.* **1 egg** (of birds, reptiles) Semon. Hdt. Ar. Call.*epigr.* Plu.; (as food) Ar. Philox.Leuc. Pl. +; (ref. to its shape) Plu.; (of Leda, fr. which Castor and Pollux were born) Sapph. ‖ PL. eggs or spawn (of fish) Hdt.
2 egg-shaped container, **egg** (laid by Night, fr. which Eros was born) Ar.; (ref. to a silver container, in which the Molionid twins were born) Ibyc.; (made fr. gum by the phoenix, as a kind of coffin) Hdt.
ὠόπ (also written ὠ ὄπ or ὠ ὄπ) *interj.* (as a signal to oarsmen) **stop!, heave to!** Ar.; (addressed to a dithyrambic poet in full flood) Ar.
—ὠοπόπ (also written ὠ ὄπ ὄπ) *interj.* (as a chant to set the rhythm of rowing) **heave ho!** Ar.
ᾠοτοκέω *contr.vb.* [ᾠόν, τίκτω] **1** (of certain animals) **lay eggs** Arist.
2 (by analogy, of fruit-bearing trees) **bear** —*olives* Emp.
ὦπα (acc.): see ὤψ
ὧπερ *dial.relatv.adv.*: see ὥσπερ
ὧπερ *dial.relatv.adv.*: see under ὅσπερ
ὠπή ῆς *f.* [reltd. ὤψ] perception or gaze; (prep.phr., ref. to persons meeting) εἰς ὠπήν *face to face* AR.
ὦπται (3sg.pf.pass.): see ὁράω
ὥρᾱ (Aeol. **ὤρᾱ**) ᾱς, Ion. **ὥρη** ης *f.* | ep.gen.pl. ὡράων, Ion. ὡρέων | **1** one of the naturally recurring periods of the year (determined by length of the day, characteristic weather, animal mating), **season** (usu. thought of as three or four) Hom. +; (ref. to a specific season, characterised by the weather, esp. spring, summer or winter) Hom. + ‖ COLLECTV.PL. seasons or climatic conditions Hdt. Pl.
2 ‖ PL. (personif.) Horai, Seasons or Hours (gatekeepers of Olympos and attendants of Zeus or Aphrodite) Il. Hes. Pi. Lyr.adesp. Ar. X. +
3 appropriate or habitual time (of the year, for a particular human activity, such as reaping, ploughing, harvesting, sailing, fighting), **season, time of year, time** Hes. Scol. Hdt. Th. Ar. Pl. +
4 one of the approximate divisions of the (solar) day, **time, hour** (sts. W.GEN. of the day or night) hHom. A. Hdt. +
5 portion of the day (fr. sunrise to sunset) or night (each divided in twelve), **hour** Plb. NT. Plu.
6 appropriate or habitual time of the day (for eating, sleeping, leaving the house, or sim.), **time, hour** (oft. W.GEN. or PREP.PHR. for sthg.) Od. Hes. Pi. Hdt. Trag. +
7 (gener.) opportune time (for doing sthg., events to happen), **right time, occasion** Od. Pi. Hdt. Trag. +; **time** or **occasion** (of an event) Od. E. NT.
8 right or good period of a human lifetime (w.connots. of youth, vigour, good looks), **time of youthfulness, freshness** or **vigour** Eleg. Carm.Pop. A. Pi. E. Ar. +; (personif., as a goddess) **Hora** Pi.
9 (gener.) time or season (of the day, night, month, or year, determined astronomically), **time** or **season** X.
10 ‖ PL. seasons or ages (denoting long duration) Emp. S. Ar.; (prep.phr.) ἐς (τὰς) ὥρας or sim. *for the time to come, for ever* Od. hHom. Ar. Theoc.
11 period of time of a limited length (during which sthg. continues), **time, while** NT.
—ὥρᾱσι (also written as if acc. **ὥρᾱς**) *loc.pl.adv.* (in phrs., as a curse) μὴ ὥρασ᾽ ἵκοισθε (or sim.) *may you not come in season, may you meet bad luck* Ar. Men.(cj.); (also ellipt.) μὴ ὥρασι Ar.
ὥρᾱ ᾱς, Ion. **ὥρη** ης *f.* [app.reltd. ὁράω] | usu. in neg.phrs. | **care, concern, regard** (freq. W.GEN. for someone or sthg.) Hes. Tyrt. Timocr. Hdt. S. Theoc.
ὡραῖος ᾱ (Ion. η) ον *adj.* **1** (of food, fruits, fish) produced at the appropriate time of year, **in season** or **ripe** Hes. Praxill. Hdt. X. ‖ NEUT.PL.SB. seasonal produce Th. Pl. X. D.(oracle)
2 (of activities, such as sailing or ploughing) undertaken at the appropriate time of year, **seasonal** Hes. Thgn.; (quasi-advbl., of Love arriving) **in due season** Thgn. ‖ FEM.SB.

appropriate season (for rain, the harvest, military campaigns) Hdt. D. AR. Plb. ‖ NEUT.IMPERS. (w. ἐστί) it is the right time —W.INF. *to do sthg*. Plu.
3 (of persons) **at a seasonable time** (of life); (of young women, their age) **ripe** (usu. W.GEN. for marriage) Thgn. Hdt. E. X.; (of a man) **of marriageable age** Hes.; (of old persons) **ready** (sts. W.GEN. for death) E. Plu.; (of a suitable age, w. πρός + ACC. for political life) Plu.; (of death after a successful life) **at the right time** X. ‖ NEUT.PL.SB. (euphem., ref. to a person's funeral rites) **things appropriate to one's age** E.
4 (of persons) **in the bloom of youth, young and beautiful** Pi. Lys. Ar. Pl. X. +; (of Iacchus) Ar.
5 (of a whitewashed tomb) **beautiful** NT.; (as the name of a temple door) NT.
ὡραιότης ητος *f.* **physical beauty** (of a person) X.
ὡραϊσμός οῦ *m.* [ὡραΐζω *beautify, adorn*] **1 youthful beauty** Plu.
2 ornamentation (worn on the body) Plu.
3 (pejor.) **embellishment** (in a style of oratory) Plu.
ὡρακιάω contr.vb. | aor. ὡρακίασα | **faint away** (fr. fear or horror) Ar.
ὡρανόθεν dial.adv.: see under οὐρανός
ὥρανος Aeol.m., **ὡρανός** dial.m.: see οὐρανός
ὥρᾱς, ὥρᾱσι advs.: see under ὥρᾱ
ὥρεα (dial.nom.acc.pl.), **ὥρεος** (dial.gen.sg.): see ὄρος
ὥρεσσι (dat.pl.): see ὄαρες
ὥρετο (ep.3sg.aor.2 mid.): see ὄρνυμαι, under ὄρνῡμι
ὡρεύω vb. [perh.reltd. ὥρᾱ] (of certain goddesses) **look after, care for** —*works* (W.DAT. *by mortal men*) Hes.
ὥρη, ὦρη Ion.*f.*: see ὥρᾱ, ὦρᾱ
ὡρη-φόρος ον adj. [ὥρᾱ, φέρω] (epith. of Demeter) **bringing the seasons** or **the seasonal fruits** hHom.
ὦρθεν (ep.3pl.aor.pass.): see ὄρνυμαι, under ὄρνῡμι
ὡρίζεσκον (iteratv.impf.): see ὀαρίζω
ὡρικός ή όν adj. [ὥρᾱ] (of a slave-girl) **of the young and beautiful kind, pretty** Ar.
—**ὡρικῶς** adv. **girlishly** —*ref. to an old woman speaking* Ar.
ὥριος ᾱ ον adj. **1 of the season** or **appropriate time of year**; (of fruits) **in season** Od. Hes. Theoc.; (of frost, rain) **seasonal** Hes.
2 (of ploughing, cutting wood, harvesting) **appropriate to the season** Hes. Theoc.; (of festivals, paean-songs) Pi. | see also οὔριος 1
3 (of marriage) **at the right time** (of life) Hes. ‖ NEUT.IMPERS. (w. ἐστί understd.) **it is the right time** —W.ACC. + INF. *for men to consider marriage* Sol.
ὥριος dial.adj.: see οὔριος
ὡρισμένος pf.pass.ptcpl.adj., **ὡρισμένως** adv.: see under ὁρίζω
Ὠρίων (ep. **Ὠρίων**), dial. **Ὠαρίων**, ωνος *m.* **1 Orion** (Boeotian giant and hunter) Od. Pi. Corinn. Call.
2 constellation of Orion, Orion Hom. Hes. E. +; (described as rising in early summer) Hes. Plb. | see also κύων 7
—**Ὠαριώνειος** ᾱ ον dial.adj. (of an athlete's physique) **comparable to Orion** Pi.
ὥρνυον (ep.impf.), **ὥρορε¹** (ep.3sg.redupl.aor.2): see ὄρνῡμι
ὥρνυτο (ep.3sg.impf.mid.), **ὦρορε²** (ep.3sg.pf.act.): see ὄρνυμαι, under ὄρνῡμι
ὦρος *m.*: see ἄωρος³
ὤρουσα (aor.): see ὀρούω
ὦρσα (ep.aor.): see ὄρνῡμι
ὦρτο (ep.3sg.aor.2 mid.): see ὄρνυμαι, under ὄρνῡμι

ὠρυγή ῆς *f.* [ὠρύομαι] **howling** (of animals, persons in distress) Plu.
ὠρυθμός οῦ *m.* **roaring** (of a lion) Theoc.
ὠρύομαι mid.vb. **1** (of wolves, dogs) **howl** Call. Theoc.; (of a lion) **roar** AR.
2 (of persons) **roar, shout out** (in grief or happiness) Hdt.; (in acclamation for an athlete) Pi.
3 (of animals, as if human) **howl** or **shriek** (in lamentation) —W.ACC. or περί + ACC. *for a dead poet* Theoc. Bion
ὥρων (Ion.impf.): see ὁράω
ὠρώρει (ep.3sg.plpf.): see ὄρνυμαι, under ὄρνῡμι
ὡς (also **ὥς, ὧς**) adv. | The wd. has five main functions: (**A**) demonstr.adv. *so, likewise*; (**B**) relatv.adv. *as, as much as, as if*; (**C**) exclam.adv. *how, oh!*; (**D**) conj. *that, so that, because*; (**E**) prep. of motion *to* (W.ACC. *a person*). |
—**A ὥς** (also **ὧς**) demonstr.adv. [reltd. ὁ] **1** (modifying a vb.) **like this, in this way, so** Hom. Lyr. Hdt. Trag. + • ὣς ἔφατο *so he spoke* Hom. Hes. hHom. AR.
2 (as correlatv. in comparisons, w.relatv.adv. B 2) ὡς ... ὥς *as ... so* Hom. + • εἴθ᾽ ὡς θυμὸς ἐνὶ στήθεσσι φίλοισιν, ὥς τοι γούναθ᾽ ἕποιτο *as is the spirit in your own breast, so may your limbs obey* Il.; (also as correlatv.w. οἷα, ὥσπερ, or sim.) Hom. +
3 (quasi-conj., in phrs.) • καὶ ὥς (ὧς) *nevertheless, even so* Hom. Hes. Th. + • οὐδ᾽ ὥς (ὧς) *not even so* Hom. Hdt. S. Th. +
4 (intensv. w.adj.) ὣς πυκνός or μαλακός *so solid* or *soft* Hom.
—**B ὡς** (postpos. **ὥς**), dial. **ὠ** relatv.adv. [reltd. ὅς¹] **1** (making a comparison) **in the same way as, as, just as** Hom. + • πάντα μάλ᾽ ἀτρεκέως ἀγορευέμεν ὡς ἐπιτέλλω *tell him all my words truly, as I command you* Il.
2 (w.correlatv.adv. ὡς A 2) ὡς ... ὥς *as ... so* Hom. +
3 (modifying ptcpls.) **as, as if** (sthg. were the case) Hom. + • λέγουσιν ἡμᾶς ὡς ὀλωλότας *they speak of us as if we were dead* A.; (w.prep.phr.) • ὡς ἐκ κακῶν *as if released from troubles* Hdt. • ὡς ἐπὶ ναυμαχίαν *as if going to battle* Th.
4 (quasi-prep., modifying a noun) **like** —W.NOM. *a god, person, object, or sim.* Hom. +; (postpos. ὥς) Hom. Trag. Call. AR. • πατὴρ δ᾽ ὣς ἤπιος ἦεν *he was kind, like a father* Od.
5 (parenth., w.vb. or phr., modifying the main cl.) **as** • ὡς ἔοικε, ὡς ἤκουσα *as it seems, as I heard* Hdt. S. E. + • ὥς ἐμοὶ δοκεῖ *as it seems to me* Hdt. Trag. Th. Att.orats. + • ὡς ἐμοί *in my view* S. • ὡς ἀπ᾽ ὀμμάτων *to judge by sight* S. • ὡς εἰπεῖν λόγῳ *as the story is* Hdt. • ὡς συντόμως εἰπεῖν *to speak briefly* Isoc. Pl. X. • ὡς ἀληθῶς *truly, in fact* Hdt. E. Att.orats. + • ὡς ἑτέρως *the other way, contrarily* Pl. D.
6 (w.superl.adv.) **as much as** Hippon. Pi. Hdt. + • ὡς μάλιστα *as much as possible* Hdt. Trag. Ar. + • ὡς τάχιστα *as quickly as possible* Hippon. + • (w. many, most) ὡς τὸ πολύ, ὡς τὸ πλεῖον, ὡς ἐπὶ τὸ πλῆθος *for the most part* Th. Att.orats. + • (w.superl.adjs., prep.phrs.) ὡς ἄριστος, ὡς ἐς ἐλάχιστον *as good as possible, as little as possible* Th. Att.orats. Pl. +
7 (distributive, w.adjs.) ὡς ἕκαστος, ὡς ἕκαστοι *each by himself or herself, severally* Pi. Hdt. Th. Arist.; (w. numbers) *as if*, **about, approximately** Hdt. +
8 (temporal) **when, as** (usu.ref. to the past, W.INDIC. or OPT.) Hom. + • ἔνωρτο γέλως ... ὡς ἴδον Ἥφαιστον *laughter rang out ... when they saw Hephaistos* Il. • (w.correlatv.) ὡς εἶδ᾽, ὡς ἀνέπαλτο *when he saw him, then he jumped up* Il. • ὡς τάχιστα (w. finite cl.) *as soon as* (sthg. happened) Hdt. X. Aeschin.
9 (ref. to location) **where** Theoc.
—**C ὡς** exclam.adv. **how!** Hom. + • ὡς οὐκ ἔστι χάρις *what a lack of gratitude there is!* Od. • φρονεῖν ὡς δεινόν *how*

terrible it is to have wisdom! S. • ὡς ἀπωλόμεσθα *now we're done for!* Ar.; (in wishes) **oh!** —W.OPT. *may someone or something perish!* Hom. S. E.

—D **ὡς** *conj*. **1** (introducing indir.cl.) **how** (sthg. was or might be the case) Hom. + • κατέλεξεν ὥς μιν θηρεύοντ' ἔλασεν σῦς *he recounted how a boar wounded him while he was hunting* Od. • μερμήριζε ... ὡς Ἀχιλῆα τιμήσῃ *he was considering how he might honour Achilles* Il. **2** (introducing statements after vbs. of thought or speech, similar to ὅτι) **the fact that, that** (sthg. is the case) Hom. + • (sts. also app. w.advbl. force) οἶσθ' ὡς πρεσβυτέροισιν Ἐρινύες αἰὲν ἕπονται *you know how* (or *that*) *Erinyes always side with the elder* Il. • (after vbs. of showing) πνεῦμα ... δείκνυσιν ὥς τι καινὸν ἀγγελεῖ κακόν *his breathing shows that he is about to announce some new disaster* E. • (w. no main vb.) δῆλον ὡς ... *it is clear that* (sthg. is the case) E. Pl. + • (indicating possibility or necessity) οὐκ ἔσθ' ὡς *there is no way that* (sthg. is the case) hHom. S. Pl. + **3** (indicating purpose) **so that, in order that** (w. ἄν or κεν + SUBJ. or OPT. sthg. might be the case) Hom. + • στείχωμεν ὡς ἂν ἐν πυρᾷ θῶμεν νεκρόν *let us go to place the corpse on the pyre* E. **4** (indicating result, W.INF.) **so that, consequently** A. Hdt. + • (of a mountain) ὑψηλὸν οὕτω ὡς τὰς κορυφὰς αὐτοῦ οἷά τε εἶναι ἰδέσθαι *so high that it is impossible to see its peaks* Hdt. **5** (indicating cause, after vbs. of emotion) **that, because** Hom. • ᾖε σύ γ' Ἀργείων ὀλοφύρεαι ὡς ὀλέκονται *do you lament for the Argives, that* (*because*) *they are being slain?* Il. **6** (introducing a reason or strong assertion) **for the fact is that, for, since, because** S. E. Ar. Pl. • τί λέγεις; ὡς οὐ μανθάνω *what are you saying?* (*I ask*) *because I don't understand* S.; (affirming or negating) **yes** or **no because** S. E. Ar.

—E **ὡς** *prep*. (ref. to persons approaching or going) **to** —W.ACC. *someone* Od.(dub.) Hdt. S. Th. + • ὡς Ἆγιν ἐπρεσβεύσαντο *they sent envoys to Agis* Th.

ὡς *dial.n.*: see οὖς

ὦσα (Ion.aor.): see ὠθέω

ὡσανεί (also **ὡς ἂν εἰ**) *adv*. [ὡσεί] (modifying a statement) **as it were, as one might say** Arist. Plb.

ὤσασκον (iteratv.aor.): see ὠθέω

ὡσ-αύτως *adv*. | also tm. ὥς δ' αὔτως (or ὡς δ' αὔτως) | **1** in like manner, **similarly, in the same way** Hom. Hdt. S. E. Pl. + **2** (quasi-prep.) **in the same way as, like** (W.DAT. someone or sthg.) Hdt.(tm.) S.

ὦσδον (dial.impf.): see ὄζω

ὡσ-εί (also **ὡς εἰ**) *adv*. | also sts. (w.pcl. τε) ὡς εἴ τε (Hom.), ὡσείτε (Pi.) | **1** (introducing a hypothetical or actual comparison) **as is** (or **would be**) **the case when** (or **if**), **as if, as though, in the same manner as** (W.INDIC., SUBJ. or OPT.) Hom. + • λαοὶ ἕπονθ', ὡς εἴ τε μετὰ κτίλον ἕσπετο μῆλα *the army followed, as sheep follow after the ram* Il. **2** (w.ptcpl.) **as if, as though** (someone were doing sthg.) Il. + • (of Ares) αἵματι φοινικόεις ὡς εἰ ζωοὺς ἐναρίζων *purple with blood, as though he were killing living men* Hes. **3** (without vb.) **as, like** Hom. + • τῶν νέες ὠκεῖαι ὡς εἰ πτερὸν ἠὲ νόημα *their ships are fast like a wing or a thought* Od. **4** (parenth., modifying a statement) **as it were** Pi. **5** (w. numbers or measures) **approximately, about** Hdt. X. NT.

ὡσί (dat.pl.): see οὖς

ὦσι (3pl.subj.): see εἰμί

ὥσ-περ (in Hom. Hes. always two wds. **ὥς περ**, sts. **ὡς ...**

περ), dial. **ὥπερ** *relatv.adv*. [ὡς B, περ¹] **1** (making a comparison) **in just the same way as, just as** Hom. + • σὺ δέ μοι δὸς ξείνιον, ὥς περ ὑπέστης *give me a gift, just as you promised* Od.; (usu. without vb.) **just like** (someone or sthg.) Hom. Eleg. + • ἄλλοι ... Ἀχαιοὶ ἐν θυμῷ βάλλονται ἐμοὶ χόλον, ὥς περ Ἀχιλλεύς *the other Achaeans are laying up anger at me in their hearts, just like Achilles* Il.; (also W.ADV. ὁμοίως *similarly*, occas. W.ADJ. ὅμοιος) A. Th. Att.orats. + **2** (introducing a specific example) **as for instance** • ὅταν γε χορὸς εἷς ἐκ τῆσδε τῆς πόλεως γίγνηται, ὥσπερ ὁ εἰς Δῆλον πεμπόμενος *when there is one chorus from this state, as for instance the one sent to Delos* X. • (to introduce a contrast) καὶ οὐδενός ὑμᾶς βιασαμένου ὥσπερ ἡμᾶς *and no one had forced you, as in our case* Th. **3** (introducing a hypothetical situation) **just as if** (w. ἄν + OPT. someone were to say or do sthg.) Att.orats. +; (more freq. w.ptcpl.) S. E. Lys. Pl. X. • ὥσπερ ἐγγελῶσα τοῖς ποιουμένοις *just as if laughing at one's deeds* S. **4** (introducing a statement or metaphor) **as it were, so to speak** Th. Ar. Pl. X. • ἐοίκοι ἂν ὥσπερ τυφλοῦ πορείᾳ *it would be like the progress of a blind person* Pl. **5** (modifying a number) οὐ μείους ὥσπερ χίλιοι *no fewer than about a thousand* Xenoph. **6** (in phrs., ref. to time) ὥσπερ εἶχε or εἶχον *just as he was or they were* (i.e. *immediately*) Hdt. S. Th. Ar. +

ὥσπερ-εί (also written **ὥσπερ εἰ**) *adv*. | also (w.pcl. ἄν) ὡσπερανεί, ὥσπερ ἂν εἰ (Att.orats. Pl. Arist.), (w. οὖν) ὥσπερ οὖν ἂν εἰ (Pl.) | **just as if** —W.INDIC., PTCPL. or OPT. *sthg. is or would be the case* Trag. +; (quasi-prep.) **like** —W. NOUN or PTCPL. *sthg.* S. Ar. Pl.

ὥσ-τε (also **ὥς τε** Hom.), dial. **ὦτε** *adv*. and *conj*. [τε¹] **1** (adv., introducing similes, w. a vbl.cl.) **just as** —*sthg. is or was the case* Hom. Sol. Lyr. A. S. AR.; (quasi-prep., w. a noun) **like** (someone or sthg.) Lyr. Trag.; (giving a reason, w. a noun) **just like** (someone, sts. W.PTCPL. doing sthg.) Hom. Hdt. **2** (conj., expressing consequence or purpose) **so as, in order** (W.INF. to do sthg., that sthg. shd. be the case) Hom. + • τοσόνδε μισεῖν ὥστε τὴν δίκην πατεῖν *to hate so much as to trample on justice* S. • πᾶν ποιοῦσιν ὥστε δίκην μὴ διδόναι *they do everything so as not to pay the penalty* Pl. • (after vbs. of wishing, commanding, or sim.) Κύπρις γὰρ ἤθελ' ὥστε γίγνεσθαι τάδε *Kypris wished that this should happen* E. • (after compar.adj.) μεῖζον ἢ ὥστε φέρειν δύνασθαι κακόν *a disaster greater than one is able to bear* (i.e. *too great*) X. • (after a noun) γέρων ἐκεῖνος ὥστε σ' ὠφελεῖν *he is an old man* (i.e. *too old*) *to help you* E. **3** (conj., expressing result) **and so, so that** (W.COMPL.CL. sthg. is the case) Hdt. + • βέβηκεν, ὥστε ... ἔξεστι φωνεῖν *he has gone, so that it is possible to speak* S. • οὕτως ἀγνωμόνως ἔχετε ὥστε ἐλπίζετε ... *you are so senseless that you hope ...* D. • βρέφος γὰρ ἦν τότε ... ὥστ' οὐκ ἂν αὐτὸν γνωρίσαιμ' ἂν εἰσιδών *he was a baby then ..., and so I would not recognise him if I saw him* E. **4** (conj., marking a strong conclusion) **so, consequently, therefore** (sthg. is or will be the case) S. + • ὥστε ... ὄλωλα *so* (*if he sees me*) *I am dead* S. • (w.imperatv.) ὥστε θάρρει *so cheer up* Pl. X.

ὠστίζομαι *mid.vb*. [reltd. ὠθέω] | fut. ὠστιοῦμαι | (of people in a crowd) **keep pushing, jostle** (sts. W.DAT. someone, each other) Ar.

ὠσφρόμην (aor.2 mid.): see ὀσφραίνομαι

ὦσχος ου (or **ὠσχός** οῦ) *m*. app. **vine plant** or **branch** Ar.(cj.) Plu.

Ὠσχοφόρια ων *n.pl.* [φέρω] festival of the vine-branch procession (at Athens), **Oskhophoria** Plu.

ὤσω (fut.): see ὠθέω

ὦτα (nom.acc.pl.): see οὖς

ὠτακουστέω *contr.vb.* [ὠτακουστής] (of soldiers, spies, or sim.) **listen carefully**, **keep one's ears open** Hdt. X. D. Plb. Plu.

ὠτ-ακουστής οῦ *m.* [οὖς, ἀκούω] one who keeps the ears open (for information, esp. covertly), **eavesdropper** Arist. Plb.(cj.)

ὠτάριον ου *n.* [dimin. οὖς] **ear** (W.GEN. of a person) NT.

ὦτε *dial.adv.*: see ὥστε

ᾧτε (dat.): see ὅστε

ὠτειλή ῆς *f.* [reltd. οὐτάω] **1 wound** (usu. fr. a weapon) Hom. E. AR. Bion
2 mark of a wound, **scar** X. Plu.

ὤτερος (dial.masc.nom.): see ἕτερος

ὠτίον ου *n.* [dimin. οὖς] **ear** (W.GEN. of a person) NT.

ὠτίς ίδος *f.* [οὖς] a kind of large bird; **bustard** X.

ὠτός (gen.), **ὤτων** (gen.pl.): see οὖς

ὠτώεις *ep.adj.*: see οὐατόεις

ωὑτός: dial. crasis for ὁ αὐτός

ὠφέλεια, Att. **ὠφελίᾱ**, ᾱς, Ion. **ὠφελίη** ης *f.* [ὠφελέω]
1 practical assistance, **help**, **aid** (for persons, esp. allies in war) Th. Ar. Att.orats. X. +; (in medical ctxt.) Pl.; (ref. to a person, W.DAT. for kin) E.
2 advantageous outcome, **gain**, **benefit**, **advantage** (of a plan, situation, course of action, sts. W.GEN. to oneself or others) Hdt. S. Att.orats. Pl. X. Arist.; (W.GEN. of a defensive wall) Hdt.
3 object gained (in war), **spoil**, **booty** Plb. Plu.; (in hunting) **prize**, **quarry** X.; **loot** (acquired by a thief) Antipho

ὠφελέω *contr.vb.* [ὄφελος] | aor. ὠφέλησα ‖ PASS.: fut. ὠφεληθήσομαι, also ὠφελήσομαι ‖ neut.impers.vbl.adj. ὠφελητέον |
1 (of persons or things) **be of use** or **help** (usu. W.ACC. to someone) Hdt. Trag. Th. Ar. + —W.DAT. Semon. Trag. Antipho —W.NEUT.ADV. *in no way, very much, or sim.* Hdt. E. Th. Isoc. —W.COGN.ACC. Pl. ‖ PASS. receive help or benefit Hdt. Trag. +
2 (of a commander) **benefit**, **enrich** —*his soldiers* (w. booty) Plu.

ὠφέλημα ατος *n.* **1** that which is useful, **benefit**, **advantage** (usu. W.DAT. to someone, ref. to physical resources) A. E. X.; (W.GEN. for one's country) X.; (ref. to hope, a good reputation) A. S.
2 (ref. to a person) **blessing** (W.DAT. to mankind) Ar.

ὠφελήσιμος ον *adj.* (of circumstances) **providing help** S.; (of information) **to one's advantage** Ar.

ὠφέλησις εως *f.* **power** or **ability to help** (someone) S.

ὠφελητέος ᾱ ον *vbl.adj.* (of a city) **to be helped** or **benefited** (W.DAT. by someone) X.

ὠφελίᾱ *f.*, **ὠφελίη** *Ion.f.*: see ὠφέλεια

ὠφέλιμος ον (also η ον Pl.) *adj.* | compar. ὠφελιμώτερος, superl. ὠφελιμώτατος | **1** (of persons) **useful**, **helpful** (to the state, a household, or sim.) Ar. Pl. X.; (W.PREP.PHR. for some purpose) Th. Pl. X.; (W.DAT. to someone) E. Th. Lys.; (of horses) Th.
2 (of circumstances, arguments, poetry, physical resources, or sim.) **beneficial**, **valuable** (sts. W.DAT. to persons or sim.) Th. Critias Att.orats. Pl. +; (w. πρός + ACC. for someone) Pl. ‖ NEUT.SB. usefulness or convenience (sts. W.DAT. for someone) Th. Pl.

—**ὠφελίμως** *adv.* | superl. ὠφελιμώτατα | **helpfully**, **advantageously** (sts. W.DAT. to someone or sthg.) Pl. X.

ὤφελλον (ep.impf.), **ὤφελον** (aor.2): see ὀφείλω

ὤφθην (aor.pass.): see ὁράω

ὤφληκα (pf.), **ὦφλον** (aor.2): see ὀφλισκάνω

ᾠχόμην (impf.mid.): see οἴχομαι

ὠχράω *contr.vb.* [ὠχρός] ‖ AOR. (of a person) turn pale (fr. fear) —W.ACC. in one's complexion Od.

ὠχρίασις εως *f.* paleness of complexion, **pallor** Plu.

ὠχριάω *contr.vb.* lack colour in the face, **be pallid** (fr. fear) Ar. Arist. Plu.; (of Socrates and his friends, fr. their unhealthy lifestyle) Ar.

ὠχρός ᾱ όν *adj.* **1** (of persons) pale of complexion, **pale**, **pallid** (fr. fear) E. Ar.; (fr. lovesickness) Theoc.; (of a sophist; of the complexion of young men, fr. their unhealthy lifestyle) Ar.; (of persons, as a sign of bad character) Plu.
2 (of a colour or shade, described as intermediate betw. white and black) perh. **pale yellow** or **brown** Arist.; (of the sun) Plu. ‖ NEUT.SB. ochre (ref. to a mixture of white and yellow) Pl.

ὦχρος ου *m.* **paleness** (of cheeks, fr. fear) Il.

ὠχρότης ητος *f.* **paleness** (of a complexion, regarded as beautiful) Pl.; (through illness) Plu.

ὤψ ὠπός *m.f.* [reltd. ὄψις] | only acc. ὦπα, also once acc.pl. ὦπας (Theoc.) and neut.pl. ὦπα (Pl.) | **1 eye** or **face**; (prep.phr.) εἰς ὦπα in the face (ref. to looking at someone) Hom.; in one's face (ref. to resembling someone) Hom. Hes.; (ref. to being terrible to look at) Od.
2 ‖ PL. **eyes** Pl. Theoc.*epigr.*

ὦψαι (2sg.pf.pass.): see ὁράω